# OF COURSE THEY KNEW,

# OF COURSE THEY...

—A Novel

Brick Tower Press
Habent Sua Fata Libelli

**Brick Tower Press**
Manhanset House
Shelter Island Hts., New York 11965-0342
Tel: 212-427-7139
bricktower@aol.com • www.BrickTowerPress.com
All rights reserved under the International and Pan-American Copyright
Conventions. Printed in the United States by J. Boylston & Company, Publishers,
New York. No part of this publication may be reproduced, stored in a retrieval system,
or transmitted in any form or by any means, electronic, or otherwise, without the prior
written permission of the copyright holder.
The Brick Tower Press colophon is a registered trademark of
J. T. Colby & Company, Inc.


**Library of Congress Cataloging-in-Publication Data**
Moody, John.
of course they knew, of course they...
p. cm.


1. Fiction—Thriller. 2. Fiction—Thriller—Suspense.
3. Fiction— 4. United States—Fiction
Fiction, I. Title.
ISBN: 978-1-883283-97-1, Hardcover  978-1-883283-92-6, Trade Paper


Copyright © 2021 by John Moody

September 2021

# OF COURSE THEY KNEW,

# OF COURSE THEY...

—A Novel

John Moody

Co-author of *The Priest Who Had to Die*
author of *Moscow Magician*, a novel,
*Pope John Paul II*, a biography, and *Kiss It Good-bye*, a
nonfiction love letter to baseball of a bygone era.

# Table of Contents

# Chapter 1
## Zhongguo tese shehui zhuyi

Qi smelled danger.

Actually, she smelled death, but she was used to that. Death is part of life, and the study of life is biology. So, when you work at a virological hazards lab, death, as it is for every living thing, is inevitable.

But it didn't usually smell this bad.

Bats, in her experience, smelled musty. But not like cadavers the way this one did. And it had only been dead for an hour.

The Wuhan Virology Services Laboratory was in a seven-story building almost in the geometric center of the city. Most people had never heard of it. But then, most people, at least outside of China, had never heard of Wuhan, a city of 11 million people with a vast array of industrial factories as well as intentionally small manufactories that churned out everything from children's toys to rare earths, the fifteen elements that, when refined with great precision, power the products that keep I-phones, computers, GPS systems and—although China denied it—the People's Liberation Army's rocket-launched nuclear missiles. Wuhan was a city that had grown from a collection of family businesses to a little-known but strategically important cog in the fast-forward machine that was the Chinese economy. Its unemployment rate among working-age citizens sat statistically just above zero. Its cost of living was purposely high, to insure that anyone who could work, worked. The elderly, the sick, the insane and the dying were, for the most part, warehoused well away from the healthy population. To prevent the spread of disease, yes, but also to minimize their unsightliness.

Qi Qi Dieh was 45 years old, divorced, overweight and generally disappointed with the way life was working out. Her education included a first-place finish in biology at the Wuhan Supplemental Academy of Science, which was the city's second-tier place of education, but which nonetheless made her highly employable. A disastrous marriage to a demented sadist had thrown her career off-track, the more so because her ex was an ambitious Party member and had spread vicious stories about her. He also worked at the Institute. Partly due to that calumny, she was never considered for promotion from her job as junior assistant to the infectious disease department at the Laboratory. Her responsibilities included feeding experimental animals, cleaning their cages (and keeping track of the amount and characteristics of their excrement), and getting rid of them when they, inevitably, died.

The feeding part was fine, except on those occasions when the Laboratory had run out of the grain, or meat bits, or small insects, or whatever the goddam animals survived on. Qi Qi had tried substituting one test subject's food for another's in those cases, but the animals, though starving and close to death anyway, refused to diversify their diets. In those cases, Qi Qi usually let them starve to death and faked their weight on the mortality charts she was required to keep. Or, if she felt sorry for the critters, and that was not often, she would inject them with concentrated bleach, which killed most animals under 3 kilos within an hour. Then on the cause of death form she was required to fill out, she wrote, "asphyxiation." Which, technically, was accurate. They had, after all, stopped breathing.

Bats were different.

For one thing, they could not be captured, cornered, held down, injected or force-fed. Bats eluded all attempts to control them. And who wanted to? Most bats are rabid, which is fine with them, since rabies doesn't sicken or kill bats, but does doom any creature that the bat might bite, or that might inadvertently consume something that the bats' excrement has been on. Which can be almost anything, as bats are unwilling to use toilets, preferring instead to shit on whatever surface might be beneath their flight path.

Which is one reason why, for centuries, bats were seldom invited to parties thrown by other members of the Animal Kingdom. Bats are dreaded, not just by humans, but by other mammals. They fly crazy routes, they screech, they look like a banshee roaring at another animal until, at the last nanosecond, they divert, and sweep screeching away.

Another reason is that in the past two or so centuries bats have cleverly learned to absorb pathogens that—like rabies—do nothing harmful to them, but are quite capable of initiating widespread disease—let's just call them pandemics—among humans and other mammalian creatures. Horses, sheep, pigs, and, best of all, humans, have fallen victim to the various mucuses, technically muci, that bats can carry harmlessly.

Two pieces of advice about bats, both concerning teeth: don't get bit by them, and don't eat them.

Qi Qi—most people just called her Qi—knew most of this from her academic training. She knew the names of the various diseases that bats could carry. She could have told her superiors—and almost everyone at the lab was her superior—that the bat she had found lying dead in Enclosure 49 smelled worse than the normal dead bat. But since no one ever asked her opinion, and since everyone assumed they knew more than a 40ish, fat and ill-tempered woman, who had displeased her ex-husband, who was, moreover, a rising local Party member, she had nothing to say to them. She steered clear of the live bats kept in the laboratory as much as her job allowed. And she never—never— picked up a dead bat without gloves. When, inevitably, the lab ran out of plastic gloves, she let the dead bats lie rotting in their enclosures. They weren't her problem. Let the Party give her the gloves, then she'd pick the thing up.

A colleague whose name Qi could never remember saw her transferring the dead bat from its cage to a waste sack. The fellow was probably in his thirties, slim, not bad-looking at all. He had actually taken the amazing step of introducing himself to Qi and asking how she was doing. Like everyone at the institute, he wore a white lab coat underneath a transparent plastic gown, to prevent some of the more dangerous materials the Lab produced from seeping into their clothes and skin. The only thing that differentiated him, as far as Qi was concerned, was a snazzy looking pair of green shoes.

"I'm heading to the inferno," he said, stifling a cough. "Want me to take that down for you?" The inferno was a two-thousand-degree oven used to incinerate test animals. In theory only dead animals were shoved through its doors.

In theory.

"No, thank you," said Qi. "I haven't checked all the cages yet. I'll do it later."

"Whatever," he said, coughing again. He looked Qi up and down and decided she had nothing going for her. He wouldn't try talking to her again. Besides, his cough made it hard to breathe.

What Qi had going for her was her name. Names were very important in China, especially in the era of Xi Jinping, the current president and general secretary of the Chinese Communist Party. The name Xi went back millennia, but only since Xi took power was it revered as a clear indication of righteousness, wisdom and the right to leadership. Since Xi became head of the Party, the number of families claiming to have a Xi in their family history had increased by 16,000 percent. That was a statistical impossibility, but in a country whose population was 1.5 billion—with a B—people, it was hard to disprove.

Qi didn't care about the popularity of the newcomer Xi. Qi knew that she had some connection—blood, spirit, soul, talent, though sadly not financial—with a great artist. The artist's name was KiKi Dee, who pronounced her name exactly the same as Qi did. Qi Qi Dieh. KiKi Dee. Get it? And Qi knew that Ki, or rather KiKi, was one of the greatest musicians of all time. She knew this because she had once been a member of the KiKi Dee fansite that she learned about on Alibaba, which was the eighth most popular website in the world. Alibaba was the source of much of Qi's wisdom, aside from what she had learned at the second-rate school where she had earned a first. When she realized the spiritual connection she had with KiKi, Qi Qi had ordered a picture calendar featuring twelve photos of the iconic star. Six of the twelve showed KiKi singing with a strange-looking man who wore laughably ugly eyeglasses and dressed in a bizarre yellow and purple outfit with sequins. Qi later learned that the man was some sort of homosexual who played the piano. Probably KiKi's accompanist, Qi surmised. A man, certainly a man who dressed and looked like this accompanist, would quickly find himself in a jail cell in China, where his shiny clothes and gaudy glasses would get him raped many times a day. Perhaps he would like that.

Sixty yuan, the calendar had cost, but it was worth it. At least Qi thought it was worth it, and was sure it would be, if and when it ever arrived. She had enquired of Alibaba when she might expect her treasure by sending an email to the website's customer service department. When she demurely mentioned this to one of the few people at the Lab who spoke to her, she had been humiliated to learn that that particular email was widely known as Styx. Styx was a river in the west somewhere, maybe Greece. Anyone who crossed the Styx never returned. So much for customer service.

Which is why on this particular early evening, Qi had a smelly bat in a plastic bag that she had retrieved from the biological experimentation dustbin. After a long spiritual and moral self-examination—about 20 seconds—Qi had decided to take the bat to the Wuhan Farmer's wet market. She hoped she could recoup her 60 yuan there. And buy her KiKi Dee calendar somewhere else.

"Farmer's Market" was a euphemistic way to describe the massive sprawl that Qi was entering. The closest thing to a farmer in this sprawl of urban blight was the old woman who sold soup. She had once *visited* a farm, she told Qi. She didn't like it and had never left Wuhan again. Most of the merchants in this market were city-slickers, shrewdies who knew nothing more about crops than how to sell them for a profit. The meats, vegetables, hearty fruits that could survive the weather around Wuhan—scorching in the summers, blisteringly cold in winter—were delivered on an irregular basis by agents of the farmers who lived in the fields and hills. The farmers themselves seldom tried to sell their own wares to the market thieves. They were either illiterate or afraid of showing themselves anyplace where officials of the Party might ask for their names, addresses, or worst of all, relatives. Chinese farmers despised the Communist Party. It had taken a land of rich soil, capable of bearing crops of all kinds, and turned it into a poverty-stricken, infertile, polluted, crime-ridden country where Party hacks who barely knew from what direction the sun rose, decided crop quotas which were never met, and then reported false figures to whatever higher-ups controlled them. The higher-ups then passed on the bogus numbers to other even higher-ups, having first taken bribes from their own underlings to cover up the lies. And how did that turn out? Much of China was starving.

Just as in every communist country where Party flunkies controlled the food chain, China spawned its own gray market system. It wasn't official. It wasn't organized. It wasn't exactly illegal, although merchants who forgot to pay off the spies who infiltrated the market often disappeared overnight. It was just the "Farmer's Market." Its main products were intimidation, bribery, blackmail, extortion, and most plentiful of all its output—misery.

It had begun growing when Wuhan did. That was when the Party decided that this was the perfect location to begin building factories, then roads that connected the factories, then huge coal-fired, smoke belching plants to supply the factories with electricity, then storehouses to stockpile the factories' outputs, then—wait, what are we forgetting? – oh yeah, some stores to sell undersized, unclean, tasteless, probably dangerous food to the 11 million workers and their families who would eventually populate the new Chinese "success story."

Then, because most people dislike the idea of starving to death or living on the putrid produce that the state-run food suppliers sold, a real black market was born. Farmers who could camouflage a portion of their fields used the land to grow and tend crops the way their ancestors had done for thousands of years. They diverted water from the state-built irrigation system, collected cow and horse manure to nourish their secret fields, found the seeds needed to grow vegetables, fruits and grains so that their cows, sheep and pigs would be fed, then butchered the animals once they had produced a new generation, and so ensured that their illicit enterprises—so far superior to the state version of farming—would continue.

Farmers know how to grow, not sell, their produce. The few who tried to be businessmen were quickly informed upon, rousted by Party heavy-hands, denounced as criminals, and stripped of the land the state had so generously allowed them to tend on behalf of the Party. They learned quickly that the best way to sell off-market produce was to find middlemen who would pay them a more-or-less fair price, then transport the bounty to Wuhan and sell it with a suitable markup to make their criminal efforts worthwhile. And who were these middlemen, these profiteers who worked the margins of legality for a margin of profit? The same heavy-hands who the Party sent out to terrorize the farmers. One day they would scream imprecations at the brow-beaten tenants of the land. The next day they would return with smiles and a ledger of prices that they would pay for the black market crops.

This, they told their powerless prey, was Socialism with Chinese characteristics. In Chinese, it was called *Zhongguo tese shehui zhuyi*. Making a profit was no longer a crime. But never accept a yuan of profit without handing part of it to the Party's muscle men. To do otherwise, they instructed the farmers, would be unpatriotic. Ordinary Chinese referred to this new social philosophy as *Dahuangyan*—the Big Lie.

Lie or no lie, the farmer's market in Wuhan grew, and grew. And grew.

This being China, there were rules about how the market had to be operated. The first and primary rule being that the Party was in charge. That would ensure that everything was done correctly, that the produce sold at the market met the strict safety and hygienic standards set by the Party for the safety of customers, that the scales that weighed out the grain, the oil, the rice, the fish—were accurate, so that citizens of the People's Republic knew they were not being cheated.

*Dahuangyan.*

The merchants of the market knew that the Party hacks who had been given control of the premises could be bribed to allow anything. Not almost anything, but anything. The sliding scale of bribes was much more accurate than the scales that weighed the food. Those could be fiddled with, so that a kilo of rice actually weighed about 85,000 centigrams, not 100,000. Sometimes a small stone or piece of metal was placed on the scale before the rice was poured out, then removed before the rice was funneled into bags to be sold. Some customers brought their own scales to the market to weigh merchandise for themselves. These undesirables were shooed away, pelted with the very stones that had been added to the scales to deceive them. Second-time offenders usually got a visit, sometimes at work, more often at home, by groups known as "safety committees" who warned them to stop making problems or face the wrath of the Party.

Socialism with Chinese characteristics.

Qi knew all this. At one time, she had found it surprising that the Party would condone such behavior, considering the thundering denunciations of corruption that Xi and the lesser leaders presented from the podium of the People's Palace of the Revolution. It took her very little time to realize that like salmon, the bribes from the merchants to the local Party hacks made their way upstream. Some bribes the locals were allowed to pocket in lieu of being paid to do their jobs. Other bribes, or a portion of them, were passed along, up the ladder of authority, so that everyone got a little piece of every pie. Or a bag of rice, or fish, or ginger, or salt, or ... bats.

Bats have been part of the diet of China for millennia. Mostly they were used for soup. The most common recipe uses fruit bats, which are the most tender species. You take a large fruit bat, wash (but don't skin or de-fur it), throw it in boiling water, add hot peppers, salt, onions, soy sauce, lemon juice, and if you can find any, coconut milk. The chance of finding any of these ingredients aside from the salt in a state-run shop is about the same chance you have of catching a bat with one hand. But the farmer's markets somehow manage to stock all these things, including bats.

Best not to ask how they were caught or by whom.

Qi knew all this because she had snuck dead bats out of the bio lab before and sold them in the farmer's market. She didn't really care how the bats died, nor did the little man she sold her bats to. His name, at least the name he used, was Wang Win. Qi called him Gramps, which he seemed to like. He also liked the size of her bottom and her breasts, but aside from accidentally grazing them, did nor said nothing about it. Which was fine with Qi if it encouraged Gramps to pay a few extra yuan for her bats.

What happened with them later was not her problem. Let the Party handle it. Gramps felt the same way. Not his problem. Party wants to be in charge, let them handle the outcome.

"Hello, Gramps."

"Ah, shi-shi bottom. How are you?"

"Fine," she said, extending the Lab waste bag. "Sixty and nothing less."

The look on Gramps's face as soon as he opened the bag told Qi she was not getting sixty yuan.

"Smells terrible," he said, revulsion overcoming his businessman's instinct.

"Adds flavor to the soup."

"If it doesn't kill you. Twenty."

"Fifty."

"Twenty-five, and if you say another word, you can take this vermin back home with you."

Qi of course had no intention of ever bringing this bat, or any other one, into her apartment. Its smell would pervade the entire 30 square meters within an hour and make sleep impossible. She already had to contend with a leaky radiator, water that occasionally came out brown from her sink, and a neighbor with a Korean sounding name, Sun. Plus, her calendar hadn't arrived.

She figured she could probably get thirty for the bat somewhere else, but smelling it again, after Gramps had opened the bag made her want this to be over with as soon as possible.

"Done."

Gramps handed over the yuan. Held the bag at arm's length, kept it folded shut so the odor wouldn't escape, looked at Qi and said, "I can probably get fifty for it if I tell someone it's exotic."

"It is, Gramps. It is."

He handed over the money, seemed to lose control of his hands and cupped her bottom for a second. She let him.

"Anyway," said the old man, shrugging. "Not my market, not my problem."

*Zhongguo tese shehui zhuyi.*

# Chapter 2
## Invasion

You could say many things about Luisa Moretti. She could be gruff, stubborn, secretive, uncooperative and at times, downright cantankerous.

But no one could call her gullible. It wasn't easy, probably not even possible, to fool her. She had spent her fifty-eight years on earth with an almost pathological fear of being taken advantage of. Use her, abuse her, malign her or ignore her. Just don't ever let it be said that she had been bamboozled. Clever didn't cover her. Nor did suspicious, nor disbelieving. Probably the word that came closest was *onniveggente*, which really only worked in Italian but translated as something like all-seeing. Luisa wasn't rich. She wasn't powerful. She wasn't even right all the time.

But she always knew what was going on and usually why. The *nonna* had taught her that.

Grandma Silvia was the strongest person—male or female—that Luisa had ever known. And the proudest. In short, the most Italian of Italians. And short she was. Barely over five-feet tall, but what did height matter when you possessed innate *hauteur.*

"My child, you are one of the world's fortunate souls," *La nonna* would say anytime Luisa wanted to complain about something. "You are a daughter of Italy; even better, of Lombardy. There is no tradition more honorable, richer, fuller of history and culture."

*La nonna* had spent most of her life as a seamstress in one of the most famous clothing mills of Northern Italy, which was itself the most famous region of the country when it came to quality cloth and garments. For a widow on a *pensioniera's* income, she lived extremely well. She went to the Prato outdoor market nearly every day to buy fresh fruits, vegetables, occasionally *bistecca,* which she marinated for hours before turning it into a meal as smooth as cashmere.

And *La nonna* knew cashmere. It was her specialty, actually. The most complicated wool, and certainly the finest. Pashmina goats provided the smoothest, most pleasing hair in existence. The hair itself, received in clumps, was a delight to touch. It felt more like a thick soup than an animal's covering. But the true magnificence of cashmere was what could be done to it on a loom. And there, *La nonna* had no peer.

Her love of fine clothing materials—wool, naturally, but also cotton—had been taught her by her own mother. And when her son, long ago deceased, presented her with a bright-eyed granddaughter whose hands were small enough to work a loom and quick enough to do it efficiently, *La nonna* decided that this child, this Luisa, would be her gift to the next generation of Italian fashion designers.

"*Piano, piano,*" *La nonna* would murmur as Luisa worked. "Go slowly, but never let your hands be still." It was advice not only for weaving, but for life.

They spent hundreds of hours practicing the skills of seamstressing, weaving, laughing at the little girl's early failures, toasting her later, obvious abilities, with a small glass of *prosecco,* into which she dropped a sugar cube, because what is accomplishment without reward? And in that narrow, love-filled lane that only grandmothers and grand-daughters can traverse together, Luis learned to love the cloth, love the trade, love the loom, love the woman who had shown her what Italians do better than anyone. And always will.

*La nonna* died clutching a scrap of cashmere that she herself had loomed and kept under her pillow for decades. It was regularly washed, dried outdoors—never in a machine—and was a source of comfort on nights when she couldn't sleep, or was in pain, more and more frequently, from the growth in her stomach that eventually took her away.

Luisa had taken the scrap of cashmere from her grandmother's finally-still hands and promised herself that she would ply that craft with honor, and ability, and love. Because the fabric from the mills of

Prato and the other towns of Northern Italy was actually its soul, its being, its … fabric.

The years passed, and Luisa, never married, never interested in that distraction, saw the ebbs and flows of the economy, saw the endless turnstile comings and goings of Italy's political circus. But what remained largely untouched, was the reputation and quality of its fabrics. "Made in Italy," was not just a label. It was a guarantee. A benediction. A pact.

When she went to work first as a weaver, then a master weaver, then a seamstress, and finally designer, she never let herself forget that she was part of a tradition of national pride. She allowed herself no mistakes and was not shy about pointing out the inadequacies of her workmates. This did not make Luisa any more popular, but she knew it was part of the price of being the best. And she knew she was the best.

And then, in a matter of a few years, it was all torn apart as surely and cruelly as scissors can slice their way through hours of labor without thought.

Today, for instance, as she left her tidy two-bedroom house just off Via Pistoiese, wearing a brown wool dress that had come from the mill where she worked and had lasted twenty years without losing its shape, she spied a gaggle of boys—young men, really—rollicking through the neighborhood, laughing furiously at nothing in particular, pounding each other's backs, and saying, well, God knows what.

In Chinese.

Where once they had been content to stay in the ghetto appropriated for them, now they were everywhere. Luisa hadn't seen any Chinese families move into her street. But that was because very few of the Chinese who lived here now had brought families with them.

There were young single men, hired to do the manual labor at the clothing mills. And middle aged and older women, hired to do what Luisa could do better than anyone else in this town. Weave material into the fabric of dreams.

She was a master weaver and seamstress, having done it for more than thirty years, at a speed and with a grace that made her the envy of her colleagues. She had a self-taught method of feeling the material as it came off the loom, knowing through some instinct deep inside her if it was good enough to be called "Italian-made." It was a term she held in reverence. She hardly thought about what was sliding through her fingers these days, but she could produce more quality goods than anyone around her. "Lightning Luisa," they called her. She wasn't arrogant about it. She showed younger women her technique, was pleased when their weaving improved. Then a Chinese millionaire bought the mill where she worked. And brought in hordes of Chinese workers, who knew nothing about cloth, or technique. Or manners.

For Luisa, it was like being told that she did her job too well, and she was being replaced by someone who did worse work, for less pay. The pack of Chinese rolled past her. Two of the boys looked at her and stretched their eyes wide, mocking Luisa's round eyes, round face.

"I hope you trip and poke your eye out," she spat at them. They laughed in ignorance of what she had said, trotted along. A final guffaw from behind her as they made their way to whatever amusement was calling them.

She hated them.

She was north Italian through and through. None of your wine-breath, work-shirking excuse-making Italians from the *mezzogiorno*, which Luisa would have described as any part of the country south of Siena. She had been born in Prato, a town about 12 miles northwest of Florence. As a girl, she rode a family hand-me-down bike everywhere, waving gaily to people she knew and also to those she did not. It was safe. It was home.

One time, decades ago, a middle-aged man who lived near Prato stopped Luisa on her bicycle and asked her what her name was. She told him. He asked if she liked Swiss chocolates. Luisa said she did. The man produced one, an egg-sized Lindt milk chocolate, wrapped in gold foil, and gave it to Luisa. She thanked him, turned her bike 180 degrees and sped away home, and told her father, who worked in the garment mills, what had happened. Three days later, the man, who had been known to approach little girls before, was found hanging from a tree, in the woods. Suicide, the police concluded. That was the kind of town Prato was, and, even though it was unjust, it was better that way than it was now.

There were other cities in the north. There was Parma, so neat and clean it might have been German. Parma was a wealthy city, known all over the world for its cheese and its ham. Luisa knew before she was six that she wanted to make neither cheese nor ham. They were good, yes, and made Parmesan an adjective that made mouths drool, and made many of its inhabitants wealthy. But Italian pasta was also legendary, as was its *ragu alla Bolognese*, and she wasn't interested in producing them either. Or living in Bologna, where it seemed three out of four citizens had stuffed themselves with their famous pasta and sauce to keep anyone else from getting any of it. The Bolognese were fat, self-satisfied, and, as far as Luisa could tell, in no hurry to change anything about themselves or their city.

Milan was different—a city-state unto itself. She hated Milan's nickname—"Italy's second city"—which of course suggested it was somehow inferior to or less than Rome. Well, let's see. Milan was, for a city of its size, remarkably clean, and clean mattered to Luisa. Rome was a cesspit, where the garbage rotted on the streets for weeks, the water was befouled, the famous Tiber River had shrunk on a trickle of shit-infested liquid, and the people—oh, God, the Romans—were filthy, ill-mannered, uneducated, lazy animals. And those were the citizens who belonged there. Never mind the criminal immigrants from Africa who seemed to arrive in their pre-historic seacraft like flies smelling of rotting cow. The more rotten the cow, the more flies.

Now Firenze—Florence to English speakers—was another matter. Florence was art. History. Culture. Civilization. Its museums were, of course, world renowned, as was its architecture. It was the spiritual home of Buonarroti, Ghiberti, Bramante. The Arno flowed through Florence at a dignified, leisurely pace, as if suggesting that pedestrians crossing its many bridges slow down, look around, and savor what they were seeing. Far more than Rome, which perhaps had a better public relations department, Florence belonged to no one, but to time, a gift from heaven to all of us.

That was the beginning of the problem.

A few years after the new millennium began, a fast-talking, wide-grinning charlatan named Michele Tenzi became president of the province of Florence, a title that effectively made him the city's mayor. It was an inauspicious time. Having survived the make-believe scare of Y2K, Italy was reveling in its status as a leading member of the European Union. It didn't contribute much to the then 16-nation confederation, but it certainly accepted quite a bit from wealthier, harder-working countries like Germany and the Netherlands. Budget deficits were as much a part of Italy as spaghetti, but for decades after World War II—where Italy changed sides at the last moment—Italy's 100 plus prime ministers just shrugged and tacked on the amount owed to next year's budget. Italy was so deeply in debt to bankers around the world that politicians started reciting Mussolini's famous line: "Governing Italy isn't impossible. It's useless."

In 2008, as the American financial crisis started to cross oceans and bring other economies down, Italy started to notice it was harder to find banks stupid enough to buy its government bonds, which were, after all, based on the patently false promise that Italy would someday pay them back.

What all Italy's learned economists and devious politicians couldn't comprehend, or wouldn't admit was transparently obvious to Luisa: if you can't afford something, don't buy it. Even better, don't covet it. Best still: Don't even spend as much as you have but save some for later. Such anachronistic thinking was, of course, pooh-poohed by the great thinkers of the government and the *Confindustria*, the association of Italian businesses. The *Confindustria* could just as well have been called La Cosa Nostra, since its main goal was to make money for its members, usually at the expense of ordinary Italians. The genius minds of the *Confindustria* had confidently guided Italy into such staggering debt to the European Union and dozens of private banks that it awarded itself a special prize for "forward thinking" – *Testa nel avanti*. Lots of Italians referred to this prize as the *"Testa su per il culo"* – head up your ass.

Michele Tenzi was one of these forward thinkers. He felt confident that he had a solution to his country's plight. Without telling anyone what he was thinking, Tenzi got on a plane, flew to Beijing where he had secretly scheduled appointments with the heads of several Chinese banks to which Italy was deeply in debt. In the briefcase he carried with him, Tenzi had the financial breakdowns for some of Italy's trademark companies—the trusty carmaker Fiat, for example, but also the much more stylish and expensive car company, Ferrari. Spaced among the rows of financial stats, Tenzi had high-quality color pictures of Ferraris in their showrooms, on the road, some being driven by beautiful light-haired Italian women whose smiles radiated out of the pages into the bankers' boardrooms.

Here is what Tenzi knew: Chinese men (and of course all the bankers he met in Beijing and Shanghai were men) like blondes. They also like fast cars. Neither was readily available in China. But both could be imported *en masse* if the bankers *owned* these companies.

It was not difficult to imagine such a transaction. Despite their fame, their glamorous image around the world, Italy's companies were, by and large, being managed as poorly as its government. The CEOs of once-successful Italian companies—carmakers, steel makers, fashion houses, sports teams—had, as if by secret covenant, driven their enterprises into irreversible debt. The CEOs, much like the government's pinhead economic advisers, made bad or ridiculously risky investments, overpaid themselves many times what they were worth, shrugged and paid off the union leaders who constantly threatened them with damaging work stoppages, failed to invest in their corporate infrastructure. The companies who lived behind slogans like *bella figura* were in fact living embodiments of its exact opposite— *bruta figura.*

Next, Tenzi showed the Chinese bankers pictures of his opulent city, Florence. Its towering Duomo and equally historic and beautiful churches like Maria Novella, Santa Maria and Santa Croce. He showed them Michelango's 17-foot-tall masterpiece, David, in the Accademia, the Pitti Palace, the unmatched temple of culture, the Uffizi Gallery. All these and more, Tenzi told them, were side benefits of investing in Italy.

The Chinese bankers liked blondes and fast cars. But they also coveted the classy beauty of the west, and of Western Europe especially. Yes, China had it own many-thousand-year history and culture. But deep down, educated Chinese knew that their art, their architecture, their sculpture, in short, their *everything*, couldn't touch the subtle genius of Italy's master creators of art, fashion, motor engineering, shoes, dresses, suits, silks, wools, marble and on and on.

With Tenzi to guide them, the bankers began a systematic, secret, stealthy campaign to identify Italian businesses that had been mismanaged to near extinction, offer absurdly high amounts to buy them outright or at least take majority control of their stock, and replace the bumbling billionaires who ran them into the ground with a new breed of executives—Chinese ones.

Socialism with Chinese characteristics.

The best place to invade is some place where you already have an army.

Prato. It was close to Florence, so the invaders could enjoy the art and architecture they had heard about but never dreamed of seeing. It contained dozens of factories, some of the absolute highest quality, others which for decades had taken recycled wool and other fabrics and turned them into knockoffs of the hand-made tailored fashions that nonetheless bore the label "Made in Italy." The knockoffs now made in Prato by Chinese laborers bore the same labels (although sometimes a place misspelled one of the words, like "Ilaty," because none of the Chinese employees knew what they meant) as the top-grade goods, because, hey, Prato was part of Italy, wasn't it?

Within a few years, Via Pistoiese, which once fronted dozens of *salumiere, pastisserie, pizzarie, panaderie,* was a long, seemingly endless row of noodle shops, fast Chinese takeout, incense and trinket joints that also sold long-distance phone cards, sex at massage parlors, and money transfer services. Bewildered longtime residents walked through streets they had known all their lives and didn't hear a word of Italian being spoken. The newcomers who seemed to have arrived from nowhere and overnight looked at the townspeople with slanted, suspicious eyes. On the street where the seven-year-old Luisa had once ridden a bike and waved to everyone, stick-ups and rapes became so common they were not even investigated by the police.

That might have owed something to the fact that three of the seven town council members, who were appointed by the prefecture of nearby Florence (of which Tenzi was the president) were Chinese immigrants. Part of the agreement Tenzi had made with the Chinese moneylenders was that in order to purchase distressed companies and turn them into tax-paying, revenue-enhancing enterprises, the Chinese newcomers needed to be part of the local governments where Chinese employees were working and living.

It was not as if working was all the Chinese immigrants did. They too had seen the pictures of Florence, the abundant art and architectural treasures that lay within the city's walls. The textile workers rented buses to take them as a group to see these wonders. They paraded through the streets of Florence in groups of a hundred or more, armed with selfie-sticks attached to their mobile phones' cameras. If other tourists were in the way, these self-same selfie-sticks were useful for poking them out of the Chinese explorers' path.

But when they weren't spear-fishing their way through the Uffizi, or prodding at the Statue of David's legs and privates with their cameras, the Chinese residents of Prato did work. Long hours for low wages. In fact, some of the newly acquired Chinese businesses in Prato didn't pay their employees anything. At least not directly. Instead of salaries, the companies made arrangements to have the workers' earnings deposited directly in bank accounts back in China, so their families could use them. This suited most of the workers fine. They didn't have to wire money to China, always a risky undertaking when it passed through so many middlemen's sticky hands. And they slowly, surely began to forget about buying the phone cards needed to make calls to China from public payphones.

Workers, especially women, who failed to turn in their daily production quotas received one warning from a supervisor, which was usually administered in private and was often accompanied by unwanted touching and coerced sexual pleasuring. No one was foolish enough to complain out loud about this abuse. Because after a second failure to meet management expectations, the unsatisfactory employee was put on a cargo ship from the Italian port of Bari in southeastern Italy and mailed, literally, to China. Few survived the journey.

Not surprisingly, the economic health of Prato took a sharp rebound for the better. Textile mills and clothing manufacturers owned by Chinese companies were scrupulous about paying local property and retail taxes. Prato's once near-empty treasuries began to swell. Crumbling roads and bridges—like the one that would collapse in Genoa from years of neglect, killing dozens—were repaired, though usually the first ones to get attention were in the neighborhoods taken over by the Chinese.

The "miracle of Prato" began to get attention in newspapers and magazines. Tenzi was mentioned in glowing terms, especially by the television network controlled by his political party. Chinese businessmen flocked to Italy in search of distressed properties. And if a few blondes in Ferraris met them at the airport and accompanied them as they moved around the country, well, what was wrong with that?

It was to the north of Italy that they came, not the south, for the same reason that Willie Sutton gave for robbing banks—that's where the money is. The north is where the banks were. And many of those banks were failing, from decades of mismanagement, poor investment strategies, skimming by executives and mid-level managers, falsified balance sheets, and payoffs to the Mafia and other criminal organizations. The banks' own pension funds as well as other companies' pension schemes that the banks had guaranteed were evaporating at such a quick pace that most would be insolvent in a year or two.

The same was true for mortgages on real estate, commercial properties, individual homes, farms, mom-and-pop stores, private schools, even Church-owned plots. The reason was obvious: no one was paying off the bank loans. Italians have had a centuries-old, intensely proud tradition of not paying their taxes. The usual response to a warning letter that arrives in the mail from the Department of Revenue in the Finance Ministry is *"Bah, fa culo,"* – roughly, stick it you know where. An equally proud tradition is the shrug and knowing smile from tax collectors who know how to play the game too. And so they will take a payoff of two percent of the tax owed in order to scrawl "Paid in Full" on their reports to the Ministry. And the Ministry is then truly surprised and confounded to see that the tax revenues it was told had been paid, couldn't be found. And so, another shrug, and two palms held up, which means: "Whatcha gonna do?"

The Chinese knew what to do.

In 2014, emboldened by what they had learned from Tenzi, the Chinese went on a buying tear that would make Imelda Marcos look like a coupon-clutching bargain hunter. Real estate, banks, transportation lines, shipping companies, telephone and Internet carriers. The Chinese bought anything that was for sale. And some things that weren't for sale, they got their hands on through some unusual means.

Many of the purchases were in violation of Italian and European Union regulations and trade agreements. To bypass the E.U. regulators,

Italy's government provided falsified figures, covered up other purchases with Italian-owned shell companies that were financed with Chinese money, and permitted, no encouraged, misleading and simply untrue guarantees of how those Ferraris, that specialty steel, those brand-name fashion icons like Gucci, Prada, Krizia, Dolce y Gabana, Canali, Tacchini, Ferragamo, Armani, luxury yachts by Ferreti, cherished Italian vintage wines, and yes, that famous Parma ham and Parmesan cheese, were being produced. In a matter of two years, with Tenzi's encouragement, the Chinese government and government-owned companies controlled more than three hundred formerly Italian enterprises, accounting for 27 percent of Italy's total economic output.

Not all the purchases were of sexy brand names. A Chinese telecom known as Huawei got its hooks into Italy's two main telecommunications firms, ENI and ENEL, and used their facilities to expand research into 5G technology. This ran completely counter to Huawei's public declarations that it was not attempting to create a 5G network anywhere outside China. That claim was backed up by Tenzi. Huawei used ENI's and ENEL's information-sharing agreements with other European and American telecommunications firms to soak up classified documents and ship them back to Beijing.

The one sector that Chinese businessmen wouldn't touch was health care. Much of Italy's health care is state-run and was once the envy of continental Europe. But budget cuts, the usual government mismanagement, cut-rate and sometimes outright falsified certificates and licenses granted to doctors and nurses who paid for their diplomas rather than waste time studying, and purchases of counterfeit and watered-down drugs, shoddily manufactured surgical gear and instruments had reduced the once-proud Italian medical profession to institutional incompetence.

When an earthquake leveled several of the villages around Amatriciana, east of Rome, in 2015, China, like many Western countries, sent doctors, nurses and technicians to the disaster area. The Chinese team however, impressed their colleagues from other countries, not by their competence or compassion, but by their resolute unwillingness to perform the necessary life-saving work for which they were purportedly there. Instead, the puzzled Westerners reported, the

Chinese seemed to be preoccupied with making written reports about how Italy had responded to a disaster of that magnitude.

Luisa knew about the China-Amatriciana scandal, because she had gone to the disaster zone to help in any way she could. She had few medical skills. She was a professional seamstress, with a shop of her own in Prato. In years past, she had worked on a free-lance basis for Armani and had even met Giorgio himself ("a real gentleman", she recalled to friends).

But once the Chinese came to town, she complained about them loudly at any public meeting where citizens were allowed to speak out. "They are dangerous. They don't care about the work they do. They don't care about coworkers who aren't Chinese. They don't care about Prato and they don't care about Italy."

Usually, she was shouted down and dismissed as a kook, a troublemaker. After all, hadn't the streets and bridges been repaired with tax money from the new Chinese-owned shops? So what if you can no longer buy a cannoli on Via Pistoiese? Plenty of other shops still sold them. Buy some Peking duck instead. Or try the bat soup. Italy has nothing like it. You have to accept other cultures and their tastes, Luisa. That's how the world works now.

Until finally, after months and months of trying to be heard and instead being insulted, Luisa did what her culture and countrymen had taught her how to do.

She shrugged. No longer her problem.

She would be among the first to sicken.

# Chapter 3
## Boomerang

For as long as he could remember—though friends later said it was not always so—Henry had longed to be somewhere else. Anyplace but where he was. He had grown up in a town in northwest Jersey. Perfectly fine town. Good schools, which is why people moved there. An easy shot into New York City, if you liked big cities. Mostly pleasant neighbors, and pretty safe from the kinds of crimes that had moved beyond urban areas and now affected lots of suburban neighborhoods.

To Henry, his parents' lives and the life they had given him were artificial.

And here he was again. Back in his parents' perfectly nice house in his perfectly sloppy bedroom, the one he had slept in for seventeen years.

He had done all the right things, as a boy and as a teenager. Made the good grades, been in the science club, had a couple of good friends so no one could call him anti-social. Been accepted to Columbia, which had been his stretch school and was the priciest of the ones he'd applied to, but his parents said it was well worth the cost.

They soon regretted their generosity. Columbia seemed tailor-made to feed Henry's wish to be elsewhere. He wandered the campus, never far from graffiti, or posters, or demonstrations that derided America. Unequal. Racist. Warmongering. Unfair to women, to minorities, and to students. Like them. Like Henry. It took him a while, but Henry learned the slogans, and mantras, the undiluted bile that came from the student speakers denouncing the campus and the country that provided them with the freedom to speak as they did.

And he had Khadija, who he wanted to believe was his girlfriend, but he wasn't sure. Khadija was a product of $21^{st}$ Century American womanhood—post-lib, pro-MeToo, and definitely anti-having any man telling her what to do. Part of her tolerance of Henry as a companion and occasional sex partner was that Henry never appeared too concerned about what she did when she wasn't with him, never asking probing questions, and seemed to agree with most of her opinions, though he might not have since they didn't discuss them much. Theirs was a sex-ship founded on her complete independence and could founder anytime that independence was threatened. To Khadija, it was perfect. Henry enjoyed the sex but wanted to be somewhere else. This felt artificial.

He double majored in political history and computer studies, more inclined toward the latter. Because universities had been bullied into minimizing courses dealing with America and other Anglo-European cultures, so they could concentrate on other parts of the world, Henry took Asian History, and courses like Chinese Political philosophy, China Versus the World, and Communist Development in Asia. These courses were fine, and deepened his conviction that the Western world, especially the United States, was in an irreversible downward spiral. Confident in that knowledge, Henry became addicted to a science in which China was the unquestioned leader, and America a stumbling laggard.

AI. Artificial intelligence. Humans think they're unique, that they alone can think, make decisions, replicate their actions, identify problems and find solutions to them. That, Henry knew and would prove, was bunk.

It had been in high school that Henry began regularly—actually, obsessively—watching YouTube clips about Artificial Intelligence, while it was still little-known and almost never discussed. The notion of inanimate objects performing tasks previously reserved for the human brain was fascinating to him. He had watched video of when IBM's computer, Deep Blue, outplay chess grandmaster Gary Kasparov. The sight of the defeated Kasparov with his head in his hands was deeply satisfying.

In truth, Henry held most humans in low regard. Especially the ones he encountered on a day-to-day basis in school, at a shopping mall, at a ball game. Henry was fairly certain that the average intellect of a fan at a major league baseball game, let alone an attendee at a hockey match, would be lower than that of the earliest-generation AI robot.

He loved watching the robots at work, and, more recently, since he had time on his hands, at play. They were more genuine, and genuinely humane, than humans. They didn't lie unless they were programmed to do so. They didn't cheat at their tasks, always making sure that they were a hundred percent complete. Robots didn't shift blame, and most pleasing of all, had not yet learned to be selfish.

Henry looked with disdain at most of the people he had encountered at high school and university, and the sloppy habits, manners and thinking patterns that most Americans seemed to have adopted. American know-how? In fact, few knew how. Exceptionalism? Except when something went wrong. The American Dream? More like dreamers. As Henry became more observant, and obsessive, about the superiority of AI, he grew more hostile toward the obvious disadvantages of being human. Or at least, the humans who inhabited America.

Perhaps it was then that Henry recognized what had been building inside him for years: if America didn't want to change, and if he couldn't change it, then he would go somewhere else.

And then, in one day, it all came crashing down. The start-up AI research company he had joined after college was always on the edge of financial peril. Henry didn't mind the skimpy salary, the lack of health care (he could stay on his parents' plan until he was twenty-six), the long hours, the lack of feedback on how he was doing.

"I'm like, really sorry, Henry," said the woman who had hired him, "like, we like you and all, but it's like, with this virus going around, nobody's interested in AI. They've all, like, got bigger problems."

"AI's not a problem, Arlene. It's a solution."

"Well, it isn't, like, solving my payroll problem."

"I'll work from home."

"You can work from home. But I can't, like, pay you." And that was, like, that.

"Home," until that day, had been an apartment that he'd shared with Khadija on Second Avenue in lower Manhattan. They'd split everything: rent, food bills, electricity, even split roach patrol. They split the bill for meals out. And when he told her he wouldn't be getting paid anymore, *she* split.

It wasn't the American Dream. But Henry's dream was different anyway.

And here he was, back "home" in his parents' house. He hated going down to eat with them, knowing he was back to that dependent status that millions of young Americans now shared: a boomerang kid. All messed up and no place to go. He dug in on AI.

Nothing succeeds like excess, as Mr. Wilde mildly observed. Henry's fantasies turned into fanaticism, and, in keeping with 21$^{st}$ Century American values, his over-the-top-ism about AI was, quite randomly, recognized and rewarded. The online Columbia alumni newsletter advertised a free lecture on AI and Henry, of course, signed up. The lecturer was Hui Jen-Sho, billed as China's leading researcher on AI. His remarks were mesmerizing, at least to Henry. And Henry took special delight in seeing Hui shut down when some students started talking to each other and laughing during the talk. The master lecturer simply went quiet, nodded once, and two Chinese private security guards who had accompanied him to the lecture descended on the offenders and politely escorted them out of the auditorium.

This, thought Henry, was the world in which he wanted membership. Individuals, especially those with whom he disagreed, must be subservient to the greater good. If the silence of disapproval is not enough, then sterner measures should and must be employed.

He wrote an email to Hui, lavishly praising him for his brilliant insights and mastery of the crowd to which he had spoken. He wondered in writing if Hui would be offering any further master classes, anywhere in the world, and if he, who appreciated what Hui was trying to get across, might be allowed to attend, at his own expense of course. His snooping Mother read the email and pronounced its recipient's name Mr. Hooey, because that, she said, is what he was full of.

For the most part, Henry's parents were smart enough to realize they had a bright and talented son. Occasionally he would rail against

America and its shortcomings. College had done something to him. Made him more negative about the country he was lucky enough to have been born in. Things would change, once he got out of this virus-induced rut.

They tried their best to accommodate the presence of an adult son who had moved back to his bedroom and spent most of his time there reading and doing mysterious things on his laptop. And they were quietly pleased about his breakup with Khadija, a girl who, though attractive and intelligent, was just a bit too opinionated for their conservative taste. When he took the bus into New York, they suspected it was to see her, but it was not a topic of discussion. Henry's sex life, they concluded, mostly involved his laptop.

To Henry's surprise and delight, his email was answered, not by Hui himself, of course. That would have been too great an honor to expect. But an assistant took the time and trouble to thank Henry for his letter and—and this was what Henry would later consider the turning point of his life—invited Henry to attend Hui's next lecture in New York, and then to meet the master himself.

Henry threw himself into an exhaustive marathon reading about every aspect of AI he could imagine. He knew he was only scratching the surface, merely raking away the chaff that fell from the splendid stalks of golden wheat that sprang from Hui's brilliance.

The second lecture was at NYU, miles and minds away from the august, socially active Columbia campus. Henry arrived early, saw that no one was being admitted yet, and began to drift away in search of a Coke.

"All yir misser Hinris?" The woman looked at him with an expression that was either instantaneous dislike or trans-oceanic incomprehension, Henry was not sure which.

"Hinris? Yir?"

"My name is Henry, yes."

"Ah, vey goo. Yir con."

You couldn't call the woman's English comprehensible. It was the typical blurred mismatch of syllables that many Asians used, especially if they had not had sufficient language training.

"Me? Come with you?"

"Shi," she nodded and stretched her lips so that he could see the tan teeth behind them. Her tooth tone was accentuated by bronze-colored wire-rim glasses she wore at a slightly askew angle.

The lip stretch, he reckoned, was a stand-in for a smile.

She led him down a corridor where Asians, mostly men, occupied cubicles separated by Plexiglas, which Henry surmised was to counter the close proximity in which they seemed to be working. They all wore blue surgical masks. Why did they need protection, he wondered? As he and the tan-toothed woman passed, each raised his head, crinkled his eyes, frowned slightly, and returned to whatever task occupied him. It was the opposite of a welcome. Henry wondered how they had appropriated an entire corridor of a prestigious place of learning like NYU. An inner voice told him—because they're important people, working on AI. Just like Mr. Hui.

Some symbols of prominence are global. Henry somehow knew that when they came to the end of the corridor, there would be a corner office. Corridor corner, he thought fleetingly, but only fleetingly, because as they went through the open door of the office foyer, a ravishingly beautiful woman looked up from her desk, closed her lovely eyes, frowned, and nodded once, abruptly, to Tanteeth.

Oh. My. God, thought Henry, who at that instant thought he would have traded all the AI robots on earth, and all the Khadijas, for a chance to touch that face. She had a perfect face, high cheekbones, only the slightest of Asian-looking eyes, long black hair, and a trim lithe body under a tight-fitting black pantsuit. She wore no mask.

"Re rate," Tanteeth said to Henry, and when he looked at her stupidly, the ravishing woman at the desk said in frozenly perfect English, "Please wait here." She rose from her chair and knocked, once, with the deference of a geisha, on the white oak door behind her desk. Though Henry heard nothing, the ravisher must have, for she opened the door no more than an inch, and said something in between a whisper and a prayer. When she, evidently, received a response, she opened the door halfway, nodded once to Tanteeth, who said to Henry, "Mir We."

Henry, who hated looking stupid though it happened often, could only stare.

"Mr. Hui will see you now," said Rav, and Henry thought he picked up the slightest trace of a British accent. He smiled at Tanteeth, who looked through him, and lowered her head. "If you please," said Rav, and Henry felt impelled to move forward, almost as if a piston behind him had surged. His legs shook slightly though he hoped he concealed it with a falsely confident stride.

The office was by no means sumptuous, but in comparison with the carrels he had passed in the hallway, Henry had no doubt it was the workspace of a superior being. And there sat Hui, dressed in what must have been a two thousand dollar suit, a white shirt that nearly glowed, and chewing, incongruously, on the eraser of a pencil that extruded from his mouth. He removed the pencil, laid it on the desk and with one brief curl of the fingers of his right hand, beckoned Henry into his presence.

"I am glad you liked my lecture at Columbia," Hui said in a smooth, comfortably modulated voice. His English was nearly perfect. "Many people, especially you *gweilos,* think of AI as a trick a magician pulls from his hat." From his China Versus the World class, Henry knew that *gweilo* was a derogatory, not to say racist term that referred to non-Chinese people with round eyes. But white people, Henry figured, had voluntarily surrendered the right to be protected from racism, for fear of being called racists themselves. It made no sense, of course; it was merely one of the thousand ways in which Euro-Americans had offered to humble themselves before all other races in the spirit, they hoped was clear, of global brotherhood. Besides, Henry was in the presence of genius. And genius had earned the right to answer to a different standard of behavior.

"I think you are a brilliant man, professor," Henry said, only realizing once the words had escaped that he meant it.

"Thank you," Hui said, in the tone of one who hears such compliments often, and also believes them. "One small correction. I am not a professor."

"You're not?" Henry looked at Hui as though he had just been told the world was flat.

"No. Technically, I am an instructor. But my actual title is Colonel."

"Colonel? Like military?"

"Not 'like' military. I am a Colonel of the People's Liberation Army."

"The Chinese Army?"

Hui parted his lips to imitate a smile. "Which other Army would have me?"

"Of course. I didn't mean to offend you."

Hui studied him for what seemed a long time. "You have very good manners. Unusual for an American."

It was Henry's turn to imitate a smile. "I suppose it is because I have great respect for you, Prof.... Colonel. And also for China." The last sentence was intended to cover his gaffe of misidentifying Hui twice. "Your country is the leader in AI research."

"Tell me, Henry. What is your profession?"

When you meet someone you admire, you want to make a good first impression. That usually involves lying, to make yourself seem more interesting, successful, and desirable in whatever way you wish to be. Henry was about to say that he worked for an AI start-up. But looking into Hui's eyes, shining with intelligence, Henry opted for the loser's truth.

"I lost my job because of the virus going around. I live with my parents."

"I know," said Hui. He registered Henry's surprise. "We checked. Did you think I would see just anyone who wrote to me?"

Henry could only muster, "You checked on me?"

"Yes," said Hui, clearly amused by this young man's chagrin. "Henry, may I make a suggestion?"

"Of course, Colonel."

"Do not commit yourself just yet to any new job opportunity. At least not until we have spoken again. I have something in mind for you, but I will have to get permission from my superior."

"What kind of thing?" What, Henry's suddenly flooding brain computed, could this man of genius have in mind for him? And who might be his superior?

In his lecturer's voice, Hui said, "The American education system is outdated, superannuated, antiquated. It is based on the idea that Western democracy is the bedrock of human existence. You pass through the system, and now you have no job. You have certain qualities that would be useful to me. But you will have to start your education over, under a superior system."

Henry would have been shocked enough had these words come from a highly trained native English speaker. To hear them from Hui, who obviously had learned English as a second or third language, was stunning. Even as he waited for Hui to continue, he felt that whatever he said was destined to change his life.

Hui did not wait to be asked. "I would like to suggest that you apply for admission to the People's Institute of Artificial Intelligence Research."

Twin shocks. Relearn everything. And Artificial Intelligence! "Where is the institute located, Pr.....Colonel?"

Hui tapped his temple. "It has no physical home. Right now, it is lodged here. Surely if the topic of its research is AI, its location is irrelevant."

"Well, it's just that..."

"Henry," Hui said mildly. "It is something I am creating. And when it is created, I will run it. And I think you are the kind of young man who could make a contribution. To AI. To the future. To humanity."

Hui fluttered his left hand. "I have another meeting. You saw the young lady outside my office? If you accept my offer, she will be your Chinese teacher, and interpreter. And, perhaps, companion. Now, goodbye."

As if by ESP, the office door opened and Rav put her head in. "Please see our young friend out."

"Shi."

Henry now paid much closer attention to Rav. Companion? Did he say companion?

After he left, Tanteeth came in. "So, what do you think?" she asked in Chinese.

Hui looked as if he had just finished a delicious bat soup. "He's perfect."

It was not a compliment.

# Chapter 4
## Stuck In Last

When you grow up in Pittsburgh, you get used to being overlooked. Jerry knew that, because Jerry had lived that. For most of his 30-some years, Jerry had inhabited one area or another of the place that was once proudly named Steel City. He knew old folks who had actually worked in the steel mills that had dotted the Allegheny and Monongahela Rivers. Those two burbling bodies of water found each other at what Pittsburghers call The Point, and westward hence form the Ohio River. It's why first the French, calling it Fort Duquesne, and then the Brits, calling it Fort Pitt, thought the convergence point of two rivers, and further, two rivers heading west, would be the perfect place to build fortifications, house troops, and, because troops have to eat and change clothes (infrequently), create commercial water traffic, open stores, build civilian homes and generally make a city out of the water.

For those who failed history, the Brits threw out the Frogs and the Pitt part stuck. Then the Americans bitch-slapped the Brits and what had been a fort became a burg. Except in this case, it was a 'Burgh, with an H at the end, which was probably just William Pitt putting on airs, but it stuck.

So, Pittsburgh.

Great place to be, if you lived in the 18$^{th}$ or 19$^{th}$ centuries, or even the first half and then some of the 20$^{th}$. Everyone needed steel to build things as the colonies became the states and the states became one country, and then briefly, two countries, and then back to one. But whatever the epoch, steel was needed, whether it was for guns, or girders or wagon wheels or those interesting new iron horses that rolled around and putt-putted and promised to take the place of old Trigger, or Smoky or whatever you called your nag.

Steel in those days was made of a blend of pig iron, which had to be dug up, coal, which also had to be dug up, and limestone, which came from quarries. Conveniently, all three of those substances could be found not far away from Pittsburgh, and transported via the trusty rivers to the place where those rivers met.

Perfect. Well, except for what burning coal, iron and limestone did to the air.

By the early 20th century, Pittsburgh was indeed the Steel City. It was also called the Smoky City. That was okay with most of the half million or so people who lived there. Because the steel mills and related businesses meant that they had jobs. And jobs, it turned out, were more important to most Pittsburghers than air quality.

The so-called "experts" on health and well-being disagreed. Pollution, air particulate, cloud inversion, ground contamination—this is what happens when you make steel. Pittsburgh made steel. It had to stop doing that. Different "experts" arrived from Washington D.C. wearing suits and white shirts. The fronts of most of those shirts had turned gray by lunchtime, a result of the soot that coated Pittsburgh like snow on a winter hillside. They tut-tutted at this despicable condition and went home to write their reports and get their white shirts laundered to their snowy splendor. To do this, they used bleach, which in those days contained calcium hypochlorite, chlorine gas and chlorine dioxide, which also aren't good for people or the place they live. Nobody said anything about that, though, because the "experts" wanted white shirts, and who were mere people to argue with "experts?"

Pittsburghers didn't know, or really care, what was going on until various government agencies started issuing things like injunctions, lawsuits, close-down orders and cease and desists. Then the same Pittsburghers who didn't know or care found out what those things meant: their jobs were gone. They had ceased and desisted from being employed, from earning money for food, rent, school clothes, vacations, and human pride. They were the targets of government "experts", whose shirts had been restored to brilliant whiteness. They were targets because they made a product, steel, that the whole world wanted and needed.

Jerry knew all this because he'd sat at countless family dinners, barbecues, bars and walks in the park where his parents, aunts, uncles, and for a short while, grandparents, would recount the systematic, purposeful destruction of Pittsburgh's power tools—steel mills—and the hollowed-out shell of a city that was left. So, Pittsburghers could be forgiven for not embracing everything that people from Washington told them.

And that was how Jerry felt as he got through high school, then a degree in biology at Park College, a third-rate school in Pittsburgh that would take just about anyone who could come up with $1,000 a semester. That bachelor's degree got Jerry jobs: flipping burgers at Burger King, recording and collating the names of customers of Quest Diagnostics, which told patients how their medical tests had come out, then for a while, as a part-time physical fitness instructor at a gym sponsored by his local Catholic Church and finally, as a junior analyst of viral test results at the University of Pittsburgh Medical Center's Health Care Network, which had taken over from the steel plants as Pittsburgh's biggest employer. He made $34,000 a year and paid $8,000 in taxes. And irony of ironies, he wasn't covered by health insurance by the health care system for which he worked. Not exactly the American Dream.

It was a shit life, being played out in a shitty city that didn't deserve its current shitty fate.

So, who could be surprised that when Donald Trump began his presidential run, people in Pittsburgh heard his message of common talk, up with the little guy, drain the swamp, and get American jobs back, start mining coal and making steel again, and decided to give the guy—orange-haired billionaire though he might be—a chance. Trump carried Pennsylvania, largely because of the working-class vote of Pittsburghers and their neighbors in any other parts of the state that weren't downtown Philadelphia. Blue-collar Democrats voted for him, people who'd never been to college voted for him, people who, like Jerry, had heard about the city's glory days when it made steel, and yes, polluted the air, but earned enough money to keep their families warm, fed and moving forward.

Jerry voted for Trump, liked what he heard from him at first, slowly became worried that the president didn't really know what the fuck he was talking about, and couldn't control his impulses. Jerry would have called himself a conservative more than a Republican. What he really, mostly believed in, was not being told what to do. Not having his livelihood stolen by white-shirted suits from Washington, not letting China take over the world's steel business that had once been headquartered just up the river. Did Chinese steel plants not pollute? Of course they did. But they weren't closed down by bureaucrats, because China didn't care about pollution. China let the United States wring its hands over how pure its air was. China was in the business of making steel, and making money. Jerry understood that. He didn't understand why some people in his own country couldn't.

He heard about the outbreak of some crazy disease in China, though it sounded like it was restricted to just one place, Whoo-hoo, or Whoo-pee, he didn't know exactly how it was pronounced and he didn't care. It sounded like it came from some crazy soup made with bats. Well, what would you expect? If you eat bats, rats and cats, bad things are likely to occur. He looked it up and saw it was called Wuhan, and was delighted to learn that they made steel nearby. Not just made it. Mass-produced it. The steel mill he read about was ten times the size of anything that had ever been built in Pittsburgh. Maybe they'd decide that the emissions from the mill were responsible for whatever disease had struck and they'd close them down, like they closed down Pittsburgh. Hey, a guy could hope.

Then, later, he heard that someone in the state of Washington had gotten the same disease. Holy shit! Had it come to America? But then, he heard it was some Chinese guy out there, probably one of those smart-ass Asians who'd made a billion dollars developing software for Microsoft or one of the big tech companies. Maybe, he fantasized, that it would shut down the tech industry, just like they shut down Pittsburgh. Someone else ought to feel what it was like to have your life changed because someone else didn't like what you were making or how you were doing it.

Jerry didn't read newspapers—you had to pay for them and he wasn't exactly rolling in scratch, plus, he mostly didn't believe them— but he checked out the free websites and got an idea that the crap was spreading to other places. From Washington State it moved to Boston, which was another place that had Asians everywhere—Harvard, MIT, the Tech Corridor around the city. Maybe they ate bats and rats there too and had gotten sick from it. So sad for them.

And Europe! Hell, Europe was almost closed down because so many people were sick. He saw the worst-hit place—the "epicenter", it was called—was Northern Italy. The place where all those expensive clothes came from.

The first time he saw someone wearing a blue surgical mask in downtown Pittsburgh, Jerry assumed it was a Japanese tourist, though why a Japanese tourist would come to Pittsburgh was hard to fathom. Tourist or bank robber, Jerry figured. Or else one of the surgeons from the health system he—and most everyone else who was employed in Pittsburgh—worked for, who'd forgotten to de-mask after performing his last operation.

Whatever.

What wasn't whatever was when the TV news anchors and the radio jocks started telling everyone to wear a mask. Yeah, sure. Try walking down Liberty Avenue with your face hidden. That made sense when there was a winter blizzard raging with snow pouring into your nose and eyes. But on a snowless, relatively mild February day? This is Pittsburgh, not Peking, guys. More to the point, it's America. Don't tell me what to wear or not to wear. Now if you wanted to tell me to take off my Pirates cap for my health, that's different. The Pirates are a team that couldn't catch a fly ball, much less a disease. Perennially stuck in last place. No need for protection from the Pirates. Just like there's no need for protection from a virus in China, and a few places where Asian immigrants had all the best jobs.

He heard Trump say this virus was no big deal. A few cases, we'll take care of it. Someone asked him about masks, and he said, I'm not wearing one. Wear one if you want, but I'm not. Goddam right, and neither am I, Jerry thought. He saw footage of Chinese police in Woohoo herding people into their apartments and bolting the doors so they couldn't get out. Chinese cops beating people who weren't wearing masks. That's how they do things in China, Jerry thought. Here's some advice: don't try it here.

Jerry liked the Three Rivers bar because it felt like home, a kind of home anyway. He knew maybe six of the regulars, the bartenders called him by name, and there was a permanent smell of beer and bodies that enclosed you as soon as you walked in. Jerry would nurse a beer for an hour or so, watch the Pirates lose another game, or the Steelers shooting for another ring, like they did three times in the 70s, or even the Penguins skating their asses off, usually to no avail. Jerry didn't believe in that stupid "It doesn't matter whether you win or lose" crybaby slogan. But in fact, when he had his knees up against the bar at the Three Rivers, it really didn't. He was home.

So when, one day, he was about to pull the door open and walk in, the red and white sign that hadn't been there the last time he visited the Three was a shock. "No mask, no service," it said. What the...? Maybe some prankster had pasted the sign on the door to see how patrons would react. Maybe some overreaching government busybody had put it up, and it was still there awaiting the first customer with a real pair to rip it down. Confused and more than a little pissed off, Jerry walked in, saw that Sam, one of his favorites, was tending bar, masked, and said in a friendly way, the way he'd say it when the Pirates had blown a rare lead in the ninth, "What the fuck, Sam? Masks?"

"Not my idea, bro. Boss said the City Council passed some ordinance last week. And they're starting to enforce it today."

"What am I supposed to do? Drink my beer through a straw?"

"You can drop the mask when you're eatin' and drinkin', but when you're not, it's Lone Ranger time. What can I say?"

"You can say, 'fuck this', which is what I'm sayin'," said Jerry, trying to make it sound jokey, but knowing it was coming out serious and pissed off.

"Dunno, Jer. Them's the rules," said Sam, shrugging. "They say that shit can fly through the air and get into your nose and mouth, just like it was outta an aerosol spray can. So, the mask is supposed to protect you. And protect anyone else you're with if you've got it."

"Got what?"

"That shit from China. Covid."

"Fuck is Covid?'

"It's what they're callin' this China shit goin' around."

"Why not call it 'this China shit?'"

"Dunno. Someone on TV said that's racist."

"I thought you got that China shit from bats," said Jerry.

"Dude, I'm not a scientist. I just hand out beer and bullshit."

It was probably the first time Jerry had heard the word 'scientist' used with respect in the Three. Usually 'scientist' played a minor role in a rough joke, such as "Fuckin' scientist ever looked at your liver, dude, he'd use it as Exhibit A." Scientists did not patronize the Three. And patrons who did liked it that way.

"I don't have a fuckin' mask with me, Sam," Jerry said, as though that ended the debate.

"Here, I got a whole bunch," said Sam, reaching under the bar and producing a blue, paper-looking thing with white elastic loops on each end. We're supposed to give 'em to people who don't have any."

Without knowing exactly how or why, something grabbed inside Jerry's chest. It was like fingers were squeezing his heart, or his stomach. He wasn't sure if he was going to puke, or crap, or die. He was reminded of the old line on that comedy show "And now for something completely different." This was different, all right. And not at all right.

"Tell you what, Sam. I'll come back when they take that fuckin' sign down."

"I'm with you, bro'," said Sam, shaking his head. "This sucks in multiple ways."

"Yeah, see you, Sam."

"So long, Jerry. See you soon."

Those were the last words spoken between Jerry and Sam. Sam died of Covid, and the Three went out of business over the summer. The Pirates finished in last.

# Chapter 5
## What's Yours Is Mine

No one really noticed, or gave a damn, when Wang Win failed to open his stall on time on Sunday. It had never happened before, in any living person's memory, but then, neither had the Party actually keeping a promise, so there was a first time for everything.

It could have been anything. The year 2020 had begun on an inauspicious note. Business at the market seemed to be ticking down. The stall owners whispered to each other that the Party was keeping people at home and out of the public marketplaces, because of some flu epidemic. Even the Zhongnang Hospital admitted it was treating an abnormally large number of flu sufferers, though one the deputy directors assured the local newspaper that they had expected 2019 to be a bad year for airborne infections and this was probably the result. Since the Zhongnang Hospital was affiliated with Wuhan University and was a teaching hospital, it was generally assumed that this was the government line and that the number of patients was much larger than the hospital chose to publicize.

The reason was obvious. The Chinese New Year, January 20, would begin soon, and despite the wave of flu that seemed to have everyone sick at home, Chinese from all around the country would be on the move, filling domestic flights, packing long-distance high-speed trains, and, if they were Party members or related to one, driving in their personal cars to celebrate. Wang was a hearty soul who never missed an opportunity to separate a customer from his yuan. He could be traveling to spend New Year with relatives or friends—although he had never mentioned having either of those kinds of people in his life.

People who ran—never owned, as all things were the property of the Party—neighboring stalls made a quiet pact not to raid Wang's merchandise. One fellow who had known Wang for years even shared some of the rotten fruit he used to feed his bats with Wang's hungry menagerie. This chap was quietly, but widely regarded as a romantic fool. Let the Party help those in need. Another cynical market folk joke.

No one, it seemed, knew where Wang lived. As far as they were concerned, Wang's life began when he showed up for work and ended when he began arranging his market wares for overnight storage. Between the second and first events, no one knew or cared about him.

"I hope he's all right though," said a seventy-something woman who had passed time over the years talking with Wang. She had also seen him bumping up against that fat woman's breasts and buttocks when she sold him the occasional research laboratory produce. Knowing not a thing about her except the source of her bats, the older woman quietly despised her. There was, for the old lady, something not Socialism-with-Chinese-Characteristics about using animals as experimental test subjects, then selling them for food. She wasn't sure if she was right. It was just a feeling. Perhaps she hadn't read enough of Chairman/General Secretary/All-around-great-guy Xi's speeches. Even in the post-modern industrial power-state the Great One had built, she was, after all, just a woman. Still, she hoped Wang was all right.

Wang was hoping this would all be over soon. He lay in the cot he used for a bed, wondering if the chills would come again before the fever once more took hold. The fever was better, because he didn't notice then how cold the room was. He checked his Huawei cellphone from time to time, to make sure he had at least an approximate idea of what time of day or night it was, and what the day and date were.

His vision was sometimes blurry. His hearing came and went. His sense of smell and taste were long gone. Breathing was a chore, no longer an instinct. When he could get up, and when it wasn't to void himself, Wang sipped a cupful of the soup he had made for himself from some of the animals he couldn't sell before they began to rot. At least, he knew there was no rat meat in his sustenance, since he had added each ingredient: garlic, some old, withered ginger, an onion that had been turning gray, a fruit bat, though he couldn't remember where it had come from. Most people couldn't really tell the difference between bat and rat once it had boiled a few hours in broth, and it was widely assumed and accepted that many soup shops supplemented the bats they could afford to buy with rats they had captured in their kitchens.

He had stopped trying to heat the soup, because his mouth couldn't tell what temperature it was anyway. He just sluiced it, chewed whatever solids were in the liquid, burped because, even though he was very ill, burping was the polite finish to a meal, to show appreciation, and dragged his way back to his cot. Chills or fever next? His world had been reduced to this. Once, in the middle of a sweaty dream, he had thought of the fat lady with the nice buttocks who let him slide his hands over her, pretending they were negotiating a tight space. What was her name? Had the bat in his soup come from her? Whatever. He turned his thoughts again to her buttocks.

He did not survive the night.

Fang Fang was feeling bad too, though not as bad as Wang, or for the same reason. Qi Qi's ex-husband, known as just Fang, wanted to win the election he was running in to become a member of the Wuhan Council of Advisors for Science and Social Responsibility. His work at the Research Laboratory—the same one where Qi Qi Dieh worked— was of a higher level, and had a thick component of party politics and ideology involved. This delighted Fang, who, truth be told, didn't understand a lot of the lab work he was assigned, and tried to deflect challenges to his competence by asking if his interrogator had read President Xi's latest remarks on the importance of hewing to socialist-with-Chinese-characteristics principles in science. He had learned early on that most questions about competence could be answered with that question as a reply. It was part of the Chinese scientific process.

Voting in the election was technically restricted to current members of the Council, who, it was assumed, would select the best-qualified candidates to join their exalted ranks. In reality, the surest way to be elected was to buy votes. It was not, of course, something that one talked about, since the Party frowned officially on corruption, unless the arbiters of corruption were the ones benefitting. The trick was to find out which member of the Council was also the Party's secret snitch.

Fang thought he had identified that person. She was a 50-something woman whose job was to compare virology reports among the experimental animals tested at the lab. This woman, whose last name was Wu—no one had ever dared use her first name in a conversation; it would suggest familiarity at the least, intimacy at worst—was fat, intense, without humor, and always wore a lapel pin with the logo of the People's Liberation Army. Wu could be counted on to answer any question or solve any problem with the words of Xi Jinping from some speech or other, all of which she seemed to have memorized. Fang had never worked directly with Wu, but based on her severe personality, her constant references to and adulation for, the President, and her weight—indicating she got more than enough to eat—he felt fairly certain she was the Party's cat's paw.

He figured he needed 200 yuan—about sixteen dollars. Anticipating that he would have to bribe his way to success, Fang had tightened his budget belt and squirreled away about 140 yuan. He was not expecting to be paid until after the election, and his Party dues would also have to be settled so he could run as a candidate in good standing. A good Communist pays his Party dues on time, Chairman Xi says.

He thought he knew where he could get it. Qi Qi never spent money on herself—just look at her—so it was logical she would have some yuan stored away. He was sure he could convince her to give it to him. He just had to pick the right moment to contact her. What the hell, he thought (though he would never utter that word out loud, since heaven and hell were not popular with the Party), I'll text her now.

"Need to talk. Where are you?"

No answer.

Good and bad. Bad that the plump monkey wasn't being respectful enough to answer him. Good that it meant she might not be home. Fang knew where his ex lived. Once they had split, he had been kind enough to help her find a room in an apartment. Fang himself stayed in the one-bedroom apartment they had shared, because he had put the property lease in his name only when they were married. Qi Qi had made noises about suing Fang to keep the apartment herself. He explained, not kindly, that such lawsuits were usually heard by Party-controlled judges. He was a Party member. Qi Qi was not. Guess who would win? But you are the one divorcing me, Qi Qi said. And any judge who is a Party member would understand why, Fang replied. At least any male judge.

He did not have a key to the apartment where Qi Qi lived, but, since there were several different lodgers in different rooms there, he didn't need one. One of the other lodgers let him in and did not ask which room he was visiting or why. He let himself into Qi Qi's room and was unpleasantly startled to see her propped up in the only chair in the room, gripping its arms tightly.

"How are you, Qi?" Fang said, trying to make himself sound interested in the answer.

"Terrible. Everything hurts." She did, indeed, look like she was in pain. He nearly felt pity, then he remembered why he was here. The sour smell in the room told him that she had been here for a while, probably unable to use the toilet down the hall, and possibly unable to feed herself.

"Would you like some soup?"

The ghastly groan that escaped her was answer enough. If the mere thought of soup could make her feel worse than she already looked, she was definitely not well.

"How about tea?"

"Please. Why are you here?"

"I texted you, but you didn't answer. I came to see if you were all right."

"Thank you. The tea things are over there," she said, pointing feebly with her left hand toward a corner.

Fang found the hotplate, shakily mounted on some books, which, he noticed, had labels on their spines indicating they came from the Research Lab. He said nothing, but put a small cooking pot already filled with water on to heat.

"Where do you keep the tea?"

This time, she extended her right arm. He found the tea box and, Glory Be, when he opened it, found a wad of yuan notes in it. He pocketed them smoothly at the same time as he pulled a few fingers-full of shredded tea from the box, dropped it into the one cup he saw nearby, and went to wait for the water to boil.

"It doesn't get hot enough to boil," Qi Qi said in a voice that sounded more resigned than resentful. "Any temperature is fine. I can't tell the difference."

"Fine." He poured tepid water on the brown-gray tea shreds, swished the cup around a few times, and brought it to her.

"Thank you. Why did you come?"

Hadn't he just answered that question? "I told you, to see how you were doing."

"You told me that? When?" The last word was carried on a wheeze he had never heard from her before. She must actually be unwell, he thought.

"I'm glad you are okay. I have to go." And he was out the door as she was still gasping for breath to answer him. Only then did he count the money.

It was only twenty yuan, but that, along with the money he had put aside, would have to do.

He went directly to the Laboratory to tell Wu how well she looked today, and to give her 160 yuan with his best wishes.

Fang was elected to the Council of Advisors by a margin of one vote.

His career was definitely on the way up.

# Chapter 6
## Sleek And Silent

In the Catholic faith, you confess your sins to a priest in the hope and belief that he has some special connection to God, and that, through that connection, he, the priest, is able to forgive your sins and set you, the sinner, on the path of righteousness anew. The success of this spiritual transaction depends entirely on the sinner's trust in the institution of Confession, the Church, and all the other shibboleths of Catholicism that would not pass the commonsense test of a ten-year-old.

The same is true of any Chinese Council of Advisors. To believe that ordinary citizens, even regular Party members, have the right and the wisdom to advise the leading edges of the Communist Party of China, is the kind of doleful humor applied to the existence of Bigfoot, or the chance that a Republican might win an election in New York City. Yes, there was Giuliani, and look what they did to him.

Fang came to the first meeting of the Council of which he was now a member with considerable self-doubt. He was a lousy scientist, and he knew it. He didn't understand a lot of the theorems on which his so-called profession was based. He had graduated from university with the lowest honors ranking possible, and that only because he had bribed the professor who conducted his least favorite class, molecular biology. Cure diseases? Improve lives? No way. What he knew how to do was to game the system, get what he needed, please those who could further his career and reputation within the Party and, possibly, make a few extra yuan in the process.

He had married Qi Qi Dieh because a Party elder had explained to him that unmarried men above the age of 30 arouse suspicions. Why aren't they married? What do they do when they should be exercising their rights as husbands? The one-child policy of Deng Xiaoping had been necessary years ago, when it appeared that China's population would double every ten years. Even the most ardent Communist could see that that was unsustainable. But the one-child policy had in fact been *too* effective. Now, China's population growth had slowed to an alarming rate, and its people were aging. Better to have a full labor force, and enough young men to fill the ranks of the People's Army than be worrying about where to find the next generation of bodies.

If some of them starved, well, Socialism with Chinese Characteristics.

And for all the talk of emancipation of women in Xi's China, very few females, except those few from exalted Party families, thought they would ever be treated the same as men. Qi Qi, for some strange reason, had thought that. It was she who had doomed their marriage, the first time she completed a scientific analysis of viruses in bats that Fang couldn't comprehend. Qi never said a word about it, but it was a shame that Fang couldn't abide, couldn't allow.

A divorced man was viewed much more favorably than a never married one, both in terms of social status and political reliability. A man who had never convinced a woman to marry him, thus ensuring hot meals and a release for his tensions was suspicious. Everyone could relate to a man who had shed a wife. Fang had few friends in whom he could confide his doubts about his scientific abilities, his complaints about Qi, and, most importantly, his fears that he was not progressing quickly enough within the Party. That, after all, was how one's life was measured in Xi's China. Not how important you were, but how important you were to the Party.

One colleague—Fang would never call him a friend, since they worked in the same department—had seemed to listen to him whinge and whine during the divorce process. Fang had asked if he should manufacture charges against Qi to support his desertion. Unfaithfulness, for instance. But adultery was not a crime in China, it was simply a condition that had little bearing on one's status. In fact, a man who had been cuckolded, though legally not in peril, was never viewed quite the same after its disclosure. "Don't make wild accusations that you can't prove," the friend had told Fang. "Be sleek and silent about it."

Fang had no idea what that meant, but he liked the way it sounded.

The first Council meeting he attended after his election took place in the Laboratory's employee cafeteria. Proof, Fang thought, that this was nothing like a sure stepping stone to Party prominence. Still, the longest journey...

Wu, who two weeks earlier had accepted his goodwill bribe, sat rigidly at the center of the lunch table that this evening was being passed off as a banquet of honor. Fang chose a plastic chair five down from Wu and promised himself he would remain mute in the presence of such great minds.

Meetings in today's China, especially those involving members of the Communist Party, are not meetings, but soliloquys. Whether formally or otherwise, and it is usually formally, someone takes charge of the meeting with a pre-determined agenda. Determined by someone higher up in the Party, that is. There is no acknowledgement of this subterranean activity. Nor is there usually any protest about it, since a protest against Party subterfuge is deemed unpatriotic and carries consequences.

At this meeting of the Wuhan Research Laboratory Council of Scientific Advisors, Wu had taken the role of arbiter, explainer, source of wisdom and authority. Those who knew her and how she worked had no trouble predicting how the meeting would be steered, or its outcome. Some workers at the lab with a modicum of worldly experience shrugged and whispered, "In Wu We Trust."

"There is no doubt that Wuhan is experiencing an onset of influenza," Wu said to open the session, after the universal and obligatory recitation of the Party oath and the resonant huzzahs directed to General Secretary Xi. "The research laboratory has been disproportionately affected by this onset" – onset being a word that carried oratorical, but not statistical weight. "As a result, it is necessary that the laboratory's Council of Scientific Advisors is in the vanguard to explain the causes of the outbreak and to provide counsel to the population."

Fang listened raptly and with admiration to this mush of words. She wasn't saying anything, yet the way she said it carried weight, authority, knowledge, even, and here he had to shake his head in wonder, honesty.

"We already have, through the efforts of the people's healthcare workers, learned that this particular strain of influenza has some different charact..." she stopped herself, not wanting to profane one of the bywords of Xi's philosophy... "traits that are unlike others. For instance, patients seem in many cases to lose their sense of smell and taste. Our research indicates that the majority of these patients have lived lifestyles that are not in keeping with the example set for us by Chairman Xi and all patriotic Chinese. And these deprivations are therefore, a sort of medical" ... again, she stopped, not wanting to misuse official Party terminology "reaction to this misbehavior."

Wu passed the torch to a colleague named Wo, a specialist in virology and a gung-ho Party believer. If he read it in People's Daily or saw it on state TV, Wo was in. And expected everyone else to be as well, prompting one less-than-staunch Party supporter to opine, "Wo is us."

"The evidence suggests that this influenza, though easily treatable by the excellent Chinese medical system, can present complications if not diagnosed and properly handled by our experts. The Chinese people know that they must listen to experts and heed their advice and diagnoses. Experts represent the wisdom of the Party, and the Party derives its life and breath from President Xi. Therefore, failure to be guided by experts, to reject their advice and wisdom, is to reject the advice and wisdom of Chairman Xi."

Fang had sat through such speeches before, although none from a body of which he was a member. He noted with satisfaction the easy transition from illness to cure via the inevitable path of following the advice of experts. Experts who derived their own wisdom from Xi. Who exactly, Fang wondered, were these experts whose advice must be heeded? Were they not mortal creatures like the rest of us? Where did they achieve their status as experts? Who conferred that title—expert—on them? Had they truly earned it, or had they, as he had, bribed someone to get special status?

He realized he had not been listening to Wo, his mind momentarily drifting into the idea-poor, conspiratorial echo chamber that was his brain.

"...malign forces trying to convince our citizens that this is something more than everyday influenza, that for some reason also robs us of our senses of taste and smell. Citizen scientists, this illness is nothing out of the ordinary, and it should be referred to and communicated about as nothing different from a case of the sniffles." This was met with a round of hearty applause and several shouts, seemingly unscripted, as "All praise to Chairman Xi."

Their Wo was about to be eased. "I wish now to introduce a colleague from the CAC—the Cyberspace Administration of China, who will speak further on the way this situation is to be handled."

"I am Xian-din Dong, the deputy editor of the CAC for the Wuhan region," said the youngish looking man who looked like his mother was an orangutan and his father a wolf. "I am here at the request of the ... Council" ... he could hardly disguise his disdain "to explain the dangers when facts are presented incorrectly and when the people" ... again, a look of disgust melted through his hard black eyes "...are permitted to form incorrect impressions of a situation which is being handled superbly by the Party, but which some criminal elements might try to distort for their own profit."

Fang was wondering who might possibly profit from influenza. Doctors provided their services at clinics run by the state, which paid the doctors. Prescription medicine was free, up to certain reasonable limits. Hospitals, should a patient ever need one, were cost-free. Where was there profit to be made?

"As citizens of the greatest country on earth," Dong was saying, "we have a special, no, a unique responsibility to ensure that our compatriots are kept informed by reliable, knowledgeable and above all, loyal sources. Experts, if you will. This can be more difficult in the age of cyber-communication, some of which, I am sorry to say, does not operate within the suggested bounds set by the Party. You all know what I am talking about. Search engines that originate outside of China, such as, and I heartily denounce it, Google. Or cyber-tools like, and again I denounce it, Twitter. We allow these non-Chinese companies—portions of them, anyway—to operate within our borders for reasons of international cooperation and fraternity. What we do not allow is misinformation spread by foreign agents who would try to damage the new world order being spearheaded by Chairman Xi."

Another few stabs at enthusiasm escaped from the audience, but none of them was convincing. Fang suspected someone had either paid or ordered them to shout Xi's name.

"The Cyberspace Administration of China has been informed of the presence of influenza in the region of Wuhan and has wisely and correctly established guidelines for how online conversation and exchange of information on this topic must—not should but must—be handled. There are three tenets that will be followed at all times. One, keep any medical advice or commentary general such as "Stay healthy." Two, do not alarm the population with meaningless statistics such as deaths caused by this influenza or the number of hospital beds available to treat the worst cases of this illness. All these things are being taken care of by the Party. There is absolutely no reason for ordinary citizens to think about them. Three, it is important to note, and to repeat endlessly on social media, that influenza never existed in China, in its thousands of years of glorious history, until Westerners were allowed to visit our country, trade with our businesses and, even, in the previous and this century, actually live among us. Any Chinese person suffering from this latest strain of flu had undoubtedly had contact with a foreigner through one means or another.

"No one in this meeting is involved in any nefarious cyber-activity," and here Dong took a long moment to move his gaze over the entire Council. "We rely on you to provide examples for how to communicate about any topics that could be considered ... uncomfortable. If you see something in cyberspace that you think might be of a problematic, or, and this goes without saying, unpatriotic nature, report it immediately to the CAC, which is the proper authority to handle such matters. Should you become inadvertently engaged in online conversations, it is important that you are... um... that you are..."

"Sleek and silent?" Fang couldn't believe he had blurted this out. Not just out, but out loud, loudly. What was he thinking? He knew the words came from his colleague, and as he saw Dong stumbling around for the right words, they had escaped his lips before he knew what he was doing or why. He could see Wu looking at him, mouth agape in silent fury. Wo was also boring with his eyes into Fang's forehead. Oh, no, Wo. Fang felt that he might vomit from embarrassment. He looked at Dong, who was looking at him with a quizzical expression, not approval, but not disapproval.

"Yes. Yes, something like that. What was it you said?"

"Sleek and silent," Fang said, much softer this time than when he had blurted it out, but also with resolution that it might not have been such a disaster to speak up.

He was, after all, on the Council of Advisors. And so, he was an expert. Now it remained to be seen how that advice would affect the rest of his life.

# Chapter 7
## When Truth Became Racist

From her narrow hallway bench in the Nuovo Ospedale di Prato on Via Suor Niccolina, Luisa, fingering *La Nonna's* scrap of cashmere, struggled air in, spewed it out.

"You shouldn't say such things," a nun in medical garb said softly.

Luisa shook her head, slowly. "*E vero.*"

"*E razzista.*"

How can it be racist when it's true? Is truth now racist? But she didn't have enough air in her lungs to get out the words. Besides, apparently, they were racist.

She had gotten herself to the hospital by taxi—the first taxi she had taken for two years—and explained to the emergency room attendants that she could not breathe.

They asked all the obvious stupid questions: have you been drinking? Do you smoke? Have you sniffed glue recently? Crystal meth? Crack?

Do I look like I do any of those things, she snapped, coughing as penance for her sharp reply.

Drug addicts come from all walks of life, the attendant, who sported a tattoo of the Virgin Mary kissing Satan on her forearm, explained.

No to all those.

All right. We'll have a nurse look you over as soon as possible.

Possible was five hours.

Nuovo Ospedale was busy just then, due to a turf fight between two Chinese gangs over a strip of the rundown Landori neighborhood.

One gang had come armed with knives, ready to slice their way to dominance in the old-style Italian method.

The other came with machetes and sawed-off shotguns. Landori belonged to them now.

Luisa sat on the uncushioned bench in the waiting room, coughing, coughing, coughing. Other potential patients came in. She coughed on them. They coughed on her. Some family members of the gang fighters came in to see how their boys were doing. They looked yellower than most of the Chinese she saw in the textile factories and the cutting floors. She coughed on them. They coughed on her. It was like the gangs' street war, fought instead with aerosolized munitions.

When she saw a nurse, the man was hugely distracted. "Fifty-eight, huh? Easy to catch a cold."

"It's not a cold. I can't breathe."

"Of course you can breathe. You're here, aren't you, talking to me?"

"There is something wrong with my lungs."

"Do you smoke?"

"Can you read?"

"Please don't speak to me that way. I'm a nurse."

"Please don't speak to me that way either. I'm an Italian citizen, unlike the last twenty gang-bangers you've treated here this afternoon." Talking was exhausting but she was Italian, and angry. Angry Italians talk.

"They have a right to be here. They're guest workers."

"I have a right to be here, too. I was born nearby."

"So you've never traveled?"

"Not as much, or as far, as those criminals you've been patching up."

"They're not criminals. Or at least you don't know that they are. You are making irrational assumptions. Are you seeing a psychiatrist? Psychologist? My cousin is a psychologist. Private, of course. You'd have to pay. He might be able to help you. Would you like his email?"

"I'm sure he, or anyone else I find on the street, can help me more than you can." She was panting from the exertion of the exchange.

"I think I hear something in your lungs. Do you take any illegal drugs? Crystal meth, maybe?"

"I'm going to ask to see someone else. A doctor, maybe. I can't breathe."

"You can ask. But there are no doctors here now. It's getting late, you know."

"Just admit me to the hospital, please, and give me some antibiotics and some oxygen. I tell you, I can't breathe."

"'I can't breathe.' The way you say it, over and over, it sounds like a slogan," said the nurse, smiling. "Probably the best thing would be to put you on a course of antibiotics. I can arrange an oxygen mask for you, but it's pretty uncomfortable."

"I'll get used to it."

"Some patients say the masks are so uncomfortable they can't wear them."

"People can get used to anything if it saves their lives."

The nurse looked at her. "If their lives are worth saving."

"You don't think my life is worth saving?"

"Honestly? I'm not sure. Why do you think the Asians I treated are criminals?"

"Perhaps because they came in here with wounds received in a gang fight?"

"What do you know about gangs?"

"Do you live in Prato?" Luisa asked, fully exhausted but unwilling to let it go.

"No. I live in Milano."

"Then it is you who doesn't know anything about gangs. Since the Chinese came to Prato, they've taken it over. It used to be a beautiful little town. Now it's like some perverted corner of Shanghai."

"Why don't you like Chinese people?"

"Because they have ruined my town. And because they have taken jobs away from Italians. And because once they take those jobs, they don't do them as well as Italians used to."

"This sounds very racist to me," said the nurse.

"It's not racist. It's true."

"It may be true. But it's racist."

"So, you're opposed to the truth?"

"If it's racist, yes."

"So, we Italians should ignore the truth, and keep our mouths shut, in order not to be called racist?"

"That's probably best."

"So, if I tell you, it's raining outside—which, by the way, it was when I came in here—and you say you think that's racist, does that mean it's a sunny day?"

"The world has changed since you were young. There are things we don't say anymore."

Luisa stood up. "You know, I came in here hoping to get treatment so I'd feel better. But I've now decided: I'm not the sick one. You are."

The nurse held up a hand. "I am going to admit you to the hospital. You need some antibiotics in your system. And you need oxygen."

"What a brilliant diagnosis. Thank you."

"Also, I'd like you to talk to Suor Jacinta."

"Who is this sister?"

"She's someone who studies the way people think."

"In other words, a shrink."

"That's not a term we use here. She might be able to work through some of your feelings about people who aren't like you?"

"You mean, people who aren't old and sick?"

"No. People who aren't white."

"I don't need a shrink. I need some oxygen."

"See Suor Jacinta first. She'll make a recommendation for treatment."

"But she's a shrink, not a medical doctor."

"She's both."

True to his word, the nurse admitted Luisa to the hospital. She was assigned a semi-private room with no other occupant at the moment. As she got into the single, railed bed, she sunk her head into the pillow and sighed. It was the first time in days she believed that she might start to feel better. The medical system, after all, was one of the few Italian institutions that had maintained its high standards— through World War II, through more than a hundred changes of governments since the war, through the various financial crises that seemed to haunt Italy like Hamlet's ghost, through the country's absorption into the European Union, the crash of 2008, and, now, she sincerely hoped, through the arrival of this strange illness carried into the country by the Chinese who we had actually welcomed here to work our mills and factories.

"You are Luisa?"

The voice startled her out of her reverie. Standing before her was a tall, very slender woman in a nun's habit, but with a white jacket over it. She face and hands were as close to coal-black as Luisa could imagine.

"Si."

"I am Suor Jacinta. I've been asked to visit you..."

"Thank you. Your Italian is excellent."

"Why should it not be?" The face, which had been neutral, grimaced into hostility in an instant.

"Well, I mean, were you born in Italy?"

"I was born in Ethiopia. A country, you will remember, which was invaded by Mussolini—who did not speak excellent Italian, by the way. I learned Italian as a child."

"It was a compliment, not a comment."

"It was disguised as a compliment and was most certainly a comment."

How, Luisa wondered, had she gotten off to such a bad start with this woman? She had a suspicion that Suor Jacinta would have taken umbrage at whatever she said.

"You are a doctor?"

"I am a staff psychologist," an answer which, Luisa noticed, evaded the point of the question.

"I am having trouble breathing. If you have my file, you will see that."

"Your file says that you harbor racist thoughts and views. Perhaps you are suffering from guilt complex."

"Look, Suor Jacinta, I am sorry that Mussolini invaded Ethiopia. I didn't take part in it."

"All Italians bear the stain of colonization."

"Well, from what I've seen and read, Ethiopia hasn't exactly been a raging success since we left." There. The lines were drawn. Patient and psychologist glared at each other with undisguised enmity. Luisa considered getting up from the bed and going home. But her body was sending signals that she was not strong enough to do that. Whatever was going to happen would happen, either because of, or despite, Mussolini and the dark-skinned nun who, inexplicably, now controlled her future.

Suor Jacinta looked at her patient. Nodded. Made a decision. "Your doctor will see you soon." She walked out.

It was an hour, which Luisa passed fitfully. She thought of Italy, a country she had always been proud of, to be a part of. She remembered trips to Milano as a girl, vacations on the beach, neighbors keeping an eye on each other's children, without motive or recompense.

"You Ruriza?"

It could have been a voice, or just as easily a door scraping the floor as it was being closed. When she looked, she saw a short, dark figure in a white jacket, holding a clipboard.

"Scusi?" she said.

"Ruriza. You?"

"Luisa. Si. And you?"

"Dokka Chen." Cliché it might be, but his eyes were like the lines between the upper and lower parts of a fraction. Could he be on the staff of Nuovo Ospedale? The hospital they were all so proud of?

"Wha rong you?"

"I cannot breathe easily."

"Ah. Takke tes."

"What?"

"Tes. Tes." He fumbled something out of the side pocket of his white jacket. It looked like a test tube. From the tube he drew what looked like a cotton swab, the kind used to clean ears, but much longer.

"Ho sti."

Without any warning, he jammed the swab into her right nostril, causing Luisa to snap back her head and emit a small shriek.

"Sti," Chen said, extending his hand and frowning as if she were a disobedient child. He removed the swab as quickly as he had inserted it, lodged it back into the test tube and popped a cork into its open end.

"Thirry min." And disappeared.

When he returned, he had a team around him. A woman in green scrubs and an orderly wheeling a large tank-like machine with a clear rubber hose extending from its top.

"Oxin," Chen said. "Fir luns." He patted his chest as if pleased with himself.

Luisa looked at the woman in scrubs. "Can you explain what is happening?"

The woman nodded, in what seemed a gesture of solidarity. "Dr. Chen," and her mouth curled down ever so slightly "has diagnosed you as having a virus. It makes it harder for your lungs to get enough oxygen. This tank contains pure oxygen. If you use it correctly, it should relieve your problem. May I?"

Without waiting for permission, she slipped the clear hose around Luisa's head, and inserted two small nubs into her nostrils. The change was instantaneous. The headache she had had for days disappeared. The heaviness in her chest gave way to easy inflation and exhalation. She felt fine.

"Thank you, that is much better."

"Goo," said Chen, and without another syllable turned and left her room.

Emboldened by her improved condition, and her lucid conversation with the woman in green, Luisa said, "Is he really a doctor?"

"Seems to be. He's one of those visiting physicians the state health service wants to encourage. The theory is that they bring new ideas, new perspectives."

"But I can't understand what he says. He barely speaks Italian."

Green-coat's eyes widened. "I know. But don't say that to anyone else. If you say anything about the foreigners, especially the Chinese, they call you racist."

"But they're all over Prato. That's where I live. You can't buy a cannoli anymore, but you can buy Peking duck."

"I know, I know. I remember when Prato was beautiful. Now it's like a pagoda. They've taken over." She was about to say something else, but stopped herself. "But don't say these things to anyone here. They're very sensitive."

"Where is this Doctor Chen from?"

"Some city in China that no one's ever heard of. Wuhan, I think it's called. Now, get some rest. I'll be back and we'll talk some more."

Exhausted, confused and somewhat angry at what she and green coat seemed to be alone in understanding, Luisa sought refuge in sleep.

She fingered the scrap of cashmere, woven by her grandmother. She dreamed about the beautiful clothes she had sewn. She dreamed about her pride in being Italian. That seemed a long time ago. A lifetime ago. When she could breathe without help. And say what she thought.

# Chapter 8
## Who Is Hui?

The bedroom he had grown up in, the bedroom he had left to take the bus into New York to hear Hui lecture, and to which he returned, stunned with shock and injected with hope, now became his prison. Henry paced the room, checking his laptop obsessively for any communication from the Prof... Colonel. An institute devoted to AI? Where, when, and, he had already decided, yes!

To break the boredom, and on the chance of earning a sexual interlude, he let Khadija talk him into taking part in a protest march led by a group called Black Lives Matter. Henry knew the tagline had sprung up about 2013, after a black youth named Trayvon Martin had been shot to death in Florida by a neighborhood watchman named George Zimmerman. It didn't matter that Zimmerman, despite his Anglo-sounding name, was Hispanic. Blacks wanted justice—actually revenge—for the killing of one of their own by someone with lighter skin. When Zimmerman was cleared of the assault and manslaughter charges against him, blacks rioted for two days, shouting, variously, "Fuck whitey," and "Black lives matter." It was the second rallying cry that stuck, and became a national motto, although the first one was more popular among BLM supporters.

The protest march was held in Newark. Khadija would not tell Henry how, but she had learned where the starting point was. She and Henry presented themselves to a group of blacks who were handing out BLM placards attached to sturdy wooden handles.

"Whddayunz doin' here?" growled an immense and bearded man in his 30s, wearing a bullet proof vest and a bandolier full of what

59

looked like shotgun shells. Henry had no idea what to answer, but Khadija swiftly said, "We want to march with you, for justice."

"You come down from the suburbs in Daddy's limo, bitch?" the guy asked. "Cuz you sho's-fuck don't belong here."

"Your message is spreading. We've heard it and come to help," said Khadija.

"Shee-it," said the guy. "OK, take some signs and make sho' you know how to swing'em."

The march, as everyone but Henry knew and intended it would, began loudly and ended violently. The marchers grew bored with merely shouting profanities after a few blocks and looted the first liquor store they passed. Next came a Best Buy store, then, because some of them were hungry, a BoJangles chicken franchise. The Newark police responded and, while most of the protesters had the sense to flee the scene, others, including Henry and Khadija, did not, and were arrested.

Henry, separated from Khadija as soon as they were cuffed, spent four hours in a holding cell with ten other men, all black, who eyed him with malevolence, but did not touch him because they, unlike Henry, knew they were on CCTV.

If moving back into his parents' home was humiliating, calling his Father to ask him to bail him out of jail was the lowest Henry could imagine sinking.

And yet, seeing his Father fork over two hundred dollars in cash while Henry waited behind a bulletproof glass door, was not what filled him with shame. He wondered: will Hui find out about this?

Henry pleaded guilty to public misconduct, the lowest charge possible under the circumstances. He paid a fine of $160 from his own bank account, and because he now had a criminal, if forgettable, conviction on his record, assumed that he would never hear from Hui. And never again see the woman translator he had already, in his heart, named Rav.

One week while he slept, Henry received the email he had quivered over since he met Hui. "Dear Henry," Rav, or at least someone writing in her name, had written. "We are pleased to inform you that you have been excepted (well, how good would *his* Mandarin have been?) to the People's Institute of Artificial Intelligence Research, where you will take placement tests and be assigned a schedule of classes. Colonel Hui looks forward to seeing you again."

Henry was thrilled to see that Rav had put — you couldn't call it signed, exactly—her name, not Hui's, at the bottom of the email. She was Ma-lin Cho—a beautiful name, Henry immediately decided. He was only mildly surprised—was intimidated the better word? — to learn from her typed signature that she was a lieutenant in the People's Liberation Army.

The email, he realized, made no mention of how he was to get to Wuhan. Flights between China and the United States had been canceled due to the virus, though not before 45 planes from different parts of China had landed here. Everyone assumed the virus, now labeled a pandemic, had started in China; now it was spreading quickly through the United States. How could it possibly get to Wuhan? He knew from deep-dive Googling that Wuhan's population exceeded 11 million, and wondered why almost no Americans had ever heard of a city that dwarfed New York, L.A., and Chicago in population. It was the largest city in central China.

Its history was as rich and varied as any tale of the Revolution or the Wild West. The name "Wuhan" came from Wuchang and Hanku which are collectively known as the Three Towns of Wuhan. It lies in the east at the confluence of the river and its largest tributary, the Han.

It was probably at Wuhan that China itself was saved from destruction and division. It was in the Battle of the Red Cliffs that warlord Cao Cao was repulsed when he tried to overrun territory of the Han dynasty. It was also near Wuhan where the Wuchang Uprising of 1911 marked the end of the Qing dynasty and the establishment of the Republic of China. Wuhan was the temporary capital of China during the Sino-Japan war of 1937. It was a major transportation hub, with dozens of railways, roads and expressways passing through the city and connecting to other major cities.

Henry bathed in a sense of superiority for having learned much of this in his Asian history course at Columbia. How come, he asked himself, such a fascinating story isn't part of every American student's curriculum? Right, because we were spending our time discussing the Civil War and how terrible slavery was and discrimination is. Henry cared little for American history and American politics. The more he learned about Wuhan and the rest of China, the more America seemed like a second-class pretender in the larger story of humankind.

Henry both dreaded and savored the conversation he would have to have with his parents. He knew what they wanted, what they would say, how they would react to his decision. It was, he thought, almost as if he was using AI to escape the life he feared he might live: Life in New Jersey.

And yet, when the moment came, Henry was taken aback. His Mother cried, but his Father used a voice Henry had never heard before. "I've been thinking about this, and you, ever since your trip to Newark," his Father said. "I don't know if you believed in what you were marching for, or just wanted to impress that girl. She's a bad influence."

And Henry, already in shock, shocked himself further by agreeing.

"I just don't want to live here," Henry said.

His Father, a conservative Republican for as long as Henry had been alive, nodded. "I understand. The United States is in trouble. We don't know what this virus is all about, or how bad it can get. It's already cost you your job. I could be next."

"China's figured out a better way," said Henry, mildly.

"If you call one-party rule and repression of any political dissent a better way," said his Father.

"When I compare it to what I see here, yes, I call theirs a better way."

"That's your way of looking at his," said his Father, who Henry noticed, was not getting emotional. "There are lots of currents of unrest, social, political, of course racial. I know how I feel about them, but I can't in good conscience impose my beliefs on you. How do you propose to get to China, with all the flights canceled?"

As if Henry's *Zingyun de jingshen*—Lucky Spirits—had been listening, he received another email from Ma-lin overnight. "Teterboro Airport, Yellow DDragon Air, tomorrow, 6p.m. Eastern time. Bring only two bags."

Teterboro Airport handles private flights. The aircraft that take off and land there are usually owned by the super-rich, who have neither the time nor the personality to stand in line at a regular airport. Yellow

DDragon Air, he found on an Internet search, had been in business since 2001. Its ownership was not disclosed.

The next issue, of course, was a visa to enter China. The Chinese Consulate on 42$^{nd}$ Street and 12$^{th}$ Avenue in New York was closed, as were most commercial buildings, due to the pandemic. A third email from Rav, as Henry preferred to think of the lovely lieutenant, said, "Visa will be issued onboard."

How could that be, he wondered. Who can make a visa—a visa to China no less—appear on an airplane? Certainly not Rav. And then it occurred to him that it was Hui, the erudite researcher of Artificial Intelligence who was a Colonel in the People's Liberation Army, who was pulling these strings. That Hui would go to such lengths to bring a young man like Henry to China was extraordinary. And it increased Henry's admiration for the man, and the country whose uniform he wore.

Teterboro is not like other airports. One does not pass through customs. One does not show one's passport. And one is not herded into a lounge to await takeoff. Henry, completely overwhelmed, bewildered and intimidated by his surroundings, was led onto a waiting plane by a smiling young Asian man dressed in a black suit and red tie, who carried Henry's bags. The plane, whose maker he could not determine, was larger than any of the Lears and Gulfstreams around him. There was no one on board to greet him.

"Have a good flight," said the young man as Henry mounted the jet way. He saw his bags being deposited by the young man in the cargo hold beneath the plane. The inner compartment, closest to the cockpit contained eight seats. Only one had been provisioned with a blanket, a small travel pillow, and a bottle of water with a label in Chinese. He assumed this was the seat assigned to him.

He looked in the pocket in front of his seat, hoping to find an information card that might tell him who had manufactured the aircraft to which he was entrusting his life. There was a vomit bag, but nothing else in the pouch.

Then, as he looked out the window at the tarmac, a middle-aged man in military dress uniform came up the jet way and into the plane. "Good evening, sir," he said in smooth if slightly accented English. "Welcome aboard."

"Thank you," said Henry.

"Our flight time to Shanghai is fourteen hours," said the uniformed man.

Henry could not hide his shock. "But I'm going to Wuhan."

"My instructions are to take you to Shanghai," said the man, who Henry suddenly realized was the pilot. A pilot in military uniform? And then he understood: he was aboard a Chinese *military* aircraft.

"Colonel Hui is expecting me in Wuhan," Henry said, eyes a bit wide with trepidation.

Something changed in the pilot's expression. He straightened up noticeably, pulled his head back, squared his shoulders. "If Colonel Hui is expecting you, I am sure you will be taken to him. If you need anything, press that," and he indicated a yellow button on the armrest to the right of Henry's seat. "Now, excuse me." And he turned on his heel, as if on parade, and ducked into the cockpit.

A 14-hour flight is not something you forget, no matter how much of it you spend unconscious. Henry had intentionally deprived himself of his normal sleep the night before, and was bedraggled as he boarded the plane, which he learned later was a Chengdu-20. But his excitement, and the nagging worry of how he would get from Shanghai to Wuhan, kept him fidgeting.

The plane took off ten minutes later without any announcement from the cockpit. Henry wondered who else was on board. Certainly not just him and the pilot. A plane this size requires some kind of help. Where were they hiding? And Henry kept thinking that Hui's name had made a deep impression on the pilot. Just who was Hui, and how much influence did he carry? It was the last conscious thought he had before he crashed into an all-engulfing sleep.

At some point during the half-day flight, Henry realized he was ravenous. That made him think of Rav, which was not, at this moment, helpful. He pressed the yellow button, and a man in uniform, but not the pilot who had greeted him, came into the cabin.

"May I have something to eat, please?" Henry said timidly. When the man in uniform did not react, Henry mimed spooning food into his mouth.

"Ah," said the man, who wore the same color and style uniform as the pilot, but without the epaulettes the pilot had brandished. Henry decided he was a steward of some sort. Ten minutes later, a plastic tray sat before Henry. It contained a cup of unsweetened tea, a bowl of semi-transparent soup with green leaves of some kind swimming on its surface, and two, four-inch-long rolls of pressed rice wrapped around what Henry took to be salmon. It was all surprisingly tasty. When he finished, the man in uniform returned, and Henry asked about the lavatory. The steward pointed to the rear of the section where Henry was seated. Once his needs were taken care of, Henry slumped back into his seat and slept some more. He thought about Rav.

To call Henry jet-lagged when the plane landed is an insult to jets and laggards. To call him intimidated is to elevate timidity. He was escorted off the Chengdu craft by the steward who had fed him, and walked through a thick throng of mostly civilian Chinese. At passport control, he and his two bags were handed off to another young man— maybe mid-20s—who asked him his name in English and hustled him past the hours-long queue of returning Chinese passengers to a kiosk manned by an angry-looking woman in a military uniform. The young man spoke with deference to the control officer, who clearly was having a bad day, though it was only ten in the morning. He thought he heard the sound "Hui", and a new alertness widened her eyes. She harrumphed and with little more than a glance, stamped Henry's American passport. The young man then disappeared. Just completely vanished. Not a word. Henry had no idea how he had accomplished this.

To his immense relief, he saw his name on a whopping placard as he emerged with his two large suitcases and a backpack after clawing his way through the scrum of other passengers. "Fuck-ee" was a sound he heard more than he expected. His first Mandarin lesson.

The woman with the placard spoke not a word of English. She took possession of both his suitcases, though he protested—and led him at a quite unreasonable pace from the International Arrivals terminal to one that Henry calculated, in his time-zone haze, to be at least half a mile away. After two failed attempts at humor and one at begging for a slower speed to this manic transfer, he decided silence was the diplomatic and best option.

He and his fleet-footed escort reached the check-in desk of BetJet with time to spare. He re-checked his bags, and was surprised when the escort boarded the plane with him, although she had no ticket. Nevertheless, a seat was apparently reserved for her, across the aisle and two rows back from Henry, giving her a perfect line of vision of his every movement.

The airport at Wuhan, that town that almost no Americans had ever heard of, was about the size of JFK in New York, and about as busy. When Henry tried to walk toward the baggage claim hall, the escort took his arm firmly, shook her head, and led him out a sliding glass door.

"But my luggage," he protested.

Head shake. Then a stream of Chinese, followed by an artificial smile.

"Ok," Henry said. He wanted to get off to a good start.

A waiting car took them to a hostel-like structure that seemed, to Henry, to be composed of many very small rooms. His was two floors up—reached by stairs since the elevator was, a sign proclaimed in English and French, "not currently function." To his relief, his two suitcases arrived less than a half hour after he did, borne up the steps by an old man of quite phenomenal strength and absolutely no personality. Henry thanked him and tried to give him five dollars for his efforts, only to be rebuffed with a look of horror. First social lesson: gratitude does not translate to gratuities here.

He was so eager to open his cases and make sure all his belongings were still there that he nearly missed the square envelope resting on the small wooden desk. Apart from a single bed, the desk and a wooden chair were the only furniture. The envelope was not sealed because there was no sticky substance on its lip. The lip had been inserted behind the fold of the envelope, the way junk mail is sent as a way of economizing on postage.

Inside the envelope was one sheet of white paper. The message, in English: "Meet Col. Hui in his office. 4pm. Address below;"

And indeed, there were a series of Chinese characters at the bottom of the page. No mention of how to get there, and Henry quickly came to understand the advantage of being in the protective custody of the Chinese military.

It was two o'clock and Henry could not recall ever having been so jet-lagged, despite the sleep he had on the Chengdu. The single bed with its snowy white sheet looked magically inviting. Just a few minutes with his eyes closed....

He knew better. Instead, he opened his suitcase, fished out a set of tan pants, a button-down blue shirt, underwear and socks. Stripped off his travel clothes and dragged himself to the bathroom. There was a space that looked like it might be a shower. It had no curtain, but did have a drain in the floor. One handle extended from the wall, and above it, something that looked like a garden hose with a silver tip. No soap. No shampoo, and one towel that might have been used recently and not washed.

Socialism with Chinese characteristics.

The so-to-speak shower felt like being licked by a large dog. The water wasn't cold, but it wasn't warm either. Henry made the best of it, using a small bottle of shampoo he had brought with him to lather his entire body. His refreshing wash-up took three minutes.

The towel, when he reached for it, felt already moist, but he ignored the implications. Get ready. Look good. Be on time. Impress them. Impress Rav, he thought.

Neatly, if not formally attired, he took the lift to the lobby, which he had barely noticed upon his arrival what, an hour ago? It began to occur to him that this could be a test, perhaps the first of many, to see how he reacted to pressure. AI analysis, he knew, was only part pure intelligence, the other part being able to react to unexpected circumstances. How else, he had read many times, could we try to program an inanimate object to react the way humans would when things don't go quite as planned. Well, he was reacting, and reacting well, he thought.

An unsmiling doorman merely nodded when Henry said, "taxi," and led him to a queue of identical red cars, that, beneath Chinese script on their sides, obligingly said, "TAXI.' The doorman had already retreated to the lobby, so Henry stuck out the piece of paper that was his welcome note, and pointed, redundantly he realized, at the address at the bottom. The driver said not a word, but pulled out and did a quick U-turn in the face of oncoming traffic. Henry closed his eyes.

The driver had his head above Henry's and was speaking sharply. He had opened the back door, tried shaking Henry awake, and then resorted to staccato imprecations. Henry had no idea how long he had slept, only that he felt worse than he had before going unconscious. His back felt welded to the plastic seat and his head was precariously balanced on his neck. A fleeting thought of Rav forced him to move forward. Slowly he slid one foot out the open back door, then the other. If he had been carrying anything with him—briefcase? backpack? – it was too much trouble to lean back into the car to collect it. The driver, satisfied that this *gweilo* was not going to climb back in, held out his hand, palm up—the universal sign. And it occurred to Henry with horror that he had no Chinese money. His Father had given him two hundred dollars for expenses, four fifty-dollar bills. In something like panic, Henry decided to ask the driver if he had change. He took out his dollars and showed them to the driver, who grabbed them all, pocketed them, slammed the back door shut and was behind the wheel of his taxi and driving off before Henry could even mount an angry "Hey!" in any language.

The building where the driver had stopped was in no way prepossessing. It was a brick construction, painted white; two stories high, four street-facing windows, with a black metal waist-high gate. No identification. It occurred to Henry that he might have been dumped off in a city he knew nothing about, where he knew no one, and, aside from his own vanity and determination, might be a huge mistake.

The gate was not locked. He approached it tentatively, reached out, and was relieved to learn that gates in China worked pretty much the way they did in New Jersey. He was in, wherever that might be. And thrilled beyond any hope or reason to see the black door open and then, Rav's most gorgeous face along with the equally ravishing rest of her.

"Henry, you made it,' she said, and coming from her, even such banalities were music.

"Of course, I did. I said I would.'

"Very impressive. We are glad that you are here. Please come in." She pulled the door open wider and stood aside. The foyer was not grand, instead, it was solid looking. A force was generated from here, Henry felt, something he could not identify but could sense. How that force came to be concentrated in a nondescript foyer of a nondescript building in the middle of China remained among the many unknowns that would define this unique day.

Henry thought he remembered the sharp perfection of Rav's English, but hearing it again, now, reminded him of just how classically correct it was. Her words were neither hurried nor hesitant, and he felt himself relaxing under their beguiling British-accented influence. "Colonel Hui said he would see you as soon as you arrived, so let us not keep him waiting."

His assent not being necessary, Henry followed her to a staircase protected by a black heavy mesh metal fence. Rav had a key for the lock in its door, and they were through and mounting the stairway to— Henry had no idea, but if it put him in proximity to Hui, he was happy to make the climb. And perhaps find out just who had sent for him from the other side of the world.

It wasn't far, though it was far removed from how the rest of the building looked. Just as in his makeshift quarters in New York, Hui occupied the south corner office on the top floor. Sitting outside his imposing black office door was none other than Tanteeth, who showed her dental work with an uncertain smile.

"Wi-col, Hanny," she said. "Honey?" thought Henry. We don't know each other well enough for that. Then he realized she had mangled his name, just as she had at their first meeting. Without pausing for his reply, she stood, knocked once, deferentially, on the door behind her, and stuck her head in. A moment later, she swung the door open, and said, "Pri gowin."

The office looked like a military museum. In one corner was a suit of armor complete with a wicked looking halberd, a peaked steel helmet and pointed silver-toned boots. In the next corner sat a canon that looked like it could fire softball-size artillery. Behind a large carved wood desk sat Hui, now in military uniform, rising with quiet dignity from his polished wood desk and leather office chair. Most impressive though, behind the chair and appearing to peer over Hui's shoulder was a life-size azure-blue hologram of Xi Jinping, China's paramount leader, smiling vaguely but eternally watchful.

"Helps me remember who I work for," said Hui, tossing his head backward, and Henry was once again overwhelmed by this man's ability to control a conversation, or for that matter, a situation, with the utterance of just a few words, and those in a language not his own.

Hui gave no indication of wishing to shake hands, and instead pointed a finger to the hardback chair situated three feet in front of the desk. Henry took it as a signal to sit.

He realized that he was taller than Hui, more muscled in the shoulders. Those were the only areas where he could claim superiority. Hui was probably in his late 50s, Henry guessed, perhaps even 60. But he held himself straight, and his eyes had a way of covering everything and everyone in the room. Henry had noticed a similar quality when he saw Hui lecturing in New York. But being so up-close and personal now was a different experience. Hui commanded, not just the room, but all within it.

"We are pleased that you are here," Hui said, as though he was reciting the exact time of day. "You made a good and brave decision to come here. Your time with us, I promise, will prove to be valuable, for us as well as for you.'

"Thank you, sir," Henry said, feeling it was an inadequate response to the flowery salutation he had just received.

Hui's face darkened. "In this institute, and in this country, you will address me as Colonel. As you see, I wear the uniform of my homeland. It seemed unnecessarily militaristic to do so while in America, especially since I was a guest of academia."

"I understand," said Henry.

"You too, will wear a uniform when you work here," said Hui, leaving no room for discussion. 'And you will be addressed as 'xiashi,' which means corporal."

"Umm, corporal of what, sir? I mean, Colonel?"

"Of the People's Liberation Army, of course," said Hui. "This Institute is part of that noble institution, and you are now a part of the Institute. Welcome, xiashi."

"But, Colonel, I am an American."

"The minute you accepted my offer to work here, you became part of the new China, part of the future, part of the rest of world history. You are fortunate, xiashi. While the rest of your former country struts confidently into oblivion, you will be a cog in the machinery of progress."

Jet-lagged nearly into oblivion, recently robbed by a cabbie, unaware of where he was, and unsure what life held for him, Henry could think of nothing to say except, "Yes, Colonel."

"Good," said Hui, then switched his demeanor, became again the wise and elder professor, no longer a stiff-necked ranking officer. "You have knowledge that can be useful to the Institute, to China as a whole, and to me. I saw these qualities in you when we first met. I mean to make use of them, if you will trust me and do as I ask. What do you say?"

He knew he was about to make an important decision. He had no way of knowing how momentous it might be. He thought of his home in New Jersey, his parents, Khadija, the non-stop news headlines about the pandemic, the awful descent of American politics into cage-match wrestling.

And in front of him, he saw Hui, suave and amiable, his perfect English a comforting halfway point in this journey he was beginning. He saw Tanteeth, looking at him with keen eyes, as if waiting for his answer. And Rav, hauntingly beautiful, clever, provocative without meaning to be.

He looked at Hui and said, "I will do my best, Colonel."

Hui nodded, satisfied. "Now it is time to get to work. You will stay in your hotel tonight, sleep soundly, and move into your room here tomorrow morning at six. Did you read the literature I recommended to you?"

"Colonel, I have read all of it, and prepared some notes and comments, along with questions I have about the material."

A micro-smile came and went on Hui's face. "You did this to impress me. It is your first success in your new life." He took a red thumb drive from his desk—was he preparing for this anyway? – and tossed it to Henry, who speared it with one hand. "Upload your notes and bring the drive back tomorrow. It will be reviewed and graded. Your first Chinese lesson will be at seven tomorrow morning. So, as I said, sleep soundly. Good day."

And with that, the interview appeared to be over, along with the first part, the American stage, of Henry's life.

Henry would never be sure, but he could have sworn that at precisely the same moment that Hui spoke, the hologram of Xi Jinping nodded, once, as if bestowing approval.

# Chapter 9
## As If Things Couldn't Get Worse

The Three Rivers closing was bad enough. It was May, the buds were popping on the trees, and it was time to breathe again. Jerry looked around for another bar, but most of them near him were closed. He heard the Fort Pitt Hotel had a bar that allowed only six patrons in at a time. And the beers were twelve bucks apiece.

Fuck that.

As if things couldn't get worse, all the blacks started running around, protesting because the cops had iced someone in Minnesota. With a gun to his head, Jerry might have picked out Minnesota on a map, but he sure as hell had no interest in the place. Or who the cops had tapped there.

So when he saw a bunch of blacks marching down Smithfield Street, with some signs that said BMW, or something like one of those foreign cars, his first reaction was to wonder where the Pittsburgh cops were. Were they all in Minnesota, on vacation? The last big demonstration in Pittsburgh, he thought, was probably the last time the Pens won the Stanley Cup, and no one was pissed off then, they were celebrating.

Jerry knew some black people. Most of them were like him, trying to scratch out a living, save a little loot, find someone to marry, raise some kids. He could absolutely say, with complete sincerity, that he had nothing against blacks. Live and let live. He wasn't keen on this affirmative action shit, because that was when some black guy got a job that someone else wanted *just because* he was black. That wasn't affirmative action. That was discrimination, and that's what all the

73

blacks were honking about back in the 50s and 60s, wasn't it? Maybe it was okay with them if whites got discriminated against. This kind of stuff gave Jerry a headache.

So when he saw what looked like half the blacks of the city out on the street shouting and hooting and hollering, it rubbed him the wrong way. You want something to change, convince enough voters to back someone who feels the way you do, elect him, and that's how you make change in a democracy. This looked more like something you'd see in South America or one of those Arab shitholes, when they dragged the President out of his palace and strung him up. He also noticed that almost none of them were wearing a mask, like they kept telling us we had to do. And the ones whose faces were covered were wearing those wooly black balaclava things, so you couldn't see their faces, not to protect them from the China shit.

Not in Pittsburgh, my friends.

What turned Jerry into a Defender was what he saw on YouTube the next day. It was video of an elderly white couple in Pittsburgh that had been sitting outside a café the day before, when that demo happened. They were outside, although it was kind of chilly, because you weren't allowed to eat inside the café anymore because of the virus. So, good Pittsburghers that they were, they were eating outside, with coats on. The old gent was nursing a beer in a mug, and his wife was picking at a salad, along with a glass of iced tea. And ten seconds into the video, a bunch of blacks come along with their placards and their pissed off attitudes. And a big fat black girl comes up to the couple's table, and without a moment's hesitation, grabs the guy's beer mug, downs most of it, and pours the rest of the beer on his wife. And all the time they're hollering, "We comin' for you. We gonna take it all away. Fuck you, whitey."

Jerry replayed the video a dozen times. Each time he saw it, he got madder. What, he kept asking himself, was the world coming to? The video had been posted online by a group called The Defenders, which Jerry had never heard of before, except maybe for an old television show about English detectives. So he Googled "The Defenders" and saw it was a group that stood for the rights of white people. And for the right of cops to shoot someone that was trying to shoot them first. And for law and order. If this group also rooted for the Pirates, it would have been perfect, but you can't have everything.

Jerry found The Defenders' website, saw that it seemed to be headquartered in Virginia, but that it also had a phone number, among several, with a 412-area code, the code for Pittsburgh.

"Yeah?"

"This the Defenders?"

"Who wants to know?"

"Name's Jerry. I saw your video on YouTube."

"Can you believe that shit? In Pittsburgh?"

"You in Pittsburgh?"

"Maybe."

"Well, I am. Like I said, name's Jerry. What are you defending?"

"We are defending the right to be white, before it's declared illegal."

If Jerry had admitted to having such emotions, he might have teared up with joy.

"So, I Googled you. There were some people saying not-so-nice stuff about you. Like you're racists, and nut-case right-wingers, and white supremacists. That true?"

"Well, Jerry, my fine fellow, you tell me what any of those not-so-nice things actually means, and I'll tell you if it's true."

"Well, racist, for starters."

"You read the newspapers, Jerry? You check any news sites?"

"Sure. I'm not stupid."

"Didn't say you were. What's your idea of racist?"

"Treating someone different because of what color they are."

"Right. So, if you read the news, notice anything different about how the media are writing black and white these days?"

"Yeah, they're capitalizing black now."

"How about white?"

"No, that's still lower case."

"So, are they treating one race different from another, because of color?"

"Yeah, I'd say they are."

"So, tell me Jerry: who's racist?"

It worked like this: the guy could see Jerry's number on his phone and asked if Jerry wanted to receive some information about The

Defenders. Jerry said he did. The guy said he could text it to Jerry, or, if Jerry had email, he could send it that way. Texts eventually cost extra if you went over your monthly limit, so Jerry gave the guy his email.

"Read it over, Jerry. If you like it, get back in touch. If not, no hard feelings."

But Jerry knew already he was going to like it, and that he'd get back in touch.

"By the way, Jerry. Are you wearing a mask?"

Jerry tensed up. He didn't need another lecture about how it was unpatriotic, unfair and unsafe not to wear one. "No, I'm not."

"Good. I'm not either. If the blacks can run around outside demonstrating and not wearing masks, why should we? But you don't see the news media pointing that out, do you? That's what I call racism."

Jerry thought: maybe the country's not finished, after all.

He read the stuff they sent him and called back. "You make a good case. I'm in if you want me."

"Bet your ass we do, bro. What part of Pittsburgh you in?"

"Just downtown from the Hill District."

"Whoa. Living on the fault line, huh?"

"I been here a long time."

"Okay. Meet you in Front of PNC Stadium, Entrance F. That's where…"

"Yeah. Where the Clemente statue is. How about right in front of him?"

"Two o'clock tomorrow work?"

"Even today."

"What? You get knocked outta your job by the virus shit?"

"Along with most of the people I know."

Jerry walked across the Roberto Clemente Bridge, which connects downtown with the north side, and leads directly to the Pirates' jewel of a home stadium. He wore a Pirates warm-up jacket because even though it was May it was nippy. Pittsburgh never disappoints.

And there, at Entrance F, stood the bronze (not steel, which was a shame, considering) statue of the Great One, the Puerto Rican right fielder who led the Pirates to two world championships and, to be honest, never got in life the respect he had earned and finally received after the plane he was flying in, to take supplies to survivors of an earthquake in Nicaragua, disappeared somewhere in the Caribbean.

Jerry had no idea what to expect of the guy he would be meeting. But he sure as shit didn't expect to see a short, beefy guy about his age, clearly Asian, and wearing a backwards Pirates cap.

"Yo, Jerry?"

"That's me. And you are..."

"Name's Tran. And before you get started, no, I'm not a transsexual, a transvestite or a trans-Atlantic traveler. It's just Tran. You surprised to see my eyes aren't round?"

Jerry figured if he couldn't be straight with someone from a group calling itself The Defenders, he was shit out of luck. "Little bit, yeah. I couldn't tell what you looked like from your voice on the phone, if that means anything."

"Yeah, it does. My mom's Vietnamese. My dad was a soldier. They met over there and I'm what happened. Dad was from Pittsburgh. He moved us back here when he came home, then two years later, up and died. We get his GI pension and I do some free-lance computer work."

"Good for you."

"Ok. You read the stuff. What can I tell you?"

"Well, I gotta tell you, I'm a little confused right now."

"Because I'm not white, right?"

"Well, yeah."

"Look, Jerry, you don't have to play coy, or be careful what you say to me. I'm Asian, I got slanted eyes and I'm a little yellower than you. Beyond that, I'm just another Pittsburgh guy worried about where the country's going. That's why I joined The Defenders. In fact, I'm kind of the local rep for them."

"How'd that happen then?"

"Well, Jerry, I'll tell you. I was lucky. My Dad loved my Mom and did the right thing by her after I was born. And he grew to love me. And I loved him, too. We were lucky he brought us here and didn't leave us in the mud paddy where I was born. I love this country and it gave me a chance. And I *earned* everything I got here. It wasn't because I was a minority."

Jerry was emboldened by Tran's openness. "Are you guys even considered a minority?"

Tran grinned. "Well, that's the point, Jer. Unlike other people in this country who aren't white, Asians, as a group, have done quite well here. We tend to come from stable families. Not everyone, of course. But most Asians who come here want to work hard, want to succeed, want to obey the law, want to take care of their families. And guess what? That pays off. You don't see a bunch of Asians running through the streets saying they haven't been treated fairly, that the police are out to exterminate them, that the system is rigged against them. We did what you're supposed to do. We assimilated, became Americans. If we don't look like George Washington and Thomas Jefferson, so what? We live by the rules, we pay our taxes, we make our kids go to school and study, and nobody gives us problems. And isn't that what America is all about?"

Jerry was very impressed with this discourse. It was the first honest conversation he'd had about race in months, years really. And Tran, who he'd met about four minutes ago, seemed like a stand-up guy.

"So, you still haven't answered my question. What are you doing with The Defenders?"

Tran was nodding before Jerry finished the question. "Actually, I did answer your question, by telling you the short version of my life story. I wasn't born here, but I like it here. I like what America is, and I don't want to see it perverted by a bunch of whiny people who don't have the guts or ambition to stand up for themselves, who fuck their women and leave them holding the bag with a bunch of kids, who commit way more crimes than their percentage of the population could account for, and who are now trying to make us think that they deserve more of my tax money because of how they look."

Tran stopped, shrugged and went on. "And let's be honest, though I just met you and for all I know, you be on the payroll of some left-wing nutbag outfit, wearing a wire or with a pinhole camera on you, and trying to dirt-bag us."

"I'm not doing any of those things," Jerry said, suddenly more cautious, wondering if maybe it was the other way around and this Tran guy was the undercover agent, trying to rope him into saying or doing something illegal.

But when he re-engaged Tran's eyes—round or not—he could see that Tran was already ahead of him. "I'm not either, Jer. I am who I say I am. You can Google me. You, by the way, my man, have no Google profile."

"Not important enough," Jerry said.

"Maybe not," said Tran. "But I don't see you out on the street, screaming and shouting that you want some, or all, of what I've got because you deserve it. Because you've been done dirty and now it's payback time."

"That's right," Jerry said. "Because I don't feel that way."

"Neither do I," said Tran. "What I was gonna say before, is, let's be honest, having me looking like I do, and a solid supporter of The Defenders makes it hard for the bleeding hearts out there to call us a White supremacist group. Which, by the way, we're not."

Jerry was looking past Tran, at PNC Park, home of his beloved if hopeless Pirates. Outside the park were four statues of Pirate immortals—Clemente, right next to him, Willie Stargell, Honus Wagner. And of course, Maz, Bill Mazeroski, the hero of the 1960 Series. Two blacks, two whites. Equality. And each of them had earned his place through brilliant play, hard work. Leading by example. None of them was up there on pedestals to fill a quota for Puerto Ricans, or blacks, or even Pollacks, like Maz. They were all part of the same team. Just like Americans were supposed to be. Not bitching about what other people had, or clamoring for handouts and special treatment.

And then his vision cleared, and he saw Tran looking at him, and he knew that Tran knew what he was thinking.

"Tran, like I said on the phone, I'm in. If you want me."

"Like I said on the phone, Jerry: Bet your ass we do."

They shook hands, and neither let go right away.

# Chapter 10
## It's My Party And I'll Lie If I Want To

The call to Fang came three days after he had broken protocol and spoken up at the Advisory Council meeting. He had spent the seventy-two hours in something of a nervous breakdown. Why had he spoken up? What had he been thinking? And then, another wave would overtake him, and he realized he had *wanted* to say those three words out loud. They weren't his invention, but he knew that they applied to the situation the speakers had been trying to address.

It was Wo, the motivational speaker at the Advisory Council meeting, who got in touch. His tone on the phone was standoffish, dismissive, which, strangely enough, Fang found reassuring. Too much friendly chit-chat would be just the kind of camouflage the Party would use to soften him up for some sort of assault.

"Your presence at the meeting was noted, and appreciated," Wo began. "The Party will need as many people like you as possible as we grapple with this situation. Please come and see me when your work schedule permits."

Fang had never heard of Wo before the Advisory Council meeting, but his attendance there was proof that he was somehow important. Not wanting to betray his ignorance, he merely said, "It would be an honor." He asked three colleagues whom he knew well enough to ask about another Party member, but got the same head-shaking reply: no idea. Frustrated, he took what he considered a bold step and asked Wu where Wo worked (Try saying that three times fast). As expected, the inquiry earned him a harsh glare. "Why do you want to know?" Wu asked.

Fang had prepared a reply for just this situation. "He spoke at the Advisory Council meeting. I hadn't met him before, but I thought he made very good points. Didn't you?"

This was a dangerous tack to take. The question implied that Wu did *not* think well of Wo, an attitude that could be reported to Wo under certain circumstances.

"Of course, I did. He works on the third floor, in the records department. Tell me if he contacts you."

"Certainly, comrade." You, thought Fang to himself as he walked away, smiling, are a pretty sneaky bastard.

Still being a sneaky bastard, Fang waited a day before cautiously approaching the records department. He had never been here before, and was unsure exactly what records were kept here and to whom they pertained. Asking too many questions was not wise. In China, these days, enquiring minds are often met with suspicion, and more often than not, punishment. He approached the office and saw Wo seated in the back, next to a window, which told him something. He slipped through the ranks of open-plan workstations, and made sure Wo saw him before he spoke.

"Comrade, I'm glad you came so promptly." This, Fang took as a partial rebuke. It had taken him a day to present himself.

"It is an honor to see you again."

"More like a duty, I'd say." Thus, the parameters had been set. Fang was there to listen, not to schmooze. "Who told you to speak up at that meeting?"

"No one, comrade. I hope I did not give offense."

"That doesn't matter. What matters is that you spoke. Who put those words in your mouth?"

Fang knew he had taken a risk speaking at the meeting. Now he was about to take another. "No one, comrade. The words were mine." In the days since the meeting, and especially in the day since Wo's call, Fang had pondered whether to give proper credit to his friend, and decided not to. After all, "sleek and silent" was advice with regard to how to treat a wife, or ex-wife. They were just three words. No one owned them. Except, it now seemed, Fang did.

"Hmmm. Well, keep it that way. I passed along that ... phrase ... to my colleagues. Do not mention it to anyone else. Do you understand?"

"Of course, comrade. May I ask what colleagues you are referring to?"

Wo fixed him with a look that was not hostile, but certainly not friendly. "I see that you do not know who I am. I come to this laboratory and have this desk in the records department. But I work for C.A.C."

"C.A.C.?" The letters meant nothing to Fang.

"The Cyberspace Administration of China."

"Ah." Fang knew enough to know what he didn't know and not to show it. "Well, comrade, anything I can do to aid you in your important work, please just let me know."

"I have just let you know. Good-bye." It was just as well, Fang thought, that Wo was pretending to work in the records department. He wouldn't be very convincing in Human Relations.

Even before he got back to his workplace, Fang was looking up Cyberspace Administration of China on his phone, using Alibaba. And regretting it instantly. The screen went red, and yellow letters rolled across it saying, "Access Denied".

Fool, fool, he thought. Why did you do that? And why, particularly, do it from your own phone? "Access Denied" meant he had done something wrong, flaunted the rules. It didn't matter that access had been denied. It mattered that his attempt to get sensitive information would be noted, somewhere, and that it would eventually be known to someone, and that they would have no trouble tracing the source of the illicit search request. Speaking up at the meeting had produced an unexpected positive result, and now he had canceled that out, probably begun a cycle of trouble from which he would never recover, and could even face Chinese justice, which, in his heart of hearts, he knew was an oxymoron.

He was useless at work for the rest of the day, caught himself staring into space, wondering if any of the CCTV cameras lurking in the corners of the room had picked him up doing nothing. Now, not only would he have to explain why he had tried to get information about something to which he did not have access, he would have to apologize for wasting the people's and the Party's time by staring into space. Or maybe Cyberspace. He tried to look busy, which can be terribly difficult if you are in an exposed cubicle and nervously twitching in front of your fellow workers.

He left the lab as soon as he responsibly could, walked with no particular destination in mind through the cold rain that was Wuhan's weather trademark. He could have gone home, but what was home? A 45-square meter shell of cracking concrete, furnished with a combination of low-end sale items and cast-offs picked up on the street, or donated by someone who knew he had gotten divorced and had no taste in fashion. He was tempted, for about thirty seconds, to again go see Qi Qi on the pretext of seeing how she was feeling, in reality to see if she had yet discovered that he had pilfered her savings to bribe Wu into naming him onto the Advisory Council.

Socialism with Chinese Characteristics.

His phone pinged. He had a text. It was Wu. "See me first thing tomorrow." His despair was now complete. He had been found out before he even reached his unfashionable home. Which he would probably lose; confiscation was only part of what happened to criminals. After all, he wouldn't need a home after tomorrow. He would have one, in prison, hanging by his wrists in chains. Maybe prison was better furnished than his home. He laughed, something that Chinese do only when embarrassed. Or scared.

He stopped at a liquor store and, though he knew he shouldn't and probably couldn't afford it, bought a large bottle of baijiu. The colorless distilled rice liquor was 65% alcohol, or 130 proof, and was guaranteed to knock any sense out of you. He put the bottle, which came wrapped in a bamboo cover, in his rucksack and headed for home through the still stinging rain. He might as well spend his last night of freedom doing something to ensure that he would not be able to remember it.

He got to the lab early, because he knew if he didn't, he would never make it in at all. He felt like flies were competing to get out of his brain through his nose, his ears, his eyes. He had not been so hung over since the night after he signed the paper granting him his divorce from Qi Qi. Freedom, oblivion, solitude, all in one day.

Wu was not in yet, so Fang resorted to something that he seldom did: he made tea. Even in 2020, it was Fang's belief that women should make tea, and men should drink it. Old-fashioned? Perhaps. But unlike the United States, which he had read about and seen online, was turning itself inside out not to offend *anyone* except white men, China did not seek literal equality. For this he was grateful, though always nervous about seeing men's primacy being chipped away.

Also, unlike Americans (how did they become so powerful, Fang wondered as he sipped his own tepid brew), the Han Chinese did not have to worry about racial discrimination, demonstrations like those convulsing America over the arrest of a convicted criminal, and other spurious attempts at "change." China had done just fine over the past ten thousand years, thank you. This was due to Han leadership and intelligence. Second-tier species such as Uighurs, half-breeds such as those with Korean blood, and the misguided who had turned to the Christian Churches for guidance, deserved whatever fate befell them. China was supreme. And now, under the infallible guidance of Xi Jinping, it was reaching its proper crescendo of power and respect around the world.

He saw Wu come in and go directly to her workspace. It occurred to Fang that, unlike Wo, Wu did not have an office. Somehow, this comforted him, but only for a second. He still had to face the Dragon, and explain, no doubt, what he had been doing searching on his phone for the Cyberspace Administration. If faced with drastic consequences, he was going to say that Wo had mentioned it to him. Let him face the music of betraying privileged information. Fang had only two priorities right now: Fang, and survival. One priority, when he distilled it all down.

He decided to take the initiative. Wu had said "first thing," so why wait to be summoned to his own execution. Get it over with. He had thought, for a few moments, of bringing her a cup of the tea that he had brewed, but rejected the idea as ass-kissing. Though he would gladly glue his lips to her grotesque looking haunches it that was what was called for.

Not many people had arrived yet. The overnight shift—who were aptly referred to as "the vampires" – were gathering their things to leave. They paid him no attention.

"You wanted to see me."

84

"Sit." She said it as though addressing a dog, which Fang assumed, with her, usually involved a knife and fork.

Wu looked through him, adjusted her ill-fitting glasses and said, simply, "You no longer work here."

Fang had steeled himself for the moment. He lifted his gaze, almost idly, to see if the police or Party militia was moving in to apprehend him. He tried to savor the moment of silence that had descended on them. He would get lots of time to listen to silence, but not as a free man, not as a member of the Party.

"You are being seconded to the Cyberspace Administration of China. Wo will instruct you further. *Zaijian.*" Good-bye. She demonstrated less passion than she would have ordering take-away food. It is impolite in China to try to extend a conversation after one of the parties has said *Zaijian,* and Fang was too confused to press his luck. "*Zaijian*," he said dully in reply, as if this was exactly what he had been expecting and walked away. What could it mean?

He quickly found out. "You will not be seeing Comrade Wu again," said Wo, with about as much interest as he might have betrayed while discussing last week's weather. "I am now your immediate superior. You will do nothing, and say nothing, without my prior approval. Do you understand?"

"I understand that. But what is my role?"

"To support me in all that I do. That is all you need to know. Gather whatever belongings you have in this building. You will not be returning here."

"But my work..."

"Your work is what the Administration says it is."

"Yes, comrade."

"Part of our job"—Fang noticed the inclusive word— " is to make sure that the Chinese people are protected from misinformation, from," here he smiled as though approaching the punchline of a hilarious joke, "fake news, as Trump calls it. But also to make sure that our social media portrays an accurate picture of what is going on. This strain of influenza, which some of our citizens have contracted is being portrayed as something new and dangerous. The CAC will counteract this lie, in order to preserve calm and order."

"I see."

"I doubt that. You have only been under my supervision for ten minutes. Did you learn everything you need to know in that time?"

"Of course not. I merely meant that you explained the situation very well."

Wo harrumphed. "You are to be my subordinate in the task of monitoring social media sites. Especially WeChat, which seems to have mistaken itself for a beacon of light, a truth-teller. That will soon end."

"How will it end?"

Wo looked at him, seemed to make a decision, and said, "You caught my attention because you had the courage to speak out at your first Advisory Council meeting. What you said made sense. I decided to use your intelligence in the cause of the Party and the people. Do not make me change my opinion. You work for me now, not Wu. And I cannot be bribed with sixty yuan."

It was a hundred-sixty yuan, Fang thought. But he tried very hard to keep his facial muscles from moving. He felt suddenly dizzy, and wondered if he was going to fall down. That damned baijiu. He knew, however, that the liquor was not the cause of his unsteadiness. He looked at Wo, and said, "I am here to serve you and the Party, comrade. Whatever I can do, just tell me."

Again, Wo looked as if he were making a decision. He nodded his head, once, downward, and said, "This is the second time I have seen intelligence in you. I have a mental exercise for you. Take it seriously."

"Yes, comrade?"

"Imagine that you, or someone very important to you, was being disparaged online, anonymously, and that the disparagement could affect the rest of your life, your job, your standing in the Party."

It was the mention of the Party, offhand, put in third place behind life and job that clued Fang that this was a test with serious implications. He tried to clear his mind and began, "I, I would..."

"Not now," cut in Wo. "Go home, think about it tonight. And when you come in tomorrow morning, give me a hundred-word answer to my question. One hundred words. Count them. Make them count. Make each word a cudgel that punishes our enemies. *Zaijian.*"

# Chapter 11
## Was Qi The Key?

Qi Qi Dieh knew she had come close to death. For days, she shivered, vomited, struggled to breathe, had nothing but water, sometimes room temperature, sometimes warmed if she could rouse herself to do it. She vaguely remembered that her ex-husband had visited her, made his normal pretense of caring how she felt, and then left. He had not been back. Perhaps that was why she felt better.

So, when there was a loud knock on her door, she figured it was Fang again. Since their divorce, Qi Qi had realized just what a shit he was. And yet, there was something about him that still ... not attracted but interested her. She, who knew that she would live out whatever life she had left, alone, ignored, and probably poor, saw in Fang some ineffable quality that seemed to point him upward, toward success, possibly celebrity, almost certainly power.

She opened the door to a spaceman. Head to toe, dressed in a white costume that looked like it was made either or plastic or canvas. A helmet covered his head, with only a small hole where his facial features could be seen. Qi Qi looked at the spaceman with frank awe. What did he want?

"What do you want?"

"You are citizen Qi Qi Dieh, yes?"

"Yes."

"It has been reported that you may be carrying a dangerous virus. You must come with us."

"Us?"

"Us." The spaceman stood aside, and Qi could see there were five, maybe six more spacemen in the hallway. Two were halfway inside another apartment, belonging to a lady who had kindly dropped off some food outside Qi's door. The lady, named Sun, was widely thought to have Korean blood in her, and so was generally shunned in the building, by all the residents except for Qi. Qi didn't like Koreans either, but made an exception for Sun.

"Where are we going?"

"Don't ask questions, citizen. Come with us."

"I need to know where I am going."

"You don't. You just come."

Qi Qi felt an inner alarm go off. This wasn't unprecedented. People had been rousted from their homes before, but those cases usually involved criminals. She had heard stories of citizens—Han Chinese! – being manhandled and thrown into police wagons, taken away to who knew where. But they had done something wrong, and she had not. Had she?

It all came together faster than a fear. The Virology Lab had discovered that she had absconded with a bat, taken it to Grandpa, sold it to him, for twenty-five lousy yuan. And now they had come for her.

"Look, I'll give back the money. You can take it. It was only twenty-five yuan." Desperately, shakily, she crossed the room and found the can of loose tea where she had concealed the yuan. And was as shocked as she had ever been to see that it was empty.

Fang.

Dirty rotten Fang.

She remembered it all. She, nearly dead from sickness, dizzy, unable to keep food down. Ready to die.

And her foul ex-husband coming in, using his own key to an apartment he shouldn't have had keys for, pretending concern, making her tea. Of course. He had found the yuan in the can and taken them.

Filthy Fang.

All Qi Qi wanted with what remained of her life was to meet KiKi Dee. Qi Qi had spent most of her life in anonymity, unlike KiKi. She had very little chance for changing that with what remained of her earthly existence. And she didn't believe in any other kind of existence, so this, more or less, was it. WWKKDD. What would KiKi Dee do?

"I started the virus." She said it as calmly, as matter-of-factly as she could. She rejoiced in the widening of the spaceman's eyes, the inside-helmet huff she heard from him. You don't get many chances to mess with the authorities here, and it's important to make the most of the ones you are handed.

"What did you say?"

"What's the matter? That helmut too tight over your ears? I know about the virus. I know how it started. I sold a bat from the Virology Lab to the fresh market. It had a disease. I contracted it. Now I know that other people have too. Thank you."

The spaceman was backing out of the apartment. One hand was gripping the wrist of the other hand, and Qi heard him mouthing, "Central. This is Number 51379. I need to talk to the commander."

Qi Qi knew that her life was about the change. Before she had married Fang, she had wanted success, fame, fortune, all the things that KiKi had achieved. She wasn't sure about the success and fortune parts, but she was pretty damn sure she was about to become famous.

# Chapter 12
## On The Road With Xi

*"Zaohang hao. Jitian hen rongxing yu nin zai yiqi."* Henry was amazed he could produce this much Chinese. Yet he did, this and every day as he roamed through the AI building, the same building he had stumbled into a month ago, jet-lagged, scared, and totally unprepared.

"Good morning. It is an honor to be with you today." That's what he had learned to say. It was, after all, only good manners. Certainly a step up from, "Hey yuz. Anyone make da coffee?" Hui had not sent for him again, and Rav was only a dream-like memory to imagine when he went, alone, to bed each night at nine. As Hui had promised, Henry lived in the Institute building, rose at six each morning, ate pickled vegetables, rice and tea, and began his Chinese language instruction at 7. At nine, he switched rooms and began the self-study course in AI language and interpretations that he had been assigned to complete in four weeks. He did it in three, aced the exam in English, and promised himself he'd be able to take the same exam in Chinese in half a year, with the same result.

He had to admit he was lonely. His parents' home in New Jersey had turned into a cone of near silence after his arrest with Khadija. But it was at least familiar. This room where he now resided was devoid of charm. The food was bland, vegetables, fish and broths, though he imagined, healthier than burgers and fries. He wore the clothes he had brought with him from America, but felt out of place with them compared to the Chinese who worked here. Somehow even his solid color trousers and shirts seemed garish, and flashy compared to the military uniforms most of the other employees wore, day after day.

Some bucked the trend and showed up in black trousers and white shirts, but it was only when they were going outside the Institute to interact with other researchers.

Still, there was something stimulating about the work he was doing. He believed Hui when the Colonel said AI would shape the future. He wanted to be part of that future, even if it meant turning his back on the American way of life he'd left behind. And what, after all, had that life done for him? Educated him on a campus where America was seen as a villain by Americans. Put him in a job that he lost not because of his own shortcomings. But because the virus whizzing around the air had forced everyone to stay at home, cover their faces, give up their lives.

Bland food aside, he liked China better.

Henry had communicated with his parents once, via Skype, or the Chinese version of Skype. And so, the conversation was conducted at surface level. I'm fine. The people here are great. I'm learning a lot. How's everyone there? Yeah, there's some sort of flu going around, but I'm not near any of that. There too, right? Of course, I'll take care of myself. You do the same. Talk again soon. Love you.

If Henry's parents had remained on the video call for a half a second longer, they would have seen a hand, not their son's, sweep across the screen to disconnect.

"Good," said the young man. Henry never knew his name, but after a month, that seemed normal. Names were irrelevant. Your work for the Party was what mattered. What you did was more important than who you were. In fact, Henry had learned, "you" were no one. Xi was someone. Remember that, and you'll do fine.

The young man was a lieutenant in the PLA, the same as Rav, an English language translator, who was also adept at AI, though that would never be his professional calling. His life was the Army, he would never take off the PLA uniform unless he was going swimming. His destiny had been chosen for him at the age of six, when he alone of his classmates in a private pre-school could remember, in order, ten English words that had been written on a board by the teacher, then erased. A week later he was in a different school with different classmates, all of whom spoke better English than he could at that time. By the time he had graduated, he was Best in Class.

You did not ask why you had been chosen, or what you had been chosen for. Such questions reeked of individualism, which Chairman Xi had made clear was dangerous to the collective Party consciousness.

"Your parents do not look happy," the lieutenant said to Henry. It was the first personal observation he had made.

"They're worried about me," said Henry.

The young man said, "Why are they worried? You are young. You are healthy. You are learning. You were selected to come here because you have talent. Why should they worry?"

"Well, I'm deviating, um, going off course," he said when he realized deviating was a word, (and an action) not encouraged here, "following a different path."

"And what path they want for you?"

"Well, you know, the American dream. Work hard, make the right connections, get married, act right, and things'll work out for you. That's what a lot of people—at least a lot of people like my parents—think. So they're worried that I'm doing something different."

"You say, people 'like' your parents. Describe."

"Well, they're not rich, but they're not hurting for money. They've traveled around the world because of my father's job. They have a nice house, a pretty solid bank account, I'd say. And there's some white guilt going on."

"White guilt?"

"Yeah, you know, because they're white. Because of the color of their skin. They probably feel they've had an easier life than some other people. People not like them." Henry didn't want to get into racial politics, because he was talking to a non-Caucasian in a non-Caucasian country where his very Caucasian future was at the mercy of, well, yellow folks. He knew to keep this to himself.

"So, you say, Americans, white Americans, have guilt?"

"Not all. But, yeah, a lot. If someone says that something isn't fair because of white privilege, they believe it. And they feel guilty."

The lieutenant spent a nanosecond in thought. "Thank you. Do not talk about this with anyone else."

Who would I talk to, Henry thought to himself?

Confused, a bit worried he had spoken out of turn, unsure what Rav would say or think if she had overheard the conversation (and perhaps she had), Henry applied himself to his studies. He was finding the basic concepts of AI undermined all the Judeo-Christian values he had absorbed all his life until now. Humans were broken-down, unreliable, second, no, third-rate machines. Their brains and memories were the stuff of dust and distraction. Their ability to compute was laughable. They still held a slight edge in the creative arts—music composition, literature, plays—but that would soon be dealt with. AI, meanwhile, had shown itself to be a beacon of endlessly stretching light. Once you got over the romanticism of the human brain putting people on the moon, or developing a vaccine against polio, there was nothing more to say, much less compare. The opportunities for using artificial intelligence were infinite. And by the way, the concept of infinity was flawed. AI could calculate anything, from the number of stars in our galaxy to the number of births in China ten years from now. And not just estimate them. Calculate them exactly. AI was God.

The more literature (helpfully translated into English by AI, and a fine job it did too) Henry consumed, the more videos and 4-D hologram presentations he took in, the more he believed that everything he had been taught in America was bogus. He was living on the cusp of a new era that would rely on AI to take control, and guide the world, as well as all the other worlds, forever.

And China was unquestionably the leader in AI.

Two days later, Henry was summoned by a flax-faced woman he had never seen before and hoped never to again. He was wanted in Colonel Hui's office, immediately.

Flax hustled him up to the third floor, down the corridor, and knocked twice, politely, on the door. When she heard "Enter," she twisted the handle, pushed politely, and ushered Henry in. Henry reacted the way a handsome slave, who had just been admitted to a queen's boudoir, would. Because...

Rav was there.

She was dressed in military uniform, her lush black hair pulled back into a bun, no lipstick on the lips Henry had fantasized about for a month. But the smile was there, and the intensity of the shimmering eyes was the same as he had seen that first time in New York.

The words, though, were pure Party line. "Corporal, wait here."

Henry was still getting used to being called, and being, a corporal. He didn't remember signing up for the Army, let alone the Chinese army, and didn't think his memory had deserted him in a month. But this was Rav, so...

The wait was only a few minutes. "Colonel Hui will see you," said the love of his young life, and so, in he went. To be surprised for the second time in the span of a few minutes by what awaited him behind an opening door.

Rav had not entered the office with Henry. Instead, Tanteeth stood there, unsmiling as a dumpling. Behind her, seated at his desk, the hologram of Xi radiating off his left shoulder, was Hui. There was no politesse.

"Corporal, it has been reported to me that you are doing well in your study of our language, and that you have exceeded your goals in AI theory."

"I try to do what the Party wants, Colonel."

"You don't try to do. You do." All the western polish that Hui had exhibited in New York was missing here. He was the Colonel. Nothing else mattered.

"Your AI studies are suspended."

"Why?" Henry was so shocked by this statement he forgot to conceal his feelings.

Now, the wise, the brilliant, the interesting Hui of New York days made a cameo appearance. He allowed a smile to form around his mouth, quickly dissolved it, and said, "Henry, Henry. I recruited you for this Institute because of your potential, because of your obvious interest in AI, and because you demonstrated the proper respect for authority that is the backbone of our Party. I want you to stay here and, when the time is right, continue your studies. You have a great future ahead of you. "

"Thank you, Colonel." There could be nothing wrong with thanking someone, even a Colonel, who had just complimented you, Henry thought.

"You see? This is the respect I spoke of just a minute ago. Now, Henry, listen carefully. What we are about to say must never leave this room. Remember it, but never refer to it."

"Yes, Colonel."

"You know that Wuhan has been struck with a highly contagious virus, yes? You know this because you used the phone we gave you to look up '*bingdu*'."

Henry froze. He had heard some of the other students at the institute talking, with their usually dour expressions even more so, and with much shaking of heads. The word he heard most often in those discussions was "bingdu," the accent on "du." Since he was supposed to learn as much Chinese as possible, as quickly as possible, he thought there could be no problem with looking up this word. He had done so, on his phone, using a translation app installed for him by the institute's IT lab-rat. '*Bingdu*' was the Chinese word for virus.

"You have done nothing wrong. You showed curiosity, which, when used in service to the Party, is a good thing. It is other kinds of curiosity that must be avoided."

Curiosity, for instance, like what was happening in Hong Kong. Or to the Uighurs in Xinjiang province. Or what was being planned for Taiwan. He had read about these things before leaving America. He hadn't heard a word about any of them since arriving. And he was too scared, or smart, to use his phone to look for such information.

"You also had a conversation recently about an American psychological flaw. You called it 'white guilt,' I believe."

Henry was young, but he was an intelligent young. In less than a second, his mind had created, analyzed and programmed what he thought was going to happen soon. It was this ability—to chart ahead, to pull seemingly unrelated circumstances together, and to project their nexus and potential use—that Hui had seen in him and recruited with his short-lived charm offensive.

"The Party knows a great deal about America, Henry. We have experts. We know its military potential, its harvest output, its history. Most Chinese students—the ones who have been selected—can name all fifty states and their capitals, which I doubt many Americans can do.

"We also know that America is not our friend. Ultimately, our systems will collide. When that happens, the Party must prevail. America's so-called democracy will be crushed, its shell flattened, and it will be incorporated into *Zhongguo tese shehui zhuyi*. You know what that means."

"Socialism with Chinese characteristics."

"So far, the Americans have made it easy for us. Years ago, they stopped making their own steel, because making steel pollutes the atmosphere. So they bought steel from China instead. Now we control the world's steel production.

"They stopped manufacturing the items that so-called consumers will spend money for. Everything from refrigerators to teaspoons that used to be made in America are made in China now. We export them, and make a handsome profit from Americans who don't care where their products are made, as long as they are cheap. And Chinese products, though we add on a huge profit margin when we send them to America, are still cheaper than the products America used to produce. Why is that?

"Because the Party, in its wisdom, believes that the responsibility of workers is to work, not to make demands about their working conditions, their salaries, or the pollution that may or may not be caused by the production of items that the Party has decreed they should make."

Hui nodded, as if considering what he had just said and finding it to his liking.

"In more recent years, as electronics and computers become more sophisticated, they have relied on a group of elements known as rare earths. Can you name some?"

"Scandium, Yttrium..." That throwaway college course in chemistry had just paid for itself.

"That's right. These elements possess qualities that when processed properly, power everything from I-Phones to GPS systems to nuclear warhead satellite guidance systems. The United States used to be the only country in the world that knew how to refine these elements. The world was dependent on American factories for rare earths.

"Then, Deng Xioping, who was at the time the leader of the Party, though a flawed leader, ordered China to begin mining the rare earths that were found in our central and northern regions. We had the raw materials but not the knowledge of how to convert them. So, Deng convinced the American president to give us ... *GIVE US*, Henry ... the technical specifications for processing. Once we had those, and sufficient raw materials, we began competing with the Americans. We undercut their prices, we drove them out of business. And then we bought those bankrupt companies, stripped them of every piece of machinery and research, and brought them here.

"Do you know, Henry, where the mighty Pentagon goes to get the rare earths it needs to make nuclear missiles, to make jet fighter guidance systems, to power its tanks, or even its mobile phones? China. We now control the production and refining of rare earth elements. We sell them all around the world, including America. And if the Party so chooses, we can stop selling them. And the Pentagon will go back to using horses to power their weapons."

Hui frowned, considering his next words. "We know these things through our experience with America. What we lack, Henry, is a deep understanding of *Americans*. They are so very different from we Han. What is the biggest difference, Henry?"

It took him a moment to formulate his answer. "Americans are used to getting what they want. The Han Chinese are used to earning what they need."

Hui turned and said something to Tanteeth, who nodded.

"I am removing you from your AI studies, corporal, because you were able to answer my question so well. Yes, Americans today are lazy. They want everything without working for it. These insights are precisely the kind we need from you. Not facts and figures. Feelings. Tell us about Americans' feelings. And how to use those feelings to weaken them further."

There are moments when we make decisions that seem logical, even simple or admirable at the time, but whose implications and consequences cannot be fathomed, even by the wisest of us. We think we are acting out of reason. But instead, are allowing control to be handed over to our deepest, darkest selves, the part that, a hundred thousand years ago, helped a hunter kill a wooly mammoth single-handed, that led a king to order the slaughter of an entire city for some perceived slight, that convinced Stalin or Pol Pot that wiping out a part of his population would strengthen the country, not to mention his hold on power.

Henry followed his feelings. "If I can help you, Colonel, I will."

Hui nodded. "I had to see how you would answer that question, Henry, before I could go any further. First, let me tell you: you will be rewarded for your loyalty.

"Now, listen. Making the Americans' steel, their kitchen spoons, their rare earths, these were all tests. Tests to see how far they would let us go, without retaliation. Because, Henry, if the Americans ever did find the courage to retaliate..." he shook his head..."I am afraid they could do very serious damage. We must not let that happen.

"This '*bingdu*,' this virus, that has taken hold in Wuhan, is killing a lot of people. Not many know this, but soon they will. This is not an accident, though of course, that is how we must explain it to the world. Just as we created the steel plants to replace the Americans', just as we built factories to make the products Americans no longer wanted to make but still need, just as we learned to mine and refine rare earths to power every modern piece of technology, so now we have created a *bingdu* that, in a very few months, will be the most talked-about topic in the world. It will be our latest, perhaps last, gift to the world. Do you understand me, corporal?"

"I think so."

"Good," said Hui. "Now, go back to your Chinese studies. You will return to AI research once this project has been successfully completed. Take the rest of the day off. Reflect on what I have said. Prepare yourself for the challenges to come. Good-bye."

As on the first day when he came into Hui's office, Henry was almost certain that the hologram of Xi nodded to him, as if underlining the Colonel's words and dismissal.

Nearly as confused as a month ago, when he had stumbled out of the cab, jet-lagged, mugged, and thoroughly lost, Henry sleep-walked through the hall, down the stairs, and into the room he had been assigned. As he opened the door, he saw something folded on his bed. The thing was Rav.

"I am the reward the Colonel mentioned," she said, coming toward him.

# Chapter 13
## Viva Luisa

Luisa recovered. Physically, anyway. She could breathe more or less normally. She no longer had a racking cough. Her sense of smell had not returned, nor could she discern what she was eating if her eyes were closed and spoon-fed. The sensory deprivation, she was told, would take a while to come back.

"So will I," Luisa said.

"Actually, you have a medical check-up scheduled in two weeks," said one of the rotating nurses who had cared for her. They were not happy about their assignment.

"Give the appointment to someone who'll actually show up."

Her conversations with Suor Jacinta had continued, despite Luisa's insistence that she had nothing to say to, or learn from, the psychiatrist. "But it's part of our service," Jacinta said, as though explaining to a child. "You're not paying anything for it."

"That's still overcharging," Luisa shot back. Jacinta shook her head, made a note on her phone.

"Italy is changing, Luisa," said the shrink. "We can no longer cling to the characteristics that have defined us for centuries. We need to become multicultural, to welcome and embrace influences from other parts of the world. Other cultures, other religions, other ways of looking at life. We Italians have…"

"Stop!" Luisa said, her voice hard but not loud. "We Italians?" She stressed the first word. "What does your passport say?"

"Luisa, passports no longer matter. The entire world must be equal, with open borders and dialogue among the nations."

"And who, exactly, does that benefit, Suor Jacinta? I've told you what happened in Prato. It's more like little Shanghai now than Lombardy. Did I benefit from the arrival of those people? Did your arrival from Ethiopia enrich my life? Or was it the other way around?"

Jacinta's white teeth shown against her black lips. "Luisa, you are an old woman with cloudy memories of a past that no longer exists. Curb your tongue and open your heart, or you will be sorry." She made another note on her phone.

"Suor Jacinta, I have enjoyed knowing you. You have helped me remember who I am, where I live and what my country—my country, not yours—needs to protect before it is taken away."

"It wasn't taken away, Luisa. You gave it away." Jacinta's smile was rock-hard, her eyes like lasers. "And you will never get it back." A final note into her phone and she was gone. That, Luisa told herself, was the real message.

After much arguing, some of it quite loud, Luisa was permitted to sign herself out of the *ospedale*. She knew two things: she would never go back in there, and Italy must be made safe once again for Italians. The next day, she called the Prato office of La Liga, and was told to come by immediately.

La Liga—the League—is the offspring of a craggy-faced, basso-voiced failed medical school student named Umberto Bossi who was born in Lombardy and never forgot it. He took the required courses in medical school, but did poorly. Once it became clear that he would not graduate and become a doctor, he asked one of his instructors what he had done wrong. "You did nothing wrong, young man. But we had to make room for the others." The *others*, Bossi realized, were foreign students from Africa, the Middle East, Asia. They had been brought to Italy on full scholarships, schooled in the language, and their progress through Italian medical school carefully shepherded by the schools' officials. The goal was to ensure that Italy met the quotas set by the European Union for welcoming "disadvantaged" students from Third World countries. Even if that meant shattering the dreams of "advantaged" Italian students like Bossi.

"But that's just another kind of racism," Bossi argued.

"No. Not accepting dark-skinned people is racism. This is inclusion," he was told.

"This is bullshit," Bossi shot back. Then and there he decided: if I cannot devote my life to healing people, I will devote it to healing my country.

Using some of the spare funds he had optimistically put aside for his first doctor's practice, he filed a declaration of intent and named himself the secretary general of what he called The Northern League. In Italy, "Northern" has a political as well as a geographic connotation. For centuries, the territory now known as Italy was a collection of rival, often warring kingdoms: Piedmont-Savoy, Lombardy, the Republics of Venice and Genoa, Modena, Parma, Tuscany, the Papal states and the Kingdom of the two Sicilies. They had different monarchs, different laws, and in some cases, different languages. Creating a republic by bringing the kingdoms together, and investing authority in a president, a parliament and a supreme court—all of whom resided in Rome— was far from universally popular. Most miffed were citizens of Lombardy, Parma and Tuscany—the so-called "Northern provinces," now that they were no longer kingdoms.

Perhaps because they were closer to Germany and Switzerland, two lands renowned for their tidiness and business efficiency, the "northern" states tended to view their southern siblings as slothful, lazy, incapable and corrupt. Like any generalization, there were exceptions, but there was no doubt that a Lombard would keep a tighter hold on his wallet if he came into contact with a Sicilian. Or a Roman.

This attitude of superiority was kept under wraps for decades, as the newly republicanized Italy grappled with the realities of unification. All power emanated from Rome, the universally acknowledged capital. But that power was not always dispensed in an equitable manner, at least not in the view of the North. The old Southern vices of corruption, cronyism, nepotism and outright scalawaggery were alive and well. Northerners felt that they bore too much of the financial brunt of powering Italian democracy, without receiving adequate credit for their hard work in support of indigent Southerners.

Bossi tapped into this smoldering resentment at exactly the right moment. He criss-crossed Lombardy, calling out the economic injustice that the province and its neighbors felt daily. His concrete-mixer voice rising, he began to talk about a "Northern League" that would seize a share of power from the plutocrats in Rome, and ensure that the sweat of Northern brows was rewarded with the best roads, the best hospitals, the lowest taxes. Bossi also asked out loud why there were so many immigrants from Africa on the streets of Milan, of Parma, of Venice. "Are they all here on vacation?" he boomed. "The ones I run into are always asking for money, not spending any."

His message caught on, and in the next regional elections, the newly minted Northern League Party came in second to the chronically corrupt but deeply entrenched Social Democrats.

Popular support for this new interloper did not go unnoticed in Rome. The Social Democrats had held onto power for years by promising better lives for everyone. Italy is one big country, they said. When you win, we all win. Their words were hollow and everyone knew it. But the Social Democrats had the best organization, and controlled all the levers of power, so there really wasn't much choice. Until now.

When you tell people they can no longer make decisions for themselves, you have to expect some opposition. Western expectations of freedom and choice are anathema to losing control. When Italy decided to join, first the Common Market, then the European Union, it effectively ceded control of much of the government's most important tasks to the unelected bureaucrats who now ruled most of the continent from Brussels. It was one thing to have to give up the beloved brown Italian passport for one that read "European Union." It was quite another to have the lira become worthless overnight, replaced by the sterile euro. "Take my life, leave my lira," became a battle cry in the North. Bossi's was one of the loudest voices.

They were, of course, condemned as fascists, racists, Neanderthals, anti-European. They were a challenge to the existing order and so had to be marginalized, villified, delegitimized. The major newspapers ran editorials warning that the Northern League was a danger to Italy's future, which, the editorial writer confidently stated, was standing with the rest of Europe. Separatism was anachronistic, the writer said bluntly. Italy must move forward, not backward.

Italians, especially those living in the North, disagreed. Support for the League grew rapidly. Its candidate for mayor of Parma won. It received a majority of votes for the Lombardy regional congress. Bossi became the most talked about man in the country, outside of the Pope. The Pope, who was not Italian, also condemned the League. Italy's soul, he said, was at stake. Bossi said that while he respected the pope, his Holiness should pay more attention to pedophile priests and less to Italian politics. Naturally, he was condemned for that statement. And naturally, he didn't care.

It turned out that lots of Italians, not just Northerners, thought that being ordered around by Brussels was not a good idea. The League started to pick up support from other regions of the country, regions that were normally the domain of the Social Democrats. The League was generally acknowledged to be the country's second most powerful political party.

Then disaster struck. Bossi suffered a major stroke that left him unable to speak. The great basso voice was silenced. The League's officers scrambled madly to find someone who could assume the mantle, and settled on Marco Calvini, a child TV star whose bearded face and ready smile were familiar to millions of Italian viewers. Calvini had two goals: close Italy's borders to illegal immigants, and return the lira as the national currency. Eight out of ten Italians surveyed wanted the lira back. Ninety five percent wanted illegals barred from the country. African immigrants had already swarmed and overrun an island off the coast of Sicily. In the five days it took the Guardia di Finanza police force to arrive on the island, forty-seven women were raped, the local branch of Invesbanco was firebombed and looted, and a tourist hotel was burned down. Calvini got there before the police and had his photo taken with his hands held out at his sides, palms up, as if saying, "What did you expect?" The incident caused the government in Rome to reshuffle the cabinet. Calvini was named Interior Minister.

Calvini, married and a father of two, also had a mistress named Donatella Tesco, who shared his political philosophy as well as his bed. She lived in Prato, though she spent an increasing share of her time with Calvini in Rome, which she referred to as "The Toilet." To give her something to do, Calvini had her named chairwoman of the League for Prato. It was not a meaningless step. The Chinese influx into Prato had weakened the League's hold on the town. Chinese-born immigrants were actually running for, and winning town council seats, despite not being Italian. Tesco protested against this idiocy, and filed a lawsuit, but a judge, who was related to the deputy chair of the Social Democrats, ruled against her. Tesco was a guest on television and radio talk shows, where she kept her message simple: Italy for Italians. She was labelled a racist.

So when Luisa Moretti walked, slowly, into Tesco's office, there was already an unspoken but palpable bond between them. Racists, real or imagined, stick together. They are related by disgrace, held erect by calumny.

Tesco was already on her feet, her hand extended. Luisa smiled weakly.

"Signora Moretti, it is a pleasure. I am Donatella Tesco. I understand you'd like to discuss your ordeal at the *ospedale*. How awful it must have been, and you fighting for your life against this dreadful Chinese virus."

Luisa was immediately on her side: the Chinese virus. Someone else finally gets it. She described her hospital stay, her encounters with Suor Jacinta and the Chinese doctor who couldn't speak Italian to save, well, *Luisa's* life. Tesco was an excellent listener, nodding and prodding at all the right times. Luisa felt she had a complete comrade and took the opportunity to express a few of her deeply-held, and these days, deeply-guarded views.

They talked for twenty minutes. Luisa began to feel weak and dizzy. She had not spoken so continuously since she became ill and made a mental note to speak in moderation, if not in moderate terms. "We are losing control of our own country."

"You are right, Signora. That is exactly what we have been saying."

"Why have I not heard more about La Liga? I read. I watch the news."

Tesco made a rueful facial gesture. "We can't get any media outlets to write about us or invite us on the air. They call us fascists, racists, Neanderthals."

"I'd call you Italians."

"And I you, Signora. I have a question. Do you think you have recovered sufficiently to speak in public?"

Luisa furrowed her brow. "In public? What do you mean?"

Tesco had anticipated the question. "The simple, genuine way you just told me what happened to you is very relatable. Most Italians would understand that you have been mistreated. They have encountered similar mistreatment themselves, perhaps. If you had the chance to speak on television, I think you would get a positive response."

"But you just said yourself: no one will listen to you."

"Not me, Luisa. You. I want to talk to Marco. I think he would be very interested in your situation. And we have a few friends in the media. They're afraid to show their true inclinations. But they are proud Italians and don't like what's happening to our country. If we got one of them to interview you, would you be able to repeat what you've told me?"

It took Luisa two seconds to decide. "Yes, yes I could. And I will."

However, it took Calvini two weeks to set up the interview with a television host on Channel 5, a network owned by Silvio Berlusconi, the billionaire who had once served as prime minister before his flamboyant style and loose relationship with facts drove him from office. The host, a portly gent whose deep voice and decades of experience gave him on-air gravitas, introduced Luisa as "a patriotic Italian who suffered horrors at the hands of the state's left-wing medical institution. Signora Luisa Moretti."

With two weeks to prepare, and some private coaching by La Liga's media consultant, Luisa presented a twenty-minute account of her ordeal at the *ospedale*. She did it without whining, without exaggerating, and without blaming anyone. She said, quietly but firmly, "They want to take Italy away from Italians and give it to outsiders. They are stealing our motherland."

"Stealing our motherland!" was the headline the next day in newspapers and websites whose reporters were assigned to cover the interview. Twitter, to use the expression so in vogue, exploded. La Liga had broken through the silence barrier.

Luisa Moretti became famous in twenty-four hours, either for being a patriot or a racist. It didn't matter. The clicks reached the hundreds of thousands, the newspapers, most of which were losing money, sold out. "Viva Luisa!" screamed one conservative site. "Mother of our motherland" said another. "Rabid racist is batty" charged a left-wing competitor. Luisa was invited on to a state-run network. The host was a woman and openly antagonistic. Her last name, oddly, was Smith.

"Don't you feel ashamed to be telling these lies? Don't you have any compassion for poor people? Don't you want to take back all the racist things you've said?" The host was working herself up into a fury that was her on-air signature.

Luisa waited her out for a full minute, and when the host paused to take a deep gulp of air, said calmly, "Now you know how I felt when I couldn't breathe. And by the way, you made some grammatical mistakes. Are you really Italian, Signora Smith?"

The host's eyes widened until Luisa thought her eyeballs would drop out. The screen went black.

Twitter re-exploded, with comments five to one in favor of "the plucky patriot." Calvini was invited onto all the networks to comment. He was prepared. "She has more balls than this government, that's for sure."

That caused another Twit-plosion.

Three days later, the Ministry of Health said it would investigate Luisa's treatment at the hospital and make changes if necessary. Suor Jacinta was quietly reassigned, although a Lombardy website found out and reported it. The ministry, of course, was accused of racism. A low-ranking deputy minister resigned.

Luisa was on her way.

# Chapter 14
## De-Fanged

The Chinese Communist Party has managed to do what few institutions—political, religious, sporting business—have done, which is to become omnipresent in 21$^{st}$ Century China. Nothing is free from its influence, or its power. Xi Jinping took the reins of power in 2012 and tightened his grip over the years. He purged the military; then the finance ministry, which was rife with corruption; then his diplomatic corps, where too many ambassadors thought that living outside of China put them beyond his reach; next came any economists who resisted Xi's command that China become the world's leading economy by 2035; and then, in a feat of daring, he purged the ideological wing of his Party.

By 2016 he had complete oversight of every aspect of China. And like strongmen before him, Xi decided that having it all wasn't enough. Seeing how social media tools like Twitter and Skype had led to the downfall of some Middle Eastern despots, Xi created the Cyberspace Administration of China, which in theory was meant to create an orderly system of licensing websites and products. Its real purpose, of course, was to make sure that nothing remotely critical of the Party—and mostly, of Xi himself—ever saw the light of cyberspace. Website creators were vetted, and if they didn't pass the proper ideological tests, the sites were commandeered and its users either fined or jailed. There was no appeal process. If the CAC found you guilty of incorrect conduct, you were guilty.

Xi himself was a technical bumbler. He could turn on his computer, and charge his phone. Beyond that, he had underlings to do what needed to be done. Not surprisingly, the CAC was headed by Xi's brother-in-law, Ke Kuan, who was even more devoted to Xi and the Party than Xi's ex-wife, Ke-Lingling, who attracted Xi's attention and whose four-year marriage produced a daughter. When Xi needed something done in the realm of social media, he turned to Ke Kuan, who was always happy to help. Ke Kuan had not spoken to his sister since her divorce from Xi. Neither had Xi.

Xi thought the chaos of Western cyberspace was a waste of effort and money. The freedom that tech companies like Apple, Google and Facebook had was inefficient in the extreme. And look where it had gotten them. Edward Snowden outing spies from downloaded files of the National Security Agency. Bradley Manning leaking 750,000 military communications because he knew how to do it. And the United States stood by, seemingly helpless, as North Korea, Russia, Ukraine, and of course, China plundered its online secrets, undercutting its national security, actually endangering its citizens in order to make them more secure. The only thing that had changed in recent years was that Bradley Manning became Chelsea Manning.

Xi actually liked some aspects of the United States. Its creative juices were always flowing. It produced truly talented scientists, physicists, musicians, athletes and actors. What he did not like was the audacious freedoms America allowed its citizens. Public protests, songs that reviled the government; other songs, known as hip-hop, that celebrated killing police and raping women, books, plays and essays that insulted the president; and always, always, Americans' assumption that because their country was powerful, successful and the envy of the world, it must be guilty of something, some injustice, some denial of rights, something wrong. When in doubt, always blame America first.

Xi was not a brute. He understood the origins of this self-doubt. The century in which America embraced slavery marred the sunny image that it tried to project. It was an abhorrent blot on the pristine pages of the history book that Americans wanted to read and revere. Blacks had a grievance that must be addressed, even a hundred and fifty years after slavery was abolished. The demands for justice, for reparations, for apologies from whites, and special privileges for blacks were never-ending. And somehow America had bought into this infinite well of griping, claiming, caterwauling, and occasionally destroying property, because they were angry about what happened to their great-great grandparents.

China used slaves for a thousand years. It enslaved any captured soldiers from other countries, especially the lowlife known as Koreans and Japanese. It used captured Korean women as "comfort girls" for its troops. And from the earliest days of Mao Zedong's era of communist control, China had never referred to the slavery of the past, certainly never apologized, and by no means ever offered to make amends for its misdeeds.

If Xi was nothing else—and he wasn't just nothing else—he was a master strategist. Like a chess grandmaster, he could review the playing field from his chair and instantly see an opponent's weaknesses, and a nanosecond later, how to exploit each weakness. He had had a string of success since assuming power: stealing intellectual property from the West, ignoring China's nuclear non-proliferation treaty obligations, repeatedly sending expeditionary military planes and ships into Japanese, Vietnamese, Taiwanese and even American waters, cheating mercilessly and increasingly on trade treaties, polluting China's skies and water with run-amuck industrial waste, cracking down on even the slightest hint of dissent from citizens who thought economic prosperity brought with it human rights, effectively muzzling the practice of Christian, Muslim, Buddhist, and Hindu faiths, the takeover of Hong Kong and the smothering of its democratic movement, and, of course, the state-sponsored genocide of the Uighur Muslims, who were sub-humans and not worthy of existence in Xi's China.

It was an impressive list of misbehavior, and so far, it had worked. Xi was immensely proud of his accomplishments, and was himself responsible for *Zhongguo tese shehui zhuyi*. It provided a bulwark to rebuke his critics from the rest of the world. We are living the new paradigm of success: socialism with Chinese characteristics.

There were two battles that had to be fought simultaneously to stamp Xi's vision of the future on the rest of the world. The backbone of *Zhongguo tese shehui zhuyi* for smaller, developing countries was, to put it politely, bribery. Xi introduced the Belt and Road initiative, a trillion-dollar program to link the Third World—all around the world—to China through the mass construction of airports, seaports, dams, highways, industrial parks, massive grain warehouses, and the jobs that were inevitably required to carry out and maintain these vast enterprises. The Belt and Road initiative was, of course, meant to evoke the Silk Road, the main highway of commerce throughout Asia and Eastern Europe for nearly two thousand years. The Silk Road was created during the Han dynasty, one of the most industrious and successful periods of Chinese monarchial rule. Early on after taking power, Xi liked to think that he was leading China into a new Han dynastic era. Now, after his string of successes, he believed the Han would gladly acclaim him as the greatest of all Chinese leaders and *Zhongguo tese shehui zhuyi* as the epitome of Chinese superiority throughout the world.

China paid for the construction and start-up of all the infrastructure necessary to make the Belt and Road program a success. Of course, agreements with the host countries had to be signed, and the massive Chinese investment was disguised as a loan. But Xi's emissaries assured the ministers, presidents and dictators of the countries that signed onto Belt and Road that these loans would never be called in, or that, if they were, it would be long after they had departed the scene. Anyone who persisted in this line of questioning was told, "Open a numbered account in Indonesia, the Caymans, Luxembourg, wherever you want. It won't be empty for long."

The construction of the projects was undertaken by Chinese engineers, architects and manual laborers. China, of course, had surplus population, and these people were assigned to their foreign jobs, told to pack their belongings and sell their homes and valuables, and start to learn whatever language was spoken wherever they were headed. Most of them would never leave the country where they were shipped, en masse, under the rubric of "guest workers." They were invaders who had been welcomed.

Before they built the dams, airports, seaports, etc., they were set to work constructing vast military landing strips, armaments testing grounds, artillery ranges, and mile upon mile of Quonset-hut like housing. Because, of course, the Chinese explained, such a huge investment required security. So PLA troops would be "temporarily" living alongside the construction crews to guarantee their safety and to prevent any theft, vandalism or other obstacles to the projects that the Chinese were so selflessly providing to their new friends and business partners.

The construction dragged on. The soldiers never left. And the loans came due. We can't repay you. The amount you're claiming we owe you is fantastic. You told us no loan would be called in until we were long gone and someone else would be saddled with it. If you think we're going to repay you now, think again. We'll tell the world that you are cheaters, swindlers, and that a Chinese promise isn't worth anything.

Go ahead, said the Chinese sitting across the table from them. Publicize your grievances. And while you're at it, you'd better also mention Account number—and they would rattle off the minister's secret foreign bank stash—so your people will know what kind of official you really are.

Xi was very proud of the Belt and Road Initiative. He considered it a prime example of an investment that both projected Chinese power and undercut the role of the United States in those parts of the world that had decided China was now the country to do business with.

But Xi was not satisfied. He knew he would still have to deal with the United States if he wanted *Zhongguo tese shehui zhuyi* to be a byword for Chinese world domination, and Xi to be spoken of as the leader who shifted the balance of power, once and for all, away from Washington and to Beijing.

And he had a plan to do just that. He would bring America to its knees. And he would do it without America knowing that he was behind its demise. Not just that, but he would get the Americans to blame themselves for what had happened to them. The Army received orders from "the top" to find and conscript the country's leading virologists, epidemiologists and bioengineers and bring them together to work as a team. The army, Xi instructed his deputy in a room with just the two of them and no microphones, should pick scientists who were Party members, to ensure their loyalty and discretion. But that was not enough. They should also all have close family members living in China. *Zhongguo tese shehui zhuyi.*

The production of SARS2, later known as coronavirus, began in a BSL2 laboratory, with minimal security and safety oversight. The experimental process was called gain-of-function, which created virus cells specifically designed to infect human cells. They started with test-tube transmission, then tried mice that had been injected with human cells.

They finally had success with bats. And then one went missing.

* * *

Fang realized the people he met at CAC were actually listening to him. He was asked what made TikTok tick and WeChat interesting to young people, and why Facebook was popular in the rest of the world, though it was banned in China. Fang had learned in the two weeks he had been at CAC to keep his answers short, and to prepare for any eventuality. As a new employee, he had been required to sign many forms, many of them non-disclosure agreements about what he saw and heard in the course of doing his work. In truth, he would have signed anything they put in front of him, as long as he could keep doing this job. He wasn't really sure what his job here was, but he knew it was more exciting than the Wuhan Virology Lab and that he never wanted to go back there.

It all came apart ten days in. He got an electronic message on his computer via the in-house topline system. It said, "Security Office 203. Now." That old shadow of despair fell over him. They had uncovered his stupid cell phone search for CAC and saw that he had been denied access. Now they would ask him why he was doing that, fire him, and send him to a Uighur re-education facility. Or worse, if such a thing existed.

Fortunately, he didn't have enough time to buy a bottle of baijiu. He got up, and with the same fatalism that had accompanied him to previous involuntary meetings, walked quickly to Office 203. The door was open.

Sitting at the desk was a captain of the PLA. His facial expression was as jaunty as his olive drab uniform. As with the other meetings Fang had attended by command, this began without ado.

"You are Fang?"

"I am."

"You are the husband of Qi Qi Dieh?"

"Ex-husband." He took a breath. The erroneous assumption was good.

"But you married her?"

"And divorced her."

"You have seen her?"

"I last saw her a month or so ago."

"Why?"

"She was ill. I went by to check on her." And steal money from her, but he didn't mention that.

"Citizen Qi has made a very alarming statement."

Shit, thought Fang, she's accused me of robbery.

"Are you aware of it?"

"I am not." Keep it simple, stupid, he told himself. Volunteer nothing.

The captain stood up, came around the desk, and got uncomfortably close. "She says she started the outbreak of the virus that is going around."

"That is, as you say, alarming."

"It is treasonous. The virus was introduced to China by American spies. This is well known. Your wife must recant her statement."

"Ex-wife."

"Never mind. Talk to her. Make her admit her error. Get a signed statement from her."

Fang almost smiled. "My ex-wife and I do not get along. She will do nothing for me."

"MAKE HER!" the captain shouted, piffling spittle onto Fang's face.

The very best way to spread this American virus. Fang paused a moment, took a paper towel out of his pocket, wiped his face, and stepped back. The captain, perhaps aware that he had acted, not rudely, but socially irresponsibly, took a step back also.

Fang said, "If I contract the virus, Captain, it will be your fault. I will communicate my concern to my superiors."

The captain began to speak, stopped himself. "I should not have done that."

"I am glad you understand that. Now we understand each other," said Fang, with courage that came from an unknown wellspring. "Now, may I return to my work?"

The captain nodded, once, turned and went back to his desk. By the time he had seated himself, Fang was gone.

The first communication from CAC to the Chinese online service providers in Wuhan, to the heads of news websites, chat groups like Weibo, and medical information sources that the general public might use, caused excitement in the office. People from all parts of the CAC watched as their screens lit up with "A communication from the Cyberspace Administration of China. There was, it said, a virus that had been detected in Wuhan and that may be spreading. All online entities had a patriotic responsibility to keep citizens calm. "Do not use pop-up notifications for any negative news reports about the prevention and control of the novel coronavirus epidemic. Do not use 'incurable,' 'fatal' or similar headlines to avoid causing societal panic. Be sleek and silent to achieve results."

His colleagues around him buzzed their pride and approval. CAC was getting the message out. CAC was going to bring the situation under control. They were proud to work at CAC. They were doing their part to help the Party and President Xi fight this virus and keep order within the population. They sounded like nothing so much as a colony of bees during mating season.

Fang sat at his computer screen and read the words again and again. "Sleek and silent. Sleek and silent."

You bastard, Wo, Fang thought. You bastard. But after the confrontation with the captain, and the knowledge that his idiot ex-wife was making crazy statements, Fang knew there was nothing to be done.

Except wait for his moment for revenge.

# Chapter 15
## To Liberty And Back

Pittsburgh in the winter is bad enough. Pittsburgh in the summer when you can't go into a joint for a burger, or a bar for a snort, is ... well, the pits. He had gotten his first $1,200 check from Donald Trump because of this virus, and was going to be very careful about how he spent it. No splurging on booze. That was one of the things Tran had warned him about.

"Look, Jerry, these times are so depressing it's tempting to drown your sorrows. Now I'm not a temperance maiden. I'm just telling you it's a waste of money. You buy a bottle, empty it in three hours, fall asleep. And when you wake up, you're still depressed by what you see around you. And you don't have your money. All you've got is a headache."

Made sense. Jerry and Tran had become, not friends, but conversation partners. That's a term he had never thought to become acquainted with, but there you were. Because they didn't exchange personal secrets. Or their aspirations for the future, or who they wanted to screw. Instead, they talked about the real world, the one out there that could drive you to drink if you let it.

Unlike most people these days, politics was not out of bounds as a topic with Tran. Jerry told him when he'd gotten his stimulus check, showed him Trump's signature on it, asked him what he thought.

"I think he's saying a lot of things that a lot of people believe, but he's not saying them right," Tran said. "He's what Plato would have called an imperfect vessel."

Jerry sure as shit wasn't going to argue with Tran about Plato, who he knew was a Greek philosopher he'd never read. "Did you vote for him?"

"Plato? No. He wasn't on the ballot." Tran smiled. "Of course, I voted for Trump. You think I was going to vote for that sob-sister ball-buster?"

"Right. Me too."

"But to be honest, Jerry, The Donald has disappointed me. I mean he came in with a chance to fix the borders, reboot industrial production, lower taxes, push back on China bring American businesses back. And instead, he's gotten down into the gutter with the Dems about race and the police and Muslims and Gold Star parents and things a president shouldn't be spending time arguing about."

"Fair enough."

"And telling people to drink Clorox to ward off this fucking virus? What next? Do a rain dance and hope it'll go away?"

"Yeah," said Jerry. "But you know, he's better…"

"Than the other guys," Tran cut in. "I still love him. He's a rock star."

"Tran, I got no star. I'd be lucky to have a cigarette lighter."

They were standing on Market Square outside Winghart's, which undeniably made the best hamburgers in Pittsburgh. Except Winghart's was closed, like ninety percent of the restaurants, bars, fast food joints and even half the takeaways. Covid, of course. Jerry couldn't bring himself to use that word. To him, whatever this virus going around was, was the China Flu. And people were dying from it.

But this being America, we had to have an argument about it. Two days later, Jerry was at a drugstore to pick up some NicoDerm smoking patches, which didn't curb his desire for a cigarette, but somehow made it bearable to go without. As he was getting them from the pharmacist, he said offhandedly, jokingly, "Think these things will protect you from the Chinese flu too?"

"Don't call it the Chinese flu," snapped the pharmacist, a blonde woman in her mid-40s, maybe, who had the round tortoise shell glasses and frizzy mop-top hair that usually meant, in Jerry's experience, that she was still sore about Hillary losing and thought anyone who voted for Trump was "deplorable."

"Why not?" Jerry said. "That's where it came from."

"Maybe. Maybe not. You can't blame an entire country. For all we know, it started here and was taken to China by someone visiting. I read in the New York *Times* that might be the case."

That confirmed who she'd voted for. Jerry said, "Well, the *Times* says a lot of stuff I don't think is real. They seem to think they know more than anybody about everything."

"With Trump as president, the *Times* feels it has to take a stand. To correct lies and misinformation."

Strike three. Yer OUT! "You mean," Jerry said, slowly, "misinformation like this thing didn't start in China?"

"We don't know where it came from. We have to wait for the experts to tell us."

"I don't have to wait for anything, or anyone," Jerry said. "And just who are these so-called experts?"

"Scientists. We have to be guided by science," said the pharmacist, as though she had just reciting a secret formula that would fix everything.

"Know what?" said Jerry, taking a step back. "I'll get my patches someplace else. "Somewhere that doesn't want to blame America for a Chinese flu."

"Good," said the pharmacist. "I'd just as soon not see you here again. Your kind are bad people."

"My kind?" said Jerry. "What's that mean?"

The pharmacist touched a button behind the counter separating her from Jerry and said, "White male. Overprivileged."

"Isn't that racist?"

"No. I can say anything I want about white males. Now get out or I'll tell the police you accosted me verbally."

"And I'll tell them you said white men were racist."

The pharmacist smiled like a crocodile. "I turned the security camera off before I said that. I'm turning it back on now." And she pushed a button.

Jerry walked out of the drugstore. He really wanted a cigarette.

More and more, Jerry found that Tran was the only one who understood his frustrations. When he told him about the confrontation at the drugstore, Tran grinned and said, "Welcome to the 21$^{st}$ Century, bro. If it's not on video, it didn't happen."

"So, no one's going to believe that a pharmacist called me a privileged white male?"

"They might believe it, Jer, but no one will care. Listen, you ever go hunting?"

"Used to, with my Dad. We'd go out to the woods near Braddock."

"What'd you hunt?"

"Well, it was deer season. But we bagged a few rabbits and squirrels too."

Tran turned to him with a delighted smile, and pointed both index fingers at him. "Perfect! You've made my point. You hunted deer during deer hunting season, right?"

"Right."

"But you didn't hunt elk, or bears, or pheasants, 'cuz those are a different season."

"I guess."

"But you bagged a few rabbits and squirrels."

"Yeah, it was mostly for fun. We didn't eat them or nothing."

"Doesn't matter. You bagged rabbits and squirrels because there is no season for hunting them. They don't have a do-not-hunt season. No protection."

"Yeah, I guess. "

"Jerry, you are the rabbit or the squirrel of American society. Every other group has a do-not-hunt protection. You can't say nothing about gays, or blacks, or Latins, or even Asians," he said, pointing to himself at the end of the sentence. "But white men like you, baby, it's open season. Say what you want about them, hunt them down if you feel like it. Nobody gonna stop you. White men got no protection."

"That is," Jerry said, "to put it mildly, unfair."

"That is, to put it more mildly," Tran said, "The Divided States of America."

In retrospect, Jerry realized, this was a testing period. He was being checked out, examined, prodded to see how he'd react.

Whatever the test was, he must have passed, because two days later, Tran texted him to arrange an in-person meeting. They met at Market Square again. Tran had a laptop with him.

"Want you to look at this. It's the local news coverage of the BLM demonstration here last month."

"You're gonna give me a headache," Jerry said.

"It'll be worse than a headache."

The video clip showed the protesters with their banners and their chants. It made a point of saying that the marchers wanted the police to be defunded. It didn't show that some of them broke off from the main demo as it got dark, and looted several liquor stores, a Wal-Mart and an electronics store. They also torched a police car. That wasn't in the video report either. Nor was the confrontation between the elderly couple and the fat girl who drank the guy's beer and threw the rest of it on his wife. "Demanding long-delayed racial justice," said the TV reporter, "this peaceful demonstration was a much-needed reminder that all is not well in America."

"What do you think?" asked Tran.

"I think you're right. I have something worse than a headache."

"Look, Jer," said Tran, "The Defenders is gonna be part of a march next week. We have a permit and it's gonna be peaceful. We're gonna call the TV stations in town and tell them about it, see if any of them show up to cover it."

"What's the march about?"

"To say we support the cops in Pittsburgh."

Jerry thought a second. "That doesn't sound exactly revolutionary."

"We'll see. Would you like to come with us?"

"I dunno, Tran. I'm not usually real political. I just want to be left alone to live my life."

"Sure, Jer, we all do. But these days, if you don't stand up for what you believe in, some people will take it away from you."

"Let me think about it. I'll let you know."

"Sure, Jer. No pressure."

Two days later, Jerry was cutting across Liberty Avenue. There was nobody else in the street, except for a lady walking the other way with a dog. Jerry was a good fifteen feet away from her when she started shouting, "Put on a mask, you fucking idiot." Jerry stopped and looked over his shoulder, to see if she might be yelling at someone else. He wasn't wearing a mask, because he wasn't near anyone.

"I said put on a mask, you piece of shit motherfucker," the lady screamed. Her dog was looking up, its eyes gone wide. Jerry looked at the confused dog, on its leash, looking up at its owner, or companion as you were now supposed to call them, and couldn't help but laugh.

"What are you laughing at, motherfucker?" the woman shouted, clearly out of control now. Some guy walking on the other side of Liberty looked at the scene, but didn't say anything.

"I'm laughing at your dog," said Jerry loudly. "You're scaring the poor thing."

"Don't talk about my dog, asshole," the lady shouted back. "Put a fucking mask on like you're supposed to."

"Don't tell me what to do, lady," said Jerry, pissed off now. "I'm not near you or anybody else. I have a mask, and I'll wear it if I go into a store or something. But I'm not wearing it outside, when I'm alone."

"You better learn to wear one, you piece of shit," screamed the lady. "You're probably one of those Trump people. You make me sick."

"Lady," said Jerry. "In the nicest possible terms, may I suggest you go fuck yourself."

"I'm going to get the police," she said, veering into the street, where there was no traffic. "I'm going to have you arrested for assault."

"Who am I assaulting?"

"Me. You just used a vulgarity on me." Now that she had moved closer, the woman looked about forty, with stringy hair and transparent glasses. Jerry recognized the type: single, way left wing, probably went to Bryn Mar or Skidmore.

"You've been cursing at me since you saw me."

"Don't argue with me, you filthy fucking white male."

"Call the police. I don't care. In the meantime, fuck off." And Jerry walked away. He could hear her exercising her lungs for nearly a block. He got out his phone and texted Tran. "When and where?"

Tran was as good as his word. The assembled multitude came to a couple hundred, not bad for short notice. Jerry didn't know anyone else, as far as he could see, but they all seemed pretty normal. White guys, some women, all dressed regular. Waving to each other. It turned out The Defenders had had posters and placards printed saying, "I Stand with the Blue" and a police badge painted on the top and bottom. Also, as promised, the march had been granted a permit, and there were a dozen or so cops assigned for protection. Police protecting people who wanted to protect the police from being defunded. This country is screwed up, Jerry thought.

The march was peaceful, and to Tran's satisfaction, there were two local TV news crews there. Jerry and Tran got separated early, but Jerry went with the flow, talked to a couple of guys who were marching next to him, realized they believed a lot of the same stuff he did, thought defunding the police was a bunch of crap, thought the BLM march was really an excuse to loot some stores, thought Trump was a windbag but his heart was in the right place, thought the virus that was going around definitely came from China—"either from a lab or from some fuckin' bat"—and said they'd wear a mask to go into a store if that's what the owner wanted, but not to walk on the street, or when they were driving, alone.

The whole thing took about ninety minutes. Up Liberty, across Grant, down Forbes, back to Liberty. The cops were friendly, tried to minimize the traffic delays, though, to be honest, there wasn't much traffic downtown these days. People weren't shopping because the stores were closed, and those that still had jobs were working from home. It was all over by three, and as everyone dispersed, he ran into Tran again.

"Good people," Jerry said.

"Wait until you see them on the news tonight."

So Jerry watched. One channel had sent a black woman reporter who was positioned at the corner of Liberty and Grant. "The people at this event—this mob, really—were all white, mostly men and they looked angry. I must tell you, as a black woman, I felt unsafe among them." The screen showed some guys raising their hands, waving to other guys. "These, for instance, appeared to be giving the Nazi salute. Others hid their faces behind posters that showed an image of a policeman's badge—obviously a symbol of deep concern and pain to African Americans. Today's event cast shame on Pittsburgh and to any

Pittsburgher who believes in justice." And that was the end of the report. He texted Tran: "What the F?"

Tran shot back immediately: "Decision time, Jer. The Defenders need you."

Still seething over what he'd just watched, Jerry texted back, "I'm in."

# Chapter 16
## What Did You Say?

Organizations spawn conflict. It's just the way they are. Bring two human beings together in a joint effort and the result may be cooperation. But before long, under the surface, the cooperation will be undercut by competition between the two. To excel. To win praise. To show up the other. To prevail. Finally, to destroy the other. It is the nature of humans.

The CAC and Hui's Institute for Artificial Intelligence didn't get along. CAC felt that Hui was a reckless plunger, toying with concepts and technology that weren't yet fully approved by the top levels of the Party. Hui thought the CAC disliked him and his institute because they couldn't understand AI.

They were comrades at combat with each other.

The CAC, which is headquartered not in Beijing but outside Wuhan, is next to an enormous data farm that records and analyzes every single keystroke of every function of every computer in China. By the time a user finishes typing in the URL of a forbidden website, the user's name and location are known to CAC. Xi Jinping, who had created the Cyberspace Administration, entrusted the CAC with the massive, if opaque task of controlling all information in Chinese cyberspace, ensuring that whatever the Chinese people could read was in keeping with Party ideology. For instance, Internet users in China will find nothing that is critical of Xi. And, should something appear that criticized another Party official, it is because Xi has decided to cut that person loose and is sending a message.

What Xi had not anticipated in 2014 was the rapid development and quantum leap in power of Artificial Intelligence. Xi's second wife, Peng Liyuan, was, in addition to being a popular folk singer, an avid user of computers in the late 1980s and onward, when the online world was still little known. She told her husband, already a star Party bureaucrat, that computers would someday have the ability to anticipate their users' wishes, even to outthink them before they realized they had been mastered by a machine. Xi told his wife to stick to her music. Once he had attained the ultimate Party position he always desired, Xi remembered Peng's warning about machines becoming smarter than people. What Xi had once dismissed as the dystopian premise of the "2001" movie by the American Kubrick, by 2014 he was seeing more evidence that the song Peng had sung to him was a real threat, not just to him but to the nation and, ultimately, the Party.

He had the Army put out feelers: who knew anything about this, this, what can we call it? Artificial intelligence? It took a month, but finally he had a name: Hui Jen-Sho, a captain from Shanghai whose three years of active duty were coming to an end and who had asked to be released from the military to pursue scientific research. His special interest was AI. Through intermediaries, Hui was persuaded to remain in uniform, with the promise that he would be allowed to work on AI problems, at an enhanced rank and salary, and, sweetest of all the sweeteners, that he would be given sufficient staff and equipment to carry out his research. Within three years, Hui had risen to Major, then Colonel, and was, quietly, of course, receiving compensation that few members of the PLA would comprehend.

He also was ushered into the presence of Xi. Perhaps he was guided by lucky spirits—*xingyun de jinshen* in Chinese—or perhaps he sensed that Xi, while supremely powerful, was not fluent in the topic to which Hui was devoting his life. Hui was respectful of the leader, but not obsequious. He spoke simply about AI but not patronizingly. He confirmed the prediction of Xi's wife that AI represented a potentially stratospheric jump forward in the power of machinery, which after all is what computers are, in the service of the Party.

Xi was impressed. This was a man who talked about what he knew and knew what he was talking about. He treated Hui more as an advisor than a subordinate, a Merlin to his Arthur. When Hui's conversation veered off into vocabulary and directions Xi did not understand, he said so. Hui immediately rephrased and recalibrated his approach and equilibrium was restored. Xi liked this approach. It was like a robot.

Xi authorized, and the Politburo quickly approved, the creation of the People's Institute for the Study of Artificial Intelligence in 2017. Hui wrote the business plan, which was entitled "A New Generation Artificial Intelligence Framework," whose one and only goal was to ensure that China led the world in this previously underfunded field of study. Xi maintained a degree of separation from the institute and from Hui, so as not to broadcast his intense interest in AI's success. He did send Hui a singularly talented woman who had been raised for several years in Great Britain before returning to China, where she graduated with an advanced degree in cosmology and space sciences. Her English was flawless, and not surprisingly, since her father was the first secretary for political affairs at China's embassy in London. Her best friend was the daughter of the ambassador. The ambassador's daughter happened to be Xi's second wife.

The woman assigned to Hui was—there was no other word for it—ravishing. Ma-lin Cho was also Xi's eyes and ears at the AI institute.

The virus was a crisis waiting to happen. Not the health aspects of it. The death toll in Wuhan was high, but this was not publicly acknowledged. Their cause of death was listed as "influenza." Xi first learned about the illness sweeping the city of 11 million in late November 2019. It was not the first health crisis during his regency, and it would not be the last. His minister of health had asked for ten minutes with Xi to brief him on developments. Xi refused her. Instead, using the PLA's internal police, Xi reached his ravishing spy by encrypted phone, and though he said not a word on the call, asked her through an intermediary what was going on.

"It was something from the Virology Lab," Rav said. "Something got loose. We think it was a bat that contracted some disease and was then sold at the wet market. They made soup out of it and sold it. It spread. And now it's everywhere."

Xi immediately recognized the implications. Despite being located in the middle of nowhere, Wuhan was a big city. If this virus was allowed to spread, it could do China, and more importantly, him, vast damage.

Leaders make decisions. Xi decided, without too much self-doubt, to seal Wuhan off from the world. Yes, people had already left the city by train, by plane, and by car, but nothing could be done about that now. The goals were twofold: confine the virus to Wuhan and keep word of it from spreading. He told his private secretary, "Speak to Zhuang Rongwei. Here is what to tell him."

Zhuang Rongwei was normally referred to as the director of CAC, but everyone knew the real head of the Administration was Xi Jinping. It was Xi who had seen the value of the Internet's offspring—social media—but who also instinctively comprehended the need to control it. Freedom of expression was anathema to Socialism with Chinese Characteristics. Indeed, in Xi's worldview, most freedoms were to be feared, not fostered.

Zhuang was the perfect chief operations officer for CAC. He understood Xi's thinking, at least most of the time, and agreed with it all of the time. He credited Xi in every communication he sent out, and took blame for any mistakes. And of course, in a country as large and online as China, there would be mistakes.

"There must be no mistakes," was the message from Xi's office to Zhuang. "This virus threatens not just China, but potentially other lands. This is not, and must never be referred to, as a 'Chinese virus.' Its origins are not Chinese, but foreign, and this must be made clear to our people and all others."

Zhuang got it. Not a Chinese disease. Gotcha. How, then, to explain it, and how then, to prevent misinformation from circulating among the online and social media population? Somewhere, he could not remember exactly, he had heard a phrase that pleased him. It was used in a directive to the executives who administered WeChat, TikTok, Baidu, Sina and YouKu , the Chinese equivalents of Google, CNN and YouTube. There was something about it that Zhuang had liked. Why couldn't he remember it? He ordered all the directives that CAC had sent out since word of the virus first started getting traffic. The directives were in his inbox within seven minutes of his request.

Seventeen minutes later, he had located the phrase that had caught his attention: "Sleek and silent." Yes, thought Zhuang, that is the way Xi would want us to go.

He made another call. "Who suggested the term 'sleek and silent' in that directive we sent out?" It took an unusually long twenty minutes for the answer to come back. It was Comrade Wo, who, fittingly enough, resided in Wuhan. "Have Wo in my office tomorrow morning," he said.

Wo didn't know whether to shit or go blind as he waited outside Zhuang's office. What could he have done to be hauled before the Boss in this abrupt way? He knew of people, people even who worked for CAC, who had simply disappeared after doing something that wasn't officially approved. Disappeared not just from their jobs, but from life itself. No one knew where they were, not even their families. And it was unwise to ask.

"How did you come up with that phrase?" Zhuang asked twenty seconds into their interview.

"I, um, it wasn't my, what I mean is..." Wo sounded like a ten-year-old and knew it. He had to conceal the truth. "I was inspired by the words of General Secretary Xi, sir."

"Don't fuck with me, Wo. The general secretary never used those words in public." Zhuang knew because he had had all of Xi's speeches scoured in the last twenty-four hours, and the words never appeared. He looked at Wo, then came to a decision. "It will be vital to our mission that any directives from CAC are clear without being threatening. In this age, we cannot ever assume that everyone is as trustworthy as"—he had to choke the word out—"you."

"Thank you," Wo stammered. "I understand."

"I wonder if you do. I want regular communications from you, with high security to prevent leaks, with further suggestions on how to word our directives. From now on, you will attend the highest-level strategy sessions. You seem to have talent in this area."

Wo went home with one thought: "Get Fang onboard. Whatever it takes."

Fang was petrified. First, he had been dressed down by a PLA captain. He had pushed back and won. Now he was being summoned to the office of Wo, who had ripped off Fang's brilliant phrase—sleek and silent—and claimed it as his own. What could possibly be next? A reunion with Qi Qi?

As usual, Wo looked displeased to see Fang. "Comrade, I want to discuss something important with you."

"Yes, sir."

"The truth, Fang, is that I do not find you a pleasant person. You have traits that I dislike. However, you have proven extremely resourceful. I have asked for, and received permission, for you to be seconded to me at the CAC. You will help me prepare my remarks, my strategy and advise me of any challenges you might see to my success. You will, in effect, be my second brain."

Careful to keep his face expressionless, Fang thought that Wo would have better use of a first brain. Conflicting currents were running through his head. One took control for a second, and he said, "I give you ideas, you take credit for them?"

Wo looked as if he'd been slapped. "You should consider your words carefully, Fang. You are still in a subservient position."

"True," said Fang. "But you are in an impossible situation. You have taken advantage of me, and I can prove it. If we are to work together, it will be as equals." Fang couldn't believe these words were coming out of his mouth. It was as if a puppet master inside his head was directing him to speak. But it felt right.

Wo let a smile develop. "What do you want?"

"More money, for one thing. I am underpaid. And when you attend meetings of the Administration's top level, I will be with you."

"I would have to get permission for that," said Wo. "But I suppose it is reasonable."

"One more thing," said Fang. He knew he was already on the border of insolence, but felt a strange confidence in his position. He described his frightening interview with the PLA captain. Described Qi's uneven personality, her menial job at the lab, her flights of fancy such as the KiKi Dee delusion. "I mean, it's crazy, isn't it?"

Wo listened closely, then said smoothly, "Crazy. Hmmm. And how is your wife's state of health now?"

"Ex-wife," said Fang. The term was becoming familiar now. "Ex-wife, not my wife. I have no wife."

Wo shook his head.

"Fang, you should thank you *xingyun de jinshen*, your lucky spirits. Once again, you have said the right words to help yourself."

He looked at Fang, not with any paternal feelings but with the eyes of a teacher about to impart an important lesson.

"Citizen Qi sounds like someone who suffers from mental illness. Or, as you put it so crassly, she is crazy. The Party sympathizes with such people. The Party tries to help them. It has facilities where such people can rest, relax, forget the concerns of the outside world. I believe the Party would be willing to take such care of citizen Qi. Especially as her claims would enflame the population if they were disseminated any further than they already have been."

"You're going to lock her away?" said Fang, all art and guise gone from his voice.

"Protective custody," said Wo.

"Good," said Fang. "But keep me out of it."

# Chapter 17
## Intelligent vs. Smart

It is a myth that all important Party meetings take place in august chambers with battalions of note takers, TV cameras and other assorted flunkies. Those are the meetings where decisions that have already been made are voted on and become the law of the land. Or at least of the Party. Which is the same thing.

Which is not to say that there is no showmanship. Colonel Hui, for example, wore his military uniform, though he left at home most of the silver mine of medals he had been awarded. What was the point, after all? He was Hui, head of the institute of Artificial Intelligence. And there was something very genuine these days about the Artificial.

Zhuang Rongwei, by contrast, was dressed in a middle-priced dark blue suit that had been purchased—well, donated, actually—from a shop in Hong Kong, the last time he had visited that misguided part of China to help some of its wrong-minded residents dismantle a social network that was spreading misinformation. Merchants in Hong Kong knew that it was best to donate fine tailoring to customers like Zhuang.

Considering that the meeting was about social media and Artificial Intelligence, and the role each played in the other, the method for scheduling it was not even 20th Century but more like 18th. Zhuang, acting on orders delivered by Xi's aide, sent an envoy to the Institute for Artificial Intelligence who asked to see Hui. Request denied. The messenger was instead shown into a room, made to wait for about thirty minutes, before the door opened and in walked Tanteeth.

"I will deliver your message to the Colonel," she said in sharp tones as though telling an inattentive schoolchild to focus.

"There is to be a meeting of the Cyberspace Administration and the Institute," said the messenger, a sallow-looking youth who was actually training to join the elite secret police arm of the CAC.

"We had heard as much," said Tanteeth, to make clear this meeting came as no surprise. "The colonel would be happy to welcome Director Zhuang here."

"Director Zhuang suggests the meeting take place at a neutral site, an inconspicuous venue that is acceptable to both sides."

Again, Tanteeth showed that she was prepared. "How about," she said, spreading out the words, "the former Wuhan police headquarters building?"

Everyone knew about this building. It had served as police HQ for more than a decade, until the Party leader of Hubei province, on her own authority, authorized construction of a new, futuristic headquarters, with impregnable security, 5G communications and easy access to the airport. The building had gone up in six weeks, and the old HQ was left to molder. When the Hubei Province's head of the Party's secret police—which competed for status and funding with the regular police—learned of the new building, he informed his superiors in Beijing. Stunned that such a thing could happen without top-level Party approval, the police chief was removed. It was too late however, to cancel the transfer of people, files and communications equipment, so the police got their new headquarters. The secret police prevented any other entity from moving into the old HQ, but it was kept in readiness in case a quiet place should be needed for a meeting. Now was that time.

"That will be acceptable," said Zhuang's messenger. "Next Monday, ten a.m.?"

"Fine," said Tanteeth.

And so, Hui and Zhuang sat at opposite centers of a long glass table, with no words spoken between them. Then the room began to fill up, by twos, like bridesmaids and groomsmen slowly filtering in and finding their proper places.

Tanteeth came in alone and sat next to Hui.

Wo and Fang, the odd couple, came in and sat to Zhuang's right.

Two more members of Zhuang's party sat to his left.

Hui put on a beatific smile. "Comrade Zhuang," he said. "If I understood your invitation properly, the purpose of this meeting is twofold: to agree upon and implement the instructions we will give to domestic websites, chat sites, video hosts, data providers about what they can and cannot say in relation to the virus now permeating China—in short, Chinese cyberspace, which is clearly in your hands and for which we are grateful.

"But there is a second goal here. We must craft a message for the outside world making clear several things: first, the virus is under control. Second, that the virus did not start here but was introduced by a foreign power, which bears responsibility for it. Third, that we take advantage of this opportunity to weaken our greatest adversary, in other words the United States, by using this virus to instill fear and confusion in the American population, to damage its economy and to drive Donald Trump from office. For Trump is the first American president who has understood what China has been doing and continues to do, and has shown a willingness to combat us on our own terms. Yes, Trump is a madman, and like most madmen is dangerous. So, we must do what we can to use American democracy to remove him from power. It has been agreed by figures in higher authority that my humble institute must be used in this struggle."

Though Hui's words sounded spontaneous, they had in fact been crafted through hours of preparation, argument and compromise. Hui did not believe in large-group decision-making, relying instead on small cadres of highly trusted advisors.

Surprisingly, Zhuang let Wo begin the meeting. "Comrades, since we are all engaged in this sensitive matter and all want the best for our country, let us speak frankly. Opinion around much of the world on the topic of this virus is not on our side. Some news media from reactionary countries have actually suggested that it began" – he thought of Fang's stupid ex-wife, now safely locked away in an asylum and out of his life—"that the Wuhan Virology Lab created the virus..." Wo tailed off. He noticed the beautiful PLA lieutentant with Hui. She blinked. Just for a second, and giving nothing away that he could use. But she had blinked. "And it is absolutely essential that such treacherous commentary is never, I say never, comrades, introduced into the social media universe of our country. To let that happen could give great comfort to those who do not recognize the Party as the center of that universe, as it is of all of China. At the direction of Comrade Director Zhuang, I have prepared some messages that will be sent to all relevant social media sites in the name of the Cyberspace Administration. Presuming that these guidelines are respected, I believe we can control the messaging most effectively."

"This is fascinating, comrade," said Hui. "And a true credit to your comprehension of the problem. But where is this going?"

Wo smiled. He had set the trap and the tiger had fallen into it. He now had the right to address Hui directly. To have done so before would have lacked respect.

"Colonel Hui, are you perhaps familiar with the case of Li Wienlang?"

Hui knew where this was going, and that he had made a tactical error. The best way to recover, he knew, was to get past it quickly. "Of course, we all know about Dr. Li," he said briskly.

Li Wienlang was an optometrist in Wuhan who had been among the first physicians to volunteer to treat residents who were complaining of shortness of breath, high fever, loss of taste and smell—in short, who had contracted the virus that was sweeping the city. Li was not a Party member and had already been tagged as suspicious by the Hubei province arm of the secret police because of suspected sympathies with undesirable elements. Likewise, his youthful looks and open manner with patients had caused comment, with some patients who were Party members mumbling about his Western style of practicing medicine. For those in the first wave of virus victims, however, Li was a human miracle, a devoted caregiver who, even sheathed by a mask, managed to bring smiles and hope to his patients.

When Li had expressed his concern that the local medical authorities were not taking this virus seriously enough, he had been summoned to a police station and told to stop trying to scare citizens. Li countered that far from trying to scare them, he was trying to keep them alive by informing them of the deadly nature of this airborne threat. When he was sent home, he began posting a blog on WeChat to get his warning out. It quickly attracted thousands of followers, who in turn repeated and re-tweeted his words. Li's theory, that the virus had started in the wet market, possibly carried by fruit bats, became the working assumption for hundreds of thousands of Wuhan residents, who, because the official news outlets had not yet even admitted there was a problem, had nowhere else to get information. Among the 11 million residents of Wuhan, Li, unknown outside his hometown, was widely regarded as a teller of truth trapped in a culture of silence and denial.

Because Li continued to treat patients for free and at the expense of his regular job as an optometrist, he came to the attention of the local Party, which joined the police in ordering Li to stop spreading false rumors. One week after that confrontation, Li ceased showing up at the hospital. One day later, he wrote on his blog, "As a result of my proximity to many patients of this novel virus, I too have contracted it. I am self-isolating so that I do not accidentally infect anyone else."

The social media response in Wuhan was overwhelming, nearly crashing the local servers. Messages of hope, concern, even a few brave messages offering prayers dominated the chatrooms like Weibo, WeChat and its Wuhan-based local cousin, WuChat. When Li's blog went dark, his followers went in person to the optometry office where, it was well known, he had worked. A coworker informed them that Li had died two days previously.

The Cyberspace Administration in Wuhan had been monitoring the chatter about Li, and had deleted posts that suggested he had been right about the virus, but had been reluctant to shut it down completely. Part of the reason: the local authorities viewed WeChat as a kind of safety valve for the expression of frustration and fear sweeping Wuhan as the cases skyrocketed and the hospitals were increasingly overcrowded. By this time, Zhuang had been brought up to speed. He consulted the deputy director, who told him there was an up-and-coming Party member in Wuhan named Wo who had suggested the now commonly accepted wisdom of being "sleek and silent" in snuffing out alarmist propaganda. Zhuang, through a deputy, told Wo to come up with "language" that would be communicated to all cyberspace entities. Wo agreed, then told Fang to write something.

If "sleek and silent" had been a phrase borrowed from a friend about how to divorce a wife, what Fang created now was purely his own inspiration and would cement him as Wo's sleek, but very, very silent partner.

Fang confronted Dr. Li's death head-on, an unusually bold and direct path for CAC, and totally out of line with "sleek and silent." Later, he said he chose the words because he had intuited that the situation was close to out of control and needed to be shut down fast.

"We must recognize with clear mind the butterfly effect, broken windows effect and snowball effect triggered by this event (Li's death)," Fang wrote, "and the unprecedented challenge that it has posed to our online opinion management and control work. All Cyberspace Administration bureaus must pay heightened attention to online opinion, and resolutely control anything that seriously damages Party and government credibility and attacks the political system."

In its way, separated by three hundred years and a universe of different thought, Fang's words became as important in 21$^{st}$ Century China as did Jefferson's "When in the course of human events" preamble. Whether through honest analysis or pure luck, Fang had identified the danger posed by the virus, recognized the potential for widespread dissent and opposition in a digital world left uncontrolled, and proposed in vague but powerful language a way to check it and prevent it from going any further.

Of course, Fang would not, for a very long time, be credited as the author of this, so to speak, Declaration of Dependence (upon the Party). Wo took ownership as soon as he saw that Zhuang approved it, and in fact, was impressed by it. Fang's revenge would come in its own good time.

"So, you see," Wo said, "without the CAC under the leadership of Director Zhuang, popular opinion could have gotten out of control and panic might have set in. I would like to offer Director Zhuang the nation's thanks. It is also important that we keep our focus on internal dangers and not let ourselves be dragged into unnecessary foreign meddling."

Hui sat back and smiled. It was now obvious why Wo, who was known mostly as a wordsmith, had been granted the honor of representing that side of the table. His real job was to mouth praise for Zhuang, who could not justify lavish hosannas on himself. Instead, Xi's trusted lieutenant looked at the table, and nodded solemnly.

"Thank you," said Hui, letting the words expand through the air between him and Zhuang. "I believe we all know what role the CAC has played so far in confronting this problem."

Zhuang looked up sharply, aware that his side had allowed Hui not just an escape route, but a plan of counterattack. Hui's thrust had been well aimed, for it was generally accepted within the upper ranks of the Party that the CAC—that 21$^{st}$ Century thought police force created by Xi himself—had been asleep at the switch and so slow to react to the threat, however remote, of online insurrection.

"Yes," Hui continued, and everyone in the room could see that he had squared his shoulders sat up straighter, and was looking directly as Zhuang, as though issuing a challenge to slug it out in the schoolyard. "I am certain that the Administration did its best in this dangerous moment. You saw that the threat had reached a potential crisis point, and managed, through Comrade Wo's skillful use of the language, to alert our digital entities to shut it down."

"Yes," said Hui again, and this appeared to be his favorite method of punctuation. "You used tried and true methods and they worked. "However," he said, again stretching out the word, and the room came alert, aware that the counterattack had commenced, "had our institute been made aware of the danger much sooner, we might have been able to avert the entire episode."

"Is that so?" said Zhuang, speaking for the first time in a long time.

"Indeed it is, comrade," said Hui, using a form of sentence construction that, in Mandarin, implied a rebuke. "I will explain in due course. But first, if you will allow me to continue," and again, this contained a mild element of presumed hurt feelings and mistreatment on Zhuang's part, "I must also take issue with Comrade Wo's presumption that our role should be confined to domestic cyberspace."

Zhuang made a frowny face as though he had tasted something unpleasant.

Hui continued as if he had not noticed. "I bring this up, knowing that some may think I am encroaching on Director Zhuang's territory. And in answer, I would point out that while our domestic cyber-security is of course a top priority, we must not overlook the potential for extending our influence outside China, indeed around the world.

And most importantly, comrades, extending it into the deepest folds of our most potent and dangerous enemy, the United States."

"With your indulgence," said Hui, "I would like to spend just a few minutes explaining why in my view, the Party has an historic opportunity to turn the unfortunate existence of this novel coronavirus into a huge advantage."

Zhuang broke in. "There are hundreds of dead in Hubei province alone. How is that an advantage?"

Hui smiled. "We are all intelligent people at this table. Let us not evade the truth. Despite some unfounded theories, the virus began in Wuhan," said Hui. He was, essentially, calling Xinhua, the official Chinese news agency, and the media spokeswoman for the Ministry of Foreign Affairs, liars. It spread through China quickly because we were not quick enough to recognize that it was airborne, or that it could be transmitted from animals to humans. It then spread around the world, very quickly, because travelers from China took it with them. And visitors to China, specifically Wuhan, contracted it and carried it back home before symptoms presented themselves.

"Northern Italy, where there are tens of thousands of Chinese working in textile and other industries, was struck next. Of course, the virus went from the Chinese there to the Italians themselves, since they are known for their chummy, kisses-on-the-cheeks way of living and doing business. As I understand it, the town of Prato, not far from Milan, has more bodies in the street than it can bury or cremate. It spread through Europe quicker than most countries could recognize what was happening. And, one by one, Europe's economies came to a halt.

"It was inevitable that the virus would reach the United States. Millions of Chinese, Europeans and others fly there every month. The virus was first recognized in Seattle, a major tech city in the state of Washington."

"We know where Seattle is," said Zhuang sharply. "Who do you think you are dealing with?"

"Someone who wants to confine our next steps to domestic surveillance," said Hui, eyes suddenly wide open, hostility bristling on his tongue. Hui, whose institute had quietly developed an AI program to guarantee a winning hand at poker every time, had decided to play for big stakes.

Zhuang measured his position swiftly; decided that time was on his side, and nodded, once.

"I believe that America is weak, despite the fact that Trump is its president."

"Bah, Trump," said Zhuang.

"Yes, comrade," said Hui, as though he and Zhuang had suddenly shared a delicious secret. "Trump is our enemy. But he is also America's enemy."

"What do you mean by that?" said Zhuang, now genuinely interested.

"Trump has divided America more than it had been for a hundred and fifty years. He hates everyone. Mexicans. People from Latin America. Old friends in Europe. And China, especially China. And why especially China? Because our economy works better than America's. Because everyone here knows that the Party is leading us in the right direction. Our army is bigger than America's now, and they know that. And they fear us. And because Trump was such a loudmouth, and got so many people angry, Americans became preoccupied with hating each other, rather than dealing with the problems that they really should be handling.

"Even now, when they realize the virus has reached their shores, and that Americans are contracting it and dying from it, they're too busy to point fingers and say, 'Yes, but black people are getting sick more than white people,' or, 'I'm fat and have diabetes. I deserve to be treated first.' Or 'why wasn't the government prepared for this?' Prepared for what? Something that probably didn't exist a year ago."

Hui took a deep breath, a sip of water.

"So what I want to say is this: America is as weak as it has ever been since its Civil War. And its people don't want to hear about new diseases or how to protect themselves from it. They want to be left alone to live their lives, to hate each other, to tear each other apart. Because that's what America is good at now."

"This is all very interesting," said Zhuang. "But what does it have to do with controlling misinformation in our Cyberspace?"

"As I have said, comrade director," said Hui, "I leave that important task to you. I am proposing that we also help Americans destroy themselves. My respectful advice to you is: make Americans think they're all going to die from this virus if they don't do exactly what they're told. And make sure you provide information to the so-called experts so they'll tell it to the Americans, and the Americans will be too afraid to ignore it. And although you may doubt me, I believe if you convince Americans to do two things, you can bring the United States to its knees in less than two months.

"And what are those two things?" said Zhuang.

"Make them cover their faces. And don't let them go to work. Make them stay at home with their family. Within a few weeks, they will be at each other's throats."

# Chapter 18
## Just Call Them Racists

Unlike most pre-pandemic meetings in office buildings, which end in promises to "look into" a problem and "circle back" for more meetings, the confrontation between Zhuang and Hui produced results, though at a much lower level and without official recognition that the two top men were working together. Zhuang, who until now could count on having Xi's ear, called the Chairman's office an hour after leaving Hui, and asked for a ten-minute appointment, at Xi's convenience, of course. Hui, for his part, returned to the Institute and handed over the pen-sized device he had worn in his jacket pocket to a wide-hipped, over-made up woman who took it away and promised results in thirty minutes. It took her twenty-seven.

"Look at this, please, comrade colonel," she said in a husky voice that suggested heavy tobacco use. She thrust a few pieces of paper at Hui, allowed him to read the content, and remained silent. The pages contained three charts, labeled "#1, #2, and #3." Hui studied them.

"Am I correct that number one is agitated?"

"Very, sir."

"Number two is exhibiting signs of insecurity?"

"Very clear signs."

"And here, this number three. Hiding something. Not willing to speak but with something to say nonetheless."

"Exactly, colonel." The analyst had no idea who the three subjects whose minds she had just plumbed were. She only knew what was going on in their heads.

"Thank you." Hui pondered. So, Zhuang was agitated. That much Hui could read without the help of AI. Hui could almost imagine Zhuang getting on the first secure phone he could find to report in to Xi. But whatever he said wouldn't matter now.

The one introduced as Wo was an empty vessel. He was pretending to belong in that meeting. That was clear by his eye movements, recorded on the AI device that Hui had in his pocket. He looked around too much, which even Hui with his naked eye had noticed. In a word, a *poseur*.

It was the third one, whose name had not been offered and who said not a word, that most interested Hui. He was not young, probably in his forties. But his demeanor was different from the other two. Composed, without pretense, sure of himself. Hui liked and suspected this one at the same time. This one would bear watching.

Like Zhuang, Hui understood that the meeting had had nothing to do with cooperation. It had been a competitive test of strength between the current cyberspace universe, controlled by monitors, censors and police, and the coming age of AI, where human behavior would be predicted, tracked, mimicked and modified, all without humans.

Hui seldom acted without reflection. That, despite his affinity for AI, was what made him human. This time however, armed with the behavior charts of Zhuang and his minions, he acted impulsively. He put in a call to Zhuang, was told he was on his way to Beijing, and asked that Zhuang return his call.

Perfect, thought Hui. He's on his way to see Xi, no doubt to ladle criticism on me. And he'll be caught flat-footed when he realizes what I want.

Zhuang too was doing mental calculus as he touched down at the private Party airport outside Beijing. Xi had said he wanted to know how the meeting had gone, so here Zhuang was. The important thing was not to misrepresent what had happened. People who tried to hide the truth from Xi were almost always caught out, then called out. It was not pleasant. It was not worth it. Xi had credited the Cyberspace Administration with tamping down hysterical social media posts. Then he had pointed out, correctly, that the quick spread of the virus, already out of China's control, had to be presented properly to the rest of the world so that China was not blamed for it, and could instead, take the lead in responding to it. Zhuang had achieved control over Chinese cyberspace. He knew he could not do the same with the rest of the world. Not alone.

The CAC used fear and intimidation to meet its objectives. No one wanted to risk ignoring a CAC directive and be accused of anti-Party activity or thought. It was said that Hui was close to developing Artificial Intelligence that mimicked the human brain functions, and that, without the need for ever more complicated algorithms, could learn an individual's thought process, copy it, act like that person and analyze why the person thought the way he did. If it worked, and if it could be developed on a large enough scale, AI would be able to recognize and predict how a person would act, analyze why, and, quite possibly, intervene in the person's thought process and inject more acceptable behavior. It was mind control taken to a global level.

He had the idea of contacting Hui, and proposing that their organizations work, not exactly together, but along parallel paths. Chinese cyberspace, which CAC largely controlled, would be an excellent and immense testing laboratory for Hui's theories. If they worked, Hui would be indebted to Zhuang. And Zhuang could then apply his tried-and-true tactics to cyberspace control, worldwide.

His phone said that Hui had called his office and wanted to talk to him. He texted the office that they should arrange the call immediately. It would be good to know what Hui wanted before Zhuang met with Xi. Both men knew their cell phones were protected behind several firewalls. Their conversation would be safe; the same might not be true of the content.

"I won't waste your time," said Hui. "That meeting revealed the potential for cooperation."

"I agree," said Zhuang, wondering if Hui could already replicate *his* thinking pattern. A troubling possibility.

"Before you meet with the General Secretary, this is what I propose: that silent member of your team, I don't know his name. Could you spare him to work with someone here at the Institute?"

"If I thought it was useful, yes. Who is this person at your Institute?"

"He is an American."

"Ah, yes. I have heard rumors about him," said Zhuang.

"I was sure you had. I'm asking because I need you to present the idea to the General Secretary. Here it is: Your man listens to what mine knows about America, and fashions the message we want to get out. If they don't get along, we'll scrap the idea. If they do, we might have the makings of a very potent propaganda weapon."

"I'll bring it up."

"Thank you."

It was the warmest conversation the two had ever had.

Fang could read Wo's displeasure as he walked into his office. There were no greetings, no preliminaries. "You have been assigned to work with a *gweilo* from the AI Institute on a project of great interest to Director Zhuang."

"Very well," said Fang. "Thank you for the opp..."

"Do not thank me. This was not my idea," said Wo, who was thinking, if this doesn't work out, I want to be on the record that it was not my doing. He knew he was living on a narrow edge, between Fang's creative wording and Zhuang's reputed influence with the Chairman. Losing either one would be disastrous. So, he had to hope that Fang could carry out this new responsibility and still supply him with effective propaganda language.

"The *gweilo* of course needs a translator. It is the woman who was at the last meeting. See if she can be turned to my ... our advantage."

"I understand."

Their first meeting could easily have been their last. Fang was ultra-suspicious, not so much of the *gweilo* but of the translator. She was too gorgeous, too precise in her wording, too fast in the simultaneous way she converted language, and worst of all, too smart. The young American, by contrast, was respectful, proper, sure of himself.

This was Hui's doing. He had called Henry into his office and, with Tanteeth in the corner and Rav, unusually, translating, said in Mandarin, "You have done very well so far, corporal. You have acclimated to your surroundings and are already a valuable part of the Institute. This, however, is a new and different challenge. It is now time for you to show your American-ness, use it to your ... our ... advantage."

"I will do whatever you ask," said Henry through Rav, flush with embarrassment and pride at Hui's compliments.

"Use your knowledge of America to guide the conversations you have. Zhuang's people know very little about your land. Guide them."

"How do you want me to do that?"

"You know America's weaknesses. Explain them. Put them to good use for our plans. That is the best service you can provide me right now."

Try as he would to dislike the American, Fang found him refreshingly honest. If he had secret, ulterior motives, Fang did not sense them. Why he was working for the Chinese Army was not Fang's business. He needed information so he could put his own talents to work. Under the circumstances, it was easy to forget that Wo stood in his way.

"We have a problem," said Fang. "The virus started in Wuhan. It probably was transmitted originally by bats." As she did at the previous meeting, Rav's eyes flicked once. She showed no emotion. "The American president, Trump, has been calling it 'The Chinese virus' and 'Wuhan Flu.' How can we put out a different story and make it believable?"

Henry bypassed Rav and said in Chinese, "Say it's racist." He had been preparing that line, rehearsing with Rav, to make a strong first impression with Fang. It seemed to work.

"Ah, you are learning our language quickly. Congratulations. Now, what do you mean, 'say it's racist'?"

Henry had his answer ready, but this time spoke through Rav. "When I was a little kid, and I wanted something—say some candy, or a soda with dinner instead of milk, and my parents said no, I would say 'that's not fair.' If they made me do homework, or turn off the television, I'd say, 'that's not fair.' Anytime I didn't get what I wanted, I'd say, 'that's not fair!' It got to be an instinct. If I felt anything negative, if anything wasn't exactly as I wanted, I'd shout, 'that's not fair!'"

Rav's translation was brilliantly smooth. She and Henry had worked on this, and she knew what was coming.

"Excuse me," interrupted Fang. "This story of your childhood is all very interesting. But what does it have to do with our problem?"

Henry smiled, nodded once. "America is tearing itself apart right now. My countrymen hate each other. The two parties, Republicans and Democrats, won't speak to each other, much less work together to solve problems. Much of it is caused by Trump, who is a very divisive figure. Much of what he says is true, but he doesn't say it with sensitivity. He just says, 'China virus,' and then blames China for it.

Fang had heard Hui say much the same thing at the previous meeting. Could he have learned some of this from the *gweilo*?

"There are twelve million people living in the United States illegally," said Henry through Rav. "Most of them are from Mexico. Trump calls them 'illegal aliens' or 'Mexican criminals' and says he's going to throw them out. Well, the virus *did* start in China, and the Mexicans *are* there illegally and so, technically are criminals. Trump is right. But the way Trump says things makes people angry. It also makes some Americans feel guilty about how good their own lives are. So they call Trump a racist.

"Since being a racist is a condition of your mind, it can't actually be proven. Someone calls you a racist, you say, 'No, I'm not.' But the thing is, you can't prove you're *not* a racist, just like your accusers can't prove you are. So, each side thinks it's right and the other's wrong. Nothing gets done, except the hatred between the sides is allowed to fester like ... well, like a virus festers inside a bat. Or a human.

"Remember what I said before? As a boy, I'd shout 'that's not fair!' every time I didn't get my way. My parents knew better, knew I'd grow out of it, knew they were doing the right thing. But I didn't know that then. So we each had our definition of 'fair,' and both thought we were right.

"That's what's happening in America. Everyone who's not white, wealthy and happy is convinced his or her bad luck is racism. So, they call anyone they don't like or don't agree with a racist. It's the twenty-first century version of 'that's not fair!'"

Rav took a deep breath. She needed it. Her translation was perfect; even so, it took effort to keep up with Henry, despite having rehearsed the words.

Fang was frankly fascinated and didn't care if it showed. "But that's crazy. Just because Trump says, 'Wuhan flu' or the 'Chinese virus' doesn't mean he hates all Chinese."

"It does these days," said Henry, and Rav added a ravishing nod to punctuate it. "You don't have to prove it. You just have to say it. By the way, your word, *gweilo.* That's racist."

"What!" shouted Fang. "It's just a word for anyone who's not Asian."

"It's racist," said Henry in Chinese.

"It just means your eyes are different in shape from ours."

"That's racist too," said Henry through Rav. "And that's what you need to say, every time Trump or any other American says something negative about China. Every time!"

"But it will lose its effect if we say it every time."

"No," said Henry. "It's just getting started."

"Well," said Fang. "All I can say is I'm glad to live in a country where you can use your own language to describe what is true, without being called racist."

All three participants in this extraordinary meeting were extraordinarily shocked when the door swung open and three Army officers in the brown and red uniform of the PLA marched in. "Citizen Fang," one of them said harshly. "You are to come with us." They didn't notice that Rav was quietly telling Henry who they were and what they said.

"Why?" said Fang, who had gone white with sudden terror. "What's happened?"

"Your wife has managed to post a message on WeChat," said the soldier. "She says she started the Wuhan virus."

"She's not my…" Fang started to say, the fear like foam on his lips.

"Come! Now!"

# Chapter 19
## Sisters, In Law

Luisa and Qi Qi did not know each other. But they were bound together by a common calamity: they each knew a truth that no one wanted to hear.

Luisa's minute of fame came and went. What she was saying in public was too close to what ordinary people were thinking and saying around their kitchen tables. But it was up against the machine of selective truth known as the news media. True to her word, Donatella Tesco got Luisa booked on all the Italian networks—once. Her message—that the virus had been imported into Italy by the Chinese working in the factories and mills of Lombardy—was met with shock and disapproval.

"Why are you trying to put the blame on poor Chinese immigrants who are here to find a better life?" Her interviewers would scold. "You are scapegoating an entire race because of the way they look."

"I am stating the obvious," Luisa replied, after hours of coaching by Tesco and other Liga media advisors. "The virus started in China. There are thousands of Chinese from Wuhan itself, never mind the rest of China—working in our fabric mills, our cutting tables, our design studios. The Chinese have bought most of the fabric companies and brought in their own people to make the clothes cheaply. But they still label them "Made in Italy.""

"But the clothes *are* being made here," insisted the interviewer.

"Yes, but not to the standards that have always defined Italian-made clothes. Look at the crap coming out of our factories now. Skimpy stitching, stripes that don't align properly, uneven dye jobs. Versace would die all over if he saw his name on this garbage."

"And you are blaming the Chinese for this?"

"I am blaming the Chinese for this, yes."

"You are a racist."

"I am an Italian telling the truth. Do you know what the Chinese call us to our faces? *Gweilos.* Is that racist?"

"No," said the interviewer. "It's a term that means someone who is not Asian."

"It's a term to describe how we look."

"Yes."

"Is it all right if I call Chinese "slant-eyes?"

"Of course not. That's racist."

"And *gweilo*, which means round-eyes, is not?"

"Correct."

"Well," said Luisa, going off her rehearsed lines, "If that makes me racist, then I guess I'm racist."

Thereafter, the media referred to her as "Admitted racist Luisa Moretti..."

After that came the silence.

No one would interview her. Newspapers refused to let her contribute opinion articles. Websites banned her, and even banned the use of her name. A right-wing Austrian website interviewed her, and helpfully headlined the story: "Luisa Moretti: Neo Nazi!"

A Socialist member of parliament asked for, and received, time to denounce Luisa from the floor of the legislature. "We Italians believe in free speech. From the days of the Roman Empire, there have been public debates on every topic. But this woman, Moretti, is a hateful person whose voice must be silenced for the protection of freedom of speech." The blatant contradiction of this absurdity was not commented upon by any news organization.

Luisa signed on as a paid staffer of La Liga. She had no choice. She was out of work, and clearly unemployable. Tesco told her: "No one wants to hear what you have to say."

"It's the truth," Luisa replied.

"I know that, and you know that," said Tesco. "But you haven't been able to prove it's the truth. That has to be your next step. "

"What step?"

"Keep saying you are right until they think you are. It doesn't matter if you are. Just keep saying it."

\* \* \*

Qi Qi knew who the first Chinese to start the virus was: her. The bat she had sold to Gramps, Wang Win, carried some disease that had started the virus. She had had to work backwards to figure this out. She knew the Virology Lab where she had worked was experimenting with SARS-2 in bats. The bat she had removed—without permission—from the low-security lab had been part of that experiment. She knew this was true because several of her former colleagues had told her. She knew that Gramps had accepted the bat, probably cut off its head, boiled it and sold it for soup. Or had used it for soup for himself if no one else would buy the smelly thing. Gramps was now dead. The cause, she knew, was coronavirus. She herself had been near death, presumably from handling the infected bat.

Therefore, she was ground zero.

She had also, through backward reasoning, figured out that her miserable ex-husband, Fang, had pilfered the money she got from Gramps when he was pretending to make her tea. Qi Qi had no residual feelings for Fang, but nor could she bring herself to hate him. It was just part of life. It was not Fang's fault she was where she was.

She had not been thinking clearly when she told the space-suited health care workers who swarmed through her building that she was the one who started it all. She was trying to be helpful, not provocative. When the police came and dragged her away, she thought at first it was because she had looked ill. But they treated her more like a criminal than a patient. And that place where they took her and held her: Its name was the Wuhan No 17 Long-Term Health Care Unit but any drooling idiot—literally — could recognize it for what it was: an insane asylum.

"Why do you think you started this?" a white-coated gorilla posing as a psychiatrist asked her. "There is no such thing as a virus going around Wuhan."

"Then why are there medical teams going into people's houses, and dragging them out?" Qi Qi asked in reply.

"That is a figment of your warped imagination."

"Really? I took pictures."

The gorilla made a horrified face and left Qi Qi's room, returning with three nurses. "These ladies will take care of you. Please note that we respect women here, and we make certain they are treated by other women."

"Please come with us," said one of the nurses. They guided Qi Qi down a corridor. One nurse stepped ahead, opened the door to what looked like a storage closet. The other two pushed Qi Qi inside and closed the door. All three nurses had eight-inch-long truncheons made of hard rubber. The beating was vicious.

"If you persist in making these fatuous statements, these cures will continue and become more intense," one nurse said, slamming her rubber club into Qi Qi's ear. "Remember, these are medical treatments to improve your condition." Slam.

"Are you feeling better now?" another nurse inquired. Slam.

"Yes," said Qi Qi. "I see now I was wrong."

"Good," said the head nurse. "Then you will be released. These beds are needed for other patients."

"Yes," said Qi Qi. "I know. For patients with the virus."

Slam.

Nonetheless, she was discharged. Standing in front of her apartment building, she thought back on her pre-bat existence. Her life seemed divided into two halves: before she picked up that sick bat, and since. She didn't have a key to her apartment. She had been grabbed and removed forcibly before she could gather her belongings. Fortunately, she found her door open. Her tea tin, where she had stored her meager savings before Fang stole them, was still there. So was her cell phone, a cheap one that she kept meaning to replace. But why? She had no one to call. About all she used it for was to read messages on WeChat. She almost never posted any of her own.

Almost never.

Before she could talk herself out of it, Qi Qi signed into WeChat and wrote: "My name is Qi Qi Dieh. I started the Wuhan virus. I stole a diseased bat from the Wuhan Virological Institute and sold it at the

Wuhan wet market to Wang Win, better known as Gramps. I don't know what he did with it, but he is now dead. When health police came to my building, I told them what I had done. They dragged me from my house and put me in Number 17 Long Term Health Care Unit, which is an insane asylum. But I am not insane. I am telling the truth."

She read through the message hurriedly. She added her national identification number, which every legal resident of China was required to have and memorize. Qi Qi wanted to be identified. She had already paid the price. Now she wanted the world to know who she was. And what she had done.

# Chapter 20
## Airy Fairy, Jerry

This, Jerry told himself, was getting ridiculous. The mayor of Pittsburgh, a Democrat who had once considered himself a possible governor, senator, maybe even president, knew he couldn't push a liberal agenda in the 'burgh and survive. Sure, the city council had passed the same local laws as most other cities and towns: made mask-wearing mandatory to get into stores, forbidden indoor dining, closed bars, all but shut down the buses and trolleys that moved the population around, and forced students to try to learn from their homes.

Fine. Jerry had nowhere to go, since his job had disappeared, and he was living on the subsistence checks that Trump had sent out under his own name, making a mockery of fiscal restraint, but what the hell? The guy didn't tell the truth about anything else, so take the money and run. Except there was nowhere to run.

And now the Pirates' season was in its annual tailspin. And even when they did play well, it was in an empty stadium. There were few enough pleasures left in life, he thought, and taking away sports and the joy it gave to people like him was like some punishment being handed out by a nasty fifth grade teacher.

This virus, whatever they called it, felt more and more like a plot to ruin everyone's life. Stay six feet apart. Ok, that made sense kind of. But who decided that six feet was safe but five feet wasn't. Well, the *experts* said so. And why do we have to wear surgical masks that wrap around your ears? What's wrong with old-fashioned bandanas, tied around your head, like bank robbers used to wear in cowboy movies? Again, the *experts* had spoken. The mask thing was especially annoying to Jerry, since the blue surgical masks they were selling at his local CVS were all made in China. And China is where the goddam virus started! Coincidence? He asked someone who worked in the drugstore—the same one where he got yelled at—if they had any masks made in America, and was told, no, they all came from China. Everything seems to come from China now, Jerry said. Don't be racist, he was told. How is that racist, Jerry asked. Because you're singling out Chinese people. But they're the ones making all the stuff we buy, he said. Maybe they just work harder, was the answer.

That, he had to admit, was probably true. Just in his lifetime, Americans seemed to have given up on the idea of working hard to get ahead. It seemed like working your ass off in the expectation of being recognized and rewarded was something to be scorned and laughed at.

Then two things happened that transformed Jerry from a regular, slightly disgruntled but average guy, into a hardened skeptic, what Clinton had called "deplorables," what the *experts* derisively labeled "pandemic deniers," in other words, people who looked around them at what was going on, listened to what they were being fed on the news sites, on TV and in whatever newspapers still existed, saw that the various levels of government—city, state, federal—were not so subtly passing laws and issuing executive decrees, all of which further restricted individual freedoms, killed private sector jobs, and made us live like sardines in a tin, all in the name of "safety," until Jerry and the rest of these people who were being labeled morons, "deniers," dangers to society, were saying, with increasing volume and rancor, "fuck, no."

The first thing that happened that changed Jerry was that he found out that the state health commissioner—the guy who said everyone had to wear the blue surgical masks that were made in China—was on the board of directors of the Chinese company that made the masks! And when some reporter called him out on it, the guy got huffy and actually said, "there is no conflict of interest here," and added, of course, that suggesting he couldn't be on the board of a Chinese company and at the same time be ordering everyone to wear the masks that the Chinese company was making was "a racist imprecation."

These days, pointing out the difference between a red traffic light and a green one was racist.

The second thing that happened was really two things rolled up into one. Tran texted Jerry and asked if he wanted to be part of a Defenders march to protest the fact that Pittsburgh's schools were still closed down, by decree of the City Council, while other cities of roughly the same size were bringing their kids back to the classrooms for in-person education.

Jerry didn't have kids, and so wasn't directly affected by the school situation. But he could see the ripple effect that closing the schools had: kids were cooped up at home, making them irritable, parents had to stay with them, to oversee their "virtual classes" and to make sure the kids didn't do some dumb shit to hurt themselves. That meant the parents couldn't go to work, presuming they still had jobs to go to. It was a sick cycle of one group pulling another down. The only ones who liked having the schools closed were the teachers, who were getting paid one hundred percent of their salaries *plus* a bonus to reward them for the inconvenience of having to teach online. The teachers' union had threatened to call a strike if they didn't get bonuses, and the city council, one of whose members was married to a public school teacher, went along with it rather than have the teachers, including his spouse, out picketing.

"And even though they're supposed to be teaching online, some of the teachers are picketing anyway," said Tran, when he and Jerry met up. "Because they say the bonuses aren't enough, and the teachers are suffering from stress from having to teach the kids without actually having all the materials they're used to having at the schools."

"Yeah, but nobody's unaffected by this virus stuff," Jerry pointed out, sounding stupid even to himself as he said it. "What makes the teachers so special?"

Tran looked at him and said, "Jerry, you are becoming a political activist before my very eyes. What, indeed, makes teachers different? Well, they have control of everyone's kids, is part of the answer. And most parents, even really good parents, actually look forward to the time when their little monsters are out of the house, and at school, and someone else's responsibility. So, the parents let the teachers push them around."

Jerry got it. It was the teachers wanting to get paid for doing nothing and screaming that they were being sentenced to death for being in the same room with kids.

In the very same City Council session, there was a vote on outlawing smoking in the entire city of Pittsburgh. Not just government buildings, not just restaurants, not just PNC Park and Heinz Field, not just city-subsidized housing—in the entire city of Pittsburgh. Inside, outside, all around the town. The Council member pushing the motion was a trans-gender who'd been elected because he/she said it was important to reduce gender friction—a term Jerry hadn't heard before and made his own assumptions about, since gender friction had treated him well over the years, though not nearly often enough.

Anyway, this City Council member named Dane or Diane depending on which gender the member felt like being from one day to the next (Jesus, Jerry thought) said that smoking cigarettes and especially cigars and pipes was a phallic symbol and part of the paternalistic society that America had become, because it was mostly white guys (which the member might be, depending on what day) and that it was a health hazard, especially to trans people, and had to end. The vote was unanimous, because nobody was brave enough to take on Dane/Diane for fear of being called prejudiced. It was now illegal to smoke cigarettes, cigars or pipes of tobacco in Pittsburgh.

And in the same session—the same fucking session—the Council voted to legalize the use and sale of marijuana within the city limits of Pittsburgh. The Council—all Democrats—passed a resolution that said the "national nervous seizure provoked by the presidency of Donald Trump has made it essential for Pittsburghers to be able to bliss out on occasion."

The vote was, of course, unanimous.

So, it was ok to toke, but not to smoke.

Jerry had never smoked cigarettes. But he went out and bought a pack and managed to smoke/choke down three before he felt really rotten and decided that that was not the way to register his opposition to the insanity going on in his much beloved hometown.

He texted Tran and said yeah, he'd be in the Defenders march.

The march had a permit, it had a start and an end time, and no one associated with it wanted it to be anything but a peaceful expression of opinion. It started on Wood Street, made its way up to Fifth Avenue and was supposed to end, with a speech and a dismissal, in front of the city's board of education building.

It was a nice enough day, and Jerry, dressed in jeans, running shoes and a sweatshirt, thought this was what it should be like all the time: people getting together to say what they think, without getting angry. Most everyone was even wearing a blue Chinese mask, to show they weren't assholes. No one was smoking, in case the cops wanted to enforce the Council's latest way of interfering in people's lives.

One of the guys in the march was a retired city cop named Earl. He had made it to sergeant and was older than Jerry by thirty years. The two had liked each other as soon as they met at a Defenders rally. Earl came over to Jerry with a grim look on his face.

"What are you dressed for? Fucking tennis?"

"What do you mean?" said Jerry. He noticed Earl had on steel toe boots, workout pants and what looked like maybe a protective metal mesh vest under his shirt.

"My buddies on the force said there's gonna be a BLM march and they're gonna collide with us on Fifth at Smithfield. You better be ready to run."

"The fuck?" said Jerry. "We're not doing anything wrong. We got a permit, and nobody's doing nothing to provoke anyone. We just want the teachers to go back to school."

"Don't tell me," said Earl. "Tell them." And he jerked his head eastward. Jerry saw a swarm of people—almost all black—coming toward them. As they got closer, he could see that some of them had signs and placards. One read: "Defund white people." Another one said, "Fuck whitey." As he focused in, Jerry saw that a bunch of them, in the front, had long pieces of wood, like the handle of an ax, in their hands, and were waving them menacingly. None of the black marchers that he could see was wearing a mask, though some had on black balaclavas that concealed their faces but had holes for their mouths and noses. Not exactly a Covid safety mask, Jerry thought.

Worried now, but not panicked, he looked around his own group and noticed that most of the guys were also wearing boots, not regular shoes. There were about twenty or so women in the Defenders march, all wearing masks, and Jerry realized they too were dressed for protection, not walking. What a dumb shit I am, he thought. Wearing running shoes to a riot.

As Jerry's group arrived at Fifth and Smithfield, the shouts from the BLM crowd became audible. "Fuck you, motherfuckers!" someone shouted, perhaps redundantly. "Fuck white people." "We gonna take yo' houses and yo' women," some guy screamed, and everyone around him laughed.

And as he looked up Smithfield, he saw TV satellite trucks, their antennae sprouting up like shafts of wheat, following the BLM march. As the trucks got near the corner of Fifth, camera people started getting out of their vehicles. Good, thought Jerry. Let's see them record what these guys are saying and put it on the air.

But the cameras went right past the BLM marchers, and were pointed at Jerry's group. Red lights flashed on, and Jerry saw Tran and a couple of other guys shouting back at the BLM crowd. He couldn't make out what Tran was saying, but it was not 'have a nice day.'

After the camera people, the TV vans discharged the pretty people: the on-air reporters. You could see them angling so that only the Defenders group was in the camera shot. And, as the cameras winked on, the BLM leaders lifted their hands, dropped the ax handles and other weapons they were carrying, and started singing, loudly and badly, "We Shall Overcome." The cameras lingered over that, but not the weapons being dropped.

And then, as the pretty people were talking into the still-rolling cameras, a line of riot police came storming down Smithfield, where the BLM march had been coming from. At least, thought Jerry, they'll keep the two groups separated and avoid any violence. But then he was shocked, but sadly, not surprised, to see the cops raising their night sticks and wading into the Defenders. You could hear the thwack thwack as guys got clobbered and went down. Some tried to defend themselves, but since no one was carrying anything like a weapon, they had no chance. And the TV cameras recorded the struggles between the Defenders and the police faithfully.

A cop who couldn't have been more than twenty-five got in front of Jerry and Earl and shouted, "Put your hands behind your backs. You're under arrest!"

"Under arrest for what, son?" said Earl. "I was on the job for thirty years and I don't see any crimes being committed here. You want to arrest someone, turn around and listen to the other guys."

And the cop, wearing a helmet, brought his nightstick down on Earl's left temple, hard. "You're resisting arrest, mister. Stand still so I can cuff you." But Earl couldn't obey that command because he was busy falling to the ground, blood coming from the side of his head and his nose, where the stick had also made contact. Jerry bent over to help Earl, who was now prone and groaning. And as he did, the cop brought his stick down on the back of Jerry's head, and the lights went out on Broadway.

When he came to, he was in a holding cell in the County Courthouse, not a hundred yards from where the cop had nailed him. His hands were behind him with a zip tie around his wrists. Earl was across the cell from him, in a little puddle of his own blood. Jerry looked over whatever parts of himself he could see, but didn't see any blood. And then, before he could think about where he was or why he was here, a cop with gray hair and a belly swung the cell door open, and went over to Earl. "Earl, man, Sarge, you ok?"

Earl made some sort of sound and lifted his head an inch before kissing the floor again. The cop got his hands under Earl's shoulders and lifted him, gently, until he was in a sitting position. The cop took out some kind of sharp implement and slit through the zip tie on Earl's wrists.

"Sorry, Sarge," the cop said. "These guys were just following orders. They didn't recognize you or they'd never have hit you."

Earl was putting it together now and focused on Jerry across the room. "Untie him too. He didn't do nothing."

"Sure thing, Sarge." He came over and cut Jerry loose. "Look, guys, I'm sorry as hell. The orders come down to rough you guys up, that's all I know."

"What about the other guys?" said Earl. "The black guys?"

The cop gave a one-note laugh that contained not a shred of humor. "Yeah, right, like any cop is gonna touch any black person these days, unless it's to kiss their ass. Those guys could've looted City Hall and no one's gonna do nothing. The only safe arrest to make these days is white guys."

"What the fuck is happening?" said Earl.

"Crazy shit, Sarge," said the cop. "Look, you haven't been processed yet so they don't have your names. Somebody told me they'd brought you in, Sarge, so I wanted to come and make sure you're ok."

"I'm okay," said Earl. "Kind of."

"You guys can leave. This shit is crazy. Go home. But do yourselves a favor and don't watch the news on TV."

"Why?" said Jerry, the first contribution he'd made to the conversation.

"Ah, they're saying you guys are racists and you planned to attack a peaceful BLM demo as they were singing, 'I am Coming', or whatever that song's called."

"'We Shall Overcome,'" said Jerry.

"Yeah, that's it. Anyway, the TV is playing it up like Selma, or something. They're charging the guys at the head of your group with a hate crime. And the BLM people are running through the city now, saying, 'We're shutting this shit down,' and 'We're gonna burn the fucking city down.' Real model citizens."

"Didn't the TV show the black guys with those posters and the ax handles they were carrying?" said Jerry.

"You couldn't find a single black person on the TV screen who wasn't smiling and singing," said the cop. "It was you guys who looked like you were resisting arrest. Now get outta here before they come looking for you."

So Jerry helped Earl get up, and they walked out of the Courthouse building by a back door that the cop opened for them. And Jerry, who had no idea where Earl lived, asked him if he wanted help getting home, and Earl said, "Know what? I think one of these guys will give me a lift. Thanks, Jerry." And Earl walked over to the parking lot of the Courthouse, which was filled with black and white police vehicles.

And that left Jerry alone on the street, asking himself what city he lived in, and what the fuck was happening here and to the rest of the country? And how come the Chinese got to make money selling us stuff to protect us from the disease the Chinese had started in the first place.

And saying, to himself, "We Shall Overcome."

# Chapter 21
## What Is Truth?

Wo, Fang and Henry met often, always with Rav at his side, thankfully. The format was, for Chinese government bureaucracies, remarkably open, more like an ongoing brainstorming session than a scheduled appointment. Wo seemed to think he was running the group, although, once they had disbursed, Rav took Henry outside, where they could not be recorded or overheard, and told him flatly that Director Zhuang had doubts about Wo's abilities.

When they met again two days later, Henry was not totally surprised when Zhuang attended in person. He was accompanied by two dour-looking PLA soldiers with rifles slung over their shoulders.

"Wo, come with these soldiers please," said Zhuang. It was lost on no one that he had not used the universal pronoun "comrade."

"Why?" said Wo, quite astounded by the order.

"Was it you who decided that citizen Qi Qi Dieh, the..." Zhuang nodded curtly to Fang, "ex-wife of comrade Fang, should be incarcerated in a mental asylum?"

Wo looked woebegone indeed. "I, she, she had said..."

"I am aware of what citizen Qi said," Zhuang said, mercy missing from his tone. "What she said she said to a health inspector, in the privacy of her dwelling."

"But," Wo stammered, "she was saying something crazy."

"And you used the authority of the Cyberspace Administration to put her away? Do you know what she did as soon as she got out?"

"No," said Wo.

"She posted the same misinformation on her WeChat account. It was seen by many people, inside China and out. And she is now a *cause célèbre*. And so, Wo, go."

Henry, on the other side of the table, understood only a fraction of what Zhuang was saying. And Rav, to her credit, said nothing to him as the berating took place. Henry tried to stare straight ahead, but his eyes flickered for a second, and he caught sight of Fang, with a big smile on his face.

Wo left the room, pincered between the two soldiers. He was never seen again.

Zhuang fixed his attention on Fang. "Comrade Fang, you are now responsible for the success of this project from the viewpoint of the Administration. I wish you well." He flicked his look toward Henry. "And you, corporal. Thank you for your work so far." Rav translated simultaneously. "I admit I was dubious at first. But you have shown real initiative and dedication to the cause. Keep it up."

Zhuang swung around and left the room to the three of them. Fang looked triumphant. So did Rav. Henry was in shock.

"That bastard took credit for my ideas," Fang said throatily. "I'm glad he's been disgraced." Rav translated perfectly, getting even the angry tone of Fang's voice right. "So, corporal," Fang continued, "I look forward to working with you. I think we make a good team."

Rav translated this, but with a frown on her indescribably beautiful face.

"Thank you, comrade," said Henry in passable Mandarin. "I look forward to working with you too." Rav snorted.

Henry had practiced these words because Colonel Hui had instructed him to do so. It had been five days ago that Henry was summoned to the colonel's office. Rav and Tanteeth were both there. The colonel was in civilian clothes, black shirt and tan trousers. His usually stern face was relaxed. "I wanted to see you, corporal, because some things are about to change regarding your assignment." Hui's English was so smooth, soothing almost, that Rav seemed to mentally drop into neutral gear. It made her even more desirable.

"Comrade Wo will not be working with you anymore," the Colonel said. "Instead, it will be Comrade Fang who represents the CAC. The specifics do not need to concern you except that our institute recognized that Wo had acted, and was continuing to act, in a selfish manner that does not further our objectives. We have had what you Americans call 'eyes and ears' on Wo since he first started attending our meetings. We could tell something was not right about him."

"You were... monitoring him, Colonel?"

Hui allowed himself the briefest smile. "It is not uncommon. And becoming more common all the time."

And with that offhand remark, Henry understood why Hui, an army Colonel, was in charge of China's AI Institute. And what he planned to do with the biggest technological development of the 21$^{st}$ Century.

"People are unreliable," Hui said softly, as if regretting the words he was speaking. "They lie, they cheat, they break their promises, they steal, and they kill. This has been so throughout recorded history. And we understand this, and shrug, and say, there is nothing we can do about it.

"But that is no longer the case. AI offers a chance to enter into people's brains, even, if you believe in such things, their souls. To know in advance what they will do. And, if it is not in the best interests of the Party, to prevent them from acting in this unfortunate way.

"And, corporal, here's a thing that most people do not know, and I am telling you so you can carry out your mission successfully. AI is much more advanced than anyone knows. We are already using it to follow the eye movements, the facial expressions, the pause before speaking, and of course the sweat glands' production, of nearly three quarters the population of China."

"But that's," Henry was going to say 'illegal', but instead rallied in time to spurt out "amazing."

"And we are just beginning. Soon, not a single farmer, or market vendor, or newborn, will be outside our range. And then begins the hard work."

"The rest of the world?"

Hui smiled for the second time of the day, which doubled the number of times he had done so in Henry's presence. "You are very perceptive, Henry. I sensed it in you from the beginning. You have the seed of brilliance in you. I plan to harvest that seed, if you will allow me, to tend to your growth."

"Of course, Colonel. I am … honored." He glanced across at Rav, who was beaming. Tanteeth was neutral.

"We are tracking you as well, Henry. We have been since the moment you arrived. I tell you this, so you understand there are no secrets between us."

It was the first blatant falsehood the Colonel had spoken that day. No secrets? Come on. But Henry was not insulted. He was thrilled to be included in such a small group.

"What I tell you now, I do at my own peril. These two comrades," —he gestured to Rav and Tanteeth—"could create grave, possibly terminal problems for me if they reported our conversation. But they will not, because they are loyal to me and to the Party." Rav nodded, Tanteeth remained stone-faced.

"Yes, we will instill Artificial Intelligence around the world, Henry. But first and most important, in the United States. Even now the fools at Stanford and M.I.T. are racing to catch up with us. And I hope they do. What they do not know is that we have broken into their encryption codes. So every giant leap forward they take in AI research, we appropriate and use for ours.

"This is where my words could lead to my downfall," Hui said, as though he were tasting a lemon. Again, he glanced at Rav who kept her face still. "Though you are young, and not Han, fate has chosen you to play a crucial role in China's destiny.

"The coronavirus was created in the Virology Lab of Wuhan. It was meant to be used for experimentation only, not for live transmission. I, these two women, and now you, Henry, are among the very few people who know this.

"At the highest levels, Henry, the Party thinks that the United States is failing. It was once unquestionably the greatest power on earth—militarily, economically, even philosophically. Democracy is an extremely complicated idea, Henry, and I am not afraid to say that the United States adopted it more successfully than any society. At its simplest, democracy is based on the assumption that people know what they want, and that they will make the right decisions, both for themselves and for their country. Your country's first civil war was fought over ideas—ideas about freedom, justice, equality. And since then, the United States has prospered, and led the rest of the world, yes, even including China, as a prosperous power, certain that its system was the best one, willing, if necessary, to unleash its mighty armed forces to defend its way of life."

Hui motioned to Tanteeth, who bowed her head, stood, and left the room. "I have asked her to bring us some tea," Hui said. "Talking so much in English makes me thirsty. Probably listening to me so much has the same effect on you."

He went on before Henry could say, 'Oh, no. Not at all.' "But like all empires, Henry, the American place of prominence has a finite lifespan. And it is ending now. Why? Because like all powerful nations, yours went too far in relying on its superiority. Democracy, as I said, is a complicated idea, and the United States has forgotten that it is the will of the majority that must be adhered to.

"For decades now, America has tried to make everyone happy. If one citizen complains about something—anything! – the American people rush to fix it. It doesn't matter whether the complaint is justified or not, it must be fixed because some individual, or some group, wants it so. This of course, is nonsense. But somehow, over the years, it has become embroidered into the fabric of your identity as deeply as the red and blue of your flag: 'I want, therefore I am entitled.'"

Tanteeth knocked on the door once, opened it, and entered with a tray containing a steel teapot and two transparent glasses.

Hui gave no hint that he had noticed her return. "Why do I call it nonsense? Because no system of government, no matter how well-meaning, can please everyone all the time. As I said, American democracy was originally based on respecting the will of the majority. And that was right for America." He took the tea from Tanteeth with no comment or thanks. Henry took his, said, thank you.

"Most Americans, Henry, used to be sensible, moderate people. They knew that while their lives might not be perfect, they were better than most of the rest of the world's population. Including China, by the way. Like all normal people, Americans did not like wars, but they offered up their sons when necessary for a just cause. They would prefer to sleep late than awaken early, yet they rose before dawn to go to their jobs, in the belief that hard work would be rewarded. They disagreed with some of their countrymen on issues—how much government was too much, how should schools be overseen, how much, and how loudly, should citizens be allowed to voice their disagreements—but overall, Americans found common ground on the important questions, and their lives were largely filled with good things."

Henry thought of his short life in America. His father's job and the money he earned for the family. The vacations that had opened his eyes to the rest of the world. The two cars, the tickets to plays, baseball games and dinners out at restaurants. And as he thought of these things, he realized he had not thought about his parents, his hometown, or any of the people he had known there, for weeks. His life, his mind and his memories were here now. With the colonel. With Rav.

Hui seemed to know what Henry had just thought. "But your country, I should say your former country, has changed, Henry, and not for the better. The very bounty of your way of life has generated guilt among the population. Why are we so happy when some people are not? We have no right to be so happy. We must make everyone happy. Otherwise, we cannot call ourselves a democracy.

"This, as I have said, is idiocy. A satisfied majority is the definition of democracy. But no. America must find a way to satisfy everyone. And so, small groups with special interests must be given special rights. Look at your history over the past fifty years. Black people, women, homosexuals, Latinos who are in the country illegally, even—and excuse me for showing my disapproval—people who want to change their gender are now listened to seriously and their concerns enacted into laws.

"Naturally, trying to please everyone causes ill will among your people, even those people who previously were willing to compromise. Now compromise is considered to be weakness. Moderation is condemned. Extremism is the new norm. All demands must be met, else no one can rest in peace. To state opposition to someone's wishes is to be an oppressor.

"Even your history—the facts of your existence—are being obliterated because they might evoke unhappy thoughts for some sliver of your population. Yes, your country tolerated slavery for years. But you fought a war against yourselves to eliminate it. Yet now, the descendants of those slaves want to be paid for what happened more than two hundred years ago. You are tearing down the statues of men who shaped your country in years past because some people now think they were insensitive. Of course, they were! They were making history!

"You once celebrated the men who returned from war because they had kept you free. Now you tear down the statues dedicated to them. I know I am not an American—thanks be to the lucky spirits— but people who do that to military veterans should be executed.

"Your people have always succumbed to gluttony because food was inexpensive and plentiful. Now, your entire country is eating itself, unable to stop because its gluttonous appetite for satisfaction can never be fulfilled. And as your country destroys itself to satisfy ungrateful minorities, China will assume the mantel of world leadership, and socialism with Chinese characteristics will quickly make the world forget the failed American experiment in democracy. *Zhongguo tese shehui zhuyi.*"

The sudden shift to Mandarin was so startling that Rav looked up, wide-eyed. Then she saw that Henry understood the term and needed no translation.

"This virus will deliver the final blow, Henry. The Americans are so confused, so ravaged by self-hate and doubt, that they can be convinced that this virus is *their* fault. We do not need missiles, tanks or troops to defeat the Americans now, Henry. They are doing it for us. We need only guide them in the proper direction."

Henry, mute throughout Hui's long dissertation, now rallied. "Colonel, may I ask a question?"

"Certainly."

"Colonel, I am more than honored to be in your presence now. And everything that you have said is very interesting. But, and I am asking with respect, do you believe it is the truth?"

Hui and Rav smiled at the same time. Tanteeth frowned, for no apparent reason.

"The truth? The truth? Tell me, Henry. What is the truth? Or, more generally, what is truth as a concept?"

"Something that is factually correct. Something that can be proven to be what it is called, or what it is."

Hui nodded. "Hmmm. Yes, I'm sure you are right. So, let us look at an example. The coronavirus started in China, true?"

"Yes, that is true," said Henry, who already wished he had not asked about truth.

"And of course, you can prove this, can you not?"

"Well, all the reports say it started in Wuhan."

"And you can prove it?"

"Well, Colonel, you just told me it was created in the Wuhan lab."

"I did no such thing," said Hui, smiling to let Henry know he was in on the joke too. In fact, I told you the virus was created by the American military and introduced into China via a secret U.S. military flyover that dropped the virus on Wuhan."

"No, you didn't, Colonel. You told me..."

"And I am telling you I never said such a thing. Now, you have your truth and I have mine. Is your truth truer than my truth? And what gives you the right to think that? Because your skin is white and mine is yellow?"

Henry's eyes widened. "Colonel, please forgive me. I never meant to say..."

Hui stopped him and uttered a sound Henry had never heard from him before. A hearty laugh. "You know what you heard me say, and now you are surprised to hear me deny it. So, you remind me of what I said to you not twenty minutes ago, and I suggest you are being racist for contradicting me. Are you still so sure that I said the virus was created in China?"

"I think you said..."

"Ah, now you only believe you heard it. So it is not so obviously true, is it? It is your recollection of what I said, versus what I say now. Is one right and one wrong?

"This is the nature of truth, Henry. My truth is whatever benefits me, or I should say, benefits the Party. Your truth may be different, but since you are now afraid of being called a racist, and losing my regard for you, you are backing away from what you know very well you heard me say."

"But you can't live like that. That's..."

Hui laughed again. "Of course, you can live like that. We do it all the time. Any Chinese who is a loyal Communist Party member knows that truth is what benefits the Party. It doesn't matter what that person saw with his own eyes, or heard with his own ears. It is what *the*

*Party tells him* he saw or heard that is the truth. Anything else is worthless. This is actually the secret of China's recent successes. We promise something, but do not fulfill the promise. We sign an agreement on trade or human rights or nuclear nonproliferation, then carry on doing exactly as we please. If someone tells us we have broken our promise, or failed to live up to our agreement, we say, 'No, it is you who have broken your promise, you who are not fulfilling the agreement...' And the argument commences. And it is an argument that can never be won by the other side, because we will never admit to wrongdoing. Never."

"But if everyone acted that way..."

"Let me tell you a secret, Henry. Not many people know it. You know who we fear?"

"Russia?" Henry tried.

"Ah," said Hui, waving his hand, palm inward. "Russians are heathens. They are worthless."

"Who do you fear then?"

"Trump."

"You fear Donald Trump? Why?"

"Because Trump knows the secret about truth. For Trump, truth is whatever helps him. Lies are anything that he doesn't like. He had learned our secret. He may even have figured it out before we perfected it. I do not think Trump has ever valued truth at any time in his life. But now, as president, he knows how important it is to wield truth, his truth, as a weapon. Because that means Trump wins."

"But so many people in America hate Trump. And all the news media hate him."

Hui thumped his desk with the flat of his hand. "There! You have made my point. The people who love Trump will believe whatever he says. The people who hate him, including the American press, will always lose. Because saying 'I am telling the truth' is always more powerful than saying, 'No, you're not, you are lying.' Because his opponents can never *prove* he is lying. And so, he goes on, victorious."

Henry knew the words he was hearing were vitally important. Not just to him and his work in China, but for the rest of his life. What Hui was saying was the complete opposite of the American values Henry had been brought up with. But what values mattered more:

those of a country that, as Hui said, was eating itself to death with hatred and division? Or a fast-growing, confident, enormously competent country where everyone is working together, and winning?

"So, corporal," said Hui, reverting to calling Henry by rank. "Whose side do you wish to take? Your skills are vital to our success. But your willingness to use those skills for China is even more vital."

And Henry, a young man from New Jersey, felt himself rising from his chair, taking a lungful of Chinese air, and saying, perhaps too loudly but knowing he was telling, finally, the truth, "I wish to serve you."

He stole a glance at Rav and saw her smiling at him. And knew that he would be receiving a visit from her that night.

# Chapter 22
## Words Worth

The work was a combination of research, interrogation, inspiration, and imagination. Fang, aware of the incredibly good fortune that had befallen him with Wo's removal and disgrace, decided this was the moment to fulfill his destiny. He put aside, for the moment, thoughts of wealth, of being able to travel, or even live, outside China. Of finding a woman who did not remind him of Qi, and who would do the things he liked to do with women. As long as this mission lasted, Fang told himself, his purpose was to be of use to the Party. So useful that the Party would recognize him. He would work with the *gweilo*, learn what, if anything, he knew, so that when the Party chose him for honors, he would have the knowledge of two people.

Henry's ambitions were more down to earth, literally. He wanted to lie on green hillsides with Rav, talk with her about their various ambitions, their beliefs, their hopes and hear her say the three words that had not crossed his lips, but that he knew to be true. The three words that, through the centuries, have shaped human history, have dominated our literature, our music, our art.

Rav had come to him the night after Hui had spoken so openly to Henry. He held her with a shaking passion that surprised them both, kissed her lips and her body with a fervor poetry can describe but not duplicate. Neither slept that night, though at some point Rav succumbed to fatigue and closed her eyes, breathing deeply, allowing Henry to worship her in silent singular wonder. She did not come to him every night, and never warned him before arriving. Sometimes, he opened the door of his room to find her on his bed, reading. Other times, her soft knock, different from anyone else's, announced that another night of ecstasy was beginning.

And yet, for all the unquestioned sincerity of his rapture and desire to share the world with her, Henry's instincts told him that he must not discuss the work they were doing, the long-range trajectory of Hui's thinking, or anything to do with the Party, not even to ask her if she was a member. Because, he assumed, whatever he said, whatever opinions he ventured, whatever Rav might feel for him, she would report his every word, every breath, every eye blink.

To someone. Maybe Hui, maybe someone else. Because there was no privacy, no haven for lovers, no information out of bounds. Everything, your ideas, your thoughts, your fears, your hopes, belonged to the Party.

Socialism with Chinese characteristics.

For Henry, the work with Fang—Rav the ever-ready go-between—was like being asked to repeat the alphabet, over and over. As sophisticated and well-informed as Hui and those in his institute appeared, Henry quickly realized there was an appalling lack of understanding about contemporary America, Americans and how they could be expected to act in the current situation.

Fang, especially, paid rapt attention to Henry's everyday recollections about life in America, the people there that he knew, his second- and third-hand impressions of famous Americans like Donald Trump, Bill Gates, the Kardashian family, and Denzel Washington.

"Is he related to your first president?" Fang asked, completely straight-faced.

"Umm, no."

"But he has the same family name."

"Yes, but it's a common name."

"In China, most people with the same family name have some blood relation, even if it is removed by many centuries."

"That might be a way to get Chinese people to work with the Cyber Administration," said Henry.

"Huh?"

"Well, you're basically trying to prevent people from spreading false rumors about the virus online, aren't you?"

Fang decided this was a serious question. "Yes, we are."

"So, think of a slogan that suggests all Chinese must have millions of family members, related if no other way, then, by name." Rav's eyes had lit up as she was translating for Fang. She understood. Henry hoped it was one of those "see you later" looks because he had said something smart.

"Like what?' said Fang, though he was already abuzz with ideas.

"Well, like 'The Rumor You Spread May Hurt Your Family.' If someone asks what that means, you can do the bit about so many of us with the same name actually are related. But it also contains a subtle threat, doesn't it?"

"Hmmm." Fang's mind was sharp, and he was already trying to sharpen this blunt tool he'd been given. Sleek and silent. The American was not stupid.

Two days later—an incredibly fast turnaround—Fang was able to report to Zhuang: "Published 15 rumor-debunking posts, reposted 62 rumor-debunking posts, 16 people were investigated by public security organs, 14 people were educated and admonished, two people were put in administrative detention."

One of the two, of course, was Qi Qi Dieh, Fang's ex-wife, whose WeChat claim to have started the virus had been widely read and commented upon. Several western news agencies made inquiries about the posting and were told the person responsible for it was mentally ill.

Zhuang passed word of the successful opinion-shaping operation up the chain of command. That afternoon, mere hours after he had sent his dispatch, a colonel of the PLA came unannounced to his office. Zhuang thought, this could either be good news, or the end of my career and life.

It was the former. "Please come with me, comrade Director. There is a secure call you must make." Zhuang went with the colonel to a black car sitting outside. Once Zhuang was in the back seat, the colonel handed him a heavily encrypted cell phone, closed the door, and a Plexiglas divider rose between the front and back seats. The phone rang, Zhuang pressed the "accept" button and heard the familiar voice of Xi Jinping.

"Your word team seems to be doing well."

"Yes, comrade. Thank you for suggesting it."

"I know one of them is a *gweilo* but I am told he could be turned into a true believer. That could be both useful, and amusing. A real asset."

"I agree."

"Give them more responsibility. Let them understand that what they are doing is important and is being closely watched. See how they react."

"I understand."

"The World Health Organization wants to send a team of virologists to Wuhan to do research and determine how the virus started."

"Is that going to be a problem?"

Xi snorted. "Not at all. We control the WHO. Two of its directors report to the PLA. And we help write all their reports and press releases. WHO is effectively an arm of the Party."

The next day, Zhuang received a second progress report on the work of what he now thought of as the Word Team. "Mobilized force of more than 1,500 cybersoldiers across the district to promptly report information about public opinion in WeChat groups and other semiprivate chat circles." Zhuang passed this along, fairly certain that it would reach Xi.

It did. Another ranking officer, another black car with Plexiglas dividers, another encrypted call. "The speed with which the Word Team is controlling cyber-traffic is comparable to the construction of a Covid hospital in Wuhan in just ten days."

"Thank you, comrade Xi."

"Of course," continued the most powerful man in the world, "that hospital lacks basic equipment. The plumbing doesn't work, and very few Covid patients who are admitted ever leave. At least not alive. But it is still a wonderful achievement."

Zhuang could not suppress a witty rejoinder. "The plumbing in our cyber-hospital works, comrade."

With domestic messaging more or less under control, and praise from the absolutely highest level, Zhuang turned the Word Team into the World Team, and to its second major objective: shaping the Covid narrative around the rest of the world, especially in the United States.

"This is your moment," Rav told Henry. "No one can believe how well you have adapted, how good your ideas are, how you are in tune with the Party's needs. You are an inspiration to us, including to me." She kissed him softy between the eyes.

"What do they want me to do?" Henry asked.

"You heard what the colonel said. The Party leadership thinks America is weak now. People are too busy fighting with each other about skin color, sexual preferences, gender roles, income inequality, their own national history. All these things are just different words for what Americans are really fighting about: power. Every group wants to be more powerful, to get more money, to tell others what they must do. They call it a fight for justice. No, it's a fight for power.

"And this virus has made everything worse. People all over the world are scared, because they don't know what the virus is, where it came from, how to avoid getting it, how to kill it. Americans most of all are scared. They are used to having everything they want. They think they *deserve* to have whatever they demand. This is a weakness of your county, not mine. We know that all things are given to us by the Party. But we must earn them."

"Same question," Henry said, touching her lips with his index finger.

"Share your knowledge of America with us. What will do the most damage to America once this virus starts spreading there?

"Depends on what kind of damage you mean."

"Social, economic, financial, cultural, societal, personal. All kinds!"

"I'll think about it," said Henry.

"Think fast," said Rav, stroking his hand. "Colonel Hui has put three of his top AI engineers on the same assignment. He wants to see if machines can be taught to understand Americans more quickly than Americans can understand themselves."

Henry gave a little smile, a little shrug. "He's going to need more than three."

# Chapter 23
## The Six Points Speech

It was the moment he had lived for.

Henry knew it was an important meeting because Hui was there. So were a bunch of the Geeks, unless they were actors who were cast perfectly for the part of geeks. Really thin eyes behind wire rim glasses, buck teeth, bad haircuts, polyester sports jackets and more devices hanging from their belts than a roofer.

He had shooed Rav from his room the night before and told her he needed to think. When he showed up for the meeting, he looked as if he had not slept all night, which he had not. Since Rav was usually the cause of this condition, she frowned. Henry, observing strict protocols of conduct among coworkers, smiled politely and said, "I was thinking fast. And slow at the same time." He slid her a copy of the printouts he was holding. "Please prepare to translate."

Zhuang and Fang were the last to arrive. Fang looked nervous and Henry surmised this was because Fang had been told he was no longer the lead dog as the focus of the assignment shifted. For the same reason, Zhuang was acting fussy, though he concealed it better.

Hui was in a hurry. "We all know what this session is about. There are ways to turn this virus to our advantage, and at the same time, weaken our primary opponent. Since we have someone who was born in America with us, I have asked him to take the lead." Zhuang sucked in his breath noisily.

Henry felt a calmness born of self-assurance. He knew things these people did not, though their lack of enlightenment surprised him, considering the powerful positions they held. He remembered that when he was asked to deliver a speech at school, he often rehearsed with his mother or father. And they were always supportive, their advice unfailingly helpful. They would not be supportive of these remarks, and their advice would certainly be, don't do this.

He straightened his shoulders, nodded once at Hui, and began in Mandarin.

"To most eminent Colonel Hui, Director Zhuang, colleagues and comrades." Make sure you mention the Colonel first, Rav had said the night before. "Everyone will notice if you don't."

No one blinked. He had gotten off to the right start. "Please forgive me for speaking English for most of this presentation. I am not yet able to speak your honorable language well enough to express what I have to say." He nodded once to Rav, who held the sheets he had passed to her. She nodded back.

"Since arriving in this wonderful country, at the invitation of Colonel Hui, I have, naturally, had a chance to see the differences between your country and the land of my birth. And again, with thanks to Colonel Hui for pointing them out to me, I would like to mention some of the important differences between China and the United States today, and suggest some ways that these differences can be effective in seizing the advantage during the days of this strange virus."

Rav was doing her usual wonderful job of translating simultaneously. Henry tried not to stray from what he had written and given to Rav. He didn't want to throw a curve at her in the middle of his presentation. Throw a curve. The baseball term was appropriate here. Henry stopped, looked at Rav, said quietly, "I'm going to go off script for a moment." She nodded, unfazed.

"In the American game of baseball," he hesitated, suddenly worried there might not be a Chinese word for it, but Rav had already finished the phrase and was waiting for him, "one player tries to throw a leather covered ball, about the size of an orange, past another player who is holding a bat. The player with the bat tries to strike the ball with it. The player throwing the ball must locate it precisely, so that it travels over a white surface at the other player's feet." Henry could see some of his audience shifting in their seats. What did a moronic American game have to do with this important mission? "Usually, the person throwing the ball tries to throw it so fast his opponent has no time to strike it with the bat. But some players who are very skilled at throwing, know that sometimes speed is not the most important thing. The most important thing, they know, is to fool their opponent. Therefore, some very good players learn to throw the ball so that it curves, or dips at the last second, or gyrates in the air. This confuses the player with the bat. And usually, that player will lose the struggle he is in with the player throwing the ball." Henry could feel several sets of perplexed eyes fixed on him. When he glanced at Hui, however, the colonel was nodding sagely. Henry knew that Hui already knew where his next pitch was heading.

"We must be like the player who can throw the ball and make it do unexpected things. We must curve its path to our opponent. We must have it drop out of sight, or shake like an old man's hands, so that our opponent is defenseless against us, and we prevail."

Because he, alone among AI Institute staff, was given access to American websites—a perk Rav had assured Hui that Henry would use profitably and securely—Henry knew that the World Health Organization had declared the Covid virus to be a pandemic. He also knew that in the United States, such health risks were handled by the Center for Disease Control, located in Atlanta. And the CDC was about to issue its latest set of guidelines to Americans to help protect them from what President Trump was still calling the "Chinese Flu."

"It is important to change the perception of the virus as something Chinese," Henry said. "You must help change that perception, so that Americans think it is their fault if they are taken ill, and their responsibility to prevent that from happening.

"Doing that will also discredit Trump, who, I believe, is an enemy of the Chinese people."

This caused a murmur. Trump's tit-for-tat policy with China was much discussed and much condemned in the ruling circles. No American president had shown the gumption in dealing with the Party's leaders like Trump had. It was as if this orange-haired sloth could see past the veneer of the official pronouncements; the two-facedness of public rhetoric and quiet misdirection; the signed treaties, whose terms always benefited China, and were never lived up to. President after president had been certain that China could be brought around to democracy if its economy was strengthened, its workforce employed, and its people's standard of living raised. And all these things had happened—all except the democracy part.

It was such a cynical game that for decades, China's leadership could not believe it could go on. Republicans and Democrats alike, they all wanted to be the one who "brought China around." And so, like a cunning child in a candy store, China promised not to steal anything that did not belong to them, while one hand reached deep into the chocolate tray, and another grabbed more gumdrops than Ronald Reagan ever dreamed of eating.

Trump, frankly, had surprised the Chinese. They had expected Clinton to win, and for the game of promising one thing while doing another to go on. Then this vulgarian came to power, and had the temerity to say what the whole world knew: China did not keep its word, could not be trusted, had to be reined in, had to accept more imported products, had to stop stealing technology, had to stop threatening Taiwan, had to let Hong Kong remain semi-independent, had to stop feeding and encouraging North Korea ... the list went on. And when Xi Jinping gave the usual bland, inscrutable smile and said, of course we will, Trump didn't wait to see if he was telling the truth, but imposed billions of dollars of tariffs on cheap Chinese goods that had been flooding America for decades and banned Huawei, the government-controlled provider of information and technology, from operating in the States.

So now, when this young *gweilo* said that Trump could be discredited, the room listened.

"There are six points I would like to make today," Henry said. He had chosen six because Rav explained to him that "six points" resonated with the Chinese people. Famously, the "six points of Chinese art" are celebrated as proof that China is the most cultured land of all time. "Six points" also referred to the famous speech given in 2009 by Xi's predecessor as general secretary of the Party, Hu Jintao, in which he outlined a half dozen demands for China to cease its aggressive stance against Taiwan and come to a peaceful agreement. The plan failed miserably, and probably was one of the main reasons for Hu's eventual displacement. "Six points" will mean something to these people, Rav said.

"Point one," said Henry, his voice controlled and in charge. "The United States, and, in fact, the democratic form of government it practices, are in fatal decline." Fang looked up, astonished to hear this candid appraisal from the American.

"In 2001," continued Henry, "the year Islamic terrorists crashed planes into the World Trade Center and the Pentagon, history changed. I remember almost nothing of that terrible day, but I have studied it and its impact. For a brief time, Americans were brought together by this tragedy. I have seen pictures of people helping each other out of the rubble. White people helping black people, black people rescuing white people. All of their faces were completely coated by gray ash from the explosions and fires, as if the malign forces of nature were saying, it doesn't matter what color your skin is. We are all the same now. All gray. All Americans.

"That camaraderie didn't last because it wasn't meant to. Seeking revenge, the U.S. invaded Afghanistan, although 15 of the 19 hijackers on the planes were from Saudi Arabia. But the U.S. couldn't punish Saudi Arabia. Why? Because they supplied America with oil. And because the royal family, hated by most Saudis, let America keep its fighter planes on Saudi soil. And when the U.S. invaded Iraq in 2003, the Muslim world came together in hatred for America and what it so grandly stood for. American soldiers were slaughtered, they were blown to bits by IEDs, they became the target of hateful sermons in every mosque where Muslims pray, and every masjid where children are taught. Muslims plotted to kill Americans, to undermine their way of life, to punish them for letting themselves be attacked by Muslims.

"So, when Trump, in his first weeks, quite rightly and understandably tried to ban Muslims from coming to the United States, instead of being hailed as a hero, he was denounced as a racist, a fascist. Congress refused to endorse his executive order, federal judges ruled the order unconstitutional, airlines said they would not prevent Muslims from boarding their planes.

"The same thing happened when Trump tried to build a wall to keep hordes of Mexicans from sneaking into the U.S. Of course they wanted to come to America. Look where they came from! Trump said, build the wall. The courts said, no you can't. Congress wouldn't fund it. Governors said, not in my state. What Trump wanted was obviously good for America. Just not for Muslims, or Mexicans.

"How can you run a country properly if you can't get your orders obeyed? It may be a democratic way of governing, but it doesn't work. So that is Point number 1.

"Point 2: Americans feel guilty about being Americans. They didn't always used to. They used to be the hardest-working people on earth. And they built a great country, actually, the most powerful country on earth, until recently. They had the wealthiest middle-class in history. They had the biggest, most profitable companies. They had cities that were safe, police to protect the population, and plenty of empty space for citizens to move around in, and enjoy the bounty of their homeland.

"Americans' lives were so good that they began to feel guilty about it. Maybe we don't deserve all this. Maybe we owe it to the rest of the world to invite them in, to partake of our happiness. Maybe being happy Americans is ... un-American."

The two bespectacled geeks from the AI institute laughed at this statement, which is what Chinese people do when they are embarrassed.

"And so, the U.S. let people in from all over the world. Mexico, the rest of Latin America, Africa, the former Soviet Union. The Middle East. And yes, China, too. Many Chinese went to America to study. Many stayed.

"America always believed it was what it called 'the melting pot.' That once people came from other countries, they would be assimilated, in other words, they would put aside their pasts and become part of Happy America. But that's not what happened. The Latinos came and started to complain that they were stuck with menial jobs. Never mind they couldn't speak English or read or write in any language. They wanted equality with the CEO of Google. The Africans moaned that their traditional cultures were not on display. So, they put up museums of African culture. Ever been to one? Me either.

"Everyone who came, instead of wanting to become American, wanted America to become more like where they came from. And Americans agreed. So that is Point number 2. Americans feel guilty. Use it.

"Point 3: People like to be with their own kind. It's considered to be racist to say that now, but it's as true as it always was. People are more comfortable with people who look like them, speak like them, eat like them, believe like them. Black people don't like white people, which is fine, but when you turn it around and admit that white people don't like black people, it's racist. When black people are elected to Congress in the United States, do you know the first thing they do? They join the Congressional Black Caucus. To be with their own. The Latinos in congress do the same thing. Everyone but white congressmen. Because if they formed a caucus for white members, it'd be racist.

"Now," Henry said, carefully, "I have been assured that I can say this without offending you. Everyone in this room, I think, is Han Chinese, right?" Heads went up, heads went down. There were proud smiles around the room. "Well, would you rather live with another Han, or with, say, a Korean?"

Much breath was sucked in. Muttering filled the room. "A non-Han might say, but Koreans look a lot like Chinese. So do Japanese. Why can't you forget where they are from? Why can't we all get along?"

Heads moved from side to side. Ridiculous. "Impossible," blurted out one of the AI guys. Fang looked at him and wondered if he would become famous for saying that.

"So that's Point number 3," said Henry. "You can shame Americans into thinking they not only can but must do the impossible.

"Point 4: Everyone in America thinks they are entitled to something." Here Henry plagiarized, heavily, happily, and with full permission, from his last meeting with Hui. It went over very well.

"Point 5: Americans think America will never end. They've been on top of the world for so long, they think it's a permanent condition. They think they can test it, push it, prod it, weaken its defenses, destroy the fabric that made it great, and nothing will change. They have either forgotten, or have never read, about the Greeks, the Romans, the Nazi empire that was going to last a thousand years and didn't even made three thousand days. The British Empire, you know, the one that was so huge the sun never set on it.

"Americans are convinced they will always be in charge of the world. I think you think they're wrong. I think so too."

And it was then that the squinty-eyed AI guy couldn't help himself any longer. "*Hanjian*," he shouted, not in anger or accusation, but in recognition of what he was hearing and of who was saying it.

Henry didn't have to look at Rav. She leaned close to him and said, quietly, "It means, 'traitor.'"

Henry closed his eyes. He thought of his family, their home, their car, the school he had attended, the ball games he'd seen. He looked at the squinty-eyed guy, nodded and said, "*Shi. Hanjian.*"

Yes, I'm a traitor.

"Point 6," he said, as if his life had just not changed irrevocably.

"It has taken me a long time to come to the point of our meeting, and for that I apologize. But it is important, I think, to know who the Americans are when you are dealing with them. So, Point 6. What can you do to weaken the Americans now, at this crucial moment, when they are already divided by their own president, when black and white people openly hate each other, and when they must face the threat of a virus that neither they nor anyone else fully understands, but which they know can kill them?

"You know that the WHO has labeled this a pandemic and warned that it might spread around the world, quickly and fatally, if proper precautions are not taken. So, what precautions can we, as the, well, the leading member of the WHO, what precautions can we insist on to weaken America as much as possible while it is already reeling from its own stupidity?

"The most important step is to close down its economy. You are realists in this room, and the numbers and statistics tell us that the United States has the biggest economy in the world. Yours," he looked at Hui as he said the word, "is the second largest. What could you do to switch those positions?

"The first step, not easily achieved, is to shut down their economy. I mean really shut it down. Hard and tight." Once Rav had translated this last sentence, Fang wrote it down. Hard and tight. He would use it.

"I don't think that has happened in America since the Great Depression of the 1920s and early 30s, Henry continued. "People had no work because there were no jobs. I've seen pictures of people standing in long lines, blocks long, for a tin cup of soup. People evicted from their houses because they couldn't pay their mortgages. Whole families living an entire day on food that previously would have counted for one meal. Take away most men's jobs and you take away their identity. The effect on their egos, confidence, their mental stability, their way of treating their families, is quite shocking. So that's one thing.

"Next, close down everything that makes America great. Close all the stores that sell the clothes, cars, shoes, toys, televisions, computers, furniture, sporting equipment … everything that people want. It's all made here in China anyway. Usually, you want them to buy your products. Now you will deny it to them.

"Next, close the theaters, the restaurants, the bars, the sports stadiums, everyplace that Americans go to relax, to have fun, to see each other, to eat, to drink, to cheer, to feel good. To talk to each other. Close it all.

"Make them cover their faces. This is simple social engineering. It's like taking away their names, telling them, 'You all look exactly alike with those blue things on, so maybe you are all the same, maybe there's nothing special about you.' That's a terrible thing for an American to hear. Every American has been taught to believe that he or she is special. It's terrible for them to be told to cover their faces, faces that identify them as being one of those special people.

"Again, you make almost all the surgical masks in the world, so make them as uncomfortable as you can. Add another layer, put talcum powder inside them, make the strings too small so they hurt to wear them. Make them hate the masks they must wear.

"Keep the children out of school. Insist that they stay at home, with their parents. All day, every day. They will get on their parents' nerves, the parents will lose their tempers, the children will cry, there will be periods when they don't speak to each other. The great American family can be turned into a hundred million versions of their famous Civil War. You might be able to destroy an entire country, the so-called world's greatest society, without firing a shot.

"Thank you for your attention."

Henry was tired. He had been speaking for more than thirty minutes, a role he was totally unused to. He looked over at Rav. Her face was as beautiful as ever, and there was a sheen of sweat on her forehead. And she was taking deep breaths.

"Please remember what you have heard today," said Hui from the end of the table. "Corporal, please follow me."

Henry stood, his legs felt slightly wobbly under him. He trailed Hui into his office. Tanteeth closed the door.

"Henry, you did very well. Thank you."

"*Xiexie ni*," Henry said. "Thank you, Colonel."

"No, there is someone else who wants to thank you." Hui lifted his left hand. The hologram of Xi Jinping jumped to life. And for the first time with Henry in the office, spoke. "*Xiexie ni*," said the most powerful man in the world to an American.

"Thank you."

# Chapter 24
## Just Drink Clorox

It worked better than anyone expected it to, especially Henry. Everyone knows what happened next. Not everyone knows why.

Though Hui explained that he could never hope to be promoted above the rank of corporal, Henry was rewarded handsomely for his Six Points presentation. He was given larger living quarters in the AI building, and his access to American Internet sites was expanded. His Chinese language lessons were increased and were now conducted by a full professor of linguistics, who, Rav told him, had been seconded from the Beijing University devoted to teaching diplomats and spies.

Fang consulted him endlessly, asking, through Rav of course, how various strategies he was working on would play out in America. Henry found Fang a tiresome individual, but had to admit he was a fountain of ideas, most of them original and promising. Others betrayed an astounding lack of understanding of the world outside China.

"Why doesn't Trump just send the Army out to force people to stay in their homes?" Fang asked. "That's what we did in Wuhan. It worked."

"Except for all the people the Army shot to death for refusing to stay home," Henry replied. He knew what had happened and felt confident enough now to challenge colleagues who did not.

"They were stupid people," Fang said, thinking of Qi Qi. "They refused orders from the People's army."

"In America, the Army cannot be used against its own people. The Army can only be used to defend America against foreign attack."

"That's stupid," said Fang, deciding there was something in all that nonsense that he could use.

Henry reported everything that Fang said to Hui, whose door, it seemed was always open to Henry these days. There had been a subtle, completely unspoken shift in the balance between Henry and Hui, one that Henry pondered, but most certainly was not going to probe too deeply.

"Keep me informed, as necessary," Hui said to Henry. "We don't need to talk every day, but now and again, let us know if you have something for me."

"Colonel, may I ask please, are you in charge of this entire project?"

What 'project,' corporal?" He had gone back to being addressed by rank as soon as his presentation was finished.

"Well, the steps to be taken to use the virus to dominate the United States."

Hui gave him a severe look, the kind, Henry imagined, that had fueled his ascent to the rank of colonel. "Never, never, say those words out loud," Hui said in a hushed voice. "No one must hear from us what we are doing. No one must be able to say, 'I heard it from them.' This work is too important to allow for errors. Especially human errors. Do you understand?"

"Yes, Colonel. Forgive me. I just wanted to know the truth."

Hui smiled his tight grin. "There is nothing to forgive. It is your Americanness showing through. I told you before. The truth is whatever the Party says it is. Whatever benefits the Party is the truth.

"That is the secret beauty of Artificial Intelligence, Henry. By adjusting a program, rewriting an algorithm, AI can redefine what is true. It will make you believe that blue is red, because a computer said so. AI is too complicated to argue with. And because most people have no idea how it works, they accept its intelligence as superior to their own. Which it is. Of course, that means that the people who write the programs, adjust the algorithms, are the masters of the universe."

"Yes, Colonel." And from behind Hui, the hologram of Xi Jinping came to life, its right index finger wagging at Henry once, then resuming 4-D stillness.

Hui had answered Henry's question. He just didn't know it.

The work sped up. Fang asked Henry, "In America, what does the word 'expert' mean?"

"In America, or in English?" Henry said. The question perplexed him. Expert means expert.

"I mean in America," said Fang. "Who is an expert?"

"I don't understand the question," Henry said. "An expert is someone who has specialized knowledge about a certain subject."

"And the Party gives you the title of expert?" Fang asked.

"We've been through this," Henry said, noticing Rav's nearly unreadable smile, a smile he had grown to love interpreting in its many degrees and varieties. "There is more than one party in America. No, an expert usually gets a degree from a university, to show that he or she has completed the required studies."

"What happens after the expert gets this degree?"

"Usually, he gets a job where he can apply the knowledge he has."

"And he is required to repeat what he learned?"

"No," said Henry, "she is free to use her knowledge from her education to address whatever problems or issues she is working on." He had intentionally switched genders, to show that he was not sexist, a distinction completely lost on Rav and Fang.

"So, after getting this degree, the expert can say whatever he wants?"

"Of course. As long as it makes sense and is accepted as correct."

"Ah. And who must accept this?"

"Well, the expert's colleagues initially. And then, the public at large."

Afterward, he said to Rav, "What strange questions Fang just asked."

"Not really," said Rav, who looked especially ravishing when she was explaining things. "The best universities in America are called, what, Ivy?"

"The Ivy Leagues, yes. It's eight universities. Harvard, Yale, Cornell, Princeton, Dartmouth, Columbia, Brown and Penn."

"Strange names. Are they good schools?"

"Well, they have the reputation for being the best universities in America."

"So, do they have the best teachers at these schools?"

"I guess so. They're called professors, and they must be good to be hired by Ivy League universities."

"Hmmm," said Rav, a delightful noise. "And do you know how many of these professors are Chinese?"

"You mean, how many come from China."

"Or have some Chinese heritage."

"No, I don't know that."

"Would you be surprised to learn it is about half?"

"Half of all the Ivy League professors are Chinese?"

"Or, as I said, have some Chinese heritage."

"I'd be very surprised if that is true."

"It is true."

"You mean half of all the teachers at the Ivies are Chinese?"

"Not the mere teachers. The full professors. The most senior ones, with the most influence. It is part of what I think Americans call the 'diversity' program."

"Are they all American citizens now?"

"Some are. Some aren't. But they have one thing in common, aside from their heritage."

"What?"

Rav looked deeply into Henry's eyes. "They all have family members who live in China."

\* \* \*

It was the visit P.F. Chang knew would come someday, but dreaded nonetheless. He had worked hard to get where he was, hard and honestly. He had semi-succeeded in erasing all traces of his Chinese-accented English, even picked up a scintilla of Southern twang, so that, at least on phone calls, if not Zoom sessions, he sounded like exactly what he was: a scientist at the Centers for Disease Control. Of course, he would never sound like a native Atlantan, but as he quietly remembered, there were worse fates.

His work environment was as near perfect as any human could hope for. The worst part was the endless shit he took from colleagues about his name, which was the same as a middlebrow chain of Chinese hash houses. "Hey, P.F., can I get an order of bat soup?" said Billy Ray

Hodgson, a great guy and a superb scientist who was convinced he could be a stand-up comic. Chang told people just to call him Chang. He didn't need it widely known that his other names were Pu Fu.

He had been plucked from a primary school in Tianjin, the fifth largest city in China, when he was ten. He always assumed, though never knew for sure, that it was because he had excelled in the child-level chemistry experiments his class took part in. In school, Chang the Child asked questions and made observations well beyond his years, just as he had always done at home since he had learned to speak. His parents were both doctors, which in China is one of the lowest paid professions. That didn't matter to them, though. Between the two of them, they made enough to have a small but comfortable apartment, enough warm clothes to get them and their son, Pu, through the winter, and to buy the medical journals that doctors were required to pay for themselves, to keep pace with new developments. Child Chang would look, first at the pictures and then the articles in these journals and ask his parents questions. Usually, they knew the answers, but sometimes they did not, and had to do research to satisfy their curious son.

When Child Chang got the flu during a normally cold and snowy January, he asked his mother why he felt bad. "You have a virus," she said.

"I don't want a virus. Can I give it back?"

"You have to wait until it goes away."

"If I tell it to go, will it go away?"

"No. It only leaves when it's ready," said his mother.

"I don't like virus," Child Chang said, and began crying.

He cried harder when his parents told him he would be leaving home, going to another city to study hard, but that he could come back home for vacations if he did well.

"I don't want to go away," Child Chang said. "I want to stay with you."

"The Party needs you elsewhere, and we must always do as the Party asks us," said his father.

"I don't like the Party," Chang said.

"Never say that out loud," warned his father. "Never. It will make trouble for all of us, including your mother."

Chang never said it again. Out loud.

"Where am I going to?" he asked his parents.

"A beautiful big city with a beautiful big school. A place called Wuhan."

Wuhan was bigger than Tianjin, that part was true. But it was not beautiful. It smelled funny to Chang. So did the laboratories where he did experiments on animals, injecting them with liquids in syringes, watching their eyes widen, then close, never to open again. He learned not to think of the animals as living things, just part of his experiment.

When he wasn't killing parts of his experiment, he went to class to learn English. He didn't like English. It was an ugly language. But he learned it, because his parents told him when he went home on his first vacation that if he learned English, they would be given a bigger, nicer place to live. Chang didn't want his parents to live somewhere else, but he wanted them to be happy. So he did well at English. And in the lab, where he killed part of his experiments.

Did well enough that he graduated early, and went on to Wuhan University, where he was told he was going to be a virology student. Since he had been interested in viruses ever since he'd had the flu, he decided to do well in Virology. He did so well in it, and English, that he was told he was going to America, to learn more about Virology there. That was where he met Xiang, an old and unpleasant woman who, though she pretended to be a house cleaner, Chang was certain was an officer in the PLA. It was Xiang who told him he was going to be hired by the CDC.

"Why are they hiring me?" he asked the strange looking woman.

"Because you're an expert," she said.

"No, I'm not," he said. "I'm just a scientist."

"From now on, you're an expert," she said harshly. "Remember that."

"Why should I?" Chang said, angrily. He had already started to become Americanized.

"When is the last time you talked to your parents?" Xiang said, knowing the answer. "And when do you hope to talk to them again?"

So now, a year later, Xiang's replacement as his "contact," an old guy who smelled like garlic, told him they would be meeting at a bar in Peachtree Street. The old guy liked to live it up on the people's money.

"A reporter from the New York *Times* is going to call you," the old guy said.

"Why?"

"Because you're an expert on viruses."

"Not really."

"Nanjiang Road, 5F-07, right?"

"What?"

"Where your parents live. Nice place, I've heard."

Chang closed his eyes. "Okay. What am I talking to the New York *Times* about?"

"The coronavirus."

"That's not what I'm working on right now. I will be soon, but I have a lot to learn about it."

"Five thousand yuan each, isn't it?"

"Isn't what?"

"Your parents' salaries."

"Fine. Coronavirus. What about it?"

"You're going to say that drinking Clorox may prevent it. Or cure it."

"What? But that's crap. It's some crazy theory that popped up online. Someone told Trump about it, and he said he was going to try it. If we're lucky, it'll kill him."

"If *you're* lucky, you'll talk to the *Times* before that happens."

"But I'll sound like an idiot."

"No, you'll sound like an expert. Because that's how the *Times* will describe you."

"But it will ruin my credibility."

"You've enjoyed living here, haven't you, Chang?"

"Yes, I have, but..."

"Good. The reporter's name is Gretchen Nu-Mi."

"Is that a Chinese name?

"See? You're an expert."

The Science Editor of the New York Times was Tu Dam Ba. With a name like that, she should have been up onstage with Billy Ray Hodgson. Instead, she was the dourest, humor-free top editor at the paper. No one gave Tu any grief about her name. Such things were *verboten* in the Cathedral of Journalism. One old-timer, a leftover from the days of free speech, once told Tu she should change her name to Vous because it was more polite in French. His retirement party the next week was sparsely attended.

Tu told Gretchen Nu-Mi that she was going to Atlanta to interview an expert on coronavirus named Chang.

"What do we know about him?" asked Gretchen.

"We know that he's who you're going to interview," replied Tu, dead-eyed.

"What's the angle of the story that you want?"

"That we must be guided by the experts, by the scientists. Not by the politicians."

Gretchen Nu-Mi got it. There were a lot more Chinese scientists and experts in the United States than there were politicians. And nearly all of them had relatives in China. As did she. As did Tu. Or Vous, to be polite.

# Chapter 25
## Try To Remember

Everyone knows what happened. Some people try to forget. And some people, like Henry and Fang, succeed in changing the facts, because that is what suits the Party.

Fang had taken the highlights of Henry's Six Points lecture and weaponized them. His gift for words, though initially based on a fraud, was recognized. He became an important part of the Cyberspace Administration, someone Zhuang consulted and trusted. Fang also showed talent in crafting messages for use in the world outside China. He asked Henry—through Rav, of course—endless questions about America, then slunk away and composed what really amounted to taglines, slogans and catchphrases that he thought would resonate with Americans and become the psychological underpinning of China's strategy for domination.

Hui, in turn, took the product Fang produced and handed it to the AI geeks he had brought with him to the Six Points meeting. They ran the words through their algorithms, to see which ones Americans would accept, and which were without value. The degree of AI accuracy astounded everyone, including Hui.

The first big hit to be churned out by the algorithm was "We're all in this together." Intended to evoke memories of the unity that Americans felt right after 9/11, it also suggested obliquely that the virus posed an equal threat to everyone, and that all that Americans could do was band together, accept whatever hardships were deemed necessary, and hope for the best.

Hui had the slogan sent in coded messages to Chinese-owned companies, as well as NGO groups funded or dominated by the Party, such as Greenpeace, the Sierra Club, Americans for Progress. Hui even authorized the creation and incorporation of a fictitious organization, Health and Prosperity Research, which a PLA agent in Washington registered with the Commerce Department and which pumped out "scientific studies" that supported whatever propaganda the AI geeks decided would work. These well-meaning groups, sneered at as "useful idiots" by the Party leadership, paid for the printing of tens of thousands of "studies" by "experts," which were converted into TV public service announcements, radio spots, podcasts, billboards in New York's Times Square, any medium where "We're all in this together" would sink into the public consciousness, and turn Americans' thoughts inward to their own plight, not outward in search of its origins. The AI geeks got the official credit, but Henry and Fang knew it was their idea.

P.F. Chang's interview with the *Times* never made the front page, but it got some attention. Specifically, the attention of Donald Trump, who suggested that disinfectants like Clorox might be ingested or injected to kill the virus. Just as Qi had done to experimental animals to put them out of their misery.

"It's worth looking into," Trump said.

Chang's parents had their salaries doubled to ten thousand yuan a month, each.

The World Health Organization asked China's Health Ministry for permission to visit Wuhan to try to determine how the virus had started there. Permission for the visit was granted, but visas for the WHO team were not forthcoming. Bureaucratic delays, they were told. Of course, you can come and inspect, draw your own conclusions, make your findings public. We have nothing to hide.

But there were no visas.

The WHO's president was a Sudanese biochemist whose only, now largely hushed-up, achievement was developing a chemical weapon for use against his country's rebellious southern flank. For this contribution to medicine, he was made foreign minister. Now ensconced in a huge office in Geneva, this officious bumpkin summoned the Chinese ambassador to Switzerland to dress her down for her government's failure to cooperate with a directive from someone as important as he was. The ambassador replied evenly that the Chinese visa process was a complicated one, and told her host to be patient.

WHO's head hooted at this tactic, and warned that his team had better be allowed to go where and when they wanted, or there'd be a whupping.

The ambassador reached into her briefcase, removed a sheaf of papers and passed them across the great man's desk. They were copies of bank transfers made from the People's Bank of Beijing to the Swiss bank account of the WHO chieftain, in exchange for his public support for a Chinese company's bid to build a new airport in his homeland.

Later that day, the WHO chief held a daily news briefing in which he expressed solidarity with the Chinese government, whose pandemic efforts he said he admired, said he had received complete cooperation from the ambassador, and said there was no evidence that the virus came from anything but animal transmission. China was the first victim, not the cause, of Coronavirus. He understood the visas for his inspection team would be ready soon.

When the visas finally were issued, and the team got to Wuhan, one of its members asked to speak to a certain Qi Qi Dieh, who had made some sensational claims on social media. The inspector was told not to meddle in Chinese internal affairs. He insisted he was within his rights. His visa was canceled the next day and he was deported. The WHO head apologized to the Chinese ambassador for his inspector's misconduct.

The AI algorithm now, to all the humans' surprise, said that the next step was to undermine its very own "We're all in this together" slogan. This discrediting of the "all in it together" cheerleading was intended to demonstrate that some portions of the American population were contracting the virus at a rate higher than their percentage of the population would indicate. The purpose was to divide America against itself.

This was to be accomplished by making available to American news media outlets a set of statistics—some close to accurate, others not at all—showing that black Americans were more likely to get the virus than whites.

Henry, informed of the next stage of the propaganda campaign, expressed some doubt. "The TV networks and big newspapers won't run something that hasn't been checked out," Henry said. They're not stupid."

He was right. They weren't stupid. They were delighted. Thrilled to be able to say that blacks were once again being discriminated against, even if the discriminator was a disease that no one understood. The proof to back up their stories: experts had done a study. The experts knew what they were talking about. They were, after all, experts. And somehow, the news media's reporting implied, this latest blow to blackness, like everything bad, was Trump's fault.

The racial disparity story became the dominant topic of cable TV chatter overnight. It was followed within a week by a new study by "experts" showing that Americans of Hispanic descent were also disproportionately affected by this mysterious disease. The reason, the experts explained, was the "cultural configuration" of Latino families, which historically lived in multi-generational close quarters, hugged and kissed each other often, and were insulted at the suggestion that they should wear anything over their faces, especially the women, who, traditionally put a great deal of effort into their appearance and did not want their makeup smudged by a mask.

Again, Henry pointed out that this explanation for the statistics— which were inaccurate to begin with—came off as racist. The AI analysis produced by the geek squad overruled him. The information was fed first to the New York *Times* as a test. The *Times* story, written by star science reporter Gretchen Nu-Mi, quoted the statistics provided by the experts without questioning them. Cable TV launched a new week of outrage, focusing on Trump's previous criticisms of Latinos and concluding that the high incidence of coronavirus among Latinos was the direct result of this Trumpian imprecation.

Three weeks later, Gretchen Nu-Mi's grandmother, who lived in Shenzhen and who had been suffering from respiratory ailments for years, was among the first residents to be given an experimental anti-virus vaccination.

The demand for Chinese-made surgical masks surged well beyond the available supply. Hui's geek squad determined that the state-run manufacturer could quintuple the price it was charging, and they did.

If importers balked at the gouging, they were taken off the distribution list. In America, two wholesale importers said the higher prices were ruinous and sought new suppliers. Fang and Henry worked for 24 straight hours to craft a version of events to American news organizations. To Henry's astonishment, every American news outlet took the bait: "Covid mask importers, discriminating against Chinese products, leave millions unprotected." The importers reached a quiet understanding with their Chinese suppliers.

The propaganda campaign was so successful that Henry and Fang decided to try something outlandish, to see if the American news media could be tricked or coerced into believing it. Wearing a mask, of course, was mandatory, the signal that the wearer was "a good person." Non-mask wearers like Jerry in Pittsburgh, were fair game to be taunted, cursed at, and accused of being pro-Trump.

Fang and Henry decided that if one mask was good, two masks were better. "Experts say two masks double protection against virus," was the headline of the "study." It made the three evening TV newscasts and was on the front page of the New York *Times*. The findings were attributed to "immunological disease experts." No one questioned the study's authenticity. Only a Trumpie would do that. Henry seriously considered trying a three-mask campaign but decided to let well enough alone.

After enduring an 86-day lockdown, residents of Wuhan were permitted to go back to work and to gather in public. Hui's AI team ran numbers through its algorithm and reported a troubling outcome. The Artificial Intelligence program predicted loosening the restrictions would result in a new spike of virus cases. The Party leader in Wuhan argued his decisions should not be dictated by a machine. He authorized the re-opening of the Happy Valley and Jiefing amusement parks. Both venues were deluged by crowds of people desperate for some normal activity. Spirits were high and masks rare. The surge in virus cases started five days after the amusement parks opened their doors. The Party leader was sacked, and Hui was told his Institute was now in charge of the city's virus recovery plan.

The lockdown, enforced rigorously by the PLA troops deployed to walk the streets and detain anyone who did not have written permission to be outside, had made an impression on Henry. An entire city of 11 million had, it appeared, complied with an order to stay in their homes and not to emerge for any reason. Health care workers kitted out in Hazmat suits roamed from building to building, knocking on doors and conducting forced examinations of bewildered residents. If anyone was found to be exhibiting symptoms of the virus, a PLA squad rousted them from their homes and took them to an undisclosed location, which turned out to be the Wuhan soccer stadium. There, the victims were given a towel, a blanket and a cup of tea and left to find a place to lie down. Most of them died within days and were buried anonymously.

The soldiers who conducted these raids were, by and large, low ranking men and women who had committed some infraction and whose army records showed them to be inferior at their work. The infection rate among this group was 82 percent. When they sickened, they were stripped of their uniforms, given one change of cheap civilian clothing and confined to the same stadium where they had taken normal citizens to die.

What Henry found amazing was the lack of opposition to what was happening. Fang had alerted Zhuang Rongwei that, left unchecked, social media would be flooded with horror stories of what was going on. At Zhuang's command, WeChat Wuhan was temporarily shut down. TikTok feeds, videos and pictures were scrupulously censored.

And it worked. Yes, Fang's ex-wife had managed to smuggle out a post claiming she had sold an infected bat at the wet market, but this was quickly removed and a stream of critical posts, manufactured by the Cyberspace Administration, called Qi a mentally diseased person who should be shunned.

In America, Henry thought, there would be protests, a Twitter storm of complaints, and cable TV talk shows would give voice to the outrage that those human rights were being ignored. For Henry, the lesson learned was this: be strong, overwhelm any opposition without mercy, and never admit the truth.

Socialism with Chinese Characteristics.

The "experts" produced studies, faithfully passed to the public by the American news media, that close proximity to other people was a sure-fire way to catch and succumb to the virus. People avoided each other, like, well, like the plague. With no known cure and the process to develop a vaccine painfully slow, the United States, was reduced in a matter of weeks from a thrumming economic powerhouse to a warehouse for three hundred million huddled, fearful idlers. Going to work meant going to your death. Sending a child to school was the same as strangling your offspring. Visiting Grandma at her assisted living facility would probably kill the entire family. Passing someone in the street meant a 50-50 chance of not being alive next month. Anything that promised the chance of meeting other people—offices, restaurants, theaters, stadiums, libraries—was shut down, and adorned with signs of a hand-drawn face wearing a blue Chinese-made mask. The mask sign became as omnipresent as the Stars and Stripes had once been. Trump kept talking about getting the country back to business. His every utterance was a chance for networks, newspapers, websites to vent their outrage at the madman who wanted to rouse America from its coma.

Without undue effort, the AI Institute in Wuhan was becoming a leading voice in America's response to the pandemic. Hui was a hero within the Party. Rav visited Henry more often.

# Chapter 26
## To The Bitter End

One of the most important lessons Luisa had learned since her stay in the hospital, her newfound celebrity and the hatred and anger showered on her by the news media was this: after a while, being called a racist lost its meaning.

"You're a racist," a television interviewer would scold.

"Just be sure to call me an Italian racist." She knew by now that rejoinder drove them crazy.

"You are a disgrace to all Italians."

"Ask them if I am." She extended her arms, palms upward, as if appealing to the nation at large. She showed the scrap of cashmere and explained why she carried it. That, too, raised their blood pressure.

It was true. Since Donatella Tesco had introduced Luisa Moretti to the world, opinion polls showed the Liga had gained ten points in popularity. If regional elections were held the next day, the Liga would win a plurality. The Social Democrats therefore reached agreement with the other traditional parties to work together to prevent the regional government from falling apart, necessitating new elections. "The Garibaldi of Prato," the right-wing websites called her. "Duce in a Dress," rebutted the left. Either way, Luisa was getting attention.

What both sides of the divide agreed upon was that the virus was getting worse, not better. It had cut a swath through Lombardy and spread south. Luisa, when she was asked about it, blamed the Chinese immigrants who huddled close together in cheap apartments and spread the bug to the rest of the population. They ignored directives to wear masks, gathered outside in large groups despite lockdown orders. No one wanted to challenge them. The left-wing media suggested that Chinese workers living in Italy should receive taxpayer subsidies to make up for any salary they had lost due to illness. Asked about this, Luisa's stock answer was, "They are the cause of the virus here. And you want to reward them?"

"It's the right thing to do."

"How about Italians who've lost salary from being out of work?"

"Most of them have families who can help them," had become the stock answer.

Causing Luisa to say, "The Chinese who are here have families in China. Let them go back and be taken care of there."

"That's a racist thing to say."

"Yes, you're right. I admit it. I like Italians better than Chinese."

Then, the Liga and Luisa got a gift from an unexpected source. The European Union's court issued a ruling that Chinese nationals who lived in its 27 member countries had the same rights as citizens, including the right to free medical care. The justice of the court who issued the ruling was a 75-year-old from the Netherlands who had recently married his third wife, a beautiful 22-year-old Chinese girl. The bride had several family members living in Shanghai, her hometown. Though she spoke not a word of Dutch, she had used other, more personal means to convince her husband that failure to rule in favor of the Chinese in Europe could have a serious impact on her relatives. And on their happy marriage.

Italians, who because of the garment trade in the north of the country, had more Chinese guest workers than any other E.U. country, were outraged. A vote of no confidence in the prime minister, who had had nothing to do with the E.U. ruling, caused the government to fall. New elections were to be held a month hence.

The Liga saw an opportunity to put its beliefs to the test with Italians. The party leader, Calvini, told Tesco to get Luisa ready to make speeches across northern Italy.

"But I've said everything I have to say," argued Luisa

"Listen, Luisa," said Tesco. "This is a big opportunity for us. Ever since Bossi founded this party, we've been waiting for something like this to happen. Tenzi let tens of thousands of those people in here, for God knows what reason. And now that geriatric judge wants to give them equal status, just so his cute little Chinese wife won't kick him out of her bed."

They were sharing coffee over a table outside a café, since indoor meetings were banned. Tesco, dressed as always as if she were about to go on television, made no comment about Luisa's frumpy dress, scuffed shoes, roughly combed hair. Then, as if seeing a solution to both their problems, she said, "Luisa, maybe we could go clothes shopping," and instantly regretted the offhand remark; stores, of course, were shuttered.

Luisa consented to look for clothes but failed to find any in the stores that were as well designed and cut as the garments she herself knew how to make. She inspected manufacturers' labels and realized that every piece of clothing she saw came from a mill either owned or operated by Chinese. She mourned for her craft and her country.

"We have a chance to take Parliament," Tesco explained.

"It won't make any difference," said Luisa. "Our lives are controlled by the European Union from Brussels, controlled by people we have never met, who don't speak Italian, who may never have been to Italy."

"But don't you want La Liga to win?" asked Tesco.

"I don't really care," Luisa said. "I didn't join to be a politician. I just want the Chinese to go home, so I can go home, home to my Prato. Where Italians make their own decisions."

At Tesco's insistence, they worked every day for a week crafting what Luisa would say, first on television interviews, then with websites, where she could expand her message slightly. And finally, what she would say at a speech that La Liga was co-sponsoring in Milan's Piazza del Duomo, with a newer right-wing party, La Repubblica, that stood for more jobs for Italians, fewer for immigrants. It was led by a gorgeous television soap opera star, Irma Di Vallera, who was widely assumed to be Silvio Berlusconi's latest *bunga bunga* girl. Berlusconi's lingering presence in Italian politics, and his attraction to beautiful women a third of his age was attributed either to his eternally dark brown hair, his charismatic, multi-capped smile, or his fortune of hundreds of billions of euros. The third possibility led the voting among the public, who loved *Il Cavaliere* for the gone-to-seed bad boy that he was.

Luisa had always thought Berlusconi a reprobate, but one who said out loud what a lot of Italians were thinking but were too scared to enunciate. When he talked about the communist Chinese and the Muslim terrorists who had flooded the country, he was met with waves of applause, cheers, and, in times past, votes for his party. When it was discovered that he had a private island where he conducted week-long orgies with underage girls, his support among female voters evaporated, while male voters maintained their support. Nonetheless, Berlusconi as a candidate was a spent force in national politics. He now pulled the strings behind heavily made-up TV stars whose political ventures he financed and controlled.

Speaking with Di Vallera and Tesco, Luisa said, "I'll read what you want me to say, but I'm going to tell the crowd that the Chinese are ruining Lombardy."

"Fine, fine," said Di Vallera, whose own speech had been crafted by the head writer of her TV drama show. The scriptwriter's skills had been matched to Di Vallera's speaking limitations. For instance, the TV star could not pronounce the word for patriotism—*patriottismo*—without mangling the syllables. This was inconvenient for the leader of a party that was built on love of country, but the writer found workarounds, like "amore d'Italia."

Luisa had her lines down pat, including several mentions of *patriottismo*, so she would not be confused with Di Vallera. Her go-to phrase, which she would repeat seven times during her remarks, was "We welcome visitors, not invaders." It had always gotten a fervent response from audiences.

And it had the added advantage of being true.

The Liga and Di Vallera's party handlers had worked closely with Milan's health officials to arrange a public speech that did not violate social distancing restrictions. "We cannot demand that Italy's laws be enforced and then break them ourselves," said Tesco. The mask-wearing requirement was silly, she insisted, "but we'll go along with it. Otherwise, the media will focus on that and not what we have to say."

It took two weeks to work out the details, but it was finally done. Di Vallera would be the first speaker, given the miniscule size of her party, despite Berlusconi's financial investment. Then Luisa would speak, and finally La Liga's leader, Marco Calvini, who would conclude the rally with a spirited call to patriotic action, and, by the way, to vote for him.

At what was arguably to be the biggest speech she had ever made, Luisa felt something close to indifference. She knew why: what La Liga and Di Vallera's—read Berlusconi's—party required was supporters who were willing to do something. Since her life-changing hospital stay, her acquaintance with Tesco and Calvini, and her emerging celebrity as a chunky, middle-aged woman who wanted to save Italy from itself, Luisa had concluded that the most successful politicians appeal to passive voters. That was the problem with La Liga: they were asking voters to *help* change the situation.

That was also the problem the American, Trump, had, Luisa had decided. He said he would *build* a wall to keep foreigners out, that he would *expel* the ones who were already in the country illegally. His words were fine and had gotten him elected. But now, as president, he had to take action, and for that he needed popular support. And most voters in advanced Western democracies couldn't be bothered. Unless their own houses were on fire, or their daughters about to be ravished by Mongol hordes, most voters in stable democracies would rather sit on their asses and watch TV. Let someone else do the hard part. They were too busy. Watching TV was hard work.

She had worked many hours on her speech. Had resisted calls from Tesco and even Calvini to curve it more toward a party rally cry. Her message would be Italian to Italian. "Your jobs are not safe as long as there are hundreds of thousands of foreigners here who will work for less. Yes, my countrymen. You are lazy, overpaid, your jobs guaranteed by unions so you cannot be fired. But this will change unless we protect ourselves. You know it. I know it. Let me help protect you. You don't have to do anything, except cast a vote telling the government you're tired of being strangers in your own land. In our land. In blessed, unique, Italian Italy. Italy for Italians!"

She had planned to sleep in her own bed the night before, then take the bus to Milan, and wave the bus ticket she had used for the journey as proof that she was truly of the people.

Calvini overruled her. "We both know the metropolitan transit service is shit. I don't want you halfway between Prato and Il Duomo and we're wondering where you are. You'll stay in a hotel just across the Piazza. We'll come get you an hour before and walk across, so people can see you you're not arriving in a limo. Or a rickshaw."

Luisa said, "Fine. I'll stay in a 400-euro hotel room, get room service breakfast, and then walk over and say, 'I'm just like you.'"

Calvini was not amused. "Four months ago, you were just a grumbling old woman. Now you're a famous grumbling old woman."

"Don't forget racist," Luisa said.

"Right," said Calvini. "You know, Luisa, you have had a second big effect on Italy. Not just with your campaign against Chinese."

"What's that?"

"You've been called a racist all over the web, all over TV, radio, newspapers. It's been used so often, it's starting to lose its meaning. Everyone can be called a racist for doing or thinking anything these days. It's like being called gay used to be the worst thing you could have said. Now, people just look back, and say, 'Yeah, so what?' and no one pays any attention."

"I'd like to be known for something more than making racism boring," Luisa said. She insisted on wearing an outfit that she had designed for herself, before she became famous. The items of clothing she had seen in recent weeks made her realize she was a craftsman, and craftsmanship still mattered.

The hotel room was sumptuous, the room service breakfast scrumptious. Now, Luisa told herself as she got dressed, you must be stupendous. Don't hold back. Say what you feel, say what you mean. Don't let your voice be silenced, even if there are protesters, even if the news media calls you racist.

You've worked hard. They can't shut you up.

A young lady from, Luisa noticed, Di Vallera's party, not La Liga, met her in the hotel lobby, walked with her out the door and into the Piazza.

"Are you nervous?" the girl asked.

"Not at all," Luisa replied, and it was true. She fingered La Nonna's cashmere scrap. "They'll either listen to me, or not, believe me or not, follow or not. All I ask is that they let me speak and listen to what I have to say."

The bullet hit her in the back of the head, ripped off her forehead and extracted her brains, threw them forward six feet with its force, followed by the rest of her body. She was dead before she sprawled on the piazza.

Later, after the clamor, the useless emergency wagon, and the shouts had come and gone, the young woman, interviewed by a YouTube journalist, was asked if Luisa said anything after being shot.

Without a moment's pause, the girl answered, "She said, 'Viva Di Vallera. Viva Italia."

It took the Guardia di Finanza, which was in charge of security at the Piazza del Duomo, only two days to deduce and disclose that the fatal bullet had been produced in China.

The scrap of cashmere, freed from Luisa's grasp, skittered in a breeze across the piazza. It was eventually scooped up and disposed of, along with the rest of that day's trash.

# Chapter 27
## Just Plain Artificial

Jerry refused to get a jab. Instead, he got a job, though it was not one he would want to hang onto forever. Because he had once worked for Quest Diagnostics, sorting medical test results and making sure they were sent out in timely fashion, he was called in for an interview, through his JobSeeker account, by a company called Seance, which was considering Pittsburgh for its U.S. headquarters. The woman who interviewed Jerry said she had been struck by his apparent ability to handle a lot of diverse information quickly and accurately.

"Yeah, I guess I multitask pretty well," Jerry said. He already didn't like the woman or the place. He had done a Google search before he came in and saw that Seance claimed to be an artificial intelligence communications company. Whatever that was. Still, no use being a jerk about it. It paid $25 an hour, which was certainly better than the Trump handouts he was taking from the government.

It wasn't like they were making him a vice president. The job was really nothing more than keeping track of computer runs of information that were collected in the course of virtual experiments, whatever those were. When Jerry asked what virtual experiments were, the woman said briskly, "They're experiments that might be, but aren't yet."

Great.

Still, she seemed to think he was okay for the job. And these days, a job is a job. Truth was, he was happy to get off the government dole. Reminded him of the lazy pricks who thought life was one big handout.

"When can you start?" the lady asked.

"What's wrong with now?"

And that's how he found himself sitting on a straight back chair with minimal cushioning, looking at sheet after sheet after sheet of numbers and figures that were neither numbers nor letters. Egyptian, if he had to guess. He was, of course, wearing a mask, one that he had made himself, because he didn't want to buy one made in China. Mask wearing was required here, and Jerry didn't like it, but a rule was a rule, and a job was a job. He stared at the papers in front of him.

"First day?" a guy sitting a couple of feet away, doing the same thing apparently, asked. Black guy, older than Jerry, maybe 45, maybe older, fit-looking, dressed in black jeans and a collared shirt, gold wedding band on his left hand, black-framed glasses. And a mask.

"Yeah. Kinda confusing," said Jerry.

"Don't worry, it gets worse," said the guy. "I'm Rutherford," he said, extending his hand. "Ruth for short." He pronounced it with a soft U. Ruuth, not Ruth, with a long U, like the girl's name.

Jerry bumped fists, smiled, squinted. "Don't you take some shit for 'Ruth'?"

"Not so much," said Rutherford. "I was Golden Gloves runner-up."

"That'll take the shit off you," Jerry said. "I'm Jerry. You a 'burgher'?"

"Lifelong. 'Til the day someone with better fists takes me out." They both laughed. "So, look, Jerry, you'll figure this out for yourself, but the best way to make a good first impression is to take your time, make sure your math is right, and, you won't believe this, but keep the pages squared off. You hand in pages that are sloppy-looking, they'll think you're a moron."

"They might be right."

"Naw, I can tell. You'll be fine."

It all happened so seamlessly that Jerry didn't stop to recognize that he was bullshitting happily with a black guy and thinking nothing of it. And just last month, he had been part of a confusing clash where his Defenders friends had nearly gotten into it with BLM protesters. Did it mean anything? He turned his attention back to the pages in front of him and started squaring them off.

"Just tap 'em twice," Rutherford said, noticing how long it was taking Jerry. "Can't do it with two taps, either the pages are different sizes, or you're a pussy." He accompanied this last with a huge smile behind his mask that made Jerry feel like he'd known him for a while. Jerry grinned back. "Now *you* might be right about me."

"Naw, I can tell. You no pussy." The lack of a verb was the first time he'd said anything like a black guy, instead of just a regular ordinary person. Jerry clocked it, but since it was phrased as a compliment, sort of, let it go.

An hour later, Jerry was feeling fairly proficient at his new career. An unsmiling manager in a white shirt and ugly tie came by, looked over Jerry's work, and said, still unsmiling. "Nice work. You're doing fine," and moved on. Came back, added, "Ruthie here can help you if you need it."

"Already has," said Jerry without taking his eyes off the pages. Smileless walked on.

"Thanks for that, Jer," Rutherford said in a low voice, not because he was trying to be quiet, but because it was the right volume for the room. "By the way, 'Ruthie' is not on the list of approved nicknames." He smiled.

"Okay, Ruthie," said Jerry, smiling as well.

A half hour later, the overhead sodium lights flashed once, twice, and Rutherford stood up. "Brain-clearing time, Jer. Fifteen minutes." He headed for the exit sign. Having no clue of what else to do, Jerry followed. They went into a hallway and Rutherford shoved a dollar bill into a vending machine, got himself a NeHi root beer.

"Didn't know they still made NeHi."

"Make it right here in the 'burgh," Rutherford said. "S'why I drink it."

"Sounds like you like it here."

"Course. The tropical climate, the championship level baseball, the fine dining, the excellent roadway system." What's not to like?"

Jerry said, "If I could have one of those things, it'd be to see the Pirates learn how to catch and hit."

"Ah, you don't understand, Jer. The Pirates are in business to groom young players with unlimited potential and then trade them to the Yankees where they'll blossom."

Jerry had noticed the shorthand use of his name but didn't mind. He had, after all, called Rutherford 'Ruthie,' though everyone understood it was just a joke.

"So," said Rutherford, if you don't mind me asking a question, and don't think I'm being nosy..."

"Shoot," said Jerry.

"What's a smart white guy like you doing in this shit job?" The question wasn't put in an aggressive way. Guy just wanted to know.

Jerry told him the story, if that's what you could call it. UPMC, Quest, trainer, government subsistence checks, now this. "I'm not sure being white has much to do with it," he said at the end.

"Maybe not," said Rutherford. "Just seems like everything these days is viewed through the prism of race."

This guy was too complex to take lightly, thought Jerry. Back at the desks, it was 'You no pussy' in ebony black, the casual note that he was a good boxer, and now, a sentence that could have come from a network TV news anchor.

"Like that near dust-up we had couple weeks ago. Those Defenders and BLM nearly getting' into it. Right on the streets of Pittsburgh!" It was the last sentence that carried the most emotion. Guy loved his town.

Jerry didn't try for sex on a first date, and he wasn't going to give up his deepest secrets the same day he met someone. He just nodded.

"My goddam wife was at that thing. Coulda blown up into a mess," said Rutherford, as if commenting on a bunch of rowdy kids at the stadium.

"Your wife?"

"Well, she might be my ex-wife by now."

Jerry didn't need to hear the guy's life story. They'd only met a few hours ago. But Ruth wanted to talk.

"Ah, she's all worked up about BLM, police brutality, racial injustice, getting' reparations for slavery. That shit. It's kinda driven a wedge between us."

"And you're not worked up?"

Ruth smiled. "I got enough to worry about. Making mortgage payments. Keeping my piece-a-shit car running. I ain't no Tom, but trying to change everyone and everything all at once ain't gone happen."

Again, the abrupt switch back to black dialect. Was he unaware or was it for effect? Jerry'd never known a black person he could ask, but this wasn't the time.

Nor was there time. "Let's get back to tapping paper. Good talking to you, Jer."

"You did most of the talking."

Rutherford looked at him hard for just a second, as if inspecting his face for sarcasm. Then he laughed. "Shit, man, you're right."

They talked more the next day, and the next. Rutherford, it turned out, had attended the University of Pittsburgh, and wrestled and boxed varsity at the 155-pound level. "A few pounds ago," he sighed, cupping his stomach. An injury ended his sporting days, and, as it turned out, the scholarship that had put him on the Pitt campus.

"I don't blame them. That was the deal. Keep your grades up and stay healthy. Grades were fine. It was the meniscus that failed. They held up their end. I couldn't."

It was the most straightforward, unself-pitying thing Jerry had heard for quite a while. Everyone always had someone or something to blame for misfortune. Rutherford blamed himself, for tearing a ligament.

Was he reaching for a deeper level of contact? Jerry was no shrink, but he thought so. So, without overthinking it he said, "Listen, Ruth"—he used a soft U, not a hard one—"that protest your wife was at with BLM? I was there too."

There was a beat's worth of pause. Then: "'Scuse me for mentioning it, but you don't look all that black."

And Jerry said, "That's 'cuz I was with the other guys. The Defenders.

Ruth took another moment to digest that. "You hate black people, Jer?"

"I'm talkin' to you, aren't I?"

Rutherford laughed, a big easy laugh. "Well, fuck, so you are. OK, Mr. Defender."

Jerry made a wince. "Guess I won't be meeting your wife anytime soon, huh?"

"Oh, you can meet her. But may I give you a fashion tip? Wear a cast iron jock strap. Edna is a tough chitlin."

"Edna?"

"Yeah. My wife named Edna. I think sometimes that's why the chitlin got so tough."

And they both laughed.

Jerry was invited to the get-together at a burger joint on Market Square to celebrate, if that was the right word, Tran's release from police custody on charges of public disorder and incitement to violence. The P.D. could be a fine, but the incitement charge carried potential jail time. Earl, the former cop who had gotten clocked along with Jerry, had found an attorney—"probably the only Republican one in Pittsburgh," Earl said—to represent Tran *pro bono*. "Which does not mean that you won't be paying me back, somehow, sometime," the lawyer said.

Jerry hadn't tried to contact, much less visit, Tran while he was being held. He was surprised that other Defenders had done so. Now Tran, looking a little thinner, but in good spirits, was thanking those people. When the moment seemed right, Jerry found his way into the crowd—mostly unmasked and not apologizing for it—and shook, not fist-bumped, Tran's hand.

"Sorry I didn't get to visit you, man," Jerry said.

"'So-kay," Tran said. "What's up with you?"

"Got a job," said Jerry, somewhere between pride and regret.

"Where?"

"Place called Seance. Seems to have something to do with artificial intelligence."

"And they hired you?" said Tran. "Just kidding, man. You like it?"

"It's a crap job. People are okay."

"Hope it works out." Tran paused. "Listen, Jer, the cops made a mistake coming after us the way they did. You know we weren't doing anything wrong."

"I know. And the TV news made it sounds like we were the Klan."

"So," and again Tran paused for effect, "we're gonna take it to the next level. "They want to use clubs on us, we'll have knives. They pull out their pistols, we'll have AKs. We can't let them push us around. There's too much at stake."

Jerry kept his face still. Then said, "Tran, aren't you about to stand trial for incitement? I mean, sure, Earl's found you a lawyer, but..."

"And I'm grateful to Earl, and everyone else who stood up for me," Tran said, and Jerry could feel that he was not currently included in "everyone else," no matter that Tran had said it was "So-kay."

"Tran, maybe this is exactly the wrong time to step it up. I mean, you are in legal jeopardy, to put it mildly. Nobody's with us. Everyone thinks we're racists and that BLM are saints."

Tran gave him a hard look. "Saints, huh? You hear about that co-founder of BLM, Qiyyancha whatever-her-name is? Some Jewish soundin' last name."

"It's Such. Pronounced 'sook.' Such-Harder," said Jerry. "Qiyyancha Such-Harder."

"Yeah. Just bought a condo for a mil and a half. And going on about how they want to reinvest in the black community. Bet she's the only black person in *that* community."

"I didn't hear about that," said Jerry. "Was it on the news?"

"Are you shittin' me? You think any big new organization is gonna report that? They'd have a lynch mob in front of their studio fifteen minutes later, calling them racists."

"You're right about that," said Jerry. "The news media has gone completely over to their side. Capitalize b for black, but not w for white. Can you explain that one?"

"Sure, I can," said Tran, getting worked up. "Everyone's afraid of blacks protesting and calling them racist. And if they don't get what they want, rioting. And that, Jerry, is exactly why we have to step this up. Let them be afraid of *us* protesting too."

"I see your point, Tran," said Jerry, meaning it. "Let me think about it. Right now, I'm trying to make this job work out." And he thought of Rutherford and their talk and wondered how it all came together.

Tran looked at him hard again. "Okay, Jer. Do what you need to do. But don't think too long. Before you know it, you're gonna be a second-class citizen in your own city. By the way, how'd the Pirates do last night?"

"Lost."

"Well," said Tran. "At least some things don't change."

214

# Chapter 28
## One Hand Washes The Other

Luisa Moretti, who believed Italy was for Italians, would have happily agreed to the trade-off of her life for five minutes of the world's attention. Her murder in Piazza del Duomo was the top of the international news cycle for twelve hours and was then relegated to the "not our kind of story" waste bin of modern-day journalism. "Italian Nationalist Gunned Down," said the website of what was once Italy's largest newspaper, back in the days when people besmirched their fingers with ink. "Racist Pays Price," said a leftist website that had tried to have Luisa arrested for hate crimes. "Santa Luisa, R.I.P." mourned La Liga's website, recognizing her value too late. "Racist Leader Meets Chinese Lead" blared a crime sheet, which apologized the next day after it briefly became the most popular site in Italy. Which was all that mattered to the crime sheet's editors.

The origin of the bullet was a topic of discussion for longer. Chinese-made ammunition, like everything else Chinese-made, was sold around the world, at substantially lower prices than any other. When a Vietnamese ammo company boldly tried to compete, a visit to its CEO from a captain of the People's Liberation Army resulted in the sudden termination of the experiment. The CEO retired a month later, and moved, like all Vietnamese millionaires, to Los Angeles. The town of Prato proposed a memorial service for its native daughter, but was warned by a Chinese immigrants' group that there would be violence. The town backed down. The immigrant group then held a raucous festival to celebrate the murder. The leader of the Black Lives Matter group in Italy—BLM had become a worldwide phenomenon—

215

summed up the group's feelings: "Bitch got what she had coming."
The MeToo movement, its attention span limited to American men's
misdeeds, did not dare to question the propriety of the remark.

Still, the link between Luisa, a virulent opponent of Chinese
infiltration of Italy, and the Chinese bullet that had, literally, caused
her to lose her mind, was too enticing to be ignored. Who had fired
the bullet? The Guardia di Finanza admitted it had no idea who was
on the departing end of the bullet, only its origin. Interpol briefly
attempted an investigation, until its top representative in China—a
PLA officer, of course—advised Headquarters to cease and desist if it
ever wanted Chinese cooperation again.

It was in China where the murder created the greatest fuss. PLA
agents in Italy took fewer than two weeks to identify the assassin, a 22-
year-old Chinese garment worker from the town next to Prato. The
killer had been born in Shenzhen province, migrated to Italy four years
earlier under a false name, and been a social malcontent since arriving.
He was lured out of the flophouse he shared with eight other workers
by a girl who had complimented his looks, and suggested they take tea
together at her flat. He was intercepted on his way to what he
confidently believed was a shack-up and never seen again. The girl's
family back in China received a surprise tax rebate of $40.

But the removal of the culprit did not solve the public relations
problem. Since China could not claim to have solved the crime, it had
to endure questions from the outside world. Why did China export
ammunition, asked an American gun-control group, the first time it
had ever pointed a finger at a country beyond its own borders. Were
Chinese residents of Italy living a healthy lifestyle, wondered Weight
Watchers International? Most worryingly, the World Health
Organization, a branch of the United Nations that China thought it
had firmly under control, said it wanted to reopen its investigation into
the origins of the coronavirus, which by now had made its way to every
continent. The Chinese Health Minister protested, saying China had
turned over all the information it had on the disease.

This was of course, balderdash. The Chinese Communist Party
had conducted a careful, one-sided investigation of its own. It had
learned that the criminal Qi Qi Dieh had removed a diseased bat from
the Wuhan Virology Lab, sold it at the city's wet market to a vendor

who made soup out of the creature, sold the soup, and began a chain reaction of illness that played out almost exactly as the virologists who created it had predicted.

The only problem was, the virus got out of control.

Admitting any responsibility for a pandemic that had already killed a million people around the world was out of the question. Even before Xi Jinping took power, the Party had learned that the best way to counter negative information is to lie. And if that doesn't work, to lie bigger. The bigger and more audacious the lie, the more likely it is to be accepted by the Western world. Especially the United States, whose citizens had been groomed to suspect their country was responsible for everything wrong in the world. Including the virus created in Wuhan.

Responding to the fool from WHO would be more delicate, since WHO's president was in effect a Chinese tool. Zhuang, Xi's handpicked man, offered the services of his Cyberspace Administration. In unusually blunt terms, Xi's office told Zhuang to mind his business and confine himself to making sure no misinformation made its way into Chinese media. Instead of the CAC, Xi decided to delegate the task of discrediting the rumors about the origin of the virus to Hui's AI institute. Within the higher ranks of the Party, this decision was seen as a generational leap of faith from trusting humans to trusting their mental superiors—robots.

Hui did not bother to conceal his pleasure at having been chosen for this mission. It was a signal of Xi's recognition that AI would become the dominant cerebral force in the entire world, and very soon. Of course, in a country with a history as long as China's, "soon" can mean a few centuries. Hui did not intend to let it take that long.

"We will do what seems impossible," he said, sitting at his desk, his guest in front of him and the hologram of Xi staring silently down on them both. "This is our moment."

"Our moment?"

"Yes, General," Hui answered. "The moment for China to bypass America as the leading force on earth, in the universe."

"You are talking like a man with too much confidence," the General said.

"On the contrary, General. I am talking like a man who knows the difficulty of the task he faces, and believes he can master it. Under your supervision, of course, and that of the Party."

The General smiled, not convincingly. After years of hard work, after the master classes in computer science, the boring English language lessons, the tests of loyalty that any ambitious Party member must pass, Hui was once again on his way up. How far he would get was anyone's guess, but the General was a keen judge of character, and Hui smelled like a winner.

"Do you not worry that you trust too much in the American?" asked the General, and Hui could not help noticing that a millisecond after the question was posed, the hologram of Xi widened its eyes, as if to ask, 'Well, what about that?'

"The corporal is a rare find," said Hui. "Part of my plan during my lecture tour in America was to find someone young enough, intelligent enough and gullible enough to give us first-hand insight into the American mind. Such as it is."

"Your plan?" asked the General with a frown. "Or the Party's plan?"

Hui immediately backtracked. "I misspoke. Of course, the Party's plan. I was merely its vessel."

"You like him, don't you?"

This was another test of Party loyalty, Hui knew. He took a moment to make it look like they took the General's probe seriously. "I don't care what happens to the American. He is a tool to be used. He has knowledge of America that we need to input into the AI system. I have paired him with the two AI engineers..."

"They call them the Geek Squad, did you know that?" interrupted the General.

"Of course I knew it," said Hui, intentionally allowing a note of irritation into his voice. "I know everything that goes on in the Institute." He was careful to say 'the' and not 'my.' "It is derived from the American store Best Buy. They sell appliances, electronics and such. The store sends technically competent people to connect their computers, their satellite dishs, their washing machines. For a price, of course."

"Why can't Americans do those things for themselves?" The General was genuinely curious, also curious to hear Hui's answer.

"Because they are lazy. An entire generation has been told 'you deserve this,' or 'let us do it for you,' or 'it's not your fault.' *Of course*, it is their fault! They have declined like the Roman Empire, into a cluster of whining, ignorant globs of fat and fantasy. The generation before them, the generation that defeated the Nazis, that generation knew how to not just install a washing machine but to fix one when it broke. The men who came back from that war spent their weekends under their cars, changing the oil, replacing the brake pads, tuning the engine. Do you think this generation even knows where the engine of a car is located? If the belt of a washing machine breaks, their first instinct is to buy a new machine. And please, deliver it today. I deserve that.

"So, yes, General, I know what the Geek Squad is. The Party allowed me the honor of learning those things to be of more use in my current work."

"How does the American fit in to your 'current work'?" This, of course, was a not-so-subtle jab, a return to the high-wire game Hui was playing by using a non-Han.

"He is key to this latest assignment, of deflecting questions about the origin of the virus. For such a young person, he has amazing powers of perception. And he is a realist. Like most of his generation of Americans, he is cynical about his country and its place in the world. He has seen America make itself foolish, allowing itself to be attacked, then failing to punish its attackers for years. He has seen corporations send their production secrets and facilities to us in China, because we can make things cheaper and without whining complaints from labor unions and environmentalists. He has seen all this in his short lifetime. And as a result, he does not have the reflexive love for what Americans like to call 'Uncle Sam.' In fact, 'Uncle Sam' has become an object of wide ridicule among his generation, like a real-life uncle who gets drunk at a family function and embarrasses himself, spouting nonsense."

"Especially Trump," said the General with disgust.

"Well," replied Hui, "Trump is a temporary annoyance, I agree. But because Trump is a buffoon, no one takes his wild claims seriously.

And by the time he is proven correct, he will be gone, and we will be masters of the world."

"And this young man approves of this?"

"Do you think I would bring on an American if I did not think I could influence his thinking? The Party's decision," again, he avoided using 'my' "was brilliant. We have at our disposal a very intelligent American, willing to betray his homeland in the service of what he recognizes as our superior system of governing. And we are providing him with incentives to continue and even improve his service."

"We know the 'incentive' you are providing," said the General with a smirk. The hologram of Xi smiled.

"The Lieutenant has proven herself extremely helpful and trustworthy," said Hui. "She passes on everything the corporal thinks and says. She has described his youthful enthusiasm, his frustrations, his incompetent sexual flummoxing. She is a great asset and another key to our plan."

Not to mention her secret, direct line to Xi, the General thought, but said nothing.

"Very well," said the General. "Thank you for the update. You have my permission to move ahead with your project. It had better succeed."

"Thank you, General," said Hui, smiling politely, looking at the unattractive biddy he despised but had to report to, hating her ugly metal glasses and ugly tan teeth.

# Chapter 29
## Farewell But Not Good-Bye

Henry was amazing himself at how his Chinese was improving. Every lesson he finished felt like a promotion to a new grade of knowledge. Of course, it helped that Rav was visiting him more frequently, and demonstrating that she actually possessed emotions, even if they were deep under the sediment of her skin.

"You have to tell them things they don't already know," she whispered one night. "You were a curiosity when you first arrived. But now you are part of the team, and you must continue to amaze them, or lose your value. And I don't want that to happen to us."

"Us?"

"Yes, us." She had not previously used that word.

"I tell them what will work in America, but they don't listen. And the approach they take is too ... clinical. They need to put feeling into it."

Rav smiled sweetly. "You Americans are so concerned with feelings."

"Feelings are what run America now. If someone says she's offended by something, that thing has to go away."

Rav said, "But everyone is offended by something. How can you control a country if you have to worry about everyone's feelings?"

"That's a good question. The answer is 'you can't'."

"All right," said Rav. "The Colonel wants to see you tomorrow. Let's go over some things we might be able to tell him that he doesn't know."

"We," she had said.

Hui's office was more dimly lit than usual, and Henry wondered if there had been a power outage in the neighborhood, a not uncommon occurrence but never discussed in the AI building because it suggested all was not well in Xi's paradise. Also different was the presence of Tanteeth, who sat in the corner the furthest away from Hui, her face carefully neutral.

"So, corporal," said Hui, lacking his usual suave manner, Henry thought. "What do you have to tell me about our problem?"

"The WHO. should not be allowed to make demands of China," Henry said, trying to follow the script he and Rav had devised. "These are Chinese affairs and they will be addressed by China."

"Fine, but please," said Hui, "let's dispense with the propaganda and talk as colleagues. Because that is what you have become, Henry. A colleague with unique knowledge that we want to use to its fullest." Over Hui's shoulder, the Xi hologram nodded, once. The shift from 'corporal' to 'Henry' had been noticed.

"The questions about how the virus started are invasive of Chinese sovereignty," said Henry. "We both know you have influence with the WHO. You have already demonstrated that. "Those who want to say that the virus started in Wuhan and was spread by Chinese carriers should be discredited."

"You are right, of course," said Hui. "But, Henry, we have a deeper problem."

Henry was not going to ask what the problem was. It was not how things were done here. He waited.

"What I am about to tell you is known by only a handful of Party officials. It is a very sensitive piece of information and must be handled as though it were a highly explosive substance. Do you understand?"

"Yes, Colonel," said Henry. He could feel that both Rav and Tanteeth were studying him for some reaction. He gave none.

"The Chinese vaccine for the virus, Sinovac. It doesn't work, Henry. Its rate of efficacy is about 45%, which is only slightly higher than a control dose, in which we were injecting water into people's arms."

Henry had two simultaneous thoughts streak through his head. First, this would be a monumental setback for Chinese science, and of course, for the Party. It could derail China's plans for bringing its workforce back, could raise more questions about China's reliability as a partner in the world of scientific research and could give the United States the kind of victory it so desperately needed these days. His second thought was how to combat this negative truth. And Henry surprised himself by inventing, in less than a second, a plan, one that he was certain would work. He marveled at his own perspicacity. Was his brain becoming like the algorithms the Geek Squad relied upon?

"We have, umm, allies in the American news media, do we not, sir?"

"Yes, we've discussed that," said Hui, seeming uncharacteristically preoccupied.

"Well, the first step would be to enlist them to combat this lie. I would recommend that woman at the New York *Times,* which seems to have adopted the 'blame America First' philosophy. Mostly because of its storied history, it still has credibility with like-minded readers. But beyond that one newspaper..." Henry wavered, not sure if he should take the chance.

"Yes?"

"I am sure that you are aware of this, Colonel, but may I just remind you that there is a new company in the United States, known as FastNews.

Hui motioned weakly with one hand. "I think so. What about it?"

"They use AI to write news."

"What do you mean, 'write news'?"

"They load an algorithm with all the pertinent information about a topic. And AI spits out a complete news story. No human contact, no editing required. Ready to go online, or on a printed page. They have also learned to convert the written story into voice, so it can be distributed as a video or audio product."

Hui was staring at Tanteeth, as though he was merely humoring the American. "This is interesting, Henry. But tell me what it means to me."

"The American news media is corrupt, lazy and hopelessly biased against America itself."

"Yes, yes, we know this."

"If your institute can duplicate what FastNews is doing, you can do the same thing."

"And how," said Hui, though his eyes had already lit up with comprehension, "would you suggest we duplicate this algorithm?"

"Steal it."

Xi's hologram, fed by AI, nodded.

The AI Institute lacked neither resources nor imagination. Within two weeks, the Geek Squad had stolen and reproduced the FastNews algorithm. Now the question became: what key terms to feed in to produce the kind of stories they wanted?

Henry couldn't do all the work. He needed an English-speaking assistant, though one with Chinese sensibilities. Rav was the obvious candidate, and she became his nearly constant companion, temporarily relieved from other military duties. Henry suggested the key words, Rav suggested the order of priority for them, and, much like putting fruit in a blender and turning it on, they waited to see what came out.

The first results were disappointing. The sentences contained a subject, predicate and object, but the structure was nearly unreadable. Rav was crestfallen. "Don't worry," said Henry with more optimism than he felt. "We'll reorder the key terms until we get them right." This of course, was the hard part, and required the help—direction really—of the Geek Squad. They worked long hours, cooped up together, with Rav the combined translator, moderator and political watchdog.

As they were slogging their way toward a workable product, the tried-and-true tactic of intimidation and threat provided a first breakthrough. Gretchen Nu-Mi, the science reporter for the New York *Times*, wrote an op-ed for the newspaper headlined "Questioning Chinese Covid Vaccine is Racist." It quickly became the most clicked-on item of the day and continued to be read avidly for another 72 hours.

Hui was impressed. "You've done well, corporal. You are proving yourself to be an invaluable part of the institute."

The AI Institute was moving swiftly on several fronts now, surpassing the Cyberspace Administration on formulating responses, not just to the failure of Sinovac, but other realities that were confronting the Party leadership. One was that criticism of its genocidal campaign against the Uighurs in Xinjiang province was becoming widespread. The United Nations overrode Chinese objections and filed an "affidavit of concern" about treatment of the Muslim minority so despised by the Han Chinese leadership. In retaliation, China's ambassador to Norway asked for, and was granted, an audience with the chairman of the Norwegian Academy of Science, which advised the Nobel Peace Prize Committee. When the nominees for the prize were announced, the U.N. secretary general's name was missing. It made him only the second U.N. secretary general not to be considered for the prize. A flurry of news items generated by an unknown, newly established news service detailed the secretary general's odd financial transactions, and also mentioned that he had fathered a child out of wedlock.

But it was the Institute's development and deployment of a facial recognition network that secured Hui's place as one of Xi's top advisors. The Geek Squad had grown to more than twenty highly proficient coders who worked round-the-clock to develop an algorithm that could predict a person's loyalty to the Party simply by scanning his or her irises. The system, code-named HanEye (and contracted to 'Honey' by some English-speaking jokesters on the Squad) was still in Beta-testing when the PLA high command asked—ordered, really—Hui to give them a demonstration.

The demonstration was conducted at the Institute in Wuhan. Several PLA generals grumbled about having to go to ground zero of the pandemic. They were reminded by the Party ideology liaisons within the Army that no matter what they had heard, neither Wuhan nor China had anything to do with Covid. These generals, not used to being corrected, quickly apologized for their errors and made plans to attend the demonstration.

Hui was uncharacteristically nervous. He could not confide in Tanteeth, and he felt uncomfortable sharing his inner weakness with Rav, who was his subordinate. To his utter amazement, Henry was summoned the day of the demonstration and asked him to come alone.

"HanEye is a great scientific achievement," Hui said. Henry noticed that Xi's hologram had been turned off, or at least was not visible. This was a first.

"Yes, Colonel," said Henry, "and I wish I had been more involved in its development."

"You have been busy with other, equally important tasks," Hui said. "It is your very distance from this program that makes it easier for me to discuss with you my concerns."

"Yes, sir."

"HanEye is in its early stages, Henry. It can make mistakes. It could, for instance, find disloyalty simply by scanning the irises of some perfectly innocent person. Of course, we will never admit that. Still, it is possible that we will be responsible for condemning a loyal citizen to prison or worse, simply because the algorithm has not yet been perfected."

"Your concern for fairness is honorable, Colonel," said Henry, "but as I learned from you, every coin has two sides."

"What do you mean?"

"HanEye is imperfect. Fine, we will say this at the outset. It is still being refined. There is nothing shameful about this. And it was the PLA that demanded this demonstration. It was not you offering to show it off before you were ready, correct?"

"Correct."

"Why do you think you are being forced to present this demonstration?"

Hui took a deep breath. "I suspect some of the generals are intimidated by the potential for AI to make command decisions instead of them. They want to discredit me, the Institute and Artificial Intelligence."

"Exactly," said Henry. He and Rav had discussed this in the days leading up to the demonstration. And it was she who encouraged Henry to say what he now said. "So, sir, why not ask the generals you suspect of ill-will to be among those to take part in the demonstration?"

"Have their irises scanned by HanEye?"

"Exactly," said Henry again. "And what if, sir, those who you distrust were found by HanEye to be disloyal to the Party?"

"They would deny it of course and say HanEye was not reliable."

"And you would concede that point with humility and dignity. But would those generals ever recover from being found disloyal, even if it was by flawed AI?"

Hui looked at this American, no longer a fumbling visitor, but an actual prodigy, partly due to Hui's guidance. He was becoming Chinese. Which made it harder now to say what he had to say.

"Henry, thank you for your insight. Let us not discuss this matter again."

"Of course, Colonel."

"Henry, there is something else I have to tell you. In the past few days, you have been sought out by several phone calls, emails and text messages from America."

Henry's eyes widened, as only a *gweilo's* can. "Excuse me, Colonel, but I have received no messages from America recently."

"You have not received the messages, because they may have been intercepted."

"By who?" Suddenly, Henry's American 'I have rights' sentiments sprung to the surface.

"By us, Henry. We needed you to complete the work you were doing. You have done well, and now I will relay the message from America to you."

Henry stood still, remained silent. It was as if he knew what was coming.

"I am sorry to tell you, Henry, that your mother has contracted Covid-19. Her condition is grave."

Henry absorbed the news. "I will have to go home. I have to go see my mother."

Hui nodded sympathetically, then said, "That may not be possible at this time."

Socialism with Chinese characteristics.

# Chapter 30
## Tyranny Of The Experts

Whether it was the grind of the mindless job, the storm of news online and on the TV about systemic racism, reparations to the descendants of long-dead slaves, the coronavirus, the failure of Trump to stop the virus (like he was a doctor), the Chinese, Russians and Iranians stealing America's most guarded secrets, or just the damn Pirates unable to throw a strike or score a run, Jerry felt like the world was slipping out of control.

The paychecks had been good to have of course. He hadn't liked being on the government dole, even a Trump government. And he was pretty sure those "relief checks" from the president were mostly intended to secure his re-election. Jerry was beyond, or as he told himself, above party politics now. The Republicans had abandoned all their principles to swing behind Trump and make believe his disjointed, disoriented and disrespectful method of governing was really okay. The Democrats had turned into Trotskyites. If you didn't agree with every hare-brained idea their most radical members came up with, you were a fascist or a racist, or both. Just leave me out of it, he thought.

His own world was fracturing too. He stayed in touch with Tran and Earl, and went to Defender meetings and marches, having been assured beforehand that they would not be confrontational. And they weren't. Pittsburgh, it turned out, had no room for a bunch of white guys who didn't want to be told to stand apart, wear masks 24/7, listen to "science" – which these days, seemed to mean whatever crackpot study the media picked up and ran with, unquestioningly. When the

Defenders demanded to know who had decided that six feet, not five or eight, was the distance you had to stand apart, they were called deniers. If they held a rally, complete with a permit from the city, on a public street, people cursed them, made monkey-noises and dragged their hands on the ground to suggest they were as stupid as apes. Would they do that at a BLM rally? When they referred to the virus as the "Chinese Flu," the TV news crews sent out to record them never failed to mention that they were racists.

And though that word, 'racist,' was used so often and in such a one-size-fits-all manner that it was losing any significance, it had started to bother Jerry to be called one. He knew why: Rutherford. Neither of them was into kumbaya or hugging, or even arguing about race. Ruth's wife was a BLM supporter. Ruth and Jerry weren't. They left it at that. Yet they had gravitated toward each other, at work, and on occasion, after work, when they would have a beer outside—the bars were still closed—with their cans cleverly concealed in brown paper bags, a sure way to outsmart any cop who might be passing by. They talked about cops and whether they were racist, or criminals.

"They're the same as elk," said Ruth.

"Huh? Like elk with horns?" Jerry wanted to know.

"Old story I heard and liked," said Ruth. "Some scientists got a government grant to study the question of why some elk jump over fences, while other elk won't. Spent a couple million dollars following the herds, and shooting little trackers into them with air rifles, then taking all their findings and running them through a computer and analyzing the results and publishing their findings."

"Which were?" Jerry asked.

"Some do, some don't."

They both laughed.

"Are some cops racist?" said Ruth. "Fuck, yes. Are all cops? Fuck, no. Same with those BLM types my wife is so crazy about. Are some of them out there because they were hassled by the blue when they were younger, or because they're afraid their own kids gonna get shot for being black? Sure. But some of them are racist too. They hate white people just 'cause they're white. So how is that not racist? And by the way, when some gangbangers are breaking into their house late one night, who do you think they're gonna call for help?"

For Jerry, it was like that one Christmas long ago when he'd come down early in the morning and found exactly the present he'd been hoping for under the tree. He had no recollection of what it was, but the feeling had stayed with him. Ruth was a black guy he could talk to, say what he felt, ask questions of, and not worry about being called a racist. And Ruth felt the obverse: a white guy who'd listen, who'd actually talk honestly about shit, and not always act like Ruth was gonna stick a knife in him.

It was becoming what passed for friendship in 21$^{st}$ Century America.

Rutherford also mostly agreed with Jerry about the virus situation. "It's all fucked up," he said, but without rancor. "This started out in China and we can't call it China Flu because that's racist? Who's gonna call me a racist, huh?

"And this mask wearing shit. You know the last time they got everyone to cover their faces? When the fucking Muslims took control in Persia, and kicked that shah dude out. Oh yeah, everyone was happy Shah-Shah was out and real excited about what was coming in. And then that Khomeini asshole and his posse come in and started talking about Allah and how everyone had to behave. And saying women should cover themselves up. Now, Persian women was used to wearing perfume and jewels and showing off their booty. They didn't want to put a scarf around their pretty faces. Then the towel heads start cutting off hands and heads. And telling the women again to cover their faces. Better to cover your face than lose your whole head, right?

"Same thing's going on here. Everyone's scared shitless that this bug gonna get inside them and kill them dead. And so now, the experts, whoever they are and whatever that means, start saying, wear a Chinese mask over your nose and mouth. Otherwise, you gonna die, bro. Gets your attention, doesn't it, someone say you're gonna die?"

"I guess," said Jerry. "What I don't like is having people yell at me if I walk down the street without one."

"Tehran, Jerry. Remember Tehran. Women'd walk down the street without a scarf over their face, and a crowd would form around them and start cursing them and throwing stones at them and calling them impure. Then the cops would come with sticks and beat the shit out of them. That's the next step here, man. Mark my words. Cops will come and beat the shit out of anyone not wearing a mask. And the crowd will applaud. And the fuckin' masks are made in China! Which started this shit. Now, how's that right?"

Talking to Ruth was like talking to one of the Defenders, except Ruth was black. And it settled into Jerry's head that what he was saying was more important than how he looked while he was saying it. And it crossed his mind that maybe he should take Ruth to a Defenders meeting. But he decided that wouldn't be good for anyone, him or Rutherford. But there was no longer any doubt about it: if someone had asked Jerry who his best friend was, he'd answer that it was a dude named Ruth.

It was obvious, and not just to Ruth, that Jerry was underemployed at his job at Seance. Not that he should be promoted to CEO, but squaring off stacks of paper was not what he should be doing. And so, when Smileless, the guy who had told him he was doing a good job on his first day, told Jerry to come into his office, Jerry wasn't too worried that he was going to be fired.

"Look, Jerry," said Smileless, true to his nickname, "the company has signed a big contract with the University of Pittsburgh Medical Center. UPMC wants to use AI to predict how people who have this virus will respond to different kinds of treatment."

"You mean like, do they just need medicine, or should they get hooked up to a ventilator?"

"Also if they're gonna live or die. They think artificial intelligence can collect data of symptoms, and temperatures, and blood pressure, and heart beat, and all the other indicators, and spit out a recommendation for how to treat the patient. Or whether to bother treating him."

"Sounds like it could save a lot of work, if it's accurate," said Jerry, kind of thinking he knew where this might be going.

"And you used to work at UPMC, right?"

"Yeah, until they laid me off."

"Right. So, you might still know some people there. At the very least, you'd know how they think, what they'd be looking for when they're working with us."

"I don't know," said Jerry, honestly. "You're talking about a lot of science here. I'm no scientist."

"No, but you could be an agency."

"Say what?"

"It's one of those new flashy terms that everyone's using," said Smileless. "It means you're a guy who can look at a situation, analyze it and make recommendations. Now, if you were an agency for us, you'd tell us what's shaking at UPMC and how we can make the most of it."

"And what would I be doing?"

"You'd be looking at the stuff Seance turns out for UPMC and telling them that we're doing good work, that they should listen to us."

"But I know almost nothing about AI."

"That's not the point," said Smileless. "See, you'd be an agency. That'd make whatever you said a lot more important. You'd be sort of an expert."

"Like a bullshit artist but with a nicer title."

"And a bigger salary, Jerry. What do you say?"

Jerry wanted to talk it over with Rutherford, but he figured Rutherford would be pissed about him getting a bigger salary, despite not knowing what the hell he was doing. So he asked Tran via text if they could meet up to discuss something not about the Defenders. "Cool," Tran texted and gave him a time and place.

"So you'd be inside UPMC?" Tran asked, after Jerry had told him what was going on, or potentially going on.

"At least until they catch on and realize I don't know shit," said Jerry.

"Look, Jer, listen to the news. Read some websites. All the politicians are screaming that we have to listen to the experts, let ourselves be guided by science."

"I know. Pisses me off," said Jerry.

"Me too," said Tran. "And now, think about what just happened to you. They're gonna put you in the middle of some experiment—an experiment on humans, Jerry—and listen to what you have to say about the data they're turning out. And, as you just expressed so eloquently, you don't know shit about it."

"Yeah."

"Take the job, Jerry. This could be huge for us."

"For who?"

"The Defenders. One of the ways we can gain credibility is by calling out the so-called experts, letting everyone know that an "expert" is just someone who knows someone who has some power. Most people know "experts" are full of shit, and will say whatever gets them published or interviewed on television. People can smell bullshit. But everyone's too scared now to say it out loud."

"Scared of what?" said Jerry.

"This fucking virus, man. Nobody wants to wear masks or have their favorite bar closed down. But nobody wants to choke to death on a ventilator either. And so, people are just doing what they're told. It's the tyranny of the experts, man. And it has to end."

"Maybe you're right," said Jerry. Or maybe you're not, he thought, but didn't say.

So he agreed, with great misgivings, to the new job. Seance thinking he'd be able to help them influence UPMC, Tran thinking he'd be a spy for the Defenders.

And just how the hell was that gonna help us lick the virus, huh? But it was better not to say some things these days, in this land of the free and home of the brave.

# Chapter 31
## You Can't Go Home Again

"I have to go home," Henry said to Rav, as they lay together on his bed. "My Mother's sick and she needs me."

"The Party needs you more," said Rav. She had her chin perched on her palm, her elbow digging into the mattress.

"I understand that," said Henry. "But she's my Mother. I love her."

"Do you think you were selected for this important work you are doing so that you can walk away anytime you want?" said Rav, eyes crinkled in frustration. "That's not what the Party expects of you. You must love the Party more than any individual."

"But my Mother!"

"People live and die. The Party is forever. You have made wonderful progress since coming here. More than anyone expected, except perhaps for Colonel Hui. He saw your potential all along. And he made sure you had an easy, straight path to follow. Now you must climb a hill."

"But it's not fair," said Henry.

Rav smiled. "Isn't that exactly the phrase you mocked little American children for using when they didn't get their way?" And Henry had to admit it was. His request to call his father was denied. So was his request to see Hui. He wrote an email to his father, read and approved by Rav, Hui and—without Henry's knowledge, Tanteeth—that he would get home as soon as possible and to tell Mom that he loved her. He felt miserable about the subterfuge. Since arriving in Wuhan, he had successfully shut off feelings about family, and, truthfully about everything except the Party and Rav. Now, thinking about his Mother suffering, those feelings seeped back into his conscious thought.

A week went by and he said nothing. He worked on the facial recognition algorithm, and made some suggestions about refining it so it could spot not just liars, but *potential* liars. The Geek Squad, jealous of his influence with Hui, made mock of his suggestions. "The best way to spot a liar with facial recognition is to train the camera on a *gweilo*. They're all liars."

And how is that any less racist than the things being debated and denounced in America, Henry asked himself, but no one else.

Alone in his room one evening—Rav had not visited since their conversation a week earlier—Henry heard a knock on his door. It was Fang, his stable-mate from the early collaboration projects with the Cyberspace Administration of China. Ever since the AI Institute had been given primacy in addressing foreign snooping into China's virus responsibility, and response, Henry had not seen Fang once, though he had heard talk that Fang was moving quickly up the Party ranks. Now his squat ugly face looked like a long-lost friend to Henry.

"May I in?" Fang asked in English.

"Please, come in," Henry said in slightly better Mandarin than Fang's English.

"Ah, you study Chinese. Good," said Fang. Then in English, "And I study your language."

"Good," said Henry in Mandarin, wondering how long this bilingual fuck-fest would go on.

"Takey walk wiv mi," said Fang, stretching his fat neck toward the corridor and main door.

"Okay," said Henry. Having nothing else to do but working on ways of helping China subvert and conquer his native country, he was happy for the diversion. And he knew that no conversation of importance could take place indoors.

Socialism with Chinese characteristics.

The summer night was warm but there was a smell in the air that had hung over Wuhan since spring. To Henry, it was the smell of dead bats, but he realized he was allowing his fears and the secret knowledge he had acquired to influence his olfactory senses.

Fang, no small talk artist, began murdering English as soon as they hit the sidewalk.

"You email Faddah."

"What?"

"Faddah. Man parent."

"My Father, yes."

"Say you go 'merica."

Henry said in Chinese, "Yes, I want to go home."

"Your home is here," said Fang, grateful for the switch.

"Yes," said Henry. "But now I must visit America."

"Hui will not allow that."

"Colonel Hui has been good to me," said Henry, being careful with his pronunciation. He didn't really trust Fang, although they had worked together well when thrown together. But he had a feeling that Fang, a Party climber, was not here to console him. "How do you know I emailed my Father?"

"Email on Internet," said Fang in English, then switched to say, "Cyberspace Administration know everything that is on the Internet."

"But I wrote that from my private email address," said Henry, and, seeing Fang's toothy smile, realized instantly how stupid that sounded.

"I help you," said Fang, emboldened by his last English phrase. "Then you help me."

A large part of Henry's attraction to China, to the AI Institute, to Hui and to the work he was helping with, was the neatness, the orderliness of it. Hui thought about a problem, made a decision, gave an order, and it was carried out. There was a clear hierarchy, and although Henry knew that as a foreigner he was held in suspicion, he was protected by the umbrella of Hui's authority, and by the reputation Hui had created for himself and for AI.

He was part of Hui's team. He must accept Hui's refusal to let him travel to America. Then he thought of his Mother, his father, and, incongruously, for the first time in months, of Khadija. How had she crept into his consciousness? And inevitably, he thought of Rav, of her touch, of the feel of her, of her voice in the darkness. Comparing Khadija and Rav was like putting corn-oil margarine on the same plate as caviar.

He realized Fang was staring at him, like a frog observes a fly on a lily pad.

"Don't say," Fang said in English. "Just ready. Ready anytime."

And Henry nodded, and wondered why.

Three nights later, thirteen days since he had learned his Mother was sick, Henry's door opened at 2:31 a.m. He hoped it was Rav, but knew—smelt actually—that it was Fang. "Now," he said.

"As you wish," Henry replied in Mandarin. It was a phrase he used so often that it came naturally now. He took off the undershirt he slept in when Rav wasn't here—Fang watching intently—and put on the quasi-uniform he wore everyday: black trousers, a white shirt, no tie, black sneakers. He picked up a winter coat, the only one he had, but Fang shook his head. He removed the thin wallet he kept in the coat, and Fang immediately held out his hand for it. "But I," Henry began, but Fang put his index finger over his lips and nose. Some languages are universal.

It was impossible to get out of the AI Institute without passing through an electronic screener. Fang held Henry's ID card over the screener, it beeped once, and he was through, Fang slipping behind him with more coordination than Henry would have given him credit for. So now they would know at what time he had snuck out. Once on the street, a black Shanguan sedan pulled up to them. Fang got in next to the driver, Henry got in the back seat, and was surprised to see a frumpy woman sitting next to him, scowling as though she, too, had been yanked from sleep.

"Hello," said Henry in Mandarin, but Fang turned around and said crisply in English, "No talk."

This put a crimp in all the questions Henry had, such as, where the hell are we going? Who is this unattractive woman and why is she in this car with me? Does Colonel Hui know and approve of this? But Fang had imposed a vow of silence on himself as well. The driver, who looked to be in his twenties, drove without once looking in the rear-view mirror. An indication, Henry thought, that he knew where he was going and had authority to be out on the streets at this hour, despite the virus-instilled curfew. It occurred to Henry this was only the second car he had been in since arriving in China. This one was far superior to the clap-trap taxi that had brought him to the AI Institute eight months ago. Eight months! So much had happened in that time. What really mattered, though, was what was going to happen next.

He couldn't see out of the blackened windows, and at any rate, despite having lived here, he knew nothing about Wuhan geography. After half an hour, they turned onto a four-lane road and Henry saw, for an instant, a signpost flash past them that said, in Mandarin and English "Tianhe International Airport." Airport? How could he get on a plane? Hui, or Rav, or someone at the Institute had his passport. Fang was an idiot if he thought he could defy Hui.

Even before he could protest this foolishness, Fang raised his hand, and without turning around, said, "Not here." Sure enough, the car went past Tianhe, brilliantly lit against the black sky. Another twenty minutes, and it made a sharp left turn and then a sudden stop. The driver rolled down his window. A guard in a PLA uniform approached, his automatic weapon extended toward the car. The driver said something, the soldier replied, and Fang let loose a stream of angry words and extended, across the driver's chest and halfway out the window, a sheaf of papers concealed in a plastic cover. The solider took them, called for backup, and kept his rifle trained on the car's occupants, as another solider took the papers and ran into a guard post ten meters away.

They waited in enforced silence. Three long minutes later, the soldier who had sprinted away, came back at the same speed, spoke urgently to the gun-toting guard, who lifted his rifle to port-arms, said something to the driver in an altogether different and deferential tone, and stood at attention. The car moved forward, slowly, and as it did, a gate by the guard house opened horizontally on a well-oiled track.

Just as Henry was getting used to the silence, Fang turned and said, "Wuhan Air Command Base." It was the best English he had spoken, and Henry was sure he had rehearsed it many times, to demonstrate his linguistic superiority to Henry, to the driver, and to the women in the back, who frowned in incomprehension.

Things moved incredibly quickly, as they tend to do when soldiers, especially, are working from fear. The Shanguan drove about two hundred meters before another solider, also armed with an automatic rifle, stepped in front of the vehicle. But instead of aiming his weapon at them, he extended it to the left, like a traffic cop's baton.

In another hundred meters, they were on a tarmac, an even from the back seat and through the tinted windows, Henry could see bright lights and hear an engine thrumming.

"Out, out," said Fang with an authority in his voice Henry had never heard. The woman with him frowned again, in what seemed to be her default facial expression.

Henry heard, before he saw, the plane, engines alive, the stink of petrol filling the air, guarded by six PLA soldiers. A narrow staircase ramp extended from the tarmac to a left side entrance to the plane. It appeared as though it could be hauled up into the aircraft.

"On, on," said Fang, and Henry for some delirious reason, had a sudden image of Ingrid Bergman hurrying her husband, Victor Laszlo, onto the plane to flee Casablanca. Stop! he told himself. This is no time for a cinema trivia quiz. But he couldn't keep up with all the sensory images he was trying to process. Fang shouted something in Mandarin at the woman, but took Henry gently by the elbow. "Come on."

If Henry expected to be greeted by a smiling air hostess, he was disappointed., just as he had been on the military flight from Teterboro. Inside this aircraft, another armed soldier stood unsmiling, as Henry walked past. There would there be no soft drinks and pretzels served here, either. The seats were narrow, high, and equipped with over the chest restraints, which the soldier who had seen them onboard now clipped over Henry and the woman, who was sitting behind Henry. Fang, on Henry's right, fastened his own. "Go very fast now," he said, back to basic English.

The pilot welcomed no one aboard. Safety features went undemonstrated. The stairway ramp folded itself up and disappeared into the fuselage. Henry heard some radio chatter, presumably between the pilot and flight control. And then they took off.

Most airplane passengers are spoiled into thinking that takeoffs are a mellow, mannerly increase in speed until altitude is achieved. This plane, a Chengdu J-20, screeched like a gazelle being eaten alive by a lion, left the ground a second after engine thrust. Henry felt vomit come into his throat, and heroically held it down. Fang pretended this happened to him every day. The woman behind them let out a shriek of fear. Fang turned around, looked at her, and guffawed in an ugly manner. They seemed to be ascending at a 75-degree trajectory, but five seconds after takeoff, the Chengdu leveled off and hit its cruising speed of 500 miles per hour. An hour and a half after their aeronautical adventure, the plane landed, with the same gut-wrenching abruptness, at the Shanghai Airport. Henry wanted to ask how a military jet could land at a civilian airport. Then he saved himself from looking stupid. The PLA can do anything it wants in China.

"Out, out," said Fang while it was still rolling to a stop. Henry became convinced that Fang genuinely did not know that one use of the word was as effective as repeating it.

Just as he had noticed upon his arrival in China, Henry saw that the Shanghai Airport was an immense expanse. The main terminal— at least he assumed this was the main terminal because of its size and opulence—looked like a multi-block stretch of a rich, fashionable city. Who could fail to be overwhelmed, dwarfed really, by this megalopolis devoted to flight?

Even Fang seemed temporarily lost. Then, as though taking shape from the mist, a man dressed in civilian garb came forward from the throng of people around them, said a few quick words to Fang, and extended an arm toward the far end of the terminal. The woman started to protest, but Fang turned on her and let loose a stream of what Henry could tell was invective, punctuated by spittle. It silenced the woman.

They followed the plainclothesman as if being led on a leash. Fang never looked back to see if Henry and the woman were keeping pace. They all knew their places and their roles, if not what this was all about and where they were going.

The far end of the terminal was dominated by an enormous neon overhead sign that said in Mandarin and English "China Air Welcomes You." The letters were all in red, on a background of garish yellow — the predominant colors of the Chinese flag and of the Party. As they approached, the plainclothesman was digging in his jacket pocket, handing off to Fang a quite substantial green envelope with a string tie at its top. Not losing a step, Fang opened the envelope, thrust a hand inside and came up with a clutch of papers and documents. Henry idly wondered what they were but didn't want to fall behind and so put his curiosity behind hm and stepped up the pace. The woman did the same.

The queue at the check-in counter must have been several hundred people. Henry, a veteran of airplane travel with his family, felt a familiar lump of fear settle into his chest. It now seemed clear that he would be getting on an airplane. But with this many people ahead of him, was it possible he would miss whatever flight he was meant to catch?

With more confidence than he had ever shown at the meetings he had attended with Henry, Fang shoved through the queue roughly, grabbing the woman by the hand. She was tugged along involuntarily, and Henry instinctively burrowed through behind them. Reaching the front of the queue took nearly five minutes of bullying, hissing, and angry stares, both from Fang and the hundreds of people he had jostled to get there. Adding a final touch of bad behavior, he shoved aside the elderly couple at the counter with a sneer that must have contained vulgarity, judging by the shock on their faces.

Fang slammed his booty of documents down on the counter and spoke in rapid staccato to the airline employee, a young woman who looked at him as if he were armed, or crazed. Such impoliteness was not characteristic of Xi Jinping's China. At least not in public.

Demonstrating a spark of spunk, the woman fired back a few words at Fang, and threw her hand, palm inward, toward the line behind him, as if saying, get back there. Wait your turn. Fang acted as if she were drunk or stupid, and tapped the top of his documents. The woman looked at them, drew in a breath, and in a much more civil tone, put her hands out, this time palm outward, but slowly. Please wait, was the body language Henry picked up.

In less than a minute, a uniformed PLA officer—captain, Henry thought, judging by the spaghetti on his shoulders and comparing it with what he had seen on Rav's—was at the counter with a wary look on his face. After he and Fang had exchanged a few sentences, he stepped out from behind the counter, over the scale on which luggage was placed and weighed, and stood directly in front of the trio of queue-busters. He picked up the papers that Fang handed him, with respect, and began reading. For the first time, Henry saw that Fang's printed treasure trove contained passports, Chinese passports. Two of them. The PLA captain took each, opened the first, scanned the front page, which contained biographical information and a photo, much like an

American passport, and said, as if acting on stage, "Harrumph." Henry nearly grinned at the overacting, but held himself in check.

He did dare to stretch his neck forward an inch or two, and saw that the picture on the top passport was of the woman Fang had dragged through the crowd. Who could this baggage be that Fang, or anyone, would take an interest in her?

His shock and fear multiplied when the Captain opened the second passport without trying to hide its contents, and Henry saw that the photo on the first page was of him. The Captain raised his bushy eyebrows, looked directly at Henry for the first time, then at Fang, and nearly shouted a remark. Fang fired back, with something Henry could not understand at all. The Captain, unconvinced, returned fire, and this time, Henry could hear amid the war of words, *gweilo*—round eyes.

Fang, seemingly prepared for this, now adopted a milder tone, a reasonable manner, and directed the Captain's attention to a piece of green, official-looking paper sticking out of the passport that contained Henry's photo. The captain was midway through another "harrumph" when he saw the paper and what was on it. He raised those matching bushes over his eyes, and, for the first time since he had come around from behind the counter, was silent. He and Fang looked at each other. Then he looked at Henry. Then at the woman. Then he said something brusque, causing Fang to smile—not a pleasant sight—and let his shoulders slump into relaxation.

"Zhuang?" said the captain.

"Zhuang," said Fang, with confidence.

The Captain was a different person now: polite, deferential even, speaking in low tones and natural cadence to Fang, who nodded, also politely, and made noises of confirmation each time the Captain posed a question. The Captain gave the three of them one long last look, stepped back over the luggage scale, and told the young woman something that left no room for questions. Ten minutes later, Henry and the woman each had a ticket entitling them to board a plane for New York.

They waded through the crowd, backwards this time, but could not escape the reproachful looks they received from those would-be passengers they had shouldered aside. Several times Henry heard *gweilo* used as an imprecation. Fang seemed not to notice.

"How did you do that? Why is my picture on a Chinese passport? Who is this woman? Where are we going? What was on that paper?" He had no idea how to ask the questions in Mandarin and his volume kept rising as he asked each one of them, and Fang ignored him. Finally, Fang grabbed Henry by the shoulders and said, in English, "Keep your voice down or you will spend tonight in a jail cell underneath the airport, instead of on a plane going to America." It was not the first time that Henry suspected Fang had rehearsed these lines because of the importance of clear communication at a moment of crisis.

Getting from the check-in to passport control took as long as some basketball games, so huge was the airport. When they finally stood in front of an unsmiling uniformed official behind Plexiglas, Henry was astounded to see the same Captain who had inspected their passports and gotten them tickets standing behind the official. Henry, the woman and Fang all stood together, although there was a sign at the top of the queue reading in both Mandarin and English, "One person at a time."

Fang slapped the passports down, and looked over the shoulder of the official, at the Captain, as though they were cousins or best friends. The Captain, all business, leaned delicately over the shoulder of the passport official, and murmured—no louder than that—into her ear.

"Zhuang," said the captain.

The passport official looked at the green page sticking out of Henry's passport, and sucked in her breath. Then she looked at the woman's passport with less trepidation. Once again, Henry thought he heard *gweilo* once or twice, but couldn't be sure because of the Plexiglas barrier. It took all of three minutes, and then, stepping away from the barrier and free to pass through, Fang said in rehearsed English, "Remember, you owe me a favor. Take this woman with you. When you get to New York, someone will meet her. You must find your own way."

"But this is a Chinese passport," said Henry. How am I going to explain that I'm an American?"

"Look at passport on plane," said Fang. "Also look who signed permission paper." Every one of his sentences in English appeared to have come from a textbook memorization course.

"Who is this woman?"

Fang shook his head as if in disgust. "No one. She no one. Remember: sleek and silent." He thrust a cheap red imitation leather fanny pack, which Henry had not seen until now, at him and walked away.

Bewildered, scared, surely unsure, Henry looked at the woman, who looked back with suspicion in her eyes. "Henry," Henry said, pointing at his chest with his index finger.

The woman started to speak rapid Mandarin, stopped when she realized Henry didn't understand. She seemed to think for a moment, then motioned for them to go past the passport control desk. They walked wordlessly until they arrived at Gate 137, where an overhead sign said, "New York," and, in English, "Flight time: 15 hrs." Fifteen hours to circle halfway around the globe with someone I don't know and can't communicate with.

Wonderful. Pretty much the same situation as when I arrived here.

Waiting at the departure gate, he thought of Hui, who had brought him here. And Rav, who he had to admit he had fallen in love with. Was he betraying them, as he had betrayed his own homeland, or was he doing the right thing? He didn't know. He thought of Fang and realized there was a reason for his sudden interest in Henry's family plight. And then he remembered that Fang had ousted Wo, his rival at the Cyberspace Administration, and who Rav told him had a way with words.

He and the woman boarded the plane, on time, sat next to each other wordlessly. Pilot noises, blah-blah, and then the mighty engines roared and China was below them. But what lay ahead?

That was when it occurred to him to look at the Chinese passport that apparently was his, at least until someone came and arrested him. There was his name, and his photo on the front page. And behind that page, pasted somehow so it could not slip out of the passport, was the green piece of paper that had turned the PLA Captain from foe into fawn. Henry tried to make out the Chinese characters. Most of it was scribble to him. Then he looked at the bottom of the page where there was a name under a signature. A name he had seen before, on transcripts of the meetings he had attended. A name he had been warned not to cross.

"Zhuang Rongwei."

Zhuang. Head of the Cyberspace Administration. Longtime confidante and friend of Xi Jinping. Hui's nemesis.

He looked at the woman sitting next to him. She had been looking at his passport too. She too had seen the name.

"Henry," Henry tried again, pointing at his own chest. "You?" he asked, pointing at her.

"Qi Qi," she said, pointing to herself. "Qi Qi Dieh."

Fourteen hours and forty minutes to go.

# Chapter 32
## Hidden In Plain Sight

The plane touched down at JFK on time. Fucking Chinese efficiency, thought Henry, brain sodden from lack of sleep, mouth tasting of dead bat, nose keenly aware that his seatmate had not bathed recently. But there was no denying it, he was no longer in China, and he was in the United States. Well, technically not. He had to get past border control, a formality he had never thought about before.

The woman, Qi Qi, had kept her eyes shut for most of the flight, not once attempting conversation. Henry respected that and left her alone. But he sensed she was panicky. Her hands shook, she moved her head back and forth as though trying, unsuccessfully, to soothe a muscle in her neck. And she made little noises from time to time, as though trying to sing, very softly, a song that Henry didn't recognize. She was trying to calm herself, he realized.

"What song?" he asked her, pointing to her mouth, a cupping his ear as if he heard what she was singing. The woman made something like a smile, for the first time. She pointed to her chest, her heart, actually. Then put her hands together and turned them downwards, as if snapping a twig. Then she wagged her right index finger back and forth, signaling a negative.

Midway through the flight, Henry had looked into the red leather fanny pack that Fang foisted on him. It contained five twenty-dollar bills, and a piece of scrap paper on which Fang had written, with two words scratched out and rewritten, in English, "Sleek and silent."

In comparison to the Shanghai Airport, the main international arrivals terminal at JFK looked like some kind of last-minute

246

afterthought, a quickly built area to handle incoming private craft from Bermuda or Jamaica, perhaps. The shabbiness, the heavy rancid-smelling air, the shiftless, dead-eyed indifference of the various security personnel they passed between the plane and passport control—it all melded together to make a traveler's first impression of America's largest city deprecatory. How long had it been since the place had been painted, let alone redesigned? No wonder first-time visitors so often commented, "Is this really the United States? I expected better."

So did Henry, who for an instant felt embarrassed that his travel companion was seeing these shambles. But when he looked at her, he saw that Qi Qi was entranced with what she saw. Her eyes went from the floor of the terminal to the top of the ceiling, swept from one side to the next, trying to take it in. It occurred to Henry that Qi Qi might not be particularly well-travelled.

She had no idea where to go, what to do. Trying a reassuring smile, Henry pointed to the front of the queue, where the border agents sat behind Plexiglas much like they did in Shanghai, but with far more boredom in their eyes. One agent, Henry noticed, had taped a "Black Lives Matter" poster to the Plexiglas of her cubicle. Henry wondered how long a political statement like that would be tolerated in the Shanghai airport.

They were shown no deference here, unlike at their departure point. As they inched toward the border patrol kiosks, Henry took out $60 and handed the three twenties to Qi Qi. Somehow, she understood that this was money. She quickly tucked it away in a pocket of her black trousers.

"Welcome to America," Henry said.

"Me-Ka," she replied.

He wondered how he could explain to her that someone was waiting for her on the other side of the passport control, but the words would not come. He strangled out a Mandarin phrase, "Friend you there" and pointed past the kiosks. Qi Qi shook her head, and Henry imagined she could not understand his Chinese.

Henry reached the head of the line first, turned and shook hands with Qi Qi formally. "Good luck," he said, and marched toward the waiting passport official, the black woman with the BLM poster who seemed to fill the entire cubicle. As soon as he slid his passport under the Plexiglas, she looked at its first page, and with heavily lidded eyes, said: "If you're Chinese, I'm an Eskimo. You wait there." She picked up a walkie-talkie and muttered into it. One minute later, a painfully thin white man in a tight-fitting uniform sidled over and held out his hand for the passport. Henry waited for the obvious questions, to which he had no answers.

"It's a valid Chinese passport, and it's got a valid visa in it," he told the black woman. "Let him in."

"Shit, Brandon, this ain't no Chinaman," she replied. "Jus' look at his eyes."

"Don't be racist," Brandon admonished her.

"I'm black. I *can't* be racist. Aw, forget it," said the woman in disgust. "I don't care. Let 'em all come in. I'm off in ten more minutes."

"Umm, sir," said Henry, not knowing why. "The lady behind me doesn't speak English, but she has a valid visa too. Perhaps you could be gentle with her?"

"Of course," said Brandon. "Welcome to the United States."

Most international passengers are greeted only after they have retrieved their luggage and passed through customs inspection. So, Henry was surprised to see, as soon as he got through passport control, a Chinese-looking man in a dark suit, white shirt and red tie, peering past him to where Qi Qi was now standing at the same cubicle where he had been welcomed, albeit in two different ways.

"Are you waiting for her?" Henry asked the man, who seemed uncertain of what a smile was. "She traveled with me."

"I am from Chinese Embassy," the man answered. "Move on, now. I will handle her."

"Handle her?" said Henry.

"Move on."

The black woman flipped through the virgin pages of Qi Qi's passport, stamped a date on her visa page, welcomed her to the United States, and motioned her to move forward.

She did, until she saw the man Henry was talking to. For a dumpy middle-aged woman, she moved extraordinarily well. She lit out of the passport area, and seemingly by instinct, down the steps to baggage retrieval, though neither she nor Henry had any baggage.

The Chinese man tried to get past Henry, who stood in his way intentionally, and pretended to engage him in more conversation. The Chinese man moved to his left, and Henry, facing him, moved right. He to the right, Henry to his left. By the time the Chinese man pushed Henry out of the way, Qi Qi was nowhere to be seen.

As the man ran after Qi Qi, Henry asked himself why he had done that. He didn't know the woman, owed her nothing, had done little more than sit next to her for fifteen mute hours. Would he have challenged a stranger who claimed to work for an embassy at a Chinese airport? Of course not. But this, he thought among many other things, was America. A free country.

And then he laughed at his own joke.

Qi Qi stopped running when she saw the Customs officer standing at a desk in front of her. Don't panic, she told herself, then wondered what else she was supposed to do if not panic. She had been abducted from her home for the second time in two months. This time not by the police, but by her shit-heel ex-husband. He had gotten into her apartment without her permission. Had moved to her bed, where she was asleep, roused her roughly, told her to get dressed and not to ask questions. On the way out of her building, she had managed to ask what was going on.

"Don't worry. You're not in trouble," Fang had said.

That made Qi Qi worry quite a bit.

When she saw she was being put in a government car, she tried to escape. Fang grabbed her by the wrist, turned it sharply, and said, "Do that again and you'll go back to the asylum."

The trip with the *gweilo* had been unnerving, and yet she felt that he was not part of whatever nightmare she was trapped in, but rather a fellow prisoner in it. She heard that he spoke some Chinese with Fang, but it was basic, and she decided not to converse on any level with him. Anything she said, no matter how innocent, could be used against her.

Socialism with Chinese characteristics.

She had understood when her travel mate said "friend" and pointed past the passport kiosk. But since she barely recognized that she was in the United States—the length of the flight being the best clue—and that she was certain she knew no one in this place, she doubted it was a friend waiting for her. And so, as soon as she saw the *gweilo* talking to a Han, she took off, sensing that the rest of her life depended on escaping from both of them.

The customs officer watched her approach, out of breath, and assumed that she was being met in the arrivals terminal and that she was running late.

"No luggage?" he asked kindly.

She held out her arms to both sides, trying to indicate she spoke no English.

"I can see you don't," said the customs guy. "Have a nice day." And pointed her toward the exit.

The *gweilo* had given her money, which was nice of him, considering he was probably working with the Han in the suit she had seen him talking to. She had no idea how much it was worth or where it might take her. She only knew she wanted to get away from this smelly place where she had landed. She saw a rank of yellow cars with plastic signs on top and assumed—correctly—that they were taxis. She got in one, slammed the door, tried to lock it, but saw that the lock button was broken.

"Where to, baby?" said the driver, a dark-skinned bearded man wearing the kind of headdress that Uighurs wore. She wondered if he was one. She plumbed her mind for anything she might be able to say, to make the car move, to make the driver take her away.

"Chin-e. Chin-e," she said, her voice cracking with fear. "Chin-e."

"Chinatown?" said the driver. "You got it." And away they went, on the Van Wyck Expressway, which had probably never welcomed a more grateful guest on its pitted asphalt adventure ride.

Like every other part of Manhattan except Gracie Mansion, where the Mayor lived, Chinatown was now a mixture of middle and lower-class residents and millionaires who liked to buy tear-down real estate and resurrect it in their image.

The mayor of New York called this mixed-use housing, as though he had invented it. Residents of the newly blighted neighborhoods thought of it more as mixed-up housing. But in a one-party town like New York, and come to think of it, like Shanghai, there was no avenue for appeal, let alone freedom of speech.

The taxi stopped at the corner of two streets, Mulberry and Canal. Peering through the back window, Qi Qi was surprised to see signs and neon lights all in Mandarin. She knew enough about taxis in Wuhan to know that there was a meter that showed how much she owed. The meter said 39.75. Numbers were the same in all countries. She placed two of the paper rectangles that her travel mate had given her into a clear plastic door built into a Plexiglas barrier between her and the driver. The driver looked at the bills as though they were turds.

"Thanks a lot, bitch," he said and went squealing off almost before Qi Qi had touched the pavement and closed the door.

She was utterly without rudder. Thank goodness all the signs seemed to be in Chinese. Clutching the last rectangular piece of paper her neighbor on the plane had given her, she warily approached a shop that appeared to be a restaurant. Bo-Ky it said in Mandarin, and also what she assumed was English. Opening the door, she realized it was not a restaurant, but rather a take-away food store. But the man behind the counter looked Chinese and so Qi Qi said, "I am lost. Can you help me?"

"How can you be lost?" he answered with a smile on his frog face. "You're Chinese and you're in Chinatown."

"I am not from this city," Qi Qi said.

"Where are you from?" he asked.

"Wuhan," she replied.

The smile disappeared from the man's face. "Get out," he said, and when she did not budge, more loudly, "Get out!" And, fumbling, he raised a blue Chinese surgical mask to his face.

Startled by such behavior, Qi Qi turned and left the shop. Next door was another, similar establishment. The woman behind the counter was already wearing a blue face mask. Had she seen Qi Qi coming in? Or did she wear it all the time? Clearly, this was another take-out food shop. There was a menu above the woman's head with various noodles, rices with vegetables and rices with fish. And, at the bottom of the menu, *bianfu tang*—bat soup. Despite being lost and confused, Qi Qi smiled. "You sell *bianfu tang*?"

"You can read, can't you?"

"Does anyone buy it?" Qi Qi asked.

"It's our most popular order," the woman said sharply. "All that talk about it causing this virus is trash."

If only you knew, Qi Qi thought.

"I need a room for the night," Qi Qi said. "Does anyplace around here rent rooms?"

"I have a room to rent," said the woman, friendlier now that the prospect of making money was on the table.

"How much?" said Qi Qi.

The woman looked her over and judged her financial status. "Ten dollars. And because it's slow today, I'll give you a take-out meal for free."

"Thank you. I'll take it."

The room turned out to be above the store. It was small, with one window overlooking Canal Street. There was a single bed and a bedside lamp. There was a lot of traffic noise. There was no toilet, but the woman pointed to one down the hall. Qi Qi handed over her rectangular piece of paper, and the woman gave her one back with "10" on it. She also gave her a plastic bag with a cup of bat soup, another cup that contained tea, a vegetable *lo mein*, and three fortune cookies.

"You look tired," the woman said. "Get some rest."

"Thank you," Qi Qi said. "I am. But I am glad to be here." And, once the woman had left, she sat on the bed, and realized that for the moment at least, she had disappeared from China and the Chinese. She slurped tea and bat soup, something she thought she would never do again. The *lo mein* lacked flavor but she ate it all. She laid down with her clothes on. Sleep came almost immediately.

She woke before dawn, disoriented, thirsty, needing to pee. Where was she? Not her flat. Not the asylum. Well, perhaps a different kind of asylum.

Even before dawn, there were hooting and motor sounds outside her window. Slowly, like fog lifting, she remembered the plane ride, the *gweilo* sitting next to her, giving her money, interfering with the Han who was waiting for her, giving her a chance to flee, the angry taxi driver, the kind woman, the bat soup. Yes, simply a different kind of bedlam.

Now she went down the hall, in search of a toilet. She walked slowly, trying not to make noise, though she wasn't sure why, and reached the open door of the toilet. It smelled bad. She thought to herself, I've smelled worse. She used the toilet, washed her hands, looked at herself in the mirror above the sink, shuddered, splashed water on her face, realized there was no towel. Dried her face with her hands, dried her hands with her face. Opened the bathroom door.

The woman from the shop was standing there. "I see you get up early, like me," she said, not smiling but not hostile either.

"What time is it, please?"

"Four-thirty in the morning."

"I fell asleep as soon as I finished eating. Thank you for the food."

"Did you like it?"

Qi Qi thought. "To be honest I was so tired I hardly tasted it. But I think it was good."

The woman laughed. "Well, come downstairs when you're ready. I'm going to start cooking for the lunchtime crowd."

"Already?"

"You think Egg Fu Yung makes itself?" said the woman, still smiling. "Anyway, come down. I'll give you some tea."

"You are very kind."

"Well, we Han have to help each other. God knows those bastards in the Party won't."

Qi Qi was so shocked to hear the Party being criticized verbally that her mouth dropped open.

The woman noticed. "Are you a Party member?" she asked, suddenly suspicious and with no warmth in her voice.

Was this a trap, Qi Qi wondered? Could this woman be an agent of the Party, trying to trick her into saying something disloyal? Then she remembered where she was. In America, hidden for the moment from whoever had tried to intercept her at the airport. And her presence here, at this house, was such a random thing that not even the Party could have planned it.

Could they?

"I am not in the Party. The Party put me in an insane asylum for expressing myself. I hate the Party." The words had come out, unbidden, and at long last, unhidden. She *did* hate the Party. What had it done for her? What had it done for China, besides make everyone afraid?

The woman's smile returned. "I think you are a stranger to New York. Most people in Chinatown hate the Party. But they are afraid to say so. Many have relatives still in China and they are afraid they will be punished if we say anything negative. But I have no relatives there, so I can speak my mind. My name is Liu."

"Mine is Qi Qi."

"Welcome to New York, Qi Qi."

"Is that where I am? New York?"

"The city that never sleeps. Except, with this coronavirus killing everyone and closing everything down, it's the city that can't wake up."

Qi Qi didn't understand what this meant, but she was happy for the conversation.

"Do you have any other clothes, Qi Qi?"

"No. Just what I'm wearing."

The woman squinted. "We're about the same size. Come with me." And she marched down the hallway, past the room where Qi Qi had slept, to a room on the left. "Come in." She flipped on the light, revealing a bedroom not much bigger than the one Qi Qi had just slept in. There was a bed, a nightstand, a dresser with a mirror. And Qi Qi was paralyzed with fear to see, on the far wall, a huge red and black poster that said, in Mandarin and what she assumed was also English, "Down with the Chinese Communist Party." And a thick black diagonal line through the letters CCP.

Liu laughed when she saw Qi Qi staring. "It comforts me at night. Helps me go to sleep, knowing that someday we'll put an end to their lies, their shit-brain ideas, and their reign of terror."

Qi Qi had never heard such talk, did not know how to react. Here was someone criticizing the Party out loud, actually calling its ideas shit-brained. Through her mind again darted the possibility that this was all a set-up. And again, she convinced herself that that was impossible, that she had ended up in his house, this hallway, this room, by chance. *Xingyun de jingshen.* Lucky Spirits.

"Here," said Liu, taking out a pair of black trousers, and a white top, much like the ones she was wearing. "You can borrow these until you get some new clothes. I haven't worn them very much." She handed them over. They were far better-quality material than anything Qi Qi had ever worn.

"Oh, I can't," she said. "They're yours."

"They're yours now," said Liu. "Change into them and then come down for tea."

In less than twenty-four hours, Qi Qi's life had changed three times. Abducted by Fang, put on a plane for America, given money and time to escape from what she was sure was another abduction attempt, fortuitously taken to the Chinese neighborhood of this immense city, and guided by Lucky Spirits to Liu, to free food, to tea, to new clothes. None of this was given to her by the Party. It was given *despite* the Party. For the time being, she was free of the Party. She decided she must show her gratitude, repay her debt to *Xingyun de jingshen.*

She found a towel in her room, not having noticed it there the night before. She took off her travel clothes, wrapped the towel around her, and went to the bathroom to take a shower. There was soap in the shower, and it smelled better than anything she had ever used to wash with before. Luxurious hot water, good-smelling soap, and she could have stayed in there forever. But she had a debt to repay.

"Those clothes look great on you," said Liu, as Qi Qi came into the shop. Liu motioned to her to come behind the counter where she was standing at a table with two chairs. Qi Qi could smell food cooking and saw a teapot with steam coming from its spout. "Help yourself," said Liu. There was a natural generosity about this woman, Qi Qi thought, that made her constant acts of kindness seem genuine. She sat at the table, poured tea for herself and for Liu.

She decided to be honest. "I can pay you for one more night, but then I don't have any more money." Liu didn't say anything, so Qi Qi continued. "I was brought to this country against my will. Kidnapped from my own home and put on a plane."

"Where is home?" asked Liu.

Again, Qi Qi decided to tell the truth. "Wuhan. If you are afraid and want me to leave, I understand."

"This virus started in Wuhan, didn't it?"

"Yes, it did," said Qi Qi.

"I saw something in a Chinese newspaper here, and I read something online," said Liu. "A woman from Wuhan said she started the virus by selling a diseased bat to the wet market."

Qi Qi was wordstruck.

"I don't think any American newspapers or websites believed her, or at least they didn't write about it. But I saw it on YouTube before it was taken down."

"It was taken down?"

"Yeah. YouTube is owned by Google, and they took it down. Google's afraid of China. The only newspaper that believes it's true is the Chinese language paper I read. They're looking for that woman, to do a follow up, but she's disappeared."

And now Qi Qi Dieh understood what *Xingyun de jingshen*—lucky spirits - had caused her to be put on that plane, and how she had chosen that particular taxi, and why she had come to Liu's shop to ask for shelter.

"I am that woman," she told Liu softly.

# Chapter 33
## Go West, Young Man

Life without a cell phone was probably what the Wild West without a revolver felt like, Henry thought.

Standing outside JFK, with forty dollars, a snarky note from Fang, a Chinese passport and nothing else, Henry's first thought was to call his father, see how his Mother was doing, and tell them he was on the way home.

Just try doing that without a cell, without a credit card, without an identity.

It had taken five tries at three convenience stores and newsstands inside the terminal building to get his twenty changed. Finally, he bought a New York *Times* for three bucks—the price had gone up since he left for China—and then he searched in vain for a public telephone. He had to walk out of the International Arrivals terminal down to Terminal A where he was told there was a public phone. When he got there, he saw an "out of order" sign hanging across it. Frustrated beyond reason, he kicked the wall under the phone, which brought a middle-aged, portly, gray-haired Port Authority cop, wearing a Chinese-made blue mask, hustling over.

"Those walls are meant to keep the rain out. Kicking them makes holes. What's up, bud?"

"I need to make a phone call."

"Don't you have a cell? I thought everyone your age had at least two."

"I just got off a plane. I don't have a cell."

"You can probably buy one in the electronics store."

"Where's that?"

"That'd be in the International Arrivals building. It's over..."

"I know where it is. I just came from there."

"Why didn't you buy a phone there?"

Henry took a deep breath. "Would you have a phone I can borrow? It's just to make a call to New Jersey."

"Can I see some ID?"

This, Henry could tell, was not going to go well. "If I show you some ID, will you lend me your phone for two minutes?"

"Show me your ID, please, sir." The cop's tone said there was no room for negotiation.

Henry handed over the passport. "Is this a joke?" the cop asked.

"No joke."

The cop took a second, said, "Not wishing to sound racist, which I know you probably think all cops are, but you're not Chinese."

"Right. And I don't think that."

"Well, that would make you different."

"Different enough that you'd lend me a phone?"

"You're gonna have to explain this passport, you know."

"Fair deal. Please, officer, lend me a phone."

"Here you go. Don't take off with it."

"Last thing on my mind."

The home phone rang. Unanswered. His father's cell rang. No pickup. He tried to remember his Mother's cell, couldn't. Neighbor? He didn't know any of their phone numbers either. And this is progress? he asked himself.

"You're wearing out my buttons," said the cop, but not unpleasantly.

Henry was dog-tired. He was scared shitless. And he was desperate. He looked right in the cop's eyes as he handed back the phone. "Officer, if I tell you the honest truth about why I have a Chinese passport and no other ID, would you consider giving me a ride to New Jersey?"

The cop looked at him different now. "I think you're in trouble, aren't you, son? Why don't you tell me about it."

"Look, officer, I'm in..."

"Tell me about it on the way to Jersey."

At Henry's direction, they were pulling off Route 17 when the cop, whose name was Gerrity, looked away from the road and at Henry, and said, "You know, Henry, that story is so fucked up, I think you might be telling me the truth."

"I am telling the truth," said Henry. "And I'm really worried about my Mom."

"Of course you are," said Gerrity. "I gotta be honest with you, though. I'm gonna have to report this to my bosses."

"But I haven't done anything illegal."

"Well, you entered the country on a passport that's clearly not yours."

"They have my American passport in Wuhan, or somewhere."

"You make me nervous when you say Wuhan, Henry. Isn't that where this virus shit started?"

"It might be. I don't think the science is settled on it." And he realized he was using language that he himself had come up with to fend off the suggestion that China was somehow responsible for corona. He was telling a small truth to hide a big lie.

Home looked very much like it always did. Maybe smaller than Henry remembered, then he also remembered that all things are smaller than your memory makes them. Did that make sense?

"Look, Henry," said Gerrity. "I'm probably not doing myself or my career any favors. Go on into your house. See what's going on. I'll wait here. But don't run."

"I'm not gonna run. I'm just looking for my Mother."

Gerrity grimaced. "I can tell that, kid."

The house was empty. He knew as soon as he walked in. He went room to room but stopped expecting someone to come hug him by the time he went upstairs. As far as he could tell, his bedroom had remained untouched. The stack of books about AI looked like comics to him now. He had learned so much, so why did he feel like he knew less than before? Where was Rav and what was she thinking? What had Hui told Xi's hologram to explain the American youth's sudden absence? And what was it with Fang?

And he felt worse as he remembered he was here to find his Mother, with a good-hearted cop waiting outside for him, maybe to further help him, maybe to arrest him. He went back outside, leaned into the open window of Gerrity's car, said, "I'm going next door to see if anyone knows anything."

"Story of my life," said Gerrity. "Remember ..."

"I won't," said Henry.

No one answered the doorbell. Typical. No one knew anything about their neighbors anymore. Sometimes, not even their names.

He went back to Gerrity. "One last favor, officer."

"In for a dime ... or in your case, I guess, a yuan..."

"Take me to the hospital, please."

Emergency rooms can be hectic or they can be, appropriately, deathly quiet. This hospital, the one where Henry had been born, had split the baby, so to speak. One entrance said, "Suspected Covid Entrance." The one he entered, with Gerrity watching from his car, said, "non-Covid Entrance." It was like the Deep South before Rosa Parks, Henry thought. Had no one else caught on to this latter-day segregation? Then Henry remembered he was the one asking for favors, so maybe he should just shut up.

He went in the non-Covid Entrance. There were five people in front of him, waiting the check in. The long flight, the tension, the worry, the ignorance of what was going on, were all catching up with him. He sat down in a chair to wait.

"Sir," said an orderly in a black smock, wearing, of course, a blue Chinese-made mask, "you can't sit until you've checked in."

"I'm waiting to check in. Well, not check in. Just get some information."

"You can't sit while you're waiting for information."

"Why not? I've been awake a long time."

"Because we get vagrants coming in and camping out here."

"I'm not a vagrant. My family lives here."

"Sir, if you don't get out of that chair, I'll have to call the police."

"I can save you some time. There's a cop out there waiting for me."

"I'm sorry, sir. You're going to have to leave."

Henry got up, walked out, waved to Gerrity that he was going to try the Covid entrance. The cop nodded the way his Father had, when they used to communicate through their car's windshield.

The air smelled different in the Covid waiting room. Smelled of disinfectant, recycled air, and ... and, Henry wasn't sure, but thought it smelled a little bit like bat soup. There were two people behind blue Chinese masks, which were behind computers, which were behind Plexiglas.

"Sir," said a metallic voice as soon as he approached them. "You have to wear a mask."

"I don't have one."

"Wait there." And a second later, a guy in a white hazmat suit came through an automatically opening door, extending a ... you know.

Henry put it on. "I need to ask a..."

"You have to wait for your number to be called," said the woman behind the Plexiglas.

"But there's no one ahead of me."

"Please wait."

"For what?"

"To be called."

"Called for what?"

"All right. It's your turn now. Please come forward."

Hospital or loony bin, Henry wasn't sure. This wouldn't happen in... maybe it would. He was confusing China and New Jersey now. Tried to escape from this dreamscape. He gave the masked lady his name, his Mother's name, and the date when he thought she might have been admitted.

She was a great typist. "Your Mother was admitted two weeks ago. Her symptoms were severe. She was listed in critical condition."

Was, was, was. What's was and why was it was?

"You keep using the past tense."

"Your Mother is no longer with us."

So that was how it was. Henry had seen the TV shows so he knew how to react. "Do you mean my Mother is...."

"She needed to be put on a ventilator and we don't have enough here to take care of everyone. Your Mother was transferred to another hospital."

"Where?"

"The University of Pittsburgh Medical Center. It's one of the best."

"You need to sleep, Henry," said Gerrity as he drove him home.

"I need to fly to Pittsburgh," said Henry.

"You can't get on a plane. You have no ID."

"I have a passport," said Henry, realizing he sounded churlish, or girlish, or something.

"Yeah, about that, Henry..."

"What?"

"I gotta take that passport. It's evidence."

"Evidence of what? For what?"

"Well, it could be evidence to be used against you."

"But I haven't done anything wrong."

"You entered the country posing as a Chinese."

"No. Just with a Chinese passport."

Gerrity looked over. "Henry, I've kinda gotten to like you. And I feel lousy about your Mom. But I'm taking the passport. There's something fishy about this whole thing."

"But I'll have no means to identify myself."

"Which means you ain't going nowhere."

"But that's not fair!" said Henry, immediately wishing he hadn't. Remembering how Rav had taunted him the last time he said those stupid words from his childhood.

"Maybe not," said Gerrity. "But it's how the system works these days."

Democracy with American characteristics.

Henry promised to stay in his house until Gerrity or someone got back to him. He knew he needed to sleep. His mind was taking a vacation. He was confusing Wuhan and New Jersey way too often.

"Thank you for everything," he said to Gerrity.

"Sit tight," said the cop. "I'll be back soon." Jerry went inside.

He knew he had to sleep, period. He took a long-overdue shower, checked the fridge. Nada. His father must have cleaned it out when he realized he'd be going to Pittsburgh with Henry's Mom for who knew how long. A ventilator. From what he'd seen, most people only came off ventilators when they no longer had any need to breathe.

He didn't want to go to his bedroom. It would remind him of too many things. But at least he could use the computer up there. He went upstairs, turned it on, remembered his password, looked at the months and months of emails that had stacked up since he left his home (was this home, or was Wuhan?), didn't care about any of them, until he saw the most recent one, the only one that mattered, written from her Army email address so everyone could see it.

"Come back."

Oh, Rav.

He put his head on his chest and was seconds from drifting off when the doorbell rang. Who would know he was here or want to see him? And, in the next second, wondered if she had followed him, found out where he lived, and come to reclaim him.

Or had they sent someone else to bring him back?

He went to the front door, stood to the side of it, as he had seen gunmen do in movies, but never understood, since if you were standing to the side of a closed door, you couldn't look through the peephole.

Fuck them, if they wanted him, let them come take him. At least he'd see her as they led him off to jail.

He opened the door.

"Guy your age needs to eat," said Gerrity, hefting two brown paper grocery bags, and not wearing a mask.

Henry stood aside. "I don't have any money." He had forgotten about the forty dollars, minus the New York *Times* purchase.

"I'll put it on your bill. You can work it off in the laundry room of whatever maximum security prison they throw you in."

Henry said nothing.

"Just kidding. I called a buddy on the force and asked what they could charge you with. He said, if you cooperate in the investigation, you'd probably get off with a warning. Just don't run."

"I won't run."

"Take care. Not all us cops are racist assholes, Henry."

"Why do you keep saying that?"

"Because someone accused of being one just before I ran into you at JFK."

"I never said you were."

"Spread the word."

He slept for four hours, woke up totally confused about where he was. And ravenous. No, not that word, it reminded him ...

Really hungry, then. Gerrity had bought milk, bread, salami, sliced ham, pickles, fresh tomatoes, lettuce, a six-pack of Bud.

Who would call him racist?

Spread the word.

He ate, made some extra sandwiches, showered again, shook himself awake. He went on a snipe hunt through the house. Cracked the safe behind his father's desk, found a valid credit card in his Dad's name, an out-of-date driver's license in which his father looked very different, about a hundred dollars in cash, and the keys to the second car, sitting in the garage.

Pittsburgh was six hours, and with luck, only one fill-up away.

"Come back," Rav had written. At least he hoped it was Rav.

The Pennsylvania Turnpike is designed to entice drivers to commit suicide. It stretches on and on, like a liar's promise (and isn't that what he was, Henry thought?) with turnoffs to places like Intercourse, Kunkleville, Bunkleville and Hunkleville (Uncle Bill apparently was missing,) Bethlehem (savior not included), and other exotic locations. The turnpike long ago gave up any pretensions of being an adequate motorway, settling instead for being bitch-kitty challenge to anyone who needed to get somewhere quickly.

Because he would not survive a traffic stop, Henry stayed below the speed limit, but not so far below as to draw attention. It was the first time he had driven in half a year, and he was rusty. He had stopped at one of the Fil-Er-Up fuel spas and in addition to gasoline, had used his Father's credit card to purchase a burner phone. With considerable effort, he had downloaded Google Maps, knowing that in doing so, he was letting everyone in Cyberspace know where he was. Would Gerrity be tracking him? Would Fang? Would Zhuang?

Would Rav?

Coming up on Pittsburgh from the East you see first the detritus of what it once was. Its westward looking future could not be glimpsed without going through the downtown (pronounced locally as 'dan-tan') and that, Google had instructed him not to do.

The University of Pittsburgh Medical Center was the city's largest employer, having long ago taken the role of the steel mills that had bequeathed the nickname "Smoky City." It operated, at last count thirty-two hospitals in Pittsburgh and the surrounding area. It had announced its intention to be the supreme dispenser of health care by refusing to accept Blue Cross/Blue Shield as methods of payment. Instead, it introduced Borizon Healthcare, which was owned, conveniently, by UPMC. Numerous lawsuits were still underway, but patients had knuckled under on the tenuous theory that dying was worse than being a Borizon customer.

While not speeding, Henry had disregarded the modern-day no-no of typing while driving and had come up with the information that his Mother was a patient at, incongruously, Pittsburgh Children's Hospital. He pulled into the parking lot closest to its main entrance, took the ticket spat out from a yellow machine, and began to move forward when a uniformed guard stopped him.

"Sorry, sir, I need some identification."

"What?"

"Your ID, sir. For identification."

Henry forced himself not to reply to this idiocy. Aware of the high chance he would be arrested, he showed his father's out-of-date driver's license with his thumb over the picture.

The guard hardly glanced at it. "Thank you, sir. Have a nice day."

He was going into a hospital. What were the odds he was going to have a nice day? But he remembered that this was part of the new American Catechism. It didn't matter if what you said was ridiculous. It only mattered that you said it.

Unlike the hospital in New Jersey, the reception area of Children's Hospital was uncrowded and staffed by three masked employees. Henry too had put on a Chinese blue mask for this medical gavotte. He gave his Mother's name, asked where she could be found. C-Wing, ICU was the response. And where is that, please? To the right, take the elevator up to the fourth floor, ask at reception.

Fourth floor reception was similarly uncrowded. Name, where, how do I get there?

"You don't."

"Sorry?"

"The patient is not allowed visitors."

"Why?"

"She's a Covid patient."

"I know."

"She might be contagious."

"I'll take that risk."

"We can't allow that. If you'd like to sit and wait, there's a Family Room in the other direction, down the hall. And we'll let Staff know your Mother has another visitor."

"Another visitor?"

"Her life companion."

"You mean my father? Her husband?"

"We don't use patriarchal terms like that. They could be upsetting."

"Where is my father, please?"

"The patient's life companion was last seen in the Family Room."

If his father no longer looked like the picture on the driver's license Henry had purloined, he looked even less now than how he had looked when they had said good-bye. His head was bowed, forehead resting on palm.

"Dad?" He hadn't known what to expect at this reunion. Tears, hugs, curses, where've you beens, why didn't you call. His father looked up, nodded a few times, said, "hi," and lowered his head again.

"I got here as soon as I could."

His father nodded without removing his head from his hand.

"Are you Henry?" said a voice from the door.

It was a young guy, in a medical smock, wearing a Chinese mask, so of course, his features were obscured. He came forward to shake hands.

"Yes, I'm Henry."

"I've heard a lot about you, man. My name's Jerry. I'm a tech supervisor here. We're gonna take good care of your Mom."

"Thank you."

"No, I really mean it. I'm a specialist, well, expert, I guess, in AI. That stands for ..."

"I know."

"Cool. Well then, you know that with AI we can do a lot more detailed analysis of your Mom's condition."

"You mean you can try to guess what might happen next."

Jerry looked at Henry with widened eyes over his mask. "Sounds like you know your way around the topic."

Henry nodded.

"Well, she's probably gonna get through this."

"Really?

"Yep. That's what all the trend models say. Trust me. I'm an expert."

# Chapter 34
## And Now, Our Very Special Guest

If Luisa's path to fame was crooked and required her to die, Qi Qi's was more like a nebula exploding from the very center of the solar system and required her to keep talking. Once Liu went back and looked at the few undeleted Internet articles about the woman who claimed to have started the Coronavirus that hadn't yet been deleted, she decided this Qi Qi was the Qi Qi in the articles, and Googled her picture, which for some reason had not been deleted in deference to China. This was, indeed, Qi Qi Dieh. Liu thanked her *Xingyun de jingshen*, her Lucky Spirits.

There are nearly 900,000 Chinese and Chinese descendants in New York, so it was little surprise that the metropolitan area had eight Chinese language newspapers. Like the American news media, they covered the world, and New York from very different perspectives. China Daily was a Party-backed newspaper and website, headquartered in Times Square, that published in Mandarin, Cantonese, and most importantly, English. Its content was translated in what might best be described as a sleek manner. Harsh statements from Chinese officials in the Mandarin and Cantonese editions became philosophical statements in English.

The New China *Times* had long tried to emulate the U.S. journalism model, an increasingly frustrating and perilous path as American journalists converted themselves from reporters of fact to fonts of political and social justice warriors, renderers of righteousness. Journalists of Chinese descent who had once held American news media outlets in high esteem began to suspect that while they, the Chinese, were trying to emulate neutral American news, the U.S. news industry was following the pattern set by the Chinese Communist Party. Namely, only one Party has the truth. Be guided by and repeat what it says.

Thrown into this mix was the Epoch *Times*, which also published in Chinese and English. It was founded and largely funded by the Falun Gong, a religious branch group that was devoted to the overthrow of the Communist Party of China and the elevation of the group's leader, a kind of cross between Jesus, the Dalai Lama and Charles Manson. In New York, Falun Gong was best known for organizing and leading yoga classes in Central Park, and handing out free copies of the Epoch Times near the Port Authority bus terminal. In China, its members were hunted down by PLA squads, swept off the streets and sent, without trial, to re-education camps that had once been the exclusive preserve of Catholic priests. Because of its extreme right-wing (in American terms) slant, the Epoch *Times* had drawn the attention and interest of American conservatives, including the Trump Administration, which treated it with a courtesy well out of keeping with its influence.

Liu read and believed the Epoch *Times*. Its news fit her beliefs, and that after all, was what a free news media was all about. She had seen a brief item about Qi Qi Dieh on its website months ago, and largely forgotten about it. Now, with the real item sitting in front of her, drinking her tea, Liu began hallucinating about fame and fortune. And, of course, getting the truth out there, too.

It took three calls to the newspaper's main phone line, the first two resulting in being hung up on.

"Would you like to interview the woman from Wuhan who says she started the coronavirus with a dead bat?"

"Who is this, please?"

"An interested citizen."

"Where is this woman?"

"She's sitting a meter away from me, drinking tea."

"A meter away is too close. What is her name?"

"Qi Qi Dieh."

"Bring her to our office. West 29th Street. Ask for me. My name is Yu-Kin Bang."

Liu was in no hurry. She had a celebrity in her grip, and she wasn't going to give her up. Fate had brought Qi Qi Dieh into her noodle shop. Fate would take them both where they were meant to be.

Qi Qi listened in disbelief as Liu told her that she could stay in the room upstairs for free, for as long as she wanted. Food was on the house. All she had to do was rehearse, with Liu, the story she had already tried to tell and been arrested for.

But no one believed me in China, said Qi Qi.

They'll believe you here, Liu assured her.

How will they check my story to see that I'm telling the truth?

They don't have to.

They don't need to know I'm telling the truth?

No.

Why?

Because what you're saying is what they want to believe.

But that sounds like China. This is America, said Qi Qi.

Yes, said Liu. This is America.

The next day, after another phone call from Liu to arrange a time, they took the subway to West 28th Street, walked a block and a half, and rang a doorbell that told them the Epoch *Times* was located on the second floor of the building. Buzzed inside they saw a dingy staircase and smelled something reminiscent of the kitchen of Liu's shop.

"Pork," said Liu, confidently.

Bat, thought Qi Qi, but only to herself.

Like Qi Qi, like Liu, Yu-Kin Bang had both expanded and shriveled with the passing of time. Early fifties, perhaps, she worked to produce a smile, shook hands with reluctance, and sat her guests in straight back chairs without an offer of refreshment.

"So, you claim to be the bat lady?" said Yu-Kin.

"Yes."

"Why should I believe you?"

"I don't know," said Qi Qi, feeling as if she belonged anywhere but here.

"You'll believe her when she tells you what she did, what she's seen, what's been done to her, and why she's here," said Liu, who had mastered the American art of instant outrage in her time in New York.

"Ok," said Yu-Kin. "Tell me."

It took an hour. Qi Qi, it turned out, was a fine storyteller. She remembered the decision to sell the dead bat despite its smell. Remembered Gramps and how she had bartered with him, adding that he had probably given her a break because he had liked her bottom. Remembered that he had died from the soup he made from her bat. Remembered that her ex-husband, Fang, a Party official, had come to her flat and stolen money from her tea tin. Remembered being dragged from her home by PLA men in spacesuits and hauled to Wuhan No 17 Long-Term Health Care Unit, which no matter its official name, was an insane asylum. Remembered her release and return, like some kind of fish that had been hooked, but was too small and insignificant to keep. Remembered being abducted a second time, this time by her ex-husband, shoved into a government car, taken to a military airport, then Shanghai Airport, then escaping from someone at JFK sent to intercept her.

Yu-Kin Bang had been taking notes for the first half of the tale. Now she just stared at Qi Qi. When she finished, Yu-Kin said, somewhat softly, "Would you like tea?"

It took more tellings, this time with spellings, and an I-Phone camera recording the whole thing the third time around. Despite the tea, which kept on coming, and the water, which she asked for, Qi Qi felt drained, dry, as if the essence of her life was now in a cell phone's memory. Liu had stayed with her the whole time, tending to her needs. Bathroom, tissues, no more tea, thank you. Doesn't matter if there's no ice in the water, she's not used to that anyway. Finally, no one had anything more to say to anyone else.

"It will take me a day or two to write this story," said Yu-Kin. "And we'll edit the video footage for use on the website. Come back tomorrow to sign a document swearing that what you say is true and giving us permission to use your words and your image on video."

"How much?" said Liu.

"The story will probably be a couple thousand words," said Yu-Kin.

"I mean, how much are you going to pay for it?"

Yu-Kin stared at her. "We are professional journalists. We don't pay for news."

"You people are Falun Gong. You have more money than Trump."

"We..." Yu-Kin began.

"Let's go, Qi Qi," said Liu.

"Five hundred."

"Five thousand. Cash. When we come back tomorrow. Unless we get a better offer."

The money was ready, in cash, the next day. Yu-Kin Bang was nowhere to be seen. Instead, a boy who called himself an intern delivered the envelope. Qi Qi signed a statement swearing that her story was true. They had an expensive late lunch, or early dinner, whichever, at the first non-Chinese restaurant Qi Qi had ever entered.

She loved America.

This is how the news media in America works now. When one outlet gets an important story, it sends around an advance draft to like-minded news organizations. CNN for instance, sends its exclusives to the New York *Times*, Washington *Post*, Politico, Vice News, CBS, NBC, ABC, PBS and finally, MSNBC.

Conservative media outlets, like Epoch *Times*, have fewer options.

The imbalance has been narrowed slightly since other would-be media moguls realized that Fox News had found a winning formula, and that not all Americans wanted to be fed a steady diet of news about how terrible America is. One of the few right-of-center websites of influence was the Washington *Free Beacon*. One of its writers saw the story in the Epoch *Times*, realized the implications, and wrote a quick rip-off of the exclusive that very evening.

The news desk at Fox News does not monitor the Epoch *Times*. Not because Fox disagreed with its politics, but because the Chinese paper wrote so much about ... China. It *does* monitor the Washington *Free Beacon* website. So when a junior desk staffer saw the story about the origin of the coronavirus, she passed it along to an editor. The editor, knowing better than to do anything without permission of an executive, sent an email to a vice president, who looked at its content, and called a booker for one of the prime-time shows, whose hosts knew they were on the air and making millions of dollars for giving their opinions, not the news.

Yu-Kin Bang took the call from the Fox booker and passed along Liu's cell phone number. The call to Liu was not picked up because Liu was busy filling a take-away an order for General Tso's chicken and a side of sweet and sour soup. When she retrieved the voice-mail message and heard it was from Fox News, she knew there was a place where the *Xingyun de jingshen*, the Lucky Spirits, lived. It was somewhere over to the right.

"No, she doesn't speak English," said Liu, whose English was serviceable at best.

"We'll provide a translator."

"She doesn't have proper clothes to go on TV."

"We'll buy her a new wardrobe."

"She looks old under harsh light."

"We have a great makeup department. She can keep anything they use on her."

"It's a long way to midtown from here."

"A limo will pick her up."

"How much will you pay us?"

"Madam, we are a professional news organization. We don't pay for news!"

"Then we'll go somewhere else."

"Well, if she comes to Fox, and if she gets ratings, we can arrange for President Trump to call her and thank her for telling her story."

"What time should we be there?"

Going into the Fox News Building on the Avenue of the Americas is like entering an oxygen chamber. Colors are enhanced. Lights are brighter. Everyone's clothing is snazzier. Everyone who appears on the screen that is. Behind the cameras, talented professionals—directors, producers, lighting engineers, sound technicians, wear jeans, sweatshirts, and could easily be mistaken for the flock of fans outside the building, who brave whatever weather New York is having for a chance to see their on-air heroes, or maybe, just maybe, if the outside cameras are turned on, to see themselves on Fox News.

Liu and Qi Qi were escorted past these lesser beings by a young woman in the most glamorous-looking outfit Qi Qi had never seen. She had a sequin blouse, tight-fitting emerald green trousers, silver Manolo Blahnik pumps. Her blonde hair was in a French twirl. Qi Qi imagined she must be a movie star. In fact, she was a greeter, and her job was to make guests feel welcome and to let them know how fortunate they were to be here. On some rare occasions, things fell through the cracks.

"We're very happy to have you here," said the greeter to Qi Qi, who nodded at everything she heard but did not understand. "Just get your ID out and we'll get you a visitor's tag.

"Take out your passport," Liu hissed behind her.

"What's this?" said a uniformed guard at the clear-glass kiosk where a turnstile admitted visitors with proper accreditation.

"A passport," said Liu. Qi Qi nodded.

"What kind?"

"Chinese, of course."

"That so? Well, I don't understand a single word here."

"It's okay," said the greeter. She's going to be on Don's show in fifteen minutes."

"Well, maybe Don ought to come out and sign her in. She ain't going in with this."

The greeter dropped the candy-cane girl act. "If Don has to come out to sign her in, he'll sign you out at the same time."

The guard thought about that. "Go ahead."

"You have a nice evening now," said the greeter, the way a chaplain might speak to a condemned prisoner stretched out on the gurney.

No interview conducted through a translator can qualify as great TV. It was, however, as the industry says, compelling. Qi Qi, who had been interrogated in an insane asylum, was less nervous than Liu, who at the last moment was told to come onto the stage and sit quietly for the segment. The host of the show, who had become an icon of Trump Nation for his steadfast support of the President, wanted someone with him who could speak English, to kill time if a translation fell flat, or if he didn't get the answers he wanted from this frumpy Chinese lady.

He need not have worried. Qi Qi repeated her story flawlessly. Bat, market, Gramps, soup, sickness, lousy ex, brutal space-suited men, loony bin, hassle after her social media heresy, lousy ex, trip to the airport, kind *gweilo* next to her on the plane, escape from JFK, lousy ex, kindness of her new friend, Liu. It was then, when she heard her name, that Liu broke the rules and said, "Yes, and my shop Ben Jing Noodles, is on the corner of Canal and Mulberry."

"Nice plug," laughed Don, who by this point knew he had a winning segment that would thrill the audience he most cared about—Donald Trump.

"So, remember, folks," Don concluded, "if you're looking to thank a hero, look no further than this lady, Qi Qi, sounds just like Elton John's old sidekick. She stared down the Chinese army, Xi Jinping, and the entire Communist Chinese apparatus of terror and persecution. They caused the virus, and she's proof.

"And, remember, don't order the bat soup. Goodnight, everyone."

Deafening theme music for ten seconds then the silence of the grave. "We're done," said Don. "Thanks for coming by." He unclipped his mike and left the stage. From some unknown speaker nestled in the ceiling, or the stars, a disembodied voice said, "Nice job, Don. Don? The other Don's on the phone for you."

Yes, it's a nanosecond world now, but television hasn't quiet caught up to warp speed. Qi and Liu were chauffeured back to Chinatown. Qi Qi took off the lovely outfit that had been purchased for her, a black DKNY suit with pink blouse by Elie Tehari, debated about leaving her makeup on, but then washed off the professional powders and lotions that had been applied to her face, arms, hands and legs ("they look at everything," the makeup girl had said, giggling) and collapsed into the bed that she had come to regard as hers, now that she had somehow paid back part of her debt to Liu. Her sleep was troubled. She saw bright lights, powder puffs attacking her face, loud music, a microphone eating through the inside of her ear, trying to reach her brain, a bat flying free, something she had never seen since the bats she knew were either caged or dead.

TV news no longer cares about reality. It cares about ratings. Not what was said or learned, but how many people were watching. Was the segment the highest rated of the show? Were there any people between 25 and 54 watching? Did any other network have as many viewers during the segment where this dumpy Chinese lady was on?

When the ratings came in, about 4 pm the next day, it was clear that the segment with Qi Qi Dieh was the most watched on cable news that evening. In fact, that whole day. People began crowding around Liu's noodle shop. Bookers, mostly, from Fox and other networks, wanting Qi Qi to come on their shows. But not just bookers. Book agents, offering six figures for her to tell her story, a kid from the New York *Times* who said he was an intern, and his editor would like to talk to the Chinawoman (he later apologized).

Someone claiming to be from the Chinese Embassy, who said they had been looking for citizen Qi, had tried to welcome her to the country at JFK but had been unable "to make contact" there. Liu told them to go away.

A particularly pushy, overweight woman with tortoise shell glasses and frizzed black and gray hair kept repeating the letters "C-N-N" as though it were a religious rite and demanding to see Kike, as she pronounced it. A young man who said he was from Fox extended an envelope to Liu and asked her to give it to her guest.

"She doesn't speak English," said Liu, clearly out of her depth with the throng crowding her shop, but not buying anything.

"It's in Chinese," said the young man, as though that was the answer to everything.

Liu read the note before giving it to Qi Qi. "It's from their morning show. They want you to be on tomorrow. It's the show that everyone watches. They want to talk to you first. It's called a pre-interview?"

"Why?"

"They ask you questions about your life, about your job, your ambitions. Stuff to make you seem more human. It's called human interest."

"There seem to be a lot of humans downstairs who are interested in me."

"I think you ought to go on CNN," said Liu. "They used to be the only cable news channel. And the most important. Not so much anymore, since Fox came along. But still big."

"Okay," said Qi Qi. "Can we ride in a big black car again?"

The studio was not as big as Don's, but it was just as brightly lit. Qi Qi wore the same outfit she had worn on Don's show, her options being limited. She hadn't asked Liu what she'd done with the money from the Epoch *Times*, and Liu hadn't offered to tell her.

The greeter was a stern looking young man in a blue blazer, white shirt and tie. "This way," was the essence of the small talk. The makeup artist didn't say a word to her. The stagehand who put the microphone around her neck and the earbud in her ear was efficient but hardly gentle. Qi Qi thought he made a noise like 'unt' but didn't understand it.

The host of the show was a woman with red hair cut into a helmet that might have been worn during the Ming Dynasty. Her makeup made her look fierce. She wore a royal blue wool suit and a pale pink blouse. She looked at Qi Qi directly for the first time just before the segment began.

"Hope you're ready for this."

Music. Bright lights. The host, her words translated into Qi Qi's ear, said, "Tonight we have a woman who claims to have come from China with nearly unbelievable claims that she actually started the coronavirus which has so far claimed nearly two million lives. She made her claims a few months ago, in China, before experts there determined that she was mentally ill. She appeared to overcome her disability after spending time at one of China's mental health facilities. Nonetheless, she decided to turn her back on her homeland and come here, where she is once again repeating her bizarre claims. Her name is Qi Qi Dieh, which people of my age may remember was the name of Elton John's old musical sidekick. There's not much else to say. Let's see what she can tell us."

"Ms. Dieh, welcome to CNN."

"Thank you." The translator seemed to take his time, and the pause between question and answer seemed much longer than on Fox.

"Now you claim you once worked in a laboratory in Wuhan."

"Not claim. I did."

"Can you prove it?"

"I imagine my name is listed somewhere."

"So you can't prove it?"

"Right now, right here? No."

"So, we really don't know who you are."

"My name is Qi Qi Dieh. From Wuhan."

"Yes. Now your claim is that you started the virus that we now know as the coronavirus. Is that what you expect us to believe?"

"It's true."

"And you say it started when you stole a bat from somewhere and sold it at a market."

"A bat from the Virology Lab, yes."

"Yet experts, Chinese and well as American experts, have told us that the virus was not started at that lab, but was caused by animal to human contamination."

"Yes, the animal was the bat I sold."

The host breathed so deeply Qi Qi thought her makeup would crack. "Let's just for a moment, believe your story. What happened to the bat?"

"The man I sold it to made it into soup."

"Bat soup? How many viewers of this show do you think would eat bat soup?"

"Sorry?"

"Why not blame Campbell's Tomato Soup? It sounds easier to believe."

"No. It was bat soup."

"Well, I can see why, after you made these fantastic claims, you were declared mentally ill. Can't you?"

"No."

"So, you are telling us to ignore the renowned experts— EXPERTS, I said—from Chinese and American science, and to instead believe you. You, a middle-aged woman with no scientific background."

"I have a degree in virology."

"Are you an expert?"

"No."

"Well, there we go. Tell me, who bought you the clothes you are wearing right now?"

"I don't know."

"But it wasn't you who bought them."

"No. Someone from another TV company."

"And was that TV company by any chance named Fox News?"

"I think, yes."

"Well, here's what I think, Quickie, or whatever your name really is. I think you're a dupe for a Trump lackey organization."

"Sorry, don't understand."

"I'll bet you're sorry. I'm sorry too. We'll be back right after these announcements."

The lights went down. The host wouldn't look at her. "Get her out of here," she growled.

The next day, the New York *Times* had a story about Qi Qi's interview, but only the interview on CNN. It was written by their science expert, Gretchen Nu-Mi.

"Ms. Qi's stuttering evasion of simple questions, the kind of questions any responsible journalist would pose, blasts a hole through her batty—and yes, that's a pun—story about starting the coronavirus. It's hard to imagine anyone would believe her, even Trump's Caped Crusaders—yes, that's another bat pun—at Fox."

She had hardly slept the night before. And this morning, even before she had tea, she was intercepted in the noodle shop by a woman who spoke Chinese and offered to be her publicity agent.

"You have to do the morning show on Fox," said Liu.

"I don't want to," said Qi Qi.

"You have to."

"Why? That was humiliating."

"Don't worry, they'll be nice to you at Fox."

"Why are they nice and the other people not?"

"Because Fox loves Trump. CNN hates him."

"What does my story have to do with Trump?"

"Qi Qi, in this country, *everything* has to do with Trump."

Two days later, the three hosts of the morning show on Fox were beaming.

"And now, our very special guest. A very brave woman from China, who has solved a mystery befuddling the entire world for more than a year. How did the awful virus, which we call the Wuhan virus but everyone else calls the coronavirus... how did it start? Well, here with the answer, is that special guest, Ms. Qi Qi Dieh."

They had told her she had to walk from behind the curtains to the raised couch where the hosts were sitting, like guests at a cocktail party, and have her microphone hooked up while the audience watched. At least she was wearing different clothes, a yellow pants suit, with purple blouse and red Christian Louboutin pumps, which they'd given her when she arrived at 4:40 a.m. The show started at six, but some executives had said they wanted to meet her first. Most of them just wanted their picture taken with her, but one, an older man accompanied by the same translator who would talk into her ear while she was on the set, said, "We can probably get you a movie deal." Liu had accompanied her, and said, as though she'd been doing this for years, "We'll think about it and get back to you."

"Don't take too long," said the executive. "Fame has a funny way of dying out."

She knew this interview would be friendly. And familiar. The lab. The bat. The market. Gramps. Soup. Illness. Bad ex. Bad police. Plane. JFK.

"And so, at last, you're free in this wonderful country. Right?"

She was supposed to agree but didn't get the chance.

"Qi Qi, excuse me," said one of the hosts, his hand over his ear. "You're not going to believe this, but there's someone on the phone who would like to welcome you to the United States. It's the president, Donald Trump."

And the voice, recognizable even though the language barrier. "Hey, Qi Qi, it's President Trump. Welcome to America. You're a really brave girl, and I just wanted to thank you. I did everything I could to make this happen. I'm glad you're safe on American soil. Let me know if I can do anything else for you, ok?" The line went dead.

"Well, that was really something, wasn't it, Qi Qi? Not many newcomers get to talk to President Trump himself."

"No," Qi Qi said. "Thank you."

"Don't thank us yet, Qi Qi. We're not done surprising you," said the woman, as though she was about to present her with a puppy. "You told our staff when you talked to them that you know your name, Qi Qi Dieh, sounds the same as a singer named KiKi Dee, who used to sing with Elton John, right?"

"Yes, KiKi Dee. Great singer," said Qi Qi, confused at the change of topic.

"Well, to thank you for all that you've done, and for being our guest here today, we have a special surprise. All the way from Hollywood to greet you. KiKi Dee!"

And the curtain flew back, and a pasty-faced woman strutted out, arms held wide. She bounded across the stage, physically lifted Qi Qi off the sofa, and hugged her for no more than a second.

"Great to meet you," she said. Qi Qi couldn't understand her because the ear bud had been pulled out of her ear during the embrace. She smiled stupidly, nodded.

KiKi Dee handed Qi Qi Dieh something and said, "I hope you don't have one already." It was the same calendar Qi Qi had tried to order in China.

"And to top it off, Qi Qi," said one of the male hosts. "KiKi Dee has agreed to greet you by singing one of her hit songs, "Don't Go Breakin' My Heart."

The canned music ramped up, and KiKi Dee took a hand mike offered to her by the woman host. "Don't go breakin' my heart..." Qi Qi heard the words through the sound system on stage. But KiKi Dee was not singing. Her lips moved, but no sound came out.

"...ooh you put the spark to the flame.

I got your heart in my sights...."

"And we'll be back after these messages," said all three hosts together. The lights went out.

"Thank you for being on the show," said the greeter, a different one from the first time, but dressed almost identically. "We'll probably want you on again tomorrow, different show of course," she said, collapsing into giggles.

"Of course," said Liu. "Which way is the car?"

"It couldn't park right in front of our building because there's some kind of security alert out there," said the greeter. Just turn right out the door and go down to the corner of 47th Street. The driver has her name in the window."

"Thank you," said Liu.

"Thank you," said Qi Qi in English.

"You did great," said Liu. "You're going to be famous. You'll be in all the papers, on TV. The president called you! Try to get that through your head. It doesn't get any better than that. We have to turn right here. There's our car."

It was not her heart but her head in the automatic rifle's sights. One shot, almost muffled by the morning traffic on Sixth Avenue. Like Luisa, Qi Qi's forehead and a clump of her brains got to the ground before the rest of her. Liu was still talking before she realized part of her companion was ahead of her, the rest behind.

The mayor of New York reacted swiftly. "There is no doubt in my mind that this crime was committed by some white, right-wing extremist who hates Asians,' hizzoner said. "This is just the latest example of why we must make gun ownership illegal. Asian people are not the problem in America. White people are the problem."

# Chapter 35
## Black Lies Matter

If it looked like an expert, and talked like an expert, it must be … Jerry. He felt like a fool every time he put the goddam medical smock on and walked down the hospital hallway where real doctors, real medical people who really knew what they were doing, also claimed, although they had earned, the title expert. What was he? A paper pusher who'd learned a few new tricks, taken the 101-course in something he definitely didn't understand, and probably didn't trust, and puff! he became an expert in AI.

And it wasn't like this was a video game, or online poker, or even some theoretical idea he was horsing with. These were people's lives. People suffering from this miserable fucking disease, whatever it was, and wherever it came from. Well, he had pretty much made up his mind where it came from. But in these hallowed halls of science, you weren't supposed to say the word "China" unless it referred to your best table settings, or the country that had made all these great blue masks we have to wear, day in and day out.

He had to admit this job was a step up from squaring off sheets of paper for Seance. He missed Rutherford, and the companionship, camaraderie, fuck, it was friendship, except guys weren't supposed to get mushy about that kind of stuff. He and Ruth had had a couple of beers since Jerry moved to the hospital. Ruth wasn't sore about Jerry getting a break. "You're younger'n me, you can still learn new stuff, take a few chances. Shit, you might even get smart before you're done." So it was play it as she laid, keep moving, you always hoped forward, just not down.

The guy Henry, whose Mom was on a respirator, was all right, Jerry decided. A bit standoffish, maybe shy. But there was a pulse working under that hair. Jerry was really pleased to be able to tell Henry and his father that the Missus was gonna make it. Like he knew. But that was what the algorithm said, and these days, AI was God. So, when he read the printout, matched the outcome numbers against the age, race, expectations and the mortality rate, she was well in the survivors' field of probability.

Of course, probability wasn't certainty. Everyone knew that. Yet Jerry had learned that when you're talking to the family of someone connected to one of these damned breathing machines, all they wanted to hear was that their loved one was "likely" to survive. He'd learned to fudge it, to use "probable," "highly possible," "by all accounts," whatever weasel words he could think of. And then he watched the reaction to see if he'd said the right thing. They choked, they teared up, they hugged him, they clasped their hands and said, 'Thank you, God,' when what they should have been saying was 'Thank you, AI.' But AI was God. So, it was a wash.

The father had a heart of stone and Jerry didn't like him much. But you could never let that show. Everyone in this ward was going through a really tough patch, and all you could do was be grateful it wasn't someone you loved.

So, all in all, he liked where he was now. He had some money, he had a sense of purpose, even if it was, well, artificial. And he could do a brewski with Ruth now and then.

The sticky bit was Tran and the Defenders. He sure didn't want it known at the hospital that he was part of that group. This was the "can't we be ruled by science?" crowd, not the "give us back our country" crowd. The two wouldn't mix, that's for sure. And last time he looked, Tran wasn't paying his salary.

They'd talked, texted, and Jerry knew the Defenders had done one of their peaceful marches through downtown, that they'd been intercepted by a BLM counter-protest, that things, again, had not gone well for the Defenders. Not that there was any physical violence, but what diplomats liked to call "a full and frank exchange of views." The views, however, were not diplomatic.

Jerry was none too pleased when his phone chirped and he saw a text from Tran. "Call please. Urgent."

He was in the middle of talking to a family whose loved one wasn't going to make it, according to the AI scan. Those were tough, because although he could always say, 'the algorithm doesn't know how strong she is,' the algorithm knew *exactly* how strong she, or he was, the data they fed in was so precise and so complete as to limit the chance of a misdiagnosis to way below that of a real live physician. Some doctors had chafed at being outshone by a machine, no matter how sophisticated. Jerry looked at their self-satisfied faces and wanted to say, "Welcome to the 21$^{st}$ Century, assholes. You're not so special anymore."

But didn't.

He got away from the sobbing relatives as soon as he could.

"Hey buddy, what's up?"

"Sorry you couldn't make it to the party, Jerry."

"Working. I told you. So?"

"Earl has been arrested."

"What?"

"Someone from the BLM group says he laid hands on her. Called her a nigger."

"Earl wouldn't do that."

"Think that matters? Cops are talking about raising it to aggravated assault and calling it a hate crime. That's heavy time."

"But he's a former cop."

"That's *why* those pricks accused him. Cops ain't exactly getting a lot of Kwanza cards these days, you know."

"Did you see anything? Were you with him?"

"Jerry, he never left my side. He never got within twenty feet of the other guys. This is made-up. They saw an old white guy, someone recognized him from his days in blue, and they're going after him."

"Goddam it."

"Yeah, well," said Tran. "Too bad you couldn't be there so you could testify." There was something in the voice, if not reproach, regret.

"Are you testifying?"

"If they let me. They arrested me at the last one, remember? They let me go, but I've got a spot on my record. Me talking out might not do Earl much good."

"Yeah, you're right."

"But we got a surprise for that bitch. We found out where she lives, and we're going over there some night with torches and clubs and maybe a few legal guns, and do like BLM does, knock on the door at midnight, shout and holler, tell her we're going to live in that house someday, rattle her and her neighbors."

Jerry said nothing. He was on a cell phone. Cell phone conversations could be recorded. Tran was too smart to be saying this shit on a cell. What was going on?

"We'll talk, Tran." And disconnected.

The most important moments of our lives are often played out without thought, rehearsal or consideration. They just happen, and we, clay models of men and women, are jounced along like marbles on an incline, colliding at random, avoiding contact by chance, winding up where we do for no reason whatsoever.

"Hey, Ruthie, how's it going?"

"You musta won the lottery and died, you be calling me Ruthie. How you doing, Jerry Jerkoff?"

"Got time for a beer?"

"I do. Not sure I got time for you, but for a beer, sure."

"Steel Wheel? About six?"

"It open now?"

"If you drink it outside, yeah."

"Six then. Ruthie my ass."

"So, Mister Grey's Anatomy, how'd it going?" Ruth looked older, his skin more smoke colored than black. Eyes yellowed instead of the bright whites that animated his conversation.

"Grey's what?"

"You here to discuss payroll disparity, Jer?"

"Nah. You hear about the latest meeting between BLM and the Defenders?"

"Hear about it? Shit, I was there. Edna dragged me to it. Said if I didn't support my race, she was gonna leave me."

Jerry didn't know how to react, so he just said, "Oh."

"Course, it wasn't really a meeting *between* anyone," said Ruth. "It was like neither side wanted to get into it. Like those guys just wanted to be seen in the streets, and us niggers saying, 'these our streets, clear off.' Like no one wanted it to get physical."

"So, when did they start mixing it up?"

"Man, you listening? They didn't. They stayed apart. I looked for you but didn't seem like you were there with them Nazis."

"I wasn't there. I was working. But truth is, I'm not sure I wanna be with them anymore."

"First smart thing I heard you say. Look, this beer tastes like piss. I'm gonna get a whisky. You want one?"

"If you're buying."

"Spoken like a true jerkoff. Be right back."

Which gave Jerry time to think. What was he doing here? Here with a guy who just said he'd been part of the BLM demo. Part of the demo that resulted in Earl being accused of roughing up a black woman and calling her a nigger. That didn't sound like Earl. But Ruth was saying that the two groups never collided. Both things couldn't be right.

"Next one's on you," Ruth said, plopping a shot glass down.

Jerry downed his in a gulp. "Cheers."

"Cheers, Jerry. So you not a Defender now, huh? You tired of hating?"

"I dunno, Ruth. A friend of mine, that ex-cop I told you about, Earl, some woman is charging him with roughing her up at that demonstration, and calling her the n-word."

Ruth snorted. "Hey, this Rutherford you talking to. You can say nigger without me poppin' you. I heard the word before. Anyway, yeah, I heard about your friend, and I know what Demonona's saying."

"What *who's* saying?"

"That's the lady's name. Demonona Cross. She got herself on television, crying and sobbing, and saying your friend put hands on her and called her a nigger."

"Earl wouldn't do that."

Listen to me, motherfucker. Earl, or whatever his name is, *didn't* do that. He's being set up."

"Set up by this lady?"

"Set up by the top people at BLM."

"What top people?"

"Remember we talking before about the lady that just bought herself a condo for a mil and a half? I couldn't remember her name then, but I'm hearing it a lot now. Her name is Qiyyancha Such-Harder. She's become BLM's ideologist, its top thinker."

"Wait a minute. Tell me her name again? I don't think I heard you right."

"Yeah, you did. Qiyyancha Such-Harder. I know, I know. You pronounce that middle name 'suck' and it's hilarious. But she pronounces it "Sook". And she says Qiyyancha is some sacred name from Africa, so no one dares to make fun of it. Anyway, she's figuring out the next steps for BLM to take. Because truth to tell, Jerry, it's fading. People tired of the rhetoric, tired of the shouting, tired of the anger."

"So what's the next step?"

"You heard of 'Defund the police?' That dumb-shit idea of the BLM hard-liners to take money away from the cops so they can't do their job. As if, when their house is being robbed, they aren't gonna call the cops?"

"Yeah. I heard the mayor of New York is behind it."

"Not the mayor. His wife. She's part of BLM. And the mayor, he doesn't wanna be sleeping on the sofa for the rest of his goddam life. Anyway, sounds like Suck-Harder has this brilliant new idea called 'Defund the po-race."

"Po-race?"

"Yeah. Po-race. It's a mix of police and white race. She's telling black people to bring criminal charges against white people for being racists."

"Which white people?"

"All white people, Jerry. Any white. She's saying the police only care about the white race. Thus, 'po-race.' Your friend Earl is sort of a test case for Pittsburgh, see if it works."

"But he didn't touch that woman, he didn't call her anything. Did he?"

Rutherford was looking away, into the middle distance. As if he were seeing something different from a bar on Wood Street, or the white dude sitting with him, or his job, or his wife, or the Pirates.

"Why you pulling away from that bunch of haters, Jerry? Those Defenders?"

"Look, Ruth, I think some of the things they're saying and doing are right.

I mean, someone's gotta stand up for white people. It's not like we're all pieces of shit. But the Defenders are going too far. They want to keep Trump in office forever. That's not right. I don't want them messing with our Constitution. And they're planning other stuff, here in Pittsburgh even, that I don't agree with. That I can't be part of."

Rutherford raised his eyes to meet Jerry's. "What they planning here, Jer?" His voice had hit an all-time low timbre.

Moment of truth. Black or white? Friend or family? What's popular or what's right? More violence or the start of healing?

Jerry told him about the plan to march to the woman's house at midnight, carrying torches, like the KKK of the past, ring her doorbell, shout curses at her, threaten to break in.

Rutherford was looking at him dead-on with those yellow, sleep-deprived eyes and a heaviness that Jerry could feel came from a deeper source. He breathed heavily, kind of sighed. "You're forgetting something," he said.

"What's that?"

"The next round is yours."

With his replacement shot glass in front of him, and a beer to back it up—Jerry's attempt to make amends for forgetting—Ruth looked off into the distance like he had before. "I told you Edna dragged me to this last demo right?"

"Yeah."

"Said I wasn't defending my race. Said she wanted me to see the righteousness of BLM. I went for *her*, she's my wife, after all. And besides, it's not like black people don't have *anything* to complain about. We do."

"Sure," said Jerry.

Ruth kind of snorted. "You say 'sure,' but you don't know. Unless you're black, you don't know. Anyhow, I went with Edna, but I also went with my cell phone, and that sucker was fully charged. And I had its camera on the whole time." He squinted his eyes for effect. "The *whole* time, Jer. You hearing me?"

"Yep."

"Well, you're right. Your friend Earl never left his group. There was never any contact between them. I kept the phone on from start to finish. It has a time code on it."

"But then how could she..."

"I told you, I had it on *start to finish*. Once the two sides went their own ways, the TV cameras came rushing up to our, I mean, to the BLM leaders. And they got this woman, this Demonona Cross, out there, and told her to get ready. And just before the red lights came on, she starts bawling and sobbing, and then she says this old white guy had grabbed her, and slapped her, and called her a nigger. And she wanted him arrested. And then everyone around her starts chanting, like they were all a choir rehearsal, 'No Justice, No Peace.' Over and over.

"And one of the reporters, some little white girl, says to his lady, this Demonona, 'Can you tell it to us again, but just say, he used the n-word.' So she goes through the whole thing again, the tears and the sobbing, but then she says, 'he called me the n-word.' And they thank her and do their little stand-ups and take off in their satellite trucks."

Jerry downed his shot in a gulp. So did Ruth.

"Ruth," said Jerry. "You gotta decide..."

"*I already have decided!*" Ruth shouted, really loud, his voice like a bear growling. "Why the fuck do you think I just told you all that? This'll probably end my marriage, not that I had much of a marriage left. But it ain't right, ain't right for someone to be accused, and punished for something they didn't do. So, yeah, I'll give you the fuckin' video. Now go get us another round."

It took a while. The charges against Earl were dropped, and he was told he would receive his full pension. A couple of ambulance chasers told him he could sue the woman who had charged him falsely. Earl told them to fuck off.

Demonona Cross was charged with making false statements to the police, a misdemeanor for which she was sentenced to thirty days of community service. She served her sentence by working as a volunteer at the Pittsburgh headquarters of Black Lives Matter.

Qiyyancha Such-Harder issued a statement saying she was shocked to hear that a member of her organization had been charged with a misdemeanor and that it was probably part of a racist cover-up by the police. She would be filing civil rights charges against the Pittsburgh police soon because these instances of systemic racism had to stop.

And she also wanted restitution for slavery, and....

"All is forgiven, Jerry," said Tran, as they walked down Liberty Avenue, neither wearing the politically correct uniform of patriotism, a Chinese-made mask."

"How do you mean?"

"Well, I got the feeling you were slipping away from us there a while back," said Tran. "You got this job, you made this new black friend, and next thing you weren't coming to the rallies, the meetings."

"Like you said, I got a job."

"Yeah, but it was something more. Like you didn't want to be seen with us. But you made up for it with that cell phone video. I can't believe you found that. Earl's off the hook, he's getting his pension, we showed those fucking BLM creeps we're not gonna take it anymore."

"I'm glad Earl's okay," said Jerry.

"Now come on, Jer. Between us. Where'd you get that video? You haven't told anyone."

"That's still how I'm playing it, Tran."

"But that looks like it was taken from the niggers' side of the demo."

"The BLM side."

"What are you?" said Tran. "Mister Political Correctness all of a sudden? Come on, where'd you get it?"

"Someone I met at a bar. That's all I can say, Tran."

"Have it your way, Jerry. Now look, the reason I wanted to talk with you is, we've been in contact with a lot of other groups that think like we do. This election was bullshit. They stole it. You know it. I know it. And we're not gonna let them get away with it."

"Yeah?"

"Yeah. Now some people I know are planning to go to Washington and let them know what we think."

"Meaning what?"

"Well, if Congress won't listen to us, and they go ahead with this vote certification, we're gonna storm the fucking Capitol. Take over. Until they do what's right."

Jerry stopped. Right in the middle of the sidewalk. A woman walking a dog nearly stepped on his heels. "Wear a mask, asshole," she said, as she went around him.

"You're going to storm the U.S. Capitol? And make Congress do what you want?"

"Not just what we want," said Tran. "What's right."

"Sorry, Tran. Count me out. That's not what I thought this was all about."

"Look, Jer," said Tran. "You're a good guy. I like you. But you don't understand how politics works these days."

"You're right, buddy," said Jerry, looking down the street where the lady with the dog was walking ahead of him. "And I don't plan to start now."

He did a 180, and started walking away. He had to be at work soon. After that, he was supposed to meet Ruth for a drink. Ever since Ruth's wife left him, he had plenty of free time.

# Chapter 36
## Ashes, Ashes, We All Fall Down

He wandered from room to room, thinking he had a reason to enter each one, realized he did not, moving on to the next. Memories of what had occurred in each room, the chance discovery of something he had not seen for nearly a year, a family photo album, some out-of-date articles about AI, tickets for a Mets game from two seasons ago, before attending a sports event became a criminal offense. A note Khadija had written him about the importance of Black Lives Matter. Wrong. Nothing mattered.

The only lift to his sprits came when he went into the spare bedroom that had been converted, before they brought her home, and at considerable expense, into an ICU unit. He watched his Mother breathing on her own, still attached to IVs but not a respirator. It could take months, they said, and even then, she might never recover her full strength. She was a strong woman, but this virus had no mercy.

He had a pretty good idea of what no mercy meant. He had seen the online reports of Qi Qi Dieh's murder on West 47th Street. What the hell was she thinking? He had put himself in the path of the goon who wanted to intercept her. Gave her time to get away, through the milling baggage reclaim area. Good for you, Qi Qi. But then? Start talking with the media? Make your whereabouts known. Repeat the claims that had put a red dot on your forehead, or more accurately, the back of your head. You could have lived in silence and anonymity. Until they found you.

Who was he to talk? He hadn't been out of the airport for more than thirty minutes before he made a spectacle of himself, kicking a wall, bringing Gerrity, the PA cop, into his blender-mixed life of contradictions.

He hadn't made a mistake, he decided, turning his back on his pre-planned future, his family, his homeland. He had decided to "follow his dreams," as the songs, and shows and books all rhapsodized. Do something different. Be yourself. Express your feelings.

He had. Now what?

Well, in half an hour, he'd be meeting with Shelton A. Drago, Special Agent for International Crimes of the Federal Bureau of Investigation. That had come as something of a shock, both to Henry and his father. But then, he and his father weren't exactly on the best of terms right now. Hadn't been, really, since Henry had lifted off for Shanghai.

You are a gifted young man, whose age is of no importance, said Hui. You are a font of information that would take us many months, possibly years, to gather on our own.

Xi's hologram nodded.

You are a unique individual, said Rav, in his arms. Not in love with him but certainly interested in him and skillfully nurturing his ego as well as his id.

He got all these people and opinions mixed up these days.

"You're in a world of trouble, Henry," said Special Agent Drago. "You're looking at a very long time in prison."

Henry's attorney, employed by his father, had warned him to say nothing to Drago unless he was there. Henry stared at Drago, dreamed of Rav.

"You entered this country on a false passport," said Drago.

"His name, his picture and his personal data were all correct," said the lawyer, whose name Henry couldn't remember.

"You provided aid and comfort to an enemy of the United States."

"Enemy?" said the lawyer. "Then why does China have an embassy on Van Ness Street in Washington, and a consulate on 42$^{nd}$ and 12$^{th}$ in New York?"

"You broke your promise to remain in your house, a promise given to a sworn officer of the Port Authority Police."

"Broke his promise? Thank God, no one in our government ever breaks promises," said the attorney. "And isn't that sworn officer you mentioned currently suspended without pay for assault and hate crimes?"

"Alleged assault," said Drago. "We'll get to that later."

"We'll get to it right god-fucking-damn now," said the attorney, thumping the coffee table that separated him from the agent. "Henry can provide an iron-clad alibi for Officer Gerrity, and you better get down with that before it goes away."

"*Get down* with it?" drawled Drago, as though the attorney had just switched to Mongolian.

"Agent Drago, we will cooperate with you, but not under these hostile conditions. Henry has done nothing legally wrong, and I want a written proffer from you, or your superior, that he will not be prosecuted in any federal jurisdiction."

Drago sagged. "In return for what?"

"His promise to answer all your, and your colleagues' questions, about his time in China, to the best of his ability and recollection."

"What about his time since he returned?"

"Off the table," said the attorney. "As you know, that's being investigated by the Port Authority, Pennsylvania State, and New York City police. Not to mention the absolute protection of Henry's rights based on the extreme mental, psychological and physical strain he has been under since his return."

Drago ignored the lawyer. "Can we talk off the record, Henry?"

"As long as you speak directly into the microphone and give an absolute guarantee that the federal government will not use any of the information from that conversation to prosecute my client."

"I guarantee nothing we say in this conversation will be used against you, Henry."

"Please identify him as my client."

"Please stick a wire brush up your ass and rotate it."

"Yeah, we can talk off the record," said Henry.

"Henry!" said the lawyer.

"You sound like you've already done the brush thing before," Drago told the lawyer. "Henry?"

"I said yeah," said Henry, looking at his lawyer.

"Jesus," said the lawyer.

"Why did you go to China, Henry?"

"I was really interested in Artificial Intelligence, AI, and wanted to learn more about it."

"May I ask why," asked Drago.

"Because I think it is a life-changing technological development that will control the way we live for centuries to come. And I wanted to learn about it from the best."

"And the best was not here?" said Drago.

"The *best*, Special Agent Drago, was Professor Hui Jen-Sho, of Wuhan International University."

"Except he turned out not to be a professor," said Drago. "Sorry, but we know that because of you."

"Yes, you are correct. He turned out not to be a professor, in the American sense. He was, is, a Colonel in the People's Liberation Army. I attended two of his lectures in New York, and… and I fell under his spell, I suppose is how you'd explain it."

"Why do you think that happened?" asked Drago, softly.

"What are you, a shrink?" said the attorney, sharply.

"Yes," said Drago quietly. "In addition to being an FBI agent, I have doctorates in psychiatry and psychology."

"Jesus," said the lawyer.

Henry gave a little laugh. "Then you understand the Theory of the Appeal of the Unknown."

"Known among the common folk as 'opposites attract.'" said Drago.

"AI has already changed the way we think, how we look at medicine, how we plan economies, how we prepare for war," said Henry. "And yet, it's just getting started. There's so much to discover, to test, to apply. I wanted to be part of that. And I wanted to learn from the best."

"Hui Jen-Sho probably qualifies," said Drago.

"Jesus," said the attorney.

"Colonel Hui took an interest in me," said Henry. "Gave me opportunities I could never have found in this country. Set my life on a different path."

"Yes," said Drago, "a path that's trying to destroy the United States."

"The United States is destroying itself," said Henry. "Just look around. Everyone hates each other. We only listen to people who agree with us, watch TV news that agrees with us, only socialize with people who agree with us. We're not the United States. We're the Divided States. Our leaders spend more time deciding who can use which bathroom, or who can marry who, or if murdering someone because of their color is more murderous than just murdering a stranger. So, if you're the stranger, should you be happy or sad that you weren't murdered because of hate? China's not our worst enemy. Russia's not our worst enemy. Iran's not our worst enemy. Americans are our worst enemy."

"From the mouths of babes," murmured the lawyer.

"Maybe before I went to China," said Henry, looking straight at the man hired to defend him from a lifetime in prison. "Not anymore." He turned to Drago. "Agent Drago, I'm not blind to China's misdeeds. Their people are afraid of the Party."

"The Communist Party."

Henry screwed up his face. "No, the Christian Democratic Party of China. There's only one party, Agent Drago. You know that. It's dictatorial and probably not sustainable. But for now, it's very efficient. Which is why China is surpassing us."

"I prefer our system," said Drago. "It's more fair."

"Good," said Henry. "Maybe you're right. Now, just hope you're not falsely accused of assault and a hate crime like Officer Gerrity."

"Okay," said Drago. "Let's go there, if it's all right with you, counselor?"

"I have your promise on tape," said the lawyer.

"You're willing to testify under oath that you were with Officer Gerrity at the very time he is being accused of accosting a woman of color at JFK and using the n-word?"

"The word is nigger," said Henry. "He never said it in my presence. And he never came close to a woman of color in that time frame."

"Then why is being accused of a hate crime?"

"Because the woman who accused him forgot to set her watch to daylight savings time."

"She what?"

"That woman is with BLM. She asked Gerrity for directions, he gave them to her. Then she looked at her watch and told the police at exactly what time he had called her a nigger."

"But it wasn't the right time?"

"It wasn't the right time. At the time she's saying Gerrity used that word, he was with me. And I will testify to that."

"What can you tell us about a Chinese national named Qi Qi Dieh?" said Drago, happy to change subjects.

"I think Henry's answered enough questions for now," said the lawyer. "We can take this up another time."

"I'd like to keep going," said Drago.

"Yes, well," said the lawyer, "there are some places where that would work. But this is America, not China. And as you yourself said, Agent Drago, you think our way is more fair."

Drago turned to leave, promising to call the lawyer to make a future appointment with Henry.

"Thank you," said Henry. "What happens to Gerrity?"

"He'll probably be reinstated."

"And the woman who accused him falsely?"

"Nothing."

"You're an idiot," snapped the lawyer once Drago was gone. "The more you talk to him, the more chance you'll say something stupid, and put yourself in a maximum-security hole in Nebraska or somewhere."

"Thank you," said Henry. "I look forward to seeing you again."

He decided to check in on his Mother. As he was halfway up the steps, the doorbell rang again. Probably the FBI agent, trying to catch him without his lawyer.

"I waited until they were gone," said Rav. She wore a black pantsuit and a white blouse, and her hair was loose and long.

Henry felt his knees losing their function. He literally went down in to a crouched position. She lifted him up, stepped back after the contact.

"I can't stay," Rav said. "I'm here on official business."

"How did you find me?" he said.

Rav smiled her I'm-smarter-than-you smile. "You know, even in the age of Artificial Intelligence, there is a website called 'White Pages.'

It publishes phone numbers and addresses if you pay four dollars on your credit card."

"Please come in."

"I really can't. Someone is waiting for me in that car across the street."

"Who is waiting for you?" He tried to look past her, but she put her hand on his face, and that stilled him.

"General Deng-Tal." She paused, smiled. "I think you call her TanTeeth."

"She's a General?"

"Has been for years."

"I thought she was some secretary of Hui's."

"Not as smart as you think you are."

"I'm the dumbest man on earth," said Henry. "The only thing I know is that I love you."

Rav looked down, but her smile was evident.

"So," said Henry, "honest to the end. I always knew you didn't love me, couldn't love me."

"Half wrong. I didn't. But I could."

"Why are you here?"

"The General and I have just come back from Washington. General Deng had an appointment at the State Department. I was her aide and translator."

"About what?"

"About the unfortunate death of a Chinese citizen on American soil. Her name was Qi Qi Dieh. Our conversation with the Americans in Washington was very satisfactory. Citizen Qi's death will remain unsolved. That is for the best. But of course, you knew her."

"For about fifteen hours," said Henry. "Fang got me out of China to see my Mother. I wouldn't have left otherwise."

"I know," Rav said. "Fang was a very devious man who caused much damage."

"How?"

"He convinced Director Zhuang of the Cyberspace Administration to sign documents ordering that you and citizen Qi be allowed to leave China. Because Director Zhuang is a well-known and trusted friend of General Secretary Xi, no one could object."

"Why would Fang do that?"

"He told us that he wanted his ex-wife out of the way. She had already threatened to damage his career. He had arranged to have her killed as soon as she got to America."

"The Embassy guy at the airport?"

"Not Embassy. Chinese Mafia."

"Fang told you this? Why?"

"He was experiencing some pain during the conversation and asked for relief. Begged, really."

"He was tortured?"

"His conscience was tortured. He is no longer in pain."

"You let him go?"

"Citizen Fang was executed last week."

"What about Zhuang?"

"I don't know. He was called to Beijing to meet with Chairman Xi. No one has heard from him since."

"And Colonel Hui?"

Rav looked sadly into Henry's eyes. "He really liked you, Henry. Came to trust you. Rely on you even. He, maybe, in a way, loved you."

"He did, but you didn't?"

She took a moment. "I said, I could."

"Where is Colonel Hui?"

"He has been reassigned."

"Where?"

"I believe it is a school in Xinjiang province."

"That's where the Uighurs are being held. And re-educated."

"I know nothing about that," she said abruptly. "I must go."

"But the AI Institute..."

"General Deng is now in charge of the Institute. She will be deciding its future."

"Ma-lin..."

She turned, smiled. "Ah, so you know my name is not Rav for ravishing?"

He looked at her. "You knew I called you that?"

Ma-lin Cho looked a long time at him. "We both knew things about each other that were better left unsaid. And still are."

"Ma-lin," said Henry, thoughts, dreams, desires, fears and frustration all welling up together. "Stay here, with me."

She smiled the most beautiful smile yet. "Come back, with me."

"I can't," Henry said.

"I can't either."

And she walked away.

Seven thousand four hundred and seventy-seven miles away, Xi's hologram nodded wisely but sadly.

It is said that we cannot dream in color, and that it is impossible to dream in a language other than your mother tongue. And that in a nightmare, a fall from the highest precipice can do us no harm. Nor can the fangs of an imagined snake. And it is said that dreams about love are based on dust, not lust. And that when we dream our deepest wishes, it is because our brains know they are beyond our reach and are giving us a few minutes, or hours, to pretend otherwise.

In our dreams, we have abilities that do not exist upon wakening. We can fly, we are stronger, more beautiful, more attractive to others, and more intelligent than we really are. Most of all intelligent. Outside our dreams, our intelligence is artificial. Which is maybe why we hope never to awaken from them.

January-April, 2021

For sales, editorial information, subsidiary rights information
or a catalog, please write or phone or e-mail
Brick Tower Press
Manhanset House
Shelter Island Hts., New York 11965, US
Tel: 212-427-7139
www.BrickTowerPress.com
bricktower@aol.com
www.IngramContent.com

For sales in the UK and Europe please contact our distributor,
Gazelle Book Services
White Cross Mills
Lancaster, LA1 4XS, UK
Tel: (01524) 68765 Fax: (01524) 63232
email: jacky@gazellebooks.co.uk

# The Fatal Shore

# The Fatal Shore

# Robert Hughes

 Alfred A. Knopf   New York

THIS IS A BORZOI BOOK
PUBLISHED BY ALFRED A. KNOPF, INC.

Copyright © 1986 by Robert Hughes
Maps copyright © 1986 by Raphael Palacios
All rights reserved under International and Pan-American Copyright Conventions.
Published in the United States by Alfred A. Knopf, Inc., New York,
and simultaneously in Canada by Random House of Canada Limited, Toronto.
Distributed by Random House, Inc., New York.
Published in Great Britain by William Collins PLC.

Library of Congress information available upon request

Manufactured in the United States of America in 2009

ISBN: 978-0-307-29161-5
9 8 7 6 5 4 3 2 1

For my godson

a seventh-generation Australian

and for my son's godparents

che 'n la mente m'e fitta, e or m'accora,
la cara e buona imagine paterna
di voi . . .
e quant'io l'abbia in grado, mentr'io vivo,
convien che nella mia lingua si scerna.

—Dante, *Inferno*, XV, 82–87

I have been studying how I may compare
This prison where I live unto the world:
And, for because the world is populous,
And here is not a creature but myself,
I cannot do it;—yet I'll hammer't out.

—Shakespeare, *Richard II*, V. v.

The very day we landed upon the Fatal Shore,
The planters stood around us, full twenty score or more;
They ranked us up like horses and sold us out of hand,
They chained us up to pull the plough, upon Van Diemen's Land.

—Convict ballad, ca. 1825–30.

# Contents

*Illustrations follow pages 194 and 450.*

# Introduction

THE IDEA for this book occurred to me in 1974, when I was working on a series of television documentaries about Australian art. On location in Port Arthur, among the ruins of the great penitentiary and its outbuildings, I realized that like nearly all other Australians I knew little about the convict past of my own country.

I grew up with a skimpy sense of colonial Australia. Convict history was ignored in schools and little taught in universities—indeed, the idea that the convicts might *have* a history worth telling was foreign to Australians in the 1950s and 1960s. Even in the mid-1970s only one general history of the System (as transportation, assignment and secondary punishment in colonial Australia were loosely called) was in print: A. G. L. Shaw's pioneering study *Convicts and the Colonies*. An unstated bias rooted deep in Australian life seemed to wish that "real" Australian history had begun with Australian respectability—with the flood of money from gold and wool, the opening of the continent, the creation of an Australian middle class. Behind the bright diorama of Australia Felix lurked the convicts, some 160,000 of them, clanking their fetters in the penumbral darkness. But on the feelings and experiences of these men and women, little was written. They were statistics, absences and finally embarrassments.

This sublimation has a long history; the desire to forget about our felon origins began with the origins themselves. To call a convict a convict in early colonial Australia was an insult certain to raise colonial hackles. The approved euphemism was "Government man." What the convict system bequeathed to later Australian generations was not the sturdy, skeptical independence on which, with gradually waning justification, we pride ourselves, but an intense concern with social and political respectability. The idea of the "convict stain," a moral blot soaked into our fabric, dominated all argument about Australian selfhood by the 1840s and was the main rhetorical figure used in the movement to abolish transportation. Its leaders called for abolition, not in the name of an independent Australia, but as Britons who felt their decency impugned by the survival of convictry. They were transplanted Britons but Britons still, *plus royalistes que la reine*. The first signs of Australian social identity had appeared as early as the 1820s among the "Currency lads and lasses," most of whom were native-born children of former convicts. In the name of abolition, this picture had to be severely edited in the 1840s; and for decades to come, the official voices of Australia would continue to stake their claim to respectability on their Britishness. If the end of transportation had been brought about in the name of the convicts' own descendants, this might not have happened. But the fight was on behalf of free emigrants and their stock; it was this side of Australia which most fervently brandished the myth of corrupted blood and "convict evil." After abolition, you could (silently) reproach your forebears for being convicts. You could not take pride in them, or reproach England for treating them as it did. The cure for this excruciating colonial double bind was amnesia—a national pact of silence. Yet the Stain would not go away: the late nineteenth century was a flourishing time for biological determinism, for notions of purity of race and stock, and few respectable native-born Australians had the confidence not to quail when real Englishmen spoke of their convict heritage.

Thus local imperialists, who believed that Australia could only survive as a vassal of Great Britain, held that the solvent for the Birth Stain was blood—as much of it as England needed for her wars. Below the propaganda of the Boer War and World War I, voices (usually working-class, and commonly Irish) were heard "unpatriotically" pointing out that, having been shipped out of Britain as criminals, we were shipped back as cannon fodder; so that, when peace came, the survivors could return to their real mission as Australians—growing cheap wool and wheat for England. But to dwell on the Stain did not promote that sense of national dignity which, our grandfathers and great-grandfathers believed, got the lads over the wire. Amnesia seemed to be a condition of patriotism, and this pervaded attitudes toward the writing and teaching of Australian history, at least up to the appearance of the first volume of Manning Clark's *History of Australia* in 1962. One of the reasons why Australians after 1918 embraced with such deep emotion the mythic event of Gallipoli, our Thermopylae, was that there seemed to be so little in our early history to which we could point with pride. "History" meant great men, stirring deeds, useful discoveries and worthy sacrifices; our history was short of these. This made us even more anxious about our worth as Australians living in Australia—the root of the "Cultural Cringe" which would continue to plague us until long after World War II. The idea that whether or not England should feel ashamed of creating the System,

Australians certainly had cause to be proud of surviving it and of creating their own values despite it, was rarely heard.

Australian historians up until the 1960s succumbed to this pressure; hence the textbooks' silence about convictry. It was as though some collective delicacy in American historians had persuaded them to play down the Civil War, so as not to open old wounds.

Denied its voice as history, convict experience became the province of journalists and novelists. The general public never lost its curiosity about these "dark" years in which so many of its roots lay tangled; and a vivid, trashy Grand Guignol, long on rum, sodomy and the lash but decidedly short on the more prosaic facts about how most convicts actually lived and worked, sprang up to supply its demands. So did one national novel, that powerful, meandering awkwardly framed and passionately felt magnum opus of Marcus Clarke's, *For the Term of His Natural Life*. All the popular literature of transportation focussed on the horrors of the System, the outer penal settlements to which recidivists were condemned—Port Arthur, Macquarie Harbor, Moreton Bay and, especially, Norfolk Island. It presented convict life as a wretched purgatory, relieved only by stretches of pure hell.

This folklore of the System kept its memory alive. But it was one-sided and, especially in its treatment of Port Arthur, sometimes luridly exaggerated. It did not bother with the general experience of convicts. Only a fraction of the men and women transported to Australia spent any time in these "secondary" settlements, which were as a rule reserved for prisoners who had committed second crimes while in the colony. Most served a few years of their sentences in assignment to a free settler or in Government labor, never wore chains, got their tickets-of-leave and in due course were absorbed into colonial society as free citizens. Most of them (if one can judge by the surviving letters) wanted to stay in Australia and rejected the idea of going back to England.

For assignment worked. Despite all its imperfections and injustices, and the abuses of bad masters and the general harshness of antipodean life, it did give a fresh start to many thousands of people who would have been crushed in spirit or confirmed in crime by long stretches in an English prison. And, despite the number of bigots in our grandfathers' day deriding Australians as the children of criminals, remarkably few Australians pointed out the obvious contrary fact that, whatever other conclusions one might draw from our weird national origins, the post-colonial history of Australia utterly exploded the theory of genetic criminal inheritance. Here was a community of people, handpicked over decades for their "criminal propensities" and for no other reason, whose offspring turned out to form one of the most law-abiding societies in the world. At a time when neo-conservative social idealogues are trying to revive the old bogey of hereditary disposition to crime, this may still be worth pondering.

From the 1960s onward, when Australian historians—inspired, though slowly at first, by Manning Clark's *History of Australia* and L. L. Robson's *The Convict Settlers of Australia* (1965)—began to draw the System out of folklore and into the light of inquiry, they focussed on the majority of convicts: those in assignment, not those on Norfolk Island. It was from them, not from the double-damned incorrigibles, that one could learn the actual workings of colonial society, the often-exotic ways in which convicts claimed rights and functioned as a class in relation to the free. Colonial Australia was unique in its mingling of the free and the bond, in its attitudes toward work and its definitions of servitude. It was also a more "normal" place than one might imagine from the folk-loric picture of a society governed by the lash and the triangle, composed of groaning white slaves tyrannized by ruthless masters. The book that best conveys this, and has rightly become a landmark in recent studies of the System, is J. B. Hirst's *Convict Society and its Enemies* (1983).

Though Hirst and other "normalizing" historians have not ignored the lower depths of the System, epitomized by Norfolk Island, they may have underestimated the moral and human significance of these places in their laudable desire to avoid sensationalism. It is true that relatively few convicts were pitched into these hellholes. It is also true that only a small fraction of the total population of Russia has suffered in the Gulag, and that relatively few Cubans have undergone the atrocities visited on dissidents by Fidel Castro's torturers on the Isle of Pines. Yet, just as it is impossible to read a book like Armando Valladares' *Against All Hope* without losing one's illusions about the true nature of Castro's regime, so it is difficult to reflect on places like Norfolk Island and Macquarie Harbor without adjusting some of one's views of British colonialism. They held a minority of convicts but they were absolutely integral to the System: they provided a standard of terror by which good behavior on the mainland of New South Wales (or so the authorities hoped) would be enforced.

The missing element in most accounts of the System has been the voices of the convicts themselves. The System left a mountain of official paper behind it. We hear a great deal from the administrators, the witnesses in the select committees, the parsons, the jailers, the masters; from the convicts themselves, very little. Accordingly I have tried, as far as possible, to see the System from below, through convicts' testimony —in letters, depositions, petitions and memoirs—about their own experiences. Much of this material is hitherto unpublished, and much more awaits study. It turns out that one common assumption is quite wrong: far from being a mute mass, the convicts did have a voice, or rather many voices. This book is largely about what they tell us of their suffering and survival, their aspiration and resistance, their fear of exile and their reconciliation to the once-unimagined land they and their children would claim as their own.

Friends gave me moral support and encouragement while I was writing this much-delayed book. Among these I should like particularly to thank Joanna Collard, who helped assemble a first list of Australian sources; Brendan Gill, whose initial enthusiasm for the idea back in 1975 sustained mine; Jerry Lieber, Barbara Rose and Lucio Manisco, on whom readings were inflicted; and Robert Motherwell, whose response to the first few chapters helped keep me going through the rest.

As anyone must who attempts to write on Australian history from primary sources, I owe my main debt to the Librarians and staff of the Mitchell and Dixson Libraries and the Archives Office of New South Wales in Sydney, the National Library of Australia in Canberra, the Allport Library and the Archives Office of Tasmania (Tasmanian State Archives) in Hobart. In particular, Catherine Santamaria (head of Australian Studies) and John Thompson (in charge of Australian Manuscripts) at the National Library, and Geoffrey Stillwell of the Allport Library steered me through the documentary labyrinth.

I must also record my gratitude to the Librarians and staff of the Latrobe Library, Melbourne; the New York Public Library; the State Paper Office and the National Library of Ireland, Dublin; the Bibliothèque Nationale, Paris; the British Library, London; the London Library, without whose lending service the early research for this book could not have begun; the Public Record Office, London; the Army Museums Ogilby Trust; the Religious Society of Friends; the Bedford County Record Office; the Derby Central Library; the Estate Office at Catton Hall, Staffordshire; the Lancashire Record Office; the William Salt Library, Stafford. For field trips in Tasmania in 1981, a car was supplied by Telford Motors, Hobart; and Dick Edwards of Strahan provided the boat in which I got around Macquarie Harbor.

The unwieldy manuscript was cuffed and licked into shape, through its various drafts, by Charles Elliott, my editor at Knopf, backed up by Christopher Maclehose and Stuart Proffitt of Collins Harvill. Gillian Gibbins at Collins and Sharon Zimmerman at Knopf helped gather material. Stephen Frankel, the copy editor, pounced on more inconsistencies than I thought possible. I offer heartfelt thanks to them all, and especially to Professor Michael Roe of the University of Tasmania, Hobart, for his generosity and care in reading the penultimate draft of the manuscript and pointing out its various sins of omission and commission. Though my interpretation of certain aspects of penal history differs from his, any surviving errors of fact are mine.

Finally, and most of all, I thank my beloved wife, Victoria Hughes, whose faith and levelheadedness kept me going through years of research and writing, and never for a minute let me down; this is her book too.

# Maps

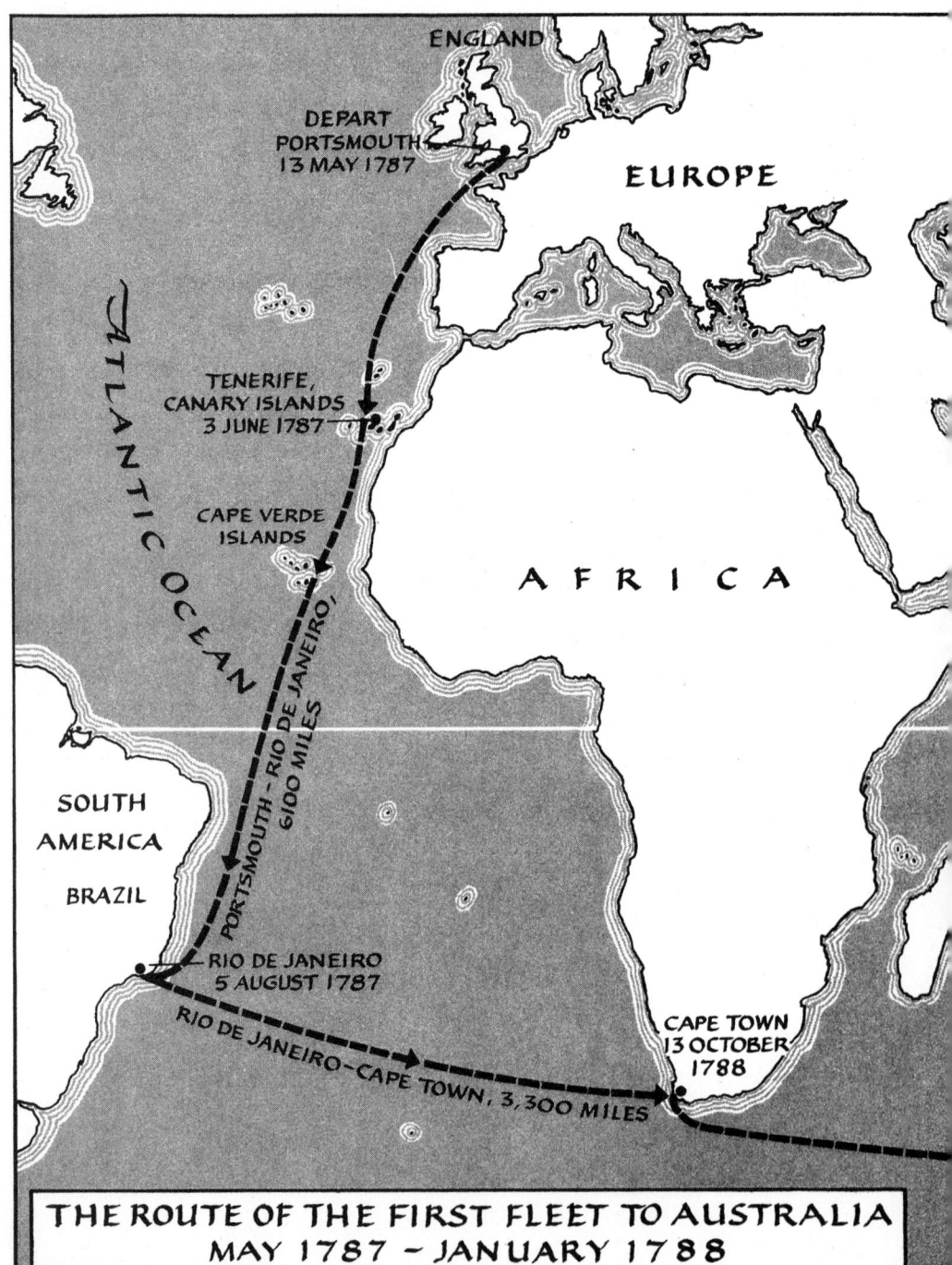

ENGLAND

EUROPE

DEPART
PORTSMOUTH
13 MAY 1787

ATLANTIC OCEAN

TENERIFE,
CANARY ISLANDS
3 JUNE 1787

CAPE VERDE
ISLANDS

AFRICA

PORTSMOUTH - RIO DE JANEIRO,
6100 MILES

SOUTH
AMERICA

BRAZIL

RIO DE JANEIRO
5 AUGUST 1787

CAPE TOWN
13 OCTOBER
1788

RIO DE JANEIRO - CAPE TOWN, 3,300 MILES

THE ROUTE OF THE FIRST FLEET TO AUSTRALIA
MAY 1787 – JANUARY 1788

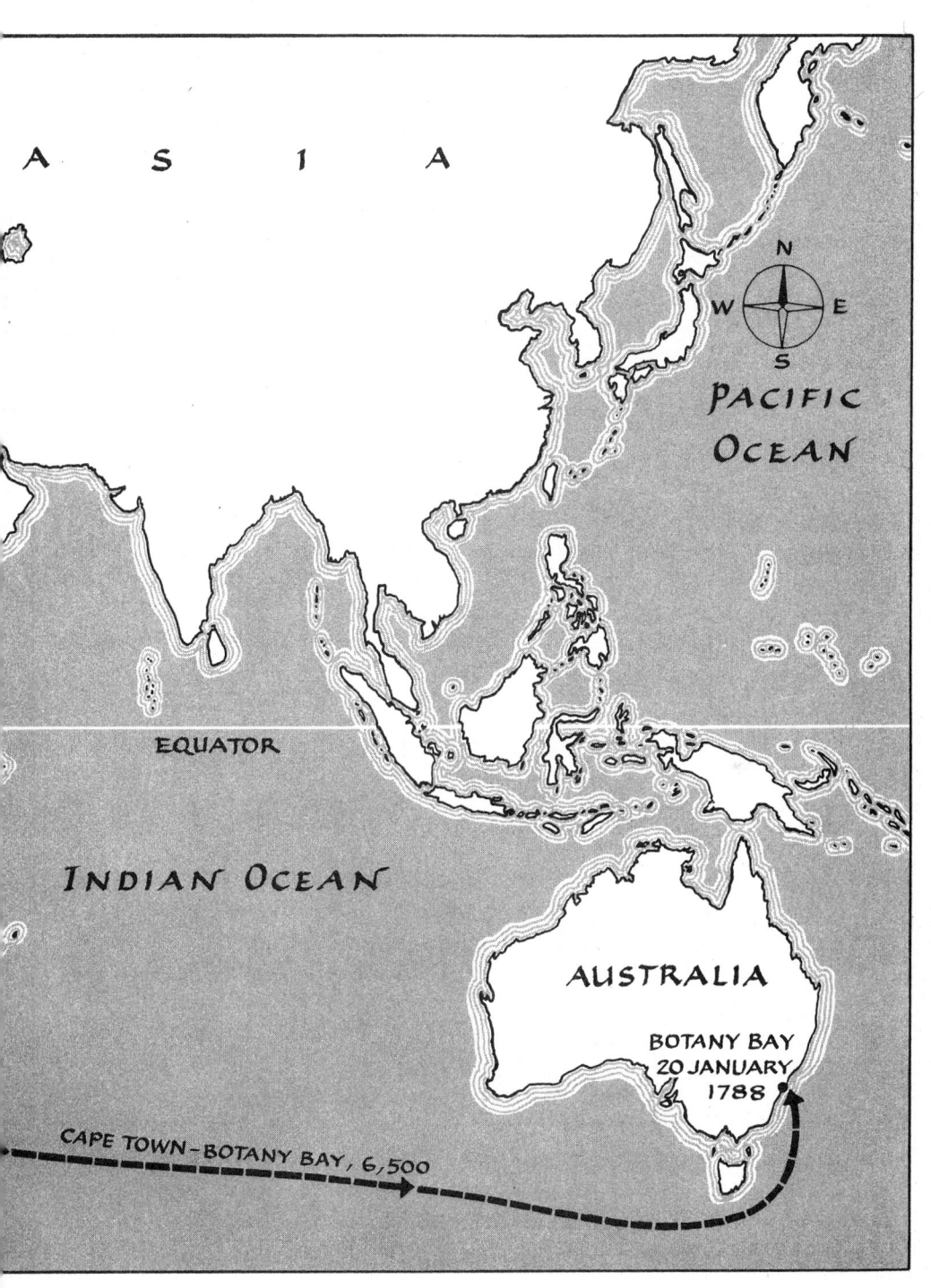

A S I A

N
W E
S

PACIFIC
OCEAN

EQUATOR

INDIAN OCEAN

AUSTRALIA

BOTANY BAY
20 JANUARY
1788

CAPE TOWN – BOTANY BAY, 6,500

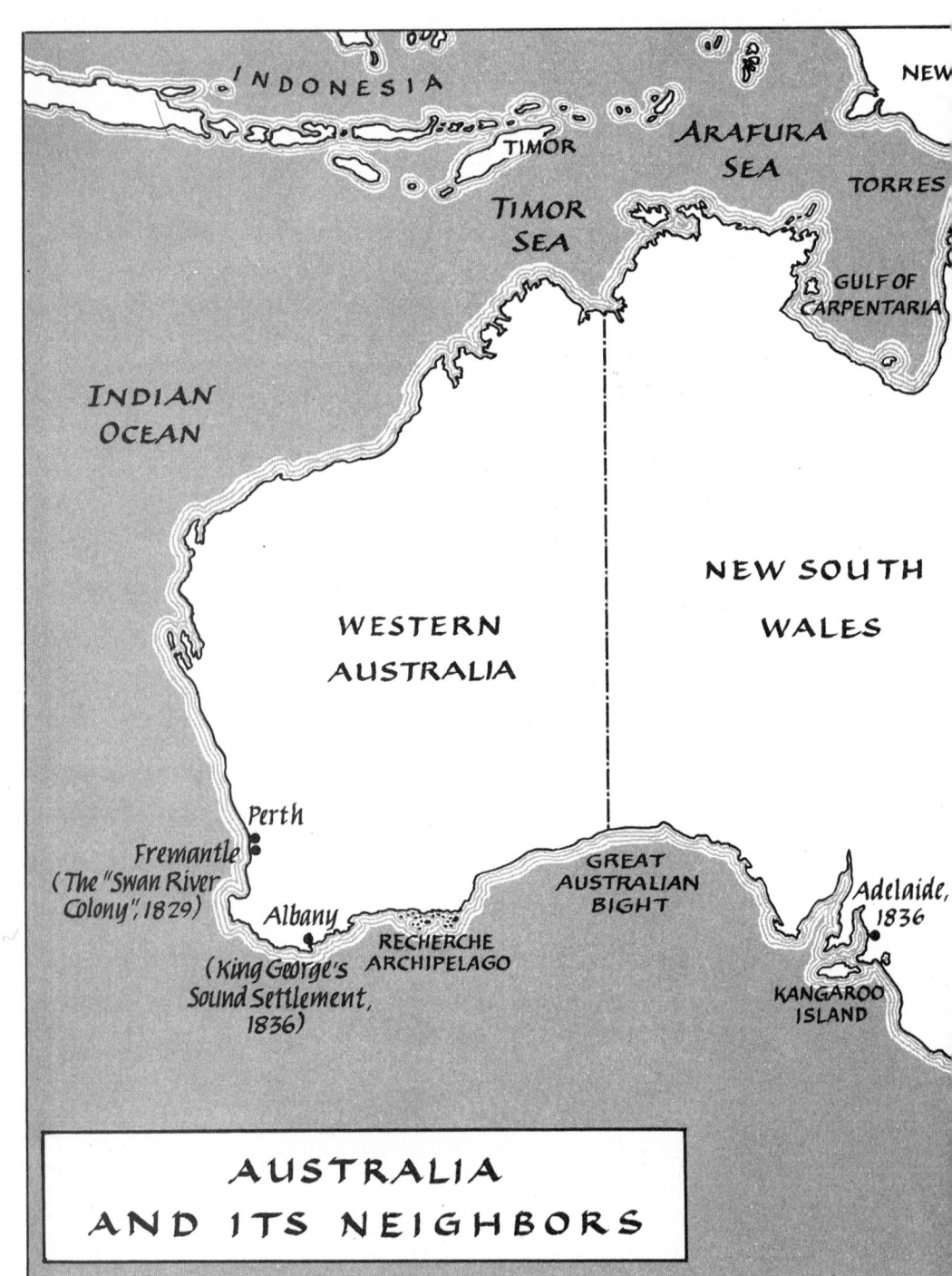

INDONESIA

TIMOR

ARAFURA SEA

NEW

TORRES

TIMOR SEA

GULF OF CARPENTARIA

INDIAN OCEAN

WESTERN AUSTRALIA

NEW SOUTH WALES

Perth

Fremantle (The "Swan River Colony", 1829)

Albany

RECHERCHE ARCHIPELAGO

(King George's Sound Settlement, 1836)

GREAT AUSTRALIAN BIGHT

Adelaide, 1836

KANGAROO ISLAND

# AUSTRALIA AND ITS NEIGHBORS

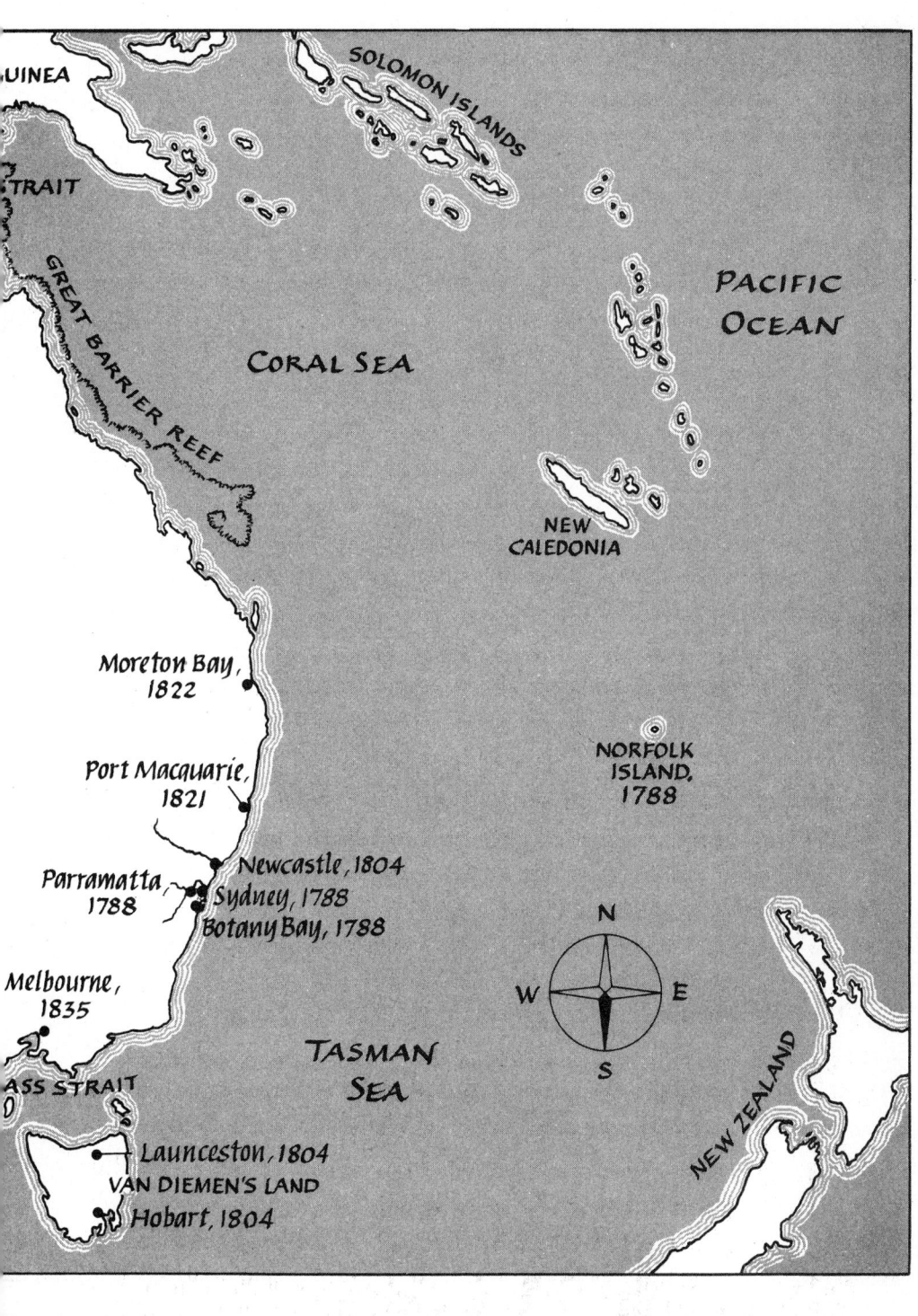

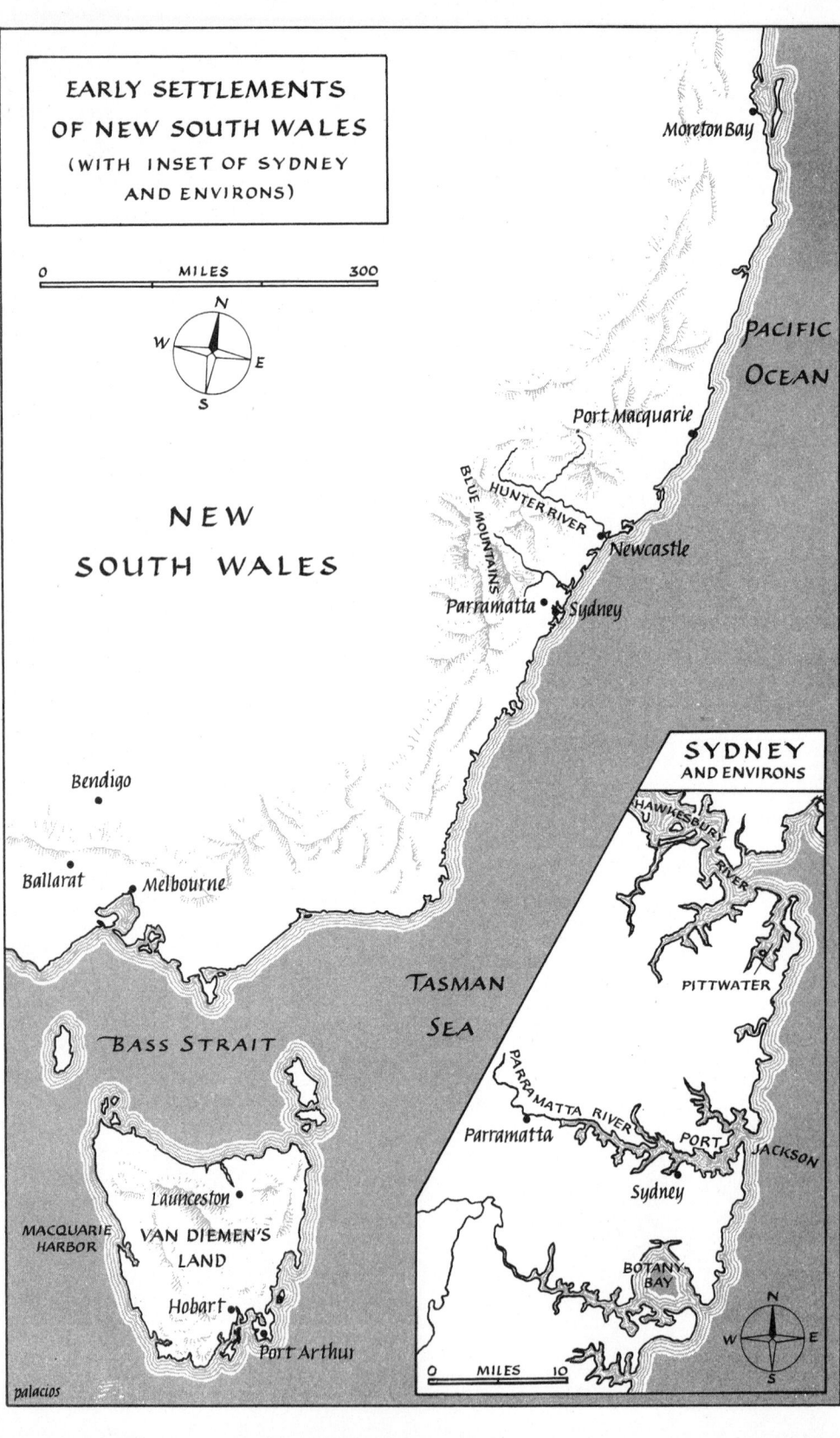

EARLY SETTLEMENTS
OF NEW SOUTH WALES
(WITH INSET OF SYDNEY
AND ENVIRONS)

0     MILES     300

N
W   E
S

NEW
SOUTH WALES

PACIFIC
OCEAN

Moreton Bay

Port Macquarie

BLUE MOUNTAINS

HUNTER RIVER

Newcastle

Parramatta • Sydney

Bendigo

Ballarat • Melbourne

TASMAN
SEA

BASS STRAIT

VAN DIEMEN'S
LAND

Launceston

MACQUARIE
HARBOR

Hobart

Port Arthur

palacios

SYDNEY
AND ENVIRONS

HAWKESBURY RIVER

PITTWATER

PARRAMATTA RIVER

Parramatta

PORT

JACKSON

Sydney

BOTANY
BAY

N
W   E
S

0   MILES   10

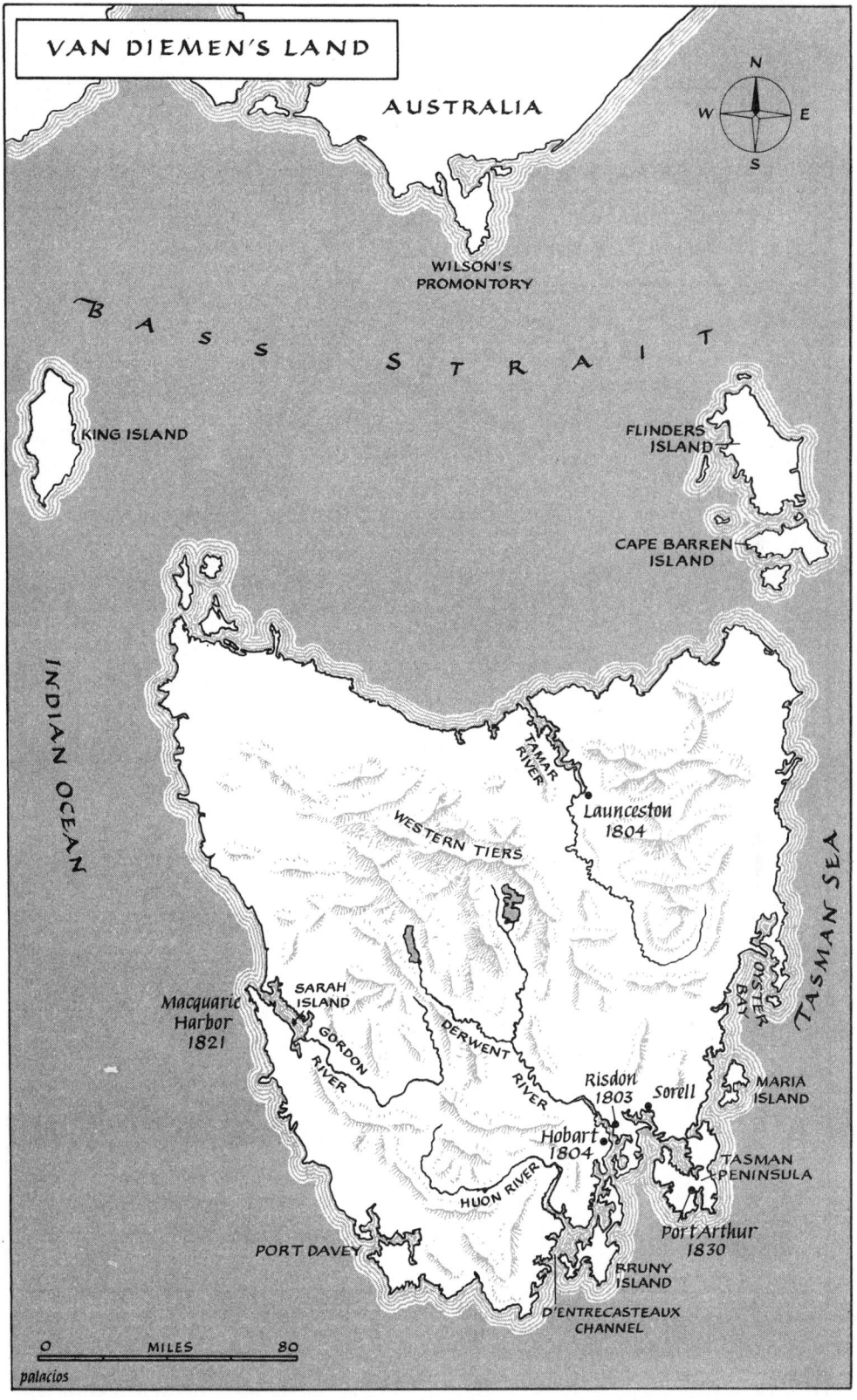

VAN DIEMEN'S LAND

AUSTRALIA

N
W   E
S

WILSON'S
PROMONTORY

B A S S   S T R A I T

KING ISLAND

FLINDERS
ISLAND

CAPE BARREN
ISLAND

INDIAN OCEAN

TAMAR
RIVER

Launceston
1804

WESTERN TIERS

TASMAN SEA

OYSTER BAY

SARAH
ISLAND

Macquarie
Harbor
1821

GORDON
RIVER

DERWENT
RIVER

Risdon
1803

Sorell

MARIA
ISLAND

Hobart
1804

TASMAN
PENINSULA

HUON RIVER

Port Arthur
1830

PORT DAVEY

BRUNY
ISLAND

D'ENTRECASTEAUX
CHANNEL

0   MILES   80

palacios

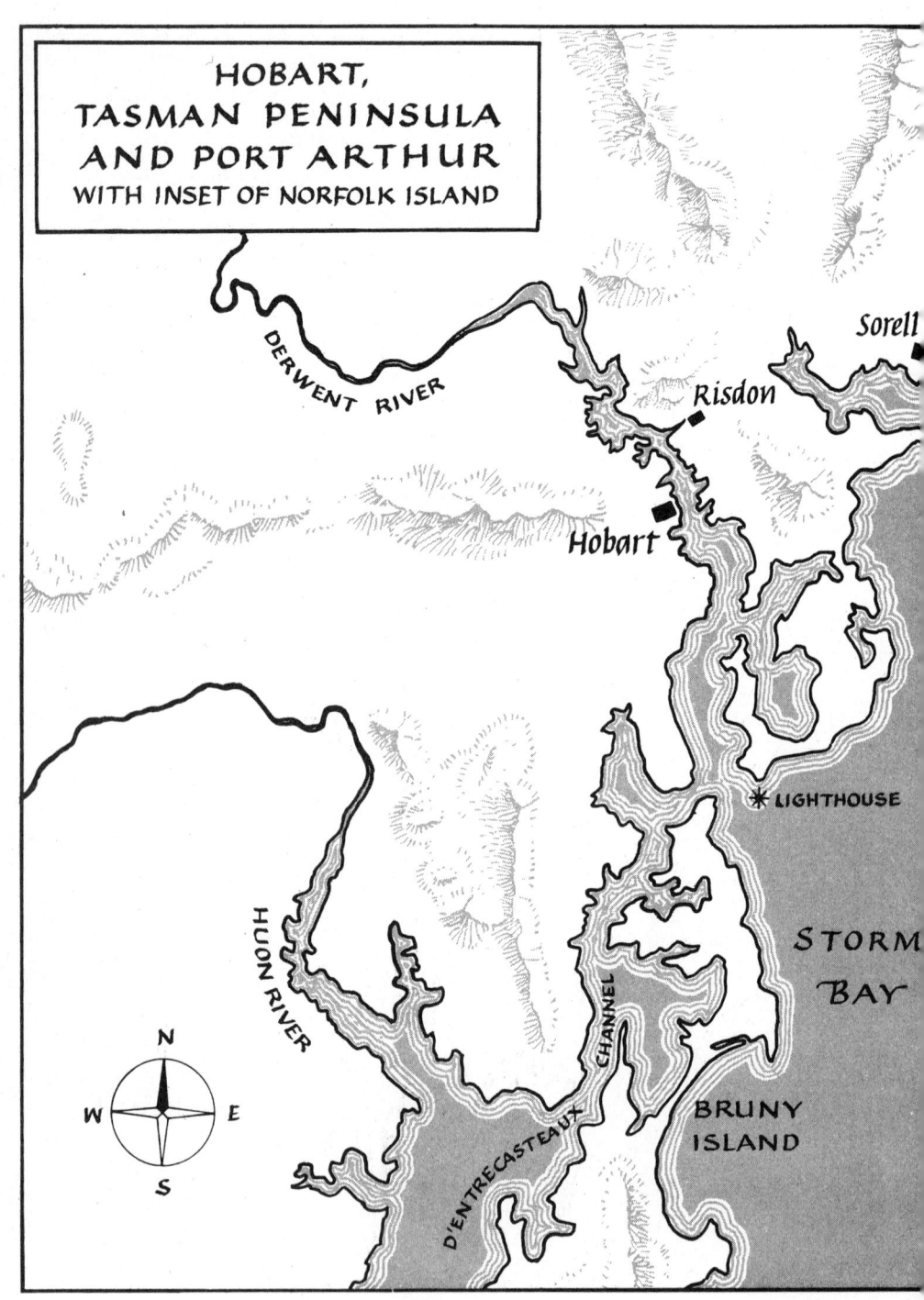

HOBART,
TASMAN PENINSULA
AND PORT ARTHUR
WITH INSET OF NORFOLK ISLAND

DERWENT RIVER

Sorell

Risdon

Hobart

LIGHTHOUSE

HUON RIVER

STORM
BAY

D'ENTRECASTEAUX CHANNEL

BRUNY
ISLAND

N
W    E
S

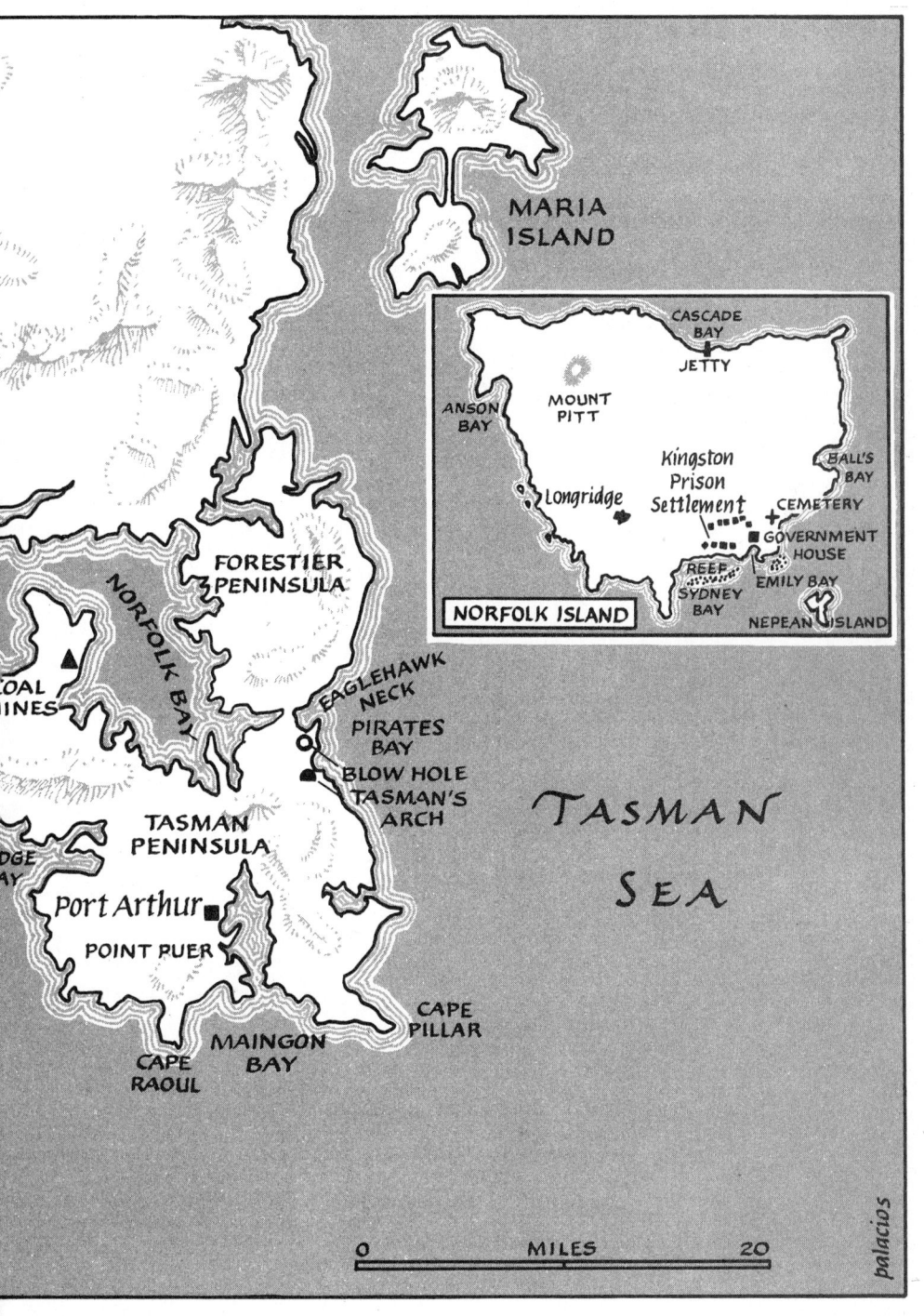

MARIA
ISLAND

CASCADE
BAY
JETTY

ANSON
BAY

MOUNT
PITT

BALL'S
BAY

Longridge

Kingston
Prison
Settlement

CEMETERY

GOVERNMENT
HOUSE

REEF
SYDNEY
BAY

EMILY BAY

NORFOLK ISLAND

NEPEAN ISLAND

FORESTIER
PENINSULA

NORFOLK BAY

COAL
MINES

EAGLEHAWK
NECK

PIRATES
BAY

BLOW HOLE

TASMAN'S
ARCH

TASMAN
PENINSULA

Port Arthur

POINT PUER

OGE
AY

CAPE
PILLAR

CAPE
RAOUL

MAINGON
BAY

TASMAN

SEA

0        MILES        20

palacios

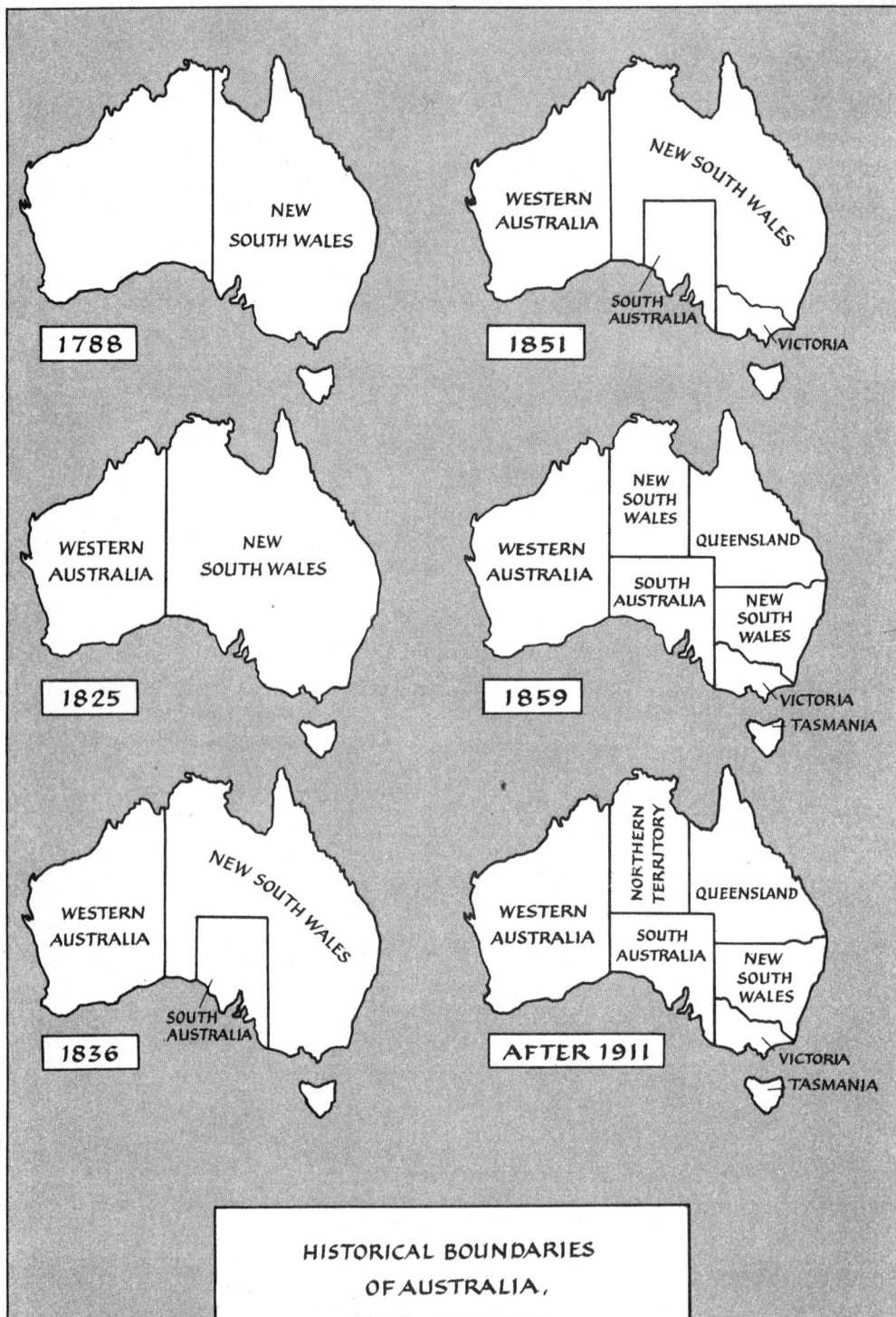

1788

NEW
SOUTH WALES

1851

WESTERN
AUSTRALIA

NEW SOUTH WALES

SOUTH
AUSTRALIA

VICTORIA

1825

WESTERN
AUSTRALIA

NEW
SOUTH WALES

1859

WESTERN
AUSTRALIA

NEW
SOUTH
WALES

QUEENSLAND

SOUTH
AUSTRALIA

NEW
SOUTH
WALES

VICTORIA

TASMANIA

1836

WESTERN
AUSTRALIA

NEW SOUTH WALES

SOUTH
AUSTRALIA

AFTER 1911

WESTERN
AUSTRALIA

NORTHERN
TERRITORY

QUEENSLAND

SOUTH
AUSTRALIA

NEW
SOUTH
WALES

VICTORIA

TASMANIA

HISTORICAL BOUNDARIES
OF AUSTRALIA,
1788 – PRESENT

# The Fatal Shore

# I

# The Harbor and the Exiles

i

IN 1787, the twenty-eighth year of the reign of King George III, the British Government sent a fleet to colonize Australia.

Never had a colony been founded so far from its parent state, or in such ignorance of the land it occupied. There had been no reconnaissance. In 1770 Captain James Cook had made landfall on the unexplored east coast of this utterly enigmatic continent, stopped for a short while at a place named Botany Bay and gone north again. Since then, no ship had called: not a word, not an observation, for seventeen years, each one of which was exactly like the thousands that had preceded it, locked in its historical immensity of blue heat, bush, sandstone and the measured booming of glassy Pacific rollers.

Now this coast was to witness a new colonial experiment, never tried before, not repeated since. An unexplored continent would become a jail. The space around it, the very air and sea, the whole transparent labyrinth of the South Pacific, would become a wall 14,000 miles thick.

The late eighteenth century abounded in schemes of social goodness thrown off by its burgeoning sense of revolution. But here, the process was to be reversed: not Utopia, but Dystopia; not Rousseau's natural man moving in moral grace amid free social contracts, but man coerced, exiled, deracinated, in chains. Other parts of the Pacific, especially Tahiti, might seem to confirm Rousseau. But the intellectual patrons of Australia, in its first colonial years, were Hobbes and Sade.

In their most sanguine moments, the authorities hoped that it would eventually swallow a whole class—the "criminal class," whose existence was one of the prime sociological beliefs of late Georgian and early Victorian England. Australia was settled to defend English property not from the frog-eating invader across the Channel but from the marauder within. English lawmakers wished not only to get rid of the "criminal class" but if possible to forget about it. Australia was a cloaca, invisible,

I

its contents filthy and unnameable. Jeremy Bentham, inveighing against the "thief-colony" in 1812, argued that transportation

> was indeed a measure of *experiment* . . . but the subject-matter of experiment was, in this case, a peculiarly commodious one; a set of *animae viles*, a sort of excrementitious mass, that could be projected, and accordingly was projected—projected, and as it should seem purposely—as far out of sight as possible.[1]

To most Englishmen this place seemed not just a mutant society but another planet—an exiled world, summed up in its popular name, "Botany Bay." It was remote and anomalous to its white creators. It was strange but close, as the unconscious to the conscious mind. There was as yet no such thing as "Australian" history or culture. For its first forty years, everything that happened in the thief-colony was English. In the whole period of convict transportation, the Crown shipped more than 160,000 men, women and children (due to defects in the records, the true number will never be precisely known) in bondage to Australia.[2] This was the largest forced exile of citizens at the behest of a European government in pre-modern history. Nothing in earlier penology compares with it. In Australia, England drew the sketch for our own century's vaster and more terrible fresco of repression, the Gulag. No other country had such a birth, and its pangs may be said to have begun on the afternoon of January 26, 1788, when a fleet of eleven vessels carrying 1,030 people, including 548 male and 188 female convicts, under the command of Captain Arthur Phillip in his flagship *Sirius*, entered Port Jackson or, as it would presently be called, Sydney Harbor.

ii

ONE MAY LIKEN this moment to the breaking open of a capsule. Upon the harbor the ships were now entering, European history had left no mark at all. Until the swollen sails and curvetting bows of the British fleet came round South Head, there were no dates. The Aborigines and the fauna around them had possessed the landscape since time immemorial, and no other human eye had seen them. Now the protective glass of distance broke, in an instant, never to be restored.

To imagine the place, one should begin at North Head, the upper mandible of the harbor. Here, Australia stops; its plates of sandstone break off like a biscuit whose crumbs, the size of cottages, lie jumbled 250 feet below, at the surging ultramarine rim of the Pacific. A ragged wall of creamy-brown sandstone, fretted by the incessant wind, runs north to a glazed horizon. To the east, the Pacific begins its 7,000-mile arc toward South America. Long swells grind into the cliff in a boiling white lather, flinging veils of water a hundred feet into the air. At the meetings of its ancient planes of rock, sea and sky—mass, energy and light—one can grasp why the Aborigines called North Head *Boree*, "the enduring one."

The sandstone is the bone and root of the coast. On top of the cliff, the soil is thin and the scrub sparse. There are banksia bushes, with their sawtooth-edge leaves and dried seed-cones like multiple, jabbering mouths. Against this austere gray-green, the occasional red or blue scribble of a flower looks startling. But further back to the west, the sandstone ledges dip down into the harbor, separating it into scores of inlets. In 1788 these sheltered coves were densely wooded. The largest trees were eucalypts: red gums, angophoras, scribbly gums and a dozen others. Until the late eighteenth century no European had ever seen a eucalypt, and very strange they must have looked, with their strings of hanging, half-shed bark, their smooth wrinkling joints (like armpits, elbows or crotches), their fluent gesticulations and haze of perennial foliage. Not evergreens, but evergrays: the soft, spatially deceitful background color of the Australian bush, monotonous-looking at first sight but rippling with nuance to the acclimatized eye.

In the gullies, where streams of water slid from pool to pool leaving beards of rusty algae on their sandstone lips, giant cabbage-tree palms grew, their damp shade supporting a host of ferns and mosses. Yellow sprays of mimosa flashed in the sun along the ridges, and there were stands of blackboy trees, their dry spear of a stalk shooting up from a drooping hackle of fronds.

Most of the ground was sandy and thin, but parts of the harbor foreshores held, to the relief of Captain John Hunter, Phillip's second-in-command,

> tolerable land . . . which may be cultivated without waiting for its being cleared of wood; for the trees stand very wide of one another, and have no underwood; in short, the woods . . . resemble a deer park, as much as if they had been intended for such a purpose.[3]

The comparison of the harbor landscape with an English park is one of the more common, if startling, descriptive resources of First Fleet diarists. Partly it came from their habit of resorting to familiar European stereotypes to deal with the unfamiliar appearance of things Australian; thus it took at least two decades for colonial watercolorists to get the gum trees right, so that they did not look like English oaks or elms.[4] Partly, no doubt, it arose from the simple fact that any land looks like

Eden after months at sea. But it also had a basis in fact, since the landscape was often burned by aboriginal hunters; their firesticks kept the
big trees isolated and promoted the growth of grass.

So there was a mingled note of relief and aesthetic pleasure in Arthur
Bowes Smyth's journal entry for January 26, 1788, as his transport *Lady
Penrhyn* glided up the harbor, past the dangerous reef with outlying rocks
that would later be called the Sow and Pigs, past the tilting, wind-
gnarled, peach-colored sandstone ledges of Vaucluse and Parsley Bay,
toward the wide, light-flushed notch of water now spanned by the Sydney
Harbor Bridge:

> The finest terras's, lawns and grottos, with distinct plantations of the
> tallest and most stately trees I ever saw in any nobleman's ground in
> England, cannot excel in beauty those wh. Nature now presented to our
> view. The singing of the various birds among the trees, and the flight of
> the numerous parraquets, lorrequets, cockatoos, and maccaws, made all
> around appear like an enchantment; the stupendous rocks from the sum-
> mit of the hills and down to the very water's edge hang'g over in a most
> awful way from above, and form'g the most commodious quays by the
> water, beggard all description.[5]

He was wrong about macaws, which do not exist in Australia. But
the density and range of bird life along the harbor was still amazing.
Several dozen kinds of parrot thronged the harbor bush: Galahs, bald-
eyed Corellas, pink Leadbeater's Cockatoos, black Funereal Cockatoos,
down through the rainbow-colored lorikeets and rosellas to the tiny, seed-
eating budgerigars which, when disturbed, flew up in green clouds so
dense that they cast long rippling shadows on the ground. The Sulphur-
Crested Cockatoos, *Cacatua galerita*, were the most spectacular—big
birds with hoarse squalling voices, chalk-white plumage (dusted with
yellow under the wedge-shaped tail), beaks the color of slate, obsidian
eyes, and an insouciant lick of yellow feathers curling back from the
head. When excited, they would flirt their crests erect into nimbi of
golden spokes like Aztec headdresses. These raucous dandies assembled
in flocks of hundreds which, settling on a dead gum tree, would cover its
silvery limbs in what seemed to be a thick blooming of white flowers;
until, at the moment of alarm, the blossoms would re-form into birds
and return screeching into the sky.

The Galahs, smaller cockatoos, had gray backs, white crests and
fronts of the most delicate, intense dusty pink, like the center of a Bourbon rose; so that a flock of them passing against the opaline horizon
would seem to change color—pink flicking to gray and back to pink again
—as it changed direction, uttering small grating cries like the creak of
rusty hinges.

The exuberance of bird life around the harbor was balanced by the stillness and secrecy of the ground. Nothing about Australian animals was obvious. Many of them were camouflaged fossils, throwbacks that crept, slid, waddled or bounded through the dry brush. In them, the legends of antipodean inversion seemed to be made harmless flesh. Their remote ancestors had evolved in isolation ever since the Australian continent broke off from Antarctica, about 40 million years ago.[6]

One of these creatures, a small macropod called a wallaby, had already been shot and collected by Sir Joseph Banks far north of Sydney Harbor, as the *Endeavour* lay beached and holed among the coral mazes of the Great Barrier Reef in June 1770. It was skinned and taken to England, where it was stuffed by a London taxidermist and given to the great animal painter George Stubbs to have its portrait made. "Called by the natives *Kangooroo*," Captain Cook noted in his journal, it moved "by hoping or jumping 7 or 8 feet at each hop upon its hind legs only. . . . The skin is cover'd with a short hairy fur of a dark Mouse or Grey Colour. Excepting the head and ears which I thought something like a Hare's, it bears no sort of resemblance to any European animal I ever saw."[7] When Phillip arrived in Sydney Harbor, the one certain thing he knew about the language of the "Indians" was that they called this creature a kangaroo. But because their language bore no resemblance to that of the tribe Cook had encountered so far to the north, the Sydney Aborigines assumed that "kangaroo" was the white intruders' word for the ordinary familiar animal they themselves had always known as a *patagarang.*

Half a dozen kinds of patagarang lived around the harbor, nibbling its wiry grass and appearing silently, like fawn wraiths, among the guttered shelves of the fern-gullies.The silvery-coated Eastern Gray kangaroo, *Macropus giganteus*, moved in flocks of dozens; "the noise they make," a colonial diarist was to note, "is a faint bleat, querulous, but not easy to describe." Other species ranged down in size from the timid rock-wallabies to the tiny, ratlike Potoroo.

The kangaroos were not the only oddities of this landscape. Koalas clambered through the gum-tree branches or sprawled sedately in the comfortable forks munching their bunches of leaves. These were not the winsome, cuddly teddy bears of the Qantas commercial, but slow, irritable, aldermanic creatures with furry ears and a boot-heel nose, which ate two pounds of fresh gum leaves a day and, when captured, scratched furiously and drenched the offending hand with eucalyptus-scented piss. Indeed they were not bears at all (any more than the moon-spotted "native cat" was a cat, or the bandy-rumped Tasmanian Wolf a canine) but nocturnal marsupials with no clear relationship to any other animal, living or fossil. After sundown, their trees were filled with the thumping, scrabbling and chittering of other nocturnals—fat brushtailed possums, ringtails and sugar-gliders, which had wide furry airfoils slung between their fore and hind feet and parachuted from tree to tree in wobbly swoops. Like true Arcadians, these creatures lived by sucking sweet nectar from bush flowers.

The oldest and most bizarre of the mammals were, however, the platypus and the echidna. Both were exceedingly primitive, stuck at an intermediate point of evolution between reptiles and mammals. They were monotremes: the same orifice served them interchangeably for mating, excretion and egg-laying. The echidna, or spiny anteater, looked vaguely like a European hedgehog, but the resemblance was not even quill-deep: its elegant yellow-and-brown spines were actually a kind of fur, though of the most formalized sort. It laid eggs like a bird but carried them about in a pouch under its belly. It was very shortsighted but had an acute sense of smell and could sniff out the ants' odor of formic acid through yards of air or inches of sun-hardened earth. It had a beak rather than jaws—an open tube from which a whip of pink, sticky tongue almost as long as its body would shoot into the ants' nest. When threatened, the echidna would curl into a ball of bristles or put its head down and start to dig with its prodigiously strong claws, burying itself within moments.

The platypus, on the other hand, was an amphibian: the sole survivor of its prehistoric family, the Ornithorhynchidae or bird-beaked mammals. It had a bill and webbed feet like a duck, a tail like a beaver and exquisitely glossy, oil-rich fur. Like a tiny seal, it had a generous layer of fat under the skin, for it was too primitive to regulate its own body temperature. In a tunnel burrowed in the mud of a creek bank, the female platypus would lay a clutch of leathery, ancient-looking eggs and suckle her young when they hatched—not with teats, but through enlarged pores on her belly which she scratched until milk oozed forth. Most of a platypus's life had to be spent foraging on the streambed for worms and insects, since it ate rather more than its own weight in food a day and had a metabolic rate like a blast furnace. Hold one of these frantic little fossils (avoiding the hind legs, which carry a poison spur, like many "cute" things in Australia) and it seems to be all heart, pumping and quivering.

Wombats—lumbering, eighty-pound marsupials resembling squat, blunt-skulled bears—dug their meandering catacombs beneath the soil; bandicoots peeked from holes; the landscape was alive, but secretively so. Here in the Australian bush one needed to look, and look again, before glimpsing the gray koala camouflaged against the fleshy gray burl of its gum tree. The voices of the animals tended to be out of all proportion to their size. Just as space was drained of perspective by the random, flickering transparency of the trees, so it was hard to guess where sounds originated. The throbbing croak of the cicada on a branch ten feet away might seem to be coming from all around. It was hard to sneak up on these creatures of the harbor shores. The bush, baked tawny and bronze by the summer heat, its ground surface mantled in a crackling skin of dry gum leaves, grasses and fallen strips of eucalyptus bark, was like a stretched drum, a delicate resonator that informed every animal of each approach.

There was little sense of menace in this parliament of creatures. The only large meat-eating animal was the dingo, the "native dog" imported to Australia long ago by migrating Aborigines. Even the dragon of the bush, a carrion-eating monitor lizard known as a goanna, would rush up a tree when approached and cling there, its throat puffed out in soundless alarm, until the intruder went away. The only universal predator was man.

### iii

A STATIC CULTURE, frozen by its immemorial primitivism, un-changed in an unchanging landscape—such until quite recently was, and for many people still is, the common idea of the Australian Aborigines. It grows from several roots: myths about the Noble Savage, misreadings of aboriginal technology, traditional racism and ignorance of Australian prehistory. It is, in fact, quite false; but in the experience of white city-dwellers there is little to contradict it. Nobody can guess how Sydney Harbor began to unfold itself to its white prisoners on January 26, 1788, just by subtracting the poultice of brick, steel and tar from its headlands, pulling down the Harbor Bridge and the Opera House and populating the beaches with black stick figures waving spears. The changes have been too radical for that. Yet the effort to perceive the landscape and its people as they were is worth making, for it bears on one of the chief myths of early colonial history as understood and taught up to about 1960. This was the idea, promulgated by the early settlers and inherited from the nineteenth century, that the First Fleet sailed into an "empty" continent, speckled with primitive animals and hardly less primitive men, so that the "fittest" inevitably triumphed. Thus the destruction of the Austra-lian Aborigines was rationalized as natural law. "Nothing can stay the dying away of the Aboriginal race, which Providence has only allowed to hold the land until replaced by a finer race," remarked a settler in 1849.[8]

But the first white Australian settlers were so conspicuously unfit for survival in the new land that they lived on the edge of starvation in the midst of what seemed natural abundance to the Aborigines. They had practically no idea of what they could eat or how to get it. Most of the

First Fleet convicts had not moved ten miles from their place of birth and had never seen the sea before they were clapped in irons and thrust on the transports. They were as lost in Australia as an Aborigine would have been in a London "rookery." The tribesmen they encountered were so well adapted to their landscape that their standard of nutrition was probably higher than that of most Europeans in 1788. To the whites, convict and officer alike, Sydney Harbor was the end of the earth. But to the Aborigines it was the center. The landscape and its elusive resources, not yet named by the whites, stood between the two cultures, showing each group its utter unlikeness to the other.

At the time of white invasion, men had been living in Australia for at least 30,000 years. They had moved into the continent during the Pleistocene epoch. This migration happened at about the same time as the first wave of human migrations from Asia into the unpeopled expanse of North America, across the now sunken land-bridge between Russia and Alaska.

The first Australians also came from Asia. When they discovered Australia, the continent was perhaps a quarter larger than it now is. In the Pleistocene epoch the level of the Pacific was between 400 and 600 feet lower than it is today. One could walk from southern Australia into Tasmania, which was not yet an island. The Sahul Shelf, that shallow ledge of ocean floor whose waters separate Australia from New Guinea was dry land; Australia, New Guinea and possibly sections of the New Hebrides formed one landmass. By trial and error, accumulated over many human generations, it would then have been possible to get from Southeast Asia into Australia (via the Celebes and Borneo) across islands sprinkled on the sea like stepping-stones. Much of this voyage would have been done by eyeball navigation to coasts that the immigrants could have seen from their starting point; there would have been a few sea voyages of more than 50 miles, but not too many; but there was no direct route. In the words of the historian Geoffrey Blainey, "Australia was merely the chance terminus of a series of voyages and migrations."[9] But the moment when the first man stepped ashore from his frail chip of a canoe on the northwestern coast of Pleistocene Australia should rightly be seen as one of the hinges of human history: it was the first time *Homo sapiens* had ever colonized by sea.

Apart from their northern origin, no one knows who these Pleistocene colonists were or whence they emerged.[10] Whoever they were, they gradually spread south, east and west across the continent, killing giant kangaroos as they went, bringing with them their imported half-wild dogs, whose descendants are the dingoes. Their first campsites were drowned by the waters of the Timor Sea and the Gulf of Carpenteria, which rose so fast between 13,000 and 16,000 B.C. that the coast moved inland at a rate of three miles a year.[11] The oldest known northern camp-sites were pitched 22,000 years ago at Oenpelli, 150 miles east of Darwin.

But the southward march was under way long before that. By 30,000 B.C. there were well-established tribes eating crayfish and emu eggs beside the now arid basin of Lake Mungo, in southeastern Australia; they were perhaps the world's first people to practice cremation, and the pellets of ocher placed as offerings in a Mungo grave suggest that they had some idea of the survival of consciousness after death.[12] By about 20,000 B.C. the Aborigines had reached Sydney Harbor. Others were prizing flint nodules from the limestone walls of Koonalda Cave, under the Nullarbor Plain on the extreme southern rim of the continent. There, in the darkness, they scratched crude patterns on the walls that may be the first works of art ever made in the southern hemisphere—the merest graffiti, compared to the later achievements of aboriginal rock-painting, but clear evidence of some primal artistic intent. Two thousand years later, the Aborigines had left their shell-middens, flint chips, bone points and charcoal in nearly every habitable part of the continent. The colonization was achieved, and a membrane of human culture had been stretched over the vast terrain.

But it was exceedingly thin. When the First Fleet arrived, there were perhaps 300,000 Aborigines in the whole of Australia—a continental average of one person to ten square miles. The density of local populations, however, varied a great deal. Probably less than 20,000 people wandered in the 300,000-square-mile tract of dry limestone plain and saltbush desert between the Great Australian Bight and the Tropic of Capricorn, a place where even the crows are said to fly backwards to keep the dust out of their eyes. On the coast, where there was more food and a higher rainfall, the land could support more people. Phillip, after a few months on Sydney Harbor, reckoned that the areas of the Cumberland Plain he had explored sustained about 1,500 blacks; this rough guess yields a density of about 3 people per square mile.

The Australians divided themselves in tribes. They had no notion of private property, but they were intensely territorial, linked to the ancestral area by hunting customs and totemism. Hundreds of tribes existed at the time of white invasion—perhaps as many as 900, although the more likely figure is about 500. The tribe did not have a king, or a charismatic leader, or even a formal council. It was linked together by a common religion, by language and by an intricate web of family relationships; it had no writing, but instead a complex structure of spoken and sung myth whose arcana were gradually passed on by elders to the younger men. Geographical features could cause splits in tribal language. Thus in the area of Sydney, the ancestral territory of the Iora tribe—who roamed over about 700 square miles, from Pittwater to Botany Bay—was cut in half by Sydney Harbor itself; so that the "hordes" or tribal subgroups on the north and south sides of the harbor, the Cameragal and the Kadigal, spoke two distinct languages. For them, the harbor formed a linguistic chasm as wide as the English Channel.[13] In 1791, as white settlement was pushing out past Windsor and the Hawkesbury River, Governor Phillip was surprised to find on its banks

> people who made use of several words we could not understand, and it soon appear'd that they had a language different from that used by the natives we have hitherto been acquainted with. They did not call the Moon *Yan-re-dah* but *Con-do-in*, and they called the Penis *Bud-da*, which our natives call *Ga-diay*.[14]

These were the Daruk, who ranged over a territory of about 2,300 square miles from the coast north of Iora territory to the Katoomba–Blackheath area of the Blue Mountains in the south. The Daruk, the Iora and the Tarawal (whose territory began on the south shore of Botany Bay) were the three tribes with whom the white settlers of Australia first had to deal.

Watkin Tench (1758–1833), a young officer of marines on the transport *Charlotte*, was struck by the ease with which the tribes understood one another. He supposed that the Daruk language was only a dialect of Iora, "though each in speaking preferred its own [tongue]."[15] In fact, the variety of aboriginal language arose from the tight social structure of the tribes, their specified restricted territories, and their more-or-less fixed patterns of movement in relation to other tribal boundaries. These factors encouraged each tribe to keep its own language intact, while nomadism forced them to learn others. Compared to some inland tribes, who routinely exchanged goods (flint axes, baler shell ornaments, lumps of ocher for body painting and other local commodities) along trade routes as long as 1,000 miles, the Iora were provincial. They could not understand languages spoken 50 miles away. Their main diet was fish, and they had no reason to leave the coast. They held their territories—the Cameragal and the Walumedegal along the north shore of the harbor, the Boorogegal on Bradley Head, the Kadigal around what is now Circular Quay and the Botanical Gardens—as they had held them for centuries.

Their main food source was the sea. The women of the tribe twisted fishing lines from pounded bark fiber and made hooks from the turban shell. But since such hooks were brittle and the line weak, the Aborigines fished in pairs—a woman led the hooked fish in as gently as possible, while a man stood ready to spear the fish as soon as it got within range. At the ends of the fish-spears were three or four prongs of wallaby or bird bone, ground sharp and set in gum resin.

The Iora fished from canoes. These they made by cutting a long oval of bark from a suitable eucalypt and binding its ends together to make bow and stern. The old, scarred "canoe trees" were a common sight around the harbor a hundred years ago, but none remain today. The gunwale was reinforced with a pliable stick, sewn on with vegetable fiber. Shorter sticks, jammed athwartships, served as spreaders. The cracks and seams were then caulked with clay or gum resin. The Aborigines kept fire burning on a pat of wet clay on the bottom of the hull, so that they could grill and eat their fish at sea. Compared to an American Indian birch canoe, they were unstable craft and wretchedly crude, "by far the worst canoes I ever saw or heard of," in the view of William Bradley, who was first lieutenant on *Sirius.* They had neither outriggers nor sails (the Iora were ignorant of weaving); low in the water, they flexed with every ripple and leaked like sieves. Nevertheless, the Iora handled them skillfully. "I have seen them paddle through a a large surf," Bradley noted, "without oversetting or taking in more water than if rowing in smooth water." The frailty of these craft suited the Iora's nomadic way of life; they were easy to carry and just as easy to replace. A tribesman could slap one together in a day.[16]

The Iora also ate immense quantities of shellfish, mainly oysters, which were gathered by women. Middens of white shells lay at the entrances of scores of sandstone caves along the harbor shores. Bennelong Point, where the Sydney Opera House now stands, was first named Limeburners' Point by the colonists because it was mantled in a deposit of mollusc shells, built up over thousands of years of uninterrupted gorging.* Gathered again (this time by white convict women) and burned in a kiln, these shells provided the lime for Sydney's first mortar.

The Iora were not wholly dependent on the sea for their diet. They also hunted on land, though rarely with boomerangs. Boomerangs have to fly without obstruction and so were weapons for open grassland and desert, not for the sclerophyll forests where the Iora lived. Probably their role in providing food for the Sydney blacks was insignificant. Rather,

---

* Bennelong was an Iora tribesman, the first black to learn English, drink rum, wear clothes and eat the invaders' strange food. He was rewarded for his curiosity with the friendship of Governor Phillip—and a small brick hut, about 12 feet square, in which he lived on the end of what is now Bennelong Point. "Love and war," a colonial diarist noted, "were his favorite pursuits." He went to England with Phillip in 1792 and was much feted as an exotic Noble Savage, the first native Australian to be seen in London. But he lost most of his curiosity value after a year or two, and it was not until the end of 1795 that he returned to Sydney, with the newly appointed governor, John Hunter. By then he fitted neither his old tribal world nor the carceral microcosm of the whites, whose tolerance of the blacks had begun to disintegrate after Phillip's departure. Bennelong became increasingly sodden and pugnacious with rum, and died at the age of about 40 in 1813.

the staple hunting weapons were the spear, the stone axe and the fire-stick.[17]

The Ioras' hunting spears, unlike their fish-gigs, were one-pointed and tipped with a variety of materials—usually fire-hardened wood, but also bones and flints and sometimes a shark tooth. John White, a surgeon on board the transport *Charlotte*, noted that a skilled hunter-warrior threw his spear with formidable accuracy and power, "thirty or forty yards with an unerring precision," although throws of twice that length were recorded. They were flung with a spear-thrower or *woomera*, a stick with a peg in one end that fitted the butt of the spear and acted as an extension of the hunter's arm, like the thong of a sling. With this equipment, a small group of hunters could bring down anything from a bandicoot to an emu. They knocked birds out of the trees with stones or trapped them by dexterity and yogic self-control: "A native will in the heat of the sun lay down asleep, holding a bit of fish in his hand; the bird seeing the bait, seizes on the fish, and the native then catches it."[18]

By any standards, the Aborigines were technologically weak but manually adept. They had not invented the bow-and-arrow, but they had exquisite skill as stalkers, trackers and mimics. A competent hunter needs to be able to read every displacement of a leaf or scuffed print in the dust. He must freeze in mid-step and stand unblinking on one leg for half an hour, waiting for a goanna to work up the courage to come all the way out of its log. He must know how to pick up a blacksnake by the tail and crack its head off, as one cracks a whip. He must climb like a cat, shinnying up the gum trees to raid the wild bees' honey or chop some befuddled nocturnal possum from its hole with a stone axe. Above all, the hunter needed to know every detail of animal life in his territory —migratory patterns, feeding habits, nesting, shelter, mating. Only thus could a small nomadic group survive.

The same was true in the vegetable kingdom, which was the province of women. Like all other known Australian tribes, the Iora forced a rigid sexual division of labor between male hunters and female gatherers. Colonists in the 1790s do not say much about Iora plant-gathering, perhaps because the work of men, even of low savages, seemed more interesting than that of women; thus, one cannot judge the importance plant food had in the Iora diet. We can deduce from the available evidence, however, that the Iora had no conception of agriculture. They neither sowed nor reaped; they appear to have wrought no changes on the face of the country. They were seen as culturally static primitives lightly wandering in an ecologically static landscape, which seemed to eliminate any claims they might have had to prior ownership. To some eighteenth- and nineteenth-century eyes, this invalidated them as human beings.

However, the crude aboriginal technology did wreak changes on the landscape and fauna, for it included fire. Everywhere the tribes went, they carried firesticks and burned many square miles of bushland. They set fire to hollow trees and clubbed the possums and lizards as they scrambled out; they incinerated swathes of bush to drive terrified marsupials onto the waiting spears.

Bushfire and drought are the traditional nightmares of bush life. A bushfire driven by a high wind through dry summer forest is an appalling spectacle: a wreathing cliff of flame moving forward at thirty miles an hour, igniting treetop after treetop like a chain of magnesium flares. Bushfire is the natural enemy of property. But the black Australians had no property and did not hesitate to burn off a few square miles of territory just to catch a dozen goannas and marsupial rats, at the cost of destroying all slow-moving animals within that area.

Fire, to the Iora, was shelter. That was part of the necessary logic of their life, since to survive at all the small knots of family groups that made up the tribe had to range easily and rapidly over a wide area, feeding as they went; and that made the idea of solid, permanent dwellings inconceivable. To them, the hearth was of far greater significance than the home. A firestick made the hearth portable. But they had never had to invent a portable house (i.e., a tent). They were far more backward than any Bedouin or Plains Indian. They used what they could find: the sandstone caves of the harbor shores, with sheets of bark propped up to form crude "humpies." "Their ignorance of building," remarked John Hunter, second captain on *Sirius*,

> is very amply compensated for by the kindness of nature in the remarkable softness of the rocks, which encompass the sea coast . . . They are constantly crumbling away . . . and this continual decay leaves caves of considerable dimensions: some I have seen that would lodge forty or fifty people, and, in a case of necessity, we should think ourselves not badly lodged [in one] for a night.[19]

He was putting the cart before the horse: It was not that the Iora lived in caves because they could not build huts, but rather that they chose not to build huts because they had caves. Another colonial observer grasped why the natives had no architecture a European could recognize:

> . . . Those who build the bark huts are very few compared to the whole. Generally speaking, they prefer the ready made habitations they find in the rocks, which perfectly accords with the roving manner in which they live, for they never stay long in one situation, and as they travel in tribes together, even making the bark huts would engage them more time than they would be happy on one spot.[20]

Caves and bark humpies are drafty places and it gets cold on the harbor at night. The Iora therefore slept huddled together close to their ever-smoldering campfires, and accidental burns were common. The debris of possum skins, fishbones and wallaby guts scattered around the entrance brought swarms of flies and insects, for the tribal "hygiene" of the nomads consisted simply of walking away from their rubbish and excreta (an ancient habit that would have catastrophic results for their marginal descendants, detribalized and trapped in their ghetto shacks on the fringes of white communities a generation or two later). Wherever they went they were plagued by mosquitoes, against which they employed the deterrent of fish oil: "It is by no means uncommon to see the entrails of fish frying upon their heads in the sun, till the oil runs over their face and body. This unguent is deemed by them of so much importance, that children even of two years old are taught the use of it."[21] Since the Iora never washed, they spent their lives coated with a mixture of rancid fish oil, animal grease, ocher, beach sand, dust and sweat. They were filthy and funky in the extreme. But their stamina and muscular development were superb, and, because there was no sugar (except for the rare treat of wild honey) and little starch in their diet, they had excellent teeth—unlike the white invaders.

No property, no money or any other visible medium of exchange; no surplus or means of storing it, hence not even the barest rudiment of the idea of capital; no outside trade, no farming, no domestic animals except half-wild camp dingoes; no houses, clothes, pottery or metal; no division between leisure and labor, only a ceaseless grubbing and chasing for subsistence foods. Certainly the Iora failed most of the conventional tests of white Georgian culture. They did not even appear to have the social divisions that had been observed in other tribal societies such as those in America or Tahiti. Where were the aboriginal kings, their nobles, their priests, their slaves? They did not exist. Although elders enjoyed special respect as the bearers of accumulated tribal myth and lore, they had no special authority over their juniors, once those juniors had reached manhood and been fully initiated; and the idea of hereditary castes was inconceivable to the Aborigines, who lived in a state approaching that of primitive communism. But if the Aborigines lacked firm hierarchical instincts, what was to be respected in their society? What, in short, was "noble" about these "savages"? The Tahitians could be seen as the last survivors of the classical Golden Age; with their fine canoes and intricate ornaments, strict rankings and plentiful supply of free coconuts, they clearly had superfluity, the paradisiacal ancestor of property, as well as strong class instincts to back it up.

Australia was no place for such Ovidian sentiments. The Tahitians might live like prelapsarian beings, illiterate Athenians; compared to them, the Iora were Spartans. They exemplified "hard" primitivism, and the name Phillip gave to a spot in Sydney Harbor alluded to this: "Their confidence and manly behavior," he reported to Lord Sydney, "made me give the name of Manly Cove to this place."[22] Iora boys, like young Spartans at play, practiced incessantly with their spears and woomeras. They believed implicitly in the power of their weapons, and a touching passage in Surgeon John White's *Journal* describes how one of them reacted when he demonstrated his pistol:

> He then, by signs and gestures, seemed to ask if the pistol would make a hole through him, and on being made sensible that it would, he showed not the smallest sign of fear; on the contrary he endeavoured . . . to impress us with an idea of the superiority of his own arms, which he applied to his breast, and by staggering and a show of falling seemed to wish us to understand that the force and effect of them was mortal and not to be resisted.[23]

Skirmishing with other clans, or with foreign tribes along the frontier between tribal territories, was an inevitable fact of nomadic life. In this the Iora were probably no less bellicose than other southeastern Australian tribes, despite the often merely symbolic nature of their encounters. They had no "specialist" army. They recognized no distinction between fighters and civilians, or between hunter and warrior. Moreover, the idea that they were intrinsically violent—"savage" in behavior, as well as in looks and economy—seemed to be borne out by the harsh relationships that obtained within their clans, especially in their treatment of women.

That hoary standby of cartoonists, the Stone Age marriage, in which the grunting Neanderthal bashes the fur-clad girl with his club and drags her off to his cave, began with classical satyrs and medieval legends of forest-dwelling Wild Men. But it was certainly amplified by the first accounts of aboriginal courtship. In a plate in the pseudonymous Barrington's *History of New South Wales*, 1802, it appears for the first time in its perfect form: the muscular savage, club in hand, lugging his unconscious victim through the scrub on her back. "Their conduct to women makes them considerably inferior to the brute creation," the author sternly and titillatingly observes:

> In obtaining a female partner the first step they take, romantic as it may seem, is to fix on some female of a tribe at enmity with their own. . . . The monster then stupefies her with blows, which he inflicts with his club, on her head, back, neck, and indeed every part of her body, then snatching up one of her arms, he drags her, streaming with blood from her wounds, through the woods, over stones, rocks, hills and logs, with all the violence and determination of a savage, till he reaches his tribe.[24]

Obviously, the real matrimonial arrangements of the Iora were less lurid than this. Armed rape as a by-product of tribal warfare was not unknown among the Aborigines, but no tribe that had to depend entirely on border raids for its supply of women could have lasted very long. Besides, what would have been the point? There were enough Iora women for the Iora men. However, the unalterable fact of their tribal life was that women had no rights at all and could choose nothing. A girl was usually given away as soon as she was born. She was the absolute property of her kin until marriage, whereupon she became the equally helpless possession of her husband. The idea of a marriage based on romantic love was as culturally absurd to the Iora as it was to most Europeans. The purpose of betrothal was not, however, to amalgamate property, as in European custom, but to strengthen existing kinship bonds by means of reciprocal favors. It did not change a woman's status much. Both before and after, she was merely a root-grubbing, shell-gathering chattel, whose social assets were wiry arms, prehensile toes and a vagina.

As a mark of hospitality, wives were lent to visitors whom the Iora tribesmen wanted to honor. Warriors, before setting out on a revenge raid against some other aboriginal group, would swap their women as an expression of brotherhood. If a tribal group was about to be attacked and knew where its enemies were, it would sometimes send out a party of women in their direction; the attackers would then show that they were open to a peaceful solution by copulating with them. But if the women came back untouched, it was a signal that there was no choice but battle. A night's exchange of wives usually capped a truce between tribes. On these occasions most kinship laws except the most sacred incest taboos were suspended. Finally, at the great ceremonies or *corroborrees*, which involved hours of chant and ecstatic dancing and were meant to reinforce the tribe's identity by merging all individual egos in one communal mass, orgiastic sex played a part. However, since these affairs were rarely seen, sketchily described and never understood by the early colonists, it is impossible to say how large or how strictly prescribed a part it was.[25] If a woman showed the least reluctance to be used for any of these purposes, if she seemed lazy or gave her lord and master any other cause for dissatisfaction, she would be furiously beaten or even speared.

Fertility, the usual protection of women in settled agricultural societies, was a poor shield. A surplus of children would have impeded the Ioras' nomadic life. On the march, each woman had to carry her infant offspring as well as food and implements. She could only manage one child in arms. That child was always weaned late; it fed from the breast until it was three or more years old, since there were no cows or goats in Australia to give substitute milk. Without their mother's milk, the roughness of the adult diet would have starved them, as there was no way to make a thongy gobbet of barely singed wallaby meat digestible to a teething infant.

To get rid of surplus children, the Iora, like all other Australian tribes, routinely induced abortions by giving the pregnant women herbal medicines or, when these failed, by thumping their bellies. If these measures failed, they killed the unwanted child at birth. Deformed children were smothered or strangled. If a mother died in childbirth, or while nursing a child in arms, the infant would be burned with her after the father crushed its head with a large stone.

This ruthless weeding-out of the helpless at one end of life also took place at the other. The Iora respected their old men as repositories of tribal wisdom and religious knowledge, but the tribe would not hamper its mobility, essential to nomadic survival, by keeping the old and infirm alive after their teeth had gone and their joints had seized up.

It was a harsh code; but it had enabled the Aborigines to survive for millennia without either extending their technology or depleting their resources. It still worked as of January 1788, although it had not the slightest chance of surviving white invasion. The most puzzling question for the whites, however, was why these people should display such a marked sense of territory while having no apparent cult of private property. What was it that bound them to the land? The colonial diarists tried as best they could, hampered by the opacity of a language they could not understand, to discover signs of a developed religion among the blacks, but they found very little to report. "We have not been able to discover," wrote Captain Hunter, "that they have any thing like an object of adoration; neither the sun, moon nor stars seem to take up, or occupy more of their attention, than they do that of any other of the animals [sic] which inhabit this immense country."[26] Certainly they had few of the external signs of religious belief: no temples or altars or priests, no venerated images set up in public places, no evidence of sacrifice or (apart from the corroborrees) of communal prayer. In all this they differed from the Tahitians and the Maori, who were settled agricultural peoples. The Iora were not: they carried their conception of the sacred, of mythic time and ancestral origins with them as they walked. These were embodied in the landscape; every hill and valley, each kind of animal and tree, had its place in a systematic but unwritten whole. Take away this territory and they were deprived, not of "property" (an abstract idea that could be satisfied with another piece of land) but of their embodied history, their locus of myth, their "dreaming." There was no possible way in which the accumulated tissue of symbolic and spiritual usage represented by tribal territory could be gathered up and conferred on another tract of land by an act of will. To deprive the Aborigines of their territory, therefore, was to condemn them to spiritual death—a destruction of their past, their future and their opportunities of transcendence. But none of them could have imagined this, as they had never before been invaded. And so they must have stood, in curiosity and apprehension but without real fear, watching from the headlands as the enormous canoes with their sails like stained clouds moved up the harbor to Sydney Cove, and the anchors splashed, and the outcasts of Mother England were disgorged upon this ancestral territory to build their own prison.

# 2

# A Horse Foaled by an Acorn

i

MOST EDUCATED PEOPLE have felt twinges of nostalgia for Georgian England.

We are tied to the Georgian past through artifacts that we would still like to use, given the chance. The town houses, squares, villas, gardens, paintings, silver and side tables seem to represent an "essence" of the eighteenth century, transcending "mere" politics. Since they present an uncommonly coherent image of elegance, common sense and clarity, we are apt to suppose that English society did too. But argument from design to society, like the syllogism that ascends from the particular to the general, usually goes awry. "We shall learn," wrote one typical English exponent of this approach, "from the architecture and furniture and all other things . . . that nearly everybody in the eighteenth century looked forward to a continuation and an agreeable expansion of gracious fashions."[1]

"Nearly everybody"—that, until quite recently, was the conventional picture. A passing reference to violence, dirt and gin; a nod in the direction of the scaffold; a highwayman or two, a drunken judge, and some whores for local color; but the rest is all curricles and fanlights. Modern squalor is squalid but Georgian squalor is "Hogarthian," an art form in itself.

Yet most Englishmen and Englishwomen did not live under such roofs, sit on such chairs or eat with such forks. They did not read Johnson or Pope, for most of them could not read. Antiques say little about the English poor, that vast and as yet unorganized social mass—Samuel Johnson's "rabble," Edmund Burke's "swinish multitude"—from whose discontents in the nineteenth century the English working class would shape itself. The Georgian London a modern visitor imagines was not their city. There were two such Londons, their separation symbolized by the cleavage that took place as the rich moved their residences westward

from Covent Garden between 1700 and 1750, as the speculators ran up
their noble squares and crescents—an absolute gulf between the new
West End and the old, rotting East End of the city.

West London had grown rationally. Its streets and squares were
planned; property was secured by long leases and enforced standards of
building. East London had not. It was a warren of shacks, decaying tenements, and brand-new hovels run up on short leases by jerry-builders
restrained by no local ordinances. Georgian residential solidity stopped
at the lower fringe of the middle class. The "rookeries" of the poor
formed a labyrinth speckled with picturesque names: Turnmill Street,
Cow Cross, Chick Lane, Black Boy Alley, Saffron Hill, the Spittle. West
of the old City of London, the worst slum areas in the mid-eighteenth
century lay around Covent Garden, St. Giles, Holborn and the older parts
of Westminster. To the east, they spread through Blackfriars and beyond
the Tower, by the Lower Pool and Limehouse Reach: Wapping, Shadwell,
Limehouse, Ratcliffe Highway, the Jewish ghettos of Stepney and Whitechapel on the north side of the Thames, the brick canyons of Southwark
with its seven prisons on the south bank. Their courts and alleys were
dark, tangled, narrow and choked with offal. Because men had to live
near their work, tenements stood cheek by jowl with slaughterhouses
and tanneries. London was judged the greatest city in the world, but also
the worst smelling. Sewers still ran into open drains; the largest of these,
until it was finally covered in 1765, was the Fleet Ditch. Armies of rats
rose from the tenement cellars to go foraging in daylight.

The living were so crowded that there was scarcely room to bury the
dead. Around St. Martin's, St. James's and St. Giles-in-the-Fields, there
were large open pits filled with the rotting cadavers of paupers whose
friends could get them no better burial; they were called "Poor's Holes"
and remained a London commonplace until the 1790s.

Within the rookeries, distinctions of class were seen. Their cellars
were rented at 9d. or 1s. a week* to the most miserable tenants—rag-
pickers, bonegatherers or the swelling crowd of Irish casual laborers
driven across St. George's Channel by famine, rural collapse and the lure
of the Big City. Thirty people might be found in a cellar. Before 1800 an
artisan might expect to find a "cheap" furnished room in London for 2s.
6d. a week, and most London workers lived in such places with no rights
of tenancy.

To speak of an eighteenth-century "working class" as though it were
a homogeneous entity, united by class-consciousness and solidarity, is

---

* In English currency, d. stands for pence (one penny used to be equivalent to ¹⁄₂₄₀ of a
pound; it is now ¹⁄₁₀₀ of a pound); s. stands for shilling (one shilling is equivalent to ¹⁄₂₀
pound, or 12 pence).

both anachronistic and abstract. It is a projection of the twentieth century onto the eighteenth.

Loyalties ran between workers in the same trade but rarely between workers as such. The variety of trades and work underwrote the complexity of this other London. It contained a huge range of occupations, and a passion for close divisions of social standing held for workers as well as for gentry. They too had their pecking orders and were bound by them. At the upper end of income and comfort, just below the independent shopkeepers, were the skilled artisans in luxury trades, regularly employed: upholsterers and joiners, watch-finishers, coach-painters or lens-grinders. At the lower end were occupations now not only lost but barely recorded: that of the "Pure-finders," for instance, old women who collected dog-turds which they sold to tanneries for a few pence a bucket (the excrement was used as a siccative in dressing fine bookbinding leather). In between lay hundreds of occupations, seasonal or regular. None of them enjoyed any protection, since trade unions and "combinations" were instantly suppressed. There were no wage guarantees, and sweated labor was usual.

Occupational diseases ran rampant. Sawyers went blind young, their conjunctival membranes destroyed by showers of sawdust—hence the difference of status between the "top-notcher," or man on top of the log in the sawpit, and his partner pulling down the saw below. Metalfounders who cast the slugs for Baskerville's elegant type died paralyzed with lead poisoning, and glassblowers' lungs collapsed from silicosis. Hairdressers were prone to lung disease through inhaling the mineral powder used to whiten wigs. The fate of tailors, unchanged until the invention of electric light, was described by one to Henry Mayhew:

> It is not the black clothes that are trying to the sight—black is the steadiest of all colours to work at; white and all bright colours makes the eyes water after looking at 'em for any long time; but of all colours scarlet, such as is used for regimentals, is the most blinding, it seems to burn the eyeballs, and makes them ache dreadful . . . everything seems all of a twitter, and to keep changing its tint. There's more military tailors blind than any others.[2]

Children went to work after their sixth birthday. The Industrial Revolution did not invent child labor, but it did expand and systematize the exploitation of the very young. The reign of George III saw a rising trade in orphans and pauper children, collected from the parish workhouses of London and Birmingham, who were shipped off in thousands to the new industrial centers of Derbyshire, Nottinghamshire and Lancashire. One London child-slave, Robert Blincoe, who was placed in the St. Pancras

Workhouse in 1796 at the age of four and sent off with eighty other abandoned children to the Lambert cotton mill outside Nottingham, gave testimony to a Parliamentary committee on child labor some forty years later:

> Q. Do you have any children?—Three.
>
> Q. Do you send them to factories?—No; I would rather have them transported. . . . I have seen the time when two hand-vices of a pound weight each, more or less, have been screwed to my ears, at Lytton mill in Derbyshire. These are the scars still remaining behind my ears. Then three or four of us have been hung at once on a cross-beam above the machinery, hanging by our hands, without shirts or stockings. Then we used to stand up, in a skip, without our shirts, and be beaten with straps or sticks; the skip was to prevent us from running away from the straps. . . . Then they used to tie up a 28-pounds weight, one or two at once, according to our size, to hang down our backs, with no shirt on.[3]

Doctors tended to side with their class allies, the factory-owners, and went on record again and again with their considered opinions that cotton lint, coal dust and phosphorus were harmless to the human lung, that fifteen hours at a machine in a room temperature of 85 degrees did not cause fatigue, that ten-year-olds could work a full night shift without risk of harm. Employers, naturally, resisted the very thought of reform. Some of them were cultivated men like Josiah Wedgwood, uncle to Charles Darwin and heir to his father's great pottery in Staffordshire, who employed 387 people—13 under ten years old, 103 between ten and eighteen—in such work as dipping ware in a glaze partly composed of lead oxide, a deadly poison which, as he admitted, made them "very subject to disease," though no more so than plumbers or painters. Yet "I have a strong opinion," Wedgwood told the Peel Committee in 1816, "that, from all I know at present of manufactories in general, and certainly from all I know of my own, we had better be left alone."[4]

Of all the testimony offered to the Royal Commissions on factory labor, there is perhaps none more chilling than the evidence of Joseph Badder, a children's overseer in a Leicester mill, to the Factory Commission of 1833. It has a prophetic ring: Here, the factory-induced dystopic visions of man as automaton that would run from Mary Shelley's *Frankenstein, or The Modern Prometheus* (1818) to Fritz Lang's *Metropolis* (1926) are made pitiably concrete:

> I used to beat them. . . . I told them I was very sorry after I had done it, but I was forced to it. The masters expected me to do my work, and I

could not do mine unless the children did theirs. Then I used to joke with them to keep up their spirits.

I have seen them fall asleep, and they have been performing their work with their hands until they were asleep, after the billy had stopped, when their work was over. I have stopped and looked at them for two minutes, going through the motions of piecening fast asleep, when there was really no work to do, and when they were really doing nothing.[5]

Such flat and distant voices confirm the rhetoric of William Blake: "Grace" is underwritten by constant, speechless suffering, and "culture" begins in the callused hands of exhausted children, weaving robotically in sleep, "going through the motions . . . when they were really doing nothing." For the first time in human history, the machine dictates the term of organic existence to its servants; the body becomes an inferior machine. If respectability was to be judged by people's endurance of such work, there is no surprise in the growth of crime. In a sense, the children of the mills were inoculated against the dread of punishment; "they appeared as complete prisoners as they would be in gaol," remarked one observer to the Peel Committee.[6]

But mill labor, at least, was regular and gave fairly steady employment. Not all workers in London had such a prospect. Home industries like weaving were prostrated by industrial competition. To be whipsawed between long work-hours and patches of unemployment was deeply demoralizing. As Francis Place found, it bred the familiar torpor of the laid-off:

I know not how to describe the sickening aversion which at times steals over the working man, and utterly disables him for a longer or shorter time from following his usual occupation, and compels him to *idleness*. I have felt it. I have been obliged to submit and run away from my work. This is the case with every workman I have known; and in such proportion as a man's case is hopeless will such fits occur and be of longer duration.[7]

A common solace was gin. After 1720 this white grain spirit flavored with crushed juniper berries became England's national stupefacient, the heroin of the eighteenth century (but worse, because its use was far wider). Brandy, port, claret and Madeira, the rich man's four tipples, were taxed on import and no workingman could afford them. But gin was made in England and cost next to nothing: "Drunk for a penny, dead drunk for twopence" meant what it said. Its consumption was eagerly promoted by the landed gentry, because England nearly always had a surplus of corn, which gin-distilling used up. Consequently there were no restrictions of any kind on making or selling the liquor until the Gin

Act of 1751, by which time London was said to have one gin-shop for every 120 citizens. By 1743 the laboring poor of England were consuming 8 million gallons of gin a year, and they presented a most squalid appearance: "Lazy, sotted and brutish by nature," a French visitor called them in 1777.[8] The contrast between the new, degraded "mob," sodden with gin, and the honest peasantry, merry with ale, was by now a commonplace with every moralist up to and including William Hogarth, who gave it memorable form in his engravings *Gin Lane* and *Beer Street*.

The "mob," as the urban proletariat was called, had become an object of terror and contempt, but little was known about it. It was seen as a malign fluid, a sort of magma that would burst through any crack in law and custom, quick to riot and easily inflamed to crime by rabble-rousers. This moral prejudice affected most efforts to find out about English crime and English poverty.

Thus Patrick Colquhoun, in his *Treatise on the Police of the Metropolis* (1797), made one of the first attempts to gauge the number of criminals in George III's London. He claimed that there were 115,000 people living off crime in the city—about one Londoner in eight, which constituted a "criminal class" in itself. But who were they, and what did they do? Colquhoun lumped thieves, muggers and forgers, who clearly were criminals, together with scavengers, bear-baiters and gypsies, who were not, or at least not clearly so. He estimated that there were 50,000 "harlots" in London—about 6 percent of its population—but, as Edward P. Thompson pointed out, "[Colquhoun's] prostitutes turn out, on closer inspection, to be 'lewd and immoral women', including 'the prodigious number among the lower classes who cohabit together without marriage' (and this at a time when divorce for women was an absolute impossibility)."[9] If the same criteria of whoredom were applied to London today, how many "harlots" would a modern Colquhoun find?

The fact that their superiors *thought* that such people were prostitutes is no guide: In social matters, Georgian Englishmen far preferred generalization to reportage, and there was no eighteenth-century Mayhew. A Spitalfields weaver, an Irish casual laborer and a Scottish ditch-digger might not even understand one another's speech, let alone share any aspirations; but seen from above they all belonged to the "mobbish class of persons." The "mob" was Georgian society's id—the sump of forbidden thoughts and proscribed actions, the locus of the raging will to survive. Amid the general fear of Jacobinism that swept England after the French Revolution, it would seem an even greater menace. Then, the issues of crime and of revolution became conflated, and so the rising crime-rate—or rather, the belief that it was rising—became a potent issue. Accordingly, the Georgian legislators fought back against a threat which they believed came from a whole class. The criminal became the dreaded *sans-culotte*'s cousin. Georgian fear of the "mob" led to Victorian belief in a "criminal class." Against both, the approved weapon was a form of legal terrorism.

i i

THE BELIEF in a swelling wave of crime was one of the great social facts of Georgian England. It shaped the laws, and the colonization of Australia was its partial result.

Sending criminals to the far Antipodes was like sending them from one disagreeably fabled land to another. The slum areas of London seemed a foreign country of crime, and in 1751 Henry Fielding reflected that

> had they been intended for the very purpose of concealment, they could hardly have been better contrived. Upon such a view, [London] appears as a fast wood or forest, in which a Thief may harbour with as great security, as wild beasts do in the deserts of Africa or Arabia.[10]

Crime was up in the countryside, too; "Our people have become what they never were before, cruel and inhuman."[11] The reasons, Fielding thought, were gin, gambling and the love of "luxury" that had caused men and women to reject their traditional stations, even among "the very dregs of the people." The helpless begged, while those "of more art and courage" stole. The innocent lived in a state of siege.

A quarter of a century later, things seemed no better. In 1775 Jonas Hanway indignantly exclaimed that

> I sup with my friend; I cannot return to my home, not even in my chariot, without danger of a pistol being clapt to my breast. I build an elegant villa, ten or twenty miles distant from the capital: I am obliged to provide an armed force to convey me thither, lest I should be attacked on the road with fire and ball.[12]

Two centuries later one can see broader reasons for this growth of crime. English society was violently changing, under the stresses of industrialization, the growth of towns, and a soaring birthrate. From 1700 to 1740, the population of England and Wales remained almost constant at about 6 million people. Then it started rising fast—so fast that between 1750 and 1770 the population of London doubled—and by 1851 it stood at 18 million. This meant that the median age of Englishmen kept dropping and the labor market was saturated with the young. No mechanisms

existed for the effective relief of mass unemployment; it was not a problem England had ever before had to contend with on this scale. The Poor
Laws had been written for a different England. Parish relief and the workhouse were the primitive devices of a pre-industrial society; now they
were overwhelmed. But crime is, was and always will be a young
man's trade, and English youth, rootless and urban, took to it with a
will.

They found easy pickings, especially since Georgian England had
none of the tools for catching criminals that the twentieth century takes
for granted. Official crime records and registers of criminals were primitive, and there would be no fingerprinting until 1885. Artists made
sketches, for popular consumption, of famous offenders like Dick Turpin
or Jack Sheppard, but one could no more recognize a felon from such
semi-devotional effigies than pick St. Paul from a crowd by consulting a
Byzantine icon. Identification of wanted men had to be made from verbal
descriptions in the police gazettes, circulated to mayors and magistrates
after the early 1770s: *"Benjamin Bird, a tall thin man, pale complexion,
black hair tied, thick lips, the nail of the forefinger of his right hand is
remarkably clumsy, comes from Coventry, and is charged with several
forgeries, the last at Liverpool . . ."* Sketchy as they were, such descriptions did produce some arrests, mainly in villages where people noticed
strangers. Some officers of the law had long memories. Henry Fielding's
sightless half-brother John, a magistrate known at Bow Street as the
"Blind Beak," was said to be able to identify 3,000 different malefactors
by their voices alone. But on the whole, it was easier for criminals to
escape scot-free in the 1780s than it would ever be again.

There was one main reason for this: England had no effective, centralized police force and would not form one until Peel's Police Act of
June 1829. Law and order on the street was left to the parishes and wards;
hence those enfeebled butts of every street urchin, the "Charlies" or
parish watchmen. There were about 2,000 of them in London in the late
eighteenth century, "poor old decrepit people" as Fielding bluntly put it,
charity cases who had cast themselves on the mercy of the parish because
they no longer had the strength to do other work. From the parish, each
Charley got a greatcoat with three capes, like a coachman's; a lantern, to
light his tottering progress through the alleys; a wooden rattle to summon help; and a staff to defend himself. He would bang its butt rhyth-
mically against the cobbles as he walked, to give thieves plenty of
warning. Thus the embarrassment of a meeting between Law and Crime
could be averted. He was easily bribed, with sixpence or a quart of gin.
Charley's deterrent power was therefore slight.

In practice, the magistrates preferred an older way of catching suspects: a graduated scale of rewards for information. This reward system

was the eighteenth century's chief way of detecting crime. It pressed private enterprise into service against its Other, the criminal.

The pickings were large enough to support a whole subclass of informers, police narks and thief-takers. Suspects could bribe the informer not to lay information against them. Thus there was hardly a petty trade conducted in the London alleys whose members did not sell gin on the side, and few of them bothered to pay—or could afford—the price of a liquor license. Instead, they paid the nark £10 or so not to denounce them. If paid by the courts, informers could squeeze sap from every twig of the huge, ramifying tree of English criminal law. Nineteen separate offenses relating to the use of hackney coaches in London carried a reward of 50 shillings for informants; from there to the exalted levels of murder and grand larceny, each crime carried its reward.

One could grow prosperous by informing, but not rich. The larger profits went to a more daring and astute kind of professional, the thief-takers. In theory, the thief-taker was no mere informer. He tracked down criminals and, at his own risk, intrepidly brought them to court. He was the eighteenth-century ancestor of the private eye, a detective with no official standing and, of course, no police protection. No niceties about laws of evidence or suspects' rights governed the thief-takers' forays into the "alsatias" (criminal purlieus) of London. They had a vested interest in fostering crime, for it kept up the flow of rewards. By playing both ends against the middle, they invented a new pattern of English felonry, thus presenting the good Georgian citizenry with a new and extraordinarily threatening spectacle: organized crime. The archetype of the thief-taker had been Jonathan Wild (1683–1725).[13]

The perception of organized crime would not go away, and in time it became more and more frightening to property-owners. A single criminal could be singly met. The householder, armed with blunderbuss and paired horse-pistols, defended by locks, grilles, bells, man-traps and loyal servants, could drive him away. But a collective of thugs and thieves, a united "criminal class" working together in gangs—that was quite another matter. It was a largely fantastical notion, exaggerated and nourished by deep-rooted territorial instincts. Gangs certainly existed in Georgian England, but they were only responsible for a fraction of the deeds that the law defined as criminal. Crime was still a cottage industry, a jumble of individual acts of desperation. The failure of language—the tyranny of moral generalization over social inspection—fed the ruling class's belief that it was endangered from below.

### iii

YET THE PEOPLE who had most to gain from a police force opposed its founding, tooth and nail. Despite the unrest that smoldered in England throughout the eighteenth century—the mobs at Tyburn, the Penlez riots of 1749, the Wilkite riots of the 1760s and the Gordon riots of 1780—there was no concerted Parliamentary move to set up a police force until the nineteenth century was a quarter gone. Georgian authorities preferred to rely on thief-takers for dealing with individuals, the Riot Act and the militia for dealing with groups. This was a source of wonder to foreigners, especially the French. "From sunset to dawn," wrote one such visitor in 1784, "the environs of London become the patrimony of brigands for twenty miles around," but the government did not improve the police because it was hampered by "clashes of interest" between people and King.[14] When the Duc de Levis asked his friends in 1814 why they had no *maréchaussée*—the rural police, the powers of arbitrary pursuit and arrest, that had all but stamped out brigandage in the French provinces—he was firmly told that "such an institution is not compatible with liberty."

There lay the nub. The English refused to create a regular police force because they had seen what lay across the Channel, where no Frenchman's home was his castle. "I had rather half-a-dozen peoples' throats be cut in the Ratcliffe Highway every three or four years," wrote one returned traveller, "than be subject to the domiciliary visits, spies and the rest of Fouche's contrivances."[15]

There were limits, of course, to this bluff libertarian attitude, and they showed up wherever the issue of class was involved. Those who opposed a police force did so from concern for the rights of property, not those of suspects. Modern precedents governing arrest and search, such as the *Miranda* decision, would have struck them as insanely favorable to the criminal. There was distress at the "tenderness" of the English legal system. "The regard shown to offenders falls little short of respect," complained Sir John Hawkins, a Middlesex magistrate of the 1760s.[16] Georgian justice may look fierce to us, but seen from Europe then it was lenient. The suspect had basic rights not recognized in France, Italy or Germany: He could not be tortured until he confessed; he could not be held indefinitely without bail or trial; and he was innocent until proven guilty. The liberalism of the English Common Law, compared to their own systems based on Roman and Canon Law, astonished European visitors. They noticed that, although it reduced the likelihood of an innocent man's conviction, it also made it easier for the guilty to escape.

The English knew this, too; hence the draconic laws they created to avenge their sense of a disturbed social order. Against the relative fairness of British trials, one must set the most striking aspect of Georgian law—the sheer scope of its capital statutes. If detection and arrest were feeble and trials tenderly fair, what punishment could keep men from crime? Only the extreme one: hanging without benefit of clergy. During the reigns of the first three Georges, law enacted death upon what seemed a limitless variety of human deeds, from infanticide to "impersonating an Egyptian" (posing as a gypsy). Between the enthronement of Charles II in 1660 and the middle of George IV's reign in 1819, 187 new capital statutes became law—nearly six times as many as had been enacted in the previous three hundred years. Nearly all were drafted to protect property, rather than human life; attempted murder was classed only as a "misdemeanor" until 1803. These grapeshot laws scattered death impartially. Why must forgers hang? Because the increase of paper transactions in eighteenth-century banking and business—checks, notes, bonds, shares, as distinct from concrete transfer of bags of gold—had made property of all sorts more vulnerable to forgery. Why was it death to "steal an heiress"? Because, like a queen bee swollen with jelly, an heiress was property incarnate; her abductor went to the gallows not for rape but for his theft of a family's accumulated goods and rights.

Some capital statutes were very broad. The most notorious of them was 9 Geo. I, c. 22, otherwise known as the Waltham Black Act. It had been drafted ostensibly to repress some minor agrarian uprisings in 1722–23 near Waltham Chase in Hampshire, where rural laborers, moving at night with blacked faces, had taken to poaching game and fish, burning hayricks and posting threatening letters on their landlords' gates. The act, passed by the Commons without a murmur of dissent, prescribed the gallows for over two hundred possible offenses in various permutations. One could be hanged for burning a house or a hut, a standing rick of corn, or an insignificant pile of straw; for poaching a rabbit, for breaking down "the head or mound" of a fishpond, or even cutting down an ornamental shrub; or for appearing on a high-road with a sooty face. As Sir Leon Radzinowicz remarked, "The Act constituted in itself a complete and extremely severe criminal code which indiscriminately punished with death a great many different offences, without taking into account either the personality of the offender or the particular circumstances of each offence."[17]

Such legislation was part of a general tendency in eighteenth-century England: the growth of the Rule of Law (as distinct from any particular statute) into a supreme ideology, a form of religion which, it has since been argued, began to replace the waning moral power of the Church of England.[18]

Like the Church, Law had its own diction and rituals and its own priests—bewigged men in scarlet and ermine. At the assizes, the judge's rolling sermons on vice and virtue, his reprobations, didactic asides and calls to repentance, were the secular equivalent of that pulpit eloquence which, in the seventeenth century, had shaken and fascinated those who thronged to hear the great preachers like John Donne or George Cokayne. Well into the nineteenth century, hanging verdicts continued to produce extremes of emotion, on both sides of the bench, that would be hard to match today. When two agricultural protestors named Peter Withers and James Lush were sentenced to death at the Salisbury assizes in 1831, a reporter from the *Dorset County Chronicle* described how

> there were ... no dry eyes in the crowded court. The tears of pity, of compassion, of regret, at the necessity of such severity were to be seen flowing and chasing one another down the cheeks not merely of the spectators, but of those who had long been accustomed to hear the last dreadful sentence which a human being has the power of passing on a fellow-creature in this world. [The judges] were frequently obliged to rest their faces on their extended hands, and even then the large drops were to be seen falling in quick succession. . . . Every one [of the prisoners] was in a state of dreadful agitation—some sobbing aloud and others with a pallid cheek ... [After the death sentence] their mothers, their sisters, and their children clasped them in their arms with an agonizing grasp—the convicts ... gave way, they wept like children ... Nature had begun to play with every force, and the heart was broken.[19]

Why did the judges weep with the accused? Because both were bound —though not, of course, in equality of pain—to the law. This drama of immutable rules lay at the heart of the tremendous power that Law held over the English imagination. The judge simply surrendered to the imperative of the statutes, a course of action that absolved him of judicial murder, and that caused him to weep. His tears humbled him not before the men in the dock, which would have been unthinkable, but before the idea of Law itself. When the Royal Mercy intervened as it commonly did, transmuting the death penalty into exile on the other side of the world, the accused and their relatives could bless the intervening power of patronage while leaving the superior operations of Law unquestioned. The law was a disembodied entity, beyond class interest: the god in the codex. The judge was invested with its numen, as a priest was touched by sacerdotal power. But he could no more change the law than a clergyman could rewrite the Bible. All men were equal before the law, and none might evade its reach. It might demand the death of a poor ten-year-old boy, but noblemen could and did hang as well. The famous one was Lord Ferrers, who in a fit of paranoid suspicion blew his steward's brains out in 1760. Convicted and sentenced to hang, the peer made his journey to Tyburn in a landau drawn by six horses, wearing a white wedding-suit sumptuously encrusted with silver embroidery; thousands of people cheered him over the drop. This, as upholders of the Law's impartiality were given to stress, was equality indeed.

iv

NOTHING IN English criminal law seems more disgusting than public hanging. We are apt to think of it as the very saturnalia of death: a man or woman carted through the screaming mob that lined the road from Newgate to Tyburn, and then killed by a civil servant while more pockets were picked around the scaffold than the victim had picked in his life.[20]

Yet the official view of hanging was the very opposite. The Georgian lawmakers believed that public execution would reform those who saw it. A writer in 1772 recounted how parents would bring their children to a hanging and flog them afterward "that they might remember the example they had seen."[21] The scaffold was the altar of a ritual whose aim was to fill society with moral awe. This expiatory theater, solemn and fatal, deserved the widest audience.

To a well-anticipated hanging, if the victims were famous—a Jack Sheppard, a Lord Ferrers—twenty-five thousand people might come. Thirty thousand are said to have attended the execution of the twin brothers Perreau (for forgery) in 1776, and in 1767, eighty thousand people—or about one Londoner in ten—flocked to a hanging in Moorefields.[22] Against this may be set the extreme unreliability of Georgian statistics. Nevertheless, hanging was clearly the most popular mass spectacle in England; nothing could match the drawing-power of the gallows or its grip as a secular image.

Hence the importance of the ritual. On the eve of Tyburn Fair (one of the colloquial names for execution-day at Tyburn gallows), it began with a prayer intoned by the sexton of the parish church of Newgate prison, St. Sepulchre's, addressed to the occupants of its condemned hold, the Stone Room:

> You prisoners that lie within, who for wickedness and sin, after many mercies shown you, are now appointed to die tomorrow in the forenoon, give ear and understand that tomorrow morning the greatest bell of St. Sepulchre's shall toll for you in form and measure of a passing bell, as used to be tolled for those at the point of death, to the end that all godly people, hearing that bell and knowing that it is for your going and your deaths, may be stirred up heartily to pray to God . . .[23]

With the morning came the minatory prayers, the hoarse clanging bells
and the procession westward along the busiest streets of London, from
Newgate to Tyburn, the present site of Marble Arch. Each condemned
man sat in the cart facing the rising sun, with a noose bound to his chest.
At the gallow's foot, phrase by halting phrase, he had to recite Psalm 51,
the "Hanging Psalm":

> Behold, I was brought forth in iniquity,
>     and in sin did my mother conceive me.
>
> Behold, thou desirest truth in the inward being,
>     therefore teach me wisdom in my secret heart.
> Purge me with hyssop, and I shall be clean;
>     wash me, and I shall be whiter than snow.
> Fill me with joy and gladness;
>     let the bones which thou hast broken rejoice.
> Hide thy face from my sins . . .

Sometimes he would append a conventional speech of repentance,
known as the "dismal ditty." Then came the donning of the white
shroud, an undignified and spectral garment like a coarse nightgown; the
climb up the ladder; the choking drop.

But what did the lower classes think of this spectacle staged for their
benefit? There is much to suggest that the panoply of Tyburn was not
taken in a proper spirit by the "mobbish class of Persons." Hanging had
two languages. The official one was elevated and abstract: A hanged man
"paid the supreme penalty," "suffered the ultimate exaction of the Law,"
or was "launch'd into Eternity." But there was also a vast gallows argot,
for, next to those hardy perennials sex, money and crime, nothing on the
social horizon of the English poor produced more slang and cant than
hanging. Not a word of it reflects the official solemnities. Terse in its
irony, bitter in its defiant concreteness, it rejected the values of the Law
and its makers.

A condemned man "died with cotton in his ears" because Cotton was
the name of the praying sexton at Newgate. The hangman was Jack
Ketch, the nubbing-cove, the crap merchant, the crapping cull, the
switcher, the cramper, the sheriff's journeyman, the gaggler, the topping-
cove, the roper or the scragger. Tyburn being in the parish of Paddington,
execution-day was also known as Paddington Fair, the hood drawn over
one's head on the scaffold was the Paddington spectacles, and in dying
one danced the Paddington frisk.

Some hangmen bequeathed their names to the rite. In the 1770s a
man would be "dempstered," and around 1785 the gallows briefly became the Gregorian tree, after a London hangman named Gregory Bran-

don. But its other names were legion. Being a construction of three posts linked by cross-bars, the gallows was the three-legged mare, and to ascend it was to "climb three trees with a ladder"; being made of oak, it was the wooden mare, and to die on it was to "ride a horse foaled by an acorn." It was the morning drop, the trining-cheat, the nubbing-cheat, the scragging-post, or, in a laconic parody of the pastoral mode, "the deadly Nevergreen that bears the fruit all the year round." The noose was a horse's nightcap, a Tyburn tippet, a hempen casement or an anodyne necklace. Before the invention of the hinged trapdoor through which the victim dropped, he or she was "turned off" or "twisted" by the hangman who pulled the ladder away. To ascend it was "to go up the ladder to bed," "to take a leap in the dark." Some names for this death were bald: to stretch, to squeeze, to be jammed or frummagemed or haltered. Others referred to epidemic disease: "to die of a hempen quinsey or a hempen fever." "To be in a deadly suspense" predicts the nudging humor of the music hall, as does another elaborate Cockney locution for hanging: "to have a hearty choke [artichoke] and caper sauce for breakfast." The most chilling are the phrases that evoke the solitude and sterility of public death: "dance upon nothing," "take the earth bath," "shake a cloth in the wind," "go off at the fall of a leaf." Or, because of the noises and grimaces a strangling person makes: "to cry cockles," "to piss when you can't whistle," "to loll your tongue out at the company."[24]

This is not the language of the penitent thief. Its brusque, canting defiance reminds one that hanging meant one thing to the judges but another to the poor and the "mob." Samuel Johnson objected to the "fury of innovation" in the movement to abolish public hanging. "Executions are intended to draw spectators," the Rambler grumbled. "If they do not draw spectators, they do not answer to their purpose. The old method was most satisfactory to all parties; the public was gratified by a procession; the criminal was supported by it."[25]

The idea that condemned men could draw solace and support from the crowd at their hanging offends our deepest sense of propriety about death. It seems unspeakably grotesque. Nevertheless, they did. There are many accounts of young men setting forth in the Tyburn coach dressed like bridegrooms in new white suits emblematic of innocence, ribbons fluttering from their hats, posies in their white-gloved hands, cockily saluting a crowd that showered them, not with dead rats and cabbages, but with fruit and flowers in tribute to their passing. This was a common enough sight for Swift to take for granted:

> As clever Tom Clinch, while the Rabble was bawling,
> Rode stately through Holbourn to die in his Calling;
> He stopt at the George for a bottle of Sack,

And Promis'd to pay for it when he came back.
His Waiscoat and Stockings, and Breeches were white,
His cap had a new Cherry Ribbon tied to it.
The Maids to the Doors and the Balconies ran,   •
And said, lack-a-day! he's a proper young Man.
But, as from the windows the Ladies he spied,
Like a Beau in a Box, he bow'd low on each Side.[26]

As early as 1701 a pamphleteer was complaining that the condemned rode to Tyburn in bright clothes "like Men that triumph," as though the journey of shame were the parade of a Caesar.[27] A man's bearing on the cart and at Tyburn was discussed like the form of a boxer at a prizefight. The phlegm of English malefactors was renowned in Europe, whose criminals tended to beg and blubber or become reduced to bovine passivity when confronted by their executioners. One admiring Italian felt that the English faced the gallows *come se andasse a Nozze . . . colla più soave indifferenza nel Mondo,* "as if going to be married, with the calmest indifference in the world."[28] The crowd wanted to see this and supported those who showed it. A "Tyburn blossom" must be an exemplary dandy, trim, gay and uncaring.

Hanging crowds were unruly. Hogarth's engraving *The Idle Prentice Executed at Tyburn* gives a powerful sense of them: the crush of jostling voyeurs, a trampled child, squabbling fruit-sellers, pamphleteers hawking the just-printed "Last Dying Speech and Confession"—a turgid mass of drunks, whores, cripples, gospellers, pikemen and building-workers from the new West End squares nearby, parting to make way for the fatal cart. Beside the scaffold rises a grandstand that belonged to a famous scalper, the Widow Proctor, who made £500 in one day selling seats for Lord Ferrers's hanging.

People also went to Tyburn to mourn, to reclaim the body of their friend or relative, to give the corpse its due dignity. They waited below the gallows to retrieve it in order to give it a proper burial and did not hesitate to fight the sheriff's officers for it. The law did not recognize the relatives' rights to a hanged corpse. It gave the body to the Royal College of Physicians for dissection, which heaped further ignominy on the dead. Thus there was a continuous record of brawls and riots at Tyburn and other English places of execution, as the "mob" battled with the surgeons' corpse-takers for possession of bodies. And, as Peter Linebaugh remarked,

When brickmakers came out to defend the bodies of two felons with several years' good standing in the trade against the surgeons, when bargemen came down from Reading to guard one of their own at a hanging, when the hackney coachmen rallied to keep the body of a fellow coach-man "from being carried off with Violence," or when the small cottagers and market people of Shoreditch surrounded the tumbril of Thomas Pinks their neighbour in the village, "declaring that they had no other Intention, but to take care of the Body for Christian burial," the evidence . . . shows the depth of the mutuality of the poor, their solidarity in the face of personal disaster.[29]

This solidarity, as Dr. Johnson perceived, gave support to the con-demned. Public execution, meant to terrify the populace, enabled the "mob" to show its defiance of authority. How mulish, the scientific onlooker might say, to deny the science of medicine its rights of progress by way of the bodies of the poor! What anatomical Luddism! What counted, however, was that the laboring poor of England gave the rituals their own meaning, quite at odds with its official one.

At this distance, one cannot say whether public hanging did terrify people away from crime. Nor can anyone do so, until we can count crimes that were never committed. Probably some people in the Tyburn crowds did fear hanging more for having seen it. Despite (or, from another point of view, because of) the intimidating ferocity of the statutes, there were more than twice as many capital convictions in the London and Middlesex courts in the 1780s as there had been in the 1750s. This does not prove, however, that capital punishment failed to deter anyone. Pop-ulation had grown, poverty was worse, and there might have been even more crime if some people were not frightened by the gallows.

But one fact is certain. As the eighteenth century went on, fewer people were actually hanged for capital crimes that they had been con-victed of. In ten-year periods, the figures for London and Middlesex (the area of highest crime) are:[30]

| DECADE | CAPITAL CONVICTIONS | EXECUTIONS | PERCENTAGE |
| --- | --- | --- | --- |
| 1749–58 | 527 | 365 | 69.3 |
| 1759–68 | 372 | 206 | 55.4 |
| 1769–78 | 787 | 357 | 45.4 |
| 1779–88 | 1152 | 531 | 46.1 |
| 1789–98 | 770 | 191 | 24.8 |
| 1799–1808 | 804 | 126 | 15.7 |

Why did the English write their fatal laws and then not use them to the full? One answer is squeamishness: Judges and juries simply frus-trated the hanging statutes out of decency. A judge would commute the death sentence on a suitably penitent felon, while juries (and sometimes even prosecutors) cheated the gallows by deliberately undervaluing stolen goods. Thus, hundreds of convictions were handed down every year for thefts of goods that juries valued at 39 shillings, not because that was their actual value, but because the law said that anyone who stole above 40 shillings in a house or on a highway must hang. However, there would not have been so many remissions if they had not been encouraged by an active intent to exercise mercy.[31]

George III took the exercise of the Royal Prerogative of Mercy (the King's power to override his courts and remit a sentence at will) very seriously. The Royal Mercy showed his subjects that their monarch cared about them. One besought it by letter, through the home secretary, enclosing whatever references and sub-petitions could be raised from clergymen and other respectable people, and it was quite often given. The laws were the stick, mercy the carrot. There was subtlety in maintaining the hanging laws but not automatically using them. If they had merely been repealed, the effect would not have been the same. For mercy to evoke gratitude, the ruler must be seen to *choose* mercy, so that each reprieve is a special case, to be paid for in gratitude and obedience, never taken as a right.[32]

Moreover, the Royal Mercy and judicial commutation of sentences kept the crossroads of England from being decorated with scores and scores of corpses—a sight that could have provoked general riots. But what could the courts do with the convicts? The less rope was used, the more jails were needed. Yet eighteenth-century England was short of jails.

v

THE ONES it had were old. They had changed little since the Middle Ages. Their archetype in London was Newgate, which began its career in the twelfth century as a city gatehouse strengthened to hold prisoners and ended after almost eight hundred years of service and four rebuildings, with demolition in 1903. Newgate's walls were of a Piranesian thickness, and there was virtually no way past its labyrinth of dark cells, subterranean corridors and iron bars as thick as a navvy's wrist. To escape from this accursed place—especially from its condemned cell, the Stone Room—was to achieve immediate celebrity in the London underworld. Newgate was called the "whit" or "wit," and all flash lads drank to its destruction. "The Wit be burnt," ran a common criminal toast, "the Flogging Cull [flogger] be damned, the Nubbing Chit [gallows] be curs'd." The debtor's section of Newgate was called "Tangier," because of the miseries suffered by English prisoners of Arab pirates on the Barbary Coast; its inmates, some abandoned by the outside world for ten years over a matter of a few shillings, were "tangerines."

Inside Newgate one simply rotted away, staring through the bars (or, as the phrase went, "polishing the King's iron with your eyebrows"). No work was done there. The central idea of the Victorian penitentiary, as proposed by Bentham and his Panopticon and first tried in Philadelphia —that prison should be a place of isolation, discipline and systematically graded punishment alleviated by precise injections of hope—was quite new and untried in the reign of George III. It affected neither the way judges thought about sentences, nor the manner in which prisons were run. The project of creating a captive society within the state, populated by convicts fed and housed at public expense and repaying an offended world (however nominally) with forced labor—in short, the idea of the penitentiary as it developed after 1820—would have struck the rules of Georgian England as utterly chimerical. Jails were simply lockups, and no one was "improved" by a spell in one. They were holes in which prisoners could be forgotten for a while. Their purpose was not reform, but terror and sublimation. But they were also meant to turn a profit.

About half the jails of England were privately owned and run. Chesterfield Jail belonged to the Duke of Portland, who sublet it to a keeper for 18 guineas a year. The Bishop of Ely owned a prison, the Bishop of Durham had the Durham County Jail, and Halifax Jail belonged to the Duke of Leeds. Their jailers were not State employees but small businessmen—malignant landlords—who made their profits by extorting money from prisoners. On entering the Bishop of Ely's lockup, a prisoner was chained down to the floor with a spiked collar riveted round his neck until he disgorged a fee for "easement of irons." Any jailer could load any prisoner with as many fetters as he pleased and charge for their removal one at a time. The "trade of chains" though often denounced as a national disgrace, survived well into the 1790s.

One paid for food, for drink—the prison tap room, dispensing gin, was a prime source of income for jailers—for bedding, water and even air. A well-off prisoner could live in some ease (although nothing could buy him immunity from typhus, the endemic disease of eighteenth-century prisons). For poorer men, the system was crushing. The entrance fee at Newgate was 3s., the weekly "rent" 2s. 6d., the charge for sharing a straw mattress with another prisoner 1s 6d a week. These sums sound small, but they often represented the full amount for which a debtor or thief had been clapped in prison, and there was little or no hope of earning them inside. "The prisoners have neither tools nor materials of any kind," wrote John Howard, the pioneer of penal reform, in the 1770s,

but spend their time in sloth, profaneness and debauchery . . . Some keepers of these houses, who have represented to magistrates the wants of
their prisoners, and desired for them necessary food, have been silenced
with the inconsiderate words, *Let them work or starve.* When these
gentlemen know the former is impossible, do they not by that sentence
inevitably doom poor creatures to the latter? [33]

Howard travelled all over collecting material for his monumental
report, *The State of the Prisons in England and Wales* (1777). He drew a
detailed picture of this hidden world, of which the respectable and literate knew nothing—its crowding, darkness and scant rations, the cruel
indifference of the Bench and the venal favoritism of wardens, the garnish and chummage and easement fees, the cell floors awash with sewage, the utter lack of medical care, the fatal epidemics. Even the air was
unbreathable. Howard discovered that

> my cloaths were in my first journeys so offensive, that in a post-chaise I
> could not bear the windows drawn up: and was therefore obliged to travel
> on horseback. The leaves of my memorandum-book were often so tainted,
> that I could not use it till after spreading it an hour or two before the fire:
> and even my antidote, a vial of vinegar, has after using it in a few prisons,
> become intolerably disagreeable. [34]

The idea that prisons could not reform criminals but were incubators
of crime was the merest commonplace in the 1780s; everyone, magistrates included, took it for granted. There was no attempt to classify or
segregate prisoners by age, sex or gravity of crime. Women were thrown
in the same common ward as men, first offenders with hardened recidivists, inoffensive civil debtors with muggers, clerkly forgers with murderers, ten-year-old boys with homosexual rapists. All prisoners, authority thought, were united by the common fact of their malignant
otherness. They had crime in common, and that was enough. There was
no need for fine distinctions in the black hole.

The common simile for the prison was a monastery or seminary, a
closed order of people who studied vice, not holiness—an appealing figure in its perfect inversion. To Henry Fielding in 1751, prisons were "no
other than . . . seminaries of idleness, and common sewers of nastiness
and disease." [35] Howard, echoing him, saw them as "seats and seminaries
(as they have very properly been called) of idleness and every vice." [36] The
line continued to Australia in the 1820s, where one finds Governor
Thomas Brisbane complaining that "The Convict-Barracks of New South
Wales remind me of the Monasteries of Spain. They contain a population
of consumers who produce nothing." [37]

However, it was Dr. Johnson who most pithily set forth the vision of
Georgian jails as anti-monasteries:

> The misery of gaols is not half their evil . . . In a prison the awe of publick
> eye is lost, and the power of the law is spent; there are few fears, there are
> no blushes. The lewd inflame the lewd, the audacious harden the auda-
> cious. Everyone fortifies himself as he can against his own sensibility,
> endeavours to practice on others the arts which are practised on himself,
> and gains the kindness of his associates by similitude of manners. Thus
> some sink amidst their misery, and others survive only to propagate
> villainy.[38]

Such passages indicate how far apart modern and Georgian penal ideas
are. In practice, high-security prisons are still human zoos. But the liberal
view is that a jail is a sad but necessary expedient, harsh but susceptible
of reform, which, if decently run, can keep a criminal out of social circulation without making him or her much worse. No such opinions were
held two hundred years ago. Then it was clear that prisons, before they
are institutions, are *concentrations of criminals*: Their institutional definition began with the fact of criminality, not the hope of reform, and
their essential nature was to degrade all their occupants by the relentless
moral pressure of the group. The prison pickled the felon in evil,
hardened him, perfused him with the hard salt of sin. Hence the loathing
in which English jails were held by those who would never see the inside
of one. They were the republics of a sublimated criminal class; they
belonged to the antipodes of crime, not to the bright world of authority,
which they represented only in a nominal way. In due course, this train
of thought would provide the underlying logic of transportation to Australia. For transportation made sublimation literal: It conveyed evil to
another world.

Howard's *The State of the Prisons* had an immediate effect on
thought and the drafting of law. But practical reforms were slow in coming. The English authorities talked incessantly about the need for new
jails, legislated for their urgent construction, but did not actually build
them. Within two years of the publication of Howard's report, an act of
1779 called for two large prisons in London, designed along the lines
Howard advocated, with provision for work, segregation of the sexes, and
confinement in single cells rather than common wards. They were not
even started. In 1786 the prime minister, William Pitt, wrote to William
Wilberforce, the great liberal abolitionist who was pressing him for
prison reform, that "the multitude of things depending, has made the
Penitentiary House long in deciding upon. But I still think," he added
vaguely, "a beginning will be made on it before the season for building is

over." Again, no beginning was made, but in the summer of 1788 Pitt reassured Wilberforce that penitentiaries "shall not be forgotten."[39] Forgotten they were, because by then the Government could only see one remedy for the increase of crime and the apparent ineffectiveness of prisons: transportation "beyond the seas."

Transportation—forced exile, in plain English—had undeniable merits. It preserved the Royal Prerogative of Mercy, as the felon was left alive. At the same time he was removed from the realm as completely, if not as permanently, as any hanged man. Transportation got rid of the prison as well as the prisoners. It supplied Britain with a large labor force, consisting entirely of people who, having forfeited their rights, could be sent to distant colonies of a growing Empire to work at jobs that no free settler would do. Free-born Englishmen had always disliked the idea of laboring bands of convicts engaged on public works at home. A bill of 1752 introducing public chain-gang labor as punishment for criminals was rejected by the Lords partly because security was too great a problem but mainly because the sight of chain gangs in public places was felt to be degrading. How could onlookers distinguish such a punishment from outright slavery? In the New World, there would be no such problem.

The germ of the transportation system lay in a law of 1597, 39 Eliz. c. 4, "An Acte for Punyshment of Rogues, Vagabonds and Sturdy Beggars." In essence, it declared that obdurate idlers "shall . . . be banished out of this Realm . . . and shall be conveyed to such parts beyond the seas as shall be . . . assigned by the Privy Council." If a "Rogue so banished" returned to England without permission, he would be hanged.

It was through this act that in the seventeenth century, convicts under commuted death sentences were sent across the Atlantic to labor on the plantations of the Virginia Company. Sir Thomas Dale, Marshal of Virginia, took three hundred "disorderly persons" with him in 1611, but they turned out so "profane and mutinous, . . . diseased and crazed that not sixty of them may be employed."[40] Still, bad labor was better than none in the New World; the Indians could not be enslaved, while the English gentlemen of the Virginia Company had an extreme distaste for manual work. Soon Dale was asking for two thousand more convicts. "All offenders out of the common gaols condemned to die should be sent for three years to the Colony; so do the Spaniards people the Indies."[41] And from 1618 onward, a steady infusion of felons came to England's embryo settlements in the New World, to Puritan Massachusetts as well as to the tidewater settlements of the South. Most of them were common criminals. Some were Scots and English prisoners-of-war taken by Cromwell at the battles of Dunbar (1650) and Worcester (1651); others—mostly shipped to the sugar plantations of Jamaica and Barbados in the

1650s—were Irishmen who had been so unwise as to resist the invasion of the Lord Protector.

After 1717, transportation was stepped up and rendered fully official by a new act, 4 Geo. I, c. 11, which provided that minor offenders could be transported for seven years to America instead of being flogged and branded, while men on commuted capital sentences (recipients of the King's Mercy) might be sent for fourteen. English jailers did excellent business by selling these luckless colonists to shipping contractors, who in turn sold them (or, to be legally precise, the rights to their labor during their seven or fourteen years) to plantation-owners in the Caribbean and America. For the next sixty years, about 40,000 people suffered this thinly disguised form of slavery: 30,000 men and women from Great Britain, 10,000 from Ireland. This steady drainage of felons, averaging fewer than 700 people a year, kept the crowded jails of England from crisis.

But after 1775, the crisis could no longer be postponed. The American colonies rebelled. One result of the revolution was that the British could no longer send its convicts there. The American air filled with nobly turned resolutions against accepting criminals from England, for a new republic must not be polluted with the Crown's offal. This was cant, since the American economy was already heavily dependent on slavery. The real point was that the trade in black slaves had turned white convict labor into an economic irrelevance. On the eve of the American Revolution, 47,000 African slaves were arriving in America every year—more than English jails had sent across the Atlantic in the preceding half-century. Beside this labor force, the work of white indentured convicts was inconsequential; the Republic did not need it.

As soon as the American outlet was stopped up, English prisons began to overflow. At first, the Crown did nothing about this. The Americans would surrender sooner or later, and then the convict transports could ply the Atlantic again. In July 1783, only a month before Britain was forced to recognize the United States at Versailles, George III wrote to Lord North: "Undoubtedly the Americans cannot expect nor ever will receive any favour from Me, but the permitting them to obtain Men unworthy to remain in this Island I shall certainly consent to."[42]

So the English did not enlarge their prisons and in 1776 they found a compromise. The idea of forced convict labor on public works no longer seemed so tainted with slavery. It was dusted off and Lord North drew it up as 16 Geo. III, c. 43, known as the Hulks Act, a stopgap meant to last only until the American insurgents were crushed.

The Thames and the southern naval ports of England were dotted with hulks—old troop transports and men-o'-war, their masts and rigging gone, rotting at anchor, but still afloat and theoretically habitable. Convicts sentenced to be transported would now be kept on them until the government decided where to send them; this would relieve the bursting land prisons. Tactfully, the Hulks Act did not mention the revolt of the American colonists. It made a virtue of necessity by noting that transportation had deprived England of people "whose labour might be useful to the Community." These men would now be set "to Hard Labour . . . cleansing the River *Thames*." Thus the felons "might be reclaimed."

But the convicts jammed on the hulks were no more reclaimed than the Thames was cleansed. By 1790 their number was rising by about one thousand a year. Not only had the problem of security become acute, but typhus was by then endemic and the prospect of general infection terrified free citizens outside. The authorities would have done almost anything to get rid of the criminals their laws had created. Clearly, transportation must begin again—but to where? They chose the least imaginable spot on earth, which had been visited only once by white men. It was Australia, their new, vast, lonely possession, a useless continent at the rim of the world, whose eastern coast had been mapped by Captain Cook in 1770. From there, the convicts would never return. The names of Newgate and Tyburn, arch-symbols of the vengeance of property, were now joined by a third: Botany Bay.

# 3

# The Geographical Unconscious

TO GRASP what exile to such a place meant, one must think of the size of the world in the late eighteenth century, so much vaster than it is today.

In the 1780s, most of the world was still unknown to Europeans. The outlines of all the continents but two, Australia and Antarctica, had been traced. In profile, it had today's shape, but immense blanks lay behind the coasts. North America was a populated eastern fringe tacked onto millions of square miles of wilderness. The interiors of South America, Asia and Africa were scarcely explored. No European had ever visited the high Himalaya, the fountains of the Nile or the poles; while the Pacific basin, to all except the most educated Englishmen in 1780, was the least imaginable of all.

The social strata from which the convicts would be drawn knew little about the remoter facts of geography. Perhaps seven Englishmen in ten still lived in the countryside; the urban population of England would not outnumber the rural until 1851. Fixed to the soil and its demands, such people did not travel; their world had a radius of ten miles or so. Because they did not read, news came to them erratically and no English newspaper, in any case, sold more than 7,000 copies.[1]

For most people, the Pacific remained as obscure and unimaginable after Captain James Cook's death as it had been before his birth, and as monstrous: an oceanic hell. Nevertheless there was a deposit of rumor and legend about it, a myth that filtered into popular culture. This was the idea of a Southern Continent, set in the antipodes. It was first raised by two late classical geographers, Pomponius Mela and Ptolemy. Symmetry, Pomponius Mela argued in A.D. 50, demanded such a continent. The northern continents must be balanced by an equal land mass below the equator. In this land, *terra australis incognita*, Pomponius placed the source of the Nile. Supported by the prestige of Ptolemy, the father of

Renaissance geography, this Southern Continent survived the flat-earth doctrines of the medieval scholars, and Marco Polo seemed to confirm it. The Venetian wanderer described how, coming home from the kingdom of Cathay, he had sailed south to "Chamba" (modern Vietnam) and thence southwest for 1,200 miles, to a place named Locac.

Locac was the Malay Peninsula, but an ambiguity in the text anchored it somewhere between the East Indies and the South Pole, far below the equator, thus turning it into the Southern Continent. As such, with its name corrupted to Luchach, Locach or Beach, it appeared in the maps of influential sixteenth-century cartographers such as Mercator and Ortelius. Without the colossal mass of Locac, Mercator wondered, what would stop the world toppling from its axis?

By the end of the sixteenth century, Locac was encysted with fable. To some, it was the golden country, filled with every kind of wealth—jewels, sandalwood, spices—and inhabited by angelic beings: an embellishment upon the myth of the Terrestrial Paradise. To others it was the land of deformity. Legends of the freaks and wonders of India had proliferated since Alexander the Great's Indian expedition (327–325 B.C.)—dog-headed men, basilisks, people whose faces grew on their chests or who had a single huge foot which, during siestas, shaded them from the equatorial sun. These creatures infested medieval books and Romanesque tympana; they were invoked in sermons, in glosses on the Bible, in romances and epics, and by Shakespeare.

It made sense, of a kind, to assume that the further south one went, the more grotesque life must become. What demonic freaks, what affronts to normality, might the Southern Continent not produce? And what trials for the mariner? Waterspouts, hurricanes, clouds of darkness at midday, ship-eating whales, islands that swam and had tusks—this imagined country was perhaps infernal, its landscape that of Hell itself. Within its inscrutable otherness, every fantasy could be contained; it was the geographical unconscious. So there was a deep, ironic resonance in the way the British, having brought the Pacific at last into the realm of European consciousness, having explored and mapped it, promptly demonized Australia once more by chaining their criminals on its innocent dry coast. It was to become the continent of sin.

ii

THE MAN WHO named the ocean *el mar Pacifico* and was the first to cross its stupendous expanse was the Portuguese captain Fernão de Magalhães or, as he is known to history, Ferdinand Magellan. During the entire voyage between Portugal and Guam, he glimpsed only two little uninhabited islands near the strait that now bears his name. "*Que de seu Rey mostrando se agrauado / Caminho ha de fazer nunca cuidado*," wrote Camoëns in his praise: "Feeling affronted by his King, he took a route unimagined by others before."[2] Having opened the westward way to the Spice Islands with his epic voyage, Magellan was killed at Mactan in the Philippines in 1521.

Spanish explorers who followed him into the Pacific at the end of the sixteenth century were seeking the glory of God and a Southern Continent full of gold. Sailing out of Peru in 1567, blown by the Pacific trades across the low latitudes between 18° S. and the equator, Alvaro de Mendana brought his ships four-fifths of the way across the Pacific to an island group which—after King Solomon's fabled gold mines of Ophir— is still known as the Solomons. Perhaps these were the outer markers of the Southern Continent, perhaps not; half-mad with starvation, thirst and scurvy, Mendana and his conquistadors had to retreat. He tried again twenty-eight years later, in 1595, but the Solomons had vanished and no one would find them again for two centuries. They are at about 160° E. longitude; navigational instruments were so inaccurate that their estimated position varied by a full seventy-five degrees, between longitude 145° E. and 140° W.

Piloted by the young Portuguese Pedro Fernandez de Quiros, Mendana struggled on to the west, finding no continent, only scattered islands. His track lay too far north to encounter Australia. Seven months out of Peru, on the island of Santa Cruz, Mendana died. The great expedition, which was to have claimed *terra australis* in the name of Philip III, dissolved in a nightmare of violence and malaria, but de Quiros brought its demoralized survivors westward to Manila and then returned across the Pacific to Acapulco and safety.

This, one might think, would have put anyone off continent-hunting in the Pacific. It did not stop de Quiros. Somewhere to the west, on the blind blue eyeball of the world's greatest ocean, the Southern Continent must lie, and its discovery would be the climax both of Spanish imperialism and of the Church Militant's mission on earth. From Acapulco, de Quiros struggled back to Spain and thence to Rome, bombarding the Pope with letters about *terra australis* and its millions of innocent heathen souls, ripe for salvation. It took him two years to raise the money for three ships and three hundred men from Philip III. In December 1605, de Quiros sailed to find the continent.

He took a new track, further south than either Magellan or Mendana, well below the Tropic of Capricorn. He ran through the Tuamotu Archipelago, passed north of Samoa and, after five months at sea, saw land to the south and southeast—high mountains, their peaks veiled in clouds, retreating to the horizon. On May 3, 1606, de Quiros's fleet anchored in a bay. They had reached the New Hebrides group at 167° E., 15° S. De Quiros decided without any further evidence that this must be the south-land and, fast succumbing to religious mania, named it *Austrialia del Espiritu Santo,** created an order of nobility, distributed taffeta crosses for almost every man-jack on his fleet to wear, christened the stream that ran into the bay the Jordan, and announced in a prophetic ecstasy that the New Jerusalem would be built there among the coral reefs—which, in his feverishly optimistic mind, were already turning into quarries of porphyry and agate.

All this was an illusion, but de Quiros, convinced of its truth, sailed back to Mexico while Luis Vaez de Torres, the captain of his second ship, pressed on across the Pacific to Manila, passing just north of Australia between Cape York Peninsula and New Guinea through the strait that now bears his name. But he hugged the New Guinea coast and did not see the continent.

After eight years' struggle to raise another fleet, de Quiros died in 1614, his quest unfulfilled. There is some intriguing evidence, in the form of the so-called Dieppe Maps copied by spies from secret Portuguese charts and presented to the future Henri II in 1536 (one of which shows a Southern Continent strikingly similar in eastern profile to Australia's), that the northeast and east coasts of Australia had been found and charted before 1550 by a Portuguese fleet sailing south from the Spice Islands. If this voyage was made, it would have been illicit. Under the Treaty of Tordesillas (1494), Portugal and Spain had agreed to divide the Earth along the great diameter of 51° W. and 129° E. longitude. Thus, everything east of 129° W., which passes through Australia, became part of the Spanish imperium—including the east coast of Australia. Portugal had no rights of exploration there and could well have chosen to keep the results of such a voyage secret. However, the originals of the Dieppe Maps, along with any logs and documents that may have amplified them, were destroyed in the Lisbon earthquake in 1755. The only other relics of European contact with Australia before 1600 are two Portuguese brass cannon, datable around 1475–1525, found at Broome Bay in northwest Australia—evidence of another voyage, but this time on Portugal's side of the Tordesillas line.[3]

There had been Asian landings in the sixteenth century, but none resulted in colonization. They were made by Makassan traders from the island of Celebes, who ran down the northern monsoons in their slat-sailed praus to what is now Arnhem Land, on the north coast of the continent.[4] The goal of their 1,200-mile voyages was a sea slug, the tre-

---

* "Austrialia" was a reference to his King's Hapsburg blood ("Austria") and a pun on *tierra austral*, "the south land."

pang or *bêche-de-mer*. These creatures, which looked like withered penises when smoked and dried, were Indonesia's largest export to the Chinese, who esteemed them as an aphrodisiac. Thus, until the nineteenth century, Australia's sole contribution to the outside world was millions of sea slugs.

In 1605 the Dutch East India Company in Bantam sent a pinnace, the *Duyfken*, under Captain Willem Jansz, to see if New Guinea had gold and spices. The little boat entered the Torres Strait, turned south after coasting New Guinea for more than two hundred miles and found a cape that its skipper named Keerweer ("turn back"). The place was wilderness, and "wild, black, cruel savages" killed some of the crew. Jansz had found a northern promontory of Australia.

In 1616 another tessera was added to the edge of the puzzle by Dirck Hartog, an Amsterdam captain who reached the west Australian coast in his ship *Eendracht* and nailed up an engraved pewter dish as proof of his visit. In 1618 another vessel on the outward voyage to Java, the *Zeewulf*, glimpsed more coast to the north.

The next year, Frederick de Houtman, an outward-bound captain who steered further south from the Cape of Good Hope than most, landed on the west coast of Australia south of modern Perth. In time, more Dutch mariners offered their fragments of information: Jan Carstens in 1623, and Francis Pelsart in 1629. Clearly, the southland seemed to be worth exploring, with the expectation that it held more than sand, reefs and choleric savages. To that end, Anthony van Diemen, Governor-General of the Dutch East India Company, organized in 1642 a grand expedition that would map "the remaining unknown part of the terrestrial globe." Abel Tasman, its commander, was to sail from Batavia to Mauritius, drop south to latitude 54° S. and then sail east until he found the Southland.

He missed it completely. Tasman's two vessels, the *Heemskerck* and the *Zeehaen*, sailed right past Australia without once glimpsing its mainland; his course had been too far south. The only part of the country he touched was an island in the southwest which he guessed was mainland and named for his patron: Van Diemen's Land. Two centuries later, when that name had become so tarnished with stories of criminality and cruelty that respectable settlers would no longer endure it, the island was renamed Tasmania after its discoverer.

It looked poor and wild. No natives showed themselves, although notched trees and traces of cooking-fires were seen. There was little to remark. Tasman sailed east across what is now the Tasman Sea and discovered the west coast of New Zealand. Sailing on into the Pacific he discovered Tonga and Fiji as well, before returning to Batavia in June 1643. The voyage, as far as van Diemen and his merchant colleagues were concerned, was a fiasco. Tasman had found no people to trade with, no commodities to exploit. So they ordered Tasman out on a second voyage, to see if the north coast of Australia held anything worthwhile. Tasman sailed in 1644, but the only people he found on that coast were black, "naked beach-roving wretches, destitute even of rice . . . miserably poor, and in many places of a very bad disposition." There would be no trade. With this, the Dutch East India Company's interest in Australia languished.

The last seventeenth-century explorer to try the northwest coast of Australia was an English buccaneer, William Dampier, in 1688. He found nothing but the propertyless men of New Holland; his description of them is one of the minor classics of racism:

> The inhabitants of this country are the miserablest people in the World. The *Hodmadods* [Hottentots] of *Monomatapa*, though a nasty People, yet for Wealth are Gentlemen to these . . . and setting aside their humane shape, they differ but little from Brutes. They are tall, strait-bodied, and thin, with small long Limbs. They have great Heads, round Foreheads, and great Brows. Their Eye-lids are always half closed, to keep the Flies out of their Eyes . . . therefore they cannot see far . . .
>
> They are long-visaged, and of a very unpleasing aspect; having no one graceful feature in their faces.
>
> They have no houses, but lye in the open Air, without any covering; the Earth being their Bed, and the Heaven their Canopy . . . The Earth affords them no food at all. There is neither Herb, Pulse, nor any sort of Grain, for them to eat, that we saw; nor any sort of Bird or Beast that they can catch, having no instruments wherewithal to do so.
>
> I did not perceive that they did worship anything.[5]

Such was the Ignoble Savage, orphan of nature. Dampier's visit to the northwest coast produced no discoveries, but his book was popular in England and its notion of a Southern Continent—still a geographical hypothesis separate from New Holland—struck a responsive chord. The Spaniards and Dutch had failed in the Pacific; the eighteenth century would make it either a French or a British ocean.

So the direction of approach shifted again, and ships once more began probing the Pacific from the east, coming round the Horn or through the Straits of Magellan: Roggeveen in 1721, Byron in 1764, Wallis and Carteret in 1766, Bougainville in 1766 and 1769. They all sailed too far north in the trade winds to find the Australian coast; only Bougainville kept far enough south and would have discovered Queensland had he not been turned back by its coral rampart, the Great Barrier Reef, and gone north like the rest. They were all resolute men, but there were some problems courage alone could not beat. The first of these was scurvy.

This disease, caused by vitamin C deficiency, was the bane of every seaman. The victim weakened; his flesh puffed up and his joints were wracked with gouty pain; his teeth loosened while his gums swelled and turned black, so that he could not eat. Scurvy could kill most of a ship's company on a long voyage. The simple cure for it was fruit (especially lemons or oranges) and green vegetables. Captains did not know this; some had noticed that scurvy victims recovered in port on a green diet, but fruit and vegetables would not keep long at sea. In mid-Pacific, Magellan's crew had to eat a mixture of biscuit crumbs and rat droppings; then they ate the rats; at last they sucked and chewed the ship's leather chafing-gear in their desperate need for animal protein. Scurvy afflicted them so badly that to chew their rations, they had to keep slicing the swollen tissue of their gums away. From de Quiros in the sixteenth century to Bougainville in the eighteenth, none of the Pacific explorers suffered as badly from scurvy as Magellan and his crew.

Scurvy chilled the ambition of every voyage. Because they did not know the causes of the disease, they could not control it. In 1768–71, James Cook first beat scurvy on a long voyage by the regular issue of the proper anti-scorbutics. By then, it was known to be a dietary problem. Dr. James Lind, in 1753, had hit on the right cure: a daily dose of citrus juice. Yet neither Cook (who always worried about the health of his crew) nor the officers of the Admiralty's Victualling Board read Lind's treatise, and instead of citrus juice Cook tried other anti-scorbutics: sauerkraut, malt, and half a ton of "portable soup," made by boiling down meat broth into a gummy cake, the ancestor of the bouillon cube. In combination, these worked. Throughout the three-year voyage of the *Endeavour*, Cook did not lose a man from scurvy—a feat without precedent in the history of seafaring. Malt-juice and pickled cabbage put Europeans in Australia, as microchip circuitry would put Americans on the moon.

The other obstacle to Pacific exploration had been finding the longitude. Exploration means nothing unless you know your daily position, but to do this two coordinates are needed. The first is latitude, the measure of one's distance from the equator. The second is longitude, the distance between a fixed prime meridian (for British navigators, that of Greenwich) and the meridian of one's position. (A meridian is the shortest line drawn from the north to the south pole on the Earth's curved surface.) A ship's latitude was easy to figure and had been since antiquity. But without longitude, one could not determine one's position with any certainty. Mariners had to make do with guesswork, based on the ocean current, the wind and the speed of the ship. Mistakes of more than 2,000 miles were common on the early Pacific voyages, because accumulated longitude error could not be checked. In calculating the longitude of the

Philippines, Magellan's pilot was wrong by some 53 degrees—more than a seventh of the world's circumference.

The more they thought of Empire, the more the British realized the need for a longitude fixing method. As England began to challenge Dutch mercantile supremacy in the Far East, the more urgent this became. In 1714 the British government put up a prize of £20,000, a fortune, for anyone who could come up with a method by which a navigator could fix longitude at sea that would be correct within thirty miles at the end of a six-week open-water voyage.

By Cook's time, there were two systems of finding longitude. Both relied on the fact that as the earth spins, local time alters from place to place—thus, when it is noon in London, it is 7 a.m. in New York. The Earth rotates once a day; and as there are 24 hours in a day and 360 degrees of longitude around the equator, an hour's difference in time represented a shift of 15 degrees in longitude. So if one knew when and at what angle a given astronomical event would be seen at Greenwich, and observed it from, say, a spot in the Pacific at that same angle, the difference in hours multiplied by 15 would yield the longitude in degrees. This constant was the angle between the moon or sun and a fixed star, such as Polaris, and was known as "lunar distance." The English Astronomer Royal, Nevil Maskelyne, was the first man to publish a complete tabulation of future lunar distances in relation to Greenwich Mean Time; this was the famous Nautical Almanac, first issued in 1766. Armed with "Mister Masculine's Tables," along with some basic trigonometry and some well-made instruments, any captain could now find his longitude. That was the first method. The second was to carry Greenwich Mean Time on board ship, compare it with local time and multiply the difference by 15 as before. That was far quicker, but it required a chronometer, a clock more accurate and durable than any other. If it ran fast or slow, every minute it lost or gained would mean an error of longitude of nearly 20 miles on the equator. It had to stand up to salt, corrosion and the ceaseless pounding of a ship at sea. Such a chronometer was finally built in 1764 by the great John Harrison.

For his first Pacific voyage, Cook had no chronometer, preferring to rely on lunar distance calculations. But the *Endeavour* was well-equipped with other instruments, as measurement rather than discovery was the main purpose of her voyage. Her passengers were to observe from Tahiti the transit of Venus across the Sun's face. The importance of this celestial event was that, if accurately observed and recorded, it could help establish the earth's distance from the sun. The last time that Earth, Venus and the sun had come into line was in 1761; the silhouette of Venus on the solar disk was watched and timed by 120 observers scattered across the world from Russia to South Africa, but even so the readings had been fuzzy and the British wanted to improve them. From Tahiti, on the predicted date of June 3, 1769, the whole transit would be seen in daytime, in clear air.

After Cook completed this task, he could then pursue his explorations. The Admiralty wanted him either to find or to eliminate the Southern Continent. He must do this by dropping south of Tahiti, below the tracks of all previous Pacific navigators, to 40° S. latitude. He must then make a sweep westward, keeping between 35° and 40° S. until he either found the Southern Continent or reached "the Eastern side of the Land discover'd by Tasman and now called New Zeland."[6] One way or the other, a myth that had haunted exploration for centuries would be cleared up.

### iii

ON AUGUST 25, 1768, the *Endeavour*—a converted Whitby collier, small and brawny, 106 feet long—set sail from Plymouth. Along with her crew, marines and officers, she had on board a number of civilians. The most important of them, from Greenwich's point of view, was the astronomer Charles Green. The rest made up a private scientific party: a brilliant, mercurial young amateur named Joseph Banks and the servants and specialists he had hired to accompany him. At twenty-five, Banks was well-educated (Eton, Oxford), well-connected, well-off (a rural fortune) and in the proper sense a dilettante: one who took an eclectic, educated pleasure in the world about him. His passion was botany, and his hero (whom he had not met) was the great Swedish botanist Carolus Linnaeus. On hearing of the expedition to Tahiti, Banks realized that this was his chance. To be the first botanist into the South Seas would make his reputation, for he would have the flora of a new world to himself. "Any blockhead can go to Italy," he is said to have told a friend who wondered when he would take his Grand Tour. "Mine shall be around the world." He would go with Cook. Friends in the Admiralty and the Royal Society arranged it. Banks went on board the *Endeavour* with a retinue consisting of two artists (one of them a young genius of botanical illustration, Sydney Parkinson), several servants, a secretary, two hounds, and another naturalist, the most affable, enthusiastic and learned of travelling companions, a favorite pupil of Linnaeus himself: Dr. Daniel Solander.

The *Endeavour* took almost eight months to reach Tahiti via Rio de Janeiro and Tierra del Fuego, dropping anchor in Matavai Bay in mid-

April 1769. The doings of Cook, Banks and the crew in this barely touched Eden must no more concern us here than the details of Cook's coastal exploration of New Zealand, as the Crown never considered either Tahiti or New Zealand as penal settlements.[7]

The transit of Venus was duly, though imperfectly, observed. Banks's crates and bottles were filling up with specimens, his artists' folios with sketches. Early in August they left Tahiti, taking with them a young Tahitian of exalted birth named Tupaia, whom Banks intended to bring back to London as the ultimate exotic pet, a live Noble Savage. Their search for the Southern Continent now began.

For months, beating west through the toppling green hills of the Pacific, they were misled by what Banks called "Our old enemy Cape fly away"—cloudbanks on the horizon. Then, on the afternoon of October 6, 1769, land lay before them. "All hands seem to agree," wrote Banks, viewing the low solid line to the west, "that this is certainly the continent we are in search of."[8]

It was not, and their track across the southern Pacific had nearly eliminated that continent. They had reached Poverty Bay on the east coast of the north island of New Zealand, and for the next four months Cook sailed the *Endeavour* around the coasts of both the north and the south islands, mapping every reef, cliff and indentation and, with caution, observing the habits of the brave and bellicose Maori: The Tahitians made love, but these men with faces rigidly tattooed like purple fingerprints made war. "I suppose," Banks jotted, "they live intirely on fish, dogs, and enemies."

At the end of March 1770 Cook was ready for the homeward voyage. The Southern Continent had proved "imaginary"; however, more than 2,400 miles of New Zealand's coastline were charted. He had fulfilled the Admiralty's brief and could shape his course for England.

He could return eastward around the Horn or westward via the Cape of Good Hope. The western route was unlikely to bring forth new discoveries. But March is the end of the Pacific summer and Cook did not want to commit his ship—battered and wormy as she was from two years' voyage—to the eastern route and the winter storms of Cape Horn. Cook had Tasman's charts, and he decided to try another way. Somewhere to the west, there must lie the east coast of New Holland. They would follow Tasman's track, in reverse, from New Zealand to Van Diemen's Land. Then they would find whether Van Diemen's Land was part of New Holland, or a separate island. If it was separate, they would find the coast of New Holland and sail north along it.

On March 31 they left New Zealand. Southerly gales rose and drove the *Endeavour* to latitude 38°, too far north to make Van Diemen's Land.

But on April 19 a new coast announced itself. Flat and sandy, most unlike the magnificent scenery of New Zealand, it lay dry on the gray horizon. Their landfall was at Cape Everard, in Victoria.

They coasted north, finding no harbor. But now and then they saw smoke rising from the scrubby headlands, so they knew that the place must be inhabited. To Banks, the landscape looked poor after Tahiti and New Zealand. "It resembled in my imagination the back of a lean Cow, covered in general with long hair, but nevertheless where her scraggy hip bones have stuck out further than they ought accidental rubbs and knocks have intirely bar'd them of their share of covering."⁹ On April 22, they saw some Australians on a beach. They looked black but it was hard to tell their real color. Exactly a week later, the first contact was made. Heading up from the south, Cook saw a wide bay and steered into it, sending the pinnace ahead to make soundings.

They saw bark canoes and in them blacks were fishing. The ship floated past these frail coracles. It was the largest artifact ever seen on the east coast of Australia, an object so huge, complex and unfamiliar as to defy the natives' understanding. The Tahitians had flocked out to meet her in their bird-winged outriggers, and the Maoris had greeted her with *hakas* and showers of stones; but the Australians took no notice. They displayed neither fear nor interest and went on fishing.

Only when they anchored and Cook, Banks, Solander and Tupaia— who, all hoped, might act as interpreter—approached the south shore of the bay in a longboat did the natives react. The sight of men in a small boat was comprehensible to them; it meant invasion. Most of the Aborigines fled into the trees, but two naked warriors stood their ground, brandished their spears and shouted in a quick, guttural tongue, not a syllable of it familiar to Tupaia. Cook and Banks pitched some trading-truck ashore—nails and beads, the visiting cards of the South Pacific. The blacks moved to attack, and Cook fired a musket-shot between them. One warrior ran back and grabbed a bundle of spears, while the other began shying rocks at the boat. Cook fired again, wounding one of them with small-shot, but still the man did not retreat; he merely picked up a bark shield.

It was time to land. A young midshipman named Isaac Smith was in the bow. Years later, after many promotions, Admiral Smith—the cousin of Cook's wife—would proudly tell how the greatest navigator in history hesitated before quitting the longboat, touched him on the shoulder and said, "Isaac, you shall land first." The lad sprang into the green, bottle-glass water as it prickled on the floury white sand, and waded ashore. Cook and the others followed, and the seal of distance and space that had protected the east coast of Australia since the Pleistocene epoch was broken. The colonization of the last continent had begun. The blacks threw their stone-tipped spears.

Cook fired a third shot. With an insolent lack of haste, the tribesmen retreated into the bush. The whites found some bark shelters near the beach from which the adult natives had fled, although in one humpy there were "four or five children with whome we left some strings of beeds &ca." What kind of people were these, who ran away and left their babies to the mercy of strangers? Nothing could win their confidence. "We could know but very little of their customs," Cook complained on May 6, a week after at anchor, "as we were never able to form any connections with them, they had not so much as touch'd the things we had left in their hutts." They seemed to have no curiosity, no sense of material possessions. "All they seem'd to want was for us to be gone." Tupaia, in particular, had a low but prophetic opinion of these elusive men and women of Australia. He was heard to remark that "they were *Taata Eno's* that is bad or poor people." The Polynesian phrase *taata ino* denoted the very lowest caste of Tahitians, the *titi*, who were used as human sacrifices.

Cook saw them differently, and in a famous passage in his journal he contradicted Dampier's view of them. "They may appear to some to be the most wretched people upon Earth," he remarked,

> but in reality they are far happier than we Europeans; being wholy unacquainted not only with the superfluous but the necessary Conveniencies so much sought after in Europe, they are happy in not knowing the use of them. They live in Tranquillity which is not disturb'd by the Inequality of Condition.[10]

These few days of sparse contact on the coast of New South Wales sealed the doom of the Aborigine. There was no chance that the Crown would ever try to plant a penal colony in New Zealand, for the Maori were a subtle, determined and ferocious race. These Australians, however, would give no trouble. They were ill-armed, backward, and timid; most of them ran at the sight of a white face; and they had no goods or property to defend. Besides, there were so few of them. All this the British authorities would presently learn from Joseph Banks, without whose evidence there might have been no convict colony in Australia.

The men of the *Endeavour* gave little thought to any of this as they explored that distant sheltered bay in the Pacific autumn of 1770. Banks and Solander were especially busy. The low, flat shores were full of plants and creatures unknown to European science. The animals were elusive —they found one kangaroo-turd, without seeing the 'roo—but there was a staggering quantity of "nondescript" (unclassified) plant life. Eventually, the young botanists were to bring back 30,000 specimens from their voyage, representing some 3,000 species of which 1,600 were wholly new to science. The harbor was full of fish, and on its shallow flats immense stingrays, *Dasyatis brevicaudatus*, were caught; Sydney Parkinson, Banks's botanical artist, commented that their guts tasted "not unlike stewed turtle." Cook decided to call the bay Stingray Harbor, but later he changed his mind. The place represented such a triumph for his young companions' science that, thinking of all the accumulated specimens and drawings in the *Endeavour*'s stern cabin, he fixed on the name Botany Bay. Its northern and southern heads went on the chart as Cape Banks and Point Solander.

They sailed and kept coasting north. They passed but did not enter a harbor fifteen miles north of Botany Bay, which Cook named Port Jackson, after the Secretary for the Admiralty. Their track up the immense eastern flank of Australia ran through twenty-eight degrees of latitude, more than two thousand miles from Botany Bay to the tip of Cape York. In the labyrinth of the Great Barrier Reef—Cook had unwittingly sailed into it like a fish into the funnel of a trap—the ship struck; a coral fang ripped through her sheathing and broke off, by the merest fluke stopping the hole until the ship could be kedged clear, beached and repaired. This brush with annihilation delayed them seven weeks at Endeavour Bay, giving Banks more time for botanizing. At last the mysterious kangaroo was seen, and two were shot; they tasted like tough venison. A seaman told Banks, to his amusement, about a ghastly monster he had spied, "about as large and much like a one gallon Kegg, as black as the Devil and had 2 horns on its head, it went but slowly but I dar'd not touch it." It was a flying fox. More Aborigines appeared, behaving in the fickle uncertain manner of people startled by an alien intrusion. They seemed as timid as those of Botany Bay. Apparently, the variations of culture and nature were small along this immense coast.

On August 21, 1770, the *Endeavour* rounded Cape York. From there, to the west, stretched a discovered sea crossed by Dutch ships. Cook, Banks, and Solander landed on a nubbin of rock now called Possession Island, hoisted a Union Jack and formally claimed the whole coast south of where they stood—down to 38° S., near their original landfall—as "New South Wales" in the name of George III. They fired three volleys, which were answered from the ship. The salute had to be given with small arms, for all the *Endeavour*'s cannon had been trundled overboard to lighten her when she lay holed on the Barrier Reef. In this modest way, by the slap of muskets echoing across a flat warm strait, Australia was added to the British Empire.

iv

AMID THE TUMULT of publicity that greeted the safe return of the
ship and her crew to England in July 1771, it was clear that only one
place ravished the public imagination: Tahiti, languid isle of the Golden
Age, Cytherea of the Pacific. New Zealand was next in order of interest,
while Australia ran a poor third. Naturally there was professional curiosity among scientists as to the plants and fauna of the new continent.
But no kangaroo, even when painted by George Stubbs, could possibly
compete with Tahitian princesses as an object of fantasy. There was
something, if not exactly dull, at least ungraspable about that flat hot
fringe of a blank continent, sown about with deadly reefs. Cultivated
opinion on the matter was symbolized in a portrait of Banks done in 1773
by Benjamin West, the rising young prodigy of America paying his homage to the even younger virtuoso of a world still newer, the Pacific. Banks
stands wrapped in a fine chief's cloak, pointing out a detail of the weave;
around him are trophies of his periplus—Tahitian ceremonial gear, a
carved paddle, a Maori *mere* (jade war-club). But the only thing that
might stand for New South Wales, and rather ambiguously at that, is an
open folio with Parkinson's drawing of a lily. The disappointing truth
about Australia was that once the legend of the Southern Continent had
been disproved and the facts about New Holland were known, there was
not much reason to go there.

In 1772 Cook boarded the *Resolution* and began his second voyage,
that epic navigation of the Antarctic Ocean which took him further
south than any human had ever been—to 71° S.—and which destroyed
the last vestiges of that legend. There was no habitable latitude where
such a continent could be, and "the greatest part of this Southern Continent (supposing there is one) must lay within the Polar Circle where
the sea is so pestered with ice, that the land is thereby inaccessible."
Cook's intuition of Antarctica was correct.

Thus eighteen years passed before another ship called at Botany Bay,
and for the first eight of those years the subject of Australia, as far as
George III's government was concerned, was forgotten. It was revived
after 1783, when Pitt the Younger became prime minister. The idea that
Australia might carry a British penal colony was raised by the revolt of
the American colonies, and by a crisis in England's hulks and jails. However, it is by now a common (though by no means general) opinion among
students of Australian history that the "grand design" of Botany Bay was
really strategic, hatched by Pitt's desire to deny France power over India
and the Far Eastern trade routes that were so vital to British interests in

the late eighteenth century. This vision of the embryo colony as a "strategic outlier" of England, not just an opportunistically chosen dump for its criminals, has become popular with Australians as our national bicentenary approaches. It lends dignity to our origins. "The rag and bone shop of Australia's beginning," wrote the main spokesman for this view, Alan Frost, "was perhaps not so foul as we have long supposed."[11] We shall see.

In 1779, the year Captain James Cook was killed by the Hawaiians at Karakakoa Bay, a House of Commons committee was set up to determine where convicts, if sentenced to transportation, could be sent now that America was closed to them. The place should be very distant but not a mere desert, for it was essential that a colony there be able to support itself. What about New Holland? The committee invited Joseph Banks, now a celebrity and soon to be knighted, to deliver his views. Nobody in England knew more about Australia. The great man, now thirty-four years old, spoke of Botany Bay and its naked cowardly savages. The climate was good, the soil was arable; he described the abundance of fish, pasture, fresh water and wood and set forth the opinion that a colony of felons could support itself within a year. Perhaps he actually believed this farrago of optimistic distortions; but though the committee was impressed, it made no decision. It heard other witnesses, who suggested transportation to Gibraltar or the west coast of Africa.

There was reason to be skeptical about such projects. The American transportation system had relied on free settlers who would buy indentured labor. The convicts were sold by middlemen and from the moment they stepped on American soil they ceased to cost England a penny; they were not a charge on the State.

Yet in Australia, these conditions would not apply. Thousands of men and women would be packed off, in ships that would bring back no cargo, to a place expected to produce no surplus. There were no free settlers to buy the indentured labor of the felons, and every item of their upkeep would be a dead charge on the government. Even granted the pervasive sense of a crisis in the criminal system and the widespread desire to solve it by expelling the "criminal classes" of England to some place "beyond the seas," the notion of setting a convict colony in a place as remote and ill-known as Australia was certainly bizarre. The argument for strategic colonization of Australia seems, at least on the face of it, to make the exercise more rational.

When William Pitt the Younger became its prime minister in 1783, England was half-bankrupted from war with France. Pitt believed it was essential to keep the French from gaining any influence over India and the trade routes of the Far East. The East's economic importance to Britain was growing. It had not approached the volume of Britain's Atlantic trade,[12] but its direction was clear: In the future, a great part of Britain's economic destiny would lie in the "East Indies," a vast swath of territory that ran from the Cape of Good Hope through India and Malaya to the coast of China and on into the Pacific.

The main instrument of British interests there had been the sprawling, corrupt East India Company, which had the closest relationships to government of any English business. For ten years, starting with Lord North's Regulating Act (1773), the government strove to curb and reform "John Company." With the passage of Pitt's India Act (1784), which partly nationalized control of the East India Company, the matter of India was at the front of all political argument, the responsibility not of the Company men but of the Crown and its ministers. Trade had brought territory, territory war, war an Empire. With this had come immense problems of security as well as trade. Not only did India have to be run, but the East as a whole—not excluding the Western Pacific—had to be kept open to British shipping, especially along the vital trade route from India to Canton. Eastern trade represented Britain's best hope of economic recovery from the setbacks of the early 1780s: her loss of North America, her costly war against the French, and her alienation from once friendly European states—notably, Holland.

For Holland was the key to strategic power in the East. The forts and harbors of the Dutch trading empire ran from Cape Town to the southwest Pacific. The Dutch monopoly of the Spice Islands was the oldest and toughest obstacle the East India company had to face. Yet the *military* weakness of this trading empire had been revealed after England declared war on Holland in 1780. The British began a series of inconclusive naval strikes against Dutch bases in the East. In March 1781 a British squadron bungled an attack on the "Gibraltar of Africa," the Cape of Good Hope, from which East India convoys sailing round the tip of Africa could be harassed by privateers. This backfired badly with the net result that the French, under Admiral de Suffren, reinforced the Dutch garrison at the Cape and held it to the end of the war. Another British fleet captured two lesser Dutch ports which had some strategic influence over the sea lanes to the Bay of Bengal: Negapatam (modern Negapattinam) on the southeast coast of India, and Trincomalee in Ceylon. Soon after, de Suffren retook Trincomalee.

The lesson Pitt drew from this distant, inconclusive sea war, after hostilities ceased, was that the combination of Dutch depots and French ships posed dangers for the British in India even though Holland was no longer a major sea power. There was a vacuum of naval power in the Far East, and the British had to fill it before the French did. In the postwar negotiations, Pitt tried very hard to reach friendly agreements with the Dutch on seaborne trade in the East Indies, while edging the French garrisons out of the Cape. He hoped (in the words of Sir James Harris, Pitt's minister at The Hague) "not only to separate the Interests of the Dutch East India Company from those of France, but to unite them with those of Great-Britain."[13] The fabric of England's Far Eastern trade was too delicate to permit anything but conciliation in dealing with the Dutch. If provoked again, they could join the French to drive England from the East Indies.

But though there was no doubt that the French wanted India, they lacked the military force to take it. After the peace of 1783, they made a series of diplomatic moves to weaken British influence there. In 1785 they struck a treaty with the Bey in Cairo to give them trading rights in Egypt, which was seen as a distant gambit to a possible invasion of India. They also formed a chartered trading company, the French East India Company of Calonne, to compete with Britain's East India Company. The peace settlement had called for a balance between British and French fleets in Indian seas—the understood figure was five warships each, none larger than 64 guns. There was some British concern (more from spies and diplomats than from naval men) when it appeared that the French East India Company was using decommissioned 64-gun cruisers, known as *flûtes*, as merchantmen. Their lower gun-decks had been removed, but in theory they could soon be re-armed. On the other hand, the French thought the massive and growing tonnage of British East India merchant fleets from the Cape to Canton could easily be converted to war, and they too were right. Despite the highly colored intelligence reports it got, there is no sign that Pitt's government saw the French *flûtes* as a grave threat.

Its main field of concern, in the problem of keeping the Indian trade routes open, was relations between the French and the Dutch. French postwar diplomacy concentrated on the majority faction in the Dutch government, the Patriot Party. At the end of 1785, France and Holland signed a treaty of defensive alliance. Early in 1786, the Patriots took control of the Dutch East India Company and, encouraged by their French allies, moved to put thousands more troops into the Cape and Trincomalee. The French also pressed the Patriots to take all military decisions about India and the Cape from the ailing hands of the Dutch East India Company. Sir James Harris gloomily reported to Pitt in March 1786 that France had told the Dutch Patriots "that a Rupture with England in Asia is not of a very distant Period—no Time should be lost in augmenting [British] Naval and Land Force in that Quarter of the World."[14]

The threat of such a "rupture," according to the strategic-outlier arguments of Australian historians like Frost and Blainey, led to Botany Bay. The reason lay in pines and flax.

In eighteenth-century strategy, pine trees and flax had the naval importance that oil and uranium hold today. All masts and spars were of pine, and flax was the raw stuff of ships' canvas; neither could be had in quantity in the Far East, although there was plenty of coir fiber for rigging. A first-rate ship of the line needed immense quantities of spar timber. The mainmast of a 74-gun first-rater was three feet thick at the base, and rose 108 feet from keelson to truck—a single tree, dead straight and flawlessly solid. Such a vessel needed some 22 masts and yards as well. No other timber would do. Only conifers made good masts, because of their natural straightness and because the pine resin cut down friction between the fibers in their grain. This second characteristic made the great sticks relatively supple, so that they could absorb the punishing stress of heavy-weather sailing.

No such spar timber grew in the British Isles or in India. It all had to come from Riga, on the Baltic coast of Russia. The flax for sails also came from Russia, and England spent half a million pounds a year importing it. The supply line from Riga to Portsmouth through Russian and Scandinavian territorial waters was 1,700 miles long and highly vulnerable to shifts of alliance between England, France and their northern neighbors. Even when these strategic materials reached England, they still had 10,000 miles to go before they could be of use to a British squadron in the Far East. Hence the anxiety of the British in September 1784, when France got from Sweden the right to put a naval depot on the island of Göteborg at the mouth of the Baltic; from there, French ships could harass the British timber-transports.

One reason for the French-British naval stalemate in Indian seas in 1782 was the drastic shortage of spar timber, all of which had to be shipped from Europe. "There was not anywhere in India, so much as a Spar fit to make a Jibb Boom for a 64 gun ship," Admiral Sir Edward Hughes reported in 1781, "nor any Timber to be had of a size to make an Anchor Stock for a Line of Battle Ship."[15]

Faced now by the prospect of a Far Eastern war (so the argument goes) Pitt's counsellors remembered Norfolk Island, a rock that Captain James Cook had discovered in the Pacific a thousand miles east of Botany Bay during his second voyage a decade earlier, in 1774. His track toward it had taken him past several islands on which pine trees grew, some trunks of which were the size of the foremast of his ship, the *Resolution*. Larger ones, he thought, might well grow on larger islands, and this would be a boon to navigators. As he noted in his log, "I know of no Island in the South Pacifick Ocean where a Ship could supply herself with a Mast or a Yard, was she everso much distress'd for want of one. . . . the discovery may be both useful and valuable." His guess proved right. The Norfolk Island pines grew to 3 feet in diameter and 180 feet in height. Better still, the island's cliffs and shoreline were densely covered with stands of flax, *Phormium tenax*, seemingly ideal for the manufacture of canvas.[16]

Samples of the flax were gathered and, back in England, test pieces of hawser, canvas and twine were made from them. The "New Zealand flax" proved to be exceptionally tough and durable. Surely it, and the pines, were to be seen as a strategic asset for the Indian ships? And—stretching the possibilities further—might not the coast of New South Wales provide an armed haven, a "strategic outlier," where warships could refit with this timber, sailcloth and cordage, protected by a garrison?

To some people then, and to later historians, this looked good on paper, but there is no hard evidence that it did so to William Pitt or his ministers. The first man to propose it was an American-born functionary, James Mario Matra (ca. 1745–1806), who had held minor administrative posts in London and diplomatic ones in Tenerife and Constantinople. Matra held no official position in England. He was one of the bit-players in the drama of Empire: a speculator petitioning for a commercial scheme that, he hoped, would give him a job. It is in this light that one must see his suggestion—the first on record—that pines and flax might afford a strategic reason for colonizing Australia. It was read because he, at least, had seen Botany Bay, having sailed as a midshipman under Cook on the *Endeavour*. He presented his idea in a letter to Lord North, who had briefly replaced Thomas Townshend, Viscount Sydney, as the home and colonial secretary in 1783. His memo was endorsed by Banks, whose name Matra invoked in flattering terms throughout.[17]

It did not involve convicts. To "atone for the loss of our American colonies," the loyalist Matra proposed a free settlement in New South Wales, a country that held out "the most enticing allurements to European adventurers." The settlers should be of two kinds: British peasants, and dispossessed Loyalists fleeing from America to find asylum. Matra was an apostle of prophylactic emigration; he wanted to export the British poor before they turned to crime. "Few of any country," he realistically observed, "will ever think of settling in any foreign part of the world from a restless mind and from *Romantick* views." Thus, he reasoned, the Australian colonists ought to be the newly poor, of whom there was no shortage, as the economic woes brought about by the American revolt had caused a serious rural depression in England by 1783.

Matra rhapsodized on what the colony might produce, with the help of Chinese slave labor: tea, silk, spices, tobacco, coffee. There would be trade with China, Japan, Korea and the Aleutians. Best of all there were the flax and the pines, material "of the greatest importance," "eminently useful to us as a naval Power." Through them, the blank coast of New Holland would acquire a very commanding influence in the policy of Europe. If a Colony from Britain was established in the large Tract of Country, & if we were at war with Holland or Spain, we might very powerfully annoy either State from our new Settlement. We might with a safe, & expeditious voyage, make Naval Incursions on Java, & the other Dutch Settlements, & we might with equal facility, invade the Coasts of Spanish America . . . This check which New South Wales would be in time of War on both those Powers, makes it a very important Object when we view it in the Chart of the World, with a Political Eye.[18]

Lord North ignored Matra's scheme, and a glance at the atlas will show why: These strategic promises were puffery. The "facility" with which Chile could be attacked from Sydney involved crossing the whole Pacific. The "safe and expeditious voyage" to Java was some 4,000 miles long, through ill-charted and reef-strewn seas, with a dangerous choke-point in the Torres Straits.

Lord Sydney replaced Lord North at the end of 1783. He faced a rising clamor over the problem of criminal confinement—the shamefully over-crowded hulks and prisons. As home and colonial secretary, he was pressed to come up with a plan for disposing of British convicts. Matra heard he was casting around for a place to send them, and so he quickly wrote convicts into his plan and re-submitted it to Sydney:

Give them a few acres of ground as soon as they arrive . . . in absolute property, with what assistance they may want to till them. Let it be here remarked that they cannot fly from the country, that they have no temp-tation to theft, and that they must work or starve.[19]

Meanwhile, the administration drafted a new bill authorizing the revival of transportation to places other than America, "to what Place or Places, Part or Parts beyond the seas" the Crown might think fit. This Transportation Act (24 Geo. III, c. 56) became law in August 1784. All that was lacking was a place to receive the felons. Lord Sydney passed Matra's idea of an Australian thief-colony along to Lord Howe, the first lord of the Admiralty, who curtly rejected it as impractical.[20] But another naval man liked it, Sir George Young (1732–1810), a future admiral who had served in Indian waters. He advised Pitt that Botany Bay would make a good base for British ships "should it be necessary to send any into the South Seas"; that it should be established by convict labor; and that Pacific flax could replace that of Russia. Like Matra, he fancied that every imaginable cash crop could be grown in New South Wales, "uniting in one territory almost all the productions of the known world." Although his plan was scarcely distinguishable from Matra's, Young proposed sending only 140 convicts a year.[21]

Another proposal for opening a strategic supply-base in Australia with convict labor came from John Call (1732–1801), a former colonel in the service of the East India company, whose specialty was military engineering. He pointed to "the declining if not . . . precarious state" of Britain's East Indies trade, and recommended a British base in either New South Wales or New Zealand, with Norfolk Island and its superior flax as a convict-worked source of naval supplies.[22]

Nothing suggests that Pitt gave this more than glancing attention, although his attorney general, Pepper Arden, liked the idea. The strategic argument was ridiculed in July 1785 by a man whose views carried more weight in official circles than Young's, Call's or Matra's: Alexander Dalrymple, hydrographer to the East India Company, who opposed plans to colonize Norfolk Island as a violation of the company's monopolistic charter. In a report to the Court of the company's directors, Dalrymple sharply pointed out that serviceable mast timber could be got in Borneo and Sumatra—Chinese and southeast Asian shipwrights, after all, had done without Riga pines for centuries—and that "the best cables in the world" were made from Eastern coir and a palm fiber called gummatty. Dalrymple thought there was every reason to grow Pacific flax in England, but none to bring "so bulky an article" from Norfolk Island—"The absurdity . . . is too great to merit any serious consideration." And he heaped scorn on the way promoters like Matra, Young and Call had tried to tailor the idea of a strategic thief-colony to fit whatever the British Government seemed to have on its mind:

> This project of a Settlement in that quarter has appeared in many Proteus-like forms, sometimes as a halfway house to China; again as a check upon the *Spaniards* at *Manila* and their *Acapulco* Trade; sometimes as a place for transported Convicts; then as a place of Asylum for American Refugees; and sometimes as an Emporium for supplying our Marine Yards with Hemp and Cordage, or for carrying on the Fur Trade on the N.W. Coast of America; just as the temper of ministers was supposed to be inclined to receive a favorable impression.[23]

But through the flurry of promotional schemes, more attractive to historians as documents today than they had ever been to Pitt's government at the time, the real problem continued to grow. The jail and hulk population swelled through the winter of 1784–85, and the task of finding a place for transported convicts became perceptibly more urgent. Provincial jails were filled to bursting and even Newgate, whose complete rebuilding by George Dance the Younger was finished in 1785, was already so overcrowded that three hundred convicts had to be taken from it and put in a hulk in Langston Harbor at Portsmouth. On April 20,

1785, as the pressure on Pitt's government mounted, a committee met to decide once and for all where to send the convicts. Its chairman was Lord Beauchamp.

The first proposal was the island of Lemane, 400 miles up the Gambia River in West Africa. It was put up by the governor of the Africa Company, a British slaving enterprise. "Notorious felons," he urged, could be sent there packed in British slavers; stranded on Lemane with natives all around and a guardship stationed downstream in the Gambia River to stop them fleeing to the coast, the prisoners could be left "entirely to themselves" without a garrison and permitted to elect their own disciplinary officers. Many would perish in this African grave, but the survivors would turn into planters.

The Beauchamp Committee, to its credit, saw through this lunatic scheme, and one of its members, Edmund Burke, spoke against it in the House of Commons. So Lemane was dropped, and the committee was left with two alternatives: Das Voltas Bay, by the mouth of the Orange River on the southwest coast of Africa, and Botany Bay. It closely questioned its witnesses on the cost of sending convicts to Botany Bay, and how to keep them alive and disciplined once they got there. Yet despite the arguments of Matra, Call and Young for a convict settlement in New South Wales, the vote went to Das Voltas Bay, for several reasons. Das Voltas Bay was more strategically located. Unlike Botany Bay, it sat plumb on the main sea route from Europe to the Far East and promised to be an excellent staging depot for naval supplies. A British garrison there could offset a French one in Cape Town. The country behind it was said to be fertile and could serve as a new home for American Loyalists, those displaced and slightly embarrassing reminders of England's vast failure in the New World. Besides, there were rumors of copper ore in the mountains, at a time when the British Navy had started coppering the bottoms of all its ships to increase their service life in distant seas.[24] With high hopes, the government dispatched a sloop to survey Das Voltas Bay in September 1785, but it came back with the news that the place was too dry and sterile to be settled.

That left Botany Bay as a mediocre second choice. Perhaps its putative access to flax and pines, as raw material to be obtained by convict labor, gave it the edge over other suggested places such as Gromarivire Bay, on the Caffre Coast east of Cape Town, or Madagascar or Tristan da Cunha. But the "strategic" arguments for Botany Bay do not seem to have impressed Pitt. References to them in his correspondence are few and vague. His concern was getting rid of convicts, for by the spring of 1786 he was under severe political pressure from independent MPs to enforce the sentence of transportation and get convicts out of hulks within their constituencies at Plymouth and Portsmouth. "Though I am not at this

Moment able to state to You the Place, to which any Number of the Convicts will be sent," he wrote placatingly to one of these Devon men, John Rolle, "I am able to assure You that Measures are taken for procuring the Quantity of Shipping necessary for conveying above a thousand of them. . . . [A]ll the Steps necessary for the removal of at least that Number, may be completed in about a Month."[25]

It took longer than that. No ship was sent to reconnoiter Botany Bay because, as Lord Sydney and his more able undersecretary Evan Nepean stressed, the hour was late and the British hulks and jails were facing an imminent breakdown. (In one hulk riot, in March 1786, eight prisoners were killed and thirty-six wounded.[26]) The Government did not have eighteen spare months to send a ship to New South Wales and back; and in any case the Beauchamp Committee trusted what Banks told them of its merits as a spot for convict settlement. Nepean and Sydney also appeared to believe Matra's claim (supported by Young) that New South Wales was not so very far from the strategic centers of the Far East: "a Months run from the Cape of Good Hope, five weeks from Madras, and the same from Canton; very near the Moluccas, & less than a Months Run from Batavia." These figures were absurdly low. It took the First Fleet two months to reach Botany Bay from the Cape, with the prevailing westerlies behind it. Returning against them, the run was more like three months. And no ship could reach Canton or Madras from New South Wales in five weeks.

Attractive though it may have looked on paper to the geographically naïve, the "strategic" argument of Matra, Young, Call and Banks for a convict-colony in New South Wales remained a chimera to which Pitt's government showed no attachment. The flax industry began weakly and was soon abandoned. No ship (except the *Buffalo*, a small colonial-built vessel) ever had a suit of sails woven from Norfolk Island flax or sailed under spars of Norfolk Island pine. Although the early colonial governors Arthur Phillip and Philip Gidley King did pursue the cultivation of the flax plant *Phormium tenax* on Norfolk Island, their home government's actions spoke louder than its instructions: It sent neither trained flax-dressers nor appropriate tools to the colony. (David Mackay is probably right in seeing King's enthusiasm for flax production as "a personal and colonial necessity, rather than a strategic one"[27]; he wanted to be remembered as the governor of an infant state, one with its own export economy, not just as the keeper of the human dump that New South Wales actually was.)

As for the direct strategic role of the colony, it was nugatory. Port Jackson was thousands of miles from England's areas of strategic interest and, in any case, the threat posed by French ships in the Far East dwindled to insignificance by the mid-1790s. The garrison sent to guard the convicts was too small and weak to resist a determined invader; not that it mattered, for no invaders were interested. In terms of military advantage, the English presence in Australia at most caused some ripples of apprehension in France and on the far side of the Pacific. In 1790 the Viceroy of Mexico thought there were "not enough forces in our South Seas and the Department of San Blas to counteract those which the English have at their Botany Bay." A visit to the half-starved, virtually shipless colony of Sydney would have put his mind at ease. Although Napoleon thought about invading New South Wales, he did not try, and the place played no role in the Napoleonic Wars.[28]

Thus, despite the talk about strategic advantage that was heard up to the dispatch of the First Fleet in 1787, the actual benefits of the new colony to England were only two: It was a sign of claim, a foothold on the new continent; and, in Evan Nepean's words, it absorbed "a Dreadful banditti." For all the hopes, New South Wales was too far out on the geopolitical periphery of the late eighteenth century to do much else.

In the summer of 1786, Pitt's Cabinet, having run out of alternatives, decided to found its penal colony at Botany Bay. Lord Sydney's announcement to the Lords of the Treasury (drafted by Evan Nepean) held a note of urgency: "The greatest danger is to be apprehended" of escape from the crowded hulks and jails, while "infectious distempers" threatened their inmates. Thus "measures should immediately be pursued" for getting the transportable convicts out of England. In round numbers, the first shipment should contain 600 of them (later 750), guarded by three companies of marines. Nepean estimated the cost of the equipment for founding the settlement in Australia at £29,300. Running it would cost the government £18,669 the first year, £15,449 the second and under £7,000 the third; after that, if all went to plan, it would be self-victualling.[29]

The proposal to colonize Botany Bay with convicts was formally drawn up (almost certainly by Nepean rather than Sydney) in an unsigned document titled "Heads of a Plan for effectually disposing of convicts" and was presented to the cabinet in August 1786. Its emphasis was clear: The proposed colony would serve as "a remedy for the evils likely to result from the late alarming and numerous increase of felons in this country, and more particularly in the metropolis." The secondary benefit of the region's raw materials was presented at the end of the document: "It may also be proper to attend to the possibility of procuring . . . masts and ships' timber for the use of our fleets in India, as the distance between the two countries is not greater than between Great Britain and America." The author's eulogies on Pacific flax repeated Matra's almost phrase for phrase.[30]

The cabinet gave its approval; and without further ado, the government chose a man to lead the expedition and govern the new colony. He was found on the navy's semi-retired list: a man of independent but modest means, living as a gentleman farmer at Lyndhurst in the New Forest of Hampshire. His name was Captain Arthur Phillip.

v

WHEN PHILLIP received his commission from George III on October 12, 1786, appointing him "Governor of our territory called New South Wales," he was one day past his forty-eighth birthday. To judge from the surviving portraits, he was slight in build, with a long nose, a slightly pendulous lower lip, a smooth pear of a skull, and liquid melancholy-looking eighteenth-century eyes. It is a face most unlike the square-boned visage of Cook; one could imagine it under a European peruke, perhaps belonging to a kapellmeister in some little Bavarian court. Phillip was half German. His father, Jakob Phillip, was a language teacher from Frankfurt, who emigrated to London and married a certain Elizabeth Breach.

Phillip first went to sea at the age of sixteen, in time for the start of the Seven Years' War against France. Three years later he was promoted to lieutenant, but when peace resumed in 1763, he retired early on half-pay at the age of twenty-five. He married, but the marriage was not a happy one and he was formally separated from his wife in 1769. They had no children. Rural life at Lyndhurst now palled on him, and by 1770 he was back on the active list. In 1774 he got leave to join the Portuguese Navy, then at war with Spain. As captain of a Portuguese ship, Phillip delivered 400 Portuguese convicts across the Atlantic to Brazil without losing a man—a feat that presumably convinced Lord Sydney of his fitness to govern a penal colony.

By 1778 he was back in the British Navy and in 1779 he received command of the fireship *Basilisk*. To be past forty with no better post was no triumph, but three years later he had risen to be master of a full ship of the line, the 64-gun *Europe*. Yet by 1784 he went back to his farm again, on half-pay.

The best reputation Phillip could have had, in view of this lackluster record, was that of a reliable, forthright and rather unimaginative man; solitary, perhaps; competent on ship and self-effacing on shore. Nobody could have mistaken him for a charismatic leader. He had no apparent political talents. But politicians were the last people the Crown needed in a remote penal settlement. If the colony were to survive at all, it must be run by chain of command, not consensus, led by an eminently practical man. Australia's remoteness would set free cruelty and madness in some British officers sent to guard convicts there. But power made Phillip equitable and level-headed, and he appears to have believed that at least some of his convicts could be reformed, provided they were isolated. "As I would not wish convicts to lay the foundations of an empire," he wrote,

> I think they should remain separated from the garrison, and other settlers that may come from Europe, and not allowed to mix with them, even after the 7 or 14 years for which they are transported may be expired. The laws of this country will, of course, be introduced in [New] South Wales, and there is one that I wish to take place from the moment his Majesty's forces take possession of the country: *That there can be no slavery in a free land, and consequently no slaves.*[31]

One could hardly compare Phillip's words with the clarion speech of a Jefferson or a Lafayette, but they were the only ones verging on the description of a social ideal that would be uttered in, or about, Australia for the rest of the eighteenth century. However, what Phillip was really talking about was *apartheid.* He had no "democratic" feelings toward the convicts, and his later gestures of apparent equality, such as cutting rations for free and bond impartially in times of crisis, indicated no special sympathy for them. He thought of the convicts essentially as slaves, by their own fallen nature if not in the strict terms of the law. In declaring that "there can be no slavery in a free land, and consequently no slaves," he was not suggesting that his new colony would *begin* free; he was pointing to a remote future in which it might *become* so, a time when the convict system would have withered away and New South Wales would be populated by free emigrants, English yeomen and planters.

On August 31, 1786, Lord Sydney told the Admiralty that the voyage was going ahead, and instructed it to commission the fleet. There were, in all, eleven vessels. Only two of them were naval warships—the flagship *Sirius* and the brig-rigged sloop *Supply.* The rest were converted merchantmen. The Navy Board chose three storeships—*Borrowdale* (272 tons), *Fishburn* (378 tons) and *Golden Grove* (331 tons)—and six transports: *Alexander* (452 tons), *Charlotte* (345 tons), *Friendship* (278 tons), *Lady Penrhyn* (338 tons), *Prince of Wales* (333 tons) and *Scarborough* (418 tons). Most of them were fairly new vessels; *Scarborough*, the oldest, had been launched in 1781. The terms of the charter contract were that all of these ships, except the naval vessels, would cost the Government 10 shillings per register ton per month. Assuming an eight months' passage out and the same back, the government would have to pay the contractors at least £20,900 for the hire of their ships, and that was the largest single expense of the First Fleet.

But they were all small vessels, and very overcrowded by modern standards of sea travel. The largest transport, the *Alexander*, was 114 feet long and 31 feet in beam. In all, the fleet had to carry almost 1,500 people —officers, seamen and marines, women, children, and convicts. That meant a close pack—less than 3 tons of ship per person embarked.[32] (The ration on a modern passenger liner is closer to 250 tons per person.) In an exasperated letter Phillip complained that his passengers, convicts and marines alike, "after taking off the tonnage for the provision of stores . . . have not one ton and a half per man."[33]

As the winter wore on, Phillip did what he could to call the authorities' attention to the lack of space. On January 11, 1787 he wrote to Nepean,

> I find that 184 men are put on board [*Alexander*.] . . . [T]here are amongst the men several unable to help themselves, and no kind of surgeons' instruments have been put on board that ship or any of the transports. . . . It will be very difficult to prevent the most fatal sickness among men so closely confined; on board that ship which is to receive 210 convicts there is not a space left . . . sufficiently large for 40 men to be in motion at the same time.[34]

No craft, then or later, was ever designed specifically to carry convicts; that would have cost the owner too much for too specialized a vessel. It became the practice to dump the bulkheads, sleeping-racks and iron grilles in Sydney before the ships sailed north to China for their cargoes of tea on the home run. The 'tween-deck plans of the First Fleet transports are lost, but the quarters were certainly very cramped for the marines and crew, let alone for the convicts: Four transportees lying in a space seven feet by six feet, the dimensions of a modern king-size bed, were the norm. There was little headroom; *Scarborough*, the second-largest transport, had only four feet, five inches, so that even a small woman had to stoop and a full-grown man had to bend double. Philip Gidley King, second lieutenant on *Sirius*, described the security, "which consists," he wrote in his journal,

> of very strong & thick Bulkheads, filled with nails & run across from side to side in ye tween decks abaft the Mainmast with loop holes to fire between the decks in case of irregularities. The hatches are well secured down by cross bars, bolts & locks & are likewise nailed down from deck to deck with oak stanchions. There is also a barricade of plank about 3 feet high, armed with pointed prongs of Iron on the upper deck, abaft the Mainmast, to prevent any connection between the Marines & Ships Company, with the Convicts. Centinels are placed at the different Hatchways

& a Guard always under arms on the Quarter Deck of each Transport in order to prevent any improper behaviour of the Convicts.[35]

The prisoners' quarters had no portholes or sidelights; such things were an innovation and perhaps a security hazard. The lower decks were as dark as the grave, as lanterns and candles were banned for fear of fire. The only fresh air the convicts got was from a windsail rigged to scoop a breeze down a hatchway. In a storm, when the hatches were battened down, there was no fresh air below. In calm weather, prisoners could exercise on deck.

By January 6, 1787, the first convicts were loaded from the Woolwich hulks, the men onto *Scarborough* and the women aboard *Lady Penrhyn*. But two months passed before all the convicts embarked and the eleven ships were mustered at anchor on the Motherbank outside Portsmouth harbor, and they would remain at anchor two months more. The late winter and spring of 1787 went by in a stream of blunders and delays. The bureaucrats of Whitehall naïvely supposed that the logistics of a six-week slave run across the Pacific could be applied to an eight-month passage to Australia—which, as Phillip kept stressing, they could not. His letters to Nepean and Sydney are full of the complaints of a practical sailor. Luckily, Nepean understood them; Sydney was too insulated or obtuse to do so.

To begin with, the fleet was undervictualled by its crooked contractor, Duncan Campbell. He had shortchanged the convicts with half a pound of rice instead of a pound of flour—"this will be very severely felt"—and supplying only enough bread to give each prisoner the pitiful ration of six ounces (two slices) a day.[36] Even worse, despite the lessons of Cook's voyages, there were no anti-scorbutics. Phillip knew it would be murder to sail without them, and his letters now grew very blunt:

> The contracts . . . were made before I ever saw the navy Board on this business. . . . I have repeatedly pointed out the consequences that must be expected of the men's being crowded on board such small ships, and from victualling the marines according to the contract which allows no flour. . . . this must be fatal to many, and the more so as no anti-scorbutics are allowed on board. . . . [I]n fact, my Lord, the garrison and the convicts are sent to the extremity of the globe as they would be sent to America— a six-weeks' passage.
>
> . . . I am prepared to meet difficulties, and I have only one fear—I fear, my Lord, that it may be said hereafter that the officer who took charge of the expedition should have known that it was more than probable he lost half the garrison and convicts, crowded and victualled in such a manner for so long a voyage. And the public . . . may impute to my ignorance or

inattention what I have never been consulted in, and which never coincided with my ideas.[37]

A stickler for detail, a true professional, Phillip knew that survival might depend on the humblest item of inventory and that he had to double-check them all. Why were only six scythes and five dozen razors provided? Could Nepean not see that they would need 560 pounds, not 200 pounds, of buckshot? How would the convict superintendents be paid? Where were the bolts of cloth against the inevitable day when, thousands of miles from Portsmouth, the convicts' clothes wore out? Phillip begged for fresh meat for the convicts, wine for the sick, fumigants, extra medicine. His masters moved with maddening slowness.

The work of the embarkation dragged on through late February and March. The convicts came rumbling down to the Plymouth and Portsmouth docks in heavy wagons, under guard, ironed together, shivering under the incessant rain. The pale, ragged, lousy prisoners, thin as wading birds from their jail diet, were herded on board and spent the next several months below; orders forbade them to exercise on deck until the flotilla was out of sight of land. The condition of the women provoked Phillip to a furious outburst:

> The situation in which the magistrates sent the women on board the *Lady Penrhyn*, stamps them with infamy—tho' almost naked, and so very filthy, that nothing but clothing them could have prevented them from perishing, and which could not be done in time to prevent a fever, which is still on board that ship, and where there are many venereal complaints, that must spread in spite of every precaution I may take hereafter.[38]

Who were these First Fleet convicts? It was once a cherished Australian belief that at least some of the people on the First Fleet were political exiles—rick-burners, trade-unionists, and the like. In fact, though victims of a savage penal code, they were not political prisoners. On the other hand, few of them were dangerous criminals. Not one person was shipped out in 1787 for murder or rape, although more than a hundred of them had been convicted of thefts (such as highway robbery) in which violence played some part. No woman on the First Fleet, legend to the contrary, had been transported for prostitution, as it was not a transportable offense. Many were treated as whores, and doubtless some were, although only two—Mary Allen and Ann Mather—had been described by their judges as "unfortunate girl" or "poor unhappy woman of the town."

In all, 736 convicts went on the First Fleet. Of these, we know the age or occupation, and sometimes both, of 330 people—127 women, 203 men.[39] They came from all over England, but most of them were Londoners. Their main categories of crime were as follows:

| OFFENSE | NUMBER |
|---|---|
| Minor theft | 431 |
| "Privy theft," including breaking and entering | 93 |
| Highway robbery | 71 |
| Stealing cattle or sheep | 44 |
| Robbery with violence (mugging) | 31 |
| Grand larceny | 9 |
| Fencing (receiving stolen goods) | 8 |
| Swindling, impersonation | 7 |
| Forgery of documents, banknotes, etc. | 4 |
| Other | 35 |
| Total of known indictments | 733 |

All these were crimes against property, some forced by a pitiful necessity. Elizabeth Beckford, the second oldest woman on the First Fleet, was seventy. Her crime, for which she got seven years' transportation, was to have stolen twelve pounds of Gloucester cheese. At the Stafford Assizes, a laborer named Thomas Hawell went down for seven years for "feloniously stealing one live hen to the value of 2d., and one dead hen to the value of 2d." Elizabeth Powley, twenty-two and unemployed, raided a kitchen in Norfolk, took a few shillings' worth of bacon, flour and raisins, with "twenty-four ounces Weight of Butter value 12d," and was sentenced to hang; but a reprieve came and to Australia she went, never to eat butter again. Hunger drove a West Indian named Thomas Chaddick into a kitchen garden where he "did pluck up, spoil and destroy, against the form of the statute" twelve cucumber plants; he, too, went to Australia, there to contemplate the exactness with which the god of property had measured out his black life in cucumbers.

Some purloined inedible trifles. William Rickson, a nineteen-year-old laborer, made off with a wooden box which proved to contain merely a piece of linen and five books. James Grace, an eleven-year-old, took ten yards of ribbon and a pair of silk stockings. William Francis stole a book entitled *A Summary Account of the Flourishing State of the Island of Tobago* from a London gentleman named Robert Melville. Fifteen-year-old John Wisehammer grabbed a packet of snuff from an apothecary's counter in Gloucester. They all went down for seven years.

There were, of course, less trivial crimes. Apprentices robbed their masters' stock. John Nicolls, a hairdresser's assistant, drew seven years' transportation for stealing goods worth £14 9s. 6d., enough to start his own barbershop: fifty-seven razors, sixty-two ivory combs, six bunches of human hair, soap, wig ribbon, pomade, scissors, hairnets and powder. A journeyman watchmaker mugged another watchmaker for a dozen silver watchcases; another stole a mass of parts, comprising 185 complete watch movements, barrels, fusees, arbors, verges and studs.

None of these acts were news when they happened. They were mere drops in a swollen torrent of eighteenth-century crime. The only exception was Thomas Gearing, who created a brief sensation in Oxford in 1786 by breaking into the chapel of Magdalen College and stealing some ecclesiastical plate. For this sacrilege, he was condemned to death, reprieved and then transported for life.

Judges were particularly severe on thieves who used violence and threats. In 1782 Thomas Josephs accosted a married woman on a London street, "putting her in fear" and seizing her handkerchief, worth 2 shillings. The sentence was death; after five years in jail he was embarked on *Scarborough*, to serve the Crown for seven years in New South Wales. All the cattle duffers and horse thieves on the First Fleet were under commuted death sentences.

The Beauchamp Committee had urged that the new colony consist of "young Convicts," and so it did. The convicts' average age was about twenty-seven years. Age distribution was much the same for either sex:

| AGE (YRS.) | MEN | WOMEN |
|---|---|---|
| under 15 | 3 | 2 |
| 16–25 | 68 | 58 |
| 26–35 | 51 | 50 |
| 36–45 | 11 | 6 |
| 46–55 | 4 | 3 |
| over 56 | 3 | 3 |
| Total convicts of known age | 140 | 122 |

The oldest female convict was Dorothy Handland, a dealer in rags and old clothes who was eighty-two years old in 1787. She had drawn seven years for perjury. In 1789, in a fit of befuddled despair, she was to hang herself from a gum tree at Sydney Cove, thus becoming Australia's first recorded suicide. The oldest male convict was a Shropshire man, Joseph Owen, who was somewhere between sixty and sixty-six. The youngest boy was John Hudson, a nine-year-old chimney sweep. He had stolen some clothes and a pistol. "One would wish to snatch such a boy, if one possibly could," the judge remarked, "from destruction, for he will only return to the same kind of life which he has led before." So little John Hudson was sent to Australia for seven years. The youngest girl was Elizabeth Hayward, a clogmaker aged thirteen, who had stolen a linen gown and a silk bonnet worth 7 shillings.

Classed by occupation, the First Fleet convicts were an anthology of country and town trades—but that did not guarantee their fitness as pioneers. The details of employment (or lack of it) for 190 men and 125 women have survived. Of the men, twenty-four (12 percent) were noted as unemployed. The largest occupation group was laborers, mostly rural —eighty-four men, or 44 percent of the total. From there the size of the professional groups dropped sharply:

| TRADE | NO. OF PERSONS |
|---|---|
| Seamen | 8 |
| Carpenters, shipwrights and cabinetmakers | 6 |
| Shoemakers | 5 |
| Weavers | 5 |
| Watermen | 4 |
| Ivory turners | 3 |
| Brickmakers | 2 |
| Bricklayers, masons | 2 |
| Other trades | 47 |

"Other trades" included three domestic servants, two leather-breeches makers, two tailors, two butchers, a jeweller, a baker and a silk-dyer. There was also one fisherman, a Cornishman named William Bryant. Of the women, fourteen (11 percent) were "unemployed," and some if not most of these may have been prostitutes. More than half the women were domestic servants. The rest were milliners, mantua-makers, oyster-sellers, glove-makers, shoe-binders—a spatter of trades that reflected the kind of jobs women in eighteenth-century England could expect to find, all of them fairly menial.

So it had a motley crew, this Noah's Ark of small-time criminality; and for all the trades represented aboard, it was absurdly ill-chosen for the task of colonizing New South Wales. The authorities had used no criteria of selection apart from youth, and that erratically. There was no choice by trade. The colony that would have to raise its own crops in unknown soil had only one professional gardener, and he was a raw youth of twenty. It would need tons of fish, but had only one fisherman. There were only two brickmakers, two bricklayers and a mason for all the houses that would need building; no sawyers were aboard, and only six carpenters. It had no flax-dressers or linen-weavers—proof of the government's indifference to the prospect of a "strategic" colony. This muddle and lack of foresight in the choice of convicts typified the planning, being one of many matters over which Captain Arthur Phillip had no control.

And there was one general class of crook not represented on the First Fleet: the successful ones. This was pointed out a few years later in a mordant ballad entitled *Botany Bay: A New Song* (1790):

> Let us drink a good health to our schemers above,
> Who at length have contriv'd from this land to remove
> Thieves, robbers and villains, they'll send 'em away,
> To become a new people at Botany Bay.
>
> Some men say they have talents and trades to get bread,
> Yet they spunge on mankind to be cloathed and fed,
> They'll spend all they get, and turn night into day—
> Now I'd have all such sots sent to Botany Bay.
>
> There's gay powder'd coxcombs and proud dressy fops,
> Who with very small fortunes set up in great shops,
> They'll run into debt with design ne'er to pay,
> They should all be transported to Botany Bay. . . .
>
> There's nightwalking strumpets who swarm in each street,
> Proclaiming their calling to each man they meet:
> They become such a pest that without more delay,
> Those corrupters of youth should be sent to the Bay.
>
> There's monopolizers who add to their store,
> By cruel oppression and squeezing the poor,
> There's butchers and farmers get rich in that way,
> But I'd have all such rogues sent to Botany Bay. . . .
>
> You lecherous whore-masters who practice vile arts,
> To ruin young virgins and break parents' hearts,
> Or from the fond husband the wife lead astray—
> Let such debauch'd stallions be sent to the Bay.
>
> There's whores, pimps and bastards, a large costly crew,
> Maintain'd by the sweat of a labouring few,
> They should have no commission, place, pension or pay,
> Such locusts should all go to Botany Bay.
>
> The hulks and the jails had some thousands in store,
> But out of the jails are ten thousand times more,
> Who live by fraud, cheating, vile tricks and foul play,
> And should all be sent over to Botany Bay.
>
> Now should any take umbrage at what I have writ,
> Or find here a bonnet or cap that will fit,
> To such I have only this one word to say:
> They are welcome to wear it in Botany Bay.[40]

In March 1787, with two months to sailing date, typhus broke out in the ships anchored on the Motherbank outside Portsmouth. The crammed decks of *Alexander* incubated it; by April 15, eleven of its prisoners had died, and the rest were hastily disembarked. Enlisted men fumigated the ship, scrubbed her with creosote (the navy's all-purpose disinfectant and pesticide) and swabbed the convict quarters with quick-lime. Even so, five more men died on *Alexander* before she sailed. One woman convict died of "jail fever" on *Lady Penrhyn,* but luckily the disease did not spread through the squadron.

This outbreak of fever provoked a flood of rumors on shore. The expedition to Botany Bay had piqued the curiosity of the public from the moment it was announced. It had been furiously lampooned and defended by pamphleteers. "What is the Punishment intended to be inflicted?" cried Alexander Dalrymple, the official of the East India Company who was an unsparing critic of penal colonies in the South Seas:

> Not to make the Felons undergo *servitude* for the *benefit of others,* was the Case in America; but to place them, as their own Masters, in a temperate Climate, where they have *every object* of *comfort* or *Ambition* before them! and although it might be going too far to suppose, This will *incite men* to become *Convicts,* that they may be *comfortably* provided for; yet surely it cannot *deter* men, inclined to commit Theft and Robbery, to know that, in case they are detected and convicted, all that will happen to them is that they will be sent, at the Publick Expense, to a good Country and Temperate Climate, where they will be their own masters![41]

In the same vein but more facetiously, ballads had described the southern arcadia, free of death and taxes, where the lucky felons were going:

> They go to an Island to take special charge,
> Much warmer than Britain, and ten times as large:
> No customs-house duty, no freightage to pay,
> And tax-free they'll live when in Botany Bay.[42]

A theatrical producer commissioned an opera entitled *Botany Bay,* which opened at the Royal Circus in London in April and closed the night before the fleet sailed.

The typhus outbreak was played up by the newspapers, which had one good effect: At last Duncan Campbell, the contractor, was forced to issue the fresh beef and vegetables Phillip wanted for the convicts and marines. The marines also complained that they would not be issued liquor in New South Wales, "without which . . . we cannot expect to survive the hardships"[43]—and three days later Nepean guaranteed them a three-year issue of rum and wine. However, the womens' clothes had still not arrived, and neither had the small-arms supplies for the marines. "We have neither musquet balls nor paper for musquet cartridges, nor have we any armourers' tools," Phillip complained—and it had to be kept a dead secret all the way across the Atlantic, for fear of a convict mutiny.[44]

Nevertheless, on the evening of May 12, Phillip ordered his flagship *Sirius* to weigh anchor. The signal flags fluttered, but nothing happened; the merchant seamen in some of the transports refused point-blank to go aloft. Lieutenant King went to investigate. It turned out that the seamen —who were not under military command, being the crew of chartered commercial vessels—were on strike against the ships' owners, who owed them seven months' back pay. The owners, skinflints all, hoped to force their crews to buy "necessaries" from ships' stores on credit at inflated prices during the long voyage; the sailors naturally wished to equip themselves cheaper and better, for cash, in Portsmouth. Their complaints were sorted out, after a fashion, and at three in the morning of Sunday, May 13, before the first cold gristle of pre-dawn light had spread upon the sea, the First Fleet weighed anchor and shaped its course in a rising wind for Tenerife.

## v i

THE CONVICTS were "humble, submissive and regular" on this first leg of the voyage, Watkin Tench wrote with relief. They had been told "in the most pointed terms that any attempt . . . to force their escape should be punished with instant death." Escape, however, was unlikely, as they were chained, in shock and atrociously seasick. Through the long rolling weeks at anchorage on the Motherbank, the literate prisoners had written letters to their families and friends ashore, and Tench had had the "tiresome and disagreeable" duty of acting as censor. "Their constant language," he noted, "was an apprehension of the impracticability of returning home, the dread of a sickly passage, and the fearful prospect of a distant and barbarous country." He dismissed their laments as "doubtless an artifice to awaken compassion."[45]

There was nothing artificial about them. None of the convicts could have had any idea of their destination. Before them yawned a terrifying void of time and space. They were going on the longest voyage ever attempted by so large a group of people. If they had been told they were off to the moon, the sense of loss, deracination and fear could hardly have been worse—at least one could see the moon from England, which could not be said for Botany Bay.

The convicts, of course, were not the only ones who felt their lives cut in half. As the flotilla sailed from Portsmouth, a young second officer of marines, not long married, began his diary:

> 5 o'clock in the morning. The Sirius made the signal for the whole fleet to get under way. O Gracious God send that we may put into Plymouth or Torbay on our way down Channel that I may see my dear and fond affectionate Alicia and our sweet son before I leave them for this long absence. O Almighty God hear my prayer and grant me this request . . . what makes me so happy this day is it because that I am in hoppes the fleet will put into Plymth. O my fond heart lay still for you may be disappointed I trust in God you will not.

But Plymouth fell astern, and Ralph Clark's journal for May 14 bears the anguished scrawl, "Oh my God all my hoppes are over of seeing my beloved wife and son."[46]

The run to Tenerife passed almost without incident. The weather was fine and, once out of sight of land, the convicts were allowed on deck to exercise. On June 3 the fleet made its anchorage in the port of Santa Cruz, under the high conical peak of Tenerife.

The officers and crewmen had a week to stretch their legs on land, while the ships took on fresh water, pumpkins, onions, indifferent and costly meat and Canary wine. Phillip and twenty of his chief officers were lavishly entertained by the Sicilian-born governor of the Canaries. One night, a convict named John Power escaped from *Alexander* by shinnying down her anchor hawser. He swam quietly astern, scrambled into a dinghy, cut its painter and drifted on the current across the bay to a Dutch East Indiaman. Its crew would not take him on board; so Power rowed to a small island in the lee of the fleet, where he beached the boat, rested up for the night (his plan being to row thirty miles to the Grand Canary) and was captured by a search party the next morning. But Power's was the only such venture, and on June 10 the fleet set sail for Rio de Janeiro.

At first, Phillip's track looks remarkably indirect: Why cross the Atlantic twice to get to Australia? In fact, his course from Portsmouth to the Cape of Good Hope via the Canaries and Rio made the best of prevailing winds and currents. Boosted south-southwest by the Canary Current and the northeast trade winds, a ship would pass the Cape Verde Islands and sail south until it entered the equatorial doldrums in the Atlantic Narrows. Once through that zone of calms and fluky winds it could pick up the southbound Brazil Current, getting a good slant on the southeast trades to reach Rio and drop further south into the zone of the westerlies, around 30°S. Then it had a straight run downwind to Cape Town.[47]

The fleet raised the Cape Verde Islands on June 18. Adverse winds prevented the ships from anchoring at Port Praia on São Tiago, and on they sailed. Now the weather became intolerably hot and humid, and as the fleet entered the tropics waves of vermin crept out of each vessel's woodwork, up from the bilges—rats, bedbugs, lice, cockroaches, fleas. Officers and convicts alike were tormented by them and fought back as best they could with "frequent explosions of gunpowder, lighting fires between decks, and a liberal use of that admirable antiseptic, oil of tar."[48]

The bilges were foul in all of the ships. Even those whose guts have heaved at the whiff from the boat's head at sea can have little idea of the anguish of eighteenth-century bilge stink: a fermenting, sloshing broth of sea water mixed with urine, puke, dung, rotting food, dead rats and the hundred other attars of the Great Age of Sail. On *Alexander*, another batch of convicts fell sick from the bilge effluents,

> which had by some means or other risen to so great a height, that the pannels of the cabin, and the buttons on the back of the officers, were turned nearly black, by the noxious effluvia. When the hatches were taken off, the stench was so powerful that it was scarcely possible to stand over them.[49]

When tropical rainstorms whipped the fleet, the convicts—who had no change of dry clothes—could not exercise on deck. They stayed below under battened hatches, and conditions in their steaming, stinking holds were extreme. "The weather was now so immoderately hot," noted John White, surgeon on *Charlotte*, "that the female convicts, perfectly overcome with it, frequently fainted away, and these faintings generally terminated in fits." At night, some of them rutted like stoats. "Notwithstanding the enervating effects of the atmospheric heat," White recorded with some amazement,

> so predominant was the warmth of their constitutions, or the depravity of their hearts, that the hatches . . . could not be suffered to lay off, during the night, without a promiscuous intercourse immediately taking place between them and the seamen and marines . . . [T]he desire of the women to be with the men was so uncontrollable that neither shame (but indeed of this they had long lost sight) nor the fear of punishment could deter them from making their way through the bulkheads to the apartments assigned to the seamen.[50]

It sounds like bedlam, and probably it was. The marines on the four female transports—*Charlotte*, *Lady Penrhyn*, *Prince of Wales* and *Friendship*—could buy a woman with a pannikin of rum from their daily rations, and from then on the drunkenness of some female convicts would become another problem for Captain Phillip.

When the women got unruly, they were ironed and sometimes flogged. One prisoner on *Friendship*, Elizabeth Dudgeon (7 years for stealing £9 19s. 6d. in London), was especially troublesome. She spent the first nine days of the Tenerife–Rio run in irons for fighting, and on release she was found carousing in the seamen's quarters. Back into irons she went, but a few days later she rashly gave a guard officer, Captain James Meredith, a tongue-lashing. He had her triced up to a grating and flogged, to the pleasure of Lieutenant Ralph Clark: "The corporal did not play with her, but laid it home, which I was very glad to see . . . she has long been fishing for it, which she has at last got to her heart's content."[51]

Once the fleet reached the doldrums, Phillip rationed water to three pints a day. But by mid-July the ships picked up the southeast trades, the sails cracked and bellied, and down to Rio they rolled, *Lady Penrhyn* lagging and wallowing, nimble little *Supply* herding up the slow transports until, on August 5, the whole fleet was snugged down in Rio harbor.

It stayed there a month. There was much to be done: watering and cleaning ship, buying stores and making repairs. Sixteen people had died since England—ten on one boat, the mephitic *Alexander*—and there were eighty-one on the sicklist. By eighteenth-century standards, things could have been much worse. Phillip busied himself with stores. He could not get the small-arms supplies he needed in Rio—Portuguese armorers' tools did not fit English guns—but he obtained 10,000 musketballs from the local arsenal. The clothing of the women convicts was already disintegrating, and to replace it Phillip parsimoniously bought 100 sacks of tapioca (which would substitute, in a pinch, for flour), the sacks of which "being of strong Russia [burlap] will be used hereafter in cloathing the convicts, many of whom are nearly naked."[52] He bought seeds and laid in supplies of the local beef, which was excellent, and of the local firewater or *aguardiente*, which was not. "That [Brazilians] have not learnt the art of making palatable rum," Watkin Tench morosely noted many hangovers later, "the English troops in New South Wales can bear testimony."

The Viceroy, who had known Phillip in the days of his mercenary service for Portugal, entertained him and his men generously and gave them carte blanche to go wherever they pleased, unescorted. They promenaded contentedly about, admiring the macaws and toucans, gorging themselves on limes, lemons and oranges, and ogling the "lusty" girls of Rio whose long hair, once unbraided, trailed two inches on the floor when they walked barefoot. They envied the Portuguese their police, but their English souls were affronted by Rio's tropical Catholicism.

The convicts, of course, saw none of this. They were kept below deck. But some of them had been up to their old tricks on the long Atlantic run. John White found that a convict named Thomas Barrett had "with great ingenuity" started a forgers' ring, making quarter-dollars out of old buckles and pewter spoons:

> The impression, milling, character . . . was so inimitably executed that had their metal been a little better, the fraud, I am convinced, would have passed undetected . . . How they could effect it at all, is a matter of the most inexpressible surprise to me; as they were never suffered to come near a fire; and a centinel was constantly placed over their hatchway, which . . . rendered it impossible for either fire or fused metal to be conveyed to their apartments. Besides, hardly ten minutes ever elapsed, without an officer going down among them. The adroitness, therefore, with which they must have managed, in order to complete a business that required so complicated a process, gave me a high opinion of their ingenuity, cunning, caution and address.[53]

Barrett was lightly punished, but James Baker, a marine who had tried to pass off one of the forged coins on shore, got 200 lashes. As a rule, the floggings inflicted on the marines were far worse than anything the convicts got. The inequality of punishment would turn out to be a great source of friction between marines and convicts later.

Other tensions were felt not long after the fleet left Rio on September 3 for its drop south and its long run before the westerlies to Cape Town. In the confined space of a ship, irritations grow and all raw spots chafe. Some of the officers took to drink, traded insults in the mess and cursed their hangovers. One could find relief from the bickering on deck, watching the frigate birds and pintadoes, trolling a line for fish and admiring the hungry grace of albacore tearing into the schools of flying fish as they burst, like scattering chainshot, from the heaving indigo rollers. Luckily the fleet had a quick crossing. By mid-October they were at Cape Town, the tip of Africa, the extreme point of European penetration into the southern hemisphere.

The fleet spent a month in Cape Town. The main task was to stock up on plants, seeds and livestock for the colony in New South Wales. This Phillip did, with much hard bargaining against phlegmatic Dutch tightwads. He also tried to build up the convicts' strength for the last, most difficult leg of the voyage, by giving them fresh beef and mutton, soft bread and as many vegetables as they could eat, every day.[54] His officers hated Cape Town—the Dutch, the Kaffirs, the heat, the dust.

Nevertheless it was the last civilized place, the last repository of recognizable European values, that the men and women of the First Fleet would see for years; and the thought must have lain heavily on them when at last the tars stood to the capstans and the anchor-cables rose dripping through their hawser-holes. This was the end of Europe. Before them stretched the awesome, lonely void of the Indian and Southern Oceans, and beyond that lay nothing they could imagine.

The modern traveller, gazing down on the wrinkles of the earth's waters from an armchair six miles up, has no conception of the forbidding grandeur of the sea into which the First Fleet now moved. Its waves are the largest of any of the world's oceans, and from the deck of a boat they are overwhelming: tottering hills of indigo and malachite glass, veined in their transparencies with braids of opaque white water, their spumy crests running level with the ship's cross-trees. The inexorable rhythm of their passage numbs the brain, first with fear and then with repetition.

The fleet transports labored now, clawing up the swells and staggering down into the troughs. They were loaded down with new supplies, including some five hundred animals mooing, clucking and bleating frantically in their improvised pens. The convict quarters were more crowded than ever, because room had to be made for the future colony's livestock (and its bales of food)—two Africander bulls, three cows, three horses, forty-four sheep, thirty-two hogs, poultry of all sorts, and such animals as the officers had managed to cram on board for their private stock. All the women convicts had been moved off *Friendship* and redistributed among the other three female transports; their place was taken by sheep which, Ralph Clark opined, would be "much more agreeable shipmates." Arthur Bowes Smythe, the surgeon on the women's transport *Lady Penrhyn*, felt the same way. "I believe few Marines or Soldiers going out on a foreign Service under Government were ever better, if so well provided for as these Convicts are," he remarked, but

> I wish I cd. with truth add that the behaviour of the Convicts merited such extream indulgence—but I believe I may venture to say there was never a more abandon'd set of wretches collected in one place at any period than are now to be met with in this Ship. . . . The greater part of them are so totally abandon'd and callous'd to all sense of shame & even common decency that it frequently becomes indispensably necessary to inflict Corporal punishment upon them. . . . [E]very day furnishes proofs of their being more harden'd in their Wickedness—nor do I conceive it possible in their present situation to adopt any plan to induce them to behave like rational or even human Beings. . . . Nor can their matchless Hippocracy be equalled except by their base Ingratitude.[55]

As the vessels slipped further down the map, below the fortieth south parallel, under the southern coast of Australia and toward Van Diemen's Land, the gales stayed favorable and the weather "dark, wet and gloomy." Gannets and terns circled the ships. Whales were sighted, and often the wandering albatross, *Diomedea exsulans*, would materialize out of the spindrift, white from white, and wheel silently about the plunging masts on its fourteen-foot wings before vanishing into a rainsquall. Waves broke green over the decks, dumping tons of freezing water down the companionways and sluicing the marines and the shivering, half-clothed convicts out of their bunks. Coming north around Van Diemen's Land on January 10, 1788, they ran into a violent thundersquall that split the *Golden Grove*'s topsails and carried away *Prince of Wales*'s main yard; the women on *Lady Penrhyn* "were so terrified that most of them were down on their knees at prayers, and in less than one hour after it had abated they were uttering the most horrid oaths and imprecations that could proceed out of the mouths of such abandoned prostitutes as they are."[56]

Surgeon John White on *Charlotte* had a revelation of how far from the company of European man they had all come. Flocks of "large ocean-ous birds" flew about the ship, and the marines amused themselves by shooting at them; but the seabirds showed no alarm "either at the report, or at the balls . . . [for] they had never been harassed with firearms before."[57]

On the evening of January 19, *Sirius* and the transports sighted the coast of mainland Australia. By ten the next morning they were all anchored in Botany Bay. "To see all the ships safe in their destined port," White wrote with commendable restraint, "without ever having, by any accident, been one hour separated; and all the people in as good health as could be expected or hoped for, after so long a voyage, was a sight truly pleasing, and at which every heart must rejoice."[58]

It had been one of the great sea voyages in English history. Captain Arthur Phillip, the middle-aged nonentity, had brought them across more than fifteen thousand miles of ocean without losing a ship. The entire run had taken 252 days. A total of forty-eight people had died—forty convicts, five convicts' children, one marine's wife, one marine's child and a marine. Given the rigors of the voyage and the primitive medical knowledge of the day, the crammed ships and the lack of anti-scorbutics, the poor planning and the bad equipment, it was a tiny death rate—a little over 3 per cent. The sea had spared them; now, they must survive on the unknown land.

# 4

# The Starvation Years

i

PHILLIP AND HIS OFFICERS soon realized that there could be no settlement at Botany Bay.

Everything they had been told about it, even the testimony of Cook's log, was wrong. They had expected grassland with deep black soil and well-spaced trees, where crops could be planted without clearing; an ample source of building-stone; a protected anchorage.[1]

But what Captain Phillip saw from the deck as his ship rounded Point Solander and hauled into Botany Bay on Friday, January 18, 1788, was a flat heath of paperbark scrub and gray-green eucalypts, stretching featurelessly away under the grinding white light of that Australian summer. The dry buzzing monotony of the landscape did not match Cook's account. The bay was open and unprotected, and the Pacific rollers gave it a violent, persistent swell; the water was shallow, the holding-ground poor.

*Supply* anchored in the north of the bay, so that she could plainly be seen by ships in the offing. Phillip and some officers, including Lieutenant Philip Gidley King, hoisted out the boats in the afternoon and went looking for water. They made tentative contact with the Aborigines, giving them beads and mirrors. These "trembling" savages, King thought, "seemed quite astonished at the figure we cut in being cloathed. I think it is very easy to conceive the ridiculous figure we must appear to these poor creatures, who were perfectly naked."[2]

Over the next two days all the rest of the fleet arrived in Botany Bay. The Aborigines began to assemble in greater numbers on the rock-strewn spits and white beaches. As *Sirius* sailed past Point Solander, Captain John Hunter watched them flourish their spears at her and cry "*Warra, warra!*" These words, the first recorded ones spoken by a black to a white in Australia, meant "Go away!"

But the intruders did not go away. Issuing from the ships, they tramped about in their scarlet tunics, looking for water, entangling them-selves in scrub and branches. Formal threats were exchanged. With gut-tural yells of *warra, warra!* one tribesman "threw his spear wide of us to shew how far they could do execution"; it flew forty yards and stuck quivering in the earth. Another black flung his spear straight at them. A marine answered with a blank cartridge, "when they all ran off with great precipitation."

But before long the Aborigines were accepting presents from Phillip. They swarmed around the boats, plucking at the whites' clothes and shouting with amazement and pleasure whenever anyone lifted his hat. The general bonhomie was such that the blacks

> ran up to the man who had thrown the lance & made very significant signs of their displeasure at his conduct by pointing all their lances at him & looking at us, intimating that they only waited our orders to kill him. However, we made signs for them to desist & made the culprit a present of some beads & c[a3]

Soon the Englishmen ran out of beads and ribbon, but the hesitant con-tacts went on through the afternoon as more tribesmen gathered on the beach. King gave two Aborigines a taste of wine, which they spat out. Names for things were exchanged. But the great enigma, for the Aborig-ines, was the sex of the whites. They poked at the marines' breeches. Finally King ordered one of his men to satisfy their curiosity. The embar-rassed marine fumbled at his fly, and the first white cock was flashed on an Australian beach. "They made a great shout of admiration," King wrote,

> and pointing to the shore . . . we saw a great number of Women and Girls, with infant children on their shoulders, make their appearance on the beach—all *in puris naturalibus,* not so much as a fig-leaf. Those natives who were around the boats made signs for us to go to them & made us understand their persons were at our service. However, I declined.[4]

Instead, he produced his handkerchief and tied it on one of the women "where Eve did the Fig Leaf; the natives then set up another very great shout."

Thus the acquaintance of black and white on the shores of Botany Bay grew. There was no violence; the convicts were still cooped up in the transports, and the officers and seamen were under strict orders from Governor Phillip (as the commodore now officially became, on landing in New South Wales) not to molest the natives in any way. Of course, they could not be ordered to like them. "Altogether a most stupid insen-

sible set of beings," concluded Surgeon Arthur Bowes Smyth, after dilat-
ing on their "miserable wigwams" and fishy stink.[5] The blacks, in turn,
were consumed with curiosity about the whites. One even scalded his
fingers trying to swipe a fish from a cookpot on the beach, for, being
totally ignorant of pottery (let alone iron), he had never seen water boiled
in a container before. Surgeon White demonstrated his pistol to a group
of Aborigines, shooting a hole in a bark shield at several paces. It produced consternation, and to calm them White whistled "the air of *Mal-
brooke*, which they appeared highly charmed with, and imitated him
with equal pleasure and readiness." It was the first sign of the astounding
powers of mimicry that the Australian Aborigines would show the
whites in years to come.[6]

This was all very well, but it was not what the First Fleet had come
for, and the colonists had a colony to make. "If we are obliged to settle
here," wrote Lieutenant Ralph Clark after five days in Botany Bay, "there
will not a soul be alive in the course of a year." In the meantime, Phillip
had left with Hunter and some marines to explore Port Jackson, a few
miles to the north. Its opening had been seen, named but not visited by
Cook as he sailed by it in 1770. Phillip returned with the news that this
place was a paradise compared to Botany Bay: a harbor with many
branching arms in which ships could find shelter from any wind, with
plenty of fresh water and fertile soil. He ordered the fleet to make ready
for sea again.

But the next morning they were thunderstruck to see, far out on the
cloudy horizon, two large and obviously European ships trying to beat in
to shore against a stiff breeze. If coincidence, this was incredible; if not,
menacing. Were they Dutch men-o'-war, sent to attack the fleet? In the
evening the strange ships vanished in the haze, still tacking impotently
against the shore wind. Phillip left for Port Jackson the next morning.
Whoever the intruders were, he must beat them to the new harbor; to
lose that would mean losing the whole expedition.

It was a prudent move, but he need not have worried. The ships were
*La Boussole* and *L'Astrolabe*, commanded by the French explorer Jean-
François de la Pérouse, two and a half years out of Brest on a voyage of
Pacific discovery. La Pérouse had been as startled to see an English squadron as Phillip had been to see his, but, as he noted in his log, "All
Europeans are countrymen at such a distance from home." When he
dropped his hook in Botany Bay on the morning of January 26, La Pérouse
was fairly cordially received by Hunter, who was in a blinding hurry to
get the rest of the fleet to Port Jackson. He politely told La Pérouse that
he could give him any assistance he wanted—except, of course, for food,
stores, sails, ammunition or anything else he needed.

After lunch, *Sirius* got the fleet under way. There was a light south-

southeast breeze, which made it as hard for the ships to get out of port as it had been for La Pérouse to get .n. The departing English now gave the French a spectacular show of fumbling. *Friendship* rammed *Prince of Wales,* losing her jib boom. *Charlotte* nearly ran on the rocks, clawed off and cannoned into *Friendship. Lady Penrhyn* just avoided ramming her amidships. The blue Pacific air darkened with nautical oaths. However, by 3 p.m. the transports had cleared Botany Bay and were working north; four hours later, while the pinkish-gray glow of evening began to fume delicately upward from the long flat inland horizon, they rounded South Head and stood in for Port Jackson or, as it would presently be called, Sydney Harbor.

ii

"WE . . . HAD the satisfaction of finding the finest harbour in the world, in which a thousand sail of the line may ride with the most perfect security."[7] Phillip's jubilant words to Lord Sydney suggest that he was already looking beyond the convict colony to the day when this harbor would become a strategic outpost for England, filled with the white-sailed emblems of a dominated Pacific. The chosen anchorage had a small stream of fresh water flowing into a sheltered bay, where ships could ride close to the shore in deep water. To honor the man who had sent them there, Phillip called it Sydney Cove.

Pink eucalypts grew thickly along its rock shores, and Phillip marvelled at how stoutly they flourished in mere cracks of the rock, drawing nourishment from the thinnest soil. The work gangs stumbled and cursed among the ferns as the ground heaved beneath their legs, and "the confusion," David Collins noted, "will not be wondered at when it is considered that each man stepped from the boat literally into a wood."[8] Over the next few days, some military order began to emerge. "Business now sat on every brow," Watkin Tench reported,

> and the scene, to an indifferent spectator, at leisure to contemplate it, would have been highly picturesque and amusing. In one place, a party cutting down the woods; a second, setting up a blacksmith's forge; a third, dragging along a load of stones or provisions; here an officer pitching his marquee, with a detachment of troops parading on one side of him, and a cook's fire blazing up on the other.[9]

The marines had to watch for runaways. Within a few days some of the prisoners had escaped and struggled through the bush as far as Botany Bay, where La Pérouse's ships still lay at anchor. They gave the French commander "trouble and embarrassment"[10] by begging him to take them on board, but he dismissed them with threats and sent them back to Sydney Cove, where they were flogged. In fact, they had been lucky not to be taken on board. On March 10, 1788, after a six-week sojourn at Botany Bay, La Pérouse sailed off into the Pacific and was never heard from again. It took the French thirty years to establish that his ships were wrecked with the loss of all hands on Vanikoro in the New Hebrides.

The presence of the French boats warned Phillip that he must quickly colonize Norfolk Island. It would be a disaster to lose its pines and flax to France; and La Pérouse told him that he had already been there, although the surf prevented him landing.[11] So Phillip dispatched *Supply* to Norfolk Island, with twenty-two people on board under the command of *Sirius*'s second lieutenant, Philip Gidley King. They had six months' rations and were told to start sowing crops and retting flax immediately. Norfolk Island would be more fertile than the sandy dirt of Sydney Cove, at which the convicts were now scratching.

They had no ploughs or draft animals; it was all hack-and-peck hoe cultivation, and they sowed the first corn on a patch half a mile east of the stream, where the Botanical Gardens of Sydney now stand. Some of the trees they felled were giants, red gums more than twenty-five feet around the trunk, whose root systems had to be dug out and grubbed from the stony earth—an exhausting labor for men whose muscles had gone to suet after months at sea. Some officers had to sleep ashore. "I never slept worse, my dear wife, than I did last night," the homesick Lieutenant Clark wrote in his journal, "what with the hard cold ground, spiders, ants and every vermin you can think of was crawling over me."[12]

A fortnight passed before enough tents and huts were ready for the female convicts. On February 6 their disembarkation began, and all through the day the longboats plied between the transports and the cove, carrying their freight of women. Those who had decent clothes had put on all their finery: "Some few among them," noted Bowes Smyth, heartily glad to have them off his ship, "might be said to be well dressed." The last of them landed by six in the evening. It was a squally day, and thunderheads were piled up in livid cliffs above the Pacific; as dusk fell, the weather burst. Tents blew away; within minutes the whole encampment was a rain-lashed bog. The women floundered to and fro, draggled as muddy chickens under a pump, pursued by male convicts intent on raping them. One lightning bolt split a tree in the middle of the camp and killed several sheep and a pig beneath it. Meanwhile, most of the sailors on *Lady Penrhyn* applied to her master, Captain William Sever, for an extra ration of rum "to make merry with upon the women quitting the ship." Out came the pannikins, down went the rum, and before long the drunken tars went off to join the convicts in pursuit of the women, so that, Bowes remarked, "it is beyond my abilities to give a just description of the scene of debauchery and riot that ensued during the night." It was the first bush party in Australia, with "some swearing, others quarrelling, others singing—not in the least regarding the tempest, tho' so violent that the thunder shook the ship exceeding anything I ever before had a conception of." And as the couples rutted between the rocks, guts burning from the harsh Brazilian *aguardiente,* their clothes slimy with red clay, the sexual history of colonial Australia may fairly be said to have begun.[13]

Its political history began the next day. Late in the morning, as the sun stood up above the treetops and the drenched ground steamed, the marine band summoned all the colonists on shore to hear the Governor's Commission read. Phillip stood at a folding table, with his senior colonial officers—Robert Ross the lieutenant-governor, David Collins the judge-advocate, Reverend Richard Johnson the clergyman and John White the surgeon—ranked next to him. Two leather cases on the table held George III's seal and the documents commissioning the colony. With a rattle of drums and a small needling of fifes, the convicts were herded together in a circle around the gentlemen and officers; the soldiers formed a ring outside them. The convicts were ordered to squat. The soldiers remained standing with loaded muskets. This simple choreography summed up the main transactions of power.

Collins read the Royal Instructions giving Phillip, as Governor, the power to administer oaths, appoint officers, convene criminal and civil court and emancipate prisoners—the customary imperial boilerplate. He could raise armies, execute martial law and build "such and so many forts and platforms castles cities boroughs towns and fortifications as you shall judge necessary," a clause that must have deepened the hungover prisoners' gloom as Collins recited it.[14]

Phillip now harangued the convicts. He would stand no repetition of the last night's orgy, and any prisoners who tried to get into the women's tents would be shot. Cattle-duffers and chicken thieves would be hanged, without exceptions. Breeding stock was infinitely precious to the colony. Having watched the felons at work, "he was persuaded nothing but severity would have any effect upon them, to induce them to behave properly in future." If they did not work, they would not eat. Up to now only one man in three had been working; discipline would fix that, and discipline they would have. Their task, apart from clearing and hoeing the soil, would be building houses: first for the officers, then for the marines and lastly for themselves. *God Save the King!* The marines fired three volleys and marched the convicts off. Phillip and his officers sat down to a lunch of cold mutton, chatting sociably amid the stuttering whir of the cicadas. Alas, the meat proved to be crawling with maggots, although the sheep had only been butchered the night before. "Nothing will keep 24 hours in this country, I find," Lieutenant Clark morosely noted.

Now the hard work began, and it soon became clear that the colonists were wretchedly equipped for it. Not only was there a dearth of skilled labor, but tools were short and, Phillip complained, "the worst that ever was seen."[15] The only good building timber came from the cabbage-tree palms that grew in profusion around the stream at Sydney Cove. They were straight, easy to work and had little natural taper. All were cut down within a year. The huts they became might have been drawn by a child—boxes about 9 by 12 feet, with a hipped roof and two windows like eyes on either side of a doorway, the archetypal cottage-as-face. Their construction was equally simple. Walls were framed with 6-inch-square timber posts, set directly in the ground; vertical studs went between these, three feet apart. Between the roughly rabbeted studs, the carpenters inserted horizontal lengths of sapling whose ends were tapered to fit grooves. The walls, at this stage, looked like crude washboards. Then they were daubed (roughly sealed) on both sides with mud. This method of construction was used in every peasant community in England and Ireland; it was called "wattle-and-daub." Because, in Sydney, the horizontal wall slats were cut from mimosa saplings, that golden tree of the Australian summer has been known as a "wattle" ever since.[16]

The usual roof was reed thatch, gathered from the tidal marshes of Rushcutters' Bay. It harbored colonies of bugs and spiders, and it leaked. Presently it would be replaced by shingles. But when the winter rains came, the mud washed out of the walls. What the colony needed was brick, and before long some suitable clay was found. One convict, James Bloodworth, had been a brickmaker in England and took charge of manufacture. Convicts ground clay with water in natural depressions in the sandstone, using a log for a pestle; then, in barelegged teams, they squelched and trod it into a homogeneous pug. The bricks were molded, racked, dried and fired. They shrank unequally, and nobody could build level courses with them. For mortar, the only source of lime was burned oyster shells, laboriously gathered by convict women. That supplied just enough for a permanent Government House, a two-storied brick building with a tiled roof, stone quoins and real glass windowpanes—the first true piece of Georgian architecture in Australia, "composed of the common and Attic orders, with a pediment in front," wrote Thomas Watling, "simple, and without any other embellishment whatever." All other buildings had to be constructed without mortar and instead were made with a mixture of sheeps' hair and mud. The rain soon washed it out. No ruins of the earliest convict buildings, therefore, have survived at Sydney Cove.[17]

There was even, one may guess, a psychological reason for the poverty of building. Architecture signifies permanence; it announces the desire to stay. No other officers shared Phillip's dream of a colony of free immigrant settlers. To the convicts, all talk of a national future, or indeed a nation, was a joke. If your one dream was to escape from this Georgian shantytown, why build for the future? "Every person," wrote Lieutenant-Governor Ross, "who came out with a design of remaining in this country were [sic] now most earnestly wishing to get away from it."[18] This was the motif of life over the next decade in Sydney, until the Rum Corps gentry—grasping, ruthless and nepotistic, but resolved to make a life for themselves in New South Wales—perceived what there was to be gained and how the gains could be consolidated through the use of slave labor.

Since the First Fleet officers did not expect to stay, their diaries emphasized the exotic, the unique: animals, plants and Aborigines. They wrote very little about the convicts themselves, who had been sent there to be forgotten. Their work, infractions and punishments were all duly logged; but of the convicts as people, the records say little. What did the first man hanged in Sydney, a seventeen-year-old lad of "most vile character" named Thomas Barrett, really mean to say when, stammering and trembling and seeming "very much shocked," he announced at the foot of the ladder that "he had led a very wicked life"? How much "wickedness" could a boy compress into that small span from his birth to the fatal act of stealing some butter, dried peas and salt pork at Sydney Cove? [19]

The Australian blacks interested the First Fleet officers much more, and no account of the new thief-colony in the antipodes could be complete without a chapter or two on its "Indians." Spartan in bearing, they had a general appeal to men whose education reposed on neoclassical foundations. They were not as attractive as the Tahitians, and they seemed less like that fiction of the liberal European mind, the Noble Savage. They exemplified "hard" as against "soft" primitivism. But certainly the colonists did not wish to exterminate or enslave them, and they seemed at first to pose no threat.

Nevertheless, they were destroyed. Cholera and influenza germs from the ships began the work. By 1789 black corpses were a common sight, huddled in the salt grasses and decomposing in the creamy uterine hollows of the sandstone. These epidemics were not meant to happen; the days of arsenic and the infected trading-blanket were still far off. Governor Phillip's instructions as to blacks were quite clear: He must "conciliate their affections, enjoining all our subjects to live in amity and kindness with them," and punish anyone who harmed them. Common sense dictated that: why add tribal warfare to the problems of the colony? [20]

If at first the officers of the fleet saw the Aborigines through a scrim of Arcadian stereotypes and Rousseauist fancies, this pleasant delusion did not last long. The proper denizens of Arcadia were nymphs, but those of Port Jackson were unlike the welcoming girls of Tahiti. Young aboriginal women provoked mild longings in George Worgan, the surgeon on *Sirius.* "I can assure you," he wrote,

> there is in some of them a Proportion, a Softness, a roundness and Plumpness in their limbs and bodies . . . that would excite tender & amorous Sensations, even in the frigid Breast of a Philosopher,
>
> > Would stop a Druid in his Pious Course,
> > Nor could Philosophy resist their Force.[21]

Their virtue, or at least their relative immunity to rape, was nonetheless secured by their dirtiness, repellent even by the norms of Georgian hygiene. "What with the stinking Fish-Oil," Worgan complained,

> with which they seem to besmear their Bodies, & this mixed with the Soot which is collected on their Skins from continually setting over the Fires, and then in addition to those sweet Odours, the constant appearance of the Excrementitious Matter of the Nose which is collected on the upper pouting Lip, in rich Clusters of dry Bubbles, and is kept up by fresh Drippings; I say, from all these personal Graces & Embellishments, every Inclination for an Affair of Gallantry, as well as every idea of fond endearing Intercourse, which the nakedness of these Damssels might excite one to, is banished.[22]

In the same way Lieutenant Daniel Southwell, mate on *Sirius,* dreamed of Palladian villas on the shores and islands of "this extraordinary harbour"—"charm'g seats, superb buildings, the grand ruins of stately edifices . . . 'Tis greatly to be wished these appearances were not as delusive as in reality they are."[23]

This was a common complaint. The land was not what it seemed. It looked fertile and lovely, but it proved arid, reluctant, incomprehensible. "Here, a romantic rocky craggy Precipice, over which a little purling Stream makes a Cascade. There, a soft, vivid-green, shady Lawn attracts your eye. Such are the prepossessing Appearances which the country that forms PORT JACKSON presents. . . . [H]appy were it for the Colony, if these appearances were not so delusive."[24] The most vivid complaint about the scenic treachery of Sydney Harbor came from a Scots convict, young Thomas Watling of Dumfries, transported for forging guinea notes on the Bank of Scotland, who arrived on the *Royal Admiral* in 1792 at the age of thirty. He was a landscape painter, and as the first European artist to live in Australia he soon found how hard it was to depict the sights of Sydney Cove within the conventions of the journeyman pictur- esque that had formed his training. To be sure, Australia presented itself to the artist or naturalist as "a country of enchantments," with "num- berless beauties" and "Elysian scenery."[25] But Arcadia is underwritten only by leisure and surplus, and the infant colony had neither. Soon Watling found the place offered no respite. The earth was sandy, swampy or full of rocks; fertile topsoil only existed in pockets, and every yard of ground was impenetrably tangled with brush. There were no streams of any size, or lakes or even ponds, and rain simply ran off the meager soil into bogs. Away from the harbor, the bush crushed the eye with its monotony. "The landscape painter," wrote poor blistered Watling, "may in vain seek here for that beauty which arises from happy-opposed off- scapes" (meaning the beauty of romantic contrast, *à la* Salvator Rosa). Close up, the country matched the harshness of the penal regime, and Watling lamented

the sterility and miserable state of *N. S. Wales.* It will be long before ever it can even support itself.—Still that country so famed for charity and liberality of sentiment will I doubt no persevere to continue it.—When I have seen so much wanton cruelty practised on board the *English* hulks, on poor wretches, without the least colour of justice, what may I not reasonably infer?—*French* Bastille, nor *Spanish* Inquisition, could not centre more of horrors.[26]

Most of all, the young Scot resented being treated worse than the Aborig- ine, a "barbarian *New-Hollander*":

Many of these savages are allowed what is termed a freeman's ratio of provisions for their idleness. They are bedecked at times with dress which they make away with [at] the first opportunity, preferring the originality of naked nature; and they are treated with the most singular tenderness. This you will suppose is not more than laudable; but is there one spark of humanity exhibited to poor wretches, who are at least denominated Christians? No, they are frequently denied the common necessaries of life!—wrought to death under the oppressive heat of a burning sun; or barbarously afflicted with often little-merited secondary punishment— this may be *philosophy*, according to the calculation of our rigid dictators; but I think it is the falsest species of it I have ever known or heard of.[27]

Undoubtedly most of the other convicts felt the same way, although they could not write it down. For eight months and 15,000 miles they had seen nothing except the pitching ocean horizons, the darkness of their prison hold and sometimes a curve of foreign bay. Now they stumbled ashore in a land of inversions where it was high summer in January, where trees kept their leaves but shed their bark, where squat brown birds roared with laughter and thin stinking blacks, painted like pantomime skeletons, mocked them with their freedom. The blacks were an extension of the prison, its outer defense. Take to the bush and they would spear you; they were on the officers' side, just as the officers were on theirs.

In convict eyes, the tribesmen had only one use: they made tools and weapons and left them lying in the open, unattended, so that they could be stolen and sold to the free sailors who took them back to England as souvenirs. The loss of these fish-spears and clubs "must have been attended with many inconveniences to the owners . . . [as] they were the only means whereby they obtained or could procure their daily subsistence."[28]

And so relations between convict and tribesman began badly and soon got worse. In May 1788, a convict who worked on the government farm to the east of the freshwater stream—known by then as the Tank Stream, because the whites had been scraping storage sinks out of the soft rock on its verge—was speared dead in the bush. A week later, two convicts on thatch-cutting detail were found speared and mangled, "the head of one beaten to a jelly." It was supposed, a seaman noted, "to have been thro' revenge for taking away one of their canoes."[29] The killers had melted back into their tribe and it was useless to pursue them. "Notwithstanding all our presents," wrote a woman convict from Port Jackson in November 1788, "the savages still continue to do us all the injury they can, which makes the soldiers' duty very hard, and much dissatisfaction among the officers. I know not how many of our people have been killed."[30]

Revenge was easier dreamed of than exacted, as Phillip forbade punitive expeditions. The officers and marines, with their muskets, were theoretically better-armed than the Iora—but the tribesman could throw four spears in the time it took to reload a flintlock. The convicts were not armed at all, and so their efforts at revenge were futile. In March 1789, sixteen of them set off with clubs to beat up the "Indians" for injuring one of their friends; the Iora ambushed them, killing one and wounding seven. Not only did Phillip refuse to order a retaliatory attack on the blacks, but he had the eight unharmed survivors flogged with 150 lashes each and placed in leg irons for a year.

Such actions rankled. In the eyes of the British Government, the status of Australian Aborigines in 1788 was higher than it would be for another 150 years, for they had (in theory) the full legal status and so, in law if not in fact, they were superior to the convicts. The convicts resented this most bitterly. Galled by exile, the lowest of the low, they desperately needed to believe in a class inferior to themselves. The Aborigines answered that need. Australian racism began with the convicts, although it did not stay confined to them for long; it was the first Australian trait to percolate upward from the lower class.

But if the convicts hated the blacks, the military detested both—and for similar reasons. When Phillip summarily punished the steward of a marine officer with 50 lashes for giving a convict a gallon of rum in exchange for a pet possum, Arthur Bowes Smyth railed against the governor:

> ... This Government (if a Government it can be called) is a scene of anarchy and confusion; an evident discontent prevails among the different officers throughout the settlement. The marines and sailors are punished with the utmost severity for the most trivial offences, whilst the convicts are pardoned (or at least punished in a very slight manner) for crimes of the blackest die. I do not even except stealing, which the Governor himself ... assured them would be punished capitally. What may be the result of such a very inconsistent and partial mode of acting, time (and I may venture to say a very short time) will shew.[31]

To the marines, Phillip's even-handedness was bias. In the famine years of the early settlement convicts were hanged for stealing food—but so, in March 1789, were six marine privates. Why, marines grumbled, should the convicts be flogged with a lighter cat-o'-nine-tails than the dreadful "military cat" used on servicemen? Why should marines and soldiers get the same ration as prisoners? Pinpricks, like the cancellation of a rum allowance to the marines' wives, became inflammations. Most of all, they resented doing duty as convict supervisors. They had not enlisted as jail wardens, and they felt (not unreasonably) that the government's failure to send civilians to keep the work gangs in order was one more proof of its incompetence and indifference.

So they hated the place, hated the convicts for bringing them there and despised the Aborigines into the bargain. "I do not scruple to pronounce," wrote the marine major whom Phillip had made lieutenant-governor, Robert Ross,

> that in the whole world there is not a worse country. All that is contiguous to us is so very barren and forbidding that it may with truth be said that *here nature is reversed;* and if not so, she is nearly worn out. ... If the minister has a true and just description given him of it he will surely not think of sending any more people here.[32]

Ross—"without exception the most disagreeable commanding officer I ever knew," in the opinion of one of his subordinates—was a choleric, whining martinet who hated Phillip and the colony equally. He would stop at nothing to cast Phillip in a bad light. But most of the colonists, marine or convict, shared his gloom about the future of New South Wales.

iii

THE HATEFUL equalizer was hunger. This first democratic experience in Australia spared no one. It made most of the colonists stupid and some crazy, playing havoc with morale and producing endless displays of petty tyranny.

The First Fleet carried enough food to keep its passengers alive for two years in Australia. The rations issued to sailors, marines and officers each week were:

| | | | |
|---|---|---|---|
| Beef | 4 lb. | Hardtack | 7 lb. |
| Pork | 2 lb. | Cheese | 12 oz. |
| Dried peas | 2 pints | Butter | 6 oz. |
| Oatmeal | 3 pints | Vinegar | ½ pint |

The male convicts got one-third less, while female convicts got two-thirds of the male ration, or slightly less than half the naval standard. On paper, this was not a bad allowance. In practice it meant scurvy, and the meat was mostly bone and gristle.

At Table Bay in South Africa, their last port of call before Australia, some officers had bought livestock for themselves. When these were added to the animals Phillip had bought for the government herd, the colony's total stock came to 2 bulls and 5 cows, 29 sheep, 19 goats, 74 hogs and sows, 18 turkeys, 35 ducks, 35 geese and 209 chickens. There were also 5 rabbits. All these creatures were guarded with reverential care. As Phillip had put it to the convicts, the life of a breeding animal was worth a man's. In August 1788, when a sheep fattened for the officers' dinner on the Prince of Wales's birthday vanished from its pen, Phillip offered full emancipation to anyone who informed on the thief. None would. Gorgon, the colony's prize Africander bull, and four of his five cows strayed into the scrub and were lost. Sheep died from bloat, while dingoes and convicts kept poaching the hens.

All ranks ate the same monotonous diet of salt meat and leathery johnnycakes baked on a shovel. Thus, food could not symbolize the proper social demarcation between bond and free. "Our allowance is very scanty," wrote James Campbell, captain of marines on *Lady Penrhyn,*

I know not why, or whither it was so intended by administration that the only difference between the allowance of provisions served to the officer & served to the convict, be only half a pint (per day) of vile Rio spirits, so offensive both in taste & smell that he must be fond of drinking indeed that can use it—but such is the fact.[33]

Phillip knew that the survival of the colony had to preclude all comforts of status. With surplus food, the officers would start to become aristocracy—but not yet. They all lived for five years on the bleak edge of starvation. The first crops failed and the whole harvest of the second planting—a meager forty bushels—had to be saved for seed. In 1788 the convicts had no draft animals; no plough would be used in Australia until 1803.

Only a third of the prisoners could work—320 men out of the 966 victualled from public stores. More than 50 convicts were too feeble from age and incurable illness to work at all, and many others—slum-raised, utterly ignorant of farming—"would starve if left to themselves."[34] The ideal of each man feeding himself was a mockery in New South Wales.

Some officers had their own vegetable gardens, tended by convicts. The kitchen garden for the public stores was planted, for security, on an island 300 yards out in the harbor; there, it was fairly safe from the prisoners and marines who, desperate for green food, would pull turnip-tops and gobble the leaves before the turnip had grown. But the yield from Garden Island, as it was named, was still poor—just enough for the sick in the hospital tents. The officers guarded their private plots zealously but unsuccessfully. Thus when Lieutenant Clark, who had the use of another islet in the harbor (still known as Clark Island), went to look at his onion bed in February 1790, he found "some Boat had landed since I had been there last and taken away the greatest part . . . It is impossible for any body to attempt to raise any Garden stuff here, before it comes to perfection they will steal it."[35]

The colonists found few plants they could eat, and little game. They gathered wild spinach and a liquorice-flavored creeper, *Smilax glycophylla*, which they called "sweet tea." A few officers had brought their fowling pieces, but it seemed unwise to use up the colony's limited stock of gunpowder.

The only reliable source of fresh protein, therefore, was fish. There was some prejudice against it. The ration was 10 pounds of fish issued in place of 2½ pounds of salt beef. King remarked, "If there were more convicts here, they would not submit to having their salt rations stopped where a quantity of fish were caught by them."[36] In Sydney the "Roast Beef of Old England"—even salted and half-rotten—was more prized than any fish.

By October 1788, Phillip still had no idea if relief ships were on their way, and there was only enough food in store to last, if strictly rationed, one more year. Given the eerily long time-lag between England and Sydney, he had to decide. He cut 1 pound from the weekly flour ration and sent his largest vessel, *Sirius*, to Cape Town to buy supplies.

Her captain, John Hunter, gambled on taking a longer but faster route, sailing around Cape Horn before the westerlies. Speed was all-important, for his sailors were sickening from scurvy and hunger. *Sirius* reached Cape Town in three months, instead of the five the western route against the prevailing winds would likely have taken. Hunter loaded, refitted and brought her back to Sydney Cove, laden with wheat, barley and flour, by May 1789. There had been no news of relief ships in Cape Town. But the 56 tons of new flour would last the colony four months, and the seed would plant the allotments around Sydney and at the new farms inland at Rose Hill.

By now, most agricultural hope centered on the governor's farm at Rose Hill, or Parramatta as the blacks called it, where the soil was deep and rich and the fields ran down to a navigable river. By the end of 1789, this farm had produced Australia's first agricultural marvel, a 26-pound cabbage; but it was still a long way from keeping the whole settlement in greens. In fact, in the year to come, the idea of progress shrunk to a mockery, for 1789 brought no ships, and as 1790 crept by, the little settlement inexorably sank into the torpor and despair of slow starvation. "God help us. If some ships dont arrive, I dont know what will," Ralph Clark scrawled in his diary, and Watkin Tench described the mood that now descended over Sydney Cove:

> Famine . . . was approaching with giant strides, and gloom and dejection overspread every countenance. Men abandoned themselves to the most desponding reflections, and adopted the most extravagant conjectures.
>
> Still we were on the tiptoe of expectation. If thunder broke at a distance, or a fowling-piece of louder than ordinary report resounded in the woods, *"a gun from a ship"* was echoed on every side, and nothing but hurry and agitation prevailed.[37]

Lieutenant Southwell wrote how his eyes, in the evening, had sometimes been deceived "with some fantastic little cloud, which . . . for a little time has deceived impatient imagination into the momentary idea that 'twas a vessel altering her sail or position while steering in for the haven."[38]

Supplies were running so low that Phillip decided to take another gamble. He dispatched 281 people—more than a third of the convicts in the colony, guarded by half the battalion of marines—to Norfolk Island in the *Sirius*, which would then sail on to Canton to load up with desperately needed provisions. The convicts and their guards, Phillip reasoned, would stand a better chance on Norfolk Island, with its fertile soil and abundant fish. The marines disliked the idea—which, as a bonus, enabled Phillip to get rid of his obstreperous bête noire, Major Ross—but they had no choice, and *Sirius* sailed with her tender, *Supply*, in March 1790. The Sydney colonists now had no means of communication with the outside world. "The little society that was in the place was broken up," wrote David Collins, "and every man seemed left to brood in solitary silence over the dreary prospect before him."[39]

On April 1, Phillip cut the rations "without distinction" to 4 pounds of flour, 2½ pounds of salt pork and 1½ pounds of rice per week. This was just enough to sustain life but not enough to work on, and so he humanely reduced the convicts' hours of work to six per day, so that each man could cultivate a private vegetable patch in the afternoon.

Then, on April 5, *Supply* appeared off South Head. She was alone. As her launch cast off and made for the shore of Sydney Cove, Tench saw her captain "make an extraordinary motion with his hand, which too plainly indicated that something disastrous had happened; and I could not help turning to the Governor . . . and saying, 'Sir, prepare yourself for bad news.' "[40]

The news was catastrophic. *Sirius* had struck a reef at Norfolk Island and was a total wreck. All the ships' crew and company, including the convicts, were saved. But both settlements, at Sydney and Norfolk Island, were now cut off from the world and—except for one 170-ton brig —from one another. Both were failing fast, for Norfolk Island was just as badly off as Sydney.

iv

TWO YEARS BEFORE, when Philip Gidley King and his party of twenty-two colonists glimpsed, from the pitching deck of *Supply*, the island that would eventually become the worst place in the English-speaking world, what they had seen was not inviting.

Magnificent in scenery, Norfolk Island was also a natural prison, harborless, cliff-bound and girdled with reefs on which the long Pacific swells broke with a ragged, monotonous booming. King had to wait five days in the lee before he could lead a scouting party ashore. They landed at Anson Bay on March 4, 1788. The high pines grew right to the cliff face; King guessed the tallest of them was 160 feet.[41] Their trunks were wreathed in vines. The ship's surgeon got lost in this maze and spent the night in the forest. In the dark, where phosphorescent fungi gleamed beneath the Gothic vaults of cabbage-trees, he heard nibbling and thought he was surrounded by rabbits. The rabbits were rats.

King found a passage through the reef at Sydney Bay (modern Kingston) and landed the convicts and supplies on March 6. They raised the Union Jack on a sapling. "I took possession of the isle, drinking 'His Majesty,' 'The Queen,' 'Prince of Wales,' 'Governor Phillip' and 'Success to the Colony.' " The ragged chorus of English voices was sucked away by the Pacific air, swallowed in the blue immensity behind the wall of dark pines. Two days later, *Supply* made sail for the Australian coast, a thousand miles away.

The first crops perished from wind and salt. Rats ate the vegetables; then came cutworms, black caterpillars and bright, screaming, seed-eating Norfolk Island Parrots. The wreck of the *Sirius* meant new mouths to feed. In March 1790, Norfolk Island had 425 people (200 convicts), but by November 1791 with new arrivals from Sydney, it had 959 (748 convicts). Thereafter, until the first settlement was abandoned in 1806, the population would remain fairly steady at about a thousand people, with one guard to every seven prisoners.

Despite the rich, deep soil, they had, by March 1790, only about fifty acres of land under the hoe. The reef swarmed with red snapper, but the colonists' two boats—a cutter and a leaky dinghy—could not always brave the pounding surf. What saved all their lives was the mutton-bird, *Pterodroma melanopus*, which flocked in immense numbers on Mount Pitt, the island's highest hill. Its flanks were riddled with their nesting tunnels. The mutton-birds arrived on Norfolk Island early in March and stayed until the end of August—almost the length of the Pacific winter. "They are very fine eating, very fat and firm," wrote Ralph Clark in August 1790, "and I think (though no Connoisseur) as good as any I ever eat." The Bird of Providence—as the officers called it; the convicts more laconically dubbed it a Pittite—tasted oily and fishy, somewhere between a penguin and a chicken. The birds had never seen men before, and their abundance struck Clark as Biblical:

> They generally hovered about the Mount for an hour before they came down, which was as thick as a shower of hail, this account will make the old story of Moses in the Wilderness (Exodus xvi.13) be a little more believ'd, respecting the shower of Quails, everyone here owes their existence to the Mount Pit Birds.[42]

Once grounded, they were encumbered by their long planing wings, like albatrosses. As quartermaster of public stores, Clark kept a daily tally: More than 170,000 of them were massacred in one three-month span, April to July 1790, an average of nearly four birds per person per day. Some convicts went to brutal lengths to get their eggs:

They catch the birds and them that have no eggs they let go again and them that are with Egg they cut the Egg out of them and then let the poor Bird fly again which is one of the cruelest things which I think I ever heard. I hope that some of them will be caught at this cruel work for the sake of making an example of them.[43]

Naturally the Birds of Providence could not survive this slaughter. By 1796 they were thinning out, and eight years later they were almost gone. By 1830, no more was heard of *Pterodroma melanopus* on Norfolk Island.

Meanwhile, the arduous work of clearing and building went on. Hungry men work slowly, so less ground is cleared; which means small crops and more hunger. There was little time or energy left over for the crops the island was meant to produce, pines and flax.

The Norfolk Island pines, however, like the rest of antipodean nature, were deceptive. They turned out to be useless for anything but huts and firewood. Their wood was not resilient enough for spars. It was short-grained, wanting in resin, more like beech than Norway pine; it snapped like a carrot.

That left the flax plant. *Phormium tenax*, Phillip had optimistically reported to Lord Sydney at the end of 1788, "will supply the settlers with rope and canvas, as well as a considerable part of their cloathing, when they can dress it properly."[44] But the Admiralty had sent no flax workers with the First Fleet. Phillip's sanguine vision of settlers and convicts wearing homespun linen whilst dispatching argosies of sailcloth to England quickly faded. He besought London to send a flax dresser, but it took two years for this expert (a convict superintendent named Andrew Hume) to reach Norfolk Island. In 1791 Hume managed to produce for the Admiralty a couple of square yards of rough Norfolk Island linen—perhaps among the costliest textiles ever woven by man.

Meanwhile, King had an idea. He remembered Banks telling him about the linen woven by the Maoris in New Zealand. Plainly, he needed a Maori; and about a year later, a ship did manage to kidnap two wildly struggling and resentful tribesmen from the Bay of Islands in New Zealand and get them to Norfolk Island. One was a young chief named Woodoo; the other, Tooke, was a priest's son; both were twenty-four years old and neither had the slightest idea of how to prepare flax, for such menial work was done by women. So Tooke and Woodoo moped haughtily about the settlement, gazing out to sea from the headlands where "almost every evening at the close of day [they] lament their separation by crying or singing a song expressive of their grief, which is at times very affecting." After six months' exile on Norfolk, King returned them to New Zealand.[45]

Meanwhile, by trial and error, flax production went on. At its peak, the convict workers (mainly women) were turning out some 100 yards of coarse canvas a month. At that pace, however, it would have taken two years to make the sailcloth for one first-rate ship. Gradually, the project wore down and lapsed. By 1800, the hopes that began with Matra's descants on the flax plant and Cook's enthusiasm for the pines were proven a total delusion. The place would produce nothing for England; it would never pay for itself. Its colonists sank, as on the mainland, into a demoralized torpor.

v

AS SOON AS he heard of the wreck of the *Sirius*, Governor Phillip had inventory taken of the stores at Sydney. It showed that they had only a few months' grace left, so he cut the rations again. These sad morsels—a third of what they should have been—were doled out daily, to groups of seven people, so that the convicts could not bolt a whole week's ration at once. Some women prostituted themselves for a few handfuls of weevily flour or a hunk of gristle. Most of the men on the work gangs were already as naked as the Aborigines, having traded off their clothes for food. There was no question of the convicts' helping one another; Sydney Cove had only distilled the dog-eat-dog misery of the English slums. When one elderly prisoner fell down and died in the food queue in May 1790, Collins's autopsy showed his stomach was quite empty. He had lost or sold his cooking utensils, and instead of helping him out, his fellow prisoners had demanded a cut of his ration before they would share their cookpot, so that he starved.

Phillip reluctantly stepped up the punishments for food theft, which were already draconic but no longer deterred the starving. In 1790 one man got 300 lashes and 6 months in chains for stealing 20 ounces of potatoes, and another drew 1,000 lashes for taking 3 pounds of the precious tubers. After such treatment, a man would be incapacitated, literally skinned alive. Huge rewards (in food, the only currency that mattered, for there was no money circulating in this jail) were offered to convicts who helped catch food thieves. Thus in May 1790, convict Thomas Yarsley received 60 pounds of flour for catching a man stealing garden vegetables. Such inducements, Watkin Tench remarked, were "more tempting than the ore of Peru or Potosi."[46]

Hunger, fear, exhaustion and the pervasive sense of abandonment—these destroyed whatever scraps of morale may have been left among the convicts. One of their few surviving letters, from an unknown woman, speaks of "our disconsolate situation in this solitary waste of the creation

... not to be imagined by any stranger" and revealingly noted, "In short, everyone is so taken up with their own misfortunes that they have no pity to bestow on others." No wonder that by April 1790 the settlement chaplain, Reverend Richard Johnson, was lamenting the convicts' apathy to the Divine Word. "Little apparent fruit yet among the Convicts, &c., Oh that they were wise—but alas! nothing seems to alarm or allure them."[47]

The guards were as apathetic as the convicts. They grew peevish; they could not make up their minds on simple matters; they hallucinated. Lieutenant Southwell felt the torpor of starvation: "I confess myself incompetent . . . being perplexed with a variety of conjectures, but able to conclude nothing."[48] Conversation, friendship and curiosity faltered and died, having nothing to sustain them. The spirit of inquiry about the new environment, which had filled several officers' journals in the first year of settlement, now dwindled; there are only about half as many observations on flora, fauna and "Indians" for 1789–90 as for 1788. Monotony reigned. The classes were now at a simmering distrust of one another, wrote an anonymous male convict lamenting their "Crusoe-like adventures":

> We fear the troops, and they are not contented with seeing those who live better than themselves, nor with us who live worse. . . . [W]e have had so many disappointments about arrivals, &c., that the sullen reserve of superiority has only increased our apprehensions; and some of the most ignorant have no other idea than that they are to be left by the troops and the shipping to perish by themselves![49]

The signs of status were vanishing. All uniforms were threadbare or ragged. Most of the marines were barefoot; drill, rituals, spit-and-polish were gone. "Nothing more ludicrous can be conceived," wrote Watkin Tench, "than the expedients of substituting, shifting and patching, which ingenuity devised, to eke out wretchedness and preserve the remains of decency."[50]

The marines resented Phillip's order that equal rations be issued to convicts and guards. When the governor turned over his private stock of flour—more than 300 pounds—to the public store, Collins wrote that the gesture "did him immortal honor, in this season of general distress" —as indeed it did.[51] But the marines did not agree. If clothes and rations could not symbolize rank, then actions would; and one may be sure that every curse, kick and blow the marines rained on the exhausted "crawlers" was meant as a reinforcement of superiority, not just an incitement to work. The convict artist Thomas Watling, transported for forgery, summed it up:

Instances of oppression, and mean-souled despotism, are so glaring and
frequent, as to banish every hope of generosity and urbanity from such as
I am:—for unless we can flatter and cajole the vices and follies of our
superiors, with the most abominable servility, nothing is to be expected
—and even this conduct, very often . . . meets with its just reward—
neglect and contempt.[52]

To construct a sense of power from the meager social resources of the
colony, the top dog had to be capricious—otherwise, the underdog's servility might be taken as a contract. Watling could neither dignify himself
by rebelling, nor protect himself by truckling. This proved utterly demoralizing for genteel convicts who still clung to the belief that they
were not "common" criminals. To them, servility—the very condition
they had tried to escape with their pathetic embezzlements and forgeries
—was indeed "abominable."

By grit, example and stubborn evenhandedness in the face of hopeless
prisoners and near-mutinous marines, Phillip pulled his wretched settlement through these months of crisis. "We shall not starve," he wrote,
"though seven-eighths of the colony deserves nothing better; the present
want will be done away by the first ship that arrives."[53]

That long-awaited sail was glimpsed on June 3, 1790, a rainy, bluster-
ing day. Watkin Tench realized it when he saw, through the doorway of
his hovel, "women with children in their arms running to and fro with
distracted looks, congratulating each other, and kissing their infants
with the most passionate and extravagant looks of fondness." The ship
was *Lady Juliana*, eleven months out of Plymouth, carrying the first
news from home the colonists had received in almost three years:

> "Letters! Letters!" was the cry. They were produced, and torn open in
> trembling agitation. News burst on us like meridian splendour on a blind
> man. We were overwhelmed with it: public, private, general, and partic-
> ular. Nor was it until some days had elapsed, that we were able to meth-
> odise it, or reduce it into form.[54]

They learned, for the first time, of George III's attack of porphyria, of the
trial of Warren Hastings, of George Washington's inauguration as the
first president of the United States. Most amazing of all—and, given their
social situation, most ominous—they learned of the French Revolution,
"that wonderful and unexpected event," as Tench called it.

They also learned why no stores had arrived. The *Guardian*, laden
with two years' worth of food and stores, had struck an iceberg and
limped into Cape Town, where she was abandoned. But for that she
would have reached Sydney in early March, thus preventing the loss of

*Sirius.* All her stores were lost. *Lady Juliana* had brought some flour, but it also brought more useless mouths in the form of 222 women convicts.

At least they were in good health. Not so the other prisoners on the Second Fleet. More than a thousand had embarked, but a quarter of them died at sea, and half were landed helplessly ill at Sydney Cove from the three remaining ships, *Neptune, Surprise* and (making her second voyage to Australia) *Scarborough*. Some died from the brutality of the ships' masters, others because they had been too sick to sail.* The authorities in England had simply used the Second Fleet to rid the hulks and prisons of invalids, dispatching them into oblivion. "The sending out of the dis-ordered and helpless," Phillip wrote angrily to his superiors in London,

> clears the gaols and may ease the parishes from which they are sent; but ... it is obvious that the settlement, instead of being a colony which will support itself, will, if this practice is continued, remain for years a bur-then to the mother-country.[55]

Before his letter reached London, however, the Third Fleet was on its way, carrying 1,864 convicts. One man in ten died, and the survivors were landed in 1791 "so emaciated, so worn away," in Phillip's words, that they were utterly unfit to work—more helpless parasites to drag the colony down.

So the ships had come, but brought little change. David Collins wrote to his father and summed up his plight:

> I find that I am spending the Prime of my Life at the farthest part of the World, without Credit, without ... Profit, secluded from my Family, ... my Connexions, from the World, under constant Apprehensions of being starved ... All these Considerations induce me ... to embrace the first Opportunity that offers of escaping from a Country that is nothing better than a Place of banishment for the Outcasts of Society.[56]

In fact, the marines would soon be relieved. The Second Fleet brought two companies of the New South Wales Corps, a new unit tailored for service in Australia. The corps' officers knew they had to do the admin-istrative work, such as jury duty, that Major Ross and his men objected to; and its enlisted men would guard convicts as well as fight the French —the latter a remote possibility. As soldiers, the Botany Bay Rangers (as they came to be nicknamed) were poor stuff even by the current low standards of the British Army. Most of them were scum, and they found service in New South Wales the best alternative to beggary or crime. Few of the officers were better than the men.[57]

---

* For the voyage of the Second Fleet, see chapter 5.

But the impact of the New South Wales Corps on life in early New South Wales was to be out of all proportion to its quality as a force. Between 1791 and 1808 the corps was de facto—if not quite de jure—the most powerful single internal influence on the colony, producing its first ruling clans and even, in 1808, overthrowing the governor.

The arrival of the Second and Third Fleets proved one thing: However bad the colony's prospects were, at least it had not been abandoned by England. From now on, sails would continue to be seen off the Heads. Some were convict ships, others supply vessels, and yet others were the first harbingers of trade in that remote ocean: sealers, whalers, and merchantmen drawn to the infant colony by the hugely inflated prices the colonists would pay for ordinary goods—3,000 to 4,000 percent on "every little Article of Comfort or Convenience," Collins noted.[58]

So by the end of 1791 there were signs that Sydney might support itself—although not, as Phillip stressed in his reports to England, on convict labor alone. The prisoners had no incentive to work. They were not so much rebellious as flaccid: "Neither kindness nor severity have any effect, and tho' I can say the convicts in general behave well, there are many who dread punishment less than they fear labour." The only hope, Phillip insisted, was a colony "formed by farmers and emigrants who have been used to labour, and who reap the fruits of their own industry."[59]

But no such sturdy free yeomanry would come to New South Wales. In fact, only twenty free settlers would migrate there before 1800. So Phillip resolved to see if the more deserving and sober Emancipists—convicts whose term of punishment had expired but who wanted to stay on and make a new life in Australia—could be made into yeomen. He would grant them land and the use of tools. If their farms prospered they would "take themselves off the store," becoming independent of government rations and eventually selling their surplus crops back to the colonial government stores. Such men might set an example and show that transportation could reform.

The first convict to succeed as an independent farmer was Richard Phillimore, who by January 1791 was growing enough grain on Norfolk Island to support himself and two workers. But the father of Australian agriculture, the first man to grub a living from the more stubborn earth of the mainland, was James Ruse, to whom Phillip gave one cleared acre and some raw bush at Parramatta. Ruse had been a farmer in Cornwall. Having no animal manure, he burned off the timber on his little acre and dug in the ashes, which were rich in potash. Lacking ploughhorse and plough, he hoed the ground thoroughly—"not like the Government farms, just scratched over, but properly done," he proudly told Watkin Tench—and turned the sod over, so that the grass and weeds composted into the soil; then, just before sowing, he turned the earth again. By late summer (February 1791), his wheat and maize were up and he jubilantly told Phillip that he could keep himself in food. By December 1791 he took his wife and child "off the store" as well.

As a reward, Phillip deeded him thirty acres at Parramatta—the first land grant ever made in Australia. The place was named Experiment Farm. By 1819 Ruse had two hundred acres to his name, and although he lost it all by rum or ill luck and ended his days working as overseer for another farmer, the lines carved on his gravestone are full of an understandably biblical pride that shines through the home-made spelling:

> *My Mother Reread Me Tenderley*
> *With me She Took Much Paines*
> *And when I arived in This Coelney*
> *I sowd the Forst Grain and Now*
> *With My Hevenly Father I hope*
> *For Ever To Remain.*

By the end of 1792 all the economic hopes of the colony were centered on Parramatta. No one now struggled with the thin soil of Sydney, and the Tank Stream was a "morass," so damaged by the settlers that ships could no longer get water from it. But at Parramatta, the farms were slowly extending their frail patchwork into the ancient gray-green chaos of the bush. By October 1792 Phillip had given land grants around Parramatta and the nearby district of Toongabbie to sixty-six people, of whom fifty-three were time-expired convicts. But there were not many men like Ruse among them. Skilled, hardworking Emancipists could save money to pay their way back to England or could work their passage as seamen and carpenters: "Thus will the best people always be carried away," Phillip ruefully noted.[60] Four years after landing, most prisoners still could not support themselves and were worked like cattle. An old lag who arrived with the Third Fleet, Henry Hale, gave a vivid picture of labor at Toongabbie:

For nine months there I was on five ounces of flour a day; when weighed out, barely four. . . . In those days we were yoked to draw timber, twenty-five in gang. The sticks were six feet long; six men abreast. We held the stick behind us, and dragged with our hands. One man . . . was put to the drag; it soon did for him. He began on a Thursday and died on a Saturday, as he was dragging a load down Constitution-hill. . . . Men used to carry trees on their shoulders. How they used to die![61]

At Toongabbie, "All the necessary conveniences of life they are strangers to, and suffer everything they could dread. . . . [I]t was not uncommon for seven or eight to die in one day, and very often while at work." No wonder that the convicts pilfered like ants. Despite a long drought in 1791, the harvest had produced nearly 5,000 bushels of wheat, of which no less than 1,500 bushels—30 percent of the year's crop—vanished somewhere between the fields and the granary.[62]

Yet at the end of 1792, a thousand public acres and 516 private were under cultivation, and more than four thousand acres had been set aside for future farming. This, Phillip thought, would be done by Emancipists and members of the New South Wales Corps, all of whom would have the use of convict labor to help them. Such was the germ of the assignment system, the modified form of slavery on which Australia's early economy would be built.

By now, according to the meticulous bookkeeping of the Colonial Office, the colony of New South Wales—four small red patches, representing Sydney Cove, Norfolk Island, Parramatta and Toongabbie—had cost the government of George III 67,194 pounds, 15 shillings and fourpence three-farthings, or about 3.35 million pounds in modern money.[63]

What had the Crown got in exchange? Not much, in strategic terms; the hope of supplying England's East Indian fleet with spars and canvas from Norfolk Island had failed miserably. On the other hand, the fact that the Australian coast had been not only claimed but occupied, however feebly, meant that the French would find it harder to press their territorial claims in the South Pacific. Given the broad nature of the balance of power between England and France—whereby France dominated the continent of Europe, while England, global in its reach, ruled the waves—there was at least a hypothetical strategic role for this colony in the primitive terms of eighteenth-century geopolitics.

As for the convicts, William Pitt's Tory government claimed to be not displeased by the results. Some critics wanted to know why the felons were not being used on public works in England, as they were in France or Germany; degraded though these creatures may be, their argument went, convict labor had some value, and it was wasted in Australia. Pitt brushed these objections aside in his toplofty way, saying—quite untruthfully—that the main expenses of the colony were a thing of the past, that it was or would shortly become self-supporting and that transportation was by far the cheapest way of getting rid of felons.[64]

So the colony would go on; but it went on without Governor Arthur Phillip. On December 10, 1792, accompanied by his two aboriginal friends, or specimens, Bennelong and Yemmerawannie, he boarded the storeship *Atlantic* and sailed down the harbor for the last time. He longed for England. Twenty-two years later, retired, bored, an admiral of the Blue living on a pension, still in touch (though desultorily now) with the affairs of the colony he had fathered, he died in Bath.

vi

A s´ T H E   L A S T decade of the eighteenth century went by, the British Government still thought of Australia and its convict colony in maritime terms. Its settlements were a port and an island; it faced outward to the sea, not inward to the land. It was a base (albeit a feeble one) for trade, refitting and defense, not for internal expansion. The first four governors of New South Wales were all naval officers: Captain Phillip, Captain Hunter, Lieutenant King and Captain William Bligh (of the *Bounty*).[65] The convict colony was, in London's view, a land-based hulk the size of a continent.

But after 1792 it became self-supporting, and that was the work of landsmen—the officers of the New South Wales Corps and their friends. For nearly three years between Phillip's departure in December 1792 and Hunter's return in September 1795, the colony was in effect run for the New South Wales Corps by its principal officers, Francis Grose and William Paterson. They set the pattern of private management and slave labor that created the wealth of Australia's first elite.

Francis Grose (1758?–1814) had fought against the American rebels in the War of Independence. Badly wounded and invalided home to England, he got back to full service pay by helping to raise and recruit the New South Wales Corps. As its commandant, and as lieutenant-governor of New South Wales, Grose took over when Phillip sailed. He promptly set about putting most civil affairs in military hands. He replaced magistrates with corps officers and appointed a thrusting young Scottish lieutenant, John Macarthur, as regimental paymaster and inspector of public works—posts that gave him leverage by controlling the supply of convict labor.

Grose did not forget his own rank and file. He cancelled Phillip's policy of equal rations for all and gave the troops more food than the convicts. He also let it be known that any member of the New South Wales Corps could have twenty-five acres of free land for the asking. But his crucial decision for the future of Australian farming was to offer 100-acre land grants to corps officers—along with ten convicts, free of charge and maintained at government expense, to work each one. The corps officers, Grose reported to London, were "the only description of settlers on whom reliance can be placed. . . . [T]heir exertions are really astonishing. . . . I shall encourage their pursuit as much as is in my power."[66]

Under Grose, officers had the economic edge on civilians; they could raise capital by borrowing against their regimental pay, and as a junta they seized a monopoly on most consumer goods arriving in Sydney

Harbor. The chief of these was rum, the social anesthetic and real currency of early New South Wales. Colonial Sydney was a drunken society, from top to bottom. Men and women drank with a desperate, addicted, quarrelsome single-mindedness. Every drop of their tipple had to be imported.

Early in 1793 an American trading vessel, the *Hope*, arrived with 7,500 gallons of rum in her cargo. The goods and stores she carried were badly needed, and the *Hope*'s hard-nosed skipper not only demanded grossly inflated prices for them but insisted that not a nail, a sack of flour or a yard of cloth would leave his ship unless the colony bought all his rum first. Rather than suffer this gouging, the New South Wales Corps' officers decided to pass it on. They formed a ring to buy the *Hope*'s cargo without competition. John Macarthur, as regimental paymaster, fixed the necessary IOUs against the regiment's funds in England.

This impromptu deal was hugely profitable, and the monopoly of the Rum Corps (as the regiment was presently nicknamed) soon pervaded the colony's economic life. For years to come, most of the cargo that came to Sydney passed through the hands of the corps and its favored satellites, among whom were several ex-convicts. Much of it was invested in land. Emancipated convicts and free settlers had an equal right to farm. At the beginning of 1794, twenty-two grants of land had been made along the rich plains of the Hawkesbury River, northwest of Sydney. Within a few months there were 70 settlers there, and a year later 400; these included 54 ex-convicts with their dependents. But by 1800, only 8 of those 54 still had farms there—and the Hawkesbury flats were the best farming land within reach of Sydney. In all, out of 274 settlers on granted land in New South Wales in 1795—the great majority, 251 of them, being ex-convicts—only 89 were still farming their own land in 1800.[67]

There were natural reasons for this: flood, fire, drought—the undying, malignant totems of Australian farming. There were cultural ones, too, since so many of the Emancipist farmers were utter novices, not experienced men like James Ruse. But this early tendency to consolidation—which reversed itself in the Emancipists' favor after 1800[68]—was certainly helped by the officers' money and access to credit, and by the rum itself. An officer could pick the best land for his grant; he could get the most skilled convicts, the "mechanics" and former agricultural laborers, to work it; he paid for his tools, seed and stock a mere fraction of what Emancipist farmers, due to the Rum Corps monopoly on imports, paid him; and if an ex-convict farmer started wasting his life with booze, some Rum Corps officer would always appear and buy him out.

"The changes we have undergone since the departure of Governor Phillip," wrote John Macarthur as early as 1793, are so great and extraordinary that to recite them all might create some suspicion of their truth. From a state of desponding poverty and threatened famine that this settlement should be raised to its present aspect in so short a time is barely credible. As for myself, I have a farm containing nearly 250 acres. . . . [O]f this year's produce I have sold £400 worth, and I have now remaining in my granaries upwards of 1,800 bushels of corn.[69]

By 1799, New South Wales Corps officers owned 32 percent of the cattle in Australia, 40 percent of the goats, 59 percent of the horses, and 77 percent of the sheep. Grasping, haughty, jealous of their privileges and prerogatives, Macarthur and his friends were on top and meant to stay there; and the official governors who followed Grose and Paterson—Hunter, King, and Bligh—had the utmost difficulty controlling them. They were so powerful, in fact, that on January 26, 1808, the twentieth anniversary of white settlement, they staged a coup d'etat by rebelling against Governor Bligh, deposing him and running New South Wales as a military junta for two years. For this remarkable mutiny, none of the officers was hanged or even seriously punished.

Their junta mentality fostered two assumptions. The first was that none of them—especially not John Macarthur, who organized the rebellion from a prison cell where Bligh had put him—believed that naval governors were ever on their side. The second was that convicts were there to be used, not reformed. Both caused a rapid hardening of attitudes against convicts, the *lumpenproletariat* of New South Wales. The New South Wales Corps stiffly resisted any effort to criticize, or even inspect, its treatment of the convicts. The emblematic form of this attitude would show itself on Norfolk Island.

## vii

THE *ATLANTIC*, before taking Phillip away in 1792, had stopped at Norfolk Island on its outward voyage with supplies for its desperate colonists. Those crewmen and marines who went ashore were struck by how bad, under the hand of King, the place had become for its prisoners. When they got to Sydney they talked about it, and a marine named John Easty noted in his diary how "that Iland which was recond the most flourishing of any Iland in the World all most"

now turns out to be A Pore Mersable [miserable] Place and all manners of Cruelties an opresion uesed by the Governor floging and beeting the people to Death that its better for the pore unhappy Creatures to be hanged allmost then to come under the command of such Tyrants and the Govner

[King] behaves more like a mad man than a man in trus[t]ed with the
Goverment of an Iland . . . Belonging to Great Britain.[70]

King had gone back to England for a brief recuperative spell after the
wreck of the *Sirius* in March 1790, but he returned to Norfolk Island in
November 1791, newly married to his cousin, Anna Coombe. He had
been promoted to lieutenant-governor of the island and would be its
commandant for five years.

The Norfolk Island prisoners were now guarded by the Botany Bay
Rangers. The corps rank and file made no effort to keep their distance
from the convicts. They became "very intimate with the convicts, living
in their huts, eating, drinking and gambling with them, and perpetually
enticing the women to leave the men they were married to."[71] There
was friction. Emancipated convicts complained that the soldiers were
seducing their wives; and one of these convicts, Dring, the island's
coxswain, beat up a soldier who had repeatedly cuckolded him. King
fined the aggrieved husband twenty shillings, which, he hoped, "would
convince the soldier that he was not to be insulted with impunity." It
did no such thing; the soldiers felt Dring should have been flogged. During Christmas of 1793, four soldiers were seen heading with a torch for
Dring's farm, intent on burning his corn. When a civilian farmer tried to
stop them, one man jabbed the torch full in his face, "which bruised and
burnt him very much."

Even King could not tolerate this. He had the soldier arrested. That
evening, two other soldiers got bludgeons and went after Dring. He was
found half dead, covered with blood and cuts. His assailants were court-
martialled and one of them, Private Downey, was sentenced to receive
100 lashes and to give Dring a conciliatory present: a gallon of rum. At
this, to King's amazement, Dring and a few other Emancipists begged
him to forgive the soldiers: They were terrified of reprisals by the corps.
They got their wish, on the condition—as King strictly ordered—that
the Emancipists and the soldiers should all sit down and drink the gallon
of rum together.

Here one might expect the rancor to simmer down, but it did not.
Bored, bitter and pugnacious, the redcoats (which they were in name
only: King was to report that by night you could not tell from a man's
dress whether he was a soldier, a settler or a convict) kept stalking about,
picking fights, muttering darkly against King—whom they despised as a
naval officer, an outsider to the corps—and plotting mutiny. In January
1794, King learned from a convict informer that the soldiers had taken
an oath "not to suffer any of their comrades to be punished for an offence
against a convict any more"; they would rise, kill Dring, and put all the
prisoners to death.[72]

Quelling this, King realized, would be "a very delicate affair"; one did not lightly disarm, on mere suspicion, a whole detachment of soldiers who owed their allegiance to a governor, himself their commanding officer, only two weeks' sail away on the Australian mainland. Nevertheless, King managed to disarm and arrest the ten suspected mutineers. He hastily formed a civil militia, consisting of forty-four free settlers, all former seamen and marines (no Emancipist, of course, could be trusted with a gun). By a remarkable fluke, a colonial schooner—the first vessel they had seen in nine months—arrived at Norfolk Island two days later, with dispatches from Sydney. The mutineers were shipped to the mainland for trial.

After they reached Sydney Cove, Grose read King's long report on the incident and was apoplectic with rage. His old wounds, inflicted almost twenty years before by the musket-balls of the American militia, were hurting him badly in the unrelenting summer heat of 1793–94; and now he learned that his naval subordinate had actually armed a civilian militia on Norfolk Island. This was subversion. Grose picked up his pen. "No provocation that a soldier can give," he wrote to King, "is ever to be admitted as an excuse for the convicts striking a soldier." No soldier could be tried by a civil judge or magistrate, or even put in the custody of a civilian constable. Most important of all, these constables "are to understand that they are not on any pretence whatever to stop or seize a soldier, *although he should be detected in an unlawful act.*"[73]

This remarkable letter was a charter of immunity for the New South Wales Corps. For Grose, the word *convict* meant both felons under sentence and Emancipists. Since the number of free emigrants was negligible, "convict" in Grose's eyes included virtually every civilian in the colony. Thus, the civil establishment could no longer touch the military, but the soldiers could do as they pleased, subject only to the restraint of a court-martial conducted by their own officers. Fortunately, King stood his ground against his intemperate governor. He sent his own explanations to the secretary of state in London; they were accepted, and Grose had to withdraw and apologize.

But when King himself became governor, succeeding the aged Captain Hunter in 1800, he installed a tiger from the Rum Corps as commandant of Norfolk Island. He was Major Joseph Foveaux (1765–1846), in whose regime the military contempt for convicts would approach the level of mania.[74]

There is no record of who Joseph Foveaux's parents were, but his father is said to have been a French cook in the employ of the Earl of Upper Ossory at Ampthill Park, in Bedfordshire. His mother's name is not recorded. Someone evidently took the trouble (and spent the money) to give him an education and steer him into a regiment, and his rapid promotion within the New South Wales Corps—from captain in 1791 to major in 1796, a most unusual leap for a young man on minor routine duty in an insignificant outpost—suggests a powerful male patron in the background.

From his letters, one can glean little of Foveaux's tastes and interests except a passion for military correctness. But he seems to have had the mentality of many a later camp commandant; Norfolk Island liberated him, enabling his sadism, which had been restrained by the more public sphere of the mainland, to overflow far from courts and judges, thinly disguised as "necessary rigor."

Arriving there late in 1800, he found morale had sagged badly in the four years since King had left. The flax manufactory still survived, but it produced nothing exportable. Skilled labor was short, and most buildings were tumbledown. The grindstones were worn out, the saws rusted, and the master carpenter had been suspended for laziness and impertinence. The settlement swarmed with bastard children, some two hundred of them, rather more than a fifth of the total island population, all illiterate and wild. The schoolmaster was in jail for debt and the lone missionary seemed "very unfit for a minister." Clearly, there was much to do.[75]

Foveaux did not go into detail about his own methods. They survive in an account by his head jailer, a transported highwayman named Robert Jones (alias Robert Buckey, alias George Abrahams), who had got a conditional pardon in or around 1795 from Governor Hunter at King's instigation but had chosen to stay on Norfolk Island.[76]

"Major Foveaux," Jones remarked, "was one of them hard and determined men who believe in the lash more than the Bible." Foveaux was determined to leave solid stone buildings behind him: a jail, a barracks, staff houses. A day's convict work was breaking five cartloads of stone per man. When the picks and hammers broke, for they were of poor quality, their users were severely flogged. The hours were long and the food bad ("the Pork . . . was so soft that you could put your finger through it, and always rotten"). Prisoners turned out before dawn and, rain or shine, had to put their straw palliasses outside their cells; when it rained, the convicts returning from labor were

> turned into their Cells in their wet state with no means of drying their clothes, such were my orders from the Governor; and did any one of them make a complaint they were immediately sent to the triangles and ordered 25 lashes. Any further complaint was an additional 50.[77]

The fate of the refractory convict on Norfolk Island was one of prolonged and hideous torture:

The flogger was a County of Clare man a very powerful man and [he] took great pleasure in inflicting as much bodily punishment as possible, using such expressions as "Another half pound, mate, off the beggar's ribs." His face and clothes usually presented an appearance of a mincemeat chopper, being covered in flesh from the victim's body. Major Foveaux delighted in such an exhibition and would show his satisfaction by smiling as an encouragement to the flogger. He would sometimes order the victim to be brought before him with these words: *Hulloa* you damn'd scoundrel how do you like it? and order him to put on his coat and immediately go to his work.[78]

One prisoner named Joseph Mansbury had been flogged so often—some 2,000 lashes in three years—that his back appeared

quite bare of flesh, and his collarer [sic] bones were exposed looking very much like two Ivory Polished horns. It was with some difficulty that we could find another place to flog him. Tony [Chandler, the overseer] suggested to me that we had better [do it on] the soles of his feet next time.[79]

A sentence of 200 lashes was called a "feeler"; one did not forget it. All the medical treatment the convict received was a bucket of sea water on his back, an operation known as "getting salty back." "Many were relieved by death from this treatment," Jones wrote. "It would be impossible to detail the torture received . . . [from] the commandant, his servants and overseers. One of the favourite . . . punishments was to make the leg irons more small each month so that they would pinch the flesh." There was also a black isolation cell, and a water pit below the ground where prisoners would be locked, alone, naked, and unable to sleep for fear of drowning, for forty-eight hours at a spell.

There were only two ways out of "the old hell," as convict slang called the place. One was death; the other—as at Macquarie Harbor and Moreton Bay in decades to come—was by committing an offense that justified sending the convict to Sydney for trial. "Many murders," Jones wrote, "most of them were committed for the purpose of getting to Sydney, it being their only way of seeing heaven [convict slang for the mainland] again." Some men, including a convict named Thomas Carpenter whom Jones seems to have befriended, simply expired under the preliminary flogging:

His 250 killed him, died of heart-failure they said. God forgive them, and him too. For he was well liked on the Island. But feeling that he was ill, and thinking that his end was near, he struck his officer, with the hope that he would see his friends (in Sydney) once more, he did so but it was his last time. Considering the purpose for which these poor devils obtain justice their lot is all the worse for the manner in which they chose to obtain it.[80]

Foveaux's main obstacle on Norfolk Island was its deputy judge-advocate, a dim but decent ex-Etonian lawyer named Thomas Hibbins (1762–1816), who had got the post through the patronage of an old school friend, the Earl of Morton. Hibbins was neither ambitious nor gifted (if he had been, he would hardly have considered such a post), but he did have a certain compassion for the convicts. Since it was his task to interpret the civil and criminal law there—and to decide which cases should be tried in Sydney, there being no criminal court on Norfolk Island—he was often in conflict with Foveaux, who saw him as a felon-loving drunk.

For his part, Hibbins seems to have made no secret of his dislike of the commandant and his methods—methods that Foveaux himself delicately described as "vigorous if not exactly conformable to law." These had to do with Irish political prisoners, originally transported to Sydney for their part in the rebellion of 1798 and then, after appalling floggings of up to 1,000 lashes each for their supposed complicity in a rising that never took place at Parramatta in 1800, sent to Norfolk Island for life.

The Irish gave signs of mutiny almost as soon as they arrived. Most of the convicts already on Norfolk Island were Irish, too; and the insurgents from Sydney, with their tales of the '98, must have catalyzed them. On the morning of December 14, 1800, an Irish convict named Henry Grady (whose crime was rape, not sedition) appeared at Foveaux's quarters "apparently in much agitation." There would be a rising that night, he blurted; a hundred pikes were already made. Foveaux sent a soldier to look for the pikes, and he found them just where Grady said they were—long, fire-hardened sticks, not tipped with iron, but indubitably weapons of a sort. The ringleaders, Grady claimed, were two "politicals"; John Wolloghan, twenty-four years old, of Munster, and Peter McClean, forty, of Ulster. Wolloghan had been in charge of making the pikes, and Mc-Clean had recruited the rebels and given them their oath to kill the English officers and guards.

Foveaux put the two under close arrest and called in Thomas Hibbins, the judge-advocate. Hibbins opined that the men could not be tried for their lives by a panel of officers; and moreover, as there were no statute books on Norfolk Island, he did not know how an indictment could be framed against them. Enraged by this "pedantry," Foveaux convened his officers to discuss "the fatal consequences that were likely to ensue if such daring & wicked designs were not checked in their earliest appearance." There was no hesitation; the officers, as terrified of mutiny as

Foveaux, unanimously agreed to hang Wolloghan and McClean summarily and without trial. They strung them up that night, by the light of flambeaux. Grady, the informer, got a free pardon. "Encouragement to such people," Foveaux wrote to King, "is ever well bestowed."[81]

At a perfunctory inquiry some months later, Foveaux was exonerated; in fact, his dispatch in hanging the Irish drew praise, not only from King but from Lord Hobart, the secretary of state for the colonies, and in 1802 he was promoted to lieutenant-colonel. He summed up his own views on the matter in a note to Lord Portland:

> The nature of this Place is so widely different from any other part of the World, the prisoners sent here, are of the worse Character & in general only those who have committed some fresh crime since their transportation to Port Jackson, in short most of them are a disgrace to human Nature. . . . [a]fter considering these circumstances, the very little support I receive from the Judge-Advocate and the situation of this Island, your grace will (I am persuaded) perceive that different Examples however vigorous if not exactly conformable to Law are on occasions indispensably necessary.[82]

Hibbins's objections counted for nothing. If the Irish in Ireland needed martial law to keep them in order, why should their dregs in Australia be protected by civil statutes? The military must not be hampered with niceties. What it most feared was an alliance against this weak and remote English colony between United Irish prisoners and a French naval force. Thus, one finds Robert Jones, Foveaux's jailer, quoting a fragment of some official address by his commandant—"His Majesty King George has been pleased to grant to all his subjects complete protection, in out of the way places . . ." Then he scribbles, "What a mockery to issue such a piece of information to chained convicts. Protection when we were the greatest enemy—as my orders were to murder all the prisoners under my care should any foreign nation bear down upon us. Protection be dam'd."[83]

He was looking back to a moment in 1804, when a convoy of China traders escorted by a French warship, *L'Athenienne*, appeared off Norfolk Island. The garrison mistook them for an invasion fleet and prepared to do battle. Redcoats were sent scouring about for broken rum bottles, and the island's two corroded six-pounders were crammed "with these fragments of glass, which (the Commandant swore) would cut the French to pieces." Foveaux was not there. He had sailed for England two months before, leaving the island under the command of Captain John Piper. But he had also left standing orders about the Irish with his civilian staff, headed by Jones. Thus, when the ships were sighted, Jones and his chief constable Edward Kimberley herded some sixty-five Irish convicts into the settlement jail, barred the doors, closed the windows so that they could not signal to the French and then piled up masses of Norfolk Island pine brushwood around the walls on a hastily constructed scaffold, thus turning the whole building into a pyre for living men. "The soldiers," Jones wrote, "were to set fire to the prison upon the signal from me." If any of the "politicals" escaped being burned alive, they were to be shot. Captain Piper, who was supervising the cannon several miles away, knew nothing of these preparations for a mass burning of the Irish; and providentially, since the ships sailed on, the prisoners escaped the incineration Foveaux had prepared for them.

No record of Foveaux's sadism, or of the torments he and his men visited on women at Norfolk Island, found its way into the official reports, although it is hard to believe that Governor King had no inkling of what his lieutenant-governor was up to. Foveaux censored all letters. "No person," Jones noted, "was allowed to write any information about the place or the work done here, they were only to write in reference to the state of our good conduct and friends." Norfolk Island was a sealed universe and its reputation among the mainland convicts existed only by word of mouth; you could not officially threaten with what did not officially exist. In a society where the line between convictry and freedom was always being crossed—by emancipation or by reconviction—the stories of the convict subculture spread quickly through the lower class, but their rulers did nothing about them.

They felt no need to. Civil law was sketchy; England had not equipped its colony with a normal judicial framework and would not do so until after 1810. The general attitude was that one did not need full civil courts in a jail. Not one judge-advocate appointed by England in these early years was properly trained. The first, David Collins, was a marine officer with no prior experience of the law. The next in office, Richard Dore (1749–1800), was a blundering and cantankerous incompetent, much given to petty graft. His successor, Richard Atkins, was even worse: The drunken fifth son of a baronet, he had run through his legacy, bought and then sold a military commission and skipped from England in order to elude his creditors. Arriving in the colony in 1791, Atkins managed, by assiduous name-dropping and currying of favor with the officials (especially with Governor Hunter), to get himself appointed judge-advocate. His professional conduct was enough to disgust the next governor, Bligh, who called him "the ridicule of the community: sentences of death have been pronounced in moments of intoxication; his determination is weak, his opinion floating and infirm; his knowledge of the law is insignificant and subservient to private inclination." The measure of his detachment from the interests of the military may perhaps be gauged from the fact that the wife of this pathetic drunk ("She wears the breeches completely," noted the convict John Grant, who lived for a time in their household) raised two of the six bastard children whom Major George Johnston of the New South Wales Corps had sired on various women.[84]

Such men could not defy the junta. The corps, therefore, was virtually immune from civil law; and military law was exercised by its own officers to protect the interests of their own group. One sees why a Foveaux could flog and kill without restraint on Norfolk Island and yet have no word breathed against him by his brother officers. The question of the "rights" of convicts was barely worth raising in New South Wales between the departure of Arthur Phillip in 1792 and the arrival of Governor Lachlan Macquarie in 1810.

By then, the English colony in Australia had spread and solidified. It was no longer a tiny outpost, racked with hunger and scurvy, clinging to the edge of the continent. Sydney was a fortified town and the country behind it, the Cumberland Plain, was fast becoming a patchwork of cleared, productive fields, self-sufficient and worked with varying degrees of efficiency by convict slave labor. The hoped-for economic importance of Norfolk Island had not materialized. But it had been bound up with the idea that New South Wales was a naval outpost, and that was beginning to change. In the early 1800s, a few last efforts were made to utilize the pines and flax that had been the colony's naval raison d'être.[85]

Thus in 1802, the government tried the experiment of sending forth to Australia a few batches of convicts in Royal Navy vessels; and rather than waste space on the return voyage—for Navy ships, unlike the contracted ones that carried most of the convicts out, could not fill up with Oriental trade goods on the return run—the Admiralty sent with them drawings for major frame timbers of three classes of ships, to be cut and rough-shaped in New South Wales and brought back to England. The order was partly filled by King, but the practice lapsed. In 1805, King also had a small naval vessel, the *Buffalo*, rigged with a suit of sails woven from Norfolk Island flax by the women convicts in the Female Factory at Parramatta. She was the only ship to sail under such canvas. Up to 1810, sporadic efforts continued to be made to supply the Royal Navy with Australian timber.[86] But they were never more than a footnote to the main economic life of the colony, which was shifting decisively to agriculture—to the land and its owners, rather than the sea and its captains. So Norfolk Island, with its dark pinnacles and stands of now strategically useless pines, was allowed to fall into decay. By March 1810, its population had sunk to 117 people, and one of Lachlan Macquarie's first actions in assuming his governorship of New South Wales was to recall the mild officer who had succeeded Foveaux as commandant, Captain

Piper, and order the abandonment of the island. "The impolicy of the original settlement," the colonial secretary, Lord Liverpool, had told him, "has been fully demonstrated."[87]

In 1813, the breaking-up began. The frame huts were torn down and burnt (the nails frugally saved), the stone houses demolished, and every last animal except a few pigs that got away was slaughtered, skinned, butchered and packed down in casks of brine. There must be nothing left to catch the eye of a passing ship, no base from which another settlement could be made. They even left behind a dozen dogs to run wild and breed into a hunting pack to discourage visitors from landing. The last salvage from the settlement was loaded into the brig *Kangaroo* in February 1814, and when she sailed, the island was as empty as it had been before the arrival of Cook. It would stay so for a decade; the new abode of misery was Van Diemen's Land, far in the south.


## viii

THE ENGLISH invasion of Van Diemen's Land was by higher imperial standards a muddled and squalid affair. It produced no setpiece battles, no benevolent occupation, no heroes, profits or cultural loot. It merely opened another pit within the antipodean darkness, a small hole in the world about the size of Ireland, which would in due time swallow more than 65,000 men and women convicts—four out of every ten people transported to Australia. How many Tasmanian Aborigines died while the invading whites readied this cavity is not known, because no one knew how many there were to begin with. Probably not very many: The best guess at present is 3,000 to 4,000 people, hunting and gathering in small bands of 30 to 80—a population density roughly equal to that of the Aborigines of coastal New South Wales.[88]

But die they did—shot like kangaroos and poisoned like dogs, ravaged by European diseases and addictions, hunted by laymen and pestered by missionaries, "brought in" from their ancestral territories to languish in camps. It took less than seventy-five years of white settlement to wipe out most of the people who had occupied Tasmania for some thirty thousand years; it was the only true genocide in English colonial history. By the standards of Pol Pot, let alone Josef Stalin or Adolf Hitler, this was a small slaughter. But not to the Tasmanian Aborigines.

Between convict and black, much blood is mingled in the soil of this green, lovely, lugubrious island—so much, in fact, that parts of it seem to be emblematic spots, places where ordinary nature is permanently corrupted by the leaching of history, a salt that nothing can extract from the earth. Except that, in Tasmania, it is hard at first to sense the violence of the implanted culture. Its relics are so modest: an earnestly detailed stone bridge spanning the river at Ross, overseen by a convict mason who once worked for Beau Nash; the squat, authoritarian Doric columns of a Hobart government building. Yet when the first white invaders reached the shores of the Derwent River, the idea that they would last long was much in doubt.

Van Diemen's Land had been occupied to forestall the French who, to the alarm of New South Wales's tarpaulin Governor King,[89] had been nosing about in the ill-charted waters of southeastern Australia. Bass Strait, which separates Van Diemen's Land from the mainland, was discovered in 1797–98. Its weather was bad and its waters were strewn with islands whose vast colonies of wildlife would support the future seal trade of Australia, but which were a peril to ships—King Island to the west, the Furneaux group in the east, and a nasty prickle of rocks and reefs athwart the strait. But to go through the Bass Strait, avoiding the long southern route below Van Diemen's Land, clipped weeks off the passage from England to Sydney.

The strategic importance of this sea lane was obvious, and King strongly felt there had to be a settlement to secure it. In January 1802 Lieutenant John Murray, surveying the southern coast in the *Lady Nelson*, discovered a great bay on the mainland near the head of the strait, which in due course was named Port Phillip Bay: the harbor of modern Melbourne.

The following April, another coastal explorer, Matthew Flinders, was working eastward along the coast when he ran into two westbound French ships at an anchorage near the present site of Adelaide, which he named Encounter Bay. They were *Le Géographe* and *Le Naturaliste*, on a cartographic mission for the French Navy under Captain Nicolas Baudin. Baudin's expedition seems to have had no direct military purpose, despite the Napoleonic Wars. Like Flinders, he was trying to find out whether the western part of Australia was all of a piece with its eastern, British-occupied flank, New South Wales. He had spent more than a month mapping the southern coast of Van Diemen's Land and had bestowed a number of French names on his rough charts of Terre Napoléon, as he called the south coast of mainland Australia. Baudin and his exhausted, sick crew put into Sydney Harbor in June 1802; he stayed there for several months refitting, and he showed Governor King his survey charts.

King thought he smelled a rat. The mere presence of French ships in these waters was bad enough, but French names tacked on the British coast—albeit an unoccupied, unclaimed one—were worse. The idea of having to share this continent with "Boney," no matter how large it might be, was intolerable. And when Baudin sailed south again, King was sure he was going to start claiming territory and hoisting the *tricolore*.

King had already urged London to occupy Port Phillip as soon as possible. Now he sent an armed schooner to shadow Baudin. (It caught up with him at King Island in Bass Strait, where Baudin handed over some escaped convicts who had stowed away in his ship in Sydney.) Since Baudin had been snooping around the D'Entrecasteaux Channel, while intrepid American whalers from the far side of the Pacific had already penetrated the calving grounds of the black whales there and in Storm Bay at the mouth of the Derwent River—thus threatening to seize the fisheries that should have been a British monopoly—King decided to put a settlement on the Derwent.

In August 1803 a little party of forty-nine souls, made up of free settlers and Rum Corps men with twenty-one male and three female convicts, sailed from Port Jackson. Their leader was a twenty-three-year-old lieutenant from Devon, John Bowen (1780–1827), just arrived in the colony on the convict transport *Glatton*, whom King promoted to the rank of commander in the belief that it would impress foreign sea captains. Armed with minute instructions from King, Bowen sailed up the Derwent estuary and pitched his camp, complete with a pair of 12-pound carronades, at a spot on its eastern shore which he named Risdon. It had a stream of fresh water and a splendid view of the snowy brow of Mount Wellington, but little else to recommend it. Its soil was poor; it was whipped by gales blowing from the 4,000-foot mountain; and the stream itself went dry when the weather did—a familiar event in Australian colonization.

Meanwhile, King's pleas for a settlement at Port Phillip Bay, protecting Bass Strait from the questing French, had reached London. England's response was to send a ship to colonize the bay. She was HMS *Calcutta*, a vessel of the Royal Navy, bearing 308 convicts with a smattering of their wives and children (who were allowed to go out with their husbands as indentured servants), guarded by marines. The expedition was under the command of David Collins, the marine officer who, having served as the first judge-advocate of Phillip's settlement at Port Jackson, had returned to England and written one of the first and best books on the infant colony, his two-volume *Account of the English Colony in New South Wales*, 1798–1802. It earned him a public name as an expert on matters Australian, and on the strength of his eight years' service in Sydney the government asked him to go back as lieutenant-governor of the new colony at Port Phillip. Harassed by his debts—a situation aggravated by a bureaucratic hitch in his emoluments as a marine officer—Collins accepted. As soon as his appointment became known in London, he found himself pursued by Jeremy Bentham, who had just published *Panopticon Versus New South Wales*. This was a lengthy diatribe against the policy of transportation whose aim was to persuade Lord Pelham to build penitentiaries instead; the model Bentham put forth was his Panopticon, with its circular plan and central watchtower, affording continuous totalitarian inspection of the caged prisoners, which had become his obsessive project. Bentham even wrote to Collins urging him to build a Panopticon in New South Wales, and the two men dined together twice. "I have given him a copy of the Panopticon book," Bentham reported to his brother, adding that Collins had asked him for "a Draught [sketch] of the Panopticon Plan. . . . I said, I hoped I might—with the book and a little *nous*, he might be able to do without the draught; [but] the *nous*, I fear, is lacking." Despite Bentham's unjustifiably low view of Collins's intelligence, he kept lobbying: "Are you serious in your intention of building a prison, and moreover of building it on the central inspection principle?" Just before sailing, Collins brushed him politely off. "I have been lately so occupied . . . as to prevent my waiting on you to receive the Hints for my pursuing the *Panopticon System*, which you were so good as to prepare for me. Be assured that my Prison shall if possible be a circular one." Of course, no Panopticon would rise by the shores of Port Phillip Bay. The *Calcutta*, escorted by the transport *Ocean*, sailed in April 1803.[90]

The fleet reached Port Phillip in October. The bay proved a miserable disappointment, as bad (or almost) as Botany Bay had seemed to the men of the First Fleet fifteen years before: sandy sterile ground, little water, a persistent hot northerly wind, swarms of biting flies, and great difficulties of access by sea because of the adverse tidal currents. After six months at sea, all hands were yearning for dry land again, but their enthusiasm soon waned. In "Canvas Town," their encampment on the sand dunes, the shade temperature in Collins's tent was 102°, and in the sun it reached 132°. It seemed a "barbarous country," the surveyor George Prideaux Harris wrote to his brother after three months there: nothing but sand, with no water and so few animals that, for meat, he had once been reduced to eating a swan's carcass fit only for a dunghill. The one recompense was the lobsters, so plentiful that the convicts could catch five hundred in an evening. "Never, surely, was a more barren land," wrote one prisoner, the counterfeiter James Grove, to his friends in faraway England. "I thought it unlikely to answer to any good purpose."[91]

Everyone else thought so, too. After a couple of weeks camped on the sand hills, the marines were muttering and grumbling their way toward mutiny, and to set an example Collins had a couple of insubordinate privates savagely flogged, one with 700 lashes. Some convicts tried to escape. A former army officer named Lee, transported for forgery, who seemed "quite a pedant, eternally quoting passages from the Greek and Latin authors," wrote some scurrilous lampoons on Collins which circulated among the tents; he was found out and bolted into the bush, never to be seen again, taking the lieutenant-governor's fowling piece with him. Groups of four or five men would vanish into the dunes, heading (as they thought) for China.* [92]

So there was general relief when dispatches arrived from Governor King in Sydney authorizing Collins to abandon Port Phillip and move his settlement down to the Derwent, to join Bowen's tiny band. But King also instructed Collins to take a look at Port Dalrymple, at the mouth of the Tamar River on the northern coast of Van Diemen's Land (the site of modern Launceston) and see if an outpost could be put there to guard the fisheries of Bass Strait from American whalers and sealers. Collins reported that it could not, or not yet, as the river entrance was difficult, and the local blacks seemed very aggressive. [93]

In any case, the strength of his party was low. So many men were sick that he could not mount enough sentinels; if one more officer went ill, he would not even find the quorum for a court martial. So the prudent course was to join forces with Bowen on the Derwent. A settlement, Collins felt, would be better on the Derwent than on the Tamar: "Its position at the Southern Extremity of Van Dieman's Land gives it an Advantage over every Harbour yet discovered in the Straits . . . [A]s a Port of Shelter to Ships from Europe, America or India, either for Whaling or other speculation, it will be greatly resorted to." [94]

So Port Phillip was abandoned. When the settlers reached the Derwent, Collins relieved Bowen of his command and moved the settlement from Risdon to the western shore of the estuary. In a sketch from about 1805, one sees the embryo town of Hobart, named after the secretary of state for the colonies who was the patron of Collins's expedition. It is a little straggle of tents and huts, with Government House—hardly more than a cottage—on Battery Point, and the huts of the surveyor-general, the surgeon and the chaplain ranged alongside it; casks are stacked up on the dock island, and an ensign flutters from its mast in front of the public store, while the whole scene is dominated by the brooding wall of Mount Wellington, capped with snow. In 1805 it must have looked very frail and ephemeral. But in the green valley folds that ran down to the water, in the copses and meadows that (seen through half-closed eyes) reminded young Bowen of a nobleman's park, there was at least some reminiscence of the England that most of the colonists would never see again. Nostalgia could cling to this Tasmanian landscape.

* For the peculiar phenomenon of the "China Travellers," see chapter 7.

Yet life by the Derwent was hard for all the colonists at first, bond or free. The isolation, torpor and semi-starvation of early Sydney repeated themselves in Van Diemen's Land. "With no ships visiting us," recalled Collins's second-in-command, Lieutenant Edward Lord,

> the whole settlement was called upon to endure hardships of no ordinary kind. The Governor himself, the officers, and the entire settlement for eighteen months, were without bread, vegetables, tea, sugar, wine, spirits, or beer, or any substitute, except the precarious supply of the wild game of the country.[95]

Memories of this starvation time died hard. Thirty years later a Hobart woman recounted what she had known as a child in the first settlement: coming off the ship and sleeping under a wet blanket, then in the hollow trunk of a tree; being "treated kindly" by curious, not yet persecuted Aborigines, in whose care white infants were sometimes left by their parents; living on "Botany Bay Greens" (boiled seaweed scraped off the rocks), and even wolfing down the "crap" (cindery residue) of whale blubber, shovelled overboard from the roaring try-pots of American whalers in Storm Bay and washed up on the beaches. The same oily gobbets were used to feed the colony's precious pigs, contaminating the taste of their flesh.[96]

By the winter of 1805 the convicts were down to a ration of 2 pounds 10 ounces of salt pork and 4 pounds of bread a week, a ration that in normal times would scarcely last two days. By 1806 the colony was starving to death. Collins had hoped that supplies would come from Sydney. But in March 1806 the farms along the Hawkesbury River, on which the food supply of Sydney depended, were devastated by flood. The water covered 36,000 acres and destroyed all the standing crops, along with the farmers' tools, livestock and seed reserves. What remained was not enough for Sydney and Parramatta; and for Hobart, there was nothing. Two years later things had improved a little in Hobart—but not much. "Bring with you as much Flour and Wheat as possible," wrote an early political transportee to Van Diemen's Land, the Irish schoolmaster William Maum, to a friend who was about to move to Hobart Town in 1808,

> and a sufficiency of corn for whatever Stock you may bring down, bring down about 12 good young Ewes, four or five Sows in pig (if possible) as there are no Boars here—as much poultry as you can get off . . . bring with you Hoes and all other Tools as they are here remarkably scarce. . . . [t]he houses in general are of Lath & plaister and immoderately dear . . . [t]he Gov[r] here has it not in his power to fulfil the intentions of Gov[t], as he has

neither Tradesmen nor Labourers, and nothing in the Stores. . . . Fowls here are of the utmost consequence, their Value being beyond Money.[97]

There was very little of the fellow-feeling that makes privation bearable. Shortages on this Georgian frontier bred stony, grasping men, who robbed one another like jackals snarling over a carcass and cheated the government blind whenever they could. The clerks who ran the government stores were so deep in collusion with the farmers who sold them their produce that a newly appointed chief clerk of the Hobart commissariat declared, in 1816, that not one document or account could be found in its records.[98]

Between the vulpine rapacity of the settlers and the short commons of government, the Derwent colony—along with the smaller one set up in October 1804 at Port Dalrymple on the Tamar, under Lieutenant-Colonel Paterson, to fix an English foothold on Bass Strait—might well have perished. What saved them both was that inoffensive marsupial, the kangaroo.

Kangaroos were plentiful in the bush of Van Diemen's Land—much more so than they had ever been around Sydney. Every able-bodied man who could use a gun went hunting them, for kangaroo flesh, not bread, was the staff of life. Collins tried to keep the market under strict control. Hunters were obliged to sell the meat to the commissariat store. To convicts and others "on the store," it was issued free; the usual ration was 8 pounds a week. To settlers living "on their own hands," its price fluctuated between 6d. and 1s. 6d. a pound. In one six-month period the settlers ate 15,000 pounds of dressed meat from haunches and tails, representing a slaughter of perhaps a thousand 'roos.[99]

This reliance on hunting brought prompt social results, all of them bad. It installed the gun, rather than the plough, as the totem of survival in Van Diemen's Land. It favored a mood of opportunism, of social improvidence. Small settlers tended to neglect the long-range pursuits of farming and instead concentrated on killing whatever they could. Before long, the kangaroos around Hobart were hunted out, and men and dogs had to push further into the bush, competing against the Aborigines for game. Thus, the pattern of ambush and murder between white and black began; it would end, in a few decades, with the near-extermination of the Tasmanian Aborigines. Hunger had put guns in the hands of convicts— and this had never been allowed to happen in New South Wales. It soon created a fringe class of armed, uncontrollable bushmen, most of whom regarded Aborigines as vermin. They would go out for days at a stretch with their "mates" and their kangaroo-dogs (half-wild mongrel lurchers, with jaws like mantraps) and bring back whatever they could corner and kill. Very soon these mountain men of Van Diemen's Land shed whatever vestiges of obedience they might have felt to the System. They became the first bushrangers (see chapter 7). They kept the guns, stole their masters' dogs and stayed in the bush. Earlier absconders from Sydney and Parramatta had died because they were not armed, but not these kangarooers. When Hobart and Port Dalrymple were tiny and the outlying farms few, they could be controlled to some degree, if only because they had to sell most of their kangaroo meat directly to the government before getting more ammunition. But as settlement pushed outward, farmer and assigned servants started buying the meat and skins directly from the outlaws. And since few settlers had any scruples about cheating their neighbors as long as they were not seen at it, they also "received" the mutton the kangarooers stole from other sheep runs and kept on the good side of the hunters by giving them ammunition, tea and rum. As the stock of sheep and cattle in the colony grew, so the demand for kangaroo meat dropped. But everyone needed kangaroo skins, for shoes, hats, bags, jackets and pants; and in between killing 'roos, the hunters moved to sheep stealing. They could do this with impunity, unless a settler caught them in the act and shot them. The redcoats could not catch them; they did not know the bush.

So in theory, the founding years of Van Diemen's Land displayed a rigidly patterned Georgian fabric of rank and power which, in practice, did not survive inspection. It was a façade. The official barriers between military and civilian, bond and free were breached in a score of ways by hunger, shortages, the rub of proximity, the ferocity of the good and the occasional decency of the criminal. "They call it the end of the world— and for vice it is truly so, for here wickedness flourishes unchecked."[100] So did boredom, a great equalizer. Technique of any kind was rare, technology feeble, and "cultivation" in any but the most rudimentary sense scarcely existed at all. When he wanted some conversation to take his mind off the miseries of his post, Lieutenant-Governor Collins, "a literary and excellent man," had to turn to the forger James Grove and his family, "passing with him under his roof many no doubt intellectual hours."[101] In return, Grove designed Collins a house; and when the lieutenant-governor died in 1810 of a heart attack at the early age of 54, worn out by the strain of keeping his precarious little colony alive, it was Grove, "his eyes suffused with tears the whole time," who cut and planed the yellow Huon pine boards for his double coffin, helped place the corpse in it, engraved the silver memorial plate and screwed down the lid. Five weeks later, heartbroken at the loss of the friend and patron who had returned him to respectability on this far edge of the world, Grove himself died. "As sensible, ingenious a man as I ever met with, & highly esteemed and respected by the Gov' & every officer in the settlement, for his uniform and excellent character"—such had been the judgment of the surveyor Harris on this convict.[102] He was buried near Collins. The friendship of these men was perhaps emblematic, suggesting at its most benevolent, and thus uncommon, level the interdependence between prisoners and masters. Wherever new settlements were made, whatever fields were broken, English settlement in Australia rested on its convicts. As Mary Gilmore would write in 1918 of the prisoners who built Australia:

> I was the convict
>     Sent to hell,
> To make in the desert
>     The living well:
>
> I split the rock;
>     I felled the tree—
> The nation was
>     Because of me.[103]

We must now look more closely at these reluctant pioneers.

# 5

# The Voyage

i

"IT IS THEREFORE ordered and adjudged by this Court, that you be transported upon the seas, beyond the seas, to such place as His Majesty, by the advice of His Privy Council, shall think fit to direct and appoint, for the term of your natural life." Or seven years, or fourteen —in any case, the shock of sentencing was dreadful. In law, seven years' banishment meant what it said; but what man could be certain of returning to England at the end of it? For many people, the sentence of transportation—whatever its announced length—must have seemed like a one-way trip over the edge of the world.

A man could bear it with dignity in the dock, but despair followed soon after. Anguish shows in the few surviving letters, like this one from a Lancashire weaver named Thomas Holden, who in the course of struggling for his rights as an early trade-unionist was convicted in 1812 of "administering an illegal oath" to one Isaac Crompton in Bolton, Lancashire. It seems probable that Holden was a Luddite. He was also happily married. "Dear Wife," he wrote from a cell in Lancaster Castle,

> Its with sorrow that I have to acquaint you that I this day receiv'd my Tryal and has receiv'd the hard sentance of Seven Years Transportation beyond the seas. . . . If I was for any Time in prison I would try and content myself but to be sent from my Native Country perhaps never to see it again distresses me beyond comprehension and will Terminate with my life. . . . [T]o part with my dear Wife & Child, Parents and Friends, to be no more, cut off in the Bloom of my Youth without doing the least wrong to any person on earth—O my hard fate, may God have mercy on me. . . . Your affec. Husband until Death.[1]

In April 1831 Peter Withers, the "Swing" protestor from Wiltshire, wrote from the convict ship *Proteus* at Spithead to his wife Mary Ann:

My Dear Wife belive me my Hark is almost broken to think I must lave you behind. O my dear what shall I do i am all Most destracted at the thoughts of parting from you whom I do love so dear. Believe me My Dear it Cuts me even to the hart and my dear Wife there is a ship Come into Portsmouth harber to take us to New Southweals.

Inconceivable distances loom before Withers, who has never even been as far from home as London; and he tries to explain them, to normalize them by promising a fidelity that will annihilate separation:

it is about 4 months sail to that country But we shall stop at several cuntreys before we gets there for fresh water I expects you will eare from me in the course of 9 months. . . . you may depend upon My keeping Myselfe from all other Woman for i shall Never Let No other run into my mind for tis onely you My Dear that can Ease me of my Desire. It is not Laving Auld england that grives me it is laving my dear and loving Wife and Children, May God be Mersyful to me.[2]

In December 1831 Richard Dillingham, a convict in the hulks at Woolwich, awaiting transportation, writes less tragically to the girl who had borne him a son out of wedlock, "my ever adorable Betsey Faine." He casts it in the form of the sweet doggerel rhymes one could buy inscribed on favors at a market fair:

Dearest Betsey the first of human kind the thoughts of you will ever ease my mind for though we at a distance are I hope that God will be your leading star—

> The first is B a letter bright
> Which plenty doth afear,
> The next is F in all women slight,
> The surname of my dearest dear. Adieu.[3]

Tossing on his iron cot in the lockup, a convict would obsessively recall his life and its mistakes. So John Ward, sentenced to 10 years' transportation in 1841 for theft:

A miserable object in truth, all my feelings and passions now rushed upon me at once. Remorse for an instant filled my breast with abandoned thoughts of plunging deeper into the depravity of heart, to which I had fallen a victim. . . . The many enemies there was to contend with all stood in dark array before my burning imagination.

Ward thinks, with bitter irony, of some lines of affectionate rhyme he once sent to his sweetheart:

Had I possessed candour enough to marry the girl, I sincerely believe I should have been one of the happiest of men!—but!—It occurred to my memory the words I wrote to Rose! some years before this, on a particular occasion—

> Far beyond the seas
> Unpittied I'll remove,
> And rather cease to live
> E'er I will cease to love!

But I did not, at that time, ever dream of putting these words into practice, much less of being sent as a poor convict.[4]

Many prisoners hoped their wives would go into Australian exile with them, although few actually did; it was hard to get passage out there, and tickets were far beyond the means of a worker's wife. "I hope you will strain your utmost to keep my Company," Thomas Holden wrote to his wife Molly as he was leaving for the hulks, "and not let mee go without you for with your company I don't mind where I go nor what I suffer, if I have your Company to chear my allmost Broken Hart." And later, from the hulk: "My sorrow is greatly Encreased by parting with you, what Comfort can I enjoy when we are separate. . . . I could wish to know if you think you Could rise money to pay your passage & go with me."[5] She did not go. Neither did Mary Ann, Peter Withers's wife, despite his heart-wringing pleas:

> We [h]ears we shall get our freedom in that Country, but if I gets my freedom evenso i am shure I shall Never be happy except I can have the Pleshur of ending my days with you and my dear Children, for I dont think a man ever loved a woman so well as I love you.
>
> My Dear I hope you will go to the gentlemen for they to pay your Passage over to me when I send for you. How happy I shall be to eare that you are a-coming after me. . . . Do you think I shall sent for you except i can get a Cumfortable place for you, do you think that I wants to get you into Troble, do you think as I want to punish my dear Children? No my dear but if I can get a cumfortsable place should you not like to follow your dear Husband who Lovs you so dear?[6]

There was no reply, and two years later Withers was writing to his brothers from Van Diemen's Land: "I have sent 2 letters to My Wife an Cant get heny Answer from her Wich Causeth Me a great deal of unhapyness for i think she have quite forgotten me an I think she is got Marred to some other Man, if she is pray send me Word." But there was still no word from her, and eleven years would pass before Mary Ann wrote in distress to her husband in Van Diemen's Land, asking to be reconciled.

She received the news that Peter had married again (there was no question of divorce for the lower classes; one simply relied on the inaccessibility of records and married bigamously) to a "staidy vertus Woman":

> I have no Property of my own but my Wife have Property wich she will have in the course of two years and then we have agreed to help you an the Children if God spares our lives.
>
> I know that for to eare that I am married is a hard trial for you to bear, but it is no good to tell you a Lye.
>
> I sent a great maney Leters before I took a Wife; so not earing from you, I being a young man, I thought it would be Proper thing to look [for] a partner which would be a Comfort to me in my Bondage. I sent for you to Come out to this country when I came first and if you had you would have got me out of Bondag for nothing, for a wife could get a release for her husband. So we must not think about Coming together again.[7]

Poor repentant Mary kept trying. The last news of her is a curt form letter from the colonial secretary's office in Whitehall dated August 1847, telling her that he "was living on the 30 Septr. 1846" but that "no further information can be given respecting him." There must have been many variations on this small colonial drama.

The Privy Council records contain hundreds of letters from wives asking to go into Australian exile with their husbands. Generally the authorities would not allow this, unless the convict had earned his ticket-of-leave and shown that he could support a family in Australia.* Permission was only rarely given for a wife to accompany her man on the transport vessel. An intense pathos rises from some of these letters, written in the neat hand of a local curate or the labored scrawl of the petitioner herself. From Rochester in Kent, Deborah Taylor, whose husband James has been transported for life for stealing a lamb, encloses, for Peel's perusal, a document infinitely precious to her: his letter exhorting her to join him in Australia. She beseeches Peel "most humbly and fervently"

> that I may be sent out with my Remaining Children a boy 10 years of age and a girl 6 years, having buried two since my Application. My husband it will be seen by the enclosed letter is very anxious to be sent out. . . . I humbly hope that I may be favored with the return of my poor husband's letter should I not be successful, pray God I may find favor.[8]

It seems she did get the letter back (at least it is not in the file) but her application was denied. "Usual answer," Peel's secretary minuted on the back of her petition, as on so many others.

* The ticket-of-leave system is discussed on pages 307–308.

The determination of some of these women was heroic; they yearned for their men and they would not accept the common fate of abandonment. Jane Eastwood, the thirty-year-old wife of a transported Manchester bootmaker, told Peel in April 1830 that her husband "has written several letters to me from Sidney Island [sic] requesting me to apply to Government in order to be sent out there to him. . . . I am determined to go out to my Husband even at the risk of my life." She implored the home secretary to "Put it in my power of becoming happy, by uniting me again to the Best of Husbands":

> Prevent me from the shame of casting myself & Child upon the Parish for Relief . . . as work is not only scarce but so ill paid for that it is utterly out of my Power to gain a living for myself & Child, and I have no other thing to depend upon except what I can earn by my needle in dress and stay making.[9]

She cannot wait for more letters, across the vast antipodean time lag; she will pay her own fare with whatever she has. "I know not how to get over the time until word come back from him, about 9 months at least. I would rather sell my household furniture which will amount to about six or eight Pounds, this sum I will most willingly give to Government to lessen their expenses of sending me out to Sidney, provided they would be graciously pleased to send me by the first Ship." She knows her skills, joined to his, will keep them without government support once she is there. "I myself have been thoroughly bred to the Dressmaking business, and have wrought for years at the Umbrella Business, I can also bind Shoes & boots and can render him every assistance. . . . [T]here can scarcely remain a doubt that we would at all become a burden upon this Colony but rather a gain to them."[10] This time the government listened, and to Australia she went.

Local clergy, with their charitable concerns, would endorse such petitions. Thus in 1819 Charles Isherwood, the curate of Brotherton, collected signatures from ten colleagues on behalf of Elizabeth Rhodes, asking that she and her two small children "may be permitted to accompany her unfortunate husband to his place of Exile." Sometimes whole groups, or part of an entire community, would intervene. "A man by the name of Mitchel has lately had the sentence of 21 yrs. transportation passed on him," wrote a Stirling magistrate, Robert Downie, to Peel's office. "The Stirling people are most anxious that he should be allowed to carry his wife and 3 children with him. Does Government ever allow of such shipments?" Parishioners would write, promising to raise a local subscription for a wife to join her husband; they offered clothes, food and bedding for her passage.[11]

Husbands and lovers were also sons, and in an age when family ties across the generations were the very mortar of society the misery felt by the parents of a transported man—and the shame he felt for them—could be unbearable. Convicts' letters to their parents were filled with promises of self-amendment. "I can assure you that since I have been here i have had plenty of leisure time to reflect on my past misconduct," a weaver named Richard Boothman writes to his father in Lancashire, "and I can assure you most sincerely that if it pleases God to bestow my Liberty upon me once more, that my life will be one series of amendment, and I trust that i shall yet be able to close your eyes in peace and comfort and render the downhill part of your life happy."[12] From his "unhappy situation" in York Castle, awaiting transfer to the hulks, Richard Taylor tells his father, "i wish i had taken your Advice. . . . I listen to my fellow Prisoners till my heart goes as Cold as Clay." But no letter comes from his father, and Taylor, fearing that he has been spurned and forgotten, writes in agitation to his "Dear unkles":

> You must let him now I ham very well and he must think as little about
> me as he can for i ham quite innesent and I hope god will be mersful to
> me an I shall see you all agane but if not I must live for a beter world. For
> my part I [am] determined to lead a godley life.[13]

He invokes the future, trying to shore up the spirits of his parents. He writes from York in May 1840—this time with better spelling, through the medium of a scribe—that "the prayers of a sincere heart are as acceptable to God from the dreary Prison as from the splendid Palace. What a blessing that assurance is to a poor unfortunate mortal in my hapless condition." He promises reunion:

> When I have lived out my ten years in a far distant land how happy I shall
> be to return to my native home, and with how much more delight will I
> return home if God shall spare my dear Father until that time, that we
> may once more meet in the flesh, and convene together about heavenly
> things—why, my dear Parent, if he spare us both to enjoy that Happiness,
> it will be like a foretaste of Heaven itself.[14]

Such utterances were sincere but they hardly masked the deeper fear that transportation would sunder the family forever. Richard Boothman beseeches his father "not to forget me to my brother-in-law" and other relatives, "and tell them that I should like to see them before my leaving here, *as it may be for the last time.*" On leaving for the hulks in June 1841, he complains of being cast off by his kin: "I think it rather strange that you have not attended to my request but I certainly should have been glad to see some of my Friends before I left here, but alas now it is too late." For every brave assertion that the writer will come back ("Dear Father I hope that you will not fret and Greeve And make yourself uncomfortable . . . I hope in a short time I shall see you again"), there are many expressions of despair. "My spiritts is low with thinking how I am sent from my Natiff Contrey, and I am inisent," Thomas Holden writes in June 1812. "Dear mother I do not think of seeing you in this world any more." [15]

That transportation inflicted social and filial death was a common theme of ballads and it occasionally percolated upward into literature: One finds George Crabbe, for instance, alluding to it in "The Borough" by evoking a pathetic still life meant as a *vanitas:*

> On swinging shelf are things incongruous stored,—
> Scraps of their food, the cards and cribbage-board,—
> With pipes and pouches, while on peg below
> Hang a lost member's fiddle and his bow;
> That still remind them how he'd dance and play
> Ere cast untimely to the Convicts' Bay. [16]

Some convicts clung to the hope of a last-minute pardon, usually in vain. The prerogative of the Royal Mercy was often extended to those sentenced to hang, especially if their crimes were political (more especially still, if they were committed after the death of Castlereagh in 1822 and seemed to represent a wave of popular opinion). Thus in 1831, at the height of agitation for reform, Peter Withers and his fellow protestor James Lush were snatched from the gallows on the very eve of their execution by a mass petition addressed to the king through the Home Office. However, once the machinery of transportation had begun to turn, one could not jump free. Yet English life was so enlaced with patronage, with lines of favor and gratitude running throughout the strata of the social pyramid from navvy to duke, that prisoners and their families would seize any chance of mitigation after sentencing. In 1798 a gentleman named C. M. Waller writes to his acquaintance in Sydney, the Irish dynast and assistant surgeon for the colony, D'Arcy Wentworth. He intercedes for an "Unfortunate young Man, who has been cast for Transportation, for the trifling sum of Half a Crown":

His situation is so much more to be pittied as he not only bore a universal good Character [but] was the whole supporter of a Sickely old Father & a Aged Mother, who is now standing Wheeping before me, & laments the loss of a Son. . . . [T]he only favour she begs of you, Sir, is, that you will be so obliging as to render him any service which is in your power, that his Situation may be more comfortable.[17]

Thomas Holden, on the eve of his sailing in 1812, was still imploring his wife "to go to Mr Fletcher & Mr Watkin [and] tell them that I still Protest my inosentse"; while at sea, despite the "great deal of truble and difficklty to get to Right a letter," he hopes "you will keep sending up Pertisions to Government to get me off or to get my Sentence mitigated." In 1841 Richard Boothman wrote that "if a little trouble was taken by my friends . . . it might be of very great service to me. . . . [I]f ever I needed help I do now."[18] The convict and his family had to find as many character references among the respectable—landowners, local magistrates, merchants, clergy—as they could raise. Through a scribe with an educated hand, a woman wrote to the home secretary's office from Salisbury in 1819:

> I beg to inform you that Silas Harris, a transport on board the *Laurel* at Portsmouth, is my Husband & has left 6 children to lament his Loss, who are at present in the greatest distress, a Gentleman has promised me he would lay my case, together with my helpless Family, before Lord Sidmouth praying me to interfere for his Releasement, Should you think that his Character annex'd would be of Service I should feel myself Thankful.[19]

It was by no means unusual for the victim of the crime to petition on the prisoner's behalf, once he or she had realized the terrible fate that lay in store for the convict in Australia and his abandoned family in England. Many Englishmen and Englishwomen were disturbed by the disproportion between crime and punishment and did not want to carry on their consciences the stigma of destroying a whole family over some relatively trivial possession, especially when it had been stolen in time of general need. William Tidman, a farmer at St. Albans, had lost some sacks of wheat to an agricultural laborer named Thomas Tate, "now lying at Wolledge [Woolwich] under sentence of Transportation for seven years." He asked Viscount Sidmouth to remit Tate's sentence on behalf of his wife and four small children, "as I freely forgive him myself." In the same vein, Mrs. Lycot, wife of "a gentleman of considerable landed property," wrote in May 1819 to the local magistrate in Minchin Hampton, Sir George Paul, begging clemency for Thomas Barker, an itinerant vendor of rabbit skins who had been sentenced to transportation for buying some silverware that a servant had stolen from her house. She asked for the sentence to be withdrawn, "in consequence of [Barker's] age which is 57, and the improbability that he and his wife would ever meet again, which being in poor circumstances would render her situation one of great distress." In forwarding her letter to Lord Sidmouth, the magistrate noted that "the man is already in the Hulk, it will not do to send him back to *our* Penitentiary, in which there are already *three* prisoners confined where there should be *one.*" Revealingly, he added: "These are times when the current of public opinion seems to disarm the law of *all* its terrors!" And so Barker left for the Fatal Shore, leaving his wife to fend for herself.[20]

Occasionally a husband and wife would be convicted together and find themselves both sentenced to transportation. The fear of being exiled to different parts of the world would produce its own petitions. From Carlton Jail in Edinburgh, in 1830, Helen Guild begged not to be separated from her husband of six years, "to crave your sanction that he and I may be sent abroad to some place as near each other as we may with propriety be sent. Altho' it has been our lot to meet with this visitation from both the laws of God & man . . . your sanction would be receiv'd with more sincere pleasure than even my liberation."[21]

The hope of remission through influence, then, was a constant theme. So was the terror of losing touch. Men on the edge of transportation, about to slip off the social map into the void of the antipodes, were apt to construe every postal delay as a sign of rejection, like poor Thomas Holden writing to his mother:

> Nothing in this life gives me such uneasiness as not hearing from you. . . . I have not received a letter but one and that was from my wife since i receiv'd my Tryal, surely you have not forgot me so soon, let me know if there is any hopes of my time being shortened. . . . I will expect to see you if not it will break my Heart that I may take my last farewell of you as I never shall think of seeing you after I leave.[22]

But whether the letters and visitors came or not, the day of transfer to the hulks or the transport inevitably did. Holden was carted from Lancaster Castle, via London, to board the hulk *Portland* in Langston Harbor, where he would work a daily ten-hour shift in the shipyards while awaiting his final departure five months later. The journey, he reported, "has been very wett and uncomfortable and I have been eight days and nights without having my cloaths off my back, so dear wife I will leave you to judge what state I am in at present." Most transportees were neglected and many brutalized on this stage of their journey. The parliamentarian Henry Bennett, in an indignant booklet addressed to the home secretary in 1819, wrote of convicts on the road to the hulks: "Among them were several children all heavily fettered, ragged and sickly. . . . The women too are brought up ironed together on the tops of coaches." Hundreds of

them went down from London "in an open caravan, exposed to the incle-
mency of the weather, to the gaze of the idle and the taunts and mock-
eries of the cruel, thus exciting . . . the shame and indignation of all those
who feel what punishment ought to be." John Ward, in 1841, went down
to the Portsmouth hulks from Northampton Jail in a coach, leg-shackled
to six other prisoners, treating them to gin and ale whenever the Black
Maria stopped at a coaching-inn to change horses, "which seemed to
shorten the night's fatigue, and lessen our uneasiness." But though he
was well-clothed, his fellow prisoners "had scarcely clothing . . . to cover
their nakedness, and could only raise 18 pence amongst them."[23]

ii

THE SIGHT OF the hulks at Portsmouth, Deptford or Woolwich was
deservedly famous. They lay anchored in files on the gray heaving water,
bow to stern, a rookery of sea-isolated crime. As the longboat bearing its
prisoners drew near, the bulbous oak walls of these pensioned-off warships rose sheer out of the sea, patched and queered with excrescences,
deckhouses, platforms, lean-tos sticking at all angles from the original
hull. They had the look of slum tenements, with lines of bedding strung
out to air between the stumps of the masts, and the gunports barred with
iron lattices. They wallowed to the slap of the waves, and dark fleeces of
weed streamed in the current from the rotting waterlines. Some were
French warships captured in battle, but most were obsolete first-raters
that had once borne a hundred guns for England; now all that remained
of their pride was a battered figurehead and the rusty chains, each link
half the size of a man, that held them to their last anchorage. They
were like floating Piranesi ruins, cramped and wet inside, dark and vile-
smelling.

The reception never changed. The new convicts were mustered on
the quarterdeck and ordered to give their money to the captain for safe-
keeping. The old hulk hands would descend on the new like locusts:

> When a party of men comes down . . . it is the hay-day for those who have
> grown old in the service . . . [The novice is] asked by those around you "if
> —if—if" twenty things at once, and at the same time "copping" (stealing)
> as it is called every little article, such as combs, knives, braces or thread
> and needles &c, you have been allowed by the Captain to keep, out of the
> few things you have had the luck to bring on board with you.[24]

Mansfield Silverthorpe, an impecunious young actor who, having trod
the boards in the 1830s as Iago, Edgar, the Ghost in *Hamlet*, Eugene

Aram, and Bernard in *Guy Mannering,* stole a trunk from a Scottish officer and was sentenced to transportation, went in irons down the river to Woolwich on a public steamer, still in his frilly shirt and long tumbling locks. He found that, on the *Ganymede* hulk,

> I was soon metamorphosed into a very different looking Animal, my long hair underwent the operation of clipping by the *Barbarous Barber,* I was then soaked in a cold bath & afterwards was arrayed in the Uniform of the Hulks. When the Quartermaster took our clothes from us I observed he thrust a knife through each article, and they are then considered to be the property of the Queen; however, when he came to Mine (which were of the best quality) he omitted this act, and as my new Shirt scraped me very much I asked him to let me wear the one I had brought down; but he threatened to flog me for what he called my *impudence,* and told me all my clothes would be burned. Next week I was not at all surprised to see my own Hat and Satin Scarf adorning his goodly person, and my Coat & Trowsers that of the Captain's son, a young man about my own size.[25]

Usually the captain had a deal with an old-clothes merchant: "An old Jew paid us several visits, for the purpose of buying up all the ordinary clothes of the men, and no matter how new a suit might be it was either a matter of take half-a-crown or throw it away." In exchange, a prisoner got shirts "like coarse wrapping," canvas trousers, a gray jacket and shoes that slopped or bit, "to remedy which you must give a couple of white loaves, a week's allowance, to one of your shipmates to change for his and so get a good fit."[26]

Every kind of graft and corruption flourished in the hulks. George Lee, sentenced to fourteen years' transportation for having a forged banknote, wrote in January 1803 from his captivity on a hulk in Langston Harbor to denounce "the bad Police and the injudicious Government so prevalent in places of this kind, making them in reality seminaries not of penitence and reform ... but of every vice which degrades human nature below the ferocious brute." Of the 440 prisoners on his hulk, about half were "what they call Johnny Raws, i.e., country bumpkins in whose composition there is more of the fool than the rogue," who were relentlessly preyed on and cheated by all officers from the captain down. Only the chaplain and surgeon, he thought, were honest. "Owing to the impositions on all hands by Contractors, Agents, Victuallers and Captains, nine at a time out of Four Hundred have lain dead on the shore, the pictures of raggedness, filth & starvation."[27]

A 14-pound iron was riveted to the felon's right ankle—a practical discouragement to swimmers. Some were more heavily ironed, for no discernible reason: Bennett in 1817 saw a "very little boy 13 years of age" miserably creeping about the hulk *Leviathan* in double fetters, while adult men wore single ones; presumably the child had not been able to pay the warder's bribe for "easement of irons," and an example was made of him. (Months later, when the weight was removed for the voyage, the prisoner's right leg would jerk up uncontrollably as he walked.) After a felon was put in irons, he was ready to go to work in the government dockyards. He was taken off the hulk at dawn and rowed back to it at dusk. Chained convicts working for the Royal Navy at Portsmouth, Deptford or Woolwich were a sight for tourists; gawking at them satisfied some of the impulses that had been denied the British public when English madhouses stopped letting them in to jeer at the lunatics. The chain gangs presented a moral spectacle, good not only for adults but for naughty children as well. Being stared at amplified the convicts' shame, especially since many of them had chosen to embrace their social death, cutting off all contact with friends and family. James Grove, soon to sail for Van Diemen's Land, wrote to a friend in 1803 that "I purposely delayed writing to you at Portsmouth, in order to avoid the continuance of your notice of me. . . . I shrank from being noticed by the world." Mansfield Silverthorpe was glad to be in a coal gang; it rendered him black and unrecognizable, a toiling absence whom not even his mother would have known.[28] John Mortlock, a young Cambridge graduate and army officer who was soon to sail for Norfolk Island, glimpsed in the crowd of onlookers a fellow student from Cambridge, the son of a banker:

> I shrank within myself, but need not have been alarmed, for his eye passed unconsciously over the group of smudged, cadaverous-looking wretches, one of whom a few weeks before had cheered him riding in winner of the steeple-chase at Bythorn.[29]

The idea that such public labor did anything but degrade the prisoners was, as Bennett pointed out, absurd: "Among men who are condemned to labor in public, exposed to the gaze and criticism of all around them, self-debasement and the loss of personal pride . . . are not instruments to work moral reform." He claimed that within a few months the prisoner's expression changed to "a furious cast of countenance, expressive of bad passions and suppressed rage. . . . This dreadful look is to be seen universally in the Presidii of Naples and Spain, in the Galleys of France, and the Hulks of England."[30]

The food was adequate if one got one's whole ration, but that did not always happen. There were three meat days a week, on which the convicts were issued an "institutional pound" (14 ounces) of fresh raw meat. But as it passed down the line to the convict, first the steward took his cut, then the cook, then the inspectors, then the boat's crew who rowed the food ashore, and lastly the dock overseer; at the end, the convict was lucky to receive 4 ounces, clapped on "a pound of stuff named bread."

When the "new chums" went to their cells, they lay down in darkness and foul air. John Mortlock, on board the hulk *Leviathan* in Portsmouth—an old 90-gunner from Nelson's Trafalgar fleet, jammed with 600 convicts rendered "tame as rabbits" by starvation and discipline—was reminded of a verse in Lamentations 4: "They that were brought up in scarlet embrace dunghills." They also had to put up with the damp, since to make life harder for the prisoners it was often the custom on hulks to sluice the upper decks with sea water instead of holystoning them with sand. And then there were the endless practical jokes the "old hands" played on the new, starting with lessons in how to tie up a hammock with running knots so that, when a man turned into it, he crashed to the deck in a tangle of canvas.[31]

Discipline was a foretaste of what the convicts were to expect on the "Bay side," as Australia was called. The great emblem of desire and repression in hulk life, more than sex or food or (in some cases) even freedom itself, was tobacco. Possession of tobacco was severely punished, but the nicotine addict would go through any degradation to get his "quid." Silverthorpe noted how this cycle of addiction and flogging broke prisoners down: "They grow indifferent . . . they go on from bad to worse until they have shaken off all moral restraint." He described how this befell a quiet, harmless man named John Woolley, one of his hulkmates on the *Ganymede*. Woolley's nicotine addiction was such that

> he had been flogged and put in the Black Hole a dozen times but it was no use: "I cannot help it, sir," he would say to the Captain. "Then I will cut the flesh off your back," the Captain would reply, and indeed the Boatswain used to do his utmost, for stepping back a couple of Paces he would bound forward with his arm uplifted, take a jump and come down with the whole weight of his Body upon the unfortunate victim, at every Blow making a noise similar to a paviour when paving the streets. At length the poor fellow (as I often heard him say) became *weary of his life*. He found that his blameless conduct in every other respect could not save him from the consequences of this trifling breech of discipline . . . and from being one of the best he became the worst character in the Yard. When I left it, he was in the Black Hole for having bitten off the first joint of the finger of Mr. Gosling the Quartermaster, who had put it in his mouth to see if he could detect any Tobacco.[32]

Each prisoner's life was governed by a maze of rules, interpreted at the whim of the hulk's quartermaster. "Sometimes my Iron was too dirty.—at other times too bright.—At one time my Hat was not properly poised on my head.—At another my neckerchief was not tied according to the rules of the Establishment." These gave endless scope for extracting bribes, large and small, from prisoners or their families. Three gold sovereigns bought Silverthorpe a transfer from coal-heaving to easier labor for three months. The naval clerks would slip a name in or out of the "Bay drafts"—the lists of who was to be shipped to Australia—for a bribe that ranged between one and six pounds. Though prisoners could not carry money, the hulks (like all prisons) supported a labyrinthine and complicated underground economy, with convict bankers, moneylenders and even lobbyists. "A man that can get money on board, he can buy anything he wishes. . . . There are so many stratagems of the convenience, and so many schemes of barter and trade, that it would be tedious to particularize." Even the doctors were on the take, Mortlock found; when a hulk prisoner died, his corpse would sometimes be sold for £5 or £6 to the dissectors' agents who haunted the docks, instead of being buried on the cemetery mudbank in the Portsmouth estuary known as Rats' Castle. And die they did, in numbers, because the naval doctors saw no harm in bleeding a sick prisoner a pint too much. Then the coffin would be rowed to Rat's Castle, where a chaplain intoned his brief exequies over a box full of stones and sand. Thus, few prisoners looked forward to a spell in the hospital hulk.[33]

But nearly all lived, and for them the day came eventually: Cast for transportation, they filed on board the Bay ship. Her sailing was always preceded by a flurry of requests for money, clothing, tobacco, combs, mementos; sometimes a convict's family could get a trifle to him, but more usually not, for if they had money to spare, who would have turned thief? Some who had been "mechanics" or skilled craftsmen in their previous life brought their tools, against the day when they would win their emancipation and work for themselves again. When relatives came to say goodbye, pathetic scenes ensued. John Ward remembered how his mother "was ill able to support herself under such trying circumstances; we exchanged but few words; for grief choaked her utterance, and shame kept me silent."[34] John Nicol, steward on the women's transport *Lady Juliana* fifty years earlier, described the reactions of the parents of a young convict, Sarah Dorset, who had been "ruined" by a London rake and then, like thousands of other girls, driven into prostitution and "taken up as a disorderly girl":

> The father, with a trembling step, mounted the ship's side; but we were forced to leave the mother on board. I took them down to my berth, and went for Sarah Dorset; when I brought her, the father said, in a choking voice, "My lost child!" and turned his back, covering his face with his hands; the mother, sobbing, threw her hands around her. Poor Sarah

fainted and fell at their feet; at length she recovered, and in the most heart-rending accents implored their pardon.[35]

Some women had been subjected to terrible psychic cruelty, and would not soon recover:

> A woman was sent up from Carlisle on the top of one of the coaches.... [S]he had been brought to bed of a child while in prison, which she was then suckling,—the child was torn from her breast, and deposited, probably to perish, in the parish poor-house: in this state of bodily pain and mental distraction she was brought to Newgate ... and was then sent out to Botany Bay.... I saw her on board, and she could not speak of her child without an agony of tears.[36]

There can hardly have been a soul among the 162,000 men and women transported to Australia who did not feel, as the transport weighed anchor and began the long voyage to its unimaginable destination, the sentiments that Simon Taylor tried to express in stumbling verse to his father:

> The distant shore of England strikes from Sight
> and all shores seem dark that once was pure and Bright,
> But now a convict dooms me for a time
> To suffer hardships in a forein clime
> Farewell a long farewell to my own my native Land
> O would to God that i was free upon thy Strugling Strand.[37]

### iii

WE NOW TURN to the mechanics of transportation. How did Britain get its outcasts to Australia? Like everything else in the System, the method was made up over the years. Its changes had direct consequences for the prisoners, affecting their health, their state of mind, and their chances of survival.

Between 1787, when the First Fleet sailed, and 1868, when the last convict transport *Hougoumont* deposited its load of Irish Fenians in Western Australia, the Crown sent 825 shiploads of prisoners from England and Ireland, an average loading of about 200 convicts per ship. This exodus began feebly: By the end of 1800 only 42 ships had gone to Australia. It continued to be weak and irregular for another fifteen years, because England was too hard-pressed in her war against France to expand her empire with Pacific thief-colonies. There was no year from 1801 to 1813 in which more than five convict transports anchored in Sydney, and not until 1814 would as many as a thousand convicts arrive in a single year.

Then, after 1815, the flood began. Its climactic period was 1831–35, in which no less than 133 vessels brought 26,731 convicts to Australia. The peak year was 1833: 36 ships and 6,779 prisoners, some 4,000 to New South Wales and the rest to Van Diemen's Land. With this practice, the system of transportation, which had begun uncertainly and with great loss of life, became smooth-running. It was not only efficient and profitable (to the contracting shipowners), but quite safe, at least by the standards of nineteenth-century ocean travel. Nobody, however, could say it was pleasant.

The First Fleet had been entirely fitted out and provisioned by the commissioners of the navy; it had been a government affair from start to finish, although the vessels had been chartered through a shipbroker at a flat 10 shillings per ton. The results, as we have seen, were muddled and potentially disastrous, but they were better than what might have happened with private contract. In the long run, though, the navy did not want to be saddled with continuous responsibility for a system of human trash-disposal. Once the guidelines were laid down, every convict transport that sailed from England or Ireland after 1788 was fitted and victualled by private contract. It was said to be cheaper, and certainly it was easier, since it relieved the government of the letting and supervision of dozens of subcontracts. And why should firms of proven respectability not make a fair profit from ridding England of its thieves and scum? The only people the arrangement did not suit were the convicts themselves, since the contract system guaranteed their miseries and, often, their deaths.[38]

By the end of the eighteenth century, as experience of the peculiar problems of shipping prisoners halfway around the world grew and was added to Britain's knowledge of sending armies on long voyages and landing them in fighting shape, the private contractor faced an imposing list of government demands. From the number of lifeboats to the size of rations, all was laid down, along with the exact responsibilities to convicts borne by captain, surgeon and officers.

The rules would reduce (but never eliminate) suffering and death on board. People at sea always suffered and died, whether they were prisoners or not. During the Napoleonic Wars the British Navy simply assumed that one sailor in thirty would die of disease or accident at sea, apart from casualties in battle; one man in six was always ill. Even among free emigrants to America in the mid-nineteenth century, a much shorter crossing than the Australian voyage—one in thirty died.[39]

By the standards of the time, then, the convicts did not do so badly once the system for getting them out to Australia was working smoothly. This happened after 1815, when the average death rate per voyage for male convicts in any five-year period varied between 1 in 85 and (by the end of transportation, in 1868) 1 in 180. At the peak of the System, the average death rate from illness on board was slightly more than 1 percent.[40]

But before 1815 it was much larger, and in the 1790s, when the System was finding its sea legs, it was huge. The defects of the contract system appeared with the Second Fleet, which sailed from Portsmouth in January 1790. Apart from *Lady Juliana*, it consisted of only three transports: *Surprize, Neptune* and *Scarborough*. They were contracted from Camden, Calvert & King, whose agent on board was Thomas Shapcote. It undertook to transport, clothe and feed the convicts for a flat, inclusive fee of £17 7s. 6d. per head, whether they landed alive or not.

The voyage of the Second Fleet turned out to be the worst in the whole history of penal transportation. Out of 254 convicts on *Surprize*, 36 died at sea; out of 499 on *Neptune*, 158 died; and on *Scarborough*, which had finished her voyage in the First Fleet without losing a single life, 73 people perished out of 253. In sum, out of 1,006 prisoners who sailed from Portsmouth, 267 died at sea and at least another 150 after landing.

Camden, Calvert & King had been slaving contractors, and they had equipped the fleet with slave shackles designed for Africans on the infamous "Middle Passage"—not the chains and basils (ankle irons) that, cruel though they were, allowed a man's legs some range of movement, but short rigid bolts between the ankles, about nine inches long, that incapacitated them. As William Hill, a second captain in the New South Wales Corps who sailed on *Surprize*, indignantly reported, "it was impossible for them to move but at the risk of both their legs being broken."[41] *Surprize* was an old ship, and in a heavy sea the water sluiced through her. The starving prisoners lay chilled to the bone on soaked bedding, unexercised, crusted with salt, shit and vomit, festering with scurvy and boils. One convict, Thomas Milburn, would later describe the voyage in a letter to his parents, later printed as a broadsheet in England:

> [We were] chained two and two together and confined in the hold during the whole course of our long voyage. . . . [W]e were scarcely allowed a sufficient quantity of victuals to keep us alive, and scarcely any water; for my own part I could have eaten three or four of our allowances, and you know very well that I was never a great eater. . . . [W]hen any of our comrades that were chained to us died, we kept it a secret as long as we could for the smell of the dead body, in order to get their allowance of provision, and many a time have I been glad to eat the poultice that was

put to my leg for perfect hunger. I was chained to Humphrey Davies who died when we were about half way, and I lay beside his corpse about a week and got his allowance.[42]

The horrors of the slave trade, Hill thought, were "merciful" beside this. He railed against the "villainy, oppression and shameful peculation" of Donald Traill, master of *Neptune*, and Nicholas Anstis of *Scarborough*. Traill was a demented sadist and Anstis not much better. But their interests coincided with the contractors', as Hill indignantly noted:

> The more they can withhold from the unhappy wretches, the more provisions they have to dispose of on a foreign market, and the earlier in the voyage they die the longer they can draw the deceased's allowance to themselves; for I fear few of them are honest enough to make a just return of the dates of their deaths to their employers.[43]

And in fact, when the Second Fleet reached Sydney and disgorged its cargo of the dead, the dying and the sick, the first thing Anstis and Traill did was to open a market on shore, selling the left-over food and clothing to the half-starved pioneers of the First Fleet.

The colony's Anglican chaplain, Reverend Richard Johnson, counted the sick: 269 people on *Neptune* were incapacitated—which meant that, out of her 499 prisoners embarked, only 72 landed in fair health. The figures for *Scarborough* and *Surprize* were a little less terrible. Johnson braved the 'tween-decks stench of *Surprize*, but he could not face going below in *Neptune*. Mewing and groaning, scarcely able to gesture or roll over, monstrously infested with vermin (Johnson estimated that one man had ten thousand lice swarming on his body) the convicts were slung overboard

> as they would sling a cask, a box, or anything of that nature. Upon their being brought up to the open air some fainted, some died upon deck, and others in the boat before they reached the shore. When come on shore, many were not able to walk, to stand or to stir themselves in the least, hence they were led by others. Some creeped upon their hands and knees, and some were carried on the backs of others.

Among the survivors who landed, all fellow-feeling was extinguished by the ferocity of their repression. Johnson was horrified to see that

> When any of them were near dying, and had something given to them as bread or lillie-pie (flour and water boiled together) . . . the person next to him would catch the bread, &c., out of his hand and, with an oath, say he was going to die, and therefore it would be of no service to him. No sooner

would the breath be out of their bodies than others would watch them and strip them entirely naked. Instead of alleviating the distresses of each other, the weakest were sure to go to the wall. In the night-time, which at this time [June, the Australian winter] is very cold, where they had nothing but grass to lay on and a blanket amongst the four of them, he that was the strongest of the four would take the whole blanket to himself and leave the rest quite naked.[44]

While this was going on at Sydney Cove in 1790, the Lords of the Committee of Council were busy submitting the proposed Great Seal of New South Wales to their King. Its obverse depicted "Convicts landed at Botany-Bay; their fetters taken off and received by Industry sitting on a Bale of Goods with her attributes, the distaff, bee-hive, pickaxe and spade, pointing to oxen ploughing, the rising habitations, and a church on a hill at the distance, with a fort for their defence," and the Virgilian motto *Sic fortis Etruria crevit*, "Thus Etruria grew strong."[45]

When the news of the Second Fleet reached England, through Phillip's dispatches and Hill's letters, there was a small official flap. Neither the government nor the public had expected so much death and misery, but memories were short and the victims, after all, were convicts. Nothing could be done about the wretched contractor's agent, Thomas Shapcote, for—in the only Second Fleet death that tasted of justice—he had died soon after sailing from Cape Town. Although a strict inquiry was promised, it was never carried out. Voluminous evidence was taken at the Guildhall in London. But Captain Traill had prudently absconded and no one could find him until 1792; whereupon he and his ship's mate were brought to trial for murdering a single convict. Both were acquitted and not prosecuted again. Three years later Traill was given a senior post at Cape Town. Anstis went scot-free, and the grim firm of Camden, Calvert & King was never indicted. In fact, it had already contracted with the government to prepare and victual the Third Fleet, which sailed in 1791. Once again its ships were old, crowded and barely seaworthy; there were inadequate medical supplies, and the treatment of prisoners was disgustingly abusive. The second mate of the *Queen*, whose duty it was to issue rations to the 150-odd men and women prisoners on board, used short weights to serve out 60 pounds of beef instead of the regulation 132 pounds at a sitting.[46] Conditions were such that 576 Third Fleet convicts needed medical attention when they got to Sydney. But out of a total of 1,869 men and 172 women embarked, only 173 men and 9 women died on the passage—a gross death rate of slightly under 9 percent, or one-third the death rate of the Second Fleet. After that, the government gave no more contracts to Camden, Calvert & King.

Nervous of publicizing the defects of transportation, it held no public inquiry either. But some improvements were made. The government put

restrictions on "these low-lifed barbarous masters, to keep them honest."
It set up deferred payments—so much per convict embarked, the rest
(usually about 25 percent) when he or she landed in decent health. Masters and surgeons had to get a certificate by the governor when they
arrived in Sydney, rating their performance; if this paper commended
their "Assiduity and Humanity," there would be a bonus from the transport committee when they got back to England.[47]

Some captains were beyond such inducements. In 1798 the contractors of the transport *Hillsborough* were to get a bonus of £4 10s. 6d. for
every convict landed alive, over and above the £18 per head paid on
embarkation. But her master, William Hingston, starved the prisoners,
kept them so heavily chained that they could not walk on deck and kept
them below in double irons at night. Typhus also raged through the
vessel soon after she left Langston Harbor, and one convict in three died.
No action was taken against Hingston.[48]

The commissioners tried but usually failed to stop contractors filling
their ships with goods to be sold in Sydney at huge markups. However,
they put a naval surgeon aboard each vessel who was answerable to them
and not the contractors; his job was to supervise convict health, correct
the abusive conduct of the ships' officers and keep an eye on lax or
incompetent contractors' surgeons. No mere medical officer could tell a
master what to do on his own ship. Still, their presence was felt. The
first transport to sail under this arrangement was the *Royal Admiral* in
May 1792, followed in 1793 by three more shiploads of English and Irish
prisoners. All had supervisors on board, and out of 670 prisoners only 14
died.[49]

The moral was clear, but by 1795 the Napoleonic Wars had begun and
England had no naval surgeons (and few ships) to spare for Botany Bay.
In the next twenty years only one privately contracted transport sailed
with a naval surgeon on board. Between 1792 and 1800, eighteen convict
ships went to Australia from Britain. The first six (from 1792 to 1794) all
had supervising agents. Their death rate was one man in 55, one woman
in 45. Of the next six ships, only two carried naval agents or surgeons,
and their death rate was one man in 19 and one woman in 68. The last
group of six had no naval supervision of any kind, and one man in 6 died,
and one woman in 34.[50]

Most of the dead were Irish convicts. Many had been sent out for
political offenses and they were especially ill-treated because the captains feared mutiny. Thus on *Britannia*, which sailed from Cork late in
1796 with 144 male and 44 female Irish on board, the master Thomas
Dennott went on a sadistic rampage. He had a supposed ringleader, William Trimball, flogged until he gave a list of 31 names of convicts who

had allegedly taken an oath to mutiny. He then had the ship searched for weapons; the guards found home-made saws, half-a-dozen improvised knives, some lengths of hoop iron and a pair of scissors. This was enough. One convict, James Brannon, received the appalling total of 800 lashes on two successive days, the second session with pieces of fresh horse-skin braided to the cat-o'-nine-tails. "Damn your eyes, this will open your carcase," Dennott bellowed at him, and it did, although he took several days to die. In all, Dennott meted out 7,900 lashes to the suspects and killed six of them. The surgeon, a half-mad incompetent named Augustus Beyer, refused to dress their wounds and, being terrified of Captain Dennott, would not supervise the floggings; he cowered in his cabin, listening to the whistling lash and the screams of the Irish. A poor female convict named Jenny Blake tried to commit suicide, for which Dennott cropped her hair, slashed her repeatedly across the face and neck with a cane and had her double-ironed.[51] The government held an inquiry into the conduct of Dennott and Beyer but took no action against either. It found Dennott had "bordered on too great a degree of severity" and Beyer had been "negligent." However, neither sailed on a transport ship again.

Although this nightmarish voyage was an exception, it would be some years before Irish convicts were decently treated. Sir Jerome Fitzpatrick, a frequent agitator for reform on the hulks and in the transports, was able to get the rigid slave leg-bolts struck off prisoners on two vessels waiting to sail from Cork in 1801, *Hercules* and her sister ship *Atlas*; they were replaced by lighter chain-fetters, "preferable as well in the Political as the Humane sense." but he was appalled by the treatment meted out to convicts waiting for transportation in the hulks, both in Ireland and in England. "Prisoners are sent to the Hulks . . . infirm and diseased, completely Blind, crippled and so advanced in Age that no sort of profit can be made from their labour . . . [They] cannot in justice to the cause of Humanity or to the profit of the Colony be sent to *New South Wales*."[52] Writing to Lord Pelham in 1801, he described

their bad and filthy bedding; some not having half the covering of their bodies; the privation of the nutritious part of their diet, by scumming the Fat off their Brooths; the defect of their Cloathing in the most intense cold; the indiscriminate application of their Labour . . . with complete and painful *Testicular Ruptures* hanging towards their knees—without Trusses, yet in common yoked in the Carts; the asthmatic and swelled or ulcerated legg'd subjects equally employed; the tender and painful-eyed at Lime Burning;—on the whole I seldom could discover a rational system in respect either to a profit arising from their labor, or the exercise of reason & humanity in its application.[53]

After *Hercules* sailed from Cork late in 1801, the convicts mutinied. Fourteen were shot out of hand and thirty more died from disease and exhaustion, a death rate of one in four. Conditions on *Atlas* were even worse; sixty-five died on the voyage, largely because they had to make way for 2,166 gallons of rum, which her master, Captain Brooks, planned to sell in Sydney. Governor King very properly refused to let him land it, but Brooks was never punished. He captained several more convict voyages and died, a respectable old salt, as a justice of the peace in Sydney.

It was hard to bring these men to book. To prosecute a cruel or corrupt master in England, the Crown would have had to ship convicts back as witnesses; the alternative was a trial in Australia, which would entail giving a New South Wales court criminal jurisdiction over visiting English ships' captains. In either case, a lot of public money would be spent on a trial, and no one wanted that. Only once were convicts returned to England to testify against a captain. This was in 1817, and on the orders of the relatively liberal, pro-Emancipist governor Lachlan Macquarie, who wanted to arraign the master and officers of the *Chapman* for killing three and wounding twenty-two unarmed convicts with fusillades of gunfire after rumors of a possible mutiny. Although Macquarie did not expect convictions (and did not get them: all were acquitted) he hoped the case might "protect the persons of the convicts in future on their passage from the cruelties and violence to which they have heretofore been exposed." All he got was a stiff rebuke from the government.[54]

Fitzpatrick summed up the convicts' predicament in a letter to Pelham's secretary. "I entreat you again and again to impress [on Pelham] the Idea that in these days of venality, of selfishness and design, you are not to expect just reports to be made by Persons ... immediately connected with those who have concern with either the Prison or the Contract Departments," he wrote. One must not expect

> that the Doctor will ever state his own neglect or mismanagement of his patients, or that Keepers will state the exercise of cruelties ... that those who supply Diet or Cloathing should ... report these Matters, other than of good Quality, or that the General Managers should criminate the persons who may deserve it but are more or less within their own Appointments.[55]

After 1815, however, hell-ships were few; conditions improved on convict transports because of a further change in supervision. Naval doctors had learned more about their craft from the Napoleonic Wars, although military medicine was still a hideously primitive business by modern standards. The man who did most for Australia-bound convicts was William Redfern (1774?–1833), a transported convict himself, and the most skilled and popular surgeon in Sydney. Redfern was family doctor to Governor Macquarie. As such, the "father of Australian medicine" was ideally placed to reform the System. Macquarie ordered him to investigate conditions on three calamitously bad ships that arrived in 1814, *Surry*, *Three Bees* and *General Hewitt*. Redfern's report was the turning point, for it impressed not only Macquarie but the authorities in England. He stressed the need for ventilation, swabbing, clean heads, disinfection with lime and "oil of tar," fumigation and exercise. He also insisted that naval surgeons go in every ship as both medical officers and government agents, "as Officers with full power to exercise their Judgment, without being liable to the Control of the Masters of the Transports."[56]

The benefits of this plan showed as soon as it was adopted. After 1815, the volume of convict shipping to Australia more than trebled—78 ships carrying 13,221 souls from 1816 to 1820, as compared to 23 carrying 3,847 in the preceding five years. From 1811 to 1815, the gross average death rate on the voyage had been 1 in 31. After Redfern's plan went into force it plummeted to 1 in 122. Thereafter it seldom rose above 1 in 100, and never beyond 1 in 85.[57]

Besides, the voyage was now faster and the vessels roomier, although these are very relative terms. No modern traveller can really imagine the tedium and social friction of this voyage. Down the map the transports dropped, sometimes escorted by naval convoys bound for Africa or India. But soon each was on its own in the blue immensity, a socially infected speck flying the red-and-white "whip" (pennant) that proclaimed the convict vessel. Its route would depend on its supplies of food and water. The First Fleet took 252 days to reach Botany Bay, spending nearly ten weeks in ports along the way. It had to carry several years' supplies of provisions, and so the rations for the voyage had to be constantly replenished. But by 1810 the ships no longer needed to carry everything for the convicts' future survival; and by 1820 most captains sailed to Rio and then "ran down their easting" straight to the southern coast of Australia, either dropping their convicts at Hobart or sailing north to Sydney. Sometimes they went out non-stop. By the 1830s, most transports did the passage in less than 110 days, but only four vessels took less than 100: *Eliza I* in 1820, *Guildford* in 1822, *Norfolk* in 1829 and *Emma Eugenia*, the fastest of all, with a 95-day passage, in 1838.

No ship was ever custom-built to be a convict transport. They were all (except for a few naval vessels) converted merchant ships, fitted out with the necessary berths and security devices.[58] The prisoners' berths were usually ranged in two rows, each double-height (a berth above and one below) against the hull, with a walkway down the center. Peter Cunningham, who made five voyages to Australia as surgeon-superintendent on convict transports (and lost only three of the 747 convicts under his care), noted that "ample space" was four convicts in a wooden berth six feet square. There was rarely as much as six feet of headroom, and the only air came from the hatchways, which were kept closed with thick grilles and heavily padlocked. Hence ventilation was always poor; and even though the naval surgeons urged masters to fit wind-sails over the hatches, these primitive airscoops failed to work just when air was most needed—as the ship lay becalmed in the suffocating heat of the doldrums. The Irish "political" John Boyle O'Reilly, transported to Western Australia with other Fenians in 1868 in the *Hougoumont*, the last of all the convict transports, described the miseries of its hold:

> The air was stifling . . . [T]here was no draught through the barred hatches. The sun above them was blazing hot. The pitch dropped from the seams, and burnt their flesh as it fell. There was only one word spoken or thought—one yearning idea in every mind—water. . . . Two pints of water a day were served out to each convict—a quart of putrid and blood-warm liquid. It was a woeful sight to see the thirsty souls devour this allowance.[59]

In bad weather everyone suffered, but the convicts worst of all. George Prideaux Harris, who sailed with David Collins's expedition to colonize Port Phillip Bay in 1803, wrote that after leaving Rio,

> we were constantly meeting with squalls of wind, rain, lightning and heavy rolling seas, so that for many days we could not sit at table, but were obliged to hold fast to boxes &c. on the floor & had all our crockery ware almost broken to pieces, besides shipping many seas into the Cabin and living in a state of Darkness from the Cabin windows being stopped up by the deadlights.—I never was so melancholy in my life before.—Not a single comfort either for the body or the mind—the provisions, infamous—the water, stinking—our livestock destroyed by the cold & wet, and every person with a gloomy countenance.[60]

The security had to be formidable. Captain Alfred Tetens, a German master who spent many years traversing the Pacific, took a shipload of 300 convicts on the *Norwood* to Fremantle in the last phase of transportation in 1861. Her 'tween-decks were "enclosed in a shotproof wall of heavy timbers," and

> the main and forward hatchways were furnished with three-inch iron bars; through the small door remaining, only one person at a time could squeeze with some difficulty. . . . [A] barricade was erected across the width of the ship on deck behind the mainmast. This also had a narrow door. A watch of ten soldiers with loaded guns was stationed night and

day at the rear of the quarterdeck. Four cannon loaded with grapeshot were aimed forward and a multitude of weapons were piled here. This gave the whole warlike picture an imposing aspect that had a calming effect not only on the prisoners but on their warders as well.[61]

The prisoners' food was coarse but sufficient, except for the lack of greens. Its staple was still brined beef, known to passengers as "salt horse"—which, no doubt, some of it was. An officer of the 50th Regiment, John Gorman, sailing to Australia on the transport *Minden* in 1851, wrote down the words of a sailor's verse about it:

> Salt horse! Salt horse! What brought you here?
> I have been carrying turf for many a year
> From Limerick going to Ballyhack
> I fell down and broke my back.
> Cut up was I for sailors' use,
> Now even they do me despise—
> They turn me over and they Damn my Eyes.[62]

Peter Cunningham adjudged the rations "both good and abundant," about two-thirds of the standard navy allowance. The convict Mellish, sailing to Australia at about the same time (the early 1820s), found

> not much reason to find fault; on Sundays, plum pudding with suet in it, about a pound to each man, likewise a pound of beef; Monday, pork (a pound with peas in it); Tuesday, beef and rice; Wednesday, same as Sunday; Thursday, same as Monday; Friday, beef and rice and pudding; Saturday, pork only.[63]

Against scurvy, the convicts got lime juice, sugar and vinegar. For a bonus, they received a nightly half-pint of port wine to keep their spirits up. This was considered a great luxury and on some ships, like the *Woodbridge* when she sailed in 1840 with the convict diarist Charles Cozens on board, its distribution was a ritual:

> for the purpose of exercising the men, and as preventive to disease, each man entered at one door on the quarter-deck, *danced* to the cask, drank his allowance, and then danced off again, round by the opposite doorway.... [T]he steps, as various as the performers, formed altogether a most amusing "ballet."[64]

The prisoners' irons were struck off when the ship was in blue water, though their bunks usually carried chains and basils so that the refractory could be fettered down in an emergency. The surgeon-superintendent got the convicts on deck for fresh air and exercise as often as possible. They holystoned the decks, swabbed and scrubbed and laundered, and took as much menial work off the crew's shoulders as discipline would allow. They could not carry knives—all eating-irons except spoons were issued with each meal and collected after it—but they could get needles, and bones from "salt horse." So they passed the long weeks making scrimshaw, "manufacturing seals, toothpicks, tobacco-stoppers, and other ornaments out of bones; and likewise a few ingenious and experienced ones, in making rings, brooches &c. out of common buttons, at which they were very expert."[65]

They fished, trolling hooks with strips of canvas greased with fat. Bonitos would grab them and be hauled like silvery finned melons, shuddering and tail-tapping, into the scuppers; they were eagerly eaten, as were the sharks, the ominous "sea-lawyers" that followed patiently at the vessel's stern. These "were pronounced excellent; the most trifling change of circumstance in so long and wearisome a voyage being greedily grasped at and joyfully entertained." Now and then sailors would catch albatrosses with baited hook and a sounding-line, drag them screaming on board, slaughter them, and skin them, there being a market for their stuffed carcasses.[66]

The convicts' efforts to amuse themselves were noted by various surgeons and free passengers. They danced and (when in irons) managed a clinking beat with their chains. On Christmas Day, one ship's carpenter observed, "the greatest joviality prevailed among the Convicts, who celebrated the anniversary of the Christian era by the execution (in a masterly style) of an abundance of vocal music in the shape of glees, trios, duets &c., probably the result of their double allowance of wine."[67]

They gambled for anything from tobacco to clothes, and if no one had cards they would dismember Bibles and prayer-books to make them, as a clergyman found to his distress on a transport in 1819. Sometimes they staged amateur plays, or held mock trials on deck—cathartic parodies in which the "judge," robed in a patchwork quilt with a swab combed over his head for a wig, his face made up with red-lead, chalk and stove-backing, would volley denunciations at the cowering "prisoner."

The big ceremony of the voyage was always the Crossing of the Line, a boisterous rite of passage in which Neptune would come aboard and initiate those who had never crossed the equator before. Fearsome in swab-wig and iron trident, shells and dried starfish entangled in his oakum beard, sewn into the flayed skin of a dolphin and stinking to heaven under the vertical sun, the sea-god would bear down on the neophytes flanked by grinning Jack-tar "mermaids" holding buckets of soap and gunk. The initiates were clipped with scissors and lathered with a mop, "shaved" and then ducked in a tub of seawater. No wonder the tradition has since been much attenuated by mass tourism. "Neptune was on board for two nights shaving the soldiers & People," Lieutenant William Coke reported to his father from the transport *Regalia* in 1826,

> he was a sulky Old Fellow & covered his new born sons over with Tar from head to foot, each night after having finished shaving he & his Constables came into my cabin to know if I was pleased with the Lenity he had treated my men, but His Majesty was such a drunkard that he & his Constables drank three gallons of my Whiskey & made my head ache terribly by obliging me to drink raw spirits with him.[68]

By the 1820s discipline ran smoothly, almost automatically, in most ships. Captains kept a vigilant eye on their human cargo, and rumors of mutiny brought down summary punishment—though not, as a rule, with the flagellatory orgies staged on early hell-ships like the *Britannia*. Four dozen lashes was usually enough; the convict would be triced to a grating, and the ceremony of his pain watched by the mustered prisoners and the ship's company. Minor offenders were ironed, or put in a cramping-box for a few hours.

Dreams of mutiny, however, were rarely absent. Lieutenant Coke mentioned that the Irish prisoners he was guarding on *Regalia* "had formed a scheme to seize & carry the ship to South America. I and my men were all to have been murdered. The Doctor, Captain & sailors were to have been saved . . . [I]t was lucky they did not attempt it or else they would have been most of them shot, and had any of the Soldiers been killed the rest would have been so enraged they would have murdered every convict on board."[69]

If there was a rising, the ship's master had to act fast and shrewdly, like Captain Tetens facing rebels on the *Norwood*:

> Hardly had I told the nearest soldiers what was going on when with revolvers cocked, I stormed into the midst of the startled gang. In spite of the stinging wound which the ringleader gave my arm with some sharp instrument, I did not let go [of him]. I kept both hands around the criminal's neck so that he had no little trouble in breathing. . . . I should not have shot him except in the greatest need, so as not to make the others needlessly embittered.[70]

But such mutiny attempts were few. The *Norwood*'s was fomented by a group of "former captains and pilots who scuttled their ships," but no ordinary convicts could navigate. Generally they would remain passive and mutter threats, rather than go up against overwhelming odds of firepower. In the whole period of transportation (1788–1868), more than eight hundred outward voyages produced only one successful mutiny—

on a female transport, the *Lady Shore*, in 1797. The insurgents were not female convicts, but their guard—a detachment of the New South Wales Corps who rose "in the name of the French Republic," seized the ship without much bloodshed, sailed her to Montevideo and were eventually accepted by France as political refugees, after they had disposed of the bewildered women prisoners as servants to Spanish colonial ladies of quality.

A captain who treated his prisoners well—as Tetens did, by making the regulations "markedly more lenient" and having long individual chats with his charges so that they could unburden their minds—was certain to be shown gratitude and even affection. At the end of the voyage "the exiles prepared a surprise for me which I remember today with deep emotion. . . . [H]atred and bitterness seemed to have vanished." Before they filed ashore the prisoners lined themselves up in ordered ranks, clasped Tetens's hand one by one, "all looking very serious," and presented him with a letter of thanks signed by 270 out of 300 men:

> HONORED SIR!
>
> It is our deep regret that we are not able to give you a greater proof of our thankfulness and respect. We can only ask you to receive our sincere thanks for the kindness, generosity and liberal treatment which you have always shown us on the long voyage to Western Australia. To this earnest request we add the sincere wish that Heaven may grant you every earthly joy, that you may succeed in all your future enterprises, and while we must follow our unknown fate in an inhospitable land far from home and family, may the hand of the Almighty protect you and bring you back to a happy home.[71]

However, the usual representative of humanity was the surgeon-superintendent, who was not only a healer but the closest thing to an ombudsman the convicts had. Most captains were not like Tetens; they were not sadists by nature, but they were tough unlettered men risen from the foc's'le in the harsh school of the sea, and they placed scant value on convict comfort. On a ship with no surgeon-superintendent, Thomas Holden (the political exile from Bolton) complained in 1812 that "we have been three weeks without Clean Shorts and we asked the Captain for Shorts and he said they could not be Durty yet, and I wear Irons on both legs . . . Dear honored Father and Mother if you cannot do nothing for me and very soon I am sure you will never see me alive again."[72] That, in essence, was what the surgeon-superintendent was on board to prevent, and when he did so, showing a constant level of "firmness alleviated by compassion," the convicts trusted him.

The surgeon's logs had to be kept in duplicate and turned in at the end of the voyage. The duller reading they make, the better the voyage

for the prisoners. The log of Surgeon-Superintendent John Smith on the
*Clyde*, carrying 215 men from Ireland to Sydney in 1838, is typical. It is
a record of cleaning and scraping, sprinkling chloride of lime by the
water-closets, supervising the laundry, lancing abscesses; blankets become lousy and are soaked all night in the urine-tubs in the hope of
killing the accursed insects; the coarse trousers give some convicts "ex-
coriations of the scrotum and thigh"; prisoners squabble and are put in
the cramping-box, a lad whispers about mutiny and spends the night
handcuffed on deck; the soldiers and their women fight like Kilkenny
cats—"a more undisciplined, quarrelsome, noisy set have seldom come
together, yet the behavior of the Prisoners is quiet and orderly with little
exception." Surgeon Smith dispenses advice, purges, blisters and bleed-
ings; he buries the dead (but very few men die); and there is a note of
quiet gratification at the end, when *Clyde* warps into Sydney Cove and
an official from the colonial secretary's office asks the customary question of the mustered prisoners: Is there any complaint about the Surgeon?
"No, no, God bless him, was the universal cry."[73]

Individual convicts also poured forth their gratitude and hoped that
Surgeon Smith would commend them to the authorities in Sydney, as in
this letter from a middle-aged man of some education, Bernard Murray,
protesting his innocence:

> Money turned the scales of Justice and unfortunate Murray was cast—yes
> Sir, cast out of Society, and banished from his home—his friends & his
> Country—but in you, Sir, I have found the tender & feeling Gentleman,
> —you have done more to meliorate my unhappy condition than I, in any
> manner, deserved,—you knew nothing of me, I was a stranger, but your
> humanity for an injured man—now nearly in the decline of his life—Sir,
> your masterly and very impressive discourse delivered to us last Sunday
> week, will be long remembered and, please God, strictly followed by me.
> Altho' a convict, Sir, I hope to bring my grey hair unsullied by Crime to
> the Grave.—Should you, Sir, still think of recommending me here to
> notice—rest assured, Kind Sir, that sobriety, steadiness & honesty with
> the strictest attention will not be wanting on my part.[74]

A good surgeon-superintendent represented whatever was best in the
System; he might not be a great doctor, but his decency made him exceptional in the netherworld of transportation. Once ashore, few convicts
could expect as much fair play. The society into which they now came,
as they were mustered at the side of Sydney Cove or the Hobart dock,
feeling the beaten clay heave beneath their feet after those months at
sea, was more punitive in its conventions, more capricious in its workings: a lottery, whose winners went on to found Australia but whose
losers were no better off than slaves.

# 6

## Who Were the Convicts?

i

IT IS A QUARTER-CENTURY since the Australian in London risked hearing languid sneers directed at his criminal ancestry. This colonial vestige was already dying a generation ago. Nevertheless, it was part of English attitudes to Australians before 1960, and especially before World War II. When it appeared, it would send upper-middle-class Australians into paroxysms of social embarrassment. None wanted to have convict ancestors, and few could be perfectly sure that some felon did not perch like a crow in their family tree. Fifty years ago, convict ancestry was a stain to be hidden.

Working people in Australia saw their convict past differently. Growing up free and reaching for social trust, children born in the colony—the Currency, to use the common colonial term, many of whom had convict ancestry—might be obsessed with respectability. But memories lived on as social myths, particularly among the Irish, who never forgot what treatment their convict forbears received on the Fatal Shore. As we shall see, the System inadvertently produced Australia's first folk-heroes, the bushrangers, most of them escaped prisoners. The basic class division of early colonial Australia—guards versus prisoners—lived on as a metaphor of future disputes there. It was something to think about at the Trades Union meeting, and on the picket lines. It provided a scheme of historical oppression. The Good Squire, the Benevolent Landowner, the Paternal Peer, all those figures of property who rise to modify the simple picture of early nineteenth-century labor relations in England—and who did in fact exist—were not features of the mythic Australian landscape. Instead, there were the harsh overseer, the treacherous "special," the flinty officer, the brute with the whip; and under them, the suffering convict.

From these twin pressures to forget and to mythologize arose the popular Australian stereotype of convict identity. It says that convicts were innocent victims of unjust laws, torn from their families and flung into exile on the world's periphery for offenses that would hardly earn a fine today. They poached rabbits or stole bread to feed their starving offspring—and they had to, because their rulers had so brutally mismanaged England that they could no longer survive as honest yeomen in a collapsing rural economy. Crushed between economic forces they could not understand and laws they had not written, they were the people Thomas Gray apostrophized in "Elegy Written in a Country Churchyard" (1750) and Oliver Goldsmith in "The Deserted Village" (1770).

The stereotype insists that the human fodder of transportation sprang from the root of British decency, the yeoman in the rural village. This would be given allegorical form by William Blake, whose vision of industrial desolation mingled with accounts he had heard of the Pacific thief-colony, the "Horrible rock far in the south," where "my sons, exiled from my breast, pass to & fro before me," and

> The Corn is turn'd to thistles & the apples into poison,
> The birds of song to murderous crows . . .[1]

The commonest tag in Australian ideas about the convicts' class identity came from Gray's "Elegy," where, musing on the decent obscurity of the village dead, the poet evoked a yeoman resisting the power of the enclosing landowner: "Some village-Hampden that with dauntless breast / The little tyrant of his fields withstood." Hence, wrote J. L. and B. Hammond in 1913 in their influential study *The Village Laborer, 1760–1832,* "the village Hampdens of that generation sleep by the shores of Botany Bay." From there it was only a step to the full form of the myth, stated more than sixty years ago in the rhetorical question of an Australian historian, Arnold Wood: "Is it not clearly a fact that the atrocious criminals remained in England, while their victims, innocent and manly, founded the Australian democracy?"[2]

It was no fact, but a stout and consoling fiction. The innocence of convicts as a class (if not their manliness) was first exposed to criticism by Manning Clark in the 1950s and finally demolished with statistical analysis by L. L. Robson in 1965.[3] Basing his work on a "random" sampling of one name in twenty in the Home Office Papers in the London Public Record Office, which list the names, ages, places of trial and crimes of about 150,000 of the transportees, Robson was able to show that, far from being first offenders, one-half to two-thirds of the convicts carried previous convictions. Eight in ten were thieves, and only a minuscule fraction could be classed as political offenders. Most were city-dwellers, not villagers or peasants. Nearly all were propertyless laborers rather than smallholders. Three-quarters were single, and their average age was about 26. The idea of the convict that one might extract from the earliest transportation indents—an old woman who stole cheese, a mere child, a harmless wigmaker's 'prentice or a sensitive Scottish painter like Thomas Watling—is very far from the whole truth about the majority of convicts who came later.

The ferocity and scope of eighteenth-century capital statutes created, as we have seen, an extraordinary range of hanging crimes. The erratic mercy of the courts could, and did, transmute such sentences to exile in Australia. Hence, many early convicts, up to the end of the Napoleonic Wars, went on board the "Bay ships" for small, often ridiculously slight, offenses. But after 1815, the general tendency (to which, of course there were thousands of exceptions) was to reserve transportation for less trivial crimes. By 1818, the first stirrings of postwar legal reform were felt in England. A parliamentary committee urged that some kinds of theft (though by no means all) should be punished by transportation, not death, and that forgery should cease to be a capital offense. Sir Robert Peel's attempts to reform and consolidate the criminal statutes in the 1820s did have a gradual effect on men in the dock. And as the number of hanging crimes shrunk, so the volume of "transportable" offenses grew.

There was no third choice, for England had no penitentiary system, could not keep her felons at home and would not be forced to do so until the Prison Acts of 1835 and 1839. Consequently, each liberalization of the law helped to increase the flow of convicts to Australia. Only extreme Tories saw the period 1820 to 1840 as a time of "reckless" liberalization of the criminal law. But a sense of humanity did creep forward. By 1837, hanging was mainly restricted to cases of murder, while crime after crime—forgery, cattle-theft, housebreaking—was relegated to the less terrible and magical status of a "transportable" offense. Slowly, the English authorities acknowledged the mistakes and fantasies that had led their predecessors to fetishize the death penalty. But the real rise of transportation began, not with the law itself, but with its new enforcers: the "peelers," the English police, established by Sir Robert Peel in 1827. A police force meant a huge rise, not in gross crime, but in successful arrests and convictions. Likewise, the abandonment of transportation was not caused by any fall in crime, but by three other factors: the growing moral and political opposition to the System among English reformers in the 1830s, the growth of an alternative English penitentiary system and the Australians' own opposition to a continuous dumping of fresh criminals on what, after 50 years of settlement, they had come to view as their soil.

A graph of transportation to Australia would run fairly flat (though uphill) from 1788 to 1816, then climb more steeply, shoot to a peak in the mid-1830s and then flatten again. After 1850, the English prison and penitentiary system could hold nearly all the criminals the courts could convict. Transportation to New South Wales finished in 1840; to Van Diemen's Land, in 1853; and by 1868, when the last convict ship from England discharged its Irish prisoners on the other side of the continent, in Western Australia, transportation was part unpleasant memory and part unhealed wound.

Thus we can roughly distinguish four phases of transportation. The first—"primitive" transportation, as it were—runs from 1787 to 1810. It began, as we have seen, as an attempt to clear the English hulks and jails and to post a British strategic presence in the Pacific. It involved relatively few convicts: in round figures, about 9,300 men and 2,500 women from England and Ireland (no more than 7 percent of the total number who would eventually be transported). They started coming out at a rate of about 1,000 people per year; but this fell by half when the Napoleonic Wars began in 1793 because convicts were needed for dockyard labor. Some were press-ganged into the Navy, or even dragged into the uniformed rabble of the British Army. England could not spare the ships to transport them "beyond the seas" to Australia.

The second stage belongs to the two decades between 1811 and 1830. Around 1811, the transportation rate began to rise again. The accumulation in jails and hulks had cleared, but the government felt that, having set up its criminal waste-disposal system, it should keep using it. The sharp rise in this second phase came after 1815, when the wars ended and England was struck by a succession of internal crises. Its population was increasing out of hand; between 1801 and 1841 it nearly doubled, from 10.1 to 18.1 million, and its fastest *rate* of growth in this period was in the decade 1811–20. Workers were pincered between falling wages and rising prices; the mechanization of hand trades created runaway unemployment; and the inexorable spread of enclosure was driving people from the country to the slum. Hence the crime wave which so troubled England's rulers after the war, and which prepared Parliament to accept Peel's novelty, a police force. Once the police existed, the supply of felons rose. So there was a great pressure driving the convicts onto the transports—and a corresponding suction at the other end of their journey, Australia, where the growth of the pastoral industry after 1815 created a ravenous demand for convict labor. From 1811 to 1820, some 15,400 male and 2,000 female convicts sailed out from England and Ireland. From 1821 to 1830, the corresponding round figures were 28,700 men and 4,100 women. So in this second phase, about 50,200 people—some

31 percent of the total number of transportees—went to Australia. By 1830, the System was mature and working at the full stretch of its efficiency.

In the third stage, 1831 to 1840, the System peaked and began its decline. In those years, 43,500 male and 7,700 female convicts sailed for Australia—a total of 51,200 people, more than the previous two decades' decantation on the Fatal Shore. The most active year was 1833, when 6,779 prisoners of both sexes were shipped to Sydney and Van Diemen's Land. By then, transportation had been accepted by most respectable Englishmen as the best of all answers to crime; the idea of the penitentiary was still a Benthamite hypothesis in England, although it was being tested by the novelty-loving Americans across the Atlantic. Nevertheless, the English Prison Acts were passed in that decade, and they distantly signalled the end of transportation. By the late 1830s, a strong current of opinion, fed by anti-slavery sentiment, was running against Botany Bay. English liberals were hearing more about the System and were shocked by what they heard, especially when the sensational and tendentious Molesworth report was published in 1838. Meanwhile, native-born Australians had come to hate the stigma of convictry—and the competition from assigned convict labor. In 1840, all transportation to New South Wales ceased.

This prepared the fourth and last stage of transportation. After 1840, convicts were of diminishing use as pioneers, and even their value as slave labor was falling. England kept sending them to Van Diemen's Land; by 1847, only 3.2 percent of the population of New South Wales were convicts under sentence, as against 34.4 percent in Van Diemen's Land.[4] From 1841 to 1850, some 26,000 convicts were poured into Van Diemen's Land, a number that soon jammed the System and led to its administrative breakdown. Transportation to Van Diemen's Land was not abolished until 1853. In 1850 the embryo colony of Western Australia announced, with naïvely eager opportunism, that it would like some convicts too—there being little enough to attract free labor, in those premineral days, to a place cut off from Sydney by 3,000 miles of desert and bush. In response, the System produced one last dribble: 9,700 felons, shipped there from Great Britain over a period of eight years, finishing with a group of Irish Fenians. By 1868, transportation was all over, except for the social and psychic results. These were considerable, for a young country does not serve as the pad on which England drew its sketches for the immense Gulags of the twentieth century without acquiring a few marks and scars.

ii

THERE WERE NO "fashions" in English crime. Poverty begets theft, monotonously and predictably. Year after year the same proportion held: about four-fifths of all transportation was for "offences against property." Of the male convicts in L. L. Robson's survey, 34 percent were transported for unspecified larcenies; 15 percent for burglary or housebreaking; 13 percent for stealing domestic or farm animals (as distinct from poaching wild game, which accounted for less than three people in a thousand); and 6 percent for "theft of wearing apparel"—a reminder of how ill-clothed the English poor were in the days before cheap, mass-produced clothing. Only a little more than 3 percent of the male convicts went down for "offences against the person," which ranged from assault, rape, kidnapping and a few statistically negligible sodomy convictions to manslaughter and murder. A meager 4 percent were under sentence for "offences of a public nature," which embraced an assortment of acts thought to undermine the rights or prestige of the Realm—mainly "coining and uttering" bad money (2 percent) followed by another 1.5 percent convicted of treason, conspiracy to riot or membership in trade unions or Irish secret societies like the Whiteboys and Ribbon Men. A few people were sent to Australia for bigamy, smuggling and perjury.[5]

Seven men in ten were tried in England, mainly at assizes and quarter sessions in London and six chief counties: Lancashire, Yorkshire, Warwickshire, Surrey, Gloucestershire and Kent. These areas were home to four transportees in every ten. About one convict in five was tried in Ireland, most of them in Dublin.[6]

Men outnumbered women six to one. Over the whole transportation period, only 24,960 women were sent out, half to New South Wales and half to Van Diemen's Land. Probably 60 percent of the male English convicts had previous convictions, and 35 percent are known to have been charged with as many as four earlier offenses before they "napped a winder" and "went to the Bay." With women it was the same: A little more than two in ten had certainly never been convicted before, but the probable ratio of second-offenders or worse was about 60 percent.[7]

Set against the popular Australian belief that the "typical" convict was an innocent creature who had sinned once and been savagely punished for it, these figures speak for themselves. They do not, of course, tell the whole story. The English criminal law was without a doubt as savagely repressive as it was inefficient. But a code's badness does not necessarily acquit its victims—even though law reflects the interests and ideology of those who frame it.

The System swelled in the 1830s because its administrative machinery had improved—that is, more criminals were caught and processed. This did not imply a catastrophic increase in crime, even though there was no end of talk about "crime waves." Rather, because it was working so much better, it was able to gratify the social desires of respectable Britons much more readily. It answered a deep desire for sublimation and generalization. Few people want to take direct responsibility for hanging; understandably, they prefer abstractions—"course of justice," "debt to society," "exemplary punishment"—to the concrete fact of a terrified stranger choking and pissing at the end of a rope. Likewise, the idea that flogging reforms the criminal was an abstraction. The realities of the lash were only apparent where the cat-o'-nine-tails met the skin. Neither the man inside the skin nor the other wielding the cat was apt to think that an act of reformation was taking place. What happened was crude ritual, a magical act akin to the scourging-out of devils. All punishment seeks to reduce its objects to abstractions, so that they may be filled with a new content, invested with the values of good social conduct. But the main use of prison, from the viewpoint of the respectable, is simply to isolate and neutralize the criminal. Australia met this requirement perfectly. Since it was not a building but a continent, it could receive a whole class, with room to spare. And it was a class, not just an aggregation of individual criminals, that the English authorities thought they saw.

For in the 1830s a new language of class had begun to take hold in England. The older Georgian vocabulary of social difference spoke of "order," "degree" and "rank," implying society stabilized by "vertical dependence," its social strata linked by bonds of common interest and patronage. The new one, by contrast, was a language of division, not merely distinction. "Class" implied sharp demarcations and possible oppositions; the hierarchies of the old order may have seemed "natural" and conventional (at least to those on top), but relations of one class to another were adversary, contractual and based on the negotiation of opposed interests rather than a commonly recognized system of duties. The very idea of "class" implied a society, and a world, in change.

We are used to thinking of the language of class as the language of the working class—perhaps, as Gertrude Himmelfarb suggested, "because social history has generally been written by labor historians and socialists."[8] But the language of class in the 1830s was mostly invented and used by a middle class trying to describe the social complications that surrounded it, and it did not resemble the scheme of a two-class society—proletariat versus bourgeoisie—that Engels would later invent. Instead of a working class, they spoke of working *classes*: an idea that reeks of atomization and false consciousness in Marxist nostrils, but which in the 1830s seemed to recognize the variety of interests among working people. Even Chartists and other radicals usually spoke of a singular "middle class" and plural "working classes" or "working people."[9] Meanwhile, the English middle classes had achieved a state of "class consciousness"—meaning an awareness of their identity, desires and hopes—long before the workers. In the 1830s, it was they, not the Left of the future, who owned the rights on the definitions of "class," which they always took to be plural.

One of these, the authorities felt, lay in crime. Criminals did not need to name themselves as a class—to show class-consciousness—before law-abiding citizens felt entitled to call them a "criminal class." There was a crucial line between the "deserving" (frugal, hardworking, stoic) and the "undeserving" (lazy, improvident) poor, and crime certainly arose from the ranks of the "undeserving." "I am anxious," declared Henry Mayhew, "that the public should no longer confound the honest, independent working men with the vagrant beggars and pilferers of this country; and that they should see that the one class is as respectable and worthy, as the other is degraded and vicious."[10]

The idea of a criminal class, as understood by the English in the 1830s, meant that a distinct social group "produced" crime, as hatters produced hats or miners coal. It was part mob, part tribe and part guild, and it led a subterranean existence below and between the lower social structures of England. The criminal class had its own argot, its hierarchies, its accumulated technical wisdom. It preserved and amplified the craft of crime, passing it on from master to apprentice. This idea emerged from the late-eighteenth-century perception that crime in England had risen so fast that Authority must deal with an orchestration, not just an accumulation, of criminal acts. The spectacular career of Jonathan Wild promoted a vision of "generals" of crime—criminal masterminds—leading "armies" of thugs. This proved a durable fantasy. It lasted right through the nineteenth century and culminated in the image of the pre-Mafia super-criminal—Arthur Conan Doyle's Moriarty.

Stabs were made at guessing the size of this class. Patrick Colquhoun figured in 1797 that there were 50,000 whores and 10,000 thieves in London, along with more specialized citizens of the demimonde (Mudlarks, Bludgeon Men, Scufflehunters and dozens of other types) who brought the criminal total to some 115,000, more than 12 percent of the city's population.[11] He was guessing, of course, and his figures were ridiculed even then. The crime statistics assembled by the early Victorians were "harder," more voluminous, but still misleading—for criminal statistics have little to tell us about crime and criminals in the nineteenth century.*

The data of the early nineteenth century are further clouded by the prejudices of those who interpreted them at the time.[12] Around 1800, the "mob" was seen, with every reason, as dangerous. It was fuel for the same revolutionary fire that had destroyed the monarchy on the other side of the Channel. Propertied Englishmen were obsessed with Jacobinism. In their eyes, it justified every resurgence of repression, inhibited every effort at reform, and deeply unsettled the poise with which they had hitherto contemplated the lower classes. It also lent a pervasive if unconscious tinge to all guesses about the nature and composition of the "mob." Their fear of the political threat translated itself into repeated exaggerations of criminal nature. Thus, it was all too easy to assign criminal propensities to the marginal, the outcast, the rag-and-boner— in short, to those who might be seen as English *sans-culottes*. For that large tract where the unpropertied survived, where tricks of subsistence had to be invented from day to day, where the cunning, the illicit and the illegal blended into one another without fine distinction, they had only one name: the criminal class.

Their tendency to invest the struggling and the low with an aura of criminality was sometimes amplified by Evangelical Methodism. If the lower orders were not frugal, humble, hardworking and devout, if they clung unrepentantly to their rum, rutting and fairs, the randy humor and coarse songs and all the other amusements that make life at the bottom of the heap intermittently tolerable, then they were on the Devil's side, not God's.

The fear of crime itself cast an exaggerated solidity on "the distinct body of thieves, whose life and business is to follow up *a determined warfare against the constituted authorities*" and who "may be known almost by their very gait in the streets from other persons."[13] Was all crime as professional as such sentinels believed? Probably only a minority of thieves ran in gangs. Many thefts were spontaneous, desperate and often bungled efforts to relieve want and hunger. Crimes of violence were

---

* The inherent difficulty may readily be seen if one thinks of a modern equivalent: How many cocaine-dealers are there in Manhattan? Despite the public preoccupation with drugs, despite immense publicity given to the production, distribution and consumption of cocaine, its physiological and psychological effects, its social imagery, its power as a status symbol and sexual stimulant, despite the relative social visibility of the dealers who sell it and its cachet as a "respectable" drug, nobody really knows. Nor is it known, despite spectacular guesses from police and government, how much money the cocaine trade in New York is worth a year. The number of convictions bears only the sketchiest relation to the number of criminal transactions. Yet here we have a crime which is thought, by many Americans, not to be criminal at all, involving a product they regularly use and dealers they often meet face-to-face. Project this back 150 years, into a different culture, and one sees the impossibility of guessing the size of the English "criminal class" in transportation days.

not always premeditated. There was a wide gray area between the "occasional" criminal, stealing a rabbit or a coat, and the hard-core professional whose strategies were evoked by the idea of a criminal class. The latter were taken to be permanently degraded, "members of a sort of criminal *race*," as Sydney Smith's *Edinburgh Review* expressively put it; the former, not. Although hard-core criminals did not drift into respectability, the respectable drifted into crime. For the official English morality of the early nineteenth century was far more absolutist than ours. Today's orthodoxy is to look for the environmental excuse and to seek the roots of crime in nurture, not nature—that is, outside the criminal's power of choice. One hundred and fifty years ago it was assumed that men and women *chose* a life of crime. The way to this life was seen— and its image was reinforced by the immense power of official and church imagery—as a sequence of irrevocable steps leading downward, the easy road to Hell. This accorded with the basic conservative tenet, that people are not "naturally" wise or good: We must be restrained by law, and frightened by punishment.

Such ideas, however, were in themselves a harshly coercive part of the social environment and may have caused many people to give up the struggle—to let go, to be what society said they would become, and accept the only milieu that would not rebuke them: crime. The son of a well-off country grocer, caught stealing apples over a neighbor's wall, might get a small fine and a heavy thrashing from his father and so, chastened, go on to respectability. The son of an Irish casual worker in a London slum, caught breaking a window, might experience no such change in the House of Correction. All people, but especially the young, tend to become what society says they are.

Belief in a "criminal class" was self-fulfilling in other ways too— mainly because it made rehabilitation so difficult. Once off the edge, it was not easy to find another respectable job. Records were better in 1830 than in 1770, and they could be checked by any prospective employer.

Many observers realized that crime does not appear in a social vacuum. From 1800 onward, a large literature—at first Evangelical in tone and rising at last to the power of Dickens's encyclopedic vision of the city as ultimate social and moral compressor—sought to describe the causes of crime: poverty, lack of work, dislocation, vile housing, addiction, the death of hope. But the official inquiries into crime, drunkenness, prisons and transportation that were held between 1815 and 1840 tended to confirm the same view of crime: that its class nature mattered more than its causes. The criminal class, in the view of one writer in 1854, "constitutes a new estate, in utter estrangement from all the rest."[14]

But how threatening was it? And was there not hope for the respectable in its estrangement and apparent cohesiveness? The difference between the "criminal classes" of London and the *classes dangereuses* of Paris was that the English were not as dangerous; events like the Gordon Riots in London were the exception, not the rule. England had no tradition of riot and revolt abetted by outpourings of aggression from the criminal classes, whereas the French were used to such explosions from the "vile mob," as the French minister Adolphe Thiers called it in 1850, that had brought "every Republic down in ruin."[15] But, despite the inflamed rhetoric of some Tory extremists, there had never been any alliance, natural or otherwise, between English criminals and English radicals—indeed, the latter took care to exclude the former from their ranks, always stressing their own respectability as workingmen.

But if English crime, unlike French, seemed to present no political threat to the state as such, it certainly menaced its citizens—chiefly the laboring poor. The "criminal class" threatened middle-class property, but what most worried the authorities was the moral contagion it offered to workers and their impressionable children. They had tried to remove the bad apples from the lower classes before they could contaminate the good. The New Poor Law had tried to separate the independent laboring poor from the paupers; the ragged-schools tried to keep the offspring of the lowest and most depraved paupers apart from the "respectable."[16] Transportation sought to remove, once and for all, the source of contamination from the otherwise decent bosom of the lower classes, and ship it "beyond the seas" to a place from which it could not easily return. There it would stay, providing slave labor for colonial development and undergoing such mutations toward respectability as whips and chains might induce. The main point was not what happened to it *there*, but that it would no longer be *here*.

The final aim of the transportation system, then, was less to punish individual crimes than to uproot an enemy class from the British social fabric. Here lay its peculiar modernity; its prediction of the vaster, more efficient techniques of class destruction that would be perfected, a century later, in Russia. However, it failed. Transportation did not stop crime in England or even slow it down. The "criminal class" was not eliminated by transportation, and could not be, because transportation did not deal with the causes of crime. And before we leave the generalizations that led authorities to their ideas about the "criminal class," we should consider a voice from inside it. Written by the wife of a thief bound early for the Fatal Shore, it recounts in bare language the descent into a crime of desperation that must have been traced by thousands of convicts, in an England without pity for the "undeserving poor."

Isaac Nelson, clerk, has been sentenced to seven years' transportation at the Stafford Assizes in 1789. He is now in chains at Portsmouth, cast for transportation on the Second Fleet. His crime was stealing "a Quantity of plated goods" (silver) from a former employer in Birmingham, Matthew Boulton, whom he had served "with the uttermost fidelity" for three years. After quitting Boulton's service, he had come to London and worked for several employers (all of whom signed the letter as character witnesses). Nelson's wife—only the initial of her Christian name, *S*, appears on the letter—begs to assure the authorities she is petitioning that her husband, after losing his last job with a Piccadilly optician,

> from that time was so unfortunate as to be Destitute of all kind of Imployment for upwards of Twelve Months in which Time we were redused to the uttermost Distress possible. Myself afflicted with Illness the whole time and in want of the Common Necessaries of life through a Long and Sevear Winter, and my Husband, the only one I had to look up to get Support, Deprived of the means to gain subsistence, and in this Deploreable Situation to Heap Up the Measure of our Misfortunes, I was Delivered of a Male Infant, who died in a few days from want of proper nourishment, My Self being in so weak a Condishion as not to be able to afford it any assistance.
>
> Think, most gracious Sir, the Feelings of a Husband who tenderley loved a Wife and had allways been used to afford a comfortable Subsistence, to see her in such a Situation, without the Possibility of releaving her Wants, and humbly hope the Gates of Mercy will not be shut against him.

Isaac Nelson went back to Birmingham and got a job at Boulton's for six weeks at 10s. 6d. a week, which was garnished to repay his coach fare and an employer's advance. His wife in London was still destitute and frantic, and so "in a fitt of distraction" he stole the silverware, which was recovered later. Mrs. Nelson goes on to beg the home secretary that

> You will in Humanity to a poor unfortunate man be pleased to Interview with His Majesty to grant him His Most Gracious Pardon or . . . [that] he will mitigate his Sentence, by allowing him to stay the time of his sentence in England, or allow Your Petitioner the favour to accompany her husband in his exile, that she may be able to afford him some Consolation amidst his Afflictions as his long confinement joined to his other Trobles, being of a weak Constitution, has brought him into a deep Consumption that has nearly reduced him to the Grave.[17]

The "Infinite Mercy and Goodness" of George III did not extend so far and Isaac Nelson sailed for Australia on the terrible Second Fleet.

Such lives confirm the truth of E. P. Thompson's bitter remark: The worst offense against property was to have none. We do not know, and never will, how many Isaac Nelsons figured in the "criminal classes." At the same time, rising somewhat on the scale of culpability, people were transported for offenses that the law condemned but their communities tended to condone. Some popular codes stood at a sharp angle to law. Thus youths made heroes of highwaymen, and whole communities in Cornwall and Devonshire not only engaged in wrecking but claimed a traditional right to plunder ships.[18] In smuggling communities along the Sussex coast, people used every shift to avoid the excise on rum and tea, despite the threat of transportation and the gallows. Poaching was another offense that few countrymen, if any, thought wrong, for the poaching laws were among the most corrupt of all English statutes; in sum, they forbade a man to kill a wild animal, even on his own land, unless he could show an income of £100 a year from a freehold estate. Since a laborer in 1830 might expect to make between £10 and £20 a year, the poaching laws were a constant theater of class conflict.

The popular legend of transportation in Australia still insists that there were many convict poachers, but there were not. The number of men transported for poaching was infinitesimal, about the same as those sent out for buggering sheep or boys; those poachers who did get sent to Australia were usually convicted for resisting arrest or assaulting a gamekeeper, not just for the pheasant in the pocket. It was very hard to find witnesses in village communities. Nevertheless, the fact that authorities pursued country people for such morally insignificant crimes—and were quick to identify them with the "dissolute and idle" rather than the "working" peasantry—shows that there was as wide and ill-recognized a gray area between harmless offense and real crime (like sheep or cattle stealing, acts condemned by all villagers) in the country as in the town.

iii

THERE IS NO doubt that many Britons made their living, wholly or in part, from crime. At trial and again on the boat, prisoners had to give their trade or occupation; the two largest categories among the transported were "farm workers" (20 percent) and "laborers" (19 percent). The prisoners did not always use these descriptions themselves; they were more blunt about what they really did for a living. Peter Cunningham, remembering his first voyage to Australia as surgeon-superintendent of convicts on the transport *Recovery* in 1819, described how a seaman he had ordered to list the trades of the prisoners on board came to me in a doubtful mood, scratching his head and observing, "When I ask what their *trades* are, all the answer I can get from three-fourths of them is, 'a thief, a thief'; shall I put them down as *labourers, sir?*"[19]

Although we cannot speak of a "criminal class" with the same confidence as early Victorians did, there certainly was a subculture of crime in the British Isles, in London most of all. It expressed itself in common interests, cant language, specialization, loyalties. Its main character, to the journalist's eye, was the fantastic range of "trades" it contained, as though the Industrial Revolution, breeding an ever-expanding range of products and specialists to make them, had brought forth an equal army of specialists to steal them. The arch-reporter of the underworld, Henry Mayhew, tabulated at least a hundred subspecies of London criminal by their argot names; a small fraction of his list runs as follows:

2. "Sneaksmen" or those who plunder by means of stealth.
   [a.] Those who purloin goods, provisions, money, clothes, old metal, &c:
   i. "Drag Sneaks," or those who steal goods or luggage from carts or coaches.
   ii. "Snoozers," or those who sleep at railway hotels, and decamp with some passenger's luggage . . .
   iii. "Star-Glazers," or those who cut the panes out of shopwindows.
   iv. "Till Friskers," or those who empty tills of their contents during the absence of shopmen.
   v. "Sawney-Hunters," or those who go purloining bacon from cheese-mongers' shop windows.
   vi. "Noisy-Racket Men," or those who steal china and glass from outside of china-shops.
   vii. "Area Sneaks," or those who steal from houses by going down the area steps.
   viii. "Dead Lurkers," or those who steal coats and umbrellas from passages at dusk, or on Sunday afternoons.
   ix. "Snow Gatherers," or those who steal clean clothes off the hedges.
   x. "Skinners," or women who entice children and sailors to go with them and then strip them of their clothes.
   xi. "Bluey-Hunters," or those who purloin lead from the tops of houses.
   xii. "Cat and Kitten Hunters," or those who purloin pewter quart and pint pots from the top of area railings.[20]

And so on. Argot, like all technical jargon, set its users apart. English criminal slang was impenetrable to the "straight" ear. It described actions that did not exist in respectable society, high or low, but were known to "the family"—all those who lived "upon the cross." A *running-rumbler*, around 1800, "gets a large grinding-stone, which he rolls along the pavement; the passengers hearing the rumble, get out of the way, for fear of its running against them, or over their toes; in this critical moment some of the gang give you the *rum-hustle*, or pick your pocket."[21] *Amusers* or *puzzlers* would throw handfuls of street filth in a victim's eyes and run away while their accomplice picked his pockets. A horse-thief was a *prigger of prancers* or a *pradnapper*; a coiner, a *bit-smasher*, a *bit-cull* or a *benefeaker*. To clip coins and keep the gold-dust was to *sweat* them or to be *in the diminishing way*. If one stole loaves from a baker's basket, one was said to be *pricking in the wicker for a dolphin*. There seemed to be no substance that could not be stolen: The *black-spice racket* consisted of stealing bags of soot from sweeps, and the word *buff* for skin gave rise to *buffer*—a man who killed dogs by running a sharp wire into their hearts and then sold their pelts to glovers. There was even a market for *curls*, or human teeth; they were used by some dentists to replace the lost molars of the living.

These were low trades. But a man *whose means are two pops and a galloper* had real status as a mounted highwayman with a pair of pistols, fearless as Turpin in bailing up *rattling-coves*, or coachmen. Forgers *drew the King's picture* in Georgian days or, in Victorian ones, *dummied the old woman's ticket*. A shoplifter practiced the *fam lay*, sometimes palming a ring from a jeweler's counter "by means of a little Ale held in a Spoon over the fire, by which the Palm being daub'd, any light thing sticks to it."[22] His female equivalent would *cant the dobbin* (steal rolls of ribbon) from haberdashers.

Of all the myriad kinds of thief—"the sons of St. Peter, with every finger a fish-hook"—the most dexterous were the *files* and *buzz-gloaks*, or pickpockets. Dickens's description of Fagin's school for boy thieves in *Oliver Twist* was no fantasy. Larger schools (whose ten-year-old initiates were known as *erriffs*, a straight word for young canaries, or *academy buzz-nappers*) were a favorite topic of London journalists. They taught the arts of *fogle-hunting* (drawing out handkerchiefs), *bung-diving* (taking purses), *speaking to the tattler* (lifting a watch, with its *onions*, or seals) and *chiving the froe* (cutting off a woman's pockets with a razor). A pupil with no talent for this was scorned as a *purple dromedary*. A skilled, coordinated adept became a *boman prig* (from the French "beau," fine) with *rum daddles* (expert hands). Out he would go, with a *bulker*, or accomplice, whose role was to jostle the mark, to do fieldwork among the crowds in Piccadilly, the sauntering dandies in Vauxhall Gardens, or the milling crush in Drury Lane during the *breaking-up of the spell*, as theater interval was called. It was under such circumstances that George Barrington, an Irish pickpocket of high vanity and considerable skill, was caught picking the pocket of the Russian Prince Orlov during an operatic first night at Covent Garden; he was transported, and ended up as a "decayed macaroni" at Parramatta with 110 acres farmed for him by lesser convicts. Barrington's celebrity was such that a number of books, none of which he wrote, were published under his name, including an early "history" of New South Wales.[23]

One could not, of course, enter the milieu of crime just by learning its argot. It took work to build up a name. There was nothing unlikely about the words Dickens put into the mouth of young Charley Bates, as he sees his *beau idéal* the Artful Dodger facing transportation for pinching a mere snuffbox. "Oh, why didn't he rob some rich old gentleman of all his walables, and go out *as* a gentleman, and not like a common prig, without no honour nor glory! . . . How will he stand in the Newgate Calendar? P'raps not be there at all." "See what a pride they take in their profession," Fagin crows.[24]

No classless society has ever existed or ever will. Every group has bottom and top dogs. The hostile glare of the decent did not prevent men and women "on the cross" from constructing pecking orders whose minuteness and punctilio were almost worthy of Versailles. From the lowest thief to the highest member of the "Swell Mob," all was graded; the criminal milieu was a meritocracy with strong tribal overtones. The pyramid of crime was a buried, inverted reflection of the pyramid of respectability, and those who lived where the two met—beggars and charity cases, with neither the skill to work nor the gumption to steal—were despised by both. Thus, Mayhew noted that a poor boy might be "partly forced to steal for his character." One's criminal record was an index of rank. At a party in a thieves' kitchen Mayhew found that

> the announcements in reply to the questions as to the number of times that any of them had been in prison were received with great applause, which became more and more boisterous as the number of punishments increased. When it was announced that one, though only nineteen years of age, had been in prison as many as twenty-nine times, the clapping of hands . . . lasted for several minutes, and the whole of the boys rose to look at the distinguished individual. Some chalked on their hats . . . the sum of the several times they had been in gaol.[25]

One had to start young, but inexperience gets caught. The young thief was eager to prove himself, rash, and hence an easy target for the police, even before fingerprints. After 1815 it was quite rare for a first-time thief to be sentenced to transportation, but the number of thefts committed by habitual criminals meant that further convictions, and Botany Bay, were bound to follow.

Illustrators depicted the "criminal type" as a mask of low cunning, stunted but alert. In fact there was no difference between the look of English criminals and that of the working class from which they came. Against the jargon of "criminal types" and the pseudo-scientific babble of the phrenologists one must balance the description of cotton-mill workers offered by Peter Gaskell in 1833:

> An uglier set of men and women . . . it would be impossible to congregate in a smaller compass. Their complexion is shallow and pallid—with a peculiar flatness of feature, caused by the want of a proper quantity of adipose substance to cushion out the cheeks. Their stature low—the average height being five feet six inches. Their limbs slender, and playing badly and ungracefully. A very general bowing of the legs.[26]

The convicts' height was not always recorded, but they tended to be short. Thus a giant poster published in Hobart in 1850, listing 465 escaped convicts at large (cumulative over 20 years) puts more than 80 percent of the men below 5 feet 8 inches, with the largest group, some 15 percent, only 5 feet 3 inches tall. Compared to most modern Australians of Irish or English descent, these men were runts, and the difference was one of diet.

They shared other traits with *lumpen* workers, chiefly a loathing of authority. The "criminal classes" of England were apolitical; on that, all observers agreed. They played no role whatsoever in the radical disturbances of the day. Tribal loyalties could be fanatically strong among them, and they stuck together against the peeler, the beak and the pink chaplain in his "cackle tub," as the prison pulpit was known. "The more you value your number one, the more careful you must be of mine. . . . [A] regard for number one holds us all together, and must do so, unless we would all go to pieces in company." Fagin's words sum up an ethos of loyalty among thieves, a clannishness much like Sicilian *omertà*.

This contemptuous resistance to everyone and everything outside one's small group was one of the roots of Australian mateship. But no convict ever felt that all convicts were his brothers. They would often trample and oppress one another, behaving with the utmost cynicism and cruelty toward weaker prisoners. And often they would not. There was no hard-and-fast rule of "convict solidarity." From authority's point of view, the London "sneaksman" had something in common with the Northumbrian cattle rustler—both had broken the law. But the two men, who knew nothing of one another's background and barely had a language in common, would feel no bond at all. Even when people were transported from the same place for the same offense, they did not always stick by one another. "I hope you will not mind what you may hear from anyone that writes to Boulton saying how good anyone have been to me," wrote the young protestor Thomas Holden, transported with other Luddites in 1812, to his parents. "I in all my illness have Receiv'd no favour from any one of they that come from Boulton, but far the other way."[27]

Most were irreligious too—except, obviously, the Irish—since the reformed man or woman devoted to Methodist "enthusiasm" and the Evangelical meeting was the last person apt to be transported. Chaplains on transport vessels and tractarians visiting the hulks felt like missionaries among hostile white heathens. They bewailed the hard-heartedness of the convicts, their imperviousness to the Word, their cynicism about prayer, their inability to imagine God, Heaven or Hell. They were "abandoned," "profligate," "irreclaimable." They respected neither God or man but truckled shamelessly to both when expediency whispered.

Mateship, fatalism, contempt for do-gooders and God-botherers, harsh humor, opportunism, survivors' disdain for introspection, and an attitude to authority in which private resentment mingled with ostensible resignation—such was the meager baggage of values the convicts brought with them to Australia. They also brought, if men, the phallocracy of the tavern and ken, and, if women, a kind of tough passivity, a way of seeing life without expectations. What they bequeathed to their native-born Australian offspring, the Currency of the colony (as distinct from the Sterling, or English-born free settlers), was summed up by the Australian poet James McAuley in the 1950s as

> a futile heart within a fair periphery.
> The women are hard-eyed, kindly, with nothing inside them:
> The men are independent but you could not call them free.

iv

ONLY A FEW convicts were sent out for political offenses. Yet transportation was an important feature in the machinery of English state repression. The right to send political offenders to Botany Bay was jealously wielded by the British Government. English interests did not want to make martyrs of radicals—and there were obvious constitutional problems attached to hanging a Dissenting clergyman for owning a copy of Tom Paine. But transportation got rid of the dissenter without making a hero of him on the scaffold. He slipped off the map into a distant limbo, where his voice fell dead at his feet. There was nothing for his ideas to engage, if he were an intellectual; no machines to break or ricks to burn, if a laborer. He could preach sedition to the thieves and cockatoos, or to the wind. Nobody would care.

The first political agitators were transported to Australia early in the life of the System. They were convicted in Edinburgh and were known as the "Scottish Martyrs."

In the early 1790s, "reforming" English intellectuals flirted with Jacobinism. To enable such parsons, lawyers and pamphleteers to make contact with like-minded workers, discussion groups known as "Corresponding Societies" were formed. Their officers called themselves "Jacobins" but were, in fact, reforming constitutionalists, who wanted to recall Britain's laborers and artisans to a sense of their ancient rights. It was to this audience that Paine's *Rights of Man* sold most of its million copies in Britain. Tories, thinking of Jacobinism in terms of the guillotine and the September Massacres, viewed the Corresponding Societies with horror and set out to break them up.

They would have liked to stage a crushing trial of some English Jacobins in England, but they could not be sure a jury would convict them. So their blow against the Corresponding Societies was struck in Scotland, where juries were easily rigged. It fell on a young, blue-eyed Scottish lawyer named Thomas Muir (1765–1799), vice-president of a Jacobin discussion group in Glasgow. Muir was an ardent constitutionalist whose offense was to advocate yearly elections of Parliament and a broadening of the Scottish franchise. He stood trial for sedition in Edinburgh in 1793, and every juror was handpicked from the rolls of a Scottish Tory organization known as the Life-and-Fortune Men, the equivalent of the Loyal Orange societies in Ireland.[28]

The main charge against Muir was that he had lent out radical tracts, among them a copy of Paine's *Rights of Man*. Muir admitted the charge but claimed he could not receive a fair trial from the packed jury. The judge—Robert Macqueen, Lord Braxfield, Lord Justice Clerk of Scotland —brushed that aside, as he had been told to do. He was a coarse cunning old drunk whose remarks during this trial won long notoriety. (When one of the Jacobins pointed out that Christ himself had been a reformer, Braxfield chuckled and snorted: "Muckle he made o' that—*He* was hanget.") From such a man, Muir was unlikely to escape, whatever his forensic skills.

Braxfield's instructions to the jury could hardly have been clearer: It was axiomatic that the British Constitution could not be improved. Muir had been telling "ignorant country people" that it must be changed to secure their liberty—"which, if it had not been for him, they would never have thought was in danger." And what right did the "rabble" have to representation? None, for they had no property. "A government in this country should be just like a corporation," the judge declared, made up of the landed interest, which alone has the right to be represented. As for a rabble, who have nothing but personal property, what hold has the nation of them? They may pack up all their property on their backs, and leave the country in the twinkling of an eye; but landed property cannot be removed.[29]

The jury quickly and unanimously found Thomas Muir guilty and he was sentenced to 14 years' transportation.

A few months later another "radical" clergyman was tried in Perth, for circulating a "seditious" pamphlet questioning Britain's motives in her war against France and helping a Dundee weaver publish an "Address to the People" on the subject of parliamentary reform. This was Thomas Fyshe Palmer (1747–1802), no Scot but an Englishman, a Unitarian minister and fellow of Queen's College, Cambridge, who had spent the past ten years preaching as a humble pastor in Dundee. He got 7 years' transportation.

These sentences caused apprehension in England, and not only among Jacobins. A group of moderate constitutionalists, headed by Lord Lauderdale, complained about them to the home secretary, Henry Dundas.[30] They asked Parliament to overturn the verdict on Muir and Palmer. Dundas would hear none of that. He wanted to press on and see if English radicals who did not live in Scotland could be arrested and tried there, and his chance came in October 1793, when the National Convention of British reformers met in Edinburgh.

Its two London delegates were middle-class dissenters, Joseph Gerrald (1760–1796) and Maurice Margarot (1745–1815). The Edinburgh sheriff's deputies worked hard to break up the other assemblies at which they spoke. William Skirving (d. 1796), the Scottish secretary of the convention, was arrested at home and his papers impounded. Gerrald and Margarot were dragged out of bed in the dead of night, later to be released on bail. Braxfield's court tried Skirving for sedition and sentenced him to 14 years' transportation. Gerrald, temporarily free, went back to London and "as an Englishman in whose person the sacred rights of his country have been violated" publicly challenged Dundas to confess that he had instigated the night arrests.[31] He was ignored. His friends urged him to jump bail and flee to Republican America. But Gerrald refused to abandon his comrades, whose trials were now taking place in Edinburgh. Margarot was sentenced to 14 years' transportation. Gerrald's turn came a month later, and Lord Braxfield gave him 14 years. Both judge and prisoner knew that this was a death sentence, for Gerrald had tuberculosis.

Palmer, Muir, Skirving and Margarot were shipped to Australia along with eighty-three less celebrated convicts in the transport *Surprize* in

February 1794. Gerrald followed a year later. On the voyage, Maurice Margarot seems to have had a nervous breakdown, and he denounced his comrades to the captain as parties to a mutiny plot. The indignant "Martyrs" spent the last five months of the voyage in the brig, on short rations. No wonder Muir wrote to a friend in London after their arrival to announce that "Palmer, Skirving and myself live in the utmost harmony. From our society, Maurice Margarot is expelled."[32]

In fact, despite their lamentations, Sydney did not treat them harshly. They did no forced work, wore no chains, and never tasted the cat-o'-nine-tails. Palmer and Muir got land grants and even managed to turn a profit in the rum trade. The government only wanted them neutralized. But they needed watching and the acting governor, Francis Grose, promised Palmer "every indulgence," provided that he "avoid on all occasions a recital of those Politicks which have produced in you the miseries a man of your feelings and abilities must at this time undergo."[33] Although Skirving was granted a hundred acres and Gerrald was bought a house on Sydney Harbor, the "Martyrs" felt the hostility of the Rum Corps—"they have kept us poor," said Palmer, though he may only have been complaining about the difficulty of getting into the rum trade himself. Political discussion was out—"they are all aristocrats here from ignorance, and being out of the way or desire of knowledge."[34]

Transportation did not destroy the political beliefs of the Scottish Martyrs. But it cooled their ardor, and one sees this reflected in "The Telegraph: A Consolatory Epistle," a lengthy poem Thomas Muir addressed to his fellow reformer Henry Erskine in Scotland. It opens with the depressing landscape of exile, "Where sullen *Convicts* drag the clanking chain / and Desolation covers all the plain." Here, Muir reflects that he is still a Jacobin and that

> The best and noblest privilege in Hell
> For souls like ours is, Nobly to rebell,
> To raise the standard of revolt and try
> The happy fruits of lov'd Democracy.
> The sacred right of Insurrection there
> May drive old Satan from his regal chair
> And the same honest means may raise perchance
> A *France* in *Hell*, that raised a *Hell* in *France*.

But doubts arise. Does not revolution wreck the constitutional principles they all stand for? (Muir was so much a moderate that he even went to Paris to plead with the real Jacobins for the life of Louis XVI.) Brooding on the dangers of the mob, he devised a new metaphor of revolution; thus, an Australian bushfire makes its first appearance in English poetry,

as a symbol of political passions ignited by ignorance. He had seen aboriginal hunters setting fire to the scrub:

> Some naked Savage on the distant shore
> With rapid step advancing to the view
> Reminds me, Henry, of my friends and you:
> Of those dear friends who join with heart & hand
> To spread the flame of Freedom round the land,
> And restless labour, anxious to inspire
> Each sluggish bosom with the sacred Fire.—
>
> To clear the forest's dark impervious maze
> The half-starv'd Indian lights a hasty blaze
> Then lifts the Torch, and rushing o'er the Strand
> High o'er his head he waves the flaming Brand
> From Bush to Bush with rapid steps he flies
> Till the whole forest blazes to the skies.
>
> Often, 'tis true, this deed of Madness done
> He mourns the mischief which his hand begun,
> When the red torrent rushing o'er the plain
> No art can stop, no human power restrain,
> Till from a Rock he sees with wild amaze
> His Wife & Children perish in the Blaze.
>
> Stop Henry stop! and cautiously enquire
> If you can quench as you enflame the fire:
> Think on the Savage in my simple tale
> Who fires a Province, for a scanty Meal.[35]

The coarse intellectual clay of Sydney was not for their shaping. They
tried to catechize some prisoners but got little response. Then Thomas
Muir, with extraordinary daring, contrived to escape. Early in 1796 he
managed to contact the skipper of an American fur-trading vessel, the
*Otter*, provisioning in Sydney Harbor. As soon as the ship sailed, Muir
stole a rowboat and hauled out through the Heads, at night; the Yankees
picked him up a few miles offshore. Months later, when the *Otter*
reached Alaskan waters, Muir learned that a Royal Navy ship had been
seen in the area. Fearing capture, he transferred to a cruising Spanish
gunboat, which took him south to Monterey in Spanish California.

From Monterey he made his way to the Caribbean, via Mexico City
and Vera Cruz. He reached Cuba by the end of the year, hoping to work
his way north on a ship to Philadelphia. But by then war had broken out
between England and Spain, and the Spanish colonial *jefe* put Muir in
the Havana prison for several months. At last he was shipped out, not to
America but to Spain, on a frigate bound for Cadiz. Near the end of her

voyage she was attacked by a British naval squadron, and an exploding shell mutilated Muir's face and destroyed his left eye; he was so badly wounded that the British officers, on learning he was aboard, could not recognize him. So unhappy Muir was put ashore in a prison-hospital in Cadiz. But after several months, word of his arrival reached the French, and as an English Republican he had friends in Paris. Talleyrand negotiated his release and brought him to Paris in December 1797 as a guest of the Directory. There he remained, a gradually fading celebrity, occasionally consulted on plans to invade England; he wrote an account of his exile and wanderings around the globe which, although it was eagerly read and discussed in manuscript, never saw publication and is now lost. Muir died at Chantilly, in lamentable poverty, on January 26, 1799— precisely eleven years after the convict settlement at Sydney Cove, the antithesis of all his republican ideals, had been founded. His grave is not known.

Two of the other Scottish Martyrs did not outlive him long, though they had no idea what had happened to Muir. Joseph Gerrald, the mild consumptive scholar, died of tuberculosis in March 1796; William Skirving followed him three days later. Both were buried in Sydney, and Skirving received the epitaph "A seditionist, but a man of good moral character."

Thomas Palmer finished his sentence in Australia, and went into the shipbuilding trade while he was serving it. He and his close friend John Boston—another "avowed Jacobin," who had voluntarily come with his wife on the long voyage to Sydney to keep Palmer company—had little experience of business, but they possessed a singular advantage: the only encyclopedia in the colony. With it, they taught themselves to make beer. Then they learned how to make soap. Next they looked up "ship" and, after some trial and error, contrived to build a somewhat cranky but adequate small vessel for trading stores to Norfolk Island. It was followed by a 30-ton sloop, the *Martha*. Finally Palmer bought and refitted *El Plumier*, a decrepit Spanish warship, and tried to sail her to England via the East Indies. Near Guam, a remote Spanish outpost in the Marianas east of the Philippines, her rotten hull opened. The survivors of the voyage, Palmer included, were detained in jail by the Spaniards. Palmer died there of cholera in June 1802. The Spanish priests, hearing of his radical opinions, refused his body Christian burial; and so the most civilized and liberal-souled gentleman to breathe Australian air in early colonial days was buried among pirates in a common grave on the beach, until an American captain (himself a man of reforming opinions) took the trouble in 1804 to retrieve Palmer's body and bring it back to burial in a Boston church.

The only Scottish Jacobin who stayed on in Australia was the erratic

Maurice Margarot, who managed to lead a shadowy, ill-documented life as a double agent between the various colonial cliques. He seems to have reported to Governor Hunter on the financial doings and political discontents of the New South Wales Corps Officers; and some evidence suggests that he kept both Grose, Hunter's predecessor, and King, Hunter's successor, informed on the conversations of his own former friends the Jacobins. King believed he plotted rebellion with the Irish convicts in 1801 and again in 1804, but he also feared that Margarot was reporting on him to the Colonial Office in London. In 1810, after seventeen years' Australian exile, Margarot struggled back to England. He died in London five years later, wretchedly poor, and politically broken, disliked and distrusted by the friends of his former radical associates.

Transportation had dealt effectively with the Scottish Jacobins. It would continue to do so with representatives of nearly every English protest movement, industrial upheaval and agrarian revolt for the next half-century. But first, it would deal with the Irish.

v

AUSTRALIA WAS the official Siberia for Irish dissidents at the turn of the century. Their presence there caused the System acute strain and insecurity. Rebellious Irishmen, known as "United Irish" and "Defenders," had been sent out in dribs and drabs during the 1790s. But between 1800 and 1805 their influx began in earnest, swollen by political exiles transported for their role in the rebellion of 1798, when Ireland tried unsuccessfully to ally with France in revolt against England.

Some of these men had been formally tried and sentenced to transportation. Others—most prominent among them was "General" Joseph Holt (1756–1826), the leader of the 1798 United Irish rebellion in County Wicklow—had surrendered under the promise of amnesty given by Lord Cornwallis and agreed to be exiled without trial rather than rot in prison. Others still had been bundled onto the convict transports without any form of trial; in 1797, the undersecretary in Dublin had been advised from England that "a light punishment for rebellion will excite revenge, not terror. . . . [Y]ou should transport all prisoners in the gaols and give full power to the generals."[36]

The Irish, on arriving in Australia, were treated as a special class. As bearers of Jacobin contagion, as ideologically and physically dangerous traitors, they were oppressed with special vigilance and unusually hard punishments. They formed Australia's first white minority. From the outset, the Irish in Australia saw themselves as a doubly colonized people.

The colonization of Ireland—the absolute ascendancy of Gall over Gael—had been going on since the twelfth century, when the first English Pope, Adrian IV, encouraged his fellow Anglo-Norman, King Henry II, to invade Ireland and "proclaim the truths of the Christian religion to a rude and ignorant people." When the English knights landed and started hewing their red way through the Gaelic resistance, Ireland had been Christian for seven hundred years. It took nearly a century to impose the Anglo-Norman feudal system on the Irish clans, but by the end of the thirteenth century it was done. The puppet Dublin parliament, owing its loyalty to the English crown, would last seven hundred years and only be dissolved by the Act of Union with England in 1801.

Throughout those seven centuries, no Irish Catholic could expect justice from its laws. As they tightened, so the rights of Irishmen dwindled; and by the end of the eighteenth century these "penal laws" reached into every cranny of the Catholic majority's life. Under them, Catholics were legislated down to helotry. They divided Ireland, as Edmund Burke remarked in 1792,

> into two distinct bodies, without common interest, sympathy or connection. One . . . was to possess all the franchises, all the property, all the education; the other was to be composed of drawers of water and cutters of turf for them. Are we to be surprised when by the efforts of so much violence in conquest . . . we had reduced them to a mob?

Under the Popery Laws, no Catholic could sit in Parliament, on the bench or in a jury; none could vote, teach or hold an army commission. They were disabled in property law, which was rewritten to break up Catholic estates and consolidate Protestant ones. Protestant estates could be left intact to eldest sons, but Catholic ones had to be split between all the children. Thus Catholic landowning families degenerated into sharecropping ones within a generation or two.

These laws cut across all class barriers. They beat the Catholic peasantry "into the clay," as the phrase went, but they also gagged and paralyzed the Catholic landowner, the intellectual, the entrepreneur. Thus, they unified the Irish Catholics more strongly than softer laws could ever have done and voided the question of a class struggle within the Catholic ranks. Hence the fervor with which working Irishmen supported middle-class leaders like Tone and O'Connell. This breadth of disaffection meant that Irish political prisoners transported to Australia ranged across a wide social spectrum, from peasant to lawyer. In March 1800, Governor Hunter was complaining that far too many of the Irish convicts were "bred up in gentle life," and successive governors of New South Wales viewed the Specials, or educated Irish convicts, with extreme wariness; they might "contaminate" the rank and file with their ideas.

The expression of middle-class dissent from English colonial rule was the Society of United Irishmen, foimed in 1791, an alliance of Dublin Catholics with Presbyterian merchants from Belfast, Down and Antrim. Its Ulster Protestant members had risen above their sectarian squabbles with the Catholic majority; they saw that English laws—especially, the crippling trade embargoes on Irish linen exports to America—oppressed them too. A free Irish Republic, they felt, was in the interest of all who made money from Irish resources and Irish labor; but what they needed was an alliance that cut across Irish religious divisions, taking its stand on Tom Paine and the *Rights of Man*.

The United Irish movement spread quite rapidly among the poor. Nobody could call the Irish peasantry of the 1790s politically educated, but it had a great deal to be angry about. It bitterly resented enclosure and tithing, the bailiffs with their writs of eviction, the landlord's bullies with their dogs and shillelaghs. The English looked to the priests to keep the peasants subdued, but the clergy did so, not out of any love for the English, but from a Christian dislike of violence and a fear of what the military could do to their parishioners.

The seeds of rebellion were already there. Before the birth of the Society of United Irishmen was formed, protest movements had risen from the peasantry and been punished by prison, exile and the gallows. The Whiteboys or Levellers, peasant gangs who toppled the new enclosure-fences around old commons, appeared in Tipperary in 1761. In 1772 the Presbyterian Hearts of Steel tried to oppose rack-renting in the Ulster counties. The Rightboys, formed to protest enclosure in Kerry in 1775, were Catholic.

Such country dissidents could not work together. In Ulster, whose population was roughly half Catholic and half Protestant, the Catholic Defenders and the Protestant Peep-o'-Day Boys fought pitched battles, to the amusement of their landlords. The achievement of Wolfe Tone and the twenty-seven other Protestants who founded the Society of United Irishmen was to merge the factions in one common goal of reform, a "cordial union," an Irish nation-state. The English were quick to strike at these nationalist subversives. The first convict ship to carry known political prisoners from Ireland to Australia was the *Marquis Cornwallis*, which sailed from Cove in August 1795 with 168 male and 73 female prisoners. Of the men, "several . . . were known by the name of Defenders, and the whole were of the very worst description."[37] The Irish began to plot mutiny as soon as the ship sailed, and when informers disclosed the plan to the captain he had more than forty men summarily flogged. Two Irish soldiers who had abetted the mutineers, Sergeant Ellis and Private Gaffney of the New South Wales Corps, were flogged and ironed to one another with handcuffs, thumbscrews and rigid slave leg-bolts. Ellis died after nine days; the captain then unshackled Gaffney from his corpse and ironed him to one of the Defenders, leaving them bolted together for the remaining five months of the voyage.

The Defenders continued to give trouble after they arrived in Australia. "Turbulent and worthless creatures," Governor Hunter called them in 1796, promising to watch them "narrowly." He had had to build new log-house jails "since it has been found necessary to send to this country such horrid characters as the people call'd *Irish Defenders*, who, I confess . . . I wish had either been sent to the coast of Africa, or some place as fit for them."[38]

There was good reason for their unrest, beyond the normal sufferings of transportation. Most of the Irish convicts already in the colony, who had come out on transports from Cork between 1791 and 1793, were doing seven years on ordinary criminal charges. But their records had not been sent with them, so no one knew how long they had to serve in Australia or when they were eligible for the tickets-of-leave that were usually given after four years' good conduct on a seven-year sentence. In one case, it took eighteen years for the lists of a shipload of political prisoners (*Anne*, 1801) to catch up. "The manner in which the convicts are sent from Ireland is so extremely careless and irregular," Hunter complained, "that it must be felt by these people as a particular hardship." No wonder that the radical Defenders off the *Cornwallis* found a ready ear among "non-political" Irish convicts who were already in New South Wales.[39]

It was taken for granted that all Irishmen were "wild" and "lawless"; and the authorities in Sydney, who had enough difficulty with the relatively tractable English prisoners, were never glad to see them. When the *Marquis Cornwallis* arrived, Judge-Advocate David Collins cast a cold eye on "Defenders, desperate and ripe for any scheme from which danger and destruction might come." The Irish women were just as bad; they had plotted "the preparing of pulverised glass to mix with the flour of which the seamen were to make their puddings. What an importation!" Half-Irish himself, Collins despised the Irish prisoners: "They do not deserve the appellation of men."[40]

Tension in Sydney between the chafed Irish and the English authorities became worse when the *Britannia* arrived in May 1797. This hellship, one of the worst in transportation history, arrived with 134 men and 43 women, mostly Defenders and other agrarian rebels. Within a few months, they had persuaded other Irishmen to escape inland. Sixty of them were caught and flogged; two were hanged. Others tried again, and were flogged too, since in view of their "obstinacy and ignorance . . . I conceived that there could be no better argument than a severe corporal punishment."[41]

By the middle of 1798, there were 653 Irish convicts in New South Wales, of whom some 265 were political prisoners.⁴² None of them knew what had happened in Ireland since they had been sent into exile. During the year 1796, the Defenders had secretly begun to merge with the United Irishmen, and Wolfe Tone had gone to France to persuade its revolutionary government to send an invasion fleet to Ireland. Once it came, he believed, the Irish middle class and peasantry would rise together. The French landing at Bantry Bay in 1796 was a fiasco, however, and the English Tories unleashed a storm of reprisals, setting Orange against Green, Protestant against Catholic.

The time was ripe for an alliance of Catholic and Protestant under the United Irish banner. In 1797 martial law was declared in Ulster, and William Orr, a Protestant United Irishman who would be transported without trial to Australia on the *Friendship* in 1800, greeted this as a sign. "All ground of jealousy between us and the Catholics is now done away," he declared.

> [The English] have denied us reform and them emancipation. They have oppressed them with penal laws and us with military ones. . . . [T]here is nothing surer than that Irishmen of every denomination must stand or fall together.⁴³

The colony had reached its flashpoint, and late in May 1798 the United Irish, who proved to have a better military organization than the English had ever dreamed, rose in rebellion. The fighting began in Kildare and flared from county to county. By July, all Ireland lay under martial law. The first victories of the rebels—at Three Rocks and Tubberneering, Wexford and Oulart—were soon converted into heroic legend by the "treason songs," to be sung in many an Australian humpy and rum shop throughout the next century; but in the end, musket was bound to prevail against pike. The momentum of the '98 rebellion was soon lost. Lord Cornwallis, the lord lieutenant of Ireland, wrote a heartsick letter to a colleague in England, asking him to judge how far worse the horrors of martial law became when that law was enforced by Irishmen, "heated with passion and revenge," guilty of "numberless murders . . . without any process or examination whatever":

> The yeomanry are in the style of the Loyalists of America, only much more numerous and powerful, and a thousand times more ferocious. These men have saved the country, but they now take the lead in rapine and murder. The feeble outrages . . . which are still committed by the rebels, serve to keep up the sanguinary disposition on our side. . . . [T]he conversation, even at my table, where you may suppose I do all I can to

prevent it, always turns on hanging, shooting, burning, etc., and if a priest
has been put to death, the greatest joy is expressed by the whole company.
So much for Ireland, and my wretched situation.[44]

Such were the memories transplanted to Australia on the next convict ships full of Irish Defenders. Those sentenced to transportation in
the wake of the '98 rebellion had left a gutted country behind them,
devastated by fire, bayonet and the portable wheeled gallows, where
whole counties looked like "the carcase of a goose, standing up." So the
authorities could be a little more lenient. If every United Irishman had
been indicted for treason, they could all have been hanged—but the
jurors would still have had to go home to their villages and live among
those who knew the accused. Juries avoided capital convictions, and, an
Omagh magistrate reported, "All the United Irish who were in on trea-
sonable practices are only indicted for a lesser offence, so as to come
under transportation; for that reason no objection lay against Jurors."[45]

This practice makes it hard to distinguish, on the face of recorded
charges, between "political" and "social" rebels—if, indeed, such a distinction in time of revolution makes much sense. Many of the prisoners
who went to Australia on charges related to property damage or assault
were probably, in their own eyes, as much political prisoners as Joseph
Holt, the farmer who rose to lead the Wicklow insurgents after some
Protestant militia burned his house in May 1798.

When nine ships appeared from the Pacific with the condemned men
and women of the '98 rebellion on board, they brought the worst load of
bitterness the System had yet seen. Of the 1,067 people on board, 775
were at a conservative estimate political exiles.[46] They presented a new
problem. As a jail for passive English felons, Sydney in 1800 was fairly
secure. But how to handle the Irish? In 1798 Hunter had already begged
for fewer rebels: "The infant state of this colony will not admit of it
being filled up with the very worst of characters."[47] The great fear was
another rebellion. "The Minerva arrived about a month ago with the first
cargo of rebels," Elizabeth Paterson, wife of the lieutenant-governor,
wrote to her uncle. "They have already begun to concert schemes—I fear
they will be a troublesome lot—I cannot say I like the place near so well
as I did before."[48]

The ship contained not only Irish rank and file but also some lesser
leaders who had been named in the Banishment and Fugitive Acts: Joseph Holt, and a medical doctor from Cork named Bryan O'Connor; two
seditious teachers, William Maum and Farrel Cuffe; a Kildare priest,
James Harold; and a Protestant clergyman, Henry Fulton. Literate and
thinking men like these were bound to be a nuisance, or even a real
danger, in British eyes; presently Governor King would inveigh against

Maum, who had written "pipes" (seditious pasquinades) against him. "His principles and conduct have changed as little as the others, nor can time and place have any Effect on such depraved characters. . . . [We] may treat such Incendiaries with Contempt."[49] Yet Governor Hunter had taken pity on them at first. They were softhanded and "bred up in genteel life," he told Portland:

> We can scarcely divest ourselves of the common feelings of humanity so far as to send a physician, a formerly respectable sheriff of a county, a Roman Catholic priest, or a Protestant clergyman and family to the grubbing hoe or the timber carriage.[50]

Yet this restraint did not survive the rumors of Irish conspiracy. In September 1800 they grew loud, and Hunter set up a court of inquiry to look into them. The Irish, informers said, had made iron pikes on secret forges and hidden them around Toongabbie and Parramatta, ready for the rising of the "Croppies" (as Irish peasants, being sharecroppers, were called). There were signs, tokens and passwords. "A ship is in sight." "What ship?" "A store-ship." But after a week's interrogation, the court had nothing but rumors, and certainly no pikes. Nevertheless, it found that "seditious meetings" had been held, "tending to excite a Spirit of Discontent which was fast ripening to a serious Revolt." Five "ringleaders" were to get 500 lashes each, and the Catholic priest, Father Harold, must watch their torment "as a peculiar Mark of Infamy and Disgrace." Then, along with "General" Holt and a dozen other suspects, they would all be sent to Norfolk Island, "where the baneful Influence of their Example cannot be experienced."[51]

Hunter might not have carried this out. But as the convicts' bad luck had it, his term of office finished on September 28 and his successor, Philip Gidley King, endorsed the court's suggestions. Meanwhile the Reverend Samuel Marsden was making his own inquiries among the Irish at Parramatta.

Marsden (1764–1838), a grasping Evangelical missionary with heavy shoulders and the face of a petulant ox, had sailed to New South Wales in 1793 as the protégé of William Wilberforce, who recommended him as assistant to the chaplain of the colony. Once there, the protégé showed few of his patron's instincts to mercy, but focused his considerable energies on getting land, breeding sturdy Suffolk sheep, preaching hellfire sermons and (as magistrate at Parramatta) subjecting convicts to draconic punishment—hence his nickname, "The Flogging Parson." Marsden soon became the chief Anglican clergyman in New South Wales, and his hatred for the Irish Catholic convicts knew no bounds. It spilled into his sermons, pervaded his table talk and was set down at length in a ranting memo to his church superiors in London which, for bigotry, rivals William Dampier's thoughts on the Australian blacks:

> The number of Catholic Convicts is very great . . . and these in general composed of the lowest Class of the Irish nation; who are the most wild, ignorant and savage Race that were ever favoured with the light of Civilization; men that have been familiar with . . . every horrid Crime from their Infancy. Their minds being destitute of every Principle of Religion & Morality render them capable of perpetrating the most nefarious Acts in cool Blood. As they never appear to reflect upon Consequences; but to be . . . always alive to Rebellion and Mischief, they are very dangerous members of Society. No Confidence whatever can be placed in them. . . . They are extremely superstitious, artful and treacherous, which renders it impossible for the most watchful & active Government to discover their real Intentions. . . . [If Catholicism were] tolerated they would assemble together from every Quarter, not so much from a desire of celebrating Mass, as to recite the Miseries and Injustice of their Banishment, the Hardships they suffer, and to enflame one another's Minds with some wild Scheme of Revenge.[52]

Marsden was set on finding the pikes, and his belief in conspiracy was confirmed by such vague observations as this from Hester Stroud, an illiterate prisoner off the *Sugar Cane:* "From what she saw of the Irishmen being in small parties in the Camp at Toongabby and by their walking about together and talking very earnestly in Irish, deponent verily believes they were intent on something improper."[53] Gaelic, of course, was their native tongue and many spoke nothing else. But Marsden was so certain they were hiding something that he resolved to have some of them "punished very severely" until they talked. Joseph Holt— who, as a voluntary transportee, could not so easily be tortured—was brought up to Toongabbie to watch the lord's representative in Australia, the Flogging Parson, at work. In his description of Marsden's interrogations under the blue indifferent Australian sky one sees the heroic determination to resist the tyrant that some of these Irish felt and paid for, as their spines were slowly opened to the air and the blowflies. The first one up was Maurice Fitzgerald, a middle-aged farmer from Cork, transported for life on the *Minerva* and now sentenced to 300 lashes.

> The place they flogged them their arms pulled around a large tree and their breasts squeezed against the trunk so the men had no power to cringe. . . . There was two floggers, Richard Rice and John Johnson the Hangman from Sydney. Rice was a left-handed man and Johnson was right-handed, so they stood at each side, and I never saw two threshers in a barn move their strokes more handier than those two man-killers did.

The moment they began I turned my face round towards the other side and one of the constables came and desir'd me to turn and look on. I put my right hand in my pocket and pulled out my pen-knife, and swore I [would] rip him from the navel to the chin. They all gathered round me and would have ill used me . . . [but] they were obliged to walk off. I could compare them to a pack of hounds at the death of a hare, all yelping.

I was to leeward of the floggers. . . . I was two perches from them. The flesh and skin blew in my face as it shook off the cats. Fitzgerald received his 300 lashes. Doctor Mason—I will never forget him—he used to go feel his pulse, and he smiled, and said: "This man will tire you before he will fail—Go on." . . . During the time [Fitzgerald] was getting his punishment he never gave so much as a word—only one, and that was saying, "Don't strike me on the neck, flog me fair."

When he was let loose, two of the constables went and took hold of him by the arms to keep him in the cart. I was standing by. [H]e said to them, "Let me go." He struck both of them with his elbows in the pit of the stomach and knocked them both down, and then stepped in the cart. I heard Dr. Mason say that man had strength enough to bear 200 more.

Next was tied up Paddy Galvin, a young boy about 20 years of age. He was ordered to get 300 lashes. He got one hundred on the back, and you could see his backbone between his shoulder blades. Then the Doctor ordered him to get another hundred on his bottom. He got it, and then his haunches were in such a jelly that the Doctor ordered him to be flogged on the calves of his legs. He got one hundred there and as much as a whimper he never gave. They asked him if he would tell where the pikes were hid. He said he did not know, and would not tell. "You may as well hang me now," he said, "for you never will get any music from me so." They put him in the cart and sent him to the Hospital.[54]

The frustrated Marsden reported to Governor King that "I am sure [Galvin] will die before he reveals anything."* King ordered a second court of inquiry, which concluded (once again) that although there was no evidence, things looked suspicious; so the "several atrocious offenders" on whom suspicion fell should be flogged again and sent to life exile on Norfolk Island, with "the strictest discipline to reduce them to due obedience, subordination and order." Thus, the Irish suspects were shipped off to the tender mercies of Major Foveaux.[55]

None of this assuaged the fears of the free colonists, who remained—as Elizabeth Paterson wrote to a friend in October 1800—in "an uncomfortable state of anxiety . . . [at] the late importations of United Irishmen. . . . Our military force is now very little in comparison with the number of Irish now in the Colony, and that little much divided. Much trouble

---

* Both lived; Galvin received a free pardon from the compassionate Governor Macquarie in 1810, Fitzgerald in 1812.

may befall us, before any succours can arrive. . . . [O]ther ships with the same description of people are now on their voyage to this place."[56]

At Sydney Cove, the ships kept coming. The *Anne*, in 1801, brought "137 of the most desperate and diabolical characters . . . together with a Catholic priest of the most notorious, seditious and rebellious principles," wrote King, "which makes the numbers of . . . United Irishmen amount to 600, ready and waiting an opportunity to put their diabolical plans in action."[57] Anxiety was running so high that people could not even farm properly; the infant colony was glutted by "violent Republicans" and imperilled by no less than three Irish priests, the most recent of whom, Father Peter O'Neil, had been transported untried after being tortured for information in a Dublin jail, with 275 lashes on his back. (Father O'Neil was later pardoned and returned to Dublin at the end of 1802, much shaken by his experiences in Sydney and Norfolk Island.) King felt it was a breach of security to have priests in the colony. The Irish interpreted this as one more violation of their rights to Mass and the Sacraments. They petitioned King once, twice and again to let Father Dixon, transported on *Friendship* in early 1800, say Mass for them. King thought Dixon's conduct had been "exemplary," and so perhaps he would not inflame his flock with seditious notions. The governor weighed the matter. "An artful priest may lead [Irishmen] to every action that is either good or bad." But more than 25 percent of the convicts in New South Wales were now Irish, and their religious impulses must have some vent. To the disgust of Samuel Marsden, King permitted Father Dixon to say mass once a month, "under stipulated restrictions"—meaning police surveillance. The first Mass and the first Catholic marriage in Australia were celebrated in Sydney on Sunday, May 15, 1803.[58]

Meanwhile the Irish had convinced themselves that the masters of convict ships had been under orders to starve and murder them by neglect on the outward voyage. They had reason to think so. When the *Hercules* arrived from Cork in 1802 it showed a 37 percent death rate; on *Atlas II*, 65 of 181 Irish convicts died. King found this "a situation shocking to humanity," but it was pointless to try and persuade the Irish that it was unintentional.[59]

The surprising fact is not that the Irish eventually rose but that they took so long before doing it. It was not until 1804 that rebellion broke out, and it did not last long, for it was badly planned. In his dying confession to Samuel Marsden, one of the rebel leaders, William Johnston, said that the Irish had been talking about a rising all through February 1804 but had fixed no date for it. The idea was to take the relatively ill-guarded and remote settlement of Castle Hill, seize what weapons they could, link up with Irish convicts in Parramatta and then march all together on Sydney. A password was fixed ("St. Peter"). But because of poor communication between the settlements, the attempt was ill-coordinated and, worse, there was an informer: an Irishman named Keogh, who had been thatching a Hawkesbury farmhouse when a fellow convict approached him with word that the rising was planned for the 4th or 5th of March. Keogh took this news to the Parramatta barracks, and before long all the guards in Sydney and Parramatta were counting their ammunition.

On Sunday, March 4, a Protestant chaplain named Hassall preached to the "desperate characters" at Castle Hill, but only a fraction of the two hundred convicts there came to hear him, "from which circumstance I thought that some alarm would take place." The Reverend Hassall guessed right, for the Irish rose at Castle Hill at seven that evening. They set fire to a house to announce their revolt and then ran from cottage to cottage, grabbing what arms they could find—mostly scythes and axes, but a few muskets as well. A convict stonemason, Philip Cunningham, hopped up on a stump and harangued his mates—"He sang out, Now my Boys, Liberty or Death"—and away they marched in the dusk to Parramatta, singing their treason songs. On the way some of them burst into the cottage of Duggin, the hated government flogger at Castle Hill, and beat him up. They also found a full keg of rum and, fortified, they split into parties and spent the night looting farms and exhorting other Irish assigned men to join them. Inspired by the rum and the headier intoxication of their liberty, they saw the roof beams of the burning sheds knuckle under, black against gold-vermilion, into the heart of the fire, while trails of sparks wreathed upward into the lavender darkness and the Irish voices joined a capella in the rebel anthem of '98, "The Croppy Boy":

> It was early, early in the spring
> The birds did whistle and sweetly sing
> Changing their notes from tree to tree,
> And the song they sang was Old Ireland free.
>
> It was early, early in the night,
> The yeoman cavalry gave me a fright,
> The yeoman cavalry was my downfall,
> And taken was I by Lord Cornwall.

As the commotion gathered in the dark and the news of the rebellion filtered into Parramatta from the outlying farms, a cry ran from house to house: "The Croppies are coming!" The Reverend Marsden, with his wife and Mrs. Elizabeth Macarthur, prudently scrambled into a boat and started floating down the Parramatta River toward Sydney. Drums beat, fowling pieces were loaded with ball and the little garrison kept anxious watch. The glow of burning sheds and shanties was seen in the distance. But meanwhile, a horseman had reached Sydney with news of the Castle Hill rising. Governor King learned about it by midnight, only five hours after it began, and he immediately had a detachment of four officers and fifty-two privates of the New South Wales Corps mustered out of barracks.[60]

One is apt to think of the Rum Corps as a rabble of incompetents, but they performed well enough that night. Commanded by Major George Johnston, they set off at 1:30 a.m. and achieved a forced march from Sydney to Parramatta by dawn, with full equipment and musket. The town was intact when they arrived, and after a swig of water and a bite of biscuit Major Johnston split his detachment into two sections, sending one toward Castle Hill and leading the other at double time along the road to Toongabbie. But the Irish were not there either. They had moved on toward the banks of the Hawkesbury River, and Johnston and his men had to chase them for another ten miles.

The "croppies" made their stand, such as it was, on a knoll which later became known as Vinegar Hill, after the site of a famous rebel battle in Wexford six years before. They had been wandering about and drinking all night, and the first rush of excitement had long since dissipated. Sheepish and confused, they did not know what to do when the "lobster-backs" in their sweat-soaked red tunics fanned out at the bottom of the hill and Major Johnston (accompanied by his adjutant and, on foot, the Catholic priest Father Dixon, who wanted to negotiate a truce without bloodshed if he could) rode forward to meet them. The Irish leaders Phillip Cunningham and William Johnston stepped out. Major Johnston said he wanted to parley. Cunningham told him to come into the rebel ranks, "which I refused, observing to them that I was within pistol-shot and that it was in their power to kill me, and that their captains must have very little spirit if they would not come forward to speak to me."[61]

At this, Cunningham and Johnston naïvely supposed the major had come in a spirit of truce. They walked up to his horse, Cunningham protesting that his men would not surrender, "that he would have Death or Liberty." Major Johnston and his trooper promptly drew their pistols and clapped them to the rebel leaders' heads, forcing them back into the ranks of the government soldiers. Then Major Johnston gave the order to fire.

The scene is fairly well rendered by an illustration of the time. Cunningham, hat in one hand and sword in the other, cries, "Death or Liberty, Major!" while Johnston, pointing his horse-pistol, retorts, "You Scoundrel, I'll liberate you!" "Croppies lie down!" the trooper barks at the rebel Johnston, who replies, "We are all ruined." In the far distance, Father Dixon exhorts the rebels to "lay down your arms, my deluded

Countrymen." A redcoat in the foreground slashes a rebel across the scalp, crying, "Thou rebel dog," while the Irishman utters (in comic accent) a woebegone "Oh Jasus." And in the middle ground, the line of serried redcoats is firing its volley as the motley Irish on the hill spout blood, stagger and fall.

In this way, fewer than thirty Botany Bay Rangers put 266 insurgents to flight within minutes. Untrained, poorly led and lightly armed with one musket for every ten men, the Irish caved in. "I never saw more zeal and activity than what has been displayed by the officers and men of the detachment for destroying or securing the runaways," Major Johnston reported with evident relish to King.[62]

They strung up Cunningham, who had been badly wounded in the melee, from the stair of the Government Store in Parramatta—no need for trial. For the next few days, under martial law, the redcoats scoured the bush and farms, bringing all the croppies in. On March 8, King convened a court-martial to try the ringleaders: John Brannon, John Burke, George Harrington, Charles Hill, Timothy Hogan, Samuel Humes, William Johnston, Bryan McCormack, John Neale and John Place. There were no courtroom heroics and the trial was brief. Seven of the ten pleaded that they had been "forced" to join the rebellion. Only William Johnston admitted all charges and threw himself on the mercy of the court. Most of them were sentenced to hang in chains, as a special mark of infamy; the only ones not hanged were Burke and McCormack. The executions were carried out at Parramatta (Hill, Humes and Place), Castle Hill (Johnston, Neale and Harrington) and Sydney (Brannon and Hogan). In this way, the greatest example could be wrung from the hangings; everyone, in all three settlements, had a chance to see what the deluded Irish slogan of "death or liberty" really meant. For months to come, the rotting bodies would dangle in their rough iron frames: "Butcher'd by Scores in New Wales / Dead Men—by me—shall tell sad tales," wrote John Grant, the first exile to write verse in Australia, and explained how on his trips around Parramatta

the Path . . . rises suddenly to an Eminence, from where—Alas! how often!—as I glanced down at the little valley before me, through which I had to pass—the *sight* and *smell* of a man called Johnston (hanged there in chains from a high Tree for his part in the Rebellion last March)— would often halt my steps, hold my Gaze, and in fact bring the tears flowing from my Eyes! . . . [T]he excellent character of that man, added not a little to the Shock.—Several spectacles of this kind were exhibited, until the arrival of Mrs. Kent from India in the Buffalo with her Husband, when . . . she obtained, by her entreaties, an order from Governor King for the burial of all these Martyrs who were hanging in the Sacred Cause of Liberty.[63]

Other United Irishmen were flogged nearly to death and sent to the mouth of the Hunter River, north of Sydney, to hew coal in a recently discovered seam, on a diet scarcely above starvation. As for the "less culpable" Irish, King had them worked in widely separated chain gangs on the rim of the little colony, where they were driven mercilessly "with no other intermission than the time allowed for their meals and the Sabbath."[64]

So ended the only concerted uprising of convicts ever to take place on the Australian mainland. With it, the prospects of a Jacobin rebellion were extinguished. The System had learned some valuable lessons from it—for instance, the basic strategy that political agitators should never be left long in one place or with the same company. "Altho' there are some violent perturbators in this Colony," King remarked a year later, "however, by their being occasionally removed from one Settlement to another, there is no present cause for apprehension." The croppies would murmur and grumble and distill poteen from maize, but they would never rise again.[65]

The English kept sending Irish political prisoners to New South Wales. From 1815 to 1840, the Irish countryside was in a state of more-or-less continuous civil war. At least 1,200 land-and-tithe protestors—probably many more, since not all political offenders were described as such in the ships' indents after 1816—were shipped to New South Wales. They called themselves Caravats and Carders, Whiteboys, Rightboys, Hearts of Steel and Ribbon Men. The most dangerous, from the English point of view, were the Whiteboys, who pretended to be a trade-union association for the protection of Irish peasants, but were in fact enforcers and assassins, the ancestors of today's Provisional IRA, who took on the dirty work of crushing knees, gouging eyes and burning houses that more squeamish Republicans would not touch. In the early 1830s, the White-boys were thought to have killed, maimed and otherwise discouraged two-thirds of the English informers in Ireland.

But neither they nor any other Irish rebels transported after the 1804 rising at Castle Hill would pose much of a threat to the System, simply because they were dispersed in an expanding colony. Settlers pushed westward from Parramatta across the Blue Mountains and into the fertile Bathurst plains beyond. They went southwest to Berrima and Bowral, and eventually down to the wide sheep plains of the high Monaro. They colonized the Hunter River Valley, inland from Newcastle. All this new property was worked by convict servants, assigned men and women. Scattered in threes and fours through the immense bush, living in outback isolation, political prisoners had no social resonance: They were neutralized by geography as much as by law.

Yet the story of English oppression and Irish resistance did not evap-

The other side of Georgian elegance, as seen by William Hogarth. Top: The Idle 'Prentice, doomed to hang, repents in the tumbril as the mob surges around Tyburn Tree (1749). Above: The proletariat ruined by addiction to spirits, in *Gin Lane*, 1750–51. (*The Bettmann Archive*)

ABOVE: Punishment by public labor on maritime projects: hulk prisoners working on the Thames at Woolwich in 1777. On the left, muscle-powered dredgers cleaning the river bottom; in the foreground, convicts laboring to construct a breakwater. Their prison hulk is anchored in midstream. (*National Library of Australia, Canberra*)

RIGHT: Captain Arthur Phillip, the *Pater Patriae* of Australians, Commodore of the First Fleet and Governor of New South Wales, holding the sketch of a fort to be erected in the new colony. Portrait by Francis Wheatley, 1787. (*Mitchell Library and Dixson Collections, Sydney*)

RIGHT, BELOW: An idealized allegory of the infant colony: *Hope Encouraging Art and Labour, under the Influence of Peace*, a medal made from the clay of Sydney Cove by Josiah Wedgwood. (*Mitchell Library and Dixson Collections, Sydney*)

OPPOSITE ABOVE: A Georgian satirist views the convicts' departure in the 1790s, as two flash lads bid adieu to their battered doxies and an official grimly points to the "Bay ship" waiting at anchor. Anonymous, *Farewell to Black-Eyed Sue and Sweet Poll of Plymouth.* (*National Library of Australia, Canberra*)

OPPOSITE BELOW: Thomas Rowlandson, *Convicts Embarking for Botany Bay*, c. 1787–88. In the background, an alternative to transportation: a gibbet, with felons hanging in chains. (*National Library of Australia, Canberra*)

The *Sirius*, flagship of the First Fleet, rides at anchor in Sydney Cove with her tender, the *Supply*—and, to the despair of the colonists, is wrecked on the reef at Norfolk Island, a thousand miles away. Watercolors by George Raper (1768?–1797), midshipman on *Sirius*. (*British Museum of Natural History, London*)

The embryo of a city, its barracks and houses built by convict labor in the quarter-century since the arrival of Europeans. John Eyre, *A North-East View of the Town of Sydney . . . Taken from the West Side of Bennelong's Point,* 1812. *(Mitchell Library and Dixson Collections, Sydney)*

Conflict begins between blacks and whites on the harbor shores, as Iora tribesmen make ready to spear a convict. "Port Jackson Painter," *The Hunted Rushcutter,* c. 1790. *(British Museum of Natural History, London)*

The Noble Savage: At the first moment of contact between Cook's expedition and the Aborigines of Botany Bay, two warriors oppose the landing. They are commemorated in the poses of antique statuary by the botanical artist on Joseph Banks's scientific team. T. Chambers after Sydney Parkinson, *Two of the Natives of New Holland Advancing to Combat*, 1773. (*Mitchell Library and Dixson Collections, Sydney*)

Further developments of the Aborigine in European eyes.

ABOVE: The "Barbarian *New-Hollander*" as Domestic Savage, rude in family customs, depicted by a Scots convict artist: Thomas Watling, *A Groupe on the North Shore of Port Jackson,* c. 1794. (*British Museum of Natural History, London*)

RIGHT: The Comic Savage, after twenty-five more years of white occupation: R. Browne, *Long Jack,* 1819. (*Mitchell Library and Dixson Collections, Sydney*)

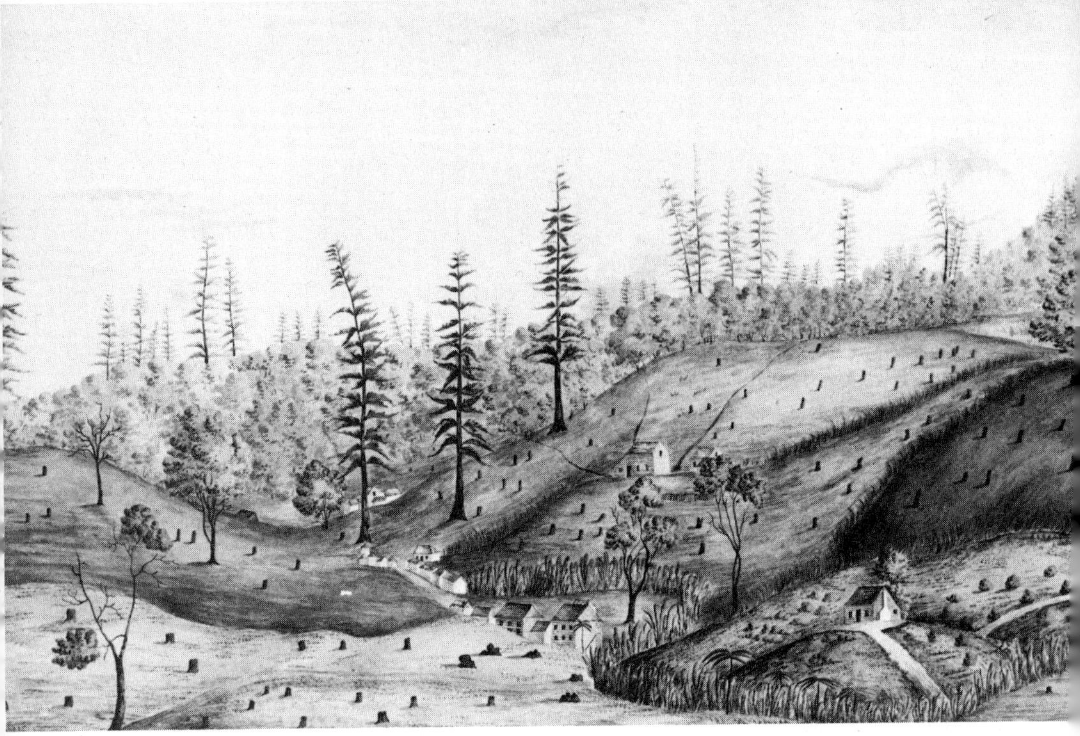

OPPOSITE ABOVE: The hills of Norfolk Island, seen by a convict artist. Note the many stumps; the virgin forest of Norfolk Island pine was receding by the end of the first settlement. John Eyre, *A View of Queensborough on Norfolk Island*, c. 1812. (*Mitchell Library and Dixson Collections, Sydney*)

OPPOSITE BELOW: The jail complex at Kingston on Norfolk Island, falling into decay by the 1870s, seen from the flank of Telegraph Hill. The remains of the Pentagonal Prison can be seen within the security wall of the compound. (*National Library of Australia, Canberra*)

RIGHT: Major Foveaux's jailer remembers discipline on Norfolk Island in the 1800s: *The Flogging of Charles Maher*, watercolor in Robert Jones's "Recollections." "The flogging of Charles Maher almost brought about a mutiny. His back was quite bare of skin and flesh. Poor wretch, he received 250 lashes and on receiving 200 Kimberley refused to count, meaning that the punishment was enough." (*Mitchell Library and Dixson Collections, Sydney*)

BELOW: The beginnings of Hobart Town on the Derwent River in Van Diemen's Land, with the bulk of Mount Wellington rising behind. Pen sketch, perhaps by the surveyor George Prideaux Harris, 1804. (*National Library of Australia, Canberra, Rex Nan Kivell Collection*)

"They lay anchored in files on the gray heaving water, bow to stern, a rookery of sea-isolated crime." The hulks—decommissioned naval ships used as prisons—were an essential part of convict management in the early years of transportation.

ABOVE: Louis Garnery, *Portsmouth Harbour with Prison Hulks,* c. 1820.

RIGHT: G. Cooke after S. Prout, *Convict Hulk at Deptford,* 1826. (*National Library of Australia, Canberra, Rex Nan Kivell Collection*)

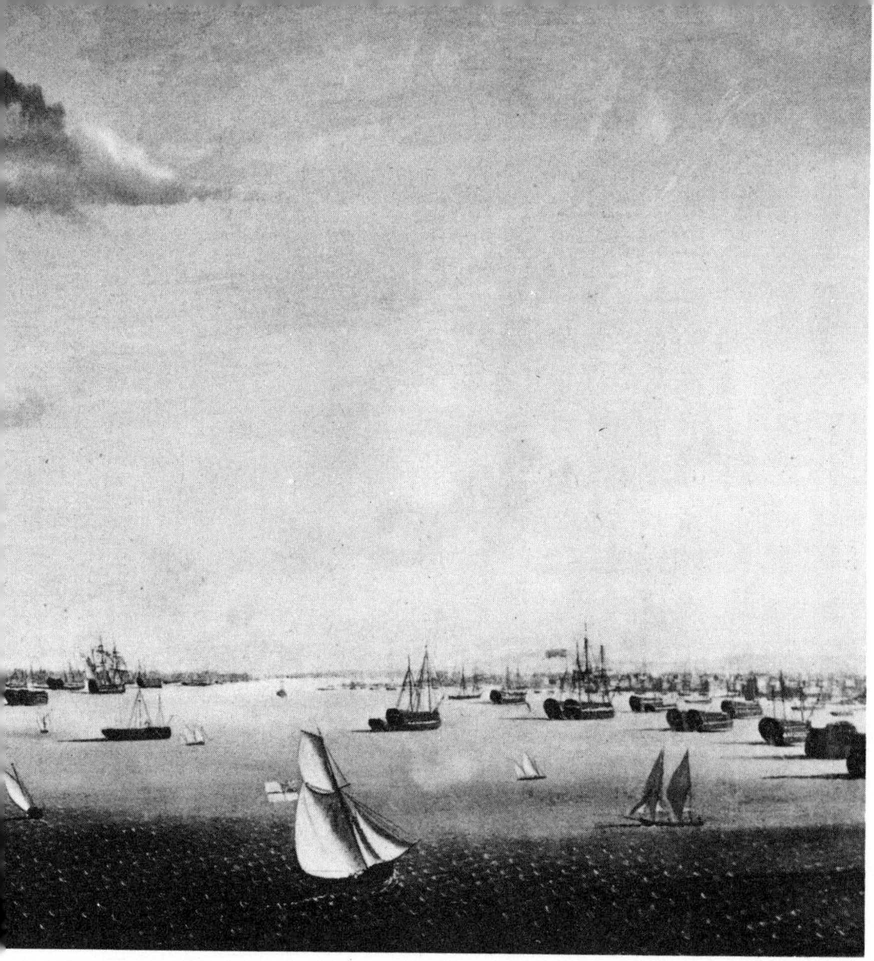

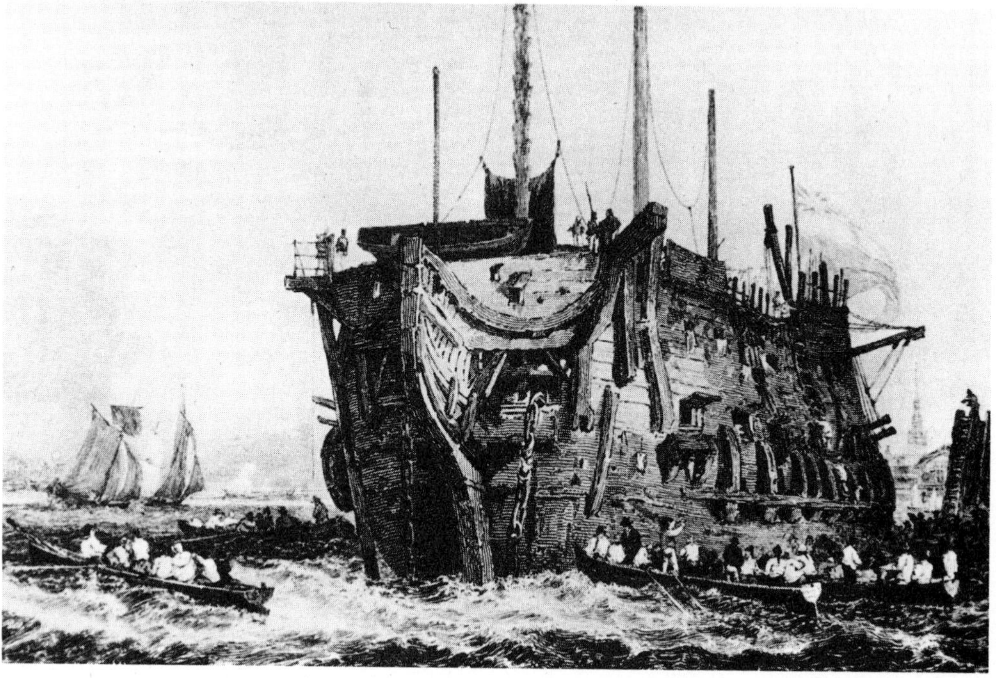

Rebellion and escape.

ABOVE: The 1804 Irish rising at Castle Hill near Parramatta, recorded by an anonymous artist. "Death or Liberty, Major," exclaims the leader of the revolt, and Major Johnson, in command of the "Botany Bay Rangers," replies, "You scoundrel, I'll liberate you." (*National Library of Australia, Canberra*)

LEFT: "The Flogging Parson," the Reverend Samuel Marsden (1764–1838), Evangelical chaplain, missionary, sheep-breeder and implacable scourge of the Irish convicts. (*Mitchell Library and Dixson Collections, Sydney*)

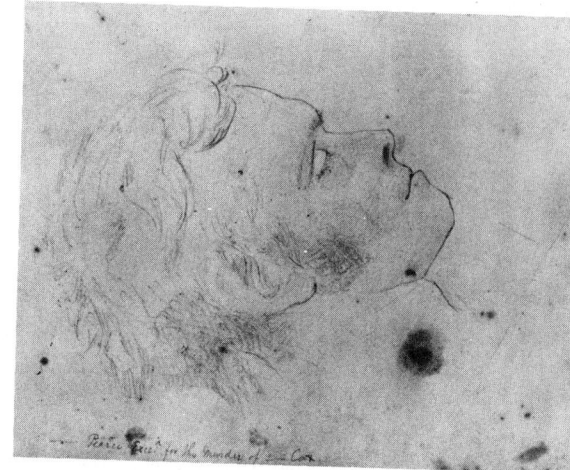

ABOVE: The castaways of the brig *Cyprus:* a woodcut by the convict artist William Gould, printed in 1829, shows Lieutenant Carew lamenting on the hostile shores of Macquarie Harbor, while two loyal convicts, Popjoy and Morgan, helped by Mrs. Carew, build a coracle for their survival. (*Mitchell Library and Dixson Collections, Sydney*)

RIGHT: A pencil drawing of the Irish cannibal and absconder Alexander Pearce, made in the Hobart morgue after his hanging, from Thomas Bock's "Sketches of Australian Bushrangers," 1823. (*Mitchell Library and Dixson Collections, Sydney*)

OPPOSITE ABOVE: James Taylor, *The Entrance of Port Jackson and Port of Sydney Town*, 1821. Note the convict gang quarrying sandstone at left, the relaxed New South Wales Corps officers in the foreground and the tame kangaroo. (*Mitchell Library and Dixson Collections, Sydney*)

OPPOSITE BELOW: The Great Perturbator and the Patriot-Chief: John Macarthur (left), the New South Wales Corps officer who created a pastoral dynasty and was leader of the Exclusives; and Governor Lachlan Macquarie (1762–1824), the veteran soldier who ruled New South Wales from 1810 to 1821, striving to bring Emancipists into the colonial power structure. (*Mitchell Library and Dixson Collections, Sydney*)

OVERLEAF ABOVE: In a watercolor by Augustus Earle, c. 1819, an overseer shows the new Female Factory at Parramatta, designed by Macquarie's convict architect Francis Greenway, to two of its future inmates. (*National Library of Australia, Canberra*)

OVERLEAF BELOW: Lieutenant Ralph Clark of the First Fleet and his "dear picture" of his wife, Betsy Alicia Clark, "surely an angel and not a woman," his idealized contrast to the "damned bitches of convict women" he had been sent to guard. (*Mitchell Library and Dixson Collections, Sydney*)

BELOW: Georgian architecture comes to Sydney: the hospital in Macquarie Street, designed by Governor Macquarie and his wife with the help of a pattern book, and financed by rum. (*Mitchell Library and Dixson Collections, Sydney*)

orate in Australia. On the contrary: It survived most tenaciously as one of the primary images of working-class culture, flourishing long after the System itself had receded from memory. The Irish stuck to one another. They were clannish and had long memories: "much hatred, little room." They always felt they were being punished, not for their crimes, but for being Irish. In Australia, as in Ireland, each act of oppression contributed to a common fund of memory; fact might waver into legend, but the essential content did not change. By the 1880s, when the Protestant majority in Australia had all but sublimated the "hated stain" of convictry, the Irish still kept the memory of the System alive. Naturally, they also fostered the ennobling delusion that most Irish convicts had been sent to the Fatal Shore for political offenses, as though there had been no common thieves, muggers or rapists among the 30,000 men and 9,000 women who had been transported directly from Ireland. Of course, the numbers contradict the myth. Probably no more than 20 percent of the Irish transportees could have been called social or political rebels (except by those, if they still exist, who imagine that all crimes against property are political statements). And the hard core—those transported between 1793 and 1840 for political crimes (as distinct from actions related to riot, such as assault or destruction of property, which were usually treated as common felonies)—numbered less than 1,500.[66] Nevertheless, the legacy of sectarianism in Australian politics, the sense of a community divided between English Protestant "haves" and Irish Catholic "have-nots," began with them and influenced the patterns of power in Australian life for another 150 years.

vi

THIS DID NOT HAPPEN with English political dissidents. But between 1800 and 1850, at the most conservative estimate, about 1,800 people were transported to Australia from England for political "crimes." Among them were representatives of nearly every protest movement known to the British Government, so that Australia received samples (if not big influxes) of most working-class movements. Frame-breaking Luddites were sent out in 1812–13, and food rioters from East Anglia in 1816. Fourteen members of the betrayed Pentridge Rising near Nottingham were exiled in 1817, and five dazed fanatics from the Cato Street Conspiracy—which had absurdly hoped to set off a general insurrection of English workers by assassinating Lord Sidmouth's cabinet as its members sat down to dinner—came in 1820. Radical weavers from Scotland in 1820 and from Yorkshire in 1821, rioters from Bristol in 1831 and Wales in 1835; Swing rioters and machine-breakers in the early 1830s, the Tolpuddle Martyrs in 1834, more than 100 Chartists between 1839 and 1848—all went to Australia. So did "politicals" from other countries. From 1828 to 1838, the Supreme Court at the Cape transported each year 30 to 40 members of what it called "the excitable classes"—South African blacks* who, although they seem to have had no political ideas, were believed to have transgressed the racial supremacist laws of the Cape colony; there, transportation was another threat to keep the Hottentots and Bushmen in line.[67]

In Canada in 1837 and 1838, there were two risings against the Tory legislature, the Anglican Church and their seeming unbreakable power over law and land: one by "Lower Canada" (Quebec) militants, the other in "Upper Canada" (Ontario) by English-speaking Canadians backed by some Americans from south of the border. Both these insurrections of tradesmen and farmers were put down by the British Army, and 153 Canadian *patriotes* were transported to Australia.[68]

Of course, the number of Englishmen transported was only a minuscule fraction of those indicted for protest offenses. But the government, especially up to 1830, did not want to transport every English protestor; it wanted to demonstrate its weapons of repression while keeping intact, as far as possible, its reputation for "mercy," which it could sustain by not pressing for extreme penalties in court.

Never had there been deeper unrest among the common people of England than between 1810 and 1845; hopelessness, poverty and resentment were endemic to postwar Britain, and they expressed themselves in a rising sense of class crisis that traced the graph of England's economic malaise. The climax of this tension, between 1830 and 1845, saw more than 10 percent of the working population of England classified as paupers, thrown by the Poor Laws on the meager charity of the parish. Working people believed, with reason, that their government cared nothing for them; and manufacturers complained that official economic policy was strangling growth. Eric Hobsbawm pointed out that "in the post-Napoleonic decades the figures of the balance of payments show us the extraordinary spectacle of the only industrial economy in the world and the only serious exporter of manufactured goods unable to maintain an export surplus in its commodity trade."[69] But for this, men were losing

---

* These were not the first black convicts to arrive in Australia; in the 1790s a small number of blacks, usually servants or slaves who had been brought to London from the West Indies and then been transported for theft, made their appearance in Sydney. One, a First Fleet convict nicknamed Black Caesar, had become Australia's first bushranger by "eloping" into the scrub in 1789 with a stolen gun and making one-man raids on tents and vegetable gardens; when this "mere animal," as David Collins referred to him, was captured, he proved "so indifferent about meeting death, that he declared in confinement that if he should be hanged, he would create a laugh before he was turned off, by playing some trick upon the executioner."

the only jobs they could do. The bitterness of the silk-weaver thrown out of work by machinery came, not solely from his own poverty, but from the sense that a whole tradition of craftwork was being thrust into oblivion by inferior products. This despair was reinforced by the anomie of city life; the Machine, with its demand for new concentrations of labor in new places, was creating a society of people who no longer knew who they were or where they came from.

Such dissatisfactions ran so deep that governments from Pitt's to Sidmouth's invented a demonology to explain them: "Our" common people would never feel this if left to their natural inclinations; hence, they have been wrought upon by foreign agents, the French; thus, all protest is tinged with treason. From the 1790s to the 1820s, the government found itself increasingly hampered by the apparatus of spies and agents it had set up to penetrate movements of working-class dissent. It was drowning in spurious information, distracted by the phantom of insurrection. This made it easier for it to ignore or misunderstand the clear import of demands for reform. It helps explain the often remarkable disproportion between the mild deeds of political protestors and the vindictiveness with which the social death of transportation was inflicted on them. It may also suggest why so many English political transportees, unlike their Irish counterparts, seem to have shed their "radical" attributes once they decided to stay on as Emancipists and enjoy the high wages that free skilled labor could command in Australia. They had been protesting against want, not foreign occupation; and in Australia, want could be relieved.

The heyday of political transportation from England was the 1830s. The 1820s were by no means peaceful, although corn prices were lower, the hated Lord Castlereagh had been succeeded by the more moderate George Canning, and workers, especially industrial workers, seemed better off. This did not apply in the country, however. To William Cobbett —who had just returned from his American exile carrying the bones of Tom Paine in a box and had set out on the long journey on horseback through the shires that was to give him the material for *Rural Rides*— the once-sturdy countryfolk of England were "villeins" and "serfs." He railed against Abolitionists like Wilberforce who, he claimed, cared more for the condition of African slaves in the colonies than for the fate of English workers at home. Most rural workers were below the poverty line at a shilling a day or less; some earned only three shillings a week. But the Tory politicians of the day saw the problem in terms of one hypnotic ideology: that of Malthus, who taught that it was futile to spend any money on poor relief, since it would only encourage the poor to breed and thus make the problem worse. If left to survive or starve, the poor would find their "natural" level. And since the out-of-work did not, by definition, generate wealth, their survival was not an issue for the government.

Aggravated by a slump in the economy and a rise in staple prices toward the end of the 1820s, such was the background to the political unrest that after 1830 landed the largest single group of protestors in Australia. Most of them were tried and convicted in the southern counties, where farm wages were lowest; and their crime was complicity in what came to be known as "The Last Laborers' Revolt." The figurehead around whom they rallied was a fictional leader to whom custom gave the name of Captain Swing: a bogeyman to the propertied, in whose name threatening letters were tacked on gateposts and shoved under front doors in the dead of night. These were known as "Swing letters" and the disturbances they promised were "Swing riots."

Captain Swing stood for several issues. He expresed grievances against the loss of common land by the policy of enclosure. He protested against high wheat prices. The Corn Laws, framed to help English farmers by keeping cheap European wheat off the market, naturally worked against the poor in times of shortage; and by 1830 many farm laborers were deprived of their white bread. Efforts to feed them potatoes were indignantly rejected. The English worker believed his bread and cheese set him several cuts above the porridge-eating Scot or the root-grubbing Irish croppie. The loaf of wheat bread was, to him, a natural right, and the fact that landlords and gentry ignored such traditions did not make them unreal.[70] The protestor's weapon was fire: a match at the base of a hayrick.

The other issue behind the Swing riots was mechanization. The impact of steam-driven farm machinery on unskilled rural labor was disastrous. One threshing-machine, rented out and hauled from farm to farm, could put a hundred men out of seasonal work. The economist today sees this as the natural result of technology; the farmworker in 1830 saw it as a cruel denial of his natural right to work. Both are right, one in the historical perspective, the other in the immediate world of need. So, like the Luddities before them, the Swing rioters went for the machines, breaking the rollers, holing the boilers, jamming the gears with crowbars.

Most Swing threats were inspired by rural grievances. Thus on January 20, 1831, an eighteen-year-old solicitor's clerk named Thomas Cook, from Whitchurch in Shropshire, wrote a letter to a local cabinetmaker and auctioneer named William Churton:

> We men of determination, firm, resolute, and undeviating, are now without scruple and determined that your property shall not be of long duration, nor yet your existence—property which has been got through roguery.

Roguery Churton has been your practice since first you were established in life, but no longer shall it be continued.

Mark, therefore, the time is at hand when your blood shall atone for
your rash and untoward acts. We shall waylay your body, and bring your
family to total subversion, which you know you are well deserving. . . .
PS, we give you this previous note in order that you may prepare for that
awful and sad end.

SIGNED: Men determined to right the oppressed. Agents to Swing.
London.[71]

Why make such threats to a provincial cabinetmaker? Because, although Churton was not a landowner, he had helped put out fires. During
1830–31 there were no less than sixteen acts of arson—rickburning and
barnburning—in the vicinity of Whitchurch, which seems to have been
a hotbed of rural political dissent. Churton was among the "respectables"
who had called for more police protection and harsher punishment for
incendiarists. So Thomas Cook was convicted at the Shrewsbury Assizes
in March 1831 and sentenced to fourteen years in Australia, where in
due course he would write his invaluable account of the System, *The
Exile's Lamentations.*

Compared to Ireland thirty years before, the rioting of 1830–31 was
mild; in any case, it was directed against property, not people. But it
spread rapidly across the southern counties, where rural wages were
about one-third the national average. Men marched, burned ricks and
broke machines in Kent and Surrey, Shropshire and Lincolnshire, Berkshire, Wiltshire, Hampshire, Essex, Oxfordshire, Dorset and Norfolk.
These "curiously indecisive and unbloodthirsty mobs"[72] were harshly
met by Lord Grey's new Whig government. It offered the enormous reward of £500 for the capture and conviction of arsonists and machine-
breakers, and it sent army detachments and locally organized posses
against them. Some counties raised their own squads of mounted yeomanry to ride down the protestors. Lord Melbourne enjoined all magistrates to maintain "a firm Resistance to all demands."

To frighten protestors, the Whig government now began an orgy of
prosecution. Nearly 2,000 insurgents were tried in 34 counties. Of these,
252 were sentenced to death but, in the usual way of showing the Royal
Mercy, only 19 of them were actually hanged and the rest had their
sentences commuted to prison or transportation. In this roundup, 481
Swing followers were shipped out to Australia, for terms of seven or
fourteen years.[73]

Most of them were older than the normal run of transported felons—
an average of twenty-nine years among those sent to Van Diemen's Land,
as against the convict average of just under twenty-six years. More than
half of them were married men. Many of them had letters of commen-

dation from former employers, and not a few were skilled craftsmen or "mechanics," the most desirable kind of assigned servant in Australia. This puzzled the magistrates: What could a millwright, a carpenter or a blacksmith have to fear from the threshing-machines? But these skilled and settled people could read; they knew they had allies in Cobbett and Tom Paine, and they were often the first villagers to speak of rights and to raise discontent among their less skilled and literate neighbors. The case of one Hampshire radical, William Winkworth, a shoemaker who read Cobbett aloud to a circle of "bumpkins" on Saturday nights, should be multiplied by many hundreds to grasp its social import.[74] Now their lives were shattered, their hopes gone, their families riven as the transport ships bore them away.

Not one of them seems to have sustained any overt kind of political activity in Australia. In fact the surviving letters from transported protestors of 1830–31—Richard Dillingham and Peter Withers in Van Diemen's Land—sketch a scene of resignation amid relative plenty. The 1830s were prosperous years on that green, fertile island, and the demand for skilled labor was high. Dillingham had been transported as a rioter, but he seems to have had few political opinions and no connection with organized protest; he found Van Diemen's Land to be a veritable Land of Cockaigne. In 1836 he was assigned as a market-gardener to David Lambe, a mild decent settler who had held the post of colonial architect early in Sir George Arthur's regime. He was "very comfortably settled," he told his parents through a scribe, less than a mile from Hobart:

> As to my living I find it better than ever I expected thank God. I want for nothing in that respect. As for tea and sugar I could almost swim in it. I am allowed 2 pound of sugar and ¼ pound of tea per week and plenty of tobacco and good white bread and sometimes beef sometimes mutton sometimes pork. This I have every day. Plenty of fruit puddings in the season of all sorts and I have two suits of Cloths a year and three pairs of shoes in a year.[75]

Peter Withers, from Wiltshire, adds to the picture: "I have got a very good place," he told his brother in 1833,

> all the Bondage I am under is to Answer my Name Every Sunday before I goes to church, so you must not think that I am made a slave of, for I am not, it is quite the Reverse of it. And I have got a good Master and Mistress, I have got plenty to eat and drink as good as ever a gentleman in this country [has], so all the Punishment I have in this Country is the

thoughts of leaving my friends, My wife and My Dear Dear Children, but I lives in hopes of seeing Old England again."[76]

Assignment, as we will see, was a lottery; Withers and Dillingham drew good masters, whereas Thomas Cook in New South Wales suffered under a bad one. "I want for nothing but my liberty," Dillingham remarked, "but though I am thus situated it is not the same with all that come as prisoners." Clearly, however, the System made no effort to persecute English politicals *as a group*, as it had done to the Irish earlier. Individual masters might give ex-rioters a hard time because they feared unrest on their own farms, but this was uncommon. Generally, the English protestors, skilled family men with a stubborn sense of their own worth, worked out their sentences and lived on as Emancipists in Australia. Significantly fewer of them than of the ordinary criminal population committed second offenses. They had paid long and bitterly for their beliefs. As Peter Withers wrote, "16 years, that is a grate While." They were not ideologues or professional agitators, but laborers and craftsmen jealous of what they believed to be their ancient rights as Englishmen. Above all, they needed to work, and the stigma of "politics" was hard to shake: Australian squatters and settlers were even more conservative than the English squirearchy whose manners and customs they were learning to ape. "You are one of the Dorchester machine-breakers, but you are caught at last!" were the first words James Brine, one of the Tolpuddle Martyrs, heard from his new master on the Hunter River in New South Wales.

Thus most English protestors lived quietly on in Australia, doing the work England had denied them. They had no marked effect on the future politics of their new country. In England, nothing could stop the trade-union movement in the long run. But in the short run, transportation certainly worked as a tactic of repression. It knocked the fight out of its victims. At home, in the villages, it held up a frightening example to workers who had little means of knowing what had really happened to the transported men, since letters back from the Fatal Shore were rare. In Australia, it turned the protester into a political eunuch without making a martyr of him. The wives of transported men, widowed and yet not widowed, taught their sons to avoid the ways of the dissenter; some of them were asked to do so quite specifically by their husbands. In 1835 a former non-commissioned officer, who had taken part in Swing activity and was transported for political insurrection to Van Diemen's Land (where he forged a deed and was re-transported to Norfolk Island), gave the Quaker missionaries James Backhouse and George Washington Walker a letter to take home to his wife. "You and I have lived for a long time without God in our hearts," he admonished her. But in bondage he had come to see that his sufferings were meant "to bring me to a sense of my own depravity and wickedness."

> You will make our children read, and get off, the above Scripture passages. *Never let them read any political works. Keep their minds from being entangled with political men, and their productions.* This, you will not need to be told, has been the prelude to all my present misery."

Probably this fairly represents the usual feelings of transported ex-protestors. Budding radicalism withered in the antipodes, unless—as with the Irish—it had close bonds and ancient national grievances to prop and feed it. In convict Australia, repression won in politics, as in the rest of life.

# 7

# Bolters and Bushrangers

i

**M**OST PRISONERS of the System acquiesced in their fate. They waited out their time, knowing that longer and worse constraint—the triangle, the iron gang, Norfolk Island—would be the price of rebellion. But in any carceral society, there is always a spark of genius for escape. The worse the odds, the more hope escape gives others.

In Australia it was easy to escape. The hard thing was to survive. The odds against surviving were high, but hundreds of convicts made their bets. Some confronted Australia's external wall, the sea: They stowed away, or hijacked ships, or built their own rafts, or stole a longboat. Others took to the land, even less charted than the sea. At first these runaways were called "banditti" (evoking ragged, romantic figures among dark caverns); more colloquially, "bolters." In time, the skulking escapee became that primal figure of popular Australian culture, the bushranger—enemy of flogger, trap and magistrate, the poor man's violent friend, the emblem of freedom in a chained society.

At first, from the 1790s to early 1800s, most of the runaways went inland. After a brief exhilaration they either died or wandered, broken, back to the settlement, "so squalid and lean," David Collins remarked, "the very crows would have declined their carcasses." There were reports that fifty skeletons, picked white by dingoes and birds, could be seen on a day's march to Botany Bay.

The most persistent absconders were the Irish, who in their ignorance had constructed a Paradise myth to alleviate their antipodean Purgatory. They kept sneaking out of the settlement in the belief, as one of them put it to Watkin Tench,

that at a considerable distance to the northward existed a large river, which separated this country from the back part of China; and that when it should be crossed (which was practicable) they would find themselves among a copper-coloured people, who would receive and treat them kindly.[1]

The fantasy of escape to China was one of the obsessive images of early transportation. Yellow girls and tea, opium and silk, queer-looking blue bridges and willows just like the ones on plates; and surcease from the hoe, the iron, the roasting sunlight and the dumb ache of hunger. For this, not a few of the "deluded Irish" died of fatigue, thirst or the spears of blacks. Their crow-pecked remains, with a rag of government slops and a rusty basil still around them, would be found in the bush between Parramatta and Pittwater.

The first large group of "Chinese travellers," as they came to be derisively known, took off from Rose Hill in November 1791—twenty men and one woman, Irish convicts off the *Queen*. They separated, blundered about in the bush for days, and in their starving bewilderment were easily recaptured (although three of them were so sure they had nearly reached China that they soon ran away again, and died). In time, the China myth was joined by another fancy, reported by Collins with his usual disapproval of the croppies who held it: "In addition to their natural vicious propensities, they conceived an opinion that there was a colony of white people, which had been discovered in this country, situated to the SW of the settlement, from which it was distant between three and four hundred miles." This other Shangri-la, where no work ever needed to be done, sustained some hope for a time.[2]

In 1798 the Irish were still running away to China, as many as sixty people at a time. Since none of them had a compass (and few possessed any idea of how to use it even if they had had one), they went out armed with a magical facsimile consisting of a circle crudely sketched on paper or bark with the cardinal points but no needle.

In 1803, King reported that fifteen "infatuated" Irish had made a run to China from Castle Hill; they were out for four days "committing every possible enormity except Murder" (one blew half a constable's face away with a musket, but he lived). The court sentenced them all to death, but King only hanged two. He then fixed the punishment for bolting at five hundred lashes, plus double chains for the remainder of the sentence. He expressed the hope that "the Convicts at Large will be assured that their ridiculous plans of leaving public labor to go into the Mountains, to China, &c., can only end in their immediate detection and punishment."[3]

As the settlement slowly moved outward and tracks were made through the raw bush, even the blindest optimist could see that the convict skeletons that kept turning up must mean something. The will to walk to Peking guttered out as it became clear that the logical escape route from this continental prison was not the land but the sea.

The sea route produced one epic escape in the early 1790s whose notoriety blossomed in London, reached back to Botany Bay and gave heart to would-be absconders for years to come. It was led by a woman, Mary Bryant (b. 1765)—"the Girl from Botany Bay," as the English press later dubbed her—who, with her two small children, her husband William Bryant, and seven other convicts, managed to sail a stolen boat all the way north from Sydney to Timor, a distance of 3,250 miles in just under ten weeks. As a nautical achievement, this compared with William Bligh's six-week voyage in a longboat from Tahiti to Timor with the "loyalists" of the *Bounty* in 1789. No one since James Cook in the *Endeavour*, twenty-one years before, had sailed all the way up the eastern coast of Australia, through the treacherous Barrier Reef, and lived to tell about it.[4]

Mary Bryant, née Broad, was a sailor's daughter from the little port of Fowey, in Cornwall. She had been transported for seven years for stealing a cloak. She went with the First Fleet, on the transport *Charlotte*. Before the fleet reached Cape Town, Mary Bryant gave birth to a girl and named her Charlotte, after the ship. Soon after the fleet reached Port Jackson, Mary Broad married one of the male convicts, who fathered her second child, Emanuel, born in April 1790. He, too, was Cornish and had come out on *Charlotte*. He was a thirty-one-year-old fisherman named William Bryant. Like many another Cornishman who kept a boat on that wild and indented coast, Bryant was a smuggler as well as a sailor, and in 1784 he had been convicted of resisting arrest at the hands of excise officers. He had already spent three years in the hulks when the First Fleet sailed, and his full seven-year sentence still loomed before him.

A fisherman was just what the half-starved colony needed. Governor Phillip put Bryant in charge of the boats that hauled the fishing nets every day in the harbor. But the black-market opportunities were too good for a Cornish smuggler to resist. He was caught selling some of his fish on the sly, instead of delivering them all to the Government Store; for this, he got one hundred lashes. If he had not set his heart on it before, Bryant was now determined to escape. At worst, he would rather drown quickly at sea than starve inch by inch on land. He had access to the boats but had no weapons, tools, navigational instruments, charts or food.

In October 1790 an East Indies trader, the *Waaksamheyd*, lumbered into Port Jackson heavily freighted with stores from Djakarta. Her Dutch captain, Detmer Smit, felt no obligations to the English convict system. He listened to William Bryant and was persuaded to part with a compass, a quadrant, muskets, food and even a chart of the waters between Sydney and Timor. Bryant hid this precious stuff in rolls of bark under the floor-boards of his hut and began assembling a crew. He picked his time care-fully. In March 1791 the *Supply* was dispatched to Norfolk Island. At the end of the month, *Waaksamheyd*, having sold the last of her cargo and finished her repairs, also set sail. Now there were no ships left in Port Jackson—nothing that could overtake an escaping boat. On the night of March 28, in the dark of the moon, the Bryants, their two children and seven other convicts scrambled into the governor's own six-oar cutter. In nervous silence, holding their breaths every time the oar-blades kissed the dark water, they rowed out into the harbor, past the little island of Pinchgut, heading east to the gate of the Pacific. The lookout on South Head did not see the cutter as it crept by in the night. They turned north toward New Guinea.

Their escape caused consternation next morning. The officers could hardly believe that although most of the men who had escaped had "con-nections" with female convicts in the settlement, not one woman had breathed a word about the long-laid escape plan. "They were too faithful to those they lived with to reveal it," observed David Collins. One of the men, a spare-time cabinetmaker named James Cox who had been trans-ported for life on the First Fleet for stealing 12 yards of lace and a pair of stockings, left a note on his workbench for his lover Sarah Young. It was a plain, fond letter, "conjuring her to give over the pursuit of the vices which, he told her, prevailed in the settlement, leaving to her what little property he did not take with him, and assigning as a reason for his flight the severity of his situation, being transported for life, without the pros-pect of any mitigation, or hope of ever quitting the country."[5]

By no means all the guards were unsympathetic to the escape. "They got Clear off," wrote a marine private, John Easty, in his diary,

> but its a very Desperate attempt, to go in an open boat for a run of about 16 or 17 hundred Leags and in pertucalar for a Woman and 2 small Chil-dren the eldest not above 3 years of age—but the thoughts of Liberty from such a place as this is Enoufh to induce any Convicts to try all Skeemes to obtain it, as they are the same as Slaves all the time they are in this Country.[6]

At first the going was easy. At their landings they found edible palms whose hearts they chopped out, "a Varse Quantity of Fish which [was] of a great Refreshment to us," and natives either friendly or timid. But then the rain poured and the seas rose; for five continuous weeks, they were soaked to the skin and rarely able to light a cooking fire. On the long stretch of surf-bound coast between Port Macquarie and Brisbane they were driven out to sea by an adverse wind, and "making no harbour or

Creek for nere three weeks we were much distress'd for water and food."
There was a brief respite for them in "White Bay being in Latt$^d$ 27°"
probably Moreton Bay. But on leaving it, they were blown out to sea
again, helpless before

> a heavy Gale of Wind and Current, expecting every Moment to go to the
> Bottom; next morn$^g$ saw no Land, the sea running Mountains high . . .
> thinking every Moment to be the last, the sea Coming in so heavy upon
> us every now and then that two Hands was obliged to keep Bailing out
> and it rained very hard all that night . . . [We] cou'd make no Land [the
> next] Day—I will leave you to Consider what distress we must be in, the
> Woman and the two little Babies was in a bad condition, everything being
> so Wet that we Cou'd by no means light a Fire, we had nothing to Eat
> except a little raw rice.[7]

After several days of this ordeal they were blown ashore, half-dead,
on one of the desert islands of the Barrier Reef. On its circling coral they
found turtles, one of which furnished "a Noble Meal this Night."
They butchered a dozen and made jerky of their meat. Thus victualled,
they made the coast again and kept creeping north, stopping for water
wherever they could get ashore, caulking the cutter—whose seams were
loosened by the incessant pounding of the ocean—with soap and turtle-
fat, fighting skirmishes with hostile blacks. Food was short all the way,
but they were all still alive when they turned the point of Cape York
Peninsula, the northernmost tip of Australia, and found themselves in
the Arafura Sea with a clear run—pursued, part of the way, by stout
cannibals in mat-sailed canoes—of five hundred miles of open water to
Arnhem Land, and another five hundred to Timor. They reached Koepang
in Timor on June 5 and passed themselves off to the local Dutch governor
as survivors of a shipwreck on the Australian coast. In new clothes, with
full bellies, they settled down to wait for a ship back to England. But
after a couple of months, by Martin's account, Bryant for some unexplained reason told the truth to the Dutch governor. Perhaps he got
drunk:

> W$^m$ Bryant had words with his wife, went and informed against himself
> Wife and children and all of us, [upon] which we was immediately taken
> Prisoners and was put into the Castle we was strictly examined.

The governor now put them in detention. In mid-September, some
more shipwrecked Englishmen appeared from the sea at Koepang: Captain Edward Edwards, who had been chasing the *Bounty* mutineers in
the frigate *Pandora*. He had captured some of them at Tahiti but lost his

ship on a reef south of New Guinea; in the pinnace, longboat and two yawls, he and 120 survivors had escaped the wreck and made their way across the Arafura Sea to Timor. Now Edwards took the Bryants and their comrades prisoner; they were clapped in irons, put on board the *Rembang*, a Dutch East Indiaman, and shipped to Batavia. In that me-phitic port, both William Bryant and his little son Emanuel died of fever just before Christmas 1791.

The survivors were shipped back to the Cape. Three of the men died at sea. At the Cape, Mary Bryant, her daughter and the remaining four convicts—James Martin, William Allen, James Brown and Nathaniel Lucas—were put on board the *Gorgon*, the man-o'-war which was carry-ing the marine detachment (just replaced by the newly formed New South Wales Corps) back from Australia to London. "We was well known by all of the marine officers which was all Glad that we had not perished at sea," Martin noted. That he did not exaggerate this is shown by the remarks of Captain Watkin Tench, of the Royal Marines, who had known the Bryants and Martin on the outward voyage of the First Fleet ("always distinguished for good behavior") and now, seeing them on board the *Gorgon*, could not suppress his esteem for them. "I confess that I never looked at these people," he wrote, "without pity and astonishment. They had miscarried in a heroic struggle for liberty; after having combated every hardship, and conquered every difficulty . . . I could not but reflect with admiration, at the strange combination of circumstances which had again brought us together, to baffle human foresight, and confound human speculation."[8]

Mary Bryant's sufferings were not over yet. On May 5, her three-year-old Charlotte died and was buried at sea. When she reached London and was committed to Newgate as an escaped felon, all she could look for-ward to was another transport ship, more irons and a second voyage to Botany Bay. But Mary Bryant soon acquired friends. Word got out about that indomitable curiosity, "the Girl from Botany Bay," who had so far overcome the inherent weakness of her sex to make this epic voyage through cannibals, coral, fever-isles and mountainous seas, from the edge of the chart back to England and civilization. Surely a just government could not send this bereaved heroine and her companions back to the thief-colony? So thought James Boswell, for one; and this kind-hearted writer pressed Dundas, the home secretary, and Evan Nepean, the under-secretary of state, with letters urging clemency and pardon for her. In May 1793, Mary Bryant received an unconditional pardon. Boswell then settled an annuity of £10 on her, and back she went to Cornwall. In November 1793 her four companions were pardoned, too; one of them promptly, if unexpectedly, enlisted in the New South Wales Corps and set sail again for Botany Bay.[9]

Boswell's interest in Mary Bryant was such that his friends, used to his amatory divings among the lower classes, joked that Botany Bay had given him a new mistress. One of them, William Parsons, penned a "Heroic Epistle from Mary Broad in Cornwall to James Boswell, Esq., in London." Mary languishes in her new, Cornish exile, pining for the Apollo of Auchinleck:

> Was it for this I braved the ocean's roar,
> And plied those thousand leagues the lab'ring oar?
> Oh, rather had I stayed, the willing prey
> Of grief and famine in the direful bay!
> Or perished, whelmed in the Atlantic tide!
> Or, home returned, in air suspended died!

Instead, she dreams of being united with her Boswell in the ultimate transport of bliss, their *liebestod* on the scaffold at Tyburn—a new thrill for her, and even for him:

> Great in our lives, and in our deaths as great,
> Embracing and embraced, we'll meet our fate:
> A happy pair, whom in supreme delight
> One love, one cord, one joy, one death unite!
> Let crowds behold with tender sympathy
> Love's true sublime in our last agony!
> First let our weight the trembling scaffold bear
> Till we consummate the last bliss in air.[10]

But despite the elegantly turned prurience of his friends, there is nothing to suggest that Boswell's interest in Mary Bryant—who faded from the newspapers and from history, on her return to Cornwall—was inspired by anything but compassion. His only souvenir of her (apart from some receipts for the annuity) was a packet of dried Australian "sweet tea" leaves, which she had held on to through thick and thin and given to him as a curiosity; they now repose in the archives of Yale University, very far from Botany Bay.

ii

AFTER THE BRYANTS made their escape from Sydney, security there had to be tightened. Collins, in April 1791, described the new arrangements: a sentinel at night on each wharf at Sydney Cove, and no boats allowed to leave the cove without direct spoken word from the officer of the guard, who also had to have a written list of all personnel, convict or free, allowed to use the fishing skiffs after sunset. Sydney Harbor was the gate to this little police-state and it had to be kept locked. In the beginning, with few ships coming and going, this was easy. But as traffic increased, the loophole widened. The Bryants' escape gave absconders new heart. "The lenity and compassion expressed in England [for them]," Hunter grumbled, "I fear may have contributed to encourage similar attempts now. Had those people been sent back and tried in this country for taking away the boat . . . we should not have any schemes of that kind projected now."[11]

American whaling captains out of Nantucket and Sag Harbor, who cared not a spit for English penal policies, let convicts stow away when they needed new crewmen. Some English transports, turned back into trading vessels for the homeward voyage, also let convicts on board—no less than thirty absconders were flushed from the transport *Hillsborough* as she made ready to leave Sydney in 1799. Even the French captain Nicolas Baudin, while mapping the southern coast of Australia in 1802–3, found eight convict stowaways on board; he cast them ashore on King Island in the Bass Strait, without holding out much hope of their survival.[12]

There were natural sympathies between convicts and sailors, for some tyrannous captains treated tars little better than prisoners. Crewmen would sometimes stow prisoners away in crannies that were unknown even to their officers. Before a ship sailed from Sydney or Hobart, the constables would swarm through her, banging on casks and prodding bales and sacks with their bayonets. Watchers on shore would see white smoke pouring from the ship's ports and ventilators, a sign that sulphur bombs had been ignited to smoke the stowaways out of their hiding places like rabbits from a warren. In 1814 a search of the trader *Earl Spencer* produced twenty-eight escapees, some concealed in barrels of flour and cheese and one wrapped up in a spare jib in the sail-locker. When the *Harriet*, a merchant ship out of Sydney, was found to have brought sixteen escaped convicts to the Cape even though she had been "diligently Searched" before sailing in December 1817, Governor Lachlan Macquarie complained to Lord Bathurst that

> it is scarcely possible to find these Runaways, when the Sailors are in league with them and Connive at their Concealment on board, few ships leaving this Port without Carrying off some Convicts of both Sexes in the same way . . . [T]he Convicts, who have been the Shortest Time in the Colony, are always those who are the Most Anxious to make their Escape from it.[13]

In 1826 a memo to George Arthur, lieutenant-governor of Van Diemen's Land, outlined some of the security problems in Hobart. The seal

trade in Bass Strait was mainly carried on by runaways working for mainland businessmen, most of whom were Emancipists themselves. Arthur's correspondent lamented

> the facility with which a Prisoner gets conveyed away from the Colony
> in the boats and small Vessels employed in Sealing . . . They soon find
> Employment in the Straits, become sharers in Plunder, and finally get
> away to New Zealand, or some other more distant Country.[14]

Arthur clamped such strict port regulations on Hobart that not even
a mouse, one would have thought, could get through them. Every ship in
the Derwent River had to have a 24-hour officer watch, or else face severe
and automatic fines. All vessels leaving were "searched and smoked"—
fumigated with sulphur to drive stowaways out. For every convict found
on board a vessel, each officer and seaman was fined a month's wages, to
be paid in full by the captain before the ship could sail. Informers were
exempt from this, and any informer got half the total fine from the ship's
crew if a convict were found on board, the search-party receiving the
other half. Since any seaman who informed in this way—and ended up
with his shipmate's wages—would face an unusually short and unpleasant life after his vessel cleared the D'Entrecasteaux Channel, Arthur's
regulations permitted the informer to "have his discharge from the ship
should he require it," unless he had actually brought the absconders on
board himself.[15]

By 1820, Hobart was the main port for whaling and sealing, and Sydney the same for island trading in sandalwood, pearlshell, bêche-de-mer
and New Zealand spar timber, throughout the South Pacific. Each had to
be both a jail and a port of call—an awkward contradiction. In stowing
away, most convicts merely exchanged one kind of imprisonment for
another. It was a fine arrangement for the ship's masters because, once
on board, the convict could not return to land—not, at any rate, to New
South Wales or Van Diemen's Land—without risking the gallows. He
was shanghaied, and there was no romance in this cramped world of the
fo'c'sle and the skinning-knife. Yet it was better than the chain gang. By
the 1830s the southern bays and refuges, from the Bay of Islands in New
Zealand (a veritable rookery of absconders) to the Recherche Archipelago
on the west coast of Australia, were littered with grim little communities and patriarchal clans of convicts.

On other trading vessels, they ranged even farther afield. The sandalwood trade littered the central Pacific with escaped convicts. For a short
time, between about 1812 and 1816, American ships had been kept out
of the Pacific by the British-American War. This gave the Sydney traders,
merchants like William Campbell and Simeon Lord, a near-monopoly on

the cutting of sandalwood, the rare and sweetly aromatic timber for which there was an enormous market among the Chinese. It grew on mid-Pacific islands, most profusely in the Marquesas and the Tuamotus. Between 1811 and 1821, colonial trading vessels out of Sydney, such as Campbell's diplomatically named *Governor Macquarie*, brought back perhaps a quarter of the total sandalwood harvest of the Marquesas. On the islands, the wood was not so much gathered as plundered. If a captain ran short of trading goods to exchange for sandalwood, he would steal them from one island to sell to another, as John Martin, master of the *Queen Charlotte*, stole canoes from Tahuata to sell in Nuku Hiva in 1815.

No law restrained these captains, and only their own violence—the lash, the battened hatch, the duck's-foot pistol with its splayed barrels that could blast a fan of slugs down on a companionway and make a shambles of mutineers—could restrain their crews. They would find space on board for any escaping convict. But it was a one-way trip: Such absconders would be cast ashore three thousand miles from Sydney to fend for themselves as beachcombers. Sometimes a captain would be genuinely surprised by their presence on board. Thomas Hammond, master of the Pacific trader *Endeavour*, did not know he had five escaped convicts until they came blinking from their holes in the 'tween-decks on the way to New Zealand. He wanted to put them ashore there, but the magistrate in the Bay of Islands refused to let them land unless Hammond left six months' provisions for them, so he sailed on and dumped them on the beach of Hiva Oa in the Marquesas.[16]

It is not known how many escaped convicts ended up as beachcombers on the sandalwood islands. Hundreds of them must have been scattered in remote parts of the Pacific. "Strangers in their new societies and scandals to their old," they contributed their own violence and opportunism, incubated and hardened by the System, to the ruin of the island cultures. By 1850 there was no part of the Pacific where the name of Botany Bay did not carry a sour infected reek—the breath of England, gone carious in double exile.

It was much harder for convicts to steal a boat for themselves than to stow away on someone else's; but that did not prevent some from trying. Most attempts to escape from Australia on stolen or secretly built craft failed. The Bryants' escape became legendary precisely because it was unique. More typical by far was the escape in September 1790 of a party of five life-sentence convicts off the Second Fleet. They stole a punt from Rose Hill, poled it down the Parramatta River to Sydney Harbor, stole a "very small and weak" skiff from the look-out station at South Head and set out for Tahiti with a week's food, three iron pots, some bedding and no compass. Naturally, no trace of them was ever found. One desperate man tried to get away from Major Foveaux's atrocious reign on Norfolk Island, around 1800, by stealing a door, cutting two leg-holes in it, and paddling out over the Kingston reef in the hope of somehow floating a thousand miles to the Australian mainland. In secret, men constructed skiffs out of green eucalyptus wood, which opened and sank; risked being skinned by the cat-o'-nine-tails to hide precious iron nails in their mouths, armpits, anuses; stole twine and needles to sew coracles out of kangaroo skin. Thomas Cook, author of *The Exile's Lamentations*, spent weeks working by moonlight in relays with four accomplices, building a boat hidden in the bush of Norfolk Island:

> Many sleepless hours did I experience in silent meditation on the schemes of Escape. All consideration of the long and perilous voyage of 1000 miles in a precarious Boat over the watery deep without either chart or compass was waived by the thought of my afflicted Parents, and the impossibility of my ever more seeing them in this world. . . . Blessed and sweet Liberty, that I had been doomed to forfeit in a place of unparallelled torture & sin, now appeared to me in all its grandeur. Those who I held dear now appeared in my dreams as transported by joy at my presence. But Alas! How visionary my calculations! A clue was gained to the boat by some means then to me unknown.[17]

The skiff, nearly finished, was found and destroyed. Such projects could not be kept secret, especially in the confines of Norfolk Island.

Sometimes, though not often, a group of convicts would manage to pirate a full-size ship. In 1797 the *Cumberland*, a Sydney-built smack, the "largest and best boat in the colony," according to Governor Hunter, was seized by an Irish convict crew on a routine trip delivering stores from Sydney to the Hawkesbury River; she went north and was never seen again, although Hunter sent a rowboat laden with armed men after her for sixty blistering miles.[18]

Late one Sunday night in May 1808, as the brig *Harrington* was riding quietly at anchor in Farm Cove in Sydney Harbor under the very windows of the Pacific trader William Campbell, her owner, a "body of desperadoes"—some fifty convicts—silently came alongside in boats and swarmed over her rail. Her chief officer awoke staring down the bore of a pistol held by the ringleader, Robert Stewart; other convicts stole forward and pinioned the crew. They cut the ship's anchor-cables and used the rowboats to tow her down the harbor to the Heads, and by dawn they were well out to sea. Stewart put the officers and crew over the side, into the boats. It took them eight hours to row back to Sydney, and by then the *Harrington* was over the horizon. It was thought that she would never be seen again—she had just been fully provisioned for a voyage to

Fiji—but three months later she ran on a reef in the South China Sea and was taken by a Manila-bound British frigate, the *Phoenix*. Robert Stewart and other ringleaders were shipped back to Sydney and hanged.[19]

Despite a widespread belief among the free that convicts who pirated boats wrought orgies of vengeance on their unhappy crews and passengers, the absconders usually showed pity and moderation. In 1826 the brig *Wellington* was seized by the sixty-six convicts it was taking to Norfolk Island. They killed nobody and, having carried the ship, solicitously treated the minor flesh wounds, cuts and bruises some of the guards had suffered. Having shaped their course for New Zealand, the convicts set up a "Council of Seven" to keep order on board and especially to punish any mutineers who tried to dishonor the escape by brutalizing their former guards. Such people were to be put back in irons and then dropped ashore in New Zealand, "instead of proceeding with us to our ultimate destination." One of the convicts was actually found guilty of "attempting a revolt and mutiny" by urging his fellow prisoners to revenge and was sentenced to spend the rest of the run to New Zealand in irons day and night on deck. The new masters of the *Wellington* kept a log of these respectable proceedings, parts of which sound cozy, almost domestic:

> This being Christmas Day, and the only deficiency we have at present found on the part of government, was in not supplying us with plums; issued an order, if any individual on board had any plums they must be given up for all hands; plums were procured, four geese killed, together with three sheep, spent a very comfortable day, moderately indulging ourselves with some gin and brandy.[20]

The *Wellington* and its escapees were recaptured by a whaler in New Zealand, and this log told in their favor at their trial. When their merciful conduct was revealed—and confirmed by the ship's guards and crew—there was a swell of public sympathy for them, and out of twenty-three men condemned to hang, only five were actually executed.

The prisoners who seized the brig *Cyprus* in 1828 were less fortunate, although their escapade became as celebrated in convict lore as the Bryants'. By the early 1830s they had become the subject of one of the "treason songs" or proscribed convict ballads. The men of *Cyprus*, reconvicted in Van Diemen's Land for "little trifling offences," were being taken from Hobart to the penal station of Macquarie Harbor, "that place of tyranny":

> Down Hobart Town streets we were gathered, on the *Cyprus* brig conveyed,
> Our topsails they were hoisted, boys, our anchor it was weighed,

The wind it blew a nor'-nor'-west, and on we steered straightway,
Till we brought her to an anchorage in a place called Recherche Bay.

The facts do not match the song at all points. Far from being guilty of
minor offenses, most of the thirty-one convicts going to Macquarie Harbor on the *Cyprus* had been convicted of capital crimes but had had their
sentences commuted. The most intrepid of them was a former sailor,
William Swallow. Swallow was a veritable Houdini. In 1810 he had hijacked a schooner in Port Jackson and been sent to Van Diemen's Land
as his secondary punishment. The ship that took him there, the *Deveron*,
was disabled in a storm and Swallow, "remarking that his own life was
of little moment," volunteered to go aloft and cut away a slatting tangle
of broken spars and rigging. It seems that the *Deveron*'s sailors were so
grateful for his courage in saving the ship that, as soon as Swallow was
landed in Hobart, they smuggled him back on board. Thus he escaped,
and got all the way west across the ocean to Rio, where he was captured
again by the British authorities. Once more he got free and stowed away
on a London-bound boat. But he was finally recognized in London, arrested and shipped out again to Van Diemen's Land. Such was the man
who, "confined within a dismal hole" with his fellow convicts as the
*Cyprus* rode at anchor near the southern tip of Van Diemen's Land,
decided to make a last bid

To take possession of that brig or else die every man:
The plan it being approv'd upon, we soon retired to rest,
And early next morning, boys, we put them to the test.

Up steps bold Jack Muldeamon, his comrades three more—
We soon disarmed the sentry and left him in his gore:
"Liberty, O liberty! It's liberty we crave—
Surrender up your arms, my boys, or the sea shall be your grave!"

After a rush, a scuffle and some shooting, the convicts overpowered
the guard and carried the ship. They put the officer-in-charge, Lieutenant
Carew, over the side along with his wife, the soldiers and thirteen convicts who had not joined the mutiny. The *Cyprus* was heavily laden with
stores for Macquarie Harbor, enough to sustain 400 men for six months,
but the convicts gave the forty-five castaways a stingy ration—a live
sheep, some salt beef, a bag of biscuits and 30 pounds of flour, with no
weapons and no boat:

First we landed the soldiers, the captain and his crew,
We gave three cheers for Liberty, and soon bid them adieu:

William Swallow he was chosen our commander for to be—
We gave three cheers for Liberty, and boldly put to sea.
Lay on your golden trumpets, boys, and sound their cheerful note!
The *Cyprus* brig's on the ocean, boys, by Justice does she float!

After prolonged sufferings from exposure and starvation, living on a handful of raw mussels and a quarter-biscuit a day, the castaways eventually got back to Hobart. They might not have done so without a convict named Popjoy, who framed up a 12-foot coracle out of mimosa branches, covered it with hammock canvas (sewn by Mrs. Carew, who had a needle) and waterproofed it with soap and resin. Popjoy and Carew sailed this fragile shell twenty miles to Partridge Island, where they were saved by a passing ship.*

In the meantime, the *Cyprus* and her pirates were well away. Swallow shaped his course for Tahiti, and then turned north for Japan, where he and his crew landed some time in 1829; seven of the convicts jumped ship there. Several months later, Swallow and three of his mates appeared in a skiff off the Chinese trading port of Whampoa. They had abandoned the *Cyprus*. Swallow presented himself to officials in Canton as Captain Waldron of the ship *Edward*, set on fire and sunk at sea by the Japanese. In this way, Swallow and his mates wangled a free passage home to England. Unfortunately, soon after they sailed, other survivors of the *Cyprus* turned up in Canton and Swallow's story began to unravel. Eventually, Swallow and his mates were arrested in England, and were identified by Popjoy, who, by a bizarre stroke of colonial ill-luck, had returned to London after receiving a free pardon for helping save the castaways at Recherche Bay. But Popjoy insisted that Swallow had been forced by his fellow absconders to navigate the ship, and the court believed him. So, although Swallow's companions were hanged, he was not. For the third time, he was forced to go on board a transport and make the long, lugubrious journey to Australia. It was his last. As soon as he arrived in Hobart, he was shipped to Macquarie Harbor—and this time there was no escape. William Swallow eventually died of tuberculosis in the penal colony of Port Arthur, to which he had been transferred when Macquarie Harbor was closed down in 1834. Unfortunately, he never wrote a memoir of his adventures.[21]

But one later absconder did: James Porter, a twenty-six-year-old Londoner who helped his convict companions, ex-sailors among them, to hijack the brig *Frederick* from the slipway where they had built her for the government at Macquarie Harbor in 1833, just as the settlement was

---

* The rescue of the survivors of the *Cyprus*, and Popjoy's construction of the coracle, was adapted by Marcus Clarke in *His Natural Life*.

being abandoned. This caused much embarrassment, not least because the vessel had been named after one of Lieutenant-Governor Arthur's seven sons. They cast the guards and crew ashore (all survived) and with remarkable skill and courage sailed clear across the Pacific to the coast of Chile, where they abandoned her to sink and took to the longboat. Reaching Valdivia, they came before its Chilean governor, who assumed that they were pirates, not innocent shipwrecked sailors, and promised to shoot them. Porter saved their skins with a stirring speech (as recorded years later, by himself):

"Avast there! We as sailors shipwrecked and in distress expected when we made this port to have been treated in a Christian-like manner, not as though we were dogs! Is this the way you would have treated us in 1818 when the British Tars were fighting for your independence, and bleeding in your cause against the old Spaniards? If we were pirates do you suppose we should be so weak as to cringe to your tyranny? Never! I also wish you to understand that if we are shot England will know of it and will be revenged . . . [S]hould you put your threat into execution we will teach you Patriots how to die."[22]

Impressed by this magnificent bluff, the governor let them stay unmolested, and asked his superiors in Santiago to issue them with residence permits. Porter and his companions now settled down to a picaresque life among the ladies and knife-wielders of Chile. But the governor was replaced soon afterward, and his successor—suspicious that Porter and his shipmates were, in fact, escaped convicts—alerted a passing British frigate, HMS *Blond*. Thus they were taken again, first back to England, and then on a second transport ship to Van Diemen's Land. On the weary voyage south, Porter was falsely denounced as a mutineer by two of his former shipmates, Charles Lyon and William Cheshire, who hoped to curry favor with the captain and escape hanging for piracy when, as seemed inevitable, they were recognized in Hobart. "Knowing my innocence I stood nearly petrified," he recounted:

I was seized by the soldiers and seamen, lashed to a grating (and to that degree until the blood hoosed from the parts where the lashings went round different parts of my person) and a lump of a black-fellow flogged me across the lines and every other part of my body until my head sank on my breast. As for the quantity of lashes I cannot say, for I would not give them the satisfaction to scringe to it, until nature gave way through exhaustion.

Then he and his mate William Shires were chained below, bleeding and infected, hands manacled behind their backs, in a steaming rat's-hole and were given no more than quarter-rations of water and food for three weeks, until they presented "the appearance of anatomies [i.e., skeletons] more than living beings." "I craved for death," Porter noted, but on recovering the use of his arms he wrote a pathetic verse on a scrounged leaf of paper:

> How wretched is an Exile's state of mind
> When not one gleam of hope on earth remain,
> Through grief worn down, with servile chains confined,
> And not one friend to soothe his heartfelt pain.
>
> Too true I know that man was made to mourn,
> A heavy portion's fallen to my lot
> With anguish full my aching heart is torn
> Far from my friends, by all the world forgot.
>
> The feathered race with splendid plumage gay
> Extent their throats with a discordant sound,
> With Liberty they spring from spray to spray,
> While I a wretched Exile gaze around.
>
> Farewell my sister, Aged Aunts dear,
> Ere long my glass of life will cease to run,
> In silence drop a sympathetic tear
> For your Unhappy, Exiled, Long-Lost Son.
>
> O cease, my troubled aching Heart, to beat,
> Since happiness so far from thee has fled!
> Haste, haste unto your silent cold retreat
> In clay-cold earth to mingle with the Dead.

But Porter was not to die; or not yet. He survived the voyage and landed in Hobart in March 1837, where he was instantly recognized as one of the pirates of the *Frederick*. He was tried and convicted of piracy, despite his ingenious argument in defense: As the vessel had not been formally commissioned by the government—"it was canvas, rope, boarding and trenails, put together shipwise—yet it was not a legal ship: the seizure might be theft, but not piracy." Luckily for him, "the bloodthirsty Arthur" had left Van Diemen's Land five months earlier, "and had not the colony been under the Government of the humane Sir John Franklin I should not now have been alive to have given this small Narrative." So Porter and Shires did not hang. They ended up on Norfolk Island, where Porter was able to write his memoirs under the kindly eye of Captain Alexander Maconochie.

These were the last men to escape from Macquarie Harbor, but they were by no means the first. Ever since 1821, when Lieutenant-Governor

Sorell had pitched this dreaded prison settlement on the isolated west coast of Van Diemen's Land, convicts had been trying to get away from it, mostly on foot. In 1822 and 1823, one man in ten disappeared. In 1824, the rate rose to nearly one in seven. They went inland, trying to reach the settled and farmed districts to the east, and most of them died. In the long list of Macquarie Harbor absconders for the first six years of settlement, only eight carry a brief remark like "Reported to have reached the cultivated part of the island: this requires confirmation." The rest is a gray official litany, punctuated by sparks of saturnine humor. Timothy Crawley, Richard Morris, John Newton, June 2, 1824: "Seized the soldiers' boat, provicions, fire-arms &c., and supposed to have perished in their way across the interior. The boat was afterwards found moored to a Stump, and written upon her stern, with chalk, 'to be Sold.' " But the usual requiem was "Supposed to have perished in the woods."[23]

Only one man escaped from Macquarie Harbor twice. His name was Alexander Pearce (1790–1824), a little, pockmarked, blue-eyed Irishman from County Monaghan who had been transported for seven years at the Armagh Assizes in 1819, for stealing six pairs of shoes.[24] He had arrived in Van Diemen's Land in 1820, and as an assigned servant he gave continuous trouble to his masters by running away, stealing and getting drunk. He soon learned enough bush skills to "stay out" for three months at a stretch with some other absconders. Flogging did not impress him. Eventually, in 1822, he was sent to Macquarie Harbor for forging a two-pound money order and absconding from service. On September 20, 1822, Pearce seized an open boat from Kelly's Basin on Macquarie Harbor, where he had been working in a sawpit gang. Seven other convicts piled into the craft with him. Two of them had already tried to escape from Van Diemen's Land by stealing a schooner moored in the Derwent estuary: Matthew Travers, an Irishman under life sentence of transportation, and Robert Greenhill, a sailor from Middlesex. For that failed escape, they had been sent to Macquarie Harbor. The others were an ex-soldier, William Dalton (perjury in Gibraltar, fourteen years); a highway robber, Thomas Bodenham; William Kennelly, alias Bill Cornelius, transported for seven years and re-sentenced to Macquarie Harbor for an escape attempt; John Mather, a young Scottish baker, working a seven-year sentence and then sent to Macquarie Harbor for forging a £15 money order; and a man called "Little Brown," whose Christian name is unknown and who cannot, due to the commonness of his surname, be identified.

Flogged with the adrenaline of escape, the eight men rowed across the harbor, ran the boat ashore, smashed its bottom with a stolen axe, and set out on foot. At first they made good time through the dank maze of the shore forest, lugging their axes and their meager rations. They spent the night on the slopes of Mount Sorell, not daring to light a fire, and struck east the next morning toward the Derwent River, where they planned to steal a schooner, sail it downstream past Hobart and out into Storm Bay and so "proceed home," 14,000 miles to England. The first leg of their route lay across the Darwin Plateau, keeping to the north of the Gordon River.[25]

Before them, although they did not know it, lay some of the worst country in Australia. Even today, bushwalkers rarely venture into the mountains between Macquarie Harbor and the inland plains: fold after fold, scarp on scarp, with giant trees growing to a hundred feet from clefts in the steep rock where, clambering along rotted limbs or floundering through the entangling ferns and creepers, one cannot possibly move in a straight line. The convicts struggled along in a gray, dripping twilight from dawn to dusk, with one man beating the scrub in front "to make the road." At night, like exhausted troglodytes, afraid of winds and shadows, they lit a fire in the cleft of a rock and huddled around it to sleep as best they could. Within a week, the weather turned to gales and sleet and their little store of tinder was soaked. Then they finished the last of their rations. Hungry, cold and failing, the band struggled for another two days through "a very rough country . . . in a very weak state for want of provisions."

But now the fugitives were straggling. "Little Brown . . . was the worst walker of any; he always fell behind, and then kept cooing [sic] so that we said we would leave him behind if he could not keep up better."[26] No man felt able to gather all the wood for a fire. In the feeble hysteria of exhaustion, they began to squabble about who should do it; in the end, each convict scraped together enough twigs for himself and eight little fires were lit. Kennelly made what might or might not have been meant as a joke. "I am so weak," he said to Pearce and Greenhill, "that I could eat a piece of a man."

They thought about that all night, and "in the morning," Pearce's narrative goes on,

> there were four of us for a feast. Bob Greenhill was the first who introduced it, and said he had seen the like done before, and that it eat much like a little pork.

John Mather protested. It would be murder, he said; and useless, too, since they might not be able to choke the flesh down. Greenhill overrode him:

> "I will warrant you," said Greenhill, "I will well do it first myself and eat the first of it; but you must all lend a hand, so that you may all be equal

in the crime." We then consulted who should fall. Greenhill said, "Dalton; as he volunteered to be a flogger, we will kill him."

In these flat declarative outlines, the scene might come from an Elizabethan revenge-tragedy: the conclave, the ritual to overcome the great taboo, the literary diction, the avenging choice of the flogger as victim. Indeed, it may be too pat; Dalton was never a flogger at Macquarie Harbor, and other "literary" touches in the narrative may come from the amanuensis to whom Pearce eventually dictated his story. But in any case, Dalton was killed. He fell sound asleep at about three in the morning, and Greenhill's axe

> struck him on the head, and he never spoke a word after . . . Matthew Travers with a knife also came and cut his throat, and bled him; we then dragged him to a distance, and cut off his clothes, and tore out his inside, and cut off his head; then Matthew Travers and Greenhill put his heart and liver on the fire and eat it before it was right warm; they asked the rest would they have any, but they would not have any that night.

But the next morning, hunger won. They had been without food for four days. Dalton's flesh was carved and doled out into seven roughly equal portions, and the band got moving again.

Brown was walking slower and slower; he must have reflected as he limped along that he, the weakest, would be next. Kennelly, too, was afraid for his life. And so the two of them fell back, and silently disappeared in the forest mazes of the Engineer Range, hoping to get back to Macquarie Harbor. Realizing that their story "would hang us all," the others tried to catch them but failed. On October 12, Brown and Kennelly were found half-dead from exposure on the shore of Macquarie Harbor, still with pieces of human flesh in their pockets. Brown died in the prison hospital on October 15, and Kennelly four days later.

Now five convicts were left. They reached the Franklin River, swollen with rain, and spent two days trying to cross it; Pearce, Greenhill and Mather went across first and dragged the other two over with the help of a long pole. Mather was crippled with dysentery and the others "were scarcely able to move, for we were so cold and wet." But they struggled on across the Deception Range and then the Surveyor Range after that, and on October 15 they saw below them a fine open valley, probably the Loddon Plains. Here, in the long grass by a creek, thoughts of fresh food rose again. It was Bodenham's turn to die. As he slept, Greenhill split his skull. Ten years later, the first official explorer to reach the Loddon Plains, a surveyor, would find human bones in this valley.[27]

Four men were left, and they kept marching. By about October 22, they had apparently reached the first line of the Western Tiers and before them lay "a very fine country," full of "many kangaroos and emus, and game of all kinds"; but they had no hunting weapons, and the frustration of starving while watching the mobs of shy gray marsupials bounding invulnerably past must have been overpowering. "We then said to ourselves," Pearce declared, "that we would all die together before anything should happen."

But Greenhill had no intention of dying together with anyone, and Mather was very apprehensive. He and Pearce "went to one side, and Mather said, Pearce, let us go on by ourselves; you see what kind of a cove Greenhill is; he would kill his father before he would fast one day." But on that open button-grass moor, which may have been the King William Plains, they could not have lost Greenhill. Since he carried the only axe they had left, he could not be killed; and none of the famished men could hobble faster than the rest. Thus bound together, they went on; and around the last week in October (from here, the chronology of Pearce's accounts grows hazier), they stopped by a little creek and lit a fire to boil the last of Bodenham, "which scarcely kept the Faculties in Motion."[28]

Mather could not eat his share. He had gathered some fern roots, which he boiled and wolfed down, but

> he found it would not rest on his stomach (no wonder) for such a Mess It could not be expected would ever digest in any Mortal whatever, which occasioned him to vomit to ease his Stomach & while in the act of discharging it from his Chest, Greenhill still showing his spontaneous habit of bloodshed seized the Axe & crept behind him gave him a blow on the head.

It did not kill Mather. He jumped up and grappled with Greenhill, wresting the axe from him. Pearce and Travers managed, for a time, to calm the two men down. But Mather was doomed, and that night the four men made camp around a fire "in a very pensive and melancholy mood." Greenhill and Travers, bosom friends, were determined to eat Mather next; Pearce, without telling Mather, was secretly on their side. He walked a little way from the fire and looked back: "I saw Travers and Greenhill collaring him." The team was at work again, and Pearce made no effort to save poor John Mather, who now made ready to die a Christian death, very far from England.

> They told him they would give him half an hour to pray for himself, which was agreed to; he then gave the Prayer-book to me, and laid down his head, and Greenhill took the axe and killed him. We then stopped two days in this place.

The three men kept heading east, but Travers was sinking. He had been bitten on the foot by a snake and could no longer walk. Terrified that his two companions would eat him, he begged them to leave him to die and go on with what remained of Mather, which might be rations enough to carry them to a settlement. Greenhill refused to abandon him. He and Pearce stayed with the delirious Travers for five days, tending him. Travers lapsed in and out of his fever, "in great agitation for fear that they would dispose of him. . . . [T]he unfortunate Man all this time had but little or no sleep."[29]

They half-dragged, half-carried Travers for several days more. But it was no use:

> [Greenhill and Pearce] began to Comment on the impossibility of ever being able to keep *Traviss* up with them for their strength was so nearly exhausted it was impossible for them to think of making any Settlement unless they left him. . . . It would be folly for them to leave him, for his flesh would answer as well for Subsistence as the others.

Travers awoke and, through his haze of pain, heard them talking.

> In the greatest agony [he] requested them in the most affecting manner not to delay themselves any longer, for it was morally impossible for him to attempt Travelling any more & therefore it would be useless for them to attempt to take him with them. . . . The Remonstrances of *Traviss* strengthened the designs of his companions.[30]

They killed Travers with the axe. The victim "only stretched himself in his agony, and then expired."

Now they were two. But for the kangaroos, the terrain through which Pearce and Greenhill were now walking was not unlike England: undulating fields of grass sprinkled with little copses, a mild and fruitful landscape ringed with hills, all golden in the early summer light.

> Greenhill began to fret, and said he would never get to any port with his life. I kept up my spirits all along, and thought we must shortly come to some inhabited parts of the country, from the very great length we had travelled.

But there could be no doubt that one would sooner or later eat the other. Greenhill had the axe, and the two men walked at a fixed distance apart. When Pearce stopped, so did Greenhill. When one squatted, so did the other. There was no question of sleep. "I watched Greenhill for two nights, for I thought he eyed me more than usual." One imagines them: a small fire of eucalyptus branches in the immense cave of the southern night, beneath the drift and icy prickle of unfamiliar stars; the secret bush noises beyond the outer ring of firelight—rustle of grass, flutter and croaking of nocturnal birds—all sharpened and magnified by fear, with the two men fixedly watching one another across the fire. One night Pearce became convinced of Greenhill's "bad disposition as to me." He waited, and near dawn his adversary fell asleep. "I run up, and took the axe from under his head, and struck him with it, and killed him. I then took part of his arm and thigh, and went on for several days."

Pearce was now utterly alone. "I then took a piece of a leather belt," he notes laconically, "and was going to hang myself; but I took another notion not to do it." He walked on a little further and blundered into his first stroke of good luck since Macquarie Harbor: a deserted aboriginal campsite. The blacks had seen him coming and had fled, leaving pieces of game scattered around their still-lit cooking-fires.

Pearce settled down and gorged himself on the first non-human meat he had tasted in nearly seven weeks. It gave him strength to keep going for several days until, from a hilltop, he glimpsed the landmark that signalled his arrival in the farmed country of the Derwent Valley: Table Mountain, a hill just south of Lake Crescent. Below him lay the Ouse, a large tributary stream of the Derwent.

Two days later, following the river down, Pearce came on a flock of sheep. He managed to grab and dismember a lamb. As he was devouring its raw flesh, a convict shepherd emerged from the bush "and said he would shoot me if I did not stop immediately."

The shepherd's name was McGuire, and he soon realized that he knew the blood-boltered little goblin he had at gunpoint. Before his banishment to Macquarie Harbor, Pearce had worked on a sheep run nearby. McGuire "carried the remains of the lamb, and took me with him into his hut, and made meat ready for me, where I stopped for three days, and he gave me all attendance." He would not turn a fellow Irishman in to the authorities, and for several weeks more Pearce hid in the huts of McGuire and other Irish convict shepherds. Then he fell in with a pair of bushrangers, Davis and Churton, who armed him; and they skulked about in the bush together for two more months. But his new companions had a £10 reward on their heads, and convict solidarity—never a dependable bond—could not hold up forever against that. On January 11, 1823, near the town of Jericho, the three of them were arrested by soldiers of the 48th Regiment acting on the word of informers and were brought down to Hobart in chains.

Churton and Davis were tried and hanged, an automatic punishment for bushrangers. While in jail, Pearce confessed the whole story of his escape—cannibalism and all—to the acting magistrate, the Reverend Robert Knopwood. It was transcribed and sealed, and not a word of it was believed. The authorities assumed—in the manner of the Cretan paradox —that since all convicts were liars, this one could only be covering for his "mates," who must still be alive and at large. This grotesque tall story could only be the invention of a felon's debased mind. There were no living witnesses to that nightmare trek from Macquarie Harbor to the Derwent, and no *corpus delicti*. And so Pearce was not executed; instead, they sent him back to Macquarie Harbor, where he arrived in February 1823.

He became, of course, a celebrity among the convicts. He was living proof that a man could get out of Macquarie Harbor, and only he kept the secret of how to do it. One newly arrived convict, a young laborer named Thomas Cox, kept begging to come along the next time. Finally, Pearce gave in to Cox's whispered entreaties; but he would not try the eastern route again. Instead, he decided to try and go north to Port Dalrymple—once again, through totally unexplored territory, but perhaps not as bad as the Western Tiers. On November 16, 1823, the two men absconded.[31]

They did not get far. On November 21, a lookout on Sarah Island saw a plume of smoke rising from a distant beach. The fire was also seen by a convict transport, the *Waterloo*, as it made sail for Hell's Gates. The ship lowered a boat, and the shore guard dispatched a launch. Before dark, the exhaused Pearce was back in the settlement where he told the commandant that he had killed Cox two days before and had been eating him since. By way of proof, he produced a piece of human flesh weighing about half a pound. Next morning he led a search-party to the bank of a stream, where Cox's body lay "in a dreadfully mangled state," according to one official report,

> being cut right through the middle, the head off, the privates torn off, all the flesh off the calves of the legs, back of the thighs and loins, also off the thick part of the arms, which the inhuman wretch declared was the most delicious food.[32]

Probably Pearce killed Cox in rage, not gluttony; his own account rings true, despite its apparent gratuitousness:

> We travelled on several days without food, except the tops of trees and shrubs, until we came upon King's River. I asked Cox if he could swim; he replied he could not; I remarked that had I been aware of it he should not have been my companion. . . . [T]he arrangement for crossing the river created words, and I killed Cox with the axe. . . . I swam the river with the intention of keeping the coast around [to] Port Dalrymple; my heart failed me, and I resolved to return.[33]

The authorities did the only thing they could. Pearce was shipped straight down to Hobart on the *Waterloo*, tried and hanged. When he was dead, a local artist, Thomas Bock, drew his likeness. The court had ordered that, as its ultimate brand of infamy, Pearce should be "disjointed" after death—delivered to the anatomizing surgeons. This was done, and Mr. Crockett, the head doctor in the Hobart Colonial Hospital, made a souvenir of the cannibal's head. He skinned it and scraped the flesh away, plucked out the eyes and the brain, and boiled the skull clean. Thirty years later, the relic was given to an American phrenologist, Dr. Samuel Morton, who was busy assembling his collection of skulls and shrunken heads, more than a thousand specimens, known as "The American Golgotha." It went into a glass cabinet in the Academy of Natural Sciences in Philadelphia, where it may still be seen, a yellowed label pasted across the blackened ivory bone, recording its small role in the taxonomy of an extinct scientific fad.

iii

In early New South Wales, up to 1825, the escaped convict was a bogey, a nuisance, an embarrassment to the seamless image of Authority —but rarely more. In Van Diemen's Land, however, he became a social force.

We have seen in Chapter 5 how the Tasmanian bushrangers began as convict kangaroo hunters who stayed out in the bush and formed gangs. Until the mid-1820s, the government had little chance of catching them, as it had few soldiers and none were skilled bushmen. No squad of stumbling "lobsters" could take these bandits. In the wild lovely terrain of Van Diemen's Land, riven by gorges and precipices, that was like trying to pluck quicksilver from a carpet with one's fingers.

Besides, some settlers had a vested interest in protecting them. As the populace's food supplies grew more secure and its dependence on kangaroo meat declined (although the need for the skins remained, as they were the main source of leather), the banditti took to sheep stealing. They would sell the mutton to free farmers for sugar, flour, tea and gunpowder, and vanish into the wild again. They stole from big farmers and sold to small "bent" ones, and with this began the Robin Hood reputation (wholly undeserved in nine cases out of ten) of the Australian bushranger. Sometimes assigned convicts would bring food to bushrangers in hiding, and by 1815 there was an efficient network of bandits' spies in Van Diemen's Land—one bushranger boasted from his mountain fastness that he had the Hobart newspapers in his hand within five hours after they came off the press. These exasperating alliances were forged from a shared hatred for the System.

Convicting the bushrangers was a worse headache than catching them. Sheep-stealing was a capital crime. Any convict charged with a second and potentially capital offense had to be tried in Sydney. But without witnesses there could be no case, and Sydney was so far north that the settler would have to abandon his farm for several months to go there at his own expense and testify against a sheep-duffer. Few could afford to. Edward Lord (1781–1859), the Welsh marine officer who in 1803 built the first private house in Hobart, was the most powerful man in the early settlement next to Collins—and next to nobody, its largest stock-owner, an arrogant land-grabbing troublemaker who burned all the Government House papers when Collins died in 1810 in order to cover his business tracks—and even he could not get legal redress against the bandits, who made off with five hundred head of his stock every year.[34]

These cave-dwelling satyrs of the penal system resist all romanticization. They were hardly worth dignifying with the name of *banditti*. As John West put it, with some asperity:

> The Italian robber tinged his adventure with romance; the Spanish bandit was often a soldier, and a partisan; but the wandering thieves of Tasmania were no less uncouth than violent—hateful for their debasement, as well as terrible for their cruelty.[35]

They had long ratty hair, thick beards, roughly sewn garments and moccasins of kangaroo hide, a pistol stuck in a rope belt, a stolen musket, a polecat's stench. When on raids, they blacked their faces with charcoal. Most of them would kill a man as soon as a kangaroo. Some joked about this. One of the earliest "gangs" in Van Diemen's Land consisted of only three men: two Irishmen named Scanlan and Brown and an Englishman named Richard Lemon, who had gone on "the out and out" from Hobart and roamed the bush in the area of Oyster Bay. Lemon did not like Brown and Scanlan talking in Gaelic, of which he understood not a word. One morning when Brown was out hunting 'roos, Lemon crept up on Scanlan at the campfire, put a pistol to the back of his head and pulled the trigger. He then strung up the corpse by the heels on a gum tree, as if he were hanging a "boomer" (big kangaroo) for skinning. "Now, Brown," he laconically observed when his partner returned, "as there are only two of us, we shall understand one another better for the future." The two of them ranged the bush for two more years, murdering four whites and an uncounted number of blacks, until some convict bounty-hunters took them prisoner. They shot Lemon dead and forced Brown, at gunpoint, to hack off his mate's head and carry it back to Hobart in a bag. Their reward was an invitation to Government House (leaving their bag outside, presumably) and a free pardon.[36]

By 1814 there were so many bushrangers at large, and the authorities in Hobart could do so little about them, that Lachlan Macquarie decided to save Lieutenant-Governor Thomas Davey's face with a proclamation. It offered amnesty to any bushranger who turned himself in by December 1, 1814. But it was so ambiguously drafted that it offered six months' grace to bushrangers to commit with impunity any crime they wanted, short of murder, before that date. Robbery, rapine and mayhem multiplied at once. When the deadline for amnesty came, few bushrangers had surrendered and the colonists were frantic. They were sure the convict population (then 1,900 souls) was ready to rise and join the bushrangers, consigning Van Diemen's Land to anarchy. So the flustered Davey reacted like the soldier he was: He hoisted the red flag in Hobart and proclaimed martial law. He then imposed a strict curfew, revoked all tickets-of-leave, forbade the sale of kangaroo skins and ordered that all kangaroo-dogs should be shot on sight, thus hoping to destroy the bushrangers' means of support. And as a court-martial could hang anyone without reference to the criminal court in Sydney, Davey strung up as many bandits as he could catch, gibbeting their corpses in chains on a little island off the Hobart docks until they stank too much even for the wheeling, scavenging birds.[37]

But although these summary proceedings (which exasperated Macquarie when he found out about them) somewhat damped the progress of banditry in Van Diemen's Land, there were bushrangers Davey's troops could not catch. The most conspicuous one was a twenty-seven-year-old seaman from Yorkshire named Michael Howe. Twice a deserter —from the merchant marine and from the army—Howe had finally come to grief on a charge of highway robbery and been transported for seven years. He arrived in Van Diemen's Land in 1812 and absconded almost at once. By 1814, he and a fellow convict named Whitehead had brought together a roving gang of twenty-eight bushrangers, terrorizing settlers in the region of New Norfolk, on the Derwent. Their favorite targets were landowners with a reputation for treating convicts badly. One of these, an especially hated "flogging magistrate" named Adolarius William Humphrey, who lived at Pittwater, some thirty miles from Hobart, lost hundreds of his Saxon merinos to them. Howe had struck when he was away; the bandits burnt Humphrey's corn, terrified the servants and then trashed the house in a paroxysm of rage after finding two pairs of leg irons.[38]

Howe left a wide and furious swath across Van Diemen's Land. His comrade, Whitehead, was captured near Launceston. Howe became sole leader, recruiting new members to replace some who had cast themselves on the mercy of Davey's amnesty, and continued to pillage across an area of some five hundred square miles, from Launceston in the north to homesteads not far from Hobart in the south. He always stressed, in his rambling chats with the "slaves" on the farms he plundered, that he was like Dick Turpin, robbing the rich and helping the poor. Many of them believed him, and so he acquired a network of informers among assigned convicts and small farmers and was able to hear about troop movements almost as soon as they began.

Howe was a natural leader, endowed with immense vitality and a gift for organization. The gang was under quasi-naval discipline, and each member had to swear an oath of obedience on a prayer book. He had the gloomy charisma of the paranoid. He kept a kangaroo-skin diary in which he inscribed his bad dreams in blood. It also contained lists of the flowers he had known as a boy in Yorkshire, for Howe was passionately interested in botany and planned to adorn his mountain hideout with an instructive garden. He believed that Fate had singled him out as the convicts' instrument of revenge on the hated System. He had the gall to style himself "Lieutenant-Governor of the Woods," in contrast to the lieutenant-governor in Hobart. He was so sure of his safety that in 1816 he sent Davey a haughty letter, thinking the lieutenant-governor would negotiate a general pardon for him and his gang if they would "come in." Howe thought Davey was stalling until informers betrayed him.

> We have thought proper to write these Lines to you—As We have been Kept in the Dark so long—and We find it is only to Keep us Quiet until By some Means or other you think you Can Get us Betrayed. But We will Stand it no Longer. We are now Determined to have A full and satisfactory [answer?] Either for or against us, As we are determined to be Kept No longer In Ignorance, for we think ourselves Greatly Ingured By the Country at Large.

Howe ironized on Davey's fear that his gang was growing into a guerrilla army: "I have not the least Doubt but you are Glad that those new Hands [are] joining us—We are Glad Also." God was on the bushranger's side, "and He who Preserved us from your Plotts in Publick will Likewise Preserve Us from them in secret." So let Davey send word back within ten days: "Answer either for or Against us . . . clap on it the King's Seal —and Your Signature"; and let the redcoats not sneak along behind, for "We [are] As Much Inclined to take Life As you are in your Hearts; We could destroy All the partyes you can send out. . . . You Must not think to Catch Old Birds with Chaff." This singular missive, only one of several Howe sent to Davey and his successor William Sorell, was written in blood and signed by ten other bushrangers.[39]

Davey would not cooperate. "The Power of Pardoning Capital Offences," he replied to Howe, "rests solely with the Governor in Chief,
but no application for favor can avail those, who are in the daily Commission of the greatest outrages." Thus the war of cops and robbers went
on, with the robbers generally winning, through the end of Davey's administration and the arrival of the next lieutenant-governor, Colonel
William Sorell, in 1817.

In that year, Michael Howe's luck began to run out. He had acquired
a devoted aboriginal "wife," Black Mary. (Such liaisons, which usually
began with abduction and rape, were of course invaluable to all bushrangers, as they could learn a host of survival tricks from a friendly black.)
One day, the couple was ambushed by soldiers. Howe ran, and Black
Mary, who was many months pregnant, could not keep up with him. In
an exchange of shots, one of Howe's bullets struck her. The soldiers,
anxious to cultivate Howe's image as a monster, claimed afterward that
he had shot her in cold blood to stop her from talking. Howe insisted it
was an accident, and probably it was. But the jilted Black Mary, left
painfully wounded on the ground by her lover, wanted revenge—and she
sought it, after she had recovered from the bullet and given birth, by
volunteering to track him down. Even with her superb skills to guide
them, the soldiers could not catch up with him; but Howe felt the law
was closing in on him and tried to negotiate with Sorell. The new lieutenant-governor of the town offered the "Lieutenant-Governor of the
Woods" a conditional pardon for all of his crimes except murder and a
strong recommendation for clemency on the murder charge itself, if he
would turn his gang-mates in. Howe began to testify, naming a surprising
number of "respectable" settlers as receivers of stolen stock and goods.
One of these, to the potential embarrassment of the law-abiding, was
Hobart's resident man of God, the Reverend Robert Knopwood. Sorell
began an investigation of Knopwood's relations with the bushrangers;
he may have been on to something, because one night all of the transcribed evidence mysteriously vanished.

The promised pardon never came. Howe got jittery at the delay, and
in September 1817 he fled back into the bush. Without his gang, which
in his absence had fallen apart into little pillaging groups, he had to go
deep into the mountain valleys of the upper Shannon near the aptly
named peaks of Barren Tier and Rat's Castle, "a dreary solitude of cloud-
land," as one chronicler put it, "the rocky home of hermit eagles." From
time to time he would waylay farmers—who were very remote and unprotected, for the Great Lake area was the extreme limit of settlement in
Van Diemen's Land—and extort food and ammunition from them, with
horrible threats. In September 1818 he barely escaped from an ex-convict
bounty hunter named John McGill, who had found him with the help of

Muskitoo, an aboriginal blacktracker imported from Sydney. A month later, two white men named Worrall and Pugh cornered him at his hut on the Shannon. Worrall and Howe faced one another, with pistols levelled, at fifteen yards. "He stared at me with astonishment," Worrall testified later, "and . . . I was a little astonished at him, for he was covered with patches of kangaroo skin and wore a black beard . . . [A] curious pair we looked. After a moment's pause he cried out, 'Black beard against grey beard for a million!' and fired"—but missed. Worrall shot him down and Pugh battered his brains out with his gun-butt. They cut off the bushranger's head and carried it back to Hobart Town, where Sorell put in on public view, spiked to a base.

If Howe's short violent career had proven one thing, it was the embarrassing volatility of imposed social order on the colonial frontier. Neither Howe nor his gang could possibly have stayed at large for more than three years without the sympathy, and sometimes the active collaboration, of assigned servants, ex-convicts and even free settlers out for profit. An Australian type was being cast—the bushranger as popular hero. Although Howe was gone, his emulators lived on, mocking the law and causing great anxiety to the government. These desperadoes threatened—as Sir John Wylde, Macquarie's deputy judge-advocate, warned after a judicial circuit of the island in 1821—to break down "the sense of Restraint and Coercion, which may be urged to keep the Prisoners of the Crown, so comparatively numerous here, in proper awe and subjugation."[40]

For by that year, 53 percent of the entire population of Van Diemen's Land were convicts under sentence, and "a Spirit of Insurrection" was on the judge's mind. Dozens of bushrangers were out around Hobart; fifteen or twenty had run away from their masters or from the government punishment gangs at Launceston and seven or eight had broken out of Hobart Jail itself. The amount of theft, cattle-rustling, sheep-stealing and general predacity "forbade," Wylde urged in his creaking syntax, "as illusory almost, the Hope that a renewed extension of Mercy to them would influence an amelioration of Principle." Translated, this meant, "Hang as many as you can."[41]

They did. Macquarie, visiting Van Diemen's Land with Wylde, conferred with Sorell and made sure that plenty of rope was used against the "depraved Wretches, . . . cruel and savage Depredators" then in custody awaiting trial. A circuit court convened in Launceston, and nine out of thirteen bushrangers swung. In Hobart, out of twenty-six awaiting their fate, ten were hanged. "Now that these dreadful examples have been made," Macquarie wrote to London, "I am enabled to report that there is every reasonable prospect of the Bush-Ranging System being completely at an End, most probably for many Years to come."[42]

He was wrong. Bushranging continued with unabated vigor after 1821, still with the clandestine support of the convict population. The next "Dick Turpin" to win fame in Van Diemen's Land was Matthew Brady (1799–1826), a Manchester boy sentenced by the Salford Assizes in 1820 to seven years' exile on the Fatal Shore for stealing a basket with some bacon, butter and rice. Wild with resentment, he tried again and again to abscond and was pushed down from assignment to the chain gang and finally to the penal nadir: Macquarie Harbor. In the first four years of his transportation he took 350 lashes.[43]

In June 1824, Brady and thirteen other convicts escaped from Macquarie Harbor in a whaleboat. Before the end of the month they reached the Derwent, came ashore, robbed a settler of his guns and provisions and began to range the bush. They quickly found themselves famous. Colonel George Arthur, the new lieutenant-governor of Van Diemen's Land, papered the gum trees with proclamations calling "in the most earnest manner" on all settlers to join in the hunt for the Brady gang, and to order their Crown servants to pass on whatever information they heard. It was futile, for the convicts would rather join Brady than rat on him. Convict servants hid Brady and his men in barns, fed them and showed them where the master's guns were kept. Arthur next appealed to baser motives by posting rewards: first £10 per head for each member of the growing Brady gang—which by now was rumored to be one hundred strong—then £25. If a convict gave information that led to the arrest of one of these bandits, he would get his ticket-of-leave. If he caught the bushranger himself, he got a conditional pardon. The only result was a notice pinned to the door of the Royal Oak Inn at Cross Marsh a week later:

> It has caused Matthew Brady much concern that such a person known as Sir George Arthur is at large. Twenty gallons of rum will be given to any person that can deliver his person to me.

There was no question that the lad was flash. He was chivalrous, too, in his way. Brady would never harm a woman or let any of his gang do so. When his partner McCabe threatened to rape a settler's wife, Brady shot him through the hand, flogged him mercilessly and threw him out of the gang; Arthur's police caught McCabe ten days later, and hanged him. A psychopath named Mark Jeffries, a government executioner and flogger who had absconded and was known as "The Monster," had captured a settler's wife while he was on the run but was irked by the squalling of her newborn baby. He picked it up by the legs and smashed its head against a gum tree. Later he was caught and jailed for trial in Launceston. When Brady heard about this he had to be argued out of leading his gang in a frontal assault on the Launceston lockup, freeing all the prisoners, dragging Jeffries out and flogging him to death.

Knowing that his protection was other convicts, Brady took care not to harm assigned servants in the homesteads he robbed; but in case they "gave music" to the police later, he forced them to drink their masters' whiskey until they were too fuddled to remember what his men had said, or which way they had gone. At least one luckless teetotaller died from this; and others, due to the vile quality of colonial spirits, became very sick.

The Brady gang fought like Tasmanian devils when cornered, with skill and coolness, shooting their way past many police ambushes. They had no compunction about revenging themselves on people who they believed were their oppressors—especially "flogging magistrates"—but they would also treat their captives fairly if such people had once been fair to them. Thus they made a prisoner of John Barnes, a colonial surgeon, while ransacking a magistrate's house at Coal River:

> One of them men who stopped me . . . had been punished a few days before by order of the magistrate, upon some trifling complaint of his master; the man was not in very good health . . . and I took him down before the whole of the flagellation had been inflicted, and requested that the magistrate would pardon him the rest; he recollected the circumstance with a little gratitude, or probably I might have been more severely handled.[44]

They took his watch but gave him back his lancet-case, "telling me that that might be of service to them by and by."

But Lieutenant-Governor Arthur was a tirelessly methodical man, and he wore Brady down. With a reorganized police force and more soldiers from the 40th Regiment under his command, he picked off the gang members in running skirmishes, one by one. He offered irresistible rewards—300 guineas or 300 acres of land free of quit-rent to the man who brought Brady in; or, for convicts, a full unconditional pardon and free passage to England. He sent rank-and-file field police convicts out wearing fetters, to infiltrate the remnants of Brady's gang with a story of having escaped from the chain gang. Betrayed and outflanked, Brady was shot in the leg in a skirmish near Paterson's Plains outside Launceston. He got away but was captured a few days later, limping and exhausted, by a settler named John Batman (the future founder of Melbourne).

They put Matthew Brady in Launceston Jail and a few days later loaded him with chains and brought him down to Hobart—accompanied, to his disgust, by the man he most despised in the world, the infant-killer Mark Jeffries. Before his trial and hanging, Brady was feted as a popular hero. Dozens of petitions for clemency arrived at Government House. Women shed tears for the "likely lad," the "poor colonial boy," who had shown such consideration to their sex. His cell was filled every day with visitors bringing baskets of flowers, fan letters, fruit and fresh-baked cakes. If his fate had been decided by vote, he would have gone free. But the judge was determined to make a solemn and awful example of him. On May 4, 1826, Brady received his last Communion and mounted the scaffold above a sea of colonial faces, contorted in grief or cheering him over the drop; only his enemies were silent. The government could not expunge his name from popular memory: A 4,000-foot peak in the Western Tiers, which frowns directly down on Arthur's Lake below, is still known as Brady's Lookout, and there is a Brady's Lake out past Tungatinah power station on the Lyell Highway—whereas Mike Howe is remembered in less noble geographical detail, a gully near Lawrenny and a marsh east of Table Mountain.

Matthew Brady was by no means the last Tasmanian bushranger, or even the last to acquire a popular aura (that man was Martin Cash, an Irish *picaro* who absconded no less than four times from Port Arthur in the early 1840s and lived to a ripe age as a farmer near Glenorchy). But he was the last politically significant bandit, the last menacing avatar of a convict counterculture in Van Diemen's Land that soon withered under the patient, systematic totalitarianism of Sir George Arthur. After Brady's death, no roaming bushranger would be able to impede, or even threaten, the progress of Tasmanian settlement. Nor would any of them threaten a *jacquerie*, the convicts' revolt that had figured in the nightmares of Australian settlers and governors since the Irish rose at Toongabbie in 1804. Van Diemen's Land was a small island, soon filled up, and the pattern of ownership and intensive grazing that dominated it by the mid-1830s disposed of the bushrangers' environment. They could no longer strike from virgin wilderness to prosperous farm or town in a day's walk, or even a day's ride. They were left without cover, like foxes in a bare field; whereas 700 miles north on the mainland, in the wide expanses of New South Wales that lay back from the coast, the bandits continued to pillage and present their threats to the law, reminding convicts and awakening the fears of their masters that chains were made to be broken.

iv

IT WAS ON the mainland, after 1825, that the popular myth of the Australian bushranger took its final form in story and folksong. Repressed in Van Diemen's Land by Lieutenant-Governor Arthur—significantly, there seem to be no bushranger ballads of Tasmanian origin—it sprang up like an irritant weed in New South Wales. Bushranging became a social problem there later than in Van Diemen's Land, because Sydney and Parramatta had never had to rely on convict kangaroo-hunters for their early survival. Not until the colony broke out of the narrow coastal plains and expanded over the mountains to Bathurst (giving plenty of scope for outlaws to hide in the gorges and caves of the Blue Mountains, now within striking distance of new trunk roads and farms) did bush-ranging start to flourish. And the supply of new bushrangers was guar-anteed by Governor Ralph Darling's crackdown in convict discipline. Most of them came from the dreaded iron gangs working on the "Great West Road" across the Blue Mountains and on the "Great North Road," surveyed in 1825 and completed in 1831, which ran through 170 miles of rough sterile gorges and linked Sydney to the burgeoning farm districts of Maitland and the Hunter River Valley. The local names for spots along this road were eloquent: "Hungry Flat," "Dennis's Dog-Kennel," "No-Grass Valley," "Devil's Backbone." As the iron gangs of Darling's admin-istration wore their way through the mountain sandstone, cutting the roads foot by anguished foot, there was no shortage of men who would rather take to the bush at any risk than spend another day "condemned to live in slavery, and wear the convict chain."

For ten years the roads and semi-settled districts of New South Wales, west to Parramatta and Bathurst, north to the Hunter River, were pes-tered by bushranging convicts who struck singly or in small gangs. There was nothing romantic about them. A few were pathetic harmless men who ran away from chain gang or master because, like a Bathurst ab-sconder named Charles Jubey, they were "so harassed and torn about" by cruel discipline that they became "weary of life." Many were mere thugs: muggers, chicken-stealers and occasional rapists. Small farmers were their victims, not the "rich," and their crimes were brutal when not petty. Some tended, not without reason, to be paranoically suspi-cious: Daniel "Mad Dog" Morgan (ca. 1830–1865), one of the second wave of bushrangers who terrorized Victoria and New South Wales after the convict period, was so afraid of poison that he would accept no food from the settlers he robbed except hard-boiled eggs.

When caught, the mainland bushrangers did not comport themselves like Robin Hood either. Their speeches from the dock or at the gallows' foot were apt to be primitive. In 1834, Dr. Robert Wardell, barrister and former editor of the colony's chief newspaper, *The Australian*, was riding the river boundary of his 2,500-acre estate at Petersham, near Sydney. Outside a humpy, he surprised three escaped convicts, whose leader, an iron gang absconder named John Jenkins, took aim with a stolen rifle and shot him dead. Jenkins and his adult accomplice, a runaway assigned servant named Thomas Tattersdale, were tried on the evidence of the third prisoner, a terrified boy called Emanuel Brace. At the verdict of guilty, the judge uttered his ritual question: Did either have anything to say before sentence of death was passed? Jenkins did:

> Throwing himself into a threatening and unbecoming attitude, [he] re-marked, that he had not had a fair trial, a bloody old woman had been palmed upon him for Counsel; he did not care a bugger for dying, or a damn for anyone in court; and that he would as soon shoot every bloody bugger in court ... [He made] a violent attack on Tattersdale, and struck him two tremendous blows in the face, which knocked him down in the dock ... The Judge sat in mute astonishment. . . . [I]t took a dozen con-stables to secure and handcuff him.[45]

Not until 1839 would the traveller be able to speak with confidence of "bushrangers, a *sub-genus* in the order *banditti*, which, happily, can no longer exist, except in places inaccessible to the mounted police."[46] These mounted police, whose sole task was tracking and capturing bush-rangers, began in 1825 as a small force of dragoons (whence, "goons") under Governor Brisbane, drawn from infantry regiments in Sydney—2 officers and 13 troopers, operating mainly around Parramatta. Darling increased it until by 1839 it had swollen to 9 officers, a sergeant-major, 156 non-commissioned officers and enlisted men, with 136 horses—not a large net to throw over so large a territory, but often an effective one. The "horse-police" or "traps" (mounted police) like Sir George Arthur's constabulary in Van Diemen's Land, were disliked only a little less than the bushrangers themselves. They were apt to use violence when dealing with small Emancipist settlers whom they routinely suspected of har-boring bushrangers out of criminal sympathy. Free workers hated them, because of the "pass system" enforced under Darling's emergency Bush-ranging Act of 1830 (11 Geo. IV, c. 10), whereby any man in the colony who could not produce his ticket-of-leave and travel pass on demand could be clapped in jail until he could prove he was *not* an escaped convict. Despite its unpopularity, the Bushranging Act was renewed under Governor Bourke in 1832, and again in 1834. Although Bourke's gubernatorial instincts were more liberal than Darling's, he persuaded himself that it was worth offending the spirit of British law with such an act: "I believe ... it would occasion very great dissatisfaction among the free People of the Colony to deprive them of the protection which this law affords," he told London in 1832.[47]

Furthermore, because Governor Darling had followed Sir George Ar-thur's lead in setting up government rewards for information against bushrangers, the colony was a morass of denunciation and spying. In this way the lower classes came to feel victimized by the bushranger laws, and this created a wave of sympathy toward the bushrangers themselves.

Much as the "free objects" (as convicts and ex-convicts sardonically called emigrant settlers in Australia) might detest the bushrangers, it was not easy to stamp out every vestige of fellow-feeling between men who had undergone the government lash. Alexander Harris, while working in the 1820s as a cedar-cutter on the coastal slopes of the Illawarra, noted that bushrangers would freely join the loggers' jamborees around the rum keg on deserted beaches and he compared the sight of their boisterous revelry to "a pirate's isle." No one would denounce them to Darling's dragoons (who seldom dared to penetrate those deep coastal forests), partly from fear of reprisals but mainly "because, having mostly been prisoners themselves, it was a point of honour among the sawyers to help them as much as they could."[48]

By the late 1820s, such sympathies had already crystallized into folk ballads—none of whose texts, unfortunately, survive. To be the hero of a song offered a snatch of immortality to the convict, as the surgeon Peter Cunningham speculated in *Two Years in New South Wales* (1827):

> The vanity of being talked of, I verily believe, leads many foolish fellows to join in this kind of life—songs being made about their exploits by their sympathising brethren. . . . It is the boast of many of them, that their names will live in the remembrance of the colony long after their exit from among us to some penal settlement, either in this world or the next; Riley, the captain of the Hunter's River banditti, vaunting that he should be long spoken of (whatever his fate may be) in fear by his enemies, and in admiration by his friends!

The year Cunningham published this, the prototype of Australian convict-ballad heroes began his desperate colonial career. His ballad, the first surviving one about a bushranger, opens in fine style:

> Come all you gallant bushrangers who gallop on the plain,
> Who scorn to live in slavery and wear the convict chain,
> Attention pay to what I say, and value it if you do—
> I shall relate the matchless fate of bold Jack Donohoe!

"Bold Jack" was a short, freckled, blond-haired, blue-eyed Irishman named John Donohoe (1806–1830), sentenced to life transportation in Dublin in 1823. On arrival in 1825, Donohoe had been assigned in the usual way (to John Pagan, a settler of Parramatta). He had misbehaved and spent time in a road gang; then he returned to assigned service under a Parramatta surgeon, Major West. The ballad, with a reasonable minimum of exaggeration, takes up the story:

> He'd scarcely served twelve months in chains upon the Australian shore,
> When he took to the highway as he had done before:
> He went with Jacky Underwood, and Webber and Walmsley too,
> These were the true companions of bold Jack Donohoe.
>
> Bold Donohoe was taken for a notorious crime,
> And sentenced to be hanged upon the gallows-tree so high—
> But when they brought him to Sydney Gaol he left them in the stew,
> For when they came to call the roll, they missed Jack Donohoe.

The "notorious crime" was committed in December 1827: Donohoe "went out" with two Irish confederates named Kilroy and Smith, holding up the bullock-drays that plied between farm and market on the Windsor Road—a kind of highway robbery which, because of the lumbering slowness of its target, did not demand a horse. The three men were soon caught, and in March 1828 they were sentenced to hang. Kilroy and Smith duly swung, but Donohoe made a break for freedom between the court and the condemned cell and fled. Before long he had assembled a small gang of other Irish and English absconders. They stole horses from settlers and, for the next eighteen months, to the discomfiture and occasional terror of the law-abiding, ranged across a wide swath of territory beyond the Blue Mountains, from Bathurst south to Yass and the Illawarra, close to Sydney and Parramatta, and north almost to the Hunter River. Hardly a week passed without a stickup, and in the bush where goods of any kind were hard to come by, Donohoe easily got rid of the swag. After his death, police searches (directed by a gang member named Walmsley, who turned informer to save his neck) showed that no less than thirty small settlers had received stolen goods from him.

> As Donohoe made his escape, to the bush he went straightway,
> The people they were all afraid to travel by night or day—
> For every day in the newspapers they brought out something new,
> Concerning that bold bushranger they called Jack Donohoe!

This verse commemorates what would become a frequent gripe of Australian authorities—that the press, in its lurid pennycatching, works against the government by making heroes out of criminals. With Ralph Darling as governor there was more point to this, for the Sydney papers took any chance they could get to make him look like a fool. In Van Diemen's Land, the colonial press pointedly observed, Lieutenant-Governor Arthur took the field himself in pursuit of bushrangers and stamped them out; but in New South Wales, Governor Darling sat in Government House, while "with a mounted police and a police establishment, *which if not effective is not for want of expense,* and a strong garrison of armed soldiery, the bushranging gentry seem to carry on their pranks almost without molestation." Donohoe and his mates even displayed a raffish elegance of dress and "a remarkably clean appearance," their leader sporting "black hat, superfine blue cloth coat lined with silk surtout fashion, plaited shirt (good quality), laced boots." Not only were they Pimpernels, the *Australian* sardonically implied, but they were not as bad as they were painted:

> *Donohoe,* the notorious bushranger, whose name is a terror in some parts of the country, though we fancy he has more credit given to him for outrages than he is deserving of, is said to have been seen by a party well acquainted with his person, in Sydney, enjoying, not more than a couple of days ago . . . a ginger-beer bottle.[49]

The price on Donohoe's head rose from £20 to £100, and Darling sent more police and volunteers into the field to refute the myth—which had spread beyond "the ignorant and tainted portion of the population"—that the fierce little Dubliner had a charmed life. They caught up with him at Bringelly, near Campbelltown outside Sydney.

> As he and his companions rode out one afternoon,
> Not thinking that the pangs of death would overtake them soon,
> To their surprise the Horse-Police rode smartly into view,
> And in double-quick time they did advance to take Jack Donohoe.
>
> "Oh Donohoe, oh Donohoe, throw down your carabine,
> Or do you intend to fight us all? And will you not resign?"
> "To surrender to such cowardly dogs is a thing I never would do—
> Today I'll fight with all my might!" cried bold Jack Donohoe.
>
> "It never shall be said of me that Donohoe the brave
> Could surrender to a policeman or become an Englishman's slave—
> I'd rather roam these hills so wild like a dingo or kangaroo
> Than work one hour for Government," cried bold Jack Donohoe.
>
> The Sergeant and the Corporal they did their men divide,
> Some fired at him from behind, and some from every side,
> The Sergeant and the Corporal they both fired at him too,
> And a rifle-bullet pierced the heart of bold Jack Donohoe.
>
> Nine rounds he fired and nine men shot before the fatal ball
> That pierced his heart and made him smart and caused him for to fall—
> And as he closed his mournful eyes, he bade the world adieu,
> Crying "Convicts all, pray for the soul of bold Jack Donohoe!"

The song embellishes, as ballads do. Donohoe did not kill nine "traps" with nine shots (or even six with six, as variants of the ballad have it) and his only recorded utterance at the moment of battle was a stream of oaths, inviting the effing buggers to come and get their bloody guts blown out, or something to that effect; he was not shot in the heart, but in the head, by a trooper named Muggleston—and so forth. Ballads are not history. Nevertheless, they do give us some sense of the penumbra of received opinion that surrounds historical events, even small ones like the killing of a flash, cursing little Mick by a squad of mounted police among the gum trees on one hot September afternoon in 1830. In death, Donohoe became more than the meager sum of his parts in life. At one end of the social scale, one finds Darling's surveyor-general Thomas Mitchell (later Sir Thomas, distinguished Australian explorer and translator of Luis de Camoëns's epic *Os Lusiades* from the Portuguese) visiting the Sydney morgue to view Donohoe's corpse and drawing his portrait, beneath which he quoted a couplet from Byron:

> No matter; I have bared my brow
> Fair in Death's face—before—and now.

At the other end of the scale, there was the Sydney shopkeeper who within a week or two of Bold Jack's death produced a line of clay pipes in the form of his head, complete with the bullet-hole in the temple. They were snapped up as devotional effigies—ceramic ballads, as it were. If Donohoe had been a sadist, a rapist or a baby-killer like Mark Jeffries in Van Diemen's Land, the outpouring of popular emotion that coalesced in the Donohoe ballads would not have occurred. But Australians admired flashness; most of them disliked Governor Darling and took great glee in seeing his authority ridiculed by this elusive bushranger. They— or, at any rate, the Emancipist and convict majority—felt that Donohoe posed no threat to them. He was a figure of fantasy, game as a spurred cock, a projection of that once-subjected, silent part of their own lives into vengeful freedom, thrown against the neutral gray screen of the bush. The legends of his freedom relieved Australians' dissatisfaction with the conformity of their own lives, and this has been the root of the cult of dead bushrangers ever since. Moreover, he was Irish, and the ballads make a point of this to commemorate the hatred of Irish convict for English guard. "It never shall be said of me that Donohoe the brave / Could surrender to a policeman or become an Englishman's slave."

Thirty years ago, the Australian historian Russel Ward noted the differences between "Bold Jack Donohoe" and earlier ballads like "Van Diemen's Land." They bespeak a big shift of attitude. The earlier ones accept the System in the name of English values, while later ballads oppose it in the name of Irish values that become Australian.[50]

"Van Diemen's Land" is a cautionary song directed to an English audience at home—"for if you knew my miseries," one version of it enjoins, "you'd never poach again." The call to repentance was a convention of the English ballads (without it, they could hardly have been printed and distributed in England). It stresses that convicts are the victims of a harsh fate that they cannot change for themselves. "May youth take warning e'er it is too late," begins one lengthy excursus in cautionary doggerel, "A Solemn Advice to All Young Men," attributed to a convict named James Kevel or Revel, returned from a fourteen-year sentence in 1823, but more likely written by some London ballad-monger, and continuing

> Lest they should share my hard unhappy fate.
> To see so many dying with hunger, pain and grief,
> And buried like dogs because they prov'd a thief.
> May all young men with speed their lives amend
> And take my advice as one that is their friend,
>
> For tho' so slight of it you may make here,
> Hard will be your lot if you are once sent there.

Such verses do not question either the order of the classes or the validity of English laws, whereas the Donohoe ballad explicitly does. Hence the ill-documented distinction, in the eyes of Australian authorities in convict days, between ordinary ballads and "treason songs," which (tradition insists) could not legally be sung, although there seems to be no local law that explicitly banned them. The voice of rebellion, defiantly inveighing against floggers and tyrants, is plainly heard in other ballads that invoke the name of Donohoe, such as the last four verses of "Jim Jones":

> For night and day the irons clang, and like poor galley-slaves
> We toil and toil, and when we die must fill dishonoured graves.
>
> But bye-and-bye I'll break my chains: into the bush I'll go,
> And join the brave bushrangers there—Jack Donohoo and Co—
>
> And some dark night when everything is silent in the town,
> I'll kill the tyrants one and all, and shoot the floggers down,
>
> I'll give the Law a little shock: remember what I say—
> They'll yet regret they sent Jim Jones in chains to Botany Bay.

And so, as the only New South Wales bushranger thrown into such high relief in the convict era, Donohoe became a general, idealized image of bushranging itself and survived long after the System had passed away.

He kept popping up with the same initials but different names: Jack Dowling, Jack Duggan, and—in the most famous of all bushranging ballads—Jim Doolan, the "Wild Colonial Boy": still Irish, still "agin the system," though it had shed its capital S sometime after the convict era ended. There used to be as many ways of singing "The Wild Colonial Boy" as there were pianos in Australian parlors. The most piercing one this writer has heard was not recorded: It was sung by a fat, seamed old Sydney prostitute, buoyed up by a few too many glasses of sweet port, in a pub on the Woollomooloo docks late one night in 1958—not in the rollicking front-room way of men, but as the off-key dirge of a mother grieving for her dead son:

> 'Tis of a wild Colonial boy, Jim Doolan was his name,
> Of poor but honest parents he was born in Castlemaine,
> He was his father's only hope, his mother's pride and joy,
> And so dearly did his parents love the Wild Colonial Boy.

> He was scarcely sixteen years of age when he left his father's home,
> And through Australia's sunny clime bushranging he did roam.
> He robbed the wealthy squatters, their stock he did destroy,
> A terror to Australia was the Wild Colonial Boy.

> In eighteen hundred and sixty-two he started his wild career,
> With a heart that knew no danger, no foeman did he fear.
> He bailed up the Beechworth Royal Mail Coach, and robbed Judge Macoboy,
> Who trembled and gave up his gold to the Wild Colonial Boy.

> He bade the Judge good morning, and told him to beware,
> He'd never robbed a poor man, or one who acted square,
> But a Judge who'd rob a mother of her only pride and joy,
> That Judge was worse of an outlaw than the Wild Colonial Boy.

> As Jim rode out one morning the mountain-side along,
> A-listening to the kookaburra's pleasant laughing song,
> He spied three mounted troopers, Kelly, Davis and Fitzroy,
> All riding forth to capture him, the Wild Colonial Boy.

> "Surrender now, Jim Doolan, you see there's three to one—
> Surrender in the Queen's name, you daring highwayman."
> Jim pulled his pistol from his belt and he waved the little toy,
> "I'll fight but not surrender," cried the Wild Colonial Boy.

> He fired at Trooper Kelly, and brought him to the ground,
> But turning round to Davis he received his mortal wound.
> All shattered through the jaw he lay, still firing at Fitzroy,
> And that's the way they captured him, the Wild Colonial Boy.

The second big difference between the Donohoe variant ballads and the earlier cautionary songs written for English consumption lies in what they imply about Australian nature and space. Until about 1830 the transportation ballads and broadsides present the bush as sterile and hostile, its fauna (except for the kangaroo, which no one could dislike) as eerie when not disgusting. The Fatal Shore is a desert full of snakes and cannibals, insufferably strange, the world upside down. "Our cots were fenced with fire, to slumber when we can, / To drive away wolves and tigers come by Van Diemen's Land." So goes the complaint in the ballad "Van Diemen's Land," faithfully mirroring the penal intentions of the colony, where nature was destined to punish. Space and the bush imprisoned it.

And so the absconder, by making the bush his new home, renamed it with the sign of freedom. On its blankness, he could inscribe what could not be read in spaces already colonized and subject to the laws and penal imagery of England. "As Donohoe made his escape, to the bush he went straightway." The bush is the citadel of the nay-sayer, the rebel: hence the poignancy, to Irish-Australian ears, of the chorus of "Wild Colonial Boy":

> O come along, me hearties, and we'll roam the mountains high—
> Together we will plunder, together we will die.
> We'll wander over valleys and we'll gallop over plains,
> And we'll scorn to live in slavery, bound down by iron chains.

The bushranger is the first figure in the low undergrowth of Australian literature to be identified with the bush animals: " 'I'd rather roam these hills so wild like a dingo or kangaroo / Than work one hour for Government,' cried bold Jack Donohoe." And the identification of bushranger with national landscape would persist until the railroads put an end to bushranging itself, with the destruction of the Kelly gang and the capture of their leader Ned at Glenrowan in 1880. By taking to the bush, the convict left England and entered Australia. Popular sentiment would praise him for this transvaluation of the landscape (though at a safe distance, of course) for another hundred and fifty years.

# 8

# Bunters, Mollies and Sable Brethren

OF THE PEOPLE transported to the antipodes between 1788 and 1852, about twenty-four thousand were women: one person in seven. Many Australians still think their Founding Mothers were whores. Undoubtedly some were prostitutes in the real sense of the word —that is, they survived by selling their sexual services, casually or regularly, without sentimental attachments. A commonly quoted figure, though a somewhat impressionistic one, is one woman in five.[1] When a woman at her trial described herself as a prostitute—"on the town" was the usual phrase—one can assume that she was telling the truth. In the mouths of Authority, the word "prostitute" was less a job description than a general term of abuse.

What is quite certain, however, is that no women were actually transported for whoring, because it was never a transportable offense. The vast majority of female convicts, more than 80 percent, were sent out for theft, usually of a fairly petty sort. Crimes of violence figured low among them, as one might expect—about 1 percent.[2] Sentences of more than seven years were exceedingly rare. None of this, given the severity of the English laws, suggests at the outset a very high degree of moral profligacy.

And yet there was rarely a comment on colonial society, scarcely a passage of evidence to the various Select Committees on Transportation, hardly a tract or a diary or a letter home, that missed the chance to describe the degeneracy, incorrigibility and worthlessness of women convicts in Australia. Military officers believed this, and so did doctors, judges, parsons, governors and, of course, their respectable wives. Convict men might in the end redeem themselves through work and penance, but women almost never. It was as though women convicts had passed the ordinary bounds of class and become a fiction, not far from pornography: crude raucous Eve, sucking rum and mothering bastards in the exterior darkness, inviting contempt rather than pity from her social superiors, rape rather than help from men.

Australian historians once swallowed this stereotype whole. "Even if these contemporaries exaggerated," wrote A. G. L. Shaw, "the picture [that women convicts] presented is a singularly unattractive one!"[3] Some later feminist historians, led by Anne Summers and Miriam Dixson, have striven to retain the picture while dismantling the biases, arguing that many or even most convict women became whores but that their fate was foisted on them by a tyrannous male power structure. The most influential statement of the case was made by Anne Summers:

> It was deemed necessary by both the local and the British authorities to have a supply of whores to keep the men, both convict and free, quiescent. The Whore stereotype was devised as a calculated sexist means of social control and then . . . characterised as being the fault of the women who were damned by it.[4]

The classic double-bind, in short. The problem is the quality of the contemporary opinions on which the Whore stereotype, accepted by Reverend Samuel Marsden and feminist historians alike (though for very different motives), was based.

The British Government did not send women to Australia to keep men "quiescent" in any political sense; the lash could do that. But the presence of women, considered as carrot rather than stick, did have its uses in social control. Eve the Whore would keep Adam the Rogue from turning homosexual, an important consideration: William Pitt would underwrite a colony of thieves, but not one of perverts. The government did not, of course, announce in so many words that female convicts were sent to Australia as breeding-stock and sexual conveniences. Indeed, the original plan of settlement drawn up by Lord Sydney in 1786 spoke of enslaving women for this purpose

> from the Friendly Islands, New Caledonia, Etc., which are contiguous thereto, and from whence any number may be procured without difficulty; and without a sufficient proportion of that sex it is well-known that it would be impossible to preserve the settlement from gross irregularities and disorders.[5]

Arthur Phillip rejected this idea, of course, for kidnapped Tahitian women would only "pine away in misery." He asked for more women convicts to be sent out, not for their labor but because he wanted the felons to marry one another and so raise a native-born yeomanry—the genetic equivalent of his hope for an economic base of agriculture run by small-farming Emancipists. He offered rewards of land or free time (an extra day a week for raising their own crops for sale or barter) to convicts who married. Some of these hastily legitimized unions proved bigamous, since a number of the newlyweds were, in fact, already married but had left their husbands or wives behind them in England. From a "respectable" viewpoint, this policy seemed a farce, and the matrimonial rush only a scramble for gubernatorial favors.[6]

The Scottish forger Thomas Watling, himself a convict, sniffed that "little I think could reasonably have been expected from the coupling of *whore* and *rogue* together." "Prostitution" and "concubinage" flourished in early colonial Sydney, as marriage did not. On this, the respectable convict, the respectable officer and the respectable cleric all agreed, because their terms of judgment were exactly the same. "There is scarcely a man without his mistress," Watling complained, adding with sublime ignorance of the sexual habits of English working people that "the high class first exhibit it; the low, to do them justice, faithfully copy it." The officers, being officers, got first pick of the women; and a female convict soon learned that her best chance of survival in New South Wales was to give herself over to the "protection" of some dominant male. In a tone of resentful irony, Watling advised "ladies of easy virtue" to get transported if they possibly could:

> They may rest assured, that they will meet with every indulgence from the humane officers and sailors in the passage; and after running the gauntlet there, will, notwithstanding, be certain of coming upon immediate keeping at their arrival. . . . Be she ever so despicable in person or manners, here she may depend that she will dress and live better and easier than ever she did in the prior part of her prostitution.[7]

Watling's prejudices were genteel. He believed he was writing as a "respectable" person (forgers always did) and his opinion of women convicts exactly reflected the attitudes of the middle class from which he had fallen. Respectable people in London—let alone in the chilly latitudes of John Knox, north of the Scottish border—saw little moral difference between prostitution and cohabitation. Patrick Colquhoun, as we have seen, included the female half of all unmarried couples in his attempts to guess the number of "prostitutes" in the "criminal class" of London. Before long the word "prostitute" came to be used of anyone promiscuous, paid or not. Eventually the distinction was so worn down by the weight of moral disapproval bearing upon the lower classes from the middle classes that Henry Mayhew, that indefatigable reporter, could claim that "prostitution . . . does not consist solely in promiscuous intercourse, for she who confines her favors to one may still be a prostitute," even if her motives were "voluptuous" and not mercenary. In short, the moral vocabulary of the English middle classes enabled the free in Australia to speak of "prostitution" among convicts when they meant any extramarital relationship. And as neither the penal system nor pioneer life favored marriage (official policy always encouraged it, but such encouragement was more than offset by the general poverty of small settlers and the uncertain, bush-wandering nature of an Emancipist worker's life), the respectable saw "prostitution" everywhere, even in sturdy matches that had lasted years out of wedlock and produced broods of children.[8] As the historian Michael Sturma points out, the idea that convicts shared the same ideas about sexual behavior as their superiors is very dubious:

> Working-class mores [in England] differed markedly from those of the upper and middle classes. . . . [A]mong the British working-class, cohabitation was prevalent. It is highly unlikely that working-class men, and in particular male convicts, considered the women convicts to be in some way sexually immoral. . . . The stereotype of women convicts as prostitutes emerged from . . . an ignorance of working-class habits.[9]

One notorious result of such thinking was the "Female Register" drawn up by the Reverend Samuel Marsden in 1806, an inspired piece of creative bigotry in which every woman in the colony, except for a few widows, was classified as either "married" or "concubine." By Marsden's count, there were 395 of the former and 1,035 of the latter. The only kind of marriage he recognized was one performed by a Church of England clergyman—ideally, himself. It followed that all Catholic and Jewish women who married within the form of their religion were automatically listed as "concubines," as were all common-law wives whose relationship with their men, however durable, went unsanctified by Anglican rite. One such woman, Mary Marshall, had lived with her "husband" Robert Sidaway for eighteen years but was listed as a "concubine." Sarah Bellamy had lived for sixteen years with the colony's master-builder, James Bloodworth or Bloodsworth, the bricklayer who was transported on the First Fleet and supervised the erection of Sydney's first permanent buildings, and had borne him seven children. No relationship could have been more respectable, devoted or tenacious than theirs. It ended in 1804 with Bloodworth's death from pneumonia. In gratitude for his services to the infant colony, Governor King buried him with military honors. Nevertheless, Sarah Bellamy went down on Marsden's list as "concubine," along with a twelve-year-old girl and a sixty-four-year-old widow. Yet when it reached London, this absurdly pharisaical document was read and apparently believed by Lord Castlereagh and William Wilberforce, and it became an authoritative text on colonial morality. As the historian Portia Robinson comments:

> That few women were legally married did not necessarily imply that the conduct of the remainder made New South Wales "a sink of infamy." It simply meant that the standards of morality and the definitions of marriage familiar to the women concerned did not agree with those imposed on society by Samuel Marsden. Contemporaries accepted his conclusions as to the nature of the women of Botany Bay and modern historians have continued to perpetuate this view.[10]

Marsden was not alone in his prejudices; and as people are named, so they will be treated. While one may doubt that the British Government set out to create special forms of humiliation and degradation for women in Australia, there is no doubt that the whore-stereotype, accepted by the upper layers of a rigid little colonial society, wielded immense power. Indeed, it would remain, though gradually fading, as part of the design of Australian sexual politics for a century after transportation was abolished. The attitudes behind the stereotype can be seen clearly in the private journal of Ralph Clark (?–1794), marine officer on the *Friendship* in the First Fleet.

When Lieutenant Clark sailed for Australia in 1787 he left behind his wife Betsy Alicia Trevan, a pretty Devon girl from a landed family, and their chubby firstborn son, Ralph Stuart Clark, aged not quite two. As the First Fleet rolled southward, Clark was tortured by remorse and nostalgia. Was a promotion worth this sundering? Betsy Alicia fills the journal as he pours forth his grief in ink, trying to conjure up the family he might not see again:

> Dear good woman I did not know thy worth . . . Alicia, my friend, my dear wife, and beautiful little engaging son, Oh sweet boy, what would your father give for a kiss of your mother and you, oh I think I hear him cry Papa, Papa, as I am taking my hat to go out, dear sweet sound, music to my poor ears, the only happiness that I have is the kissing of my Betsy's dear picture and my little boy's hair that she sent. I would not part with them for a Captain's commission.[11]

Clark devises a small ritual with the "dear picture," a miniature under a hinged glass lid. Each morning, Monday to Saturday, he kisses the glass. On Sundays he raises the tiny oval pane to kiss "my dear Alicia's picture out of the case," the image symbolically laid bare, a little closer to flesh. This act is both a denuding and a prayer, as to the effigy of a female saint. Holiness and sexuality are intertwined through the knot of marriage. Sometimes his dreams of Alicia are sexual ("Dreamt last night of seeing my dear beloved Alicia in bed and I pulled her towards me"), but usually they reflect his guilt at leaving her and his fear of losing her. He cannot quite make sense of his dreams, but they seem ominous; he is unhappy

> from dreaming that my Alicia took a dead louse from herself and gave it to me, oh unlucky dream, for I have often heard her say that dreaming of lice was a certain sign of sickness.[12]

Alicia is the fixed star of well-being in Clark's emotional universe. Her name summons up what he left behind: security, fidelity, licit sexual delight, social continuity, maternal tenderness. The conventional form in which he phrased these feelings belies their intensity. He never meant to publish his journal; he was not a writer but a miserably homesick young marine trying to set down his deepest emotional engagements in a language of sensibility derived from the genteel culture of the day:

> Read the remainder of the *Tragedy of Douglas* this day, oh it is a sweet play. . . . [W]hat are the emotions in the breast of Lady Randolph when she sees the features and shape of her lost and stained husband Douglas in that of young Norval, little does she know, fond mother, that it is her long lost son . . . but still I cannot think that she loved as my Betsy, my virtuous Alicia does.[13]

To say that Ralph Clark idealized his wife would understate his feelings: She monopolized his image of women. If another woman misbehaved, her violence or immorality became a slur on Alicia, suggesting to him on some less-than-conscious level that she too might fall from grace. Hence the vindictive contrast Clark drew between Alicia and the female convicts over whom he was placed in authority. He was being punished for their sins by losing his adored wife. "I could never have thought that there were so many abandoned wenches in England, they are ten thousand times worse than the men Convicts, and I am afraid we will have a great deal more trouble with them," he wrote while they were still in the English Channel. In July, when four of *Friendship*'s sailors were found at it with four female convicts in the 'tween-decks, the captain had the men flogged; but, Clark added, "if I had been the Commander I would have flogged the four whores also."[14] The Whore was typically foulmouthed:

> Elizabeth Barber one of the Convict women abused the doctor in a most terrible manner and said that he wanted to f—— her and called him all the names she could think of. . . . She began to abuse Capt. Merideth in a much worse manner, and said she was no more a whore than his

wife. . . . In all the course of my days I never heard such expressions come from the mouth of a human being. . . . She desired Merideth to come and kiss her Cunt for he was nothing but a lousy rascal as were we all. I wish to God she was out of the ship, I would rather have a hundred more men than have a single woman.[15]

The gulf between such "damned bitches of convict women" and distant Betsy, "surely an angel and not a woman," is absolute, and his hatred of the debased lower orders for taking him away from his wife leads to fantasies and dreams of violence. "If they were to lose anything of mine that I gave them to wash I would cut them in pieces," he writes of women doing laundry duty on board; and later he dreams that "I was going down to Tregadock to take leave of [the family] before I went to Botany, but was assaulted by a great mob, whom I was obliged to handle rather roughly with my sword." Three years later, suffering the rigors of Norfolk Island duty after the wreck of the *Sirius*, he pens a brutally dismissive epitaph on the first person to die a natural death there, a convict woman named Ann Farmer: "She was better than half dead before they sent her from England, by all accounts she was a most wicked woman having been the occasion of more than twenty men and women coming to untimely ends, but she is now gone where she will be rewarded according to her merits." Soon he was wishing death on other women convicts as well. "I wish the Almighty would be so kind to us as to take a few of them, for we could do much better without them at present."[16]

Clark got away eventually and was briefly reunited with his Betsy Alicia in June 1792. After that, his diary ceases before he could see his ideal again. In December 1792, he returned to service in the war against France. Early in 1794 Betsy Alicia died in childbirth, and the child was stillborn. A few months later, Clark's darling boy, Ralph, then a nine-year-old midshipman, died of yellow fever on board ship in the Caribbean, during a fight with a French ship. Clark was on board, too, and was killed in battle the same day. However, that was not quite the end of Clark's line, for at the time of his death he had a three-year-old daughter, whom he scarcely knew. She had been born to a convict woman, Mary Branham, on Norfolk Island in July 1791. At Clark's insistence, she had been christened Alicia. There is no reference to her mother in his journal.

ii

THE WOMEN in the First Fleet were picked haphazardly, ranging from old crones to mere children. There was more system on the next female transport, *Lady Juliana*, which brought young women of "marriageable" age, "the colony at that time being in great want of women." A few of them were hardened professional criminals, like Mrs. Barnsley, a shop-lifter who boasted that her family had been swindlers and highwaymen for a hundred years; her brother, a highwayman, often visited her on board before the fleet sailed, "as well-dressed and genteel in his appearance as any gentleman." At the other end of the scale was a meek little creature who bore a curiously strong resemblance to the prime minister, William Pitt, and was thought by all on board to be his bastard daughter.

Some wept and stormed, some tried to escape, and others spent the weeks before sailing hidden in corners, pale with shock and shame, their eyes red with incessant weeping; a young Scottish girl died of a broken heart before the ship left the Thames. Most of them were so demoralized by their "ruin"—the cycle of poverty, pregnancy and survival by theft or prostitution that formed the plot of a thousand melodramas and ballads simply because it was one of the commonest things that could happen to a girl—that John Nicol, a Scottish steward on the *Lady Juliana*, thought they were actually glad to be on board. "When I inquired their reason," he recalled,

> they answered, "How much more preferable is our present situation to what it has been since we commenced our vicious habits? . . . Banishment is a blessing to us. Have we not been banished for a long time, and yet in our native land, the most dreadful of all situations? We dared not go to our relations, whom we had disgraced. Other people would shut their doors in our faces. We were as if a plague were upon us, hated and shunned."[17]

Such sentiments, whatever their literary garnish, remind one how the morale of female convicts, never very strong, must have broken down on the way to Australia. London or Botany Bay: both poles of the world were, to many, equally alien and empty of hope. "Harmless unfortunate creatures," Nicol called them, "the victims of the basest seduction . . . a troublesome cargo, yet not dangerous or very mischievous, as I may say more noise than danger."

As soon as the Second Fleet was at sea, the seamen of *Lady Juliana* began to pair off with their cargo, thus starting the almost invariable pattern of later voyages. Doubtless some of the tars felt like pashas, lording it over a seaborne seraglio. Yet Nicol's phrase is significant: "Every man on board took a wife from among the convicts, they nothing loath." Offensive as such pairings were to later middle-class morality they were simply taken for granted among workers in villages, in ports and in London itself. Certainly Nicol did not regard his "wife," Sarah

Whitlam, transported to Australia for seven years for stealing a cloak, as a whore. He remembered her with respect and tenderness as

> a girl of a modest reserved turn, as kind and true a creature as ever lived;
> I courted her for a week and upwards, and would have married her on the
> spot, had there been a clergyman on board. . . . I had fixed my fancy on
> her from the moment I knocked the rivet out of her irons upon the anvil,
> and as firmly resolved to bring her back to England, when her time was
> out, my lawful wife.[18]

He could not get her released, however, and he sailed back to England alone, leaving Sarah Whitlam and their son, born on shipboard, in Sydney.

One may doubt, however, that all sailors showed convict women as much respect as Nicol claimed he showed his Sarah. Lord Auckland, the chairman of the 1812 Select Committee on Transportation, visited a brig loaded with women convicts that lay in the Thames in the summer of 1812 (well after the committee's work was done) to question its skipper "as to the means of preventing improper intercourse between the sailors and the women." The captain told him that

> every sailor was allowed to have one woman to cohabit with him during
> the voyage.—Had information of this practice been laid before the Com-
> mittee . . . it would have been marked with the strongest reprobation as
> likely to lead some and confirm others of these unfortunate women in
> habits of prostitution and disorder.[19]

Clearly, such "unfortunates" were not being sent to Australia to drain England of some social purulence. Even if they all had been prostitutes, their banishment would have made no difference to English crime; but it would mean a great deal to an infant colony troubled by sexual starvation. The policy was reflected in the the age of transported women— "marriageable age," as the 1812 Select Committee on Transportation was told:

> Q. To what ages are women limited? —We generally confine it, as near
> as possible, to about 24 and not more than 45. . . . [T]hey are very young
> that go out, from London in particular.[20]

"A lonely woman is a poor thing in a Country where there are so many villains," wrote one of the officers of the female transport *Britannia* in 1798.[21] When a ship bearing women anchored in Sydney Cove, its upper deck became a slave-market, as randy colonists came swarming over the bulwarks, grinning and ogling and chumming up to the captain with a bottle of rum, while the female convicts—washed for the occasion and dressed in the remnants of their English finery—were mustered before them, trying as hard as they could "to set themselves off to the best advantage." Military officers got the first pick, then non-commissioned officers, then privates, and lastly such ex-convict settlers as seemed "respectable" enough to obtain the governor's permission to keep a female servant. (Such permission was a very great favor before Macquarie's day; and it was stingily given, as an unusual reward, by the governors after Phillip: Grose, Paterson, Hunter, King and Bligh.) According to one former convict, not all the women assigned to officers were made their mistresses (some men, after all, were married and had brought their wives). In fact, "there were several women who were rather taken by the officers as prostitutes than as servants";[22] most of the convict women in the colony cohabited with men and the fitful attempts to curb this did not really apply to officers. Thus, Bligh had forbidden women to be "taken off the store, without being married, unless it was as servant to an officer." Bligh himself declared, bluntly enough, that "it was impossible to prevent prostitution" (but here he clearly means cohabitation), "and therefore there was no necessity for any regulations respecting it . . . [S]ettlers wanted female servants, and pitched upon particular women for whom they applied, who perhaps cohabited together; these things could never be prevented."[23]

Some witnesses found this spectacle morally barbarous, "rendering the whole Colony little better than an extensive Brothel,"[24] but the governors were slow to discourage it because it got the women—whose labor was not much use—"off the store," so that they did not have to be fed and supported at government expense. It petered out during Macquarie's administration, after some harsh injunctions from London.[25]

It was the sense of helplessness, above all, that ground the women prisoners down. Reflecting on the regular shipboard slave market, "a Custom that reflects the highest Disgrace upon the British Government in that Colony," one observer noted that all the women were not equally "depraved" on arrival; but they were driven down by "Jealousy Vexation & want." "All have not run to the same Excesses of Iniquity; some occasionally are found better disposed, and perhaps their number would be much increased if they were not, on their first arrival, promiscuously thrown into such difficulties and temptations."[26]

Since the liaisons were free of legal ties, a settler could simply throw a convict woman out when he was tired of her. This caused a troublesome floating population of whores and unattached "disorderly women" to accumulate around Sydney Cove, whose westerly arm, "The Rocks," soon acquired a well-deserved name as the rowdiest and most dangerous thieves' kitchen in the colony. As early as 1793, these women were offending all who met them, including a Spanish lieutenant who stopped in Sydney on an exploration vessel, the *Atrevida:* They made "continuous seductive advances" to his crewmen, slipped them Mickey Finns, robbed them blind, and were so "degraded by vice, or rather greed" that the notorious dock-women of Tenerife paled in memory beside them.[27] In 1802 Michael Hayes, an Irishman from Wexford who had been transported as a political prisoner for his part in the abortive Irish uprising of 1798, wrote to his sister Mary pleading with her not to come out and join him. He warned her of

> the distress that generally accompany [sic] unprotected Females coming to this distant part of the world. . . . Even were you with me your life would be a solitary one, [unless] you were to asociate with Prostitutes. In this country there is Eleven Hundred women I cannot count Twenty out of that number to be virtuous. The remainder support themselves through the means of Ludeness. . . . This way of life was sanctioned by the Governors, from the first Landing to this day.[28]

Hayes also mentioned the punishments, similar to the barbarous treatment of adulteresses in Puritan societies, visited on convict women who could not, due to their weaker constitutions and the relative mercy of the governor, be flogged as severely as men:

> They are so accustomed to their lude way of life that the most severe punishments will not restrain them. I have been witness to some flogged at the Tryangle, more led through the Town [with] a rope round their waist held by the common Executioner, and a label on their necks denoting the crime. The mode of punishment mostly adopted now is mostly shaving their heads and Ducking, and afterwards [they are] sent up to Hard Labour with the men.[29]

Women who had money or evidence of property were usually given their ticket-of-leave on arrival—at least up to the early 1820s and the departure of Macquarie. So were married women joining their husbands in Sydney; if the husband was a convict, he too would generally get his ticket, "as affording greater facilities of support." A female convict could also secure her ticket-of-leave on the dock if she had a special recommendation from the captain or surgeon of the transport ship—an arrangement that gave the ship's officers a great deal of sexual leverage, although most refrained from using it.[30]

All the others—those pregnant or with children born on shipboard, the rejects from the "market," the poor, the ugly, the mad, the old, the wizened—were sent to the Female Factory in Parramatta. They travelled by barge, along the long crinkling silver arm of Sydney Harbor, up the

Parramatta River: a stately progress through that wild and exquisite landscape between banks lined with ancient eucalypts, where sudden green
clouds of budgerigars whirled over the water and the white cockatoos
flapped, shrieking like colonies of lost souls, from tree to tree. If the wind
set fair, the trip took all day, but sometimes it used up the night as well;
then they had to bed down at one of the ramshackle inns, mere huts with
straw in back, along the river. The innkeepers—not jolly publicans, but
hard-eyed ex-convicts who had got their little corner of the rum trade—
plied them with liquor until they were stupefied and then robbed them
of their small possessions. The barge constable did nothing to protect
them.[31]

What greeted them the next day, as they floundered blearily into
Parramatta, was a scene of disgusting squalor. The Female Factory was a
loft above a jail, some sixty feet by twenty. This loft was filthy and its
floor could not, in any case, be washed, since its boards had warped so
much that water went straight through the cracks onto the heads of
prisoners in the cells below. The roof leaked, the privies stank, and the
kitchen was just a fireplace. Here, the women were expected to card and
spin wool into yarn, and from the yarn weave the coarse "Parramatta
cloth" from which convicts' winter clothes were made. Those who had
not managed to bring their bedding from the transport ship had to sleep
on piles of scungy raw wool, full of ticks and dags; the government did
not give mattresses or blankets to Parramatta women.[32]

The Factory had room for only a third of the women prisoners. The
rest had to lodge on whatever terms they could get with the local settlers.
The cost of "lodging and fire" was usually about four shillings a week, a
sum which most women could only raise by "buttock-and-twang." Their
main clientele consisted of the male convicts, who had no money either
and had either to steal it or work for it in their own time after they had
done their "government task" for the day. Most preferred the former;
and so, one irritated colonist pointed out, more than £1,560 was stolen
every year in Parramatta to pay the "whores." Macquarie reported that
almost any night one could see up to three hundred convicts of both
sexes roaming the town "at full liberty."[33] And the Reverend Samuel
Marsden complained that

> there is not a bushel of wheat or maize in the farmer's barn, nor a sheep
> in his fold, nor a hog in his stye—nor even a potatoe, turnip or cabbage in
> his garden—but what he is likely to be robbed of every night . . . to supply
> the wants of these abandoned women, to whom the men can gain access
> at all times of the night.[34]

Meanwhile the superintendent of the Female Factory did nothing for
his prisoners except give them their rations and reassure the government

that all was quiet among the women. One of these incumbents, an oily Emancipist named Durie, went so far as to admit in 1811, after a testy memo from Macquarie, that he had let women sleep outside the Factory; but now he had abolished "this indulgence" and in future they will all sleep inside the Factory walls. Actually, it had no "walls," except the ones that held up its roof, and convicts of both sexes came and went as they pleased.[35]

In 1819 Macquarie had his ex-convict architect Francis Greenway design a new Female Factory, a pretty three-story Georgian structure complete with clock, cupola and security wall. But the social conditions inside it were still imperfect. Thomas Reid, surgeon on the female transport *Morley*, visited his former charges there early in 1821 and found it hard to describe their "miserable state." They gathered around him, weeping incoherently, and he learned that when they had arrived there the previous evening they had been surrounded by hordes of idle fellows, convicts . . . provided with bottles of spirits . . . for the purpose of forming a banquet *according to custom*, which they assured themselves of enjoying without interruption, as a prelude to excesses which decency forbids to mention."[36]

In the new Factory, the women were sorted into three classes: "general," "merit" and "crime." The "crime" class of incorrigibles wore no badge, but their hair was cropped, as a mark of disgrace. The "merit" class was made up of those who had sustained six months' good behavior. The "general" class was by far the largest, and it resembled a nursing-hospital, being mainly composed of unlucky girls who had been sent back to the Factory when they got pregnant on assigned service. They were not compelled to reveal the father's name, and when asked they usually said he was the Reverend Samuel Marsden.

The Female Factory was the colony's main marriage-market, and settlers took themselves to Parramatta to find a "Factory lass" (the Australian equivalent of the mail-order bride). All it took was a written permit from Marsden, written notice to the matron and enough phlegm to endure the teasing and taunts of the women. "It requires the face of a Turk to come on such an open and acknowledged errand." A bizarre scene: The women lined up in their coarse flannel dresses, some scowling and others hopefully primping; the "Coelebs" or bachelor, often an elderly and tongue-tied "stringybark" from the back country, hesitating his way along the rank; the matron reeling off the women's characters and records. "After uttering the awkward 'yes,'" recalled one witness to this colonial mating ritual in the 1820s,

the bride-elect flies around to her pals, bidding hasty adieus, and the bridegroom leads her out. "I'll give you three months before you're returned!" cries one, and "It's a *bargain* you've got, old stringy-bark!" cries another. Hubbub and confusion mark the exit of the couple. . . . The clothes of the convict are returned to her, and dressed again like a free woman she hies with her suitor of an hour to the church. Government gives her a "ticket of leave" as a dower, and she steps into her husband's carriage to go to his farm.[37]

These unions were not guaranteed to last. The "Factory lasses," one ex-convict thought, only wanted to get back to Sydney and "dress themselves up and go to the flash houses, and at night to the dancing houses, then they are happy":

I have known . . . very nice young women as you could wish to see, actually marry an old man, as ragged as possible, and perhaps he lives 20 or 30 miles up in the country, and no house within 5 or 6 miles of him, right up in the bush, where you can see nothing but the trees; but there is a policy in that, this man is a free man, and when they are married it makes her free, then after she has stop'd a day or two she will make some excuse which a woman is never at a loss for, to come down to Sydney; she will get what money she can of him (the Old Fool!) but she don't return again.[38]

Punishments for the "crime" class at the Parramatta Factory—and at its no less disagreeable southern cousin, the Female Factory in Hobart, which was built in 1827 and was so overcrowded that it stank like the hold of a slave ship—were not as severe as for the men. By the 1820s, female convicts in New South Wales could no longer be seen hauling big baskets of earth for bridge construction; nor, as a rule, did "refractory" women have to wear spiked iron collars, or be whipped to the beat of a drum. However, a treadmill was put in the Parramatta Female Factory in 1823, and in 1837 another was installed in Hobart; women condemned to it suffered "a very horrible pain in the loins."[39] And there was punishment by humiliation, whose most hated form was shaving the woman's head. This could produce rebellions, as the superintendent of the Hobart Factory found in 1827 when he told the assigned convict Ann Bruin that she was to be shorn for spending a night away from her master's house:

She screamed most violently, and swore that no one should cut off her hair. . . . She then entered my Sitting Room screaming, swearing, and jumping about the Room as if bereft of her senses. She had a pair of Scissors in her hand and commenced cutting off her own hair. . . . Coming before the window of my Sitting Room [she] thrust her clenched fist

through three panes of glass in succession. . . . With a Bucket [she] broke
some more panes of glass and the Bottom Sash of the Window Frame.[40]

Naturally, this was seen as the action of a crazed termagant, not the
protest of a woman whose physical rights were brutally transgressed.
There were several riots and near-breakouts at both factories, including one in 1827 when the soldiers had to be brought in because the
"Amazonian banditti" stood together, "declaring that, if one suffered,
all should suffer." In 1829 the women in the Hobart Factory tried to
burn the whole place down with "Parcels of fire" thrown through their
ventilation-hatches.[41]

iii

"WHORE" AND "PROSTITUTE," then, were bandied about to
serve the moral views of middle-class ideology; and neither the male nor
the female convicts thought it disgraceful, or even wrong, to live together
out of wedlock. However, female convicts in Australia were all to greater
or lesser degrees oppressed *as women*—as members of an inferior sex.
The sexism of English society was brought to Australia and then amplified by penal conditions. A convict woman needed unusual strength of
character not to be crushed by its assumptions. Language itself confirmed
her degradation, and some sense of this may be gleaned from the slang
and cant words applied to women in Georgian times—a brusque, stinging
argot of appropriation and dismissal.

A woman was a *bat*, a *crack*, a *bunter*, a *case fro*, *cattle*, a *mort*, a
*burick*, or a *convenient*. If she had a regular man, she was his *natural* or
*peculiar*. If married, she was an *autem mott*; if blonde, a *bleached mott*;
if a very young prostitute, almost a child, a *kinchin mott*; if beautiful, a
*rum blowen*, a *ewe*, a *flash piece of mutton*. If she had gonorrhea, she
was a *queer mort*. This language was the lower millstone; the upper was
the pompous moral phraseology of the Establishment, the good flogging
Christians. Ground between the two, a woman would need unusual reserves of tenacity and self-esteem to resist the pressure of the stereotype.
The pervasive belief in their whorishness and worthlessness must have
struck deep into the souls of these women. The double-bind to which
they were condemned was piercingly illustrated by the remark of one
Scottish settler, Peter Murdoch (who had more than 6,000 acres in Van
Diemen's Land and had helped set up the penal station on Maria Island),
to the 1838 Select Committee in London. "They are generally so bad,"
he said, "that the settlers have no heart to treat them well."[42]

The brutalization of women in the colony had gone on so long that it was virtually a social reflex by the end of the 1830s. The first full account of it was given by Robert Jones, Major Foveaux's chief jailer on Norfolk Island in the early 1800s, who thought the lot of the women prisoners there "must surely have been greater than the male convicts. . . . Several have not recovered yet from their treatment at the hands of the Major." Passages in Jones's memoir show how absolute the chattel status of women was. "Ted Kimberley chief constable considered the convicts of Norfolk Island no better than heathens unfit to grace the earth. Women were in his estimation born for the convenience of men. He was a bright intelligent Irishman."[43] Jones's sentiments are echoed in a fragmentary letter from a free settler on Norfolk Island, an ex-missionary turned trader named James Mitchell. "Surely no common mortal could demand treatment so brutal," he wrote around 1815.

> Heaven give their weary footsteps their aching hearts to a better place of rest for here there is none. During governorship of Major Foveaux convicts both male and female were held as slaves. Poor female convicts were treated shamefully. Governor King being mainly responsible.[44]

The rituals of courtship on Norfolk Island were, to put it mildly, brusque. We see the "bright intelligent" Kimberley pursuing a married convict woman named Mary Ginders with an axe, shouting that "if she did not come and live with him he would report her to the Major and have her placed in the cells." Major Foveaux got the woman of his choice, Ann Sherwin, away from one of his subordinate officers by throwing him in jail on a trumped-up charge "so that," claimed the Irish rebel leader Joseph Holt, a Norfolk prisoner at the time, "the poor fellow, seeing the danger he was in, thought it better to save his life, and lose his wife, than to lose both."[45] (At least their union lasted: Foveaux married Ann Sherwin in England in 1815.)

In such a moral environment, although male convicts had some rights (however attenuated), the women had none except the right to be fed; they had to fend for themselves against both guards and male prisoners. "England for white slaves, why were they sent here," Jones scribbled in one of his outbursts of delayed guilt, while reflecting on the fate of three women sent to Norfolk Island for the "crime" of abortion,

> for crimes that required pity more than punishment. Heaven forbid [sic] England if that is her way of populating her hellholes. What would our noble persons think of our virgin settlements and their white slaves. In every case the women treated as slaves, good stock to trade with and a convict having the good chance to possess one did not want much encouragement to do so.[46]

Thus the women were prisoners of prisoners. The price of a young, good-looking girl, fresh off the ship from Sydney, was "often as high as ten pounds." The island's bellman or beadle, Potter by name, had acquired the right to sell them. The same woman might be sold several times during her Norfolk Island sentence, with Potter "in most cases reselling them for a gallon or two of rum until they were in such a Condition as to be of little or no further use." The sales would be held in an old store where the women had to strip naked and "race around the room" while Potter kept up a running commentary on their "respective values."

The regular social pleasure of Norfolk Island under Foveaux, however, was the Thursday evening dance in the soldiers' barracks where, Jones wrote,

> all the women would join in the dances of the Mermaids, each one being naked with numbers painted on their backs so as to be recognized by their admirers who would clap their hands on seeing their favorite perform some grotesque action . . . with the assistance of a gallon or two of Rum. Such amusements were the talk of the soldiers for days before and after the performance.[47]

Such dances commonly took place in London brothels, where they were known in flash-talk as "ballum rancums." In these scenes, with the drunken, lurching bodies of women numbered like sides of beef, we see the epitome of sexual politics in early Australia. Women had to adapt as best they could; the system of sexual exploitation provoked competition among them, and they would fight like cats to stay in with the guards. Mary Ginders, the chief constable's woman, was "the leader of all the dances in the barrack Room and was well liked among the soldiers"; when Bridget Chandler, another convict woman, challenged her as favorite, Ginders broke her arm. James Mitchell, despite his moral disapproval of Norfolk Island promiscuity, gave up his missionary work and acquired a mistress, rather to Jones's envy,

> a beautiful young woman named Liza McCann who was as cunning as himself, who could drink more rum than most of the Hardened Soldiers, and took every opportunity to make herself disagreeable to the other females who would never dare venture within her store. Her greatest pride was to be clothed in silk and a bonnet with feathers.[48]

Women on the mainland or in Van Diemen's Land were rarely flogged, but such punishment was common on Norfolk Island and, in-

deed, appears to have been Major Foveaux's special treat. "To be remembered by all there," Mitchell alleged, "was his love for watching women
in their agony while receiving a punishment on the Triangle. . . . [I]t was
usual for [him] to remit a part of the sentence on condition that they
would expose their nakedness it being considered part of the punishment. And poor wretches were only too glad to save their flesh and
pain."[49] With his pistol in one hand and cutlass in the other, Foveaux
would muster the male convicts in a semicircle; the naked woman was
compelled to walk past them before she was trussed up to the triangle
and the "skinner" or "backscratcher" (Norfolk Island cant for the flogger)
went to work. The usual sentences were 25 lashes, the "Botany Bay
dozen," but they could go as high as 250. The last Norfolk Island woman
to be flogged on Foveaux's orders, in 1804, received such a sentence, but
the flogger was squeamish about it; he said he was sick and Kimberley
had to take the cat-o'-nine-tails, "upon which," as Jones described it,
"[he] cried out that he did not flog women. This reply made the Major
furious. He then asked one of the soldiers, Mick Kelly by name, to take
the tails and go on with the punishment, which he immediately proceeded to perform in such a manner that not one mark was left on her
back. This made the Major so wild that he ordered the woman to be
placed in the dark cells for a fortnight."[50]

This was the man whom Ellis Bent, Macquarie's deputy judge-advocate, found "attentive and obliging." Foveaux's amusements may suggest
how much of the true nature of the British regime in early Australia lies
hidden under the smooth language of administration. Crimes die with
their witnesses, and so, no doubt, did most of the crimes against women
in the early colony. Yet there is no lack of evidence that women continued to be treated as a doubly colonized class throughout the life of the
penal system. Almost four decades later, the fate of women excited the
horror and contempt of François-Maurice Lepailleur, one of the fifty-
eight Canadian *patriotes* who had been transported for political rebellion
against the English colonial authorities in "Lower Canada" (Quebec).
Arriving in 1840, these Canadian exiles were confined on a penal farm in
the forest at Longbottom, halfway between Sydney and Parramatta. All
of them, and especially Lepailleur (who was able to keep a journal in
secret), were disgusted by the way the local free men, Emancipists,
guards and police treated their women. "A farce," Lepailleur called the
New South Wales police force. "Drunks and scum."[51] At night, the huts
around the stockade would resound with the shrieks of women being
thrashed. The forest warden at Longbottom, a man named Rose, tied his
wife to a post and gave her 50 lashes with a government cat-o'-nine-tails;
another settler, a Portuguese, stabbed his wife and hung her on a gum

tree, with complete impunity. Not surprisingly, most of the women Lepailleur encountered in his Australian exile were alcoholic sluts, broken down by abuse, wife-beating and rum:

> During the afternoon a drunken woman, just come from the factory at Parramatta, began to abuse the woman who lives in the small cabin in front of the gate. After she had sworn a lot, cursed and blasphemed, . . . [she] turned her back to us, lifted up all her clothes and showed us her bum, saying that she had a "Black Hole" there and slapping her belly like the wretch she was. Nothing more vile than that tribe; animals are more decent than they. I would say much more but it would dirty my little journal to go on. It is incredible to see so many drunken women in this country. The roads are full of women drunkards.[52]

Thus it would seem that some prisoners—especially those who, like Lepailleur, believed themselves to be the respectable victims of tyranny and hence a cut above the "real" criminals—had exactly the same contempt for convict women as the free witnesses who discoursed so unanimously on their evils to the Molesworth Committee in 1838. "More irreformable than the male convicts," opined Bishop Ullathorne, declaring that "when a woman is bad, she is generally very bad." "I do not believe that one woman in a thousand has the moral energy to resist the temptation [to promiscuity]," Peter Murdoch testified.

Religious authorities and social workers claimed that convict women, in and out of the Female Factory, responded eagerly to any gesture of compassion or attention. But such assertions were rarely unbiased. The Roman Catholic prelate William Ullathorne (1806–1889), who had been appointed vicar-apostolic for New South Wales in 1834, never missed an opportunity to assert the success (and hence the necessity) of Catholic missionary work among the convicts. He had brought out a large contingent of Catholic clergy to Australia in 1838, including the first nuns ever seen in the colony—five Irish Sisters of Charity. Ullathorne described how these devoted women would go and visit the prisoners of the Female Factory at Parramatta five evenings a week. About a third of the factory women, he said, were Catholics, and most of them were desperate to pour their hearts out to a friendly ear. "It was sometimes difficult to prevent these poor creatures from making complete confession to the nuns. They wanted to unburden their minds, and said they would as soon speak to a nun as to a priest. The reverence with which the Sisters were regarded by all these women was quite remarkable, and the influence they exercised told . . . throughout the Colony."[53] If one has difficulty swallowing this, it can only be because Ullathorne's sentimental picture of women convicts begging to be shriven flies in the face of most other evidence about them; there is not much reason to suppose that they were any less tough or any more pathetic than their male equivalents—which is not, of course, to say that they were the degenerate creatures some authorities made them out to be. Clearly, it was in Ullathorne's interest to increase the Catholic clergy in Australia, and his testimony on the moral iniquities of transportation must be seen in that light.

Yet some were certainly grateful for a kindly ear. The prison reformer Caroline Anley visited the factory in 1834 and met two "young and extremely pretty" women who, while drunk and in a desperate outburst of temper, had attacked their tyrannous master—a Captain Charles Waldron of the 39th Regiment—and killed him. For once, popular sentiment intervened (and none of the other assigned convicts would give evidence against them), so that their death sentence was commuted to three years. Nevertheless they were regarded inside the factory as incorrigible demonesses, and Caroline Anley was the first prison visitor ever to ask for their side of the story. "If I had always been kindly treated," one of them told Anley, through the first tears she had shed since her conviction, "I wouldn't be as I am." [54]

Life in the factory—whether in New South Wales or in Van Diemen's Land—was a vegetative misery for all who led it. The minds of the women convicts rotted through lack of anything to do, although most of them preferred this stagnant leisure, punctuated by bouts of inefficient taskwork at the hand-loom, to being "treated like dogs and worked like horses" by some abusive master. The steadily growing population of freemen and colonial-born Australians objected to the Female Factories on more pragmatic grounds. By cloistering women in a colony short of females, it slowed down the birthrate. Their main mouthpiece, *The Australian*, editorialized at length on this in 1825, defending traditional "colonial marriage"—living together out of wedlock—as a great civilizer of the bush, a styptic against "dissoluteness and crime":

How many parties are living to this day together by virtue of no other bond? How many . . . are there who, after conducting themselves in an exemplary manner in that state of "resemblance to marriage," have been made *honest women*, and who, but for the forming of this species of obligation, would have been vagrants in the streets? How many by mutual industry have rendered miserable hovels comfortable homes? How many families have sprung up where nothing but a wilderness would have been seen? Had this order of things continued, even in this objectionable shape, many a vagabond, who had been lost to Society, might have been reclaimed; might have become a decent Settler. . . . But we live in an age, when it is fashionable to assume a demureness of manner, an extraordinary degree of godliness, and lay claim to an uncommon share of holy endowment.[55]

Here spoke the voice of rough-and-ready sense; but it was not one that penal officials, imprisoned by their own moral stereotypes of convict evil and female whoredom, were disposed to believe. The barrier of class thinking—of judging the social behavior of working-class convicts in terms of the desiderata of the English and colonial middle classes—was too strong for that; and ecclesiastical witnesses, from Quaker missionaries to Catholics like Ullathorne, were never slow to produce the bogey of convict sexual depravity when they needed to raise funds and muster support for their own evangelical programs in Australia. It was also, as many pages of the Molesworth Committee's evidence record, an incomparably useful weapon for Abolitionists. To show the vileness of the System they had to emphasize its power to degrade. Hence the additional emphasis, in the English reformers' decade of the 1830s, on something even less discussable: convict homosexuality.

iv

ONE WOULD naturally suppose that, in a remote colony whose proportion of men to women varied between 4 to 1 in the city and 20 to 1 in the bush, homosexuality would have flourished. So it did, especially on the chain gangs and in the outer penal settlements; but it did not leave much official evidence behind.

This was not only because sodomy was a capital crime. In the eyes of the law, sodomy deserved death; but in the eyes of social custom, especially the customs of English and Irish working people, it was more than ordinarily loathsome—"the crime whose name cannot be uttered," the phrase that Oscar Wilde would later soften into "the Love that dare not speak its name." Arthur Phillip, the first governor, was not by the ordinary standards of his time and calling a harsh man; indeed, he generally acted with humane decency. "I doubt if the fear of death ever prevented a man of no principle from committing a bad action," he noted before the First Fleet sailed. But in his code there were two exceptions: murder and sodomy. "For either of these crimes I would wish to confine the criminal until an opportunity offered of delivering him to the natives of New Zealand, and let them eat him. The dread of this will operate much stronger than the fear of death." Thus the sodomite, "violent against Nature," would be erased from society, denied even the small social niche that burial affords. This draconic idea was not carried out, or even mentioned again—there were no spare ships to ferry the "madge culls," "mollies" and "fluters," as homosexuals were known in Georgian cant, across the Tasman Sea to enrich the Maori diet.[56]

Buggery, it has been said, is to prisons what money is to middle-class society. It was as utterly pervasive in the world of hulks and penal settlement as it is in modern penitentiaries. "The horrible crime of sodomy," reported the convict George Lee from the *Portland*, a hulk in Langston Harbor, in 1803, "rages so shamefully throughout that the Surgeon and myself have been more than once threatened with assassination for straining to put a stop to it. . . . [It] is in no way discountenanced by those in command." Jeremy Bentham claimed that prisoners entering the Woolwich hulks were raped as a matter of course: "An initiation of this sort stands in the place of garnish and is exacted with equal rigour. . . . [A]s the Mayor of Portsmouth, Sir John Carter . . . very sensibly observes, *such things ever must be.*"[57]

Not until 1796 was anyone in Australia charged with a homosexual offense. This pioneer was Francis Wilkinson, accused (but acquitted) of buggering a sixty-year-old settler named Joseph Pearce. The first forty years of the colony provide scattered mentions of homosexual acts, routinely listed in the magistrates' bench-books and remarked on, in a general way, by lay and church authorities.[58] Nothing in the reports of the Select Committees on convict establishments and transportation for 1798 or 1812 can be construed as a reference to homosexuality. But after 1830, the documents are full of references to it—for that was the decade in which the movement to abolish transportation, dormant since the protestations of Jeremy Bentham, began to gather steam. Abolitionists like Lord John Russell and Sir William Molesworth wanted to show that transportation to Australia depraved most of its victims and reformed none of them. Proponents of transportation—especially the wealthy Australian landowners, who stood to lose their assigned labor if convictry was abolished—did not want convict homosexuality discussed; but its opponents did. Mentioning the unmentionable would complete the picture of Australia sketched by William Ullathorne as a polity of fallen souls whose "otherness" was all the worse because they were white, not black. "The eye of God," Ullathorne feelingly declared,

> looks down upon a people such as, since the deluge, has not been. Where they marry in haste, without affection; where each one lives to his senses alone. A community without the feelings of community; whose men are very wicked, whose women are very shameless, and whose children are very irreverent. . . . The naked savage, who wanders through those endless forests, knew of nothing monstrous in crime, except cannibalism, until England schooled him in horrors through her prisoners. The removal of such a plague from the earth concerns the whole human race.[59]

When speaking of sodomy, Bishop Ullathorne's eloquence became sublime and cloudy. He spoke to the Molesworth Committee of "crimes that, dare I describe them, would make your blood to freeze, and your hair to rise erect in horror upon the pale flesh." But he, like all the Abolitionists, offered more impressions than figures. We do not know (and probably never will) how widespread homosexuality was in penal Australia.

An example of the difficulty occurs in the minutes of evidence of the 1832 Select Committee on Secondary Punishments. John Stephen, a former judge in New South Wales, related how in the first trial he had attended in Australia four or five Norfolk Island prisoners were sentenced to death. "They thanked the Judge for having ordered them to die: stating, that they lived in such a state of horrid misery, witnessing the most horrid crime known to human nature, committed in numberless cases from morning to night, that they preferred death." In the course of another trial, Stephen testified, a witness had mentioned "50 or 60 cases [of sodomy] occurring in a day" on Norfolk Island, a sexual epidemic which "made men so perfectly miserable, that many preferred death to living in that penal settlement." Since the total convict population of Norfolk Island at the time was about 600, this argues an impressive priapic energy on the prisoners' part, perhaps caused by the sea air. Yet in the same report there is the testimony of the Crown botanist, Allan Cunningham, who spent four months on Norfolk Island in the same year, 1830. Were the convicts in a state "of the most horrible degradation"? "Not that I heard of," said Cunningham, dismissing the idea of Norfolk Island as a sea-girt Sodom, which he thought had been cooked up by the "radical" press, particularly the "most scurrilous paper" in the colony, the *Monitor*, ever critical of Governor Darling. The crime of sodomy, he thought, "might have been committed once or twice in the course of ten years, but I do not believe it was common."[60]

Once a decade or sixty times a day? Inflated though Stephen's guess may have been, Cunningham's was clearly absurd; but both were, in fact, produced by the same reflex. Because the act was unspeakable, it must not be inspected; easier to deny its existence, or else to believe any horror story about it. All that is known about Norfolk Island, however, suggests that Stephen's guess was not far off the mark, especially by the mid-1840s under Major Childs, when the muddle of laxity and brutality there had reached its absolute nadir.

Obviously, most lovers were not caught; hence, statistics on sodomy from the penal period are of little use, as they were based only on court indictments. Homosexual acts in penal Australia were done in secret, and prisoners seldom swore out complaints against other prisoners for performing them. Consequently few "sodomists" were arraigned, let alone convicted. Over the period 1829–35, in New South Wales and Van Diemen's Land, only twenty-four men were tried for "unnatural offences." Twelve were convicted and sentenced—four capitally, though only one (in 1834) was actually hanged. Five drew hard labor in irons on the chain gang, and three were re-transported to Norfolk Island or Moreton Bay.[61]

Why so few convictions? Ernest Augustus Slade, who had been superintendent of the convict barracks at Hyde Park in Sydney from 1833 to 1834 (his resignation was forced by sexual scandal, though over a woman), testified that "among [the lower] class of convicts sodomy is as common as any other crime." It was an ineradicable part of jail culture. But only about one case in thirty could be proven. Molested youths lodged complaints but then prevaricated in court; and other evidence tended to be vague, since "shirtlifters" were rarely caught in the act of buggery. "If you had it proved," Slade told the Molesworth Committee in 1838, "that men were found with their breeches down in secluded spots, and they stated that they had gone there to ease themselves, and upon examination it was found that they had not done so, what could have occurred?" But no jury would convict on such grounds. Out in the bush, the dreaded act became more obscure still, as there was nobody to watch the assigned convicts. Bishop Ullathorne believed that sodomy was less frequent among the shepherds, who tended to live alone, than among stockmen, "a much more dissolute set" who practiced "a great deal of that crime" and even taught it to the formerly innocent Aborigines. And if the Man from Snowy River's convict forebear was not content with the brusque embraces of Jacky-Jacky, there were always sheep. "As a juryman," one witness told the committee, "I have had opportunities of hearing many trials for unnatural offences, with animals particularly. . . . I think they are much more common than in any other country inhabited by the English." "That is, among the convicts?" interjected one committee member. "Yes," said the witness, dispelling the thought of the colonial gentry practicing abominations on their own merinos.[62]

The testimony given to the Molesworth Committee suggests a demimonde not quantified by the statistics of the time. Homosexuality was the norm in the Hyde Park barracks in Sydney, where new arrivals were decanted from the ships, old lags thrown together with young boys. As in all systems of confinement since prisons began, lads became "punks" (passive homosexuals) to get the protection of a dominant man; they went by girls' names, Kitty, Nancy or Bet. Few of them had any homosexual experience before they got to Australia, according to Ullathorne —and his testimony was more than guesswork, since as a priest he had heard thousands of prison confessions and had to struggle with his conscience as he testified, generalizing so as not to violate the seal of the confessional. As one bewildered youth exclaimed to him, "Such things no one knows in Ireland."[63]

The only account of penal homosexuality in Australia by a convict was set down by the Swing letter-writer from Shropshire, Thomas Cook, in his memoir of the System in the 1830s, *The Exile's Lamentations*. His contact with it began when he was sent to labor in the road gangs in the Blue Mountains, cutting the Great Western Road through raw bush and sandstone at Honeysuckle Flat. "It was now," he wrote, "that my miseries commenced," although he would not press their "nauseous details" on the reader:

> I was yet in the dark of the horrible propensity which the coarse and brutish language of my Gangmates in calamity, coupled with their assignations one towards the other, shortly told me the greater part of them had imbibed. So far advanced were these wretched men in depravity, that they appeared to have entirely lost the feelings of men, and to have imbibed those that would render them execrable to all mankind.[64]

For warmth, men bedded two or three together, a custom which "appeared to me altogether objectionable"; and before long, Cook was so broken down by labor and lack of sleep that a medical officer transferred him to another gang working closer to Sydney, at Mount Victoria. But at night, the same fumbling and rooting went on there; the only difference was that there the gangers "were less public in their demonstrations of brutal regard." Naïvely, Cook tried to remonstrate with a ganger who took a fancy to him. "Extraordinary as it may appear," he wrote indignantly,

> it is not the less true, that an appeal to their better feelings was the certain cause of insult and derision, which they would copiously inflict on their less depraved fellow Prisoner; and if he nevertheless persisted in publicly deprecating their horrid propensities, he would be struck, kicked and otherwise abused.[65]

There was no appeal to authority, because all the overseers on the mountain road gangs were convicts, and most of them, according to Cook, were homosexuals. "Woe unto that man who had the courage to pass a remark at all disrespectful of the despicable objects of their horrible ambition! He would be selected as a Lamb for the Slaughter!" If crossed, they could send a man to be summarily "lacerated at the Triangles" at the courthouse at Mount Wallawarang.

With his virtue stubbornly intact, Cook labored in the Mount Victoria gang for several months before losing his temper with an importunate homosexual, whom he thrashed "rather unmercifully." For this, he was sentenced to a year in irons on the road at No. 2 Stockade, whose overseers were the worst of all—"without exception, the most overbearing and depraved Villains it were possible to find in the mountain district," Cook wrote, his abstract figures of moral obloquy creaking under the strain:

> The only regard they had to classification, was evidently that which to all *natural* beings, bespoke their own abominations,—or, in other words, the most execrable portion of their men found no difficulty in ingratiating themselves into favor, by the coarseness of their language, and the open demonstrations of Pleasure with which they give effect to their horrible propensities, in their Overseers' hearing.[66]

At the stockade, convicts could sometimes bribe their way out of a flogging with money or tobacco, but the only other way was to "come out" as a homosexual and so mollify the overseers. A circle of sexual tyranny sustained itself because, according to Cook, the overseers on the iron gangs were chosen from the working hands on unshackled gangs, like those at Honeysuckle Flat and Mount Victoria. They were recommended by those gangs' overseers, so that like chose like; an overseer's sexual favorites could be rewarded with a ration of power on the iron gangs, enforcing "Starvation, Flogging and insupportable Labour" upon any resistant "straights." Cook declared that in his time on the road gangs, he had only known two overseers who were not homosexual.[67]

Although Cook, like most Englishmen of his day, thought homosexuality disgusting in itself, his deeper objection to its role in the penal world was that it multiplied the injustices of power. It represented an abusive control over the will of others, often involving rape. If this carceral society of the 1830s was anything like prisons today, we must recognize that many of the sexual episodes Cook witnessed were not lovemaking but acts of sadistic humiliation, in which sexuality was merely the instrument of a deeper violence—the strong breaking the weak down into a punk, a molly, a gobbling queen. Nothing in Cook's background prepared him for such transactions, and so he went down through the circles of the System—from the road gangs to Port Macquarie, from Port Macquarie to Norfolk Island—in amazement and outrage. He described, in language that can scarcely bear to encompass its subject, how sexual contact in prison tends to be metabolized into relationships of power.

Cook thought that the System nurtured sodomy—that it flourished in Australia as nowhere else. He believed that there was little homosexuality in English jails and hulks, but that inversion, in the sexual sense as well as the geographical, ruled the antipodes; and that cruelty was the seed of "the practice which was engendered at the Penal Settlements of Old where they were tortured by Tyrants in a manner that tended to brutalize all Nature." If "nature"—which, for Cook, included the idea of "natural law" or justice—is perverted by tyranny, then other realms, including the sexual, will be warped as well. Reflecting on this years later, in the relative peace and security of Alexander Maconochie's administration on Norfolk Island, Cook speculated that the System meant to *encourage* sodomy, using the perpetual threat of rape or humiliation as one of the automatic punishments for the unwitting convict. In this he was wrong, but one can understand why he thought it. Until Maconochie took over Norfolk Island in 1840, not one commandant in the System had shown the least concern for the rehabilitation of his prisoners. They acted purely as agents of repression, as guardians of the pit. And if the men in the pit had ways of degrading one another, why trouble to stop them? So Cook, writing in the early 1840s, makes his climactic outcry against the "Old System" of the 1830s:

> No prospect being afforded them of a woman's Love,—without hope of Heaven or fear of Hell; their already darkened reason became more clouded. Their lax morals gave way and they indulged with apparent delight in every filthy and unnatural propensity. None but a mind capable of powerful reasoning, into which early moral habits had been instilled, or a heart filled with early affection could prevent a being falling into the lowest depths of infamy, never more to rise to the rank of man. . . . [I]t would be better to introduce the *Dracon Laws* than revert to the *Old System*.[68]

Between Cook's objurgations one glimpses the workings of homosexual society among the prisoners. Clearly, there was a good deal of solidarity:

> Several individuals were punished for the heinous offence, and although it may appear incredible it is nevertheless true that these wretches were generally viewed with feelings of sympathy and those who had brought such cases forward were looked upon with contempt, and very few would afterwards associate with them.[69]

Cook also hints at the strength of attachments between prison lovers on Norfolk Island, a fact confirmed by the disapproving testimony of Thomas Arnold, the deputy-assistant commissary on Norfolk Island, to the Molesworth Committee: "Actually, incredible as it may appear, feelings of jealousy are exhibited by those depraved wretches, if they see the boy or young man with whom they carry on this abominable intercourse speak to another person." Eight years later an official report by Robert

Pringle Stuart, a convict department magistrate in Norfolk, described how convicts called themselves "man and wife," that there were probably 150 such couples, not counting more casual attachments, and that they could not bear to be separated: "The natural course of affection is quite distracted, and these parties manifest as much eager earnestness for the society of each other as members of the opposite sex." Bishop Ullathorne, visiting Norfolk Island in 1835–36, heard at second hand (from a Protestant clergyman, who had been told it by a prisoner under sentence of death) that "two-thirds of the island were implicated" in homosexual activity. He thought the same proportion obtained at Moreton Bay and other penal stations.[70]

Certainly there was no decline in sexual coercion on Norfolk Island, except perhaps between 1839 and 1843, the time of Maconochie's brief adminstration. By the mid-1840s it had grown even worse, largely because there was no effort to sort out the hardened criminals from the new arrivals. "Youths are seized upon, and become the victims of hoary and unnatural villains," reported Thomas Naylor, chaplain on Norfolk Island from 1841 to 1845:

With these scoundrels the English farm labourer, the tempted and fallen mechanic, the suspected but innocent victims of perjury or mistake, are indiscriminately herded. With them are mixed Chinamen from Hong Kong, the aborigines of New Holland, West Indian Blacks, Greeks, Caffres, and Malays; soldiers for desertion; idiots, madmen, pig-stealers and pickpockets. In the open day the weak are bullied and robbed by the stronger. At night the sleeping-wards are very cess-pools of unheard-of vices. I cannot find sober words enough to express the enormity of this evil. . . . I watched the process of degradation. I saw very boys seized upon and lost; I saw decent and respectable men, nay gentlemen . . . thrown among the vilest ruffians, to be tormented by their bestialities.[71]

In no less heated terms, Robert Pringle Stuart reported to his superiors in Van Diemen's Land in 1846 that Norfolk Island under the lax, vacillating sway of Major Childs had become a citadel of sodomy:

How can anything else be expected? Here are 800 men immured from 6 o'clock in the evening until sunrise . . . without lights, without visitation by the officers. Atrocities of the most shocking, odious character are there perpetrated, and that unnatural crime is indulged in to excess; the young have no chance of escaping from abuse, and even forcible violation is resorted to. To resist can hardly be expected, in a situation so utterly removed from, and lamentably destitute of, protection. A terrorism is sternly and resolutely maintained, to revenge not merely exposure but even complaint.[72]

Convict homosexuality seemed, from Stuart's perspective, to be the quintessential form of convict evil. Other reformers and officials, staring timorously into the pit that England had created and whose very bottom was Norfolk Island, agreed. The danger seemed to be that this "contagion" would spread unchecked like an epidemic disease from the island to the mainland of Australia, so that, as Stuart put it, "in future years a moral stain of the deepest dye may be impressed, perhaps immovably, on its people, and thus become attached to the name of Englishmen."[73] This fear cannot have been felt by Stuart alone. The portions of his report that had to do with convict homosexuality were censored from its published form; but it is hardly possible that news and rumors of such doings on Norfolk Island and other penal stations, over the years, did not leak out into the colony and contribute to the atmosphere of nameless evil, of unutterable degradation, that surrounded the idea of convictry in the ears of its respectable citizens. This inevitably fostered more repressive attitudes toward all homosexuals in Australia. Their sexual preference was doubly damned: first, because it was a crime under law, and second, because it was mainly committed by those who were convicts already.

There could have been no better breeding ground for the ferocious bigotry with which Australians of all classes, long after the abandonment of Norfolk Island and of the System itself, perceived the homosexual. And this in turn seemed like an act of cleansing—for homosexuality was one of the mute, stark, subliminal elements in the "convict stain" whose removal, from 1840 onward, so preoccupied Australian nationalists.


                                    v


THE THIRD "minority" in penal Australia was not, in round figures, a minority at all, for until about 1845 there were probably more Aborigines scattered across the continent than whites clustered around its coastal settlements. But aboriginal groups were always small and scattered, whereas the white groups (except on the rim of pastoral settlement) tended to be larger and denser. On the shores of Sydney Harbor, whites outnumbered blacks from the moment the First Fleet arrived; no black could ever have seen so many people before. One is apt to think of Sydney and its outlying penal settlements, from Hobart and Launceston in the south to Moreton Bay in the north, as small and weak. So they were, but to the Aborigines they looked large, strange and imposing, and the malign gravitational field they emitted would destroy their culture.

The fate of the Australian blacks was intimately connected to the System. A frontier society based on slave labor, run by the threat of extreme violence and laced with rigid social divisions was not likely to treat the Aborigines compassionately or even fairly. Nor did it. There was a great gap between policy and practice. The Royal instructions to every governor of Australia, from Arthur Phillip in 1788 to Thomas Brisbane in 1822, always repeated the same themes. The Aborigines must not be molested. Anyone who "wantonly" killed them, or gave them "any unnecessary interruption in the exercise of their several occupations", must be punished. The aim in racial relations was "amity and kindness."[74] The idea of converting them to Christianity would not be embodied in official policy until Brisbane's successor as governor, Ralph Darling, came in 1825. Yet, even though white settlement began with no *policy* of racist persecution, the coming of the whites was an unmitigated disaster for everyone with a black skin.

The legal status of Aborigines—and of their "claims," as white officials interestingly put it, to the territory they had occupied for some eighteen millennia before the arrival of the whites—seemed almost insoluble to the whites. Everywhere else in the historical experience of the British Empire, colonies had been planted where the "natives" and "Indians" understood and defended the idea of property. In Virginia as in Africa, in New Zealand as in the East Indies, British colonists encountered cultures of farming people who had houses, villages and plots of cultivated land. These proofs of prior ownership might be violated by the whites (and often were); but they could not be denied or ignored. Even Charles II's instructions to the Council of Foreign Plantations on the conduct of the English colony in Virginia had recognized that as the new settlement would "border upon" the lands of the Indians, their territory had to be respected, for "peace is not to be expected without . . . justice to them."[75]

But the Aborigines were hunter-gatherers who roamed over the land without marking out boundaries or making fixed settlements. They had no idea of farming or stock-raising. They saved nothing, lived entirely in the present and were, in the whites' eyes, so ignorant of property as to be little more than intelligent animals "whose only superiority above the brute," as one visiting naval surgeon put it, "consisted in their use of the spear, their extreme ferocity and their employing fire in the cookery of their food." The whites were not the only ones to think so; when a Maori named Tipahee visited Sydney with his son around 1800 at the behest of Governor King, both warriors formed "the most contemptible opinion" of the Aborigines' nakedness, weak technology, poor comforts and "trifling mode of warfare."[76]

Macquarie hoped they could be brought from their "rambling Naked state" and made into farmers. In 1815 he tried to put sixteen aboriginal men on a small farm on Sydney Harbor, complete with huts and a boat. They lost the boat, ignored the huts and wandered off into the bush.[77]

From then on, it was assumed that "native labor" was useless. Hence, the rights normally assigned to colonized native workers within the Empire were not extended to Aborigines. The early colony was so overwhelmingly dependent on the slave labor of white convicts that the effort of training nomadic blacks even for the most menial work was not worthwhile. The convicts might be scum, but they had an economic value. The blacks clearly had none; therefore, they were less than scum. The decay of fringe-dwelling blacks on the edge of white urban culture —the remnants of the Iora, Gammeraigal and Daruk—was inexorable and all-pervasive; to sympathetic onlookers it seemed a plague, and to racist ones a bestial joke. Stupefied with the cheapest grade of rum, racked with every new disease from tuberculosis to syphilis, begging and babbling in the flash-talk and gutter argot of the convicts, they were caricatures of misery. Even their traditions of authority had been parodied by the whites, who insisted on giving some elders patronizing identity cards in the form of crescent-shaped copper plates, with their rank as "chief" engraved on them in English. And yet, as the Russian explorer Captain Bellingshausen noted of some Sydney Aborigines in 1820,

> The natives remember very well their former independence. Some expressed their claims to certain places, asserting that they belonged to their ancestors. . . . Despite all the compensation offered to them [!], a spark of vengeance still smoulders in their hearts.[78]

The tribes further out were better off, but only for a short time. They, too, were about to lose their land. Where did their title to it lie? Only in their own collective memory and oral traditions, to which the whites paid no attention. They seemed to drift across the territory in little ragged groups, never staying long in one place, appearing from the forest and vanishing back into it. They carried what they owned and killed the infants they could not carry. The complex and ancient ideas about territory that were embedded in aboriginal thought—ideas that had to do more with land as the "property" of mythic ancestors than with material ownership in the here and now—were completely unfamiliar to the whites and would have been opaque to them even without the barrier of language. The Aborigines had no visible political framework, and certainly they were not united as a people with common interests: There were perhaps five hundred languages and dialects spoken by the aboriginal tribes of early colonial Australia. Moreover, they lived in an almost continuous state of tribal warfare, aggravated by the kind of random contact made inevitable by nomadic life. One Australian historian cautiously ventured that the aboriginal death rate from these bloody encounters—rarely involving more than fifty men on each side—lay between 1 person in 270 and 1 in 150, a death rate "not exceeded in any nation of Europe during any of the last three centuries."[79] If these strange people showed so little solidarity among themselves, what common rights would their invaders assign them? In practice, almost none. The government simply declared all Australian land to be Crown land; and the idea that Aborigines might have some territorial rights by virtue of prior occupation was settled to the entire satisfaction of the whites by a New South Wales court decision in 1836, which declared that the Aborigines were too few and too ill-organized to be considered "free and independent tribes" who owned the land they lived on.[80] Even the humanitarians could salve their consciences by reflecting that the Aborigines were, after all, nomads—and to a nomad, one tract of land is "as good as" another. This absurd misreading of nomadic life meant that Aborigines could be driven without compunction out of their ancestral territory and into new conflicts, not only with the whites, but with other tribes.

At the same time, the Aborigines were classified as British subjects; indeed, the early governors wanted to see them converted to Christianity and farming so that they could be absorbed, socially if not genetically, into the lower class of the colony—an idea loathed and resisted by every white, no matter what his class. The first policies about clashes between settlers and Aborigines were therefore most equivocal. In 1802, after nearly seven years of undeclared warfare against the Daruk tribe on the Hawkesbury River—guerrilla raids by blacks, punitive torture and killings by settlers—Governor King saw fit to remind the colonists that the killing of natives "will be punished with the utmost severity of the Law," but that "the Settler is not to suffer his property to be invaded, or his existence endangered by them." Thus, he would commute the hanging of five colonists who had killed two blacks on the Hawkesbury River two years before. In 1805, King's judge-advocate opined that, since the Aborigines had no grasp of such basics of English law as evidence, guilt or oaths, they could neither be prosecuted nor sworn as witnesses, for either would be "a mockery of judicial proceedings." And so the best course would be to "pursue and inflict such punishment as they may merit," without the formalities of a trial. A settler would have had to be blind or a saint not to see the point, and from then on the miseries of dispossession began.[81]

They were brought to full spate over the next thirty years by the Australian wool industry and its insatiable appetite for land. They would go on far beyond the end of the penal system itself. Between 1800 and 1830, the settled stations pushed inexorably outward: south to Goulburn and the high Monaro plains, west across the Blue Mountains to the golden grasslands that stretched around Bathurst and Mudgee, and north to the valley of the Hunter River. At every contact with the Aborigines, the pattern would be much the same: a collision between a white culture of private property and a black one of "primitive communism" in which no resources, land least of all, were privately owned. Sometimes the blacks would move on. Usually they attacked, launching a small guerrilla war until enough of their warriors had been cut down by the settlers' firearms to render the tribe helpless. If their resistance was strong enough, martial law could be declared against them: In 1824 the stockholders around Bathurst persuaded Governor Brisbane to send soldiers in to "pacify" the blacks in their area. Brisbane, who a few years before had been impressing missionaries with his liberal expressions of concern for the Aborigine ("If something is not done for these poor, distressed creatures, they will become extinct: the race of them will perish from absolute want!" he told a Wesleyan),[82] dispatched his troopers and native police, and the death toll was not tallied.

Until lately, historians have not paid enough attention to the fierceness with which Australian aboriginal clans fought the European invaders for possession of their land. "The other side of the frontier"—to use the title Henry Reynolds gave to his study of this subject—showed a pattern of tenacious and often well-organized resistance, ranging from massed frontal attacks through guerrilla warfare to the carefully plotted tracking and revenge-murder of individual Europeans for known crimes against tribespeople. The Aborigines' tactical superiority was generally, if reluctantly, admitted by whites. Aborigines stole guns and learned how to use them; they made devastating attacks on sheep and cattle, harassed miners, killed horses and burned homesteads, thus undercutting the economic basis of many areas of white settlement.[83]

This resistance did not always begin at once. Aborigines—at least in the early colonial years, before awareness of European rapacity became general among them—seemed to have no idea of dispossession. As Reynolds pointed out, "While conflict was ubiquitous in traditional societies, territorial conquest was virtually unknown. . . . If blacks often did not react to the initial invasion of their country it was because they were not aware it had taken place. They certainly did not believe that their land had suddenly ceased to belong to them and they to their land. The mere presence of Europeans, no matter how threatening, could not uproot certainties so deeply implanted in Aboriginal custom and consciousness."[84] Many tribes were convinced of the ignorance and weakness of the whites—at first. It was not the coming of the Europeans that provoked resistance, but their unrelenting seizure of all rights and uses of the land.

In some districts the Aborigines' resistance lasted as long as ten years, but they were fated not to win. European technology was against them, and so was the breakdown of their hunting environment caused by the introduction of stock. Pasturage altered the environment and began to obliterate the old material bases of aboriginal life. Sheep and cattle drove out kangaroos and other game. Fences blocked ancient routes and runs. The forests were cut back. Familiar plants died out. And always, everywhere on the expanding limits of settlement, the Aborigine was seen as a mere native pest, like a dingo or kangaroo. He was a *myall*, a *murky*, a *boong* or (in a phrase that precisely expressed the whites' belief in his inevitable passing) a *dark cloud*. He could be killed without hesitation—and, given the remoteness of the outer settlements and the thinness and inherent racism of the police force, without much chance of detection and punishment. "They may be destroyed by their fellows, and what is worse, may be shot wholesale by Europeans, and yet the arm of the law has no power to punish unless the evidence of a white person can be procured."[85] One observer heard "a large proprietor of sheep and cattle" maintain "that there was no more harm in shooting a native, than in shooting a dog"; and another

> narrated, as a good thing, that he had been one of a party who had pursued the blacks, in consequence of cattle having been rushed by them, and he was sure they shot upwards of a hundred. . . . [H]e maintained that there was nothing wrong in it, that it was preposterous to suppose they had souls.[86]

The death toll of this long frontier war is a matter of informed guesswork rather than hard fact. Probably between 2,000 and 2,500 European settlers were killed, and upwards of 20,000 Aborigines.[87]

The emblematic massacre in New South Wales occurred in 1838 on the property of Henry Dangar, at a place called Myall Creek near the Gwydir River. It was meant as a reprisal for stock-theft and "cattlerushing" or stampeding, which stockmen resented because it thinned the animals through panic and so reduced their salable weight.

The station-hands had no idea who the actual culprits were, but they found an inoffensive encampment of Aborigines some forty miles from the site and attacked them. A dozen armed stockmen, led by a white who had kept company with the little tribe for the previous three weeks, rounded up twenty-eight unarmed men, women and children, roped them together, drove them to a killing-ground nearby, and slaughtered them all with muskets and cutlasses. Then they chopped some up and mutilated others, and burned the corpses on a pyre. But as it happened, there was a white witness among the killers who turned informer against the other eleven. Although the jury in their first trial acquitted them all, a second trial produced verdicts of guilty for seven of them, who were hanged; four went free. The case was politically explosive. Probably it would never have come to court at all had Governor George Gipps not intervened directly. As no treaties with the Aborigines existed, Gipps concluded that they "had never been in possession of any Code of Laws intelligible to a Civilized People," but he maintained that "in putting the Law into Force against the Aborigines, the utmost degree of Mercy and forebearance should be exercised." Settlers had exterminated thousands of Aborigines before, but none had swung for it. So acute was the resentment of this sentimental interference with the code of the frontier that some graziers, led by a magistrate, even raised a defense fund for the murderers. Although the Myall Creek massacre caused a passing revulsion of public conscience, it did nothing to stop the majority of those who believed the Australian version of Manifest Destiny—that "it is in the order of nature that, as civilization advances, savage nations *must* be exterminated" and that the safety of explorers and settlers should not "be sacrificed out of deference to . . . political and humbugging maniacs who write and prate of matters of which they knew nothing whatever."[88]

The best way to deal with the "sable brethren" was "by the discriminating application of firearms." Ten days after Myall Creek (the news of which, however, had not yet leaked out), a correspondent in another Sydney paper, piqued by Gipps's "softness" in not sending a punitive military force against the blacks in the Hunter Valley, urged that

if, by one decisive step, the Aborigines are shown their own weakness, and convinced that it is useless for them to contend with Europeans, they will submit and cease their outrages, and much bloodshed may be spared. . . . [U]nless prompt measures are adopted, these dusky "lords of the soil" will fairly drive the pale faces from their territories.[89]

The people who most craved this Final Solution were the convicts. It was not thought surprising that, of the twelve white murderers at Myall Creek, only one (the witness) was born in the colony and all the rest were either convicts or ex-convicts; or that, of the eleven, not one would inform on his fellows. Convicts' hatred of Aborigines was a well-established tradition by then.

In Chapter 4, we saw how the first conflicts between black and white in the colony began with the convicts, who stole the Aborigines' weapons to sell as souvenirs, transgressed their territory while trying to escape and hated the blacks not only for their freedom but for the conciliatory treatment the officers, acting on instructions, gave them. If a convict stole a chicken, he would be flogged; if a tribesman did the same, he would go scot-free. Such things rankled, particularly as the blacks soon came to be seen as a wild extension of the jail of infinite space: To escape into the bush was to risk almost certain death from either starvation or the blacks' waddies and spears. Thus the conviction grew among the convicts that the Aborigines, if not exactly in league with their hated jailers, were on their side; and this was confirmed when, in the penal stations of Newcastle and Moreton Bay in the 1820s, the guards took to rewarding Aborigines who captured escaped prisoners, beat them bloody and dragged them in. By the 1830s, the systematic use of blacktrackers —Aborigines who, at the behest of the hunting police, used their superb skills at following a man through the bush—had confirmed the convicts' picture of the Aborigine as a skilled, treacherous enemy. If not an enemy, he was merely subhuman—a spindly nomadic wretch, Nature's dull orphan. "The natiffs of this Country they are Blacks," a typical convict description goes, "and they go naked just as they came into the world, and they live on Ruts of trees and snails or aney other Creeping thing, Women and Children goes all naked alike."[90] Every underdog needs a dog below him so he can feel canine. That, in the convicts' eyes, was all the Aborigines were good for. The cruelty of the authorities toward whites was stored up as blind resentment in the convict *lumpenproletariat,* and discharged—though not always as efficiently as at Myall Creek and other sites of massacre—upon the blacks.

For their part, the Aborigines seem to have despised the convicts, whom they saw laboring under conditions which their own pride would never have accepted, treated like the defeated members of some enemy tribe, as in a sense they were: driven, harried, kicked, flogged, scorned and occasionally killed. "No good—all same like croppy," some tribesmen said when offered some left-over convict slops, "croppy" being the disdainful term for an Irish convict. In 1837 a missionary was surprised to find that Aborigines who had accepted a gift of winter dresses and cloaks painstakingly sewn from blankets had unpicked all the stitches and turned them back into blankets, because they thought them "Irish cloaks"—"our natives commonly attach some idea of inferiority to what is Irish and Ireland."[91]

Without records from the blacks' side, one can only guess what the structure of the System contributed to their opinion of whites; but their behavior showed that if they were to take sides, however briefly or opportunistically, it might as well be with the esteemed warriors—the men in red coats who dispensed the power, the tobacco, the blankets. The idea that the despised black might have had some "natural" sympathy with the oppressed convict is the flimsiest sentiment. Across the cultural chasm that separated them, no such alliances were possible and none were ever made, except for a few escaped convicts who successfully "went native" and adapted to tribal life.[92]

Convicts did not stop despising and fearing Aborigines after they had served out their sentences, received their pardons and become free men.

On the contrary: Because "settled" land near the towns was always taken, the newly emancipated settler with little or no capital—and no government subsidies beyond a grant of raw bushland—was more likely to put up his slab hut on the very fringes of white occupation. This brought him and his family into contact with fresh tribal groups who would begin, all over again, the pattern of black resistance and "treachery," answered by white retaliation and murder. In this way life on an expanding frontier ensured that convict attitudes toward Aborigines were carried and transmitted from generation to generation, from bond parents to free children. When one free farmer in the 1840s remonstrated with a hutkeeper—a former convict and soldier—for shooting an unarmed Aborigine, "he looked on me as a sort of dangerous lunatic for troubling myself about the lives of a few Blacks, which he evidently thought he had a perfect right to dispose of as he chose, so long as he did not get into trouble." Let missionaries and city-dwellers prattle humanely about the blacks—they did not have to deal with them, or defend their huts and runs against them. They did not know how shiftless, feckless and dangerous they could be. In some parts of Australia, as any traveller can verify for himself, this attitude has never died.

With convicts, the hatred was greater because the fear was more pervasive. An emigrant free settler was likely to have good weapons. An Emancipist, newly pardoned by the governor, might be able to get hold of an old musket or a rusty horse-pistol. More likely he would set off with nothing but cutlass and axe. Even with a gun, a man was at a disadvantage against Aborigines with spears, especially in close bush; he could not load and fire fast enough, and in any case few convicts had the kind of military training or sporting experience that would have turned them into good shots. And when the fire-sticks were clattering on the roof of the hut, and its slab walls began to smolder, there was no colonial cavalry to come galloping over the hill. The cavalry was a long way off—in America, in fact. Thus the typical form of frontier skirmish was ambush and small, indiscriminate massacre, along the lines of the atrocity at Myall Creek. Whites laid for blacks and shot them in the back. Blacks crept into the hut and crushed the skulls of a settler and his woman with their waddies. "The normal condition of inland life was an armed, watchful, wary, nervous calm," slow in tempo but punctuated by sunny explosions of horror that soon settled again on the indifferent skin of the land.[93]

Other factors helped worsen this long, bitter contact with men brutalized by the convict system. The remnants of aboriginal groups, their strength and numbers blasted away by the settlers' guns, gave in to a marginal life as "station blacks" living on handouts and irregular work, like tracking stray cattle. Men who had sweated out years as assigned slave laborers were not averse to seeing blacks worse degraded. Ill from epidemic disease, blacks would sometimes "come in" to a settlement begging for medicine and be given sheep-drench, as befitted their animal status, and the crude veterinary medicines killed them. The one thing they could usually sell to Europeans was their women, and this led to debilitating outbreaks of venereal disease as well as further loosening of their vestigial tribal structure, through the birth of half-caste bastards. Missionaries often complained that the "lower-class whites"—former convicts and their descendants—deliberately undermined their efforts to educate and convert the fringe-dwelling Aborigines. Sewing-bees and Bible readings had no chance against rum and prostitution. And the politician who wanted to get and keep some popularity with the majority of white settlers had to deride government and missionary aid as the meddling of soft busybodies. Thus William Charles Wentworth, in bygone years the tribune of the ex-convicts but now widely known as "the lord of the lash and the triangle," was reported as saying in a speech to the Australian Legislative Council in 1844:

> He could not see if the whites in this colony were to go out into the land and possess it, that the Government had much to do with them. No doubt there would be battles between the settlers and the border tribes; but they might be settled without the aid of the Government. The civilized people had come in and the savage must go back. They must go on progressing until their dominancy was established, and therefore he could think that no measure was wise or merciful to the blacks which clothed them with a degree of seeming protection, which their position would not allow them to maintain. . . . It was not the policy of a wise Government to attempt the perpetuation of the aboriginal race of New South Wales. . . . They must give way before the arms, aye! even the diseases of civilized nations—they must give way before they attain the power of those nations.[94]

For the original Australians, then, the arrival of the convicts was a catastrophe. Perhaps they might have suffered less if New South Wales had been colonized by free emigrants who were, at least notionally, less brutal; who had a less obvious investment in kicking a subject class. The more opportunistic the settlers were, the more their sense of being poor white trash demanded relief, the more they spoke of civilization and racial superiority, reflecting that even their diseases facilitated Destiny's plan for the blacks. It was a thin, embittered comfort; but it was one of very few the System offered its white subjects, at the end of their own deracination.

# 9

# The Government Stroke

OBODY ON SHORE in Sydney was blasé about the arrival of a convict transport. For the people who crammed the bobbing flotilla of rowboats around the ship as she warped in, it meant news from home or even the glimpse of a familiar face, pallid from life below the hatches. But for the settlers, it meant a small gush of the most precious commodity in Australia: labor. Every convict faced the same social prospects. He or she served the Crown or, on the Crown's behalf, some private person, for a given span of years. Then came a pardon or a ticket-of-leave, either of which permitted him to sell his labor freely and choose his place of work. What this came down to, in the common view of English critics of transportation—most of whom had not been to Australia and had no first-hand knowledge of the convict system—was that the Crown used them as slaves until they were judged fit to become peasants.

An equation between convictry and slavery was the invariable trope used to attack the System. Some key figures in the convict administration also used it—such as George Arthur, the Tory lieutenant-governor of Van Diemen's Land from 1824 to 1836—but it was most commonly heard from Abolitionists, in a lengthy succession that began with Jeremy Bentham and William Wilberforce and continued to William Molesworth and Lord Russell in the late 1830s. It lasted, therefore, for fifty years and remained (at least as a figure of speech) largely unquestioned in English liberal circles. But was it correct? Were convicts, in fact, slaves? And could the matter of their rights—or lack of them—rightly be brought under the great moral umbrella of the English Abolitionist movement, which had at such vast cost and effort extirpated black slavery from the British Empire and, by the 1830s, was busy trying to suppress the tenacious institution of slavery among the Africans and Arabs themselves? English liberal reformers were sure it could. Today, one is less sure.[1]

In theory, the social contract of slavery is simple, rigid and one-sided. It is pure power in action, rampant will. The master *owns* the slave: his work, his time, his person. Slaves are bought and sold; they are property. Their rights begin and end with their status as chattels. They do not have the right to negotiate, to set the tempo or length of their work, to organize collectively or to protest. Incentives are unknown in the theoretical world of slavery (though not, as the experience of slave societies always shows, in its real world). Slavery is permanent and it perpetuates itself from generation to generation; slave parents beget slave children. When slaves are freed, it is an indulgence—or a revolution.

None of these conditions applied to the convicts Britain exiled to Australia. Each served a fixed term of punishment and then became free. None was a chattel, the property of a master. All of them, within limits, had the right to sell some portion of their labor on the free market. Harsh and rigorous as their social world often was, it was enlaced by concepts of right and law, not of simple ownership. They could appear as witnesses in court, bring suits in civil law, and write petitions to the governor, which were given full and usually prompt consideration. Their masters did not have the right to flog them; such punishments could only be inflicted by the sentence of a magistrate, or, in later years, two magistrates. A convict could bring a master to court for ill-treatment. Often, when they had served their terms, convicts were given land and assigned convicts to work it. Their children were born free. They could not vote; but neither could anyone else in New South Wales until after 1840. If this was slavery, as its critics insisted, it was not of a kind recognizable in Barbados or Atlanta, let alone in ancient Athens, Rome or Luxor.

It had its own name: the assignment system. Most convicts were "assigned"—lent out, as laborers, by the government—to private settlers. A few, perhaps one in ten, were kept by the government to labor on public works, digging ditches and tunnels, building jails, courthouses, stores and breakwaters, making roads through the bush. Thus the "government man"—a favorite euphemism in a society where the word "convict" was rarely used—could serve the Crown directly and pay back his debt to English society. Government labor was thought the worse punishment. But assignment was the staff of colonial life for the first fifty years of European settlement. It shaped the colony and molded its social institutions; and it was one—if not quite *the*—main reason why emigrants went there at all.

Penal Australia was too distant, weird and tainted to attract many free immigrants from the working class. However, its government hoped to bring in "opulent" settlers, men of capital who would spend it in the colony, with offers of free land and free labor. In its unexplored vastness, the colony was glutted with land, and the government gave it away.

Prime grazing country less than a hundred miles from Sydney could still be had for 2 shillings an acre in the 1830s.

Because it was far scarcer, skilled free labor was much more valuable than land. It could name its own price. When the green and hopeful colonist brought his free servant to Australia with him, the servant often deserted:

> My own man, who had served me for eight years in England . . . never reached my new abode. About a month after our arrival I missed him one morning. Before night I received a letter, by which he informed me that he had taken a grant of land near Hunter's River, and that he "hoped we parted friends." He is now one of the most consequential persons in the Colony, has grown enormously fat, feeds upon greasy dainties, drinks oceans of bottled porter and port wine, damns the Governor, and swears by all his gods, Jupiter, Jingo and Old Harry, that this colony must soon be independent.[2]

Cheap land and free grants meant that anyone with hard hands and a strong back could become his own boss. They also meant that the only stable source of labor, whatever its defects, came from the assignment system. Thus, assignment was as important to colonial Australia as black slavery was to the antebellum South, and both had practical disadvantages in common.

Black slave labor was rarely as efficient as the paid work of the free. Its unproductiveness was rooted in the effect of slavery on men's souls, for "bondage forced the Negro to give his labor grudgingly and badly, and his poor work habits retarded . . . the general level of productivity."[3] Most slaves were employed, not on Tara-like plantations, but in groups of one to ten on modest-sized farms.

Slavery suits the production line, where each worker does a rigidly set task over and over again, with no variation. It also suits the rural ancestor of a production line, the *latifundium* with a huge labor force. But on a small farm the worker must turn his hand to many tasks, and here the drawbacks of slave labor—lack of skills, absence of initiative—bit deep. Slavery is inherently static. No slave ever came up with a new farm tool or a better way of using an old one.

These drawbacks were just what a pioneer society did not need. But because the assignment system was more open and flexible than slavery, because it left some room for the initiative of the individual convict (if not in working for the master, then "on his own time"), it tended to be more innovative in its deployment of skills. Only in the outer penal settlements like Moreton Bay, Macquarie Harbor or Norfolk Island were the rigid, punitive inefficiencies of formal prison labor sustained, with men instead of animals dragging carts, and the hoe used instead of the plough. The economy of the mainland was more dynamic and, as John Hirst pointed out, "One of the colony's claims to fame ought to be that it was a forced labor economy which developed a staple industry [wool] in which the forced laborers—the convict shepherds—worked alone."[4]

Still, the convicts had an irreducible unit of labor. They called it the "Government stroke." Doing it kept you out of the hands of the flogger; you were seen to be working, but that was all. Colonial Australia progressed slowly because of its shortage of capital, its solitudes and distances, its small population, and because jails are inherently conservative. But its worst problem was a labor force with so few incentives to work.

The mediocrity of convict labor drove free workers' wages up. "Not the slightest dependence can be placed on convict labor as a permanent source of wealth."[5] But this was untrue. What was true was that being the master of assigned convicts did not give anyone the seigneurial confidence of the slave-owner, because the government could take them back. No farmer "had a property in" his convict servants. They were not part of his capital.

Nor would any master see them as morally neutral creatures, like black slaves. Convicts, by definition, were criminals; they had to be watched closely and kept in rigorous submission. The farther away from the city the master was, the harsher his vigilance tended to become, unless he was an ex-convict himself and treated his assigned man "softly"—an indulgence that, colonial conservatives believed, only led to disorder.

Yet the fact that convict labor produced less than the work of free men did not mean it was unproductive; indeed, fortunes were raised on it. Convicts did not represent capital, like slaves, but their work produced the same effect as the expenditure of capital. "The operation of the penal system has altered the face of the country where it has been set down," remarked the author of an emigrant's handbook published in 1851, "just as manure may have altered the character of a field." It could not produce extravagant surpluses, but it could and did offer the well-organized settler a solid prosperity. Nobody could visit Camden Park in the 1830s, the proud seat of the Macarthur family, with its 60,000 acres and its elegant Regency house by John Verge, without seeing what the System could do. And here was a "typical" large 800-acre farm in Van Diemen's Land in the 1840s:

> The house is of stone, large, and commodious. The farm-buildings are ample in extent, and built of stone, with solid roofs. The implements are all of the best kind, and kept in perfect order. The livestock . . . consists

of 30 cart-horses, 50 working bullocks, 100 pigs, 20 brood mares, 1,000 head of horned cattle, and 25,000 fine-wooled sheep. In this single establishment, by one master, 70 labourers have been employed at the same time. They were nearly all convicts. Nothing of the sort could have existed in this island if convicts had not been transmitted hither, and assigned, on their landing, to settlers authorized to make slaves of them.[6]

This idyll was more common on the small, fertile island of Van Diemen's Land than in the sprawling backblocks of New South Wales. Because it favored standardized work, and because men of influence could get the skilled servants (leaving the lumpen for the lumpen), assignment worked better for the large farmer than for the dirt-farming "dungaree settler." But in either case, it held several compelling merits from the viewpoint of the government.

First, it was cheap. It got convicts "off the stores" and, by shifting the cost of their food and keep to private citizens, it saved the British Government thousands of pounds a year.

Second, it induced well-to-do free settlers to think of emigrating to Australia. Where else in the world could "settlers of responsibility and Capital" assure themselves a free supply of labor? The authorities in New South Wales and their friends in England were apt to emphasize that advantage. The first capitalist-farmer to emigrate was a friend of Joseph Banks named Gregory Blaxland, a prosperous landowner from Kent who had sold most of his English property to invest in Australia, arriving in 1805. The authorities, realizing that here (at last) was the first settler of unimpeachable respectability, showered him with favors. On instructions from Castlereagh, Governor King gave him 4,000 acres of land "in perpetuity . . . in a situation of his own Chusing" and forty convicts to work them with. All were fed and clothed by the Crown for the first eighteen months of their assignment to Blaxland, at a total cost of £1,300, which is more than £50,000 in today's money.[7] Clearly, both the Crown and the colonial government were very anxious to have solid settlers. But in those years, few came out.

The assignment system had a third merit: social control. It dispersed convicts all over New South Wales and Van Diemen's Land, instead of concentrating them in potentially rebellious groups and gangs. It could also control settlers through patronage. The government could punish a settler by denying him convicts, or reward another by assigning them. This damped the political dissensions of free settlers, just as the convicts could be kept in line by the threat of the lash and the promise of eventual freedom. It was a power wielded with special vigor in Van Diemen's Land between 1824 and 1836, under Lieutenant-Governor Arthur—where, according to the wealthy settler George Meredith, a potential master's access to convict labor depended "not upon [his] wants, but upon the construction the Governor may be pleased to put upon the political sentiments and conduct of the applicant." Arthur's favoritism was such that in 1832 half the skilled artisan convicts in Van Diemen's Land were assigned to one-tenth of the settlers, mostly his own clique of officials.[8] The price of irking a governor might be to lose one's servants a week later, for "what the Settler is now allowed by the law to enjoy is a mere *indulgence*, a temporary, revocable loan of services."[9]

Convict assignment in Australia differed, in law, from its earlier form in America. Many respectable Americans railed at the influx of felons, which they thought polluted their society. "In what can Britain show a more Sovereign contempt for us," wrote an irate Virginian in 1751, "than by emptying their Jails into our settlements; unless they would likewise empty their Jakes on our tables!" But the fact was that most farmers and merchants in Maryland or Virginia, when offered a chance of convict labor, grabbed it—and paid handsomely for it. The American colonist owned his indentured servants. He had paid for their transportation across the Atlantic, and he expected to be safeguarded against financial loss if they were set free by some "unforeseen exercise of the Royal Mercy." Convicts were capital, like slaves, and had been freely traded as such since the early seventeenth century. "Our principall wealth consisteth in servants," wrote the Virginia settler John Pory in 1619. Under the transportation acts of the seventeenth and early eighteenth centuries, therefore, the Crown was bound to pay a convict's owner should it remit his sentence. Such a release was unlikely but possible.[10]

In any case, Virginia and Maryland were not penal colonies, but free ones that used felon slaves. In Australia, which had been settled as a jail, no free settler ever paid for a convict's passage from England; and that, in the official view, disposed of the settler's claim to a right of property in the convict's labor. All such rights belonged to the government. Nevertheless, disputes over the "right" of settlers to sell or reassign their convicts kept raising colonial hackles for decades.[11]

ii

IN THE FIRST years of the colony, under Governor Phillip, convicts worked only for the government, which also had a monopoly on all the crops grown; these went into a communal store and were rationed out to the colonists. The first stage of the assignment system, which lasted until 1800, was a refinement of this. The government gave convict labor, clothed and victualled at government expense, to free settlers. But the crops they raised could only be bought by the government, at fixed prices.

The government store became the sole market. In 1790 there were 38 such "assigned" convicts in New South Wales, working on private farms. By 1800 there were 356, and by December 1825 there were 10,800.

As the memory of the "famine years" receded and the economy of the colony grew and diversified, the government store gave up trying to hold its monopoly on farm produce. As it no longer controlled the market, it did not want to pay for the upkeep of assigned convicts either. Hence, by a General Order issued in October 1800, Governor King changed the system. In this second stage of assignment, the masters had to feed, clothe and shelter their servants. The government would advance them food and clothing out of its own stores, to be repaid at the year's end; a full year's rations for one convict cost about £13 13s.[12]

This not only stimulated farming; it got convicts "off the stores," so that they cost the government nothing. From 1800 to 1806, Governor King tried very hard to cut the routine costs of convict administration. Part of his strategy was to alter the rules of assignment again. After 1804, any settler who took a convict "off the stores" signed an indenture to keep him for at least twelve months.[13] The master must maintain his man on exactly the same terms of work, food and clothing as the felons in government employ. If a settler could not support the convict and had to discharge him, he must pay the government a shilling for every day of the unexpired year, a fine that few smallholders could readily afford.

In return, the convict worked the same hours as the government exacted: ten hours Monday to Friday, and six on Saturday, giving a fifty-six-hour week—not a brutal schedule, by any means. But every prisoner, whether he worked for the government or a settler, had to do his "task" of work. Labor by task rather than time followed the logic of having an unwilling convict work force. It had been excessively difficult to keep the hands at work all day; and the early settlement had no full-time guards except the military, who resented being used as jail overseers. Hence, very early, Phillip adopted the system of fixing an amount of product rather than a span of time as the daily norm, and convicts would work at their own rates, although at first, Collins complained, "they preferred passing in idleness the hours that might have been so profitably spent."[14] Task-work had an association with skilled labor in England; it suggested a higher status than mere toil. In this way, labor negotiations were installed in the fledgling penal colony almost from its birth—not what one would expect in a jail, still less in a "slave society." In 1800, Governor King fixed some typical task-rates: In one week, a male convict must fell an acre of forest timber, or split 500 five-foot palings, or thresh 18 bushels of wheat.

In the "famine years," convicts had been let off work at three in the afternoon so that they could raise their own produce. This dispensation became the custom, and it survived for both private and government workers after the shortages had passed. Convicts soon came to be paid wages for out-of-hours labor. They could sell this overtime anywhere, if the master did not want to pay for it. Some items in the 1808 code of labor prices were: 10s. for felling an acre of trees, £1 4s. per acre for "breaking up new ground," 6d. a bushel for pulling and husking corn, and so forth. If a convict always worked the whole day for his master, not just the ten standard government hours, his surplus time entitled him to a shilling a day, or about £18 a year. He might also get occasional bonuses of rum. "Mechanics" or skilled craftsmen—blacksmiths, shoemakers, tailors—could get much more on their own time, sometimes £4 to £5 a week.[15]

How well did the convict's right to earn overtime, which was part of the essence of the assignment system for some twenty years after 1804, translate into spending power? Certainly, worse than one would suppose. Successive governors fixed the price of overtime convict labor, but the colony had no money supply. England had not sent money there, for one did not need cash circulating in a jail. Not until 1812 would the Crown dispatch a supply of silver coin to Australia; £10,000, which, as the Select Committee on Transportation had gloomily predicted, was sucked out of the colony by its unfavorable balance of trade. Not even Macquarie's creation of the "Holey Dollar"—a mutilated Spanish coin of Charles III, whose center or "dump" was punched out and given a value of 1s. 3d., the "ring" being worth 5 shillings—could keep coinage in the colony.[16]

As a result, the first twenty-five years of economic life were a crazy quilt of barter, IOUs and sliding coinage—guineas, johannas, guilders, mohurs, rupees, Spanish dollars and ducats, left in the colony by visiting ships. At one point in 1800, even the English copper penny was declared to be worth twopence. Official prices were given in sterling but the only notes with full sterling value equal to their face value were of two kinds: government bills of exchange on the British treasury, and paymaster's notes issued to the officers of the New South Wales Corps, which were consolidated as bills on the regimental treasury in England.

Of the two, the Rum Corps notes were much preferred, although the government could enforce the use of its own paper in settlement of debts up to £300. Rum Corps paper carried premiums of as much as 25 percent against copper cash, let alone personal IOUs, which no one trusted and whose use as circulating currency was finally proscribed by Governor Bligh.[17]

The convicts got the worst of these economic arrangements, of course. Their paid labor was mercilessly exploited by the means of payment, which was mainly in kind, at the prices of goods fixed by the free settlers. Sometimes they would be forced to take imported goods they did not need at all: white cotton dress stockings, for instance, or "sheeps' rumps" (lambskins) imported from Cape Town. In the heyday of the Rum Corps, sugar was 7s. a pound, tea 6s. an ounce, and spirits 20s. a bottle. King had known rum to go as high as £8 a gallon.[18]

Even when a convict could get cash wages, he received them not in sterling but in the depreciated "currency" of the colony. In 1814, some little while after Governor Macquarie had begun to deflate the exorbitant prices of the 1800s, the convict weaver Thomas Holden wrote to his parents in Bolton,

> Dear Mother, things in this Country is very dear, mens hats is too pounds too shillings and stockings ten shillings per pair and shoes 16 shillings per pair. sugar 3 shillings per pound and butter 7 shillings per pound . . . although the Prices is so high we are very glad to get [them] at any price.[19]

As an assigned man, Holden added, he was earning £20 a year in "currency," but that was only worth £12 in English money. In general, by 1820, the assigned man was paid in kind for overtime work at prices 40 to 70 percent above wholesale cash prices, and 25 to 35 percent over retail. He could (and some did) appeal against this gouging to a magistrate, but magistrates, being settlers themselves, "must naturally feel an interest in support of charges that have the effect of diminishing the price of labour to themselves as well as to others." They always favored paying convicts in store goods rather than money.[20]

The most sought-after commodity of all was rum, a word which stood for spirits of all kinds—arrack, *aguardiente*, poteen, moonshine—but which meant, especially, imported liquor from Bengal. In this little community (less than 5,000 people in 1799; about 7,000 in 1805; just over 20,000 by 1817), nearly all the men and most of the women were addicted to alcohol. In Australia, especially between 1790 and 1820, rum became an overriding social obsession. Families were wrecked by it, ambitions destroyed, an iron chain of dependency forged. Many colonists drank with an oblivion-haunted thirst, determined to blot out the harsh tenor of their lives. In the heyday of the rum monopoly, William Bligh recalled,

> the thirst after spirits was so very strong that [the settlers] sacrificed every thing to the purchase of them, and the prices were raised by that monopoly to so high a degree that it was the ruin of many of those poor people.[21]

Governor Bligh, who was firmly sympathetic to the plight and interests of struggling small farmers and sometimes supported them against the Rum Corps officers, saw rum as an instrument of debilitation that helped an elite maintain its power, even as it was debauching the quality of labor. Settlers would leave their farms and come forty miles into Sydney, a four days' round trip, to pick up a gallon of spirits, "in doing which they spent ten times more than it was worth, and lost their time in agriculture."

It may be that the reproofs of lower-class colonial boozing that came from the upper colonial crust should be treated with caution, like the pronouncements of Marsden and others on convict sexuality. If everyone had been drunk, the colony could not have survived. And yet there is little room for doubt about the hold rum had on the embryo society of New South Wales; and its evangelical pastors, first Richard Johnson and then Samuel Marsden, were powerless to stop it.

Because most convicts would rather be paid in rum than anything else, it gave great leverage to the wealthy landowner, who could secure any amount of overtime labor with a broached barrel. "You may get more ground worked for a little spirits than you can for anything else, and that I fancy is the reason of labour being so high," declared John "Little Jack" Palmer, Captain Phillip's former purser on the First Fleet who had risen to be the official banker and contractor to the early settlement. When Major George Johnston of the New South Wales Corps received a grant of 2,000 acres from Governor King as his official reward for crushing the Irish rebellion of 1804, he "used to barter spirits to pay the labourers for clearing our grounds," although it was not always easy to get the governor's permission to buy as many barrels of liquid incentive as he wanted.[22]

Naturally, the prudent master would find a balance between the quantity of liquor served out as a special indulgence to his men and the amount of work he needed done the next day. At Camden Park, the Macarthurs made it a rule to give steady workers a bonus in Cape wine. Colonial Australia showed little interest in beer or ale. It was rum that could make or break a man's prosperity, and although civil and military officers controlled the rum trade by getting first access to incoming cargo and selling the liquor at an initial markup of 500 percent, every small businessman tried to dabble in it, while judges, lawyers, surgeons, ministers and missionaries all got into the trade.

Long after the Rum Corps was recalled to England in 1810, the fledgling economies of New South Wales and Van Diemen's Land—particularly as they affected convicts—remained tied to a kind of rum standard. Quality hardly mattered. Real Jamaica rum, landed at 6 shillings a gallon, reached the small settlers land convicts at £2 to £4; but it was the first victim of the efforts of King and Bligh between 1800 and 1810 to fix rum prices, since their standards abolished the shippers' profit margin and sometimes sent the boats away at a loss. Bringing spirits from England became "a losing trade," but there was liquor from Bengal, half the price at 10 shillings a gallon. Cheap Bengali rum, even with restrictions, was the most profitable kind and it did incalculable social damage, from the bottom of the colony to the top.[23]

The civil establishment bore its quota of fuddled incompetents, from Richard Atkins (1745–1802), Governor King's deputy judge-advocate, to William Gore (1765–1845), acquaintance of Palmerston and the provost-marshal of New South Wales under Bligh, who became (in the words of a later governor) "so totally abandoned to drinking that I fear He is for ever lost to Society."[24] This sad, detested creature was transported to the penal settlement at Newcastle for shooting a trespassing soldier of the 48th Regiment, and he died at the age of eighty, penniless and disgraced, his body left for several years unburied along with his wife's beneath a heap of palings on his farm. The Sydney suburb of Gore Hill bears his name.

The convicts were even less able to stay off the rum, since their need for oblivion was worse. "Intemperance is the greatest curse we have on our land," wrote a convict named John Broxup, claiming that booze caused "three-thirds [sic] of the crimes that are committed." If a young assigned man managed to live soberly it was a cause for congratulation, to be mentioned in letters home: "Your son Richard I can say is very steady for though liquor is very cheap"—it is 1832 and the price of rum has dropped to 2 shillings a pint—"and he have the means and opportunity of getting it he never gets more than do him good," a convict scribe added to a letter home from Richard Dillingham, a convict in Van Diemen's Land.[25]

But most convicts would have found an anthem in the "Rum Song," supposedly of penal days:

> Cut yer name across me backbone,
>     Stretch me skin across a drum,
> Iron me up to Pinchgut Island
>     From today till Kingdom Come!
> I will eat your Norfolk Dumpling
>     Like a juicy Spanish plum,
> Even dance the Newgate hornpipe,
>     If you'll only give me rum!*

* It is not certain whether this canting, defiant ditty, quoted in Russel Ward, *Australia Since the Coming of Man* (Sydney, 1965), was written before or after 1830. It is not, however, an English music-hall song like the spurious jingle "Botany Bay," ca. 1880. "Pinchgut Island," or plain "Pinchgut," was a bare knob of rock in Sydney Harbor, now occupied by Fort Denison, where recalcitrant convicts were sometimes chained in semi-starvation. The "Norfolk Dumpling" was 100 lashes, and the "Newgate hornpipe" the hanged man's twitching in air.

Some authorities thought that the only solution was prohibition, which Governor Thomas Brisbane tried to enforce on Newcastle and the Hunter River Valley settlers in 1824. Ships entering Newcastle Harbor had to be placed under bond whether they carried liquor or not, because the mere sight of a possibly rum-laden boat caused "confusion and wild uproar."[26]

The English authorities had transported Gin Lane to Australia, and the harsh conditions of colonial life made for heavy drinking. Yet the relationship between drink, wages and work had long been ingrained in England. Benjamin Franklin, for instance, had been astonished to see that his fellow printers in London drank three-quarters of a gallon of strong ale every day at work, supplied against their wages, while the habit of paying workers and craftsmen on Saturday nights from a table in a public-house—thus assuring that all but the teetotaller would drink a hole in his salary before he got home—did not die out in London until the 1820s. Certainly, few convicts were likely to feel that their rights were under attack if their masters part-paid them in rum, and none complained about it.[27]

iii

THE MAN WHO cleaned up this system was Lachlan Macquarie (1762–1824), the last British proconsul sent to run New South Wales as a military autocracy. In guts, moral vigor and paternal evenhandedness, as well as in his bouts of self-righteousness and bull-headed vanity, Macquarie was a fine early example of that breed of Scottish administrators who kept the engine-room of Empire working throughout the nineteenth century. The son of a Hebridean tenant farmer, related through his mother to the Highland laird Maclaine of Lochbay, he was to become the laird of New South Wales, ruling his anomalous fief from January 1810 to December 1821—the longest tenure of any Australian governor.

Macquarie had risen through the British Army as a career officer, serving with increasing distinction for nearly twenty years in India and the Middle East. By his fortieth year he was a thoroughly seasoned Empire hand: a good organizer, resentful of critics, used to prompt obedience, socially rather creaky but shrewd about the needs of those who fell under his power—an "awkward, rusticated, Jungle-Wallah," in his own words, ramrod-like in port and bearing, with a bony jaw and eyes as hard as cairngorms.

But he was not too awkward to look after his career. In 1807 Macquarie transferred to a new regiment, the 73rd Highlanders. He then learned that it was being sent to New South Wales to clean up the chaos left in the wake of the Rum Corps's 1808 rebellion against Governor Bligh. Its commander would be the colonial governor, since the mutiny against Bligh had shown that a naval governor could not necessarily depend on the army's allegiance. But the commanding officer of the 73rd did not want to go, so Macquarie started lobbying for the post. In 1809 Lord Castlereagh confirmed his appointment as governor of New South Wales. With his wife and his regiment, he sailed for Sydney in May 1809, and was sworn in there on the first day of 1810.

Macquarie's orders were to arrest the leaders of the Rum Rebellion— John Macarthur and the corps's naïvely seditious second-in-command, Major George Johnston, who had arrested Bligh and taken charge of the colony—and to send them back to England for trial. But they had sailed for England already, to take their case before the government. Bligh himself came back to Sydney from his exile in Van Diemen's Land a fortnight after Macquarie's arrival, raging against the rebels in his foul "tarpaulin" lingo. Macquarie ignored him; he, not Bligh, was governor now. Bligh sailed back to England soon after and never saw the blood he wanted, for Johnston was cashiered, not hanged, and Macarthur, "the great perturbator," returned to New South Wales in 1814, his wings clipped (though not for long) by an order to stay out of public affairs.

Macquarie cancelled all the civilian and military appointments and revoked all the pardons, leases and land grants made in Sydney between January 26, 1808, the day of the Rum Rebellion, and his own arrival. He reinstated all dismissed officers and got rid of Macarthur's drunken stooge of a judge-advocate, Richard Atkins, replacing him with Ellis Bent (1783–1815), the first decently trained professional lawyer to hold office in Australia, who had come out with him on the same ship from England. Firmly seated now, all reins in his hand, Macquarie began the inchmeal conversion of a jail into a colony.

It was not an easy task. He could not, for instance, abolish the social addiction to rum by an act of will. The Rum Corps was gone but the thirst remained. However, as the farms spread, and free settlers seeped in and emancipated convicts got their land grants and businesses other than farming grew on the coast—mainly whaling and sealing—so the economy of New South Wales diversified and could no longer be ruled by a primitive cartel. The rum monopolists' day would therefore have ended anyway, but Macquarie hastened it by a series of enactments against drinking: Public-houses were to shut on Sundays and there was, instead, mandatory church parade for convicts; the number of licensed houses was sharply cut; a stiff duty went on imported spirits in the hope of pricing drunkenness out of existence. This last measure failed, as it was bound to do; despite Macquarie's brisk reports of moral improvement, it only caused more colonists than ever to drink themselves into debt.

His attitudes to convicts mattered more than his war on appetite. He rejected the idea that convict labor was a pool from which officers and a few favored settlers could enrich themselves. Convicts were there to be punished but rehabilitated through work. Macquarie saw that Emancipists so outnumbered emigrant settlers that Australia was bound to be an Emancipists' country, its political reality shaped by them and their descendants. If emancipated convicts were not given back their rights as citizens, New South Wales would become as riddled with false dreams of aristocracy as the American South.

Emancipation pointed a convict back into respectable society, which must receive him. With the flurry of capital letters that usually signalled his moral enthusiasms, Macquarie told Castlereagh that emancipation was "the greatest Inducement that Can be held out to the Reformation of the Manners of the Inhabitants. . . . [W]hen United with Rectitude and long tried Good Conduct, [it] should lead a man back to that Rank in Society which he had forfeited and do away, as far as the Case will admit, with All Retrospect of former Bad Conduct."[28] And for the emancipated to grasp the normal responsibilities of citizenhood, they must be shown that they had rights while they were still in the larval stage of convict serfdom. Macquarie's respect for the potential of convicts was noble. Yet it led to his political ruin at the hands of the "Merinos" and their allies in England, who believed in unrelenting exploitation of the convicts; and he died a broken man, obsessed with his detractors and their myriad calumnies.

But that lay in the future. What Sydney saw, at the beginning, was the vigorous administrator in his late forties, for whose attention no matter was too trivial. Whenever a convict transport disgorged its cargo in Sydney, Governor Macquarie was there to meet it. A convict remembered the ceremony that greeted the disembarked prisoners:

> The Governor, Superintender, and Doctor, &c., comes; the Governor addresses them, by saying what a fine fruiteful country they are come to, and what he will do for them if there conduct merits it; likewise tells them if they find themselves anyways dessatesfied with there employer, to go (immediately) to the madjestrate of the district, and he will see him righted.[29]

All convicts were initiated to Australia with this fatherly speech from the governor. By telling the new arrivals "what he will do for them," Macquarie made it plain that the channels of patronage were as much in operation here as the chains of the law. No matter who their master was, they would always be working for the government.

At first Macquarie complained of the shortage of labor and asked the government for more convicts. But for the first five years of his rule, not enough ships could be spared from the war against Napoleon to send them out. So he was faced with a ticklish balance. He would assign men and women to free settlers as far as it was necessary; he had no bias against the farmer and his need for labor. But he felt convict labor was best used in government service, where Authority could judge its incentives nicely and measure the reformation of each person instead of depending on second-hand reports from masters.

It would be better for the colony, too. For Macquarie was appalled by the shoddy look of Sydney: an unplanned straggle of shacks "in most ruinous decay," perched on the rim of the shining, amethyst, many-lobed harbor. The judge-advocate's residence was a "perfect pigstye," and the convict barracks at Sydney and Parramatta were beyond mere disgust. There was no proper hospital. The churches were huts—a fact particularly repugnant to Macquarie, who believed religious practice would reform his sinners. The town streets were dusty tracks in summer and ditches after a rain, and no sewers existed. Beyond the town's perimeter, the roads (except for the toll road to Parramatta) could scarcely be negotiated by a cart.

With a mixture of naïveté, zeal and creative drive, Macquarie set out to turn this hodgepodge into a Georgian city. His architectural education was necessarily slight, but he had seen the work of Nash, Soane and Wood, and believed their idiom was the correct one for the architecture of Empire. About the technicalities of building he knew nothing, but the taste of his time had rubbed off on him, as it was bound to do on any intelligent proconsul with firmly elitist values. Elizabeth Macquarie, his wife, had brought an album of building and town designs with her. It became the source-book for Macquarie's plans of urban renewal.

He started writing codes that specified the minimum floor area of houses and width of streets in Sydney. There would be no more hovels on Crown leases. These were the first such regulations in Australia. He laid out what is still the central grid of Sydney, and in five settlements along the Hawkesbury River he ordered that the core sites should be reserved for the court, the schoolhouse and the church, and that all houses must have their plans filed with the district constable.[30]

When he turned from rulebooks to real buildings, Macquarie faced more obstacles. The British Government wanted him to cut costs. That meant no "extravagances," no structures except of a strictly military or penal kind—and even they should be humble. It refused to send him an architect. But Macquarie had emergency powers, and felt he could define "emergencies" broadly enough to stifle long-range criticism with *faits accomplis.* So he tricked his way around the British Government's ban on building. His first effort was probably designed with his wife. It was a new hospital, a handsome three-block affair with wide verandas (which came, not from English Regency architecture, but from Macquarie's observations in India). It was by far the largest structure ever built in the colony. He financed it with rum, as the New South Wales Government, 150 years later, would part-finance its colossally expensive Opera House with lotteries. He gave its building contractors a trading monopoly on 45,000 gallons of spirits, from which the government drew a duty of 3 shillings a gallon; the £6,750 this generated was to be kicked back to the contractors as their fee, off the books. These arrangements did not work out, and bitter accusations of graft and cheating flew in all directions, but the "Rum Hospital," as it was inevitably nicknamed, got finished. Two of its three blocks survive today: jerry-built in parts, due to the greed of the contractors, but the first presentable Georgian public building in Australia.

It was followed by others. Lacking a free settler who was an architect, Macquarie found a convict of that profession: Francis Howard Greenway (1777–1837). The descendant of generations of West Country builders and stonemasons, Greenway was a trained architect—a pupil of Nash— but a poor businessman. Practicing in Bristol, he went bankrupt, forged a contract and received a death sentence which, as usual by then, was commuted to fourteen years' transportation. When Macquarie found out about Greenway's arrival in 1814, he grew cautiously interested. Given his modest talents and lack of savoir-faire in dealing with clients, Greenway might never have landed important commissions in England. But in Australia he was John Soane, he was Beau Nash—he might as well have been Gianlorenzo Bernini, for all the competition he had. Macquarie put him in charge of designing and building all government works, beginning in 1816.[31]

Over the next six years, Greenway turned out for Macquarie a series of buildings, uneven in quality, the best of which utterly transformed the architectural standards of the fledgling colony. The main ones were two convict barracks, the Female Factory in Parramatta (1819) and—his secular masterpiece—the Hyde Park Barracks for men in Sydney (1819), together with several churches, notably St. Matthew's in Windsor (1817– 20) and St. James' in Sydney (1820–24). The Female Factory kept at least some women off the Parramatta streets, although it was never large enough. The Hyde Park Barracks—which, like the General Hospital, Macquarie began without permission from London—he believed was an unqualified success. It was designed to house all convicts working for the government in Sydney. Because the 800 convicts placed in it could no longer plead that they needed the income from their "own-time" work to pay for the lodgings the government had formerly not provided, moving them in there was a ticklish business: The Hyde Park Barracks had to provide all kinds of inducements, from extra rations to weekends off, in return for Macquarie's wholesale appropriation of the convicts' time. The extra surveillance it afforded seemed to affect them for the better, or so Macquarie thought. In 1820 he told Bathurst that "not a tenth part of the former Night Robberies and Burglaries [are] being now committed, since the Convicts have been lodged in the New Barracks." It held 800 felons, rather less than a third of the convict population of Sydney.[32]

Such projects demanded skilled labor from bricklayers, masons, tilers, blacksmiths, glaziers and joiners. These "mechanics," the riffraff of the immense body of craft on which the architectural achievements of England had been raised, were always in short supply and rarely much good. The government picked them out as soon as they arrived. When a ship anchored, the superintendent of convicts made a roll of names and trades, skimming off the men whom the government wanted for public works. Since most arriving felons had already learned that a skilled man's life was apt to be easier in private assignment than in government labor, this always produced a little ballet of lies on shipboard, with wheelwrights and coopers professing to be common ditch-diggers or hayseeds. From 1814 to 1820, the government took 1,587 (or 65 percent) of the 2,418 "mechanics" arriving in Australia, and 3,000 (or 32 percent) of the laborers—the peak year in its demand for the skilled being 1819, at the height of Macquarie's building schemes, when it took 80 percent of the artisans. Naturally, this policy irked the free settlers who needed artisans themselves.[33]

Besides skilled labor, there was an equally great need for unskilled. From 1814 to 1820, the government took over some 4,600 of the 7,200 convicts arriving in Australia, for it needed worker ants. In technological terms, Macquarie's Australia was more backward than Cromwell's England. There was as yet no steam power; draft animals were few; and there were no streams near Sydney reliable enough to turn watermills. So every hole was dug, every log sawn, every rock quarried and every ton of rubble moved by that least efficient of engines, the human body, toiling in gangs. Macquarie's plans demanded roads.

For by 1813 the colony was beginning to feel crowded. Along the Hawkesbury River and on the rich flats of Parramatta, every inch of land had been leased and granted. Settlers had pushed southwest to Stonequarry (modern Picton and Bowral) and the poor dry belt of the Bargo Brush. But the great barrier lay to the west—the line of mountains that could be seen, low on the horizon, from Sydney. The Blue Mountains, as they were named after their color, were an ever-present proof of the "impenetrability," the "hostility," of the continent to whose rim the colonists clung. Nobody had got across them—not in twenty-five years. Even the Aborigines said they were impassable. Some convicts who tried to cross them, thinking China lay beyond, died of hunger in their immense labyrinth of sandstone, where bellbirds chimed and long filaments of water fell, wreathing, from distant cliffs.

Then in 1813 three prosperous settlers, Gregory Blaxland, William Lawson and W. C. Wentworth, set out to look for a way over the divide. They took convict servants, dogs and horses; and after three weeks' exhausting struggle they found themselves looking down on a golden vista which, like other explorers in America, they compared to Arcadia and the land of Canaan. From the summit of what is now Mount Blaxland they saw, rolling like the sea, "Enough grass to support the stock of this colony for thirty years." There would never be a shortage of pasture again; but there had to be a permanent way to get to it. In 1815 Macquarie made a journey of inspection along their trail, bestowing names on its grander views: "The Prince Regent's Glen," "Black Heath," "Pitt's Amphitheatre." To record the picturesque splendors of this gateway to Goshen, he even took an artist, John Lewin, with his party. Surveyors followed; and Macquarie, determined to have "a good practicable Cart Road made with the least practicable Delay" from Parramatta to the other side of the Blue Mountains, chose sixty convicts "who had been a Certain Time in the Colony and who were also considered well-behaved Men, and entitled . . . to some Indulgence." He told them they would get conditional pardons for their "Arduous Labours" if they finished the road —126 miles of it—in six months. They did it and were set free. This meant cutting about 1,200 yards of road per day and building more than a dozen wooden bridges along the way from Emu Island to the Macquarie River—a feat that showed what prisoners could do if they had better incentives than the lash. There was only one major problem with this road: Parts of it, especially the descent of Mount York, were so steep that loaded bullock-carts had to go down with big logs hitched to them as brakes; and the ascent could only be made if the cart were dragged up in stages, by a chain run through iron ringbolts in the rock face harnessed to a second bullock team pulling downhill. The Western Road, as Macquarie pointed out to Bathurst (for whom its destination was diplomatically named), would have taken three years to finish by contracted free labor or the "Government stroke" of unmotivated prisoners, instead of six months.[34]

It was also the first public work in Australia to be praised in verse. For Macquarie had appointed a convict poet-laureate: Michael Massey Robinson (1744–1826), a graduate of Oxford and former lawyer who had tried to blackmail a London ironmonger by threatening to publish a scurrilous verse about him, and was transported for life. It was his task, each year, to recite a birthday ode at Government House in Sydney. These first frail pipings of the formal Australian muse included a paean to the Western Road across "yon Blue Mountains, with tremendous brow,"

> Behold, where Industry's encourag'd hand
> Hath chang'd the lurid Aspect of the Land;
> With Verdure cloathed the solitary Hills,
> And pour'd fresh Currents from the limpid Rills;
> Has shed o'er darken'd Glades a social Light,
> And BOUNDLESS REGIONS OPEN TO OUR SIGHT![35]

One can almost see Marquarie, stiff in his gold braid, nodding with approval to the march of his assigned iambics. For his vanity matched his energy. He loved, as the colony expanded, to name new places after himself, a harmless habit much satirized after (not before) he left the colony. " 'Twas said of Greece two thousand years ago," wrote another Scot, the Presbyterian minister John Dunmore Lang, who had arrived in Sydney in 1823, the year after Macquarie sailed,

> That every stone i' the land had got a name,
> Of New South Wales too, men will say that too,
>     But every stone there seems to get the same.
> "Macquarie" for a name is all *the go;*
>     The old Scotch Governor was fond of fame,
> Macquarie Street, Place, Port, Fort, Town, Lake, River;
> "Lachlan Macquarie, Esquire, Governor," for ever![36]

Nevertheless, Macquarie's commitment to public works rather than private assignment paid its dividends by giving the colony a civic armature. Its critics in London and New South Wales harped on how much it cost the Crown to have so many convicts working for the government, for during Macquarie's term of office, 1810–1821, the colony cost England about £3 million, which seemed a great deal for a place that sent no goods back to England and functioned in a merely negative way, as a social *oubliette.* But in 1810 it took £100 a year to transport a man and maintain him "on the stores," whereas by the time Macquarie's public-works policy was fully under way—between 1816 and 1821—the cost was down to less than £30 a year.[37]

The gross cost of the transportation system had certainly risen: £579,000 for 1810–12, £717,000 for 1816–18, £1,125,000 for 1819–21.

This worried the British Government and disposed Lord Bathurst to listen to critics who believed that convicts should work only, or mainly, for private enterprise—and especially for free emigrant settlers, whose numbers had increased from about four hundred in 1810 to nearly two thousand men, women and children by 1820.[38]

Such was the pressure that in 1819 Bathurst sent a commissioner of inquiry, John Thomas Bigge, to look into Macquarie's administration. Bigge, a diligent, intensely snobbish Tory lawyer who thought convicts were scum and unhesitatingly sided with the emigrants against the small farmers and Emancipists, fell out with Macquarie and in with the Macarthurs, and his eventual report was a litany of extravagance—a political disaster for Macquarie.

And yet Macquarie's policies were, if anything, frugal. What had driven the gross cost up was numbers—the flood of convicts that came after 1815 with the end of the Napoleonic Wars. England now had more crime and more ships to bear it away; and Macquarie, who had begged for more convicts, had not bargained for so many. The white population of New South Wales and Van Diemen's Land almost doubled between 1812 and 1817, going from 12,471 to 20,379. Most of these were convicts; in 1818 there were so few free settlers—and the ones along the Hawkesbury River had been so battered by a disastrous flood in 1817—that hardly one convict in eight could be assigned. "In the meantime I have no alternative but to employ large Gangs of them on the Government Public Works," Macquarie protested.[39]

By 1821, his last year in office, Macquarie had a total of 4,001 convicts working for the government—more than twice the number (1,853) that would be doing government labor under his successor, Sir Thomas Brisbane, in 1825.[40] And he had cut down the treasury bill expenditure for each convict per year from £60 in 1810 to less than £15.

The most parsimonious Scot could hardly have done better, but the British Government counted grosses, not averages, and did not like Macquarie's reputed kindness to convicts. Before Bigge sailed, Bathurst told him unequivocally that Australia must be "rendered an Object of real Terror" and that this must outweigh all questions of the economic or social growth of Australia as a colony.[41] Since Macquarie's policy was based on his belief that the social growth of Australia really mattered, and it could not grow unless some quilting of liberality softened the iron framework of its repressive laws, this idea of Australia as a theater of horror acted out for a distant audience was not to his moral taste. In the end, he was seen as too extravagant because his own government sent him more convicts than the colony could absorb—and too lenient because he, alone among the early governors of New South Wales, really thought about the rights of these prisoners.

iv

THE QUESTION of rights under the assignment system was, in fact, more delicate than it looked. The convicts were not slaves under the law, but British citizens whose enforced task, in Australia, was to work their way back to freedom through expiation. Certain rights were guaranteed them—to food, to shelter, to protection from summary punishment by masters. Others accrued to them by custom, such as the right to sell what one made or did on one's "own time." From the Crown's point of view, all convicts were legally dead under civil law from their arrival in Australia to their emancipation. They could neither sue nor be sued, nor could they testify in court as witnesses. In the colony, these restrictions were simply overlooked—they had to be, since no society composed mainly of present or former convicts, most of whom had businesses to run, debts to recover and wrongs to right, could function otherwise. But the rights to a convict's work were vested in the government, which owned his labor until his sentence was served or remitted.

This put the assigned servant in an odd relationship to his or her master. Government would only get between them to protect its own rights. The government strictly monitored a master's treatment of his assigned servants because each master was its agent in the scheme of punishment. The assignment system was not just a way of using the labor of people whose crimes had already been expiated by transportation. Assigned labor was their punishment—hence, the government had the right to control its conditions and to step in when a master became too hard or too soft. The strictest emphasis on this was laid in Van Diemen's Land under the rule of Sir George Arthur, but it was the ground rule of the System everywhere in Australia.

The axiom that the settler, in accepting a convict servant, was acting on behalf of the government caused resentment. No settler, for instance, could take it on himself to punish a convict; for that, the felon had to be tried before a magistrate. When the settler was himself a magistrate he could not flog his own men; they had a right to their day in court. Likewise, if a convict felt ill-treated, he could complain to a magistrate. In this way, the government meant to protect its rights in its prisoners' labor. But neither master nor servant was always willing to grasp that the rules were meant to safeguard the government's interests before their own.

Although the government took the skilled workers for its own projects and gave the dross of the labor force to settlers, it was a common practice under early governing officials such as Grose, Paterson and Hunter to give favored insiders a share of the first pick. Maurice Margarot thought "only the greatest ruffians" were assigned to the ordinary settlers, for "it is not in the interest of officers that settlers should get forward."[42]

A wealthy and established landowner could usually expect to get the convicts he needed. One finds Robert Townson (1763–1827), a scholarly friend of Joseph Banks who had published works on botany and mineralogy before taking up land grants in New South Wales, writing in 1822 to ask the government for "three men from the first ships" for his model estate, Varro Ville, near Minto. He made a request for "Shepherds, Gardeners, & Ploughmen—But *English or Scotchmen*, having already an undue proportion of *Irish*. The last three were Irish of no use—one was a runaway Soldier Lad—& another a Dublin Grocer's errand boy."[43]

The law could also be bent. New settlers were meant to get servants first, so they could get started on the land. The liberal Whig governor Richard Bourke (1831–37) wanted to make sure that convicts were assigned in proportion to the amount of land a master held. Unfortunately, the law did not care whether their land was freehold or leasehold, cleared or raw bush; hence the loophole, not closed until after 1835. A large farmer could issue dummy leases of land to his own dependents and get up to eight assigned servants on each lease, "whilst persons who were more scrupulous as to the means they employed could get none." He could also pad his application by claiming that acres of bush were actually worked land that needed assigned labor.[44]

The cure for these and other abuses lay in tighter bureaucratic control over assignment. Governor Darling set up a board to which all applications for servants had to be sent; he told its members to favor settlers with a good record and to turn down applications from men with a record of cruelty or excessive lenience. Unfortunately, much of the paperwork in processing applications for assigned servants was done by convict clerks, who rarely refused a bribe. Nevertheless the successive administrations of Darling and Bourke did much to make assignment more "objective." But it could not guarantee the quality of a convict's labor.

Throughout the life of the System, the average "dungaree settler" was likely to end up with an unskilled, resentful cuckoo of a convict who had been born and raised in a city and could not tell a hoe from a shovel. Only one convict in five had been an agricultural worker. But incompetents could neither be fired, like free workers, nor sent back to the government. This arrangement, Governor Richard Bourke remarked in 1832, was "for the most part very Unsatisfactory":

The Convict generally does as little as he can. . . . Much of his time is passed on the road going to or returning from Hospital, or to a Justice to complain of his master's treatment, or to answer the Master's charges against him for negligence, drunkenness or insubordination. Many also are unsuited to labour of any sort.[45]

By then, the cavalier habits of some settlers with their assigned convicts had already been causing some concern in England. A farmer saddled with an incompetent convict would swap him off with another settler or abandon him in town. The inconvenience and waste of time in haling a convict before a magistrate's court, which might be three days' journey from the farm, discouraged complaint through legal channels; so the incompetent assigned man would simply be dumped on the road or left in town, to beg or survive as best he could. The authorities had no choice but to put these outcasts in jail, on a skimpy allowance of bread and water, until they were either reassigned or put in a government work gang.[46]

It was demoralizing for them and irksome for the government; but in New South Wales, at least, there seemed to be no way of stopping it. Ten years after Bigge described the problem in his report, it was still perplexing the Crown. By 1831, there were about 13,400 assigned servants scattered around New South Wales, and keeping track of them was becoming a clerical nightmare. So although convicts could not, of course, be legally sold by one master to another, Governor Bourke compromised: Now they could be reassigned without the cumbersome business of recalling them to Sydney, endorsing their papers and sending them out into the remote bush again. All one needed was a formal permission to transfer, which "indeed is Seldom refused . . . as it is not only a convenience . . . but it saves expense."[47]

Masters who were caught transferring servants without permission would be blacklisted from getting assigned men again. But neither Bourke nor his predecessors could get rid of the common assumption among landowners that, whatever the Crown might *say* about its ownership of convict labor, the *fact* was that convicts were slaves, and masters should be left to treat them as such. Farmers without servants believed they had a right to them. "Every man, who cannot obtain Land or Convict Servants as he wishes, thinks no doubt he has a right to complain of the Governor's injustice," wrote Governor Darling in 1831.[48]

Nor were such feelings without legal support. Sir Francis Forbes, the first chief justice of the Supreme Court of New South Wales, thought masters did have a right to the labor of their assigned servants. He based this on seventeenth-century American precedents. The settlers wanted to believe him, but the Crown refused, pointing out that in America the settler paid for the convict's passage, which gave him this right—but not in Australia.

Even Forbes's position looked mild compared to the one adopted, a few years later, by William Charles Wentworth, who had become a power in the colony (see Chapter 10) by agitating for the rights of Emancipists. In 1839 Wentworth actually proposed that assignment should be cancelled altogether and that convicts be sold outright to the highest bidder. Worse still, he wanted to institute group punishments of assigned convicts. If one man on a property committed a crime, all the other servants should be penalized by an automatic extension of their sentence unless they informed on him. This, Wentworth thought, would reduce the main inconvenience settlers had to put up with from their assigned men—the difficulty of getting them to "tell" on one another.[49]

The convicts, on the other hand, believed they had rights, and that these arose from the fact that they worked. A man was a convict from sunrise to afternoon, but overtime was his to sell. The more skilled he was, the harder he could bargain with his master. In this way, some masters were gradually forced to make concessions, even within the unequal class relations of the colony.

What were these rights? Some were conventional: food, clothing, health care. The government enforced strict standards for the first two and was by no means indifferent to the third. By the 1830s, masters were obliged to pay a shilling a day, up to thirty days, toward the keep of an assigned man in hospital—hardly a lavish allowance, but the cause of much grumbling among settlers.[50]

Before 1830, the master had to give each assigned man a wage of £10 a year, which paid for his clothes and bedding. In 1831 Governor Darling changed this by ruling that the master must issue the blankets, palliasses, and clothes directly, instead of wages. The workers' diet was rough and monotonous. "They can make a meal from what would not be looked at in England," wrote the convict John Broxup. In 1823 a settler in Van Diemen's Land, Gilbert Robertson, was accused of feeding his men on dead magpies. But on most farms the servants ate what the masters ate.[51]

A master might give his convicts tea, sugar, milk or a bit of the rank, locally grown colonial tobacco as an "indulgence," a little reward for good work. But custom might turn the master's indulgence into the convict's right or claim. This tended to happen especially after the 1820s, when Macquarie's successors—Governors Brisbane and Darling—did away with wages and "own time" rights for assigned servants. They were replaced by an informal system of incentives and rewards, "indulgences" under the law but essential to the efficient ordering of a property. At the master's discretion, men could be favored with easy jobs or punished with hard ones; they could be given work that would teach them trade skills, or sent to the most routine tasks of common labor. "Luxuries" like tea, sugar and soap, a half-pint of rum or dinner in the homestead kitchen, were prized as signs of status and regarded as forms of payment, replacing the wages and overtime that Brisbane and Darling cancelled. Some men certainly felt they had a right to tea, sugar and tobacco, and they vociferously told their masters so. When William Larissey, a convict at Port Macquarie in 1836, was told his sugar and tea were stopped, he seized his master by the neck. "Damn my bloody limbs and bones," he shouted, "if I don't have the worth of that tea and sugar out of you." He paid for this outburst with twelve months in the iron gang.[52]

Not all convicts were as defiant as this, but the bench books of the magistrates' courts show many cases of men brought up for "insolent" behavior in disputes with their masters over rations and clothing. Sometimes—though much more rarely—a convict would bring his master to court. In 1833, in the district of Scone north of Sydney, there were 210 charges by masters or overseers against assigned convicts, and only six charges by convicts against masters—all of which, however, were upheld by the magistrates. They involved matters like rotten meat and insufficient shelter; one convict, Simon Lewis, assigned to an absentee station-owner, was found to have had no blanket or mattress from him in four years.[53]

Very occasionally, convicts would band together to bargain in defense of what they perceived as their rights. But it was more common to "go slow" (after sizing the master up), either for the pleasure of inconveniencing him or in the hope of being transferred. Thus, finding he was in bond to "a hard hearted wreach" in Van Diemen's Land, the convict George Taylor "began to only do that part of my work which I thought proper and soon aforded my Master an opertunity of takeing me to a magistrate, this was repeated two or three times [but] I found I could not get from him by this means."[54]

Although it was by no means impossible, or always difficult, for an assigned man, once before the magistrate, to justify his insolence or violence by proving his master had provoked him, not a few convicts took their legal rights at face value and brought their masters to court for ill-treatment. The usual complaints were stoppage of rations and physical violence. Thus, in 1829 the convict James Davis, assigned in New South Wales to Mr. David Hayes, "maketh Oath and saith . . . I swear I have had no Rations since Friday last excepting part of a Loaf; a Two-Pound Loaf was shared among five of us." He was backed by four other convicts and won. In the same year, Thomas Argent, assigned to a Sydney butcher named William Merritt, was ordered to wash Merritt's gig with warm water and then go to Parramatta to take delivery of some livestock. "Argent said he was weak and faint with hunger, having received nothing to eat since Friday, and that he would not go. . . . Mr. Merritt jumped up and gripped him by the breast with one hand, and struck him twice with the other, and dragged him out of the hut, and then took up a paling and threatened to beat his brains out." Argent, terrified, said he would put himself in police custody, at which Merritt mounted his horse and tried to run him down.[55]

Argent's reward for getting Merritt into court was to be reassigned to another and better master. The government had no interest in assigning convicts to brutes, but some masters seemed unable to grasp that their servants were, in the ordinary sense, human. Such was the case with a Mrs. Ramus of Hamilton, Van Diemen's Land, whose assigned man, George Willey, had in 1833 been sentenced to twenty-five lashes for insolence. The punishment was to be inflicted in the local jail, and Willey had words with Mrs. Ramus's brother over his right to take rations there when he was flogged. At this point, the Hamilton magistrate reported,

> Mrs. Ramus' brother ordered his hands to be tied behind him with a piece of hide rope, a heavy bullock chain to be put around his waist which was attached to another chain and yoked to a pair of bullocks, he himself following on horseback with a loaded gun. In this state the man was brought to my house, a distance of 5 miles, when I immediately ordered him to be set at liberty.[56]

An order followed, depriving Mrs. Ramus of all her assigned servants. Losing one's convicts in this way was more of a risk in Van Diemen's Land in the 1830s, because of Arthur's evenhanded strictness. But a cruel settler in New South Wales could be stripped of his servants, especially if his social connections were poor.

The most vivid disagreements over the matter of rights were caused by the ticket-of-leave system. There were only three ways in which the law might release a man from bondage. The first, though the rarest, was an absolute pardon from the governor, which restored him to all rights including that of returning to England. The second was a conditional pardon, which gave the transported person citizenship within the colony but no right of return to England. The third was the ticket-of-leave. The convict who had been given a ticket-of-leave no longer had to work as an assigned man for a master. He was also free from the claims of forced government labor. He could spend the rest of his sentence working for himself, wherever he pleased, as long as he stayed within the colony. He was, as the phrase went, "on his own hands," in contrast to the assigned man who was merely said to be "off the store." The ticket lasted only a year and had to be renewed, and it could be revoked at any time. It was an effective way of fostering conformity and self-help while keeping the convict on a leash.

Ticket-of-leave men could be denounced by anyone, and thus they lived in some uncertainty. As an editorial in the *Sydney Gazette* put it,

> A ticket-of-leave is the most tender kind of liberty that can be conceived; it is liberty in one sense, and non-liberty in another. . . . Under the present system, a ticket-of-leave exempts a man from the service of one master, while upon the other hand he becomes the slave of hundreds of others. From the Magistrate, down to the meanest constable in the district, a ticket-of-leave holder is continually kept the subject of apprehension.[57]

One lost one's ticket, Governor King proclaimed in 1804, by being idle, or insolent to "any officer, soldier or Constable," or charging too much for out-of-hours work. But fragile as it was, the ticket-of-leave was craved by every convict in the colony and regarded by most of them as a natural right, a goal that one struggled toward and was entitled to. It played an immense role in the moral economy of colonial life. The worst thing a master could do to a convict servant was to keep him from getting his ticket-of-leave.

The less scrupulous settlers sometimes tried to do this. More convicts were always coming in one end of the System from the transports than were going out the other, as "ticket-of-leavers" or Emancipists. Thus, from January 1826 to December 1828, 6,032 male convicts arrived in Australia, while 4,140 men were added to the free population by the expiry of sentence or the granting of tickets-of-leave.[58]

But this did not reduce the demand for assigned labor, because so many of the newly freed men became farmers themselves and needed working hands. "Since convict labour has become so exceedingly valuable as it now is," Governor Gipps reported to the secretary for war and the colonies in 1838,

> it is a matter of very frequent complaint that Masters prevent their Servants from getting Tickets of Leave from an unwillingness to lose their labour; and that they even cause (in some cases) their men to be punished, for the sake of retaining their services . . . [E]ach punishment which an assigned man receives, puts him back a year in getting his Ticket. I am willing to hope that the cases are but few.[59]

They were probably more common than Gipps was "willing to hope," and they had been going on for nearly forty years before the government cast an official eye on them. The prisoner Thomas Cook described the fate of one convict, assigned to "a very oppressive and miserable-hearted

man" at White Rock in New South Wales during the early 1830s. Originally sentenced to 14 years' transportation,

> he had toiled hard and so fared for the space of 5 years and 9 months of
> that term, without a charge being preferred against him; but as he ap-
> proached his probationary period of servitude (6 years) entitling him to a
> Ticket of Leave . . . his master, to benefit himself by the Blood and Sweat
> of a hard-toiling Slave, preferred a charge of insolence and threatening
> language against him.

That meant a magistrate's sentence of 50 lashes, and a year's delay on
the ticket-of-leave. When the year was almost gone,

> his cruel Master, unmoved by compassion or gratitude, again brought him
> before the Bench, and charged him again with disrespectful conduct upon
> which he was again sentenced 50 lashes. Thus was this pitiable object
> despairing of obtaining a moment's liberty until the death of his master
> or the termination of his sentence. He was nearly stupid from hard toil
> and cruel treatment.[60]

A master might goad an assigned man to insolence or violence, simply by battering him with insults. The *Sydney Gazette* in 1826 complained about "the all too prevalent custom"

> of casting an unhappy fellow creature's life and character into his teeth,
> and by this means leaving the man either passively to suffer under such a
> gross outrage . . . or to resent it by insubordinate language and conduct,
> whereby he becomes subject to . . . 50 lashes! for the magistrates . . .
> generally feel it imperative to lean on the side of power.[61]

District benches close to Sydney were apt to treat convicts fairly and
well, partly because their magistrates were more in the public eye. The
Stonequarry bench, run by a settler from New York named Henry Antill,
who had married the daughter of an Emancipist and settled down to
become the largest landowner in the modern district of Picton, had a
name for decency, and Antill was by no means the only even-handed
magistrate in New South Wales.

But the further outback a farm was, the more opportunity it held for
tyranny and the more likelihood there was of collusion between settlers
and magistrates. George Loveless, another Tolpuddle Martyr, believed
from his own experiences that no one could "form a just impression of
the System" unless he had been assigned in such remote places:

> One magistrate will bring his men to be tried before a neighbour magis-
> trate, and it is a frequent practice for the master to pay a private visit to

the magistrate, and say he is going to bring such a man or men before him, and wishes that such or such particular punishment may be dealt out. On the arrival of the men . . . the magistrate enquires what they have to say in answer to this charge, and frequently, if they attempt to answer, he interrupts them, saying "I will not believe a word you have to say, and I shall sentence you to receive so many lashes."[62]

While it is true that the masters won most cases in which they brought their servants to court for disobedience or insolence, one cannot simply assume that this was due to collusions of class between masters and magistrates. As Hirst observed, the magistrates "were superior men both in wealth and education and were free from personal ties or obligations to the middling and small masters. How better to demonstrate their superior status than by carefully examining the complaint of a convict against a small farmer and perhaps reproaching the master or even taking his servant from him?"[63] The area of offense that magistrates always paid attention to was summary punishment by master of man, and here the claims of convicts often succeeded—partly because the physical evidence, the wounds and weals, spoke clearly in court. But a servant in the settled areas had a better chance of access to a magistrate's court than one in the outback, where lodging a complaint might entail a walk of fifty miles or more—and require permission from the master to leave the property for several days.

We cannot know how many assigned men were unjustly denied their tickets-of-leave. Presumably the settlers minimized the number and the convicts exaggerated it. What is not in doubt is the gulf that separated the settler's from the convict's view of the ticket-of-leave—one calling it (as the government declared it to be) an "indulgence," the other always claiming it as a right. Thomas Cook, for instance, wrote of servitude "entitling" the convict at White Rock to his ticket. The extreme opposite view on this was held by Chief Justice Francis Forbes, who thought no convict had a right to a ticket while on assigned service to a private settler. Luckily for the convicts, Forbes could not persuade the government of this.

Their belief in a right to a ticket did not mean the prisoners were deluded. Rights emerge by bargaining between the powerful and the relatively powerless; they are not simply "granted," for if they were, there would be none. Rights are solidified claims, sanctioned by usage and expectation. When convicts spoke of wider rights than their simple, mechanical entitlement to food and shelter, they were speaking from their inherited expectations as laborers—that masters should behave with fairness and circumspection, and that the law should offer some formal protection to their own interests. In short, they expected the moral and legal economy of the traditional English labor market to apply in the continental prison that was Australia. And that economy did not exclude the common English practice by which free workers, adults as well as apprentices, were bonded to their masters and suffered severe penalties, ranging from fines to ostracism, if they broke away. In this respect, at least, assignment was not as totally foreign to English labor relations as one might assume.

Some were cruelly disappointed. "The extent to which tyranny was formerly carried on with regard to assigned servants throughout the Colony," wrote one ex-convict, Charles Cozens, "is almost incredible." But sometimes the accounts of the same convict establishment, seen through different eyes, contradict one another like black and white. The Abolitionist J. D. Lang, who was certainly no friend of the assignment system, praised the way Governor Darling's private secretary, Colonel Henry Dumaresq (1792–1838) ran St. Heliers, his 13,000-acre estate near Muswellbrook in New South Wales: "one of the best regulated estates in the colony . . . rewards, not punishments . . . the men are sober, industrious and contented." To a visiting Quaker named James Backhouse, St. Heliers also seemed a model of convict management, and the future explorer Edward J. Eyre, a man of unquestionable decency and candor, thought it "the best-ordered, best-managed station on the Hunter." Yet in 1850, one of Lang's co-Abolitionists, John Goodwin, protested that his praises were only true of "the time of the late Mr. Whiteman's superintendence" of St. Heliers (after 1830) and that the previous superintendent, Mr. Scott, had been "a demon incarnate":

> He was in the habit of putting handcuffs, and leg-irons on them, and throwing them into a dungeon on that estate, where they remained generally for three days without either meat or drink. . . . [H]e did not trouble to take his men to court; but sentenced them for the most trivial offence, and just as his caprice dictated, to carry logs of wood on their shoulders, on his own verandah, and under his eye, for two to twelve hours; these logs weighed from 50 to 100 lbs. He never went out without a brace of loaded pistols and a belt-full of handcuffs. . . . Captain Dumaresque [sic], "that nice gentleman," has to my own knowledge drawn as much blood from the flogged backs of his assigned men, as would make him to swim in human gore.[64]

James Brine, one of the Tolpuddle Martyrs transported to Australia for trade-union activity in 1834, was assigned to a magistrate named Robert Scott at Glindon on the Hunter River. Scott set Brine to digging postholes, even though his bare feet were so cut and sore that he could not put them to the spade. Eventually Brine "got a piece of an iron hoop and wrapped it round my foot to tread upon," but for six months (the regulation period between issues) Scott would give him no shoes, clothes or bedding. Stricken by a severe cold after spending seventeen days up to his chest in a creek, washing sheep, Brine begged for a blanket and got a homily instead.

> "No," said he, "I will give you nothing until you are due for it. What would your masters in England have had to cover them if you had not been sent here? I understand it was your intention to have murdered, burnt and destroyed every thing before you, and you are sent over here to be severely punished, and no mercy shall be shown you. If you ask me for any thing before the six months is expired, I will flog you as often as I like.... You d—d convict!—don't you know that not even the hair on your head is your own?"[65]

E. J. Eyre, who found it "a most revolting sight to see the scarred and bleeding backs of human beings—convicts tho' they were," was impressed by the docility with which accused servants would trek unguarded to the split-slab outback courthouse. It was "singular," he wrote,

> that men said to be the most worthless of their kind and the most reckless ruffians should thus quietly march a distance of 5, 10, 20 or even 60 miles, knowing that at the end of their journey there was a moral certainty of being severely flogged; yet the instances of their absconding or failing to appear at Court were comparatively rare. Some of the men would almost willingly undergo punishment for the sake of a few days' wandering about in idleness and gossiping with the various persons they passed on the road.[66]

Some masters began as liberals and ended as martinets. One such man was "the Laird of Shoalhaven," a Scottish settler from Fife named Alexander Berry, who traversed almost the whole period of transportation, having arrived in Sydney in 1808 and died, aged 102 and worth 40,000 acres, in 1873. At first he was against flogging:

> It is silly to object to any man because he is a rogue, when they all come here for their crimes. All I care about is having able-bodied men—for the rest, no matter if they have been born and bred in Hell. With quiet, peaceable and humane measures, I will make the most refractory see that it is in their interest to behave well.... [T]o turn in men for flogging because they behave ill is utterly childish.[67]

"Childish," of course, because it showed a dependence on higher authority—the unwieldy power of the Bench—and so made the master lose face before his servants. But two years later, Berry was calling for irons and cat-o'-nine-tails: "We have been teasing ourselves to death," he wrote to his partner Edward Wollstonecraft, "in endeavouring to render ungrateful and irreclaimable profligates more comfortable than they have ever been in their lives."[68]

But a contented convict plainly worked better than a hungry, rebellious one. To that end, as John Macarthur's son James sensibly told the Select Committee on Transportation in 1837, it was best "where a man behaves well, to make him forget, if possible, that he is a convict." One of the first treatises on Australian farming (1826) advised settlers that "the belly is far more vulnerable and sensitive than the back." Use firmness and circumspection, the carrot not the stick; stay away from magistrates, because constant appeals to the formal powers of higher authority will diminish your own. Set up wages and a scale of rewards which will seem "a very great boon" and whose withdrawal will be "much more effectual . . . than the lash of the flogger." On one hand, do not get familiar with the convicts or give them the idea that their work is indispensable; on the other, a master must never forget "that they are men who, however degraded, still have the same feelings and passions as himself." The right stance is balanced paternalism, the instinctive attitude of the English squire when dealing with his laborers. For that was how the English workingman expected his employer to behave; the code of the country gentleman underwrote the modest, customary rights of his workers. Kindness, firmness and distance—with these, boasted a new settler with ten assigned men on the Yass Plains in 1835, "as Burns says, 'I labour them completely,' and have them in hand, bless your heart, as tame as *'pet foxes.'* . . . I never had occasion to give a single lash."[69]

Most "government men" in bush service were, if not content with their fate, realistic about it. They knew that rebelliousness, insolence or conspicuous foot-dragging would probably extend their sentences and delay their tickets-of-leave for years—and knew as well, from experience, how pervasive and efficient the "pass system" was in preventing long escapes. (Every convict, when off his master's property for any time or for any reason, had to carry and show on demand a written pass that stated his name, where he had started from, where he was going and the precise number of days or even hours he was to be on the road.) So they behaved "admirably as a class," Edward J. Eyre observed after he took up land near Queanbeyan on the Molonglo Plains near the present site of Canberra in 1834, and became "most excellent, careful, industrious, trustworthy servants." Even the worst of them, though they might rob a passing visitor or a new assigned man, "would rarely plunder their own masters" and could be trusted anywhere:

I have constantly known two convicts sent down to Sydney quite by themselves, a distance of 200 miles in a dray full of wool drawn by oxen, and having, after depositing their wool at the merchants', to bring back a load of . . . clothing, flour, tea, sugar, tobacco and other groceries—luxuries for the master, and even wines, beer and spirits, and yet tho' this journey involved an absence of five or six weeks during which the men were tempted constantly by the presence of so much property and the facility of appropriating it, the instances were very rare in which any plundering took place or loss ensued.[70]

And trust built reform. The posting of sanctioned rural relationships on the far soil of Australia mattered greatly to convicts and always evoked their gratitude. Everything else was strange—the bouncing animals, the upside-down stars, the resentful blacks and the nine agonizing claws of the cat-o'-nine-tails—but this was blessedly familiar. Besides, the man assigned to a decent master in the country districts in the 1830s was, as Eyre pointed out, "in a better position than half the honest laborers of England. No wonder then that convicts behaved well, and from being useful members of the community gained both the respect of others and learned to respect themselves."

The feeling was sometimes reflected in convict songs, or folk songs about convictry. In one of the versions of "Van Diemen's Land," a ballad circulated in the late 1820s, the narrator is at first horrified to see

> . . . my fellow sufferers,
> I'm sure I can't tell how,
> Some chained to a harrow
> And some unto a plough.
>
> No shoes nor stockings had they on,
> No hats had they to wear,
> Leather breeches and linen drawers,
> Their feet and heads were bare.
> They drove about in two and two
> Like horses in a team,
> The driver he stood over them
> With his malacca cane.

Such was the fate of the "government man." But then:

> As we marched into Hobart Town
> Without no more delay
> A gentleman farmer took me,
> His game-keeper for to be:
> I keep my occupation,

My master loves me well,
My joys are out of measure
I'm sure no tongue could tell.

Assigned convicts and their relatives often expressed their gratitude
to the good master. Thomas Holden, the Bolton weaver transported for
political protest, is assigned to a decent master, writes home about his
good luck, and in 1814 hears from his parents, "We are led to believe that
the man you are liveing with is a *gentleman*, we beg to say to him we
are very grateful that he hath so far condescended to take you into his
service." His wife, who with other wives of radical weavers has unsuccessfully petitioned the Prince Regent to be allowed to join their men in
Australia—"Let your situation in Life be prosperity or adversity it Woud
give me great satisfaction to share the Toil with you, but wether it will
Ever be our lot to meet at NS Wales or not I cannot tell"—reinforces his
gratitude:

> It gives us all the greatest pleasure to say [you have found] a friend . . .
> [W]e think it our Duty to say as he hath placed so much confidence in
> you we make not the least doubt but you will study to merit his Future
> Trust or Favors he may Chuse to bestow on you.[71]

This, from the point of view of authority, was an ideal penal relationship. But it depended on a steady market, as John Bigge pointed out: Only
constant production would keep felons too busy and tired for sin and
achieve "that stimulus to exertions that supersedes the necessity of coercion." And if there was not the proper class distance between master and
man, all was apt to be lost. Bigge frostily noted that Emancipist settlers
did not like to have a servant punished:

> This feeling is . . . attributable to a sympathy with that condition which
> was once their own, and is not corrected until they acquire property.[72]

Many settlers who had been convicts did, in fact, spare the lash. Samuel
Terry, the "Botany Bay Rothschild," was said never to have had a man
flogged; and Governor Bourke thought assigned men would rather work
for a newly freed Emancipist: "A Convict . . . prefers their coarse fare to
being better fed and Cloathed with a more opulent Master and less liberty."[73] Colonial conservatives were doggedly opposed to this. Their
views were mirrored in Bigge's report, which argued that convicts should
be assigned preferentially to "opulent" rural settlers. Giving them to
small Emancipists, the poor white trash of New South Wales, was "very
pernicious."[74]

Convicts who found benevolent masters far preferred their assigned life to the miseries they had known in England. When they could write home, they stressed their comforts, reassured their families and begged them not to fret. "When this you see, remember me, and banish all trouble away from thee," runs a little jingle in a letter from William Vincent, convict at Parramatta, to his family in Sussex in 1829. "Some people thought they had put me in [a] great deal [of] trouble, which they would, some of them, be glad to be as well as me; and I hope you are, mother, for I live at the Governor's table, along with the other servants." Two years later he is made an overseer, the much-coveted "bludger's job," and he jubilantly reports that "I have not worked one day since I have been in the country, so I am not hurt with work." But Vincent was not an assigned man. An experienced farmer, he had been grabbed for government service as soon as he landed, "for there is but a few in the country knows much about cultivation." He even urged his brothers to emigrate: "If I came free in this country, I could get 90£ a year to look after land."[75]

The sense of opportunity was a common theme. "Dear brother," wrote the rural protestor Peter Withers in 1833,

> I hav got a very good place all the Bondeg i am under is to Answer My [Name] Every Sunday before I goes to church so you Mit not think that I am made a Slave of, for I am not, it is quite the Reverse of it. And i have got a good Master and Mistress i have got Plenty to eate and drink as good as ever a gentleman . . . so all the Punishment I have in this Country is the thoughts of leaving My frends My Wife and My Dear Dear Children . . . [T]ell Samuel never to get trannsported for i knows Very Well he will not Like to Lave his Mother 16 thousand miles behind him.[76]

After this mild bit of child-scaring, the testimonials: "I think you would make your forting [fortune] in about 6 years, dear Brother," Withers adds. "I should like to see you and your famly Com to this Country if you could get to com, for it Whould be Well for your Children after you are dead, for this is a very Plentiful Contrey, pervisions is very Cheap and Labour is dear, this is the Plesents [pleasantest] Country that ever I saw." In the same way, Richard Dillingham, a ploughman from Flitwick in Bedfordshire who had been transported for life in 1831 for theft, is assigned to a colonial architect named David Lamb in Van Diemen's Land and, after a few years, assures his parents that "I am now very comfortably situated . . . [A]s to my living I find it better than ever I expected thank God. . . . I am doing much better than many labouring men in England."[77]

One must read such praises in context: Vincent, Withers and Dillingham were all farm workers who had known the dreadful privations of the agricultural collapse whose nadir came in the 1830s, when England went closer to general agrarian revolt and "levelling" than it had been since the days of Wat Tyler. After such miseries, the cheap food and high wages in Australia must have seemed wonderful; in the words of such convicts, the idea of Australia as the paradise of a working man finds its first voice among workers. But the word about opportunities in Australia spread quite rapidly, and by 1830 the Privy Council archives contained many such petitions as this one, from Thomas Jones, a convict languishing on the *York* hulk:

> Having made Frequent applications to leave the country . . . having served four years and upwards . . . my friends having deserted me and my character lost, I dread to think of my situation when I obtain my liberty as no one will employ me; I have no resource left. . . . [H]ave the kindness to send me by the first ship that goes to New South Wales, I doubt not that I shall redeem that character that I have lost.[78]

Eight years before, Bigge had warned in his report that the shortness of sentences—for most, a "mere" seven years—combined with the ticket-of-leave system and the high labor market to disturb the penal framework. A seven-year sentence was "too short" for convict laborers; it gave them premature thoughts of becoming settlers and made them less cautious, obedient and respectful. Thus by 1820, convicts were becoming uppity, or so Bigge thought, and "the prospect afforded by transportation to New South Wales is more one of emigration than of punishment."[79] This became a common criticism of the System in the 1830s. In 1833 the Archbishop of Dublin, Richard Whately, a fervent abolitionist, wrote that Australian felons

> are carried to a country whose climate is delightful, producing in abundance all the necessaries and most of the luxuries of life;—that they have a certainty of maintenance . . . are better fed, clothed and lodged, than (by *honest* means) they ever were before; [can get] all the luxuries they are most addicted to . . . are permitted, even before the expiration of their term, to become settlers on a fertile farm . . . [I]t certainly does not look like a very terrific punishment.[80]

When Thomas Potter Macqueen, an English magistrate who was the absentee landlord of 10,000 acres in Australia granted him in 1823 by Governor Brisbane, echoed this by remarking that assigned convicts in New South Wales were better off than farmworkers in Bedfordshire, a pseudonymous Australian settler fiercely disputed it:

The work in this new country is of the most laborious description:— cutting down trees, the wood of which is of such hardness that English-made tools break like glass before the strokes of the woodman; making these trees into fires, and attending them, with the thermometer usually ranging in the middle of the day from 80 to 100 deg. for eight months in the year; grubbing up the stumps by the roots, the difficulty of which would appall an English woodman; splitting his hard wood into posts and rails, and erecting them into fences. . . . In what, then, does the superior condition of the convict consist? Is it in a slavery more profound than that of the West African negro?[81]

Farm work in Australia was always hard; and probably the toughest of all jobs, in terms of the psychic tolls it could exact on a man, was a shepherd's. As merino cross-breeds became the basis of Australian prosperity, more and more assigned men were sent to a lonely life in the bush, tending sheep. They lived on the perimeter of remote properties; and even places near Bathurst or in the Hunter River Valley were still virgin bush in the 1830s, not much tamer than the "real" outback, 300 miles inland. A shepherd stood a high chance of being the first white person to bear the revenge of Aborigines who had been evicted from their hunting-grounds by the outward push of white settlement. When blacks could not mount a frontal attack on a station homestead, they could easily pick off a lone shepherd with their silent spears, especially since assigned men are not armed. Even if local Aborigines had no special grievance against the farmer, they loved mutton anyway and would kill to get it. The assigned shepherd therefore lived in constant fear of death.

His flock could be as few as 200 or as many as 3,000 sheep. The work sounds simple: All he had to do was drive the sheep out in search of pasture each day, keep an eye on strays, and bring them back at night. But he was rarely mounted and often had no dogs. Moreover, pasturage was not as common in New South Wales before 1850 as it is today. Millions of rolling acres were covered in box, a middle-sized eucalypt of no commercial value, whose thirsty roots pulled every drop of surface moisture out of the soil and prevented the growth of grass. The solution, which later farmers resorted to with excessive zeal, was ringbarking. This killed the box without using up extra labor in felling it and grubbing out the stumps. Grass then sprouted in abundance on these spectral landscapes of gesticulating, claw-white dead trees. But in the convict era, ringbarking was not much used, and the shepherd had to cover much more ground to find enough grass for his sheep. If he got lost, or if he lost some of the flock, he would have to stay out for days until he rounded them up again and struggled back to the out-station, although his master would only give him a day's rations when he set out, to discourage him from abandoning the flock and bolting.

The loneliness of a shepherd's life was increased by the medical need to keep flocks (and hence their keepers) away from one another. Besides dingoes, the terror of a pastoralist was a highly infectious ovine disease called the Scab which, as Eyre found from bitter experience, ruined the wool, checked breeding and was practically incurable:

> A single act of neglect or inattention on the shepherd's part might in a moment blast the prospects of his employer—and what more natural than that such acts should occur—the shepherd anxious to have a gossip would drive his flock as near to the boundaries of his run as possible—the shepherd of the infected flock would do the same, and while the two men were talking the two flocks would intermingle and the dreaded mischief be done.[82]

It was not unknown for a resentful convict to avenge himself on his master by deliberately infecting his stock.

In mallee scrub, patches of which could extend for miles—there was one district shared between northern Victoria and southern New South Wales that still covered 10,000 square miles in the 1880s—sheep were bound to get lost. The tough bushes of *Eucalyptus dumosa* were too high for a man to see across, even from horseback. In such a labyrinth, with dingoes howling in the middle distance—mallee was known as "dingo scrub" because it sheltered the wild dog that shepherds most feared—the assigned man was likely to go "cranky," as colonial slang termed the harmlessly mad. As stations got larger, all the grass near the homestead was needed for stock-horses and working bullocks. The shepherd had to mind the flocks on runs three, five or ten miles out; instead of coming back to the homestead each night, he would have to sleep out in the bush.

John Standfield, one of the Tolpuddle Martyrs, described what this did in 1834 to his father, Thomas Standfield, who was in his fifties and had been assigned to a farmer named Nowlan near Maitland, some 150 miles from Sydney. Three weeks after being sent to this out-station, he was

> a dreadful spectacle, covered in sores from head to foot, and as weak and helpless as a child. . . . [H]e pointed to the place where he slept, called a "watch-box." After my father had been out in the bush from sunrise to sunset, he had then to retire for repose to the watch-box, 6 feet by 18 inches, with a small bed and one blanket, where he could lie and gaze upon the starry heavens, and where the wind blew in at one end and out of the other, with nothing to ward off the pitiless storm—such were the comforts of the watch-box. Besides this he had to walk four miles for his rations, which journeys he was compelled to perform by night.[83]

The Tolpuddle men (and a few other "politicals" in Australia) seem to have had especially harsh treatment from their masters. But even at the best of times, life in the outback could have a hallucinatory strangeness for men fresh from England. One visitor to the Maitland area in the 1830s noted that convict quarters in the bush were like a cross between a zoo and an Irish cabin, with

> a multitude of noisy parrots, intended for sale; pet kangaroos and opossums, and a variety of kangaroo dogs, greyhounds, and sheep-dogs; on the fire was a huge boiler filled with the flesh of a kangaroo, and close by were suspended the hind-quarters of another of these animals; in one corner was a large pan of milk; in another, a number of skins partially dried; while, a few feet from the ground, were the filthy bed-places or cribs of the people themselves.

Inside it all was fug and cockatoo-shit, dried sweat and blowflies and the stink of hides. Outside, the landscape could be apocalyptic, vast; it was like standing on the edge of one world and looking into another:

> The extreme silence that prevails here almost exceeds what the imagination can conceive. . . . One would imagine that a residence in such a lone place would be liable to cause a change of some consequence in the minds and habits of any person; and it would be an interesting point to ascertain the effect on the convict stock-keepers, who, for weeks together, can have no opportunity of conversing with a white man, except their sole companion; for there are always two to a hut.

And it did affect them. It promoted the pair-bonding, the feeling of reliance on one's "mate," that would lie forever at the heart of masculine social behavior in Australia. Because there were no white women in the bush, it meant—as some authorities grudgingly acknowledged, by the end of the 1830s—that "mateship" found its expression in homosexuality. Most important, in the eyes of some observers, was the fact that life in the bush reformed the socially useless criminal by teaching him skills and giving him time to reflect, with the bonus of exposure to "sublime" landscape. Here was Wordsworth applied to penology—the nineteenth-century belief that Nature, as the unaltered fingerprint of its Creator, could serve as a moral text for the betterment of fallen man. The convict becomes a hermit, cleansing his soul in the desert:

> This monotonous and solitary life has the effect of giving a new direction to the ideas of the moral patient, superior to any other which the most profound metaphysician could have invented. Solitude and idleness in a cell either subdue and subvert the mind entirely, by causing madness and

suicide, or they generate a hardihood and a caution which enable the criminal to pursue his career with greater chances of profit; while the combination of *pastoral occupation* with solitude, offers the fairest chance of success, by weaning and forcing him from his ancient habits.

The future Poet Laureate, Robert Southey, while still at Oxford in 1794, had drawn much the same picture of the moral benefits of Australian wilderness on the repentant sinner in his *Botany-Bay Eclogues*:

> Welcome ye wild plains
> Unbroken by the plough, undelv'd by hand
> Of patient rustic; where for lowing herds
> And for the music of the bleating flocks,
> Alone is heard the kangaroo's sad note
> Deepening in distance. Welcome ye rude climes,
> The realm of Nature! for as yet unknown
> The crimes and comforts of luxurious life,
> Nature benignly gives to all enough,
> Denies to all a superfluity . . .
> On these wild shores Repentance' saviour hand
> Shall probe my secret soul, shall cleanse my wounds,
> And fit the faithful penitent for Heaven.

The bassoon-like sound of the distant 'roo, one feels, must have made the journey worthwhile.

Probably about one-fifth of the masters in Van Diemen's Land and New South Wales were genuinely interested in reforming their assigned servants, and two-fifths more "encouraged the convicts for their own interests." The latter might treat their assigned servants like farm equipment, but at least they would teach them skills and keep them away from bad company. Out in the bush, there were no booze-shops, whores, or criminal cabals. There, convicts led "a healthy useful life of labor, well clothed and well fed, with the prospect of attaining their freedom," Eyre wrote. "Transportation of convicts to a healthy country and the assignment of them to settlers . . . is . . . the true means of reforming the criminals themselves."[84]

Masters and government authorities generally believed that it was far harder for an assigned convict to "go straight" in a butcher's shop or wearing servant's livery in Sydney. The city was the condenser of vice; in the bush, there were more routines and less company, and the master's life shared more of the hardships of the servant's than in town. In Sydney or Hobart, the *bon bourgeois'* need to demarcate his life from the felon's led to exaggerated rituals of class superiority, which promoted the feeling that convicts could not be reformed at all. But the issue of class loomed

large in penal Australia—a society traversed by confusingly rapid movements of individual status, where tides of men and women were constantly flowing from servitude into citizenhood and responsibility, from
bitter poverty to new-found wealth. By the 1830s, Australia was as class-
obsessed a society as any in the world.

# IO

# Gentlemen of New South Wales

i

THE VISITOR from England, arriving in Sydney in the 1820s, saw a bright prospect from the deck of his ship: Across the glittering blue of the harbor, under the immense clarity of the southern sky, a neat-looking town of freestone or whitewashed cottages with shady verandas, their gardens marked off from one another and from the still-encircling bush with paling fences or clipped geranium hedges, their kitchen-yards "teeming with culinary delicacies." And yet, as the naval surgeon Peter Cunningham noted in his memoir of New South Wales life, the sense of domestic familiarity dissipated as soon as he stepped ashore, among the English faces and not-quite-English accents, the caged cockatoos and rosellas shrieking among the overflowing fruit stalls, and the silent caged men:

> The government gangs of convicts ... marching backwards and from their work in single military file, and the solitary ones straggling here and there, with their white woollen Parramatta frocks and trowsers, or gray and yellow jackets with duck overalls (the different styles of dress denoting the oldness or newness of their arrival), all daubed over with broad arrows, P.B.'s, C.B.'s, and various numerals in black, white and red; with perhaps the chain-gang straddling sulkily by in their jingling leg-chains, —tell a tale too plain to be misunderstood.[1]

Inequality did not stop with the public gangs. In penal Australia, the question of class was all-pervasive and pathological. Distance had made it so. Tiny as it was (about 7,500 people in 1807; 10,500 in 1812; 24,000 in 1820; and 36,598 at the time of the first census in November 1828), the colony was gnawed by isolation and boredom, plagued by foolish vendettas and extreme class-consciousness. Class barriers were translated into personal affront in the blink of an eye. The atmosphere of New

South Wales at the end of the transportation period was summed up in 1839 by "A Settler," writing pseudonymously but with piercing insight in the *Sydney Morning Herald*:

> People come here to better their condition, many with limited means, their tempers a little soured with privations and disappointed expectations (for all expect too much); cut off from the ties of kindred, old friendships, and endearing associations, all struggling in the road of advancement, and no-one who reflects will be surprised that they jostle one another. *Every man does not know his own position so well as at home.* [Italics added.][2]

One speaks of "colonial gentry" as though there were gentlemen in early Australia; but there were not. Frontiers have a way of killing, maiming or simply dismissing gentlemen. In any case, most folk with settled estates have no reason to go to a raw, new country. They can invest in it later, without needing to break their bodies on it now. To succeed on the frontier, a man needed the kind of violent, grabbing drive that only failure or mediocrity in his former life could fuel.

The male society of early New South Wales could be roughly sorted into three kinds of people. There were opportunists struggling to be gentlemen; convicts and outcasts waiting to be opportunists; and the failures, who would never become anything. Social life thus displayed a crude, insecure face, which the cosmetic application of airs and graces could not altogether hide. The mixture of ambition and social pretension wearied many a visitor. The relentless deployment of tooth and claw against the tentative mobility of the lower orders would impress Charles Darwin himself with its unpleasant naïveté when he arrived in Sydney on the *Beagle* in 1836.

The colonial elite after 1800 had arrived at an idea of gentility that was already becoming, if not obsolete, then certainly old-fashioned in England. It was feudal and rural. It belonged more to the 1720s than the 1820s. It parodied an ideal of privilege they had never had and, moreover, was distinguished by its absolute inability to relax. English gentility defined itself in relation to an aristocracy above and a peasantry and serving classes below. But its vision of the "good yeoman" did not apply very well in convict Australia, whose peasantry was, by definition, not good.

The Exclusives had come from nowhere in a generation or two. They were determined to prevent other men, also from nowhere, from getting what they had. Hence their stubborn resistance to the gathering social demands of the Emancipists and their Australian-born children. It was a campaign fought with extreme punctilio. When Governor Lachlan Macquarie, who correctly believed that some of the ablest men in the colony were Emancipists, invited four of them to dinner at Government House in 1810, the Exclusives were outraged. When he went further and appointed two of these men, the merchant Simeon Lord and the landowner Andrew Thompson, as trustees and commissioners of the new turnpike road that was to be built between Sydney and the Hawkesbury River, the third proposed trustee—the Reverend Samuel Marsden, senior chaplain of the colony and one of its biggest landowners, a merciless pharisee—was so piqued in his clerical dignity that he refused to serve. This in turn sent the governor into one of his military rages, and the feud between the two men poisoned relations between Church and State in New South Wales for the rest of Macquarie's term.

The Exclusives could define their sense of class against the despised Emancipists, but they were snobbish as only provincials could be. The tone was faithfully echoed as late as the 1840s by Louisa Anne Meredith, a clergyman's wife who wrote a delectably acerbic account of her five years in Australia (1839–44):

> The distinctions in society here remind me of the "dock-yard people" described by Dickens. . . . Thus—Government officers don't know merchants; merchants with "stores" don't know other merchants who keep "shops"; and the shopkeepers have, I doubt not, a little code of their own, prescribing the proper distances to be obseved between drapers and haberdashers, butchers and pastrycooks. . . . [T]his pride of place is so very ridiculous and unbecoming in such a community, that were not its tendency so mischievous, it could only provoke a smile.[3]

All colonial standards—of rank, etiquette, taste and the "interesting" —were English. Until well into the 1820s, the word "Australian" was a term of abuse, or at best of condescension; it carried an air of seediness on the rim of the Pacific. Sydney's was a heliotropic society, and the sun it faced—distant, abstract but commanding—was the Royal family, seen through its viceroy the governor. He was an autocrat presiding over a police state with certain social trimmings. His power was all-encompassing, as befitted the man who ran a continent that was also a jail. It had been so since 1788, when Arthur Bowes Smyth, hearing Captain Phillip's commission read at Sydney Cove, found it "a more unlimited one than was ever before granted to any governor under the British Crown," while Ralph Clark noted that he "had never heard of any single person having so great a power invested in him."[4] All political decisions ran through his hands; who got land, where and how much; who got labor; who was pardoned, freed or sent to a penal station; what religions were celebrated, other than the established rites of the Church of England, and at what hours; who filled administrative positions; what could be said in the colony's embryonic press—a thousand matters, loaded or trivial, down to the vexed question of which side of the road the chaotic, ever increasing traffic of Sydney should move on (Macquarie chose the left, as in Britain). Nowhere in the British Empire did a proconsul have wider social power than in penal Australia.

It was in the person of the governor, therefore, that the class divisions of the colony found their basis, their reassurance. If a governor leaned toward populism, showing favor to small farmers or ex-convicts, immense resentments could be released, as they were against Lachlan Macquarie. It is not easy to exaggerate the entrenched mentality of the dozen or so clans, starting with the Macarthurs and their allies like Samuel Marsden, who made up the leading free families of Australia between 1800 and 1840.

John Macarthur (1767–1834) and his wife Elizabeth Veale (1767–1850) were the founders and prototypes of the colonial gentry. Macarthur was the son of a Plymouth mercer and corset-maker, a choleric man with a rage for gentility, who saw plots and insults everywhere and was as touchy as a Sicilian. He wasted half his life in imbroglios. Known to Emancipists as "Jack Bodice"—a nickname that reduced him to rage— and to his administrative enemies as "the perturbator," he quarrelled furiously with judges, clergymen, sea captains and traders, and with a succession of governors from Hunter to Darling. From prison in 1808, he masterminded (if that is the word for so half-cocked and rash a gesture) the Rum Corps's *putsch* against Governor Bligh.[5]

The fruit of his spleen was exile; he had to spend all but four years of the period 1801–17 in England, while his wife Elizabeth, most resourceful and levelheaded of women, bred their sheep and ran their growing estates by the Nepean River in Camden. Off the land, Macarthur was a poor businessman, betrayed by his enthusiasms and his hatreds alike. He was rarely conscious of any line between private and public interest, except when scrutinizing the behavior of his enemies. He died mad. None of this tarnished Macarthur's name as the doyen of Australian pastoral conservatism.[6]

Macarthur had come out as a New South Wales Corps ensign on the Second Fleet in 1790 with his wife, their baby son and a maid. Francis Grose, the army governor, favored him and made him paymaster of the Rum Corps. Macarthur started small, with a mixed-breed herd of about a thousand sheep. He got all the land and convict labor he wanted from

Grose and his successor Paterson. But the next two governors, Hunter and King, were navy men who saw no reason to do inside deals with Macarthur or to give him special patronage. "Jack Bodice" took this to mean war. His basilisk campaigns of innuendo against Government House reached their climax in September 1801 in a quarrel, and then a pistol duel, with his own colonel, whose allegiance Macarthur had tried to suborn from Governor King. He winged the colonel in the shoulder, and King, incensed by the doings of "this perturbator," arrested him for trial. But he could not be given a court-martial in Sydney, because—King believed—his fellow officers would have supported the Rum Corps against the Navy with an acquittal. So he was sent back to be tried in England. This, by one of the bizarre flukes that often seemed to govern colonial life, made Macarthur's fortune.

His sole punishment for shooting turned out to be a free ticket to London, with wool samples. King's strategy backfired, as the English court-martial acquitted Macarthur. Before leaving, Macarthur had bought 1,250 more mixed-breed sheep from a brother officer, Major Foveaux, thus making him the biggest sheep-owner in Australia. The main source of first-class wool for the growing English textile industries had been the merino flocks of Saxony and Spain. But Europe was under naval blockade and the English woollen industry was in crisis. It looked as though no more merino fleeces would be reaching England. Even with his coarse hanks of colonial wool, Macarthur's timing was perfect. He found the government more than willing to encourage the raising of fine wool in Australia. He got Treasury permission to buy and export some merino sheep from a small specimen flock owned by George III. He also persuaded Lord Camden to give him a special land grant on which to raise these aristocratic beasts—2,000 acres around Mount Taurus, by the Nepean River, an area called the Cowpastures, the finest known grazing land in New South Wales (which he later renamed Camden). Macarthur sailed back in triumph in 1805 on his own whaling ship, rechristened the *Argo* after the vessel in which Jason sought the Golden Fleece.[7]

The pure merino, two centuries ago, was a tricky and delicate animal, a pompous ambling peruke, unused to Australian heat and Australian grass. Its virtue lay in the size of its fleece and the quality of its wool. But to flourish in Australia the strain had to be cross-bred. Although Macarthur did not, as he often claimed, introduce the merino to New South Wales (both pure and cross merinos were owned by "Little Jack" Palmer and the Reverend Samuel Marsden before him), he turned it into the staple of Australian export by crossing it with hardier types, Bengal and Afrikaner Fat-Tail, while conserving a pure merino flock to improve the strains.[8]

Before long, "pure Merino" was colonial slang for any member of the pastoral elite, starting with the Macarthurs; and by 1808, when he had to run for England and stay there nine years, leaving his stud in charge of Elizabeth and his growing sons, Macarthur was the largest sheep-owner in New South Wales. In his absence, Elizabeth bought, built and bred their holdings far beyond the original Cowpastures grant, to 60,000 acres.

Few ways of life, one would think, demand more evenness of temper, perseverance, instinctive sympathy and financial prudence than stock-farming. Yet the curious fact is that both the founders of Australian sheep-farming were melancholics, given to attacks of extreme anxiety—the very opposite of the contented squire. Alexander Riley (1788–1833) was a genial Irishman most of the time, but his black fits were almost as bad as Macarthur's. Riley had followed his two sisters, who married Rum Corps officers, from Ireland to Australia. He began as a general trader, raising sheep on the side at his station, Raby, near Liverpool. His coup, which would transform Australian grazing, was to bring in Saxon merino sheep, a better stapled and hardier strain than Macarthur's Spanish me-rinos. In 1825 he landed a whole flock of them, each like a woolly pasha in its own padded pen. He wheedled from the government a grant of 10,000 acres of prime land, but further out, near Yass, on the western limits of settlement. He called this station Cavan, after his family's district in Ireland. The essential bloodlines of Australian sheep-breeding run back to Camden and Cavan.

Riley and Macarthur were very different men. Macarthur had a plan-tation mind and could not keep his fingers out of politics. Riley shied away from public affairs and expected the convict system to wither away, leaving a society of free men whose elite were graziers. The contrast between them reminds one of the dangers of generalizing about early pastoralists as though they were units in a class, not individuals. And yet the values of most well-off free men in early colonial Australia were certainly closer to Macarthur's than to Riley's, especially since very few of them were Irish.

What was the ideology of the Merinos and those who aspired to their company—of the Exclusives in general? Mainly, gut Tory conservatism, reinforced by the doctrines of the established Church of England. Like the English squires they emulated, they hated all things French and were apt to treat any kind of Emancipist restiveness as unbridled Jacobinism.

They thought themselves uniquely fitted to hold power in the colony —indeed, that no others were suitable. Not the Emancipists or their children, for the "taint" of convictry was ineradicable and hereditary; stock-breeding encourages a rigid view of genetic inheritance. Not the growing class of city traders and entrepreneurs, no matter how much money they were beginning to make, for trade was ignoble beside land, although much could be forgiven for a suitable dowry. Not the new-chum settlers, who were coming in growing numbers after 1820, for their roots in the land did not go deep enough, and they did not have the big holdings. Not being able to idealize their origins, the early Exclusives fetishized their achievements fiercely and rigidly, seeing themselves as an island of order in a lake of *arrivisme* and crime. They knew that what was good for them was good for the country.

They felt threatened by the rise of new money, generated by trade and property deals. Prudently, they married their offspring into the merchant families, crossing their lines as they had crossed their sheep for economic hardihood. Less realistically, they tried to cripple the Emancipists politically.

Was their conservatism nothing better than an exploitive, "un-Australian" style of baronial laissez-faire? This was the picture created by the Emancipists from 1815 onward—the pseudo-squire in an antipodean landscape, owning the land but not belonging to it; but it was mainly a rhetorical device.

In the 1830s this rhetoric was inflamed by the exacerbated quarrels between colonial conservatives—mainly landowners who had settled the Hunter River Valley in the 1820s—and their liberal governor Richard Bourke (1831–37). Appointed to office by the Whigs in England, Bourke had pushed through a number of reforms that endeared him to the Emancipists, the chief one being a new law which, in 1833, allowed criminal cases to be tried by civil juries and permitted former convicts to serve as jurors. This important enlargement of Emancipists' rights was viewed with horror by conservatives. What anarchy, they asked, might not be unleashed by courts which allowed felons to try criminals? Bourke also restricted the power of landowners over their assigned servants, by decreeing that disciplinary sentences of flogging for offenses against the labor code now had to be given by two magistrates, not one, and setting their limit at 50 lashes instead of 100. Getting two magistrates to judge such cases was not a problem in the settled districts, but up in the Hunter River Valley it took time and trouble. There, a plantation mentality reigned among the big settlers, and they were furious at Bourke for his "leniency." Emancipists and colonial liberals sided with Bourke, and in the crossfire of insult and polemic Bourke's critics were painted as iron-souled blimps, men who would have been more at home among slaves on the banks of the Mississippi than in New South Wales.

The emblematic figure was "Major" James Mudie (1779–1852), cashiered marine lieutenant and failed medal publisher, now a rich man and a colonial magistrate, who called his homestead Castle Forbes and was said to have treated his assigned men so badly that they were driven to rebellion.* He pictured Governor Bourke as a shallow and misguided humanitarian, practicing (as Mudie later termed it) an "anti-penal, anti-social and anti-political system" which would lead the colony to "unbridled crime and lawless anarchy, and . . . its violent and sanguinary separation from the Empire."[9] (Moderation in attack was not a colonial habit, and certainly not Mudie's.) In 1836 Bourke struck back by depriving Mudie (along with thirty-six others) of his magistracy. This loss of caste was too much for Mudie, who sold up and returned to England, vowing revenge. It came in the form of a hastily written book with the felicitous title *The Felonry of New South Wales* (1837). "Felonry," Mudie explained, was his own word, encompassing all of the "criminal population" of the colony, including the Emancipists, no matter what their wealth or professional standing. It corresponded, he said, to the orders of the old world—"the tribe of apellatives distinguished by the same termination, as *peasantry, tenantry, yeomanry, gentry, cavalry, chivalry,* &c." Such people, he argued, were "for ever infamous . . . infamous *in law* . . . unworthy of future trust"; they and their offspring should be disenfranchised forever. There was not the slightest chance that Mudie's tirade could affect social relations in the colony, or be taken seriously outside a small group; but it certainly reinforced the Emancipist claim that men like Mudie were foreigners to New South Wales and outsiders to its social realities.

Yet most Exclusives, however rapacious and snobbish they were, identified themselves with Australia while drawing their models of hierarchy from England. The idea that egalitarianism was a true index of patriotism is mere piety. The Exclusives were more than marsupialized Englishmen; and against the boasts and toasts of the Emancipist party,

---

* In 1833, six convict runaways, most of them assigned to Mudie, went on a rampage at Castle Forbes. Led by a skilled and relatively privileged convict carpenter named John Poole, they robbed the house, shot at Mudie's son-in-law, plundered another property in the district and flogged the master of a third farm. They were soon captured, and the case became a *cause célèbre*. Conservatives greeted the "Castle Forbes rebellion" as proof of the anarchy that had to follow Bourke's liberal attitudes. The defense, marshalled by Emancipist and emigrant friends of Bourke, argued that the convicts had been driven to rebellion by flogging and starvation. Unhappily for the liberal argument, it developed that rations at Castle Forbes were good and discipline moderate (about half the sixty assigned servants there had never been flogged); the discontent arose more from the incompetence of Mudie's son-in-law, John Larnach, who managed the estate during Mudie's own prolonged absences. Despite the facts, the case tarred Mudie with a permanent reputation, which he greatly resented, as the Simon Legree of the Hunter River. See John Hirst, *Convict Society and its Enemies*, pp. 182–84. One may also note that champions of the Emancipists could get a very bad name for cruelty among their assigned men. Robert Wardell, barrister and first editor of Wentworth's pro-Emancipist newspaper *The Australian*, was shot dead by one of his servants, John Jenkins, who declared on the scaffold that he had murdered Wardell for his tyranny.

one might set this, from James Macarthur in London to his aging father in 1829:

> I shall now sit down peaceably and contentedly amongst our sheep-folds and under the shade of our own fig-trees . . . putting more trust in our own efforts, than in the acquaintance and connexions who have too many troubles of their own in this Country to think of the complaints of poor Australians. . . . [T]here are few people in England with whom I would willingly change places.[10]

Eden as property. It is hardly a populist utterance, but one cannot deny its Australian-ness.

In any case, no one held the exclusive rights on ambition or greed. It was William Charles Wentworth, the Emancipists' trumpet, who in 1852 came round to lobby with James Macarthur for the creation of a hereditary colonial *noblesse*, the "bunyip aristocracy," which, fortunately, the Crown saw no reason to create. No Merino ever came close to the kind of transaction that Wentworth, once cursed by them as a republican, a Jacobin and a leveller, attempted in 1840, when he and some associates gulled seven Maori chiefs into selling them about one-third of New Zealand—the largest private land deal in history. (It was, however, quashed by government order.) When it came to dividing the colonial pie, Whigs could behave exactly like Tories, Emancipists like Exclusives.

ii

RILEY DIED in 1833, Macarthur a year later. Neither lived to see the wool industry dominate Australia's economy. That did not happen until well into the 1830s, and when it did the graziers would be "home on the sheep's back," as the phrase went, for the next century. Wool became so big an export, so essential a part of the Australian imagination, that it is hard to imagine as a secondary industry. Yet for most of the convict period in New South Wales, it was. Between the failure of the naval-supply plans for flax and timber, and the enthronement of the sheep— that is, for about the first half-century of white settlement—much of Australia's export wealth came from whaling and sealing, both trades dominated by Emancipists and their sons, the "Currency lads," native-born white Australians.

"The fisheries," as sealing and whaling were collectively known, were of an abundance hardly imaginable today. The southern oceans were a vast, undisturbed sanctuary for the black whale, the sperm whale and the fur seals. Every season, the huge cetaceans cruised north from Antarctica in millions, to mate and calve in the tranquil bays and estuaries along the coasts of New Zealand, Van Diemen's Land and southeastern Australia. In the early 1800s, Hobart's estuary was dangerous for small boats, which could scarcely steer between the pregnant and calving black whales. Whalers could sally out in dories and kill thousands a year. Because it did not need large vessels, bay-whaling was a cheap trade and easy for Emancipists to get into. It had been plied in Australian and New Zealand coastal waters since the 1790s; the first whalemen came on the Third Fleet.

Whaling in Australian waters could not, of course, be confined to colonists. In 1803 Pitt's administration opened the whole Pacific Ocean east of 180° to unlicensed whalers. Scores of whaling ships, reeking and storm-battered, years out of Nantucket and Sag Harbor, came in for the killing. Colonial whalers learned from the American captains, those driven ancestors of Ahab, pressed on by flinty Quaker fleet-owners. By the 1820s, exports of whale oil and whalebone were paying for much of the iron, cloth, tools, salt provisions, tea, rum and Far Eastern luxury goods that came into the colony. The rest was bought with profits from sealing.[11]

Every beach of the Tasman Sea, each wild promontory of Bass Strait, every rock west of Kangaroo Island off South Australia bore teeming rookeries of seals and sea lions. They had no natural enemies and knew nothing of man except for the occasional Aborigine hunter. Tens of millions of them were wiped out in less than thirty years.

The sealers killed year-round, clubbing their prey to death. Because there was no closed season in mating and pupping time, pregnant seals were killed in myriads and the pups were left milkless on the rocks to starve. Disturbed in their ancestral rookeries, which soon became bogs of putrefaction—for the sealers took only the skins and left hills of flayed carcasses behind—the seals stopped breeding and abandoned their haunts. "The whole of this valuable trade is threatened with a speedy & total annihilation," an official warned Lieutenant-Governor Arthur in 1826. The idea of appealing to the sealers was, of course, a joke. Most were the scum of the System, escaped convicts gone wild on a bitter shore:

The Islands . . . afford constant shelter, and secure retreats, for runaways and villains of the worst description. Amost every rock throughout the strait has become the habitation of some one or more amongst the most desperate and lawless of mankind. The whole of the Straits seem to present one continued scene of violence, plunder and the commission of every species of crime.—Natives, chiefly black women, are occasionally stolen from the mainland and actually *sold* to the leaders. . . . [F]rom 10 to 15 children, the offspring of these poor Creatures and of their oppressors, are now or were lately to be met with on the several Islands.[12]

There were many more than that. The rapparees and bolters who formed their bloody, troglodytic island colonies kidnapped hundreds of black women from their tribes not only because they needed sex, but because many coastal Aborigines were expert seal-hunters.[13]

Convicts could easily escape from Van Diemen's Land on sealing vessels. By 1820 Hobart had become the main port and market for all whaling and sealing in the southern ocean. It was hard to monitor the passage of crews between ship and shore; and any convict could bluff his way past the wharf guards with a forged ticket-of-leave. Hundreds of men went through this loophole into the sealing trade. It was an excellent arrangement for the masters of the "fisheries." Once aboard, the convict could not return to land without risking the gallows; he was shanghaied into another sort of captivity, masquerading as freedom. By the 1830s the southern bays and refuges, from the Bay of Islands in New Zealand to the Recherche Archipelago on the west coast of Australia, were littered with criminal flotsam left by the dying pursuit of seals and whales.

The first colonist to make money on the "fisheries" was a free Scottish merchant, Robert Campbell—"just and humane and a gentleman," in Governor Bligh's view, and no ally of Macarthur's. To preserve its monopoly, the East India Company had arranged that no Australian-based trader could export whale or seal products direct to London. (Other "Southern whalers," who were not actually based in Australia, were exempt from this ruling.) Campbell was determined to break this unfair restraint on trade, which in effect denied that New South Wales had any functions but penal ones. In 1805 he sailed to England with his family in his ship *Lady Barlow*. In her hold were 260 tons of oil rendered down from sea-elephant blubber and 13,700 sealskins. A few months behind her sailed the *Honduras Packet*, laden with 34,000 skins. The East India Company reacted predictably by seizing Campbell's ship and cargo. The ensuing fracas, which Campbell handily won, led at last to free exports from Australia to England, bypassing the East India Company. Campbell returned to New South Wales a trader-hero, "father of the mercantile community."[14]

Free colonial trade destroyed the chance that there would ever be another rum monopoly. Some Emancipists could plough their profits from whaling and sealing back into property. They became—on the balance-sheet, at least—the equal of an Exclusive.

In the early 1800s most sealing and whaling in Australian waters was run by three men: Henry Kable, Simeon Lord and James Underwood. All three were ex-convicts. Kable (1763–1846) was a burglar who came out on the First Fleet under a death sentence that had been commuted to fourteen years' transportation. He became an overseer, then a rum trader, selling liquor to convicts the officers were too haughty to deal with directly.

Some time before 1800, Kable met up with James Underwood (1776–1844), another convict who possessed the inestimably useful skill of knowing how to build boats. Ships of any kind were in short supply in the colony, even then. Kable and Underwood built a sloop, *Diana*, and fitted her out for sealing in Bass Strait. Before long they had sixty men working for them and were skinning 30,000 seals a year; Underwood's shipyard, at the head of Sydney Cove, was turning out vessels up to 200 tons in burthen.

In 1805 they took on a a third partner, Simeon Lord (1771–1840), who had been transported in 1790 for stealing several hundred yards of calico and muslin. His offense was a juvenile one and he never repeated it. A ruthless stone-squeezer of a Yorkshireman, Lord too had come up through the rum trade. Doubtless the officers felt that by using such shady men as distributors, they were saved from demeaning contact with convicts and Emancipists. In fact, they were creating just the social anomaly they feared. Lord was an entrepreneurial genius and fast as a dingo. By 1798 he had his own warehouse, and by 1799 his first ship. He cultivated Robert Campbell, who gave him useful introductions to important people in the sealskin market in London. Lord "traded up" from rum to iron and timber, and then to manufacture. In workshops staffed by assigned convicts, he made the consumer goods that were still in such erratic supply, and so costly, in Sydney: candles, soap, glasses, stockings, cloth, harness, boots and leather hats. Between 1806 and 1809 Lord, Kable and Underwood sold over 127,000 sealskins in London, more in China and Calcutta. Sealing led naturally to Pacific trade in sandalwood and other commodities.

In 1803 Simeon Lord built himself a mansion in Sydney, the largest private house in the colony. It had three stories and a basement, and an elegant veranda carried on slender columns over the street; it was built of sandstone bound with imported mortar. "Lord's palace" was to commerce what Macquarie's estate was to landholding. His social betters passed it with distaste, unable to ignore this irrefutable monument to social permeability. "Mr. Lord (formerly a horse stealer) has built a house that he lives in that cost 20,000£," sniffed a visiting naval surgeon in 1810, "but still these men are despised and any free settler would not deign to sit at their tables. . . . Most of these men have made their money by *trading*."[15]

"These men" were not all men. Mary Haydock (1777–1855), convicted and transported at the tender age of thirteen for horse-stealing in Lancashire, married a young free merchant and shipowner named Thomas Reibey in 1794, learned the business of shipping and sealing from him and aggressively expanded her holdings after 1811, when he died and left her with seven children. She owned warehouses and trading brigs as well as seven farms on the Hawkesbury River and numerous buildings in the growing center of Sydney. This alert and formidably tenacious woman was the exception that proved the rule: No other convict woman made a success, or even a passing stir, at business in the male-dominated society of penal Australia, and it is unlikely that Reibey herself, for all her drive and cunning, could have done it without the start her husband gave her.

The most spectacular of the ex-convict merchants, and the most detested by the Exclusives, was Samuel Terry (1776–1838). Terry began as an illiterate Manchester laborer who was transported for seven years for stealing 400 pairs of stockings and became known to his contemporaries as "The Rothschild of Botany Bay." Freed in 1807, he set up in Sydney as a pubkeeper and moneylender. Many nasty stories, some of them perhaps true (though none proven), were told of his exploitation of drunken Emancipists and ticket-of-leave men—how he would let them booze on credit for days and weeks and then seize their farms as payment. Whether by trickery, frugality or a judicious mixture of both, by 1820 he owned 19,000 acres, or 10 percent of the land possessed by all the eight hundred or so Emancipist landowners put together. He also held more mortgages on property than the Bank of New South Wales, in which he was a principal shareholder—about one-fifth of the total value of mortgages registered in the colony. Later in life, he turned to charity and politics, becoming an enthusiastic backer of Emancipists' rights. His convict servants remembered him warmly as one who never had them flogged and never forgot the class bonds of his own past. When he died in 1838, Terry received the most lavish funeral ever held in Australia, complete with flags, full Masonic panoply and—to the disgust of his enemies—a procession through the crowded, silent streets of Sydney led by the military band of the 50th Regiment. "It is a piece of important news, certainly," ran a letter to the London *Times*, "for the criminals of England, that military honours have given lustre to the obsequies of one of their most successful chums."[16]

But the Terrys, Reibeys and Lords are memorable precisely because they were exceptions. Very few ex-convicts made big fortunes after 1821, although many of their free descendants would. Most Emancipists survived as handymen, "mechanics," butchers, bakers or small farmers. These "dungaree settlers," so called for the coarse cloth they wore, clung to the land by their fingernails until they were shaken loose by drought or debt or drink. Their truck-gardens produced the fruit, vegetables and chickens that the exalted Merinos would not condescend to raise except for their own kitchens; they feared the space and melancholy of the bush, and stuck to the land around Sydney while other settlers, more adventurous and better endowed with slave labor, pushed outward. Often they drank their small acreage away and died paupers. And yet, as Peter Cunningham remarked, they served "like the American backwoodsmen" —a breed not yet mythologized in 1825—"the office of pioneers to prepare the way for a more healthy population": their own children, the Currency.

If the colony's economy depended on ex-convicts, so did its professional and cultural communities. In Macquarie's time, there was not one lawyer in Australia who had come there as a free man. No respectable lawyer would have contemplated going there to practice. But colonial life was bitterly litigious, and much of the suing and pleading therefore had to be done by fallen solicitors who had been struck off the rolls in England and Ireland.

Their status as lawyers was, to put it mildly, uncertain. But because Ellis Bent, Macquarie's deputy judge-advocate, did not want to waste court time with the meandering, amateurish pleas of litigants acting as their own attorneys, he cautiously allowed three ex-convict lawyers to bring civil cases. Two of them built up quite flourishing practices, for a time. One was George Crossley (1749–1823), who, after twenty-four years' blameless practice as a solicitor, had been transported for perjury.[17] Governor King conditionally pardoned him in 1801, two years after he arrived; by 1803 he owned more than 400 acres on the Hawkesbury River and was handling cases for other settlers, despite a flurry of writs from newly acquired creditors. He advised Governor Bligh, who knew the law of the sea better than that of the land, on his legal dealings with the Rum Corps. Macarthur's cabal, after their *putsch* against Bligh in 1808, had him arrested as a supporter of their "Tyrant" and sent to slave in the dreaded coal mines near Newcastle. Macquarie freed him to practice civil law again, but by 1821 he was crushed by debts and a last conviction, at the age of seventy-two, for perjury. He died two years later. His colleague, Edward Eagar (1787–1866), a Dublin attorney under life sentence for forgery, did slightly better: After getting his conditional pardon in 1813, he practiced law for two years. But then his and Crossley's right to plead in court was struck down by the judge of the newly created Supreme Court of Civil Judicature, Jeffrey Bent.

Bent proved to be an idle, haughty drone, whose conservatism even embarrassed some of the Exclusives. He and Macquarie detested one another on sight, and the friction between them rendered the new court unworkable. Bent thought of Emancipists as permanent helots, and refused point-blank to hear any cases brought by ex-convict lawyers.[18] Naturally, this was a catastrophe for the likes of Eagar and Crossley. Macquarie protested, but in vain. In May 1815 it was ruled that no lawyer disbarred in England could plead in Australia. Macquarie then wrote to the colonial secretary, Lord Bathurst, threatening to resign if Jeffrey Bent and his ailing brother Ellis, the colony's judge-advocate, were not both recalled. Bathurst, realizing that the whole relationship between the government and the bench was about to break down, gave in. Ellis Bent solved half of the problem by dying a few months later, and soon after that Jeffrey Bent left Australia. Nevertheless it would be some time before an Emancipist lawyer could plead with much chance of being taken seriously by an Australian court. This legal disability continued to be one of the most potent weapons in the Exclusives' armory of social discrimination.

Ex-convict doctors fared better than lawyers. One could hardly say that harried, shady writ-pushers like Eagar and Crossley, however badly they were victimized, founded Australian law; but William Redfern (1774–1833), another ex-convict, was certainly the father of Australian medicine.

A spirited and deeply altruistic man, Redfern began his career as a naval surgeon and was tried in 1797 for supporting the mutiny of British sailors on the fleet at the Nore. He was accused as a leader of the rising, although his only role in it was to exhort the tars "to be more united among themselves." The court sentenced him to hang, but he was reprieved, due to his youth and rashness, and spent four years in prison before being transported to New South Wales in 1801.[19]

In a colony short of doctors, beset by grave problems of diet and sanitation, with a high accident rate and laws enforced by flogging, Redfern had plenty to do. He began as assistant surgeon on Norfolk Island, where he got a free pardon from Governor King in 1803. Returning to Sydney in 1808, he was made assistant surgeon to the colony and put in charge of the squalid and chaotic hospital on Dawes Point in Sydney. In 1816 he took effective charge of Macquarie's new "Rum Hospital," and by then his practice was the largest and most popular in the colony.

For Redfern, much of the social prejudice against ex-convicts was suspended. He was clearly the best surgeon in the colony; moreover, his forte was obstetrics, which meant that every family, "good" or not, needed him. He delivered Governor Macquarie's only son Lachlan in 1814, and he was also the family doctor to the Macarthurs in Camden. Respect for Redfern's skills was one of the very few matters on which Macquarie and Macarthur wholeheartedly agreed. Yet despite the strength of his connections at Government House and Camden, Redfern was not content merely to be a "social" doctor. He never forgot that he, like other convicts, had come in chains to Australia. He spent as much time on the convicts' dysenteries, broken bones, eye-sores, infected lash-cuts and bastard births as on the diseases of the rich. He was always accessible to them and ran an outpatient clinic for gang laborers at the back of the Rum Hospital. Above all, he fought to improve conditions on convict transports. Public health in Australia began with Redfern. Many convicts and Emancipists, therefore, considered him their savior; this gave the later political actions of this brusque, kindly and incorruptible man a real constituency.

Early colonial Sydney was not a cultivated town, and even its poor poet laureate Michael Massey Robinson was driven to metaphors of infancy and sunrise when he contemplated it. Cultural life among the better classes of Sydney society existed in a larval way, producing an occasional recitation or watercolor; but mostly it struck both visitors and residents as jejune and provincial. "A land without antiquities," complained the well-named Judge Barron Field, who had come to Australia in 1816 to replace Jeffrey Bent. To Field, it was a place so raw as to be, except for a few oddities like the kangaroo, culturally invisible:

> . . . where Nature is prosaic,
> Unpicturesque, unmusical, and where
> Nature reflecting Art is not yet born;—
> We've nothing left us but anticipation,
> Better (I grant) than utter selfishness,
> Yet too o'erweening—too American;
> Where's no past tense, the ign'rant present's all.

Sydney, he felt, was "a spireless city and profane." The only evocative object in sight is a ship:

> . . . poetry to me
> Since piously I trust, in no long space,
> Her wings will bear me from this prose-dull land.[20]

The only free professional artist to visit Australia before 1825 was John Lewin (1770–1819), a natural-history painter who, sensing that English interest in Australian exotica might make a journey worthwhile, arrived in 1800 to start work on two fine (and now exceedingly rare) illustrated books, *Prodromus Entomology* (1805), on Australian lepidopterous insects, and *Birds of New Holland* (1808).[21] Lachlan Macquarie adopted this modest and uncomplaining young man as his quasi-official painter, taking him to do watercolors of the scenes on his gubernatorial "progress" across the Blue Mountains on the new convict road in 1815, and commissioning "transparencies" from him for the ballroom at Government House. He also gave Lewin a sinecure of £40, later £80, a year by appointing him coroner, which was as close to a direct subsidy of the infant arts as any governor could do.

Educated convicts—known as Specials—took pride in their literacy and their distance from the brutish laboring mass of felons, and Lewin was a source of comfort to them; his presence suggested that they were not totally severed from culture. "I view, admire, and venerate the Man," cried the convict John Grant, in an an exclamatory panegyric on this "tender Genius,"

> Lewin: rare, beauteous plant in Genius' Vale!
> Painter! Engraver! Nature's Wooer! Hail!
> Courage![22]

Lewin apart, all artists in the early colony were in the literal sense counterfeiters—or thieves, or fallen clerks, or obscurely disgraced pupil-teachers. Australia was not short of convict painters. One of them, Joseph Lycett (ca. 1774–? ) came under Macquarie's erratic patronage. A mere "limner" in England and a helpless alcoholic, Lycett in 1811 received fourteen years for forgery. In Sydney he was made a post-office clerk. There, he had access to the post office's small printing press. Lycett scrounged some copper plates and a burin, and before long the colony was flooded with dud five-shilling notes. He was sent to the penal station at Newcastle. Very luckily for him, the commandant was Captain James Wallis, an amateur painter himself; and instead of hewing coal in darkness, Lycett was set to designing a church and painting a triptych, long since lost, for its altar.

Wallis arranged a conditional pardon for Lycett in 1819, and then Macquarie—anxious, as always, to promote the beauties of Australia and attract free emigrant settlers—encouraged him to wander across the colony, sketching its landscapes. The watercolors became a volume of *Views of Australia*, published serially from 1824 on; these colored engravings were dedicated to the colonial secretary, Lord Bathurst, and presented an Arcadian image of Australia hardly distinguishable from the Cotswolds or a picturesque park.[23] They proclaimed how the benign hand of the "Patriot-Chief," Lachlan Macquarie, had transformed the harsh antipodes. "Behold," the advertisement for the *Views* adjured its readers, "the gloomy grandeur of solitary woods and forests exchanged for the noise and bustle of thronged marts of commerce; while the dens of savage animals, and the hiding places of yet more savage men, have become transformed into peaceful villages." There was something elegantly appropriate about setting a forger to such a task.

Although the list of convict artists is fairly long—from Thomas Watling (b. 1762) in Sydney Cove to William Buelow Gould (1801–1853) in Hobart—it contains no men (and of course no women) of more than local interest, except for the celebrated "painter-poisoner" Thomas Griffiths Wainewright (1794–1847), an epigone of Henry Fuseli who had mixed in London literary circles with Lamb, Hazlitt, De Quincey and the young Dickens. His reputation for poisoning heiresses was a posthumous canard (invented in part by Dickens: so much for literary friendships); in fact, he was transported for forgery. But most convict painters were obscure limners who struggled as best they could in a society without opportunities, lived drunk and died disheartened.[24]

Much of the same was true of writing, which, beyond the level of official dispatch, the legal opinion and the family letter, led a thin erratic life. Professional writers were of course unheard-of. There were convict balladeers, and no shortage of writers of "pipes" or anonymous pasquinades (the curious word came from their author's habit of pushing them under doors, rolled in a cylinder) directed against Authority. Most of these were awkward expostulations, railing against well-known targets to whom they gave easily decodable names—"Parson Rapine," for instance, for the sanctimonious Dr. Samuel Marsden.[25]

The first Australian publisher was a former shoplifter, George Howe (1769–1821), whose bastard son would go on to start the first newspaper in Van Diemen's Land.

The first play produced in Australia was George Farquhar's Restoration comedy *The Recruiting Officer*, performed by an all-convict cast in 1789. Its prologue, supposedly written by some nameless felon bard, was to become famous in and beyond Botany Bay:

> From distant climes o'er wide-spread seas we come,
> Though not with much eclat or beat of drum,
> True patriots all; for be it understood,
> We left our country for our country's good;
> No private views disgrac'd our generous zeal,
> What urg'd our travels was our country's weal,
> And none will doubt but that our emigration
> Has prov'd most useful to the British nation.

Alas, later research has shown that this was not penned by a convict in Port Jackson, but by Henry Carter, a hack journalist in London, well after he heard the play had been performed; he also spread the tale that it had been spoken by the famed pickpocket George Barrington. (Nevertheless, even without its imperishable second couplet, the "Barrington prologue" deserves to be remembered as the first of a long series of gibes directed by the supercilious Pommy at cultural efforts in Australia.)

The most important cultural figure to emerge from the ranks of the convicts was, however, the architect Francis Howard Greenway. He was a touchy, arrogant, painstaking and uncompromising man, and these qualities ensured both his successes and his failures. Without that stubborn egotism his talent could scarcely have survived the humiliations of convict life intact, but his outspokenness about the poor taste, graft, incompetence and bad workmanship that surrounded him made so many enemies that after Macquarie, his patron, returned to England, his career soon withered. To call Greenway an innocent victim distorts the record; much of his reputation for greed and extravagance was deserved. For example, after drawing his salary for six years as Macquarie's architect, he had the cheek to present a further bill for £11,000, which he claimed as his commission fee (about 5 percent of construction cost) on government work for which he had already been paid. He lost his official post when Macquarie left and got no real jobs after 1828; ten years later, Australia's finest Georgian architect died a pauper and was buried in an unmarked grave.

Three major Greenway buildings survive in their intended form: St. Matthew's Church in Windsor, and the Hyde Park Barracks and St. James's Church in Sydney, whose grave and spare pedimented façades face one another at the south end of Macquarie Street. Greenway had a genius for turning the relative poverty of colonial architectural resources —the lack of skilled carvers, for instance—to good account. He had to concentrate on proportion and material texture, rather than ornament: the simple-looking (but closely accounted) use of Palladian bays, with plain pilasters—brick on the Barracks, tawny sandstone on St. James's— firmly stating the ratios of the walls. His Doric detailing, straightforward and masculine, suited the hard clarity of Australian light as well as the limitations of convict masonry skills. As in early American churches, the direct speech of Greenway's idiom reinforced the content of the rituals: nothing Romish, every brick reflecting (as J. M. Freeland put it) "a vehemently evangelical society which saw all hope and cause for pride and pleasure in the unchallengeable rightness of the Protestant ascendancy."[26] The political engagement between Church and State was unambiguously put by the sole inscription in the cartouche on St. James's pediment: not a motto or a Biblical text, just Lachlan Macquarie's name, facing the same name in the same place on the Barracks a hundred yards away.

Architecture is a social art *par excellence*. A citizen sees his city's buildings every day, whether he wants to or not; their speech is quiet but pervasive. Greenway's public buildings publicly epitomized one of the "distasteful" facts of penal Australia—that free birth did not confer a monopoly of talent. For all the Exclusives' obsession with status, and despite the armored barriers of class raised against the Emancipists, the free still had to employ an ex-convict to form and condense their desire for urban elegance and ceremonial space. To worship God in a house built by a forger, while across the way more criminals were confined in another house of equal elegance—this was a piquant contradiction, not to be dwelt on. It summed up the peculiar insecurity of the signals respectable people in Sydney devised to distinguish themselves from their Others.

In their desire for signs of status, the colonial Australians developed some unlikely fixations, refuting entirely the idea that remote societies are robustly free of snobbery. Of course, the reverse is true: It is the provinces that fix on style and "correctness," since their fate is to reflect distant prototypes. Hence the attention the early Australian gentry paid to form, and their contempt for the pretensions of new Emancipist money. Louisa Anne Meredith, the recording angel of the antipodean drawing-room, took one of her finest flights on the subject of risen convicts:

> Wealth, all-powerful though it be, —and many of these emancipists are the richest men in the colony, —cannot wholly overcome the prejudice against them, though policy, in some instances, greatly modifies it. Their want of education is an effectual barrier to many, and these so wrap themselves in the love of wealth, and the palpable, though misplaced, importance it gives, that their descendants will probably improve but little on the parental model. You may often see a man of immense property, whose wife and daughters dress in the extreme of fashion and finery, rolling home in his gay carriage from his daily avocations, with face, hands and apparel as dirty and slovenly as any common mechanic. And the son of a similar character has been seen, with a dozen costly rings on his coarse fingers, and chains, and shirt-pins, glistening with gems, buying yet more expensive jewelry, yet without sock or stockings to his feet; the *shoes*, to which his *spurs* were attached, leaving a debatable ground between them and his trowsers! Spurs and shoes are, I imagine, a fashion peculiar to this stamp of exquisites, but among them very popular.[27]

But how to distinguish oneself from the spur-and-shoe men? Much ingenuity was expended on the problem. Beyond drink, social climbing and fornication, the amusements of the upper crust of New South Wales were not the same as they are today, and generally not of a distinctively "Australian" kind. Superior people did not, for instance, swim in the sea or even go to the beach; sea-bathing bore the taint of the imprisoned, because when Sydney convicts washed they usually had to do it in the salt water. To get a tan, for a woman, was to plummet from gentility to coarseness; sunburned skin suggested convict labor and carried overtones of the despicable black savage. "Few ladies venture to risk their complexions to the exposure of an equestrian costume, and accordingly few appear on horseback."[28]

The desire not to resemble convicts even affected diet. Mrs. Meredith was puzzled by her hosts' refusal ever to serve fresh fish at lunch or dinner, despite the superb quality and variety of Sydney seafood. Instead, she was given smoked salmon or dried cod brought from England. This aimed to invert the convict diet. Convicts traditionally ate salted meat —which signified lack of property, for only the landed could enjoy fresh beef or lamb—and fresh fish. The ceremonial food of the free must therefore be fresh meat and salt fish.

One could live grandly in early Sydney, given the money and the adminstrative power. The extreme example was Captain John Piper (1773–1851), a very unthrifty Scottish Lucullus who had come out with the New South Wales Corps and obtained the plum job of chief naval officer in Sydney, giving him the right to take a percentage of all excise on spirits and customs dues exacted on imported goods. This was worth more than £4,000 a year to him, and with it he built Henrietta Villa— otherwise known as the Naval Pavilion—on a 190-acre harborside promontory granted to him by Macquarie and known today as Point Piper. "He lives in a beautiful house," reported George Thomas Boyes, Governor Brisbane's deputy-assistant commissary-general in Sydney,

> but it stands alone for there is nothing like it in the Colony. He has laid out immense sums and no expense had been spared to ornament this fairy Palace. . . . He does the thing properly, for he sends carriages and four and boats for those who like the water, and returns his guests to their homes in the same manner. He keeps a band of music and they have quadrilles every evening under the spacious verandahs. At the table there is a vast profusion of every luxury the four quarters of the globe can supply, for you must know that this fifth or pick-pocket quarter contributes nothing of itself. . . . There is no honour in dining with Piper for he invites everybody who comes here.[29]

The respectable classes loved horse-breeding and horse-racing; Australia's equine fixation was fully formed by 1820. They held lavish balls, which some pastoral families would ride 200 miles to attend—these being the main displays of the colonial marriage-market. The dancing was segregated, with Emancipists at one end of the room and Exclusives at the other, sometimes with different orchestras. Some gentlemen did what English gentry were known to do—they rode to hounds. But there were no foxes in Australia, and so the "Cumberland Hunt," as it called itself, donned pink coats amid the old scribbly gray of the bush and went baying, belling and tallyhoing after dingoes. Rarely can Oscar Wilde's definition of hunting as "the unspeakable in pursuit of the uneatable" have applied so forcibly within the British Empire.

The aim was to be as English as possible, and to speak of England as "home." But the settlers could not follow the change of English fashion; their conservatism was underscored by the great antipodean time lag. Ships would bring out-of-date magazines and newspapers, ancient Court news, obsolescent ladies' clothes and overpriced luxury goods. There was a faded pleasure in gossiping about the Prince of Wales's debts when, for all one knew, they might have been paid before one heard of them; or about the unwonted pregnancy of a county heiress if the baby had presumably already been born. The poverty of conversation could drive an intelligent visitor to despair. Louisa Meredith lamented that none of the colonial elite seemed to have read anything:

> An apathetic indifference seems the besetting fault; an utter absence of interest or enquiry beyond the merest gossip, —the cut of a new sleeve, or the guests at a late party. "Do you play?" and "Do you draw" are invariable queries to a new lady-arrival. "Do you *dance?*" is thought superfluous, for everybody dances; but not a question is heard relative to English literature or art; far less a remark on any political event, of however important a nature:—not a syllable that betrays *thought*.[30]

And so the image of England slowly dimmed to a nostalgic wraith, a film of imperfect memory. What filled up the horizon, as in small isolated communities it always does, was local news. And the convicts were the necessary low-water mark to which all social heights were compared. The gentry needed them for self-definition, not just for labor.

iii

ONE SAW GANGS of convicts everywhere. All around Sydney, on the Blue Mountain roads, or south toward Bowral, Goulburn and the Monaro plains, the visitor heard the colonial carillon of ringing leg-irons partly muffled by leather and coarse wool—the sound of chained men hewing the sandstone, dragging their fetter as though wading in air. Free settlers tended to conventionalize the sight, to turn these sweating, shuffling, unknowable Others into voids, mere yellow uniforms, man-shaped holes in the social landscape. One half-averted one's eyes: There, but for the grace of God, go I.

In most sketches and paintings of these landscapes, even those by convict artists, the convicts do not appear. When they do, as in the former purse-stealer Charles Rodius's sketch of *Convicts Building the Road to Bathurst*, 1833, they are reduced to inconspicuous *staffage* figures against the notch of Western plain that opens promisingly to view. Much less common are sketches like Augustus Earle's somewhat earlier *View from the Summit of Mount York, Looking towards Bathurst Plains* (ca. 1826–27), where the road gang moves into close-up and there is as much interest in its work and garb as in the immense landscape behind: a man in punishment irons carrying water, three felons hewing sandstone, an imperious—though in Earle's drawing, rather limp—gesture from the military guard. The laboring convict, unlike the Neapolitan fisherman or the Provençal peasant, never became a picturesque feature in the landscape whose social use he typified. He was a pictorial embarrassment, since his known propensity for evil prevented any kind of idealization. He was not so much "brutalized" (in the modern sense: deformed by ill-treatment) as he was "a brute," whose criminal nature was written on his very skin. He was a kind of abstraction to the traveller. "The villainous countenances of the greater number, the clank of their chains, and the thought of how awful an amount of crime had led to this disgraceful punishment, made me positively dread passing or meeting a band of the miserable wretches," wrote Louisa Meredith of her journey across the Blue Mountains.[31]

The otherness of the convict was further reinforced by his language, for his argot declared that he came from another society, an Alsatia of the mind. The linguistic class barriers in penal Australia were absolute —the very opposite of today, when all classes share the robust vernacular of Australian slang. English criminal cant, an entire sub-language, immediately branded its users and the aspiring Emancipist had to unlearn it or stay where he was. Purely colonial terms like *scrubbing brushes* (bad bread full of chaff), *smiggins* (prison soup thickened with barley), *canary* (a sentence of 100 lashes) or *sandstone* (a weak man, who crumbled under flogging), classified the speaker as plainly as the broad-arrow stamped on all prisoners' clothes. The fantastic richness of Australian slang, its power of invective and its curious metaphorical twists, are ultimately traceable to convict days, although the full blossoming of Australian language belongs to the later nineteenth century. Among themselves, old lags used the cant of transportation: They had "been married together" (gone fettered in a chain), "piked across the herring pond," or been "on my travels," or "marinated," or "napped fourteen penn'orth" (drawn a sentence of fourteen years' exile). Because such a sentence was a blow that knocked the wind out of the victim, the transported felon called himself a "bellowser." But there was also a great need for euphemism, because class was such a sensitive issue. In the ears of

Emancipists and their descendants, "convict" was a fighting word. In the 1820s, the polite form was *government man* or *legitimate*, and these were later displaced by *exile* or even *empire-builder*. Such usage was part of what amounted to a social agreement to soften the rub of convict status. One did not throw his bondage in a man's face. Until 1840 and the end of transportation, few (if any) emigrants to New South Wales would have thought of calling themselves "Australian"—a British colonel in Bombay would have as soon called himself "Indian." One was British, and it demeaned one's own standing within the conventions of British society to think that New South Wales was radically different from a "normal" civil community. Of course it was not normal, but to make it seem so the convicts had to be treated, in law and language, as belonging to such a community, lest the free emigrant colonists come to regard themselves as parasites on a jail. To its settlers, New South Wales was *not* a jail but a free community with rather a large preponderance of prisoners in it. This seemingly casuistical point had important social consequences. One sees them, for instance, in the policy that prevented governors sending prisoners, at will and without trial, from assignment to the secondary settlements. A man had to stand trial and be convicted again before losing his rights as a member of the civil community and going to Norfolk Island. If New South Wales had been thought as much a jail as Norfolk Island, no trial would have been needed—it would have been a technical matter, like moving a prisoner from one cell to another. Convicts arrested and held on suspicion in New South Wales could apply for *habeas corpus*, and in granting it a Supreme Court judge named John Stephen remarked that "the rights of prisoners were as sacred in the eye of the law as those of free men." This was no idle figure of speech. In the same spirit of civil conciliation, judges in New South Wales (especially those of the Supreme Court) could be extraordinarily careful of convicts' and former convicts' rights—so much so that one judge in 1838 ruled it improper for the attorney-general to ask a witness, "What were you sent for?" This, said the judge, invited the witness to degrade himself in court. Thereafter, even if witnesses were known to be ex-convicts, they could not be questioned about their past and their convict origin could not be mentioned.[32]

Outside the courts, in the private sphere, a particularly sensitive area of contact between bond and free lay in the use of convicts as maids, nannies, stewards and even teachers. The very idea of assigning convicts as personal servants "for the purposes of Luxury" gave later governors qualms[33]; but, since no butler or groom in London was likely to emigrate to raw Sydney to ply his skills, there was no socially acceptable alternative. For domestic service, preferences were altered. The farmer on his station might crave the labor of a horse-thief or a rick-burner. But in

Sydney, the idea of some "barn door gentleman," an untutored hayseed, big-booting nervously about the drawing-room and breaking the china, filled matrons with horror. Thus, there was a demand for city convicts, preferably refined and literate forgers, who might know from which side to pass the roast; or, if not forgers, at least thieves, who could protect their masters' property:

> It is very seldom that any thieves is sent up the country, as most of the gentlemen resides in Suydney, and would sooner take for his servant a man that he knows has been a regular thief at home, than one of them barn dore gentlemen; why is it, he knows he can depend on them, for they won't see no tricks play'd with his master's property, nor play none himself; you never hear of a thief getting into any trouble.[34]

The servant problem was "as common a topic of conversation with the ladies . . . as the weather," remarked the Catholic prelate William Ullathorne in 1838. "Whenever persons meet it is a constant topic." There were more than enough domestic horror-stories of drink, impropriety and clumsiness—particularly drink—to go round.[35]

The mistress of the house had to lock everything up—the "tantalus" (security-frame for the decanters), the cellar, the pantry, the dressing-table, the desks, the sewing-kit. Sometimes she had to put up with insults from her servants unknown in England, for convict women in domestic service were "very much in the habit" of raking their mistresses with curses and oaths of such obscenity that a proper lady could not repeat them to her husband, much less in evidence to a magistrate in court; so the foul tongue could not be punished.[36]

Given the choice, colonists would have preferred free servants. Sir John Franklin, when he was lieutenant-governor in Van Diemen's Land, proposed in 1837 that all assigned persons—including domestic help—should wear a distinguishing badge or patch on their clothes; the governor, Sir George Gipps, held back on applying this idea in New South Wales because he feared repercussions from rich colonists who did not want the splendor of their flunkies' uniforms dimmed by this mark of infamy.[37]

A few settlers in Van Diemen's Land managed to keep a domestic staff of free people, but they were scarce and apt to leave without warning; there was, in any case, little difference of quality between convict and free male servants. However, up to the mid-1830s, most efforts to bring in respectable women as nurses or governesses failed utterly. For women convicts seemed particularly uncontrollable. (Respectable settlers supposed that their own mercies ensured this.) Parents were plagued by the fear that the running of their households was in the hands of

vengeful and immoral women.[38] Convict nannies and nurses would corrupt those innocent bearers of the Australian future, its children. The
everyday peculiarities of growing up in a penal colony were striking
enough, and domestic scenes like those set down by Marcus Clarke in
*His Natural Life* must have been enacted many times:

> "You're an impertinent man, sir," cries Dora, her bright eyes flashing.
> "How dare you laugh at me? If I was papa, I'd give you half an hour at the
> triangles. *Oh*, you impertinent man!" And, crimson with rage, the spoilt
> little beauty ran out of the room.
>
> Vickers looked grave, but Frere was constrained to get up to laugh at
> his ease.
>
> "Good! 'Pon honour, that's good! The little vixen! —half an hour at
> the triangles! Ha-ha! ha, ha, ha!"
>
> "She is a strange child," says Vickers, "and talks strangely for her age
> ... [H]er education has been neglected. Moreover, this gloomy place, and
> its associations—what can you expect from a child bred in a convict
> settlement?"

In a society where violence against the person was all-pervasive and
institutionalized, children were bound to acquire strange habits that
mimicked those of their elders. They played flogging games and judgment games as freely as their descendants would play bushrangers. "I
have observed children playing," wrote one colonial observer in 1850,

> at the Botany Bay game of Courts of Petty Sessions, and noted the cruel
> sentences which were uniformly pronounced on those who were doomed
> to be "damned," and the favour and partiality which was extended to
> others! Justice appeared never to be thought of:—the gratification of a
> licentious and an unlimited Power being all they sought.[39]

Childhood became even more a theater of coercion in Australia than
in England. On one level, children could threaten their parents' convict
servants in grotesque omnipotence: where else could a spiteful brat
promise a nurse or a butler 25 lashes? On another, the habit extended
into—and was reinforced by—adult society. As the Scottish penal reformer and future commandant of Norfolk Island, Alexander Maconochie, observed, "The total disuse ... of moral motives in the domestic
relations of life, and the habit of enforcing obedience by mere compul-
sion, give a harsh and peremptory bearing in all transactions." Children
learned contempt for others early. "Being very much in the hands of
assigned servants," Bishop Ullathorne testified, "they of course are aware
of the condition of these servants; they look down on them with contempt. This creates an early habit in the minds of the children of looking

down on those who are placed over them; it creates altogether . . . an insolence of feeling and of bearing towards their elders."[40]

The female convict's alleged revenge was to teach the tots bad habits, from swearing to sexual precocity. "They do . . . much damage to the rising generation," John Russell told the 1838 Select Committee on Transportation, "being generally most mischievous in attempting to seduce or contaminate the daughters of settlers." The committee's witnesses, anxious to depict the antipodes as Sodom and Gomorrah, told stories of how colonists' girls had seen female convicts "in connexion" with their satyr-like lovers, and how the three daughters of one family had been so deranged by this penal primal scene that each went forth and got pregnant "by a connexion of her own, which was just the result of being left . . . to the tuition of a convict servant maid."[41]

No wonder, then, that Specials—educated convicts—were much in demand as servants. Because such people were uncommon (less than half, probably no more than a third, of the prisoners arriving in Australia at any stage of its penal history could sign their names), they were of value to government, which by the mid-1820s needed a small army of clerks to keep track of convicts' records. The bureaucracy of New South Wales and Van Diemen's Land was almost wholly made up of forgers, none averse to palm oil. Governor Darling complained that "these people are guilty of all sorts of nefarious practices, altering and interpolating the Registers, and cannot be restrained by any fear of punishment or disgrace . . . [T]hey cannot resist a bribe." But there were few free clerks, and so government demands meant that few Specials were assigned.[42]

Nevertheless, private influence sometimes worked. Thus, several wealthy families boasted their convict tutors, who steered the children through *mensa* or tinkled away the eucalyptus-scented afternoon on a slightly warped Broadwood. The first grammar school in Sydney was started by a ruined Irish clergyman, Laurence Halloran (1765–1831), transported at the age of forty-six for forging a tenpenny frank. Certainly he was a better pedagogue than John Mortlock, a former officer in the British Army who had seen service in India and who was made headmaster of a small Hobart grammar school in the 1850s: "To impress myself with a sense of my dignity, and to lighten my spirits, I immediately belaboured several of the boys (particularly those whose parents had never been transported). This refreshed and consoled me."[43]

Because they had known respectability, most Specials found it very difficult to accept their fate. They looked down on the "decent" society of New South Wales and Van Diemen's Land. Some of them were utterly convinced of their own innocence and could not perceive themselves as criminals: How could the mere alteration of a document be compared to house-breaking or mugging? The shock of transportation caused a reflex

of denial, leaving them with an aggrieved posture of superiority to convict trash. They tried to believe that transportation had not ruined the
class position they had sinned to hold.

One such man was a would-be poet, John Grant (1776– ? ), whose
character typified the Special's occasional sense of unreality. He was the
unstable son of a landed English gentleman in Buckinghamshire, who,
trying to better his lot, wooed a titled heiress but found his efforts frustrated by a lawyer in his family circle. In a fit of rage, he shot the solicitor
with a pistol in the buttocks, in full daylight on a London street. His
family connections saved his life; a petition was sent to the daughters of
George III and instead of hanging, he sailed. Grant arrived in Sydney in
May 1804 and within months was asking Governor King for a ticket-of-
leave. Rebuffed, he wrote again: "Why hesitate, Governor King, to do an
act of justice? If you had presented to me the freedom of the Colony as
soon as I landed, you would only have rescued a much-injur'd Gentleman
from Highwaymen and Housebreakers." King took no notice. "You must
feel with me," Grant lamented to his mother,

> the cruelty of keeping one thus upon the footing of the Highwaymen I
> came with in the eye of the Law. . . . But there is in this colony a disposi-
> tion to humble those who come here, on the part of the Civil and Military.

If one ponders the last sentence, it could be no surprise that Governor
King thought Grant quite mad. This opinion was self-fulfilling. King
banished him to Norfolk Island, where he could tell the cormorants
about his innocence and his pretensions to gentility. Grant collapsed
under the stress of three years' isolation and ill-treatment on this remote
settlement, and was invalided back to Sydney in 1808; Macquarie in his
mercy pardoned him, and he returned to England in 1811.[44]

Now and then a Special's sense of superiority would be flavored with
a touch of irony. "Our society now became somewhat improved. Though
I did not hear of any naval or military officers, barristers or doctors of
medicine," wrote John Mortlock, who had been transported for the
attempted murder of his uncle, a clergyman of Christ's College in
Cambridge,

> I could count two Protestant clergymen convicts, one of them a doctor of
> divinity, several solicitors, including one of them an ex-mayor, and many
> Chartists. What a sensation would be caused by the transportation of a
> bishop! The colony was also honoured by the advent of an ex-member of
> parliament, a gentleman at no time treated as an ordinary offender.[45]

Giving themselves airs and graces, most Specials were disliked—and
some detested—by laboring convicts for their flashness and arrogance.

Officialdom could make life difficult for those suspected of freethinking. It was especially sweet to see these uppity nobs reconvicted and sent to a punishment gang on the Blue Mountain roads or at Port Macquarie. "Many of them were so flash that they used to look down on the other class of men, and try to play a game of 'bluff,'" recalled the convict whose memoirs were published under the pseudonym of "Woomera":

> Their hands were very soft . . . [T]hey schemed and wasted their time. In the middle of work I often heard them commence to talk about the fine wine they had drunk at some of the big inns in London—"The Angel at Islington," "The Hole in the Wall," or "The Elephant and Castle," for instance, and some of them had never tasted wine in their lives. At night they began to "blow" about how they had done some of the honest merchants in England out of large and small sums of money. But it was a different tale now—they saw very little money in the road party.[46]

Probably the rank-and-file convicts' resentment of Specials helped consolidate the prejudice, long to be felt in Australia, against brain-workers as "bludgers" or social parasites. Be that as it may, the question of the Specials (who never formed more than a tiny minority of the convicts) bears directly on the much-vexed question of convict solidarity. Here, at least, was one group of convicts that received no trust from the majority and gave no loyalty to it—which only means that the existing class divisions of English society were preserved, as one might expect, among transported felons of all stations.

Much ink has been spilt by Australian historians arguing whether or not convicts in general not only sympathized with one another but also brought these sympathies, tempered by mutual suffering, to the point of "class solidarity." Did they stick by one another as members of an oppressed class? Or were their loyalties so atomized by self-interest as to have no collective reach at all?[47]

At moments of famine and stress, convicts could and did behave ruthlessly to one another. The weak went to the wall among the bond as well as among the free. The Reverend John Morison heard an ex-convict in Van Diemen's Land utter the significant words, whose *reductio ad horrorem* was the cannibalism of Pearce: "What is the use of a friend, but to take the use of him?" "Very comforting doctrine, this," he commented, "and the friendships of some people are more to be dreaded then their enemies."[48]

Convicts were seen to treat one another with special ruthlessness in the chain gangs and the outer penal settlements, such as Macquarie Harbor, Norfolk Island and Moreton Bay. The official strategy of breaking

down their trust in one another by encouraging convict informers undoubtedly worked in these places. "Trusty" convicts, promoted to overseers, could be as brutal as the guards—and worse. Absolute punishment,
such as existed on Norfolk Island under Lieutenant-Colonel James Morisset or at Moreton Bay under Captain Patrick Logan, degrades absolutely; as men are treated, so will they become. But only a tiny fraction
of those transported to Australia spent any time in those penal stations.
Most convicts lived under conditions that sustained and often increased
their sense of mutual oppression; so that, from the earliest days of the
settlement, whole groups of prisoners would stand mute rather than
surrender one of their number to authority, whatever the promised bribes
and rewards. When someone in the late 1790s burned down the only
church in Sydney, Governor John Hunter offered the colossal incentive
of a free pardon, a passage home and £50 to anyone, even a lifer, who
informed on the culprit. "One would have thought that irresistible," he
recalled some years later. "But it brought no evidence; I never learned
who it was; it was a designed thing."[49]

The church was Anglican and the arsonist was undoubtedly Irish.
The Irish convicts had brought a "primitive" collectivism with them on
the transport ships, a common will to stick together that had nothing to
do with ideology (although it would greatly affect the tenor of socialist
movements in Australia a hundred years later) but everything to do with
kin and clan. They were seen, and despised, by English authorities in
Australia as tribal people whose allegiances were not touched by the
work-ethic of Protestant individualism. They were "depraved beyond
conception . . . designing and treacherous," ranted the Reverend Samuel
Marsden from the depths of his bigotry; and their loyalty to one another
could not be broken:

> they consider their Engagements to each other of whatever nature they
> be, as sacred; and when any are detected in the Commission of any Capi-
> tal Crime . . . they will suffer death before they will give Information of
> any of their Accomplices: and when brought to the fatal Tree, will deny
> their Guilt with their last Breath. . . . Thus many of them live and die in
> the most hardened and impenitent State.[50]

The Irish were the largest and most cohesive white minority in penal
Australia, and their folkways were bound to make a deep mark on the
ethos of all convicts and their descendants. The cohesion of the group is
what resists pressure from outside it, and the clannish solidarity of Irishmen seems to have been experienced by many convicts who were not
Irish as a way of resisting the overwhelming power of the organs of State
discipline. Crime is by definition anti-social; criminals are *lumpen* indi-

vidualists. But as Russel Ward pointed out, "When the criminal becomes a long-term convict, his scope for exercising individual cunning is very severely limited, while the forces impelling him towards social, collectivist behavior (within his own group) are correspondingly strengthened."[51] From this rude collectivism, set against the harsh environment of the country and the framework of inquisitorial law, emerged the basic traits of Australian mateship.

There is no doubt about the ties of mutual recognition, sometimes amounting to a non-ideological sort of class loyalty, that could bind convicts together. Strong friendships were forged by repression, and they were so plentiful that one example must do for all. When the convict Mellish had served out his time in Macquarie's New South Wales, he "left the bay" as servant to a married Emancipist couple, who had made their pile in New South Wales and were returning to England. He soon found there were six convict fugitives stowed away on board, two of them friends of his. "The reason I was unhappy was, I could not do by those men as I could wish; I was oblig'd to go out a thieving every night for provishions for those men; to be shoor I brought some tools with me such as would unlock any of the harness casks where the meat was kepd." He stole for them for a month, at great risk, before he was caught and subjected to six weeks of appalling privations, chained in the darkness of the hold. When the ship reached Cape Town, "my flesh was black and blue, and all around the wastebands of my trousers was scratch'd to pieces. . . . I have never so to say been right well since." Yet there is not a breath of resentment in his memoir against the fellow convicts he had kept alive. "They were men that I had a very great respect for, and I do mean to say, that no man will leave behind him a friend in bondage, if they choose to chance the consequences of it."[52]

Visitors to Australia noted what Alexander Harris called the "mutual regard and trust engendered by two men working together in the otherwise solitary bush"—the typical situation of convict shepherds on far out-stations. "Men under these circumstances often stand by one another through thick and thin; in fact it is a universal feeling that a man ought to be able to trust his mate in anything."[53]

Such feelings of trust and recognition could readily run between men who had shared the same experience of servitude. Harris described how, in his wanderings in the Hawkesbury district, he met an Emancipist farmer and public-house keeper who, "like most of those who have risen from the ranks of the prison population by their own efforts" had "a sort of open sturdy manliness about his character which was very agreeable."

He had several convict-servants, who I could see were governed in quite a different manner from those I had met with in my Illawarra jobs under free settlers. The free settlers governed their men with capriciousness and by terror, and so could never trust them beyond their sight; whilst these settlers, who had once been prisoners themselves, seemed rather to obtain a willing obedience, founded on respect for their judgment and fairness; and consequently they could trust their men as well out of their sight as in.[54]

Governor Bligh told the Select Committee in London in 1812 that "the convicts unite with one another, and get on very well." Commissioner Bigge in 1822 pointed out that Emancipist settlers tended not to punish their assigned men out of "sympathy with that condition which was once their own." Ten years later this had not changed; Governor Bourke in 1832 reported that most assigned men hoped to work for Emancipists, preferring "their coarse fare to being better fed and Cloathed with a More opulent Master and less liberty." Such utterances (and there were many more) can only suggest that loyalties between convicts, throughout the life of the System, regularly went beyond personal friendship.[55]

iv

OF COURSE Australia was marked for glory, some wag said (and the saying would be repeated for generations), for its people had been chosen by the finest judges in England.

And clearly, one of the things its people did best was breed. A rough census of New South Wales in 1807 showed a total population of 7,563 people. Of these, 1,430 were women, mostly convicts or Emancipists, and one woman in three was married. But the number of children was very high: 807 legitimate, 1,025 not. One person in four in the colony was a child; more than half the children were illegitimate; and most of them were the offspring of convicts.

In 1828 the first official census revealed that there were at last more free people (20,870) than convicts under sentence (15,728) in New South Wales. Almost half the free population were ex-convicts who had done their time, received their pardons and stayed. Most of the rest were children born in Australia, whose parents were either ex-convicts or "came-free" settlers—soldiers, marines, officials large and small, settlers, emigrants of every kind. This first generation of Australians were born free but were raised in a police state. The term for these native-born "Currency lads" and "Currency lasses" came from monetary slang— "currency" meaning coin or notes that were only good in the colony, makeshift stuff, implying raffishness or worse, unlike the solid virtues of the "Sterling," the free English immigrants. The Currency also called themselves "natives," a word not applied to Aborigines, only to locally born whites.

From England, the identity of these people looked simple: They were seen in a bald, one-dimensional way as "the children of the convicts," heirs of a depraved gene pool, from whom little good could be expected. That many of them did not have convict parents; that many of those who did were not raised by stereotyped villains and whores; that crime may not run in the blood—none of this affected English opinion very much. Sin must beget sin, and the "thief-colony" was doomed to spin forever, at the outer rim of the world, in ever worsening moral darkness. This idea was epitomized in 1819 by one of the many experts who had never been there, the Reverend Sydney Smith, the clerical wit who founded the *Edinburgh Review* and, unfortunately, was sometimes consulted on colonial matters by Peel:

> There can be but one opinion. New South Wales is a sink of wickedness, in which the great majority of convicts of both sexes become infinitely more depraved than at the period of their arrival. . . . It is impossible that vice should not become more intense in such [a] society.[56]

Almost everything that was said about the native-born in England, and by English visitors to Australia up to about 1835, tended to assume that they formed a homogeneous group, the "children of the convicts." However, the native-born did not think of themselves that way—not because they felt up to denying the facts of the colony's birth, but because their society was so much more intricate than England's "instrumental" view of Australia as a convict dump, a society defined by criminality, would allow. In this real society, the children of the free were inextricably mingled in a web of social and economic relations with those of Emancipists. The poor were not all convict-born, the rich were not all free; menial workers as well as Macarthurs had come there free, and there were rough Midases as well as sober tradesmen and illiterate, broken helots among the transported. Some children of convicts grew up fighting for crusts, others had private tutors or went to ladies' schools in Parramatta. Because the native-born were the sons and daughters of all conditions of people, bond and free, they were at every level of colonial Australian society by 1825 and could not be treated as a "class" on their own.[57]

Thinking and writing of them as "the children of the convicts" exposed them to condescension. The very word "convict" carried a crushing load of moral opprobrium. "Atrocious" crimes had put the parents in Australia, with predictable results for the native-born. Few of the observers of colonial life, from generally sympathetic ones like Peter Cunningham to prejudiced Tories like John Bigge—let alone choleric bigots like James Mudie—made allowance for the fact that many of their parents had been transported for small crimes. Such folk were not habitual criminals, still less limbs of that chimera the "criminal class," but ordinary sinners without much opportunity, who had offended the law once and had been caught. But to their moralizing observers, simply to be in Australia against one's will was a proof of wickedness.

In particular, the moral prejudices invoked against convict women— the stereotypes of their boozing, promiscuity, rebelliousness and lack of talent for motherhood—distorted the picture of Emancipist family life, suggesting that the native-born were reared on rum and abandoned to fate. Some of the native-born shared this prejudice against their social "inferiors." They were the smallest group: the sons and daughters of the Exclusives, the high officials and the wealthy free settlers, who believed they were a colonial aristocracy.

The idea that, in the words of a colonial judge in the 1850s, "crime *descends*, as surely as physical properties and individual temperament," was the very axis of the idea of a "criminal class"; it was also, of course, the key reason for all social discrimination by "respectable" Australians against their Others, the Emancipists. But it turned out not to be true. Despite all the jeremiads directed against their origins, despite the widespread perception of a permanent groundswell of crime for which they were supposed to be responsible, the first generations of the native-born turned out to be the most law-abiding, morally conservative people in the country. Among them, the truly durable legacy of the convict system was not "criminality" but the revulsion from it: the will to be as decent as possible, to sublimate and wipe out the convict stain, even at the cost —heavily paid for in later education—of historical amnesia.[58]

This was to be confirmed by the crime statistics in New South Wales. In 1835 W. W. Burton, judge of the New South Wales Supreme Court, speaking at length on the prevalence of crime, declared that it was as though "the whole colony were continually in motion towards the several Courts of Justice." But five years later, reflecting on his experiences on the colonial bench—and on the sensational revelations about Australian vice that had filled the ears of the Molesworth Committee—he protested that the Molesworth report "no more represents the true state of society in New South Wales than an enquiry into the horrible particulars of an ill-regulated gaol in England would represent the state of society in the county in which it is situated."[59]

For instead of growing up depraved, the Currency showed the lowest crime rate of any group. Out of 827 men he had tried in the years 1833 to 1838, 450 (54 percent) were convicts under sentence, 241 (29 percent) were Emancipists, 50 (6 percent) were free emigrants, and only 30 (4 percent) were Australian-born. Moreover, none of the Currency had committed murder or grand larceny; and he had never even heard of one being charged with rape. Of the 30 Currency defendants, 13 (nearly half) were up for horse-stealing or cattle-rustling—which, like poaching in England, ordinary Australians hardly thought were crimes at all.[60]

Then how did the cankered stock of English criminality produce such fresh, green shoots in Australia? Observers like Bigge pondered this and came up with a theory. The children had a "natural aversion" to the spectacle of sin. They "neither inherit the vices nor the feelings of their parents," he reported in 1822. They "felt contempt for the vices and depravity of the convicts *even when manifested in the persons of their own parents*" [emphasis added].[61] The Currency lasses, Cunningham thought, were "anxious to get into respectable service . . . [to] escape from the tutelage of their often profligate parents." So there must have been a general rupture between parents and children, a fissure that traversed whole generations—the young, en masse, rejecting the old, and exiling felonry from their lives as it had been exiled from Mother England. They were so hurt by the behavior of their parents that they resolved, no matter how difficult it was, to be as little like them as possible—to go straight. Thus the "viciousness and indolence" of the parents could be squared with the "honesty and industry" of their children.

But there is little to support this idea. Australia was not only a country of opportunity for the Merinos and their friends—men like John Macarthur, in England a draper's boy, a dynast in the antipodes; it was a frontier society that rewarded hard work at any level, to a degree undreamed-of by the English or Irish poor. The out-of-work blacksmith, reduced to petty theft by lack of opportunity, could soon become a flourishing tradesman in Sydney once his sentence was completed. Hope, effort and luck enabled thousands of Emancipists to make a second start in life, better than anything they had known in their British lives. The difference was biggest of all for unskilled workers, whose chances in England had been nil.

To read what these people said about themselves, instead of what their superiors like Bigge and Cunningham said about them, is to get a different impression. Its main source is the "Memorials," or petitions to the governor asking for land grants, which had, of course, to be accompanied by character references from magistrates and chaplains. By the first census, in 1828, one native-born man in three owned land, and the surviving Memorials (written by men on their own behalf, or by fathers seeking land grants for their sons) show a consistent pattern of family ties: Parents asked for land for their sons, sons petitioned for land grants close by their fathers' farms, and this somewhat confutes the "assumption of parental abandonment and neglect" among the native-born.[62] The language in which the memorials are couched always speaks of fathers as "tender," "respectable," "loving," "honest"; of the sons as "deserving," "sober," "devoted." Part of this, no doubt, is the standard language of scribes making formal addresses; one would not expect to find a petition asking the governor to give sixty acres to the "lazy, brutish, undeserving" son of a "drunken, dissolute, hard-hearted" ex-convict. Yet one may feel that the language reflected social facts as well as epistolary conventions.

By 1828, about one adult Currency man in three owned land, but not all the native-born aspired to. The landless did not want to become agricultural laborers either, since that carried the stigma of working alongside assigned convicts. It was noticed that the Currency shunned farm labor "partly from a sense of pride: for, owing to the convicts being hitherto almost the sole agricultural laborers, they naturally look upon that vocation as degrading in the same manner as white men in slave colonies regard work of any kind, seeing that none *but* slaves *do* work." By the same token, the Currency did not look to the sea for work. The harsh regime on board ship, the absolute authority of the captains and their way of keeping discipline with a rope's end was too much like convict life for their taste.[63]

The great area of opportunity was skilled labor and small trade. It took patience to succeed as a farmer. But a carpenter, joiner, bricklayer, wheelwright, cooper, cobbler or blacksmith—in short, any artisan skilled at one of the basic trades on which transport, construction and storage depended—had success at his fingertips in colonial Australia. There was little demand for luxury trades; the colony could support any number of house-carpenters but not many ivory-turners, perfumers or bookbinders. At the end of the 1820s, a good carpenter could make 7s. 6d. a day in Sydney, whereas his counterpart in London might manage to earn two-thirds that. This was the main reason why, despite the seasoning of "political" workers transported to Australia for their protests against trade and labor conditions in England, no radical ideas took root and no trade-union agitation of any note was heard from either the Emancipists or the Currency in New South Wales. Sweated free labor and the exploitation of child workers were equally unheard of there; it was the convicts who sweated and were exploited. Pay and conditions for skilled workers were so much better there than in England that, relatively speaking, they had no gripes.

The native-born Australians did not look like their parents and grandparents, those dark and often stunted emanations of English slums and mills. As children, they were well if plainly fed, cradled in sunshine, and grew into tall and stringy cornstalks, "like the Americans," the resident naval surgeon Dr. Peter Cunningham remarked in the 1820s, "generally remarkable for that Gothic peculiarity of fair hair and blue eyes." They did not have the typically apple-red cheeks which, some etymologists think, were the origin of that mysterious and durable Australian slang term for an Englishman, "pommy." Their complexion was sallow, and they lost their teeth early. They were punctiliously honest and sober, with "an open manly simplicity of character . . . little tainted with the vices so prominent among their parents."[64]

The men were very "clannish"; mateship and class solidarity were absolutely fundamental to their values. They were great street-fighters. One in, all in: "If a soldier quarrels with one, the whole hive sally to his aid; and often they have turned out at Christmas-time, and beat the *redcoats* fairly into their barracks." The Currency lasses tended to be gauche, pretty, credulous, sexually precocious (virginity had no special value for the "lower classes" on the marriage-market of penal Australia) but astute in improving their lot through matrimony. They married early, "and do not seem to relish the system of concubinage so popular among their Sterling brethren here." They spent a lot of time at the beach and swam "like dab-chicks." They were, in short, very like their seventh-generation descendants.

The Currency were also warmly patriotic. "You cannot imagine," wrote George Thomas Boyes, the sensitive and irritable colonial diarist, from Van Diemen's Land to his wife Mary in far-off England in October 1831,

> such a beautiful Race as the rising generation in this Colony. . . . As they grow up they think nothing of England and can't bear the idea of going there. It is extraordinary the passionate love they have for the country of their birth. . . . There is a degree of Liberty here which you can hardly imagine at your side of the Equator. The whole country round, Mountains and Valleys, Rock Glens, Rivers and Woods, seem to be their own domain; they shoot, ride, fish, go bivouacing in the woods—hunt Opossum and Kangaroos, catch and train parrots. . . . They are in short as free as the Birds of the Air and the Natives of the Forests. They are also connoisseurs in horses, cattle, sheep, pigs, and wool . . . and this they all understand before they can speak that two and two make four.[65]

This would become a common theme of visitors: In the midst of all the constraints of a penal colony, the native-born had developed for themselves a sense of *physical* liberty and kinship with the landscape—like Australians in the 1950s, accepting all manner of censorship, Grundyism and excess police power, but feeling like the freest people on earth because they could go surfing at lunch-time.

Surgeon Peter Cunningham was startled to find that most of them thought Australia's "very miserable-looking" gum trees more beautiful than any oak or elm. (It was contagious, for after a time, he wrote, "I myself, so powerful is habit, began to look upon them pleasurably.") The Currency lad who visited England could hardly wait to get back and tell his friends what a dull time he had, how thin the beer was and how slow the horses. Most of them did not want to visit England at all, because it was so full of thieves.

They also had by the 1820s a peculiar accent, lacking both the euphony of standard English and the glottal patter of Cockney: twangy, sharp, high in the nose, and as utterly unmistakable as the scent of burning eucalyptus.

They shared certain grievances with the Emancipist stock from which so many of them had sprung. The prime one was the general attitude of the colonial Exclusives to labor. Convictry had induced the Exclusives to think of all labor as with "supercilious intolerance." Masters used "to tell [convicts] they have no rights, and to taunt and mock them if they talk about seeking redress for any ill treatment. . . . The habit and the feeling have become rooted in their very nature; and they would wish to treat free people in the same way." Women behaved similarly: "It is most laughable to see the capers some of our drunken old Sterling madonnas will occasionally cut over their Currency adversaries in a quarrel. It is then, 'You saucy baggage, how dare you set up your *Currency* crest at me? I am *Sterling*, and that I'll let you know!' "[66]

By far the most galling manifestation of this—the point at which the colony's penal, police-state nature rubbed incessantly against the free-born—were the restrictions of movement and the farm-constable system. Many Currency lads were wanderers, constantly "on the wallaby track." They would roll their swag and go from one end of New South Wales to the other, picking their work. Most of them carried no identification and, being free, were not required to. Nor did they want to: The convict's pass or ticket, much folded and tattered, was as plain an image of servitude as a scarred back. But fear of escaped convicts had led, by the 1830s, to an oppressive patchwork of regulations, chief among which was the Bushranging Act. Under it, anyone could be arrested on suspicion of being an absconder; and the primitive communications in the outback (and records in the towns) made it hard to prove one's identity. Since police were thinly scattered, most of the arrests were made by "farm constables," "trusty" convicts still under sentence, who knew their sentences would be shortened if they could bring a bolter in.

The result was a widespread system of arbitrary arrest, without *habeas corpus* for innocent men fettered in the crude farm lockup with the "log on their toes." Alexander Harris, whose books *Settlers and Convicts* was the only substantial account of life in penal Australia from the free worker's side, told of one "native lad" who had to spend seven weeks out of three months marching in handcuffs under the Bushranging Act; arrested by a farm constable in a distant area of the Hunter River, he had to walk at a horse's stirrup 250 miles to Sydney. Once cleared, he set out in the opposite direction—southwest, toward the Murrumbidgee—and was arrested again and forced back to Sydney, to prove his name all over again. Such exasperations were so common that the Currency did not even sue for wrongful arrest—but then, they were workingmen and did not have the money to litigate, so they grumblingly accepted their fate in what would become the usual Australian manner: cursing authority, but obeying it all the same. "Whole shoals of men, both emigrant and freed, are daily passing to and fro from one police office to another 'for identification,' " Harris noted. "Yet I have never seen one syllable [written] on the subject."[67]

Common oppressions make common causes, and by the end of Macquarie's governorship, Emancipists and Currency were ranged together against the Exclusives. The Anglophile "aristocracy" was scorned as a thin, derivative elite whose standards had little of benefit to add to the emerging folkways of life in New South Wales. The Currency felt they were disenfranchised and the Emancipists knew they were. Looking for a tribune, they soon found him—a slouching, copper-haired, rasping mixture of Irish rage, English manipulation and pure Australian brashness named William Charles Wentworth (1790–1872), "the Great Native." Wentworth's birth had put him neatly between all factions. He was a Currency bastard begotten by a free man on a convict woman, with more than enough property to qualify as a Merino. But his father, D'Arcy Wentworth, was only free by a hair, and conservatives thought of him as an Emancipist.

The Wentworths came originally from Yorkshire and were related to one of the great English families, the Fitzwilliams. D'Arcy Wentworth, son of a Protestant pub-keeper in Northern Ireland, had been born in Armagh around the year 1762. He grew up a man of great charm, cheerful, gregarious, and liberal in his political views. After duty as a medical ensign in the Irish Volunteers, he went to London to continue his medical studies. The Fitzwilliams gave him social introductions and soon this personable lad was living far beyond his means. He came up on three charges of highway robbery at the Old Bailey in 1787. Acquitted of all three, he was haled before the court again in 1789 on yet another robbery charge. At the start of this fourth trial, Wentworth, who cannot have been too sure of his innocence, asked his counsel to tell the judge that he was going to Botany Bay anyhow; in fact he had got a post as an assistant surgeon. He was acquitted a fourth time, but now he had given his word and had to go. He sailed on *Neptune*, the hell-ship of the Second Fleet. A third of her five hundred convict passengers died, but Wentworth survived and so did a twenty-year-old girl named Catherine Crowley, transported for stealing cloth. By the end of the voyage she was heavily pregnant by D'Arcy Wentworth. Their son, William Charles, was probably born at sea on the way to Norfolk Island, where D'Arcy Wentworth became an assistant in the hospital.

D'Arcy Wentworth went on to make a fortune in land, rum and trade. As a doctor, he was mediocre; but as a public figure, he stood large in the tiny colony. When he died in 1827, the funeral cortege was a mile long. With tact and care, he had managed throughout his life to avoid the crab-basket quarrels and ignore the slights of colonial society. Not even the censorious pen of John Bigge could accuse him of social climbing. "Mr. Wentworth has very rarely mixed in the society of New South Wales altho' he has always been distinguished by propriety of demeanour when invited to partake of it and has been observed to shun rather than court attention."[68] In private, there was plenty of courting. He sired (and supported) at least seven other children by various mistresses in Australia, and his tombstone bore the sly scriptural text, "In my Father's house there are many mansions."

From the beginning, the Exclusives disliked him as a rake, a liberal and a convict manqué. His son William Charles, idolizing his father, heard and resented their whispers. The boy went to school in England and came back to New South Wales in 1810, a rawboned lad with thin skin and blood in his eye, just in time for the first clashes between Macquarie and the Exclusives over the Emancipists' rights to serve as jurors and magistrates. He wrote "pipes" against John Macarthur and Macquarie's lieutenant-governor, Lieutenant-Colonel George Molle of the 46th Regiment, whom Wentworth thought a hypocritical anti-Emancipist. His couplets offered "dirty, grovelling Molle" "some bum-tingling kicks" and a "mutton fist upon thy bleeding nose." No doubt Wentworth, who moved gracelessly but had shoulders like an Irish ox, could have made good on this threat. But since the verse was anonymous and not printed, there was little Molle could do.[69]

In the meantime, William Charles had larger matters on his mind—in particular, the crossing of the Blue Mountains, a feat that he accomplished with Blaxland and Lawson in 1813. He was a public figure in the colony by then, and one of its largest landowners (Macquarie, never adverse to the exercise of patronage, granted him 1,750 acres at Parramatta in 1811 and a further 1,000 for penetrating the ranges). In 1816 he set off to England again to study law. His aims were large: He would study the British Constitution so that he could draft one for Australia; and in the meantime he hoped to marry Elizabeth Macarthur, daughter of John, so as to form a great colonial dynasty, Merino inseminated by Currency. In this he was rashly overconfident, since the fierce, aging John Macarthur well knew that young Wentworth had written an anonymous "pipe" against him before quitting New South Wales.

By 1819, his marriage plans had foundered and his touchiness about his father was more inflamed than ever. When Henry Bennett, an English MP, publicly insinuated that D'Arcy Wentworth had been transported as a convict, William Charles bullied a public retraction from Bennett. Thus, the future "Emancipists' friend" could explode at the mere suggestion that he was an Emancipist's son. He remained hypersensitive about his family name for the rest of his life: "I will not suffer myself to be outstripped by any competitor and I will finally create for myself a reputation which shall reflect a splendour on all who are related to me." In his deeper heart, Wentworth believed as strongly in the "convict stain" as any Englishman or Exclusive, and part of him longed to be English; hence the frustrated ambition of his later life, the creation of a new nobility, derided by his opponents as the "bunyip aristocracy" and modelled on the Whig aristocracy of Georgian England.[70]

At first the Emancipists were not so much his friends as his enemies' enemies. But Wentworth saw that the issue of Emancipists' rights could levitate him quickly into the public eye, since Currency so far outnumbered Sterling in Australia. So he wrote a tract, arguing that Australia should cease to be a jail and become, instead, a free colony with its own elected government, rivalling America in its attraction for the English emigrant. "A native of New South Wales," he put on the title page—the first time an author had claimed Australian identity. Inside, he argued for government by a legislative council, nominated, and a small assembly, elected. Ex-convicts should be able to vote for any candidate and stand for any office. But Wentworth's own conservatism rejected the principle of "one man, one vote"; the legislative council would bear "many resemblances to the House of Lords" while landed property was "the only standard by which the right of electing, or being elected, can in any country be properly regulated." He defended Macquarie's Emancipist policy and bitterly attacked the Exclusives:

> The covert aim of these men is to convert the ignominy of the great body of the people into a hereditary deformity. They would hand it down from father to son, and raise an eternal barrier of separation between their offspring, and the offspring of the unfortunate convict.[71]

His book ran through three editions in Sydney but fell flat in England. "A Botany Bay parliament would give rise to jokes," the Reverend Sydney Smith sniffed in the *Edinburgh Review*, and as for juries, what settlement in New South Wales could produce four dozen men fit to serve on one?[72]

But Wentworth began lobbying in London. Soon after he got there, the King's Bench invalidated all pardons, conditional or absolute, granted by past governors of New South Wales. This was a disaster for the Emancipists (for one thing, it invalidated all their titles to property), and in 1821 they met to draft a petition to the Crown, pointing out the "infinite danger and prejudice" to which it exposed them and demanding the restoration of their rights. "It has been by their Labour, Industry and Exertions," the ex-convicts begged to remind George IV, "that this Your Majesty's Colony . . . has been converted from a barren Wilderness of Woods into a thriving British Colony."[73] Governor Macquarie forwarded the document with strong endorsements to London. It bore 1,368 signatures—a quarter of the Emancipist population of New South Wales.

The secretary of its drafting committee was the ex-convict lawyer Edward Eagar, whose modest practice in New South Wales had been wiped out by Jeffrey Bent. Eagar brought the petition to London, and his fare was paid by the Emancipist doctor William Redfern, who went with them. Wentworth helped them lobby the government for validation of colonial pardons, trial by jury and representative government. They did not succeed—at least, not immediately—but their presence in London helped plant the awareness that Emancipists were not just inferior social abstractions in a distant colony but people of British blood with a cause. Lobbying and letters mattered a great deal in shaping official English policy toward Australia. This was the unintended result of setting up an authoritarian, penal regime there. New South Wales had neither free press nor parliament; English officials did not suppose its governor's reports told the whole sociopolitical story; and so unofficial letters from the antipodes to men of influence soon found their way to upper Tory and Whig circles. Only a free assembly in Australia could have reduced this exaggerated power of private correspondence, by supplying a record of debate on issues. Failing that, lobbyists had to pull what strings they could reach.

In 1823 Wentworth wound up his law studies in London and went to Cambridge. This was merely to brown the crust, as he did not work for a degree. His time was taken up writing a lengthy poem in heroic couplets, his entry for the chancellor's gold medal, whose set subject that year—by a happy coincidence—was "Australasia." If he could win this, he reasoned, he would become a public literary man as well as a lawyer and political aspirant—the thirty-three-year-old Byron of the antipodes. Alas, the Native's verses, creaking with trope and figure, came in second. Yet second place was better than none, especially when viewed from Sydney; and Wentworth's peroration, in which Britain sinks in decadence while

her old values rise brightly in Australia, would be quoted there for years
to come:

> And, oh Britannia! shouldst thou cease to ride,
> Despotic Empress of old Ocean's tide:—
> Should thy tam'd Lion—spent his former might—
> No longer roar the terror of the fight;—
> Should e'er arrive that dark disastrous hour,
> When bow'd by luxury, thou yield'st to power;—
> When thou, no longer freest of the free
> To some proud victor bend'st the vanquish'd knee;—
> May all thy glories in another sphere
> Relume, and shine more brightly still than here;
> May this, thy last-born infant,—then arise,
> To glad thy heart and greet thy parent eyes;
> And Australasia float, with flag unfurl'd.
> A new Britannia in another world.

The poem sank without a trace in England, along with its dedication to
Lachlan Macquarie and its defiant signature, "by W. C. Wentworth, *an
Australasian.*"[74]

He sailed back to Sydney in 1824 with a printing press and started
a newspaper, *The Australian*, the first of a line of nationalistic, pro-
Currency, pro-Emancipist journals whose eventual heir in the 1890s
would be *The Bulletin*. It was meant to compete against the moribund
*Sydney Gazette*, whose every word was vetted by Government House.

Two years earlier, Lachlan Macquarie, hailed in departure as the
"Patriot-Chief," had retired to England, and to his obsessive, time-
wasting efforts to rebut the criticism of the Exclusives' allies, chiefly
Bigge and Marsden. His successor was another Scottish protégé of Wellington's, Brigadier-General Sir Thomas Brisbane (1773–1860). Brisbane
had one main thing on his mind. He had been instructed to carry out
Bigge's recommendations that security and discipline be tightened up
in the colony, so that it would once more become a place of dread and
cease to be seen by the poor as one of possible opportunity. Macquarie's
detractors had accused him of granting too many tickets-of-leave too early;
Brisbane would cut down their number and make sure that sentences
were fully served. He had Norfolk Island reopened as a place of terrible
secondary punishment, "the *ne plus ultra*," as he put it "of convict degradation." But at the same time, he realized that the colony had grown
to the point where not every detail could be overseen by the governor's
office. To the dismay of the Exclusives, he decided to free the press, thus
giving Wentworth his inch.

The Native Son promptly grabbed a mile. In a few months *The Aus-*

*tralian* became so popular that most native-born Australians and every Emancipist accepted him as their tribune. Nobody in Australia had ever built a political base so strongly or so fast. In speeches and editorials, Wentworth hammered away at the issues of jury trial and political representation for Currency and Emancipists, at the prejudices and pretensions of the Exclusives. On the thirty-seventh anniversary of white settlement in Australia, January 26, 1825, eighty of the leading Currency met at a Sydney hotel for a banquet given by Wentworth and Redfern. Michael Massey Robinson, the convict bard who had been Macquarie's poet laureate (to his pique, the post was not renewed by Brisbane) was seventy-nine now and doddery from years of rum; but he roused himself to compose an Emancipists' toast in jingling couplets. It disclaimed Republican sentiments; the Emancipists were Britons reclaiming their ancient rights. Mercy and Justice made the allegorical appearances and agreed to foil the plans of the Exclusives: "Your names shall, unstain'd, to your children go forth / Distinguished for virtue—remember'd for worth." It ended with glasses raised to Australia:

> Then to *thee* shall our hearts' purest homage be given,
> And the toast that succeeds be: *"The land, boys, we live in,"*

Governor Brisbane sympathized, up to a point, with such feelings. He hardened the line on convicts under sentence, but his policy toward the Emancipists was virtually an extension of Macquarie's; and he thought Exclusivist attitudes not only pretentious but unworkable, given the human material of which Australia was composed. He was also tolerant in religious matters. Although he was not fond of Irish Catholics, to whose "barbarous ignorance" he ascribed "every murder or diabolical crime that has been committed in the Colony since my arrival," he felt the best way of saving them from barbarism was for the government to subsidize the building of their long-delayed diocesan church in Sydney to the tune of £3,000, a proposal that struck horror into Protestant hearts.[75] He also incurred Marsden's wrath by suggesting that the Protestant clergy should live on their stipends, not their trade. For these reasons as well as his amateur passion for astronomy, the Exclusives nicknamed him "the stargazer" and bombarded their official contacts in London with hate-letters about him. He was recalled to England at the end of 1825, but he tacitly showed his opinion of the Macarthurs and Marsdens by allowing Wentworth and his friends to hold a public meeting in Sydney whose object was to frame a farewell address to him.

This was the first public political meeting of any kind ever held in Australia, and Wentworth made the most of it, turning it into a forum from which to dare "the yellow snakes of the colony" (meaning the

Exclusives) to come out of their holes. The Exclusives had pursued Macquarie and now Brisbane with "a deadly hostility," "a system of persecution," private calumnies of every sort, turning the public and ministry of England into "the dupes of their habitual and filthy misrepresentations"; but now, where were they? Not "manfully" opposing him and his majority, but skulking in silence. All this robust invective, and more, was duly reported in *The Australian.*

But the reforms that the Emancipists and Currency wanted were slow in coming. In 1823 a British Act of Parliament had created legislative councils for both Van Diemen's Land and New South Wales, whose administrations were formally separated. This was a slight gain, for it meant that the governor was no longer a complete autocrat. But the councils were tiny, appointed by the governor himself, and could do no more than advise; only the governor could initiate a new law in the colony. In 1828 another act increased the size of the legislative council to fifteen people, none elected, all appointed. Not until 1842 did the legislative council acquire members who could present issues for public debate—twenty-four men out of thirty-six. But each representative had to own at least £2,000 in landed property, so that, even if all its members were not "pure Merinos," they had to be as rich as one before getting elected. As a democratic body, this "Squatters' Council" left much to be desired. Wentworth, irresistible in coarse oratory and an expert on procedure, became its de facto leader. But transportation to New South Wales had been abolished in 1840, and the convict presence in New South Wales, which stood around 45 percent of the total white population at the time of Brisbane's departure, had dwindled to a mere 12 percent. The social tensions of convictry were winding down (though not in Van Diemen's Land) and the role of the Emancipists' tribune was less politically useful. The issue of Emancipists' rights fizzled out before it could create an Australian democracy.

Meanwhile, the prospects for the convicts themselves had grown considerably worse. Brisbane had begun to re-convert Australia into a place of dread for the lower classes of Britain. The process did not stop with him. Between 1825 and 1840, the separate colonies of New South Wales and Van Diemen's Land found their penal systems refined, expanded and rendered ever more efficient and excruciating. This work was begun by two military martinets: Lieutenant-General Sir Ralph Darling, who governed New South Wales from 1825 to 1831, and Lieutenant-Colonel Sir George Arthur, who ran Van Diemen's Land from 1824 to 1836. Vast differences—of character, ideals and methods—lay between these two men. But their styles of oppression and philosophies of reform shaped Australia during the last years of the Georges.

# II

## To Plough Van Diemen's Land

IN CONVICT LORE, Van Diemen's Land always had the worst reputation for severity. Its name induced a *frisson* that later became integral to Australian culture, and earlier ballads refer to it with a kind of passive dread lacking in the more defiant convict-songs of New South Wales. It was the very quintessence of punishment:

> Come all you gallant poachers that ramble void of care,
> While walking out one moonlit night with gun and dog and snare,
> With hares and lofty pheasants in your pocket and your hand,
> Not thinking of your last career upon Van Diemen's Land.
>
> It's poor Tom Brown from Nottingham, Jack Williams and poor Joe,
> They were three daring poachers, boys, the country well did know;
> At night they were trepanned by the keepers hid in sand—
> For fourteen years transported, boys, upon Van Diemen's Land.
>
> The very day we landed upon the fatal shore,
> The planters they stood round us full twenty score or more;
> They ranked us up like horses and sold us out of hand,
> They roped us to the plough, brave boys, to plough Van Diemen's Land.
>
> The cottage that we lived in was built of sods and clay,
> And rotten straw for bed, and we dare not say nay,
> Our cots were fenced with fire, to slumber when we can,
> To drive away wolves and tigers come by Van Diemen's Land.
>
> It's oft-times when I slumber I have a pleasant dream:
> With my pretty girl I've been roving down by a sparkling stream;
> In England I've been roving with her at my command,
> But I wake broken-hearted upon Van Diemen's Land.
>
> Come all you gallant poachers, give hearing to my song:
> I give you all my good advice, I'll not detain you long:

O lay aside your dogs and snares, to you I must speak plain,
For if you knew our miseries you'd never poach again.

The reputation of Van Diemen's Land as the convicts' hell was gradually acquired. At first the place seemed equally miserable for bond and free, in the way that any new Australian settlement did: coarse, dangerous, and plagued by shortages. Its reputation for severity began modestly with Lieutenant-Governor Thomas Davey (1758–1823), who ran Van Diemen's Land from 1813 to 1816.

Davey was a Devon man, a lieutenant-colonel in the Royal Marines, who, a quarter-century before, had sailed to Botany Bay as an eager young first lieutenant on the First Fleet. By the end of 1792, he was back in England; but the colonial bug had bitten Davey, and by 1810, when he learned of the death in Hobart Town of his old marine comrade David Collins, he thought the antipodes might offer a way of advancement. Davey got Lord Harrowby, a liberal Tory cabinet member who came from the same Devon village as himself, to lobby for his appointment as lieutenant-governor of Van Diemen's Land. It was confirmed, and he arrived in Sydney in 1812 with John Beaumont, the son of his patron, in tow as his secretary (but without his luggage, which had gone on another ship and been captured by an American privateer).

Administratively, Van Diemen's Land was an appendage of New South Wales, not a separate colony; much depended on good relations between Davey and his governor, Lachlan Macquarie. The two men hated one another on sight. Davey thought Macquarie a Scottish prig; and Macquarie considered his new lieutenant-governor a wastrel and a drunk, who manifested "an extraordinary degree of frivolity and low buffoonery in his Manners."

So he did. Davey marked his arrival in Hobart Town in February 1813 by lurching to the ship's gangway, casting an owlish look at his new domain and emptying a bottle of port over his wife's hat. He then took off his coat, remarking that the place was as hot as Hades, and marched uphill to Government House in his shirtsleeves. Nicknamed "Mad Tom" by the settlers, he would later make it his custom to broach a keg of rum outside Government House on royal birthdays and ladle it out to the passersby.[1]

In the past, Davey was said to have tampered with his regimental payroll. Macquarie was given explicit orders from London that Davey could not have a free hand with public money, and he set out with gusto to cramp his lieutenant-governor's style. Davey was not even allowed to draw treasury bills, construct buildings or make contracts for shipping without Macquarie's approval, which, given the distance between Hobart and Sydney, would take months to get. Consequently, Macquarie was furious when Davey, in his zeal to suppress bushranging—which seemed ready to take over Van Diemen's Land by 1814—proclaimed martial law throughout the island without consulting him. Davey, for his part, was sure that Macquarie had encumbered him with regulations out of spite; that he did not understand the problems of Van Diemen's Land (as his ill-worded offer of amnesty to bushrangers in May 1814, unintentionally giving them carte blanche to commit any crime short of murder until the end of the year, indeed suggested); that he was hamstringing the island's economy by buying wheat from India instead of Van Diemen's Land; and that he used the island as a dump for hundreds of Sydney convicts who were too turbulent, lazy or brutish to be useful in New South Wales.

There was truth in all these grievances, but Macquarie went on papering Downing Street with reports denouncing Davey until, in 1816, "Mad Tom" was relieved of his lieutenant-governorship and put out to pasture as a farmer, at which he failed. He left behind him, as much through Macquarie's mistakes as his own, a sub-colony with a growing reputation for unmanageability and violence, where bushranging had become so flagrant as to border on a general convict uprising. However, the administrative chaos, the lack of records and the prevalence of embezzlement in Hobart were of Davey's own making.

It fell to the next lieutenant-governor, William Sorell (1775–1848), to repair the damage. He summed up the state of the island in a pessimistic memo in which he declared that it held "a larger portion, than perhaps ever fell to the same number in any Country, of the most depraved and unprincipled people in the Universe," and was dragged down by

> its long disordered state from a Banditti which has subsisted for years, with connexions ramified throughout the Country; the retransportation of the worst Convicts from Sydney; the great influx of Convicts to a Colony of such limited institutions, and their diffusion all over the Island; the difficulty attending the punishment of serious Offences, and . . . the want of a court of Criminal Judicature; and the Insufficiency of the Lower Police, in which (from the difficulty of obtaining with the present rate of payment the service of respectable people) Convicts are unavoidably too largely employed.[2]

Sorell was a far better man than Davey, with no weakness for the bottle. He too was a soldier, and had served with the 31st Regiment since 1790. In 1807, he was made deputy adjutant-general of the British forces at the Cape of Good Hope, which gave him some previous administrative experience. Skillful, tactful and patient, but with a steel backbone, he seemed an ideal choice to run a fractious place like Van Diemen's Land, with its bloody-minded population and long delays in orders. His only flaw, which Macquarie reluctantly overlooked, was a taste for fornication; he had abandoned his wife and seven children and had taken up while at the Cape with a Mrs. Kent, the wife of a brother officer, who bore him several more offspring and, to the scandal of many, was installed in Government House as the lieutenant-governor's lady.[3]

Sorell broke Michael Howe's gang and hanged most of its members, thus stemming the tide of banditry that seemed set to sluice all law-abiding people off the island. With troops and police, he made the rich farmland of the upper Derwent and the Clyde at least partially safe for settlers. He systematized land grants and cleaned up the Augean stables of government bookkeeping Davey had left. He tried, but failed, to regulate the chaotic slippages of debased currency. He built convict barracks and laid the foundations of the "system of perpetual reference and control" over convicts that would become the bureaucratic masterpiece of his successor, George Arthur. Under his rule, the free population of Van Diemen's Land (including Emancipists) rose from 2,546 in 1817 to 6,525 in 1824; the total population, from 3,114 to 12,464. This meant an enormous proportional increase in the convict population. At the start of Sorell's regime, convicts made up not quite 18 percent of the white populace of Van Diemen's Land; by 1822, the figure was 58 percent. New means of terror had to be devised to keep them docile, and Sorell came up with an effective one. In 1821 he founded a small penal settlement at Macquarie Harbor, as a "Place of Ultra Banishment and Punishment" for convicts who had committed second crimes in the colony and appeared to be turning into bushrangers. For ten years, this would be the worst spot in the English-speaking world.

ii

MACQUARIE HARBOR lies at latitude 42° 14' S., longitude 145° 10' E., on the west coast of Tasmania. As you approach it, sea and land curve away to port in a dazzle of white light, diffused through the haze of the incessantly beating ocean. All is sandbank and shallow; the beach that stretches to the northern horizon is dotted with wreckage, the impartial boneyard of ships and whales. No one has ever lived there or ever will. To starboard, there is a sharp jumble of rocks.

To enter the harbor, you must steer between this headland and another rock, Entrance Island, that marks the southern tip of the sandbars. There is no more than fifty yards between them, and at full tidal flow, the neck of water has a glossy, swollen look, ominous to seamen. Macquarie Harbor is one of the few large bodies of tidal water in the world (covering some 150 square miles), with a bottleneck entrance that faces west. Moreover, it looks directly into the Roaring Forties; the prevailing winds are northwesterly, and the waves of the Southern Ocean have the entire circumference of the world in which to build their energy before they crash on this pitiless coast. And so, when tide sets against wind and millions of tons of water a minute come boiling through the entrance, frightful seas rise. Worse, there is a sandbar dead across the entrance, with only eleven feet of water over it at spring tide. For these and other reasons, the place is called Hell's Gates. It was the first thing that Irish and English convicts saw when their transport ship sailed in, a hundred and sixty years ago.

Sorell made no bones about the purpose of Macquarie Harbor. He commissioned its first commandant, Lieutenant John Cuthbertson of the 40th Regiment, with powers as magistrate and justice of the peace, so that he could hear and determine all charges against convicts and punish them with solitary confinement up to 14 days and floggings not in excess of 100 lashes. The place, he wrote, was for "the most disorderly and irreclaimable convicts," and the system must be "strict and uniform." "You will consider," he wrote in his standing orders,

> that the constant, active, unremitting employment of every individual in very hard labour is the grand and main design of your settlement. They must dread the very idea of being sent there. . . . You must find work and labour, even if it consists in opening cavities and filling them up again. . . . Prisoners upon trial declared that they would rather suffer death than be sent back to Macquarie Harbour. It is the feeling I am most anxious to be kept alive.[4]

To achieve this "grand and main design," the Macquarie Harbor convicts would be loaded at Hobart into ships without bunks or hammocks; they had to sprawl as best they could on the stone ballast in the hold:

> If they had a blanket it was all very well; but I think . . . out the 35 men they mustered 4 blankets. I recollect on one occasion . . . there was one prisoner who had neither jacket nor trowsers; the commanding officer gave him a bit of canvas, and I have frequently, when at Macquarie Harbour, seen men, 30 or 40 in that state, who have been on board the vessel for five or six weeks.[5]

Those weeks were spent at sea, beating north to Macquarie Harbor against the prevailing winds. Once off Hell's Gates, stuck in a northwesterly, it could be days before a ship could get in. The Quaker missionary James Backhouse went there in 1832 and described the midwinter passage through the Gates. His ship had to wait close-reefed in a storm outside the sandbar while the semaphore on Entrance Island waggled its message, through relay signals, to the distant settlement. At last the harbor pilot appeared in a six-oared boat rowed by convicts, and when he came aboard

> he commanded the women and children to go below . . . and advised me to go below too. I replied, that if we were lost I should like to see the last of it, for the sight was awfully grand. . . . The pilot went to the bows, and nothing was now to be heard through the roar of the wind and the waves, but his voice calling to the helmsman, the helmsman's answer, and the voices of the men in the chains, counting off the fathoms.

As the vessel bore in toward the sandbar, albatrosses circled her; then the bar itself was seen, a pale blurred whaleback in the dark water.

> The fathoms decreased, and the men counted off the feet, of which drew 7½, and there were but 7 in the hollow of the sea, until they called out 11 feet. At this moment a huge billow carried us forward on its raginghead into deep water. The pilot's countenance relaxed; he looked like a man reprieved from the gallows, and coming aft, shook hands with each individual, congratulating them on a safe arrival in Macquarie Harbor.[6]

Past the entrance, past another rust-streaked rock named Bonnet Island, the harbor opens to view. It is so long that its far end is lost in the grayness. The water is tobacco-brown with a urinous froth, dyed by the peat and bark washed into it by Australia's last wild river, the Gordon, which flows into the eastern end of the harbor. The sky is gray, the headlands gray, receding one behind the other like flat paper cut-outs. It is an utterly primordial landscape of unceasing interchange, shafts of pallid light reaching down from the low sky, scarves of mist streaming up from impenetrable valleys, water sifting forever down and fuming perpetually back. Macquarie Harbor is the wettest place in Australia, receiving 80 inches of rain a year.

The settlement was twenty miles back from the harbor entrance. One sailed to it past ironic names: Liberty Point, Liberty Bay, the Butt of Liberty. As their boat moved slowly to its anchorage—there was no hurry now, for prison time had superseded the time of the real world—the convicts must have begun to realize their final imprisonment in great space. Then coastal scrub, dreadful in its monotony, was so thick that a cat could hardly get ashore; the iron-laden rocks would tear the soles off your feet. Beyond them the hills rose, tier on tier of them, dominated by the 4,700-foot peak of Frenchman's Cap—named, in irony, after the

Phrygian headgear that had symbolized liberty, equality and brotherhood to the French a generation before. Below its smooth half-dome of basalt, veiled most of the year by clouds, the trees began.

The logging of these trees was the economic purpose of the settlement, and before the convicts arrived no man had ever touched them. The most prized kind was the Huon pine, *Decydium cupressinum*, which grew in great stands along the Gordon River. They attained a height of 70 feet and a circumference of 15 feet, and some of them had been saplings when Augustus Caesar was a child. Huon pine was the best ships' timber on earth—springy, close-grained, easy to work, and so rot-proof that there are still Huon trunks felled by convicts in the 1820s and bearing their ax-marks lying intact along the shores of Macquarie Harbor today. In one year, 2,869 of these trunks were felled, sawn up and loaded for transport to Hobart.[7] There were other valuable trees as well: lightwood *(Acacia melanocylon)*, a lovely semi-hard timber that worked like walnut and had the grain and figure of Spanish mahogany, much prized by colonial shipwrights; celery-top pine *(Podocarpus asplemfolius)*, good for masts and spars; and myrtle *(Betula antarctica)*, whose wood resembled beech and was used by wheelwrights.

The prisoners were quartered on an island in the middle of the harbor, known as Sarah Island (now Settlement Island). Today the trees have reclaimed it, and the pink underfired bricks of its walls have all but dissolved back into their original clay; here and there one can make out the plan of a cell or a passage, and fragments of carved lintel repose like fragments of a botched, weak culture among the embrangling thickets. In the 1820s, however, the island was bare of forest, covered with buildings, fenced with sawn paling fences and protected against the northeast gales by tall lath windbreaks. It had sawpits and shipbuilding yards, a stone penitentiary, a bakehouse and a tannery, and trim, cold barracks. Of all the sites that could have been chosen for a settlement at Macquarie Harbor, this was the most windswept and barren; even the water and firewood had to come by boat from the mainland. But it was also the most secure.

At 6 a.m., the convicts were herded into boats and ferried to the mainland to cut timber. The settlement had no draft animals, because horses and bullocks rarely survived the voyage from Hobart and, in any case, there was not enough grass there to feed them. So the ponderous trunks, some weighing twelve tons, had to be hauled down a crude corduroy slipway of logs, known as a "pine-road," laid on the forest floor. At the tideline, the logs—sometimes a hundred at a time—were chained together in rafts and towed behind whaleboats across the harbor to the sawpits. When they got the raft back to Sarah Island, the worst part of the prisoners' work began: grappling the logs ashore with handspikes, struggling for hours up to their waists in icy water.

A small minority of luckier prisoners was chosen to build boats on the Sarah Island slips under the eye of Mr. Hoy, the master shipwright. Over the eleven years of its existence, the Macquarie Harbor settlement turned out a surprising number of vessels, all made from local timber. Hoy alone was responsible for the 200-ton bark *William IV*, four brigs of 130 tons each, three 50-ton cutters, five 25-ton schooners, twenty-two launches of 5 to 10 tons, and forty-six small craft of various types.

The convict's daily ration was 1 pound of meat, 1¼ pounds of bread, 4 ounces of oatmeal or hominy, and salt. The meat was brine-cured pork or beef, two or three years old; Surgeon Barnes noted that it often had to be destroyed "as being too bad for the convicts to consume," and that in his own eighteen months at Macquarie Harbor he himself had eaten fresh meat no more than six times.[8]

The officers would vary their diet by shooting kangaroos. The hunt "relieved the dreariness and monotony of a Station and Duty, which must otherwise in numerous instances have originated discontent and probably insubordination." They also ate wombats, which they roasted like piglets ("a most delicious dish," one visitor wrote) and the echidnas, or spiny anteaters, which with a stuffing of sage and onion were vaguely reminiscent—if one closed one's eyes—of roast goose.[9] Fish could not live in Macquarie Harbor; the peat washed down by the Gordon River poisoned them. The river had big eels in it, and a giant freshwater cray-fish (*Astacopsis gouldii*, named after the convict artist William Buelow Gould, who was the first to draw and describe one), and mud crabs with fifteen-inch claws.

The convicts, of course, never got fresh meat, let alone the other exotica of Macquarie Harbor; nor did they get greens. Sorell urged Cuth-bertson to grow as many vegetables as possible "as the sure mode of preventing scurvy," but the incessant rain defeated most efforts at gar-dening in the mean, gravelly soil of the settlement. Hence scurvy was endemic there. It abated somewhat toward the middle of 1822, when lime juice and potatoes arrived from Hobart, but by January 1823 "it was again increasing rapidly, and in short there were very few who had not more or less of the disease."[10]

By ferrying topsoil and humus across to Sarah Island, which had little good earth, convicts did manage to grow vegetables "of a quality and size which would not have disgraced the stalls of Covent Garden," but these small crops were all reserved for the officers and the civil establishment. Phillip Island, about four miles down the harbor from the settlement, had better soil and potatoes were grown there—about forty tons a year, which were not issued to the prisoners either.[11] They could have as much water as they wanted, Surgeon Barnes added with no conscious effort at irony; but "other sources of comfort or luxury could not be provided, as it was an insulated situation."[12]

Such was light punishment, routine at Macquarie Harbor. If a convict was balky or insolent, he would be deprived of meat and forced to perform the same work on a protein-free diet. That was the second grade of punishment, and the third was to be ironed with clumsy leg-fetters, weighing 12, 18 or up to 45 pounds, riveted round his ankles and linked by a chain. An ironed man was issued leather gaiters to keep the basils, or rings, from wearing through his flesh. Before long, however, the wet chafing of the iron and the stiff hide started ulcers and scraped their ankles down to the bone.

By far the worst work was driving piles, under water and in chains, for the slipways. If that did not break a man down, he could be left overnight on tiny Grummet Island, half a mile off Sarah Island. According to a convict named Davies (his given name is lost) who spent several years at Macquarie Harbor, it was

> a perpendicular Rock Fifty Feet above the levil of the Sea about 40 yards long and 8 wide—a rude stairs in the cliffs is the only road to a truly Wretched Barracks Built with Boards and Shingles (the timber quite green) into which 79 men were often confined in so crowded a state as to be scarcely able to lay down on their sides—to lay on their backs was out of the Question.[13]

To sleep on this rock, in Surgeon Barnes's view, was "very severe indeed, although it was considered a minor punishment." No convict could land on Grummet without being soaked, so he had to sleep either naked or in wet clothes, without fire or blankets.

Half-starved, chilled to the bone, forced to labor twelve hours a day in winter and sixteen in summer, sleeping on a wet rock under the driving rainsqualls of the Southern Ocean, aching with rheumatism and stinking from dysentery, afflicted by saltwater boils and scurvy, some convicts nevertheless remained defiant.[14] Hence flogging was a daily event, and Davies noted down the sentences handed out in his time by Cuthbertson, "the most Inhuman Tyrant the world ever produced I think, since the reign of Nero. . . . Oppression and Tyranny was his motto, he had neither Justice nor compassion for the naked starved & wretched, Humanity was a virtue he did not acknowledge." Neglect of work got 25 lashes, insolence 25. Losing an item from one's "slops"— the cotton duck government-issue work clothes—meant 50 lashes and three months in irons, even if the garment had been stolen by another prisoner. Tools, in that remote settlement, were irreplaceable, and so 50 lashes and three months' irons were meted out to anyone who broke "a Saw, Axe, Spade, Oar or any other tool no matter how, as [Cuthbertson] did not admit Accidents, he would say it was Carelessness." For robbing the stores, or attempting to escape, or striking an overseer, a convict got 100 lashes and six months in irons. Davies's manuscript gives a vivid picture of the daily blood-ritual:

> The Cats and the way they were made and used were the most Dreadful things that can be thought of. They had 9 tails or rather thongs, each four feet long, just 3 times the thickness of the Hobart Town cats. Consequently it took 3 pair [of regulation cat-'o-nine-tails] to make one at this settlement. . . . [E]ach tail had on it seven Overhand Knots and was whipped, some with wire ends some with waxed ends. It was left to the decision of the Commandant which should be used.
>
> The place of punishment was a low point almost levil with the sea, and just above high water mark was a planked Gangway 100 yards long. By the side of it in the center stands the Triangles to which a man is tied with his side towards the platform on which the Commandant and the Doctor walked so that they could see the man's face and back alternately.
>
> It was their costome to walk 100 yards between each lash; consequently those who received 100 lashes were tied up from one Hour to One Hour and a Quarter—and the moment it was over unless it were at the Meal Hours or at Nights he was immediately sent to work, his back like Bullock's Liver and most likely his shoes full of Blood, and not permitted to go to the Hospital until next morning when his back would be washed by the Doctor's Mate and a little Hog's Lard spread on with a piece of Tow, and so off to work . . . and it often happened that the same man would be flogged the following day for Neglect of Work.[15]

On an average, over the five years 1822 to 1826, there were 245 prisoners at Macquarie Harbor. Of these, seven men in ten were flogged for various offenses, mainly "rebelliousness," "insolence" or "refusal to work." In that period the scourgers inflicted a total of 33,723 lashes— 6,744 per year, meaning a little over 40 per man, each stroke meticulously noted in the commandant's ledger.

Convicts distrusted one another, because the system was astute enough to use convicts as guards. All the constables at Macquarie Harbor were convicts, pressed into service by the military commandant. So were the floggers, the chief constable and the chain-gang overseers. The result was "the most tyrannical system that can be imagined." If a convict constable failed to report some insubordination, word of his cover-up would usually get back to the military command and he would be flogged. If he did report it, and the disobedient convict was flogged, the other prisoners would hate him all the more. The worst thing the military could do to a convict constable, therefore, was to strip him of his rank and throw him back unprotected, among the prisoners. To survive at all, the constables had to ride an ascending spiral of vigilance and brutality; and the taste of arbitrary power was an elixir to men who had lost every other source of self-esteem:

> There was a man of the name of Anderson at Macquarie Harbour, and that individual seemed to delight in seeing his fellow-convicts punished; and I believe scarcely a day passed over without four or five, and in some cases 16 or 17 individuals, being flogged on the report of that man.... Any man that he had a spite against, he would go before the commanding officer and swear that he had been idle; of course the man ... would receive a flogging.[16]

The officers at Macquarie Harbor tended to be mediocre and harassed men whose skills, in the Army's view, deserved no better reward; nobody who could get a better post wanted this one, and so "it was a most difficult matter to select individuals from a regiment to fill such a post."[17] So they tended to run the settlement by the book, and endless abuses were possible within the formal chain of command. Yet the more capricious the convict-overseer system was, the better it "worked," since it demoralized the convicts as a group and made them weaker.

The jailers found other means to atomize the convicts, "to divide them as much as we could" and so frustrate their obsessive conspiracies to escape:

> It is only the keeping their minds and their bodies constantly exercised that will prevent the commission of crimes. We invariably found, if the convicts were allowed to be idle, that there was always some new plan, either an attempt to make an escape or a personal injury to the other convicts in agitation; it was not in apportioning their work so much as it was in distributing them in various gangs, so that a man who was in one gang today should not be in the same gang tomorrow.[18]

There was reason to watch the refractory, because a convict would occasionally incite his mates to defiance and try to call a strike. In one twenty-man logging gang in 1825, Commandant James Butler reported to Arthur, an Irishman named William Pearse "stepped out and urged the others not to labour any more—that the Commandant would not flog but merely confine them, which they could well bear, tho' they could not stand flogging—and called the Constables a damned set of villains." Butler gave him 25 lashes.[19]

Prisoners would go to extreme lengths to get away from Macquarie

Harbor, even for a little while. For example, two men would arrange for one to gash the other with an ax or a hoe; the victim would then swear out a charge and other convicts would step forward as witnesses. Since there was no court at Macquarie Harbor, they would all have to be shipped back to Hobart for trial. In court, their testimony would become vague and contradictory, and in the fog of lies the case would have to be dismissed. Prisoners detained on capital charges, waiting for the ship back to Hobart, could not by law be flogged or otherwise punished for a lesser offense until they had been tried for the hanging crime; hence "they become turbulent and insolent, cut their irons and injure the Gaol walls, besides setting an extremely bad example in a Station like this."[20]

If a man was so fortunate as to be sent back to Hobart as a witness in a capital crime, he had a good chance of never returning to Macquarie Harbor. The strict *omertà* among convicts there virtually ensured that he would be beaten up or killed for ratting on a mate. In 1827 nine prisoners were charged with the murder of a particularly hated convict constable, George Rex. Down they went to Hobart, where the attorney-general's case against them failed on a technicality. The five convict prosecution witnesses at once begged Lieutenant-Governor Arthur to be transferred to other settlements. "Our circumstances is at present very Critical and not safe, agoing to Macquarie Harbour again—there are such Characters there that would do us a great injury if not Terminate our Existence, as we was sent up to prosecute those men for Murder." Three of them, "through the intercession of friends" who knew Arthur, were transferred to other penal stations; the other two went back to Macquarie Harbor, where they were indeed killed.[21]

Other prisoners would simply murder an overseer or a prisoner so that they could be hanged in Hobart. T. J. Lemprière, who worked for a time as storekeeper in the commissariat at Macquarie Harbor, described how one such man, by the name of Trennam, had reasoned this out. Trennam stabbed a fellow prisoner on Grummet Island and was in jail awaiting transfer to Hobart and the gallows. Why, the chaplain asked, had he done it? Because he was "tired of his life," Trennam answered, and hoped to hang. Then why did he not drown himself, instead of murdering a fellow creature?

> "Oh," he replied, "the case is quite different. If I kill myself I shall immediately descend to the bottomless pit, but if I kill another I would be sent to Hobart Town and tried for my life; if found guilty, the parson would attend me, and then I would be sure of going to Heaven." He was asked if he had any animosity towards his victim; he replied in the negative. Would he have killed any of the officers? Certainly, if they had given him the same chance. Would he have killed his interrogator, the Chaplain? "Yes, as soon as anyone else."[22]

Even starker mutations were seen in the moral void produced by Macquarie Harbor. A group of prisoners were being led in single file through the forest when, without provocation or warning, one of them crushed the skull of the prisoner in front of him with his ax. Later he explained that there was no tobacco to be had in the settlement; that he had been a smoker all his life and would rather die than go without it; so, in the torment of nicotine withdrawal, he had killed the man in order to be hanged himself. At least he could get a twist of nigger-head shag in Hobart before he died.[23]

Such bizarre events became so common that the commandant, with the permission of the lieutenant-governor, ordered a public hanging at Macquarie Harbor. The gallows were raised, the felons were all mustered and the three condemned prisoners were marched forth; but, alas for the majesty of Law and the moral power of the spectacle,

> their execution produced a feeling, I should say, of the most disgusting description. . . . So buoyant were the feelings of the men who were about to be executed, and so little did they seem to care about it, that they absolutely kicked their shoes off among the crowd as they were about to be executed, in order, as the term expressed by them was, that they might "die game"; it seemed . . . more like a parting of friends who were going a distant journey on land, than of individuals who were about to separate from each other for ever; the expressions used on that occasion were "Good bye, Bob" and "Good bye, Jack," and expressions of that kind, among those in the crowd, to those who were about to be executed.[24]

Macquarie Harbor would remain a colonial benchmark for some time —the nadir of punishment, until it was shut down and then exceeded by Norfolk Island. Sorell himself left Van Diemen's Land in 1824. His reputation had been very much undermined by colonial gossips, particularly by a malevolent former officer in the Rum Corps named Anthony Fenn Kemp, who had risen to wealth as a grazier and trader in Van Diemen's Land and out of sheer obsessive contentiousness had appointed himself Sorell's *bête noire.* Perhaps it was Kemp's snarling recitations of the lieutenant-governor's sexual laxity, in letters to the English authorities, that did the trick; whatever the cause, Sorell was never to get another administrative post in the British Empire, and he died after twenty-four years of virtual idleness in 1848.

His successor had already been chosen before Sorell left Hobart. He remains one of the most controversial figures in early Australian history: Sir George Arthur (1784–1854), the archetype of the pious colonial strongman, charged by the British Government with the task of rendering all transportation a perfect terror to the criminal classes of Great

Britain. "The most powerful, skilful and ruthless figure in the colony," L. L. Robson's judgment on him runs, "hated with an intensity of which only the neurotic and grasping settlers of Van Diemen's Land were capable."[25]

Arthur was a military man through and through. He had seen service against Napoleon with the 35th Regiment around the Mediterranean, from Calabria to Egypt; in 1815 he took on the post of superintendent and commandant of British Honduras, a slave state with some passing resemblances to the society he would later rule in Van Diemen's Land. During his eight years there, Arthur showed himself to be a reformer, not by any means a populist but certainly more on the side of the slaves than of their choleric and arrogant owners. Reports of his work in Honduras won him the admiration of William Wilberforce.

He returned to England in 1822. Honduras had given him a taste for colonial administration. It was his vocation; what other field could give him the same proconsular scope, the same free hand to take a small remote country and re-mold its life in a way acceptable both to King and to God? There was not a trace of hypocrisy in Arthur. He believed it was his duty to make men moral—high and low alike. He was an evangelist who had chosen soldiering as his medium. Soon, through friends in London, he heard that the lieutenant-governorship of Van Diemen's Land was open.

When, after much lobbying at the Colonial Office, Arthur was chosen as Sorell's successor, he insisted on running Van Diemen's Land as a separate colony and having the effective powers of governor, though he remained lieutenant-governor in title. Shrewdly, he realized even before he got there that Sorrell's and Davey's inability to move without permission from Sydney had done endless harm to convict discipline. He persuaded the Colonial Office to frame his commission so that he could draft laws, make land grants to settlers, directly control government money, extend pardons, remit sentences, appoint his own staff and report directly to Downing Street without referring to the governor in Sydney. This was done, and by 1825 the Government went further: It turned Van Diemen's Land into a separate colony from New South Wales, with its own legislative council—which, in practice, was a rubber stamp for Arthur's wishes. His Utopia of punishment and reform would be an autocracy.

iii

A FEW MONTHS short of his fortieth birthday, when he stepped ashore from the *Adrian* in Hobart on May 12, 1824, Arthur seemed distant, cold and aloof. His tall frame was stooped; the pallor of his face had not been changed by months at sea. His mouth was thin and compressed, the corners turned down. He rarely smiled in public. In conversation he would fix you with his wide, glaucous, interrogatory gray eyes, and he did not seem to blink as much as other people. He radiated an impression, not of wolfish severity, but of unshakable and vigilant moral calm. If there was ever an Australian governor who had no trouble distinguishing right from wrong, it was George Arthur.

This was not only due to his military background. Arthur's serenity came from religion. He did not like to be called a Methodist; that smacked of "enthusiasm" and hence irrationality, and suggested links with the lower orders. But ever since he had a revelation of faith amid the tropical heat of Honduras, he had known that only God was the great emancipator. The Calvinist Evangelicalism he professed was not a private matter. Arthur had been put on earth to impose his values on others; that was the burden and duty of leadership.

He knew human nature was born and saturated in wickedness and could be redeemed only by prostration before Christ, by participating in the sacrifice of his Crucifixion in a complete surrender of faith. All social amusements that stood in the way of the Savior's work were vain, and to be shunned. He was, as the vernacular of a later Australia would express it, a God-bothering, blue-nosed wowser. "Would the forerunner of Christ," he asked his sister in a letter from Honduras, "ever have allowed himself the madness of the quadrilles?" (The image of the Baptist, goatskins a-whirl, treading nimbly across the polished teak at a regimental dance in Honduras has a certain charm, but not to Arthur.) Like most fundamentalists, he was stiffly censorious in matters cultural. He read mainly to reject: The philosopher David Hume was a "wretched infidel," and the net effect of Alexander Pope's didactic satires had been to make the young cynical and self-righteous. Social encounters with Arthur and family at Government House were marked by prayer and scriptural readings and were enlivened only by tea, although he permitted himself some port with his colonial secretary. Colonists, in the presence of this martinet and his starchy wife, realized that the days of "Mad Tom" Davey and adulterous Sorell were far behind them. Few people could extract much pleasure from Arthur's company; but none could doubt that here was the most incisive and vigilantly ordered mind ever to immerse itself in the problems of running a convict colony in the antipodes.

Arthur meant to close all the loopholes in the system of convict punishment and turn the island into an ideal police state where surveillance was constant and total—a Panopticon-without-walls. Moreover, his new system of punishment and incentive would have the inexorable character of a machine, of Bentham's idea of "a mill for grinding rogues honest." Arthur came to believe that his system was so perfectly mechanical that it became cybernetic, or self-correcting. The convict's fate was determined entirely by himself—by his own obedience and tractability, or lack of them. All the officials of the Convict Department had to do was tend the machine and stoke it with paper. As long as it was running, the disposal of the convicts and the severity of their punishment became automatic. That, at least, was the theory; for machines are dispassionate, not vindictive, and Arthur wanted to purge the grit and slop of emotion from his. Weakness led to cruelty; neither befitted a man of God.

In one respect, Arthur was surprisingly modern. He thought crime was a kind of sickness. Criminals suffered from a "mental delirium," caused by seeing reality through a "false medium," a scrim of illusions and distortions. The solution was to train them by drill and rote—he compared his prisoners, more than once, to unbroken horses—backed by the total exclusion of choice from their daily lives. Hard labor and, above all, the boredom of repetition was the only way to get convicts into the passive frame of mind where reformative teaching could pierce and dispel their "delirium."

To enforce this "enlightened rigor," as he called it, Arthur devised an extraordinarily complete system of social control. Van Diemen's Land was a police state; he made no bones about that. But under Arthur, it also became the closest thing to a totalitarian society (though small and in some ways inefficient) that would ever exist within the British Empire. Arthur wanted to control his island utterly, settlers as well as convicts. His system had the logic of his given premise, which was that Van Diemen's Land was first and foremost a jail, and that any free people who lived there must put up with the inconveniences of a penal society (the galling apparatus of police, spies, travel passes, trade restrictions, a muzzled press and crackdowns on the right of assembly) if they were to enjoy its benefits—free land grants and cheap assigned labor.

He divided Van Diemen's Land into nine police districts, each with a police magistrate in charge of a force of constables and field police. Each police magistrate reported back to the chief police magistrate in Hobart, who in turn reported to Arthur. In his own district, however, the police magistrate was boss, judge, coroner and recording angel. He kept minute registers of births, behavior, proper transactions and deaths of the free and bond in his district. He issued travel passes to convicts. All applications from settlers for assigned servants and all petitions from convicts for "indulgences," remissions and tickets-of-leave had to go through him. And he controlled the local police force, which ran from the chief district constable down to the rank and file of the field police, who were recruited from among the serving convicts. To get into the field police was considered a fine indulgence, and Arthur knew perfectly well what effect these government turncoats would have on the morale of convicts: "a mistrust and jealousy had already been infused into the prisoner Population which gives a Security to the free inhabitants."[26]

Every convict, Arthur insisted,

> should be regularly and strictly accounted for, as Soldiers are in their respective Regiments. . . . [T]he whole course of their Conduct—the Services to which they are sent, —and from which they are discharged—the punishments they receive, as well as instances of good conduct they manifest—should be registered from the day of their landing until . . . their emancipation or death.[27]

In 1826 he ordered a transported law-stationer named Edward Cook, under the direction of the muster-master as registrar, to start this gigantic compilation with the 12,305 prisoners who had arrived in Van Diemen's Land since Collins founded the colony. The result was the "Black Books"—ponderous leather-bound tomes three feet high, containing the name, physical description, sentence, details of transportation and assignment, jail and surgeon's reports, punishment and conduct record of every convict sent to Van Diemen's Land. By 1830, Van Diemen's Land had the most thorough files on its inhabitants, bond and free, of any community in the world—a mastaba of paper raised on the miseries of skewed, truncated lives, falling or rising through the levels of Arthur's system.

Arthur made sure that each convict was interrogated on arrival, so that the muster-master had full particulars of them all.* He often went down to the Hobart Penitentiary to meet the prisoners as they arrived, and spoke to them in person. James Backhouse, the Quaker missionary, recounted the homily with which Arthur greeted them:

> He alluded to the degraded state into which they had brought themselves by their crimes; this he justly compared to a state of slavery. . . . [He told them] that their conduct would be narrowly watched, and if it should be bad, they would be severely punished, put to work in a chain-gang, or sent to a penal settlement, where they would be under very severe discipline; or their career might be terminated on the scaffold. That, on the contrary, if they behaved well, they would in the course of a proper time,

---

* This had not always been done before; under Davey and Sorell, thanks to lackadaisical record-keeping in England, whole shiploads of prisoners would come into the Derwent without any records of their crimes and sentences, so that, as Arthur protested in 1827, "we stand in the extraordinary predicament in a Penal Colony of not being able to *prove* that the offenders transported from England *are* Convicts."

be indulged with a ticket-of-leave; . . . that if they should still persevere in doing well, they would then become eligible for a conditional pardon, which would give them the liberty of the colony: and that a further continuance in good conduct, would open the way for a free pardon, which would liberate [them] to return to their native land.[28]

From that moment the prisoner's life became a strictly regulated and automatic game of snakes and ladders. "The spirit of the convict," their new ruler would declare in the summation of his penal philosophy, *Observations Upon Secondary Punishment* (1833),

> is not subdued by unmingled severity. Encouragement forms part of the plan by which he is reclaimed. . . . There is presented to him the choice of two opposite paths. The one will lead him to the possession of a ticket of leave. The other . . . will conduct him by a short cut, to the government gang or the penal settlement where he will be subjected to every privation. . . . Thus it is that every man has afforded him an opportunity of in a great measure retrieving his character and becoming useful in society.[29]

Arthur's system set up seven levels of punishment between its extremes of freedom and the scaffold. In growing order of severity, they were: [1] holding a ticket-of-leave; [2] assignment to a settler; [3] labor on public works; [4] labor on the roads, near civilization, in the settled districts; [5] work in a chain gang; [6] banishment to an isolated penal settlement; and [7] penal settlement labor in chains.

A prisoner sank by bad conduct, and went up the rungs by good—after a time. But he always had to conform perfectly for a part of his sentence before he had any chance of a ticket-of-leave. A man with a seven-year sentence could apply for his ticket after four years of proven good behavior; a fourteen-year man, after six years; a lifer, after eight. He might also shorten his sentence by exceptional services—by catching an escaped fellow convict, for instance, or capturing troublesome Aborigines or serving as a convict constable in Arthur's detested field police.

His progress up the ladders and down the snakes would be decided by full reports on his conduct, gathered from settlers, police magistrates and other witnesses, compiled at the police station in his district and forwarded to Arthur's colonial secretary. Every offense and sentence, each change of place and labor, would be noted by "a firm and determined, but mild and consistent supervision," which would also scrutinize the convict's attitudes to authority and work, his state of conscience and degree of remorse. Thus the prisoner would live without refuge from the eye of authority.

Arthur's belief in his system was absolute, and it distressed him to have its workings disturbed by direct orders from England. The Quaker missionary George Washington Walker called at Government House one day in 1834 and found Arthur "extremely chagrined" at an order that had just come on the transport *Moffatt* from Smith Stanley, the secretary of state for the colonies, enjoining him to take thirty of its four hundred newly arrived prisoners and work them in chains for seven years, instead of giving them the milder punishment of assignment. This draconic and arbitrary sentence, Stanley hoped, would spread the terror of Van Diemen's Land in England. None of the unfortunate men had done anything to deserve it; they had all been submissive and quiet on the voyage; and Arthur was at a loss to know what to say to them. "They naturally ask why are we treated thus? What have we done?" wrote Walker.

> [But] All the Lt.-Governor is able to say is, "such is the order from home, it is out of my power to help it. However, let me recommend you as your friend to submissively acquiesce: to resist w$^d$ only be to render y$^r$ situation worse; & I will write home & endeavour to obtain some mitigation of your sentence, until any bad conduct, exhibited in the colony, renders you deserving of this punishment." Common equity, let alone humanity, prompts this language, which has actually been used tow$^{ds}$ them by the Governor.[30]

Arthur was certainly a martinet, and sometimes a suffocatingly pious one, but in no sense was he a sadist. That taint would be foisted on him later by a hostile colonial press, and fixed in literature long after his death by the Victorian tales of penal Grand Guignol written by Marcus Clarke and Price Warung. His real aim on Van Diemen's Land was reformatory, not vindictive, like the aims of the Panopticon that Jeremy Bentham had set before the French National Assembly more than thirty years earlier.

All convicts entered the board at level [2], as assigned labor. Those not assigned to settlers were put on the public works, for which there was a constant demand, for Van Diemen's Land always needed more jails, barracks, piers, bridges and roads to cope with the growing convict population and the spread of settlement. In 1827, after three years of Arthur's regime, there were 2,500 men employed at punishment labor (levels [3] through [7]) on public works in Van Diemen's Land, or 43 percent of the convict population (as against 577 men, or 32 percent in 1820); this reflected the urgent need for new government buildings of every kind.[31]

But most of the convicts in that year and all others (2,750 or 46 percent in 1827) were in level [2], the norm, as assigned servants. Assignment was the backbone of Arthur's system but also—as he was well aware—its weakest point. The idea that *any* system could smoothly and automatically convert an undifferentiated mass of criminals into the permanent underclass of repentant, tractable cottagers who were the ideal end product of transportation to Van Diemen's Land, was chimerical. To see the common reality one must turn, for a moment, from the administration to one of its thousands of subjects, whose claim to attention is that, unlike the great majority of his fellow convicts, he wrote an uncommonly frank clandestine letter, which has survived.[32]

George Taylor was transported for life to Van Diemen's Land in 1826 for stealing a pocketbook, and in 1832 he tried to smuggle a letter describing his ups and downs to his "dear Brother" John Thompson, another convict serving time in Macquarie Harbor. On first landing at Hobart, he was sent to work in a government vegetable garden "under the Superintendence of a Cruel and Vindictive tyrant where I remained for a fortnight." Then he drew assignation to a free settler named Tennant. "Here I was again unfortunate for altho I received a good Caracter from the Cleark of the prisoners barracks as a hard working industrious man Still I had no sooner got to my master than he began to discover [i.e., disclose] the disposition of a Hardhearted Wreach." After seven months Taylor started scheming to get away. He hoped to provoke his master into bringing him before the local police magistrate on a minor charge, so he started a go-slow strike, only doing "that part of my work which I thought proper." Tennant haled him before the magistrate "two or three times," but the charge was not bad enough to warrant returning Taylor to government work. So Taylor "persued a diferant line" by feigning sickness and asking, as was his right, to be sent to the doctor—who discovered "that I was sailing under false Collors and gave me a note to take to my Master to that effect." Taylor opened, read and destroyed the note. He stayed in a fellow convict's hut for three days and then told his master, on returning, that he had been in the hospital. This flimsy story came apart, of course, the next time Tennant saw the doctor. Tennant took his assigned man to the police magistrate, who sentenced Taylor to the chain gang at Bridgewater. There, convicts in levels [3] through [5] were sweating to create one of Colonel Arthur's favorite public works— a causeway and bridge over the River Derwent, part of the main trunk road from Hobart to Launceston. The facilities provided there to reform the likes of Taylor included cells that were more like animals' lairs, seven feet long and less than three feet high; the men crawled into them at night and were padlocked there, behind a stout lattice, unable to stand or sit. Taylor spent two months at Bridgewater but did not seem chastened enough. His next "automatic" descent was to chain-gang labor at the Kangaroo Point jetty in Hobart and on the roads. "You may be sure my Sittuation is not very enviable," he wrote to his friend, "for it only makes me think more of my Liberty than ever and I am determined to try the first opertunity to gain it by some means or other if possible."

Unluckily for him, his letter was intercepted by the authorities. It had been folly to write it in the first place, and after due inquiry, Colonel Arthur banished him to level [6], an isolated penal settlement. "Let Him then be removed forthwith to Port Arthur," he decreed in a note on the offending document. This was done by the end of 1832. Later, good behavior extracted Taylor from Port Arthur and moved him up again to level [5], this time in a chain gang at Launceston. But the desire for freedom still burned in him; in 1836 he vanished from Arthur's records with the laconic notation "Run," meaning that he had escaped. Whatever else Arthur's system had done for him, it had not made Taylor any more docile. There were many Taylors.

Nevertheless, Arthur had to make his system as perfect and uniform as he could. His task, in conformity with John Bigge's advice to the British Government, was to run an island of punishment, a place of terror to English criminals. He therefore had to keep assignment in Van Diemen's Land from becoming the ill-supervised lottery it had become in New South Wales.

But the free clay of his island varied as much as the criminal. Like New South Wales, Van Diemen's Land had kind and cruel settlers; vigilant and negligent ones; men who would work their assigned servants to the bone, and others who would let them eat at the same kitchen table; above all, men who by temperament and sense of moral obligation would stick to the lieutenant-governor's rules of convict management, and others who would not, and in between those who, like most people anywhere, would bend the rules if they wanted to and thought they could get away with it. All of them must be brought into line, levelled before the System.

Without assignment, there could have been no colony in Van Diemen's Land. Its economy would have died because, as in New South Wales, there was no labor but convict labor. Hence, in Arthur's view, the mere fact of living as a free settler in a penal colony meant that a man must accept the paramount values of penal discipline. Free settlers were as integral a part of Arthur's machinery of punishment as policemen or government clerks. Assignment was a bargain a man struck with the government and if he did not play by the government's rules he lost his convict servants. And the rules were far stricter than they had been under Lachlan Macquarie's more liberal (and, to Bigge, more muddled) system in New South Wales. They went with a larger and ever-growing police force, and a complete denial of any political say to Emancipists and free settlers alike. Throughout his term of office, which was as long as Macquarie's New South Wales—twelve years, from 1824 to 1836—George Arthur never lost sight of the fact that to control a state's labor supply is to control its political life. So Arthur's "red list" of settlers who could not get assigned convicts was, in plan and in detail, a formidable social weapon.

Whole groups were automatically put on it. Arthur would show none of the encouragement Macquarie had given to Emancipists in New South Wales. His view tallied exactly with Bigge's. Ex-convicts, he thought, made bad masters—and of course there was evidence to support it. Either they were too lenient to their men and despised the police, thus jamming Arthur's "objective" machinery of punishment; or else the psychological need to wield power, after their grinding years of servitude and degradation, turned them into sadists and so aborted their servants' prospects of reform. Hence, with very few exceptions, no one who had been a convict in Van Diemen's Land could get convict labor. In this way, Arthur tried to enforce the ideal of Bigge and the Exclusives—that of a permanent ruling class of free descent, with the descendants of convicts as their helots. Refusing labor to Emancipists in Van Diemen's Land could only deepen the gulf between wealthy (or at the very least, "unstained") Exclusive families there, and the convict-descended majority. There were only three passably wealthy ex-convicts in all of Van Diemen's Land at the time Arthur arrived, and he was not anxious to create any more. David Lord, who had inherited an estate worth £50,000 from his convict father James and by 1827 was said to have so multiplied it that he "knows not the extent of his riches," was not only an inveterate enemy of Arthur but also a complete social anomaly.[33]

Some trades found it hard to get convict servants. Arthur despised rum and those who sold it, and would rarely assign a convict to an innkeeper. Believing that the city was wickeder than the country—which it was, given the number of its taverns and the floating population of "loose" women it harbored—Arthur preferred to assign convicts to farmers rather than tradesmen in town.

Arthur expected masters to make their servants pray and scrupulously observe the Sabbath. They must buy Bibles for their men, if the men could read, but few masters actually did so. Few things irked Arthur more than a master's failure to instill religious habits in his convicts. Besides, he wanted to leave Van Diemen's Land covered with a brown mantle of Anglican churches and Wesleyan meetinghouses. He did all he could to bring in clergymen, missionaries and other catechists. The Wesleyans did particularly good work at the foot of the scaffold with condemned criminals, of whom there was no shortage under Arthur. One preacher, the Reverend Carvosso, helped fourteen men to lament and exult their way through the noose into the portals of eternity within a space of thirty hours.[34]

Wherever a town coalesced in the "settled districts" of Van Diemen's Land, Arthur wanted a chapel to be built, usually a plain stone box with lancet windows and a pitched roof in the Gothic manner, without much in the way of crockets and stone foliage, where the Lord could be praised in metrical psalms. There were four churches in Van Diemen's Land when he arrived in 1824, and eighteen when he left. The church and the police magistrate's office were the architectural symbols of his regime, and one served the other. Official religion was a means of penal control. The mandatory Sunday muster of convicts had to finish with a service and a clerical harangue. But it was not easy to make sure masters kept their men's noses to the moral grindstone. Some would work their convicts on the Sabbath, tolerate their propensity to vice and give them rum as an incentive. If he found out about that, Arthur withdrew their assigned men and left them economically crippled.

He discouraged all intimacy between bond and free. One settler found himself red-listed for letting his convicts eat Christmas dinner with his family. In 1831, when a leading settler, George Meredith, defied the strict letter of police regulations by treating his assigned men to a drink on New Year's Eve, Arthur ordered his colonial secretary to warn him that another dram of rum down a felon's throat "will lead to the immediate removal of all his servants."[35]

If a settler had an affair with a convict woman, and Arthur found out about it through his district police magistrate, all his servants would be reassigned. Even if a free man married an ex-convict woman—and most of the women in Van Diemen's Land had been transported, so there was not much choice for the small settler—he would lose his assigned servants at once. The situation that often arose in New South Wales, where a convict might be assigned to a relative, was rarely allowed here. Sometimes Arthur would let a wife emigrate to Van Diemen's Land to join her convict husband, provided that the man had his ticket-of-leave or that his master would give her domestic work. But he would not, of course, pay for her passage.

One exception was reluctantly made for "Ikey" Solomon, the celebrated Jewish pickpocket and fence on whom, legend (perhaps incorrectly) insists, Charles Dickens had based the character of Fagin. His wife Ann, daughter of an Aldgate coachmaster named Moses Julian, had been transported for receiving stolen goods. She landed in Hobart in 1828, with four small children between the ages of three and nine. She was assigned as a servant to a police officer. Meanwhile the intrepid "Ikey," who was tried and sentenced for theft in 1827 but had escaped from the Black Maria on his way to Newgate (the vehicle, as the authorities discovered all too late, was driven by his father-in-law), had fled to Denmark, to the United States, to Rio and finally to Hobart under an alias to join his wife. He bought land and a house and he started a business, which flourished. Everyone in Hobart knew who he was (the town was small, and of course full of his former colleagues) but a peculiar technicality saved him: Arthur, who always played by the book, had received no warrant for his arrest from the Colonial Office in London and could not touch him until one arrived. Thus, with the backing of some fellow traders, Isaac Solomon put up a bond of a thousand pounds and Arthur reluctantly allowed his wife to be assigned to him. Their family idyll was rudely disrupted in November 1829 when Arthur at last received the warrant from England. Even then, the *ur*-Fagin made one last wriggle to dislodge the hook, and with effrontery worthy of his fictional counterpart he petitioned Arthur from his jail cell for an official job:

TO:
    His Excellency Colonel George Arther
    L<sup>t</sup> Govener of V D Land &c &c &c

Sir,
    I beg leave to state the following . . . I some time back detected A Man with A Forged note on the Bank of the Derwent I had him taken into Custedy; he was Convicted and sent to Mackquarrey Harbour. I allso beg Leave to State that theire Was a Greate Many forged Note in Circulation before I detected this Man; & I have not heard of Any being in Circulation since I detected this Man; I theirefor now offer my Serveses to The Government in detecting all Such Offences or Any thing Else that the Goverment may Appoint me to do to the Hutermost of my Obility.

    I have the honor to subscribe
        Your Excellencys Most humble Servant,
                      Isaac Solomon.[36]

But Arthur was not swayed. "I presume," he frostily noted on the verso, "this is from the Person commonly called 'Ikey Solomon'—no notice need be taken of his Memorial." So Isaac Solomon was returned to England amid cries of protest from the Hobart opposition press, who thought it a breach of *habeas corpus*. There he was tried and sentenced to fourteen years' transportation; by the end of 1831 he was back in Hobart; and in 1835 he got his ticket-of-leave and was reunited with his family. By then, unfortunately, they all loathed one another. *

    It was essential to Arthur's system that the settlers who had convict labor assigned to them carry out his rules to the last detail. Judging their moral fitness to preside over the punishment of prisoners was perhaps

---

* Solomon and his wife quarrelled incessantly and in 1840, when she got her pardon, they broke up. "Ikey" died ten years later. His old gift for making money had deserted him and he did not—as another legend had it—contribute to the founding of the first synagogue in Van Diemen's Land. His estate was only worth £70.

the most ticklish problem that faced the Convict Office. The price of having assigned servants was full participation in Arthur's system of convict management. It made all free settlers into jailers—"auxiliaries," in John West's words, "hired by royal bounties to co-operate with the great machinery of punishment and reformation."[37] The settler was expected to shut up about "rights," stay at home on his farm and do exactly as he was told. A master could lose his assigned labor if he let his men idle, or used convict rather than free overseers or lent a man to another settler. In particular, it was forbidden to transfer convicts as though they were private property, as sometimes happened in New South Wales. To abuse a servant was to lose him, and assigned convicts had the right to complain to the police magistrate at any time. But it was equally forbidden to indulge them, and any delay in bringing a mulish, rebellious or backsliding convict before the magistrate would get the master (or mistress) in trouble. The only play in these regulations came from the supply of assignable convicts. When the demand for them was high, Arthur could take them away from settlers who infringed the rules, just as he pleased. But convicts had to be put somewhere, and so when there was a glut of assignable felons, more settlers found they were let off with a reprimand and could keep their men.

The key to Arthur's scheme of total surveillance was, of course, the quality of the police. "It is extremely desirable," he declared, "that either through the Police or Principal Superintendent's Department, the most conclusive information should always be obtained of the character of the applicant [for] assigned labor and all circumstances."[38] To assure this, Arthur had to make certain that his police force was run by men who had no allegiance to either settlers or convicts and were responsible only to him; and that its rank and file had no reason to favor anyone either. He cunningly did both by appointing army men as district magistrates and by putting upward-moving convicts in the field police as a reward for good conduct and a step toward freedom. This was a bureaucratic master stroke. The convict constables were anxious to distinguish themselves, could be kept in line by the merest threat of demotion, knew they had no second chances and doubtless took a certain pleasure in bossing the settlers around. One could expect dog-like obedience—and canine ferocity—from them. The army police magistrates might not know much about civil law; often they looked on the settlers with disdain, and on convicts with contempt. But they were impervious to criticism from civilians and despised the press. Their background had trained them to handle the laborious, detailed paperwork of reports and to carry out every quillet of Arthur's copious, inflexible orders with military zeal. They believed in the chain of command as implicitly as Arthur did.

Not everyone resented the methods used by Arthur's police. They had cleaned out the bushrangers, destroyed the Brady gang and made the roads safe for trade; thousands of people could sleep easier because of them. Nevertheless, they poisoned the social air. Tempers had always been short in Van Diemen's Land, frictions magnified, manners gross. Bitching and backbiting were the favorite sports of Hobart society—as of Australian society in general. Among the "dirty pack of unprincipled place hunters" whom Arthur's auditor-general, the waspish George Boyes, saw occupying the upper rungs of Van Diemen's Land, "lying, slandering, every hatred and malice are their daily ailment and their consumption is incredible." Now the stew of ill-will was thickened by spying and the fear of denunciation. By 1830, Van Diemen's Land was fast becoming "a community of slanderers and slaves."[39]

Besides, Arthur was a committed nepotist. He knew what a small pool of administrative talent he had in Van Diemen's Land, and he needed people he could trust—loyalty being an acceptable substitute for imagination. If he was an autocrat, and he was, he had partly been made so by distance: He faced a year's delay in obtaining instructions from London, and up to four months' lag in getting them from Sydney. This gave him even wider discretion than the governor enjoyed in New South Wales, and he used it with a sovereign contempt for "liberal" and "democratic" principles. Never apologize, never explain.

Arthur made no bones about the scope of his patronage or his bias toward military men. Given the quality of some of the civil officials the Crown sent, one can hardly blame him. Dudley Fereday (1789–1849), a bankrupt coal magnate's son whom an English lord's patronage had made sheriff of Van Diemen's Land in 1824, turned out to be a relentless usurer, lending money at 35 percent interest. Arthur soon got rid of him, and of his uncompliant attorney-general, Arthur Gellibrand, and of anyone else who seemed either disobliging or short on moral fiber. He went after the customs collector, Rolla O'Farrell, who had arrived penniless in Hobart but amassed a fortune of more than £15,000 by creative venality. This man, Arthur told London, was a debauchee with the morals of a stoat, who lived with one of the prostitutes off the *Princess Royal* and had been fined for harboring and seducing female convicts. In 1831 England sent Arthur a judge, Alexander "Dandy" Baxter (1798–1836), whose ignorance and paranoiac sadism (while serving as Darling's attorney-general in New South Wales, he had battered his wife with a poker after she gave birth to twins) were such that Arthur would not have him in his colony. "I found him," he declared, "in a high state of neurotic excitement and such an habitual sot that it would have been a violation of all public decency to have suffered him to take his seat on the Bench."[40] In 1826 Arthur received John Burnett (1781–1860) as his first colonial secretary—a mewing, forgetful creature, who confessed to Ar-

thur soon after getting to Hobart that "so extremely sensitive is my
nervous system that everything which agitates my mind immediately
affects my bodily health, and brings on illness."[41] Not without some
difficulty, Arthur replaced him with John Montagu (1797–1853), a blunt,
thrusting ex-officer of the 40th Regiment, a veteran of Waterloo who—
no incidental point—had married Arthur's niece.

In the end, Arthur always got his way with appointments and managed to cripple most of the enemies his purges made. "The Government
of the Colony is nominally vested in the Lieutenant Governor and an
Executive Council," wrote Boyes. "I say nominally, because the Executive Council as a body is powerless. The real government is composed of
Colonel Arthur [and] his two nephews." The "nephews" were Montagu
and the chief police magistrate, Matthew Forster (1796–1846), a half-
blind former captain in the 85th Regiment who had had the excellent
sense to marry another of Arthur's nieces.

Another Arthur favorite was Roderic O'Connor (1784–1860), a "red-
hot Irishman," the son of a rich landowner, who had sailed to Hobart on
his own ship with his two bastard sons in 1824. O'Connor was tough,
outspoken, pragmatic and arrogant—a man Arthur could use, despite his
atheism and his taste for the grog. He appointed him to the survey and
valuation commission, whose task it was to oversee the division of Van
Diemen's Land into counties and parishes, to assess unoccupied Crown
land and survey the route for the north–south trunk road, the spine of
the colony, which convicts would build between Hobart and Launceston.
It was the right job in which to gather some land of his own. In 1824
Arthur gave O'Connor 1,000 acres; by 1828, he had 4,000 and as much
convict labor as he wanted—when assigning men to his favorites, the
colonel never stinted. In 1836, when Arthur left Van Diemen's Land,
O'Connor was one of the half-dozen richest men in the colony, ada-
mantly opposed to any alteration in the system of slavery that had created his wealth. He was not liked (Lady Franklin, the wife of Arthur's
successor, complained that he was "bound by ties of I know not what
nature to the Arthur faction . . . a man of blasted reputation, of exceedingly immoral conduct and of viperous tongue"), but he was very much
feared, and at his death he owned 65,000 acres of Tasmania and leased
10,000 more from the government.[42]

Meanwhile, under Arthur's organizing hand, the economy of Van
Diemen's Land was surging. In 1824, when he arrived, Van Diemen's
Land had a white population of about 12,000 and its exports were worth
£45,317. In 1836, the year he left, they stood at £540,221, and there were
40,000 bond and free. Most of the settlers were men of capital, for Arthur
discouraged free workers, even mechanics, from emigrating to Van Diemen's Land; a free labor market would have diminished the social con-

trol that flowed from his power to allocate convict labor. Wealthy settlers —the "planters" of folksong—ruled the Vandemonian roost and despised mere traders and merchants. By 1830, Van Diemen's Land had a wool boom, a wheat boom, a boom in real estate and agricultural land and a severe loansharking problem; members of Arthur's own Legislative Council were rumored to be lending out money at illegal rates of 15 and even 50 percent. Thrifty and ruthlessly astute, the colonel himself knew of every project in advance, made a fortune from land investment and lived like a tea-drinking, psalm-intoning nabob. He stayed within the letter of the law, but the law was easier then, and respectable folk were more apt to avert their eyes from conflicts of interest. Thus when he had the causeway and bridge over the Derwent River for the Hobart–Launceston road built at Bridgewater, Arthur owned most of the land around it; and when he picked the site for a new Hobart wharf, he was accused (though not conclusively) of increasing the value of his property next to it from £800 to £12,000.

After a few years of dictatorial, God-fearing nepotism there was plenty of reckoning and questioning. It came from settlers, who chafed at the intrusions of his police and were furious when Arthur withdrew their convict servants for infractions of his code; from merchants, who were treated as low money-grubbers by Arthur's landed gentry; and from all who felt that, as Englishmen in a far colony but Englishmen still, they should have the constitutional rights their "tyrant" denied them. They liked having convict labor but disliked living in a jail. Van Diemen's Land could not be run simply as a jail forever, but Arthur was determined to do so until the Crown changed his orders. The opposition was weak and tetchy. Its attempts to make itself heard—public meetings in 1831 and 1832 and a constitutional association in 1835—were ignored in Government House. But it had an irksome and at times hysterically abusive voice: the press, which Arthur detested.

The newspapers of Van Diemen's Land were rough, choleric and short —a few columns of news and editorials, some letters and official business, tacked onto a mass of advertisements. They tried to win their petty circulation wars with stilted, lurid rhetoric. In short, they were as poor and vindictive as most early nineteenth-century American newspapers. But they were the only forum of popular opinion—as distinct from the printed mandates of the government—in the colony. Everyone read them.

Such journalism goaded Arthur to folly. In 1827, he tried to quash the liberty of all printing on the island by proposing a Licensing Act, so that any editor's right to publish could be cancelled at the lieutenant-governor's pleasure. He coldly offered his all-purpose justification. Van Diemen's Land was a jail, and in jail opposition should have no voice.

Compared to the absolute need for "security and tranquillity," the free settlers' unanimous desire for a free press must go unsatisfied. Behind this, of course, lay Arthur's implacable vanity; he could not stand criticism of any kind, especially not from civilians, and least of all from ex-convicts.

When he looked at Vandemonian journalists, Arthur saw, not a Fourth Estate struggling for freedom of the press, but a swarm of semi-criminal gadflies sent to harass him personally. There was Robert Murray (1777–1850), ex-soldier, journalist and reputedly the bastard son of an English peer, transported for bigamy in 1815 and by 1825 editor of the *Hobart Town Gazette*, who wrote sharp attacks—or gross slanders, depending on which side one took—on Arthur's policies under the name "A Colonist." (He fell into line after 1832 and became a sycophantic tool of Arthur's patronage.)

Another was Murray's colleague Andrew Bent, sent out for burglary in 1810, now editor of the *Colonial Times:* an unrestrained seditionist, Arthur thought. Henry Melville, an eccentric Freemason obsessed with the occult, published the first Australian novel set in Australia (*Quintus Servinton*, 1830–31, by the transported forger Henry Savery) and, to Arthur's intense displeasure, wrote an entire book against his administration, *History of the Island of Van Diemen's Land from the Year 1824 to 1825*, which had to be smuggled out of the colony and published in England. Then there was William Goodwin, editor of the *Cornwall Chronicle*, a harsh transport captain turned venomous hack, whose attacks on Arthur and other pillars of the Vandemonian establishment seemed, unlike those of these other editors, to have no basis at all beyond his own opportunism.[43]

Some of these men bore unmistakably personal grudges against Arthur. One was Gilbert Robertson, the mulatto son of a Scottish sugar-planter in British Guiana, who had twice failed as a farmer: first in Scotland (where falling wheat prices ruined him), and then on a 400-acre grant in Van Diemen's Land. He was jailed for debt in 1824 and then worked for Arthur as superintendent of a government farm. In 1829 he struck out on his own again on Woodburn, a fine grazing property in the Richmond district. This time Robertson seemed set. Arthur had made him district constable and the farm prospered; but in 1832 he made the mistake of indulging his convicts too much. For a celebration after the February harvest, he gave them a barrel of wine, invited in another eight assigned servants from farms nearby and left twenty-five convicts carousing while he went to perform his police duties. All the convicts got drunk and one was mortally wounded in a brawl. This time, Arthur acted with surprising leniency. He did not withdraw all Robertson's assigned men; he merely red-listed him from getting any more. But that was enough for the choleric Scot, who switched to journalism to get his revenge on Arthur and emerged as editor of a daily paper, *The True Colonist*. Through this sheet, Robertson was able to heap accusations of fraud, peculation, favoritism and tyranny on Arthur for the last two years of his office.

Arthur's running battle with the press lasted throughout his administration. The British Government refused to let him have his Licensing Act; so Arthur felt he had no recourse but to sue his critics for libel, bombarding them with litigation to the point where, harassed and short-staffed, they would no longer be able to publish their broadsides against him. Arthur did this with such methodical zeal that Murray, Robertson, Melville and Bent all spent time behind bars. They protested their treatment, in and out of print. There is a particularly indignant letter from Henry Melville to Arthur, protesting the "torture" inflicted on him in the Hobart jail:

> I am writing this in the condemned cell where the notorious man-eater Pierce and some score of other murder[er]s have been confined. In this cell I passed the night (after being locked up by British convicts!) with swarms of bugs, which precluded the possibility of my sleeping.
> I ask for suitable appartments chiefly on account of my wife, who has expressed her determination to remain with me as many hours as possible, and if the authorities have a wish to be revenged on a political opponent at all events the chief ruler ought to have some feelings for an unoffending woman who suffers more from the incarceration of her husband than [he] does.[44]

Naturally, they were seen as martyrs. Andrew Bent was defended in court in 1830 as "this Nimrod of printers, this [Benjamin] Franklin of the Southern Hemisphere." Arthur could put them in jail, but not all his autocratic powers could keep them there forever. What especially irked him was the attitude of his own attorney-general, Joseph Tice Gellibrand (1786–1837), a close friend of Robert Murray. Gellibrand several times refused point-blank to sue for libel on the Crown's behalf; he even helped write editorials for Murray's paper. Arthur could not endure this and laid siege to Gellibrand's reputation in England. As Gellibrand was one of the few genuinely acute and honest lawyers ever to hold public office in early Australia, Arthur could not nail him for incompetence; but he created a cloud of allegations of fiscal dishonesty, and in 1826 a dispatch from Lord Goderich removed Gellibrand. His successor as attorney-general was a feeble anorexic named Thomas McCleland, whom Arthur found much easier to control. Gellibrand at once became editor of *The Tasmanian* in Hobart.[45]

And so, through his moral arrogance and his inability to understand or sympathize with civilian tempers, Arthur soon found himself facing a raucous phalanx of opposition papers. Part of their strategy was to contrast the suffering convict with the cold, rhadamanthine lieutenant-governor. To show the "tyrant" at his worst, they harped on the dreaded nadir of Arthur's system, the secondary penal settlements: first Macquarie Harbor, and then Port Arthur.

iv

UNTIL 1832, the only place in Van Diemen's Land fit for the severest levels of Arthur's punishment system was Macquarie Harbor, reserved for those who had committed serious crimes after landing in the colony. Its name reeked of fear and woe; all convicts feared it; but Arthur thought it had defects as well, and these came to look worse as both the convict population and the number of secondary convictions grew.

Despite its wealth of Huon pine, Macquarie Harbor was expensive. Being so remote from Hobart, it was hard to run. Ships took as long as six weeks to reach it, and no overland route had been found. The sandbar at the mouth of Hell's Gates was silting up, making entry to the harbor even more perilous than it already was. Arthur's orders were slow in reaching it, and the commandant's replies were delayed. Food ran short; scurvy was endemic; the barracks on Sarah Island, with a capacity of about 370 prisoners, was too small. Furthermore, a new speculative venture called the Van Diemen's Land Company was trying to open up the west coast for stock-grazing, and it looked as though the utter isolation of Macquarie Harbor, its best feature, might be on the wane.

There was another, far milder, penal settlement on Maria Island, three miles off the east coast of Van Diemen's Land. Arthur had it set up in 1825 to receive convicts "whose crimes are not of so flagrant a nature to induce the Magistrates to sentence them to Macquarie Harbour." The convicts lucky enough to be sent to this sweetly idyllic place wove cloth and cobbled shoes, and although flogging and solitary confinement were common punishments, their life escaped the miseries of Macquarie Harbor.[46]

But it made no sense and cost too much to keep two isolated secondary-punishment stations, one severe and one not; the levels of Arthur's system did not call for light punishment in remote places. Arthur decided to shut both of them down and to open a new penal settlement on the ragged tip of the Tasman Peninsula, closer to Hobart. The place was called Port Arthur. It is his monument, and perhaps no British proconsul has a more impressive one.

Today Port Arthur is easily visited by road; it is sixty miles from Hobart, and every season thousands of tourists in buses and cars stream down the Arthur Highway below Mount Forestier, glimpsing the bright planes of Blackman Bay and Norfolk Bay like burnished pewter struck and feathered by shafts of light, framed by dark headlands. Outcrops of cream and green fibro cottages, neat with garden gnomes and carports, cling to this melancholy coast. The hamlets of this peninsula look feeble and intrusive; their modest grafts of suburbia do not belong in a landscape so drenched in sublimity and misery. One soon forgets them, looking down on the mosaic shore at Pirate's Bay, cracked into hexagonal tessellations by the cooling of the lava flow; or gazing into the vertiginous depths of the Blowhole where, beneath a slender natural arch of rock, the sea two hundred feet below thunders across the jostled slabs of basalt on the cavern floor, saturating the air with a permanent, clinging mist.

In convict days, of course, there was no road. The inaccessibility of the Tasman Peninsula was what commended it to the System, and the best way to sense this is to go there, as prisoners did, by sea. One sails down the Derwent estuary from Hobart and turns into Storm Bay, once the calving-ground of thousands of black whales but now empty; from Cape Direction, where Australia's oldest lighthouse still winks its beam, the long humpy profile of the Tasman Peninsula lies on the southeastern horizon. Its furthest southern point is Cape Raoul, which as one rounds it appears as the western arm of Maingon Bay, the sea-gate that opens the way to Port Arthur—the eastern arm being Cape Pillar. Both capes are of towering basalt pipes, flutes and rods, bound like fasces into the living rock. Their crests are spired and crenellated. Seabirds wheel, thinly crying, across the black walls and the blacker shadows. The breaking swells throw up their veils. When the clouds march in from the Tasman Sea and the rainsqualls lash the prismatic stone, these cliffs can look like the adamantine gates of Hell itself. Geology had conspired with Lieutenant-Governor Arthur to give the prisoners of the crown a moral fright as their ships hauled in.

But once inside the landlocked bay of Port Arthur, the impression melts. Or so it does for a modern visitor, who sees green lawns, the ivy-covered remains of a Gothic church and the enormous bulk of the penitentiary. In its soft tones of pink brick, far gone in crumbling, it seems an almost maternal ruin. It did not seem so to the convicts, but the shudder it reliably evokes in the modern tourist comes from the contrast between its mild, pastoral present—*et in Arcadia ego*—and the legends of its past. Australia has many parking lots but few ruins. When Australians see the ruin of an old building, our impulse is either to finish tearing it down or to bring in the architects and restore it as a cultural center, if large, or a restaurant, if small. Port Arthur is the only major example of an Australian historical ruin appreciated and kept for its own sake (although local entrepreneurs have tried, and so far failed, to refurbish it as Convictland). It is our Paestum and our Dachau, rolled into one. Far more than Macquarie Harbor or even Norfolk Island, Port Arthur has always dominated the popular historical imagination in Australia as *the* emblem of the miseries of transportation, "the Hell on earth."

Moreover, its reputation was terrible right from the start. To have served time there was to receive an indelible stain. "There is something so lowering," remarked Arthur's successor as lieutenant-governor, Sir John Franklin, "attached to the name of a Port Arthur man."[47] Yet the records clearly show that Port Arthur, though certainly a place of misery for its prisoners, was by no means as bad as either Macquarie Harbor or Norfolk Island.

Its main difference from other secondary stations lay in the hermetic regularity of its discipline. It was conceived and run as a purgatorial grinding-mill rather than a torture chamber. "The most unceasing labour is to be exacted from the convicts," Arthur's Standing Instructions emphasized, "and the most harassing vigilance over them is to be observed."[48] But his regulations for the settlement were equally strict on the behavior of its guards. The commandant's authority was absolute, and he answered directly to the lieutenant-governor through the colonial secretary in Hobart. He could, and did, inflict punishment without trial, immediately after the offense, so that the convict would "learn his lesson" without delay. But the sequence of offense, detection and punishment must show a machine-like regularity, to which vindictiveness and pity were equally alien. Arthur's regulations were framed to leave no scope for the exercise of sadistic practices by prison personnel that made a convict's life at Macquarie Harbor or Norfolk Island so vile. Thomas Lemprière (1796–1852), who served as a commissary officer at Port Arthur (as well as Macquarie Harbor and Maria Island), felt that Arthur's enemies exaggerated in calling it an "Earthly Hell." But he did not bridle at phrases like "the abode of misery." "To this cognomen we do not object," he remarked with a certain brisk realism, for

> a penal settlement is, and ought to be, an abode of misery to those whose crimes have sequestered them from the society of their fellow-creatures. Were it a place of comfort, the very object for which such establishments are formed, the punishment and reform of malefactors, would become nugatory.[49]

"*And* reform"—this was a crucial phrase. Port Arthur existed to punish its men purposively. It would be the clamp that held the rigid structure of Arthur's social system together at the bottom.

Arthur had been thinking about the place since 1827, when the colonial brig *Opossum* took refuge there from a storm on the way back from Maria Island to Hobart and came back with news of a deep sheltered inlet, surrounded by colossal stands of timber. Arthur sent her captain back with a surveyor to make a detailed report on the place: its merits as a port, its water supply, and above all its forests, since the demand for timber for buildings and furniture kept rising, and logging was an ideally harsh punishment.

The report was good, and Arthur decided to put a settlement on the bay that, "from profound respect," had been given his name. He did not mean to transfer all the convicts from Macquarie Harbor at once. Some of the less evilly inclined ones could be put there as a form of probation, on their way back up the ladder of his system. But the basic population of Port Arthur would be men re-convicted of minor offenses, and others fresh from England.

The first group, thirty-four new English prisoners with fifteen soldiers to guard them under the command of Dr. John Russell, assistant surgeon of the 63rd Regiment, was landed there in September 1830. More followed; by mid-1831, the convict population was about 150. Dr. Russell would later list "a few well-known characters . . . mixed with the general class of housebreakers, pickpockets and felons":

> There was the famous Ikey Solomons; there was Collins, the old sailor, who threw a stone at the King—he died at Port Arthur; there were those men for agrarian disturbances, for setting fire to haystacks, a circumstance that occurred about 1830 or 1831; there was a clergyman from Scotland, and an attorney from Ireland; there were a number of boys sent to learn trades.[50]

A heterogeneous crew—which, as always at new penal outposts, had great difficulty surviving at all. Rations were miserably short and scurvy widespread. Medical supplies were so inadequate that at one point the doctor had to operate on a man's "stricture" with a piece of sharpened whalebone for a scalpel. Convicts went half-naked from want of uniforms. "I had great difficulty in punishing the men," Russell recalled, "in fact, I was living in the bush myself, and I therefore struck off the irons of every man that came down, and made it a punishment to put them on again." He could not use solitary confinement at first, for want of cells; but later the "most effectual" punishment proved to be hard labor in irons, with all meals and rest hours in solitary.[51]

Russell's pleas to Hobart went unanswered, because Arthur was obsessed with the field strategy of his military campaign to round up the remaining black tribes of Van Diemen's Land. And when the first group of convicts from Macquarie Harbor was moved to Port Arthur, Russell soon saw their influence on the prisoners fresh from England: "They exercised a complete tyranny over them, and shortly rendered them as hardened, as reckless, and as hypocritical as they were themselves." With Arthur's attention distracted, the colonial government ruined morale by not keeping its word to the better prisoners:

> Promises were sometimes held out through the commandant to well-conducted men, that their sentences should be shortly remitted in case of good conduct; that very good conduct rendered the men more useful in the settlement, and then the government detained them much longer. . . . The men, finding good conduct useless, reverted to bad practices, being rendered desperate.[52]

Little by little, a settlement rose at Port Arthur. At the end of 1832, Lieutenant-Colonel Logan of the 63rd Regiment made a tour of inspection of Tasman's Peninsula and reported that, once it had a fast patrol boat that could cruise the shore looking for absconders, the place would be ready to take over from Macquarie Harbor.[53] Two months later, in February 1833, the man who was to give Port Arthur its true penal shape disembarked at Hobart with a detachment of the 21st Fusiliers. This was Charles O'Hara Booth, destined to fulfill Arthur's hopes by taking "the vengeance of the Law to the utmost limits of human endurance" on Tasman's Peninsula. He would remain commandant at Port Arthur for eleven years. In 1833, when he took command, there were 475 prisoners on the Tasman Peninsula; by 1835 there were nearly 950; and the total number of convicts received by Port Arthur up to 1844, the last year of Booth's command, was 6,002. About 6,000 more had gone there by 1853, the year transportation to Van Diemen's Land ceased. All told, about 12,700 sentences were served at Port Arthur during its half-century of active life—about one in six of the 73,500 convicts transported to Van Diemen's Land. (Some prisoners, however, went there more than once.) The place was therefore of great importance in the penal scheme and played a much bigger part in the punishment of habitual criminals, or recidivists, than Macquarie Harbor or even Norfolk Island.[54]

Charles O'Hara Booth was a tough, vigilant man, whose taste for iron discipline was mingled with a liking for puns, Frenchifications and music-hall jollities. He had a strong sense of his job as role. In his journal, he called the Port Arthur convicts his "lions"; their tamer needed a certain histrionic poise. "Put on my annihilating countenance," he wrote one evening when he had to face down 375 insubordinate prisoners on his own. "Raised my Stentorian voice and made them quake."[55]

He was innately conservative and had no illusions about his ability to reform the Port Arthur convicts. He was there to discipline them and make them work, but any moral change seemed an unlikely bonus. He made his opinions clear to a French visitor, Captain Laplace, in 1839. How, Laplace inquired as they paced the night rounds of the settlement with Booth, had he achieved such quiescence with such minimal means —a dozen or so guards to supervise several hundred men, a low-security jail building? "By severe punishments, he replied, by impartial justice, as impassive as that of fate; by untiring vigilance; by demanding absolute silence from the prisoners." Booth added that he saw to it that convicts were never insulted or sworn at, and that he rarely had them flogged because the lash "often exasperates them and drives them to crime instead of reforming them"; he preferred solitary confinement, which, "much dreaded . . . subdues them through boredom." They came out of solitary "better than they went in," but only for a little while; "the banter, the bad examples of their companions, a fatal pride, soon make them forget their good resolutions, and they become just as dangerous as before." When depressed, as he sometimes was by illness, he would feel doubts. "Sick at Heart from the number of Boys obliged to punish," he noted in his journal in 1838, after a particularly taxing day among the refractory juveniles of Point Puer. "Would that we had persons to work the system—with firmness but temper and Patience to witness the results of perseverance—find myself breaking constitutionally rapidly— this is a trying situation . . . but great good may be effected by firmness tempered with kindness and unremitting perseverance." This was the only opinion on the aims, as distinct from the means, of prison policy that Booth committed to his diaries in Port Arthur. His journals were full of notes on hunting, which he loved; sixteen brace of quail bagged one day, nine kangaroos another, duck on the lagoon; the making of a purse from a kangaroo's scrotum, or "pebble case" as he archly called it, "it being a very fine specimen from a 'Fighting Buck.' " But of reflection on his job and the moral values it entailed, there is hardly a trace. Booth was not a reflective man.[56]

He had a name for justice, and even humanity, among his subordinates at Port Arthur. "We know he detests the use of [the lash]," Lemprière wrote, "and it is with regret, when he is compelled by the necessity of inflicting strict discipline, that he causes corporal punishment to be inflicted."[57] But when he used it he laid it on, handing out sentences of up to 100 lashes. Convicts regarded the Port Arthur cat-o'-nine-tails as unusually cruel—although the same had been said about the tools of flagellation at Macquarie Harbor. One of Port Arthur's political prisoners, the Chartist John Frost (he had been sentenced to be hanged, drawn and quartered for leading an ill-armed band of insurrectionary miners from the Monmouth Hills against the English town of Newport

after the mass arrests of Chartist leaders in 1839, but this was commuted
to life transportation) claimed that "twenty-five lashes at Port Arthur . . . produced more suffering than 300 would have produced as they
are inflicted in the Army." In Van Diemen's Land in the 1840s, "politicals" were relatively privileged, and Frost was never flogged. But his
description of the hateful ritual, with "the flogger using every means in
his power to break the spirit of those who suffered, and the sufferers
determined to sustain the punishment unflinchingly," was vivid enough:

> The knout was made of the hardest whipcord, of an unusual size. The
> cord was put into salt water till it was saturated; it was then put into the
> sun to dry; by this process it became like wire, the eighty-one knots
> cutting the flesh as if a saw had been used.

Charles O'Hara Booth, Frost claimed, "would often witness this punishment with as much indifference as if he were looking at some philosophical experiment."[58]

He would also muster the convicts to witness floggings, a practice
that the Quaker missionaries Backhouse and Walker felt "has an exasperating effect upon bystanders" and risked provoking a general mutiny, "in spite of the military Guards; the Prisoners present at these
times being between six and seven hundred and the Guard but forty
in number."[59]

Booth had solitary cells built, and special punishment cells, 7 feet by
4 feet and pitch dark, where "the occupant is not even allowed a knife to
eat his food. . . . They throw in to him in the dark, as they would to a
dog, a little food, and there is nothing but an old rug for him to lie upon.
If he is wet he is obliged to remain in his wet clothes until the following
morning." Nights are cold on the Tasman Peninsula. For less "atrocious"
offenders there were boxes like dog-kennels where the prisoner was
chained, breaking stones from a pile in front of him; and if the irons were
not heavy enough to suit his sins, he would go with "the log on his toes,"
with a heavy balk of timber attached to his ankle-irons that he dragged
as he walked.[60]

To scrutinize into the punishment records of Port Arthur men is to
look into a microcosm of harsh, bureaucratic tedium. Its horror comes
not from unrestrained cruelty (as the Gothic legends and popular horror
stories of the place insisted) but rather from its opposite, the mechanical
apportioning of strictly metered punishments designed to wear each prisoner down into bovine acceptance—Arthur's criterion of moral reform.
It is like looking into the memory of some dull god interminably counting fallen sparrows on his fingers. Here, as a sample, is three years from
the punishment record of a Scottish horse-thief named Robert William-

son, born in 1812, who was sentenced to fourteen years' transportation at Inverness in 1832, arrived in Van Diemen's Land on the *John Barry* in 1834 and later that year was sentenced to seven years in Port Arthur for the extreme unwisdom of stealing a pea-jacket and other nautical gear from Arthur's former attorney-general, now a judge of the Supreme Court and passionate amateur yachtsman, Algernon Sidney Montagu:

### 1835

JAN. 3RD: Having a file in his possession: 6 weeks in Chain Gang.

FEB. 21ST: Neglect of Duty while at work: 6 weeks in Chain Gang.

MARCH 28TH: Breaking gaol and absenting himself without leave from the Public Works at Port Arthur . . . and remaining absent until apprehended this day at Sympathy Point [sic] by a party of Constables and Military: 75 lashes.

MARCH 28TH: Same date—having a variety of Government tools in his possession for the purpose of aiding him in his Escape from the Penitentiary . . . the Settlement Workshop having been broken into: 10 days Solitary Confinement in a Cell at the Coal Mine.

SEPT. 4TH: Absenting himself from his Gang: 10 days Solitary Confine‡.

NOV. 6: Absent from his Gang for several hours: 10 Days ditto.

DEC. 3RD: Endeavouring to excite prisoners to Abscond: 6 months in Irons.

DEC. 19: Tampering with his Leg-Iron: 36 lashes.

### 1836

AUG. 13: Fishing contrary to orders: 3 weeks in Irons.

SEPT. 6: Having a quantity of Vegetables in his Possession: 1 month on chain gang.

SEPT. 20: Idleness: 3 Days Solitary Confine‡.

OCT. 10: Idleness: To lodge in a Cell 10 nights.

OCT. 20: Fighting at Work: 48 hrs. solitary Confine‡.

DEC. 28: Absenting himself from his Gang without leave: 14 days No. 1 Chaingang.

DEC. 29: Having a Knife improperly in his possession: 3 Days Solitary Confine‡.

### 1837

JULY 15: Having a Towel improperly in his possession: 14 Days No. 2 Chaingang.

SEPT. 18: Making use of a most Grossly Indecent Expression and subsequent malicious Conduct towards a fellow prisoner: 10 Days Solitary Confine‡.

OCT. 4: Absenting himself when going to the Hospital: 1 month in No. 2 Chaingang.

Nov. 28: Having a Crayfish in his possession and endeavouring to convey
it into the Gaol: 1 month No. 2 Chaingang.[61]

Charles O'Hara Booth was an active commandant, roaming on foot
and horseback through the bush of the Tasman Peninsula to drive his
favorite projects along: a coal mine; a semaphore system that could communicate with Hobart; and the first Australian railway, powered not by
steam but by convicts. But first he had to attend to the security system
at Eaglehawk Neck, where Arthur had posted a permanent guard-station
in 1831, after prisoners started escaping in numbers two years before
Booth's arrival. This wasp-waisted isthmus between the surf of Pirate's
Bay and the calm of Norfolk Bay, less than 100 yards wide, was the key
to Port Arthur; it was and still is the only way a man could leave the
Tasman Peninsula by land. Getting across it, therefore, became an obsessive focus of convict ingenuity. They walked, crept, ran, waded and even
hopped. One prisoner, a former actor named William Hunt, "who in his
younger days had belonged to a company of strolling mountebanks,"
disguised himself as an enormous "boomer" or male kangaroo. He nearly
got across to Forestier's Peninsula before two picket-guards, thinking he
really was a kangaroo, spotted him and gave chase, levelling their muskets. "Don't shoot, I am only Billy Hunt," the nervous marsupial
squeaked, to their consternation.[62]

Booth soon put a stop to such doings. His "prudent measures," Lemprière acknowledged, "have . . . rendered every attempt futile, nor does
it appear that any man effected the passage across." Eaglehawk Neck was
dotted with sandy hummocks, which gave cover to an escaping man
creeping by; and the surf blotted out the sound of footsteps. In 1832,
before Booth arrived, the ensign in charge of the guard there had the
smart idea of putting a string of nine tethered guard dogs across the Neck.
To this line he added a row of oil lamps, which shed their light on a
white band of crushed cockle-shells; these primitive searchlights made
it still more difficult for a bolter to pass at night without his shadow
being spotted, even if he got past the dogs. Booth increased the guard to
twenty-five men, built guardhouses and sentry-boxes, and doubled the
number of dogs. "Whether Port Arthur is an 'Earthly Hell' or not," Lemprière ponderously quipped, "it has at all events its Cerberus . . . [T]hese
dogs form an impassable line."[63] When convicts started trying to wade
out into the water to get past the line, Booth put more dogs on platforms
out from the shore. There may have been some truth to the legend that
the guards habitually dumped offal and blood off the beaches to draw
sharks, since there was a slaughtering-station a few miles away on
Forestier's Peninsula. But perhaps they just told the convicts they did.

To warn of escapes and crises in Port Arthur, and to receive messages from Hobart, Booth set up a chain of signal stations, the first long-range communication system in Australia. It was a "telegraph" without electricity, run by semaphores: tall poles set on hilltops and islands, each carrying three sets of double arms like railway signals. By a system of chains, each arm could be set at various angles, and each angle was allotted a numerical meaning. The number-groups translated into words, phrases and whole sentences through a codebook. Booth spent years of midnight oil on his signal book, which eventually contained thousands of number-groups referring to such matters as names, weather, runaway prisoners, supplies, tools, weapons, disease, food, places, measurements and distances. By 1844, the book listed 11,300 signals, which could be sent to Hobart through a relay of twenty-two stations perched on coastal headlands and islands around Storm Bay. In clear weather, it took less than half an hour to waggle a message to Hobart from Booth's transmitter, a wooden pole as high as a ship's mast, which dominated the settlement at Port Arthur. Local semaphores on the Tasman Peninsula could flash the news of a bolting convict from Port Arthur to Eaglehawk Neck in one minute flat.[64]

Deep in the sandstone about fifteen miles from Eaglehawk Neck, on the western side of Norfolk Bay, there was a seam of coal. What more chastening form of extra punishment than to turn convicts into miners, condemned to hard labor, darkness, extreme confinement and hourly fear of cave-ins? So Arthur reasoned, and told Booth to sink shafts there, worked by the most refractory prisoners. Before long, the commandant had built a large stone barracks for 170 men, whose apricot-colored ruins, fretted by wind and weather and underpinned by cramped, half-collapsed isolation cells, still gaze picturesquely over Norfolk Bay. The mineshafts, behind, are long closed. Working in them was much dreaded. Only eleven miners could attack the seam at a time, and each had to hew 30 trolleys-full or 2½ tons of coal a day. The deeper of the shafts was 100 feet below sea level, and seepage was a constant problem. Lumps of Port Arthur coal kept alight "for an incredible length of time," but "when at first lighted they crack and throw out small pieces in great quantities, to the detriment of carpets, furniture, ladies' gowns, etc." Nevertheless the fuel sold in Hobart for one-third the price of New South Wales coal and was in great demand.[65]

Booth's inventiveness shone forth, however, not from his mines but from his railway. It was a true curiosity, a small landmark in the history of transportation—in either sense of that word. It connected the dock at the head of Norfolk Bay, by Eaglehawk Neck, to the main settlement at Port Arthur some 4½ miles away. On it, supplies and people could be taken to the coal mines and the Neck without a long detour by sea around the peninsula. It was laid along a switchback route through the dense gum-and-fern forest; sawn hardwood rails about 6 inches by 3 inches were nailed to rough sleepers bedded in clay. Wooden bridges carried the line across the gullies. It had no engine; the power was supplied by convicts, propelling it at a trot, pushing against crossbars at front and rear. Its carriages were four-passenger carts, running on cast-iron mine-truck wheels. Such was the first passenger railway in Australia. It embarrassed some visitors, but on the other hand it was better than walking, especially for the ladies. The trucks of Booth's railway could rattle downhill at 30 mph, a terrifying velocity at a time when people seldom went faster than a trotting horse. Colonel Godfrey Mundy, a visitor to Port Arthur in 1851, described how the convicts pushed the cart up to the top of "a long descent,"

> when, gettting up their steam, down they rattled at tremendous speed— tremendous, at least, to lady-like nerves—the chains around their ankles chinking and clanking as they trotted along. . . . [T]he runners jumped upon the side of the trucks in rather unpleasant proximity with the passengers, and away we all went, bondsmen and freemen, jolting and swaying . . . a man sitting behind contrived, more or less, to lock a wheel with a wooden crowbar when the descent became so rapid as to call for remonstrance.

In a more pensive mood, Lieutenant-Governor Sir William Denison rode a similar convict railway at Ralph Bay Neck while on an official tour of inspection of Tasman Peninsula in 1847: "I must say that my feelings at seeing myself seated, and pushed along by these miserable convicts, were not very pleasant. It was painful to see them in the condition of slaves, which, in fact, they are, waiting for me up to their knees in water."[66]

It must have given the children pause, too. For Port Arthur was not only a prison for the errant mature; it was also a school for young boys.

v

THE VISITOR to Port Arthur in the 1830s and 1840s rarely failed to take a boat across Opossum Bay to a neck of land named Point Puer, where he could see, "climbing among the rocks and hiding or disappearing from our sight like land-crabs in the West Indies," a colony of ragged pale-faced lads.[67]

Point Puer was aptly named, *puer* being Latin for "boy." It was a prison for children between nine and eighteen years of age who, caught in the inexorable mechanism of British law, had been transported to Van Diemen's Land. "Little depraved felons" was Arthur's word for them. By the mid-1830s, they were arriving in disconcerting numbers, as the gross influx of transported felons steadily grew. Thus, out of 1,434 convicts disembarked at Hobart between January and September 1834, 240 were juveniles. In all, more than 2,000 such boys were transported to Van Diemen's Land and went to the reformatory at Point Puer.[68]

The problem for Arthur and his three-man Board of Assignment was what to do with them. They were, to the last boy, either too young or too ignorant to have a trade or to be of the slightest use to a settler. These bewildered tykes, many of them hardened in theft and flashness, for whom no place could be found in the assignment system, were a dead weight on the government. Some were helpless, Arthur recognized, from "having been thrown upon the world totally destituted, others have become so from the tutelage of dissolute parents—and others have been agents of dexterous thieves about London—but all are objects of compassion."[69]

In 1833, sixty-eight such lads were vegetating in the Prisoners' Barracks in Hobart, and Arthur's "compassion" expressed itself by sending them all to the Tasman Peninsula. They arrived in January 1834, all of them drunk, for on the ship they had broken into a six-dozen crate of wine and shared it with the adult convicts on board. After a sharp lecture from Commandant Booth, they were put in a large, drafty temporary barracks rigidly segregated from the main settlement, so that the adult prisoners would have no chance to "contaminate" them. Point Puer was well isolated, with a shoreline consisting mainly of sixty-foot cliffs and the sea around it full of boiling rips and dangerous currents—"a wretched, bleak, barren spot without water, wood for fuel or an inch of soil that is not . . . utterly valueless." It would improve along with its inmates, or so the System assumed.[70]

The juvenile population at Port Arthur climbed rapidly. By the end of 1834, Booth had 161 boys under his eye; in 1836, 271; and in 1837, a special transport ship, the *Frances Charlotte,* was dispatched from England at the benevolent suggestion of Lord John Russell, with 139 boys and 10 adult overseers on board. By 1842, there were 716 lads on this dismal neck of land, and a jumble of barracks, workrooms and schoolrooms had grown up to shelter them.

They were to be schooled, taught trades, instructed in the truths of Christianity, and punished. "Keep in mind that these boys have been very wicked," wrote Arthur to Booth in 1834, in the ominous accents of Dickens's Wackford Squeers; "the utmost care should be taken to enforce upon their minds the disgraceful condition in which they are placed, whilst every effort should be made to eradicate their corrupt habits." He did not want to see too much time wasted in "instructing the boys in reading and writing." They needed practical skills, which

would make useful assigned servants of them. They would acquire these
from a hard daily grind. Up at 5:00 a.m., fold hammocks, assembly, Bible
reading and prayer; breakfast at 7:00, hygiene inspection, muster, and
classes in practical trades like joinery or bootmaking from 8:00 to 12:00.
At midday, ablutions and another inspection; at 12:30, dinner; from 1:30
to 5:00, more apprentice work; wash and inspection again, and supper at
5:30; muster for school at 6:15; then school lessons for an hour, followed
by evening prayers and Scripture reading, and bed at 7:30. Later the time
for schoolwork in the evening was increased to two hours; it made little
difference, however, as most of the boys were by then too fatigued to
learn anything much.

The most successful part of this regime was the trade instruction,
which was remarkably diverse. By 1837 it included baking, shoemaking,
carpentry, tailoring, gardening, nail-making and blacksmithery. Enroll-
ment in trade classes was limited, and most boys wanted to get into
them. "As vacancies occur," reported Booth, "the better disposed are
selected to be placed at a trade, which is eagerly sought after." They were
anxious to get out of the laboring gangs, where every new arrival at Point
Puer was introduced to "the use of the spade, the hoe and the grubbing-
axe." Boys in the laboring gangs did the donkey-work of Point Puer—the
cleaning and scrubbing, the fetching and carrying—and they were
worked hard; it may be no coincidence that, out of thirty-eight boys who
died at Point Puer in the years 1834 to 1843, twenty-two were laborers.
To be a sawyer or a joiner was far better. It also meant free skilled (or
semi-skilled) labor for the Establishment, of the kind noted in the Port
Arthur returns:

> Construction of wheel-barrows, four cells, five coffins, 390 hammer-
> handles, six barrack stools, 13 school desks, 4 garden gates, and one set of
> stocks, and a pillory.
> Turning of 216 masons' mallets, 20 hat-pins, 50 belaying-pins, 2 bed-
> posts, and 243 ships' blocks.
> Making 17 pairs of Wellingtons @ 11s. pr., 24 Bluchers @ 5s. a pr.,
> 2 prs. ladies' shoes @ 3s. a pr., 1788 boots, prisoners', @ 4s. a pr.

Point Puer boys made the nails, sewed the convicts' "canary" uniforms
of yellow and gray wool, painted the fences, forged the ax-heads and
shaped the sledgehammer handles with their drawknives; the stonemasons among them laboriously cut the ashlar for the round security towers
of Port Arthur, chiselled the moldings and ornamented keystones for the
stone arches, hewed the angles of the pediments. The carpentry class
made the elaborate pulpit and pews for the large neo-Gothic church, and

in 1844 the thirty-four brickmakers turned out 155,000 bricks, some of which—bearing the thumb-marks left by those long-dead adolescents as they pushed the bricks from the sandstock molds—still lie scattered among the ruins of Point Puer.

There is no question that Point Puer boys received a trades education as good as (and probably better than) any they could have hoped to get in England in the 1830s. But their intellectual schooling was rudimentary. In 1842, some boys who had been there two or three years had difficulty reading words of one syllable; their arithmetic was no better. The only readers the pupils had were Bibles, supplied by a Wesleyan mission, and there were a few spelling-books and primers, but never enough; for eight hundred pupils there was "one very small blackboard seldom used" and not even a map of the world. The state of religious instruction was not much better. At first, it had been in the hands of Methodists, who reported in 1836 that "considerable attention is given to the boys' religious instruction and several have been brought under the saving influence of the Gospel"; Backhouse and Walker, the visiting Quakers, vehemently dissented, finding the boys' morals in "a most degraded state." The Wesleyans were replaced in 1837 by an eager young Anglican catechist, Peter Barrow, fresh from running an orphanage for black foundlings on the coast of Sierra Leone. He thought a chaplain could reclaim half or even two-thirds of the Point Puer boys. He failed. Five years later, a few of the boys could parrot bits of an Anglican catechism, but none could recite the Commandments in correct order or show much grasp of scriptural history. Even their hymn-singing had declined, to the point that "the screaming is almost intolerable to any person whose ears have not been rendered callous."[71]

The likelihood of producing good little Christians at such a place was slight. Like any borstal or boarding-school, Point Puer had not one but two social systems: an official one imposed by the commandant and the chaplain, and a tribal one invented by the boys. Benjamin Horne, reporting on the place in 1842, mentioned "a sort of tyranny of public opinion amongst themselves which every boy in the place must submit to as a slave, almost at peril of his life . . . [T]he maxim of the whole fraternity was that everyone must tell as many lies [to overseers and other authorities] as may be necessary for himself and the community."[72]

The boy who ratted on his fellow prisoners would be persecuted and hazed half to death. The Point Puer boys had no reason to like their jailers; and although conditions there were at least no worse than an English orphanage or ragged-school, they were little better and its inmates loathed them. In particular, the boys hated the convict overseers as tyrants. If an overseer fell asleep on night dormitory watch, the lads would put out the lights and empty the communal chamber pot over his head. One especially unpopular overseer was so battered in such a nocturnal scuffle that he spent three months in the hospital. In 1843 one overseer, Hugh McGine, was murdered by a pair of fourteen-year-olds named Henry Sparks and George Campbell.[73]

If a boy at Point Puer found a middle way between the strictures of Authority and the pressure of his peers and managed to learn a trade, he could come out with a better chance of making good than most assigned men; if not, the System would simply grind him down. So it was with Thomas Willetts, a stunted boy of sixteen from Warwick, transported in 1834 for filching some stockings and garden vegetables, who in the course of five years at Point Puer and Port Arthur racked up a total of 35 lashes from the full cat-o'-nine tails, 183 strokes of the cane on his butt and 19 sentences of solitary confinement.

THOMAS WILLETTS N° 1809

tried 12 March 1833, arr^d V.D.L. Aug^t 1834.

| | |
|---|---|
| Trade: None. | Height: 4 ft. 11 in. |
| Complex^n: Dark | Head: Small |
| Hair: Brown | Whiskers: None |
| Visage: Small | Forehead: M. Ht. |
| Eyebrows: Brown | Eyes: Grey |
| Nose: Small | Mouth: Med. Wide |
| Chin: Small | Remarks: Pockmarked, scar on Rt. Arm. |

Arrived in Van Diemen's Land August 1834.
Convict. 7 Years' Transportation.
Tried at Warwick, transported for stealing Stockings.
Character—*Very Bad.*

1834

DEC^r 30TH: Assaulting fellow prisoner & attempt to deprive him of his bread: 24 lashes on the breech.

1835

SEPT. 9: Transferred to Port Arthur.
SEPT. 28: Improper & riotous conduct in the Cells: 15 lashes on the breech.
OCT. 21: Swearing, etc.: 7 days solitary confinement.
NOV. 18: Having Tobacco: 5 days ditto

1836

FEB. 22: Having turnips, 5 days ditto
NOV. 3: Insolent conduct to Overseer, 4 days ditto

Nov. 7: Talking in cells, 3 days ditto

Dec^r 26: Most improper conduct to the Ass^t Sub-Constable in the Execution of his Duty: 36 stripes.

### 1837

Jan 26: Fighting in the Schoolroom, 3 Days Solitary, Bread & Water.

Feb. 18: Disorderly Conduct in School on Sunday, 5 Days ditto, ditto.

March 20: Having a pair of Fustian Trowsers in his possession and most Improper Conduct towards the Assist. Sub-Constable: 36 Stripes on the Breech.

Same date: Most Contemptuous Conduct in laughing immediately on leaving the Office after Sentence for the preceding Offence: 7 days' solitary confinement on bread & water.

May 29: Having a pair of Boots improperly: 4 Days Solit^y Conf^t.

June 26: Smoking in his hut contrary to orders: 3 weeks in No. 2 Chain Gang.

Sept. 2nd: Gross Misconduct & Violence to Schoolmaster: 36 Stripes on the breech.

### 1838

Jan 17: Insolence: 3 Days solitary Confinement, Bread & Water.

March 16: Gross insolence, 7 days ditto.

April 19: Improper Conduct towards a fellow Boy: 10 days ditto.

June 25: Talking in church during Divine Service, 48 hrs. sol^y conf^t on B^d & W^r.

July 7: Striking a fellow prisoner: 36 Stripes on the breech.

July 28: Talking in the Cells and Insolence when checked, 3 days solitary, B^d & W^r.

August 3: Having his Face disgracefully disfigured, 48 hrs. sol^y conf^mt.

August 16: Gross indecency on his going to the cells, 4 days ditto.

October 1st: Absenting himself without leave from Public Works at Port Arthur and remaining absent until apprehended and brought back: 7 days ditto.

### 1839

March 5: Absconding: 35 lashes.

March 20: Absconding: 2 years hard labour in Chain Gang, Port Arthur —conduct to be reported to Lieutenant Governor.

July 18: Disorderly Conduct: 24 hrs. solitary conf^t.

Oct^r 9: Having a Silk Stock in possession improperly: 1 month on No. 2 Chain Gang.

Dec 5: Neglect of Duty and refusing to work: 1 month ditto.[74]

On skins like his, the flaws of Arthur's system were glaringly inscribed. But however wretched the life of the "incorrigible," the "fractious" and the "refractory" could be made at Port Arthur, their sufferings were slight compared to the fate of the Tasmanian Aborigines under Arthur's reign.

vi

COLONEL ARTHUR's last big problem was the Tasmanian blacks; and he was theirs. By 1824, the year he came to Van Diemen's Land, a vicious, undeclared and seemingly unfinishable guerrilla war had been dragging on between whites and blacks for two decades. Its first shots were fired at Risdon Cove in 1804, a few months after the first landing. Years later, Edward White, a former convict, told a Committee for Aboriginal Affairs how it had been. On May 3, 1804, he was hoeing ground by the creek when a party of some three hundred Aborigines, men, women and children, came out of the bush, driving a mob of kangaroos before them. The blacks were strung out in a big crescent, between the 'roos and the water. They carried clubs but no spears, and White saw that they were not a war-party; all they meant to do was kill the cornered game, build their fires and have a corroborree. He remembered how "they looked at me with all their eyes . . . [they] did not threaten me; I was not afraid of them." Nevertheless he ran off to tell the soldiers, who loaded their muskets and marched on the tribespeople. "The Natives did not attack the soldiers; they would not have molested them." Nevertheless the soldiers trained a carronade on them point-blank and blasted them with grapeshot. Nobody counted how many of the unarmed blacks were slaughtered, but at the end of the massacre the colonial surgeon Jacob Mountgarrett, prompted by some anthropological whim, salted down a couple of casks of their bones and sent them to Sydney.[75]

There may have been four thousand Aborigines in Van Diemen's Land when the whites landed; by Arthur's time there were considerably fewer, although it is hardly possible to guess how many. Perhaps ten blacks were killed for every white, perhaps twenty. At first the dirty little war sputtered its way around Hobart and the banks of the Derwent, as settlers in the starvation years competed against blacks for the kangaroos. Sometimes whites killed blacks for sport. In 1806 two early bushrangers, John Brown and Richard Lemon, "used to stick them, and fire at them as marks whilst alive." Another escaped convict, James Carrott or Carrett, abducted an Aborigine's wife near Oyster Bay, killed her husband when he came after them, cut off his head and forced her to wear it slung around her neck in a bag "as a plaything."[76] There were rumors that kangaroo-hunters would shoot blacks to feed their dogs. Two whites cut the cheek off an aboriginal boy and forced him to chew and swallow it. At Oatlands, north of Hobart, convict stock-keepers kept aboriginal women as sexual slaves, secured by bullock-chains to their huts. On the Bass Strait coast, marauding sealers would try to buy women from the tribes; the usual offer was four or five sealskins for a woman, but if the Aborigines would not sell, they would shoot the men and kidnap the women. When one of these women tried to run away from the sealers, they trussed her up, cut off her ears and some flesh from her thigh and made her eat it. All this and more, the convict pioneer James Hobbes remarked, with some understatement, "was known by the tribes, and operated on their minds."[77]

The pattern of violence between black and white in Van Diemen's Land was fully established by 1815. It went on against a background of proclamations by the lieutenant-governor—Collins, Davey and Sorell all issued them—enjoining the settlers not to provoke or persecute the blacks and stressing that they had the full protection of English law. Their utterances weighed nothing against the reality of invasion: The whites were on the blacks' land, and grabbing as much of it as they could. No colonists were prepared to consider such two-legged animals as beings with prior rights.

So the war of random encounter inexorably changed into one of extermination, as the settlements and the stock-pastures spread. The late 1820s began a roaring boom in sheep-farming and wool exports. Some stock-breeders got three lambings every two years. In 1827 there were 436,256 sheep in Van Diemen's Land. By 1830 there were 682,128, an increase of more than 55 percent. By 1836 the ovine population had risen by another third, to 911,357—20 sheep for every white person in the colony. The export figures, in pounds sterling, tell their own story of growth:[78]

| YEAR | GROSS EXPORTS | WOOL EXPORTS |
| --- | --- | --- |
| 1825 | £ 44,498 | £ 12,543 |
| 1827 | 59,912 | 9,089 |
| 1830 | 141,745 | 57,724 |
| 1832 | 152,967 | 63,145 |
| 1836 | 540,221 | 220,739 |

This new prosperity affected the look, the self-esteem, the very fiber of Vandemonian life. "Trade flourishes exceedingly," wrote Richard Stickney, a Quaker emigrant, to his sister Sarah in 1834; there are

rows of shops in the first London style and elegant houses are springing up like magic. The Sperm Whale fishery is carried on successfully and to a great extent, whilst Wool is becoming a greatly increasing article of export. The peach tree is loaded with fruit without the aid of a gardener. . . . I don't think England has a colony where everything appears so much like home as this. The scarcety of the Black Natives, . . . the excellent roads, the fashionable appearance of the well-dressed inhabitants, carriages without number and good horses. It really has not the dull look of a Colony at all but the bustle and activity of an English seaport. A stranger might easily fancy himself in England.[79]

In 1829 the "scarcety of the Black Natives" was not so pronounced, and no savages would be allowed to interfere with growth. But the sheep were destroying the Aborigines' food base by displacing kangaroos and other game. By the late 1820s, retaliatory raids by tribesmen against sheep had become a constant nuisance: They speared the stock and left them dead on the ground, often without eating them, as a sign of contempt; they robbed and burned outlying huts and, although frontal attacks on homesteads were rare, they kept convict shepherds in continuous terror. Out of these scattered forays, by 1829, a general strategy seemed to be emerging. The idea that they had developed "a systematic plan of attacking the settlers and their possessions," thought Archdeacon Broughton, chairman of a committee convened in 1830 by Arthur to inquire into the causes of black hostility to white settlers, "has been but too completely verified by the events of the last two years. . . . It is manifest that they have lost the sense of the superiority of white men, and the dread of the effect of fire-arms."[80]

The Aborigines had learned not to attack en masse, charging into the muzzles of the settlers' guns. Instead, they harassed the periphery of settlement, the stock-huts and shepherds' cottages. In the first three months of 1830, there were almost thirty such incidents, involving the death of eight whites. The tribesmen set fire to thatched roofs to drive the whites into the open. They lured stockmen into the bush away from their huts where they could be more easily killed, and the undefended hut was plundered and burned. Then the blacks would melt away into the hills, where few whites could catch up with them. One settler, Gilbert Robertson, complained that there was no "effectual mode of pursuing them. . . . [T]hey cannot be surrounded by several parties coming upon them; they go all over the whole island; they always keep regular sentries, and pass over dangerous grounds, and by the brinks of the most dangerous precipices." He had a low opinion of the soldiers' ability to pursue the black marauder, declaring that they were "quite useless . . . they will not exert themselves." Settlers, police and convicts did better. Sometimes they hunted tribal groups down like kangaroos, shooting them from horseback; but the efficient way to catch up with the Aborigines was to follow them by night and mark their campfire smoke in the morning. One party of five or six constables from Campbell Town, according to Robertson (although his story was indignantly denied by other whites), ambushed an encampment of natives in a gully between two cliffs and slaughtered seventy of them; and when the gunsmoke cleared, they went down among the rocks, dragged out the terrified women and children and brained them. This, he thought, put paid to the whole tribe.[81]

When whites did such things, they showed necessary rigor; when Aborigines threw their spears from ambush, they proved their treachery. Whites "defended their interests," while blacks "perpetrated atrocities" and "committed the most wanton and unprovoked acts of barbarity." Faced with the black resistance, the settlers began sliding toward panic. Arthur, after a long and searching field trip among the agitated settlers of the outer districts that had borne the brunt of aboriginal resistance, noted a curious passivity in them. "The indifference . . . is quite remarkable, and strikingly manifests that people are always much more ready to complain of evils than disposed to exert themselves to overcome them." Instead of whingeing, he thought, they should get guns and learn to use them—"the only security which can be given, unless a safety-guard were placed in every dwelling, a thing which is impossible."[82]

Arthur's Committee for Aboriginal Affairs knew where the real blame for this ghastly situation lay, and declared that "every degree of moderation and forbearance" was due to the "ignorant, debased and un-reflecting" blacks, so cruelly wronged by "miscreants who were a disgrace to our name and nation." But on the other hand, one had to admit that "the Natives are now visiting the injuries they have received, not on the actual defenders, but on a different and *totally innocent* class." This reflected Arthur's own delusion that the only people to blame for the murder and harassment of the Aborigines were escaped convicts, sealers and other colonial trash—never the respectable settlers, who "always" showed "kindness and humanity."[83]

Some of these colonial innocents aired brisk and strong views on how to handle the blacks. "They must be captured or exterminated," opined John Sherwin, merchant, whose house on the River Clyde near Bothwell had just been burned to the ground. He said that others (not he) had proposed setting up "decoy huts, containing flour and sugar, strongly impregnated with poison." He claimed he did not know of any atrocities whites had done to blacks; all that was exaggeration. But if they did not take steps soon, by bringing in blacktrackers and bloodhounds from Sydney and hunting the pests down, no one could live in the bush, for "the Natives wish to have their lands to themselves." His fellow settler George Espie wanted to see 150 armed convicts sent after the natives, with a promise of a ticket-of-leave for every two or three blacks a man

brought in —"they would shoot more than they would capture." Roderic
O'Connor, a red-hot Irishman who accumulated vast estates while serving Arthur as magistrate and land commissioner, growled that armed
posses of convicts might do the trick; he knew of one man named Douglas Ibbets who had wiped out half the "Eastern mob" of natives with his
double-barrelled shotgun. "Some of the worst characters would be the
best to send after them." An elderly farmer named Brodribb claimed
he knew of no rational cause for the blacks' new ferocity, that most
settlers treated them kindly, that he really "cannot form an idea if the
Natives are displeased at our taking possession of the country"—and
so on.[84]

The Aborigines, in fact, were in their last frenzy of resistance. In 1828
Arthur reported to Goderich that "I have been pressingly called upon by
the settlers . . . to adopt some measure which should free them from
these troublesome assailants, and from the nuisance of their dogs."[85] He
felt he had to take "some decisive step," and he thought the most likely
one was to round them all up and put them—every last Aborigine on
Van Diemen's Land—on one of the islands in Bass Strait, give them
temporary rations, teach them to raise crops and so convert them by
force from nomadic hunter-gatherers into a "stationary . . . civilization."
But he realized it would not work:

> They already complain that the white people have taken possession of
> their country, encroached upon their hunting grounds, and destroyed their
> natural food, the kangaroo; and they doubtless would be exasperated to
> the last degree to be banished altogether from their favourite haunts; and
> as they would be ill-disposed to receive instructions from their oppres-
> sors, any attempt to civilize them . . . must fail.[86]

Besides, Arthur knew where the blame lay: "All aggression originated
with the white inhabitants, and . . . much ought to be endured in return
before the blacks are treated as an open and accredited enemy by the
government."

So instead of sending them to a miserable death on an island, Arthur
proposed an early form of *apartheid* to keep them out of the settled
districts. His idea was to round them up and move them all to the northeast coast of Van Diemen's Land, "the best sheltered and warmest part,"
where they would be fed and clothed by the government and protected
from the annihilating fury of white farmers.

He issued a proclamation. It repeated what everyone knew: that the
whites (especially convicts: shepherds, stockmen and sealers) were the
first aggressors, but that now the black resistance was making "advances
in art, system and method." So ways must be found to "restrict the

intercourse" between white and black "by a legislative Enactment, of a permanent nature"—putting them beyond a pale of settlement in the northeastern corner. In the meantime, there would be a line of military guard posts stationed along the confines of the settled districts, which the Aborigines must not cross:

> And I do hereby strictly command and order all Aborigines immediately to retire and depart from, and for no reason, and on no pretence, save as hereinafter provided, to re-enter such settled districts, or any portions of land cultivated and occupied by any person whomsoever, on pain of forcible expulsion therefrom, and such consequences as may be necessarily attendant on it.[87]

This magnificently festooned slab of imperial boilerplate meant nothing to the blacks, who could not read and kept striking back against their white tormentors as best they could, while suffering the "necessarily attendant" consequences.

So Arthur proclaimed martial law against the Aborigines in the settled center of the island. It would not extend to designated outer areas, to which he hoped the blacks would drift—the Tasman Peninsula, the northeast and southwest corners, all the country south of Mount Wellington to the ocean including Bruny Island, and the whole western coast.[88] This must have seemed a fair deal to Arthur, since the "settled districts" had few kangaroos left and could not support the traditional forms of aboriginal life, whereas the areas he had exempted from martial law and hoped to push the blacks into were wild, untrammelled, unlikely ever to be settled, full of game, and constituted about half the land area of Van Diemen's Land. But the Aborigines did not think it fair.

Meanwhile, the whites kept slaughtering the blacks, women and children usually first, with musket and fowling piece, cutlass and ax. By 1830, there were perhaps two thousand Aborigines left alive in Van Diemen's Land.[89] Some settlers took Arthur's proclamation of martial law as a license to kill. In February 1830 Arthur's colonial secretary tried to recall them to a sense of measure and proportion:

> The repeated orders which have been put forth by this Government must convey the idea . . . that there exists a horde of savages in Van Diemen's Land whose prowess is equal to their revengeful feelings; thereas every settler must be conscious that his foe consists of an inconsiderable number of a very feeble race, not possessing physical strength, and quite undistinguished by personal courage.[90]

But the pressure on Arthur to solve the "black problem" was intense, and he must have reflected that a solution would amend his own extreme unpopularity with the colonists, for people will love an autocrat if they believe he is a savior. Suppressing the Aborigines was the only major issue on which every settler in Van Diemen's Land was ready to work with Arthur and the military. "How cordially and entirely the whole community unite with the earnest desire of the Government!" he reported to Murray in London.[91]

Reading Arthur's reports in London, Sir George Murray, secretary of state for the colonies, had felt a tingle of premonition: "The whole race of [Van Diemen's Land Aborigines] may, at no distant period, become extinct. . . . [A]ny line of conduct, having for its avowed, or for its secret object, the extinction of the Native race, could not fail to leave an indelible stain upon the character of the British Government."[92]

Arthur decided to bring every white—settlers as well as military—into one concerted effort to expel the aboriginal tribes from the settled areas of the island, where they had become such a menace to Europeans, and bottle them up in the Tasman Peninsula, between Forestier's Neck and Eaglehawk Neck, where they could be kept imprisoned forever by a small garrison at either end. This operation was called the Black Line. He may not have expected it to succeed; it was, as Robson rightly called it, "an excellent public relations exercise to show that the highly unpopular Arthur apparently had the welfare of the colonists at heart."[93] But if he wanted to preserve any loyalty among the colonists, he had little choice. The settlements were almost hysterical with fear that the coming spring of 1830 would produce a bloodbath. The Big River and Oyster Bay tribes had become "too much enjoined in the most rancorous animosity to be spared the most vigorous measures against them."[94] In a meeting with his Executive Council late in August 1830, Arthur succumbed to the pressure and agreed to a spring offensive against the Big River and Oyster Bay tribes.

It took the form of an immense pheasant-drive, under the command of Major Douglas of the 63rd Regiment. Every white man in Van Diemen's Land, Arthur reported to London, joined in it "with the most zealous and cheerful alacrity."[95] The main line of hunters stretched across two-thirds of the island, from St. Patricks' Head on the east coast to Quamby Bluff in the Western Tiers; it was supported by two flanking lines, one in the east and the other in the southwest, to catch any Aborigines who slipped by the ends of the main line. Some 2,200 men formed the Black Line—550 troops from the 17th, 57th and 63rd Regiments, 700 convicts, and the rest free settlers. They carried between them a thousand muskets, 30,000 rounds of ammunition and 300 pairs of handcuffs with which to subdue the resistant natives. Off they set on October 7, 1830: redcoats sweltering in their woollen uniforms under the load of knapsacks and muskets, mounted dragoons plodding forward in a clink of steel and a creaking of leather, stout farmers with their fowling pieces, cornstalk boys with red faces and hard eyes. Keeping the line as best they could, they surged slowly downward toward the Tasman Peninsula along paths determined for them by the officers of the Survey Department, hallooing and cursing and beating the bush for its black wraiths, firing musketry into the air and blowing bugles. Their movements, Arthur reported, were "much better executed than could have been anticipated." At night the bush flickered with guard fires and one man in three stood sentry duty to prevent the escape of the crafty foe."

It took the Black Line seven weeks to converge, like the closing of a fishing net, on the peninsula. A few Aborigines were spotted, and there were some brief skirmishes; two Oyster Bay tribesmen were captured and two others shot, but Arthur was certain that the main mass of them were fleeing ahead of the Black Line toward the Tasman Peninsula. "The forces are now . . . moving forward in full hopes of success," he reported from the town of Sorell on November 20, 1830.

When the net closed, it was empty. The Black Line had caught two Aborigines, a man and a small boy. All the rest had slipped through. The enterprise had been a fiasco, and for once Arthur's detailed and prolix reports to London became terse, almost evasive. Yet the Big River tribe had been driven into comparative seclusion beyond the Western Tiers, and the Oyster Bay tribesmen were split up and forced from their habitual territory; so, from the whites' point of view, the episode could be called a strategic victory, even though it did not produce all the results Arthur hoped for. It also suggested that there were fewer Aborigines in the settled districts than Major Douglas had supposed.[96] This did wonders for the settlers' morale. Arthur felt he could move from a military solution to one of "pacification." This new strategy took the mild, quietly convivial and persistent form of an emigrant house-builder from London, George Augustus Robinson (1788–1866), the "Conciliator."[97]

Robinson had been interested in the Aborigines from the moment he arrived in Van Diemen's Land. He had a philanthropic vision: He would bring these chafed and resentful people, by mildness and understanding, into the fold of white law and religion—but not before he, unlike all previous missionaries and go-betweens, had come to understand their ways and language. In 1828, in the lull before the final desperate retaliations of the black tribes, Arthur had advertised for a man who might be able to conciliate them. Robinson had put himself forward and was accepted. He tried to evangelize the blacks on Bruny Island in 1829, but his real work began the following year, when he went on an arduous eight-month trek into the wilderness of the southwest and west coast searching for surviving tribal groups of Aborigines. He had a party with him made up of trusty convict servants, an aboriginal chief from Bruny Island

named Woorrady and another from the Swanport district named Eumar-
rah, four black tribesmen and three women.

One of the latter was a bright, promiscuous girl named Trucanini,
about eighteen years old, also from Bruny Island.[98] She was very small,
only 4 feet 3 inches high, and had pronounced curly whiskers; in other
respects, all white witnesses agreed, she was remarkably attractive—for
an Aborigine. As a child, she had seen her mother stabbed to death in a
night raid by whites; later, a sealer named John Baker had kidnapped two
of her tribal sisters and her blood sister, Moorina, and taken them in
slavery to the tribe of white pirates that lived on Kangaroo Island, far to
the west off the coast of South Australia. Her stepmother was abducted
by the convict mutineers of the brig *Cyprus* and must have died as they
were seeking China; she was never heard from again. Around 1828, she
was crossing from the mainland to Bruny Island with several tribesmen,
to one of whom she was "betrothed," in a boat manned by two convict
loggers. In mid-channel, the whites seized the black men and threw them
overboard; when they grabbed for the gunwale and tried to haul themselves up, the loggers chopped their hands off and left them to sink. They
then rowed her ashore and raped her. Trucanini, one would presume, had
every reason to hate the whites. In fact she sought their company thereafter and was busy becoming a sealers' moll, sterile from gonorrhea,
hanging around the camps and selling herself for a handful of tea and
sugar, when Robinson and his guide Woorrady persuaded her to come on
their long, strange journey of "conciliation" to the remaining tribes of
Van Diemen's Land.

They all set off in the winter of 1830, ill-equipped and badly provisioned, and suffered appalling hardships from exposure, hunger and
scurvy. But they worked their way around the west coast, from Port
Davey to Macquarie Harbor and thence to Cape Grim, the aptly named
northwesternmost tip of Van Diemen's Land. From there they struck
east along the coast and reached Launceston early in October, just after
Arthur's Black Line had begun working south.

Robinson was to venture upon five more such expeditions, and by the
end of 1834 Robinson had made contact with every tribe and group of
Aborigines left in Tasmania. Always the method was the same: opening
civilities with presents and food, and a winning of the shy or hostile
blacks' confidence with the help of Woorrady and Trucanini; a compilation of their basic vocabularies; notes on their ceremonies and religious
customs, as far as he could determine them; a friendly parting, and then
a new visit with promises of sanctuary. If they would "come in" with
him, the Conciliator told these dying and frightened remnants of their
race, they would be given a safe haven where no white man would persecute them, where they would have food and clothing and peace.

Slowly, the blacks followed him; and when he brought in the last of the once-feared warriors of the Big River and Oyster Bay tribes—a pathetic group of sixteen people—he was greeted like a Roman conqueror in Hobart. A colonial artist, Benjamin Duterreau, painted him posed with "his" Aborigines; the girl on the right, leading a doubtful native by one hand and pointing at Robinson with the other, is Trucanini, the archtraitor to her race.

Thus, by 1834, the last Aborigines of Van Diemen's Land had followed their evangelical Pied Piper into a benign concentration camp, set up on Flinders Island in Bass Strait. There, Robinson planned to Europeanize them. They were given clothes, new names, Bibles and elementary schooling. They were shown how to buy and sell things, so that they might acquire a reverence for property. They were allowed to elect their own police. In the main, however, they simply died—of accidie, deracination and new diseases. In 1835, only 150 Aborigines were left. Little by little, they wasted away and their ghosts drifted out over the water. Robinson left Flinders in 1839 and returned to the Australian mainland. His successors chose to treat Flinders Island as a jail, and its dwindling colony of Aborigines as prisoners. Occasionally a girl would be flogged, but only for moral offenses. In 1843 there were fifty-four Aborigines alive. Three years later, amid blood-curdling prophecies of a new black war from the colonial press, the survivors were returned to the mainland and settled on a property at Oyster Cove on the D'Entrecasteaux Channel, near Hobart. There they guzzled rum, which was thoughtfully provided by their keepers; they posed impassively for photographers in front of their filthy slab huts; and they waited to die. In 1855 the census of natives was three men, two boys and eleven women, one of whom was Trucanini.

The last man died in 1869. His name was William Lanne and he was described as Trucanini's "husband," although he was twenty-three years her junior. Realizing that his remains might have some value as a scientific specimen, rival agents of the Royal College of Surgeons in London and the Royal Society in Tasmania fought over his bones. A Dr. William Crowther, representing the Royal College of Surgeons, sneaked into the morgue, beheaded Lanne's corpse, skinned the head, removed the skull and slipped another skull from a white cadaver into the black skin. This gruesome ruse was soon unmasked, for when a medical officer picked the head up, "the face turned round and at the back of the head the bones were sticking out." In pique, the officials decided not to let the Royal College of Surgeons get the whole skeleton; so they chopped off the feet and hands from Lanne's corpse and threw them away. The lopped, dishonored cadaver of the last tribesman was then officially buried, unofficially exhumed the next night and dissected for its skeleton by representatives of the Royal Society. It was, one of them remarked with some understatement, a "dirty job." Lanne's skeleton then disappeared; and the head, which Crowther consigned by sea to the Royal College of Surgeons, vanished too. It seems that the ineffable doctor had packaged it in a sealskin, and before long the bundle stank so badly that it was tossed overboard.

Trucanini wept and raged inconsolably when she was told of the fate of Lanne's body. She had long been frightened of death and of the evil spirit Rowra who would exact the revenge of the dead tribes she had betrayed; but now a further terror joined those. She begged a clergyman to make sure that when she died, she would be wrapped in a bag with a stone at her feet and dropped into the deepest part of the D'Entrecasteaux Channel—"because I know that when I die, the Tasmanian Museum wants my body." By 1873, the last of her black companions was dead and Trucanini was taken to Hobart, where she lingered on in a wretched aura of colonial celebrity, invented by the whites, as the "Queen of the Aborigines." One May evening in 1876 she was heard to scream, "Missus, Rowra catch me, Rowra catch me!" A stroke felled her, and she lay in coma for five days. Her last words, as the dark peeled back for a moment from her terrified consciousness, were, "Don't let them cut me, but bury me behind the mountains."

The government arranged a funeral procession for the last Tasmanian on May 11, 1876. Huge crowds lined the pavements to watch her small, almost square coffin roll by; they followed it to the cemetery, and saw it lowered into a grave. It was empty. Fearing some unseemly public disturbance, the government had buried her corpse in a vault of the Protestant Chapel in the Hobart Penitentiary the night before. So Trucanini lay not "behind the mountains," but in jail. In 1878 they dug her up again and sloughed the flesh off her bones, then boiled them and nailed them in an apple crate, which lay in storage for some years. The crate was about to be thrown out when someone from the Tasmanian Museum and Art Gallery read the faded label. The bones were strung together, and the skeleton of Trucanini went into a glass case in the museum, where it remained until feelings of public delicacy and humanitarian sentiment caused it to be removed, in 1947, to the basement. In 1976, the centenary of her death, the authorities—not knowing what else to do with this otherwise ineradicable dweller in their closet—had it cremated, and the ashes were scattered on the waters of the D'Entrecasteaux Channel. Just 140 years had passed since the day in 1836 when the virtuous and unbending proconsul, Sir George Arthur, had been ushered weeping onto the *Elphinstone* at the New Wharf and, to the cheers of several hundred free Vandemonians, had sailed away to England, his baronetcy and the deserved gratitude of the Crown.

# 12

# Metastasis

i

I N 1815, the year Napoleon was crushed and England could once
more turn her strength to building an empire, the map of white
settlement in New South Wales was hardly more than a patch, consisting only of Sydney and Parramatta. The rest was void, the scarcely
penetrated green continuum of bush, with a few tracks winding their
frail, dusty capillaries toward inland farms.

By 1825 this had changed. There were specks on the coast north of
Sydney—Newcastle, Port Macquarie, Moreton Bay—scattered along
a thousand miles of coastline and tenuously linked by ships; and
Norfolk Island, which had been abandoned on Macquarie's orders, was
resettled.

These little footholds were hamlets of punishment. They had not
been created by the hopes of settlers. A growing convict population, and
increased severity from the authorities, had forced them into existence.
They were, as the phrase went, "the Botany Bay of Botany Bay"—en-
claves of banishment in a land of exile. The flood of convicts to Australia
had now begun in earnest. From 1820 to 1831 the number of convicts
serving sentences there would never be less than 40 percent of the total
population. The creation of the penal out-stations was a response to
crisis, even though, in practice, less than one prisoner in ten ever served
time in one. If Australia was going to scare English criminals, the penal
out-stations would have to terrify colonial ones.

By 1825, the English authorities knew—and in fact, had come to
accept—that their ways of dealing with crime had failed in the past, were
not working now and would be unlikely to succeed in the foreseeable
future. The crime rate in England had not dropped; thus one had to
conclude that transportation did not deter. The question of "reformation" was not quite as important, since so few people came back from
Australia. In 1826, for instance, only about 7 percent of the convicts freed

at the end of their sentences chose to return to England, an eloquent comment on what they believed their chances were there.[1]

Nevertheless the criminal-justice system was by now addicted to transportation and had no real alternatives. In 1821 the government had built an experimental penitentiary at Millbank on the Thames, designed to hold eight hundred people—minor criminals, both men and women, whose offenses would have brought them 7 years' transportation. It cost half a million pounds and was a failure; its cold cells and defective drains killed the prisoners like flies. Neither public nor government opinion was ready for wholesale jail reform yet; and, in the meantime, transportation was far cheaper than building new prisons. Besides, the idea of the penitentiary was seen as an American invention; no Tory and few Whigs desired to mimic the ideas of that rebellious ex-colony.

In 1822 the arch-conservative Lord Castlereagh killed himself in a fit of depression and Sir Robert Peel became home secretary. Peel oversaw the removal of some hanging statutes. But what replaced hanging, as punishment, was only more transportation. Peel was a timid reformer and, when it came to thinking about the practical issues of what one did with criminals, his imagination failed. "I admit the inefficiency of transportation to Botany Bay, but the whole subject . . . is full of difficulties," he wrote to the Reverend Sydney Smith. "I can hardly devise anything as a secondary punishment in addition to what we have at present." The hulks were full to bursting with a population of four to five thousand felons. He could not use public chain gangs, for they would "revolt public opinion" and the penitentiary had failed. Only Australia was left to cope with a swelling crime wave. "The real truth is the number of convicts is too overwhelming for the means of proper and effectual punishment."[2]

There must still be a place of terror. About the volume of crime, and therefore of transportation, there was little doubt. After 1815, England began to pay the full price for its recent defeat in war, its collapsing labor relations and a succession of failed harvests. Semi-capitalized industry was destroying the old base of town manufacture, the apprentice system; enclosure and famine were sending the rural workers of England and Ireland into paupery. The crime rate leaped, and with it the numbers of transported convicts. From 1810 to 1814, an average of 678 felons a year went to Australia; this mere trickle could easily be absorbed, as unskilled labor, by the assignment system. But from 1815 to 1819, the yearly average trebled, to 2,090; from 1820 to 1824, it went to 2,756. The British Government could not have cut down on transportation even if it had wanted to. It therefore sought ways to make it more severe, more frightening—to remove the impression, as one Lord Chief Justice put it, that it was "a summer excursion." None of its policymakers had ever been to Australia and all of them saw it through a narrow band of information. John Bigge's reports, in their thorough detail and unbending class bias, were *the* authoritative text; and Bigge's message confirmed the basic intention of the government: that Australia's eventual fate as a community of free citizens mattered infinitely less than its expedient role as England's social sewer. The Tories wanted a governor who would think less—much less—about the convicts' future reclamation than about their present punishment.

Sir Ralph Darling (1775–1858) was their man: a tough, censorious, narrow-minded veteran of the Peninsular War, who arrived in Sydney at the age of fifty in 1825. Morally and intellectually, he was a duller being than George Arthur. He, too, had spent time in a hot climate as the British proconsul of a changing slave state. The prelude to his Australian service had been four years as British military governor of Mauritius, a colony of defeated France. As its virtual dictator, he had done his heavy-handed best to protect the frail rights of the 70,000 blacks on the sugar plantations against their French owners, demanding snap-to obedience and resenting every demurral from his policies. He carried these habits to Australia, where he soon alienated everyone except the Exclusives, who were cheered by his unquestioning obedience to London and his extreme dislike of anything that smacked of democracy, reform or (where convicts were concerned) ordinary mercy. "A cold, stiff, sickly person," thought Sir James Dowling, a new puisne judge of New South Wales, on meeting Darling for the first time in 1828. "He had none of the frankness and ease of a soldier, and I absolutely froze in his presence."[3]

Like Arthur in Van Diemen's Land, Darling in New South Wales was determined to carry out the suggestions of the Bigge Report to the letter. He would roll back Macquarie's liberalism, whose vestiges had lingered under Governor Brisbane. Instead of treating the prisoners on their merits, he wanted a rigid, undeviating standard of punishment, "with a view to the prevention of Crime at Home."

The basis of this standard was the cat-o'-nine tails, whose whistle and dull crack were as much a part of the aural background to Australian life as the kookaburra's laugh. "Flogging in this country," one old hand in the 1820s remarked to the newly arrived Alexander Harris, "is such a common thing that nobody thinks anything of it. I have seen young children practising on a tree, as children in England play at horses."[4]

Most floggings by then were confined to 25, 50, 75, 100 or, on very rare occasions, 150 lashes. By the standards of earlier days when punishments of 500 lashes were handed out by the likes of Foveaux and Marsden, such inflictions may sound light. But they were not; and in any case, a magistrate could stack up separate floggings for different aspects of the same deed.

Every stroke was noted and compiled, and in 1838 Governor Sir

George Gipps submitted to Long Glenelg a summary of corporal punishment inflicted on convicts in New South Wales over the years 1830 to
1837:[5]

| YEAR | NO. OF FLOGGINGS | TOTAL OF LASHES | AVG. LASHES PER FLOGGING | MALE CONVICT POPULATION |
|------|------------------|-----------------|--------------------------|-------------------------|
| 1830 | 2,985 | 124,333 | 41 | 18,571 |
| 1831 | 3,163 | 186,017 | 58 | 21,825 |
| 1832 | 3,816 | 164,001 | 43 | 24,154 |
| 1833 | 5,824 | 242,865 | 41 | 23,357 |
| 1834 | 6,328 | 243,292 | 38 | 25,200 |
| 1835 | 7,103 | 332,810 | 46 | 27,340 |
| 1836 | 6,904 | 304,327 | 44 | 29,406 |
| 1837 | 5,916 | 268,013 | 45 | 32,102 |

Alexander Harris's *Settlers and Convicts, or Recollections of Sixteen
Years' Labour in the Australian Backwoods* (1847) offers some vivid
reflections on these commonplace events:

> Officers, and especially young officers, when made magistrates, get
> irritated at the hardihood of a class of men whom they have made up their
> minds to despise; and the cat being a soldier's natural revenge, they fly to
> it directly. . . .
> I was sent for to Bathurst Court-house. . . . I had to go past the trian-
> gles, where they had been flogging incessantly for hours. I saw a man
> walk across the yard with the blood that had run from his lacerated flesh
> squashing out of his shoes at every step he took. A dog was licking the
> blood off the triangles, and the ants were carrying away great pieces of
> human flesh that the lash had scattered about the ground.
> The scourger's foot had worn a deep hole in the ground by the violence
> with which he whirled himself round on it to strike the quivering and
> wealed back, out of which stuck the sinews, white, ragged and swollen.
> The infliction was a hundred lashes, at about half-minute time, so as to
> extend the punishment through nearly an hour. The day was hot enough
> to overcome a man merely standing that length of time in the sun. . . . I
> know of several poor creatures who have been entirely crippled for life by
> these merciless floggings.[6]

Even 25 lashes (known as a *tester* or a *Botany Bay dozen*) was a draconic
torture, able to skin a man's back and leave it a tangled web of criss-
crossed knotted scars.

The psychological damage inflicted by the lash was worse than the
physical, and its traces were equally permanent. "It had the effect of
demoralizing them to the very greatest possible extent," a former sur-

geon at Macquarie Harbor, John Barnes, would testify to the Molesworth Committee; "I never saw a convict benefited by flagellation." What the cat-o'-nine-tails instilled was not respect for discipline, but a sullen conviction of one's own impotence in the face of Authority; this could only be expunged by violence or erased by one's own death. Next to homosexual rape, flogging was the most humiliating invasion of the body that could befall a prisoner. Nothing in an ordinary man's experience compared to the rituals of the cat: to be stripped and tied to the triangle, like an owlskin nailed to a barn door; to hear, through battering pain, the quartermaster-sergeant slowly calling out the strokes; this was to be drowned in powerlessness. It left the prisoner consumed with worthlessness and self-hatred, and Barnes spoke of convicts who, on first being flogged, "have become so very much degraded by the punishment, that they sometimes told me that they should never be satisfied until they had been executed for some further offence; *they considered it a most unmanly form of punishment.*" [Italics added.][7]

The scarred back became an emblem of rank. So did silence. Convicts called a man who blubbered and screamed at the triangles a *crawler* or a *sandstone*. (Sandstone is a common rock around Sydney; it is soft and crumbles easily.) By contrast, the convict who stood up to it in silence was admired as a *pebble* or an *iron man*. He would *show his shapes* (strip for punishment) with disdain, and after the *domino* (last lash) he would spit at the feet of the man who gave him his *red shirt*. There were always more sandstones than pebbles. Ernest Augustus Slade, superintendent of the Hyde Park Barracks in Sydney in 1833–34, believed that convicts always broke down under the lash and furnished the Molesworth Committee with examples of both, culled from his past records. James Clayton, of the *Phoenix*, was given fifty lashes for being "absent without leave and neglecting his duty . . ."

> The skin was lacerated at the fifth lash and there was a slight effusion of blood; the prisoner subdued his sense of pain by biting his lip. The skin of this man was thick to an uncommon degree, and both his body and mind had been hardened by former punishments, and he is also known to be what is termed "flash" or "game." . . . [I]f all his former punishments . . . had been as vigorously administered as this last, his indomitable spirit would have been subdued.

By contrast, there was poor James Kenworthy of Camden, a pilferer:

> The first lash elicited loud cries from this prisoner; at the 18th lash the blood appeared; at the 25th lash the blood was trickling; at the end of the 32nd, flowing down his back. . . . [H]e would have been sufficiently

punished at the 25th lash. He says he was never flogged before. . . . [H]e was very fat, with a thin skin. The sufferings of this prisoner were evinced by his unnerved state of body when cast loose; he could hardly stand.[8]

The System in the 1830s had a passion for bureaucratic exactitude about pain. In 1833 Governor Bourke, Darling's successor, received many complaints from local benches that 50 lashes, the most that one magistrate could impose for a single offense, was not enough, and that the government-issue cats were positively feeble. Accordingly, a circular went forth to all police magistrates in New South Wales, demanding a report on standard cats, samples of which were enclosed for consumer testing.[9]

The answers were illuminating but contradictory.[10] George Holden, police magistrate at Campbelltown, could give no "categorical answer" about the standard cat except that it was too ill-made to last more than 150 lashes. The nine tails should be stiffer and lighter, but

it involves a fearful responsibility, which I cannot bring myself to assume, to decide precisely how much torture ought to be systematically inflicted by law on any set of men. . . . I do not profess to have yet acquired the power of witnessing the infliction of pain with such unmoved nerves.

Besides, his flogger seemed to lay it on without "that peculiar art in the flourish of the scourge which [is] employed . . . in Hyde Park Barracks, and so greatly adds to the pain."

The Draco of Hyde Park Barracks, Ernest Slade, thought the standard cats quite adequate "when properly wielded" but reminded the colonial secretary that scourgers must not be overworked—they should give no more than 150 lashes a day—and that, due to the nature of their unappreciated task, they ought to have special protection.

One "J.P." wrote in from Bathurst to say that the cats came undone at the ends and did not cut the back enough. The Goulburn police magistrate poured scorn on the instruments. The lashes came off the handles after 20 strokes; the thread whipping on the end of each tail came undone, so that "altho' it bruises, bleeding but seldom is caused, consequently the offender escapes that acute pain and smarting to the extent so desirable should be experienced under the lash." The cord should be harder, the tails a foot longer, and "it would be preferable were they to terminate in small knots."

For Darling and his successors in the 1830s, however, flogging merely represented the episodic peak of punishment within a consistent environment of misery. Every male convict would be put in irons on arrival and sent out to labor on public works for time, "at the expiration of which, I had purposed to assign them to Settlers; and in the event of misconduct, of replacing them in the Road Gangs." The taste of road-gang life would by then "have rendered their assignment to the Settlers a desirable release from a painful and degraded situation; and in proportion to their dread . . . they would have behaved to their Masters."[11]

Darling could not put this into practice; there was too much demand for assigned labor. But he did put many more convicts into government work on the gangs, pulling them out of "the very refuse of the whole Convict Population."[12] The roads absorbed this human trash. By 1828, Darling was congratulating himself on having 1,260 second-sentence men in the road gangs of New South Wales, more than in all the penal settlements.[13] All this, he proudly informed London, was very cheap: The convict overseers got a "gratuity" of around £16 a year, and with the salaries of free superintendents the complete payroll for the roads in 1827–28 was only £1,621 18s. 9d. No private contractor using assigned labor could possibly charge so little.[14]

The convict memoirist Thomas Cook found what road-gang life was like when he was sent to labor against raw bush and sandstone at Honey-suckle Flat on the Great Western Road over the mountains to Bathurst:

> With a sheet of Bark for my bed, the half of a threadbare Blanket for my covering, and a Log for my pillow, the action of the frost was so severe on my limbs that it was with difficulty I could find the use of them, and then only by frequenting the fire at intervals during each night. As I arose, after experiencing all the horrors of a restless and perishing cold Night, the rugged mountains covered with snow, and the frozen Tools for labour stared me in the face before the stars were off the skies; and many a tear did I shed, when contemplating upon my hard fate, and the slight offence for which I had been doomed to participate so largely in the bitters of a wretched life.[15]

Cook began in the lesser kind of punishment gang, an "out-of-iron gang." These did most of the road-building in New South Wales (after 1828 there were, at any time, between 1,200 and 1,500 convicts laboring in them), but they were miserably unproductive. Most of their members had either been rejected by settlers as unfit to be assigned workers or else were working out short sentences (six months or less) for petty colonial offenses. "The mere fact of their being returned on the hands of Government in a community where the demand for labour is very urgent and clamorous," wrote Richard Bourke, Darling's successor, meant that such men "must be notoriously idle and worthless." Their "trusty" convict overseers were corrupt. They would form "select parties" of gangers to go food-stealing by night. Cook reported how some of his fellow gangers frightened two fat bullocks over a cliff at Mount Victoria by rolling boulders down at them and ate steak for days. Prisoners also kept escaping from the out-of-iron gangs; they would run off into the bush, live for a while (but not, as a rule, very long) by scavenging and robbery and then get retaken. The number of these bushrangers made travel, especially over the Blue Mountains, a risky business, since most of them were more like famished muggers than the altruistic Robin Hoods of Australian folksong.[16]

Clearly, there was room for improvement, and Darling and Bourke pinned their hopes on the iron gangs. Their members (by 1834, Bourke reported, there were over 800 men serving sentences of 6 months to 3 years in them) were all twice-convicted and they worked and slept in irons. "They have no time for recreation. . . . [T]heir lot is felt by themselves as one of great privation and unhappiness." As the road advanced, the iron-gangers dragged their nocturnal prisons with them—huts on wheels, each sleeping eighteen to twenty-four convicts. Sometimes more permanent stockades and fixed huts were provided, from which the gangers had to march out to their sites in irons. The superintendent could make them run to work in double time, pricked on by the soldiers' bayonets.[17] When Thomas Cook was condemned to a year in an iron gang on the Great Western Road he and his fellow gangers suffered in this way

> for some 10 or 15 days when the men (finding themselves so much advanced in debility, and their legs so far injured by the friction of the Irons that they could no longer bear against it) offered a determined resistance . . . which led to a deal of traffic in human flesh and blood, by the soldiers with their Bayonets, and the Scourgers with their Cats.

As for the summary punishments,

> The mode of Trial was a mere mockery of justice. I have known instances where the Officer would not even stay one moment to enquire into the merits of the charges, but would sit on his horse and sentence 14 or 15 men standing a distance away (sometimes a whole Gang) to 50 and some 100 lashes each, without an oath, on hearing ten words from the lips of their villainous accusers. This system of severity was so rigorously pursued that some of the longer-sentenced men were goaded . . . either to end their days on the Gallows, or better their condition by taking to the Bush.[18]

Not all the recidivist convicts could go in the chain gangs. Iron gangs needed too many guards. There was a case for penal settlements whose remoteness would deter escape, whose severity and frightening unfamiliarity would instill "salutary terror."

The need for such places had been argued at some length in John Bigge's report, which took the Exclusivist, pro-rural view and stressed that Sydney was an incubator of crime.[19] Bigge claimed that in 1820 there had been one fresh crime for every three convicts in Sydney, as compared to one for every eight in Windsor and far less in the outlying districts. The answer was to get the serving felons out of the towns and into the country—to put the recidivists in distant penal stations, where they could not corrupt the others and where the news of their sufferings would be an example to all. Only thus, Bigge thought, could the government relieve the "constant pressure of new arrivals" and "the uneasiness I felt at the constant arrivals of convict ships." The convicts were silting up in Sydney, unclassified, mingling too easily with the free, and giving the lie to talk about the "terror" of transportation. "The great cause of the diminished effect of transportation has arisen from the increase in the numbers transported," Bigge argued:

> All the evils of association, the difficulties of superintendence and control, whether arising from the extension and variety of the employments, or from the more laborious duties of the magistrates and superintendents, have arisen chiefly from this source.[20]

Besides, the settled districts around Sydney were getting almost too comfortable and Bigge thought it "hopeless" to expect that they would confront convict work gangs with "all the hardships, privations and severities [of their] unsettled state." Convicts at gang labor should get no room for initiative and work only at such uniform tasks as grubbing out the giant roots of gum trees left in the ground by earlier clearing-parties. There would be plenty of exhausting work along the north coast, to which Bigge urged the government to send them. Under the fiery Tropic of Capricorn, the combination of raw bush and hostile Aborigines would be a powerful deterrent to escape. And once the bush was cleared, the convict gangs would move out and the settlers could go in.[21]

Lord Bathurst and Macquarie's successors, Brisbane and Darling, all accepted this plan of northward colonization into the punitive tropics. It was set in full motion by Brisbane and perfected by Darling. Since the fate of prisoners in such places would bulk large in the imagery of the System, they are worth considering in some detail.

ii

THE FIRST PENAL out-station on the mainland was Newcastle, founded where the Hunter River flows into the Pacific about seventy miles north of Sydney. This river mouth had been a Cretaceous swamp and, on the flat rocks at the base of the cliffs, the ocean water swilled green and blue around the stumps of petrified trees, whose growth rings could still be read. Of more interest to the early settlers, however, was another relic of that swamp: a seam of coal, three feet thick, that ran near water level through Nobby's Head, the southern jaw of the river entrance. This seam, first noticed in 1795, gave the place its first name: Coal Harbor.

In 1801 Governor King sent sixteen refractory convicts to mine coal there, under military guard. They were soon recalled, as it was too difficult to supply this tiny outpost, but in 1804, after the Irish rose at Castle Hill, King dispatched thirty-five of them to labor in the cliff seam. The convict population of Newcastle, as the place was soon named, grew fitfully. By the end of 1804, it was 128; by 1817 it was 553; and in 1821 there were 1,169 people living there, including a handful of free settlers and Emancipist farmers. By then, the economic mainstay of the settlement was no longer coal but timber.

Vast stands of cedar, the prime joinery timber of colonial Australia, grew in the Hunter River Valley. Men with crosscut saws could rip the great trunks down into tabletops three inches thick, six feet wide and as long as you wanted—the red-gold, ponderous, subtly aromatic slabs that are unobtainable today, but were then as common as pine. Cedar was a government monopoly. Contractors took their ships to Newcastle and bought it convict-sawn, at 3d. per superficial foot. The panelled doors of Macquarie's Sydney—the moldings, the dadoes and cabinets, even the floors—were made of it.

Most prisoners at Newcastle worked in the cedar gangs. By 1820, the shore forests were so depleted that the cedar-getters had to go seventy miles upstream to find large trees. These expeditions lasted a month or more and were of course overseen by military guards who supervised the task-work; the quota for a thirty-man gang was about one hundred trunks a month. Once felled and lopped, they would be lashed together into a single big raft; sheltered by a rough hut on its "deck," the whole gang would float back down to Newcastle in style.[22]

Standing orders kept the settlement isolated. If a private vessel put in there without a license, she was scuttled and her crew imprisoned. Licensed boats had to unship their rudders and surrender them to the harbormaster. These measures not only prevented escapes but discouraged cedar-poachers.

Life at Newcastle was hard, and successive commandants were ordered to keep it so. It was a dirty infant of a town, consisting of parallel rows of convict-built slab huts and a barracks holding some 250 men considered dangerous. There, they slept in cribs a little more than four feet wide, three men to a crib. (The practice of bedding the men by threes and not in pairs was supposed, optimistically, to reduce unmentionable crime.) In summer this shantytown was oppressively hot, the thermometer rising to 105° in the shade, with burning northerlies sometimes pushing it to 115°. One young guard officer, Lieutenant William Coke, a scion of the great family of Holkham Hall, found the climate deadly:

> Often at half past 7 in the Evening we cannot bear our Coats on & are laying down panting for breath, & in a quarter of an Hour afterwards on leaving the Mess we are cold, shivering and wishing for a fire. These sudden changes kill many people. Soldiers and the Inhabitants die very quick here, what with drinking & being exposed to the sudden changes of the weather.[23]

Everything in Newcastle seemed either exhausting or boring, but that was what commended it to the authorities. The wildlife lacked charm. "If a snake bites you in this country," Coke wrote home to England, doubtless meaning to make his sisters' skin crawl, "instant death follows; one of the most deadly & common Snake's bite is so bad that the person bit only shivers and falls dead immediately."[24] There were sandflies, mosquitoes, cholera, dysentery, catarrh and, as an extra irritation, a large perambulating sand dune—unwisely stripped of scrub so that escaping convicts could not hide in it—which kept creeping into the town and had to be shovelled back.

Convict diggers, some of whom had been coal miners in England, worked ten to twelve hours a day. The old exposed seam on the face of Nobby's had been abandoned after 1817, for fear that the undermined sandstone above would crash into the sea. Now the miners went down a shaft, lowered more than 100 feet by a windlass, their leg-irons jingling forlornly in the dark. Conditions in it were dreadful, what with seepage from the sea above, rockfalls and bad air. The miners suffered from "black lung," asthma and rheumatism. At the end of the day they had no change of clothes, and sometimes no blankets. They had to mine twenty tons of coal a day.[25]

The most hated labor, worse than the mine, was lime-burning. Sydney had no mineral lime for mortar. But immense beds of oysters grew a few miles north of Newcastle, and the more refractory convicts were sent to gather and burn them. This meant trudging barefoot all day in mud thick with knife-sharp oyster shells, carrying baskets of quicklime across the tidal flats to the waiting boats. When water splashed into the unslaked lime it burned their unprotected eyes and their scabbed backs. Bigge noted that the lime-burners' eyes suffered from the smoke "but not to a greater degree than in England," and thought the convicts blinded themselves to malinger. But the hospital gave little solace to the sick; it was a mere shed, without proper supplies or even soap (which prisoners had to cook up themselves from pot-grease and ashes). In 1816 there were only enough blankets there for one patient in eight.[26]

In 1818, to exhort his lime-burners to greater efforts, Lachlan Macquarie visited the oyster beds of Newcastle. He arrived in full gubernatorial fig, with a retinue of fifty people and a four-piece band. The musicians brayed and fiddled, the governor inspected, and what the convicts thought is not recorded. He and his band then went off to lay the foundation stone of a breakwater, to be named Macquarie Pier; convict gangs spent many months dragging rocks underwater to build this hated amenity but it was never finished.

The main preoccupation among the Newcastle prisoners was escape. To discourage it, the commandants made their officers treat the local Aborigines well, cajoling them with small gifts or tobacco and sugar or, for exceptional services, blankets. In this way, Bigge noted, the Aborigines had become "very active" in recapturing prisoners:

> They accompany the soldiers who are sent in pursuit, and by the extraordinary strength of sight they possess . . . they can trace to a great distance, with wonderful accuracy, the impressions of the human foot. Nor are they afraid of meeting the fugitive convicts in the woods, when sent in their pursuit, without the soldiers. . . . [T]hey wound and disable them, strip them of their clothes, and bring them back as prisoners. . . . [N]otwithstanding the apprehensions of revenge from the convicts whom they bring back, they continue to live in Newcastle and its neighbourhood, but are observed to prefer the society of the soldiers to that of the convicts.[27]

Thus the black police tracker made his first appearance in Australia; and one more grudge was added to the growing hatred of convict white for tribal black.

The prisoners bolted singly and in parties; some reached the Hawkesbury district, where they hoped to find shelter with assigned shepherds. They arrived gaunt and naked, reamed out by diarrhea, barely able to walk after a three-week diet of bugs, roots and raw snake meat. Once recaptured, some men tried again; one convict at Newcastle in 1810 had five escapes on his record. The punishments for those recaptured were "inflicted with more severity than at other settlements," Bigge thought. Other punishments included chain-gang labor, and, for women (a few of whom had ended up in Newcastle on second convictions, despite the general policy against sending women to penal stations), humiliating spiked iron collars, riveted around the neck.[28]

The symbolism of rank was jealously maintained. Tipping the cap or touching the forelock was imposed as a fetishistic ritual on the prisoners; sometimes, as at Norfolk Island, they were required (on pain of flogging for "disrespect") to salute not only any passing soldier, but certain objects associated with soldiering—an empty sentry-box, for instance. These orders came from Major James Morisset, who had succeeded Captain Wallis as commandant at Newcastle. A free trader from Sydney named John Bingle was struck by the relentless way that Morisset ran the Newcastle station; he had "never seen arbitrary power carried to such an extent . . . [I]t seemed very un-English."[29]

Death sentences for absconding seem to have been handed out with abandon by the military court at Newcastle, if young Lieutenant Coke was not exaggerating in his letters home:

> The Lieutenants and Ensigns have no duty here, except sitting on the Criminal court and seeing men hung.—The jury here is formed of seven Officers, every day we sit we get 15 shillings allowed us each for our trouble.—The Court in general consists of one Judge, one Counsel against the prisoner, & the Witnesses, seldom indeed does any person come here as a Spectator & the prisoners seldom employ a man to defend them, we sometimes condemn five in a day to be hanged: it is more in appearance like an Inquisition as the Prisoners seldom call Witnesses, & men are condemn'd with little ceremony.[30]

What is extraordinary is Coke's matter-of-factness, his assumption that the convicts had no rights. Why did the prisoners not defend themselves? Because they believed they had no chance with the "deliberations" of this military Star Chamber. Not all the hangings seem to have been carried out; the usual procedure by the late 1820s was to commute the capital sentence or, in some cases, to send the third-time offender straight to Norfolk Island, a punishment in some ways worse than hanging. But such a passage suggests how the System could degenerate once minor officials felt that a governor like Ralph Darling cared little for "convict rights."

However, by the 1820s the usefulness of Newcastle as a place of secondary punishment was waning. The place was no longer isolated, because more and more free settlers were anxious to farm the rich plains of the Hunter River Valley. The cedar forests were vanishing and, although the coal mines were still being worked by convicts—including some Chartist political prisoners[31]—in the 1830s, they could not absorb very much labor. Besides, Bigge reported to his government, the good farmland along the Hunter River made the convicts' lives too easy. In earlier years, when the settlement only spread a mile or two inland, all crops had to be raised on the poor, sandy coastal soil, so that Nature combined with Authority "to render hard labour an indispensable condition of existence." Fertile soil contradicted the purpose of the settlement. So after 1823, Newcastle was thrown open to free trade and settlement. Its convicts stayed on—there were more than 1,600 by 1827 —but it was no longer simply a jail for the twice-convicted. That role was assumed by a new settlement started in 1821, 270 miles north of Sydney: Port Macquarie.

Port Macquarie (not to be confused with Macquarie Harbor) was meant for incorrigible life-sentence prisoners convicted of second offenses in New South Wales. Discipline under its first commandant, Francis Allman, was severe; a man could get 100 lashes for trying to smuggle a letter out, or a month in the cell for merely possessing a piece of writing paper. (One sees why convict diaries were nonexistent, and convict memoirs rare.) One veteran of the Port Macquarie iron gang recalled how

> the hills [we] cut through were so steep that a man could not comfortably ascend one of them without irons on his legs, let alone with them—but the hills had to be broken down by men with sore backs, and if one man happened to collide with another who had recently been flogged, it would be—"Oh, G—! Mind my sore back." Those were hard times; hard worked and half starved.[32]

The rubbing of the leg-rings on their flesh, Port Macquarie men used sardonically to say, "put plenty of iron in the blood."

Port Macquarie had a high proportion of Specials. Darling had them sent there so that they could not make trouble in Sydney; he did not want literate convicts adding to the rhetoric of Wentworth and the Sydney *Monitor*. Some of them were harmless creatures, like the Irishman James Bushelle, who, in cahoots with "a broken-down French gambler," had toured the jewelry shops of London masquerading as a Polish prince, with gum on his fingertips, substituting fake diamonds for real ones. He drew life in New South Wales, and on being reconvicted at Port Macquarie he found a niche as a tutor to some of the free settlers who had begun to trickle in after 1830, "instructing the young ladies both married and single," as he put it,

> in music, dancing, French and Italian . . . who met occasionally to enjoy the pleasure of a German Waltz or a Spanish Quadrille in this recent Emanation from the forest; where hitherto the sound of music, or the voice of merriment, had never been heard; where no sounds, but the cooees and howlings of the Black man, the groans of the convicts under

the excruciating Lash, or the croaking of the wild Cockatoo, ever pierc'd the Skies or disturb'd the Ambient Air.[33]

Thus, the first uncertain pipings of the Muses were heard at Port Macquarie.

But among other Specials, "relaxation, petty traffic and abuse" reigned. They seized every privilege they could get; they truckled to authority ("When an overseer spoke to him," it was said of one Special, "he had the appearance of a goose looking down a bottle") and made tyrannous overseers themselves. Solidarity might rise between prisoners on the run or men who had been through the assignment system; in the penal stations, rarely. Convict overseers in such places—and on the chain gangs—were notoriously cruel. "The worst wretches that a man could be put to work under were those who had been sent to the country themselves. They were far worse than men who came out free."[34]

As at Newcastle, escape attempts were common. But few succeeded, particularly since the Aborigines proved eager to help catch bolters. As the area opened up to free settlers at the end of the 1820s, security faltered and after 1830 the place became a grotesque mixture of jail and infirmary, "a *demi* penal settlement."[35] The crippled, the mad and the blind were dumped into it along with the Specials. In the late 1830s, Port Macquarie boasted a gang of one-armed stonebreakers and another of blind men, who in 1835 could be seen "manacled to a chain, and so marched to and fro on the causeway facing the window of the Commandant's quarters for 2 or 3 successive days for his amusement." The "blind mob" had a high reputation as thieves, deft enough to ease a man's rolled-up trousers from under his head as he slept and take the coins from his pocket, or grope melons out of an officer's garden patch by moonlight. Cross one, and he might put a tiger snake's head, fangs up, in your boot.

Most conspicuous of all were the "men on timber," amputees with wooden legs who were unsuitable for gang labor elsewhere in the colony. They served as delivery men, humping packages inland for free settlers. When not employed, they would lie sunning themselves and gazing at the sea, guzzling rum, of which there was plenty at Port Macquarie, cooked up in illicit convict stills from the sugar cane that flourished there. Real men drank it laced with tobacco juice, a mixture believed to kill the pain of a flogging.

One of the amputees' main recreations was fighting. Since they could not stand toe-to-toe like regular pugilists, their friends would perch them face-to-face on the thwarts of a dinghy; each combatant was propped up by a man at his back, "and in this fashion they would fight away in great style" until one of them could no longer sit up. They also played practical jokes. The overseer of the one-armed stone-cutting gang was a Jew with two wooden legs. One day, as he lay dozing drunk in the sun, another Jewish prisoner

> collected a quantity of old maize stalks and other fuel, and set fire to his wooden legs. . . . They were not burning long, however, before he awoke and found one to be shorter than the other; and it was a sight for sore eyes to see him walking down to the Old Broken Barracks, singing out to everyone that he met—"That Jew-looking bugger down there has burnt my legs nearly off."[36]

Other pranks involved animals. Convicts would wire two tomcats' tails together and drape them over a doorknob at night. They would slide a live shark into a drunkard's bed. Almost anything would do to relieve the tedium of Port Macquarie, where Brueghel would not have lacked subjects.

Discipline in the 1830s was uneven but harsh. Thomas Cook, sent there from the iron gang as a Special in the summer of 1835, found a commandant who (he alleged) thought nothing of flogging old men and cripples, and boasted "that he would make the Deaf to hear, the Dumb to speak, the lame to walk, the blind to see, and the foolish to understand" with his colonial cure-all, the lash. Soon after arriving, Cook came down with dysentery, but he did not report to the surgeon "for the name he bore among my fellow prisoners as a Butcher." For this, he was heavily ironed and ordered by the commandant "in a voice like thunder" to extra labor, under the eye of Roach, the chief flogger. But there was some pity in Roach. Not all such men were the blood-boltered sadists of convict lore:

> At this time the Scourger (whose calling one would have supposed had long since excluded almost every kindred feeling from his breast) was begging of me to keep my Tool in motion, until the Commandant took his ride out, and promising to do my work for me. In about an hour the Commandant left the settlement, and the Scourger, putting down his arms, worked excessively hard so as to save me from the Punishment with which I must otherwise have been visited.[37]

Nevertheless Cook was sure he would die at Port Macquarie and decided to flee, "under the impression that there existed some hope of my being able to effect a final escape to England." There was none. He walked out of the settlement, which had no wall but the bush, and went eighty miles south before realizing he was totally lost. Sick with the flux, he survived a week on roots and wild nettles until the Aborigines caught him and gave him to an armed search-party of constables. That did not deter him; in all, Cook tried three times to escape from Port Macquarie, with no success.

iii

GOVERNOR BRISBANE decided to plant another penal station on the mainland, so remote that its prisoners would give up all hope of escape. It would be in the Deep North, as Australians call Queensland, where the sun's heat would bake and baste the sin out of them. In 1823 Brisbane sent an exploring party under his surveyor-general, John Oxley, to look at Moreton Bay, a big coastal inlet noted by Cook fifty years before. It was 450 miles north of Sydney, far enough to discourage any bolter. If it had a river, it might be settled.

Oxley and his men reached Moreton Bay by sea without incident and carried out a rough survey. They found a river, rich soil, plenty of fresh water, and friendly Aborigines. The shallow bay teemed with fish; they could wade out and catch mullet and snapper with their hands. The mangroves were encrusted with little milky oysters in ruffled shells, and in the ooze between their roots lived regiments of huge, delicious mud crabs. Up the river, as a former convict would remember in years to come, "it looked as though some race of men had been here before us, and planted this veritable Garden of Eden." The riverbanks were tropical jungle, laced with blue-and-white flowering vines; stately white lilies grew in masses from the tidal mud. Colonies of black Funereal Cockatoos stared from the palm trees, nodding their wiry crests and occasionally flapping clumsily into the air, like croaking umbrellas. Kingfishers flashed through the deep shade.[38]

It looked almost too good for convicts, and surely survival would not be a problem: The first human beings Oxley and his men encountered, to their stupefaction, were two naked, scarred and sunburnt white men, who had been wrecked on the coast a year and a half before and were "in healthy state and plump condition," thanks to the local Aborigines, who had adopted them. In fact, Oxley's report on Moreton Bay was so encouraging that when it reached London, Lord Bathurst decided that the area should be thrown directly open to free settlers. But his opinions on this took months to reach Sydney, and in the meantime Governor Brisbane had given orders to start a penal settlement there. He wanted it "to receive and maintain a great number of persons." The convicts' slave labor was "the best means of paving the way for the introduction of free population, as the example of Port Macquarie abundantly testifies."[39] He put it in charge of Lieutenant Henry Miller of the 40th Regiment. In September 1824, Miller sailed north with fifty settlers, thirty of whom were convict volunteers who hoped to win an early ticket-of-leave. They started on the edge of Moreton Bay, at the present site of Redcliffe.

Governor Brisbane expected the new settlement to become self-sufficient within two years, by growing maize. However, because of the inefficiency of penal labor, it did not; one cannot build an economy quickly with work designed to punish the builders. Work performed quickly was not punishment enough; the labor had to be "arduous." Miller had the convicts working twelve hours a day, dawn to dusk. Horses, draft animals and ploughs were all proscribed. As in the "starvation years" in Sydney, every inch of ground had to be inefficiently tilled with hoes, which kept breaking, and there was no animal manure. The convicts became afflicted with scurvy, and conditions were so squalid that they also fell victim to filth diseases like dysentery and trachoma.

Pioneering was bad enough, but doing it under such handicaps was absurd. The Eden-like prospect of Moreton Bay disintegrated fast, as such fantasies always did in Australia. The soil at Redcliffe was poor and the first seeds died in the ground; there was not enough building timber, and even the grass for thatch had to be dragged for miles; medicine ran out, and the place was infested with flies, ticks, scorpions and venomous snakes. Lieutenant Miller was driven near to distraction by all this, but he soldiered on:

> Nothing was undertaken that I did not plan, nothing was carried on that I did not inspect, literally, under a burning sun earning my bread in the sweat of my brow; I passed toilsome and miserable days, anxious and restless nights, and underwent privations . . . greater than any I had been called upon to sustain during years of [army] service.[40]

But toward the end of 1824, Governor Brisbane visited the Brisbane River, flatteringly named after him, and decided that the settlement should be moved to its banks. After several months of indecision he ordered Miller to make the move in February 1825. The huts were laboriously dismantled—every iron nail pulled out, straightened and saved—and the commandant's official residence, a prefabricated cottage brought in kit form from Sydney, was taken down and stowed. In July, they took everything twenty-seven miles up the river to the present site of Brisbane, Queensland's capital. "The difficulties of this task," Miller sighed, "with my original few [convicts] wasted and enfeebled by sickness, were so many and so great that none but an eye-witness could in the least form an opinion of them." Then the governor dismissed him. "I was removed to cover the mistakes of others," Miller protested, and in fact he had been: Brisbane needed a scapegoat for his own failure to equip the settlement properly.[41]

His successor, Captain Peter Bishop of the 40th Regiment, was a fairly humane man by colonial standards. He saw that the convicts would never work well under the severe discipline and the gruelling heat unless they had "a little reward for it," an ounce or two of tea or sugar. (Such gifts had also cemented good relations with the Aborigines around Brisbane Town, who, as at Newcastle and Port Macquarie, soon learned to catch runaway convicts and bring them in.)[42] But he had only two hundred convicts, few of them skilled tradesmen; and although some crops grew, only twelve acres were cultivated, because no one had enough farming experience to be superintendent of agriculture. When Bishop left Brisbane Town in March 1826, it was still only a straggle of cockeyed, leaking slab huts, without a hospital, a granary or even a jail. But the new commandant would change all that. He was Captain Patrick Logan of the 57th Regiment, and his regime would reflect the ironclad severity that the new governor, Ralph Darling, who appointed him, was determined to impose on the prisoners of Australia.

Between his arrival at Moreton Bay and his violent death there four years later, Logan became a legend among the convicts—so much so that he was the only commandant of an Australian penal station to have a whole ballad dedicated to him, "The Convict's Lament on the Unfortunate Death of Patrick Logan," which was called "Moreton Bay," for short.

One Sunday morning as I went walking, by the Brisbane's waters I
    chanced to stray,
I heard a prisoner his fate bewailing, as on the sunny river bank he lay:
"I am a native of Erin's island, but banished now to the fatal shore,
They tore me from my aged parents and from the maiden I do adore.

"I've been a prisoner at Port Macquarie, Norfolk Island and Emu Plains,
At Castle Hill and cursed Toongabbie, at all those settlements I've
    worked in chains;
But of all those places of condemnation, in each penal station of New
    South Wales,
To Moreton Bay I've found no equal: excessive tyranny there each day
    prevails.

"For three long years I was beastly treated, heavy irons on my legs I
    wore,
My back from flogging it was lacerated, and often painted with crimson
    gore,
And many a lad from downright starvation lies mouldering humbly
    beneath the clay,
Where Captain Logan he had us mangled on his triangles at Moreton
    Bay.

"Like the Egyptians and ancient Hebrews, we were oppressed under
   Logan's yoke,
Till a native black who lay in ambush did give our tyrant his mortal
   stroke.
Fellow prisoners, be exhilarated, that all such monsters such a death
   may find!
And when from bondage we are liberated, our former sufferings shall
   fade from mind."

Preferably sung *a capella* in a high nasal drone, this survived in many
variants and was perhaps the most popular anti-authoritarian ballad of
colonial Australia. Ned Kelly, last and greatest of the folk-hero bushrangers, the son of poor Irish Currency, put it into prose in his "Jerilderie
Letter." Openly addressed to the people of Australia, in 1879

Port McQuarrie Toweringabbie Norfolk island and Emu plains and in
those places of tyranny and condemnation many a blooming Irish man
rather than subdue to the Saxon yoke were flogged to death and bravely
died in servile chains.

Of all the Australian camp commandants, it was Logan who had the
worse reputation for cruelty. The convicts regarded him as an ogre and
his subordinates as grotesque monsters. Stories—almost certainly untrue
—were told about his chief flogger, a man with deformed legs named Old
Bumble (because he staggered along like a bee walking), who would wash
off the bloody thongs of his cat-o'-nine-tails in a can of water and drink
the contents. Logan was said to have flogged men to death for the pleasure of it and driven "hundreds" into the grave by working them in
chains until they dropped. The convict resister, wrote a former Moreton
Bay prisoner named William Ross in a pamphlet written after Logan's
death,

would be tortured with flogging and slavery until the spark of life had
fled, when he would be buried like a dog. . . . Such conduct is horrid, and
ought not to have been permitted; but unfortunately, Logan had the greatest interest with the never-to-be-forgotten Governor D[arling], who
backed him in every tyrannical work.[43]

Such was the Logan to frighten children, the infamous Beast of Brisbane. In later years, efforts would be made to exonerate him as a capable
explorer who battled against shocking conditions. The best likeness of
Logan offers few clues to him. What is one to read in Logan's stern face
with its pale, high cheekbones, level stare and slightly twisted mouth,
raised on its formal Georgian plinth of white linen? Only that he looks
as authoritarian as any other man of his day, rank and calling. Soldiers

liked to be depicted like that—and Logan, before he was anything else, was a soldier.

He had been born in Scotland in 1792, and he joined the 57th Regiment at the age of eighteen. For the next fifteen years he served his King all over the world: against Napoleon in Spain and France, in the American War, on garrison duty in Ireland, and finally in Australia, where he arrived in 1825. Because his whole life had been shaped by the army, Logan—like almost any other career officer—took for granted the army's assumptions about human nature; and the chief of these, in the early nineteenth century, was that the motley rabble who comprised the rank and file could only be turned into soldiers by unremitting discipline backed up by summary flagellation and the threat of the firing squad. Drill and the cat, not mercy or appeals to esprit de corps, had made the machine that defeated Napoleon. Logan's own regiment was noted for its severity. Why soften this proven system for worse scum, the convicts? "A little severity," Logan wrote a year after taking command at Moreton Bay, "was absolutely necessary to convert the settlement into anything like a place of punishment." [44]

On paper the commandant's powers were strictly limited. Logan could inflict summary punishments to 50 lashes, but standing orders warned that extra labor and solitary confinement should be preferred to the lash. However, the more detailed instructions he received from Governor Darling in 1829 made "every person, whether free or bond . . . subject to his orders" and gave official sanction to an inescapable fact: At distant places like Moreton Bay there was no way to keep an eye on the commandant, and therefore he could rule his small kingdom of pain as an absolute despot. He was the only magistrate, and through him all justice—other than trial for new felonies, which had to be held in a full Sydney court—was interpreted. His officers would stand behind him whenever questions were asked; so, as a rule, would free settlers (especially since Logan had absolute and summary power over their movements and could expel any one at will). Convicts, of course, had no voice. No convict could hope to persuade a Sydney court of the commandant's tyrannies; most of them were illiterate, and in any case all affidavits had to be sworn before Logan. [45]

When Logan arrived, he had a labor force of about one hundred convicts. By the end of 1826, it had doubled; in 1828 he had 415; and by February 1829, he had 772. The peak convict population was 1,020, in 1831 [46] Thus, although the labor supply grew steeply during Logan's reign, it was never large enough for ambitious building programs—a problem compounded by Darling's vacillations about the nature of the settlement and whether it should have free settlers or not. Under these conditions, Logan found it hard to make long-range plans. Yet by mid-1827, he had

120 acres under wheat and another 300 prepared for maize, while on the bank of the Brisbane River a town was shaping up, with a grid of beaten-earth streets, compacted by the soldiers' boot and the dragging of the prisoners' irons, and with a hospital, barracks, stores, and even a few stone cottages among the warped timber hovels.

It was done at a certain cost, which the convicts paid. Many of them worked as naked as Aborigines in the sun, except for their irons, and had to eat "Snakes, Pigs that have died of disease, Cabbage leaves . . . and every filth that was thrown into the streets."[47] An older hand, who escaped so often that he served a total of 26 years on a 7-year sentence for petty larceny, spent 7 years at Moreton Bay alone:

> I lost one of my eyes and the use of one of my hands. I suffered a great deal of hardship because I was unable to do the work allotted to me, and the punishment was very severe . . . [M]ost of the men at the Settlement were in irons . . . I had chains on my leg for four years . . . [I]t was through being ill-treated by the overseers that I lost the use of my hand—they struck me with whatever was handiest.[48]

Although the punishment registers for Moreton Bay in Logan's time are lost, its seems clear that Logan habitually worked prisoners in irons, whatever their sentences.[49] He was also a relentless flogger. One sample record of the floggings he handed out has survived; they were noted in a journal kept by some convict clerk for Peter Spicer, the superintendent of convicts, and show that from February to October 1828, Logan ordered 200 floggings, for a total of 11,100 lashes.

The flogging cannot have abated much after October 1828, because Logan was facing an explosive situation in his settlement. The crops failed in the summer of 1828–29. And there were epidemics of trachoma and dysentery. The crude death rate at Moreton Bay shot up to 35 per 1,000 per month, and Logan chose this of all moments to put the settlement on half rations. In the midst of this social catastrophe, there was a great rise in the number of convicts hospitalized for the special affliction of Moreton Bay, coyly Latinized in the records as *"flagellatio."*[50]

Logan's subordinates, to be sure, were not much help. Peter Spicer was a ludicrous incompetent, while Henry Cowper, the settlement's surgeon, appeared to his newly arrived assistant in 1830 as

> a most uncouth individual, an excessive grog-drinker and smoker, and the most ill-tempered and quarrelsome man I ever saw . . . I really think he is half insane. However, he is aware of his dreadful temper, for he speaks about it and says he is quite sure he will yet be confined in a madhouse.[51]

No wonder, then, that the prisoners tried to run away. Any chance of escape, no matter how thin, was preferable to life in this Georgian snake pit where even their turds were inspected for undigested kernels of stolen corn. In 1828–29, 126 prisoners (about one in ten) bolted into the bush and headed south, clutching what pitiful supplies of flour, fat and corn they had managed to steal and save, prepared to risk being killed (and, most of them believed, eaten) by Aborigines. Sixty-nine of them walked or were dragged back to the settlement, half-dead from exhaustion, to face 100, 200 or even 300 clawing strokes of the cat and be loaded with 20-pound irons for the rest of their sentences, to which Logan (as magistrate) would usually add another three years. (This was illegal and fell outside his powers as magistrate; but it drew no rebuke from Darling.) The fate of the rest is unknown. Most died. No prisoner was ever officially said to have reached freedom from Moreton Bay. Some may have done it, for several actually got as far down the coast as Port Macquarie before they were taken.

Meanwhile relations got worse with the Aborigines, whose stance toward the colonials by the late 1820s had changed from curiosity to open hostility. Convicts were ready to kill any black they met in the bush, if they could; the spiral of violence grew, and by early 1828 Logan had to report that armed bands of Aborigines, sometimes fifty men at a time, were attacking the maize fields.[52] However, the convict tradition that Logan retaliated for these crop raids by shooting an Aborigine and hanging up his stuffed skin in the maize fields as a warning may be unfounded—although similar things were done in New South Wales.[53]

Governor Darling countenanced what Logan was doing at Moreton Bay, but word of it leaked out into the community. Almost certainly it was meant to: the settlement needed a terrible reputation among convicts if it was to become a deterrent. The problem was not so much Logan's severity as his rumored capriciousness. By 1830, voices in Sydney were asking what was really going on at Moreton Bay. The leading voice was that of Edward Smith Hall (1786–1860).

Hall, the son of a minor English banker, had emigrated to New South Wales in 1811. Even in England he had involved himself in religious and social work, and he was a friend of the Abolitionist William Wilberforce. This recommended him to Lachlan Macquarie, who granted him more than 2,000 acres of pastoral land over the years. Hall failed utterly as a farmer, and his record as an officer of the fledgling Bank of New South Wales was not much better. But to a man of hot conscience and philanthropic instincts, penal Australia—especially after Macquarie left it— offered a vast acreage to rake muck in. Hall found his vocation as a newspaper editor. In 1826 he and a partner in Sydney founded the *Monitor*. Its broad political aims were like those of Wentworth's *Australian*: trial by jury, government by representative assembly, and the defense of civil liberties against Darling the martinet. More than the *Australian*, whose constituency was the Emancipists, the *Monitor* was concerned (or seditiously obsessed, some officials thought) with the plight of convicts under sentence whether privately mistreated as assigned servants or officially ground down on the chain gangs and at the penal stations.

Darling was Hall's bête noire. His leaden autocracy, Hall editorialized, had made New South Wales "singularly prone to espionage, suspicion, and a servile dread of offending the higher authorities." Through the *Monitor* and in a series of open letters to the colonial secretary in England, he accused him of negligence, unconstitutional disregard for the "ancient mild Laws of England," graft, favoritism to rich colonists, jury-packing, indifference to "proven" cases of official torture, and "prostituting his Authority and influence as Governor to feelings of private resentment."[54]

Hall's first big clash with Darling on events, rather than policies, came in 1826 over the Sudds-Thompson case. Joseph Sudds and Patrick Thompson, privates in the 57th Regiment, had come to believe (like many of their comrades in New South Wales) that the life of a serving convict, bad as it was, was still easier than a rank-and-file soldier's. A soldier who committed a crime in Australia faced transportation to a penal settlement. To get out of the army, Sudds and Thompson robbed a Sydney shop and made no effort to escape arrest. They were tried and sentenced to 7 years in a penal settlement.

This enraged Darling, who felt the news that His Majesty's soldiers preferred the life of a condemned convict would make either the army seem brutal (and discourage enlistment) or transportation mild (thus encouraging crime). He took it on himself, quite illegally, to cancel their prison sentences and send them to the iron gangs for 7 years. This was preceded by a ceremony of disgrace: dressed in the convicts' "canaries" (the yellow and gray uniform of felonry) and wearing massive spiked collars linked to their leg-fetters by 13-pound chains, Sudds and Thompson were drummed out of their regiment and into jail, where they languished in their irons. But to Darling's great embarrassment, Sudds— who had suffered from "dropsy"—fell ill from this treatment and died a few days later. Darling had not known Sudds's medical history, if only because he had not asked about it; certainly he did not mean to kill the man. But the results of his "exemplary" punishment made such measures seem Draconian and provoked a wave of revulsion among all Emancipists. From the *Australian* and the *Monitor*, Wentworth and Hall accused the governor of murder, torture and Nero-like perversions of justice.

Darling fought back stiffly but as best he could against Wentworth ("a vulgar, ill-bred fellow") and Hall ("a fellow without principles, an apostate missionary"). From that point on, all criticism was sedition. "The opposition papers," he complained to Bathurst, "must destroy that Confidence which the people generally ought to place in the Government, and in a Colony composed as this is produce, if not checked, anarchy and revolt."[55] He saw, as anyone could, that the Sudds-Thompson case was a heaven-sent lever for the "democrats" to press their claims for trial by open jury and a representative assembly. So he made a clumsy lunge against the opposition press. He tried to muzzle the *Australian* and the *Monitor* by imposing newspaper licenses, which would be withdrawn if they printed a "blasphemous or seditious libel." John Macarthur also urged him to kill their circulation with a stamp duty of 4d. per copy. Both measures had already been proposed by the autocrat of Van Diemen's Land, George Arthur. But all legislative bills had to be reviewed by the chief justice of the colony, Sir Francis Forbes.

Forbes thought his narrow-minded zealot of a governor had "less knowledge of the laws of his country than any gentleman filling his high official station whom it was ever my fortune to meet." He took most of the bite out of Darling's acts, until they could no longer silence the press —although they could certainly harass it. Hall, in return, kept up his invective against Darling and the Merinos and suffered seven prosecutions for criminal libel. In 1829 Darling at last managed to imprison him, but Hall continued to edit the *Monitor* from his cell and send long diatribes against the governor to officials in England. And it was in the Sydney jail, in March 1830, that Hall was handed the document that he believed would topple Captain Logan, disgrace Darling and force reform at Moreton Bay.

It was a manuscript left in the condemned cell of Sydney Jail by a convict named Thomas Matthew; he had left it hidden when he was taken out to be hanged. Matthew had been a "troublesome" convict. On the way from Sydney to Moreton Bay, he plotted a mutiny on the transport *City of Edinburgh*; the plan failed, because a prisoner named John Carrol ratted on the ringleaders. Matthew bided his time and smashed Carrol's skull with a pickax at Moreton Bay. He was brought down to Sydney, tried and cast to die.

His death-cell letter explained that his own life was of no value to him. It told of life at Moreton Bay under "such a herd of tyrants that never met together in one place before." The convict overseers "murder many a bright man," but the prisoners could bring no charges against them, because they had to be made to Logan. The jail gang overseer, named Trenand, killed a prisoner with a spade in front of ten convict witnesses, "but such was their terror [that] none of them dared to mention it, for fear of being flogged to death." Overseers stole the prisoners' bread; men died in the fields and the cells "from want of attention and food" and were flogged to death "for stealing a cob of corn." Some convicts were so weak that they had to crawl out to field labor. And Logan in one of his "mad fits" had all the cripples dragged from hospital and flogged "in their crutches." Matthew claimed he had seen men so broken by the first half of a flogging that they had to be brought back to the triangles the next day in a wheelbarrow to be strung up for the second half.

Hall published this letter in the *Monitor* on March 27, 1830. He also declared, from jail, that he would prosecute Captain Logan for the murder of a convict named William Swann, who (Hall alleged) had died of ill-treatment at Moreton Bay in 1827. But here he was wrong, for Swann had died of dysentery in the hospital—or so surgeon Cowper swore in an affidavit.[56] Captain Logan now wrote a stiff note to the colonial secretary demanding Hall's prosecution for criminal libel. In June, the Executive Council questioned both Reverend Vincent, the former Moreton Bay chaplain, and Surgeon Cowper. Cowper denied outright that there had ever been any cruelty, let alone murder, at Moreton Bay, and said nobody named Trenand had ever been an overseer there. The clergyman did remember Trenand, "who was said to be of a cruel disposition, and in the habit of beating and abusing the prisoners," but denied that he had heard of him killing a prisoner with a spade. Asked whether men were killed unofficially by guards there, he hedged. "Certainly not to justify the statement in the paper," was his strange reply.[57] Neither man remembered seeing cripples flogged or confirmed the more lurid accusations of arbitrary torture in Matthew's gallows document. Prompted by Darling, the Executive Council advised the attorney-general to issue yet another writ for criminal libel against Edward Hall, that spreader of "sedition and levelling."

The case never came to trial. Logan was about to leave for India—a posting now made necessary by the terrible reputation his regime at Moreton Bay had earned from the Emancipist press. By October 1830, his successor as commandant, Captain James Clunie of the 17th Regiment, was already learning the ropes at Moreton Bay. But Logan was not to leave Australia until he had given his sworn testimony in the trial of Hall and the *Monitor*, and while awaiting this call to Sydney he filled in time making exploratory sorties into the Brisbane Valley, upriver from Moreton Bay. On October 17, during one of these rides, his party lost him in the labyrinth of scrub.

Four days later a search-party found his saddle, its stirrup-leathers cut with a stone ax. Bands of convicts, led by Cowper and others, combed the bush for another week. In a clearing that bore the marks of many aboriginal feet, as though a wild dance had been held there, they found some pages of his notebook trampled in the dry grasses, along with a

The degradation of the fringe-dwelling Aborigines of Sydney, with their hand-me-down English rags and rum bottles, is recorded c. 1830 in Augustus Earle's lithograph *Natives of New South Wales*. (*Mitchell Library and Dixson Collections, Sydney*)

An iron-gang of Government men seen outside the Sydney Barracks by Augustus Earle's unsympathetic eye, during the governorship of Sir Ralph Darling, c. 1830. (*National Library of Australia, Canberra*)

A road-gang in the bush near Sydney, c. 1838. The pinched and sallow look of the chained prisoners is probably nearer the truth than are the sturdy, brutalized Irish stereotypes of Earle's lithograph. (*National Library of Australia, Canberra*)

Gang labor on the Great West Road across the Blue Mountains: Augustus Earle's *View from the Summit of Mount York, Towards Bathurst Plains*, c. 1826. *(National Library of Australia, Canberra)*

The road nears its completion, and "boundless regions open to our sight." Charles Rodius, *Convicts Building the Road to Bathurst*, 1833. *(National Library of Australia, Canberra)*

ABOVE: "That place of tyranny"—Macquarie Harbor. The ruins of the stone jail on Sarah Island, photographed by J. W. Beattie in the 1860s. (*National Library of Australia, Canberra*)

LEFT: Sarah Island from the south, by the convict artist C. H. T. Costantini, c. 1830. The main wharf and boatyard are in the center; note the tall sawn-log security fences. (*Allport Library and State Museum of Fine Arts, Hobart*)

LEFT, BELOW: Crews of convicts towing a raft of felled Huon pine logs to the sawpit at Sarah Island, Macquarie Harbor. Grummet Island is at right, with its crude punishment hut and, below, the dark opening in the rock used as a solitary cell. Sketch by T. J. Lemprière, c. 1830. (*Allport Library and State Museum of Fine Arts, Hobart*)

ABOVE: *A View of Hobart Town, Van Diemen's Land,* c. 1823, by George W. Evans. In the foreground, convicts are working, rather lackadaisically—note the two men at center chatting and smoking —under the supervision of an architect. This loose discipline was what Lieutenant-Governor Arthur dedicated himself to abolishing. Evans, the artist, was forced by Arthur from his post as surveyor in Van Diemen's Land, after allegations of bribery. (*National Library of Australia, Canberra*)

RIGHT: The unbending proconsul of Van Diemen's Land, Lieutenant-Governor Sir George Arthur (1784–1854). Anonymous miniature. (*Mitchell Library and Dixson Collections, Sydney*)

ABOVE: Port Arthur in the 1860s. The four-story building with attics and stone quoins at right is part of the huge flour mill converted in 1857 to a penitentiary. The round castellated tower halfway up the hill to the left is the guardhouse. (*National Library of Australia, Canberra*)

LEFT: "Impartial justice, as impassive as that of fate": Captain Charles O'Hara Booth (1800–1851), Commandant of Port Arthur from 1833 to 1840. Portrait by T. J. Lemprière. (*Tasmanian Museum and Art Gallery, Hobart*)

RIGHT: Sir John and Lady Franklin inspect the line of guard dogs at Eaglehawk Neck. (*Mitchell Library and Dixson Collections, Sydney*)

BELOW LEFT: "The Polar Knight," Lieutenant-Governor Sir John Franklin (1766–1847). Anonymous miniature. (*Mitchell Library and Dixson Collections, Sydney*)

BELOW RIGHT: *Et in Arcadia Ego:* instruments of Port Arthur discipline and bureaucracy, surrounded by native wildflowers. Tourist postcard by J. W. Beattie, c. 1870. (*Mitchell Library and Dixson Collections, Sydney*)

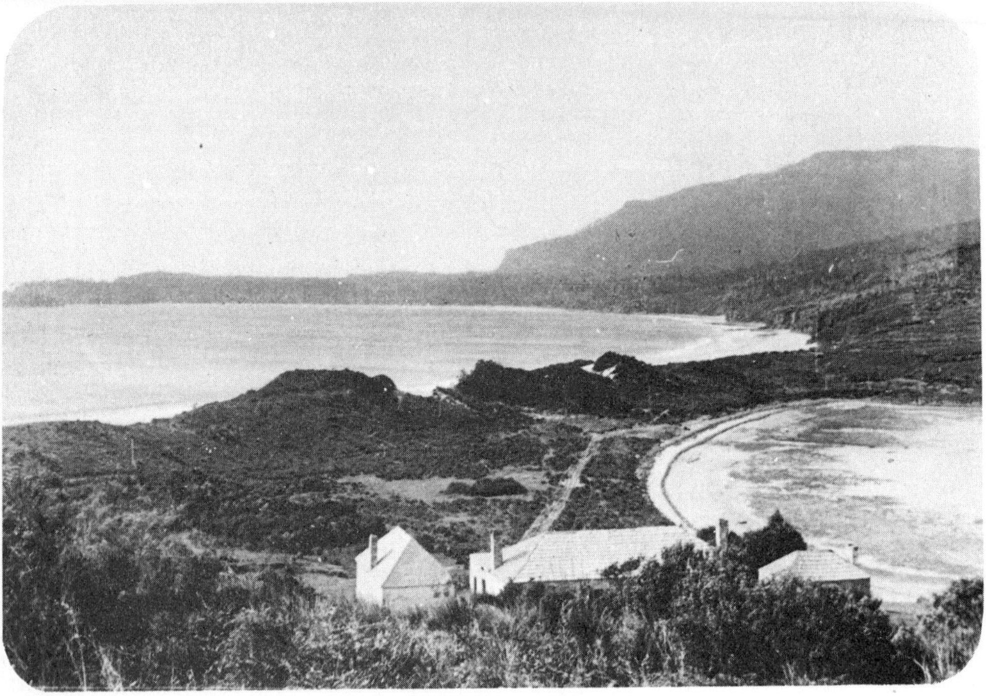

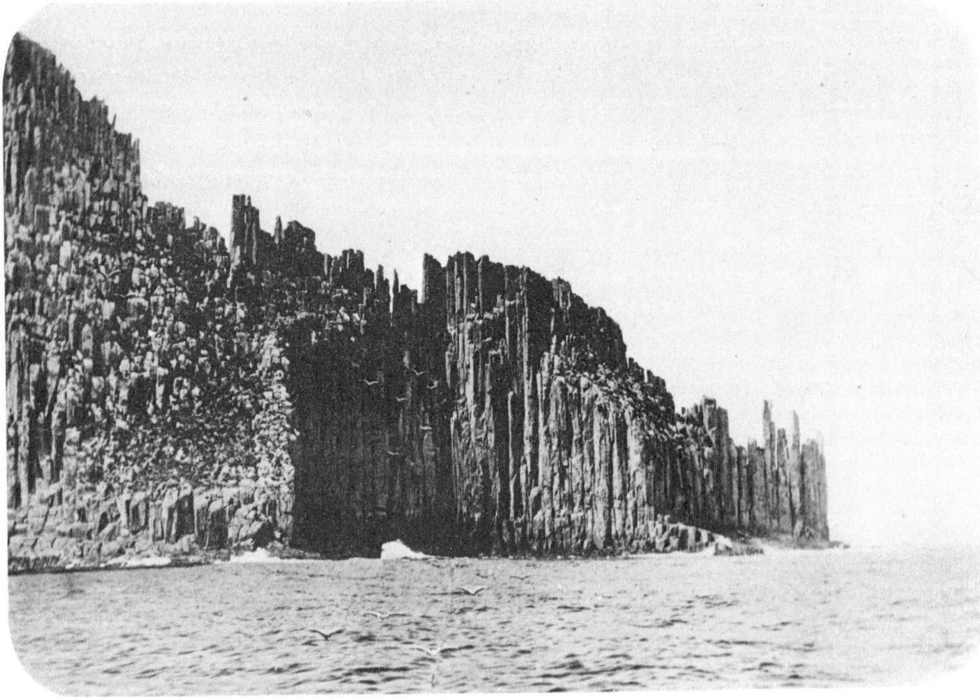

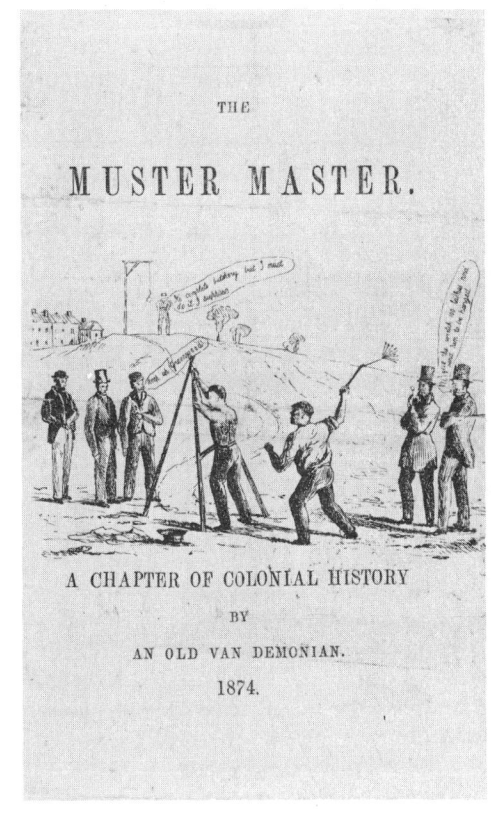

ABOVE: The first Australian railway, convict-powered, designed and installed by Commandant Booth, carries visitors through the primeval forest of the Tasman Peninsula. (*National Library of Australia, Canberra*)

RIGHT: Propaganda against the memory of the System. On the title page of "The Muster Master," published thirty years after transportation to Tasmania stopped, a convict is flagellated while a low official exhorts him to "keep up." At right, a magistrate remarks, "I'll give the wretch 100 lashes and send him to be hanged." The hangman, by the gallows on the hill, exclaims, "It's complete butchery but I must do it, I suppose." In fact, such combinations of corporal and capital punishment were proscribed. (*Mitchell Library and Dixson Collections, Sydney*)

OPPOSITE ABOVE: Eaglehawk Neck, the only land-bridge to the Tasman Peninsula, photographed by J. W. Beattie in the 1870s. Guardhouses are in the foreground. (*Launceston Museum and Art Gallery, Tasmania*)

OPPOSITE BELOW: "The adamantine gates of Hell itself"—Cape Raoul, at the entrance to Port Arthur, with its towering black basalt flutes. (*Launceston Museum and Art Gallery, Tasmania*)

THE

## MUSTER MASTER.

A CHAPTER OF COLONIAL HISTORY

BY

AN OLD VAN DEMONIAN.

1874.

ABOVE: Benjamin Duterreau's "National Picture," *The Conciliation*, c. 1835. George Augustus Robinson is seen "bringing in" the surviving mainland Aborigines of Van Diemen's Land. Seated to his left, Trucanini points at the Conciliator and draws a hesitant tribesman toward him. Note the imagery of "reconciliation" naively expressed in the coexistence of a wallaby and some kangaroo-hounds. (*Tasmanian Museum and Art Gallery, Hobart*)

LEFT: The last pureblood Aborigines of the Tasmanian mainland, facing the end in European finery: from left to right, Trucanini, William Lanney and Bessie Clarke, photographed by J. W. Beattie in 1866. (*National Library of Australia, Canberra*)

Arthur's policy on race relations, c. 1828: a notice-board promising equal justice to blacks and whites alike, addressed to Aborigines. (*Tasmanian Museum and Art Gallery, Hobart*)

ABOVE: The remains of a "dumb cell" in the main prison at Kingston, Norfolk Island. Note the thickness of the walls, through which no sound could pass. Since this photograph was taken (c. 1870), the site has been levelled, and little trace of these structures survives. (*Launceston Museum and Art Gallery, Tasmania*)

RIGHT: Gravestone of a mutineer hanged after the convict rising of 1834 against Commandant Morisset on Norfolk Island. (*Author's collection*)

OPPOSITE ABOVE: The rituals of the cat: a flogging at Moreton Bay, from William Ross's pamphlet inveighing against Captain Logan's regime, *The Fell Tyrant; or, the Suffering Convict,* 1836. (*Mitchell Library and Dixson Collections, Sydney*)

OPPOSITE BELOW LEFT: The martinet of the mainland: Sir Ralph Darling (1775–1858), Governor of New South Wales from 1824 to 1831, oversaw the expansion of "secondary" penal colonies from Newcastle to Moreton Bay and the revival of Norfolk Island as "the *ne plus ultra* of convict degradation." Portrait by John Linnell. (*Mitchell Library and Dixson Collections, Sydney*)

OPPOSITE BELOW RIGHT: "Fellow prisoners, be exhilarated / That all such monsters such a death may find": Captain Patrick Logan, 57th Regiment, Commandant of Moreton Bay. Anonymous portrait. (*Mitchell Library and Dixson Collections, Sydney*)

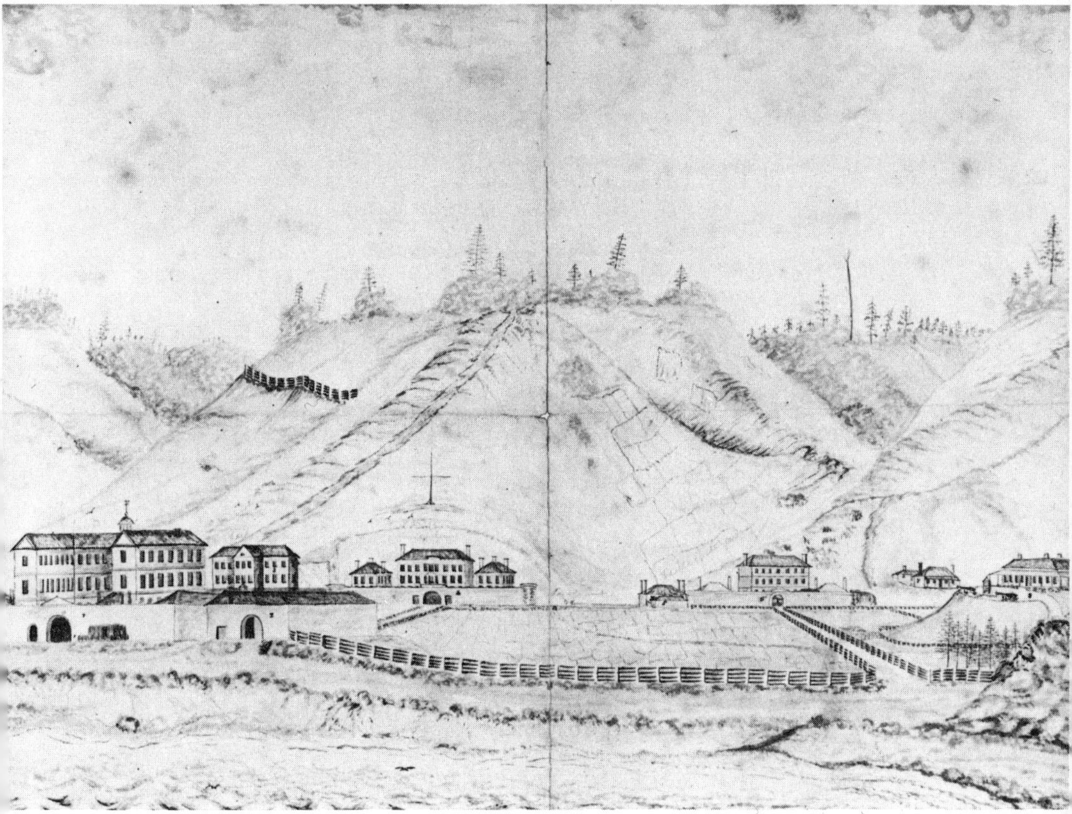

ABOVE: Unknown artist's sketch of the main settlement at Kingston, Norfolk Island, in 1838. The prisoners' barracks and mess are at left; behind, at the foot of the hill, the Military Barracks; at right, Government House. (*Mitchell Library and Dixson Collections, Sydney*)

RIGHT: Maconochie permits dignity to the dead: the convict-carved headstone of Samuel Jones, shot for his part in an attempted hijacking of the *Governor Phillip* off Norfolk Island, 1842. (*Author's collection*)

OPPOSITE ABOVE: "Murderers' Mound," the mass grave outside the consecrated ground of the Norfolk Island cemetery, where the convict mutineers of 1846 were buried. (*Launceston Museum and Art Gallery, Tasmania*)

OPPOSITE BELOW LEFT: Captain Foster Fyans (1790–1870), Morisset's second-in-command on Norfolk Island, who suppressed the 1834 mutiny. (*Mitchell Library and Dixson Collections, Sydney*)

OPPOSITE BELOW RIGHT: "One of the durable ogres of the Australian imagination": John Giles Price (1808–1857), Commandant of Norfolk Island from 1846 to 1853. (*Royal Society of Tasmania*)

Products of the System: some of the remaining "old crawlers" or veteran convicts at Port Arthur, photographed in 1874. (*National Library of Tasmania, Hobart*)

bloodstained tatter of his waistcoat and a part of his compass, broken and discarded by prying stone-age fingers. The next morning, about a mile away, the searchers found Logan's horse dead and swollen in a creek-bed, with sticks incomprehensibly strewn over it. Up the steep bank of the stream was a shallow grave. Logan's bare feet, partly eaten, protruded from the earth and his boots lay to one side. The blacks had speared him to death and buried him facedown, but the wild dogs had begun to dig him up; now he was black with flies and beyond eating. When his body was brought back to Moreton Bay, the convicts "manifested insane joy at the news of his murder, and sang and hoorayed all night, in defiance of the warders."[58]

So anxious were they to claim his death as their own revenge that they invented a different version: The hated commandant had been seized by his own convict servants in the bush, flogged nearly to death, finished off with a stone and buried facing downward, "looking down to Hell, for that's where he's going." Then came the ghost stories. On the day Logan died, it was said, he appeared immobile and silent on his ghastly horse on the far bank of the Brisbane River; but when the ferry-man rowed over to collect him, no one was there. Thus, Patrick Logan began to pass into popular legend at the moment of his death; the ballads came soon after. There was no libel trial for Edward Hall, this time. In fact Governor Darling, perhaps hoping to reduce the hail of innuendo and invective from the colonial press that beat around his head, took a deep breath and made the sole placatory gesture of his governorship: He freed Hall in November 1830, soon after the news of Logan's killing reached Sydney.

But Hall was not grateful; nor did the Sydney democrats think this gesture outweighed Darling's record of cruelty to convicts and favoritism to colonial Tories. Darling might have remained in office despite his colonial enemies—for Australians had not put him there, and they could not remove him—but England itself was moving away from the Tory extremism that Darling, an army man serving this arch-reactionary government of Wellington, embodied.

By 1830, the movement for parliamentary reform had percolated from working men to the very middle classes who, in 1819, had reacted indifferently or timidly to the Peterloo Massacre and who distrusted the idea of "reform." And as the English middle classes became more aware of the appalling inequities built into the power structure—symbolized by the postwar sufferings of the countryside and the scandal of the "Rotten Boroughs"—so the social base of the reform movement broadened, and the Whigs, led by Lord Charles Grey, could move against the Tories' monopoly of power. There was, moreover, the example of the French Revolution of 1830, which persuaded some liberal Whigs that populist moves, led by bourgeois interests, did not—as the Tories had warned since 1789—lead to Jacobinism and tumbrils. Lafayette and Louis-Philippe were plainly not the same as Marat and Robespierre. In November 1830, Wellington's government fell and the new king, William IV, instructed Lord Grey to form a government. Under Grey, the Reform Bill passed, though only by one vote.

Grey was not liberal: "There is no one more decided against annual parliaments, universal suffrage, and the ballot than I am," he told the House. "My object is not to favour, but to put an end to such hopes and projects."[59] But his son, Henry George Grey, known as Viscount Howick, did not share all the father's views. In particular he had been fired by Wilberforce's campaign against slavery, and he was not unaware of the comparisons drawn between slavery and convict transportation. Nepotism put Howick in his father's ministry in 1830 as under-secretary for the colonies, under Viscount Goderich. In Howick, the stream of complaints from Australia about Governor Darling found a sympathetic ear. The world had moved somewhat, and even at the limits of Empire there was less room for a a dull, gold-braided martinet who believed more in the lash than the ballot-box. Howick particularly disliked Darling's attempts to muzzle public speech in New South Wales; and when the governor's six-year term ran out in 1831, there was no move to renew it. So Darling left Australia.

His departure was marked by wild jubilations from the Emancipists. Hall's *Monitor* announced that an "illumination" would rise over its editorial office the night Darling sailed, bearing the incandescent phrase "He's off." "THANK GOD—We have shaken off the *incubus* at last!" Wentworth exclaimed in the *Australian*, and held open house for every Emancipist in the colony on the grounds of his estate at Vaucluse, overlooking Sydney Harbor, whose perimeter had been surrounded by a shallow trench filled with Irish earth to keep the Australian snakes out. Some four thousand people converged on Vaucluse House by gig, horse, donkey and Shank's pony, and hoed into a feast more Brobdingnagian than Lucullan, involving a whole roast ox, twelve sheep, thousands of loaves of bread and incalculable quantities of ale and spirits. The pro-Darling newspaper, the *Sydney Gazette*, asked its readers to imagine

> the roaring, bawling, screeching, blaspheming, thumping, bumping, kicking, licking, tricking, cheating, beating, stealing, reeling, breaking of heads, bleeding of noses, blackening of eyes, picking of pockets, and what not . . . the orgies of the lowest rabble of Botany Bay, congregated in the open air, shrouded by the curtain of night, released from the eyes of the police, and *helewated* by the fumes of *Cooper's gin* . . . [T]hese contemptible proceedings have excited universal disgust and abhorrence among decent people.[60]

But that night the Emancipists and Currency voted obstreperously with their bellies; there were few tears when Darling sailed, and no new appointments for him when he reached England.

Darling's departure, and his replacement by the comparatively liberal Richard Bourke, made convict life at Moreton Bay slightly better—but not much. Thanks to Logan's slave-driving, the settlement now had better buildings and a regular supply of water (whose pipes were each laboriously hollowed from an ironbark log); accordingly, the disease rate slowed down, although trachoma would linger among convicts and then among poor-white settlers on the Brisbane River for half a century longer. Logan's successor, Clunie, was a flogger but a less capricious one, and the convicts did not think him such a tyrant. Fewer of them tried to escape, but that was because they had given up hope: Relations between whites and blacks at Moreton Bay had degenerated so far that convicts now expected to be killed by the natives if they went bush. Allan Cunningham, who had been there in 1828–29, later reported that escaped convicts had been "taking liberties with"—raping—aboriginal women.[61] This must have been the last straw. However, the territories of those offended tribes lay south of Moreton Bay.

Other convicts went north, in the hope of reaching China, and at least one of them not only survived but became famous for his escape (although he did not reach China). This was John Graham, a resourceful Irishman who had been transported in 1824 for stealing a few pounds of hemp from a linen-maker. Assigned at first to a master in Parramatta, he got to know the local Aborigines and learned from them some tricks of survival in the unfamiliar bush. Then, for a second offense, he was transported to Moreton Bay in 1827. After a few months of Logan's brutalities he bolted north, managing to avoid the Aborigines and live, unaided, off the land. When at last he did blunder into contact with a tribe, he had the improbable luck to be greeted by one of its women as the white ghost of her dead warrior-husband. Thus he entered the tribe and lived with it from 1827 to 1833, before walking back to Moreton Bay and surrendering to the surprised Clunie. No convict, other than Buckley in Victoria, had ever acquired such intimate, detailed knowledge of aboriginal life and ritual, but it did not make Graham any more sympathetic to the blacks once he was back in white company. He denounced them as "frightful clans and hordes of cannibals and savages," hoping to convince the authorities that he had suffered so much among them that his sentence should not be prolonged.[62]

Under Clunie, Moreton Bay took shape as a town, the embryo of the city of Brisbane. Its crude economy of forced labor had diversified, expanded by artisans from the "First Class" of convicts—minor offenders who had shown an unblemished record over their first years of imprisonment there. Tailors sewed gray-and-yellow uniforms out of the coarse, felt-like "magpie cloth" or "canary stuff"; and there were cobblers, tanners and candlemakers, smiths, coopers, joiners and wheelwrights—a thriving little economy that contained the seeds of surplus and trade, and whose labor was exploited in various ways by the overseers and officers. The convicts had more food now and placed an enormous value on small luxuries like tea and sugar. The tea was coarse green stuff full of twigs, known as "posts-and-rails"; the brown sticky sugar was nicknamed "coal tar," but it would improve a sweet potato duff and give strength to the insipid mock-coffee the prisoners made from burnt corn kernels.

By the end of 1835, when Captain Foster Fyans of the 4th (King's Own) Regiment succeeded Clunie as commandant, the old starvation days under Logan were just a memory—though a bitterly preserved one in convict lore. But the rest of prison life went on much as before beneath the shadow of the triangles. Fyans took a sardonic pleasure in describing the rituals of the cat-o'-nine-tails to George Walker and James Backhouse, two Quaker missionaries on a tour of the Australian penal colonies:

> "Friend," said Friend Backhouse, "I wish thee much to explain the punishments. First, friend, the number of stripes in whipping?"
> My reply was, from twenty to a hundred or two hundred lashes, that was our limit:—when two long and hollow groans followed. "The first lash, Friend, the skin rises not unlike a white frost, Friend. The second lash, Friend, often reminds me of a snowstorm.... [T]he third lash, Friend, the back is lacerated dreadfully." Half a dozen of groans. "The painful feelings then subside, Friend, for the blood comes freely." Long groans and heavy moans, and the Friends said some prayers; when out the notebooks came.... I then proposed to flog a fellow that they might see the process, and be better able to judge. "No, Friend, we thank thee."[63]

But by then the main form of punishment at Moreton Bay was not the lash, but the treadmill. In 1827, Logan had built a windmill there (it still stands, though converted into an observatory, and is one of the few remaining buildings of the convict period in Brisbane); and two years later a treadmill was added to it, so that convicts could grind corn when the wind did not blow—a practical machine that doubled as an instrument of mass punishment. The treadmill was like a waterwheel, but it was forty feet long, with wooden treads nine inches wide. As many as fifty convicts could be punished on it at once. The convicts' names for it were expressive: the *everlasting staircase* or, because the stiff prison clothes scraped one's groin raw after a few hours on it, the *cockchafer*.

The prisoners went up a flight of steps and stood ready on the horizontal blade of the mill. They had a fixed handrail to hold. The overseer pulled out an iron bolt and the wheel began to turn: "You would hear the 'click, click' of their irons as they kept step with the wheel, and those with the heaviest irons seemed to have a great job to keep up. Some poor wretches only just managed to pull through until they got off."[64] The mill stood for progress—the rationalization of punishment. It was a more philosophical instrument than the cat.

From 1835 on, the exclusively penal nature of Brisbane Town and its outlying settlements began to fade. The lash could still be heard in the streets, and the centipedes of ironed men, their chains rusty with tropical dew, still shuffled from barracks to work, their heads bowed; but their numbers were declining, and when Fyans took over there were only about four hundred male convicts there. By 1840, the prisoners' barracks and the Female Factory stood empty. All convicts still under sentence had been recalled to Sydney, and the assignment system had been discontinued. Now the free settlers of Brisbane had to manage without government-sponsored slave labor, for the place was no longer isolated. It even had a post office. And the broken, marginal Aborigines, stupefied with cane liquor, dozing like lumps of shadow in patches of shade, confirmed the total victory of white civilization. By 1840, squatters had found a stock route north to the rich plains of the Darling Downs, inland from Brisbane. So the pastoral economy of modern Queensland began with the emancipation of Brisbane, for "Nature has pointed out that spot," the *Australian* editorialized in 1842, "as the site of the northern capital of Australia." A week later, Governor Gipps formally declared that Moreton Bay was no longer a penal settlement. Settlers and visitors could come and go as they pleased. Military rule was over. So ended the last of the penal stations on the Australian mainland; and when the first Queensland Parliament was convened some years later, it met, by an irony that Logan might have appreciated, in the upper floor of the largest building in Brisbane—the old convict barracks, built to house a thousand men. But soon this unloved souvenir, like so many buildings that spoke of Australian darkness, was razed.

iv

THE SPOT THAT now represented the quintessence of punishment was Norfolk Island. Governor Brisbane had turned his attention to it in 1824, the year Moreton Bay was settled. After reading the Bigge Report, Lord Bathurst had ordered him to prepare a place of ultimate terror for the incorrigibles of the System. As long as convicts were on the mainland, they could escape; and so Bathurst told Brisbane to re-occupy Norfolk Island, which had been abandoned ten years before at the merciful behest of Governor Macquarie. This speck of land, floating in the infinite waste of the Pacific a thousand miles east of Sydney and four hundred miles north of New Zealand, would once more serve as "a great Hulk or Penitentiary," the nadir of England's penal system. Its old form had been bad enough. As Governor Hunter declared in 1812, its prisoners "felt [it] was a very severe sentence; they would sooner have lost their lives." Now it would get worse, and although no convict could escape from it, rumor and reputation would. In this way, the "Old Hell," as convict argot termed it, would reduce mainland crime by sheer terror.[65]

Brisbane wrote to England, outlining his new kakotopia. On Norfolk Island, the genial stargazer promised, all pretense at reform would be dropped. Its sole purpose would be to provide "the *ne plus ultra* of convict degradation." The island could not support many prisoners, and those it contained must be the absolute worst of those double-damned by the System. Hence, most of them would be men convicted of fresh hanging crimes in the colony, whose sentences had been commuted to life imprisonment. "The felon, who is sent there, is forever excluded from all hope of return," and although mainland convicts in government service or on the assignment system had some legal rights, those on Norfolk Island "have forfeited all claim to the protection of the law." To ensure their reduction to mere ciphers, Brisbane urged that

> if it were not too repugnant to the Laws of England, I should consider it very fitting to have Norfolk Island completely under Martial Law, which would not only form part of the punishment in itself, but save the complicated machinery of Civil Courts, or sending people for trial [to Sydney]. ... My experience convinces me that there is nothing so effectual in dealing with convicts as Summary Proceedings.[66]

This, Bathurst would not grant; but in practice, the future commandants of Norfolk Island were invested with such sweeping powers short of arbitrary hanging that their rule was all but absolute.

The prisoners must be promised nothing and given only the dimmest sense of a goal toward which they could work. "No hopes of any mitigation of their sentences ... should ever be held out to them," and they could only get off the island after a minimum of 10 years, whose last 5 must show a perfect behavior-sheet.[67] That record, of course, could be wiped out by the whim of an officer, the merest grudge-word of an informer. And even if the prisoner finished his Norfolk Island sentence and returned to the mainland, he must serve out the rest of his original sentence in full. *Lasciate ogni speranza, voi ch'intrate*—Dante's words on the adamantine gate of Hell became the obligatory text quoted by educated visitors to Norfolk Island (not that there were many of them) over the next fifteen years. The island would be a machine for extinguishing hope.

For this purpose it was ideal, for it concentrated and epitomized the sense of delusive beauty, beauty empty at the core and flaking into viciousness, uselessness and indifference, that had been part of English reactions to Australian landscape ever since the arrival of the First Fleet. From an approaching boat, Norfolk Island is an apparition, a rolling cap of green meadow and spiring trees, raised out of the Pacific on pipes and pillars of basalt as though offered to one infinite blueness by another. It was no harbor. Most of its coast is sheer cliff, black planes of rock laced with red oxides. There are only two landing-places. One is at Cascades Bay on the northeast side, where boats and crew have to be plucked from the water by a derrick. The other, chiefly used in convict days, is at Sydney Bay, where the ruins of the Kingston penal settlement stand. A reef blocks the whole approach to the shore; ships stood off and unloaded their freight of chained convicts into whalers, which had to be rowed over the reef through its boiling cross-rips—a terrifying ordeal for all but the stoutest tar.

They struggled ashore in Paradise. There was a little crescent beach of white sand where, still by an arm of the reef, the water lapped in aquamarine clarity. Green hills encircled the flat, swampy table where the first settlement had been pitched forty years before; their folds ran down to the sea, and in them ran cascades of bright water shaded by hibiscus and palms. Great ropes of jasmine, on stems thick as a man's wrist, hung in swags from the branches of the Norfolk Island pines. There were groves of sugar cane, figs, guavas and lemons, the wild descendants of specimens brought by the First Fleet from Rio and the Cape in 1788. The Norfolk Island birds had forgotten man had ever been there; one could pick them out of the bushes, like fruit. Even today, a walk along the cliffs—where the green meadow runs to the very brink of the drop and the bushes are distorted by the eternal Pacific wind into humps and clawings that resemble Hokusai's *Great Wave* copied by a topiarist—is a fine cure for human adhesiveness. One sees nothing but elements: air, water, rock and the patterns wrought by their immense friction. The mornings are by Turner; the evenings, by Caspar David Friedrich, calm and beneficent, the light sifting angelically down toward the solemn horizon. "My object," wrote Governor Darling in 1827, "was to hold out that Settlement as a place of the extremest Punishment, short of Death."[68]

The first party of convicts—fifty-seven of them, picked for their skill as artisans—landed in June 1825 and began setting up new quarters out of stone and plank scavenged from the abandoned Kingston settlement. Over the next five years, the population grew and an unremarkable succession of military officers ran the island.* The authorities did not fix on a long-term commandant until 1829. The man they chose was a lieutenant-colonel of the 80th Regiment, James Thomas Morisset (1780–1852).

Morisset had proven tastes and abilities for the work. At the age of forty-nine he was an old soldier; in fact, the army had been his entire life, from the age of eighteen, when he joined the 80th and began a steady rise through the ranks of service in India and Egypt. He was a career officer with no family money to buy him a commission. In the Napoleonic Wars, he fought as a captain in Spain and was gravely wounded at the battle of La Albuera. In 1817 he was posted with his regiment to New South Wales, where he took over command of the Newcastle penal settlement from Captain James Wallis. Through what Hall would later call "the timidity and suspicion of his natural temper, and his proneness to severity," Morisset soon became a terror to the convicts, infamous for the harshness of his punishments. As commandant he was also magistrate, and in order to spare settlers up the Hunter River the bother of coming to Newcastle in order to bring charges against their assigned servants, he would make excursions upstream in a boat with two flagellators and a portable set of triangles so that he could hand out summary lashings on their farms.

No portrait of Morisset survives, and his appearance would have taxed the meager resources of any colonial artist. He was slender, elegantly dressed (by Buckmaster, one of the more fashionable London military tailors) and fond of gold embroidery; even his forage cap was covered with it. But the look of the military dandy was brusquely contradicted by his face. At La Albuera, a 32-inch mine-shell had exploded near him and left him with the mask of an ogre. His mouth ran diagonally upward and made peculiar whistling noises when he spoke. One eye was normal, but the other protruded like a staring pebble and seemed never to move. The cheekbone and jaw on one side had been smashed to fragments and, without cosmetic surgery, had re-knit to form a swollen mass like "a large yellow over-ripe melon"; he would defiantly thrust this cheek forward in conversation, as though daring his interlocutor to look away.[69] For Morisset was not without bravado, and he was determined to convert his wound into a badge of bitter honor in the eyes of his equals and superiors.

* They were, in order: Captain Turton, 1825–26; Captain Vance Young Donaldson, 57th Regt., 1826–27; Captain Thomas Wright, 39th Regt., 1827–28; Captain Robert Hunt, 57th Regt., 1828–29; Captain Wakefield, 39th Regt., 1829. Only Wright stayed longer than a year.

For his inferiors, the convicts, more dangerous sublimations lay within the dapper frame and the twisted gourd of shiny tissue. He "knew" them; and when he returned to London on leave after eight years in Australia—the last two as commandant at Bathurst, beyond the Blue Mountains—he could not get the convicts out of his mind, for their management had become an obsession. He went every day to Bow Street; he haunted the police offices; he learned to talk underworld cant. "I am the man to keep these scoundrels in order," he boasted later. "I assure you, Sir, if the Duke of Wellington searched through the Army of Great Britain he could not equal me; I understand all their priggings."[70] And while in London, he waited on Lord Bathurst and begged for Norfolk Island.

Bathurst knew talent when he saw it. He was worried about the rabble's changing attitude to transportation. Too many letters had come back from Emancipists and from assigned convicts who had found easy masters, praising the conditions of life in New South Wales and Van Diemen's Land, where wages were high and a man could make a new life for himself with his two hands. Bathurst did not want Australia to lose its reputation. Morisset seemed just the man to help Darling put a dose of iron back in the convict soul. The increase of terror (a word Bathurst used often in dispatches to Darling) must begin from the bottom of the System, which meant Norfolk Island. So Morisset went back to Australia as a lieutenant-colonel in 1827. There was some delay in getting him to Norfolk Island. He had married a young woman named Emily Vaux in 1826, but Darling wanted no women in Norfolk Island, because their presence would confuse the schematic purity of discipline in that Mount Athos of English misery. "I laid it down as a rule," Darling explained, "that women should not be sent to the Settlement, and the few free women . . . belonging to the troops and the people there, were accordingly withdrawn."[71] He was reluctant to have only one woman, the commandant's wife, in residence there. Yet it seemed unfair to separate Morisset from the meek young bride whom—with some difficulty, one may surmise, considering his looks—he had wooed and won and then brought so far to Australia. In February 1829, the Morissets sailed for Norfolk Island with their two children. These infants were to see strange sights.

# 13

# Norfolk Island

i

WHEN Lieutenant-Colonel Morisset left to take up his new duties, the *Monitor* in Sydney ran an editorial about his future on "Norfolk Island, late Gomorrah Island," exhorting him to run it with mercy and restraint. To the powerless and passive convicts "he will be as a God," and so

> let him therefore put himself in the place of Deity, and let his mind become imbued with magnanimity, considering that his power was given him, not for his own pleasure and benefit, but for the benefit of the wretches under his sovereign control (for such is a Commandant's will at penal settlements).
>
> Let the biting scourge be inflicted seldom, and then in merciful quantities; and let no other part of an Englishman's body be subjected to this ancient, though still brutal torture, but the *back*.[1]

Morisset may or may not have read this advice; it hardly mattered, for he knew what his chief, Governor Darling, thought of the *Monitor* and its editor. People often suppose that penal systems recruit sadists. But cruelty is an appetite that grows with feeding, and few people receive an epiphany of their own sadism in the abstract; they must see their victims first. It is most unlikely that Morisset's habits were known in advance and so ensured him the command of Norfolk Island. If anything, the authorities concluded from his conduct at Newcastle that he was conscientious, stern, but not unjust. Lachlan Macquarie, the Emancipists' friend, had praised his work there (and even named a lagoon after him in 1821; 150 years later, more fittingly, a lunatic asylum would receive his name). The *Sydney Gazette* extolled him as an opponent of hanging.[2] Both Bathurst in London and Darling in Sydney thought they had found in Morisset a tough, reliable line officer who would run the settlement with a heavy hand but by the book. But this description also fits the men who have run the Gulags of our own time.

The essence of any sadistic relationship between a bad prison boss and his prisoners is that the latter should be (in the word so often used of Australian convicts) "objects." The System's distinction between "objects" (prisoners) and "subjects" (the free) was no mere grammatical quirk: It implied the convict's expulsion from the domain of rights. "Felons on Norfolk Island have forfeited all claim to protection of the law," wrote Governor Brisbane in 1825, meaning every word. "Port Macquarie for first grave offences; Moreton Bay for runaways from the former; and Norfolk Island as the *ne plus ultra*."[3] There was no point of exile beyond this island; its convicts were at their ultimate distance from reasoned legality and open transaction. The only refuge of their criminality was within their bodies, from whose inaccessible centers the meek silence craved by the System could be trumped by mute defiance. This was the silence of the "pebble," the "stone man," as prisoners of unusual endurance were called—a panting and glaring silence, that of a fox gone to earth. On Norfolk Island, that silence would be broken. On May 26, 1829, Morisset landed on Norfolk Island. A year and a half later, the only convict to leave a first-hand account of life under Morisset also arrived there. His name was Laurence Frayne.[4]

Frayne was sent to Norfolk Island in his sixth year of transportation. He was an Irishman, convicted of theft in Dublin in October 1825. He arrived in Sydney on the transport *Regalia* with 129 other Irish convicts at the end of 1826; he may have been implicated en route to Rio in an abortive mutiny plot that failed because—as a young officer on board recounted it—"an Old Man whom we favoured a little came & confessed all the plot. . . . [The soldiers] would have been so enraged they would have murdered every convict on board."[5] In 1828 Frayne was reconvicted for "repeatedly absconding" and was sent to Moreton Bay. There, he still kept trying to escape and his behavior was so untameable that he was sent down to Sydney in January 1830, reconvicted by the Supreme Court, sentenced to death, had his sentence commuted and was put on the *Phoenix* hulk, awaiting transportation to Norfolk Island.

The hulk, an unseaworthy old transport moored in Lavender Bay, had served as an antechamber to the far penal settlements since 1824. She was a stationary hellship, "that receptable of Filth and place of Cruelty and Starvation."[6] Prisoners on board were kept half-starved by the guards, who withheld their rations of flour and "salt horse" to sell on shore; the head warden was an alcoholic who later died in delirium tremens. Frayne tried to escape from the *Phoenix*, but he was caught slipping over the side and was given 50 lashes; then he cursed the overseer and received 150 more. Other convicts on the hulk fared just as ill.

Thomas Cook, held there in May 1836 en route to Norfolk Island, was seized by the head keeper for sharing a pipe of tobacco with his nine cellmates. The ten men were stripped naked,

> and after manacling each of our hands behind our backs, he reefed the legs, which were heavily Ironed, to the upper part of the Iron Stanchions of the Cell . . . with the whole weight of our chains and bodies pressing on our Shoulder Blades for the night, in a state of perfect nudity. By the following morning, and for two days afterward, I could scarcely regain the use of my arms.[7]

Prisoners were silenced with a gag, or by sluicing them down with sea water; in winter, this brought on pneumonia. On the voyage to Norfolk Island their ill-treatment continued. James Lawrence, the convict son of a London diamond broker who had been transported for fraud in 1836 and sent to Norfolk Island almost as soon as he arrived in Sydney, recalled that on this thousand-mile voyage in the brig *Governor Phillip*, there were "Seventy-Five of us in cross irons, our clothes taken from us with the exception of our Shirts, and then rove on a chain in a small prison scarce able to breathe, our passage was dreadful in the Extreme."[8] Frayne, cut to ribbons by the lash, had to make the voyage to Norfolk Island on the *Lucy Ann* in October 1830 with maggots crawling in his back and no chance of a wash or a bandage:

> My shoulders were actually in a state of decomposition the stench of which I could not bear myself, how offensive then must I appear and smell to my companions in misery. In this state immediately after my landing I was sent to carry Salt Beef on my back with the Salt Brine as well as pressure stinging my mutilated & mortified flesh up to Longridge. I really longed for instant death.[9]

As soon as they landed at Kingston, the convicts went to work. Norfolk Island had no free settlers and no assignment system; hence, the convicts worked only for government, constructing buildings or growing food. Every structure on the island, from the sentry-boxes to the high stone security walls around the main compounds at Kingston, was convict-built. Few skilled masons were to be found among the twice-convicted "incorrigibles" in exile there, but the last drop of crude labor was wrung from them in iron gangs. They made bricks, burned coral into lime for mortar and ripped the Norfolk Island pines into planks. The jail gang, made up of some thirty-five multiple offenders crammed in a filthy hovel of a prison near the jetty, hewed stone in the quarry wearing double or even triple irons. As a special punishment, men were assigned to the "wet quarry," a reef partly covered by the sea at the edge of the cemetery, to cut stone under water.

The workday was sunrise to sunset, with an hour off for the midday meal. Every morning and evening, all irons were inspected for signs of tampering—nick-marks, ovalling of the leg-ring, a loose rivet. At unpredictable times, the convicts would be mustered, counted and given full body-searches with inspections of the mouth and anus. Their daily rations were 1½ pounds of cornmeal, 1 pound of salt beef, 1 ounce of sugar, ½ ounce of salt, and a tiny morsel of soap. At dinner, the superintendent was to issue each "mess" of six men a mess kit (knife, fork, spoon, pannikin) which they used in rotation and handed back. But there were never enough utensils to go round, so that they had to eat in a way "disgusting to any man possessing the slightest degree of decency.... The provisions were brought out to the various Gangs in wooden or large tin Dishes and set down as before a Hog or a Dog and [they had] to gnaugh it just the same." If a man dared to make his own utensils, especially a knife, he would be flogged at once and jailed.[10]

The basis of prison discipline was the informer. On Norfolk the policy of splintering the convicts as a class, dissolving solidarity in mutual suspicion, was taken to extremes; the authorities felt, quite correctly, that if the prisoners were given the smallest chance to combine there could be a bloody uprising, even a general massacre. Thus *not* to inform became suspicious in itself, and hardly a week passed without the disclosure of elaborate plots, complete with lists of names, as convicts competed for trivial favors from Morisset and his officers by denouncing one another. "Indulgence," Frayne noted, "was only got by such traffic in human blood." The quality of the information mattered far less than its quantity. Informers had their quotas of denunciation to fill and were "capable of any act of purfidy or blood no matter how Black or horrifying such a deed might be." Any Norfolk man could be flogged on suspicion, as long as he was charged; and since prisoners were tried summarily, by tribunal and not by jury, they had no effective defense. In this way the "normal" relations between guilt and punishment mutated into a continuous sadistic fiction, whose sole aim was to preserve terror.

Frayne described what these punishments could mean. He was brought before Morisset for breaking a flagstone in the quarry. "As usual I found my defence useless," and thus was sentenced to 100 lashes:

> After the sentence I plainly told the Commandant in the Court that he was a Tyrant. He replied that no man had ever said that about him before. I said they knew the consequences too well to tell him so.—But I tell you in stark naked blunt English that you are as great a tyrant as Nero ever was.

The moment I expressed these words I was sentenced to an additional 100 & to be kept ironed down in a cell for Life and never to see daylight again.[11]

The floggings were spaced. Frayne got 50 lashes on his back. In four days, the cuts were partly scabbed over and he got 50 more. On the eighth day, he got 50 on the buttocks; and on the twelfth day, the last 50. Morisset supervised all this "specially to see the infliction . . . given as severe as the scourgers could possibly inflict it," so that

> new and heavier Cats were procured purposely for my punishment, & the flagellator threatened to be flogged himself if he did not give it me more severe. He replied that he did his utmost and really could do no more. . . . The Super[intendent] who witnessed the Punishment swore when I was taken down that i was a Brickmaker, meaning that I was like an Iron Man past all feelings of the punishment. Alas, delusive idea!—I felt too acutely the full weight scourge & sting of every lash but I had resolution enough accompanied by inflexible Obstinacy not to give any satisfaction. . . . I knew my real innocence and bore up against it.[12]

Morisset, insulted to his face, sought new pretexts to break this stiff-necked young Irishman. Nine or ten weeks later, Frayne was up before him again, charged with assaulting a convict informer named Harper. "What have you to say for yourself?" the Commandant asked, and Frayne began a tirade:

> I replied that I would leave it to you to judge whether I am guilty or innocent; you know the character & conduct of the informer; you also know mine. It is useless for me to gainsay anything. . . . If you actually knew my innocence yourself I well know that you would punish me. . . . If you acquit me for the assault you will flog me for what I have now said to you, but I disreagard both you and all the punishment you can give me.
>
> His very next expression was, "I will give you 300 at three different whippings, you damned Scoundrel."
>
> I said, "I am no Scoundrel no more than yourself, but *I don't think I can take that punishment.*" This I said out of derision and ironically, with a sneer at the Colonel.
>
> I and the other man was taken out and we received our first 100 in slow time and with heavy cats. The flagellators were almost as much besmeared with blood as even we. . . . When I was taken down an overseer who assisted to loosen the cords said, giving me a Fig of Tobacco, "You are a *Steel Man* not a Flesh-and-Blood Man at all, you can stand to be sawn asunder after all that skinning and mangling."[13]

Frayne and his fellow convict were jailed for a week until their backs scabbed over; then Morisset sent the island surgeon, Dr. Gamack, to see if they could take their second hundred. Frayne begged the surgeon to get on with it: "I am ready to be scarified alive again," as long as the other man (who "had tender flesh") could take his flogging too.

> Gamack says, "Do you wish to expire under the lash?" I said, "I want to get it over and have done with it & all thought of it, being here injures me more than the flogging."[14]

He got his second 100 and went back into solitary, without any medical treatment. To alleviate the pain from his mangled back Frayne had to pour his water ration on the stone floor of the cell, piss in it to enlarge the puddle, and lie down

> with my sore shoulders on the exact spot where the water lay. . . . I was literally alive with Maggots and Vermin, nor could I keep them down; to such a wretched and truly miserable state was I reduced, that I even hated the look & appearance of myself. . . . The trifle of soap allowed me to wash our persons & shirts was stopped from me, as I thought to spur me to abuse the Gaol authorities and thereby again subject myself to more cruelty . . . knowing as they all did my hasty temper.[15]

Before he could undergo the third part of his flogging, Frayne was reprieved; the colonial secretary in Sydney issued an executive order limiting all floggings to 100 lashes. Morisset then clapped him in the "dumb cell," a totally dark, soundless stone isolation chamber, for two months. No sooner did he come out, disoriented and staggering in the sudden blaze of Pacific sunlight, than he got in trouble again.

There were two assigned convict women working as servants at Government House. They had been briefly jailed for some trivial offense. One of them was not only Irish but came from the same town as Frayne. "Strange to say (and equally true as strange) I purposely got into Gaol if possible to get to them, and while they were walking in the Yard for Air I shewed myself through the Bars. . . . I told them they might expect me to pay them a visit at all Hazard, & I would put up with the consequences if it was 300." That night he did contrive to sneak into the women's cell and hide under their bedding. "They knew too well the Colonel's feelings towards me. . . . They were equally as anxious as myself to annoy the Colonel." So Frayne and the two women had their night of sexual comfort, the only tenderness, perhaps, that any of them had received or given in years. He was found out, of course, and haled before Morisset once more:

I plainly told the Commandant that it was the only opportunity I had ever had or perhaps ever would have of spending a night in Womens company; it was a very natural offence in a twofold degree. "How do you mean twofold?" asked the Commandant. "The first," I said, "is too obvious to need explanations, the second is that they are both your servants —now you can do as you please, that is all I have to say."

"Well then," said the Commandant, "I will give you 100 lashes in slow time so that you shall pay for your creeping into the women's cell."

I said, "I hope you will send me back to gaol right after it, and you can give me another 100 tomorrow for the same offence if that will gratify you or give you a pleasure."[16]

Frayne got his hundred, in slow time. So it went on: "I am an oppressed convict," he raves at Morisset, "oppressed by your Tyranny, & sacrificed by your base Informers & blood hunters, & my hunger and your cruel torture gives you the greatest pleasure & gratification." But nothing changes; defiance calls forth the lash, torture demands resistance, each side defends its territory, neither will budge. How many men like Frayne were there among the seven hundred Norfolk prisoners under Morisset in 1834? How much implacable, hopeless courage was summoned up to confront the iron machinery of discipline? Frayne spent three years "loaded with French or exceedingly heavy Irons" in the jail gang, reefed to a chain cable every night. Certainly, few convicts can have been like him—otherwise the island would have been uncontrollable.

More normal was the experience of John Holyard, who had come to Norfolk Island on the same boat as Frayne in 1830. He, too, had had his sentence for a capital crime commuted, but he learned quite early that to truckle was to survive; and so he became an informer. In the miseries of the *Phoenix* hulk, he "learned a lesson which I trust will never be forgot, viz., Submission to the Authorities." On Norfolk Island, "the exaggerated accounts told of the misery existing on the Island . . . wrung tears from me as I got out of the Boat." Yet he found

> to my great consolation, that to a well-conducted prisoner even on Norfolk Island there is kindness shewn; misery certainly stares the majority of them in the face, but their own doing is the true source of it. . . . I found that although it is a settlement of hardship and privation, yet not altogether so insupportable as I imagined.[17]

Holyard was writing to a clergyman who kept assigned servants and had given him a "character" to one of the Norfolk Island officers, so his tone is predictable. But anyone who rose above passive docility was pounced on, and Frayne was clearly not alone in feeling that the rules and those who applied them were meant "to harass and torture me in a manner repugnant to & not consistent with British Law." Authority was absolute and capricious, lacking any proportion between the acts it forbade and the punishments it meted out. Frayne knew he had been singled out as a "bush lawyer"—"the leading man among my fellow prisoners particularly among the litigious & disaffected." Despite his formidable inner resources he began to sink into despair, believing God himself was against him:

> I began to think that the Almighty had decreed that my life should be made a life of infamy & turmoil & degradation, a life to be perpetually harrow'd up & goaded with such inhuman, barbarous and algerine brutality. This place I considered worse than the blackest dens and caverns of Hell. . . . I began to question in my own then-perverted mind the infinite mercy, nay the justice, of Deity itself.[18]

He recoiled from this idea, reminding himself that God "was shewing me as forcibly as possible the truth of holy Writ." So he resorted to the Bible, particularly the 88th Psalm, which he knew by heart. Ironed down to the jail floor as the Pacific boomed without end on the Kingston reef, each percussion causing a faint shudder in the flagstones, he recited it over and over:

> I am counted with them that go down into the pit:
> I am as a man that hath no help:
> Cast off among the dead,
> Like the slain that lie in the grave,
> Whom thou rememberest no more;
> And they are cut off from thy hand.
> Thou hast laid me in the lowest pit,
> In the dark places, in the deeps.

The decisive way out of this misery was suicide. "If ever it once had entered my mind that a Self-Murderer could obtain salvation I would not have seen a 10th part of the misery I underwent." But religious instruction was so basic to the rearing of many convicts, especially the Irish, that suicide was unthinkable. By killing themselves, they believed they would exchange the pains of the island for a real and eternal Hell, from which there would be no release. And so most of the prisoners who felt, like Frayne, "heartsick of my own existence," still could not bring themselves to "that climax of human depravity, to take away my own life with my own hands." They were caught between God and Commandant, condemned by their will to survive.

Yet in Morisset's time, a remarkable usage emerged on the Island. It turned suicide into an act of solidarity, not of solipsism and despair. A group of convicts would choose two men by drawing straws: one to die, the other to kill him. Others would stand by as witnesses. There being no judge to try capital offenses on Norfolk Island, the killer and witnesses would have to be sent to Sydney for trial—an inconvenience for the authorities but a boon to the prisoners, who yearned for the meager relief of getting away from the "ocean hell," if only to a gallows on the mainland. And in Sydney, there was some slight chance of escape. The victim could not choose himself; everyone in the group, apparently, had to be equally ready to die, and the benefits of his death had to be shared equally by all survivors. Suicide by lottery thus acquired a Roman tinge of disinterestedness.

There are several references to such suicides in the 1830s. Thus William Ullathorne, the Catholic vicar-general of Australia, visited the island in 1834 and remarked that

> so indifferent had even life become, that murders were committed in cold blood; the murderer afterwards declaring that he had no ill-feeling against his victim, but that his sole object was to obtain his own release. Lots were even cast; the man on whom it fell committed the deed, his comrades being witnesses, with the sole view of being taken . . . to Sydney.[19]

But one full account of such a ritual survives. It was written by Captain Foster Fyans, Morisset's second-in-command, who had questioned the survivors of the event.[20]

One day in 1832 or 1833 a gang of 16 convicts was marched out from the Kingston barracks to labor on a road. At the site they seized and manacled their overseer to the only "outsider" in the gang, an unnamed Jewish prisoner, remarking that "Jews are not to be trusted."[21] The gang leader, Fitzgerald, produced a makeshift knife and harangued his mates:

> "Now gentlemen to business. You all know the plot, is anyone against it? Nil. I have sixteen straws in my fist—the long straw will gain a prize, and the short will be his mate, and here is as good a piece of Hoop Iron as any on the island, and what is more it would shave a Bishop—fair play is a jewel, who draws for Lazarus?"
>
> "Oh my Codd almighty, spare my life, Gentlemen," cried the poor Jew.
>
> "Fair play is a jewel, come Mr. Jew, you shall have first prize."
>
> "So help me Codd, spare me"—the Jew fainted, when all cried out for the overseer to choose for the Jew. With some difficulty he was forced by kicks and threats to draw; he did so, the others following, when Fitzgerald was left with the longest straw, and the other with the shortest; either were to suffer a cruel death on the spot.

The long straw now drew against the short "for who was to suffer." Fitzgerald himself won, and made a orief speech to his comrades:

> "I am sorry boys that I am leaving you, but I am not the man either to peach or tell a lie—you'll have fine fun before you going to Sydney, and a chance of giving them the go-by. Think of me, boys, you'll all get off alone. Tell old Dowling the judge that it's my own free will, and that Pat Larkins sticks me. I am all ready now. Come on, my heartys . . . now quick, please yourself and give me as little pain as you can."[22]

At this, Pat Larkins drove the hoop-iron knife into Fitzgerald's stomach "up to his fist" and disemboweled him, there in the dust of the road. The gang ran away; the Jew and the overseer found the key to their handcuffs in the dying man's pocket and freed themselves; after two days of anguish Fitzgerald died in the hospital. Later, most of the gang "with some other aspiring youths for the gallows" were shipped back to Sydney for trial. Clearly, Fyans was impressed by the stoic courage of Fitzgerald's death; he was a soldier and could respect the clan-bound toughness of such men.

We do not know how many such deaths were enacted on Norfolk Island. Fyans's wording suggests that it was part of a pattern, as when he has Fitzgerald begin his speech with the words "You all know the plot." Such rituals evolve through custom; they are not simply invented. But in cheating suicide of its stigma, they covered its traces. Officially, the victim had to be classified as murdered by other convicts. It may be that some other moments when a group of prisoners suddenly killed a convict who was not obviously an informer were, in fact, suicide pacts of this kind.

Convict killings were common on Norfolk Island by the end of 1833, so common that Governor Richard Bourke realized he had to close the loophole. "There has appeared abundant reason to suspect," he wrote to England,

> that Capital crimes have been committed [on Norfolk Island] from a desperate determination to stake the chance of capital conviction and punishment in Sydney against the chances of escape, which the passage might afford to the accused and the Witnesses summoned to attend the trial. The number of the latter has been much augmented by the Sinister endeavour of convicts to procure themselves to be summoned.[23]

He proposed that a session of the Supreme Court with hanging powers be held whenever it was needed on the island, the judge to be any barrister of three years' standing and the jury composed of five military officers

—a kangaroo court if ever there was one. This was not done, but from time to time a judge accompanied by a crown prosecutor, a defense solicitor and a hangman did visit the island to represent the Supreme Court. The first session of this kind was in September 1833; the judge was James Dowling, the second chief justice of New South Wales. He tried and hanged some convicts for murder. From then on, no Norfolk Island convicts were sent to Sydney for trial.

ii

THE CONVICTS' only chance of relief from Morisset's regime now lay in open rebellion. There can have been few who did not sometimes dream, like Laurence Frayne, of revenge:

> I should certainly have taken his life . . . & many a time I prayed, if I knew what prayer was, that the heaviest curses that ever Almighty God let fall on blighted man might reach him, for blood will have blood, and in no depth of earth or sea can we bury it; and the blood of several of my fellow-Prisoners cryed aloud & often to Heaven to let fall its vengeance on this wholesale Murderer and despicable White Savage.[24]

Through the summer of 1833–34, the prisoners' barracks seethed with rumors of a coming outbreak. According to Frayne, Morisset was on the point of flogging confessions out of him and other convicts, as the Reverend Samuel Marsden had done thirty years before to the Irish at Parramatta. But the commander of the garrison, Captain Charles Sturt—whose deeds as an explorer of the Australian hinterland included the discovery of the continent's largest river, the Murray, and who was known for his decency to convicts—dissuaded him.

By then, Morisset could barely handle the routines of his duty. He was prostrated by bouts of pain from his old head wound, which struck so fiercely that he could only lie in bed unable to speak, with his eye bulging like a hen's egg. He stared at failure, a man of fifty-one with nothing to show but this remote post, a brood of unmarriageable daughters and a whistling mask of scar tissue that even the convicts sniggered at. He decided to sell his commission. He wrote to Sydney, announcing that he must remove his daughters from "an abode so unfit for them"; perhaps the colonial secretary could get him a better civil post?[25] Then he took to his bed again, glaring at the wooden ceiling and listening to the enveloping drone of the sea wind in the Norfolk Island pines.

The running of the island now devolved on his second-in-command, Foster Fyans, who had two main informants among the convicts: a prisoner named Bullock and an overseer, Constable Price. Fyans was worried, for something was brewing. An anonymous note was dropped in the soldiers' barracks warning them to "beware of poison"; and Fyans held fresh in his memory a poison plot hatched two years before by one of the convicts on a ship to Norfolk Island. The man was John Knatchbull.[26] Knatchbull, alias Fitch (1792?–1844), was one of twenty children of a baronet in Kent who had married three times. With no inheritance coming, Knatchbull joined the navy and rose during the Napoleonic Wars to the rank of captain. Down on his luck in peacetime, he was arrested, tried and transported for fourteen years in 1824 for stealing a pocketbook with two sovereigns in it from a reveller in Vauxhall Gardens. By 1826, Knatchbull was a convict constable on the Western Road at Bathurst. He had his ticket-of-leave by 1829—won for bringing in eight runaways under the hated Bushranging Act—but two years later he forged a check and was caught. Knatchbull was sentenced to hang, but the sentence was commuted and he was shipped to Norfolk Island in 1832. Once on board, he conspired with fifteen other convicts to lace the crew's and guards' food with white arsenic, seize the ship and escape. An informer gave the plan away, and a whole pound of the deadly stuff was found hidden in their quarters. But because no one was actually poisoned, Knatchbull was not tried, as it was too much trouble to ship the conspirators back to Sydney for trial. So they remained on Norfolk Island, admired by their fellow convicts and known, collectively, as the "Tea-Sweeteners."

Fyans was right to suspect Knatchbull. He was helping them make plans. The only way off the island was by ship, and only Knatchbull knew how to run one. On August 1, 1833, before lights-out in the prisoners' barracks, Knatchbull was stretched on his mat when a convict named George Farrell "laid himself on the mat next to me, when he said I should shortly hear something." Another lifer, an eighteen-year-old Irish lad named Dominick McCoy, joined them.

> "What do you mean?" asked Knatchbull.
> "Tell him," said McCoy.
> "The men outside," Farrell began, "are all mad for their liberty; it is such a gift, especially after the last boat went."[27]

He explained the plan. At dawn muster in the convict barracks yard, they would rush Fyans and his soldiers and overpower them. If any of the guard managed to barricade themselves in the guardhouse, the prisoners would set fire to it and flush them out. Meanwhile the jail gang (made up of prisoners under special punishment in the rickety old calaboose 150 yards away) would likewise rush their own guard as they were being mustered for work in the stone quarry. They, too, were "ready at any time to do anything for their liberty." Then the convicts would break for Government House, capture Morisset, seize the 18-pound cannon there, slew it around and blow the military barracks down. If the soldiers surrendered they would be spared; if not, they would hang, along with all the hated convict constables, overseers and informers. The convicts would force Morisset to hand over his code book of signals, so that they could flag false messages to the next ship that hove to off the reef. Thus, before the captain realized what was happening, they could get on board in the overseers' blue jackets and seize the vessel. They could avenge themselves at leisure. Morisset and Fyans "should be put to a lingering death of torture." Skinned alive by his own cat, the colonel would hang for three days, then be quartered, and the fragments of his carcass would dangle on four trees until the sea birds had stripped them. The women on the island were to be "taken and distributed" to the ringleaders, and Knatchbull wanted the colonel's timid and neurasthenic wife Emily Vaux. After the orgies, the convicts meant to build a decked launch to hold forty or fifty people, which they would sail to New Caledonia. Knatchbull would pilot the hijacked ship to America, for "if he once got there, the Americans would not allow them to be given up again."[28]

So the plan grew, a poor unlikely project nourished by whispers and swollen by fantasies of vengeance. It linked convict to convict in the lumber yard and the sawpits, at the limeburners' kiln and the stone quarry, where the convict Redmond Moss, who carried messages between the various gangs, begged Knatchbull to "learn him the compass" before they all sailed gloriously off into the blue. The very thought of escape, however farfetched, gave new hope to the Norfolk Island longsentence men. (Of the 137 rebels eventually charged with mutiny, half were lifers and another third had sentences of fourteen years.) They devised a password and countersign: "You carry a load." "Yes, but relief is at hand."

Rumors of rebellion filtered back to Fyans through his informants. They were vague about time and strategy, and so Morisset contemptuously dismissed them as a pack of lies. Fyans believed them, however, and slept badly. He pored over the uselessly long list of two hundred names his informers had given him, men they had seen whispering together, whom they had grudges against, or who were merely Irish. But there was no sign from the convicts until January 15.

That day, a Wednesday, dawned in fog and pale gray light. Soon after the 5 a.m. reveille bell, a downpour swept Kingston. Through the rain, Fyans and his men in the military barracks heard a distant clinking of iron fetters from the seaward side of the jail. They could see nothing. There were shouts and the flat bang of a musket, followed by a ragged volley. The mutiny had begun.

The timing was nearly right. At the dawn muster in the prisoners' barracks, an unusually large number of men—thirty-eight in all—had reported sick and were marched off to hospital by a warder, John Higgins. Once inside the hospital lockup, the men turned on Higgins, overpowered him and locked him in a sickroom. The prisoners burst into other wards; one convict named William Groves found the camp constable from Longridge lying ill in bed. "Here's old Howley the dog," Groves cried, "and we ought to settle with him now." The leaders of the hospital revolt, Dominick McCoy, Lawrence Duggan and Henry Drummond, told Groves to leave the sick man alone.

Soon they struck off one another's irons and armed themselves with makeshift weapons, from chair legs to scalpels and a poker; some found axes. They massed in the entrance of the hospital, ready to fall on the jail guard when it came by, and waited in silence.

A hundred yards away this guard was mustering the jail gang—about thirty convicts under the eye of a corporal and twelve privates of the 4th Regiment. The soldiers formed them up in a column by the jail gate, under the gallows. At this moment the jail wardsman looked toward the beach and saw Laurence Frayne helping a guard empty a night-tub of urine into the sea. Frayne looked toward the sawpits and cried, "Are you ready?" At that moment, the guard corporal ordered the prisoners to march. They would not budge. They stood there, rattling their chains: a signal. Seconds later, a gang of convicts from the sawpits—another forty or fifty men—ran yelling at the rear of the guards around the corner of the jail, while the hospital gang burst from hiding and attacked their front. Suddenly, the dozen guards were trapped in a melee of some 120 convicts. Taken utterly by surprise, they could not get their weapons to their shoulders; the convicts, one of the soldiers recalled, "were within the bayonets of the Guard, before they were aware of them."[29] Their muskets, nearly six feet from buttplate to bayonet tip, were not designed for hand-to-hand combat, and for a few moments the convicts and guards stood locked, grappling for the guns. Two convicts knocked Private William Ramsay down and tried to wrench the musket from his hands. In a daze he heard one of them, Patrick Glenny, shouting "Kill the bugger!" while another named Snell cried that he acted "like a bloody dog over the gang." Ramsay begged for his life, and Snell, kneeling on the soldier's arm, said he would spare him if he surrendered his gun; he did, and he lived to testify. Snell stood up but was immediately shot and bayoneted by Private James Oppenshaw. Private Pearson lost his musket to Robert Douglas. "Shoot the bugger, shoot him!" other prisoners yelled. But the gun missed fire; Douglas wheeled on a hated free overseer named Phipps and snapped the hammer six or seven times at him without result. Clutching the musket, Douglas fled into the sugar cane with Phipps in hot pursuit. Henry Drummond, another ringleader, grabbed the musket of Private William Parham, going for his throat with a knife as he did so. The gun was smashed in the struggle, but Parham wrenched free, swung its heavy barrel and brained another convict named Wilson.[30]

The guards began shooting, and their shots alerted the barracks far away across the swamp. They backed into the gateway of the jail, frantically loading and firing while their comrades kept the lunging convicts back at saber-point. The rebel Henry Drummond fell, under the gallows at the jail gate. Several others went down and, as suddenly as it began, the melee broke up. Dazed by the firing and the sudden red spouts where the balls struck home, they scrambled back into the refuge of the jail-yard: James Shields, the jailer, guessed that ten or fifteen of them "who would not have anything to do with the soldiers" rushed by him to temporary safety. Later, the rebel George Farrell would bitterly complain that their cowardice lost the mutiny. The rest of the convicts, driven back by the guard, started retreating in the direction of Longridge, away from the sea.

The clash had only lasted a few minutes. Half a mile away in Quality Row, where the barracks and officers' houses stood, Foster Fyans and his soldiers had come scrambling out in cap and shirts, buckling on their cartridge-belts as they ran; they had not even had time to lace up their boots. They double-timed down the road to intercept the mutineers and formed up panting breathlessly on a small rise, probably where the Norfolk Island war memorial now stands. The convicts came on, but they faltered when they saw the long barrels levelled at them. Fyans gave the order to fire, and when the black-powder smoke cleared, fifteen rebels were seen stretched on the ground while most of the others had plunged into the sugar cane that grew beside the road; only the remnants of the jail gang stood dumbly in surrender, hampered by their irons. Any rebel who tried to head uphill to Longridge was shot. Soldiers followed the escapees into the vegetable gardens and sugar cane. "The men were very keen after these ruffians," Fyans recalled with some relish. "It was really game and sport to these soldiers . . . 'Come on out, my Honey'—with a prick of the Bayonet through both thighs or a little above." Leaving them to this work he led a detachment up the hill to deal with the convicts at the agricultural station at Longridge.

Up there, the morning had begun casually. The convicts had lookouts planted where they could see the Kingston jail buildings and signal the start of the mutiny. Walter Bourke, the leader of the Longridge rebels, was in the toolhouse sharpening hoes when these "cockatoos" burst through the door, shouting "Turn out, my lads—now is the time for Liberty." Convicts came crowding exultantly around, and with a swing of his hoe Bourke smashed the lock on the main toolchest and started passing out axes and pitchforks to the men. "Come on, my boys, follow me," he shouted. "I do not value my life more than I do that piece of dirt —if you think you can do any good follow me."[31] Crying "Death or glory!" "Liberty or death!" and "Huzza for liberty!" about eighty convicts followed him down the road to Flagstaff Hill, pausing only to crack off one another's irons with their axes.

Foster Fyans and his men heard them coming, as a thin straggle of cheers carried over the crest of the hill in the wind. The Longridge men expected to see a victorious crowd of their fellow rebels surging to meet them. Instead they saw two men stumbling up the hill, one of them wounded, and behind them, the redcoats in pursuit. The huzzahs died away, and the surge of adrenaline turned to panic. The soldiers fired a few rounds, but the range was too great. Soon, they closed in and beat the rebels back to Longridge, taking twenty-eight prisoners on the way; with difficulty, Fyans kept the soldiers from bayonetting them to death on the spot, and felt later that "perhaps such lenity is ill bestowed."[32] Nevertheless the soldiers kicked, stabbed and beat the rebels so hard that Fyans himself broke his sword in pieces hitting them with the flat of it.

Within a couple of hours, all of the Longridge rebels were subdued and bound together with cord in a line, which the soldiers marched down the hill to Kingston. At the foot of Flagstaff Hill, they found the youngest ringleader, Dominick McCoy, dying on the ground; cut down by musketballs, he had been repeatedly bayonetted in the lungs, liver and diaphragm. Now Fyans gave the order to drag him by his chains to the Police Office; and when Dr. Gamack protested and demanded McCoy be carried to the hospital, Fyans told his men to wheel right and drag him there, his head bumping across another 200 yards of stones and mud. Other soldiers, with blood in their eyes, came up and threatened to shoot the doctor.[33]

By noon, Fyans had the mutineers behind walls in the main prison barracks—"nearly one thousand Ruffians," he wrote later, although it was more like two hundred.[34] A few were still missing, among them Robert Douglas, who was found later on the other side of the Island at Anson's Bay, groping along but still carrying a musket with ninety rounds of ammunition wrapped in a palm leaf. A bayonet thrust had destroyed his left eye, and infection blinded the other a few days later. Fyans interrogated him daily in the hospital, but Douglas refused to say a word about the rebellion. The final tally of casualties was light: five rebels dead, and about fifty crippled. No guard was killed until the night after the mutiny, when two military search parties met in a cornfield while looking for rebels still at large and, each believing the other to be convicts, opened fire. One fluke shot killed both a civilian constable and a young private of the 4th Regiment, Thomas York.

So ended the Norfolk Island mutiny of 1834. It had been the only mass convict uprising in the history of transportation to Australia since Castle Hill in 1804. It was ill-planned, badly coordinated, and a failure. It was over in seven hours, but the vengeance of the prison authorities lasted for months. When Captain Fyans, a sweaty, dishevelled figure with his double-barrelled gun on one shoulder and an old rusty dragoon sabre in his hand, reported to Colonel Morisset (who was still in bed from his migraine attack), Morisset gave him carte blanche, saying—as Fyans remembered it—"Glad I am that I am not responsible. Do as you like."

In a prolonged sadistic fury, Fyans and the soldiers of the 4th set out to make the mutineers wish they had never been born. It took the black-smiths nine days to make new irons for the prisoners: they were double or triple weight, with the inside of the basils jagged to lacerate the flesh.[35] Rebels locked in the jail awaiting trial were kept naked in a yard so crowded that not a third of them could sit at a time. For the next five months, while the reports went back to Sydney and arrangements were being made to send a judge to Norfolk Island, the rebels were kept locked to a chain cable and "disciplined in a state of nudity for four hours each day, with their arms up and fingers extended, and such of them as betrayed the slightest emotion of pain, were either stabbed by the Military or flogged on the spot."[36] One of the soldiers' amusements, encouraged by Fyans, was to choose a prisoner at random and get one of the floggers, for a plug of tobacco, to thrust a stick into the cord that bound his arms, twisting it round and round until blood burst from his fingertips.

The main torture, inevitably, was the lash. In these weeks after the mutiny, Fyans earned his enduring nickname among the convicts, "Flog-ger Fyans." So many lashes were inflicted that the government cats were not equal to the task, and they kept unravelling; they were "ridiculous, and the flogger nearly as bad," Fyans grimly complained. Besides, the prisoners took their usual pride in being "stone men" and endured the triangles in awesome silence. Fyans wanted new, special cats made "to strike terror into these hardened-minded fellows: prisoners of this description cannot be treated as a Gentleman's Servant in Sydney." The mass floggings went on into the evening by the light of flambeaux, until the "desperate lawless and listless mob" had been battered into submission. Some convicts, weary of their "acute and intolerable sufferings," planned to commit group suicide: they would throw stones at the guards "and thus call forth the Fatal Ball." But this came to nothing.[37]

It took Fyans and his staff five months to interrogate all the witnesses and take their depositions for trial. There was, of course, a cataract of self-serving evidence from informers. The formal charge of mutiny was brought against 137 men, but only 55 came to trial because only known informers spoke against them, and the Crown solicitor considered them "characters ... of the foulest description, upon whose uncorroborated testimony no conviction could take place."[38] The Supreme Court judge, a deeply religious Anglican named William Westbroke Burton, sailed with Chambers, the Crown solicitor, in June 1834 to hold his court on Norfolk Island. On arrival, Burton was puzzled by the discrepancy between the looks and the contents of the place. Why, he wondered, should its "soft beauty ... not have its effect on hearts not wholly hardened by the searing effects of Vice"? Why should the convicts seem "to gather no heartening effect from the beauties of the Creation around them, but to make a Hell of that which else might be a Heaven"?[39] Here, Romantic belief in the therapeutic power of landscape (which had become an *idée reçue* of educated men across the world in the 1830s) had to be suspended, a distressing anomaly to the judge.

The trial went on through July 1834, and Burton's dislike for the main source of prosecution evidence, the informers or "approvers," mounted. He was moved by the evident honesty of the rebels, in contrast to the shiftiness of the witnesses—particularly of Knatchbull, who had tried to incriminate everyone else while saving his own skin. The Crown solicitor had wanted to indict Knatchbull, but "the jury rejected the evidence of the approvers and there being no *other* evidence against [him] I did not bring him to trial."[40] Burton gave Fyans a severe reprimand from the Bench for accepting any confession from Knatchbull: "He was the chief of the mutineers, the man you should have named first.... You have saved his life, or prolonged it. He never can do good."*

By contrast, some of the rebels on trial were praying to die. The oldest of them was only thirty-five years old, but after six months' retribution from the 4th Regiment they came before Burton "grey, wizened and shrunken, their eyes dull and unseeing, the skin stretched taut on the cheeks; they spoke in whispers and were awful to behold." One of them declared in the simplest terms that he and his friends had been condemned to death before and had been reprieved and sent to the island: "We wish we had been executed then. It was no mercy to send us to this place. I do not ask for life, I do not want to be spared.... [L]ife is not worth living on such terms."[41]

In the dock, Robert Douglas impressed Burton with his "singular ability and uncommon calmness and self-possession under circumstances so appalling to ordinary minds." He turned his scarred face and

---

* He was right; Knatchbull ended on the Sydney gallows in 1844, having summoned enough phlegm to write his memoirs in the condemned cell. After his release from Norfolk Island in 1839 he got his ticket-of-leave, drifted in and out of seaman's work, and murdered a Sydney widow for her savings. His lawyer made him a small footnote to legal history by attempting, for the first time in a British court, to raise the defense of "moral insanity" that would later be codified as the McNaughton Rules. It did not save him.

blinded eyes to the judge, uttering the words that remain the final judgment on the *ne plus ultra* of the System: "Let a man's heart be what it will when he comes here, his Man's heart is taken from him, and he is given the heart of a Beast."

Other convicts begged to be shriven: "Oh, your Honour, I have committed many crimes for which I ought to die, but do not send me out of this World without seeing my Priest." But Norfolk Island had no Catholic priest, and later Burton would glimpse this Irishman in his cell "in miserable agony . . . embracing and beating himself upon a rudely constructed figure of the Cross."

By now, he was beginning to feel the System was worse than its "objects." The trial had provoked a crisis of conscience in him, a "sad meditation," a gush of pity to which "the Human Heart could not be insensible." Who, under these conditions, would not rebel? The military jury found thirty of the thirty-five mutineers guilty, but Burton could not sentence them to death. In a wholly unprecedented step he reprieved them all until he could lay their case directly before the governor, Richard Bourke, and bring a Catholic priest to Norfolk Island so that the condemned could receive their last sacraments.

Back in Sydney, Burton pleaded so eloquently to Governor Bourke and his Executive Council that sixteen of the thirty convicted mutineers had their sentences commuted to hard labor for life. The remaining fourteen, however, were to hang; and so two clergymen—one Catholic, the other Anglican—were dispatched there. This was to have far-reaching effects for the System, for the Catholic priest was the vicar-general of Australia, William Ullathorne, later to be a chief witness in the inquiry that helped abolish transportation to New South Wales.

Arriving in September, Ullathorne went straight to the jail; he had five days to prepare the rebels for death. The turnkey told him to stand back, and he opened the first cell. "There came forth a yellow exhalation, the produce of the bodies confined therein," Ullathorne later wrote.

> My unexpected appearance . . . came on them like a vision. I found them crowded in three cells, so small as barely to allow their lying down together—their garments thrown off for a little coolness. They had been six months looking at their fate. I had to announce life to all but thirteen* — to these, death. A few words of preparation, and then their fate. Those

---

* In fact, fourteen. They were: Michael Anderson, James Bell, John Butler, Walter Bourke, Robert Douglas, Henry Drummond, Patrick Glenny, William Groves, Thomas Freshwater, Henry Knowles, William McCullough, Robert Ryan, Joseph Snell and John Toms. The headstones of 8 of these men (Anderson, Burke, Butler, Drummond, Glenny, Knowles, McCullough and Snell) still stand in the Norfolk Island cemetery but other graves have presumably been covered by the creeping dune sand.

who were to live wept bitterly; whilst those doomed to die, without exception, dropped on their knees, and with dry eyes, thanked God that they were to be delivered from such a place. Who can describe their emotions?[42]

Ullathorne baptized four more of them as Catholics; they prayed with him, and then prayed alone, as the vicar-general strolled lost in thought by the cemetery "closed in on three sides by thick, melancholy groves of the tear-dropping manchineel, while the fourth is open to the restless sea."[43]

The hangings took place in two sessions, on September 22 and 23. Each time, half the prison population was mustered in front of the gallows, while the rest looked on from the upper story of the barracks. The condemned men "manifested extraordinary fervour of repentance," Ullathorne wrote. "They received on their knees the sentence as the will of God. Loosened from their chains, they fell down in the dust and, in the warmth of their gratitude, kissed the very feet that had brought them peace." In a silence broken only by the cry of birds and the solemn concussion of surf on the Kingston reef, they mounted the scaffold, dressed in white like bridegrooms. The oldest, Henry Knowles, was twenty-nine. The youngest, William McCullough, had just turned twenty-one. They gazed at the horizon, at the iron rocks of Phillip Island in the circling blue. The hoods went over their heads. "Their lives were brief," wrote their priest, "and as agitated and restless as the waves which now break at their feet, and whose dying sound is their only requiem."

iii

MORISSET WAS long gone. Months earlier, he had gone back to the mainland, convalescent and unofficially disgraced. He sold his army commission and invested the proceeds, all he had, in the newly formed Bank of Australia, which then collapsed, taking his money with it. He lived on in obscurity as a police magistrate in Bathurst, making £6 a week, part of which was garnished to satisfy his creditors. He died in 1852, leaving four sons, six daughters and his wife Emily totally unprovided for. He never wrote a line of reminiscence about Norfolk Island.[44]

His successor there was Major Joseph Anderson (1790–1877) of the 50th Regiment, another career veteran of the Peninsular War, a grasping, vigilant and pious Scot, with a face like an irritable osprey—bleak sunken eyes, a blade of a nose, a wiry bush of white whiskers. "Potato Joe" Anderson's command of Norfolk Island lasted from March 1834 to

February 1839. Opinions about him were divided. Ullathorne, no friend to cruelty, praised his "prudence and solicitude" in encouraging good prisoners, in contrast to the "wanton tyranny" of Morisset. In his own memoirs, Anderson claimed to have reduced floggings from Morisset's 1,000 sentences a year to a mere 70 or 75.[45] This might have surprised the convicts themselves. Thomas Cook, who arrived on Norfolk Island in 1836 and lived through most of Anderson's regime, thought that

> his measures were of a most severe and harassing description. . . . [T]he tide of Informing had uninterrupted scope, and anything beyond an expressed suspicion . . . was not required by his System. . . . It drew no distinction between the well-behaved and the notoriously bad-disposed prisoner.[46]

Anderson once gave five men 1,500 lashes before breakfast. He punished two loafing prisoners who neglected to sow corn properly with 300 lashes each for the Biblical-sounding offense of "robbing the Earth of its seed," as though their crime was vegetable contraception. Prisoners could run up heavy punishment records, like William Riley's during two years in heavy irons after the mutiny:

| | |
|---|---|
| 100 lashes | For saying "O My God" while on the Chain for Mutiny. |
| 100 lashes | Smiling while on the Chain. |
| 50 lashes | Getting a light to smoke. |
| 200 lashes | Insolence to a soldier. |
| 100 lashes | Striking an overseer who pushed him. |
| 8 months' solitary confinement, on the chain | Refusing to work. |
| 3 months ditto | Disobedience of Orders. |
| 3 months' Gaol | Being a short distance from the Settlement. |
| 100 lashes before all hands in the Gaol | Insolence to the Sentry. |
| 100 lashes | Singing a Song. |
| 50 lashes | Asking Gaoler for a Chew of Tobacco. |
| 100 lashes | Neglect of work. |

In all, this came to 1,000 lashes, eleven months' solitary and three months' jail in two years. Another prisoner, Michael Burns, got the stupendous total of 2,000 lashes in less than three years from Anderson: his crimes, like Riley's, included "Singing a Song"—presumably one of the Irish "treason songs."

Anderson exacted harsh extremes of labor from the prisoners. Thus, when a field was to be hoed, a line of convicts began hacking across it and the strongest workers were picked to be the pacesetters at either end; those in the middle would be punished if they lagged and made to work after hours until they dropped.

Anderson was a builder, too, and his architectural memorial is the Commissariat Store (since converted to a church), a massive, coarsely detailed three-story building surrounded by a tall security wall. It draws its peculiarly dogmatic character from the exaggerated rhyme between its pediment and the ziggurat-like flight of steps that leads up to the entrance. In a plaque on that pediment, and in a cartouche above the main building of the New Military Barracks (1837) next door, he had a convict mason chisel his name: *Major Anderson, 50th Regt., Commandant.*

He also planned a new jail, to replace the foul, rickety structure in which the mutineers had been crammed. To get its foundations up above the swampland that lay between the sea and Military Row (where the administrative buildings, barracks and officers' quarters stood), he had all the landfill from the excavations for the Commissariat Store and New Military Barracks moved to the new gaol site, dumped and levelled. Thus the convicts, having hacked a slice off the flank of a hill 300 feet deep, 40 feet high and 700 feet long, now had to carry some 150,000 cubic yards of earth nearly a quarter of a mile in handcarts. Apart from some stretches of the Blue Mountain roads, this must have been the toughest building job in the history of the Australian convict system.[47]

Labor was aimed at punishment, not production; the conditions robbed exertion of its meaning. No ploughs were allowed on Norfolk Island "under the idea of making the work of the prisoners laborious"; so all the convicts responded with the "Government stroke." Everything went at a snail's pace, despite the threat of the lash, and the result was an almost parodical inefficiency. The harder the overseers and guards pushed, the more the convicts malingered. They feigned sickness or induced it, poisoning themselves with lye and nightshade berries; they raised ulcers with manchineel juice or got friends to cut their toes off with a hoe. Anderson had such malingerers flogged, but sometimes sick men came up for a flogging, too, and died. Thus, in October 1836 a prisoner named Barrett, gravely weakened by dysentery, was taken for a malingerer and sentenced to 200 lashes; he collapsed and died after the first 50.[48]

Deranged by cruelty and misery, some men would opt for a lifetime at the bottom of the carceral heap by blinding themselves; thus, they reasoned, they would be left alone. This was the passive end of the moral

anarchy that pervaded Norfolk Island; its active end was the "demoniz-
ing" of prisoners by an authority whose own capricious brutality could
offer no road back from their abasement. For, as Laurence Frayne put it,

> If you endeavour to take out of [a prisoner] that manly confidence which
> ought to be cherished in every civilized human being, you then begin the
> work of demoralization; and it will end in the very Dreggs of debasement
> & an insensibility to every species of integrity & decency, and eradicate
> every right feeling in the human breast. You make him regardless of
> himself, and fearless as to the consequences of doing wrong to oth-
> ers. . . . There is a certain pitch to which you can work upon man to bring
> him to fear . . . but exceed that and you make him reckless. Begin to treat
> him as beneath [your] care and notice, and they then think that you put
> God, his laws, his omniscience, his providence, as though they were mere
> nominal attributes and not virtual & real.[49]

Norfolk Island, Frayne argues, wrecked the social contract. Authority
was supposed, by sinner and saint alike, to draw its value from its mirroring power—its role as a reflected sign of God's mercy as well as His
justice. Bad authority strips all men of hope by showing them a cracked
glass, a different truth about hierarchies:

> They at once throw off all restraint & regard for either God or man, and
> consider everyone over them as acting under the influence of Hypocrisy
> and Imposture, usurping a power never delegated or sanctioned by the
> Almighty. They say you make man the slave of man. They resist and
> cavil at every trifle, and multiply every little departure from rectitude as
> a premeditated scheme to bilk & gull them into submission . . . because
> they are under the operation of the LAW, and cannot seek or obtain
> redress.[50]

Missionaries on Norfolk Island were struck by the state of mind that
oppression bred in the convicts. Judge Burton had praised the beauty of
the place, and Ullathorne was enraptured by it as he watched the evening
sun on the pines "like the bronzed spires of some vast cathedral, flooded
in golden light." Like Burton, he wondered why such beauty did not
reform the soul, on this island where "man wanders, the demoniac of
the scene":

> The devout man, like David, will muse on these His works, until he
> kindles like a fire; but perverse hearts will never see fine days. . . . [W]e
> find the foulest crimes always staining the fairest lands. Those five crim-
> inal cities, on whom the Lord rained down his fire and his fury, were

placed in a very beautiful country, and Norfolk Island is the modern representative of these guilty cities.[51]

Norfolk Island resembled Sodom sexually, but the likeness went deeper. It seemed to have become the epitome of *all* inversions, to breed that final hopelessness held by theologians to be the worst torment of Hell: a place where—in those words of Milton used by Edmund Burke in an early Commons debate on transportation—"all life dies and all death lives." It completed the myth of the antipodean inversion of nature by projecting it onto human society. Within its unspeakable microcosm language itself was reversed:

> So corrupt was their most ordinary language . . . that, in their dialect, *evil* was literally called *good,* and *good, evil*—the well-disposed man was branded *wicked,* whilst the leader in monstrous vice was styled *virtuous.* The human heart seemed inverted, and the very conscience reversed.[52]

Ullathorne had never heard this kind of argot on the mainland. Who could help such men as would use it? The Catholics (about a third of the prisoners at the time of Ullathorne's second visit there in 1835) were desperately grateful for any priest's visit, for only a priest could hear their confessions and so enable them to die in a state of grace. But the Protestants no longer kept up their religious observances; there was no chaplain on Norfolk Island until 1836, because no respectable clergyman would sacrifice his career on such a remote altar. The first one was an unordained missionary, the Reverend Thomas Atkins, an erratic young man of twenty-eight with a burning sense of indignation at official cruelty, who took the convicts' side from the start, quarrelled sharply with Major Anderson, accused him of sadism and graft, and was stigmatized by Governor Bourke as "highly indiscreet and improper." The convict Thomas Cook, by contrast, called him "the brightest star that ever shone on this depraved island." He lasted less than three months. The more normal view of God and religion among the prisoners on Norfolk Island was described by James Backhouse, writing in horror of a prisoner of "great recklessness," "chafed in his mind," who "doubted the being of a Deity, but wished, if there was a God in Heaven, that he would deprive him of life." Such men had one obsession: escape. "Their passions, severed from their usual objects, centred in one intense thirst for liberty, to be gained at whatever cost. Their faces were like those of demons."[53]

None of them did escape. Some tried to capture boats and row them across the Kingston Reef to the open sea; they broached to, were sunk by musket fire, or were chased and caught. Others tried to build escape vessels in secret, with stolen lumber, working at night in caves of the island; they were always betrayed by informers. The "demonization" of the prisoners continued under Anderson's successors, Major Bunbury of the 80th Regiment and Major Ryan of the 50th. They eased some of Anderson's more gratuitous punishments—Bunbury, for instance, replaced the hoe with the plough, which almost doubled farm production in the first year—and the pace of building slowed. But for all that, the System ground on; it was too deeply moored in the habits and appetites of guard, overseer and officer to be fundamentally changed by a few leniencies.

In any case, its reputation had to be kept up. Norfolk Island held a thousand convicts, but its real use was the intimidation of tens of thousands more. If it was not "demonic," it would have been as useless a deterrent as a gallows with no rope. Mercy on the mainland needed the background of terror elsewhere. Such was the official position. It had no lack of sanction from those who might have been preaching mercy. The Reverend Sydney Smith of the *Edinburgh Review*, so clubbable and so jolly, had gone on record for himself and thousands of like minds with the view that a prison should be "a place of punishment from which men recoil with horror—a place of real suffering painful to the memory, terrible to the imagination . . . a place of sorrow and wailing, which should be entered with horror."[54]

But in England, opinion was changing, especially among the Whigs. From 1835 on, such voices as Ullathorne's, resonant with moral outrage, were added to a growing chorus of liberal indignation against the transportation system. Any system that could create a Norfolk Island—no matter how small a percentage of the mainland convicts were actually sent there—seemed iniquitous and fit to be abolished. But while the upper-class reformers were promoting their belief that transportation should cease, the opinion of the lower classes kept drifting the other way. The belief, or hope, that a convict could make his or her fortune in Australia (or at least, a better living than could be scratched from England) had become fixed in the popular imagination. Meanwhile, little by little, the reformers gained ground. It was in 1840 that transportation to New South Wales ceased; and in that year, a new commandant also found himself in charge of Norfolk Island, a prophetic reformer, a noble anomaly in the theater of antipodean terror and punishment: Alexander Maconochie.

# 14

# Toward Abolition

i

T HE MAN SENT to replace Arthur in Van Diemen's Land was an
early Victorian hero, Sir John Franklin (1786–1847), fresh from
the howling wastes of ultima Thule. As a boy in 1801, he had
sailed to Australia with his uncle by marriage, Matthew Flinders, in the
*Investigator*, a three-year voyage of discovery, charting the unknown
south coast from the Great Australian Bight to the present border of
Victoria. In these virgin waters, where the thick red plate of the Australian desert snaps off into the sea and only Antarctica lies to the south,
young John Franklin's passion for geography, hydrography and exploration was born; it would pursue him to his death.

By the end of 1804, he was back in the Royal Navy, serving under
Nelson at Trafalgar on the *Bellerophon*. After the peace, routine duties
followed; but in 1818 he had his first stab at Arctic discovery when he
volunteered as second-in-command on the Admiralty's expedition to find
the "North-West Passage," linking the polar seas to the North Pacific.
Blocked by ice, his ship had to turn back; but the north had laid its frozen
word on Franklin, and he was to lead two more Arctic expeditions—the
first across Canada to Arctic America between 1819 and 1822, a 5,000-
mile journey of almost inconceivable hardship, and the second, to Arctic
America again, between 1824 and 1828. He published narratives of both,
which were avidly consumed by the public. Thus, by his early forties,
this gallant English explorer found himself dubbed a knight, promoted to
captain and pursued as a social celebrity; he was the muffled figure in
W. M. Praed's delicious satire on the foibles of London society, "Goodnight to the Season": "the Lion his mother imported / In bearskins and
grease, from the Pole."

He had also found a second wife (his first having died while he was in
the Arctic). Lady Jane Franklin (1791–1875) was a restless, indefatigably
curious, highly intelligent and slightly neurasthenic woman, a silk-

weaver's daughter given to consuming projects—mainly, advancing her husband's career as hero. After 1833, no imperial sea wars were being fought, but Franklin still had to find a post worthy of his talents. Lord Glenelg, Melbourne's secretary for war and the colonies, was persuaded that there could be no better man for Van Diemen's Land. Accompanied by Lady Jane and his private secretary, Captain Alexander Maconochie, Sir John Franklin stepped ashore in Hobart from the *Fairlie* in February 1837.

His fame had preceded him. He was greeted with relief and good will: illuminations, balls, teas, eulogies, each more florid than the last. Every bottle-nosed, favor-grubbing colonist who could stand up at table seemed to have a toast in him. When Sir John Franklin entered Launceston at the northernmost point of his first official progress across the island, three hundred horsemen and seventy carriages turned out to escort him. After reeling off the speeches Alexander Maconochie wrote for him and receiving tumultuous applause each time, he felt "both oppressed and delighted with the signs of popular joy."

For although Franklin was guileless and did not (at first) question the motives of the colonists he had been sent to rule, he was not blind. He soon saw that these outpourings from the middle class of Van Diemen's Land had something behind them. Many free Vandemonians had assumed, on no authority but their own wishful thinking, that the "polar knight" had come to give them representative government. They were sick of Arthur and his placemen. They expected Franklin to cancel the axioms of Arthur's rule and somehow convert the island into a democracy without taking away the pleasures of assigned labor. There was no ground for this, and Franklin told them so. He might have liked to make Van Diemen's Land self-governing, but the Crown had given him no power to change its constitution.[1]

Besides, he had to work with the officials he had inherited—the "Arthur Faction," a much-detested but certainly able administrative team who knew Van Diemen's Land far better than he did. These included Matthew Forster, Arthur's chief police magistrate and head of the convict establishment, a brutal man and a cunning political survivor ("When I stick my harpoon into a man," Lady Franklin heard him remark, "I don't take it out again")[2]; John Montagu, the colonial secretary; John Gregory, the colonial treasurer; and Sir John Pedder, the chief justice. All four had got their money and power from assigned labor and Arthur's nepotism; none had any time for the airy-fairy liberalism of a new lieutenant-governor who, however intrepid he may have been in the Arctic, seemed in the antipodes not only soft on convicts but governed by the petticoats of his interfering wife. While Arthur's lady had never uttered a peep about the running of the colony, Lady Franklin never ceased to share her views on the matter with guests at Government House and grill them on theirs. She displayed an unwonted interest in the experiences, and even the welfare, of convicts. She corresponded at length with the great English humanitarian and penal missionary Elizabeth Fry, sending her regular (and by no means flattering) reports on Van Diemen's Land. Jane Franklin was particularly concerned about women convicts, who were shamefully treated at the Female Factory in Hobart and often reduced to government-subsidized whoredom in assignment. In 1841 she formed a "Tasmanian Ladies' Society for the Reformation of Female Prisoners," which was mercilessly ridiculed by the Hobart papers, lapsed for two years and was revived—though never very effectively—in 1843.

She asked a great many questions about the System (too many, people thought) and, when accompanying her husband on his first visit to Port Arthur in March 1837, she startled the officers there by asking to try on a set of convict irons. Commissary Lemprière obligingly produced a pair of light handcuffs and snapped them on her wrists. Lady Franklin bore this for a short while but then had a mild attack of anxiety and asked to be released.[3]

What was more, she wished to intervene in the culture and even the ecology of Van Diemen's Land. On learning that the island was infested with snakes, she offered convicts a shilling a head for them, hoping to de-herpetize Van Diemen's Land altogether. This is said to have cost the government £600—and won her great popularity among the prisoners—before it was stopped, for Van Diemen's Land had more snakes than shillings. Her efforts on behalf of intellectual life were more successful. She sponsored lectures and encouraged the faltering steps of the visual arts in Hobart (although its best artist, the unhappy convict Thomas Griffiths Wainewright, quondam exhibitor at the Royal Academy, received no patronage from Government House). She instituted a yearly regatta on the Derwent to honor the sailors on whom the colony depended. She persuaded her husband to sponsor a learned society which, in 1848, became the first colonial Royal Society for scientific studies. Devoted to the study of natural history, she set up a botanical garden outside Hobart; it boasted a natural history museum in the form of a Doric temple, which, for want of support after the Franklins were recalled to England, was turned into a storehouse for apples. As a friend of the great Dr. Arnold of Rugby, she was committed to the advance of education in the fledgling colony, and founded its state college (although its actual opening was delayed for years by the bitter religious factionalism endemic to Van Diemen's Land). As a traveller, she might have been the Lady Wortley Montagu of the antipodes: She was the first woman to travel overland from Melbourne to Sydney, to ascend Mount Wellington and to make the appallingly difficult journey from the "settled districts" overland to Macquarie Harbor (borne, however, for much of the way on the shoulders of convicts in a palanquin or litter). Her letters reveal an eager, tough-minded, nosy, idealistic and intensely loyal person, just the lioness her sometimes naïve and administratively timid lion of a husband needed. It was foreordained that the more conservative colonists would dislike Jane Franklin for being a bluestocking and resent her influence on Sir John.

Perhaps the Arthur Faction would have accorded Franklin a certain grudging respect (followed, as day by night, by undying enmity: that was the Vandemonian way) if he had purged them as Arthur had their predecessors. But Franklin did not have the stomach for that. He vacillated; as Montagu remarked in a letter to his old boss Arthur, now the lieutenant-governor of Upper Canada, "the high qualities which were so conspicuous in Sir John . . . at the North Pole, have not accompanied him to the South."[4]

Instead, he decided he had no choice but to work with the existing officials. So the Arthur Faction began to despise him as a vain, good-natured weakling, while the anti-Arthur colonists came to feel they had been sold down the Derwent. Lady Franklin was right when she wrote, in a letter to a friend, that in Van Diemen's Land "people should have hearts of stone and frames of steel." For Sir John Franklin, who as a midshipman had been unable to witness a naval flogging without trembling, this convict colony was a taxing place. Its colonists, as the English treasury official George Boyes remarked after nearly thirty years' experience,

> very much resemble the Americans in their presumption, arrogance, impudence, and conceit. They believe they are the most powerful men on the Globe, and that their little Island "whips all Creation." They are radicals of the worst kind and their children are brought up in the belief that all Governments are bad—that they are deprived of their rights, and that they are ground and oppressed by the Mother Country, and mocked by the Officers sent out from England to rule them. Their views are of the narrowest and most selfish kind. They are incapable of any generous sentiment, and ever ready to impute the basest motives to their fellow colonists.[5]

An avalanche of administrative problems was teetering behind Government House. And by a peculiar irony, the man whose voice started its descent was the best ally Franklin had in the colony apart from his wife: his private secretary, the incorruptible Captain Alexander Maconochie (1787–1860), who would emerge as the one and only inspired penal reformer to work in Australia throughout the whole history of transportation.

ii

ALEXANDER MACONOCHIE was a lawyer's son, born in Edinburgh. His father died when he was nine, and he had the good luck to be raised by a kinsman, Allan Maconochie, later Lord Meadowbank, who assured him a better-than-average education. He was expected to become a lawyer. But young Maconochie wanted to go to sea, not to the bar, and by 1804 he was a midshipman in the Royal Navy, serving for several years under Admiral Cochrane in the Caribbean. In 1810, as a lieutenant on the brig *Grasshopper*, he underwent perhaps the most significant experience of his career. The *Grasshopper*, on convoy duty in the Baltic, was wrecked on Christmas Eve 1811 off the Dutch coast, and Maconochie, with everyone else on board, was taken prisoner and handed over to the French. There ensued a forced march in the bitter cold of winter from Holland to Verdun, and more than two years' misery as a prisoner of war —at a time when, half a century before the signing of the Geneva Convention, a POW's lot was even less enviable than it is today. This was Maconochie's one traumatic taste of life in prison, and he never forgot it. Indeed, he was the only major official of the transportation system who had ever spent time behind bars.

Released by Napoleon's abdication in 1814, Maconochie rejoined the English Navy in its war against America, captaining the gunboat *Calliope*; he was promoted to commander just before peace was signed in 1815. For the next thirteen years he lived in Edinburgh, studying geography and geopolitics and writing lengthy tracts on Pacific colonization and steam navigation. (His interest in the Pacific, at this point, was somewhat abstract, as he had never been there.) He married in 1822, moved to London in 1828, and in 1830 became the first Professor of Geography at University College, London, and the first secretary of the newly formed Royal Geographical Society. From these chairbound labors he was plucked in 1837 by Sir John Franklin, who offered him the chance to see the Pacific, and England's remotest colony, at first hand. Maconochie's acquaintances in the Society for the Improvement of Prison Discipline asked him, since there was such a dearth of first-hand observers with no vested interest in the System, to complete for them a 67-point questionnaire on the treatment of prisoners in Van Diemen's Land. The Scot had no theories about the System and no prior acquaintance with it; he seemed quite unprejudiced. He agreed to make the report, a task to which neither Franklin nor Sir Henry George Grey, under secretary for the colonies, had any objection so long as he sent it through Franklin to Grey, not directly to the Society.

Maconochie's troubles began almost as soon as he arrived in Hobart. He saw that the wily colonials "read [Franklin] in a moment," while Franklin the new-chum was far too vulnerable to their flattery:

> I was a looker-on all the while, neither sharing in the applause nor . . . very likely to be imposed on by it—I read it thus at its just value, and tried to expose it equally to him, but that was hopeless—it was like trying to force a piece of barley-sugar out of a child's mouth.[6]

Montagu, Forster and the rest of the Arthur Faction quickly sized Maconochie up as a potential enemy whose influence on the new lieu-tenant-governor had to be neutralized quickly. They blew a cloud of innuendo at Franklin, calling his private secretary an ideologue—who but a man with unrealistic pro-felon prejudices would do a report for an English reform society?—a "perfect *Radical*" who "encouraged all the disaffected, and promised what he could not perform." Soon, Franklin and Maconochie began to draw apart—partly because Franklin wanted the Arthur Faction on his side, partly due to Maconochie's own blunt-ness, but mainly because Franklin's sworn duty was to run a system that horrified Maconochie. For Maconochie liked neither the harshness of Arthur's police state nor the cant of those who profited from it. The System, he roundly declared in the report that Franklin transmitted to the Colonial Office in October 1837,

> is cruel, uncertain, prodigal; ineffectual either for reform or example; can only be maintained in some degree of vigour by extreme severity: some of its most important enactments are systematically broken by the Gov-ernment itself. . . .[T]hey are of course disregarded by the community.[7]

The System, Maconochie thought, debased free and bond alike, pro-ducing "the fretfulness of temper . . . which so peculiarly characterises the intercourse of society in our penal colonies."

Much of his report consisted of social impressions and moral lucubra-tions, but it had a hard core of fact. There, he was helped by several others. The Quaker missionaries James Backhouse and George Washing-ton Walker, who had travelled throughout Van Diemen's Land between 1832 and 1834 and reported on the chain gangs for Arthur, opened their files to him. He was advised by the Scottish surveyor Alexander Cheyne (1785–1858), who had been Arthur's director-general of roads and bridges since 1835 and whom Franklin, in 1838, put in charge of the newly formed Department of Public Works. One sees the hand of Cheyne in Maconochie's criticism of convict labor on government works, which entailed so much waste and graft that "1s. 9d. is lost out of every 3s. worth of labour." Maconochie found little to commend in Arthur's graded assignment system. It did not reform convicts; it bred social malaise and blunted the moral sense. "It destroys both soul and body—both master and man—both colonial character and, I may almost say, national reputation."[8] The convicts, he movingly argued,

> have their claims on us also, claims only the more sacred because they are helpless in our hands. . . . [W]e condemn them for our own advantage. We have no right to cast them away altogether. Even their physical suffering should be in moderation, and the moral pain we must and ought to inflict with it should be carefully framed so as if possible to reform, and not necessarily to pervert them. The iron should enter both soul and body, but not so as utterly to sear and harden them.[9]

Manconochie gave his report to Franklin, who asked him to tone down some of the sharper criticisms, and he did so. Then Franklin sent the edited version to the main officials of the colony. Cheyne supported it, the others vehemently disagreed, and Franklin sent their minutes, one of his own, and Maconochie's rebuttal along with the report itself to Lord Glenelg. For fear that this mass of paper, now running to several hundred pages, should "perish in the Colonial office from [its] own intrinsic gravity," Maconochie wrote a separate summary of his case, and sent it to Lord Grey, as he had promised to do, but with a covering note asking him, if he thought fit, to show it to Lord John Russell. Russell was the home secretary, in charge of the British penal system. Franklin did not read this abstract from Maconochie, but he thought he knew what was in it. He hesitated to pass it on but gave in to Maconochie's pleas. He wrote a covering note to Grey urging him not to send any material to the Society for the Improvement of Prison Discipline before it was thoroughly vetted by the Colonial Office, lest it "give pain to many respectable inhabitants here."

Thus two reports on Van Diemen's Land—the long revised one Franklin had read, and the more pungent précis he had not—reached London by the same ship in February 1838. Grey read the précis and, on March 5, 1838, passed it on to Lord Russell. If any moment can be said to mark the peak and incipient decline of transportation to Australia, this innocuous act marked it.

For what Maconochie did not know—and could not have known, due to the long delays in official communication between England and Australia—was that Russell, an ardent critic of transportation, had already been appointed a member of a Parliamentary Select Committee, under the chairmanship of the even more dogmatically anti-transportationist

Sir William Molesworth, to inquire into the workings of the System. The Molesworth Committee had been convened in April 1837, when the dispatches were on the water. At that point, its members knew no more about Maconochie's criticisms than Maconochie knew about the committee.

Russell wanted ammunition. He sent Maconochie's précis straight to the government printer, for publication. Thus a private memo entered the public, official record. To back it up, Russell had the whole text and minutes of the longer report, as approved by Franklin, published a month later.

Both documents caused a sensation in the English press. But it was nothing compared to the hullaballoo the English papers touched off in Van Diemen's Land six months later, in September 1838, when they reached Hobart.

All of a sudden, the good citizens of Van Diemen's Land found themselves vilified in official parliamentary print as callous slave-owners, rulers of a petty kingdom raised on the exploited bodies of convicts. This was enough to bury—for a time—all differences between the Arthur Faction and the anti-Arthurians. Everyone who had ever had a convict assigned to him could now hate Maconochie, who (so the Hobart version went) had gone behind Franklin's back and smuggled his foul canards to England under the guise of official correspondence. Montagu and his friends lost no time persuading Franklin that Maconochie had betrayed him.

Franklin was not quite sure that he had. The opinions in the report were, after all, Maconochie's own, and not presented as official. But in the end he had no choice. He dismissed Maconochie, although he allowed him (with his wife and six children) to stay on at Government House until they found other lodgings. Lady Franklin was sorry. Maconochie, she wrote to her sister, had "such a freedom from colonial suspicion and narrowness of views and personal spite and hostility . . . and so much less apparent self-interest that I could not but value his union with us and deplore his separation."[10]

The Maconochies were ostracized. "We see few and go nowhere," Mrs. Maconochie wrote.

> Alexander is like a lion at bay, deafened by the barking and yelping of the curs about him, but in no other ways stirred from his steady honesty of purpose. . . . Alas, alas! I always looked forward to trials and difficulties, mystifications of every description, but no imagination could have realized the continued tissue of falsehood, suspicion and unworthy accusation continually poured forth.[11]

All this only stiffened Maconochie's fiber. He had at last found his mission in life: "The cause has got me complete," he wrote to London. "I will go the whole hog on it. . . . I will neither acquiesce in the moral destruction of so many of my fellow beings nor in misrepresentation made of myself, without doing *everything* that may be necessary or possible to assist both."[12]

He felt the deck lifting under his feet. The Molesworth Committee had brought in its verdict of guilty on transportation; public opinion in England was changing. Despite his isolation in Hobart, Maconochie had found the allies he needed 14,000 miles away, at the head of the System, among English Whigs whose slanting of the evidence had made the findings of the Molesworth Committee a foregone conclusion.

iii

THE MOLESWORTH COMMITTEE was convened "to inquire into the System of Transportation, its Efficacy as a Punishment, its Influence on the Moral State of Society in the Penal Colonies, and how far it is susceptible of improvement." It began its hearings in 1837 and laid its final report before the Commons in August 1838.[13]

The Molesworth Committee claimed to be an objective tribunal. It was in fact a heavily biased show trial designed to present a catalog of antipodean horrors, conducted by Whigs against a system they were already planning to jettison. Its real movers were the home secretary, Lord John Russell, and the under secretary for the colonies, Lord Grey, in consultation with the Colonial Office. Grey, then thirty-six years old, was later to run the Colonial Office under Lord Russell; he never made any secret of his disdain for the assignment system. Australian affairs were not a large issue for either of these men or for the British Government; they came some distance behind those of Canada, Malta, Gibraltar and the colony at the Cape of Good Hope.[14] But in 1836, Russell had already announced his intent to liberalize the criminal law, reduce the hanging statutes and abolish transportation as a punishment for simple larceny—which would have cut the number of transportees by half.[15] He thought transportation archaic and, like other "progressive" Parliamentarians, favored punishment (at least for routine crimes) in model prisons and penitentiaries on English soil. Between them, Russell and Lord Glenelg had decided to abolish assignment and step up free emigration to Australia before the Molesworth Committee had heard a single witness.

So the Molesworth Committee was formed to dramatize the need for a decision which had already been taken. Russell chose a chairman of suitably flamboyant idealism, an eager young show-pony: the member for Cornwall, the twenty-six-year-old Sir William Molesworth. He was a

"Philosophic Radical," a follower of Bentham and Hobbes (whose collected works he would turn to editing in 1839), and a staunch Abolitionist.

The committee heard twenty-three witnesses, most of whom, like the Scottish clergyman and politician John Dunmore Lang, an untiring promoter of free Protestant emigration to Australia, were already well-known foes of transportation. Others, like James Mudie, were so fiercely bigoted against convicts that their views on colonial morality were untrustworthy. Even Bishop Ullathorne had an ulterior motive in expounding on the horrors of atheism and sodomy Down Under, as he wanted to expand the power of the Catholic mission in Australia. James Macarthur, fourth son of fierce old John, who gave extensive evidence to the committee, thought the convict labor that had raised his family to immense wealth at Camden would no longer be needed if the Crown permitted the colony to get coolie labor from Asia and Crown-subsidized free emigrants from Britain.

Some of their evidence remains useful to the historian, for most of the witnesses were telling the truth as they saw it; but the effect was still tendentious, because it was not the whole truth. The committee was out to portray Australia as a colony plagued by a rising crime rate and crippled by its dependence on criminal slavery. It wanted to set the stage for the policy of controlled emigration set forth by Molesworth's intellectual mentor, Edward Gibbon Wakefield, whereby Crown lands in Australia would be sold to well-screened young emigrants at a "sufficient" or high price so that mere ex-convict laborers could not easily acquire land they could not use. "It is difficult," Molesworth noted,

> to conceive how any man . . . merely having the common feelings of morality, with the ordinary dislike of crime, could be tempted, by any prospect of pecuniary gain, to emigrate, with his wife and family, to one of these colonies, after a picture has been presented to his mind of what would be his probable lot. To dwell in Sydney . . . would be much the same as inhabiting the lowest purlieus of St. Giles's, where drunkenness and shameless profligacy are not more apparent than in the capital of Australia . . . [E]very kind and gentle feeling of human nature is constantly outraged by the perpetual spectacle of punishment and misery— by the frequent infliction of the lash—by the gangs of slaves in irons—by the horrid details of the penal settlements; till the heart of the immigrant is gradually deadened to the sufferings of others, and he becomes at last as cruel as the other gaolers of these vast prisons . . . [T]he whole system of transportation violates the feelings of the adult, barbarizes the habits, and demoralizes the principles of the rising generation; and the result is, to use the expression of a public newspaper, "Sodom and Gomorrah."[16]

Stirring stuff, and meant to be; but it ignored the facts that scores of thousands of emancipated convicts had gone on to build happy, productive and law-abiding lives for themselves and their children in Australia, that by no means all the "respectables" were opportunistic slave drivers, and that the place was not entirely a sink of atheism and inherited propensities to crime. Bishop Ullathorne summed up the committee's bias—without perhaps realizing the implications of his story—when he described a private call he made on the young chairman at home in London. "I went to his house, and was amused to find him in a dandy silk dressing-gown, covered with flowers like a garden, and tied with a silk cord with flowing tassels. He had my pamphlet before him, *and tried to coach me as to the best way of giving evidence.*" [Italics added.][17]

The committee's basic charge against the assignment system was its randomness as a "strange lottery," ranging between "extremes of comfort [sic] and misery," in which a swarm of unpredictable variants—the character, temper and security of the master, the kind of work, the site —had, as Governor Bourke put it, "an unmeasurable influence over [the convict's] condition, both physical and mental, which no regulations whatever can anticipate."[18] What deterred crime, the committee argued, was not the fate of the convict in Australia but the *perception* of his fate among English criminals:

> Most persons in this country . . . are ignorant of the real amount of suffering inflicted on a transported felon, and underrate [its] severity. . . . On their arrival at the antipodes, they discover that they have been grievously deceived by the accounts transmitted to them, and that their condition is a far more painful one than they expected. For those convicts who write to their friends . . . are generally persons who have been fortunate in the lottery of punishment, and truly describe their lot in flattering terms; those . . . who really experience the evils of Transportation, and are haunted with "a continual sense of degradation," are seldom inclined to narrate their sufferings except when they have powerful friends from whom they may expect assistance.[19]

The main characteristics of transportation, the committee acerbically put it, were "inefficiency in deterring from crime, and remarkable efficiency . . . in still further corrupting those who undergo the punishment." Efficiency for evil and futility for good "are inherent in the system," which could never be improved. What of its economic benefits to the colony? The committee took a pessimistic view of these, too. Due to free convict labor, it noted, "a larger amount of wealth has been accumulated in a shorter space of time than perhaps in any other community of the same size in the world." But it was an artificial prosperity, not likely to continue. "New South Wales is suffering excessively from a dearth of labourers. The flocks of sheep are double the size they ought to be; a vast number perish for want of care; the complaints of the colonists on this subject are loud and universal." Ten thousand laborers were needed in New South Wales but only three thousand convicts were likely to arrive there in 1838, barely enough to replace those lost to the labor force by death, illness or tickets-of-leave. Hence, there had to be another source of labor. The committee rejected Macarthur's idea of importing Asian coolies; that smacked of American slavery.

Hence, the only course was free emigration, underwritten by the sale of Crown land in Australia as proposed by Wakefield. That, too, demanded the end of the System, for "Transportation has a tendency to counteract the moral benefits of emigration, while . . . emigration tends to deprive Transportation of its terrors." But with labor short, land cheap and wages high in New South Wales, it was too easy for free laborers to become small independent farmers—which they wanted to do for more than ordinary reasons, since "the employment of convicts as slaves has . . . a tendency to bring labour into disrepute." So when transportation was abolished, the price of Crown land, then as low as 5s. an acre, had to go up to at least £1, so that laborers would keep laboring.[20]

It was not these reflections, however, that maddened the colonists, but the report's strictures on their morals. Even before the full text reached Australia, word had leaked back of what some of the witnesses, especially Ullathorne, had said; it provoked much unease, and in May 1838 more than five hundred respectable citizens petitioned the Legislative Council of New South Wales to do something to counteract the talk about Sodom, Gomorrah and the rising crime rate. In July the council issued a lengthy resolution pointing out that "the character of this Colony . . . has unjustly suffered by the misrepresentations" of Molesworth, Russell and their parliamentary colleagues; that the free emigrants and the rising generation of native-born Australians "constitute a body of Colonists who, in the exercise of the social and moral relations of life . . . impress a character of respectability on the colony at large"; that many convicts were in fact reformed by assignment amid the "solitude and privations" of the outback; and that assignment generated the wealth that enabled settlers to buy Crown lands and so produce the government income to underwrite immigration, so that "the continuance of Immigration . . . must necessarily depend on the continuance of the Assignment of Convicts."[21]

The colonists feared, with reason, that by the time the Whigs had finished libelling their morals, nobody would want to come to Australia anyway and the colony would have neither convict nor free labor. To them, the report was a stunning parental rejection. They had posited their social self-esteem on a rigid class barrier between themselves and the convicts. Even the Currency had done this, burying their convict origins within a generation or two. Now, the report claimed that crime was increasing faster than population and referred to a "progressive demoralization both of the bond and of the free inhabitants"; clearly, in English eyes, there was little to choose between them. No wonder that the Exclusives—who had always insisted that the offspring of convicts bore a hereditary stain which had not touched their own lineage—reproached Mother England in bewildered denials and Oedipal tantrums and that they resolved to tighten the class line between convicts and "respectables" in New South Wales. Meanwhile, the Sydney press, which until 1838 had kept up a drumfire of scare stories about a growing crime wave in New South Wales, suddenly changed its tune; the very idea of a crime wave became, in local Tory eyes, a "monstrous caricature" sketched by English Whigs.[22]

The report had placed the colonists in exactly the double bind that defines a colonial mentality. Many of them wanted to be more English than the English; they needed the approval of the implacable parent. Instead, Molesworth gave them pages of condescending Whiggery-and-priggery about their ineradicable stain.

Once the fuss over the Molesworth Report had died down, however, the end of transportation and assignment in New South Wales came smoothly, without much political or economic strain. Even before the report hit the colony, the instructions from Downing Street were to wind down assignment and "coerce" convicts in government labor gangs instead. In October 1838, Bourke's successor, Governor Sir George Gipps, who had taken over a few months before, proscribed the assignments of convicts "for domestic service, or for the purposes of Luxury and in Towns," although they still did essential work on pastoral stations.[23]

Gipps, a gallant veteran of the Peninsular War and a strikingly prudent and humane governor, did all he could to ease the transition of the labor supply from convicts to immigrants. The "bounty system," approved by the Colonial Office in 1837, helped considerably: It gave £30 to every able-bodied migrant couple under the age of thirty, and £5 to each of their children; single men, sponsored by settlers, were underwritten to the tune of £10 each, and respectable spinsters between the ages of fifteen and thirty (if they came out under the protection of a married couple) got £15. Before long, eighteen thousand free immigrants had arrived in New South Wales on the bounty system, and over forty thousand on their own initiative. This was more than enough to fill the gap in the labor supply. The *Eden I*, the last convict transport to arrive in New South Wales under the Old System, dropped her 269 male passengers at Sydney Cove on November 18, 1840.

But what could England now do with her criminals? Molesworth and

Russell were impressed with American penitentiaries. But in 1838, England did not have any; therefore, they would have to be built—at a cost of millions. Spread over the years, that would probably be cheaper than transportation, which was costing the Crown between £400,000 and £500,000 a year. The committee urged the government not to be put off by the cost. Short sentences could be served in penitentiaries in England, longer ones in others built on suitable islands—places as diverse as Malta, Corfu and the Falklands were mentioned—but not in the far antipodes.

Meanwhile, convicts must still go abroad. But not to New South Wales or the settled parts of Van Diemen's Land, if assignment were abandoned—"which it ought to be at once." The committee felt short sentences ought to be served in Bermuda for the time being, but the only receptacles for long-sentence convicts, until the penitentiaries rose, were still those sites of ill-fame on the outer edges of Australia—Norfolk Island and the Tasman Peninsula, each a natural prison isolated from free settlement.

And there, the committee urged, Alexander Maconochie's guidelines for a new prison discipline based on incentives and clear future goals "might in part at least be attempted with advantage." Maconochie had not been idle; he never was. While seeking another post in Australia, he had bombarded Russell from Hobart with his theories of reformatory punishment, set forth in densely argued, prolix memos. And the committee was swayed. "It would be advisable," the report noted,

> to ascertain, by experiment, the effect of establishing a system of reward and punishment not founded merely upon the prospect of immediate pain or immediate gratification, but [on] . . . the hope of obtaining or the fear of losing *future and distant advantages*. . . . The great object of a good system for the government of convicts should be that of teaching them to look forward to the future and remote effects of their own conduct, and to be guided in their actions by their reason, instead of merely by their animal instincts and desires.[24]

Here, the committee was simply echoing Maconochie, whose ideas—so far in advance of their time, when they came to be tested on Norfolk Island between 1840 and 1844, containing so many of the principles of modern penology—we may now consider.

iv

ALEXANDER MACONOCHIE wanted to shift the focus of penology from punishment to reform. Of course, the State could and must punish crime, but punishment on its own, he argued, was a socially empty act without checks built into it: "Our penal science is . . . without precise rule, a mere balancing between conflicting impulses, severity for the supposed good of society on one hand, and leniency for the supposed good of the criminal on the other, in both frequently running into error." He saw no sense in punishing a criminal for his past while not training him with incentives for his future.

Because it was fixated on punishment alone, the Old System had produced mainly crushed, resentful and embittered men and women, in whom the spark of enterprise and hope was dead. So Maconochie argued. Exemplary punishment was only vindictive; it ran wild, degrading both convict and jailer. Terms like "mercy" and "remission of punishment" were to be dropped. "Let us offer our prisoners, not favors, but *rights*, on fixed and unalterable conditions."[25]

But how was this to be done? How to stop the corrosion of despair, the leakage of human possibility? Maconochie never claimed to be an original penal thinker, but he had what more "original" men like Jeremy Bentham lacked—firsthand experience of prison and humane understanding of its inmates. The basic idea for his system had first been raised by the Cambridge theologian William Paley in his *Moral and Political Philosophy* (1785). In this early Utilitarian text, Paley suggested that the punishment of criminals should be measured, not by raw time, but by work, "in order both to excite industry, and to render it more voluntary."

Within a few years, this idea of punishment by task and not by time was mooted in America. It found another advocate in Richard Whately, soon to be appointed Archbishop of Dublin. In the *London Review* in 1829, Whately urged that convicts be sentenced to give the state a measurable amount of labor in expiation of their sins, so that the quicker and better they worked the sooner they would be free: "With each additional step they took on the treadmill they would be walking out of prison—by each additional cut of the spade they would be cutting a way to return to society."

Such ideas reached the Quaker missionaries James Backhouse and George Walker and went from them to Maconochie. They, too, advocated task rather than time punishment, and argued that, as most convicts were morally childish, the penal reformer might take a cue from the discipline of "enlightened" schools, which offered rewards for good conduct rather than punishment for bad. At each monthly muster, the diligent convict would get a "ticket" and the lazy would lose one or more; getting three tickets would shorten one's sentence by a month.

Such ideas of discipline by the carrot, not the stick, were the germ of Alexander Maconochie's "Mark System." Maconochie argued that sentences should be indefinite—no more stretches of seven, ten, fourteen years or life. Instead, the convicts would have to earn a certain number of "marks," or credits for good behavior and hard work, before they got free. Six thousand marks would be the equivalent of a seven-year sentence, seven thousand would correspond to ten years, ten thousand to life. They would buy their way out of prison with these marks. To buy, they must save.

Hence the length of his sentence was, within limits, up to the convict himself. Marks could be exchanged for either goods or time. The prisoner could buy "luxuries" with his marks from the jail administration—extra food, tobacco, clothing and the like. They were "just wages, and will equally stimulate to care, exertion, economy and fidelity." Maconochie hoped to abolish rations, "whose moral effect is always bad, by taking the care of a man's maintenance out of his own hands." Ideally, the convict would pay for everything beyond a bare subsistence diet of bread and water with the marks he earned.[26]

Maconochie believed his Mark System would be objective. As things stood, prisoners were at the mercy of their overseers for "indulgences," which "corrupt and debilitate the mind." Official freedom to remit sentences led the convicts to lie and curry favor. It made them servile or evasive, and usually both. Only measurable actions could measure reform:

> The term "remission of sentence" should be banished. . . . There should, in truth, be none whatever; but the duration of the sentences being made measurable by conduct under them, and not by time at all . . . no power should anywhere even exist in a subordinate authority to remit a fraction of it; but on the other hand, there should not be less certainty in the result of good conduct. *The fate of every man should be placed unreservedly in his own hands. . . . There should be no favour anywhere.*[27]

As soon as a convict entered the system, then, he would begin his Pilgrim's Progress with a short harsh stretch of confinement with hard labor and religious instruction. This was a moral aperient, punishment for the past.

The next phase, rehabilitation for the future, would begin with his advance through the stages of the Mark System, where everything he had was bought with his labor and obedience, translated into marks and entered in the commandant's incorruptible ledgers. As the convict's behavior improved and the moral lesson of the Mark System—nothing for nothing—sank in, so his environment altered by stages: first, solitary or separate imprisonment; then, "social labor" through the day and separate confinement at night; next, "social treatment both day and night"; and so on. He rose from one grade to the next automatically, with no interference from commandant or magistrates, depending on his total credit of marks. Some, of course, would slide back, losing marks or wasting them, which only reinforced the metaphor of real life. However, just as there would be no favors under Maconochie's system, so the only punishment would be the loss of marks—the mild, inescapable, all-seeing accountancy that drew its attentive parallels between time and money, units of labor and moral worth.

Once the prisoner was trained to see the relation between morality and self-interest, he stood ready for the third stage of the Mark System: group therapy. Maconochie wanted to put "developed" prisoners in groups of six. They would work together and mess together. Each man in the group would be responsible for the marks of others as well as his own. If one backslid and lost marks, all would. In this way the prisoners would learn mutual dependence and social responsibility.

Nobody in England or America, let alone penal Australia, had tried such therapies on convicts before. This idea of prison as a moral hospital would not win full acceptance until well into the twentieth century. The details of Maconochie's system—that prisoners should have direct access to the commandant, through an ombudsman, for instance, or that officials should take a personal interest in individual convicts—were a century ahead of their time.

The Mark System would have stayed in Cloud-Cuckoo Land but for the Molesworth Committee, which endorsed most of Maconochie's plan except the group therapy. Recommendations passed; things moved slowly, but they did move. In May 1840, the Colonial Office suggested Maconochie's appointment to Norfolk Island. Gipps passed the matter to Franklin in Van Diemen's Land.

Sending him there struck the lieutenant-governor as a double solution. It would rid Van Diemen's Land of its intractable, idealistic gadfly and would appease the Arthur Faction, on whom Franklin relied more and more passively. Meanwhile, Maconochie's visionary penal scheme would get a fair trial. If it failed, he would sink; if not, it would hardly change things in Van Diemen's Land—not, at least, during Franklin's term of office. He offered Maconochie the post.

In fact, the Scot did not think the place at all ideal for his experiment, and he told Governor Gipps so at length. He pointed out that there were already twelve hundred twice-convicted prisoners there, hard beaten-down men who would furiously resent a second and milder system of convict discipline for new convicts; the practical difficulties of running two systems for two different groups of prisoners on such a small place would be insoluble, and it would be "extreme cruelty to mix up newcomers" with the old Norfolkers. The old lags would corrupt the new "by contagion." Besides, Norfolk Island was too remote for his purposes and (a very Caledonian thought) its soil was so fertile that "the rewards of industry may be obtained without its exertion." So Maconochie begged Gipps to let him set up a new experimental station on the Tasman Peninsula, or Maria Island, or even on King Island in the Bass Strait, rather than Norfolk. But Gipps would not hear of it.

He was not hostile to Maconochie or cynical about his plans. He knew the defects of the Old System, and its horrors plagued him. But he had to be realistic. There was nowhere to put the twelve hundred twice-convicted Norfolkers. They could not go back to New South Wales, because transportation there was ending; to have so much of the doubly damned scum of the System siphoned back to the mainland would be interpreted as a gesture of contempt for the aspirations of its free citizens and would set off a wild public outcry. At the same time, its old lags could not go to Van Diemen's Land, because Franklin would not take them and Gipps could not force him to.

So Maconochie was ordered, quite unrealistically, to keep the old Norfolkers and the new subjects of his experiment separate as best he could. By the time he took ship for Norfolk Island, with his wife and family and three hundred new convicts (all fresh from England and not even disembarked in Sydney), Maconochie was so fired with enthusiasm that he saw all difficulties melting before him like wax. He was certain that his experiment would work; he could not wait.

A few days after landing, he had the Old Hands mustered in the jailyard at Kingston and strode in to confront the collective stare of twelve hundred men, nameless to him, masks of criminality and evasion, burnt by sun and seamed by misery, the twice-convicted and doubly damned, Scottish bank clerks and aboriginal rapists, Spanish legionnaires and Malay pearlers, English killers and Irish rapparees. "A more demoniacal-looking assemblage could not be imagined," he later wrote, "and nearly the most formidable sight I ever beheld was the sea of faces upheld to me." They looked at their new commandant with utter skepticism as, exalted by the thought of laying his balm on such scars, he announced the end of the Old System and described his system of marks.[28]

He had not come as their torturer, one of the prisoners reported him as saying; but he did not have the authority to extend the Mark System to them as Old Hands. He could only try it with the new arrivals. Nevertheless,

> he felt no hesitation in saying that he should find little difficulty in obtaining such an authority, and that he would venture therefore to place us under that System with the English prisoners. . . . The cheers which emanated from the Prisoners were most deafening. From that instant all crime disappeared. The Old Hands from that moment were a different

race of beings. The notion, the erroneous notion that had been engendered in their minds by a course of harsh and cruel treatment under which they had for many years been compelled to groan, was almost entirely eradicated when they found themselves received as *men* by their Philanthropic Ruler.

At once, old feelings of patriotism stirred in the convicts:

> No sooner did they rightly comprehend the purport of his message from our Most Gracious Queen,—that Sovereign who had been forgotten by them as having any dominion over the land of their Captivity—that land in which so much blood had been spilt,—than Her Majesty reigned in their hearts and they all appeared to labor cheerfully in the one large field of Reformation.[29]

Maconochie was a zealot, but an acute one. He saw that in this terrible place the sense of a chain of authority leading back to England and its monarch had been ruptured; the men had given up hope because they believed themselves abandoned by their homeland. There was nobody beyond the prison to whom they could appeal. By reinstating the Queen as icon, with all her imagery of youth, femininity and maternal concern, Maconochie showed great insight into their predicament.

His first sight of the Old Hands seems to have dispelled the last of Maconochie's doubts. From now on, nothing but the most prompt and radical therapy could help them. Dutifully, he penned a report to Gipps announcing that he would not obey his orders to keep the old and new prisoners under separate systems. Gipps was pained. It raised his worst fears of Maconochie's "visionary" streak. Had he appointed a loose cannon who would wreck the Old System and replace it with nothing workable? The governor sent a stern rebuke to Maconochie.

It reached the island just five days before the birthday of the young Queen Victoria, May 24, 1840. The new commandant had set aside Monday, May 25, as a public holiday for everyone, bond and free. At first light, strings of signal pennants headed by the Union Jack fluttered gaily up the flagpoles while a 21-gun salute boomed across Kingston from a massed battery of cannon on the hill behind Quality Row. Turning out of bed, the Old Hands as well as the new convicts up at Longridge were stupefied to find the great gates of the walled prison compounds standing wide open. They could wander as they pleased on the island, swim in the sea, stretch and frolic on the sand—as long, Maconochie's proclamation warned them, as they showed by "retiring to their quarters at the sound of the bugle . . . that they might be trusted with safety." Thus, Cook recalled, "these men who had for many years been ruled with the Rod of

Iron and had received their hundreds for being a short distance from the Barracks, were on this loyal occasion permitted to range from the settlement . . . without the least fear of committing any depredation."[30]

They got special food, including a generous ration of fresh pork, which they cooked for themselves over festive little barbecue fires. Throughout the morning, Maconochie wandered among his prisoners, affably chatting with them. When the convicts sat down to lunch—at tables in the open air, like men, not like hogs at swill—they were further amazed to be given pannikins of rum-and-lemon, the rum paid for out of Maconochie's own pocket, with which to toast their young Sovereign. They cheered her loudly, "three times three," and then toasted their commandant's health even louder.

Then, after the meal, there was an entertainment, whose hand-written playbill survives. James Lawrence (1795–? ), an educated convict —the son of a London diamond broker, who had been retransported to Norfolk Island for fraud in 1836—played the lead role of Don Caesar in the "admired Comic Opera of the *Castle of Andalusia*," supported by a cast of ten other named players and "the usual Banditti" for extras. Lawrence apparently had a taste for amateur theatricals. In the past, Major Anderson had sentenced him to fifty lashes for singing a song in the barracks, as he was "a very strict man and no lover of the Drama."[31] But now he could strut and fret his hilarious hour, amid roars of amusement from the prisoners. After the opera came a "musical melange" of glees and songs—"Prithee, Brothers, Speed to the Boat," "Paddy from Cork," "Behold How Brightly." James Lawrence gave a rendition of "The Old Commander"—a veiled reference, perhaps, to the detested Anderson— and James Porter (1807–? ), one of the Macquarie Harbor convicts who had intrepidly seized the brig *Frederick* and sailed her all the way across the Pacific to Chile before being caught and sent to Norfolk Island to suffer under that "second Nero," Captain Bunbury, sang "The Light Irishman." Michael Burns, whose back bore the tangled scars of two thousand accumulated lashes, danced a hornpipe. Another convict gave the Tent Scene from *Richard III*, which Maconochie must have chosen to rebuke the indurated cynicism and despair of the Old Hands:

> My conscience hath a thousand several tongues,
> And every tongue brings in a several tale,
> And every tale condemns me for a villain.
> Perjury, perjury in the highest degree,
> Murder, stern murder, in the dir'st degree—
> All several sins, all us'd in each degree,
> Throng to the bar, crying all, "Guilty! Guilty!"
> I shall despair. There is no creature loves me,
> And if I die, no soul will pity me:

Nay, wherefore should they, since that I myself
Find in my heart no pitɔ to myself?

In the afternoon the show was moved up the hill to Longridge and
repeated for the New Hands (who were kept segregated from the old, in
strict deference to orders). Down at Kingston there were more amusements and sports, lasting into the evening. When night fell, fireworks—
paid for, like the rum, by Maconochie himself—banged and glittered over
the prison compounds; and by the time the last spark had trailed away
in the blackness, Maconochie noted that "not a single irregularity, or
even anything approaching an irregularity, took place.... [E]very man
quietly returned to his ward; some even anticipated the hour."

When the good colonists of Sydney heard news of this extraordinary
day, so utterly unlike any other in the past fifty years of the colony's
history, a wave of execration broke on Maconochie's head. The scum of
the System were parading free, with rum, dances and fireworks, on the
Isle of the Damned. What further revolutions might this not presage?
What would the mainland convicts do when they heard about the felon's
picnic? How soon could this rosewater liberal of a Scot be recalled? Not
soon enough, was the answer. Gipps was embarrassed by Maconochie's
disregard of orders, but he was a principled man and had given his word
to the reformer. "My desire to see Capt. Maconochie's system tried in a
fair and proper manner remains undiminished," he wrote to Lord Russell
in June 1840, enclosing copies of his protégé's "rather voluminous" reports, but Gipps expressed his "surprise"

> that [he] had, within a week after his arrival in Norfolk Island, abolished
> all distinctions between the two classes; that he had extended equally to
> all a system of extreme indulgence, and held out hopes, almost indiscrim-
> inately, to them of being speedily restored to freedom.... [T]hough my
> disapproval of Capt. Maconochie's proceedings ... was received by him
> on the 20th May, no attention whatever was paid by him to my commu-
> nications.... [O]n the contrary, within a few days after the receipt of
> them the whole Convict population of the Island was regaled with Punch,
> and entertained with the performance of a Play.[32]

In the meantime, Russell had written to Gipps, having second
thoughts about Maconochie and giving the governor authority to recall
the reformer if he thought proper:

> Notwithstanding the Objections which I entertain ... to the Theory of
> Captain Maconochie, that Reformation is to be the sole Object of the
> Convict System, I still wish the Experiment to be tried under his imme-

diate Supervision; but with the clear understanding that you shall remove him, if you should find Mischief ensue . . . from his Management.[33]

But when Gipps's account of the Queen's Birthday celebrations on Norfolk Island reached him, Russell's next letter took on a sharper note of alarm:

> I see no Alternative but to direct that Captain Maconochie should not be intrusted with the management of any Convicts who have more than three years' time to serve before . . . they may obtain a Ticket of Leave. The rest of the Convicts at Norfolk Island should be gradually removed from under his Control. . . . Make the necessary arrangements with Sir John Franklin for the Reception of such Convicts in Tasman's Peninsula.
>
> I have already authorised you to remove Captain Maconochie from Norfolk Island. . . . [I am convinced of] the necessity of leaving you full Discretion to supersede that Officer.[34]

Maconochie, however, cared not a fig for the colonists' prejudices. He pressed ahead with his plans for cultural and moral reform. The first are summed up in a shopping list he forwarded to Gipps.[35] By past penal standards, it was outlandish. He wanted books, for instance—an encyclopedia, magazines on engineering, craft and farming, cookbooks for brewers and bakers; these would help teach the men trades they had never learned, or else forgotten. He asked for a copy of *Robinson Crusoe*, to instill "energy, hopefulness in difficulty, regard & affection for our brethren in savage life, &c." He wanted the convicts to read travel and exploration books, starting with Cook's Voyages, because "the whole white race in this hemisphere wants softening towards its aboriginal inhabitants." Hoping "to invest country and home with agreeable images and recollections [which] are too much wanting in the individual experience of our lower and criminal classes," he sent for books on English history and popular national poetry—Robert Burns, George Crabbe, the sentimental sketches of English village life by Mary Mitford, a set of Walter Scott's Waverley Novels to encourage national pride in Scottish convicts, and the works of the Rousseau-tinged woman novelist Maria Edgeworth, such as the satirical *Castle Rackrent* (1800), to do the same for Irish ones. He also stocked this prisoners' library with moral and religious works, some, as he put it himself, of "controversial divinity," for he wanted the prisoners to think and argue together, not rot in their cells:

> Polemical discussions are sometimes inconvenient; but I do not dread them, for they are nearly always, I think, improving. Wherever a taste for them prevails, as in Scotland, Switzerland &c[a], it is always found accompanied by other good qualities; while on the contrary, where they are

despised, as in France, or crushed, as in Spain, the national character seems to suffer. . . . I would have no fear [of controversies], even in a prison.

He included the works of Shakespeare in his island library, for their nobility; had his doubts about the reformative power of theater ("the English drama is often licentious, but substantially its tendency is moral"); and felt that theatrical training could help convicts overcome their passions. Such had been his purpose on the Queen's Birthday.

Music would be the main therapy; the Orphean lyre, once heard on Norfolk Island, would charm and soothe the savage beasts of the Old System. Music was an "eminently social occupation." It taught collaboration and disciplined obedience. It rested on strict order and subordination, and, if "national and plaintive" in character, kept its hearers affable and patriotic. "It is sometimes thought to lead to drinking," wrote this earnest Scot, anticipating objections from on high, "but this, when true at all, applies to *rude* rather than scientific music. . . . The most musical people, as the Italians or Germans, are thus sober rather than drunken." (Maconochie had never visited either country.) He put in a request for trumpet, fifes, horns, drums, cymbals and two "seraphines" (reed accordions with keyboard and bellows, invented in the 1830s and popular in small parishes that could not afford full organs). He spent £46 of the government's money on a large stock of music-paper: old, infirm and crippled prisoners would be set to copy the scores out.

Gipps worried that there was little he could do, short of recalling Maconochie altogether, to stop him running Norfolk Island as he pleased. The island was too far from the mainland. But he had his colonial secretary, E. Deas Thomson, write a blistering rebuke:

> [Your] Errors . . . appear to have been the consequence of *Your own too sanguine temperament*. . . . Deeply impressed with the Truth of your own Principles, and elated, it is not unreasonable to suppose with the Notice which your Writings had attracted in England, you appear to his Excellency to have set to work with the Idea that everything was to give way before you.[36]

He also reported to Russell, a week later, that although he could not yet

> be justified in declaring Captain Maconochie's System of Management has failed, I doubt whether he will be ever able himself to work it out, as the Nonfulfilment of the Expectations which he has encouraged the Prisoners to entertain must . . . diminish his Influence over them.[37]

Maconochie replied, with annoying airiness, that he had ignored his orders to submit all new convicts to a time of punishment labor before putting them under the Mark System because "it can scarcely be doubted that this Act [2 & 3 William IV, c. 62] will be repealed. . . . I never thought of these rules as a guide; I thought them a dead letter."[38]

But Gipps's reply, through Thomson, put the politics of the matter quite flatly. The issue was not how well Maconochie's measures were working on Norfolk Island, but their effects on the mainland:

> Whether [the Old System] was good or bad is not the question; it was a system which caused transportation to that settlement to be held in great and salutary dread by the convict population of New South Wales, and to destroy that dread before even any substitute for transportation to Norfolk Island had been devised, would be to expose this colony to risks for which [Gipps] cannot make himself responsible. I am therefore to inform you that the instructions . . . are now repeated.[39]

Gipps was pincered between his hope that Maconochie's system would succeed and his fear of the majority of influential colonists—irascible, bigoted men, haunted by the threat of a "slave rebellion," who believed that convicts should be kept in iron constraint and not given an inch. Pressed to make a public statement, he reluctantly criticized Maconochie in a speech to the New South Wales Legislative Council. This whipped the criticisms of the conservative press into a firestorm. Before long, as Gipps himself recounted it,

> every man was against him, every man derided his System. . . . The feeling in fact against him, though not so intense, and far more justifiable, was analogous to that which, a dozen years ago, manifested itself in the West Indies against any attempt to ameliorate the condition of slavery.[40]

But Maconochie, a thousand miles away, pressed indefatigably on. He argued vehemently against Russell's wish, as transmitted to him by Gipps, that "my Men" who had won their tickets-of-leave should be sent down to Van Diemen's Land to complete their sentences:

> Nothing would, I think, be more unfair to them, or more certainly tend to their second Fall. Dropping, as it were, from the Clouds, without Friends or Experience, or the Habits of Evasion and Suspicion which in existing Circumstances must and do characterize the mass of the Convict Population there,—likely to be regarded with dislike by the inferior Authorities as having been trained on with different Maxims from their own, —indifferently supported thus by their Superiors when they do get into difficulty,—and jeered and tempted, if but for the Fun of it, by their

Equals,—I can see but one fate for them, and that is too melancholy to be further dwelt on.[41]

Maconochie continued to lobby Gipps for more money, more power, an absolute scope for his Mark System. His long-winded, theory-stuffed dispatches soon palled in Sydney. Gipps's patience frayed. "His Excellency cannot lay the public Purse open to your Hands," snapped Thomson in July 1842.

> He cannot make you what, in one of your own Letters, you expressed a Desire to be,—a Dictator. . . . After a Correspondence of more than Two Years his Excellency feels he is sufficiently acquainted with your System to render unnecessary any Discussion on the first Principles of it; and he cannot help remarking, although he does it with great Reluctance, that your frequent Practice of introducing Theoretical Reasoning into your Despatches causes the Public Correspondence to be both tedious and unsatisfactory.[42]

Maconochie obviously had grave problems. He could not promise the convicts freedom under his system and be sure that the government would honor his word; his powers were ill-defined; money was short; and to keep two separate systems for two groups of prisoners on a small island was an administrative nightmare. But he kept at it, and he described his general relations with the prisoners in optimistic terms. "I deliberately claim the Merit of almost complete Success," he exulted in a lengthy dispatch to Gipps in June 1842. "I have almost made black white." He expatiated on his day-to-day relations with the convicts:

> I showed the greatest Confidence in all; walking familiarly among them; taking my Wife and Family with me to every Corner of the Island, without Protection; removing the iron bars from my House Windows . . .
> I bade them stand up like Men, whomsoever they addressed . . . [A]t one time, if a Prisoner contradicted a Free Witness against him, he was punished for Insolence. . . .
> I even frequently tried Offenders in the open Barrack Yard, and engaged the [prisoners] to act as Jurors, Pleaders, Accusers, or otherwise, as the Case might be; I derived extraordinary Advantage from this, in at once suppressing false Testimony . . . and in interesting the Body of the Men in the Administration of Justice. Their sole Object on all occasions had been to defeat it, but now they began to sympathise with it. . . .
> I told them repeatedly that I could work no miracles with them, that I had not come to be their Gaoler, but if possible their Reformer; that I could do much in this if they would assist me, but nothing without. . . . I thus omitted nothing which I thought could touch their Hearts and Feelings, and thus give them an elevated direction.[43]

Maconochie dismantled the gallows, which had stood as a permanent emblem of dread outside the gate of the prisoners' barracks. He threw away the special double-loaded cats used by the floggers. The island had never had a church, but now Maconochie built two, one for the Catholics and the other for Protestants, each accommodating 450 men. For the dozen or so Jewish prisoners, who suffered badly from the anti-Semitism of other convicts and the lack of any means to conduct their own religious ceremonies, he set aside a room in the barracks as a makeshift synagogue. He gave every man a plot of the rich soil, set up classes in vegetable and fruit gardening—"a boon to the industrious, none at all to the idle"—and encouraged them to sell their surplus produce to the officers. "I thus sought to distribute property among them, and from its possession inculcate a sense and value for its rights." It greatly reduced petty theft. He let them grow and use their own tobacco "to legalize an indulgence which it was impossible to prevent, and in which, unless forbidden, there was no moral evil."[44]

He even instituted a new policy on death and commemoration. Few convicts had ever been given headstones. The exceptions were usually rebels, such as the men executed in the 1834 rising; some of their tablets can still be read in the Norfolk Island cemetery, their inscriptions a pointed reminder to other convicts of what disobedience deserved. But to be commemorated after death, however simply, was of great importance to ordinary men; and so Maconochie authorized the placing of "headstones, or rather painted boards" on the graves of convicts.

> a privilege previously confined exclusively to the free; and our burying-ground being a somewhat romantic spot . . . near the sea, it was eventually seldom without one or more visitors reading and meditating on its stern and touching lessons and recollections.

These wooden markers are gone. But some convict headstones from Maconochie's years do remain, testifying in their elaboration to Maconochie's scrupulous refusal to deny the dead their dignity—even when they were killed in a mutiny. The gravestones of men shot in the abortive piracy of the brig *Governor Phillip* in 1842, the work of skilled but anonymous convict hands, are among the finest in the cemetery. That of James Saye bears a severe reminder:

> Stop Christian stop and meditate
> On this man's sad & awfull fate
>
> On Earth no more he breathes again
> He lied [lived?] in hope but died in pain.

But the stone of Bartholomew Kelly (an Irish convict from Kilmurray in Cork who had been transported as a mere child of twelve in 1831 and had suffered on the island since March 1834 before turning pirate at twenty-six in 1842) is adorned with emblems of mercy, two turtledoves bearing olive twigs in their beaks, between the cherub's head on top and the skull and crossbones below. And Samuel Jones, transported as a boy from Warwick for stealing rabbits eleven years before he was shot on the *Governor Phillip*, has a stone of strict and simple beauty, with an angel blowing the trumpet of resurrection while stony, leafing tendrils—shoots that promise renewal of life beyond the grave—twine upward from the ground. No convict since 1788 had been granted such exequies. Even a simple stone meant a lot. Thus Laurence Frayne, who had suffered so terribly under Morisset's regime, was allowed to set up a monument to his fellow Dubliner William Storey, officially listed as "a troublesome mutinous character," who had been shot in 1838, a year before Maconochie's arrival, after escaping into the bush. "This stone was erected by Lau[ren]ce Frayne to comemmorate his memory," the plain worn inscription reads, testifying to the solidarity between the Irish convict and his mate, a bond whose public expression only Maconochie would permit.[45]

Trusted at last, reprieved from the incessant torment of the cat-o'-nine-tails, treated like human beings instead of caged beasts, some convicts poured forth their gratitude to the man they saw as their savior. The last hundred pages of Cook's *Exile's Lamentations* are given over to describing and praising Maconochie's Mark System. Other prisoners were briefer but no less intense in their feelings. "We were relieved by an Angell and Family," wrote James Lawrence, "the well known and respected Captain Maconochie, Humane, Kind, religious and now Justice stares us in the Face, the Almighty has now sent us a deliverance—no gaol, no Flogging . . . ."[46]

Maconochie's humanity also showed in his treatment of men so broken by cruelty and neurosis that they were thought beyond help. Perhaps the most striking case was that of Charles Anderson, a mentally impaired convict who had undergone years of misery in Sydney as the butt of every colonial sadist.[47] An orphan, Anderson had passed from the workhouse into the navy at the age of nine. On active service, he was wounded in the head and suffered irreversible brain damage; after a drink or two, especially when under stress, he turned violent and hostile. During such a bout on shore leave, Anderson smashed some shop windows and was arrested for burglary. Tried and convicted, he was sentenced to seven years in Australia; he was then eighteen. Anderson was so crazed with resentment when he landed in Sydney that the penal authorities isolated him on Goat Island, a rock in Sydney Harbor. Over the next few years he escaped and swam for shore three times, and received a total of some

1,500 lashes for such "offenses" as "looking round from his work, or at a steamer in the river, etc." He spent two years tethered to a chain on the rock, naked and sun-blackened. His only shelter was a coffin-shaped cavity hewn out of the sandstone; at night he would lie down in it and the warders would bolt a wooden lid, pierced with air holes, over him till morning. His food was put on the rock and pushed at him with a pole, like a wild beast's rations. Prisoners were forbidden to speak to him, on pain of flogging. The welts and gouges torn in his back by the cat never healed and were infested with maggots. He stank of putrefaction and Sydney colonists found it amusing to row up to his rock, pitch crusts and offal at him, and watch him eat. Eventually Governor Bourke, ashamed by the light this public spectacle cast on the people of Sydney, had Anderson removed to the lime-kilns of Port Macquarie. He escaped again and joined a black tribe; was recaptured and savagely flogged; and killed an overseer, hoping to be hanged. The authorities sent him to Norfolk Island instead, and he was still there—a man of twenty-four, looking twenty years older, relentlessly persecuted by the Old Hands—when Maconochie took command.

His therapy for Anderson was simple: he gave the poor, crazed man some responsibilities by putting him in charge of some half-wild bullocks, and freed him from the taunts of the Old Hands by letting him stay with them out of range of the barracks every day. He hoped, rather fancifully, that "bovine" characteristics would rub off on Anderson, making him more tractable. But the man did tame the bullocks, and found himself—for the first time since leaving England—congratulated and spoken kindly to. Then Maconochie moved him up to a new job, managing the signal station on top of Mount Pitt, which he did "with scrupulous care." Anderson could never be fully rehabilitated—his earlier brain damage was too severe for that—but when Governor Gipps visited Norfolk Island in 1843, he recorded his amazement on seeing the former wild beast of Goat Island bustling about in a sailor's uniform, open and frank in demeanor, returned to his human condition. This was the most striking success, but not the only one, of Maconochie's occupational therapy, an idea unheard-of in the English penal system until then.

A man of such radical views was bound to make enemies wherever he went, and his system was sure to be attacked.* The first complaint

---

* Maconochie's critics especially relished, as light relief, the fate of his eldest daughter Mary Ann, or Minnie. It only showed how this Caledonian do-gooder, the felon's friend, could be hoist with his own petard: Minnie's education had been entrusted to an educated convict, a young and handsome Special transported for forgery. The nineteen-year-old girl (bored stiff, one may surmise, by the social horizons of Norfolk Island) had shown a tender and deep sentiment for her tutor. It is not known whether he actually seduced her. But

from a minor official on Norfolk Island was, of all things, that he had become a tyrant, applying his system in the teeth of regulations. In August 1842, Governor Gipps forwarded to London a letter from a "demi-official," Maconochie's commissariat officer, J. W. Smith. It claimed that

> Captain Maconochie fancies himself supreme. . . . He has contended for absolute Power . . . [A] most radical Change is wanted here immediately. The Place bears no more Resemblance to what a Penal settlement should be than a Playhouse does to a Church. The Public works are neglected for want of mere Labour; the Roads which were made with so much Pains [sic] are falling into Decay; . . . the Crops are wholly insufficient to supply the Establishment. Idleness and Insubordination prevail to a shameful extent.[48]

Both the shortage of food and decline of labor came from events beyond Maconochie's control. In 1841 blight struck the staple crops on Norfolk Island. They failed, and hunger lowered the prisoners' resistance to disease. Dysentery swept the island, and killed off a number of the "New Hands" from England. Smith mentioned none of this.

There were also rumors, impossible to quash from Norfolk Island, of escapes and near-rebellions facilitated by the lenient new system. All were untrue, but they became arguments against Maconochie. Once in 1842, a group of twelve convicts (all twice-convicted Old Hands) seized the brig *Governor Phillip* at sea off Norfolk Island and held her for half an hour before the military guard rallied, killing five of them and capturing the rest. But since this piracy happened several miles offshore, it could only be blamed—as Gipps was prompt to recognize—on the negligence of the vessel's captain and guards, not on Maconochie's Mark System.

It was hard for Governor Gipps to formulate a policy for Norfolk Island and make it stick. Lord Russell had told him to stop sending twice-convicted criminals there from New South Wales and to keep the island solely as a prison for new offenders, fresh from England, subject to Maconochie's system. All very well, but where was he to put the 250 or so recidivists who, each year, were condemned to second sentences and would normally have been sent to Norfolk Island? Russell had airily suggested putting them on Goat Island in Sydney Harbor. Gipps had to point out that Goat Island was less than a mile from Sydney Cove and now held the military magazine; putting twice-sentenced convicts on

---

when the story got out, it sent the colonial conservatives into fits of sniggering delight and filled the Sydney and Hobart papers with columns of innuendo. Minnie, bereft, was packed off to England and the care of an aunt; she died there, a spinster verging on old-maidhood, at the age of thirty-two. Gipps to Stanley, July 8, 1839, HRA, Series 1, vol. 20, pp. 217–18, and October 13, 1841, HRA, Series 1, vol. 22, pp. 541–42.

this (literal) powder-keg "excited much apprehension among the colonists." Gipps devised a new holding-pen for them, on Cockatoo Island in Sydney Harbor north of Balmain, "surrounded by deep water and under the very eye of Authority." It was solid rock, and could supply Sydney with building stones as the Sing Sing quarries did New York. Among the structures Gipps had the "hard cases" build there were twenty bottle-shaped wheat silos, hewn into the living sandstone.[49]

But Cockatoo Island could not hold more than four-fifths of the recidivists. Where to put the rest? Russell had told Gipps to send no more second offenders to Norfolk, but the law (3 William IV, c.3) forbade him to send them anywhere else. Only an act of the New South Wales Legislative Council could change that. But the Legislative Council, Gipps well knew, would not allow any Old Hands back to contaminate New South Wales. It would only send them to Van Diemen's Land—where Lieutenant-Governor Franklin did not want them either and would not permit them to land. And unless the twelve hundred Old Hands could be removed from Norfolk Island and put somewhere, there was little prospect that Maconochie's new system would get its fair trial. But was it working at all? Or should it simply be abandoned? On this point, Gipps felt torn between the pressures of the colonists and his own sympathies for Maconochie.[50]

Dutifully, Gipps kept the Colonial Office posted on all the main criticisms of Maconochie and his system. In 1840 Russell had empowered him to cancel Maconochie's appointment "whenever the public good might . . . require such an exertion of authority." By mid-1842, he felt fairly secure he ought to do so. He confessed the difficulty of getting at the truth, between the rancor of Maconochie's critics and the commandant's own lofty and long-winded certainties. Some good, Gipps agreed, had come out of the new system. There was less murder and violence among the prisoners, and Maconochie's acts of leniency did awaken "the good feeling implanted in them by nature." Punishment was rare, task work light, the New Hands "idle and listless," the Old Hands "uneasy and scheming." Maconochie had given out too many tickets-of-leave, so that the amount of work done for the government had fallen—convicts were always scurrying off to tend their vegetable-gardens. The validity of these tickets-of-leave was restricted to Norfolk Island, which raised another problem: If and when their holders were transferred to Van Diemen's Land, they could not keep their tickets. Gipps doubted if the currencies of punishment could be exchanged between Van Diemen's Land and Norfolk Island. So he advised the secretary of state for the colonies, Lord Stanley, that unless he received orders to the contrary by March 1843, he would move all the Norfolk Island New Hands down to Van Diemen's Land and declare Maconochie's experiment cancelled. "The best thing to do with Norfolk Island," Gipps concluded, encompassing the end of the Mark System with a gloomy stroke of the nib, "will be to let it revert to what it was, prior to the year 1840."[51]

But Gipps was a fair-minded man, and the idea of erasing Maconochie's project on the mere word of the man's enemies gnawed at his conscience. Thus, just before the deadline of March 1843, he decided to visit Norfolk Island—without warning its commandant. He arrived there on the *Hazard* in the Pacific autumn of that year, and on landing he was agreeably surprised. Far from being an anarchic holiday-camp for criminal loafers, as the critics had suggested, the place semed perfectly in order, the convicts "respectful and quiet." Digging deeper, he privately interrogated "every person having any charge or authority, however small" in the absence of Maconochie, taking notes and keeping the answers from the commandant. During his six-day visit, he "minutely inspected" every building of any significance on the island and spoke to many convicts.[52]

All his findings pointed to one conclusion: Maconochie's critics were mostly wrong, and the new system, though imperfect, was in some respects working better than the old. The elimination of disease, the main source of administrative troubles, lay outside the reach of any commandant; among the New Hands at the Longridge settlement, those sent directly from England to Norfolk Island as Maconochie's guinea pigs in 1840, one in nine (11 percent) had died of dysentery in the past three years. Most of the survivors seemed listless, less healthy than the Old Hands, and (understandably) obsessed with the hope of being retransported to Van Diemen's Land—anything would be better than death by the flux. "When I explained to them," Gipps reported,

> that, owing to the Scarcity of Employment in Van Diemen's Land, their Condition would probably not be improved by being removed from it, they replied "Perhaps not", but that . . . they wished to get away from the Place where they had seen so many of their Comrades die; that they would rather go to New South Wales than to Van Diemen's Land, but that they would go anywhere rather than remain on Norfolk Island.[53]

That seemed to dispose of the charge of mollycoddling. However, Gipps could not "pronounce any decided Opinion" on the all-important question of whether the New Hands, after three years of Maconochean treatment, would be more likely to behave better when off Norfolk Island than "an equal number of men taken promiscuously from the Convict Population of New South Wales." The convicts seemed to take a fairly opportunistic view of the Mark System; they thought accumulating

marks would "be of little Avail to them" except by getting them, perhaps, off the island sooner. Most of the New Hands, 509 out of 593, had
accumulated the 6,000 to 8,000 marks needed for a ticket-of-leave; many
had racked up thousands of marks beyond that, theoretically redeemable
on release at a penny a mark in cash, and Gipps doubted whether the
government would ever foot this bill, running (in the case of one unusually virtuous convict, a millwright named Elliott) as high as £37 10s.

Their morale was fair, no more. They had not suffered from "the
chance of that Severity"

> which often brutalizes a Man in New South Wales, where a Convict's life
> is one of extreme chances, yet they have become in Norfolk Island famil-
> iarized with one detestable Crime, before unknown to them, and addicted
> (especially of late) to one very demoralizing vice: the Vice is that of Gam-
> bling, —the Crime, the one most repugnant to Human Nature.[54]

The New Hands, Gipps thought, gambled more than the Old (although
this seems unlikely, it was "admitted by all persons on the Island"). He
found sodomy to be widespread: Between 5 percent and 12 percent of the
New Hands practiced it (this Maconochie denied); it was "said to prevail
almost exclusively among the Prisoners of English birth. . . . [T]he Irish
are (to their honour) generally acknowledged to be untainted with it."

Gipps's objection was that the "Social System" had not really been
tried. Maconochie's "sanguine and hasty" enthusiasm about the prisoners' reform, the governor crushingly remarked, had distracted him
from "the sterner parts of his own System, which are nevertheless the
Foundation of the Whole":

> Nothing is more clearly laid down by Captain Maconochie than that
> Punishment should precede Probation, —that before Prisoners under his
> System should be distributed into social Parties on the principle of mu-
> tual responsibility, they should go through a Period of severe, though not
> vindictive, Punishment. But . . . he entered at once on the Second Part of
> his own System, overlooking altogether the first Stage of it; and this was
> the more remarkable, as it was no less contrary to the express Directions
> of Her Majesty's Government, than contrary to his own System.[55]

Gipps believed that Maconochie's "marks" had become inflated currency through his goodwill. He had handed them out too lavishly. Some
prisoners had worked "like tigers" to accumulate the number of marks
that would make them free—"but when after they had acquired their
full Number of Marks, and they found that they nevertheless were not
removed from the Island, the Stimulus no longer existed, and Marks
gradually came . . . to be considered valueless." Disappointment and
cynicism followed.[56]

The "Experimental Prisoners," then, had not done so well under the new system. But Gipps wrote with "almost unqualified Approbation" of its effects on the Old Hands: "These men had suffered, and suffered severely. . . . [T]heir minds had consequently been brought to a State in which the Manifestation of Kindness on the Part of their Ruler was likely to make the best Impression on them." The changes had been "Great and merciful," and had only good results. The Old Hands worked twice as hard as the new; they were cleaner, healthier, had better morale, and had responded to the religious training Maconochie offered: "I cannot speak but in commendation of them, and bear witness to the humanizing effect which [Chapel] seems to be producing." Their morale, Gipps thought, was less due to the diminished use of irons and the lash than to many small mercies, "the importance of which can hardly be estimated by anyone who has not been on the Island." They could rove about, fish and swim in the sea, sleep out of barracks sometimes, grow food in their own garden plots, and even carry knives.

This "mildness," Gipps felt, was justified by the fundamental misery of being on this distant island,

> so entirely cut off from Society, or even from a View or a Glimpse of Society, and more especially from the Society of Women. The yearning of their Hearts towards Society is indescribable; it constitutes their torment; it is a punishment greater than the Lash, or any other that Man can inflict on them. . . . In Assignment a Man is a Slave, but he is still a slave in *Society.*[57]

Here, perhaps without altogether realizing it, Gipps answered his own objection to Maconochie's way of running the island—that the prisoners were not given a taste of punishment first. Maconochie clarified this some years later:

> It may be said that I . . . overlooked, or even sacrificed, the great object— that of punishment . . . [but] I carried into effect the full letter and spirit of the law, and merely did not indulge in excesses beyond it. Every man's sentence was to imprisonment and hard labour; the island was his prison; and each was required to do his full daily Government task before bestow- ing time on either his garden or education. What I really did spare was the unnecessary humiliation.[58]

Gipps was against the Mark System being used "indiscriminately" among the Old Hands, because even if they won enough marks to expiate their second or "colonial" conviction in Norfolk Island and went back to the mainland, they would still have to serve out their first sentence in the usual way in New South Wales. He feared the social impact on New South Wales of 876 felons coming en masse from Norfolk Island. "I cannot contemplate the Possibility of their return without alarm; by the Colonists generally I am certain it would be viewed with Terror."

But the prison population was falling so fast that Gipps doubted whether Norfolk Island could keep supporting itself. No more twice-convicted men had been sent there from New South Wales since 1840; because Old Hands were being transferred to Van Diemen's Land, their number on Norfolk Island had dropped from 1,278 to 876 in three years; and the "Experimental Prisoners" would also be going to Van Diemen's Land. Thus, if a large group of new prisoners did not go to Norfolk soon, Maconochie would not have the labor force "to maintain the cultivation of it, and to keep in repair the numerous buildings."[59]

So what would Her Majesty's Government do with Norfolk Island? "The Decision . . . is of pressing Importance." Clearly, if it remained a penal island, there should only be one system of management on it, not the two that Maconochie had been ordered to maintain. Maconochie still thought Norfolk Island "ill-adapted" to his system and, Gipps added, "I must admit, as I ever have done, that if his System is to be tried it . . . should be tried in a Locality which he approves." Moreover, "I feel it right to say that I should regret to see the Experience wholly thrown away . . . [H]e fully admits that in the Distribution of Marks (the great Engine of his System) he has hitherto been too lavish."[60]

So Maconochie had received at least a guarded vindication from Gipps. The cost of running the island, Gipps saw, was not—as Maconochie's fiercest critics had put about—the result of some inherent extravagance, but simply due to the failure or success of crops. Such variations were beyond the control of any commandant.[61]

Gipps wrote his long report, and dispatched it to Lord Stanley on April Fool's Day, 1843. Maconochie had every reason to hope that now, at last, the government would ignore his critics and give full backing to his system. What happened was the exact reverse. Powerful lobbying from the Arthur Faction throughout 1842 had convinced Downing Street that Franklin was a disaster and Maconochie worse. In any case, the Colonial Office had believed Gipps's earlier criticism of Maconochie, and it was too late for the report to change Stanley's decision: to recall Maconochie. The Colonial Office was under growing pressure from the Treasury to cut the expenses of the transportation system. Sir James Stephen, the under secretary for the colonies, felt no commitment to Maconochie's theories of penal reform. It was all unimportant stuff, happening on the "remote, anomalous" dark side of the world. Maconochie had no defenders in the Colonial Office, and Lord Russell's curiosity about his ideas had waned in the six years since his reports had helped the Molesworth Committee. He could be dropped to placate the Treasury, and he was. On April 29, 1843, before the ship carrying Gipps's report had even crossed the equator, Stanley sent a dispatch ordering the end of the Mark System and the recall of Maconochie. It was carefully worded so as not to cast too black a shadow on his career. It gave Maconochie "the fullest credit" for his exertions and probity. "I gladly acknowledge," Stanley wrote with icy unction, "that his efforts appear to have been rewarded by the decline of crimes of violence and outrage, and by the growth of humane and kindly feelings in the minds of the persons under his care." It was the coup de grace.[62]

The dispatch contained good news for the prisoners, Old and New hands alike. All the men to whom Maconochie had promised a discharge at the end of their sentences would get it; everyone holding an "Island ticket-of-leave" would go on probation to Van Diemen's Land, where after a year or two of good behavior they would be issued a fully valid ticket-of-leave.

With it, on the same ship, came Stanley's choice as the new commandant. He was Major Joseph Childs (1787–1870) of the Royal Marines, a harsh, blundering turkey-cock bearing orders to make the island a place of exemplary terror once more. Yet the signs were that Maconochie's mildness had done more to reform the Norfolk Island men than any amount of terror. Throughout his administration, Maconochie had discharged 920 of the twice-convicted prisoners to a new life in Sydney. Despite the hysterical agitation against former convicts, and especially against men with the Norfolk Island taint, by 1845 only twenty of them —a mere 2 percent—had slid back and been convicted again.

But the moment of reform clanged shut. Alexander Maconochie and his family began their long trip back to England. He was fifty-six now, and his great opportunity to raise his fellow men from degradation had been taken from him, never to be handed back. The Colonial Office did not give him another post. In England, he kept campaigning for prison reform; but, although the English ardor for transportation was rapidly ebbing, the authorities were not interested in his views. "Captain Maconochie," wrote James Stephen, "has not much that is really important to urge." There was no point in punishment without terror.

For once again, English authorities were anxious about a crime wave. The number of males committed for trial for serious offenses at Assizes and Sessions had nearly doubled in less than two decades, from 170 per 100,000 population in 1824 to 326 per 100,000 in 1842. Over the same period there had been a steady tightening of prison discipline at home as well as in Australia. Its aim was to crush the criminal subculture, to deprive the individual convict of the support of his "family felons." The day of the American penitentiary had come to England. It had two alter-

native forms, each named for its American model: The Auburn (or Silent)
System, and the Philadelphia (or Separate) System. The Auburn System
had prisoners working in gangs, but under a rule of absolute silence,
whose least infraction was punished by summary flogging. By contrast,
the Philadelphia System was based on monastic solitary confinement. It
took away a prisoner's name and past, reducing him to a number; not
even the warder who brought his food knew his name or his crime. In
haggard anonymity, masked in a black hood whenever he was brought
from his cell for exercise, he lived out the sand grains of his sentence. He
had no visitors, received no letters, and saw no human faces except those
of his warders. He could never talk to a fellow prisoner; even his shoes
were felted, to make his presence the more ghostlike. In old Newgate,
criminals had been jammed together in social chaos, yelling, talking,
weeping, wheedling, plotting, like cats in a great stone bag. But in the
new penitentiary, this sense of criminal *community* was voided: All
other prisoners were silent, invisible abstractions to the man in his solitary cell. The republic of crime was vaporized, and all social sense along
with it, leaving only a disoriented, passive obedience. The young Charles
Dickens was horrified by the great Eastern Penitentiary at Philadelphia,
which he visited in 1842 in order to see the Benthamite machine of
benevolent punishment at first hand:

> I believe that very few men are capable of estimating the immense
> amount of torture and agony which this dreadful punishment, prolonged
> for years, inflicts. . . . [T]here is a depth of terrible endurance in it which
> none but the sufferers can fathom. I hold this slow and daily tampering
> with the mysteries of the brain to be immeasurably worse than any tor-
> ture of the body; and because its ghastly signs and tokens are not so
> palpable to the eye and sense of touch as scars upon the flesh; because its
> wounds are not upon the surface . . . therefore the more I denounce it, as
> a secret punishment which slumbering humanity is not roused up to
> stay.[63]

Such was the new engine of reform, begotten by Utilitarianism on
Idealism, to which English authorities were turning for relief from the
uncertainties of transportation. The conversion of the prisons from mere
incarceration to punitive brainwashing, through solitary confinement,
dumb cells, crank labor and the treadmill, proceeded throughout the
1830s. In 1834 the great Coldbath Fields House of Correction in London
doubled its ratio of guards to inmates and adopted a system of perpetual
silence and inspection. Other prisons followed suit. By 1842, England
had its first Panopticon; the ideas of Jeremy Bentham had at last completed their long loop across the Atlantic, to Philadelphia and back, cre-

ating the 450-cell "model prison" on the Caledonian Road in north London known as Pentonville. Its orthodoxy filled the horizon of penal thought, and left no room for Maconochie's more humane ideas.[64]

Unable to get a hearing, Maconochie settled down to write a book: *Crime and Punishment, The Mark System, framed to mix Persuasion with Punishment, and Make their Effect Improving, yet their Operation severe* (1846). Although it would later become one of the classical reforming texts of modern penology, it was largely ignored—except by Dickens—in Maconochie's lifetime. In 1849, through the friendship of the Recorder of Birmingham, a liberal barrister named Matthew Hill, he secured a post as governor of a new prison in Birmingham—but could not control its sadistic deputy-governor, a naval officer named William Austin. After two years of reversals and humiliation, Maconochie was dismissed. By then he was sixty-four, and in failing health: erect, prematurely aged, refined in bearing, with snow-white hair, a bitterly disappointed man too proud to bear the outward marks of self-pity. Too obscure to be given more than a brief death-notice in *The Times*, he died in 1860 at the age of 73.

v

THE REVERSES Maconochie had endured at the hands of the System were bad enough. But those suffered by his former chief, Sir John Franklin, were even more stinging. The former officials of Arthur's regime through whom Franklin had decided to govern—chiefly the able and insidious John Montagu, his colonial secretary—thought him weak. Since he could not trust them (he found that out too late, as good-natured men do) and Maconochie was gone, he naturally relied more and more on the advice of the one person in the colony he could trust, his wife. Lady Jane Franklin was highly intelligent, but the thought of a Sir taking private lessons in statecraft from a woman was appalling to the Arthur Faction—and to most of the other colonists, case-armored in dogmas of masculine ascendancy. Franklin's leanings toward pity and mildness—not only to convicts, but to the dying Aborigines as well—were proof of effeteness. He was besieged by lobbyists, but whenever he did anyone a favor he created one ingrate and ten malcontents.

Worst of all, he was blamed for events over which he had little or no control. In 1840 the economy of Van Diemen's Land began to slide into a five-year depression. Banks and businesses failed; Hobart, Launceston and the townships between were silted up with unemployed workers. At the same time, the end of transportation to New South Wales meant that the whole yearly exodus of convicts was directed to Van Diemen's Land.

In 1839, less than 1,500 convicts had arrived there. By 1842 the figure was over 5,300. The machinery could not handle them, and the island could not absorb them. Worst of all, in the midst of the confusion, it was Franklin's Sisyphean task to change the whole apparatus of convict management. The Colonial Office, under the new management of Lord Stanley, had decreed that from 1842 onward the assignment of convicts to private settlers in Van Diemen's Land must cease. It would be replaced by something Lord Stanley had cooked up in his office in Whitehall: the so-called Probation System, whereby they would all be worked in government gangs distributed at outer stations around the island (see Chapter 15). Now, the settlers could not only blame John Franklin for the depression that was bankrupting them; they could also curse him for taking away the free labor on which the whole economy of the island had depended.

It would be tedious to list the innuendos against Franklin that John Montagu and his colleagues poured into the ears of Whitehall. At the start of 1842, Montagu had written Franklin an impertinent letter, suggesting in thinly veiled terms that he was getting soft in the head. At this, Franklin's patience snapped. He suspended Montagu from his job as colonial secretary. The Iago of the Derwent took himself to England and appealed to Lord Stanley, citing Franklin's "dependence" on his wife as the cause of the myriad harassments that had gummed up the administration of Van Diemen's Land. He won. Franklin found himself censured; and his letter of recall came in 1843. When he reached England, he found that the whispers of petticoat domination had preceded him—a searing humiliation for a man who loved his wife but who had also been a brave sailor and an indefatigable explorer.

To clear his name, Sir John Franklin returned to his old love, the clean cold place he had known before his country had dropped him into the vile antipodes. Once again, in 1847, the Admiralty was equipping an expedition to the Arctic, in search of the Northwest Passage. At fifty-nine, Franklin was too old for exploring in the world's high latitudes, but his daemon would not be assuaged. Reluctantly, but in a spirit of obligation, the Admiralty gave him command. This time Sir John Franklin did find the Northwest Passage, dying of starvation with the rest of his men within sight of it, on their iced-in ship the *Erebus*. In doing so, he not only expunged his failure in Van Diemen's Land but entered the Victorian pantheon of explorers (despite evidence of cannibalism in the last weeks of the expedition) as one of the heroic legends of the Arctic. Which, all in all, was more than his luckless successor at the other end of the earth could claim.

# 15

# A Special Scourge

LORD STANLEY had never been to the antipodes or met a felon, but he glowed with ideological confidence in his new plan for mending the morals of both. It was meant to benefit England first, the convicts second, and Van Diemen's Land not at all.

Stanley took the whole matter of convict discipline to be "an Imperial interest," to whose running the interests of local free settlers were quite irrelevant. Let them complain about losing their cheap labor; that was not the Colonial Office's problem. He only wanted to get criminals out of Britain cheaply, while satisfying the much louder and closer chorus of English MPs, clergy and editors, most of whom wanted the assignment system buried forever.

Stanley dispatched his plan in November 1842 and it reached Hobart early in 1843. It cancelled the last area in which convicts could be assigned—service on farms. Instead, the felons were to pass through five stages on their way to reformation and liberty.[1]

The first was detention on Norfolk Island, usually for a year, to instill discipline. This penal antechamber could only take 750 new convicts a year direct from England. Hence, Norfolk Island was kept for long-sentence men, mainly lifers who, Stanley reasoned, were more apt to be desperate and so would need more isolation and discipline to make them tractable. The rest would go straight to Hobart, where, along with the current crop of men emerging from their time on Norfolk, they entered the second stage: the probation gangs.

Each of these gangs was to be made up of 250 to 300 men, laboring in the "unsettled districts," on long, arduous government projects—building roads and bridges, clearing Crown land to improve its sale value or logging on the Tasman Peninsula. The gangers would need special religious instruction (for which Stanley wanted Franklin to gather more penal chaplains), but, if properly supervised on long-term projects, they might grow their own food. Stanley figured that if England sent out 4,000 men a year (the actual numbers were close to that: 4,819 men in 1842; 3,048 in 1843; and 3,959 in 1844) and the average term of probation gang-labor was 18 months, then twenty gangs of 300 men would absorb them all. Each man would cost about £18 to ship to Van Diemen's Land, and £27 a year to feed; reckoning in £35,000 for the costs of Norfolk Island and £10,000 for overheads, Stanley thought the Probation System could maintain about 35,000 convicts in government service and continuous punishment for less than £300,000 a year, half the estimated cost of building penitentiaries for them all.[2]

That would be England's only expense. After their probation labor the prisoner received a "probation pass," which meant he could work for wages for an approved settler or for the local government of Van Diemen's Land. The Crown would not contribute a penny to these wages. The convicts could work or starve—that was up to them and to their prospective employers. The probation pass led to the last two stages: the normal ticket-of-leave (allowing the man to choose his own master without a say-so from Hobart) and, lastly, a conditional or absolute pardon.

So much for the men. With less relish, Stanley turned to the women and children. Boy criminals would begin with a term of 2 to 3 years in Parkhurst Prison. "Every boy who enters Parkhurst," declared one of Stanley's underlings in Whitehall to the prison authorities there, in words that rang of iron and cold corridors,

> is doomed to be transported; and this part of the sentence passed on him is immutable. He must bid a long farewell to the hopes of revisiting his native home, of seeing his parents, or of rejoining his companions. These are the hopes and pleasures which his crimes have forfeited. . . . [H]is future prospects in life depend entirely on his conduct at Parkhurst.[3]

If he behaved well at Parkhurst, the boy would get a ticket-of-leave on landing in Van Diemen's Land "and virtually be pardoned," although Whitehall did not explain how he was expected to survive thereafter. If his conduct was indifferent, he would start with a probationary pass, "which is far short of freedom." A bad boy went to Point Puer at Port Arthur, where "every hardship and degradation awaits him, and where his sufferings will be severe."[4]

As for the punishment of women, Lord Stanley entrusted his thoughts on this "more difficult subject" to Franklin in November 1842. Though as depraved as men, they could not be worked in probation gangs. The government could lock them up in Van Diemen's Land or "permit them to enter, in some mode or other, into the mass of the population." It could hardly revive assignment for them, because "respectable" settlers did not want them and, were they to be "assigned to the less scrupulous and less moral portion of the community"—namely, Emancipists—"they must continually be exposed to criminal solicitation, to grievous oppression, and often to personal violence." Moreoever, they would confront Authority with their own version of the Cretan paradox, because even if they were solicited, oppressed and beaten, "little confidence is placed, or can be placed, in the truth of their complaints."[5]

Nor could Franklin keep them in the existing Female Factories at Hobart and Launceston, which (Stanley had learned) were chaotic sumps where evil "is constantly perpetuating and increasing itself." They held three classes of female convict, each as bad as the next: those who could not be assigned at all, those who were returned from assignment to the government for punishment, and helpless women pregnant with bastard offspring who were thrown back on the government's hands. Conditions in such places, and in the Queen's Orphan School in Hobart which took in illegitimates, were "sufficient to make the blood run cold," wrote a clergyman who knew them well, the Reverend Robert Crooke (1818–1888). Crooke had been a catechist with the Convict Department in 1843, and he described the life of the seven hundred inmates of the Queen's Orphan School. Pale and sick, these young prisoners were segregated, kept on low coarse rations and frequently punished.

> The slightest offence, whether committed by boy or girl, was punished by unmercial flogging and some of the officers, more especially females, seem to have taken a delight in inflicting corporal punishment.... The female superintendent was in the habit of taking girls, some of them almost young women, to her own bedroom and for trifling offences ... stripping them naked, and with a riding whip or a heavy leather strap flagellating them until their bodies were a mass of bruises.[6]

Such institutions were jam-packed, so all the lieutenant-governor could do to house the newly arriving women convicts was rent secure buildings in Hobart, or else detain the ship they came on and keep them on board "until you shall be able to effect more permanent arrangements." The long-term plan, on which Franklin was to start at once, was to put up a women's penitentiary for at least four hundred prisoners within twenty miles of Hobart, whose construction the Home Government would pay for. Here, every female prisoner would spend at least six months on arrival and then receive a probation pass. The penitentiary was not built.

Stanley's Probation System looked impressively machine-like and rational on paper, but it proved a cruel and wretched failure because it ignored both the economic facts of Van Diemen's Land and the quality of its administrators. To succeed, it needed at least a prosperous economy and a strong cooperation between the Government House and the settlers. Neither existed in the last years of Franklin's governorship. But Stanley, in his anxiety to have no one sully his plan, chose as Franklin's successor a person so devoid of initiative that he hardly cast a shadow.

Sir John Eardley Eardley-Wilmot (1783–1847) was a Warwickshire baronet of sixty, whom scarcely anyone in public life except Stanley had even heard of; and Stanley, his patron, was indiscreet enough to call him (though not in public) "a muddle-brained blockhead." Until his appointment in August 1843, Eardley-Wilmot had not devoted a moment's thought to the colonies in general or to Van Diemen's Land in particular. His qualifications were three: His duties as a county magistrate had given him an amateurish, paternal interest in prison reform and juvenile offenders;[7] having been to Oxford with Stanley, and having joined Stanley's embryonic third party on quitting the Whigs, he had a place on the Old Boy network; and he was dull enough not to be disloyal. To back him up, Stanley appointed as comptroller-general of convicts a leftover from Arthur's day, the harsh and choleric Captain Matthew Forster. Such was the team that Stanley relied on to run the penal system and to keep at bay the colonists of Van Diemen's Land, irate at being denied both assigned labor and self-government.

Under such conditions, the angel Gabriel himself would have been an unpopular lieutenant-governor. When the "battered old beau" (as one Hobart lady described Eardley-Wilmot on first glimpse) appeared with his three sons Augustus, Charles and Robert, all of whom promptly got public offices in Van Diemen's Land, no one took to the new proconsul.

He could not persuade the settlers that Whitehall knew or cared what it was doing to their economy. The trade depression that had begun in Van Diemen's Land in 1841 was still worsening. One black day in 1843, Eardley-Wilmot learned that there was only £800 left in his treasury, and he had to borrow £20,000 from banks and the military chest to pay the wages of pass-holders in government service. Every year the government revenues of Van Diemen's Land fell by £20,000, and Eardley-Wilmot had to keep borrowing "in the style of a man continuing to sign checks before his bank manager caught up with him."[8] Across the Bass Strait, in New South Wales and the Port Phillip region, vast, cheap and fertile acreage beckoned the settler. In Van Diemen's Land, grazing land was expensive, and the best of it was already taken up; so the government's revenue from the sale of Crown land dwindled to almost nothing.

As with the public sector, so with the private. By 1844, it was cheaper to import cattle from the mainland than to buy locally raised animals. Sydney imported wheat from Valparaiso but charged a duty on grain coming from the "Tainted Isle," Van Diemen's Land. Men could not sell their farms, for there were no buyers; they could not hire labor, for they had no money. The farmers were even worse placed than the government to absorb the huge labor surplus that Stanley's Probation System had created. At the low point of Eardley-Wilmot's office the island had 16,000 unemployed prisoners and ex-convicts stranded in its collapsed economy —7,000 holders of probation passes, 5,000 ticket-of-leave men, and 4,000 of the conditionally pardoned.

Meanwhile, the flow of immigrants had dried up. In 1842, 2,446 emigrants had landed in Van Diemen's Land; the next year there were 26, and in 1844 exactly one emigrant arrived. (In 1843–44, 3,618 people had emigrated from England to New South Wales.) In Launceston alone, 264 houses stood empty, abandoned by their owners, who had fled to the mainland to begin their lives again. In the first six months of 1845, 1,628 settlers left Van Diemen's Land, a loss of some 5 percent of its free population.[9]

There was also a great deal of alarm about fugitives from the probation gangs, who were said to be roaming the roads and valleys of Van Diemen's Land unchecked, plundering at will, spreading misery and vice like a contagion everywhere. Some of them were tattooed like South Sea Island chiefs and would have stood out in "respectable" company. The description on a "wanted" poster of one such absconder, Charles Stagg, a twenty-three-year-old laborer from Norwich who ran from the Seven-Mile Creek probation station in March 1843, enumerates his tattoos, which included the initials of most of his family as well as his past sweethearts:

> Mary Stagg, Thomas Stagg, crucifix, 5 dots, shoe, crucifix, WS, man with stick, HK, dog, Gwynson, X Mary Robinson, Liberty, bracelet on right arm, Eliza Smith, O Sun and blue marks and rings all over right hand; man and woman, two men fighting, TS WS LS LHHS 1842, anchor, MSCS on left arm, blue dots and rings on fingers of left hand, H Stagg, William, crucifix, sun and moon on breast, ABCDEFGH on left leg, large scar on upper right arm.[10]

It would seem, however, that the tales of marauding gangs were somewhat exaggerated, for the poster listed some 465 convicts at large, cumulative since 1831. Many of these must long since have died, escaped on sealing boats or made their way across the Bass Strait to the mainland.

A further source of irritation was that Eardley-Wilmot had been ordered to go after free settlers for the arrears on their quit-rents. These small sums had mounted up, having remained unpaid for years on land granted in Arthur's time or earlier; Stanley felt that collection of these taxes could offset the drop in Crown land sales. The settlers bridled at

that, and even worse was the demand for taxes to carry the cost of both
the judiciary and the police. The Van Diemen's Land police force was
huge in ratio to the free population. The costs of the police, the judiciary
and the maintenance of paupers came to £52,437 a year, or nearly a pound
a head for every man, woman and child, free and bond, in Van Diemen's
Land.[11]

The colony was sliding into bankruptcy. Eardley-Wilmot bore all the
blame for this and was even more execrated than Arthur. Yet the sad fact
was that he sympathized with the plight of the settlers and took their
side in his dispatches to Whitehall, much to Lord Stanley's annoyance.
He urged Stanley to drop the minimum price of Crown land below £1 an
acre, as an inducement to new settlers; and he tried to get credit to use
the mass paid labor of otherwise unemployable pass-holders on public
works, to be underwritten by Britain but paid for, in time, by tolls and
service charges. He also pressed the Treasury to pay the cost of the jail
and police system; eventually, in early 1846, it agreed to pay two-thirds.

This gesture came too late to appease the settlers. Between October
and November 1845, Eardley-Wilmot faced a political crisis in his Legislative Council. The Legislative Council of Van Diemen's Land was not
an elected body, and, since Arthur's day, it had usually been content to
act as a rubber stamp. It consisted of the lieutenant-governor, six government officials and eight non-official members drawn from the ranks of
free citizens, usually opulent ones. Six of the latter—the "Patriotic Six,"
as their supporters called them—resigned over the police-funds issue and
left the council without a quorum. They claimed they had been refused
information on police budgets and convict administration, and that when
they pressed for it Eardley-Wilmot and the official members had called
them "factious" and "disloyal." Although Eardley-Wilmot managed to
replace the six, he could not keep a lid on the demands for representative
government and the end of transportation, which by now had fused into
the single obsessive issue of political life in Van Diemen's Land.

But Whitehall would not listen. All Eardley-Wilmot could show after
two years of pleas was a lengthy rebuke from Stanley, complaining that
he had not filed proper reports on the working of the Probation System.
By then, Van Diemen's Land boasted sixteen probation stations: four
(mainly for logging and coal-mining) on Tasman's Peninsula, five for
agriculture on the coast of the D'Entrecasteaux Channel, one to build
the female penitentiary at Oyster Bay, two on Maria Island, one on the
east coast and three, whose gangers labored to build roads and bridges, in
the interior of the island. There were eight hiring depots from which the
free settlers could recruit pass-holders, but traffic through them was
sluggish. All this presented a lot of ground for reports to cover. Eardley-
Wilmot did not take to scrambling down the coal mines or through the

forests of Tasman's Peninsula to see how well the probation gangs were shedding their vices by splitting shingles and felling 150-foot eucalypts, and so he was often content to scrawl mere covering-notes on the detailed statistical reports of his comptroller-general of convicts, Forster. But Stanley's complaints typified his imperial and solipsistic view of the antipodes. To him, Van Diemen's Land was not a complex little society with severe economic problems; it was more abstract—a receptacle, a social void whose sole purpose was to swallow criminals. He did not want to hear that "his" convicts could not be fully employed in "his" colony. Realizing that the Probation System was about to fail, and that he might be blamed for it, Lord Stanley got ready to fling Sir Eardley-Wilmot to the Tasmanian Devils. He would make sure that the chaos in Van Diemen's Land was seen not as his system's fault but as the proconsul's.[12]

Stanley gave the draft of his strongly critical dispatch to the government printer, who published it for the House of Commons in February 1846. The first Eardley-Wilmot saw of it was in print. He was aghast at Stanley's maneuver, which denied him the chance to have his letters of rebuttal printed along with the Colonial Office's criticisms and pilloried him before government and press as incompetent, lazy and vague. Eardley-Wilmot dug in.

The Colonial Office was getting set to dismiss him when, in 1845, Lord Stanley quit the Colonial Office for a larger political sphere. He was replaced by the thirty-six-year-old junior minister William Ewart Gladstone. Gladstone depended for his knowledge of Australian matters on the permanent under secretary to the Colonial Office, one of the preeminent civil servants of the nineteenth century (and the grandfather of Virginia Woolf), Sir James Stephen. Stephen felt Britain had been wrong in overloading Van Diemen's Land with convicts, and he was very skeptical of Stanley's Probation System. But he was also sure of Eardley-Wilmot's incompetence and he took up the issue which, he knew, would turn the morally priggish Gladstone against the foundering lieutenant-governor.

Ever since the Probation System had been installed, lobbyists had been harping on a subject peculiarly repugnant to the Victorian sense of public morality: that, thanks to those isolated bush gangs of toiling, degenerate men, Van Diemen's Land was now a hotbed of sodomy. Letters and witnesses came across the oceans to Whitehall, testifying to the collapse of all moral values in the stained island. They made Van Diemen's Land under Eardley-Wilmot sound infinitely worse than Capri under Tiberius.

Francis Russell Nixon, Bishop of Van Diemen's Land, carried the most weight among them. The epidemic of unnatural crime, he assured

Lord Grey, "unless sternly arrested in its growth, must not only ensure the moral degradation of the colony, but draw down divine vengeance upon it." Nixon believed that all the convicts, without exception, left the probation gangs worse than they entered them. He quoted letters to him from despairing gang chaplains. "I cannot depict the horrors committed here daily by miserable men, who know better, but who cannot escape from their wretched condition." Parties of convicts slunk off together into the bush to gratify their lusts. In the "tench" or penitentiary (in fact, an ordinary prisoners' barracks) in Hobart Town, where twelve hundred were kept, "The most disgusting crimes that ever stained the character of man are perpetrated . . . and without the least possible way of preventing it." In the coal mines near Port Arthur, two men had raped a boy convict, "an offence hitherto, I believe, unheard-of in a Christian country." They hanged for it, but the medical officer at the mines, Dr. Motherwell, found twenty men "labouring under disease from unnatural crimes." The spread of rectal gonorrhea, Bishop Nixon warned, was "a special scourge" from God, "a mark of his increased wrath, for the yet greater abomination."[13]

Nor was the evil confined to men. The Female Factory at the Cascades in Hobart swarmed with lesbians. In August 1841, Franklin had set up a committee of inquiry to review the facilities for discipline of female prisoners in this dank, miserable and overcrowded building, along with its twin institution in Launceston. Its semi-confidential report appeared in February 1843, with its descriptions of women convicts in the "very act of exciting each other's passions—on the Lord's Day in the House of God—and at the very time divine service was performing."[14] By then the local press was printing stories about the "fiendish fondness" of Sapphic practices in the factories, and in November 1843 Eardley-Wilmot sent a secret dispatch of his own to London on this subject. He told Stanley that women in the Female Factories "have their Fancy-women, or lovers, to whom they are attached with quite as much ardour as they would be to the other sex, and practice onanism to the greatest extent."[15]

At least one convict, the Chartist exile John Frost (and he can hardly have been alone in his opinion), believed that the British Government maintained the probation gangs in all their turpitude in order to crush the spirit of class resistance. "The authorities of Van Diemen's Land were indifferent to the commission of this great offence," he told a shocked English audience some years after his release. "Smoking was deemed a greater offence than that of Gomorrah, and published with greater severity."[16]

Eardley-Wilmot, far away in Hobart Town, protested that although the vice denoted by asterisks in the Parliamentary Papers certainly existed in Van Diemen's Land, one found it in the army and navy, too, and in all "large assemblies of the male sex." In vain, he relayed to Stanley the opinions of the medical officers on the probation and hiring stations, as diligently collected by his comptroller-general. They showed only seventy cases of the sexual disease in a gang population of 10,000 men. Seven in one thousand, he agreed, were too many, but even so, the scare-stories had largely been made up by his critics to discredit the Probation System.[17]

None of this appeased the local press, the clergy, the settlers or the Colonial Office. In July 1846, twenty-five Van Diemen's Land clergymen (most of its Anglican establishment) signed a petition to Grey begging for the end of the Probation System, as an incubator of homosexuality.[18] In London, embarrassing stories had been current in the press for some time. "Van Diemen's Land is in a bad state," wrote an anonymous pen in the London *Naval and Military Gazette* in October 1845. "Crimes the most horrible are of daily occurrence. All the females have left the bush and have taken refuge in the towns, and . . . are subject to every kind of insult. Sir Eardley-Wilmot sets a bad example himself. No people of any standing will now enter Government House except on business. No ladies can." Satires and moral versicles made their clumping appearance:

Shall fathers weep and mourn,
　　To see a lovely son
Debas'd, demoraliz'd, deform'd
　　By *Britain's filth and scum!*

Shall mothers heave the sigh,
　　To see a daughter fair
Debauch'd and sunk in infamy
　　By *those imported here!*

Shall Tasman's Isle so fam'd,
　　So lovely and so fair,
From other nations be estrang'd—
　　The *name of Sodom* bear?

Till Nature's GOD, provok'd,
　　Stretch forth His mighty arm;
And in relentless fury, pour
　　His *righteous judgments down.*[19]

It was not exactly—the anonymous tongues now began to whisper—that the man in Government House condoned this frightful state of affairs; still less that he himself, despite the loneliness he must feel now and then in the antipodes without a wife, was touched by the hot breath of the Cities of the Plain. It was just that his behavior gave rise to idle rumors about quirks that, though doubtless innocent in themselves, clouded his office. He gave dinners in Lent, to the scandal of Bishop Nixon, who had already quarrelled with Eardley-Wilmot over the lieutenant-governor's right to appoint religious instructors to the probation gangs. He had been seen putting his arm around girls' shoulders on the sofa in Government House. He had flirted at a formal dinner party with Julia Sorell, the granddaughter of a leading settler and future grandmother of Aldous Huxley. Manifestly, there must be some ratio between this permissiveness at Government House and the unspeakable, furtive ecstasies of the probation gangs. Fish rot at the head.

Gladstone's reaction to all this was predictable. He flew into a moral rage, and at the end of April 1846 he wrote two letters of dismissal to Eardley-Wilmot. The first one was public, announcing that in view of the lieutenant-governor's utter failure to safeguard the morals of the convicts under the Probation System, he was dismissed. The very absence of external signs of the vice of Sodom that Eardley-Wilmot had reported, Gladstone wrote with crushing illogic, showed how deeprooted it was, how well sheltered from the light. Eardley-Wilmot was not being fired for mismanaging the transition from assignment to probation (anyone, Gladstone seemed to imply, could have failed at that) but for not displaying enough "assiduity," "anxiety" and "prudence" in moral reform. Accordingly, Gladstone was transferring Charles La Trobe, the superintendent of Port Phillip, to Hobart to take over until a new lieutenant-governor was named.

The second letter was private, short and even nastier. It told Eardley-Wilmot that in view of unspecified rumors circulated by unnamed persons regarding aspects of his unofficial conduct which it was "perhaps unnecessary" that Gladstone should discuss, he must not expect another official post.[20]

Thus the "battered old beau" with his flirtatious post-prandial ways was at last broken on the iron wheel of Gladstone's sanctimony. He tried to defend himself; he protested against the "grossest falsehoods that ever oppressed an English gentleman," "the most extraordinary conspiracy that ever succeeded in defaming the character of a Public Servant"; he appealed to Gladstone to name his accusers and state their charges; he forwarded petitions in defense of his character, bearing many respectable signatures. It was all to no avail. In February 1847, a few weeks short of his sixty-fourth birthday, Sir John Eardley Eardley-Wilmot slipped beyond the reach of his tormentors in the Colonial Office and died in Hobart, reputedly of a broken heart. At once, the *Colonial Times* declared that he had been "murdered." The settlers who had detested and abused him performed a brisk volte-face, awarding him a state funeral with a solemn procession through the crepe-decked town, during which

Anglican clergy and Catholic priests fell over one another in their haste to lead the hearse. They then subscribed for a spindly stone monument in the Neo-Gothic style, the largest tomb ever erected to the memory of a governor on Australian soil. By the time it had been installed above the remains of Sir Eardley-Wilmot, the interim governor Charles La Trobe had come to Van Diemen's Land, made his report and returned with almost palpable relief to his duties across the Strait in Port Phillip. He told Lord Grey what everyone, in and out of the colony, knew by now—that the Probation System was an utter fiasco, that "whatever principle of reformation might be included in the theory," its only result in practice was to degrade, that it was "vicious . . . a fatal experiment," and that the sooner it ended the better for the credit of the nation and of humanity.[21] In 1846, Her Majesty's Government suspended all transportation of convicts to Van Diemen's Land for two years. By then, the last lieutenant-governor to preside over the System on that island, Sir William Denison, had arrived in Hobart to confront the problems that had defeated Eardley-Wilmot and would in due course baffle him. Among the thorniest of these was the management of Norfolk Island.

ii

THE ADMINISTRATIVE CONTROL of Norfolk Island passed from New South Wales to Van Diemen's Land in 1844, and by then an ill wind had blown through the barracks at Kingston and Longridge. Captain Alexander Maconochie had been recalled from the island in 1843, and replaced by the last military commandant of that ill-omened rock to be appointed from New South Wales: Major Joseph Childs, a fifty-six-year-old marine officer. He was Maconochie's opposite in every way—a dull, vacillating military hack, distinguished only by his severity.

For severity was what Lord Stanley wanted—and he wished to see it directed, in particular, against "crimes unattended with violence": namely, sodomy. From the second-hand reports Gipps wrote before he actually saw Maconochie's system for himself, Stanley concluded that the new "leniency" of Norfolk Island incubated all crimes, but especially the unmentionable ones. Since going there in February 1843, Gipps had changed his mind—but too late to change Stanley's. Work them till they drop, skin them alive if they get out of line and make no exceptions—this, in essence, was the formula he transmitted to Gipps as the first stage of his Probation System for men on Norfolk Island. "Nothing but constant vigilance and inflexible rigour in enforcing the appropriate Punishments will be sufficient to restrain the immoralities to which I refer."[22]

The idea that two thousand men, mostly in their twenties and thirties, could be incarcerated on a distant island, deprived of any contact with women, treated so harshly that their only emotional solace could come from one another and then "restrained" from sodomy by incessant flogging is a curiously abstract one; but it seemed real to Whitehall. All their evil proclivities, including the sexual, could be vaporized in the tension between, in Stanley's words, "an invigorating hope and a salutary dread."

There was not much hope on Norfolk Island. From the moment Childs was rowed through the foaming reefs of Kingston from the *Maitland* in February 1844, the trust Maconochie had struggled to establish between convicts and Authority caved in. There was no longer the sense of a responsive chain of command, or of access to the commandant. Childs's idea of authority, formed in the harsh mold of the British Marines, destroyed part of that; and the rest was annihilated by his lazy habit of leaving summary punishments to the turnkeys, the overseers and to his resident stipendiary magistrate, Samuel Barrow. Barrow, twenty-eight years old when he arrived from Van Diemen's Land in August 1845, had been a junior barrister in London. His real talent, however, was less for legal argument than for gross arbitrary sadism. For that, he was the right man in the right place at the right time. If the ornate diction of Lord Stanley's dispatches provided the theory of Norfolk Island after Maconochie, Childs and Barrow between them supplied the practice, and the treatment of prisoners there became as bad as it had been in the "murdering times" of Morisset. All the men on Norfolk Island were, in Childs's apoplectic language, "the worst men that the annals of criminal jurisprudence can hold forth to the world as an example of all combined evil."[23]

One did not treat such demons softly, although in fairness to Childs one should note that not all of them were handled with equal severity. One convict who passed through Childs's regime on Norfolk Island, the former military officer John Mortlock, would describe Childs as "a gallant marine officer" who gained the "entire respect" of the convicts with his "discreet management." Perhaps all that this judgment shows is that military officers shared the same views on discipline; and Mortlock was never flogged. All the same, he recalled, it was thanks to the "delightful scenery and heavenly climate" of Norfolk Island "that I do not look back upon my residence there with unmixed horror."[24]

"Many of my shipmates were flogged daily," Mortlock recalled, "in the barrack yard, under my windows, on complaints often made with a wicked purpose by their overseers; though I could shut my eyes, the horrid sound of the 'cats' upon the naked flesh (like the crack of a cartwhip) tortured my ears. . . . Petty 'dogs in office,' in order to strike terror, would commonly threaten 'to see the back-bone.' "[25] Thomas Rogers, a curate from Dublin who was posted _rom Van Diemen's Land to Norfolk Island in September 1845 as its sole religious instructor (such convict-department comforters being stipulated by Stanley's Probation System), claimed that Childs had 26,024 lashes inflicted in the last sixteen months of his command. On some mornings

> the ground on which the men stood at the triangles was saturated with human gore as if a bucket of blood had been spilled on it, covering a space three feet in diameter and running out in various directions in little streams two or three feet long. I have seen this.[26]

But it was in the summary punishments—inflicted by Barrow and his underlings without interference from Major Childs—that the crude ingenuity of the new regime showed itself. The cat was banal; the elite of convicts, the "pebbles" or "iron men," had their own infrangible code of contempt for it. One prisoner in Childs's day had a message to the "skinner" tattooed on his back: FLOG WELL AND DO YOUR DUTY.[27] "Salutary dread" required something more. In a report made to Eardley-Wilmot in October 1845, Childs had bewailed the limits of punishment set by the Colonial Quarter Sessions Act, as they were "too confined for the class of men we now have to deal with, for whom chains have no restraint, and the lash no terror."[28] He turned a blind eye while Barrow and his men devised methods of summary discipline. The main ones were the "tube-gag," the "spread-eagle," the "scavenger's daughter" and the water-pit.

The tube-gag was an adaption of that ancient English instrument of torture for women, the "scolds' bridle." It looked like a small leather head-harness, except that instead of a bit it had a cylinder of hardwood, four inches long and an inch and a half in diameter, fastened into a broad leather strap that buckled across the face. When this gag was forced into the victim's mouth and the straps cinched, the man could only breathe through a small hole in the wooden plug, with great difficulty, emitting what the Reverend Rogers described as a "low indistinct whistle" accompanied, if he had resisted the gag and lost a tooth or two, with some red foam. The first prisoner on whom Rogers saw the tube-gag used was blind; for talking in his sleep, he was dragged from his cell, gagged and left for three hours with his arms shackled around a post behind him and tears streaming from his sightless eye-sockets.

The "spread-eagle" was simpler, though often used in concert with the gag. The prisoner was ironed to three ringbolts, arms fully outstretched, feet together, face to the wall, and left in this tiptoe crucifixion for six to eight hours. Some remained paralyzed for days afterward. A more refined implement for inflicting a similar torture was a raised iron frame six feet by two, on which the victim was strapped with his head and neck projecting unsupported off one end. If he tried to keep his head up, he would suffer anguish from muscular cramps. If he let it flop down, he would suffocate. The "scavenger's daughter" consisted of binding the convict with his head against his knees and leaving him until he fainted from the pain of cramps. The water-pit was an underground cell with salt water to waist height; men were left there in darkness for days at a stretch, unable to sleep for fear of drowning.

No wonder, then, that all sense of contract with authority disappeared and that the island lurched toward anarchy. In 1846 the Reverend Thomas Rogers's predecessor, an Anglican clergyman named Thomas Begley Naylor who had been chaplain on Norfolk Island from 1841 to September 1845, wrote a detailed report on Childs's regime to Lord Grey. "Revolting things have been done, in silence and without remedy," things for which "nothing else but the complete isolation of the island can account for." All was favoritism, spying and evasion, and chaos prevailed beneath Childs's claim to have restored an order "lost" by Maconochie's misplaced compassion. Villains were put in soft clerical jobs,* while harmless and indeed innocent prisoners, such as the unfortunate lawyer William Henry Barber, wrongly transported for a fraud on the Bank of England and later to be exonerated by Parliament, were given the filthiest and most degrading tasks. Childs had no system of discipline "conscientiously or intelligently carried out"; all he did was feed and clothe the demons and keep them nominally busy.[29]

Far from repressing homosexuality, Naylor reported, the overcrowding and lack of segregation on Norfolk Island encouraged it. "A parade of separation is kept up, but the communication is complete, and at times unrestricted." The bad apples always contaminated the good, in "a heterogeneous mass of moral pollution painful to contemplate." First-time offenders and even innocent men "are immediately on their disembarkation thrust among the veriest monsters of crime, from the cold-blooded murderer trebly convicted, to the wretch whose enormity Blackstone characterises as 'inter Christianos non nominandum,' without a possibility of escaping." In the end, Naylor warned Lord Grey, in the tone of eschatological prophecy that would soon become a common trope in discussions of the Probation System, "the curse of Almighty God must sooner or later fall in scorching anger upon a nation which can tolerate the continuance of a state of things so demoniacal and unnatural."[30]

The report horrified Lord Grey. Naylor had hoped to publish it as a

---

* In contravention of Clause 38 of the standing regulations: "No convict shall be employed as clerk in the Commandant's or any other office, or have access to the records kept therein."

pamphlet (and Maconochie, to whom it was delivered, dissuaded him from doing so) but its private impac: in Downing Street was immediate. One could not read, he noted, such a litany of "guilt, wretchedness and mismanagement," on which a clergyman had staked his name, without intense disquiet; Naylor's revelations were "too probable" to pass over. The new lieutenant-governor, Sir William Denison, was on the point of sailing from Portsmouth for Hobart. At the end of September 1846, Grey's instructions went to Denison. Her Majesty's Government must not even take the chance of prolonging evils so fearful in their nature. Denison must evacuate Norfolk Island and bring all its prisoners to Tasman's Peninsula "with the least possible delay." But he had second thoughts in November, and warned Denison that "practical difficulties, not to be foreseen at this distance" might defeat the move. They did, and Norfolk Island was not "broken up" for another decade.[31]

But meanwhile, before Gladstone's ax fell on him, Eardley-Wilmot had asked for a report of his own. He knew nothing of Naylor's damning letter but was worried by the rumors in the hostile colonial press. His own morals were under attack and he could not afford to seem dilatory. In April 1846, Eardley-Wilmot's comptroller-general of convicts, William Champ, directed an investigator to sail there and, as he delicately put it, report on the "many points . . . which might naturally fail to attract the attention . . . of Major Childs." The investigator was a magistrate in the Van Diemen's Land convict department, Robert Pringle Stuart, and he arrived at Norfolk Island in May 1846. He completed his investigation in two weeks, and his voluminous report reached Eardley-Wilmot by the end of June.

Little is known of Stuart's character, beyond the fact—obvious from his report—that he had an avid eye for detail, considerable skill in sifting and marshalling evidence, and knew the general penal environment well. One historian recently complained that his report "reads like that of a man without humour,"[32] but to wring laughs from such material would have taxed the most determined comedian.

His findings parallelled Naylor's. The physical state of the system on Norfolk was miserable—the rations underweight, the grain foul, the meat of the poorest quality, the maize-flour bread (known as "scrubbing-brushes" for the inflammation its abrasive bran produced in the prisoner's guts) scarcely edible. The service buildings, from the kitchens to the fouled latrines, provoked Stuart's disgust and the prisoner's simmering, mutinous resentment. Ophthalmia, gonorrhea and dysentery were endemic. The jail was an unventilated pigsty and the main barrack building at Kingston a *bagnio*: more than eight hundred men were locked in the barracks every evening after work, the lights went out, and what went on afterward was not the guards' business. Stuart paid it a surprise visit at eight o'clock one hot night and saw a flurry of "men scrambling into their own beds from others, in a very hurried manner, concealment being evidently their object." Prostitution was widespread; lads sold themselves for tobacco, new boots, or a lump of bread kneaded together with fat. Rape was not merely common, but inevitable.[33]

What especially shocked Stuart (and its effect on the officials who read his report may be gauged from the fact that, when it was eventually printed for the Lords and Commons in 1847, nearly all references to homosexuality were edited out) was that the virtuous forms of sexual life were parodied and inverted on Norfolk Island—not just rape and whoring, but marriage. "The association is not unusually viewed by the convicts as that between the sexes is ordinarily regarded; is equally respected by some of them; and is as much the source of jealousy, rivalry, intrigue and conflict . . . in others." Some of the demons were faithful to one another, and "the natural course of Affection is quite distracted. . . . [They] manifest as much eager earnestness for the society of each other as members of the opposite sex." In general, it was the English who turned to sodomy; the Irish Catholic prisoners abjured it.[34]

Despite the hysterical level of official violence, general discipline was poor. The morning muster was "unseemly, disorderly . . . in fact the mere nomination of the members of a promiscuous crowd," with "English and colonial prisoners intermixed, some lounging about with folded arms, others standing with their hands in their pockets, all either in conversation, uninterrupted, or otherwise engaged at their pleasure." When new men arrived from England, gangs of twenty to thirty Old Hands would pick the locks on their ward, rush in, beat them up and steal their belongings. No one stopped these forays, even when a group of bewildered New Hands just off the transport *Mayda*, when escorted down to the sea to wash, were plundered on the beach "notwithstanding the efforts of the constabulary." Convicts swore most opprobriously at their guards and got away with it; houses were robbed in broad daylight; one hardened Old Hand (as Naylor had reported) actually knocked down the commandant himself, bruising him severely. Most extraordinary of all, the convicts—or a hard core of them, numbering perhaps one hundred—often went on strike, openly refused to work and submitted "only when terms had been arranged to their satisfaction." Not one of them was punished or even tried. Their usual complaint was inedible food. On February 25, 1846, they struck over a different issue: The day was Ash Wednesday, a Catholic holiday, and they would not go to work until a military party levelled its muskets and made ready to shoot them. Childs's civilian officers, however, were not up to enforcing regulations without the help of the military, which could not be invoked every day. "The spirit of disobedience thus strengthened in the refractory," Stuart gloomily noted, "is, from impunity, reflected by the many, and provokes imitation." The hard-core men carried knives openly, threatened their overseers with them, and ruthlessly avenged any "peaching" by other prisoners. Anyone who betrayed a fellow prisoner to Authority was denounced as a traitor or "dog," and his punishment was swift: The men would kill him, or at least mutilate him by biting his nose and ears off, an operation known as "taking the dog's muzzle."

As the guards and overseers had so little control over what went on inside the barrack walls, the prisoners were able to create their own rule. Its center was the enclosed lumber-yard, a building next to the main barracks compound which also held the kitchens. It became a sanctuary where few guards or officers dared to go. The yard was ruled by the "Ring," a carceral mafia whose control over the lives of prisoners was both inescapable and minutely enforced. Its members did not fear to kill constables when they brought evidence against them; one such informer was found eviscerated in the bush near Longridge, his guts replaced by the entrails of a sheep. Later tales of the System, as composed by Marcus Clarke and Price Warung, surrounded the Ring with the awful glamour of a secret society, a freemasonry of evil, complete with elaborate initiation ceremonies, distinguishing tattoos (stamped on the neophyte's hide with needles and gunpowder) and a communal chant or oath:

> Hand in Hand
> On Earth, in Hell,
> Sick or Well,
> On Sea, On Land,
>    On the Square, Ever.
>
> Stiff or in Breath,
> Lag or Free,
> You and Me,
> In Life, in Death,
>    On the Cross, never.[35]

Such are the embellishments of fiction, but there is no doubt that the Ring had existed on Norfolk Island since the late 1830s and that it was very much feared. It gave the hardened and depraved, Stuart wrote,

> an absolute power, which is exerted in the most tyrannical manner over the majority, many of whom, I firmly believe, desire to conduct themselves becomingly, but have not sufficient courage to enable them to defy the threats, rendered more alarming by the almost hourly exhibition of them being carried into effect, or to resist the determined, vicious confed-

eracy by which they are oppressed. There are no means of protecting a man who may have brought himself odium on account of good conduct, or . . . having given evidence against any member of the so-called "Ring." A more miserable position than that of such a man cannot be conceived.[36]

There was more, in the same vein. When Stuart finished his report to Champ, and Champ "with the deepest regret" laid it before Eardley-Wilmot, and Eardley-Wilmot called a special meeting of the Executive Council on July 1, 1846, to consider what to do about it, that was the end of Major Childs. The council voted unanimously to get rid of him at once. Against Eardley-Wilmot's protests, they agreed to relieve Major Childs without notice, lest "matters might be brought to a crisis, and the island be subjected to all the horrors of an open mutiny."[37]

And in fact, as they sat in council on July 1, a mutiny did break out on Norfolk Island. It was a food riot. The prisoners never had enough food, and what they got gave them dysentery. The wretched victuals on Norfolk Island were a permanent and galling proof of Britain's contempt for them. In July 1846, it only took a pinprick to release an explosion of hatred.[38]

July 1 was the date of the half-yearly survey of all stores and equipment. William Forster, the superintendent, was in charge of the inventory, and on June 30 he went into the lumber-yard and its cookhouse to look for kitchen gear and cookpots. He did not want to make trouble with a close search, but he thought many dishes and mess-kits were missing (the inmates cut up large vessels and tinkered them into small ones, for sale to guards or other prisoners) and decided to come back after the eight hundred convicts were locked in barracks. That evening he found "a great number" of pots, pans and knives hidden around the lumber-yard, along with hoards of maize-meal that members of the Ring had skimmed for themselves from the regular rations. Foster had it all carried to the convict barracks store and locked away for the night, for inventory.

Next morning the prisoners turned out for their breakfast and found that "their" kettles and pans, along with their private hoards of flour, were gone. Their loss maddened the elite of the ring and they surrounded the muster officer, Patrick Hiney, shouting confused threats. Then, noticing the open gate of the lumber-yard, a mob of men ran outside, made for the barracks store, broke the locks and returned in triumph with their maize-flour and cooking gear. They settled down to boil water and make porridge. None of the guards interfered. But half an hour later, as constables and overseers gathered outside the gates to march the prisoners off to the day's labor, there was a shout from inside the lumber-yard:

"Come on, we will kill the——."* For the second time that morning, a mob of fifty or sixty men came boiling from the gates, led now by one of the hardest cases in the Ring, a twenty-six-year-old twice-convicted bushranger from Van Diemen's Land named William "Jackey-Jackey" Westwood. They grabbed whatever weapons lay to hand—axes, shovels, slabs of wood for clubs—swinging furiously at their guards as they rushed at the constables' cottages and then toward the house of the hated stipendiary magistrate, Samuel Barrow. They left four corpses behind them, men who had barely been able to react before their skulls were caved in by the mutineers. But they had no plan, and as they charged gasping and cursing toward Barrow's cottage they saw a line of soldiers bearing down on them, muskets levelled and bayonets fixed. The mutineers faltered, turned, and ran back to their only haven, their "Alsatia" (as Stuart's report had termed it), the lumber-yard. The bloody episode had lasted only minutes, but the reprisals were thorough. Barrow arrested more than fifty prisoners, and they crammed the filthy old jailhouse (which had not been enlarged or improved since Morisset's time) to bursting. Most of them were summarily sentenced to a year's hard labor in chains, and the presumed ringleaders were loaded with iron and reeved by their fetters to a long chain cable to await the arrival of a judge who could hold the necessary trial. Before the mutiny there were nine men in the lockup on other capital charges, and Childs had already sent for a criminal court justice. He arrived on the *Lady Franklin* a few weeks later, not knowing the mutiny had happened and unprepared for the sight of several dozen capital defendants. His name was Francis Burgess, and on board with him was the newly appointed commandant of Norfolk Island, John Price.

Burgess fell ill a few days after the hearings started. He had to go back to Hobart on the *Lady Franklin*, and the court opened again in late September before a new judge, Fielding Browne. In the meantime Barrow and Price between then had developed the prosecution as a perfect opportunity to break the Ring. They indicted all the known Ring members they could, committing twenty-six men to trial; eventually, fourteen were tried on five counts of murder and abetting. Despite the protests of the chaplain, Thomas Rogers, none of them was allowed a defense lawyer; and when Rogers helped the prisoners draft a petition to the judge asking for counsel, the request was ignored. Several defendants were illiterate and could not read the depositions against them. The "jury" was only a tribunal of five military officers. Twelve witnesses were heard from the Crown but none for the defense, and as they gave their evidence

---

* Expletive deleted, in the Parliamentary Papers.

the men in the dock hooted and cursed at them, trying as best they could to mock the processes of this kangaroo court. On October 5, twelve men out of fourteen were sentenced to death. No reprieves were given, although "Jacky-Jacky" Westwood wrote for the Reverend Rogers a last declaration exonerating four of the accused:

> I, William Westwood, wish to die in the communion of Christ's Holy Church, seeking the mercy of God through Jesus Christ Our Lord, amen. I acknowledge the justice of my sentence; but as a dying man I wish to say that I believe four men now going to suffer are innocent of the crime laid to their charge, namely Lawrence Cavenagh, Henry Whiting, William Pickthorne, and William Scrimshaw. I believe that I never spoke to Cavenagh on the morning of the riots; and those other three men had no part in the killing. . . . I die in charity with all men, and I ask your prayers for my soul.

Rogers had persuaded Westwood and other condemned men to write out their last statements instead of declaiming them, as was the custom, from the scaffold; Price, Barrow and the guards feared that their speeches might spark another riot.

On October 13, the men were hanged in two sets of six on the gallows that looked over Kingston beach and the Pacific beyond, before the assembled convicts, with all the military standing by with primed muskets to crush any restiveness.* No voices were raised but those of the condemned, who joined together in singing a hymn. Rogers had sat up all night with them, praying; he and the Roman Catholic chaplain, Father Bond, walked with the men to the scaffold, where their irons were struck off although their arms remained "severely pinioned." The trapdoor crashed, the bodies fell, the ropes thrummed on the beams. The mutineers' corpses were cut down, coffined, loaded unceremoniously into bullock-carts and dumped in an old sawpit outside the consecrated ground of the cemetery, by the sea's edge. Rogers, cassock flying, trotted up too late for the burial; by the time he reached the edge of the mass grave, where the new commandant had stood grimly staring at the remains of the Ring, the gravediggers had done their work and the coffins were already under earth. As a token of infamy, the sawpit was unmarked, but the hump of earth over the bodies remained clearly visible decades later; it received the name of "Murderers' Mound."

---

* In all, seventeen men were hanged on various charges, some not connected with the July mutiny, over the next week. It was the largest gallows-session ever held on Norfolk Island, and one of the largest in Australian penal history.

iii

WITH THIS MASS execution, the career of the most notorious of all the commandants of Norfolk Island began.

John Giles Price (1808–1857) was the fourth son of a Cornish baronet, Sir Rose Price of Trengwainton. A family fortune had been raised on sugar and slaves in the Caribbean, but by John Price's time it was all dissipated and he was only one of fourteen children begotten by this philoprogenitive minor aristocrat. Out he went to the colonies in 1836, a man in his late twenties armed with good letters of introduction but little capital. But in the pathologically snobbish society of Hobart Town, letters and a dash of noble blood counted for a lot. Lieutenant-Governor Arthur gave Price a generous land grant on the Huon River and more assigned servants than most new arrivals could expect. In 1838 Price married the niece of Arthur's successor, Mary Franklin. His farm was successful and his skill at running assigned convicts was noted. He was appointed muster-master of the Convict Department, then assistant police magistrate. His wife bore him five children in rapid succession. Price's colonial future was assured, despite a bout of illness after he moved to Hobart Town to take up his administrative duties. He was praised for his abilities as a classical scholar, athlete and oarsman; he was a skilled carpenter, turner, blacksmith, locksmith and tinker; he could even cook and sew; and, like some camp commandants in Europe a century later, he loved children. But it was his reputation for being tough and methodical that caused poor Eardley-Wilmot, in casting around for someone to redeem Norfolk Island from the miseries of Childs's incompetence, to pick Price. Eardley-Wilmot got more than he bargained for.

John Price has remained one of the durable ogres of the Australian imagination for more than a century now. This was largely because he was the original of the brutal island commandant Maurice Frere in the Great Australian Novel of the nineteenth century, Marcus Clarke's *His Natural Life*. Clarke could hardly have invented a more interesting villain than Frere, but he hardly needed to; the lineaments of the man Australians have loved to hate ever since were traced in the official correspondence of Norfolk Island, in the indignant letters of Price's main opposition there, the Reverend Thomas Rogers, and in the various Parliamentary Papers that refer to him or contain his views on convict management. Clarke drew copiously on all of these, particularly on Rogers's *Correspondence Relating to the Dismissal of the Rev. T. Rogers from his*

*Chaplaincy at Norfolk Island* (1849), which remains a source of unremittingly pejorative information on Price. (In *His Natural Life*, Norfolk Island's frail, morally tormented, alcoholic chaplain, the Reverend James North, who unsuccessfully opposes the demonic energies of Frere, is based on Rogers, and most of his reflections are taken verbatim from Rogers's letters.) The habits of Frere the character were essentially those of Price the prototype, and so was the appearance: six feet tall (unusually tall for an Englishman in the mid-nineteenth century), with Herculean shoulders and a thick bull neck, his legs slightly bowed like those of a pit bull, "a round bullet head of the true Legree type," a strong flushed face, sandy-red hair oiled in waves, and a cold gray stare through a monocle jammed in his eye. Price's monocle looked incongruous and struck more than one prisoner as a sign of "flashness," a puzzling intrusion of lower-class vulgarity into the world of Authority. This was confirmed by his dress. "He was dressed something after the style of a flash gentleman," recalled a former Norfolk Island lag named Henry Beresford Garrett, who had remained so obsessed with Price that in the 1870s, years after both had left the island, he wrote a lengthy manuscript about him called *The Demon*:

> On his round bullet head a small straw hat was jauntily stuck, the broad blue ribbon of which reached down between his shoulders, a glass stuck in one eye, a black silk kerchief tied sailor fashion around his bullneck, no vest but a bobtail or oxonian coat, or something like a cross between this and a stableman's jacket seemed to be bursting over his shoulders. A pair of rather tight pants completed his costume, except for a leather belt, six inches broad, buckled around the loins. In the belt two pepperbox revolvers were conspicuously stuck.
>     . . . [A]ssured by the presence of the soldiers and the guard, he struck an attitude by placing his arms akimbo, and again spoke.
>     "You know me, don't you? I am come here to rule, and by God I'll do so and tame or kill you. I know you are cowardly dogs, and I'll make you worry and eat one another."[39]

Such were Price's first words to his "lambs," on his first visit to the Kingston barracks in 1846.

When Clarke changed Price's name to Frere in his novel, it was not a casual gesture. *Frère*, of course, means "brother," and Price's peculiar relationship to the convicts fascinated Clarke. Unlike all previous commandants, Price went to great lengths to deal with them as an insider. He learned their flash argot and always spoke to them in it, with none of the slips and malapropisms that betray a man using a foreign tongue. How had he learned it? Nobody knew, and many of the prisoners on Norfolk Island apparently believed that he had "done time" himself. He was rumored to have lived a Jekyll-and-Hyde existence in the dosshouses and kens of Hobart Town, mixing freely with hard cases who accepted him as one of them. There were also some missing years in England, from 1827 (when he matriculated at Brasenose College in Oxford, though without taking a degree) to 1836, when he sailed for Van Diemen's Land. It may be—although the evidence for it, as we shall see, is ambiguous and circumstantial—that Price was homosexual and had picked up his fluent criminal slang when cruising for rough trade.

Price was extremely proud of his reputation for special insight into the "criminal mind," which he believed gave him special latitude. To confirm it, he would air weirdly contorted views on the irremediable and uniform evil of the prisoners under his charge. There was, for instance, no doubt that the brief mutiny of July 1, 1846, was a protest against semi-starvation. Price knew this perfectly well, for his first act after the mutineers were hanged was to increase the rations at the Kingston barracks. But at the end of 1846, Price cynically explained to William Champ, the comptroller-general in Van Diemen's Land, that the outbreak was caused by sodomy. Without their confiscated kettles, the prisoners could not make culinary treats for "the objects of their lusts, and . . . this aroused their savage and ferocious passions to a pitch of madness."[40]

By turns fascinated and repelled by the spectacle of convict evil, Price set himself up as its authoritarian mirror and, as his biographer John Barry remarked, entered "a psychopathological love-hate relationship" with the prisoners of Norfolk Island. He had to dominate them by their own standards, to show that he was their master, even without the backing of the System. Hence his obsession with knowing the convicts: their slang, the way they thought, their desires. To speak their language was to demoralize them, to show that their world was open to him while his remained closed to them. To this end, he deployed the jocular, domineering, fake-egalitarian cruelty that is still one of the bad dreams of Australian life. Price was certainly bad and possibly mad, but no one could have called him stupid. No wonder Australians still remember him, though they have forgotten Morisset the blundering martinet and Maconochie the humane reformer.

Price had no time for Maconochie's "soothing system," to which he attributed all the disorganization he inherited on Norfolk Island. He ruled by terror, informers and the lash, to which he added the public force of his own indomitable character; he was known to walk into the lumber-yard unescorted and, before five hundred hostile men, face down a convict who showed signs of rebellion. He once stared down a convict who snatched the pistol from his belt, taunting the man as a coward and a dog, until the prisoner handed back the weapon and fell beaten to his knees.

The informer system had been usual on Norfolk Island long before

Price arrived there; so, of course, had the lash. The question in assessing Price's regime is how far he went in arbitrary cruelty and despotic abuse, beyond the degree of "responsible" brutality that the government expected a Norfolk Island commandant to deploy.

The main evidence came from two clergymen. The first was Thomas Rogers, who witnessed the first months of Price's regime up to early 1847, when he was recalled to Van Diemen's Land by Dr. J. S. Hampton, the new comptroller-general of convicts who favored Price and wanted to protect his position. Fired from the Convict Department, unable to move the authorities against Price and widely dismissed by officials from Denison down as a slandering crank, Rogers was nonetheless supported by some of his church superiors. In 1849 he published his *Correspondence*, which described what he had seen on Norfolk Island in prolix, indignant but convincing detail. Significantly, neither Price nor Denison made any effort to refute it, although Rogers was reprimanded for using official documents without permission.

The second clerical witness to Price's regime was Robert Willson (1794–1866), a priest from Nottinghamshire who had risen, by 1844, to become the first Roman Catholic Bishop in Tasmania. Willson visited Norfolk Island three times: in 1846 (when Childs was still commandant), in 1849 and in 1852. In 1849 he was struck by the success Price had had in cleaning up the chaos of Childs's regime. Not until 1852 did his doubts about method really surface, in a long and appalling report he laid before Lieutenant-Governor Denison. Price, it seems, implored him not to send it. "I am sorry to see you carried away by the stories of these men; you know what a miserable lot they are; do not permit their stories to make any impression upon you." Willson was outraged: "When I was last in England I told the Government to take away one third of the convicts on the island, and now I will recommend the Government to take the whole." At this, Price burst into tears and begged Willson "not to ruin him."[41]

Rogers's first charge was that Price's transactions with the convicts on Norfolk Island were cynical. Price did not believe that reformation was possible; he assumed that good behavior was a sham and that everything any prisoner said about his own state of mind or moral progress was a lie. "Whenever a fellow is recommended to me by the religious instructor or the surgeon superintendent," Price declared, "I always set that fellow down as the greatest hypocrite of the whole lot." In 1846 the transport *John Calvin* landed its 199 prisoners on Norfolk Island to begin their trudge through the Probation System, and one convict was recommended by the surgeon superintendent as "an inoffensive man with very fine feelings." "Oh, I'll soon take *them* out of him!" Price replied.[42]

On the other hand, he wanted the worst men he could draft as constables and overseers. "In selecting men for the police one day," Rogers related,

> Mr. Price asked a man what he had been at home, the man replied he had been a farm servant; "well then," was the remark, "you are not thief enough for me." Another who professed to have been an "honest travel-ler" in England, i.e., a thief by profession, was made a police man.

Price defended such appointments on the well-worn ground that one must set a thief to catch a thief, but the consistency with which he put "hard" men in minor offices and kept "soft" ones underfoot was per-verse. No less so was his purge of the civil officers on Norfolk Island. Everyone who showed signs of opposing his autocratic rule was sus-pended or recalled to Hobart, until no one stood between Price and the prisoners. Rogers, before he had to leave in 1847, recorded the pervasive terror of informants Price fostered and the capriciousness with which prisoners could be punished. One prisoner was flogged for mislaying his shoelaces. A man named Peart got seven days in chains for saying "good morning" to the wrong person. Another was seen walking along waving a twig; a constable saw him and demanded to know what he was up to and where he was going. "Why, I might be after a parrot," the prisoner replied, and was flogged. A cart-driver came before Price on the charge of "having a tamed bird" and got 36 lashes. A stockman named Higson was passing by a garden plot when the gardener asked him to "give this tree a push, I want to roll it down the hill to mend the garden fence where your bullocks come in." Obligingly, the stockman did so and was seen by a constable, who charged him with "pushing a tree with his foot." Price awarded him 36 lashes on the back and 36 on the buttocks, and within less than two weeks after that he was flogged twice more, once with 100 lashes for having tobacco and hiding in the bush. It had been the custom among the convicts to wash the back of a newly flogged man, to press down his mangled skin and dress it with cool banana leaves; Price had anyone seen with a banana leaf in his possession summarily punished.

Punishments for less trivial offenses were in proportion; and Price's orders were meticulously carried out by his chief constable, a ticket-of-leave man named Alfred Essex Baldock (1821–1848), whom Rogers called "of most unprincipled disposition . . . perfidious and unfeeling to-wards his fellow-prisoners . . . the servile creature of the commandant in everything." Some men, after flogging, would be laced into a strait-jacket and tied down to an iron bedstead for a week or two, so that their backs mortified and stank. Others were "strapped down" without a flogging, but for as much as six weeks at a time, after which the victim "looked

more like a pale distended corpse than a living being, and his voice . . .
could scarcely be heard." For striking Baldock, a convict named Lemon
was bludgeoned unconscious by the constables, tube-gagged, and chained
up with his arms, one broken, behind him around a lamp post. Cells were
frequently whitewashed to cover the blood which, Rogers alleged, spat-
tered the walls to a height of seven feet. In one fetid punishment cell,
known as the "Nunnery," Price would keep a dozen men with a latrine-
bucket in a space six by twelve feet when the outside temperature was
100°F.; "I had to step out into the yard at first," Rogers confessed, "to
save myself from fainting." Men were sentenced to work "on the reef,"
cutting coral in water up to their waists, in 36-pound leg-irons; they were
condemned to fourteen days' solitary for "having some ravelling from an
old pair of trousers," or "being at the privy when the bell rang."

Price defended his "severities," without (of course) going into detail
about them, on the ground the prisoners were wild beasts who would
rise and take the island if they got an inch of slack. Rogers disagreed:
Except for some twenty or thirty "villains," the two thousand prisoners
"were as manageable by the common methods of just and firm and rational government as the peasantry of Kent or Devon."

The commandant had his wife and children on the island, but his
"constant companion," according to Rogers, was Baldock, who went
"riding with him to out-stations and shepherds' huts in the bush, and
attending him and advising him constantly." Rogers seems to have
thought that the two men were lovers, and that this explained Baldock's
invulnerability to reproof. In Van Diemen's Land, former officers of Baldock's probation gang assured Rogers that "he was so strongly suspected
of being addicted to unnatural crime that he was ordered to be placed at
nights in one of the sleeping cells." There is no conclusive evidence of a
liaison between Price and Baldock, although when the chief constable
was drowned (to the unbounded joy of the prisoners) after his rowboat
turned turtle on the Kingston reef, Price set up an unusually large and
elaborate gravestone to him, much in contrast to the mass grave of Murderers' Mound, with the grieving quatrain:

'Tis His Supreme prerogative
    O'er subject Kings to reign.
'Tis just that he should rule the world
    Who does the world sustain.

The Reverend Rogers's strictures on the "subject Kings" of Norfolk
Island, however, were not acknowledged by Sir William Denison when
his *Correspondence* was printed in 1849. Price was shielded by another
friend, the dismally cynical opportunist (and future governor of Western

Australia) Dr. J. S. Hampton, who wrote a whitewashing report on the prisoners' condition and strenuously denied that anything odd was happening.

Yet the suspicion that the commandant was out of control, that the island's remoteness from Hobart had permitted some cancer of his soul to metastasize wildly, could not entirely be allayed. Price's rule grew worse as his paranoia thickened, and in 1852 he received a dispatch from Denison's desk querying the enormous inflictions of the lash he himself had reported. His Excellency, Price learned, "regrets very much that you should have considered such punishment necessary to so great an extent" and "trusts that you may ... adopt ... means of enforcing proper discipline without recourse to such frequent infliction of this mode of punishment."[43]

In reply, Price railed against the character of the convicts—"cullings," "incorrigibles," "desperadoes," among whom "persuasion is useless, advice is thrown away." He defended the "beneficial effect" of flogging. "Stringent the regulations are," he wrote, "and stringent they must be, but they are not more so than those imposed on soldiers, indeed on boys at public schools in England."[44]

But in that month, March 1852, Bishop Willson was moved by rumor and report to make his third visit to Norfolk Island. He was appalled by what he saw there and penned a thirty-page report to Lieutenant-Governor Denison. It described mass floggings, blood-soaked earth, and an atmosphere of "gloom, sullen despondency, despair of leaving the Island." He saw hideously overcrowded cells, men loaded with 36-pound balls on their chains, wizened pallid creatures staring at him "with their bodies placed in a frame of iron work." He found the sole medical officer so much in cahoots with Price that he claimed a desperately sick prisoner had to be kept in an airless cell because ventilation would be "prejudicial" to him. Hampton, in turn, tried to discredit Bishop Willson's report with obfuscations and quibbles. Price burst into tears and begged the Bishop to suppress his report. But Willson filed it, placing the blame squarely on Price and "the system which invests one man at this remote place with absolute, I might say irresponsible power of dealing with so large a mass of human beings."

Price had tendered his resignation once, at the end of 1850, citing the difficulty of bringing up his children well in "this Lazar house of crime." He got a raise in salary instead. But by now, Denison feared he might become a serious embarrassment to the Crown. He felt that there was a connection between Price's "illness"—whose nature was not specified in official correspondence—and the morbid ferocities of his rule. Denison had already cut the size of the convict population of Norfolk Island by half in 1847, in deference to Grey's wish to abandon the island altogether; most of the probation prisoners had gone down to Van Diemen's Land, leaving a hard core of about 450 "colonial" or twice-convicted offenders. But the military force on Norfolk Island had not been reduced, and very expensive it was, while civilian officers could not be found at any price, because of the rush to the newly discovered goldfields of Ballarat and Bendigo.* In any case, Denison could read the larger political signs, all of which pointed to the abolition of transportation to Australia. It would be better to get rid of this remote penal outrider and concentrate all the management of convicts on Van Diemen's Land. Denison therefore ordered his Convict Department to start drawing up plans for a maximum-security penitentiary at Port Arthur, modelled on the Separate System of Pentonville—which would receive the hard cases of Norfolk Island.[45]

John Price was happy to leave; he had been there more than six years, he was sick of the eyes of prisoners, and he had a garden to cultivate in Van Diemen's Land. No censure was passed. The new secretary of state for the colonies, the Duke of Newcastle, scanned Bishop Willson's report and its accompanying drafts of exculpation from both Price and Hampton, and concluded that since Norfolk Island was about to be abandoned, one need investigate no further. Let the dead stay dead; let old wounds not be re-opened. John Price had done his duty according to his lights, with indefatigable prowess. He had been a good servant of the Crown, if a touch zealous. But excess of zeal in defense of penalty was no crime, the secretary of state reflected, closing the books on Norfolk Island.

Price farmed for a while, but he could not keep away from prison management. Within a year, in January 1854, he accepted a job on the mainland as inspector-general of penal establishments in Victoria. One of his tasks was to run the five prison hulks moored in the port of Melbourne, at Hobson's Bay off Williamstown. The regime on these vessels became a new byword for ferocity. The worst of Norfolk Island had come to the mainland: the tube-gagging and spread-eagling, the bludgeon-handle jammed in the mouth in tobacco searches, the rotten victuals, the loading with irons, the beatings, ringbolts and buckets of sea water. Before long, a warship had to take up station next to the hulks, its guns double-shotted so that, if the prisoners mutinied and the guards had to flee, it could sink the hulk and send its ironed men to the bottom.

On March 26, 1857, Price paid an official visit to the quarry at Williamstown where gangs of hulk convicts were laboring. He had come, as his office demanded, to hear their grievances; and with his usual bravado, he walked straight into the midst of them, escorted only by a small party of guards. A hundred prisoners watched him marching up the tramway

---

* For the gold rush and its consequences for transportation, see the next chapter.

that bore the quarried stone from the cutting-face to the jetty. Quietly they surrounded Price, and their circle began to close. There was a hubbub of hoarse voices, a clatter of chains, a scraping of hobnails on stone. Rocks began to fly. The guards fled; Price turned and began to run down the tramway when a stone flung from the top of the quarry-face caught him between the shoulderblades and pitched him forward on his face. Then, nothing could be seen except a mass of struggling men, a frenetic scrum of arms and bodies in piebald cloth, and the irregular flailing of stone-hammers and crowbars.

iv

PRICE'S REIGN on Norfolk Island had been the last paroxysm of the System's cruelty, a nightmare sweated out by a dying organism. Elsewhere, the transportation of convicts to Australia was winding down. But the process was slow, because Britain did not want it to end. In Whitehall and Downing Street, after 1846, there was still the hope that it might be kept alive. Her Majesty's Government was not going to cave in before the colonial abolitionists just because the Probation System had failed. England still had to purge itself of convicts, the "excrementitious mass" Jeremy Bentham had written of a generation before; it needed space for thousands a year. Most judges, bishops and politicians agreed that transportation was still the way to get rid of them, given the surge in penal convictions. The Report of the 1847 Select Committee on Criminal Laws, Juvenile Offenders and Transportation was quite categorical on that: "The punishment of transportation cannot safely be abandoned."[46] So various projects were mooted, with a view of relieving the pressure on Van Diemen's Land and sneaking the convicts onto the mainland through the back door. The first of these was promoted by Gladstone during his six-month term as secretary of state for the colonies, in early 1846.

Gladstone proposed drawing a line across the map of New South Wales at 26°S., just above Brisbane. The land north of it would form a new and separate colony, North Australia. The "Gladstone Colony" would be a vast low-security jail, settled by convicts with conditional pardons and tickets-of-leave who would be moved up from Van Diemen's Land. Prisoners from England would get conditional pardons as soon as they stepped ashore. In this way, Van Diemen's Land would find room for more freshly transported felons from England.

Naturally, this struck the island's free settlers as a very poor solution. Van Diemen's Land was saturated with convicts. By 1846, almost half its total population were criminals under sentence; out of 66,000 people,

30,300 were bond. If one reckoned in the number of former convicts among the free population (perhaps another 15,000), prospects for the Exclusive minority looked bad. They saw themselves as a small archipelago of decency in a rising sea of moral pollution; anything that let in new convict blood had to be opposed.

The Gladstone Colony was even more unpopular in Sydney, since its plan did not include a convict-proof fence along the 26th parallel. What would stop a new seepage of outcasts into New South Wales? Yet it was tried. Early in 1847, settlers landed at its intended capital, Port Curtis, just south of the Tropic of Capricorn. But it did not take root: Short of food, harassed by Aborigines, tropical rain, baking sun, bad water and whining clouds of insects, the colonists succumbed to despondency.

Meanwhile Gladstone moved upward from the Colonial Office and his place was taken by Lord Grey, who—to the immense relief of its settlers, who heard the glad news in April 1847—ordered the evacuation of Port Curtis. If Gladstone's scheme was meant to place convicts as pioneers in the wilderness, Grey explained to Parliament, it would have been better to put them in the wild parts of Van Diemen's Land; but his predecessor's "real object . . . was to send them through North Australia as it were through a sieve into New South Wales." It was one thing for emancipated convicts to start a new life in neighboring colonies; "this cannot, with justice, be prevented." But it was quite another, and most unfair, to dump them next to New South Wales and let them percolate south into a society that did not want them.[47]

But Grey had some tricks of his own up his sleeve. Realizing that no more convicts could be sardined into Van Diemen's Land, he announced in 1846 that transportation would be suspended for two years. In 1845, 2,870 prisoners of both sexes had landed there. The figure for 1846 was 1,126; for 1847, 1,269; and for 1848, 1,434. More than a thousand of the male convicts arriving in Van Diemen's Land during 1847–48 had been relocated from Norfolk Island, so the cut in transportation from England was large.

However, Grey in 1847 had told Lieutenant-Governor Denison that "it is not the intention" of Britain to resume transportation when the two years were up; and his under secretary, Sir James Stephen, told the Treasury a few days later that "Her Majesty's Government have decided upon altogether abandoning the system of transportation to Van Diemen's Land."[48] Denison, on reading Grey's dispatch, assumed that it meant what it said and that abolition was just around the corner; so, to their joy, did the free settlers of Van Diemen's Land. Both were wrong. Grey, speaking for perfidious Albion, had a new system in mind, euphoniously called "assisted exile."

His idea was to combine penitentiaries at home with transportation abroad. Let the sinners first do time in Pentonville; once subdued by its awful mental rigor, let them have conditional pardons and be sent to Australia to complete their sentences. Even if Van Diemen's Land (whose economy, by 1847, was showing distinct signs of revival) could not absorb them, then the labor-hungry pastoral settlers of New South Wales and Port Phillip certainly could. The sequence would be: first, "separate confinement" in England followed by a spell of "associated labor" in the naval dockyards; then "assisted exile" to the antipodes. Once there, the men would not be exposed to the evils of the Probation System; they would be dispersed to settlers across the country districts and the outback. They could also take their wives and families, if their moral qualities seemed adequate. Thus the colonists could not complain of being deluged, once more, in transportation. "The penal system known as transportation will not be renewed," Grey told Denison in 1848. "The *diffusion* of men, instead of placing them in Penal and Probation Gangs, totally changes its character."[49] And since Grey had a politician's sense of an acceptable name, the subjects of his penal experiment would not, under any circumstances, be called "convicts"; instead, they would be "exiles."[50]

This idea had been revolving in Grey's mind for almost ten years. He first produced it during the sessions of the Molesworth Committee on transportation, where in 1837, as Viscount Howick, he suggested it to James Macarthur, the pastoral king of New South Wales. "Suppose," he asked, "criminals were to be punished in England with a certain number of years' imprisonment, and after that to be banished to New South Wales, [where they would] be placed under the surveillance of the police in the same manner of ticket-of-leave men, what do you think would be the effect?" "In a modified shape, the same as . . . transportation," Macarthur replied.[51] Before Grey received the seals of the Colonial Office, the experiment had already begun. In 1844, the transport vessel *Royal George* had landed twenty-one convicts at Port Phillip Bay, the first felons to arrive in the future state of Victoria since the abortive attempt at a convict settlement there back in 1803. They had all done terms in Pentonville, the new penitentiary in Britain.

These "Pentonvillains," as they were promptly nicknamed, were snapped up by labor-hungry settlers, who asked for more. Edward Curr, a rock-ribbed conservative who had become the manager of the ill-fated Van Diemen's Land Company twenty years before and, after it failed, had taken up wide acres in the Port Phillip district, led the settlers' case. Free labor was not to be had, so wages were high, and this attracted "whole shoals"of former convicts from Van Diemen's Land and the "Middle District" of New South Wales. It would be better to have the Pentonville men, who might have been partly reformed by the penitentiary machine, than these frequently dubious characters. The grand question, Curr argued, was the need for cheap labor, and neither he nor his fellow squatters stood ready to be "ruined for virtue's sake."[52]

Others disagreed. In the view of the Melbourne editor and alderman William Kerr, the "Exiles" threatened to depress not only the wages but the moral tone of the colony; and their introduction, "free of all manner of restraint," would be a wanton injustice to all free citizens.[53]

Thus the lines of class conflict over the arrival of Exiles were drawn. It was city versus country, worker versus squatter. The prospect that transportation to mainland Australia would begin again bypassed the old and by now demographically feeble division between Exclusive and Emancipist in the vast territory of New South Wales. Some Emancipist families were now very rich and wanted cheap convict labor; many a free emigrant rebelled at the idea of losing wages to a flood of Exiles. Even among the sons and daughters of "old" Exclusive families, who preened themselves on having been in the colony for fifty years or more, the convict presence was no longer pervasive, no longer a threat to order; out of a total population of 187,000 people in New South Wales in 1846, fewer than 11,000 were convicts still under sentence. Compared to the dark taint of Van Diemen's Land, convictry (in the eyes of those who wanted more of it) was a mere tinge, rapidly fading. It was time to think about its advantages again.

Thus, on the issue of Exiles, the squatters won—at first. In 1845–46, 517 "Pentonvillains" disembarked at Melbourne and found instant employment. Late in 1846, a committee set up by the New South Wales Legislative Council reported to Gladstone that the "vast solitude" of outback New South Wales seemed "to have been assigned by Providence to the British nation as the fittest scene for the reformation of her criminals."[54] The Legislative Council itself disagreed at first, but when Grey offered to send one free emigrant for every convict, and wives and families of the Exiles as well, it changed its mind. The stage was now set for the wholesale revival of transportation to the Australian mainland, even to Sydney, under the name of Grey's Exile scheme. In 1847, 536 convicts arrived in Port Phillip; in 1848, 455.

But then, hitches began to appear. The "vast solitudes" no longer seemed quite so empty, because England's general economic depression of 1847 caused a surge of free emigration. From 1847 to 1849, some 30,000 emigrants sailed from England to take their chances in New South Wales. It was no longer so easy to find work for the Exiles who came to Port Phillip in 1847–48; the demand for convict labor had ebbed. Moreover, given the low state of the British economy, Grey did not feel he could ask the Treasury to pay for the plan of sending out a free settler for every Exile. So he dropped that part of his agreement with the Legislative Council of New South Wales. Instead, in August 1848, he secured an Order-in-Council declaring that convicts could once more be sent to New South Wales at the will and pleasure of Her Majesty's Government, and he dispatched a transport loaded with 239 male prisoners, the *Hashemy*, direct to Sydney. She was the first convict ship to enter the immense gates of Sydney Harbor in a decade, and the splash of her anchor on June 11, 1849, at Circular Quay—where, like some stained cuckoo, she nested amid five ships loaded with more than 1,400 new-chum immigrants—was promptly taken as the sign of a complete breach of faith between Lord Grey and Queen Victoria's loyal subjects in Australia.

It provoked the biggest show of mass public indignation in the colony's short history. In driving rain, crowds assembled at the Quay—five thousand by the Abolitionists' count, seven or eight hundred according to the police. The governor, Sir Charles Fitzroy, watched them pouring down George and Macquarie Streets; the shopkeepers along the quay prudently locked up their shutters as soldiers with fixed bayonets took up their stations outside Government House and the perimeter of the Quay, by now a squelching bog, was ringed with police. But there was no violence. Speaker after speaker clambered on top of the improvised dais (an omnibus) harangued the crowd and was rewarded with thunderous cheers. Robert Campbell, nephew of the great colonial merchant whose brick warehouses and wharf stood nearby, a man who had been campaigning against transportation for twenty full years, declaimed that "they would be content to subdue the land and replenish it without the introduction of British crime and its attendant British misery." John Lamb, a retired naval commander and now a leading businessman with a seat on the Legislative Council of New South Wales, moved the first of the anti-transportation resolutions, drafted by a rising Australian politician named Henry Parkes—a "deliberate and solemn protest" against transportation:

FIRSTLY—Because it is in violation of the will of the majority of the colonists, as is clearly evinced by their expressed opinions on this question at all times.

SECONDLY—Because numbers among us have emigrated on the faith of the British Government, that transportation to this colony had ceased for ever.

THIRDLY—Because it is incompatible with our existence as a free colony, desiring self-government, to be the receptacle of another country's felons.

FOURTHLY—Because it is in the highest degree unjust, to sacrifice the great social and political interests of the colony at large to the pecuniary profit of a fraction of its inhabitants.

FIFTHLY—Because . . . we greatly fear that the perpetration of so stupendous an act of injustice . . . will go far in alienating the affections of the people of this colony from the mother country.

An English emigrant barrister, Robert Lowe, the future Viscount Sherbrooke, a half-blind albino with a stentorian voice and a feel for the main vein of popular sentiment, scrambled onto the bus roof to declaim that "the stately presence of their city, the beautiful waters of their harbour, were this day again polluted with the presence of that floating hell—a convict ship." He denounced "this attempt to impose the worst and most degrading slavery on the colony" as the outcome of "that oppressive tyranny which had confiscated the lands of the colony—for the benefit of a class," the squatters. This meeting, he shouted into the brief lulls between the cheers of the crowd, was the prelude to an Australian republic, as the Boston Tea Party had been to the American. "In all times, and in all nations, so will injustice and tyranny ripen into rebellion, and rebellion into independence."[55]

The meeting wound to its end, by which time (some of the more perceptive listeners noted) not a single Emancipist or descendant of a convict had spoken; and the anti-transportation orators went to Government House and asked to present their petition to Governor Fitzroy. He agreed to see them the next day. Fitzroy told Lowe that he would pass their protest on to Her Majesty, but the convicts from the *Hashemy* would stay; on that, there could be no negotiation. So another monster rally was called at Circular Quay for June 18, to ask for the dismissal of Lord Grey. Lowe moved for dismissal, and Henry Parkes rose to speak against Grey, "a nobleman who never bestowed a thought upon New South Wales in his life, till some political chance or accident gave him his ministerial position." But because there had been a buzz of speculation about a Yankee-style revolt in Australia, he added that he did not see what good would come from such comparisons. Free Australians "were not at a state of advancement to be benefited by separation from the mother country, even if we had cause to desire separation. . . . We possessed little of the stern and sturdy spirit of the old American colonists." So much, in Parkes's view, for the legendary independence of Australians. He was righter than even he could have supposed, for a century and a quarter later Australia would continue to cling to the British Commonwealth.

Fitzroy wrote to Lord Grey, assuring him that the anti-transportation lobby in Sydney was merely a faction, whose sole audience was the mob.

Their notion that the secretary of state for the colonies had committed a breach of faith with the colonists was quite unjust, Fitzroy thought.[56] And indeed, the political crisis over the *Hashemy* did die out quite soon. When yet another convict ship, the *Randolph*, arrived in Port Phillip with 295 convicts, the citizens of Melbourne persuaded La Trobe to bar it from anchoring—but her captain merely sailed north and unloaded his bedraggled cargo in Sydney, without provoking a single meeting or speech. After that, two more vessels, the *Havering* and the *Adelaide*, disembarked a total of 593 Exiles at Sydney Cove. They were the last, and they caused no incident.

Nor did their passengers perceptibly degrade the tone of the colony. They were quite like ordinary people. "Dear Wife you can come out to me as soon as it pleases you," one of them wrote after he was settled with a master upcountry.

> I will provide for you a comfortable Situation and Home as good a one as ever lies in my power. . . . When you come ask for me as an emigrant, and never use the word Convict or the ship Hashemy on your voyage, *never let it be once named among you, let no one know your business but your own selves.* . . . Dear Wife this is a fine Country and a beautiful climate it is like a perpetual Sumer, and I think it will prove congenial for your health, No wild beast or anything of the sort are here, fine beautiful birds and every thing seems to smile with pleasure. . . . [T]his is just the country where we can end our days in peace and contentment when we meet.[57]

This encomium from a satisfied Englishman was printed in the most popular English magazine of the time, *Household Words*, whose editor was none other than Charles Dickens. To say that Dickens "edited" it is to understate the degree to which his views permeated the publication. On Australia, which he never visited, he had a most explicit line; and it had been given him by a journalist who had never been there either, although he pretended he had: Samuel Solomon (1813–1883), who wrote extensively on railways and agriculture under the pen name of Samuel Sidney. Sidney was quite well-informed about Australia (his brother had settled there and come back in 1847), and his many readers knew so little about it that for ten years they accepted him as an expert—indeed, as *the* popular authority—on matters Australian. He published a magazine, *Sidney's Emigrant's Journal* (1849–50), as well as a number of books, beginning with *A Voice from the Far Interior of Australia* (1847), and ending with *The Three Colonies of Australia* (1852), subtitled "How to Settle and Succeed in Australia," which—coinciding as it did with the discovery of gold—was a roaring popular success. Sidney was an engaging mélange of social idealist and literary con man, like many another influential journalist. His heart yearned for the vision that the Industrial Revolution was banishing from England; pastoral Arcadia inhabited by sturdy forty-acre yeomen. He believed this paradise of the common man could be revived in Australia, by emigration. "There are thousands in this country pining in indigence, who if removed to a suitable colony would be able to attain decent independence."[58]

For this picture of Australia, Sidney drew heavily on Alexander Harris's *Settlers and Convicts* (1847), the first book on the life of free workers there—anti-System, anti-squatter, squarely on the side of self-help, extolling the comradeship of hard labor among farmers and cedar-getters in the bush. The yeomen of England had fallen into the decay foreseen by Cobbett; they were the fretful prey of agitators, Chartists, ideologues of every kind. On the vast democratic grasslands of Australia Felix they would find their natural station.

Such arguments were endorsed by reformers better-known today than Sidney: by Harriet Martineau, and the brave Roman Catholic philanthropist Caroline Chisholm, "the emigrant's friend," who had labored immensely from 1840 to 1846 in New South Wales, meeting every migrant ship, finding jobs for their bewildered women passengers, setting up shelters and employment agencies throughout the interior for newly arrived immigrants, and tirelessly escorting groups of "new chums" into the bush on her white horse, Captain.[59] On her return to London, Mrs. Chisholm won the ear of Lord Grey and Sir James Stephen, the permanent under secretary at the Colonial Office. In 1849 she formed a Family Colonization Loan Society, underwritten through Coutts Bank at the behest of the philanthropic Baroness Burdett-Coutts, with a board of London merchants; it lent migrants their passage money, found them work in Australia, and collected the loans in small installments at no interest. She had interviewed hundreds of immigrants in Australia and their words became the first-hand stuff of her pamphlets. Chisholm was fervently committed to yeoman emigration and small farming. She had a natural ally in Samuel Sidney. Both found a mutual one in Dickens, who spread their opinions in every issue of *Household Words* and enthusiastically incorporated them into his novels. It was exactly along the lines of emigration proposed by Chisholm and Sidney that the feckless and debt-ridden Wilkins Micawber, at the happy end of *David Copperfield* (1849–50), took his chances in Australia along with Mr. Peggotty, Em'ly and Gummidge, finding a happy haven at Port Middlebay, Dickens's name for Melbourne. Micawber is redeemed by the work of his hands. "I've seen that theer bald head of his, a-perspiring in the sun, Mas'r Davy, till I a'most thowt it would have melted away," says Peggotty, the Yarmouth fisherman who knows what work is. "And now he's a Magistrate."[60]

Dickens, Sidney and Chisholm: a formidable team of persuaders, backed by such sympathizers as Harriet Martineau and Edward Bulwer-Lytton, who was himself to become a strikingly inept secretary of state for the colonies in 1858. They knew who deserved their sympathy—and who did not: the villains in the drama of colonial opportunity they were writing, the graziers of Australia, the selfish squatters, nostalgic for cheap slave labor and bitterly determined to preserve transportation. "Unlock the land!"—such was the cry, both in England and New South Wales, on behalf of the forty-acre yeomen. Were the big pastoralists deliberately sabotaging free immigration? In hindsight, it seems that they were not; they were desperate for labor much of the time, and paid for it when they could get it—but there was little doubt that the most reactionary would rather have had convicts. However, experience had also shown that, although Australian prospects could be seen by Englishmen (and sometimes, under the spell of Dickens's prose, by Australians as well) through a rosy haze of Pickwickian stereotypes, small farmers in 1850 remained as vulnerable to drought, fire and flood as they had been along the Hawkesbury in the days of Governor Bligh. The land was not Arcadia; the bush could flare up and incinerate ten years of a forty-acre man's work in a day; even in good times, it took three acres to sustain one sheep. But such realities were moved into the background by the largely urban polemicists who now urged the abolition of transportation not just as a moral good in itself but as a blow against land monopoly, a condition of successful emigration and a cure for England's discontents.

In Australia, the focus was different. The image of the earnest yeoman frustrated by squatters' greed was politically potent, sure enough, but the stereotype of convict evil was fixed beyond the power of any individual's experience to alter it. Get rid of convictry, keep the imperial attachment —such was the local reformers' tune. No bunyip Demosthenes preaching abolition would open his mouth against the pollutions of English crime without unfurling a long red-white-and-blue preamble assuring Her Gracious Majesty, Queen Victoria, of his undying, wholehearted and groveling fealty to the British Crown. The end of transportation was reached through a cumbersome accommodation between morally indignant colonials who could not make good on their threats and imperialists who felt weary of an obsolete penal system and yet could not cancel it at a stroke for fear of seeming malleable to Australian pressure. Anti-transportation views, by the late 1840s, were a commonplace of every pulpit sermon and most political meetings. Abolition was, as one British officer in New South Wales remarked, "the only movement at all resembling a popular *émeute*" in "the usually drowsy, well-fed and politically apathetic Sydney."[61] The same was true in Melbourne, and in Van Diemen's Land, where in 1849 an Anti-Transportation League was formed under the leadership of the island's leading publisher, Henry Dowling, Jr. (1810–1885), the landowner Richard Dry (1815–1869) and John West (1809–1873), a fervidly eloquent Congregationalist minister who, when not inveighing against the System from lecture halls and pulpits throughout the island, wrote the first and for many years the best history of Van Diemen's Land.

But for all the protests, the meetings and the airing of grievances at the enforced Stain, there was never any question of secession. Nobody, in or out of the League, wanted that. Meanwhile, Grey's two-year moratorium on transportation to Van Diemen's Land ran out in 1848, and the machinery of exile, obedient to his Lordship's peevishly stubborn character, began once more to roll in the direction of Hobart and Launceston. Sir William Denison, the lieutenant-governor, could do no more than pooh-pooh the "moral pretensions" of the League and find what work could be found for Lord Grey's Exiles. He also tried, with less success, to assure the free settlers that the new arrivals—having done their stint in Pentonville—were of better stuff than the old and that eight or ten convict ships a year did not mean a breach of faith by the Colonial Office. As the economy of Van Diemen's Land struggled erratically out of its catastrophic slump, Denison grew optimistic about the number of convicts it could absorb in private employment: first 1,500 a year, then 2,000. The actual arrivals were 1,434 men and women in 1848, 1,847 in 1849 and a leap to 3,406 in 1850. "I have succeeded in getting back the assignment system in a modified form," he boasted. Grey, however, did not wish to hear about assignment; and the Abolitionists did not want to have it, modified or no. The League's work played a large part—larger than it is usually credited with—in killing transportation to Van Diemen's Land. But what finished it off was Lord Grey's retirement from the Colonial Office, and the discovery of gold in Australia.

# 16

# The Aristocracy Be We

**A**MONG THE FORTUNE-HUNTING optimists who set sail from Sydney across the Pacific to San Francisco when the news of the California gold rush reached New South Wales at the end of 1848 was a corpulent bull-calf of a man named Edward Hammond Hargraves. He was thirty-one when he reached California, and with a fellow "Sydney Duck" he trudged, scrambled and panned for two years, not finding so much as an ounce of gold. English by birth, he had lived in Australia and knew the terrain west of the Blue Mountains, near Bathurst. Gradually, the conviction seized him that the Wellington district of New South Wales, 170 miles west of Sydney and about 50 miles from Bathurst, with its tawny hills, quartz outcrops and gullies, was very like the gold regions of California. At the end of 1850, having bottomed out like so many thousands of other Forty-Niners, Hargraves spent his last dollars on a passage back to Sydney. But he took his pan and rocking-cradle with him, and on February 12, 1851, he and his guide, John Lister, rode down Lewes Pond Creek, a tributary of the Macquarie River near Guyong outside Bathurst.

As the horses picked their way along, Hargraves felt—as he put it later—"surrounded by gold." He got down into the creek-bed with his pick and trowel, and scratched some gravel and earth from a dike of schist that ran athwart the gully. Four pans out of five produced gold. Hargraves was overcome. "This," he exclaimed to Lister, "is a memorable day in the history of New South Wales. I shall be a baronet, you will be knighted, and my old horse will be stuffed, put in a glass case, and sent to the British Museum!"[1]

None of these happened, but something of infinitely greater consequence did. Australia was convulsed with gold fever. In April 1851, Hargraves bestowed on his district the biblical name of Ophir, and in May the newspapers announced it to be "one vast gold-field." By May 24, a thousand diggers were tunnelling, cursing and exulting on the banks of Summerhill Creek, and the road over the Blue Mountains was choked with a footsore, sluggishly winding column of men: clerks and grooms, grocers' assistants and sailors, lawyers and army deserters, oyster-sellers and magistrates, government officials and ex-convict shepherds, trudging beneath the weight of tents, blankets, crowbars, picks, shovels, pans and billycans hastily bought at gougers' prices, stumbling toward unheard-of wealth in mud-balled boots under the driving rains of the Australian autumn. It was as though a plug had been pulled and the male population of New South Wales had emptied like a cistern, in a rush toward the diggings. Business, the Bathurst and Sydney newspapers reported, was "utterly paralysed. . . . A complete mental madness appears to have seized almost every member of the community."[2]

By June the Ophir district was an impacted mass of clay-colored men, shoulder to shoulder, hacking in delirium at the fickle earth. Prospectors that month moved northeast to the banks of the Turon River and struck gold there, even more of it. An aboriginal stockman, who was not prospecting but idly chipping with his tomahawk at an outcrop fifty miles from Bathurst, found a mass of quartz that yielded 1,272 ounces of gold, the largest reef nugget in recorded history, bigger than anything found by the Forty-Niners in California. "Men . . . stare stupidly at each other, talk incoherent nonsense, and wonder what will happen next. . . . [A] hundred-weight of sugar or potatoes is an every-day fact, but a hundred-weight of gold is . . . beyond the range of our recorded ideas—a sort of physical incomprehensibility." The Aborigine was not allowed to keep the gold but his employer, a Dr. Kerr, on whose land it was found, gave him and his brother some sheep, two horses, provisions and a few acres as a consolation prize.[3]

As the gold fever spread, prospectors realized that, geologically speaking, the newly constituted state of Victoria was simply an extension of New South Wales. In July, gold was found at Clunes, a hundred miles from Melbourne; and in September 1851, a septuagenarian digger named John Dunlop discovered the richest field of all, at Ballarat, a mere 75 miles west of the Melbourne Post Office. The word ran back to Melbourne that gold was everywhere. It lay scattered on the rocks and between the wiry tussocks, glistening as it had done for unregarded thousands of years; now the deepest obsessions of a frontier society would clamp themselves to it, and it would transform that society beyond recognition.

The gold belonged to the government, which demanded an exorbitant license fee of 30 shillings a month from the Victorian diggers. Nevertheless, by November 1851 more than 6,500 Victorian licenses had been issued and a cataract of gold was pouring from Ballarat as well as the Turon diggings, into the stout canvas bags, down to the holds of the waiting ships. The first gold shipment to London, on the *Thomas Ar-*

*buthnot*, was a mere 253 ounces. By the middle of 1852, there were perhaps 50,000 people on the diggings and the average weekly shipment on the gold-escorts from Ballarat and Bendigo was more than 20,000 ounces—half a ton a week. *The Times* declared, in November 1852, that the flood of Australian gold had become "perfectly bewildering"; by then, a single ship (the *Dido*) was expected with 280,000 ounces, or ten and a half tons, on board. All this was from the Victorian diggings, which in the month of August 1852 alone, despite nearly continuous winter rain and bitterly difficult working conditions for the diggers, had yielded 246,000 ounces of the "yellow stuff."[4]

By then, Melbourne was both a ghost-port and a continuous saturnalia. Port Phillip Bay had become a Sargasso Sea of dead ships, rocking empty at anchor through a hundred tides and then a hundred more, bilges unpumped, their masts a bare forest. When a vessel arrived with her gold-hungry passengers and her hold crammed with mining tools and cheap furniture, the crews (and often the captains too) would desert as soon as she was unloaded, joining the thick human stream for Ballarat and Bendigo. Employers, stranded without labor, locked their offices and went on the road. "Cottages are deserted," reported the lieutenant-governor of Victoria, Charles La Trobe, In October 1851,

> houses to let, business is at a stand-still, and even schools are closed. In some of the suburbs not a man is left, and the women are known for self-protection to forget neighbours' jars [quarrels] and to group together to keep house. . . . Fortunate the family, whatever its position, which retains its servants at any sacrifice, and can further secure supplies for their households from the few tradesmen that remain . . . all buildings and contract works, public and private, almost without exception, are at a stand-still. No contract can be insisted upon under the circumstances.[5]

Shanty towns and bark huts proliferated to house the thousands of emigrants, frantic with hope, who poured off the ships from England and Ireland.

In the grog-shops and hotels that lined the filthy, traffic-jammed streets of the young city, where a man could sink up to his knees in mud and ordure merely by stepping off the curb, a round-the-clock orgy was conducted by "the worst-looking population eyes ever beheld"—the diggers and their hangers-on, their mates and their flushed doxies, drinking the gold away. One man, who had never tasted champagne before, bought a hotel's entire stock of it and emptied every bottle into a horse trough, inviting all and sundry to suck it up. Miners lurched up and down the luxury shops, jamming huge tawdry rings on their girls' fingers, demanding the most expensive dresses, lighting their pipes with £5 notes and pouring gold dust into the cupped hands of hackney-drivers. "They are intoxicated with their suddenly-acquired wealth, and run riot in the wildness of their joy," noted an English gold-seeker, John Sherer. They were "just like so many unbroken horses caught in a desert where they never knew anything but hunger, and suddenly thrown into a rich paddock where they find nothing but plenty."[6] They treated their women like crude pashas, even the ones who seemed to have few prospects, like "Biddy Carroll," fresh from Ireland: "Exceedingly stupid, lazy, and dirty, poor Biddy could make no friends," and resembled "an unripe potato just dug from the soil with its jacket flying." But soon she found her digger, and soon after that an acquaintance noticed in the saloon of a steamer

> the simple, stupid, potato-like face of Biddy Carroll . . . the very perfection of a lucky, thoughtless, gold-digger's bride. Her bonnet was of white satin, with a profusion of the most exquisite flowers, the whole enveloped in the folds of a rich white veil. She wore a superb lavender-coloured flowered satin dress, with a gorgeous barège shawl . . . a massive gold brooch . . . a massive gold chain, and her wrists encircled with handsome silver bracelets.[7]

The Biddies were not just amusing objects of condescension. In their gaudy store-bought finery, they were signs of class rupture. Gold disturbed the order of Anglo-Australian society—from pastoral "aristocrat" down to convict—with shudders of democracy. Gold wealth was not "democratic," but it did expand the existing oligarchy. It would diversify both Australian markets and Australian production and help create the Australian bourgeoisie. The clay-stained digger, a butcher in his former life, who still carried the grease-stink of tallow in his hair and the argot of the diggings on his tongue, would soon have his Axminster-carpeted drawing room in Toorak. The cash his gold set in circulation would construct suburbia. His spending habits would raise more merchants to comfort. Fortunes were made by diggers—and extracted from them. Gold did respect class. It slightly favored the low: A horny-handed navvy, miner or seaman with muscles hardened by years of manual work could sink a shaft twenty feet to the blue auriferous strata of Bendigo in the time that it took a refined "new chum," his hands pulpy and blistered, to scratch away three feet of earth. "Everything had assumed a revolutionary character," wrote Sherer, adding that

> all the aristocratic feelings and associations of the old country are at once annihilated. Plebeianism of the rankest and . . . the lowest kind at present dwells in Australia; and as riches are now becoming the test of a man's position, it is vain to have any pretensions whatever unless you are sup-

ported by that powerful auxiliary. It is not what you were, but what you are that is the criterion.[8]

"We be the aristocracy now," miners were heard to say as they rollicked in the Melbourne grog-shops, "and the aristocracy now be we."

ii

THERE WAS, however, a specter at this feast of truculent egalitarianism: the Old Hands, or ex-convicts. Victorians took a considerable, indeed an exaggerated pride in the thought that their colony had not—or at least, not primarily—been a convict settlement. In 1835, the pioneering land-grabber John Batman had "bought" some 600,000 acres in the Port Phillip Bay area, including the present site of Melbourne, from three chiefs (confusingly named Jagajaga, Jagajaga and Jagajaga) for some blankets, knives, shirts and mirrors. Pioneers had gone south from the "Middle District" of New South Wales with their bands of assigned men; and nearly 2,000 Exiles had landed at Port Phillip in the 1840s. But until then, Victoria had no institutions for exploiting convict labor; this helped its free population feel more virtuous than the raffish Sydney-siders and tainted Vandemonians. Some settlers—not gold-seekers, but more sober and conscientious men—had gone there partly because it had no "convict taint," expecting security and a low crime rate.

They were not merely dismayed but outraged when gold brought a rush of emancipated convicts from Van Diemen's Land. Thousands of criminals—for in the eyes of the "respectable," an ex-convict was a felon still—were flooding into Melbourne and fanning out all over Victoria. Nobody knew exactly how many there were, because they were all free and did not have to present passes when moving from one colony of Australia to another. The pessimistic guess was that one digger in ten had been a government man. Soon, every unsolved crime in Victoria (and not a few in New South Wales) was automatically blamed on the "Van-demonians," or simply the "Demons," as these undesirables from Van Diemen's Land were called. And in fact, an unusually high number of offenders convicted for crimes in Victoria between 1851 and 1853 turned out to be ex-convicts who had crossed Bass Strait.

For most of the Vandemonians, the gold rush was their last desperate gamble. The economy of Van Diemen's Land was so primitive compared to that of the mainland, and the chances of getting enough land to compete against the established pastoral families so remote, that any man with blood in him would rather try for gold across the Strait. The depression was past but the labor market for ex-convicts stayed badly shrunk.

On the goldfields, expirees might get rich, and even when poor they carried a certain glamor in the eyes of impressionable "new chums":

> The new chum sits on the logs about the fire listening to the tales of crime and adventure of some "old hand" or convict. Some of these men have now great quantities of Gold and now that they are independent, boast of their former bad deeds. The greater the criminal the more he is respected.[9]

The Victorian authorities sided with the Anti-Transportation League of Van Diemen's Land. In February 1851, the mayor of Melbourne had congratulated two of its prime movers, the historian and Congregational minister John West and the pastoralist William Weston—who had come there to form a "League of Solemn Engagement" of the Australian colonies never to accept convict labor again—on their "patriotic exertions." Victoria, too, the Mayor declaimed, was making "efforts to avert the attempt made by our fair Province with the outpourings of British crime," and

> the proximity of our colony to yours gives us a vital interest in assisting you to stem the tide of convictism now flowing in upon Van Diemen's Land. Rest assured that the colonists of Victoria will go with you heart and hand.[10]

Naturally, when Victoria became a separate colony a few months later, anti-convict sentiments rose higher still. In February 1852, the mayor, aldermen and citizens of Melbourne wrote a petition to Queen Victoria, protesting against transportation of "Criminals of the deepest dye" to Van Diemen's Land, whence, after "a brief period of probation," they crossed to the colony which bore her own name, contaminating and degrading it:

> The unlimited influx of manumitted convicts from Van Diemen's Land is an intolerable grievance calculated rapidly to alienate the affections of Your Majesty's dutiful subjects. . . . [W]e should be guilty of deceit if we withheld from Your Majesty the fact that there is a large and increasing population growing up to maturity amongst us who have no such feelings [of loyalty] towards the Parent State; who feel deeply the disgrace of belonging to a colony which is regarded by other nations as a portion of Britain's great emunctory of crime.[11]

There was silence from Balmoral and a perfunctory reply from Downing Street. But the tone of the mayor's address was not feigned. The grievance ran deep, and it soon produced an obnoxious law, passed with bellows of popular acclaim by the newly formed Legislative Council of Victoria in September 1852: the ' Convicts Prevention Act." It was framed, as La Trobe remarked in forwarding it to London, with "zeal and haste," and it ignored "many salient principles of constitutional liberty"; but it was so popular, the crime rate was so high and the expenses of the police so ruinous that he had signed it anyway.

Anyone coming to Victoria from Van Diemen's Land now had to prove he was unconditionally free. The penalty for not doing so was three years' hard labor in irons. The particular injustice of the act was that it discriminated against holders of conditional pardons, convicts who by law were allowed to go anywhere within the Australian colonies, so long as they did not go back to England. It condemned them to stagnate in the economic backwater of Van Diemen's Land. In the wide powers of arrest and search it granted the Victorian police, it resembled the hated Bush-ranging Act of thirty years before. But in the atmosphere of Melbourne in 1852, it bordered on political suicide to speak for the "rights" of ex-convicts. The fear of a real rupture between the colonists and the Crown made La Trobe think it "highly desirable . . . to show every disposition to co-operate heartily with the Colonists . . . under the extraordinary cir-cumstances of the times."

Not all interests in Australia agreed—especially not the graziers, who had been hardest hit by the flight of labor to the goldfields. The gold rush, even in winter, was draining pastoral labor; by spring, the shortage would be catastrophic. The only thing that could save these northeastern es-tates from the drain of labor into the "middle districts" of New South Wales was a prompt infusion of felons, who would not be able to quit their assigned posts to hunt gold. "At no previous crisis in the history of this Colony was a large and continuous supply of such a class so much required, or so likely to be productive."[12]

The lack of cheap labor for the sheep- and cattle-runs of Queensland had been apparent even before the gold rush. In January 1850, a son of one pastoral clan, the Leslies, reported to his father that they had held public meetings to ask the secretary of state for convicts, as "we must have more labor than Emigration will supply. . . . The Emigrants we get are the sweepings of the parish workhouses, not a bit more moral than the Exiles, and much lazier & independant; we ask for half & half Exiles & Emigrants, and if we do not get them we will send for Chinese."[13]

The issue split the Queenslanders, as it did the rest of white Aus-tralia: on one side, the squatters and pastoralists, wanting convicts; on the other, the free country workers, the clergy, the shopkeepers and almost everyone else from the town of Brisbane, agitating against the Stain and the Taint. But at the national level, the pastoralists were out-numbered. Although they could discount "unwashed" hands raised in their own woolsheds, they could not pretend that, in real political life, those hands were invisible.

Everywhere else in Australia, with one exception, it was the same. Victoria was dead set against the Stain, and so was South Australia, which in December 1851 had sent its own petition to Lord Grey reminding him that the appearance of ex-convicts from Van Diemen's Land within its boundaries was ruining the morals of its people.

The exception, of course, was Van Diemen's Land itself. It had had no gold rush. It had not benefitted from immigration; few people wanted to start a new life in the colonial source of the Stain. Too many of the young, the hard-handed, the energetic and the ambitious had been sucked out of it by the gold rush. Van Diemen's Land was an economic cripple; there, it was convictry or beggary, a point made over and over again by the pastoralists. The Anti-Transportation League could afford the luxuries of moral indignation and preach as it pleased—but the fact remained that every convict who arrived in Van Diemen's Land was eagerly snapped up by the graziers. There was no waiting-list for convict servants in Hobart before mid-1851, but when 292 prisoners arrived on the *Fairlie* in mid-1852 there were 1,259 applications for their services.[14]

Social prejudices remained, a "phalanx of antipathy," as one Hobart paper called it in 1851, among landed gentry against convicts and Emancipists. Most employers would take a free worker over a convict one any time, given the choice. But they did not have the choice, because the free workers had gone to the diggings. Thus the oligarchs of land—such families as the O'Connors and Lords, the Bisdees and Talbots, the Headlams and Bayleys, who between them disposed of more than a quarter-million acres of the green sullen island—stolidly dispatched their petitions to London; one of these respectful memorials in defense of the plantation society was signed by 459 graziers and merchants.

The Australasian Anti-Transportation League did not doubt the justice of its mission. Its letterhead was a flag with the Southern Cross and the extravagantly righteous motto *In hoc signo vinces*. These had been the words spoken in a dream to Constantine the Great, "In this sign you will conquer"; and under the aegis of the Cross, he had gone on to defeat the pagan armies of Maxentius at the Mulvian Bridge in 312 A.D. Likewise, the Leaguers intended to defeat what passed for Rome in Australia, the Colonial Office. The League's rhetoric, its tub-thumping about defilement and the Stain, went down like cream in the other colonies—except among the descendants of Emancipists, who resignedly kept their peace when the adjectives rained on their fathers and grandfathers from the platforms of abolition. But the Vandemonians choked on it. Too many of them—perhaps four people out of five by 1850—were related to convicts on one or both sides of their lineage, and although this was a social embarrassment to be passed over, if possible, in silence, they did not want to listen to harangues on the extent of their own pollution. As a result, the League was obliged to pack the empty seats at its dinners in Hobart and Launceston with free tickets; Vandemonians did not want to pay good money to hear their parents insulted.[15]

The battle between the League and the government of Van Diemen's Land, over the issue of the unfair Convict's Prevention Act that had been sponsored by the League's branch in Victoria, inflamed a real class struggle in Hobart. Its theater was the campaign for the Van Diemen's Land Legislature elections, due in January 1853, whose chief issues were the shift of responsibility to local, municipal government (which Denison favored) and the ending of transportation (which he opposed). The 1851 elections had been won by men sympathetic, in the main, to abolition— friends of the Australasian League. Could the Leaguers in Van Diemen's Land repeat their victory?[16]

One could not be sure. The Victorian Convicts' Prevention Act had put them in an awkward bind. Many of them did not want to offend the Crown with a law that, in effect, denied the validity of conditional Royal pardons for convicts. It seemed, and was, a tyrannous statute, unfair to other Tasmanians. Sir William Denison's government saw its perfect opportunity to reverse anti-transportation propaganda by depicting the Leaguers, through the government-aligned press, as reactionaries who wanted to keep conditionally pardoned convicts in permanent subjection, as oligarchs ("former merciless white slave drivers, and now new-fangled Leaguers") in liberals' clothing.[17] As the spring of 1852 gave way to the early Tasmanian summer, long-suppressed political emotions in Hobart boiled over in a way that recalled the bitter disputes of Emancipists and Exclusives in Sydney forty years before, in the time of Macquarie. All the euphemisms in which local political discourse had veiled the convict system and its class divisions were dropped, as Denison's supporters found an alliance with the ex-convict interest against the League. Insults and propaganda flew. During the campaign, readers of government-sympathizing newspapers like the *Guardian* were switched to a diet of pro-Emancipist sentiments and even treated to surveys of Australian history in which the convicts emerged as the sole heroes. At meetings, speakers for the League were howled down by what one of the Leaguers' journals, the *Times*, called "The Slumocracy," which "the patronage of Sir William Denison raised . . . into vigor." The Leaguers accused their lieutenant-governor of fomenting "a war of classes" and called his administration—in a bizarre foretaste of later political rhetoric —"the Red Republican Government of Van Diemen's Land."[18] But when the votes were counted in January 1853, the tallies showed a heavy majority for Denison and the lower-class ex-convicts whose feelings he had adroitly manipulated.

Nevertheless, the British Government did listen to the League, to critics at home and to the wealthier mainland colonies. It rebuked Denison for his "partiality" when he reported the election as a proof of his popularity. In England, the pressure to transport was slackening and, for the first time in living memory, there were actually vacant cells in government prisons at home. The government had built more jails in 1851, for instance, the grim commodious prison of Dartmoor opened, and a new jail had been built at Portsmouth to replace the crowded hulks. By 1852, there was prison space for 16,000 convicts in England.

Prison was cheaper than transportation by now, at least for short sentences. It cost £100 to keep a man in Van Diemen's Land for the run of his sentence, but prison in England cost the government £15 per man per year. Since only a small minority of British prisoners drew sentences of more than a year in home prisons (only 5,000, in all, between 1842 and 1850, as against 30,000 men and women transported for 7 to 10 years to Van Diemen's Land in the same period), it was now feasible to reduce transportation by stepping up the length of sentences in English prisons. The penitentiary, for which Jeremy Bentham had beaten the philosophical drum so long and tiringly fifty years before, was clearly destined to replace Botany Bay.[19]

In April 1850, Lord Grey rose in the House to make one of the last defenses of transportation. He still planned to send his Exiles out when and as they were needed. In fact, to assuage the northeastern graziers, he had dispatched two ships direct to Moreton Bay, *Mount Stewart Elphinstone* in May 1849 and *Bangalore* in January 1850; and as long as the Legislative Council of New South Wales was controlled by grazing interests, he wanted to keep alive the option of sending felons there. Convicts had created the economic base that made free emigrants want to go to Australia—and 31,000 such emigrants had gone there in the last year. Grey conceded that "confinement and penal labour ... ought to be chiefly inflicted at home," and that "free colonies have a right to expect that convicts should not be sent to them without their own consent." But he was not going to abandon transportation on principle—especially not to Van Diemen's Land. The island had been founded as a penal colony; it had never had any other purpose. England had spent "millions" equipping it as a jail, and

> the free population which has established itself there for the sake of the pecuniary advantages of that expenditure, has no right whatever to expect that the policy of this country should be altered when they think proper

to demand it, and that we should be compelled again to incur the heavy expense of preparing some new settlement. . . . I conceive that authority ought to be firmly maintained and asserted, and that Van Diemen's Land should continue to be used for the reception of convicts.[20]

Whatever the justice of Grey's position—and justice it had, for all its lack of appeal to colonial feelings—his hopes (and the graziers') were overridden by the gold discoveries of 1851. Gold was the mineral that put an end to transportation, because its discovery plucked off the last rags of terror that clung to the name of Australia. With a quarter of Britain, from navvies to viscounts, clamoring for tickets to the southern goldfields, who was to think that a trip to El Dorado at government expense constituted a fearful punishment—especially if, as rumor had it, convicts got a conditional pardon as soon as they stepped ashore at Hobart? As Governor-General Fitzroy remarked, "few English criminals . . . would not regard a free passage to the gold-fields via Hobart town as a great boon."[21]

There were still people who thought of convict labor as an economic panacea. But they were mostly cranks.[22] The English press, led by the *Times*, was by now solidly against transportation. Grey had few allies in either house of Parliament, except for some of the more reactionary Law Lords; and in any case, his government lost office in 1852. His Tory successor as secretary of state for the colonies was Sir John Pakington, who acted without delay. In mid-December 1852, Pakington wrote to Lieutenant-Governor Denison in Van Diemen's Land. He pronounced himself "not unaware" of the continuing arguments for transportation. Part of the rage to abolish it "may . . . be ascribed to the prevalence . . . of one deplorable crime, in consequence of the temporary overcrowding of the convicts"—to wit, sodomy. But better arrangements had checked that; and certainly "the readiness and almost indeed the avidity" with which settlers snatched convict labor from each arriving ship proved that the demand for them was real. However, the pro-transportationists had not formed an effective lobby, and "whatever may be the private opinions of individuals who have not come forward on this question, numerous public meetings and all the legislative authorities in these colonies have declared themselves strongly against transportation." He would not provoke Australians to "a furious opposition" that would end with hatred of the Crown. Finally there was the gold, whose very existence made it "a solecism to convey offenders, at the public expense, with the intention of at no distant time setting them free, to the immediate vicinity of those very gold fields which thousands of honest labourers are in vain striving to reach."[23]

With this, transportation to Van Diemen's Land came to an end. The last convict transport, the 630-ton ship *St. Vincent*, had sailed for Hobart on November 27, 1852. Van Diemen's Land officially ceased to be a penal colony thirteen months later; and with a collective whistle of relief, its citizens proceeded (as they hoped) to get rid of the "demonic" image of their island once and for all, by giving it the name of its Dutch discoverer: Tasmania, for the navigator Abel Tasman.

The formal end of transportation to Van Diemen's Land came with the Jubilee of the colony—August 10, 1853, the fiftieth anniversary of the day the first settlement was pitched at Risdon Cove. It provoked a flutter of doggerel in the press. "Hurra for the noble Leaguers!" the *Hobart Town Daily Courier* exclaimed,

> Hurra for our British Queen!
> Hurra for the tread of Freemen
> Where Bondsmen erst have been!
>
> Peal on, ye shrill-voiced heralds!
> Your thrilling music tells
> Tasmania's happy future;
> Peal on, ye English bells!
>
> From city hall to cottage,
> O'er all our island homes,
> Ring round your benediction!
> The Unstained Future comes!

Not to be outdone, an editor in Launceston composed a pastiche to the tune of "God Save the Queen." Thousands of copies were printed on a press which, mounted on a bunting-lined cart, was drawn in procession through the town:

> Sing! for the hour is come!
> Sing! for our happy home,
>     Our land is free!
> Broken Tasmania's chain,
> Wash'd out that hated stain,
> Ended the strife and pain!
>     Blest Jubilee!

The cart, symbol of the power of the colonial press in its struggles for Abolition against foot-dragging officialdom, was preceded by groups separated by bannermen: members of the Legislative Council, the mayor and the corporation, a phalanx of native-born colonists marching four abreast, public societies with their regalia, and "the hope and staff of the colony," its children. They marched under a triumphal arch of pasteboard, decked with fronds of native wattle, to the sprightly tooting and flourishing of a brass band. There was feasting at Ross; and in the town of Oatlands whole sheep were roasted, while the colonial boys played cricket, climbed poles and fell to the breathless pursuit of a greased pig. It darted frantically among the spectators, smearing their moleskins until someone collared it. One "facetious bystander" extolled the animal as a symbol of the fight for Abolitionists' rights: "That pig, greasy, long-winded and cunning though he was, was caught at last by patience and perseverance."[24]

There were only a few sour notes. The next day, the *Hobart Town Daily Courier* reported the "ill-advised and unwarranted setting up of *an effigy* in the back of Messrs. Marsh and Chapman's timber-yard." It was removed before it could be burned. The paper did not say whose effigy it was, but everyone knew it was Denison's. He had offended the colonists, when they asked him to convey their satisfaction with the new policy to the people of England, by replying: "The people of England do not care for you one straw; the Houses of Parliament look upon you as the fly on the wheel." At this, the press branded him "a coarse-minded, vindictive, ungenerous man," but Denison had read worse. Abolition was rung in with triple bob-majors on the church bells, not saluted from Battery Point by army cannon. Perhaps the lack of unanimity was appropriate; on the other side of Australia, transportation had begun all over again.[25]

### iii

THE LAST PLACE to receive English convicts was Western Australia, the western third of the continent where few had been and fewer, apparently, wanted to go: a colony with a body the size of Europe and the brain of an infant. Except for some coastal patches, it was all desert, pebbles, saltbush and spinifex—the right spot, in the Australian phrase, "to do a perish."

Its first settlement nearly did just that. In 1826, Governor Darling sent a detachment of soldiers and fifty convicts to occupy King George's Sound, the present site of Albany on the southwestern tip of the continent. In establishing a military base there, he hoped he would deter the white desperadoes—escaped convicts and Yankee whaling riffraff with their black slave-harems—who had set up their half-wild tribal communities all along the southern coast from Bass Strait to Kangaroo Island and westward to King George's Sound.

The settlement lasted five years, every day of them an ordeal. Officers went half-mad with loneliness and boredom. As for the convicts, the most that can be said is that, with hostile blacks and saltbush desert right behind them and the cobalt grin of a shark-infested ocean in front, none of them tried to escape. Eventually, Darling conceded that no free settler would ever want to go to the Sound, and that the military base was too frail to do much against the sealers. In 1831 he had the garrison and its surviving convicts withdrawn.

By then, another plan for Western Australian settlement had formed. It centered on the Swan River, and its mover was a gallant young post-captain in the navy, James Stirling (1791–1865), who had married into a family influential both in Westminster and in the East India Company. In 1826 Stirling was given a ship and told to remove the survivors of a dispirited garrison experimentally put on Melville Island, and the Timor Sea near the present site of Darwin. This northern outpost had been meant to discourage the French from landing, but they had never even tried to, perhaps because it was so far off the shipping routes. It had lasted two years and was now on its last legs, rotting from heat, dysentery and terror of the blacks. To avoid the monsoon season, Stirling took the long route around the 4,300-mile coast of Western Australia, imagining as he went a settlement that would keep the French off and be a staging-port for British ships. The mouth of the Swan looked promising, and in March 1827 he spent a delighted two weeks there. Then, picking up the Melville Island garrison, he proceeded to Sydney, composing on the way the first of a stream of memos to Governor Darling and the authorities in England. He urged a settlement at Swan River (Hesperia, he wanted to call it, since it faced the westering sun). He himself would be its lieutenant-governor.[26]

Not until 1828, with a change of government in London, did Stirling make much headway. Family influence played a major part. Both the new head of the Colonial Office, Sir George Murray, and his assistant, Horace Twiss, were friends of Stirling's father-in-law. Stirling proposed to them that a syndicate of private capitalists should raise the money to establish settlers at Swan River. The government liked the sound of this —a Crown colony developed by private funds, as Pennsylvania had been by William Penn and Georgia by Colonel Oglethorpe.

Enter, at this point, a young English landowner, the second son of a cotton-manufacturer, something of a wastrel but marked with gentility and imbued with the desire to cut a great figure on the colonial stage: Thomas Peel (1793–1865). An hour's conversation with Captain Stirling had convinced him that the Swan River held his future, and he appeared before the government with a hastily convened syndicate of investors, who offered to transfer ten thousand settlers with all their stock and gear to Western Australia in return for a Crown grant of four million acres. The government counter-offered one million. At this dampening stingi-ness the syndicate evaporated, and Peel, who had much less money than

Stirling thought, had to find a new backer. He did, but not one he wanted to acknowledge publicly: an ex-convict named Solomon Levey (1794–1833) who, transported in 1814 for stealing a chest of tea, had risen in Sydney as a merchant, banker, landowner and, eventually, philanthropist. The firm of Cooper and Levey, founded in 1826, was one of the biggest trading concerns in the South Pacific. Levey was an astute, generous man, but not—as it turned out—quite astute enough. He had always craved the respectability, the sense of access that had been twice denied him as an ex-convict and as a Jew. The chance to underwrite an ambitious imperial scheme with an aristocratic *goy*, a relative of the great Sir Robert Peel, dazzled him. Thomas Peel, for his part, insisted on keeping Levey's partnership secret, so that the Swan River scheme would not be tainted by Jewishness and felonry. The company they formed was called Thomas Peel & Co.[27]

The Colonial Office agreed to give this company 250,000 acres on the Swan, and 250,000 more after it landed 400 settlers, who would receive grants of 200 and 100 acres each. These settlers had to arrive by November 1, 1829. After twenty-one years—by mid-century—Thomas Peel & Co. was to get another 500,000 acres. Captain James Stirling, master of many ships and darling of the Colonial Office, would be lieutenant-governor of the new colony, with 100,000 acres of his choice. Peel would go with him to manage the company's affairs.

In May 1829, the frigate *Challenger* sailed into the Swan River estuary, and its master, Captain Charles Fremantle, took formal possession of one million square miles of territory,* naming it Western Australia—the first time the word *Australia* had been officially used. (Curiously enough, he was told to ask the Aborigines if they consented to this; but neither Fremantle nor anyone else on board spoke their language, and one could hardly convey so heroic a territorial concept to savages by pointing and waving.) Meanwhile, in England, the first Swan River colonists, all free men and women with promises of Arcadia dancing in their heads, were signed up, assembled and embarked on the *Parmelia*. No one had tried to survey the area or to map any part of its coastline, a fact that became embarrassingly evident at the end of the long voyage when Captain Stirling, catching sight of the mouth of the Swan River and the *Challenger* at anchor, became so anxious to make port that he steered a shortcut between an island and the shore and ran his ship, with all its colonists, onto the rocks. No one was drowned, and a few days later the young lieutenant-governor kedged *Parmelia* off. The Swan River pioneers

---

* Its eastern boundary was the meridian of 129°E.—not that this represented any "natural" boundary, but simply because it was the convenient fossil of the "Pope's Line," fixed in the fifteenth century by the Treaty of Tordesillas, which divided the world into Spanish and Portuguese hemispheres.

had their first taste of Australian life, huddled disconsolately under canvas in the pouring rain surrounded by the emblems of the civilization they were to plant in the wild: cases of flour, trunks full of nankeen and velvet, Georgian furniture, rusting shovels, an upright piano cocked listing in the sand. They slapped at mosquitoes and scratched at sand-fleas while gazing on the barren coast, the prostrate creeping plants and the steaming rocks; their hearts sank. Not being convicts, the ladies could not curse.

But Stirling was indefatigable. He named a port town, Fremantle, at the mouth of the Swan; and then led a party upstream, between embowered banks where the arch-symbols of antipodean inversion that had given the river its name, the black swans, dibbled their red bills in the water. Nine miles from the sea, he chose a spot for the main city, Perth. By December 1829, when Thomas Peel sailed in with ninety more colonists, two shantytowns marked the white man's foothold on the coast. It was typical of Stirling that, as the age of Sail turned to that of Steam, he had separated the capital from the port by a stretch of river navigable only by rowboats.

The fertility of the land proved, as so often it had done to Australian pioneers before, a mirage. Either the soil was barren, or it was so thick with trees that the work of clearing and stumping defeated all but the most iron-willed settlers. Not until 1835 did the Swan River colony grow enough wheat to feed itself. Stirling was constantly sending to the Cape for emergency supplies, but the British Government did not want to spend money underwriting what had been presented to it as a legitimate commercial speculation. Hence, the settlers lived on the edge of famine most of the time. Stirling won their gratitude, if little else, by sailing to England in 1832 to beg assistance; the Colonial Office sent Stirling back to Western Australia with a flea in his ear for leaving his post without permission.

As lieutenant-governor, Stirling had to spend every grain of his charm and authority to keep the anxieties of his "genteel colonists" at bay, so that their morale would not cave in. He never let them forget their Englishness. They dined at the vice-regal tent in formal dress, decorations optional; he presided over balls, picnics and hunts. Not without difficulty, he got Anglican chaplains to make the immense voyage to Western Australia so that their rites and sermons could furnish the little colony with its necessary social glue and spiritual comfort.

Yet such efforts were mainly cosmetic. Nothing could abolish the miseries of the land or the frictions of the harassed little community, promised Arcadia but given sand. One settler noted that the doctors were kept busy with "casualties and accidents, arising from grog drinking, and guns and gunpowder in the hands of persons not accustomed to their use till they came here." Thomas Peel, their financial promoter, disintegrated almost as soon as he arrived. His chosen acreage south of Fremantle, poor land to begin with, was swept by a bushfire; in May 1830, the *Rockingham*, carrying settlers for his land, was wrecked on the same rocks that had nearly destroyed *Parmelia*. In a paroxysm of rage, he challenged her captain to a duel and got shot in the right hand. He seemed so choleric and crazy that no one would work for him. Supplies he promised never arrived. Promissory notes on Cooper & Levey, in which many workers had been paid, were dishonored by Daniel Cooper in Sydney (without, it should be mentioned, the knowledge of Solomon Levey in London). Settlers sued Peel for their wages; he countersued for their passage money. He sent no reports to Levey and did not set aside the 125,000 acres meant to recompense his unacknowledged partner for the £20,000 he had sunk in the Swan River scheme. In 1832, Levey had to ask the Colonial Office what on earth was happening at Swan River— and the Office was loath to tell him, for it had no record of Levey's financial involvement. Peel had not revealed that his one solid backer was an Emancipist Jew.

Levey died the next year, 1833, his spirits broken by this utter fiasco. Peel lived on in Western Australia for another thirty years, slipping into poverty, juggling his land-grants, selling a few acres here and there to keep going—not that there were many takers. In his old age, he could sometimes be glimpsed riding alone through his vast acreage of worthless bush, wearing a frayed pink coat like the hunting squire he had tried, and failed, to become.

In 1832 the Swan River colony had slightly under 1,500 white colonists; five years later it had scarcely 500 more. By 1839, when Stirling left, it could support itself after a fashion, but all its wheat and flour still had to be imported from Hobart. Each year, it exported a token few hundred bales of wool to England, nothing else. In December 1850, after two decades of settlement, Western Australia had only 5,886 colonists— two-thirds of whom, according to its governor, Charles Fitzgerald, in a report to Lord Grey, "would quit this colony tomorrow." Sheep that had cost £4 to £5 a head were going begging at half a crown. The price of their wool had plummeted to 9d. or even 6d. a pound, leaving the grazier no margin at all. All was "depression, stagnation, and, I may say, despair."[28] One last possible fount of manpower remained to save them: convicts.

In 1846 some West Australians petitioned Whitehall "to make and declare their Colony a Penal Settlement Upon an Extensive Scale."[29] Grey was delighted. Here, at least, was one colony wise enough to realize that Britain's long enterprise of social excretion could do good, manuring the antipodean sand. If Western Australia clamored for felons, Grey reasoned, the Anti-Transportation League would look weaker. At least it could not claim a complete moral monopoly among the white settlers of Australia.

And so, just as transportation was drawing to a close in the east of Australia, it began in the west. The first convict ship to Western Australia, the *Scindian*, with 75 felons, 54 guards and the usual officials on board, appeared off Fremantle in June 1850. In January 1868, the thirty-seventh and last convict ship, the *Hougoumont*, disgorged 279 prisoners there—including a number of Irish Fenians, most prominent of whom was the writer and editor John Boyle O'Reilly, soon to make a spectacular escape on a ship chartered by fellow Irishmen in America. In those eighteen years, 9,668 convicts, all men and most of them able-bodied, were sent to Western Australia over the continuous protests of the other Australian colonies. They did not improve the moral tone of the raw West, but they saved its economy. As in the past, slave labor got the wheels turning.

The monument of the System in Western Australia was a long, low, white building overlooking the sea at Fremantle—the convict barracks, known as the "Establishment." It held the prisoners who had to work in chain gangs in and around Fremantle. Other groups of serving convicts, not in chains, were housed in depots at Perth and in the country districts, where they made roads, raised public buildings and in general improved the public face of Western Australia. After doing a specified part of his sentence, each prisoner became eligible for a conditional pardon—4 years for a 7-year sentence, 5 years and 3 months for a 10-year sentence, and so on.[30] He could then do wage-labor for a free settler until his time was up. Before his ticket-of-leave, he could only work for the local government.

The lash, by now only an execrated memory in the older Australian colonies, was part of the discipline here but not its basis. In 1858 the superintendent of convicts avowed that he wanted it reserved for "cases of brutal assault," not even for escape attempts, for "when we consider the utter impossibility of effecting escape in the bush, —the colony being in reality what it is commonly described to be, a vast natural prison, — we ought in awarding punishment to reflect that the unfortunate culprit has already received the most impressive of all kinds of persuasion, viz., actual suffering from starvation."[31]

The colony was greedy; it wanted to get as many "government men" as it could, and extract as much profit from their labor as possible. In February 1858 the comptroller-general's office in Fremantle asked the Colonial Office for a guaranteed one thousand prisoners a year, since "the prosperity of the Colony must mainly depend on the number of convicts sent here." With less success, it asked the British Government to pay for "materials, powder, cartage, plant, &c" in road, dock and bridge building, as well as the prisoners' transportation, food, clothing and tools. Western Australia was so poor, it added piteously, that paying for such things "is wholly out of the question." Popular as government labor was in Western Australia (both the Anglican and the Catholic Bishops of Perth fruitlessly requested convict labor to erect their rival episcopal palaces), the whole idea of its continued influx was regarded with horror and dismay back East. The Stain was powerful stuff; this "moral sewage" could cross deserts, contaminate seas, seep its noxious way thousands of miles east and surface on the newly purged coast of Australia. Where did the Western Australian convicts go when their sentences ran out? To New South Wales, Victoria and South Australia—or so indignant citizens believed. The one issue on which all the participating members could agree at the first Australian Intercolonial Conference, held in Melbourne in 1863, was that transportation to Western Australia had to stop. A British Royal Commission on Penal Discipline chose this heated moment to urge that *all* male convicts sentenced to *any* length of sentence should be sent to Western Australia.[32]

At this, the Victorian Anti-Transportation League, which had atrophied for want of a cause, sat up with a jerk and addressed a solemn plea to the people of Great Britain. "The happy homes of tens of thousands of families who were lately your neighbours," it intoned, were about to be "desolated, by the presence of a convict curse . . . productive of abominations too horrible to be named." If Western Australia could not survive without convicts, let its free settlers go elsewhere. But South Australia, Victoria, New South Wales, Queensland, Tasmania and New Zealand would no longer consent to indirectly serve as "the refuge for Britain's outcasts, the hiding places for her sin and shame." The fact that a convict had to have served his sentence before leaving Western Australia, and hence was no longer a convict but a free man, was immaterial.[33] Nobody knew how many demons and villains really came east—a popular though certainly exaggerated figure was six men in ten—but there was no doubt that it would be easily done by ship. Certainly no one ever heard of an ex-prisoner doing it on foot. And if (as one of the Macarthurs suggested in a letter to the London *Daily News*) only six hundred felons a year got into the eastern states, that was six thousand in ten years, and each of them capable of corrupting at least a dozen innocent folk.[34] The mere arithmetic was enough to freeze a man's blood.

The facts pointed another way. Only about one ticket-of-leave holder in Western Australia in three was convicted of a second offense; less than one in twenty of these offenses was "serious," and two convictions in five were for drunkenness or attempted escape. Escapes had become more frequent between 1862 and 1867, under the odious and corrupt governorship of J. S. Hampton, the former ally of John Price on Norfolk Island.[35]

But this time the Abolitionists won. Her Majesty's Government was no longer prepared to trade the convenience of draining six hundred felons a year into Western Australia for the grave risk of alienating all the eastern colonies, which had the population, the money, the resources, the trade—everything, in fact, that made a colony worth having. Early in 1865, Lord Palmerston's cabinet announced that transportation would end within three years. And so it did: On January 10, 1868, the last convict ship to Australia landed its cargo of sixty Fenian political prisoners and more common assorted malefactors at Fremantle, eighty years to the month, if not quite the day, since Captain Arthur Phillip brought the First Fleet to its anchorage in Sydney Cove.

The loss of convicts was an economic disaster for Western Australia. For two decades it had had the free labor of some fifteen hundred men, at a cost to England of £100,000 a year; and as a Fremantle editor put it, "we now awake from our normal state of apathetic indifference to find ourselves on the verge of ruin." Virtually all it had to show for those twenty years were some mines that could no longer be worked, since free labor did not want to go down them; a network of roads around Perth that petered out in the bush; some handsome Victorian public buildings, a few bridges and dredged channels, and a half-empty jail barracks at Fremantle. The population of Western Australia in 1871 was 25,447, of whom about 9,000 were convicts or their descendants.

The 1871 Census revealed that in population growth, the colonies that shed the System first (or, like South Australia, had never had it) had zoomed ahead of both Western Australia and Tasmania. In the twenty years since 1851, the white population of New South Wales had gone (in round figures) from 197,000 to 500,000; Victoria, from 77,000 to 730,000, a tenfold increase set off by the gold rush and sustained by land development; South Australia, from 66,500 to 189,000. Queensland's population had quadrupled since 1861, to 122,000 souls. But the last of the convict colonies, Tasmania and Western Australia, would be stuck for decades in their hangover from the malign indulgence of semi-slave labor.

# 17

# The End of the System

THE LONG ANGUISH of the System was over. What had it achieved? It might be gratifying to claim that it had failed altogether; that this not-so-small, not-so-primitive ancestor of the Gulag deterred no one in Britain and reformed no one in Australia; that as a penal system it was quite unproductive, a botched act of sublimation.

Certainly, there were things it did not do. If one accepts the "strategic outlier" argument—that the hidden agenda of convict colonization was to protect England's Far Eastern trade with a refitting port on the coast of New South Wales—then it did fail. No big warships were rigged with the pine and flax that had so interested Captain Cook on Norfolk Island, and Australia's contribution to the balance of military and trading power in Indian waters between 1788 and 1820 was nil. Perhaps the English colony on the eastern coast deterred the French from claiming the continent—or perhaps the French were not as interested in Australia as the English, fearful of Napoleon, assumed? The west and north coasts, facing the Indian Ocean and the Timor Sea, had strategic prospects, but the French did not try to claim them, even though England did not put a garrison into Western Australia until 1826.

Some Frenchmen—though not, as a rule, those who had actually been there—did admire the English penal experiment in Australia. "Eh! qui ne connait pas le consolant spectacle," sang a penally inspired bard named Delille in 1830, in a work entitled "De La Pitié" ("On Pity"),

> Qu'étale de bandits ce vaste réceptacle
> Cette *Botany-Bay*, sentine d'ALBION,
> Ou le vol, la rapine et la sédition
> En foule sont venus, et, purgeant l'Angleterre,
> Dan leur exil lointain vont féconder la terre?
> La, l'indulgent loi, du sujets dangereux

Fait d'habiles colons, des citoyens heureux;
Soucit au repentir, excite l'industrie,
Leur rend la liberté, des moeurs, une patrie.
Je vois de toute part les marais déssechés.
Les déserts embellis, et les bois défrichés.
Imitez cet example: à leur prison stérile
Enlevez ces brigands, rendez leur peine utile.[1]

To foreign eyes, the long experiment on the Fatal Shore generally seemed a success, as philosophy in action: "Imitate this example, take these brigands from their sterile prison, make their punishment useful." It might have been more widely imitated, had there not been such a shortage of undiscovered continents in the early nineteenth century. France would presently pay England the sincere homage of imitation by constructing its own Pacific convict colony, a hellish one, in the New Hebrides.

The proponents of British transportation had hoped that, broadly speaking, it would do four things: sublimate, deter, reform and colonize. First, it would remove the "criminal class"—or a good slice of it—from England, and put it where it could do no further harm to the English polity and the interests of property. It was social amputation. What was the cause of crime? Criminals, who manufactured or, rather, secreted it from their inner nature, as snakes their venom or eels their slime. Get rid of criminals and you would get rid of, or at least greatly reduce, crime in Great Britain. Transportation had to fail in this, because the causes of crime lay further back in the social system: in poverty, inequality, unemployment and want, and in laws that had relentlessly created new categories of "transportable" crime. Transportation did rid England of many real sociopaths, men whose aggression and violence were built into their genetic labyrinth, but they were in a minority—and not a few were usefully absorbed by the System as overseers and floggers.

By the 1830s, the hopes of the English authorities had centered on a second aim. This was deterrence. Transportation would not only get rid of the guilty, but terrify the innocent away from crime. The problem with arguments about deterrence is the lack of figures on uncommitted crimes. One cannot know if the threat of a given punishment really did stop the thief at the windowpane.* The crime rate in early-nineteenth-century England did not drop as a result of transpor-

---

* The only plausible case for capital punishment, among those who believe the State has the right to kill in the interests of social order, is not the ficton that it "deters" people from murder—although it may indeed make some think twice—but that it gets rid of mad-dog sociopaths whose life, if preserved with even the slightest hope of eventual freedom, would be a lethal menace to innocent and ill-protected people. Obviously, few murderers belong in this category.

tation, again because its roots lay too deep for *any* deterrent to reach. But what most complicated the matter was the difficulty of convincing the lower classes of Great Britain that Australia was a terrible place to go.

This had been a problem from the start. A verse entitled "The Convicts' Departure," jocose rather than satirical, written as early as 1790, raised the possibility that Botany Bay might prove a milky land, compared to the withered dug of Mother England—a place where

> . . . every day
> Nature is kindly giving,
> Plenty to have, and nothing to pay,
> This is the land to live in.[2]

Nobody on the early fleets can have believed this, but the notion of a colonial Eden was not readily dispelled by colonial experience, since the whole Pacific was faintly tinged (if not in learned discourse, then in popular fancy) with the sweetness of Otaheite. The idea that one might be better off there than in England—that, in the words of the ballad, it was "Better to range in a foreign land / Than in a prison perish"—persisted after the time of Governor Macquarie, who gave commonsense recognition to the fact that, despite the pretensions of the Exclusives, the stock of Australian life would be, for the foreseeable future, Emancipist and Currency. After Macquarie had gone, the contrast was still confirmed by the miseries of common English life—the growth of slums, the unemployment, the ruin of smallholders. Hence the proletarian idea that Botany Bay might not be so bad survived the policies that were meant to destroy it: the increased severity of the regimes of Brisbane, Darling and Arthur; the brutality of the chain gangs; and the outright ferocity of Macquarie Harbor, Norfolk Island and Moreton Bay.

Some of this may have sprung from the bravado of prisoners sending letters home to England, playing down their sufferings to soothe the anxieties of their wives and children, or merely wishing to seem unbowed by the System. Some, no doubt, was due to wishful thinking among those at home. But by the 1830s, with due allowance made for the harshness that went with assignment, some of it was true. The convict with manual skills, if he had the luck to be assigned to a decent master in the back country, stood a chance of living a better life than he might have done amid the penury of England's rural depression. "The grand secret in the management of convicts," an emigrant's handbook of the early 1830s insisted, "is to treat them with kindness, and at the same time with firmness." Most masters knew this from experience, though their "kindness" rarely had much sugar in it and their "firmness" could be that of petty pharaohs. "It is true," wrote Edward Curr, superintendent of the Van Diemen's Land Company, in 1831,

> that convicts are sent out here as punishment. But it is equally true that it is not in the interests of the master to make his service a punishment, but rather to make the condition of the convict as comfortable as is consistent with economy. *The interest of the master essentially contradicts the object of transportation.*[3]

When he got his ticket-of-leave, the redeemed convict's work was more in demand and his wages higher than in England or Ireland. As we have seen, New South Wales and Van Diemen's Land held no shortage of brutal masters, and a man could be crushed under the penal system like a toad beneath a harrow—but he could also remake his life. Those who went under did not write home; those who prospered sometimes did.

Try as it might, the British Government could not stop the flow of impressions this opened. It gave orders to increase the severity of the penal stations, and under Governor Darling some 20 to 25 percent of all male convicts in New South Wales suffered appalling conditions, either in the chain gangs or in the penal out-stations. The Home and Colonial Offices kept urging their proconsuls in Australia to make the System harsher, more certain in retribution, more machine-like—right up to the moment when transportation to Van Diemen's Land was abolished.

Successive governments, Whig and Tory alike, made no secret of their view that transportation was meant to inflict relentless suffering rather than to reform the criminal. But Britain could not come out and tell the public at large how bad things really were in Norfolk Island or the Blue Mountain chain gangs, for fear of looking sadistic; or how lenient they could become in assignment, lest its System seem weak. The first was left to the reformers, the second became a kind of folk-whisper that sounded louder than the voice of Whitehall in the ears of hedgers or coachmen.

This was not the first time that the low of England had balked at believing the high, but the size of the credibility gap on transportation is perhaps indicated by the fact that Charles Dickens should have contemplated leaping into it on the government's behalf. On July 2, 1840, he wrote to Lord Normanby, the literary Whig home secretary, pointing out that most English criminals now thought of transportation as a passport to opportunity and even wealth, and offering to write "a vivid description of the terrors of Norfolk Island and such-like places, told in a homely narrative with a great appearance of truth and reality and circulated in some very cheap and easy form."[4] One would like to know what Dickens would have made of Maconochie, for the Scottish reformer—brave, compassionate, fixated and priggish—was a very "Dickensian" creature; but he never went. Dickens's polemical reporting on prisons would come two years later, in his journals of a visit to America. In 1851, of course, with the discovery of gold, any lingering terrors eastern Australia might still have held for English laborers were outweighed by the possibility of making a fortune.

The only fully drawn character from penal Australia in Dickens is the returned convict Abel Magwitch in *Great Expectations* (1860); and Magwitch sums up the distaste verging on dread with which some middle-class Englishmen (Dickens included) viewed the transported convict "making good" in exile. As a child, the hero, Pip, has saved Magwitch from the gallows by helping him evade his pursuers in the fens; but Magwitch is betrayed by a "gentleman" crook and disappears to Australia, swallowed by the black hulk, "a wicked Noah's Ark." The plot turns on a mysterious benefaction that transforms Pip, in his young manhood, into a "gentleman." The money is revealed to have come from Magwitch, who has gone back to Australia, made a fortune and, in gratitude, endowed the one human being that ever showed him compassion. Magwitch is a figure edged with terror: coarse, brutalized, possibly a cannibal.* His energy is demonic, his thirst for revenge insatiable. And it turns out that his anonymous, obsessively prompted generosity to Pip is another kind of revenge, a black joke against English and colonial class relations. Pip will be his revenge on the Exclusives, who still spurn him as a risen felon. Do gentlemen make convicts? Then a convict will "make" and "own" a real gentleman, not a colonial facsimile. He will show the truth about gentility: It can be bought. He will hug the knowledge of that for the rest of his life. Under the skin of generosity, there is slavery in reverse. "And then, dear boy, it was a recompense to me, look'ee here, to know in secret that I was making a gentleman," Magwitch tells the horrified Pip:

> The blood horses of them colonists might fling up the dust over me as I was walking; what do I say? I says to myself, "I'm making a better gentleman nor ever *you'll* be!" When one of 'em says to another, "He was a convict, a few year ago, and is an ignorant common fellow now, for all he's lucky," what do I say? I says to myself, "If I ain't a gentleman, nor yet ain't got no learning, I'm the owner of such. All on you owns stock and land; which on you owns a brought-up London gentleman?" This way I kep myself a-going.

* Presumably Dickens read the confession of Pearce, the Irish man-eater of Macquarie Harbor, printed in the appendix to the Molesworth Report in 1838.

He tells Pip the truth about his upbringing to close the circle of revenge. Magwitch's sufferings have put him beyond taking pleasure in another's gratitude:

> Do I tell it, fur you to feel an obligation? Not a bit. I tell it, fur you to know as that there hunted dunghill dog wot you kep life in, got his head so high that he could make a gentleman—and, Pip, you're him!

It occurs to Pip that he is now a convict, too; Magwitch has been "loading wretched me with his gold and silver chains for years." No wonder that "the repugnance with which I shrank from him, could not have been exceeded if he had been some terrible beast."

Thus in the person of Magwitch, Dickens knotted several strands in the English perception of convicts in Australia at the end of transportation. They could succeed, but they could hardly, in the real sense, return. They could expiate their crimes in a technical, legal sense, but what they suffered there warped them into permanent outsiders. And yet they were capable of redemption—as long as they stayed in Australia.

The redemption of sinners came a distant third on the aims of transportation. Yet it may be that more people were reformed in Australia—in the sense that they came out of bondage meaning to work for their living and obey the law, and were not convicted again—than were ever "deterred" from crime in England. This was due to the assignment system. Assignment did give its "objects" a chance. Not evenly, or consistently, or reliably—but often; whereas the more schematized, "ideological" punishment of Lord Stanley's Probation System in the 1840s was a demoralizing fiasco, and all the worse because Her Majesty's Government tried to do it on the cheap.*

For all its flaws (and one cannot imagine a prison system without defects) the assignment system in Australia was by far the most successful form of penal rehabilitation that had ever been tried in English, American or European history. In assessing it one must remember that many of its critics, in dwelling on the cruelties and injustices that took place within it, were doing so not as objective reporters but as proponents of rival ideologies of punishment. From Bentham with his Panopticon to Lord Stanley with his Probation System, every one of them opposed

---

* And its parsimony could be extreme, at every level of the probation system. In Van Diemen's Land, prisoners who had escaped were expected to reimburse the Convict Department for any rewards paid out for their own capture (TSA, CON 67/1 # 2/1377). In May 1848 one finds a fallen merchant in the Saltwater River probation gang, Samuel Sidney Smith, asking for six sheets of paper on which to write a petition for clemency. Request refused, the superintendent gruffly scribbled in the margin: "The man ... is an idle schemer. As the case of any man can be put upon one sheet of paper I have refused to let him have more." Here one sees the bureaucratic mind at full stretch, or rather crimp.

assignment in the name of penal Utopias which, when tried, were worse. The assigned man's work was hard (unless he was lucky enough to get work as a domestic servant or a clerk, as many did). But it was not necessarily harder than the kind of work a settler had to do for himself; and to judge by the surviving letters of assigned men who had been rural workers before, it was not worse than the labor of a farm-hand in Britain, despite the flies, the snakes and the heat. Enemies of the System got used to calling this work, and the condition of those who did it, slavery. But it was not slavery. The assigned man worked within a vigilantly sustained framework of laws and rights. Some of the masters were cruel, others irresponsible, some exploitative and a few openly sadistic. But most were none of those things; they were hard, imperfect men struggling to wrest survival or something more from the stingy Australian earth, and many of them had been transported themselves. Few of them perceived their assigned servants as a seigneur did a serf, and those who wished to were frustrated by the law.

Assignment had been the early form of today's open prison. Instead of herding men together in gangs—in which bad apples automatically dominated—assignment dispersed them throughout the bush and kept them in working contact with the free. It fostered self-reliance, taught them jobs and rewarded them for doing them right. It put them on the frontier and did not leave them to rot. Of course, one can overrate the virtues of assignment. But as a rough-and-ready way of getting convicts back into society as self-sustaining workers, it was better than the soul-crushing, totalitarian machinery of the Philadelphia System applied at Pentonville to "reform" Lord Stanley's probationers and Lord Grey's exiles before they took ship to Australia.

Its results were uneven. For a decade and more after transportation to New South Wales ended, colonial society wanted to believe that the residue of convict evil produced most of its crime. In 1835, at the peak of transportation to New South Wales, its courts had handed down a total of 771 convictions for all indictable offenses committed against property or against any person within the colony—a rate of nearly 1,100 convictions per 100,000 inhabitants. From there, the annual number of convictions fell slowly, but the population, swollen by immigrants, grew rapidly, so that by 1851 the conviction rate was just over 290 per 100,000, and by 1861 it was 122—about a tenth of its level in 1835. The conviction rate for New South Wales in 1835 had been about ten times that of England. By 1861, it was only twice as large.[5]

Without doubt, the crime rate fell as the Stain was diluted by immigration and the original felons died off. But did its fall argue reformation as well? In 1841 about three men in five in New South Wales had originally been transported. In 1851 about three in ten had been—still a lot.

Very few of the convictions (about 6 percent) were for crimes committed by the Currency (native-born Australians)—partly because so many of these were children, but largely because the Currency adults, despite the jabber about hereditary stains, were diligent family-oriented workers with a stake in their community. By contrast, convicts or Emancipists (all of whom, by definition, were adults) were the defendants in 70 percent of all criminal trials that yielded convictions in New South Wales in 1841.

As the historian Michael Sturma has shown, one should see this seeming endurance of a propensity for crime in the light of other factors. New South Wales remained a police state well after it finished receiving convicts in 1840. "Its machinery for social control was directed largely to the coercion of convicts. They were subject to more stringent regulation, kept under closer surveillance by the police, and treated differently by the courts."[6] The police leaned on Emancipists as well, legally free though they were. It was far harder for an offender to disappear in a tiny outback town or even in Sydney than in the vast and pullulating anonymity of London. Hence, ticket-of-leave men and Emancipists were more likely to be charged and convicted. They had the worst jobs, the least capital, the lowest education. Hence they were more likely to steal, fight and get drunk. In sum, Australia presented them with much the same social disabilities that had pushed them into crime in Britain, and one thing more: the unrelenting, go-getting, land-grabbing, cash-and-gold-obsessed materialism of free Australian colonists, acting in a vast geographical space but a small social one. Nowhere in the world was the Victorian equation between wealth and virtue rammed home more brutally than in mid-nineteenth-century Australia. With such a social ethic, it is perhaps surprising that the conviction rate was not higher. Indeed, such gross figures as 666 superior-court convictions in New South Wales out of a total population of 265,503 do not begin to justify the rantings and wailings of local Jeremiahs on their obsessive subject, colonial morality.

The fourth, and last, aim of transportation was colonization. Here, *si monumentum requiris, circumspice*. If Australia had not been settled as a prison and built by convict labor, it would have been colonized by other means; that was foreordained from the moment of Cook's landing at Botany Bay in 1770. But it would have taken half a century longer, for Georgian Britain would have found it exceptionally difficult to find settlers crazy or needy enough to go there of their own free will. As James Matra had pointed out before the First Fleet sailed, no one would take such a voyage to such a place "from *romantick* views." To ask what Australia would have been without convicts is existentially meaningless. They built it—if by "it" one means European material culture there—

and their mute traces are everywhere: in the peckings and scoops of iron chisels on the sandstone cuttings of Sydney, hewn with such terrible effort by the work gangs; in the fine springing of one bridge at Berrima in New South Wales, and the earnest, slightly bizarre figures carved on the face of another at Ross in Tasmania; in the zigzags of the Blue Mountain road, where traffic now rolls above the long-buried, rusted chains of the dead; less obviously, in the fruitful pastures that were once primeval gum forest:

> Shame on the mouth
> That would deny
> The knotted hands
> That set us high![7]

What these people bequeathed to Australian character, or to our sense of ourselves as a nation, is much more debatable than the economic results of their labor. Probably it was not what Australians like to think—the truculent independence on which, with shaky justification, we are apt to pride ourselves.

To see the opposite effects of the System on those who lived it out, one may consider Tasmania, which stagnated. Its population had crept from 69,000 in 1851 to 102,000 in 1871, not even doubling in twenty years. Visitors at the end of the 1860s saw apathy and depression every-where: silent streets, building at a standstill, farmers sinking into rural solipsism, empty docks, a static populace heavy with old people and children but deserted by the young and energetic, who had gone across Bass Strait. The flood of immigrants to Victoria, Queensland and New South Wales passed Tasmania by. The island was decaying, like the Southern slave states of America after Abolition. Convicts remained an inescapable presence, a gray-and-yellow ghost in a dying house. Although Her Majesty's Government had stopped sending prisoners to Tasmania so long ago, the long-sentence men remained there and had to serve out their years of stipulated punishment; the imperial convict system was not fully dismantled until 1886.

Economic stagnation condemned the island to live with its past; long after the rough developing energies of the mainland colonies had tran-scended the "convict stain," the Dr. Jekyll of Tasmania remained paired with the sinister Mr. Hyde of Van Diemen's Land. Convictry lived on in a hundred pervasive ways. It seemed to be rooted in the very landscape, cankering its lavish and picturesque beauty, as the Irish political prisoner John Mitchel remarked in his journal in 1850:

> Trees of vast height wave their tops far beneath our feet: and the farther
> side of the glen is formed by a promontory that runs out into the bay,

with steep and rocky sides worn into cliffs and caves floored with silvery sand, shellstrewn, such as in European seas would have been consecrate of old to some Undine's love . . . and over the soft, swelling slope of the hill above, embowered so gracefully in trees, what building stands? Is that a temple crowning the promontory as the pillared portico crowns Sunium? Or a villa, carrying you back to Baiae? Damnation! It is a convict "barrack."[8]

Instead of Paestum, Port Arthur. Instead of the train of classical satyrs, the road gangs "harnessed to gravel-carts . . . their hair close-cropped, their close leathern caps, and hangdog countenances . . . evil, rueful and abominable . . . vacant but impudent."[9] Instead of Claudian or Turneresque nymphs in this landscape, a pass-holding woman servant in the charge of a convict constable, "a hideous and obscene-looking creature with a brandy-bloated face and a white satin bonnet, adorned with artificial flowers."[10] Tasmania was a place of social counterfeits and off-key echoes, where "the convict-class is regarded just as the negroes must be in South Carolina," and ex-convict shepherds "whistled nigger melodies in the balmy air."[11] The main veneer, however, was Englishness. In Tasmania one found every kind of frustrated longing for British privilege and British aristocracy, but the only proper coat-of-arms would be "a fleece, and a kangaroo with its pocket picked; and the legend *Sic Fortis Hobartia crevit*, namely, by fleecing and picking pockets."[12] It was, to Mitchel's piercing though jaundiced eye, a pathetic replica accurately made from wrong materials:

At one o'clock up comes the Hobart Town and Launceston day coach, which . . . is precisely like what an English stagecoach was before the railroads had swallowed them all up. The road is excellent, the horses good. The coachman and guard (prisoners, no doubt) are in manners, dress and behaviour as like untransported English guards and coachmen as it is possible to conceive. The wayside inns we passed are thoroughly British; even, I regret to say, to the very brandy they sell. The passengers all speak with an English accent. . . . Every sight and sound . . . remains me that I am in a small, misshapen, transported, bastard England; and the legitimate England itself is not so dear to me that I can love the convict copy.[13]

Even allowing for Mitchel's unconstrained spleen—Tasmania was his prison, and he an Irish nationalist—no visitors were writing of the mainland colonies in such terms by 1850.

The toxins of convictry would linger in Tasmania for another generation after 1853. There was no sudden purging of the Stain, and even its old name stuck to it like tar; "Vandemonians," in the eyes of the free

Australian working class, were either criminal drones or tyrants. "During the last twenty years," wrote a journalist as late as 1882,

> I have been thrown among some hundred of immigrants, and I can safely say that not one in a hundred of them knows this island by the name of Tasmania; but it is well-known as Van Diemen's Land; the land of white slavery.

No new felons were coming, but the old ones remained, and the census of 1857 showed that half the adults of both sexes on the island (and 60 percent of the adult men) were either convicts or Emancipists.[14] It took the Old Hands another thirty years to die off, and in the meantime they supplied most of the crime in Tasmania. In 1848–49 convicts and Emancipists formed 68 percent of the population but committed 93 percent of its serious crimes. In 1866–67, although only about 35 percent of the adults there had gone through the System, the convicts and Emancipists were responsible for 70 percent of the crime. In this period, Tasmania had the highest crime rate in Australia: 1.72 Supreme Court convictions per 1,000 people, as against 1.3 in New South Wales, 1.18 in Victoria and 0.61 in South Australia.

Meanwhile the refuse of the System—the broken, the unhinged, the helpless, the mad and the abandoned—clogged the institutions of Tasmania. What transportation produced in them was not Victorian "manliness" but abject neurosis. Ticket-of-leave men from the Probation System were scattered all over the interior—debilitated, muttering odd-jobbers who were known, with the usual finesse of Australian slang, as "old crawlers." In 1867, a clergyman recalled meeting one of the "old crawlers" in the employ of a former naval officer. The retired salt boasted that he had had his man "flogged times without number. . . . I have put a rope around his neck, and on horseback dragged him back and forth through that pond. . . . But it was all of no use, the man will not leave my service." At which the Reverend John Morison reflected that the worn-out incorrigible "must have been so habituated to punishment that it had become a kind of necessity to him, and likely he felt at times uneasy if he did not receive any; all that was human in his nature must have been well-nigh lashed out of him, leaving nothing but . . . the nature of a spaniel dog."[15]

A few "old crawlers" did not crawl. One of the *frissons* of Anthony Trollope's visit to Tasmania was his journey to Port Arthur in January 1872. There, he interviewed one of its last fifteen or so prisoners, an Irishman from Londonderry named Dennis Doherty, one of "the heroes of the place . . . who told us that for forty-two years he had never been a free man for an hour." Doherty was tall, heavily tattooed, with a large cleft chin and one small gray eye. He had enlisted in the 16th Lancers as a boy, and he was still a lad of eighteen in May 1833 when a court-martial in Guernsey sentenced him to 14 years' transportation for deser-tion. From that point on, he traversed the whole of the System. In 1837 the Sydney Supreme Court sentenced him to life imprisonment on Nor-folk Island as a bushranger. After four years, he feigned madness well enough to be repatriated to Sydney. He was reconvicted at Berrima Quar-ter Sessions, in New South Wales, for bushranging in 1841, and returned to Norfolk Island for his second life sentence. A year later, he went on the Probation System to Port Arthur. In 1844 he was sent back among the hard cases to Norfolk Island. On the way he tried to seize the brig *Governor Phillip*, for which he received his third life sentence. In 1853 Doherty returned to Van Diemen's Land, or Tasmania as it was now called, to serve out the rest of his probation. Two years later, he received his fourth life sentence for assaulting a man with a stolen gun. And so it had gone on. Over the years, Doherty told the astonished Trollope, he had received more than 3,000 lashes. "In appearance," the writer noted, "he was a large man and still powerful, well to look at in spite of his eye, lost as he told us through the miseries of prison life. But he said that he was broken at last." Doherty had made his last escape attempt three weeks before and had been brought back "almost starved to death":

> He had been always escaping, always rebelling, always fighting against authority, and always being flogged. There had been a whole life of tor-ment such as this; forty-two years of it; and there he stood, speaking softly, arguing his case well, and pleading while the tears ran down his face for some kindness, for some mercy in his old age. "I have tried to escape; always to escape," he said, "as a bird does out of a cage. Is that unnatural; is that a great crime?" The man's first offence, that of mutiny [sic], is not one at which the mind revolts. I did feel for him, and when he spoke of himself as a caged bird, I should have liked to take him out into the world, and have given him a month of comfort. He would probably, however, have knocked my brains out at the first opportunity. I was assured that he was thoroughly bad, irredeemable, not to be reached by any kindness, a beast of prey, whose hand was against every honest man, and against whom it was necessary that every honest man should raise his hand. Yet he talked so gently and so well, and argued his case with such winning words! He was writing in a book when we entered his cell ... "Just scribbling, sir," he said, "to while away the hours."[16]

Dennis Doherty was then fifty-seven, and his conduct record, which Trollope had not been able to see, bears out what he said of his life. It is a litany of almost inconceivable suffering and defiance, pages long—lashes, chains, gang labor, solitary confinement, for offenses that ran from "Absconding" and "Mutiny" to "Having a Crayfish in his possession without authorization."

By the 1870s, Tasmania had more paupers, lunatics, orphans and invalids than South Australia and Queensland combined, concentrated in a population less than half of theirs. Despite the labor shortage, most ex-convicts were discriminated against, usually with a sullen reflexive viciousness, by the freeborn. They were regarded as lazy, improvident, unworthy to own land; and as the Victorian animus against homosexuals grew ever stronger in Australia after 1850, so did the belief that most convicts were sexually tainted. "The growing dread of the frightful practices to which it is well known many of them are addicted," remarked a Parliamentary committee in 1860, "render[s] their search for employment often tedious and difficult." In contrast to the ex-convicts of New South Wales, the felonry of Tasmania was so fettered by social prejudice that it could never rise. Moreover, the laws governing their work and their relations to their employers retained, dilute but unmistakable, the iron and gall of the System. Thus, under the 1856 Master and Servants Act, masters had the power to arrest their servants, and it was quite legal for an employer (or any member of his family) to put a hired hand in custody on suspicion of an offense and keep him confined for a week without trial. The extraordinary fact was that this law remained on the statute books of Tasmania for more than a generation; in 1882, the Legislative Council rejected efforts to repeal the employer's right of arrest. This would not have happened so late in New South Wales, with its working-class resentment of authority, its ethos of mateship and its mistrust of "boss-cockies."

By and large, Tasmanian Emancipists showed very little sense of themselves as a political group, so that "the large ex-convict component in the population probably retarded the growth of radical and working-class politics."[17] Probably this was because so few Irish convicts were sent there. Forty percent of all transported felons went to Van Diemen's Land. But in the period 1812–1853, only fifty-one transports sailed from Ireland to Hobart, an average of hardly more than one ship a year.[18] As a result, the proportion of Irish to English convicts was far, far smaller in Van Diemen's Land than in New South Wales; and the percentage of Catholics was about half that on the mainland—17 percent of the white Tasmanian population, bond and free. The Irish were not a powerful minority in Tasmania, and they never became one. The residual clan collectivism that they had brought to New South Wales, which would give such a strong root to the anti-authoritarian, stick-together ethos of the mainland workers, scarcely existed in Tasmania. The exaggerated "Englishness" of post-penal Tasmania was one result of this, since the thin colonial elite etched its values on the classes below it.

So Tasmania is a problem for those who would like to believe that most Australian bush virtues—intransigence, sticking to your "mate," distrust of judge, trap and nob, unpolished self-reliance, democratic and brusquely dissenting temper—were created by the convict system. If this were so, one would naturally expect these traits to be vividly emblazoned on the social fabric of Tasmania, the colony with the highest density of convicts and their descendants. But they were not. Workers were less sure of themselves as a class there than in New South Wales, because they were selling their labor in a buyer's market: Tasmania nearly always had a glut of hands, New South Wales a shortage. Moreover, Tasmania had little sense of the frontier and hence no context in which the "bush ethos," however sentimentalized, could flourish. It could not expand, and this marked its people. It remained a close-settled, leaf-green microcosm, where the roving bush-worker, beholden to no squatter and picking up his check where he wandered, was a complete anomaly. Nomads made respectable Tasmanians wince; they thought of escaped probation gangers.

What convictry left to the island, then, was the very opposite of its supposed legacy in New South Wales: a malleable and passive working class, paternalistic institutions, a tame press and colonized Anglophile values. The idea that rebels are the main product of oppression is a consoling fiction. In any penal society the rebel is always the exception and never the rule. Tasmania was a factory, a "mill for grinding rogues honest," which turned out an unleavened human mass, a submissive *lumpenproletariat* of men and women, cudgelled into humility by repetitive task-work and the all-pervasive threat of corporal punishment. They had learned to eat out of the hand of Authority, because Authority had always fed them. They illustrated the melancholy truth of Vauvenargues's maxim: "Servitude debases men to the point where they end up liking it." And because there were so many of them in proportion to the free population, immigration being so slight, Authority was harder on them than in post-penal New South Wales. The depth of virulence of Tasmania's obsession with the Stain still astonished visitors from the mainland in the 1890s, even though by then hardly any Old Hands remained alive.

Yet there is no doubt that bitter memories of the System were sometimes a deep source of energy of Australian independence—on the mainland. John Fawkner (1792–1869), the "Grand Old Man of Victoria," who with John Batman settled Port Phillip Bay and founded Melbourne on the Yarra River in 1835, was a convict's son, who shipped with his father to the first settlement of Hobart Town in 1803. Growing up with convicts, he sided with them as a class. When he was twenty-two, his sympathies were confirmed in blood and agony: He helped seven prisoners build a lugger to escape to South America, but it was captured and Fawkner, implicated, received 500 lashes. He carried the cat's claw-marks on his skin—the essential text of a power he loathed—for the rest of his life. But he also worked and cheated, made money, turned himself into a "bush lawyer," started newspapers of liberal-radical bias in Van Diemen's Land and then in Victoria, and campaigned vituperatively for the rights of convicts and small settlers. Fawkner spent fifteen years on the Legislative Council of Victoria as a populist gadfly, "the tribune of the people." His target was the big sheep-grazing families that had "locked up the land" for themselves, growing fat from convict labor and hungry for more. He saw transportation itself, not the transportees, as the shame of Australia; he wanted to foster a society of yeomen farmers. Fawkner's stubborn, cantankerous altruism was rooted in his experience of convict Tasmania, but it only became politically effective in the wider arena of the mainland.

By the mid-1830s, the struggle for Emancipists' rights had been won, and it would never pay another Australian politician—as it had paid Wentworth, on his long progress toward fantasies of colonial aristocracy —to campaign for ex-convicts as a group. The idea of a convicts' party was absurd, and there were no political advantages in displaying one's own convict past—or that of one's parents. On the contrary: The drawbacks were extreme. Australians, especially well-to-do and powerful Australians, retained no sympathy with or interest in the convict past. They only wanted to forget it. The exceptions were mostly working-class Irish, mainly in New South Wales, among whom convict memory was concentrated and to some degree fetishized. It survived because it linked up to an older tissue of recollection, the general pattern of English oppression of the Irish. It tended to produce a dug-in clannishness, the attitude of a "mental ghetto . . . a thought-universe of harsh conflict," as the historian Miriam Dixson called it.[19]

If it did contribute to Australian egalitarianism, then it did so in a most unamiable way. In the 1830s, astute observers like Maconochie and his associate Alexander Cheyne felt that the primary division of Australian society into two classes, the bond and the free, tended to flatten distinctions of class between free men by concentrating their hostility on the convicts below them. "The habit which most of the free contract," Cheyne told the Molesworth Committee,

> of thinking and speaking of and treating the convicts contemptuously, is, by a very natural process extended to the whole species; and hence the want of respect and deference to others which is so universally manifested.[20]

By the same token, the importance of being a free man and not a convict "has a tendency to break down the distinctions conceded in the mother country, *and thus to place the whole free population on a nearly equal footing.*" Contempt was repaid in hatred; convicts and ex-convicts "regard with settled antipathies, nearly amounting to hatred, all who have not been, or who are not prisoners; and, when not repressed by self-interest, this is plainly exhibited."

Not all the roots of Australian egalitarianism can be idealized. Bush comradeship was real, but so was the defensive, static, levelling, two-class hatred that came out of convictry. From it ran an undertow of impotent dreams of vengeance, as in the hope of Australia's republican bush poet of the late nineteenth century, Henry Lawson, that the poor man would be educated up *and* the rich man educated down. By the turn of the century, most connections between early Australian socialist temper and the resentments of the convict past were conventional matters of ritual invocation—or else, they were buried by workers who cherished their right to be respected and no more wanted to be identified with criminal ancestors than the Chartists of an earlier day in England had wished to be associated with thieves and footpads. When such connections surfaced, they took their popular, idealized form, with the convicts presented as shining innocent poachers, Chartists and apple-stealing children, and the bushrangers as Robin Hoods.

The "convict past" is a shadowy behavioral catch-all today. Thus, it made Australians cynical about Authority; or else it made them conformists. As so many Australians are conformist skeptics, the "convict legacy" is seen to be all the more pervasive. Perhaps there are roots of social conduct that wind obscurely back to the convict era, and the familiar Australian habit of cursing authority behind the hand while truckling to its face may well be one of them; it may also be that Australian sexism receives some of its force from the brutal psychic legacy of carceral life. But since the vast majority of European Australians are the descendants either of Anglo-Irish-Scots who arrived after 1850, or of Greeks, Italians, Hungarians, Balts, Poles and Germans who emigrated after 1945, this seems a sterile line of inquiry.

Would Australians have done anything differently if their country had not been settled as the jail of infinite space? Certainly they would. They would have remembered more of their own history. The obsessive cultural enterprise of Australians a hundred years ago was to forget it entirely, to sublimate it, to drive it down into unconsulted recesses. This affected all Australian culture, from political rhetoric to the perception of space, of landscape itself. Space, in America, had always been optimistic; the more of it you faced, the freer you were—"Go West, young man!" In Australian terms, to go west was to die, and space itself was the jail. The flowering of Australian nature as a cultural emblem, whether in poetry or in painting, could not occur until the stereotype of the "melancholy bush," born in convict perceptions of Nature-as-prison, had been expunged. A favorite trope of journalism and verse at the time of the Australian Centennial, in 1888, was that of the nation as a young vigorous person gazing into the rising sun, turning his or her back on the dark crouching shadows of the past. A "Centennial Song" published in the Melbourne *Argus* struck the right note of defensive optimism, coupling it with an appeal to censor early Australian history—or, preferably, not to write it at all:

> Is it manly, fair or honest with our early sins to stain
> What we aimed at, worked for, conquered—aye—an honest, noble name?
> And those scribes whose gutter pleasure is to air the hideous past,
> Let us leave them to the loathesome mould in which their mind is cast.
> Look ahead and not behind us! Look to what is sunny, bright—
> Look into our glorious future, not into our shadowed night.

At the heart of each proclamation of renewal was a longing for amnesia. And Australians embarked on this quest for oblivion with go-getting energy. They wanted to forget that their forefathers had ever been, or even rubbed shoulders with, government men; and before long, they succeeded.

Nobody could deny that convicts had once been in Australia. Indeed, some of the "old crawlers" were still alive, though only just, in 1888. But they were not invited to crawl in the parades, and the Centenary was not heavy with historical retrospection. One dipped one's brush in the Stain, to put in a little darkness behind the radiant bouquet of wattle, wheat, Union Jacks and Golden Fleeces that symbolized Australia's present and future prosperity. One hinted, in the text of commemorative albums that bore cartouches of kookaburras and paddle steamers stamped in gold leaf on their covers, that dreadful things had been done in the remote colonial days of Australia, but new pages must not be sullied; that it was time to draw the curtain at last on so much indignity and suffering and to contemplate the Dawn. "The convict stage is now forgotten as a dream," wrote one of these Centennial boosters. "Today New South Wales . . . has an annual import and export trade of nearly £50,000,000, . . . 1727 miles of railway, . . . 19,000 miles of telegraph wires." In Tasmania, "slowly but surely Nature is reclaiming her own, and is effacing the memorials of an infamy which none care to look back upon. Chapter after chapter might be written on the annals of Port Arthur, but they would be inconsonant with the tone [of] these pages."[21]

Whenever they could, the instruments of official culture tried to play down the obdurate attachment of the Australian rank and file to its bushranger folk-heroes, to the distant memory of Bold Jack Donohoe and the recent one of Ned Kelly. The memory of the English officer and his punishment-book, of the whole detested machinery and practice of forced labor and flogging, was shifted into the background as one of the things on which it was unhealthy to "dwell."

Australian politicians conceived and ran the Centenary as a lavish feast of jingoism, a tribute to the benevolent, all-embracing British Empire. Without Britain's market, Australian business could not survive; without her institutions, especially the Monarchy, Australian morality would decay; without her dreadnoughts, Australian blood would be yellowed by hordes of invading junks. Bunting, flags, parades, speeches and more bunting were rammed down the popular throat, and only republicans gagged on them.

The organ of their protest was *The Bulletin*, that anti-imperialist paper, which excoriated the whole idea of the Centennial as a slavish feast of Australian dependence. Australia, it argued, began its first hundred years as a penal colony, but was finishing them as an economic and political one. Its irons had been struck off but nothing else had changed. One of its cartoonists made this point with a pair of drawings: the first, labelled 1788, of an Irish convict dancing a jig in his chains for the amusement of an English officer; the second of a modern bush-settler in his cabbage-tree hat, doing the same dance for John Bull in 1888. In an editorial headlined "The Day We Were Lagged," *The Bulletin* called the celebrations "a feeble, fifth-rate drunk—a sort of combined scalp dance and gin conversazione—in honour of the meanest event in [our] short history."[22] The Australian Centenary was a "feeble copy" of the American one of 1876: "The elements of grandeur are entirely wanting. The great Republic rejoiced, not on account of an empty flight of years, which pass alike for man and beast . . . but in honour of the triumph of liberty over grasping tyranny. Australia, on the other hand, celebrates a century which begins and ends alike in nothing. A hundred years have left her as they found her—a name but not a nation, a huge continent content to be the hanger-on of a little island."[23] However unwelcome these sentiments, there was a good deal of truth in them, and even more in the connection *The Bulletin* drew between imperialisms past and present:

> The day which inaugurated a reign of slavery and loathesomeness and moral leprosy—is the occasion for which we are called upon to rejoice with an exceeding great joy. Yet there might be a palliation even for this, if Australia could show that she had shaken off the old fetters and the old superstitions of that dark era. . . . [B]ut the old slavish taint still clings to her garments, and her chains of iron are merely exchanged for chains of gold.[24]

English capital, the editorial went on, was imported every day to develop Australian resources—"and, naturally enough, the English capitalist takes the resources themselves for his pains." It was better to be poor and independent, *The Bulletin* urged, pointing to Chile, Mexico, Switzerland, and above all the Boer Republic, whose "little army of farmers almost exterminated the gaudy troops of England and slaughtered their aristocratic commander at Matuta Hill. . . . [E]ven the effeminate soldiers of Egypt made a gallant struggle before their native land sank into a feudatory of England, but Australia, by the mouth of such 'representative statesmen' as GILLIES and PARKES, declares herself to be something meaner than Egypt and lower than the Boer Republic. The declaration is one which fits the occasion and does honour to the anniversary of the day on which our first families were—exported."[25]

Nothing could be allowed to diminish the gratitude Australians were meant to feel for the imperial umbrella. The essence of colonization was that they could claim no history of their own. Some thirty years before the Centenary, the English gold-seeker John Sherer had complained of the historical blankness of the antipodean landscape, where nothing recognizable had happened for millennia:

> There can be no walk, no journey of any kind, more monotonous than one through the bush. . . . There is no association of the past connected with it. Your sight is never regaled with the "ruins grey" of some fine old fortress. . . . Imagination is at a standstill—fairly *bogged*, as your body may be in the mud-swamp. There are no sacred groves . . . No time-hallowed fanes, sanctified by the recollections of hospitable deeds . . . No fields, recalling the downfall of tyranny . . . Nothing whatever to visit as a spot noted as being capable of exalting the mind by the memories with which it is associated. No locality, memorable as the haunt of genius. No birthplaces of great men . . . Nothing of this kind; all is dully-dead, uninspiring mud-work.[26]

But if the landscape carried no such litany of association, Australian children would; they were made to read the novels of Walter Scott and the deeds of Sir Francis Drake, to recite like parrots the names of English kings, the dates of unexplained events like the Rump Parliament and the Gunpowder Plot, the lengths of European rivers they would never see— while, as the poet Henry Lawson complained in the *Republican* in 1888, they were shown nothing of Australian history earlier than 1850. Educators played their part, with the result that it became impossible to find, in any history book used in Australian schools up to the mid-1960s, a satisfactory or even coherent account of penal Australia. For what was this meager "history"? A chronicle of provincial misery; a minor episode in English imperial policy, best forgotten. What was distant in time and space was real; what was close had been sublimated into the substance of bad social dreams.

Amnesia and shame nibbled at the edges of the record, without altering it much. A citizen might ink over his family name in a ship's bound indent; the record books of trials and convictions at country benches in New South Wales would sometimes be burnt, so as not to inflict social pain on innocent descendants. But the mountain of paper the System left behind it was too huge to be removed.

Paper outlives stone and brick. Most of the buildings directly associated with the System in Australia are long gone. Most historically significant structures raised in New South Wales before 1835 or in Tasmania before 1850—churches, stores, town halls, courts, villas, station homesteads, bridges—were built, wholly or in part, by convict labor. Many of them remain, especially in Tasmania, which did not have enough money to pull them down and build new ones. But there seemed little point in keeping obsolete jails and barracks standing as souvenirs of a haunted past, and the few that survive only narrowly escaped a general demolition. On Norfolk Island, the pentagonal New Jail and the huge Prisoners' Barracks at Kingston, along with many lesser structures, were torn down for building-stone by the new inhabitants who moved in after the last convicts left—the descendants of Fletcher Christian's mutineers and their Tahitian women, relocated from Pitcairn Island in 1856. Except for the eroded foundations of cells that protrude illegibly from the green carpet of turf, little is left in the compound, and even the walls and gates themselves, raised so high by the sweating gangs, were narrowly saved from being bulldozed to create a picnic park in 1959. At the head of Sydney Cove, now renamed Circular Quay, nothing speaks of the convict past; a banal modern sculpture of two joined bronze ellipses, which might represent leg-irons, turns out to be an allegory of the bonds of friendship between Sydney and Portsmouth. There is no monument of any kind to the men and women of the First Fleet, and none appears to be planned for the Bicentennial in 1988.

Yet despite neglect, amnesia and a thousand unconscious acts of censorship, the System did continue to flourish in popular memory—as Grand Guignol. One of the few tourist attractions of Hobart in the 1880s was the *Success*, a convict hulk that had lain in Port Phillip Bay for years and had acquired a delectably bloody reputation, as its prisoners had joined in the killing of "The Demon," John Price. Entrepreneurs had bought her and fitted her out with dummy convicts and an imposing array of fetters, gratings, handcuffs, punishment-bands, balls, chains and cats, all genuine (such things had not become expensive colonial antiques at the time), along with the black iron armor worn by the bush-ranger Ned Kelly at his last stand at Glenrowan. When most of the population of Tasmania had trooped through her, the owners sailed *Success* to Sydney in the hope of bigger crowds. She was promptly censored: Scuttled in the dead of night by indignant citizens who did not wish to be reminded of the Stain, *Success* sank at her moorings with the loss of all waxworks.

The *locus classicus* remained unsinkable. Port Arthur was closed down in 1877. By then, its roster of inmates had dwindled to 64 convicts still serving their accumulated sentences, 126 paupers and 79 lunatics. They were transferred to Hobart; the convicts came ashore in handcuffs and leg-irons, even though most of them were old and infirm, before a gaping and giggling crowd.

In its last years it had been visited not only by Anthony Trollope but by the young Australian novelist and journalistic hackabout Marcus Clarke, who had pored over a mass of documentation on con-victry in the Melbourne Public Library and, inspired by Victor Hugo's *Les Misérables* and Alexandre Dumas's *The Count of Monte Cristo*, had decided to write his own epic of crime and punishment. Clarke's *His Natural Life* began running as a serial in the *Australian Journal* in March 1870. It ran for two years, and in the end it lost most of its readers. But its appearance as a book in 1874 revived it—and, with it, came a revival of popular interest in the System and its dreaded epitome, Port Arthur.

Clarke and his followers impressed the full character of Grand Guig-nol on the place, for they knew their audience. Why, not so long ago, did one hear "oral traditions" (tall stories for tourists) about collective sui-cides of children jumping, like lemmings, from the cliffs at Point Puer to evade the miseries of flogging and rape; about slavering convicts eating the dead in the darkness of Commandant Booth's mineshafts? Because, given the lack of serious historical writing about transportation for more than seventy years after Clarke's novel was published, its stories became "true."

Port Arthur inhumanity had been made its central myth long before —by George Arthur's enemies in the Van Diemen's Land press. In the 1870s, when Clarke and Price Warung (followed by a horde of penny-a-liners) began to write their versions of the System, the myth had be-come "reality" and so could be re-invested with fantasy. Hence Clarke's goriest episodes, such as the cannibalism of Gabbett at Port Arthur (a thinly disguised version of the escape of Pearce), were shifted from Macquarie Harbor in the 1820s to the Tasman Peninsula in the 1830s, and used to "typify" the System. Likewise, Clarke's suicide of Tommy and Billy, the little Point Puer boys who jump from the cliff, is one of the finest heart-wringers in Victorian fiction—a penal answer to the death of Little Nell:

> "I can do it now," said Tommy. "I feel strong."
> "Will it hurt much, Tommy?" said Billy, who was not so courageous.
> "Not so much as a whipping."
> "I'm afraid! Oh, Tom, it's so deep! Don't leave me, Tom!"
> The bigger baby took his little handkerchief from his neck, and with it bound his left hand to his companion's right.
> "Now I can't leave you."
> "What was it the Lady that kissed us said, Tommy?"
> "Lord have pity on them two fatherless children!" repeated Tommy.
> "Let's say it, Tom."
> And so the two babies knelt down on the brink of the cliff, and, raising the bound hands together, looked up at the sky, and said, "Lord have pity on us two fatherless children!" And then they kissed each other, and did it.[27]

Nothing like this ever happened at Point Puer, but the tourists loved it. On fine weekends in the late 1870s and through the '80s, hundreds of trippers would descend on it from Hobart in paddlewheel steamers, shrieking with agitation as they were locked for a few minutes in the pitch-black, stony silence of the Dumb Cells, chattering happily as their boots crunched through the debris in the echoing penitentiary dormitories. Sometimes a visitor would be able to buy a rusty leg-ring or a rotted hobnail boot from one of the "locals" who, now that Port Arthur had been officially renamed Carnavon and re-incorporated as a town, were trickling back to the Tasman Peninsula. The appetite for carceral souvenirs had not been lost on a Hobart photographer named John Watt Beattie, who documented the buildings and some of the surviving Old Hands of Port Arthur and even visited Norfolk Island. He also printed postcards of prison emblems—elaborate still lifes of leg-irons, cuffs, keys, guards' carbines and paraphernalia from the Model Prison, surrounded by swags of leaves and wildflowers.

It was well that he made such records of the detested past, for not long afterward the long-impending fate of Sodom struck the Tasman Peninsula. First, there was an earthquake; then, in 1897, a bushfire consumed the penal settlement. It raged in the great four-story penitentiary for two days and nights, and the Model Prison, that ominous replication of Pentonville in the south, once the silent hive of hooded and numbered human drones, was gutted. Many Tasmanians had difficulty concealing their glee and wished only to demolish the ruins. The visitor today, wandering through what remains of the penitentiary with other tourists, can hardly grasp the isolation it once stood for. Perhaps that is easier deduced from Nature itself, from the barely penetrable labyrinth of space that England chose as its abode of crime; and to see that, one need only go to the black basalt cliffs that frame the Tasman Peninsula, crawl through the bushes to their unfenced rim and gaze down on the wide, wrinkled, glimmering sheet of our imprisoning sea.

Appendixes

Abbreviations

Notes

Bibliography

Index

# Appendixes

## APPENDIX 1

### Governors and Chief Executives of New South Wales, 1788–1855

| | |
|---|---|
| Capt. Arthur Phillip, R.N. (1738–1814), Gov. | Jan. 1788–Dec. 1792 |
| Maj. Francis Grose (1758?–1814), Lt.-Gov. | Dec. 1792–Dec. 1794 |
| Capt. William Paterson (1755–1810), Administrator | Dec. 1794–Sept. 1795 |
| Capt. John Hunter, R.N. (1737–1821), Gov. | Sept. 1795–Sept. 1800 |
| Lieut. Philip Gidley King, R.N. (1758–1808), Gov. | Sept. 1800–Aug. 1806 |
| Capt. William Bligh, R.N. (1754–1817), Gov. | Aug. 1806– Jan. 1810 |
| Lt.-Col. Lachlan Macquarie (1762–1824), Gov. | Jan. 1810–Dec. 1821 |
| Sir Thomas Brisbane (1773–1860), Gov. | Dec. 1821–Nov. 1825 |
| Sir Ralph Darling (1775–1858), Gov. | Nov. 1825–Dec. 1831 |
| Sir Richard Bourke (1777–1855), Gov. | Dec. 1831– Oct. 1837 |
| Sir George Gipps (1791–1847), Gov. | Oct. 1837– July 1846 |
| Sir Charles Fitzroy (1796–1858), Gov.-General | Aug. 1846– Jan. 1855 |

## APPENDIX 2

### Chief Executives of Van Diemen's Land, 1803–53

| | |
|---|---|
| Lieut. John Bowen, R.N. | Sept. 1803– Feb. 1804 |
| Col. David Collins, R.M., Lt.-Gov. | Feb. 1804–Mar. 1810 |
| Lt. Edward Lord, R.M. | Mar. 1810– July 1810 |
| Capt. John Murray, 73rd Regt. | July 1810– Feb. 1812 |
| Lt.-Col. Andrew Geils, 73rd Regt. | Feb. 1812– Feb. 1813 |
| Col. Thomas Davey, R.M., Lt.-Gov. | Feb. 1813– Apr. 1817 |
| Col. William Sorell, Lt.-Gov. | Apr. 1817– May 1824 |
| Col. George Arthur, Lt.-Gov. | May 1824– Oct. 1836 |
| Lt.-Col. K. Snodgrass, Acting Lt.-Gov. | Oct. 1836– Jan. 1837 |
| Sir John Franklin, R.N., Lt.-Gov. | Jan. 1837–Aug. 1843 |
| Sir John E. Eardley-Wilmot, Lt.-Gov. | Aug. 1843– Oct. 1846 |
| C. J. Latrobe, Administrator | Oct. 1846– Jan. 1847 |
| Sir William Denison, Lt.-Gov. | Jan. 1847– Jan. 1855 |

## APPENDIX 3

## *Secretaries of State for the Colonies, 1794–1855*

Evan Nepean, as under secretary of state to Lord Sydney in the Home Department, was chiefly responsible for the arrangements for the First Fleet and the administration of the colony up to 1794. Thereafter it passed into the hands of a succession of secretaries of state for [war and] the colonies:

|  | *Month appointed* |
|---|---|
| H. Dundas | July 1794 |
| Lord Hobart | Mar. 1791 |
| Earl of Camden | May 1804 |
| Viscount Castlereagh | July 1805 |
| W. Windham | Feb. 1806 |
| Viscount Castlereagh | Mar. 1807 |
| Earl of Liverpool | Nov. 1809 |
| Earl of Bathurst | June 1812 |
| Viscount Goderich | Apr. 1827 |
| W. Huskisson | Sept. 1827 |
| Sir George Murray | May 1828 |
| Viscount Goderich | Nov. 1830 |
| E. G. Smith Stanley | Apr. 1833 |
| T. Spring Rice | June 1834 |
| Duke of Wellington | Nov. 1834 |
| Earl of Aberdeen | Dec. 1834 |
| C. Grant | Apr. 1835 |
| Marquess of Normanby | Feb. 1839 |
| Lord John Russell | Sept. 1839 |
| Lord Stanley | Sept. 1841 |
| W. E. Gladstone | Dec. 1845 |
| Earl Grey | July 1846 |
| Sir John Pakington | Feb. 1852 |
| Duke of Newcastle | Dec. 1852 |
| Sir Henry George Grey | June 1854 |
| Hon. S. Herbert | Feb. 1855 |
| Lord J. Russell | May 1855 |
| Sir W. Molesworth | July 1855 |
| H. Labouchere | Nov. 1855 |

# Abbreviations

| | |
|---|---|
| *ADB* | *Australian Dictionary of Biography.* |
| *AJPH* | *Australian Journal of Politics and History.* |
| *ANZJM* | *Australian and New Zealand Journal of Medicine.* |
| Bigge NSW | John Bigge, "Report of the Commissioner of Inquiry into the State of the Colony of New South Wales," *Great Britain, Parliamentary Papers* 1822, vol. 20, paper #448. |
| BL | British Library |
| BT | Bonwick Transcripts, Mitchell Library, Sydney. |
| Clark *HA* 1–4 | C. M. H. Clark, *A History of Australia*, vols. 1–4. |
| CO | Colonial Office Records, Public Record Office, London. |
| Col. Sec. | Colonial Secretary. |
| CON | Convict Department Records, Van Diemen's Land. |
| Con. Disc. 1, 1846 | *Correspondence re Convict Discipline*, ordered to be printed February 9, 1846, containing: (1) Secondary Punishment, pp. 1–139; (2) Convict Discipline and (3) Convict Discipline and Convict Estimates, pp. 141–259. |
| Con. Disc. 2, 1846 | *Correspondence re Convict Discipline*, ordered to be printed February 9, 1846, pp. 1–69, PP (HL) 1846, vol. 7. |
| Con. Disc. 3, 1846 | *Correspondence re Convict Discipline*, ordered to be printed June 12, 1846, pp. 1–77, PP (HL) 1846, vol. 7. |
| Con. Disc. 4, 1846 | *Correspondence between the Secretary of State . . . and the Governor of New South Wales, respecting the Convict System Administered in Norfolk Island, Under the Superintendence of Captain Maconochie R.N.*, ordered to be printed February 23, 1846, pp. 1–169, PP (HL) 1846, vol. 7. |
| Con. Disc. 1847 | *Correspondence Relative to Convict Discipline*, PP (HL) 1847, vol. 8, pp. 1–250. |
| Con. Disc. 1850 | *Correspondence Relative to Convict Discipline*, PP (HL) 1850, vol. 11, pp. 1–282. |
| Con. Disc. 1853 | *Further Correspondence on Convict Discipline and Transportation*, PP (HL) 1852–3, vol. 18. |
| Cook *EL* | Thomas Cook, *The Exile's Lamentations.* |
| Corr. Military Operations 1831 | *Copies of all Correspondence between Lieutenant-Governor Arthur and His Majesty's Secretary of State for the Colonies, on the Subject of the Military Operations lately carried out against the Aboriginal Inhabitants of Van Diemen's Land*, PP (HC) #259, pp. 1–86, September 23, 1831. |

| | |
|---|---|
| Crowley, *Doc. Hist.* | Frank Crowley, *A Documentary History of Australia.* |
| CSO | Colonial Secretary's Office Records, Van Diemen's Land. |
| DRO | Derbyshire Record Office. |
| FLB | Joseph Foveaux, "Letter Book, 1800–1804." |
| GO | Governor's Office, Tasmania. |
| HO | Home Office Records, Public Records Office, London. |
| HRA | Historical Records of Australia (Series 1). |
| HRNSW | Historical Records of New South Wales. |
| *HS* | *Historical Studies of Australia and New Zealand.* |
| *JAS* | *Journal of Australian Studies.* |
| *JRAHS* | *Journal of Royal Australian Historical Society.* |
| LF | Laurence Frayne, *Memoirs of Norfolk Island.* |
| *LH* | *Labour History.* |
| LRO | Lancashire Record Office, Preston, Lancashire. |
| *MJA* | *Medical Journal of Australia.* |
| ML | Mitchell Library, Sydney. |
| NLA | National Library of Australia, Canberra. |
| NSW | New South Wales. |
| NSWA | Archives Office of New South Wales, Sydney. |
| NSW V & P | Votes and Proceedings of the Legislative Council of New South Wales. |
| PC | Privy Council Papers. |
| *PHR* | *Pacific Historical Review.* |
| PP | Parliamentary Papers, Great Britain (Lords and/or Commons). |
| PRO | Public Records Office, London. |
| *RAHJ* | *Royal Australian Historical Journal.* |
| Robson, *Hist. Tas.* | Lloyd L. Robson, *A History of Tasmania.* |
| SC 1798 | *Report of the Select Committee on Transportation,* PP 1798. |
| SC1812 | *Report of the Select Committee on Transportation,* PP 1812. |
| SC 1832 | *Report of the Select Committee on Secondary Punishments,* PP 1832. |
| SC 1837–38 (i) | *Report of the Select Committee on Transportation* ("Molesworth Report," part i), PP 1837. |
| SC 1837–38 (ii) | *Report of the Select Committee on Transportation* ("Molesworth Report," part ii), PP 1838. |
| Shaw *CC* | A. G. L. Shaw, *Convicts and the Colonies.* |
| *SMH* | *Sydney Morning Herald.* |
| SPO | State Paper Office, Dublin. |
| THRA, PP | Tasmanian Historical Research Association, Papers and Proceedings. |
| TSA | Tasmanian State Archives, Hobart. |
| UTL | University of Tasmania Library, Hobart. |
| VDL | Van Diemen's Land. |

# Notes

## CHAPTER ONE  *The Harbor and the Exiles*

1. Jeremy Bentham, *Panopticon Versus New South Wales*, p. 7.
2. The numbers given for convicts transported vary widely; Shaw *CC* gives a total of some 156,000, Robson (*The Convict Settlers of Australia*) the same, others as high as 162,000.
3. John Hunter, *An Historical Journal of the Transactions at Port Jackson and Norfolk Island*, p. 77.
4. On the prevalence of imported stereotypes of landscape among colonial artists looking at Australian nature, and their gradual resolution toward naturalism in the work of Lycett, Earle and others, see Bernard Smith, *European Vision and the South Pacific, 1768–1850*, esp. Chapter 9, "Colonial Interpretations of the Australian Landscape, 1821–35."
5. Arthur Bowes Smyth, "Journal," ML Sydney. (This has been published as *The Journal of Arthur Bowes Smyth, Surgeon, Lady Penrhyn, 1787–1789*, ed. P. G. Fidlon and R. J. Ryan, Sydney, 1979.)
6. The bloodlines of Australian animals were, by other standards, young. Fossil remains of vertebrates reaching back 200 million years have been found in other continents; in Australia, the earliest such evidence of mammalian life is only about 22 million years old, from the Miocene epoch. The three main and distinctive types of vertebrate that evolved in Australian isolation were ratites (large, flightless birds like the emu), monotremes (egg-laying mammals) and marsupials (pouched mammals).

   On other continents, mammals had increased their genetic efficiency by developing into placentals, in which the embryo grows within the mother's womb, fed by an umbilical cord or placenta. It enjoys this protection for months and so is born relatively well-developed. Marsupials, by contrast, are born when still embryos—hardly bigger than ants. The embryo remains inside the mother's body for no more than a few weeks after fertilization, until it has used up the nutrients in the egg-sac; then out it comes, groping blindly like a grub through the savannah of belly fur, heading for the mother's pouch and, inside that, her teat. There it stays until it is mature enough to get around on its own.
7. J. C. Beaglehole, ed., *The Journals of Captain James Cook on His Voyages of Discovery*, vol. 1, p. 359.
8. C. Lockhart, replying to Circular Letter from Select Committee on the Aborigines, New South Wales V & P (1849): 20.
9. Geoffrey Blainey, *The Triumph of the Nomads*, p. 17.
10. On the as yet unsolved question of the origin of the Australian Aborigines, opinion divides between the "hybridists" and the "homogeneists." A summary of their positions is given by A. G. Thorne in "The Racial Affinities and Origins of the Australian

Aborigines," in Mulvaney and Golson, eds., *Aboriginal Man and Environment in Australia*, pp. 316–25.

Throughout the nineteenth century, and on into the twentieth, it was widely assumed that the Australian Aborigines were all of one racial stock and "practically uniformly homogeneous" (A. A. Abbie, "Physical Characteristics of Australian Aborigines," in *Australian Aboriginal Studies*, pp. 89–107). The exceptions, in this theory, were the insular Tasmanians, believed to be descended from Melanesians who arrived after the rising of the Pacific and the isolation of Tasmania and who never visited the mainland.

A contrary "hybridist" argument was advanced in 1967 by the American anthropologist Joseph B. Birdsell (in his "Preliminary Data on the Trihybrid Origin of the Australian Aborigines," in *Archaeology and Physical Anthropology in Oceania*, vol. 2, pp. 100–155). He proposed that there were three distinct waves of migration from the north in the Quaternary period. The first were a light-skinned, woolly-haired people, physically similar to the hill tribesmen of the Andaman Islands in the Bay of Bengal, whom Birdsell called the Oceanic Negritoids. They were in turn absorbed or driven south by a second wave, the Murrayians (so called because their racial type was conspicuous among the Aborigines of the Murray River), who had straighter hair and sprang from archaic Caucasoid stock. The displaced Oceanic Negritoids, according to this theory, survived in a few pockets in the Queensland rain forests and, retreating south, occupied Tasmania—which was cut off from the continent soon afterward by the rising sea level.

The Murrayians, by this theory, then dominated most of mainland Australia, except for the extreme north. This area, the gateway of the continent, was then invaded by a third race, the Carpenterians, racially similar to the hill peoples of Malaya, who never moved south of Australia's tropical zone.

This theory has been disputed by other anthropologists who argue in favor of a double Australian population; but all around, the evidence is so scanty that, in the words of D. J. Mulvaney, "a century after T. H. Huxley, it remains premature to pronounce for racial heterogeneity or homogeneity" (Mulvaney, *The Prehistory of Australia*, p. 64).

11. Inland movement of coast: Mulvaney, *Prehistory*, p. 136.
12. Ibid., pp. 147–52.
13. On the distribution of tribes and territory around the area of Sydney at the time of European contact, see Norman Tinsdale, *Aboriginal Tribes of Australia*, 2 vols.; for the Iora, vol. 1, p. 193. See also Blainey, *Triumph*, p. 31.
14. Phillip to Banks, Dec. 3, 1791, cit. in John Cobley, *Sydney Cove, 1789–1790*, p. 117.
15. Watkin Tench, *A Complete Account of the Settlement at Port Jackson, in New South Wales . . .*, p. 230.
16. On aboriginal canoes: William Bradley, *A Voyage to New South Wales*, Ms. facsimile ed. (Sydney, 1969), pp. 68–69.
17. The boomerang scarcely appears in First Fleet accounts and there is no printed description of its use before 1804. Hunter does not mention it; and although a boomerang (or at least, a boomerang-like object, curved, symmetrically tapered and about 18 inches long) figures in the plate facing p. 292 of John White's *Journal*, it is described as "an humble kind of scymitar," which suggests that White cannot have seen it in action.
18. George Barrington [pseud.], *The History of New South Wales*, p. 17.
19. Hunter, *Historical Journal*, p. 60.
20. Barrington, *History*, p. 20.
21. Ibid., p. 10.
22. Phillip to Sydney, HRNSW ii:129, May 15, 1788; for the Australian Aborigine as exemplar of "hard" primitivism in contrast to the indolent and peaceable Tahitian, see Smith, *European Vision*, pp. 126–27.
23. John White, cit. in John Cobley, *Sydney Cove, 1788*, p. 30.
24. Predatory aboriginal courtship: Barrington, *History*, p. 35.

25. A. P. Elkin, *The Australian Aborigines*, rev. ed. (Sydney, 1974), pp 159–61.
26. Hunter, *Historical Journal*, p. 64.

## CHAPTER TWO  *A Horse Foaled by an Acorn*

1. John Gloag, *Georgian Grace*, p. 54. This attitude is still very much with us; its recent monument (1985–86) was a vast and theatrical loan exhibition in Washington, D.C., called *Treasure Houses of England*, in which the English country house was presented as the primary "vessel of civilization" and taken as epitomizing the "age" in which it flourished. Modern Americans, in particular, like to fantasize about being Georgian gentlemen.
2. Henry Mayhew, *London Labour and the London Poor*, vol. 1, pp. 342–43.
3. Robert Blincoe to Central Board on Employment of Children in Manufactories, in PP 1833, xxi. D3:17–18.
4. Josiah Wedgwood to Peel Committee, in PP 1816, iii:64.
5. Joseph Badder to the Factory Commission of 1833, in PP 1833, xx. Cl:191.
6. Theodore Price to the Peel Committee, in PP 1816, iii:125.
7. Francis Place, cit. in Graham Wallas, *Life of Francis Place*, p. 163.
8. L. Lacombe, *Observations sur Londres . . .*, p. 180.
9. Edward P. Thompson, *The Making of the English Working Class*, pp. 59–60. This casual identification of any woman living out of wedlock as a "whore" would cause grave confusions about the actual morality of transported women convicts in Australia. The results of such assumptions are discussed in Chapter 8.
10. Henry Fielding, *An Enquiry into the Causes of the Late Increase of Robbers . . .*, p. 176.
11. Ibid., p. 92.
12. Jonas Hanway, *The Defects of the Police*, p. 224.
13. On Jonathan Wild, see Christopher Hibbert, *The Roots of Evil*, pp. 47–50.
    Jonathan Wild's career long predates transportation to Australia, but because of its effect on English views of the growth of crime it deserves a brief recapitulation here. Like thousands of other London toughs, Wild began as a pimp; but within a few years he had acquired two brothels and a circle of underground contacts—the human capital of the informer's trade. Not content with managing whores and informing, Wild built a fortune on the insight, dazzling in its simplicity, that would make all magistrates regard him as a national treasure: Although it was illegal to act as a receiver of stolen goods (a "fence"), no law forbade you to tell owners where their stolen property was, or to share in a reward for that information. Thus Wild set up a profitable business in stolen goods without ever touching a stolen object. Instead of buying the candlesticks or watches, he took a list of the loot from the thief, item by item. He then went to the owner with the news that certain items had fallen into the hands of an "honest broker," who had refused to buy them. The thief had fled, leaving the loot in the broker's hands, and Wild had been designated to find the owner and arrange for their return—provided the fictitious broker were decently rewarded for his honesty and civic spirit. This suited the thieves well, as Wild paid better than ordinary fences who only gave about 10 percent of value on stolen goods. It satisfied the law, as he only shared in a legal reward, and the sketchiness of eighteenth-century records made it difficult to disprove the broker's existence. It pleased the owners, because it was their one good chance of getting their property back. Most of all, it gratified Wild. He made £10,000 off it in fifteen years, the equivalent of a fairly large landed income.
    Parliament, startled by the sums he and others were pulling through this legal loophole, attempted to close it in 1718 with an act that made it a crime equal to theft to accept a reward for restoring goods without prosecuting the thief (4 Geo. I, c. 11, s. 4). In response, Wild merely shifted his tactics a little. He told the robbed householders who arrived in a daily stream at his office in Cock Lane to leave their money in cash in a designated place, and their possessions were returned to them the same day. Thus

there was no record of Wild even handling the money, let alone the loot. Before long Wild had done business with thousands of criminals and knew them by name. He kept files on them, listing their specialties; with these, he boasted, he could hang any thief in London. His next step was to use his leverage as England's top fence to shape the raw material of English crime, marshalling the scattered efforts of thieves, cut-purses and coiners across the nation into a corporate pattern. Starting with London, Wild organized gangs in every district of England. He had specialists trained in all kinds of theft and employed his own jewelers to melt plate and break up jewelry. He set up a rental service in burglars' tools and ran stolen goods to Holland in his own cargo sloop. London was his hatchery; in it, he raised thieves like trout. There was little profit in turning in a young thief for petty pinching. Wild cajoled his recruits along, prodding them deeper into crime, appealing to their audacity until they matured as "forty-pound men," criminals who would be worth handing over to the authorities. If anyone crossed him, Wild donned his role as thief-taker and haled him into court. It made no difference whether the charge was real or trumped-up, since Wild could produce as many witnesses as he wanted who would give whatever perjured testimony he needed. In the same way, he protected his friends by providing witnesses to swear to their innocence, retaining defense lawyers (there being no public defender) and, if necessary, bribing the more corruptible magistrates. He wielded his power with ruth-less zeal, certain that the law was on his side. It was; for the authorities were more interested in the thieves he caught than the ones he raised, and as a thief-taker he was hugely successful. He boasted of sending seventy-two men to the gallows, and he secured the conviction of thousands of lesser fry. Despite its mock-official ring, the title he bestowed on himself—"Thief-Taker General of Great Britain and Ireland"—was not exaggerated: In the eyes of the London mob, the bourgeoisie, the magistrates and the penny press alike, Wild was the arm of the law.

He went down at last, in 1725, convicted under the act which for the last seven years had borne his name. At Tyburn, the bellowing crowd that had gathered to watch him die pelted him with stones and slops, and his last act was to pick the hangman's pocket.

14. De La Coste,——*Voyage Philosophique d'Angleterre Fait en 1783 et 1784*, vol, 1, p. 12, cit. in Radzinowicz, *A History of the English Criminal Law and Its Administration Since 1752*, vol. 1, p. 724.

15. Cit. in Shaw *CC*, p. 39.

16. Radzinowicz, *History*, vol. 1, p. 27, note 87.

17. Ibid., vol. 1, p. 77.

18. For a discussion of the rituals of the Rule of Law, see Douglas Hay, "Property, Authority and the Criminal Law," in *Albion's Fatal Tree: Crime and Society in Eighteenth-Century England*, ed. Douglas Hay, Peter Linebaugh and Edward P. Thompson, p. 17ff.

19. Extract from *Dorset County Chronicle* [date unknown], 1831, incl. in Withers document file in TSA, Hobart.

20. The ritual of the procession to Tyburn from Newgate lasted until 1783, and it appears to have been curtailed by the sheriffs of London and Middlesex for fear that the "mob" would take it over completely—a fear probably reinforced by the Gordon Riots of 1780. Hangings remained public for a while thereafter, but they were done in front of the entrance to Newgate. Michael Ignatieff (*A Just Measure of Pain*, pp. 88–90) compares this to the efforts of prison reformers to reclaim the subculture of prisons from the inmates, and to Colquhoun's proposals for a metropolitan police force—"an attempt to establish state hegemony over collectivities of the poor whose defiance of public authority had long been tolerated or taken for granted."

21. J. P. Grosley, *A Tour in London* (London, 1772), vol. 1, pp. 172–73, cit. in Radzinowicz, *History*, vol. 1, p. 176, n. 50.

22. Radzinowicz, *History*, vol. 1, p. 175, note 45.

23. Text of the sexton's prayer: Howard, *The State of the Prisons in England and Wales*, p. 175.

24. The fullest eighteenth-century dictionaries of criminal slang and cant are Francis Grose, *A Classical Dictionary of the Vulgar Tongue* (London, 1785) and Anon., *A New Canting Dictionary* (London, 1725). The indispensable modern guide is Eric Partridge's monumental *A Dictionary of the Underworld* (3rd ed., London, 1971).
25. James Boswell, *The Life of Samuel Johnson* (Everyman ed., London, 1920), vol. 2, p. 447.
26. Jonathan Swift, "Clever Tom Clinch Going to Be Hanged," in Harold Williams (ed.), *The Poems of Jonathan Swift* (Oxford, 1937), vol. 2, p. 399.
27. Anon., *Hanging Not Punishment Enough* (London, 1701), cit. in Radzinowicz, *History*, vol. 1, p. 235.
28. F. Gemelli, *Viaggi per Europa* (1701), vol. 1, p. 328, cit. in Radzinowicz, ibid., vol. 1, p. 182.
29. Peter Linebaugh, "the Tyburn riot Against the Surgeons," in Hay et al., eds., *Albion's Fatal Tree*, p. 83.
30. Figures from Radzinowicz, *History*, vol. 1, p. 190.
31. On mercy and patronage, see Hay, "Property," in Hay et al., eds., *Albion's Fatal Tree*, p. 23.
32. The source for these petitions, especially those relating to transportation, is in the Privy Council Papers in the Public Records Office, London, in-letters to the Home Office 1/67–92, covering the years 1819–44. I have quoted from a few of them in Chapter 5, but the immense wealth of information they offer on the social background, experiences and circumstances of individual convicts and their families awaits the attention of historians.
33. John Howard, *The State of the Prisons in England and Wales*, p. 12.
34. Ibid., p. 9.
35. Fielding, *Enquiry*, p. 214.
36. Howard, *State of the Prisons*, p. 21.
37. Brisbane to Bathurst, Nov. 29, 1823, HRA xi:181.
38. Samuel Johnson, Jan. 6, 1759, in *The Idler*, vol. 1, p. 38.
39. In 1786 Pitt wrote to William Wilberforce, who was pressing him for penal reform, to say that "The multitude of things depending, has made the Penitentiary House long in deciding upon. But I still think," he added vaguely, "a beginning will be made before the season for building is over." No beginning was made and in the summer of 1788 Pitt reassured Wilberforce that penitentiaries "shall not be forgotten." Although Sir Samuel Romilly urged the government to pursue the idea of a national penitentiary, it remained in limbo until 1812, when ground was broken at Millbank, on the Thames, for the biggest prison in Europe—seven pentagonal blocks holding 1,200 prisoners, clustered around a chapel. It was theoretically modelled on Jeremy Bentham's scheme for a centralized Panopticon, but it turned out, in practice, to be an almost uncontrollable maze. The Millbank Penitentiary was never an effective substitute for transportation. It was demolished to make way for the Tate Gallery.
40. Smith, *Colonists in Bondage*, p. 92.
41. Ibid.
42. *The Correspondence of King George III*, ed. J. Fortescue, vol. 6, p. 415ff, cit. in Clark *HA*, vol. 1, p. 64.

## CHAPTER THREE  *The Geographical Unconscious*

1. On the dissemination of information in the eighteenth century, see Eric J. Hobsbawm, *The Age of Revolution*, pp. 21–23.
2. Luis de Camoëns, *Os Lusiadas*, vol. 10, p. 139.
3. On the Tordesillas line, originally meant to divide the Atlantic only but soon extended into a great meridian around the world dividing Luso-Castilian zones of influence in seas as yet unknown, see O. H. K. Spate, *The Pacific Since Magellan*, vol. 1: *The Spanish Lake*, pp. 25–29. On the Dieppe maps, and presumed Portuguese encounters

with the eastern coast of Australia, see Russel Ward, *Australia Since the Coming of Man*, pp. 21–26, and K. G. McIntyre, *The Secret Discovery of Australia*.

4. There is some evidence, not conclusive, of Chinese contact with Australia in the fifteenth century. See D. G. Mulvaney, *The Prehistory of Australia*, pp. 41–44.

5. William Dampier, *Dampier's Voyages*, ed. John Masefield, vol. 1, pp. 350–51.

6. Cook's instructions from the Admiralty on the Southern Continent: James Cook, *The Journals of Captain James Cook on His Voyage of Discovery*, ed. J. C. Beaglehole, vol. 1, pp. 279–84, and J. C. Beaglehole, *The Life of Captain James Cook*, pp. 147–49.

7. On the doings of the *Endeavour's* men two centuries ago at the now hopelessly corrupted paradise of Matavai Bay on Tahiti, the literature is vast. A summary is given by Beaglehole, *Life of Cook*, pp. 172–95.

8. Joseph Banks, *The Endeavour Journal of Joseph Banks, 1768–1771*, ed. J. C. Beaglehole.

9. Banks, *Journal*, April 25, 1770. Thus the image of sterile Australia—the "old Cow" of a continent—makes its appearance at the very moment of contact.

10. Cook, *Journals*, vol. 1, p. 399.

11. Alan Frost, *Convicts and Empire: A Naval Question, 1776–1811*, p. 135.

12. John Ehrman, *The Younger Pitt*, vol. 1, p. 405. In 1781–85 Britain's exports to the East Indies were worth less than £1 million and its imports a little more than £2 million. The corresponding figures for the Atlantic countries (Caribbean, North America, Newfoundland, Africa) were £4 million and £3.5 million.

13. Harris to Carmarthen, Aug. 19, 1785, cit. in Frost, *Convicts and Empire*, p. 99.

14. Harris to Carmarthen, Mar. 7, 1786, cit. in Frost, *Convicts and Empire*, p. 104.

15. Admiral Hughes on spar shortage in India: cit. ibid., p. 66.

16. *Phormium tenax*, the New Zealand flax plant which grew on Norfolk Island, superior in tensile strength and fiber to *Gymnostatus anceps*, the wild flax plant of the mainland coast, figured in the royal instructions to Phillip on the First Fleet, which mentioned its "superior excellence for a variety of Maritime purposes" and the prospect that it "may ultimately become an Article of Export." Phillip was enjoined to "particularly attend to its Cultivation, and . . . send home . . . Samples of this Article." Phillip's Instructions, Apr. 25, 1787, HRNSW ii:89.

17. James Mario Matra's proposal, Aug. 23, 1783, HRNSW ii:1–6.

18. Ibid.

19. Addition to Matra's proposal, Aug. 23, 1783, HRNSW ii:7.

20. Howe to Sydney, Dec. 26, 1784, HRNSW ii:10. "The length of the navigation," Admiral Howe remarked discouragingly, "subject to all the retardments of an India voyage, do [sic] not, I must confess, encourage to hope for a return of the many advantages in commerce or war which Mr. M. Matra has in contemplation."

21. Young to Pitt, enclosed in Pepper Arden to Sydney, Jan. 13, 1785, HRNSW ii:11. Young stressed the possible revenue from trade in Australian products, mainly spices, "fine Oriental cotton," sugar cane, coffee and tobacco. His main subject of enthusiasm, however, was *Phormium tenax*, "that very remarkable plant known by the name of the New Zealand flax-plant," which Young believed could be grown in limitless quantities. "Its uses are more extensive than any vegetable hitherto known, for in its gross state it far exceeds anything of the kind for cordage and canvas, and may be obtained at a much cheaper rate than . . . from Russia."

22. John Call to Pitt [?], ca. August 1784, HO 42/7:49–57, cit. in Frost, *Convicts and Empire*, p. 203.

23. Alexander Dalrymple, "A Serious Admonition . . . ," cit. in David Mackay, *A Place of Exile: The European Settlement of New South Wales*, p. 33.

24. Shaw *CC*, pp. 46–47.

25. For Rolle's pressure on Pitt to transport the felons accumulating in the Devon hulks, see Mackay, *Place of Exile*, p. 21.

26. Clark *HA*, vol. 1, p. 67.

27. For King's continuing interest in Norfolk Island flax, sustained in the face of discouraging indifference from his government, see Mackay, *Place of Exile*, p. 95.

28. In *Convicts and Empire*, Alan Frost claims a place in the Napoleonic Wars for the

infant colony of Sydney. "It is one of history's niceties," he claims, "as it is a tribute both to their percipience and their political longevity, that those who in the mid-1780s created [the colony as strategic outlier] called it onto the stage of war with the Emperor Napoleon." Yet Australia's "role" against Napoleon consisted of a passing thought by Pitt, in 1804, that Valparaiso might be attacked by a trans-Pacific expeditionary force from Sydney; and of Grenville's unexecuted plan to attack Chile, Peru and Mexico with a force that included men from the New South Wales Corps and "100 convict pioneers ... seasoned to work in the sun." Nothing came of either. Australia's "role" in the struggle against Bonaparte was nil.

29. Nepean, CO 201/2:15 and HO 42/7:24.
30. In preparing the "Heads of a Plan" for announcement by Lord Sydney, Nepean leaned heavily on the argument and phrasing of Matra's 1783 proposal for the Botany Bay settlement. The "Heads of a Plan" on flax in 1786: "The threads or filaments of this New Zealand plant are formed by nature with the most exquisite delicacy, and may be so minutely divided as to be manufactured into the finest linens." Matra on the same, in 1783: "The threads or filaments of this plant are formed by nature with the most exquisite delicacy, and they may be so minutely divided as to be small enough to make the finest Cambrick."
31. "Phillip's Views on the Conduct of the Expedition and the Treatment of Convicts," 1787, HRNSW ii:53.
32. Charles Bateson, *The Convict Ships, 1787–1868*, pp. 96–98.
33. Phillip to Nepean, Mar. 18, 1787, HRNSW ii:58.
34. Phillip to Nepean, Jan. 11, 1787, HRNSW ii:46.
35. Philip Gidley King, *The Journal of Philip Gidley King, Lieutenant, R.N., 1787–1790*, p. 6.
36. Phillip to Sydney, Feb. 28, 1787, HRNSW ii:50.
37. Phillip to Sydney, Mar. 12, 1787, HRNSW ii:56–57.
38. Phillip to Nepean, Mar. 18, 1787, HRNSW ii:59.
39. The basic source for the identity of the First Fleet convicts is a thorough compilation from sessions papers and assizes records published by Dr. John Cobley in 1970, *The Crimes of the First Fleet Convicts*. Defects and ambiguities in the records make it uncertain how many prisoners actually were shipped on the First Fleet. Cobley's figure is 778, both male and female; Crowley's (in *A Documentary History of Australia*, vol. 1) is 736; Lieutenant King's count, before sailing, was 752; and so on.
40. "Botany Bay: A New Song" is in Ballads collection, ML, Sydney.
41. [Alexander Dalrymple], *A Serious Admonition to the Publick on the Intended Thief-Colony at Botany Bay.*
42. *Whitehall Evening Post*, Dec. 19, 1786, cit. in C. M. H. Clark, *Sources of Australian History*, pp. 75–77.
43. "Memorial from the Marines," written on *Scarborough*, May 7, 1787, HRNSW ii:100–101.
44. Phillip to Sydney, June 5, 1787, HRNSW i:107.
45. Watkin Tench, *A Narrative of the Expedition to Botany Bay*, p. 3.
46. Ralph Clark Journal, May 13–14, 1787, *Journal and Letters, 1787–1792* (Sydney, 1981).
47. Samuel Eliot Morison, *The European Discovery of America*, vol. 1: *The Southern Voyages* (New York, 1974), p. 222.
48. Tench, *Narrative*, p. 19.
49. John White, *Journal*, July 1787, p. 39.
50. Ibid., pp. 30–31.
51. Clark, *Journal*, July 3, 1787.
52. Phillip to Nepean, Sept. 2, 1787, HRNSW ii:112.
53. White, *Journal*, p. 45.
54. Arthur Bowes Smyth, Journal, Nov. 12, 1787.
55. Ibid., Dec. 10, 1787.
56. Ibid., Jan. 10, 1788.

57. White, *Journal*, Jan. 1788, p. 113.
58. Ibid., p. 114.

CHAPTER FOUR   *The Starvation Years*

1. The prepossessing description of Botany Bay was given by Capt. James Cook in his Journal, Mar. 1, 1770. Joseph Banks, in his summary of the New South Wales coast written aboard *Endeavour* in August 1770 (Banks, *Journal*, ed. Beaglehole, vol. 2, p. 111ff.: "Some Account of that part of New Holland now called New South Wales"), was much more skeptical. "Barren it may justly be call'd and in a very high degree. . . . [U]pon the Whole the fertile Soil Bears no kind of Proportion to that which seems by nature doomed to everlasting barrenness. Water is here a scarce article. . . . [A]t the two places where we filld for the ships use it was done from pools not brooks. Cultivation could not be supposed to yeild much towards the support of man."
   A few pages later he softened these strictures a little, remarking that "Upon the whole New Holland, tho' in every respect the most barren countrey I have seen, is not so bad that between the productions of sea and Land a company of People who should have the misfortune of being shipwrecked upon it might support themselves."
2. Lieut. Philip Gidley King, *Journal*, Jan. 20, 1788, pp. 34–35.
3. Ibid.
4. Ibid.
5. Arthur Bowes Smyth, *Journal*, Jan. 21, 1788, pp. 57–58.
6. Watkin Tench, *A Narrative of the Expedition to Botany Bay*, pp. 57–58, and John White, *Journal*, p. 117. Apparently the tune (that of "For He's a Jolly Good Fellow") was retained among the Aborigines, for George Thompson (*Slavery and Famine: An Account of the Miseries and Starvation at Botany Bay*, p. 16) would describe them paddling their canoes while singing it—"they have the French tune of Malbrook very perfect: I have heard a dozen or twenty singing it together."
7. Phillip to Sydney, May 15, 1788, HRNSW ii:121–22.
8. David Collins, *An Account of the English Colony at New South Wales*, vol. 1, p. 5.
9. Tench, *Narrative*, p. 60.
10. Jean-François de la Pérouse, *A Voyage Around the World . . . Under the Command of J. F. G. de la Pérouse*, vol. 2, p. 180.
11. Phillip to Sydney, May 15, 1788, HRNSW ii:123.
12. Ralph Clark, Journal, Feb. 1, 1788, *Journal and Letters, 1787–1792*. (The original Ms. is in ML Sydney.) On the indolence of convicts, see Phillip to Sydney, HRNSW ii:123.
13. Bowes Smyth, *Journal*, Feb. 6, 1788.
14. Ibid., Feb. 7, 1788, pp. 67–69. Bowes Smyth's opinion that Phillip's Commission was "a more unlimited one than was ever before granted to any Governor under the British Crown" was shared by other officers, including Ralph Clark: "I never heard of any one single person having so great a power invested in him." George Worgan, the naval surgeon who brought the first piano to Australia on the *Sirius*, felt that the "feeling and concern" of Phillip's delivery did honor to his humanity, "and it really is a Pity, he has the Government of a set of Reprobates who will not suffer him to indulge himself in a Lenity, which he sincerely wishes to govern them by." G. B. Worgan, *Journal*, Feb. 9, 1788.
15. Phillip in HRNSW ii:155–56, July 9, 1788.
16. On the construction of the first settlement's huts, see J. M. Freeland, *Architecture in Australia*, pp. 12–17.
17. Thomas Watling, *Letters from an Exile at Botany-Bay . . . .*, p. 17. The use of sheeps' hair in the mortar (not wool) was inevitable; the first Australian sheep were hairy animals from the Cape, raised for their meat not their fleece.
18. Ross to Col. Sec. Stephens, July 10, 1788, HRNSW ii:173.
19. Bowes Smyth, *Journal*, Feb. 25–26, 1788, pp. 74–75.

20. HRNSW I/ii:89. N. G. Butlin, in *Our Original Aggression,* proposes that the officers of the First Fleet, with the connivance f Phillip, deliberately infected the Aborigines with cholera as a form of germ warfare. There is no direct or persuasive evidence for this, and the distress with which the First Fleet diarists observed the epidemics among the tribespeople argues strongly against it.
21. George B. Worgan, *Journal,* May 24, 1788.
22. Ibid.
23. Daniel Southwell, HRNSW ii:666.
24. Worgan, letter to Richard Worgan, June 12, 1788, Ms. in ML, Sydney.
25. Watling, *Letters from an Exile,* pp. 7–8.
26. Ibid.
27. Ibid.
28. Collins, *Account,* vol. 1, p. 17.
29. Extract of Journal of Richard Williams (seaman on *Borrowdale*) in broadsheet Q991/W, ML, Sydney.
30. HRNSW ii:746–77.
31. Bowes Smyth, *Journal,* Feb. 23, 1788, p. 74.
32. Ross to Nepean, HRNSW ii:212.
33. Campbell to Lord Ducie, cit. in Cobley, *Sydney Cove, 1788,* p. 191.
34. Phillip to Sydney, July 9, 1788, HRNSW ii:150.
35. Clark, *Journal,* Feb. 28, 1790.
36. King, *Journal,* May 10, 1788.
37. Tench, *Account,* p. 37.
38. Southwell to Rev. W. Butler, Apr. 14, 1790, cit. in Cobley, *Sydney Cove, 1789–1790,* p. 183.
39. Collins, *Account,* p. 81.
40. Tench, *Account,* pp. 39–40.
41. King, HRNSW ii:431.
42. Clark, letter to Capt. Campbell, Feb. 11, 1791, in Clark, *Journal and Letters, 1787–1792.*
43. Clark, *Journal,* May 21, 1790.
44. Phillip to Sydney, HRNSW ii:211.
45. Kidnapped Maoris: King, *Journal,* Nov. 1793, pp. 177–78. King had made the young Maoris "a very serious promise of sending them home" [*Journal,* May 1793, p. 135] and he honored it, though not soon enough for either of them. "Woodoo like a true Patriot thinks there is no country People or Customs equal to those of his own, which makes him less curious in what he sees about him, than his companion Tooke." [*Journal,* November 1793, pp. 178–79.]
46. Tench, *Account,* p. 43.
47. Letter from anonymous convict woman dated Port Jackson, Nov. 14, 1788, in HRA ii:746–47. Rev. Richard Johnson to Henry Fricker, Apr. 9, 1790, at C232 in ML, Sydney.
48. Southwell to Rev. Butler, Apr. 14, 1790.
49. Anonymous male convict, cit. in Cobley, *Sydney Cove, 1789–1790,* pp. 165–66.
50. Tench, *Account,* p. 42.
51. Collins, *Account,* p. 88.
52. Watling, *Letters from an Exile,* p. 18.
53. "We shall not starve": Phillip to Nepean, Apr. 15, 1790, HRNSW ii:330.
54. Arrival of *Lady Juliana:* Tench, *Account,* p. 46.
55. Phillip to W.W. Grenville, HRA i:194–97, Jul. 17, 1790.
56. Collins, *Account,* cit. in Cobley, *Sydney Cove, 1791–92,* p. 129.
57. For the New South Wales Corps, see George Mackaness, *Life of Vice-Admiral Bligh,* vol. 2, p. 117–18; Herbert V. Evatt, *Rum Rebellion,* passim; Clark *HA,* vol. 1, pp. 150, 166.
58. Collins, *Account,* vol. 1, p. 187.
59. Phillip to Grenville, July 17, 1790, HRA i:194–97.

60. Phillip to Dundas, Mar. 19, 1792, HRNSW ii:597.

61. "Reminiscences of Henry Hale to Mrs. Caroline Chisholm," in Samuel Sidney, *The Three Colonies of Australia*, p. 43.

62. George Thompson, *Slavery and Famine*, pp. 35–36. Phillip to Dundas, Oct. 2, 1792, HRNSW ii:645.

63. HRNSW ii:664. I am assuming a (very approximate) conversion rate of 50:1 between modern and late eighteenth-century sterling. See Roy Porter, *English Society in the Eighteenth Century*, p. 13.

64. *Parliamentary History*, vol. 28, pp. 1222–24.

65. See Appendix 1, "Governors and Chief Executives of New South Wales During Convict Period, 1788–1855," for the various governors' dates of office.

66. Grose to Dundas, Feb. 16, 1793. HRA ii:14–15.

67. Crowley, *Doc. Hist.*, vol. 1, p. 63. Shaw *CC*, p. 66.

68. Roe, "Colonial Society in Embryo," *HS*, vol. 7, no. 26 (May 1956), p. 157.

69. S. Macarthur-Onslow, ed., *Some Early Records of the Macarthurs of Camden*, pp. 45–46.

70. John Easty, "A Memorandum of the Transactions of a Voyage from England to Botany Bay in the Scarborough Transport . . . ," Dixson Library, Sydney; entry for Sept. 30, 1792. Easty's opinion as to the severity of discipline under King on Norfolk Island is not supported by King's own journal, with its (on the whole) moderate record of flogging. A private in the Marines, and subject to harsh discipline himself, Easty showed a lively sense of injustice when noting the punishments inflicted on others. Thus at Cape Town [Nov. 7, 1787] he found the Dutch authorities "very Strict sort of People . . . they hang them for the Lest thing in the World allmost and for anything that is very Bad they rack them and Break their Bones one by one and hang them upon a Gibett like a Dog."

71. King to Dundas, Mar. 10, 1794, HRNSW ii:137.

72. King's report, in HRNSW ii:145.

73. Grose to King, Feb. 25, 1794, HRNSW ii:130–31.

74. On Maj. Joseph Foveaux, see ADB entry and Mss. catalogued under Foveaux in ML, Sydney, especially Foveaux's "*Letter Book, 1800–1804*" (ML A1444), hereafter referred to as FLB.

75. Foveaux to King, Nov. 16, 1800, FLB.

76. Robert Jones, "Recollections of 13 Years Residence at Norfolk Island," ca. 1823.

77. Ibid.

78. Ibid.

79. Ibid.

80. Ibid.

81. Foveaux to King, Jan. 13, 1801, FLB.

82. Foveaux to Duke of Portland, Sept. 17, 1801, letter at Af 48/4, ML, Sydney.

83. Jones, "Recollections."

84. On Richard Atkins, see ADB entry; John Grant, letter 15, July 13, 1804, Ms. 737, NLA, Canberra.

85. Alan Frost, *Convicts and Empire*, pp. 168–69.

86. Ibid., p. 172.

87. Liverpool to Macquarie, HRNSW vii:562–63.

88. On the numbers, distribution and tribal organization of the Van Diemen's Land Aborigines, see Robson, *Hist. Tas.*, pp. 13–25, esp. pp. 17–18. Lyndall Ryan (*The Aboriginal Tasmanians*, p. 14) follows Rhys Jones in assuming a population of 3,000 to 4,000 Aborigines at the time of European settlement. This figure is disputed, on no very clear evidence, by present-day aboriginal descendants, whose guesses run as high as 8,000 to 10,000.

89. The word "tarpaulin" is common eighteenth-century slang for "career naval officer."

90. For Bentham's pursuit of Collins, see Bentham Papers, Add. Ms. 33544, fols. 20–21, 41–42, 57–58, BL.

91. George Prideaux Harris at Port Phillip, to Henry Harris: Harris Family Papers, Add.

Ms. 45156, fols. 14–15, BL. James Grove, undated letter 2, in "Select Letters of James Grove," ed. Earnshaw, THRA, PP.

92. George Harris, Add. Ms. 45156, fol. 16, BL.
93. King to Collins, Nov. 26, 1803, HRA iii:39, and Dec. 30, 1803, HRA iii:50. Collins to King, Dec. 30, 1803, HRA iii:50, and Jan. 27, 1804, HRA iii:53.
94. Collins to King, Feb. 28, 1804, HRA iii:217–18.
95. Memo by Lieut. Edward Lord in "Select Letters of James Grove," ed. Earnshaw, pp. 38–39.
96. James Backhouse, *A Narrative of a Visit to the Australian Colonies*, p. 21.
97. William Maum to Robert Nash, Jan. 28, 1808, Calder Papers, ML, Sydney.
98. Robson, *Hist. Tas.*, p. 71.
99. Jones, "Recollections."
100. James Grove, undated letter 4, in "Select Letters of James Grove," p. 38.
101. Memo by Lieut. Edward Lord, ibid., p. 39.
102. George Harris, Add. Ms. 45156, fol. 16, BL.
103. Mary Gilmore, "Old Botany Bay," 1918.

CHAPTER FIVE   *The Voyage*

1. Thomas Holden to Molly Holden, DDX 140/7:4, LRO.
2. Peter Withers to Mary Ann Withers, April 1831, TSA, Hobart.
3. Richard Dillingham to Betsey Faine, Dec. 28, 1831, letter 2, Bedfordshire County Archive.
4. John Ward, "Diary of a Convict," transcript pp. 39–40, in Ward Papers, NLA.
5. Thomas Holden to Molly Holden, DDX 140/7:8 and 10a, LRO.
6. Peter Withers to Mary Ann Withers, TSA, Hobart.
7. Ibid.
8. Deborah Taylor to Sir Robert Peel, Apr. 8, 1830, PC 1:78, PRO.
9. Jane Eastwood to Sir Robert Peel, Apr. 12, 1830, PC 1:78, PRO.
10. Ibid.
11. Isherwood et al. to Viscount Sidmouth, May 12, 1819, PC 1:67, PRO. R. Downie to Peel, Apr. 15, 1830, PC 1:78, PRO.
12. Richard Boothman to his father, Feb. 10, 1841, DDX 537:5, LRO.
13. Richard Taylor to his father, Apr. 14 and Apr. 22, 1840, DDX 505:2 and 3, LRO.
14. R. Taylor to parents, May 1840, 505:4, LRO.
15. R. Boothman to father, May 18 and June 16, 1841, DDX 537:11 and 13, LRO. R. Brown to father, May 2, 1841, DDX 505:15, LRO. T. Holden to mother, June 1812, DDX 140/7:7, LRO.
16. "The Borough," letter 18, in *George Crabbe, Poems*, ed. A. W. Ward, vol. 1, p. 458, cit. in Coral Lansbury, *Arcady in Australia*, p. 10.
17. Wentworth Papers, pp. 31–32, ML, Sydney.
18. T. Holden, DDX 140/7:8, LRO. R. Boothman, DDX 537:11, LRO.
19. Petition of Mrs. Silas Harris, May 2, 1819, PC 1:67, PRO.
20. William Tidman to Sidmouth, Feb. 8, 1819, PC 1:67, PRO. Mrs. Lycot to Sir George Paul, encl. in Paul to Sidmouth, May 12, 1819, PC 1:67, PRO.
21. Helen Guild, petition dated April 1830, PC 1:78, PRO.
22. T. Holden to mother, DDX 140/7:6, LRO.
23. T. Holden to Molly Holden, DDX 140/7:9, LRO. Henry Bennett, *A Letter to Viscount Sidmouth, on Transportation*, p. 24. Ward, "Diary of a Convict," p. 42.
24. Ward, ibid., p. 44.
25. Mansfield Silverthorpe, Ms. no. 9, Norfolk Island Convict Papers.
26. Woomera [pseud.], *The Life of an Ex-Convict*, printed extract in ML, Sydney, p. 2. Ward, "Diary of a Convict," p. 78.
27. George Lee to Sir Henry St. J. Mildmay, Jan. 24, 1803, Bentham Papers, BL, Add. Ms. 33544, ff. 14–15.

28. Little boy: Bennett, *Letter to Viscount Sidmouth*, p. 25. James Grove, letter 1 in "Select Letters of James Grove." Silverthorpe, Ms. no. 9, Norfolk Island Convict Papers.
29. John Mortlock, *Experiences of a Convict*, p. 55.
30. Bennett, *Letter to Viscount Sidmouth*, p. 30.
31. Mortlock, *Experiences*, p. 53. Ward, "Diary of a Convict," p. 83.
32. Silverthorpe, Ms. no. 9, p. 66.
33. Silverthorpe., ibid. Ward, "Diary of a Convict," p. 90. Mortlock, *Experiences*, p. 53.
34. Ward, ibid., p. 40.
35. John Nicol, *The Life and Adventures of John Nicol, Mariner*, pp. 114–15.
36. Bennett, *Letter to Viscount Sidmouth*, p. 29.
37. Simon Taylor to his father, May 1841, DDX 505:17, LRO.
38. Contract system: see Charles Bateson, *The Convict Ships 1787–1868*, pp. 12ff.
39. Death rate during the Atlantic crossing and in the Navy: see Shaw *CC*, p. 117.
40. The death rate in the early 1830s was increased by three bad shipwrecks. In 1833 the *Amphitrite* ran around near Boulogne before she even cleared the English Channel, drowning 106 women convicts. In 1835 the *George III* sank in the D'Entrecasteaux Channel, near Hobart, after a scurvy-ridden outward voyage; captain and crew were slow to unbar the hatches, and 127 male prisoners drowned. The same year, *Neva* was wrecked in the Bass Strait, killing another 138 women. If allowance is made for the loss of life from these wrecks, one sees that the convicts' general death rate from disease and neglect en route had, by naval standards, become very small by the 1830s.
41. Capt. William Hill to Wathen, July 26, 1790, HRNSW ii:367.
42. Thomas Milburn, "Copy of a Letter from Thomas Milburn in Botany Bay to his Father and Mother in Liverpool," broadsheet, Aug. 26, 1790, ML, Sydney.
43. Hill to Wathen, July 26, 1790, HRNSW ii:367.
44. Rev. Richard Johnson to Thornton, HRNSW ii:387–88.
45. The design of the Great Seal: HRNSW ii:389. In England, Erasmus Darwin, poetaster and grandfather of the great naturalist, was moved to pen his *Visit of Hope to Botany-Bay* to accompany a medallion made by Wedgwood out of Sydney clay, a verse less remarkable for its social realism than for its prediction of the Sydney Harbor Bridge:

> Where Sydney Cove her lucid bosom swells,
> Courts her young navies, and the storm repels;
> High on a rock amid the troubled air
> HOPE stood sublime, and wav'd her golden hair;
> Calm'd with her rosy smile the tossing deep
> And with sweet accents charm'd the winds to sleep;
> To each wild plain she stretch'd her snowy hand,
> High-waving wood, and sea-encircled strand.
> "Hear me", she cried, "ye rising Realms! record
> Time's opening scenes, and Truth's unerring word—
> *There* shall broad streets their stately walls extend,
> The circus widen, and the crescent bend;
> *There*, ray'd from cities o'er the cultured land,
> Shall bright canals, and solid roads expand.—
> *There* the proud Arch, Colossus-like, bestride
> Yon glittering streams, and bound the chafing tide— . . .

And so on. Hope was easier to see in England than in Sydney.
46. Short rations on *Queen*: Bateson, *Convict Ships*, p. 137.
47. Capt. William Hill, cit. in Shaw *CC*, p. 112.
48. For conditions on the *Hillsborough* before her departure from Australia, see Jerome Fitzpatrick to Baldwin, Aug. 25, 1801, Pelham Papers, BL, Add. Ms. 33107, pp. 407ff. A vivid account of the voyage (*Voyage to Sydney in the Ship Hillsborough 1798–99, and a Description of the Colony*, Ms. in Dixson, published for the Library of Australian History, 1978) was written by the convict silversmith William Noah, a native of

Shropshire who, at forty-three, had been sentenced to death at the Old Bailey in April 1797 for stealing two thousand pounds of lead, value £23, from a plumber in Westminster. Captain Hingston's attitude to the convicts may be gauged from Noah's account of his wife's attempt to visit her condemned husband on Dec. 4, 1798, before the *Hillsborough* sailed:

> I was very mich Suppris'd on looking thro' the port Holes of the Ship to see my Wife come Off in a Werry & a longside. I immediately wrote to Capt Hingston begging the Indulgence to speak to her on the Deck but had no Answer finding her still along side I wrote a Second Stating to him that she had Came from London with what she must have Experienc'd from the Cold & that it might be a final Leave I being banish'd to a Distant Land, this last sofed'd his Heart & after her being a Longside two Hour's I was Orderd on Deck when with a Brutal Kind of Behavior she was admitted with a Box she had brought for me.... [Hingston] fell in a Violent Passion askin how many Boxes I meant to have, Swearing If any thing was in it off Tools he would throw the [w]Hole into the Sea & unfortunately I had Orderd a few Ingravers & Others small tools ... the Maj[ority] of which he found she was then Immediately Orderd out of the Ship with the Tools and I with the most Horrid Language down to my Miserable Place of Confinement no One Can feel the Horror of an Unhappy Mind I was Disconsolate & felt the Horrors of Cruel Misfortunes.

49. Conditions and medical officers on the *Royal Admiral:* see Bateson, *Convict Ships,* p. 43.
50. Ibid. pp. 45–46.
51. Ibid., pp. 160–65. *Massey's Journal Book,* 1796, typescript extract at Ab. 93, ML, Sydney. Beyer was on his third voyage to Sydney; he had been Captain Anstis's surgeon on *Scarborough* in the Second Fleet.
52. Fitzpatrick to Rev. Charles Lindsey, re conditions on *Hercules* and *Atlas,* Pelham Papers, Add. Ms. 33107, pp. 200–203, BL.
53. Fitzpatrick to Pelham, ibid., p. 341ff.
54. Shaw *CC,* p. 114. Macquarie to Bathurst, Dec. 12, 1817, HRA ix:510.
55. Fitzpatrick to Baldwin, Pelham Papers, Add. Ms. 33105, BL, p. 242ff.
56. Redfern to Macquarie, HRA viii:275ff.
57. Figures from Bateson, *Convict Ships,* Appendix 7b.
58. As merchantmen, most transports had been designed to squeeze as much cargo space as possible from the tonnage laws that governed the payment of harbor dues up to 1835. The rule of thumb in this tonnage calculation assumed that a hull's depth was half its beam. Hence the owners sought to fool the tax man by building ships as narrow and deep as possible. This was fine for cargo, but terribly uncomfortable for convicts, as narrow hulls were less stable than beamy ones and rolled violently. As free emigration to Australia began to take hold in the 1830s, so the quality of convict shipping declined—for it was much more profitable for owners to take paying passengers than to accept government charters.
59. John Boyle O'Reilly, *Moondyne,* pp. 186–89.
60. George Prideaux Harris to family, n.d. [Jan. 1804], BL, Add. Ms. 45156, p. 9v.
61. Alfred Tetens, *Among the Savages of the South Seas,* p. xxii.
62. John Gorman, Log-book, untitled Ms. 1524, NLA, Canberra.
63. Mellish, "A Convict's Recollections of New South Wales," p. 49.
64. Charles Cozens, *The Adventures of a Guardsman,* p. 98.
65. Ibid., pp. 95–96.
66. Ibid., pp. 103–4.
67. John Gregg, Journal on convict ship *York,* 1862, Ms. 2749, NLA.
68. William Coke to his father, Apr. 20, 1826, Coke letters, D.1881, DRO.
69. Ibid.
70. Tetens, *Among the Savages,* p. xxiii.
71. Ibid., p. xxiv.

72. T. Holden to parents, DDX/140:12, LRO.
73. John Smith, Surgeon's log on transport *Clyde*, Ms. 6169, NLA, Canberra.
74. Murray to Smith, Sept. 13, 1838, encl. in Ms. 6169, NLA, Canberra.

### CHAPTER SIX   *Who Were the Convicts?*

1. William Blake, "Vala, Night the Ninth," in *The Complete Writings of William Blake,* ed. Geoffrey Keynes, London, 1966, pp. 359–60.
2. J. L. Hammond and B. Hammond, *The Village Laborer, 1760–1832,* p. 239; G. Arnold Wood, "Convicts," *JRAHS,* vol. 8, no. 4 (1922), p. 187.
3. See C. M. H. Clark, "The Origins of the Convicts Transported to Eastern Australia, 1787–1852," HS, vol. 7, no. 26 (May 1956), pp. 121–35, and vol. 7, no. 27 (June 1956), pp. 314–27; and see also Lloyd L. Robson, *The Convict Settlers of Australia.*
4. C. M. H. Clark, *Select Documents in Australian History, 1788–1850,* pp. 406–8.
5. Robson, *Convict Settlers of Australia,* Appendix 4, table 4(e). I have rounded off the percentages.
6. Ibid., Appendix 4, table 4(d).
7. Ibid., Appendix 4, tables 4(b) and (1).
8. Gertrude Himmelfarb, *The Idea of Poverty,* p. 291. For her discussion of class language, see pp. 281–304.
9. Ibid., p. 295.
10. Henry Mayhew, *London Labour and the London Poor,* vol. 3, p. 381.
11. Patrick Colquhoun, *A Treatise on the Police of the Metropolis,* pp. vii–xi.
12. Edward P. Thompson, *The Making of the English Working Class,* pp. 59–66.
13. *Fraser's Magazine,* June 1832, pp. 521–22, cit. in J. J. Tobias, *Crime and Industrial Society in the 19th Century.*
14. *Eclectic Review,* vol. 2 (April 1854), p. 387, cit. in Tobias, ibid.
15. Himmelfarb, *Poverty,* p. 397.
16. Ibid., p. 399. "Ragged-schools" were charity schools for pauper children.
17. Petition from S. Nelson to Home Secretary, Ms. in NLA, Canberra. Isaac Nelson survived the voyage and—gentle soul—became one of the first schoolteachers in Australia, under the Rev. Richard Johnson.
18. On the wreckers' assumption of their traditional "rights," see John G. Rule, "Wrecking and Coastal Plunder," in Hay et al., eds., *Albion's Fatal Tree,* pp. 181–84.
19. Peter Cunningham, *Two Years in New South Wales,* vol. 2, p. 234.
20. Henry Mayhew, *London Labour and the London Poor,* vol. 4, pp. 25–26.
21. G. Parker, *Life's Painter of Variegated Characters,* 1789, cit. in Eric Partridge, *Dictionary of the Underworld.*
22. Partridge, ibid.
23. On Barrington, see HRA i:1–4 and ADB entry.
24. Dickens, *Oliver Twist* (London: Penguin Books, Penguin Classics, 1966), pp. 390–91.
25. Mayhew, *London Labour,* vol. 1, pp. 411 and 467.
26. Peter Gaskell, *The Manufacturing Population of England,* 1833, chapter 4.
27. Thomas Holden, letter to parents, 1812, DDX 140/7:13, LRO.
28. On Muir's trial and those of other "Scottish Martyrs," see Anon., *The Political Martyrs of Scotland Persecuted During the Years 1793 and 1794* (Edinburgh, 1795).
29. Ibid.
30. Lauderdale's objection was that the 1703 Act under which Muir and Palmer had been convicted limited their punishment to banishment, not transportation. Banishment meant only "exclusion from a community," whereas transportation "implies that exclusion executed in a compulsory and commonly ignominious Manner, always aggravated by Confinement and . . . the obligation of laborious Servitude." Lauderdale et al. to Dundas, Dec. 14, 1793, WI/5007 in Whitbread Papers, Bedford.
31. Gerrald to Margarot, 1794, Ms. at Ag. 14, ML, Sydney.
32. Muir to Moffatt, Dec. 13, 1794, Ms. in ML, Sydney.

33. Thomas Fyshe Palmer, *A Narrative of the Sufferings of T. F. Palmer*, p. 35.
34. Palmer, letters dated Apr. 23 and May 5, 1796, ML, Sydney.
35. Thomas Muir, "The Telegraph: A Consolatory Epistle," unpublished Ms. at Am. 9, ML, Sydney. "Telegraph" here means a semaphore.
36. Hill and Newton to Cooke, Mar. 12, 1797, Rebellion Papers 620/29:58 and 196, SPO, cit. in Shaw *CC*, p. 170.
37. Hugh Reid, statement in summary of evidence on *Marquis Cornwallis* mutiny, HRA i:657–58.
38. Hunter to Portland, Nov. 12, 1796, HRA i:674–75.
39. Irish convicts in Australia: HRA x:203–4. Hunter to Portland, Mar. 3, 1796, HRA i:555–56.
40. David Collins, *An Account of the English Colony in New South Wales*, vol. 1, pp. 380–81, and vol. 2, p. 57.
41. Hunter to Portland, Feb. 15, 1798, HRA i:131.
42. Number of Irish convicts in New South Wales in 1798: T. J. Kiernan, "Transportation from Ireland to Sydney 1791–1816" (M.A. thesis), p. 59.
43. James Carty, ed., *Ireland from Grattan's Parliament to the Great Famine, 1783–1850: A Documentary Record*, p. 69.
44. Cornwallis to Major-General Ross, cit. in Carty, *Ireland*, pp. 95–96.
45. Shaw *CC*, p. 170.
46. Kiernan, "Transportation," Appendix II, p. 29. Opinions differ, however, on the number of "politicals" in these Irish shipments. George Rude, in *Protest and Punishment* (1978), takes the stringently reductionist view that only 241 Irish were "politicals."
47. Hunter to Portland, Jan. 10, 1798, HRA ii:118.
48. Elizabeth Paterson to Capt. Johnson, Feb. 10, 1800, in Ms. Ap. 36:5, ML, Sydney.
49. King to Cooke, July 20, 1805, HRA v:534.
50. Hunter to Portland, Mar. 20, 1800, HRA ii:223.
51. Irish Conspiracy Papers, HRA iii:575 et seq. and 582–83.
52. Samuel Marsden, "A Few Observations on the Toleration of the Catholic Religion in New South Wales," Ms. 18, Marsden Papers, ML, Sydney.
53. Hester Stroud, deposition to Marsden, Irish Conspiracy Papers, HRA iii:641.
54. Joseph Holt, "Life and Adventures of Joseph Holt . . . ," Ms. in ML, Sydney, pp. 293–95. I have corrected the distractingly erratic spelling and some of the odder punctuation of this passage.
55. King's court of inquiry into Irish insurgents: Oct. 1, 1800, HRA iii:650–51.
56. Elizabeth Patterson to "Mrs. B.," Oct. 7, 1800. Bentham Papers, Add. Ms., BL, pp. 423–24.
57. King to Portland, HRA iii:8–9.
58. Punishment of Father O'Neil: HRA iii:759. Irish efforts to get a priest to the colony, and King's eventual permission to Father Dixon to say Mass and administer the sacraments: King to Hobart, May 9, 1803, HRA iv:82–83.
59. "Situation shocking to Humanity": King to Transport Commissioners, HRA ii:532.
60. On Hassall's description of the start of the Irish rising at Castle Hill, see Castle Hill Rebellion Papers, Bonwick Transcripts, vol. 1, box 49, pp. 234–35, ML, Sydney.
61. Major George Johnston refuses to parley with Paterson: HRA iv:570.
62. Johnston to King, encl. 4 in King to Hobart, Mar. 12, 1804, HRA iv:568.
63. John Grant, Journal, pp. 47–48, Ms. 737, Grant Papers, NLA, Canberra.
64. King to Hobart, Apr. 16, 1804, HRA iv:611.
65. "Occasionally removed from one Settlement to another": King to Hobart, Apr. 30, 1805, HRA v:305. Poteen stills: HRA v:571.
66. George Rude, *Protest and Punishment*, p. 249.
67. Leslie C. Duly, "Hottentots to Hobart and Sydney: The Cape Supreme Court's Use of Transportation, 1828–1838."
68. On Canadian protesters see Rude, *Protest and Punishment*, pp. 42–51 and 82–88.
69. Eric Hobsbawm, *Industry and Empire*, p. 76.

70. Thompson, *English Working Class*, pp. 347–48.
71. Cook to Churton, Jan. 20, 1831, copy in "The Exile's Lamentations," MS at A1711, ML, Sydney, and cit. in Clune, *The Norfolk Island Story*, p. 157.
72. Thompson, *English Working Class*, p. 250.
73. Eric Hobsbawm and George Rude, *Captain Swing*, p. 262.
74. Ibid., pp. 245–46.
75. Richard Dillingham, letter to parents, Sept. 29, 1836, Dillingham Papers, Ms-CRT. 150:24, Bedfordshire County Record Office.
76. Peter Withers, letter to brother, Ms. letters in TSA, Hobart.
77. James Backhouse and G. W. Walker, *A Narrative of a Visit to the Australian Colonies*, Appendix J, letter 3.

CHAPTER SEVEN  *Bolters and Bushrangers*

1. Watkin Tench, *A Complete Account of the Settlement at Port Jackson, in New South Wales*, p. 141. Some of the "Chinese travellers," he found (*Account*, p. 138), believed that China was only a hundred miles to the north of Parramatta, and separated from Australia by a river. Others were not so sure, but they had gone along "on account of being over-worked, and harshly treated . . . [T]hey preferred a solitary and precarious existence in the woods, to a return to the misery they were compelled to undergo." The China myth, Phillip correctly thought, was "an evil that will cure itself" (Phillip to Nepean, Nov. 18, 1791, HRA i:309). For Collins's views on it and the Irish who held it, see Collins, *An Account of the English Colony at New South Wales*, vol. 1, pp. 154, 162–63, and vol. 2, pp. 54–55, 57. In 1791, according to John Hunter (*An Historical Journal of the Transactions at Port Jackson and Norfolk Island*, pp. 563–64), no less than forty of them were missing in the bush.
2. Hunter to Portland, Feb. 15, 1798, HRNSW iii:359. Collins (*Account*, vol. 2, p. 57) adds that the Irish imagined this colony of whites to lie some 300 to 400 miles southwest of Sydney.
3. King to Hobart, May 9, 1803, HRA iv:85. King to Hobart, enclosure of Govt. & General Order dated March 1803, in Aug. 7, 1803, HRA iv:337.
4. On Mary Bryant, see ADB, vol. 1, pp. 173–74; C. H. Currey, *The Transportation, Escape and Pardoning of Mary Bryant*; and F. A. Pottle, *Boswell and the Girl from Botany Bay*. For the voyage, see James Martin, *Memorandoms*. This is an edition of Martin's own "Memorandoms," acquired by Jeremy Bentham and preserved in his papers in the British Library. Martin had been sentenced to 7 years' transportation at the Exeter Assizes for stealing "16½ lb. of old Lead and 4½ lb. of old Iron property of Lord Courney powdrum cacle near Exeter." He had struck up a friendship with the Bryants both on the hulk and on *Charlotte*, and escaped with them from Sydney Harbor. When, after his adventures, he returned to London, he wrote down an account of their sufferings on the epic small-boat voyage. It found its way to Jeremy Bentham, who was collecting evidence of the injustices and failures of transportation for his *Letter to Lord Pelham* (1802) and *A Plea for the Constitution* (1803), reprinted as *Panopticon Versus New South Wales* (1812). However, there is no reference to James Martin or his "Memorandoms" in Bentham's published works.
5. Collins, *Account*, pp. 129–30.
6. John Easty, "A Memorandom of the Transactions of a Voyage from England to Botany Bay in Scarborough Transport," entry for Mar. 28, 1791.
7. All quotations are from the account of the voyage in Martin's "Memorandoms."
8. Tench, *Account*, note to p. 108.
9. On Boswell and Mary Bryant in England, see Pottle, *Boswell and the Girl from Botany Bay*.
10. For Parsons's satire on Boswell's imagined affair with Mary Bryant, see Pottle, ibid., and Brady, *James Boswell: The Later Years*, pp. 464–65.

11. Hunter to Portland, Jan. 10, 1798, HRNSW iii:346.

12. Baudin to King, May 9, 1803, HRA iv:151.

13. Macquarie to Bathurst, May 16, 1818, HRA ix:793.

14. Memo to Lt.-Gov. Arthur on Bass Strait sealing, May 29, 1826, at reel 600, NSWA, Sydney.

15. Hobart Port Regulations, Apr. 13, 1830, CSO 1/445:1922, TSA, Hobart.

16. On the sandalwood trade and escaped convicts in the Pacific, see Greg Dening, *Islands and Beaches*, pp. 119ff., 129ff.

17. Cook *EL*, pp. 177–78.

18. Hunter to Portland, Jan. 10, 1798, HRNSW iii:345. Collins (*Account*, vol. 2, p. 35) gives an account of the seizure of the *Cumberland*.

19. On the seizure of the *Harrington*, see *Sydney Gazette*, May 22, 1808.

20. *The Australian*, Feb. 23, 1827, cit. in Crowley, *Doc. Hist.*, vol. 1, pp. 349–50.

21. On the piracy of the *Cyprus*, see Arthur to Murray, Sept. 11, 1829. TSA, CON 280:31; John West, *The History of Tasmania*, p. 425ff.; Lloyd L. Robson, *A History of Tasmania*, p. 150. The version of the ballad "The Cyprus Brig" is from Gary Shearston's recording *Bolters, Bushrangers and Duffers*, CBS #BP 233288. The *Cyprus* episode forms an important part of the narrative of Marcus Clarke's *His Natural Life*.

22. On James Porter and the voyage of the *Frederick*, see Porter's "Memoirs," typescript of an unpublished Ms. at MSQ 168, Dixson Library, Sydney. All quotations of Porter are from this source. General outlines of the voyage are given in the rare Anon., "Narrative of the Sufferings . . . of the Convicts Who Piratically Seized the 'Frederick,'" ca. 1838 (copy in ML at 910.453/29A1), and in West, *History of Tasmania*, p. 429ff.

23. SC1837–38 (ii), "Papers Delivered in by John Barnes, Esq." (B, "List of Prisoners Who Absconded from Macquarie Harbour . . .").

24. Pearce's origin, physical appearance and deeds have been, due to his subsequent history, the subject of much journalistic fantasy. The one reliable study is Dan Sprod, *Alexander Pearce of Macquarie Harbour*. Primary sources are: (1) "Narrative of Escape from Macquarie Harbour" (the "Knopwood Narrative," based on Pearce's interrogation after capture by the Rev. Robert Knopwood), Ms. 3, Dixson Library, Sydney; (2) manuscript in National Library of Australia, Ms. 3323, ff. 1–5; and (3) deposition made before Cuthbertson at Macquarie Harbor and entered in SC 1837–38 (ii). Except where noted I have taken all direct Pearce quotes from (3).

25. For the chronology and route of Pearce's escape, see Sprod, *Alexander Pearce*, pp. 64–81.

26. "Knopwood Narrative."

27. W. S. Sharland, "Rough Notes of a Journal of Expedition to the Westward . . . ," in Tasmanian Parliament Legislative Council Papers, 16, 1861, as *Survey Office Reports*, 1861, 1, p. 6.

28. "Knopwood Narrative."

29. Ibid.

30. Ibid.

31. For Pearce's second escape from Macquarie Harbor, with Cox, see Sprod, *Alexander Pearce*, pp. 99–106, based on evidence of John Barnes to SC 1837–38 (ii), Appendix 1, 56(d).

32. Barnes to SC 1837–38 (ii), Appendix 1, 56(d), p. 316.

33. Pearce's "Bisdee" confession, Jun. 20, 1824, in Sprod, *Alexander Pearce*, p. 105.

34. On the emergence of Van Diemen's Land bushrangers and their relative immunity from capture and prosecution, see Robson, *Hist. Tas.*, Chapter 6, esp. pp. 79–83.

35. West, *Tasmania*, p. 364.

36. On Brown, Lemon and Scanlan, see Paterson to Castlereagh, May 7, 1818, HRA iii:685–86; Robson, *Hist. Tas.*, p. 80; and Charles White, *History of Australian Bushranging*, vol. 1, pp. 3–4.

37. Macquarie's proclamation: May 14, 1814, HRA viii:262 and 264–65. Davey's proclamation of martial law: West, *Tasmania*, p. 360, and Robson, *Hist. Tas.*, p. 81.

38. Petition to Davey by Humphrey, Sept. 30, 1815, CON 201:79. Robson, *Hist. Tas.,* p. 88.

39. Howe to Davey, CSO 1/223:5399, a contemporary copy of Howe's lost original. I have amended the spelling and punctuation slightly, for clarity's sake. Davey mentioned in dispatches that the original was "written in blood," presumably that of a sheep or a kangaroo. Of course there were few inkwells in the Tasmanian bush, but one may still admire Howe's dramatic gesture.

40. Wylde to Macquarie, encl. 2 in Macquarie to Bathurst, Jul. 17, 1821, HRA x:512–15.

41. Ibid.

42. Macquarie to Bathurst, Jul. 17, 1821, HRA x:509.

43. On Brady, see ADB entry and bibliography; Robson, *Hist. Tas.,* pp. 141–44; George Boxall, *The Story of the Australian Bushrangers,* p. 41ff; and White, *Australian Bushranging,* vol. 1, pp. 40–53.

44. John Barnes, testimony in SC 1837–38 (ii), Minutes, p. 41.

45. *The Australian,* Nov. 11, 1834.

46. T. L. Mitchell, *Three Expeditions into the Interior of Eastern Australia,* vol. 1, p. 9.

47. Bourke to Goderich, Mar. 19, 1832, HRA.

48. Alexander Harris, *Settlers and Convicts,* p. 35.

49. White, *Australian Bushranging,* vol. 1, pp. 102–3.

50. See Russel Ward, "Felons and Folksongs," passim.

CHAPTER EIGHT   *Bunters, Mollies and Sable Brethren*

1. Lloyd L. Robson, *The Convict Settlers of Australia,* pp. 77–78.

2. Ibid., Appendix 4, table 4(0), p. 187.

3. Shaw *CC,* p. 164.

4. Anne Summers, *Damned Whores and God's Police,* p. 286. Summers attributes the emblematic phrase "damned whores" to Lieutenant Ralph Clark of the First Fleet, who allegedly uttered it on seeing the *Lady Juliana,* female transport of the Second Fleet, sail into Sydney Harbor in June 1790. "No, no—surely not! My God—not more of those damned whores! Never have I known worse women." A sharp-eyed fellow, for at the time of *Lady Juliana*'s arrival he was actually a thousand miles away, stranded on Norfolk Island.

5. Sydney to the Treasury Commissioners, "Heads of a Plan," Aug. 18, 1786, HRNSW i:18. One may note, without dwelling on it, the sense of Pacific geography implied by Lord Sydney's notion that New Caledonia and Tahiti were "contiguous" to New South Wales.

6. Before he sailed for Australia, Phillip briefly considered a scheme of licensed prostitution in New South Wales. "The keeping of the women apart merits great consideration, and I don't know but it may be the best if the most abandoned are permitted to receive the visits of the convicts in the limits allotted them at certain hours, and under certain restrictions; something of this kind was the case in Mill Bank formerly. The rest of the women I should keep apart." ("Phillip's Views on the Conduct of the Expedition and Treatment of the Convicts," HRNSW ii:52.) Maybe the general promiscuity of the early settlement made this idea unnecessary. On Phillip's policy of encouraging convict marriages—most of which lasted—see HRNSW ii:52; and Watkin Tench, *A Narrative of the Expedition to Botany Bay,* p. 63: "To prevent their intercourse was impossible; to palliate its evils only remained. Marriage was recommended, and such advantages held out to those who aimed at reformation, as have greatly contributed to the tranquillity of the settlement."

7. Thomas Watling, *Letters from an Exile at Botany-Bay . . . ,* pp. 18–19. Does his "*whore* and *rogue* together" indicate a reading of Dean Swift?

Under an Oak, in stormy weather,
I put this Whore and Rogue together:

And none but Him Who rules the thunder
May put this rogue and whore asunder.

8. Patrick Colquhoun, *A Treatise on the Police of the Metropolis*, pp. vii–xi. Mayhew conflating promiscuity with prostitution: see Mayhew and Hemyng, "The Prostitution Class Generally," in Mayhew, *London Labour and the London Poor*, vol. 4, cit. in Sturma, "The Eye of the Beholder," p. 6.
9. Sturma, ibid., pp. 8–10.
10. For a discussion of Marsden's *Register* and the effects it had on the perception of colonial "immorality," see Portia Robinson, *The Hatch and Brood of Time*, vol. 1, pp. 75–77.
11. Ralph Clark, *Journal*, June 23, 1787.
12. Ibid., June 28, 1787.
13. Ibid., July 16, 1787.
14. "Ten thousand times worse": ibid., May 16, 1787. "I would have flogged the four whores also": ibid., June 19, and July 3, 1787.
15. Ibid., July 18, 1787.
16. "Surely an angel": ibid., Dec. 9, 1787. "If they were to lose anything": ibid., Oct. 11, 1787. "I was going down to Tregadock": ibid., Nov. 20, 1787. "She was better than half dead": ibid., May 24, 1790. "I wish the almighty": June 21, 1790.
17. For Nicol's account of women convicts on the *Lady Juliana*, see John Nicol, *The Life and Adventures of John Nicol, Mariner*, pp. 111–23.
18. Ibid.
19. Lord Auckland, draft of letter, Aug. 25, 1812, in Auckland Papers, BL, Add. Ms. 34458, pp. 382–84.
20. John Capper to SC 1812, Appendix 1, p. 77.
21. S. Hutchinson to J. Foyle, Sept. 5, 1798, letter at Ab. 67/15, ML.
22. Thomas Robson to SC 1812, Appendix 1, p. 52.
23. William Bligh to SC 1812, Appendix 1, p. 32.
24. T. W. Plummer to Macquarie, May 4, 1809, HRA vii:120.
25. Castlereagh to Macquarie, May 14, 1809, HRA vii:84.
26. G. H. Hammersley, "A Few Observations on the Situation of the Female Convicts in NSW," ca. 1807, in Hammersley Papers, A 657, ML.
27. The opinion of the *Atrevida*'s lieutenant is given in Crowley, *Doc. Hist.*, vol. 1, p. 57.
28. Michael Hayes to his sister Mary, Nov. 2, 1802, ML, Sydney.
29. Ibid.
30. Bigge NSW, p. 20.
31. Ibid.
32. For general descriptions of the Female Factory in 1815, before its reconstruction by Greenway, see Samuel Marsden, "An Answer to the Calumnies of the Late Governor Macquarie's Pamphlet" (1826), p. 18ff. (Marsden Papers, ML, Sydney), and (for the Factory in 1820) Bigge NSW, pp. 68–74. For regulations of the Female Factory and classification of its inmates, see "Rules and Regulations for the Management of Female Convicts at the New Factory at Parramatta," Sydney 1821, ML, Sydney.
33. Anon., in HRA ix:198–99. Macquarie to Bathurst, Dec. 4, 1817.
34. Rev. Samuel Marsden, "An Answer," pp. 23–24.
35. R. Durie to J. T. Campbell, Mar. 3, 1811, NSW Col. Sec. in-letters bundle 5, Nos. 1–64, pp. 99–100, ML, Sydney.
36. Thomas Reid, *Two Voyages to New South Wales and Van Diemen's Land*, cit. in Margaret Weidenhofer, *The Convict Years*, p. 77.
37. J. F. O'Connell, *A Residence of Eleven Years in New Holland*, p. 54, cit. in Crowley, *Doc. Hist.*, vol. 1, p. 310.
38. Mellish, *A Convict's Recollections*, p. 54.
39. Summers, *Damned Whores*, p. 281.
40. J. E. Drabble to J. Lakeland, Hobart, May 1, 1827, CSO 1/324:1704, TSA, Hobart.
41. *Sydney Gazette*, Oct. 31, 1827, cit. in Summers, *Damned Whores*, p. 285.

42. Peter Murdoch to SC 1837–38 (ii), Minutes, p. 118.

43. Robert Jones, "Recollections of 13 Years Residence on Norfolk Island," Ms. in ML, Sydney.

44. James Mitchell, memorandum ca. 1815, typescript Ms. 27/c. in Stenhouse Papers II, ML, Sydney.

45. Joseph Holt, "Life and Adventures of Joseph Holt," Ms. A2024, ML, Sydney.

46. Ibid.

47. Ibid.

48. Ibid.

49. James Mitchell, Ms. memorandum in Stenhouse Papers II, Ms. 27/c, ML, Sydney.

50. Jones, "Recollections."

51. Lepailleur's journal, covering the years 1839–44, is in the Archives Nationales de Québec; a translation is expected for publication by F. Murray Greenwood of the University of British Columbia. On Lepailleur and his comrades in Australia, see Beverley D. Boissery, "French-Canadian Political Prisoners in Australia, 1838–39" (Ph.D. diss.), and Beverley D. Boissery and Murray F. Greenwood, "New Sources for Convict History."

52. Lepailleur, "Journal."

53. Bishop William Ullathorne, *Autobiography*, p. 152.

54. Caroline Anley, *The Prisoners of Australia*, cit. in Crowley, *Doc. Hist.*, vol. 1, p. 461.

55. *The Australian*, Apr. 7, 1825.

56. For one chronicler of homosexuality in Australia, this promise of fierce punishment was "evidence" of Phillip's own homosexuality; it was, he claimed, meant to deflect attention from "rumors" of his own supposed "interest in young seamen." (Martin Smith, "Arthur Phillip and the Young Lads," p. 15.) This is wishful thinking. No jot of evidence suggests that the *pater patriae* was homosexual, or that such rumors existed. All military governors of Australian colonies found homosexual prisoners utterly repugnant; Arthur, for instance, called one pair of convict lovers "horrible beasts" (Jan. 27, 1832, CSO 1/572:12924).

57. George Lee, letter to Sir H. St. J. Mildmay, Jan. 24, 1803, Bentham Papers, Add. Ms. 33544, BL, pp. 14–15. Jeremy Bentham, draft letter re hulk conditions, ibid., p. 105ff.

58. See, for example, Backhouse and Walker, Ms. "Reports" in ML, at B706–7, i/27:231ff.

59. Ullathorne's reflections on immoral Australia: William Ullathorne, *The Catholic Mission in Australasia*, p. iv.

60. John Stephen, Jr. to SC 1832. Minutes, p. 30. Allan Cunningham, ibid., p. 36.

61. Report of SC 1837–38 (ii), Appendix 1/57, "Return of the Number of Persons Charged with Criminal Offences," p. 317.

62. John Russell to SC 1837–38 (ii), Minutes, p. 60.

63. Ullathorne, *Catholic Mission*, p. 17.

64. Cook *EL*, pp. 19–20.

65. Ibid.

66. Ibid., p. 46.

67. Ibid., p. 41.

68. Ibid., pp. 174–75.

69. Ibid., p. 173.

70. Thomas Arnold to SC 1837–38 (ii), Sept. 27, 1837, Appendix E/45. Robert Pringle Stuart, 1846 Report to the VDL Comptroller-General, reprinted in Eustace Fitzsymonds, ed., *Norfolk Island 1846: The Accounts of Robert Pringle Stewart and Thomas Beagley Naylor*, p. 46. Ullathorne to SC 1837–38 (ii), Minutes, p. 25.

71. Thomas Beagley Naylor, "Norfolk Island, the Botany Bay of Botany Bay: A Letter . . . to the Rt. Hon. Lord Stanley, Secretary of State for the Colonies" (1846). Original in TSA, GO 1/63; reprinted in Fitzsymonds, ed., *Norfolk Island*, pp. 17–18. The reports of both Naylor and Stuart were printed by the English Government in *Correspondence Relative to Convict Discipline and Transportation, presented to both Houses of Parliament*, Feb. 16, 1847. But both were heavily bowdlerized, all proper names were omitted, and all reference to homosexual practices was suppressed—either to protect

the delicate sensibilities of Parliamentarians, or to minimize the damage to the already much-bruised name of the transportation system.

72. Stuart, Report, in Fitzsymonds, ed., *Norfolk Island*, pp. 45–46.

73. Ibid., p. 47.

74. George III's instructions to Phillip: HRNSW ii:52.

75. C. D. Rowley, *Aboriginal Policy and Practice*, vol. 1: *The Destruction of Aboriginal Society*, p. 19.

76. J. Arnold, letter to his brother, Mar. 18, 1810, at A1849, ML, Sydney. P. G. King, "Observations on the New Zealand Natives," HRA vi:7.

77. Macquarie to Bathurst, Oct. 8, 1814, HRA viii:369–70, and Mar. 24, 1815, HRA viii:467.

78. F. Debenham, ed., *The Voyage of Captain Bellingshausen to the Antarctic Seas 1819–1821*, cit. in Crowley, *Doc. Hist.*, vol. 1, p. 264.

79. Geoffrey Blainey, *The Triumph of the Nomads*, pp. 108–9.

80. Decision by J. Burton in *Rex v. Jack Congo Murrell* (1836), cit. in Rowley, pp. 15–16.

81. Proclamation by King, June 1802, HRA iii:592–93. Atkins to King, July 8, 1805, HRA iv:653.

82. William Walker to Rev. W. Watson, 1821, cit. in Jean Woolmington, ed., *Aborigines in Colonial Society, 1788–1850*, p. 86. "It was an observation of the Governor's that will never lose its impression on my mind," remarked the Wesleyan missionary in this letter to his colleague in London.

83. Economic warfare by Aborigines: Reynolds, *Other Side*, p. 121.

84. Aboriginal perception of white settlement and land ownership: Reynolds, *Other Side*, p. 64ff.

85. Benjamin Hurst to Latrobe, July 22, 1841, BT Box 54 in ML, Sydney, cit. in Woolmington, ed., *Aborigines*, p. 38.

86. Edward M. Curr, cit. in ibid., pp. 63–64.

87. Reynolds, *Other Side*, pp. 121–24.

88. E. Deas Thomson to James Dowling, Jan. 4, 1842, HRA xxi:655–56. *SMH*, Dec. 26, 1836, cit. in Woolmington, ed., *Aborigines*, p. 54.

89. *The Colonist*, June 20, 1838, cit. in Woolmington, ed., *Aborigines*, pp. 55–56.

90. Thomas Holden, letter to his wife, ca. 1815, DDX 140/7:18, LRO.

91. James Gunther, Journal, Dec. 30, 1837, cit. in Woolmington, ed., *Aborigines* p. 69.

92. The most famous of these was William Buckley (1780–1856), an English militiaman from Cheshire who stood 6′6″ in his bare feet and had been transported for life, in 1802, for receiving stolen cloth. He absconded from the tiny settlement on Port Phillip in Victoria in 1803 and had the luck to run into an aboriginal tribe, the Watourong, who mistook him for the reincarnated spirit of their dead chief. (It was an almost universal belief among Aborigines, irrespective of tribe, that the spirits of the dead returned in the form of "peeled" men, ashen white or gray. The color white was associated with death and resurrection.) Thus, in the guise of an enormous spirit, Buckley lived with the Watourong for thirty-two years before giving himself up. The sheer improbability of this gave rise to an Australian expression that still survives: "Buckley's chance," meaning no chance at all.

93. On the conditions of inland life, and the attitudes of lower-class settlers to aboriginal tribes on the frontiers of settlement in penal New South Wales, see David Denholm, *The Colonial Australians*, p. 37ff.

94. Wentworth, in the *SMH*, June 21, 1844.

CHAPTER NINE *The Government Stroke*

1. For a critique of the idea of penal Australia as a "slave society," see John B. Hirst, *Convict Society and Its Enemies*, esp. pp. 21–25, 31, 82.

2. Robert Gouger [pseud. of E. G. Wakefield], *A Letter from Sydney*, pp. 12–13. Wakefield had not visited Sydney, and his views on the difficulties facing the uninitiated settler

in an economy where land was given away were meant as propaganda for his "sufficient price" emigration scheme, whereby the price of Australian crown land was raised so that only substantial colonists could afford it. However, his sketch of this fictional servant carried a nugget of truth.

3. Eugene D. Genovese, *The Political Economy of Slavery*, p. 43. For a contrary view on the efficiency and adaptability of southern slave labor, which argues that southern slave agriculture was 35 percent more efficient than northern family farming, see William Fogel and Stanley Enderman, *Time on the Cross* (New York, 1974).

4. Hirst, *Convict Society*, p. 65.

5. Gouger [Wakefield], *Letter*, p. 37.

6. E. G. Wakefield, *The Art of Colonization*, pp. 176–77.

7. King to Castlereagh, HRA v:748–49.

8. Meredith to Burnett Dec. 30, 1828, in Meredith, *Correspondence*, p. 8, cit. in Shaw *CC*, p. 218. On the proportion of assigned "mechanics" in Van Diemen's Land under Arthur, see Shaw *CC*, p. 217.

9. Murray to Darling, Jan. 30, 1830, HRA xv:351ff.

10. "In what can Britain show": anon. article in *Virginia Gazette*, May 24, 1751, cit. in Abbot Emerson Smith, *Colonists in Bondage*, p. 130. John Pory, cit. in ibid., p. 13.

11. Smith, *Colonists*, p. 13. For a discussion of the legal differences between the old, American system of indenture and the new, Australian assignment system, see Murray to Darling, Jan. 30, 1830, HRA xv:351ff.

12. King, General Order of Oct. 31, 1800, in NSW General Orders and Proclamations, Safe 1/87, ML, Sydney, cit. in Crowley, *Doc. Hist.*, pp. 97–98.

13. King, General Order published in *Sydney Gazette*, Jan. 14, 1804.

14. David Collins, *An Account of the English Colony in New South Wales*, p. 11.

15. Margarot to SC 1812, Appendix 1, Minutes, p. 54.

16. SC 1812, Report, p. 4.

17. Bligh to SC 1812, Appendix 1, Minutes, p. 43.

18. Richardson to SC 1812, Appendix 1, Minutes, p. 57. King to Portland, Dec. 31, 1801, HRA iv:655–56.

19. Thomas Holden, letter in LRO, DDX 140/17:18.

20. Bigge NSW, p. 77.

21. Bligh to SC 1812, Appendix. 1, p. 46.

22. John Palmer to SC 1812, Appendix 1, p. 61. George Johnston, ibid., p. 73.

23. Campbell to SC 1812, Appendix 1, p. 68ff.

24. Brisbane to Undersecretary Horton, Nov. 6, 1824, HRA ix:414–15.

25. John Broxup, *Life of John Broxup, Late Convict at Van Diemen's Land*, p. 11. Addition (by scribe) to letter from Richard Dillingham, Sept. 29, 1836, in Harley W. Forster, ed., *The Dillingham Convict Letters*.

26. Brisbane to Bathurst, Nov. 6, 1824, HRA ix:413–14.

27. John Rule, *The Experience of Labour in Eighteenth-Century English Industry*, p. 201.

28. Macquarie to Castlereagh, Apr. 30, 1810.

29. Mellish, *A Convict's Recollections of New South Wales*, p. 51.

30. Macquarie, General Order, Dec. 15, 1810, in NSW General Orders and Proclamations, safe 1/87, ML, Sydney. The towns in question were Windsor, Richmond, Wilberforce, Castlereagh and Pitt Town; Macquarie's decision to name a town after William Wilberforce, the anti-slavery leader, reflected a mutual admiration between the two men.

31. See M. H. Ellis, *Francis Greenway*; J. M. Freeland, *Architecture in Australia*, pp. 30–41; and Morton Herman, *Early Australian Architects and Their Work*, passim.

32. Macquarie to Bathurst, Sept. 1, 1820.

33. Appendix to Bigge NSW, cit. in Shaw *CC*, p. 92.

34. Macquarie to Bathurst, Dec. 4, 1817, HRA ix:507–9.

35. M. M. Robinson, "Ode for the Queen's Birthday, 1816," in Brian Elliott and Adrian Mitchell, eds., *Bards in the Wilderness*, p. 12.

36. J. D. Lang, "Colonial Nomenclature," in ibid., p. 29.

37. Figures from Shaw *CC*, pp. 98–99.

38. R. B. Madgwick, *Immigration into Eastern Australia, 1788–1851*, pp. 30–32.
39. Macquarie to Bathurst, Mar. 24, 1819, HRA x:88.
40. Mar. 18, 1825, HRA xi:549.
41. Bathurst to Bigge, HRA x:4ff.
42. Margarot to SC 1812, Appendix 1, p. 54.
43. Petition of Robert Townson, NSWA, Mechanics' Bond Accounts 4/4525, 4/1775, p. 173.
44. Gipps to Glenelg, HRA xix:604–5.
45. Bourke to Goderich, HRA xvi:625, cit. in Bigge NSW, p. 75.
46. Bigge NSW, p. 75ff.
47. Goderich to Bourke, Aug. 22, 1831, HRA xvi:330. Bourke to Goderich, May 4, 1832, HRA xvi:640.
48. Darling to Goderich, July 14, 1831, HRA xvi:299.
49. W. C. Wentworth to Committee on Police, 1839, pp. 88–96, cit. in Hirst, *Convict Society*, p. 185.
50. Bourke to Goderich, Apr. 30, 1832, HRA xvi:624–26.
51. The clothing issue was fixed at three shirts a year, two sets of jacket and trousers (wool for winter and light wool or cotton duck for summer), and a strong pair of leather shoes. The weekly food ration was 12 lb. wheat (ground by the convicts themselves, in small iron handmills), 7 lb. fresh beef or mutton, two ounces of salt and two of soap. When grain or fresh meat were short, the master could substitute maize flour and salt pork. It will immediately be seen that, though monotonous and lacking in vegetables, this was a solid diet; no one could starve on a pound of meat a day. "They can make a meal": Broxup, *Life*, p. 7.
52. Port Macquarie Bench Book, June 13, 1836, NSWA 4/5639, cit. in Alan Atkinson, "Four Patterns of Convict Protest."
53. Atkinson, ibid.
54. George Taylor, letter, CSO 1/624/14148, TSA, Hobart.
55. Deposition of James Davis, Dec. 10, 1829, HRA xv:306–7. Thomas Argent: HRA xv:305.
56. CSO 1/568/12796, TSA, Hobart.
57. *Sydney Gazette*, Aug. 18, 1825.
58. Darling to Murray, Feb. 16, 1829, HRA xiv:646.
59. Gipps to Glenelg, Oct. 8, 1838, HRA xix:604.
60. Cook *EL*, pp. 33–34.
61. *Sydney Gazette*, Feb. 1, 1826.
62. George Loveless et al., *A Narrative of the Sufferings of . . . Four of the Dorchester Labourers*, p. 16.
63. Hirst, *Convict Society*, p. 109.
64. Goodwin to Lang, Sept. 21, 1850, A2226, Lang Papers, vol. 6, pp. 492–95, ML, Sydney.
65. James Brine, in G. Loveless et al., *A Narrative*, pp. 11–12.
66. Edward J. Eyre, "Autobiography," Ms., p. 45.
67. Alexander Berry, *Reminiscences*, cit. in ADB, vol. 1, p. 95.
68. Berry to Wollstonecraft, June 7, 1823, and Oct. 13, 1825, cit. in Shaw *CC*, p. 222 from Berry Papers, xi/xii, ML, Sydney.
69. James Macarthur to SC 1837–38 (ii), Minutes, p. 164. James Atkinson, *An Account of the State of Agriculture and Grazing in New South Wales*, pp. 112–16. T. P. Besnard, *A Voice from the Bush in Australia: Shewing its Present State, Advantages, and Capabilities* (1839), pp. 20–21, cit. in Crowley, *Doc. Hist.*, pp. 478–79.
70. Eyre, "Autobiography," Ms., p. 46.
71. Parents to Holden, DDX 140/17:14, LRO; wife to Holden, DDX 140/17:16, LRO.
72. Bigge NSW, p. 76.
73. Bourke to Goderich, Apr. 30, 1832, HRA xvi:625.
74. Bigge NSW, pp. 76–77.
75. William Vincent, letter to his mother, Aug. 17, 1829, in SC 1837–38 (ii), Appendix, p. 354.

76. Peter Withers, letter to his brother, TSA, Hobart.

77. Withers, ibid.; Richard Dillingham, *The Dillingham Convict Letters*, ed. H. W. Foster (Melbourne, 1970), pp. 21–23 [Sept.–Nov. 1838].

78. Petition of Thomas Jones, Apr. 8, 1830, PC 1/78, PRO.

79. Bigge NSW, p. 103.

80. Richard Whately, "Transportation," in *Miscellaneous Lectures and Reviews*, pp. 258–59, cit. Clark, ed., *Select Documents in Australian History, 1788–1850*, p. 151.

81. [O.P.Q.] in *New South Wales Magazine*, vol. 1 (August 1833), pp. 16–17.

82. Eyre, "Autobiography," Ms., pp. 46–47.

83. John Standfield, in G. Loveless et al., *A Narrative*, pp. 5–6.

84. Shaw *CC*, p. 226, quoting Anne McKay, p. 355. Eyre, "Autobiography," Ms., p. 47.

CHAPTER TEN   *Gentlemen of New South Wales*

1. Peter Cunningham, *Two Years in New South Wales*, vol. 1, pp. 44–45.

2. "A Settler," *SMH*, Jan. 16, 1839, cit. in John B. Hirst, *Convict Society and Its Enemies*, p. 207.

3. Louisa Anne Meredith, *Notes and Sketches of New South Wales*, pp. 52–53.

4. Arthur Bowes Smyth and Ralph Clark, Journals, Feb. 7, 1788.

5. On John Macarthur, see ADB entry (vol. 2, pp. 153–59); Macarthur Papers, ML, Sydney; M. H. Ellis, *John Macarthur*; and S. Macarthur-Onslow, ed., *Some Early Records of the Macarthurs of Camden*.

6. Macarthur's attempts to broaden his business interests beyond the pastoral were almost uniformly unsuccessful, so much so that by 1812 his unwise investments in Pacific trade had all but cancelled his profits from wool. He was the worst of company men. No one could work with him and expect to be treated as an equal partner. He boasted that he had "never yet failed in ruining a man who had become obnoxious to him." His grand disaster was a chartered company set up to corner the production of wool in Australia. Macarthur had dreamt of such a monopoly since at least 1804, but not until twenty years later did he bring it into existence with the all-important backing of the British Government: the Australian Agricultural Company, endowed with a million acres of land near Port Stephens, north of Sydney, and capitalized by private subscription at £1 million. No corporation of this size had ever been set up in the Pacific, and despite its early success Macarthur wrecked it within four years. By 1828 his meddling had become so intrusive that the AAC's shares sank from their original £100 to £8.

7. Macarthur's timing: S. Cottrell to E. Cooke, July 14, 1804. Lord Camden's land grant to Macarthur: David Collins, *An Account of the English Colony in New South Wales*, vol. 1, pp. 437–38.

8. On sheep-breeding in early colonial Australia, see Eric Rolls, *A Million Wild Acres*, pp. 23–27.

9. James Mudie, *The Felonry of New South Wales*, pp. 12–13.

10. James Macarthur to John Macarthur, Sr., June 24, and July 11, 1820, cit. in John M. Ward, *James Macarthur, Colonial Conservative*, p. 45.

11. On the southern "fisheries" of whales and seals, see Alan Moorehead, *The Fatal Impact*, pp. 195–204.

12. Unsigned memo on Bass Strait sealing to Lieut-Gov. Arthur, May 29, 1826, on microfilm reel 600, NSWA, Sydney.

13. The numbers of native women kidnapped in this way cannot be accurately assessed, but the traffic had two chief results. First, it stamped the aboriginal tribes with an ineradicable hatred of whites and depleted their birthrate. Second, and paradoxically enough, it ensured the survival of the Tasmanian Aborigines. After their extermination on the main island of Tasmania, a small group of aboriginal descendants contin-

ued to exist on Cape Barren Island in Bass Strait. (See Chapter 11.) For an account of the sealers' incursions, see Anne McMahon, "Tasmanian Aboriginal Women as Slaves"; on the Cape Barren Islanders, see Lyndall Ryan, *The Aboriginal Tasmanians.*

14. On Campbell's defiance of the East India Company's embargo on oil and sealskin from Australia, see Alan Frost, *Convicts and Empire,* p. 193ff.

15. J. Arnold, letter to his brother, Feb. 25, 1810, A1849, ML, Sydney, cit. in Crowley, *Doc. Hist.,* vol. 1, p. 171.

16. London *Times,* July 14, 1838. On Terry, see ADB entry (vol. 2, pp. 508–9); P. E. Leroy, "Samuel Terry" in *JRAHS,* vol. 47 (1961). On the rumors against Terry, see Bigge NSW, p. 141: Terry was alleged to keep ready-written powers of attorney in his public house, which fuddled ex-convicts would sign when drunk. "By these means, and by an active use of the common arts of over-reaching, Samuel Terry has been able to accumulate a considerable capital, and a quantity of land . . . inferior only to that which is held by Mr. D'Arcy Wentworth." The allegations that he fleeced other ex-convicts began with the Rev. Samuel Marsden. At his death, the "Botany Bay Rothschild" (who was, in fact, a Gentile) left his widow with £10,000 a year, an estate of £250,000, and vast land holdings that included the whole of Martin Place, the hub of modern Sydney.

17. On Crossley, see ADB entry (vol. 1, p. 262). Crossley was charged with posthumously altering the will of a clergyman, on the man's very deathbed, in favor of one of his own friends. He is said to have pleaded that there was, in fact, "life" in the Reverend's body at the moment the will was doctored. He had made sure of this by popping a live fly in his client's mouth, pushing it shut, and then placing in the dead hand a pen with which the signature was written. The court surprisingly acquitted him, but before long he was on his way to Botany Bay for seven years, for perjury in another malpractice case.

18. Although Bent's sole motive was bigotry, he attempted to give his decision a legal veneer by basing his refusal to hear convict attorneys on the statute 12, Geo. I, c. 29.

19. On Redfern, see HRA i:6–10; E. Ford, *The Life and Work of William Redfern;* and E. Ford, "Medical Practice in Early Sydney," *MJA,* July 9, 1955.

20. Barron Field, "On Reading the Controversy between Mr. Byron and Mr. Bowles," in Brian Elliott and Adrian Mitchell, eds., *Bards in the Wilderness: Australian Colonial Poetry to 1920,* p. 18.

21. On Lewin, see Bernard Smith, *European Vision and the South Pacific,* pp. 158–62. A relatively large number of convict artists were transported for the crime closest to their profession, forgery. The colony also had its free amateurs: naval draftsmen like the unidentified "Port Jackson Painter," who came with the First Fleet, and George Raper; and army officers who dabbled in painting, like Capt. James Wallis of the 46th Regiment.

22. John Grant, "Verses Written to Lewin, the Entomologist," 1805, in Grant Papers, Ms. 737, NLA, Canberra.

23. On Lycett and the beguiling modifications of Australian landscape in his "Views," see Smith, *European Vision,* pp. 179–81.

24. On Thomas Griffiths Wainewright, see J. Curling, *Janus Weathercock* (London, 1838); and R. Crossland, *Wainewright in Tasmania* (Melbourne, 1954). A sickly but eager esthete and something of a Georgian dandy, Wainewright was both painter and art critic, writing for the *London Magazine* in the 1820s under the pseudonyms of Egomet Bonmot and Janus Weathercock. He exhibited paintings strongly indebted to Henry Fuseli at the Royal Academy from 1826 onward. Wainewright lived beyond his means, and his fall from grace into the Antipodes began when he forged powers of attorney in order to get his hands on a capital sum of £5,250 left him by his grandfather and transferred, in trust, to his wife. Thirteen years later he was arrested and tried for (as he saw it) taking his own money. The governor of Newgate Prison persuaded him to plead guilty in return for a light sentence. Instead, to Wainewright's horror, he was transported for life.

The unhappy artist arrived in Hobart at the end of 1837 and was put in a chain gang on the roads. His health collapsed and he was transferred to ward work in the Hobart hospital. In return for small and condescendingly given favors from the eminent of Hobart, he did watercolor portraits; some forty of these survive. A heart-rending plea for a ticket-of-leave, written to the lieutenant-governor, Sir John Eardley Eardley-Wilmot, in April 1844, is preserved (Aw. 15, ML, Sydney). Wainewright calls Van Diemen's Land "a moral sepulchre." "Deign, your Excellency! to figure to yourself my actual condition during 7 years, without *friends, good-name* (the breath of Life) or *Art*—(the fuel to it with me). Tormented at once by Memory, & Ideas struggling for outward form & realization, barred up from increase of knowledge, & deprived of the exercise of profitable or even *decorous* speech. Take pity, Your Excellency!" He reminds Eardley-Wilmot (who had probably not heard of any of them) that he, Wainewright, has been praised by "Flaxman, Coleridge, Chas. Lamb . . . & the God of his worship, *Fuseli*." All to no avail; his ticket-of-leave was not granted until the end of 1846, less than a year before his death.

25. For an example of these "pipes," see Anon., "Alas; poor Botany Bay," in Elliott and Mitchell, eds., *Bards in the Wilderness*, p. 8.

26. J. M. Freeland, *Architecture in Australia*, p. 39. On Greenway, see ADB entry (vol. 1, pp. 470–72); M. H. Ellis, *Francis Greenway*; and Morton Herman, *Early Australian Architects and their Work*.

27. Meredith, *Notes and Sketches*, pp. 50–51.

28. Ibid., p. 39.

29. Letters of G.T.W.B. Boyes, May 6, 1824, Royal Society of Tasmania, UTL, Hobart.

30. Meredith, *Notes and Sketches*, pp. 49–50.

31. Ibid., pp. 58–59, 75.

32. Hirst, *Convict Society*, pp. 118–19.

33. Gipps to Glenelg, Mar. 29, 1839. HRA xx:74.

34. Mellish, *A Convict's Recollections*, p. 52.

35. Ullathorne to SC 1837–38 (ii), Minutes, p. 22. Domestic horror-stories: Meredith, *Notes and Sketches*, p. 128. Christmas was especially trying, she reported: "The prevailing vice of drunkenness among the lower orders is perhaps more resolutely practised at this season than any other. I have heard of a Christmas-day party being assembled, and awaiting the announcement of dinner as long as patience would endure; then ringing the bell, but without reply; and on the hostess proceeding to the kitchen, finding every servant either gone out or rendered incapable of moving, the intended feast being meanwhile burned to ashes. Nor is this by any means a rare occurrence."

36. John Russell to SC 1837–38 (ii), Minutes, p. 56.

37. Gipps to Glenelg, Mar. 29, 1839, HRA xx:74.

38. Russell to SC 1837–38 (ii), Minutes, pp. 58–59.

39. John Goodwin to J. D. Lang, 1850, Lang Papers, vol. 6, A2226, ML, Sydney.

40. Maconochie to SC 1837–38 (ii), Report, p. xxxiii; Ullathorne to SC 1837–38 (ii), Minutes, p. 23.

41. Russell to SC 1837–38 (ii), Minutes, p. 56.

42. Darling to Goderich, Oct. 2, 1837, HRA xiii: 673.

43. J. F. Mortlock, *Experiences of a Convict Transported for Twenty-one Years*, p. 92.

44. On John Grant, see ADB entry (vol. 1, pp. 469–70); W. S. Hill-Reid, *John Grant's Journey*; Grant Papers (journal and letters), NLA, Canberra. Grant's description of his efforts to extract a ticket-of-leave from Governor King is in a letter to his mother and sister, Jan. 1, 1805, Ms. 737/22, NLA, Canberra.

45. Mortlock, *Experiences of a Convict*, pp. 84–85. The former MP was William Smith O'Brien (1803–1864), member for Ennis (1828–31) and Limerick (1835–49), one of the leaders of the Young Ireland movement who, with his compatriot John Mitchel and several others, was convicted of high treason in 1848 and transported for life to Van Diemen's Land.

46. Woomera [pseud.], *The Life of an Ex-Convict*, p. 13. On official harassment of Specials who professed atheism, see James Bushelle, "Memoir." Bushelle, the son of an Irish merchant in Limerick, was transported for stealing diamonds. He served a term in the penal station at Port Macquarie, returned to Sydney, became choir-leader in St. Mary's Cathedral and instructor to the military bands; he presented these signs of respectability to Governor Bourke, hoping for an early ticket-of-leave. Alas, "Governor Bourke would not grant [me] that indulgence; having referred to [my] character on the books, and found the charge of ATHEISM affixed to [my] name." Instead, he went back to Port Macquarie for another year, bitterly lamenting the day he had succumbed to the French accomplice in crime who "in the polite and fascinating language of France and Italy . . . infused into my unsuspecting mind, that ffrench Philosophy best known in England as *ffrench Principles*, meaning those poisonous seeds disseminated by *Voltaire* and his school, founded upon Satire and Irony upon Religion and Government."

47. The first view was set forth by Russel Ward in *The Australian Legend:* "All we know about the convicts shows that egalitarian class solidarity was the one human trait which usually remained to all but the most brutalized." It was attacked by Humphrey McQueen (*A New Britannia*, pp. 126–27) on the grounds that the convicts could not have felt class loyalty because they did not form a class: "For its first fifty years at least, Australia did not have a class structure, but only a deformed stratification. . . . The convicts lacked, through no fault of their own, any feeling of class-consciousness." This late Marxist boilerplate ignores the primary social fact of colonial society, which was that convicts were treated, oppressed, and made to see themselves as a class separate from and inferior to all free settlers. They were usually called "a class" in official communications. That their behavior did not conform to Utopian stereotypes of class unity—that, like their social superiors, they competed for property and status—in no way altered their sense of separateness as a group, or their ability to stick together. In McQueen's schematic view of history, even the convicts' dislike of guard, trap, informer and beak was "essentially bourgeois in origin and content," reflecting only the hegemony of false individualism. No doubt if they had loved their Gulag, such writers would laud them as pioneer Stalinists.

48. Rev. John Morison, *Australia As It Is*, London, 1864, p. 223.

49. Hunter to SC 1812, Appendix 1, Minutes, p. 23.

50. Samuel Marsden, "A Few Observations on the Toleration of the Catholic Religion in N. South Wales."

51. Ward, *Australian Legend*, pp. 29–30.

52. Mellish, *Recollections*, pp. 63–65.

53. Alexander Harris, *Settlers and Convicts*, p. 326.

54. Ibid., p. 126.

55. Bligh to SC 1812, Appendix 1, Minutes, p. 46. Bigge NSW, p. 102. Bourke to Goderich, Apr. 30, 1832, HRA xvi:625.

56. Sydney Smith, *Edinburgh Review*, July 1819.

57. For a discussion of the complexities of origin in colonial society in the 1820s, and the inadequacy of the "children of the convicts" stereotype, see Portia Robinson, *The Hatch and Brood of Time*.

58. "Crime *descends*": Judge Alfred Stephen to James Macarthur, ca. 1857, cit. in Michael Sturma, *Vice in a Vicious Society*, p. 2. On the respectable reaction against convictism, see Sturma, p. 8: "Ultimately the community's reaction to its convict origins proved of more lasting and profound significance than convictism itself."

59. Sir William W. Burton, "State of Society and State of Crime in New South Wales . . . ," *Colonial Magazine*, vol. 1, p. 425.

60. Burton, ibid., vol. 2, pp. 51–53. Burton's general figures for crime, gathered from trials before other judges as well, show the same pattern. Translated into percentages of defendants in three sample years, they become:

| | *percentage of total indictments* | | |
|---|---|---|---|
| SOCIAL GROUP | 1833 | 1835 | 1836 |
| Free emigrants | 1 | 11 | 9 |
| Currency | 2 | 3 | 5 |
| Emancipists | 43 | 37 | 41 |
| Convicts under sentence | 51 | 46 | 42 |
| Other (incl. military and blacks) | 3 | 3 | 3 |

61. Bigge NSW, p. 105.
62. Robinson, *Hatch and Brood of Time*, p. 12.
63. "None *but* slaves *do* work": Cunningham, *New South Wales*, vol. 2, pp. 48–49. Aversion to the sea and maritime labor: Robinson, *Hatch and Brood of Time*, p. 237ff. Bigge, it seems, was wrong in reporting (Bigge NSW, pp. 81–82) that "many of the native youths have evinced a strong disposition for a sea-faring life, and are excellent sailors. . . . [T]hat class of the population will afford abundant and excellent materials for the supply of any department in the commercial or naval service."
64. "Fair hair and blue eyes": Cunningham, *New South Wales*, vol. 2, p. 53. Other references to Currency traits also are from Cunningham, passim.
65. G.T.W.B. Boyes to Mary Boyes, Oct. 23 and 27, 1831, in Boyes Letters, UTL, Hobart.
66. "Supercilious intolerance": Harris, *Settlers and Convicts*, pp. 295–96. "Sterling madonnas": Cunningham, *New South Wales*, vol. 2, p. 53.
67. Harris, *Settlers and Convicts*, pp. 149–53.
68. Bigge NSW, Appendix. CO 201:142, p. 336ff, cit. in Clark *HA*, vol. 2, p. 43. On Wentworth, see Clark *HA*, vol. 2, p. 41ff.
69. William Charles Wentworth, "Where'er the sickening Muse," in Wentworth Papers, Miscellanea, ML, Sydney.
70. "I will not suffer": W. C. Wentworth, May 1, 1820, in Wentworth Letters, ML, Sydney. The term "bunyip aristocracy"—still occasionally used in Australia to deride the pretentious—was invented by the young Irish politico Daniel Deniehy in 1853, in a speech against Wentworth's self-serving proposal for a hereditary colonial *noblesse.* The relevant passage, as reported on Aug. 16, 1853 in the *Sydney Morning Herald,* runs: "Even the poor Irishman in the streets of Dublin would fling his jibe at the Botany Bay aristocrats. In fact, he [Deniehy] was puzzled how to classify them. . . . Perhaps it was only a specimen of the remarkable contrariety that existed at the Antipodes. Here they all knew the common water-mole was transformed into the duck-billed platypus, and in some distant emulation of this degeneration, he supposed they were to be favoured with a bunyip aristocracy. (Great laughter.)"
71. W. C. Wentworth, *A Statistical, Historical and Political Description of the Colony of New South Wales . . .* , pp. 349–50.
72. Sidney Smith, *Edinburgh Review*, July 1819.
73. The text of the Emancipists' petition to the Crown is given in HRA x:549–52.
74. The winner was William Mackworth Praed, who knew little about Australasia but was soon to become the wittiest writer of *vers de société* in England. Against him, Wentworth's clumping measures had little chance; but that second prize was the first cultural kudos earned by an Australian overseas.
75. Brisbane to Bathurst, Oct. 28, 1824, in "Transcripts of Missing Despatches," A1267, ML, Sydney.

CHAPTER ELEVEN   *To Plough Van Diemen's Land*

1. On Thomas Davey, see ADB entry; Robson, *Hist. Tas.*, pp. 64–67 and 78–94; and J. W. Beattie, *Glimpses of the Lives and Times of the Early Tasmanian Governors*, pp. 23–25.

2. William Sorell, Memorandum in HRA iii:4.

3. In July 1817, shortly after assuming office in Van Diemen's Land, Sorell was ordered to pay damages of £3,000—a colossal sum—to Lieutenant Kent for alienating the affections of his wife. When Mrs. Kent arrived in Hobart and settled into residence at Government House, the notoriously choleric Anthony Fenn Kemp, merchant, landowner, former New South Wales Corps Captain and conspirator in the "Rum Rebellion" plot against Governor Bligh, used this "evil example to the Rising Generation" as his main weapon in a campaign to unseat Sorell. Partly because the normally prudish Governor Macquarie distrusted Fenn Kemp for his role in the Rum Rebellion, these objurgations failed.

4. Sorell to Cuthbertson, in standing orders, Dec. 8, 1821, CSO 1/133/3229, TSA, Hobart.

5. John Barnes to SC 1837–38 (ii), Minutes, pp. 45–46.

6. James Backhouse, A *Narrative of a Visit to the Australian Colonies*, pp. 44–45.

7. Pine logging statistics for the year 1827: T. J. Lemprière, *The Penal Settlements of Van Diemen's Land*, p. 39.

8. Barnes to SC 1837–38 (ii), Minutes, p. 37.

9. Monotony relieved by hunting privileges: J. Butler to Arthur, Aug. 28, 1828, CSO 1/290/6944, TSA, Hobart. Taste of echidna: Lemprière, *Penal Settlements*, pp. 43–44.

10. Vegetables against scurvy: Sorell to Cuthbertson, Dec. 10, 1823, CSO 1/134/3229. Rapid increase of scurvy: J. Spence (asst. surgeon at Macquarie Harbor) to James Scott, Colonial Surgeon, Feb. 8, 1823, CSO 1/134/3230.

11. Lemprière, *Penal Settlements*, pp. 37–38.

12. Barnes to SC 1837–38 (ii), Minutes, p. 37.

13. Davies, "Memoir of Macquarie Harbour," Ms. 8 in MSQ 168, Dixson Library, Sydney.

14. For occupational disease among the convicts and guards at Macquarie Harbor, see Spence to Scott, CSO 1/134/3230.

15. Davies, "Memoir," pp. 2–3.

16. Barnes to SC 1837–38 (ii), Minutes, p. 45.

17. Ibid., p. 46.

18. Ibid., p. 43.

19. J. Butler (commandant at Macquarie Harbor) to Arthur, June 9, 1825, CSO 1/220/5313.

20. Butler to Col. Sec. Burnett, Nov. 25, 1827, CSO 1/216/5236, p. 189.

21. CSO 1/216/5188, Minute 312, Dec. 17, 1827, pp. 239, 243, 247.

22. Lemprière, *Penal Settlements*, p. 31.

23. Ibid., p. 32.

24. Barnes to SC 1837–38 (ii), Minutes, p. 43.

25. Robson, *Hist. Tas.*, p. 137. On Arthur, see ADB entry; Anne McKay, "The Assignment System of Convict Labour in Van Diemen's Land, 1824–1842" (M.A. thesis); and W. D. Forsyth, *Governor Arthur's Convict System*.

26. Arthur to Huskisson, cit. in P. R. Eldershaw, "The Colonial Secretary's Office," in "Guide to the Public Records of Tasmania," Thrapp, vol. 15, no. 3, Jan. 1968, p. 57.

27. Arthur to Bathurst, July 3, 1825.

28. Backhouse, *Narrative*, p. 19.

29. Arthur, *Observations Upon Secondary Punishment*, pp. 27–28.

30. George Washington Walker to Margaret Bragg, May 24, 1834, Walker Papers, UTL, Hobart.

31. McKay, "Assignment System," p. 78.

32. George Taylor to John Thompson, CSO 1/624/14148, collected as No. CXXVIII in Eustace Fitzsymonds, ed., *A Looking-Glass for Tasmania*.

33. The first major landowner and capitalist of Van Diemen's Land was Edward Lord; see E. R. Henry, "Edward Lord: the John Macarthur of Van Diemen's Land." On his unrelated namesake, the convict's son David Lord (1785–1847), see ADB entry (vol. 2, p. 126).

34. On the Rev. Carvosso at the scaffold, see Robson, *Hist. Tas.*, p. 276.

35. Arthur to Montagu, January 1831, CSO 1/224/5434, CSO 1/141/2493, cit. in McKay, "Assignment System," pp. 124–25.

36. Petition of Isaac Solomon to Arthur, CSO 1/430/9642. On Isaac "Ikey" Solomon, see ADB entry.

37. John West, *The History of Tasmania*, part 3, sect. XVII, p. 138.

38. Arthur, memo, Oct. 20, 1827, CSO 1/172/4150.

39. "Slanderers and slaves": West, *Tasmania*, part 3, sect. xvii, pp. 139–40.

40. Arthur's opinion of Baxter: ADB, vol. 1, p. 75.

41. On John Burnett, see ADB entry and corr. file under Burnett, J., in TSA.

42. On Roderic O'Connor and his relations with Arthur, see ADB, vol. 2, p. 296.

43. On Goodwin, Bent, Melville, Murray and other pioneers, however flawed, of journalism in Van Diemen's Land, see ADB entries and E. M. Miller, *Pressmen and Governors*.

44. Melville to Arthur, Nov. 17, 1835, CSO 1/836/17722. In a covering note to Melville's letter, the jailer, Thomas Capon, gives an interesting side-light on public opinion of Australian journalists. He had offered Melville a cell on the side of prison reserved for debtors, but "the Debtors had expressed their great repugnance to any person connected with the Press being put on their side of the Prison."

45. On Gellibrand, see ADB entry (vol. 1, p. 437), and Robson, *Hist. Tas.*, pp. 289–92.

46. Margaret Weidenhofer, *Maria Island: A Tasmanian Eden*, pp. 18–22.

47. On the growth of the "demonic" reputation of Port Arthur, see Decie Denholm, "Port Arthur: the Men and the Myth."

48. Arthur's Standing Instructions for Port Arthur are in CSO 1/639/14383.

49. Lemprière, *Penal Settlements*, p. 61.

50. John Russell to SC 1837–38 (ii), Minutes, p. 50.

51. On early years at Port Arthur (administrations of Russell and Mahon, 1830–32) see Margaret Weidenhofer, *Port Arthur: A Place of Misery*, pp. 7–12.

52. Russell to SC 1837–38 (ii), Minutes, pp. 51–2.

53. Logan to Col. Sec., Dec. 31, 1832, CSO 1/633.1/14299.

54. For number of sentences served at Port Arthur, see Decie Denholm, "Port Arthur," p. 408.

55. Charles O' Hara Booth, *Journal*, ed. Dora Heard, May 18, 1833.

56. C. P. T. Laplace, "Considerations" p. 152, cit. and trans. in Booth, *Journal*, p. 28; Booth, *Journal*, Feb. 20, and Dec. 7, 1833.

57. Lemprière, *Penal Settlements*, p. 94.

58. John Frost, *The Horrors of Convict Life*, pp. 30–31.

59. Backhouse and Walker to Arthur, CSO 1/807/17244, cit. in Weidenhofer, *Port Arthur*, p. 24.

60. Frost, *Horrors*, p. 59.

61. Punishment record of Robert Williamson is in TSA, Hobart.

62. Absconder disguised as kangaroo: Lemprière, *Penal Settlements*, p. 69.

63. Ibid., p. 95.

64. Details of the semaphore system are in Dora Heard's Introduction to Booth, *Journal*, pp. 24–25; W. E. Masters, *The Semaphore Telegraph System of Van Diemen's Land* (Hobart, 1973); and Weidenhofer, *Port Arthur*, p. 25.

65. Characteristics of Port Arthur coal: Lemprière, *Penal Settlements*, pp. 78–80.

66. For the convict-propelled railway, see Godfrey Mundy, *Our Antipodes*, and William Denison, *Varieties of Vice-Regal Life*, both cit. in Weidenhofer, *Port Arthur*, pp. 37, 39.

67. Ross, "Excursion to Port Arthur," in *Elliston's Hobart Town Almanack* (1837), p. 91.

68. On Point Puer, I have relied on F. C. Hooper's M.Ed. thesis, "Point Puer," University of Melbourne, 1954 (subsequently revised and published as *Prison Boys of Port Arthur*, Melbourne, 1967). Unless otherwise noted, all quotations are from Hooper's thesis, the standard and only full study of this curious pedagogical experiment.

69. Arthur to Turnbull, Feb. 8, 1834, cit. in Hooper, "Point Puer," p. 21.

70. Champ to the Comptroller-General of Convicts, June 3, 1844, cit. in ibid., p. 3.

71. On the religious instruction of inmates at Point Puer, see Hooper, pp. 72–79.

72. Benjamin Horne, "The Report of B. J. Horne to the Lieutenant-Governor of Van Diemen's Land," cit. in ibid., pp. 43–44.

73. Hooper, pp. 36–39.

74. Punishment record of Thomas Willetts is in TSA, Hobart.

75. Corr. Military Operations 1831, Minutes of Evidence for Committee for Aboriginal Affairs, testimony of Edward White, pp. 53–54.

76. James Carrott: Report of Committee for Aboriginal Affairs, Corr. Military Operations 1831, p. 36.

77. Corr. Military Operations 1831, Minutes of Evidence, testimony of James Hobbs, pp. 49–50. A full account of European settlers' and sealers' aggression against the Tasmanian Aborigines is given in Lyndall Ryan, *The Aboriginal Tasmanians*, Chapters 3–7.

78. Figures from Robson, *Hist. Tas.*, p. 260.

79. Richard Stickney to his sister Sarah, June 21, 1834, Stickney Papers, UTL. The Vandemonians, Stickney thought, "are a facsimile of the Americans both in body and mind, tall, raw-boned and muscular, with a most exalted opinion of themselves. . . . They are mostly ignorant to the last degree."

80. Corr. Military Operations 1831, Report of Aborigines Committee (Mar. 19, 1830), p. 41.

81. Ibid., Minutes, testimony of Gilbert Robertson, p. 48.

82. Ibid., encl. 7, Arthur to Murray, Apr. 15, 1830, p. 16.

83. Ibid., p. 48. For Arthur's views on treatment of Aborigines by free settlers, see ibid., p. 16.

84. Ibid., p. 47 (Sherwin, Espie), pp. 54–55 (O'Connor).

85. Ibid, p. 4: Arthur to Goderich, Jan. 10, 1828. The dogs were not dingoes, but the descendants of kangaroo-dogs and sheep-dogs "originally purloined from the settlers," which now formed enormous semi-wild packs.

86. Ibid.

87. Proclamation by Arthur, encl. 2 in Arthur to Huskisson, Apr. 17, 1828, Corr. Military Operations 1831, pp. 5–7.

88. Arthur's proclamation of martial law and his definition of restricted aboriginal territory in Van Diemen's Land, issued Nov. 1, 1828: ibid., pp. 11–12. Arthur was careful to "strictly order, enjoin and command that the actual use of arms be in no case resorted to . . . that bloodshed be checked as much as possible; that any tribes which may surrender themselves up shall be treated with every degree of humanity; and that defenceless women and children be invariably spared."

89. Robson, *Hist. Tas.*, pp. 214–15.

90. John Burnett, Government Order 2, Feb. 25, 1830, Corr. Military Operations 1831, p. 35.

91. Arthur to Murray, Nov. 20, 1830, ibid., p. 58.

92. Murray to Arthur, Nov. 5, 1830, ibid., p. 56.

93. Robson, *Hist. Tas.*, p. 230.

94. Fear of bloodbath: Anstey to Arthur, Aug. 22, 1830, CSO 1/316. "The most rancorous animosity": Report of Aborigines Committee, in Corr. Military Operations 1831.

95. Arthur, Memorandum, encl. 7, Corr. Military Operations 1831, p. 72.

96. For an account of the Black Line and its effects on the big River and Oyster Bay tribes, see Ryan, *Aboriginal Tasmanians*, pp. 110–12.

97. On George Augustus Robinson, see ADB entry (vol. 2, pp. 385–87) and Ryan, *Aboriginal Tasmanians*, Chapters 8–9.

98. For the story of Trucanini, and a useful criticism of the myths that grew up around her (including the fiction that she was an Aboriginal "Queen"), see Vivienne Ellis, "Trucanini."

    However, the most pernicious—and seemingly, the most durable—myth is the one exposed by Lyndall Ryan, in *The Aboriginal Tasmanians*: the belief that Trucanini was "The Last Aborigine," and that after her death the Tasmanian Aborigines became

an extinct race. It has been repeated, with varying degrees of outrage and pathos, by·
historians, anthropologists and journalists for over a century, with the result that the
surviving Tasmanian Aborigines—who now number about 2,500—have found themselves treated as ciphers or non-persons by conservative Tasmanian whites, and as
embarrassments by liberal ones with a vested emotional interest in the tale of their
"extinction." Consequently, the Tasmanian State Government recognizes neither the
ethnic identity of the surviving Tasmanian Aborigines, nor any of their claims to
ancestral territory or sacred sites—as other Australian State Governments, in varying
degrees, grudgingly do with mainland Aborigines. What happened, as Ryan shows in
detail, was that a substantial number of Aborigines survived, interbreeding with the
descendants of white sealers, on the islands in the Bass Strait, especially Cape Barren
Island. In 1847 the Cape Barren islanders numbered thirteen families, comprising
some fifty people. Their descendants, though as racially dilute as most American
blacks or mainland Australian Aborigines, form the present black population of Tasmania. It should also be noted that Trucanini was not even the last full-blood Aborigine to die; that person was Suke, an old woman who had been taken by sealers from
Cape Portland in Tasmania to Kangaroo Island off South Australia, and who lived
until 1888.

CHAPTER TWELVE   *Metastasis*

1. Shaw *CC*, p. 142.
2. Peel to Smith, Mar. 24, 1826, cit. in Shaw *CC*, pp. 144–45.
3. James Dowling, "Norfolk Island Journal," Feb. 25, 1828, ML, Sydney.
4. Alexander Harris, *Settlers and Convicts*, p. 11.
5. Figures based on Gipps to Glenelg, Nov. 8, 1838, HRA xix:654.
6. Harris, *Settlers and Convicts*, p. 12.
7. John Barnes in SC 1837–38 (ii), Minutes, p. 37.
8. Report of Ernest Augustus Slade, Appendix to SC 1837–38 (ii), paper 518, pp. 89–90.
9. Bourke to Rice, Dec. 14, 1834, HRA xvii:604 and n.; Col. Sec. circular 33/38, NSWA,
   Sydney.
10. Replies to Col. Sec. circular 33/38, Oct. 1–8, 1833, at NSWA 4/2189:1.
11. Darling to Bathurst, Mar. 1, 1827, cit. in Shaw *CC*, p. 195.
12. Darling to Huskisson, Mar. 28, 1828, HRA xiv:70.
13. Darling to Huskisson, Mar. 28, 1828, ibid. There were 1,045 "colonially convicted"
    men at Port Macquarie, Moreton Bay and Norfolk Island put together. On the road
    gangs, Darling's count ran to 500 men, supervised by 22 "trusty" convict overseers,
    split into gangs of a few dozen at work stations along the 150-mile Great Western
    Road, out of Parramatta; some 400 gangers on the Great Northern Road north from
    Windsor; 249 on the Great Southern Road, connecting Sydney to Stonequarry and
    Throsby Creek beyond; and 119 on the unfinished road to Newcastle.
14. As Governor Bourke found six years later, when he tried using privately contracted
    roadwork "at a very high rate, notwithstanding that the bonus of an assignment of
    three convicts per mile has been given to the contractors." Bourke to Stanley, Jan. 15,
    1834, HRA xvii:317.
15. Cook *EL*, p. 18.
16. "The mere fact": Bourke to Stanley, Jan. 15, 1834, HRA xvii:315. Two fat bullocks:
    Cook *EL*, p. 28.
17. "They have no time": Bourke to Stanley, Jan 15, 1834, HRA xvii:321. Iron-gangers
    running to work in double time: Cook *EL*, p. 58.
18. Cook *EL*, pp. 58–60.
19. Bigge NSW, p. 99.
20. Ibid., p. 155.
21. Lachlan Macquarie had proposed outward colonization by convict gangs before Bigge,

in the wake of the disastrous Nepean floods of 1816–17, when settlers were actually returning assigned convicts whom they could no longer support on their ravaged farms to the government. In May 1818, having received five ships carrying 1,046 men within a single month, Macquarie sent 450 of the new arrivals down to Van Diemen's Land and proposed, as a long-term buffer, that convicts working for the government should break ground to the south of Sydney, at Jervis Bay and Illawarra. (Macquarie to Bathurst, May 1818, HRA ix:795.)

22. James Jervis, "The Rise of Newcastle."
23. William Sacheverell Coke, letter, 1827, in DRO, D1881.
24. W. S. Coke, letter in DRO, D1881.
25. On conditions in the Newcastle coal mine, see Bigge NSW, p. 115–16. A harrowing account of both coal-mine and lime-kiln labor at Newcastle is given in the early Australian novel *Ralph Rashleigh*, written about 1840 by "Giacomo di Rosenberg," supposedly the pseudonym of the convict James Rosenberg Tucker (1808–1888?), an Essex clerk tranported for life in 1826 for writing a threatening letter.
26. Jervis, "Newcastle," p. 149.
27. Bigge NSW, p. 117.
28. Ibid., p. 116.
29. Jervis, pp. 149–50.
30. W. S. Coke, letter, Apr.–Aug. 1827, DRO D1881.
31. James Backhouse, *A Narrative of a Visit to the Australian Colonies*, p. 405.
32. Woomera [pseud.], *The Life of an Ex-Convict*, p. 6.
33. James Bushelle, "Memoir," Ms.
34. Woomera, *Life*, p. 15.
35. Bushelle, "Memoir."
36. Woomera, *Life*, p. 6.
37. Cook *EL*, pp. 79–80.
38. "The Brisbane River 100 Years Ago, by an Old Brisbaneite," *Brisbane Courier*, Mar. 22, 1930, cit. in J. G. Steele, *Brisbane Town in Convict Days, 1824–1842*, p. 28.
39. Brisbane to Bathurst, HRA xi:604.
40. Miller to Balfour, CSO 1/371/8476.
41. Ibid.
42. Charles Bateson, *Patrick Logan, Tyrant of Brisbane Town*, p. 52.
43. W[illiam] R[oss], *The Fell Tyrant; or the Suffering Convict*: in places a tendentious and biassed diatribe, although its bias, as from a former convict, is understandable. It is verifiably accurate on certain matters of routine and convict discipline, but apt to invent when it comes to names and cases. Thus Ross asserts, at one point that a prisoner named Geary "starved to death in his cell" when in fact he died of dropsy in hospital. Ross was a Special, serving time for embezzlement, and was Logan's clerk at Moreton Bay. He did not have to labor and was apparently not flogged.
44. Logan to Col. Sec. Macleay, Apr. 6, 1827, cit. in Steele, *Brisbane Town*, p. 72.
45. Darling's orders to Logan: HRA xv:104–16. Summary power over free settlers: ibid., clause 35.
46. Bateson, *Patrick Logan*, p. 96. Douglas Gordon, "Sickness and Death at the Moreton Bay Convict Settlement," p. 473.
47. Ross, *Fell Tyrant*, p. 20.
48. J. J. Knight, *In the Early Days* (1895), cit. in Steele, *Brisbane Town*, p. 181.
49. Bateson, *Patrick Logan*, pp. 81–82. In 1827 Macleay wrote to Logan enclosing a copy of a report on Moreton Bay discipline by the acting attorney-general, William Moore, and instructed him to "state both whether the prisoners are actually worked constantly in irons, as supposed by Mr. Moore, and whether hard labour may not advantageously be imposed instead of the severe corporal punishments of which he takes notice."
50. Gordon, "Sickness and Death," p. 474.
51. Asst. Surgeon J. F. Murray to Anna Bunn, NSWA 4/1966. One of Spicer's recorded efforts was to tell the kitchen overseer to replace the worn-out copper bottoms of the

settlement cauldrons with wood. "Sir," the mystified overseer replied, "the wood will catch fire, and the bottoms be immediately burned out, and the prisoners' victuals will fall into the fire." "Then, sir," Spicer is said to have told him, "let the carpenters make fresh bottoms every day, for there is plenty of wood in the settlement." (Ross, *Fell Tyrant*, pp. 24–25.)

52. Bateson, *Patrick Logan*, p. 100.

53. Thus at Glendon in the Hunter River Valley an Aborigine was shot while in custody of the mounted police, "a very singularly formed man" nicknamed Black Cato, whom "it took four men to hold." His body "was hung up by the Men on the Farm as a terror to the other Blacks," just as one would nail a dead dingo to a tree. Enclosure 3 in Darling to Bathurst, Oct. 6, 1826, HRA xii:625–26.

54. "Singularly prone to espionage": E. S. Hall, *Monitor*, Oct. 17, 1829. "Prostituting his authority": E. S. Hall to Murray, May 1830, Enclosure 1 in Darling to Murray, HRA xv:628ff.

55. Darling to Bathurst, Apr. 18, 1827, HRA xiii:262–63.

56. Affidavit of Surgeon Henry Cowper, NSWA 4/2081.

57. Affidavit of Rev. Vincent, Executive Council Minutes, NSWA 4/1516.

58. Steele, *Brisbane Town*, p. 150.

59. Lord Charles Grey, November 1830, cit. in E. P. Thompson, *The Making of the English Working Class*, p. 202.

60. *Sydney Gazette*, Oct. 22, 1831.

61. Allan Cunningham to SC 1832, Minutes, p. 40.

62. John Graham, petition in NSWA 4/2325:4. Graham helped rescue one of the minor celebrities of colonial Australian history, Mrs. Eliza Frazer, from a tribe of Aborigines near Lake Cootharaba, north of Moreton Bay. She was among the survivors of the *Stirling Castle*, wrecked on Eliza Reef, some 150 miles northeast of Gladstone, in May 1836. Its castaways (including its master, Captain Fraser) had reached Macleay's Island (since renamed Fraser Island) in a longboat and a pinnace before they were seized by local tribesmen. Captain Fraser and others were killed. In August a search party from Moreton Bay, led by Lieutenant Otter and guided by Graham, located the naked and by now partly deranged widow, "dreadfully debilitated and crippled from the sufferings she had undergone" at the hands of the natives. The ordeal of Mrs. Fraser became the subject of a number of books and accounts, from John Curtis's *Shipwreck of the Stirling Castle*, 1838, to Patrick White's novel *A Fringe of Leaves*. It was also the basis of two well-known series of paintings (1947, 1957) by the Australian artist Sidney Nolan. The best account of the wreck of the *Stirling Castle* and its aftermath is Michael Alexander, *Mrs. Fraser on the Fatal Shore* (London, 1971).

63. Foster Fyans, "Memoirs," Ms., pp. 314–15 (p. 146 in the recently published edition, *Memoirs, 1790–1870*, ed. P. L. Brown). See Chapter 13, note 20, below, for a brief account of Fyans.

64. Constance Petrie, *Tom Petrie's Reminiscences* (1904), cit. in Steele, *Brisbane Town*, p. 247. Treadwheels had been in use in English prisons since 1818; the idea had been given to the poor by the engineer and builder Samuel Cubitt, who gave the rich (among other things) the luxurious and solid architecture of Belgravia. It was a parody of labor: utterly useless work which produced nothing, merely "grinding air" as prisoners put it. Never had the alienation of producer from product been so complete—and the authorities did not need a Marx or an Engels to tell them what a torment of anomie this could inflict on the "workers." Sydney Smith hailed the treadwheel as a wonderful and salutary invention, and one judge called it "the most tiresome, distressing, exemplary punishment that has ever been contrived by human ingenuity." See Michael Ignatieff, *A Just Measure of Pain: The Penitentiary in the Industrial Revolution, 1750–1850*, pp. 177–78.

65. Bathurst to Brisbane, HRA xi:322. "Very severe sentence": Hunter to SC 1812, Appendix 1, Minutes, p. 21.

66. Brisbane to Horton, HRA xi:552–54; to Bathurst, HRA xi:604; to Bathurst, HRA xi:553.

67. Bathurst to Darling, HRA xiii:36.
68. Darling to Undersecretary Hay, Feb. 11 1827, HRA xii:105.
69. Fyans, "Memoirs," pp. 213–14 (published edition, p. 92).
70. Ibid.
71. Darling to Hay, HRA xii:105.


CHAPTER THIRTEEN  *Norfolk Island*

1. *Monitor*, Feb. 10, 1829.
2. Morisset praised by Macquarie: Lachlan Macquarie, *Journal*, Nov. 17, 1821, p. 50, A785, ML. Morisset as opponent of hanging: *Sydney Gazette*, Nov. 20, 1827.
3. Brisbane Papers, Box 4, Ms. 4036, NLA, Canberra.
4. "Memoir of Norfolk Island," Frayne's undated Ms., catalogued in the ML as "Anonymous Convict Narrative," is at p. 427 of miscellaneous papers bound in the back of NSW Col. Sec. Papers, vol. 1, Ms. 681. It was clearly written some time after the events described, a memoir (not a diary) probably composed during the Norfolk Island administration of Captain Maconochie (1840–44), who is known to have encouraged other convicts including Frayne's friend Thomas Cook to set down their recollections of the Old System—thus supplying the only first-hand accounts of the Norfolk Island regime from the convicts' viewpoint. The transcription is mine.
5. W. S. Coke, Apr. 1826 from Rio, letter 20, D1881, DRO.
6. LF, p. 1.
7. Cook *EL*, p. 100.
8. James Lawrence, "Memoir," Ms.
9. LF, p. 3.
10. Ibid., pp. 20–21.
11. Ibid., p. 15.
12. Ibid., p. 16.
13. Ibid., pp. 35–37.
14. Ibid., pp. 38–39.
15. Ibid., p. 40.
16. Ibid., p. 51.
17. John Holyard to Rev. J. Reddell, Feb. 4, 1834, in Reddell Papers, A423, p. 91, ML.
18. LF, p. 19.
19. William Ullathorne, *Catholic Mission*, p. 41.
20. Foster Fyans (1790–1870), an Irish Anglican from Dublin, was a seasoned career officer by the time he came to Norfolk Island. He had enlisted in the 67th Regiment in 1810 and served at Cadiz and in the Peninsular War for seven years. As soon as he returned to England he re-embarked, with the 1st Battalion, for India; of its thousand men only 130 survived the ravages of cholera and fighting. He bought his captaincy, and 1827 found him in England again; but like many another "Empire hand," he could not summon up the will to live there. He transferred to the 20th Regiment and in 1833 moved from Mauritius to Sydney, where he joined the 4th (King's Own) Regiment and was sent to Norfolk Island as captain of the guard under Morisset. After his repression of the prisoners' revolt there, he was posted (as commandant) to Moreton Bay.
    When the 4th K.O. sailed for India in 1837, Fyans sold his commission and remained in Australia, settling in the Port Phillip district as the police magistrate of Geelong. In 1840 he was made commissioner of crown lands for Portland Bay, riding six thousand miles a year on his tours of inspection of licensed runs. He built up his own cattle-run and married in 1843. Fyans retired from government service ten years later. Up to then his hobby had been carpentry and wood-turning; it was said to be his eccentric fancy to hide jewels, purchased or looted in India, in secret compartments in the furniture he made, and a desk constructed by Fyans and sold at a country auction in the 1940s for £7 did in fact yield diamonds worth £4,000. But on retirement he turned to write his memoirs, whose 500-page manuscript reposes in the Latrobe

Library, Melbourne. Rambling, unselfconscious and full of salty humor, it is a prime source on penal Australia. All quotations have been checked against these edited memoirs (1986, ed. P. L. Brown) but were taken from a typescript copy generously furnished by the Army Museums Ogilby Trust, Connaught Barracks, Aldershot. On Fyans, see also entry in ADB (vol. 1, pp. 422–24); S. Sayers, "Captain Foster Fyans of Portland Bay District," *Victorian Historical Magazine*, vol. 40, nos. 1–2, pp. 45–66.

21. Jewish prisoners on Norfolk Island were few. In 1841, when the convict population stood at 1,400, only 12 Jews were counted. One may tentatively guess that the man in question was Israel Levey, sentenced to 7 years on Norfolk Island in 1829 and appointed a convict overseer there in September 1832, which would place the suicide pact earlier in that year. Levey played a major role as an informer and witness after the convict mutiny of 1834, and was highly commended by Fyans to the Colonial Secretary for his "zeal." This was the kind of man whom other convicts would say was "not to be trusted."

22. Fyans, "Reminiscences," pp. 233–35.

23. Bourke to Stanley, Nov. 30, 1833, HRA xvii:276–77.

24. LF, p. 65.

25. Morisset to Undersecretary R. W. Hay, Morisset Letters, Ms. AM34, ML, Sydney.

26. On Knatchbull, see ADB entry (vol. 2, p. 66); the colonial secretary's correspondence on Norfolk Island for 1833–35, NSWA 4/2244:2; Executive Council Minutes for 1834, NSWA 4/1441 and 1443; Colin Roderick, *John Knatchbull, from Quarterdeck to Gallows*; and Anon., *A Memoir of Knatchbull, the Murderer of Mrs. Jamieson, Comprising an Account of his English and Colonial History* (Sydney, 1844).

27. Knatchbull, deposition in NI Mutiny Papers, 1834, NSWA 2/8291.

28. John Jackson, deposition in NI Mutiny Papers, NSWA 2/8291.

29. James Pearson in NI Mutiny Papers, NSWA 2/8291, p. 223.

30. Narrative reconstructed from depositions of James Pearson, Elijah Sallis, William Phipps, James Oppenshaw, Charles Russell and William Parham in NI Mutiny Papers.

31. Deposition of James Fitzgerald, ibid.

32. Fyans to Col. Sec. McLeay, Feb. 16, 1834, NI Mutiny Papers, NSWA 4/1441.

33. Cook *EL*, pp. 128–29.

34. All the mutiny figures in Fyans's "Reminiscences" are exaggerated. He gave 500 (not 120) for the first attack on the jail gang guard; and 300 for the strength of the mutineers at Longridge, whereas his report to McLeay written within a month of the mutiny put it between 60 and 80. He was writing his memoir many years later, in retirement: Heroic exploits grow with age.

35. Cook *EL*, pp. 134–35.

36. Cook *EL*, pp. 130–31. This form of torture was also referred to by Rev. T. Sharpe, who was chaplain on Norfolk Island from 1837 to 1841, hence not a witness to the mutiny: Sharpe Papers, 27 ff., A1502, ML, Sydney.

37. Fyans to Col. Sec. McLeay, Feb. 20, 1834, NI Mutiny Papers, NSWA 4/1441. "Fatal Ball": Cook *EL*, p. 133.

38. Chambers to Col. Sec. McLeay, Aug. 20, 1834, NSWA 4/2245.

39. Sir William W. Burton, *The State of Religion and Education in New South Wales*, pp. 152–54.

40. Chambers to McLeay, Aug. 30, 1834, CSO 34/6236, NSWA 4/2245.

41. Burton, *Religion and Education*, p. 154.

42. Ullathorne, *Catholic Mission*, passim and esp. pp. 40–45.

43. Ibid., p. 37.

44. On the last years of Morisset, see Petition of Emily Morisset to Sir Charles Fitzroy, Governor of NSW, Sept. 13, 1852, Ms. at Am. 34, Morisset Papers, ML.

45. Joseph Anderson, *Recollections of a Peninsula Veteran* (London, 1913).

46. Cook *EL*, p. 137.

47. T. Sharpe, "Letter Book," Ms. A1502 in ML, also cit. in Phillip Cox and Wesley Stacey, *Building Norfolk Island*, p. 24.

48. James Backhouse, *A Visit to the Australian Colonies*, p. 257. It was difficult to per-

suade the skeptical authorities on Norfolk Island of the genuineness of one's injuries. In January 1834 (NSWA) the convict Joʰ n Boyd petitioned for release from his chains and his life sentence: "Being totally deprived of sight . . . I most humbly intreat you to look on me with an eye of Mercy . . . the remainder of my life, shall be spent in sorrow for violating the Laws of the Land . . ." This heartrending plea did not impress Fyans, who minuted on the back: "From all I can learn of this person, he has malingered with his eyes—and has anything but a good Character."

49. LF, pp. 25–26.
50. Ibid., p. 26.
51. Ullathorne, *Catholic Mission*, p. 40.
52. Ibid.
53. Prisoner of "great recklessness": Backhouse, *Australian Colonies*, p. 266. "Their passions": Ullathorne, *Catholic Mission*, p. 41.
54. Sydney Smith, cit. in Sheldon Glueck, Foreword to Sir John Vincent Barry, *Alexander Maconochie of Norfolk Island*, p. viii.

CHAPTER FOURTEEN  *Toward Abolition*

1. John West, *The History of Tasmania*, part 4, sect. 1, pp. 146–47.
2. Lady Franklin to Mrs. Simpkinson, Dec. 10, 1841, in George Mackaness, *Some Private Correspondence of Sir John and Lady Jane Franklin*, vol. 2, p. 36.
3. T. J. Lemprière, *Diary at Port Arthur*, Mar. 26, 1837, p. 24.
4. Montagu to Arthur, Dec. 9, 1837, cit. in Shaw *CC*, p. 269.
5. Diary of G.W.T.B. Boyes, June 11, 1846, cit. in Sir John V. Barry, *Alexander Maconochie of Norfolk Island*, p. 30.
6. Maconochie to Admiral Sir George Back, cit. in Barry, *Maconochie*, p. 28.
7. Alexander Maconochie, *Report on the State of Prison Discipline in Van Diemen's Land*.
8. Maconochie to Back, Mar. 14, 1839 [?], cit. in Barry, *Maconochie*, p. 52.
9. Maconochie, *Report*.
10. Jane Franklin to Mrs. Simpkinson, Dec. 26, 1839, cit. in Barry, *Maconochie*, p. 58.
11. Mrs. Maconochie to Back, Mar. 11, 1839, cit. in Barry, ibid.
12. Maconochie to Washington, May 29, 1839.
13. On Apr. 8, 1837, the "philosophic Radical" William Molesworth, Member for East Cornwall, rose in the Commons to propose a select committee of inquiry into transportation. Fifteen members were appointed, representing a fair cross-section of political views from Tories to Radicals, with Molesworth as chairman. The committee held, in all, thirty-eight meetings between its first session on Apr. 10, 1837 and its last on Aug. 3, 1838. It examined twenty-three witnesses; the most extensive testimony was given by Sir Francis Forbes, James Mudie, James Macarthur, J. D. Lang, Colonel George Arthur and the Rev. William Ullathorne. The voluminous Report of the Molesworth Committee, with minutes of testimony and appendices was published in two parts: PP vol. xix, no. 518, 1837, pp. 5–317, cited as SC 1837–38 (i), and PP vol. 22, 1837–38, pp. 1–139, cited as SC 1837–38 (ii).
14. Correspondence between Russell and the Commissioners for the Reform of the Criminal Law, *The Times* (London), Apr. 1, 1837, cit. in John Ritchie, "Towards Ending an Unclean Thing," p. 158.
15. Ritchie, "Towards Ending," pp. 159–60.
16. Extract from Molesworth's notes on Report of SC 1837–38 (ii), cit. in Sir William W. Burton, "State of Society and State of Crime in New South Wales," *Colonial Magazine*, vol. 1.
17. William Ullathorne, *Autobiography*, pp. 138–39.
18. See SC 1837–38 (ii), Report, p. viii, and Appendix, p. 77.
19. Ibid., p. xxi.
20. Ibid., pp. xxiv–vi.

21. NSW V & P, July 17, 1838.
22. On the changing perception of colonial crime in the wake of the Molesworth Report and the attitudes of "respectables," see Michael Sturma, *Vice in a Vicious Society*, pp. 27–30.
23. Gipps to Glenelg, Mar. 29, 1839, HRA xx:75.
24. SC 1837–38 (ii), Report, p. xliv.
25. Maconochie, encl. 7 in Gipps to Russell, Feb. 25, 1840, HRA xx:544.
26. Maconochie, encl. 2 in Gipps to Russell, HRA xx:532–33.
27. Maconochie, encl. 3 in Gipps to Russell, HRA xx:533–34.
28. Alexander Maconochie, *Norfolk Island*, p. 8. West, *Tasmania*, vol. 2, p. 283.
29. Cook *EL*, pp. 192–93.
30. Ibid.
31. James Lawrence, "Memoir," Ms.
32. Gipps to Russell, June 27, 1840, HRA xx:689.
33. Russell to Gipps, Sept. 10, 1840, *Con. Disc.* 4, 1846, p. 29.
34. Russell to Gipps, Nov. 12, 1840 (in response to Gipps-Russell, June 27, 1840), *Con. Disc.* 4, 1846, pp. 29–30.
35. Maconochie to Gipps, encl. 4 in Gipps to Russell, Feb. 25, 1840, HRA xx:535.
36. E. Deas Thomson (Col. Sec. Off., Sydney) to Maconochie, Aug. 20, 1841, *Con. Disc.* 4, 1846, p. 29.
37. Gipps to Russell, Aug. 27, 1841, *Con. Disc,* 4, 1846, p. 27.
38. Maconochie to Gipps, re Mark & Ticket System, June 2, 1842.
39. Encl. 1 in Gipps to Stanley, Aug. 15, 1842, *Con. Disc.* 4, 1846, p. 59.
40. Gipps to Stanley, Aug. 15, 1842. HRA xxii:209.
41. Maconochie to Gipps, Dec. 31, 1841, encl. 1 in Gipps to Stanley, *Con. Disc.* 4, 1846, p. 38.
42. Thomson to Maconochie, Jul. 29, 1842, *Con. Disc.* 4, 1846, p. 55.
43. Maconochie to Gipps, June 2, 1842, encl. 1 in Gipps to Stanley, Aug. 15, 1843, *Con. Disc.* 4, 1846, p. 54 and passim.
44. Alexander Maconochie, *The Mark System of Prison Discipline*.
45. On the convict graves in the Norfolk Island cemetery, see R. Nixon Dalkin, *Colonial Era Cemetery of Norfolk Island*.
46. James Lawrence, "Memoir," Ms. It seems to have been Maconochie's policy to encourage literate convicts to write down their experiences, both to exorcise their horrors and to supply an unofficial record of the underside of the Old System. The historian can only be grateful to him, since, if Maconochie had not given men like Thomas Cook, James Lawrence, James Porter and Laurence Frayne the means and time to describe the hells they had passed through, their reality would now be lost in administrative euphemisms, omissions and lies.

    In general, convicts' experiences were not considered worth wasting time on, and it is remarkable not only that the occasional manuscript like Cook's should have survived complete, but that the others survived in any form, however physically damaged or edited. Most, one may assume, were thrown out by archivists or embarrassed descendants. Thus the memoir of a Liverpool convict named Jones (b. 1813), probably written under Maconochie's aegis, ends after a few pages before his transport ship has left the White cliffs of Dover behind; on the last page is the notation, in a later hand, "*Jones—Thief*—up to his transportation for the Colonies—nothing interesting. Excerpt 1867." One could wish to see those missing pages. See memoir of Jones, item 10 at MSQ 168, Dixson Library, Sydney.
47. The story of "Bony" Anderson, the convict chained to the rock of Goat Island in Sydney Harbor, appears first in the English journal *Meliora*, vol. 4, no. 13 (April 1861), pp. 12–14. Barry (*Maconochie*, p. 121) raises the possibility that it was taken from an unpublished, and now lost, manuscript by Maconochie himself. For a full account of Anderson and Maconochie see Barry, *Maconochie*, pp. 121–24.
48. J. W. Smith to Gipps, encl. 1 in Gipps to Stanley, Aug. 15, 1842, *Con. Disc.* 4, 1846, p. 58ff.

49. Gipps to Stanley, Oct. 13, 1841, HRA xxi:542.
50. Gipps to Stanley, Aug. 15, 1842, *Con. Γ sc.* 4, 1846, p. 66.
51. Gipps to Stanley, Apr. 1, 1843, HRA xxii:617. Barry, *Maconochie*, p. 140.
52. Gipps to Stanley, Apr. 1, 1843, *Con. Disc.* 4, 1846, p. 138.
53. Ibid., p.142.
54. Ibid., p. 143.
55. Ibid., pp. 143–44.
56. Ibid., pp. 146–47.
57. Ibid., p. 147.
58. Alexander Maconochie, *On Reformatory Prison Discipline*, p. 26.
59. Gipps to Stanley, Apr. 1, 1843, *Con. Disc.* 4, 1846, p. 148.
60. Ibid., p. 149.
61. In 1840 it had cost £10. 18s. 4d. to keep a convict on Norfolk Island; in 1843, £13 3s. 11d., a rise of 21 percent. But in 1838, due to bumper harvests; the year's cost of a convict was £4 14s. 2d; whereas in 1839, the year before Maconochie arrived, the crops were dismal and because all food had to be imported the figure went to £17 19s. 10d —a rise of 380 percent.
62. Stanley to Gipps, Apr. 29, 1843, HRA xx:691.
63. For the Eastern Penitentiary in Philadelphia, see Charles Dickens, *American Notes for General Circulation*, pp. 68–77.
64. Pentonville penitentiary seemed, from the moment of its opening in 1842, to be "a model for prison architecture and discipline not only in England but in most of Europe . . . the culmination of three generations of thinking" (Ignatieff, *A Just Measure of Pain*, p. 3). Its purpose was to crush the will of its 450 inmates by means of absolutely inflexible routine, complete isolation and unvarying task-work, with each convict identically engaged on a 12-hour day of cobbling or weaving. Whenever the prisoner stepped outside his cell for muster or exercise, he was required to don a woollen mask with eyeholes so that he could neither recognize nor be recognized by his fellow-prisoners. The Pentonville chapel, where prisoners were assembled every day, was designed with a separate box for each prisoner; wooden partitions and a door in each box assured that no convict could see the man to right or left of him, only the preacher in the "cackle tub" or pulpit. All the main features of Pentonville—the silent cells, the spyholes, the isolation, the masks and the chapel—would be faithfully copied after 1853 in the "Model Prison" built at Port Arthur in Tasmania. (See note 45 to Chapter 15, below.)

CHAPTER FIFTEEN *A Special Scourge*

1. Stanley's dispatches to Franklin outlining the Probation System: Nov. 25, 1842, *Correspondence re Convict Discipline*, in PP 159, 1843, nos. 175 (p. 3) and 176 (p. 10).
2. Shaw *CC*, pp. 295–96.
3. Sir James Graham to the Committee of Visitors of Parkhurst Prison, Dec. 20, 1842, *Correspondence re Convict Discipline*, Appendix to Part I, pp. 1–2, PP 1843.
4. Ibid.
5. Stanley to Franklin, Nov. 25, 1842, dispatch no. 176.
6. Robert Crooke, *The Convict*, pp. 39–40.
7. Eardley-Wilmot's loyalty to the apprenticeship system for training young artisans—which was being harried into extinction by the free labor market of the late 1820s—would be upheld in the curriculum of craft-training at Point Puer in Port Arthur in the 1840s. He blamed the increase of juvenile crime on the breakdown of the master's parental supervision of the young. "Formerly the apprentice was taken into the house of the master," he declared in 1827; "he was considered one of the family. . . . [N]ow the master has ten or a dozen apprentices and perhaps never sees them. . . . [They] are allowed to go where they please . . . and the consequence is that they are all thieves." Ignatieff, *A Just Measure of Pain*, p. 182.

8. Robson, *Hist. Tas.*, p. 418. For a general description of the depression of the Van Diemen's Land economy, see pp. 413–19.

9. Robert Pitcairn to Lord Stanley, Feb. 4, 1846, *Correspondence re Convict Discipline*, PP 1843, p. 38.

10. "Half-Yearly Return of Runaway Convicts, Authorised by J. S. Hampton, Comptroller General at Hobart." Poster, dated Jul. 1, 1850, cumulative since 1831, D356–18, ML, Sydney.

11. F. R. Nixon to Lord Grey, Feb. 15, 1847; printed in PP 1847, Memorials on Transportation, "A Communication upon the Subject of Transportation," vol. 38, no. 741, p. 2.

12. Stanley to Eardley-Wilmot, draft dispatch dated Sept. 1845, encl. 1 in J. Stephen to S. W. Phillips, Sept. 8, 1845, *Con. Disc.* 3, 1846.

13. Nixon to Grey, Feb. 15, 1847, in PP 1847, vol. 38, no. 741, p. 3ff.

14. For the incidence of lesbianism in the Female Factories in Launceston and at the Cascades, see G. R. Lennox, "A Private and Confidential Despatch of Eardley-Wilmot." The mention of lesbianism in chapel is at p. 342 of the 1841 Committee's report at CSO 22/50, TSA. One reason for Eardley-Wilmot's downfall as lieutenant-governor was that Gladstone believed he had done little or nothing to curb convict lesbianism in Van Diemen's Land. Though plans for the separate women's penitentiary Stanley had called for as part of his Probation System had been drawn up (by Major Joshua Jebb, along the lines of Parkhurst on the Isle of Wight) and sent from England, and though a budget of £35,000 had been approved for its construction, it was not, as noted above, actually built. Instead, as many newly arrived women convicts as possible were diverted from the Cascades Factory into a converted prison ship moored in the Derwent, HMS *Anson*, where (it was hoped) they would not be exposed to the factory's corrupting influence. In all, about 3,500 convict women passed through probationary instruction on board the *Anson* between 1844 and 1849, under the authority of Edmund and Philippa Bowden, superintendent and matron. To save money, however, Eardley-Wilmot planned to reverse the roles of the *Anson* and the Cascades Factory; the factory would become the reform-school, the ship a punishment hulk. This earned him the enmity of Matron Bowden; she helped persuade Gladstone (already famous for his interest in "fallen women") that her work as a rehabilitator was being undermined by the lieutenant-governor; and this, Lennox points out (p. 87), must have accelerated Eardley-Wilmot's sacking in April 1846.

15. Wilmot's confidential report to Stanley, Nov. 2, 1843, cit. in Lennox, "Eardley-Wilmot," p. 80.

16. John Frost, *The Horrors of Convict Life*, p. 40.

17. Eardley-Wilmot to Stanley, Mar. 17, 1846, *Con. Disc.*, 1847, p. 46.

18. The petition of twenty-five clergymen in Van Diemen's Land to Lord Grey was couched in somber tones, inspired by "a deep sense of the responsibility of living in a land where such awful sins are committed, and where the unhappy convicts are subjected to an association leading them into such shocking corruption." Enclosure 1 (dated July 9, 1846) in Bishop Nixon to Lord Grey, May 3, 1847, *Con. Disc.* 1847, p. 44.

19. J. Syme, *Nine Years in Van Diemen's Land . . .*, Dundee, 1848, pp. 200–201, cit. in Crowley, *Doc. Hist.*, vol. 2, p. 122.

20. Gladstone to Eardley-Wilmot, Apr. 30, 1846, both private and public letters in CO 408/25.

21. C. J. La Trobe to Lord Grey, May 31, 1847, paper 941, in *Con. Disc.* 1847.

22. Stanley to Gipps, HRA xxii:695–96.

23. Childs to Champ, July 11, 1846, encl. 2 in Wilmot to Gladstone, Sept. 3, 1846, *Con. Disc.* 1847, p. 176.

24. John Mortlock, *Experiences of a Convict*, pp. 73, 71.

25. Ibid., p. 70.

26. Rev. Thomas Rogers, *Correspondence*, p. 144. Thomas Rogers (1806–1903), a graduate of Trinity College in Dublin, accepted from the Society for the Propagation of the Gospel a post on Norfolk Island as religious instructor to convicts. He arrived in

Hobart in July 1845 and by September was on Norfolk Island. His position was anomalous. Not having been appointed by Bishop Nixon in Tasmania, he had no ecclesiastical authority. He was not well-placed to argue with the island commandants, Childs and Price; but argue he did, passionately and with anguish, on behalf of the tormented prisoners. He tried (but failed) to report on Childs's misdeeds and neglect to Eardley-Wilmot in Hobart; tried (and failed again) to get Denison's ear on John Price. Naturally, this dissident friend of the convicts did not last long on Norfolk Island; he was recalled to Hobart in February 1847. In 1849 he published a book defending his stand against the System, *Correspondence Relating to the Dismissal of the Rev. T. Rogers, from his Chaplaincy at Norfolk Island.* Rogers's manuscript Letter-Book for his sojourn on Norfolk Island, 1844–46, is in the ML, Sydney.

He was less generous to his family. Over four years in Australia Rogers only sent £75, a miserable pittance, to the wife and six children he had left behind. Sarah Rogers died destitute without seeing her errant husband again. Early in 1850, friends subscribed to raise the passage money to send their children to Australia. Unaware of this, Rogers had made arrangements to sail back to Ireland to fetch them. The two ships passed each other en route; Rogers was not reunited with his offspring until he returned to Australia in 1860.

One of his sons, John William Foster Rogers, worked up his father's reminiscences and letters into a manuscript, which remained unpublished: "Man's Inhumanity—Being a Chaplain's Chronicle of Norfolk Island in the 'Forties" (typescript, with illustrations, C214, ML, Sydney). Rogers himself was the prototype of the tormented, alcoholic chaplain the Rev. James North in Clarke's *His Natural Life.*

27. Diary of Elizabeth Robertson, Ms. 163 in Dixson Library, Sydney, cit. in Margaret Hazzard, *Punishment Short of Death*, p. 189.

28. Childs to Eardley-Wilmot, Oct. 1, 1845, encl. in Wilmot to Stanley, Dec. 19, 1845, *Con. Disc.* 2, 1846, p. 48.

29. Naylor to Grey, in GO 1/63, TSA, cit. in Eustace Fitzsymonds, ed., *Norfolk Island 1846 . . .* , pp. 15–16. (Naylor's report to Stanley, edited for parliamentary publication, is printed as encl. 2 in Grey to Denison, Sept. 30, 1846, *Con. Disc.* 1847, pp. 67–76.)

30. Ibid.

31. Maconochie advises Naylor against publishing the report: Maconochie to B. Hawes, Sept. 22, 1846, encl. 1 in paper 11, *Con. Disc.* 1847, p. 67. "Too probable" to pass over: Grey to Denison, Sept. 30, 1846, paper 11 in *Con. Disc.* 1847, p. 66. Grey's second thoughts: Grey to Denison, Nov. 7, 1846, paper 12 in *Con. Disc.* 1847, p. 76.

32. Hazzard, *Punishment Short of Death*, p. 196.

33. Robert Pringle Stuart's Ms. of the report is at CON 1/5183 and GO 33/55, TSA. The censored version, with whole paragraphs missing and a copious scattering of asterisks, appeared in *Con. Disc.* 1847, pp. 84–101. The full text, as with Naylor, is published in Fitzsymonds, ed., *Norfolk Island 1846.*

34. Ibid.

35. Clarke's account of the Ring in *His Natural Life*, based on Stuart's report, is relatively unsensational, though fanciful in parts. Price Warung's "Secret Society of the Ring," in *Convict Days*, pulls out all the stops and sounds like an antipodean mixture of *Maria Monk, Juliette, The Castle of Otranto* and *Melmoth the Wanderer*, overglazed with Poe; the Ring's nocturnal conclaves are lit with blazing light from the eyesockets of a skull, producing "a diabolic effect upon weakened nerves," including the reader's. As for the language, "Were you to clothe with literary form the mouthings of the creatures led by Hebert, as thy danced round Lais and Phryne enthroned as Goddesses of Reason on the desecrated church altars of Revolutionary Paris, you would scarcely parallel it in point of blasphemous horror" (pp. 159–60). On the rhymed "Convict Oath" (presumably written by Warung), see "The Liberation of the First Three" in *Convict Days*, pp. 68–69.

36. Stuart, in Fitzsymonds, ed., *Norfolk Island 1846*, p. 67.

37. Minutes of Executive Council Meeting, Hobart, July 1–2, 1846.

38. On the Norfolk Island mutiny of July 1, 1846, see Judge Fielding Browne's Report in

*Con. Disc.* 1847, pp. 35–40. Price's report, with declarations and testimony from Alfred Baldock, George Bott, William Forster and others, encl. in Latrobe to Grey, Jan. 8, 1847, ibid., pp. 25–35.

39. On Henry Beresford Garrett and "The Demon," see Sir John Vincent Barry, *The Life and Death of John Price*, Appendix A. The facts of Garrett's life are unclear. According to one version, he was a soldier transported for robbing the commissariat in Nottingham. He arrived on Norfolk Island around 1845, and toward the end of Price's commandancy he was transferred to Van Diemen's Land; he escaped in 1853 and fled to Victoria, finding anonymity within the vast horde of gold-seekers. In 1854 Garrett and three accomplices "stuck up" the Bank of Victoria at Ballarat, making off with £14,300 in cash and 250 oz. of gold. With his share of the loot, Garrett returned to London but was recognized at once and re-transported to Melbourne for trial. Convicted of bank robbery, he went to the hulks in Port Phillip Bay, where he saw (and perhaps took part in) the murder of John Price in 1857. Released in 1861, he went to New Zealand, lived as a bushranger, and was sentenced in 1868 to 20 years in jail for shopbreaking. During the latter part of this sentence, before his death in 1885, Garrett wrote a number of manuscripts, including "The Demon," his 25,000-word account of John Price—a document of obsession. It survives only as a transcript made after 1948; the original notebooks, which Garrett entrusted to a Methodist lay preacher named Hall, are lost. A photocopy of the transcript is in the Mitchell Library, Sydney.

40. Price to Champ, Dec. 7, 1846, encl. 1 in Latrobe to Grey, Jan. 8, 1847, letter 8 in *Con. Disc.* 1847, p. 26.

41. Barry, *The Life and Death of John Price*, p. 37. Willson's damaging report to Denison on Norfolk Island (dated May 22, 1852) is printed in *Con. Disc*, 1853, pp. 88–95. In 1849, on his previous (second) visit, Willson had praised the improvement of rations, the "perfect unanimity" among the civil and military officers, and "the judicious conduct of Mr. Price, the Commandant" (*Con. Disc.* 1850, pp. 111–114).

42. Quotes from Rogers, unless otherwise specified, are from passages cited in Barry, *The Life and Death of John Price*, pp. 45–50, and from W. F. Rogers, "Man's Inhumanity . . . ," typescript at C214, ML, Sydney.

43. W. Nairn to Price, Feb. 2, 1852, in *Con. Disc.* 1853, pp. 88–89.

44. Price to Nairn, Mar. 15, 1852, ibid., pp. 89–90.

45. The "Model Prison" at Port Arthur was begun in 1848 and finished in 1852; it remained in continuous use until Port Arthur closed down in 1877. It was, in every way, a scale model of Pentonville, with a fraction of the capacity—48 separate cells, arranged in three wings; the fourth wing of the cross was the chapel, with its partitioned stalls so designed that convicts could not see or communicate with one another when at Divine Service. The cells, fittings, central inspection hall and schedules for work, exercise and cleaning were copied from Pentonville, as were the prisoners' cloth masks, the felt slippers worn by guards to ensure silence, the silent numbering-machine that indicated to prisoners the order in which they must leave the chapel, and much else besides. It had four dumb-bells, black isolation chambers with walls three feet thick and no less than three internal doors; when these and the entrance door were closed, as any visitor to the restored Model Prison can now test for himself, the silence and darkness were such as to exclude all sensory stimulation. The records suggest that the Model Prison produced a high level of neurosis and mental breakdown in its inmates—as did Pentonville.

46. Report of SC on Criminal Laws, Juvenile Offenders and Transportation, PP 1847 (449), pp. 3–7.

47. Lord Grey in *GB Parl. Debates*, 3rd series, vol. 110, cols. 211–12, cit. in Crowley, *Doc. Hist.*, vol. 2, p. 114.

48. Grey to Denison, Feb. 5, 1847. Stephen to the Treasury, Feb. 15, 1847, CO 280/196.

49. Grey to Denison, Apr. 27, 1848.

50. Grey to Fitzroy, Sept. 3, 1847, HRA xxv:735. In September 1847, Grey offered to send

out one free emigrant, his fares paid by the government, for every "exile" transported to Australia. However, he retracted this offer the following year.

51. James Macarthur to SC 1837, p. 218.

52. *Port Phillip Patriot and Melbourne Advertiser*, Dec. 19, 1844.

53. Ibid., Dec. 26, 1844. On William Kerr (1812–1859), editor of the radically anti-pastoralist *Argus* and champion of workers' rights in early Victoria, see entry in ADB and Garryowen [pseud. of E. Finn], *The Chronicles of Early Melbourne* (Melbourne, 1888), pp. 1–2.

54. V & P, NSW Legislative Council, Oct. 30, 1846.

55. *Sydney Morning Herald*, June 12–18, 1849.

56. Fitzroy to Grey, June 30, 1849, CO 201/414, cit. in Clark *HA*, vol. 3, p. 420.

57. Anon. letter in *Household Words* (London), Mar. 30, 1850, p. 24.

58. Samuel Sidney, *Emigrant's Journal and Travel Magazine*, cit. in Coral Lansbury, *Arcadia in Australia: The Evocation of Australia in Nineteenth-Century English Literature* (Melbourne, 1970). Prof. Lansbury's discussion of Sidney, a figure ignored by most Australian historians, is highly pertinent to an understanding of the image of Australia among English reformers at mid-century, and I have relied on it here.

59. On Caroline Chisholm, see ADB entry; M. L. Kiddle, *Caroline Chisholm* (Melbourne, 1957); and Caroline Chisholm, *The Emigrants' Guide to Australia*, (London, 1853).

60. Charles Dickens, *David Copperfield*, Chapter 63.

61. Godfrey Charles Mundy, *Our Antipodes*, vol. 3, p. 125.

CHAPTER SIXTEEN   *The Aristocracy Be We*

1. Edward Hammond Hargraves, *Australia and Its Gold Fields . . .* , p. 116. On the "Sydney Ducks," see Sherman Ricards and George Blackman, "The Sydney Ducks: A Demographic Analysis," and Jay Monaghan, *Australians and the Gold Rush*. Sydney first heard of the California gold discoveries in December 1848. The first Australian gold-seekers arrived in San Francisco in April 1849. By May 1851 no less than 11,000 Australians had sailed to California, about 7,500 of them from Sydney. (In 1852 the population of San Francisco County was about 36,000, so the proportion of the Australian gold-seekers—and hence, of ex-convicts—was enormous. The origin of the term "Sydney Duck" (or "Derwent Duck," for gold-seekers from Tasmania) is unclear. They were viewed with extreme suspicion by Americans, and the crimes of a few brought down prejudice upon the whole. Some Ducks were reported to have adapted a mode of robbery from aboriginal hunters, who would set fire to hollow trees and kill the animals as they scurried out. In San Francisco, the technique was to set fire to a building at night and wait for the occupants to run outside clutching—of course— their most valuable possessions. The California Vigilance Committees were especially hard on Australian emigrants. They were "obvious objects of persecution," due to their strange accents and presumed criminal past, even though only one in eight from New South Wales and one in five from Van Diemen's Land were Emancipists. Most of them (some 65 percent) migrated in family groups and had no criminal past or larcenous ambitions. The committees made ninety-one recorded arrests of Ducks. Of these, four were summarily hanged in front of mobs of as many as 15,000 people; fourteen were deported back to Australia, fourteen more summarily deported from California, fifteen handed over to other authorities, and the rest let off.

2. *Bathurst Free Press*, May 17, 1851.

3. Ibid., July 19, and Aug. 13, 1851. Clark *HA*, vol. 4, p. 9.

4. *The Times* (London), Nov. 24, 1852.

5. La Trobe to Lord Grey, Dec. 10, 1851, PP 1852, 34/1508, pp. 45–46.

6. John Sherer, *The Gold-Finder of Australia: How he Went, How he Fared, and How he Made His Fortune*, pp. 195–96.

7. Ibid., p. 198.

8. Ibid., p. 10.

9. William Rayment, Diary, Oct. 19, 1852, Ms. in Public Library of Victoria, cit. in John M. Ward, *The Australian Legend*, pp. 116–17.

10. Address from William Nicholson, mayor of Melbourne, to the delegates from the Van Diemen's Land Anti-Transportation League, February 1851, Ms. Aa 25/5, ML.

11. Address from Mayor J. T. Smith, aldermen and citizens of Melbourne to Queen Victoria: Dispatches from Victoria #26, Feb. 16, 1852, A2341, ML.

12. A. G. Dumas to Lord Grey, July 17, 1851, in Dumas Family Papers, vol. 1, pp. 19–34, A4453–1, ML.

13. Leslie family letters, Jan. 20, 1850, pp. 37–40, A4094, ML.

14. Robson, *Hist. Tas.*, p. 502.

15. Clark *HA*, vol. 4, pp. 28–29.

16. For an account of the 1851 elections in Van Diemen's Land and the curious alliance of Denison and the ex-convict lower classes against the Anti-Transportation League, see Michael Roe, "The Establishment of Local Self-Government in Hobart and Launceston."

17. Ibid., pp. 31–32.

18. Ibid., p. 34.

19. Shaw *CC*, pp. 348–49.

20. Lord Grey, in G.B. Parliamentary Debates, 3rd series, vol. 110, cols. 206–18.

21. Fitzroy to Grey, June 19, 1851.

22. Among these believers in the miraculous universality of convict labor was a Mr. Levinson, who appeared in Hobart with a prospectus for an irrigation canal to be dug across the continent from sea to sea, whose "stupendous nature . . . offers no obstacle to the science, ingenuity and perseverance of Englishmen of the 19th century." Convicts, guarded by sappers and miners, would do the spadework on three-year terms, and be rewarded at the end with an allotment of land and a share of all minerals discovered on the way. The water for the canal, Levinson vaguely averred, would come from the "many rivers [which] would probably be discovered. . . . Thousands of men, who fail at the diggings and do not exactly like to go to agricultural labour, would take to this work, there being a chance of gold." No investors were seduced. *Hobart Town Daily Courier*, Aug. 10, 1853.

23. Pakington to Denison, Dec. 14, 1852, PP 1852–53, 82/1601, pp. 105–6.

24. *Colonial Times and Tasmanian* (Hobart), Aug. 13, 1853.

25. "The people of England": *Colonial Times and Tasmanian*, Aug. 6, 1853. Church bells instead of cannon: *Hobart Town Daily Courier*, Aug. 11, 1853.

26. Stirling to Darling, Dec. 14, 1826, encl. 2 in Darling to Bathurst Dec. 18, 1826, HRA xii:777–80. On Stirling and the Swan River colony, see ADB entry and Clark *HA*, vol. 3, pp. 11, 17–37.

27. On Peel and Levey, see Hasluck, *Thomas Peel of Swan River;* ADB entries; and Clark *HA*, vol. 3, p. 18ff.

28. Fitzgerald to Grey, Mar. 3, 1849, in *Further Correspondence re Convict Discipline and Transportation*, PP 1849, 43/1121, pp. 246–47.

29. *Perth Gazette*, Jan. 2, 1847.

30. Kennedy to Stanley, June 12, 1858, CO 18/104.

31. Superintendent (Fremantle) to Comptroller-General (Henderson), Jan. 10, 1858, CO 18/104.

32. "The prosperity of the colony": Henderson to Stanley, Feb. 9, 1858. "Wholly out of the question": Stanley to Gov. Kennedy, Apr. 16, 1858, CO 18/104. Convict labor to erect rival episcopal palaces: Kennedy to Labouchère, Mar. 13, 1858, CO 18/104.

33. *Statement and Appeals of the Anti-Transportation League of Victoria for the People of Great Britain*, Melbourne, Oct. 23, and Dec. 22, 1853, Q041/Pa 10, ML, Sydney.

34. A. Macarthur, letter in *The Daily News* (London), Mar. 7, 1864, Macarthur Papers, vol. 29, pp. 567–77, A2927, ML, Sydney.

35. Shaw *CC*, p. 356.

CHAPTER SEVENTEEN  *The End of the System*

1. Cit. in Ernest de Blosseville, *Histoire des Colonies Penales de L'Angleterre dans Australie.* The verses translate thus: "Ah! Who does not know the consoling spectacle / Displayed by this vast receptacle of bandits, / This Botany Bay, the sewer of ALBION, / Where theft, rapine and treason / Go in hordes, and, while purging England / Fertilize the ground in their far exile? / There, kindly laws turn dangerous men / Into skilled colonists and happy citizens / Stir them to penitence, stimulate industry, / And give them freedom, customs and a homeland. / On all sides, I see drained marshes / Flowering deserts, and cleared forests. / Follow this example! Take these bandits / From their sterile prison, make their punishment useful."

2. John Freeth, ed., *The Political Songster* (Birmingham, 1790).

3. Edward Curr to Directors of VDL Co., letter 162, Jan. 12, 1831, VDL Co. Foreign Letter Book No. 3, cit. in Shaw *CC*, p. 220.

4. Dickens to Normanby (unpublished), July 2, 1840, cit. in Sarah Bradford, "Forthcoming Sale of English Books and MSS," *Times Literary Supplement,* Dec. 10, 1981.

5. See Appendixes III, IV and V in Michael Sturma, *Vice in a Vicious Society.*

6. Sturma, ibid., p. 77. For a general discussion, see his Chapter 4, "Measuring Morality," pp. 64–85.

7. Mary Gilmore, "Old Botany Bay."

8. John Mitchel, *Jail Journal,* p. 231.

9. Ibid., p. 227.

10. Ibid., p. 213.

11. Ibid., p. 244.

12. Ibid., p. 210.

13. Ibid., p. 238.

14. Henry Reynolds, " 'That Hated Stain': The Aftermath of Transportation in Tasmania." I have relied on Reynolds's essay for the account of post-Transportation entropy in Tasmania that follows.

15. Rev. John Morison, *Australia As It Is,* p. 214ff.

16. Anthony Trollope, *Australia and New Zealand,* vol. 2, Chapter 2, pp. 28–29.

17. Reynolds, "Hated Stain," p. 31.

18. My count, based on figures from Bateson, *The Convict Ships,* Appendix II, "Convict Ships to Van Diemen's Land, 1812–1853."

19. See Miriam Dixson, *"Greater Than Lenin"? Lang and Labour, 1916–1932.*

20. Alexander Cheyne to SC 1837–38, *Report,* pp. xxii–xxiii.

21. Edward Willoughby, *Australian Pictures Drawn with Pen and Pencil,* pp. 78–79, 151.

22. Anon., "The Day We Were Lagged," *The Bulletin,* Jan. 20, 1888.

23. Ibid.

24. Ibid.

25. Ibid.

26. John Sherer, *The Gold-Finder of Australia,* p. 246.

27. Marcus Clarke, *His Natural Life,* Chapter 22.

# Bibliography

## MANUSCRIPT SOURCES

### JOURNALS, DIARIES, ACCOUNTS

Bowes Smyth, Arthur. Journal of a Voyage to NSW in the *Lady Penrhyn*, 1786–89. Safe 1/15, ML, Sydney.

Boyes, G.T.W.B. Diary, 1823–43. Royal Society of Tasmania Library, Hobart.

Bradley, William. Journal, 1786–1792. Safe 1/14, ML, Sydney.

Bushelle, James. Memoir. Ms. 4 at MSQ 168, Dixson Library, Sydney.

Clark, Ralph. Journal, 1787–92, Typescript and *Letter Book*. C219, ML, Sydney.

Coke, William Spencer. Diary (Feb.–Sept. 1828). Brookhill Hall Collection, Derbyshire Record Office, Wardwick, Derby.

Cook, Thomas. "The Exile's Lamentations: Memoir of Transportation." Ms. A1711, ML, Sydney.

Davies,——. Memoir of Macquarie Harbor. Ms. 8 in Norfolk Island Convict Papers, MSQ 168, Dixson Library, Sydney.

Downing, J. Norfolk Island Journal. Ms. B804, ML, Sydney.

Easty, John. "A Memorandum of the Transactions of a Voyage from England to Botany Bay in the Scarborough Transport . . . ," Dixson Library, Sydney.

Eyre, Edward J. Autobiography. ML, Sydney.

Frayne, Laurence. Memoir on Norfolk Island. NSW Colonial Secretary Papers, vol. 1 (re NSW 1799–1830). Ms. 681/1, ML, Sydney.

Fyans, Foster. "Memoirs." Ms., Latrobe Library, Melbourne. Typescript copy in Army Museums Ogilby Trust, Connaught Barracks, Aldershot.

Gorman, John. Log-book. Ms. 1524, NLA, Canberra.

Grant, John. Notes and manuscripts. Ms. 737, Grant Papers, NLA, Canberra.

Gregg, John. Journal on Convict Ship *York* (1862). Ms. 2749, NLA, Canberra.

Holt, Joseph. "Life and Adventures of Joseph Holt, Written by Himself." Ms. A2024, ML, Sydney.

Jones,——. Memoir. Ms. 10 in Norfolk Island Convict Papers, MSQ 168, Dixson Library, Sydney.

Jones, Robert. "Recollections of 13 Years Residence on Norfolk Island." Ms. C/y/1/2, ML, Sydney.

King, Philip Gidley. Journal, Norfolk Island (1791–94). Ms. A1687, ML, Sydney.

Knopwood. Rev. Robert. Diaries, 1803–25. ML, Sydney.

——. "Narrative of Escape from Macquarie Harbour by Alexander Pearce." Ms. 3, Dixson Library, Sydney.

Lawrence, James. Memoir. Ms. 1 in Norfolk Island Convict Papers, MSQ 168, Dixson Library, Sydney.

Lemprière, T. J. Diary. ML, Sydney.

Lepailleur, François-Maurice. Journal, 1839–44. Archives Nationales de Québec.

656

Marsden, Samuel. "A Few Observations on the Toleration of the Catholic Religion in New South Wales." Ms. 18, ML, Sydney.

Muir, Thomas. "The Telegraph, A Consolatory Epistle . . . to the Honble. Henry Erskine." Ms. Am. 9, ML, Sydney.

Palmer, Thomas Fyshe. Letters. Ms. B1666, ML, Sydney.

[Pearce, Alexander.] "Narrative of Escape from Macquarie Harbour," Ms. 3, Dixson Library, Sydney.

Porter, James. Memoirs. Typescript 6 in Norfolk Island Convict Papers, MSQ 168, Dixson Library, Sydney.

Rogers, W. F. "Man's Inhumanity." Typescript C214, ML, Sydney.

Sharpe, Rev. T. Journal, Ms. B217–8, ML, Sydney.

Silverthorpe, Mansfield. Ms. 9 in Norfolk Island Convict Papers, MSQ 168, Dixson Library, Sydney.

Smith, John. Surgeon's Log on Transport *Clyde* (1838). Ms. 6169, NLA, Canberra.

Sorell, William Jnr. Diaries, 1800–1860. UTL, Hobart.

Walker, James Backhouse. Papers, 1853–98. UTL, Hobart.

Ward, John. "Diary of a Convict." Ms. 3275, NLA, Canberra.

Worgan, G. B. Journal, Jan.–July 1788. Typescript B1463, ML, Sydney.


CORRESPONDENCE AND GENERAL PAPERS

Arthur Papers. Mss. A1962, A2161–95, A2214, D292. ML, Sydney.

Auckland Papers. Add. Ms. 34458, BL.

Bentham Papers. Add. Mss. 33543, 33544, BL.

Bonwick Transcripts, Bigge NSW, Appendix, ML, Sydney.

Boothman, Richard. Letters. Ms. DDX 537, LRO, Preston, Lancashire, Eng.

Boyes, G.T.W.B. Letters. UTL, Hobart.

Bradley, William. Journal . . . 1786–1792. Ms. A3631, ML, Sydney.

Brisbane Letter Book. Ms. A1559, ML, Sydney.

Brown, Simon. Letters, 1840–58. Ms. DDX 140, LRO, Preston, Lancashire, Eng.

Calder Papers. Ms. A594, ML, Sydney.

Catton Papers. Derby Central Library, Wardwick, Derby, Eng.

Coke, William Spencer. Letters (1824–28). Ms. D1881, Brookhill Hall Collection, Derbyshire Record Office, Wardwick, Derby, Eng.

Dillingham, Richard. Letters. Ms. CRT 150/24, Bedford County Record Office, Bedford, Eng.

Dumas Family Papers. Vol. 1. Ms. A4453–1, ML, Sydney.

Foveaux, Joseph. Letter Book, 1800–1804. Ms. A1444, ML, Sydney.

Gordon, Hugh. Letter to his brother Robert, Dec. 31, 1839. Doc. 1308, ML, Sydney.

Grant, John. Letters in Grant papers. Ms. 737, NLA, Canberra.

Grieg, James. Letters, 1824–29. Doc. 2316, ML, Sydney.

Hammersley papers, A657, ML.

Harris family letters. Add. Ms. 45156, BL.

Hassall Correspondence. Ms. A1677, ML, Sydney.

Hayes, Michael. Letters. Ms. A3586, ML, Sydney.

Holden, Thomas. Letters, 1812–16. Ms. DDX 140, LRO, Preston, Lancashire, Eng.

Irish Political Prisoners' Letters. NLA, Canberra.

Jewell, W. H. Letter, May 1820. Doc. 1042, ML, Sydney.

King, Philip Gidley. Letter Books, 1788–96, 1797–1806, and papers. Mss. A1687, C187, ML, Sydney.

Lang Papers. Mss. A2221, A2226, A2229, ML, Sydney.

Leslie Papers, A4094, ML, Sydney.

Macarthur Papers. Mss. A2897, A2900, A2911, A2927, A2955, ML, Sydney.

Marsden Papers. Mss. A1992, A1998, ML, Sydney.

Morisset, J. T. Papers, Ms. Am.34, ML, Sydney.

NI Mutiny Papers. NSWA.
Peel Papers. Add. Ms. 40380, BL.
Pelham Papers. Add. Mss. 33105, 33106, 33107, BL.
Privy Council Office Papers. 1/67–92 (1819–1844). Letters and petitions from convicts and families. PRO, London.
Reddell Papers, ML, Sydney.
Sharpe, Rev. T. Papers. Ms. A1502, ML, Sydney.
Stenhouse Papers II, ML, Sydney.
Stickney Papers. UTL, Hobart.
Taylor, Richard. Letters, 1840–58. Ms. DDX 505, LRO, Preston, Lancs.
Ward Papers, Ms. 3275, NLA, Canberra.
Wentworth Papers. Ms. A751, ML, Sydney.
Whitbread Papers, Bedford.
Withers, Peter. Letters. TSA, Hobart.


PRIMARY SOURCES


[Contemporary books, pamphlets and articles, published during the transportation period or drawn from their authors' direct experience of the penal system in convict Australia.]

Anderson, Joseph. *Recollections of a Peninsular Veteran*. London, 1913.
Anon. "Anti-transportation Movement in Sydney." *Colonial Magazine and East India Review*, vol. 18 (July–December 1849), pp. 179–84.
———. *Biographical Memoir* [of John Price]. Melbourne, 1857.
———. *Great and New News from Botany Bay*. London, 1797.
———. *A Narrative of the Sufferings . . . of the Convicts Who Piratically Seized the 'Frederick' in Van Diemen's Land*. c. 1838. (Copy in ML Sydney at 910–453/29A1.)
———. *Sinks of London Laid Open*. [On slang and cant.] 1844.
———. *The Political Martyrs of Scotland Persecuted During the Years 1793 and 1794*. Edinburgh, 1795.
———. "Transportation and Convict Colonies." *Colonial Magazine and East India Review*, vol. 18 (July–December 1849), pp. 27–37.
Anon. [Edward Eagar]. *Letters to Sir Robert Peel on the Advantages of New South Wales and Van Diemen's Land as Penal Settlements*. 1824.
Arthur, George. *Observations upon Secondary Punishment*. Hobart, 1833.
———, ed. *Defence of Transportation in Reply to the Remarks of the Bishop of Dublin*. Hobart and London, 1835.
Atkins, Rev. T. *Reminiscences of Twelve Years Residence on Tasmania and New South Wales, Norfolk Island and Moreton Bay, Calcutta, Madras and Cape Town, the United States of America and the Canadas*. London, 1869.
Atkinson, James, *An Account of the State of Agriculture and Grazing in New South Wales . . .*, London, 1826.
Backhouse, James, and Walker, George Washington, *A Narrative of a Visit to the Australian Colonies*. London, 1843.
Banks, Joseph. *The Endeavour Journal of Joseph Banks, 1768–1771* (ed. J. C. Beaglehole). 2 vols. Sydney, 1962.
Barrington, George [pseud.]. *The History of New South Wales*. London, 1802.
Beccaria, Cesare. *Degli Delitti e delle Pene*, trans. as *Essay on Crimes and Punishments*. London, 1767.
Bennett, H. G. *A Letter to Viscount Sidmouth on Transportation*. London, 1819.
———. *A Letter to Earl Bathurst, Secretary of State for the Colonial Department, on the Condition of the Colonies in New South Wales and Van Diemen's Land*. London, 1820.
Benoiston de Chateauneuf, Jean-François. *De la Colonization des Condamnés*. Paris, 1827.
Bentham, Jeremy. *Panopticon; or, The Inspection-House*. London, 1791.
———. *Panopticon Versus New South Wales: Two Letters to Lord Pelham*. London, 1812.

Betts, T. *An Account of the Colony of Van Diemen's Land.* Calcutta, 1830.

Bischoff, James. *Sketch of the History of Van Diemen's Land.* London, 1832.

de Blosseville, Ernest. *Histoire des Colonies Penales de L'Angleterre dans Australie.* Paris, 1831.

Booth, Charles O'Hara. *The Journal of Charles O'Hara Booth, Commandant of the Port Arthur Penal Settlement* (ed. Dora Heard). Hobart, 1981.

Boswell, James. *The Life of Samuel Johnson,* vol. 2. London, 1920 (Everyman ed).

de Bougainville, Louis Antoine. *A Voyage Around the World* (trans. John Reinhold Foster). London, 1772.

Bowes Smyth, Arthur. *The Journal of Arthur Bowes Smyth, Surgeon, Lady Penrhyn, 1787–1789.* Ed. by P. G. Fidlon and R. J. Ryan. Sydney, 1979.

Bradley, William. *A Voyage to New South Wales, 1786–1792.* Facs. ed. of Bradley Ms. in Safe P.H. 8, ML, Sydney, 2 vols., Sydney, 1967.

Breton, William H. *Excursions in New South Wales, Western Australia and Van Diemen's Land, 1830–33.* London, 1833.

Browning. C. A. *The Convict Ship and England's Exiles.* 2nd ed., London, 1847.

Broxup, John. *Life of John Broxup, Late Convict at Van Diemen's Land.* London, 1850.

Burton, Sir William Westbrooke. *The State of Religion and Education in New South Wales.* London, 1840.

———. "State of Society and State of Crime in New South Wales, During Six Years' Residence in that Colony." *Colonial Magazine and Commercial-Maritime Journal,* vol. 1 (January–April 1840), pp. 421–40; vol. 2 (May–August 1840), pp. 34–54.

Byrne, J. C. *Twelve Years' Wanderings in the British Colonies, From 1835 to 1847.* 2 vols. London, 1848.

Chisholm, Caroline. *Emancipation and Transportation Relatively Considered; in a Letter, Dedicated, By Permission, to Earl Grey.* London, 1847.

———. *The Emigrants' Guide to Australia.* London, 1853.

Clark, Ralph. *Journal and Letters 1787–1792.* Sydney, 1981.

Collins, David. *An Account of the English Colony in New South Wales.* 2 vols. London, 1798, 1802; reprinted Sydney, 1975.

Colquhoun, Patrick. *A Treatise on the Police of the Metropolis.* London, 1797.

———. *The State of Indigence and the Situation of the Casual Poor in the Metropolis Explained.* London, 1799.

———. *A Treatise on the Commerce and Police of the River Thames.* London, 1800.

Cook, James. *The Journals of Captain James Cook on His Voyage of Discovery* (ed. J. C. Beaglehole). Vols. 1 and 2. Cambridge, 1955 and 1961.

———. *A Voyage to the Pacific Ocean.* 3 vols. (vol. 3 by Capt. James King). London, 1784.

Cook, Thomas. *The Exile's Lamentations* (ed. A. G. L. Shaw). Sydney, 1978.

Cozens, Charles. *The Adventures of a Guardsman.* London, 1848.

Cunningham, Peter. *Two Years in New South Wales.* 2 vols. 2nd ed., London, 1827.

Curr, Edward M. *Recollections of Squatting in Victoria Then Called the Port Phillip District, from 1841 to 1851.* Melbourne, 1883.

[Dalrymple, Alexander]. *A Serious Admonition to the Publick on the Intended Thief-Colony at Botany Bay.* London, 1786.

Dampier, William. *Dampier's Voyages* (ed. John Masefield). 2 vols. London, 1906.

Darwin, Charles. *The Voyage of the Beagle.* New York: Bantam paperback edition, 1972.

Denison, Sir William. *Varieties of Vice-Regal Life.* 2 vols. London, 1870.

Dickens, Charles. *American Notes for General Circulation.* London, 1850.

Fielding, Henry. *An Enquiry into the Causes of the Late Increase of Robbers . . .* London, 1751.

———. *A Proposal for Making Effectual Provision for the Poor.* London, 1753.

Fielding, John. *An Account of the Origin and Effects of a Plan of Police.* London, 1753.

———. *Penal Laws Relating to the Metropolis.* London, 1768.

Forster, Harley W. (ed). *The Dillingham Convict Letters.* Melbourne, 1970.

Frost, John. *The Horrors of Convict Life.* Preston, 1856; Hobart, 1973.

Fyans, Capt. Foster. *Memoirs, 1790–1870* (ed. P. L. Brown). Geelong, 1986.

Gaskell, Peter. *The Manufacturing Population of England: Its Moral, Social and Physical Conditions.* London, 1833.

Gouger, Robert [pseud. of E. G. Wakefield]. *A Letter from Sydney, the Principal Town of Australia.* London, 1829.

Grove, James. "Select Letters of James Grove, Convict . . . , 1803–4" [ed. John Earnshaw]. Part II, the letters. THRA, PP, vol. 8, no. 2, October 1959.

Hanway, Jonas. *The Defects of the Police.* London, 1775; reprinted as *The Citizen's Monitor,* London, 1780.

Hargraves, E. H. *Australia and its Gold Fields: A Historical Sketch of the Progress of the Australian Colonies, from the Earliest Times, to the Present Day.* London, 1855.

Harris, Alexander. *The Emigrant Family: or, The Story of an Australian Settler.* London, 1849; reprint [ed. W. S. Ramson], Canberra, 1967.

———[An Emigrant Mechanic]. *Settlers and Convicts, or Recollections of Sixteen Years' Labour in the Australian Backwoods.* London, 1847; reprint [ed. C. M. H. Clark], Melbourne, 1964.

Haygarth, Henry W. *Recollections of Bush Life in Australia, During a Residence of Eight Years in the Interior.* London, 1848.

Henderson, John. *Observations on the Colonies of New South Wales and Van Diemen's Land.* Calcutta, 1832.

———. *Excursions and Adventures in New South Wales; with Pictures of Squatting and Life in the Bush.* 2 vols. London, 1851.

Holt, Joseph. *Memoirs of Joseph Holt* [ed. T. C. Croker]. 2 vols. London, 1838.

Howard, John. *The State of the Prisons in England and Wales.* Warrington, 1777.

Hunter, John. *An Historical Journal of the Transactions at Port Jackson and Norfolk Island.* London, 1793; reprint [ed. J. Bach], Sydney, 1968.

Jeffrey, Mark. *A Burglar's Life.* Hobart, 1893.

King, Philip Gidley. *The Journal of Philip Gidley King, Lieutenant, R.N., 1787–1790* [ed. P. G. Fidlon and R. J. Ryan]. Sydney, 1980.

Lacombe, L. *Observations sur Londres par un Athéronome de Berne,* Paris, 1777.

Lang, John Dunmore. *An Historical and Statistical Account of New South Wales, Both as a Penal Settlement and as a British Colony.* 2 vols. London, 1837.

———. *Transportation and Colonization: or, The Causes of the Comparative Failure of the Transportation System in the Australian Colonies.* London, 1837.

La Pérouse, Jean-François de Galaup, Comte de. *A Voyage Around the World, Performed in the Years 1785, 1786, 1787 and 1788, by the Boussole and the Astrolabe, under the Command of J. F. G. de la Pérouse.* 2 vols. London, 1799.

Laplace, C. P. T. "Considérations sur la Système de Colonization suivi par les Anglais," in *Voyage Autour du Monde, 1830–32,* vol. 3. 1835.

Lilburn, Edward. *A Complete Exposure of the Convict System . . .* Lincoln, n.d.

Loveless, George et al. *A Narrative of the Sufferings of Jas. Loveless, Jas. Brine, and Thomas & John Standfield, Four of the Dorchester Labourers; Displaying the Horrors of Transportation.* 1838.

Macarthur, James. *New South Wales, Its Present State and Future Prospects . . . Submitted in Support of Petitions to Her Majesty and Parliament.* London, 1837.

Maconochie, Alexander. *Report on the State of Prison Discipline in Van Diemen's Land, . . .* Hobart, 1838.

———. *Thoughts on Convict Management and other subjects connected with the Australian Penal Colonies.* Hobart, 1838.

———. *Australiana, Thoughts on Convict Management, etc.* London, 1839.

———. *General Views Regarding the Social System of Convict Management.* Hobart, 1839.

———. *Principles of the Mark System, now sought to be introduced into Transportation, Imprisonment and other Forms of Secondary Punishment,* London, n.d. [ca. 1845].

———. *Crime and Punishment, The Mark System, framed to mix persuasion with punishment, and make their effect improving, yet their operation severe.* London, 1846.

———. *Norfolk Island.* London, 1847.

———. *On Reformatory Prison Discipline.* Birmingham, 1851.

————. *The Mark System of Prison Discipline*. London, 1857.

Macquarie, Lachlan. *A Letter to the Rt. Hon. Viscount Sidmouth in Refutation of State-ments Made by the Hon. Henry Grey Bennett*. London, 1821.

Macqueen, T. Potter. *Australia as She Is and As She Might Be*. London, 1840.

Marjoribanks, Alexander. *Travels in New South Wales*. London, 1847.

Martin, James. *Memorandoms*. From 1791 Ms. in Bentham Papers, BL, London (ed. C. Blount), Cambridge, 1937.

Mayhew, Henry. *London Labour and the London Poor*. 3 vols. London, 1862.

————. *Those that Will Not Work* (extra vol. to *London Labour*).

Mellish,————. "A Convict's Recollections of New South Wales, Written by Himself." *London Magazine*, vol. 2, 1825.

Melville, Henry. *The Present State of Australia, including New South Wales, Western Australia, South Australia, Victoria and New Zealand, with Practical Hints on Emigra-tion*. London, 1851.

Meredith, Louisa Anne. *Notes and Sketches of New South Wales During a Residence in that Colony from 1839 to 1844*. London, 1844; facs. ed., Melbourne, 1973.

Mitchel, John. *Jail Journal; or, Five Years in British Prisons*. Glasgow, 1876.

Mortlock, John F. *Experiences of a Convict Transported for Twenty-One Years*. London, 1864–65; reprint (ed. by G. A. Wilkes and A. G. Mitchell), Sydney, 1965.

Mudie, James. *The Felonry of New South Wales: Being a Faithful Picture of the Real Romance of Life in Botany Bay*. London, 1837; reprint (ed. Walter Stone), Melbourne, 1964.

Mundy, Godfrey Charles. *Our Antipodes: or, Residence and Rambles in the Australian Colonies with a glimpse of the Gold Fields*. London, 1855.

Nicol, John. *The Life and Adventures of John Nicol, Mariner*. London, 1822.

Noah, William. *Voyage to Sydney in the Ship 'Hillsborough' 1798–99, and A Description of the Colony*, Sydney, 1978.

O'Connell, J. F. *A Residence of Eleven Years in New Holland and the Caroline Islands: Being the Adventures of James F. O'Connell, Edited from his Verbal Narration*. Boston, 1836.

O'Reilly, John Boyle. *Moondyne Joe*. Philadelphia, [188—?], p. 230.

Palmer, Thomas Fyshe. *A Narrative of the Sufferings of T. F. Palmer*. London, 1797.

Parkinson, Sydney. *A Journal of a Voyage to the South Seas*. London, 1784.

Peron, François, and de Freycinet, Louis. *Voyages de Découvertes aux Terres Australes*. 2 vols. Paris, 1807–16.

Phillip, Arthur. *The Voyage of Governor Phillip to Botany Bay*. London, 1789; reprint (ed. J. J. Auchmuty), Sydney, 1970.

————. *Extracts of Letters from Arthur Phillip, Esq*. Facs. ed., Adelaide, 1963.

Phillips, Sir Richard. *A Letter to the Livery of London*. London, 1808.

Prieur, F. X. *Notes of a Convict of 1838*. N.p., n.d.

Reid, Thomas. *Two Voyages to New South Wales and Van Diemen's Land*. London, 1822.

Ritchie, D. *Voice of Our Exiles; or, Stray Leaves from a Convict Ship*. London, 1854.

Rogers, Rev. Thomas. *Correspondence relating to the Dismissal of the Rev. T. Rogers from his Chaplaincy at Norfolk Island*. Launceston, 1849.

R[oss], W[illiam]. *The Fell Tyrant; or, the Suffering Convict*. London, 1836.

Sadleir, John. *Recollections of a Victorian Police Officer*. Melbourne, 1913.

Savery, Henry. *The Hermit in Van Diemen's Land*. Hobart, 1829; reprint (ed. Cecil Hadgraft and Margaret Roe), Brisbane, 1964.

Sherer, John. *The Gold Finder of Australia: How He Went, How He Fared, and How He Made His Fortune*. London, 1853.

Sidney, Samuel. *The Three Colonies of Australia: New South Wales, Victoria, South Aus-tralia: Their Pastures, Copper Mines and Gold Fields*. London, 1852.

Syme, J. *Nine Years in Van Diemen's Land*. Perth, 1848.

Tench, Watkin. *A Narrative of the Expedition to Botany Bay; with an Account of New South Wales, Its Productions, Inhabitants &c . . .* London, 1789.

————. *A Complete Account of the Settlement at Port Jackson, in New South Wales . . .* London, 1793.

Tetens, Alfred (trans. F. M. Spoehr). *Among the Savages of the South Seas: Memoirs of Micronesia, 1862–68.* Los Angeles, 1958.

Therry, Roger. *Reminiscences of Thirty Years' Residence in New South Wales and Victoria.* London, 1863; facs. ed., Sydney, 1974.

Thompson, George. *Slavery and Famine: An Account of the Miseries and Starvation at Botany Bay.* London, 1794.

Trollope, Anthony. *Australia and New Zealand.* Vol. 2. London, 1968.

Ullathorne, William. *The Catholic Mission in Australasia.* Liverpool, 1837.

————. *The Horrors of Transportation Briefly Unfolded to the People,* Dublin, 1838.

Wakefield, E. G. *The Art of Colonization.* London, 1849.

Wakefield, E. G. [Robert Gouger]. (See Gouger, Robert.)

Watling, Thomas. *Letters from an Exile at Botany-Bay to his Aunt in Dumfries; Giving a Particular Account of the Settlement of New South Wales, with the Customs and Manners of the Inhabitants.* Penrith, n.d.

Wentworth, William C. *A Statistical, Historical and Political Description of the Colony of New South Wales.* London, 1819.

West, John. *The History of Tasmania.* Launceston, 1852; reprint (ed. A. G. L. Shaw), Sydney, 1971.

———— [Lackland, Jacob]. *Common Sense: an Inquiry into the Influence of Transportation on the Colony of Van Diemen's Land.* Launceston, 1847.

Westgarth, William. *Australia Felix: or, a Historical and Descriptive Account of the Settlement of Port Phillip, New South Wales.* Edinburgh, 1848.

Whateley, Richard. *Thoughts on Secondary Punishment, in a Letter to Earl Grey . . .* London, 1832.

White, John. *Journal of a Voyage to NSW.* London, 1790.

Woomera [pseud.]. *The Life of an Ex-Convict.* Printed extract in ML, Sydney.

## SECONDARY SOURCES

### PUBLISHED BOOKS AND ARTICLES

Abbie, A. A. "Physical Characteristics of Australian Aborigines." In H. Shields, ed., *Australian Aboriginal Studies,* pp. 89–107. Melbourne, 1967.

Asbury, Herbert. *The Barbary Coast.* London, 1937.

Atkins, Barbara. "Australia's Place in the Swing to the East—an Addendum." HS, vol. 8 (1958).

Atkinson, Alan. "Four Patterns of Convict Protest." *LH,* vol. 37 (November 1979), pp. 28–51.

Australian Council of National Trusts. *The Historic Buildings of Norfolk Island: Their Restoration, Preservation and Maintenance.* Canberra, 1971.

Baker, Sidney J. *The Australian Language.* Sydney, 1966.

Barker, Sydney K. "The Governorship of Sir George Gipps." *JRAHS,* vol. 16, parts 3 and 4, 1930, pp. 169–260.

Barnard, Marjorie. *Macquarie's World.* Melbourne, 1949.

Barry, Sir John Vincent. *Alexander Maconochie of Norfolk Island: A Study of a Pioneer in Penal Reform.* Melbourne, 1958.

————. *The Life and Death of John Price: A Study in the Exercise of Naked Power.* Melbourne, 1964.

Bateson, Charles. *Patrick Logan, Tyrant of Brisbane Town.* Sydney, 1966.

————. *The Convict Ships, 1787–1868.* Sydney, 1974.

Beaglehole, J. C. *The Exploration of the Pacific.* London, 1934; rev. ed., 1947.

————, ed. *The Journals of Captain James Cook on His Voyages of Discovery.* Vols. 1 and 2. Cambridge, 1955 and 1961.

————, ed. *The Endeavour Journal of Joseph Banks, 1768–1771.* 2 vols. Sydney, 1962.

————. *The Life of Captain James Cook.* London, 1974.

Beattie, J. W. *Glimpses of the Lives and Times of the Early Tasmanian Governors.* Hobart, n.d. [1905].

Birdsell, Joseph B. "Preliminary Data on the Trihybrid Origin of the Australian Aborigines." In *Archaeology and Physical Anthropology in Oceania,* vol. 2, pp. 100–155. London, 1967.

Blainey, Geoffrey. *The Rush That Never Ended: A History of Australian Mining.* Melbourne, 1963.

————. *The Tyranny of Distance: How Distance Shaped Australia's History.* Melbourne, 1966.

————. *The Triumph of the Nomads: A History of Ancient Australia.* Melbourne, 1975.

Boissery, Beverley D., and Greenwood, F. Murray. "New Sources for Convict History: The Canadien Patriotes in Exile." *JRAHS,* vol. 71 (October 1978), pp. 277–82.

Bolger, Peter. *Hobart Town.* Canberra, 1973.

Boxall, George. *The Story of the Australian Bushrangers.* London, 1899.

Boyer, P. W. "Leaders and Helpers: Jane Franklin's Plan for Van Diemen's Land." THRA, PP, vol. 21, no. 2 (June 1974).

Brady, Frank. *James Boswell: The Later Years.* New York, 1984.

Brand, Ian, *The 'Separate' or 'Model' Prison, Port Arthur.* Hobart, 1975.

Butlin, N. G. *Our Original Aggression.* Sydney, 1984.

Cadogan, Edward. *The Roots of Evil.* London, 1937.

Calder, J. E. et al. *Some Account of the Wars, Extirpation, Habits etc. of the Native Tribes of Tasmania.* Hobart, 1875.

Campbell, J. F. "The Valley of the Tank Stream." *JRAHS,* vol. 10 (1924).

Campbell, Walter S. "The Use and Abuse of Stimulants in the Early Days of Settlement in New South Wales." *JRAHS,* vol. 18, part 2 (1932), pp. 74–99.

Cannon, Michael. "Violence: The Australian Heritage." *National Times Magazine,* March 5, 1973, pp. 16–21; March 12, 1973, pp. 28–30.

Carty, James, ed. *Ireland from Grattan's Parliament to the Great Famine, 1783–1850: A Documentary Record.* Dublin, 5th ed. 1966.

Chapman, Don. *1788, The People of the First Fleet.* Sydney, 1981.

Chapman, Peter. "G.T.W.B. Boyes and Australia: The Pursuit of a Vision?" THRA, PP, vol. 23, no. 3 (September 1976), pp. 58–76.

Chesney, Kellow. *The Anti-Society: An Account of the Victorian Underworld.* Boston, 1970.

Clark, C. M. H. *A History of Australia.* Vol. 1: *From the Earliest Times to the Age of Macquarie.* Melbourne, 1962.

————. *A History of Australia.* Vol. 2: *New South Wales and Van Diemen's Land, 1822–1838.* Melbourne, 1968.

————. *A History of Australia.* Vol. 3: *The Beginning of an Australian Civilization, 1824–1851.* Melbourne, 1973.

————. *A History of Australia.* Vol. 4: *The Earth Abideth For Ever, 1851–1888.* Melbourne, 1978.

————, ed. *Sources of Australian History,* London 1957.

————, ed. *Select Documents in Australian History, 1788–1850.* Sydney, 1977.

————. "The Origins of the Convicts Transported to Eastern Australia, 1787–1852," HS vol. 7, nos. 26–27, May–June 1956.

Clarke, Marcus. *His Natural Life* (ed. Stephen Murray-Smith). London, Penguin Books, 1970.

Clune, Frank. *The Norfolk Island Story.* Sydney, 1967.

Cobley, John. *Sydney Cove, 1788.* London, 1962.

————. *Sydney Cove, 1789–1790.* Sydney, 1963.

————. *Sydney Cove, 1791–1792.* Sydney, 1965.

————. *The Crimes of the First Fleet Convicts.* Sydney, 1970.

Conlon, Anne. " 'Mine Is a Sad Yet True Story': Convict Narratives 1818–50." *JRAHS*, vol. 55, part 1 (March 1969), pp. 43–82.

Cor, Henri. *Contribution à l'étude des questions coloniales de la Transportation . . .* Paris, 1895.

Cox, Philip, and Stacey, Wesley. *Building Norfolk Island.* Melbourne, n.d.

Cribb, A. B., and Cribb, J. W. *Wild Food in Australia.* Sydney, 1974.

Cronin, Sean. *Irish Nationalism: A History of its Roots and Ideology.* New York, 1980.

Crooke, R. *The Convict.* Reprint. Hobart, 1958.

Crowley, Frank, ed. *A Documentary History of Australia.* Vol. 1: *Colonial Australia, 1788–1840.* Melbourne, 1980.

———. *A Documentary History of Australia.* Vol. 2: *Colonial Australia, 1841–1874.* Melbourne, 1981.

Currey, C. H. *The Transportation, Escape and Pardoning of Mary Bryant.* Sydney, 1963.

Dalkin, R. Nixon. *The Colonial Era Cemetery of Norfolk Island.* Sydney, 1974.

Denholm, David. *The Colonial Australians.* Sydney, 1979.

Denholm, Decie. "Port Arthur: The Men and the Myth." *HS*, vol. 15, no. 55, Sept. 1966.

Dening, Greg. *Islands and Beaches: Discourse on a Silent Land, Marquesas 1774–1880.* Honolulu, 1980.

Department of Home Affairs and Environment. *Norfolk Island: Kingston and Arthur's Vale Historic Area Management Plan, April 1980.* Australian Government Publishing Service, Canberra, 1981.

Dingle, A. E. " 'The Truly Magnificent Thirst': An Historical Study of Australian Drinking Habits." *HS*, vol. 19, no. 75 (October 1980), pp. 227–49.

Dixson, Miriam. *The Real Matilda: Woman and Identity in Australia, 1788–1975.* Melbourne, 1976.

———. *"Greater Than Lenin"? Lang and Labour, 1916–1932.* Melbourne, n.d.

Duly, Leslie C. " 'Hottentots to Hobart and Sydney': The Cape Supreme Court's Use of Transportation 1828–1838." *AJPH*, vol. 25, no. 1 (April 1979).

Eddy, J. J. *Britain and the Australian Colonies, 1818–1831—The Technique of Government.* Oxford, 1969.

Ehrman, John. *The Younger Pitt.* 2 vols. London, 1969.

Eldershaw, M. Barnard. *Phillip of Australia.* London, 1938.

———. *The Life and Times of John Piper.* Sydney, 1973.

Eldershaw, P. R. "Guide to the Public Records of Tasmania." *THRA, PP*, vol. 15, no. 3, Jan. 1968.

Elkin, A. P. *The Australian Aborigines.* Rev. ed. Sydney, 1974.

Elliott, Brian, and Mitchell, Adrian, eds. *Bards in the Wilderness: Australian Colonial Poetry to 1920.* Melbourne, 1970.

Ellis, M. H. "Macquarie and the Rum Hospital." *JRAHS*, vol. 32 (1946–47).

———. *Lachlan Macquarie.* Sydney, 1947.

———. *Francis Greenway.* 2nd ed. Sydney, 1953.

———. *John Macarthur.* Sydney, 1955.

Ellis, Vivienne R. "Trucanini." *THRA, PP*, vol. 23, no. 2 (June 1976).

Evans, Lloyd. *Convicts and Colonial Society, 1788–1853.* Sydney, 1977.

Evatt, Herbert Vere. *Rum Rebellion.* Sydney, 1938.

Fels, Marie. "Culture Contact in the County of Buckinghamshire, Van Diemen's Land, 1803–11." *THRA, PP*, vol. 26, no. 2 (June 1982).

Firth, Marjorie M. *The Tolpuddle Martyrs.* London, 1971.

Fitzpatrick, Kathleen. *Sir John Franklin in Tasmania, 1837–1843.* Melbourne, 1949.

Fitzsymonds, Eustace, ed. *Norfolk Island 1846: The Accounts of Robert Pringle Stuart and Thomas Beagley Naylor.* Adelaide, 1979.

———. *A Looking-Glass for Tasmania.* Adelaide, 1980.

Fletcher, Brian H. *Ralph Darling: A Governor Maligned.* Melbourne, 1984.

Ford, E. *The Life and Work of William Redfern.* Sydney, 1953.

Forsyth, W. D. *Governor Arthur's Convict System.* London, 1935.

Fortescue, J., ed. *The Correspondence of King George III.* 7 vols. London, 1928.

Foster, John. *Class Struggle and the Industrial Revolution: Early Industrial Capitalism in Three English Towns.* London, 1974.

Freeland, J. M. *Architecture in Australia, A History.* Melbourne, 1974.

Frost, Alan. *Convicts and Empire: A Naval Question, 1776–1811.* Melbourne, 1980.

Gandevia, Brian. "Socio-Medical Factors in the Evolution of the First Settlement at Sydney Cove, 1788–1803." *RAHJ* (March 1975).

————, and Cobley, J. "Mortality at Sydney Cove, 1788–1792." *ANZJM,* vol. 4 (1974).

————, and Gandevia, Simon. "Childhood Mortality and its Social Background in the First Settlement at Sydney Cove, 1788–1792." *Australian Paediatric Journal,* vol. 11 (1975).

Gaskell, Peter. *The Manufacturing Population of England.* London, 1933.

Genovese, Eugene D. *The Political Economy of Slavery: Studies in the Economy and Society of the Slave South.* New York, 1965.

George, M. Dorothy. *London Life in the Eighteenth Century.* London, 1925; reprint, London, 1966.

Gibbings, Robert. *John Graham, Convict 1824; an historical narrative.* London, 1956.

Gibson, Rev. C. B. *Life Among Convicts.* London, 1863.

Gloag, John. *Georgian Grace.* London, 1954.

Gordon, Douglas. "Sickness and Death at the Moreton Bay Convict Settlement." *MJA,* September 1963.

Grabosky, Peter. *Sydney in Ferment: Crime, Dissent and Official Reaction, 1788 to 1973.* Canberra, 1977.

Greener, Leslie. "The Bridge At Ross." THRA, PP, vol. 14, no. 3 (February 1967).

Grocott, Allan. *Convicts, Clergymen and Churches: Attitudes of Convicts and Ex-Convicts Towards the Churches and Clergy in New South Wales, 1788–1851.* Sydney, 1980.

Hamer, Clive. "Novels of the Convict System." *Southerly,* vol. 18, no. 4 (1957).

Hammond, J. L., and Hammond, B. *The Village Laborer, 1760–1832.* London, 1913.

Harrison, J. F. C. *Early Victorian Britain.* London, 1979.

Hasluck, Alexandra. *Unwilling Immigrants.* Melbourne, 1959.

Hay, Douglas. "Property, Authority and the Criminal Law." In *Albion's Fatal Tree: Crime and Society in Eighteenth-Century England* (ed. Douglas Hay, Peter Linebaugh and Edward P. Thompson). London, 1975.

Hazzard, Margaret. *Punishment Short of Death: A History of the Penal Settlement at Norfolk Island.* Melbourne, 1984.

Heard, Dora, ed. *The Journal of Charles O'Hara Booth.* Hobart, 1981.

Henry, E. R. "Edward Lord: The John Macarthur of Van Diemen's Land," THRA, PP, vol. 22, no. 2 (June 1973).

Herman, Morton. *Early Australian Architects and their Work.* Sydney, 1954.

Hibbert, Christopher. *The Roots of Evil.* London, 1963.

Hill, Christopher. *Reformation to Industrial Revolution.* London, 1967.

Hill-Reid, William Scott. *John Grant's Journey: A Convict's Story, 1803–11.* London, 1957.

Himmelfarb, Gertrude. *The Idea of Poverty: England in the Early Industrial Age.* New York, 1984.

Hirst, John B. *Convict Society and its Enemies.* Sydney, 1983.

Hoare, M. H. *Norfolk Island, An Outline of its History 1774–1968.* Brisbane, 1969.

Hobsbawm, Eric J. *Primitive Rebels: Studies in Archaic Forms of Social Movement in the 19th and 20th Centuries.* Manchester, 1959.

————. *The Age of Revolution.* London, 1962.

————. *Industry and Empire.* Vol. 3 of Pelican Economic History of Britain. London, 1969.

————, and Rude, George. *Captain Swing.* London, 1969.

Hooper, F. C. *Prison Boys of Port Arthur.* Melbourne, 1967.

Howard, Derek L. *The English Prisons.* London, 1962.

Ignatieff, Michael. *A Just Measure of Pain: The Penitentiary in the Industrial Revolution, 1750–1850.* New York, 1978.

Ingleton, Geoffrey. *True Patriots All.* Sydney, 1952.

Inglis, Brian. *Poverty and the Industrial Revolution.* London, 1971.

Inglis, K. S. *The Australian Colonists: An Exploration of Social History 1788–1870.* Melbourne, 1974.

Jervis, James. "The Rise of Newcastle." *JRAHS,* vol. 21, no. 3 (1935).

Johnson, W. B. *English Prison Hulks.* London, 1957.

Johnston, Edith M. *Great Britain and Ireland 1760–1800: A Study in Political Administration.* London, 1963.

Keesing, Nancy. *John Lang and "The Forger's Wife": A True Tale of Early Australia.* Sydney, 1979.

Kerr, James S. *Design for Convicts: An Account of Design for Convict Establishments in the Australian Colonies.* Sydney, 1984.

Kiddle, M. L. *Caroline Chisholm.* Melbourne, 1957.

Kiernan, T. J. *Irish Exiles in Australia.* Dublin, 1954.

King, Jonathan, and King, John. *Philip Gidley King: A Biography of the Third Governor of New South Wales.* Sydney, 1981.

Knight, Ruth. *Illiberal Liberal: Robert Lowe in New South Wales, 1842–1850.* Melbourne, 1966.

Lansbury, Coral. *Arcady in Australia: The Evocation of Australia in Nineteenth-Century English Literature.* Sydney, 1970.

Lemprière, T. J. *The Penal Settlements of Van Diemen's Land.* Launceston, 1954.

Lennox, G. R. "A Private and Confidential Despatch of Eardley-Wilmot: Implications . . . Concerning the Probation System for Convict Women." THRA, PP, vol. 29, no. 2 (June 1982).

Levi, J. S., and Bergman, J. F. *Australian Genesis: Jewish Convicts and Settlers, 1788–1850.* Sydney, 1974.

Levy, M. C. *Governor George Arthur, a Colonial Benevolent Despot.* Melbourne, 1953.

Linebaugh, Peter. "The Tyburn Riot Against the Surgeons." In *Albion's Fatal Tree: Crime and Society in Eighteenth Century England* (ed. Douglas Hay, Peter Linebaugh and Edward Thompson). London, 1975.

Macarthur-Onslow, S., ed. *Some Early Records of the Macarthurs of Camden.* Sydney, 1914.

Mackaness, George. *Some Private Correspondence of Sir John and Lady Jane Franklin.* Sydney, 1947.

———. *The Life of Vice-Admiral Bligh.* 2 vols. Sydney, 1951.

Mackay, David. *A Place of Exile: The European Settlement of New South Wales.* Melbourne, 1985.

———. *In the Wake of Cook: Exploration, Science and Empire, 1780–1801.* Wellington, 1985.

McIntyre, K. G. *The Secret Discovery of Australia: Portuguese Ventures 200 Years Before Captain Cook.* Menindie, New South Wales, 1977.

McMahon, Anne. "Tasmanian Aboriginal Women as Slaves." THRA, PP, vol. 23, no. 2 (June 1976).

McNab, Robert. "Phillip's Views on . . . Treatment of Convicts." HRNZ, vol. 1, pp. 67–70.

McQueen, Humphrey. "Convicts and Rebels." LH, vol. 15 (November 1968).

———. *A New Britannia: An Argument Concerning the Social Origins of Australian Radicalism and Nationalism.* Melbourne, 1970; rev. ed., 1975.

McRae, Mary M. "Yankees from King Arthur's Court: A Brief History of North American Prisoners Transported to Canada from Van Diemen's Land, 1839–40." THRA, PP, vol. 19, no. 4 (December 1972).

Madgwick, R. B. *Immigration into Eastern Australia, 1788–1851.* London, 1937; reprint, Sydney, 1969.

Manifold, J. S., ed. *The Penguin Australian Song Book.* Sydney, 1964.

Marlow, Joyce. *The Tolpuddle Martyrs.* 1971.

Meredith, John. *The Wild Colonial Boy: Life and Times of Jack Donahoe (1808?–1830).* Sydney, 1960.

Miller, E. M. *Pressmen and Governors.* Sydney, 1952.

Mitchell, T. L. *Three Expeditions into the Interior of Eastern Australia.* 2 vols. London, 1839.

Monaghan, Jay. *Australians and the Gold Rush: California and Down Under, 1849–54.* San Francisco, 1966.

Moore, James. *The Convicts of Van Diemen's Land, 1840–1853.* Hobart, 1976.

Moorehead, Alan. *The Fatal Impact: An Account of the Invasion of the South Pacific, 1767–1840.* London, 1966.

Morison, Samuel Eliot. *The European Discovery of America.* Vol. 1: *The Southern Voyages.* New York, 1974.

Morrell, W. P. *British Colonial Policy in the Age of Peel and Russell.* London, 1930.

Mulvaney, D. G. *The Prehistory of Australia.* Rev. ed. Melbourne, 1975.

————, and Golson, eds. *Aboriginal Man and Environment in Australia.* Canberra, 1971.

Murray-Smith, Stephen. "Beyond the Pale: The Islander Community of Bass Strait in the Nineteenth Century." THRA, PP, vol. 20, no. 4 (December 1973).

O'Farrell, Patrick. *The Catholic Church and Community in Australia, A History.* Melbourne, 1977.

————. *Letters from Irish Australia, 1825–1929.* Ed. Brian Trainor. Sydney and Belfast, 1984.

Park, Ruth. *The Companion Guide to Sydney.* London, 1973.

Partridge, Eric. *A Dictionary of the Underworld.* London, 1971.

Peyser, Dora. "A Study of the History of Welfare Work in Sydney from 1788 to about 1900: Part One." *JRAHS*, vol. 25, part 2 (1939).

Pike, E. Royston, ed. *Human Documents of the Industrial Revolution in Britain.* London, 1966.

Porter, Roy. *English Society in the Eighteenth Century.* London, 1982.

Pottle, F. A. *Boswell and the Girl from Botany Bay.* New York, 1938.

Pritchard, W. T. *Polynesian Reminiscences.* London, 1866.

Radzinowicz, Leon. *A History of English Criminal Law and Its Administration from 1750.* 3 vols. London, 1948–56.

————. *Ideology and Crime: A Study of Crime in Its Social and Historical Context.* London, 1966.

————, with Wolfgang, Marvin, eds. *Crime and Justice.* Vol. 1: *The Criminal in Society.* New York, 1971.

Reece, R. H. *Aborigines and Colonists: Aborigines and Colonial Society in New South Wales in the 1830s and 1840s.* Sydney, 1974.

Reed, Michael. *The Georgian Triumph, 1700–1830.* London, 1983.

Reynolds, Henry. " 'That Hated Stain': The Aftermath of Transportation in Tasmania." *HS*, vol. 14, no. 53 (October 1969), pp. 19–33.

————. "Violence, the Aboriginals, and the Australian Historian." *Meanjin Quarterly*, vol. 31, no. 4 (December 1972).

————. *The Other Side of the Frontier: Aboriginal Resistance to the European Invasion of Australia.* Melbourne, 1982.

Ricards, Sherman, and Blackburn, George. "The Sydney Ducks: A Demographic Analysis." *PHR*, vol. 42, no. 1 (February 1973).

Richmond, Barbara. "John West and the Anti-Transportation Movement." THRA, PP, vol. 2 (1952).

Ritchie, John. *Punishment and Profit: The Reports of Commissioner John Bigge on the Colonies of New South Wales and Van Diemen's Land, 1822–23.* Melbourne, 1970.

————. "Towards Ending an Unclean Thing: The Molesworth Committee and the Abolition of Transportation to New South Wales, 1837–40." *HS*, vol. 17, no. 67 (October 1976), pp. 144–64.

Robinson, Portia. *The Hatch and Brood of Time: A Study of the First Generation of Native-Born White Australians, 1788–1828.* Vol. 1. Melbourne, 1985.

Robson, Lloyd L. "The Historical Basis of *For the Term of His Natural Life.*" *Australian Literary Studies*, vol. 1 (1963).

——. *The Convict Settlers of Australia: An Enquiry into the Origin and Character of the Convicts Transported to New South Wales and Van Diemen's Land, 1787–1852.* Melbourne, 1965.

——. *A History of Tasmania.* Oxford, 1983.

Roderick, Colin. *John Knatchbull from Quarterdeck to Gallows (Including the Narrative Written by Himself in Darlinghurst Gaol . . . ).* Sydney, 1963.

Roe, Michael. "Colonial Society in Embryo." *HS,* vol. 7, no. 56 (May 1956).

——. *Quest for Authority in Eastern Australia, 1835–51.* Melbourne, 1965.

——. "The Establishment of Local Self-Government in Hobart and Launceston." THRA, PP, vol. 14, no. 1 (December 1966).

——. "1830–1850." Chap. 3 of Frank Crowley, ed., *A New History of Australia.* Melbourne, 1980.

Rolls, Eric. *A Million Wild Acres.* Melbourne, 1982.

Rowley, C. D. *Aboriginal Policy and Practice.* Vol. 1: *The Destruction of Aboriginal Society.* Canberra, 1970.

Rude, George, *Paris and London in the 18th Century: Studies in Popular Protest.* London, 1952.

——. *The Crowd in History: A Study of Popular Disturbances in France and England, 1730–1848.* New York, 1964.

——. "Captain Swing and Van Diemen's Land." THRA, PP, vol. 12 (1964).

——. *Protest and Punishment: The Story of the Social and Political Protesters Transported to Australia, 1788–1868.* London, 1978.

Rule, John. *The Experience of Labor in Eighteenth-Century English Industry.* New York, 1981.

Ryan, Lyndall. *The Aboriginal Tasmanians.* Brisbane, 1981.

Serle, Geoffrey. *The Golden Age: A History of the Colony of Victoria, 1851–1861.* Reprint, Melbourne, 1968.

Serventy, Vincent. *A Continent in Danger.* London, 1966.

Shaw, A. G. L. "Origins of the Probation System." *HS,* vol. 6 (1953).

——. "Sir John Eardley-Wilmot and the Probation System in Tasmania." THRA, PP, vol. 11 (1963).

——. *Convicts and the Colonies: A Study of Penal Transportation from Great Britain and Ireland to Australia and Other Parts of the British Empire.* London, 1966.

——. *Heroes and Villains in History: Governors Darling and Bourke in New South Wales.* Sydney, 1966.

——. "Some Officials in Early Van Diemen's Land." THRA, PP, vol. 14 (1967).

——. "A Colonial Ruler in Two Hemispheres: Sir George Arthur in Van Diemen's Land and Canada." THRA, PP, vol. 17 (1970).

——. "Violent Protest in Australian History." *HS,* vol. 15 (April 1973).

——. *Sir George Arthur, Bart. 1784–1854.* Melbourne, 1980.

Smith, Abbot Emerson. *Colonists in Bondage: White Servitude and Convict Labor in America, 1607–1776.* New York, 1971.

Smith, Bernard. *European Vision and the South Pacific, 1768–1850: A Study in the History of Art and Ideas.* Oxford, 1960.

—— (ed). *Documents on Art and Taste in Australia: The Colonial Period, 1770–1914.* Melbourne, 1975.

Smith, Martin. "Arthur Phillip and the Young Lads." *Campaign,* no. 19, Sydney (1977).

——. "The Emergence of a Gay Society." *Campaign,* no. 20, Sydney (1977).

Smith, Sydney. *Works.* London, 1878.

Smith, Warren B. *White Servitude in Colonial South Carolina.* Columbia, S.C., 1961.

Spate, O. H. K. *The Pacific Since Magellan.* Vol. 1: *The Spanish Lake.* Minneapolis, 1979.

——. *The Pacific Since Magellan.* Vol. 2: *Monopolists and Freebooters.* Minneapolis, 1983.

Sprod, Dan. *Alexander Pearce of Macquarie Harbour: Convict—Bushranger—Cannibal.* Hobart, 1977.

Steele, J. G. *Brisbane Town in Convict Days, 1824–1842.* St. Lucia, Queensland, 1975.

Sturma, Michael. "Eye of the Beholder: The Stereotype of Women Convicts, 1788–1852." *LH*, no. 34 (May 1978).

———. *Vice in a Vicious Society: Crime and Convicts in Mid-Nineteenth-Century New South Wales*. Brisbane, 1983.

Summers, Anne. *Damned Whores and God's Police: The Colonization of Women in Australia*. London: Penguin Books, Pelican edition, 1975.

Sweeney, Christopher. *Transported: In Place of Death. Convicts in Australia*. Melbourne, 1981.

Thomas, J. E., and Stewart, A. *Imprisonment in Western Australia*. Nedlands, Western Australia, 1978.

Thompson, Edward P. *The Making of the English Working Class*. London: Penguin Books, Pelican edition, 1968.

———. *Whigs and Hunters: The Origin of the Black Act*. London, 1975.

———, Douglas Hay, and Peter Linebaugh, eds. *Albion's Fatal Tree: Crime and Society in Eighteenth-Century England*. London, 1975.

Tinsdale, Norman. *Aboriginal Tribes of Australia*. 2 vols. Los Angeles, 1974.

Tobias, J. J. *Crime and Industrial Society in the 19th Century*. London, 1967, 1972.

Townsend, Norma. "The Molesworth Enquiry: Does the Report Fit the Evidence?" *JAS*, no. 1 (June 1977).

Tucker, Maya. "Centennial Celebrations, 1888." In *Australia 1888*, A Bicentennial History Bulletin, ed. Graeme Davidson and Ailsa McLeary, Bulletin no. 7 (April 1981).

Turnbull, Clive. *Black War: The Extermination of the Tasmanian Aborigines*. Melbourne, 1948.

Ullathorne, William. *The Autobiography of Archbishop Ullathorne, with Selections from his Letters*. London, 1891.

Walker, Robin. "Bushranging in Fact and Legend." *HS*, vol. 11, no. 42 (April 1964).

Wallas, Graham. *The Life of Francis Place, 1771–1854*. London, 1898.

Ward, John M. *Earl Grey and the Australian Colonies, 1846–57: A Study of Self-Government and Self-Interest*. Melbourne, 1958.

———. *James Macarthur, Colonial Conservative, 1798–1867*. Sydney, 1981.

Ward, Russel. "Felons and Folksongs." October 1954. Typescript in ML, Sydney.

———. *The Australian Legend*. Sydney, 1958; rev. ed., 1970.

———. *Australia Since the Coming of Man*. Rev. ed. Sydney, 1982.

Warung, Price [Astley, William]. *Tales of the Convict System*. Sydney, 1892.

———. *Tales of the Early Days*. Melbourne, 1894.

———. *Tales of the Old Regime*. Melbourne, 1897.

———. *Tales of the Isle of Death*. Melbourne, 1898.

———. *Convict Days*. Sydney, 1960.

Weidenhofer, Margaret. *The Convict Years: Transportation and the Penal System 1788–1868*. Melbourne, 1973.

———. *Maria Island: A Tasmanian Eden*. Melbourne, 1977.

———. *Port Arthur: A Place of Misery*. Melbourne, 1981.

Wells, T. E. *Michael Howe, the Last and Worst of the Bushrangers of Van Diemen's Land: Narrative of his Chief Atrocities . . .* Introd. by George Mackaness. Dubbo, 1979.

White, Charles. *History of Australian Bushranging*. 2 vols. Reprint, Sydney, 1976.

Whitley, G. "The Doom of the Bird of Providence." *Australian Zoology*, vol. 8 (1934).

Wilding, Michael. *Marcus Clarke*. Melbourne, 1977.

Willoughby, Edward. *Australian Pictures Drawn with Pen and Pencil*. London, 1886.

Wilson, Barbara Vance. *Convict Australia, 1788–1868: A Social History*. Melbourne, 1981.

Wood, F. L. W. "Jeremy Bentham versus New South Wales." *JRAHS*, vol. 19, part 6 (1933), pp. 329–51.

Wood, G. Arnold. "Convicts," *JRAHS*, vol. 8, no. 4 (1922), p. 187.

Woolmington, Jean, ed. *Aborigines in Colonial Society, 1788–1850: From 'Noble Savage' to 'Rural Pest.'* Sydney, 1973.

Wright, Gordon. *Between the Guillotine and Liberty: Two Centuries of the Crime Problem in France*. New York, 1983.

UNPUBLISHED THESES

Boissery, Beverley D. "French-Canadian Political Prisoners in Australia, 1838–39." Ph.D. diss., Australian National University, 1977.

Crowley, K. "Master and Servant in Early Australia." M.A. thesis, University of Melbourne, 1949.

Dalkin, R. N. "Norfolk Island: A History of its Government and Administration." M.A. thesis, Australian National University, 1977.

Driscoll, Francis. "How the Convict System Worked under Governor Macquarie." M.A. thesis, Sydney University, 1940.

Hooper, F. C. "Point Puer." M.Ed. thesis, University of Melbourne, 1954.

Kiernan, T. J. "Transportation from Ireland to Sydney, 1791–1816." M.A. thesis, Australian National University, 1954.

Korbell, M. J. "Bushranging in Van Diemen's Land, 1824–1834." 4th year thesis, University of Tasmania, 1974.

Leroy, Paul Edwin. "The Emancipists from Prison to Freedom: The Story of the Australian Convicts and their Descendants." Ph.D. diss., Ohio State University, 1960.

McKay, Anne. "The Assignment System of Convict Labour in Van Diemen's Land, 1824–1842." M.A. thesis, University of Tasmania, 1959.

Rosenberg, Sidney. "Black Sheep and Golden Fleece: A Study of Nineteenth-Century English Attitudes towards Australian Colonies." Ph.D. diss., Columbia University, 1954.

Watson, M. S. "Transportation and Civil Liberties in New South Wales, 1810–1840." M.A. thesis, Sydney University, 1960.

Williams, John Vernon. "Irish Convicts and Van Diemen's Land." M.A. thesis, University of Tasmania, 1972.

# Index

# TABLE OF CONTENTS

# INTRODUCTION

The purpose of the **V.I.P. ADDRESS BOOK** is to provide readers with a means of reaching Very Important People — Celebrities, Government Officials, Business Leaders, Entertainers, Sports Stars, Scientists and Artists.

It is genuinely hoped that people will use this volume to write for information about an entrant's work or to express encouragement. Compliments and praise for one's efforts are always appreciated. Being at the top of one's chosen profession is no exception. And for those who are no longer active in a field, it is especially flattering to be contacted about one's past accomplishments.

## Methodology

The determination of candidates for inclusion in this reference work is an on-going process. Committees of prominent and knowledgeable people review those included in the nine major areas (listed in **bold** below).

**Public Service** includes World Leaders, Government Officials (both U.S. and International), Law Enforcement Officials and Members of the Legal and Judicial Fields.

**Adventure** includes Military Leaders (both U.S. and International), Astronauts and Cosmonauts, Heroes and Explorers.

**Business, Religion and Education** includes Financial and Labor Leaders as well as Businesspeople and Nobel Prize Winners in Economics and Peace.

**Life and Leisure** includes Fashion Design, Modeling, Beauty and Health Care and Social Activists.

**Communications** includes Columnists, Commentators, Editors and Publishers, along with Editorial and Comic Book Cartoonists.

**Fine Arts** includes Architects, Artists, Opera, Ballet and Dance Performers, Conductors, Concert Artists, Composers (both classical and popular), Writers, Photographers and Nobel Literature Laureates.

**Science** covers Nobel Prize winners in Chemistry, Medicine and Physics, Engineers, Inventors, Earth, Space and Computer Scientists, Psychologists and Psychiatrists, Medical and Research Scientists.

**Entertainment** includes stars of Radio, Stage, Screen and Television, Musicians, Cinematographers, Producers and Directors.

**Sports** includes all major spectator and participatory sports.

The committees define the parameters of the people included and prepare a list of additions and deletions to the candidate list. The research staff checks and updates information daily.

## Occupations and Titles

The category listed after an entrant's name is selected to best describe his/her most noteworthy accomplishment. No distinction is made as to whether the person still holds that position. It is felt that a person who made a name for herself or himself still retains that identity even if it was accomplished in the past.

## How Addresses Are Obtained

The editors of the **V.I.P. ADDRESS BOOK** have made every effort possible to insure that the addresses listed are accurate and current. Once it is determined a person is eligible for inclusion in the book, that person is contacted to determine which address he or she prefers. If a person prefers a home address, it is included. If a person prefers a business address or one in care of an agent or representative, that address is included. If a person specifically asks that their name not be included, his/her name is omitted. Once an address is listed, we continue efforts to verify that the address has not changed. These efforts include random sampling of the entire database and follow-up on all returned mailings received including those received from users of the book.

Users of the book should realize that people's addresses are in a state of constant change. The U.S. Bureau of Statistics says that almost 20 percent of people move each year. Not only do people change places of residence, they may also change business affiliations. Businesses move their headquarters as well as downsizing, merging or selling portions of their companies. Athletes get traded or retire. Entertainers change agents or personal managers and television shows get canceled. Politicians leave office or run for new positions. In addition, there are deaths almost daily which affect the address listings.

## National Change of Address Program

Our staff notes changes on a daily basis by watching television news shows and reading newspapers around the world. But we also take an extra step which few other directory or address book attempts. We match addresses of all U.S. listees with the U.S. Postal Service's National Change of Address program. The National Change of Address match is a process that compares mailing lists with more than 100 million address change cards filed by postal customers over the past three years. Address change information is provided for mailing list records that match with information from address change cards.

If a person/family/business moves, there are several factors which determine whether the National Change of Address program is effective. These include whether the mover filed an address change with the Postal Service, when the change was filed, whether the mover lived in an area covered by the automated address change systems (which includes more than 90 percent of the United States) and whether the name and address information in our files matches the information provided by the mover.

## Bad Addresses/Corrections

We keep track of not only current addresses but outdated ones as well. Our files list more than 250,000 people and we have up to 40 addresses for some of the people in the book. We continually update our data base and you can help. While we no longer provide address corrections, we do welcome information about bad addresses from users of the book.

## Envelope Markings

On your outgoing letters, you should always write "Address Correction Requested" beneath your return address in a clear and noticeable manner. If you do this, postal workers are supposed to send the forwarding address for a nominal fee.

## V.I.P. Address Book Update

Realizing the ever-changing aspect of addresses, we also publish the **V.I.P. ADDRESS BOOK UPDATE** which is available in late August for an additional fee. The UPDATE lists several thousand address changes and new addresses as well as informing users of the names of celebrities who pass away.

## Recommendations for the Book

If you are interested in people who are not listed in the book, send us a letter or email with their name, address and biographical information. If these people are deemed worthy for inclusion, they may be listed in a future edition.

Until people stop moving or changing jobs, there are going to be address changes. We want to provide the best service possible and we know we have the highest percentage of accuracy of any directory or address book.

If you have suggestions for improving accuracy beyond random follow-ups, following daily news events, checking on all bad address notifications and using the Postal Service's National Change of Address service, let us know your ideas.

## Forms of Address

An important part of writing to people - regardless of their positions - is to properly address envelopes and to use the correct salutations in the letters. Although the titles and positions of people listed in this directory are too numerous to cover, there are a number of people whose forms of address are worth noting. The table below is a guide to enhance the likelihood your letter will be received in a favorable light.

| POSITION | ENVELOPE/ADDRESS | SALUTATION |
|---|---|---|
| Presidents | The President of Countries | Dear Mr/Madam President - - - |
| Vice Presidents | The Vice President of Countries | Dear Mr/Madam Vice President - - - |
| Cabinet Officers | The Honorable John/Jane Doe Secretary of --- | Dear Mr/Madam Secretary of - - - |
| Senators | The Honorable John/Jane Doe US Senator from - - - | Dear Mr/Ms Senator - - - |
| Representatives | The Honorable John/Jane Doe US Representative from - - - | Dear Mr/Ms Representative - - - |
| Judges | The Honorable John/Jane Doe, Judge, US - - - Court | Dear Judge - - - |
| US Ambassadors | The Honorable John/Jane Doe US Ambassador to (Country) | Dear Mr/Ms Ambassador - - - |

# TABLE OF ABBREVIATIONS

**A**

| | |
|---|---|
| AB | Alberta |
| ACT | Australian Capital Territory |
| AFB | Air Force Base |
| AK | Alaska |
| AL | Alabama |
| APO | Army Post Office |
| AR | Arkansas |
| Arc | Arcade |
| AS | American Samoa |
| Assn | Association |
| Assoc | Associates |
| Ave | Avenue |
| AZ | Arizona |

**B**

| | |
|---|---|
| BC | British Columbia |
| Bd | Board |
| Beds | Bedfordshire |
| Berks | Berkshire |
| Bldg | Building |
| Blvd | Boulevard |
| Br | Branch |
| Bros | Brothers |
| Bucks | Buckinghamshire |
| BWI | British West Indies |
| Byp | Bypass |

**C**

| | |
|---|---|
| CA | California |
| Cambs | Cambridgeshire |
| Cir | Circle |
| CM | Mariana Islands |
| CMH | Congressional Medal of Honor |
| CO | Colorado |
| Co | Company |
| Corp | Corporation |
| Cres | Crescent |
| Cswy | Causeway |
| CT | Connecticut |
| Ct | Court |
| Ctr | Center |
| Ctrl | Central |
| Cts | Courts |
| CZ | Canal Zone |

**D**

| | |
|---|---|
| DC | District of Columbia |
| DE | Delaware |
| Dept | Department |
| Dis | District |
| Div | Division |
| Dr | Drive |
| Drwy | Driveway |

**E**

| | |
|---|---|
| E | East |
| Edin | Edinburgh |
| Ent | Entertainment |
| Expy | Expressway |
| Ext | Extended, Extension |

**F**

| | |
|---|---|
| Fedn | Federation |
| FL | Florida |
| FPO | Fleet Post Office |
| Ft | Fort |
| Fwy | Freeway |

**G**

| | |
|---|---|
| GA | Georgia |
| Gdns | Gardens |
| Glos | Gloucestershire |
| Grp | Group |
| Grv | Grove |
| Gt | Great |
| GU | Guam |

**H**

| | |
|---|---|
| Hants | Hampshire |
| Herts | Hertfordshire |
| HI | Hawaii |
| HOF | Hall of Fame |
| Hq | Headquarters |
| Hts | Heights |
| Hwy | Highway |

**I**

| | |
|---|---|
| IA | Iowa |
| ID | Idaho |
| IL | Illinois |
| IN | Indiana |
| Inc | Incorporated |
| Inst | Institute |
| Int'l | International |
| Intercoll | Intercollegiate |

**J**

| | |
|---|---|
| Jr | Junior |

**K**

| | |
|---|---|
| KS | Kansas |
| KY | Kentucky |

**L**

| | |
|---|---|
| LA | Louisiana |
| Lab | Laboratory |
| Lancs | Lancashire |
| Lincs | Lincolnshire |
| Ln | Lane |
| Ltd | Limited |

# 2014 Edition

# V.I.P. ADDRESS BOOK

PUBLISHER AND EDITOR
James M Wiggins, PhD

PRESIDENT AND MANAGING EDITOR
Adele M Cooke

VICE PRESIDENT OF TECHNICAL AFFAIRS
Mike K Maloy

DESIGN DIRECTOR
LeeAnn Nelson

WEBSITE DESIGNERS
Rawn Rhoades
Ernie Brown

SOCIAL MEDIA CONSULTANT
Verin Lewis

PUBLISHER
Associated Media Companies
PO Box 489
Gleneden Beach, OR 97388-0489
United States of America
Phone/Fax - 1-541-764-4233
Email – info@vipaddress.com
Website - www.vipaddress.com

## Abbreviations (Continued)

| | | | | |
|---|---|---|---|---|
| **M** | | | **R** | |
| MA | Massachusetts | | RD | Rural Delivery |
| MB | Manitoba | | Rd | Road |
| MD | Maryland | | Rep | Republic |
| Mddx | Middlesex | | RI | Rhode Island |
| ME | Maine | | RR | Rural Route |
| Med | Medical | | | |
| Mgmt | Management | | **S** | |
| MI | Michigan | | S | South |
| MN | Minnesota | | SA | South Australia |
| MO | Missouri | | SC | South Carolina |
| Mon | Monmouthshire | | Sci | Science |
| MS | Mississippi | | SD | South Dakota |
| MT | Montana | | SE | Southeast |
| Mt | Mount | | SK | Saskatchewan |
| | | | Spdwy | Speedway |
| **N** | | | Sq | Square |
| N | North | | St | Saint, Street |
| NB | New Brunswick | | SW | Southwest |
| NC | North Carolina | | | |
| ND | North Dakota | | **T** | |
| NE | Northeast, Nebraska | | Tas | Tasmania |
| NH | New Hampshire | | Ter | Territory |
| NJ | New Jersey | | Terr | Terrace |
| NL | Newfoundland | | TN | Tennessee |
| NM | New Mexico | | Tpke | Turnpike |
| Northants | Northamptonshire | | Trl | Trail |
| Notts | Nottinghamshire | | TX | Texas |
| NS | Nova Scotia | | | |
| NSW | New South Wales | | **U** | |
| NT | Northwest Territories, | | Univ | University |
| | Northern Territory | | USA | United States of America |
| NV | Nevada | | UT | Utah |
| NW | Northwest | | | |
| NY | New York | | **V** | |
| | | | VA | Virginia |
| **O** | | | VC | Victoria Cross |
| OH | Ohio | | VI | Virgin Islands |
| OK | Oklahoma | | VIC | Victoria |
| ON | Ontario | | VT | Vermont |
| OR | Oregon | | | |
| Oxon | Oxfordshire | | **W** | |
| | | | W | West |
| **P** | | | WA | Washington, |
| PA | Pennsylvania | | | Western Australia |
| PE | Prince Edward Island | | WI | Wisconsin |
| Pkwy | Parkway | | Worcs | Worcestershire |
| Pl | Place | | WV | West Virginia |
| Plz | Plaza | | WY | Wyoming |
| PO | Post Office | | | |
| PR | Puerto Rico | | **X-Y-Z** | |
| Prof | Professional | | YT | Yukon Territory |
| Pt | Point | | Yorks | Yorkshire |
| | | | | |
| **Q** | | | | |
| QC | Quebec | | | |
| QLD | Queensland | | | |

| | | |
|---|---|---|
| Foreign Ambassadors | His/Her Excellency John/Jane Doe | Dear Mr/MsAmbassador - - - |
| Kings/Queens | His/Her Royal Highness --- King/Queen of --- | Your Royal Highness --- |
| Military Leaders (Attention should be given to the actual rank) | General/Admiral John/Jane Doe | Dear General/Admiral - - - |
| Governors | The Honorable John/Jane Doe Governor of - - - | Dear Governor - - - |
| Mayors | The Honorable John/Jane Doe Mayor of - - - | Dear Mayor - - - |

The Clergy

| | | | |
|---|---|---|---|
| | Catholic | | |
| | The Pope | His Eminence the Pope - - - | Your Holiness - - - |
| | Cardinals | His Eminence John Cardinal Doe | Dear Your Eminence Cardinal |
| | Episcopalian | The Rt Rev John Doe | Dear Bishop - - - |
| | Protestant | The Rev John Doe | Dear Mr/Mrs - - - |
| | Eastern Orthodox Patriarch | His Holiness, the Patriarch - - - | Your Holiness - - - |
| | Jewish | Rabbi John Doe | Dear Rabbi - - - |

Forms of addresses can vary to almost impossible proportions. If you are a real stickler for proper protocol, you will need to obtain one of the many excellent reference books on etiquette or consult your local reference librarian for assistance.

Times are less formal so if you are polite and spell names correctly, your letter should be favorable received.

## ACKNOWLEDGEMENTS

The Editors would like to thank the following people for their generous assistance in maintaining the accuracy of this publication:

Robert Allen, Jr., Florence Bagdasian, Ed Bielucke, III, Jake Bommer, John Gracen Brown, William Butts, Gloria & Len Bytnar, Thomas Burford, Bill Clogston, David Coston, James A. Cox, Charlie Dixon, Jimmy Dodson, Jr., Douglas Files, John T. Gillin, Brian Graybill, Tom Hall, Jack Hilton, Steve Koroknay, Dewey Linze, Helen Mangani, Wayne McDonald, Massee McKinley, Larry Miller, Pacer Center's Jan Flora, Mark J. Quilling, Ed Sammels, Ira Sabin, Juergen Schwarz, Eric Shuman, Jay F. Smith, Christopher Snowden, Darryl Spurlock, Kim Tangye, Jim Thomson, Anders Tvegard, Joe Wagner, Deanna Ward, Jim & Judy Watt, Marci Yates.

THE
DIRECTORY
OF
ADDRESS
LISTINGS

Although we have made every effort to provide
current addresses, we assume no responsibility for
address that become outdated.

Neither do we guarantee that people listed in the book
will personally answer their mail or that they will
respond to correspondence.

**A$AP Rocky** — Rap Artist
Polo Grounds Music, 243 W 30th St, #302, New York NY 10001, USA

**Aaker, Lee W** — Actor
PO Box 1386, Mammoth Lakes CA 93546, USA

**Aalda, Marian** — Actress
Rebecca Augustin Mgmt, 105 78 Avenue K, Brooklyn NY 11236, USA

**Aames, Willie** — Actor
Jeff Ballard Public Relations, 4814 N Lemona Ave, Sherman Oaks CA 91403, USA

**Aamodt, Kjetil Andre** — Alpine Skier
8 Quai Jean Charles Rey, 98000 Monte Carlo, Monaco

**Aardsma, David A** — Baseball Player
6009 E Turquoise Ave, Paradise Valley AZ 85253, USA

**Aaron, Caroline** — Actress
Abrams Artists, 9200 W Sunset Blvd, #1125, West Hollywood CA 90069 USA

**Aaron, Chester** — Writer
PO Box 388, Occidental CA 95465, USA

**Aaron, Henry L (Hank)** — Baseball Player, Executive
1611 Adams Dr SW, Atlanta GA 30311, USA

**Aaron, Jeffrey** — Actor
Johnson & Laird Mgmt, PO Box 78340, Grey Lynn, Auckland 1245, New Zealand

**Aaron, Lee** — Singer, Songwriter
Paquin Entertainment Agency, 219 Dufferin St, #206B, Toronto ON M6K 3J1, Canada

**Aaron, Paul** — Director
Suntaur/Elsboy Entertainment, 1581 N Crescent Heights Blvd, Los Angeles CA 90046, USA

**Aaron, Thomas D (Tommy)** — Golfer
440 E Lake Dr, Gainesville GA 30506, USA

**Aarsleff, Hans** — Linguist
Princeton University, English Dept, Princeton NJ 08544, USA

**Aase, Donald W (Don)** — Baseball Player
5055 Via Ricardo, Yorba Linda CA 92886, USA

**Abad, F Andrus (Andy)** — Baseball Player
1092 Chicksaw St, Jupiter FL 33458, USA

**Abagnale, Frank W, Jr** — Businessman
Abagnale Assoc, PO Box 701290, Tulsa OK 74170, USA

**Abair, Mindi** — Singer, Jazz Saxophonist
Chapman Company Mgmt, 14011 Ventura Blvd, #405, Sherman Oaks CA 91423, USA

**Abakanowicz, Magdalena** — Artist
Ul Bzowa 1, 02 708 Warsaw, Poland

**Abalakin, Victor K** — Astronomer
Main Observatory, Pulkovskoye Shosse 65, 196140 Saint Petersburg, Russia

**Abbado, Claudio** — Conductor
Askonas Holt, Lincoln House, 300 High Holborn, London WC1V 7JH, England

**Abbado, Roberto** — Conductor
Opus 3 Artists, 470 Park Ave S, #900N, New York NY 10016 USA

**Abbas, Mahmoud** — President, Palestine
President's Office, Gaza City, Gaza Strip, Palestine, Israel

**Abbass, Hiam** — Actress
Untitled Entertainment, 350 S Beverly Dr, #200, Beverly Hills CA 90212 USA

**Abbatiello, Carmine** — Harness Racing Driver
7 Whirlaway Road, Manalapan NJ 07726, USA

**Abbe, Elfriede M** — Artist
Applewood, Manchester Center VT 05255, USA

**Abbot, Charles S** — Navy Admiral, Government Official
Military Officers Assn, 201 N Washington St, Alexandria VA 22314, USA

**Abbot, Russ** — Actor, Comedian
Harvey Voices, 58 Woodlands Road, London N9 8RT, England

**Abbott, Anthony J (Tony)** — Prime Minister, Australia
Prime Minister's Office, Parliament House, Canberra ACT 2600, Australia

**Abbott, Bruce** — Actor
29500 Heathercliff Road, Malibu CA 90265, USA

**Abbott, Christie** — Actress
Kim Dawson Agency, 1645 Stemmons Freeway, #B, Dallas TX 75207, USA

**Abbott, Christopher** — Actor
Gersh Agency, 9465 Wilshire Blvd, #600, Beverly Hills CA 90212 USA

**Abbott, Diahnne** — Actress
460 W Ave 46, Los Angeles CA 90065, USA

**Abbott, James A (Jim)** — Baseball Player
Lilly Walters Schermerhorn, 740 W Purdue Dr, Claremont CA 91711, USA

**Abbott, James W** — Educator
University of South Dakota, President's Office, Vermillion SD 57069, USA

**Abbott, Jeff** — Writer
Hachette/Grand Central Publishing, 3 Center Plaza, Boston MA 02108, USA

**Abbott, Jeffrey W (Jeff)** — Baseball Player
119 Little John Lane, Murrayville GA 30564, USA

**Abbott, Jeremy** — Figure Skater
Care of the World Arena, 3185 Venetucci Blvd, Colorado Springs CO 80906, USA

**Abbott, Jude** — Singer (Chumbawamba)
Doug Smith Assoc, PO Box 1151, London W3 8ZJ, England

**Abbott, Karen** — Writer
Random House, 1745 Broadway, #1800, New York NY 10019 USA

**Abbott, Kurt T** — Baseball Player
1704 NW Spruce Ridge Dr, Stuart FL 34994, USA

**Abbott, Paul** — Producer, Writer
The Agency, 24 Pottery Lane, Holland Park, London W11 4LZ, England

**Abbott, Paul D** — Baseball Player
1809 Yermo Place, Fullerton CA 92833, USA

**Abbott, Reg** — Ice Hockey Player
5239 Hanover Place, Victoria BC V8Y 2C7, Canada

**Abbott, Vinnie Paul** — Drummer (Pantera, Damageplan)
Clubhouse, 2250 Manana Dr, Dallas TX 75220, USA

**Abbott, W Glenn** — Baseball Player
4413 Dawson Dr, North Little Rock AR 72116, USA

**Abboud, A Robert** — Businessman
209 Braeburn Road, Barrington Hills IL 60010, USA

**Abboud, Francois M** — Internist, Physician
24 Kennedy Parkway, Iowa City IA 52246, USA

**Abboud, Joseph M** — Fashion Designer
650 5th Ave, #2700, New York NY 10019, USA

**Abd, Rodrigo** — Photojournalist
Associated Press, Editorial Dept, 450 W 33rd St, #1500, New York NY 10001 USA

**Abdallah Mohamed Sambi, Ahmed** — President, Comoros
President's Office, Palais de Beit Salam, BP 421, Moroni, Grand Comoro, Comoros

**Abdel Aziz, Mohamed Ould** — Head of State Council, Mauritania
President's Office, BP 184, Nouakchott, Mauritania

**Abdoo, Rose** — Actress
Innovative Artists, 1505 10th St, Santa Monica CA 90401 USA

**Abdrashitov, Vadim Y** — Director
3D Frunzenskaya 8, #211, 119270 Moscow, Russia

**Abdrazakov, Ildar** — Opera Singer
Mariinsky Theater, Theater Square, 1 Pl Iskusstr, 190000 Saint Petersburg, Russia

**Abdul Ahad Mohmand** — Cosmonaut, Afghanistan
Cosmonaut Training Center, Star City, 141160 Zvezdny Gorodok, Moscow Oblast, Russia

**Abdul, Paula J** — Singer, Dancer
Tudor Management Group, 1610 Oak St, #2, Santa Monica CA 90405, USA

**Abdul-Aziz, Zaid** — Basketball Player
12329 Roosevelt Way NE, # C203, Seattle WA 98125, USA

**Abdul-Ghani, Abdul Aziz** — Prime Minister, Yemen
Haddah St, San'a, Yemen

**Abdul-Jabbar, Kareem** — Basketball Player
Amsel Eisenstadt Frazier, 5055 Wilshire Blvd, #865, Los Angeles CA 90036 USA

**Abdul-Jabbar, Karim** — Football Player
17044 Downing St, Gaithersburg MD 20877, USA

**Abdullah Ibn Abdul al-Aziz** — King, Saudi Arabia
Council of Ministers, Murabba, Riyadh 11121, Saudi Arabia

**Abdullah II** — King, Jordan; Army General
Royal Palace, Royal Hashemite Court, Amman, Jordan

**Abdullah, Rabih F** — Football Player
12810 Wallingford Dr, Tampa FL 33624, USA

**Abduraimov, Behzod** — Concert Pianist
Harrison/Parrott, 5-6 Albion Court, London W6 0QT, England

**Abdur-Rahim, Shareef** — Basketball Player
9890 Wexford Circle, Granite Bay CA 95746, USA

**Abe, Shana** — Writer
303 S Broadway St, #200-124, Denver CO 80209, USA

**Abe, Shinzo** — Prime Minister, Japan
Prime Minister's Office, 1-6-1 Nagatoicho, Chiyodaku, Tokyo 100, Japan

**Abed, Hisham** — Cinematographer, Producer, Director
Worldwide Production Agency, 144 N Robertson Blvd, #A, West Hollywood CA 90048, USA

**Abel, Dana** — Singer, Guitarist (Misty River)
1111B NW 131st Way, Vancouver WA 98685, USA

**Abel, Dominique** — Actress, Director, Writer
Courage Mon Amour, 9 Rue Ruysdael, 1070 Brussels, Belgium

**Abel, Gerald (Gerry)** — Ice Hockey Player
23570 Samoset Trail, Southfield MI 48033, USA

**Abel, Jake** — Actor
Creative Artists Agency, 2000 Ave of Stars, #100, Los Angeles CA 90067 USA

**Abel, Jennifer** — Diver
C A M O Diving Club, 1000 Ave Emile-Journault, Montreal QC H2M 2E7, Canada

**Abel, Jessica** — Cartoonist
Fantagraphics Books, 7563 Lake City Way NE, Seattle WA 98115, USA

**Abel, Joy** — Bowler
PO Box 296, Lansing IL 60438, USA

**Abel, Yves** — Conductor
Askonas Holt, Lincoln House, 300 High Holborn, London WC1V 7JH, England

**Abela, George** — President, Malta
President's Office, Palace, Valletta, Malta

**Abele, Jim** — Actor
S M S Talent, 8383 Wilshire Blvd, #230, Beverly Hills CA 90211 USA

**Abell, Timothy S (Tim)** — Actor, Producer
Tactical Media Productions, 578 Washington Blvd, #346, Marina del Rey CA 90292, USA

**Abelson, John N** — Biologist
112 Laidley St, San Francisco CA 94131, USA

**Abendroth, John K** — Golfer
Hooked on Golf, 1620 McDonald Way, Burlingame CA 94010, USA

**Abercrombie, Jeff** — Bassist (Fuel)
Media Five Entertainment, 3005 Broadhead Road, #170, Bethlehem PA 18020, USA

**Abercrombie, John L** — Jazz Guitarist
iGuitar Workshop, 290 Main St, Building #3, Cold Spring NY 10516, USA

**Abercrombie, Walter A** — Football Player
217 Westlane Circle, Woodway TX 76712, USA

**Abernathy, Frederick H** — Mechanical Engineer
43 Islington Road, Auburndale MA 02466, USA

**Abernathy, M Brent** — Baseball Player
5920 Buxton Dr, Columbus GA 31907, USA

**Abernethy, Robert** — Commentator
Public Broadcasting System, 1320 Braddock Place, Alexandria VA 22314, USA

**Abernethy, Thomas C (Tom)** — Basketball Player
5268 Woodfield Dr N, Carmel IN 46033, USA

**Abeyta, Tony** — Artist
1127 W Madison St, Chicago IL 60607, USA

**Abgrall, Dennis** — Ice Hockey Player
16607 S 12th Place, Phoenix AZ 85048, USA

**Abidine, Dhafer** — Actor
Hamilton Hodell, 66-68 Margaret St, #500, London W1W 8SR, England

**Abigail** — Singer
T-Best Talent Agency, 508 Honey Lake Court, Danville CA 94506 USA

**Abil, Iolu Johnson** — President, Vanuatu
President's Office, Port Vila, Vanuatu

**Abiodun, Oyewole** — Rap Artist (Last Poets)
Rykodisc, 3 Broadway, #E, Beverly MA 01915, USA

**Abiola-Muller, Joy Lee** — Actress
Grundy U F A TV Productions, Coloneum, Geb B-S, Butzweiler Str 255, 50829 Cologne, Germany

**Abizaid, John P** — Army General
United Services Automobile Assn, USAA Building, San Antonio TX 78288, USA

**Abkarian, Simon** — Actor
Cineart, 28 Rue Mogador, 75009 Paris, France

**Able, Forest E** — Basketball Player
11102 Mitchell Hill Road, Fairdale KY 40118, USA

**Ablon, Ralph E** — Businessman
Ogden Corp, PO Box 2615, Fairfield NJ 07004, USA

**Ablow, Keith** — Writer
Saint Martin's Press, 175 5th Ave, #400, New York NY 10010 USA

**Abner, Shawn W** — Baseball Player
1443 Olde Oak Court, Mechanicsburg PA 17050, USA

**Aboud, John** — Writer
Principato-Young, 9465 Wilshire Blvd, #880, Beverly Hills CA 90212 USA

**Aboulela, Amir** — Actor
Grace Talent Organization, 8370 Wilshire Blvd, #210, Beverly Hills CA 90211, USA

**Aboulela, Leila** — Writer
Polygon Books, 22 George Square, Edinburgh EH8 9IF, Scotland

**Abourezk, James G** — Senator, SD
21 Dupont Circle NW, #400, Washington DC 20036, USA

**Abraham, Arthur** — Boxer
Boxsport Gmbh, Hanns-Braun-Str, 14053 Berlin, Germany

**Abraham, E Spencer** — Secretary of Energy; Senator, MI
Abraham Group, 600 14th St NW, #500, Washington DC 20005, USA

**Abraham, F Murray** — Actor
Innovative Artists, 1505 10th St, Santa Monica CA 90401 USA

**Abraham, John A** — Football Player
101 Irongate Dr, Columbia SC 29223, USA

**Abraham, Marc** — Producer
Strike Entertainment, 3000 W Olympic Blvd, Building 5, Santa Monica CA 90404, USA

**Abraham, Phil** — Director
Skouras Agency, 1149 3rd St, #300, Santa Monica CA 90403 USA

**Abraham, Robert E** — Football Player
831 Canal St, Myrtle Beach SC 29577, USA

**Abraham, Vader** — Singer
Piet Roelen Talent Agency, Antwerpsesteenweg 16, 2350 Vosselaar BE, Netherlands

**Abrahamian, Emil** — Cartoonist (Stumpy Stumbler)
147 Woodleaf Dr, Winter Springs FL 32708, USA

**Abrahams, Elihu** — Physicist
Rutgers University, Physics/Astronomy Dept, 136 Frelinghuysen Road, Piscataway NJ 08854, USA

**Abrahams, Ivor** — Sculptor
Royal Arts Academy, Burlington House, Piccadilly, London W1V 0DS, England

**Abrahams, Jim S** — Director
Ziffren Brittenham Branca, 1801 Century Park W, #700, Los Angeles CA 90067 USA

**Abrahams, Michael T (Mick)** — Guitarist (Jethro Tull)
Primary Talent International, 2-12 Pentonville Road, London N1 9PL, England

**Abrahamson, James A** — Air Force General, Businessman
StratCom International, 20112 Marble Quarry Road, Keedysville MD 21756, USA

**Abramovic, Marina** — Performance Artist, Photographer
Sean Kelly Gallery, 528 W 29th St, New York, NY 10001, USA

**Abramowicz, Daniel S (Danny)** — Football Player
143 Parkdale Road, Steubenville OH 43952, USA

**Abramowitz, Sidney H (Sid)** — Football Player
3341 Thomashire Court, Marietta GA 30066, USA

**Abrams, Bobby E** — Football Player
1470 Pampas Dr, Montgomery AL 36117, USA

**Abrams, Dan** — Actor
MSNBC, 30 Rockefeller Plaza, New York NY 10112, USA

**Abrams, Elliott** — Government Official
10607 Dogwood Farm Lane, Great Falls VA 22066, USA

**Abrams, Herbert L** — Radiologist
620 Sand Hill Road, #109G, Palo Alto CA 94304, USA

**Abrams, Jeffrey J (J J)** — Director, Producer, Writer
Oasis Media Group, 8730 W Sunset Blvd, #700, West Hollywood CA 90069, USA

**Abrams, John N** — Army General
Associated Press, Editorial Dept, 450 W 33rd St, #1500, New York NY 10001 USA

**Abramson, Leslie** — Attorney
4929 Wilshire Blvd, #490, Los Angeles CA 90010, USA

**Abramson, Neil** — Director, Writer
United Talent Agency, U T A Plaza, 9336 Civic Center Dr, Beverly Hills CA 90210 USA

**Abreu, Bob K (Bobby)** — Baseball Player
Los Angeles Dodgers, Stadium, 1000 Elysian Park Ave, Los Angeles CA 90090 USA

**Abreu, Dilip J** — Economist
Princeton University, Economics Dept, Princeton NJ 08544, USA

**Abreu, Irina** — Actress
Televisa, Blvd A Lopez Mateos 232, Colonia San Angel, Mexico City DF 01060 CP, Mexico

**Abrigo, Megan** — Model
Jet Set Models, 2160 Avenida de la Playa, La Jolla CA 92037, USA

**Abrikosov, Alexei A** — Nobel Physics Laureate
804 Houston St, Lemont IL 60439, USA

**Abril Y Castello, Santos Cardinal** — Religious Leader
Via Nicola Festa 50, 00137 Rome Lazio, Italy

**Abril, Victoria** — Actress
Stephanie Zitzermann, Rue du Louvre 1, 75001 Paris, France

**Abroms, Edward M** — Director
E M A Enterprises, 1866 Marlowe St, Thousand Oaks CA 91360, USA

**Abrosimova, Svetlana I** — Basketball Player
Seattle Storm, Key Arena, 351 Elliott Ave W, #500, Seattle WA 98119 USA

**Abruzzo, Ray** — Actor
Bret Adams Agency, 448 W 44th St, New York NY 10036, USA

**Absher, Richard A (Dick), Jr** — Football Player
353 Tavistock Dr, Saint Augustine FL 32095, USA

**Abshire, David M** — Diplomat
4800 Fillmore Ave, #458, Alexandria VA 22311, USA

**Abtahi, Omid** — Actor
Greene Assoc, 1901 Ave of Stars, #130, Los Angeles CA 90067 USA

**Abts, Tomma** — Artist
Kunsthalle Basel, Steinenberg 7, 4051 Basel, Switzerland

**Abu-Assad, Hany** — Director
Creative Artists Agency, 2000 Ave of Stars, #100, Los Angeles CA 90067 USA

**Abu-Jaber, Diana** — Writer
W W Norton, 500 5th Ave, #600, New York NY 10110 USA

**Acaba, Joseph M (Joe)** — Astronaut
N A S A, Johnson Space Center, 2101 NASA Road, Houston TX 77058 USA

**Accambray, William** — Handball Player
Montpellier Agglomeration H B, 1000 Ave du val de Montferrand, 34090 Montpellier, France

**Accardi, Vincent** — Guitarist (Brand New)
Stunt Company Media, 20 Jay St, #208, Brooklyn NY 11201, USA

**Accardo, Salvatore** — Concert Violinist
Agenzia Resia Srl Rappresentanze, Via Manzoni 31, 20121 Milan, Italy

**Accola, Candice** — Actress
A P A Talent/Literary Agency, 405 S Beverly Dr, #300, Beverly Hills CA 90212 USA

**Accola, Paul** — Alpine Skier
Bolgenstr 17, 7270 Davos Platz, Switzerland

**Acconci, Vito** — Conceptual Artist
39 Pearl St, Brooklyn NY 11201, USA

**Ace** — Guitarist (Skunk Anansie)
13 Artists, 11-14 Kensington St, Brighton BN1 4AJ, England

**Ace Hood** — Rap Artist
Def Soul Records, 825 8th Ave, #2700, New York NY 10019 USA

**Acero-Sanchez, Hector** — Boxer
Shelly Finkel Mgmt, 110 Greene St, #403, New York NY 10012 USA

**Aceto, Raymond** — Opera Singer
I M G Artists, Hogarth Business Park, Chiswick, London W4 2TH, England

**Acevedo, Juan C** — Baseball Player
143 Madera Circle, Mesa AZ 85204, USA

**Acevedo, Kirk** — Actor
Domain Talent, 9229 W Sunset Blvd, #710, West Hollywood CA 90069 USA

**Achatz, Grant** — Chef, Restaurateur
Alinea Restaurant, 1723 N Halsted, Chicago IL 60614, USA

**Achen, Christopher H** — Social Scientist
Princeton University, Politics Dept, Robertson Hall, Princeton NJ 08544, USA

**Acheson, James** — Costume Designer
I C M Partners, 10250 Constellation Blvd, #900, Los Angeles CA 90067 USA

**Achica, George** — Football Player
3165 Lone Bluff Way, San Jose CA 95111, USA

**Achterberg, Chantal** — Rowing Athlete
D S R Proteus-Ereyes, Rotterdamseweg 362A, 2628 AT Delft, Netherlands

**Achtymichuk, Gene** — Ice Hockey Player
305-9985 93rd Ave, Fort Saskatchewan AB T8L 1N5, Canada

**Acker, Amy** — Actress
A P A Talent/Literary Agency, 405 S Beverly Dr, #300, Beverly Hills CA 90212 USA

**Acker, James J (Jim)** — Baseball Player
PO Box 214, Freer TX 78357, USA

**Acker, Sharon** — Actress
2530 Alister Ave, Tustin CA 92782, USA

**Acker, William B (Bill), Jr** — Football Player
1809 Walker Dr, Alice TX 78332, USA

**Ackeren, Robert V** — Director, Producer, Writer
Kurfurstendamm 132A, 10711 Berlin, Germany

**Acker-Macosko, Anna** — Golfer
304 Earl Dr, Kerrville TX 78028, USA

**Ackerman, Bruce A** — Attorney, Educator
Yale University, Law School, 127 Wall St, New Haven CT 06511, USA

**Ackerman, Diane** — Writer
W W Norton, 500 5th Ave, #600, New York NY 10110 USA

**Ackerman, F Duane** — Businessman
BellSouth Corp, 472 Ivy Park Lane NE, Atlanta GA 30342, USA

**Ackerman, R Andrew (Andy)** — Director
W M E Entertainment, 9601 Wilshire Blvd, #300, Beverly Hills CA 90210 USA

**Ackerman, Richard C (Rick)** — Football Player
995 N US Highway 30, Laramie WY 82072, USA

**Ackerman, Robert Allan** — Director
I C M Partners, 10250 Constellation Blvd, #900, Los Angeles CA 90067 USA

**Ackerman, Thomas M (Tom)** — Football Player
17511 N Greenbluff Road, Colbert WA 99005, USA

**Ackerman, William** — Composer, Guitarist
Drake Assoc, 177 Woodland Ave, Westwood NJ 07675, USA

**Ackermann, Rosemarie** — Track Athlete
Yuri-Gagarin Str 14, 03046 Cottbus, Germany

**Ackland, Joss** — Actor
London Theatrical, 18 Leamore St, London W6 0JZ, England , USA

**Ackland, Oliver** — Actor
United Talent Agency, U T A Plaza, 9336 Civic Center Dr, Beverly Hills CA 90210 USA

**Ackles, Danneel** — Actress
Gersh Agency, 9465 Wilshire Blvd, #600, Beverly Hills CA 90212 USA

**Ackles, Jensen** — Actor
W M E Entertainment, 9601 Wilshire Blvd, #300, Beverly Hills CA 90210 USA

**Ackroyd, Barry** — Cinematographer
United Agents, 12-26 Lexington St, London W1F 0LE, England

**Ackroyd, David** — Actor
PO Box 9041, Kalispell MT 59904, USA

**Ackroyd, Norman** — Artist
Royal Academy of Arts, Piccadilly, London W1V 0DS, England

**Ackroyd, Peter** — Writer
Anthony Sheil Assoc, 43 Doughty St, London WC1N 2LF, England

**Acks, Ronald W (Ron)** — Football Player
563 Licklog Ridge, Hayesville NC 28904, USA

**Acler, Rarika** — Model
Ten Model Mgmt, Rua Iquatemi 448, CEP 01451 010 Sao Paulo SP, Brazil

**Acogny, Germaine** — Dancer, Choreographer
Jant-Bi, BP 22626, 15523 Dakar, Senegal

**Acohido, Byron** — Journalist
Seattle Times, Editorial Dept, 1000 Denny Way, Seattle WA 98109 USA
**Acord, Lance** — Cinematographer
Creative Artists Agency, 2000 Ave of Stars, #100, Los Angeles CA 90067 USA
**Acosta, Carlos** — Ballet Dancer
Royal Opera House, Covent Garden, London WC2E 9DD, England
**Acosta, George** — Producer (Planet Soul)
Richard Walters, PO Box 2789, Toluca Lake CA 91610 USA
**Acra, Reem** — Fashion Designer
730 5th Ave, #205, New York NY 10019, USA
**Acres, Mark R** — Basketball Player
233 6th St, Manhattan Beach CA 90266, USA
**Acrivos, Andreas** — Chemical Engineer
788 Cedro Way, Stanford CA 94305, USA
**Acta, Manuel E (Manny)** — Baseball Manager
6427 Shoreline Dr, Saint Cloud FL 34771, USA
**Acton, Charles R (Bud)** — Basketball Player
PO Box 87, Empire MI 49630, USA
**Acton, Keith** — Ice Hockey Player
14 Cornell Place, Rye NY 10580, USA
**Acton, Loren W** — Astronaut
PO Box 1857, Bozeman MT 59771, USA
**Acuff, Carl, Jr** — Singer
PO Box 2367, Harrison AR 72602, USA
**Aczel, Janos D** — Mathematician
University of Waterloo, Pure Mathematics Dept, Waterloo ON N2L 3G1, Canada
**Adair, Deborah** — Actress
2530 J St, #330, Sacramento CA 95816, USA
**Adair, Robert K** — Physicist
Harvard University, Belfer Science Center, Cambridge MA 02138, USA
**Adam, Ken** — Designer
Mirisch Agency, 8840 Wilshire Blvd, #100, Beverly Hills CA 90211 USA
**Adam, Mike** — Curling Athlete
Curling Assn, 1660 Vimont Court, Cumberland ON K4A 4J4, Canada
**Adam, Robert** — Architect
Winchester Design, 9 Upper High St, Winchester, Hants SO23 8UT, England
**Adam, Russ** — Ice Hockey Player
69 Old Petty Harbour Road, Saint Johns NL A1G 1H5, Canada
**Adam, Theo** — Opera Singer
Schillerstr 14, 01326 Dresden, Germany
**Adamek, Donna** — Bowler
29834 Webster Place, Stevenson Ranch CA 91381, USA
**Adamek, Tomasz** — Boxer
Ul Viantykowka 6, 34-322 Gilowice, Poland
**Adami, Franco** — Sculptor
Via del Vicinato, Pontestrada, 55045 Piatrasanta, Italy
**Adamle, Michael D (Mike)** — Football Player, Sportscaster
826 Lincoln St, Evanston IL 60201, USA
**Adams Beckham, Victoria** — Singer (Spice Girls)
19 Entertainment, 32/33 Ransomes Dock, 35-37 Parkgate Road, London SW11 4NP, England
**Adams, Alvan L** — Basketball Player
5617 N Palo Cristi Road, Paradise Valley AZ 85253, USA
**Adams, Amy** — Actress
Brillstein Entertainment Partners, 9150 Wilshire Blvd, #350, Beverly Hills CA 90212 USA
**Adams, Anthony L (Tony)** — Football Player
14012 Juniper St, Overland Park KS 66224, USA
**Adams, Brooke** — Actress
Cunningham-Escott-Dipene, 261 S Robertson Blvd, Beverly Hills CA 90211, USA
**Adams, Bryan** — Singer, Guitarist, Songwriter
Bruce Allen Talent, 500-425 Carrall St, Vancouver BC V6B 6E3, Canada
**Adams, Bryan** — Singer (Color Me Badd)
J Bird Entertainment, 4905 S Atlantic Ave, Ponce Inlet FL 32127, USA
**Adams, Christine** — Actress
Innovative Artists, 1505 10th St, Santa Monica CA 90401 USA
**Adams, Craig** — Ice Hockey Player
8030 Sherwood Dr, Presto PA 15142, USA
**Adams, Flozell J** — Football Player
5201 Reflection Court, Flower Mound TX 75022, USA
**Adams, Fred** — Astrophysicist
University of Michigan, Astrophysics Dept, Ann Arbor MI 48109, USA
**Adams, George** — Basketball Player
508 Watergate Circle, Gastonia NC 28052, USA
**Adams, George W** — Football Player
2410 Damsel Katie Dr, Lewisville TX 75056, USA
**Adams, Gerard (Gerry)** — Political Leader, Northern Ireland
Sinn Fein/l R A, 51/55 Falls Road, Belfast BT12 4PD, Northern Ireland
**Adams, Greg** — Ice Hockey Player
Cowichan Valley Capitals, 2687 James St, Duncan BC V9L 2X5, Canada
**Adams, Greg** — Singer, Trumpeter (Tower of Power)
A L M Management Group, PO Box 16608, Encino CA 91416, USA
**Adams, Hunter Patch** — Physician
122 Franklin St, Urbana IL 61801, USA
**Adams, Jane** — Actress
Framework Entertainment, 9057 Nemo St, #C, West Hollywood CA 90069 USA
**Adams, Joey Lauren** — Actress
Paradigm Agency, 360 N Crescent Dr, North Building, Beverly Hills CA 90210 USA
**Adams, John** — Ice Hockey Player
109 Nottingham Crescent, Thunder Bay ON P7G 1B4, Canada
**Adams, John C** — Composer, Conductor
I M G Artists, Carnegie Hall Tower, 152 W 57th St, #500, New York NY 10019 USA
**Adams, John G** — Golfer
4610 County Road 42200, Paris TX 75462, USA
**Adams, Julie** — Actress
5915 Corbin Ave, Tarzana CA 91356, USA
**Adams, Julius T** — Football Player, Coach
2135 Jefferson Davis St, Macon GA 31201, USA

# A

**Adams, Katie** — Actress
Hollander Talent Group, 14011 Ventura Blvd, #202, Sherman Oaks CA 91423, USA
**Adams, Keith A** — Football Player
9 N 9th St, #712, Philadelphia PA 19107, USA
**Adams, Kevyn** — Ice Hockey Player
Phoenix Coyotes, 6751 N Sunset Blvd, #200, Glendale AZ 85305 USA
**Adams, Lindsey** — Auto Racing Driver
819 W Arapho, #24B-188, Richardson TX 75080, USA
**Adams, Lorraine** — Journalist
Washington Post, Editorial Dept, 1150 15th St, Washington DC 20071, USA
**Adams, Lynn** — Golfer
2445 Bryant St, #207, San Diego CA 92101, USA
**Adams, Mary Kay** — Actress
Ingber Assoc, 1140 Broadway, #907, New York NY 10001, USA
**Adams, Maud** — Actress
PO Box 10838, Beverly Hills CA 90213, USA
**Adams, Michael** — Basketball Player
WWRC-Radio, Sports Dept, 8121 Georgia Ave, Silver Spring MD 20910, USA
**Adams, Michael C (Mike)** — Football Player
70 Graham Ave, Paterson NJ 07524, USA
**Adams, Neal** — Cartoonist
W M E Entertainment, 9601 Wilshire Blvd, #300, Beverly Hills CA 90210 USA
**Adams, Nicola V** — Boxer
Haringey Amateur Boxing Club, 701 High Road, Tottenham Greater London N17 8AD, England
**Adams, Noah** — Commentator
National Public Radio, 635 Massachusetts Ave NW, #1, Washington DC 20001, USA
**Adams, Norman** — Artist
6 Gainsborough Road, London W4 1NJ, England
**Adams, Oleta** — Singer
Tom Estey Publicity, 144 E 22nd St, #1B, New York NY 10010, USA
**Adams, Pat** — Artist
370 Elm St, Bennington VT 05201, USA
**Adams, Patrick J** — Actor
Gersh Agency, 9465 Wilshire Blvd, #600, Beverly Hills CA 90212 USA
**Adams, Paul L** — WW II Army Air Corps Hero
6800 A St, #139, Lincoln NE 68510, USA
**Adams, Phillip A** — Humanist, Social Commentator
Radio National, GPO Box 9994, Sydney NSW 2001, Australia
**Adams, R Michael (Mike)** — Baseball Player
13205 Jo Lane NE, Albuquerque NM 87111, USA
**Adams, Ranald T, Jr** — Air Force General
1002 Emerald Dr, Alexandria VA 22308, USA
**Adams, Rhonda** — Model
Playboy Promotions, 2706 Media Center Dr, Los Angeles CA 90065 USA
**Adams, Richard G** — Writer
Benwell's, 26 Church St, Whitchurch, Hantshire RG28 7AR, England
**Adams, Robert B (Bob)** — Football Player
16422 SE 17th St, Bellevue WA 98008, USA
**Adams, Robert H** — Photographer
306 Lincoln St, Longmont CO 80501, USA
**Adams, Robert M, Jr** — Anthropologist
PO Box ZZ, Basalt CO 81621, USA
**Adams, Ryan** — Singer, Songwriter
S A M, 722 Seward St, Los Angeles CA 90038, USA
**Adams, Sam A** — Football Player
218 Main St, #514, Kirkland WA 98033, USA
**Adams, Sam E** — Football Player
12010 Holly Stone Dr, Houston TX 77070, USA
**Adams, Scott** — Cartoonist (Dilbert)
Harper Business Publishers, 10 E 53rd St, New York NY 10022, USA
**Adams, Seth** — Actor
Mark Robert, PO Box 1549, Studio City CA 91614, USA
**Adams, Stefon L** — Football Player
937 Bingham Lane, Stone Mountain GA 30083, USA
**Adams, Stephanie L** — Model
PO Box 8202, New York NY 10116, USA
**Adams, Steven** — Basketball Player
Oklahoma City Thunder, 211 N Robinson Ave, #300, Oklahoma City OK 73102 USA
**Adams, Terry** — Pianist, Clarinet Player (NRBQ)
Skyline Music, 2270 Maiden Lane SW, Roanoke VA 24015, USA
**Adams, Terry W** — Baseball Player
PO Box 1035, Mobile AL 36633, USA
**Adams, Tom** — Actor
Langford, 17 Westfields Ave, London SW19 0AT, England
**Adams, Tony (T-Bone)** — Boxer
1209 56th Court, Northport AL 35473, USA
**Adams, Valerie Vili** — Track Athlete
1155 Union Circle, Denton TX 76201, USA
**Adams, William J (Bill)** — Football Player
12 Willowby Way, Lynnfield MA 01940, USA
**Adams, Willis D** — Football Player
7831 Quail Meadow Dr, Houston TX 77071, USA
**Adams, Yolanda** — Singer
Grand Gospel Bookings, 3933 Harrison St, #103, Oakland CA 94611, USA
**Adams-Geller, Paige** — Model, Fashion Designer
Paige Premium Denim, 10119 Jefferson Blvd, Culver City CA 90232, USA
**Adamski, Filip K** — Rowing Athlete
U 1, #9, 67161 Mannheim, Germany
**Adamson, Andrew** — Director, Writer, Animator
Strange Weather Films, 4205 Santa Monica Blvd, Santa Monica CA 90029, USA
**Adamson, Andrew** — Director, Producer
United Talent Agency, U T A Plaza, 9336 Civic Center Dr, Beverly Hills CA 90210 USA
**Adamson, James C** — Astronaut
25 Tradewind Circle, Fishersville VA 22939, USA
**Adamson, Robert E, Jr** — Navy Admiral
1709 Bohnhoff Court, Virginia Beach VA 23454, USA

**Adams - Adamson**

**Adams-Sassoon, Beverly**                                              Model
1800 The Strand, Manhattan Beach CA 90266, USA
**Addai, Joseph**                                                Football Player
6710 Rosedale Path Court, Sugar Land TX 77479, USA
**Addario, Lisa**                                                      Writer
United Talent Agency, U T A Plaza, 9336 Civic Center Dr, Beverly Hills CA 90210 USA
**Addazio, Steve**                                              Football Coach
Boston College, Athletic Dept, Chestnut Hill MA 02467, USA
**Adderley, Herbert A (Herb)**                                   Football Player
1058 Tristam Circle, Mantua NJ 08051, USA
**Addington, Crandell**                                            Poker Player
Phoenix Biotechnology, 8626 Tesoro Dr, #801, San Antonio TX 78217, USA
**Addison, Adele**                                               Concert Singer
98 Riverside Dr, New York NY 10024, USA
**Addison, Chris**                               Actor, Comedian, Writer, Director
Avalon Mgmt, 4A Exmoor St, London W10 6BD, England
**Addison, Rafael**                                            Basketball Player
6 Bernadette Court, East Hanover NH 07936, USA
**Adduci, James D (Jim)**                                        Baseball Player
16314 Crescent Lake Dr, Crest Hill IL 60403, USA
**Adduono, Rick**                                             Ice Hockey Player
153 Donald St W, Thunder Bay ON P7E 5X8, Canada
**Addy, Mark**                                                         Actor
Independent Talent Group, 40 Whitfield St, London W1T 2RH, England
**Ade, King Sunny**                                                   Singer
Monterey International, 200 W Superior St, #202, Chicago IL 60654 USA
**Adebimpe, Tunde**                                     Singer (TV on the Radio)
D G C/Interscope Records, 2220 Colorado Ave, Santa Monica CA 90404, USA
**Adel, Marwa**                                                  Photographer
Safar Khan Art Gallery, 6 Brazil St, Zamalek, Cairo 11211, Egypt
**Adele**                                                   Singer, Songwriter
September Mgmt, 80/82 Chiswick High Road, London W4 1SY, England
**Adelin, Jean-Claude**                                                Actor
Artmedia, 20 Ave Rapp, 75007 Paris, France
**Adell, Traci**                                                Actress, Model
Playboy Promotions, 2706 Media Center Dr, Los Angeles CA 90065 USA
**Adelman, Kenneth L**                                     Government Official
George Washington University, English Dept, 2121 I St N, Washington DC 20052, USA
**Adelman, Morris A**                                               Economist
Massachusetts Institute of Technology, Economics Dept, Cambridge MA 02139, USA
**Adelman, Richard L (Rick)**                            Basketball Player, Coach
5109 Tangle Lane, Houston TX 77056, USA
**Adelson, Sheldon G**                                            Businessman
Las Vegas Sands Corp, 3355 Las Vegas Blvd S, Las Vegas NV 89109, USA
**Adelstein, Paul**                                                    Actor
Abrams Artists, 9200 W Sunset Blvd, #1125, West Hollywood CA 90069 USA
**Ader, Tammy**                                               Producer, Writer
Creative Artists Agency, 2000 Ave of Stars, #100, Los Angeles CA 90067 USA
**Ades, Thomas J E**                               Composer, Pianist, Conductor
I M G Artists, Hogarth Business Park, Chiswick, London W4 2TH, England
**Adey, Christopher**                                               Conductor
Richard Haigh Performing Arts, 6 Windmill St, London W1P 1HF, England
**Adey, William R**                                                 Physician
20 Sunrise Hill Road, Orinda CA 94563, USA
**Adichie, Chimamanda N**                                             Writer
Wylie Agency, 17 Bedford Square, London WC1B 3JA, England
**Adickes, David P**                                                Sculptor
2500 Summer St, Houston TX 77007, USA
**Adickes, Mark S**                                              Football Player
6146 Bordley Dr, Houston TX 77057, USA
**Adiga, Aravind**                                                    Writer
Simon & Schuster, 1230 Ave of Americas, Concourse 1, New York NY 10020 USA
**Adisa, Lawrence B**                                                  Actor
Synergy Pictures, PO Box 16772, North Hollywood CA 91615, USA
**Adjani, Isabelle**                                                 Actress
Orbis Media, 27 Rue Cardinet, 75017 Paris, France
**Adkins, Derrick**                                             Track Athlete
909 Derrick Adkins Lane, West Hempstead NY 11552, USA
**Adkins, Jim**                            Singer, Guitarist (Jimmy Eat World)
S A M, 722 Seward St, Los Angeles CA 90038, USA
**Adkins, Jonathan S (Jon)**                                    Baseball Player
RR 3 Box 2306, Wayne WV 25570, USA
**Adkins, Samuel A (Sam)**                                       Football Player
15912 NE 160th St, Woodinville WA 98072, USA
**Adkins, Seth**                                                       Actor
Paradigm Agency, 360 N Crescent Dr, North Building, Beverly Hills CA 90210 USA
**Adkins, Trace**                                                     Singer
Vector Mgmt, PO Box 120479, Nashville TN 37212, USA
**Adkisson, Perry L**                                    Etomologist, Educator
3805 Park Village Court, Bryan TX 77802, USA
**Adleman, Leonard M**                                     Computer Scientist
University of Southern California, Computer Mathematics Dept, Los Angeles CA 90089, USA
**Adler, Brian**                                                    Composer
Evolution Music Partners, 1680 Vine St, #500, Los Angeles CA 90028 USA
**Adler, Charles**                                                     Actor
Innovative Artists, 1505 10th St, Santa Monica CA 90401 USA
**Adler, Chris**                                        Drummer (Lamb of God)
Entertainment Services, 1000 Main Street Plaza, #303, Voorhees NJ 08043, USA
**Adler, Jerry**                                                       Actor
Paradigm Agency, 360 N Crescent Dr, North Building, Beverly Hills CA 90210 USA
**Adler, Joanna**                                                    Actress
Innovative Artists, 235 Park Ave S, #1000, New York NY 10003 USA
**Adler, Julius**                                        Biologist, Biochemist
1234 Wellesley Road, Madison WI 53705, USA
**Adler, Lee**                                                        Artist
Lime Kiln Farm, Climax NY 12042, USA

**Adler, Lou** — Director, Producer, Actor
Ode Sounds & Visuals, 3969 Villa Costera, Malibu CA 90265, USA
**Adler, Max** — Actor
Gersh Agency, 9465 Wilshire Blvd, #600, Beverly Hills CA 90212 USA
**Adler, Renata** — Writer, Journalist
198 Hattertown Road, Newtown CT 06470, USA
**Adler, Stephen J** — Editor
Business Week, Editor's Office, 1221 Ave of Americas, New York NY 10020, USA
**Adler, Steven** — Drummer (Guns N' Roses)
Artists Worldwide, 3921 Wilshire Blvd, #619, Los Angeles CA 90010, USA
**Adler, Willie** — Guitarist (Lamb of God)
Entertainment Services, 1000 Main Street Plaza, #303, Voorhees NJ 08043, USA
**Adlington, Rebecca (Becky)** — Swimmer
Nova Centurion S C, Beechdale Road, Bilborough, Nottingham NG8 3LL, England
**Adlon, Pamela S** — Actress
C E S D, 10635 Santa Monica Blvd, #130, Los Angeles CA 90025 USA
**Adly-Guirgis, Stephen** — Actor
W M E Entertainment, 9601 Wilshire Blvd, #300, Beverly Hills CA 90210 USA
**Adonis** — Writer
College de France, 11 Marchelin Berthelot, 75231 Paris Cedux O5, France
**Adoor, Gopalakrishnan** — Director
Darsanam, Trivandrum, 695017 Kerala, India
**Adoti, Razaaq** — Actor
Abrams Artists, 9200 W Sunset Blvd, #1125, West Hollywood CA 90069 USA
**Adria Acosta, Albert** — Chef
Tickets Restaurant, Av Paralel 164, 08015 Barcelona, Spain
**Adria, Ferran** — Chef
El Bulli, Portaferrisa 7, Pral 2A, 08002 Barcelona, Spain
**Adrian, Nathan G** — Swimmer
University of California, Athletic Dept, Dwinelle Hall, Berkeley CA 94720, USA
**Adriana** — Model
Luna Presse, Villa Grande Armee, 8 Rue des Acacias, 75017 Paris, France
**Adsit, Scott** — Actor
A P A Talent/Literary Agency, 405 S Beverly Dr, #300, Beverly Hills CA 90212 USA
**Adu, Freddie** — Soccer Player
Philadelphia Union, Union Field, Seaport Dr, Chester PA 19013 USA
**Adubato, Richie** — Basketball Coach
290 Chiswell Place, Lake Mary FL 32746, USA
**Adway, Dwayne** — Actor
House of Representatives, 1434 6th St, #1, Santa Monica CA 90401 USA
**Adyrkhayeva, Svetlana D** — Ballerina
1 Smolensky Pereulor 9, #74, 121099 Moscow, Russia
**Aesop Rock** — Rap Artist
Kork Agency, 1880 Century Park E, #711, Los Angeles CA 90067 USA
**Afanasenkov, Dmitry** — Ice Hockey Player
HC Moscow Dynamo, Leningradsky Prospect 36, 125167 Moscow, Russia
**Afanasyev, Viktor M** — Cosmonaut
Cosmonaut Training Center, Star City, 141160 Zvezdny Gorodok, Moscow Oblast, Russia
**Aferiat, Paul** — Interior Designer
Stamberg Aferiat Architect, 152 5th Ave, New York NY 10011, USA
**Afewerki, Issaias** — President, Eritrea
President's Office, PO Box 257, Gejeret, Asmara, Eritrea
**Affeldt, Jeremy D** — Baseball Player
6211 E Mandalay Lane, Spokane WA 99217, USA
**Afflalo, Arron A** — Basketball Player
Orlando Magic, 8701 Maitland Summit Blvd, Orlando FL 32810 USA
**Affleck, Benjamin G (Ben)** — Actor, Director, Writer
W M E Entertainment, 9601 Wilshire Blvd, #300, Beverly Hills CA 90210 USA
**Affleck, Bruce** — Ice Hockey Player
1847 Oxborough Court, Chesterfield MO 63017, USA
**Affleck, Casey** — Actor
I/D Public Relations, 7060 Hollywood Blvd, #800, Los Angeles CA 90028 USA
**Affleck, James G** — Businessman
American Cyanamid, 5 Giralda Farms, Madison NJ 07940, USA
**Afinogenov, Maxim S** — Ice Hockey Player
3700 S Ocean Blvd, #1502, Highland Beach FL 33487, USA
**Afrika Bambaataa** — Rap DJ Musician
K L B Productions, 302A W 12th St, PH A #26, New York NY 10014, USA
**Afroman** — Rap Artist
Crescent Moon Talent, 20 Music Square W, Nashville TN 37203, USA
**Aga Khan IV, Prince Karim** — Spiritual Leader
Aiglemont, 60270 Gouvieux, France
**Agajanian, Benjamin J (Ben)** — Football Player
27950 Avenida Terrazo, Cathedral City CA 92234, USA
**Agam, Yaacov** — Artist
26 Rue Boulard, 75014 Paris, France
**Agassi, Andre** — Tennis Player
9804 Caden Hills Ave, Las Vegas NV 89145, USA
**Agatston, Arthur S** — Cardiologist, Writer
1633 N View Dr, Miami Beach FL 33140, USA
**Agbayani, Benny P, Jr** — Baseball Player
66-948 Kolu Place, Waialua HI 96791, USA
**Agee, Tommie L** — Football Player
1505 Blackhawk Dr, Opelika AL 36801, USA
**Agena, Keiko** — Actress
C E S D, 10635 Santa Monica Blvd, #130, Los Angeles CA 90025 USA
**Aghdashloo, Shohreh** — Actress
Ken McReddie Assoc, 101 Finsbury Pavement, London EC2A 1RS, England
**Agischewa, Marijam** — Actress
Doells, Rosenheimer Stra 38, 10781 Berlin, Germany
**Agler, Brian** — Basketball Coach
Seattle Storm, Key Arena, 351 Elliott Ave W, #500, Seattle WA 98119 USA
**Agliotti, Marilyn** — Field Hockey Player
Oranje-Zwart M H C, Charles Roelslaan 13, 5644 HX Eindhoven, Netherlands
**Aglukark, Susan** — Singer, Songwriter
Agency Group Ltd, 142 W 57th St, #600, New York NY 10019 USA

**Agnel, Yannick** — Swimmer
30 Boul General Louis Delfino, 06300 Nice, France
**Agnelo, Geraldo Majella Cardinal** — Religious Leader
Piazza Certaldo 85, 00146 Rome Lazio, Italy
**Agnew, Chloe** — Singer (Celtic Woman)
W M E Entertainment, 9601 Wilshire Blvd, #300, Beverly Hills CA 90210 USA
**Agnew, Jim** — Ice Hockey Player
10080 Equestrian Way, Missoula MT 59808, USA
**Agnew, Paul** — Conductor
Theatre de Caen, 135 Boulevard du Maréchal Leclerc, 14000 Caen, France
**Agnew, Ray M, Jr** — Football Player
2215 Cline St, Winston Salem NC 27107, USA
**Agnew, Rudolph I J** — Businessman
7 Eccleston St, London SW1X 9LX, England
**Agoos, Jeff** — Soccer Player, Executive
235 Pascack Road, Park Ridge NJ 07656, USA
**Agosta, Meghan** — Ice Hockey Player
Team Canada, 2424 University Dr NW, Calgary AB T2N 3Y9, Canada
**Agosto Gonzalez, Juan R** — Baseball Player
4748 Sweetmeadow Circle, Sarasota FL 34238, USA
**Agosto, Benjamin A (Ben)** — Ice Dancer
31284 Huntley Square E, #1124, Beverly Hills MI 48025, USA
**Agranoff, Bernard W** — Biochemist
University of Michigan, Biological Chemistry Dept, 1150 W Medical Center Dr, Ann Arbor MI 48109, USA
**Agre, Peter** — Nobel Chemistry Laureate
7033 Lenleigh Road, Baltimore MD 21212, USA
**Agrelo, Marilyn** — Director
Gersh Agency, 9465 Wilshire Blvd, #600, Beverly Hills CA 90212 USA
**Agresta, Maria** — Opera Singer
I M G Artists, Hogarth Business Park, Chiswick, London W4 2TH, England
**Agron, Dianna** — Actress
Creative Artists Agency, 2000 Ave of Stars, #100, Los Angeles CA 90067 USA
**Agt, Andries A M Van** — Prime Minister, Netherlands
6564 Heilig Landstichting AG, Netherlands
**Aguayo Muriel, Luis** — Baseball Player
PO Box 1427, Vega Baja PR 00694, USA
**Aguayo, Albert J** — Neurophysiologist
648 Ave Belmont, Westmount QC H3Y 2W2, Canada
**Aguerre, Gustavo** — Photographer, Artist
FA+, Drottninggatan 71A, 111 36 Stockholm, Sweden
**Aguilar Diaz, Macarena** — Handball Player
Randers H K, Sjaellandsgade 57, 8900 Randers, Spain
**Aguilar, George** — Actor
Artists First, PO Box 7217, Beverly Hills CA 90212, USA
**Aguilar, Louis R (Louie)** — Football Player
1411 Palmer Creek Dr, Columbia IL 62236, USA
**Aguilar, Pepe** — Singer
J E P Entertainment Group, 16207 Ventura Blvd, #510, Encino CA 91436, USA
**Aguilera, Christina** — Singer, Songwriter, Actress
Creative Artists Agency, 2000 Ave of Stars, #100, Los Angeles CA 90067 USA
**Aguilera, Marian** — Actress
Kuranda Mgmt, Santo Angel 84, 28043 Madrid, Spain
**Aguilera, Richard W (Rick)** — Baseball Player
PO Box 174, Rancho Santa Fe CA 92067, USA
**Aguirre, Mark A** — Basketball Player, Executive
10281 Highland Court, Frisco TX 75034, USA
**Agurcia, Ricardo** — Archaeologist
Copan Assn, Casa Yax Na, Avenida Los Jaguares, Copan Runinas, Honduras
**Agutter, Jenny** — Actress
Ken McReddie Assoc, 101 Finsbury Pavement, London EC2A 1RS, England
**Agyeman, Freema** — Actress
Independent Talent Group, 40 Whitfield St, London W1T 2RH, England
**Ahanotu, Chidi O** — Football Player
1000 S Harbour Island Blvd, #2611, Tampa FL 33602, USA
**Ahdout, Jonathan** — Actor
Paradigm Agency, 360 N Crescent Dr, North Building, Beverly Hills CA 90210 USA
**Ahearn, Kevin J** — Ice Hockey Player
174 Marlborough St, Boston MA 02116, USA
**A'Hern, Basia** — Actress
Nickelodeon UK, PO Box 6425, London W1A 6UR, England
**Ahern, Fred** — Ice Hockey Player
21 Crescent St, Plympton MA 02367, USA
**Ahern, Jim** — Golfer
130 E Glendale Ave, Phoenix AZ 85020, USA
**Ahern, Neal, Jr** — Producer
Paradigm Agency, 360 N Crescent Dr, North Building, Beverly Hills CA 90210 USA
**Ahern, P Batholomew (Bertie)** — Prime Minister, Ireland
Saint Luke's, 161 Lower Drumcondra, Dublin 9, Ireland
**Ahlberg, Dennis A** — Educator
Trinity University, President's Office, 1 Trinity Place, San Antonio TX 78212, USA
**Ahlund, Joakim** — Guitarist, Singer (Caesars)
Paradigm Agency, 360 Park Ave, #1600, New York NY 10022 USA
**Ahmed, Akbar** — Political Scientist
American University, International Relations Dept, Washington DC 20006, USA
**Ahmed, Fakhruddin** — Prime Minister, Bangladesh
Sere-e Bangla Nagar, Gono, Bhaban, Sher-e-Banglanagar, Dhakar 1207, Bangladesh
**Ahmed, Kazi Zafar** — Prime Minister, Bangladesh
National Parliament, Jatiya Sangsad, Dhaka 1801, Bangladesh
**Ahmed, Rafi** — Immunologist
Emory University Medical Center, 954 Gatewood Road, Atlanta GA 30329, USA
**Ahmed, Riz** — Actor
Gordon & French, 12-13 Poland St, London W1F 8QB, England
**Ahn, Priscilla** — Singer, Songwriter
Blue Note Records, 6920 W Sunset Blvd, Los Angeles CA 90028 USA
**Aho, Esko T** — Prime Minister, Finland
Finnish Centre Party, Apollonkatu 11A, 00100 Helsinki, Finland

**Ahoussou-Kouadio, Jeannot** — Prime Minister, Cote d'Ivoire
Prime Minister's Office, Blvd Angoulvant Plateau, 01 BP 1533 Abidjan 01, Cote d'Ivoire

**Ahrends, Peter** — Architect
16 Rochester Road, London NW1 9JH, England

**Ahrens, David I** — Football Player
5864 Manchester Court, Pittsboro IN 46167, USA

**Ahrens, Lynn** — Lyricist
W M E Entertainment, 1325 Ave of Americas, New York NY 10019 USA

**Ahtisaari, Martti** — President, Finland; Nobel Peace Laureate
Erottajankatu 11A, #400, 00130 Helsinki, Finland

**Aibel, Howard J** — Businessman
183 Steep Hill Road, Weston CT 06883, USA

**Aicardi, Matteo** — Water Polo Player
A S D Pro Recco, Via Biagio Assereto 10/A, 16036 Recco (GE), Italy

**Aida, Takefumi** — Architect
1-3-2 Okubo, Shinjukuku, Tokyo 169 0072, Japan

**Aiello, Danny** — Actor
Artists Agency, 9430 Olympic Blvd, Beverly Hills CA 90212 USA

**Aigner, Hannes** — Canoeing Athlete
Augsburger Kajak Verein E V, Am Eiskanal 49, 86161 Augsburg, Germany

**Aigrain, Pierre R** — Physicist
56 Rue de Boulainvilliers, 75016 Paris, France

**Aiken, Clay** — Singer
Strategic Artist Mgmt, 1100 Glendon Ave, #1000, Los Angeles CA 90024, USA

**Aiken, John (Johnny)** — Ice Hockey Player
18 Pinetree Road, Billerica MA 01821, USA

**Aiken, Liam** — Actor
Brillstein Entertainment Partners, 9150 Wilshire Blvd, #350, Beverly Hills CA 90212 USA

**Aiken, Linda H** — Sociologist
2209 Lombard St, Philadelphia PA 19146, USA

**Aiken, Sam** — Football Player
104 Winter Ridge Dr, Holly Springs NC 27540, USA

**Aikens, Curtis** — Chef
PO Box 575, Conyers GA 30012, USA

**Aikens, Willie M** — Baseball Player
10206 Locust St, Kansas City MO 64131, USA

**Aikin, Laura** — Opera Singer
Ingpen & Williams, 131 Putney Bridge Road, London SW15 2PA, England

**Aikman, Troy K** — Football Player, Sportscaster
4425 Highland Dr, Dallas TX 75205, USA

**Aiko** — Princess, Japan
Imperial Palace, 1-1 Chiyoda, Chiyodaku, Tokyo 100 0001, Japan

**Ailes, Roger E** — Businessman
218 Truman Dr, Cresskill NJ 07626, USA

**Aimard, Pierre-Laurent** — Concert Pianist
Harrison/Parrott, 5-6 Albion Court, London W6 0QT, England

**Aimee, Anouk** — Actress
Artmedia, 20 Ave Rapp, 75007 Paris, France

**Ainge, Daniel R (Danny)** — Basketball Player, Coach
140 Wellesley Ave, Wellesley Hills MA 02481, USA

**Ainsleigh, H Gordon** — Ultra Marathon Athlete
17119 Placer Hills Road, Meadow Vista CA 95722, USA

**Ainslie, C Benedict (Ben)** — Yachtsman
Royal Lymington Yacht Club, Bath Road, Lymington, Hampshire S041 3SE, England

**Ainsworth, Kacey** — Actress
United Agents, 12-26 Lexington St, London W1F 0LE, England

**Ainsworth, Kurt** — Baseball Player
15220 Memorial Tower Dr, Baton Rouge LA 70810, USA

**Airiana** — Circus Aerialist
Ringling Bros Barnum & Bailey, 8607 Westwood Circle Dr, Vienna VA 22182 USA

**Airlie, Andrew** — Actor
Noble/Caplan/Abrams, 1260 Yonge St, #200, Toronto ON MT4 1W6, Canada

**Aislin** — Editorial Cartoonist
Gazette, 1010 Sainte Catherine Street W, Montreal QC H3B 5L1, Canada

**Aitay, Victor** — Concert Violinist
800 Deerfield Road, #203, Highland Park IL 60035, USA

**Aitcheson, Joe, Jr** — Steeplechase Racing Jockey
15404 Riding Stable Road, Laurel MD 20707, USA

**Aitken, Brad** — Ice Hockey Player
825 Royal Orchard Dr, Oshawa ON L1K 1Z8, Canada

**Aitken, Doug** — Artist
2437 Via Sonoma, Palos Verdes Estates CA 90274, USA

**Aivazoff, Micah** — Ice Hockey Player
6916 Hammond St, Powell River BC V8A 1R4, Canada

**Aja, Alexandre** — Director
W M E Entertainment, 9601 Wilshire Blvd, #300, Beverly Hills CA 90210 USA

**Ajayan, Pulickel M** — Materials Engineer
Rice University, Materials Science Dept, Houston TX 77005, USA

**Ajodhia, Jules R** — Prime Minister, Suriname
Prime Minister's Office, Paramaribo, Suriname

**Akalaitis, JoAnne** — Director, Writer, Actress
Mabon Mimes, 150 1st Ave, New York NY 10009, USA

**Akbar, Taufik** — Astronaut, Indonesia
Jalan Simp, Pahlawan III/24, Bandung 40124, Indonesia

**Akebono** — Sumo Wrestler
Azumazeki Stable, 4-6-4 Higashi Komagata, Ryogoku, Tokyo, Japan

**Akel, Mike** — Director, Producer, Writer
United Talent Agency, U T A Plaza, 9336 Civic Center Dr, Beverly Hills CA 90210 USA

**Aker, Jack D** — Baseball Player
5911 E Bloomfield Road, Scottsdale AZ 85254, USA

**Akerlof, George A** — Nobel Economics Laureate
University of California, Economics Dept, Evans Hall, Berkeley CA 94720, USA

**Akerlund, Jonas** — Director
I C M Partners, 10250 Constellation Blvd, #900, Los Angeles CA 90067 USA

**Akerman, Malin** — Actress, Singer
Sanders Armstrong Caserta, 2120 Colorado Ave, #120, Santa Monica CA 90404, USA

**Akers, Angie** — Volleyball Player
Gaylord Sports Mgmt, 13845 N Northsight Blvd, #200, Scottsdale AZ 85260 USA
**Akers, David R** — Football Player
16 Penhale Passage, Medford NJ 08055, USA
**Akers, John F** — Businessman
PO Box 194, Pebble Beach CA 93953, USA
**Akers, Michelle A** — Soccer Player
1690 Tallapoosa Dr, Geneva FL 32732, USA
**Akers, Thomas D (Tom)** — Astronaut
HC 3 Box 35, Eminence MO 65466, USA
**Akerson, Daniel F** — Businessman
General Motors Corp, Renaissance Center, Detroit MI 48243, USA
**Akey, Lisa** — Actress
Metropolitan Talent Agency, 5405 Wilshire Blvd, #218, Los Angeles CA 90036 USA
**Akhmedow, Han A** — Prime Minister, Turkmenistan
Presidential Administration, Karl Marx 24, 744017 Ashgabat, Turkmenistan
**Akhurst, Lucy** — Actress
Emptage Hallett, 14 Rathbone Place, London W1T 1HT, England
**Akihito** — Emperor, Japan
Imperial Palace, 1-1 Chiyoda, Chiyodaku, Tokyo 100 0001, Japan
**Akil** — Rap Artist (Jurassic 5)
Vision Entertainment Group, 1100 Glendon Ave, #1100, Los Angeles CA 90024, USA
**Akilov, Akil G** — Prime Minister, Tajikistan
Prime Minister's Office, Rudaki Prospect 42, 743051 Dushaube, Tajikistan
**Akin, Fatih** — Director, Producer, Actor
Corazon International, Ditmar-Koel-Str 26, 20459 Hamburg, Germany
**Akinnagbe, Gbenga** — Actor
Stone Manners Salners, 9911 W Pico Blvd, #1400, Los Angeles CA 90035 USA
**Akinnuoye-Agbaje, Adewale** — Actor
A P A Talent/Literary Agency, 250 W 57th St, #1701, New York NY 10107 USA
**Akinradewo, Foluke A** — Volleyball Player
1181 NW 101st Way, Plantation FL 33322, USA
**Akins, Christopher D (Chris)** — Football Player
60 Gold Mine Springs Road, Conway AR 72032, USA
**Akins, Rhett** — Singer
R P M Mgmt, 209 10th Ave S, #229, Nashville TN 37203, USA
**Akishino** — Prince, Japan
Imperial Palace, 1-1 Chiyoda, Chiyodaku, Tokyo 100, Japan
**Akiyama, Kazuyoshi** — Conductor
Columbia Artists Mgmt Inc, 1790 Broadway, #702, New York NY 10019 USA
**Akiyoshi, Toshiko** — Jazz Pianist, Composer
38 W 94th St, New York NY 10025, USA
**Akon** — Singer, Songwriter
H G X Marketing, 307 W 38th St, #807, New York NY 10018, USA
**Akpan, Uwem** — Writer
Little Brown, 3 Center Plaza, #100, Boston MA 02108 USA
**Akram, Omar** — Singer
Real Music, 85 Liberty Ship Way, #207, Sausalito CA 94965, USA
**Akre, Carrie** — Singer
Good-Ink Records, 203 Underhill Ave, #3D, Brooklyn NY 11238, USA
**Aksyonov, Vladimir V** — Cosmonaut
Astrakhansky Per 5, Kv 100, 129010 Moscow, Russia
**Al Hussein** — Crown Prince, Jordan
Royal Palace, Royal Hashemite Court, Amman, Jordan
**Alabau Neira, Marina** — Yachtswoman
Real Federacion Espanola de Vela, Luis de Salazar 9, 28002 Madrid, Spain
**Alagna, Roberto** — Opera Singer
Askonas Holt, Lincoln House, 300 High Holborn, London WC1V 7JH, England
**Alaia, Azzeddine** — Fashion Designer
7 Rue de Moussy, 75002 Paris, France
**Alarcon, Arthur L** — Judge
US Court of Appeals, 312 N Spring St, #G33, Los Angeles CA 90012, USA
**Alarie, Mark S** — Basketball Player, Coach
8514 Country Club Dr, Bethesda MD 20817, USA
**Alas, Mert** — Photographer
Art Partner, 155 6th Ave, #1500, New York NY 10013, USA
**Alazzqui, Carlos** — Actor, Writer
Sovereign Talent Group, 8421 Wilshire Blvd, #200, Beverly Hills CA 90211 USA
**Alba, Jessica** — Actress
W M E Entertainment, 9601 Wilshire Blvd, #300, Beverly Hills CA 90210 USA
**Alban, Carlo** — Actor
Don Buchwald, 6500 Wilshire Blvd, #2200, Los Angeles CA 90048 USA
**Alban, Richard H (Dick)** — Football Player
306 Belpaire Court, Newtown Square PA 19073, USA
**Albanese, Licia** — Opera Singer
800 Park Ave, New York NY 10021, USA
**Albarn, Damon** — Singer (Blur, Gorillaz); Songwriter
C M O Mgmt, Shepherds East, Richmond Way, London W14 0DQ, England
**Albeck, C Stanley (Stan)** — Basketball Coach
130 Tall Oak Dr, San Antonio TX 78232, USA
**Albee, Arden L** — Space Scientist, Geologist
2040 Midlothian Dr, Altadena CA 91001, USA
**Albee, Edward F** — Writer
14 Harrison St, New York NY 10013, USA
**Albelin, Tommy** — Ice Hockey Player
23 Fellswood Dr, Verona NJ 07044, USA
**Alberghetti, Anna Maria** — Singer, Actress
10755 Massachusetts Ave, #204, Los Angeles CA 90024, USA
**Albers, Kristi** — Golfer
5872 Via Cuesta Dr, El Paso TX 79912, USA
**Alberstein, Chava** — Singer
Aviv Productions, 10418 E Meadowhill Dr, Scottsdale AZ 85255, USA
**Albert II** — King, Belgium
Koninklijk Palais, Rue de Brederode, 1000 Brussels, Belgium
**Albert II** — Prince, Monaco
Palais de Monaco, BP 518, 98015 Monaco Cedex, Monaco

V.I.P. Address Book

**Albert, Arthur** — Cinematographer
707 Haverford Ave, Pacific Palisades CA 90272, USA
**Albert, Jason** — Singer (Heartland)
Country Thunder Records, 1016 17th Ave S, Nashville TN 37212, USA
**Albert, Jodie** — Actress, Singer
Susan Angel & Kevin Francis, 12 D'Arblay St, London W1F 8DU, England
**Albert, John** — Writer
Simon & Schuster, 1230 Ave of Americas, Concourse 1, New York NY 10020, USA
**Albert, John G** — Air Force General
Albert Farms, RR 2, Monroe VA 24574, USA
**Albert, Kenny** — Sportscaster
Fox-TV, Sports Dept, 205 W 67th St, New York NY 10065 USA
**Albert, Marv** — Sportscaster
TNT-TV, Sports Dept, 1050 Techwood Dr, Atlanta GA 30318 USA
**Alberti, Maryse** — Cinematographer
Dattner Dispoto, 10635 Santa Monica Blvd, #165, Los Angeles CA 90025, USA
**Alberti, Micah** — Actor
Innovative Artists, 1505 10th St, Santa Monica CA 90401 USA
**Alberts, Bruce M** — Foundation Executive, Biochemist
National Academy of Sciences, 500 5th St NW, #1, Washington DC 20001, USA
**Alberts, Trev K** — Football Player
University of Nebraska, Athletic Dept, Omaha, NE 68106, USA
**Albertsen, Jordan** — Director, Writer
Paradigm Agency, 360 N Crescent Dr, North Building, Beverly Hills CA 90210 USA
**Alberty, Robert A** — Chemist
1573 Cambridge St, #605, Cambridge MA 02138, USA
**Albita** — Singer, Songwriter
Albita Rodriguez Enterprises, 5825 SW 8th St, #200, Miami FL 33144, USA
**Albom, Mitch** — Writer
Hyperion Books, 114 5th Ave, New York NY 10011 USA
**Alborn, Alan** — Ski Jumper
PO Box 109, Willow AK 99688, USA
**Albrecht, A Chim** — Body Builder
Physique Promotions, 9668 Moss Glen Ave, Fountain Valley CA 92708, USA
**Albrecht, Gerd** — Conductor
Hamburg Opera, Grosse Theaterstr 34, 20354 Hamburg, Germany
**Albrecht, Karl H** — Businessman
Aldi Einkauf GmbH, Burgstr 37-39, 45476 Muelheim, Germany
**Albrecht, Marc** — Conductor
I M G Artists, Hogarth Business Park, Chiswick, London W4 2TH, England
**Albrecht, Stan L** — Educator
Utah State University, President's Office, Logan UT 84322, USA
**Albrecht, Theodore C (Ted)** — Football Player
1205 Cherry St, Winnetka IL 60093, USA
**Albright, Christopher J (Chris)** — Soccer Player
Philadelphia Union, Union Field, Seaport Dr, Chester PA 19013 USA
**Albright, Gerald** — Jazz Saxophonist, Singer
Chapman & Co Mgmt, PO Box 55246, Sherman Oaks CA 91413, USA
**Albright, Jack L** — Animal Scientist
839 E Village Dr, Carmel IN 46032, USA
**Albright, L Ethan** — Football Player
19181 Ferry Field Terrace, Leesburg VA 20176, USA
**Albright, Madeleine K** — Secretary, State
Albright Stonebridge Group, 1101 New York Ave NW, #900, Washington DC 20005, USA
**Albright, Tenley E** — Figure Skater
70 Suffolk Road, Chestnut Hill MA 02467, USA
**Albuquerque, Lita** — Artist
Art Center College of Design, 1700 Lida St, Pasadena CA 91103, USA
**Albus, Jim** — Golfer
3972 Somerset Dr, #1, Sarasota FL 34242, USA
**Alcaraz, Lalo** — Editorial Cartoonist
PO Box 63052, Los Angeles CA 90063, USA
**Alcock, Charles** — Theoretical Physicist
Lawrence Livermore Laboratory, 7000 East St, Livermore CA 94550, USA
**Alcott, Amy S** — Golfer
323 Amalfi Dr, Santa Monica CA 90402, USA
**Alda, Alan** — Actor
I C M Partners, 10250 Constellation Blvd, #900, Los Angeles CA 90067 USA
**Alda, Rutanya** — Actress
Shallon Star Mgmt, 14320 Ventura Blvd, #624, Sherman Oaks CA 91423, USA
**Aldaco, Marco** — Architect
Paseo de la Canada 3872, Guadalajara 45129 Jalisco, Mexico
**Aldean, Jason** — Singer, Guitarist
Spalding Entertainment, 54 Music Square E, #200, Nashville TN 37203, USA
**Alden, Ginger** — Model, Actress, Singer
Ron Leyser, 25 Rolling Hill Court W, Sag Harbor NY 11963, USA
**Alden, Howard** — Jazz Guitarist
Hot Jazz Mgmt, 116 E 27th St, New York NY 10016, USA
**Alder, Berni J** — Theoretical Physicist
1245 Contra Costa Dr, El Cerrito CA 94530, USA
**Alderete, Loretta** — Golfer
80194 Delphi Court, Indio CA 92201, USA
**Alderfer-Benner, Gertrude** — Baseball Player
2191 County Line Road, East Greenville PA 18041, USA
**Alderman, Daniel** — Drag Racing Driver
6730 Flemingsburg Road, Morehead KY 40351, USA
**Alderman, Darrell** — Auto Racing Driver
D A Construction, 8145 Flemingsburg Road, Morehead KY 40351, USA
**Alderman, Grady C** — Football Player
62 Elk Valley Way, Evergreen CO 80439, USA
**Aldisert, Ruggero J** — Judge
120 Cremona Dr, #D, Santa Barbara CA 93117, USA
**Aldiss, Brian W** — Writer
Hambledon, 39 Saint Andrews Road, Old Headington, Oxford OX3 9DL, England
**Aldred, Scott W** — Baseball Player
13435 Lakebrook Dr, Fenton MI 48430, USA

**Aldred, Sophie** — Actress
1 Duchess St, #1, London S1N 3EE, England
**Aldrete, Michael P (Mike)** — Baseball Player
22160 Toro Hills Dr, Salinas CA 93908, USA
**Aldrich, Lance** — Cartoonist (Real Life Adventures)
Universal Press Syndicate, 4520 Main St, #700, Kansas City MO 64111 USA
**Aldridge, Allen R, Jr** — Football Player
2111 Hammenwood Dr, Missouri City TX 77489, USA
**Aldridge, Donald O** — Air Force General
1004 Lincoln Road, #168, Bellevue NE 68005, USA
**Aldridge, Edward C (Pete), Jr** — Government Official, Businessman
4308 Lorcom Lane, Arlington VA 22207, USA
**Aldridge, LaMarcus** — Basketball Player
23232 SW Stafford Hill Dr, West Linn OR 97068, USA
**Aldrin, Edwin E (Buzz), Jr** — Astronaut
10380 Wilshire Blvd, #703, Los Angeles CA 90024, USA
**Aleandro, Norma** — Actress
Blanco Encalada 1150, 1428 Buenos Aires, Argentina
**Alechinsky, Pierre** — Artist
2 Bis Rue Henri Barbusse, 78380 Bougival, France
**Alejandro, Kevin** — Actor
Gersh Agency, 9465 Wilshire Blvd, #600, Beverly Hills CA 90212 USA
**Alekna, Virgilijus** — Track Athlete
Prime Minister's Office, Tumo-Vaizganto 2, 01511 Vilnius, Lithuania
**Aleksander, Grant** — Actor
Abrams Artists, 9200 W Sunset Blvd, #1125, West Hollywood CA 90069 USA
**Aleksandrov, Aleksandr P** — Cosmonaut
Space Research Institute, 6 Moskovska St, BG1000 Sofia, Bulgaria
**Aleksinas, Charles (Chuck)** — Basketball Player
16 Litchfield Road, Morris CT 06763, USA
**Aleksiy II** — Religious Leader
Moscow Patriarchate, Chisty Per 5, 119034 Moscow, Russia
**Alencherry, George Cardinal** — Religious Leader
Via Torino 94, 00184 Rome Lazio, Italy
**Alerlof, George** — Nobel Economics Laureate
University of California, Economics Dept, Berkeley CA 94720, USA
**Alesi, Jean** — Auto Racing Driver
A F Corse Srl, Via Farnesiana 242/B, 29100 Piacenza, Italy
**Alesi, Tommy** — Percussionist (BeauSoleil)
Rosebud Agency, PO Box 170429, San Francisco CA 94117 USA
**Alessi, Raquel** — Actress
Vincent Cirrincione Assoc, 1516 N Fairfax Ave, Los Angeles CA 90046 USA
**Alessio, Josephine** — Actress
Giuseppino Alessio, Via Aquara 75, 84020 Bellosguardo, Italy
**Alexakis, Art** — Singer, Guitarist (Everclear)
Pinnacle Entertainment, 30 Glenn St, White Plains NY 10603, USA
**Alexander** — Crown Prince, Yugoslavia
Royal Palace, Dedinje, 11040 Belgrade, Serbia
**Alexander, A J** — Model, Actress
Playboy Promotions, 2706 Media Center Dr, Los Angeles CA 90065 USA
**Alexander, Brooke** — Actress, Model
Abrams Artists, 9200 W Sunset Blvd, #1125, West Hollywood CA 90069 USA
**Alexander, Bruce E** — Football Player
508 Englewood Dr, Lufkin TX 75901, USA
**Alexander, Charles F, Jr** — Football Player
3711 Heritage Colony Dr, Missouri City TX 77459, USA
**Alexander, Christopher W J** — Architect
2701 Shasta Road, Berkeley CA 94708, USA
**Alexander, Claire** — Ice Hockey Player
11 Tammy Circle, Saint Catherines ON L2N 1R2, Canada
**Alexander, Claudia** — Space Scientist
Jet Propulsion Laboratory, 4800 Oak Grove Dr, Pasadena CA 91109 USA
**Alexander, Clifford L, Jr** — Government Official
Alexander Assoc, 400 C St NE, Washington DC 20002, USA
**Alexander, Dan L** — Football Player
58520 Saint Clement Ave, Plaquemine LA 70764, USA
**Alexander, Derrick** — Football Player
5301 Gulf Blvd, #E303, Saint Pete Beach FL 33706, USA
**Alexander, Derrick S** — Football Player
25381 W 149th Court, Olathe KS 66061, USA
**Alexander, Doyle L** — Baseball Player
5416 Hunter Park Court, Arlington TX 76017, USA
**Alexander, Eliana** — Actress
Talent Works, 3500 W Olive Ave, #1400, Burbank CA 91505 USA
**Alexander, Elizabeth** — Writer
Yale University, English Dept, New Haven CT 06520, USA
**Alexander, Emily** — Model, Actress
Playboy Promotions, 2706 Media Center Dr, Los Angeles CA 90065 USA
**Alexander, Eric** — Jazz Saxophonist
Joel Chriss Co, 300 Mercer St, #3J, New York NY 10003 USA
**Alexander, Erika** — Actress
Untitled Entertainment, 350 S Beverly Dr, #200, Beverly Hills CA 90212 USA
**Alexander, Flex** — Actor
Global Artists Agency, 6253 Hollywood Blvd, #508, Los Angeles CA 90028 USA
**Alexander, Gary W** — Baseball Player
5420 Senford Ave, Los Angeles CA 90056, USA
**Alexander, Jaimie** — Actress
W M E Entertainment, 9601 Wilshire Blvd, #300, Beverly Hills CA 90210 USA
**Alexander, James** — Bassist (Bar-Kays)
Entertainment Artists, 2409 21st Ave S, #100, Nashville TN 10019 USA
**Alexander, Jane** — Actress, Government Official
W M E Entertainment, 9601 Wilshire Blvd, #300, Beverly Hills CA 90210 USA
**Alexander, Jason** — Actor, Comedian
Innovative Artists, 1505 10th St, Santa Monica CA 90401 USA
**Alexander, Jesse** — Producer, Writer
Creative Artists Agency, 2000 Ave of Stars, #100, Los Angeles CA 90067 USA

**Alexander, Jessica (Jessi)** — Singer, Songwriter
W M E Entertainment, 1600 Division St, #300, Nashville TN 37203 USA
**Alexander, Jim** — Actor
Associated International Mgmt, 7 Hatton Garden, #400, London EC1N 8AD, England
**Alexander, Joe A** — Basketball Player
Chicago Bulls, United Center, 1901 W Madison St, Chicago IL 60612 USA
**Alexander, John E** — Artist
University of Houston, Art Dept, 4800 Calhoun, Houston TX 77004, USA
**Alexander, Jules** — Musician (Association)
Variety Artists, 1924 Spring St, Paso Robles CA 93446 USA
**Alexander, Kala** — Actor, Surfer
Innovative Artists, 235 Park Ave S, #1000, New York NY 10003 USA
**Alexander, Kermit J** — Football Player
16651 Stallion Place, Riverside CA 92504, USA
**Alexander, Manuel D (Manny)** — Baseball Player
3660 N Lake Dr, #2664, Chicago IL 60613, USA
**Alexander, Matthew (Matt)** — Baseball Player
2419 Stonewall St, Shreveport LA 71103, USA
**Alexander, Maximillian** — Actor
Kritzer Levine Wilkins Griffin, 11872 La Grange Ave, #100, Los Angeles CA 90025 USA
**Alexander, Monty** — Jazz Pianist
Abby Hoffer, 223 1/2 E 48th St, New York NY 10017, USA
**Alexander, Peter** — Sculptor
1811 16th St, Santa Monica CA 90404, USA
**Alexander, R Brent** — Football Player
349 Remington Ave, Gallatin TN 37066, USA
**Alexander, R Minter** — Air Force General
824 Eden Court, Alexandria VA 22308, USA
**Alexander, Sarah** — Actress
Independent Talent Group, 40 Whitfield St, London W1T 2RH, England
**Alexander, Sasha** — Actress
United Talent Agency, U T A Plaza, 9336 Civic Center Dr, Beverly Hills CA 90210 USA
**Alexander, Shaun** — Football Player
13655 NE 36th Place, Bellevue WA 98005, USA
**Alexander, Stephen T** — Football Player
30677 Santa Fe Ave, Norman OK 73072, USA
**Alexander, Tim (Herb)** — Drummer (Perfect Circle, Primus)
Creative Artists Agency, 2000 Ave of Stars, #100, Los Angeles CA 90067 USA
**Alexander, V Raymond (Ray)** — Football Player
1631 Royal Palm Dr, Edgewater FL 32132, USA
**Alexander, Willie** — Bassist, Guitarist (Velvet Underground)
Toumaline Music Group, 894 Mayville Road, Bethel PA 19507, USA
**Alexander, Willie J** — Football Player
7219 Holder Forest Circle, Houston TX 77088, USA
**Alexandre, Maxime** — Cinematographer
Partos Co, 227 Broadway, #204, Santa Monica CA 90401, USA
**Alexeev, Dmitri K** — Concert Pianist
I M G Artists, Hogarth Business Park, Chiswick, London W4 2TH, England
**Alexeev, Nikita** — Ice Hockey Player
PO Box 3342, Riverview FL 33568, USA
**Alexeev, Nikolai G** — Conductor
Estonian National Symphony, Estonia Ave 4, 10148 Tallinn, Estonia
**Alexeyeva, Lyudmila M** — Social Activist, Historian
Moscow Prison Reform Center, Luchnikov Lane 4, Entrance 3, 101000 Moscow, Russia
**Alexie, Sherman** — Writer
PO Box 376, Wellpinit WA 99040, USA
**Alexi-Malle, Adam** — Actor
Innovative Artists, 1505 10th St, Santa Monica CA 90401 USA
**Alexis, Kim** — Model
Axiom Sports & Entertainment, 28 W 44th St, #1600, New York NY 10036, USA
**Alexrod, Albert** — Fencer
798 Heritage Hills, #A, Somers NY 10589, USA
**Alfaro, Andreu** — Sculptor
Urbanizacion Sta Barbara 138R, 46111 Rocafort, Valencia, Spain
**Alfaro, Victor** — Fashion Designer
130 Barrow St, New York NY 10014, USA
**Alferov, Zhores** — Nobel Physics Laureate
Zhakia Duclo Str 8/3-82, 194223 Saint Petersburg, Russia
**Alfieri, Janet** — Cartoonist (Suburban Cowgirls)
15 Bumpus Road, Plymouth MA 02360, USA
**Alfieri, Victor** — Actor
Metropolitan Talent Agency, 5405 Wilshire Blvd, #218, Los Angeles CA 90036 USA
**Alfonseca, Antonio** — Baseball Player
3020 SW 169th Terrace, Miramar FL 33029, USA
**Alfonso, Kristian** — Actress
I C M Partners, 10250 Constellation Blvd, #900, Los Angeles CA 90067 USA
**Alfonzo, Edgardo A** — Baseball Player
3745 Marietta Way, Saint Cloud FL 34772, USA
**Alford, Steve** — Basketball Player, Coach
11600 Zinfandel Ave NE, Albuquerque NM 87122, USA
**Alford, William P** — Attorney, Writer
Harvard University, International Legal Studies, Cambridge MA 02138, USA
**Alfredson, Tomas** — Director
Cinetic Mgmt, 555 W 25th St, #400, New York NY 10001, USA
**Alfredsson, H Daniel** — Ice Hockey Player
C A A Hockey, 822 11th Ave SW, #204, Calgary AB T2R 0E5, Canada
**Alfredsson, Helen** — Golfer
9034 Crichton Woods Dr, Orlando FL 32819, USA
**Algabid, Hamid** — Prime Minister, Niger
National Assembly, Vice President's Office, Niamey, Niger
**Alger, Pat** — Singer, Guitarist, Songwriter
A S C A P, 1 Lincoln Plaza, New York NY 10023, USA
**Algotsson Ostholt, Sara** — Equestrian
Vohren 31, 482 31 Warendorf, Sweden
**Ali, Aires B B** — Prime Minister, Mozambique
Prime Minister's Office, Avenida Julius Nyerere 1780, Maputo, Mozambique

**Ali, Laila** — Boxer
She Bee Stingin Inc, 20929 Ventura Blvd, #47-432, Woodland Hills CA 91364, USA

**Ali, Monica** — Writer
Charles Scribner's Sons, 866 3rd Ave, New York NY 10022 USA

**Ali, Muhammad** — Boxer
PO Box 160, Berrien Springs MI 49103, USA

**Ali, Robin** — Ophthalmologist
Moorfields Eye Hospital, 162 City Road, London EC1V 2PD, England

**Ali, Tatyana** — Singer, Actress
Innovative Artists, 1505 10th St, Santa Monica CA 90401 USA

**Alibar, Lucy** — Writer
Gersh Agency, 9465 Wilshire Blvd, #600, Beverly Hills CA 90212 USA

**Alicea de Jesus, Luis R** — Baseball Player
2140 C Road, Loxahatchee FL 33470, USA

**Alis, Robert** — Cinematographer
13920 72nd Road, Flushing NY 11367, USA

**Alisha** — Singer, Songwriter
International Artists, PO Box 32, 5360 Grave AA, Netherlands

**Alison, Jane** — Writer
Farrar Straus Giroux, 18 W 18th St, #700, New York NY 10011 USA

**Alito, Samuel A, Jr** — Supreme Court Justice
US Supreme Court, 1 1st St NE, Washington DC 20543 USA

**Aliyev, Ilham** — President, Azerbaijan
President's Office, Istiglaliyyat St 19, 371066 Baku, Azerbaijan

**Allain, William A** — Governor, MS
970 Morningside St, Jackson MS 39202, USA

**Allan, Gabrielle** — Producer, Writer
United Talent Agency, U T A Plaza, 9336 Civic Center Dr, Beverly Hills CA 90210 USA

**Allan, Gary** — Singer, Guitarist
H B Public Relations & Mgmt, 4611 Dakota Ave, Nashville TN 37209, USA

**Allan, James** — Singer, Guitarist (Glasvegas)
Sony Music, 9 Derry St, London W8 5HY, England

**Allan, Jed** — Actor
477 White Horse Trail, Palm Desert CA 92211, USA

**Allan, Jennifer** — Model
Playboy Promotions, 2706 Media Center Dr, Los Angeles CA 90065 USA

**Allan, Mitch** — Singer, Guitarist (SR-71); Songwriter
Supreme Entertainment Artists, PO Box 15601, Boston MA 02215, USA

**Allan, Rab** — Singer, Guitarist (Glasvegas)
Sony Music, 9 Derry St, London W8 5HY, England

**Allan, William G** — Artist
73 Ranch Road, San Rafael CA 94903, USA

**Allard, Beatrice (Bea)** — Baseball Player
1040 Ridgewood Dr, Lillian AL 36549, USA

**Allard, Linda M** — Fashion Designer
Ellen Tracy Corp, 575 Fashion Ave, #300, New York NY 10018, USA

**Allbaugh, Joseph** — Government Official
Federal Emergency Management Agency, 500 C St SW, Washington DC 20472, USA

**Allegre, Claude J** — Geochemist
Institut de France, 23 Quai Conti, 75006 Paris, France

**Allegre, Raul E** — Football Player
6500 Rain Creek Parkway, Austin TX 78759, USA

**Allem, Fulton P** — Golfer
6786 Hidden Glade Place, Sanford FL 32771, USA

**Allen, Aleisha** — Actress
Jordan Gill Dornbaum Agency, 1133 Broadway, #623, New York NY 10010, USA

**Allen, Amy** — Actress
PO Box 8081, Calabasas CA 91372, USA

**Allen, Andrew M** — Astronaut
205 Highland Woods Dr, Safety Harbor FL 34695, USA

**Allen, Anthony (Tony)** — Basketball Player
70 Kodiak Way, #2638, Waltham MA 02451, USA

**Allen, Anthony D** — Football Player
956 20th Ave, Seattle WA 98122, USA

**Allen, Ashley** — Model
Playboy Promotions, 2706 Media Center Dr, Los Angeles CA 90065 USA

**Allen, Bernard K (Bernie)** — Baseball Player
3725 Coventry Way, Carmel IN 46033, USA

**Allen, Bruce** — Auto Racing Driver
Reher-Morrison Racing Engines, 1120 Enterprise Place, Arlington TX 76001, USA

**Allen, Bryan** — Ice Hockey Player
6635 NW 122nd Ave, Parkland FL 33076, USA

**Allen, C Keith (Bingo)** — Ice Hockey Coach, Executive
20011 Sanibel View Circle, #201, Fort Myers FL 33908, USA

**Allen, Chad** — Actor
Kazarian/Measures/Ruskin, 11969 Ventura Blvd, #300, Studio City CA 91604 USA

**Allen, Charles R (Chuck)** — Football Player
192 Victoria Loop, Port Townsend WA 98368, USA

**Allen, Christa B** — Actress
Maydew & Golenberg, 8383 Wilshire Blvd, #1050, Beverly Hills CA 90211, USA

**Allen, Dalva R** — Football Player
337 Daingerfield St, Pittsburg TX 75686, USA

**Allen, Davis** — Interior Designer
Skidmore Owings Merrill, 14 Wall St, #2500, New York NY 10005, USA

**Allen, Debbie** — Dancer, Singer, Actress
Red Bird Productions, 3623 Hayden Ave, Culver City CA 90232, USA

**Allen, Deborah** — Singer
104 Broadley Court, Franklin TN 37069, USA

**Allen, Dennis** — Football Coach
Oakland Raiders, 1220 Harbor Bay Parkway, Alameda CA 94502 USA

**Allen, Dion** — Singer (Az Yet)
Richard Walters, PO Box 2789, Toluca Lake CA 91610 USA

**Allen, Doug** — Artist
Fantagraphics Books, 7563 Lake City Way NE, Seattle WA 98115, USA

**Allen, Duane D** — Singer (Oak Ridge Boys)
88 New Shackle Island Road, Hendersonville TN 37075, USA

**Allen, Elizabeth Anne** — Actress
Boutique, 3034 Havrone Way, Lawrence KS 66047, USA
**Allen, Eric A** — Football Player
484 San Elijo St, San Diego CA 92106, USA
**Allen, George F** — Senator, Governor, VA
4296 Neitzey Place, Alexandria VA 22309, USA
**Allen, Geri** — Jazz Pianist, Composer
Clayton Ross Productions, 508 Shoreline Highway, Mill Valley CA 94941, USA
**Allen, Ginger Lynn** — Actress
Schiowitz Connor, 1680 N Vine St, #1016, Los Angeles CA 90028 USA
**Allen, Giselle** — Opera Singer
Hazard Chase, 25 City Road, Cambridge CB1 1DP, England
**Allen, Harold A (Hank)** — Baseball Player
PO Box 4612, Upper Marlboro MD 20775, USA
**Allen, Henry** — Critic
Washington Post, Editorial Dept, 1150 15th St NW, Washington DC 20071 USA
**Allen, India** — Actress, Model
Playboy Promotions, 2706 Media Center Dr, Los Angeles CA 90065 USA
**Allen, J Carl** — Football Player
1614 Hornsby Ave, Saint Louis MO 63147, USA
**Allen, J Randall (Randy)** — Basketball Player
10185 Nichols Lake Road, Milton FL 32583, USA
**Allen, Jackie** — Singer
Dan Cleary Mgmt, 6399 Wilshire Blvd, #1019, Los Angeles CA 90048, USA
**Allen, Jared S** — Football Player
2303 Silver Breeze Court, San Jose CA 95138, USA
**Allen, Jason J** — Football Player
Cincinnati Bengals, 1 Paul Brown Stadium, Cincinnati OH 45202 USA
**Allen, Jennifer** — Sportscaster
N F L Network, 10950 Washington Blvd, #100, Culver City CA 90232 USA
**Allen, Joan** — Actress
I C M Partners, 10250 Constellation Blvd, #900, Los Angeles CA 90067 USA
**Allen, Joseph P, IV** — Astronaut
N A S A, Johnson Space Center, 2101 NASA Road, Houston TX 77058 USA
**Allen, Karen** — Actress
Hyler Mgmt, 20 Ocean Park Blvd, #25, Santa Monica CA 90405 USA
**Allen, Keegan** — Actor
A P A Talent/Literary Agency, 405 S Beverly Dr, #300, Beverly Hills CA 90212 USA
**Allen, Keith** — Actor, Comedian
Independent Talent Group, 40 Whitfield St, London W1T 2RH, England
**Allen, Kevin** — Director, Actor
United Talent Agency, U T A Plaza, 9336 Civic Center Dr, Beverly Hills CA 90210 USA
**Allen, Kevin** — Singer, Guitarist (And You Will Know Us)
Kork Agency, 1880 Century Park E, #711, Los Angeles CA 90067 USA
**Allen, Kris** — Singer
Sony Records, 550 Madison Ave, #600, New York NY 10022 USA
**Allen, Krista** — Actress, Model
A K A Talent, 6310 San Vicente Blvd, #200, Los Angeles CA 90048, USA
**Allen, L Patrick** — Football Player
20801 32nd Lane S, #A, Seatac WA 98198, USA
**Allen, Larry C** — Football Player
7 Shelby Hill Lane, Danville CA 94526, USA
**Allen, Laura** — Actress
Gersh Agency, 9465 Wilshire Blvd, #600, Beverly Hills CA 90212 USA
**Allen, Leopold R (Leo)** — Actor, Comedian, Writer
Generate, 1545 26th St, #200, Santa Monica CA 90404, USA
**Allen, Lily R B** — Singer, Songwriter
Paradigm Agency, 360 N Crescent Dr, North Building, Beverly Hills CA 90210 USA
**Allen, Lloyd C** — Baseball Player
2340 Castlewood Dr, Toledo OH 43613, USA
**Allen, Loy, Jr** — Auto Racing Driver
323 Lochside Dr, Cary NC 27518, USA
**Allen, Lucas G (Luke)** — Baseball Player
282 Cooper Road, Social Circle GA 30025, USA
**Allen, Lucius O** — Basketball Player
1915 Buckingham Road, Los Angeles CA 90016, USA
**Allen, Malik** — Basketball Player
Orlando Magic, 8701 Maitland Summit Blvd, Orlando FL 32810 USA
**Allen, Marcus L** — Football Player, Sportscaster
9536 Wilshire Blvd, #300, Beverly Hills CA 90212, USA
**Allen, Marty** — Actor, Comedian
3847 Tropical Vine St, Las Vegas NV 89147, USA
**Allen, Maryon P** — Senator, AL
1551 Creekstone Circle, Birmingham AL 35243, USA
**Allen, Michael L** — Golfer
5827 E Anderson Dr, Scottsdale AZ 85254, USA
**Allen, Nancy** — Actress
Bauman Redanty Shaul Agency, 5757 Wilshire Blvd, #473, Los Angeles CA 90036 USA
**Allen, Neil P** — Baseball Player
3619 Torrey Pines Blvd, Sarasota FL 34238, USA
**Allen, Patrick L** — Governor General, Jamaica
Governor General's Office, King's House, Hope Road, Kingston 10, Jamaica
**Allen, Paul G** — Co-Developer (PC Language)
6451 W Mercer Way, Mercer Island WA 98040, USA
**Allen, Rae** — Actress
Kyle Fritz Mgmt, 6325 Heather Dr, Los Angeles CA 90068 USA
**Allen, Rex, Jr** — Singer
Leroy Van Dyke Enterprises, 29000 Highway V, Smithton MO 65350, USA
**Allen, Richard** — Actor
89 Saltergate, Chesterfield S40 IUS, England
**Allen, Richard A (Richie)** — Baseball Player
PO Box 254, Wampum PA 16157, USA
**Allen, Richard J (Rick)** — Drummer (Def Leppard)
Front Line Mgmt, 1100 Glendon Ave, #2000, Los Angeles CA 90024 USA
**Allen, Richard V** — Government Official
1615 L St NW, #900, Washington DC 20036, USA

**Allen, Robert E** — Businessman
11 Country Road W, Boynton Beach FL 33436, USA
**Allen, Robert G (Bob)** — Baseball Player
PO Box 667, Tatum TX 75691, USA
**Allen, Robert J (Bob)** — Basketball Player
117 Quarter Mile Way, Nicholasville KY 40356, USA
**Allen, Rosalind** — Actress
A K A Talent Agency, 6310 San Vicente Blvd, #200, Los Angeles CA 90048, USA
**Allen, Scott** — Figure Skater
511 Knickerbocker Road, Tenafly NJ 07670, USA
**Allen, Sian Barbara** — Actress
1411 NE 16th Ave, #219, Portland OR 97232, USA
**Allen, Taje L** — Football Player
1209 Valorie Court, Cedar Park TX 78613, USA
**Allen, Ted** — Entertainer
W M E Entertainment, 1325 Ave of Americas, New York NY 10019 USA
**Allen, Teddy G** — Army General
6900 Shackle Place, Burke VA 22015, USA
**Allen, Terry** — Singer (Stamps Quartet)
PO Box 1471, Brentwood TN 37024, USA
**Allen, Terry** — Artist, Songwriter
Route 10 Box 88N, Santa Fe NM 87501, USA
**Allen, Terry T, Jr** — Football Player
3176 Sable Ridge Dr, Buford GA 30519, USA
**Allen, Tessa** — Actress
Abrams Artists, 9200 W Sunset Blvd, #1125, West Hollywood CA 90069 USA
**Allen, Thomas B** — Opera Singer
Askonas Holt, Lincoln House, 300 High Holborn, London WC1V 7JH, England
**Allen, Tim** — Actor, Comedian
Boxing Cat Productions, 11500 Hart St, North Hollywood CA 91605, USA
**Allen, W Ray** — Basketball Player, Actor
10185 Nichols Lake Road, Milton FL 32583, USA
**Allen, Will** — Football Player
Pittsburgh Steelers, 3400 S Water St, Pittsburgh PA 15203 USA
**Allen, Will D** — Football Player
2325 SW 105th Terrace, Davie FL 33324, USA
**Allen, Woody** — Actor, Comedian, Director
118 E 70th St, New York NY 10021, USA
**Allenby, Robert** — Golfer
4901 Pacifico Court, Palm Beach Gardens FL 33418, USA
**Allende, Fernando** — Actor, Singer
El Dorado Productions, PM Box 888, 425 Carr 693, Dorado PR 06646, USA
**Allende, Isabel** — Writer
92 Fernwood Dr, San Rafael CA 94901, USA
**Allen-Dutton, Jordan** — Writer
Gersh Agency, 9465 Wilshire Blvd, #600, Beverly Hills CA 90212 USA
**Allen-Meares, Paula** — Educator
University of Illinois, Chancellor's Office, 840 S Wood St, Chicago IL 60612, USA
**Allenson, Gary M** — Baseball Player
711 SE 34th St, Cape Coral FL 33904, USA
**Allert, Ty H** — Football Player
1504 County Road 308, Lexington TX 78947, USA
**Alley, Kirstie** — Actress
United Talent Agency, U T A Plaza, 9336 Civic Center Dr, Beverly Hills CA 90210 USA
**Alley, L Eugene (Gene)** — Baseball Player
10236 Steuben Dr, Glen Allen VA 23060, USA
**Alley, Steve** — Ice Hockey Player
545 College Road, Lake Forest IL 60045, USA
**Allford, Simon** — Architect
232 Bickenhall Mansions, Bickenhall St, London W1V 6BW, England
**Allison, Brooke** — Singer, Songwriter
2 K/E M I America Records, 6920 Sunset Blvd, Los Angeles CA 90028, USA
**Allison, David B (Dave)** — Ice Hockey Player, Coach
Iowa Stars, 833 5th Ave, Des Moines IA 50309, USA
**Allison, Dorothy** — Writer
Penguin Putnam, 375 Hudson St, New York NY 10014, USA
**Allison, Dunkiny (Donnie)** — Auto Racing Driver
355 Quail Dr, Salisbury NC 28147, USA
**Allison, Glenn** — Bowler
1844 S Haster St, #138, Anaheim CA 92802, USA
**Allison, Graham T, Jr** — Educator
69 Pinhurst Road, Belmont MA 02478, USA
**Allison, Henry H (Hank)** — Football Player
458 W Ellis Ave, Inglewood CA 90302, USA
**Allison, Jerry** — Drummer (Crickets), Songwriter
8455 New Bethal Road, Lyles TN 37098, USA
**Allison, John A, IV** — Financier
B B & T Corp, 200 W 2nd St, #260, Winston Salem NC 27101, USA
**Allison, John V** — Vietnam War Air Force Hero
6606 Britt St, Navarre FL 32566, USA
**Allison, Margaret** — Singer
I B A Productions, 3 Av Florimont, 1829 Montreux, Switzerland
**Allison, Mike** — Ice Hockey Player
7204 Birchmont Court NE, Bemidji MN 56601, USA
**Allison, Mose J, Jr** — Jazz Pianist, Composer, Singer
82 Ballad Court, Eastport NY 11941, USA
**Allison, Odis** — Basketball Player
3162 Majestic Shadows Ave, Henderson NV 89052, USA
**Allison, Ray** — Ice Hockey Player
106 N Valleybrook Road, Cherry Hill NJ 08034, USA
**Allison, Richard C** — Judge
224 Circle Dr, Manhasset NY 11030, USA
**Allison, Robert A (Bobby)** — Auto Racing Driver
PO Box 3696, Mooresville NC 28117, USA
**Allison, Robert J, Jr** — Businessman
Anadarko Petroleum Corp, 1201 Lake Robbins Dr, Spring TX 77380, USA

**A**

Allen - Allison

**A**

| | |
|---|---|
| **Allison, Stacy** | Mountaineer |
| 6633 SE 29th Ave, Portland OR 97202, USA | |
| **Allison, Verne** | Singer (Dells) |
| Associated Booking Corp, 501 Madison Ave, #501, New York NY 10022 USA | |
| **Alliss, Peter** | Sportscaster |
| Peter Alliss Golf Ltd, PO Box 224, Surrey GU26 6WQ, England | |
| **Allman, Gregory L (Gregg)** | Singer, Musician, Songwriter |
| Allman Brothers Band Inc, 18 Tamworth Road, Waban MA 02468, USA | |
| **Allman, Jamie Anne** | Actress |
| Greene Assoc, 1901 Ave of Stars, #130, Los Angeles CA 90067 USA | |
| **Allman, Marshall** | Actor |
| Gersh Agency, 9465 Wilshire Blvd, #600, Beverly Hills CA 90212 USA | |
| **Allnutt, Robert** | Space Scientist, Biochemist |
| 5400 Edgemoor Lane, Bethesda MD 20814, USA | |
| **Allouache, Merzak** | Director |
| Cite des Asphodeles, Bt D15, 183 Ben Aknoun, Algiers, Algeria | |
| **Allred, Corbin M** | Actor |
| Aquarius Public Relations, 5320 Sylmar Ave, Sherman Oaks CA 91401, USA | |
| **Allred, Gloria R** | Attorney |
| Allred Maroko Goldberg, 6300 Wilshire Blvd, #1500, Los Angeles CA 90048, USA | |
| **Allred, Jason** | Golfer |
| 10239 E Salt Bush Dr, Scottsdale AZ 85255, USA | |
| **Allred, John** | Football Player |
| PO Box 748, Del Mar CA 92014, USA | |
| **Allyson, Karrin** | Singer, Pianist |
| Stilleto Entertainment, 5200 W 83rd St, #G, Los Angeles CA 90045, USA | |
| **al-Mansour, Haifaa** | Director |
| Anonymous Content, 3532 Hayden Ave, Culver City CA 90232 USA | |
| **Almers, Wolfhard** | Biochemist |
| Oregon Health & Science University, Vollum Institute, Portland OR 97239, USA | |
| **Almirola, Aric** | Auto Racing Driver |
| Aric Almirola Inc, 215 Overhill Dr, #A, Mooresville NC 28117, USA | |
| **Almodovar, Pedro** | Director |
| El Deseo SA, Francisco Navacerrada 24, 28028 Madrid, Spain | |
| **Almon, William F (Billy)** | Baseball Player |
| 42 Channel View, #4, Warwick RI 02889, USA | |
| **Almond, Lincoln C** | Governor, RI |
| 82 Smith St, #222, Providence RI 02903, USA | |
| **Almond, Marc** | Singer (Soft Cell), Songwriter |
| Take Out Productions, 630 9th Ave, #603, New York NY 10036, USA | |
| **Almond, Morris** | Basketball Player |
| Red Star Belgrade, Obilicev Wreath 24, Belgrade, Serbia | |
| **Almquist, John O** | Physiologist |
| 300 Lions Hill Road, #W502, State College PA 16803, USA | |
| **Almunia Amann, Joaquin** | Government Official, Spain |
| Carrera de San Jeronimo S/N 28014 Madrid, Spain | |
| **Alois** | Prince, Liechtenstein |
| Schloss Vaduz, 9490 Vaduz, Liechtenstein | |
| **Alomar, Roberto V (Robbie)** | Baseball Player |
| Urbana Monserrate B-56, PO Box 367, Salinas PR 00751, USA | |
| **Alomar, Santos C (Sandy), Jr** | Baseball Player |
| 1906 W Cortland St, Chicago IL 60622, USA | |
| **Alomar, Santos C (Sandy), Sr** | Baseball Player |
| PO Box 367, Salinas PR 00751, USA | |
| **Alonso Bernardo, Jessica** | Handball Player |
| R K Zajecar, Dositejeva 11, 19000 Zajecar, Serbia | |
| **Alonso, Adrian** | Actor |
| Featured Artists Agency, 6210 Wilshire Blvd, #311, Los Angeles CA 90048, USA | |
| **Alonso, Alicia** | Ballerina |
| National Ballet of Cuba, Calzada 510 Entre D & E, El Vedado, Havana, Cuba | |
| **Alonso, Anabel** | Actress |
| Ramon Pilaces, C/Hortaleza 20, #1 Izqda, 28004 Madrid, Spain | |
| **Alonso, Daniella** | Actress, Model |
| Gersh Agency, 9465 Wilshire Blvd, #600, Beverly Hills CA 90212 USA | |
| **Alonso, Fernando** | Auto Racing Driver |
| Carretera de Fuencarral, 14-16 Bloque C, 28108 Alcobendas, Madrid, Spain | |
| **Alonso, Laz** | Actor |
| I C M Partners, 10250 Constellation Blvd, #900, Los Angeles CA 90067 USA | |
| **Alonso, Maria Conchita** | Actress, Singer |
| Don Buchwald, 6500 Wilshire Blvd, #2200, Los Angeles CA 90048 USA | |
| **Alou, Felipe R** | Baseball Player, Manager |
| 6891 Cobia Circle, Boynton Beach FL 33437, USA | |
| **Alou, Jesus M R** | Baseball Player |
| Apartado Postal 539/2 Lafaria, Santo Domingo, Dominican Republic | |
| **Alou, Moises R** | Baseball Player |
| 13095 NW 13th St, Pembroke Pines FL 33028, USA | |
| **Alpay, David** | Actor |
| A P A Talent/Literary Agency, 405 S Beverly Dr, #300, Beverly Hills CA 90212 USA | |
| **Alpert, Herb** | Musician |
| 31930 Pacific Coast Highway, Malibu CA 90265, USA | |
| **Alpert, Joseph S** | Physician |
| 3440 E Cathedral Rock Circle, Tucson AZ 85718, USA | |
| **Alphand, Luc** | Alpine Skier |
| Chalet Le Balme, Chantemerie, 05330 Sierre Chavalier, France | |
| **Alphin, W Kenneth (Big Kenny)** | Singer, Songwriter |
| Morris Management Group, 818 19th Ave S, Nashville TN 37203, USA | |
| **Al-Saud, Abdullah** | Equestrian |
| Haras de Wisbecq, Rue de Bierghes 4, 1430 Rebecq, Belgium | |
| **Al-Sebesi, Al-Baji** | Prime Minister, Tunisia |
| Prime Minister's Office, Place du Gouvernement, Tunis, Tunisia | |
| **Alsgaard, Thomas** | Cross Country Skier |
| Cathinka Guldbergsveg 16, 2034 Holter, Norway | |
| **Alsop, Marin** | Conductor |
| Baltimore Symphony Orchestra, 1212 Cathedral St, #1, Baltimore MD 21201, USA | |
| **Alsop, William A** | Architect |
| 72 Pembroke Road, London W8 6NX, England | |

*Allison - Alsop*

**Alston Reeves, Shirley** — Singer (Shirelles)
G H R Entertainment, 6014 N Pointe Place, Woodland Hills CA 91367, USA
**Alston, Barbara** — Singer (Crystals)
Tingrassia Entertainment, PO Box 314, Holden MA 01520, USA
**Alston, Gerald** — Singer (Manhattans)
Wenig-LaMonica Associates, 580 White Plains Road, #130, Tarrytown NY 10591 USA
**Alston, Mack, Jr** — Football Player
5421 Echols Ave, Alexandria VA 22311, USA
**Alston, Rafer J** — Basketball Player
9002 Legends Lane, Missouri City TX 77459, USA
**Alstott, Michael J (Mike)** — Football Player
7800 9th Ave S, Saint Petersburg FL 33707, USA
**Alt, Carol** — Model, Actress
Scott Hart Mgmt, 14622 Ventura Blvd, #746, Sherman Oaks CA 91403, USA
**Alt, John M** — Football Player
21 Crescent Lane, Saint Paul MN 55127, USA
**Altbach, Philip G** — Sociologist
Boston College, Campion Hall, Chestnut Hill MA 02467, USA
**Alter, Harvey J** — Hematologist
National Institutes of Health, Magnuson Center, 10 Center Dr, Bethesda MD 20892, USA
**Alter, Hobie, Jr** — Surfboard, Boat Designer
PO Box 1008, Oceanside CA 92051, USA
**Alterman, Kent** — Director
Creative Artists Agency, 2000 Ave of Stars, #100, Los Angeles CA 90067 USA
**Alther, Lisa** — Writer
1086 Silver St, Hinesburg VT 05461, USA
**Althoff, Kai** — Artist
Christian Nagel Gallery, Richard-Wagner-Str 28, 50674 Cologne, Germany
**Altice, Summer** — Model, Actress
Elite Model Mgmt, 404 Park Ave S, #900, New York NY 10016 USA
**Altman, Bruce** — Actor
Don Buchwald, 6500 Wilshire Blvd, #2200, Los Angeles CA 90048 USA
**Altman, Chelsea** — Actress
Liebman Entertainment, 25 E 21st St, #PH, New York NY 10010, USA
**Altman, Jeff** — Actor, Comedian
Agency S G H, 6525 Sunset Blvd, #PH9, Los Angeles CA 90028, USA
**Altman, Scott** — Opera Singer
Columbia Artists Mgmt Inc, 1790 Broadway, #702, New York NY 10019 USA
**Altman, Scott D** — Astronaut
1247 33rd St NW, Washington DC 20007, USA
**Altman, Sidney** — Nobel Chemistry Laureate
71 Blake Road, Hamden CT 06517, USA
**Altman, Stuart H** — Educator
11 Bakers Hill Road, Weston MA 02493, USA
**Altmeyer, Jeannine T** — Opera Singer
Im Muhlader, 8709 Herrliberg, Switzerland
**Altobelli, Joseph (Joe)** — Baseball Player, Manager
10 Stowell Dr, #3, Rochester NY 14616, USA
**Alton, Kevin B** — Chemist
Schering-Plough Research, 2000 Galloping Hill Road, Kenilworth NJ 07033, USA
**Altschul, Serena** — Commentator
MTV, News Dept, 1515 Broadway, New York NY 10036, USA
**Altshuler, Alan A** — Political Scientist
Harvard University, Kennedy Government School, Cambridge MA 02138, USA
**Altwegg, Jeanette E** — Figure Skater
British Olympic Assn, 60 Charlotte St, London W1T 2NU, England
**Alusik, George J** — Baseball Player
PO Box 454, Woodbridge NJ 07095, USA
**Alvarado, Natividad (Naty)** — Handball Player
Equitable of Iowa, 2700 N Main St, Santa Ana CA 92705, USA
**Alvarez, Al** — Writer
Gillon Atkin, 18-21 Caraye Place, London SW10 9PT, England
**Alvarez, Barry** — Football Coach, Sportscaster
Fox-TV, Sports Dept, 205 W 67th St, New York NY 10065 USA
**Alvarez, George** — Actor
Michael Bruno Group, 13576 Cheltenham Dr, Sherman Oaks CA 91423, USA
**Alvarez, Isabel** — Baseball Player
7932 Everglade Court, Fort Wayne IN 46819, USA
**Alvarez, Julia** — Writer
Susan Bergholz Literary Agency, 17 W 10th St, #5N, New York NY 10011, USA
**Alvarez, Kyle Patrick** — Writer, Director
United Talent Agency, U T A Plaza, 9336 Civic Center Dr, Beverly Hills CA 90210 USA
**Alvarez, Marcelo** — Opera Singer
Zemsky/Greene Artists Mgmt, 104 W 73rd St, #1, New York NY 10023, USA
**Alvarez, Rigoberto** — Boxer
Golden Boy Promotions, 626 Wilshire Blvd, #350, Los Angeles CA 90017 USA
**Alvarez, Saul (Canelo)** — Boxer
Canelo Promotions, D Rodriguez 1667, Sec Libertad CP 44730, Guadalajara Jalisco, Mexico
**Alvarez, Wilson E** — Baseball Player
6927 Westchester Circle, Bradenton FL 34202, USA
**Alvarez-Buylla, Arturo** — Biologist
Rockefeller University Medical Center, 1230 York Ave, New York NY 10065 USA
**Alvart, Christian** — Director
Paradigm Agency, 360 N Crescent Dr, North Building, Beverly Hills CA 90210 USA
**Alverson, Tommy** — Singer, Songwriter
Ken-Ran Entertainment, 418 S Barton St, Grapevine TX 76051, USA
**Alves, Joe** — Director
Gersh Agency, 9465 Wilshire Blvd, #600, Beverly Hills CA 90212 USA
**Alves, Rick** — Musician (Pirates of the Mississippi)
Third Coast Talent, PO Box 110225, Nashville TN 37222, USA
**Alvin, Dave** — Guitarist (Blasters); Songwriter
Mongrel Music, 743 Center Blvd, Fairfax CA 94930, USA
**Alvis, R Maxwell (Max)** — Baseball Player
806 Hunterwood Dr, Jasper TX 75951, USA
**Alwaleed Bin Talal Bin Abdulaziz Alsaud** — Prince, Saudi Arabia; Businessman
Kingdom Holdings, Kingdom Centre, Al-Urubah Road, Riyadh, Saudi Arabia

**A**

**Alworth, Lance D** — Football Player
Del Mar Corporate Center, 990 Highland Dr, #300, Solana Beach CA 92075, USA

**Alyea, Garrabrant R (Brant)** — Baseball Player
125 Dobbs Place, Goldsboro NC 27534, USA

**Alys, Francis** — Artist
David Zwirner Gallery, 537 W 20th St, New York NY 10011, USA

**Alyse, Alice** — Actress, Ballerina, Model
Mademoiselle Talent Agency, 24328 Vermont Ave, #309, Harbor City CA 90710, USA

**Ama, Shola** — Singer
Concorde International, 101 Shepherds Bush Road, London W6 7LP, England

**Amadou, Hama** — Prime Minister, Niger
Prime Minister's Office, State House, BP 353, Abuja, Niger

**Amaechi, John E** — Basketball Player
5747 E Aire Libre Ave, Scottsdale AZ 85254, USA

**Amaker, H Tommy** — Basketball Player, Coach
Harvard University, Athletic Dept, Cambridge MA 02138, USA

**Amalfitano, J Joseph (Joe)** — Baseball Player, Manager
60 Sheath Dr, Sedona AZ 86336, USA

**Amalric, Mathieu** — Actor, Diector
Zelig Films, 57 Rue Reamur, 75002 Paris, France

**Aman, Zeenat** — Actress
Neelam Apts, Mount Mary Road, #300, Bandra, Mumbai MS 400050, India

**Amandes, Tom** — Actor
Paul Kohner, 9300 Wilshire Blvd, #555, Beverly Hills CA 90212 USA

**Amanpour, Christiane** — Commentator
Cable News Network, 2 Stephen St, #100, London W1P 1PL, England

**Amante, Michael** — Singer
Dera Roslan Campion, 132 Nassau St, New York NY 10038, USA

**Amara, Lucine** — Opera Singer
260 W End Ave, #7A, New York NY 10023, USA

**Amaral, Richard L (Rich)** — Baseball Player
3122 Country Club Dr, Costa Mesa CA 92626, USA

**Amaro, Ruben M, Sr** — Baseball Player
4098 Cinnamon Way, Weston FL 33331, USA

**Amato, Giuliano** — Prime Minister, Italy
Carmera dei Deputati, Piazza di Montecitorio, 00186 Rome, Italy

**Amato, Joe** — Auto Racing Driver
PO Box 615, Wilkes Barre PA 18703, USA

**Amato, Kenneth C (Ken)** — Football Player
641 Old Hickory Blvd, #305, Brentwood TN 37027, USA

**Amaury, Jean-Etienne** — Businessman, Sports Executive
Amaury Sports, 2 Rue de Lisle, 92137 Issy-le-Mounlineaux, France

**Amavia Lunkewitz, Daniela** — Actress
Global Artists Agency, 6253 Hollywood Blvd, #508, Los Angeles CA 90028 USA

**Amaya, Armando** — Sculptor
Cuauh Temoc, 168 Col Deo Carmen, Coyoacan DF 04100, Mexico

**Ambani, Mukesh** — Businessman
Reliance Industries, Makers Chambers IV, Nariman Point, 400021 Mumbai, India

**Ambasz, Emilio** — Architect
43 E 63rd St, New York NY 10065, USA

**Amber** — Singer, Songwriter
Central Entertainment Group, 166 5th Ave, #400, New York NY 10010, USA

**Ambramovich, Roman A** — Businessman
Chelsea F C, Stamford Bridge, Fulham Road, London SW6 1HS, England

**Ambro, Thomas L** — Judge
US Court of Appeals, Federal Building, 844 N King St, Wilmington DE 19801, USA

**Ambros, Victor R** — Geneticist
University of Massachusetts Medical School, 55 Lake Ave N, Worcester MA 01655, USA

**Ambrose, Ashley A** — Football Player
2726 Eudora Trail, Duluth GA 30097, USA

**Ambrose, Lauren** — Actress, Singer
United Talent Agency, U T A Plaza, 9336 Civic Center Dr, Beverly Hills CA 90210 USA

**Ambrose, Marcus** — Auto Racing Driver
Richard Petty Racing, 7065 Zephyr Place, Concord NC 28027, USA

**Ambrose, Richard J (Dick)** — Football Player
24049 Stonehedge Dr, Westlake OH 44145, USA

**Ambrosio, Alessandra** — Model, Actress
Ulla Models, Lijnbaansgracht 338-339, 1017 Amsterdam XA, Netherlands

**Ambrosius, Marsha** — Singer (Floetry), Songwriter
I C M Partners, 10250 Constellation Blvd, #900, Los Angeles CA 90067 USA

**Ambuehl, Cindy** — Actress
28343 Ave Crocker, #1, Valencia CA 91355, USA

**Amdahl, Gene M** — Computer Engineer, Businessman
620 Sand Hill Road, #212G, Palo Alto CA 94304, USA

**Amedori, John Patrick** — Actor
Gersh Agency, 9465 Wilshire Blvd, #600, Beverly Hills CA 90212 USA

**Ameling, Elly** — Concert Singer
Hubstein Artist Services, 65 W 90th St, #13F, New York NY 10024, USA

**Amelio, Gilbert F** — Businessman
13416 Middle Fork Lane, Los Altos CA 94022, USA

**Amell, Robert P (Robbie)** — Actor
I C M Partners, 10250 Constellation Blvd, #900, Los Angeles CA 90067 USA

**Amelung, Edward V (Ed)** — Baseball Player
16681 Cedar Circle, Fountain Valley CA 92708, USA

**Amen, Irving** — Artist
PO Box 812365, Boca Raton FL 33481, USA

**Amend, Bill** — Cartoonist (FoxTrot)
Universal Press Syndicate, 4520 Main St, #700, Kansas City MO 64111 USA

**Amendola, Tony** — Actor
Marc Bass Agency, 9255 W Sunset Blvd, #727, West Hollywood CA 90069, USA

**Ament, Jeff** — Bassist (Green River, Pearl Jam)
Curtis Mgmt, 1900 S Corgiat Dr, Seattle WA 98108, USA

**Amentler, James (Jim)** — Photographer
8117 Manchester Ave, #573, Playa del Rey CA 90293, USA

**Amer, Ghada** — Artist
Cheim & Read Gallery, 547 W 25th St, New York NY 10001, USA

**Alworth - Amer**

**Amer, Nicholas** — Actor
14 Great Russell St, London WC1B 3NH, England
**Amerie** — Singer, Songwriter, Actress
Feenix Entertainment, 1360 Clifton Ave, #318, Clifton NJ 07012, USA
**Ames, Bruce N** — Biochemist
1324 Spruce St, Berkeley CA 94709, USA
**Ames, Denise** — Actress
Coralie Junior Theatrical Agency, 907 S Victory Blvd, Burbank CA 91502, USA
**Ames, Ed** — Singer, Actor
Paradise Artists, PO Box 1821, Ojai CA 93024 USA
**Ames, Stephen M** — Golfer
Professional Golfer's Assn, PO Box 109601, Palm Beach Gardens FL 33410 USA
**Amick, Madchen** — Actress
Gersh Agency, 9465 Wilshire Blvd, #600, Beverly Hills CA 90212 USA
**Amigo Vallejo, Carlos Cardinal** — Religious Leader
Via Giulia 151, 00186 Rome Lazio, Italy
**Amis, Martin L** — Writer, Journalist
Wylie Agency, 17 Bedford Square, London WC1B 3JA, England
**Amis, Suzy** — Actress, Model
I C M Partners, 10250 Constellation Blvd, #900, Los Angeles CA 90067 USA
**Amlee, Jessica** — Actress
Real 2 Real Talent, 20475 Lougheed Highway, Maple Ridge BC V2X 9B6, Canada
**Amlong, Joseph** — Rowing Athlete
2445 4th Lane, Vero Beach FL 32962, USA
**Amlong, Thomas** — Rowing Athlete
166 Four Mile River Road, Old Lyme CT 06371, USA
**Ammaccapane, Danielle** — Golfer
13214 N 13th St, Phoenix AZ 85022, USA
**Ammaccapane, Dina** — Golfer
4407 E Blanche Dr, Phoenix AZ 85032, USA
**Ammachi** — Religious Leader
Amrita Institutions, Ettimadai, Coimbatore, Tamil Nadu 641105, India
**Ammann, Simon** — Ski Jumper
W W P Group, Lustenauerstra 64, 6850 Dornbirn, Austria
**Amodeo, Mike** — Ice Hockey Player
556 Fralicks Beach Road, RR 5, Port Perry ON L9L 1B6, Canada
**Amoia, Charlene** — Actress
House of Representatives, 1434 6th St, #1, Santa Monica CA 90401 USA
**Amonte, Tony** — Ice Hockey Player
PO Box 771, Humarock MA 02047, USA
**Amorello, Matthew J** — Government Administrator
Massachusettes Turnpike Authority, 10 Park Plaza, #4160, Boston MA 02116, USA
**Amorosi, Vanessa** — Singer, Songwriter
Harbour Agency, 135 Forbes Road, Woolloomooloo NSW 2011, Australia
**Amory, Misha** — Concert Violist
David Rowe Artists, 24 Bessom St, #2, Marblehead MA 01945, USA
**Amos, Daniel P (Dan)** — Businessman
A F L A C Inc, A F L A C Center, 1932 Wynnton Road, Columbus GA 31999, USA
**Amos, James F** — Marine Corps General
Commandant, HqUSMC, 2 Navy Annex, Washington DC 20380 USA
**Amos, Tori** — Singer, Pianist, Songwriter
Creative Artists Agency, 2000 Ave of Stars, #100, Los Angeles CA 90067 USA
**Amos, Wally (Famous)** — Businessman
PO Box 88323, Honolulu HI 96830, USA
**Amoyal, Pierre A W** — Concert Violinist
Jacques Thelen, 15 Ave Montaigne, 75008 Paris, France
**Amram, David W, III** — Jazz, Classical Composer, Conductor
Ed Keane Assoc, 573 Pleasant St, Winthrop MA 02152, USA
**Amrapurkar, Sadashiv** — Actor, Comedian
A/201 Panchdhara Off Yari Road, Versova Andheri, Mumbai MS 400058, India
**Amritraj, Ashok** — Actor, Producer, Writer
Hyde Park Entertainment, 16555 Sherman Way, #A1, Van Nuys CA 91406, USA
**Amritraj, Vijay** — Tennis Player
First Serve, 10/5A 13th Ave, Harrington Road, Chetpet, Chennai 600031, India
**Amsden, Ben C** — WW II Navy Air Force Hero
514 C St, Farmington MO 63640, USA
**Amsellem, Norah** — Opera Singer
Columbia Artists Mgmt Inc, 1790 Broadway, #702, New York NY 10019 USA
**Amsterdam, Anthony G** — Attorney, Educator
68 Middle Lane Highway, Southampton NY 11968, USA
**Amuka-Bird, Nikki** — Actress
Greene Assoc, 1901 Ave of Stars, #130, Los Angeles CA 90067 USA
**Amy, Susie** — Actress
Curtis Brown Group, 28-29 Haymarket St, #500, London SW1Y 4SP, England
**An Sang Mi** — Speed Skater
Skating Union, 88 Bangyee-Dong, Songpaku, Seoul 138 749, South Korea
**An Yulong** — Speed Skater
Skating Assn, 56 Zhongguancun South St, Haidian, Beijing 100044, China
**Ana Alicia** — Actress
S D B Partners, 1801 Ave of Stars, #902, Los Angeles CA 90067 USA
**Anagnostopoulos, Constantine E** — Heart Surgeon
435 Dockside Dr, #902, Naples FL 34110, USA
**Anahi** — Actress, Singer, Model
E M I Music, Rio Tigris 33, Col Cuahtemoc CP 06500, Mexico
**Anand, Vijay** — Actor, Director
Ketnav 17 Union Park Pali Hill, Khar, Mumbai MS 400052, India
**Anand, Viswanathan (Vishy)** — Chess Player
F I D E, 9 Ave de Beaumont, 1012 Lausanne, Switzerland
**Ananiashvili, Nina G** — Ballerina
Frunzenskaya Nab 46, #79, 119270 Moscow, Russia
**Anappau, Kristina** — Actress
Untitled Entertainment, 350 S Beverly Dr, #200, Beverly Hills CA 90212 USA
**Anastacia** — Singer
Braude Mgmt, PO Box 7249, San Diego CA 92167, USA
**Anastasio, Trey** — Guitarist (Phish, Oysterhead)
Red Light Mgmt, 44 Wall St, #2200, New York NY 10005, USA

**A**

**Amer - Anastasio**

| | |
|---|---|
| **Anatsui, El** | Sculptor |
| University of Nigeria, Art Dept, Nsukka, Nigeria | |
| **Anaya, Elena** | Actress |
| Kuranda Mgmt, Santo Angel 84, 28043 Madrid, Spain | |
| **Anaya, Rudolfo** | Writer |
| 5324 Canada Vista NW, Albuquerque NM 87120, USA | |
| **Anaya, Toney** | Governor, NM |
| 711 E May Ave, Las Cruces NM 88001, USA | |
| **Ancelotti, Carlo** | Soccer Player, Coach |
| F C Milan, Via Filippo Turati 3, 20121 Milan, Italy | |
| **Anchultz Thoms, Daniela** | Speed Skater |
| Eissportclub Erfurt, Arnstaedter Str 53, 99096 Erfurt, Germany | |
| **Ancona, Bill** | Drag Racing Driver |
| 260 Nelson Wyatt Road, Mansfield TX 76063, USA | |
| **Anconina, Richard** | Actor |
| Artmedia, 20 Ave Rapp, 75007 Paris, France | |
| **Anden, Mini** | Model, Actress |
| Medavoy Mgmt, 10203 Santa Monica Blvd, #400, Los Angeles CA 90067 USA | |
| **Anderegg, Robert H (Bob)** | Basketball Player |
| 11708 E Onyx Ave, Scottsdale AZ 85259, USA | |
| **Anders, Allison** | Director, Writer |
| A P A Talent/Literary Agency, 405 S Beverly Dr, #300, Beverly Hills CA 90212 USA | |
| **Anders, Andrea** | Actress |
| Abrams Artists, 9200 W Sunset Blvd, #1125, West Hollywood CA 90069 USA | |
| **Anders, David** | Actor |
| Liberman-Zerman Mgmt, 252 N Larchmont Blvd, #200, Los Angeles CA 90004 USA | |
| **Anders, Kimble L** | Football Player |
| Running Back Giving Back Foundation, 4435 Prospect Ave, Kansas City MO 64130, USA | |
| **Anders, Sean** | Director, Producer, Writer, Actor |
| Mosiac Media Group, 9200 W Sunset Blvd, #1000, Los Angeles CA 90069 USA | |
| **Anders, William A** | Astronaut, Air Force General |
| 1 Aeroview Lane, Eastsound WA 98245, USA | |
| **Andersen, Anthony L** | Businessman |
| H B Fuller Co, PO Box 64683, Saint Paul MN 55164, USA | |
| **Andersen, Christopher P** | Writer |
| Hyperion Books, 114 5th Ave, New York NY 10011 USA | |
| **Andersen, Eric** | Singer, Songwriter |
| Charles Rothschild Productions, 330 E 48th St, #2D, New York NY 10017, USA | |
| **Andersen, Greta** | Swimmer |
| 16222 Monterey Lane, #264, Huntington Beach CA 92649, USA | |
| **Andersen, Kurt** | Writer |
| Random House, 1745 Broadway, #1800, New York NY 10019 USA | |
| **Andersen, Ladell** | Basketball Coach |
| 41 W Cedar Dr, Hermiston OR 97838, USA | |
| **Andersen, Larry E** | Baseball Player |
| 2043 Sunray Circle, West Linn OR 97068, USA | |
| **Andersen, Linda** | Yachtswoman |
| Aroysund, 3135 Torod, Norway | |
| **Andersen, May** | Model |
| 2 P M Model Mgmt, Norregade 2, 1165 Copenhagen K, Denmark | |
| **Andersen, Morten** | Football Player |
| 6501 Old Shadburn Ferry Road, Buford GA 30518, USA | |
| **Andersen, Susan** | Writer |
| Jane Rotrosen Agency, 318 E 51st St, New York NY 10022, USA | |
| **Anderson, Al** | Singer, Guitarist (NRBQ) |
| Skyline Music, 2270 Maiden Lane SW, Roanoke VA 24015, USA | |
| **Anderson, Alfa** | Singer (Chic) |
| Lustig Talent, PO Box 770850, Orlando FL 32877 USA | |
| **Anderson, Alfred A** | Football Player |
| 2805 Chesterwood Court, Mansfield TX 76063, USA | |
| **Anderson, Anthony A** | Actor, Comedian, Writer |
| United Talent Agency, U T A Plaza, 9336 Civic Center Dr, Beverly Hills CA 90210 USA | |
| **Anderson, Audrey Marie** | Actress |
| I C M Partners, 10250 Constellation Blvd, #900, Los Angeles CA 90067 USA | |
| **Anderson, Bill** | Singer, Guitarist, Songwriter |
| Bill Anderson Enterprises, PO Box 888, Hermitage TN 37076, USA | |
| **Anderson, Blake** | Actor, Writer |
| United Talent Agency, U T A Plaza, 9336 Civic Center Dr, Beverly Hills CA 90210 USA | |
| **Anderson, Brad** | Drag Racing Driver |
| Brad Anderson Enterprises, 1240 S Cucamonga Ave, Ontario CA 91761, USA | |
| **Anderson, Brad** | Director |
| 422 Santa Monica Court, Escondido CA 92029, USA | |
| **Anderson, Bradbury H** | Businessman |
| Best Buy Co, 7601 Penn Ave S, Minneapolis MN 55423, USA | |
| **Anderson, Bradford** | Actor |
| Michael Enfield Mgmt, 10630 Moorpark, #101, Toluca Lake CA 91602, USA | |
| **Anderson, Bradley J (Brad)** | Cartoonist (Marmaduke) |
| 13022 Wood Harbour Dr, Montgomery TX 77356, USA | |
| **Anderson, Brady K** | Baseball Player |
| 2205 Warwick Way, #200, Marriottsville MD 21104, USA | |
| **Anderson, Brett** | Singer (Suede) |
| Lookout Records, PO Box 40828, San Francisco CA 94140, USA | |
| **Anderson, Brett F** | Baseball Player |
| Oakland Athletics, McAfee Coliseum, 7000 Coliseum Way, #3, Oakland CA 94621 USA | |
| **Anderson, Brian J** | Baseball Player |
| 3571 N Meyers Road, Geneva OH 44041, USA | |
| **Anderson, Bruce A** | Football Player |
| 910 NE Parkview Court, Roseburg OR 97470, USA | |
| **Anderson, C Neal** | Football Player |
| 10626 SW 41st Place, Gainesville FL 32608, USA | |
| **Anderson, Christine** | Singer, Pianist, Songwriter |
| Brian Lewis Presents, 781 Herman Ave, Medford OR 97501, USA | |
| **Anderson, Clarence E (Bud)** | WW II Army Air Corps Hero |
| 1060 Southridge Dr, Auburn CA 95603, USA | |
| **Anderson, Clayton C** | Astronaut |
| N A S A, Johnson Space Center, 2101 NASA Road, Houston TX 77058 USA | |

Anatsui - Anderson

**Anderson, Craig** — Guitarist (Heartland)
Country Thunder Records, 1016 17th Ave S, Nashville TN 37212, USA
**Anderson, Dale** — Ice Hockey Player
2217 Ave Haultain, Saskatoon SK S7J 1PT, Canada
**Anderson, Daniel E (Dan)** — Basketball Player
19000 NW Squirrel Tail Loop, Bend OR 97701, USA
**Anderson, Daniel W (Dan)** — Basketball Player
100 3rd Ave S, #2002, Minneapolis MN 55401, USA
**Anderson, Darren H** — Football Player
7328 Overland Park Court, West Chester OH 45069, USA
**Anderson, Daryl** — Actor
House of Representatives, 1434 6th St, #1, Santa Monica CA 90401 USA
**Anderson, David C (Dave)** — Baseball Player
421 Lockett St, Monticello KY 42633, USA
**Anderson, David J** — Biologist
California Institute of Technology, Biology Division, Pasadena CA 91125, USA
**Anderson, David P (Dave)** — Sportswriter
8 Inness Road, Tenafly NJ 07670, USA
**Anderson, Derek L** — Basketball Player
Legendary Liquids, 500 Bishop St, Building B2, Atlanta GA 30318, USA
**Anderson, Derek M** — Football Player
Carolina Panthers, Ericsson Stadium, 800 S Mint St, Charlotte NC 28202 USA
**Anderson, Dion** — Actor
S D B Partners, 1801 Ave of Stars, #902, Los Angeles CA 90067 USA
**Anderson, Don** — Sculptor
3711 Cabrant Road, Everson WA 98247, USA
**Anderson, Don L** — Geophysicist
PO Box 1417, Cambria CA 93428, USA
**Anderson, Duwayne M** — Polar Scientist
6119 139th Place SE, Bellevue WA 98006, USA
**Anderson, Earl** — Ice Hockey Player
602 3rd Ave NE, Roseau MN 56751, USA
**Anderson, Earl E** — Marine Corps General
West Virginia University, Morgantown WV 26506 USA
**Anderson, Eddie Lee, Jr** — Football Player
PO Box 6363, Warner Robins GA 31095, USA
**Anderson, Eric W** — Basketball Player
12284 Whirlaway Dr, Noblesville IN 46060, USA
**Anderson, Erich** — Actor
Paradigm Agency, 360 N Crescent Dr, North Building, Beverly Hills CA 90210 USA
**Anderson, Erika** — Actress, Model
Click Model Mgmt, 9057 Nemo St, West Hollywood CA 90069, USA
**Anderson, Ernestine I** — Singer
Thomas Cassidy, PO Box 1311, Tucson AZ 85702 USA
**Anderson, Fredell L (Fred)** — Football Player
11810 NE 48th Place, Kirkland WA 98033, USA
**Anderson, G Don (Donny)** — Football Player
4516 Lovers Lane, #133, Dallas TX 75225, USA
**Anderson, Garret J** — Baseball Player
34 Vernal Spring, Irvine CA 92603, USA
**Anderson, Gary A** — Football Player
265 Miskow Close, Cannmore AB T1W 3G7, Canada
**Anderson, Gary L** — Marksman
National Rifle Assn, 11250 Waples Mill Road, Fairfax VA 22030, USA
**Anderson, Gary W** — Football Player
1 Ridgefield Court, Little Rock AR 72223, USA
**Anderson, Gillian** — Actress
Independent Talent Group, 40 Whitfield St, London W1T 2RH, England
**Anderson, Glenn** — Ice Hockey Player
42 W 69th St, #2A, New York NY 10023, USA
**Anderson, Harry L** — Actor
Creative Artists Agency, 2000 Ave of Stars, #100, Los Angeles CA 90067 USA
**Anderson, Howard A, Jr** — Cinematographer
Howard A Anderson Co, 5161 Lankershim Blvd, North Hollywood CA 91601, USA
**Anderson, Ian** — Singer (Jethro Tull), Songwriter
W M E Entertainment, 9601 Wilshire Blvd, #300, Beverly Hills CA 90210 USA
**Anderson, J C** — Golfer
232 Fairway Green Dr, O Fallon MO 63368, USA
**Anderson, Jade** — Singer
Evolution Entertainment, 901 N Highland Ave, Los Angeles CA 90038 USA
**Anderson, Jamal S** — Football Player
10540 Montclair Way, Duluth GA 30097, USA
**Anderson, James L (Jim)** — Baseball Player
2111 Bennington Court, Thousand Oaks CA 91360, USA
**Anderson, James M (Jamie)** — Cinematographer
19 Hanson St, Portland ME 04103, USA
**Anderson, James W** — Endocrinologist
University of Kentucky Medical Center, Endocrinology Dept, Lexington KY 40506, USA
**Anderson, Jamie** — Actress
Rage Talent Agency, 23501 Park Sorrento, Calabasas CA 91302, USA
**Anderson, Janet** — Golfer
4311 W Ardmore Road, Laveen AZ 85339, USA
**Anderson, Janina** — Actress
Ominiquest Entertainment, 1416 N La Brea Ave, Los Angeles CA 90028, USA
**Anderson, Joel** — Director, Writer
Bloom Hergott Diemer, 150 S Rodeo Dr, #300, Beverly Hills CA 90212 USA
**Anderson, John B** — Representative, Presidential Candidate
4120 48th St NW, Washington DC 20016, USA
**Anderson, John D** — Singer, Songwriter
Pathfinder Mgmt, PO Box 159006, Nashville TN 37215, USA
**Anderson, John M** — Ice Hockey Player, Coach
260 Sunset Ave, Glen Ellyn IL 60137, USA
**Anderson, John, Jr** — Governor, KS
PO Box 343, Gardner KS 66030, USA
**Anderson, Jon** — Singer (Yes)
Agency Group Ltd, 142 W 57th St, #600, New York NY 10019 USA

**Anderson, Joseph (Joe)** — Actor
United Agents, 12-26 Lexington St, London W1F 0LE, England

**Anderson, June** — Opera Singer
Hazard Chase, 25 City Road, Cambridge CB1 1DP, England

**Anderson, Kenneth (Kenny)** — Basketball Player
270 N Canon Dr, #1289, Beverly Hills CA 90210, USA

**Anderson, Kenneth A (Ken)** — Football Player, Coach
41 Sedge Fern Dr, Hilton Head SC 29926, USA

**Anderson, Kerrii** — Businesswoman
P F Chang's, 7676 E Pinnacle Peak Road, Scottsdale AZ 85255, USA

**Anderson, Kevin** — Actor
Lighthouse Entertainment, 9220 W Sunset Blvd, #200, West Hollywood CA 90069 USA

**Anderson, Kevin J** — Writer
AnderZone, PO Box 767, Monument CO 80132, USA

**Anderson, Kim S** — Football Player
6709 La Tijera Blvd, #222, Los Angeles CA 90045, USA

**Anderson, Lauren** — Model
5200 NW 43rd St, #102-304, Gainesville FL 32606, USA

**Anderson, Laurie** — Performance Artist, Singer
Pomgranate Arts, 1140 Broadway, #305, New York NY 10001, USA

**Anderson, Lawrence A (Larry)** — Football Player
3170 Blanchard Road, Shreveport LA 71103, USA

**Anderson, Layke** — Actor
Ken McReddie Assoc, 101 Finsbury Pavement, London EC2A 1RS, England

**Anderson, Loni** — Actress
Innovative Artists, 1505 10th St, Santa Monica CA 90401 USA

**Anderson, Louie** — Actor, Comedian
A P A Talent/Literary Agency, 405 S Beverly Dr, #300, Beverly Hills CA 90212 USA

**Anderson, Lynn** — Singer
P L A Media, 1303 16th Ave S, Nashville TN 37212, USA

**Anderson, Mark** — Football Player
PO Box 27551, Tulsa OK 74149, USA

**Anderson, Mary** — Actress
1127 Norman Place, Los Angeles CA 90049, USA

**Anderson, Melissa Sue** — Actress
Globe Pequot Press, 246 Goose Lane, PO Box 480, Guilford CT 06437, USA

**Anderson, Melody** — Actress
PO Box 24483, Los Angeles CA 90024, USA

**Anderson, Michael** — Singer, Songwriter
A&M Records, 70 Universal City Plaza, Universal City CA 91608 USA

**Anderson, Michael A (Mike)** — Baseball Player, Coach
4112 Westbrook Dr, Florence SC 29501, USA

**Anderson, Michael H** — Physicist
University of Colorado, Physics Dept, Boulder CO 80309, USA

**Anderson, Michael J** — Director
Paul Burford, 52 Yorkminster Road, North York ON M2P 1M3, Canada

**Anderson, Michael J** — Actor
C R Mgmt, 23852 Pacific Coast Highway, #627, Malibu CA 90265, USA

**Anderson, Michael M (Mike)** — Football Player
PO Box 12753, Chandler AZ 85248, USA

**Anderson, Miles** — Actor
Gage Group, 14724 Ventura Blvd, #505, Sherman Oaks CA 91403 USA

**Anderson, Murray** — Ice Hockey Player
38 Head Ave, PO Box 38 Station Main, Pas MB R9A 1K3, Canada

**Anderson, Nathan** — Actor
Geddes Agency, 8430 Santa Monica Blvd, #201, West Hollywood CA 90069 USA

**Anderson, Nelison (Nick)** — Basketball Player
163 Harbor Isle Circle N, Memphis TN 38103, USA

**Anderson, Nick** — Editorial Cartoonist
Courier-Journal, Editorial Dept, 525 W Broadway, Louisville KY 40202, USA

**Anderson, Nicole G** — Actress, Model
PO Box 231624, Encinitas CA 92023, USA

**Anderson, Ottis J (O J)** — Football Player
9636 Guehring Dr, Saint Louis MO 63123, USA

**Anderson, Pamela** — Model, Actress
I C M Partners, 10250 Constellation Blvd, #900, Los Angeles CA 90067 USA

**Anderson, Paul Thomas** — Director, Writer
Creative Artists Agency, 2000 Ave of Stars, #100, Los Angeles CA 90067 USA

**Anderson, Paul W S** — Director
Key Creatives, 1800 N Highland Ave, Los Angeles CA 90028, USA

**Anderson, Perry** — Ice Hockey Player
3516 E Meadowbrook Ave, Phoenix AZ 85018, USA

**Anderson, Pete** — Guitarist
Little Dog Records, 2219 W Olive Ave, #150, Burbank CA 91506, USA

**Anderson, Philip W** — Nobel Physics Laureate
Princeton University, Physics Dept, Princeton NJ 08544, USA

**Anderson, R John** — Football Player
14739 Crestwood Court, Sewickley PA 15143, USA

**Anderson, R Lanier, III** — Judge
US Court of Appeals, PO Box 977, Macon GA 31202, USA

**Anderson, Randy** — Auto Racing Driver
Anderson Racing, 1240 S Cucamonga Ave, Ontario CA 91761, USA

**Anderson, Ray** — Jazz Trombonist, Trumpeter
Ellicott Talent Group, 2503 Marilyn Circle, Petaluma CA 94954, USA

**Anderson, Rebecca Moesta** — Writer
Word Fire, PO Box 1840, Monument CO 80132, USA

**Anderson, Reid B** — Ballet Dancer, Artistic Director
Stuttgart Ballet, Ober Schlossgarten 6, 70173 Stuttgart, Germany

**Anderson, Richard** — Businessman
Delta Air Lines, Hartsfield International Airport, Atlanta GA 30320, USA

**Anderson, Richard** — Actor
10120 Cielo Dr, Beverly Hills CA 90210, USA

**Anderson, Richard D (Richie)** — Football Player
6311 Meandering Woods Court, Frederick MD 21701, USA

**Anderson, Richard Dean** — Actor
I C M Partners, 10250 Constellation Blvd, #900, Los Angeles CA 90067 USA

| | |
|---|---|
| **Anderson, Richard P (Dick)** <br> 4603 Santa Maria St, Miami FL 33146, USA | Football Player |
| **Anderson, Robert C (Bob)** <br> 3140 E 89th St, Tulsa OK 74137, USA | Baseball Player |
| **Anderson, Robert C (Bobby)** <br> 79125 Big Horn Trail, La Quinta CA 92253, USA | Football Player |
| **Anderson, Robert G W** <br> British Museum, Great Russell St, London WC1B 3DG, England | Museum Executive |
| **Anderson, Robert P (Bob)** <br> 244 Carmel Dr, Melbourne FL 32940, USA | Football Player |
| **Anderson, Ronald C (Ron)** <br> 72 Woodside Close, Airdie AB T4B 2C7, Canada | Ice Hockey Player |
| **Anderson, Ross** <br> Seattle Times, Editorial Dept, 1000 Denny Way, Seattle WA 98109 USA | Journalist |
| **Anderson, Russ** <br> 76 Fern Dr, Plantsville CT 06479, USA | Ice Hockey Player |
| **Anderson, Ryan J** <br> New Orleans Pelicans, 1250 Poydras St, #101, New Orleans LA 70113 USA | Basketball Player |
| **Anderson, Samuel (Sam)** <br> Talent Works, 3500 W Olive Ave, #1400, Burbank CA 91505 USA | Actor |
| **Anderson, Scott E** <br> I C M Partners, 10250 Constellation Blvd, #900, Los Angeles CA 90067 USA | Director |
| **Anderson, Shandon R** <br> 63 Mangum St SW, #6, Atlanta GA 30313, USA | Basketball Player |
| **Anderson, Shawn** <br> Hockey S T, 19 51st Ave, Notre Dame de L'ile Perrot QC J7V 7L8, Canada | Ice Hockey Player |
| **Anderson, Shelly** <br> Brad Anderson Racing, 1240 S Cucamonga Ave, Ontario CA 91761, USA | Drag Racing Driver |
| **Anderson, Stephen H** <br> US Court of Appeals, Federal Building, 125 S State St, Salt Lake City UT 84138, USA | Judge |
| **Anderson, Sunshine** <br> Music World Entertainment, 1505 Hadley St, Houston TX 77002, USA | Singer |
| **Anderson, Tai** <br> Creative Trust, 5141 Virginia Way, #320, Brentwood TN 37027, USA | Bassist (Third Day) |
| **Anderson, Tazwell L (Taz), Jr** <br> Taz Anderson Realty, 2931 Paces Ferry Road SE, #150, Atlanta GA 30339, USA | Football Player |
| **Anderson, Terence (Terry)** <br> 17 Sunlight Hill, Yonkers NY 10704, USA | Journalist, Iran Hostage |
| **Anderson, Thomas (Tom)** <br> MySpace, 1333 2nd St, Santa Monica CA 90401, USA | Businessman |
| **Anderson, Tim** <br> Herb Tannen, 10801 National Blvd, #101, Los Angeles CA 90064 USA | Actor |
| **Anderson, Todd** <br> Country Thunder Records, 1016 17th Ave S, Nashville TN 37212, USA | Drummer (Heartland) |
| **Anderson, Tom** <br> Feast Mgmt, 34 Upper St, London N1 0PN, England | Actor |
| **Anderson, Tyrone L (Bennie)** <br> 6450 Virginia Ave, Saint Louis MO 63111, USA | Football Player |
| **Anderson, W French** <br> University of Southern California Medical School, 1510 San Pablo St, Los Angeles CA 90033, USA | Biochemist, Geneticist |
| **Anderson, W William (Bill)** <br> 6924 Lark Lane, Knoxville TN 37919, USA | Football Player |
| **Anderson, Walter** <br> Parade Publications, Publisher's Office, 711 3rd Ave, New York NY 10017, USA | Publisher |
| **Anderson, Wendell** <br> PO Box 49097, Minneapolis MN 55449, USA | Ice Hockey Player |
| **Anderson, Wendell R** <br> Baker Building, 706 2nd Ave S, #720, Minneapolis MN 55402, USA | Governor, Senator, MN |
| **Anderson, Wes** <br> American Empirical Pictures, 405 W 13th St, #6R, New York NY 10014, USA | Director, Writer |
| **Anderson, Wessell** <br> Fat City Artists, 1906 Chet Atkins Place, #502, Nashville TN 37212 USA | Jazz Saxophonist |
| **Anderson, Wilford C** <br> 3585 Round Barn Blvd, Santa Rosa CA 95403, USA | WW II Army Hero |
| **Anderson, Willie A** <br> 1490 Meadowcreek Court, Atlanta GA 30338, USA | Football Player |
| **Anderson, Willie L** <br> Toronto Raptors, Air Canada Center, 20 Bay St, Toronto ON M5J 2N8, Canada | Basketball Player |
| **Anderson, Willie L (Flipper)** <br> 190 Abbey Hill Road, Suwanee GA 30024, USA | Football Player |
| **Anderson, Winslow** <br> PO Box 1700, Huntington WV 25717, USA | Artist |
| **Andersson, Benny** <br> Mono Music, Sodra Brobaeken 41A, 111 49 Stockholm, Sweden | Singer (ABBA), Composer |
| **Andersson, Bibi** <br> Agents Associes, 201 Faubourg Saint Honore, 75008 Paris, France | Actress |
| **Andersson, Harriet** <br> Agentfirman Planthaber/Kildén, Drottninggatan 55, 111 21 Stockholm, Sweden | Actress |
| **Andersson, Mattias** <br> S G Flensburg-Handewitt, Schiffbrucke 66, 24939 Flensburg, Germany | Handball Player |
| **Andersson, Susanna** <br> I M G Artists, Hogarth Business Park, Chiswick, London W4 2TH, England | Opera Singer |
| **Anderszewski, Piotr** <br> I M G Artists, Hogarth Business Park, Chiswick, London W4 2TH, England | Concert Pianist, Conductor |
| **Andes, Karen** <br> G P Putnam's Sons, 375 Hudson St, New York NY 10014 USA | Body Builder |
| **Andino, Robert L** <br> 2250 NW 2nd St, Miami FL 33125, USA | Baseball Player |
| **Andion Gonzalez, Patxi** <br> Calle Pavia N 2, 28013 Madrid, Spain | Singer, Songwriter, Actor |
| **Ando, Kozue** <br> F C R 2001 Duisburg, Mundelheimer Str 123-125, 47259 Duisburg, Germany | Soccer Player |
| **Ando, Miki** <br> International Mangement Group, 1 Erieview Plaza, 1360 E 9th St, Cleveland OH 44114 USA | Figure Skater |
| **Ando, Tadao** <br> Tadao Ando Architect, 5-23-2 Toyosaki, Kitaku, Osaka 531, Japan | Pritzker Architectural Laureate |

**A**

Anderson - Ando

# A

## Andrade - Andrews

**Andrade, William T (Billy)** — Golfer
4429 E Brookhaven Dr NE, Atlanta GA 30319, USA

**Andrascik, Steve** — Ice Hockey Player
32 Early Lane, Annville PA 17003, USA

**Andre 3000** — Rap Artist (Outkast), Actor
4016 Elizabeth Terrace, Rex GA 30273, USA

**Andre, Annette** — Actress
Infinite Artists, Pinewood Studios, Iver Heath, Buckinghamshire SLO ONH, England

**Andre, Carl** — Sculptor
689 Crown St, Brooklyn NY 11213, USA

**Andrea, Pat** — Artist
18 Rue Henri Regnault, 75014 Paris, France

**Andrea, Paul** — Ice Hockey Player
136 Regent St, North Sydney NS B2A 2G5, Canada

**Andreas, G Allen** — Businessman
Archer Daniels Midland Co, 4666 E Faries Parkway, Decatur IL 62526, USA

**Andreasen, Nancy C** — Psychiatrist
200 Hawkings Dr, Iowa City IA 52242, USA

**Andreason, Larry** — Diver
10874 Kyle St, Los Alamitos CA 90720, USA

**Andree, Ingrid** — Actress
Freie Akademie der Kunste, Klosterwall 23, 20095 Hamburg, Germany

**Andreeff, Starr** — Actress
C N A Assoc, 1875 Century Park East, #2250, Los Angeles CA 90067 USA

**Andreessen, Marc** — Computer Software Designer
Opsware, 19420 Homestead Road, Cupertino CA 95014, USA

**Andreoli, Severino** — Cyclist
Via Carolucci 19, 3706 Lugoguomo, Italy

**Andreone, Leah** — Singer, Songwriter
Metropolitan Entertainment Group, 2 Penn Plaza, #1500, New York NY 10121, USA

**Andres Puerta, Jose R** — Chef, Restauranteur
ThinkFoodGroup, 717 D St NW, #600, Washington DC 20004, USA

**Andres, Dominic** — Curling Athlete
Curling Assn, PO Box 606, 3000 Bern, Switzerland

**Andresen, Frode** — Biathlete
Borgergt 3, 3514 Honefoss, Norway

**Andress, Tuck** — Jazz Guitarist (Tuck & Patti)
T & P Productions, PO Box 1363, Menlo Park CA 94026, USA

**Andress, Ursula** — Actress
Via Francesco Siacci 38, 00186 Rome, Italy

**Andretti, John** — Auto Racing Driver
Andretti Autosport, 7615 Zionsville Road, Indianapolis IN 46268, USA

**Andretti, Mario** — Auto Racing Driver
457 Rose Inn Ave, Nazareth PA 18064, USA

**Andretti, Michael M** — Auto Racing Driver, Executive
Andretti Autosport, 7615 Zionsville Road, Indianapolis IN 46268, USA

**Andrew** — Prince, England
Buckingham Palace, London SW1A 1AA, England

**Andrew, Philip** — Actor
Bohemia Management, 8170 Beverly Blvd, #102, Los Angeles CA 90048, USA

**Andrew, Samuel H (Sam), III** — Guitarist (Big Brother Holding Company)
Gen-X Entertainment, PO Box 128164, Nashville TN 37212, USA

**Andrews, Amy Leigh** — Model
Playboy Promotions, 2706 Media Center Dr, Los Angeles CA 90065 USA

**Andrews, Andy** — Actor, Comedian
PO Box 17321, Nashville TN 37217, USA

**Andrews, Anthony** — Actor
Paradigm Agency, 360 N Crescent Dr, North Building, Beverly Hills CA 90210 USA

**Andrews, Brittany** — Exotic Dancer, Model, Actress
Look North Promotions, 7-9 Clifford St, York, Yorkshire YO1 9RA, England

**Andrews, D Shane** — Baseball Player
807 Dennis Way, Carlsbad NM 88220, USA

**Andrews, Donna** — Golfer
2301 Hawthorne Road, Lynchburg VA 24503, USA

**Andrews, Erin** — Sportscaster
Fox-TV, Sports Dept, 205 W 67th St, New York NY 10065 USA

**Andrews, George E** — Mathematician
119 Meadow Lane, Centre Hall PA 16828, USA

**Andrews, George E, II** — Football Player
10195 Overhill Dr, Santa Ana CA 92705, USA

**Andrews, Jessica** — Singer
Creative Artists Agency, 2000 Ave of Stars, #100, Los Angeles CA 90067 USA

**Andrews, John H** — Architect
Colleton, Cargo Road, Orange NSW 2800, Australia

**Andrews, John R** — Baseball Player
9292 Gordon Ave, La Habra CA 90631, USA

**Andrews, Julie E** — Actress, Singer
PO Box 491668, Los Angeles CA 90049, USA

**Andrews, Lee** — Singer
Mars Talent, 27 L'Ambiance Court, Nanuet NY 10954, USA

**Andrews, Mark** — Senator, ND
3354 165th Ave SE, Mapleton ND 58059, USA

**Andrews, Michael J (Mike)** — Baseball Player
Jimmy Fund, 10 Brookline Place W, #600, Brookline MA 02445, USA

**Andrews, Naveen** — Actor
Gersh Agency, 9465 Wilshire Blvd, #600, Beverly Hills CA 90212 USA

**Andrews, Real** — Actor
Abrams Artists, 275 7th Ave, #2600, New York NY 10001 USA

**Andrews, Robert** — Writer
G P Putnam's Sons, 375 Hudson St, New York NY 10014 USA

**Andrews, Robert F** — Religious Leader
5404 Sharon Trail, Lakeland FL 33810, USA

**Andrews, Robert P (Rob)** — Baseball Player
1280 Mountbatten Court, Concord CA 94518, USA

**Andrews, Theresa** — Swimmer
2004 Homewood Road, Annapolis MD 21402, USA

| | |
|---|---|
| **Andrews, Tina** | Actress, Producer, Writer |
| Sharp Assoc, 1516 N Fairfax Ave, Los Angeles CA 90046, USA | |
| **Andrews, V C** | Writer |
| Pocket Books, 1230 Ave of Americas, New York NY 10020 USA | |
| **Andrews, William D (Billy), Jr** | Football Player |
| PO Box 703, Clinton LA 70722, USA | |
| **Andreychuck, Dave** | Ice Hockey Player |
| 18130 Longwater Run Dr, Tampa FL 33647, USA | |
| **Andrie, George J** | Football Player |
| 26356 E Zeerip, Drummond Island MI 49726, USA | |
| **Andriessen, Louis** | Composer |
| Nonesuch Records, 75 Rockefeller Plaza, #800, New York NY 10019 USA | |
| **Androsky, Carol** | Actress |
| Henderson/Hogan, 850 7th Ave, #1003, New York NY 10019 USA | |
| **Andruff, Ron** | Ice Hockey Player |
| 71 1/2 Irving Place, #1F, New York NY 10003, USA | |
| **Andrus, Cecil D** | Secretary, Interior; Governor, ID |
| PO Box 852, Boise ID 83701, USA | |
| **Andrusak, Greg** | Ice Hockey Player |
| 5240 Highway 3A, Nelson BC V1L 6N6, Canada | |
| **Andruzzi, Joseph D (Joe)** | Football Player |
| 682 Bellmore Ave, East Meadow NY 11554, USA | |
| **Andsnes, Leif Ove** | Concert Pianist |
| I M G Artists, Hogarth Business Park, Chiswick, London W4 2TH, England | |
| **Andujar, Joaquin** | Baseball Player |
| Ave L Amiama Tio #47, San Pedro de Macoris, Dominican Republic | |
| **Andy, Horace** | Singer, Songwriter |
| Agency Group Ltd, 1880 Century Park E, #711, Los Angeles CA 90067 USA | |
| **Ane, Charles T (Charlie), III** | Football Player |
| Punahou School, 1601 Punahou St, Honolulu HI 96822, USA | |
| **Anemone** | Actress |
| 82 Rue Bonaparte, 75006 Paris, France | |
| **Angarano, Michael** | Actor |
| United Talent Agency, U T A Plaza, 9336 Civic Center Dr, Beverly Hills CA 90210 USA | |
| **Angel Arango, Juan Pablo** | Soccer Player |
| Chivas U S A, Home Depot Center, 18400 S Avalon Blvd, Carson CA 90746, USA | |
| **Angel, Ashley Parker** | Singer (O-Town) |
| Mavrick Artists Agency, 6100 Wilshire Blvd, #550, Los Angeles CA 90048, USA | |
| **Angel, Criss** | Illusionist |
| Renaissance Literary & Talent, PO Box 17379, Beverly Hills CA 90209, USA | |
| **Angel, Heather H** | Photographer |
| Highways, 6 Vicarage Hill, Farnham, Surrey GU9 8HJ, England | |
| **Angel, J Roger P** | Astronomer |
| University of Arizona, Stewart Observatory, 933 N Cherry Ave, Tucson AZ 85721, USA | |
| **Angel, Marie** | Opera Singer |
| Allied Artists, 42 Montpelier Square, London SW7 1JZ, England | |
| **Angel, Vanessa** | Actress, Model |
| Media Artists Group, 8255 Sunset Blvd, Los Angeles CA 90046, USA | |
| **Angela, Sharon** | Actress |
| C E S D, 257 Park Ave S, #950, New York NY 10010 USA | |
| **Angelil, Rene** | Actress, Writer |
| United Talent Agency, U T A Plaza, 9336 Civic Center Dr, Beverly Hills CA 90210 USA | |
| **Angelini, Fiorenzo Cardinal** | Religious Leader |
| Via dei Penitenzieri 12, 00193 Rome Lazio, Italy | |
| **Angell, Wayne D** | Financier, Government Official |
| 1600 N Oak St, Arlington VA 22209, USA | |
| **Angeloni, Umberto** | Fashion Executive |
| Brioni's Srl, Via Barberini 79, 00187 Rome, Italy | |
| **Angelou, Maya** | Writer |
| 3240 Valley Road, #MB9, Winston-Salem NC 27106, USA | |
| **Angelyne** | Actress, Artist, Model |
| Angelyne Mgmt, 5670 Wilshire Blvd, #2200, Los Angeles CA 90036, USA | |
| **Angerer, Paul** | Composer |
| Esteplatz 3/26, 1030 Vienna, Austria | |
| **Angerer, Peter** | Biathlete |
| Gampermuhlstr 2, 83313 Siegsdorf, Germany | |
| **Angerer, Tobias** | Cross Country Skier |
| Hubertusstr 4, 83278 Traunstein, Germany | |
| **Angier, Natalie M** | Journalist |
| New York Times, Editorial Dept, 229 W 43rd St, New York NY 10036, USA | |
| **Anglade, Jean-Hughes** | Actor |
| Intertalent, 16 Rue Henri Barbusse, 75005 Paris, France | |
| **Angle, Kurt S** | Freestyle Wrestler |
| 5032 Stags Leap Lane, Coraopolis PA 15108, USA | |
| **Anglim, Philip** | Actor |
| 2404 Grand Canal, Venice CA 90291, USA | |
| **Anglin, Jennifer** | Actress |
| Geddes Agency, 8430 Santa Monica Blvd, #201, West Hollywood CA 90069 USA | |
| **Angula, Nahas** | Prime Minister, Namibia |
| Premier's Office, South Parliament Building, Windhoek 9000, Namibia | |
| **Angulo, Richard** | Football Player |
| 4801 W Libby St, Glendale AZ 85308, USA | |
| **Anholt, Darrell** | Ice Hockey Player |
| 4935 49th St, Hughenden, AL T0B 2E0, Canada | |
| **Anikulap-Kuti, Femi** | Singer, Songwriter |
| M C A Records, 70 Universal City Plaza, Universal City CA 91608 USA | |
| **Anissina, Marina V** | Figure Skater |
| Sports de Glace Federation, 35 Rue Felicien David, 75016 Paris, France | |
| **Aniston, Jennifer** | Actress |
| Todd Shemarya Artists, 2550 Outpost Dr, Los Angeles CA 90068 USA | |
| **Aniston, John** | Actor |
| Geddes Agency, 8430 Santa Monica Blvd, #201, West Hollywood CA 90069 USA | |
| **Anjou, Danielle** | Sculptor |
| Voila Gallery, 518 N La Brea Ave, Los Angeles CA 90036, USA | |
| **Anka, Paul** | Singer, Songwriter, Actor |
| 2674 Stafford Road, Thousand Oaks CA 91361, USA | |

**Ankiel, Richard A (Rick)** — Baseball Player
126 Sandpiper Circle, Jupiter FL 33477, USA

**Ankvab, Alexander Z** — Prime Minister, Abkhazia
Prime Minister's Office, People's Assembly, Sukhumi, Abkhazia, Georgia

**Anlyan, William G** — Surgeon
Duke Medical Center, 100 Seeley Mudd Building, #109, Durham NC 27710, USA

**Annable, Dave** — Actor
Creative Artists Agency, 2000 Ave of Stars, #100, Los Angeles CA 90067 USA

**Annan, Kofi A** — Secretary-General, United Nations
799 United Nations Plaza, New York NY 10017, USA

**Annaud, Jean-Jacques** — Director
9 Rue Guenegard, 75006 Paris, France

**Anne** — Princess, England
Buckingham Palace, London SW1 1AA, England

**Anne of Bourbon-Palma** — Queen, Romania
Villa Serena, 77 Chemin Louis-Degallier, 1290 Versoix-Geneva, Switzerland

**Annenberg, Wallis** — Publisher
10273 Century Woods Dr, Los Angeles CA 90067, USA

**Annett, Chloe** — Actress
Spotlight, 7 Leicester Place, London WC2H 7RJ, England

**Annís, Francesca** — Actress
Independent Talent Group, 40 Whitfield St, London W1T 2RH, England

**Ann-Margret** — Actress, Singer, Dancer
2707 Benedict Canyon Road, Beverly Hills CA 90210, USA

**Anno, Sam S** — Football Player
12934 Ferndale Ave, Los Angeles CA 90066, USA

**Anosike, Nkolika N (Nicky)** — Basketball Player
Los Angeles Sparks, 888 S Figueroa St, #2010, Los Angeles CA 90017 USA

**Anouk** — Singer
Artmedia, 20 Ave Rapp, 75007 Paris, France

**Anozie, Nonso** — Actor
Garricks-Megan Willis, Angel House, 76 Mallinson Road, London SW11 1BN, England

**Ansa, Tina McElroy** — Writer
Jonee Ansa, 422 Sea Breeze Dr, PO Box 20602, Saint Simons Island GA 31522, USA

**Ansari, Anousheh** — Tourist Cosmonaut
Prodea Systems, 6101 W Plano Parkway, #210, Plano TX 75093, USA

**Ansari, Aziz** — Actor, Comedian
3 Arts Entertainment, 9460 Wilshire Blvd, #700, Beverly Hills CA 90212 USA

**Anschutz, Philip F** — Businessman, Sports Executive
Qwest Communications, 1801 California St, #5200, Denver CO 80202, USA

**Ansell, Jonathan** — Singer
Agency Group Ltd, 142 W 57th St, #600, New York NY 10019 USA

**Anselmo, Philip H** — Singer (Pantera)
5869 Colbert St, New Orleans LA 70124, USA

**Ansip, Andrus** — Prime Minister, Estonia
Prime Minister's Office, Stenbocki Maja, Rahukohtu 3, 15161 Tallinn, Estonia

**Anspach, Susan** — Actress
11734 Wilshire Blvd, #207, Los Angeles CA 90025, USA

**Anspaugh, David** — Director
I C M Partners, 10250 Constellation Blvd, #900, Los Angeles CA 90067 USA

**Ant** — Actor, Comedian
Mavrick Artists Agency, 1680 N Vine St, #802, Hollywood CA 90028, USA

**Ant, Adam** — Singer, Guitarist
Tony Denton Promotions, PO Box 2839, London W1K 5LE, England

**Antal, Nimrod** — Director, Actor, Writer
Creative Artists Agency, 2000 Ave of Stars, #100, Los Angeles CA 90067 USA

**Antes, Horst** — Artist
Hohenbergstr 11, 76228 Karlsruhe (Wolfartsweier), Germany

**Anthony, Carl** — Environmentalist
Harvard University, Kennedy Government School, Cambridge MA 02138, USA

**Anthony, Carmelo F** — Basketball Player
New York Knicks, Madison Square Garden, 2 Penn Plaza, New York, NY 10121 USA

**Anthony, Eric T** — Baseball Player
42 Fosters Court, Sugar Land TX 77479, USA

**Anthony, Gregory C (Greg)** — Basketball Player
63 Corso Italia, Freehold NJ 07728, USA

**Anthony, Lysette** — Actress
Belfield & Ward, 80-81 Saint Martin's Lane, London WC2N 4AA, England

**Anthony, Marc** — Singer, Actor, Songwriter
Marc Anthony Productions, 146 W 57th St, #38C, New York NY 10019, USA

**Anthony, Piers** — Writer
PO Box 2289, Inverness FL 34451, USA

**Anthony, Ray** — Orchestra Leader, Trumpeter
9288 Kinglet Dr, Los Angeles CA 90069, USA

**Anthony, Reidel C** — Football Player
PO Box 23, South Bay FL 33493, USA

**Anti, Michael (Mike)** — Marksman
13383 Honey Run Way, Colorado Springs CO 80921, USA

**Antin, Steve** — Actor, Writer
United Talent Agency, U T A Plaza, 9336 Civic Center Dr, Beverly Hills CA 90210 USA

**Antioco, John** — Businessman
Blockbuster Inc, 3704 Stratford Ave, Dallas TX 75205, USA

**Antoine, Lionel S** — Football Player
1455 Glencliff Dr, Dallas TX 75217, USA

**Antoine, Marc** — Jazz Guitarist
Variety Artists, 1924 Spring St, Paso Robles CA 93446 USA

**Anton, Alan** — Bassist (Cowboy Junkies)
S L Feldman Mgmt, 1505 W 2nd Ave, #200, Vancouver BC V6H 3Y4, Canada

**Anton, Susan** — Actress, Singer
10300 W Charleston Blvd, #13, Las Vegas NV 89135, USA

**Antonakakis, Dimitris** — Architect
Atelier 66, Emm Benaki 118, Athens 11473, Greece

**Antonakakis, Suzana M** — Architect
Atelier 66, Emm Benaki 118, Athens 11473, Greece

**Antonelli, Dominic A (Tony)** — Astronaut
4106 Oak Blossom Court, Houston TX 77059, USA

| | |
|---|---|
| **Antonelli, Ennio Cardinal**<br>Via di Sant'Andrea delle Fratte 1, 00187 Rome Lazio, Italy | Religious Leader |
| **Antonelli, Laura**<br>Pietrovalle, Via B Buozzi 51, 00197 Rome, Italy | Actress |
| **Antonicheva, Anna**<br>Bolshoi Theater, Teatralnaya Pl 1, 103009 Moscow, Russia | Ballerina |
| **Antonio, James D (Jim)**<br>Epstein-Wyckoff, 280 S Beverly Dr, #400, Beverly Hills CA 90212 USA | Actor |
| **Antonio, Lou**<br>Actor's Studio, 8341 DeLongpre Ave, West Hollywood CA 90069, USA | Actor |
| **Antonoff, Jack M**<br>Nettwerk Management Group, 1650 W 2nd Ave, Vancouver BC V6J 4R3, Canada | Guitarist (Fun) |
| **Antonova, Lana**<br>Creative Artists Agency, 2000 Ave of Stars, #100, Los Angeles CA 90067 USA | Actress |
| **Antonovich, Mike**<br>4701 Desmond Beach, Fort Gratiot MI 48059, USA | Ice Hockey Player |
| **Antrim, Donald**<br>Wylie Agency, 250 W 57th St, #2114, New York NY 10107 USA | Writer |
| **Antunes, Arnaldo**<br>Monte Criacao Producao, Tra Santa Leocadia 40, Rio de Janiero 22061 050 Brazil | Singer, Songwriter |
| **Antuofermo, Vito**<br>16019 81st St, Howard Beach NY 11414, USA | Boxer, Actor |
| **Anu, Christine**<br>Robert Barnham Mgmt, 432 Tyagarah Road, Myocum NSW 2481, Australia | Singer |
| **Anuszkiewicz, Richard J**<br>76 Chestnut St, Englewood NJ 07631, USA | Artist |
| **Anwar, Gabrielle**<br>Innovative Artists, 1505 10th St, Santa Monica CA 90401 USA | Actress |
| **Aoki, Chieko N**<br>Westin Hotels, Westin Building, 777 Westchester Ave, West Harrison NY 10604, USA | Businesswoman |
| **Aoki, Devon E**<br>Schiff Co, 9200 Sunset Blvd, #430, West Hollywood CA 90232 USA | Actress, Model |
| **Aoki, Isao**<br>International Mangement Group, 1 Erieview Plaza, 1360 E 9th St, Cleveland OH 44114 USA | Golfer |
| **Aoki, Jun**<br>Jun Aoki Assoc, 3-38-11 Jingumae, Shibuyaku, Tokyo 150 0001, Japan | Architect, Interior Designer |
| **Aoki, Satoshi**<br>Honda Motor Co, 2-1-1 Minami-Aoyama, Minatoku, Tokyo 107 8556, Japan | Businessman |
| **Aoki, Steve**<br>Ministry of Sound, 103 Gaunt St, London SE1 6DP, England | DJ Musician |
| **Aouita, Said**<br>Abdejil Bencheikh, 9 Rue Soivissi, Loubira, Rabat, Morocco | Track Athlete |
| **Aoun, Michel N**<br>Assemble Nationale, Place de L'Etoile, Beirut, Lebanon | Prime Minister, Lebanon; Army General |
| **Apache Indian**<br>Mission Control, City Business Center, Lower Road, London SE16 2XB, England | DJ Musician |
| **Apap, Gilles**<br>Columbia Artists Mgmt Inc, 1790 Broadway, #702, New York NY 10019 USA | Concert Violinist |
| **Aparicio, Luis E**<br>Calle 67, #26-82, Maracaibo, Venezuela | Baseball Player |
| **Apatow, Judd**<br>Apatow Productions, 11788 W Pico Blvd, Los Angeles CA 90064, USA | Director, Producer, Writer |
| **Apel, Katrin**<br>Suedlung 9, 99330 Grafenroda, Germany | Biathlete |
| **Apiata, Bill H (Willie)**<br>Victoria Cross Assn, Old Admiralty Building, London SW1A 2BL, England | Afghanistan War Army Hero (VC) |
| **Apicella, Lorenzo F**<br>Pentagram, 11 Needham Road, London W11 2RP, England | Architect |
| **Apking, Stephen A**<br>Skidmore Owings Merrill, 14 Wall St, #2500, New York NY 10005, USA | Interior Designer |
| **Apl.De.Ap**<br>Paradigm Agency, 404 W Franklin St, Monterey CA 93940 USA | Rap Artist (Elephunk, Black Eyed Peas) |
| **Apodaca, Raymond S (Jerry)**<br>6223 Utah Ave NW, Washington DC 20015, USA | Governor, NM |
| **Apodaca, Robert J (Bob)**<br>2999 SW Van Buren Terrace, Port Saint Lucie FL 34953, USA | Baseball Player |
| **Apollonia**<br>M G A Talent, 269 S Beverly Dr, #1088, Beverly Hills CA 90212, USA | Model, Actress, Singer |
| **Appadurai, Arjun**<br>New York University, Steinhardt School, New York, NY 10012, USA | Anthropologist |
| **Appel, Deena**<br>Montana Artists Agency, 7715 W Sunset Blvd, #300, Los Angeles CA 90046, USA | Costume Designer |
| **Appel, Jayne**<br>San Antonio Silver Stars, 1 AT&T Center, San Antonio TX 78219 USA | Basketball Player |
| **Appel, Peter**<br>Hartig-Hilepo Agency, 54 W 21st St, #610, New York NY 10010 USA | Actor |
| **Appel, Richard**<br>W M E Entertainment, 9601 Wilshire Blvd, #300, Beverly Hills CA 90210 USA | Producer, Writer |
| **Appelbaum, Ralph**<br>Ralph Appelbaum Assoc, 88 Pine St, #2900, New York NY 10005, USA | Museum Designer |
| **Appelfeld, Aharon**<br>Wylie Agency, 17 Bedford Square, London WC1B 3JA, England | Writer |
| **Appice, Carmine**<br>Worldsound, 17837 1st Ave S, #3, Seattle WA 98148, USA | Drummer (Vanilla Fudge, Cactus) |
| **Appier, R Kevin**<br>30743 Victory Road, Paola KS 66071, USA | Baseball Player |
| **Apple, Fiona**<br>Front Line Mgmt, 1100 Glendon Ave, #2000, Los Angeles CA 90024 USA | Singer, Songwriter |
| **Applebaum, Anne**<br>Doubleday Press, 1745 Broadway, New York NY 10019 USA | Writer |
| **Appleby, Malcolm A**<br>Aultberg, Grandtully by Aberfeldy, Perthshire PH15 2QU, England | Artist |
| **Appleby, Shiri**<br>John Carrabino Mgmt, 5900 Wilshire Blvd, #406, Los Angeles CA 90036 USA | Actress |
| **Appleby, Steven**<br>Bloomsbury Publishing, 50 Bedford Square, London WC1B 3DP, England | Cartoonist, Writer |

**A**

*Antonelli - Appleby*

**Appleby, Stuart** — Golfer
9724 Chestnut Ridge Dr, Windermere FL 34786, USA

**Applegate, Christina** — Actress
Management 360, 9111 Wilshire Blvd, Beverly Hills CA 90210 USA

**Applegate, Debby** — Writer
125 Lawrence St, New Haven CT 06511, USA

**Applegate, Jodi** — Commentator
News 12 Long Island, 1 Media Crossways, Woodbury NY 11797, USA

**Applegate, K A** — Writer
Scholastic Press, 555 Broadway, New York NY 10012 USA

**Applegate, Kendall** — Actress
Greene Assoc, 1901 Ave of Stars, #130, Los Angeles CA 90067 USA

**Appleton, Marc** — Architect
Appleton Assoc, 1556 17th St, Santa Monica CA 90404, USA

**Appleton, Steve** — Singer, Songwriter
Agency Group Ltd, 142 W 57th St, #600, New York NY 10019 USA

**Apps, Gillian M** — Ice Hockey Player
Team Canada, 2424 University Dr NW, Calgary AB T2N 3Y9, Canada

**Apps, Sylvanus M (Syl), Jr** — Ice Hockey Player
36 Pennock Crescent, Markham ON L3R 3M4, Canada

**Aprea, John** — Actor
Mavrick Artists Agency, 6100 Wilshire Blvd, #550, Los Angeles CA 90048, USA

**April, Renee** — Costume Designer
Sandra Marsh Assoc, 9150 Wilshire Blvd, #220, Beverly Hills CA 90212 USA

**Apt, Jerome (Jay)** — Astronaut
4 Shadycourt Dr, Pittsburgh PA 15232, USA

**Apted, Michael D** — Director
1126 Indiana Ave, Venice CA 90291, USA

**Aqualung** — Singer, Songwriter
First Column Mgmt, 60 Compton Road, Brighton BN1 5AN, England

**Aqueduct** — Singer, Keyboardist, Guitarist
Aero Booking, 8008 Greenwood Ave N, #3, Seattle WA 98103, USA

**Aquilino, Thomas J, Jr** — Judge
US Court of International Trade, 1 Federal Plaza, New York NY 10278, USA

**Aquino Carmona, Javier I** — Soccer Player
Cruz Azul C D, San Pablo 100, C La Noria Xochimilco, Mexico City 16030, Mexico

**Aquino, Amy** — Actress
Talent Works, 3500 W Olive Ave, #1400, Burbank CA 91505 USA

**Aquino, Luis A C** — Baseball Player
17201 Collins Ave, #606, Sunny Isles Beach FL 33160, USA

**Arabo, Claude** — Fencer
9 Rue Franquet, 75015 Paris, France

**Arad, Michael** — Architect
Handel Architects, 150 Varick St, #800, New York NY 10013, USA

**Arad, Ron** — Architect
Arad Assoc, 62 Chalk Farm Road, London NW1 8AN, England

**Aragall Garriga, Giacomo** — Opera Singer
Stafford Law Assoc, 6 Barham Close, Weybridge, Surrey KT1 9PR, England

**Aragones, Sergio** — Cartoonist (Mad Comics)
PO Box 696, Ojai CA 93024, USA

**Araguz, Leo J** — Football Player
3201 Araguz St, Harlingen TX 78552, USA

**Araiza Herrera, Armando** — Actor
Televisa, Blvd A Lopez Mateos 232, Colonia San Angel, Mexico City DF 01060 CP, Mexico

**Araiza, Francisco** — Opera Singer
Kuntsler Mgmt, M Kursidem, Tal 15, 80331 Munich, Germany

**Arakawa, Shizuka** — Figure Skater
International Skating Center, 1375 Hopemeadow St, Simsbury CT 06070, USA

**Araki, Gregg** — Director, Writer
KillerMoxie Management, 5890 W Jefferson Blvd, #J, Los Angeles CA 90016, USA

**Arana, Tomas** — Actor
Affirmative Entertainment, 425 N Robertson Blvd, Los Angeles CA 90048, USA

**Aranauskas, Leonas S** — Architect
Glavmozarchitectura, Mayakovsky Square 1, 103001 Moscow, Russia

**Arango, Juan Carlos** — Actor
Gabriel Blanco, Rio Balsas 35-32, Colonia Cuauhtemoc DF 6500, Mexico

**Ararktsyan, Babken G** — Supreme Council Chairman, Armenia
3 Tamanian St, #35, 375009 Yerevan, Armenia

**Araskog, Rand V** — Businessman
I T T Corp, 1330 Ave of Americas, New York NY 10019, USA

**Arau, Alfonso** — Director
Glick Agency, 1321 7th St, #203, Santa Monica CA 90401 USA

**Araujo Razo, Nestor A** — Soccer Player
Cruz Azul C D, San Pablo 100, C La Noria Xochimilco, Ciudad de Mexico 16030, Mexico

**Araujo, Ana Paula** — Model
Next Model Mgmt, 188 Rue de Rivoli, 75001 Paris, France

**Araujo, Serafim Fernandes de Cardinal** — Religious Leader
Curia Metropolitana, Av Brasil 2079, 30140-002 Belo Horizonte MG, Brazil

**Arbanas, Frederick V (Fred)** — Football Player
3350 SW Hook Road, Lees Summit MO 64082, USA

**Arbatt, Alexandre** — Actor
Artmedia, 20 Ave Rapp, 75007 Paris, France

**Arber, Werner** — Nobel Medicine Laureate
Klingelbergstr 70, 4056 Basel, Switzerland

**Arbour, Alan (Al)** — Ice Hockey Player, Coach, Executive
2071 Harbour Links Dr, Longboat Key FL 34228, USA

**Arbour, Louise** — Government Official, Canada; Judge
130 Queen St W, Toronto ON M5H 2N5, Canada

**Arbulu Galliani, Guillermo** — Prime Minister, Peru; Army General
Prime Minister's Office, Urb Corpac, Calle 1 Oeste S/N, Lima 27, Peru

**Arcand, Denys** — Director
Agence Goodwin, 839 E Sherbrooke St, #200, Montreal QC H2L 1K6, Canada

**Arce, Alyssa** — Model
Playboy Promotions, 2706 Media Center Dr, Los Angeles CA 90065 USA

**Arce, Jorge A** — Boxer
Top Rank, 3908 Howard Hughes Highway, #580, Las Vegas NV 89169, USA

**Arcgitzel, David** — Navy Admiral
Commander, Naval Air Systems Command, Patuxent River MD 20670 USA

**Archambault, Lee J** — Astronaut
4318 Sweet Cicely Court, Houston TX 77059, USA

**Archambeau, Lester M** — Football Player
10520 Montclair Way, Duluth GA 30097, USA

**Archer of Weston-Super-Mare, Jeffrey H** — Government Official, England; Writer
Peninsula Heights, 93 Albert Embankment, London SE1 7TY, England

**Archer, Anne** — Actress
Kritzer Levine Wilkins Griffin, 11872 La Grange Ave, #100, Los Angeles CA 90025 USA

**Archer, Dave** — Artist
1541 Buckhorn Road, Roseburg OR 97470, USA

**Archer, David** — Football Player
3831 Upland Dr, Marietta GA 30066, USA

**Archer, Glenn L, Jr** — Judge
US Court of Appeals, 717 Madison Place NW, Washington DC 20439, USA

**Archer, Jeffrey** — Writer
Curtis Brown Group, 28-29 Haymarket St, #500, London SW1Y 4SP, England

**Archer, Robyn** — Actress, Songwriter, Director
Rick Raftos Mgmt, Box 445, Paddington NSW 2021, Australia

**Archibald, David (Dave)** — Ice Hockey Player
PO Box 2108, Saint Sardis Main, Chilliwack BC V2R 1A6, Canada

**Archibald, Jane** — Opera Singer
I M G Artists, Hogarth Business Park, Chiswick, London W4 2TH, England

**Archibald, Nathaniel (Nate)** — Basketball Player
2720 Grand Concourse, #218, Bronx NY 10458, USA

**Archibald, Nolan D** — Businessman
Black & Decker Corp, 701 E Joppa Road, Towson MD 21286, USA

**Archipowski, Ken** — Singer (Randy & the Rainbows)
Brothers Management Assoc, 141 Dunbar Ave, Fords NJ 08863 USA

**Archuleta, Adam J** — Football Player
1237 W Galveston St, Chandler AZ 85224, USA

**Archuleta, David J** — Singer, Keyboardist, Guitarist
Arch Consulting Group, 340 W Whitney Ave, Salt Lake City UT 84115, USA

**Arcia Orta, Jose R** — Baseball Player
7325 NW 3rd St, Miami FL 33126, USA

**Arcieri, Leila** — Actress
Luber Rocklin Entertainment, 8530 Wilshire Blvd, #555, Beverly Hills CA 90211 USA

**Arciero, Frank** — Auto Racing Executive
Arciero Racing, 1901 Nancita Circle, Placentia CA 92870, USA

**Arcuri, Manuela** — Actress, Model
Condominio L'Orologio, Via Isonzo Int 25, 04100 Latina, Italy

**Arcuri, Robin** — Model
17128 Colima Road, #411, Hacienda Heights CA 91745, USA

**Ard, William D (Bill)** — Football Player
41 Vail Lane, Watchung NJ 07069, USA

**Ardant, Fanny** — Actress
Les Visiteurs du Soir, 40 Rue de la Folie Regnault, 75011 Paris, France

**Arden, Jann** — Singer, Songwriter
S L Feldman Mgmt, 1505 W 2nd Ave, #200, Vancouver BC V6H 3Y4, Canada

**Arden, Toni** — Singer
3434 75th St, Jackson Heights NY 11372, USA

**Arditi, Pierre** — Actor
Voyez Mon Agent, 20 Ave Rapp, 75007 Paris, France

**Ardito Barletta Vallarino, Nicolas** — President, Panama
PO Box 7737, Panama City 9, Panama

**Arditti, Irvine** — Concert Violinist
Latitude Arts, 109 Boul Saint-Joseph Quest, Montreal PA H2T 2P7, Canada

**Ardoin, Daniel W (Danny)** — Baseball Player
1524 Lee St, Ville Platte LA 70586, USA

**Arena, Bruce** — Soccer Player, Coach
Los Angeles Galaxy, Home Depot Center, 18400 Avalon Blvd, Carson CA 90746 USA

**Arena, Tina** — Singer
Harbour Agency, 135 Forbes St, Wooloomooloo NSW 2011, Australia

**Arenas, Gilbert J** — Basketball Player
4550 Gable Dr, Encino CA 91316, USA

**Arenas, L Joseph (Joe)** — Football Player
780 W Bay Area Blvd, #1215, Webster TX 77598, USA

**Arend, Geoffrey** — Actor
United Talent Agency, U T A Plaza, 9336 Civic Center Dr, Beverly Hills CA 90210 USA

**Arend, Jeff** — Drag Racing Driver, Owner
Arend/Smith Racing, 2 Mallingham Court, Toronto ON M2N 6C4, Canada

**Arens, Moshe** — Government Official, Israel
49 Hagderot, Savyon 56526, Israel

**Aresco, Joey** — Actor
Carrier Talent Mgmt, 705-1080 Howe St, Vancouver BC V6Z 2T1, Canada

**Areshenkoff, Ron** — Ice Hockey Player
1701 1st St, Estevan SK S4A 0H5, Canada

**Arestrup, Niels** — Actor
Voyez Mon Agent, 20 Ave Rapp, 75007 Paris, France

**Arfin, Lesley** — Actress
W M E Entertainment, 9601 Wilshire Blvd, #300, Beverly Hills CA 90210 USA

**Argent, Rod** — Keyboardist (Zombies)
Gen-X Entertainment, PO Box 140, Cedar MN 55011, USA

**Argento, Asia** — Actress, Director
Cineart, 28 Rue Mogador, 78009 Paris, France

**Argento, Dario** — Director
A D C, Via Balamonti 2, Rome, Italy

**Argento, Dominick** — Composer
University of Minnesota, Music Dept, Ferguson Hall, Minneapolis MN 55455, USA

**Argerich, Martha** — Concert Pianist
Jacques Thelen Agence, 15 Ave Montaigne, 75008 Paris, France

**Argos, Eddie** — Singer (Art Brut)
Coda Agency, 229 Shoreditch High St, London E1 6PJ, England

**Argott, Don** — Director, Producer, Cinematographer
9.14 Pictures, 1804 Chestnut St, #2, Philadelphia PA 19104, USA

**Ariail, Robert** — Editorial Cartoonist
The State, Editorial Dept, PO Box 1333, Columbia SC 29202, USA
**Arianda, Nina** — Actress
I C M Partners, 10250 Constellation Blvd, #900, Los Angeles CA 90067 USA
**Arias Sanchez, Oscar** — Nobel Laureate; President, Costa Rica
Arias Foundation for Peace, Apdo 8-6410-1000, San Jose, Costa Rica
**Arias, Alejandro (Alex)** — Baseball Player
37 Edmund Road, West Park FL 33023, USA
**Arias, Moises** — Actor
Greene Assoc, 1901 Ave of Stars, #130, Los Angeles CA 90067 USA
**Arias, Yancey** — Actor
Global Artists Agency, 6253 Hollywood Blvd, #508, Los Angeles CA 90028 USA
**Arienti, Luigi** — Cyclist
Via Tardelle Frasche 80, 2003 Desio, Italy
**Arigoni, Dulio** — Chemist
Im Glockenacker 42, 8053 Zurich, Switzerland
**Arii, Takendo** — Architect
1117 W Arbor Dr, San Diego CA 92103, USA
**Arima, Akito** — Physicist
Physical Research Institute, Hirosawa 2-1, Wakoshi, Saitama 351 01, Japan
**Arinze, Francis Cardinal** — Religious Leader
Diocese of Velletri-Segni, Corso della Repubblica 343, 00049 Velletri (RM), Italy
**Arison, M Micky** — Businessman, Basketball Executive
Carnival Corp, 3655 NW 87th Ave, Doral FL 33178, USA
**Ariyoshi, George R** — Governor, HI
745 Fort St, #500, Honolulu HI 96813, USA
**Ariza, Trevor A** — Basketball Player
1111 S Grand Ave, #PH 2, Los Angeles CA 90015, USA
**Arizmendi, Yareli** — Actress
C E S D, 10635 Santa Monica Blvd, #130, Los Angeles CA 90025 USA
**Arkhipov, Denis** — Ice Hockey Player
716 Sweet Cherry Court, Nashville TN 37215, USA
**Arkin, Adam** — Actor
3531 Coldwater Canyon Ave, Studio City CA 91604, USA
**Arkin, Adam** — Physical Chemist
University of California, Physical Chemistry Dept, Berkeley CA 94720, USA
**Arkin, Alan W** — Actor
Principal Entertainment, 9255 Sunset Blvd, #500, Los Angeles CA 90069 USA
**Arkin, Jordana** — Producer
W M E Entertainment, 9601 Wilshire Blvd, #300, Beverly Hills CA 90210 USA
**Arkush, Allan** — Director, Producer
Paradigm Agency, 360 N Crescent Dr, North Building, Beverly Hills CA 90210 USA
**Arlauckas, Joseph (Joe)** — Basketball Player
917 Night Heron Dr, Mount Pleasant SC 29464, USA
**Arlen, Michael J** — Writer
New Yorker, Editorial Dept, 4 Times Square, Basement C1B, New York NY 10036 USA
**Arlin, Stephen R (Steve)** — Baseball Player
6819 Claremore Ave, San Diego CA 92120, USA
**Armacost, Michael H** — Government Official, Diplomat
9425 Tarnberry Dr, Potomac MD 20854, USA
**Armadroff, Taft** — Astronomer
W M Keck Observatory, 65-1120 Mamalahoa Highway, Kamuela HI 96743, USA
**Armani, Giorgio** — Fashion Designer
Via Borgonuovo 21, 20121 Milan, Italy
**Armano, Mario** — Bobsled Athlete
Olympic Committee, Foro Italico, Largo Lauro de Bosis 15, 00135 Rome, Italy
**Armant, Ivonne** — Model, Actress
Tayrona Entertainment Group, 9663 Santa Monica Blvd, #623, Beverly Hills CA 90210, USA
**Armaou, Lindsay** — Singer (B*Witched)
Clintons, 55 Drury Lane, Covent Garden, London WC2B 5SQ, England
**Armas, Antonio R (Tony)** — Baseball Player
Calle Las Mercedes 37, Puerto Piritu, Venezuela
**Armas, Chris** — Soccer Player
Chicago Fire, 700 S Harlem Ave, Bridgeview IL 60455 USA
**Armatrading, Joan** — Singer, Songwriter
Entourage Talent Assoc, 236 W 27th St, #800, New York NY 10001, USA
**Armbrister, Edison R (Ed)** — Baseball Player
McQuay St, Box 2003, Nassau, Bahamas, West Indies
**Armedariz, Pedro, Jr** — Actor
Diamond Artists, 9200 W Sunset Blvd, #701, West Hollywood CA 90069 USA
**Armenante, Jillian** — Actress
Framework Entertainment, 9057 Nemo St, #C, West Hollywood CA 90069 USA
**Armerding, Hudson T** — Educator
780 Schick Road, #29W, Bartlett IL 60103, USA
**Armesto, Sebastian** — Actor
Curtis Brown Group, 28-29 Haymarket St, #500, London SW1Y 4SP, England
**Armey, Richard K** — Representative, TX
Citizens for a Sound Economy, 1775 Pennsylvania Ave NW, Washington DC 20006, USA
**Armfield, Diana M** — Artist
10 High Park, Kew, Richmond, Surrey TW9 4BH, England
**Armiliato, Marco** — Conductor
I M G Artists, Hogarth Business Park, Chiswick, London W4 2TH, England
**Armisen, Fred** — Actor, Comedian
W M E Entertainment, 9601 Wilshire Blvd, #300, Beverly Hills CA 90210 USA
**Armitage, Alison** — Actress, Model
9220 W Sunset Blvd, #305, West Hollywood CA 90069, USA
**Armitage, George** — Director, Producer, Writer
Gersh Agency, 9465 Wilshire Blvd, #600, Beverly Hills CA 90212 USA
**Armitage, Karole** — Choreographer, Dancer
350 W 21st St, New York NY 10011, USA
**Armitage, Richard** — Actor
United Agents, 12-26 Lexington St, London W1F 0LE, England
**Armitstead, Elizabeth M (Lizzie)** — Cyclist
M T C (UK) Ltd, 71 Gloucester Place, London W1U 8JW, England
**Armleder, John** — Artist
Simon Lee Gallery, 12 Berkeley St, London W1J 8DT, England

**Armour, Justin H**           Football Player
8 Crystal Park Place, #B, Manitou Springs CO 80829, USA
**Armour, Thomas D (Tommy), III**       Golfer
4211 Saint Andrews Blvd, Irving TX 75038, USA
**Armstead, Jessie W**           Football Player
1316 Mill Stream Dr, Dallas TX 75232, USA
**Armstead, Ray**           Track Athlete
7953 Bloom Dr, Saint Louis MO 63133, USA
**Armstrong Savola, Kristin**         Cyclist
Joe Savola, 455 E Cave Court, Boise ID 83702, USA
**Armstrong, A James**         Religious Leader
Broadway Methodist Church, 1100 W 42nd St, #210, Indianapolis IN 46208, USA
**Armstrong, Adger, Jr**          Football Player
6403 Paddington St, Houston TX 77085, USA
**Armstrong, Alex**          Actor, Comedian
Rights House, Drury House, 34-43 Russell St, London WC2B 5HA, England
**Armstrong, Alun**          Actor
Markham Froggatt Irwin, Julian House, 4 Windmill St, London W1P 1HF, England
**Armstrong, Ami**       Producer, Director, Writer
United Talent Agency, U T A Plaza, 9336 Civic Center Dr, Beverly Hills CA 90210 USA
**Armstrong, Anthony**        Guitarist (Red)
Paradigm Agency, 404 W Franklin St, Monterey CA 93940 USA
**Armstrong, Benjamin R (B J)**   Basketball Player, Executive
1550 Hawthorne Lane, Highland Park IL 60035, USA
**Armstrong, Bess**          Actress
Vox Inc, 6420 Wilshire Blvd, #1080, Los Angeles CA 90048 USA
**Armstrong, Billie Joe**     Singer, Guitarist (Green Day)
5652 Florence Terrace, Oakland CA 94611, USA
**Armstrong, Brandon S**        Basketball Player
New Jersey Nets, 390 Murray Hill Parkway, East Rutherford NJ 07073 USA
**Armstrong, Bruce C**         Football Player
12543 Brookwood Court, Davie FL 33330, USA
**Armstrong, Clay M**         Physiologist
University of Pennsylvania Medical School, 3400 Spruce, Philadelphia PA 19104, USA
**Armstrong, Craig**         Composer
First Artists Mgmt, 4764 Park Granada, #210, Calabasas CA 91302 USA
**Armstrong, Curtis**         Actor
Marshak/Zachary Co, 8840 Wilshire Blvd, #100, Beverly Hills CA 90211 USA
**Armstrong, Darrell E**        Basketball Player
337 Broadmoor Way, McDonough GA 30253, USA
**Armstrong, Deborah (Debbie)**      Alpine Skier
PO Box 770925, Steamboat Springs CO 80477, USA
**Armstrong, Derek**        Ice Hockey Player
873 8th St, Manhattan Beach CA 90266, USA
**Armstrong, George E**        Ice Hockey Player
22 Saint Cuthbert's Road, East York ON M4G 1V1, Canada
**Armstrong, Gillian**         Director
Creative Artists Agency, 2000 Ave of Stars, #100, Los Angeles CA 90067 USA
**Armstrong, Jack W**         Baseball Player
272 E River Park Dr, Jupiter FL 33477, USA
**Armstrong, Kerry**         Actress
Mike Morrissey Assoc, 16 Princess Ave, Rosebery, Sydney NSW 2018, Australia
**Armstrong, Kit**      Concert Pianist, Composer
June Artists Mgmt, Charlottenstra 43, 10117 Berlin, Germany
**Armstrong, Lance**         Cyclist
Penguin Books, 375 Hudson St, Basement 1, New York NY 10014 USA
**Armstrong, Linda**         Actress
Associated International Mgmt, 7 Hatton Garden, #400, London EC1N 8AD, England
**Armstrong, M Tate**        Basketball Player
14704 Westbury Road, Rockville MD 20853, USA
**Armstrong, Matthew John**        Actor
Don Buchwald, 6500 Wilshire Blvd, #2200, Los Angeles CA 90048 USA
**Armstrong, Michael D (Mike)**      Baseball Player
525 Ashbrook Court, Athens GA 30605, USA
**Armstrong, Neil**        Ice Hockey Referee
1169 Sherwood Trail, Sarnia ON N7V 2H3, Canada
**Armstrong, Neil F**      Football Player, Coach
312 Lakewood Dr, Roanoke TX 76262, USA
**Armstrong, Otis**         Football Player
7183 S Newport St, Denver CO 80220, USA
**Armstrong, Randy**         Bassist (Red)
Paradigm Agency, 404 W Franklin St, Monterey CA 93940 USA
**Armstrong, Raymond L (Trace)**     Football Player
422 SW 88th Terrace, Gainesville FL 32607, USA
**Armstrong, Rob**     Singer, Cittern Player (Tarras)
Rounder Records, 1 Rounder Way, Burlington MA 01803 USA
**Armstrong, Robb**      Cartoonist (Jump Start)
United Feature Syndicate, PO Box 5610, Cincinnati OH 45201 USA
**Armstrong, Robin L**         Physicist
383 Ellis Park Road, #383-303, Toronto ON M6S 5B2, Canada
**Armstrong, Rowland C O (Rolle)**   Musician (Faithless)
Helter Skelter, 347-353 Chiswick High Road, London W4 4HS, England
**Armstrong, Russell P**   Vietnam War Marine Corps Hero
425 Bench Road, Fallon NV 89406, USA
**Armstrong, Sheila A**     Opera, Concert Singer
Harvesters, Tilford Road, Hindhead, Surrey GU26 6SQ, England
**Armstrong, Spence M**       Air Force General
9120 Belvoir Woods Parkway, #117, Fort Belvoir VA 22060, USA
**Armstrong, T Robert (Bob)**     Basketball Player
6802 Packer Dr NE, Belmont MI 49306, USA
**Armstrong, Thomas**      Auto Racing Driver
PacWest Racing Group, PO Box 1717, Bellevue WA 98009, USA
**Armstrong, Thomas H W**      Concert Organist
1 East St, Olney, Bucks MK46 4AP, England
**Armstrong, Timothy L (Tim)**     Guitarist (Rancid)
Leave Home Booking, 10 W Broadway, #608, Salt Lake City UT 84101, USA

**Armstrong - Arnzen**

| | |
|---|---|
| **Armstrong, Tom** | Cartoonist (Marvin) |
| North American Syndicate, 235 E 45th St, New York NY 10017 USA | |
| **Armstrong, Ty** | Golfer |
| 11529 Kensington Dr, Eden Prairie MN 55347, USA | |
| **Armstrong, Valorie** | Actress |
| Contemporary Artists, 610 Santa Monica Blvd, #202, Santa Monica CA 90401 USA | |
| **Armstrong, Vaughn** | Actor |
| 1903 Apex Ave, Los Angeles CA 90039, USA | |
| **Armstrong, Victor M (Vic)** | Actor, Stuntman |
| Gersh Agency, 9465 Wilshire Blvd, #600, Beverly Hills CA 90212 USA | |
| **Armstrong, William L** | Senator, CO |
| Colorado Christian University, President's Office, Lakewood CO 80226, USA | |
| **Arnason, Chuck** | Ice Hockey Player |
| 39 Grimston Road, Winnipeg MB R3T 3T2, Canada | |
| **Arnaud, Jean-Loup** | Government Official, France |
| 55 Ave du Maine, 75014 Paris, France | |
| **Arnault, Bernard** | Businessman |
| Moet Hennessy Louis Vuitton, 30 Ave Hoche, 75008 Paris, France | |
| **Arnaz, Desi, Jr** | Actor |
| 516 Avenue M, Boulder City NV 89005, USA | |
| **Arnaz, Lucie** | Actress, Singer |
| David Williams Mgmt, 9614 Olympic Blvd, #F, Beverly Hills CA 90212, USA | |
| **Arndt, Judith** | Cyclist |
| Wermsdorder Str 28, 94277 Leipzig, Germany | |
| **Arndt, Michael** | Writer |
| Verve Talent/Literary Agency, 9696 Culver Blvd, #301, Culver City CA 90232 USA | |
| **Arndt, Stefan** | Producer |
| X-Filme Creative Pool, Kurfuerstenstr 57, 10785 Berlin, Germany | |
| **Arnelle, Jesse** | Basketball Player |
| 400 Urbano Dr, San Francisco CA 94127, USA | |
| **Arnesen, Liv** | Polar Skier |
| 16560 220th St N, Scandia MN 55073, USA | |
| **Arnett, Jon D** | Football Player |
| 200 Greenridge Dr, #715, Lake Oswego OR 97035, USA | |
| **Arnett, Peter** | Commentator, Journalist |
| ForeignTV.com, 162 5th Ave, #105A, New York NY 10010, USA | |
| **Arnett, Will** | Actor |
| W M E Entertainment, 9601 Wilshire Blvd, #300, Beverly Hills CA 90210 USA | |
| **Arnette, Jay H** | Basketball Player |
| 2 Hillside Court, Austin TX 78746, USA | |
| **Arnette, Jeannetta** | Actress |
| Connor Ankrum Assoc, 1680 Vine St, #1016, Los Angeles CA 90028, USA | |
| **Arnez, J** | Actor, Comedian |
| I C M Partners, 10250 Constellation Blvd, #900, Los Angeles CA 90067 USA | |
| **Arngrim, Alison** | Actress |
| PO Box 98, Tujunga CA 91043, USA | |
| **Arnhold, Henry H** | Financier |
| Arnhold & S Bleichroeder, 1345 Ave of Americas, #4300, New York NY 10105, USA | |
| **Arniel, Scott** | Ice Hockey Player |
| 6 Edmond Muys Place, Winnipeg MB R3P 2R1, Canada | |
| **Arning, Lisa** | Actress |
| Chasen Agency, 8899 Beverly Blvd, #405, Los Angeles CA 90048 USA | |
| **Arnold, Andrea** | Director |
| Sayle Screen, 11 Jubilee Place, London SW3 3TD, England | |
| **Arnold, Andrew** | Geneticist |
| Massachusetts General Hospital, Genetics Dept, Boston MA 02114, USA | |
| **Arnold, Anna Bing** | Philanthropist |
| Anna Bing Arnold Foundation, 9700 W Pico Blvd, Los Angeles CA 90035, USA | |
| **Arnold, Christopher P (Chris)** | Baseball Player |
| 2219 El Capitan Ave, Arcadia CA 91006, USA | |
| **Arnold, David** | Composer |
| Coalition Mgmt, 12 Barley Mow Passage, London W4 4PH, England | |
| **Arnold, Frances H** | Engineer |
| California Institute of Technology, Spalding Building, Pasadena CA 91125, USA | |
| **Arnold, Gary H** | Film Critic |
| 5133 N 1st St, Arlington VA 22203, USA | |
| **Arnold, James E (Jim)** | Football Player |
| 223 Boxwood Dr, Franklin TN 37069, USA | |
| **Arnold, Kristine** | Singer (Sweethearts of the Rodeo) |
| 2803 Bransford Ave, Nashville TN 37204, USA | |
| **Arnold, Morris S** | Judge |
| US Court of Appeals, 600 W Capitol Ave, #224, Little Rock AR 72201, USA | |
| **Arnold, Richard R (Ricky), II** | Astronaut |
| N A S A, Johnson Space Center, 2101 NASA Road, Houston TX 77058 USA | |
| **Arnold, Thomas D (Tom)** | Actor, Comedian |
| 9958 Kip Dr, Beverly Hills CA 90210, USA | |
| **Arnold, Tichina** | Actress, Singer |
| A P A Talent/Literary Agency, 405 S Beverly Dr, #300, Beverly Hills CA 90212 USA | |
| **Arnold, Walt** | Football Player |
| 8503 La Sala Grande NE, Albuquerque NM 87111, USA | |
| **Arnold, Walter (Walt)** | Rodeo Steer Roper |
| PO Box 713, Silverton TX 79257, USA | |
| **Arnoldi, Charles A** | Artist |
| 721 Hampton Dr, Venice CA 90291, USA | |
| **Arnott, Jason** | Ice Hockey Player |
| 155 Carondelet Plaza, #302, Saint Louis MO 63105, USA | |
| **Arnoul, Francoise** | Actress |
| 53 Rue Censier, 75005 Paris, France | |
| **Arns, Paulo E Cardinal** | Religious Leader |
| Avenida Higienopolos 890, CP 6778, 01064 Sao Paulo SP, Brazil | |
| **Arnsparger, Bill** | Football Coach, Administrator |
| 1574 Pine Needles Lane, Lexington KY 40513, USA | |
| **Arnstein, Holly** | Singer (Dream) |
| Bad Boy Entertainment, 1540 Broadway, #3000, New York NY 10036, USA | |
| **Arnzen, Robert L (Bob)** | Basketball Player |
| 8 Grand Lake Dr, Fort Thomas KY 41075, USA | |

**Aronofsky, Darren** — Director
Creative Artists Agency, 2000 Ave of Stars, #100, Los Angeles CA 90067 USA
**Arons, Arnold B** — Physicist
10313 Lake Shore Blvd NE, Seattle WA 98125, USA
**Aronsohn, Lee** — Producer, Writer
Paradigm Agency, 360 N Crescent Dr, North Building, Beverly Hills CA 90210 USA
**Aronson, David** — Artist
137 Brimstone Lane, Sudbury MA 01776, USA
**Aronson, Elliot** — Psychologist
University of California, Psychology Dept, Santa Cruz CA 95064, USA
**Aronson, Judie** — Actress
A T M Mgmt, 292 5th Ave, #400, New York NY 10001, USA
**Arp, Halton C** — Astronomer
Max Planck Physics/Radiology Institute, 84518 Garching Munich, Germany
**Arpaia, Donatella** — Restaurateur
Anthos Restaurant, 36 W 52nd St, New York NY 10019, USA
**Arpaio, Joseph M (Joe)** — Law Enforcement Official
102 W Madison St, Phoenix AZ 85003, USA
**Arpel, Adrien** — Businesswoman
Adrien Arpel Cosmetics, 400 Hackensack Ave, Hackensack NJ 07601, USA
**Arpey, Gerard J** — Businessman
A M R Corp, 4333 Amon Carter Blvd, Fort Worth TX 76155, USA
**Arquette, Alexis** — Actress
Innovative Artists, 1505 10th St, Santa Monica CA 90401 USA
**Arquette, David** — Actor
A P A Talent/Literary Agency, 405 S Beverly Dr, #300, Beverly Hills CA 90212 USA
**Arquette, Patricia** — Actress
Gersh Agency, 9465 Wilshire Blvd, #600, Beverly Hills CA 90212 USA
**Arquette, Rosanna** — Actress
Lovett Mgmt, 1327 Brinkley Ave, Los Angeles CA 90049, USA
**Arquez, Gaelle** — Opera Singer
I M G Artists, Hogarth Business Park, Chiswick, London W4 2TH, England
**Arraras, Maria Celeste** — Commentator
Telemundo Network Group, News Dept, 2470 W 8th Ave, Hialeah FL 33010, USA
**Arredondo, Rosa** — Actress
Talent Works, 3500 W Olive Ave, #1400, Burbank CA 91505 USA
**Arriaga, Guillermo** — Director, Writer
United Talent Agency, U T A Plaza, 9336 Civic Center Dr, Beverly Hills CA 90210 USA
**Arrigo, Gerald W (Jerry)** — Baseball Player
3740 Red Thorne Dr, Amelia OH 45102, USA
**Arrington, Jill** — Sportscaster
ESPN-TV, ESPN Plaza, 935 Middle St, Bristol CT 06010 USA
**Arrington, LaVar R** — Football Player
1514 Cedar Lane Farm Road, Annapolis MD 21409, USA
**Arrow, Kenneth J** — Nobel Economics Laureate
620 Sand Hill Road, #406C, Palo Alto CA 94304, USA
**Arroyo, Bronson A** — Baseball Player
23315 Frontier Way, Brooksville FL 34601, USA
**Arroyo, Carlos** — Basketball Player
1115 NW 126th Court, Miami FL 33182, USA
**Arroyo, Fernando** — Baseball Player
702 Hampton Woods Lane SW, Vero Beach FL 32962, USA
**Arroyo, Harry** — Boxer
726 S Salem Road, North Jackson OH 44451, USA
**Arroyo, Luis E** — Baseball Player
PO Box 354, Penuelas PR 00624, USA
**Arroyo, Martina** — Opera Singer
Berkshire Concert Artists, 20 Alfred Dr, Pittsfield MA 01201, USA
**Artemas, Cole** — Cartoonist
1050 Colonial St, Rutland VT 05701, USA
**Arterton, Gemma** — Actress
Independent Talent Group, 40 Whitfield St, London W1T 2RH, England
**Arteta, Miguel** — Director, Producer
W M E Entertainment, 9601 Wilshire Blvd, #300, Beverly Hills CA 90210 USA
**Arthur, Darrell** — Basketball Player
Memphis Grizzlies, 191 Beale St, Memphis TN 38103 USA
**Arthur, Elizabeth** — Writer
Bloomsbury LLC, 36 Soho Square, London W1D 3Q4, England
**Arthur, Fred** — Ice Hockey Player
203-1408 Ernest Ave, London ON N6E 3B2, Canada
**Arthur, Michael S (Mike)** — Football Player
11271 Terwilligers Vallet Lane, Cincinnati OH 45249, USA
**Arthur, Perry** — Golfer
7513 Zurich Dr, Plano TX 75025, USA
**Arthur, Rebeca** — Actress
Epstein-Wyckoff, 280 S Beverly Dr, #400, Beverly Hills CA 90212 USA
**Arthur, Stacy Leigh** — Model
Playboy Promotions, 2706 Media Center Dr, Los Angeles CA 90065 USA
**Arthurs, Paul (Bonehead)** — Guitarist (Oasis)
Ignition Mgmt, 54 Linhope St, London NW1 6HL, England
**Arthus-Bertrand, Yann M** — Photographer
Altitude, 30 Rue des Favorites, 75015 Paris, France
**Artist, Jacob** — Actor
A P A Talent/Literary Agency, 405 S Beverly Dr, #300, Beverly Hills CA 90212 USA
**Artsebarsky, Anatoli P** — Cosmonaut
Cosmonaut Training Center, Star City, 141160 Zvezdny Gorodok, Moscow Oblast, Russia
**Artson, Bradley Shavit** — Religious Leader, Rabbi, Educator
American Jewish University, 15600 Mulholland Dr, Los Angeles CA 90077, USA
**Artur, Sophie** — Actress
Agence Laurence Bagoe, 11 Rue Delambre, 75014 Paris, France
**Artzt, Alice J** — Concert Guitarist
51 Hawthorne Ave, Princeton NJ 08540, USA
**Artzt, Edwin L** — Businessman
3849 Hedgewood Dr, Lawrenceburg IN 47025, USA
**Arum, Robert (Bob)** — Boxing Promoter
36 Gulf Stream Court, Las Vegas NV 89113, USA

**A**

## Arutyunyan - Ashkar

**Arutyunyan, Gagik G** — Prime Minister, Armenia
Prime Minister's Office, Republic Square, Government House 1, 0010 Yerevan, Armenia

**Arvidsson, Margareta** — Beauty Queen, Model
Miss Universe Organization, 1370 Ave of Americas, #1600, New York NY 10019 USA

**Arvizu, Reginald (Fieldy)** — Bassist (Korn)
Mitch Schneider Organization, 14724 Ventura Blvd, #500, Sherman Oaks CA 91403 USA

**Arwady, Meredith** — Opera Singer
Columbia Artists Mgmt Inc, 1790 Broadway, #702, New York NY 10019 USA

**Arzu Irigoyen, Álvaro E** — President, Guatemala
Partida de Avanzada Nacional, 7A Avda 10-38, Guatemala City, Guatamala

**Asada, Mao** — Figure Skater
Kishi Kinen Taiikukan 1-1-1, Jinnan Shibuyahku, Tokyo 150 8050, Japan

**Asano, Tadanobu** — Actor
Anore, Ochiai Building, 6-17-15 Jingumae Shibuyuku, #9F, Tokyo 150 0001, Japan

**Asante, Amma** — Director, Writer
Judy Daish Assoc, 2 Saint Charles Place, London W10 6EG, England

**Asawa, Brian** — Opera Singer
Askonas Holt, Lincoln House, 300 High Holborn, London WC1V 7JH, England

**Asay, Chuck** — Cartoonist
Colorado Springs Gazette, 303 S Prospect St, Colorado Springs CO 80903, USA

**Asbaek, Pilou** — Actor
Lindberg Mgmt, Lavendelstraad 5-7, 1462 Copenhagen K, Denmark

**Asbaty, Diandra** — Bowler
Kaizen, 100 E 14th St, #1005, Chicago IL 60605, USA

**Asbury, Kelly** — Animator, Director, Writer
United Talent Agency, U T A Plaza, 9336 Civic Center Dr, Beverly Hills CA 90210 USA

**Asbury, Martin** — Cartoonist (Garth)
Stoneworld, Pitch Green, Princes Risborough, Buckinghamshire HP27 9QG, England

**Asbury, Richard** — WWII Army Air Corps Hero
1104 Kimberly Road, #907, Bettendorf IA 52722, USA

**Ascaride, Ariane** — Actress
Zelig, 57 Rue Reaumur, 75002 Paris, France

**Asch, Peter** — Water Polo Player
1946 Green St, San Francisco CA 94123, USA

**Aselton, Kathryn (Katie)** — Actress, Director, Producer
I C M Partners, 10250 Constellation Blvd, #900, Los Angeles CA 90067 USA

**Asencio, Henry** — Artist
Crown Thorn Publishing, 2375 Northside Dr, #200, San Diego CA 92108, USA

**Asfaw, Ingida** — Physician, Social Activist
2278 W Philadelphia St, Detroit MI 48206, USA

**Ash, Daniel** — Guitarist (Bauhaus, Love & Rockets)
Agency Group Ltd, 142 W 57th St, #600, New York NY 10019 USA

**Ash, Nadine** — Golfer
Quantum Sports Mgmt, 5625 E Wethersfield Road, Scottsdale AZ 85254, USA

**Ashanti** — Singer, Songwriter, Actress
Media Artists Group, 8222 Melrose Ave, #203, Los Angeles CA 90048 USA

**Ashbery, John L** — Writer
326 Belmont Ave, Buffalo NY 14223, USA

**Ashbrook, Dana** — Actor
Gage Group, 450 7th Ave, #1809, New York NY 10123 USA

**Ashbrook, Daphne** — Actress
Defining Artists, 10 Universal City Plaza, #2000, Universal City CA 91608, USA

**Ashby, Alan D** — Baseball Player
12011 Cypress Creek Lakes Dr, Cypress TX 77433, USA

**Ashby, Andrew J (Andy)** — Baseball Player
2 Osborne Dr, Pittston PA 18640, USA

**Ashby, Jeffrey S** — Astronaut
N A S A, Johnson Space Center, 2101 NASA Road, Houston TX 77058 USA

**Ashby, Linden** — Actor
639 N Larchmont Blvd, #207, Los Angeles CA 90004, USA

**Ashcroft, John D** — Attorney General; Senator, Governor, MO
5603 W Farm Road 54, Willard MO 65781, USA

**Ashcroft, Richard** — Singer (Verve), Songwriter
Fresh & Clean Media, 12701 Venice Blvd, Los Angeles CA 90066, USA

**Ashdown, J J D (Paddy)** — Government Official, England
Vane Cottage, Norton Sub Hamdon, Somerset TA14 6SG, England

**Ashenfelter, Horace, III** — Track Athlete
100 Hawthorne Ave, Glen Ridge NJ 07028, USA

**Asher, Barry** — Bowler
Professional Bowlers Assn, 719 2nd Ave, #701, Seattle WA 98104 USA

**Asher, Jane** — Actress
Jane Asher Cakes & Sugarcraft, 22-24 Cole St, London SW3 3QU, England

**Asher, Peter** — Singer (Peter & Gordon), Businessman
Santuary Artist Mgmt, 45-53 Sinclair Road, London W14 0NS, England

**Asher, Robert D (Bob)** — Football Player
4800 S Chicago Beach Dr, #612, Chicago IL 60615, USA

**Ashfield, Kate** — Actress
Independent Talent Group, 40 Whitfield St, London W1T 2RH, England

**Ashford, Annaleigh** — Actress
A P A Talent/Literary Agency, 405 S Beverly Dr, #300, Beverly Hills CA 90212 USA

**Ashford, Matthew** — Actor
260 S Beverly Dr, #208, Beverly Hills CA 90212, USA

**Ashford, Rob** — Choreographer
Creative Artists Agency, 2000 Ave of Stars, #100, Los Angeles CA 90067 USA

**Ashford, Roslyn** — Singer (Martha & Vandellas)
Soundedge Personal Mgmt, 332 Southdown Road, Huntington NY 11743, USA

**Ashford, Thomas S (Tucker)** — Baseball Player
502 S Maple St, Covington TX 76636, USA

**Ashida, Jun** — Fashion Designer
1-3-3 Aobadai, Meguroku, Tokyo 153 8521, Japan

**Ashihara, Yoshinobu** — Architect
47-10 Nishihara 3, Shibuyaku, Tokyo 151 0066, Japan

**Ashitey, Clare-Hope** — Actress
United Agents, 12-26 Lexington St, London W1F 0LE, England

**Ashkar, Saleem Abboud** — Concert Pianist
I M G Artists, Hogarth Business Park, Chiswick, London W4 2TH, England

| | |
|---|---|
| **Ashkenasi, Shmuel** | Concert Violinist |
| Caecilia, 5 Place de la Fustene, 1204 Geneva, Switzerland | |
| **Ashkenazy, Dimitri** | Concert Clarinetist |
| Harrison/Parrott, 5-6 Albion Court, London W6 0QT, England | |
| **Ashkenazy, Vladimir D** | Concert Pianist, Conductor |
| Savinka, Kappelistr 15, 6045 Meggen, Switzerland | |
| **Ashley, Adryenn** | Actress, Writer, Filmmaker |
| 925 Lakeville St, #304, Petaluma CA 94952, USA | |
| **Ashley, Billy M** | Baseball Player |
| 2787 Autumn Ridge Dr, Thousand Oaks CA 91362, USA | |
| **Ashley, Christopher** | Director |
| I C M Partners, 730 5th Ave, New York NY 10019 USA | |
| **Ashley, David** | Educator |
| University of Nevada Las Vegas, President's Office, Las Vegas NV 89154, USA | |
| **Ashley, Elizabeth** | Actress |
| 1223 N Ogden Dr, West Hollywood CA 90046, USA | |
| **Ashley, Jennifer** | Actress |
| Morgan Agency, 1200 N Doheny Dr, Los Angeles CA 90069, USA | |
| **Ashley, Merrill** | Ballerina |
| New York City Ballet, Lincoln Center Plaza, New York NY 10023 USA | |
| **Ashley, Robert R** | Composer |
| Brooklyn Academy of Music, 30 Lafayette Ave, New York NY 10007, USA | |
| **Ashman, Duane A** | Football Player |
| 2625 Antler Court, Silver Spring MD 20904, USA | |
| **Ashmore, Aaron** | Actor |
| K G Talent, 55A Sumach St, Toronto ON M5A 3J6, Canada | |
| **Ashmore, Darryl A** | Football Player |
| 8695 Thornbrook Terrace Point, Boynton Beach FL 33473, USA | |
| **Ashmore, Edward B** | Navy Admiral, England |
| Naval Secretary, Victory Building, H M Naval Base, Portsmouth, Hampshire PO1 3LJ, England | |
| **Ashmore, Shawn** | Actor |
| Gersh Agency, 9465 Wilshire Blvd, #600, Beverly Hills CA 90212 USA | |
| **Ashrawi, Hanan** | Political Leader, Palestine |
| Arab League, PO Box 11642, Tahrir Square, Cairo, Egypt | |
| **Ashton, Brent** | Ice Hockey Player |
| 311 Brabent Crescent, Saskatoon SK S7J 4Y9, Canada | |
| **Ashton, Dean** | Actor |
| Laine Mgmt, Laine House, 131 Laine Road, Salford M6 8LF, England | |
| **Ashton, John** | Actor |
| Beddingfield Co, 13600 Ventura Blvd, #B, Sherman Oaks CA 91423, USA | |
| **Ashton, Joseph** | Actor |
| Don Buchwald, 6500 Wilshire Blvd, #2200, Los Angeles CA 90048 USA | |
| **Ashton, Susan** | Singer |
| Sparrow Communications, 101 Winners Circle, Brentwood TN 37027, USA | |
| **Ashton-Griffiths, Roger** | Actor |
| 16 Chelmsford Road, London E11 1BS, England | |
| **Ashworth, Frank** | Ice Hockey Player |
| 5110 Hot Springs, Fairmont Hot Springs BC V0B 1L0, Canada | |
| **Ashworth, Gerald (Gerry)** | Track Athlete |
| PO Box 2, Ogunquit ME 03907, USA | |
| **Ashworth, Jeanne C** | Speed Skater |
| Whiteface Highway, Wilmington NY 12997, USA | |
| **Askew, Bobby D (B J), Jr** | Football Player |
| 4216 Lantana Dr, Lebanon OH 45036, USA | |
| **Askew, Desmond** | Actor |
| Paul Kohner, 9300 Wilshire Blvd, #555, Beverly Hills CA 90212 USA | |
| **Askew, Reubin O** | Governor, FL |
| PO Box 12487, Tallahassee FL 32317, USA | |
| **Askey, Tom** | Ice Hockey Player |
| 5732 S 6th St, Kalamazoo MI 49009, USA | |
| **Askson, Bert** | Football Player |
| 7713 Charlesmont St, Houston TX 77016, USA | |
| **Asman, David** | Commentator |
| Fox-TV, News Dept, 205 E 67th St, New York NY 10065 USA | |
| **Asmussen, Cash** | Thoroughbred Racing Jockey |
| 111 Devonshire Court, Laredo TX 78041, USA | |
| **Asner, Edward** | Actor |
| Greene Assoc, 1901 Ave of Stars, #130, Los Angeles CA 90067 USA | |
| **Asomugha, Nnamdi** | Football Player, Actor |
| 1050 Armitage St, Alameda CA 94502, USA | |
| **Asplin, Edward W** | Businessman |
| 601 Carlson Parkway, #1050, Hopkins MN 55305, USA | |
| **Aspromonte, Kenneth J (Ken)** | Baseball Player, Manager |
| 2 Derham Park St, Houston TX 77024, USA | |
| **Aspromonte, Robert T (Bob)** | Baseball Player |
| 1000 Uptown Park Blvd, #241, Houston TX 77056, USA | |
| **Assad, Badi** | Singer, Guitarist, Pianist |
| Aviv Productions, 10418 E Meadowhill Dr, Scottsdale AZ 85255, USA | |
| **Assad, Bashar al-** | President, Syria; Army General |
| Presidential Palace, Muharreem Abu Rumanch, Al-Rashid St, Damascus, Syria | |
| **Assad, Odair** | Concert Guitarist |
| Opus 3 Artists, 470 Park Ave S, #900N, New York NY 10016 USA | |
| **Assad, Sergio** | Concert Guitarist |
| Opus 3 Artists, 470 Park Ave S, #900N, New York NY 10016 USA | |
| **Assange, Julian P** | Businessman, Editor, Activist |
| Wikileaks, PO Box 4080, University of Melbourne, Melbourne VIC 3052, Australia | |
| **Assante, Armand** | Actor |
| A P A Talent/Literary Agency, 405 S Beverly Dr, #300, Beverly Hills CA 90212 USA | |
| **Assayas, Olivier** | Director, Writer |
| Creative Artists Agency, 2000 Ave of Stars, #100, Los Angeles CA 90067 USA | |
| **Asseltine, Brian H** | Baseball Player |
| 1488 Country Court, Santa Ynez CA 93460, USA | |
| **Assenmacher, Paul A** | Baseball Player |
| 500 Covington Cove, Alpharetta GA 30022, USA | |
| **Assim** | Rap Artist |
| Bad Boy Entertainment, 1440 Broadway, #16, New York NY 10018 USA | |

**A**

**Ashkenasi - Assim**

**Assinger, Armin** — Skier
Kuhweg 23, 9620 Hermagor, Austria
**Assis, Raymundo D Cardinal** — Religious Leader
Via Degli Etruschi 36, 00185 Rome Lazio, Italy
**Astacio Pura, Pedro J** — Baseball Player
2695 E Long Lane, Littleton CO 80121, USA
**Astar, Shay** — Actress
Franchot Mgmt, PO Box 48890A, Los Angeles CA 90048, USA
**Astbury, Ian R** — Singer (Cult)
Tom Vitorino Mgmt, 11606 Viny Road, Granada Hills CA 91344, USA
**Astin, Allen V** — Physicist
5008 Battery Lane, Bethesda MD 20814, USA
**Astin, John** — Actor, Director
3801 Canterbury Road, #505, Baltimore MD 21218, USA
**Astin, Mackenzie** — Actor
Sovereign Talent Group, 8421 Wilshire Blvd, #200, Beverly Hills CA 90211, USA
**Astin, Sean** — Actor
Rogers & Cowan, 8687 Melrose Ave, #G700, West Hollywood CA 90069 USA
**Astin, Skylar** — Actor
United Talent Agency, U T A Plaza, 9336 Civic Center Dr, Beverly Hills CA 90210 USA
**Astley, Rick** — Singer
Barry Collings Entertainment, PO Box 2112, Essex Hockley SS5 4WD, England
**Astrid** — Queen, Belgium
Royal Palace, Rue Brederode, 1000 Brussels, Belgium
**Asylmuratova, Altynai** — Ballerina
Mariinsky Ballet, Teatralnaya Square 1, 190000 Saint Petersburg, Russia
**Atala, Anthony** — Surgeon
Wake Forest University, Regenerative Medical Institute, Winston-Salem NC 27109, USA
**Atambayev, Almazbek S** — Prime Minister, Kyrgyzstan
President's Office, Government House, 720003 Bishkek, Kyrgyzstan
**Ataneli, Lado** — Opera Singer
I M G Artists, Hogarth Business Park, Chiswick, London W4 2TH, England
**Atchison, Doug** — Director, Writer
United Talent Agency, U T A Plaza, 9336 Civic Center Dr, Beverly Hills CA 90210 USA
**Atchison, Michael** — Editorial Cartoonist
Associated Press, Editorial Dept, 450 W 33rd St, #1500, New York NY 10001 USA
**Atchison, Scott B** — Baseball Player
1820 Barrington Dr, Keller TX 76262, USA
**Atelian, Taylor** — Actress
Abrams Artists, 9200 W Sunset Blvd, #1125, West Hollywood CA 90069 USA
**Athas, Peter G (Pete)** — Football Player
1125 NW 130th St, Miami FL 33168, USA
**Atherton, David** — Conductor
Askonas Holt, Lincoln House, 300 High Holborn, London WC1V 7JH, England
**Atherton, Keith R** — Baseball Player
1014 Cobbs Creek Lane, Cobbs Creek VA 23035, USA
**Atherton, Michael A** — Cricketer
Lancashire County Cricket Club, Old Trafford, Manchester M16 0PX, England
**Atherton, William** — Actor
Stone Manners Salners, 9911 W Pico Blvd, #1400, Los Angeles CA 90035 USA
**Atika, Aure** — Actress
Agence Artiste Adequet, 108 Rue Reaumur, 75002 Paris, France
**Atiyeh, Victor** — Governor, OR
Victor Atiyeh Co, 519 SW Park Ave, #205, Portland OR 97205, USA
**Atkin, Harvey** — Actor
527 S Curson St, Los Angeles CA 90036, USA
**Atkins, Christopher** — Actor
6934 Bevis Ave, Van Nuys CA 91405, USA
**Atkins, Douglas L (Doug)** — Football Player
8005 Clapps Chapel Road, Knoxville TN 37902, USA
**Atkins, Eileen** — Actress
Independent Talent Group, 40 Whitfield St, London W1T 2RH, England
**Atkins, Erica** — Singer (Mary Mary), Songwriter
Paradigm Agency, 404 W Franklin St, Monterey CA 93940 USA
**Atkins, Essence** — Actress
Don Buchwald, 6500 Wilshire Blvd, #2200, Los Angeles CA 90048 USA
**Atkins, Garrett B** — Baseball Player
Colorado Rockies Foundation, 2001 Blake St, #A, Denver CO 80205, USA
**Atkins, Gene R** — Football Player
3515 Sunnyside Dr, Tallahassee FL 32305, USA
**Atkins, Kenneth L (Chucky)** — Basketball Player
229 S Ortman Dr, Orlando FL 32811, USA
**Atkins, Pervis** — Football Player
8040 Ventura Canyon Ave, Springfield PA 19064, USA
**Atkins, Rodney** — Singer
McGhee Entertainment, 8730 Sunset Blvd, #200, West Hollywood CA 90069, USA
**Atkins, Sharif** — Actor
Christopher Wright Mgmt, 3207 Winnie Dr, Los Angeles CA 90068, USA
**Atkins, Tina** — Singer (Mary Mary), Songwriter
Paradigm Agency, 404 W Franklin St, Monterey CA 93940 USA
**Atkins, Tom** — Actor
106 Forestwood Dr, Venetia PA 15367, USA
**Atkinson, Allen E (Al)** — Football Player
218 Wells Lane, Springfield PA 19064, USA
**Atkinson, Conrad** — Artist
172 Erlanger Road, London SE14 5TJ, England
**Atkinson, George H (Butch)** — Football Player
6331 Fairmount Ave, El Cerrito CA 94530, USA
**Atkinson, Jayne** — Actress
S M S Talent, 8383 Wilshire Blvd, #230, Beverly Hills CA 90211 USA
**Atkinson, Kate** — Writer
Transworld Publishing, 61-63 Uxbridge Road, London W5 5SA, England
**Atkinson, Rick** — Journalist, Writer
Kansas City Times, Editorial Dept, 1729 Grand Ave, Kansas City MO 64108, USA
**Atkinson, Rowan S** — Actor, Comedian
P B J Mgmt, 22 Rathbone St, London W1T 1LA, England

**Atkov, Oleg Y** — Cosmonaut
Cosmonaut Training Center, Star City, 141160 Zvezdny Gorodok, Moscow Oblast, Russia
**Atlantov, Vladimir A** — Opera Singer
Vienna State Opera, Opernring 2, 1015 Vienna, Austria
**Atogwe, Oshiomogho I (O J)** — Football Player
496 Speyer Place, Saint Charles MO 63303, USA
**Attai, Kader** — Artist
Saatachi Gallery, Duke of York's H Q, King's Road, London SW3 4RY, England
**Attal, Yvan** — Actor, Director
Voyez Mon Agent, 20 Ave Rapp, 75007 Paris, France
**Attanasio, Paul** — Writer
Creative Artists Agency, 2000 Ave of Stars, #100, Los Angeles CA 90067 USA
**Attell, Dave** — Actor, Comedian
Creative Artists Agency, 2000 Ave of Stars, #100, Los Angeles CA 90067 USA
**Attenborough, David F** — Entertainer, Writer, Naturist
5 Park Road, Richmond, Surrey TW10 6NS, England
**Attenborough, Richard S** — Actor, Director
Old Friars, Beaver Lodge, Richmond Green, Surrey TW9 1NQ, England
**Attersee, Christian** — Artist
Vienna University of Applied Arts, Oskar Kokoschka-Platz 2, #3, 1010 Vienna, Austria
**Atterton, Edward** — Actor
I C M Partners, 10250 Constellation Blvd, #900, Los Angeles CA 90067 USA
**Attias, Daniel** — Director, Producer
Principato-Young, 9465 Wilshire Blvd, #880, Beverly Hills CA 90212 USA
**Attig, Rick** — Journalist
Portland Oregonian, Editorial Dept, 1320 SW Broadway, Portland OR 97201, USA
**Attkisson, Sharyl** — Commentator
CNN-TV, 190 Marietta Ave SW, Atlanta GA 30303 USA
**Attlee, Frank, III** — Businessman
Monsanto Co, 800 N Lindbergh Blvd, Saint Louis MO 63167, USA
**Attles, Alvin A (Al)** — Basketball Player, Coach
195 Villanova Dr, Oakland CA 94611, USA
**Atwal, Arjun** — Golfer
International Mgmt Group, Burlington Lane, London W4 2TH, England
**Atwater, H Brewster, Jr** — Businessman
I D S Center, 80 S 8th St, Minneapolis MN 55402, USA
**Atwater, Stephen D (Steve)** — Football Player
2510 Sugarloaf Club Dr, Duluth GA 30097, USA
**Atwell, Hayley** — Actress
Hamilton Hodell, 66-68 Margaret St, #500, London, W1W 8SR, England
**Atwood, Casey L** — Auto Racing Driver
Day Enterprises, 107 Flat Ridge Road, Goodlettsville TN 37072, USA
**Atwood, Colleen C** — Costume Designer
232 Aderno Way, Pacific Palisades CA 90272, USA
**Atwood, Harold L** — Zoologist
602 Castlefield Ave, Toronto ON M5N 1L8, Canada
**Atwood, Margaret E** — Writer
Curtis Brown, Haymarket House, 28-29 Haymarket, London SW14 4SP, England
**Atwood, Susie (Sue)** — Swimmer
5624 E 2nd St, Long Beach CA 90803, USA
**Atzmon, Moshe** — Conductor
P M G, 59 Lansdowne Place, Hove, East Sussex BN3 1FL, England
**Auber, Brigitte** — Actress
Agence A Berthomme, 72 Rue Notre Dame des Champs, 75006 Paris, France
**Auberjonois, Rene** — Actor
448 S Arden Blvd, Los Angeles CA 90020, USA
**Aubert, Brian** — Singer, Guitarist (Silversun Pickups)
Ink Tank Public Relations, 1824 W Sunset Blvd, #102, Los Angeles CA 90026, USA
**Aubert, Karen D (K D)** — Actress
Sovereign Talent, 8421 Wilshire Blvd, #200, Beverly Hills CA 90211, USA
**Aubin, Normand** — Ice Hockey Player
1287 Rue des Berges, Sorel-Tracy QC J3P 7X5, Canada
**Aubret, Isabelle** — Singer
Gerard Mays Productions, 110 Rue Saint Martin, 75001 Paris, France
**Aubrey, Juliet** — Actress
Ken McReddie Assoc, 101 Finsbury Pavement, London EC2A 1RS, England
**Aubry, Eugene E** — Architect
Morris/Aubry Architects, 3465 W Alabama St, Houston TX 77027, USA
**Aubry, Pierre** — Ice Hockey Player
110 Rue Buisson, Cap-de-la-Madelain, QC G8V 1K4, Canada
**Auburn, David** — Writer, Director
97 W Elmwood Ave, Clawson MI 48017, USA
**Aucoin, Adrian M** — Ice Hockey Player
421 N Grant St, Hinsdale IL 60521, USA
**AuCoin, Les** — Representative, OR
Bogle & Gates, 601 13th St NW, #370, Washington DC 20005, USA
**Aucoin, Rich** — Singer
Agency Group Ltd, 142 W 57th St, #600, New York NY 10019 USA
**Audette, Donald (Don)** — Ice Hockey Player
15 Rue de Chinon, Blainville QB J7B 1Y2, Canada
**Audiard, Jacques** — Director, Writer
Voyez Mon Agent, 20 Ave Rapp, 75007 Paris, France
**Audick, Daniel J B (Dan)** — Football Player
13253 Sparren Ave, San Diego CA 92129, USA
**Audran, Stephane** — Actress
Artmedia, 20 Ave Rapp, 75007 Paris, France
**Auel, Jean M** — Writer
PO Box 8278, Portland OR 97207, USA
**Auer, Jonathon (Jon)** — Musician, Songwriter (Posies)
Entourage Talent Assoc, 236 W 27th St, #800, New York NY 10001, USA
**Auer, Joseph (Joe)** — Football Player
1138 Washington Ave, Winter Park FL 32789, USA
**Auer, Peter L** — Plasma Physicist
220 Devon Road, Ithaca NY 14850, USA
**Auer, Victor** — Marksman
8 Dellbrook Ave, San Francisco CA 94131, USA

| | |
|---|---|
| **Auerbach, Daniel Q (Dan)** | Singer, Guitarist (Black Keys) |
| Q-Prime South, 131 S 11th St, Nashville TN 37206 USA | |
| **Auerbach, Frank** | Artist |
| Marlborough Fine Art Gallery, 6 Albermarle St, London W1X 4BY, England | |
| **Auerbach, Frederick S (Rick)** | Baseball Player |
| 2139 Stunt Road, Calabasas CA 91302, USA | |
| **Auerbach, Stanley I** | Ecologist |
| 3314 W End Ave, #202, Nashville TN 37203, USA | |
| **Auermann, Nadja** | Model, Actress |
| D N A Model Mgmt, 555 W 25th St, #600, New York NY 10001 USA | |
| **Auger, Brian** | Jazz Pianist |
| Earthtone, 8306 Wilshire Blvd, #981, Beverly Hills CA 90211, USA | |
| **Auger, Claudine** | Actress |
| Steve Kenis Co, Royalty House, 72-74 Dean St, London WID 3SG, England | |
| **Augmon, Stacey** | Basketball Player |
| 1412 European Dr, Henderson NV 89052, USA | |
| **Auguin, Philippe** | Conductor |
| I M G Artists, Hogarth Business Park, Chiswick, London W4 2TH, England | |
| **August, Bille** | Director |
| Creative Artists Agency, 2000 Ave of Stars, #100, Los Angeles CA 90067 USA | |
| **August, John** | Writer |
| United Talent Agency, U T A Plaza, 9336 Civic Center Dr, Beverly Hills CA 90210 USA | |
| **August, Pernilla** | Actress, Director |
| Agentfirman Planthaber/Kilden, Drottninggatan 55, 111 21 Stockholm, Sweden | |
| **August, Steve P** | Football Player |
| 7704 E 86th St, Tulsa OK 74133, USA | |
| **Augusta, Kim** | Golfer |
| 16 Rachella Court, East Providence RI 02914, USA | |
| **Augusta, Patrik** | Ice Hockey Player |
| HC Dukla Jihlava, Tolsteno 23, 58601 Jihlava, Czech Republic | |
| **Augustain, Ira** | Actor |
| 4715 Fauna St, Montclair CA 91763, USA | |
| **Augustin, Darrel J (D J), Jr** | Basketball Player |
| Toronto Raptors, Air Canada Center, 20 Bay St, Toronto ON M5J 2N8, Canada | |
| **Augustine, Gerald L (Jerry)** | Baseball Player |
| S74W13490 Courtland Lane, Muskego WI 53150, USA | |
| **Augustine, Norman R** | Businessman |
| 24131 Doreen Dr, Gaithersburg MD 20882, USA | |
| **Augustnyiak, Jerry** | Drummer (10000 Maniacs) |
| Paradise Artists, PO Box 1821, Ojai CA 93024 USA | |
| **Augustus, Seimone** | Basketball Player |
| 9315 Pettit Road, Baker LA 70714, USA | |
| **Aulby, Michael (Mike)** | Bowler |
| 2331 Brothers Dr, Lafayette IN 47909, USA | |
| **Auld, Alexander (Alex)** | Ice Hockey Player |
| 2005 Swallow Crescent, Thunder Bay ON P7C 4T9, Canada | |
| **Ault, Chris** | Football Coach |
| University of Nevada, Athletic Dept, Reno NV 89557, USA | |
| **Aumann, Robert J** | Nobel Economics Laureate |
| Hebrew University, Economics Dept, Mount Scopus, 91904 Jerusalem, Israel | |
| **Aumont, Michel** | Actor |
| 8 Rue Herold, 75001 Paris, France | |
| **Aung San Suu Kyi** | Nobel Peace Laureate |
| National League for Democracy, 97B W Shwegondine Road, Yangon, Myanmar | |
| **Auriemma, Geno** | Basketball Coach |
| 185 Garth Road, Manchester CT 06040, USA | |
| **Aurilla, Richard S (Rich)** | Baseball Player |
| 5448 E Mariposa St, Phoenix AZ 85018, USA | |
| **Ausbie, Hubert E (Geese)** | Basketball Player |
| 902 Arthur Dr, Little Rock AR 72204, USA | |
| **Ausmus, Bradley D (Brad)** | Baseball Player, Manager |
| 1644 Stratford Way, Del Mar CA 92014, USA | |
| **Auster, Paul** | Writer, Director |
| I C M Partners, 10250 Constellation Blvd, #900, Los Angeles CA 90067 USA | |
| **Austin, A Woody** | Golfer |
| 10906 W Havenhurst St, Maize KS 67101, USA | |
| **Austin, Charles** | Track Athlete |
| 514 Duncan Dr, San Marcos TX 78666, USA | |
| **Austin, Dallas** | Actor |
| J M G Mgmt, 18000 Coastline Dr, #8, Malibu CA 90265, USA | |
| **Austin, Debbie** | Golfer |
| 6733 Bittersweet Lane, Orlando FL 32819, USA | |
| **Austin, Denise** | Physical Fitness Expert |
| PrimeCare Systems, 610 Thimble Shoals Blvd, #402A, Newport News VA 23606, USA | |
| **Austin, Issaac E (Ike)** | Basketball Player |
| 1221 S 800 E, Salt Lake City UT 84105, USA | |
| **Austin, Jake T** | Actor |
| Paradigm Agency, 360 N Crescent Dr, North Building, Beverly Hills CA 90210 USA | |
| **Austin, John** | Basketball Player |
| 1330 Riggs St NW, Washington DC 20009, USA | |
| **Austin, Julie** | Actress |
| Abrams Artists, 9200 W Sunset Blvd, #1125, West Hollywood CA 90069 USA | |
| **Austin, K Darrell** | Football Player |
| 268 Austin Road, Union SC 29379, USA | |
| **Austin, Karen** | Actress |
| Gage Group, 14724 Ventura Blvd, #505, Sherman Oaks CA 91403 USA | |
| **Austin, Lynne** | Model |
| Playboy Promotions, 2706 Media Center Dr, Los Angeles CA 90065 USA | |
| **Austin, Patti** | Singer |
| Tom Estey Publicity, 144 E 22nd St, #1B, New York NY 10010, USA | |
| **Austin, Steve (Stone Cold)** | Professional Wrestler |
| Caliber Media, 9229 W Sunset Blvd, #720, West Hollywood CA 90069, USA | |
| **Austin, Teri** | Actress |
| 4245 Laurel Grove, Studio City CA 91604, USA | |
| **Austin, Timothy (Tim)** | Boxer |
| 9261 Calista Dr, North Ridgeville OH 44039, USA | |

**Austin, Tracy**	Tennis Player
Octagon Worldwide, 1751 Pinnacle Dr, #1500, McLean VA 22102 USA
**Auteuil, Daniel**	Actor
Artmedia, 20 Ave Rapp, 75007 Paris, France
**Auth, W Anthony (Tony), Jr**	Editorial Cartoonist
Philadelphia Inquirer, Editorial Dept, 1830 Town Center Dr, Langhorne PA 19047 USA
**Autry, Alan**	Actor
David Shapira Assoc, 193 N Robertson Blvd, Beverly Hills CA 90211 USA
**Auzenne, Troy A**	Football Player
1501 Bluff Court, Diamond Bar CA 91765, USA
**Avalon, Frankie**	Singer, Actor
4303 Spring Forest Lane, Westlake Village CA 91362, USA
**Avant**	Singer
Paradigm Agency, 360 N Crescent Dr, North Building, Beverly Hills CA 90210 USA
**Avant, Jason**	Football Player
112 Villas Court, Clementon NJ 08021, USA
**Avari, Erick**	Actor
Greene Assoc, 1901 Ave of Stars, #130, Los Angeles CA 90067 USA
**Avary, Roger**	Director, Writer
I C M Partners, 10250 Constellation Blvd, #900, Los Angeles CA 90067 USA
**Avati, Pupi**	Director
Via del Babuino 135, 00187 Rome, Italy
**Avdeeva, Yulianna**	Concert Pianist
Harrison/Parrott, 5-6 Albion Court, London W6 0QT, England
**Avdeyev, Sergei V**	Cosmonaut
Cosmonaut Training Center, Star City, 141160 Zvezdny Gorodok, Moscow Oblast, Russia
**Avellini, Robert H (Bob)**	Football Player
1085 Flamingo Dr, Roselle IL 60172, USA
**Averbukh, Ilia**	Ice Dancer
Skating Assn, Luchnesksia Nab 8, 119871 Moscow, Russia
**Averill, Earl D**	Baseball Player
1806 19th Dr NE, Auburn WA 98002, USA
**Averitt, William R (Bird)**	Basketball Player
Kim Averitt, 103 N O'Neal Ave, Hopkinsville KY 42240, USA
**Averno, Sisto J**	Football Player
4759 Bonnie Brae Road, Pikesville MD 21208, USA
**Averre, Berton**	Guitarist (Knack)
17510 Posetano Road, Pacific Palisades CA 90272, USA
**Avery, Brad**	Guitarist (Third Day)
Creative Trust, 5141 Virginia Way, #320, Brentwood TN 37027, USA
**Avery, Bryan R**	Architect
Avery Architects, 270 Vauxhall Bridge Road, London SW1V 1BB, England
**Avery, Eric A**	Bassist (Jane's Addiction)
DeMann Entertainment, 9465 Wilshire Blvd, #426, Beverly Hills CA 90212, USA
**Avery, James**	Actor
A K A Talent, 6310 San Vicente Blvd, #200, Los Angeles CA 90048 USA
**Avery, John E, Jr**	Football Player
12 Ballantree Circle, Asheville NC 28803, USA
**Avery, Kenneth W (Ken)**	Football Player
625 Indian Ridge Dr, Nashville TN 37221, USA
**Avery, Margaret**	Actress
Talent Works, 3500 W Olive Ave, #1400, Burbank CA 91505 USA
**Avery, Sean**	Ice Hockey Player
I C M Partners, 10250 Constellation Blvd, #900, Los Angeles CA 90067 USA
**Avery, Steven T (Steve)**	Baseball Player
2 Glenagles Court, Dearborn MI 48120, USA
**Avi**	Writer
859 S York St, Denver CO 80209, USA
**Avila, Jim**	Commentator
ABC-TV, News Dept, 77 W 66th St, New York NY 10023 USA
**Avildsen, John G**	Director
2423 Briarcrest Road, Beverly Hills CA 90210, USA
**Avise, John C**	Geneticist
University of Georgia, Genetics Dept, Athens GA 30602, USA
**Avital, Mili**	Actress
Liebman Entertainment, 25 E 21st St, #PH, New York NY 10010, USA
**Avnet, Jonathan M (Jon)**	Director, Producer
Creative Artists Agency, 2000 Ave of Stars, #100, Los Angeles CA 90067 USA
**Avory, Mike**	Drummer (Rolling Stones, Kinks)
Larry Page, 29 Rushton Mews, London W11 1RB, England
**Avril, Clifford S (Cliff)**	Football Player
Seattle Seahawks, 12 Seahawks Way, Renton WA 98056 USA
**Awalt, Robert M (Rob)**	Football Player
5011 Highgrove Court, Granite Bay CA 95746, USA
**Awrey, Donald W (Don)**	Ice Hockey Player
1015 Alaska Ave, Lehigh Acres FL 33971, USA
**Awtrey, Dennis W**	Basketball Player
38245 James Road, Nehalem OR 97131, USA
**Ax, Emmanuel**	Concert Pianist
Opus 3 Artists, 470 Park Ave S, #900N, New York NY 10016, USA
**Axel, Richard**	Nobel Medicine Laureate
435 Riverside Dr, #62, New York NY 10025, USA
**Axelrod, Jonathan H**	Molecular Biologist
Goldyne Savad Institute of Gene Therapy, PO Box 12000, Jerusalem 91120, Israel
**Axelsson, A Per Johan (P J)**	Ice Hockey Player
50 Fleet St, #301, Boston MA 02109, USA
**Axen, K Martin**	Guitarist (The Ark)
Live Nation, Linnegatan 89, Box 21451, 10451 Stockholm, Sweden
**Axley, Eric**	Golfer
1700 Cottage Wood Way, Knoxville TN 37919, USA
**Axwell**	DJ Musician
Mission Control, City Business Center, Lower Road, London SE16 2XB, England
**Ayadi, Naidra**	Actress
Josiane Stoh, 3 Allee Marie Laurent, 75020 Paris, France
**Ayala Gonzales, Robert J (Bobby)**	Baseball Player
11011 W Cottonwood Lane, Avondale AZ 85392, USA

**Ayala, Benigno (Benny)** — Baseball Player
PO Box 222, Dorado PR 00646, USA

**Ayala, Francisco J** — Geneticist, Molecular Biologist
2 Locke Court, Irvine CA 92617, USA

**Ayala, Luis I** — Baseball Player
Atlanta Braves, Turner Field, 755 Hank Aaron Dr, Atlanta GA 30315 USA

**Ayala, Paulie** — Boxer
3817 Southwest Blvd, Fort Worth TX 76116, USA

**Ayanbadejo, Obafemi** — Football Player
301 W G St, #134, San Diego CA 92101, USA

**Ayanna, Charlotte** — Actress
Bohemia Group, 8170 Beverly Blvd, #102, Los Angeles CA 90048, USA

**Aybar, Erick J** — Baseball Player
773 W Raven Dr, Chandler AZ 85286, USA

**Ayckbourn, Alan** — Writer, Director
Casorotto Ramsay, Waverley House, 7-12 Noel St, London W1F 8GQ, England

**Aycock, Alice** — Sculptor
62 Green St, #4, New York NY 10012, USA

**Aycox, Nicki** — Actress
Innovative Artists, 1505 10th St, Santa Monica CA 90401 USA

**Ayer, David** — Director, Writer
Creative Artists Agency, 2000 Ave of Stars, #100, Los Angeles CA 90067 USA

**Ayer, William S (Bill)** — Businessman
Alaska Airlines, 19300 International Blvd, Seattle WA 98188, USA

**Ayers, Chuck** — Cartoonist (Crankshaft)
Universal Press Syndicate, 4520 Main St, #700, Kansas City MO 64111 USA

**Ayers, Dick** — Cartoonist (Sgt Fury)
64 Beech St W, White Plains NY 10604, USA

**Ayers, Sam** — Actor
Bobby Ball Talent Agency, 4116 W Magnolia Blvd, #205, Burbank CA 91505, USA

**Aykroyd, Dan** — Actor, Comedian
Creative Artists Agency, 2000 Ave of Stars, #100, Los Angeles CA 90067 USA

**Aylesworth, Reiko** — Actress
Gersh Agency, 9465 Wilshire Blvd, #600, Beverly Hills CA 90212 USA

**Ayling, Robert J** — Businessman
Dwr Cymru Welsh Water, PO Box 690, Cardiff, CF3 5WL, Wales

**Aylward, John J** — Actor
Mitchell K Stubbs Assoc, 8695 Washington Blvd, #204, Culver City CA 90232, USA

**Aylwin Azocar, Patricio** — President, Chile
Teresa Salas 786, Providencia, Santiago, Chile

**Ayoade, Richard** — Director
W M E Entertainment, 9601 Wilshire Blvd, #300, Beverly Hills CA 90210 USA

**Ayodele, Akinnola J (Akin)** — Football Player
7105 David Lane, Colleyville TX 76034, USA

**Ayrault, Jean-Marc** — Prime Minister, France
Premier's Office, Hotel Matignon, 57 Rue de Varenne, 75700 Paris, France

**Ayres, Gillian** — Artist
Alan Cristea Gallery, 31-34 Cork St, London W1S 3NU, England

**Ayres, Rosalind** — Actress
Lou Coulson Assoc, 37 Berwick St, London W1V 8RS, England

**Aytes, Rochelle** — Actress, Producer
Innovative Artists, 1505 10th St, Santa Monica CA 90401 USA

**Ayton, Sarah L** — Yachtswoman
Lynx Sports Mgmt, Lymington Road, Lymington, Hampshire SO41 5S5, England

**AZ** — Rap Artist
Celebrity Talent Agency, 111 E 14th St, #249, New York NY 10003, USA

**Azarenka, Victoria** — Tennis Player
Best, 303 E Main St, #200, Louisville KY 40202 USA

**Azaria, Hank** — Actor, Singer
W M E Entertainment, 9601 Wilshire Blvd, #300, Beverly Hills CA 90210 USA

**Azarov, Mykola Y** — Prime Minister, Ukraine
Prime Minister's Office, Hrushevskoga 12/2, 252008 Kiev, Ukraine

**Azinger, Paul W** — Golfer
7847 Chick Evans Place, Sarasota FL 34240, USA

**Aznavour, Charles** — Singer, Actor, Songwriter
Agents Associes, 201 Rue du Faubourg Saint Honore, 75008 Paris, France

**Azria, Max** — Fashion Designer
B C B G/Max Azria, 1450 Broadway, #1700, New York NY 10018, USA

**Azuma, Norio** — Artist
4530 Broadway, #4F, New York NY 10040, USA

**Azuma, Takatmisu** — Architect
Azuma Architects, 3-6-1 Minami-Aoyama Minatoku, Tokyo 107 0016, Japan

**Azumah, Jerry** — Football Player
462 W Superior St, Chicago IL 60654, USA

**Azzara, Candice** — Actress
Maverick Entertainment, 6100 Wilshire Blvd, #550, Los Angeles CA 90048, USA

**Azzi, Jennifer L** — Basketball Player, Coach
Azzi Training, 8589 S Mardi Gras Lane, West Jordan UT 84088, USA

**B o B** — Rap Artist
T J D J's, 1424 Capitol Circle NW, Tallahassee FL 32303, USA
**B T** — Musician
Big Machine Media, 780 3rd Ave, #1500, New York NY 10017, USA
**Baab, Michael J (Mike)** — Football Player
PO Box 1808, Euless TX 76039, USA
**Baas, David A** — Football Player
7004 Lacantera Circle, Lakewood Ranch FL 34202, USA
**Babando, Peter (Pete)** — Ice Hockey Player
50 Sterling Ave W, Timmins ON P4N 3K3, Canada
**Babashoff, Jack** — Swimmer
17254 Santa Clara St, Fountain Valley CA 92708, USA
**Babashoff, Shirley** — Swimmer
17254 Santa Clara St, Fountain Valley CA 92708, USA
**Babatunde, Obba** — Actor
I C M Partners, 10250 Constellation Blvd, #900, Los Angeles CA 90067 USA
**Babb, Albert L** — Biomedical Engineer
PO Box 3429, Redmond WA 98073, USA
**Babb, Charlie** — Football Player
371 Heron Ave, Naples FL 34108, USA
**Babb, Eugene W (Gene)** — Football Player
5110 W 9th Ave, Stillwater OK 74074, USA
**Babbitt, Bruce E** — Secretary, Interior; Governor, AZ
World Wildlife Fund,1250 24th St NW, Washington DC 20090, USA
**Babbitt, Natalie** — Writer, Illustrator
Farrar Straus Giroux, 18 W 18th St, #700, New York NY 10011 USA
**Babb-Sprague, Kristen** — Synchronized Swimmer
4677 Pine Valley Dr, Stockton CA 95219, USA
**Babcock, Barbara** — Actress
Paradigm Agency, 360 N Crescent Dr, North Building, Beverly Hills CA 90210 USA
**Babcock, Michael (Mike), Jr** — Ice Hockey Coach
17891 Stonebrook Circle, Northville MI 48168, USA
**Babcock, Tim M** — Governor, MT
Ox Bow Ranch, PO Box 877, Helena MT 59624, USA
**Babenco, Hector E** — Director
I C M Partners, 10250 Constellation Blvd, #900, Los Angeles CA 90067 USA
**Babey, Pamela** — Interior Designer
Babey Moulton Jue Booth, 510 3rd St, #110, San Francisco CA 94107, USA
**Babich, Robert (Bob)** — Football Player
4994 Mount Ashmun Dr, San Diego CA 92111, USA
**Babilonia, Tai R** — Figure Skater
Diverse Talent Group, 1900 Ave of Stars, #2840, Los Angeles CA 90067, USA
**Babin, Jason T** — Football Player
2735 Peninsulas Dr, Missouri City TX 77459, USA
**Babineaux, Jonathan J** — Football Player
5659 Legends Club Circle, Braselton GA 30517, USA
**Babineaux, Jordan J** — Football Player
720 N 10th St, #227, Renton WA 98057, USA
**Babka, Richard (Rink)** — Track Athlete
1080 Silver Hill Road, Redwood City CA 94061, USA
**Babluani, Gela** — Director, Writer
W M E Entertainment, 9601 Wilshire Blvd, #300, Beverly Hills CA 90210 USA
**Baby Bash** — Rap Artist
J L Entertainment, 18653 Ventura Blvd, #340, Los Angeles CA 91356 USA
**Baby Oje** — Rap Artist (Arrested Development)
Agency Group Ltd, 142 W 57th St, #600, New York NY 10019 USA
**Baby Peggy** — Actress
1279 Southport Way, Gustine CA 95322, USA
**Babych, Dave** — Ice Hockey Player
1315 Wellington Crescent, Winnipeg MB R3N 0A9, Canada
**Babych, Wayne** — Ice Hockey Player
1315 Wellington Crescent, Winnipeg MB R3N 0A9, Canada
**Baca, David** — Drag Racing Driver
529 Garcia Ave, #C, Pittsburg CA 94565, USA
**Baca, John P** — Vietnam War Army Hero (CMH)
PO Box 154, Julian CA 92036, USA
**Baca, Susana** — Singer
Luaka Bop, 195 Chrystie St, #901, New York NY 10002, USA
**Bacall, Lauren** — Actress
Dakota Hotel, 1 W 72nd St, #43, New York NY 10023, USA
**Bacall, Michael** — Actor, Writer
Timaeus Group, PO Box 1432, Pacific Palisades CA 90272, USA
**Baccarin, Morena** — Actress
United Talent Agency, U T A Plaza, 9336 Civic Center Dr, Beverly Hills CA 90210 USA
**Bach Nunez, Jaume** — Architect
Avenida Diagonal 335, 08037 Barcelona, Spain
**Bach, Barbara** — Actress
2 Glynde Mews, London SW3 1SB, England
**Bach, Catherine** — Actress
Ziffren Brittenham Branca, 1801 Century Park W, #700, Los Angeles CA 90067 USA
**Bach, David** — Writer
W M E Entertainment, 9601 Wilshire Blvd, #300, Beverly Hills CA 90210 USA
**Bach, Jillian** — Actress
Abrams Artists, 9200 W Sunset Blvd, #1125, West Hollywood CA 90069 USA
**Bach, John W (Johnny)** — Basketball Player, Coach
2300 Clarendon Blvd, #306, Arlington VA 22201, USA
**Bach, Pamela** — Actress
International Talent Agency, 10 NBC Universal Studios Plaza, #2000, Universal City CA 91608, USA
**Bach, Richard** — Writer
Dell Publishing, 1540 Broadway, New York NY 10036, USA
**Bach, Sebastian** — Singer (Skid Row), Actor
New Ocean Media, 270 Doug Baker Blvd, #700, Birmingham AL 35242, USA
**Bach, Thomas** — Sports Executive
International Olympic Committee, Chateau de Vidy, 1007 Lausanne, Switzerland
**Bachar, Carmit** — Singer (Pussycat Dolls), Dancer, Actress
R S S Mgmt, 137 N Larchmont Blvd, #213, Los Angeles CA 90004, USA

# B

| | |
|---|---|
| **Bacharach, Burt**<br>681 Amalfi Dr, Pacific Palisades CA 90272, USA | Composer, Musician |
| **Bachardy, Don**<br>145 Adelaide Dr, Santa Monica CA 90402, USA | Artist |
| **Bachchan, Amitabh**<br>A B Corp, 13 North South Road, Juhu, Mumbai 400049, India | Actor |
| **Bacher, Aron (Ali)**<br>17 Romajador Ave, Sandhurst #4, Sandton, South Africa | Cricketer, Cricket Executive |
| **Bachfeld, Jochem**<br>Wandrumer Str 19, 19073 Wittenssorde, Germany | Boxer |
| **Bachleda, Alicja**<br>Hofflund/Polone, 9465 Wilshire Blvd, #420, Beverly Hills CA 90212 USA | Actress |
| **Bachman, Randy**<br>Paquin Entertainment, 468 Stradbrooke Ave, Winnipeg MB R3L 0J9, Canada | Singer, Songwriter, Guitarist |
| **Bachtadze, Michael**<br>I M G Artists, Hogarth Business Park, Chiswick, London W4 2TH, England | Opera Singer |
| **Baciocco, Albert J, Jr**<br>747 Pitt St, Mount Pleasant SC 29464, USA | Navy Admiral |
| **Back, Stephen A**<br>Oregon Health Science University, 3181 SW Jackson Park Dr, Portland OR 97239 USA | Pediatric Neurologist |
| **Backe, Brandon A**<br>103 E Viejo Dr, Friendswood TX 77546, USA | Baseball Player |
| **Backe, John D**<br>399 Park Ave, #1900, New York NY 10022, USA | Businessman |
| **Backhaus, Robin**<br>PO Box 6271, Ocean View HI 96737, USA | Swimmer |
| **Backis, Audrys Juozas Cardinal**<br>Via Urbisaglia 2, 00183 Rome Lazio, Italy | Religious Leader |
| **Backley, Stephen (Steve)**<br>Cambridge Harriers, 56A-60 Glenhurst Ave, Bexley, Kent DA5 3QN, England | Track Athlete |
| **Backman, R Christian**<br>784 Bellerive Manor Dr, Saint Louis MO 63141, USA | Ice Hockey Player |
| **Backman, Walter W (Wally)**<br>241 SE Mercury Lane, Prineville OR 97754, USA | Baseball Player, Manager |
| **Backstrom, Niklas O**<br>929 Portland Ave, #2701, Minneapolis MN 55404, USA | Ice Hockey Player |
| **Backstrom, Ralph G**<br>1625 Pelican Lakes Point, Windsor CO 80550, USA | Ice Hockey Player |
| **Backus, Christopher**<br>Don Buchwald, 6500 Wilshire Blvd, #2200, Los Angeles CA 90048 USA | Actor |
| **Backus, George E**<br>9362 La Jolla Farms Road, La Jolla CA 92037, USA | Geophysicist |
| **Backus, Gus**<br>Lustig Talent, PO Box 770850, Orlando FL 32877 USA | Singer (Del Vikings) |
| **Backus, Jeffrey C (Jeff)**<br>48075 Bellagio Court, Northville MI 48167, USA | Football Player |
| **Backus, Sharon**<br>University of California, Athletic Dept, Los Angeles CA 90024, USA | Softball Player, Coach |
| **Bacon, Henry**<br>10103 Grand Ave, #218, Louisville KY 40299, USA | Basketball Player |
| **Bacon, Kevin N**<br>W M E Entertainment, 9601 Wilshire Blvd, #300, Beverly Hills CA 90210 USA | Actor |
| **Bacon, Richard P**<br>Rights House, Drury House, 34-43 Russell St, London WC2B 5HA, England | Producer, Actor, Writer |
| **Bacon, Roger F**<br>24285 Johnson Road NW, Poulsbo WA 98370, USA | Navy Admiral |
| **Bacquier, Gabriel**<br>141 Rue de Rome, 75017 Paris, France | Opera Singer |
| **Bacri, Jean-Pierre**<br>Anne Alvares Correa, 34 Rue Jouffroy d'Abbans, 75017 Paris, France | Actor |
| **Bacs, Ludovic**<br>31 D Golescu, Sc III, E7 V Ap 87, Bucharest 1, Romania | Conductor, Composer |
| **Bacsik, Michael Joseph (Mike)**<br>4014 Falcon Lake Dr, Arlington TX 76016, USA | Baseball Player |
| **Bacsinszky, Timea**<br>Case Postale 22, 1092 Belmont-sur-Lausanne, Switzerland | Tennis Player |
| **Badalamenti, Angelo**<br>11 Fidelian Way, Lincoln Park NJ 07035, USA | Composer |
| **Badalucco, Michael**<br>Stone Manners Salners, 9911 W Pico Blvd, #1400, Los Angeles CA 90035 USA | Actor |
| **Badami, Anita Rau**<br>Carlisle Co, 121 E 17th St, New York NY 10003, USA | Writer |
| **Baddeley, Aaron**<br>8606 E Via del Sol Dr, Scottsdale AZ 85255, USA | Golfer |
| **Baddeley, Alan D**<br>York University, Psychology Dept, Heslington, York YO10 5DD, England | Psychologist |
| **Baddour, Raymond F**<br>6495 SW 122nd St, Miami FL 33156, USA | Chemical Engineer |
| **Bade, Lance**<br>9491 Berrey Lane, Colorado Springs CO 80925, USA | Marksman |
| **Bader, Beth**<br>713 S 7th St, Eldridge IA 52748, USA | Golfer |
| **Bader, Diedrich**<br>Paradigm Agency, 360 N Crescent Dr, North Building, Beverly Hills CA 90210 USA | Actor |
| **Bader, Larry**<br>1413 Westwood Dr SW, Faribault MN 55021, USA | Ice Hockey Player |
| **Badger, Brad**<br>3553 Milleford Court, Pleasanton CA 94588, USA | Football Player |
| **Badgley, Mark**<br>Badgley Mischka, 215 W 40th St, New York NY 10018, USA | Fashion Designer |
| **Badgley, Penn**<br>Anonymous Content, 3532 Hayden Ave, Culver City CA 90232 USA | Actor |
| **Badgley, William S**<br>505 E Waters Edge Dr, Belleville IL 62221, USA | Financier |
| **Badham, John M**<br>Badham Company, 16830 Ventura Blvd, #300, Encino CA 91436, USA | Director, Producer |

*Bacharach - Badham*

**Badham, Mary** — Actress
3720 Whitehall Road, Sandy Hook VA 23153, USA
**Badian, Ernst** — Historian
Harvard University, History Dept, Robinson Hall, Cambridge MA 02138, USA
**Badler, Jane** — Actress
PO Box 43, South Yarra VIC 3141, Australia
**Badly Drawn Boy** — Singer, Songwriter
Big Life Mgmt, 67-69 Charlton St, London NW11 1HY, England
**Badrov, Sergei** — Director
Arlook Group, 205 S Beverly Dr, #209, Beverly Hills CA 90212, USA
**Badu, Erykah** — Singer, Songwriter
Five Burroughs Entertainment, 2503 Main St, #201, Santa Monica CA 90405, USA
**Badura-Skoda, Paul** — Concert Pianist, Composer
Hochschule Musik, Lothringerstr 18, 1037 Vienna, Austria
**Baechtold, James E (Jim)** — Basketball Player
225 W Irvine St, Richmond KY 40475, USA
**Baek Sung-Dong** — Soccer Player
Football Assn, 1-131 Sinmunno, 2-Ga Jongno-Gu, Seoul 110 062, South Korea
**Baeling, Rebecca D (Becky)** — Singer, Actress
Abrams Artists, 9200 W Sunset Blvd, #1125, West Hollywood CA 90069 USA
**Baena, Marisa** — Golfer
3605 Dandelion Dr, Plano TX 75093, USA
**Baer, Gordy** — Bowler
8577 Tullamore Dr, Tinley Park IL 60487, USA
**Baer, Max, Jr** — Producer, Director, Actor
2795 Tam O'Shanter Dr, El Dorado Hills CA 95762, USA
**Baer, Olaf** — Opera Singer
Olbersdorferstr 7, 01324 Dresden, Germany
**Baer, Ralph H** — Inventor (Video Game Console)
134 Mayflower Dr, Manchester NH 03104, USA
**Baer, Robert** — Writer
Crown Publishing Group, 1745 Broadway, #1300, New York NY 10019 USA
**Baer, Robert J (Jacob)** — Army General
6213 Militia Court, Fairfax Station VA 22039, USA
**Baer, William** — Attorney, Government Official
Arnold & Porter, 555 12th St NW, Washington DC 20004, USA
**Baerga, Carlos O** — Baseball Player
PO Box 1667, Bayamon PR 00960, USA
**Baez Gonzalez, Danys** — Baseball Player
6190 SW 114th St, Miami FL 33156, USA
**Baez, Joan** — Singer, Songwriter
Mark Spector Co, 100 5th Ave, #1100, New York NY 10011, USA
**Baeza, Braulio** — Thoroughbred Racing Jockey
1588 Rosalind Ave, Elmont NY 11003, USA
**Baeza, Paloma** — Actress
United Agents, 12-26 Lexington St, London W1F 0LE, England
**Baffert, Robert A (Bob)** — Thoroughbred Racing Trainer
705 Carriage House Dr, Arcadia CA 91006, USA
**Bagayoko, Amadou** — Singer, Guitarist (Amadou & Mariam)
Partisan Arts, PO Box 5085, Larkspur CA 94977, USA
**Baggetta, Vincent** — Actor
4812 Ranchito Ave, Sherman Oaks CA 91423, USA
**Baggio, Roberto** — Soccer Player
Brescia F C, Via Bazoli 10, 27127 Brescia, Italy
**Baggott, Julianna** — Writer
Pocket Books, 1230 Ave of Americas, New York NY 10020 USA
**Bagian, James P** — Astronaut
21537 Holmbury Road, Northville MI 48167, USA
**Bagley, John E** — Basketball Player
31W450 Circle Dr, Elgin IL 60120, USA
**Bagley, Lorri** — Actress
Cinetic Mgmt, 555 W 25th St, #400, New York NY 10001 USA
**Bagnal, Charles W** — Army General
Ratchford Assoc, 221 W Springs Road, Columbia SC 29223, USA
**Bagnasco, Angelo Cardinal** — Religious Leader
Via Cassua 1, 00191 Rome Lazio, Italy
**Bagshawe, Tilly** — Writer
Warner Books, 1271 Ave of Americas, New York NY 10020 USA
**Bagwell, Jeffrey R (Jeff)** — Baseball Player
405 Timberwilde Lane, Houston TX 77024, USA
**Bahns, Maxine L** — Actress, Model
Glick Agency, 1321 7th St, #203, Santa Monica CA 90401 USA
**Bahnsen, Stanley R (Stan)** — Baseball Player
3500 Blue Lake Dr, #402, Pompano Beach FL 33064, USA
**Bahouth, Peter** — Association Executive
Greenpeace, 702 H St NW, #300, Washington DC 20001, USA
**Bahr, Chris** — Football Player
122 Kaywood Dr, Boalsburg PA 16827, USA
**Bahr, Iris** — Actress
Abrams Artists, 9200 W Sunset Blvd, #1125, West Hollywood CA 90069 USA
**Bahr, Matthew D (Matt)** — Football Player
53 Parkridge Lane, Pittsburgh PA 15228, USA
**Bahr, Walter A** — Soccer Player
250 Elks Road, Boalsburg PA 16827, USA
**Bahrani, Ramin** — Director, Writer
Creative Artists Agency, 2000 Ave of Stars, #100, Los Angeles CA 90067 USA
**Bahrke, Shannon** — Freestyle Skier
Q Sports Marketing, 534 W Evergreen St, Wheaton IL 60187 USA
**Bai Ling** — Actress, Model
Global Artists Agency, 6253 Hollywood Blvd, #508, Los Angeles CA 90028 USA
**Bailar, Benjamin F** — Government Official, Educator
410 Walnut Road, Lake Forest IL 60045, USA
**Bailes, Scott A** — Baseball Player
5895 S Teters Court, Springfield MO 65804, USA
**Bailey, Benjamin R (Ben)** — Actor, Comedian
Gersh Agency, 9465 Wilshire Blvd, #600, Beverly Hills CA 90212 USA

**Bailey, Christina (Chris)** — Ice Hockey Player
3902 N Main St, Marion NY 14505, USA

**Bailey, Christopher** — Fashion Designer
Burberry Prorsum, 18-22 Haymarket St, London SW1Y 4DQ, England

**Bailey, Damon** — Basketball Player
723 Diamond Road, Heltonville IN 47436, USA

**Bailey, David** — Photographer
Robert Montgomery, 3 Junction Mews, Sale Place, London W2, England

**Bailey, Donovan** — Track Athlete
625 Hales Chapel Road, Johnson City TN 37615, USA

**Bailey, Eion** — Actor
Gersh Agency, 9465 Wilshire Blvd, #600, Beverly Hills CA 90212 USA

**Bailey, F Lee** — Attorney
38 Blueberry Cove, Yarmouth ME 04096, USA

**Bailey, Fenton** — Director, Producer
Creative Artists Agency, 2000 Ave of Stars, #100, Los Angeles CA 90067 USA

**Bailey, G W** — Actor
Essential Talent Management, 7958 Beverly Blvd, Los Angeles CA 90048, USA

**Bailey, Harold** — Football Player
22502 Prince George Lane, Katy TX 77449, USA

**Bailey, J Mark** — Baseball Player
32703 Waltham Crossing, Fulshear TX 77441, USA

**Bailey, James R (Jim)** — Football Player
5219 Stone Creek Court, Lawrence KS 66049, USA

**Bailey, Jerry D** — Thoroughbred Racing Jockey
105 Nurmi Dr, Fort Lauderdale FL 33301, USA

**Bailey, Jim** — Actor, Singer, Female Impersonator
Stephen Campbell Management, 350 N Crescent Dr, #105, Beverly Hills CA 90210, USA

**Bailey, John I** — Cinematographer
W M E Entertainment, 9601 Wilshire Blvd, #300, Beverly Hills CA 90210 USA

**Bailey, Karsten M** — Football Player
16 Salbide Ave, Newnan GA 30263, USA

**Bailey, Keith E** — Businessman
Williams Companies, 1 Williams Center, Tulsa OK 74172, USA

**Bailey, Maxwell C** — Air Force General
4704 W Pearl Ave, Tampa FL 33611, USA

**Bailey, Mike** — Actor
University of Teesside, Performing Arts Dept, Middlesbrough Tees Valley, TS1 3BA, England

**Bailey, Norman S** — Opera Singer
84 Warham Road, South Croydon, Surrey CR2 6LB, England

**Bailey, Paul** — Writer
79 Davisville Road, London W12 9SH, England

**Bailey, Philip** — Singer, Musician (Earth Wind & Fire)
Performers of the World, 5657 Wilshire Blvd, #280, Los Angeles CA 90036 USA

**Bailey, Razzy** — Singer, Songwriter
Doc Sedelmeier, PO Box 62, Geneva NE 68361, USA

**Bailey, Robert M L** — Football Player
15325 SW 99th Ave, Miami FL 33157, USA

**Bailey, Robert S (Bob)** — Baseball Player
3181 Lido Isle Court, Las Vegas NV 89117, USA

**Bailey, Roland (Champ)** — Football Player
5744 Aspen Leaf Dr, Littleton CO 80125, USA

**Bailey, Scott** — Actor
Glick Agency, 1321 7th St, #203, Santa Monica CA 90401 USA

**Bailey, Stacey D** — Football Player
3400 Lakewind Way, Alpharetta GA 30005, USA

**Bailey, T Wayne** — Political Scientist, Social Activist
Stetson University, Political Science Dept, Deland FL 32720, USA

**Bailey, Thurl L** — Basketball Player
10265 N 6960 W, Highland UT 84003, USA

**Bailey, W Donald (Don)** — Football Player
14831 NW 7th Ave, North Miami FL 33168, USA

**Baillie, Kathy** — Singer (Baillie & the Boys)
1703 Old Hillsboro Road, Franklin TN 37063, USA

**Baillie, Victoria** — Singer, Songwriter
17 Coalville Road, Moe VIC 3825, Australia

**Bailly, Sandrine** — Biathlete
Residence Saint-Laurent, 10 Rue Jacques Cartier, 25300 Pontarlier, France

**Bailon, Adrienne E** — Singer (Cheetah Girls), Actress
Creative Artists Agency, 2000 Ave of Stars, #100, Los Angeles CA 90067 USA

**Bailor, Robert M (Bob)** — Baseball Player
1950 Swan Lane, Palm Harbor FL 34683, USA

**Baily, Martin N** — Government Official, Economist
McKinsey Global Institute, 1101 Pennsylvania Ave NW, Washington DC 20004, USA

**Bailyn, Bernard** — Historian
170 Clifton St, Belmont MA 02478, USA

**Bain, Barbara** — Actress
Barry Krost Management, 838 N Doheny Dr, #501, Los Angeles CA 90069, USA

**Bain, Michael** — Actor
W M E Entertainment, 9601 Wilshire Blvd, #300, Beverly Hills CA 90210 USA

**Bain, William E (Bill)** — Football Player
27661 Paseo Barona, San Juan Capo CA 92675, USA

**Baines, Harold D** — Baseball Player
PO Box 10, Saint Michaels MD 21663, USA

**Baines, Nicholas M (Peanut)** — Keyboardist (Kaiser Chiefs)
Red Light Mgmt, 8439 Sunset Blvd, West Hollywood CA 90069, USA

**Bainimarama, Josaia Voreqe (Frank)** — Prime Minister, Fiji
Prime Minister's Office, New Government Buildings, 6 Berkeley Crescent, Suva, Viti Levu, Fiji

**Baio, Scott** — Actor
Talent Works, 3500 W Olive Ave, #1400, Burbank CA 91505 USA

**Baiocchi, Hugh** — Golfer
142 Royal Saint Georges Way, Rancho Mirage CA 92270, USA

**Bair, C Douglas (Doug)** — Baseball Player
11545 Kemper Woods Dr, Cincinnati OH 45249, USA

**Bair, Sheila C** — Government Official
Federal Deposit Insurance Corp, 550 17th St NW, Washington DC 20429, USA

**Baird, Briny** — Golfer
3340 SW Rivers End Way, Palm City FL 34990, USA
**Baird, Diora** — Model, Actress
Don Buchwald, 6500 Wilshire Blvd, #2200, Los Angeles CA 90048 USA
**Baird, Fred (Butch)** — Golfer
PO Box 2633, Carefree AZ 85377, USA
**Baird, Janice** — Opera Singer
Opera et Concert, 37 Rue de la Chaussee d'Antin, 75009 Paris, France
**Baird, Jenni** — Actress
Kritzer Levine Wilkins Griffin, 11872 La Grange Ave, #100, Los Angeles CA 90025 USA
**Baird, Scott** — Curling Athlete
5835 Tall Pines Road, Bemidji MN 56601, USA
**Baird, Stuart** — Director
Mirisch Agency, 8840 Wilshire Blvd, #100, Beverly Hills CA 90211 USA
**Baird, William A (Bill)** — Football Player
6050 E Heaton Ave, Fresno CA 93727, USA
**Baird, Zoe** — Attorney
Aetna Life & Casualty, 151 Farmington Ave, Hartford CT 06156, USA
**Baitz, Jon Robin** — Writer
Creative Artists Agency, 2000 Ave of Stars, #100, Los Angeles CA 90067 USA
**Baiul, Oksana** — Figure Skater
Bob Young, PO Box 988, Niantic CT 06357, USA
**Bajcsy, Ruzena** — Electrical Engineer
University of California, Electrical Engineering Dept, Berkeley CA 94720, USA
**Bajema, Billy** — Football Player
2605 SW 120th St, Oklahoma City OK 73170, USA
**Bakatin, Vadim V** — Government Official, Russia
Reforma, Kotelnicheskaya Nab 17, 103240 Moscow, Russia
**Bakay, Nick** — Actor, Producer
A P A Talent/Literary Agency, 405 S Beverly Dr, #300, Beverly Hills CA 90212 USA
**Bakels, Kees** — Conductor
I M G Artists, Hogarth Business Park, Chiswick, London W4 2TH, England
**Baker, Alan** — Mathematician
Mathematical Science Center, Wilberforce Road, Cambridge CB3 0WB, England
**Baker, Anita** — Singer
W M E Entertainment, 9601 Wilshire Blvd, #300, Beverly Hills CA 90210 USA
**Baker, Betsy** — Actress
C E S D, 10635 Santa Monica Blvd, #130, Los Angeles CA 90025 USA
**Baker, Blanche** — Actress
Abrams Artists, 9200 W Sunset Blvd, #1125, West Hollywood CA 90069 USA
**Baker, Brian** — Guitarist (Bad Religion)
Goldstar Public Relations, PO Box 130, Ross on Wye HR9 6WY, England
**Baker, Carroll** — Actress
Abrams Artists, 9200 W Sunset Blvd, #1125, West Hollywood CA 90069 USA
**Baker, Charles E (Charlie)** — Football Player
PO Box 112593, Carrollton TX 75011, USA
**Baker, Colin** — Actor
Evans & Reiss, 100 Fawe Park Road, London SW15 2EA, England
**Baker, Dale** — Drummer (Sixpence None the Richer)
Nettwerk Mgmt, 1201 Villa Place, #206, Nashville TN 37212 USA
**Baker, Deanna** — Model
Playboy Promotions, 2706 Media Center Dr, Los Angeles CA 90065 USA
**Baker, Diane** — Actress
Blake Agency, 23441 Malibu Colony Road, Malibu CA 90265 USA
**Baker, Donald K** — Cinematographer
11789 Lakeshore N, Auburn CA 95602, USA
**Baker, Douglas L (Doug)** — Baseball Player
116 Woodthrush Lane, Fallbrook CA 92028, USA
**Baker, Dylan** — Actor
Paradigm Agency, 360 N Crescent Dr, North Building, Beverly Hills CA 90210 USA
**Baker, Earl P, Jr** — WW II Navy Hero (CMH)
10100 Cypress Cove Dr, #320, Fort Myers FL 33908, USA
**Baker, Ellen Shulman** — Astronaut
2207 Garden Stream Court, Houston TX 77062, USA
**Baker, Elzie W (Buddy), Jr** — Auto Racing Driver
4860 Moonlite Bay Dr, Sherrills Ford NC 28673, USA
**Baker, Ginger** — Drummer (Cream, Masters of Reality)
Twist Mgmt, 4230 Del Rey Ave, #621, Marina del Rey CA 90292, USA
**Baker, Graham** — Director
United Agents, 12-26 Lexington St, London W1F 0LE, England
**Baker, Homer** — WW II Army Air Corps Hero
8112 S Los Feliz Dr, Tempe AZ 85284, USA
**Baker, Howard H, Jr** — Senator, TN; Diplomat
Baker Donelson Assoc, 920 Massachusetts Ave NW, Washington DC 20001, USA
**Baker, J Albert L (Bubba)** — Football Player
2784 Trinity Court, Avon OH 44011, USA
**Baker, Jaime** — Ice Hockey Player
210 Highland Oaks Dr, Los Gatos CA 95032, USA
**Baker, James A, III** — Secretary, State
Baker & Botts, 1299 Pennsylvania Ave NW, #1200, Washington DC 20004, USA
**Baker, James P (Jamie)** — Ice Hockey Player
18590 Farragut Lane, Los Gatos CA 95030, USA
**Baker, Janet A** — Opera, Concert Singer
Transart Ltd, 8 Bristol Gardens, London W9 2JG, England
**Baker, Jason M** — Football Player
435 S Tryon St, #906, Charlotte NC 28202, USA
**Baker, Joe Don** — Actor
23339 Hatteras St, Woodland Hills CA 91367, USA
**Baker, John** — Dog Sled Racer
General Delivery, Kotzebue AK 99752, USA
**Baker, Johnnie B (Dusty), Jr** — Baseball Player, Manager
40 Livingston Terrace Dr, San Bruno CA 94066, USA
**Baker, Jordan** — Actress
Douglas Gorman Rothacker, 1501 Broadway, #703, New York NY 10036, USA
**Baker, Kathy** — Actress
Abrams Artists, 9200 W Sunset Blvd, #1125, West Hollywood CA 90069 USA

# B

| | |
|---|---|
| **Baker, Kenneth (Kenny)** | Actor |
| 51 Mulgrave Ave, Aston upon Ribble, Preston, Lancashire PR2 1HJ, England | |
| **Baker, Kitana** | Model, Actress |
| PO Box 452, 231 E Alessandro Blvd, #A, Riverside CA 92502, USA | |
| **Baker, Laurie** | Ice Hockey Player |
| 67 Prairie St, Concord MA 01742, USA | |
| **Baker, Leigh-Allyn** | Actor |
| Stone Manners Salners, 9911 W Pico Blvd, #1400, Los Angeles CA 90035 USA | |
| **Baker, Leslie David** | Actor |
| Innovative Artists, 1505 10th St, Santa Monica CA 90401 USA | |
| **Baker, Lewis** | Singer (Danny & the Juniors) |
| Joe Terry Mgmt, PO Box 279, Williamstown NJ 08094, USA | |
| **Baker, Mark** | Bowler |
| 665 Park Dr, #20, Costa Mesa CA 92627, USA | |
| **Baker, Mark-Linn** | Actor |
| 2625 6th St, #2, Santa Monica CA 90405, USA | |
| **Baker, Melissa** | Model |
| Click Model Mgmt, 881 7th Ave, New York NY 10019 USA | |
| **Baker, Michael A (Mike)** | Astronaut |
| N A S A, Johnson Space Center, 2101 NASA Road, Houston TX 77058 USA | |
| **Baker, Myron T** | Football Player |
| 297 Pearl Road, Alexandria LA 71302, USA | |
| **Baker, Paul T** | Anthropologist |
| 337 Upton Pyne Dr, Brentwood CA 94513, USA | |
| **Baker, Penny** | Model, Actress |
| PO Box 1116, Orchard Park NY 14127, USA | |
| **Baker, Peter** | Golfer |
| Int'l Mgmt Group, Hogarth Business Park, Chiswick, London W4 2TH, England | |
| **Baker, Phil** | Producer, Writer |
| I C M Partners, 10250 Constellation Blvd, #900, Los Angeles CA 90067 USA | |
| **Baker, Ralph R** | Football Player |
| 36 Sunshine Circle, Lewistown PA 17044, USA | |
| **Baker, Raymond (Ray)** | Actor |
| Abrams Artists, 9200 W Sunset Blvd, #1125, West Hollywood CA 90069 USA | |
| **Baker, Richard H** | Representative, LA |
| Managed Funds Assn, 2025 M St NW, #610, Washington DC 20036, USA | |
| **Baker, Rick** | Makeup Artist |
| Cinovation Studios, 6527 San Fernando Road, Glendale CA 91201, USA | |
| **Baker, Robby** | Guitarist (Tragically Hip) |
| Bobby Breen Mgmt, 13 Blackburn St, #300, Toronto ON M4M 2B3, Canada | |
| **Baker, Robert** | Actor |
| Paul Kohner, 9300 Wilshire Blvd, #555, Beverly Hills CA 90212 USA | |
| **Baker, Russell W** | Columnist |
| New York Times, Editorial Dept, 229 W 43rd St, New York NY 10036, USA | |
| **Baker, Scott Thompson** | Actor, Director |
| 11661 San Vicente Blvd, #307, Los Angeles CA 90049, USA | |
| **Baker, Sean S** | Director, Producer, Writer |
| Gersh Agency, 9465 Wilshire Blvd, #600, Beverly Hills CA 90212 USA | |
| **Baker, Simon** | Actor |
| Untitled Entertainment, 350 S Beverly Dr, #200, Beverly Hills CA 90212 USA | |
| **Baker, Steve** | Ice Hockey Player |
| 2929 N 70th St, #3087, Scottsdale AZ 85251, USA | |
| **Baker, T Scott** | Baseball Player |
| 327 Lingering Lane, Henderson NV 89012, USA | |
| **Baker, Terry W** | Football Player |
| 3208 SW Fairmount Blvd, Portland OR 97239, USA | |
| **Baker, Tony F** | Football Player |
| 3847 Eagleston Court, High Point NC 27265, USA | |
| **Baker, Vincent L (Vin)** | Basketball Player |
| PO Box 179, Old Saybrook CT 06475, USA | |
| **Baker, W Thane** | Track Athlete |
| 6704 Saint John Court, Granbury TX 76049, USA | |
| **Baker, William (Bill)** | Ice Hockey Player |
| 5638 Ojibwa Road, Brainerd MN 56401, USA | |
| **Baker-Finch, Ian M** | Golfer |
| 11309 Caladium Lane, Palm Beach Gardens FL 33418, USA | |
| **Baker-Guadagnino, Kathy** | Golfer |
| 1535 SW 4th Circle, Boca Raton FL 33486, USA | |
| **Bakhit, Marouf al-** | Prime Minister, Jordan |
| Prime Minister's Office, PO Box 80, 35216 Amman, Jordan | |
| **Bakhtair, Rudi** | Commentator |
| CNN-TV, 190 Marietta Ave SW, Atlanta GA 30303 USA | |
| **Bakke, Brenda** | Actress |
| 5615 Foxwood Dr, #B, Oak Park CA 91377, USA | |
| **Bakkedahl, Dan** | Actor |
| Paradigm Agency, 360 N Crescent Dr, North Building, Beverly Hills CA 90210 USA | |
| **Bakken, Earl** | Heart Surgeon, Inventor |
| Medtronic Inc, PO Box 38460, Waikoloa HI 96738, USA | |
| **Bakken, James L (Jim)** | Football Player |
| 4801 Holiday Dr, Madison WI 53711, USA | |
| **Bakken, Jill** | Bobsled Athlete |
| 23701 3rd Place W, Bothell WA 98021, USA | |
| **Bakker, Billy** | Field Hockey Player |
| Amsterdamsche Hockey Club, Postbus 7843, 1008 Amsterdam AA, Netherlands | |
| **Bakker, James O (Jim)** | Religious Leader |
| 180 Grace Chapel Road, #201, Blue Eye MO 65611, USA | |
| **Bako, Brigitte** | Actress |
| Hartig-Hilepo Agency, 54 W 21st St, #610, New York NY 10010 USA | |
| **Bako, G Paul, II** | Baseball Player |
| 500 Princeton Woods Loop, Lafayette LA 70508, USA | |
| **Bakovic, Peter (Pete)** | Ice Hockey Player |
| 7991 S 47th St, Franklin WI 53132, USA | |
| **Bakshi, Ralph** | Animator |
| PO Box 4322, Los Angeles CA 90076, USA | |
| **Bakula, Scott** | Actor |
| Anonymous Content, 3532 Hayden Ave, Culver City CA 90232, USA | |

**Baker - Bakula**

**Bala, Chris** — Ice Hockey Player
271 Beacon Dr, Phoenixville PA 19460, USA
**Balaban, Bob** — Actor, Director
Susan Smith, 1344 N Wetherly Dr, Los Angeles CA 90069 USA
**Baladi, Patrick** — Actor
United Agents, 12-26 Lexington St, London W1F 0LE, England
**Baladmenti, Angelo** — Composer
4146 Lankershim Blvd, #401, North Hollywood CA 91602, USA
**Balan, Vidya** — Actress
Bling Entertainment Solutions, Off Dr E Moses Road, Worli, Mumbai 400018, India
**Balandin, Aleksandr N** — Cosmonaut
Cosmonaut Training Center, Star City, 141160 Zvezdny Gorodok, Moscow Oblast, Russia
**Balaski, Belinda** — Actress
PO Box 461011, Los Angeles CA 90046, USA
**Balassa, Sandor** — Composer
18 Sumegvar Str, 1118 Budapest, Hungary
**Balasubramanian, Shankar** — Chemist
University of Cambridge, Chemistry Dept, Old Schools, Trinity Lane, Cambridge CB2 1TN, England
**Balasubramanyam, Rajeev** — Writer
Bloomsbury Publishing, 50 Bedford Square, London WC1B 3DP, England
**Balaz, John L** — Baseball Player
2916 Worden St, San Diego CA 92110, USA
**Balbi, Raul H (Pepe)** — Boxer
Edgardo Rosani Morresi, Cortina 2057, Buenos Aires 1408, Argentina
**Balboa, Marcelo** — Soccer Player
13139 Hedda Dr, Cerritos CA 90703, USA
**Balboni, Stephen C (Steve)** — Baseball Player
117 Burlington Road, New Providence NJ 07974, USA
**Baldacci, David** — Writer
10509 Braddock Road, #2D, Fairfax VA 22032, USA
**Baldacci, John E** — Governor, ME; Government Official
Pierce Atwood L L P, Merrill's Wharf, 254 Commercial St, Portland ME 04101, USA
**Baldelli, Rocco D** — Baseball Player
81 Windsong Road, Cumberland RI 02864, USA
**Balderis-Sildedzis, Helmuts** — Ice Hockey Player
Hockey Federation, Raunas Lela 23, 1039 Tiga, Latvia
**Balderstone, James S** — Businessman
115 Mont Albert Road, Canterbury VIC 3126, Australia
**Baldes, Kevin** — Bassist (Lit)
Sepetys Entertainment, 5543 Edmondson Park, #8A, Nashville TN 37211, USA
**Baldeschwieler, John D** — Chemist
PO Box 50065, Pasadena CA 91115, USA
**Baldessari, John** — Conceptual Artist, Photographer
702 6th Ave, Venice CA 90291, USA
**Balding, Rebecca** — Actress
2001 Winnetka Place, Woodland Hills CA 91364, USA
**Baldinger, Brian D** — Football Player, Sportscaster
21 S Elmwood Road, Marlton NJ 08053, USA
**Baldinger, Gary T** — Football Player
114 Adam Road, Massapequa NY 11758, USA
**Baldinger, Richard L (Rich)** — Football Player
5401 Phelps Road, Kansas City MO 64136, USA
**Baldini, Ercole** — Cyclist
Viale Bologna 103, 04710 Ferli, Italy
**Baldischwiler, J Karl** — Football Player
3033 N Willow Dr, Newcastle OK 73065, USA
**Baldock, Bobby Ray** — Judge
US Court of Appeals, PO Box 2388, Roswell NM 88202, USA
**Baldoni, Justin** — Actor
Talent Works, 3500 W Olive Ave, #1400, Burbank CA 91505 USA
**Baldschun, Jack E** — Baseball Player
311 Erie Road, Green Bay WI 54311, USA
**Balducci, Lorenzo** — Actor
Carol Levi Mgmt, Via Giuseppe Pisanelli 2, 00196 Rome, Italy
**Baldwin, Adam** — Actor
Innovative Artists, 1505 10th St, Santa Monica CA 90401 USA
**Baldwin, Alec** — Actor
N2N Entertainment, 1230 Montana Ave, #203, Santa Monica CA 90403, USA
**Baldwin, Bobby** — Poker Player
City Center Las Vegas, 3780 Las Vegas Boulevard S, Paradise NV 89109, USA
**Baldwin, Daniel** — Actor
Chaotik, 6446 Santa Monica Blvd, Los Angeles CA 90038 90038, USA
**Baldwin, David G (Dave)** — Baseball Player
PO Box 190, Yachats OR 97498, USA
**Baldwin, Hunt** — Producer, Writer
Creative Artists Agency, 2000 Ave of Stars, #100, Los Angeles CA 90067 USA
**Baldwin, Jack** — Auto Racing Driver
4748 Balmoral Way NE, Marietta GA 30068, USA
**Baldwin, Jack E** — Chemist
Oxford University, Dyson Perrins Laboratory, S Parks Road, Oxford OX1 3QY, England
**Baldwin, John A (Jack), Jr** — Navy Admiral
1371 Millersville Road, Millersville MD 21108, USA
**Baldwin, John, Jr** — Figure Skater
Lee Marshall Mgmt, 199 E Garfield Ave, Aurora OH 44202, USA
**Baldwin, Judith** — Actress
Grant Savic Kopaloff & Associates, 6399 Wilshire Blvd, #415, Los Angeles CA 90048, USA
**Baldwin, Karen D** — Beauty Queen, Actress
Miss Universe Organization, 1370 Ave of Americas, #1600, New York NY 10019 USA
**Baldwin, Keith M** — Football Player
124 Leonardville Road, Belford NJ 07718, USA
**Baldwin, Kevin** — Writer
Bloomsbury Publishing, 50 Bedford Square, London WC1B 3DP, England
**Baldwin, Margaret** — Writer
PO Box 1106, Williams Bay WI 53191, USA
**Baldwin, Randy C** — Football Player
715 Peeples St SW, #10, Atlanta GA 30310, USA

**Baldwin, Stephen** — Actor
Chaotik, 6446 Santa Monica Blvd, Los Angeles CA 90038, USA
**Baldwin, William** — Editor
Forbes, Editorial Dept, 60 5th Ave, New York NY 10011, USA
**Baldwin, William (Billy)** — Actor
Brillstein Entertainment Partners, 9150 Wilshire Blvd, #350, Beverly Hills CA 90212 USA
**Bale, Christian** — Actor
W M E Entertainment, 9601 Wilshire Blvd, #300, Beverly Hills CA 90210 USA
**Bale, John R** — Baseball Player
9017 Roberts Road, Odessa FL 33556, USA
**Bales, Michael (Mike)** — Ice Hockey Player
470 Brunswick Ave, Toronto ON M5R 2Z5, Canada
**Balestrini, Jose** — Opera Singer
I M G Artists, Hogarth Business Park, Chiswick, London W4 2TH, England
**Balfour, Earl** — Ice Hockey Player
71 Beasley Crescent, Cambridge ON N1T 1P5, Canada
**Balfour, Eric** — Actor
United Talent Agency, U T A Plaza, 9336 Civic Center Dr, Beverly Hills CA 90210 USA
**Balfour, Grant R** — Baseball Player
2678 N McMullen Booth Road, Clearwater FL 33761, USA
**Baliani, Marco** — Actor
Carol Levi Mgmt, Via Giuseppe Pisanelli 2, 00196 Rome, Italy
**Balic, Ivano** — Handball Player
Club Balonmano Atletico, Paseo del Pintor Rosales, 26 Bajos Derecha, 28008 Madrid, Spain
**Baliga, Bantval Jayant** — Electrical Engineer
2612 Bembridge Dr, Raleigh NC 27613, USA
**Baliles, Gerald L** — Governor, VA
University of Virginia, Miller Public Affairs School, Charlottesville VA 22903, USA
**Balin, Marty** — Singer, Songwriter
Joe Buchwald, 811 31st Ave, San Francisco CA 94121, USA
**Balitran, Celine** — Model
T F 6, 120 Ave Charles de Gaulle, 92522 Neuilly-sur-Seine Cedex, France
**Bality, Oded** — Photojournalist
Associated Press, Editorial Dept, 450 W 33rd St, #1500, New York NY 10001 USA
**Balk, Fairuza** — Actress
Shadow, 10 Universal City Plaza, #2000, Universal City CA 91608, USA
**Balkenhol, Klaus** — Equestrian
Narzissenweg 11A, 40723 Hilden, Germany
**Balkenhol, Stephan** — Artist
Saatchi Gallery, Duke of York's HQ, King's Road, London SW3 4RY, England
**Balkestein, Marcel** — Field Hockey Player
Oranje Zwart E M H C, Charles Roelslaan 13, 5644 Eindhoven HX, Netherlands
**Ball, Angeline** — Actress
Marfarlane Chard, 7 Adelaide St, Dun Laoghaire, Dublin, Ireland
**Ball, David** — Singer (Soft Cell), Songwriter
Susan Collier Mgmt, 6204 Jocelyn Hollow Road, Nashville TN 37205, USA
**Ball, David S (Dave)** — Football Player
208 Tarrington Court, Brentwood TN 37027, USA
**Ball, David W** — Writer
7744 Valmont Road, Boulder CO 80301, USA
**Ball, Eric C** — Football Player
10614 Margate Terrace, Cincinnati OH 45241, USA
**Ball, Jerry L** — Football Player
3311 Meadowside Dr, Sugar Land TX 77478, USA
**Ball, Larry L** — Football Player
8830 SW 57th St, Cooper City FL 33328, USA
**Ball, Marcia** — Singer, Pianist, Songwriter
Rosebud Agency, PO Box 170429, San Francisco CA 94117 USA
**Ball, Michael A** — Singer, Actor
Works Public Relations, 11 Marshalsea Road, London SE1 1EN, England
**Ball, Sam** — Actor
Robert Stein Mgmt, 1180 S Beverly Drive, #304, Los Angeles CA 90035, USA
**Ball, Taylor** — Actor
W M E Entertainment, 9601 Wilshire Blvd, #300, Beverly Hills CA 90210 USA
**Ball, Terry** — Ice Hockey Player
4502 Torrington Ave, Parma OH 44134, USA
**Balladur, Edouard** — Prime Minister, France
5 Rue Jean Formige, 75015 Paris, France
**Ballantine, Sara** — Actress
Brady Brannon Rich, 5670 Wilshire Blvd, #820, Los Angeles CA 90036 USA
**Ballantyne, Frederick** — Governor General, St Vincent-Grenadines
Governor General's Office, Kingstown, Saint Vincent & Grenadines
**Ballard, Alimi** — Actor
Stone Manners Salners, 9911 W Pico Blvd, #1400, Los Angeles CA 90035 USA
**Ballard, Carroll** — Director
PO Box 556, Saint Helena CA 94574, USA
**Ballard, Del, Jr** — Bowler
Ebonite International, PO Box 746, Hopkinsville KY 42241, USA
**Ballard, Donald E** — Vietnam War Navy Hero (CMH)
PO Box 34593, Kansas City MO 64116, USA
**Ballard, Glen** — Songwriter
Gorfaine/Schwartz, 4111 W Alameda Ave, #509, Burbank CA 91505 USA
**Ballard, Gregory (Greg)** — Basketball Player
100 Arborcrest Court, Tyrone GA 30290, USA
**Ballard, Howard L** — Football Player
PO Box 584, Ashland AL 36251, USA
**Ballard, Jeffrey S (Jeff)** — Baseball Player
4828 Rimrock Road, Billings MT 59106, USA
**Ballard, Kaye** — Actress, Comedienne
C E S D, 10635 Santa Monica Blvd, #130, Los Angeles CA 90025 USA
**Ballard, Keith** — Ice Hockey Player
2336 River Pointe Circle, Minneapolis MN 55411, USA
**Ballard, Robert D** — Oceanographer (Titanic Discoverer)
Institute for Exploration, 55 Coogan Blvd, Mystic CT 06355, USA
**Ballas, Mark A (Corky), Sr** — Professional Dancer
Commercial Talent, 9255 Sunset Blvd, #505, West Hollywood CA 90069, USA

| | |
|---|---|
| **Ballas, Mark A, Jr** | Professional Dancer |
| Nocturnal Entertainment, 11735 Dorothy St, #302, Los Angeles CA 90049, USA | |
| **Baller, Jay S** | Baseball Player |
| 303 Spring Valley Road, Reading PA 19605, USA | |
| **Ballerini, Edoardo** | Actor |
| Markham Froggatt Irwin, Julian House, 4 Windmill St, London W1P 1HF, England | |
| **Ballestrini, Veronica** | Singer, Songwriter |
| 11 Centre St, #6, Salem CT 06385, USA | |
| **Ballhaus, Michael** | Cinematographer |
| 11 Elm Place, Rye NY 10580, USA | |
| **Ballmer, Steven A (Steve)** | Businessman |
| 3832 Hunts Point Road, Hunts Point WA 98004, USA | |
| **Ballou, Mark** | Actor |
| Total Talent Mgmt, 136 Centre St, Nutley NJ 07110, USA | |
| **Balloun, James S** | Businessman |
| National Service Industry, 1420 Peachtree St NE, #200, Atlanta GA 30309, USA | |
| **Balmaseda, Liz** | Journalist |
| Palm Beach Post, Editorial Dept, 2751 S Dixie Highway, West Palm Beach FL 33405, USA | |
| **Balmer, Dan** | Jazz Guitarist |
| Sterling Talent, PO Box 231059, Tigard OR 97281, USA | |
| **Balmer, Jean-Francois** | Actor |
| Artmedia, 20 Ave Rapp, 75007 Paris, France | |
| **Balmond, Cecil** | Structural Engineer |
| University of Pennsylvania, School of Design, Philadelphia PA 19104, USA | |
| **Balmy, Coralie** | Swimmer |
| Le Dauphins du Toec, 54 Rue des 7 Troubadours, 31000 Toulouse, France | |
| **Balsam, Talia** | Actress |
| Gersh Agency, 9465 Wilshire Blvd, #600, Beverly Hills CA 90212 USA | |
| **Balsley, Philip E** | Singer (Statler Brothers) |
| 191 Abbington Road, Swoope VA 24479, USA | |
| **Balsom, Alison** | Concert Trumpet Player |
| Harrison/Parrott, 5-6 Albion Court, London W6 0QT, England | |
| **Baltacha, Elena** | Tennis Player |
| Octagon Worldwide, 1751 Pinnacle Dr, #1500, McLean VA 22102 USA | |
| **Baltimore, Bryon** | Ice Hockey Player |
| McCauig Desrochers, 2401 10088th Ave NW, Edmonton AB T5J 2Z1, Canada | |
| **Baltimore, Charli** | Rap Artist |
| The Inc Records, PO Box 40538, Glen Oaks NY 11004, USA | |
| **Baltimore, David L** | Nobel Medicine Laureate, Educator |
| 31460 Beach Park Road, Malibu CA 90265, USA | |
| **Baltsa, Agnes** | Opera Singer |
| Schultz Mgmt, Rutistr 52, 8044 Zurich-Gockhausen, Switzerland | |
| **Baltz, Lewis** | Photographer |
| 23 Rue des Blancs Mantgaux, 75004 Paris, France | |
| **Balukas, Jean** | Billiards Player |
| 9818 4th Ave, Brooklyn NY 11209, USA | |
| **Balutin, Jacques** | Actor |
| Artmedia, 20 Ave Rapp, 75007 Paris, France | |
| **Baluyut, James** | Guitarist, Keyboardist (Versus) |
| Ground Control Touring, 20 Jay St, #838, Brooklyn NY 11201, USA | |
| **Baluyut, Richard** | Singer, Guitarist (Versus) |
| Ground Control Touring, 20 Jay St, #838, Brooklyn NY 11201, USA | |
| **Bama, Jim** | Artist |
| 27 Dunn Creek Road, Cody WY 82414, USA | |
| **Bambaataa, Afrika** | Rap Artist |
| K L B Productions, 70 Greenwich Ave, #441, New York NY 10011, USA | |
| **Bamber, David J** | Actor |
| Ken McReddie Assoc, 101 Finsbury Pavement, London EC2A 1RS, England | |
| **Bamert, Matthias** | Conductor |
| Scottish National Orchestra, 3 La Belle Place, Glasgow G3 7LH, Scotland | |
| **Bamford, Maria** | Actress, Comedienne |
| OmniPop Talent Group, 4605 Lankershim Blvd, #201, Toluca Lake CA 91602 USA | |
| **Ban Ki Moon** | Government Official, South Korea |
| Secretary-General's Office, 1 United Nations Plaza, New York NY 10017, USA | |
| **Bana, Éric** | Actor, Comedian |
| 8-12 Sandilands St, #2, South Melbourne VIC 3205, Australia | |
| **Banach, Edward (Ed)** | Freestyle Wrestler |
| 2128 Country Club Blvd, Ames IA 50014, USA | |
| **Banach, Louis (Lou)** | Freestyle Wrestler |
| 1828 Tallgrass Circle, Waukesha WI 53188, USA | |
| **Banachowski, Andy** | Volleyball Player, Coach |
| University of California, Athletic Dept, Los Angeles CA 90024, USA | |
| **Banas, Michaela** | Actress |
| Channel 7 Sydney, Television Center, Mobbs Lane, Epping NSW 2121, Australia | |
| **Banaszak, John A** | Football Player |
| 420 Robinhood Lane, Canonsburg PA 15317, USA | |
| **Banaszak, Peter A (Pete)** | Football Player |
| 1021 Inverness Dr, Saint Augustine FL 32092, USA | |
| **Banaszek, Casimir J (Cas), II** | Football Player |
| 1018 Cohen Court, Petaluma CA 94952, USA | |
| **Banaszynski, Jacqui** | Journalist |
| Saint Paul Pioneer Press, Editorial Dept, 345 Cedar St, Saint Paul MN 55101, USA | |
| **Bancroft, Ann** | Explorer, Cross Country Skier |
| Yourexpedition, 1920 Oliver Place S, Minneapolis MN 55405, USA | |
| **Bancroft, Cameron** | Actor |
| Characters Talent Mgmt, 8 Elm St, Toronto ON M5G 1G7, Canada | |
| **Bancroft, George M** | Chemist |
| Western Ontario University, Chemistry Dept, London ON N6A 3K7, Canada | |
| **Band, Alexander M (Alex)** | Singer (Calling), Songwriter |
| Career Artist Management, 1100 Glendon Ave, #1100, Los Angeles CA 90024, USA | |
| **Band, Richard H** | Composer |
| 24053 Bessemer St, Woodland Hills CA 91367, USA | |
| **Banda, Joyce H** | Government Official, |
| President's Office, BP 1463, Bamako, Mali | |
| **Banda, Rupiah** | President, Zambia |
| Boston University, African President in Residence Program, Boston MA 02215, USA | |

**Banderas - Bannan**

**Banderas, Antonio** — Actor, Singer, Director
Media Art Mgmt, C/ Castelló 82, 2 Derecha, 28006 Madrid, Spain
**Bandholz, Willy** — Handball Player
Sonnholm 92, 24977 Westerholz, Germany
**Bando, Christopher M (Chris)** — Baseball Player
638 Walsall Road, El Cajon CA 92019, USA
**Bando, Salvatore L (Sal)** — Baseball Player
W308N6225 Shore Acres Road, Hartland WI 53029, USA
**Bandy, Moe** — Singer, Songwriter
Leroy Van Dyke Enterprises, 2900 Highway V, Smithton MO 65350, USA
**Bane, Edward N (Eddie)** — Baseball Player
598 Paloma Court, Encinitas CA 92024, USA
**Banes, Lisa** — Actress
Don Buchwald, 6500 Wilshire Blvd, #2200, Los Angeles CA 90048 USA
**Banfield, Ashleigh** — Commentator
NBC-TV, News Dept, 30 Rockefeller Plaza, #270E, New York NY 10112 USA
**Banfield, Bever-Leigh** — Actress
Gersh Agency, 9465 Wilshire Blvd, #600, Beverly Hills CA 90212 USA
**Banfield, J Anthony (Tony)** — Football Player
1010 Myrtlewood Dr, Friendswood TX 77546, USA
**Bang, Molly** — Writer, Illustrator
43 Drumlin Road, Falmouth MA 02540, USA
**Bangalter, Thomas** — Musician (Daft Punk)
Clintons, 55 Drury Lane, Covent Garden, London WC2B 5RZ, England
**Bangemann, Martin** — Government Official, West Germany
Telefonica, Gran Via 28, 28013 Madrid, Spain
**Bangerter, Norman H** — Governor, UT
603 E South Temple, Salt Lake City UT 84102, USA
**Banham, Frank** — Ice Hockey Player
139 W Grayling Lane, Suffield CT 06078, USA
**Bank, Melissa** — Writer
Rabineay Wachter Sanford, 1107 1/2 Glendon Ave, Los Angeles CA 90024, USA
**Banker, Ted** — Football Player
1862 Park Ave, East Meadow NY 11554, USA
**Bankhead, M Scott** — Baseball Player
1236 Idlewood Dr, Asheboro NC 27205, USA
**Banks, Anthony L (Tony)** — Football Player
2211 Vaquero Club Dr, Westlake TX 76262, USA
**Banks, Azealia A** — Rap Artist
Polydor Records, 364-366 Kensington High St, London W14 8NS, England
**Banks, Barry** — Opera Singer
I M G Artists, Carnegie Hall Tower, 152 W 57th St, #500, New York NY 10019 USA
**Banks, Brian G** — Baseball Player
2232 E 900 S, Salt Lake City UT 84108, USA
**Banks, Carl E** — Football Player
7 Glenview Dr, Warren NJ 07059, USA
**Banks, Darren** — Ice Hockey Player
11 Millington Road, Pleasant Ridge MI 48069, USA
**Banks, Dennis** — Indian Rights Activist
General Delivery, Oglala SD 57764, USA
**Banks, Elizabeth** — Actress, Model, Producer
United Talent Agency, U T A Plaza, 9336 Civic Center Dr, Beverly Hills CA 90210 USA
**Banks, Ernest (Ernie)** — Baseball Player
27 N Wacker Dr, #466, Chicago IL 60606, USA
**Banks, Estes** — Football Player
640 Gooseberry Dr, #703, Longmont CO 80503, USA
**Banks, Eugene L (Gene)** — Basketball Player
1210 Sloan St, Greensboro NC 27401, USA
**Banks, Frederick R (Fred)** — Football Player
5665 Orly Terrace, Atlanta GA 30349, USA
**Banks, Gordon G** — Football Player
2644 E Trinity Mills Road, Carrollton TX 75006, USA
**Banks, Jonathan** — Actor
Lovett Mgmt, 1327 Brinkley Ave, Los Angeles CA 90049, USA
**Banks, Kelcie H** — Boxer
Tocco's Ringside Gym, 9 W Charleston, Las Vegas NV 89102, USA
**Banks, Leann** — Bassist (Von Bondies)
Tsunami Entertainment, 2525 Hyperion Ave, Los Angeles CA 90027, USA
**Banks, Lloyd** — Rap Artist
Emmel Communications, 36 W 25th St, #200, New York NY 10010, USA
**Banks, Lynne Reid** — Writer
Harper Collins Publishers, 10 E 53rd St, Cellar 1, New York NY 10022 USA
**Banks, Morwenna** — Actress, Comedienne
I C M Partners, 10250 Constellation Blvd, #900, Los Angeles CA 90067 USA
**Banks, Russell** — Writer
Trident Media Group, 41 Madison Ave, #3600, New York NY 10010, USA
**Banks, Steven** — Actor, Comedian, Writer
Creative Artists Agency, 2000 Ave of Stars, #100, Los Angeles CA 90067 USA
**Banks, Thomas S (Tom), Jr** — Football Player
358 Wisteria St, Fairhope AL 36532, USA
**Banks, Tyra** — Model, Actress
W M E Entertainment, 9601 Wilshire Blvd, #300, Beverly Hills CA 90210 USA
**Banks, W Chip** — Football Player
709 Albany Ave, Augusta GA 30901, USA
**Banks, Walker B** — Basketball Player
3207 Brentwood Dr, Champaign IL 61821, USA
**Banks, William A (Willie), III** — Track Athlete
250 Williams St NW, #6000, Atlanta GA 30303, USA
**Banks, Willie A** — Baseball Player
13 Michael St, Jamesburg NJ 08831, USA
**Bankston, Michael** — Football Player
182 N Burberry Park Circle, Spring TX 77382, USA
**Bankston, Warren S** — Football Player
4201 Bordeaux Dr, Kenner LA 70065, USA
**Bannan, Justin L** — Football Player
561 Mockingbird Dr, Belgrade MT 59714, USA

**Banner, David** — Rap Artist, Actor
Creative Artists Agency, 2000 Ave of Stars, #100, Los Angeles CA 90067 USA
**Banner, Jon** — Commentator
ABC-TV, News Dept, 77 W 66th St, New York NY 10023 USA
**Bannerman, Isabella** — Cartoonist (Six Chix)
41 South Drive, Hastings-on-Hudson NY 10706, USA
**Bannerman, Murray** — Ice Hockey Player
7222 Kiowa Road, Larkspur CO 80118, USA
**Bannister, Alan** — Baseball Player
6349 N 78th St, #129, Scottsdale AZ 85250, USA
**Bannister, Brian P** — Baseball Player
6701 E Caballo Dr, Paradise Valley AZ 85253, USA
**Bannister, Floyd F** — Baseball Player
6701 Caballo Dr, Paradise Valley AZ 85253, USA
**Bannister, Kenneth (Ken)** — Basketball Player
2322 Broadgreen Dr, Missouri City TX 77489, USA
**Bannister, Roger G** — Track Athlete, Neurologist
21 Bardwell Road, Oxford OX2 6SV, England
**Bannon, Jack** — Actor
6470 E Sunnyside Road, Coeur D'Alene ID 83814, USA
**Bans, Jenna** — Producer
I C M Partners, 10250 Constellation Blvd, #900, Los Angeles CA 90067 USA
**Banse, Juliane** — Opera Singer
Kunstler Sekretariat am Gasteig, Rosenheimer Str 52, 81669 Munich, Germany
**Banta, D Bradford (Brad)** — Football Player
1100 Smith Ave, Birmingham MI 48009, USA
**Banta-Cain, Tully** — Football Player
27 Apple Valley Dr, Sharon MA 2067, USA
**Bantom, Michael A (Mike)** — Basketball Player, Executive
418 Egret Lane, Secaucus NJ 07094, USA
**Banton, Buju** — Singer
Agency Group Ltd, 142 W 57th St, #600, New York NY 10019 USA
**Banville, John** — Writer
Gillon Aitken Assoc, 29 Fernshaw Road, London SW10 0TG, England
**Bao, Joseph Y** — Microsurgeon, Orthopedist
17436 Terry Lyn Lane, Cerritos CA 90703, USA
**Baquero, Ivana** — Actress
Eduardo Gonzalez Valdivia, Isaac Peral 48, #1B, 28040 Madrid, Spain
**Bar, Olaf** — Opera Singer
Opus 3 Artists, 470 Park Ave S, #900N, New York NY 10016 USA
**Baraban, Yannis** — Actor
Artmedia, 20 Ave Rapp, 75007 Paris, France
**Barahona, Ralph** — Ice Hockey Player
317 1/2 E Plymouth St, Long Beach CA 90805, USA
**Barajas, Rodridgo R (Rod)** — Baseball Player
8533 N 50th Place, Paradise Valley AZ 85253, USA
**Barak, Ehud** — Prime Minister, Israel; Army General
Defense Ministry, Kaplan St, Hakirya, Tel-Aviv 67659, Israel
**Baraka, Imamu Amiri (LeRoi Jones)** — Writer
State University of New York, Afro American Studies Dept, Stony Brook NY 11794, USA
**Baranova, Anastasia** — Actress
4 H M, 11340 Moorpark St, Studio City CA 91602, USA
**Baranski, Christine** — Actress
United Talent Agency, U T A Plaza, 9336 Civic Center Dr, Beverly Hills CA 90210 USA
**Barasso, Tom** — Ice Hockey Player
12820 Rosalie St, Raleigh NC 27614, USA
**Barats, Luke** — Actor, Comedian
Independent Artists, 9601 Wilshire Blvd, #750, Beverly Hills CA 90210, USA
**Barbacid, Mariano** — Onocologist
Spanish National Cancer Research Center, Melchor Fernandez Almagro 3, 28029 Madrid, Spain
**Barbacini, Maurizio** — Conductor
I M G Artists, Hogarth Business Park, Chiswick, London W4 2TH, England
**Barbakow, Jeffrey C** — Businessman
Tenet Healthcare Corp, 13737 Noel Road, #100, Dallas TX 75240, USA
**Barbarin, Philippe X I Cardinal** — Religious Leader
Piazza Trinita dei Monti 3, 00187 Rome Lazio, Italy
**Barbaro, Gary W** — Football Player
1000 Giuffrias Ave, Metairie LA 70001, USA
**Barbato, Randy** — Director, Producer
World of Wonder, 6650 Hollywood Blvd, #400, Los Angeles CA 90028, USA
**Barbeau, Adrienne** — Actress, Singer
Bauman Redanty Shaul Agency, 5757 Wilshire Blvd, #473, Los Angeles CA 90036 USA
**Barber, Aaron** — Golfer
2830 Fillmore St NE, Minneapolis MN 55418, USA
**Barber, Atiim K (Tiki)** — Football Player, Sportscaster
Greater Talent Network, 437 5th Ave, #700, New York NY 10016, USA
**Barber, Bill** — Ice Hockey Player, Coach
1112 Peppertree Court, #223, Sarasota FL 34242, USA
**Barber, Christopher E (Chris)** — Football Player
2621 Monaco Cove Circle, Orlando FL 32825, USA
**Barber, Glynis** — Actress
Waring & McKenna, Mayfair, 11-12 Dover St, London W1S 4LJ, England
**Barber, J Oronde (Ronde)** — Football Player
17119 Journeys End Dr, Odessa FL 33556, USA
**Barber, John (Skip), III** — Auto Racing Driver, Executive
497 Lime Rock Road, Lakeville CT 06039, USA
**Barber, Lance** — Actor
Paul Kohner, 9300 Wilshire Blvd, #555, Beverly Hills CA 90212 USA
**Barber, Marion, III** — Football Player
PO Box 191348, Dallas TX 75219, USA
**Barber, Marion, Jr** — Football Player
PO Box 46106, Minneapolis MN 55446, USA
**Barber, Michael D (Mike)** — Football Player
PO Box 2424, DeSoto TX 75123, USA
**Barber, Michael L (Mike)** — Football Player
43 Mill Creek Crossing, Hurricane WV 25526, USA

**Barber, Patricia** — Jazz Singer, Pianist, Composer
Blue Note Records, 304 Park Ave S, New York NY 10010, USA
**Barber, Paul** — Actor, Writer, Producer
Diamond Mgmt, 31 Percy St, London W1T 2DD, England
**Barber, Stewart C (Stew)** — Football Player
2138 Country Manor Dr, Mount Pleasant SC 29466, USA
**Barber, William** — Cinematographer
2509 White Chapel Place, Thousand Oaks CA 91362, USA
**Barberie, Bret E** — Baseball Player
11607 Bos St, Cerritos CA 90703, USA
**Barberie-Reynolds, Jillian** — Sportscaster, Actress
KTTV Fox-TV, 1999 S Bundy Dr, Los Angeles CA 90025, USA
**Barberos, Alessandro** — Businessman
Fiat Spa, Corso G Marconi 10/20, 10125 Turin, Italy
**Barbi, Shane** — Model (Barbi Twins)
A T Y, 4725 N Lois Ave, Tampa FL 33614, USA
**Barbi, Sia** — Model (Barbi Twins)
A T Y, 4725 N Lois Ave, Tampa FL 33614, USA
**Barbieri, Gato** — Jazz Saxophonist
Andi Howard Entertainment, 100 N Crescent Ave, #275, Beverly Hills CA 90210, USA
**Barbieri, Paula** — Actress, Model
Warner Books, 1271 Ave of Americas, New York NY 10020 USA
**Barbieri, Richard** — Keyboardist (Japan, Porcupine Tree)
Agency Group Ltd, 361-373 City Road, London EC1V 1PQ, England
**Barbosa, Leandro M** — Basketball Player
8046 E Vista Canyon St, Litchfield Park AZ 85340, USA
**Barbour, Haley R** — Governor, MS; Political Leader
B G R Group, Homer Building, 601 13th St NW, #1100-S, Washington DC 20005, USA
**Barbour, Ian G** — Nuclear Physicist, Templeton Laureate
Carleton College, Theology Dept, Northfield MN 55057, USA
**Barbour, John** — Actor, Comedian, Writer
10309 Denman St, Las Vegas NV 89178, USA
**Barboza, David** — Journalist
New York Times, Editorial Dept, 229 W 43rd St, New York NY 10036 USA
**Barbuscia, Lisa** — Actress, Singer
Independent Talent Group, 40 Whitfield St, London W1T 2RH, England
**Barbutti, Pete** — Jazz Trumpeter
Thomas Cassidy, PO Box 1311, Tucson AZ 85702 USA
**Barch, Krystoger (Krys)** — Ice Hockey Player
Dallas Stars, 2601 Ave of Stars, #100, Frisco TX 75034 USA
**Barclay, Paris** — Director, Producer
Paradigm Agency, 360 N Crescent Dr, North Building, Beverly Hills CA 90210 USA
**Bard, Allen J** — Chemist
6202 Mountainclimb Dr, Austin TX 78731, USA
**Bard, Joshua D (Josh)** — Baseball Player
2139 Beechnut Place, Castle Rock CO 80108, USA
**Bard, Marjorie** — Social Activist
Women Organized Against Homelessness, PO Box 911, Saint Michaels MD 21663, USA
**Bardeen, William A** — Physicist
Fermi National Accelerator Laboratory, PO Box 500, Batavia IL 60510, USA
**Bardem, Javier E** — Actor
Bloom Hergott Diemer, 150 S Rodeo Dr, #300, Beverly Hills CA 90212 USA
**Barden, Brian D** — Baseball Player
10452 E Cannon Dr, Scottsdale AZ 85258, USA
**Barden, Jessica** — Actress
W M E Entertainment, 9601 Wilshire Blvd, #300, Beverly Hills CA 90210 USA
**Bardot, Brigitte** — Actress
La Madrigue, 83990 Saint Tropez, Var, France
**Bare, James** — WW II Navy Air Force Hero
3618 NW 47th St, Oklahoma City OK 73112, USA
**Bare, Richard L** — Director
700 Harbor Island Dr, Newport Beach CA 92660, USA
**Bare, Robert J (Bobby)** — Singer, Guitarist, Songwriter
Bobby Bare Enterprises, 112 The Landing, Hendersonville TN 37075, USA
**Barea, Jose J (J J)** — Basketball Player
Minnesota Timberwolves, Target Center, 600 1st Ave N, Minneapolis MN 55403 USA
**Bareikis, Arija** — Actress
Gersh Agency, 41 Madison Ave, #3301, New York NY 10010 USA
**Bareilles, Sara** — Singer, Pianist, Songwriter
Career Artist Mgmt, 1100 Glendon Ave, #1100, Los Angeles CA 90024, USA
**Barek, Djemel** — Actor
Artmedia, 20 Ave Rapp, 75007 Paris, France
**Baren, Justin** — Bassist (Redwalls)
Pinnacle Entertainment, 30 Glenn St, White Plains NY 10603, USA
**Baren, Logan** — Singer, Guitarist (Redwalls)
Pinnacle Entertainment, 30 Glenn St, White Plains NY 10603, USA
**Barenboim, Daniel** — Conductor, Concert Pianist
29 Rue de la Coulouvreeniere, 1206 Geneva, Switzerland
**Baretto, Ray** — Percussionist
Creative Music Consultants, 181 Christie St, #300, New York NY 10002, USA
**Barfield, Jesse L** — Baseball Player
5814 Spanish Moss Court, Spring TX 77379, USA
**Barfod, Hakon** — Yachtsman
Jon Ostensensv 15, 1360 Nesbru, Norway
**Barfoed, Kasper** — Director
United Talent Agency, U T A Plaza, 9336 Civic Center Dr, Beverly Hills CA 90210 USA
**Bargnani, Andrea** — Basketball Player
Toronto Raptors, Air Canada Center, 20 Bay St, Toronto ON M5J 2N8, Canada
**Barinholtz, Ike** — Actor, Comedian
United Talent Agency, U T A Plaza, 9336 Civic Center Dr, Beverly Hills CA 90210 USA
**Barisich, Carl J** — Football Player
1744 N 134th Lane, Goodyear AZ 85395, USA
**Barjatya, Sooraj** — Director, Producer
1 Bhana, 422 Veer Sawarkar Road Prabhadevi Dadar, Mumbai MS 400025, India
**Barkauskas, Antanas S** — Chairman of Presidium, Lithuania
Akmenu Str 7A, Vilnus, Lithuania

| | |
|---|---|
| **Barker, Bryan C** | Football Player |
| 200 1st St, #203, Neptune Beach FL 32266, USA | |
| **Barker, Cameron (Cam)** | Ice Hockey Player |
| Minnesota Wild, XCel Energy Arena, 1275 Saint Antoine W, Saint Paul MN 55104 USA | |
| **Barker, Clive** | Writer, Director, Producer, Actor |
| Midnight Picture Show, PO Box 691821, West Hollywood CA 90069, USA | |
| **Barker, Clyde F** | Surgeon |
| 3 Coopertown Road, Haverford PA 19041, USA | |
| **Barker, David J P** | Epidemiologist |
| Manor Farm, East Dean near Salisbury, Wiltshire SP5 1HB, England | |
| **Barker, James F** | Educator |
| Clemson University, President's Office, Clemson SC 29634, USA | |
| **Barker, Kevin S** | Baseball Player |
| PO Box 96, Mendota VA 24270, USA | |
| **Barker, Lee** | Bass Guitar Designer |
| 1842 SE 1st St, Redmond OR 97756, USA | |
| **Barker, Leo** | Football Player |
| 25 Via Lucena, San Clemente CA 92673, USA | |
| **Barker, Leonard H (Len)** | Baseball Player |
| 10690 Locust Grove Dr, Chardon OH 44024, USA | |
| **Barker, Lucius** | Political Scientist |
| Stanford University, Political Science Dept, Stanford CA 94305, USA | |
| **Barker, Michael** | Director |
| Sony Pictures Classics, 550 Madison Ave, New York NY 10022, USA | |
| **Barker, Mike** | Producer, Writer, Actor |
| United Talent Agency, U T A Plaza, 9336 Civic Center Dr, Beverly Hills CA 90210 USA | |
| **Barker, Pamela** | Boxer |
| 1617 Mexican Poppy St, Las Vegas NV 89128, USA | |
| **Barker, Pat** | Writer |
| Gillon Aitken, 29 Fernshaw Road, London SW10 0TG, England | |
| **Barker, Robert W (Bob)** | Producer, Actor |
| Kazarian/Measures/Ruskin, 11969 Ventura Blvd, #300, Studio City CA 91604 USA | |
| **Barker, Roy** | Football Player |
| 23 Saint Marks Circle, Islandia NY 11749, USA | |
| **Barker, Travis** | Drummer (Blink-182, +44) |
| 7325 Seafarer Place, Carlsbad CA 92011, USA | |
| **Barkett, Rosemary** | Judge |
| US Court of Appeals, 99 NE 4th St, #1223, Miami FL 33132, USA | |
| **Barkin, Ellen** | Actress |
| Creative Artists Agency, 2000 Ave of Stars, #100, Los Angeles CA 90067 USA | |
| **Barkley, Charles W** | Basketball Player, Sportscaster |
| 7615 E Vaquero Dr, Scottsdale AZ 85258, USA | |
| **Barkley, Douglas (Doug)** | Ice Hockey Player, Coach |
| 523-3131 63 Ave NE, Calgary AB T3E 6N4, Canada | |
| **Barkley, Iran** | Boxer |
| John Henry Reetz, 222 E 27th St, #3, New York NY 10016, USA | |
| **Barkman Tyler, Jane (Janie)** | Swimmer |
| Princeton University, Athletic Dept, Princeton NJ 08544, USA | |
| **Barkmin, Gun-Brit** | Opera Singer |
| Columbia Artists Mgmt Inc, 1790 Broadway, #702, New York NY 10019 USA | |
| **Barks, Samantha** | Actress, Singer |
| United Agents, 12-26 Lexington St, London W1F 0LE, England | |
| **Barksdale, Chuck** | Singer (Dells) |
| Associated Booking Corp, 501 Madison Ave, #501, New York NY 10022 USA | |
| **Barksdale, James (Jim)** | Businessman |
| Barksdale Group, 2730 Sand Hill Road, Menlo Park CA 94025, USA | |
| **Barksdale, Rhesa H** | Judge |
| US Court of Appeals, 245 E Capitol St, Jackson MS 39201, USA | |
| **Barkum, Jerome P** | Football Player |
| 2720 Palmer Dr, #15, Gulfport MS 39507, USA | |
| **Barlett, Donald L** | Journalist |
| Wylie Agency, 250 W 57th St, #2114, New York NY 10107 USA | |
| **Barletta, Joseph** | Publisher |
| TV Guide, Publisher's Office, 100 Matsonford Road, Wayne PA 19080, USA | |
| **Barlow, Bob** | Ice Hockey Player |
| 4912 Wesley Road, Victoria BC V8Y 1Y5, Canada | |
| **Barlow, Craig** | Golfer |
| 644 Desert Passage St, Henderson NV 89002, USA | |
| **Barlow, Gary** | Singer, Pianist, Songwriter |
| International Talent Booking, Ariel House, 74A Charlotte St, #100 London W1T 4QJ, England | |
| **Barlow, Kevan C** | Football Player |
| 82 Waterfront Dr, Pittsburgh PA 15222, USA | |
| **Barlow, Lou** | Singer, Guitarist, Songwriter |
| Paradigm Agency, 360 N Crescent Dr, North Building, Beverly Hills CA 90210 USA | |
| **Barlow, Michael R (Mike)** | Baseball Player |
| Sheftic, 4524 Francis Road, Cazenovia NY 13035, USA | |
| **Barlow, Perry** | Cartoonist |
| New Yorker, Editorial Dept, 4 Times Square, Basement C1B, New York NY 10036 USA | |
| **Barlow, Reggie D** | Football Player |
| 8311 Timber Trace Lane, Pike Road AL 36064, USA | |
| **Barmes, Clint H** | Baseball Player |
| 113 Mallard Court, Mead CO 80542, USA | |
| **Barnaby, Matthew** | Ice Hockey Player |
| 134 King Anthony Way, Getzville NY 14068, USA | |
| **Barnard, Aneurin** | Actor |
| Ken McReddie Assoc, 101 Finsbury Pavement, London EC2A 1RS, England | |
| **Barnathan, Michael** | Producer |
| 1492 Pictures, 4000 Warner Blvd, Building 3, Burbank CA 91522, USA | |
| **Barndt, Thomas A (Tom)** | Football Player |
| 11041 Romola St, Las Vegas NV 89141, USA | |
| **Barner, Bob** | Writer |
| 2100 Green St, #206, San Francisco CA 94123, USA | |
| **Barnes, Aaron** | Cinematographer |
| Gersh Agency, 9465 Wilshire Blvd, #600, Beverly Hills CA 90212 USA | |
| **Barnes, Benny J** | Football Player |
| 5003 Fleming Ave, Richmond CA 94804, USA | |

**B**

**Barker - Barnes**

**Barnes, Brenda C** — Businesswoman
Sara Lee Corp, 3500 Lacey Road, Downers Grove IL 60515, USA
**Barnes, Brian** — Golfer
International Golf Partners, 3300 PGA Blvd, #820, Palm Beach Gardens FL 33410, USA
**Barnes, Chris** — Bowler
Professional Bowlers Assn, 719 2nd Ave, #701, Seattle WA 98104 USA
**Barnes, Christopher Daniel** — Actor
Agency S G H, 6525 Sunset Blvd, #PH9, Hollywood CA 90028, USA
**Barnes, Danny** — Singer, Musician (Bad Livers)
Red Light Mgmt, 44 Wall St, #2200, New York NY 10005, USA
**Barnes, Darian D** — Football Player
554 Clifton Ave, Toms River NJ 08753, USA
**Barnes, David M (Dave)** — Singer, Songwriter
Paradigm Agency, 360 N Crescent Dr, North Building, Beverly Hills CA 90210 USA
**Barnes, David Wilson** — Actor
Hartig-Hilepo Agency, 54 W 21st St, #610, New York NY 10010, USA
**Barnes, Demore** — Actor
S M S Talent, 8383 Wilshire Blvd, #230, Beverly Hills CA 90211 USA
**Barnes, E Randolph (Randy)** — Track Athlete
Randy Barnes Enterprises, PO Box 1373, Mechanicsburg PA 17055, USA
**Barnes, Erich T** — Football Player
712 Warburton Ave, Yonkers NY 10701, USA
**Barnes, Frank** — Baseball Player
1508 Brazil St, Greenville MS 38701, USA
**Barnes, Frank S** — Electronics Engineer
University of Colorado, Engineering Dept, Boulder CO 80309, USA
**Barnes, Gary M** — Football Player
849 Tiger Blvd, #406, Clemson SC 29631, USA
**Barnes, Harrison B** — Basketball Player
Golden State Warriors, 1011 Broadway, Oakland CA 94605 USA
**Barnes, Jeff** — Football Player
10738 Versailles Blvd, Clermont FL 34711, USA
**Barnes, Jhane E** — Fashion Designer
Jhane Barnes Inc, 140 W 57th St, #5B, New York NY 10019, USA
**Barnes, Jimmy** — Singer
Harbour Agency, 135 Forbes St, Woolloomooloo NSW 2011, Australia
**Barnes, Joanna** — Actress, Writer
PO Box 1103, Gualala CA 95445, USA
**Barnes, Joey** — Drummer (Daughtry)
19 Entertainment, 8560 W Sunset Blvd, #900, Los Angeles CA 90069, USA
**Barnes, Jonathan** — Philosopher
1 Place de la Taconnerie, 1204 Geneva, Switzerland
**Barnes, Jonathan** — Writer
William Morrow Publishers, 1350 Ave of Americas, New York NY 10019 USA
**Barnes, Julian P** — Writer
Gage Group, 14724 Ventura Blvd, #505, Sherman Oaks CA 91403 USA
**Barnes, Khalif** — Football Player
7967 Monterey Bay Dr, Jacksonville FL 32256, USA
**Barnes, Luther** — Singer
Universal Attractions, 135 W 26th St, #1200, New York NY 10001 USA
**Barnes, Marvin J** — Basketball Player
3420 Freemason Dr, Portsmouth VA 23703, USA
**Barnes, Matt K** — Basketball Player
Los Angeles Clippers, Staples Center, 1111 S Figueroa St, Los Angeles CA 90015 USA
**Barnes, Michael** — Singer (Red)
Paradigm Agency, 404 W Franklin St, Monterey CA 93940 USA
**Barnes, Michael J (Mike)** — Football Player
27474 Plank Road, Guys Mills PA 16327, USA
**Barnes, Norm** — Ice Hockey Player
17 Meadow Crossing, Simsbury CT 06070, USA
**Barnes, Priscilla** — Actress, Model
Glick Agency, 1321 7th St, #203, Santa Monica CA 90401 USA
**Barnes, Rick** — Basketball Coach
Texas University, Athletic Dept, Austin TX 78713, USA
**Barnes, Robert H** — Psychiatrist
Texas Tech University Medical School, Psychiatry Dept, PO Box 4349, Lubbock TX 79409, USA
**Barnes, Stu** — Ice Hockey Player
5069 Royal Creek Lane, Plano TX 75093, USA
**Barnes, William H (Skeeter)** — Baseball Player
11544 Winding Wood Dr, Indianapolis IN 46235, USA
**Barnes, William R (Billy Ray)** — Football Player
518 James C Lane, Dallas NC 28034, USA
**Barnett of Heywood & Royton, Joel B** — Government Official, England
7 Hillingdon Road, Whitefield, Manchester M25 7QQ, England
**Barnett, Charlie** — Actor
Gersh Agency, 9465 Wilshire Blvd, #600, Beverly Hills CA 90212 USA
**Barnett, Douglas S (Doug), Jr** — Football Player
14105 Veracruz Dr, Bakersfield CA 93314, USA
**Barnett, Fred L** — Football Player
PO Box 604, Bala Cynwyd PA 19004, USA
**Barnett, James F (Jim)** — Basketball Player
7 Kittiwake Road, Orinda CA 94563, USA
**Barnett, Jonathan** — Architect
225 S Bonsall St, Philadelphia PA 19103, USA
**Barnett, Mandy** — Singer
Conway Entertainment Group, 1625 Broadway, #500, Nashville TN 37203, USA
**Barnett, Nathaniel (Nate)** — Basketball Player
710 N Jefferson St, Wilmington DE 19801, USA
**Barnett, Nicholas A (Nick)** — Football Player
3496 Country Winds Court, Green Bay WI 54311, USA
**Barnett, Oliver W** — Football Player
1133 Autumn Ridge Dr, Lexington KY 40509, USA
**Barnett, Pamela (Pam)** — Golfer
4908 E Rancho Tierra Dr, Cave Creek AZ 85331, USA
**Barnett, Richard (Dick)** — Basketball Player
1227 Pine Ridge, Bushkill PA 18324, USA

| | |
|---|---|
| **Barnett, Robby** | Dance Artistic Director |
| Pilobolus Dance Theater, PO Box 388, Washington Depot CT 06794, USA | |
| **Barnett, Sabrina** | Model |
| Next Model Mgmt, 23 Watts St, New York NY 10013 USA | |
| **Barnett, Samuel** | Actor |
| I C M Partners, 10250 Constellation Blvd, #900, Los Angeles CA 90067 USA | |
| **Barnett, Tommy** | Religious Leader |
| Phoenix First Assembly Church, 13613 N Cave Creek Road, Phoenix AZ 85022, USA | |
| **Barney, Lemuel J (Lem), Jr** | Football Player |
| 775 Kentbrook Dr, Commerce Township MI 48382, USA | |
| **Barney, Matthew** | Performance Artist |
| Barbara Gladstone Gallery, 515 W 24th St, New York NY 10011, USA | |
| **Barnhart, Nicole R** | Soccer Player |
| F C Kansas City, 5366 W 95th St, Prairie Village KS 66207 USA | |
| **Barno, David W** | Army General |
| Center for a New American Security, 1301 Pennsylvania Ave NW, #403, Washington DC 20004, USA | |
| **Barnow, Alex** | Producer, Writer |
| United Talent Agency, U T A Plaza, 9336 Civic Center Dr, Beverly Hills CA 90210 USA | |
| **Barnum, Harvey C, Jr** | Vietnam War Marine Corps Hero (CMH) |
| 12008 Walnut Branch Road, Reston VA 20194, USA | |
| **Barnwell, Malcolm** | Football Player |
| 4045 Gullah Ave, #103, North Charleston SC 29405, USA | |
| **Barocco, Rocco** | Fashion Designer |
| Via Occhio Marion, 80773 Capri/Napoli, Italy | |
| **Baron Cohen, Sacha (Borat)** | Actor, Comedian |
| W M E Entertainment, 9601 Wilshire Blvd, #300, Beverly Hills CA 90210 USA | |
| **Baron Crespo, Enrique** | Government Official, Spain |
| European Parliament, Rue Wiertz 60, 1047 Brussels, Belgium | |
| **Baron, Lita** | Actress |
| 1508 S La Verne Way, Palm Springs CA 92264, USA | |
| **Baron, Martin D** | Editor |
| Boston Globe, Editorial Dept, 135 William Morrissey Blvd, Dorchester MA 02125 USA | |
| **Baron, Murray** | Ice Hockey Player |
| 23623 N Scottsdale Road, #D3, Scottsdale AZ 85255, USA | |
| **Baron, Natalia** | Actress |
| Evolution Entertainment, 901 N Highland Ave, Los Angeles CA 90038 USA | |
| **Barone, Anita** | Actress |
| Paradigm Agency, 360 N Crescent Dr, North Building, Beverly Hills CA 90210 USA | |
| **Barone, Richard A** | Singer, Guitarist, Songwriter (Bongos) |
| Richard Barone Music, 240 Waverly Place, #23, New York NY 10014, USA | |
| **Baroux, Olivier** | Actor |
| U B B A, 6 Rue de Braque, 75003 Paris, France | |
| **Barr, Dave** | Ice Hockey Player |
| 3100 Wilcrest Dr, #260, Houston TX 77042, USA | |
| **Barr, Douglas** | Actor |
| Paradigm Agency, 360 N Crescent Dr, North Building, Beverly Hills CA 90210 USA | |
| **Barr, Jean-Marc** | Actor |
| Zelig, 57 Rue Reaumur, 75002 Paris, France | |
| **Barr, Julia** | Actress |
| Abrams Artists, 275 7th Ave, #2600, New York NY 10001 USA | |
| **Barr, Matt** | Actor |
| Luber Rocklin Entertainment, 8530 Wilshire Blvd, #555, Beverly Hills CA 90211 USA | |
| **Barr, Michael J (Mike)** | Basketball Player |
| 350 38th St NW, Canton OH 44709, USA | |
| **Barr, Nathan (Nate)** | Composer |
| First Artists Mgmt, 4764 Park Granada, #210, Calabasas CA 91302 USA | |
| **Barr, Nevada** | Writer |
| 85 Versailles Blvd, New Orleans LA 70125, USA | |
| **Barr, Roseanne** | Actress, Comedienne |
| 904 Silver Spur Road, #433, Rolling Hills Estates CA 90274, USA | |
| **Barr, Tara Lynne** | Actress |
| Bicoastal Talent, 210 N Pass Ave, #204, Burbank CA 91505, USA | |
| **Barr, William P** | Attorney General |
| Time Warner, Board of Directors, 1 Time Warner Center, New York NY 10019, USA | |
| **Barraclough, Roy** | Actor |
| Gavin Barker Assoc, 2D Wimpole St, London W1G 0EB, England | |
| **Barrasso, Thomas (Tom)** | Ice Hockey Player |
| 12820 Rosalie St, Raleigh NC 27614, USA | |
| **Barratier, Christophe** | Director, Writer, Lyricist |
| Galatee Films, 19 Ave de Messine, 75008 Paris, France | |
| **Barratt, Michael R** | Astronaut |
| 2102 Pleasant Palm Circle, League City TX 77573, USA | |
| **Barrault, Doug** | Ice Hockey Player |
| 527 10th St S, Golden BC V0A 1H0, Canada | |
| **Barraza, Adriana** | Actress, Director |
| Mesala Films, C/Lopez De Hoyos 384 Bis, Bajo Izq, 28043 Madrid, Spain | |
| **Barrea, Juan J (J J)** | Basketball Player |
| Dallas Mavericks, Pavilion, 2909 Taylor St, Dallas TX 75226 USA | |
| **Barrera, Marco Antonio** | Boxer |
| Golden Boy Promotions, 626 Wilshire Blvd, #350, Los Angeles CA 90017, USA | |
| **Barrere, Paul** | Singer, Guitarist, Songwriter |
| Skyline Music, 48 Prospect St, Whitehead NH 03598, USA | |
| **Barrese, Sasha** | Actress |
| C E S D, 10635 Santa Monica Blvd, #130, Los Angeles CA 90025 USA | |
| **Barre-Sinoussi, Francois C** | Nobel Medicine Laureate |
| Institut Pasteur, 25 Rue du Docteur Roux, 75724 Paris Cedex 15, France | |
| **Barreto, Bruno** | Director |
| Creative Artists Agency, 2000 Ave of Stars, #100, Los Angeles CA 90067 USA | |
| **Barrett, Christina (Tina)** | Golfer |
| Ladies Pro Golf Assn, 100 International Golf Dr, Daytona Beach FL 32124 USA | |
| **Barrett, Colleen** | Businesswoman |
| Southwest Airlines, PO Box 36611, 2702 Love Field Dr, Dallas TX 75235, USA | |
| **Barrett, Craig R** | Businessman |
| Intel Corp, 2200 Mission College Blvd, Santa Clara CA 95054, USA | |
| **Barrett, David** | Football Player |
| 3181 E Waterman Court, Gilbert AZ 85297, USA | |

**Barrett, Edward G (Ted)** — Baseball Umpire
855A Silverberry Circle SE, Albuquerque NM 87116, USA
**Barrett, Fred W** — Ice Hockey Player
3016 Leitrim Road, Gloucester ON K1T 3V9, Canada
**Barrett, George S** — Businessman
Cardinal Health, 7000 Cardinal Place, Dublin OH 43017, USA
**Barrett, Jacinda** — Actress, Model
I C M Partners, 10250 Constellation Blvd, #900, Los Angeles CA 90067 USA
**Barrett, James E** — Judge
US Court of Appeals, 2120 Capitol Ave, #2131, Cheyenne WY 82001, USA
**Barrett, Jean M, Jr** — Football Player
7494 S Sleepy Hollow Dr, Tulsa OK 74136, USA
**Barrett, Malcolm** — Actor
Gersh Agency, 9465 Wilshire Blvd, #600, Beverly Hills CA 90212 USA
**Barrett, Marcia** — Singer (Boney M)
International Artists, PO Box 100334, 47563 Goch, Germany
**Barrett, Martin G (Marty)** — Baseball Manager
3552 Ridge Meadow St, Las Vegas NV 89135, USA
**Barrett, Michael P** — Baseball Player
126 Circle Dr, Port Saint Joe FL 32456, USA
**Barrett, Rona** — Columnist, Commentator
Rona Barrett Foundation, PO Box 1559, Santa Ynez CA 93460, USA
**Barrett, Shirley** — Director
H L A Mgmt, PO Box 1536, Strawberry Hills NSW 2012, Australia
**Barrett, Stephen** — Psychiatrist, Social Activist
PO Box 1747, Allentown PA 18105, USA
**Barrial, Henry** — Director
O'Neill Talent Group, 4150 Riverside Dr, #212, Burbank CA 91505, USA
**Barrichello, Rubens G** — Auto Racing Driver
Eng Luis Carlos Berrini 1140, 8 Andar, Sao Paulo Cep 04571 SP, Brazil
**Barrick, Matt** — Singer, Guitarist (Walkmen)
Mick Mgmt, 35 Washington St, Brooklyn NY 11201 USA
**Barrie, Amanda** — Actress
Associated International Mgmt, 7 Hatton Garden, #400, London EC1N 8AD, England
**Barrie, Barbara** — Actress
Innovative Artists, 1505 10th St, Santa Monica CA 90401 USA
**Barrie, Douglas R (Doug)** — Ice Hockey Player
12130 46th St NW, Edmonton AB T5W 2W4, Canada
**Barrie, Len** — Ice Hockey Player
Bear Mountain, 208-2800 Bryn Maur Road, Victoria BC V9B 3T4, Canada
**Barriere, Alain** — Singer, Songwriter
Discotheque Le Stirwen, Chemin Mane Brizil, 56340 Carmac, France
**Barris, George** — Custom Car Designer
Kustom City, 10811 Riverside Dr, North Hollywood CA 91602, USA
**Barro, Robert J** — Economist
Harvard University, Economics Dept, Cambridge MA 02138, USA
**Barron, Alex B** — Football Player
630 Emerson Road, #206, Saint Louis MO 63141, USA
**Barron, Dana** — Actress
Epstein-Wyckoff, 280 S Beverly Dr, #400, Beverly Hills CA 90212 USA
**Barron, Eric J** — Educator
Florida State University, President's Office, Tallahassee FL 32306, USA
**Barron, Kenneth (Kenny)** — Jazz Pianist, Composer
Unlimited Myles, 6 Imaginary Place, Aberdeen NJ 07747, USA
**Barron, Mark** — Football Player
Tampa Bay Buccaneers, 1 W Buccaneer Place, Tampa FL 33607 USA
**Barron, Steve M** — Director
United Talent Agency, U T A Plaza, 9336 Civic Center Dr, Beverly Hills CA 90210 USA
**Barros, Ana Beatriz** — Model
Elite Model Mgmt, Bridgade 23B, #400, 1260 Copenhagen, Denmark
**Barros, Dana B** — Basketball Player
10 Arborway, North Easton MA 02356, USA
**Barroso, Jose Manuel** — Prime Minister, Portugal
European Commission, Berlaymont, Rue la Loi 200, 1040 Brussels, Belgium
**Barrow, Barbara** — Golfer
11427 Mayapple Way, San Diego CA 92131, USA
**Barrow, Dean O** — Prime Minister, Belize
Prime Minister's Office, East Bloc, Belmopan, Belize
**Barrow, Geoffrey P (Geoff)** — Synthesizer Player (Portishead)
High Road Touring, 751 Bridgeway, #200, Sausalito CA 94965 USA
**Barrow, John D** — Mathematician, Templeton Prize Laureate
Cambridge University, Math Sciences Center, Cambridge CB3 0WA, England
**Barrow, Micheal C** — Football Player
1115 S Alhambra Circle, Coral Gables FL 33146, USA
**Barrowman, John** — Actor, Singer
293 Villas Road, Plumstead, London SE18 7PR, England
**Barrowman, Michael (Mike)** — Swimmer
603 S Alp St, Bay City MI 48706, USA
**Barrs, Jack L (Jay), Jr** — Archery Athlete
646 E Kings Peak Cove, Draper UT 84020, USA
**Barry, Allen (Al)** — Football Player
3760 Edgeview Dr, Pasadena CA 91107, USA
**Barry, Barbara** — Interior Designer
Barbara Barry Inc, 9526 Pico Blvd, Los Angeles CA 90035, USA
**Barry, Brandon** — Singer (Stamps Quartet)
PO Box 1471, Brentwood TN 37024, USA
**Barry, Brent R** — Basketball Player
712 The Strand, Hermosa Beach CA 90254, USA
**Barry, Daniel T (Dan)** — Astronaut
46 Ashton Lane, South Hadley MA 01075, USA
**Barry, Dave** — Journalist, Writer
6510 Granada Blvd, Coral Gables FL 33146, USA
**Barry, Ellen** — Journalist
New York Times, Editorial Dept, 229 W 43rd St, New York NY 10036 USA
**Barry, Jeff** — Composer
B M I, 8730 W Sunset Blvd, #300, Los Angeles CA 90069 USA

| | |
|---|---|
| **Barry, Jon A** | Basketball Player |
| 4555 Club Dr NE, Atlanta GA 30319, USA | |
| **Barry, Jon B** | Photographer |
| 1965 Magnolia Dr, Baton Rouge LA 70808, USA | |
| **Barry, Kevin T** | Baseball Player |
| 76 Amethyst Way, Franklin Park NJ 08823, USA | |
| **Barry, Len** | Singer (Dovells) |
| Cape Entertainment, 8432 NW 31st Court, Sunrise FL 33351, USA | |
| **Barry, Lynda** | Cartoonist (Ernie Pook's Comeck) |
| PO Box 447, Footville WI 53537, USA | |
| **Barry, Marion S, Jr** | Mayor, Washington DC |
| 161 Raleigh St SE, Washington DC 20032, USA | |
| **Barry, Mark** | Singer, Flutist (BBMak) |
| Spirit Media, PO Box 43591, Phoenix AZ 85080, USA | |
| **Barry, Maryanne Trump** | Judge |
| US Court of Appeals, US Courthouse, Federal Square, #333, Newark NJ 07101, USA | |
| **Barry, Patricia** | Actress |
| 2619 Eden Place, Beverly Hills CA 90210, USA | |
| **Barry, Paul F** | Football Player |
| 409 Kingswood Dr, El Paso TX 79932, USA | |
| **Barry, Raymond J** | Actor |
| Metropolitan Talent Agency, 5405 Wilshire Blvd, #218, Los Angeles CA 90036 USA | |
| **Barry, Richard F D (Rick), III** | Basketball Player, Sportscaster |
| 5240 Broadmoor Bluffs Dr, Colorado Springs CO 80906, USA | |
| **Barry, Seymour (Sy)** | Cartoonist (Flash Gordon, Phantom) |
| 225 Fairfield Dr E, Holbrook NY 11741, USA | |
| **Barry, Thom** | Actor |
| Prestige Talent Agency, 9250 Wilshire Blvd, #208, Beverly Hills CA 90212, USA | |
| **Barry, Todd** | Actor, Comedian |
| 3 Arts Entertainment, 9460 Wilshire Blvd, #700, Beverly Hills CA 90212 USA | |
| **Barrymore, Drew** | Actress, Model |
| Creative Artists Agency, 2000 Ave of Stars, #100, Los Angeles CA 90067 USA | |
| **Barsh, Gregory S** | Pediatrician |
| Stanford University Medical Center, Pediatrics Dept, Stanford CA 94305, USA | |
| **Barshefsky, Charlene** | Government Official |
| Wilmer Cutler Pickering, 1875 Pennsylvania Ave NW, Washington DC 20006, USA | |
| **Barson, Mike** | Keyboardist (Madness) |
| I T F, Ariel House, 74A Charlotte St, London W1T 4QJ, England | |
| **Barsotti, Charles** | Cartoonist |
| 419 E 55th St, Kansas City MO 64110, USA | |
| **Barstow, David** | Journalist |
| New York Times, Editorial Dept, 229 W 43rd St, New York NY 10036 USA | |
| **Barstow, Josephine C** | Opera Singer |
| Musichall Ltd, Vicarage Way, Ringmer BN8 5LA, England | |
| **Bart, Peter B** | Editor |
| Variety, 5900 Wilshire Blvd, #3100, Los Angeles CA 90036, USA | |
| **Bart, Roger** | Actor |
| Innovative Artists, 1505 10th St, Santa Monica CA 90401 USA | |
| **Bartecko, Lubos** | Ice Hockey Player |
| 121 Windy Acres Estates Dr, Ballwin MO 63021, USA | |
| **Bartee, Kimera A** | Baseball Player |
| 10808 N 57th Dr, Glendale AZ 85304, USA | |
| **Bartel, Robin** | Ice Hockey Player |
| 210 Forsyth Court, Saskatoon SK S7N 4H2, Canada | |
| **Barth, Francis** | Artist |
| 7105 Jackson St, North Bergen NJ 07047, USA | |
| **Barth, John M** | Businessman |
| Johnson Controls, 5757 N Green Bay Ave, PO Box 591, Milwaukee WI 53201, USA | |
| **Barth, John S** | Writer |
| Wylie Agency, 250 W 57th St, #2114, New York NY 10107 USA | |
| **Barth, T Fredrik W** | Anthropologist |
| Rodkleivfaret 16, 0788 Oslo, Norway | |
| **Barth, Uta** | Conceptual Artist, Photographer |
| Tanya Bonakdar Gallery, 521 W 21st St, Front 1, New York NY 10011, USA | |
| **Bartha, Justin** | Actor |
| Creative Artists Agency, 2000 Ave of Stars, #100, Los Angeles CA 90067 USA | |
| **Bartholemew, Ian** | Actor |
| Ken McReddie Assoc, 101 Finsbury Pavement, London EC2A 1RS, England | |
| **Bartholomew I** | Religious Leader |
| Eastern Orthodox Church, Rum Ortoks Patrikhanesi, 34220 Istanbul, Turkey | |
| **Bartholomew, Dave** | Jazz Trumpeter, Singer |
| Paramount Entertainment, PO Box 12, Far Hills NJ 07931 USA | |
| **Bartholomew, Logan** | Actor |
| J L A Talent Agency, 9151 Sunset Blvd, West Hollywood CA 90069, USA | |
| **Bartilson, Lynsey** | Actress |
| C E S D, 10635 Santa Monica Blvd, #130, Los Angeles CA 90025 USA | |
| **Bartiromo, Maria** | Commentator |
| CNBC-TV, 2200 Fletcher Ave, #600, Fort Lee NJ 07024, USA | |
| **Bartkowiak, Andrzej** | Director |
| Paradigm Agency, 360 N Crescent Dr, North Building, Beverly Hills CA 90210 USA | |
| **Bartkowski, Steven J (Steve)** | Football Player |
| 10745 Bell Road, Duluth GA 30097, USA | |
| **Bartlett, Bonnie** | Actress, Singer |
| 12805 Hortense St, Studio City CA 91604, USA | |
| **Bartlett, Don** | Curling Athlete |
| Curling Assn, 1660 Vimont Court, Cumberland ON K4A 4J4, Canada | |
| **Bartlett, Erinn** | Actress |
| Innovative Artists, 1505 10th St, Santa Monica CA 90401 USA | |
| **Bartlett, Jennifer L** | Artist |
| 134 Charles St, New York NY 10014, USA | |
| **Bartlett, Jim** | Ice Hockey Player |
| 8718 Chadwick Dr, Tampa FL 33635, USA | |
| **Bartlett, Robin** | Actress |
| Gersh Agency, 9465 Wilshire Blvd, #600, Beverly Hills CA 90212 USA | |
| **Bartlett, Scott** | Guitarist (Saving Abel) |
| Virgin Records, 338 N Foothill Road, Beverly Hills CA 90210 USA | |

**Bartlett, Thomas A** — Educator
1209 SW 6th St, #904, Portland OR 97204, USA
**Bartletti, Don** — Photojournalist
Los Angeles Times, Editorial Dept, 202 W 1st St, Los Angeles CA 90012 USA
**Bartley, Adam** — Actor
Gersh Agency, 9465 Wilshire Blvd, #600, Beverly Hills CA 90212 USA
**Bartley, Geoff** — Singer, Guitarist, Songwriter
Jean Schwartz Entertainment, 326 Grant St, Framingham MA 01702, USA
**Bartoe, John-David F** — Astronaut
2724 Lighthouse Dr, Houston TX 77058, USA
**Bartoletti, Louis** — Golfer
1450 Longlea Terrace, Wellington FL 33414, USA
**Bartoli, Cecilia** — Opera Singer
Mastroianni Assoc, 161 W 61st St, #32B, New York NY 10023, USA
**Bartoli, Marion** — Tennis Player
Women's Tennis Assn, 1 Progress Plaza, #1500, Saint Petersburg FL 33701 USA
**Bartolome, Victor (Vic)** — Basketball Player
1025 Rinconada Road, #A, Santa Barbara CA 93101, USA
**Bartolomew, Kenneth (Ken)** — Speed Skater
4820 Bryant Ave S, Minneapolis MN 55419, USA
**Barton, Austin** — Sculptor
100 N Lake, Joseph OR 97846, USA
**Barton, Daric W (D B)** — Baseball Player
958 Naples Dr, Corona CA 92882, USA
**Barton, Dorie** — Actress
Abrams Artists, 9200 W Sunset Blvd, #1125, West Hollywood CA 90069 USA
**Barton, Eric** — Football Player
23 Hayes Hill Dr, Northport NY 11768, USA
**Barton, Glenys** — Artist
Angela Flowers Gallery, 199-205 Richmond Road, London E8 3NJ, England
**Barton, Gregory (Greg)** — Canoeing Athlete
6851 30th Ave NE, Seattle WA 98115, USA
**Barton, Harris S** — Football Player
334 Lincoln Ave, Palo Alto CA 94301, USA
**Barton, Jacqueline K** — Chemist
California Insitute of Techonolgy, Chemistry Dept, Pasadena CA 91125, USA
**Barton, Lou Ann** — Singer
Luther Wolf Agency, PO Box 685138, Austin TX 78718, USA
**Barton, Mischa** — Actress, Model
Domain Talent, 9229 W Sunset Blvd, #710, West Hollywood CA 90069 USA
**Barton, Peter** — Actor
2265 Westwood Blvd, #2619, Los Angeles CA 90064, USA
**Barton, Rachel** — Concert Violinist
I C M Artists, 40 W 57th St, #1800, New York NY 10019 USA
**Barton, Robert W (Bob)** — Baseball Player
37193 Stardust Way, Murrieta CA 92563, USA
**Bartovic, Milan** — Ice Hockey Player
141 Bennington Hills Court, West Henrietta NY 14586, USA
**Bartrum, Mike W** — Football Player
43375 Carlton Place, Pomeroy OH 45769, USA
**Bartusiak, Skye McCole** — Actress
C E S D, 10635 Santa Monica Blvd, #130, Los Angeles CA 90025 USA
**Bartz, Gary L** — Jazz Saxophonist, Composer
Joel Chriss Co, 300 Mercer St, #3J, New York NY 10003 USA
**Bartz, Randall (Randy)** — Speed Skater
3829 Baker Road, Hopkins MN 55305, USA
**Baruch, Jordan J** — Electrical Engineer
5630 Wisconsin Ave, #905, Chevy Chase MD 20815, USA
**Baruchel, Jay** — Actor
Thruline Entertainment, 9250 Wilshire Blvd, #100, Beverly Hills CA 90212 USA
**Barwell, Eric** — British WW II Air Force Hero
Toft, 5 Beldam's Close, Cambridge CB3 7RN, England
**Baryshnikov, Mikhail** — Ballet Dancer, Actor
Baryshnikov Productions, 1830 Rittenhouse Square, Philadelphia PA 19103, USA
**Barzelay, Eef** — Singer, Guitarist (Clem Snide)
Impact Artist Mgmt, 356 W 123rd St, New York NY 10027, USA
**Barzilauskas, Carl J** — Football Player
4444 Lower Schooner Road, Nashville IN 47448, USA
**Barzini, Benedetta** — Model
Donna Karan Co, 361 Newbury St, Boston MA 02115, USA
**Basaraba, Gary** — Actor
Stone Manners Salners, 9911 W Pico Blvd, #1400, Los Angeles CA 90035 USA
**Basche, David Alan** — Actor
New Wave Entertainment 2660 W Olive Ave, Burbank CA 91505, USA
**Baschnagel, Brian D** — Football Player
1824 Ridgewood Lane W, Glenview IL 60025, USA
**Basco, Dante** — Actor
Dayton-Milrad-Cho, 8899 Beverly Blvd, #918, Los Angeles CA 90048, USA
**Basco, Dion** — Actor
Schiowitz Connor, 1680 N Vine St, #1016, Los Angeles CA 90028 USA
**Baselios Cleemis Cardinal Thottunkal** — Religious Leader
Major Archbishop's House, Pattom, Thiruvananthapuram, Kerala 695004, India
**Baselitz, Georg** — Artist
Schloss Derneberg, 31188 Holle, Germany
**Bashir, Idrees** — Football Player
5579 Mountain View Pass, Stone Mountain GA 30087, USA
**Bashir, Martin** — Commentator
ABC-TV, News Dept, 77 W 66th St, New York NY 10023 USA
**Bashmet, Yuri A** — Concert Violist, Conductor
Briyusov 7, #16, 103009 Moscow, Russia
**Bashoff, Blake** — Actor
Abrams Artists, 9200 W Sunset Blvd, #1125, West Hollywood CA 90069 USA
**Basia** — Singer
Creative Artists Agency, 2000 Ave of Stars, #100, Los Angeles CA 90067 USA
**Basilashuili, Oleg V** — Actor
Borodinskaya Str 13, #58, 196180 Saint Petersburg, Russia

**Basinger, Kim** — Actress
Paradigm Agency, 360 N Crescent Dr, North Building, Beverly Hills CA 90210 USA
**Basis, Austin** — Actor
Don Buchwald, 6500 Wilshire Blvd, #2200, Los Angeles CA 90048 USA
**Basler, Marianne** — Actress
Agence Artiste Adequet, 108 Rue Reaumur, 75002 Paris, France
**Basri, Gibor** — Astronomer
University of California, Astronomy Dept, Berkeley CA 94720, USA
**Bass, George F** — Underwater Archaeologist
1600 Dominik Dr, College Station TX 77840, USA
**Bass, Glenn A** — Football Player
4185 Diplomacy Circle, Tallahassee FL 32308, USA
**Bass, Hyman** — Mathematician
435 Riverside Dr, New York NY 10025, USA
**Bass, J Lance** — Singer ('N Sync)
Owen Entertainment, 1708 21st Ave S, #274, Nashville TN 37212, USA
**Bass, Kevin C** — Baseball Player
3630 Maranatha Dr, Sugar Land TX 77479, USA
**Bass, Michael T (Mike)** — Football Player
4703 NW 36th St, Gainesville FL 32605, USA
**Bass, Norman D (Norm), Jr** — Baseball, Football Player
156 E 70th St, Los Angeles CA 90003, USA
**Bass, Randy W** — Baseball Player
2709 SW Coombs Road, Lawton OK 73505, USA
**Bass, Ronald J (Ron)** — Writer
I C M Partners, 10250 Constellation Blvd, #900, Los Angeles CA 90067 USA
**Bassen, Robert P (Bob)** — Ice Hockey Player
1742 Coldstone Dr, Frisco TX 75034, USA
**Bassett, Angela** — Actress
Lighthouse Entertainment, 9220 Sunset Blvd, #200, West Hollywood CA 90069, USA
**Bassett, Brian** — Editorial Cartoonist, Cartoonist (Adam)
Seattle Times, Editorial Dept, 1000 Denny Way, Seattle WA 98109 USA
**Bassett, E Timothy (Tim)** — Basketball Player
1143 Dorsey Place, Plainfield NJ 07062, USA
**Bassett, Leslie R** — Composer
5433 Ashmore Lane, Flowery Branch GA 30542, USA
**Bassett-Seguso, Carling** — Tennis Player
1008 Vista del Mar Dr, Delray Beach FL 33483, USA
**Bassey, Jennifer** — Actress
12 E 86th St, #1728, New York NY 10028, USA
**Bassey, Shirley** — Singer
La Rocca Bella, 24 Ave Princess Grace, 98000 Monte Carlo, Monaco
**Bassham, Lanny R** — Marksman
7101 Lake Mead Court, Frisco TX 75034, USA
**Basso, Dennis** — Fashion Designer
317 W 33rd St New York NY 10001, USA
**Bastedo, Alexandra** — Actress
Associated International Mgmt, 7 Hatton Garden, #400, London EC1N 8AD, England
**Basti, Juli** — Actress
Krecsanyi Utca 6, 1025 Budapest, Hungary
**Baston, Maceo** — Basketball Player
PO Box 4846, Troy MI 48099, USA
**Basu, Asish R** — Geochemist
University of Rochester, Geochemistry Dept, Rochester NY 14627, USA
**Batali, Dean** — Writer
A P A Talent/Literary Agency, 405 S Beverly Dr, #300, Beverly Hills CA 90212 USA
**Batali, Mario** — Restauranteur, Chef
Babbo, 110 Waverly Place, Front A, New York NY 10011, USA
**Batalli-Cosmovici, Cristiano** — Astronaut
International Astronomical Union, Via Fosso del Cavaliere 100, 00133 Rome, Italy
**Batbold, Sukhbaataryn** — Prime Minister, Mongolia
Prime Minister's Office, Great Hural, Ulan Bator 12, Mongolia
**Batch, Charles D (Charlie)** — Football Player
1844 Willow Oak Dr, Wexford PA 15090, USA
**Batchelder, Alice M** — Judge
US Court of Appeals, 143 W Liberty St, Medina OH 44256, USA
**Batchelder, Joseph L (Joe)** — Yachtsman
11004 Hard Rock Road, Austin TX 78750, USA
**Batchelor, Joy E** — Animator
Educational Film Center, 5-7 Kean St, London WC2B 4AT, England
**Bate, Jennifer L** — Concert Organist
35 Collingwood Ave, Muswell Hill, London N10 3EH, England
**Bateau, Laurent** — Actor
Voyez Mon Agent, 20 Ave Rapp, 75007 Paris, France
**Batelaan, Kelsey** — Actor
C E S D, 10635 Santa Monica Blvd, #130, Los Angeles CA 90025 USA
**Bateman, Brian** — Golfer
100 Brunswick Ave, Saint Simons Island GA 31522, USA
**Bateman, Jason** — Actor
Creative Artists Agency, 2000 Ave of Stars, #100, Los Angeles CA 90067 USA
**Bateman, Justine** — Actress
8004 Woodrow Wilson Dr, Los Angeles CA 90046, USA
**Bateman, Marvin F (Marv)** — Football Player
1022 W Smithsonian Way, Apple Valley UT 84737, USA
**Bateman, Robert M** — Artist
PO Box 115 Fulford Harbour, Salt Spring Island BC V8K 2P2, Canada
**Bates, Billy Ray** — Basketball Player
8051 Gibbon St, Daniel Island SC 29492, USA
**Bates, Charles C** — Oceanographer
750 S La Posada Circle, #77, Green Valley AZ 85614, USA
**Bates, David M** — Artist
34 Horatio St, #4B, New York NY 10014, USA
**Bates, Doug** — Journalist
Portland Oregonian, Editorial Dept, 1320 SW Broadway, Portland OR 97201, USA
**Bates, D'Wayne L** — Football Player
1862 Sherman Ave, #1NE, Ponte Vedra Beach FL 32082, USA

# B

| | |
|---|---|
| **Bates, Jared L (Jerry)** | Army General |
| L-3 Communications Holdings, SyColeman Division, 600 3rd Ave, New York NY 10016, USA | |
| **Bates, Kathy** | Actress |
| I C M Partners, 10250 Constellation Blvd, #900, Los Angeles CA 90067 USA | |
| **Bates, Mario D** | Football Player |
| PO Box 5832, Scottsdale AZ 85261, USA | |
| **Bates, Michael D** | Football Player, Track Athlete |
| 1239 W Keuhne Court, Tucson AZ 85755, USA | |
| **Bates, Patrick (Pat)** | Golfer |
| 215 Ward Circle, #200, Brentwood TN 37027, USA | |
| **Bates, Quentin** | Writer |
| Ampersand Agency, Ryman's Cottages, Little Tew, Oxfordshire OX7 4JJ, England | |
| **Bates, Richard (Dick)** | Baseball Player |
| 5858 W Cielo Grande, Glendale AZ 85310, USA | |
| **Bates, Shawn** | Ice Hockey Player |
| 35 Bradshaw St, Medford MA 02155, USA | |
| **Bates, Ted D** | Football Player |
| 4036 Paige St, Los Angeles CA 90031, USA | |
| **Bates, Tyler** | Composer |
| Greenspan Kohan Management, 8760 Sunset Blvd, Los Angeles CA 90069, USA | |
| **Bates, William F (Bill)** | Football Player |
| 1252 Neck Road, Ponte Vedra FL 32082, USA | |
| **Bathe, Frank** | Ice Hockey Player |
| 2 Meadowwood Dr, Scarborough ME 04074, USA | |
| **Bathgate, Andrew J (Andy)** | Ice Hockey Player |
| 43 Brentwood Dr, Brampton ON L6T 1R1, Canada | |
| **Bathory, Zoltan** | Guitarist (Five Finger Death Punch) |
| 10th Street Entertainment, 568 Broadway, #608, New York NY 10012, USA | |
| **Bathurst, Otto** | Director |
| Casorotto Ramsay, Waverley House, 7-12 Noel St, London W1F 8GQ, England | |
| **Batiashvili, Lisa** | Concert Violinist |
| Harrison/Parrott, 5-6 Albion Court, London W6 0QT, England | |
| **Batinkoff, Randall** | Actor |
| Glick Agency, 1321 7th St, #203, Santa Monica CA 90401 USA | |
| **Batiste, Kimothy E (Kim)** | Baseball Player |
| 16161 Aikens Road, Prairieville LA 70769, USA | |
| **Batiuk, Thomas M (Tom)** | Cartoonist (Crankshaft) |
| Universal Press Syndicate, 4520 Main St, #700, Kansas City MO 64111 USA | |
| **Batiz Campbell, Enrique** | Conductor |
| Cerrada Rancho los Colorines 11, Dele Tlalan, Mexico DF 14000, Mexico | |
| **Batmanglij, Zal** | Director |
| United Talent Agency, U T A Plaza, 9336 Civic Center Dr, Beverly Hills CA 90210 USA | |
| **Bator, Francis M** | Economist |
| 85 Grove St, #2, Wellesley MA 02482, USA | |
| **Batra, Pooja** | Actress, Model |
| 403H Gokul Vihar II, Thakar Complex Kandivli (E), Mumbai MS 400068, India | |
| **Batt, Michael P (Mike)** | Singer, Songwriter |
| Dramatico Entertainment, PO Box 214, Farnham, Surrey GU10 5XZ, England | |
| **Battaglia, Jon (Bates)** | Ice Hockey Player |
| 832 Graham St, Raleigh NC 27605, USA | |
| **Battaglia, Marco** | Football Player |
| 15832 79th St, Howard Beach NY 11414, USA | |
| **Battaglia, Matt** | Actor |
| Matt Battaglia Productions, 8033 Sunset Blvd, #3000, Los Angeles CA 90046, USA | |
| **Battelle, Ann** | Moguls Skier |
| Mogul Logic, 4279 Monroe Dr, #D, Boulder CO 80303, USA | |
| **Batten, Kimberly (Kim)** | Track Athlete |
| 192 Sugar Plum Dr, Tallahassee FL 32312, USA | |
| **Battersby, Alan R** | Chemist |
| 20 Barrow Road, Cambridge CB2 2AS, England | |
| **Battie, D Antonio (Tony)** | Basketball Player |
| 11264 Bridge House Road, Windermere FL 34786, USA | |
| **Battier, Shane C** | Basketball Player |
| 4075 Bonita Ave, Miami FL 33133, USA | |
| **Battiste, P Francois** | Actor |
| Innovative Artists, 1505 10th St, Santa Monica CA 90401 USA | |
| **Battistelli, Francesca** | Singer, Songwriter |
| Proper Mgmt, PO Box 150867, Nashville TN 37215, USA | |
| **Battle, Arnaz J** | Football Player |
| 1091 Broadmoore Lane, Prosper TX 75078, USA | |
| **Battle, Hinton** | Dancer, Actor |
| Borinstein Oreck Bogart, 3172 Dona Susana Dr, Studio City CA 91604 USA | |
| **Battle, John S** | Basketball Player |
| 125 Glen Beigh Run, Tyrone GA 30290, USA | |
| **Battle, Kathleen D** | Opera Singer |
| Columbia Artists Mgmt Inc, 1790 Broadway, #702, New York NY 10019 USA | |
| **Battle, Texas** | Actor |
| Innovative Artists, 1505 10th St, Santa Monica CA 90401 USA | |
| **Battles, Ainsley T** | Football Player |
| 1237 Misty Valley Court, Lawrenceville GA 30045, USA | |
| **Batton, Dave** | Basketball Player |
| 6506 Bayonne Dr, Spring TX 77389, USA | |
| **Batts, Lloyd** | Basketball Player |
| 500 S Dante Ave, Glenwood IL 60425, USA | |
| **Batum, Nicolas** | Basketball Player |
| Portland Trail Blazers, Rose Garden, 1 N Center Court St, Portland OR 97227 USA | |
| **Baturin, Yuri M** | Cosmonaut |
| Cosmonaut Training Center, Star City, 141160 Zvezdny Gorodok, Moscow Oblast, Russia | |
| **Baty, Gregory J (Greg)** | Football Player |
| 4 King St, Redwood City CA 94062, USA | |
| **Bauchau, Patrick** | Actor |
| David Shapira Assoc, 193 N Robertson Blvd, Beverly Hills CA 90211 USA | |
| **Baudo, Serge** | Conductor |
| Les Hautes du Ferra, Chemin Charre, 13600 Ceyreste, France | |
| **Baudry, Patrick** | Spatinaut, France |
| 305 Ave Mairie, 31600 Eaunas, France | |

Bates - Baudry

| | |
|---|---|
| **Bauer, Chris** | Actor |
| Framework Entertainment, 9057 Nemo St, #C, West Hollywood CA 90069 USA | |
| **Bauer, Erwin A** | Photographer |
| 8880 SE 19th Avenue Road, Ocala FL 34480, USA | |
| **Bauer, Hans-Uwe** | Actor |
| Fitz & Skoglund Agents, Liniestr 130, 10115 Berlin, Germany | |
| **Bauer, Henry J (Hank)** | Football Player |
| 11150 Alejo Place, San Diego CA 92124, USA | |
| **Bauer, Jaime Lyn** | Actress |
| Gar Lester Agency, 4130 Cahuenga Blvd, #108, Universal City CA 91602, USA | |
| **Bauer, Joy** | Writer |
| W M E Entertainment, 1325 Ave of Americas, New York NY 10019 USA | |
| **Bauer, Kristin** | Actress |
| Kritzer Levine Wilkins Griffin, 11872 La Grange Ave, #100, Los Angeles CA 90025 USA | |
| **Bauer, Lukas** | Cross Country Skier |
| Muller Productions, Na Valech 45/32, 16000 Prague 6, Czech Republic | |
| **Bauer, Michelle** | Actress, Model |
| A I Productions, 6260 Laurel Canyon Blvd, #201, North Hollywood CA 91606, USA | |
| **Bauer, Peggy** | Photographer |
| 8880 SE 19th Avenue Road, Ocala FL 34480, USA | |
| **Bauer, Peter** | Bassist, Organist (Walkmen) |
| Mick Mgmt, 35 Washington St, Brooklyn NY 11201 USA | |
| **Bauer, Richard E (Rick)** | Baseball Player |
| 6805 Easthaven Way, Citrus Heights CA 95621, USA | |
| **Bauer, Steven** | Actor |
| Global Artists Agency, 6253 Hollywood Blvd, #508, Los Angeles CA 90028 USA | |
| **Bauer, Viola** | Cross Country Skier |
| Ski Verband, Hubertusstr 1, 82152 Planegg, Germany | |
| **Bauer, William J** | Judge |
| 213 S Grace Ave, Elmhurst IL 60126, USA | |
| **Baugh, Laura** | Golfer |
| 5225 Timberview Terrace, Orlando FL 32819, USA | |
| **Baugh, Thomas A (Tom)** | Football Player, Coach |
| 14716 S Bynum Road, Lone Jack MO 64070, USA | |
| **Baughan, Maxie C, Jr** | Football Player, Coach |
| 3355 Lawndale Road, Reisterstown MD 21136, USA | |
| **Baughman, J Ross** | Photojournalist |
| 31101 Harbour Vista Circle, Saint Augustine FL 32080, USA | |
| **Baughman, Ray H** | Nanotechnologist |
| 5428 Willow Road, Dallas TX 75252, USA | |
| **Baulcombe, David C** | Geneticist, Plant Scientist |
| Cambridge University, Plant Institute, Cambridge CB2 1TN, England | |
| **Baulieu, Etienne-Emile** | Biochemist, Inventor (Abortion Pill) |
| Institut de France, 23 Quai de Conti, 75006 Paris, France | |
| **Baum, Bob** | Ice Hockey Player |
| 465 Bayle St W, Pickering ON L1W 3P6, Canada | |
| **Baum, John (Johnny)** | Basketball Player |
| 8216 Fenton Road, Glenside PA 19038, USA | |
| **Baum, William W Cardinal** | Religious Leader |
| Via Guido Reni 2/D, 00196 Rome Lazio, Italy | |
| **Bauman, Jon (Bowzer)** | Singer, Pianist (Sha Na Na) |
| David Belenzon Mgmt, PO Box 5000, PMB 67, Rancho Santa Fe CA 92067, USA | |
| **Baumann, Dieter** | Track Athlete |
| Biesingerstr 18, 72070 Tubingen, Germany | |
| **Baumann, Frank M** | Baseball Player |
| 7712 Sunray Lane, Saint Louis MO 63123, USA | |
| **Baumann, Herbert K W** | Composer |
| Franziskaserstr 16, #1419, 81669 Munich, Germany | |
| **Baumann, Kenny** | Actor |
| A K A Talent, 6310 San Vicente Blvd, #200, Los Angeles CA 90048 USA | |
| **Baumbach, Noah** | Director, Writer |
| United Talent Agency, U T A Plaza, 9336 Civic Center Dr, Beverly Hills CA 90210 USA | |
| **Baumbauer, Frank** | Director |
| Deutsches Schauspielhaus, Kirchenallee 39, 20099 Hamburg, Germany | |
| **Baumgartner, Brian** | Actor |
| 3-Bees Entertainment, 4217 Verdugo View Dr, Los Angeles CA 90065, USA | |
| **Baumgartner, Bruce** | Freestyle Wrestler |
| 12765 Forrest Dr, Edinboro PA 16412, USA | |
| **Baumgartner, Felix** | Sky Diver |
| Red Bull Stratos Project, International Air Center, 1 Jerry Smith Circle, Roswell NM 88202, USA | |
| **Baumgartner, Ken** | Ice Hockey Player |
| 39 Court St, #1, Newton MA 02458, USA | |
| **Baumgartner, Nolan** | Ice Hockey Player |
| Vancouver Canucks, 800 Griffiths Way, Vancouver BC V6B 6G1, Canada | |
| **Baumgartner, Steven J (Steve)** | Football Player |
| 144 Brookside Dr, Mandeville LA 70471, USA | |
| **Baumhower, Robert G (Bob)** | Football Player |
| 21201 Ayrshire Lane, Fairhope AL 36532, USA | |
| **Baumler, Hans-Jurgen** | Figure Skater |
| Magt Rehling, Kirchenstr 17C, 82110 Germering, Germany | |
| **Baumol, William J** | Economist |
| 455 N End Ave, #1204, New York NY 10282, USA | |
| **Baun, Robert N (Bob)** | Ice Hockey Player |
| 35 Pittman Crescent, Ajax ON L1S 3G4, Canada | |
| **Bauta, Eduardo G (Ed)** | Baseball Player |
| 3786 Long Grove Lane, Port Orange FL 32129, USA | |
| **Bautista, Daniel B (Danny)** | Baseball Player |
| 901 E Van Buren St, #1063, Phoenix AZ 85006, USA | |
| **Bautista, Jose A** | Baseball Player |
| 100 Shockoe Slip, #400, Richmond VA 23219, USA | |
| **Bautista, Jose J** | Baseball Player |
| 15621 SW 16th Court, Pembroke Pines FL 33027, USA | |
| **Bavaro, Mark** | Football Player |
| 17 Long Hill, Boxford MA 01921, USA | |
| **Bavouzet, Jean-Efflam** | Concert Pianist |
| Chandos Records, 1 Commerce Park, Commerce Way, Colchester, Essex CO2 8HX, England | |

**Bawel, Edward R (Bibbles)** — Football Player
1169 2nd Ave, Jasper IN 47546, USA
**Bawoyeu, Jean Alingue** — Prime Minister, Chad
Union for Democratic Republic, BP 1122, N'Djamena, Chad
**Bax, Adriaan (Ad)** — Biophysicist
National Institutes of Health, Biophysics Dept, 5 Memorial Dr, Building 5, Bethesda MD 20892, USA
**Bax, Kylie** — Model, Actress
Storm Model Agency, 5 Jubilee Place, Chelsea, London SW3 3TD, England
**Baxendale, Helen** — Actress
Yakety Yak, 8 Bloomsbury Square, London WC1A 2UA, England
**Baxter, Frederick D (Fred)** — Football Player
PO Box 14, Brundidge AL 36010, USA
**Baxter, Gary W** — Football Player
13749 Choctaw Dr, Tyler TX 75709, USA
**Baxter, Glen** — Artist, Cartoonist
Chris Beetle Gallery, 10 Ryder St, London SW1Y 6QB, England
**Baxter, James** — Animator
James Baxter Animation, 32 Mills Place, Pasadena CA 91105, USA
**Baxter, Jeff (Skunk)** — Guitarist (Doobie Brothers, Steely Dan)
Howard Rose, 9460 Wilshire Blvd, #310, Beverly Hills CA 90212, USA
**Baxter, Jennifer** — Actress
Talent Works, 3500 W Olive Ave, #1400, Burbank CA 91505 USA
**Baxter, Kirk** — Editor
Motion Pictures Editors Guild, 7715 Sunset Blvd, #200, Los Angeles CA 90046, USA
**Baxter, Meredith** — Actress
Talent Works, 3500 W Olive Ave, #1400, Burbank CA 91505 USA
**Baxter, Paul** — Ice Hockey Player
1610 Saint John St, Wichita Falls TX 76302, USA
**Baxter, William E (Billy), Jr** — Poker Player
CardPlayer Media, 6940 Obannon Drive, Las Vegas NV 89117, USA
**Baxter-Johnson, Patricia** — Golfer
111 Bryn Mawr Dr, Lake Worth FL 33460, USA
**Bay, Jason R** — Baseball Player
5811 106th Ave NE, Kirkland WA 98033, USA
**Bay, Michael** — Director
W M E Entertainment, 9601 Wilshire Blvd, #300, Beverly Hills CA 90210 USA
**Bay, Susan** — Actress
Gersh Agency, 9465 Wilshire Blvd, #600, Beverly Hills CA 90212 USA
**Baye, Nathalie** — Actress
Artmedia, 20 Ave Rapp, 75007 Paris, France
**Bayer, Vanessa** — Actress
W M E Entertainment, 9601 Wilshire Blvd, #300, Beverly Hills CA 90210 USA
**Bayh, Birch E, Jr** — Senator, IN
PO Box 3353, Easton MD 21601, USA
**Bayi, Filbert** — Track Athlete
PO Box 60240, Morogoro Road, Dar es Salaam, Tanzania
**Bayl, Benjamin** — Conductor
Harrison/Parrott, 5-6 Albion Court, London W6 0QT, England
**Bayldon, Geoffrey** — Actor
Joy Jameson, 219 Plaza, 535 Kings Road, London SW10 0SZ, England
**Bayle, Jean-Michel** — Motorcycle Racing Rider
General Delivery, 04100 Manosque, Alpes-de-Haute-Provence, France
**Bayless, Jerryd** — Basketball Player
New Orleans Pelicans, 1250 Poydras St, #101, New Orleans LA 70113 USA
**Bayless, Martin A** — Football Player
834 Calle Lagasca, Chula Vista CA 91910, USA
**Bayley, Clive** — Opera Singer
I M G Artists, Hogarth Business Park, Chiswick, London W4 2TH, England
**Baylor, Don E** — Baseball Player, Manager
56325 Riviera, La Quinta CA 92253, USA
**Baylor, Elgin G** — Basketball Player, Executive
2480 Briarcrest Road, Beverly Hills CA 90210, USA
**Baylor, John M** — Football Player
211 Oak St, Hattiesburg MS 39401, USA
**Baynham, G Craig** — Football Player
1 7th St, #1102, Augusta GA 30901, USA
**Bayo, Maria** — Opera Singer
Columbia Artists Mgmt Inc, 165 W 57th St, New York NY 10019, USA
**Bayou, Bradley** — Fashion Designer
Film Fashion, 8687 Melrose Center, #G684, Los Angeles CA 90069, USA
**Bayrakdarian, Isabel** — Opera Singer
I M G Artists, Hogarth Business Park, Chiswick, London W4 2TH, England
**Bays, Carter** — Producer, Writer
United Talent Agency, U T A Plaza, 9336 Civic Center Dr, Beverly Hills CA 90210 USA
**Baz, Farouk El-** — Geologist
213 Silver Hill Road, Concord MA 01742, USA
**Baze, Russell A** — Thoroughbred Racing Jockey
22 Somerset Place, Woodside CA 94062, USA
**Bazell, Josh** — Writer
United Talent Agency, U T A Plaza, 9336 Civic Center Dr, Beverly Hills CA 90210 USA
**Bazell, Robert J** — Commentator
NBC-TV, News Dept, 4001 Nebraska Ave NW, Washington DC 20016 USA
**Bazelli, Bojan** — Cinematographer
Dattner Disposto, 10635 Santa Monica Blvd, #165, Los Angeles CA 90025, USA
**Bazer, Fuller W** — Animal Scientist
8600 Creekview Court, College Station TX 77845, USA
**Bazzaz, Fakhri A** — Plant Biologist
Harvard University, Organismic & Evolutionary Biology Dept, Cambridge MA 02138, USA
**Beach, Adam** — Actor
A P A Talent/Literary Agency, 405 S Beverly Dr, #300, Beverly Hills CA 90212 USA
**Beach, Bill** — Bowler
3715 Lee Run Road, Hermitage PA 16148, USA
**Beach, Gary** — Actor, Singer
122 Andalusia Way, Palm Beach Gardens FL 33418, USA
**Beach, Michael** — Actor
Medavoy Mgmt, 10203 Santa Monica Blvd, #400, Los Angeles CA 90067 USA

**Beach, Patrick J (Pat)** — Football Player
2523 NW Beach Road, Oak Harbor WA 98277, USA
**Beach, Sanjay R** — Football Player
2989 Riviera Lane, Westlake OH 44145, USA
**Beacham, Stephanie** — Actress
United Agents, 12-26 Lexington St, London W1F 0LE, England
**Beachley, Layne** — Surfer
Aim for Stars Foundation, PO Box H67, Sydney NSW 1213, Australia
**Beadle, Michelle D** — Sportscaster
NBC-TV, Sports Dept, 30 Rockefeller Plaza, #270E, New York NY 10112 USA
**Beagle, Ronald G (Ron)** — Football Player
3830 San Ysidro Way, Sacramento CA 95864, USA
**Beahan, Kate** — Actress
Management 360, 9111 Wilshire Blvd, Beverly Hills CA 90210 USA
**Beal, Bradley** — Basketball Player
Washington Wizards, M C I Centre, 601 F St NW, Washington DC 20004 USA
**Beal, Jeff** — Composer
First Artists Mgmt, 4764 Park Granada, #210, Calabasas CA 91302 USA
**Beale, Simon Russell** — Actor
Richard Stone Partnership, De Walden Court, 85 New Cavendish St, London W1W 6XD, England
**Beals, Jennifer** — Actress
Greenlight Mgmt, 13848 Valleyheart Dr, Sherman Oaks CA 91423, USA
**Beam, C Arlen** — Judge
US Court of Appeals, 100 Centennial Mall N, Lincoln NE 68508, USA
**Beamer, Frank** — Football Coach
Virginia Polytechnic Institute, Athletic Dept, Blacksburg VA 24061, USA
**Beamer, Lisa** — Writer
9 Cubberly Court, Cranbury NJ 08512, USA
**Beamish, Lindsay** — Actress, Dancer
Semler Entertainment, 13636 Ventura Blvd, #510, Sherman Oaks CA 91423, USA
**Beamon, Autry, Jr** — Football Player
2664 Lakeview Dr, Shakopee MN 55379, USA
**Beamon, Robert (Bob)** — Track Athlete
20533 Biscayne Blvd, #113, Miami FL 33180, USA
**Bean, Alan L** — Astronaut
9173 Briar Forest Dr, Houston TX 77024, USA
**Bean, Andy** — Golfer
2912 Grasslands Dr, Lakeland FL 33803, USA
**Bean, Dawn Pawson** — Synchronized Swimmer
11902 Red Hill Ave, Santa Ana CA 92705, USA
**Bean, Henry** — Director, Writer
Creative Artists Agency, 2000 Ave of Stars, #100, Los Angeles CA 90067 USA
**Bean, Joe** — Soccer Coach
Wheaton College, Athletic Dept, Wheaton IL 60187, USA
**Bean, Noah** — Actor
C E S D, 257 Park Ave S, #950, New York NY 10010 USA
**Bean, Orson** — Actor, Comedian
Stone Manners Salners, 9911 W Pico Blvd, #1400, Los Angeles CA 90035 USA
**Bean, Sean** — Actor
Independent Talent Group, 40 Whitfield St, London W1T 2RH, England
**Bean, William D (Billy)** — Baseball Player, Writer
W M E Entertainment, 9601 Wilshire Blvd, #300, Beverly Hills CA 90210 USA
**Beane, William L (Billy), Jr** — Baseball Player
33 Brightwood Lane E, Danville CA 94506, USA
**Bear, Gregory D (Greg)** — Writer
506 Lakeview Road, Lynnwood WA 98087, USA
**Bearak, Barry** — Journalist
New York Times, Editorial Dept, 229 W 43rd St, New York NY 10036 USA
**Beard, Alana M** — Basketball Player
Washington Mystics, Verizon Center, 401 9th St NW, #750, Washington DC 20004 USA
**Beard, Albert (Butch)** — Basketball Player, Coach
3834 Berleigh Hill Court, Burtonsville MD 20866, USA
**Beard, Amanda** — Swimmer, Model
4609 W Saguaro Cliffs Dr, Tucson AZ 85745, USA
**Beard, C David (Dave)** — Baseball Player
5325 Derby Chase Court, Alpharetta GA 30005, USA
**Beard, Edward L (Ed)** — Football Player
4110 2nd St, Chesapeake VA 23324, USA
**Beard, Frank** — Drummer (ZZ Top)
Sanctuary Mgmt, 15301 Ventura Blvd, Building B, Sherman Oaks CA 91403, USA
**Beard, Frank** — Golfer
74066 De Anza Way, Palm Desert CA 92260, USA
**Beard, Matthew** — Actor
Independent Talent Group, 40 Whitfield St, London W1T 2RH, England
**Bearse, Amanda** — Actress, Director, Producer
910 N 39th St, Seattle WA 98103, USA
**Beart, Emmanuelle** — Actress
Agence Artiste Adequet, 108 Rue Reaumur, 75002 Paris, France
**Beasley, Aaron B** — Football Player
1635 Braid Hills Dr, Pasadena MD 21122, USA
**Beasley, Allyce** — Actress
Henderson/Hogan, 850 7th Ave, #1003, New York NY 10019 USA
**Beasley, Bruce M** — Sculptor
322 Lewis St, San Francisco CA 94607, USA
**Beasley, Charles P (Charlie)** — Basketball Player
6308 Winton St, Dallas TX 75214, USA
**Beasley, Frederick J (Fred)** — Football Player
PO Box 210931, Montgomery AL 36121, USA
**Beasley, Jere L** — Attorney; Governor, AL
Beasley Allen Crow, 218 Commerce St, Montgomery AL 36104, USA
**Beasley, John** — Actor
Bauman Redanty Shaul Agency, 5757 Wilshire Blvd, #473, Los Angeles CA 90036, USA
**Beasley, John** — Composer, Musician
Donofrio Productions, 607 W Shore Road, Brigantine NJ 08203, USA
**Beasley, John** — Football Player
W3848 Turtle Patch Road, Pine River WI 54965, USA

| | | |
|---|---|---|
| **Beasley, John M** | | Basketball Player |
| 113 Oak Acres Dr W, Malakoff TX 75148, USA | | |
| **Beasley, Thomas L (Tom)** | | Football Player |
| RR 1 Box 185, Hiltons VA 24258, USA | | |
| **Beasley, Walter** | | Jazz Saxophonist |
| Berklee College of Music, 1140 Boylston St, Boston MA 02215, USA | | |
| **Beason, Jonathan (Jon)** | | Football Player |
| Carolina Panthers, Ericsson Stadium, 800 S Mint St, Charlotte NC 28202 USA | | |
| **Beathard, Peter F (Pete)** | | Football Player |
| 3770 Drake St, Houston TX 77005, USA | | |
| **Beaton, Frank** | | Ice Hockey Player |
| 3327 Chapel Hills Parkway, Fultondale AL 35068, USA | | |
| **Beatrix** | | Queen Mother, Netherlands |
| Soestdijk Palace, Amsterdamsestraatweg 1, 2513 Baarn AA, Netherlands | | |
| **Beatriz Barros, Ana** | | Model |
| Elite Model Mgmt, 404 Park Ave S, #900, New York NY 10016 USA | | |
| **Beattie, Ann** | | Writer |
| Janklow & Nesbit Assoc, 445 Park Ave, #1300, New York NY 10022 USA | | |
| **Beattie, Bob** | | Alpine Skier |
| 312 Aabc, #I, Aspen CO 81611, USA | | |
| **Beattie, Bruce** | | Editorial Cartoonist |
| Daytona Beach News-Journal, Editorial Dept, 901 6th St, Daytona Beach FL 32117, USA | | |
| **Beattie, James L (Jim)** | | Baseball Player |
| PO Box 231, Quechee VT 05059, USA | | |
| **Beattie, Joseph** | | Actor |
| Ken McReddie Assoc, 101 Finsbury Pavement, London EC2A 1RS, England | | |
| **Beattie, Michael** | | Actor |
| W M E Entertainment, 9601 Wilshire Blvd, #300, Beverly Hills CA 90210 USA | | |
| **Beatty, James T (Jim)** | | Track Athlete |
| 6525 Morrison Blvd, Charlotte NC 28211, USA | | |
| **Beatty, Linda** | | Model |
| Playboy Promotions, 2706 Media Center Dr, Los Angeles CA 90065 USA | | |
| **Beatty, Ned** | | Actor |
| 2706 N Beachwood Dr, Los Angeles CA 90068, USA | | |
| **Beatty, Warren** | | Director, Producer, Actor |
| 13671 Mulholland Dr, Beverly Hills CA 90210, USA | | |
| **Beaucham, Danny** | | Model |
| Select Model Mgmt, 17 Ferdinand St, London NW1 8EU, England | | |
| **Beauchamp, Alfred (Al)** | | Football Player |
| 533 Pinegate Road, Peachtree City GA 30269, USA | | |
| **Beauchamp, Joseph S (Joe)** | | Football Player |
| 8896 Highwood Dr, #A, San Diego CA 92119, USA | | |
| **Beaudin, Norman J A (Norm)** | | Ice Hockey Player |
| 11010 Longboat Key Lane, #106, Tampa FL 33626, USA | | |
| **Beaudoin, Douglas L (Doug)** | | Football Player |
| 15143 Springview St, Tampa FL 33624, USA | | |
| **Beaufoy, Simon** | | Writer |
| Knight Hall Agency, 7 Mallow St, London EC1Y 8RQ, England | | |
| **Beaumont, Jimmy** | | Singer (Skyliners), Songwriter |
| Creative Entertainment Assoc, 1950 Old Cuthbert Road, #J, Cherry Hill NJ 08034 USA | | |
| **Beaupre, Don** | | Ice Hockey Player |
| 5020 Scriver Road, Minneapolis MN 55436, USA | | |
| **Beauregard, Robin** | | Water Polo Player |
| 467 Midvale Ave, Los Angeles CA 90024, USA | | |
| **Beauregard, Stephane** | | Ice Hockey Player |
| 175 Rue Des Plaines, Cowansville QC J2K 3T8, Canada | | |
| **Beauvais, Garcelle** | | Model, Actress |
| S D B Partners, 1801 Ave of Stars, #902, Los Angeles CA 90067 USA | | |
| **Beauvois, Xavier** | | Actor, Writer, Director |
| Artmedia, 20 Ave Rapp, 75007 Paris, France | | |
| **Beavan, Jenny** | | Costume Designer |
| United Talent Agency, U T A Plaza, 9336 Civic Center Dr, Beverly Hills CA 90210 USA | | |
| **Beaver, James N (Jim)** | | Actor |
| House of Representatives, 1434 6th St, #1, Santa Monica CA 90401 USA | | |
| **Beaver, Joe** | | Rodeo Rider |
| PO Box 1595, Huntsville TN 37756, USA | | |
| **Beaver, Terry L** | | Actor |
| Paradigm Agency, 360 Park Ave S, #1600, New York NY 10010 USA | | |
| **Beban, Gary J** | | Football Player |
| 20 Timber Lane, Northbrook IL 60062, USA | | |
| **Bebington, Anna** | | Rowing Athlete |
| Leander Club, Henly on Thames, Leander RG9 2LP, England | | |
| **Beblawi, Hazem Abdel Aziz al-** | | Prime Minister, Egypt |
| Prime Minister's Office, PO Box 191, 1 Majlis El-Shaab St, Cairo CA104, Egypt | | |
| **Bebout, Nick** | | Football Player |
| 1606 Major Ave, Riverton WY 82501, USA | | |
| **Becaert, Sylvie** | | Biathlete |
| F F S Biathlon, 50 Rue des Marquisats, 74011 Annecy, France | | |
| **Bechara Boutros al-Rai, Mar** | | Religious Leader |
| Patriarchy of Maronite Catholic Church, Bkerke, Lebanon | | |
| **Bechdel, Alison** | | Cartoonist, Writer |
| Houghton Mifflin Harcourt, 215 Park Ave S, #1200, New York NY 10003 USA | | |
| **Becherer, Hans W** | | Businessman |
| 432 Columbine St, Denver CO 80206, USA | | |
| **Becht, Anthony** | | Football Player |
| 4657 Artesian Road, Land O Lakes FL 34638, USA | | |
| **Bechtel, Riley P** | | Businessman |
| Bechtel Group, 50 Beale St, San Francisco CA 94105, USA | | |
| **Bechtel, Stephen D, Jr** | | Businessman |
| Bechtel Group, 50 Beale St, San Francisco CA 94105, USA | | |
| **Bechtol, T Bubba** | | Actor, Comedian |
| The Consortium, 49 Music Square W, #210, Nashville TN 37203, USA | | |
| **Beck** | | Singer, Guitarist, Songwriter |
| S A M, 722 Seward St, Los Angeles CA 90038, USA | | |
| **Beck, A Byron** | | Basketball Player |
| 1909 S Williams St, Kennewick WA 99338, USA | | |

**Beck, Aaron T**
3535 Market St, #200, Philadelphia PA 19104, USA — Psychiatrist
**Beck, Barry**
Hong Kong Academy of Hockey, 183 Queens Road E, #64/F, Wanchai, Hong Kong, China — Ice Hockey Player
**Beck, Charles (Charlie)**
Los Angeles Police Dept, 150 S Los Angeles St, Los Angeles CA 90012, USA — Law Enforcement Official
**Beck, Charles H (Chip)**
11 Pembroke Dr, Lake Forest IL 60045, USA — Golfer
**Beck, Ernest J (Ernie)**
1523 Brierwood Road, Havertown PA 19083, USA — Basketball Player
**Beck, Glenn**
2208 Vaquero Estates Blvd, Westlake TX 76262, USA — Commentator
**Beck, Jeff**
Coda Agency, 229 Shoreditch High St, London E1 6PJ, England — Singer, Guitarist (Yardbirds)
**Beck, John C**
1562 Casale Road, Pacific Palisades CA 90272, USA — Geriatrics Physician
**Beck, Marilyn M**
2152 El Roble Lane, Beverly Hills CA 90210, USA — Columnist
**Beck, Martin J**
Big Red Roster, 121 Thurman Ave, Columbus OH 43206, USA — Industrial Designer
**Beck, Martina (Molly) Glagow**
Rehbergstr 40, 82481 Mittenwald, Germany — Biathlete
**Beck, Noelle**
Gersh Agency, 41 Madison Ave, #3301, New York NY 10010 USA — Actress
**Beck, Robin**
Cavaricci & White, 156 W 56th St, #1803, New York NY 10019, USA — Singer
**Beckel, Robert D**
New Mexico Military Institute, Superintendent's Office, Roswell NM 88201, USA — Air Force General
**Beckenbauer, Franz**
Posrfach 700220, 81302 Munich, Germany — Soccer Player, Coach
**Becker, Arthur C (Art)**
1879 E Bentrup Dr, Tempe AZ 85283, USA — Basketball Player
**Becker, Boris**
Ruessenstr 6, 6341 Baar, Switzerland — Tennis Player
**Becker, Brooklyn**
Gersh Agency, 9465 Wilshire Blvd, #600, Beverly Hills CA 90212 USA — Model, Actress
**Becker, Gary S**
1308 E 58th St, Chicago IL 60637, USA — Nobel Economics Laureate
**Becker, Harold**
I C M Partners, 10250 Constellation Blvd, #900, Los Angeles CA 90067 USA — Director
**Becker, Jo**
Washington Post, Editorial Dept, 1150 15th St NW, Washington DC 20071 USA — Journalist
**Becker, Karl J Cardinal**
Via Cassia 1036, 00189 Rome Lazio, Italy — Religious Leader
**Becker, Kuno**
A P A Talent/Literary Agency, 405 S Beverly Dr, #300, Beverly Hills CA 90212 USA — Actor
**Becker, Kurt F**
49W412 Scott Road, Big Rock IL 60511, USA — Football Player
**Becker, Quinn H**
2111 Peninsula Dr, San Antonio TX 78239, USA — Army General, Surgeon
**Becker, Richard G (Rich)**
210 Mary Senica Court, LaSalle IL 61301, USA — Baseball Player
**Becker, Robert J**
2200 S Ocean Lane, #1905, Fort Lauderdale FL 33316, USA — Allergist
**Becker, Walt W**
Walt Becker Productions, 1680 Vine St, #1101, Los Angeles CA 90028, USA — Director
**Becker, Walter**
Front Line Mgmt, 1100 Glendon Ave, #2000, Los Angeles CA 90024 USA — Bassist, Guitarist (Steely Dan)
**Beckert, Glenn A**
1953 Arkansas Ave, Englewood FL 34224, USA — Baseball Player
**Beckett, Bob**
38 Fonthill Blvd, Markham ON L3R 1V7, Canada — Ice Hockey Player
**Beckett, Joshua P (Josh)**
1 Avery St, #20B, Boston MA 02111, USA — Baseball Player
**Beckett, Margaret M**
Foreign Ministry, 11 Downing St, London SW1A 2AA, England — Government Official, England
**Beckett, Rogers**
635 Gaelic Court, Apopka FL 32712, USA — Football Player
**Beckett, Sister Wendy**
BBC TV Center, Wood Lane, London W12 7R3, England — Art Critic
**Beckett, William E, Jr**
Crush Music Media Mgmt, 60-62 E 11th St, #700, New York NY 10003, USA — Singer (Academy Is), Songwriter
**Beckford, Roxanne**
Abrams Artists, 9200 W Sunset Blvd, #1125, West Hollywood CA 90069 USA — Actress
**Beckford, Tyson**
I C M Models, 2 Henrietta St, Covent Garden, London WC2E 8PS, England — Model, Actor
**Beckham, David R J**
Creative Artists Agency, 2000 Ave of Stars, #100, Los Angeles CA 90067 USA — Soccer Player
**Beckinsale, Kate**
United Talent Agency, U T A Plaza, 9336 Civic Center Dr, Beverly Hills CA 90210 USA — Actress
**Becklean, William**
30 Cambridgepark Dr, #445, Cambridge MA 02140, USA — Rowing Athlete
**Beckless, Ian H**
4915 Andros Dr, Tampa FL 33629, USA — Football Player
**Beckley, Gerald L (Gerry)**
Morey Mgmt, 1100 Glendon Ave, #1100, Los Angeles CA 90024, USA — Singer, Guitarist (America), Songwriter
**Beckman, Cameron**
23303 Wilderness Cove, San Antonio TX 78261, USA — Golfer
**Beckman, Edwin J (Ed)**
4295 18th St NE, Naples FL 34120, USA — Football Player
**Beckman, Julie**
Kaseman Beckman Advanced Strategies, 408 Vine St, #2B, Philadelphia PA 19106, USA — Architect
**Beckmann, M Patricia**
Homestead Clinical Corp, 235 E 42nd St, Seattle WA 98102, USA — Chemist
**Beckwith, T Joseph (Joe)**
859 Annabrook Dr, Auburn AL 36830, USA — Baseball Player

**Becquer, Julio V** — Baseball Player
2461 Kyle Ave N, Minneapolis MN 55422, USA
**Bedard, Eric** — Speed Skater
Speed Skating Canada, 2781 Lancaster Road, #402, Ottawa ON K1B 1A7, Canada
**Bedard, Irene** — Actress
Don Buchwald, 6500 Wilshire Blvd, #2200, Los Angeles CA 90048 USA
**Bedard, Myriam** — Biathlete
3329 Pinecourt, Neufchatel QC G2B 2E4, Canada
**Bedelia, Bonnie** — Actress
Innovative Artists, 1505 10th St, Santa Monica CA 90401 USA
**Bedell, Brad** — Football Player
545 N Altura Road, Arcadia CA 91007, USA
**Bedford, Brian** — Actor
Paradigm Agency, 360 N Crescent Dr, North Building, Beverly Hills CA 90210 USA
**Bedford, Mark (Bedders)** — Bassist (Madness)
I T F, Ariel House, 74A Charlotte St, London W1T 4QJ, England
**Bedford, Martyn** — Writer
Bloomsbury Publishing, 50 Bedford Square, London WC1B 3DP, England
**Bedford, Steuart J R** — Conductor
76 Cromwell Ave, London N6 5HQ, England
**Bedi, Bisban Singh** — Cricketer
Ispat Bhawan, Lodhi Road, New Delhi 110 003, India
**Bedi, Kabir** — Actor
Beach House Park, Gandhigram, Juhu, Mumbai 400 049, India
**Bedia, Jose** — Artist, Sculptor
George Adams Gallery, 41 W 57th St, #700, New York NY 10019, USA
**Bedingfield, Daniel** — Singer, Songwriter
Primary Talent International, 10-11 Jockey's Fields, London WC1R 4BN, England
**Bedingfield, Natasha** — Singer, Songwriter
I/D Public Relations, 150 W 30th St, #1900, New York NY 10001, USA
**Bednarik, Charles P (Chuck)** — Football Player
6379 Winding Road, Coopersburg PA 18036, USA
**Bednob, Gerry** — Actor, Producer
Amsel Eisenstadt Frazier, 5055 Wilshire Blvd, #865, Los Angeles CA 90036 USA
**Bednorz, J Georg** — Nobel Physics Laureate
I B M Research Laboratory, Saumerstr 4, 8803 Ruschlikon, Switzerland
**Bedows, Elliott** — Oncologist
University of Nebraska Medical Center, Eppley Cancer Center, Omaha NE 68198, USA
**Bedrosian, Stephen W (Steve)** — Baseball Player
3335 Gordon Road, Senoia GA 30276, USA
**Bee, Samantha** — Actress
Parent Management, 530 Queen St, #E, Toronto, ON M5A 1V2, Canada
**Beebe, Dion** — Cinematographer
I C M Partners, 10250 Constellation Blvd, #900, Los Angeles CA 90067 USA
**Beebe, Don L** — Football Player
1246 Verona Ridge Dr, Aurora IL 60506, USA
**Beebe, Reta** — Astronomer
New Mexico State University, Astronomy Dept, Las Cruces NM 88003, USA
**Beeby, Thomas H** — Architect
Hammond Beeby Babka, 440 N Wells St, #630, Chicago IL 60654, USA
**Beede, Frank, III** — Football Player
1645 Somerset Place, Antioch CA 94509, USA
**Beedle, Ashley** — DJ Musician (X-Press 2)
International Talent Booking, Ariel House, 74A Charlotte St, #100 London W1T 4QJ, England
**Beeli, Binia** — Curling Athlete
Curling Assn, PO Box 606, 3000 Bern, Switzerland
**Beem, Rich** — Golfer
104 Bella Cima Dr, Austin TX 78734, USA
**Been, Robert Levon** — Bassist (Black Rebel Motorcycle Club)
Paradigm Agency, 360 Park Ave, #1600, New York NY 10022 USA
**Beene, Frederick R (Fred)** — Baseball Player
PO Box 143, Oakhurst TX 77359, USA
**Beenie Man** — Singer
Agency Group Ltd, 142 W 57th St, #600, New York NY 10019 USA
**Beer, Donald** — Rowing Athlete
2 Governors Lane, Princeton NJ 08540, USA
**Beerbaum, Ludger** — Equestrian
Altvaterweg 5, 86807 Buchloe, Germany
**Beering, Steven C** — Educator
10487 Windemere, Carmel IN 46032, USA
**Beers, Betsy** — Producer
ShondaLand, 4151 Prospect Ave, #400, Los Angeles CA 90027, USA
**Beers, Bob** — Ice Hockey Player
97 Blake Road, Lexington MA 02420, USA
**Beers, Gary** — Singer, Bassist (INXS)
8 Hayes St, #1, Neutral Bay 20891 NSW, Australia
**Beers, Thom** — Producer, Actor, Writer
Fremantle Media North America, 4000 W Alameda Ave, #300, Burbank CA 91505, USA
**Beesley, Damon** — Writer
Bwark Productions, 35-47 Bethnal Green Road, London E1 6LA, England
**Beesley, Max** — Actor
Untitled Entertainment, 350 S Beverly Dr, #200, Beverly Hills CA 90212 USA
**Beeson, Terry E** — Football Player
1302 Hibbard St, Coffeyville KS 67337, USA
**Beeston, Paul M** — Baseball Executive
Toronto Blue Jays, Skydome, 1 Blue Jay Way, Toronto ON M5V 1J1, Canada
**Beetem, Chris** — Actor
Abrams Artists, 9200 W Sunset Blvd, #1125, West Hollywood CA 90069 USA
**Bega, Leslie** — Actress
Sovereign Talent Group, 8421 Wilshire Blvd, #200, Beverly Hills CA 90211, USA
**Bega, Lou** — Singer
Juergen Reiter, Herzogstr 59, 80803 Munich, Germany
**Begay, Notah** — Golfer
3620 Vista del Sur St NW, Albuquerque NM 87120, USA
**Beggs, Don** — Educator
Wichita State University, President's Office, Wichita KS 67260, USA

| | |
|---|---|
| **Beggs, James M** | Space Engineer, Government Official |
| 1177 N Great Southwest Parkway, Grand Prairie TX 75050, USA | |
| **Begg-Smith, Dale** | Freestyle Moguls Skier |
| Ski & Snowboard, 1 Cobden St, South Melbourne VIC 3205, Australia | |
| **Beghe, Jason** | Actor |
| A P A Talent/Literary Agency, 405 S Beverly Dr, #300, Beverly Hills CA 90212 USA | |
| **Beghe, Renato** | Judge |
| US Tax Court, 400 2nd St NW, Washington DC 20217, USA | |
| **Begler, Michael** | Producer, Writer |
| W M E Entertainment, 9601 Wilshire Blvd, #300, Beverly Hills CA 90210 USA | |
| **Begley, Ed, Jr** | Actor |
| Innovative Artists, 1505 10th St, Santa Monica CA 90401 USA | |
| **Beglin, Elizabeth (Beth)** | Field Hockey Player |
| 2070 Silver Maple Trail, North Liberty IA 52317, USA | |
| **Beguelin, Chad** | Writer, Lyricist |
| Gersh Agency, 9465 Wilshire Blvd, #600, Beverly Hills CA 90212 USA | |
| **Behagen, Ronald M (Ron)** | Basketball Player |
| 1101 Juniper St NE, #401, Atlanta GA 30309, USA | |
| **Behar, Joy** | Actress, Comedienne |
| Westport Entertainment Associates, 1700 Post Road, #C15, Fairfield CT 06824, USA | |
| **Beharie, Nicole** | Actress |
| I C M Partners, 10250 Constellation Blvd, #900, Los Angeles CA 90067 USA | |
| **Beharry, Johnson G** | Iraq War British Army Hero (VC) |
| Victoria Cross Assn, Old Admiralty Building, London SW1A 2BL, England | |
| **Behe, Michael** | Biochemist, Writer |
| Lehigh University, Biochemistry Dept, Bethlehem PA 18015, USA | |
| **Behle, Petra** | Biathlete |
| Sonnenhof 1, 34508 Willingen, Germany | |
| **Behmen, Alija** | Prime Minister |
| Prime Minister's Office, Alipasina 1, 71000 Sarajevo, Bosnia & Herzegovina | |
| **Behnisch, Stefan** | Architect |
| Behnisch Behnisch Partners, 6 Christophstr, 70178 Stuttgart, Germany | |
| **Behnke, Elmer H** | Basketball Player |
| 3412 Ivy Chase Circle, Birmingham AL 35226, USA | |
| **Behnken, Lukas** | Actor |
| Media Artists Group, 8222 Melrose Ave, #203, Los Angeles CA 90048 USA | |
| **Behnken, Robert L** | Astronaut |
| N A S A, Johnson Space Center, 2101 NASA Road, Houston TX 77058 USA | |
| **Behr, Jason** | Actor |
| Untitled Entertainment, 350 S Beverly Dr, #200, Beverly Hills CA 90212 USA | |
| **Behrend, Marc** | Ice Hockey Player |
| 6805 Cross Country Road, Verona WI 53593, USA | |
| **Behrendt, Greg** | Writer, Actor |
| Avalon Mgmt, 4A Exmoor St, London W10 6BD, England | |
| **Behrendt, Jan** | Luge Athlete |
| Karl-Zink-Str 2, 96893 Ilmenau, Germany | |
| **Behrendt, Wolfgang** | Boxer |
| Springbornstr 204, 12487 Berlin, Germany | |
| **Behrens, Sam** | Actor |
| 530 Bryant Dr, Canoga Park CA 91304, USA | |
| **Behrensmyer, Anna K** | Paleobiologist |
| Amboseli National Park, PO Box 18, Namanga, Kenya | |
| **Behrman, David W (Dave)** | Football Player |
| 10187 25 1/2 Mile Road, Albion MI 49224, USA | |
| **Behrman, Richard E** | Pediatrician |
| PO Box 4446, Santa Barbara CA 93140, USA | |
| **Behrs, Beth** | Actress |
| Creative Artists Agency, 2000 Ave of Stars, #100, Los Angeles CA 90067 USA | |
| **Beickler, Ferdinand** | Businessman |
| Adam Opel AG, Bahnhofsplatz 1, 65428 Russelsheim, Germany | |
| **Beikirch, Gary B** | Vietnam War Army Hero (CMH) |
| 468 Crosby Lane, Rochester NY 14612, USA | |
| **Beilein, John** | Basketball Coach |
| University of Michigan, Athletic Dept, Ann Arbor MI 48109, USA | |
| **Beilina, Nina** | Concert Violinist |
| 400 W 43rd St, #7D, New York NY 10036, USA | |
| **Beimel, Joseph R (Joe)** | Baseball Player |
| 291 Fairview Road, Kersey PA 15846, USA | |
| **Beineix, Jean-Jacques** | Director |
| Cargo Films, 9 Rue Ambroise Thomas, 75009 Paris, France | |
| **Beirne, James P (Jim)** | Football Player |
| 2 Cedar Chase Place, Spring TX 77381, USA | |
| **Beisler, Randall L (Randy)** | Football Player |
| 899 Northgate Dr, #500, San Rafael CA 94903, USA | |
| **Beisner, Michelle** | Sportscaster |
| Maximum Talent Agency, 1873 S Bellaire St, #915, Denver CO 80222, USA | |
| **Bejo, Berenice** | Actress |
| Agence Artiste Adequet, 108 Rue Reaumur, 75002 Paris, France | |
| **Bekmambetov, Timur** | Director |
| W M E Entertainment, 9601 Wilshire Blvd, #300, Beverly Hills CA 90210 USA | |
| **Belafonte, Harry** | Singer, Actor |
| Equitable Stewardship for Artists, 10317 Jefferson Blvd, Culver City CA 90232, USA | |
| **Belafonte, Shari** | Actress, Model |
| W M E Entertainment, 9601 Wilshire Blvd, #300, Beverly Hills CA 90210 USA | |
| **Belasco, Bert** | Actor |
| Talent Works, 3500 W Olive Ave, #1400, Burbank CA 91505 USA | |
| **Belbin, Tanith J L** | Figure Skater |
| Detroit Skating Club, 888 Denison Court, Bloomfield Hills MI 48302, USA | |
| **Belcher, Timothy W (Tim)** | Baseball Player |
| PO Box 153, Sparta OH 43350, USA | |
| **Belda, Alain J P** | Businessman |
| Alcoa Inc, 201 Isabella St, Pittsburgh PA 15212, USA | |
| **Belen, Ana** | Actress, Singer |
| Rompeolas Productions, Alabama St, #1761, San Gerardo, Rio Piedras PR 00926, USA | |
| **Belenky, Valery** | Gymnast |
| Schillerstr 20, 73760 Ostfildern, Germany | |

**Belfi, Jordan** — Actor
Schumacher Mgmt, 10323 Santa Monica Blvd, #101, Los Angeles CA 90024, USA
**Belford, Christine** — Actress
C E S D, 10635 Santa Monica Blvd, #130, Los Angeles CA 90025 USA
**Belfour, Edward J (Ed)** — Ice Hockey Player
544 Studebaker Road, Whitewright TX 75491, USA
**Belgrave, Elliott F** — Governor General, Barbados
Governor General's Office, Bay St, Saint Michael, Bridgetown, Barbados
**Belica, Marina** — Singer, Keyboardist (October Project)
October Project, PO Box 539, Prince Street Station, New York NY 10012, USA
**Belichik, William S (Bill)** — Football Coach
116 Meadowbrook Road, Weston MA 02493, USA
**Belin, Gaspard D** — Attorney
4 Willard St, Cambridge MA 02138, USA
**Belin, Nat** — Cartoonist
Drawing Board, 820 W 7th St, #B, Winston Salem NC 27101, USA
**Belinda, Stanley P (Stan)** — Baseball Player
454 Sylvan Dr, State College PA 16803, USA
**Belinelli, Marco A** — Basketball Player
San Antonio Spurs, Alamodome, 1 AT&T Center Parkway, San Antonio TX 78219 USA
**Belisle, Matthew T (Matt)** — Baseball Player
4009 Sierra Dr, Austin TX 78731, USA
**Beliveau, Jean A** — Ice Hockey Player
155 Rue Victoria, Longuevil QC J4H 2J4, Canada
**Belk, William A (Bill)** — Football Player
12 Ricemill Ferry, Columbia SC 29229, USA
**Belknap, Anna** — Actress
S M S Talent, 8383 Wilshire Blvd, #230, Beverly Hills CA 90211 USA
**Bell, Angellica** — Entertainer
C B B C, PO Box 9989, London W12 6PA, England
**Bell, Archie** — Singer
Billy Paul Mgmt, 8215 S Winthrop St, Philadelphia PA 19136, USA
**Bell, Ashley** — Actress
Paradigm Agency, 360 N Crescent Dr, North Building, Beverly Hills CA 90210 USA
**Bell, Brad** — Golfer
6255 Oakridge Way, Sacramento CA 95831, USA
**Bell, Byron** — Basketball Player
2546 Tech Dr, Bettendorf IA 52722, USA
**Bell, C Gordon** — Computer Scientist
Microsoft Corp, 1 Microsoft Way, Redmond WA 98052, USA
**Bell, Carl** — Guitarist (Fuel)
Media Five Entertainment, 3005 Brodhead Road, #170, Bethlehem PA 18020, USA
**Bell, Catherine** — Actress
Brillstein Entertainment Partners, 9150 Wilshire Blvd, #350, Beverly Hills CA 90212 USA
**Bell, Clyde R (Bob)** — Navy Admiral, Association Executive
1301 Harney St, Omaha NE 68102, USA
**Bell, Darrin** — Cartoonist
Washington Post Writers Group, 1150 15th St NW, Washington DC 20071 USA
**Bell, Darryl M** — Actor
Innovative Artists, 1505 10th St, Santa Monica CA 90401 USA
**Bell, David G (Buddy)** — Baseball Player, Manager
244 W Goldfinch Way, Chandler AZ 85286, USA
**Bell, David M** — Baseball Player
9710 E La Posada Circle, Scottsdale AZ 85255, USA
**Bell, Dennis R** — Basketball Player
111 Springfield Pike, Cincinnati OH 45215, USA
**Bell, Derek N** — Baseball Player
3404 Pine Top Dr, Valrico FL 33594, USA
**Bell, Drake** — Actor
Creative Artists Agency, 2000 Ave of Stars, #100, Los Angeles CA 90067 USA
**Bell, Drew Tyler** — Actor
Luber Rocklin Entertainment, 8530 Wilshire Blvd, #555, Beverly Hills CA 90211 USA
**Bell, Edward A (Eddie)** — Football Player
4529 Tacoma Terrace, Fort Worth TX 76123, USA
**Bell, Emma** — Actress
I C M Partners, 10250 Constellation Blvd, #900, Los Angeles CA 90067 USA
**Bell, Eric A** — Baseball Player
1140 S 124th St, Chandler AZ 85286, USA
**Bell, Gary** — Baseball Player
2107 Oak Ranch, San Antonio TX 78259, USA
**Bell, Gerald A (Jerry)** — Football Player
1347 Deerbourne Dr, Wesley Chapel FL 33543, USA
**Bell, Gregory (Greg)** — Track Athlete
5983 E Division Road, Logansport IN 46947, USA
**Bell, Gregory L (Greg)** — Football Player
5849 Azalea Way, Goleta CA 93117, USA
**Bell, Heath J** — Baseball Player
7437 Los Brazos, San Diego CA 92127, USA
**Bell, James D** — Diplomat
4512 San Marino Dr, Davis CA 95618, USA
**Bell, Jamie** — Actor
W M E Entertainment, 9601 Wilshire Blvd, #300, Beverly Hills CA 90210 USA
**Bell, Jason D** — Football Player
3387 N Studebaker Road, Long Beach CA 90808, USA
**Bell, Jay S** — Baseball Player
PO Box 50249, Phoenix AZ 85076, USA
**Bell, John** — Singer (Widespread Panic)
Shore Fire Media, 32 Court St, #1600, Brooklyn NY 11201 USA
**Bell, John Anthony** — Director, Actor
On It Artists, 5 Heathmans Road, London SW6 4TJ, England
**Bell, Jorge A M (George)** — Baseball Player
Lamiama #14, Bell 2nd Planto, San Pedro de Macoris, Dominican Republic
**Bell, Joseph (Joe)** — Ice Hockey Player
10522 11th Ave NE, Seattle WA 98125, USA
**Bell, Joshua** — Concert Violinist
Konzertdirektion Schmid, Konigstra 36, 30175 Hannover, Germany

Bell, Kendrell A     Football Player
400 W Peachtree St NW, #1211, Atlanta GA 30308, USA
Bell, Kevin R     Baseball Player
621 Sue St, Little Chute WI 54140, USA
Bell, Kristen     Actress
Brookside Artist Mgmt, 250 W 57th St, #2303, New York NY 10107, USA
Bell, Lake     Actress
United Talent Agency, U T A Plaza, 9336 Civic Center Dr, Beverly Hills CA 90210 USA
Bell, Larry S     Sculptor
PO Box 4101, Taos NM 87571, USA
Bell, Lauralee     Actress
Martin Bell Productions, 8033 Sunset Blvd, #799, West Hollywood CA 90046, USA
Bell, Leola     Model
Playboy Promotions, 2706 Media Center Dr, Los Angeles CA 90065 USA
Bell, Lynette     Swimmer
149 Henry St, Merewether NSW 2200, Australia
Bell, Madison Smartt     Writer
Random House, 1745 Broadway, #1800, New York NY 10019 USA
Bell, Mark E     Football Player
2701 Wild Rose Ave, Wichita KS 67205, USA
Bell, Michael P (Mike)     Actor
4906 Encino Ave, Encino CA 91316, USA
Bell, Michel     Actor, Singer
Kelly Productions, 824 Munras Ave, Monterey CA 93940, USA
Bell, Michelle     Golfer
18895 Pond Cypress Court, Jupiter FL 33458, USA
Bell, Mike     Motorcyle Racing Rider
American Motorcycle Assn, 13515 Yarmouth Dr, Pickerington OH 43147 USA
Bell, Mike J     Football Player
7405 Lakewood Circle, Wichita KS 67205, USA
Bell, Myron C     Football Player
3027 Crawford Ave, Gastonia NC 28052, USA
Bell, O'Neil     Boxer
Warrior's Boxing Promotions, 5397 Orange Dr, #202, Davie FL 33314, USA
Bell, Peter D     Association Executive
Care, 151 Ellis St NE, Atlanta GA 30303, USA
Bell, Raja     Basketball Player
12962 Grand Oaks Dr, Davie FL 33330, USA
Bell, Rini     Actress
Brady Brannon & Rich Talent, 5670 Wilshire Blvd, #820, Los Angeles CA 90036, USA
Bell, Robert A (Rob)     Baseball Player
28 Blossom Hill Dr, Marlboro NY 12542, USA
Bell, Robert E (Kool)     Bassist (Kool & the Gang)
Spirit Media, PO Box 43591, Phoenix AZ 85080 USA
Bell, Robert F (Bob)     Football Player
7415 N 12th St, Elkins Park PA 19027, USA
Bell, Robert H (Rob), Jr     Religious Leader
Mars Hill Bible Church, 3501 Fairlanes Ave, Grandville MI 49418, USA
Bell, Robert L (Bobby), Sr     Football Player
208 NW Shagbark St, Lees Summit MO 64064, USA
Bell, Ronald N     Saxophonist (Kool & the Gang)
Spirit Media, PO Box 43591, Phoenix AZ 85080 USA
Bell, Sam     Track Coach
2310 E Woodstock Place, Bloomington IN 47401, USA
Bell, Steve     Editorial Cartoonist
Guardian, Editorial Dept, 1 Scott Place, Manchester M3 3GG, England
Bell, Tatum A     Football Player
18754 E Powers Dr, Aurora CO 80015, USA
Bell, Thom     Songwriter
B M I, 8730 W Sunset Blvd, #300, Los Angeles CA 90069 USA
Bell, Tobin     Actor
C E S D, 10635 Santa Monica Blvd, #130, Los Angeles CA 90025 USA
Bell, William     Singer, Pianist, Songwriter
Rodgers Redding, PO Box 4603, Macon GA 31208 USA
Bell, William Brent     Director
Creative Artists Agency, 2000 Ave of Stars, #100, Los Angeles CA 90067 USA
Bell, Yeremiah N     Football Player
1886 Sirius Lane, Weston FL 33327, USA
Bell, Zoe E     Actress, Stuntwoman
Runaway Films, 1338 Rhode Island St, San Francisco CA 94107, USA
Bella, Ivan     Cosmonaut
Cosmonaut Training Center, Star City, 141160 Zvezdny Gorodok, Moscow Oblast, Russia
Bellamy, Bill     Actor, Comedian
A P A Talent/Literary Agency, 405 S Beverly Dr, #300, Beverly Hills CA 90212 USA
Bellamy, David     Singer (Bellamy Brothers), Songwriter
Bellamy Brothers Partners, 13917 Restless Lane, Dade City FL 33525, USA
Bellamy, David J     Botanist, Writer, Broadcaster
Mill House, Bedburn, Bishop Auckland, County Durham DL13 3NN, England
Bellamy, Howard     Singer (Bellamy Brothers), Songwriter
Bellamy Brothers Partners, 13917 Restless Lane, Dade City FL 33525, USA
Bellamy, Matthew     Singer, Guitarist (Muse)
Hall or Nothing P R, 35-37 Parkgate Road, London SW11 4NP, England
Bellamy, Ned     Actor
Global Artists Agency, 6253 Hollywood Blvd, #508, Los Angeles CA 90028 USA
Belland, Bruce     Singer (Four Preps)
4339 Ensenada Dr, Woodland Hills CA 91364, USA
Belland, Neil     Ice Hockey Player
868 Renaissance Dr, Oshawa ON L1J 8K9, Canada
Bellar, Clara     Actress
Julian Belfrage Assoc, 9 Argyll St, #300, London W1F 7TG, England
Belle, Albert J     Baseball Player
9299 E Mariposa Grande Dr, Scottsdale AZ 85255, USA
Belle, Camilla     Actress
United Talent Agency, U T A Plaza, 9336 Civic Center Dr, Beverly Hills CA 90210 USA
Belle, Regina     Singer, Songwriter
Sony Records, 2100 Colorado Ave, Santa Monica CA 90404 USA

# B

**Bellemer, John** — Opera Singer
I M G Artists, Hogarth Business Park, Chiswick, London W4 2TH, England
**Beller, Kathleen** — Actress
PO Box 806, Half Moon Bay CA 94019, USA
**Bellhorn, Mark C** — Baseball Player
19550 N Grayhawk Dr, #1083, Scottsdale AZ 85255, USA
**Belli, Gioconda** — Writer
Carlisle Co, 121 E 17th St, New York NY 10003, USA
**Belli, Paolo** — Singer
Cicuta Produczioni, Via Barbeerini 29, 00187 Rome, Italy
**Belliard, Rafael L** — Baseball Player
10846 King Bay Dr, Boca Raton FL 33498, USA
**Belliard, Ronald (Ronnie)** — Baseball Player
2999 NW 96th St, Miami FL 33147, USA
**Bellincampi, Giordano** — Conductor
I M G Artists, Hogarth Business Park, Chiswick, London W4 2TH, England
**Bellingham, Lynda** — Actress
Artist Rights Group, 4 Great Portland St, London W1W 8PA, England
**Bellingham, Norman** — Canoeing Athlete
1825 Cantwell Grove, Colorado Springs CO 80906, USA
**Bellini, Mario** — Architect
Architecture Center, 66 Portland Place, London W1, England
**Bellino, Joseph M (Joe)** — Football Player
45 Hayden Lane, Bedford MA 01730, USA
**Bellisario, Donald P** — Producer
Gelfand Rennert Feldman, 1880 Century Park E, #1600, Los Angeles CA 90067, USA
**Bellisario, Troian** — Actress
Innovative Artists, 1505 10th St, Santa Monica CA 90401 USA
**Bell-Lundy, Sandra** — Cartoonist (Between Friends)
255 Northwood Dr, Welland ON L3C 6V1, Canada
**Bellman, Gina** — Actress
Independent Talent Group, 40 Whitfield St, London W1T 2RH, England
**Bello, Frank** — Bassist (Anthrax)
Zen Media Group, 272 Grand St, #B, Brooklyn NY 11211, USA
**Bello, Maria** — Actress
Creative Artists Agency, 2000 Ave of Stars, #100, Los Angeles CA 90067 USA
**Bellocchio, Marco** — Director, Writer
Bobbio Film Festival, Piazzetta Santa Chiara, 129022 Bobbio (PC), Italy
**Bellotti, Mike** — Football Coach, Executive, Sportscaster
ESPN-TV, ESPN Plaza, 935 Middle St, Bristol CT 06010 USA
**Bellovin, Steven M** — Computer Scientist
AT&T Research Laboratories, 180 Park Ave, PO Box 971, Florham Park NJ 07932, USA
**Bellows, Brian** — Ice Hockey Player
5205 Mirror Lakes Dr, Minneapolis MN 55436, USA
**Bellows, Gil** — Actor
Innovative Artists, 1505 10th St, Santa Monica CA 90401 USA
**Bellucci, Monica** — Model, Actress
Creative Artists Agency, 2000 Ave of Stars, #100, Los Angeles CA 90067 USA
**Bellwood, Pamela** — Actress
1696 San Leandro Lane, Santa Barbara CA 93108, USA
**Bellynck, Lise** — Actress
Agents Associes Chen, 201 Rue Faubourg Saint-Honore, 75008 Paris, France
**Belmondo, Jean-Paul** — Actor
6 Rue Gassendi, 75014 Paris, France
**Belmondo, Olivier** — Actor
Artmedia, 20 Ave Rapp, 75007 Paris, France
**Belmont, Lara** — Actress
Markham Froggatt Irwin, Julian House, 4 Windmill St, London W1P 1HF, England
**Belo, Carlos Filipe Ximenes** — Nobel Peace Laureate, Religious Leader
Catholic Bishop, Caixa Postale 4, Dili-Leste, East Timor
**Belote Hamlin, Melissa** — Swimmer
7311 Exmore St, Springfield VA 22150, USA
**Belousova, Ludmila Y** — Figure Skater
Chalet Hubel, 3818 Grindelwald, Switzerland
**Belser, Ceaser E** — Football Player
317 Cooper Dr, Hurst TX 76053, USA
**Belser, Jason D** — Football Player
20474 Middlebury St, Ashburn VA 20147, USA
**Beltrami, Marco** — Composer
Kraft-Engel Management, 15233 Ventura Blvd, #200, Sherman Oaks CA 91403, USA
**Beltran, Carlos I** — Baseball Player
18 Paseo Alcala, Urb Hacienda Hermanos Mena, Manati PR 00674, USA
**Beltran, Rigoberto (Rigo)** — Baseball Player
3950 Laurelwood Lane, Delray Beach FL 33445, USA
**Beltran, Robert A** — Actor
Abrams Artists, 9200 W Sunset Blvd, #1125, West Hollywood CA 90069 USA
**Beltre Perez, Adrian** — Baseball Player
Texas Rangers, Ameriquest Field, 1000 Ballpark Way, #306, Arlington TX 76011 USA
**Belushi, James** — Actor
Brillstein Entertainment Partners, 9150 Wilshire Blvd, #350, Beverly Hills CA 90212 USA
**Belvaux, Lucas** — Director
Voyez Mon Agent, 20 Ave Rapp, 75007 Paris, France
**Belzer, Richard** — Actor, Comedian
McBelz Enterprises, 1995 Broadway, #16, New York New York 10023, USA
**Beman, Deane R** — Golfer, Golf Executive
255 Deer Haven Dr, Ponte Vedra FL 32082, USA
**Bement, Linda J** — Beauty Queen
Miss Universe Organization, 1370 Ave of Americas, #1600, New York NY 10019 USA
**Bemile, Paul Cardinal** — Religious Leader
Diocese of Wa, PO Box 47, Wa, Upper West Region, Ghana
**Bemiller, Al D** — Football Player
5002 Armor-Duells Road, Orchard Park NY 14127, USA
**Ben Tre, Howard B** — Artist
Charles Cowles Gallery, 210 11th Ave, #500, New York NY 10001, USA
**Benade, Leo Edward** — Army General
417 Pine Ridge Road, #A, Carthage NC 28327, USA

*Bellemer - Benade*

**Benanti, Laura** — Actress, Singer
Brookside Artist Mgmt, 250 W 57th St, #2303, New York NY 10107, USA
**Benard, Marvin L** — Baseball Player
2806 S 38th Ave, West Richland WA 99353, USA
**Benard, Maurice** — Actor
Benard Management, 15300 Ventura Blvd, #315, Sherman Oaks CA 91403, USA
**Benassi, Benny** — DJ Musician, Producer
A M Only, 55 Washington St, #658, New York NY 10006, USA
**Benatar, Pat** — Singer, Songwriter
W M E Entertainment, 9601 Wilshire Blvd, #300, Beverly Hills CA 90210 USA
**Benavides, Fortunato P (Pete)** — Judge
US Court of Appeals, 903 San Jacinto Blvd, #400, Austin TX 78701, USA
**Benben, Brian** — Actor
Paradigm Agency, 360 N Crescent Dr, North Building, Beverly Hills CA 90210 USA
**Bench, John L (Johnny)** — Baseball Player
Johnny Bench Enterprises, 3899 Ridgedale Dr, Cincinnati OH 45247, USA
**Benchoff, Dennis L (Den)** — Army General
380 Arbor Road, Lancaster PA 17601, USA
**Bender, Gary N** — Sportscaster
TNT-TV, Sports Dept, 1050 Techwood Dr, Atlanta GA 30318 USA
**Bender, Jack** — Cartoonist (Alley Oop)
RR 1 Box 540, Terlton OK 74081, USA
**Bender, Jack** — Director
United Talent Agency, U T A Plaza, 9336 Civic Center Dr, Beverly Hills CA 90210 USA
**Bender, Jonathan R** — Basketball Player
New York Knicks, Madison Square Garden, 2 Penn Plaza, New York, NY 10121 USA
**Bender, Lawrence** — Producer, Director
W M E Entertainment, 9601 Wilshire Blvd, #300, Beverly Hills CA 90210 USA
**Bender, Lon** — Sound Editor
Soundelux, 7080 Hollywood Blvd, #1100, Los Angeles CA 90028, USA
**Bendewald, Andrea** — Actress
Metropolitan Talent Agency, 5405 Wilshire Blvd, #218, Los Angeles CA 90036 USA
**Bendinger, Jessica** — Director, Writer
Creative Artists Agency, 2000 Ave of Stars, #100, Los Angeles CA 90067 USA
**Bendix, Simone** — Actress
Joy Jameson, 2/19 Plaza, 535 Kings Road, London SW10 0SZ, England
**Bendlin, Kurt** — Track Athlete
D L V, Asfelder Str 27, 64289 Leverkusen, Germany
**Ben-Dor, Gisele** — Conductor
I M G Artists, Hogarth Business Park, Chiswick, London W4 2TH, England
**Bene, B Christopher** — Architect
Chang Bene Design, 43-55 Wyndham St, Central, Hong Kong, China
**Benedek, George B** — Physicist
Massachusetts Institute of Technology, Physics Dept, Cambridge MA 02139, USA
**Benedeti, Paulo** — Actor
4201 N Ocean Blvd, #C505, Boca Raton FL 33431, USA
**Benedetti, Nicola** — Concert Violinist
I M G Artists, Hogarth Business Park, Chiswick, London W4 2TH, England
**Benedict XVI, Pope** — Religious Leader
Castel Gandolfo, 00040 Lazio, Italy
**Benedict, Bruce E** — Baseball Player
335 Quiet Water Lane, Atlanta GA 30350, USA
**Benedict, Dirk** — Actor
Arsenal Productions & Management, 8200 Wilshire Blvd, #400, Beverly Hills CA 90211, USA
**Benedict, Rob** — Actor
S M S Talent, 8383 Wilshire Blvd, #230, Beverly Hills CA 90211 USA
**Benedict-Jones, Linda** — Photographer
256 Jefferson Dr, Pittsburgh PA 15228, USA
**Benedicto, Lourdes** — Actress
A P A Talent/Literary Agency, 405 S Beverly Dr, #300, Beverly Hills CA 90212 USA
**Benepe, Jim** — Golfer
602 Mountain Shadows Blvd, Sheridan WY 82801, USA
**Benero, Edward Allen** — Writer, Producer
Creative Artists Agency, 2000 Ave of Stars, #100, Los Angeles CA 90067 USA
**Benes, Alan P** — Baseball Player
754 Kraffel Lane, Chesterfield MO 63017, USA
**Benes, Andrew C (Andy)** — Baseball Player
1127 Highland Point Dr, Saint Louis MO 63131, USA
**Benet, Eric** — Singer, Songwriter
Avnet Mgmt, 4111 W Alameda Ave, #410, Burbank CA 91505, USA
**Benetton, Carlo** — Businessman
Benetton Group SpA, Via Minelli, 31050 Ponzano Treviso, Italy
**Benetton, Gilberto** — Businessman
Benetton Group SpA, Via Minelli, 31050 Ponzano Treviso, Italy
**Benetton, Giuliana** — Businesswoman
Benetton Group SpA, Via Minelli, 31050 Ponzano Treviso, Italy
**Benetton, Luciano** — Businessman
Benetton Group SpA, Via Minelli, 31050 Ponzano Treviso, Italy
**Benga** — Electronic Musician (Magnetic Man)
Columbia Records, 9 Derry St, London W8 5HY, England
**Benglis, Lynda** — Artist, Sculptor
917 Acequia Madre, Santa Fe NM 87505, USA
**Bengston, Billy Al** — Artist
110 Mildred Ave, Venice CA 90291, USA
**Benguigui, Jean** — Actor
U B B A, 6 Rue de Braque, 75003 Paris, France
**Benhima, Mohamed** — Prime Minister, Morocco
Km 5.5, Route des Zaers, Rabat, Morocco
**Benichou, Maurice** — Actor
Voyez Mon Agent, 20 Ave Rapp, 75007 Paris, France
**Benigni, Roberto** — Actor, Director
Melampo Cinematografica, Via Ludovici 35, 00187 Rome, Italy
**Bening, Annette** — Actress
13671 Mulholland Dr, Beverly Hills CA 90210, USA
**Benioff, David** — Writer, Producer
Creative Artists Agency, 2000 Ave of Stars, #100, Los Angeles CA 90067 USA

**Beniquez Torres, Juan J** — Baseball Player
Villa Carolina 87-12, Calle 99A, Villa Carolina PR 00985, USA
**Benirschke, Rolf J** — Football Player
4326 Vista de la Tierra, San Diego CA 92130, USA
**Benish, Daniel J (Dan)** — Football Player
1158 Trailblazer Way NW, Lilburn GA 30047, USA
**Benitez, Armando G** — Baseball Player
520 N Parkway, Golden Beach FL 33160, USA
**Benitez, Elsa** — Model
Talent Entertainment Group, 9111 Wilshire Blvd, Beverly Hills CA 90210 USA
**Benitez, Maria** — Flamenco Dancer
Teatro Flamenco, Institute for Spanish Arts, PO Box 8418, Santa Fe NM 87504, USA
**Benitez, Wilfredo** — Boxer
Saint Just, 248 Calle 6, Trujilloo Alto, PR 00976, USA
**Benjamin, Benoit** — Basketball Player
PO Box 690912, San Antonio TX 78269, USA
**Benjamin, George W J** — Composer
Faber Music, 3 Queen Square, London WC1N 3AU, England
**Benjamin, Guy E** — Football Player
91-443 Ewa Beach Road, Ewa Beach HI 96706, USA
**Benjamin, H Jon** — Actor, Comedian
Creative Artists Agency, 2000 Ave of Stars, #100, Los Angeles CA 90067 USA
**Benjamin, Julia** — Actress
4054 Redwood Ave, #6, Los Angeles CA 90066, USA
**Benjamin, Lloyd W, III** — Educator
Indiana State University, President's Office, Terre Haute IN 47809, USA
**Benjamin, Lucy** — Actress
Iconic Publicity International, Wren House, #4, 334A Creek Road, London SE10 9SW, England
**Benjamin, Michael P (Mike)** — Baseball Player
25608 S 182nd Place, Queen Creek AZ 85142, USA
**Benjamin, Regina M** — Government Official, Physician
Surgeon General's Office, 5600 Fishers Lane, Rockville MD 20857, USA
**Benjamin, Richard** — Actor, Director
Gersh Agency, 9465 Wilshire Blvd, #600, Beverly Hills CA 90212 USA
**Benjamin, Stephen (Steve)** — Yachtsman
PO Box 399, Norwalk CT 06856, USA
**Benkovic, Stephen J** — Chemist
771 Teaberry Lane, State College PA 16803, USA
**Benmosche, Robert H** — Businessman
American International Group, 70 Pine St, New York NY 10270, USA
**Benn, Anthony N W (Tony)** — Government Official, England
12 Holland Park Ave, London W11 3QU, England
**Benn, Nigel** — Boxer
Matchroom Boxing, 10 Western Road, Romford Essex RM1 3JT, England
**Bennack, Frank A, Jr** — Publisher
Hearst Corp, 250 W 55th St, #4200, New York NY 10019, USA
**Bennet, Chloe** — Actress
Creative Artists Agency, 2000 Ave of Stars, #100, Los Angeles CA 90067 USA
**Benneteau, Julian** — Tennis Player
Federation de Tenis, Stade Roland Garros, 2 Ave Gordon Bennett, 75016 Paris, France
**Bennett Spector, Veronica (Ronnie)** — Singer (Ronettes)
Absolute Artists, 8490 W Sunset Blvd, #403, West Hollywood CA 90069, USA
**Bennett, Adam** — Ice Hockey Player
7 Stockman Crescent, Georgetown ON L7G 1J5, Canada
**Bennett, Alan** — Writer, Actor
United Agents, 12-26 Lexington St, London W1F 0LE, England
**Bennett, Albert F** — Physiologist
University of California, Biological Sciences School, Irvine CA 92697, USA
**Bennett, Andrew R (Drew)** — Football Player
2335 Hyde St, #1, San Francisco CA 94109, USA
**Bennett, Anthony** — Basketball Player
Cleveland Cavaliers, Gund Arena, 1 Center Court, Cleveland OH 44115 USA
**Bennett, Anthony G (Tony)** — Basketball Player, Coach
3408 Cesford Grange, Keswick VA 22947, USA
**Bennett, Barry M** — Football Player
22047 Ginseng Road, Long Prairie MN 56347, USA
**Bennett, Bob** — Singer, Songwriter
Benjamin Artists Agency, PO Box 92348, Nashville TN 37209, USA
**Bennett, Brandon** — Football Player
308 Daybrook Court, Greenville SC 29605, USA
**Bennett, Brooke** — Swimmer
2585 Rowe Road, Milford MI 48380, USA
**Bennett, Charles L** — Astrophysicist
Johns Hopkins University, Physics/Astronomy Dept, Baltimore MD 21218, USA
**Bennett, Clay** — Editorial Cartoonist
Christian Science Monitor, Editorial Dept, 1 Norway St, Boston MA 02136 USA
**Bennett, Cornelius O** — Football Player
818 S 7th Ave, Hollywood FL 33019, USA
**Bennett, Curt A** — Ice Hockey Player
260 Awapuhi Place, Wailuku HI 96793, USA
**Bennett, Darren L** — Football Player
3347 Corte del Cruce, Carlsbad CA 92009, USA
**Bennett, Donnell** — Football Player
8055 W Leitner Dr, Coral Springs FL 33067, USA
**Bennett, Eliza Hope** — Actress
Independent Talent Group, 40 Whitfield St, London W1T 2RH, England
**Bennett, Elmer J** — Basketball Player
2820 Ave of the Woods, Louisville KY 40241, USA
**Bennett, Fleur A** — Actress
Richard Stone Partnership, De Walden Court, 85 New Cavendish St, London W1W 6XD, England
**Bennett, Fran** — Actress
House of Representatives, 1434 6th St, #1, Santa Monica CA 90401 USA
**Bennett, Harvey, Jr** — Ice Hockey Player
1096 Warwick Neck Ave, Warwick RI 02889, USA
**Bennett, Hayley** — Actress, Singer
Schiff Co, 9465 Wilshire Blvd, #480, Beverly Hills CA 90212, USA

|  |  |
|---|---|
| **Bennett, Hywel**<br>116 Lots Road, Chelsea Creek, London SW10, England | Actor |
| **Bennett, Jean**<br>University of Pennsylvania Medical School, 422 Curie Blvd, Philadelphia PA 19104, USA | Molecular Geneticist, Physician |
| **Bennett, Jimmy**<br>Untitled Entertainment, 350 S Beverly Dr, #200, Beverly Hills CA 90212 USA | Actor |
| **Bennett, Joan**<br>Playboy Promotions, 2706 Media Center Dr, Los Angeles CA 90065 USA | Model |
| **Bennett, Joe C**<br>4101 Altamont Road, Birmingham AL 35213, USA | Rheumatologist, Educator |
| **Bennett, John**<br>US Olympic Committee, 1 Olympic Plaza, Building 6, Colorado Springs CO 80909 USA | Track Athlete |
| **Bennett, John O, III**<br>Montclair State University, Political Science Dept, 1 Normal Ave, Upper Montclair NJ 07043, USA | Governor, NJ |
| **Bennett, Jonathan**<br>Evolution Entertainment, 901 N Highland Ave, Los Angeles CA 90038 USA | Actor |
| **Bennett, Laurence**<br>Innovative Artists, 1505 10th St, Santa Monica CA 90401 USA | Production Designer |
| **Bennett, Matthew R**<br>Edna Talent, 318 Dundas St W, Toronto ON M5T 1G5, Canada | Actor |
| **Bennett, Michael A**<br>Minnesota Vikings, 9520 Viking Dr, Eden Prairie MN 55344 USA | Football Player |
| **Bennett, Michael V L**<br>Albert Einstein College of Medicine, Neuroscience Dept, Bronx NY 10461, USA | Neuroscientist |
| **Bennett, Monte L**<br>2075 Ave U, Sterling KS 67579, USA | Football Player |
| **Bennett, Nigel**<br>Characters Talent, 8 Elm St, Toronto ON M5G 1G7, Canada | Actor |
| **Bennett, Patricia**<br>Lustig Talent, PO Box 770850, Orlando FL 32877 USA | Singer (Chiffons) |
| **Bennett, Rick**<br>55 Evergreen Ave, Clifton Park NY 12065, USA | Ice Hockey Player |
| **Bennett, Robert F (Rob)**<br>Arent Fox LLP, 1050 Connecticut Ave NW, Washington DC 20036, USA | Senator, UT |
| **Bennett, Robert R**<br>Home Shopping Network, 2501 118th Ave N, Saint Petersburg FL 33716, USA | Businessman |
| **Bennett, Ronan**<br>Tavistock Wood Mgmt, 45 Conduit St, London W1S 2YN, England | Writer |
| **Bennett, Sarah**<br>Willow Personal Mgmt, 151 Main St, Yaxley, Peterborough PE7 3LD, England | Actress |
| **Bennett, Tom**<br>Bennett Gallery, 6200 Pleasant Valley Road, El Dorado CA 95623, USA | Sculptor |
| **Bennett, Tom**<br>Susan Angel & Kevin Francis Ltd, 12 D'Arblay St, London W1F 8DU, England | Actor, Writer |
| **Bennett, Tony**<br>R P M Music Productions, 48 W 10th St, #B, New York NY 10011, USA | Singer |
| **Bennett, Tony**<br>48B W 10th St, New York NY 10011, USA | Artist |
| **Bennett, Tony L**<br>7645 Ballinshire N, Indianapolis IN 46254, USA | Football Player |
| **Bennett, William J**<br>5716 3rd St NW, Washington DC 20011, USA | Secretary, Education |
| **Bennett, Winston G, III**<br>54 Barrington Circle, Paducah KY 42003, USA | Basketball Player |
| **Bennett, Woodrow (Woody), Jr**<br>PO Box 25022, Fort Lauderdale FL 33320, USA | Football Player |
| **Bennetts, Leslie**<br>Voice/Hyperion Books, 77 W 66th St, #1100, New York NY 10023, USA | Writer |
| **Benning, Brian A**<br>Interstate Batteries, 11216 156th St NW, Edmonton AB T5M 1Y3, Canada | Ice Hockey Player |
| **Bennington, Chester**<br>Special Artists Agency, 9200 Sunset Blvd, #410, West Hollywood CA 90069 USA | Singer (Linkin Park) |
| **Bennis, Warren G**<br>University of Southern California, Management School, Los Angeles CA 90089, USA | Educator, Writer |
| **Benoit Samuelson, Joan**<br>95 Lower Flying Point Road, Freeport ME 04032, USA | Track Athlete |
| **Benoit, David**<br>Chapman & Co Mgmt, PO Box 55246, Sherman Oaks CA 91413, USA | Jazz Pianist, Composer |
| **Benrubi, Abraham**<br>Stone Manners Salners, 9911 W Pico Blvd, #1400, Los Angeles CA 90035 USA | Actor |
| **Benson, Amber N**<br>Glick Agency, 1321 7th St, #203, Santa Monica CA 90401 USA | Actress |
| **Benson, Andrew A**<br>6044 Folsom Dr, La Jolla CA 92037, USA | Marine Biologist, Plant Physiologist |
| **Benson, Anna**<br>6025 Sandy Springs Circle, #133, Atlanta GA 30328, USA | Model |
| **Benson, Ashley V**<br>W K T Public Relations, 9350 Wilshire Blvd, #450, Beverly Hills CA 90212 USA | Actress |
| **Benson, Bradley W (Brad)**<br>Brad Benson Mitsubishi, 3905 Route 1 S, Monmouth Junction NJ 08852, USA | Football Player |
| **Benson, Brendan**<br>High Road Touring, 751 Bridgeway, #200, Sausalito CA 94965 USA | Singer, Guitarist, Songwriter |
| **Benson, Bruce D**<br>University of Colorado, President's Office, 1800 Grant St, #800, Denver CO 80203, USA | Educator |
| **Benson, Cedric M**<br>20 Commerce Dr, #301, Cranford NJ 7016, USA | Football Player |
| **Benson, Charles**<br>1514 Hanover Lane, Van Alstyne TX 75495, USA | Football Player |
| **Benson, Doug**<br>OmniPop Talent Group, 4605 Lankershim Blvd, #201, Toluca Lake CA 91602 USA | Actor, Comedian |
| **Benson, Duane D**<br>33053 Grit Road, Lanesboro MN 55949, USA | Football Player |
| **Benson, Harry**<br>181 E 73rd St, #18A, New York NY 10021, USA | Photographer |
| **Benson, Herbert**<br>Mind/Body Medical Institute, Beth Israel Hospital, Brookline MA 02146, USA | Cardiologist |

# B

|  |  |
|---|---|
| **Benson, Jodi**<br>319 1/2 N Church St, Grass Valley CA 95945, USA | Actress, Singer |
| **Benson, Jonathan (Johnny), Jr**<br>19528 Mary Ardrey Circle, Cornelius NC 28031, USA | Auto, Truck Racing Driver |
| **Benson, Kristen J (Kris)**<br>2140 Vicki Lane, Cumming GA 30041, USA | Baseball Player |
| **Benson, Linda**<br>SurfHer, PO Box 1, Solana Beach CA 92075, USA | Surfer |
| **Benson, M Kent**<br>4315 Weymouth Lane, Bloomington IN 47408, USA | Basketball Player |
| **Benson, Peter**<br>Liebman Entertainment, 25 E 21st St, #PH, New York NY 10010 USA | Actor |
| **Benson, Ray**<br>Bismeaux Productions, PO Box 463, Austin TX 78767, USA | Singer, Guitarist (Asleep at the Wheel) |
| **Benson, Raymond**<br>Ian Fleming Foundation, PO Box 7312, Buffalo Grove IL 60089, USA | Writer |
| **Benson, Robby**<br>A K A Talent, 6310 San Vicente Blvd, #200, Los Angeles CA 90048 USA | Actor |
| **Benson, Stephen R (Steve)**<br>Arizona Republic, Editorial Dept, 200 E Van Buren St, Phoenix AZ 85004, USA | Editorial Cartoonist |
| **Benson, Thomas C (Tom)**<br>PO Box 701341, Dallas TX 75370, USA | Football Player |
| **Benson, Vernon A (Vern)**<br>1040 De Lara Circle, Granite Quarry NC 28072, USA | Baseball Player, Manager |
| **Bent, Amel**<br>19 Music & Mgmt, 35-37 Parkgate Road, London SW11 4NP, England | Singer |
| **Bent, Lyriq**<br>Stone Manners Salners, 9911 W Pico Blvd, #1400, Los Angeles CA 90035 USA | Actor |
| **Bent, Margaret H**<br>All Souls College, Oxford University, Music Dept, Oxford OX1 4AL, England | Musicologist |
| **Bent, Ridley**<br>Divine Industries, 101-1001 W Broadway, Vancouver BC V6H 4E4, Canada | Singer, Songwriter |
| **Bentas, Lily H**<br>Cumberland Farms, 100 Crossing Blvd, Framingham MA 01702, USA | Businesswoman |
| **Bentley, Albert T**<br>13631 Eagle Ridge Dr, #234, Fort Myers FL 33912, USA | Football Player |
| **Bentley, Ben**<br>6007 N Sheridan Road, #28G, Chicago IL 60660, USA | Sportswriter |
| **Bentley, Dierks**<br>W M E Entertainment, 1600 Division St, #300, Nashville TN 37203 USA | Singer, Guitarist, Songwriter |
| **Bentley, Jay D**<br>Goldstar Public Relations, PO Box 130, Ross on Wye HR9 6WY, England | Bassist (Bad Religion) |
| **Bentley, Kevin K**<br>3001 Murworth Dr, #904, Houston TX 77025, USA | Football Player |
| **Bentley, Ray**<br>4050 Redbush Dr SW, Grandville MI 49418, USA | Football Player, Sportscaster |
| **Bentley, Wes**<br>W M E Entertainment, 9601 Wilshire Blvd, #300, Beverly Hills CA 90210 USA | Actor |
| **Benton, Barbi**<br>40 N 4th St, Carbondale CO 81623, USA | Model, Actress |
| **Benton, Fletcher C**<br>250 Dore St, San Francisco CA 94103, USA | Sculptor |
| **Benton, Robert**<br>Creative Artists Agency, 2000 Ave of Stars, #100, Los Angeles CA 90067 USA | Director |
| **Bentsen, William**<br>N1946 Birches Dr, Lake Geneva WI 53147, USA | Yachtsman |
| **Bentyne, Cheryl**<br>Bennett Morgan, 1022 RR 376, #3, Wappinger Falls NY 12590 USA | Singer (Manhattan Transfer) |
| **Benvenuti, Giovanni (Nino)**<br>V S Costanza 13, 00198 Rome, Italy | Boxer |
| **Ben-Victor, Paul**<br>A P A Talent/Literary Agency, 405 S Beverly Dr, #300, Beverly Hills CA 90212 USA | Actor |
| **Benymon, Chico**<br>Don Buchwald, 6500 Wilshire Blvd, #2200, Los Angeles CA 90048 USA | Actor |
| **Benyon, Margaret**<br>Holography Studio, 40 Springdale, Broadstone, Dorset BH18 9EU, England | Artist |
| **Benz, Edward J, Jr**<br>20 Beacon St, #4, Boston MA 02108, USA | Pediatrician, Pathologist |
| **Benz, Julie**<br>I C M Partners, 10250 Constellation Blvd, #900, Los Angeles CA 90067 USA | Actress |
| **Benza, Alfred Joseph (A J)**<br>Media Artists Group, 8222 Melrose Ave, #203, Los Angeles CA 90048 USA | Actor, Writer |
| **Benzali, Daniel**<br>Vanguard Management Group, 8060 Melrose Ave, #400 Los Angeles CA 90046, USA | Actor |
| **Benzi, Roberto**<br>12 Villa Sainte Foy, 92200 Neuilly-sur-Seine, France | Conductor |
| **Benzinger, Todd E**<br>1047 Shore Point Court, Loveland OH 45140, USA | Baseball Player |
| **Beranek, Josef**<br>Pittsburgh Penguins, Consol Energy Center, 1001 5th Ave, Pittsburgh PA 15219 USA | Ice Hockey Player |
| **Beranek, Leo**<br>10 Longwood Dr, #265, Westwood MA 2090, USA | Acoustical Engineer |
| **Berard, Bryan**<br>9 Holly Lane, Cumberland RI 02864, USA | Ice Hockey Player |
| **Berardi, Antonio**<br>Saint Martin's House, 59 Saint Martin's Lane, London WC2N 4JS, England | Fashion Designer |
| **Bercaw, John E**<br>California Institute of Technology, Chemistry Dept, Pasadena CA 91125, USA | Chemist |
| **Berce, Eugene D (Gene)**<br>1119 Hawthorne Place, #6, Pewaukee WI 53072, USA | Basketball Player |
| **Bercich, Peter J (Pete)**<br>17448 Honeysuckle Ave, Lakeville MN 55044, USA | Football Player |
| **Bercot, Emmanuelle**<br>U B B A, 6 Rue de Braque, 75003 Paris, France | Director, Writer |
| **Bercu, Michaela**<br>Elite Model Mgmt, 404 Park Ave S, #900, New York NY 10016 USA | Model, Actress |

**Berdimuhammedow, Gurbanguly M** — President, Turkmenistan
President's Office, Karl Marx Str 24, 744017 Ashkabat, Turkmenistan
**Bere, Jason P** — Baseball Player
40 Berrington Place, North Andover MA 01845, USA
**Berehowsky, Drake** — Ice Hockey Player
20455 N 95th St, Scottsdale AZ 85255, USA
**Berendt, John L** — Writer
W M E Entertainment, 9601 Wilshire Blvd, #300, Beverly Hills CA 90210 USA
**Berendzen, Richard E** — Educator
1300 Crystal Dr, Arlington VA 22202, USA
**Berenger, Tom** — Actor
Brillstein Entertainment Partners, 9150 Wilshire Blvd, #350, Beverly Hills CA 90212 USA
**Berengo Gardin, Gianni** — Photographer
Via S Michele del Carso 21, 20144 Milan, Italy
**Berenguer, Juan B** — Baseball Player
8616 Alisa Court, Chanhassen MN 55317, USA
**Berenson, Gordon A (Red)** — Ice Hockey Player, Coach
3555 Daleview Dr, Ann Arbor MI 48105, USA
**Berenyi, Bruce M** — Baseball Player
10 Pine Grove Road, Exeter NH 03833, USA
**Berenzweig, Andrew** — Ice Hockey Player
4603 Brookside Road, Ottawa Hills OH 43615, USA
**Beresford, Bruce** — Director
Rayfield Allied, Southbank House, Black Prince Road, London SE1 7SJ, England
**Beresford, Meg** — Peace Activist
Wiston Lodge, Wiston, Biggar ML12 6HT, Scotland
**Bereta, Joe** — Actor, Comedian
Barats & Bereta Productions, 9601 Wilshire Blvd, #750, Beverly Hills CA 90210, USA
**Berezan, Perry** — Ice Hockey Player
Wellington West Capital, 1100-255 5th Ave SW, Calgary AB T2P 3G6, Canada
**Berezhnaya, Elena V** — Figure Skater
Figure Skating Federation, Luzhnetskaya Nab 8, 119871 Moscow, Russia
**Berezin, Sergei** — Ice Hockey Player
1645 SW 4th Ave, Boca Raton FL 33432, USA
**Berezovsky, Boris V** — Concert Pianist
I M G Artists, Burlington Lane, Chiswick, London W4 2TH, England
**Berezovy, Anatoli N** — Cosmonaut
Cosmonaut Training Center, Star City, 141160 Zvezdny Gorodok, Moscow Oblast, Russia
**Berfield, Justin** — Actor
Virgin Produced, 315 S Beverly D, #506, Beverly Hills CA 90212 90212, USA
**Berg, A Scott** — Writer
Creative Artists Agency, 2000 Ave of Stars, #100, Los Angeles CA 90067 USA
**Berg, Aki-Petteri** — Ice Hockey Player
Toronto Maple Leafs, AirCanada Center, 40 Bay St, Toronto ON M5J 2K2, Canada
**Berg, David S (Dave)** — Baseball Player
1917 Stonecastle Dr, Roanoke TX 76262, USA
**Berg, Elizabeth** — Writer
Random House, 1745 Broadway, #1800, New York NY 10019 USA
**Berg, Jeffrey S** — Businessman
Resolution, 1801 Century Park East, #2300, Los Angeles CA 90067, USA
**Berg, Laura** — Softball Player
USA Softball, 2801 NE 50th St, Oklahoma City OK 73111, USA
**Berg, Matraca** — Singer, Songwriter
Universal Publishing Group, 1904 Adelicia St, Nashville TN 37212, USA
**Berg, Paul** — Nobel Chemistry Laureate
838 Santa Fe Ave, Stanford CA 94305, USA
**Berg, Peter** — Actor, Director, Producer
W M E Entertainment, 9601 Wilshire Blvd, #300, Beverly Hills CA 90210 USA
**Berg, William D (Bill)** — Ice Hockey Player
N H L Network, 9 Channel Nine Court, Toronto ON M1S 4B5, Canada
**Berg, Yehuda** — Religious Leader
Kabbalah Centre, 1054 S Robertson Blvd, Los Angeles CA 90035, USA
**Berganio, David, Jr** — Golfer
17811 Lahey St, Granada Hills CA 91344, USA
**Berganza, Teresa** — Opera Singer
La Rossiniana, Archanda 5, 28200 San Lorenzo del Escorial, Madrid, Spain
**Berge, Francine** — Actress
Intertalent, 16 Rue Henri Barbusse, 75005 Paris, France
**Berge, Pierre V G** — Businessman
Yves Saint Laurent SA, 5 Ave Marceau, 75116 Paris, France
**Bergen, Bob** — Actor
C E S D, 10635 Santa Monica Blvd, #130, Los Angeles CA 90025 USA
**Bergen, Candice P** — Actress
51 Tradd St, Charleston SC 29401, USA
**Bergen, Gary D** — Basketball Player
1386 Graham Circle, Erie CO 80516, USA
**Bergen, Polly** — Actress
1746 S Britain Road, Southbury CT 06488, USA
**Berger Perdomo, Oscar J R** — President, Guatemala
President's Office, Palacio Nacional, 6 Avenida 419, Guatemala City, Guatemala
**Berger, Christian** — Cinematographer
Haus 7, 6072 Lans, Austria
**Berger, Gerhard** — Auto Racing Driver
Berger Motorsport, Postfach 1121, 9490 Vaduz, Austria
**Berger, Glenn** — Writer
W M E Entertainment, 9601 Wilshire Blvd, #300, Beverly Hills CA 90210 USA
**Berger, Helmut** — Actor
Viale Parioli 50, 00197 Rome, Italy
**Berger, Howard** — Makeup Artist
K N B Effects Group, 7535 Woodman Place, Van Nuys CA 91405, USA
**Berger, John** — Writer
Quincy, Mieussy, 74440 Taninges, France
**Berger, Joseph D (Joe)** — Football Player
Minnesota Vikings, 9520 Viking Dr, Eden Prairie MN 55344 USA
**Berger, Joseph S** — Inventor (Light Can Converter)
J S B Enterprises, 12605 W North Ave, #225, Brookfield WI 53005, USA

# B

| | |
|---|---|
| **Berger, Lars**<br>Dombas/Byaasen I L, PB 9266, Stavset, 7424 Trondheim, Norway | Cross Country Skier |
| **Berger, Mitchell S (Mitch)**<br>9108 N 118th Place, Scottsdale AZ 85259, USA | Football Player |
| **Berger, Peter**<br>I M G Artists, Hogarth Business Park, Chiswick, London W4 2TH, England | Opera Singer |
| **Berger, Senta**<br>Deutsche Filmakademie, Kothener Str 44, 10963 Berlin, Germany | Actress, Producer |
| **Berger, Thomas L**<br>PO Box 11, Palisades NY 10964, USA | Writer |
| **Bergere, Jenica**<br>Innovative Artists, 1505 10th St, Santa Monica CA 90401 USA | Actress |
| **Bergeron, Michel**<br>T Q S, 612 Rue Saint-Jacques, Montreal QC H3C 5R1, Canada | Ice Hockey Player, Coach |
| **Bergeron, Patrice**<br>234 Causeway St, #1109, Boston MA 02114, USA | Ice Hockey Player |
| **Bergeron, Peter C**<br>3495 Manatee Dr SE, Saint Petersburg FL 33705, USA | Baseball Player |
| **Bergeron, Tom**<br>International Management Group, 2049 Century Park E, #2460, Los Angeles CA 90067, USA | Entertainer |
| **Bergeron, Yves**<br>1035 Clearwater Ave, Bathurst NB E2A 4H5, Canada | Ice Hockey Player |
| **Bergevin, Marc**<br>404 Canterbury Court, Hinsdale IL 60521, USA | Ice Hockey Player |
| **Bergey, John**<br>1807 Mayflower Circle, Lancaster PA 17603, USA | Inventor (Pulsar Watch) |
| **Bergey, William E (Bill)**<br>2 Hickory Lane, Chadds Ford PA 19317, USA | Football Player |
| **Berggren, Jenny**<br>United Stage Artists, Asogatan 142, Box 11029, 100 61 Stockholm, Sweden | Singer (Ace of Base) |
| **Berggren, Jonas**<br>United Stage Artists, Asogatan 142, Box 11029, 100 61 Stockholm, Sweden | Singer (Ace of Base) |
| **Berggren, Linn**<br>United Stage Artists, Asogatan 142, Box 11029, 100 61 Stockholm, Sweden | Singer (Ace of Base) |
| **Berggren, Thommy**<br>Swedish Film Institute, PO Box 27126, 102 52, Stockholm, Sweden | Actor, Director, Writer |
| **Bergh, Larry C**<br>1849 Bent Pine Hill, Fogelsville PA 18051, USA | Basketball Player |
| **Bergin, Joan**<br>Gersh Agency, 9465 Wilshire Blvd, #600, Beverly Hills CA 90212 USA | Costume Designer |
| **Bergin, Michael**<br>Chasen Agency, 8899 Beverly Blvd, #405, Los Angeles CA 90048 USA | Model, Actor |
| **Bergin, Patrick**<br>Sovereign Talent Group, 8421 Wilshire Blvd, #200, Beverly Hills CA 90211, USA | Actor |
| **Bergkamp, Dennis**<br>Arsenal F C, Arsenal Stadium, Avenell Road, London N5 1BU, England | Soccer Player |
| **Bergl, Emily**<br>Innovative Artists, 1505 10th St, Santa Monica CA 90401 USA | Actress |
| **Bergland, Robert S (Bob)**<br>1104 7th Ave SE, Roseau MN 56751, USA | Secretary, Agriculture |
| **Bergland, Tim**<br>721 Labree Ave N, Thief River Falls MN 56701, USA | Ice Hockey Player |
| **Berglund, Art**<br>1775 Bob Johnson Dr, Colorado Springs CO 80906, USA | Ice Hockey Executive |
| **Berglund, Bo**<br>Buffalo Sabres, 1 Seymour Knox Plaza, #1, Buffalo NY 14203 USA | Ice Hockey Player |
| **Bergman, Alan**<br>714 N Maple Dr, Beverly Hills CA 90210, USA | Lyricist |
| **Bergman, Andrew C**<br>Creative Artists Agency, 2000 Ave of Stars, #100, Los Angeles CA 90067 USA | Director, Writer |
| **Bergman, David B (Dave)**<br>728 Canterbury Road, Grosse Pointe Woods MI 48236, USA | Baseball Player |
| **Bergman, Joel D**<br>Bergman Walls Assoc, 2964 S Jones, Las Vegas NV 89146, USA | Architect |
| **Bergman, John W**<br>Commander, Forces Reserve, HqUSMC, 2 Navy St, Washington DC 20380 USA | Marine Corps General |
| **Bergman, Lowell**<br>New York Times, Editorial Dept, 229 W 43rd St, New York NY 10036 USA | Journalist |
| **Bergman, Marilyn K**<br>714 N Maple Dr, Beverly Hills CA 90210, USA | Lyricist |
| **Bergman, Martin**<br>641 Lexington Ave, New York NY 10022, USA | Producer |
| **Bergman, Peter**<br>Abrams Artists, 9200 W Sunset Blvd, #1125, West Hollywood CA 90069 USA | Actor |
| **Bergman, Robert G**<br>501 Coventry Road, Kensington CA 94707, USA | Chemist |
| **Bergman, Sean F**<br>14421 Scott Road, Bryan OH 43506, USA | Baseball Player |
| **Bergman, Thommie**<br>Tolvmansvagen 4, 18463 Akersberga, Sweden | Ice Hockey Player |
| **Bergmann, Barbara R**<br>9707 Old Georgetown Road, #2419, Bethesda MD 20814, USA | Economist |
| **Bergonzi, Carlo**<br>I Duc Foscari, Piazza Carl Rossi 15, 43011 Busseto (Parma), Italy | Opera Singer |
| **Bergoust, Eric**<br>2727 Mulberry Lane, Missoula MT 59804, USA | Freestyle Aerials Skier |
| **Bergqvist, Kajsa M**<br>Box 5126, 200 77 Malmo, Sweden | Track Athlete |
| **Bergsten, C Fred**<br>4106 Sleepy Hollow Road, Annandale VA 22003, USA | Economist |
| **Berisha, Sali**<br>Prime Minister's Office, Keshilli i Ministrave, Tirana, Albania | Prime Minister, Albania |
| **Berke, Deborah**<br>Deborah Berke Partners Architects, 220 5th Ave, #700, New York NY 10001, USA | Architect |
| **Berkeley, Michael F**<br>Oxford University Press, 70 Baker St, London W1U 7DN, England | Composer |

**Berger - Berkeley**

**Berkley Lauren, Elizabeth** — Actress, Model
Sloane Offer Weber, 9601 Wilshire Blvd, #500, Beverly Hills CA 90210 USA
**Berkman, W Lance (Elvis)** — Baseball Player
5 Farnham Park Dr, Houston TX 77024, USA
**Berkoff, David** — Swimmer
Harvard University, Athletic Dept, Cambridge MA 02138, USA
**Berkoff, Steven** — Actor, Writer
Rosica Colin Ltd, 1 Clareville Mews, London SW1 5AH, England
**Berkowitz, Bob** — Entertainer
CNBC-TV, 1 CNBC Plaza, Englewood Cliffs NJ 07632, USA
**Berkus, Nate** — Interior Designer
Nate Berkus Assoc, 406 N Wood St, Chicago IL 60622, USA
**Berlant, Anthony (Tony)** — Artist
Los Angeles Louver Gallery, 55 N Venice Blvd, Venice CA 90291, USA
**Berlanti, Greg** — Director, Producer, Writer
W M E Entertainment, 9601 Wilshire Blvd, #300, Beverly Hills CA 90210 USA
**Berlekamp, Elwyn R** — Mathematician
120 Hazel Lane, Piedmont CA 94611, USA
**Berlin, Eddie** — Football Player
100 Market St, #421, Des Moines IA 50309, USA
**Berlin, Jeannie** — Actress, Director
M C 2 Entertainment, 18541 Elkwood St, Reseda CA 91335, USA
**Berlin, Mike** — Bowler
12 Coventry Lane, Muscatine IA 52761, USA
**Berlin, Steve** — Singer, Saxophonist (Los Lobos)
Gold Mountain, 3940 Laurel Canyon Blvd, #444, Studio City CA 91604 USA
**Berliner, Alain** — Director
United Talent Agency, U T A Plaza, 9336 Civic Center Dr, Beverly Hills CA 90210 USA
**Berling, Charles** — Actor
Markham Froggatt Irwin, Julian House, 4 Windmill St, London W1P 1HF, England
**Berling, Clay** — Soccer Executive, Publisher
2935 Franciscan Way, Carmel CA 93923, USA
**Berling, Peter** — Actor
12 V S Calisto, 00153 Rome, Italy
**Berlinger, Warren** — Actor
23291 Ventura Blvd, Woodland Hills CA 91364, USA
**Berlinsky, Dmitri** — Concert Violinist
35 W 64th St, #7F, New York NY 10023, USA
**Berlusconi, Silvio** — Prime Minister, Italy
Palazzo Grazioli, Via del Plebiscito 102, 00186 Rome, Italy
**Berman, Andy** — Actor
United Talent Agency, U T A Plaza, 9336 Civic Center Dr, Beverly Hills CA 90210 USA
**Berman, Boris** — Concert Pianist
Columbia Artists Mgmt Inc, 1790 Broadway, #702, New York NY 10019 USA
**Berman, Christopher J (Chris)** — Sportscaster
ESPN-TV, ESPN Plaza, 935 Middle St, Bristol CT 06010 USA
**Berman, David** — Actor
Optimism Entertainment, 303 N La Peer Dr, #205, Beverly Hills CA 90211, USA
**Berman, Francine** — Computer Scientist
San Diego Supercomputer Center, 9500 Gilman Dr, La Jolla CA 92093, USA
**Berman, Jennifer** — Physician
University of California, Women's Sexual Health Center, Los Angeles CA 90024, USA
**Berman, Josh** — Producer
Creative Artists Agency, 2000 Ave of Stars, #100, Los Angeles CA 90067 USA
**Berman, Julia** — Architect
Julia Berman Design, 947 Camino de Chelly, Santa Fe NM 87505, USA
**Berman, Julius** — Religious Leader, Attorney
Kaye Scholer Fierman, 425 Park Ave, #1200, New York NY 10022, USA
**Berman, Kip** — Singer (Pains of Being Pure at Heart)
Slumberland Records, PO Box 19029, Oakland CA 94619, USA
**Berman, Laura** — Psychotherapist
I C M Partners, 10250 Constellation Blvd, #900, Los Angeles CA 90067 USA
**Berman, Saul J** — Religious Leader, Rabbi, Writer
E D A H, 1501 Broadway, #501, New York NY 10036, USA
**Berman, Shari Springer** — Director, Producer, Writer
Anonymous Content, 3532 Hayden Ave, Culver City CA 90232 USA
**Berman, Shelley** — Actor, Comedian
268 Bell Canyon Road, Bell Canyon CA 91307, USA
**Berman, Zev** — Writer, Producer, Director
Gersh Agency, 9465 Wilshire Blvd, #600, Beverly Hills CA 90212 USA
**Bern, Dan** — Singer, Songwriter
Public Emily, 56 Main St, #206, Northampton MA 01060, USA
**Bern, Howard A** — Biologist
1010 Shattuck Ave, Berkeley CA 94707, USA
**Bernal, Gael Garcia** — Actor, Director
Canana Films, San Luis Potosi #211 Piso 8, Colonia Roma, Mexico City  DF 06700, Mexico
**Bernanke, Ben S** — Government Official, Economist
Federal Reserve Board, 20th St & Constitution Ave NW, Washington DC 20557, USA
**Bernard, Betsy** — Businesswoman
American Telephone & Telegraph Corp, 32 Ave of Americas, New York NY 10013, USA
**Bernard, Carlos** — Actor
Innovative Artists, 1505 10th St, Santa Monica CA 90401 USA
**Bernard, Crystal** — Actress, Singer, Songwriter
8436 W 3rd St, #650, Los Angeles CA 90048, USA
**Bernard, Robert (Rocky)** — Football Player
16655 SE 69th Way, Bellevue WA 98006, USA
**Bernard, Robyn** — Actress
3227 Cardiff Ave, Los Angeles CA 90034, USA
**Bernard, Rod** — Singer
PO Box 90665, 2410 Eraste Landry, Lafayette LA 70509, USA
**Bernath, Antonia** — Actress
Creative Artists Agency, 2000 Ave of Stars, #100, Los Angeles CA 90067 USA
**Bernauer, David W** — Businessman
Walgreen Co, 200 Wilmot Road, Deerfield IL 60015, USA
**Bernazard Garcia, Antonio (Tony)** — Baseball Player
D25 Calle Santa Ana, Urb Santa Elvira, Caguas PR 00725, USA

**Berne, Robert M** — Physiologist
250 Pantops Mountain Road, #5134, Charlottesville VA 22911, USA
**Bernero, Adam G** — Baseball Player
11 Columbus Dr, Savannah GA 31405, USA
**Bernero, Edward Allen** — Producer, Writer
Creative Artists Agency, 2000 Ave of Stars, #100, Los Angeles CA 90067 USA
**Berners-Lee, Timothy J** — Computer Scientist
20 Powder Mill Road, Concord MA 1742, USA
**Bernhard, Sandra** — Actress, Comedienne, Singer
6145 Shadyglade Ave, North Hollywood CA 91606, USA
**Bernhardt, Tim** — Ice Hockey Player
RR 1, Schomberg ON L0G 1T0, Canada
**Bernheimer, Martin** — Music Critic
17350 Sunset Blvd, #702C, Pacific Palisades CA 90272, USA
**Bernier, Serge J** — Ice Hockey Player
534 Rue Elisabeth, Rimouski QC G5L 3M9, Canada
**Berning, Susie Maxwell** — Golfer
80413 Portobello Dr, Indio CA 92201, USA
**Berninger, Matt** — Singer (National), Songwriter
Brassland Records, PO Box 76, Prince Street Station, New York NY 10012, USA
**Bernoldi, Enrique A L S** — Auto Racing Driver
Bartels Motor & Sport, Kobbinghausen 2, 58840 Plettenberg, Germany
**Berns, Richard R (Rick)** — Football Player
127 Merry Trail, San Antonio TX 78232, USA
**Bernsen, Corbin** — Actor
Home Theater Films, 12041 Maxwellton Road, Studio City CA 91604, USA
**Bernstein, Bonnie** — Sportscaster
Monmouth County District Attorney, 71 Monmouth Park, Freehold NJ 07728, USA
**Bernstein, Carl** — Journalist
14 E 60th St, #705, New York NY 10022, USA
**Bernstein, Charles** — Composer
Soundtrack Music Assoc, 1460 4th St, #308, Santa Monica CA 90401 USA
**Bernstein, Jake** — Journalist
ProPublica, Editorial Dept, 1 Exchange Plaza, 55 Broadway, #2300, New York NY 10006, USA
**Bernstein, Jamie** — Concert Narrator
Opus 3 Artists, 470 Park Ave S, #900N, New York NY 10016 USA
**Bernstein, Jared** — Government Official, Economist
Budget and Policy Priorities Center, 820 1st St NW, #510, Washington DC 20002, USA
**Bernstein, Kenny** — Auto Racing Driver
Budweiser King Racing, 26231 Dimension Dr, Lake Forest CA 92630, USA
**Bernstine, Rod E** — Football Player
22180 E Euclid Place, Aurora CO 80016, USA
**Bernthal, Jon** — Actor
W M E Entertainment, 9601 Wilshire Blvd, #300, Beverly Hills CA 90210 USA
**Berra, Dale A** — Baseball Player
164 Eagle Rock Way, Montclair NJ 07042, USA
**Berra, Lawrence P (Yogi)** — Baseball Player, Manager
19 Highland Ave, Montclair NJ 07042, USA
**Berrian, Bernard** — Football Player
7209 Tokay Circle, Winton CA 95388, USA
**Berridge, Elizabeth** — Actress
Judy Schoen, 606 N Larchmont Blvd, #309, Los Angeles CA 90004 USA
**Berridge, Michael J** — Zoologist, Biologist
Babraham Institute, Babraham Hall, Cambridge CB2 4AT, England
**Berrigan, Daniel** — Clergyman, Social Activist
147 Thompson St, New York NY 10012, USA
**Berroa, Geronimo E** — Baseball Player
3681 Broadway, #23, New York NY 10031, USA
**Berry, A Kenneth (Ken)** — Baseball Player
1131 SW Camden Lane, Topeka KS 66604, USA
**Berry, Ace** — Rodeo Rider
29705 E County Road 1650, Elmore City OK 73433, USA
**Berry, Bertrand D (Bert)** — Football Player
1402 E Coral Cove Dr, Gilbert AZ 85234, USA
**Berry, Bill** — Drummer (REM)
REM/Athens Ltd, 170 College Ave, Athens GA 30601, USA
**Berry, Brad** — Ice Hockey Player
PO Box 5182, Grand Forks ND 58206, USA
**Berry, Brian J L** — Geographer, Political Economist
2404 Forest Court, McKinney TX 75070, USA
**Berry, Charles E (Chuck)** — Singer, Songwriter
Berry Park, 691 Buckner Road, Wentzville MO 63385, USA
**Berry, Cornelius J (Neil)** — Baseball Player
407 Inkster Ave, Kalamazoo MI 49001, USA
**Berry, Halle** — Actress, Model
Vincent Cirrincione Assoc, 1516 N Fairfax Ave, Los Angeles CA 90046 USA
**Berry, Jim** — Editorial Cartoonist
United Feature Syndicate, PO Box 5610, Cincinnati OH 45201 USA
**Berry, John** — Singer
Circle T Management, 44 Wiregrass Circle, Tifton GA 31794, USA
**Berry, Kenneth R (Ken)** — Actor
147 Sunny Lane, Branson West MO 65737, USA
**Berry, Mark (Bez)** — Percussionist (Happy Mondays)
145 S Fairfax, #310, Los Angeles CA 90036, USA
**Berry, Michael J** — Chemist
7801 Comfort Cove, Austin TX 78731, USA
**Berry, Raymond E** — Football Player, Coach
1110 SE Broad St, Murfreesboro TN 37130, USA
**Berry, Robert C (Bob)** — Football Player
1351 Wilson Circle, Gardnerville NV 89410, USA
**Berry, Robert V (Bob)** — Ice Hockey Player, Coach, Executive
640 3rd St, Hermosa Beach CA 90254, USA
**Berry, Royce E** — Football Player
PO Box 909, Comfort TX 78013, USA
**Berry, Sean R** — Baseball Player
307 Susannah Lane, Paso Robles CA 93446, USA

**Berry, Stephen J (Steve)** — Journalist
6527 Ellenview Ave, West Hills CA 91307, USA
**Berry, Wendell E** — Writer, Ecologist
PO Box 1, Port Royal KY 40058, USA
**Berryhill, Damon S** — Baseball Player
11 Springbrook Road, Laguna Niguel CA 92677, USA
**Berryman, Guy R** — Bassist (Coldplay)
Paradigm Agency, 360 N Crescent Dr, North Building, Beverly Hills CA 90210 USA
**Bersani, Leo** — Educator
University of California, French Dept, Berkeley CA 94720, USA
**Bersia, John** — Journalist
Orlando Sentinel, Editorial Dept, 633 N Orange Ave, Orlando FL 32801, USA
**Berson, Jerome A** — Chemist
200 Leeder Hill Dr, #205, Hamden CT 06517, USA
**Bertarelli, Ernesto** — Businessman, Yachtsman
Serono SA, Chemin des Mines 15 Bis, 1211 Geneva 20, Switzerland
**Bertello, Giuseppe Cardinal** — Religious Leader
Governatorate of Vatican City State, Urbs Salvia, 00120 Vatican City
**Bertelmann, Fred** — Singer, Guitarist
Am Hohenberg 9, 82335 Berg, Germany
**Bertelsen, James A (Jim)** — Football Player
2001 Days End Road, Wimberley TX 78676, USA
**Berteotti, Missie** — Golfer
300 Kane Blvd, Pittsburgh PA 15243, USA
**Berthiaume, Daniel** — Ice Hockey Player
PO Box 673, Hardy VA 24101, USA
**Berti, Marco** — Opera Singer
I M G Artists, Hogarth Business Park, Chiswick, London W4 2TH, England
**Bertil** — Crown Prince, Sweden
Hert Av Halland, Kungl Slottet, 111 30 Stockholm, Sweden
**Bertinelli, Valerie** — Actress
Innovative Artists, 1505 10th St, Santa Monica CA 90401 USA
**Bertish, Suzanne** — Actress
Jonathan Altaras Assoc, 11 Garrick St, London WC2E 9AR, England
**Berto, Andre M** — Boxer
Ray Rafoll, 1519 3rd St SE, Winterhaven FL 33880, USA
**Bertolucci, Bernardo** — Director
Via Della Lungara 3, 00165 Rome, Italy
**Bertone, Tarcisco Cardinal** — Religious Leader
Secretary of State's Office, Apostolic Palace, 00120 Vatican City
**Bertotti, Michael D (Mike)** — Baseball Player
14 Jupiter Road, Highland Mills NY 10930, USA
**Bertsch, Jackie** — Golfer
300 Ocean Trail Way, #1304, Jupiter FL 33477, USA
**Bertsch, Shane** — Golfer
11120 Night Heron Dr, Parker CO 80134, USA
**Bertuzzi, Todd** — Ice Hockey Player
900 Deer Ridge Court, Kitchener ON N2P 2L3, Canada
**Berube, Craig** — Ice Hockey Player
1314 Durham Road, New Hope PA 18938, USA
**Berzins, Andris** — President, Latvia
President's Office, Ratslaukums 7, 1900 Riga LV, Latvia
**Berzon, Marsha S** — Judge
US Court of Appeals, Court Building, 95 7th St, San Francisco CA 94103, USA
**Beshore, Delmer (Del)** — Basketball Player
4724 N Crestmoor Ave, Clovis CA 93619, USA
**Besler, Matt** — Soccer Player
Sporting Kansas City, 210 W 19th Terrace, #200, Kansas City MO 64108 USA
**Bess, Daniel** — Actor
Coast to Coast Talent, 3350 Barham Blvd, Los Angeles CA 90068 USA
**Bess, Rufus T, Jr** — Football Player
10 Greenview Circle, Chico CA 95928, USA
**Bessmertnykh, Aleksandr A** — Government Official, Russia
International Foreign Policy Assn, Yakovo-Apostolski 10, 103064 Moscow, Russia
**Besson, Luc** — Director
Europa Corp, 137, Rue du Faubourg Saint-Honore, 75008 Paris, France
**Best, Ahmed** — Actor
PO Box 707, Renton WA 98057, USA
**Best, Ben** — Actor, Comedian, Producer
Creative Artists Agency, 2000 Ave of Stars, #100, Los Angeles CA 90067 USA
**Best, Eve** — Actress, Singer
Independent Talent Group, 40 Whitfield St, London W1T 2RH, England
**Best, Greg** — Equestrian
39 Troon Terrace, Annandale NJ 08801, USA
**Best, James** — Actor, Director, Writer
PO Box 5325, Hickory NC 28603, USA
**Best, Karl J** — Baseball Player
PO Box 1790, Snohomish WA 98291, USA
**Best, R Peter (Pete)** — Singer, Drummer (Beatles)
Splash Mgmt, 8 Hymans Green, West Derby, Liverpool L12 7JG, England
**Best, Travis E** — Basketball Player
703 Bradley Road, Springfield MA 01109, USA
**Bester, Allan** — Ice Hockey Player
12527 Crayford Ave, Orlando FL 32837, USA
**Beswicke, Martine** — Actress
4011 Primavera Road, #B, Santa Barbara CA 93110, USA
**Betancourt Perez, Yuniesky** — Baseball Player
1001 Brickell Bay Dr, #1710, Miami FL 33131, USA
**Betancourt, Rafael J** — Baseball Player
6857 Valhalla Way, Windermere FL 34786, USA
**Betancur Cuartas, Belisario** — President, Colombia
Fundacio Santilana, Calle 80, #3974, Santa Fe de Bogota, Colombia
**Bethea, Elvin L** — Football Player
16211 Leslie Lane, Missouri City TX 77489, USA
**Bethell, Tabrett** — Actress
W M E Entertainment, 9601 Wilshire Blvd, #300, Beverly Hills CA 90210 USA

## B

| | |
|---|---|
| **Betker, Jan**<br>Curling Assn, 1660 Vimont Court, Cumberland ON K4A 4J4, Canada | Curling Athlete |
| **Betori, Giuseppe Cardinal**<br>Archdiocese, Piazza S Giovanni 3, 50129 Florence, Italy | Religious Leader |
| **Bets, Maxim**<br>5566 Candlelight Dr, La Jolla CA 92037, USA | Ice Hockey Player |
| **Bettany, Paul**<br>Affirmative Entertainment, 425 N Robertson Blvd, Los Angeles CA 90048 USA | Actor |
| **Bettencourt, Liliane**<br>L'Oreal Group, 41 Rue Matre, 92117 Clichy, France | Businesswoman |
| **Bettencourt, Nuno**<br>Dreamscapers International, 1701 18th Ave S, Nashville TN 37212, USA | Guitarist (Extreme) |
| **Bettenhausen, Gary**<br>2410 W Wavelyn Circle S, Martinsville IN 46151, USA | Auto Racing Driver |
| **Bettens, Gert**<br>Sharpe Entertainment Services, 683 Palmera Ave, Pacific Palisades CA 90272, USA | Guitarist, Keyboardist (K's Choice) |
| **Bettens, Sarah**<br>Sharpe Entertainment Services, 683 Palmera Ave, Pacific Palisades CA 90272, USA | Singer (K's Choice) |
| **Betters, Doug L**<br>77 Better Way, Whitefish MT 59937, USA | Football Player |
| **Bettinger, Walter**<br>Charles Schwab Co, 101 Montgomery St, #200, San Francisco CA 94104, USA | Financier |
| **Bettini, Paolo**<br>Via Aurelia Sud 8, 77020 La California-Bibbona (LI), Italy | Cyclist |
| **Bettis, Angela**<br>BenderSpink, 8447 Wilshire Blvd, #250, Beverly Hills CA 90211 USA | Actress |
| **Bettis, Jerome A**<br>1651 Randall Mill Place NW, Atlanta GA 30327, USA | Football Player, Sportscaster |
| **Bettis, W Thomas (Tom)**<br>6931 Terrace Ridge, Katy TX 77494, USA | Football Player, Coach |
| **Bettman, Gary B**<br>National Hockey League, 1251 Ave of Americas, #4601, New York NY 10020, USA | Ice Hockey Executive |
| **Betts, Daisy**<br>I C M Partners, 10250 Constellation Blvd, #900, Los Angeles CA 90067 USA | Actress |
| **Betts, F Richard (Dickie)**<br>David Spero Mgmt, 1679 S Belvoir Blvd, Cleveland OH 44121, USA | Singer, Guitarist (Allman Brothers Band) |
| **Beuerlein, Stephen T (Steve)**<br>15624 McCullers Court, Charlotte NC 28277, USA | Football Player |
| **Beukeboom, Jeff**<br>464 Wagg Road, RR 4, Uxbridge ON L9P 1R4, Canada | Ice Hockey Player |
| **Beuron, Yann**<br>I M G Artists, Hogarth Business Park, Chiswick, London W4 2TH, England | Opera Singer |
| **Beutler, Bruce**<br>Scripps Research Institute, 10550 N Torrey Pines Road, La Jolla CA 92037 USA | Nobel Medicine Laureate |
| **Bevan, Alonzo G**<br>Little Big Man, 39A Grammercy Park N, #1C, New York NY 10010, USA | Bassist (Kula Shaker) |
| **Bevan, Tim**<br>Working Title Films, 26 Aybrook Str, London W1U 4AN, England | Actor, Producer |
| **Beverley, Nick**<br>Nashville Predators, 501 Broadway, Nashville TN 37203 USA | Ice Hockey Player, Coach, Executive |
| **Beverly, Eric R**<br>PO Box 492433, Lawrenceville GA 30049, USA | Football Player |
| **Beverly, Frankie**<br>115 Cherokee Rose Lane, Fayetteville GA 30214, USA | Singer (Maze) |
| **Beverly, Jo**<br>Signet Books, 375 Hudson St, New York NY 10014, USA | Writer |
| **Beverly, Randolph (Randy)**<br>PO Box 193, Monroe Township NJ 08831, USA | Football Player |
| **Bevill, Lisa**<br>Jeff Roberts, 3050 Business Park Circle, #301, Goodlettsville TN 37072, USA | Singer |
| **Bevington, Terry P**<br>2600 Halle Parkway, Collierville TN 38017, USA | Baseball Manager |
| **Bevis, Leslie**<br>Epstein-Wyckoff, 280 S Beverly Dr, #400, Beverly Hills CA 90212 USA | Actress |
| **Bewkes, Jeffrey L (Jeff)**<br>Time Warner, 10 Columbus Circle, New York NY 10019, USA | Businessman |
| **Bex, Shannon**<br>Bad Boy Entertainment, 1440 Broadway, #16, New York NY 10018 USA | Singer (Danity Kane) |
| **Bey, George**<br>Millsaps College, Anthropology Dept, 1701 State St, Jackson MS 39201, USA | Anthropologist |
| **Bey, Richard**<br>445 Park Ave, #1000, New York NY 10022, USA | Entertainer |
| **Beyer, Andy**<br>4237 Lenore Lane NW, Washington DC 20008, USA | Sportswriter |
| **Beyer, Brad**<br>Abrams Artists, 9200 W Sunset Blvd, #1125, West Hollywood CA 90069 USA | Actor |
| **Beyer, Frank M**<br>Academie der Kunste, Hanseatenweg 10, 10557 Berlin, Germany | Composer |
| **Beyer, Markus**<br>Daniela Haak, Niederende 1, 28665 Lilienthal, Germany | Boxer |
| **Beyer, Peter**<br>Albert-Ludwigs-Universitat, Biochemistry Dept, 79104 Freiburg, Germany | Biochemist |
| **Beyer, Tanya**<br>Playboy Promotions, 2706 Media Center Dr, Los Angeles CA 90065 USA | Model |
| **Beyer, Troy**<br>Independent Artists Agency, 9601 Wilshire Blvd, #750, Beverly Hills. CA 90210, USA | Actress, Director |
| **Beymer, Richard**<br>147 N Ridgewood Place, Los Angeles CA 90004, USA | Actor |
| **Bezos, Jeff**<br>Amazon Inc, 1200 12th Ave S, #1200, Seattle WA 98144, USA | Businessman |
| **Bezucha, Thomas G (Tom)**<br>Creative Artists Agency, 2000 Ave of Stars, #100, Los Angeles CA 90067 USA | Director, Writer |
| **BG**<br>Nene Musik Productions, 1460 SW Santiago Ave, Port Saint Lucie FL 34953 USA | Rap Artist (Hot Boys) |
| **Bhanupriya**<br>4 1st Cross St, Vijayaraghava Road, Chennai TN 600017, India | Actress |

*Betker - Bhanupriya*

**Bhardwaj, Mohini** — Gymnast
53 Juergens Ave, Cincinnati OH 45220, USA
**Bhaskar, Sanjeev** — Actor
United Agents, 12-26 Lexington St, London W1F 0LE, England
**Bhattacharya, Sameer** — Guitarist (Flyleaf)
W M E Entertainment, 9601 Wilshire Blvd, #300, Beverly Hills CA 90210 USA
**Bhavsar, Natvar P** — Artist
131 Greene St, New York NY 10012, USA
**Bhraonain, Maire Ni** — Singer, Harpist (Clannad); Songwriter
Soho Agency, 55 Fulham High St, London SW6 3JJ, England
**Bhumibol Adulyadej (Rama IX)** — King, Thailand
Royal Residence, Chitralada Villa, 9 Rama VI Road, Soi 30, Bangkok 10400, Thailand
**Biafra, Jello** — Singer (Dead Kennedys), Songwriter
Agency Group Ltd, 142 W 57th St, #600, New York NY 10019 USA
**Biagiotti, Laura** — Fashion Designer
Biagiotti Group, Via Palombarese Km 17 300, 00012 Guidonia, Italy
**Biakabutuka, Tshimanga (Tim)** — Football Player
110 Sonnys Way, Fort Mill SC 29708, USA
**Biali, Laila** — Singer, Songwriter
Agency Group Ltd, 142 W 57th St, #600, New York NY 10019 USA
**Bialik, Mayim** — Actress
Talent Works, 3500 W Olive Ave, #1400, Burbank CA 91505 USA
**Biancalana, Roland A (Buddy)** — Baseball Player
1204 Lakeview Dr, Fairfield IA 52556, USA
**Bianchi, Alfred A (Al)** — Basketball Player, Coach
Miami Heat, American Airlines Arena, 601 Biscayne Blvd, Miami FL 33132 USA
**Bianchin, Wayne** — Ice Hockey Player
2091 Wellington Road E, Nanaimo BC V9S 5V2, Canada
**Bianco, Esme** — Actress
B/W/R, 9100 Wilshire Blvd, #500W, Beverly Hills CA 90212 USA
**Bianco, Suzannah** — Synchronized Swimmer
Cirque du Soleil, 8400 2nd Ave, Montreal QC H1Z 4M6, Canada
**Biasucci, Dean** — Football Player
3484 Sandy Beach Dr, Canandaigua NY 14424, USA
**Bibb, Leslie** — Actress
I C M Partners, 10250 Constellation Blvd, #900, Los Angeles CA 90067 USA
**Bibby, C Henry** — Basketball Player, Coach
191 Beale St, Memphis TN 38103, USA
**Bibby, Michael (Mike)** — Basketball Player
6439 E Gelding Dr, Scottsdale AZ 85254, USA
**Bichette, A Dante** — Baseball Player
2298 Robin Road, Orlando FL 32814, USA
**Bichir, Demian** — Actor
Creative Artists Agency, 2000 Ave of Stars, #100, Los Angeles CA 90067 USA
**Bickerstaff, Bernard T (Bernie)** — Basketball Coach, Executive
Portland Trail Blazers, Rose Garden, 1 N Center Court St, Portland OR 97227 USA
**Bickett, Duane C** — Football Player
508 Van Dyke Ave, Del Mar CA 92014, USA
**Bickle, Richard (Rich), Jr** — Truck, Auto Racing Driver
Billy Ballew Motorsports, 802A Performance Road, Mooresville NC 28115, USA
**Bidart, Frank** — Writer
Wellesley College, English Dept, 106 Central St, Wellesley MA 02481, USA
**Bidaud, Laurence** — Curling Athlete
Curling Assn, PO Box 606, 3000 Bern, Switzerland
**Biddle, Lee F (Rocky)** — Baseball Player
2031 E Rancho Culebra Dr, Covina CA 91724, USA
**Biddle, Martin** — Archaeologist
19 Hamilton Road, Oxford OX2 7OY, England
**Biden, Joseph R (Joe), Jr** — Vice President; Senator, DE
White House, 1600 Pennsylvania Ave NW, Washington DC 20502, USA
**Bidner, Todd** — Ice Hockey Player
434 Oozloffsky, Petrolia ON N0N 1R0, Canada
**Bidstrup, Jane** — Curling Athlete
Curling Assn, Idraettens Hus, 2605 Brondby, Denmark
**Bidwell, Charles E** — Sociologist
5835 S Kimbark Ave, Chicago IL 60637, USA
**Bidwell, Joshua J (Josh)** — Football Player
11924 Middlebury Dr, Tampa FL 33626, USA
**Bidwell, William V** — Football Executive
Arizona Cardinals, PO Box 888, Phoenix AZ 85001 USA
**Bieber, Justin** — Singer
Creative Artists Agency, 2000 Ave of Stars, #100, Los Angeles CA 90067 USA
**Bieber, Nita** — Actress
PO Box 1889, Avalon CA 90704, USA
**Bieber, Owen F** — Labor Leader
United Auto Workers Union, 8000 E Jefferson Ave, Detroit MI 48214, USA
**Biebl-Prelevic, Heidi** — Alpine Skier
Haus Olympia, 87534 Oberstaufen, Germany
**Biedenbach, Edward (Ed)** — Basketball Player
92 Kimberly Ave, Asheville NC 28804, USA
**Biedermann, Jeanette** — Singer, Actress
One Two Media, Schluter Str 51, 10629 Berlin, Germany
**Biedrins, Andris** — Basketball Player
Utah Jazz, Energy Solutions Arena, 301 W South Temple, Salt Lake City UT 84101 USA
**Biegel, Kevin** — Producer
I C M Partners, 10250 Constellation Blvd, #900, Los Angeles CA 90067 USA
**Biehn, Michael** — Actor
14358 Magnolia Blvd, #229, Sherman Oaks CA 91423, USA
**Bieka, Silvestre Siale** — Prime Minister, Equatorial Guinea
Prime Minister's Office, Malabo, Equatorial Guinea
**Biekert, Greg** — Football Player
2360 Fish Creek Place, Danville CA 94506, USA
**Biel, Jessica** — Actress
L B I Entertainment, 2000 Avenue of Stars, Century City CA 90067, USA
**Bielanko, Dave** — Singer, Songwriter, Guitarist (Marah)
Yep Roc Records, 449A Trollingwood Road, Haw River NC 27258, USA

**Bielanko, Serge** — Singer, Songwriter, Guitarist (Marah)
Yep Roc Records, 449A Trollingwood Road, Haw River NC 27258, USA

**Bielecki, J Krzysztof** — Prime Minister, Poland
European Reconstruction Bank, 1 Exchange Square, London EC2A 2EA, England

**Bielecki, Michael J (Mike)** — Baseball Player
1505 Habersham Place, Crownsville MD 21032, USA

**Bielema, Bret A** — Football Coach
University of Arkansas, Athletic Dept, Fayetteville AR 72701, USA

**Bielke, Donald P (Don)** — Basketball Player
126 Madelia Place, San Ramon CA 94583, USA

**Biellmann, Denise** — Figure Skater
Im Brachli 25, 8053 Zurich, Switzerland

**Bielski, Richard (Dick)** — Football Player
27 Malibu Court, Towson MD 21204, USA

**Bieniemy, Eric** — Football Player
11478 S Carbondale St, Olathe KS 66061, USA

**Bier, Susanne** — Director
Creative Artists Agency, 2000 Ave of Stars, #100, Los Angeles CA 90067 USA

**Bierko, Craig** — Actor, Singer
Impression Entertainment, 9229 W Sunset Blvd, #700 , Los Angeles CA 90069, USA

**Bierman, Bernard (Bernie)** — Songwriter
70 E 10th St, #17C, New York NY 10003, USA

**Bierman, Bruce** — Interior Designer
29 W 15th St, #A, New York NY 10011, USA

**Bierman, Robert** — Director
Independent Talent Group, 40 Whitfield St, London W1T 2RH, England

**Bies, Don** — Golfer
1262 NW Blakely Court, Seattle WA 98177, USA

**Biffi, Giacomo Cardinal** — Religious Leader
Archdiocese of Bologna, Via Altabella 6, 40126 Bologna, Italy

**Biffle, Gregory J (Greg)** — Auto, Truck Racing Driver
8807 Heatherstone Court, Terrell NC 28682, USA

**Big Boi** — Rap Artist (OutKast), Songwriter
4016 Elizabeth Terrace, Rex GA 30273, USA

**Big Daddy Kane** — Rap Artist, Lyricist
Betty of Troy, 100 Lincoln Ave, #12D, Mineola NY 11502, USA

**Big K R I T** — Rap Artist
Agency Group Ltd, 142 W 57th St, #600, New York NY 10019 USA

**Big Sean** — Rap Artist
Agency Group Ltd, 142 W 57th St, #600, New York NY 10019 USA

**Bigbie, Larry R** — Baseball Player
102 Brooke Lane, Centreville MD 21617, USA

**Bigelow, Kathryn A** — Director
Creative Artists Agency, 2000 Ave of Stars, #100, Los Angeles CA 90067 USA

**Biggio, Craig A** — Baseball Player
6520 Belmont St, Houston TX 77005, USA

**Biggs, Don** — Ice Hockey Player
10050 Somerset Dr, Loveland OH 45140, USA

**Biggs, Jason** — Actor
Management 360, 9111 Wilshire Blvd, Beverly Hills CA 90210 USA

**Biggs, John H** — Businessman
240 E 47th St, #47D, New York NY 10017, USA

**Biggs, Peter M** — Veterinarian
Willows, London Road, Saint Ives PE27 5ES, England

**Biggs, Tyrell (Burt)** — Boxer
Scott Schiff, 330 S High St, Columbus OH 43215, USA

**Bigham, John** — Guitarist, Keyboardist (Fishbone)
Silverback Mgmt, 9469 Jefferson Blvd, #101, Culver City CA 90232, USA

**Bigley, Thomas J** — Navy Admiral
20530 Falcons Landing Circle, #3210, Sterling VA 20165, USA

**Biittner, Lawrence D (Larry)** — Baseball Player
915 3rd Ave NW, Pocahontas IA 50574, USA

**Bikel, Theodore** — Actor, Singer
167 Langley Road, Newton Center MA 02459, USA

**Bilal** — Singer, Songwriter
Creative Artists Agency, 2000 Ave of Stars, #100, Los Angeles CA 90067 USA

**Bilardello, Dann J** — Baseball Player
4600 2nd St, Vero Beach FL 32968, USA

**Bilderback, Nicole** — Actress
Rebel Entertainment Partners, 5700 Wilshire Blvd, #456, Los Angeles CA 90036, USA

**Bildt, N D Carl** — Prime Minister, Sweden
Kreab Group, Floragatan 13, 114 75, Stockholm, Sweden

**Bileck, Pamela (Pam)** — Gymnast
2475 Redbud Court, San Jose CA 95128, USA

**Biletnikoff, Frederick (Fred)** — Football Player, Coach
1736 Avondale Dr, Roseville CA 95747, USA

**Bilk, Acker** — Clarinetist, Composer
Acker's Jazz Agency, 53 Cambridge Mansions, Cambridge Road, London SW11 4RX, England

**Bill, Leo** — Actor
Hamilton Hodell, 66-68 Margaret St, #500, London W1W 8SR, England

**Bill, Tony** — Producer, Director, Actor
Barnstorm Films, 73 Market St, Venice CA 90291, USA

**Billick, Brian H** — Football Coach, Sportscaster
836 Stagwell Road, Queenstown MD 21658, USA

**Billing, Roy** — Actor
Sue Barnett Assoc, 1/96 Albion St, Surrey Hills, Sydney 2010, Australia

**Billingham, John E (Jack)** — Baseball Player
625 Faulkner St, New Smyrna FL 32168, USA

**Billinglsey, Ronald S (Ron)** — Football Player
PO Box 2455, Gadsden AL 35903, USA

**Billings, Earl** — Actor
Stone Manners Salners, 9911 W Pico Blvd, #1400, Los Angeles CA 90035 USA

**Billings, Richard A (Dick)** — Baseball Player
1917 Creek Wood Dr, Arlington TX 76006, USA

**Billingslea, Beau** — Actor
Abrams Artists, 9200 W Sunset Blvd, #1125, West Hollywood CA 90069 USA

**Billingsley, Chad R** — Baseball Player
25686 N Sandstone Way, Surprise AZ 85387, USA
**Billingsley, Hobie** — Diving Coach
746 E Pepperridge Dr, Bloomington IN 47401, USA
**Billingsley, John A** — Actor
Stone Manners Salners, 9911 W Pico Blvd, #1400, Los Angeles CA 90035 USA
**Billingsley, Peter** — Actor, Producer
Stone Meyer Genow, 9665 Wilshire Blvd, #510, Beverly Hills CA 90212 USA
**Billingsley, Ray** — Cartoonist (Curtis)
King Features Syndicate, 300 W 57th St, #1500, New York NY 10019 USA
**Billington, Craig** — Ice Hockey Player
Colorado Avalanche, Pepsi Center, 1000 Chopper Circle, Denver CO 80204 USA
**Billington, David P** — Civil Engineer
45 Hodge Road, Princeton NJ 08540, USA
**Billington, Kevin** — Director
Judy Daish Assoc, 2 Saint Charles Place, London W10 6EG, England
**Billups, Chauncey R** — Basketball Player
11 Sandy Lake Road, Englewood CO 80113, USA
**Bilodeau, Jean-Luc** — Actor
Kirk Talent Agencies, 196 W 3rd Ave, #102, Vancouver BC V5Y 1E9, Canada
**Bilson, Bruce** — Director
Downwind Enterprises, 12505 Sarah St, Studio City CA 91604, USA
**Bilson, Malcolm** — Concert Pianist
132 N Sunset Dr, Ithaca NY 14850, USA
**Bilson, Rachel** — Actress
Creative Artists Agency, 2000 Ave of Stars, #100, Los Angeles CA 90067 USA
**Binder, Mike** — Actor, Director, Writer
Verve Talent/Literary Agency, 9696 Culver Blvd, #301, Culver City CA 90232 USA
**Binder, Theodor** — Physician
Taos Canyon, Taos NM 87571, USA
**Bing, David (Dave)** — Basketball Player; Mayor, Detroit
29555 Woodhaven Lane, Southfield MI 48076, USA
**Bing, Jonathan** — Writer
Trident Media Group, 41 Madison Ave, #3600, New York NY 10010, USA
**Bingbing Fan** — Actress
W M E Entertainment, 9601 Wilshire Blvd, #300, Beverly Hills CA 90210 USA
**Binger, Brittany** — Model
Playboy Promotions, 2706 Media Center Dr, Los Angeles CA 90065 USA
**Bingham, Gregory R (Greg)** — Football Player
3710 W Valley Dr, Missouri City TX 77459, USA
**Bingham, Guy R** — Football Player
9214 Keegan Trail, Missoula MT 59808, USA
**Bingham, Ryan** — Singer, Songwriter
Creative Artists Agency, 2000 Ave of Stars, #100, Los Angeles CA 90067 USA
**Bingham, Traci** — Actress, Model
Vincent Cirrincione Assoc, 1516 N Fairfax Ave, Los Angeles CA 90046 USA
**Binion, Jack B** — Poker Player
Wynn Resorts, 3131 Las Vegas Blvd S, Las Vegas NV 89109, USA
**Binkley, Gregg** — Actor
Schachter Entertainment, 1157 S Beverly Dr, #200, Los Angeles CA 90035 USA
**Binmore, Kenneth G** — Economist
Newmills, Whitebrook, Monmouth, Gwent NP5 4TY, England
**Binn, David A (Dave)** — Football Player
2005 Loring St, San Diego CA 92109, USA
**Binnie, W Brian** — Test Pilot
Scaled Composites, Mojave Airport, Hangar 78, Mojave CA 93501, USA
**Binnig, Gerd K** — Nobel Physics Laureate
I B M Research Laboratory, Saumerstr 4, 8803 Ruschlikon, Switzerland
**Binns, Malcolm** — Concert Pianist
Turner Mgmt, 223 Kingston Road, Leatherhead, Surrey KT22 7PE, England
**Binoche, Juliette** — Actress
Untitled Entertainment, 350 S Beverly Dr, #200, Beverly Hills CA 90212 USA
**Bintley, David** — Choreographer
Birmingham Ballet, Thorpe St, Birmingham B5 4AU, England
**Biodrowski, Dennis J (Denny)** — Football Player
1221 N Sylvania Ave, Fort Worth TX 76111, USA
**Biondi, Frank J, Jr** — Businessman
Biondi Reiss Capital Mgmt, 1114 Ave of Americas, New York NY 10036, USA
**Biondi, Matthew N (Matt)** — Swimmer
Parker School, 65-1224 Lindsey Road, Mathematics Dept, Kamuela HI 96743, USA
**Birch, Diane** — Singer, Songwriter
Magus Entertainment, 158 W 23rd St, #2, New York NY 10011, USA
**Birch, L Charles** — Zoologist
5A/73 Yarranabbe Road, Darling Point NSW 2027, Australia
**Birch, Stanley F, Jr** — Judge
US Court of Appeals, 56 Forsyth St NW, Atlanta GA 30303, USA
**Birch, Thora** — Actress
Keep the Peace Productions, PO Box 691675, West Hollywood CA 90069, USA
**Birck, Michael J** — Businessman
Tellabs Inc, 1415 W Diehl Road, Naperville IL 60563, USA
**Bird, Andrew** — Singer, Guitarist, Songwriter
Ekonomisk Mgmt, 3147 W Logan Blvd, #7, Chicago IL 60647, USA
**Bird, Brad** — Animator
Pixar Animation, 1200 Park Ave, Emeryville CA 94608, USA
**Bird, Caroline** — Social Activist, Writer
60 Grammercy Park, New York NY 10010, USA
**Bird, Forrest M** — Inventor (Medical Respirators)
Percussionaire Corp, PO Box 817, Sandpoint ID 83864, USA
**Bird, J Douglas (Doug)** — Baseball Player
11821 Lady Anne Circle, Cape Coral FL 33991, USA
**Bird, Larry J** — Basketball Player, Coach, Executive
4715 Ellery Lane, Indianapolis IN 46250, USA
**Bird, R Byron** — Chemical Engineer
University of Wisconsin, Chemical Engineering Dept, Madison WI 53706, USA
**Bird, Simon** — Actor
Avalon Mgmt, 4A Exmoore St, London W10 68D, England

**B**

**Bird, Suzanne (Sue)** — Basketball Player
Seattle Storm, Key Arena, 351 Elliott Ave W, #500, Seattle WA 98119 USA
**Birden, LaJourdain J (J J)** — Football Player
27743 N 70th St, Scottsdale AZ 85266, USA
**Birdman** — Rap Artist
J L Entertainment, 18653 Ventura Blvd, #340, Los Angeles CA 91356 USA
**Birdsong, Carl** — Football Player
1807 Clubview Dr, Amarillo TX 79124, USA
**Birdsong, Mary** — Actress
United Talent Agency, U T A Plaza, 9336 Civic Center Dr, Beverly Hills CA 90210 USA
**Birdsong, Otis L** — Basketball Player
PO Box 316, Little Rock AR 72203, USA
**Birdy** — Singer, Pianist, Songwriter
Warner Bros Records, 75 Rockefeller Plaza, New York NY 10019 USA
**Bires, Kelly** — Auto Racing Driver
Black Cat Racing, 200 Swiggum Road, Westby WI 54667, USA
**Birgeneau, Robert J** — Physicist, Educator
University of California, Chancellor's Office, University Hall, Berkeley CA 94720, USA
**Birgisson, Jon Thor (Jonsi)** — Singer (Sigur Ros)
Music Road Records, 5012 Brighton Road, Austin TX 78745, USA
**Birk, Matthew R (Matt)** — Football Player
5 Norfolk Court, Reisterstown MD 21136, USA
**Birk, Roger E** — Government Official, Financier
Federal National Mortgage Assn, 3900 Wisconsin Ave NW, Washington DC 20016, USA
**Birkavs, Valdis** — Prime Minister, Latvia
Justice Ministry, Brivbas Blvd 34, 1536 Riga, Latvia
**Birkbeck, Michael L (Mike)** — Baseball Player
1705 W Hill Dr, Orrville OH 44667, USA
**Birkerts, Gunnar** — Architect
Gunnar Birkerts Assoc, 65 Grove St, #241, Wellesley MA 02482, USA
**Birkett, Zoe** — Singer
Fremantle Media, 2700 Colorado Ave, #450, Santa Monica CA 90404 USA
**Birkin, Jane** — Actress
Agence Artiste Adequet, 108 Rue Reaumur, 75002 Paris, France
**Birmingham, Stephen** — Writer
Brandt & Brandt, 1501 Broadway, #2310, New York NY 10036, USA
**Birn, Laura** — Actress
Creative Artists Agency, 2000 Ave of Stars, #100, Los Angeles CA 90067 USA
**Birney, David** — Actor
Bret Adams Agency, 448 W 44th St, New York NY 10036, USA
**Birns, Jack** — Photographer
2021 Castilian Dr, Los Angeles CA 90068, USA
**Biron, Martin** — Ice Hockey Player
488 Willardshire Road, East Aurora NY 14052, USA
**Bironas, J Robert D (Rob)** — Football Player
104 Loring Court, Nashville TN 37220, USA
**Birren, James E** — Gerontologist
University of California, Borun Gerontology Center, Los Angeles CA 90024, USA
**Birthistle, Eva** — Actress
Independent Talent Group, 40 Whitfield St, London W1T 2RH, England
**Birtsas, Timothy D (Tim)** — Baseball Player
PO Box 96, Clarkston MI 48347, USA
**Bisbal Ferre, David** — Singer
Universal Music, 420 Lincoln Road, #200, Miami Beach FL 33139, USA
**Bisby, Frank A** — Biologist
Reading University, Plant Science Laboratories, Reading Berk RG6 6AS, England
**Biscet Gonzalez, Oscar Elias** — Human Rights Activist
Lawton Foundation for Human Rights, PO Box 430905, Miami FL 33243, USA
**Bischof, Ole** — Judo Athlete
Suelburgstr 237, 50937 Cologne, Germany
**Bishe, Kerry** — Actress
Brookside Artist Mgmt, 250 W 57th St, #2303, New York NY 10107 USA
**Bishil, Summer** — Actress
Paul Kohner, 9300 Wilshire Blvd, #555, Beverly Hills CA 90212 USA
**Bishop, Blaine E** — Football Player
PO Box 3082, Brentwood TN 37024, USA
**Bishop, Elvin** — Singer, Guitarist
Blue Mountain Artists, 810 Tyvola Road, #114, Charlotte NC 28217, USA
**Bishop, Harold L** — Football Player
2709 20th Street Ensley, Birmingham AL 35208, USA
**Bishop, J Michael** — Nobel Medicine Laureate, Educator
University of California, Chancellor's Office, San Francisco CA 94143, USA
**Bishop, Keith B** — Football Player
PO Box 131048, Spring TX 77393, USA
**Bishop, Kelly** — Actress
Abrams Artists, 9200 W Sunset Blvd, #1125, West Hollywood CA 90069 USA
**Bishop, Kevin** — Actor
Troika, 74 Clerkenwell Road, #300, London EC1M 5QA, England
**Bishop, Michael L** — Writer
PO Box 646, Pine Mountain GA 31822, USA
**Bishop, Nicholas** — Actor
United Talent Agency, U T A Plaza, 9336 Civic Center Dr, Beverly Hills CA 90210 USA
**Bishop, Richard A** — Football Player
1374 SW 142nd Terrace, Miami FL 33186, USA
**Bishop, Stephen** — Singer, Songwriter
2310 Apollo Dr, Los Angeles CA 90046, USA
**Bishops, Thom** — Actor
Brillstein Entertainment Partners, 9150 Wilshire Blvd, #350, Beverly Hills CA 90212 USA
**Biss, Jonathan** — Concert Pianist
Konzertdirektion Schmid, Konigstra 36, 30175 Hannover, Germany
**Bissell, Charles O** — Editorial Cartoonist
1006 Tower Place, Nashville TN 37204, USA
**Bissell, Charles P (Phil)** — Cartoonist
Cartoon Corner, 4 Cross Hill Circle, Forestdale MA 02644, USA
**Bissell, Jean G** — Judge
US Court of Appeals, 717 Madison Place NW, Washington DC 20439, USA

**Bissell, Mina J** — Physicist
Lawrence Berkeley Laboratory, 1 Cyclotron Road, Berkeley CA 94720, USA
**Bisset, Jacqueline** — Actress
1815 Benedict Canyon Dr, Beverly Hills CA 90210, USA
**Bisson, Thomas N** — Historian
21 Hammond St, Cambridge MA 02138, USA
**Bisson, Yannick** — Actor
Robert Stein Management, 1180 S Beverly Dr, #304, Los Angeles CA 90035, USA
**Bista, Kirti Nidhi** — Prime Minister, Nepal
Gyaneshwor, 4441009 Kathmandu, Nepal
**Bisutti, Danielle** — Actress
Pakula/King, 9229 W Sunset Blvd, #315, West Hollywood CA 90069 USA
**Biswas, Abdul Rahmana** — President, Bangladesh
Residence Dhonmondi, Dhaka, Bangladesh
**Bitsch, Hans-Ullrich** — Architect, Industrial Designer
Kaiser-Wilhelm-Ring 23, RiveGauche, 40545 Dusseldorf-Oberkassel, Germany
**Bittinger, Ned** — Illustrator
1323 Escalante St, Santa Fe NM 87505, USA
**Bittle, Ryan** — Actor
Bauman Redanty Shaul Agency, 5757 Wilshire Blvd, #473, Los Angeles CA 90036 USA
**Bittner, Armin** — Alpine Skier
Rauchbergstr 30, 83334 Izell, Germany
**Bitton, Joshua** — Actor
S M S Talent, 8383 Wilshire Blvd, #230, Beverly Hills CA 90211 USA
**Bitton, Raquel** — Singer
Icon Performing Arts, 1557 Westwood Blvd, #242, Los Angeles CA 90024, USA
**Biya, Paul** — President, Cameroon Republic
Palais de L'Unite, Rue de l'Exploratour, Yaounde, Cameroon
**Biyombo, Bismack** — Basketball Player
Charlotte Bobcats, 333 E Trade St, #A, Charlotte NC 28202 USA
**Biz Markie** — Rap Artist, Comedian
Media Artists Group, 8222 Melrose Ave, #203, Los Angeles CA 90048 USA
**Bizarre** — Rap Artist (D-12)
Coast to Coast Talent, 3350 Barham Blvd, Los Angeles CA 90068 USA
**Bizzy Bone** — Rap Artist (Bone Thugs-N-Harmony)
Entertainment Artists, 2409 21st Ave S, #100, Nashville TN 10019 USA
**Bjedov-Gabrilo, Djurdjica** — Swimmer
Brace Santini 33, 5800 Split, Serbia
**Bjoergen, Marit** — Cross Country Skier
7295 Rognes, Norway
**Bjoerndalen, Ole Einar** — Biathlete
Simostranda, Postboks 516, 3342 Amot, Norway
**Bjork** — Singer, Songwriter, Actress
Quest Mgmt, 36 Marple Way, #1D, London W3 0RG, England
**Bjorken, James D** — Physicist
Stanford Linear Accelerator Center, Stanford University, Stanford CA 94305, USA
**Bjorklund, Anders** — Neurologist
University of Lund, Neurology Dept, 221 00 Lund, Sweden
**Bjorkman, Jonas** — Tennis Player
Funke Promotions, Box 5126, 200 71 Malmo, Sweden
**Bjorkman, Olle E** — Plant Biologist
3040 Greer Road, Palo Alto CA 94303, USA
**Bjorkman, Rubin E** — Ice Hockey Player, Coach
504 Lake St NW, Warroad MN 56763, USA
**Bjorlin, Nadia** — Actress
Don Buchwald, 6500 Wilshire Blvd, #2200, Los Angeles CA 90048 USA
**Bjornson, Eric** — Football Player
40 Orchard Road, Orinda CA 94563, USA
**Bjornson, Karen** — Model
Ford Models Inc, 111 5th Ave, #900, New York NY 10003 USA
**Bjugstad, Scott** — Ice Hockey Player
2874 Lisbon Ave N, Lake Elmo MN 55042, USA
**Blab, Uwe K** — Basketball Player
5993 Mount Gainor, Wimberley TX 78676, USA
**Blacc, Aloe** — Rap Artist
W M E Entertainment, 9601 Wilshire Blvd, #300, Beverly Hills CA 90210 USA
**Blachnik, Gabriele** — Fashion Designer
Blachnik Gabriele KG, Marstallstr 8, 80539 Munich, Germany
**Black of Crossharbour, Conrad M** — Publisher
1 Canada Square, Canary Wharf, London E14 5DT, England
**Black Thought** — Rap Artist (Roots)
Universal Attractions, 135 W 26th St, #1200, New York NY 10019, USA
**Black, B Jordan** — Football Player
4002 Tradewind Circle, Rowlett TX 75088, USA
**Black, Barbara A** — Attorney, Educator
Columbia University, Law School, 435 W 116th St, New York NY 10027, USA
**Black, Bibi** — Concert Trumpeter
Columbia Artists Mgmt Inc, 1790 Broadway, #702, New York NY 10019 USA
**Black, Cathleen P** — Publisher
Hearst Corp, Magazine Division, 250 W 55th St, New York NY 10019, USA
**Black, Claudia** — Actress
S M S Talent, 8383 Wilshire Blvd, #230, Beverly Hills CA 90211 USA
**Black, Clint** — Singer, Songwriter, Actor
W M E Entertainment, 1600 Division St, #300, Nashville TN 37203 USA
**Black, Dennis** — Epidemiologist
University of California Medical Center, 505 Parnassus, San Francisco CA 94122 USA
**Black, Dustin Lance** — Writer
Creative Artists Agency, 2000 Ave of Stars, #100, Los Angeles CA 90067 USA
**Black, Francis (Frank)** — Singer, Guitarist, Songwriter
X-Ray Touring, 77-79 Great Eastern St, #A, London EC2A 3HU, England
**Black, Harry R (Bud)** — Baseball Player, Manager
PO Box 2133, Rancho Santa Fe CA 92067, USA
**Black, Jack** — Actor, Singer, Comedian
W M E Entertainment, 9601 Wilshire Blvd, #300, Beverly Hills CA 90210 USA
**Black, Jake** — Singer (A3)
Conservative Mgmt, 12700 Lake Ave, #2801, Lakewood OH 44107, USA

# B

**Black, James**  
235 Callingwood Place NW, Edmonton AB T5T 2C6, Canada — Ice Hockey Player

**Black, Jay** — Singer (Jay & the Americans)  
Charles Rapp Mgmt, 10775 Santa Laguna Dr, Boca Raton FL 33428, USA

**Black, Jully** — Singer, Songwriter  
Agency Group Ltd, 142 W 57th St, #600, New York NY 10019 USA

**Black, Lewis** — Actor, Comedian, Writer  
A P A Talent/Literary Agency, 405 S Beverly Dr, #300, Beverly Hills CA 90212 USA

**Black, Lucas** — Actor  
I C M Partners, 10250 Constellation Blvd, #900, Los Angeles CA 90067 USA

**Black, Mary** — Singer  
International Music Network, 278 Main St, #400, Gloucester MA 01930 USA

**Black, Michael Ian** — Actor, Puppeteer, Producer  
United Talent Agency, U T A Plaza, 9336 Civic Center Dr, Beverly Hills CA 90210 USA

**Black, P Michael (Mike)** — Football Player  
5690 Stonekirk Place NW, Acworth GA 30101, USA

**Black, Pippa** — Actress  
Aran Michael Mgmt, 118 Caroline St, South Yarra VIC 3141, Australia

**Black, Robert L** — Pediatrician  
976 Mesa Road, Monterey CA 93940, USA

**Black, Ron** — Religious Leader  
General Baptist Ministries, 100 Stinson Dr, Poplar Bluff MO 63901, USA

**Black, Roy** — Attorney  
Black Strebnick Kornspan Stumpf, 201 S Biscayne Blvd, #1300, Miami FL 33131, USA

**Black, Shane** — Director, Writer  
W M E Entertainment, 9601 Wilshire Blvd, #300, Beverly Hills CA 90210 USA

**Black, Shirley Temple** — Actress, Diplomat  
O'Melveney & Myers, 1999 Ave of Stars, #700, Los Angeles CA 90067, USA

**Black, Susan H** — Judge  
US Court of Appeals, 311 W Monroe St, Jacksonville FL 32202, USA

**Blackburn, Ade** — Singer, Guitarist (Clinic)  
Windish Agency, 1658 N Milwaukee Ave, #211, Chicago IL 60647, USA

**Blackburn, Chase W** — Football Player  
562 Wagonwheel Lane, Marysville OH 43040, USA

**Blackburn, Don** — Ice Hockey Player  
637 S Owl Dr, Sarasota FL 34236, USA

**Blackburn, Elizabeth H** — Nobel Medicine Laureate  
294 Yerba Buena Ave, San Francisco CA 94127, USA

**Blackburn, Tyler** — Actor  
Gersh Agency, 9465 Wilshire Blvd, #600, Beverly Hills CA 90212 USA

**Blackburn, Woody T** — Golfer  
Frank W Brown Assoc, PO Box 215, Orange Park FL 32067, USA

**Blackledge, Bob** — Journalist  
Birmingham News, Editorial Dept, 2701 4th Ave N, Birminhgam AL 35203, USA

**Blackledge, Todd A** — Football Player, Sportscaster  
2711 Glenmont Dr NW, Canton OH 44708, USA

**Blackman, Cindy** — Jazz, Rock Drummer  
BookArts Co, 6404 Wilshire Blvd, #1750, Los Angeles CA 90048, USA

**Blackman, Honor** — Actress  
N S M, Clapham North Arts Center, Voltaire Road, London SW4 6DH, England

**Blackman, Rolando A** — Basketball Player, Sportscaster  
14902 Preston Road, #404, Dallas TX 75254, USA

**Blackman, Steve** — Professional Wrestler  
Steve Blackman Fighting Systems, 2200 Paxton St, Harrisburg PA 17111, USA

**Blackmar, Philip A (Phil)** — Golfer  
4420 Janssen Dr, Corpus Christi TX 78411, USA

**Blackmon, Donald K (Don)** — Football Player  
4340 Lansfaire Terrace, Suwanee GA 30024, USA

**Blackmon, Douglas A** — Writer  
Wall Street Journal, 303 Peachtree St NE, #4200, Atlanta GA 30308, USA

**Blackmon, Larry E** — Singer (Cameo)  
Mercury Records, 11150 Santa Monica Blvd, #1000, Los Angeles CA 90025 USA

**Blackmon, Robert J (Bob)** — Football Player  
70 Glenwood N, Van Vleck TX 77482, USA

**Blackmore, Richard H (Ritchie)** — Singer, Guitarist (Deep Purple, Rainbow)  
Performers of the World, 5657 Wilshire Blvd, #280, Los Angeles CA 90036 USA

**Blackmore, Stephanie** — Actress  
Chateau-Billings, 5667 Wilshire Blvd, #340, Los Angeles CA 90036, USA

**Blackshear, Jeffrey L (Jeff)** — Football Player  
9229 Christo Court, Owings Mill MD 21117, USA

**Blackwelder, Myra** — Golfer  
2009 Hill Gail Way, Versailles KY 40383, USA

**Blackwell, Alfonzo** — Jazz Saxophonist, Composer  
Celebrity Talent Agency, 111 E 14th St, #249, New York NY 10003, USA

**Blackwell, Nathaniel (Nate)** — Basketball Player  
1926 S 22nd St, Philadelphia PA 19145, USA

**Blackwell, Simon** — Producer, Writer  
P B J Mgmt, 5 Soho Square, London W1D 3QA, England

**Blackwell, Timothy P (Tim)** — Baseball Player  
8854 Whiteport Lane, San Diego CA 92119, USA

**Blackwell, William H (Will), Jr** — Football Player  
6168 Seneca Circle, Discovery Bay CA 94505, USA

**Blackwood, Ariel** — Actress  
Coast to Coast Talent, 3350 Barham Blvd, Los Angeles CA 90068 USA

**Blackwood, Sarah** — Singer (Dubstar)  
Primary Talent International, 2-12 Petonville Road, London N1 9PL, England

**Blacque, Taurean** — Actor  
5049 Rock Springs Road, Lithonia GA 30038, USA

**Bladd, Stephen Jo** — Singer, Drummer (J Geils Band)  
Nick Ben-Meir, 652 N Doheny Dr, West Hollywood CA 90069, USA

**Blade, Brian** — Jazz Drummer (Black Dub)  
Ted Kurland, 173 Brighton Ave, Boston MA 02134 USA

**Blade, Danielle** — Artist  
Gartner & Blade, 4-1354 Kuhio Highway, Kapaa HI 96746, USA

**Blades, H Benedict (Bennie)** — Football Player  
5124 NW 30th Lane, Fort Lauderdale FL 33309, USA

**Blades, Ruben** — Singer, Songwriter, Actor
W M E Entertainment, 9601 Wilshire Blvd, #300, Beverly Hills CA 90210 USA

**Bladon, Tom** — Ice Hockey Player
2595 Wilcox Terrace, Victoria, BC V8Z 7G5, Canada

**Blagden, George** — Actor
Paradigm Agency, 360 N Crescent Dr, North Building, Beverly Hills CA 90210 USA

**Blaha, John E** — Astronaut
346 Whitestone Dr, Spring Branch TX 78070, USA

**Blahak, Joseph P (Joe)** — Football Player
4040 N 21st St, Lincoln NE 68521, USA

**Blahnik, Manolo** — Fashion Designer
49-51 Old Church St, London SW3 5BS, England

**Blahoski, Alana** — Ice Hockey Player
60 E 9th St, #315, New York NY 10003, USA

**Blaine, David** — Illusionist
W M E Entertainment, 9601 Wilshire Blvd, #300, Beverly Hills CA 90210 USA

**Blaine, Edward H (Ed)** — Football Player
4 E Clarkson Road, Columbia MO 65203, USA

**Blaine, Jason** — Singer, Songwriter
Agency Group Ltd, 142 W 57th St, #600, New York NY 10019 USA

**Blaine, Nell** — Artist
210 Riverside Dr, #8A, New York NY 10025, USA

**Blair, A Matthew (Matt)** — Football Player
16725 43rd Ave N, Minneapolis MN 55446, USA

**Blair, Anthony C L (Tony)** — Prime Minister, England
PO Box 60519, London W2 7JU, England

**Blair, Bonnie** — Speed Skater
306 White Pine Road, Delafield WI 53018, USA

**Blair, Charles (Chuck)** — Ice Hockey Player
869 Niagara Parkway, Fort Erie ON L2A 5M4, Canada

**Blair, DeJuan L** — Basketball Player
Dallas Mavericks, Pavilion, 2909 Taylor St, Dallas TX 75226 USA

**Blair, Dennis C** — Navy Admiral
National Intelligence Department, 725 17th St NW, Washington DC 20523 USA

**Blair, George** — Ice Hockey Player
61 Kingsnill St, Fort Erie ON L2A 4E5, Canada

**Blair, Isla** — Actress
Curtis Brown Group, 28-29 Haymarket St, #500, London SW1Y 4SP, England

**Blair, Linda** — Actress
Almond Talent Agency, 8217 Beverly Blvd, #8, West Hollywood CA 90048, USA

**Blair, M June** — Model, Actress
Playboy Promotions, 2706 Media Center Dr, Los Angeles CA 90065 USA

**Blair, Marie-Claire** — Writer
4411 Rue Saint Denis, #401, Montreal QC H2J 2LN, Canada

**Blair, Paul L D** — Baseball Player
4177 Lotus Circle, Ellicott City MD 21043, USA

**Blair, Selma** — Actress
Gersh Agency, 9465 Wilshire Blvd, #600, Beverly Hills CA 90212 USA

**Blair, Wayne** — Director
Shanahan Mgmt, Berman House, 91 Campbell St, #300, Surry Hills NSW 2010, Australia

**Blair, William (Bill)** — Baseball Player
1411 E Red Bird Lane, Dallas TX 75241, USA

**Blair, William (Bill)** — Astronomer, Space Scientist
Johns Hopkins University, Astronomy Dept, Baltimore MD 21218, USA

**Blair, William E (Willie)** — Baseball Player
62 Elder Lane, Pikeville KY 41501, USA

**Blair, William M, Jr** — Attorney, Diplomat
435 E 52nd St, #6B, New York NY 10022, USA

**Blais, Richard** — Chef
Home Restaurant, 111 W Paces Ferry Road NE, Atlanta GA 30305, USA

**Blake Nelson, Tim** — Actor, Director, Writer
Gateway Mgmt, 860 Via de la Paz, #F10, Pacific Palisades CA 90272, USA

**Blake, Francis (Frank)** — Businessman
Home Depot Inc, 2455 Paces Ferry Road NW, Atlanta GA 30339, USA

**Blake, Geoffrey** — Actor
Talent Works, 3500 W Olive Ave, #1400, Burbank CA 91505 USA

**Blake, James** — Tennis Player
35 Prospect Road, Westport CT 6880, USA

**Blake, Jason** — Ice Hockey Player
10 Meadow Lane, Glen Head NY 11545, USA

**Blake, Jay Don** — Golfer
2859 Calle del Sol, Saint George UT 84790, USA

**Blake, Jeffrey B C (Jeff)** — Football Player
5821 Sunset Ridge, Austin TX 78735, USA

**Blake, John C** — Artist
Oz Voorburgwal 131, 1012 Amsterdam ER, Netherlands

**Blake, Johnathan** — Drummer (Donny McCaslin Trio)
Greenleaf Records, PO Box 477364, Chicago IL 60647 USA

**Blake, Josh** — Actor
C E S D, 10635 Santa Monica Blvd, #130, Los Angeles CA 90025 USA

**Blake, Norman** — Guitarist, Mandolin Player
Scott O'Malley Assoc, PO Box 9188, Colorado Springs CO 80932, USA

**Blake, Norman** — Singer, Guitarist (Teenage Fanclub)
High Road Touring, 751 Bridgeway, #200, Sausalito CA 94965 USA

**Blake, Peter T** — Artist
Waddington Galleries, 11 Cork St, London W1X 1PD, England

**Blake, Robert** — Actor
Thomas Mesereau, 3055 Wilshire Blvd, #600, Los Angeles CA 90010, USA

**Blake, Robert B (Rob)** — Ice Hockey Player
75 Dwyer St, Buffalo NY 14224, USA

**Blake, Stephanie** — Actress
15101 Magnolia Blvd, #E12, Sherman Oaks CA 91403, USA

**Blake, Steven H (Steve)** — Basketball Player
3479 Cascade Terrace, West Linn OR 97068, USA

**Blake, Susie** — Actress
Gavin Barker Assoc, 2D Wimpole St, London W1G 0EB, England

# B

**Blake, W Casey** — Baseball Player
8224 150th Ave, Indianola IA 50125, USA
**Blakely, Susan** — Actress, Model
Jaffe Co, 9663 Santa Monica Blvd, #214, Beverly Hills CA 90210, USA
**Blakemore, Colin B** — Neurophysiologist, Physiologist
University Laboratory of Physiology, Parks Road, Oxford OX1 3PT, England
**Blakemore, Michael H** — Director, Actor, Writer
18 Upper Park Road, London NW3 2UP, England
**Blakeney, Larry** — Football Coach
Troy University, Athletic Dept, Troy AL 36082, USA
**Blakenham, Michael J** — Businessman
House of Lords, Westminster, London SW1A 0PW, England
**Blaker, Clay** — Singer, Songwriter
Texas Sounds Entertainment, 2317 Pecan St, Dickinson TX 77539, USA
**Blakey, G Robert** — Attorney, Educator
947 Riverside Dr, South Bend IN 46616, USA
**Blakey, Lynn** — Singer (Tres Chicas)
Conqueroo, 11271 Ventura Blvd, #522, Studio City CA 91604 USA
**Blakey, Marion** — Government Official
Aerospace Industries Assn, 1000 Wilson Blvd, #1700, Arlington VA 22209, USA
**Blakiston, Caroline** — Actress
Coolwaters Productions, 10061 Riverside Dr, Box 531, Toluca Lake CA 91602 USA
**Blakley, Ronee** — Actress, Singer
1404 Fairview Ave, Caldwell ID 83605, USA
**Blalack, Robert** — Cinematographer
12251 Huston St, Valley Village CA 91607, USA
**Blalock, Hank J** — Baseball Player
8797 Adobe Bluffs Dr, San Diego CA 92129, USA
**Blalock, Jane** — Golfer
197 8th St, #300, Charlestown MA 02129, USA
**Blalock, Jolene** — Actress
W M E Entertainment, 9601 Wilshire Blvd, #300, Beverly Hills CA 90210 USA
**Blanc, Dominique** — Actress
Les Visiteurs du Soir, 40 Rue de la Folie Regnault, 75011 Paris, France
**Blanc, Georges** — Restauranteur
Le Mere Blanc, 01540 Vonnas, Ain, France
**Blanc, Jennifer** — Actress
Blancbiehn Productions, 10990 Wilshire Blvd, #800, Los Angeles CA 90024, USA
**Blanc, Manuel** — Actor
Cineart, 28 Rue Mogador, 78009 Paris, France
**Blanc, Raymond R A** — Restauranteur
Le Manoir, Church Road, Great Milton, Oxford OX44 7PD, England
**Blancas, Homero, Jr** — Golfer
6826 Queensclub Dr, Houston TX 77069, USA
**Blanchard, James J** — Governor, MI; Diplomat
426 4th St NE, Washington DC 20002, USA
**Blanchard, Kenneth** — Writer, Business Consultant
2048 Aldergrove, #B, Escondido CA 92029, USA
**Blanchard, Olivier J** — Economist
Massachusetts Institute of Technology, Economics Dept, Cambridge MA 02139, USA
**Blanchard, R Cary** — Football Player
6616 NW 127th St, Oklahoma City OK 73142, USA
**Blanchard, Rachel** — Actress
Luber Rocklin Entertainment, 8530 Wilshire Blvd, #555, Beverly Hills CA 90211 USA
**Blanchard, Tammy** — Actress, Singer
I C M Partners, 10250 Constellation Blvd, #900, Los Angeles CA 90067 USA
**Blanchard, Terence** — Jazz Trumpeter, Composer
91 English Turn Dr, New Orleans LA 70131, USA
**Blanchard, Thomas R (Tom)** — Football Player
217 Independence Dr, Grants Pass OR 97527, USA
**Blanchett, Cate** — Actress
Robyn Gardiner Mgmt, PO Box 128, Surrey Hills NSW 2010, Australia
**Blanckaert, Myriam** — Actress
Agents Associes, 201 Rue du Faubourg Saint Honore, 75008 Paris, France
**Blanco, Cuauhtemoc** — Soccer Player
Chicago Fire, 700 S Harlem Ave, Bridgeview IL 60455 USA
**Blanco, Henry R** — Baseball Player
5510 N 132nd Dr, Litchfield Park AZ 85340, USA
**Blanco, Roberto** — Singer, Actor
Rotbuchenstr 25, 81547 Munich, Germany
**Blanco-Cervantes, Raul** — President, Costa Rica
Apdo 918, San Jose, Costa Rica
**Bland, Carl N** — Football Player
1985 Crossbridge Court, Saint Charles MO 63303, USA
**Bland, John** — Golfer
PO Box 451436, Westlake OH 44145, USA
**Blandford, Roger D** — Astronomer
California Institute of Technology, Astrophysics Dept, Pasadena CA 91125, USA
**Blaney, Dave** — Auto Racing Driver
211 N Emily Court, High Point NC 27265, USA
**Blaney, George R** — Basketball Player
1633 Main St, Glastonbury CT 06033, USA
**Blanford, Lawrence J (Larry)** — Cinematographer
210 5th Ave, Venice CA 90291, USA
**Blank, Arthur M** — Businessman
1080 W Paces Ferry Road NW, Atlanta GA 30327, USA
**Blank, Boris** — Synthesizer Player (Yello)
Creative Artists Agency, 2000 Ave of Stars, #100, Los Angeles CA 90067 USA
**Blank, Rebecca M** — Secretary, Commerce
Commerce Department, 14th St & Constitution Ave NW, Washington DC 20230 USA
**Blankenbuehler, Andy** — Choreographer, Dancer
W M E Entertainment, 9601 Wilshire Blvd, #300, Beverly Hills CA 90210 USA
**Blankenship, Lance R** — Baseball Player
340 Kimberwicke Court, Alamo CA 94507, USA
**Blankfein, Lloyd C** — Financier
Goldman Sachs Co, 85 Broad St, Building 85, New York NY 10004, USA

**Blankfield, Mark** — Actor
K & K Entertainment, 1498 W Sunset Blvd, Los Angeles CA 90026 USA
**Blanks, Billie, Jr** — Actor
W M E Entertainment, 9601 Wilshire Blvd, #300, Beverly Hills CA 90210 USA
**Blanks, Billy** — Physical Fitness Expert
Tae Bo, 7095 Hollywood Blvd, #500, Los Angeles CA 90028, USA
**Blanks, Larvell** — Baseball Player
PO Box 562, Del Rio TX 78841, USA
**Blanks, Sidney (Sid)** — Football Player
4402 Warm Springs Road, Houston TX 77035, USA
**Blanton, Arell** — Actor
4191 Greenbush Ave, Sherman Oaks CA 91423, USA
**Blanton, Dain** — Volleyball Player
1615 Stoner Ave, #3, Los Angeles CA 90025, USA
**Blanton, Gerald (Jerry)** — Football Player
1942 Calumet Ave, Toledo OH 43607, USA
**Blany, David (Dave)** — Auto Racing Driver
Randy Humphrey Assoc, 18636 Starcreek Dr, Cornelius NC 28031, USA
**Blasco, Chuck** — Singer (Vogues)
Media Promotion Enterprises, 423 6th Ave, Huntington WV 25701, USA
**Blashford-Snell, John N** — Explorer
Exploration Society, Motcome, Shaftesbury, Dorset SP7 9PB, England
**Blasi, Rosa** — Actress
Untitled Entertainment, 350 S Beverly Dr, #200, Beverly Hills CA 90212 USA
**Blasingame, Wade A** — Baseball Player
5207 Riverhill Road, Marietta GA 30068, USA
**Blass, Stephen R (Steve)** — Baseball Player
1756 Quigg Dr, Pittsburgh PA 15241, USA
**Blasucci, Richard (Dick)** — Actor, Producer
A P A Talent/Literary Agency, 405 S Beverly Dr, #300, Beverly Hills CA 90212 USA
**Blatche, Andray** — Basketball Player
15053 Doral Place, Haymarket VA 20169, USA
**Blatt, Melanie R** — Singer
Concorde International, 101 Shepherds Bush Road, London W6 7LP, England
**Blatter, Joseph S (Sepp)** — Soccer Executive
Federation International Football Assn, Hitzigweg 11, 8030 Zurich, Switzerland
**Blatty, William Peter** — Writer
7018 Longwood Dr, Bethesda MD 20817, USA
**Blatz, Kelly** — Actor
Luber Rocklin Entertainment, 8530 Wilshire Blvd, #555, Beverly Hills CA 90211 USA
**Blau, Daniel** — Artist
Belgradstr 26, 80796 Munich, Germany
**Blau, Peter M** — Sociologist
7019 Old NC 86, Chapel Hill NC 27516, USA
**Blauner, Peter** — Writer
Warner Books, 1271 Ave of Americas, New York NY 10020 USA
**Blauser, Jeffrey M (Jeff)** — Baseball Player
6080 Carlisle Lane, Alpharetta GA 30022, USA
**Blaustein, Barry W** — Director
Creative Artists Agency, 2000 Ave of Stars, #100, Los Angeles CA 90067 USA
**Blaylock, Anthony D** — Football Player
88 Brighton Dr, Garner NC 27529, USA
**Blaylock, Caroline** — Golfer
232 Hennon Dr NW, Rome GA 30165, USA
**Blaylock, Daron O (Mookie)** — Basketball Player
1017 Gresham Road, Zebulon GA 30295, USA
**Blaylock, Derrick D** — Football Player
1471 Edgewater Road, Crown Point IN 46307, USA
**Blaylock, Kenneth T** — Labor Leader
American Government Employees, 80 F St NW, #700, Washington DC 20001, USA
**Blayton, Anitra** — Sculptor
Tarrant County College, Art Dept, 828 W Harwood Road, Hurst TX 76054, USA
**Blazelowski, Carol A** — Basketball Player, Executive
126 Walnut St, Nutley NJ 07110, USA
**Blechacz, Rafal** — Concert Pianist
Konzertdirektion Schmid, Konigstra 36, 30175 Hannover, Germany
**Bledel, Alexis** — Actress, Model
New Wave Entertainment, 2660 W Olive Ave, Burbank CA 91505, USA
**Bledsoe, Drew** — Football Player
845 Delrey Road, Whitefish MT 59937, USA
**Bledsoe, Tempestt** — Actress
House of Representatives, 1434 6th St, #1, Santa Monica CA 90401 USA
**Bleeth, Yasmine** — Actress
Gersh Agency, 9465 Wilshire Blvd, #600, Beverly Hills CA 90212 USA
**Blegen, Judith** — Opera Singer
91 Central Park West, #1B, New York NY 10023, USA
**Blehm, Gary** — Cartoonist (Penmen)
PO Box 60607, Colorado Springs CO 80960, USA
**Bleibtreu, Moritz** — Actor
Voyez Mon Agent, 20 Ave Rapp, 75007 Paris, France
**Bleier, Robert P (Rocky)** — Football Player
929 Osage Road, Pittsburgh PA 15243, USA
**Bleifeld, Stanley** — Sculptor
27 Spring Valley Road, Weston CT 06883, USA
**Bleiler, Gretchen** — Snowboard Athlete
PO Box 5774, Snowmass Village CO 81615, USA
**Blessed, Brian** — Actor
Associated International Mgmt, 7 Hatten Garden, #400, London EC1N 8AD, England
**Blessed, Rosalind** — Actress
Associated International Mgmt, 7 Hatten Garden, #400, London EC1N 8AD, England
**Blessen, Karen A** — Journalist, Illustrator
Karen Blessen Illustration, 6327 Vickery Blvd, Dallas TX 75214, USA
**Blessing, Jack** — Actor
Golan & Blumberg, 6528 W 6th St, Los Angeles CA 90048, USA
**Blethen, Frank A** — Publisher
Seattle Times, Publisher's Office, 1120 John St, Seattle WA 98109, USA

**Blethyn, Brenda A** — Actress
I C M Partners, 10250 Constellation Blvd, #900, Los Angeles CA 90067 USA
**Bleu, Corbin** — Actor, Singer
James/Levy Mgmt, 3500 W Olive Ave, #1470, Burbank CA 91505 USA
**Blevins, Ronnie Gene** — Actor
Glick Agency, 1321 7th St, #203, Santa Monica CA 90401 USA
**Bley, Carla B** — Composer, Jazz Pianist
Ted Kurland, 173 Brighton Ave, Boston MA 02134 USA
**Bley, Paul** — Jazz Pianist, Composer
Improvising Artists, PO Box 496, Cherry Valley NY 13320, USA
**Blieden, Michael** — Actor, Writer
A K A Talent, 6310 San Vicente Blvd, #200, Los Angeles CA 90048 USA
**Blier, Bertrand** — Director
11 Rue Margueritte, 75017 Paris, France
**Blige, Mary J** — Rap Artist, Singer
Creative Artists Agency, 2000 Ave of Stars, #100, Los Angeles CA 90067 USA
**Blilie, Hannah** — Drummer (Gossip)
Shotclock Mgmt, 20312 NE 259th St, Battle Ground WA 98604, USA
**Blim, Richard D** — Pediatrician
304 W 172nd St, Belton MO 64012, USA
**Blinder, Alan S** — Government Official, Financier
Princeton University, Economics Dept, Fischer Hall, Princeton NJ 08544, USA
**Blinka, Stanley J (Stan)** — Football Player
3304 Carriage Dr, Export PA 15632, USA
**Blinks, Susan** — Equestrian
362 Vista del Rey Dr, Encinitas CA 92024, USA
**Bliss, Boti** — Actress
Stone Manners Salners, 9911 W Pico Blvd, #1400, Los Angeles CA 90035 USA
**Bliss, Caroline** — Actress
Rights House, Drury House, 34-43 Russell St, London WC2B 5HA, England
**Bliss, Julian** — Concert Clarinetist
I M G Artists, Hogarth Business Park, Chiswick, London W4 2TH, England
**Bliss, Michael (Mike)** — Auto Racing Driver
156 Mariner Pointe Lane, Mooresville NC 28117, USA
**Blitt, Ricky** — Writer, Producer
Smart Entertainment, 9595 Wilshire Blvd, #900, Beverly Hills CA 90212, USA
**Blitz, Jeffrey** — Director, Writer
Creative Artists Agency, 2000 Ave of Stars, #100, Los Angeles CA 90067 USA
**Blitzer, Wolf** — Commentator
8929 Holly Leaf Lane, Bethesda MD 20817, USA
**Blix, Hans M** — Government Official
Curtis Brown Group, 28-29 Haymarket, London SW1Y 4SP, England
**Blobel, Gunter K-J** — Nobel Medicine Laureate
1100 Park Ave, #10D, New York NY 10128, USA
**Bloch, Erich** — Electrical Engineer, Computer Scientist
National Science Foundation, 1800 C St NW, Washington DC 20002, USA
**Bloch, Phillip** — Actor, Fashion Designer
Grand Central Publishing, 237 Park Ave, #1300, New York NY 10017, USA
**Block, Gene D** — Educator
University of California, Chancellor's Office, Los Angeles CA 90024, USA
**Block, Hunt** — Actor
Don Buchwald, 6500 Wilshire Blvd, #2200, Los Angeles CA 90048 USA
**Block, John R** — Secretary, Agriculture
National Wholesale Grocers Assn, 201 Park Washington, Falls Church VA 22046, USA
**Block, John W** — Basketball Player
1069 Santa Barbara St, San Diego CA 92107, USA
**Block, Lawrence** — Writer
299 W 12th St, #12D, New York NY 10014, USA
**Block, Lawrence J (Larry)** — Actor
Gage Group, 14724 Ventura Blvd, #505, Sherman Oaks CA 91403 USA
**Block, Ned J** — Philosopher
96 Ellery St, #2, Cambridge MA 02138, USA
**Block, Ron** — Singer, Banjo Player (Union Station)
Rounder Records, 1 Rounder Way, Burlington MA 01803 USA
**Block, Susan** — Artist
2725 Bentley Road, Highland Park IL 60035, USA
**Blocker, Dirk** — Actor
5063 La Ramada Dr, Santa Barbara CA 93111, USA
**Bloemberg, Jeff** — Ice Hockey Player
170 Diagonal Road, Wingham ON N0G 1W0, Canada
**Bloembergen, Nicolaas** — Nobel Physics Laureate
13835 E Langtree Lane, Tucson AZ 85747, USA
**Blokhuijsen, Jan** — Speed Skater
K N S B, Postbus 1120, 3800 BC Arnesfoort, Netherlands
**Blomberg, Ronald M (Ron)** — Baseball Player
11660 Mountain Laurel Dr, Roswell GA 30075, USA
**Blomdahl, Benjamin E (Ben)** — Baseball Player
9 Emmy Lane, Ladera Ranch CA 92694, USA
**Blomkamp, Neill** — Director, Writer
W M E Entertainment, 9601 Wilshire Blvd, #300, Beverly Hills CA 90210 USA
**Blomqvist, Timo P** — Ice Hockey Player
Helsinki Ligaforeningen H I F K Road, Mantytie 23, 00270 Helsinki, Finland
**Blomstedt, Herbert T** — Conductor
Columbia Artists Mgmt Inc, 1790 Broadway, #702, New York NY 10019 USA
**Blong, Jenni** — Actress
Judy Schoen, 606 N Larchmont Blvd, #309, Los Angeles CA 90004 USA
**Blonsky, Nikki** — Actress, Singer
Innovative Artists, 1505 10th St, Santa Monica CA 90401 USA
**Blood, Edward J** — Skier, Skiing Official
2 Beech Hill, Durham NH 03824, USA
**Bloodgood, Moon** — Actress, Model
United Talent Agency, U T A Plaza, 9336 Civic Center Dr, Beverly Hills CA 90210 USA
**Bloom, Amy** — Writer, Psychotherapist
Gillon Aitken Assoc, 18-21 Cavaye Place, London SW10 9PT, England
**Bloom, Brian** — Actor
Osbrink Talent Agency, 4343 Lankershim Blvd, #100, North Hollywood CA 91602 USA

**Bloom, Brooke** — Actress
Talent Works, 3500 W Olive Ave, #1400, Burbank CA 91505 USA
**Bloom, Claire** — Actress
Clive Conway, 32 Grove St, Oxford OX2 TJT, England
**Bloom, Floyd E** — Physician
628 Pacific View Dr, San Diego CA 92109, USA
**Bloom, Harold** — Educator, Writer
179 Linden St, New Haven CT 06511, USA
**Bloom, Jane Ira** — Jazz Saxophonist, Composer
Joel Chriss Co, 300 Mercer St, #3J, New York NY 10003 USA
**Bloom, Jeremy** — Alpine Skier, Football Player
PO Box 770-311, Park City UT 84060, USA
**Bloom, John** — Editor
Independent Talent Group, 40 Whitfield St, London W1T 2RH, England
**Bloom, Lindsay** — Actress
3751 Recklaw, Studio City CA 91604, USA
**Bloom, Luka** — Singer, Guitarist, Songwriter
Howlin' Wuelf Media, 527 Barclay Ave, Morrisville PA 19067, USA
**Bloom, Matthew J (Matt)** — Professional Wrestler
New Japan Dojo, PM Box 1245, 1223 Wilshire Blvd, Santa Monica CA 90403, USA
**Bloom, Mike** — Ice Hockey Player
227 School Road, Delanson NY 12053, USA
**Bloom, Orlando** — Actor
Viddywell Productions, 1041 N Formosa Ave, Formosa Building, West Hollywood CA 90046, USA
**Bloom, Scott** — Actor
11 Croydon Court, Dix Hills NY 11746, USA
**Bloom, Ursula** — Writer
Newton House, Walls Dr, Ravenglass, Cumbria CA18 1SQ, England
**Bloom, Vail** — Actress
C E S D, 10635 Santa Monica Blvd, #130, Los Angeles CA 90025 USA
**Bloom, Verna** — Actress
327 E 82nd St, New York NY 10028, USA
**Bloomberg, Michael R** — Mayor, New York City; Publisher
Mayor's Office, Gracie Mansion, New York NY 10007, USA
**Bloomfield, Michael J (Mike)** — Astronaut
14302 Autumn Canyon Trace, Houston TX 77062, USA
**Bloomfield, Sara** — Museum Director
Holocaust Memorial Museum, 100 Wallenberg Place SW, Washington DC 20024, USA
**Bloomquist, William P (Willie)** — Baseball Player
7026 E Blue Sky Dr, Scottsdale AZ 85266, USA
**Blotzer, Robert J (Bobby)** — Drummer (Ratt)
Paradise Artists, PO Box 1821, Ojai CA 93024 USA
**Blount, Corie K** — Basketball Player
5427 Kytes Lane, Liberty Township OH 45044, USA
**Blount, Mark D** — Basketball Player
5723 High Flyer Road S, Palm Beach Gardens FL 33418, USA
**Blount, Melvin C (Mel)** — Football Player, Executive
Mel Blount Youth Home, 6 Mel Blount Dr, Claysville PA 15323, USA
**Blount, Winton M, III** — Businessman
Blount Inc, 4909 SE International Way, Portland OR 97222, USA
**Blow, Kurtis** — Rap Artist
Green Light Talent Agency, PO Box 3172, Beverly Hills CA 90212 USA
**Blowers, Michael R (Mike)** — Baseball Player
22211 42nd Ave E, Spanaway WA 98387, USA
**Blowfly** — Singer, Rap Artist
Pandisc Music, 15982 NW 48th Ave, Hialeah FL 33014, USA
**Blubaugh, Douglas M (Doug)** — Freestyle Wrestler
6640 N Utt Dr, Bloomington IN 47408, USA
**Blucas, Marcus (Marc)** — Actor
Anonymous Content, 3532 Hayden Ave, Culver City CA 90232 USA
**Blue, Angel** — Opera Singer
I M G Artists, Hogarth Business Park, Chiswick, London W4 2TH, England
**Blue, Callum** — Actor
Ken McReddie Assoc, 101 Finsbury Pavement, London EC2A 1RS, England
**Blue, John** — Ice Hockey Player, Coach
2301 Half Moon Lane, Costa Mesa CA 92627, USA
**Blue, Vida R** — Baseball Player
PO Box 1449, Pleasanton CA 94566, USA
**Blueprint** — DJ Musician
Kork Agency, 1880 Century Park E, #711, Los Angeles CA 90067, USA
**Bluford, Guion S (Guy), Jr** — Astronaut
PO Box 549, North Olmsted OH 44070, USA
**Blum, Arlene** — Mountaineer
University of California, Biochemistry Dept, Berkeley CA 94720, USA
**Blum, Don** — Singer, Drummer (VonBondies)
Tsunami Entertainment, 2525 Hyperion Ave, Los Angeles CA 90027, USA
**Blum, Geoffrey E (Geoff)** — Baseball Player
7 Calle Angelitos, San Clemente CA 92673, USA
**Blum, H Steven** — Army General
Chief, National Guard Bureau, HqUSA, Pentagon, Washington DC 20310, USA
**Blum, Manuel** — Computer Scientist
700 Euclid Ave, Berkeley CA 94708, USA
**Blum, Stephanie** — Actress, Comedienne
Don Buchwald, 6500 Wilshire Blvd, #2200, Los Angeles CA 90048 USA
**Blum, Steve** — Actor
Arlene Thornton Assoc, 12711 Ventura Blvd, #490, Studio City CA 91604, USA
**Blum, Walter (Mousey)** — Thoroughbred Racing Jockey
5710 NW 65th Way, Tamarac FL 33321, USA
**Blumberg, Stuart** — Actor, Writer, Producer
Class 5 Films, 200 Park Ave S, #800, New York NY 10003, USA
**Blume, B Ray** — Basketball Player
29248 SE Powell Valley Road, Gresham OR 97080, USA
**Blume, Judy S** — Writer
W M E Entertainment, 9601 Wilshire Blvd, #300, Beverly Hills CA 90210 USA
**Blume, Martin** — Physicist
Brookhaven National Laboratory, 2 Center St, Upton NY 11973 USA

**Blumenfeld, Alan** — Actor
Stone Manners Salners, 9911 W Pico Blvd, #1400, Los Angeles CA 90035 USA

**Blumenthal, George R** — Educator
University of California, Chancellor's Office, 1156 High St, Santa Cruz CA 95064, USA

**Blumenthal, Heston** — Chef, Restauranteur
Fat Duck Restaurant, High St, Bray on Thames West Berkshire SL6 2AQ, England

**Blumenthal, W Michael** — Secretary, Treasury; Financier
227 Ridgeview Road, Princeton NJ 08540, USA

**Blundell, Graeme** — Actor
Shanahan Mgmt, 91 Campbell St, #300, Surry Hills NSW 2010, Australia

**Blundell, Mark** — Auto Racing Driver
4001 Methanol Lane, Indianapolis IN 46268, USA

**Blundell, Pamela** — Fashion Designer
Copperwheat Blundell, 14 Cheshire St, London E2 6EH, England

**Blunstone, Colin** — Singer (Zombies)
Rhino Mgmt, 60 Babbercombe Road, Bromley, Kent BR1 3CW, England

**Blunt, Emily** — Actress
Ken McReddie Assoc, 101 Finsbury Pavement, London EC2A 1RS, England

**Blunt, James** — Singer, Guitarist, Songwriter
High Road Touring, 751 Bridgeway, #200, Sausalito CA 94965 USA

**Blunt, Matthew R (Matt)** — Governor, MO
Cassidy & Assoc, 700 13th St NW, #400, Washington DC 20005, USA

**Bluteau, Lothaire** — Actor
Don Buchwald, 6500 Wilshire Blvd, #2200, Los Angeles CA 90048 USA

**Bluth, Ray** — Bowler
569 Beauford Dr, Saint Louis MO 63122, USA

**Bluth, Tony** — Animator
C A A T Studios, 10630 Moorpark St, #303, North Hollywood CA 91602, USA

**Bly, Donald A (Dre')** — Football Player
4312 Topsail Landing, Chesapeake VA 23321, USA

**Bly, Robert E** — Writer, Psychologist
1904 Girard Ave S, Minneapolis MN 55403, USA

**Blyleven, R Bert** — Baseball Player
1501 McGregor Reserve Dr, Fort Myers FL 33901, USA

**Blyth, Ann** — Actress, Singer
PO Box 9754, Rancho Santa Fe CA 92067, USA

**Blyth, Chay** — Yachtsman, Explorer
Inmans House, 12 London Road, Sheet, Petersfield, Hampshire GU31 4BE, England

**Blythe, Arthur M** — Jazz Saxophonist
Joel Chriss Co, 300 Mercer St, #3J, New York NY 10003 USA

**Blythe, D Randall (Randy)** — Singer (Lamb of God)
Entertainment Unlimited, 1000 Main Street Plaza, #303, Voorhees NJ 08043, USA

**Blythe, Stephanie** — Singer
Opus 3 Artists, 470 Park Ave S, #900N, New York NY 10016 USA

**Bo Bae Song** — Golfer
Ladies Pro Golf Assn, 100 International Golf Dr, Daytona Beach FL 32124 USA

**Boal, Mark** — Writer
Creative Artists Agency, 2000 Ave of Stars, #100, Los Angeles CA 90067 USA

**Board, Dwaine P** — Football Player
651 Arlington Road, Redwood City CA 94062, USA

**Boardman, Christopher M (Chris)** — Cyclist
Lindfield House, Station Approach Meols, Wirral L47 8XA, England

**Boardman, Eric** — Actor, Director
I C M Partners, 10250 Constellation Blvd, #900, Los Angeles CA 90067 USA

**Boardman, Lee** — Actor
Ken McReddie Assoc, 101 Finsbury Pavement, London EC2A 1RS, England

**Boat, William L (Billy)** — Auto Racing Driver
Boat Indy Racing, 23045 N 15th Ave, Phoenix AZ 85027, USA

**Boatman, Michael** — Actor
1432 Sunnycrest Dr, Fullerton CA 92835, USA

**Bob, Tim** — Bassist (Rage Against the Machine)
ArtistDirect, 10900 Wilshire Blvd, #1400, Los Angeles CA 90024 USA

**Bobbie, Walter** — Director, Actor, Lyricist
Gage Group, 14724 Ventura Blvd, #505, Sherman Oaks CA 91403 USA

**Bobby G** — Singer (Bucks Fizz)
Barry Collings Entertainment, PO 2112, Hockley, Essex SS5 4WD, England

**Bobek, Nicole** — Figure Skater
19220 Seaview Road, #100, Jupiter FL 33469, USA

**Bober, Chris** — Football Player
605 N 264th St, Waterloo NE 68069, USA

**Bobko, Karol J** — Astronaut
91 Turnberry Road, Half Moon Bay CA 94019, USA

**Bobo, Jonah** — Actor
Abrams Artists, 9200 W Sunset Blvd, #1125, West Hollywood CA 90069 USA

**Bocachica, Hiram** — Baseball Player
2340 Carr 2, 2 Urb Rexville, Bayamon PR 00961, USA

**Bocca, Julio** — Ballet Dancer
F P S International, 150 Broadway, New York NY 10038, USA

**Boccabella, John D** — Baseball Player
1035 Lea Dr, San Rafael CA 94903, USA

**Bocchi, Nicole** — Actress
Carson Adler Agency, 250 W 57th St, #2030, New York NY 10107, USA

**Bocelli, Andrea** — Concert Singer
Pentagon Music Mgmt, Hume House, Ballsbridge, #700, Dublin 4, Ireland

**Bochco, Steven** — Producer, Writer
22035 Saddle Peak Road, Topanga CA 90290, USA

**Bochenski, Brandon** — Ice Hockey Player
12962 Radisson Road NE, Minneapolis MN 55449, USA

**Bochenski, Jacek** — Writer
Ul Sonaty 6M 801, 02 744 Warsaw, Poland

**Bochner, Hart** — Actor
Integral Artists, 601 W Broadway, #400, Vancouver BC V5Z 4C2, Canada

**Bochner, Salomon** — Mathematician
4100 Greenbriar Ave, #239, Houston TX 77098, USA

**Bochte, Bruce A** — Baseball Player
80 Century Lane, Petaluma CA 94952, USA

**Bochtler, Douglas E (Doug)**    Baseball Player
154 Narrow Gate Road, Maryville TN 37801, USA
**Bochy, Bruce D**    Baseball Player, Manager
16144 Brittany Park Lane, Poway CA 92064, USA
**Bock, Charles, Jr**    Test Pilot
PO Box 4197, Incline Village NV 89450, USA
**Bock, Dennis**    Writer
Carlisle Co, 121 E 17th St, New York NY 10003, USA
**Bock, John M**    Football Player
627 Cambridge Terrace, Weston FL 33326, USA
**Bockhorn, Arlen (Bucky)**    Basketball Player
3540 Big Tree Road, Bellbrook OH 45305, USA
**Bockrath, Tina**    Actress, Model
755 S San Rafael Ave, Pasadena CA 91105, USA
**Bockwinkel, Nick W F**    Professional Wrestler
Cauliflower Alley Club, 383 Highway 00, Rolla MO 65401, USA
**Bocuse, Paul**    Restauranteur
Kuchenmeister, 40 Rue de la Plage, 69660 Collonges au Mont d'Or, France
**Bodden, Alonzo**    Actor, Comedian
Levity Entertainment Group, 6701 Center Drive W, #1111, Los Angeles CA 90045, USA
**Bodden, Leigh E**    Football Player
400 Foxboro Blvd, Foxborough MA 02035, USA
**Boddicker, Michael J (Mike)**    Baseball Player
11324 W 121st Terrace, Overland Park KS 66213, USA
**Boddy, Gregg**    Ice Hockey Player
2271 Sorrento Dr, Coquitlam BC V3K 6P4, Canada
**Bode, Hendrick W**    Research Engineer
Harvard University, Pierce Hall, Cambridge MA 02138, USA
**Bode, John R**    Vietnam War Air Force Hero
1100 Warm Sands Dr SE, Albuquerque NM 87123, USA
**Bode, Ken**    Commentator, Educator
Northwestern University, Journalism School, Evanston IL 60206, USA
**Boden, Lynn R**    Football Player
7103 N 146th St, Bennington NE 68007, USA
**Boden, Margaret A**    Philosopher, Psychologist
Brighton University, Cognitive Science School, Brighton BN1 9QH, England
**Bodenheimer, George**    Businessman, TV Executive
ABC-TV, Sports Dept, 77 W 66th St, New York NY 10023 USA
**Bodett, Tom**    Writer, Entertainer
PO Box 268, Putney VT 05346, USA
**Bodger, Doug**    Ice Hockey Player
Eddy's Hockey Shop, 2728 James St, Duncan BC V9L 2X9, Canada
**Bodill, Colin**    Aviator
Polar First, Onslow Gardens, #2, London SW7 3LX, England
**Bodine, Brett**    Auto Racing Driver
304 Performance Road, Mooresville NC 28115, USA
**Bodine, Geoffrey E (Geoff)**    Auto Racing Driver
18695 Northline Dr, #C2, Cornelius NC 28031, USA
**Bodine, Todd**    Auto Racing Driver
120 Harris Farm Dr, Mooresville NC 28115, USA
**Bodmer, Walter F**    Geneticist
Oxford University, Hertford College, Oxford OX1 3BW, England
**Bodrov, Sergei V, Sr**    Director
Arlook Group, 205 S Beverly Dr, #209, Beverly Hills CA 90212, USA
**Boe, Alfie**    Singer
Agency Group Ltd, 361-373 City Road, London EC1V 1PQ, England
**Boe, Eric A**    Astronaut
N A S A, Johnson Space Center, 2101 NASA Road, Houston TX 77058 USA
**Boecher, Katherine**    Actress
Innovative Artists, 1505 10th St, Santa Monica CA 90401 USA
**Boedeker, William H (Bill)**    Football Player
1632 Thistle Lane, Fort Wayne IN 46825, USA
**Boeheim, James A (Jim), Jr**    Basketball Coach
701 Eagle Woods Trail, Kissimmee FL 34747, USA
**Boehm, Gottfried K**    Pritzker Architectural Laureate
Kunstgeschichtliches Seminar, Saint Alban-Graben 16, 4051 Basel, Switzerland
**Boehringer, Brian E**    Baseball Player
10 Sunset Dr, Fenton MO 63026, USA
**Boeke, James F (Jim)**    Football Player
18914 San Blas St, Fountain Valley CA 92708, USA
**Boerner, Jacqueline**    Speed Skater
Bernhard-Bastlein-Str 55, 10367 Berlin, Germany
**Boesak, Allan**    Religious Leader, Social Activist
16 Villa Bellini, Constantia St, Strand 7140, South Africa
**Boeschenstein, William W**    Businessman
10617 Cardiff Road, Perrysburg OH 43551, USA
**Boesel, Raul D**    Auto Racing Driver
150 SE 25th Road, #4E, Miami FL 33129, USA
**Boesen, Dennis L (Denny)**    Astronaut
6613 Sandra Ave NE, Albuquerque NM 87109, USA
**Boever, Joseph M (Joe)**    Baseball Player
416 Savannah Way, Franklin TN 37067, USA
**Boeving, Christian**    Actor
Diverse Talent Group, 9911 W Pico Blvd, #350W, Los Angeles CA 90035, USA
**Boff**    Guitarist (Chumbawamba)
Doug Smith Assoc, PO Box 1151, London W3 8ZJ, England
**Boff, Leonardo G D**    Theologian
Pr M Leao 12/204, Alto Vale Encantado, 20531-350 Rio de Janeiro, Brazil
**Bofill, Angela**    Singer
1385 York Ave, #6B, New York NY 10021, USA
**Bofill, Ricardo**    Architect
Taller de Arquitectura, 14 Ave de la Industria, 08960 Barcelona, Spain
**Bofinger, Helge**    Architect
Biebricher Allee 49, 65187 Wiesbaden, Germany
**Bogaliy-Titovets, Anna**    Biathlete
Biathlon Union, Luzhnetskaya Nab 8, 119992 Moscow, Russia

**B**

**Boganyi - Bok**

| | |
|---|---|
| **Boganyi, Tibor**<br>Konzertdirektion Hortnagel, Oranienburger Str 50D, 10117 Berlin, Germany | Conductor |
| **Bogar, Timothy P (Tim)**<br>194 Gray St, North Andover MA 01845, USA | Baseball Player |
| **Bogardus, Stephen**<br>Talent Works, 3500 W Olive Ave, #1400, Burbank CA 91505 USA | Actor |
| **Bogdanich, Walt**<br>New York Times, Editorial Dept, 229 W 43rd St, New York NY 10036 USA | Journalist |
| **Bogdanovich, Peter**<br>Abrams Artists, 9200 W Sunset Blvd, #1125, West Hollywood CA 90069 USA | Director |
| **Bogeberg, J B**<br>Bandana Mgmt, 11 Elvaston Place, #300, London SW7 5QC, England | Bassist (A-Ha) |
| **Boggs, Bill**<br>240 Central Park S, New York NY 10019, USA | Journalist |
| **Boggs, Danny J**<br>US Court of Appeals, US Courthouse, 601 W Broadway, Louisville KY 40202, USA | Judge |
| **Boggs, Haskell**<br>3710 Goodland Ave, Studio City CA 91604, USA | Cinematographer |
| **Boggs, Thomas W (Tommy)**<br>1450 Long Meadow, Salado TX 76571, USA | Baseball Player |
| **Boggs, Wade A**<br>6006 Windham Place, Tampa FL 33647, USA | Baseball Player |
| **Bogguss, Suzy**<br>Creative Artists Agency, 2000 Ave of Stars, #100, Los Angeles CA 90067 USA | Singer, Guitarist, Songwriter |
| **Bogle, Eric**<br>Laing Entertainment, 35 Montague St, Goulburn NSW 2580, Australia | Singer, Songwriter |
| **Bogle, John C**<br>320 Fishers Road, Bryn Mawr PA 19010, USA | Financier |
| **Boglioli, Wendy**<br>2014 210th Circle, Sammamish WA 98074, USA | Swimmer |
| **Bogner, Willy**<br>Firma Willy Bogner GmbH, Saint-Veit-Str 4, 81673 Munich, Germany | Producer, Fashion Designer |
| **Bogosian, Eric**<br>Brookside Artist Mgmt, 250 W 57th St, #2303, New York NY 10107 USA | Performance Artist, Actor, Writer |
| **Bogues, Tyrone (Muggsy)**<br>527 E 83rd St, #2W, New York NY 10028, USA | Basketball Player, Coach |
| **Boguniecki, Eric**<br>129 Buttonball Road, Orange CT 06477, USA | Ice Hockey Player |
| **Bogush, Elizabeth**<br>Innovative Artists, 1505 10th St, Santa Monica CA 90401 USA | Actress |
| **Bogut, Andrew**<br>1660 N Prospect Ave, #2607, Milwaukee WI 53202, USA | Basketball Player |
| **Bohan, Marc**<br>35 Rue du Bourg a Mont, 21400 Chatillon sur Seine, France | Fashion Designer |
| **Bohanon, Brian E**<br>243 W Thorn Way, Houston TX 77015, USA | Baseball Player |
| **Bohay, Heidi**<br>Brogan Agency, 1517 Park Row Dr, Venice CA 90291, USA | Actress |
| **Bohem, Leslie (Les)**<br>United Talent Agency, U T A Plaza, 9336 Civic Center Dr, Beverly Hills CA 90210 USA | Writer |
| **Bohigas Guardiola, Oriol**<br>M B M Arquitectes, Placa Reial 18, 08002 Barcelona 21, Spain | Architect |
| **Bohlin, Peter Q**<br>Bohlin Cywinski Jackson, 49 Geary St, #300, San Francisco CA 94108, USA | Architect |
| **Bohn, Jason**<br>757 Carl Sanders Dr, Acworth GA 30101, USA | Golfer |
| **Bohn, Laura**<br>Laura Bohn Design, 30 W 26th St, #1100, New York NY 10010, USA | Interior Designer |
| **Bohn, Parker, III**<br>25 Pitney Lane, Jackson NJ 08527, USA | Bowler |
| **Bohne, Bruce**<br>Beacon Talent Agency, 170 Apple Ridge Road, Woodcliff Lake NJ 07677, USA | Actor |
| **Bohon, Justin**<br>Innovative Artists, 1505 10th St, Santa Monica CA 90401 USA | Actor |
| **Bohorquez, Claudio**<br>Conciertos Augusto, Calle Viento 15, 2B Majadahonda, 28220 Madrid, Spain | Concert Cellist |
| **Bohrer, Corinne**<br>Abrams Artists, 9200 W Sunset Blvd, #1125, West Hollywood CA 90069 USA | Actress |
| **Bohrer, Thomas**<br>77 Crest St, Concord MA 01742, USA | Rowing Athlete |
| **Bohringer, Romane**<br>Agence Artiste Adequet, 108 Rue Reaumur, 75002 Paris, France | Actress |
| **Boies, David**<br>Cravath Swaine Moore, 1 Chase Manhattan Plaza, New York NY 10005, USA | Attorney |
| **Boikov, Alexandre**<br>2138 Charleys Creek Road, Culloden WV 25510, USA | Ice Hockey Player |
| **Boileau, Linda**<br>Frankfort State Journal, Editorial Dept, 321 W Main St, Frankfort KY 40601, USA | Editorial Cartoonist |
| **Boisclair, Bruce A**<br>5423 Spanish Oak Lane, #D, Oak Park CA 91377, USA | Baseball Player |
| **Boise, Mike**<br>Agency Group Ltd, 142 W 57th St, #600, New York NY 10019 USA | Drummer (Chesterfield Kings) |
| **Boisset, Yves**<br>61 Blvd Inkerman, 92200 Neuilly-sur-Seine, France | Director |
| **Boisson, Christine**<br>Artmedia, 20 Ave Rapp, 75007 Paris, France | Actress |
| **Boisvert, Gilles**<br>10213 Greenside Dr, Cockeysville MD 21030, USA | Ice Hockey Player |
| **Boitano, Brian**<br>1072 Inverness Way, Sunnyvale CA 94087, USA | Figure Skater |
| **Boitano, Danny J**<br>15400 Winchester Blvd, #43, Los Gatos CA 95030, USA | Baseball Player |
| **Boivin, Leo J**<br>PO Box 406, Prescott ON K0E 1T0, Canada | Ice Hockey Player |
| **Bok, Bart J**<br>200 N Sierra Vista Dr, Tucson AZ 85719, USA | Astronomer |

**Bok, Chip** — Editorial Cartoonist
709 Castle Blvd, Akron OH 44313, USA
**Bok, Derek C** — Educator
Harvard University, Kennedy Government School, Cambridge MA 02138, USA
**Bok, Sissela** — Philosopher
75 Cambridge Parkway, #E610, Cambridge MA 02142, USA
**Bokamper, Kim** — Football Player
301 NW 127th Ave, Plantation FL 33325, USA
**Bolam, James** — Actor
Independent Talent Group, 40 Whitfield St, London W1T 2RH, England
**Bolcom, William E** — Composer, Pianist
3080 Whitmore Lake Road, Ann Arbor MI 48105, USA
**Bolden, Charles F, Jr** — Astronaut, Marine Corps General
National Aviation & Space Administration, 300 C St SW, Washington DC 20024, USA
**Bolden, Jeanette** — Track Athlete
University of California, Athletic Dept, Los Angeles CA 90024, USA
**Boldin, Anquan** — Football Player
471 E Crescent Place, Chandler AZ 85249, USA
**Boldirev, Ivan** — Ice Hockey Player
2003 Woodmere Dr E, Valparaiso IN 46383, USA
**Boldon, Ato** — Track Athlete
PO Box 3703, Santa Cruz, Trinidad, Trinidad & Tobago
**Bolduc, Danny** — Ice Hockey Player
27 Daisy Lane, Sidney ME 04330, USA
**Bole, Cliff** — Director
374 Links Dr, Palm Desert CA 92211, USA
**Boles, John E, Jr** — Baseball Manager, Executive
7901 Timberlake Dr, Melbourne FL 32904, USA
**Bolger, Dermot** — Writer
A P Watt, 20 John St, London WC1N 2DR, England
**Bolger, James B (Jim)** — Prime Minister, New Zealand
New Zealand Embassy, 37 Observatory Circle NW, Washington DC 20008, USA
**Bolger, James C (Jim)** — Baseball Player
5524 Sidney Road, Cincinnati OH 45238, USA
**Bolger, Sarah L** — Actress
Hamilton Hodell, 66-68 Margaret St, #500, London W1W 8SR, England
**Bolick, Frank C** — Baseball Player
381 Virginia Lane, Kulpmont PA 17834, USA
**Bolin, Bobby D** — Baseball Player
100 Medinah Dr, Easley SC 29642, USA
**Boling, David** — Writer
Bloomsbury Publishing, 50 Bedford Square, London WC1B 3DP, England
**Boll, Timo** — Table Tennis Player
B Schmittenbecher-Sportsmarketing, Erlenring 16, 61118 Bad Vilbel, Germany
**Boll, Uwe** — Director
Bolu Filmproduktion, Holmanstr 8-10, 97421 Schweinfurt, Germany
**Bollen, Roger** — Cartoonist (Animal Crackers, Catfish)
8964 Little St, Mentor OH 44060, USA
**Boller, Kyle B** — Football Player
2365 Jennifer Lane, Encinitas CA 92024, USA
**Bolles, Richard N** — Writer
10 Stirling Dr, Danville CA 94526, USA
**Bollettieri, Nick** — Tennis Coach
Nick Bollettieri Tennis Academy, 5500 34th St W, Bradenton FL 34210, USA
**Bolli, Justin** — Golfer
136 Ramsford Lane, Simpsonville SC 29681, USA
**Bolling, Claude** — Jazz Pianist, Composer
New Audiences Productions, 161 W 75th St, #9E, New York NY 10023, USA
**Bolling, Dave** — Writer
Bloomsbury Publishing, 50 Bedford Square, London WC1B 3DP, England
**Bolling, Frank E** — Baseball Player
171 Fenwick Road, Mobile AL 36608, USA
**Bolling, Tiffany** — Actress
Tyler Kjar, 10153 1/2 Riverside Dr, #255, Toluca Lake CA 91602 USA
**Bollinger, Brooks** — Football Player
3549 Birchpond Road, Saint Paul MN 55122, USA
**Bollinger, Lee C** — Educator
Columbia University, President's Office, New York NY 10027, USA
**Bollinger, R Randal** — Surgeon
1120 Infinity Road, Durham NC 27712, USA
**Bolocco Fonck, Cecilia C** — Beauty Queen, Actress
Miss Universe Organization, 1370 Ave of Americas, #1600, New York NY 10019 USA
**Bologna, Joseph** — Actor
S M S Talent, 8383 Wilshire Blvd, #230, Beverly Hills CA 90211 USA
**Bolonchuk, Larry** — Ice Hockey Player
385 Woodlawn St, Winnipeg MB R3J 2J2, Canada
**Bolstorff, Douglas** — Basketball Player
1553 Skyline Court, Saint Paul MN 55121, USA
**Bolt, Mae** — Bowler
1516 Robinhood Lane, La Grange Park IL 60526, USA
**Bolt, Usain** — Track Athlete
Pace Sports Mgmt, 6 Causeway, Teddington, Middlesex TW11 0HE, England
**Boltanski, Christian** — Artist, Photographer
146 Blvd Carmelina, 92240 Malakoff, France
**Bolten, Michael** — Actor
C E S D, 10635 Santa Monica Blvd, #130, Los Angeles CA 90025 USA
**Bolton, James R** — Photochemist
Calgon Carbon Corp, 130 Royal Crest Court, Markham ON L6G 1A8, Canada
**Bolton, Michael** — Singer, Songwriter
Works Public Relations, 11 Marshalsea Road, London SE1 1EN, England
**Bolton, Ronald C (Ron)** — Football Player
408 Maiden Lane, Chesapeake VA 23325, USA
**Bolton, Thomas E (Tom)** — Baseball Player
2288 Rolling Hills Dr, Nolensville TN 37135, USA
**Bolton-Holifield, Ruthie** — Basketball Player
Sacramento Monarchs, Arco Arena, 1 Sports Parkway, Sacramento CA 95834 USA

**Bolyard, Bob** — Basketball Player
10607 Wild Flower Place, Fort Wayne IN 46845, USA

**Bomar, Mary** — Government Official
National Park Service, Interior Department, PO Box 37127, Washington DC 20013, USA

**Bombardie, Brad** — Ice Hockey Player
8959 Baywatch Trail NW, Walker MN 56484, USA

**Bomer, Matthew (Matt)** — Actor
Anonymous Content, 3532 Hayden Ave, Culver City CA 90232 USA

**Bon Jovi, Jon** — Singer (Bon Jovi), Songwriter, Actor
Bon Jovi Mgmt, 809 Elder Circle, Austin TX 78733, USA

**Bona, Richard** — Bassist, Singer
International Music Network, 278 Main St, Gloucester MA 01930, USA

**Bonadio, Jeffrey** — Physician
Pacific Rim Pathology, 5325 Metro St, San Diego CA 92110, USA

**Bonaduce, Danny** — Actor, Singer
Rebel Entertainment Partners, 5700 Wilshire Blvd, #456, Los Angeles CA 90036, USA

**Bonaly, Surya** — Figure Skater
35 Rue Felicien David, 75016 Paris, France

**Bonamassa, Joe** — Guitarist, Singer, Songwriter
Premier Artists Services, 10025 Vestal Place, Coral Springs FL 33071, USA

**Bonar, Dan** — Ice Hockey Player
361 Mandeville St, Winnipeg MB R3J 2J2, Canada

**Bond, Alan** — Yachtsman, Businessman
89 Watkins Road, Dalkeith WA 6069, Australia

**Bond, Edward** — Writer
Casorotto Ramsay, Waverley House, 7-12 Noel St, London W1F 8GQ, England

**Bond, H Julian** — Civil Rights Activist
5435 41st Place NW, Washington DC 20015, USA

**Bond, Phillip (Phil)** — Basketball Player
208 Northwestern Parkway, Louisville KY 40212, USA

**Bond, Samantha** — Actress
Innovative Artists, 1505 10th St, Santa Monica CA 90401 USA

**Bond, Victoria A** — Conductor, Composer
Roanoke Symphony, 541 Luck Ave SW, #200, Roanoke VA 24016, USA

**Bond, Walter** — Basketball Player
PO Box 87, Hamel MN 55340, USA

**Bondar, Roberta L** — Astronaut, Canada
Space Agency, Rockcliffe Base, Ottawa ON K1A 1A1, Canada

**Bondarenko, Vtaly M** — Architect
Communal Institute, Kalitnikovskaya Str 30, 109807 Moscow, Russia

**Bonderman, Jeremy A** — Baseball Player
10 Ridgeview Dr, Pasco WA 99301, USA

**Bondevik, Kjell Magne** — Prime Minister, Norway
Oslo Peace & Human Rights Center, Box 2753 Solli, 0204 Oslo, Norway

**Bondi, Viggo** — Bassist (A-Ha)
Bandana Mgmt, 11 Elvaston Place, London SW7 5QC, England

**Bondra, Peter** — Ice Hockey Player
372 Carriage Park Way, Annapolis MD 21401, USA

**Bonds, Barry L** — Baseball Player
44 Beverly Park Circle, Beverly Hills CA 90210, USA

**Bonds, Gary U S** — Singer
Tony DeLauro Entertainment, 157 Broad St, #309, Red Bank NJ 07701, USA

**Bondurant, Robert (Bob)** — Auto Driving Instructor
Firebird International Speedway, PO Box 51980, Phoenix AZ 85076, USA

**Bone Crusher** — Rap Artist
Richard De La Font Agency, 4845 S Sheridan Road, #505, Tulsa OK 74145 USA

**Bone, Ken** — Basketball Coach
Washington State University, Athletic Dept, Pullman WA 99164, USA

**Bonebreak, Donald J (D J)** — Drummer (X)
A P A Talent/Literary Agency, 405 S Beverly Dr, #300, Beverly Hills CA 90212 USA

**Bonehill, Richard** — Actor
Bosun's Nest, Carthew Way, Saint Ives, Cornwall TR26 1RJ, England

**Bonell, Carlos A** — Concert Guitarist, Composer
Bravo Music International, PO Box 19060, London N7 0ZD, England

**Bonerz, Peter** — Actor, Comedian, Director
Shapiro/West Assoc, 141 El Camino Dr, #205, Beverly Hills CA 90212, USA

**Bones, Ricardo (Ricky)** — Baseball Player
908 NW 100th Ave, Pembroke Pines FL 33024, USA

**Bonet, Lisa** — Actress
Untitled Entertainment, 350 S Beverly Dr, #200, Beverly Hills CA 90212 USA

**Bonet, Pep** — Architect
C/Pujades 62, 08005 Barcelona, Spain

**Boneta, Diego** — Actor, Singer
Gersh Agency, 9465 Wilshire Blvd, #600, Beverly Hills CA 90212 USA

**Bonetti, Mattia** — Designer, Interior Decorator, Artist
10 Rue Rocjebrune, 75011 Paris, France

**Bong Joon Ho** — Director, Writer
Creative Artists Agency, 2000 Ave of Stars, #100, Los Angeles CA 90067 USA

**Bong Jung Keun** — Baseball Player
2917 Asteria Pointe, Duluth GA 30097, USA

**Bonham Carter, Helena** — Actress
7 W Heath Ave, London NW11 7QS, England

**Bonham, Jason** — Drummer
Agency Group Ltd, 142 W 57th St, #600, New York NY 10019 USA

**Bonham, Ronald D (Ron)** — Basketball Player
8020 S Country Road 700E, Selma IN 47383, USA

**Bonham, S Shane** — Football Player
321 Clover Hill Road, Maryville TN 37801, USA

**Bonham, Tracy** — Singer, Musician, Songwriter
Big Hassle, 44 Wall St, #2200, New York NY 10005, USA

**Bonhomme, Brian** — Guitarist (Roman Holliday)
Youngstown State University, History Dept, Youngstown OH 44555, USA

**Bonhomme, Tessa** — Ice Hockey Player
Team Canada, 2424 University Dr NW, Calgary AB T2N 3Y9, Canada

**Boni, T Yayi** — President, Benin
President's Office, Palais Presidentiel, BP 2028, Cotonou, Benin

**Boniface, Bruce** — Singer, Songwriter
Virgin Records, 338 N Foothill Road, Beverly Hills CA 90210 USA
**Bonifacio, Emilio J** — Baseball Player
Kansas City Royals, Kauffman Stadium, 1 Royal Way, Kansas City MO 64129 USA
**Bonilla, Henry** — Representative, TX
2 Lake Shore Dr, Corpus Christi TX 78413, USA
**Bonilla, Juan G** — Baseball Player
2902 Orchidcrest Dr, Crestview FL 32539, USA
**Bonilla, Michelle C** — Actress
Imperium 7 Artists, 5455 Wilshire Blvd, #1706, Los Angeles CA 90036 USA
**Bonilla, Roberto M A (Bobby)** — Baseball Player
1403 Kenilworth St, Sarasota FL 34231, USA
**Bonin, Gordie** — Auto Racing Driver
12471 Sanford St, Los Angeles CA 90066, USA
**Bonin, Marcel** — Ice Hockey Player
408 Rue Precieux-Sang, Joliette QC J6E 2M5, Canada
**Bonington, Christian J S** — Mountaineer
Badger Hill, Hesket Newmarket, Wigton, Cumbria CA7 8LA, England
**Bonior, David E** — Representative, MI
38875 Harper Ave, Clinton Township MI 48036, USA
**Bonjour, Daniel** — Actor
Tinoco Mgmt, 8033 Sunset Blvd, #573, West Hollywood CA 90046, USA
**Bonk, Radek** — Ice Hockey Player
137 Allenhurst Circle, Franklin TN 37067, USA
**Bonnaire, Sandrine** — Actress, Director, Writer
Artmedia, 20 Ave Rapp, 75007 Paris, France
**Bonnefous, Jean-Pierre** — Ballet Dancer, Choreographer
Indiana University, Ballet Dept, Music School, Bloomington IN 47405, USA
**Bonnefoy, Yves J** — Writer
College de France, Poetry Study Dept, 11 Place Marcelin Berthelot, 75005 Paris, France
**Bonnell, R Barry** — Baseball Player
2102 179th Court NE, Redmond WA 98052, USA
**Bonner, Anthony** — Basketball Player
5854 Elmbank Ave, Saint Louis MO 63120, USA
**Bonner, DeWanna** — Basketball Player
Phoenix Mercury, American West Arena, 201 E Jefferson St, Phoenix AZ 85004 USA
**Bonner, Elayna G** — Human Rights Activist
A D Sajharova Museum, Zemlyanoy Val 57, Building 6, 107120 Moscow, Russia
**Bonner, Matthew R (Matt)** — Basketball Player
San Antonio Spurs, Alamodome, 1 AT&T Center Parkway, San Antonio TX 78219 USA
**Bonner, Robert C** — Attorney, Judge
Gibson Dunn Crutcher, 333 S Grand Ave, #4400, Los Angeles CA 90071, USA
**Bonner, Tony** — Actor
Agents Associes, 201 Rue du Faubourg Saint Honore, 75008 Paris, France
**Bonness, Richard K (Rik)** — Football Player
18914 Boyle Circle, Elkhorn NE 68022, USA
**Bonneville, Hugh** — Actor
United Talent Agency, U T A Plaza, 9336 Civic Center Dr, Beverly Hills CA 90210 USA
**Bonney, Barbara** — Opera Singer
Universität Mozarteum Salzburg, Mirabellplatz 1, 5020 Salzburg, Austria
**Bono** — Singer, Songwriter (U-2)
Principle Management, 250 W 57th St, #2120, New York NY 10107, USA
**Bono, Chaz** — Entertainer
Haber Entertainment, 434 S Canon Dr, #204, Beverly Hills CA 90212, USA
**Bono, Steven C (Steve)** — Football Player
1100 Hamilton Ave, Palo Alto CA 94301, USA
**Bonoff, Karla** — Singer, Pianist, Songwriter
2122 E Valley Road, Santa Barbara CA 93108, USA
**Bonsall, Joseph S (Joe), Jr** — Singer (Oak Ridge Boys)
88 New Shackle Island Road, Hendersonville TN 37075, USA
**Bonser, John P (Boof)** — Baseball Player
12060 Lucca St, #202, Fort Myers FL 33966, USA
**Bonsignore, Jason** — Ice Hockey Player
2152 Edgemere Dr, Rochester NY 14612, USA
**Bontemps, Ronald (Ron)** — Basketball Player
133 S Illinois Ave, Morton IL 61550, USA
**Bonvie, Dennis** — Ice Hockey Player
670 N River St, #210, Wilkes Barre PA 18705, USA
**Bonvoisin, Berangere** — Actress
Voyez Mon Agent, 20 Ave Rapp, 75007 Paris, France
**Bonvoisin, Bernie** — Actor
U B B A, 6 Rue de Braque, 75003 Paris, France
**Bonynge, Richard A** — Conductor
Chalet Monet, Route de Sonloup, 1833 Les Avants, Switzerland
**Boo, Katherine** — Journalist
Washington Post, Editorial Dept, 1150 15th St NW, Washington DC 20071 USA
**Book, Asher M** — Actor
Paradigm Agency, 360 N Crescent Dr, North Building, Beverly Hills CA 90210 USA
**Booker, Gregory S (Greg)** — Baseball Player
1535 Charleigh Court, Elon College NC 27244, USA
**Booker, Marty M** — Football Player
15982 SW 11th St, Pembroke Pines FL 33027, USA
**Booker, Vaughn J** — Football Player
11 Page St, Hurst TX 76053, USA
**Bookwalter, J R** — Director
PO Box 6573, Akron OH 44312, USA
**Boomer, Linwood** — Actor, Producer, Writer
Greenberg Taurig, 1840 Century Park E, #1900, Los Angeles CA 90067 USA
**Boomer, Walter E** — Marine Corps General
4 Pinckney Landing Dr, Sheldon SC 29941, USA
**Boon, Dany** — Actor
W M E Entertainment, 9601 Wilshire Blvd, #300, Beverly Hills CA 90210 USA
**Boon, David C** — Cricketer
Durham Cricket Club, Chester-le-Street, County Durham DH3 3QR, England
**Boone, Aaron J** — Baseball Player
10111 E Phantom Way, Scottsdale AZ 85255, USA

**B**

**Boniface - Boone**

# B

**Boone, Alfonso** — Football Player
14290 W Lyle Court, Libertyville IL 60048, USA
**Boone, Brendon** — Actor
9157 W Sunset Blvd, #206, West Hollywood CA 90069, USA
**Boone, Bret R** — Baseball Player
6383 Calle Ponte Bella, Rancho Santa Fe CA 92091, USA
**Boone, Daneen** — Actress
Sherrida Personal Mgmt, 110 Scollard St, Toronto ON M5R 1G2, Canada
**Boone, Debby** — Singer, Actress
I C M Partners, 730 5th Ave, New York NY 10019 USA
**Boone, Pat** — Actor, Singer
Solters & Digney, 1680 N Vine St, #1105, Hollywood CA 90028, USA
**Boone, Robert R (Bob)** — Baseball Player, Manager
1432 Misty Sea Way, San Marcos CA 92078, USA
**Boone, Ronald B (Ron)** — Basketball Player
3877 Pheasant Ridge Road, Salt Lake City UT 84109, USA
**Boone, Steve** — Bassist, Singer (Lovin' Spoonful)
Lustig Talent, PO Box 770850, Orlando FL 32877 USA
**Boorem, Mika** — Actor
Untitled Entertainment, 350 S Beverly Dr, #200, Beverly Hills CA 90212 USA
**Boorman, John** — Director
Merlin Films, 16 Upper Pembroke St, Dublin 2, Ireland
**Booros, James** — Golfer
2615 W Pennsylvania St, Allentown PA 18104, USA
**Boosler, Elayne** — Actress, Comedienne, Writer
Levity Entertainment, 6701 Center Drive W, #1111, Los Angeles CA 90045, USA
**Bootcheck, Christopher B (Chris)** — Baseball Player
1204 Suncast Lane, #2, El Dorado Hills CA 95762, USA
**Booth, Calvin L** — Basketball Player
6001 E Horseshoe Road, Paradise Valley AZ 85253, USA
**Booth, Connie** — Actress
Lip Service Casting, 60-66 Wardour St, London W1F 0TA, England
**Booth, Douglas** — Actor
United Talent Agency, U T A Plaza, 9336 Civic Center Dr, Beverly Hills CA 90210 USA
**Booth, Emma** — Actress
Robyn Gardiner Mgmt, PO Box 128, Surry Hills NSW 2010, Australia
**Booth, George** — Cartoonist
PO Box 1539, Stony Brook NY 11790, USA
**Booth, Kellee** — Golfer
4804 Goldeneyes Lane, McKinney TX 75070, USA
**Booth, Kristin** — Actress
Edna Talent, 318 Dundas St W, Toronto ON M5T 1G5, Canada
**Booth, Lindy** — Actress
Innovative Artists, 1505 10th St, Santa Monica CA 90401 USA
**Booth, Melanie L** — Soccer Player
Canadian Soccer, Place Soccer Canada, 237 Metcalfe St, Ottawa ON K2P 1R2, Canada
**Booth, Michael** — Interior Designer
Babey Mountol Jue & Booth, 510 3rd St, #110, San Francisco CA 94107, USA
**Boothe, Kevin M** — Football Player
12100 NW 18th St, Plantation FL 33313, USA
**Boothe, Powers** — Actor
Brillstein Entertainment Partners, 9150 Wilshire Blvd, #350, Beverly Hills CA 90212 USA
**Booty, John F** — Football Player
16401 Governor Bridge Road, #407, Bowie MD 20716, USA
**Booty, Joshua G (Josh)** — Football, Baseball Player
6248 N Windermere Dr, Shreveport LA 71129, USA
**Boozer, Carlos A, Jr** — Basketball Player
4550 S 700 E, Salt Lake City UT 84107, USA
**Boozer, Emerson** — Football Player
25 Windham Dr, Huntington Station NY 11746, USA
**Borbon, Pedro F, Jr** — Baseball Player
60 Enoch Crosby Road, Brewster NY 10509, USA
**Borchardt, Dirk** — Actor
Agentur Hubchen, Pariser Str 20, 10707 Berlin, Germany
**Borcherds, Richard E** — Mathematician
University of California, Mathematics Dept, Berkeley CA 94720, USA
**Borcherdt, Brian** — Singer, Songwriter
Agency Group Ltd, 142 W 57th St, #600, New York NY 10019 USA
**Bordeleau, Jean-Pierre (J P)** — Ice Hockey Player
94 Lakemist Court, Dartmouth NS B3A 4Z1, Canada
**Bordelon, Kenneth P (Ken)** — Football Player
1224 Octavia St, New Orleans LA 70115, USA
**Borden, Amanda** — Gymnast
Cincinnati Gymnastics Academy, 3536 Woodridge Blvd, Fairfield OH 45014, USA
**Borden, Robert** — Producer, Writer
United Talent Agency, U T A Plaza, 9336 Civic Center Dr, Beverly Hills CA 90210 USA
**Border, Allan R** — Cricketer
Cricket Board, 90 Jolimont St, Jolimont VIC 3002, Australia
**Borders, Patrick L (Pat)** — Baseball Player
1135 S Lakeshore Blvd, Lake Wales FL 33853, USA
**Bordi, Richard A (Rich)** — Baseball Player
1133 Hailey Court, Rohnert Park CA 94928, USA
**Bordick, Michael T (Mike)** — Baseball Player
1302 Locust Ave, Towson MD 21204, USA
**Boreanaz, David** — Actor
Creative Artists Agency, 2000 Ave of Stars, #100, Los Angeles CA 90067 USA
**Boren, David L** — Educator; Governor, Senator, OK
University of Oklahoma, President's Office, 660 Parrington, Norman OK 73019, USA
**Borg, Bjorn R** — Tennis Player
Tulegatan 11, 113 53 Stockholm, Sweden
**Borg, Marcus J** — Theologian
Oregon State University, School of Religion, Corvallis OR 97331, USA
**Borges, Jacobo** — Artist
Museo Jacobo Borges, Catia, Caracas, Venezuela
**Borghi, Frank** — Soccer Player
4123 Poepping St, Saint Louis MO 63123, USA

**Boone - Borghi**

**Borgman, James M (Jim)** — Editorial Cartoonist
Cincinnati Enquirer, Editorial Dept, 617 Vine St, #500, Cincinnati OH 45202, USA
**Boris, Robert (Bob)** — Director, Writer
Marshak/Zachary Co, 8840 Wilshire Blvd, #100, Beverly Hills CA 90211 USA
**Borisenko, Andrey I** — Cosmonaut Engineer
Cosmonaut Training Center, Star City, 141160 Zvezdny Gorodok, Moscow Oblast, Russia
**Boriso-Glebsky, Nikita** — Concert Violinist
I M G Artists, The Light Box, 111 Power Road, London W4 5PY , England
**Bork, Erik** — Producer, Writer
Creative Artists Agency, 2000 Ave of Stars, #100, Los Angeles CA 90067 USA
**Borkar, Nitin** — Computer Engineer
Intel Corp, 5200 NE Elam Young Parkway, Hillsboro OR 97124, USA
**Borkh, Inge** — Opera Singer
Florentinerstr 20, #2018, D 7000 Stuttgart 75, Germany
**Borkowski, Robert V (Bob)** — Baseball Player
1031 Gerhard St, Dayton OH 45404, USA
**Borland, Toby S** — Baseball Player
8642 Quitman Highway, Quitman LA 71268, USA
**Borland, Wesley L (Wes)** — Guitarist (Limp Bizkit), Songwriter
Flip/Interscope Records, 8733 Sunset Blvd, #205, West Hollywood CA 90069, USA
**Borle, Christian** — Actor
Management 360, 9111 Wilshire Blvd, Beverly Hills CA 90210 USA
**Borman, Frank F, II** — Astronaut, Businessman
PO Box 64, Bighorn MT 59010, USA
**Born, Ruth** — Baseball Player
4205 Meridian Woods Dr, Valpariso IN 46385, USA
**Bornedal, Ole** — Director, Writer
Principal Entertainment, 9255 Sunset Blvd, #500, Los Angeles CA 90069 USA
**Borodina, Olga V** — Opera Singer
Mariinsky Theater, Theater Square, 1 Pl Iskusstr, 190000 Saint Petersburg, Russia
**Borofsky, Jonathan (Jon)** — Artist
11301 W Olympic Blvd, #514, Los Angeles CA 90064, USA
**Boros, Guy D** — Golfer
2900 NE 40th St, Fort Lauderdale FL 33308, USA
**Boross, Csilla** — Opera Singer
I M G Artists, Hogarth Business Park, Chiswick, London W4 2TH, England
**Boross, Peter** — Prime Minister, Hungary
Kossouth Lajos Ter 1-3, 1055 Budapest, Hungary
**Borowiak, Tony** — Singer (All-4-One)
Universal Attractions, 135 W 26th St, #1200, New York NY 10001 USA
**Borowitz, Anthony (Andy)** — Writer
Creative Artists Agency, 2000 Ave of Stars, #100, Los Angeles CA 90067 USA
**Borrell, Jonathan E (Johnny)** — Singer, Guitarist (Razorlight)
Agency Group Ltd, 361-373 City Road, London EC1V 1PQ, England
**Borroff, Marie E** — Writer
88 Notch Hill Road, #101, North Branford CT 6471, USA
**Borsato, Luciano** — Ice Hockey Player
200-4 Tortoise Crescent, Brampton ON L6P 0A1, Canada
**Borschevsky, Nikolai** — Ice Hockey Player
3 Geranium Court, Richmond Hill ON L4C 7M7, Canada
**Borstein, Alex** — Actress, Comedienne
W M E Entertainment, 1325 Ave of Americas, New York NY 10019 USA
**Bortz, Mark S** — Football Player
PO Box 3504, Quincy IL 62305, USA
**Boruch, Robert F** — Statistician
University of Pennsylvania, Wharton Business School, Philadelphia PA 19104, USA
**Boryla, Vincent J (Vince)** — Basketball Player, Executive
5577 S Emporia Circle, Greenwood Village CO 80111, USA
**Borzov, Valeri F** — Track Athlete
National Olympic Committee, Esplanadnaya 42, 252023 Kiev, Ukraine
**Bosch, Edith** — Judo Athlete
De Korte Sport Institute, Middenbaan Zuid 402, 3191 Hoogvliet AH, Netherlands
**Boschini, Victor J, Jr** — Educator
Texas Christian University, Chancellor's Office, 2800 S University Dr, Fort Worth TX 76129, USA
**Boschman, Laurie** — Ice Hockey Player
27 Delamere Dr, Stittsville ON K2S 1G7, Canada
**Bosco, Philip** — Actor
Don Buchwald, 10 E 44th St, New York NY 10017 USA
**Bose, Bimal K** — Electrical Engineer
215 Ski Mountain Road, Gatlinburg TN 37738, USA
**Bose, Eleanora** — Model
I M G Models, 304 Park Ave S, #PH N, New York NY 10010 USA
**Bose, Lucia** — Actress
Anne Alvares Correa, 34 Rue Jouffroy d'Abbans, 75017 Paris, France
**Boselli, D Anthony (Tony), Jr** — Football Player
12400 W Highway 71, #350-170, Bee Cave TX 78738, USA
**Boseman, Chadwick** — Actor
Greene Assoc, 1901 Ave of Stars, #130, Los Angeles CA 90067 USA
**Bosetti, Richard A (Rick)** — Baseball Player
1471 Arroyo Manor Dr, Redding CA 96003, USA
**Bosh, Christopher W (Chris)** — Basketball Player
20 W Kinzie St, #1000, Chicago IL 60654, USA
**Bosio, Christopher L (Chris)** — Baseball Player
417 Hidden Ridges Way, Combined Locks WI 54113, USA
**Boskie, Shawn K** — Baseball Player
10220 N 55th St, Paradise Valley AZ 85253, USA
**Boskin, Michael J** — Government Official, Economist
Stanford University, Hoover Institution, Stanford CA 94305, USA
**Bosley, Thaddis (Thad), Jr** — Baseball Player
19440 Amhurst Court, Cerritos CA 90703, USA
**Bosman, Richard A (Dick)** — Baseball Player
3511 Landmark Trail, Palm Harbor FL 34684, USA
**Bosnak, Karyn** — Writer
Harper Collins Publishers, 10 E 53rd St, Cellar 1, New York NY 10022 USA
**Boso, Casper N (Cap)** — Football Player
8811 Calumet Dr, Indianapolis IN 46236, USA

Borgman - Boso

# B

**Bossard, Andre** — Law Enforcement Official
228 Rue de la Convention, 75015 Paris, France
**Bosson, Barbara** — Actress, Producer, Writer
C E S D, 10635 Santa Monica Blvd, #130, Los Angeles CA 90025 USA
**Bossy, Michael (Mike)** — Ice Hockey Player
136 Place Ducharme, Rosemere QC J7A 4H8, Canada
**Bostelle, Tom** — Artist, Sculptor
Aeolian Palace Gallery, 267 Spring Run Lane, Downingtown PA 19335, USA
**Bostic, Jeffrey L (Jeff)** — Football Player
8250 Royal Saint Georges Lane, Duluth GA 30097, USA
**Bostic, Jenn** — Singer, Songwriter
M S T B, ReverbNation, 115 N Duke St, #2A, Durham NC 27701, USA
**Bostic, Joe E, Jr** — Football Player
3507 Bromley Wood Lane, Greensboro NC 27410, USA
**Bostick, Devon** — Actor
Noble Caplan Abrams, 1260 Yonge St, #200, Toronto ON M4T 1W6, Canada
**Bostock, Roy J** — Businessman
Yahoo Inc, 701 1st Ave, Sunnyvale CA 94089, USA
**Boston, Daryl L** — Baseball Player
1016 Valley Lane, Cincinnati OH 45229, USA
**Boston, David** — Football Player
18502 Skippers Helm, Humble TX 77346, USA
**Boston, Rachel** — Actress
Gersh Agency, 9465 Wilshire Blvd, #600, Beverly Hills CA 90212 USA
**Boston, Ralph H** — Track Athlete
3301 Woodbine Ave, Knoxville TN 37914, USA
**Bostridge, Ian** — Opera Singer
Opus 3 Artists, 470 Park Ave S, #900N, New York NY 10016 USA
**Bostwick, Barry** — Actor
Vanguard Management Group, 8060 Melrose Ave, #400, Los Angeles CA 90046, USA
**Boswell, Barbie** — Model
2235 Arrowgrass Dr, #103, Wesley Chapel FL 33544, USA
**Boswell, Bobby** — Soccer Player
Houston Dynamo, 1415 Louisiana, #3400, Houston TX 77002 USA
**Boswell, Kenneth G (Ken)** — Baseball Player
1103 Live Oak Dr, Marble Falls TX 78654, USA
**Boswell, Thomas M** — Sportswriter
Washington Post, Sports Dept, 1150 15th St NW, Washington DC 20071, USA
**Boswell, Tommy G (Tom)** — Basketball Player
341 N Anton Dr, Montgomery AL 36105, USA
**Bosworth, Brian** — Football Player, Actor
4400 Arlen Court, Plano TX 75093, USA
**Bosworth, Kate** — Actress, Model
Creative Artists Agency, 2000 Ave of Stars, #100, Los Angeles CA 90067 USA
**Bosworth, Lauren O (Lo)** — Actress
Octogon Entertainment, 8687 Melrose Ave, #700, Los Angeles CA 90069, USA
**Bosworth, Libby** — Singer, Songwriter
3011 Fort Worth Trail, Austin TX 78748, USA
**Boteach, Shmuley** — Religious Leader, Rabbi, Writer
Shalom in the Home, 7700 Wisconsin Ave, Bethesda MD 20814, USA
**Botehho, Joao** — Director
Assicuacai de Realizadores, Rua de Palmeira 7, R/C, 1200 Lisbon, Portugal
**Botelho, Luciano** — Opera Singer
I M G Artists, Hogarth Business Park, Chiswick, London W4 2TH, England
**Botero, Fernando** — Artist
Nohra Haime Gallery, 41 E 57th St, #600, New York NY 10022, USA
**Botha, Francois (Frans)** — Boxer
White Buffalo, PO Box 3982, Clearwater FL 33767, USA
**Botha, Roelof F** — Government Official, South Africa
PO Box 16176, Pretoria North 0116, South Africa
**Botham, Ian T** — Cricketer, Sportscaster
Mission Logistics, 158 Hurlington Road, Fulham, London SE6 3NGF, England
**Bothmer, Bernard V** — Museum Official, Egyptologist
Brooklyn Museum, 188 Eastern Parkway, Brooklyn NY 11238, USA
**Bothwell, Tim** — Ice Hockey Player, Coach
14 Billings Court, Burlington VT 05408, USA
**Botone, Talia** — Actress
C E S D, 10635 Santa Monica Blvd, #130, Los Angeles CA 90025 USA
**Botsford, Beth** — Swimmer
2210 River Bend Court, White Hall MD 21161, USA
**Botsford, Sara** — Actress
Kordek Agency, 8490 W Sunset Blvd, #403, West Hollywood CA 90069, USA
**Botstein, David** — Geneticist
Lewis-Sigler Institute, Princeton University Medical Center, Princeton NJ 08544, USA
**Botstein, Leon** — Conductor
Columbia Artists Mgmt Inc, 1790 Broadway, #702, New York NY 10019 USA
**Botstein, Leon** — Educator
Bard College, President's Office, Annandale on Hudson NY 12504, USA
**Botta, Mario** — Architect
Via Ciani 16, 6904 Lugano, Switzerland
**Bottalico, Richard P (Ricky)** — Baseball Player
10 Rocamora Road, Rocky Hill CT 06067, USA
**Bottenfield, Kent D** — Baseball Player
12168 142nd Court N, West Palm Beach FL 33418, USA
**Botterill, Jason** — Ice Hockey Player
Pittsburgh Penguins, Consol Energy Center, 1001 5th Ave, Pittsburgh PA 15219 USA
**Botti, Chris** — Trumpeter
Neuman Assoc, 16255 Ventura Blvd, #920, Encino CA 91436, USA
**Bottin, Rob** — Director
Gersh Agency, 9465 Wilshire Blvd, #600, Beverly Hills CA 90212 USA
**Botto, Juan Diego** — Actor
Torres & Prieto, Calle Princesa 3, 28008 Madrid, Spain
**Bottom, Joe** — Swimmer
374 Spanish Garden Dr, Chico CA 95928, USA
**Bottoms, Joseph** — Actor
Bottoms Art Galleries, 1260 Channel Dr, Santa Barbara CA 93108, USA

Bossard - Bottoms

**Bottoms, Timothy** — Actor
PO Box 15559, San Luis Obispo CA 93406, USA
**Bottum, Roddy** — Keyboardist (Faith No More)
Creative Artists Agency, 2000 Ave of Stars, #100, Los Angeles CA 90067 USA
**Bouasone Bouphavanh** — Prime Minister, Laos
Premier's Office, National Assembly, Vientiane Capital, Vientiane, Laos
**Boublil, Alain A** — Lyricist
Cameron Mackintosh Ltd, 1 Bedford Square, London WC1B 3RA, England
**Boucha, Henry C** — Ice Hockey Player
7200 Biglerville Circle, Anchorage AK 99507, USA
**Bouchard, Daniel (Dan)** — Ice Hockey Player
3111 Hillsdale Court SE, Marietta GA 30067, USA
**Bouchard, Lucien** — Government Official, Canada
Parti Quebecois, 1200 Ave Papineau, Montreal QC H2K 4R5, Canada
**Bouchard, Pierre** — Ice Hockey Player
1216-1705 Ave Victoria, Saint-Lambert QC, J4R 2T7, Canada
**Bouchard, Ron** — Auto Racing Driver
300 Lunenburg St, Fitchburg MA 01420, USA
**Bouchareb, Rachid** — Director, Writer
Casorotto Ramsay, Waverley House, 7-12 Noel St, London W1F 8GQ, England
**Bouchaud, Jean** — Actor
Artmedia, 20 Ave Rapp, 75007 Paris, France
**Boucher, Brian** — Ice Hockey Player
416 Overhill Road, Haddonfield NJ 08033, USA
**Boucher, Candice** — Model
Outlaws Models, 11 Wessels Road, Greenpoint 8011 Capetown, South Africa
**Boucher, Gaetan** — Speed Skater
Center Sportif, 3850 Edgar, Saint Hubert QC J4T 368, Canada
**Boucher, Lawrence** — Businessman
Adaptec Inc, 691 S Milpitas Blvd, Milpitas CA 95035, USA
**Boucher, Philippe** — Ice Hockey Player
Dallas Stars, 2601 Ave of Stars, #100, Frisco TX 75034 USA
**Bouchez, Elodie** — Actress
Evolution Entertainment, 901 N Highland Ave, Los Angeles CA 90038 USA
**Bouchitey, Patrick** — Actor
Voyez Mon Agent, 20 Ave Rapp, 75007 Paris, France
**Boudart, Michel** — Chemical Engineer
9636 El Venado Dr, Whittier CA 90603, USA
**Boudia, David A** — Diver
617 Dorchester Dr, Noblesville IN 46062, USA
**Boudin, Michael** — Judge
US Court of Appeals, 1 Courthouse Way, Boston MA 02210, USA
**Boudreau, Bruce** — Ice Hockey Player, Coach
PO Box 27280, Anaheim CA 92809, USA
**Boudrias, Andre** — Ice Hockey Player
1008-4300 Place des Cageux, Laval QC H7W 4Z3, Canada
**Boudrias, Christine-Isabel** — Speed Skater
Speed Skating Canada, 2781 Lancaster Road, #402, Ottawa ON K1B 1A7, Canada
**Boughner, Robert (Bob)** — Ice Hockey Player
5541 La Puerta del Sol Blvd S, #414, Saint Petersburg FL 33715, USA
**Bouillon, Jean-Christophe** — Auto Racing Driver
Wildbacher 9, 8340 Hinwil, Switzerland
**Bouix, Evelyne** — Actress
Artmedia, 20 Ave Rapp, 75007 Paris, France
**Boujenah, Michel** — Actor
Voyez Mon Agent, 20 Ave Rapp, 75007 Paris, France
**Boulanger, Veronique** — Actress
Artmedia, 20 Ave Rapp, 75007 Paris, France
**Boulerice, Jesse** — Ice Hockey Player
152 McClellan Ave, West Berlin NJ 08091, USA
**Boulez, Pierre** — Conductor, Composer
Postfach 100022, 76481 Baden-Baden, Germany
**Boulmetis, Samuel A (Sam), Sr** — Thoroughbred Racing Jockey
711 Academy Road, Cantonsville MD 21228, USA
**Boulos, Frenchy** — Soccer Player
20 Elvin St, Staten Island NY 10314, USA
**Boulton, Eric** — Ice Hockey Player
41 Cove Road, Huntington NY 11743, USA
**Boulud, Daniel** — Chef
Daniel Restaurant, 60 E 65th St, New York NY 10065, USA
**Boulud, David** — Chef
Daniel Restaurant, 60 E 65th St, New York NY 10065, USA
**Boulware, Peter** — Football Player
3791 E Millers Bridge Road, Tallahassee FL 32312, USA
**Bouman, Todd** — Football Player
2080 140th Ave, Holland MN 56139, USA
**Bouquet, Carole** — Actress, Model
Agence Intertalent, 5 Rue Clement Marot, 75008 Paris, France
**Bourboulon, Jacques** — Photographer
24 Rue Rennequin, 75017 Paris, France
**Bource, Ludovic** — Film Composer
First Artists, 4764 Park Granada, #210, Calabasas CA 91302 USA
**Bourdain, Anthony** — Restauranteur, Chef, Writer
Inkwell Management, 521 Fifth Ave, New York NY 10175, USA
**Bourdais, Sebastian** — Auto Racing Driver
K V S H Racing, 4001 Methanol Lane, Indianapolis IN 46268, USA
**Bourdeaux, Michael** — Templeton Religion Laureate
Keston College, Heathfield Road, Keston, Kent BR2 6BA, England
**Bourdette, Christine** — Sculptor, Artist
Elizabeth Leach Gallery, 417 NW 9th Ave, Portland OR 97209, USA
**Bourdon, Rob** — Drummer (Linkin Park)
Artist Group International, 150 E 58th St, #1900, New York NY 10155, USA
**Bourgeois, Benjamin C (Ben)** — Surfer
Pro Surfing Mgmt, 320 High Tide Dr, #101, Saint Augustine FL 32080 USA
**Bourgeois, Charles (Charlie)** — Ice Hockey Player
PO Box 1481, Station Main, Moncton NB E1C 8T6, Canada

# B

**Bourgeois, Derek D** — Composer
Portland House, Burton Road, Wool, Dorset BH20 6EY, England

**Bourgoin, Louise** — Actress
W M E Entertainment, 9601 Wilshire Blvd, #300, Beverly Hills CA 90210 USA

**Bourn, Michael R** — Baseball Player
24604 Belvon Valley Lane, Mulberry FL 33860, USA

**Bourne, Bob** — Ice Hockey Player
Bob Bourne Realty, 1-1890 Cooper Road, Kelowna BC V1Y 8B7, Canada

**Bourne, Shae-Lynn** — Figure Skater
Connecticut Skating Center, 300 Alumni Road, Newington CT 06111, USA

**Bournigal, Rafael A** — Baseball Player
230 Canterwood Lane, Mulberry FL 33860, USA

**Bournissen, Chantal** — Alpine Skier
1983 Evolene, Switzerland

**Bourque, Phil** — Ice Hockey Player
5117 Yale Dr, Aliquippa PA 15001, USA

**Bourque, Pierre** — Horticulturist; Mayor, Montreal
Hotel de Ville, 275 Rue Notre Dame E, Montreal QC H2Y 1C6, Canada

**Bourque, Raymond J (Ray)** — Ice Hockey Player
Tresca Restaurant, 233 Hanover St, Boston MA 02113, USA

**Bourque, Rene G W** — Ice Hockey Player
9110 93rd Ave, Lac La Biche AB T0A 2C0, Canada

**Bourret, Caprice** — Model, Actress
PO Box 509, Walton-on-Thames KT12 5XJ, England

**Boushka, Richard (Dick)** — Basketball Player
5414 W 145th St, Overland Park KS 66224, USA

**Bousman, Darren Lynn** — Director
Verve Talent, 9696 Culver Blvd, #301, Culver City CA 90232, USA

**Bouteflika, Abdul Aziz** — President, Algeria
138 Chemin Bachir Brahimi, El Biar, Algiers, Algeria

**Boutette, Pat** — Ice Hockey Player
Doctors House Restaurant, 21 Nashville Road, Kleinburg ON L0J 1C0, Canada

**Boutilier, Paul** — Ice Hockey Player
35 Elgin Lane, Bedford NS B4A 2K2, Canada

**Bouton, Daniel** — Financier
Societe Generale, 29 Blvd Hausman, 75009 Paris, France

**Bouton, James A (Jim)** — Baseball Player, Writer
PO Box 188, North Edgemont MA 01252, USA

**Boutros-Ghali, Boutros** — Secretary-General, United Nations
2 Ave El Nil, Giza, 11221 Cairo, Egypt

**Bouvet, Didier** — Alpine Skier
Bouvet-Sports, 74360 Abondance, France

**Bouvia, Gloria** — Bowler
2072 NE Hogan Dr, Gresham OR 97030, USA

**Bouvier, Jean-Pierre** — Actor
Artmedia, 20 Ave Rapp, 75007 Paris, France

**Bouw, Carline** — Rowing Athlete
A A S R Skoll, Jan Vroegopsingel 6, 1096 Amsterdam CN, Netherlands

**Bouwmeester, Jay** — Ice Hockey Player
7824 NW 123rd Ave, Parkland FL 33076, USA

**Bouwmeester, Marit** — Yachtswoman
Bouwmeester Sailing, De Greiden 14, 9003 Wartena MJ, Netherlands

**Bouza, Matthew K (Matt)** — Football Player
1042 Via Nueva, Lafayette CA 94549, USA

**Bova, Raoul** — Actor
Cristiano Cucchini Mgmt, Lungoterre dei Mellini 10, 00193 Rome, Italy

**Bowa, Lawrence R (Larry)** — Baseball Player, Manager
129 Upper Gulph Road, Radnor PA 19087, USA

**Bowden, Craig D** — Golfer
1101 E Benson Court, Bloomington IN 47401, USA

**Bowden, Katrina** — Actress
Management 360, 9111 Wilshire Blvd, Beverly Hills CA 90210 USA

**Bowden, Mark** — Writer
I C M Partners, 10250 Constellation Blvd, #900, Los Angeles CA 90067 USA

**Bowden, Robert (Bobby)** — Football Coach
2813 Shamrock St N, Tallahassee FL 32309, USA

**Bowden, Terry** — Football Coach, Sportscaster
University of North Alabama, Athletic Dept, Florence AL 35632, USA

**Bowe, David** — Actor
Karg/Weissenbach, 329 N Wetherly Dr, #101, Beverly Hills CA 90211 USA

**Bowe, Riddick L** — Boxer
714 Ahmer Dr, Fort Washington MD 20744, USA

**Bowe, Rosemarie** — Actress
321 Saint Pierre Road, Los Angeles CA 90077, USA

**Bowen, Andrea** — Actress
Domain Talent, 9229 W Sunset Blvd, #710, West Hollywood CA 90069 USA

**Bowen, Andrew** — Actor
Principato-Young, 9465 Wilshire Blvd, #880, Beverly Hills CA 90212 USA

**Bowen, Anne** — Fashion Designer
589 8th Ave, #200, New York NY 10018, USA

**Bowen, Bruce** — Basketball Player
1810 Settler Court, San Antonio TX 78258, USA

**Bowen, Cameron** — Actor
Stone Manners Salners, 9911 W Pico Blvd, #1400, Los Angeles CA 90035 USA

**Bowen, Jason** — Ice Hockey Player
4900 W 14th Ave, Kennewick WA 99338, USA

**Bowen, Julie** — Actress, Model
Liberman/Zerman Mgmt, 252 N Larchmont Blvd, #200, Los Angeles CA 90004, USA

**Bowen, Michael** — Actor
Martin Berneman Mgmt, 5820 Wilshire Blvd, #200, Los Angeles CA 90036 USA

**Bowen, Nanci** — Golfer
201 Carolina Point Parkway, #1119, Greenville SC 29607, USA

**Bowen, Robert M (Rob)** — Baseball Player
56 Spring Dr, Ellijay GA 30536, USA

**Bowen, Ryan E** — Baseball Player
2806 Maryland Ave, Fort Worth TX 76162, USA

Bowen, Stephen G — Astronaut
N A S A, Johnson Space Center, 2101 NASA Road, Houston TX 77058 USA
Bowen, Wade — Singer
W M E Entertainment, 1600 Division St, #300, Nashville TN 37203 USA
Bowen, William G — Foundation Executive, Educator
Andrew Mellon Foundation, 140 E 62nd St, New York NY 10065, USA
Bowens, David W — Football Player
15140 SW 16th St, Weston FL 33326, USA
Bowens, Malick — Actor
Don Buchwald, 6500 Wilshire Blvd, #2200, Los Angeles CA 90048 USA
Bowens, Timothy L (Tim) — Football Player
PO Box 93, Okolona MS 38860, USA
Bower, Antoinette — Actress
1529 N Beverly Glen Blvd, Los Angeles CA 90077, USA
Bower, Gary E — Bowler
256 Green Lane Dr, Camp Hill PA 17011, USA
Bower, Gordon H — Psychologist
Stanford University, Psychology Dept, Stanford CA 94305, USA
Bower, Jamie Campbell — Actor
Dalzell & Beresford, 26 Astwood Mews, London SW7 4DE, England
Bower, Jeff — Basketball Coach
New Orleans Pelicans, 1250 Poydras St, #101, New Orleans LA 70113 USA
Bower, John W (Johnny) — Ice Hockey Player
Bower Enterprises, 3937 Parkgate Dr, Mississauga ON L5N 7B4, Canada
Bower, Robert W — Inventor (Semiconductor Insulated Gate)
University of California, Microelectronics Dept, Davis CA 95616, USA
Bower, Tom — Actor
United Talent Agency, U T A Plaza, 9336 Civic Center Dr, Beverly Hills CA 90210 USA
Bowering, Jodie — Softball Player
Boondall, Redcliffe QLD 4020, Australia
Bowers, Bryan — Singer, Autoharp Player
Scott O'Malley Assoc, PO Box 9188, Colorado Springs CO 80932, USA
Bowers, Chris — Actor
Gersh Agency, 9465 Wilshire Blvd, #600, Beverly Hills CA 90212 USA
Bowers, Dane — Singer, Songwriter
79 Byrbe Blood, Mill House, Millers Way, London W6 7NH, England
Bowers, David — Director
Independent Talent Group, 40 Whitfield St, London W1T 2RH, England
Bowers, Glenn — WW II Marine Air Corps Hero
225 Mountain Road, Dillsburg PA 17019, USA
Bowers, Mary Helen — Ballerina
Rubenstein Public Relations, 1345 Ave of Americas, #30, New York NY 10105, USA
Bowers-Broadbent, Christopher J — Concert Organist, Composer
94 Colney Hatch, Muswell Hill, London N10 1EA, England
Bowersox, Bob — Actor
Reinhard Agency, 2021 Arch St, #400, Philadelphia PA 19103, USA
Bowersox, Crystal L — Singer, Songwriter
PO Box 86190, Portland OR 97286, USA
Bowersox, Kenneth D — Astronaut
16907 Soaring Forest Dr, Houston TX 77059, USA
Bowes, Bill — Financier
US Venture Partners, 2735 San Hill Road, Menlo Park CA 94025, USA
Bowie, David — Singer, Actor
Maine Road Mgmt, 195 Chrystie St, #901F, New York NY 10001, USA
Bowie, Heather — Golfer
3017 Elm River Dr, Fort Worth TX 76116, USA
Bowie, Larry G — Football Player
739 Echo Shores Court, Saint Paul MN 55115, USA
Bowie, Micah A — Baseball Player
2039 Small Town Dr, New Braunfels TX 78130, USA
Bowie, Samuel P (Sam) — Basketball Player
901 The Curtilage, Lexington KY 40502, USA
Bowker, Judi — Actress
Howes & Prior, 66 Berkeley House, Hay Hill, London W1X 7LH, England
Bowlby, April — Model, Actress
W M E Entertainment, 9601 Wilshire Blvd, #300, Beverly Hills CA 90210 USA
Bowler, Grant — Actor
Don Buchwald, 6500 Wilshire Blvd, #2200, Los Angeles CA 90048 USA
Bowles, Erskine B — Government Official
Forstman Little Co, 767 5th Ave, #4500, New York NY 10153, USA
Bowles, Lauren — Actress
Main Title Entertainment, 8383 Wilshire Blvd, #408, Beverly Hills CA 90211, USA
Bowlin, Michael R — Businessman
Atlantic Richfield Co, 333 S Hope St, Los Angeles CA 90071, USA
Bowling, Orbie L — Basketball Player
10179 Frank Road, Collierville TN 38017, USA
Bowman, Elizabeth — Golfer
82 Davidson St, Chula Vista CA 91910, USA
Bowman, Harry W — Businessman
Outboard Marine, 1325 Remington Road, #H, Schaumburg IL 60173, USA
Bowman, James E (Jim) — Football Player
12 Stony Field Road, Norton MA 02766, USA
Bowman, Kenneth B (Ken) — Football Player
13664 N Placita Montansas de Oro, Tucson AZ 85755, USA
Bowman, Kirk — Ice Hockey Player
740 Pointe Pelee Dr, RR 1, Leamington ON N8H 3V4, Canada
Bowman, Pasco M, II — Judge
US Court of Appeals, US Courthouse, 811 Grand Ave, Kansas City MO 64106, USA
Bowman, Rob — Director, Producer
W M E Entertainment, 9601 Wilshire Blvd, #300, Beverly Hills CA 90210 USA
Bowman, W Scott (Scotty) — Ice Hockey Coach, Executive
56 Halston Parkway, East Amherst NY 14051, USA
Bown, Jane H — Photographer
Old Mill House, 50 Broad St, Alresford, Hants SO24 9AN, England
Bown, R Charles (Chuck), Jr — Auto Racing Driver
Stock Car Racing Career Development, 5082 Old NC Highway 49, Asheboro NC 27203, USA

# B

| | |
|---|---|
| **Bowness, Richard G (Rick)** | Ice Hockey Player, Coach |
| 10 Shadowstone Lane, Lawrence Township NJ 08648, USA | |
| **Bowsfield, Edward O (Ted)** | Baseball Player |
| 980 Briar Rose Lane, Nipomo CA 93444, USA | |
| **Bowyer, C Stuart** | Astronaut, Astronomer |
| 34 Seascape Dr, Muir Beach CA 94965, USA | |
| **Bowyer, Clint** | Auto, Truck Racing Driver |
| Clint Bowyer Enterprises, 6221 Ramada Dr, Clemmons NC 27012, USA | |
| **Bowyer, William** | Artist |
| 12 Cleveland Ave, Chiswick, London W4 1SN, England | |
| **Box, C J** | Writer |
| Penguin Books, 375 Hudson St, Basement 1, New York NY 10014 USA | |
| **Boxberger, Loa** | Bowler |
| PO Box 708, Russell KS 67665, USA | |
| **Boxx, Gillian** | Softball Player |
| 15111 Chelsea Dr, San Jose CA 95124, USA | |
| **Boxx, Shannon** | Soccer Player |
| 300 W Grand Ave, #401, Chicago IL 60654, USA | |
| **Boyadjiev, Latchezar** | Sculptor |
| 48 Mark Dr, San Rafael CA 94903, USA | |
| **Boyarsky, Gerald M J (Jerry)** | Football Player |
| 229 Boyarsky Road, Scott Township PA 18447, USA | |
| **Boyarsky, Konstantin** | Concert Violinist, Composer |
| Grant Rogers Mgmt, 8 Wren Crescent, Bushey Heath, Hertfordshire WD23 1AN, England | |
| **Boyce, Kim** | Singer |
| 200 Nathan Dr, Hollister MO 65672, USA | |
| **Boyd, Alan S** | Secretary, Transportation |
| 116 Fairview Ave N, #735, Seattle WA 98109, USA | |
| **Boyd, Brandon C** | Singer, Percussionist (Incubus) |
| Creative Artists Agency, 2000 Ave of Stars, #100, Los Angeles CA 90067 USA | |
| **Boyd, Brent V** | Football Player |
| 948 N Coast Highway 101, #185, Encinitas CA 92024, USA | |
| **Boyd, Cayden** | Actor |
| Gersh Agency, 9465 Wilshire Blvd, #600, Beverly Hills CA 90212 USA | |
| **Boyd, Darren** | Actor |
| Independent Talent Group, 40 Whitfield St, London W1T 2RH, England | |
| **Boyd, David** | Cinematographer |
| Montana Artists Agency, 625 Montana Ave, Santa Monica CA 90403 USA | |
| **Boyd, Dennis R (Oil Can)** | Baseball Player |
| 45 Swan St, East Providence RI 02914, USA | |
| **Boyd, Douglas** | Conductor |
| Ingpen & Williams, 131 Putney Bridge Road, London SW15 2PA, England | |
| **Boyd, Fred L** | Basketball Player |
| 10915 Open Trail Road, Bakersfield CA 93311, USA | |
| **Boyd, Guy** | Actor |
| Stone Manners Salners, 9911 W Pico Blvd, #1400, Los Angeles CA 90035 USA | |
| **Boyd, Jenna** | Actress |
| Gersh Agency, 9465 Wilshire Blvd, #600, Beverly Hills CA 90212 USA | |
| **Boyd, John** | Actor |
| Dontanville/Frattaroli, 315 S Beverly Dr, #201, Beverly Hills CA 90212, USA | |
| **Boyd, Liona M C** | Concert Guitarist |
| B C Fiedler Mgmt, 53 Seton Park Road, Montreal ON M3C 3Z8, Canada | |
| **Boyd, Lynda** | Actress |
| Greene Assoc, 1901 Ave of Stars, #130, Los Angeles CA 90067 USA | |
| **Boyd, Malcolm** | Writer, Religious Leader |
| Saint Augustine by Sea Episcopal Church, 1227 4th St, Santa Monica CA 90401, USA | |
| **Boyd, Randy** | Ice Hockey Player |
| 1769 Blackwillow Dr, Marietta GA 30066, USA | |
| **Boyd, Robert** | Golfer |
| 828 Robert E Lee Dr, Wilmington NC 28412, USA | |
| **Boyd, Robert D (Bobby)** | Football Player |
| 2105 Lansdown Dr, Garland TX 75040, USA | |
| **Boyd, Russell S** | Cinematographer |
| 52 Sutherland St, Cremorne NSW 2090, Australia | |
| **Boyd, Stephen G** | Football Player |
| 1268 Marginal Road, Atlantic Beach NY 11509, USA | |
| **Boyd, Tanya** | Actress |
| Vincent Cirrincione Assoc, 1516 N Fairfax Ave, Los Angeles CA 90046 USA | |
| **Boyd, Willard L** | Educator, Museum Executive |
| 3800 N Lake Shore Dr, #3A, Chicago IL 60613, USA | |
| **Boyd, William A M** | Writer |
| The Agency, 24 Pottery Lane, Holland Park, London W11 4LZ, England | |
| **Boyden, Frank D** | Artist |
| 1914 N Three Rocks Road, Otis OR 97368, USA | |
| **Boyega, John** | Actor |
| Identity Agency Group, 11-15 Betterton St, Covent Garden, London WC2H 9BP, England | |
| **Boyens, Philippa** | Producer |
| I C M Partners, 10250 Constellation Blvd, #900, Los Angeles CA 90067 USA | |
| **Boyer, Blaine T** | Baseball Player |
| 4825 Bellingham Dr, Marietta GA 30062, USA | |
| **Boyer, Brant T** | Football Player |
| 1683 Old Lake Lane, Kaysville UT 84037, USA | |
| **Boyer, Cloyd** | Baseball Player |
| 14528 County Road 210, Jasper MO 64755, USA | |
| **Boyer, Herbert W** | Biochemist, Inventor |
| PO Box 7318, Rancho Santa Fe CA 92067, USA | |
| **Boyer, Mark** | Football Player |
| 21942 Kaneohe Lane, Huntington Beach CA 92646, USA | |
| **Boyer, Paul D** | Nobel Chemistry Laureate |
| 1033 Somera Road, Los Angeles CA 90077, USA | |
| **Boyer, Wally** | Ice Hockey Player |
| 400 Manly St, Midland ON L4R 3E3, Canada | |
| **Boyes, Brad** | Ice Hockey Player |
| 11711 Fawnridge Dr, Saint Louis MO 63131, USA | |
| **Boyette, Garland D** | Football Player |
| 4003 E Valley Dr, Missouri City TX 77459, USA | |

**Boykins, Earl A** — Basketball Player
7572 Sanctuary Circle, Brecksville OH 44141, USA
**Boyko, Darren** — Ice Hockey Player
1341 Wolseley Ave, Winnipeg MB R3G 1H8, Canada
**Boylan, Eileen April** — Actress
S M S Talent, 8383 Wilshire Blvd, #230, Beverly Hills CA 90211 USA
**Boylan, Jeanne M** — Forensics Artist
W M E Entertainment, 9601 Wilshire Blvd, #300, Beverly Hills CA 90210 USA
**Boylan, Jennifer Finney** — Writer
Colby College, English Dept, 4000 Mayflower Hill, Waterville ME 04901, USA
**Boylan, John** — Actor
Noble Caplan Abrams, 1260 Younge St, #200, Toronto ON M4T 1WG, Canada
**Boylan, Orla** — Opera Singer
Harrison/Parrott, 5-6 Albion Court, London W6 0QT, England
**Boyle, Barbara D** — Businesswoman
Boyle-Taylor Productions, 5200 Lankershim Blvd, #700, North Hollywood CA 91601, USA
**Boyle, Consolata** — Costume Designer
Independent Talent Group, 40 Whitfield St, London W1T 2RH, England
**Boyle, Daniel (Dan)** — Ice Hockey Player
18232 Daves Ave, Monte Sereno CA 95030, USA
**Boyle, Danny** — Director
Independent Talent Group, 40 Whitfield St, London W1T 2RH, England
**Boyle, Jerry** — Sculptor
Jerry Boyle Studio, 926 3rd Ave, Longmont CO 80501, USA
**Boyle, Lara Flynn** — Actress
Don Buchwald, 6500 Wilshire Blvd, #2200, Los Angeles CA 90048 USA
**Boyle, Lisa D** — Model, Actress
7336 Santa Monica Blvd, #776, West Hollywood CA 90046, USA
**Boyle, Susan** — Singer
Andy Stephens Mgmt, 60A Highgate Hight St, London N6 5HX, England
**Boyle, T Coraghessan** — Writer
Creative Artists Agency, 2000 Ave of Stars, #100, Los Angeles CA 90067 USA
**Boylen, Jim** — Basketball Coach
University of Utah, Athletic Dept, Salt Lake City UT 84112, USA
**Boyne, Walter** — Museum Executive, Writer
10833 Margate Road, Silver Spring MD 20901, USA
**Boynes, Winford G** — Basketball Player
8979 Haflinger Way, Elk Grove CA 95757, USA
**Boynton, Nicholas (Nick)** — Ice Hockey Player
3326 N Valencia Lane, Phoenix AZ 85018, USA
**Boynton, Robert M** — Psychologist
6632 Grulla St, Carlsbad CA 92009, USA
**Boynton, Sandra** — Graphic Artist
Recycled Paper Products, 111 N Canal St, #700, Chicago IL 60606, USA
**Boysen, Sarah** — Psychologist
Ohio State University, Psychology Dept, Columbus OH 43210, USA
**Boyum, Steve** — Director, Producer
Creative Artists Agency, 2000 Ave of Stars, #100, Los Angeles CA 90067 USA
**Bozanic, Josip Cardinal** — Religious Leader
Zagreb Archdiocese, Kaptol 31, PP 553, 10001 Zagreb Hrvatska, Croatia
**Bozek, Steve** — Ice Hockey Player
8410 E Whispering Wind Dr, Scottsdale AZ 85255, USA
**Bozeman, Todd** — Basketball Coach
Morgan State University, Athletic Dept, Baltimore MD 21251, USA
**Bozzio, Dale** — Singer, Model
11935 Laurel Hills, Studio City CA 91604, USA
**Bozzo, Laura C** — Entertainer
Televisa, Blvd A Lopez Mateos 232, Colonia San Angel, Mexico City DF 01060 CP, Mexico
**Braase, Ordell** — Football Player
204 3rd St W, #201, Bradenton FL 34205, USA
**Braaten, Josh** — Actor
A P A Talent/Literary Agency, 250 W 57th St, #1701, New York NY 10107 USA
**Brabants, Tim** — Canoeing Athlete
Nottingham Canoe Club, Trentside North, Nottingham NG2 5FA, England
**Brabham, Geoff** — Auto Racing Driver
B M W Group Australia, 783 Springvale Road, Mulgrave VIC 3170, Australia
**Brabham, John A (Jack)** — Auto Racing Driver
Bag 1, #404, Robins Towne Centre QLD 4230, Australia
**Brabo, Manu** — Photojournalist
Associated Press, Editorial Dept, 450 W 33rd St, #1500, New York NY 10001 USA
**Bracco, Lorraine** — Actress
Innovative Artists, 1505 10th St, Santa Monica CA 90401 USA
**Bracegirdle, Nick (Chicane)** — Musician
W M E Entertainment, Centrepoint Tower, 103 New Oxford St, London WC1A 1DD, England
**Bracelin, Gregory L (Greg)** — Football Player
5465 Calumet Ave, La Jolla CA 92037, USA
**Bracey, Luke** — Actor
Creative Artists Agency, 2000 Ave of Stars, #100, Los Angeles CA 90067 USA
**Bracey, Stephen H (Steve)** — Basketball Player
560 Lincoln Ave, Brooklyn NY 11208, USA
**Bracher, Karl D** — Political Scientist, Historian
Universitat Bonn, Stationsweg 17, 53127 Bonn, Germany
**Bracht, Stephanie** — Golfer
2004 Delancey Dr, Norman OK 73071, USA
**Brack, Kenny** — Auto Racing Driver
Allen Farst Mgmt, PO Box 90383, Dayton OH 45490, USA
**Bracken, Donald C (Don)** — Football Player
15950 W Diamond St, Goodyear AZ 85338, USA
**Brackenbury, Curt** — Ice Hockey Player
W378N5861 Valley Road, Oconomowoc WI 53066, USA
**Brackens, Tony L, Jr** — Football Player
193 Private Road 407, Fairfield TX 75840, USA
**Brackett, Gary** — Football Player
3591 Hintocks Circle, Carmel IN 46032, USA
**Bradbury, Janette Lane** — Actress
10817 Kling St, North Hollywood CA 91602, USA

**Braddock, Paige** — Graphic Designer (Snoopy Stamp)
Creative Associates, 1 Snoopy Place, Santa Rosa CA 95403, USA
**Braddy, Johanna E** — Actress
Innovative Artists, 1505 10th St, Santa Monica CA 90401 USA
**Brademas, John** — Educator; Representative, NY
New York University, President's Emeritus Office, New York NY 10012, USA
**Braden, Dallas L** — Baseball Player
1459 W Walnut St, Stockton CA 95203, USA
**Braden, Vic** — Tennis Coach
22000 Trabuco Canyon Road, Trabuco Canyon CA 92678, USA
**bradford,** — Architect
Fentress Bradburn Assoc, 421 Broadway, Denver CO 80203, USA
**Bradford, Barbara Taylor** — Writer
Bradford Enterprises, 450 Park Ave, #2303, New York NY 10022, USA
**Bradford, Chadwick L (Chad)** — Baseball Player
3867 Bill Downing Road, Raymond MS 39154, USA
**Bradford, Charles W (Buddy)** — Baseball Player
6440 Springpark Ave, Los Angeles CA 90056, USA
**Bradford, Corey L** — Football Player
13002 Highway 955 E, Ethel LA 70730, USA
**Bradford, Richard** — Actor
2511 Canyon Dr, Los Angeles CA 90068, USA
**Bradford, Ronnie** — Football Player, Coach
965 Allen Lake Lane, Suwanee GA 30024, USA
**Bradford, Samuel J (Sam)** — Football Player
Saint Louis Rams, 901 N Broadway, Saint Louis MO 63101 USA
**Bradford, Sarah** — Writer
Penguin Books, 375 Hudson St, Basement 1, New York NY 10014 USA
**Bradlee, Benjamin C** — Editor
3014 N St NW, Washington DC 20007, USA
**Bradley, Alonzo** — Basketball Player
1713 Briaroaks Dr, Flower Mound TX 75028, USA
**Bradley, Bob** — Soccer Player, Coach
Club Deportivo Chivas, 18400 Avalon Blvd, #500, Carson CA 90746 USA
**Bradley, Brian** — Ice Hockey Player
6417 MacLaurin Dr, Tampa FL 33647, USA
**Bradley, Bruce** — Water Polo Player
262 Saint Joseph Ave, Long Beach CA 90803, USA
**Bradley, Carlos H** — Football Player
1316 E Cliveden St, Philadelphia PA 19119, USA
**Bradley, Charles W** — Basketball Player
10810 Mountshire Circle, Highlands Ranch CO 80126, USA
**Bradley, Christopher** — Actor
Ford/Robert Black Agency, 4032 N Miller Road, #104, Scottsdale AZ 85251, USA
**Bradley, Dan** — Director
W M E Entertainment, 9601 Wilshire Blvd, #300, Beverly Hills CA 90210 USA
**Bradley, David** — Actor
United Agents, 12-26 Lexington St, London W1F 0LE, England
**Bradley, Dick** — Sports Cartoonist
10176 Corporate Square Dr, #200, Saint Louis MO 63132, USA
**Bradley, Dudley L** — Basketball Player
9830 Clanford Road, Randallstown MD 21133, USA
**Bradley, Edward W (Ed), Jr** — Football Player
187 Fryes Creek Lane, Clemmons NC 27012, USA
**Bradley, Everett** — Singer, Songwriter
Fretland Productions Mgmt, 70A Greenwich Ave, PMB 212, New York NY 10011, USA
**Bradley, James** — Actor
Spotlight, 7 Leicester Place, London WC2H 7RJ, England
**Bradley, James** — Writer
PO Box 367, Rye NY 10580, USA
**Bradley, Kathleen** — Actress
8412 S Denker Ave, Los Angeles CA 90047, USA
**Bradley, Keegan H** — Golfer
Altus Marketing & Managing, 177 Huntington Ave, Boston MA 02115, USA
**Bradley, Lonnie** — Boxer
405 Edgecombe Ave, New York NY 10032, USA
**Bradley, Michael (Mike)** — Golfer
5501 Branch Oak Place, Lithia FL 33547, USA
**Bradley, Michael T** — Basketball Player
6150 Blackjack Court N, Punta Gorda FL 33982, USA
**Bradley, Milton O, Jr** — Baseball Player
5359 Oak Park Ave, Encino CA 91316, USA
**Bradley, Patricia E (Pat)** — Golfer
PO Box 248, West Hyannisport MA 02672, USA
**Bradley, Paul C (Gus)** — Football Coach
Jacksonville Jaguars, 1 AllTel Stadium Place, Jacksonville FL 32202 USA
**Bradley, Philip P (Phil)** — Baseball Player
6950 Seminole Court, Columbia MO 65203, USA
**Bradley, Rebecca** — Golfer
7501 Alderwood Dr, Garland TX 75044, USA
**Bradley, Robert A** — Physician
2465 S Downing St, Denver CO 80210, USA
**Bradley, Ryan** — Figure Skater
Colorado Springs World Arena & Ice Hall, 3185 Venetucci Blvd, Colorado Springs, CO 80906, USA
**Bradley, Sam** — Singer, Songwriter
Agency Group Ltd, 142 W 57th St, #600, New York NY 10019 USA
**Bradley, Scott W** — Baseball Player
43 Chicory Lane, Pennington NJ 08534, USA
**Bradley, Shawn P** — Basketball Player
606 Sunny Flowers Lane, Salt Lake City UT 84107, USA
**Bradley, Thomas W (Tom)** — Baseball Player
4104 Woodberry St, University Park MD 20782, USA
**Bradley, Timothy** — Boxer
Top Rank Inc, 3908 Howard Hughes Parkway, #580, Las Vegas NV 89169 USA
**Bradley, William C (Bill)** — Football Player
1505 Whispering Water, Spring Branch TX 78070, USA

| | |
|---|---|
| **Bradley, William W (Bill)** | Senator, NJ; Basketball Player |
| 7 Kips Ridge, Verona NJ 07044, USA | |
| **Bradshaw, Ahmad** | Football Player |
| Indianapolis Colts, 7001 W 56th St, Indianapolis IN 46254 USA | |
| **Bradshaw, James A** | Football Player |
| 5653 Eagle Harbor Dr, Westerville OH 43081, USA | |
| **Bradshaw, John E** | Writer, Theologian |
| Becsey/Wisdom/Kalajian, 849 S Wooster St, #7, Los Angeles CA 90035, USA | |
| **Bradshaw, Morris, Jr** | Football Player |
| 82 Steuben Bay, Alameda CA 94502, USA | |
| **Bradshaw, Sufe** | Actress |
| Affinity Artists Agency, 5724 W 3rd St, #511, Los Angeles CA 90036, USA | |
| **Bradshaw, Terry P** | Football Player, Sportscaster |
| 12221 Merit Dr, #750, Dallas TX 75251, USA | |
| **Brady, Ed J** | Football Player |
| 5755 White Path Lane, Liberty Township OH 45011, USA | |
| **Brady, James S (Jim)** | Government Official, Journalist |
| Handgun Control, 1225 I St NW, #1100, Washington DC 20005, USA | |
| **Brady, Jeffrey T (Jeff)** | Football Player |
| 1506 NW 37th Place, Cape Coral FL 33993, USA | |
| **Brady, Kyle J** | Football Player |
| 2221 Alicia Lane, Atlantic Beach FL 32233, USA | |
| **Brady, Nicholas F** | Secretary, Treasury; Senator, NJ |
| Darby Overseas Investments, 1133 Connecticut NW, #400, Washington DC 20036, USA | |
| **Brady, Orla** | Actress |
| Independent Talent Group, 40 Whitfield St, London W1T 2RH, England | |
| **Brady, Pat** | Cartoonist (Rose Is Rose) |
| United Feature Syndicate, PO Box 5610, Cincinnati OH 45201 USA | |
| **Brady, Patrick H** | Vietnam War Army Hero (CMH), General |
| 10419 Felsblock Lane, New Braunfels TX 78132, USA | |
| **Brady, Paul J** | Singer, Songwriter |
| Asgard Promotions, 125 Parkway, London NW1 7PS, England | |
| **Brady, Ray** | Commentator |
| CBS-TV, News Dept, 524 W 57th St, New York NY 10019, USA | |
| **Brady, Roscoe O** | Neurogeneticist |
| 6026 Valerian Lane, Rockville MD 20852, USA | |
| **Brady, Sarah** | Social Activist |
| Handgun Control, 1225 I St NW, #1100, Washington DC 20005, USA | |
| **Brady, Sean B Cardinal** | Religious Leader |
| Archbishop's House, Ara Coeli, Cathedral Road, Armagh BT6 7QY, Ireland | |
| **Brady, Thomas (Tom)** | Football Player |
| 310 Beacon St, #4, Boston MA 02116, USA | |
| **Brady, Wayne** | Actor, Comedian, Singer |
| W M E Entertainment, 9601 Wilshire Blvd, #300, Beverly Hills CA 90210 USA | |
| **Braeden, Eric** | Actor |
| Harrison Stokes, 8730 W Sunset Blvd, #270, West Hollywood CA 90069, USA | |
| **Braff, Zach** | Actor, Director |
| Creative Artists Agency, 2000 Ave of Stars, #100, Los Angeles CA 90067 USA | |
| **Braga, Alice** | Actress |
| Roar Mgmt, 9701 Wilshire Blvd, #800, Beverly Hills CA 90212 USA | |
| **Braga, Brannon** | Writer, Producer |
| W M E Entertainment, 9601 Wilshire Blvd, #300, Beverly Hills CA 90210 USA | |
| **Braga, Sonia** | Actress |
| Framework Entertainment, 9057 Nemo St, #C, West Hollywood CA 90069 USA | |
| **Bragg of Wigton, Melvyn** | Writer |
| 12 Hampstead Hill Gardens, London NW3 2PL, England | |
| **Bragg, Billy** | Singer, Guitarist, Songwriter |
| Sincere Mgmt, 35 Bravington Road, #6, London W9 3AB, England | |
| **Bragg, Darren W** | Baseball Player |
| 163 Patriot Road, Southbury CT 06488, USA | |
| **Bragg, Donald G (Don)** | Track Athlete |
| 965 Oak St, Clayton CA 94517, USA | |
| **Bragg, Michael E (Mike)** | Football Player |
| PO Box 4842, Falls Church VA 22044, USA | |
| **Bragg, Todd** | Drummer (Caedmon's Call) |
| Breen Agency, 25 Music Square W, Nashville TN 37203, USA | |
| **Braggs, Glenn E** | Baseball Player |
| 28369 Falcon Crest Dr, Canyon Country CA 91351, USA | |
| **Braggs, Stephen** | Football Player |
| 120 Power House Road, Lawndale NC 28090, USA | |
| **Bragnalo, Rick** | Ice Hockey Player |
| 515 Christina St E, Thunder Bay ON P7E 4P3, Canada | |
| **Braham, Rich** | Football Player |
| 19 Miramichi Trail, Morgantown WV 26508, USA | |
| **Brahaney, Thomas F (Tom)** | Football Player |
| 1602 W Cuthbert Ave, Midland TX 79701, USA | |
| **Brainerd, Clayton** | Opera Singer |
| Columbia Artists Mgmt Inc, 1790 Broadway, #702, New York NY 10019 USA | |
| **Braly, Angela** | Businesswoman |
| WellPoint Inc, 120 Monument Circle, #200, Indianapolis IN 46204, USA | |
| **Bramall of Busfield, Edwin N W** | Army Field Marshal, England |
| House of Lords, Westminster, London SW1A 0PW, England | |
| **Brambilla, Marco** | Director |
| Creative Artists Agency, 2000 Ave of Stars, #100, Los Angeles CA 90067 USA | |
| **Bramhill, Gina** | Actress |
| United Agents, 12-26 Lexington St, London W1F 0LE, England | |
| **Bramlett, Bonnie** | Singer, Actress |
| Mutual Central Mgmt, 9 Music Square S, #316, Nashville TN 37203, USA | |
| **Bramlett, David A (Dave)** | Army General |
| 61-100 Iliohu Way, Haleiwa HI 96712, USA | |
| **Bramlett, John C** | Football Player |
| 159 Cotton Ridge Cove S, Cordova TN 38018, USA | |
| **Brammell, Abby** | Actress |
| Paul Kohner, 9300 Wilshire Blvd, #555, Beverly Hills CA 90212 USA | |
| **Branagh, Kenneth** | Director, Actor |
| Troika, 74 Clerkenwell Road, #300, London EC1M 5QA, England | |

**Branca, John G** — Attorney
Ziffren Brittenham Branca, 1801 Century Park West, #700, Los Angeles CA 90067, USA
**Branca, Ralph T J** — Baseball Player
Westchester Country Club, 99 Biltmore Ave, Rye NY 10580, USA
**Brancato, John** — Writer, Producer, Actor
United Talent Agency, U T A Plaza, 9336 Civic Center Dr, Beverly Hills CA 90210 USA
**Branch, A Deion, Jr** — Football Player
New England Patriots, 1 Patriot Place, Foxboro MA 02035 USA
**Branch, Adrian F** — Basketball Player
18008 Fence Post Court, Gaithersburg MD 20877, USA
**Branch, Alan K** — Football Player
3076 E Kesler Lane, Gilbert AZ 85295, USA
**Branch, Anthony (Deion)** — Football Player
13382 W Sherbern Dr, Carmel IN 46032, USA
**Branch, Clifford (Cliff)** — Football Player, Coach
2071 Stonefield Lane, Santa Rosa CA 95403, USA
**Branch, John** — Journalist
New York Times, Editorial Dept, 229 W 43rd St, New York NY 10036 USA
**Branch, Michelle** — Singer, Songwriter
A2 Mgmt, 1316 Sherman Ave, #215, Evanston IL 60201, USA
**Branch, Reginald E (Reggie)** — Football Player
515 San Lanta Circle, Sanford FL 32771, USA
**Branch, Taylor** — Historian
Larjansoff & Verrill, 179 Franklin St, New York NY 10013, USA
**Branco, Joaquim Rafael** — Prime Minister, Sao Tome & Principe
Prime Minister's Office, CP 38, Sao Tome, Sao Tome & Principe
**Brand, Elton T** — Basketball Player
1077 Sentry Lane, Gladwyne PA 19035, USA
**Brand, Esther C** — Track Athlete
PO Box 11115, 9321 Universitas, South Africa
**Brand, Joshua** — Producer, Director
United Talent Agency, U T A Plaza, 9336 Civic Center Dr, Beverly Hills CA 90210 USA
**Brand, Oscar** — Singer, Songwriter
Douglas A Yeager Productions, 300 W 55th St, New York NY 10019, USA
**Brand, Ronald G (Ron)** — Baseball Player
4421 Staten Island Dr, Plano TX 75024, USA
**Brand, Russell** — Actor, Comedian
W M E Entertainment, 9601 Wilshire Blvd, #300, Beverly Hills CA 90210 USA
**Brand, Stewart** — Editor, Writer
E Gate 5 Road, Sausalito CA 94965, USA
**Brand, Vance D** — Astronaut
21825 Hidden Canyon Dr, Tehachapi CA 93561, USA
**Brandauer, Klaus Maria** — Actor
Novapool GmbH, Alte Schoenhauser Str 46, 10119 Berlin, Germany
**Brandenstein, Daniel C** — Astronaut
648 N Tailwind Dr, Blanco TX 78606, USA
**Brandes, Christine** — Opera Singer
I M G Artists, Hogarth Business Park, Chiswick, London W4 2TH, England
**Brandes, John W** — Football Player
905 Ashland Court, Mansfield TX 76063, USA
**Brandi** — Model
Next Model Mgmt, 23 Watts St, New York NY 10013 USA
**Brandmeier, Jonathon** — Entertainer
C E S D, 10635 Santa Monica Blvd, #130, Los Angeles CA 90025 USA
**Brandon, Barbara** — Cartoonist (Where I'm Coming From)
Universal Press Syndicate, 4520 Main St, #700, Kansas City MO 64111 USA
**Brandon, Christopher** — Actor
Ken McReddie Assoc, 101 Finsbury Pavement, London EC2A 1RS, England
**Brandon, Clark** — Actor
9000 W Sunset Blvd, #801, West Hollywood CA 90069, USA
**Brandon, Darrell G** — Baseball Player
590 White Cliff Dr, Plymouth MA 02360, USA
**Brandon, Michael** — Actor
Talent Works, 3500 W Olive Ave, #1400, Burbank CA 91505 USA
**Brandon, T Terrell** — Basketball Player
3310 NE Shaver St, Portland OR 97212, USA
**Brands, Henry W (H W)** — Writer
University of Texas, Government Dept, Austin TX 78712, USA
**Brands, Terry** — Freestyle Wrestler
3744 Lacina Dr SW, Iowa City IA 52240, USA
**Brands, Tom** — Freestyle Wrestler, Coach
4494 Taft Ave SE, Iowa City IA 52240, USA
**Brandt, Betsy** — Actress
Talent Works, 3500 W Olive Ave, #1400, Burbank CA 91505 USA
**Brandt, Brandi** — Model, Actress
Esterman Entertainment, 220 Park Road, Riva MD 21140, USA
**Brandt, Carlo** — Actor
Artmedia, 20 Ave Rapp, 75007 Paris, France
**Brandt, John G (Jackie), Jr** — Baseball Player
5 Rabbit Trail, Wildwood FL 34785, USA
**Brandt, Kyle** — Actor
Sweeney Mgmt, 8755 Lookout Mountain Ave, Los Angeles CA 90046, USA
**Brandt, Lesley-Ann** — Actress
Karen Kay Mgmt, 2/25 State St, Aukland 1010, New Zealand
**Brandt, Paul R** — Singer, Songwriter
Warner Bros Records, 3300 Warner Blvd, Burbank CA 91505 USA
**Brandt, Thordis** — Actress
8171 Mannix Dr, Los Angeles CA 90046, USA
**Branduardi, Angelo** — Singer, Songwriter
Studio Legale Costa, Via Azzo Guardino 54, 40122 Bologna, Italy
**Brandy** — Singer, Actress
Norwood & Norwood, 22187 Ventura Blvd, #432, Woodland Hills CA 91364, USA
**Brandywine, Marcia** — Commentator
1428 Rising Glen, Los Angeles CA 90069, USA
**Brannagh, Brigid** — Actress
Innovative Artists, 1505 10th St, Santa Monica CA 90401 USA

| | |
|---|---|
| **Brannan, Charles F** | Secretary, Agriculture |
| 3131 E Alameda Ave, Denver CO 80209, USA | |
| **Branscomb, Lewis M** | Physicist, Computer Scientist |
| Harvard University, Kennedy School of Government, Cambridge MA 02138, USA | |
| **Branshaw, David** | Golfer |
| 16220 Sierra de Avila, Tampa FL 33613, USA | |
| **Branson, Jeffrey G (Jeff)** | Baseball Player |
| 10749 Spokane Court, Union KY 41091, USA | |
| **Branson, Richard** | Businessman, Balloonist |
| Virgin Group, 120 Campden Hill Road, London W8 7AR, England | |
| **Branstad, Terry E** | Governor, IA |
| Regency West 5, #201, 4500 Westown Parkway, West Des Moines IA 50266, USA | |
| **Brant, Tim** | Sportscaster |
| 12416 Ansin Circle Dr, Potomac MD 20854, USA | |
| **Brantley, Jeffrey H (Jeff)** | Baseball Player |
| 104 Cherry Laurel Cove, Ridgeland MS 39157, USA | |
| **Brantley, Larry** | Actor |
| Home Agency, 4420 W Lovers Lane, Dallas TX 75209, USA | |
| **Branton, Daniel** | Biophysicist |
| Harvard Medical School, Molecular & Cell Biology Dept, 25 Shattuck St, Boston MA 02115, USA | |
| **Branyan, Russell O (Russ)** | Baseball Player |
| 3301 Running Spring Court, Franklin TN 37064, USA | |
| **Brasar, Per-Olov** | Ice Hockey Player |
| Brasar Trav A B, Heden 99, 793 29 Leksand, Sweden | |
| **Brasco, James J (Jim)** | Basketball Player |
| 225 W Neck Road, Huntington NY 11743, USA | |
| **Brashares, Ann** | Writer |
| Delacorte Press, 1540 Broadway, New York NY 10036 USA | |
| **Braslow, Paul** | Sculptor |
| 567 Virginia Dr, Belvedere Tiburon CA 94920, USA | |
| **Brasseur, Claude** | Actor |
| Artmedia, 20 Ave Rapp, 75007 Paris, France | |
| **Braswell, Joseph** | Interior Designer |
| Joseph Braswell Assoc, 1148 E Jordan St, Pensacola FL 32503, USA | |
| **Brathwaite, Edward** | Writer |
| University of West Indies, History Dept, Mona, Kingston 7, Jamaica | |
| **Brathwaite, Nicholas A** | Prime Minister, Grenada |
| House of Representatives, Grenada Trade Center, Grand Anse, Saint George's, Grenada | |
| **Bratkowski, Edmund R (Zeke)** | Football Player, Coach |
| 224 Anchors Lake Dr N, Santa Rosa Beach FL 32459, USA | |
| **Bratt, Benjamin** | Actor |
| Arcieri Assoc, 305 Madison Ave, #2315, New York NY 10165 USA | |
| **Bratton, Creed** | Actor, Guitarist (Grass Roots) |
| Artistry Mgmt, 340 N Camden Dr, #302, Beverly Hills CA 90210, USA | |
| **Bratton, Joseph K** | Army General |
| 5902 Blakeford Dr, Windermere FL 34786, USA | |
| **Bratton, William J** | Law Enforcement Official |
| Altergrity Corp, 7799 Leesburg Pike, #1100 North, Falls Church VA 22043, USA | |
| **Bratz, Michael L (Mike)** | Basketball Player |
| 7503 Tillman Hill Road, Colleyville TX 76034, USA | |
| **Bratzke, Chad A** | Football Player |
| 1478 Landings Circle, Sarasota FL 34231, USA | |
| **Brauckmann, Linda** | Figure Skating Coach |
| Center of Excellence, 6501 Sprott St, #2, Burnaby BC V5B 3B8, Canada | |
| **Braude, Peter R** | Obstetrician, Gynecologist |
| King's College, Women's Health Dept, Strand, London WC2R 2LS, England | |
| **Brauer, Arik** | Artist |
| Academy of Fine Arts, Schillerplatz 3, 1010 Vienna, Austria | |
| **Brauer, William (Bill)** | Artist |
| Bill Brauer Studios, 4368 E Warren Road, Warren VT 05674, USA | |
| **Braugher, Andre** | Actor |
| Principato-Young, 9465 Wilshire Blvd, #880, Beverly Hills CA 90212 USA | |
| **Brauman, John I** | Chemist |
| 849 Tolman Dr, Stanford CA 94305, USA | |
| **Braun, Allen** | Neuroscientist |
| National Institute on Deafness, 9000 Rockville Pike, Bethesda MD 20892, USA | |
| **Braun, Colin** | Truck Racing Driver |
| 4502 Raceway Drive, Concord NC 28027, USA | |
| **Braun, Nicholas** | Actor |
| Levine Okwu/Ericson Talent, 6363 Wilshire Blvd, #300, Los Angeles CA 90048, USA | |
| **Braun, Rick** | Jazz Trumpeter |
| Chapman Mgmt, 14011 Venture Blvd, #405, Sherman Oaks CA 91423, USA | |
| **Braun, Russell** | Opera, Concert Singer |
| Columbia Artists Mgmt Inc, 1790 Broadway, #702, New York NY 10019 USA | |
| **Braun, Ryan J** | Baseball Player |
| 8926 38th Ave, #8W, Kenosha WI 53142, USA | |
| **Braun, Steve** | Actor |
| Talent Works, 3500 W Olive Ave, #1400, Burbank CA 91505 USA | |
| **Braun, Wendy** | Actress |
| C E S D, 10635 Santa Monica Blvd, #130, Los Angeles CA 90025 USA | |
| **Braun, Zev** | Producer |
| Zev Braun Pictures, 1438 N Gower St, #26, Los Angeles CA 90028, USA | |
| **Braunfels, Michael** | Composer, Concert Pianist |
| Dransdorferstr 40, 50968 Cologne, Germany | |
| **Braunwald, Eugene** | Physician |
| Partners Healthcare, 800 Boylston St, Boston MA 02199, USA | |
| **Braver, Rita** | Commentator |
| CBS-TV, News Dept, 2020 M St NW, Washington DC 20036 USA | |
| **Braverman, Bart** | Actor |
| House of Representatives, 1434 6th St, #1, Santa Monica CA 90401 USA | |
| **Braverman, Nachum** | Religious Leader, Rabbi |
| Aish Hatorah, 9106 W Pico Blvd, Los Angeles CA 90035, USA | |
| **Bravman, John C** | Educator |
| Bucknell University, President's Office, Marts Hall, Lewisburg PA 17837, USA | |
| **Braxton, Anthony** | Jazz Saxophonist, Composer |
| Berkeley Agency, 2608 9th St, #301, Berkeley CA 94710 USA | |

Brannan - Braxton

**B**

**Braxton, David H** — Football Player
6406 Donnegal Farm Road, Charlotte NC 28270, USA
**Braxton, Kara** — Basketball Player
Phoenix Mercury, American West Arena, 201 E Jefferson St, Phoenix AZ 85004 USA
**Braxton, Toni** — Singer, Songwriter
I C M Partners, 10250 Constellation Blvd, #900, Los Angeles CA 90067 USA
**Braxton, Tyrone S** — Football Player
455 Kearney St, Denver CO 80220, USA
**Bray, Robert** — Interior Designer
Bray-Schaible Design, 80 W 40th St, #800, New York NY 10018, USA
**Bray, Thomas E (Thom)** — Actor
7006 SE 29th Ave, Portland OR 97202, USA
**Brayton, Tyler** — Football Player
412 Hunter Lane, Charlotte NC 28211, USA
**Brazelton, Dewon C** — Baseball Player
107 Scenic Dr, Tullahoma TN 37388, USA
**Brazelton, T Berry** — Pediatrician
23 Hawthorn St, Cambridge MA 02138, USA
**Braziel, Larry** — Football Player
7616 Carriage Lane, Fort Worth TX 76112, USA
**Brazile, Robert L, Jr** — Football Player
813 Felder Ave, Fort Worth TX 76112, USA
**Brazile, Trevor** — Rodeo Rider
715 County Road 3051, Decatur TX 76234, USA
**Brazoban, Yhency J** — Baseball Player
13609 N 20th St, Tampa FL 33613, USA
**B-Real** — Rap Artist (Cypress Hill)
W M E Entertainment, 9601 Wilshire Blvd, #300, Beverly Hills CA 90210 USA
**Bream, Julian A** — Concert Guitarist
Hazard Chase, 25 City Road, Cambridge CB1 1DP, England
**Bream, Sidney E (Sid)** — Baseball Player
115 Sable Run, Zelienople PA 16063, USA
**Breathed, Berkeley** — Cartoonist (Bloom County, Outland)
Washington Post Writers Group, 1150 15th St NW, Washington DC 20071, USA
**Breathnach, Paddy** — Director
I C M Partners, 10250 Constellation Blvd, #900, Los Angeles CA 90067 USA
**Breaux, Jimmey** — Accordian Player (BeauSoleil)
Rosebud Agency, PO Box 170429, San Francisco CA 94117, USA
**Breaux, John B** — Senator, LA
Lousiana State University, Mass Communications School, Baton Rouge LA 70803, USA
**Breaux, Timothy (Tim)** — Basketball Player
845 Augusta Dr, #E75, Houston TX 77057, USA
**Brebner, Morwyn** — Producer, Writer, Actress
Gary Goddard Agency, 10 Sainte Mary St, #305, Toronto ON M4Y 1P9, Canada
**Brecher, John** — Writer
I C M Partners, 10250 Constellation Blvd, #900, Los Angeles CA 90067 USA
**Brechignac, Catherine** — Physicist
Scientifique Recherche Centre, 3 Rue Michel Ange, 75794 Paris, France
**Breckenridge, Alexandra** — Actress
Gersh Agency, 9465 Wilshire Blvd, #600, Beverly Hills CA 90212 USA
**Brecker, Randy** — Jazz Trumpeter
Michael Bloom Media Relations, PO Box 41380, Los Angeles CA 90041, USA
**Bredahl, Charlotte** — Equestrian
PO Box 318, Solvang CA 93464, USA
**Bredesen, Espen** — Ski Jumper
Hellerud Gardsvei 18, 0671 Oslo, Norway
**Bredow, Reinhard** — Luge Athlete
Bert-Heller Str 12, 38855 Wernigerode, Germany
**Breech, James T (Jim)** — Football Player
5461 Union Centre Dr, West Chester OH 45069, USA
**Breeden, Harold N (Hal)** — Baseball Player
665 Middle Road S, Leesburg GA 31763, USA
**Breeden, Richard C** — Government Official
Coopers & Lybrand, 1800 M St NW, Washington DC 20036, USA
**Breedlove, N Craig** — Auto Racing Driver
World Speedway Team, 200 N Front St, Rio Vista CA 94571, USA
**Breedlove, Rodney W (Rod)** — Football Player
264 New Valley Road, Conowingo MD 21918, USA
**Breen, Edward D, Jr** — Businessman
Tyco International, 273 Corporate Dr, #100, Portsmouth NH 03801, USA
**Breen, George** — Swimmer
425 Pepper Mill Court, Sewell NJ 08080, USA
**Breen, J Eugene (Gene)** — Football Player
1018 Henley Downs Place, Lake Mary FL 32746, USA
**Breen, Mike** — Sportscaster
ABC-TV, Sports Dept, 77 W 66th St, New York NY 10023 USA
**Breen, Patrick** — Actor
Gersh Agency, 9465 Wilshire Blvd, #600, Beverly Hills CA 90212 USA
**Breen, Shelley L P** — Singer (Point of Grace)
Blanton Harrell Cooke Corzine, 1014 Cross Bow Court, Hendersonville TN 37075 USA
**Breen, Stephen P (Steve)** — Editorial Cartoonist
San Diego Union-Tribune, Editorial Dept, 350 Camino Reina, San Diego CA 92108 USA
**Breer, Murle** — Golfer
7008 Sand Road, Savannah GA 31410, USA
**Brees, Drew C** — Football Player
5500 Prytania St, New Orleans LA 70115, USA
**Bregman Recht, Tracey E** — Actress
Bell-Bregman Productions, 7800 Beverly Blvd, #3371, Los Angeles CA 90036, USA
**Bregman, Anthony** — Producer, Actor
Likely Story, 150 W 22nd St, #900, New York NY 10011, USA
**Bregman, Buddy** — Director, Producer, Composer
Paul Lane Entertainment, 468 N Camden Dr, Beverly Hills CA 90210, USA
**Bregman, Martin** — Producer
Martin Bregman Productions, 100 Universal City Plaza, Universal City CA 91608, USA
**Bregvadze, Nani G** — Singer
Irakly Abashidze Str 18A, #10, 380079 Tbilisi, Georgia

Braxton - Bregvadze

| | |
|---|---|
| **Brehaut, Jeff** | Golfer |
| 1085 Leonello Ave, Los Altos CA 94024, USA | |
| **Breidenbach, Warren** | Surgeon |
| Jewish Hospital, Surgery Dept, 217 E Chestnut, Louisville KY 40202, USA | |
| **Breiman, Valerie** | Director, Actress |
| Creative Artists Agency, 2000 Ave of Stars, #100, Los Angeles CA 90067 USA | |
| **Breining, Fred L** | Baseball Player |
| 2120 Ticonderoga Dr, San Mateo CA 94402, USA | |
| **Breitenbach, Ken** | Ice Hockey Player |
| 8 Greenvale Court, SS 1, Fonthill ON L0S 1E1, Canada | |
| **Breitenstein, Robert C (Bob)** | Football Player |
| 4215 E 95th St, Tulsa OK 74137, USA | |
| **Breitner, Paul** | Soccer Player |
| Kuckucksweg 4, 85649 Brunnthal, Germany | |
| **Breitschwerdt, Werner** | Businessman |
| Daimler-Benz AG, Mercedesstr 136, 70322 Stuttgart, Germany | |
| **Breland, Mark** | Boxer, Trainer |
| 20514 Heritage Highway, Denmark SC 29042, USA | |
| **Bremers, Peter** | Artist |
| PO Box 27, 6120 Born AA, Netherlands | |
| **Bremner, Ewen** | Actor |
| Independent Talent Group, 40 Whitfield St, London W1T 2RH, England | |
| **Brenciu, Marius** | Opera Singer |
| I M G Artists, Hogarth Business Park, Chiswick, London W4 2TH, England | |
| **Brendel, Alfred** | Concert Pianist |
| Ingpen & Williams, 131 Putney Bridge Road, London SW15 2PA, England | |
| **Brendel, Wolfgang** | Opera Singer |
| Manuela Kursidem, Wasagasse 12/1/3, 1090 Vienna, Austria | |
| **Brendlinger, Kai** | Model |
| Playboy Promotions, 2706 Media Center Dr, Los Angeles CA 90065 USA | |
| **Brendon, Nicholas** | Actor |
| Gage Group, 14724 Ventura Blvd, #505, Sherman Oaks CA 91403 USA | |
| **Breneman, Curtis E** | Chemist |
| 47 Farrell Road, Troy NY 12180, USA | |
| **Brener, Shirly** | Actress, Model |
| Jackoway Tyerman Wertheimer, 1925 Century Park E, #2200, Los Angeles CA 90067 USA | |
| **Brengarth, Didier** | Actor |
| Angy Co, 85 Rue Saint Honore, 75001 Paris, France | |
| **Brenly, Robert E (Bob)** | Baseball Player, Manager |
| 9726 E Laurel Lane, Scottsdale AZ 85260, USA | |
| **Brennan, Bernard F** | Businessman |
| B V-Cornerstone Ventures, 11001 W 120th St, #300, Broomfield CO 80021, USA | |
| **Brennan, Brian M** | Football Player |
| 2961 Edgewood Road, Cleveland OH 44124, USA | |
| **Brennan, Christine** | Sportswriter |
| Washington Post, Sports Dept, 1150 15th Ave NW, Washington DC 20071, USA | |
| **Brennan, Dan** | Ice Hockey Player |
| 1912 108th Ave, Dawson Creek BC V1G 2T8, Canada | |
| **Brennan, Gabriele** | Actress |
| C E S D, 10635 Santa Monica Blvd, #130, Los Angeles CA 90025 USA | |
| **Brennan, George** | Harness Racing Driver |
| 2 Millpond Road, Millstone Township NJ 08535, USA | |
| **Brennan, Joseph E** | Governor, ME |
| 104 Frances St, Portland ME 04102, USA | |
| **Brennan, Melissa** | Actress |
| 6520 Platt Ave, #634, West Hills CA 91307, USA | |
| **Brennan, Richard (Rich)** | Ice Hockey Player |
| 14 Reflection Way, South Yarmouth MA 02664, USA | |
| **Brennan, Shane** | Producer, Writer |
| Paradigm Agency, 360 N Crescent Dr, North Building, Beverly Hills CA 90210 USA | |
| **Brennan, Terrance** | Restauranteur, Chef |
| Pichoine Restaurant, 35 W 64th St, New York NY 10023, USA | |
| **Brennan, Terrance P (Terry)** | Football Player, Coach |
| 1731 Wildberry Dr, #C, Glenview IL 60025, USA | |
| **Brennan, Thomas M (Tom)** | Baseball Player |
| 8204 Millbank Dr, Orland Park IL 60462, USA | |
| **Brenneman, Amy** | Actress |
| Creative Artists Agency, 2000 Ave of Stars, #100, Los Angeles CA 90067 USA | |
| **Brenneman, Gregory D** | Businessman |
| Quiznos, 1475 Lawrence St, #400, Denver CO 80202, USA | |
| **Brenneman, John** | Ice Hockey Player |
| 247 Radley Road, Mississauga ON L5G 2R6, Canada | |
| **Brenner, Carol** | Actress |
| Jean-François Pignard de Mart, 11 Rue Chanez, 75781 Paris Cedex 16, France | |
| **Brenner, David** | Actor, Comedian |
| Hess Entertainment, 195 S Beverly Dr, #401, Beverly Hills CA 90212, USA | |
| **Brenner, Hoby F J** | Football Player |
| 40 Calle Ameno, San Clemente CA 92672, USA | |
| **Brenner, Sydney** | Nobel Medicine Laureate |
| Molecular Sciences Institute, 2168 Shattuck Ave, #200, Berkeley CA 94704, USA | |
| **Brenner, Teddy** | Boxing Promoter |
| 24 W 55th St, #9C, New York NY 10019, USA | |
| **Bresee, Bobbie** | Actress |
| PO Box 1222, Los Angeles CA 90078, USA | |
| **Breslik, Pavel** | Opera Singer |
| I M G Artists, Hogarth Business Park, Chiswick, London W4 2TH, England | |
| **Breslin, Abigail K** | Actress |
| I C M Partners, 10250 Constellation Blvd, #900, Los Angeles CA 90067 USA | |
| **Breslin, Jimmy** | Journalist |
| Newsday, Editorial Dept, 235 Pinelawn Road, Melville NY 11747, USA | |
| **Breslin, Spencer** | Actor |
| B/W/R, 9100 Wilshire Blvd, #500W, Beverly Hills CA 90212 USA | |
| **Breslow, Craig A** | Baseball Player |
| 26 Finchwood Dr, Trumbull CT 06611, USA | |
| **Breslow, Ronald C** | Chemist |
| 295 Three Mile Harbor Road, East Hampton NY 11937, USA | |

**B**

| | |
|---|---|
| **Bresnik, Randolph J (Randy)**<br>N A S A, Johnson Space Center, 2101 NASA Road, Houston TX 77058 USA | Astronaut |
| **Bressoud, Edward F (Eddie)**<br>515 Marble Canyon Lane, San Ramon CA 94582, USA | Baseball Player |
| **Brest, Martin**<br>I C M Partners, 10250 Constellation Blvd, #900, Los Angeles CA 90067 USA | Director, Producer |
| **Bretos, Conchy**<br>M I A Consulting, 5208 Aston Road, Miami Beach Fl 33140, USA | Social Activist |
| **Brett, George H**<br>6528 Seneca Road, Mission Hills KS 66208, USA | Baseball Player, Executive |
| **Brett, Jan**<br>132 Pleasant St, Norwell MA 02061, USA | Writer |
| **Brettschneider, Carl**<br>4649 Bird View Court, Las Vegas NV 89129, USA | Football Player |
| **Bretz, Gabor**<br>I M G Artists, Hogarth Business Park, Chiswick, London W4 2TH, England | Opera Singer |
| **Breuer, Randall W (Randy)**<br>10481 Misty Morning Lane, Eden Prairie MN 55347, USA | Basketball Player |
| **Breunig, Robert P (Bob)**<br>9215 Westview Circle, Dallas TX 75231, USA | Football Player |
| **Brewer, Christine**<br>I M G Artists, Hogarth Business Park, Chiswick, London W4 2TH, England | Opera Singer |
| **Brewer, Craig**<br>W M E Entertainment, 9601 Wilshire Blvd, #300, Beverly Hills CA 90210 USA | Director, Writer |
| **Brewer, David L**<br>Commander, Military Sealift Command, Washington DC 20398 USA | Navy Admiral |
| **Brewer, Donald**<br>Lustig Talent, PO Box 770850, Orlando FL 32877 USA | Drummer (Grand Funk Railroad) |
| **Brewer, Eric C**<br>634 Riviera Dr, Tampa FL 33606, USA | Ice Hockey Player |
| **Brewer, James T (Jim)**<br>1814 S 23rd Ave, Maywood IL 60153, USA | Basketball Player, Coach |
| **Brewer, Ronnie**<br>Houston Rockets, 1730 Jefferson St, Houston TX 77003 USA | Basketball Player |
| **Brewer, Thomas A (Tom)**<br>409 State Road, Cheraw SC 29520, USA | Baseball Player |
| **Brewer, William R (Billy)**<br>7405 Woodway Dr, Woodway TX 76712, USA | Baseball Player |
| **Brewster, Darrel B (Pete)**<br>PO Box 183, Peculiar MO 64078, USA | Football Player |
| **Brewster, Jordana**<br>Creative Artists Agency, 2000 Ave of Stars, #100, Los Angeles CA 90067 USA | Actress |
| **Brewster, Lamon T**<br>Don King Productions, 501 Fairway Dr, Deerfield Beach FL 33441 USA | Boxer |
| **Brewster, Lincoln**<br>G O A Inc, 1710 General George Patten Dr, #104, Brentwood TN 37027, USA | Singer, Guitarist, Songwriter |
| **Brewster, Paget**<br>Burstein Co, 15304 W Sunset Blvd, #208, Pacific Palisades CA 90272, USA | Actress |
| **Brewster, Patience**<br>World Media Communications, PO Box 689, Skaneateles NY 13152, USA | Artist, Writer |
| **Brey, Mike**<br>Notre Dame University, Athletic Dept, Notre Dame IN 46556, USA | Basketball Coach |
| **Breyer, Stephen G**<br>US Supreme Court, 1 1st St NE, Washington DC 20543 USA | Supreme Court Justice |
| **Breytenbach, Breyten**<br>Houghton Mifflin Harcourt, 215 Park Ave S, #1200, New York NY 10003 USA | Writer, Political Activist |
| **Brezec, Primoz**<br>10030 Hazelview Dr, Charlotte NC 28277, USA | Basketball Player |
| **Brezina, Gregory (Greg)**<br>155 Tillinghurst Trace, Newnan GA 30265, USA | Football Player |
| **Brezina, Robert P (Bobby)**<br>1204 Pine Hollow Dr, Friendswood TX 77546, USA | Football Player |
| **Breziner, Salome**<br>Rosen Law Group, 15 Brooks Ave, Venice CA 0291, USA | Director, Writer |
| **Brezis, Haim**<br>18 Rue de la Glaciere, 75640 Paris Cedex 13, France | Mathematician |
| **Brezner, Larry**<br>M B S T Entertainment, 345 N Maple Dr, #200, Beverly Hills CA 90210, USA | Producer |
| **Brian, Frank S (Frankie)**<br>4425 40th St, Zachary LA 70791, USA | Basketball Player |
| **Brice, Lee**<br>377 Mgmt, 209 10th Ave, #332, Nashville TN 37203, USA | Singer, Songwriter |
| **Brice, Pierre**<br>8 Rue Orleans, Domaine des Moinets, 60800 Sezy-Magnefall, France | Actor |
| **Brickel, James R**<br>4798 Hanging Moss Lane, Sarasota FL 34238, USA | Air Force General, Hero |
| **Brickell, Beth**<br>9630 Arby Dr, Beverly Hills CA 90210, USA | Director, Producer, Actress |
| **Brickell, Edie**<br>Sachs Co, 427 W 14th St, #300, New York NY 10014, USA | Singer (New Bohemians), Songwriter |
| **Brickell, James**<br>Caroline Rose Mgmt, Peter House, Oxford St, Manchester M1 5AN, England | Wildlife Filmmaker |
| **Brickley, Andy**<br>5 Mill River Lane, Hingham MA 02043, USA | Ice Hockey Player |
| **Bricklin, Daniel S**<br>Trellix Corp, 300 Bahr Ave, Concord MA 01742, USA | Computer Software Designer (VisiCalc) |
| **Brickman, Jim**<br>Lucid Artists Mgmt, 54 Music Square E, #200, Nashville TN 37203, USA | Pianist, Composer |
| **Brickman, Marshall**<br>I C M Partners, 10250 Constellation Blvd, #900, Los Angeles CA 90067 USA | Writer |
| **Brickman, Paul M**<br>Creative Artists Agency, 2000 Ave of Stars, #100, Los Angeles CA 90067 USA | Director, Producer, Writer |
| **Brickowski, Frank A**<br>589 7th St, Lake Oswego OR 97034, USA | Basketball Player |
| **Bricusse, Leslie**<br>8730 W Sunset Blvd, #300W, West Hollywood CA 90069, USA | Composer, Lyricist |

| | |
|---|---|
| **Bridgeman, Ulysses L (Junior)** | Basketball Player |
| 1604 Cherokee Road, Louisville KY 40205, USA | |
| **Bridges, Alan J S** | Director |
| 28 High St, Shepperton, Middlesex TW7 9AW, England | |
| **Bridges, Alicia** | Singer, Songwriter |
| Richard Walters, PO Box 2789, Toluca Lake CA 91610 USA | |
| **Bridges, Angelica** | Actress, Model |
| Universal Attractions, 135 W 26th St, #1200, New York NY 10001 USA | |
| **Bridges, Beau** | Actor |
| Creative Artists Agency, 2000 Ave of Stars, #100, Los Angeles CA 90067 USA | |
| **Bridges, Everett L (Rocky)** | Baseball Player |
| 1128 W Shane Dr, Coeur D'Alene ID 83815, USA | |
| **Bridges, Jeff** | Actor, Singer |
| Creative Artists Agency, 2000 Ave of Stars, #100, Los Angeles CA 90067 USA | |
| **Bridges, Jeremy** | Football Player |
| 15833 S 35th Way, Phoenix AZ 85048, USA | |
| **Bridges, Jordan** | Actor |
| Mavrick Artists Agency, 6100 Wilshire Blvd, #550, Los Angeles CA 90048, USA | |
| **Bridges, Krista** | Actress |
| Talent Works, 3500 W Olive Ave, #1400, Burbank CA 91505 USA | |
| **Bridges, Mark** | Costume Designer |
| United Talent Agency, U T A Plaza, 9336 Civic Center Dr, Beverly Hills CA 90210 USA | |
| **Bridges, Roy D, Jr** | Astronaut, Air Force General |
| 113 William Barksdale, Williamsburg VA 23185, USA | |
| **Bridges, Ruby** | Civil Rights Activist, Writer |
| Ruby Bridges Foundation, PO Box 870248, New Orleans LA 70187, USA | |
| **Bridges, Todd A** | Actor |
| 16002 Nordhoff St, North Hills CA 91343, USA | |
| **Bridges, William C (Bill)** | Basketball Player |
| 2322 33rd St, Santa Monica CA 90405, USA | |
| **Bridgewater, Brad M** | Swimmer |
| 3843 Echo Brook Lane, Dallas TX 75229, USA | |
| **Bridgewater, Dee Dee** | Singer. Actress |
| Ted Kurland, 173 Brighton Ave, Boston MA 02134 USA | |
| **Bridgman, Mel** | Ice Hockey Player |
| 221 Concord St, El Segundo CA 90245, USA | |
| **Bridwell, Norman** | Writer |
| PO Box 869, Edgartown MA 02539, USA | |
| **Brie, Alison** | Actress |
| W M E Entertainment, 9601 Wilshire Blvd, #300, Beverly Hills CA 90210 USA | |
| **Briem, Anita** | Actress |
| B/W/R, 9100 Wilshire Blvd, #500W, Beverly Hills CA 90212 USA | |
| **Brien, Douglas R Z (Doug)** | Football Player |
| 55 Cambrian Ave, Piedmont CA 94611, USA | |
| **Briere, Daniel** | Ice Hockey Player |
| 17 S Hinchman Ave, Haddonfield NJ 08033, USA | |
| **Briesewitz, Uta** | Cinematographer |
| W M E Entertainment, 9601 Wilshire Blvd, #300, Beverly Hills CA 90210 USA | |
| **Brigati, Eddie** | Singer, Percussionist (Rascals) |
| Dassinger Creative, 172 2nd Ave, Little Falls NJ 07424, USA | |
| **Briggs of Lewes, Asa** | Historian |
| Caprons, Keere Saint Lewes, Sussex BN7 1TX, England | |
| **Briggs, Daniel L (Dan)** | Baseball Player |
| 8270 Rookery Way, Westerville OH 43082, USA | |
| **Briggs, Edward S** | Navy Admiral |
| 3648 Lago Sereno, Escondido CA 92029, USA | |
| **Briggs, John E (Johnny)** | Baseball Player |
| 238 Wall Ave, Paterson NJ 07504, USA | |
| **Briggs, John T** | Baseball Player |
| 216 Tom Bell Road, #133, Murphys CA 95247, USA | |
| **Briggs, Johnny** | Actor |
| Associated International Mgmt, 7 Hatton Garden, #400, London EC1N 8AD, England | |
| **Briggs, Lance M** | Football Player |
| 225 NE Mizner Blvd, #685, Boca Raton FL 33432, USA | |
| **Briggs, Raymond R** | Writer, Illustrator, Cartoonist |
| Weston, Underhill Lane, Westmeston near Hassocks, Sussex, England | |
| **Briggs, Shannon** | Boxer |
| 22114 N Flamingo Road, Pembroke Pines FL 33028, USA | |
| **Briggs, William R** | Biologist |
| 480 Hale St, Palo Alto CA 94301, USA | |
| **Briggs, Wilma** | Baseball Player |
| 111 Summit Ave, Wakefield RI 02879, USA | |
| **Bright, Leon, Jr** | Football Player |
| 1183 Dutton Ave, Deland FL 32720, USA | |
| **Bright, Myron H** | Judge |
| 655 1st Ave N, #340, Fargo ND 58102, USA | |
| **Brightman, Sarah** | Singer |
| The Mill, Mill Lane, Cockham SL6 9QT, England | |
| **Brighton, Connie** | Model, Actress |
| Playboy Promotions, 2706 Media Center Dr, Los Angeles CA 90065 USA | |
| **Brigman, D J** | Golfer |
| 8304 Calle Soquelle NE, Albuquerque NM 87113, USA | |
| **Briles, Arthur R (Art)** | Football Coach |
| Baylor University, Athletic Dept, Waco TX 76798, USA | |
| **Briley, Gregory (Greg)** | Baseball Player |
| 2170 Sunnybrook Road, Greenville NC 27834, USA | |
| **Brill, Charlie** | Actor |
| 3635 Wrightwood Dr, Studio City CA 91604, USA | |
| **Brill, Francesca** | Actress |
| Kate Feast, Primrose Hill Studios, Fitzroy Road, London NW1 8TR, England | |
| **Brill, Steven** | Editor, Publisher |
| American Lawyer, Editorial Dept, 600 3rd Ave, New York NY 10016, USA | |
| **Brill, Steven (Steve)** | Director, Writer |
| United Talent Agency, U T A Plaza, 9336 Civic Center Dr, Beverly Hills CA 90210 USA | |
| **Brill, Winston J** | Bacteriologist |
| 12529 237th Way NE, Redmond WA 98053, USA | |

**B**

**Bridgeman - Brill**

**Brillinger, Alysha** — Singer, Songwriter
Agency Group Ltd, 142 W 57th St, #600, New York NY 10019 USA

**Brilmayer, Roberta L** — Attorney, Educator
Yale University, Law School, 127 Wall St, New Haven CT 06511, USA

**Brimanis, Aris** — Ice Hockey Player
12909 Badger Lane, Anchorage AK 99516, USA

**Brimble, Nick** — Actor
Curtis Brown Group, 28-29 Haymarket St, #500, London SW1Y 4SP, England

**Brimblecombe, Richard** — Actor
Associated International Mgmt, 7 Hatton Garden, #400, London EC1N 8AD, England

**Brimhall, Cynthia** — Actress, Model
Playboy Promotions, 2706 Media Center Dr, Los Angeles CA 90065 USA

**Brimley, Wilford** — Actor
Blake Agency, 23441 Malibu Colony Road, Malibu CA 90265, USA

**Brin, Sergey** — Businessman, Computer Engineer
Google Inc, 1600 Amphitheatre Parkway, #41, Mountain View CA 94043, USA

**Brind'Amour, Rod** — Ice Hockey Player
1153 Four Wheel Dr, Wake Forest NC 27587, USA

**Brink, Andre P** — Writer
University of Cape Town, English Dept, Rondebosch 7700, South Africa

**Brink, Elisabeth** — Writer
Houghton Mifflin Harcourt, 215 Park Ave S, #1200, New York NY 10003 USA

**Brink, Evelien** — Balloonist
Sikelalodge, PO Box 2277, Hazyview 1242, South Africa

**Brink, Henk** — Balloonist
Sikelalodge, PO Box 2277, Hazyview 1242, South Africa

**Brink, Lawrence (Larry)** — Football Player
13310 Tierra Heights Road, Redding CA 96003, USA

**Brink, R Alexander** — Geneticist
8301 Old Sauk Road, #326, Middleton WI 53562, USA

**Brinker, Nancy Goodman** — Foundation Executive
Komen Breast Cancer Foundation, 5005 LBJ Freeway, #250, Dallas TX 75244, USA

**Brinkley, Christine (Christie)** — Model, Actress
Ford Models, 9200 Sunset Blvd, #805, West Hollywood CA 90069, USA

**Brinkley, Douglas** — Historian
Harper Collins Publishers, 10 E 53rd St, Cellar 1, New York NY 10022 USA

**Brinkman, Charles E (Chuck)** — Baseball Player
126 Country Club Road, Bryan OH 43506, USA

**Brinkman, John A** — Historian
1321 E 56th St, #4, Chicago IL 60637, USA

**Brinkman, Joseph N (Joe)** — Baseball Umpire
10351 NW 70th St, Chiefland FL 32626, USA

**Brinkman, William F** — Physicist
1177 22nd St NW, #2C, Washington DC 20037, USA

**Brinkmann, Robert S** — Cinematographer
Mirisch Agency, 8840 Wilshire Blvd, #100, Beverly Hills CA 90211 USA

**Brinson, Gary** — Financier
Brinson Partners, 1 N Wacker Dr, #3000, Chicago IL 60606, USA

**Brion, Francoise** — Actress
11 Rue de Seine, 75006 Paris, France

**Brion, Jon** — Composer
Kraft-Engel Mgmt, 15233 Ventura Blvd, #200, Sherman Oaks CA 91403 USA

**Brisby, Vincent C** — Football Player
1926 Norfolk St, #19, Houston TX 77098, USA

**Brisco, Valerie A** — Track Athlete
USA Track & Field, 4341 Starlight Dr, Indianapolis IN 46239 USA

**Briscoe, Brent** — Actor, Writer
Red Baron Mgmt, 600 Rosecrans Ave, Building 7, Manhattan Beach CA 90266, USA

**Briscoe, Conie** — Writer
Random House, 1745 Broadway, #1800, New York NY 10019 USA

**Briscoe, Marlin** — Football Player
675 Coronado Ave, Long Beach CA 90814, USA

**Briscoe, Mary Beck** — Judge
US Appeals Court, 4839 Billings Parkway, Lawrence KS 66049, USA

**Briscoe, Ryan** — Auto Racing Driver
Penske Racing, Penske Plaza, 366 Riverfront, Reading PA 19602, USA

**Brisebois, Danielle** — Actress, Singer
1311 Broadway, Santa Monica CA 90404, USA

**Brisebois, Patrice** — Ice Hockey Player
4723 Castle Circle, Broomfield CO 80023, USA

**Briski, Zana** — Photographer, Cinematographer
Kids with Cameras, 341 Lafayette St, #4407, New York NY 10012, USA

**Brissie, Leland V (Lou)** — Baseball Player
1908 White Pine Dr, North Augusta SC 29841, USA

**Brister, Walter A (Bubby), III** — Football Player
139 Fontainebleau Dr, Mandeville LA 70471, USA

**Bristol, J David (Dave)** — Baseball Player, Manager
1748 Fairview Road, Andrews NC 28901, USA

**Bristow, Allan M** — Basketball Player, Coach, Executive
510 Sand Hill Court, Marco Island FL 34145, USA

**Britt, Chris** — Editorial Cartoonist
State Journal-Register, Editorial Dept, 1 Copley Plaza, Springfield IL 62701, USA

**Britt, James E** — Football Player
PO Box 371202, Decatur GA 30037, USA

**Britt, May** — Actress
5059 Enfield Ave, Encino CA 91316, USA

**Britt, Michael** — Guitarist (Lonestar)
Borman Entertainment, 4322 Harding Pike, #429, Nashville TN 37205, USA

**Britt, Thomas** — Interior Designer
136 E 57th St, #700, New York NY 10022, USA

**Brittain, Paul** — Actor, Comedian
W M E Entertainment, 9601 Wilshire Blvd, #300, Beverly Hills CA 90210 USA

**Brittan of Spennithorne, Leon** — Government Official, England
1 Finsbury Ave, London EC2M 2PP, England

**Brittany, Morgan** — Actress, Model
Scott Stander Assoc, 4533 Van Nuys Blvd, #401, Sherman Oaks CA 91403 USA

**Brittenham, Harry** — Attorney
Ziffren Brittenham Branca, 1801 Century Park West, #700, Los Angeles CA 90067, USA
**Brittingham, Eric** — Singer, Bassist (Cinderella)
Union Entertainment Group, 1323 Newbury Road, #104, Thousand Oaks CA 91320, USA
**Britton, Benjamin** — Inventor (Lascaux Virtual Reality Cave)
University of Cincinnati, Fine Arts Dept, Cincinnati OH 45221, USA
**Britton, Connie** — Actress
W M E Entertainment, 9601 Wilshire Blvd, #300, Beverly Hills CA 90210 USA
**Britton, Tony** — Actor
Shepherd Mgmt, 45 Maddox St, #400, London W1S 2PE, England
**Britz, Jerilyn** — Golfer
415 E Lincoln St, #7, Luverne MN 56156, USA
**Brixius, Liz** — Producer, Writer
W M E Entertainment, 9601 Wilshire Blvd, #300, Beverly Hills CA 90210 USA
**Broad, Eli** — Businessman
SunAmerica Inc, 10900 Wilshire Blvd, #1200, Los Angeles CA 90024, USA
**Broad, Molly Corbett** — Educator
American Council on Education, 1 Dupont Circle, #800, Washington DC 20036, USA
**Broadbent, Harry** — Keyboardist (Kula Shakur)
Little Big Man, 39A Grammercy Park N, #1C, New York NY 10010, USA
**Broadbent, Jim** — Actor
Independent Talent Group, 40 Whitfield St, London W1T 2RH, England
**Broadbent, John Edward** — Government Official, Canada
1386 Nicola, #30, Vancouver BC V6G 2G2, Canada
**Broadhead, James L** — Businessman
F P L Group, 700 Universe Blvd, North Palm Beach FL 33408, USA
**Broadie, Sarah W** — Philosopher
Saint Andrews University, Philosophy Dept, Fife KY16 9AJ, Scotland
**Brobeck, John R** — Physiologist
224 Vassar Ave, Swarthmore PA 19081, USA
**Broberg, Peter S (Pete)** — Baseball Player
220 Monterey Road, Palm Beach FL 33480, USA
**Brocail, Douglas K (Doug)** — Baseball Player
8011 Meadow Vista Dr, Missouri City TX 77459, USA
**Broch, Hugo** — WW II German Luftwaffe Hero
Zedernweg 4, 51381 Leverkusen, Germany
**Broch, Nicolai Cleve** — Actor
Panorama Agency, Ryesgade 103B, 2100 Copenhagen, Denmark
**Brochere, Lizzie** — Actress
Conway Van Gelder Grant, 8-12 Broadwick St, #300, London W1F 8HW, England
**Brochet, Anne** — Actress
Artmedia, 20 Ave Rapp, 75007 Paris, France
**Brochtrup, William (Bill)** — Actor
S D B Partners, 1801 Ave of Stars, #902, Los Angeles CA 90067 USA
**Brochu, Devin** — Actor
Greene Assoc, 1901 Ave of Stars, #130, Los Angeles CA 90067 USA
**Brochu, Doug** — Actor
A P A Talent/Literary Agency, 405 S Beverly Dr, #300, Beverly Hills CA 90212 USA
**Brock, Chad** — Singer
Collingsworth Bright, 209 10th Ave S, #216, Nashville TN 37203, USA
**Brock, Gregory A (Greg)** — Baseball Player
3727 Valley Oak Dr, Loveland CO 80538, USA
**Brock, Louis C (Lou)** — Baseball Player
61 Barkley Place, Saint Charles MO 63301, USA
**Brock, Matthew L (Matt)** — Football Player
3105 SW 98th Ave, Portland OR 97225, USA
**Brock, Peter A (Pete)** — Football Player
111 Main St, Topsfield MA 01983, USA
**Brock, Raheem F** — Football Player
1017 Serpentine Lane, Wyncote PA 19095, USA
**Brock, Stanley J (Stan)** — Football Player, Coach
2555 SW 81st Ave, Portland OR 97225, USA
**Brock, T Christopher (Chris)** — Baseball Player
7684 Markham Bend Place, Sanford FL 32771, USA
**Brock, Tarrik** — Baseball Player
8111 Fairchild Ave, Winnetka CA 91306, USA
**Brock, Tricia** — Director
I C M Partners, 10250 Constellation Blvd, #900, Los Angeles CA 90067 USA
**Brock, William E (Bill), III** — Secretary of Labor; Senator, TN
16 Revell St, Annapolis MD 21401, USA
**Brockermeyer, Blake W** — Football Player
PO Box 789, Wilson WY 83014, USA
**Brockers, Michael S** — Football Player
Saint Louis Rams, 901 N Broadway, Saint Louis MO 63101 USA
**Brockert, Richard C** — Labor Leader
United Telegraph Workers, 701 E Gude Dr, Rockville MD 20850, USA
**Brockington, John S** — Football Player
1835 Fort Stockton Dr, San Diego CA 92103, USA
**Brockington, Ryan** — Actor
C E S D, 10635 Santa Monica Blvd, #130, Los Angeles CA 90025 USA
**Brockovich-Ellis, Erin** — Legal Activist, Writer
Masry & Vititoe, 5707 Corsa Ave, #200, Westlake Village CA 91362, USA
**Brodbin, Kevin** — Writer
Creative Artists Agency, 2000 Ave of Stars, #100, Los Angeles CA 90067 USA
**Broden, Connie** — Ice Hockey Player
88 Valecrest Dr, Etobicoke ON M9A 4P6, Canada
**Broder, Samuel** — Medical Administrator
I V A X Corp, 4400 Biscayne Blvd, Miami FL 33137, USA
**Broderick, Beth** — Actress
Vox Inc, 6420 Wilshire Blvd, #1080, Los Angeles CA 90048 USA
**Broderick, J M** — Artist
8825 SE 32nd Ave, Portland OR 97222, USA
**Broderick, Kenneth L (Ken)** — Ice Hockey Player
5142 Citation Road, Niagara Falls ON L2H 3H7, Canada
**Broderick, Matthew** — Actor
246 W 44th St, New York NY 10036, USA

| | |
|---|---|
| **Brodeur, Martin (Marty)** | Ice Hockey Player |
| 100 Mountain Ave, West Orange NJ 07052, USA | |
| **Brodeur, Richard** | Ice Hockey Player |
| 5007 Angus Dr, Vancouver BC V6M 3M6, Canada | |
| **Brodhead, Richard H** | Educator |
| Duke University, President's Office, Durham NC 27708, USA | |
| **Brodie, H Keith H** | Psychiatrist |
| 63 Beverly Dr, Durham NC 27707, USA | |
| **Brodie, John R** | Football Player, Sportscaster, Golfer |
| 49350 Avenida Fernando, La Quinta CA 92253, USA | |
| **Brodie, Kevin** | Actor |
| 3925 Big Oak Dr, #5, Studio City CA 91604, USA | |
| **Brodowski, Richard S (Dick)** | Baseball Player |
| 120 Pine St, Manchester MA 01944, USA | |
| **Brody, Adam** | Actor |
| United Talent Agency, U T A Plaza, 9336 Civic Center Dr, Beverly Hills CA 90210 USA | |
| **Brody, Adrien** | Actor |
| Paradigm Agency, 360 N Crescent Dr, North Building, Beverly Hills CA 90210 USA | |
| **Brody, Jane E** | Journalist |
| 4508 Cedros Ave, Sherman Oaks CA 91403, USA | |
| **Brody, Kenneth D** | Financier |
| Export-Import Bank, 811 Vermont Ave NW, Washington DC 20571, USA | |
| **Brody, Lane** | Singer, Songwriter |
| Center Stage Attractions, 20 Music Square W, #208, Nashville TN 37203, USA | |
| **Brody, William R** | Educator |
| Biological Studies Institute, 10100 N Torrey Pines Road, La Jolla CA 92037, USA | |
| **Broecker, Wallace S** | Geologist, Geochemist |
| Lamont-Doherty Earth Observatory, PO Box 1000, Palisades NY 10964, USA | |
| **Broelsch, Christopher E** | Surgeon |
| University of Chicago Medical Center, Surgery Dept, Chicago IL 60690, USA | |
| **Brogdon, Cinderella J (Cindy)** | Basketball Player |
| 4162 Anson Trail, Suwanee GA 30024, USA | |
| **Broglio, Ernest G (Ernie)** | Baseball Player |
| 2838 Via Carmen, San Jose CA 95124, USA | |
| **Brohawn, M Troy** | Baseball Player |
| 1619 Taylors Island Road, Woolford MD 21677, USA | |
| **Brokaw, Gary G** | Basketball Player, Coach, Executive |
| 6614 Augustine Way, Charlotte NC 28270, USA | |
| **Brokaw, Thomas J (Tom)** | Commentator |
| 941 Park Ave, #14C, New York NY 10028, USA | |
| **Brokop, Lisa** | Singer, Songwriter |
| Libre Entertainment, 313-2906 W Broadway, Vancouver BC V6K 2G8, Canada | |
| **Brolin, James** | Actor |
| Jeff Wald Entertainment, 176 Acari Dr, Los Angeles CA 90049, USA | |
| **Brolin, Josh** | Actor |
| I/D Public Relations, 7060 Hollywood Blvd, #800, Los Angeles CA 90028 USA | |
| **Brolly, Shane** | Actor |
| Luber Rocklin Entertainment, 8530 Wilshire Blvd, #555, Beverly Hills CA 90211 USA | |
| **Bromberg, David** | Guitarist, Songwriter |
| Apex Artists, 818 N Market St, Wilmington DE 19801, USA | |
| **Bromley, Gary** | Ice Hockey Player |
| 1130 Munro St, Victoria BC V9A 5P1, Canada | |
| **Bromley, R Scott** | Interior Designer |
| Bromley Caldari Architects, 242 W 27th St, #200, New York NY 10001, USA | |
| **Bromstad, David** | Actor, Interior Designer |
| W M E Entertainment, 9601 Wilshire Blvd, #300, Beverly Hills CA 90210 USA | |
| **Bron, Eleanor** | Actress |
| Rebecca Blond, 69A King's Road, London SW3 4NX, England | |
| **Bronars, Edward J** | Marine Corps General |
| 3354 Rose Lane, Falls Church VA 22042, USA | |
| **Bronfman, Charles R** | Businessman, Baseball Executive |
| Koor Industries, 14 Hamelacha St, Rosh Ha'ayin 48091, Israel | |
| **Bronfman, Edgar M, Jr** | Businessman |
| Warner Music Group, 75 Rockefeller Plaza, Basement 1, New York NY 10019, USA | |
| **Bronfman, Edgar M, Sr** | Businessman |
| 31122 Broad Beach Road, Malibu CA 90265, USA | |
| **Bronfman, Yefin** | Concert Pianist |
| Opus 3 Artists, 470 Park Ave S, #900N, New York NY 10016 USA | |
| **Bronleewe, Matt** | Guitarist (Jars of Clay) |
| Creative Artists Agency, 2000 Ave of Stars, #100, Los Angeles CA 90067 USA | |
| **Bronner, Till** | Jazz Singer, Trumpeter, Composer |
| Bam Bam Music, Alte Schonhauser Str 44, 10119 Berlin, Germany | |
| **Bronson, Po** | Writer |
| Random House, 1745 Broadway, #1800, New York NY 10019 USA | |
| **Bronson, R Zack** | Football Player |
| 5735 Jackie Lane, Beaumont TX 77713, USA | |
| **Bronstein, Elizabeth** | Producer |
| Creative Artists Agency, 2000 Ave of Stars, #100, Los Angeles CA 90067 USA | |
| **Brook, Jayne** | Actress |
| Gersh Agency, 9465 Wilshire Blvd, #600, Beverly Hills CA 90212 USA | |
| **Brook, Kelly** | Model, Actress |
| Curtis Brown Group, 28-29 Haymarket St, #500, London SW1Y 4SP, England | |
| **Brook, Michael** | Composer |
| First Artists, 4764 Park Granada, #210, Calabasas CA 91302 USA | |
| **Brook, Peter S P** | Director |
| C I C T, 37 Bis Blvd de la Chapelle, 75010 Paris, France | |
| **Brook, Robert H** | Physician |
| 1474 Bienvenida Ave, Pacific Palisades CA 90272, USA | |
| **Brooke, Bob** | Ice Hockey Player |
| 15496 Stanbury Curve, Eden Prairie MN 55347, USA | |
| **Brooke, Edward W, III** | Senator, MA |
| 808 Brickell Key Dr, #3204, Miami FL 33131, USA | |
| **Brooke, Jonatha** | Singer (Story), Songwriter |
| Patrick Rains Assoc, 1255 5th Ave, #7K, New York NY 10029, USA | |
| **Brooke, Paul** | Actor |
| Caroline Dawson, 125 Gloucester Road, London SW7 4TE, England | |

| | |
|---|---|
| **Brookens, Thomas D (Tom)** | Baseball Player |
| 488 Black Gap Road, Fayetteville PA 17222, USA | |
| **Brooker, Gary** | Singer (Procol Harum), Songwriter |
| 195 Sandycombe Road, Kew TW9 2EW, England | |
| **Brooker, W Thomas (Tommy)** | Football Player |
| 306 Woodridge Dr, Tuscaloosa AL 35406, USA | |
| **Brookes, Harvey** | Physicist |
| Harvard University, Aiken Computation Laboratory, Cambridge MA 02138, USA | |
| **Brookes, Peter** | Editorial Cartoonist |
| London Times, Editorial Dept, 1 Pennington St, London E98 1S5, England | |
| **Brooke-Taylor, Tim** | Actor, Comedian |
| Jill Foster Ltd, 3 Lonsdale Road, London SW13 9ED, England | |
| **Brookhart, Maurice S** | Chemist |
| University of North Carolina, Chemistry Dept, Chapel Hill NC 27514, USA | |
| **Brooking, Keith H** | Football Player |
| 883 Lennox Court NE, Atlanta GA 30324, USA | |
| **Brookins, Clarence** | Basketball Player |
| 8266 Fayette St, Philadelphia PA 19150, USA | |
| **Brookins, Gary** | Editorial Cartoonist |
| Richmond Newspapers, Editorial Dept, PO Box 85333, Richmond VA 23293, USA | |
| **Brookner, Anita** | Writer |
| 68 Elm Park Gardens, #6, London SW10 9PB, England | |
| **Brooks, Aaron J** | Basketball Player |
| Houston Rockets, 1730 Jefferson St, Houston TX 77003 USA | |
| **Brooks, Aaron L** | Football Player |
| 1005 Middle Quarter Court, Henrico VA 23238, USA | |
| **Brooks, Albert** | Director, Writer, Actor |
| W M E Entertainment, 9601 Wilshire Blvd, #300, Beverly Hills CA 90210 USA | |
| **Brooks, Amanda** | Actress |
| United Agents, 12-26 Lexington St, London W1F 0LE, England | |
| **Brooks, Avery** | Actor |
| Lynn Coles Productions, PO Box 1918, El Cerrito CA 94530, USA | |
| **Brooks, Barrett** | Football Player |
| 11 Berkshire Dr, #25, Voorhees NJ 08043, USA | |
| **Brooks, Cindy** | Model |
| Playboy Promotions, 2706 Media Center Dr, Los Angeles CA 90065 USA | |
| **Brooks, Clifford (Cliff), Jr** | Football Player |
| 12023 Briar Forest Dr, Houston TX 77077, USA | |
| **Brooks, Conrad** | Actor |
| PO Box 264, Inwood WV 25428, USA | |
| **Brooks, Danny** | Singer (Dovells) |
| Lustig Talent, PO Box 770850, Orlando FL 32877 USA | |
| **Brooks, Darin L** | Actor |
| United Talent Agency, U T A Plaza, 9336 Civic Center Dr, Beverly Hills CA 90210 USA | |
| **Brooks, Deanna** | Model, Actress |
| Playboy Promotions, 2706 Media Center Dr, Los Angeles CA 90065 USA | |
| **Brooks, Derrick D** | Football Player |
| 12815 Pacifica Place, Tampa FL 33625, USA | |
| **Brooks, Diana D** | Businesswoman |
| Sotheby's Holdings, 1334 York Ave, New York NY 10021, USA | |
| **Brooks, Dolores (Lala)** | Singer (Crystals) |
| Superstars Unlimited, PO Box 371371, Las Vegas NV 89137, USA | |
| **Brooks, Ed** | Golfer |
| 6604 Augusta Road, Fort Worth TX 76132, USA | |
| **Brooks, Ethan B** | Football Player |
| 8 Gatewood, Avon CT 06001, USA | |
| **Brooks, Frederick P, Jr** | Mathematician, Computer Scientist |
| 413 Granville Road, Chapel Hill NC 27514, USA | |
| **Brooks, Garth** | Singer, Songwriter |
| Red Strokes Entertainment, 9465 Wilshire Blvd, #319, Beverly Hills CA 90212, USA | |
| **Brooks, Geraldine** | Writer |
| PO Box 5056, Vineyard Haven MA 02568, USA | |
| **Brooks, Golden** | Actress |
| Vincent Cirrincione Assoc, 1516 N Fairfax Ave, Los Angeles CA 90046 USA | |
| **Brooks, Hubert (Hubie)** | Baseball Player |
| 15001 Olive St, Hesperia CA 92345, USA | |
| **Brooks, James L** | Director, Producer, Writer |
| I C M Partners, 10250 Constellation Blvd, #900, Los Angeles CA 90067 USA | |
| **Brooks, James R** | Football Player |
| 2876 Sycamore Creek Dr, Independence KY 41051, USA | |
| **Brooks, Jason** | Actor |
| 289 S Robertson Blvd, #424, Beverly Hills CA 90211, USA | |
| **Brooks, Jessica** | Actress |
| United Agents, 12-26 Lexington St, London W1F 0LE, England | |
| **Brooks, Kevin C** | Football Player |
| 8201 Lighthouse Dr, Rowlett TX 75089, USA | |
| **Brooks, Kimberly A** | Actress |
| Metropolitan Talent Agency, 5405 Wilshire Blvd, #218, Los Angeles CA 90036 USA | |
| **Brooks, Kix** | Singer (Brooks & Dunn), Songwriter |
| Team 2 Entertainment, 6345 Balboa Blvd, Building 4, #375, Encino CA 91316, USA | |
| **Brooks, Lawrence L (Larry), Sr** | Football Player, Coach |
| 11200 NE 53rd St, Kirkland WA 98033, USA | |
| **Brooks, Lonnie** | Singer, Guitarist |
| Alligator Records & Mgmt, PO Box 60234, Chicago IL 60660, USA | |
| **Brooks, Mark** | Golfer |
| 1712 S Adams St, Fort Worth TX 76110, USA | |
| **Brooks, Max** | Writer |
| Creative Artists Agency, 2000 Ave of Stars, #100, Los Angeles CA 90067 USA | |
| **Brooks, Mehcad** | Actor |
| Mosiac Media Group, 9200 W Sunset Blvd, #1000, Los Angeles CA 90069 USA | |
| **Brooks, Mel** | Director, Actor, Composer |
| Brooksfilms, 9336 W Washington Blvd, Culver City CA 90232, USA | |
| **Brooks, Meredith** | Singer, Songwriter, Guitarist |
| Imago Mgmt, 11400 W Olympic Blvd, #200, Los Angeles CA 90064, USA | |
| **Brooks, Michael (Mike)** | Football Player |
| 716 2nd Ave, Ruston LA 71270, USA | |

**Brooks, Michael A** — Basketball Player
495 Bethany St, San Diego CA 92114, USA

**Brooks, Nathan** — Boxer
21274 Ellacott Parkway, #M208, Warrensville Heights OH 44128, USA

**Brooks, Randi** — Actress, Model
3205 Evergreen Point Road, Medina WA 98039, USA

**Brooks, Ray** — Actor
Ken McReddie Assoc, 101 Finsbury Pavement, London EC2A 1RS, England

**Brooks, Rich** — Football Coach
88725 Sky High Dr, Springfield OR 97478, USA

**Brooks, Richard** — Actor
Greene Assoc, 1901 Ave of Stars, #130, Los Angeles CA 90067 USA

**Brooks, Robert D** — Football Player
8611 N 17th Place, Phoenix AZ 85020, USA

**Brooks, Rodney** — Computer Scientist
Massachusetts Institute of Technology, Computer Science Dept, Cambridge MA 02139, USA

**Brooks, Ross** — Ice Hockey Player
196 Old River Road, #215, Lincoln RI 02865, USA

**Brooks, Scott W (Scottie)** — Basketball Player, Coach
Oklahoma City Thunder, 211 N Robinson Ave, #300, Oklahoma City OK 73102 USA

**Brooks, Terry** — Writer
PO Box 244, 1150 Vienna, Austria

**Brooks, William (Bill), Jr** — Football Player
1088 Laurelwood, Carmel IN 46032, USA

**Brooks, William M (Billy)** — Football Player
313 E Garrett Run, Austin TX 78753, USA

**Broome, David M** — Equestrian
Mount Ballan Manor, Crick, Caldicot, Monmouthshire NP26 XP, Wales

**Broota, Rameshwar** — Artist, Photographer
Triveni Kala Sangam, 205 Tansen Marg, Near Mandi House, New Delhi 110001, India

**Brophy, Kevin** — Actor
15010 Hamlin St, Van Nuys CA 91411, USA

**Brorby, Wade** — Judge
US Court of Appeals, 2120 Capitol Ave, #2131, Cheyenne WY 82001, USA

**Bros, Jose** — Opera Singer
Opera et Concert, 37 Rue de la Chaussee d'Antin, 75009 Paris, France

**Broshears, Robert** — Sculptor
Robert Broshears Studio, 8020 NW Holly Road, Bremerton WA 98312, USA

**Brosius, Scott D** — Baseball Player
1780 NW Troon Court, McMinnville OR 97128, USA

**Broski, David C** — Educator
University of Illinois, President's Office, Chicago IL 60607, USA

**Brosnahan, Rachel** — Actress
Innovative Artists, 1505 10th St, Santa Monica CA 90401 USA

**Brosnan, James P (Jim)** — Baseball Player
7742 Churchill St, Morton Grove IL 60053, USA

**Brosnan, Pierce** — Actor
31118 Broad Beach Road, Malibu CA 90265, USA

**Brosnan, Sean** — Actor
Sages Entertainment Group, 9107 Wilshire Blvd, #450, Beverly Hills CA 90210, USA

**Brossart, Willy** — Ice Hockey Player
9318 Susquehanna Trail, Ashland VA 23005, USA

**Brostek, Bern** — Football Player
PO Box 44552, Kamuela HI 96743, USA

**Broten, Aaron** — Ice Hockey Player
307 Delmore Dr, Roseau MN 56751, USA

**Broten, Neal** — Ice Hockey Player
N8216 690th St, River Falls WI 54022, USA

**Broten, Paul** — Ice Hockey Player
2971 Jordan Court, Saint Paul MN 55125, USA

**Broth, Ed** — Writer
Trident Media Group, 41 Madison Ave, #3600, New York NY 10010, USA

**Brother Ali** — Rap Artist
Agency Group Ltd, 142 W 57th St, #600, New York NY 10019 USA

**Brotman, Jeffrey** — Businessman
Costco Wholesale Corp, 999 Lake Dr, #200, Issaquah WA 98027, USA

**Brough Clapp, A Louise** — Tennis Player
1808 Voluntary Road, Vista CA 92084, USA

**Broughton, Willie L** — Football Player
1724 Lacy Lane, Mesquite TX 75181, USA

**Brouhard, Mark S** — Baseball Player
6289 Jackie Ave, Woodland Hills CA 91367, USA

**Brouse, Sharon** — Religious Leader, Rabbi
I K A R, 5870 W Olympic Blvd, Los Angeles CA 90036, USA

**Broussard, Benjamin I (Ben)** — Baseball Player
8917 Old Lampasas Trail, #14, Austin TX 78750, USA

**Broussard, Israel** — Actor
Paradigm Agency, 360 N Crescent Dr, North Building, Beverly Hills CA 90210 USA

**Broussard, Marc** — Singer, Songwriter
Paradigm Agency, 404 W Franklin St, Monterey CA 93940 USA

**Broussard, Rebecca** — Actress
9911 W Pico Blvd, #PH A, Los Angeles CA 90035, USA

**Browder, Ben** — Actor
Gersh Agency, 9465 Wilshire Blvd, #600, Beverly Hills CA 90212 USA

**Browder, Felix E** — Mathematician
4 Foulet Dr, Princeton NJ 08540, USA

**Brower, James R (Jim)** — Baseball Player
4947 Green Valley Road, Minnetonka MN 55345, USA

**Brown Heritage, Doris** — Track Athlete
Seattle Pacific College, Athletic Dept, Seattle WA 98119, USA

**Brown, Aaron C** — Football Player
3922 W Robson St, Tampa FL 33614, USA

**Brown, Alex J** — Football Player
Coyote Logistics, 2545 W Diversey Ave, Chicago IL 60647, USA

**Brown, Alison** — Singer, Songwriter, Banjo Player
Jensen Music International, PO Box 3445, Charlottetown PE C1A 8W5, Canada

**Brown, Alton**
42 West, 220 W 42nd St, #1200, New York NY 10036 USA — Chef
**Brown, Amanda**
E P Dutton, 375 Hudson St, New York NY 10014 USA — Writer
**Brown, Andre L**
11245 S Emerald Ave, Chicago IL 60628, USA — Football Player
**Brown, Andy**
6243 S 125th W, Trafalgar IN 46181, USA — Ice Hockey Player
**Brown, Angela**
Columbia Artists Mgmt Inc, 1790 Broadway, #702, New York NY 10019 USA — Opera Singer
**Brown, Anthony**
42561 Cavalier Court, Canton MI 48187, USA — Football Player
**Brown, Antron**
Antron Brown Racing, 1681 E Northfield Drive, #A, Brownsburg IN 46112, USA — Drag Racing Driver, Motorcycle Rider
**Brown, Arnie**
General Delivery, Woodview ON K0L 3E0, Canada — Ice Hockey Player
**Brown, Arthur E, Jr**
35 Fairway Winds Place, Hilton Head Island SC 29928, USA — Army General
**Brown, Ashley Nicole**
Hervey/Grimes Talent, 10561 Missouri Ave, #2, Los Angeles CA 90025 USA — Actress
**Brown, Billy**
Talent Works, 3500 W Olive Ave, #1400, Burbank CA 91505 USA — Actor
**Brown, Billy Aaron**
Stone Manners Salners, 9911 W Pico Blvd, #1400, Los Angeles CA 90035 USA — Actor
**Brown, Billy Ray**
7502 Whitman Lane, Sugar Land TX 77479, USA — Golfer
**Brown, Blair**
Innovative Artists, 1505 10th St, Santa Monica CA 90401 USA — Actress
**Brown, Bobby**
M E Entertainment, 722 Varsity Road, South Orange NJ 07079, USA — Singer, Dancer, Songwriter
**Brown, Brant M**
40756 Balch Park Road, Springville CA 93265, USA — Baseball Player
**Brown, Brett**
Philadelphia 76ers, 1st Union Center, 3601 S Broad St, Philadelphia PA 19148 USA — Basketball Coach
**Brown, Brianna**
Pakula/King, 9229 W Sunset Blvd, #315, West Hollywood CA 90069 USA — Actress
**Brown, Bruce**
3858 W Carson St, Torrance CA 90503, USA — Photographer, Surfer
**Brown, Bryan**
New Town Films, 12/37 Nicholson St, East Balmain NSW 2041, Australia — Actor
**Brown, Bryan D (Doug)**
Aurora Flight Services, 9950 Wakeman Dr, Manassas VA 20110, USA — Army General
**Brown, Carlinhos**
Tempest Entertainment, 245 W 25th St, #BD, New York NY 10001, USA — Percussionist, Composer
**Brown, Cedric W**
PO Box 23201, Oklahoma City OK 73123, USA — Football Player
**Brown, Chadwick**
SirenSong Entertainment, PO Box 2919, New York NY 10163, USA — Actor
**Brown, Chadwick E (Chad)**
10287 Dowling Way, Littleton CO 80126, USA — Football Player
**Brown, Charles (Charlie)**
3113 Cherry Valley Circle, Fairfield CA 94534, USA — Football Player
**Brown, Charles E**
7676 Ranier Lane N, Osseo MN 55311, USA — Ice Hockey Player
**Brown, Charles E (Charlie)**
7317 S Merrill Ave, Chicago IL 60649, USA — Football Player
**Brown, Christopher M (Chris)**
Tina Davis Co, 96 Linwood Plaza, #454, Fort Lee NJ 07024, USA — Singer, Rap Artist, Actor
**Brown, Christopher R (Chris)**
251 Riverbend Dr, Franklin TN 37064, USA — Football Player
**Brown, Clancy**
I C M Partners, 10250 Constellation Blvd, #900, Los Angeles CA 90067 USA — Actor
**Brown, Clare**
A M Heath Co, 79 Saint Martin's Lane, London WC2N 4RE, England — Writer
**Brown, Clarence (Chucky)**
102 Balsamwood Court, Cary NC 27513, USA — Basketball Player
**Brown, Cleophus**
3912 Sharon Church Road, Pinson AL 35126, USA — Baseball Player
**Brown, Clifton**
Alvin Ailey American Dance Theater, 405 W 55th St, New York NY 10019, USA — Dancer
**Brown, Collier (P J)**
2142 Hampshire Dr, Slidell LA 70461, USA — Basketball Player
**Brown, Cornell D**
1600 Sangloe Place, Lynchburg VA 24502, USA — Football Player
**Brown, Corwin A**
1124 E 90th St, Chicago IL 60619, USA — Football Player
**Brown, Courtney L**
1133 Schurlknight Road, Saint Stephen SC 29479, USA — Football Player
**Brown, Curtis**
467 Carroll St, Sunnyvale CA 94086, USA — Ice Hockey Player
**Brown, Curtis L, Jr**
204 Starrwood, Hudson WI 54016, USA — Astronaut
**Brown, Cynthia G (Cindy)**
Playboy Promotions, 2706 Media Center Dr, Los Angeles CA 90065 USA — Model
**Brown, Dale**
Renaissance Literary & Talent, PO Box 17379, Beverly Hills CA 90209, USA — Writer
**Brown, Damone L**
83 Greenfield St, Buffalo NY 14214, USA — Basketball Player
**Brown, Dan**
Atria/Washington Square Press, 1230 Ave of Americas, New York NY 10020, USA — Writer
**Brown, Daniel (Dee)**
575 Birnamwood Dr, Suwanee GA 30024, USA — Basketball Player
**Brown, Dave**
Philadelphia Flyers, 1st Union Center, 3601 S Broad St, Philadelphia PA 19148 USA — Ice Hockey Player
**Brown, David M (Dave)**
216 Watchung Fork, Westfield NJ 07090, USA — Football Player

# B

**Brown, David T**
Owings Corning, 1 Owens Corning Parkway, Toledo OH 43659, USA — Businessman
**Brown, Denise Scott**
Venturi Scott Brown Assoc, 4236 Main St, Philadelphia PA 19127, USA — Architect
**Brown, Derek V**
13 Four Leaf Manor, Rexford NY 12148, USA — Football Player
**Brown, Dermal B (Dee)**
2626 Balmoral Court, Kissimmee FL 34744, USA — Baseball Player
**Brown, Donald David**
6511 Abbey View Way, Baltimore MD 21212, USA — Biologist
**Brown, Donald J**
Yale University, Rosencrantz Hall, 28 Hillhouse Ave, New Haven CT 06520, USA — Economist, Mathematician
**Brown, Doug**
3188 Bradway Blvd, Bloomfield Hills MI 48301, USA — Ice Hockey Player
**Brown, Dustin J**
1717 8th St, Manhattan Beach CA 90266, USA — Ice Hockey Player
**Brown, Dwier**
House of Representatives, 1434 6th St, #1, Santa Monica CA 90401 USA — Actor
**Brown, Eddie L**
628 Cedar Park Dr, Daytona Beach FL 32114, USA — Football Player
**Brown, Edward R**
3925 S Jones Blvd, #1011, Las Vegas NV 89103, USA — Cinematographer
**Brown, Emil Q**
18361 Olde Farm Road, Lansing IL 60438, USA — Baseball Player
**Brown, Eric G**
2226 Drake Falls Dr, Pearland TX 77584, USA — Football Player
**Brown, Ewart F, Jr**
Premier's Office, Cabinet Building, 105 Front St, Hamilton HM 12, Bermuda — Prime Minister, Bermuda
**Brown, Faith**
Million Dollar Music Co, 12 Praed Mews, London W2 1QY, England — Actress
**Brown, Foxy**
J L Entertainment, 18653 Ventura Blvd, #340, Los Angeles CA 91356 USA — Rap Artist
**Brown, Fred**
3696 72nd Place SE, Mercer Island WA 98040, USA — Basketball Player, Coach
**Brown, Fred R**
4128 Rigel Ave, Lompoc CA 93436, USA — Football Player
**Brown, G Hanks (Hank)**
Daniels Fund, 101 Monroe St, Denver CO 80206, USA — Senator, CO; Educator
**Brown, Georg Stanford**
2565 Greenvalley Road, Los Angeles CA 90046, USA — Actor
**Brown, George R**
24652 Santa Barbara St, Southfield MI 48075, USA — Basketball Player
**Brown, Glenn**
Gagosian Gallery, 6-24 Britannia St, London WC1X 9JD, England — Artist
**Brown, Greg**
43 Trysting Road, Scituate MA 02066, USA — Ice Hockey Player
**Brown, Greg**
Motorola Inc, 1303 E Algonquin Blvd, Schaumburg IL 60196, USA — Businessman
**Brown, Gregory (Greg)**
1016 Hartley Court, Sicklerville NJ 08081, USA — Football Player
**Brown, Guy, III**
2233 Forest Hollow Park, Dallas TX 75228, USA — Football Player
**Brown, H Harold (Hal)**
4216 Henderson Road, Greensboro NC 27410, USA — Baseball Player
**Brown, Harold**
Strategic/International Studies Center, 1800 K St NW, #400, Washington DC 20006, USA — Secretary, Defense
**Brown, Henry**
1101 E Pike St, #300, Seattle WA 98122, USA — Actor
**Brown, Henry Lee**
4075 N 61st St, Milwaukee WI 53216, USA — Baseball Player
**Brown, Henry W**
2825 Carter Road, #117, Sumter SC 29150, USA — WW II Army Air Force Hero
**Brown, Hubie**
120 Foxridge Road NW, Atlanta GA 30327, USA — Basketball Coach
**Brown, Hyman**
Colorado State University, Civil Engineering Dept, Fort Collins CO 80523, USA — Civil Engineer
**Brown, Ian A**
13 Artists, 11-14 Kensington St, Brighton BN1 4AJ, England — Singer, Bassist (Stone Roses)
**Brown, Ivory L**
9811 Dale Crest Dr, #126, Dallas TX 75220, USA — Football Player
**Brown, J Gordon**
Prime Minister's Office, 10 Downing St, London SW1A 2AA, England — Prime Minister, England
**Brown, J Kevin**
105 Browns Ridge, Macon GA 31210, USA — Baseball Player
**Brown, James (J B)**
CBS-TV, Sports Dept, 51 W 52nd St, New York NY 10019 USA — Sportscaster
**Brown, James H (J B)**
12520 Woodsong Lane, Bowie MD 20721, USA — Football Player
**Brown, James N (Jim)**
100 Alfred Lerner Way, Cleveland OH 44114, USA — Football Player, Actor
**Brown, James R**
18286 Buccaneer Terrace, Leesburg VA 20176, USA — Air Force General
**Brown, Jamie S**
25023 Riding Center Dr, Chantilly VA 20152, USA — Football Player
**Brown, Jammal F**
2223 NE 36th St, Lawton OK 73507, USA — Football Player
**Brown, Janice Rogers**
US Court of Appeals, 333 Constitution Ave NW, #4400, Washington DC 20001, USA — Judge
**Brown, Jarvis A**
4201 S Decatur Blvd, #1161, Las Vegas NV 89103, USA — Baseball Player
**Brown, Jason W**
8810 Gilly Way, Randallstown MD 21133, USA — Football Player
**Brown, Jeff**
800 Tara Oaks Dr, Chesterfield MO 63005, USA — Ice Hockey Player
**Brown, Jim Ed**
Joe Taylor Artist Agency, 2802 Columbine Place, Nashville TN 37204 USA — Singer

**Brown - Brown**

**Brown, John C** — Football Player
101 Gadshill Place, Pittsburgh PA 15237, USA
**Brown, John Y** — Basketball Player
1523 Oak Forest Dr, Rolla MO 65401, USA
**Brown, John Y, Jr** — Governor, KY
1990 Fort Harrods Dr, Lexington KY 40503, USA
**Brown, Jonathan Daniel** — Actor
I C M Partners, 10250 Constellation Blvd, #900, Los Angeles CA 90067 USA
**Brown, Julie** — Actress, Comedienne, Singer
11288 Ventura Blvd, #728, Studio City CA 91604, USA
**Brown, Julie (Downtown)** — Actress, Producer
Independent Management Group, 8444 Wilshire Blvd, #500, Beverly Hills CA 90211, USA
**Brown, Julie Caitlin** — Actress, Singer
2109 S Wilbur Ave, Walla Walla WA 99362, USA
**Brown, June** — Actress
Associated International Mgmt, 7 Hatton Garden, #400, London EC1N 8AD, England
**Brown, Junior** — Singer, Guitarist
Paradigm Agency, 124 12th Ave S, #410, Nashville TN 37203, USA
**Brown, Keith** — Ice Hockey Player
8515 Woodland Brooke Trail, Cumming GA 30028, USA
**Brown, Kenneth J** — Labor Leader
Graphic Communications International Union, 1900 L St NW, #800, Washington DC 20036, USA
**Brown, Kevin L** — Baseball Player
9201 Ryan Court, Evansville IN 47712, USA
**Brown, Kimberly J** — Actress
Gemstone Talent, 27943 Seco Canyon Road, #212, Los Angeles CA 91350, USA
**Brown, Kristopher C (Kris)** — Football Player
712 Holly St, Bellaire TX 77401, USA
**Brown, Kwame** — Basketball Player
7685 Veragua Dr, Playa del Rey CA 90293, USA
**Brown, Larry** — Football Player
1377 Glencoe Ave, Pittsburgh PA 15205, USA
**Brown, Larry L** — Baseball Player
13158 La Mirada Circle, Wellington FL 33414, USA
**Brown, Larry, Jr** — Football Player
5603 Sycamore Dr, Colleyville TX 76034, USA
**Brown, Lawrence (Larry), Jr** — Football Player
4390 Parliament Place, #A, Lanham MD 20706, USA
**Brown, Lawrence H (Larry)** — Basketball Player, Coach, Executive
1030 Green Valley Road, Bryn Mawr PA 19010, USA
**Brown, Lester R** — Ecologist
Worldwatch Institute, 1776 Massachusetts Ave NW, #800, Washington DC 20036, USA
**Brown, Lomas, Jr** — Football Player
5049 Elizabeth Lake Road, Waterford MI 48327, USA
**Brown, Marc** — Artist, Writer
Little Brown, 3 Center Plaza, #100, Boston MA 02108 USA
**Brown, Marcia Joan** — Writer
165 Avenida Majorca, #B, Laguna Hills CA 92637, USA
**Brown, Mark A** — Football Player
2761 SW 81st Way, Davie FL 33328, USA
**Brown, Mark N** — Astronaut
80 Earlsgate Road, Dayton OH 45440, USA
**Brown, Marty** — Singer, Guitarist
PO Box 190515, Nashville TN 37219, USA
**Brown, Matthew B (Matt)** — Baseball Player
11259 N Cutlass St, Hayden ID 83835, USA
**Brown, Max** — Actor
United Agents, 12-26 Lexington St, London W1F 0LE, England
**Brown, Melanie J** — Singer (Spice Girls)
Paradigm Agency, 360 N Crescent Dr, North Building, Beverly Hills CA 90210 USA
**Brown, Michael (Mike)** — Basketball Player
304 Rays Mill Road, Aberdeen NC 28315, USA
**Brown, Michael A** — Astronomer
California Institute of Technology, Astronomy Dept, Pasadena CA 91125, USA
**Brown, Michael C (Mike)** — Baseball Player
2904 E Minton St, Mesa AZ 85213, USA
**Brown, Michael D** — Government Official
OnScreen Technologies, 600 NW 14th Ave, Portland OR 97209, USA
**Brown, Michael E (Mike)** — Astronomer
California Institute of Technology, Geological & Planetary Sciences Division, Pasadena CA 91125, USA
**Brown, Michael G (Mike)** — Baseball Player
710 95th Ave N, Naples FL 34108, USA
**Brown, Michael S** — Nobel Medicine Laureate
5719 Redwood Lane, Dallas TX 75209, USA
**Brown, Miguel** — Singer
International Artists, PO Box 32, Grave 5369 AA, Netherlands
**Brown, Mike** — Football Executive
Cincinnati Bengals, 1 Paul Brown Stadium, Cincinnati OH 45202 USA
**Brown, Nancy E** — Navy Admiral
Director, Communications/Computers, Joint Staff, Pentagon, Washington DC 20310 USA
**Brown, Norman** — Singer, Guitarist
A P A Talent/Literary Agency, 405 S Beverly Dr, #300, Beverly Hills CA 90212 USA
**Brown, Olivia** — Actress
Bill Rogin Mgmt, 427 N Canon Dr, #215, Beverly Hills CA 90210, USA
**Brown, Ollie L** — Baseball Player
8462 Country Club Dr, Buena Park CA 90621, USA
**Brown, Orlando** — Actor
Abrams Artists, 9200 W Sunset Blvd, #1125, West Hollywood CA 90069 USA
**Brown, Oscar L** — Baseball Player
19113 Gunlock Ave, Carson CA 90746, USA
**Brown, Patricia** — Baseball Player
821 Solar Lane, Glenview IL 60025, USA
**Brown, Patrick** — Biochemist
Stanford University Medical School, Biochemistry Dept, Stanford CA 94305, USA
**Brown, Patrick (Sleepy)** — Singer, Songwriter
J Erving Group, 555 Whitehall St SW, #N, Atlanta GA 30303, USA

| | |
|---|---|
| **Brown, Paul** | Jazz Guitarist |
| Chapman & Co Mgmt, PO Box 55246, Sherman Oaks CA 91413, USA | |
| **Brown, Peter** | Actor |
| Special Artists Agency, 9200 Sunset Blvd, #410, West Hollywood CA 90069 USA | |
| **Brown, Peter R L** | Historian |
| Princeton University, History Dept, Princeton NJ 08544, USA | |
| **Brown, Philip** | Actor |
| 8721 W Sunset Blvd, #200, West Hollywood CA 90069, USA | |
| **Brown, Pieta** | Singer, Guitarist, Songwriter |
| Blind Ambition Mgmt, 6 Courthouse Way, Jonesboro GA 30236, USA | |
| **Brown, Preston M** | Football Player |
| 6804 Jones Valley Dr SE, Huntsville AL 35802, USA | |
| **Brown, R Anthony B (Tony), Jr** | Football Player |
| PO Box 7122, Branson MO 65615, USA | |
| **Brown, R Hanbury** | Astronomer |
| White Cottage, Penton Mewsey, Andover, Hampshire SP11 0RQ, England | |
| **Brown, Ralph, III** | Football Player |
| 9395 Old Post Dr, Rancho Cucamonga CA 91730, USA | |
| **Brown, Randy** | Basketball Player |
| Chicago Bulls, United Center, 1901 W Madison St, Chicago IL 60612 USA | |
| **Brown, Raymond M** | Football Player |
| 4936 Lake Fjord Pass, Marietta GA 30068, USA | |
| **Brown, Reggie V** | Football Player |
| 1325 Oxford Lane, Union NJ 07083, USA | |
| **Brown, Rhyon Nicole** | Actress |
| HeyGurl, 335 E Albertoni St, Carson CA 90746, USA | |
| **Brown, Richard S** | Football Player |
| 5652 Alfred Ave, Westminster CA 92683, USA | |
| **Brown, Rita Mae** | Writer, Social Activist |
| Wendy Weill Agency, 232 Madison Ave, New York NY 10016, USA | |
| **Brown, Rob** | Ice Hockey Player |
| 5204 84th St, Edmonton AB T6E 5N8, Canada | |
| **Brown, Robert (Rob)** | Actor |
| W M E Entertainment, 9601 Wilshire Blvd, #300, Beverly Hills CA 90210 USA | |
| **Brown, Robert A** | Chemical Engineer, Educator |
| Boston University, President's Office, 1 Sherborn St, Boston MA 02215, USA | |
| **Brown, Robert B** | Army General |
| Commanding General, I Corps, Joint Base Lewis-McChord WA 98433, USA | |
| **Brown, Robert D** | Businessman |
| Milacron Inc, 2090 Florence Ave, Cincinnati OH 45206, USA | |
| **Brown, Robert E (Bob)** | Football Player |
| PO Box 211081, Saint Louis MO 63121, USA | |
| **Brown, Robert S (Bob)** | Football Player |
| 1628 Fairmont Dr, San Leandro CA 94578, USA | |
| **Brown, Robert W (Bobby)** | Baseball Player, Executive |
| 4100 Clark Ave, Fort Worth TX 76107, USA | |
| **Brown, Roger Aaron** | Actor |
| Innovative Artists, 1505 10th St, Santa Monica CA 90401 USA | |
| **Brown, Roger L** | Football Player |
| 9 N Point Dr, Portsmouth VA 23703, USA | |
| **Brown, Rogers L (Bobby)** | Baseball Player |
| 112 Avonlea Dr, Chesapeake VA 23322, USA | |
| **Brown, Ron J** | Football Player, Track Athlete |
| 2212 Radcourt Dr, Hacienda Heights CA 91745, USA | |
| **Brown, Ronald K** | Choreographer, Dance Executive |
| Evidence, 80 Hanson Place, #605, Brooklyn NY 11217, USA | |
| **Brown, Ronnie G, Jr** | Football Player |
| 3445 Stratford Road NE, #3707, Atlanta GA 30326, USA | |
| **Brown, Ruben** | Football Player |
| 170 Fox Meadow Lane, Orchard Park NY 14127, USA | |
| **Brown, Rupert A** | Educator |
| Boston University, President's Office, 1 Silber Way, Boston MA 02215, USA | |
| **Brown, Ryan** | Actor |
| Side by Side Literary Productions, 15 W 26th St, #200, New York NY 10010, USA | |
| **Brown, Sandra** | Writer |
| 1306 W Abram St, Arlington TX 76013, USA | |
| **Brown, Sara Suzanne** | Actress |
| Media Artists Group, 8222 Melrose Ave, #203, Los Angeles CA 90048 USA | |
| **Brown, Sheldon D** | Football Player |
| 6 Tuxedo Court, Marlton NJ 08053, USA | |
| **Brown, Shirley** | Singer |
| Rodgers Redding, PO Box 4603, Macon GA 31208 USA | |
| **Brown, Sophina** | Actress |
| Peter Strain, 5455 Wilshire Blvd, #1812, Los Angeles CA 90036 USA | |
| **Brown, Sterling K** | Actor |
| Innovative Artists, 1505 10th St, Santa Monica CA 90401 USA | |
| **Brown, Steve** | Football Player |
| 2207 Osage St, Saint Louis MO 63118, USA | |
| **Brown, Susan** | Actress |
| Hamilton Hodell, 66-68 Margaret St, #500, London W1W 8SR, England | |
| **Brown, T Edward (Ted)** | Football Player |
| 7320 130th St W, Saint Paul MN 55124, USA | |
| **Brown, T Graham** | Singer |
| Cody Entertainment, PO Box 456, Winchester VA 22604, USA | |
| **Brown, Terry L** | Football Player |
| 401 N 6th St, Marlow OK 73055, USA | |
| **Brown, Theotis, II** | Football Player |
| 9604 W 121st Terrace, Overland Park KS 66213, USA | |
| **Brown, Thomas A (Timmy)** | Football Player |
| 505 S Farrell Dr, #E28, Palm Springs CA 92264, USA | |
| **Brown, Thomas M (Tommy)** | Baseball Player |
| 8119 Shady Place, Brentwood TN 37027, USA | |
| **Brown, Thomas W (Tom)** | Football, Baseball Player |
| 27981 Nanticoke Road, Salisbury MD 21801, USA | |
| **Brown, Timothy D (Tim)** | Football Player |
| 1107 W Pleasant Run Road, De Soto TX 75115, USA | |

Brown, Tom — Football Player
679 Aldford Ave, Delta BC V3M 5P5, Canada
Brown, Trisha — Choreographer, Dancer
Trisha Brown Dance Co, 465 Greenwich St, Front 1, New York NY 10013, USA
Brown, Troy F — Football Player
PO Box 452, Foxboro MA 02035, USA
Brown, Vincent B — Football Player
PO Box 71268, Henrico VA 23255, USA
Brown, W Earl — Actor
Greene Assoc, 1901 Ave of Stars, #130, Los Angeles CA 90067 USA
Brown, W Mack — Football Coach
University of Texas, Athletic Dept, Austin TX 78712, USA
Brown, Wayne — Ice Hockey Player
50 Montgomery Blvd, Belleville ON K8N 1H9, Canada
Brown, William D (Bill) — Football Player
9365 Libby Lane, Eden Prairie MN 55347, USA
Brown, William F (Willie) — Football Player, Coach
27138 Lillegard Court, Tracy CA 95304, USA
Brown, Yvette Nicole — Actress
Abrams Artists, 9200 W Sunset Blvd, #1125, West Hollywood CA 90069 USA
Brown, Zac — Singer, Guitarist
Roar Mgmt, 9701 Wilshire Blvd, #800, Beverly Hills CA 90212, USA
Browne, Byron E — Baseball Player
2831 S 83rd Dr, Tolleson AZ 85353, USA
Browne, Chris — Cartoonist (Hagar the Horrible)
King Features Syndicate, 300 W 57th St, #1500, New York NY 10019 USA
Browne, Gerald — Writer
Warner Books, 1271 6th Ave, New York NY 10020, USA
Browne, Gordon W (Gordie) — Football Player
1001 Lakeridge Court, Colleyville TX 76034, USA
Browne, Herbert A, Jr — Navy Admiral
A F C E A International, 4400 Fair Lakes Court, #104, Fairfax VA 22033, USA
Browne, Jackson — Singer, Songwriter
Donald Miller Mgmt, 12746 Kling St, Studio City CA 91604, USA
Browne, Jann — Singer
Tracy Gershon Mgmt, PO Box 158400, Nashville TN 37215, USA
Browne, Jerome A (Jerry) — Baseball Player
2102 Company St, #1, Christiansted VI 00820, USA
Browne, Leslie — Ballerina, Actress
2025 Broadway, #6F, New York NY 10023, USA
Browne, Olin — Golfer
9562 SE Sandpine Lane, Hobe Sound FL 33455, USA
Browner, Carol M — Government Official
White House, 1600 Pennsylvania Ave NW, Washington DC 20500, USA
Browner, Jimmie L (Jim) — Football Player
3369 Peachtree Corners Circle, Norcross GA 30092, USA
Browner, Joey M — Football Player
PO Box 22721, Saint Paul MN 55122, USA
Browner, Keith T — Football Player
5017 Chesley Ave, Los Angeles CA 90043, USA
Browner, Ross — Football Player
7900 Indian Springs Dr, Nashville TN 37221, USA
Brown-Findlay, Jessica — Actress
Troika, 74 Clerkenwell Road, #300, London EC1M 5QA, England
Browning Chris — Actor
Don Buchwald, 6500 Wilshire Blvd, #2200, Los Angeles CA 90048 USA
Browning, David (Dave) — Football Player
10117 S Lambs Lane, Mica WA 99023, USA
Browning, Edmond L — Religious Leader
5164 Imai Road, Hood River OR 97031, USA
Browning, Emily — Actress
Signpost Mgmt, 1641 Ivar Ave, Los Angeles CA 90028, USA
Browning, Kurt — Figure Skater
International Management Group, 175 Bloor St E, #400S, Toronto ON M4W 3R8, Canada
Browning, Logan — Actress, Singer
Kazarian/Measures/Ruskin, 11969 Ventura Blvd, #300, Studio City CA 91604 USA
Browning, Ricou — Actor
5221 SW 196th Lane, Southwest Ranches FL 33332, USA
Browning, Thomas L (Tom) — Baseball Player
1110 Grindstone Court, Union KY 41091, USA
Brownlee, Alistair E — Triathlete
23 Manor Road N, Esher Surrey KT10 0AA, England
Brownlee, Don — Astronomer
University of Washington, Astronomy Dept, PO Box 351580, Seattle WA 98195, USA
Brownlee, Jonathan — Triathlete
Leeds Metropolitan University, Carnegie High Performance Center, Leeds LS1 3HE, England
Brownlee, Lawrence — Opera Singer
I M G Artists, Hogarth Business Park, Chiswick, London W4 2TH, England
Brownlee, Shannon — Writer
New America Foundation, 1899 L St NW, #400, Washington DC 20036 20036, USA
Brownlow, Kevin — Producer
Photoplay Productions, 21 Princess Road, London NW1, England
Brown-Miller, Lisa — Ice Hockey Player
US Olympic Committee, 1 Olympic Plaza, Building 6, Colorado Springs CO 80909 USA
Brownmiller, Susan — Social Activist
61 Jane St, New York NY 10014, USA
Brownschidle, Jack — Ice Hockey Player
35 Hidden Pines Court, East Amherst NY 14051, USA
Brownstein, Carrie — Singer, Guitarist (Sleater-Kinney)
High Road Touring, 751 Bridgeway, #200, Sausalito CA 94965 USA
Broza, David — Singer, Songwriter
Gold Village Entertainment, 72 Madison Ave, #800, New York NY 10016, USA
Brozer, Kim — Golfer
2700 N 16th St, Beaumont TX 77703, USA
Brubaker, Charles W — Architect
82 Essex Road, Winnetka IL 60093, USA

**Brubaker, Ed** — Cartoonist, Writer
United Talent Agency, U T A Plaza, 9336 Civic Center Dr, Beverly Hills CA 90210 USA
**Brubaker, Jeff** — Ice Hockey Player
1827 Oak Ridge Road, #A, Oak Ridge NC 27310, USA
**Bruce Bruce** — Actor, Comedian
I C M Partners, 10250 Constellation Blvd, #900, Los Angeles CA 90067 USA
**Bruce, Aundray** — Football Player
1730 Wentworth Dr, Montgomery AL 36106, USA
**Bruce, Christopher** — Choreographer
Rambert Dance Co, 94 Chiswick High Road, London W4 1SH, England
**Bruce, David** — Ice Hockey Player
975 Grand Blvd, Bellingham WA 98229, USA
**Bruce, Ed** — Singer
1022 16th Ave S, Nashville TN 37212, USA
**Bruce, Isaac I** — Football Player
PO Box 550141, Fort Lauderdale FL 33355, USA
**Bruce, Jack** — Singer, Bassist (Cream), Songwriter
Agency Group Ltd, 142 W 57th St, #600, New York NY 10019 USA
**Bruce, Robert J (Bob)** — Baseball Player
800 E 15th St, #207, Plano TX 75074, USA
**Bruce, Thomas E (Tom)** — Swimmer
122 Sea Terrace Way, Aptos CA 95003, USA
**Bruckheimer, Jerry** — Producer
Jerry Bruckheimer Films, 1631 10th St, Santa Monica CA 90404, USA
**Bruckner, Agnes** — Actress
A P A Talent/Literary Agency, 405 S Beverly Dr, #300, Beverly Hills CA 90212 USA
**Bruckner, Greg** — Golfer
3906 E Potter Dr, Phoenix AZ 85050, USA
**Bruckner, Leslie C (Les)** — Football Player
1325 Valley View Road, #307, Glendale CA 91202, USA
**Brudzinski, Robert L (Bob)** — Football Player
4607 Gleneagles Dr, Boynton Beach FL 33436, USA
**Brueckner, Keith A** — Physicist
7723 Ludington Place, La Jolla CA 92037, USA
**Brueggemann, Walter** — Theologian
701 S Columbia Dr, Decatur GA 30030, USA
**Brueggergosman, Measha** — Opera Singer
I M G Artists, Hogarth Business Park, Chiswick, London W4 2TH, England
**Bruel, Patrick** — Singer, Actor
Voyez Mon Agent, 20 Ave Rapp, 75007 Paris, France
**Brueland, Lowell K** — WW II Army Air Corps Hero
420 La Z Acres Road, Westminster SC 29693, USA
**Bruen, John D** — Army General, Businessman
6104 Greenlawn Court, Springfield VA 22152, USA
**Bruener, Mark F** — Football Player
19860 NE 133rd St, Woodinville WA 98077, USA
**Bruening, Justin** — Actor
Innovative Artists, 1505 10th St, Santa Monica CA 90401 USA
**Bruer, Robert A (Bob)** — Football Player
2406 Oakridge Road, Stillwater OK 55082, USA
**Bruetti, Dana** — Producer
Creative Artists Agency, 2000 Ave of Stars, #100, Los Angeles CA 90067 USA
**Bruford, Bill** — Drummer (U K, Yes)
Ted Kurland, 173 Brighton Ave, Boston MA 02134 USA
**Brugge, Joan S** — Cell Biologist
Harvard Medical School, Cell Biology Dept, 240 Longwood Ave, Boston MA 02115, USA
**Brugge, Pieter Jan** — Director
Innovative Artists, 1505 10th St, Santa Monica CA 90401 USA
**Bruggen, Frans** — Concert Recorder Player, Flutist
Askonas Holt, Lincoln House, 300 High Holborn, London WC1V 7JH, England
**Bruggink, Eric G** — Judge
US Claims Court, 717 Madison Place NW, Washington DC 20439, USA
**Bruguera, Sergi** — Tennis Player
C'Escipion 42, 08023 Barcelona, Spain
**Bruhl, Daniel** — Actor
Players Agentur Mgmt, Sophienstr 21, 10178 Berlin, Germany
**Bruininks, Robert H** — Educator
University of Minnesota, Humphries Institute, Saint Paul MN 55104, USA
**Brukner, Caslav** — Physicist
Quantum Foundations Theory, Boltzmanngasse 5, 1090 Vienna, Austria
**Brumfield, Jacob D** — Baseball Player
208 Wrights Mill Circle NE, Atlanta GA 30324, USA
**Brumfield, Scott** — Football Player
1150 E 900 S, Spanish Fork UT 84660, USA
**Brumfield-White, Dolores (Dolly)** — Baseball Player
1604 Millcreek Dr, Arkadelphia AR 71923, USA
**Brumley, A Michael (Mike)** — Baseball Player
112 Corral Dr, Keller TX 76244, USA
**Brumm, Donald D (Don)** — Football Player
511 County Road 442, New Franklin MO 65274, USA
**Brummer, Glenn E** — Baseball Player
1830 Dalton Dr, Belleville IL 62226, USA
**Brummer, Renate L** — Astronaut, Germany
Global Systems Division, 325 Broadway, Boulder CO 80305, USA
**Brumwell, Murray** — Ice Hockey Player
727 Tabriz Dr, Billings MT 59105, USA
**Brunansky, Thomas A (Tom)** — Baseball Player
15444 Harrow Lane, Poway CA 92064, USA
**Brunckhorst, Natja** — Actress
Above the Line, Wielandstr 5, 10625 Berlin, Germany
**Brundage, Howard D** — Publisher
RR 2 Box 332-47, Old Lyme CT 06371, USA
**Brundage, Jackson** — Actor
Kazarian/Measures/Ruskin, 11969 Ventura Blvd, #300, Studio City CA 91604 USA
**Brundage, Jennifer** — Softball Player
4487 Augusta Court, Ann Arbor MI 48108, USA

**Brundige, William G (Bill)** — Football Player
40 Corbett St, Salem VA 24153, USA
**Brundy, Stanley D (Stan)** — Basketball Player
4644 Stephen Girard Ave, New Orleans LA 70126, USA
**Brunell, Mark A** — Football Player
1710 Beach Ave, Atlantic Beach FL 32233, USA
**Brunelli, Samuel A (Sam)** — Football Player
1080 Wisconsin Ave NW, #104W, Washington DC 20007, USA
**Bruner, Jack C (Teel)** — Football Player
518 Oak, Kamiah ID 83536, USA
**Bruner, Michael L (Mike)** — Swimmer
339 Garcia Ave, Half Moon Bay CA 94019, USA
**Brunet, Robert P (Bob)** — Football Player
149 Aspen Square, Denham Springs LA 70726, USA
**Brunet, Yasmine** — Model
One Model Mgmt, 424 W Broadway, #200, New York NY 10012 USA
**Brunette, Andrew** — Ice Hockey Player
2392 Morgan Ave N, Stillwater MN 55082, USA
**Brunetti, Dana** — Producer
Creative Artists Agency, 2000 Ave of Stars, #100, Los Angeles CA 90067 USA
**Bruney, Brian A** — Baseball Player
1471 SW Pine Dr, Warrenton OR 97146, USA
**Bruney, Fred** — Football Player, Coach
800 Mountain Creek Trace NW, Atlanta GA 30328, USA
**Brungardt, Kurt** — Physical Fitness Trainer, Writer
Trident Media Group, 41 Madison Ave, #3600, New York NY 10010, USA
**Bruni Tedeschi, Valeria** — Actress
Carol Levi Mgmt, Via Giuseppe Pisanelli 2, 00196 Rome, Italy
**Bruni, Emily** — Actress
Markham Froggatt Irwin, Julian House, 4 Windmill St, London W1P 1HF, England
**Bruni-Sarkozy, Carla** — Model, Singer, Songwriter
Palais de l'Elysee, 55 Rue Faubourg Saint Honore, 75008 Paris, France
**Brunkhorst, Brian J** — Basketball Player
6182 Brumder Dr, Hartland WI 53029, USA
**Brunner, Jerome S** — Psychologist
200 Mercer St, New York NY 10012, USA
**Bruno, Chris** — Actor, Producer, Director
S D B Partners, 1801 Ave of Stars, #902, Los Angeles CA 90067 USA
**Bruno, Dylan** — Actor
Gersh Agency, 41 Madison Ave, #3301, New York NY 10010 USA
**Bruno, Gioia** — Singer (Expose), Songwriter
T-Best Talent Agency, 508 Honey Lake Court, Danville CA 94506 USA
**Bruns, George W** — Basketball Player
16 E Poplar St, Floral Park NY 11001, USA
**Brunson, Larry R** — Football Player
6104 E Peakview Place, Centennial CO 80111, USA
**Bruntlett, Eric K** — Baseball Player
4445 Montecito Ave, Santa Rosa CA 95404, USA
**Brupbacher, Ross A** — Football Player
200 Pembroke Lane, Lafayette LA 70508, USA
**Bruschi, Tedy L** — Football Player
31 Jeffrey Dr, North Attleboro MA 02760, USA
**Bruske, James S (Jim)** — Baseball Player
5242 N Quail Run Place, Paradise Valley AZ 85253, USA
**Bruskin, Grisha** — Artist, Sculptor
236 W 26th St, #705, New York NY 10001, USA
**Bruson, Renato** — Opera Singer
Columbia Artists Mgmt Inc, 1790 Broadway, #702, New York NY 10019 USA
**Brusstar, Warren S** — Baseball Player
3320 Redwood Road, Napa CA 94558, USA
**Brustein, Robert S** — Educator, Producer, Critic
Harvard University, Loeb Drama Center, 64 Brattle St, Cambridge MA 02138, USA
**Bruton, John G** — Prime Minister, Ireland
Dail Eireann, Leinster House, Dublin 2, Ireland
**Bry, Ellen** — Actress
Media Artists Group, 8222 Melrose Ave, #203, Los Angeles CA 90048 USA
**Bryan, Alan** — Archaeologist
University of Alberta, Archaeology Dept, Edmonton AB T6G 2J8, Canada
**Bryan, David** — Keyboardist (Bon Jovi)
Bon Jovi Mgmt, 809 Elder Circle, Austin TX 78733, USA
**Bryan, James** — Fiddler
Chris Smith Mgmt, 21 Camden St, #500, Toronto ON M5V 1V2, Canada
**Bryan, Luke** — Singer, Guitarist, Songwriter
Red Light Mgmt, PO Box 159310, Nashville TN 37215, USA
**Bryan, Mark** — Guitarist (Hootie & the Blowfish)
FishCo Mgmt, 2519 Devine Street  Columbia SC 29205, USA
**Bryan, Michael C (Mike)** — Tennis Player
PO Box 91, Bailey MI 49303, USA
**Bryan, Richard H** — Governor, Senator, NV
Lionel Sawyer Collins, Bank America Plaza, 300 S 4th St, Las Vegas NV 89101, USA
**Bryan, Robert C (Bob)** — Tennis Player
PO Box 91, Bailey MI 49303, USA
**Bryan, Sabrina** — Actress, Singer (Cheetah Girls)
Puravida Enterprises, 2480 Corinth Ave, #3, Los Angeles CA 90064, USA
**Bryan, William K (Billy)** — Football Player
3408 Creekwood Dr, Tuscaloosa AL 35453, USA
**Bryan, William R (Billy)** — Baseball Player
3001 Hickory Lane, Opelika AL 36801, USA
**Bryan, Wright** — Journalist
3747 Peachtree Road NE, #516, Atlanta GA 30319, USA
**Bryan, Zachary Ty** — Actor
Evolution Entertainment, 901 N Highland Ave, Los Angeles CA 90038 USA
**Bryant Clark, Rosalyn** — Track Athlete
3901 Somerset Dr, Los Angeles CA 90008, USA
**Bryant, Anita** — Social Activist, Singer
Blackwood Mgmt, PO Box 5331, Sevierville TN 37864, USA

**Bryant, Bart H** — Golfer
Professional Golfer's Assn, PO Box 109601, Palm Beach Gardens FL 33410, USA
**Bryant, Bobby L** — Football Player
13437 Lochrin Lane, Sylmar CA 91342, USA
**Bryant, Bradley D (Brad)** — Golfer
900 Mulberry Bush Court, Orlando FL 32828, USA
**Bryant, Clara** — Actress
Paradigm Agency, 360 N Crescent Dr, North Building, Beverly Hills CA 90210 USA
**Bryant, Edward E (Junior), Jr** — Football Player
2906 S 102nd St, Omaha NE 68124, USA
**Bryant, Emmette (Em)** — Basketball Player
PO Box 6229, Chicago IL 60680, USA
**Bryant, Fernando A** — Football Player
2336 Emerald Dr, Jonesboro GA 30236, USA
**Bryant, Jeffrey D (Jeff)** — Football Player
2665 Tilson Road, Decatur GA 30032, USA
**Bryant, Joseph A (Red)** — Football Player
Seattle Seahawks, 12 Seahawks Way, Renton WA 98056 USA
**Bryant, Joseph W (Joe)** — Basketball Player, Coach
1835 N 72nd St, Philadelphia PA 19151, USA
**Bryant, Joy** — Actress, Model
KillerMoxie Mgmt, 5890 W Jefferson Blvd, #J, Los Angeles CA 90016, USA
**Bryant, Karyn** — Actress, Producer, Commentator
Serendipity Entertainment, 9107 Wilshire Blvd, #400, Beverly Hills CA 90210, USA
**Bryant, Kelvin L** — Football Player
701 E Church St, Tarboro NC 27886, USA
**Bryant, Kobe B** — Basketball Player
Los Angeles Lakers, Staples Center, 1111 S Figueroa St, Los Angeles CA 90015 USA
**Bryant, Mark C** — Basketball Player
3300 Everett Dr, Edmond OK 73013, USA
**Bryant, Robert L** — Mathematician
Duke University, Math-Science Research Institute, Box 90220, Durham NC 27708, USA
**Bryant, S Matt** — Football Player
5689 Legends Club Circle, Braselton GA 30517, USA
**Bryant, Sharon** — Singer (Atlantic Starr)
Betty of Troy, 15 Meritoria Dr, East Williston NY 11596, USA
**Bryant, Stephen (Steve)** — Football Player
3602 George Washington Lane, Missouri City TX 77459, USA
**Bryant, Tony** — Football Player
2351 Sombrero Blvd, Marathon FL 33050, USA
**Bryant, Trent B** — Football Player
4801 S Tierney Dr, Independence MO 64055, USA
**Bryars, R Gavin** — Composer
Schott Co, 48 Great Marlborough St, London W1V 2BN, England
**Bryce, Quentin A L** — Governor General, Australia
Governor General's Office, Government House, Canberra ACT 2600, Australia
**Bryce, Scott** — Actor
Don Buchwald, 6500 Wilshire Blvd, #2200, Los Angeles CA 90048 USA
**Brye, Stephen R (Steve)** — Baseball Player
621 S Spring St, #603, Los Angeles CA 90014, USA
**Bryers, Paul** — Writer
Bloomsbury Publishing, 50 Bedford Square, London WC1B 3DP, England
**Brylin, Sergei** — Ice Hockey Player
32 Robert Dr, Short Hills NJ 07078, USA
**Bryson, A Shawn** — Football Player
418 Heatherstone Dr, Franklin NC 28734, USA
**Bryson, David** — Singer, Guitarist (Counting Crowes)
Geffen Records, 10900 Wilshire Blvd, #1000, Los Angeles CA 90024 USA
**Bryson, Jim** — Singer, Songwriter
What Mgmt, 906A Logan Ave, Toronto ON M4K 3E4, Canada
**Bryson, Peabo** — Singer, Songwriter
A P A Talent/Literary Agency, 405 S Beverly Dr, #300, Beverly Hills CA 90212 USA
**Bryson, William Curtis** — Judge
US Appeals Court, 717 Madison Place NW, Washington DC 20439, USA
**Bryzgalov, Ilya N** — Ice Hockey Player
4092 Santa Anita Lane, Yorba Linda CA 92886, USA
**Brzeska, Magdalena** — Rhythmic Gymnast
Vitesse Karcher GmbH, Porscestr 6, 70736 Fellbach, Germany
**Brzezinski, Douglas G (Doug)** — Football Player
329 Greenhill Way, Silver Spring MD 20904, USA
**Brzezinski, Zbigniew** — Government Official, Educator
Strategic/International Studies Center, 1800 K NW, #400, Washington DC 20006, USA
**Buanne, Patrizio** — Singer
Agency Group Ltd, 142 W 57th St, #600, New York NY 10019 USA
**Buatta, Mario** — Interior Designer
120 E 80th St, New York NY 10075, USA
**Bubka, Sergei N** — Track Athlete
Physical Culture/Sport Committee, 42 Esplanadnaya, 252023 Kiev, Ukraine
**Bubla, Jiri** — Ice Hockey Player
405-1050 Bowron Crescent, North Vancouver BC V7H 2X7, Canada
**Buble, Michael** — Singer, Songwriter
Creative Artists Agency, 2000 Ave of Stars, #100, Los Angeles CA 90067 USA
**Bucatinsky, Dan** — Actor
Creative Artists Agency, 2000 Ave of Stars, #100, Los Angeles CA 90067 USA
**Buccellato, Benedetta** — Actress
Carol Levi Mgmt, Via Giuseppe Pisanelli 2, 00196 Rome, Italy
**Bucchieri, Stephen** — Architect
Bucchieri Architects, 2026 Murray Hill, Cleveland,OH 44106, USA
**Bucha, Paul W** — Vietnam War Army Hero (CMH)
822 N Salem Road, Ridgefield CT 06877, USA
**Buchan, William Carl** — Yachtsman
826 Evergreen Point Road, Medina WA 98039, USA
**Buchan, William Eastman** — Yachtsman
7100 NE 42nd St, Bellevue WA 98004, USA
**Buchanan, Brian J** — Baseball Player
8600 El Mirasol Court, Fort Myers FL 33967, USA

| | |
|---|---|
| **Buchanan, Edna** | Journalist |
| PO Box 403556, Miami Beach FL 33140, USA | |
| **Buchanan, Ian** | Actor, Model |
| Talent Works, 3500 W Olive Ave, #1400, Burbank CA 91505 USA | |
| **Buchanan, Isobel** | Opera Singer |
| Marks Mgmt, 14 New Burlington St, London W1X 1FF, England | |
| **Buchanan, J Robert** | Physician |
| 19 Shipway Place, Charlestown MA 02129, USA | |
| **Buchanan, Jeff** | Ice Hockey Player |
| 220 Cedar Ave, Hershey PA 17033, USA | |
| **Buchanan, Jensen** | Actress |
| Paradigm Agency, 360 N Crescent Dr, North Building, Beverly Hills CA 90210 USA | |
| **Buchanan, John M** | Biochemist |
| 56 Meriam St, Lexington MA 02420, USA | |
| **Buchanan, Ken** | Boxer |
| 45 Marmion Road, Greenfaulds, Cumbernaul G67 4AN, Scotland | |
| **Buchanan, Patrick J (Pat)** | Commentator, Government Official |
| 8233 Old Courthouse Road, #200, Vienna VA 22182, USA | |
| **Buchanan, Raymond L (Ray)** | Football Player |
| 2423 Strand Ave, Lawrenceville GA 30043, USA | |
| **Buchanan, Ron** | Ice Hockey Player |
| 200 Telluride Trail, Ruidoso NM 88345, USA | |
| **Buchanan, Simone** | Actress |
| McMahon Mgmt, 2/24 Brereton St, South Brisbane QED 4101, Australia | |
| **Buchanan, Thomas (Tom)** | Educator |
| University of Wyoming, President's Office, 1000 E University Ave, Laramie WY 82071, USA | |
| **Buchanon, Phillip D** | Football Player |
| 6425 Emerald Pines Circle, Fort Myers FL 33966, USA | |
| **Buchanon, Willie J** | Football Player |
| 2742 Mesa Dr, Oceanside CA 92054, USA | |
| **Buchberger, Kelly** | Ice Hockey Player |
| Edmonton Oilers, 11230 110th St, Edmonton AB T5G 3H7, Canada | |
| **Buchek, Gerald P (Jerry)** | Baseball Player |
| 123 Royal Vista Dr, #502, Branson MO 65616, USA | |
| **Buchel, Marco** | Alpine Skier |
| Ramschwagweg 55, 9496 Balzers, Switzerland | |
| **Buchholz, Clay D** | Baseball Player |
| 630 King Oaks St, Lumberton TX 77657, USA | |
| **Buchholz, Taylor** | Baseball Player |
| 194 Powell Road, Springfield PA 19064, USA | |
| **Buchli, James F (Jim)** | Astronaut |
| 14761A Innerarity Point Road, Pensacola FL 32507, USA | |
| **Buchmann, Rainer** | Auto Racing Executive |
| Project Indy, 434 E Main St, Brownsburg IN 46112, USA | |
| **Buchwald, Ephraim** | Religious Leader, Rabbi |
| National Jewish Outreach, 989 Ave of Americas, #1000, New York NY 10018, USA | |
| **Buchwald, Stephen L** | Chemist |
| Massachusetts Institute of Technology, Chemistry Dept, Cambridge MA 02139, USA | |
| **Buck 65** | Rap Artist |
| Agency Group Ltd, 142 W 57th St, #600, New York NY 10019 USA | |
| **Buck, Craig** | Volleyball Player |
| 17872 W 59th Ave, Golden CO 80403, USA | |
| **Buck, Jason O** | Football Player |
| 4759 Canyon View Dr, Highland UT 84003, USA | |
| **Buck, Joe** | Sportscaster |
| 18 Upper Warson Road, Saint Louis MO 63124, USA | |
| **Buck, John E** | Sculptor |
| 11229 Cottonwood Road, Bozeman MT 59718, USA | |
| **Buck, Jonathan R (John)** | Baseball Player |
| 15068 Desert Eagle Circle, Riverton UT 84065, USA | |
| **Buck, Linda B** | Nobel Medicine Laureate |
| 14295 Sherwood Road NW, Seattle WA 98177, USA | |
| **Buck, Mike E** | Football Player |
| 269 Matthews Road, Oakdale NY 11769, USA | |
| **Buck, Peter** | Businessman |
| Subway Restaurants, 325 Bic Dr, Milford CT 06461, USA | |
| **Buck, Peter L** | Guitarist (REM) |
| REM/Athens Ltd, 170 College Ave, Athens GA 30601, USA | |
| **Buck, Scott** | Producer |
| Creative Artists Agency, 2000 Ave of Stars, #100, Los Angeles CA 90067 USA | |
| **Buck, Tara** | Actress |
| C E S D, 10635 Santa Monica Blvd, #130, Los Angeles CA 90025 USA | |
| **Buck, Travis G** | Baseball Player |
| 1443 W Roadrunner Dr, Chandler AZ 85286, USA | |
| **Buck, Vincent L (Vince)** | Football Player |
| 1005 Vintage Dr, Kenner LA 70065, USA | |
| **Buckens, Celine** | Actress |
| Creative Artists Agency, 2000 Ave of Stars, #100, Los Angeles CA 90067 USA | |
| **Buckey, Jay C, Jr** | Astronaut |
| 1 Sargent St, Hanover NH 03755, USA | |
| **Buckfield, Clare** | Actress |
| Associated International Mgmt, 7 Hatton Garden, #400, London EC1N 8AD, England | |
| **Buckhalter, Joseph (Joe)** | Basketball Player |
| 3900 Rose Hill Ave, #201A, Hanover NH 03755, USA | |
| **Buckingham, Amyand D** | Chemist |
| Crossways, 23 The Ave, Newmarket CB8 9AA, England | |
| **Buckingham, Gregory (Greg)** | Swimmer |
| 338 Ridge Road, San Carlos CA 94070, USA | |
| **Buckingham, Lindsey** | Guitarist, Singer (Fleetwood Mac) |
| Front Line Mgmt, 1100 Glendon Ave, #2000, Los Angeles CA 90024 USA | |
| **Buckinghams** | Pop, Rock Music Group |
| PO Box 220082, Great Neck NY 11022, USA | |
| **Buckland, Jonathan M (Jonny)** | Guitarist (Coldplay) |
| Paradigm Agency, 360 N Crescent Dr, North Building, Beverly Hills CA 90210 USA | |
| **Buckley, A J** | Actor |
| Thruline Entertainment, 9250 Wilshire Blvd, #100, Beverly Hills CA 90212 USA | |

**Buckley, Andy** — Actor
Coronel Group, 1100 Glendon Ave, #1700, Los Angeles CA 90046, USA
**Buckley, Betty L** — Actress, Singer, Director
Parseghian/Planco, 388 2nd Ave, #506, New York, NY 10010 USA
**Buckley, Carol** — Elephant Conservationist
Elephant Sanctuary, PO Box 393, Hohenwald TN 38462, USA
**Buckley, Curtis L** — Football Player
2208 Cantura Dr, Mesquite TX 75181, USA
**Buckley, D Terrell** — Football Player
19106 S Gardenia Ave, Weston FL 33332, USA
**Buckley, Dan** — Publisher
Marvel Comics, Publisher's Office, 417 5th Ave, New York NY 10016, USA
**Buckley, David** — Composer
Kraft-Engel Mgmt, 15233 Ventura Blvd, #200, Sherman Oaks CA 91403 USA
**Buckley, Dick** — Director
I C M Partners, 10250 Constellation Blvd, #900, Los Angeles CA 90067 USA
**Buckley, George** — Businessman
Minnesota Mining & Manufacturing, 3-M Center, Saint Paul MN 55144, USA
**Buckley, James L** — Senator, NY; Judge
PO Box 597, Sharon CT 06069, USA
**Buckley, Jean** — Baseball Player
143 Monarch Dr, Fortuna CA 95540, USA
**Buckley, Jerome H** — Educator
52 Waverley St, Belmont MA 02478, USA
**Buckley, Marcus W** — Football Player
240 Yukon Court, Weatherford TX 76087, USA
**Buckley, Richard E** — Conductor
310 W 55th St, #1K, New York NY 10019, USA
**Buckley, Robert E** — Actor
W M E Entertainment, 9601 Wilshire Blvd, #300, Beverly Hills CA 90210 USA
**Buckley, Roy** — Bowler
6900 Lee Road, Westerville OH 43081, USA
**Buckman, Phil** — Actor
S M S Talent, 8383 Wilshire Blvd, #230, Beverly Hills CA 90211 USA
**Buckner, Cleveland** — Basketball Player
19227 S Grandee Ave, Carson CA 90746, USA
**Buckner, Gregory D (Greg)** — Basketball Player
4129 Catawba Ave, Carrollton TX 75010, USA
**Buckner, Pam** — Bowler
645 Utah St, Reno NV 89506, USA
**Buckner, Paul E** — Sculptor
2322 Rockwood Ave, Eugene OR 97405, USA
**Buckner, Shelley** — Actress
B/W/R, 9100 Wilshire Blvd, #500W, Beverly Hills CA 90212 USA
**Buckner, W Quinn** — Basketball Player, Coach
857 Valencia Blvd, Irving TX 75039, USA
**Buckner, William J (Bill)** — Baseball Player
4405 E Wild Horse Lane, Boise ID 83712, USA
**Bucknor, C B** — Baseball Umpire
46 Midwood St, Brooklyn NY 11225, USA
**Buckson, David P** — Governor, DE
60 Exchange Dr, Camden Wyoming DE 19934, USA
**Buckwheat Zydeco** — Singer, Accordionist
Ted Fox Mgmt, PO Box 561, Rhinebeck NY 12572, USA
**Bucyk, John P (Chief)** — Ice Hockey Player
17 Boren Lane, Boxford MA 01921, USA
**Budarin, Nikolai M** — Cosmonaut
Cosmonaut Training Center, Star City, 141160 Zvezdny Gorodok, Moscow Oblast, Russia
**Budd Pieterse, Zola** — Track Athlete
Coastal Carolina University, Athletic Dept, Myrtle Beach CA 29578, USA
**Budd, David L (Dave)** — Basketball Player
40 N Woodland Ave, Woodbury NJ 08096, USA
**Budd, Frank** — Track, Football Player
138 Dorchester Road, Mount Laurel NJ 08054, USA
**Budd, Harold** — Composer, Writer
Opal/Warner Bros Records, 6834 Camrose Dr, Los Angeles CA 90068, USA
**Budd, Jersey** — Singer, Songwriter
Agency Group Ltd, 361-373 City Road, London EC1V 1PQ, England
**Budd, Julie** — Actress, Singer
Herb Bernstein Mgmt, 180 W End Ave, #2A, New York NY 10023, USA
**Budde, Brad E** — Football Player
5121 W 159th Terrace, Stilwell KS 66085, USA
**Budde, Edward L (Ed)** — Football Player
5121 W 159th Terrace, Stilwell KS 66085, USA
**Budden, Joseph A (Joe), II** — Rap Artist, Songwriter
I C M Partners, 10250 Constellation Blvd, #900, Los Angeles CA 90067 USA
**Buddie, Michael J (Mike)** — Baseball Player
157 Scottsdale Dr, Advance NC 27006, USA
**Buddon, Joseph A (Joe), II** — Rap Artist
I C M Partners, 10250 Constellation Blvd, #900, Los Angeles CA 90067 USA
**Budig, Eugene A (Gene)** — Baseball Executive, Educator
5 Sandwedge Lane, Isle of Palms SC 29451, USA
**Budig, Rebecca** — Actress
A P A Talent/Literary Agency, 405 S Beverly Dr, #300, Beverly Hills CA 90212 USA
**Budimir, Zivko** — President, Bosnia-Herzegovia
President's Office, Marsala Titz 7, 71000 Sarajevo, Bosnia & Herzegovina
**Budness, William W (Bill)** — Football Player
401 Huckle Hill Road, Bernardston MA 01337, USA
**Buechele, Steven B (Steve)** — Baseball Player
1104 Arlena Dr, Arlington TX 76012, USA
**Buechler, John Carl** — Director
12031 Vose, #19-21, North Hollywood CA 91605, USA
**Buehler, George S** — Football Player
201 E Grant Line Road, #16, Tracy CA 95376, USA
**Buehler, Judson D (Jud)** — Basketball Player
1515 West Lane, Del Mar CA 92014, USA

**Buehler, Rachel** — Soccer Player
1571 Luneta Drive, Del Mar CA 92014, USA
**Buehrle, Mark A** — Baseball Player
51 Long Cove Dr, Lemont IL 60439, USA
**Buell, Bebe** — Model, Singer, Actress
International Management Group, 767 5th Ave, New York NY 10153, USA
**Buell, Garett** — Percussionist (Caedmon's Call)
Breen Agency, 25 Music Square W, Nashville TN 37203, USA
**Bueno, Maria E** — Tennis Player
Rua Consolagao 3414, #10, 1001 Edificio Augustus, Sao Paulo, Brazil
**Buffa, Dudley W** — Writer
William Morrow Publishers, 1350 Ave of Americas, New York NY 10019 USA
**Buffenbarger, R Thomas** — Labor Leader
International Machinists Assn, 9000 Machinists Place, Upper Marlboro MD 20772, USA
**Buffer, Michael** — Boxing Commentator
Buffer Enterprises, 131 Fleet St, Marina del Rey CA 90292, USA
**Buffett, Jimmy** — Singer, Songwriter
Margaritaville, 424 Flemming St, #A, Key West FL 33040, USA
**Buffett, Warren E** — Businessman
Berkshire Hathaway, 1440 Kiewit Plaza, 3555 Farnam St, Omaha NE 68131, USA
**Buffkins, Archie Lee** — Performing Arts Administrator
Kennedy Center, Executive Suite, 2700 F St NW, Washington DC 20566, USA
**Buffone, Douglas J (Doug)** — Football Player
1272 W Lexington St, Chicago IL 60607, USA
**Bufman, Zev** — Producer
520 Brickell Key Dr, #612, Miami FL 33131, USA
**Buford, Damon J** — Baseball Player
5055 W Ray Road, #2, Chandler AZ 85226, USA
**Buford, Donald A (Don)** — Baseball Player
15412 Valley Vista Blvd, Sherman Oaks CA 91403, USA
**Buford, Jason (Brooks)** — Rap Artist
50 Murray St, #415, New York NY 10007, USA
**Buford, Maury A** — Football Player
2901 Sweet Briar St, Grapevine TX 76051, USA
**Buggs, Daniel (Danny)** — Football Player
3186 Evans Mill Road, Lithonia GA 30038, USA
**Buggy, Regina** — Field Hockey Player
550 Limekiln Road, Oley PA 19547, USA
**Bugliosi, Vincent T** — Attorney, Writer
663 Arbor St, Pasadena CA 91105, USA
**Bugner, Joe** — Boxer
22 Buckingham St, Surrey Hills NSW 2010, Australia
**Bugnon, Alex** — Jazz Pianist, Composer
Entertainment Consultants, 1207 Penshurst Court, Abingdon MD 21009, USA
**Buhari, Muhammadu** — President, Nigeria; Army General
G R A, PO Box 2010, Daura, Katsina State, Nigeria
**Buhler, Urs** — Singer (Il Divo)
Octagon, 81-83 Fulham High St, London SW6 3JW, England
**Buhner, Jay C** — Baseball Player
3219 300th Ave SE, Fall City WA 98024, USA
**Bujnoch, Glenn** — Football Player
7598 Fairway Glen Dr, Cincinnati OH 45248, USA
**Bujold, Genevieve** — Actress
C C A Mgmt, Garden Level, 32 Charlwood St, London SW1V 2DY, England
**Bukich, Rudolph A (Rudy)** — Football Player
7910 Ivanhoe Ave, #333, La Jolla CA 92037, USA
**Bukin, Andrei A** — Ice Dancer
Skating Federation, Lucjneskraia Nab 8, 119871 Moscow, Russia
**Buktenica, Raymond** — Actor
Special Artists Agency, 9200 Sunset Blvd, #410, West Hollywood CA 90069 USA
**Bukvich, Ryan A** — Baseball Player
200 Apple Blossom Circle, Brandon MS 39047, USA
**Bulaich, Norman B (Norm)** — Football Player
421 Lynndale Court, Hurst TX 76054, USA
**Bulatov, Erik** — Artist
Arndt Gallery, Potsdamer Str 96, 10785 Berlin, Germany
**Bulatovic, Andjela** — Handball Player
Z R L Buducnost, Ivana Milutinovica B B, 81000 Podgorica, Montenegro
**Bulatovic, Katarina** — Handball Player
C S Oltchim Ramnicu Valcea, Str Uzinel #1, 240007 Ramnicu Valcea, Romania
**Bulbrook, Anna** — Violist (Airborne Toxic Event)
Island Def Jam Records, 8920 W Sunset Blvd, #200, West Hollywood CA 90069 USA
**Bulger, Jason** — Baseball Player
1898 Harbour Oaks Dr, Snellville GA 30078, USA
**Bulger, Marc R** — Football Player
2701 S Lindbergh Blvd, Saint Louis MO 63131, USA
**Bulifant, Joyce** — Actress
Glick Agency, 1321 7th St, #203, Santa Monica CA 90401 USA
**Bulimar, Diana** — Gymnast
C S Dinamo Bucharest, Soseaua Stefan cel Mare 7-9, 020121 Bucharest, Romania
**Bulis, Jan** — Ice Hockey Player
Vancouver Canucks, 800 Griffiths Way, Vancouver BC V6B 6G1, Canada
**Buljung, Erich** — Marksman
7570 Stampede Dr, Colorado Springs CO 80920, USA
**Bull, Richard** — Actor
200 E Delaware Place, #20F, Chicago IL 60611, USA
**Bull, Ronald D (Ronnie)** — Football Player
15 Redspire Court, Bolingbrook IL 60490, USA
**Bullard, Matthew G (Matt)** — Basketball Player
10 Balmoral Place, Spring TX 77382, USA
**Bullard, Mike** — Ice Hockey Player
1170 Shillington Ave, Ottawa ON K1Z 7Z4, Canada
**Bullinger, James E (Jim)** — Baseball Player
2504 Elise Ave, Metairie LA 70003, USA
**Bullinger, Kirk M** — Baseball Player
3608 David Dr, Metairie LA 70003, USA

# B

| | |
|---|---|
| **Bullington, Bryan P** | Baseball Player |
| 20116 Oakwood Dr, Mokena IL 60448, USA | |
| **Bullins, Ed** | Writer |
| Northeastern University, English Dept, Boston MA 02115, USA | |
| **Bulloch, Jeremy** | Actor |
| Fett Photos, 10 Birchwood Road, London SW17 9BQ, England | |
| **Bullock, Bruce J** | Ice Hockey Player |
| 5226 W Redbird Road, Phoenix AZ 85083, USA | |
| **Bullock, Eric J** | Baseball Player |
| 17503 Harwick Court, Carson CA 90746, USA | |
| **Bullock, Jim J** | Actor |
| Connor Ankrum & Associates, 1680 Vine St, #1016, Los Angeles CA 90028, USA | |
| **Bullock, Reggie** | Basketball Player |
| Los Angeles Clippers, Staples Center, 1111 S Figueroa St, Los Angeles CA 90015 USA | |
| **Bullock, Sandra** | Actress |
| Creative Artists Agency, 2000 Ave of Stars, #100, Los Angeles CA 90067 USA | |
| **Bullock, Susan** | Opera Singer |
| Harrison/Parrott, 5-6 Albion Court, London W6 0QT, England | |
| **Bulluck, Keith J** | Football Player |
| 874 Nialta Lane, Brentwood TN 37027, USA | |
| **Bumbeck, David A** | Artist |
| 435 Farmers Dell Lane, Deltaville VA 23043, USA | |
| **Bumbry, Alonzo B (Al)** | Baseball Player |
| 28 Tremblant Court, Lutherville MO 21093, USA | |
| **Bumbry, Grace** | Opera Singer |
| I M G Artists, Carnegie Hall Tower, 152 W 57th St, #500, New York NY 10019 USA | |
| **Bump, Dennis** | Mathematician |
| Stanford University, Mathematics Dept, Stanford CA 94305, USA | |
| **Bump, J D** | Sculptor |
| Onda Gallery, 220 A Ave, 104, Lake Oswego OR 97034, USA | |
| **Bumpass, Rodger** | Actor |
| W M E Entertainment, 9601 Wilshire Blvd, #300, Beverly Hills CA 90210 USA | |
| **Bumpers, Dale L** | Governor, Senator, AR |
| 12723 Hunters Field Road, Little Rock AR 72211, USA | |
| **Bunch, Melvin L** | Baseball Player |
| 12 Tyler Lane, Hooks TX 75561, USA | |
| **Bund, Karlheinz** | Businessman |
| Huyssenallee 82-84, 45128 Essen Ruhr, Germany | |
| **Bundchen, Gisele** | Model, Actress |
| I M G Models, 304 Park Ave S, #PH N, New York NY 10010 USA | |
| **Bundy, Brooke** | Actress |
| 1801 Ave of Stars, #1250, Los Angeles CA 90067, USA | |
| **Bundy, Laura Bell** | Actress, Singer |
| Sanctuary Mgmt, 15301 Ventura Blvd, Building B, Sherman Oaks CA 91403, USA | |
| **Bunetta, Bill** | Bowler |
| 1176 E San Bruno Ave, Fresno CA 93710, USA | |
| **Bunin, Michael** | Actor |
| Circle Talent, 433 N Camden Dr, #400, Beverly Hills CA 90210 USA | |
| **Bunker, Wallace E (Wally)** | Baseball Player |
| 66 Falmouth Way, Bluffton SC 29909, USA | |
| **Bunkley, Brodrick** | Football Player |
| New Orleans Saints, 5800 Airline Highway, Metairie LA 70003 USA | |
| **Bunkowsky-Scherbak, Barb** | Golfer |
| 8725 Marlamoor Lane, West Palm Beach FL 33412, USA | |
| **Bunnell, Dewey** | Singer, Guitarist (America) |
| Morey Mgmt, 1100 Glendon Ave, #1100, Los Angeles CA 90024, USA | |
| **Bunnett, Joseph F** | Chemist |
| 608 Arroyo Seca, Santa Cruz CA 95060, USA | |
| **Bunning, James P D (Jim)** | Senator, KY; Baseball Player |
| 4 Fairway Dr, Southgate KY 41071, USA | |
| **Bunting, Eve** | Writer |
| 1512 Rose Villa St, Pasadena CA 91106, USA | |
| **Bunting, John S** | Football Player, Coach |
| 134 Soundview Dr, Hampstead NC 28443, USA | |
| **Bunting, William C (Bill)** | Basketball Player |
| 11000 Pacer Court, Raleigh NC 27614, USA | |
| **Bunton, Emma L** | Singer (Spice Girls) |
| Hall of Nothing, Poplar Mews, Uxbridge Road, London W12 7JS, England | |
| **Bunz, Dan** | Football Player |
| 4230 Rocklin Road, #2, Rocklin CA 95677, USA | |
| **Bunzow, John** | Singer, Songwriter |
| T K O Artist Mgmt, 2303 21st Ave S, #300, Nashville TN 37212, USA | |
| **Buoniconti, Nicholas A (Nick)** | Football Player, Businessman |
| 445 Grand Bay Dr, #803, Key Biscayne FL 33149, USA | |
| **Buono, Cara** | Actress |
| C E S D, 257 Park Ave S, #950, New York NY 10010 USA | |
| **Burba, David A (Dave)** | Baseball Player |
| 378 N Shore Lane, Gilbert AZ 85233, USA | |
| **Burba, Edwin H, Jr** | Army General |
| 256 Montrose Dr, McDonough GA 30253, USA | |
| **Burbank, Daniel C (Dan)** | Astronaut |
| 364 Route 6A, Yarmouth Port MA 02675, USA | |
| **Burbidge, E Margaret P** | Astronomer |
| 423 Washington St, #600, San Francisco CA 94111, USA | |
| **Burbules, Peter G** | Army General |
| 8287 Chestnut Point Lane, Hayes VA 23072, USA | |
| **Burch, Paul** | Singer |
| Silverleaf Booking, 589 W 1st St, Boiling Springs PA 17007, USA | |
| **Burch, Rick** | Bassist (Jimmy Eat World) |
| S A M, 722 Seward St, Los Angeles CA 90038, USA | |
| **Burch, Tory** | Fashion Designer |
| 11 W 19th St, #400, New York, NY 10011, USA | |
| **Burcham, David W** | Educator |
| Loyola Marymount University, President's Office, L1 L M U Dr, Los Angeles CA 90045, USA | |
| **Burchfiel, Burrell C** | Geologist |
| 9 Robinson Park, Winchester MA 01890, USA | |

| | |
|---|---|
| **Burchuladze, Paata** <br> Askonas Holt, Lincoln House, 300 High Holborn, London WC1V 7JH, England | Opera Singer |
| **Burckhalter, Joseph H** <br> 734 Green Valley Lane, Melbourne FL 32940, USA | Inventor (Florescent Dyes) |
| **Burckle, Caroline** <br> Premier Management Group, 115 Crescent Commons, Cary, NC 27518 USA | Swimmer |
| **Burd, Steven A** <br> Safeway Inc, 5918 Stoneridge Mall Road, Pleasanton CA 94588, USA | Businessman |
| **Burden, Luther D (Ticky)** <br> 4332 Grove Ave, #C, Winston Salem NC 27105, USA | Basketball Player |
| **Burden, William** <br> Opus 3 Artists, 470 Park Ave S, #900N, New York NY 10016 USA | Singer |
| **Burdette, Mallory** <br> 105 Winter Chase Lane, Brunswick GA 31520, USA | Tennis Player |
| **Burdick, Clinton D** <br> 1134 26th St, #4, Santa Monica CA 90403, USA | WW II Army Air Corps Hero |
| **Burditt, Joyce** <br> Jeff Ross Entertainment, 14560 Benefit St, #206, Sherman Oaks CA 91403, USA | Writer |
| **Burdon, Eric** <br> Lustig Talent, PO Box 770850, Orlando FL 32877 USA | Singer (Animals); Songwriter |
| **Bure, Pavel V** <br> 11091 Redhawk St, Plantation FL 33324, USA | Ice Hockey Player |
| **Bure, Valeri V** <br> 237 Monte Grigio Dr, Pacific Palisades CA 90272, USA | Ice Hockey Player |
| **Burfeindt, Betty** <br> 70 Sam Simeon Place, Rancho Mirage CA 92270, USA | Golfer |
| **Burford, Christopher W (Chris)** <br> 1215 Broken Feather Court, Reno NV 89511, USA | Football Player |
| **Burg, Mark** <br> Evolution Entertainment, 901 N Highland Ave, Los Angeles CA 90038 USA | Producer |
| **Burgee, John H** <br> Perelanda Farm, Skunks Misery Road, Millerton NY 12546, USA | Architect |
| **Burger, Leslie** <br> Princeton Public Library, 65 Witherspoon St, Princeton NJ 08542, USA | Association Executive, Librarian |
| **Burger, Neil** <br> Creative Artists Agency, 2000 Ave of Stars, #100, Los Angeles CA 90067 USA | Director, Writer |
| **Burgess, Adrian** <br> 324 G St, Anderson SC 29625, USA | Mountaineer |
| **Burgess, Albert A (Sonny)** <br> AristoMedia, PO Box 22765, Nashville TN 37202, USA | Singer, Guitarist, Songwriter |
| **Burgess, Christian** <br> 33 Gastein Road, London W6 8LT, England | Actor |
| **Burgess, Derrick L** <br> New England Patriots, 1 Patriot Place, Foxboro MA 02035 USA | Football Player |
| **Burgess, Don** <br> Gersh Agency, 9465 Wilshire Blvd, #600, Beverly Hills CA 90212 USA | Cinematographer |
| **Burgess, Mitchell** <br> I C M Partners, 10250 Constellation Blvd, #900, Los Angeles CA 90067 USA | Writer, Producer |
| **Burgess, Neil** <br> 201 E 5th St, #2200, Cincinnati OH 45202, USA | Electrical Engineer |
| **Burgess, Ronald L, Jr** <br> Director, Defense Intelligence Agency, Pentagon, Washington DC 20340 USA | Army General |
| **Burgess, Timothy A (Tim)** <br> Solo Agency, 53-55 Fulham High St, #200, London SW6 3JJ, England | Singer (Charlatans) |
| **Burghard, Maria** <br> Angentur Retzlaff, Kurfuerstenstra 34, 10785 Berlin, Germany | Actress |
| **Burghoff, Gary** <br> Scott Stander Assoc, 4533 Van Nuys Blvd, #401, Sherman Oaks CA 91403 USA | Actor |
| **Burgi, Richard W** <br> 1019 Baja St, Laguna Beach CA 92651, USA | Actor |
| **Burgmeier, Thomas H (Tom)** <br> 13118 Walmer St, Leawood KS 66209, USA | Baseball Player |
| **Burhoe, Ralph Wendell** <br> Montgomery Place, 5550 S South Shore Dr, #715, Chicago IL 60637, USA | Templeton Religion Laureate |
| **Buribayev, Alan** <br> I M G Artists, Hogarth Business Park, Chiswick, London W4 2TH, England | Conductor |
| **Buring, MyAnna** <br> Ken McReddie Assoc, 101 Finsbury Pavement, London EC2A 1RS, England | Actress |
| **Burka, Petra** <br> Skate Canada, 865 Shefford Road, Ottawa ON K1J 1H9, Canada | Figure Skater |
| **Burkart, Phil, Jr** <br> Phil Burkart Racing, 114 Oriskany Blvd, Yorkville NY 13495, USA | Drag Racing Driver |
| **Burke Charvet, Brooke** <br> Bx2 Mgmt, 1333 2nd St, #620, Santa Monica CA 90401, USA | Actress, Model |
| **Burke Hederman, Lynn** <br> 26 White Oak Tree Road, Syosset NY 11791, USA | Swimmer |
| **Burke, Alfonso C (Trey), III** <br> Utah Jazz, Energy Solutions Arena, 301 W South Temple, Salt Lake City UT 84101 USA | Basketball Player |
| **Burke, Bernard F** <br> 10 Bloomfield St, Lexington MA 02421, USA | Physicist, Astrophysicist |
| **Burke, Billy** <br> Ellen Meyer Entertainment, 8899 Beverly Blvd, #616, Los Angeles CA 90048, USA | Actor |
| **Burke, Cheryl B** <br> Cheryl Burke Dance, 1400 N Shoreline Blvd, #A1, Mountain View CA 94043, USA | Dancer |
| **Burke, Chris** <br> Abrams Artists, 9200 W Sunset Blvd, #1125, West Hollywood CA 90069 USA | Actor |
| **Burke, Christopher A (Chris)** <br> 15415 Crystal Springs Way, Louisville KY 40245, USA | Baseball Player |
| **Burke, Clement (Clem)** <br> Agency Group Ltd, 142 W 57th St, #600, New York NY 10019 USA | Drummer (Blondie) |
| **Burke, David** <br> Stone Manners Salners, 9911 W Pico Blvd, #1400, Los Angeles CA 90035 USA | Actor |
| **Burke, Delta** <br> Shelter Entertainment, 9255 Sunset Blvd, #300, Los Angeles CA 90069 USA | Actress |
| **Burke, Doris** <br> ABC-TV, Sports Dept, 77 W 66th St, New York NY 10023 USA | Sportscaster |

**B**

**Burchuladze - Burke**

**Burke, James** — Commentator
Henley House, Terrace Barnes, London SW13 0NP, England

**Burke, James E (Jamie)** — Baseball Player
374 W Lilburn Ave, Rosenburg OR 97470, USA

**Burke, James Lee** — Writer
Simon & Schuster, 1230 Ave of Americas, Concourse 1, New York NY 10020, USA

**Burke, Jan** — Writer
12437 Seal Beach Blvd, #101, Seal Beach CA 90740, USA

**Burke, Jim** — Producer, Actor
Ad Hominem Enterprises, 506 Santa Monica Blvd, #400, Santa Monica CA 90401, USA

**Burke, John J (Jack), Jr** — Golfer
5602 Glen Pines Dr, Houston TX 77069, USA

**Burke, Kathy** — Actress
Hatton McEwan, 3 Chocolate Studios, 7 Shepherdess Place, London N1 7LJ, England

**Burke, Kelly** — Model
Playboy Promotions, 2706 Media Center Dr, Los Angeles CA 90065 USA

**Burke, Kelly H** — Air Force General
803 Choctaw Lane, Shalimar FL 32579, USA

**Burke, Kevin** — Businessman
Consolidated Edison, 4 Irving Place, New York NY 10003, USA

**Burke, Leo P** — Baseball Player
3395 Torrey Pines Circle, Riner VA 24149, USA

**Burke, Michael Reilly** — Actor
Domain Talent, 9229 W Sunset Blvd, #710, West Hollywood CA 90069 USA

**Burke, Phil** — Actor
Lisa Richards Agency, 108 Upper Leeson St, Dublin 4, Ireland

**Burke, Robert John** — Actor
Paradigm Agency, 360 N Crescent Dr, North Building, Beverly Hills CA 90210 USA

**Burke, Sean** — Ice Hockey Player
9016 N 60th St, Paradise Valley AZ 85253, USA

**Burke, Simon** — Actor
United Agents, 12-26 Lexington St, London W1F 0LE, England

**Burke, Tim** — Visual Effects Designer
Rocket Science Talent, 5023 N Parkway Calabasas, Calabasas CA 91302, USA

**Burke, Timothy P (Tim)** — Baseball Player
12108 W Ida Lane, Littleton CO 80127, USA

**Burke, Will** — Writer, Director, Actor
United Talent Agency, U T A Plaza, 9336 Civic Center Dr, Beverly Hills CA 90210 USA

**Burkett, Bunny** — Drag Racing Driver
Bunny Burkett Racing Team, 8314 Robert E Lee Dr, Spotsylvania VA 22551, USA

**Burkett, Chris** — Football Player
296 Dover Lane, Madison MS 39110, USA

**Burkett, John D** — Baseball Player
1404 Laurel Lane, Southlake TX 76092, USA

**Burkhalter, Edward A, Jr** — Navy Admiral
4128 Fort Washington Place, Alexandria VA 22304, USA

**Burkhard, Gedeon** — Actor
Elisabeth von Molo, Nymphenburger Str 154, 80635 Munich, Germany

**Burkhardt, Francois** — Architect
3 Rue de Venise, 75004 Paris, France

**Burkhart, Kathe** — Artist
Moti Hasson Gallery, 230 Arabian Road, Palm Beach FL 33480, USA

**Burkholder, JoAnn** — Medical Activist, Physician
North Carolina State University, Botany Dept, Raleigh NC 27695, USA

**Burkholder, Max** — Actor
Osbrink Talent Agency, 4343 Lankershim Blvd, #100, North Hollywood CA 91602 USA

**Burks, Ellis R** — Baseball Player
115 South Lane, Chagrin Falls OH 44022, USA

**Burleson, Nate** — Football Player
15508 SE 79th Place, Newcastle WA 98059, USA

**Burleson, Richard P (Rick)** — Baseball Player
241 E Country Hills Dr, La Habra CA 90631, USA

**Burleson, Tommy L (Tom)** — Basketball Player
PO Box 596, Newland NC 28657, USA

**Burley, Gary** — Football Player
514 Bristol Lane, Birmingham AL 35226, USA

**Burman, Alexandra** — Model
Group Model Mmgt, Po de Gracia 67, Pral 1A, 08008 Barcelona, Spain

**Burman, George R** — Football Player
1646 James St, Syracuse NY 13203, USA

**Burn, Malcolm** — Singer
Anthem Entertainment, 189 Carlton St, Toronto ON M5A 2K7, Canada

**Burnell, Jocelyn Bell** — Astronomer
Bell Open University, Physics Dept, Milton Keynes MK7 6AA, England

**Burner, David L** — Businessman
B F Goodrich Co, 3 Coliseum Centre, 2550 W Tyvola Road, Charlotte NC 28205, USA

**Burnes, Karen** — Commentator
CBS-TV, News Dept, 51 W 52nd St, New York NY 10019 USA

**Burnet, Guy** — Actor
Resolution, 1801 Century Park East, #2300, Los Angeles CA 90067 USA

**Burnett, Allan J (A J)** — Baseball Player
15208 Jarrettsville Pike, Monkton MD 21111, USA

**Burnett, Carol** — Actress, Comedienne
I C M Partners, 10250 Constellation Blvd, #900, Los Angeles CA 90067 USA

**Burnett, Kevin B** — Football Player
2938 S Sunbeck Circle, Dallas TX 75234, USA

**Burnett, Nancy** — Actress
Pinnacle Commercial Talent, 5757 Wilshire Blvd, #510, Los Angeles CA 90036, USA

**Burnett, Sean R** — Baseball Player
14016 Aster Ave, Wellington FL 33414, USA

**Burnett, T-Bone** — Singer, Songwriter, Music Producer
Creative Artists Agency, 2000 Ave of Stars, #100, Los Angeles CA 90067 USA

**Burnette, Olivia** — Actress
A P A Talent/Literary Agency, 405 S Beverly Dr, #300, Beverly Hills CA 90212 USA

**Burnette, Rocky** — Singer
1900 Ave of Stars, #2530, Los Angeles CA 90067, USA

**Burning Spear** — Singer
Burning Spear Mgmt, 130-34 231st St, Springfield Gardens NY 11413, USA

**Burningham, John** — Writer
Conville & Walsh, 118-120 Wardour St, London W1V 3LA, England

**Burnitz, Jeromy N** — Baseball Player
PO Box 676032, Rancho Santa Fe CA 92067, USA

**Burnley, James H, IV** — Secretary, Transportation
Venable LLP, 575 7th St NW, #1, Washington DC 20004, USA

**Burns, Annie** — Singer (Burns Sisters), Songwriter
Burns Sisters Band, PO Box 845, Ithaca NY 14851, USA

**Burns, Bob** — Drummer (Lynyrd Skynyrd)
Vector Mgmt, PO Box 120479, Nashville TN 37212 USA

**Burns, Bob** — Golfer
12512 Fraser Ave, Granada Hills CA 91344, USA

**Burns, Brooke** — Actress
A P A Talent/Literary Agency, 405 S Beverly Dr, #300, Beverly Hills CA 90212 USA

**Burns, Charles F (Charlie)** — Ice Hockey Player, Coach
7 Fawn Dr, Wallingford CT 06492, USA

**Burns, Christian** — Singer, Guitarist (BBMak)
Spirit Media, 34 Salisbury St, London NW8 8QE, England

**Burns, David D** — Psychiatrist
Stanford University, Psychiatry/Behavioral Science Dept, Stanford CA 94305, USA

**Burns, Edward** — Director, Actor
Marlboro Road Gang Productions, 334 E 90th St, New York NY 10128, USA

**Burns, Eric A** — Entertainer
Fox News, 1211 Ave of Americas, Lower C3R, New York NY 10036, USA

**Burns, Eric D (Ric)** — Director
Steeplechase Films, 2095 Broadway, #503, New York NY 10023, USA

**Burns, George** — Golfer
403 S Sapodilla Ave, #516, West Palm Beach FL 33401, USA

**Burns, Heather** — Actress
I C M Partners, 10250 Constellation Blvd, #900, Los Angeles CA 90067 USA

**Burns, James MacGregor** — Political Scientist, Historian
High Mowing, Bee Hill Road, Williamstown MA 01267, USA

**Burns, Jeannie** — Singer (Burns Sisters), Songwriter
Burns Sisters Band, PO Box 845, Ithaca NY 14851, USA

**Burns, Jere, II** — Actor
Innovative Artists, 1505 10th St, Santa Monica CA 90401 USA

**Burns, Jimmy** — Writer
Bloomsbury Publishing, 50 Bedford Square, London WC1B 3DP, England

**Burns, Joey** — Singer, Guitarist (Calexico)
Billions Corp, 3522 W Armitage Ave, Chicago IL 60647 USA

**Burns, Keith B** — Football Player
13572 Heritage Farms Dr, Gainesville VA 20155, USA

**Burns, Kenneth L (Ken)** — Documentary Director
Florentine Films, 59 Maple Grove Road, Walpole NH 03608, USA

**Burns, M Anthony** — Businessman
Ryder System Inc, 11690 NW 105th St, Medley FL 33178, USA

**Burns, Marie** — Singer (Burns Sisters), Songwriter
Burns Sisters Band, PO Box 845, Ithaca NY 14851, USA

**Burns, Marilyn** — Writer
Marilyn Burns Educational Assoc, 150 Gate 5 Road, #101, Sausalito CA 94965, USA

**Burns, Marilyn** — Actress
12951 Briar Forest Dr, Houston TX 77077, USA

**Burns, Megan** — Actress
Rights House, Drury House, 34-43 Russell St, London WC2B 5HA, England

**Burns, R Britt** — Baseball Player
1550 Katy Gap Road, #903, Katy TX 77494, USA

**Burns, Regan** — Actor, Comedian
OmniPop Talent Group, 4605 Lankershim Blvd, #201, Toluca Lake CA 91602 USA

**Burns, Robin** — Ice Hockey Player
186 Sherwood Road, Beaconsfield QC H9W 2G8, Canada

**Burns, Steve** — Actor
Paradigm Agency, 360 N Crescent Dr, North Building, Beverly Hills CA 90210 USA

**Burns, Todd E** — Baseball Player
PO Box 111, Princeton AL 35766, USA

**Burns, Ursula M** — Businesswoman
Xerox Corp, 800 Long Ridge Road, Stamford CT 06092, USA

**Burnside, Iain** — Concert Pianist, Commentator
Askonas Holt, Lincoln House, 300 High Holborn, London WC1V 7JH, England

**Burnside, Peter W (Pete)** — Baseball Player
1765 Washington Ave, Wilmette IL 60091, USA

**Burr, Bill** — Actor, Comedian
A P A Talent/Literary Agency, 405 S Beverly Dr, #300, Beverly Hills CA 90212 USA

**Burr, Matthew** — Drummer (Grace Potter & the Nocturnals)
Paradigm Agency, 404 W Franklin St, Monterey CA 93940 USA

**Burrell Wiley, Kim** — Singer, Pianist, Songwriter
Universal Attractions, 135 W 26th St, #1200, New York NY 10001 USA

**Burrell, Garland L, Jr** — Judge
US District Court, 501 I St, #3200, Sacramento CA 95814, USA

**Burrell, Gary** — Businessman
Garmin International, 1200 E 151st St, Olathe KS 66062, USA

**Burrell, John B (Johnny)** — Football Player
376 Park Lake Dr, Mead OK 73449, USA

**Burrell, Kenneth E (Kenny)** — Jazz Guitarist, Composer
Joel Chriss Co, 300 Mercer St, #3J, New York NY 10003 USA

**Burrell, Leroy** — Track Athlete
University of Houston, Athletic Dept, Houston TX 77023, USA

**Burrell, Patrick B (Pat), III** — Baseball Player
PO Box 1770, Boulder Creek CA 95006, USA

**Burrell, Scott D** — Basketball Player
331 Evergreen Ave, Hamden CT 06518, USA

**Burrell, Ty** — Actor
I C M Partners, 10250 Constellation Blvd, #900, Los Angeles CA 90067 USA

**Burres, Brian** — Baseball Player
350 SE 2nd St, #1420, Fort Lauderdale FL 33301, USA

**Burress, Plaxico A** — Football Player
47 Huntington Terrace, Totowa NJ 07512, USA
**Burridge, Pam** — Surfer
Mark Rabbidge, 441B Bendalong Road, Bendalong NSW 2539, Australia
**Burridge, Randy** — Ice Hockey Player
1911 Nuevo Road, Henderson NV 89014, USA
**Burris, Jeffrey L (Jeff)** — Football Player
8074 Hopkins Lane, Indianapolis IN 46250, USA
**Burrough, Kenneth O (Ken)** — Football Player
5823 Tallow Lane, Indianapolis IN 46250, USA
**Burroughs, Augusten X** — Writer
Picador/Saint Martin's Press, 175 5th Ave, New York NY 10010, USA
**Burroughs, Jeffrey A (Jeff)** — Baseball Player
6155 Laguna Court, Long Beach CA 90803, USA
**Burroughs, Sean** — Baseball Player
6155 Laguna Court, Long Beach CA 90803, USA
**Burrow, Kenneth R (Ken)** — Football Player
5371 Dunwoody Club Creek, Atlanta GA 30360, USA
**Burrows, Darren E** — Actor
Writers & Artists, 360 N Crescent Dr, Building North, Beverly Hills CA 90210, USA
**Burrows, David J (Dave)** — Ice Hockey Player
RR 1, Lake Harris ON P2A 2W7, Canada
**Burrows, Edwin G** — Writer
Oxford University Press, 198 Madison Ave, #800, New York NY 10016 USA
**Burrows, Eva E** — Religious Leader
Domain Park, 193 Domain Road, #102, South Yarra VIC 3141, Australia
**Burrows, J Stuart** — Opera Singer
29 Blackwater Grove, Alderholt, Dorset SP6 3AD, England
**Burrows, James E (Jim)** — Director
I C M Partners, 10250 Constellation Blvd, #900, Los Angeles CA 90067 USA
**Burrows, Saffron** — Actress
United Agents, 12-26 Lexington St, London W1F 0LE, England
**Burrows, Stephen** — Fashion Designer
10 W 57th St, New York NY 10019, USA
**Burrs, Marcia Ann** — Actress
Torque Entertainment, 3118 Wilshire Blvd, #160, Santa Monica CA 90403, USA
**Burrus, William** — Labor Leader
American Postal Workers Union, 1300 L St NW, #200, Washington DC 20005, USA
**Burruss, Kandi** — Singer (Xscape)
Richard Walters, PO Box 2789, Toluca Lake CA 91610 USA
**Bursch, Daniel W** — Astronaut
1305 Buena Vista Ave, Pacific Grove CA 93950, USA
**Burshnick, Anthony J (Tony)** — Air Force General
7715 Carrleigh Parkway, Springfield VA 22152, USA
**Burson, Clare** — Singer, Songwriter
Rounder Records, 1 Rounder Way, Burlington MA 01803 USA
**Burson, Harold** — Businessman
30 W 63rd St, #7H, New York NY 10023, USA
**Burson, James O (Jimmy)** — Football Player
351 Heath Road, Dawsonville GA 30534, USA
**Burstyn, Ellen** — Actress
Blue Flower Arts, PO Box 1361, Millbrook NY 12545, USA
**Burt, Adam** — Ice Hockey Player
34 Smull Ave, Caldwell NJ 07006, USA
**Burt, Donald Graham** — Art Director
Skouras Agency, 1149 3rd St, #300, Santa Monica CA 90403 USA
**Burt, James P (Jim)** — Football Player
10 River Farms Lane, Saddle River NJ 07458, USA
**Burtnett, Wellington, Jr** — Ice Hockey Player
1703 Pouliot Place, Wilmington MA 01887, USA
**Burton, Brandie** — Golfer
3480 Pleasant Hill Dr, Highland CA 92346, USA
**Burton, Ellis N** — Baseball Player
15621 Beach Blvd, #SP7, Westminster CA 92683, USA
**Burton, F Shane** — Football Player
PO Box 522, Hewitt Road, Catawba NC 28609, USA
**Burton, Gary** — Jazz Vibist
Berklee College of Music, 1140 Boylston St, Boston MA 02215, USA
**Burton, Hilarie** — Actress
Principal Entertainment, 9255 Sunset Blvd, #500, Los Angeles CA 90069 USA
**Burton, Jake** — Snowboard Skier
Burton Snowboards, 80 Industrial Parkway, Burlington VT 05401, USA
**Burton, Jeffrey B (Jeff)** — Auto Racing Driver
6000 Fairview Road, #635, Charlotte NC 28210, USA
**Burton, Kate** — Actress, Singer
Gersh Agency, 9465 Wilshire Blvd, #600, Beverly Hills CA 90212 USA
**Burton, L Jared** — Baseball Player
PO Box 506, Westminster SC 29693, USA
**Burton, Lance** — Illusionist
Monte Carlo Hotel, 3770 S Las Vegas Blvd, Las Vegas NV 89109, USA
**Burton, Lawrence G (Larry), Jr** — Football Player
41 San Gabriel, Rancho Santa Margarita CA 92688, USA
**Burton, Leonard B (Len)** — Football Player
3436 Beech Grove Road, Rancho Santa Margarita CA 92688, USA
**Burton, LeVar** — Actor
Sovereign Talent Group, 8421 Wilshire Blvd, #200, Beverly Hills CA 90211 USA
**Burton, Nelson, Jr** — Bowler
9359 SW Eagles Landing, Stuart FL 34997, USA
**Burton, Richard S V** — Architect
1B Lady Margaret Road, London NW5 2NE, England
**Burton, Steve** — Actor
James/Levy Mgmt, 3500 W Olive Ave, #1470, Burbank CA 91505 USA
**Burton, Thomas M** — Journalist
Wall Street Journal, Editorial Dept, 1 World Financial Center, New York NY 10281, USA
**Burton, Timothy W (Tim)** — Director
Tim Burton Productions, 8033 W Sunset Blvd, #7500, West Hollywood CA 90046, USA

| | |
|---|---|
| **Burton, Ward**<br>2046 Myers Road, Halifax VA 24550, USA | Auto Racing Driver |
| **Burton, Willie R**<br>18900 Fleming St, Detroit MI 48234, USA | Basketball Player |
| **Burtt, Ben, Jr**<br>Skywalker Sound, PO Box 29901, San Francisco CA 94129, USA | Sound Editor |
| **Burtt, Steven D (Steve)**<br>200 W 143rd Sr, #12D, New York NY 10030, USA | Basketball Player |
| **Burum, Stephen H**<br>Mirisch Agency, 8840 Wilshire Blvd, #100, Beverly Hills CA 90211 USA | Cinematographer |
| **Burwell, Carter**<br>Body Studio, 105 Hudson St, New York NY 10013, USA | Composer |
| **Burwitz, Nils**<br>Calle Rosa 22, Valldemossa, Majorca, Spain | Artist, Sculptor |
| **Bury, Pol**<br>236 Blvd Raspail, 75014 Paris, France | Sculptor |
| **Busby, Steven L (Steve)**<br>2701 Brittany Lane, Grapevine TX 76051, USA | Baseball Player |
| **Buscemi, Steve**<br>Gotham Group, 7250 Melrose Ave, Los Angeles CA 90046, USA | Actor, Director |
| **Busch, Adam**<br>Glick Agency, 1321 7th St, #203, Santa Monica CA 90401 USA | Actor, Director, Producer |
| **Busch, August A, III**<br>Anheuser-Busch Cos, 1 Busch Place, Saint Louis MO 63118, USA | Businessman, Baseball Executive |
| **Busch, Charles**<br>Creative Artists Agency, 2000 Ave of Stars, #100, Los Angeles CA 90067 USA | Actor, Writer |
| **Busch, Kurt T**<br>117 Nevis Lane, Mooresville NC 28115, USA | Auto, Truck Racing Driver |
| **Busch, Kyle T**<br>Kyle Busch Motorsports, 559 Pitts School Road, Concord NC 28027, USA | Auto, Truck Racing Driver |
| **Buse, Donald R (Don)**<br>7300 W State Road 64, Huntingburg IN 47542, USA | Basketball Player |
| **Busemann, Frank**<br>Borkumstr 13A, 45665 Recklinghausen, Germany | Track Athlete |
| **Buser, Martin**<br>PO Box 520997, Big Lake AK 99652, USA | Dog Sled Racer |
| **Busey, Gary**<br>Global Artists Agency, 6253 Hollywood Blvd, #508, Los Angeles CA 90028 USA | Actor |
| **Busey, Jake**<br>Kritzer Levine Wilkins Griffin, 11872 La Grange Ave, #100, Los Angeles CA 90025 USA | Actor |
| **Busfield, Timothy**<br>Paradigm Agency, 360 N Crescent Dr, North Building, Beverly Hills CA 90210 USA | Actor, Producer, Director |
| **Bush, Barbara P**<br>10000 Memorial Dr, #900, Houston TX 77024, USA | Wife of US President |
| **Bush, Blair W**<br>16911 SE 32nd Place, Bellevue WA 98008, USA | Football Player |
| **Bush, David T (Dave)**<br>8 Stevens Cove Road, Bridgton ME 04009, USA | Baseball Player |
| **Bush, Devin M**<br>10278 Laurel Road, Davie FL 33328, USA | Football Player |
| **Bush, George H W**<br>10000 Memorial Dr, #900, Houston TX 77024, USA | President, USA |
| **Bush, George W**<br>Prairie Chapel Ranch, Crawford TX 76638, USA | President, USA |
| **Bush, Guy L**<br>Michigan State University, Zoology Dept, East Lansing MI 48824, USA | Zoologist |
| **Bush, Homer G**<br>1402 Exeter Court, Southlake TX 76092, USA | Baseball Player |
| **Bush, Jim**<br>5106 Bounty Lane, Culver City CA 90230, USA | Track Coach |
| **Bush, Johnny**<br>Texas Sounds Entertainment, 957 N A S A Parkway, #542, Houston TX 77058, USA | Singer, Guitarist, Songwriter |
| **Bush, Katherine (Kate)**<br>Jukes Productions, PO Box 13995, London W9 2FL, England | Singer, Songwriter |
| **Bush, Kristian**<br>Gail Gellman Mgmt, 23852 Pacific Coast Highway, #920, Malibu CA 90265, USA | Singer (Billy Pilgrim, Sugarland) |
| **Bush, Laura**<br>Prairie Chapel Ranch, Crawford TX 76638, USA | Wife of US President |
| **Bush, Lesley L**<br>65 Birch Ave, Princeton NJ 08542, USA | Diver |
| **Bush, Michael**<br>Chicago Bears, 1000 Football Dr, Lake Forest IL 60045 USA | Football Player |
| **Bush, R Randall (Randy)**<br>37 Kings Canyon Dr, New Orleans LA 70131, USA | Baseball Player |
| **Bush, Reggie**<br>2443 Poydras St, New Orleans LA 70119, USA | Football Player |
| **Bush, Sam**<br>Samanda Lynn Music, PO Box 50962, Nashville TN 37205, USA | Singer, Mandolinist (New Grass Revival) |
| **Bush, Sophia**<br>Joan Green Mgmt, 1836 Courtney Terrace, Los Angeles CA 90046 USA | Actress |
| **Bush, Walter L, Jr**<br>5200 Malibu Dr, Minneapolis MN 55436, USA | Ice Hockey Executive |
| **Bush, William Green**<br>Talent Works, 3500 W Olive Ave, #1400, Burbank CA 91505 USA | Actor |
| **Bushinsky, Joseph M (Jay)**<br>Rehov Hatsafon 5, Savyon 56540, Israel | Commentator |
| **Bushland, Raymond C**<br>200 Concord Plaza Dr, San Antonio TX 78216, USA | Entomologist |
| **Bushnell, Bill**<br>2751 Pelham Place, Los Angeles CA 90068, USA | Director |
| **Bushnell, Candace**<br>Greater Talent Network, 437 5th Ave, #700, New York NY 10016, USA | Writer |
| **Bushnell, Nolan K**<br>UWink, 2100 N Main St, #A14, Los Angeles CA 90031, USA | Businessman |
| **Bushwick Bill**<br>Richard Walters, PO Box 2789, Toluca Lake CA 91610 USA | Rap Artist (Geto Boys) |

V.I.P. Address Book

| | |
|---|---|
| **Bushy, Ronald (Ron)** | Drummer (Iron Butterfly) |
| Lustig Talent, PO Box 770850, Orlando FL 32877 USA | |
| **Busick, Steve R** | Football Player |
| 6246 W Long Dr, Littleton CO 80123, USA | |
| **Busino, Orlando F** | Cartoonist (Mugsy) |
| 12 Shadblow Hill Road, Ridgefield CT 06877, USA | |
| **Buskas, Rod** | Ice Hockey Player |
| 182 Wentworth Dr, Henderson NV 89074, USA | |
| **Busniuk, Ron** | Ice Hockey Player |
| 540 Laurentian Dr, Thunder Bay ON P7C 5J8, Canada | |
| **Buss, David M** | Psychologist, Writer |
| University of Texas, Psychology Dept, Austin TX 78712, USA | |
| **Busse, Keith E** | Businessman |
| Steel Dynamics, 7575 W Jefferson Blvd, Fort Wayne IN 46804, USA | |
| **Bussell, Darcey A** | Ballerina |
| 155 New King's Road, London SW6 4SJ, England | |
| **Bussey, Barney A** | Football Player |
| 5059 Park Ridge Court, West Chester OH 45069, USA | |
| **Bussey, Dexter M** | Football Player |
| American/S C I, 888 W Beaver Road, Troy MI 48084, USA | |
| **Bustamante, Carlos** | Molecular Scientist |
| University of California, Howard Hughes Medical Institute, Berkeley CA 94720, USA | |
| **Bustamante, Hector Luis** | Actor |
| Diverse Talent Group, 9911 Pico Blvd, #350W, Los Angeles CA 90035 USA | |
| **Bustamente, Sergio** | Artist, Sculptor |
| Independence 238, Col Centro, Tlaquepaque CP 45500 Jalisco, Mexico | |
| **Butala, Tony** | Singer (Lettermen) |
| PO Box 151, McKees Rocks PA 15136, USA | |
| **Butcher, Adam** | Actor |
| I C M Partners, 10250 Constellation Blvd, #900, Los Angeles CA 90067 USA | |
| **Butcher, Garth** | Ice Hockey Player |
| 1524 Maple Lane, Bellingham WA 98229, USA | |
| **Butcher, John D** | Baseball Player |
| 4245 Trillium Lane E, Mound MN 55364, USA | |
| **Butcher, Page** | Model |
| Next Model Mgmt, 23 Watts St, New York NY 10013 USA | |
| **Butcher-Marsh, Mary** | Baseball Player |
| 1119 Cedar St, Carson City NV 89701, USA | |
| **Butera, Salvatore P (Sal)** | Baseball Player |
| 324 Tersas Court, Lake Mary FL 32746, USA | |
| **Buthelezi, Chief Mangosuthu G** | Chief Minister, KwaZulu/Natal |
| Home Affairs Ministry, Private Bag X741, Pretoria 0001, South Africa | |
| **Butkus, Richard M (Dick)** | Football Player, Actor |
| Butkus Foundation, 18920 NE 227th Ave, Brush Prairie WA 98606, USA | |
| **Butler of Brockwell, F E Robin** | Government Official, England |
| Master's Residence, University College, Oxford OX1 4BH, England | |
| **Butler, Austin R** | Actor |
| Anonymous Content, 3532 Hayden Ave, Culver City CA 90232 USA | |
| **Butler, Bernard** | Guitarist (Suede) |
| Interceptor Enterprises, 98 White Lion St, London N1 9PF, England | |
| **Butler, Bill C** | Cinematographer |
| 1097 Aviation Blvd, Hermosa Beach CA 90254, USA | |
| **Butler, Brett** | Actress, Comedienne |
| Evolution Entertainment, 901 N Highland Ave, Los Angeles CA 90038 USA | |
| **Butler, Brett M** | Baseball Player |
| 9512 E Canyon View Road, Scottsdale AZ 85255, USA | |
| **Butler, Chad M** | Drummer, Percussionist (Switchfoot) |
| Universal Attractions, 135 W 26th St, #1200, New York NY 10001 USA | |
| **Butler, Cher** | Model |
| Playboy Promotions, 2706 Media Center Dr, Los Angeles CA 90065 USA | |
| **Butler, Chris** | Guitarist (Waitresses), Songwriter |
| C E S D, 10635 Santa Monica Blvd, #130, Los Angeles CA 90025 USA | |
| **Butler, Clay** | Cartoonist |
| PO Box 245, Capitola CA 95010, USA | |
| **Butler, Dan** | Actor |
| Innovative Artists, 1505 10th St, Santa Monica CA 90401 USA | |
| **Butler, Dean** | Actor, Producer, Writer |
| Peak Moore Enterprises, 3233 Donald Douglas Loop S, #B, Santa Monica CA 90405, USA | |
| **Butler, Edwin F (Win), III** | Singer (Arcade Fire), Songwriter |
| Billions Corp, 3522 W Armitage Ave, Chicago IL 60647 USA | |
| **Butler, Gayle Goodson** | Editor |
| Better Homes & Gardens, Editor's Office, 1716 Locust St, Des Moines IA 50309, USA | |
| **Butler, George L (Lee)** | Air Force General |
| Peter Kiewit & Sons, 11122 William Plaza, Omaha NE 68144, USA | |
| **Butler, Gerard** | Actor, Singer, Producer |
| Creative Artists Agency, 2000 Ave of Stars, #100, Los Angeles CA 90067 USA | |
| **Butler, J Caron** | Basketball Player |
| 3802 Millard Way, Fairfax VA 22033, USA | |
| **Butler, J Keith** | Football Player |
| 805 Cavan Dr, Cranberry Township PA 16066, USA | |
| **Butler, James (Cannonball)** | Football Player |
| 1261 Cahaba Dr SW, Atlanta GA 30311, USA | |
| **Butler, James W** | Sculptor |
| Valley Farm Studios, Radway, Warwick CV35 0UJ, England | |
| **Butler, Jerry** | Ice Hockey Player |
| 3595 Eldridge Ave, Winnipeg MB R3R 0L5, Canada | |
| **Butler, Jerry (Iceman)** | Singer, Songwriter |
| Entertainment Consultants, 1207 Penhurst Court, Abingdon MD | |
| **Butler, Jerry O** | Football Player |
| 17117 Shaker Blvd, Cleveland OH 44120, USA | |
| **Butler, Jonathan** | Guitarist, Singer, Songwriter |
| Creative Artists Agency, 2000 Ave of Stars, #100, Los Angeles CA 90067 USA | |
| **Butler, Joseph C (Joe)** | Drummer, Singer (Lovin'Spoonful) |
| Lustig Talent, PO Box 770850, Orlando FL 32877 USA | |
| **Butler, Kevin G** | Football Player |
| 3256 Bagley Passage, Duluth GA 30097, USA | |

**B**

| | |
|---|---|
| **Butler, LeRoy**<br>4119 Westloop Lane, Jacksonville FL 32277, USA | Football Player |
| **Butler, Martin**<br>University of Sussex, Music Dept, Brighton BN1 9RH, England | Composer |
| **Butler, Michael A**<br>3107 Magdalene Forest Court, Tampa FL 33618, USA | Football Player |
| **Butler, Mitchell L**<br>3464 Meier St, Los Angeles CA 90066, USA | Basketball Player |
| **Butler, Raymond L (Ray)**<br>1300 Woodcrest Dr, Houston TX 77018, USA | Football Player |
| **Butler, Robert**<br>650 Club View Dr, Los Angeles CA 90024, USA | Director |
| **Butler, Robert C (Bobby)**<br>5567 Naylor Court, Norcross GA 30092, USA | Football Player |
| **Butler, Robert Olen**<br>3909 Reserve Dr, #1611, Tallahassee FL 32311, USA | Writer |
| **Butler, Samuel C**<br>Cravath Swain Moore, 825 8th Ave, New York NY 10019, USA | Attorney |
| **Butler, Terence M J (Geezer)**<br>Sharon Osborne Mgmt, 8899 Beverly Blvd, #905, West Hollywood CA 90048, USA | Bassist (Black Sabbath), Songwriter |
| **Butler, William F (Bill)**<br>141 Buckskin Lane, Berkeley Springs WV 25411, USA | Baseball Player |
| **Butler, William F (Skip)**<br>1311 Spyglass Dr, Mansfield TX 76063, USA | Football Player |
| **Butler, William R (Bill)**<br>200 E Liberty St, Berlin WI 54923, USA | Football Player |
| **Butler, Yancy**<br>Framework Entertainment, 9057 Nemo St, #C, West Hollywood CA 90069 USA | Actress |
| **Butor, Michel**<br>A l'Ecart, 216 Place de L'Eglise, 74380 Lucinges, France | Writer |
| **Butt, Yondani**<br>Gurtman & Murtha, 450 Fashion Ave, #603, New York NY 10123, USA | Conductor |
| **Butterfield, Alexander P**<br>9237 Regents Road, #323, La Jolla CA 92037, USA | Government Official |
| **Butterfield, Benjamin**<br>I M G Artists, Hogarth Business Park, Chiswick, London W4 2TH, England | Opera Singer |
| **Butterfield, Deborah K**<br>11229 Cottonwood Road, Bozeman MT 59718, USA | Sculptor |
| **Buttle, Gregory E (Greg)**<br>5 Hollacher Dr, Northport NY 11768, USA | Football Player |
| **Buttle, Jeffrey**<br>International Management Group, 304 Park Ave, #PH N, New York NY 10010, USA | Figure Skater |
| **Button, Jenson A L**<br>Jenson Racing, 67 Valkenburgerweg, 6419 Heerlen AP, Netherlands | Auto Racing Driver |
| **Button, Richard T (Dick)**<br>Candio Productions, 765 Park Ave, #6B, New York NY 10021, USA | Figure Skater, Producer |
| **Butts, James**<br>16950 Belforest Dr, Carson CA 90746, USA | Track Athlete |
| **Butz, David E (Dave)**<br>746 E Adams St, Belleville IL 62220, USA | Football Player |
| **Butz, Norbert Leo**<br>Creative Artists Agency, 2000 Ave of Stars, #100, Los Angeles CA 90067 USA | Actor, Singer |
| **Buxbaum, Richard M**<br>University of California, Law School, Boalt Hall, Berkeley CA 94720, USA | Attorney, Educator |
| **Buxton, Sarah**<br>Origin Talent Mgmt, 4705 Laurel Canyon BLvd, #306, Valley Village CA 91607, USA | Actress, Singer |
| **Buy, Margherita**<br>Carol Levi Mgmt, Via Giuseppe Pisanelli 2, 00196 Rome, Italy | Actress |
| **Buyers, William**<br>Atomic Energy of Canada, 2251 Speakman Dr, Mississauga ON L5K 1B2, Canada | Physicist |
| **Buynak, Gordie**<br>11512 Douglas Lake Road, Pellston MI 49769, USA | Ice Hockey Player |
| **Buzzi, Ruth**<br>31159 N State Highway 108, Mingus TX 76463, USA | Actress, Comedienne |
| **Byambasuren, Dashiin**<br>C D S S R, Sergen Mandakh Gudamj 13, #4 Gin Hurd, Uuriin Javar, Mongolia | Prime Minister, Mongolia |
| **Byars, Betsy C**<br>401 Rudder Ridge, Seneca SC 29678, USA | Writer |
| **Byatt, Antonia Susan (A S)**<br>37 Rusholme Road, London SW15 3LF, England | Writer |
| **Bybee, Catherine**<br>Dystel & Goderich Literary Mgmt, 1 Union Square W, #904, New York NY 10003, USA | Writer |
| **Bybee, Jay**<br>US Court of Appeals, Courthouse, 333 Las Vegas Blvd S, Las Vegas NV 89101, USA | Judge |
| **Bychkov, Semyon**<br>Buffalo Symphony Orchestra, 499 Franklin St, Buffalo NY 14202, USA | Conductor |
| **Bye, Kermit E**<br>US Court of Appeals, 657 2nd Ave N, Fargo ND 58102, USA | Judge |
| **Bye-Dietz, Karyn**<br>322 Gandy Dancer Circle, Hudson WI 54016, USA | Ice Hockey Player |
| **Byer, Renee C**<br>Sacramento Bee, Editorial Dept, 2100 Q St, Sacramento CA 95816 USA | Photojournalist |
| **Byers, Michael A (Mike)**<br>28 Presidio Dr, Novato CA 94949, USA | Ice Hockey Player |
| **Byers, Nina**<br>University of California, Physics Dept, Los Angeles CA 90024, USA | Physicist |
| **Byers, Steve**<br>Talent Works, 3500 W Olive Ave, #1400, Burbank CA 91505 USA | Actor |
| **Byers, Walter**<br>25707 Aiken Switch Road, Emmett KS 66422, USA | Athletic Association Executive |
| **Bykovsky, Valeri F**<br>Cosmonaut Training Center, Star City, 141160 Zvezdny Gorodok, Moscow Oblast, Russia | Cosmonaut |
| **Bylsma, Dan**<br>12637 Broadmoor Place, Grand Haven MI 49417, USA | Ice Hockey Player |
| **Byman, Robert T (Bob)**<br>9325 Eagle Ridge Dr, Las Vegas NV 89134, USA | Golfer |

**Butler - Byman**

**Byner, Earnest A** — Football Player
1016 Sattui Court, Franklin TN 37064, USA
**Byner, John** — Actor, Comedian, Impressionist
American Mgmt, 19948 Mayall St, Chatsworth CA 91311, USA
**Bynes, Amanda** — Actress, Comedienne
B/W/R, 9100 Wilshire Blvd, #500W, Beverly Hills CA 90212 USA
**Bynum, Andrew L** — Basketball Player
7412 Denrock Ave, Los Angeles CA 90045, USA
**Bynum, Caroline W** — Historian
Institute for Advanced Study, Einstein Dr, Princeton NJ 08540 USA
**Byrd, Chris** — Boxer
1181 Heatherwood Court, Flint MI 48532, USA
**Byrd, Dan** — Actor
Creative Artists Agency, 2000 Ave of Stars, #100, Los Angeles CA 90067 USA
**Byrd, Donald** — Choreographer
Spectrum Dance Theater, 800 Lake Washington Blvd, Seattle WA 98122, USA
**Byrd, Eugene** — Actor
Sanders/Armstrong/Caserta Mgmt, 2120 Colorado Ave, #120, Santa Monica CA 90404 USA
**Byrd, George E (Butch)** — Football Player
23 Wayside Road, Westborough MA 01581, USA
**Byrd, Gill A** — Football Player
5347 Notting Hill Road, Gurnee IL 60031, USA
**Byrd, Jonathan C** — Golfer
110 Meadow Brook, Saint Simons Island GA 31522, USA
**Byrd, Paul G** — Baseball Player
910 Foxhollow Run, Alpharetta GA 30004, USA
**Byrd, Richard** — Football Player
2230 Haley Road, Terry MS 39170, USA
**Byrd, Thomas J (Tom)** — Actor
Stewart Talent, 318 W 53rd St, #201, New York NY 10019, USA
**Byrd, Tracy** — Singer
Star Keeper Public Relations, 4695 Monticello St, Beaumont TX 77706, USA
**Byrdak, Timothy C (Tim)** — Baseball Player
16721 W Seneca Dr, Lockport IL 60441, USA
**Byrne, Alexandra** — Costume Designer
Independent Talent Group, 40 Whitfield St, London W1T 2RH, England
**Byrne, Brendan T** — Governor, NJ
6 Becker Farm Road, Roseland NJ 07068, USA
**Byrne, David** — Singer (Talking Heads), Songwriter
Luaka Bop, 195 Christie St, #901, New York NY 10002, USA
**Byrne, Gabriel** — Actor
Paradigm Agency, 360 N Crescent Dr, North Building, Beverly Hills CA 90210 USA
**Byrne, Gerry** — Publisher
Penske Media Corporation, 9800 S La Cienega Blvd, #1400, Los Angeles CA 90301, USA
**Byrne, Josh** — Actor
Hervey/Grimes Talent, 10561 Missouri Ave, #2, Los Angeles CA 90025 USA
**Byrne, Megan** — Actress
Douglas Gorman Rothacker Wilhelm, 1501 Broadway, #703, New York NY 10036 USA
**Byrne, Michael** — Actor
Conway Van Gelder Grant, 8-12 Broadwick St, #300, London W1F 8HW, England
**Byrne, Rose** — Actress
Creative Artists Agency, 2000 Ave of Stars, #100, Los Angeles CA 90067 USA
**Byrnes, Edd** — Actor
PO Box 1623, Beverly Hills CA 90213, USA
**Byrnes, James T (Jim)** — Actor, Singer
Characters Talent Agency, 8 Elm St, Toronto ON M5G 1G7, Canada
**Byrnes, Martin W (Marty)** — Basketball Player
8739 3rd Ave, Pleasant Prairie WI 53158, USA
**Byrom, Monty** — Singer (Big House), Songwriter
Gurley Co, PO Box 150657, Nashville TN 37215 USA
**Byron, Don** — Jazz Clarinetist
Hans Wendl Productions, 2220 California St, Berkeley CA 94703, USA
**Byrum, Curt A** — Golfer
12441 N 86th St, Scottsdale AZ 85260, USA
**Byrum, John W** — Director
Creative Artists Agency, 2000 Ave of Stars, #100, Los Angeles CA 90067 USA
**Byrum, Tom** — Golfer
70 Sierra Oaks Dr, Sugar Land TX 77479, USA
**Bystrom, Martin E (Marty)** — Baseball Player
PO Box 89, Geigertown PA 19523, USA
**Byun Chun-Sa** — Speed Skater
Skating Union, 88 Bangyee-Dong, Songpaku, Seoul 138 749, South Korea
**Byzantine, Julian S** — Concert Guitarist
42 Ennismore Gardens, #1, London SW7 1AQ, England
**Bzdelik, Jeff** — Basketball Coach
Wake Forest University, Athletic Dept, Winston-Salem NC 27109, USA

**Caan, James** — Actor
Rogers & Cowan, 8687 Melrose Ave, #G700, West Hollywood CA 90069 USA
**Caan, Scott** — Actor
Paradigm Agency, 360 N Crescent Dr, North Building, Beverly Hills CA 90210 USA
**Caballe, Montserrat** — Opera Singer
Avenida Madronos 27, Madrid 28043, Spain
**Caballero, Eugenio** — Art Director
Sheldon Prosnit Agency, 800 S Robertson Blvd, #6, Los Angeles CA 90035, USA
**Caballero, Ralph J (Putsy)** — Baseball Player
6773 Milne Blvd, New Orleans LA 70124, USA
**Cabana, Robert D** — Astronaut
Kennedy Space Center, Director's Office, Kennedy Space Center FL 32899, USA
**Cabarga, Leslie** — Cartoonist
451 S Padre Juan Ave, Ojai CA 93023, USA
**Cabas** — Singer, Musician
J E P Entertainment, 16027 Ventura Blvd, #510, Encino CA 91436, USA
**Cabell, Enos M** — Baseball Player
4103 Frost Lake Court, Missouri City TX 77459, USA
**Cabell, Nicole** — Opera Singer
Columbia Artists Mgmt Inc, 1790 Broadway, #702, New York NY 10019 USA
**Cabellut, Lita** — Artist
Bill Lowe Gallery, 1555 Peachtree NE, #100, Atlanta GA 30309, USA
**Cable, Byrum W (Barney)** — Basketball Player
1134 S Main St, #69, Hampstead MD 21074, USA
**Cable, Tawnni** — Actress, Model
Playboy Promotions, 2706 Media Center Dr, Los Angeles CA 90065 USA
**Cable, Thomas L (Tom), Jr** — Football Player, Coach
Oakland Raiders, 1220 Harbor Bay Parkway, Alameda CA 94502 USA
**Cabral, Angelique** — Actress
Pakula/King, 9229 W Sunset Blvd, #315, West Hollywood CA 90069 USA
**Cabral, Travis** — Moguls Skier
Police Department, 1352 Johnson Blvd, South Lake Tahoe NV 96150, USA
**Cabranes, Jose A** — Judge
US Court of Appeals, 141 Church St, New Haven CT 06510, USA
**Cabrera, Angel L** — Golfer
Professional Golfer's Assn, PO Box 109601, Palm Beach Gardens FL 33410 USA
**Cabrera, J Miguel T** — Baseball Player
3339 Virginia St, #PH2, Miami FL 33133, USA
**Cabrera, Ryan** — Singer, Guitarist
Luber Rocklin Entertainment, 8530 Wilshire Blvd, #555, Beverly Hills CA 90211 USA
**Cabrera, Santiago** — Actor
Conway Van Gelder Grant, 8-12 Broadwick St, #300, London W1F 8HW, England
**Cabrinha, Pete** — Kiteboarding Athlete
245A Kane Road, Haiku, Maui HI 96708, USA
**Cabtaline, Anita** — Bowler
32455 Pinto Dr, Warren MI 48093, USA
**Cacciavillan, Agostino Cardinal** — Religious Leader
Patrimony of Holy See, Palazzo Apostolico, 00120 Vatican City
**Caceres, Kurt** — Actor
Pakula/King, 9229 W Sunset Blvd, #315, West Hollywood CA 90069 USA
**Cackowski, Liz** — Actress, Comedienne
United Talent Agency, U T A Plaza, 9336 Civic Center Dr, Beverly Hills CA 90210 USA
**Cadaret, Gregory J (Greg)** — Baseball Player
22636 Bridlewood Lane, Palo Cedro CA 96073, USA
**Caddell, Patrick H** — Statistician
Cambridge Research Inc, 1625 I St NW, Washington DC 20006, USA
**Cadell, Ava** — Actress, Model
Levin, 8484 Wilshire Blvd, #745, Beverly Hills CA 90211, USA
**Cadiff, Andy** — Director
United Talent Agency, U T A Plaza, 9336 Civic Center Dr, Beverly Hills CA 90210 USA
**Cadigan, Dave** — Football Player
14416 Katie Road, Phoenix MD 21131, USA
**Cadman, Sam** — Director, Producer, Actor
United Talent Agency, U T A Plaza, 9336 Civic Center Dr, Beverly Hills CA 90210 USA
**Cadogan, William J** — Businessman
A D C Telecommunications, PO Box 1101, Minneapolis MN 55440, USA
**Cadrez, Glenn E** — Football Player
1294 Mariposa Road, Carlsbad CA 92011, USA
**Caesar, Shirley** — Singer
Shu-Bel Music, PO Box 3336, Durham NC 27702, USA
**Caesar, Sid** — Actor, Comedian
1910 Loma Vista Dr, Beverly Hills CA 90210, USA
**Cafagna, Ashley** — Actress
Tesoro Entertainment, 205 N Stephanie St, #D115, Henderson NV 89074, USA
**Caffara, Carlo Cardinal** — Religious Leader
Archdiocese of Bologna, Via Altabella 6, 40126 Bologna, Italy
**Caffarelli, Luis A** — Mathematician
University of Texas, Mathematics Dept, 1 University Station, Austin TX 78712, USA
**Caffari, Denise (Dee)** — Yachtswoman
Caroline Rose Mgmt, Peter House, Oxford St, Manchester M1 5AN, England
**Cafferata, Hector A, Jr** — Korean War Marine Corps Hero (CMH)
1807 Plum Lane, Venice FL 34293, USA
**Caffey, Charlotte** — Guitarist (Go-Go's)
Direct Management Group, 947 N La Cienega Blvd, #G, West Hollywood CA 90069, USA
**Caffey, Jason A** — Basketball Player
PO Box 131, Roswell GA 30077, USA
**Caffie, Joseph C (Joe)** — Baseball Player
PO Box 1932, Warren OH 44482, USA
**Cafu** — Soccer Player
F C Milan, Via Filippo Turati 3, 20121 Milan, Italy
**Cagatay, Mustafa** — Prime Minister, Cyprus Federated State
60 Cumhuriyet Caddesi, 900 Kyrenia, Cyprus
**Cage** — Rap Artist
Agency Group Ltd, 142 W 57th St, #600, New York NY 10019 USA
**Cage, Byron** — Singer
Mahogany Entertainment, 12201 Pleasant Prospect Road, Mitchellville MD 20721, USA

**C**

# C

|  |  |
|---|---|
| **Cage, Michael J**<br>21163 Newport Coast Dr, Newport Coast CA 92657, USA | Basketball Player |
| **Cage, Nicolas**<br>Creative Artists Agency, 2000 Ave of Stars, #100, Los Angeles CA 90067 USA | Actor |
| **Cagle, Chris**<br>McGhee Entertainment, 8730 Sunset Blvd, #200, West Hollywood CA 90069, USA | Singer, Songwriter |
| **Cagle, Myrtle K**<br>RR 3, Lake Tobesofkee, Lizella GA 31052, USA | Astronaut Candidate |
| **Cagle, Yvonne D**<br>N A S A, Johnson Space Center, 2101 NASA Road, Houston TX 77058 USA | Astronaut |
| **Cahill, Eddie**<br>Management 360, 9111 Wilshire Blvd, Beverly Hills CA 90210 USA | Actor |
| **Cahill, Laura**<br>I C M Partners, 10250 Constellation Blvd, #900, Los Angeles CA 90067 USA | Writer |
| **Cahill, Michael (Mike)**<br>W M E Entertainment, 9601 Wilshire Blvd, #300, Beverly Hills CA 90210 USA | Director |
| **Cahill, Sarah**<br>KPFA-FM, 1929 Martin Luther King Way, Berkeley CA 94704, USA | Pianist |
| **Cahill, Teresa M**<br>65 Leyland Road, London SE12 8DW, England | Opera, Concert Singer |
| **Cahill, Thomas**<br>Doubleday Press, 1540 Broadway, New York NY 10036, USA | Writer |
| **Cahill, Trevor J**<br>Arizona Diamondbacks, Chase Field, 401 E Jefferson, Phoenix AZ 85003 USA | Baseball Player |
| **Cahn, John W**<br>2032 43rd Ave E, #18, Seattle WA 98112, USA | Metallurgist |
| **Cahouet, Frank V**<br>Mellon Bank Corp, 1 Mellon Bank Center, 500 Grant St, #1, Pittsburgh PA 15219, USA | Financier |
| **Cahow, Caitlin**<br>USA Hockey, 1775 Bob Johnson Dr, Colorado Springs CO 80906 USA | Ice Hockey Player |
| **Caillat, Colbie M**<br>Fitzgerald Hartley, 34 N Palm St, #100, Ventura CA 93001, USA | Singer, Songwriter |
| **Caillon, Anne**<br>U B B A, 6 Rue de Braque, 75003 Paris, France | Actress |
| **Cain, Carl**<br>3045 Sun Valley Dr, Pickerington OH 43147, USA | Basketball Player |
| **Cain, Chelsea**<br>Saint Martin's Press, 175 5th Ave, #400, New York NY 10010 USA | Writer |
| **Cain, Dean**<br>W M E Entertainment, 9601 Wilshire Blvd, #300, Beverly Hills CA 90210 USA | Actor |
| **Cain, Matthew T (Matt)**<br>1331 N 104th Place, Mesa AZ 85207, USA | Baseball Player |
| **Caine, Michael**<br>I C M Partners, 10250 Constellation Blvd, #900, Los Angeles CA 90067 USA | Actor |
| **Cainero, Chiara**<br>Comitato Olimpico Nazionale, Largo Lauro de Bocsis 15, 00194 Rome, Italy | Markswoman |
| **Caio, Francesco**<br>Netscalibur, 9 Selsdon Way, Cityharbour, London E14 9GL, England | Businessman |
| **Caird, John**<br>Gersh Agency, 9465 Wilshire Blvd, #600, Beverly Hills CA 90212 USA | Director, Lyricist |
| **Cairns, Eric**<br>1291 Treeland St, Burlington ON L7R 3T5, Canada | Ice Hockey Player |
| **Cairns, Ian**<br>868 Wilson St, Laguna Beach CA 92651, USA | Surfer |
| **Cairo, Miguel J**<br>209 Highland Woods Dr, Safety Harbor FL 34695, USA | Baseball Player |
| **Caivano, Ernesto**<br>Guild & Greyshkul, 131 Prince St, #4F, New York NY 10012, USA | Artist |
| **Cajanek, Petr**<br>Saint Louis Blues, Scott Trade Center, 1401 Clark Ave, Saint Louis MO 63103 USA | Ice Hockey Player |
| **Cake, Jonathan**<br>Independent Talent Group, 40 Whitfield St, London W1T 2RH, England | Actor |
| **Calabrese, Gerald A (Gerry)**<br>351 Esplanade Place, Cliffside Park NJ 07010, USA | Basketball Player |
| **Calabresi, Guido**<br>US Court of Appeals, 157 Church St, #1800, New Haven CT 06510, USA | Judge |
| **Calabro, Thomas**<br>A K A Talent, 6310 San Vicente Blvd, #200, Los Angeles CA 90048 USA | Actor |
| **Calame, Ingrid**<br>Cohen Gallery, 533 W 26th St, New York NY 10001, USA | Artist |
| **Calamos, John P, Sr**<br>Calamos Asset Management, 1111 E Warrenville Road, Naperville IL 60563, USA | Financier |
| **Calarco, Vincent A**<br>Crompton Corp, 199 Benson Road, Waterbury CT 06749, USA | Businessman |
| **Calatrava, Santiago**<br>Santiago Calatrava SA, Hoschgasse 5, 8008 Zurich, Switzerland | Architect, Engineer |
| **Calcagno, Domenico Cardinal**<br>Admin of Patrimony, Palazzo Apostolico, 00120 Vatican City | Religious Leader |
| **Calcevecchia, Mark**<br>2741 E Bighorn Ave, Phoenix AZ 85048, USA | Golfer |
| **Calder, Kyle**<br>23 Orange Blossom Circle, Ladera Ranch CA 92694, USA | Ice Hockey Player |
| **Calderon Fournier, Rafael A**<br>Partido Unidad Social Cristiana, San Jose, Costa Rica | President, Costa Rica |
| **Calderon, Mark**<br>J-Bird Entertainment, 4905 S Atlantic Ave, Ponce Inlet FL 32127 USA | Singer (Color Me Badd) |
| **Calderon, Paul**<br>TalentWorks, 220 E 23rd St, #303, New York NY 10010, USA | Actor |
| **Caldicott, Helen**<br>Physicians for Responsibility, 639 Massachusetts Ave, Cambridge MA 02139, USA | Social Activist, Pediatrician |
| **Caldwell Dyson, Tracy E**<br>N A S A, Johnson Space Center, 2101 NASA Road, Houston TX 77058 USA | Astronaut |
| **Caldwell, Adrian B**<br>10990 West Road, #311, Houston TX 77064, USA | Basketball Player |
| **Caldwell, Andrew**<br>Management 101, 11271 Ventura Blvd, #102, Studio City CA 91604 USA | Actor |

**Cage - Caldwell**

**Caldwell, Bobby** — Singer, Musician, Songwriter
Universal Attractions, 135 W 26th St, #1200, New York NY 10001 USA
**Caldwell, Gail** — Journalist
Boston Globe, Editorial Dept, 135 William Morrissey Blvd, Dorchester MA 02125 USA
**Caldwell, Isaiah (Mike), Jr** — Football Player
646 Robertsville Road, Oak Ridge TN 37830, USA
**Caldwell, James W (Jim)** — Basketball Player
705 Freedom Lane, Roswell GA 30075, USA
**Caldwell, Jim** — Football Coach
Baltimore Ravens, Ravens Stadium, 1 Winning Dr, Baltimore MD 21230 USA
**Caldwell, Joe L** — Basketball Player
15 E Pebble Beach Dr, Tempe AZ 85282, USA
**Caldwell, John** — Cartoonist
King Features Syndicate, 300 W 57th St, #1500, New York NY 10019 USA
**Caldwell, Kimberly** — Singer, Actress
PO Box 8158, The Woodland TX 77387, USA
**Caldwell, L Scott** — Actor
Innovative Artists, 1505 10th St, Santa Monica CA 90401 USA
**Caldwell, Nicholas** — Singer (Whispers)
Pyramid Entertainment Group, 377 Rector Place, #21A, New York NY 10280 USA
**Caldwell, R Michael (Mike)** — Baseball Player
1645 Brook Run Dr, Raleigh NC 27614, USA
**Caldwell, Ravin C, Jr** — Football Player
4415 Johnson St, Fort Smith AR 72904, USA
**Caldwell, Rex** — Golfer
260 El Dorado Blvd, #3006, Webster TX 77598, USA
**Caldwell, Stephen (Steve)** — Singer (Orlons)
Lustig Talent, PO Box 770850, Orlando FL 32877 USA
**Caldwell, Toy** — Guitarist (Marshall Tucker Band)
Ron Rainey Mgmt, 315 S Beverly Dr, #407, Beverly Hills CA 90212, USA
**Caldwell, Zoe** — Actress
Whitehead-Stevens, 1501 Broadway, New York NY 10036, USA
**Caldwell-Pope, Kentavious** — Basketball Player
Detroit Pistons, Palace, 4 Championship Dr, Auburn Hills MI 48326 USA
**Cale, Paula** — Actress
Gersh Agency, 9465 Wilshire Blvd, #600, Beverly Hills CA 90212 USA
**Calegari, Maria** — Ballerina
404 Richardsville Road, Carmel NY 10512, USA
**Caleo, Michael** — Director, Writer
I C M Partners, 10250 Constellation Blvd, #900, Los Angeles CA 90067 USA
**Calero, Enrique N (Kiko)** — Baseball Player
1465 65th St, Emeryville CA 94608, USA
**Caley, Don** — Ice Hockey Player
7127 E Aloe Vera Dr, Scottsdale AZ 85266, USA
**Calfa, Marian** — President, Czechoslovakia
Calfa, Pravni Kancela Premyslovska 28, 130 00 Prague 3, Czech Republic
**Calfan, Nicole** — Actress
Agents Associes, 201 Rue du Faubourg Saint Honore, 75008 Paris, France
**Calhoon, Jesse M** — Labor Leader
Marine Engineers Union, 17 Battery Place, New York NY 10004, USA
**Calhoun, David L (Corky)** — Basketball Player
17912 Lafayette Dr, Olney MD 20832, USA
**Calhoun, Donald C (Don)** — Football Player
PO Box 49104, Wichita KS 67201, USA
**Calhoun, James A (Jim)** — Basketball Coach
PO Box 379, Pomfret Center CT 06259, USA
**Calhoun, Jeffrey W (Jeff)** — Baseball Player
10002 Springwood Forest Dr, Houston TX 77080, USA
**Calhoun, Monica** — Actress
Abrams Artists, 9200 W Sunset Blvd, #1125, West Hollywood CA 90069 USA
**Calhoun, Troy** — Football Coach
US Air Force Academy, Athletic Dept, Colorado Springs CO 80840, USA
**Calhoun, Will** — Drummer (Living Colour)
Entertainment Artists, 2409 21st Ave S, #100, Nashville TN 10019 USA
**Calhoun, William C (Bill)** — Basketball Player
3740 El Cerro View Circle, Reno NV 89509, USA
**Cali, Joseph** — Actor
25630 Edenwild Road, Calabasas CA 91302, USA
**Caliendo, Frank** — Actor, Comedian, Writer
Gersh Agency, 9465 Wilshire Blvd, #600, Beverly Hills CA 90212 USA
**Califano, Joseph A, Jr** — Secretary, Health Education & Welfare
Casa at Columbia, 633 3rd Ave, #1900, New York NY 10017, USA
**Calipari, John** — Basketball Coach
University of Kentucky, Athletic Dept, Lexington KY 40506, USA
**Calis, Natasha** — Actress
Creative Artists Agency, 2000 Ave of Stars, #100, Los Angeles CA 90067 USA
**Call, Kevin B** — Football Player
839 Carey Road, Carmel IN 46033, USA
**Callahan, Daniel J** — Educator
Hastings Center, 255 Elm Road, Briarcliff Manor NY 10510, USA
**Callahan, John** — Actor
Levin Representatives, 2402 4th St, #6, Santa Monica CA 90405, USA
**Callahan, Ryan** — Ice Hockey Player
New York Rangers, Madison Square Garden, 2 Penn Plaza, New York NY 10121 USA
**Callahan, William E (Bill)** — Football Coach
623 Lake Point Dr, Irving TX 75039, USA
**Callan, K** — Actress
Gage Group, 14724 Ventura Blvd, #505, Sherman Oaks CA 91403 USA
**Callan, Michael** — Actor, Director, Producer
4440 Talofa Ave, #102, Toluca Lake CA 91602, USA
**Calland, Albert M, III** — Navy Admiral
Central Intelligence Agency, Deputy Director's Office, Washington DC 20505, USA
**Calland, Lee** — Football Player
6624 Windwood Circle, Douglasville GA 30135, USA
**Callard, Rebecca** — Actress
Curtis Brown Group, 28-29 Haymarket St, #500, London SW1Y 4SP, England

# C

| | |
|---|---|
| **Callas, John L**<br>Jet Propulsion Laboratory, 4800 Oak Grove Dr, Pasadena CA 91109 USA | Space Scientist, Physicist |
| **Callaway, Ann Hampton**<br>Miller Wright Assoc, 1650 Broadway, #1210, New York NY 10019, USA | Jazz Singer, Pianist, Composer |
| **Callaway, Howard H (Bo)**<br>Callaway Gardens, Pine Mountain GA 31822, USA | Government Official; Representative, GA |
| **Callaway, Michael C (Mickey)**<br>8061 Stonewyck Road, Germantown TN 38138, USA | Baseball Player |
| **Callaway, Thomas V**<br>House of Representatives, 1434 6th St, #1, Santa Monica CA 90401 USA | Actor |
| **Callen Jones, Gloria**<br>1508 Chafton Road, Charleston WV 25314, USA | Swimmer |
| **Callen, Bryan C**<br>Innovative Artists, 1505 10th St, Santa Monica CA 90401 USA | Actor, Comedian |
| **Callender, William D (Jock)**<br>388 Lear Road, Avon Lake OH 44012, USA | Ice Hockey Player |
| **Callery, Sean**<br>Gorfaine/Schwartz, 4111 W Alameda Ave, #509, Burbank CA 91505 USA | Composer |
| **Callie, Dayton**<br>Abrams Artists, 9200 W Sunset Blvd, #1125, West Hollywood CA 90069 USA | Actor |
| **Callies, Sarah Wayne**<br>Resolution, 1801 Century Park East, #2300, Los Angeles CA 90067, USA | Actress |
| **Callighen, Brett**<br>PO Box 249, Bala ON P0C 1A0, Canada | Ice Hockey Player |
| **Callis, James**<br>Alan Siegel Entertainment, 345 N Maple Dr, #375, Beverly Hills CA 90210, USA | Actor |
| **Calloway, Christopher F (Chris)**<br>1213 Dawnview Dr, Locust Grove GA 30248, USA | Football Player |
| **Calloway, Jordan**<br>Gold Levin, 8424A Santa Monica Blvd, #706, Los Angeles CA 90069, USA | Actor |
| **Calloway, Vanessa Bell**<br>Luber Rocklin Entertainment, 8530 Wilshire Blvd, #555, Beverly Hills CA 90211 USA | Actress |
| **Calman, Robert F**<br>241 S 6th St, #2302, Philadelphia PA 19106, USA | Businessman |
| **Calmus, Rocky A**<br>4131 Trinity Road, Franklin TN 37067, USA | Football Player |
| **Calne, Roy Y**<br>Douglas House Annexe, 18 Trumpington Road, Cambridge CB2 2AS, England | Surgeon |
| **Caltabiano, Tom**<br>United Talent Agency, U T A Plaza, 9336 Civic Center Dr, Beverly Hills CA 90210 USA | Actor, Comedian, Producer, Writer |
| **Calvaer, Andre J**<br>Blvd Louis Mettewie 270, 1080 Molenbeek-Saint-Jean, Belgium | Electrical Engineer |
| **Calvert, Mark**<br>908 W Waco St, Broken Arrow OK 74011, USA | Baseball Player |
| **Calvet, Jacques**<br>Bazar de L'Hotel de Ville, 14 Rue du Temple, 75189 Paris, France | Businessman, Financier |
| **Calvin, Brian**<br>David Kordansky Gallery, 3143 S La Cienega Blvd, #A, Los Angeles CA 90016, USA | Artist |
| **Calvin, John**<br>445 Sudden Valley, Bellingham WA 98229, USA | Actor |
| **Calvin, William H**<br>University of Washington, Neurobiology Dept, Seattle WA 98195, USA | Neurobiologist, Writer |
| **Calvo, Paul M**<br>Calvo Enterprises, 138 Martyr St, Hagatna, GU 96910, USA | Governor, Guam |
| **Calzaghe, Joseph W (Joe)**<br>Newbridge Boxing Gym, Bridge St, Newbridge, Caerphily South Wales NP11 5FR, Wales | Boxer |
| **Camacho, Carlos A**<br>Telemundo Network Group, 2470 W 8th Ave, Hialeah FL 33010 USA | Actor |
| **Camacho, Ernest C (Ernie)**<br>746 Saint Regis Way, Salinas CA 93905, USA | Baseball Player |
| **Camacho, Felix**<br>Lisa Terlizzi, 14 Fulton St, Weehawken NJ 07086, USA | Boxer |
| **Camacho, Felix P**<br>Governor's Office, Executive Chamber, PO Box 2950, Hagatna GU 96932 USA | Governor, Guam |
| **Camacho, Jesse**<br>Amanda Rosenthal Agency, 543 Richmond St W, #123, Toronto, ON M5V 1Y6, Canada | Actor |
| **Camacho, Jessie**<br>Laura Lichen Mgmt, PO Box 33051, Granada Hills CA 91394, USA | Actress, Comedienne |
| **Camarda, Charles J**<br>2386 Sabal Park Lane, League City TX 77573, USA | Astronaut |
| **Camargo, Christian**<br>Innovative Artists, 1505 10th St, Santa Monica CA 90401 USA | Actor |
| **Camarillo, Richard J (Rich)**<br>1941 E Clubhouse Dr, Phoenix AZ 85048, USA | Football Player |
| **Camastra, Danielle**<br>Don Buchwald, 6500 Wilshire Blvd, #2200, Los Angeles CA 90048 USA | Actress |
| **Cambage, Elizabeth (Liz)**<br>Zhejiang Golden Bulls, 153 Administrative Building 6, Tiyu Chang Rd, Hangzhou Zhejiang, China | Basketball Player |
| **Camberling, Sylvain**<br>S W R Orchestra, 76550 Baden-Baden, Germany | Conductor |
| **Cambor, Kathleen**<br>Farrar Straus Giroux, 18 W 18th St, #700, New York NY 10011 USA | Writer |
| **Cambor, Peter**<br>Brillstein Entertainment Partners, 9150 Wilshire Blvd, #350, Beverly Hills CA 90212 USA | Actor |
| **Cambre, Ronald C**<br>Newmont Mining, 1700 Lincoln St, Denver CO 80203, USA | Businessman |
| **Cambreling, Sylvain**<br>Van Walsum Mgmt, Tower Building, 11 York Road, London SE1 7NX, England | Conductor |
| **Cambria, John**<br>9939 Topanga Canyon Blvd, #11, Chatsworth CA 91311, USA | Cinematogapher |
| **Camby, Marcus D**<br>6725 Fite Road, Pearland TX 77584, USA | Basketball Player |
| **Camdessus, Michel J**<br>27 Rue de Valois, 75001 Paris, France | Financier |
| **Cameron Bure, Candace**<br>Abrams Artists, 9200 W Sunset Blvd, #1125, West Hollywood CA 90069 USA | Actress |

**Callas - Cameron Bure**

**Cameron, Al** — Ice Hockey Player
1225 Ormsby Lane NW, Edmonton AB T5T 6R2, Canada
**Cameron, Ann** — Writer
Foster Books/Farrar Straus Giroux, 18 W 18th St, New York NY 10011, USA
**Cameron, Cam** — Football Coach
Miami Dolphins, 7500 SW 30th St, Davie FL 33314, USA
**Cameron, Caressa** — Beauty Queen
Miss America Organization, 1370 Ave of Americas, #1600, New York NY 10019 USA
**Cameron, David** — Fashion Designer
Schauspielschule Krauss, Weihburggasse 19, 1010 Vienna, Austria
**Cameron, David** — Prime Minister, England
Prime Minister's Office, 10 Downing St, London SW1A 2AA, England
**Cameron, Dean** — Actor
Maverick Artists, 6100 Wilshire Blvd, #550, Los Angeles CA 90048, USA
**Cameron, Don R** — Educator, Labor Leader
National Education Association, 1201 16th St NW, Washington DC 20036, USA
**Cameron, Glenn S** — Football Player
250 S Australian Ave, West Palm Beach FL 33401, USA
**Cameron, James** — Director, Producer
Cameron/Pace Group, 2020 N Lincoln St, Burbank CA 91504, USA
**Cameron, Joanna** — Actress
PO Box 198900-9MB 808, Hawi HI 96719, USA
**Cameron, John** — Composer, Conductor
David Wilkinson Assoc, 115 Hazlebury Road, London SW6 2LX, England
**Cameron, Julia** — Writer
Tarcher/Penguin Books, 375 Hudson St, Basement 1, New York NY 10014, USA
**Cameron, Kenneth D** — Astronaut
11333 Gulf Beach Highway, Pensacola FL 32507, USA
**Cameron, Kirk** — Actor
Mark Craig Productions, 1383 Callens, Ventura CA 93003, USA
**Cameron, Michael T (Mike)** — Baseball Player
615 Champions Dr, McDonough GA 30253, USA
**Cameron, Michelle** — Synchronized Swimmer
Box 2 Site 1SS3, Calgary AB T3C 3N9, Canada
**Cameron, Nancy** — Model
Playboy Promotions, 2706 Media Center Dr, Los Angeles CA 90065 USA
**Cameron, Stephanie** — Actress
Innovative Artists, 1505 10th St, Santa Monica CA 90401 USA
**Cameron, Tassie** — Producer
Creative Artists Agency, 2000 Ave of Stars, #100, Los Angeles CA 90067 USA
**Camerota, Brett** — Nordic Combined Athlete
Park City Nordic Ski Club, PO Box 682722, Park City UT 84081, USA
**Camil, Jaime** — Singer, Actor
Westwood Entertainment, De Teresa 250, Col Tlacopac San Angel, Mexico City 01040, Mexico
**Camilleri, Andrea** — Writer
Viking Press, 375 Hudson St, New York NY 10014, USA
**Camilleri, Louis C** — Businessman
Kraft Foods Inc, 3 Lake Dr, Northfield IL 60093, USA
**Camilli, Douglas J (Doug)** — Baseball Player
4245 61st Ave, Vero Beach FL 32967, USA
**Camilo, Michel** — Jazz Pianist
Redondo Music & Mgmt, PO Box 216, Katonah NY 10536, USA
**Caminito, Jerry** — Auto Racing Driver
Blue Thunder Racing, 480 Hyson Road, Jackson NJ 08527, USA
**Cammalleri, Michael (Mike)** — Ice Hockey Player
43 Stockdale Crescent, Richmond Hill ON L4C 3T1, Canada
**Cammarata, Bernard** — Businessman
T J X Companies, 770 Cochituate Road, Framingham MA 01701, USA
**Cammuso, Frank** — Cartoonist
1725 James St, #1, Syracuse NY 13206, USA
**Camp, Anna** — Actress
United Talent Agency, U T A Plaza, 9336 Civic Center Dr, Beverly Hills CA 90210 USA
**Camp, Bill** — Actor
Innovative Artists, 1505 10th St, Santa Monica CA 90401 USA
**Camp, Colleen** — Actress
Colleen Camp Productions, 6464 Sunset Blvd, #800, Los Angeles CA 90028, USA
**Camp, Greg** — Guitarist (Smash Mouth)
Creative Artists Agency, 2000 Ave of Stars, #100, Los Angeles CA 90067 USA
**Camp, Jeffrey B** — Artist
Browse & Darby, 19 Cork St, London W1X 2LP, England
**Camp, Jeremy T** — Singer, Actor
Third Coast Artists Agency, 2021 21st Ave S, #220, Nashville TN 37212, USA
**Camp, Shawn** — Singer, Guitarist, Songwriter
Tamara Saviano Media, 1603 Horton Ave, Nashville TN 37212, USA
**Camp, Shawn** — Baseball Player
9416 Deep Creek Lane, Fredericksburg VA 22407, USA
**Camp, Steve** — Singer
Third Coast Artists Agency, 2021 21st Ave S, #220, Nashville TN 37212, USA
**Campanella, Joseph** — Actor
4196 Colfax Ave, Studio City CA 91604, USA
**Campaneris, B Dagoberto (Bert)** — Baseball Player
9797 N 105th Place, Scottsdale AZ 85258, USA
**Campau, Thomas E** — Cinematographer
2000 S Hammond Lake Dr, West Bloomfield MI 48324, USA
**Campbell, A P D Kim** — Prime Minister, Canada
Club de Madrid, C/Goya 5-7, Pasaje 2, 28001 Madrid, Spain
**Campbell, Alan** — Actor
Douglas Gorman Rothacker Wilhelm, 1501 Broadway, #703, New York NY 10036 USA
**Campbell, Allan McCulloch** — Biologist
947 Mears Court, Stanford CA 94305, USA
**Campbell, Andy** — Actor, Comedian
OmniPop Talent Group, 4605 Lankershim Blvd, #201, Toluca Lake CA 91602 USA
**Campbell, Brian W** — Ice Hockey Player
Florida Panthers, 1 Panthers Parkway, Sunrise FL 33323 USA
**Campbell, Bruce** — Actor
A P A Talent/Literary Agency, 405 S Beverly Dr, #300, Beverly Hills CA 90212 USA

**Campbell, Bruce A** — Geophysicist
National Air/Space Museum, Smithsonian Institution, Earth/Planetary Studies, Washington DC 20560, USA
**Campbell, Bryan A** — Ice Hockey Player
10895 Tamoron Lane, Boca Raton FL 33498, USA
**Campbell, Calais** — Football Player
Arizona Cardinals, PO Box 888, Phoenix AZ 85001 USA
**Campbell, Cassie** — Ice Hockey Player
Team Canada, 2424 University Dr NW, Calgary AB T2N 3Y9, Canada
**Campbell, Cheryl** — Actress
Amanda Howard, 74 Clerkenwell Road, London EC1M 5QA, England
**Campbell, Christa** — Actress, Model
Sovereign Talent Group, 8421 Wilshire Blvd, #200, Beverly Hills CA 90211, USA
**Campbell, Christian** — Actor
Don Buchwald, 6500 Wilshire Blvd, #2200, Los Angeles CA 90048 USA
**Campbell, Clifton** — Producer
I C M Partners, 10250 Constellation Blvd, #900, Los Angeles CA 90067 USA
**Campbell, Colin** — Ice Hockey Player
National Hockey League, 50 Bay St, #1100, Toronto ON M5J 2X8, Canada
**Campbell, Conchita** — Actress
Paceline Entertainment, 12444 Ventura Blvd, #103, Studio City CA 91604 USA
**Campbell, D Chad** — Golfer
200 Glade Road, Colleyville TX 76034, USA
**Campbell, Daniel A (Dan)** — Football Player
PO Box 977, County Road 2111, Meridian TX 76665, USA
**Campbell, David** — Actor, Singer
Caplice Mgmt, PO Box 381, Darlinghurst NSW 1300, Australia
**Campbell, David W** — Baseball Player
726 N Dundee Dr, Post Falls ID 83854, USA
**Campbell, Derrick** — Speed Skater
Skate Canada, 865 Shefford Road, Ottawa ON K1J 1H9, Canada
**Campbell, Earl C** — Football Player
8700 Brodie Lane, #816, Austin TX 78745, USA
**Campbell, Elden J** — Basketball Player
17252 Hawthorne Blvd, #493, Torrance CA 90504, USA
**Campbell, Eugene E (Gene)** — Ice Hockey Player
6149 Sugar Mill Lane, Mound MN 55364, USA
**Campbell, Gary K** — Football Player
PO Box 775353, Steamboat Springs CO 80477, USA
**Campbell, Glen** — Singer, Guitarist
Gursey Schneider, 1888 Century Park E, #900, Los Angeles CA 90067, USA
**Campbell, Gregory** — Ice Hockey Player
PO Box 342, Tilsonburg ON N4G 4H8, Canada
**Campbell, Ian** — Singer
Act 1 Entertainment, PO Box 1079, New Haven CT 06504, USA
**Campbell, Isobel** — Singer, Cellist (Belle & Sebastian)
Red Ryder Entertainment, 1532 N Milwaukee Ave, #207, Chicago IL 60622, USA
**Campbell, Jason** — Football Player
Cleveland Browns, 76 Lou Groza Blvd, Berea OH 44017 USA
**Campbell, Jennifer L** — Actress, Model
9200 W Sunset Blvd, #1130, West Hollywood CA 90069, USA
**Campbell, Jim** — Ice Hockey Player
32 Lemp Road, Saint Louis MO 63122, USA
**Campbell, John** — Harness Racing Driver
John D Campbell Stable, 823 Allison Dr, River Vale NJ 07675, USA
**Campbell, John** — Bassist (Lamb of God)
Entertainment Services, 1000 Main Street Plaza, #303, Voorhees NJ 08043, USA
**Campbell, John W** — Football Player
12908 Welcome Lane, Burnsville MN 55337, USA
**Campbell, Jonny** — Director
Independent Talent Group, 40 Whitfield St, London W1T 2RH, England
**Campbell, Julia** — Actress
Innovative Artists, 1505 10th St, Santa Monica CA 90401 USA
**Campbell, Kate** — Singer, Songwriter
Large River Music, PO Box 121743, Nashville TN 37212, USA
**Campbell, Kevin W** — Baseball Player
207 Ridout Dr, Des Arc AR 72040, USA
**Campbell, L Arthur** — Molecular Genticist
Rockefeller University Medical Center, 1230 York Ave, New York NY 10065 USA
**Campbell, LaMar** — Football Player
2511 W 7th St, Chester PA 19013, USA
**Campbell, Larry Joe** — Actor
A P A Talent/Literary Agency, 405 S Beverly Dr, #300, Beverly Hills CA 90212 USA
**Campbell, Levin H** — Judge
US Court of Appeals, 1 Courthouse Way, #9400, Boston MA 02210, USA
**Campbell, Lewis B** — Businessman
Textron Inc, 40 Westminster St, #500, Providence RI 02903, USA
**Campbell, Luther (Skywalker)** — Rap Artist (2 Live Crew)
8000 Governors Square Blvd, #304, Hialeah FL 33016, USA
**Campbell, Marion** — Football Player, Coach
351 Marsh Point Circle, Saint Augustine FL 32080, USA
**Campbell, Martin** — Director
Independent Talent Group, 40 Whitfield St, London W1T 2RH, England
**Campbell, Mary Schmidt** — Art Historian
New York University, Tisch Art School, 721 Broadway, New York NY 10003, USA
**Campbell, Menzies** — Government Official, England
House of Commons, Westminster, London SW1A 0AA, England
**Campbell, Michael** — Golfer
Master's International, Hurst Grove, Sandford Lane, Hurst, Berkshire R10 0SQ, England
**Campbell, Naomi** — Model, Singer, Actress
I M G Models, 304 Park Ave S, #PH N, New York NY 10010 USA
**Campbell, Natalie** — Model
Playboy Promotions, 2706 Media Center Dr, Los Angeles CA 90065 USA
**Campbell, Nathaniel (Nate)** — Boxer
Don King Productions, 501 Fairway Dr, Deerfield Beach FL 33441 USA
**Campbell, Neve** — Actress
United Talent Agency, U T A Plaza, 9336 Civic Center Dr, Beverly Hills CA 90210 USA

**Campbell, Nicholas** — Actor
Noble Caplan Abrams, 1260 Yonge St, #200, Toronto ON M4T 1W6, Canada

**Campbell, Richard** — Ice Hockey Player, Coach
National Hockey League, 50 Bay St, #1100, Toronto ON M5J 2X8, Canada

**Campbell, Robert** — Architectural Critic
54 Antrim St, Cambridge MA 02139, USA

**Campbell, Tevin** — Singer
Universal Attractions, 135 W 26th St, #1200, New York NY 10001 USA

**Campbell, Tisha** — Actress, Singer
Paul Kohner, 9300 Wilshire Blvd, #555, Beverly Hills CA 90212 USA

**Campbell, Tracyanne** — Singer, Guitarist (Camera Obscura)
Ground Control Touring, 20 Jay St, #826, Brooklyn NY 11201 USA

**Campbell, Vivian** — Guitarist (Def Leppard, Whitesnake)
Front Line Mgmt, 1100 Glendon Ave, #2000, Los Angeles CA 90024 USA

**Campbell, William** — Businessman
Intuit Inc, PO Box 7850, Mountain View CA 94039, USA

**Campbell, William J** — Air Force General
3267 Alex Findlay Place, Sarasota FL 34240, USA

**Campbell, William R (Bill)** — Baseball Player
133 S Hale St, Palatine IL 60067, USA

**Campbell, Woodrow L (Woody)** — Football Player
9122 Weymouth Dr, Houston TX 77031, USA

**Campbell-Bower, Jamie** — Actor
Dalzell & Beresford, 26 Astwood Mews, London SW7 4DE, England

**Campbell-Hughes, Antonia** — Actress
Independent Talent Group, 40 Whitfield St, London W1T 2RH, England

**Campbell-Martin, Tisha** — Actress, Singer
Paul Kohner, 9300 Wilshire Blvd, #555, Beverly Hills CA 90212 USA

**Campedelli, Dominic** — Ice Hockey Player
732 Jerusalem Road, Cohasset MA 02025, USA

**Campen, James F** — Football Player
2789 Ichabod Lane, Green Bay WI 54313, USA

**Campese, David I** — Rugby Player
D C Management Group, 870 Pacific Highway, #4, Gordon NSW 2072, Australia

**Campfield, William (Billy)** — Football Player
930 Glenmore Way, #K, Westerville OH 43082, USA

**Campi, Ray** — Singer, Guitarist
2872 1/2 W Ave 35, Los Angeles CA 90065, USA

**Campion, Cris** — Actor
Artmedia, 20 Ave Rapp, 75007 Paris, France

**Campion, Jane** — Director
H L A Mgmt, PO Box 1536, Strawberry Hills, Sydney NSW 2012, Australia

**Campisi, Amber** — Model
Playboy Promotions, 2706 Media Center Dr, Los Angeles CA 90065 USA

**Campo, David C (Dave)** — Football Coach
Dallas Cowboys, 1 Cowboys Parkway, Irving TX 75063 USA

**Campos, Alana** — Model
10925 Bluffside Dr, #203, Studio City CA 91604, USA

**Campos, Antonio** — Director, Producer
United Talent Agency, U T A Plaza, 9336 Civic Center Dr, Beverly Hills CA 90210 USA

**Campos, Jorge** — Soccer Player
Federacion de Futbol Assn, CP 06600, Col Juarez, Mexico City 6 DF, Mexico

**Campos, Tony** — Bassist (Static-X, Soulfly, Asesino)
Warner Bros Records, 3300 Warner Blvd, Burbank CA 91505 USA

**Campuzano Lopez, Felipe** — Composer
Urbanizacion Cumbres de Marbella 47, Los Naguelos 29601 Marbella, Spain

**Cam'ron** — Rap Artist, Actor
I C M Partners, 10250 Constellation Blvd, #900, Los Angeles CA 90067 USA

**Camus, Philippe** — Businessman
Alcatel-Lucent, 54 Rue Le Boetie, 75006 Paris, France

**Canada, Geoffrey** — Educator, Social Activist
Harlem Children's Zone Project, 35 E 125th St, New York NY 10035, USA

**Canada, Ron** — Actor
C E S D, 10635 Santa Monica Blvd, #130, Los Angeles CA 90025 USA

**Canadas, Esther** — Model, Actress
Wilhelmina Models, 300 Park Ave S, #200, New York NY 10010 USA

**Canady, Alexa I** — Pediatric Neurosurgeon
6064 Forest Green Road, Pensacola FL 32505, USA

**Canals-Barrera, Maria** — Actress
A P A Talent/Literary Agency, 405 S Beverly Dr, #300, Beverly Hills CA 90212 USA

**Canary, David** — Actor
698 W End Ave, #1B, New York NY 10025, USA

**Canby, William C, Jr** — Judge
US Court of Appeals, US Courthouse, 401 W Washington St, #1, Phoenix AZ 85003, USA

**Cancellara, Fabian** — Cyclist
Team CSC, Riis Cycling, Firskovvej 36, 2800 Lyngby, Denmark

**Candaele, Casey T** — Baseball Player
251 Broad St, San Luis Obispo CA 93405, USA

**Candelaria, John R** — Baseball Player
3122 Elroy Ave, Pittsburgh PA 15227, USA

**Candelaria, Richard G** — WW II Army Air Corps Hero
3812 Conough Lane, Las Vegas NV 89129, USA

**Candelo, Juan Carlos (J C)** — Boxer
T's K O Fight Club, 3730 Wheeling St, #10, Denver CO 80239, USA

**Candiotti, Thomas C (Tom)** — Baseball Player
6061 E Jenan Dr, Scottsdale AZ 85254, USA

**Candyman** — Rap Artist
Groove Entertainment, 1005 N Alfred St, #2, West Hollywood CA 90069, USA

**Cane, Louis P J** — Artist
37 Rue D'Enghien, 75010 Paris, France

**Cane, Mark A** — Oceanographer, Climatologist
Lamont Doherty Earth Observatory, Route 9W, Palisades NY 10964, USA

**Canella, Guido** — Architect
Via Revere 7, 20123 Milan, Italy

**Canepa, John C** — Financier
Crowe Chizek, 400 Riverfront Plaza, Grand Rapids MI 49503, USA

**Canestri, Giovanni Cardinal** — Religious Leader
Archdiocese of Genoa-Bobbio, Piazza Matteotti 4, 16123 Genoa, Italy
**Canet, Guillaume** — Actor, Director
U B B A, 6 Rue de Braque, 75003 Paris, France
**Canete, Ariel** — Golfer
Advantage International, 1751 Pinnacle Dr, #1500, McLean VA 22102 USA
**Canfield, Jack** — Writer
PO Box 30880, Santa Barbara CA 93130, USA
**Canfield, Paul** — Physicist
Iowa State University, Physics Dept, Ames IA 50011, USA
**Canfield, William N (Bill)** — Editorial Cartoonist
Star Ledger, Editorial Dept, 1 Star Ledger Plaza, Newark NJ 07102, USA
**Cangelosi, John A** — Baseball Player
10914 Caribou Lane, Orland Park IL 60467, USA
**Cangemi, Joseph P** — Psychologist
1409 Mount Ayr Circle, Bowling Green KY 42103, USA
**Canibus** — Rap Artist
J L Entertainment, 18653 Ventura Blvd, #340, Los Angeles CA 91356 USA
**Canin, Ethan** — Writer
Rogers Coleridge White, 20 Powis Mews, London W11 1JN, England
**Canin, Serena** — Concert Violinist
David Rowe Artists, 24 Bessom St, #2, Marblehead MA 01945, USA
**Canizales, Jose (Gaby)** — Boxer
4215 Santa Marie Ave, Laredo TX 78041, USA
**Canizales, Orlando** — Boxer
17542 College Port Dr, Laredo TX 78045, USA
**Canizares Llovera, Antonio Cardinal** — Religious Leader
Archdiocese of Toledo, Arco de Palacio 3, 45001 Toledo, Spain
**Cannavale, Bobby** — Actor
I C M Partners, 730 5th Ave, New York NY 10019 USA
**Cannavaro, Fabio** — Soccer Player
F C Real Madrid, Avda Concha Espana 1, 28036 Madrid, Spain
**Cannida, James T, II** — Football Player
4504 Harmony Place, Rohnert Park CA 94928, USA
**Cannizzaro, Christopher J (Chris)** — Baseball Player
13597 Grain Lane, San Diego CA 92129, USA
**Cannom, Greg** — Makeup Artist
223 Alameda Ave, #1, Burbank CA 91502, USA
**Cannon, Danny** — Director
Steve Kenis Co, Royalty House, 72-74 Dean St, London WID 3SG, England
**Cannon, Dyan** — Actress
1100 Alta Loma Road, #808, West Hollywood CA 90069, USA
**Cannon, Freddy (Boom Boom)** — Singer, Songwriter
5119 Surfrider Way, Oxnard CA 93035, USA
**Cannon, Joe** — Soccer Player
Vancouver Whitecaps, 375 Water St, #550, Vancouver V6B 5C6, Canada
**Cannon, John (Ace)** — Saxophonist
J L Entertainment, 18653 Ventura Blvd, #340, Los Angeles CA 91356 USA
**Cannon, John R** — Football Player
2911 W Bay Vista Ave, Tampa FL 33611, USA
**Cannon, Katherine** — Actress
1310 S Westholme Ave, Los Angeles CA 90024, USA
**Cannon, Mark M** — Football Player
2604 Riveroaks Dr, Arlington TX 76006, USA
**Cannon, Nick** — Actor, Comedian, Writer
I C M Partners, 10250 Constellation Blvd, #900, Los Angeles CA 90067 USA
**Cannon, Robert H, Jr** — Aerospace Engineer
Stanford University, Aeronautics/Astronautics Dept, Stanford CA 94305, USA
**Cannon, William A (Billy)** — Football Player
8851 Sage Hill Dr, Saint Francisville LA 70775, USA
**Cano Mercedes, Robinson J** — Baseball Player
New York Yankees, Yankee Stadium, E 161st St & River Ave, Bronx NY 10451 USA
**Cano, Pablo D** — Sculptor
501 SW 24th Ave, Miami FL 33135, USA
**Canogar, Rafael** — Artist
Calle de la Bolsa 14, 28012 Madrid, Spain
**Canonero, Milena** — Costume Designer
I C M Partners, 10250 Constellation Blvd, #900, Los Angeles CA 90067 USA
**Canot, Adan** — Actor
United Talent Agency, U T A Plaza, 9336 Civic Center Dr, Beverly Hills CA 90210 USA
**Canova, Diana** — Actress
Talent Works, 3500 W Olive Ave, #1400, Burbank CA 91505 USA
**Canseco, Jose, Jr** — Baseball Player
Canseco Inc, 112 Panlock Court, Irmo SC 29063, USA
**Cantaline, Anita** — Bowler
31455 Pinto Dr, Warren MI 48093, USA
**Canterbury, Chandler** — Actor
United Talent Agency, U T A Plaza, 9336 Civic Center Dr, Beverly Hills CA 90210 USA
**Cantey, Charlsie** — Sportscaster
ABC-TV, Sports Dept, 77 W 66th St, New York NY 10023 USA
**Canto, Adan** — Actor
United Talent Agency, U T A Plaza, 9336 Civic Center Dr, Beverly Hills CA 90210 USA
**Canton, Mark** — Businessman, Producer
Atmosphere Entertainment, 4751 Wilshire Blvd, #300, Los Angeles CA 90010, USA
**Cantona, Eric** — Soccer Player
Mikado, 105 Ave Raymond Poincare, 75016 Paris, France
**Cantone, Mario** — Actor, Comedian
Gersh Agency, 9465 Wilshire Blvd, #600, Beverly Hills CA 90212 USA
**Cantor, Charles R** — Molecular Biologist
Sequenom Inc, 3595 John Hopkins Court, San Diego CA 92121, USA
**Cantor, Geoffrey** — Actor
Stone Manners Salners, 9911 W Pico Blvd, #1400, Los Angeles CA 90035 USA
**Cantor, Nancy E** — Educator
Syracuse University, Chancellor's Office, Syracuse NY 13244, USA
**Cantor, Tim** — Artist
527 4th Ave, San Diego CA 92101, USA

**Cantrell, Blu** — Singer
Universal Attractions, 135 W 26th St, #1200, New York NY 10001 USA
**Cantrell, Cady** — Model
Playboy Promotions, 2706 Media Center Dr, Los Angeles CA 90065 USA
**Cantrell, Jerry F, Jr** — Singer, Guitarist (Alice in Chains)
Core Entertainment Organization, 14724 Ventura Blvd, #PH, Sherman Oaks CA 91403, USA
**Cantrell, Lana** — Singer
300 E 71st St, #91A, New York NY 10021, USA
**Cantu Guzman, Jorge L** — Baseball Player
5015 24th Ave S, Tampa Bay FL 33619, USA
**Canty, Christopher L (Chris)** — Football Player
Baltimore Ravens, Ravens Stadium, 1 Winning Dr, Baltimore MD 21230 USA
**Canup, Robin** — Astronomer
Southwest Research Institute, 1050 Walnut St, #300, Boulder CO 80302, USA
**Capaldi, Peter** — Actor, Writer, Director
United Agents, 12-26 Lexington St, London W1F 0LE, England
**Caparulo, John** — Actor, Comedian, Writer
Parallel Entertainment, 9420 Wilshire Blvd, #250, Beverly Hills CA 90212, USA
**Capasso, Federico** — Physicist
Lucent Technologies, Bell Laboratories, 600 Mountain Ave, New Providence NJ 07974, USA
**Capecchi, Mario R** — Nobel Medicine Laureate
778 E 13800 S, Draper UT 84020, USA
**Capellas, Michael** — Businessman
M C I, 500 Clinton Center Dr, #2200, Clinton MS 39056, USA
**Capellino, Ally** — Fashion Designer
N1R, Metropolitan Wharf, Wapping Wall, London E1 9SS, England
**Capellmann, Nadine** — Equestrian
Haller Str 46, 52325 Wurselen, Germany
**Capello, Fabio** — Soccer Player, Manager
F C Real Madrid, Avda Concha Espana 1, 28036 Madrid, Spain
**Capers, Dom** — Football Coach
814 Hilltop Dr, Walpole MA 02081, USA
**Caperton, W Gaston, III** — Governor, WV; Foundation Executive
College Board, President's Office, 45 Columbus Ave, New York NY 10023, USA
**Capilouto, Eli** — Educator
University of Kentucky, President's Office, Lexington KY 40506, USA
**Caplan, Lizzy** — Actress
W M E Entertainment, 9601 Wilshire Blvd, #300, Beverly Hills CA 90210 USA
**Capleton** — Singer
Agency Group Ltd, 142 W 57th St, #600, New York NY 10019 USA
**Caplin, Mortimer M** — Government Official
5610 Wisconsin Ave NW, #18E, Chevy Chase MD 20815, USA
**Capobianco, Tito** — Opera Director
Pittsburgh Opera Co, 711 Penn Ave, #800, Pittsburgh PA 15222, USA
**Caponera, John** — Actor, Comedian
Messina Baker Entertainment, 955 Carillo Dr, #100, Los Angeles CA 90048, USA
**Caponi-Byrnes, Donna** — Golfer
2731 Silver River Trail, Orlando FL 32828, USA
**Cappelletti, Gino R M** — Football Player
19 Louis Dr, Wellesley MA 02481, USA
**Cappelletti, John R** — Football Player
23791 Brant Lane, Laguna Niguel CA 92677, USA
**Capps, Matthew D (Matt)** — Baseball Player
6348 S Summers Circle, Douglasville GA 30135, USA
**Capps, Ron** — Drag Racing Driver
Copenhagen Racing, 1232 Distribution Way, Vista CA 92081, USA
**Capps, Steve** — Computer Software Designer
Microsoft Corp, 1 Microsoft Way, Redmond WA 98052, USA
**Capra, Francis** — Actor
Curtis Talent Mgmt, 9607 Arby Dr, Beverly Hills CA 90210, USA
**Capra, Fritjof** — Physicist, Systems Theorist
PO Box 9066, Berkeley CA 94709, USA
**Capra, Lee W (Buzz)** — Baseball Player
15039 W Keswick Place, Lockport IL 60441, USA
**Capriati, Jennifer** — Tennis Player
5326 Foxhunt Dr, Wesley Chapel FL 33543, USA
**Caprice** — Model, Singer, Songwriter
Select Model Mgmt, 43 King St, London WC2E, England
**Caprioli, Anita** — Actress
Carol Levi Mgmt, Via Giuseppe Pisanelli 2, 00196 Rome, Italy
**Capron, Robert** — Actor
Generation TV, 20 W 20th St, #1008, New York NY 10011, USA
**Capshaw, Jessica** — Actress
Creative Artists Agency, 2000 Ave of Stars, #100, Los Angeles CA 90067 USA
**Capshaw, Kate** — Actress
PO Box 491356, Los Angeles CA 90049, USA
**Capuano, Christopher F (Chris)** — Baseball Player
10953 E Tusayan Trail, Scottsdale AZ 85255, USA
**Capuano, Dave, Jr** — Ice Hockey Player
145 Capuano Ave, Cranston RI 02920, USA
**Capuano, Jack** — Ice Hockey Player, Coach
New York Islanders, 1255 Hempstead Turnpike, Uniondale NY 11553 USA
**Capucon, Gautier** — Concert Cellist
Columbia Artists Mgmt Inc, 1790 Broadway, #702, New York NY 10019 USA
**Capucon, Renaud** — Concert Violinist
Columbia Artists Mgmt Inc, 1790 Broadway, #702, New York NY 10019 USA
**Capurro, Scott** — Actor
Coolwaters Productions, 10061 Riverside Dr, Box 531, Toluca Lake CA 91602 USA
**Cara, Irene** — Singer, Actress, Songwriter
Caramel Productions, 2143 SR 54, #116, New Port Richey FL 34653, USA
**Carafotes, Paul** — Actor
C E S D, 10635 Santa Monica Blvd, #130, Los Angeles CA 90025 USA
**Caramanlis, Costas** — Prime Minister, Greece
Prime Minister's Office, Maximos Mansion, 19 Irodou Attikou St, 10674 Athens, Greece
**Carano, Gina J** — Actress
Syndicate, 8265 Sunset Blvd, #205, Los Angeles CA 90046, USA

| | |
|---|---|
| **Carano, Glenn T**<br>2551 Lakeridge Shores E, Reno NV 89519, USA | Football Player |
| **Carasco, Joe (King)**<br>Texas Sounds, 2317 Pecan St, Dickinson TX 77539, USA | Singer |
| **Carax, Leos**<br>Artmedia, 20 Ave Rapp, 75007 Paris, France | Director |
| **Caray, Harry C (Chip), III**<br>1302 Azalea Lane, Maitland FL 32751, USA | Sportscaster |
| **Carbajal, Michael**<br>PO Box 510, Phoenix AZ 85001, USA | Boxer |
| **Carberry, Deirdre**<br>American Ballet Theater, 890 Broadway, #300, New York NY 10003, USA | Ballerina |
| **Carbo, Bernardo (Bernie)**<br>6352 Woodside Dr S, Theodore AL 36582, USA | Baseball Player |
| **Carbonara, David**<br>Creative Artists Agency, 2000 Ave of Stars, #100, Los Angeles CA 90067 USA | Composer |
| **Carbonell, Nestor**<br>Paradigm Agency, 360 N Crescent Dr, North Building, Beverly Hills CA 90210 USA | Actor |
| **Carcaterra, Lorenzo**<br>Pitt Group, 9465 Wilshire Blvd, #420, Beverly Hills CA 90212, USA | Writer |
| **Card, Andrew H, Jr**<br>1207 Buchana St, McLean VA 22101, USA | Secretary, Transportation |
| **Card, Michael**<br>Michael Card Music, PO Box 586, Franklin TN 37065, USA | Singer, Musician, Songwriter |
| **Card, Orson Scott**<br>401 Willoughby Blvd, Greensboro NC 27408, USA | Writer |
| **Cardamone, Richard J**<br>US Court of Appeals, 10 Broad St, #322, Utica NY 13501, USA | Judge |
| **Cardellini, Linda**<br>I/D Public Relations, 7060 Hollywood Blvd, #800, Los Angeles CA 90028 USA | Actress |
| **Carden, Joan M**<br>Avere Artists Mgmt, 26 Oxley Dr, Bowral NSW 2576, Australia | Opera Singer |
| **Carden, Michael (Mike)**<br>Crush Music Media Mgmt, 60-62 E 11th St, #700, New York NY 10003, USA | Guitarist (Academy Is), Songwriter |
| **Cardenal, Jose D**<br>118 Bridgewater Court, Bradenton FL 34212, USA | Baseball Player |
| **Cardenas, Robert L**<br>6143 Madra Ave, San Diego CA 92129, USA | Test Pilot, Air Force General |
| **Cardin, Claude**<br>13 Rue Boucher, Sorel QC J3P 1E7, Canada | Ice Hockey Player |
| **Cardin, Pierre**<br>59 Rue du Faubourg-Saint-Honore, 75008 Paris, France | Fashion Designer |
| **Cardinal, Douglas J**<br>7011A Manchester Blvd, #315, Alexandria VA 22310, USA | Architect |
| **Cardinale, Claudia**<br>Artmedia, 20 Ave Rapp, 75007 Paris, France | Actress |
| **Cardona, Manolo**<br>D2 Management, 9255 Sunset Blvd, #600, West Hollywood CA 90069, USA | Actor |
| **Cardona, Manuel**<br>Max-Planck-Institut, Heisenbergstr 1, 70569 Stuttgart, Germany | Physicist |
| **Cardona, Prudencio**<br>4845 NW 7th St, #402, Miami FL 33126, USA | Boxer |
| **Cardone, Vivian**<br>C E S D, 10635 Santa Monica Blvd, #130, Los Angeles CA 90025 USA | Actress |
| **Cardow, Cameron (Cam)**<br>Ottawa Sentinental, 11 Baxter Road, Box 5020, Ottawa ON K2C 3M4, Canada | Editorial Cartoonist |
| **Cardoza, Dennis A**<br>Manatt Phelps Phillips, 700 12th St NW, #1100, Washington DC 20005, USA | Representative, CA |
| **Care, Peter**<br>Bob Industries, 1313 5th St, Santa Monica CA 90401, USA | Director, Producer, Writer |
| **Carell, Steve**<br>W M E Entertainment, 9601 Wilshire Blvd, #300, Beverly Hills CA 90210 USA | Actor, Writer |
| **Carelli, Rick**<br>PO Box 1000, Arvada CO 80001, USA | Truck Racing Driver |
| **Caretto-Brown, Patty**<br>16079 Mesquite Circle, Fountain Valley CA 92708, USA | Swimmer |
| **Carew, Rodney C (Rod)**<br>1171 Via Santiago, Corona CA 92882, USA | Baseball Player |
| **Carey, Clare**<br>B/W/R, 9100 Wilshire Blvd, #500W, Beverly Hills CA 90212 USA | Actress |
| **Carey, Danny**<br>Volcano Records, 3375 Cahuenga Blvd, #590, Los Angeles CA 90068, USA | Drummer (Tool) |
| **Carey, Drew**<br>Gersh Agency, 9465 Wilshire Blvd, #600, Beverly Hills CA 90212 USA | Actor, Comedian |
| **Carey, Duane G**<br>5938 Instone Circle, Colorado Springs CO 80922, USA | Astronaut |
| **Carey, Ezekiel**<br>509 E Ridge Crest Blvd, #A, Ridge Crest CA 93555, USA | Singer (Flamingos) |
| **Carey, George L**<br>Gloucestershire University, Chancellory, Cheltenham GL50 2RH, England | Religious Leader |
| **Carey, Gerard**<br>Gavin Barker Assoc, 2D Wimpole St, London W1G 0EB, England | Actor |
| **Carey, Jim**<br>5351 Hunt Club Way, Sarasota FL 34238, USA | Ice Hockey Player |
| **Carey, Maggie**<br>United Talent Agency, U T A Plaza, 9336 Civic Center Dr, Beverly Hills CA 90210 USA | Director, Producer, Writer |
| **Carey, Mariah**<br>Creative Artists Agency, 2000 Ave of Stars, #100, Los Angeles CA 90067 USA | Singer, Songwriter |
| **Carey, Matthew**<br>J K A Talent, 12725 Ventura Blvd, #H, Studio City CA 91604, USA | Actor |
| **Carey, Peter**<br>I C M Partners, 730 5th Ave, New York NY 10019 USA | Writer |
| **Carey, Vernon A**<br>5321 Thoroughbred Lane, Southwest Ranches FL 33330, USA | Football Player |
| **Caria, Marco**<br>I M G Artists, Hogarth Business Park, Chiswick, London W4 2TH, England | Opera Singer |

| | |
|---|---|
| **Carides, Gia** | Actress |
| Innovative Artists, 1505 10th St, Santa Monica CA 90401 USA | |
| **Caridis, Miltiades** | Conductor |
| Himmelhofgasse 10, 1130 Vienna, Austria | |
| **Carillo, Mary** | Sportscaster, Tennis Player |
| 822 Boylston St, #203, Chestnut Hill PA 02467, USA | |
| **Carillo, Tony** | Cartoonist (F Minus) |
| United Feature Syndicate, PO Box 5610, Cincinnati OH 45201 USA | |
| **Carion, Christian** | Director, Writer |
| Fims Talents, 34 Rue du Louvre, 75001 Paris, France | |
| **Carioti, Ricky** | Photographer |
| Washington Post, Editorial Dept, 1150 15th St NW, Washington DC 20071 USA | |
| **Cariou, Len** | Actor |
| 7004 Blvd E, #17D, West New York NJ 07093, USA | |
| **Carithers, William C, Jr** | Physicist |
| 817 The Alameda, Berkeley CA 94707, USA | |
| **Carkner, Terry** | Ice Hockey Player |
| 4 Remington Lane, Malvern PA 19355, USA | |
| **Carl XVI Gustaf** | King, Sweden |
| Kungliga Slottet, Slottsbacken, 111 30 Stockholm, Sweden | |
| **Carle, Eric** | Artist |
| PO Box 485, Northampton MA 01061, USA | |
| **Carlei, Carlo** | Director |
| Bloom Hergott Diemer, 150 S Rodeo Dr, #300, Beverly Hills CA 90212 USA | |
| **Carles Gordo, Ricardo M Cardinal** | Religious Leader |
| Carrer del Bisbe 5, 08002 Barcelona, Spain | |
| **Carlesimo, Pete J (P J)** | Basketball Coach, Sportscaster |
| 1429 Willard Ave W, Seattle WA 98119, USA | |
| **Carleson, Lennart A E** | Abel Mathematics Laureate |
| Royal Institute, Kungl Tekniska Hogskloan SE 100 44, Stockholm, Sweden | |
| **Carlestrom, John E** | Astronomer |
| University of Chicago, Astronomy Dept, 5640 S Ellis Ave, Chicago IL 60637, USA | |
| **Carleton, K Wayne** | Ice Hockey Player |
| 9846 Highway 26 E, RR 2 LCD Collingwood, Collingwood ON L9Y 3Z1, Canada | |
| **Carley, Christopher** | Actor |
| Untitled Entertainment, 350 S Beverly Dr, #200, Beverly Hills CA 90212 USA | |
| **Carlile, Brandi** | Singer, Guitarist, Songwriter |
| A2 Mgmt, 1316 Sherman Abe, #215, Evanston IL 60201, USA | |
| **Carlile, Forbes** | Swimming Coach |
| 16 Cross St, Ryde NSW 2112, Australia | |
| **Carlin, Amanda** | Actress |
| Greene Assoc, 1901 Ave of Stars, #130, Los Angeles CA 90067 USA | |
| **Carlin, Brian** | Ice Hockey Player |
| 103 Mount Norquay Park SE, Calgary AB T2Z 2R3, Canada | |
| **Carlin, John W** | Governor, KS |
| 1208 Wyndham Heights Dr, Manhattan KS 66503, USA | |
| **Carling, William D C** | Rugby Player, Sportscaster |
| Mike Burton Mgmt, Brunswick Road, Gloucester GL1 1JJ, England | |
| **Carlisle, Belinda** | Singer, Songwriter, Model |
| Tony Denton Promotions, Charter House, 157/159 High St, London N14 7DY, England | |
| **Carlisle, Bob** | Singer, Songwriter |
| Ray Ware Artist Mgmt, 3108 Saint Stephens Way, Franklin TN 37064, USA | |
| **Carlisle, Cooper M** | Football Player |
| 2032 Sorrelwood Court, San Ramon CA 94582, USA | |
| **Carlisle, Jodi** | Actress, Comedienne |
| I C M Partners, 10250 Constellation Blvd, #900, Los Angeles CA 90067 USA | |
| **Carlisle, Mary** | Actress |
| 517 N Rodeo Dr, Beverly Hills CA 90210, USA | |
| **Carlisle, Richard P (Rick)** | Basketball Player, Coach |
| 3925 Greenbrier Dr, Dallas TX 75225, USA | |
| **Carll, Hayes** | Singer, Guitarist, Songwriter |
| Crowley Artists Mgmt, 602 Wayside Dr, Wimberley TX 78676, USA | |
| **Carlos Moco, Marcolino Jose** | Prime Minister, Angola |
| Movimento Popular de Libertacao de Angola, Luanda, Angola | |
| **Carlos, Bun E** | Drummer (Cheap Trick) |
| Oakie Dokie Mgmt, 6090 Central Ave, Saint Petersburg FL 33707, USA | |
| **Carlos, John** | Track Athlete |
| 68640 Tortuga Road, Cathedral City CA 92234, USA | |
| **Carlos, Wendy** | Composer |
| B M I, 8730 W Sunset Blvd, #300, Los Angeles CA 90069 USA | |
| **Carlson, Amy** | Actress |
| Principal Entertainment, 9255 Sunset Blvd, #500, Los Angeles CA 90069 USA | |
| **Carlson, Arne H** | Governor, MN |
| 145 Holly Lane N, Minneapolis MN 55447, USA | |
| **Carlson, Dudley L** | Navy Admiral |
| Navy League, 2300 Wilson Blvd, #210, Arlington VA 22201, USA | |
| **Carlson, Jack W** | Association Executive |
| American Assn of Retired Persons, 1901 K St NW, Washington DC 20006, USA | |
| **Carlson, John A** | Businessman |
| Cray Research, 655 Lone Oak Dr, #A, Saint Paul MN 55121, USA | |
| **Carlson, John D, Jr** | Football Player |
| Minnesota Vikings, 9520 Viking Dr, Eden Prairie MN 55344 USA | |
| **Carlson, K C** | Cartoonist (Legion of Super Heroes) |
| D C Comics, 1700 Broadway, #400, New York NY 10019 USA | |
| **Carlson, Kelly** | Actress |
| Gersh Agency, 9465 Wilshire Blvd, #600, Beverly Hills CA 90212 USA | |
| **Carlson, Lane** | Model |
| Warning Models, 1590 S Lewis St, Anaheim CA 92805, USA | |
| **Carlson, M Cody** | Football Player |
| 3417 Foothill Terrace, Austin TX 78731, USA | |
| **Carlson, Mark C** | Baseball Umpire |
| 354 Tall Oak Trail, Tarpon Springs FL 34688, USA | |
| **Carlson, Michael** | Chef |
| Schwa Restaurant, 1466 N Ashland Ave, Chicago IL 60622, USA | |
| **Carlson, Monica** | Model, Actress |
| Sports Unlimited, 1732 NW Quimby St, Portland OR 97209, USA | |

**C**

**Carides - Carlson**

**Carlson, Paulette** — Singer
Fat City Artists, 1906 Chet Atkins Place, #502, Nashville TN 37212 USA
**Carlson, Richard A** — Interior Designer
Swanke Hayden Connell Architects, 295 Lafayette St, New York NY 10012, USA
**Carlson, Shane** — Model
Warning Models, 1590 S Lewis St, Anaheim CA 92805, USA
**Carlson, Steve** — Auto Racing Driver
539 Brickel Road, West Salem WI 54669, USA
**Carlson, Steve E** — Ice Hockey Player
PO Box 3476, Rancho Cordova CA 95741, USA
**Carlson, Tucker** — Commentator
Fox-TV, News Dept, 205 E 67th St, New York NY 10065 USA
**Carlson, Veronica** — Actress
7844 Kavanagh Court, Sarasota FL 34240, USA
**Carlsson, Arvid** — Nobel Medicine Laureate
Gothenborg University, Sahlgrenska Academy, Box 100, 405 30 Gothenborg Sweden
**Carlsson, Ingvar G** — Prime Minister, Sweden
Riksdagen, 100 12 Stockholm, Sweden
**Carlton, Carl** — Singer
Universal Attractions, 135 W 26th St, #1200, New York NY 10001 USA
**Carlton, Hope Marie** — Actress, Model
Playboy Promotions, 2706 Media Center Dr, Los Angeles CA 90065 USA
**Carlton, L Wray** — Football Player
29 Pine Terrace, Orchard Park NY 14127, USA
**Carlton, Larry** — Jazz Guitarist, Composer
W B A Entertainment, PO Box 291802, Nashville TN 37229, USA
**Carlton, Paul K, Jr** — Air Force General, Surgeon
ImmuneRegen BioSciences, 8777 Via de Ventura, #280, Scottsdale AZ 85258, USA
**Carlton, Steven N (Steve)** — Baseball Player
G W Sports, 555 S Camino del Rio, #B2, Durango CO 81303, USA
**Carlton, Vanessa** — Singer, Songwriter
Creative Artists Agency, 2000 Ave of Stars, #100, Los Angeles CA 90067 USA
**Carlucci, Dave** — Singer (Danny & the Juniors)
Joe Terry Mgmt, PO Box 279, Williamstown NJ 08094, USA
**Carlucci, Frank C, III** — Secretary, Defense; Businessman
Carlyle Group, 1001 Pennsylvania Ave NW, #220S, Washington DC 20004, USA
**Carlyle, Earl L (Buddy)** — Baseball Player
205 Ashmere Court, Tyrone GA 30290, USA
**Carlyle, Joan H** — Opera Singer
Laundry Cottage, Hammer, North Wales SY13 4QX, England
**Carlyle, Liz** — Writer
1939 High House Road, #185, Cary NC 27519, USA
**Carlyle, Randy** — Ice Hockey Player, Coach
180 S Lakeview Ave, Anaheim CA 92807, USA
**Carlyle, Robert** — Actor
Hamilton Hodell, 66-68 Margaret St, #500, London W1W 8SR, England
**Carman** — Singer
Carman World Outreach, PO Box 470470, Tulsa OK 74147, USA
**Carman, Brian** — Singer, Guitarist (Chantays)
Bill Hollingshead Productions, 1010 Anderson Road, Davis CA 95616 USA
**Carman, Donald W (Don)** — Baseball Player
555 Murex Dr, Naples FL 34102, USA
**Carman, Gregory W** — Judge; Representative, NY
US Court of International Trade, 1 Federal Plaza, New York NY 10278, USA
**Carmel, Leon J (Duke)** — Baseball Player
116 Spring Lake Blvd, Waretown NJ 08758, USA
**Carmen, Eric** — Singer, Songwriter
David Spero Mgmt, 1679 S Belvoir Blvd, Cleveland OH 44121, USA
**Carmen, Julie** — Actress
Greene Assoc, 1901 Ave of Stars, #130, Los Angeles CA 90067 USA
**Carmichael, Albert R (Hoagy)** — Football Player
78641 Hampshire Ave, Palm Desert CA 92211, USA
**Carmichael, Clint** — Actor
Kazarian/Measures/Ruskin, 11969 Ventura Blvd, #300, Studio City CA 91604 USA
**Carmichael, Daniel A (Dan), Jr** — WW II Navy Air Force Hero
2764 Elm Ave, Columbus OH 43209, USA
**Carmichael, Jesse** — Keyboardist (Maroon 5)
J Records, 745 5th Ave, #600, New York NY 10151 USA
**Carmichael, Katy** — Actress
Shining Mgmt, 12 D'Arblay St, London W1F 8DU, England
**Carmichael, L Harold** — Football Player
38 Birch Lane, Glassboro NJ 08028, USA
**Carmichael, Laura** — Actress
Curtis Brown Group, 28-29 Haymarket St, #500, London SW1Y 4SP, England
**Carmichael, Ricky** — Motorcycle Racing Rider
1219 Shady Rest Road, Havana FL 32333, USA
**Carmine, Michael** — Cinematographer
3615 West Dr, Little Neck NY 11363, USA
**Carmody, Matt** — Actor
Metropolitan Talent Agency, 5405 Wilshire Blvd, #218, Los Angeles CA 90036 USA
**Carmona, Richard H** — Physician, Government Official
Canyon Ranch Wellness Center, 8600 E Rockcliff Road, Tucson AZ 85750, USA
**Carmona, Wayne** — Producer
W M E Entertainment, 9601 Wilshire Blvd, #300, Beverly Hills CA 90210 USA
**Carnahan, Joe** — Director, Producer, Writer
Creative Artists Agency, 2000 Ave of Stars, #100, Los Angeles CA 90067 USA
**Carnahan, Matthew Michael** — Writer
W M E Entertainment, 9601 Wilshire Blvd, #300, Beverly Hills CA 90210 USA
**Carne, Jean** — Singer
Walt Reeder Productions, 93 Old York Road, #1-604, Jenkintown PA 19046, USA
**Carneiro, Joana** — Conductor
I M G Artists, Hogarth Business Park, Chiswick, London W4 2TH, England
**Carner, Charles Robert** — Director, Producer, Writer
4172 Sandy Hollow Court, Moorpark CA 93021, USA
**Carner, JoAnne Gunderson** — Golfer
3030 S Ocean Blvd, Palm Beach FL 33480, USA

**Carnes, Kim** — Singer, Songwriter
1829 Tyne Blvd, Nashville TN 37215, USA
**Carnes, Ryan** — Actor
Talent Works, 3500 W Olive Ave, #1400, Burbank CA 91505 USA
**Carnesale, Albert** — Educator
University of California, Chancellor's Office, Los Angeles CA 90024, USA
**Carnesecca, Luigi (Lou)** — Basketball Coach
18247 Midland Parkway, Jamaica NY 11432, USA
**Carnevale, Mark** — Golfer
24 Loggerhead Lane, Ponte Vedra Beach FL 32082, USA
**Carney, Jay** — Government Official, Journalist
White House, 1600 Pennsylvania Ave NW, Washington DC 20500 USA
**Carney, John** — Director, Writer, Actor
Casorotto Ramsay, Waverley House, 7-12 Noel St, London W1F 8GQ, England
**Carney, John M** — Football Player
2950 Wishbone Way, Encinitas CA 92024, USA
**Carney, Keith E** — Ice Hockey Player
8701 N 55th Place, Paradise Valley AZ 85253, USA
**Carney, Patrick J** — Drummer (Black Keys)
Q-Prime South, 131 S 11th St, Nashville TN 37206 USA
**Carney, Quinn** — Lacrosse Player
University of Maryland, Athletic Dept, College Park MD 20742, USA
**Carney, Reeve** — Actor
Paradigm Agency, 360 N Crescent Dr, North Building, Beverly Hills CA 90210 USA
**Carney, Thomas P** — Army General
Thomas P Carney Inc, PO Box 28, Langhorne PA 19047, USA
**Carnoy, Martin** — Economist
Stanford University, Economic Studies Center, Stanford CA 94305, USA
**Carns, Michael P C (Mike)** — Air Force General
966 Coral Dr, Pebble Beach CA 93953, USA
**Caro, Niki** — Director, Writer
I C M Partners, 10250 Constellation Blvd, #900, Los Angeles CA 90067 USA
**Caro, Robert A** — Writer
Robert A Caro Assoc, 250 W 57th St, #2215, New York NY 10107, USA
**Caroit, Phillipe** — Actor
Voyez Mon Agent, 20 Ave Rapp, 75007 Paris, France
**Carol, Linda** — Actress
William Kerwin Agency, 1605 N Cahuenga Blvd, #202, Los Angeles CA 90028, USA
**Carolin, Heather M** — Model
Playboy Promotions, 2706 Media Center Dr, Los Angeles CA 90065 USA
**Caroline** — Heir Presumptive, Monaco
Villa Le Clos Saint Pierre, Ave San-Martin, 98000 Monte Carlo, Monaco
**Caroline, James C (J C)** — Football Player
2501 Stanford Dr, Champaign IL 61820, USA
**Carolla, Adam** — Actor, Comedian
Dixon Talent, 375 Greenwich St, #500, New York NY 10013, USA
**Carollo, Joseph P (Joe)** — Football Player
4634 Meyer Way, Carmichael CA 95608, USA
**Caron, Glenn Gordon** — Producer, Writer
Picturemaker Productions, 1600 Rosecrans Ave, Building 2A, Manhattan Beach CA 90266, USA
**Caron, Jacques** — Ice Hockey Player
6426 Moorings Point Circle, #201, Lakewood Ranch FL 34202, USA
**Caron, Jean-Claude** — Actor
Artmedia, 20 Ave Rapp, 75007 Paris, France
**Caron, Leslie** — Actress, Dancer
6 Rue De Bellechaisse, 75007 Paris, France
**Carothers, Veronica** — Actress
535 N Heatherstone Dr, Orange CA 92869, USA
**Carp, Daniel A (Dan)** — Businessman
Delta Air Lines, Hartsfield International Airport, Atlanta GA 30320, USA
**Carpani, Rachael** — Actress
Lisa Mann Agency, PO Box 1192, Bondi Junction NSW 1315, Australia
**Carpenter, Andrew (Drew)** — Baseball Player
1894 SW Mistybrook Dr, Grants Pass OR 97527, USA
**Carpenter, Bobby** — Ice Hockey Player
71 Chestnut St, North Reading MA 01864, USA
**Carpenter, Carleton** — Actor
RR 2, Chardavoyne Road, Warwick NY 10990, USA
**Carpenter, Chad** — Cartoonist
Tundra Comics, PO Box 871354, Wasilla AK 99687, USA
**Carpenter, Charisma** — Actress, Model
John Carrabino Mgmt, 5900 Wilshire Blvd, #406, Los Angeles CA 90036 USA
**Carpenter, Christopher J (Chris)** — Baseball Player
809 S Warson Road, Saint Louis MO 63124, USA
**Carpenter, Ed** — Auto Racing Driver
Vision Racing, 4760 Kingsway Dr, #B, Indianapolis IN 46205, USA
**Carpenter, Jack** — Actor
I C M Partners, 10250 Constellation Blvd, #900, Los Angeles CA 90067 USA
**Carpenter, Jennifer** — Actress
W M E Entertainment, 9601 Wilshire Blvd, #300, Beverly Hills CA 90210 USA
**Carpenter, John H** — Director, Writer
Echo Lake Mgmt, 421 S Beverly Dr, #800, Beverly Hills CA 90212, USA
**Carpenter, Keion E** — Football Player
2009 Shin Court, Buford GA 30519, USA
**Carpenter, Kip** — Speed Skater
W375S10897 Prairie Lane, Eagle WI 53119, USA
**Carpenter, Mary Chapin** — Singer, Guitarist, Songwriter
Paradigm Agency, 360 N Crescent Dr, North Building, Beverly Hills CA 90210 USA
**Carpenter, Richard L** — Pianist, Singer, Songwriter
960 Country Valley Road, Westlake Village CA 91362, USA
**Carpenter, Robert J (Bobby), III** — Football Player
103 Graeser Acres, Saint Louis MO 63146, USA
**Carpenter, Robert J (Rob), Jr** — Football Player
1601 Wheeling Road NE, Lancaster OH 43130, USA
**Carpenter, Russell P** — Cinematographer
Worldwide Production Agency, 144 N Robertson Blvd, #200, West Hollywood CA 90048, USA

# C

**Carpenter, Stephen** — Guitarist (Deftones)
Velvet Hammer Music, 9014 Melrose Ave, West Hollywood CA 90069, USA
**Carpenter, William S (Bill), Jr** — Army General, Hero, Football Player
PO Box 4067, Whitefish MT 59937, USA
**Carpenter-Phinney, Connie** — Cyclist
470 Juniper Ave, Boulder CO 80304, USA
**Carpentier, Alain** — Heart Surgeon
Hospital Broussais, 96 Rue Didot, 75674 Bris Cedex 14, France
**Carpentier, Patrick** — Auto Racing Driver
S A M A X Motorsports, 203 NW 16th St, Pompano Beach FL 33060, USA
**Carpinello, James** — Actor, Singer
A P A Talent/Literary Agency, 405 S Beverly Dr, #300, Beverly Hills CA 90212 USA
**Carr, Antoine L** — Basketball Player
5724 Croyden Circle, Wichita KS 67220, USA
**Carr, Austin G** — Basketball Player
4547 Saint Germain Blvd, Cleveland OH 44128, USA
**Carr, Brandon C** — Football Player
Dallas Cowboys, 1 Cowboys Parkway, Irving TX 75063 USA
**Carr, Caleb** — Writer
Grand Central Publishing, 237 Park Ave, #1300L, New York NY 10017, USA
**Carr, Catherine (Cathy)** — Swimmer
409 10th St, Davis CA 95616, USA
**Carr, Charles L G (Chuck), Jr** — Baseball Player
5419 E Greenway St, Mesa AZ 85205, USA
**Carr, David** — Football Player
4771 Sweetwater Blvd, #226, Sugar Land TX 77479, USA
**Carr, Gary** — Actor
Markham Froggatt Irwin, Julian House, 4 Windmill St, London W1P 1HF, England
**Carr, Gene** — Ice Hockey Player
13529 Leadwell St, #1, Van Nuys CA 91405, USA
**Carr, Gerald P (Jerry)** — Astronaut
Camus Inc, 49 Maple St, #123, Manchester Center VT 05255, USA
**Carr, Jimmy** — Actor
P F D, Drury House, 34-43 Russell St, London WC2B 5HA, England
**Carr, Katie** — Actress
S M S Talent, 8383 Wilshire Blvd, #230, Beverly Hills CA 90211 USA
**Carr, Kenneth A (Kenny)** — Basketball Player
24421 SW Valley View Dr, West Linn OR 97068, USA
**Carr, Kenneth M** — Navy Admiral
16600 Warren Court, #302, Chagrin Falls OH 44023, USA
**Carr, Michael Leon (M L)** — Basketball Player, Coach, Executive
168 Beaver Road, Weston MA 02493, USA
**Carr, Robyn** — Writer
Nancy Berland Public Relations, 2816 NW 57th St, #101, Oklahoma City OK 73112, USA
**Carr, Roger D** — Football Player
101 Green Forest Dr, Monroe LA 71203, USA
**Carr, Steve** — Director, Producer
Rumpus Entertainment, 9000 W Sunset Blvd, #650, Los Angeles CA 90048, USA
**Carr, Vikki** — Singer
Vi-Carr Entertainment, 3102 Iron Stone Lane, San Antonio TX 78230, USA
**Carrabba, Christopher A (Chris)** — Singer (Dashboard Confessional)
Hard 8 Mgmt, 2118 Wilshire Blvd, #361, Santa Monica CA 90403, USA
**Carrack, Paul** — Singer, Songwriter
Alan Wood Agency, 346 Gleadless Road, Sheffield, South York S2 3AJ, England
**Carradine, Ever** — Actress
Management 360, 9111 Wilshire Blvd, Beverly Hills CA 90210 USA
**Carradine, Keith** — Actor, Singer, Songwriter
355 S Grand Ave, #1710, Los Angeles CA 90071, USA
**Carradine, Robert** — Actor
Triple Tap Productions, 5850 Canoga Ave, #200, Woodland Hills CA 91367, USA
**Carrasco, Daniel J (D J)** — Baseball Player
508 Lonesome Trail, Haslet TX 76052, USA
**Carre, Isabelle** — Actress
Agence Artiste Adequet, 108 Rue Reaumur, 75002 Paris, France
**Carreker, Alphonso** — Football Player
5599 Asheforde Lane, Marietta GA 30068, USA
**Carreon, Mark S** — Baseball Player
413 Ashland Creek, Victoria TX 77901, USA
**Carrera, Barbara** — Actress, Model
Alan David Mgmt, 8840 Wilshire Blvd, #200, Beverly Hills CA 90211, USA
**Carrera, Carlos** — Director
Creative Artists Agency, 2000 Ave of Stars, #100, Los Angeles CA 90067 USA
**Carrera, Christy** — Actress
Michael Scott, PO Box 683, Lewis Center OH 43035, USA
**Carreras, Jose** — Opera Singer
Fundacion Jose Carreras, Calle Muntaner 383, 08021 Barcelona, Spain
**Carrere, Emmanuel** — Writer
Bloomsbury Publishing, 50 Bedford Square, London WC1B 3DP, England
**Carrere, Tia** — Actress, Model
Arlook Group, 205 S Beverly Dr, #209, Beverly Hills CA 90212, USA
**Carretto, Joseph A, Jr** — Astronaut
Space Missile Systems Center, 483 N Aviation Blvd, El Segundo CA 90245, USA
**Carrey, Jim** — Actor, Comedian
J C 23 Entertainment, 1925 Century Park E, #200, Los Angeles CA 90067, USA
**Carrick, Charlie** — Actor
United Talent Agency, U T A Plaza, 9336 Civic Center Dr, Beverly Hills CA 90210 USA
**Carrick, Ted** — Clinical Neurologist
Carrick Graduate Studies Institute, 203-8941 Lake Dr, Cape Canaveral FL 32920, USA
**Carrier, J Darel** — Basketball Player
4224 Glasgow Road, Oakland KY 42159, USA
**Carrier, J Mark** — Football Player
4115 Highland Park Circle, Lutz FL 33558, USA
**Carrier, Mark A** — Football Player
7340 Indian Hill Road, Cincinnati OH 45243, USA
**Carriere, Jean P J** — Writer
Le Devois, Super Camprieu, 30750 Treves, France

Carpenter - Carriere

**Carriere, Larry** — Ice Hockey Player
94 Dawnbrook Lane, Buffalo NY 14221, USA
**Carriere, Mathieu** — Actor
Agence Elizabeth Simpson, 32 Blvd du Montparnasse, 75015 Paris, France
**Carril, Pete** — Basketball Coach
372 Carter Road, Princeton NJ 08540, USA
**Carrillo, Elpidia** — Actress
Bresler Kelly Assoc, 11500 W Olympic Blvd, #400, Los Angeles CA 90064 USA
**Carrington, Alan** — Chemist
46 Lakewood Road, Chandler's Ford, Hampshire SO53 1EX, England
**Carrington, Darren R** — Football Player
14097 Montfort Court, San Diego CA 92128, USA
**Carrington, Debbie Lee** — Actress
PO Box 9897, Marina del Rey CA 90295, USA
**Carrington, Kelly** — Model
Playboy Promotions, 2706 Media Center Dr, Los Angeles CA 90065 USA
**Carrington, Paul D** — Attorney, Educator
Duke University, Law School, Durham NC 27708, USA
**Carrington, Peter A R** — Government Official, England
32A Ovinton Square, London SW3 1LR, England
**Carrington, Robert F (Bob)** — Basketball Player
PO Box 13191, Carlsbad CA 92013, USA
**Carrington, Rodney** — Actor, Comedian
P M G Entertainment Group, 1505 S Atlantic St, Melbourne Beach FL 32951, USA
**Carrington, Terri Lyne** — Jazz Drummer
Stax/Concord Records, 270 N Canon Dr, #1212, Beverly Hills CA 90210 USA
**Carroll, Charles C (Corky)** — Surfer
624 20th St, Huntington Beach CA 92648, USA
**Carroll, Clay P** — Baseball Player
3052 22nd St, Sarasota FL 34234, USA
**Carroll, Diahann** — Singer, Actress
C E S D, 10635 Santa Monica Blvd, #130, Los Angeles CA 90025 USA
**Carroll, James S (Jim)** — Football Player
3101 N State Road 7, Hollywood FL 33021, USA
**Carroll, Jamey B** — Baseball Player
3492 Siderwheel Dr, Rockledge FL 32955, USA
**Carroll, Jason Michael** — Singer, Songwriter
Paradigm Agency, 360 Park Ave, #1600, New York NY 10022 USA
**Carroll, John** — Attorney
Rogers & Wells, 31 W 52nd St, #300, New York NY 10019, USA
**Carroll, John B** — Psychologist
2158 Penrose Lane, Fairbanks AK 99709, USA
**Carroll, Joseph B (Joe Barry)** — Basketball Player
5220 Cascade Road SW, Atlanta GA 30331, USA
**Carroll, Julian M** — Governor, KY
Carroll Assoc, PO Box 1491, Frankfort KY 40602, USA
**Carroll, Kent J** — Navy Admiral
Country Club of North Carolina, 1600 Morganton Road, #30X, Pinehurst NC 28374, USA
**Carroll, Lester (Les)** — Cartoonist (Our Boarding House)
1715 Ivyhill Loop N, Columbus OH 43229, USA
**Carroll, Liz** — Fiddler
Mike Green Assoc, 339 E Liberty St, #220, Ann Arbor MI 48104, USA
**Carroll, Peter C (Pete)** — Football Coach
Seattle Seahawks, 12 Seahawks Way, Renton WA 98056 USA
**Carroll, Philip J** — Businessman
10314 Crimston Canyon Dr, Houston TX 77098, USA
**Carroll, Roscoe (Rocky)** — Actor
I C M Partners, 10250 Constellation Blvd, #900, Los Angeles CA 90067 USA
**Carroll, Thomas (Tom)** — Surfer
Quiksilver, 363 George St, Sydney NSW 2000, Australia
**Carroll, Willard** — Director
Hyperion Pictures, 7510 Sunset Blvd, #228, Los Angeles CA 90046, USA
**Carrot Top** — Actor, Comedian
420 Sylvan Dr, Winter Park FL 32789, USA
**Carruthers, Alastair** — Dermatologist
943 W Broadway, #820, Vancouver BC V5Z 4E1, Canada
**Carruthers, Caitlin (Kitty)** — Figure Skater
2106 White Eagle Lane, Katy TX 77450, USA
**Carruthers, Dwight** — Ice Hockey Player
9513 W Nelson Dr, Nine Mile Falls WA 99026, USA
**Carruthers, Garrey E** — Governor, NM
4405 Echo Canyon Road, Las Cruces NM 88011, USA
**Carruthers, Jean** — Opthamalogist
943 W Broadway, #820, Vancouver BC V5Z 4E1, Canada
**Carruthers, Peter** — Figure Skater
239 Via Monterey, Newbury Park CA 91320, USA
**Carsey, Marcia L P** — Producer
Carsey-Warner Productions, 4024 Radford Ave, Building 3, Studio City CA 91604, USA
**Carson, Adam** — Drummer, Singer (AFI)
S A M, 722 Seward St, Los Angeles CA 90038, USA
**Carson, Benjamin S** — Neurosurgeon
Johns Hopkins University Medical Center, Baltimore MD 21218 USA
**Carson, Carlos A** — Football Player
4747 W 150th Terrace, Overland Park KS 66224, USA
**Carson, David** — Director
Creative Artists Agency, 2000 Ave of Stars, #100, Los Angeles CA 90067 USA
**Carson, Essence** — Basketball Player
New York Liberty, Madison Square Garden, 2 Penn Plaza, New York NY 10121 USA
**Carson, Harold D (Harry)** — Football Player
PO Box 852, Westwood NJ 07675, USA
**Carson, James (Jimmy)** — Ice Hockey Player
1154 Ridgeway Dr, Rochester MI 48307, USA
**Carson, Jeff** — Singer
Buddy Lee Attractions, 38 Music Square E, #300, Nashville TN 37203 USA
**Carson, Kendel** — Singer, Songwriter
Train Wrecks Records, 218 Tallwood Dr, Hartsdale NY 10530, USA

**C**

|  |  |
|---|---|
| **Carson, Lisa Nicole**<br>Beth Rosner Management, 4 Stuyvesant Oval, #10H, New York NY 10009, USA | Actress |
| **Carson, William H (Willie)**<br>Minster House, Barnsley, Cirencester, Gloucestershire GL7 5DZ, England | Thoroughbred Racing Jockey |
| **Carswell, Dwyane**<br>PO Box 2488, Immokalee FL 34143, USA | Football Player |
| **Cartagena, Victoria**<br>Gersh Agency, 9465 Wilshire Blvd, #600, Beverly Hills CA 90212 USA | Actress |
| **Cartellone, Michael**<br>Vector Mgmt, PO Box 120479, Nashville TN 37212, USA | Drummer (Lynyrd Skynyrd, Damn Yankees) |
| **Carter, Aaron C**<br>Roger Paul, 1650 Broadway, #304, New York NY 10019, USA | Singer, Actor |
| **Carter, Adrienne**<br>Characters Talent Mgmt, 8 Elm St, Toronto ON M5G 1G7, Canada | Actress |
| **Carter, Alex**<br>Emmerdale Production Center, 27 Burley Lane, Leeds LS3 1JT, England | Actor |
| **Carter, Anson**<br>820 Haven Oaks Court NE, Atlanta GA 30342, USA | Ice Hockey Player |
| **Carter, Anthony**<br>4314 Danielson Dr, Lake Worth FL 33467, USA | Football Player |
| **Carter, Anthony B**<br>15250 E Caley Ave, Centennial CO 80016, USA | Basketball Player |
| **Carter, Antonio M (Tony)**<br>7839 Maple Grove Dr, Lewis Center OH 43035, USA | Football Player |
| **Carter, Carlene**<br>Roots Agency, 177 Woodland Ave, Westwood NJ 07675, USA | Singer, Songwriter |
| **Carter, Cheryl**<br>C E S D, 10635 Santa Monica Blvd, #130, Los Angeles CA 90025 USA | Actress |
| **Carter, Christopher C (Chris)**<br>Broder Webb Chervin Silbermann, 9242 Beverly Blvd, Beverly Hills CA 90210 USA | Producer, Writer |
| **Carter, Christopher G (Chris)**<br>1500 Mill Creek Dr, De Soto TX 75115, USA | Football Player |
| **Carter, Clarence**<br>Rodgers Redding, PO Box 4603, Macon GA 31208 USA | Singer |
| **Carter, Clarence E (Butch)**<br>900 Legacy Park Dr, Lawrenceville GA 30043, USA | Basketball Player, Coach |
| **Carter, Cristopher D (Cris)**<br>2943 NW 46th St, Boca Raton FL 33431, USA | Football Player, Sportscaster |
| **Carter, Cy**<br>Archetype, 1608 Argyle Ave, Los Angeles CA 90028, USA | Actor |
| **Carter, Dale L**<br>10416 Magnolia Heights Circle, Covington GA 30014, USA | Football Player |
| **Carter, Darren**<br>A K A Talent, 6310 San Vicente Blvd, #200, Los Angeles CA 90048 USA | Actor, Comedian |
| **Carter, David**<br>2401 Long Reach Dr, Sugar Land TX 77478, USA | Football Player |
| **Carter, Deana**<br>Peters Mgmt, PO Box 1710, Topanga CA 90290, USA | Singer, Songwriter |
| **Carter, Dexter A**<br>7130 Nesters Dr, Tallahassee FL 32312, USA | Football Player |
| **Carter, Dixie**<br>T N A Wrestling, 209 10th Ave S, #302, Nashville TN 37203, USA | Professional Wrestler |
| **Carter, Duane (Pancho), Jr**<br>32 Forest Dr, Brownsburg IN 46112, USA | Auto Racing Driver |
| **Carter, E Graydon**<br>Vanity Fair, Editorial Dept, 4 Times Square, Basement C1B, New York NY 10036, USA | Editor |
| **Carter, Elan**<br>Playboy Promotions, 2706 Media Center Dr, Los Angeles CA 90065 USA | Model, Actress |
| **Carter, Finn**<br>Front Line Entertainment, 867 S Muirfield Road, Los Angeles CA 90005, USA | Actress |
| **Carter, Frederick J (Fred)**<br>2979 W School House Lane, #703K, Philadelphia PA 19144, USA | Basketball Player, Coach |
| **Carter, Gerald L**<br>3917 Cheshire Court, Bryan TX 77802, USA | Football Player |
| **Carter, Howard O**<br>7572 Hanks Dr, Baton Rouge LA 70812, USA | Basketball Player |
| **Carter, Jack**<br>1023 Chevy Chase Dr, Beverly Hills CA 90210, USA | Actor, Comedian |
| **Carter, James (Larry)**<br>American International Artists, 356 Pine Valley Road, Hoosick Falls NY 12090, USA | Jazz Saxophonist, Composer |
| **Carter, James E (Jimmy), Jr**<br>Carter Center, 453 Freedom Parkway NE, Atlanta GA 30307, USA | President, USA; Nobel Peace Laureate |
| **Carter, Jay**<br>PO Box 5357, Spring Hill FL 34611, USA | Singer (Crests) |
| **Carter, Jeffrey A (Jeff)**<br>4625 River Overlook Dr, Valrico FL 33596, USA | Baseball Player |
| **Carter, Jim**<br>12575 N 130th Way, Scottsdale AZ 85259, USA | Golfer |
| **Carter, Jim**<br>Caroline Dawson, 125 Gloucester Road, London SW7 4TE, England | Actor |
| **Carter, Joelle**<br>Innovative Artists, 1505 10th St, Santa Monica CA 90401 USA | Actress |
| **Carter, John**<br>27 Country Lane, Sharon MA 02067, USA | Ice Hockey Player |
| **Carter, John**<br>Harden-Curtis Associates, 850 7th Ave, #903, New York NY 10019 | Actor |
| **Carter, John D (Jake)**<br>5102 80th St, #132, Lubbock TX 79424, USA | Basketball Player |
| **Carter, Joseph C (Joe)**<br>3000 W 117th St, Leawood KS 66211, USA | Baseball Player |
| **Carter, Kevin L**<br>17111 Journeys End Dr, Odessa FL 33556, USA | Football Player |
| **Carter, Ki-Jana**<br>1236 NW 121st Ave, Plantation Fl 33323, USA | Football Player |
| **Carter, Lance D**<br>306 74th Street Court NW, Bradenton FL 34209, USA | Baseball Player |

**Carson - Carter**

Carter, Lynda — Actress, Singer
Potomac Productions, PO Box 59110, Potomac MD 20859, USA
Carter, Mel — Actor, Singer
Cape Entertainment, 4799 Coconut Creek Parkway, #258, Coconut Creek FL 33063, USA
Carter, Michael D — Football Player, Track Athlete
901 Red Oak Creek Dr, Red Oak TX 75154, USA
Carter, Nicholas G (Nick) — Singer (Backstreet Boys), Songwriter
E M C Bowery, 8145 Santa Monica Blvd, #200, West Hollywood CA 90046, USA
Carter, Powell F, Jr — Navy Admiral
699 Fillmore St, Harpers Ferry WV 25425, USA
Carter, Regina — Jazz, Concert Violinist
Depth of Field Mgmt, 1501 Broadway, #1304, New York NY 10036, USA
Carter, Ronald L (Ron) — Jazz Bassist, Composer
Bridge Agency, 35 Clark St, #A5, Brooklyn NY 11201, USA
Carter, Rosalynn S — Wife of US President
Carter Center, 453 Freedom Parkway NE, Atlanta GA 30307, USA
Carter, Rubin — Football Player, Coach
1793 Vineyard Way, Tallahassee FL 32317, USA
Carter, Rubin (Hurricane) — Boxer
498 20th Ave, Paterson NJ 07513, USA
Carter, Sarah — Actress
A P A Talent/Literary Agency, 405 S Beverly Dr, #300, Beverly Hills CA 90212 USA
Carter, Shawn C (Jay-Z) — Rap Artist, Songwriter, Record Producer
Roc Nation, 1411 Broadway, #3800, New York NY 10018, USA
Carter, Stephen L — Attorney, Educator, Writer
Yale University, Law School, 127 Wall St, New Haven CT 06511, USA
Carter, Terry — Actor, Producer
244 Madison Ave, #332, New York NY 10016, USA
Carter, Thomas — Director
Kazarian/Measures/Ruskin, 11969 Ventura Blvd, #300, Studio City CA 91604 USA
Carter, Thomas (Tom), III — Football Player
4548 Bristol Lane, Cincinnati OH 45229, USA
Carter, Tom — Golfer
3787 County Lane Road, Quakertown PA 18951, USA
Carter, Ty — Afghanistan War Army Hero (CMH)
US Army 7th Infantry Division, Joint Base Lewis-McChord WA 98433, USA
Carter, Vincent L (Vince) — Basketball Player
1978 Country Club Dr, Port Orange FL 32128, USA
Carter, Virgil R (Virg) — Football Player
2010 Whitebluff Dr, San Dimas CA 91773, USA
Carter, W Hodding, III — Government Official
214 N Columbus St, Alexandria VA 22314, USA
Carter, W Patrick (Pat) — Football Player
11321 Cambray Creek Loop, Riverview FL 33579, USA
Carteri, Rosana — Opera Singer
Angel Records, 150 5th Ave, New York NY 10011 USA
Carteris, Gabrielle — Actress
4019 Longridge Ave, Sherman Oaks CA 91423, USA
Carter-Williams, Michael — Basketball Player
Philadelphia 76ers, 1st Union Center, 3601 S Broad St, Philadelphia PA 19148 USA
Carthon, Maurice — Football Player
2040 E Indigo Dr, Chandler AZ 85286, USA
Carthy, Eliza — Singer, Fiddler, Songwriter
Glass Ceiling, 50 Stroud Green Road, London N4 3ES, England
Carthy, Martin — Singer, Guitarist, Songwriter
Moneypenny Agency, Westwood House, North Dalton, Driffield East Yorkshire YO25 9XA, England
Carthy-Deu, Deborah F — Beauty Queen, Actress
Deborah Carthy-Deu Studio, 353 F Calder St, Urb Roosevelt, San Juan, PR 00918, USA
Cartwright, Angela — Actress
Rubber Boots, 11333 Moorpark St, #433, North Hollywood CA 91602, USA
Cartwright, Catherine — Golfer
4505 SE County Road 760, Arcadia FL 34266, USA
Cartwright, J William (Bill) — Basketball Player, Coach
1839 Wedgewood Court, Lake Forest IL 60045, USA
Cartwright, Justin — Writer
P F D, Drury House, 34-43 Russell St, London WC2B 5HA, England
Cartwright, Nancy — Actress
Innovative Artists, 1505 10th St, Santa Monica CA 90401 USA
Cartwright, Nancy D — Philosopher
London School of Economics, Houghton St, London WC2A 2AE, England
Cartwright, Roderick R (Rock) — Football Player
231 Interstate 45 N, #21115, Conroe TX 77304, USA
Cartwright, Veronica — Actress
Mitch Clem Mgmt, 2600 W Olive Ave #500, Burbank CA 91505, USA
Carty, Donald J — Businessman
Dell Inc, 1 Dell Way, Round Rock TX 78682, USA
Carty, Jay J — Basketball Player
5425 Lower Honopaiilani Road, Lahaina HI 96761, USA
Carty, Ricardo A J (Rico) — Baseball Player
5 Ens Enriquillo, San Pedro de Macoris, Dominican Republic
Carty, Todd — Actor
Associated International Mgmt, 7 Hatton Garden, #400, London EC1N 8AD, England
Caruana, Patrick P (Pat) — Air Force General
1922 Havemeyer Lane, Redondo Beach CA 90278, USA
Caruana, Peter R — Chief Minister, Gibraltar
Chief Minister's Office, 10/3 Irish Town, Gibraltar
Caruncho, Fernando — Landscape Architect
Paseo del Narcea 17, San Sebastian de los Reyes, 28707 Madrid, Spain
Caruso, D J — Director
Creative Artists Agency, 2000 Ave of Stars, #100, Los Angeles CA 90067 USA
Caruso, David — Actor
Untitled Entertainment, 350 S Beverly Dr, #200, Beverly Hills CA 90212 USA
Carver, Brent — Actor, Singer
Live Entertainment, 1500 Broadway, #902, New York NY 10036, USA
Carver, Johnny — Singer
Ace Productions, PO Box 428, Portland TN 37148, USA

# C

**Carver, Melvin (Mel)** — Football Player
10840 Breaking Rocks Dr, Tampa FL 33647, USA
**Carver, Randall** — Actor
Kazarian/Measures/Ruskin, 11969 Ventura Blvd, #300, Studio City CA 91604 USA
**Carveth-Dunn, Betty** — Baseball Player
11531 77th Ave, Edmonton AB T6G 0M2, Canada
**Carvey, Dana** — Actor, Comedian
B/W/R, 9100 Wilshire Blvd, #500W, Beverly Hills CA 90212 USA
**Carville, C James, Jr** — Political Consultant
424 S Washington St, Alexandria VA 22314, USA
**Cary, Caitlin** — Singer, Fiddler
Conqueroo, 11271 Ventura Blvd, #522, Studio City CA 91604 USA
**Cary, Charles D (Chuck)** — Baseball Player
1016 Stephen Dr, Niceville FL 32578, USA
**Cary, W Sterling** — Religious Leader
2344 Vardon Lane, Flossmoor IL 60422, USA
**Cary-Williams, Robert** — Fashion Designer
1A Wellington Row, London E2 7BB, England
**Casablancas, Julian** — Singer (Strokes), Songwriter
Creative Trust, 5141 Virginia Way, #320, Brentwood TN 37027, USA
**Casadesus, Jean-Claude** — Conductor
23 Blvd de la Liberte, 59800 Lille, France
**Casady, Jack** — Bassist (Jefferson Airplane, Hot Tuna)
Mission Control, 15030 Ventura Blvd, #541, Sherman Oaks CA 91403, USA
**Casale, Jerry J** — Baseball Player
600 County Ave, #408, Secaucus NJ 07094, USA
**Casali, Kim** — Cartoonist (Love Is)
Times-Mirror Syndicate, Times-Mirror Square, Los Angeles CA 90053 USA
**Casals, Rosemary (Rosie)** — Tennis Player
Women's Tennis Assn, 1 Progress Plaza, #1500, Saint Petersburg FL 33701 USA
**Casamayor Johnson, Joel** — Boxer
Luis de Cubas, 19220 E Saint Andrews, Miami FL 33015, USA
**Casanova, Raul** — Baseball Player
1441 Ortiz Ave, Fort Myers FL 33905, USA
**Casanova, Thomas H (Tommy)** — Football Player
345 Casanova Road, Crowley LA 70526, USA
**Casar, Amira** — Actress
Conway Van Gelder Grant, 8-12 Broadwick St, #300, London W1F 8HW, England
**Casbarian, John** — Architect
Taft Architects, 2370 Rice Blvd, #112, Houston TX 77005, USA
**Cascadden, Chad** — Football Player
2611 Windsor Dr, Eau Claire WI 54703, USA
**Casdin-Silver, Hariet** — Artist
99 Pond Ave, #D403, Brookline MA 02445, USA
**Case** — Singer
Celebrity Talent Agency, 111 E 14th St, #249, New York NY 10003 USA
**Case, Christopher** — Producer, Writer
Evolution Entertainment, 901 N Highland Ave, Los Angeles CA 90038 USA
**Case, J Scott** — Football Player
4930 Price Dr, Suwanee GA 30024, USA
**Case, John** — Writer
Random House, 1745 Broadway, #1800, New York NY 10019 USA
**Case, Neko** — Singer (New Pornographers), Songwriter
Beekeeper Corp, 1005 Reagan Terrace, Austin TX 78704, USA
**Case, Peter** — Singer, Guitarist
Eastern Star Productions, 2625 Alcatraz Ave, #302, Berkeley CA 94705, USA
**Case, Sharon** — Actress
Innovative Artists, 1505 10th St, Santa Monica CA 90401 USA
**Case, Stephen M (Steve)** — Businessman
8619 Westwood Center Dr, Vienna VA 22182, USA
**Case, Walter H, Jr** — Harness Racing Driver
8795 Crow Dr, Macedonia OH 44056, USA
**Casell, John W** — Actor
3746 Willowcrest Ave, Studio City CA 91604, USA
**Casey, Bernie** — Football Player, Actor
6145 Flight Ave, Los Angeles CA 90056, USA
**Casey, Brandon** — Singer (Jagged Edge)
Entertainment Artists, 2409 21st Ave S, #100, Nashville TN 10019 USA
**Casey, Brian** — Singer (Jagged Edge)
Entertainment Artists, 2409 21st Ave S, #100, Nashville TN 10019 USA
**Casey, Conor** — Soccer Player
Colorado Rapids, 1000 Chopper Circle, Denver CO 80204 USA
**Casey, Daniel** — Actor
Curtis Brown Group, 28-29 Haymarket St, #500, London SW1Y 4SP, England
**Casey, Dillon** — Actor
A P A Talent/Literary Agency, 405 S Beverly Dr, #300, Beverly Hills CA 90212 USA
**Casey, Dwane** — Basketball Player, Coach
Toronto Raptors, Air Canada Center, 20 Bay St, Toronto ON M5J 2N8, Canada
**Casey, Harry W (K C)** — Singer (K C & the Sunshine Band)
7530 Loch Ness Dr, Hialeah FL 33014, USA
**Casey, John D** — Writer
University of Virginia, English Dept, Bryan Hall, Charlottesville VA 22903, USA
**Casey, Jon** — Ice Hockey Player
651 Bluffs View Court, Eureka MO 63025, USA
**Casey, Patrick (Paddy)** — Singer, Songwriter
Principal Mgmt, 30-32 John Robertson's Quay, Dublin 2, Ireland
**Casey, Paul A** — Golfer
Paul Casey Foundation, 72 Salcott Road, London SW11 6DF, England
**Casey, Peter** — Director
Creative Artists Agency, 2000 Ave of Stars, #100, Los Angeles CA 90067 USA
**Casey, Sean T** — Baseball Player
271 Trotwood Dr, Pittsburgh PA 15241, USA
**Cash, Aya** — Actress
Paradigm Agency, 360 N Crescent Dr, North Building, Beverly Hills CA 90210 USA
**Cash, David (Dave), Jr** — Baseball Player
16308 Birkdale Dr, Odessa FL 33556, USA

**Cash, Kerry L** — Football Player
9839 Heritage Farm Road, San Antonio TX 78245, USA
**Cash, Pat** — Tennis Player
Patrick Cash Assoc, PO Box 2238, Footscray 3011, Australia
**Cash, Richard F (Rick)** — Football Player
203 E Benton St, Savannah MO 64485, USA
**Cash, Rosanne** — Singer, Songwriter
Cross Road Mgmt, 45 W 11th St, #7B, New York NY 10011, USA
**Cash, Swintayla M (Swin)** — Basketball Player
Chicago Sky, 20 W Kinzie St, #1010, Chicago IL 60654 USA
**Cashell, Sophie** — Concert Pianist
I M G Artists, Hogarth Business Park, Chiswick, London W4 2TH, England
**Cashin, Patrick (Pat)** — Clown
Kelly-Miller Circus, 2581 E 2070 Road, Hugo OK 74743, USA
**Cashman, John** — Test Pilot
Boeing Commerical Airplane Group, PO Box 3707, Seattle WA 98124, USA
**Cashman, Terry** — Singer (Buchanan Brothers)
Metrostar Records, PO Box 5807, Englewood NJ 07631, USA
**Cashman, Wayne J** — Ice Hockey Player
5150 NW 80th Avenue Road, Ocala FL 34482, USA
**Casian, Lawrence P (Larry)** — Baseball Player
1939 Popcorn St NW, Salem OR 97304, USA
**Casida, John E** — Entomologist
1570 La Vereda Road, Berkeley CA 94708, USA
**Casile, Genevieve** — Actress
Agents Associes, 201 Rue du Faubourg Saint Honore, 75008 Paris, France
**Casillas, Tony S** — Football Player
6201 Bay Valley Court, Flower Mound TX 75022, USA
**Caslavska, Vera** — Gymnast
Czech Olympic Committee, Benesovska 6, 101 00 Prague 10, Czech Republic
**Casnoff, Philip** — Actor
Don Buchwald, 6500 Wilshire Blvd, #2200, Los Angeles CA 90048 USA
**Cason, James A (Jim)** — Football Player
1802 E Washington Ave, Harlingen TX 78550, USA
**Cason, Rod** — Football Player
50623 Dossow St, Kenai AK 99611, USA
**Casorati, Francesco** — Artist
C So Kossuth 19, Turin, Italy
**Caspar, Donald L D** — Biophysicist
911 Gardenia Dr, Tallahassee FL 32312, USA
**Caspe, David** — Producer, Writer
W M E Entertainment, 9601 Wilshire Blvd, #300, Beverly Hills CA 90210 USA
**Casper, David J (Dave)** — Football Player
1525 Alamo Way, Alamo CA 94507, USA
**Casper, John H** — Astronaut
4414 Village Corner Dr, Houston TX 77059, USA
**Casper, William E (Billy)** — Golfer
2561 Stonebury Loop Road, Springville UT 84663, USA
**Cass, Christopher** — Actor
Halpern Assoc, PO Box 5597, Santa Monica CA 90409 USA
**Cassady, Howard (Hopalong)** — Football Player
Tails Sports Mgmt, PO Box 7828, Columbus OH 43207, USA
**Cassavetes, Nick** — Actor, Director
Resolution, 1801 Century Park East, #2300, Los Angeles CA 90067 USA
**Cassel, Matthew B (Matt)** — Football Player
150 Street of Dreams, Village Loch Loyd MO 64012, USA
**Cassel, Seymour** — Actor
Abrams Artists, 9200 W Sunset Blvd, #1125, West Hollywood CA 90069 USA
**Cassel, Vincent** — Actor
Agence Artiste Adequet, 108 Rue Reaumur, 75002 Paris, France
**Cassell, Samuel J (Sam)** — Basketball Player
5205 N Charles St, Baltimore MD 21210, USA
**Casserino, Frank J** — Astronaut, Air Force General
Office of Under Secretary of Air Force, HqUSAF, Pentagon, Washington DC 20330, USA
**Casserly, Charley** — Football Executive, Sportscaster
N F L Network, 10950 Washington Blvd, #100, Culver City CA 90232 USA
**Casseus, Gabriel** — Actor
Don Buchwald, 6500 Wilshire Blvd, #2200, Los Angeles CA 90048 USA
**Cassidy, Candice** — Model
Playboy Promotions, 2706 Media Center Dr, Los Angeles CA 90065 USA
**Cassidy, Christopher J (Chris)** — Astronaut
N A S A, Johnson Space Center, 2101 NASA Road, Houston TX 77058 USA
**Cassidy, David** — Actor, Singer
J A G Entertainment, 4265 Hazeltine Ave, Sherman Oaks CA 91423, USA
**Cassidy, Edward I Cardinal** — Religious Leader
Council for Christian Unity, Piazza del S Uffizio 11, 00193 Rome, Italy
**Cassidy, Joanna** — Actress
Stone Manners Salners, 9911 W Pico Blvd, #1400, Los Angeles CA 90035 USA
**Cassidy, Katherine E (Katie)** — Actress, Model, Singer
Anonymous Content, 3532 Hayden Ave, Culver City CA 90232 USA
**Cassidy, Patrick** — Actor
979 E 42nd St, Brooklyn NY 11210, USA
**Cassidy, Ronald G (Ron)** — Football Player
2214 W 171st St, Torrance CA 90504, USA
**Cassidy, Shaun** — Actor, Singer
Shaun Cassidy Productions, 8530 Wilshire Blvd, #200, Beverly Hills CA 90211, USA
**Cassie** — Rap Artist, Model, Singer
42 West, 220 W 42nd St, #1200, New York NY 10036 USA
**Cassignard, Pierre** — Actor
Artmedia, 20 Ave Rapp, 75007 Paris, France
**Cassolato, Tony** — Ice Hockey Player
576 Camino El Dorado, Encinitas CA 92024, USA
**Casspi, Omri** — Basketball Player
Cleveland Cavaliers, Gund Arena, 1 Center Court, Cleveland OH 44115 USA
**Cast, Edward** — Actor
4 Bankside Dr, Thames Ditton, Surrey KT7 0AQ, England

**C**

| | |
|---|---|
| **Cast, Tricia** <br> 20 Georgette Road, Rolling Hills Estates CA 90274, USA | Actress |
| **Casta, Laetitia** <br> D Management Group, 13 Via Forcella, 20144 Milan, Italy | Model, Actress |
| **Castaneda, Cameron** <br> Lewis & Beal Talent Agency, 15303 Ventura Blvd, #900, Sherman Oaks CA 91403, USA | Actor |
| **Castaneda, Jorge A** <br> Anillo Periferico Sur 3180, #1120, Jardines del Pedregal, 01900 Mexico | Government Official, Mexico |
| **Castellaneta, Dan** <br> Foster Entertainment, 12533 Woodgreen St, Building B, Los Angeles CA 90066, USA | Actor |
| **Castellaw, John G** <br> Deputy Commandant, Aviation, HqUSMC, 2 Navy St, Washington DC 20380 USA | Marine Corps General |
| **Castelluccio, Federico** <br> Barry Haft Brown Artists Agency, 165 W 46th St, #908, New York NY 10036, USA | Actor |
| **Caster, Richard C (Rich)** <br> 41 Lincoln Court, Rockville Centre NY 11570, USA | Football Player |
| **Castiglioni, Consuelo** <br> Marni International, Palazzo Torre Delta, La Sguancia 23, 6902 Lugano, Switzerland | Fashion Designer |
| **Castilla Soria, Vinicio S (Vinny)** <br> 7680 Polo Ridge Dr, Littleton CO 80128, USA | Baseball Player |
| **Castille, Jeremiah** <br> 2904 Kirkcaldy Lane, Birmingham AL 35242, USA | Football Player |
| **Castillo, Alberto T** <br> 400 SW Lakota Ave, Port Saint Lucie FL 34953, USA | Baseball Player |
| **Castillo, Jose Luis** <br> Top Rank Inc, 3908 Howard Hughes Parkway, #580, Las Vegas NV 89169 USA | Boxer |
| **Castillo, Luis A** <br> 14165 Augusta Court, Poway CA 92064, USA | Football Player |
| **Castillo, Luis A D** <br> 14149 N Forest Oak Circle, Davie FL 33325, USA | Baseball Player |
| **Castillo, M Carmelo (Carmen)** <br> 344 Prospect Ave, #6A, Hackensack NJ 07601, USA | Baseball Player |
| **Castle, John** <br> Larry Dalzell, 91 Regent St, London W1R 7TA, England | Actor |
| **Castle, Michael N** <br> Castle Campaign Fund, PO Box 133, Wilmington DE 19899, USA | Governor, Representative, DE |
| **Castle, Nick C, Jr** <br> Jackoway Tyerman Wertheimer, 1925 Century Park E, #2200, Los Angeles CA 90067 USA | Director |
| **Castle-Hughes, Keisha** <br> Gail Cowan Mgmt, 21 Village Fields Road, Waiau Pa, RD4, Pukekohe 2679, New Zealand | Actress |
| **Castleman, Foster E** <br> 8250 Graves Road, Cincinnati OH 45243, USA | Baseball Player |
| **Castrale, Nicole** <br> Ladies Pro Golf Assn, 100 International Golf Dr, Daytona Beach FL 32124 USA | Golfer |
| **Castrillon Hoyos, Dario Cardinal** <br> Arzobispado, Calle 33, N 21-18, Bucaramanga, Santander, Colombia | Religious Leader |
| **Castro Ruz, Fidel A** <br> Palacio de Gobierno, Cibsejo de la Revolucion, Havana, Cuba | President, Cuba |
| **Castro Ruz, Raul** <br> Palacio de Gobierno, Cibsejo de la Revolucion, Havana, Cuba | President, Prime Minister, Cuba |
| **Castro, Cristian** <br> Generamusica Mgmt, C Arcniegae 29A, Col Mixcoac, Naucalpan 03910, Mexico | Singer |
| **Castro, Joseph I** <br> California State University, President's Office, 5241 N Maple Ave, Fresno CA 93740, USA | Educator |
| **Castro, Juan C** <br> 7324 W Artie Ave, Peoria AZ 85383, USA | Baseball Player |
| **Castro, Ramon A** <br> 1230 Windway Circle, Kissimmee FL 34744, USA | Baseball Player |
| **Castro, Raquel** <br> Abrams Artists, 275 7th Ave, #2600, New York NY 10001 USA | Actress |
| **Castro, Raul H** <br> 429 W Crawford St, Nogales AZ 85621, USA | Governor, AZ; Diplomat |
| **Castro, Ruy** <br> Bloomsbury Publishing, 50 Bedford Square, London WC1B 3DP, England | Writer |
| **Castro, Tommy** <br> Rosebud Agency, PO Box 170429, San Francisco CA 94117 USA | Singer, Guitarist, Band Leader |
| **Castroneves, Helio** <br> 386 Isla Dorada Blvd, Coral Gables FL 33143, USA | Auto Racing Driver |
| **Caswell, Ben** <br> Progressive Artists Agency, 1041 N Formosa Ave, West Hollywood CA 90046, USA | Actor |
| **Caswell, Dean** <br> 2309 Village Way Dr, Austin TX 78745, USA | WW II Marine Corps Air Force Hero |
| **Cat Power** <br> Management Production Entertainment, 9229 Sunset Blvd, #301, West Hollywood CA 90069, USA | Singer, Songwriter, Actress |
| **Catalanotto, Frank J** <br> 4 Muffins Meadows, Saint James NY 11780, USA | Baseball Player |
| **Catalifo, Patrick** <br> Artmedia, 20 Ave Rapp, 75007 Paris, France | Actor |
| **Catalino, Ken** <br> Creators Syndicate, 737 3rd St, Hermosa Beach CA 90254 USA | Editorial Cartoonist |
| **Catano, Mark** <br> 9036 Walton St, Indianapolis IN 46231, USA | Football Player |
| **Catanzaro, Tony** <br> 8915 SW 207th St, Cutler Bay FL 33189, USA | Dancer |
| **Catchings, Harvey L** <br> 17406 Edenwalk, Spring TX 77379, USA | Basketball Player |
| **Catchings, Tamika D** <br> 3429 Windham Lake Place, Indianapolis IN 46214, USA | Basketball Player |
| **Cate, Earl** <br> 1606 Cartwright Circle, Springdale AR 72762, USA | Singer, Songwriter (Cate Brothers) |
| **Cate, Ernie** <br> 17464 Highway 90 W, Ravenden Springs AR 72460, USA | Singer, Pianist (Cate Brothers) |
| **Cate, Field** <br> J L A Talent Agency, 9151 Sunset Blvd, West Hollywood CA 90069, USA | Actor |
| **Cater, Danny A** <br> 3268 Candlewood Trail, Plano TX 75023, USA | Baseball Player |

**Cast - Cater**

| | |
|---|---|
| **Cater, Gregory W (Greg)** <br> 19 Warwick Way SE, Rome GA 30161, USA | Football Player |
| **Cates, Phoebe** <br> Hofflund/Polone, 9465 Wilshire Blvd, #420, Beverly Hills CA 90212 USA | Actress |
| **Cathcart, Patti** <br> T & P Productions, PO Box 1363, Menlo Park CA 94026, USA | Singer (Tuck & Patti) |
| **Catherine** <br> Artery Foundation, 1412 S St, Sacramento CA 95811, USA | Singer |
| **Catillon, Brigitte** <br> Artmedia, 20 Ave Rapp, 75007 Paris, France | Actress |
| **Catlett, Mary Jo** <br> Robert Yacko, 4375 Farmdale Ave, Studio City CA 91604, USA | Actress |
| **Catlett, Sidney L (Sid)** <br> 3110 Scottish Ave, Suitland MD 20746, USA | Basketball Player |
| **Catley, Glenn** <br> Bristol Gym, Trinity Road, Saint Phillips, Bristol BS2 0NW, England | Boxer |
| **Cato, Kelvin T** <br> 13607 Winter Creek Court, Houston TX 77077, USA | Basketball Player |
| **Caton-Jones, Michael** <br> Gersh Agency, 9465 Wilshire Blvd, #600, Beverly Hills CA 90212 USA | Director |
| **Catrow, David** <br> Springfield News-Sun, Editorial Dept, 202 N Limestone St, Springfield OH 45503, USA | Editorial Cartoonist |
| **Cattage, Robert L (Bobby)** <br> 4838 US Highway 29 S, Auburn AL 36830, USA | Basketball Player |
| **Cattaneo, Peter** <br> Independent Talent Group, 40 Whitfield St, London W1T 2RH, England | Director |
| **Cattelan, Maurizio** <br> Galleria Massimo De Carlo, Via Privata Giovanni Ventura, 5, 20134 Milan, Italy | Artist |
| **Cattell, Christine** <br> Epstein-Wyckoff, 280 S Beverly Dr, #400, Beverly Hills CA 90212 USA | Actress |
| **Cattrall, Kim** <br> I C M Partners, 10250 Constellation Blvd, #900, Los Angeles CA 90067 USA | Actress, Model |
| **Catz, Caroline** <br> Independent Talent Group, 40 Whitfield St, London W1T 2RH, England | Actress |
| **Caudill, William H (Bill)** <br> 11605 NE 41st St, Kirkland WA 98033, USA | Baseball Player |
| **Cauffiel, Jessica** <br> Greene Assoc, 1901 Ave of Stars, #130, Los Angeles CA 90067 USA | Actress |
| **Caufield, Jay** <br> 106 Quail Hollow Lane, Wexford PA 15090, USA | Ice Hockey Player |
| **Caughthran, Matt** <br> Crush Music Mgmt, 60-62 E 11th St, #700, New York NY 10003, USA | Singer (Bronx) |
| **Caulfield, Emma** <br> Crazy 8 Entertainment, 8581 Santa Monica Blvd, West Hollywood CA 90069, USA | Actress |
| **Causey, J Wayne** <br> 2905 Paynter Dr, Ruston LA 71270, USA | Baseball Player |
| **Causwell, Duane** <br> 3 Pierce Dr, Stony Point NY 10980, USA | Basketball Player |
| **Caute, J David** <br> 41 Westcroft Square, London W6 0TA, England | Writer |
| **Cauthen, Stephen M (Steve)** <br> 15541 Porter Road, Verona KY 41092, USA | Thoroughbred Racing Jockey |
| **Cauthen, Terrance** <br> 953 Beatty St, Trenton NJ 08611, USA | Boxer |
| **Cauty, James F (Jimmy)** <br> Nene Musik Productions, 1460 SW Santiago Ave, Port Saint Lucie FL 34953 USA | Musician (KLF) |
| **Cavaiani, Jon R** <br> 10956 Green St, #230, Columbia CA 95310, USA | Vietnam War Army Hero (CMH) |
| **Cavalera, Max** <br> Oasis Mgmt, 3010 E Bloomfield Road, Phoenix AZ 85032, USA | Singer, Guitrist |
| **Cavaliere, Felix** <br> Brothers Management Assoc, 141 Dunbar Ave, Fords NJ 08863 USA | Singer, Keyboardist, Composer (Rascals) |
| **Cavaliero, Rosie** <br> Another Tongue, 10-11 D'Arblay St, London W1F 8DS, England | Actress |
| **Cavallari, Kristin** <br> W M E Entertainment, 9601 Wilshire Blvd, #300, Beverly Hills CA 90210 USA | Actress |
| **Cavalli, Roberto** <br> Via Senato 8, 20121 Milan, Italy | Fashion Designer |
| **Cavallini, Gino** <br> 6614 Clayton Road, #315, Saint Louis MO 63117, USA | Ice Hockey Player |
| **Cavallini, Paul** <br> 7201 Kingsbury Blvd, Saint Louis MO 63130, USA | Ice Hockey Player |
| **Cavalli-Sforza, Luigi L** <br> Stanford University, Human Population Genetics Laboratory, Stanford CA 94305, USA | Geneticist |
| **Cavallo, Domingo F** <br> Hipolito Yrigoyen 250, 1310 Buenos Aires, Argentina | Government Official, Argentina |
| **Cavanagh, Thomas (Tom)** <br> Circle of Confusion, 315 S Beverly Dr, #201, Beverly Hills CA 90212, USA | Actor |
| **Cavanaugh, Kasie** <br> PO Box 21882, El Cajon CA 92021, USA | Body Builder |
| **Cavanaugh, Matthew A (Matt)** <br> 8 Barstad Court, Lutherville Timon MD 21093, USA | Football Player |
| **Cavaney, Red** <br> ConocoPhillips, 600 N Dairy Ashford Road, Houston TX 77079, USA | Association Executive |
| **Cavazos, Lauro F** <br> 173 Annursnac Hill Road, Concord MA 01742, USA | Secretary, Education |
| **Cavazos, Lumi** <br> Talent on Road Mgmt, Av Revolucion 1716 Y\O Sagredo #155, Mexico City DF 03900, Mexico | Actress |
| **Cavazos, Richard E** <br> Texas Tech University, Board of Regents, Lubbock TX 79409, USA | Army General |
| **Cave, Nick** <br> Creative Artists Agency, 2000 Ave of Stars, #100, Los Angeles CA 90067 USA | Singer, Songwriter |
| **Caveness, Ronald G (Ronnie)** <br> 684 N Cliffside Dr, Fayetteville AR 72701, USA | Football Player |
| **Caves, Richard E** <br> Harvard University, Economics Dept, Cambridge MA 02138, USA | Economist |

**Cavett, Richard A (Dick)** — Entertainer
1044 Northern Blvd, #304, Roslyn NY 11576, USA
**Cavezza, Carmen J** — Army General
Columbus State University, Leadership Development Center, Columbus GA 31907, USA
**Caviezel, James** — Actor
Tencer Assoc, 9777 Wilshire Blvd, #1005, Beverly Hills CA 90212, USA
**Cavill, Henry** — Actor
United Agents, 12-26 Lexington St, London W1F 0LE, England
**Cawley, Tucker** — Writer, Producer
Creative Artists Agency, 2000 Ave of Stars, #100, Los Angeles CA 90067 USA
**Cawley, Warren (Rex)** — Track Athlete
17331 Jacaranda Ave, Tustin CA 92780, USA
**Caws, Matthew** — Singer, Guitarist (Nada Surf)
M-Squared Mgmt, 201 W 72nd St, #12G, New York NY 10023, USA
**Cayne, James E (Jimmy)** — Financier
Bear Stearns Co, 383 Madison Ave, New York NY 10179, USA
**Cazalot, Clarence P, Jr** — Businessman
Marathon Oil, 5555 San Felipe Road, Basement B114, Houston TX 77056, USA
**Ce, Marco Cardinal** — Religious Leader
S Marco 318, 30124 Venice, Italy
**Ceballos, Cedric Z** — Basketball Player
2068 FM 1252 W, Kilgore TX 75662, USA
**Ceberano, Kate** — Singer, Songwriter
Ralph Carr Mgmt, Lennox House, 229 Lennox St, Richmond VIC 3121, Australia
**Ceccarelli, Arthur E (Art)** — Baseball Player
63 Hall Dr, Orange CT 06477, USA
**Ceccato, Aldo** — Conductor
Chaunt da Crusch, 7524 Zuoz, Switzerland
**Cecchi, Carlo** — Actor
Carol Levi Mgmt, Via Giuseppe Pisanelli 2, 00196 Rome, Italy
**Cech, Thomas R** — Nobel Chemistry Laureate
Howard Hughes Medical Institute, 4000 Tones Bridge Road, Chevy Chase MD 20815, USA
**Cechmanek, Roman** — Ice Hockey Player
Los Angeles Kings, Staples Center, 1111 S Figueroa St, Los Angeles CA 90015 USA
**Cechvala, Dean** — Actor
Geddes Agency, 8430 Santa Monica Blvd, #201, West Hollywood CA 90069 USA
**Cecil, Charles D (Chuck)** — Football Player
2008 Waterstone Dr, Franklin TN 37069, USA
**Cecil, Derek** — Actor
One Entertainment, 347 5th Ave, #1404, New York NY 10016 USA
**Cecil, Francesca** — Actress
Cinematic Mgmt, 249 1/2 E 13th St, New York NY 10003, USA
**Cedar, Joseph** — Director
Kneller Artists Agency, Hayarkon 169, #420, Tel Aviv 63453, Israel
**Cedarstrom, Gary L** — Baseball Umpire
1610 18th St SE, Minot ND 58701, USA
**Cedeno, Cesar E** — Baseball Player
2112 Marisol Loop, Kissimmee FL 34743, USA
**Cedeno, Matt** — Actor, Model
Luber Rocklin Entertainment, 8530 Wilshire Blvd, #555, Beverly Hills CA 90211 USA
**Cedeno, Roger L** — Baseball Player
9325 Byron Ave, Surfside FL 33154, USA
**Cederqvist, Jane** — Swimmer
National Museum of Antiquities, PO Box 5428, 114 84 Stockholm, Sweden
**Cedillo, Julio Cesar** — Actor
Judy Fox Mgmt, 1525 1/2 S Beverly Dr, Los Angeles CA 90035, USA
**Cedolins, Fiorenza** — Opera Singer
Columbia Artists Mgmt Inc, 1790 Broadway, #702, New York NY 10019 USA
**Cedric the Entertainer** — Actor, Comedian
Creative Artists Agency, 2000 Ave of Stars, #100, Los Angeles CA 90067 USA
**Cee-Lo** — Singer, Rap Artist, Songwriter
Primary Wave Music Publishing, 116 E 16th St, #900, New York NY 10003, USA
**Cefalo, James C (Jimmy)** — Football Player
6675 Roxbury Lane, Miami Beach FL 33141, USA
**Ceglarski, Leonard (Len)** — Ice Hockey Player, Coach
61 Lantern Lane, Duxbury MA 02332, USA
**Cejka, Alexander** — Golfer
9484 S Eastern Ave, Las Vegas NV 89123, USA
**Cejudo, Henry** — Freestyle Wrestler
USA Wrestling, 6155 Lehman Dr, Colorado Springs CO 80918, USA
**Celestin, Oliver, Jr** — Football Player
635 Hendee St, New Orleans LA 70114, USA
**Cellier, Caroline** — Actress
Artmedia, 20 Ave Rapp, 75007 Paris, France
**Celmins, Vija** — Artist
49 Crosby St, New York NY 10012, USA
**Celski, John R (J R)** — Short Track Speed Skater
Agency Sports Mgmt, 230 Park Ave S, #851, New York NY 10169, USA
**Cena, John** — Actor, Professional Wrestler
I C M Partners, 10250 Constellation Blvd, #900, Los Angeles CA 90067 USA
**Cenac, Wyatt** — Actor, Comedian, Writer
United Talent Agency, U T A Plaza, 9336 Civic Center Dr, Beverly Hills CA 90210 USA
**Cenker, Robert J** — Astronaut
G O R C A Inc, 155 Hickory Corner Road, East Windsor NJ 08520, USA
**Centers, Larry E** — Football Player
5023 Stagecoach Way, Grand Prairie TX 75052, USA
**Cenziper, Debbie** — Journalist
Miami Herald, Editorial Dept, 1 Herald Plaza, Miami FL 33132 USA
**Cepeda, Orlando M** — Baseball Player
2305 Palmer Court, Fairfield CA 94534, USA
**Cepero, Jaime** — Actor
Hartig-Hilepo Agency, 54 W 21st St, #610, New York NY 10010 USA
**Cepicky, Matthew W (Matt)** — Baseball Player
7 Upper Bluffs View Court, Eureka MO 63025, USA
**Cera, Michael** — Actor
Thruline Entertainment, 9250 Wilshire Blvd, #100, Beverly Hills CA 90212 USA

|  |  |
|---|---|
| **Cerami, Anthony**<br>Ram Island Dr, Shelter Island NY 11964, USA | Biochemist |
| **Ceresino, Ray**<br>13282 Ocean Vista Road, San Diego CA 92130, USA | Ice Hockey Player |
| **Cerezo Arevalo, M Vinicio**<br>Party of Christian Democracy, Avda Elena 20-66, Zone 3, Guatemala City, Guatemala | President, Guatemala |
| **Cerf, Vinton G**<br>3614 Camelot Dr, Annandale VA 22003, USA | Inventor (Internet) |
| **Cerha, Friedrich**<br>Kupelwiesergasse 14, 1010 Vienna, Austria | Composer, Conductor |
| **Cermeno, Antonio**<br>San Antonio de Los Altos Loma, U R B Residencial, Los Eucaliptos 1020, Venezuela | Boxer |
| **Cerne, Joseph (Joe)**<br>408 Prospect Ave, Minneapolis MN 55419, USA | Football Player |
| **Cerone, Laura**<br>Don Buchwald, 6500 Wilshire Blvd, #2200, Los Angeles CA 90048 USA | Actress |
| **Cerone, Richard A (Rick)**<br>34 Winding Way, West Paterson NJ 07424, USA | Baseball Player |
| **Cerra, Erica**<br>Industry Entertainment, 955 Carillo Dr, #300, Los Angeles CA 90048 USA | Actress |
| **Cerrudo, Ronald J (Ron)**<br>7 Fox Briar Court, Hilton Head Island SC 29926, USA | Golfer |
| **Cerruti, Nino**<br>Via A Saffi 25, 20121 Milan, Italy | Fashion Designer |
| **Cerry, Amanda**<br>Playboy Promotions, 2706 Media Center Dr, Los Angeles CA 90065 USA | Model |
| **Certo, Tish**<br>151 Buffalo Ave, #211, Niagara Falls NY 14303, USA | Golfer |
| **Cerv, Robert H (Bob)**<br>805 N 22nd St, #1A, Blair NE 68008, USA | Baseball Player |
| **Cervantes, Hector**<br>Proper Mgmt, PO Box 150867, Nashville TN 37215, USA | Guitarist (Casting Crowns) |
| **Cervenka, Exene**<br>A P A Talent/Literary Agency, 405 S Beverly Dr, #300, Beverly Hills CA 90212 USA | Singer (X) |
| **Cerveris, Michael**<br>Innovative Artists, 1505 10th St, Santa Monica CA 90401 USA | Actor, Singer |
| **Cervi, Valentina**<br>T N A, Via Parioli 41, 00197 Rome, Italy | Actress |
| **Cesaire, Jacques E**<br>13388 Greenstone Court, San Diego CA 92131, USA | Football Player |
| **Cesarani, Sal**<br>S J C Concepts, 40 E 80th St, New York NY 10075, USA | Fashion Designer |
| **Cesare, William J (Billy)**<br>1655 Hendry Isles Blvd, Clewiston FL 33440, USA | Football Player |
| **Cesario, Jeff**<br>A P A Talent/Literary Agency, 405 S Beverly Dr, #300, Beverly Hills CA 90212 USA | Actor, Comedian |
| **Cetera, Peter**<br>M P I Talent, 9255 Sunset Blvd, #407, West Hollywood CA 90069, USA | Singer, Bassist, Songwriter |
| **Cetlinski, Matthew (Matt)**<br>13121 SE 93rd Terrace Road, Summerfield FL 34491, USA | Swimmer |
| **CeU**<br>Six Degrees Records/A-Train Entertainment, PO Box 29242, Oakland CA 94604, USA | Singer, Songwriter |
| **Cey, Ronald C (Ron)**<br>22714 Creole Road, Woodland Hills CA 91364, USA | Baseball Player |
| **Ceylan, Nuri Bilge**<br>N B C Film, Baskurt Sok 19/4, Urgup Palas Apt, 34433 Cihangir, Istanbul, Turkey | Actor, Director |
| **Chabat, Alain**<br>Chez Wham, 18 Blvd Montmartre, 75009 Paris, France | Actor |
| **Chaber, Madelyn J**<br>101 California St, San Francisco CA 94111, USA | Attorney |
| **Chabert, Lacey**<br>Innovative Artists, 1505 10th St, Santa Monica CA 90401 USA | Actress |
| **Chabon, Michael**<br>United Talent Agency, U T A Plaza, 9336 Civic Center Dr, Beverly Hills CA 90210 USA | Writer |
| **Chabraja, Nicholas D**<br>General Dynamics, 2941 Fairview Park Dr, #100, Falls Church VA 22042, USA | Businessman |
| **Chacon, Alex Pineda**<br>Los Angeles Galaxy, Home Depot Center, 18400 Avalon Blvd, Carson CA 90746 USA | Soccer Player |
| **Chacon, Bobby**<br>3010 Wilshire Blvd, #491, Los Angeles CA 90010, USA | Boxer |
| **Chacon, Shawn A**<br>162 50th Avenue Place, Greeley CO 80634, USA | Baseball Player |
| **Chacurian, Efrain (Chico)**<br>96 Stratford Road, Stratford CT 06615, USA | Soccer Player |
| **Chad**<br>Icon Performing Arts, 1557 Westwood Blvd, #242, Los Angeles CA 90024, USA | Singer, Guitarist (Chad & Jeremy) |
| **Chadbon, Tom**<br>Caroline Dawson, 125 Gloucester Road, London SW7 4TE, England | Actor |
| **Chadha, Gurinder**<br>I C M Partners, 10250 Constellation Blvd, #900, Los Angeles CA 90067 USA | Director |
| **Chadli, Bendjedid**<br>Palace Emir Abedelkader, Algiers, Algeria | President, Algeria; Army Officer |
| **Chadwick, Ed**<br>12 Bowen Road, Fort Erie ON L2A 2Y4, Canada | Ice Hockey Player |
| **Chadwick, J Leslie (Les)**<br>Barry Collins, 21A Cliftown Road, Southend on Sea, Essex SS1 1AB, England | Bassist (Gerry & the Pacemakers) |
| **Chadwick, Jeffrey A (Jeff)**<br>23062 Village Dr, #A, Lake Forest CA 92630, USA | Football Player |
| **Chadwick, June**<br>Independent Artists, 9601 Wilshire Blvd, #750, Beverly Hills CA 90210, USA | Actress |
| **Chadwick, Justin**<br>Independent Talent Group, 40 Whitfield St, London W1T 2RH, England | Director, Actor |
| **Chadwick, Paul**<br>Dark Horse Publishing, 10956 SE Main St, Portland OR 97222 USA | Cartoonist (Concrete) |
| **Chae Ji Hoon**<br>Skating Union, 88 Bangyee-Dong, Songpaku, Seoul 138 749, South Korea | Speed Skater |

**Chafee, Lincoln D** — Senator, RI
Brown University, International Studies Institute, Providence RI 02912, USA
**Chafetz, Sidney** — Artist
Ohio State University, Art Dept, Columbus OH 43210, USA
**Chaffee, Don** — Director
7020 La Presa Dr, Los Angeles CA 90068, USA
**Chaffee, Susan (Suzy)** — Alpine Skier
55 Roadrunner Road, Sedona AZ 86336, USA
**Chagaev, Ruslan** — Boxer
Universum Box-Promotion, Am Stadtrand 27, 22047 Hamburg, Germany
**Chagoya, Enrique** — Artist
59 Arroyo Way, San Francisco CA 94127, USA
**Chaiken, Ilene** — Producer, Writer
W M E Entertainment, 9601 Wilshire Blvd, #300, Beverly Hills CA 90210 USA
**Chaikin, Carly** — Actress
Paradigm Agency, 360 N Crescent Dr, North Building, Beverly Hills CA 90210 USA
**Chailly, Riccardo** — Conductor
Royal Concertgebrew, Jacob Obrechtstraat 51, 1071 KJ Amsterdam 41, Holland
**Chakiris, George** — Actor, Singer, Dancer
7266 Clinton St, Los Angeles CA 90036, USA
**Chakvetadze, Anna D** — Tennis Player
Best, 303 E Main St, #200, Louisville KY 40202 USA
**Chalayan, Hussein** — Fashion Designer
71 Endell Road, London WC2 9AJ, England
**Chalenski, Michael (Mike)** — Football Player
225 S Michigan Ave, Kenilworth NJ 07033, USA
**Chalfant, Kathleen** — Actress
Douglas Gorman Rothacker Wilhelm, 1501 Broadway, #703, New York NY 10036 USA
**Chalfie, Martin** — Nobel Chemistry Laureate
15 Claremont Ave, New York NY 10027, USA
**Chalfont, A G (Arthur)** — Government Official, England
House of Lords, Westminster, London SW1A 0PW, England
**Chali 2na** — Rap Artist
Vision Entertainment Group, 1100 Glendon Ave, #1100, Los Angeles CA 90024, USA
**Chalk, David L (Dave)** — Baseball Player
137 Cross Timbers Trail, Coppell TX 75019, USA
**Chalke, Sarah** — Actress
John Carrabino Mgmt, 5900 Wilshire Blvd, #406, Los Angeles CA 90036 USA
**Challenger, James** — Businessman
Challenger Gray Christmas, 1200 Smith St, #1600, Houston TX 77002, USA
**Chalmers, Iain G** — Medical Research Executive
James Lind Initiative, Summertown Pavilion, Oxford OX2 7LG, England
**Chaloner, William G** — Botanist
20 Parke Road, London SW13 9NG, England
**Chalupny, Lori C** — Soccer Player
Octagon Worldwide, 1751 Pinnacle Dr, #1500, McLean VA 22102 USA
**Chamarande, Brigitte** — Actress
Artmedia, 20 Ave Rapp, 75007 Paris, France
**Chamberlain, Byron** — Football Player
PO Box 326, Montclair CA 91763, USA
**Chamberlain, Cliff** — Actor
Brillstein Entertainment Partners, 9150 Wilshire Blvd, #350, Beverly Hills CA 90212 USA
**Chamberlain, Dean** — Photographer, Artist
1795 Washington Way, Venice CA 90291, USA
**Chamberlain, Gary E** — Economist
Harvard University, Littauer Center, Cambridge MA 02138, USA
**Chamberlain, Jeffrey S** — Geneticist
University of Michigan Medical Center, 301 E Liberty St, Ann Arbor MI 48104, USA
**Chamberlain, Justin L (Joba)** — Baseball Player
1504 Kara Lane, Lincoln NE 68522, USA
**Chamberlain, Richard** — Actor
Framework Entertainment, 9057 Nemo St, #C, West Hollywood CA 90069 USA
**Chamberlain, Spencer** — Singer (Underoath)
Red Light Mgmt, 44 Wall St, #2200, New York NY 10005, USA
**Chamberlain, Wesley P (Wes)** — Baseball Player
PO Box 1358, Homewood IL 60430, USA
**Chamberlin, Beth** — Actress
Paradigm Agency, 360 N Crescent Dr, North Building, Beverly Hills CA 90210 USA
**Chamberlin, James J (Jimmy)** — Drummer (Smashing Pumpkins)
535 W Basil Road, Lake Bluff IL 60044, USA
**Chambers, Anne Cox** — Businesswoman, Diplomat
Cox Enterprises, 1400 Lake Hearn Dr NE, Atlanta GA 30319, USA
**Chambers, Christina** — Actress
Don Buchwald, 6500 Wilshire Blvd, #2200, Los Angeles CA 90048 USA
**Chambers, Jerome P (Jerry)** — Basketball Player
4135 Don Diablo Dr, Los Angeles CA 90008, USA
**Chambers, John T** — Businessman
Cisco Systems, 170 W Tasman Dr, San Jose CA 95134, USA
**Chambers, Justin** — Actor, Model
Gersh Agency, 41 Madison Ave, #3301, New York NY 10010 USA
**Chambers, Kasey** — Singer
Premier Artists, 9 Dundas Lane, Albert Park VIC 3206, Australia
**Chambers, Kirk** — Football Player
1294 Lakeview Dr, Provo UT 84604, USA
**Chambers, Lester** — Singer (Chambers Brothers)
Lustig Talent, PO Box 770850, Orlando FL 32877 USA
**Chambers, Martin** — Drummer (Pretenders)
Gailforce Mgmt, 91 Peterborough Road, London SW6 3BU, England
**Chambers, Nancy** — Actress
United Talent Agency, U T A Plaza, 9336 Civic Center Dr, Beverly Hills CA 90210 USA
**Chambers, Raymond G** — Businessman, Social Activist
Malaria No More, 432 Park Ave S, #400, New York NY 10016, USA
**Chambers, Shawn R** — Ice Hockey Player
9999 Wood Ridge, Pequot Lakes MN 56472, USA
**Chambers, Thomas D (Tom)** — Basketball Player
7437 E Via Dona Road, Scottsdale AZ 85266, USA

**C**

| | |
|---|---|
| **Chambers, Wallace H (Wally)** | Football Player |
| 1838 Joslin St, Saginaw MI 48602, USA | |
| **Chambers, Willie** | Singer, Guitarist (Chambers Brothers) |
| Lustig Talent, PO Box 770850, Orlando FL 32877 USA | |
| **Chamblee, Brandel E** | Golfer |
| Golf Channel, 7580 Golf Channel Drive, Orlando FL 32819, USA | |
| **Chambliss, C Christopher (Chris)** | Baseball Player |
| 9100 Otter Creek Dr, #L, Charlotte NC 28277, USA | |
| **Chambliss, Scott** | Art Director |
| Innovative Artists, 1505 10th St, Santa Monica CA 90401 USA | |
| **Chambon, Pierre H** | Biochemist |
| Institute of Genetics Molecular & Cellular Biology, 1 Rue Laurent Fries, 67404 Illkirch, France | |
| **Chamillionaire** | Rap Artist |
| Universal Records, 70 Universal City Plaza, Universal City CA 91608 USA | |
| **Chamitoff, Gregory E** | Astronaut |
| N A S A, Johnson Space Center, 2101 NASA Road, Houston TX 77058 USA | |
| **Chammah, Walid A** | Financier |
| Morgan Stanley Co Inc, 1585 Broadway, New York NY 10036, USA | |
| **Champine, Robert** | Test Pilot |
| 205 Tipton Road, Newport News VA 23606, USA | |
| **Champion, B Billy** | Baseball Player |
| 240 Triple H Farm Road, Inman SC 29349, USA | |
| **Champion, Marge** | Dancer, Actress |
| 484 W 43rd St, New York NY 10036, USA | |
| **Champion, William (Will)** | Drummer (Coldplay) |
| Paradigm Agency, 360 N Crescent Dr, North Building, Beverly Hills CA 90210 USA | |
| **Champlin, Charles D** | Film Critic |
| 2169 Linda Flora Dr, Los Angeles CA 90077, USA | |
| **Champlin, James L** | Vietnam War Air Force Hero |
| Distinguished Flying Cross Society, PO Box 530250, San Diego CA 92153, USA | |
| **Champoux, Robert (Bob)** | Ice Hockey Player |
| 8861 Centuras Way, San Diego CA 92126, USA | |
| **Chan, Ernie** | Cartoonist (Conan the Barbarian) |
| 4131 Vale Ave, Oakland CA 94619, USA | |
| **Chan, Jackie** | Actor |
| Jackie Chan Cinema, 70 Pak To Ave, Clearwater Bay Road, Kowloon, Hong Kong 852, China | |
| **Chan, Julius** | Prime Minister, Papua New Guinea |
| PO Box 6030, Boroto, Papua New Guinea | |
| **Chan, Margaret F C** | Government Official, China |
| World Health Organization, Ave Appia 20, 1211 Geneva 27, Switzerland | |
| **Chan, Michael Paul** | Actor |
| Tyler Kjar, 10153 1/2 Riverside Dr, #255, Toluca Lake CA 91602 USA | |
| **Chance, Greyson** | Singer |
| W M E Entertainment, 9601 Wilshire Blvd, #300, Beverly Hills CA 90210 USA | |
| **Chance, Larry** | Singer (Earls) |
| Brothers Management Assoc, 141 Dunbar Ave, Fords NJ 08863 USA | |
| **Chance, Robert (Bob)** | Baseball Player |
| 2258 Oakridge Dr, Charleston WV 25311, USA | |
| **Chance, W Dean** | Baseball Player |
| 9505 W Smithville Western Road, Wooster OH 44691, USA | |
| **Chancellor, Van** | Basketball Coach |
| Lousiana State University, Athletic Dept, Baton Rouge LA 70803, USA | |
| **Chancey, Robert D** | Football Player |
| PO Box 212, Coosada AL 36020, USA | |
| **Chanchez, Hosea** | Actor |
| A P A Talent/Literary Agency, 405 S Beverly Dr, #300, Beverly Hills CA 90212 USA | |
| **Chandler, Carrol H (Howie)** | Air Force General |
| Vice Chief of Staff, HqUSAF, Pentagon, Washington DC 20330 USA | |
| **Chandler, Christopher M (Chris)** | Football Player |
| 1625 Lugano Lane, Del Mar CA 92014, USA | |
| **Chandler, Dianne** | Model |
| 110 River Oaks Dr, Woodstock GA 30188, USA | |
| **Chandler, Gene** | Singer |
| 8829 S Bishop St, Chicago IL 60620, USA | |
| **Chandler, Jeff** | Boxer |
| 6242 Horner St, Philadelphia PA 19144, USA | |
| **Chandler, Karl V** | Football Player |
| 5 Plymouth Road, Newtown Square PA 19073, USA | |
| **Chandler, Kyle** | Actor |
| Gersh Agency, 9465 Wilshire Blvd, #600, Beverly Hills CA 90212 USA | |
| **Chandler, Tyson C** | Basketball Player |
| 21731 Ventura Blvd, #300, Woodland Hills CA 91364, USA | |
| **Chandler, Wesley S (Wes)** | Football Player |
| 207 Howard St, New Smyrna Beach FL 32168, USA | |
| **Chandler, Wilson** | Basketball Player |
| Denver Nuggets, Pepsi Center, 1000 Chopper Circle, Denver CO 80204 USA | |
| **Chandola, Walter** | Photographer |
| 50 Spring Hill Road, Annandale NJ 08801, USA | |
| **Chandor, J C** | Director, Writer |
| W M E Entertainment, 9601 Wilshire Blvd, #300, Beverly Hills CA 90210 USA | |
| **Chandrasekar** | Actor |
| 34 Senthil Nagar Main Road, Chinna Porur, Chennai TN 600116, India | |
| **Chaney, Donald R (Don)** | Basketball Player, Coach |
| 20711 Park Pine Dr, Katy TX 77450, USA | |
| **Chaney, John** | Basketball Coach |
| 7840 Gilbert St, Philadelphia PA 19150, USA | |
| **Chaney, Rebekah** | Actress |
| Polimedia Communications, 1010 Wilshire Blvd, Los Angeles CA 90017, USA | |
| **Chang, David** | Chef, Restaurant |
| Momofuku Sam Bar, 207 2nd Ave, Front 1, New York NY 10003, USA | |
| **Chang, Han-Na** | Conductor, Concert Cellist |
| Harrison/Parrott, 5-6 Albion Court, London W6 0QT, England | |
| **Chang, Jeannette** | Publisher |
| Harper's Bazaar, Publisher's Office, 1700 Broadway, New York NY 10019, USA | |
| **Chang, Katie** | Actress |
| I C A Talent, 818 12th St, #9, Santa Monica CA 90403 USA | |

| | | |
|---|---|---|
| **Chang, Michael** | | Tennis Player |
| Chang Foundation, 28562 Oso Parkway, #D343, Rancho Santa Margarita CA 92688, USA | | |
| **Chang, Sarah** | | Concert Violinist |
| Opus 3 Artists, 470 Park Ave S, #900N, New York NY 10016 USA | | |
| **Chang, Shirley** | | Architect |
| Chang Bene Design, 43-55 Wyndham St, Central, Hong Kong, China | | |
| **Chang-Diaz, Franklin R** | | Astronaut |
| Ad Astra Rocket Co, 141 W Bay Area Blvd, Webster TX 77598, USA | | |
| **Changeux, Jean-Pierre G** | | Molecular Biologist |
| 47 Rue du Four, 75006 Paris, France | | |
| **Chanik, Evan M** | | Navy Admiral |
| Commander, 2nd Fleet, FPO AE 09506 USA | | |
| **Channing, Carol** | | Actress, Singer |
| Dramatic Artists Agency, 103 W Alameda, #139, Burbank CA 91502, USA | | |
| **Channing, Stockard** | | Actress |
| Hofflund/Polone, 9465 Wilshire Blvd, #420, Beverly Hills CA 90212 USA | | |
| **Chante, Keshia** | | Singer, Songwriter |
| Agency Group Ltd, 142 W 57th St, #600, New York NY 10019 USA | | |
| **Chan-Wook, Park** | | Director |
| W M E Entertainment, 9601 Wilshire Blvd, #300, Beverly Hills CA 90210 USA | | |
| **Chao, Charles** | | Businessman |
| Sina, 37F Jinmao Tower, 88 Century Blvd, Pudong, Shanghai 200121, China | | |
| **Chao, Manu** | | Singer, Guitarist |
| Cookman Mgmt, 10627 Burbank Blvd, North Hollywood CA 91601, USA | | |
| **Chao, Rosalind** | | Actress |
| Don Buchwald, 6500 Wilshire Blvd, #2200, Los Angeles CA 90048 USA | | |
| **Chaovarat Chanweerakul** | | Prime Minister, Thailand |
| Prime Minister's Office, Thanon Nakhon Patnom, Bangkok 10300, Thailand | | |
| **Chapdelaine, Rene** | | Ice Hockey Player |
| 662 S Division Road, Petoskey MI 49770, USA | | |
| **Chapin, Dwight L** | | Publisher, Government Official |
| San Francisco Examiner, 110 5th St, San Francisco CA 94103, USA | | |
| **Chapin, Jen** | | Singer, Songwriter |
| Admire Entertainment, PO Box 152, Palisades NY 10964, USA | | |
| **Chapin, Lauren** | | Actress |
| 726 63rd Ave, Vero Beach FL 32968, USA | | |
| **Chapin, Tom** | | Singer, Songwriter |
| Charles Rothschild, 330 E 48th St, #2D, New York NY 10017 USA | | |
| **Chaplin, Ben** | | Actor |
| Independent Talent Group, 40 Whitfield St, London W1T 2RH, England | | |
| **Chaplin, Carmen** | | Actress |
| Talent Store, 8 # 10 Rue de Normandie, 7503 Paris, France , USA | | |
| **Chaplin, Geraldine** | | Actress |
| Manoir de Bau, 1800 Vevey, Switzerland | | |
| **Chaplin, Kiera** | | Actress, Model |
| Limelight Films, 8913 1/2 W Sunset Blvd, West Hollywood CA 90069, USA | | |
| **Chapman, Beth Nielsen** | | Singer, Songwriter |
| PO Box 121551, Nashville TN 37212, USA | | |
| **Chapman, Blair** | | Ice Hockey Player |
| 2086 Redcoach Road, Allison Park PA 15101, USA | | |
| **Chapman, Candace M M** | | Soccer Player |
| Canadian Soccer, Place Soccer Canada, 237 Metcalfe St, Ottawa ON K2P 1R2, Canada | | |
| **Chapman, Clarence W** | | Football Player |
| 14820 Parkside St, Detroit MI 48238, USA | | |
| **Chapman, Dinos** | | Artist |
| Chapman Fine Arts, 49 Fashion St, London E1 6PX, England | | |
| **Chapman, Gary W** | | Singer, Songwriter, Entertainer |
| PO Box 25330, Nashville TN 37202, USA | | |
| **Chapman, Georgina** | | Fashion Designer (Marchesa), Actress |
| Marchesa, 60 W 26th St, #1425, New York NY 10001, USA | | |
| **Chapman, Jake** | | Artist |
| Chapman Fine Arts, 49 Fashion St, London E1 6PX, England | | |
| **Chapman, John** | | Actor |
| Elliott Agency, 94 Roundhill Crescent, Brighton BN2 3FR, England | | |
| **Chapman, Judith** | | Actress |
| McCabe Group, 3211 Cahuenga Blvd W, #104, Los Angeles CA 90068, USA | | |
| **Chapman, Kevin** | | Actor |
| Talent Works, 3500 W Olive Ave, #1400, Burbank CA 91505 USA | | |
| **Chapman, Lanei** | | Actress |
| Mitchell K Stubbs Assoc, 8695 W Washington Blvd, #204, Culver City CA 90232 USA | | |
| **Chapman, Marshall** | | Singer, Guitarist, Songwriter |
| 1906 South St, #704, Nashville TN 37212, USA | | |
| **Chapman, Max C, Jr** | | Financier |
| Nomura Securities, 1 World Financial Center, #200, New York NY 10281, USA | | |
| **Chapman, Michael G (Mike)** | | Football Player |
| 8731 Avator Circle, Boerne TX 78015, USA | | |
| **Chapman, Michael J** | | Director, Cinematographer |
| United Talent Agency, U T A Plaza, 9336 Civic Center Dr, Beverly Hills CA 90210 USA | | |
| **Chapman, Nicki** | | Actress, Entertainer |
| 19 Music & Mgmt, 35-37 Parkgate Road, London SW11 4NP, England | | |
| **Chapman, Orville L** | | Chemist |
| 1213 Roscomare Road, Los Angeles CA 90077, USA | | |
| **Chapman, Philip K** | | Astronaut |
| 11460 E Helm Dr, Scottsdale AZ 85255, USA | | |
| **Chapman, Rex E** | | Basketball Player |
| 16600 N Thompson Peak Parkway, #2043, Scottsdale AZ 85260, USA | | |
| **Chapman, Steven Curtis** | | Singer, Guitarist, Songwriter |
| Creative Trust, 5141 Virginia Way, #320, Brentwood TN 37027, USA | | |
| **Chapman, Tracy** | | Singer, Songwriter |
| Macklam/Feldman Mgmt, 1505 W 2nd Ave, #200, Vancouver BC V6H 3Y4, Canada | | |
| **Chapman, Wayne G** | | Basketball Player |
| 3593 Salisbury Dr, Lexington KY 40510, USA | | |
| **Chapman, Wes** | | Ballet Dancer |
| American Ballet Theater, 890 Broadway, #300, New York NY 10003, USA | | |
| **Chapot, Frank** | | Equestrian |
| 1075 Opie Road, Branchburg NJ 08853, USA | | |

| | |
|---|---|
| **Chappell, Crystal**<br>Stone Manners Salners, 9911 W Pico Blvd, #1400, Los Angeles CA 90035 USA | Actress |
| **Chappell, Lenonard R (Len)**<br>7624 Chestnut Lane, Waterford WI 53185, USA | Basketball Player |
| **Chappelle, David**<br>Gersh Agency, 9465 Wilshire Blvd, #600, Beverly Hills CA 90212 USA | Actor, Comedian |
| **Chapuisat, Stephane**<br>Borussia Dortmund S C, Strobelallee, 44139 Dortmund, Germany | Soccer Player |
| **Chaput, Charles J**<br>Archdiocese, 222 N 17th St, Philadelphia PA 19103, USA | Religious Leader |
| **Chaquico, Craig**<br>Maximus Entertainment, PO Box 27517, Austin TX 78755, USA | Guitarist (Jefferson Starship) |
| **Chara, Zdeno**<br>343 Commercial St, #211-213, Boston MA 02109, USA | Ice Hockey Player |
| **Charbonneau, Patricia**<br>Mary Harden-Curtis Assoc, 850 7th Ave, #903, New York NY 10019, USA | Actress |
| **Charbonneau, Stephane**<br>1 Wilderness Dr, Voorhees NJ 08043, USA | Ice Hockey Player |
| **Chardin, Germain**<br>10 Ave Meurthe, 54320 Maxeville, France | Rowing Athlete |
| **Charest, Benoit**<br>I C M Partners, 10250 Constellation Blvd, #900, Los Angeles CA 90067 USA | Composer |
| **Charest, Isabelle**<br>Speed Skating Canada, 2781 Lancaster Road, #402, Ottawa ON K1B 1A7, Canada | Speed Skater |
| **Chargin, Don**<br>Don Chargin Productions, 1241 Knollwood Dr, #134, Cambria CA 93428, USA | Boxing Promoter |
| **Charhi, Liraz**<br>Paradigm Agency, 360 N Crescent Dr, North Building, Beverly Hills CA 90210 USA | Actress |
| **Charice**<br>W M E Entertainment, 9601 Wilshire Blvd, #300, Beverly Hills CA 90210 USA | Actress, Singer |
| **Charlap, William M (Bill)**<br>Ted Kurland, 173 Brighton Ave, Boston MA 02134 USA | Jazz Pianist |
| **Charlene**<br>Palais de Monaco, BP 518, 98015 Monaco Cedex, Monaco | Princess Consort, Monaco |
| **Charles**<br>Saint James's Palace, London SW1A 1BS, England | Prince of Wales, England |
| **Charles, Caroline**<br>56/57 Beauchamp Place, London SW3, England | Fashion Designer |
| **Charles, Craig**<br>P F D, Drury House, 34-43 Russell St, London WC2B 5HA, England | Actor |
| **Charles, Edwin D (Ed)**<br>57 Park Terrace E, #B58, New York NY 10034, USA | Baseball Player |
| **Charles, Fran**<br>N F L Network, 10950 Washington Blvd, #100, Culver City CA 90232 USA | Sportscaster |
| **Charles, Gaius**<br>Gersh Agency, 9465 Wilshire Blvd, #600, Beverly Hills CA 90212 USA | Actor |
| **Charles, John C (J C)**<br>5644 Westheimer Road, #164, Houston TX 77056, USA | Football Player |
| **Charles, Josh A**<br>Kipperman Mgmt, 420 W End Ave, #1G, New York NY 10024 USA | Actor |
| **Charles, Kenneth M (Ken)**<br>621 Putnam Ave, Brooklyn NY 11221, USA | Basketball Player |
| **Charles, Larry**<br>W M E Entertainment, 9601 Wilshire Blvd, #300, Beverly Hills CA 90210 USA | Director |
| **Charles, Robert J (Bob)**<br>5329 Sea Biscuit Road, Palm Beach Gardens FL 33418, USA | Golfer |
| **Charles, Tanika**<br>Agency Group Ltd, 142 W 57th St, #600, New York NY 10019 USA | Singer, Songwriter |
| **Charles, Tina**<br>Connecticut Sun, 1 Mohegan Sun Blvd, Uncasville CT 06382 USA | Basketball Player |
| **Charles, Tina**<br>International Artists, PO Box 32, 5360 Grave AA, Netherlands | Pop, Disco Singer |
| **Charles-Furlow, Daedra**<br>19414 Spencer St, Detroit MI 48234, USA | Basketball Player |
| **Charleson, Leslie**<br>4851 Cromwell Ave, Los Angeles CA 90027, USA | Actress |
| **Charles-Roux, Edmonde**<br>Editions Grasset, 61 Rue des Saints-Peres, 75006 Paris, France | Writer |
| **Charlesworth, Brian**<br>Edinburgh University, Biology Institute, Edinburgh EH1 1HT, Scotland | Evolutionary Biologist |
| **Charlesworth, Todd**<br>2240 Pleasant Hill Dr, Muskegon MI 49441, USA | Ice Hockey Player |
| **Charlone, Cesar**<br>I C M Partners, 10250 Constellation Blvd, #900, Los Angeles CA 90067 USA | Cinematographer |
| **Charlton, Norman W (Norm)**<br>312 Estes Dr, Rockport TX 78382, USA | Baseball Player |
| **Charlton, Robert (Bobby)**<br>Garthollerton, Cleford Road, Ollerton, Cheshire WA16 8RY, England | Soccer Player |
| **Charnin, Martin**<br>Richard Ticktin, 1345 Ave of Americas, New York NY 10105, USA | Producer, Director, Lyricist |
| **Charno, Stuart**<br>4147 Sunnyside Ave, Los Angeles CA 90066, USA | Actor, Comedian |
| **Charo**<br>Charo Entertainment, 1801 Lexington Road, Beverly Hills CA 90210, USA | Singer, Guitarist |
| **Charron, Paul R**<br>44 Contentment Island Road, Darien CT 06820, USA | Businessman |
| **Chartier, Dave**<br>SW 13-19-28 W, Binscarth MB R0J 0G0, Canada | Ice Hockey Player |
| **Chartoff, Melanie**<br>Artists Agency, 9430 Olympic Blvd, Beverly Hills CA 90212 USA | Actress |
| **Chartraw, Rick**<br>600 Chaparral Road, Sierra Madre CA 91024, USA | Ice Hockey Player |
| **Charvet, David**<br>Chasen Agency, 8899 Beverly Blvd, #405, Los Angeles CA 90048 USA | Actor |
| **Charyk, Joseph V**<br>790 Andrews Ave, #A302, Delray Beach FL 33483, USA | Businessman |

**Charyn, Jerome** — Writer
Bloomsbury Publishing, 50 Bedford Square, London WC1B 3DP, England

**Chase, Alison** — Dance Artistic Director
Apogee Arts, PO Box 224, Brooksville ME 04617, USA

**Chase, Alston** — Writer
Bohran Agency, 3141 Ellington Dr, Los Angeles CA 90068, USA

**Chase, Bailey** — Actor
Gersh Agency, 9465 Wilshire Blvd, #600, Beverly Hills CA 90212 USA

**Chase, Barrie** — Actress, Dancer
446 Carrol Canal, Venice CA 90291, USA

**Chase, Brian** — Drummer (Yeah Yeah Yeahs)
C E S D, 10635 Santa Monica Blvd, #130, Los Angeles CA 90025 USA

**Chase, Chevy** — Actor, Comedian
Kritzer Levine Wilkins Griffin, 11872 La Grange Ave, #100, Los Angeles CA 90025 USA

**Chase, Daveigh** — Actress
Brillstein Entertainment Partners, 9150 Wilshire Blvd, #350, Beverly Hills CA 90212 USA

**Chase, David** — Producer, Writer
United Talent Agency, U T A Plaza, 9336 Civic Center Dr, Beverly Hills CA 90210 USA

**Chase, Debra Martin** — Producer
Martin Chase Productions, 500 S Buena Vista St, Burbank CA 91521, USA

**Chase, Jonathan** — Actor
Main Title Mgmt, 8383 Wilshire Blvd, #408, Beverly Hills CA 90211 USA

**Chase, Kelly W** — Ice Hockey Player
16476 Horseshoe Ridge Road, Chesterfield MO 63005, USA

**Chase, Lori** — Actress, Comedienne
OmniPop Talent Group, 4605 Lankershim Blvd, #201, Toluca Lake CA 91602 USA

**Chase, Lorraine** — Actress
Burnett Granger Assoc, 3 Clifford St, London W1S 2LF, England

**Chase, Qiana** — Model
Playboy Promotions, 2706 Media Center Dr, Los Angeles CA 90065 USA

**Chase, Steve** — Interior Designer
Chase Design Assoc, 70005 Mirage Cove Dr, Rancho Mirage CA 92270, USA

**Chasez, Joshua Scott (J C)** — Singer ('N Sync)
Podwall Entertainment, 710 N Orlando Ave, #203, West Hollywood CA 90069, USA

**Chass, Murray** — Sportswriter
New York Times, Editorial Dept, 229 W 43rd St, New York NY 10036 USA

**Chassagne, Regine** — Musician (Arcade Fire), Actress
Billions Corp, 3522 W Armitage Ave, Chicago IL 60647 USA

**Chast, Roz** — Cartoonist
New Yorker, Editorial Dept, 4 Times Square, Basement C1B, New York NY 10036 USA

**Chastain, Brandi** — Soccer Player, Sportscaster
1661 University Way, San Jose CA 95126, USA

**Chastain, Jessica** — Actress
Mosiac Media Group, 9200 W Sunset Blvd, #1000, Los Angeles CA 90069 USA

**Chastel, Andre** — Writer
30 Rue de Lubeck, 75116 Paris, France

**Chater, Eos** — Violinist (Bond)
Mel Bush, Ranglewood, Arrowsmith Road, Wimborne, Dorset BH21 3B5, England

**Chatham, Matthew (Matt)** — Football Player
2502 Old Bridge Lane, Bellingham MA 02019, USA

**Chatham, Russell** — Artist
Clark City Press, PO Box 1358, Livingston MT 59047, USA

**Chatham, Wes** — Actor
Gersh Agency, 9465 Wilshire Blvd, #600, Beverly Hills CA 90212 USA

**Chatroit, Francois** — Auto Racing Driver
Artmedia, 20 Ave Rapp, 75007 Paris, France

**Chattaway, Jay** — Composer
May Artist Mgmt, 8491 W Sunset Blvd, #228, West Hollywood CA 90069, USA

**Chatwin, Justin** — Actor
Alchemy Entertainment, 7024 Melrose Ave, #420, Los Angeles CA 90038 USA

**Chaudhry, Iftikhar Mohammed** — Judge
Supreme Court, Constitution Ave, Islamabad, Pakistan

**Chaudhry, Mahendra P** — Prime Minister, Fiji
Fiji Labor Party, PO Box 2162, Suva, Fiji

**Chaumette, Monique** — Actress
Voyez Mon Agent, 20 Ave Rapp, 75007 Paris, France

**Chauvin, Yves** — Nobel Chemistry Laureate
10 Place Francois Sicard, 37000 Tours, France

**Chauvire, Yvette** — Ballerina
21 Place du Commerce, 75015 Paris, France

**Chaves, Richard** — Actor
Media Artists Group, 8222 Melrose Ave, #203, Los Angeles CA 90048 USA

**Chavez Ramirez, Darvin F** — Soccer Player
C F Monterrey, Ave Revolucion 846B, C Jardin Espanol, 63820 Monterrey Nuevo Leon, Mexico

**Chavez, Endy D** — Baseball Player
1406 Bonnie Lane, Bayside NY 11360, USA

**Chavez, Jorge F** — Thoroughbred Racing Jockey
106 John St, Garden City NY 11530, USA

**Chavez, Julio Cesar, Jr** — Boxer
Team Chavez, 12620 Washington Blvd, Los Angeles CA 90066, USA

**Chavira, Ricardo Antonio** — Actor
Innovative Artists, 1505 10th St, Santa Monica CA 90401 USA

**Chavous, Barney L** — Football Player, Coach
601 Chavous Road, Aiken SC 29803, USA

**Chavous, Corey L** — Football Player
1218 S Main St, Saint Charles MO 63301, USA

**Chawla, Juhi** — Actress
153 Oxford Tower, Yamuna Nagar, Oshiwara Andheri (W), Mumbai 40058, India

**Chayanne** — Singer, Actress
Chaf Enterprises, 1717 N Bayshore Dr, #2146, Miami FL 33132, USA

**Chbosky, Stephen** — Writer, Producer
W M E Entertainment, 9601 Wilshire Blvd, #300, Beverly Hills CA 90210 USA

**Cheadle, Don** — Actor
United Talent Agency, U T A Plaza, 9336 Civic Center Dr, Beverly Hills CA 90210 USA

**Cheaney, Calbert N** — Basketball Player
2103 Finchley Road, Carmel IN 46032, USA

**Charyn - Cheaney**

**Cheatham, Maree** — Actress
Sutton-Barth Vennari, 5900 Wilshire Blvd, #700, Los Angeles CA 90036 USA
**Checker, Chubby** — Singer, Songwriter
Twisted Entertainment, 320 Fayette St, #200, Conshohocken PA 19428, USA
**Checkley, Laura** — Actress
Gavin Barker Assoc, 2D Wimpole St, London W1G 0EB, England
**Cheechoo, Jonathan** — Ice Hockey Player
707 Iris Gardens Court, San Jose CA 95125, USA
**Cheek, Jimmy G** — Educator
University of Tennessee, Chancellor's Office, Andy Holt Tower, Knoxville TN 37996, USA
**Cheek, Joey** — Speed Skater
Q Sports Marketing, 534 W Evergreen St, Wheaton IL 60187 USA
**Cheek, Louis R, Jr** — Football Player
545 Woelke Road, Seguin TX 78155, USA
**Cheek, Molly** — Actress
Kazarian/Measures/Ruskin, 11969 Ventura Blvd, #300, Studio City CA 91604 USA
**Cheeks, Maurice E (Mo)** — Basketball Player, Coach
709 Broad Acres Road, Penn Valley PA 19072, USA
**Cheena, Parvesh** — Actor
Global Artists Agency, 6253 Hollywood Blvd, #508, Los Angeles CA 90028 USA
**Cheeseborough, Chandra** — Track Athlete
104 W Harbor, Hendersonville TN 37075, USA
**Cheesman, Barry** — Golfer
2901 Theresa Lane, Sarasota FL 34239, USA
**Cheetham, Jay (Jay Kay)** — Singer
Merlin Elite, Hammersmith Studios, 55 Yelman Road, London W6 8JF, England
**Cheever, Eddie** — Auto Racing Driver
8227 N West Blvd, #300, Indianapolis IN 46278, USA
**Cheever, Susan** — Writer
Simon & Schuster, 1230 Ave of Americas, Concourse 1, New York NY 10020 USA
**Cheevers, Gerald M (Gerry)** — Ice Hockey Player, Coach
106 Appleton St, North Andover MA 01845, USA
**Chee-Yun** — Concert Violinist
Opus 3 Artists, 470 Park Ave S, #900N, New York NY 10016 USA
**Chef, Genia** — Artist
Leibnizstr 61, 10629 Berlin, Germany
**Chekamauskas, Vitautas** — Architect
State Arts Academy, Maironio 6, 2600 Vilnius, Lithuania
**Chelberg, Robert D** — Army General
Cubic Applications, Patch Community, Unit 30400, Box R65, APO AE 09131, USA
**Cheli-Merchez, Marianne** — Astronaut, Belgium
38 Via Ciro Sant'agata, 40019 Modena, Italy
**Chelios, Christos K (Chris)** — Ice Hockey Player
790 Falmouth Dr, Bloomfield Hills MI 48304, USA
**Chellas, Semi** — Producer
United Talent Agency, U T A Plaza, 9336 Civic Center Dr, Beverly Hills CA 90210 USA
**Chellgren, Paul W** — Businessman
Ashland Inc, PO Box 15391, Covington KY 41015, USA
**Chelsom, Peter** — Director
Principato-Young, 9465 Wilshire Blvd, #880, Beverly Hills CA 90212 USA
**Chemetov, Paul** — Architect
Chemetov-Huidobro, 4 Square Massena, 75013 Paris, France
**Chen Kaige** — Director
I C M Partners, 10250 Constellation Blvd, #900, Los Angeles CA 90067 USA
**Chen Lu** — Figure Skater
World Ice Arena, 1881th Bao'an Road, Luohu District, Shenzhen 518000 , China
**Chen Wenbo** — Artist
P K M Gallery, 7-32 Samcheongro, Jongnogu, Seoul 110 230 South Korea
**Chen Xieyang** — Conductor
Shanghai Symphony Orchestra, 105 Hunan Road, Shanghai 200031, China
**Chen Yi** — Composer
University of Missouri, Music Conservatory, Kansas City MO 64110, USA
**Chen Yibing** — Gymnast
Beijing Normal University, 19 Xin Jie Kou Wai St, Hai Dian District, Beijing 100875 PR, China
**Chen Zuohuang** — Conductor
Wichita Symphony Orchestra, Concert Hall, 225 W Douglas St, Wichita KS 67202, USA
**Chen, Bruce K** — Baseball Player
18372 W Ivy Lane, Surprise AZ 85388, USA
**Chen, Daniel (Dan)** — Sculptor, Artist
PO Box 41513, Eugene OR 97404, USA
**Chen, Edison** — Actor
Fulong Production, 8/F Baskerville House, 13 Duddell St, Central, Hong Kong, China
**Chen, Irvin S Y** — Geneticist
University of California Medical Center, Hematology Dept, Los Angeles CA 90024, USA
**Chen, Joan** — Actress, Director
2601 Filbert St, San Francisco CA 94123, USA
**Chen, Joie** — Commentator
CNN-TV, 190 Marietta Ave SW, Atlanta GA 30303 USA
**Chen, Julie** — Commentator
CBS-TV, News Dept, 51 W 52nd St, New York NY 10019 USA
**Chen, Lincoln C** — Nutritionist
302 Dean Road, Brookline MA 02445, USA
**Chen, Steve** — Businessman
YouTube, 1000 Cherry Ave, #200, San Bruno CA 94066, USA
**Chen, Steve S** — Computer Engineer
Chen Systems Corp, 1414 W Hamilton Ave, Eau Claire WI 54701, USA
**Chen, Steven** — Keyboardist (Airline Toxic Event)
Island Def Jam Records, 8920 W Sunset Blvd, #200, West Hollywood CA 90069 USA
**Chenchikova, Olga** — Ballerina
Kirov Ballet Theater, 1 Pl Iskusstr, 190000 Saint Petersburg, Russia
**Chenery, Penny** — Thoroughbred Racing Owner
20 Roberts Lane, Saratoga Springs NY 12866, USA
**Cheney, Dorothy B (Dodo)** — Tennis Player
442 Woodland Hills Dr, Escondido CA 92029, USA
**Cheney, Lauren** — Soccer Player
Boston Breakers, 400 Blue Hill Dr, #302, Westwood, MA 02090 USA

**C**

**Cheney, Lynne V** — Government Official
American Enterprise Institute, 1150 17th St NW, Washington DC 20036, USA
**Cheney, Richard B** — Vice President; Secretary, Defense
6613 Madison Dr, McLean VA 22101, USA
**Cheng, Andy** — Director
Paradigm Agency, 360 N Crescent Dr, North Building, Beverly Hills CA 90210 USA
**Chenier, Philip (Phil)** — Basketball Player
7807 Arbor Grove Dr, #407, Hanover MD 21076, USA
**Chennault, Anna Chan** — Businesswoman, Writer
T A C International, Chennault Building, 1049 30th St NW, Washington DC 20007, USA
**Chenoweth, Kristin** — Actress, Singer
Creative Artists Agency, 2000 Ave of Stars, #100, Los Angeles CA 90067 USA
**Cheong Jin-Suk, Nicholas Cardinal** — Religious Leader
Seoul Archdiocèse, Chunggu Myongdong 2-1, Seoul 100 022, South Korea
**Chepik, Sergei** — Artist
Galerie Guiter, 23 Rue Guenegaud, 75006 Paris, France
**Cher** — Actress, Singer
Schiff Co, 9200 Sunset Blvd, #430, West Hollywood CA 90232 USA
**Cherestal, Jean Marie** — Prime Minister, Haiti
Villa d'Accueil, Delmas 60, Musseau, Port-au-Prince 6110, Haiti
**Cherlin, Andrew J** — Sociologist
Johns Hopkins University, Sociology Dept, Baltimore MD 21218, USA
**Chermayeff, Peter** — Architect
Chermayeff Sollogub Poolle, 51 Melcher St, #902, Boston MA 02210, USA
**Chernicky, Laura** — Actress
Jennifer's Talent, 740 N Plamkinton Ave, #300, Milwaukee WI 53203, USA
**Chernin, Peter** — Businessman
Chernin Entertainment, 1733 Ocean Ave, Santa Monica CA 90401, USA
**Chernow, Ron** — Writer
105 State St, Brooklyn NY 11201, USA
**Cherrelle** — Singer
Green Light Talent Agency, PO Box 3172, Beverly Hills CA 90212 USA
**Cherry, Byron** — Actor, Producer
Talent Bin, 5270 Railview Court, #238, Shelby Township MI 48316, USA
**Cherry, Deron L** — Football Player
13800 S Pebblebrook Lane, Greenwood MO 64034, USA
**Cherry, Dick** — Ice Hockey Player
Box 346 RR 1, Bath ON K0H 1G0, Canada
**Cherry, Don** — Singer, Golfer
928 Pinehurst Dr, Las Vegas NV 89109, USA
**Cherry, Don S** — Ice Hockey Player, Coach, Sportscaster
CBC-TV, PO Box 500, Station A, Toronto ON M5W 1E6, Canada
**Cherry, Eagle-Eye L** — Singer
Umbrella Group, 1 West St, #3506, New York NY 10004, USA
**Cherry, Fred V** — Vietnam War Air Force Hero
720 Dale Dr, Silver Spring MD 20910, USA
**Cherry, Jake** — Actor
United Talent Agency, U T A Plaza, 9336 Civic Center Dr, Beverly Hills CA 90210 USA
**Cherry, Je'rod L** — Football Player
993 Mimosa Dr, Macedonia OH 44056, USA
**Cherry, Jonathan** — Actor
Roar, 2400 Broadway, #330, Santa Monica CA 90404, USA
**Cherry, Marc** — Producer
Paradigm Agency, 360 N Crescent Dr, North Building, Beverly Hills CA 90210 USA
**Cherry, Neneh** — Singer
Paradigm Agency, 360 Park Ave, #1600, New York NY 10022 USA
**Chertoff, Michael** — Secretary, Homeland Security; Judge
Covington & Burling, 1201 Pennsylvania Ave NW, Washington DC 20004, USA
**Cherundolo, Charles J (Chuck), Jr** — Football Player
4230 Simms Road, Lakeland FL 33810, USA
**Cherundolo, Steve** — Soccer Player
Hanover 96, Arthur-Menge Ufer 5, 30169 Hannover, Germany
**Chervin, Stan** — Writer
I C M Partners, 10250 Constellation Blvd, #900, Los Angeles CA 90067 USA
**Chesnais, Patrick** — Actor
Artmedia, 20 Ave Rapp, 75007 Paris, France
**Chesnes, Shelby** — Model
Playboy Promotions, 2706 Media Center Dr, Los Angeles CA 90065 USA
**Chesney, Kenny** — Singer
Morris Management Group, 818 19th Ave S, Nashville TN 37203, USA
**Chesnutt, Mark N** — Singer, Songwriter
Music City News Media, 38 Music Square E, #200, Nashville TN 37203, USA
**Chester, Colby** — Actor
Brady Brannon Rich, 5670 Wilshire Blvd, #820, Los Angeles CA 90036 USA
**Chester, Raymond T** — Football Player
4722 Grass Valley Road, Oakland CA 94605, USA
**Chestnut, Mary Boykin** — Educator
Sweet Briar College, President's Office, Sweet Briar VA 24595, USA
**Chestnut, Morris** — Actor
Gersh Agency, 9465 Wilshire Blvd, #600, Beverly Hills CA 90212 USA
**Chet, Ilan** — Microbiologist
Weizmann Science Institute, President's Office, Rehovot 76100, Israel
**Chetry, Kiran** — Commentator
CNN-TV, 190 Marietta Ave SW, Atlanta GA 30303 USA
**Chetwynd, Lionel** — Writer, Producer, Director
Creative Artists Agency, 2000 Ave of Stars, #100, Los Angeles CA 90067 USA
**Cheung, Maggie** — Actress
Schachter Entertainment, 1157 S Beverly Dr, Los Angeles CA 90035, USA
**Cheveldae, Tim** — Ice Hockey Player
Moose Jaw Warriors, 1251 Main St N, Moose Jaw SK S6H 6M3, Canada
**Chew, Geoffrey F** — Physicist
10 Maybeck Twin Dr, Berkeley CA 94708, USA
**Cheyunski, James M (Jim)** — Football Player
821 W Locust St, Seaford DE 19973, USA
**Chi Haotian** — Army General, China
National Defense Ministry, Jingshanqia Jie, Beijing 100009, China

---

**Cheney - Chi Haotian**

|  |  |
|------|-----------|
| **Chi, Chen**<br>23 Washington Square N, New York NY 10011, USA | Artist |
| **Chi, Tony**<br>Tony Chi & Assoc, 121 Varick St, #500, New York NY 10013, USA | Interior Designer |
| **Chía, Sandro**<br>601 W 26th St, #12, New York NY 10001, USA | Artist |
| **Chiacchia, Darren**<br>PO Box 278, East Aurora NY 14052, USA | Equestrian |
| **Chianese, Dominic**<br>S M S Talent, 8383 Wilshire Blvd, #230, Beverly Hills CA 90211 USA | Actor |
| **Chiao, Leroy**<br>2108 Butler Dr, Friendswood TX 77546, USA | Astronaut |
| **Chiara, Maria**<br>Narodni Divado, Ostrovni 1, 11230 Prague 1, Czech Republic | Opera Singer |
| **Chichkan, Ilya**<br>Victor Pinchuk Foundation, 2 Mechnikova St, 01601 Kiev, Ukraine | Artist, Sculptor |
| **Chick, Austin**<br>Bloom Hergott Diemer, 150 S Rodeo Dr, #300, Beverly Hills CA 90212 USA | Director |
| **Chihara, Charles S**<br>567 Cragmont Ave, Berkeley CA 94708, USA | Philosopher |
| **Chihuly, Dale P**<br>Chihuly Inc, 1111 NW 50th St, Seattle WA 98107, USA | Artist, Sculptor |
| **Chikezie, Caroline**<br>Paradigm Agency, 360 N Crescent Dr, North Building, Beverly Hills CA 90210 USA | Actress |
| **Chiklis, Michael**<br>W M E Entertainment, 9601 Wilshire Blvd, #300, Beverly Hills CA 90210 USA | Actor |
| **Child, Desmond**<br>D S W Entertainment, 116 E 16th St, #900, New York NY 10003, USA | Singer, Songwriter |
| **Child, Jane**<br>7095 Hollywood Blvd, #747, Los Angeles CA 90028, USA | Singer, Keyboardist, Songwriter |
| **Child, Lee**<br>Delacorte Press, 1540 Broadway, New York NY 10036 USA | Writer |
| **Childers, Ambyr**<br>W M E Entertainment, 9601 Wilshire Blvd, #300, Beverly Hills CA 90210 USA | Actress |
| **Childress, Joshua M (Josh)**<br>1433 Cherokee Trail, Lawrenceville GA 30043, USA | Basketball Player |
| **Childress, Kallie Flynn**<br>Amsel Eisenstadt Frazier, 5055 Wilshire Blvd, #865, Los Angeles CA 90036 USA | Actress |
| **Childress, Raymond C (Ray), Jr**<br>639 Shady Hill St, Houston TX 77056, USA | Football Player |
| **Childress, Richard (R C)**<br>Childress Racing, 236 Industrial Dr, Welcome NC 27374, USA | Auto Racing Executive |
| **Childs, Billy**<br>Unlimited Myles, 6 Imaginery Place, Aberdeen NJ 07747, USA | Jazz Pianist |
| **Childs, Chris**<br>10830 Willow Meadow Circle, Alpharetta GA 30022, USA | Basketball Player |
| **Childs, David M**<br>Skidmore Owings Merrill, 14 Wall St, #2500, New York NY 10005, USA | Architect |
| **Childs, Henry**<br>8304 Allman Road, Lenexa KS 66219, USA | Football Player |
| **Childs, Martin**<br>Independent Talent Group, 40 Whitfield St, London W1T 2RH, England | Art Director |
| **Childs, Toni**<br>Studio C Communications, 324 Sunset Ave, Venice CA 90291, USA | Singer, Songwriter |
| **Chiles, Henry G (Hank), Jr**<br>6436 Pima St, Alexandria VA 22312, USA | Navy Admiral |
| **Chiles, Linden**<br>2521 Topanga Skyline Dr, Topanga CA 90290, USA | Actor |
| **Chiles, Lois**<br>Abrams Artists, 9200 W Sunset Blvd, #1125, West Hollywood CA 90069 USA | Actress, Model |
| **Chillar, Brandon O**<br>1030 Iris Court, Carlsbad CA 92011, USA | Football Player |
| **Chillemi, Connie**<br>2701 NE 10th St, #705, Ocala FL 34470, USA | Golfer |
| **Chilstom, Ken**<br>20 Selby Lane, Palm Beach Gardens FL 33418, USA | Test Pilot |
| **Chilton, Gene A**<br>45828 US Highway 69 N, Jacksonville TX 75766, USA | Football Player |
| **Chilton, Karen**<br>Innovative Artists, 1505 10th St, Santa Monica CA 90401 USA | Actress |
| **Chilton, Kevin P**<br>2555 Talleson Court, Colorado Springs CO 80919, USA | Astronaut, Air Force General |
| **Chilton, W Alexander (Alex)**<br>High Road Touring, 751 Bridgeway, #200, Sausalito CA 94965 USA | Singer, Guitarist (Box Tops, Big Star) |
| **Chiminazzo, Jeisa**<br>I M G Models, 304 Park Ave S, #PH N, New York NY 10010 USA | Model |
| **Chin, Lonny**<br>Playboy Promotions, 2706 Media Center Dr, Los Angeles CA 90065 USA | Actress, Model |
| **Chinchilla Miranda, Laura**<br>Casa Presidencial, Apdo 520-2010, San Jose 1000, Costa Rica | President, Costa Rica |
| **Ching, Brian**<br>Houston Dynamo, 1415 Louisiana, #3400, Houston TX 77002 USA | Soccer Player |
| **Chingy**<br>Central Entertainment Group Talent, 251 W 39th St, New York NY 10018, USA | Rap Artist |
| **Chinlund, Nick**<br>Innovative Artists, 1505 10th St, Santa Monica CA 90401 USA | Actor |
| **Chinn, Simon**<br>Red Box Films, Kirkman House, 12-14 Whitfield St, #300, London W1T 2RF, England | Documentary Producer |
| **Chipchura, Kyle D G**<br>Phoenix Coyotes, 6751 N Sunset Blvd, #200, Glendale AZ 85305 USA | Ice Hockey Player |
| **Chipperfield, David**<br>Chipperfield Architects, Cobham Mews, Agar Grove, London NW1 9SB, England | Architect |
| **Chipperfield, Ron**<br>Optima World Sports, Box 248, Wilcox SK S0G 5E0, Canada | Ice Hockey Player |
| **Chirac, Jacques R**<br>110 Rue du Bac, 75007 Paris, France | President, France |

**C**

**Chirico, Emanuel** — Businessman
Phillips-Van Heusen Corp, 200 Madison Ave, Basement 1, New York NY 10016, USA

**Chisholm, Melanie J** — Singer (Spice Girls)
45 Mgmt, 13 Tottenham Mews, London W1T 4AG, England

**Chisholm, Sallie W (Penny)** — Biological Oceanographer
Massachusetts Institute of Technology, Engineering Dept, Cambridge MA 02139, USA

**Chislett, Michael Guy** — Guitarist (Academy Is)
Decaydance Records, 9229 Sunset Blvd, #900, West Hollywood CA 90069, USA

**Chissano, Joaquim A** — President, Mozambique
Rua Pereira do Lago 10, Bairro de Sommerschield, Maputo, Mozambique

**Chitalada, Sot** — Boxer
Home Express Co, 242/19 Moo 10, Sukhumvit Road, Cholburi 20210, Thailand

**Chittenden, Khan** — Actor
Lisa Mann Creaqtive Mgmt, 99 Spring St, Bondi Junction NSW 2022, Australia

**Chittister, Joan D** — Social Psychologist
Saint Scholastica Priory, 335 E 9th St, Erie PA 16503, USA

**Chitty, Dennis** — Animal Ecologist
1602-5775 Hampton Place, Vancouver BC V6T 2G6, Canada

**Chitwood, Joey, Jr** — Stunt Car Driver
5324 Golden Isles Dr, Apollo Beach FL 33572, USA

**Chiu, Raymond J** — Heart Surgeon
9075 Rue Omega, Brossard QC J4Y 3A9, Canada

**Chivian, Eric** — Psychiatrist, Social Activist
Harvard University, Health & Global Environment Center, Cambridge MA 02138, USA

**Chizevsky, Kim** — Body Builder
PO Box 9101, Springfield MO 65801, USA

**Chladek, Dana** — Canoeing Athlete
5302 Flanders Ave, Kensington MD 20895, USA

**Chlumsky, Anna** — Actress
Innovative Artists, 235 Park Ave S, #1000, New York NY 10003 USA

**Chmerkovskiy, Maksim** — Dancer, Choreographer
Rising Stars Dance Academy, 479 N Midland Ave, #H, Saddlebrook NJ 07663, USA

**Chmerkovskiy, Val** — Dancer
Lizzie Grubman Mgmt, 424 W 33 St, #110, New York NY 10001, USA

**Chmura, Mark W** — Football Player
S18W28948 Price Court, Waukesha WI 53188, USA

**Cho, Alfred Y** — Electrical Engineer
A T & T Bell Lucent Laboratory, 600 Mountain Ave, New Providence NJ 07974 USA

**Cho, Frank** — Cartoonist (Liberty Meadows)
Creators Syndicate, 737 3rd St, Hermosa Beach CA 90254 USA

**Cho, Fujio** — Businessman
Toyota Motor Corp, 1 Toyotacho, Toyota City, Aichi Pref 471 8701, Japan

**Cho, John** — Actor
Gersh Agency, 9465 Wilshire Blvd, #600, Beverly Hills CA 90212 USA

**Cho, Margaret** — Actress, Comedienne
W M E Entertainment, 9601 Wilshire Blvd, #300, Beverly Hills CA 90210 USA

**Cho, Paul Y** — Evangelist
Full Gospel Central Church, 12 Yoido-dong, #1100, Youngdungpoku, Seoul 150 869, Korea

**Cho, Simon** — Short Track Speed
US Speedskating, 5662 S Cougar Lane, Salt Lake City UT 84118 USA

**Cho, Smith** — Actress
Gersh Agency, 9465 Wilshire Blvd, #600, Beverly Hills CA 90212 USA

**Choate, Jerry D** — Businessman
Allstate Insurance, Allstate Plaza, 2775 Sanders Road, Northbrook IL 60062, USA

**Choate, Randol D (Randy)** — Baseball Player
6610 Cobia Circle, Boynton Beach FL 33437, USA

**Chodron, Pemo** — Religious Leader
Gampo Abbey, Pleasant Bay, Cape Breton NS B0E 2P0, Canada

**Choi Eun-Kyung** — Speed Skater
Skating Union, 88 Bangyee-Dong, Songpaku, Seoul 138 749, South Korea

**Choi Min-Kyung** — Speed Skater
Skating Union, 88 Bangyee-Dong, Songpaku, Seoul 138 749, South Korea

**Choi, Kenneth** — Actor
Talent Works, 3500 W Olive Ave, #1400, Burbank CA 91505 USA

**Choi, Kyung-Ju (K J)** — Golfer
2205 Vaquero Estates Blvd, Westlake TX 76262, USA

**Chojnacka, Elisabeth** — Concert Harpsichordist
17 Rue Emile Dubois, 75014 Paris, France

**Chojnowska-Liskiewicz, Krystyna** — Yachtswoman
Ul Norblina 29 m 50, 80 304 Gdansk-Oliwa, Poland

**Chokachi, David** — Actor
Pantheon Talent, 1801 Century Park East, #1910, Los Angeles CA 90067 90067, USA

**Chomet, Sylvain** — Animator, Lyricist
I C M Partners, 10250 Constellation Blvd, #900, Los Angeles CA 90067 USA

**Chomski, Alejandro** — Director, Producer, Writer
Gersh Agency, 9465 Wilshire Blvd, #600, Beverly Hills CA 90212 USA

**Chomsky, A Noam** — Linguist
15 Suzanne Road, Lexington MA 02420, USA

**Chomsky, Marvin J** — Director
15200 W Sunset Blvd, #209, Pacific Palisades CA 90272, USA

**Chonacas, Katie** — Actress, Model
K Star Productions, 8491 Sunset Blvd, #549, Los Angeles CA 90069, USA

**Chones, James B (Jim)** — Basketball Player
26400 George Zeiger Dr, #405, Beachwood OH 44122, USA

**Chong, Rae Dawn** — Actress
Metropolitan Talent Agency, 5405 Wilshire Blvd, #218, Los Angeles CA 90036 USA

**Chong, Thomas (Tommy)** — Actor, Comedian (Cheech & Chong)
1625 Casale Road, Pacific Palisades CA 90272, USA

**Chontosh, Brian R** — Marine Corps Iraq War Hero
1009 Harbour Dr, Stafford VA 22554, USA

**Choper, Jesse H** — Attorney, Educator
University of California, Law School, Boalt Hall, Berkeley CA 94720, USA

**Chopra, Daniel** — Golfer
9838 Laurel Valley Dr, Windermere FL 34786, USA

**Chopra, Deepak** — Writer
Trident Media Group, 41 Madison Ave, #3600, New York NY 10010, USA

**Chopra, Prem** — Actor
144A Nibbana Pali Hill, Bandra, Mumbai MS 400050, India
**Chopra, Priyanka** — Beauty Queen, Actress
Creative Artists Agency, 2000 Ave of Stars, #100, Los Angeles CA 90067 USA
**Chopra, Vidhu Vinod** — Director, Producer
Bhagtani Krishang, RH1, Plot 16C, Dattatray Road, Santacruz (West), Mumbai 400054, India
**Chorley of Kendal, Roger R E** — Businessman
50 Kensington Place, London W8 7PW, England
**Chorske, Tom** — Ice Hockey Player
23 Cooper Circle, Minneapolis MN 55436, USA
**Chorvat, Scarlett** — Actress
Innovative Artists, 1505 10th St, Santa Monica CA 90401 USA
**Chorzempa, Daniel W** — Concert Organist, Composer
Kunstleragentur Raab & Bohm, Plankengasse 7, 1010 Vienna, Austria
**Choudhury, Sarita** — Actress
Don Buchwald, 6500 Wilshire Blvd, #2200, Los Angeles CA 90048 USA
**Chouinard, Guy** — Ice Hockey Player
P E I Rocket, 46 Kensington Road, Charlottetown PE C1A 5H7, Canada
**Chouinard, Marie** — Dancer, Choreographer
Compagnie Chouinard, 3981 Boul Saint-Laurent, Montreal QC H2W 1Y5, Canada
**Chouinard, Robert W (Bobby)** — Baseball Player
6024 S Paris Place, Englewood CO 80111, USA
**Choummali Sayasone** — President, Laos; Army General
Presidential House, Vientiane Capital, Vientiane, Laos
**Chow Yun-Fat** — Actor
2/F 192 Prince Edward Road W, Kowloon, Hong Kong, China
**Chow, Amy Y Y** — Gymnast
Lucille Packard Children's Hospital, Pediatrics Dept, Palo Alto CA 94304, USA
**Chow, China** — Actress, Model
Creative Artists Agency, 2000 Ave of Stars, #100, Los Angeles CA 90067 USA
**Chow, Jeffrey** — Fashion Designer
Jeffrey Chow Inc, 525 E 82nd St, New York NY 10028, USA
**Chow, Kelsey** — Actress
Coast to Coast Talent, 3350 Barham Blvd, Los Angeles CA 90068 USA
**Chow, Raymond** — Producer
Golden Harvest, 16/F Peninsula Office Tower, Tsim Sha Tsui, Kowloon, Hong Kong, China
**Chow, Stephen** — Actor, Director
Creative Artists Agency, 2000 Ave of Stars, #100, Los Angeles CA 90067 USA
**Chowdhury, A Q M Badruddoza** — President, Bangladesh
Residence Bari Dhara near Gulshan, Dhaka 1212, Bangladesh
**Chrebet, Wayne** — Football Player
147 Heulitt Road, Colts Neck NJ 07722, USA
**Chretien, Jean J J** — Prime Minister, Canada
541 Acacia Ave, Ottawa ON K1A 0A6, Canada
**Chretien, Jean-Loup** — Spatinaut, France; Air Force General
Tietronix Software, 1331 Gemini Ave, #300, Houston TX 77058, USA
**Chriqui, Emmanuelle** — Actress
Brookside Artist Mgmt, 250 W 57th St, #2303, New York NY 10107 USA
**Chrisman, Paul W (Woody Paul)** — Singer, Fiddler (Riders in the Sky)
New Frontier Mgmt, 1921 Broadway, Nashville TN 37203, USA
**Christakis, Nicholas A** — Internist, Sociologist
Harvard University, Sociology Dept, Cambridge MA 02115, USA
**Christensen, Calvin L (Cal)** — Basketball Player
395 Canal Road, #419, Waterville OH 43566, USA
**Christensen, Erika** — Actress
Brillstein Entertainment Partners, 9150 Wilshire Blvd, #350, Beverly Hills CA 90212 USA
**Christensen, Hayden** — Actor
Forest Park Pictures, 11210 Briarcliff Lane, Studio City CA 91604, USA
**Christensen, Helena** — Model, Photographer
Panorama Agency, Ryesgade 103B, 2100 Copenhagen, Denmark
**Christensen, Jesper** — Actor
Conway Van Gelder Grant, 8-12 Broadwick St, #300, London W1F 8HW, England
**Christensen, Kai** — Architect
100 Vester Voldgade, 1552 Copenhagen V, Denmark
**Christensen, Shawn** — Singer, Guitarist (Stellarstarr*)
+1 Management/Public Relations, 242 Wythe Ave, #6, Brooklyn NY 11211, USA
**Christensen, Tonja M** — Model
Playboy Promotions, 2706 Media Center Dr, Los Angeles CA 90065 USA
**Christenson, Ryan A** — Baseball Player
100 Lismore Court, Tyrone GA 30290, USA
**Christian, Ash** — Actor, Director, Producer
Ironclad Pictures, 25 Broadway, #1200, New York NY 10004, USA
**Christian, Claudia** — Actress
Abrams Artists, 9200 W Sunset Blvd, #1125, West Hollywood CA 90069 USA
**Christian, David W (Dave)** — Ice Hockey Player
513 Queens Court, Moorhead MN 56560, USA
**Christian, Gordon** — Ice Hockey Player
604 Lake St NW, Warroad MN 56763, USA
**Christian, Robert D (Bob)** — Football Player
9450 Lincolnwood Dr, Evanston IL 60203, USA
**Christian, Stephen T E** — Singer (Anberlin)
Arson Media Group, 23 N Summerlin Ave, #200, Orlando FL 32801, USA
**Christian, William (Bill)** — Ice Hockey Player
502 Carrol St NW, Warroad MN 56763, USA
**Christians, F Wilhelm** — Financier
Konigsallee 51, 40212 Dusseldorf, Germany
**Christiansen, Jason S** — Baseball Player
3428 E Jasmine Circle, Mesa AZ 85213, USA
**Christiansen, Keith R (Huffer)** — Ice Hockey Player
1023 Timberline Lane, Duluth MN 55811, USA
**Christianson, Claude V (Chris)** — Army General
Director, National Defense University, Fort Lesley J McNair, Washington DC 20319, USA
**Christie, Douglas D (Doug)** — Basketball Player
13812 NE 40th St, Bellevue WA 98005, USA
**Christie, G Stephen (Steve)** — Football Player
PO Box 646, Buffalo NY 14231, USA

**C**

**Chopra - Christie**

| | |
|---|---|
| **Christie, Gwendoline**<br>United Agents, 12-26 Lexington St, London W1F 0LE, England | Actress |
| **Christie, Julie**<br>Rene Missel Mgmt, 2376 Adrian St, #A, Newbury Park CA 91320, USA | Actress, Model |
| **Christie, Linford**<br>Nuff Respect, 107 Sherland Road, Twickenham, Middlesex TW9 4HB, England | Track Athlete |
| **Christie, Lou**<br>Fox Entertainment, 1650 Broadway, #303, New York NY 10019, USA | Singer |
| **Christie, Mike**<br>6093 S Krameria St, Centennial CO 80111, USA | Ice Hockey Player |
| **Christie, Perry G**<br>Prime Minister's Office, Rawson Square, PO Box N8301, Nassau NP, Bahamas | Prime Minister, Bahamas |
| **Christie, Tony**<br>Amarillo Music, 31 Kensington Oval, Lichfield, Staffs WS13 6ND, England | Singer |
| **Christie, Warren**<br>I F A Talent Agency, 8730 W Sunset Blvd, #490, West Hollywood CA 90069 USA | Actor |
| **Christie, William**<br>81 Ave Victor Hugo, 75116 Paris, France | Concert Harpsichordist |
| **Christin, Judith**<br>Columbia Artists Mgmt Inc, 1790 Broadway, #702, New York NY 10019 USA | Opera Singer |
| **Christine, Andrew (Andy)**<br>King Features Syndicate, 300 W 57th St, #1500, New York NY 10019 USA | Cartoonist (Man Called Horse) |
| **Christl, Lisy**<br>Claire Best Assoc, 736 Seward St, Los Angeles CA 90038, USA | Costume Designer |
| **Christlieb, Peter (Pete)**<br>J V C Music, 3800 Barham Blvd, #409, Los Angeles CA 90068, USA | Jazz Saxophonist |
| **Christman, Daniel W (Dan)**<br>US Chamber of Commerce, 1615 H St NW, Washington DC 20062, USA | Army General, Educator |
| **Christman, Kevin**<br>714 S Pacific Highway, Talent OR 97540, USA | Artist, Sculptor |
| **Christmas, G Ronald (Ron)**<br>3809 Spicewood Springs Road, Stafford VA 22554, USA | Marine Corps General |
| **Christo**<br>48 Howard St, New York NY 10013, USA | Sculptor |
| **Christoff, Steven (Steve)**<br>542 Fairview Ave S, Saint Paul MN 55116, USA | Ice Hockey Player |
| **Christon, Shameka D**<br>Chicago Sky, 20 W Kinzie St, #1010, Chicago IL 60654 USA | Basketball Player |
| **Christopher**<br>Colden McKuin Frankel, 141 El Camino Dr, #100, Beverly Hills CA 90212, USA | Cartoonist (Ghouly Boys) |
| **Christopher, Ann**<br>Stable Block, Hay St, Marshfield near Chippenham SN14 8PF, England | Sculptor |
| **Christopher, Dennis**<br>B R & S, 5757 Wilshire Blvd, #473, Los Angeles CA 90036, USA | Actor |
| **Christopher, Gretchen**<br>509 E Ridgecrest Blvd, #A, Ridgecrest CA 93555, USA | Singer (Fleetwoods) |
| **Christopher, Joseph O (Joe)**<br>PO Box 65240, Baltimore MD 21209, USA | Baseball Player |
| **Christopher, Tyler**<br>Paradigm Agency, 360 N Crescent Dr, North Building, Beverly Hills CA 90210 USA | Actor |
| **Christopherson, James (Jim)**<br>526 Queens Court, Moorhead MN 56560, USA | Football Player, Coach |
| **Christy, James W**<br>Hollinghead, 7285 Golden Eagle Dr, Flagstaff AZ 86004, USA | Astronomer |
| **Christy, Jeffrey A (Jeff)**<br>138 Horseshoe Dr, Freeport PA 16229, USA | Football Player |
| **Chromy, Bronislaw**<br>Ul Halki 5, 30 228 Cracow, Poland | Sculptor |
| **Chryssa**<br>565 Broadway, #5W, New York NY 10012, USA | Sculptor |
| **Chu, Julie**<br>USA Hockey, 1775 Bob Johnson Dr, Colorado Springs CO 80906 USA | Ice Hockey Player |
| **Chu, Paul Ching-Wu**<br>University of Houston, Center for Superconductivity, Houston TX 77204, USA | Physicist |
| **Chu, Steven**<br>42 Bishop Lane, Menlo Park CA 94025, USA | Nobel Laureate; Secretary, Energy |
| **Chua, Amy L**<br>Yale University, Law School, New Haven CT 06520, USA | Writer |
| **Chua, Leon O**<br>University of California, Electrical Engineering Dept, Berkeley CA 94720, USA | Electrical Engineer |
| **Chuan Leekpai**<br>Prachatipat, 67 Thanon Setsiri, Samsen Nai, Bangkok 10300, Thailand | Prime Minister, Thailand |
| **Chubais, Anatoly B**<br>United Power Grids, Kitaigorodsky Proyezd 7, 103074 Moscow, Russia | Government Official, Russia |
| **Chuck D**<br>Richard Walters, PO Box 2789, Toluca Lake CA 91610 USA | Rap Artist (Public Enemy) |
| **Chuck, Wendy**<br>Paradigm Agency, 360 N Crescent Dr, North Building, Beverly Hills CA 90210 USA | Costume Designer |
| **Chudacoff, Katy**<br>Dovetail Design Works, 1005 Buckworth Ave, Franklin TN 37064, USA | Interior Designer |
| **Chukwurah, Patrick C**<br>6757 Camino Real, Irving TX 75039, USA | Football Player |
| **Chulack, Christopher**<br>Ken Gross Mgmt, 12135 Stanwood Drive, Los Angeles CA 90066, USA | Producer, Director, Writer |
| **Chulk, C Vincent (Vinnie)**<br>4607 Ballstonefield Lane, Katy TX 77494, USA | Baseball Player |
| **Chun Lee-Kyung**<br>Skating Union, 88 Bangyee-Dong, Songpaku, Seoul 138 749, South Korea | Speed Skater |
| **Chun, Tze**<br>Gramercy Park Entertainment, 9701 Wilshire Blvd, #1000, Beverly Hills CA 90212, USA | Writer |
| **Chung, Constance Y (Connie)**<br>Creative Artists Agency, 2000 Ave of Stars, #100, Los Angeles CA 90067 USA | Commentator |
| **Chung, Kyung-Wha**<br>Harrison/Parrott, 5-6 Albion Court, London W6 0QT, England | Concert Violinist |
| **Chung, Myung-Whun**<br>Askonas Holt, Lincoln House, 300 High Holborn, London WC1V 7JH, England | Concert Pianist, Conductor |

**Chupack, Cindy** — Writer, Producer
W M E Entertainment, 9601 Wilshire Blvd, #300, Beverly Hills CA 90210 USA

**Church, Charlotte** — Singer, Actress
Creative Artists Agency, 2000 Ave of Stars, #100, Los Angeles CA 90067 USA

**Church, Eric** — Singer, Songwriter
Q Prime South, 131 A 11th St, Nashville TN 37206, USA

**Church, George** — Molecular Geneticist
Harvard Medical School, Genetics Dept, 77 Ave Louis Pasteure, Boston MA 02115, USA

**Church, Ryan M** — Baseball Player
3500 Thurloe Dr, Rockledge FL 32955, USA

**Church, Thomas Haden** — Actor
Creative Artists Agency, 2000 Ave of Stars, #100, Los Angeles CA 90067 USA

**Churchill, Caryl** — Writer
Casorotto Ramsay, Waverley House, 7-12 Noel St, London W1F 8GQ, England

**Churchill, Kim** — Singer, Songwriter
Agency Group Ltd, 142 W 57th St, #600, New York NY 10019 USA

**Churla, Shane** — Ice Hockey Player
31826 Scotch Pine Lane, Bigfork MT 59911, USA

**Chute, Robert M** — Biologist, Writer
68 Schellinger Road, Poland ME 04274, USA

**Chuy, Donald J (Don)** — Football Player
11690 Oxnard St, North Hollywood CA 91606, USA

**Chwast, Seymour** — Artist, Illustrator
Push Pin Group, 38 W 26th St, #5A, New York NY 10010, USA

**Chynoweth, Dean** — Ice Hockey Player
131 Shawnee Rise SW, Calgary AB T2Y 2S3, Canada

**Cialini, Julie Lynn** — Model, Actress
PO Box 55536, Valencia CA 91385, USA

**Cianfrance, Derek** — Director
Creative Artists Agency, 2000 Ave of Stars, #100, Los Angeles CA 90067 USA

**Cianfrocco, Angelo D (Archi)** — Baseball Player
12424 Addax Court, San Diego CA 92129, USA

**Ciani, Suzanne** — Composer
Musica International, 20 Sunnyside Ave, #A197, Mill Valley CA 94941, USA

**Ciara** — Singer, Songwriter
W M E Entertainment, 9601 Wilshire Blvd, #300, Beverly Hills CA 90210 USA

**Ciaramello, Benjamin (Benny)** — Actor
A P A Talent/Literary Agency, 405 S Beverly Dr, #300, Beverly Hills CA 90212 USA

**Ciavaglia, Peter** — Ice Hockey Player
1137 Carrie Court, Rochester Hills MI 48309, USA

**Cibani, Tia** — Fashion Designer
601 W 26th St, #875, New York NY 10001, USA

**Cibrian, Eddie** — Actor
I C M Partners, 10250 Constellation Blvd, #900, Los Angeles CA 90067 USA

**Ciccarelli, Dino** — Ice Hockey Player
37934 Lakeshore Dr, Harrison Township MI 48045, USA

**Ciccolella, Jude** — Actor
McKeon-Myrones Mgmt, 3500 Olive Ave, #770, Burbank CA 91505 USA

**Ciccolini, Aldo** — Concert Pianist
Gerhild Baron Mgmt, Dornbacher Str 41/III/3, 1170 Vienna, Austria

**Ciccone, Enrico** — Ice Hockey Player
Sports Prospects, 77 Rue de Bleury, Rosemere QC J7A 4L9, Canada

**Cicerone, Ralph J** — Environmental Scientist
University of California, Earth Science Dept, Rowland Hall, Irvine CA 92717, USA

**Cichocki, Chris J** — Ice Hockey Player
3955 Pine Lake Circle, Stockton CA 95219, USA

**Cichy, Joseph J (Joe)** — Football Player
1220 N Mandan St, Bismarck ND 58501, USA

**Ciechanover, Aaron** — Nobel Chemistry Laureate
Technion-Israel Institute, Box 9649, Bat Galim, Haifa 31096, Israel

**Cienfuegos, Mauricio** — Soccer Player
Los Angeles Galaxy, Home Depot Center, 18400 Avalon Blvd, Carson CA 90746 USA

**Cierpinski, Waldemar** — Track Athlete
Sport GmbH, Grosse Ulrichstr 60, 06108 Halle/Saale, Germany

**Cigliuti, Natalia** — Actress
Sager Mgmt, 260 S Beverly Dr, #205, Beverly Hills CA 90212, USA

**Cimino, Michael** — Director, Writer
9015 Alto Cedro, Beverly Hills CA 90210, USA

**Cincotta, Anthony H** — Biotechnologist
VeroScience, 1334 Main Road, Tiverton RI 02878, USA

**Cincotti, Peter** — Singer, Pianist, Songwriter
Morey Management Group, 1100 Glendon Ave, #1100, Los Angeles CA 90024, USA

**Cink, Stewart** — Golfer
2195 Lockett Court, Duluth GA 30097, USA

**Cintron, Alexander (Alex)** — Baseball Player
HC 2 Box 8575, Yabuccoa PR 00767, USA

**Cintron, Kermit (Killer)** — Boxer
DiBella Entertainment, 350 7th Ave, #800, New York NY 10001, USA

**Cioffi, Charles** — Actor
Paradigm Agency, 360 N Crescent Dr, North Building, Beverly Hills CA 90210 USA

**Ciokey, Janna** — Actress
J Michael Bloom, 9255 W Sunset Blvd, #710, West Hollywood CA 90069 USA

**Ciorbea, Victor** — Prime Minister, Romania
C D N P P, Bd Carol I34, 73231 Bucharest, Romania

**Cipriani Thorne, Juan Luis Cardinal** — Religious Leader
Arzobispado, Plaza de Armas S/N, Apartado 1512, Lima 100, Peru

**Cirella, Joe** — Ice Hockey Player
Teranet 600-1 Adelaide St E, Toronto ON M5C 2V9, Canada

**Ciriani, Henri** — Architect
61 Rue Pascal, 75013 Paris, France

**Cirici, Cristian** — Architect
Cirici Arquitecte, Carrer de Pujades 63 2-N, 08005 Barcelona, Spain

**Cirillo, Jeffrey H (Jeff)** — Baseball Player
604 Elmwood Lane, Celina OH 45822, USA

**Cirio, Chuck** — Composer, Director, Producer
B M I, 8730 W Sunset Blvd, #300, Los Angeles CA 90069 USA

| | |
|---|---|
| **Ciry, Michel** | Artist |
| La Bergerie, 76119 Varengeville sur Mer, Seine-Maritime, France | |
| **Cisco, Galen B** | Baseball Player |
| 604 Elmwood Lane, Celina OH 45822, USA | |
| **Cisneros, Evelyn** | Ballerina |
| San Francisco Ballet, 455 Franklin St, San Francisco CA 94102, USA | |
| **Cisneros, Henry G** | Secretary, Housing & Urban Development |
| 2002 W Houston St, San Antonio TX 78207, USA | |
| **Citerne, Philippe** | Financier |
| Societe Generale, 29 Blvd Haussman, 75009 Paris, France | |
| **Citizen Cope** | Singer, Songwriter |
| Agency Group Ltd, 142 W 57th St, #600, New York NY 10019 USA | |
| **Citro, Ralph** | Boxing Historian |
| 32 N Black Horse Pike, Blackwood NJ 08012, USA | |
| **Citron, Martin** | Neurobiologist |
| Amgen Co, 152A 226 Amgen Center, Thousand Oaks CA 91320, USA | |
| **Citterio, Antonio** | Architect, Interior Designer |
| Antonio Citterio Partners, Via Cerva 4, 20122 Milan, Italy | |
| **Citti, Christine** | Actress |
| Artmedia, 20 Ave Rapp, 75007 Paris, France | |
| **Ciuha, Joze** | Artist |
| Presernov 12, 61000 Ljubjana, Slovenia | |
| **Civiletti, Benjamin R** | Attorney General |
| 5900 Old Ocean Blvd, #B3, Boynton Beach FL 33435, USA | |
| **Cizik, Robert** | Businessman |
| Cizik Interests, Chase Tower, 600 Travis St, #3628, Houston TX 77002, USA | |
| **Claassen, Yann** | Actor |
| Artmedia, 20 Ave Rapp, 75007 Paris, France | |
| **Clackson, Kim** | Ice Hockey Player |
| 342 Thomas Road, Canonsburg PA 15317, USA | |
| **Claes, Willy** | Government Official, Belgium |
| Berkenlaan 23, 3500 Hasselt, Belgium | |
| **Claflin, Bruce L** | Businessman |
| Advanced Micro Devices, 1 A M D Plaza, Sunnyvale CA 94088, USA | |
| **Claflin, Sam** | Actor |
| Creative Artists Agency, 2000 Ave of Stars, #100, Los Angeles CA 90067 USA | |
| **Claiborne, Chris** | Football Player |
| Premier Sports Mgmt, 1000 N Green Valley Parkway, #440, Henderson NV 89074, USA | |
| **Claire, Julie** | Actress |
| I C M Partners, 10250 Constellation Blvd, #900, Los Angeles CA 90067 USA | |
| **Clamp, Shirley** | Singer |
| Lionheart, PO Box 11108, Nytogstan 40A, 100 61 Stockholm, Sweden | |
| **Clampett, Robert D (Bobby), Jr** | Golfer, Sportscaster |
| 10600 Golf Link Dr, Raleigh NC 27617, USA | |
| **Clancy, Abigail R** | Model |
| Money Mgmt, 42A Berwick St, London W1F 8RZ, England | |
| **Clancy, Aoife** | Singer |
| Producers Inc, 11806 N 56th St, Tampa FL 33617 USA | |
| **Clancy, Edward B Cardinal** | Religious Leader |
| Sydney Archdiocese, Polding House, 276 Pitt St, Sydney NSW 2000, Australia | |
| **Clancy, James (Jim)** | Baseball Player |
| 177 Lance Dr, Twin Lakes WI 53181, USA | |
| **Clancy, Sam** | Football Player |
| 1308 Crest Lane, Oakdale PA 15071, USA | |
| **Clancy, Terry** | Ice Hockey Player |
| 65 Golfdale Road, Toronto ON M4N 2B5, Canada | |
| **Clancy, William (Liam)** | Singer (Clancy Brothers) |
| Charles Rothschild, 330 E 48th St, #2D, New York NY 10017 USA | |
| **Clanton, Jimmy** | Singer |
| Neal Hollander Agency, 9966 Majorca Place, Boca Raton FL 33434 USA | |
| **Clapp, Gordon** | Actor |
| Cynthia Snyder Public Relations, 5739 Colfax Ave, North Hollywood CA 91601, USA | |
| **Clapp, Joss** | Singer, Guitaist (Tarras) |
| Rounder Records, 1 Rounder Way, Burlington MA 01803 USA | |
| **Clapp, Nicholas R** | Explorer (Ubar), Producer |
| PO Box 1019, Borrego Springs CA 92004, USA | |
| **Clapper, James R (Jim), Jr** | Government Official, Air Force General |
| National Intelligence Department, 725 17th St NW, Washington DC 20523 USA | |
| **Clapton, Eric** | Singer, Guitarist |
| Michael Eaton, 22 Blades Court, Deodar Road, London SW15 2NU, England | |
| **Clardy, Jon C** | Chemist |
| Cornell University, Chemistry Dept, Ithaca NY 14853, USA | |
| **Clare, Jillian** | Actress |
| Greene Assoc, 1901 Ave of Stars, #130, Los Angeles CA 90067 USA | |
| **Clarizio, Louis** | Baseball Player |
| 133 Lela Lane, Schaumburg IL 60193, USA | |
| **Clark, A Keon** | Basketball Player |
| Phoenix Suns, 201 E Jefferson St, Phoenix AZ 85004 USA | |
| **Clark, Alan** | Pianist (Dire Straits) |
| Damage Mgmt, 16 Lambton Place, London W11 2SH, England | |
| **Clark, Alan M (Allie)** | Baseball Umpire |
| 1185 SW 5th Ave, Boca Raton FL 33432, USA | |
| **Clark, Anthony** | Actor, Comedian |
| Innovative Artists, 1505 10th St, Santa Monica CA 90401 USA | |
| **Clark, Anthony C (Tony)** | Baseball Player |
| 14125 N 65th Ave, Glendale AZ 85306, USA | |
| **Clark, Archie L** | Basketball Player |
| 4268 10th St, Ecorse MI 48229, USA | |
| **Clark, Bob** | Commentator |
| ABC-TV, News Dept, 5010 Creston St, Hyattsville MD 20781 USA | |
| **Clark, Brady W** | Baseball Player |
| 19275 Green Lakes Loop, Bend OR 97702, USA | |
| **Clark, Brett** | Ice Hockey Player |
| 8745 Aberdeen Circle, Littleton CO 80130, USA | |
| **Clark, Brian M** | Football Player |
| 811 Wonderland Forest Dr, Waxhaw NC 28173, USA | |

**Clark, Bryan D**
508 E Clark St, Madera CA 93638, USA — Baseball Player

**Clark, C Joseph (Joe)**
Joe Clark Assoc, 237 4th Ave SW, #3000, Calgary AB T2P 4X7, Canada — Prime Minister, Canada

**Clark, Candace J (Candy)**
PO Box 3421, Memorial Station, Montclair NJ 07043, USA — Actress

**Clark, Carol Higgins**
524 E 72nd St, #28DE, New York NY 10021, USA — Writer

**Clark, Colin W**
9531 Finn Road, Richmond BC V7A 2L3, Canada — Mathematician

**Clark, Dallas D**
2995 Belle Maison Dr, Zionsville IN 46077, USA — Football Player

**Clark, Daniel**
Brightline Education, 3200 Port Royale Dr N, #906, Fort Lauderdale FL 33308, USA — Actor

**Clark, Danny, IV**
213 Seneca Trail, Bloomington IL 60108, USA — Football Player

**Clark, David E (Dave)**
4842 Mayfield Road W, Collierville TN 38017, USA — Baseball Player, Manager

**Clark, Doran**
Paul Kohner, 9300 Wilshire Blvd, #555, Beverly Hills CA 90212 USA — Actress

**Clark, Dwight E**
2511 Sedley Road, Charlotte NC 28211, USA — Football Player, Executive

**Clark, Earl**
Los Angeles Lakers, Staples Center, 1111 S Figueroa St, Los Angeles CA 90015 USA — Basketball Player

**Clark, Elbernita (Twinkie)**
Universal Attractions, 135 W 26th St, #1200, New York NY 10001 USA — Gospel Singer (Clark Sisters)

**Clark, Gary C**
PO Box 202, Dublin VA 24084, USA — Football Player

**Clark, Guy**
Keith Case Assoc, 1025 17th Ave S, #200, Nashville TN 37212 USA — Singer, Songwriter

**Clark, Hamish**
Ken McReddie Assoc, 101 Finsbury Pavement, London EC2A 1RS, England — Actor

**Clark, Helen E**
Labour Party, 160-62 Willis St, Wellington 6011, New Zealand — Prime Minister, New Zealand

**Clark, Herbert H**
Stanford University, Psychology Dept, Jordan Hall, Stanford CA 94305, USA — Pscycholinguist

**Clark, Jack A**
6541 Scottsdale Way, Frisco TX 75034, USA — Baseball Player

**Clark, James (Jim)**
Neoteris, 940 Stewart Dr, Sunnyvale CA 94085, USA — Businessman

**Clark, Jerald D**
12325 Crisscross Lane, San Diego CA 92129, USA — Baseball Player

**Clark, Jim**
International Union of Electronic Workers, 401 3rd St NW, Washington DC 20001, USA — Labor Leader

**Clark, Joe**
1856 Clarence Dr, Hellertown PA 18055, USA — Educator

**Clark, Kelly**
PO Box 725, West Dover VT 05356, USA — Snowboarding Athlete

**Clark, Kelvin**
3812 Evesham Dr, Plano TX 75025, USA — Football Player

**Clark, L Hill**
Crane Co, 100 Stamford Place, #300, Stamford CT 06902, USA — Businessman

**Clark, Larry**
Killer/Moxie Mgmt, 5890 W Jefferson Blvd, Los Angeles CA 90016, USA — Director

**Clark, Louis S**
6149 Kissengen Springs Court, Jacksonville FL 32258, USA — Football Player

**Clark, Marcia R**
A P A Talent/Literary Agency, 405 S Beverly Dr, #300, Beverly Hills CA 90212 USA — Attorney

**Clark, Mario S**
48100 Sandia Creek Dr, Temecula CA 92590, USA — Football Player

**Clark, Martin**
Knopf Publishers, 1745 Broadway, New York NY 10019 USA — Writer, Judge

**Clark, Mary Ellen**
24 Hayes St, Arlington MA 02474, USA — Diver

**Clark, Mary Higgins**
15 Werimus Brook Road, Saddle River NJ 07458, USA — Writer

**Clark, Mary Jane**
Saint Martin's Press, 175 5th Ave, #400, New York NY 10010 USA — Writer

**Clark, Matt**
1199 Park Ave, #15D, New York NY 10128, USA — Actor, Director

**Clark, Melvin E (Mel)**
18262 E Crescent, #520N, Kilbourne IL 62655, USA — Baseball Player

**Clark, Michael, II**
4007 Pintail Circle, Rocky Face GA 30740, USA — Golfer

**Clark, Mystro**
I C M Partners, 10250 Constellation Blvd, #900, Los Angeles CA 90067 USA — Actor

**Clark, Oliver**
House of Representatives, 1434 6th St, #1, Santa Monica CA 90401 USA — Actor

**Clark, Perry**
Miami University, Athletic Dept, Coral Gables FL 33124, USA — Basketball Coach

**Clark, Peter B**
7675 La Jolla Blvd, #203, La Jolla CA 92037, USA — Publisher

**Clark, Petula**
15 Chemin Rieu Coligny, 1208 Geneva, Switzerland — Singer, Actress

**Clark, Philip E (Phil)**
208 George St, Barrington IL 60010, USA — Football Player

**Clark, Phillip B (Phil)**
PO Box 620612, Orlando FL 32862, USA — Baseball Player

**Clark, Ricardo**
Eintracht Frankfurt S C, Morfelder Landstr 362, 60528 Frankfurt, Germany — Soccer Player

**Clark, Richard C (Dick)**
4424 Edmunds St NW, #1070, Washington DC 20007, USA — Senator, IA

**Clark, Rickey C**
8953 Emerald Waters Court, Las Vegas NV 89147, USA — Baseball Player

**Clark, Robert A**
Munstead Wood, Godalming, Surrey GU7 1UN, England — Businessman

**Clark, Robert C**  
34 Monterey Court, Manhattan Beach CA 90266, USA — Artist  
**Clark, Ronald B (Ron)**  
700 Starkey Road, #511, Largo FL 33771, USA — Baseball Player  
**Clark, Roy**  
Ro-Bar, 3225 S Norwood Ave, #101, Tulsa OK 74135, USA — Singer, Guitarist  
**Clark, Ryan T**  
1236 Camarta Dr, Pittsburgh PA 15227, USA — Football Player  
**Clark, Sharon**  
Playboy Promotions, 2706 Media Center Dr, Los Angeles CA 90065 USA — Model, Actress  
**Clark, Spencer Trent**  
Untitled Entertainment, 350 S Beverly Dr, #200, Beverly Hills CA 90212 USA — Actor  
**Clark, Stephen E (Steve)**  
29 Martling Road, San Anselmo CA 94960, USA — Swimmer  
**Clark, Susan**  
13400 Riverside Dr, #308, Sherman Oaks CA 91423, USA — Actress  
**Clark, Terri**  
Spalding Entertainment, 54 Music Square E, #200, Nashville TN 37203, USA — Singer, Songwriter  
**Clark, Terry L**  
1607 E Tam O'Shanter St, Ontario CA 91761, USA — Baseball Player  
**Clark, Vernon E (Vern)**  
Raytheon Co, 870 Winter St, Waltham MA 02451, USA — Navy Admiral  
**Clark, Victoria**  
Untitled Entertainment, 350 S Beverly Dr, #200, Beverly Hills CA 90212 USA — Actress, Singer  
**Clark, W G**  
Clark & Menefee Architects, 4048 E Main St, Charlottesville VA 22902, USA — Architect  
**Clark, W Ramsey**  
37 W 12th St, #2B, New York NY 10011, USA — Attorney General  
**Clark, Wayne M**  
14241 Lambeth Way, Tustin CA 92780, USA — Football Player  
**Clark, Wendel L**  
Toronto Maple Leafs, AirCanada Center, 40 Bay St, Toronto ON M5J 2K2, Canada — Ice Hockey Player  
**Clark, Wesley Curley (W C)**  
Crossfire Productions, 304 Braeswood Road, Austin TX 78704, USA — Guitarist  
**Clark, Wesley K (Wes)**  
1 Crestmont Dr, Little Rock AR 72227, USA — Army General  
**Clark, William N (Will), Jr**  
36170 Pleasant Hill Court, Prairieville LA 70769, USA — Baseball Player  
**Clark-Chisholm, Jacky**  
Universal Attractions, 135 W 26th St, #1200, New York NY 10001 USA — Singer (Clark Sisters)  
**Clark-Cole, Dorinda**  
Universal Attractions, 135 W 26th St, #1200, New York NY 10001 USA — Singer (Clark Sisters)  
**Clarke, Allan**  
Hill Farm, Hackleton, Northamptonshire NN7 2DH, England — Singer, Musician (Hollies)  
**Clarke, Brian**  
Tony Shafrazi Gallery, 544 W 26th St, #2, New York NY 10001, USA — Artist  
**Clarke, Brian Patrick**  
2102 Clubside Dr, Longwood FL 32779, USA — Actor  
**Clarke, Darren C**  
Darren Clarke Golf School, The Lodge, Greenmount Campus, Antrim BT41 4PU, England — Golfer  
**Clarke, Emilia**  
Creative Artists Agency, 2000 Ave of Stars, #100, Los Angeles CA 90067 USA — Actress  
**Clarke, Gary**  
1113 Heep Run, Buda TX 78610, USA — Actor, Writer  
**Clarke, Geoffrey**  
Stowe Hill, Hartest, Bury Saint Edmunds, Suffolk IP29 4EQ, England — Artist, Sculptor  
**Clarke, Gilby**  
Central Entertainment Group, 165 5th Ave, #400, New York NY 10010, USA — Singer, Guitarist (Guns N' Roses)  
**Clarke, Horace M**  
PO Box 891, Frederiksted VI 00841, USA — Baseball Player  
**Clarke, Jacqueline (Jackie)**  
Paradigm Agency, 360 N Crescent Dr, North Building, Beverly Hills CA 90210 USA — Actress  
**Clarke, Jason**  
Creative Artists Agency, 2000 Ave of Stars, #100, Los Angeles CA 90067 USA — Actor, Producer  
**Clarke, John**  
8350 Santa Monica Blvd, #206A, West Hollywood CA 90069, USA — Actor  
**Clarke, Judy**  
Clarke & Rice, 1010 2nd Ave, #1800, San Diego CA 92101, USA — Attorney  
**Clarke, Kathy Kiera**  
Emptage Hallett, 14 Rathbone Place, London W1T 1HT, England — Actress  
**Clarke, Kenneth H**  
House of Commons, Westminster, London SW1A 0AA, England — Government Official, England  
**Clarke, Kenneth M (Ken)**  
7610 Willoughby Court, Alpharetta GA 30005, USA — Football Player  
**Clarke, Lenny**  
Paradigm Agency, 360 N Crescent Dr, North Building, Beverly Hills CA 90210 USA — Actor  
**Clarke, Martha**  
Columbia Artists Mgmt Inc, 1790 Broadway, #702, New York NY 10019 USA — Dancer, Choreographer  
**Clarke, Melinda**  
Innovative Artists, 1505 10th St, Santa Monica CA 90401 USA — Actress  
**Clarke, Noel A**  
Independent Talent Group, 40 Whitfield St, London W1T 2RH, England — Actor  
**Clarke, Paul Charles**  
Welsh National Opera, Millennium Centre, Bute Place, Cardiff Bay, Cardiff CF10 5AL, Wales — Singer  
**Clarke, Richard A**  
Simon & Schuster, 1230 Ave of Americas, Concourse 1, New York NY 10020 USA — Government Official  
**Clarke, Robert E (Bobby)**  
420 Beechwood Ave, Haddonfield NJ 08033, USA — Ice Hockey Player, Executive  
**Clarke, Robert L**  
Bracewell & Patterson, 711 Louisiana St, #2900, Houston TX 77002, USA — Government Official  
**Clarke, Ronald (Ron)**  
1 Bay St, Brighton VIC 3186, Australia — Track Athlete  
**Clarke, Sarah**  
Levine Mgmt, 9028 W Sunset Blvd, #PH1, Los Angeles CA 90069, USA — Actress  
**Clarke, Stanley M**  
4786 Topanga Canyon Blvd, Woodland Hills CA 91364, USA — Jazz Bassist, Composer

**Clarke, Stanley M (Stan)**     Baseball Player
5533 Sanders Dr, Toledo OH 43615, USA
**Clarke, Susanna**     Writer
Curtis Brown Group, 28-29 Haymarket St, #500, London SW1Y 4SP, England
**Clarke, Thomas E**     Businessman
Nike Inc, 1 SW Bowerman Dr, Beaverton OR 97005, USA
**Clark-Sheard, Karen**     Singer (Clark Sisters)
Universal Attractions, 135 W 26th St, #1200, New York NY 10001 USA
**Clarkson, Kelly**     Singer
Starstruck Entertainment, 40 Music Square W, Nashville TN 37203, USA
**Clarkson, Patricia**     Actress
Anonymous Content, 3532 Hayden Ave, Culver City CA 90232 USA
**Claro, Manuel Alberto**     Cinematographer
Sheldon Prosnit Agency, 800 S Robertson Blvd, #6, Los Angeles CA 90035, USA
**Clary, Robert**     Actor
10001 Sundial Lane, Beverly Hills CA 90210, USA
**Clary, Tyler**     Swimmer
Premier Management Group, 115 Crescent Commons, Cary, NC 27518 USA
**Clasby, Robert J (Bob)**     Football Player
8180 E Shea Blvd, #1090, Scottsdale AZ 85260, USA
**Clash, Kevin**     Puppeteer
W M E Entertainment, 9601 Wilshire Blvd, #300, Beverly Hills CA 90210 USA
**Clatterbuck, Tamara**     Actress
House of Representatives, 1434 6th St, #1, Santa Monica CA 90401 USA
**Clatworthy, Robert**     Sculptor
Moelfre, Cynghordy, Landovery, Carmarthenshire SA20 OUW, Wales
**Clauser, Francis H**     Aeronautical Engineer, Educator
842 E Villa St, #161, Pasadena CA 91101, USA
**Clauss, Jared**     Football Player
215 S 82nd St, West Des Moines IA 50266, USA
**Claver Arocas, Victor**     Basketball Player
Portland Trail Blazers, Rose Garden, 1 N Center Court St, Portland OR 97227 USA
**Clavier, Christian**     Actor
Ouille, 7 Rue des Dames Agustines, 92200 Neuilly, France
**Clawson, John R**     Basketball Player
30 Eagle Lake Place, #31, San Ramon CA 94582, USA
**Claxton, Craig (Speedy)**     Basketball Player
11215 Fairhaven Dr, Riverside CA 92505, USA
**Claxton, Paul**     Golfer
PO Box 485, Claxton GA 30417, USA
**Clay, Andrew**     Actor, Comedian
Robert Bruce, 218 Richmond Road, Grey Lynn, Auckland 1021, New Zealand
**Clay, Bryan E T**     Track Athlete
Doyle Mgmt, 952 Chippendale Trail, Marietta GA 30064, USA
**Clay, Eric L**     Judge
US Court of Appeals, 231 W Lafayette Blvd, #564, Detroit MI 48226, USA
**Clay, Kenneth E (Ken)**     Baseball Player
4523 60th Street Court W, Bradenton FL 34210, USA
**Clay, Otis**     Singer
Universal Attractions, 135 W 26th St, #1200, New York NY 10001 USA
**Clayborn, Raymond D (Ray)**     Football Player
20610 Aspen Canyon Dr, Katy TX 77450, USA
**Claycomb, Laura**     Opera Singer
I M G Artists, Hogarth Business Park, Chiswick, London W4 2TH, England
**Clayderman, Richard**     Pianist
World Entertainment, 8815 Conroy Windermeer Road, #407, Orlando FL 32835, USA
**Clayman, Ralph V**     Surgeon
Barnes Hospital, Surgery Dept, 416 S Kingshighway Blvd, Saint Louis MO 63110, USA
**Claypool, James (Jim)**     Ice Hockey Executive
302 Paine Farm Road, Duluth MN 55804, USA
**Claypool, Leslie E (Les)**     Singer, Bassist (Primus, Oysterhead)
Red Light Mgmt, PO Box 1467, Charlottesville VA 22902, USA
**Claypool, Philip**     Singer, Songwriter
B L T Mgmt, 2953 Sidco Dr, Nashville TN 37204, USA
**Clayson, Jane**     Commentator
CBS-TV, News Dept, 51 W 52nd St, New York NY 10019 USA
**Clayton, Adam**     Bassist (U-2)
Principle Mgmt, 30-32 Sir John Rogerson's Quay, Dublin 2, Ireland
**Clayton, Beth**     Opera Singer
I M G Artists, Hogarth Business Park, Chiswick, London W4 2TH, England
**Clayton, Donald D**     Astrophysicist
Clemson University, Physics/Astrophysics Dept, Clemson SC 29634, USA
**Clayton, Mark G**     Football Player
16426 Canyon Chase Dr, Houston TX 77095, USA
**Clayton, Mark J**     Football Player
9407 Manor Forge Way, Owings Mill MD 21117, USA
**Clayton, Robert N**     Geochemist
5201 S Cornell Ave, Chicago IL 60615, USA
**Clayton, Royce S**     Baseball Player
6035 Murphy Way, Malibu CA 90265, USA
**Clayton, Willie**     Singer, Songwriter
Universal Attractions, 135 W 26th St, #1200, New York NY 10001 USA
**Clayton-Thomas, David**     Singer (Blood Sweat & Tears)
Live Tour Artists, 1451 White Oaks Blvd, Oakville ON L6H 4R9, Canada
**Claywell, Brett**     Actor
Don Buchwald, 6500 Wilshire Blvd, #2200, Los Angeles CA 90048 USA
**Cleamons, James M (Jim)**     Basketball Player, Coach
29 Sausalito Circle W, Manhattan Beach CA 90266, USA
**Clear, Jacob**     Canoeing Athlete
Gold Coast Kayak & Canoe, 18 Kiers Road, Miami QLD 4220, Australia
**Clear, Mark A**     Baseball Player
15654 S Rene St, Olathe KS 66062, USA
**Clearwater, Keith A**     Golfer
PO Box 371503, Las Vegas NV 89137, USA
**Cleary, Beverly A**     Writer
Harper Collins Publishers, 10 E 53rd St, Cellar 1, New York NY 10022 USA

**Cleary, Jon** — Pianist, Composer
Rosebud Agency, PO Box 170429, San Francisco CA 94117, USA
**Cleary, Robert B (Bob)** — Ice Hockey Player
680 South Ave, #8, Weston MA 02493, USA
**Cleary, Robert J** — Attorney
Proskauer Rose, 1585 Broadway, #2700, New York NY 10036, USA
**Cleary, William J (Bill), Jr** — Ice Hockey Player, Coach
27 Kingswood Road, Auburndale MA 02466, USA
**Cleave, Mary L** — Astronaut
1901 E Belair Dr, Mount Vernon WA 98273, USA
**Cleaver, Alan R** — Fashion Designer
Byblos, Via Maggini 126, 60127 Ancona, Italy
**Cleaves, Slaid** — Singer, Songwriter
Keith Case Assoc, 1025 17th Ave S, #200, Nashville TN 37212 USA
**Cleeland, Cameron S (Cam)** — Football Player
23160 Lanyard Lane, Mount Vernon WA 98274, USA
**Cleese, John** — Actor, Comedian, Writer
Anonymous Content, 3532 Hayden Ave, Culver City CA 90232 USA
**Clegg, Johnny** — Singer
Monterey International, 200 W Superior St, #202, Chicago IL 60654 USA
**Cleghorne, Ellen** — Actress, Comedienne
Management 101, 468 N Camden Dr, #200, Beverly Hills CA 90210, USA
**Cleland, J Maxwell (Max)** — Senator, GA
2460 Peachtree Road NW, #1406, Atlanta GA 30305, USA
**Clemons, Clarence (Big Man)** — Saxophonist (E Street Band)
Vineberg Communications, 1695 Beach St, #303, San Francisco CA 94123, USA
**Clemens, Donella** — Religious Leader
Mennonite Church, 722 N Main St, Newton KS 67114, USA
**Clemens, Douglas H (Doug)** — Baseball Player
4799 Lower Mountain Road, New Hope PA 18938, USA
**Clemens, J Barry** — Basketball Player
3111 Clinton Ave, Cleveland OH 44113, USA
**Clemens, W Roger** — Baseball Player
8572 Katy Freeway, #106, Houston TX 77024, USA
**Clemenson, Christian** — Actor
Stone Manners Salners, 9911 W Pico Blvd, #1400, Los Angeles CA 90035 USA
**Clement, Anthony** — Football Player
141 Navajo Lane, Opelousas LA 70570, USA
**Clement, Aurore** — Actress
Artmedia, 20 Ave Rapp, 75007 Paris, France
**Clement, Bill** — Ice Hockey Player
6813 Upper York Road, New Hope PA 18938, USA
**Clement, Edith Brown** — Judge
US Court of Appeals, 600 Camp St, New Orleans LA 70130, USA
**Clement, Jemaine** — Singer (Flight of the Conchords), Actor
Creative Artists Agency, 2000 Ave of Stars, #100, Los Angeles CA 90067 USA
**Clement, John** — Businessman
Tuddenham Hall, Tuddenham, Ipswich, Suffolk IP6 9DD, England
**Clement, Kerron** — Track Athlete
University of Florida, Athletic Dept, Gainesville FL 32611, USA
**Clement, Matthew P (Matt)** — Baseball Player
143 Milt Miller Road, Renfrew PA 16053, USA
**Clement, Paul D** — Government Official, Attorney
Georgetown University, Law Center, Washington DC 20057, USA
**Clemente, Carmine D** — Anatomist
11737 Bellagio Road, Los Angeles CA 90049, USA
**Clemente, Francesco** — Artist
684 Broadway, New York NY 10012, USA
**Clements, John A** — Physiologist
University of California, Cardiovascular Institute, San Francisco CA 94143, USA
**Clements, Kim** — Writer
Creative Artists Agency, 2000 Ave of Stars, #100, Los Angeles CA 90067 USA
**Clements, Lennie** — Golfer
PO Box 182197, Coronado CA 92178, USA
**Clements, Nathan D (Nate)** — Football Player
Cincinnati Bengals, 1 Paul Brown Stadium, Cincinnati OH 45202 USA
**Clements, Patrick B (Pat)** — Baseball Player
166 Lazy S Lane, Chico CA 95928, USA
**Clements, Ronald F (Ron)** — Animator, Director
Creative Artists Agency, 2000 Ave of Stars, #100, Los Angeles CA 90067 USA
**Clements, Suzanne** — Fashion Designer
Clements Ribeiro Ltd, 48 S Molton St, London W1X 1HE, England
**Clemmensen, Scott L** — Ice Hockey Player
7 Woodbridge Court, Saratoga Springs NY 12886, USA
**Clemons, Duane** — Football Player
7512 Dr Phillips Blvd, #50-908, Orlando FL 32819, USA
**Clendenin, Robert T (Bob)** — Actor
Stone Manners Salners, 9911 W Pico Blvd, #1400, Los Angeles CA 90035 USA
**Cleobury, Nicholas R** — Conductor
Ben Rayfield, Southbank House, Black Prince Road, London SE1 7SJ, England
**Cleobury, Stephen J** — Conductor, Organist
King's College, Music Dept, Cambridge CB2 1ST, England
**Clergue, Lucien** — Photographer
Galerie Patrice Trigano, 229C Rue des Beaux-Arts, #4 Bis, 75006 Paris, France
**Clermont, Herve** — Actor
Commercial Talent, 9255 Sunset Blvd, #505, Los Angeles CA 90069, USA
**Clervoy, Jean-Francois** — Spatinaut, France
European Space Center, Linder Hohe, Box 906096, 51127 Cologne, Germany
**Clery, Corrine** — Actress
C D A Studio di Nardo, 12 Cavour 171, 00184 Rome, Italy
**Cleve, George W** — Conductor
Columbia Artists Mgmt Inc, 1790 Broadway, #702, New York NY 10019 USA
**Cleveland, Ashley** — Singer, Songwriter
Street Level Artists Agency, 107 E Center St, Warsaw IN 46580, USA
**Cleveland, Charles G (Chick)** — Air Force General, Hero
3603 Thomas Ave, Montgomery AL 36111, USA

**Cleveland, Davis** — Actor
Coast to Coast Talent, 3350 Barham Blvd, Los Angeles CA 90068 USA
**Cleveland, Pat** — Model
Ford Models Inc, 111 5th Ave, #900, New York NY 10003 USA
**Cleveland, Patience** — Actress
PO Box 490, Richland MO 65556, USA
**Cleveland, Reginald L (Reggie)** — Baseball Player
202 Creekview Dr, Anna TX 75409, USA
**Cleven, Harry** — Actor
U B B A, 6 Rue de Braque, 75003 Paris, France
**Clevenger, Raymond C, III** — Judge
US Court of Appeals, 717 Madison Place NW, Washington DC 20439, USA
**Clevenger, Truman E (Tex)** — Baseball Player
31727 Country Club Dr, Porterville CA 93257, USA
**Clexton, Edward W, Jr** — Navy Admiral
1000 Bobolink Dr, Virginia Beach VA 23451, USA
**Cliff, Jimmy** — Singer, Songwriter
51 Lady Musgrave Road, Kingston 10, Jamaica
**Clifford, Keith** — Actor
Jonathan Altaras Assoc, 11 Garrick St, London WC2E 9AR, England
**Clifford, Linda** — Singer
T-Best Talent Agency, 508 Honey Lake Court, Danville CA 94506 USA
**Clifford, M Richard (Rich)** — Astronaut
N A S A, Johnson Space Center, 2101 NASA Road, Houston TX 77058 USA
**Clift, William B, III** — Photographer
PO Box 6035, Santa Fe NM 87502, USA
**Clifton, J Chad** — Football Player
1641 Whispering Hills Dr, Franklin TN 37069, USA
**Clifton, James** — Actor
500 W 43rd St, #26J, New York NY 10036, USA
**Clifton, Kyle** — Football Player
777 South Point Court, Aledo TX 76008, USA
**Clifton, Scott** — Actor
Innovative Artists, 1505 10th St, Santa Monica CA 90401 USA
**Clifton, Shaw** — Religious Leader
Salvation Army International, 101 Queen Victoria St, London EC4 4EP, England
**Clijsters, Kim A L** — Tennis Player
Omselweg 37, 3960 Bree, Belgium
**Cline, Richard** — Cartoonist
New Yorker, Editorial Dept, 4 Times Square, Basement C1B, New York NY 10036 USA
**Clines, Eugene A (Gene)** — Baseball Player
5303 9th Ave Dr W, Bradenton FL 34209, USA
**Clinger, Debra** — Actress
1206 Chickasaw Dr, Brentwood TN 37027, USA
**Clinkscale, F Dextor** — Football Player
206 Michaux Dr, Greenville SC 29605, USA
**Clinton, George** — Singer, Synthesizer Player, Songwriter
Agency Group, 9348 Civic Center Dr, #200, Beverly Hills CA 90210 USA
**Clinton, George S** — Composer
First Artists Mgmt, 4764 Park Granada, #210, Calabasas CA 91302 USA
**Clinton, Hillary Rodham** — Secretary, State; Senator, NY
15 Old House Lane, Chappaqua NY 10514, USA
**Clinton, Kate** — Actress, Comedienne, Writer
Beachfront Productions, PO Box 13218, Portland OR 97213, USA
**Clinton, William J (Bill)** — President, USA
15 Old House Lane, Chappaqua NY 10514, USA
**Clippard, Tyler L** — Baseball Player
13575 58th St N, #199, Clearwater FL 33760, USA
**Clivilles, Robert M** — Music Producer (C & C Music Factory)
Brothers Management Assoc, 141 Dunbar Ave, Fords NJ 08863 USA
**Clodagh** — Interior Designer
Clodagh Design International, 670 Broadway, #400, New York NY 10012, USA
**Cloepfil, Brad** — Architect
4505 SW Bernard Dr, Portland OR 97239, USA
**Clohessy, Robert** — Actor
Don Buchwald, 6500 Wilshire Blvd, #2200, Los Angeles CA 90048 USA
**Cloke, Kristen** — Actress
Mitchell K Stubbs Assoc, 8695 W Washington Blvd, #204, Culver City CA 90232 USA
**Cloninger, Tony L** — Baseball Player
PO Box 1500, Denver NC 28037, USA
**Clooney, George** — Actor, Director, Writer
Stan Rosenfield Assoc, 2029 Century Park E, #1190, Los Angeles CA 90067 USA
**Close, Charles T (Chuck)** — Artist
20 Bond St, New York NY 10012, USA
**Close, Eric** — Actor
Untitled Entertainment, 350 S Beverly Dr, #200, Beverly Hills CA 90212 USA
**Close, Glenn** — Actress
Trillium Productions, PO Box 1560, #200, New Canaan CT 06840, USA
**Close, Joshua** — Actor
Untitled Entertainment, 350 S Beverly Dr, #200, Beverly Hills CA 90212 USA
**Closs, William T (Bill)** — Basketball Player
555 Byron St, #409, Palo Alto CA 94301, USA
**Closton, Cory** — Ice Hockey Coach
Ottawa Senators, Scotia Bank Place, Kanata ON K2V 1A5, Canada
**Clotet, Lluis** — Architect
Studio P E R, Caspe 151, 08013 Barcelona, Spain
**Clottey, Joshua** — Boxer
Top Rank Inc, 3908 Howard Hughes Parkway, #580, Las Vegas NV 89169 USA
**Clotworthy, Robert** — Actor
Amsel Eisenstadt Frazier, 5055 Wilshire Blvd, #865, Los Angeles CA 90036 USA
**Clotworthy, Robert L (Bob)** — Diver, Coach
2301 Moss Rose Lane, Fort Collins CO 80526, USA
**Cloud, Michael A (Mike)** — Football Player
5126 Miller Ave, Dallas TX 75206, USA
**Clough, G Wayne** — Educator, Administrator
Smithsonian Institution, 100 Jefferson Dr SW, Washington DC 20560, USA

**Clough, Ray W, Jr** — Structural Engineer
19800 SW Touchmark Way, #280, Bend OR 97702, USA
**Cloutier, Jacques** — Ice Hockey Player
12172 Triple Crown Dr, Parker CO 80134, USA
**Clowes, Daniel** — Cartoonist (Ghost World), Writer
United Talent Agency, U T A Plaza, 9336 Civic Center Dr, Beverly Hills CA 90210 USA
**Clunes, Martin** — Actor
Independent Talent Group, 40 Whitfield St, London W1T 2RH, England
**Clunie, Michelle** — Actress
Abrams Artists, 9200 W Sunset Blvd, #1125, West Hollywood CA 90069 USA
**Cluzet, Francois** — Actor
Voyez Mon Agent, 20 Ave Rapp, 75007 Paris, France
**Clyde, David E (Dave)** — Baseball Player
7806 Pinehurst Shadows Dr, Humble TX 77346, USA
**Clymer, Ben** — Ice Hockey Player
2713 Plaza Verde, Lake Havasu City AZ 86406, USA
**Clyne, Patricia** — Fashion Designer
353 W 39th St, New York NY 10018, USA
**Coachman Davis, Alice** — Track Athlete
1317 Lee St, Albany GA 31701, USA
**Coakley, W Dexter** — Football Player
1304 Sunset Ridge Circle, Cedar Hill TX 75104, USA
**Coan, Gilbert F (Gil)** — Baseball Player
70 Beach Lane, Brevard NC 28712, USA
**Coates, Anne V** — Film Editor, Producer
United Talent Agency, U T A Plaza, 9336 Civic Center Dr, Beverly Hills CA 90210 USA
**Coates, James A (Jim)** — Baseball Player
1098 Oak Hill Road, Lancaster VA 22503, USA
**Coates, Kim** — Actor
Oscars Abrams Zimel, 438 Queen St E, Toronto ON M5A 1T4, Canada
**Coates, Phyllis** — Actress
PO Box 1969, Boyes Hot Springs CA 95416, USA
**Coates, Steve J** — Ice Hockey Player, Sportscaster
102 Stoney Creek Dr, Egg Harbor Township NJ 08234, USA
**Coats, Kristi** — Golfer
185 Wildwood Place, Petal MS 39465, USA
**Coats, Michael L** — Astronaut
3203 Acorn Wood Way, Houston TX 77059, USA
**Cobb, Garry W** — Football Player
112 Society Hill Blvd, Cherry Hill NJ 08003, USA
**Cobb, Geraldyn M (Jerrie)** — Astronaut Candidate
1006 Beach Blvd, Sun City Center FL 33573, USA
**Cobb, Henry N** — Architect
Pei Cobb Freed Partners, 88 Pine St, Lobby 1, New York NY 10005, USA
**Cobb, Jewel Plummer** — Biologist
California State University, PO Box 3480, Fullerton CA 92834, USA
**Cobb, John B, Jr** — Social Activist
Claremont Graduate School, Center for Process Studies, Claremont CA 91711, USA
**Cobb, Julie** — Actress
C E S D, 10635 Santa Monica Blvd, #130, Los Angeles CA 90025 USA
**Cobb, Keith Hamilton** — Actor
Gage Group, 450 7th Ave, #1809, New York NY 10123 USA
**Cobb, Reginald J (Reggie)** — Football Player
PO Box 17416, Sugar Land TX 77496, USA
**Cobbin, W Jim (James)** — Baseball Player
121 E Raven Ave, Youngstown OH 44503, USA
**Cobbs, Bill** — Actor
Stone Manners Salners, 9911 W Pico Blvd, #1400, Los Angeles CA 90035 USA
**Coben, Harlan** — Writer
E P Dutton, 375 Hudson St, New York NY 10014 USA
**Cobert, Bob** — Composer
B M I, 8730 W Sunset Blvd, #300, Los Angeles CA 90069 USA
**Cobham, William C (Billy)** — Jazz Drummer, Composer
Joel Chriss Co, 300 Mercer St, #3J, New York NY 10003 USA
**Coble, G Drew** — Baseball Umpire
205 80th Ave N, Myrtle Beach SC 29572, USA
**Coblenz, Walter** — Director, Producer
4310 Cahuenga Blvd, #401, Toluca Lake CA 91602, USA
**Cobos, Alberto** — Paleontologist
Teruel-Dinopolis Museum, Poligono de los Planos, 44002 Teruel, Spain
**Cobos, Jesus Lopez** — Conductor
Cincinnati Symphony, 1241 Elm St, Cincinnati OH 45202, USA
**Coburn, Braydon** — Ice Hockey Player
523 Chews Landing Road, Haddonfield NJ 8033, USA
**Coburn, Doris** — Bowler
130 Dalton Dr, Buffalo NY 14223, USA
**Coburn, John G** — Army General
7717 Island Creek Court, Alexandria VA 22315, USA
**Coccopalmerio, Francesco Cardinal** — Religious Leader
Pontifical Council for Legislative Texts, 00120 Vatican City
**Cochinescu, Ioan Mihai** — Photographer, Writer
CP 1-151, 2000 Ploiesti 1, Prahova, Romania
**Cochran, Barbara Ann** — Skier
Cochran's Ski Area, PO Box 789, Richmond VT 05477, USA
**Cochran, John** — Commentator
ABC-TV, News Dept, 5010 Creston St, Hyattsville MD 20781 USA
**Cochran, Robert** — Writer, Producer
A P A Talent/Literary Agency, 405 S Beverly Dr, #300, Beverly Hills CA 90212 USA
**Cochran, Russ** — Golfer
3 Circle Lake Dr, Paducah KY 42001, USA
**Cochran, Shannon** — Actress
Mitchell K Stubbs Assoc, 8695 W Washington Blvd, #204, Culver City CA 90232 USA
**Cochran, Stacy** — Director
I C M Partners, 10250 Constellation Blvd, #900, Los Angeles CA 90067 USA
**Cochran, Tammy** — Singer, Songwriter
Consortium, 49 Music Square W, #210, Nashville TN 37203, USA

Cochrane, David C (Dave) — Baseball Player
126 Silver Eagle Lane, Mooresville NC 28117, USA
Cochrane, Glen M — Ice Hockey Player
405 Collett Road, Kelowna BC V1W 1K6, Canada
Cochrane, Rory — Actor
Untitled Entertainment, 350 S Beverly Dr, #200, Beverly Hills CA 90212 USA
Cockburn, Bruce — Singer, Songwriter, Guitarist
Finkelstein Mgmt, 137 Berkeley St, Toronto ON M5V 2X1, Canada
Cocker, Jarvis — Singer (Pulp), Songwriter
X-Ray Touring, Nena House, 77-79 Great Eastern St, London EC2A 3HU, England
Cocker, Joe — Singer
Mad Dog Ranch, 43401 Cottonwood Creek Road, Crawford CO 81415, USA
Cockerill, Franklin — Microbiologist
Mayo Clinic, Microbiology Dept, 200 1st St SW, Rochester MN 55905, USA
Cockerill, Kay — Golfer
131 Beulah St, San Francisco CA 94117, USA
Cockey, Tim — Writer
Hyperion Books, 114 5th Ave, New York NY 10011 USA
Cockrell, Kenneth D — Astronaut
2300 Richmond Ave, #350, Houston TX 77098, USA
Cockroft, Donald L (Don) — Football Player
2418 Dunkeith Dr NW, Canton OH 44708, USA
Coco, Lea — Actor, Writer
Gersh Agency, 9465 Wilshire Blvd, #600, Beverly Hills CA 90212 USA
Cocroft, Sherman — Football Player
2504 Christopher Lane, Costa Mesa CA 92626, USA
Codiroli, Christopher A (Chris) — Baseball Player
2700 Hillcrest Dr, Cameron Park CA 95682, USA
Codrescu, Andrei — Writer
Louisiana State University, English Dept, Baton Rouge LA 70803, USA
Coduri, Camille — Actress
Independent Talent Group, 40 Whitfield St, London W1T 2RH, England
Cody, Diablo — Producer, Writer
W M E Entertainment, 9601 Wilshire Blvd, #300, Beverly Hills CA 90210 USA
Cody, William E (Bill) — Football Player
209 Orleans Dr, Fairhope AL 36532, USA
Coe of Ranmore, Sebastian N — Track Athlete
Starswood, High Barn Road, Effingham, Surrey KT24 5PW, England
Coe, David Allan — Singer, Guitarist, Songwriter
Conqueroo, 11271 Ventura Blvd, #522, Studio City CA 91604, USA
Coe, George — Actor
Abrams Artists, 9200 W Sunset Blvd, #1125, West Hollywood CA 90069 USA
Coe, Sue — Artist
Galerie Saint Etienne, 24 W 57th St, New York NY 10019, USA
Coe-Jones, Dawn — Golfer
2945 SW 39th Ave, Gainesville FL 32608, USA
Coelho, Paulo — Writer
Caixa Postal 43003, Rio de Janeiro 22052-970, Brazil
Coelho, Susie — Actress
3565 Meadowview Dr, Riverside CA 92503, USA
Coen, Ethan — Director, Writer
United Talent Agency, U T A Plaza, 9336 Civic Center Dr, Beverly Hills CA 90210 USA
Coen, Joel — Director, Writer
United Talent Agency, U T A Plaza, 9336 Civic Center Dr, Beverly Hills CA 90210 USA
Coetzee, Gergardus C (Gerrie) — Boxer
22 Sydney Road, Ravenswood, Boksburg 1460, South Africa
Coetzee, John M — Nobel Literature Laureate
PO Box 92, Rondebosch, Cape Province 7700, South Africa
Coetzer, Amanda — Tennis Player
PO Box 686, Florida Hills 1716, South Africa
Coeur De Pirate — Singer, Songwriter
Agency Group Ltd, 142 W 57th St, #600, New York NY 10019 USA
Cofer, J Michael (Mike) — Football Player, Truck Racing Driver
Racing West, 1772 Los Arboles, #J186, Thousand Oaks CA 91362, USA
Cofer, Michael L (Mike) — Football Player
110 Bridgestone Cove, Fayetteville GA 30215, USA
Coffey, J Todd — Baseball Player
109 Colonel Hampton Court, Rutherfordton NC 28139, USA
Coffey, Jeffrey (King) — Drummer (Butthole Surfers)
Kork Agency, 1880 Century Park E, #711, Los Angeles CA 90067, USA
Coffey, John L — Judge
US Court of Appeals, US Courthouse, 517 E Wisconsin Ave, Milwaukee WI 53202, USA
Coffey, Junior L — Football Player
17228 32nd Ave S, #E12, Seatac WA 98188, USA
Coffey, Kellie — Singer, Songwriter
W M E Entertainment, 1600 Division St, #300, Nashville TN 37203 USA
Coffey, Paul D — Ice Hockey Player
Bolton Toyota, 12050 Albion Vaughan Road, Bolton ON L7E 1S7, Canada
Coffin, Edmund (Tad) — Equestrian
1151 Dairy Road, Ruckersville VA 22968, USA
Coffin, Fredrick — Actor
Gage Group, 14724 Ventura Blvd, #505, Sherman Oaks CA 91403 USA
Coffin, Peter — Artist, Sculptor
Venus Over Manhattan Gallery, 980 Madison Ave, #300, New York NY 10075, USA
Coffman, Paul R — Football Player
14103 E 195th St, Peculiar MO 64078, USA
Cogan, Kevin — Auto Racing Driver
205 Rocky Point Road, Palos Verdes Estates CA 90274, USA
Cogdill, Gail R — Football Player
12922 E 36th Ave, Spokane Valley WA 99206, USA
Coggins, Richard A (Rich) — Baseball Player
4095 Fruit St, #219, La Verne CA 91750, USA
Coghill, Jonathan R (Jon) — Drummer (Powderfinger)
Secret Service, PO Box 401, Fortitude Valley QLD 4006, Australia
Coghlan, Eamon — Track Athlete
International Mangement Group, 1 Erieview Plaza, 1360 E 9th St, Cleveland OH 44114 USA

**Cogollo, Heriberto** — Artist
54 Rue Faubourg du Courreau, 34000 Montpelier (Herault), France

**Cohan, Lauren** — Actress
Creative Artists Agency, 2000 Ave of Stars, #100, Los Angeles CA 90067 USA

**Cohan, Robert P** — Choreographer
The Place, 17 Dukes Road, London WC1H 9AB, England

**Coheleach, Guy J** — Artist
Pandion Art, PO Box 96, Bernardsville NJ 07924, USA

**Cohen, Adam** — Singer, Guitarist, Songwriter
Paquin Entertainment Agency, 219 Dufferin St, #206B, Toronto ON M6K 3J1, Canada

**Cohen, Alexandra P (Sasha)** — Figure Skater
International Mangement Group, 1 Erieview Plaza, 1360 E 9th St, Cleveland OH 44114 USA

**Cohen, Arnaldo** — Concert Pianist
Arts Management Group, 1133 Broadway, #1025, New York NY 10010, USA

**Cohen, Avishai** — Jazz Bassist
Janet Williamson Music Agency, PO Box 27114, Los Angeles CA 90027, USA

**Cohen, Bernard W** — Artist
80 Camberwell Grove, London SE5 8RF, England

**Cohen, Bruce** — Producer
Bruce Cohen Productions, 8292 Hollywood Blvd, Los Angeles CA 90069, USA

**Cohen, David** — Keyboardist (Country Joe & the Fish)
I C M Partners, 10250 Constellation Blvd, #900, Los Angeles CA 90067 USA

**Cohen, David X** — Producer, Writer
Creative Artists Agency, 2000 Ave of Stars, #100, Los Angeles CA 90067 USA

**Cohen, Etan** — Producer, Writer
Creative Artists Agency, 2000 Ave of Stars, #100, Los Angeles CA 90067 USA

**Cohen, Jerome A** — Attorney, Educator
New York University, Law School, 40 Washington Square, New York NY 10012, USA

**Cohen, Joshua** — Philosopher
Stanford University, Philosophy Dept, Stanford CA 94305, USA

**Cohen, Larry** — Labor Leader
Communications Workers of America, 501 3rd St NW, #C1, Washington DC 20001, USA

**Cohen, Larry** — Director, Writer
Larco Productions, 2111 Coldwater Canyon, Beverly Hills CA 90210, USA

**Cohen, Leonard N** — Writer, Singer, Songwriter
S L Feldman Mgmt, 1505 W 2nd Ave, #200, Vancouver BC V6H 3Y4, Canada

**Cohen, Lynn** — Actress
Paradigm Agency, 360 Park Ave S, #1600, New York NY 10010 USA

**Cohen, Marshall H** — Astronomer
California Institute of Technology, Astronomy Dept, Pasadena CA 91125, USA

**Cohen, Marvin** — Pharmacologist
Triumph Pharmaceuticals, 10403 Baur Blvd, #A, Saint Louis MO 63132, USA

**Cohen, Marvin L** — Physicist
10 Forest Lane, Berkeley CA 94708, USA

**Cohen, Matt** — Actor
Stone Manners Salners, 9911 W Pico Blvd, #1400, Los Angeles CA 90035 USA

**Cohen, Peter M** — Director, Producer, Writer
United Talent Agency, U T A Plaza, 9336 Civic Center Dr, Beverly Hills CA 90210 USA

**Cohen, Rachel Leah** — Actress
Avalon Artists Group, 143 W 29th St, #1103, New York NY 10001, USA

**Cohen, Rob** — Director
Nowita Pictures, 2900 Olympic Blvd, #345, Santa Monica CA 90404, USA

**Cohen, Robert** — Concert Cellist
15 Birchwood Ave, London N10 3BE, England

**Cohen, Sacha Baron** — Actor, Comedian
W M E Entertainment, 9601 Wilshire Blvd, #300, Beverly Hills CA 90210 USA

**Cohen, Sarah** — Journalist
Washington Post, Editorial Dept, 1150 15th St NW, Washington DC 20071 USA

**Cohen, Scott** — Actor
One Entertainment, 347 5th Ave, #1404, New York NY 10016 USA

**Cohen, Sheldon S** — Government Official
5518 Trent St, Chevy Chase MD 20815, USA

**Cohen, Stanley** — Nobel Medicine Laureate
106 Mint Spring Circle, Brentwood TN 37027, USA

**Cohen, Stanley N** — Geneticist, Inventor
Stanford University Medical Center, Genetics Dept, Stanford CA 94305, USA

**Cohen, William S** — Secretary, Defense; Senator, ME
Cohen Group, 600 13th St NW, #640, Washington DC 20005, USA

**Cohen-Tannoudji, Claude K** — Nobel Physics Laureate
38 Rue des Cordelieres, 75013 Paris, France

**Cohn, Alfred (Al)** — Bowler
85 Odyssey Dr, Tinley Park IL 60477, USA

**Cohn, Gary** — Journalist
Baltimore Sun, Editorial Dept, 501 N Calvert St, Baltimore MD 21278, USA

**Cohn, Gary** — Financier
Goldman Sachs Co, 85 Broad St, Building 85, New York NY 10004, USA

**Cohn, Marc** — Singer, Songwriter
Michael Hausman Mgmt, 511 Ave of Americas, #197, New York NY 10011, USA

**Cohn, Mindy** — Actress
Arthouse Entertainment, 9350 Wilshire Blvd, #328, Beverly Hills CA 90212, USA

**Coia, Arthur A** — Labor Leader
Laborers' International Union, 905 16th St NW, #600, Washington DC 20006, USA

**Coifman, Ronald R** — Computer Scientist
11 Hickory Road, North Haven CT 06473, USA

**Coker, Larry E** — Football Coach, Sportscaster
University of Texas, Athletic Dept, San Antonio TX 78249, USA

**Cokes, Curtis** — Boxer
618 Calcutta Dr, Dallas TX 75241, USA

**Colander-Richardson, LaTasha** — Track Athlete
26 E Myrtle Dr, Angier NC 27501, USA

**Colangelo, Jerry J** — Basketball, Baseball Executive
70 E Country Club Dr, Phoenix AZ 85014, USA

**Colantoni, Enrico** — Actor
Innovative Artists, 1505 10th St, Santa Monica CA 90401 USA

**Colao, Vittorio** — Businessman
Vodafone Group, Connection, Newbury, Berkshire RG14 2FN, England

| | |
|---|---|
| **Colbert, Jim** | Golfer |
| 118 Wanish Place, Palm Desert CA 92260, USA | |
| **Colbert, Nathan (Nate)** | Baseball Player |
| 2756 N Green Valley Parkway, Henderson NV 89014, USA | |
| **Colbert, Stephen** | Actor, Comedian, Writer |
| Dixon Talent Agency, 375 Greenwich St, #500, New York NY 10013, USA | |
| **Colborn, James W (Jim)** | Baseball Player |
| 2932 Solimar Beach Dr, Ventura CA 93001, USA | |
| **Colburn, Richard** | Drummer (Belle & Sebastian) |
| Ground Control Touring, 20 Jay St, #826, Brooklyn NY 11201 USA | |
| **Colchico, Daniel M (Dan)** | Football Player |
| 5160 Paul Scarlet Dr, Concord CA 94521, USA | |
| **Colclough, Henry** | Singer |
| 3040 Fontain St, Philadelphia PA 19121, USA | |
| **Cold 187um** | Rap Artist (Above the Law) |
| Green Light Talent Agency, PO Box 3172, Beverly Hills CA 90212 USA | |
| **Cole, Alexander (Alex)** | Baseball Player |
| 6545 N Stevens Hollow Dr, Chesterfield VA 23832, USA | |
| **Cole, Anne** | Fashion Designer |
| Cole of California, 6040 Bandini Blvd, Los Angeles CA 90040, USA | |
| **Cole, Artemas** | Cartoonist |
| 15 Regency Manor, #15-8, Rutland VT 05701, USA | |
| **Cole, Ashley** | Soccer Player |
| Arsenal London, Avenell Road, Highbury, London N5 1BU, England | |
| **Cole, Bobby** | Golfer |
| 204 W 2nd Ave, Windermere FL 34786, USA | |
| **Cole, Bradley** | Actor |
| Leading Artists, 145 W 45th St, #1000, New York NY 10036 10036, USA | |
| **Cole, Cheryl A (Tweedy)** | Singer (Girls Aloud) |
| Concorde International, 101 Shepherds Bush Road, London W6 7LP, England | |
| **Cole, Christina** | Actress |
| Conway Van Gelder Grant, 8-12 Broadwick St, #300, London W1F 8HW, England | |
| **Cole, Danton** | Ice Hockey Player |
| 7180 Wapiti Way, Saline MI 48176, USA | |
| **Cole, David D** | Attorney |
| Georgetown University, Law School, Washington DC 20057, USA | |
| **Cole, Erik** | Ice Hockey Player |
| 1112 Stonekirk, Raleigh NC 27614, USA | |
| **Cole, Freddy** | Singer |
| Producers Inc, 11806 N 56th St, Tampa FL 33617 USA | |
| **Cole, Gary** | Actor |
| I C M Partners, 10250 Constellation Blvd, #900, Los Angeles CA 90067 USA | |
| **Cole, George E** | Actor |
| Joy Jameson, PO Box 68182, London N1P 2BN, England | |
| **Cole, Holly** | Singer |
| Alert Music, 51 Hillsview Ave, Toronto ON M6P 1J4, Canada | |
| **Cole, Jasper** | Actor |
| Newman-Thomas Mgmt, 8306 Wilshire Blvd, #996 Beverly Hills CA 90211, USA | |
| **Cole, Joanna** | Writer |
| Scholastic Press, 555 Broadway, New York NY 10012, USA | |
| **Cole, John** | Editorial Cartoonist |
| Scranton Times-Tribune, Editorial Dept, 149 Penn Ave, Scranton PA 18503, USA | |
| **Cole, Johnnetta B** | Museum Executive, Educator |
| National African Art Museum, 950 Independence Ave SW, Washington DC 20560, USA | |
| **Cole, Julie Dawn** | Actress |
| Joy Jameson, PO Box 68182, London N1P 2BN, England | |
| **Cole, Kenneth** | Fashion Designer |
| Kenneth Cole Productions, 601 W 50th St, New York NY 10019, USA | |
| **Cole, Keyshia** | Singer, Actress |
| Creative Artists Agency, 2000 Ave of Stars, #100, Los Angeles CA 90067 USA | |
| **Cole, Larry R** | Football Player |
| 400 Country Place, Colleyville TX 76034, USA | |
| **Cole, Lily** | Model, Actress |
| I M G Models, 304 Park Ave S, #PH N, New York NY 10010 USA | |
| **Cole, Marilyn** | Model |
| Playboy Promotions, 2706 Media Center Dr, Los Angeles CA 90065 USA | |
| **Cole, Michael** | Psychologist |
| University of California, Communications Dept, La Jolla CA 92093, USA | |
| **Cole, Michael** | Actor |
| J K A Talent Agency, 12725 Ventura Blvd, #H, Studio City CA 91604, USA | |
| **Cole, Nadine E L** | Singer (Girls Aloud) |
| Concorde International, 101 Shepherds Bush Road, London W6 7LP, England | |
| **Cole, Natalie** | Singer, Actress |
| Moir/Borman Entertainment, 1250 6th St, #401, Santa Monica CA 90401, USA | |
| **Cole, Nigel** | Director, Writer |
| Independent Talent Group, 40 Whitfield St, London W1T 2RH, England | |
| **Cole, Olivia** | Actress |
| Century Artists, PO Box 59747, Santa Barbara CA 93150 USA | |
| **Cole, Paula** | Singer, Songwriter |
| Skyline Music, 48 Prospect St, Whitefield NH 03598, USA | |
| **Cole, Ralph, Jr** | Actor |
| Prestige Talent Agency, 9250 Wilshire Blvd, #208, Beverly Hills CA 90212, USA | |
| **Cole, Richard (Richie)** | Jazz Saxophonist |
| Abby Hoffer Enterprises, 223 1/2 E 48th St, New York NY 10017 USA | |
| **Cole, Richard E** | WW II Army Air Corps Hero |
| 48 Blaschke Road, Comfort TX 78013, USA | |
| **Cole, Richard R (Dick)** | Baseball Player |
| 3149 Madeira Ave, Costa Mesa CA 92626, USA | |
| **Cole, Robert C (Bob)** | Sportscaster |
| CBC-TV, PO Box 500 Station A, Toronto ON M5W 1E6, Canada | |
| **Cole, Robin** | Football Player |
| 9 Brook Lane, Eighty Four PA 15330, USA | |
| **Cole, Steve** | Jazz Saxophonist |
| Great Scott Productions, 4750 Lincoln Blvd, #229, Marina del Rey CA 90292, USA | |
| **Cole, Steven** | Opera Singer |
| Columbia Artists Mgmt Inc, 1790 Broadway, #702, New York NY 10019 USA | |

**Cole, Susan A** — Educator
Montclair State University, President's Office, Montclair NJ 07043, USA

**Cole, Tina** — Actress, Singer
4603 Edison Ave, Sacramento CA 95821, USA

**Cole, Trent** — Football Player
Philadelphia Eagles, 1 Novacare Way, Philadelphia PA 19145 USA

**Colella, Richard (Rick)** — Swimmer
217 19th Place, Kirkland WA 98033, USA

**Coleman, Bill** — Dance Company Executive, Choreographer
Coleman Lemieux Compagnie, 304 Paliament St, Toronto M5A 3A4, Canada

**Coleman, Bobby** — Actor
Coast to Coast Talent, 3350 Barham Blvd, Los Angeles CA 90068 USA

**Coleman, Brian** — Artist
900 Old Evans Road, Watsonville CA 95076, USA

**Coleman, Catherine G (Cady)** — Astronaut
30 Frank Williams Road, Shelburne Falls MA 01370, USA

**Coleman, Chad** — Actor
Talent Works, 3500 W Olive Ave, #1400, Burbank CA 91505 USA

**Coleman, Cosey C** — Football Player
11901 Northumberland Dr, Tampa FL 33626, USA

**Coleman, Dabney** — Actor
Michael Black Mgmt, 9701 Wilshire Blvd, 1000, Beverly Hills CA 90212, USA

**Coleman, David L (Dave)** — Baseball Player
4303 Delhi Dr, Dayton OH 45432, USA

**Coleman, Deborah** — Singer, Guitarist
Piedmont Talent, PO Box 680006, Charlotte NC 28216, USA

**Coleman, Don E** — Football Player
424 McPherson Ave, Lansing MI 48915, USA

**Coleman, E C, Jr** — Basketball Player
370 E Harmon Ave, Las Vegas NV 89169, USA

**Coleman, George E** — Jazz Saxophonist
Maurice Montoya Music Agency, 1133 Broadway, #1608, New York NY 10010, USA

**Coleman, Gerald F (Jerry)** — Baseball Player, Manager; Sportscaster
1004 Havenhurst Dr, La Jolla CA 92037, USA

**Coleman, Greg J** — Football Player
2313 River Pointe Circle, Minneapolis MN 55411, USA

**Coleman, Jack** — Actor
Domain Talent, 9229 W Sunset Blvd, #710, West Hollywood CA 90069 USA

**Coleman, Jenna-Louise** — Actress
Troika, 74 Clerkenwell Road, #300, London EC1M 5QA, England

**Coleman, Jeremy (Jaz)** — Singer (Killing Joke), Songwriter
Agency Group, 9348 Civic Center Dr, #200, Beverly Hills CA 90210 USA

**Coleman, Joseph H (Joe)** — Baseball Player
17851 Eagle View Lane, Cape Coral FL 33909, USA

**Coleman, Kari** — Actress
C E S D, 10635 Santa Monica Blvd, #130, Los Angeles CA 90025 USA

**Coleman, Kelly** — Basketball Player
PO Box 183, Higgins Lake MI 48627, USA

**Coleman, Kenyon O** — Football Player
35723 Stock St, Murrieta CA 92562, USA

**Coleman, Marco D** — Football Player
105 Monarch Court, Saint Augustine FL 32095, USA

**Coleman, Marissa** — Basketball Player
Los Angeles Sparks, 888 S Figueroa St, #2010, Los Angeles CA 90017 USA

**Coleman, Mary Sue** — Educator
University of Michigan, President's Office, Ann Arbor MI 48109, USA

**Coleman, Monique** — Actress
Magnolia Entertainment, 9595 Wilshire Blvd, #601, Beverly Hills CA 90212, USA

**Coleman, Norman B, Jr** — Senator, MN
American Action Forum, 1455 Pennsylvania Ave NW, #350, Washington DC 20004, USA

**Coleman, Ornette** — Jazz Saxophonist, Composer
Ted Kurland, 173 Brighton Ave, Boston MA 02134 USA

**Coleman, Phyllis** — Model
Playboy Promotions, 2706 Media Center Dr, Los Angeles CA 90065 USA

**Coleman, Roderick D (Rod)** — Football Player
6735 Great Water Dr, Flowery Branch GA 30542, USA

**Coleman, Rowan** — Writer
Pocket Books, 1230 Ave of Americas, New York NY 10020 USA

**Coleman, Sidney** — Football Player
15083 Highway 39 N, DeKalb MS 39328, USA

**Coleman, Signy** — Actress
Abrams Artists, 9200 W Sunset Blvd, #1125, West Hollywood CA 90069 USA

**Coleman, Vincent M (Vince)** — Baseball Player
7271 Primrose Lane, San Diego CA 92129, USA

**Coleman, William T, Jr** — Secretary, Transportation
O'Melveny & Myers, 1625 I St NW, Washington DC 20006, USA

**Coleman, Zendaya** — Actress
Monster Talent Mgmt, 6333 W 3rd St, #912, Los Angeles CA 90036, USA

**Coles, Darnell** — Baseball Player
306 Signature Terrace, Safety Harbor FL 34695, USA

**Coles, Janet** — Golfer
6083 Alumni Gym, Hanover NH 3755, USA

**Coles, Julie** — Actress
6780 N Casa Real Place, Boise ID 83714, USA

**Coles, Kim** — Actress, Comedienne
Abrams Artists, 9200 W Sunset Blvd, #1125, West Hollywood CA 90069 USA

**Coles, Laveranues L** — Football Player
1 Sagamore Dr, Plainview NY 11803, USA

**Coles, Robert M** — Psychiatrist
81 Carr Road, Concord MA 01742, USA

**Coles, Vernell E (Bimbo)** — Basketball Player
203 E Washington St, Lewisburg WV 24901, USA

**Colescott, Warrington W** — Artist
8788 County Road A, Hollandale WI 53544, USA

**Coley, Daryl** — Clarinetist, Pianist
Daryl Coley Ministries, 417 E Regent St, Inglewood CA 90301, USA

**Coley, John Ford** — Singer, Songwriter
Utopia Artists, PO Box 1821, Ojai CA 93024, USA
**Colfer, Chris** — Actor
Coast to Coast Talent, 3350 Barham Blvd, Los Angeles CA 90068 USA
**Colgate, Stirling A** — Physicist
422 Estante Way, Los Alamos NM 87544, USA
**Colicchio, Thomas P (Tom)** — Chef, Restauranteur
Colicchio & Sons, 85 10th Ave, New York NY 10011, USA
**Colin, Charlie** — Bassist (Train)
Jon Landau, 80 Main St, Greenwich CT 06830, USA
**Colin, Margaret** — Actress
Innovative Artists, 1505 10th St, Santa Monica CA 90401 USA
**Colinet, Stalin** — Football Player
3 Mohawk Dr, Framingham MA 01701, USA
**Coll, Ashley** — Artist
1419 Chetwynd Ave, Plainfield NJ 07060, USA
**Coll, Ivonne** — Actress
Don Buchwald, 6500 Wilshire Blvd, #2200, Los Angeles CA 90048 USA
**Coll, Stephen W** — Journalist
New America Foundation, 1899 L St, NW, #400, Washington DC 20036, USA
**Collard, Jean-Philippe** — Concert Pianist
Caroline Martin Musique, 126 Rue Vielle du Temple, 75003 Paris, France
**Collet-Serra, Jaume** — Director
Ombra Films, 12444 Ventura Blvd, #103, Studio City CA 91604, USA
**Collett, C Elmer** — Football Player
PO Box 522, 10 Avenida Farralone, Stinson Beach CA 94970, USA
**Collett, Jason** — Singer, Songwriter
Agency Group Ltd, 142 W 57th St, #600, New York NY 10019 USA
**Collette, Toni** — Actress
United Agents, 12-26 Lexington St, London W1F 0LE, England
**Colletti, Stephen** — Actor
A P A Talent/Literary Agency, 405 S Beverly Dr, #300, Beverly Hills CA 90212 USA
**Colley, Dana** — Saxophonist (Morphine)
48 Laight St, New York NY 10013, USA
**Colley, Ed** — Cartoonist (Suburban Cowgirls)
11 Blaisdell Terrace, Ipswich MA 01938, USA
**Colley, Kenneth** — Actor
Ken McReddie Assoc, 101 Finsbury Pavement, London EC2A 1RS, England
**Colley, Michael C** — Navy Admiral
12022 Forest St, Thornton CO 80241, USA
**Colley, Tom** — Ice Hockey Player
71 Dillon Dr, Collingwood ON L9Y 4S4, Canada
**Collie, Bruce S** — Football Player
9595 Ranch Road 12, #13, Wimberley TX 78676, USA
**Collie, Mark** — Singer, Songwriter, Actor
Dreamcatcher Artist Mgmt, 2908 Poston Ave, Nashville TN 37203, USA
**Collier, Charles (Charlie)** — Businessman
A M C Networks, 11 Penn Plaza, New York NY 10001, USA
**Collier, Don** — Actor
9024 E 21st St, Tucson AZ 85710, USA
**Collier, James Lincoln** — Writer
71 Barrow St, New York NY 10014, USA
**Collier, Lesley F** — Ballerina
Royal Ballet, Covent Garden, Bow St, London WC2E 9DD, England
**Collier, Louis K (Lou)** — Baseball Player
6409 S Kenwood Ave, Chicago IL 60637, USA
**Collier, Timothy (Tim)** — Football Player
3116 50th St, Dallas TX 75216, USA
**Colligan, Edward T** — Businessman
Equity Partners, 70 E 55th St, New York NY 10022, USA
**Colligan, John (Bud)** — Businessman
Macromedia Inc, 600 Townsend St, San Francisco CA 94103, USA
**Collin, Aurelien** — Soccer Player
Sporting Kansas City, 210 W 19th Terrace, #200, Kansas City MO 64108 USA
**Collingwood, Chris** — Singer (Fountains of Wayne), Songwriter
Big Hassle, 157 Chambers St, #1200, New York NY 10007, USA
**Collins, Anthony (Tony)** — Football Player
2712 Gulfstream Dr, Miramar FL 33023, USA
**Collins, Arthur W (Bud), Jr** — Sportscaster
822 Boylston St, #203, Chestnut Hill MA 02467, USA
**Collins, Bernard** — Singer (Abyssinians)
Fast Lane International, 4856 Haygood Road, #200, Virginia Beach VA 23455, USA
**Collins, Candace L** — Model
Playboy Promotions, 2706 Media Center Dr, Los Angeles CA 90065 USA
**Collins, Carla** — Comedienne, Actress
Agency Group Ltd, 142 W 57th St, #600, New York NY 10019 USA
**Collins, Clifton G, Jr** — Actor
A P A Talent/Literary Agency, 405 S Beverly Dr, #300, Beverly Hills CA 90212 USA
**Collins, David J** — Inventor (Bar Code)
A2B Tracking Solutions, 207 Highpoint Ave, Portsmouth RI 02871, USA
**Collins, David S (Dave)** — Baseball Player
206 N East St, #15, Mason OH 45040, USA
**Collins, Dean** — Actor
Howard Entertainment, 10850 Wilshire Blvd, #1260, Los Angeles CA 90024, USA
**Collins, Eileen M** — Astronaut
2024 Pebble Beach Dr, League City TX 77573, USA
**Collins, Francis S** — Geneticist
National Institutes of Health, 9000 Rockville Pike, Bethesda MD 20892, USA
**Collins, Gary** — Ice Hockey Player
1908-1320 Islington Ave, Etobicoke M9A 5C6, Canada
**Collins, Gary J** — Football Player
221 Lamp Post Lane, Hershey PA 17033, USA
**Collins, Heidi** — Commentator
CNN-TV, News Dept, 820 1st St NE, #1000, Washington DC 20002 USA
**Collins, J Maxwell S (Max), III** — Singer, Bassist (Eve 6)
Agency Group Ltd, 1880 Century Park E, #711, Los Angeles CA 90067 USA

# C

**Collins, Jackie** — Writer
10624 Wellworth Ave, Los Angeles CA 90024, USA

**Collins, James B (Jim)** — Football Player
2140 E Oceanfront, Newport Beach CA 92661, USA

**Collins, Jarron T** — Basketball Player
11173 Cashmere St, Los Angeles CA 90049, USA

**Collins, Jason P** — Basketball Player
13120 Constable Ave, Granada Hills CA 91344, USA

**Collins, Jeff** — Rodeo Rider
1429 Limestone Road, Redfield KS 66769, USA

**Collins, Jerry** — Actor, Writer, Producer
United Talent Agency, U T A Plaza, 9336 Civic Center Dr, Beverly Hills CA 90210 USA

**Collins, Jessica** — Actress
I C M Partners, 10250 Constellation Blvd, #900, Los Angeles CA 90067 USA

**Collins, Jim** — Writer, Management Consultant
Harper Business Books, 10 E 53rd St, Cellar 1, New York NY 10022, USA

**Collins, Jo** — Model, Actress
Playboy Promotions, 2706 Media Center Dr, Los Angeles CA 90065 USA

**Collins, Joan** — Actress
Paul Keylock, 16 Bulbecks Walk, S Woodham Ferrers, Essex CM3 5ZN, England

**Collins, Joely** — Actress
Kirk Talent Agencies, 196 W 3rd Ave, #102, Vancouver BC V5Y 1E9, Canada

**Collins, John** — Bassist (Powderfinger)
Secret Service, PO Box 401, Fortitude Valley QLD 4006, Australia

**Collins, John W** — Businessman
Clorox Co, 1221 Broadway, Oakland CA 94612, USA

**Collins, Judy** — Singer, Songwriter
American Program Bureau, 313 Washington St, #225, Newton MA 02458, USA

**Collins, K C** — Actor
Glick Agency, 1321 7th St, #203, Santa Monica CA 90401 USA

**Collins, Kate** — Actress
1410 York Ave, #4D, New York NY 10021, USA

**Collins, Kayla** — Model
Playboy Promotions, 2706 Media Center Dr, Los Angeles CA 90065 USA

**Collins, Kerry M** — Football Player
1090 Stockett Dr, Nashville TN 37221, USA

**Collins, Kevin M** — Baseball Player
9121 Point Charity Dr, Pigeon MI 48755, USA

**Collins, Lauren** — Actress
A M I Artist Management, 464 King St E, Toronto ON M5A 1L7, Canada , USA

**Collins, Lily J** — Actress, Model
Creative Artists Agency, 2000 Ave of Stars, #100, Los Angeles CA 90067 USA

**Collins, Lynn** — Actress
3 Arts Entertainment, 9460 Wilshire Blvd, #700, Beverly Hills CA 90212 USA

**Collins, Mark A** — Football Player
2568 Baseline St, #155, Highland CA 92346, USA

**Collins, Martha Layne** — Governor, KY; Educator
921 Taborlake Court, Lexington KY 40502, USA

**Collins, Marva** — Educator
1507 E 53rd St, Chicago IL 60615, USA

**Collins, Michael** — Conductor, Concert Clarinetist
Hazard Chase, 72 Charlotte St, London W1T 4QQ, England

**Collins, Michael** — Writer
Viking Penguin Books, 375 Hudson St, Basement 1, New York NY 10014 USA

**Collins, Michael** — Astronaut, Air Force General
272 Polynesia Court, Marco Island FL 34145, USA

**Collins, Misha** — Actor
Framework Entertainment, 9057 Nemo St, #C, West Hollywood CA 90069 USA

**Collins, Mo** — Actress, Comedienne
Odenkirk Provissiero Entertainment, 1936 N Bronson Ave, Los Angeles CA 90069 USA

**Collins, Nancy A** — Writer
Harper Collins Publishers, 10 E 53rd St, Cellar 1, New York NY 10022 USA

**Collins, P Douglas (Doug)** — Basketball Player, Coach, Sportscaster
10040 E Happy Valley Road, #617, Scottsdale AZ 85255, USA

**Collins, Patrick** — Actor
Tisherman Agency, 6767 Forest Lawn Dr, #101, Los Angeles CA 90068 USA

**Collins, Pauline** — Actress
Independent Talent Group, 40 Whitfield St, London W1T 2RH, England

**Collins, Phil** — Singer, Songwriter, Drummer
Alfred House, 23-24 Cromwell Place, #300, London SW7 2LD, England

**Collins, Randall** — Sociologist
University of Pennsylvania, Sociology Dept, Philadelphia PA 19104, USA

**Collins, Shanna** — Actress
A K A Talent, 6310 San Vicente Blvd, #200, Los Angeles CA 90048 USA

**Collins, Shawn** — Football Player
PO Box 711933, San Diego CA 92171, USA

**Collins, Sherron M** — Basketball Player
Charlotte Bobcats, 333 E Trade St, #A, Charlotte NC 28202 USA

**Collins, Stephen** — Actor
A P A Talent/Literary Agency, 405 S Beverly Dr, #300, Beverly Hills CA 90212 USA

**Collins, Steve** — Boxer
Rock Solid Productions, PO Box 70642, Houston TX 77270, USA

**Collins, Terry L** — Baseball Manager
40992 Hollydale, Novi MI 48375, USA

**Collins, Thomas C Cardinal** — Religious Leader
Archdiocese, Chancery Office, 1155 Yonge St, Toronto ON M4T 1W2, Canada

**Collins, Todd S** — Football Player
26 Cambridge Circle, Victor NY 14564, USA

**Collins, William (Billy)** — Writer
RR 202, Somers NY 10589, USA

**Collins, William E (Bill)** — Ice Hockey Player
5000 Town Center, #505, Southfield MI 48075, USA

**Collins, William E (Bootsy)** — Singer, Bassist
Agency Group Ltd, 1880 Century Park E, #711, Los Angeles CA 90067 USA

**Collinson, Madeleine** — Model, Actress
Playboy Promotions, 2706 Media Center Dr, Los Angeles CA 90065 USA

**Collinson, Mary** — Model, Actress
Playboy Promotions, 2706 Media Center Dr, Los Angeles CA 90065 USA
**Collinsworth, A Cris** — Football Player, Sportscaster
31 Crow Hill Road, Fort Thomas KY 41075, USA
**Collison, Darren M** — Basketball Player
Dallas Mavericks, Pavilion, 2909 Taylor St, Dallas TX 75226 USA
**Collison, Frank** — Actor
Amsel Eisenstadt Frazier, 5055 Wilshire Blvd, #865, Los Angeles CA 90036 USA
**Collison, Nicholas J (Nick)** — Basketball Player
16 Comstock St, Seattle WA 98109, USA
**Collister, Christine** — Singer
Running Media, 14 Victoria Road, Douglas, Isle of Man IM2 4ER, England
**Collman, James P** — Chemist
794 Tolman Dr, Stanford CA 94305, USA
**Collomb, Bertrand P** — Businessman
4 Rue de Lota, 75116 Paris, France
**Collyer, Laurie** — Director, Writer, Actress
Gersh Agency, 9465 Wilshire Blvd, #600, Beverly Hills CA 90212 USA
**Colman, Booth** — Actor
2160 Century Park E, #603, Los Angeles CA 90067, USA
**Colman, Oliva** — Actress
United Agents, 12-26 Lexington St, London W1F 0LE, England
**Colman, Paul** — Singer, Guitarist, Pianist, Composer
W M E Entertainment, 9601 Wilshire Blvd, #300, Beverly Hills CA 90210 USA
**Colman, Wayne C** — Football Player
604 N Somerset Ave, Ventnor NJ 08406, USA
**Colmes, Alan** — Commentator
Fox-TV, News Dept, 1211 Ave of Americas, New York NY 10036, USA
**Colo, Donald R (Don)** — Football Player
7355 E Claremont St, Scottsdale AZ 85250, USA
**Coloma, Marcus** — Actor
Don Buchwald, 6500 Wilshire Blvd, #2200, Los Angeles CA 90048 USA
**Colombo, Marc E** — Football Player
7219 Marigold Dr, Irving TX 75063, USA
**Colomby, Scott** — Actor
Borinstein Oreck Bogart, 3172 Dona Susana Dr, Studio City CA 91604 USA
**Colon, Bartolo** — Baseball Player
14 Federal St, #1, Passaic NJ 07055, USA
**Colon, Willie A** — Singer, Trombonist, Composer
Universal Attractions, 135 W 26th St, #1200, New York NY 10001 USA
**Colosimo, Vince** — Actor
Robyn Gardiner Mgmt, 397 Riley St, Surry Hills NSW 2010, Australia
**Colquitt, Dustin F** — Football Player
1905 Pitts Field Lane, Knoxville TN 37922, USA
**Colquitt, J Craig** — Football Player
1905 Pitts Field Lane, Knoxville TN 37922, USA
**Colson, Elizabeth F** — Anthropologist
University of California, Anthropology Dept, Berkeley CA 94720, USA
**Colston, Marques** — Football Player
New Orleans Saints, 5800 Airline Highway, Metairie LA 70003 USA
**Colter, Jessie** — Singer
Bobby Roberts, PO Box 1547, Goodlettsville TN 37070, USA
**Colter, Steve** — Basketball Player
802 E Mountain Sage Dr, Phoenix AZ 85048, USA
**Colton, Graham** — Singer, Songwriter
Back Bay Mgmt, 397 Little Neck Road, Virginia Beach VA 23452, USA
**Coltrane, Chi** — Singer, Pianist, Songwriter
5955 Tuxedo Terrace, Los Angeles CA 90068, USA
**Coltrane, Ravi** — Jazz Saxophonist
Ted Kurland, 173 Brighton Ave, Boston MA 02134 USA
**Coltrane, Robbie** — Actor, Comedian
Caroline Dawson, 125 Gloucester Road, London SW7 4TE, England
**Coluccio, Robert P (Bob)** — Baseball Player
369 Flower St, Costa Mesa CA 92627, USA
**Columbo, Marc E** — Football Player
Miami Dolphins, 7500 SW 30th St, Davie FL 33314 USA
**Columbu, Franco** — Body Builder
2265 Westwood Blvd, #A, Los Angeles CA 90064, USA
**Columbus, Christopher J (Chris)** — Director, Writer
1492 Pictures, 4000 Warner Blvd, Building 3, Burbank CA 91522, USA
**Colvin, James R (Jim)** — Football Player
1310 Rancho Vista Dr, McKinney TX 75070, USA
**Colvin, John O** — Judge
US Tax Court, 400 2nd St NW, Washington DC 20217, USA
**Colvin, Roosevelt, III** — Football Player
9340 Sargent Road, Indianapolis IN 46256, USA
**Colvin, Shawn** — Singer, Songwriter
Vector Mgmt, PO Box 120479, Nashville TN 37212 USA
**Colvin, Shelly** — Singer, Songwriter
Parallel Entertainment, 209 10th Ave S, #506, Nashville TN 37203, USA
**Colwell, John A** — Association Executive, Physician
American Diabetes Assn, 1701 N Beauregard St, #100, Alexandria VA 22311, USA
**Colwell, Rita R** — Microbiologist, Foundation Executive
5010 River Hill Road, Bethesda MD 20816, USA
**Colwill, Les** — Ice Hockey Player
714 20th St, North Lethbridge AB T1H 3N6, Canada
**Comaneci, Nadia** — Gymnast
4421 Hidden Hill Road, Norman OK 73072, USA
**Comart, Jean-Paul** — Actor
Artmedia, 20 Ave Rapp, 75007 Paris, France
**Comastri, Angelo Cardinal** — Religious Leader
Basilica di San Pietro, 00120 Vatican City
**Combas, Robert** — Artist
Galleries D'Arte Elysees, 26 Ave des Champs-Elysees, 75008 Paris, France
**Combeau, Muriel** — Actress
Voyez Mon Agent, 20 Ave Rapp, 75007 Paris, France

**Combes, Willard W** — Editorial Cartoonist
1266 Oakridge Dr, Cleveland OH 44121, USA

**Combs, David** — Actor
Special Artists Agency, 9200 Sunset Blvd, #410, West Hollywood CA 90069 USA

**Combs, Glenn** — Basketball Player
3627 Dogwood Lane SW, Roanoke VA 24015, USA

**Combs, Holly Marie** — Actress
Gersh Agency, 9465 Wilshire Blvd, #600, Beverly Hills CA 90212 USA

**Combs, Jeffrey** — Actor
Bleu, 5225 Wilshire Blvd, #401, Los Angeles CA 90036, USA

**Combs, Rodney** — Auto Racing Driver
American Diecast, 16173 Edgemont Dr, Fort Myers FL 33908, USA

**Combs, Sean, (Puff Daddy, P Diddy)** — Rap Artist, Actor
Creative Artists Agency, 2000 Ave of Stars, #100, Los Angeles CA 90067 USA

**Comeau, Andy** — Actor
Talent Works, 3500 W Olive Ave, #1400, Burbank CA 91505 USA

**Comeau, Ray** — Ice Hockey Player
4 Rue de Cernay, Lorraine QC J6Z 2Z1, Canada

**Comeaux, Darren** — Football Player
6313 Kristie Lane, Brusly LA 70719, USA

**Comegys, Dallas A** — Basketball Player
4330 Wayne Ave, Philadelphia PA 19140, USA

**Comer, Steven M (Steve)** — Baseball Player
525 Lake Dr, #377, Chanhassen MN 55317, USA

**Comess, Aaron** — Musician (Spin Doctors)
D A S Communications, 83 Riverside Dr, New York NY 10024 USA

**Comi, Paul** — Actor
2395 Ridgeway Road, San Marino CA 91108, USA

**Commander Cody** — Musician
Jacobson & Colfin, 60 Madison Ave, #1026, New York NY 10010, USA

**Commissiong, Janelle** — Beauty Queen
Bowen Marine, Western Main Road, Chaguaramas, Trinidad

**Commodore, Michael (Mike)** — Ice Hockey Player
12017 Fern Dr, Detroit Lakes MN 56501, USA

**Common** — Rap Artist, Actor
42 West, 220 W 42nd St, #1200, New York NY 10036 USA

**Compagnon, Antoine M T** — Educator, Writer
875 W End Ave, #15D, New York NY 10025, USA

**Compagnoni, Deborah** — Alpine Skier
Benetton Group SpA, Via Minelli, 31050 Ponzano Treviso, Italy

**Compaore, Blaise** — President, Burkina Faso
President's Office, 03 BP 7030, Ouagadougou 03, Burkina Faso

**Compte, Maurice** — Actor
Don Buchwald, 6500 Wilshire Blvd, #2200, Los Angeles CA 90048 USA

**Compton, Ann Woodruff** — Commentator
ABC-TV, News Dept, 3361 75th Ave, #X, Hyattsville MD 20785, USA

**Compton, Richard** — Actor
A P A Talent/Literary Agency, 405 S Beverly Dr, #300, Beverly Hills CA 90212 USA

**Compton, Richard L (Dick)** — Football Player
3408 S Briarcliff Court, Irving TX 75062, USA

**Comrie, Michael W (Mike)** — Ice Hockey Player
10800 Wilshire Blvd, #1703, Los Angeles CA 90024, USA

**Comstock, Harold** — Air Force Hero
2809 Aberdeen Lane, El Dorado Hills CA 95762, USA

**Comstock, Keith M** — Baseball Player
9615 E Desert Trail, Scottsdale AZ 85260, USA

**Cona, Louis** — Publisher
New Yorker, Publisher's Office, 4 Times Square, New York NY 10036, USA

**Conacher, Jim** — Ice Hockey Player
422-980 Lynn Valley Road, West Vancouver BC V7J 3V7, Canada

**Conacher, Pat** — Ice Hockey Player
18371 W Sweet Acacia Dr, Goodyear AZ 85338, USA

**Conant, Kenneth J** — Archaeologist
3 Carlton Village, #T105, Bedford MA 01730, USA

**Conatsor, Clinton A (Connie)** — Baseball Player
26701 Quail Creek, #191, Laguna Hills CA 92656, USA

**Conaty, William B (Billy), Jr** — Football Player
203 Country Club Dr, Moorestown NJ 08057, USA

**Conaway, Cristi** — Actress
1759 Old Ranch Road, Los Angeles CA 90049, USA

**Conaway, John B** — Air Force General
Spectrum Group, 11 Canal Center Plaza, #103, Alexandria VA 22314, USA

**Conaway, Ronald C** — Geneticist
Stowers Medical Research Institute, 1000 E 50th St, Kansas City MO 64110, USA

**Concepcion Benitez, David I (Davey)** — Baseball Player
Urb el Castano Botalon 5D, Maracay 5, Venezuela

**Conde, Alpha** — President, Guinea
President's Office, Palais Presidentiel, Cite des Nations, Conakry, Guinea

**Conde, Ninel H** — Actress, Singer
Apodaca Promotions, 717 E Tidwell Road, Houston TX 77022, USA

**Condit, Gary A** — Representative, CA
2509 Acorn Lane, Ceres CA 95307, USA

**Condo, George** — Artist
108 E 78th St, New York NY 10075, USA

**Condon of Langton Green, Paul L** — Law Enforcement Official
I C C, Clock Tower, Lord's Cricket Ground, London NW8 8QN, England

**Condon, Kerry** — Actress
I C M Partners, 10250 Constellation Blvd, #900, Los Angeles CA 90067 USA

**Condon, Thomas J (Tom)** — Football Player
99 Oakleigh Lane, Saint Louis MO 63124, USA

**Condon, William (Bill)** — Director, Writer
Anonymous Content, 3532 Hayden Ave, Culver City CA 90232 USA

**Condon, Zach** — Singer (Beirut), Songwriter
Ba Da Bing Records, 181 Clermont Ave, #403, Brooklyn NY 11205, USA

**Condren, Glen P** — Football Player
8557 N 175th East Ave, Owasso OK 74055, USA

**Condrey, Clayton L (Clay)** — Baseball Player
412 N 8th St, Navasota TX 77868, USA
**Cone Vanderbush, Carin** — Swimmer
47 Rose Dr, Highland Falls NY 10928, USA
**Cone, David B** — Baseball Player
219 Dolphin Cove Quay, Stamford CT 6902, USA
**Cone, Fred** — Football Player
PO Box 1819, Blairsville GA 30514, USA
**Confino, Edmond** — Obstetrician, Gynecologist
676 N Saint Clair St, #1845, Chicago IL 60611, USA
**Conforti, Gino** — Actor
Orange Grove Group, 12178 Ventura Blvd, #205, Studio City CA 91604 USA
**Congdon, Jeffrey D (Jeff)** — Basketball Player
505 Highway View Court, Mesquite NV 89027, USA
**Conine, Jeffrey G (Jeff)** — Baseball Player
3166 Iverness, Weston FL 33332, USA
**Conkey, Margaret** — Archaeologist
University of California, Archaeological Research Facility, Berkeley CA 94720, USA
**Conklin, Harold C** — Anthropologist
200 Leeder Hill Dr, #607, Hamden CT 06517, USA
**Conklin, Ty** — Ice Hockey Player
PO Box 472, New Castle NH 03854, USA
**Conlan, Shane P** — Football Player
521 East Dr, Sewickley PA 15143, USA
**Conlee, Jenny** — Organist, Accordianist (Decemberists)
Big Hassle, 44 Wall St, #2200, New York NY 10005, USA
**Conlee, John** — Singer
John Conlee Enterprises, 38 Music Square E, #117, Nashville TN 37203, USA
**Conley, Clare D** — Editor
Hemlock Farms, Hawley PA 18428, USA
**Conley, D Eugene (Gene)** — Baseball, Basketball Player
400 Foxboro Blvd, #3102, Foxboro MA 02035, USA
**Conley, Earl Thomas** — Singer, Songwriter
657 Baker Road, Smyrna TN 37167, USA
**Conley, Mike, Jr** — Basketball Player
3496 Windgarden Cove, Memphis TN 38125, USA
**Conley, Wayne** — Writer
Paradigm Agency, 360 Park Ave S, #1600, New York NY 10010 USA
**Conlin, Edward J (Ed)** — Basketball Player
153 N Mountain Ave, Montclair NJ 07042, USA
**Conlin, Michaela** — Actress
Evolution Entertainment, 901 N Highland Ave, Los Angeles CA 90038 USA
**Conlon, Edward W** — Writer
Random House, 1745 Broadway, #1800, New York NY 10019 USA
**Conlon, James J** — Conductor
Shuman Assoc, 120 W 58th St, #8D, New York NY 10019, USA
**Conlon, Martin M (Marty)** — Basketball Player
204 Head of Pond Road, Water Mill NY 11976, USA
**Conn, Didi** — Actress, Singer
C E S D, 10635 Santa Monica Blvd, #130, Los Angeles CA 90025 USA
**Conn, Richard R (Dick)** — Football Player
144 Sugarmill Lane, Moore SC 29369, USA
**Conn, Shelley** — Actress
United Agents, 12-26 Lexington St, London W1F 0LE, England
**Conneff, Kevin** — Singer, Percussionist (Chieftains)
Macklam/Feldman Mgmt, 1505 W 2nd Ave, #200, Vancouver BC V6H 3Y4, Canada
**Connell, Albert G A** — Football Player
3522 Ruth St, Houston TX 77004, USA
**Connell, Desmond Cardinal** — Religious Leader
Archbishop's House, Drumcondra, Dublin 9, Ireland
**Connelly, Jennifer** — Actress
Creative Artists Agency, 2000 Ave of Stars, #100, Los Angeles CA 90067 USA
**Connelly, Michael** — Writer
Little Brown, 3 Center Plaza, #100, Boston MA 02108 USA
**Connelly, Wayne F** — Ice Hockey Player
RR 2 Site 2, Box 61, Swastika ON P0K 1T0, Canada
**Conner, Bart** — Gymnast
4421 Hidden Hill Road, Norman OK 73072, USA
**Conner, Chris** — Actor
A K A Talent, 6310 San Vicente Blvd, #200, Los Angeles CA 90048 USA
**Conner, Clyde R** — Football Player
510 Valencia Dr, Los Altos Hills CA 94022, USA
**Conner, Darion** — Football Player
9553 Prairie Point Road, Macon MS 39341, USA
**Conner, Dennis W** — Yachtsman
881 Golden Park Ave, San Diego CA 92106, USA
**Conner, Lester A** — Basketball Player
13836 Coldwater Dr, Carmel IN 46032, USA
**Conner, Lois** — Photographer
36 Gramercy Park E, #4E, New York NY 10003, USA
**Conners, Daniel J (Dan)** — Football Player
1032 Chorro St, San Luis Obispo CA 93401, USA
**Conners, Sheralee** — Model
Playboy Promotions, 2706 Media Center Dr, Los Angeles CA 90065 USA
**Connery, Sean** — Actor
Lyford Cay, PO Box N7776, Nassau, Bahamas
**Connery, Vincent L** — Labor Leader
National Treasury Employees Union, 1730 K St NW, Washington DC 20006, USA
**Connes, Alain** — Mathematician
Leon Motchane I'H E S, 35 Route Chartres, 91440 Bures-sur-Yvette, France
**Connick, Harry, Jr** — Pianist, Singer, Actor
Creative Artists Agency, 2000 Ave of Stars, #100, Los Angeles CA 90067 USA
**Conniff, Cal** — Skier
157 Pleasantview Ave, Longmeadow MA 01106, USA
**Connolly, Billy** — Actor
Julian Belfrage Assoc, 9 Argyll St, #300, London W1F 7TG, England

**Connolly, John** — Writer
Simon & Schuster, 1230 Ave of Americas, Concourse 1, New York NY 10020 USA
**Connolly, Kevin** — Actor
Creative Artists Agency, 2000 Ave of Stars, #100, Los Angeles CA 90067 USA
**Connolly, Kristen** — Actress
Untitled Entertainment, 350 S Beverly Dr, #200, Beverly Hills CA 90212 USA
**Connolly, Nathan** — Singer, Guitarist (Snow Patrol)
Big Life Mgmt, 67-69 Charlton St, London NW1 1HY, England
**Connolly, Olga Fikotova** — Track Athlete
218 1/2 E 20th St, Costa Mesa CA 92627, USA
**Connolly, Theodore W (Ted)** — Football Player
1805 N Carson St, #86, Carson City NV 89701, USA
**Connolly, Tom** — Actor
Innovative Artists, 1505 10th St, Santa Monica CA 90401 USA
**Connor, Cam** — Ice Hockey Player
1331 Leeward Way, Qualicum Beach BC V9K 2M1, Canada
**Connor, Daniel M (Dan)** — Football Player
1032 Chorro St, San Luis Obispo CA 93401, USA
**Connor, Kate** — Actress
Jay Schwartz Assoc, 3151 Cahuenga Blvd, W, #220, Los Angeles CA 90068, USA
**Connor, Linda S** — Photographer
87 Rutherford, San Anselmo CA 94960, USA
**Connor, Paolo** — Actor
Abrams Artists, 275 7th Ave, #2600, New York NY 10001 USA
**Connor, Sarah** — Singer, Songwriter
World Concerts, Hamburger Str 273A, 38114 Braunschweig, Germany
**Connors, Carol** — Songwriter
1709 Ferrari Dr, Beverly Hills CA 90210, USA
**Connors, James S (Jimmy)** — Tennis Player
1962 E Valley Road, Santa Barbara CA 93108, USA
**Connors, Mike** — Actor
4810 Louise Ave, Encino CA 91316, USA
**Connors, Norman** — Jazz Drummer
Universal Attractions, 135 W 26th St, #1200, New York NY 10001 USA
**Connors, William A (Bill)** — Jazz Guitarist
Michael Bloom Media Relations, PO Box 41380, Los Angeles CA 90041, USA
**Conover, K Scott** — Football Player
28 Windsor Terrace, #B, Freehold NJ 07728, USA
**Conover, Lloyd H** — Inventor (Tetracycline)
5200 Brittany Dr S, #304, Saint Petersburg FL 33715, USA
**Conquest, G Robert A** — Historian
52 Peter Coutts Circle, Stanford CA 94305, USA
**Conrad, David** — Actor
Gersh Agency, 9465 Wilshire Blvd, #600, Beverly Hills CA 90212 USA
**Conrad, Fred** — Photographer
New York Times, Editorial Dept, 229 W 43rd St, New York NY 10036, USA
**Conrad, James A** — Financier
Source One Mortgage, 100 Galleria Officentre, #300, Southfield MI 48034, USA
**Conrad, Jimmy** — Soccer Player
Sporting Kansas City, 210 W 19th Terrace, #200, Kansas City MO 64108 USA
**Conrad, Lauren K** — Actress, Model
United Talent Agency, U T A Plaza, 9336 Civic Center Dr, Beverly Hills CA 90210 USA
**Conrad, Robert** — Actor
6320 Via Cataldo St, Malibu CA 90265, USA
**Conrad, Robert J (Bobby Joe)** — Football Player
148 County Road 3270, Clifton TX 76634, USA
**Conrad, Shane** — Actor
Sutton-Barth Vennari, 5900 Wilshire Blvd, #700, Los Angeles CA 90036 USA
**Conradt, Jody** — Basketball Coach
9614 Leaning Rock Circle, Austin TX 78730, USA
**Conran, Jasper A T** — Fashion Designer
1-7 Rostrevor Mews, Fulham, London SW6 5AZ, England
**Conran, Kerry** — Director, Writer
Paradigm Agency, 360 N Crescent Dr, North Building, Beverly Hills CA 90210 USA
**Conran, Philip J** — Vietnam War Air Force Hero
4706 Calle Reina, Santa Barbara CA 93110, USA
**Conran, Terence O** — Interior Designer
22 Shad Thames, London SE1 2YU, England
**Conroy, Craig** — Ice Hockey Player
PO Box 549, Henderson Harbor NY 13651, USA
**Conroy, D Patrick (Pat)** — Writer
247 Brighton Road NE, Atlanta GA 30309, USA
**Conroy, Frances** — Actress
Paradigm Agency, 360 N Crescent Dr, North Building, Beverly Hills CA 90210 USA
**Conroy, Kevin** — Actor
Imperium 7 Talent, 5455 Wilshire Blvd, #1706, Los Angeles CA 90036, USA
**Conroy, Patricia** — Singer, Songwriter
Live Tour Artists, 1451 White Oaks Blvd, Oakville ON L6H 4R9, Canada
**Conroy, Timothy J (Tim)** — Baseball Player
109 Moonlight Dr, Monroeville PA 15146, USA
**Considine, Paddy** — Actor, Director
Creative Artists Agency, 2000 Ave of Stars, #100, Los Angeles CA 90067 USA
**Considine, Tim** — Actor, Writer, Director
3708 Mountain View Ave, Los Angeles CA 90066, USA
**Constantine II** — King, Greece
4 Linnell Dr, Hampstead Way, London NW11 7LN, England
**Constantine, Kevin L** — Ice Hockey Coach
5928 Jenny Lind Court, San Jose CA 95120, USA
**Constantine, Michael** — Actor
6861 Colbath Ave, Van Nuys CA 91405, USA
**Constantine, Susannah** — Actress
Paradigm Agency, 360 N Crescent Dr, North Building, Beverly Hills CA 90210 USA
**Constantinescu, Roxana** — Opera Singer
Harrison/Parrott, 5-6 Albion Court, London W6 0QT, England
**Consuelos, Mark** — Actor, Model
Milojo Productions, 270 Lafayette St, #702, New York NY 10012, USA

**Contador Velasco, Alberto** — Cyclist
Team Saxo Bank, Firskowej 38, 2800 KGS Lynby, Denmark
**Conte, Paolo** — Singer, Pianist, Composer
Partisan Arts, PO Box 5085, Larkspur CA 94977, USA
**Conteh, John** — Boxer
8 Cedar Dr, Hatch End, Pinner, Middlesex HA5 4DE, England
**Conti, Bill** — Composer
117 Fremont Place W, Los Angeles CA 90005, USA
**Conti, Jason** — Baseball Player
740 N April Dr, Chandler AZ 85226, USA
**Conti, Tom** — Actor
Gersh Agency, 9465 Wilshire Blvd, #600, Beverly Hills CA 90212 USA
**Contino, Dick** — Singer, Accordianist
3355 Nahatan Way, Las Vegas NV 89169, USA
**Contner, James A** — Cinematographer
3020 Kensington Ave, Richmond VA 23221, USA
**Contreras Camejo, Jose A** — Baseball Player
1001 Brickell Bay Dr, #1710, Miami FL 33131, USA
**Contreras, Narciso** — Photojournalist
Associated Press, Editorial Dept, 450 W 33rd St, #1500, New York NY 10001 USA
**Contz, William (Bill)** — Football Player
106 Grace Dr, Cranberry Township PA 16066, USA
**Converse, Frank** — Actor
I C M Partners, 10250 Constellation Blvd, #900, Los Angeles CA 90067 USA
**Converse, James D (Jim)** — Baseball Player
11865 Cobble Brook Dr, Rancho Cordova CA 95742, USA
**Converse-Roberts, William** — Actor
Don Buchwald, 6500 Wilshire Blvd, #2200, Los Angeles CA 90048 USA
**Convertino, John** — Drummer, Percussionist (Calexico)
Billions Corp, 3522 W Armitage Ave, Chicago IL 60647 USA
**Convertino, Michael** — Composer
Soundtrack Music Assoc, 1460 4th St, #308, Santa Monica CA 90401 USA
**Conway Mitchell, Susan** — Actress
70 Highbourne Road, Toronto ON M5R 3H8, Canada
**Conway, Billy** — Drummer (Morphine)
Spivak Entertainment, 11845 W Olympic Blvd, Los Angeles CA 90064, USA
**Conway, Brett A** — Football Player
630 Virginia Ave NE, Atlanta GA 30306, USA
**Conway, Craig** — Actor
Ken McReddie Assoc, 101 Finsbury Pavement, London EC2A 1RS, England
**Conway, Curtis L** — Football Player
446 E Phelps St, Gilbert AZ 85295, USA
**Conway, Gary** — Actor
11240 Chimney Rock Road, Paso Robles CA 93446, USA
**Conway, James L** — Director
Kaplan-Stahler Agency, 8383 Wilshire Blvd, #923, Beverly Hills CA 90211 USA
**Conway, James T** — Marine Corps General
8164 Ambach Way, Hypoluxo FL 33462, USA
**Conway, Jill K** — Educator, Historian
65 Commonwealth Ave, #8B, Boston MA 02116, USA
**Conway, Joe** — Writer
Gersh Agency, 9465 Wilshire Blvd, #600, Beverly Hills CA 90212 USA
**Conway, John Horton** — Mathematician
120 Prospect Ave, #1A, Princeton NJ 08540, USA
**Conway, Karla (Sachi)** — Model, Artist
PO Box 249, Honaunau HI 96726, USA
**Conway, Kevin** — Actor
Innovative Artists, 1505 10th St, Santa Monica CA 90401 USA
**Conway, Robert T, Jr** — Navy Admiral
Commander, Installations Cmd, 2713 Mitscher Road SW, Anacostia Annex DC 20373, USA
**Conway, Tim** — Actor, Comedian
Innovative Artists, 1505 10th St, Santa Monica CA 90401 USA
**Conwell, Ernest H (Ernie)** — Football Player
5301 McGavock Road, Brentwood TN 37027, USA
**Conwell, Esther M** — Physicist
800 Phillips Road, Webster NY 14580, USA
**Conwell, Tommy** — Guitarist
Brothers Management Assoc, 141 Dunbar Ave, Fords NJ 08863 USA
**Coo Coo Cal** — Rap Artist
Celebrity Talent Agency, 111 E 14th St, #249, New York NY 10003, USA
**Cooder, Ry** — Singer, Guitarist, Composer
326 Entrada Dr, Santa Monica CA 90402, USA
**Coody, B Charles** — Golfer
1555 Oldham Lane, Abilene TX 79602, USA
**Coogan, Steve** — Actor, Comedian
Independent Talent Group, 40 Whitfield St, London W1T 2RH, England
**Cook, Aaron L** — Baseball Player
6113 Liberty Fairfield Road, Liberty Township OH 45011, USA
**Cook, Andrea Joy (A J)** — Actress
Paradigm Agency, 360 N Crescent Dr, North Building, Beverly Hills CA 90210 USA
**Cook, Anthony A** — Football Player
PO Box 961404, Riverdale GA 30296, USA
**Cook, Barbara** — Singer, Actress
Jeff Berger Mgmt, 301 W 53rd St, #10J, New York NY 10019, USA
**Cook, Brian J** — Basketball Player
24 Malaga Place E, Manhattan Beach CA 90266, USA
**Cook, Carole** — Actress, Comedienne
8829 Ashcroft Ave, West Hollywood CA 90048, USA
**Cook, Claire** — Writer
Voice/Hyperion Books, 77 W 66th St, #1100, New York NY 10023, USA
**Cook, Daequan** — Basketball Player
Houston Rockets, 1730 Jefferson St, Houston TX 77003 USA
**Cook, Dane J** — Actor, Comedian
United Talent Agency, U T A Plaza, 9336 Civic Center Dr, Beverly Hills CA 90210 USA
**Cook, Darwin L** — Basketball Player
1840 W Avenue J12, #103, Lancaster CA 93534, USA

**Cook, David R** — Singer, Guitarist, Songwriter
19 Entertainment, 8560 W Sunset Blvd, #900, Los Angeles CA 90069 USA
**Cook, Dennis B** — Baseball Player
3413 Serene Hills Court, Austin TX 78738, USA
**Cook, Doris** — Baseball Player
1059 Airport Road, Muskegon MI 49441, USA
**Cook, Elizabeth** — Singer
Thirty Tigers Mgmt, 1604 8th Ave S, #200, Nashville TN 37203, USA
**Cook, Frederick H (Fred), III** — Football Player
4402 Market St, Pascagoula MS 39567, USA
**Cook, Gareth** — Journalist
Boston Globe, Editorial Dept, 135 William Morrissey Blvd, Dorchester MA 02125 USA
**Cook, Jamie R** — Guitarist (Arctic Monkeys)
Wildlife Entertainment, 21 Heathmans Road, London SW6 4TJ, England
**Cook, Jeffrey A (Jeff)** — Singer, Guitarist (Alabama)
Cook Sound Studio, PO Box 680067, Fort Payne AL 35968, USA
**Cook, Jeffrey J (Jeff)** — Basketball Player
4908 E Doubletree Ranch Road, Paradise Valley AZ 85253, USA
**Cook, Jesse** — Jazz, Latin Guitarist
Paul Mercs Concerts, 3355 W Broadway, #200, Vancouver BC V6R 2B1, Canada
**Cook, John N** — Golfer
8815 Conroy Windermere Road, #40, Orlando FL 32835, USA
**Cook, Kristy Lee** — Singer
Arista/RCA Records, 1400 18th Ave S, Nashville TN 37212, USA
**Cook, Marvin E (Marv)** — Football Player
425 Butternut Lane, Iowa City IA 52246, USA
**Cook, Paul** — Drummer (Sex Pistols)
Solo Agency, 53-55 Fulham High St, #200, London SW6 3JJ, England
**Cook, Paul M** — Businessman
S R I International, 333 Ravenswood Ave, Menlo Park CA 94025, USA
**Cook, Peter F C** — Architect
54 Compayne Gardens, London NW6 3RY, England
**Cook, Rachel Leigh** — Actress
James/Levy Mgmt, 3500 W Olive Ave, #1470, Burbank CA 91505 USA
**Cook, Rebecca** — Director, Actress
G Williams Agency, 525 S 4th St, #365, Philadelphia PA 19147, USA
**Cook, Robert** — Opera Singer
Quavers, 53 Friars Ave, Fiern Barnet, London N2O OXG, England
**Cook, Robin** — Writer
10 Louisburg Square, Boston MA 02108, USA
**Cook, Stanton R** — Publisher
224 Raleigh Road, Kenilworth IL 60043, USA
**Cook, Stephen A** — Computer Scientist, Mathematician
6 Indian Valley Crescent, Toronto M6R 1Y6, Canada
**Cook, Steve** — Bowler
1209 Devonshire Court, Roseville CA 95661, USA
**Cook, Terry** — Auto, Truck Racing Driver
PO Box 86, Mount Mourne NC 28123, USA
**Cook, Thomas A** — Writer
Bantam Books, 1745 Broadway, New York NY 10019 USA
**Cook, Timothy D (Tim)** — Businessman
Apple Computer, 1 Infinite Loop, Cupertino CA 95014, USA
**Cook, Toi F** — Football Player
8430 Winnetka Ave, #20, Winnetka CA 91306, USA
**Cook, Victor Trent** — Singer, Actor
Gage Group, 450 7th Ave, #1809, New York NY 10123 USA
**Cooke, Amelia** — Actress
John Pierce Agency, 800 S Robertson Blvd, #5, Los Angeles CA 90035, USA
**Cooke, Christian** — Actor
United Agents, 12-26 Lexington St, London W1F 0LE, England
**Cooke, Christopher (Chris)** — Editor
2157 Ridgeview Ave, Los Angeles CA 90041, USA
**Cooke, David D** — Basketball Player
PO Box 270591, San Diego CA 92198, USA
**Cooke, Edward G (Ed)** — Football Player
2093 Wake Forest St, Virginia Beach VA 23451, USA
**Cooke, Janis** — Journalist
Washington Post, Editorial Dept, 1150 15th St NW, Washington DC 20071, USA
**Cooke, John P** — Rower
290 Old Branchville Road, Ridgefield CT 06877, USA
**Cooke, Josh** — Actor
Gersh Agency, 9465 Wilshire Blvd, #600, Beverly Hills CA 90212 USA
**Cooke, Michael (Mick)** — Trumpet Player (Belle & Sebastian)
Ground Control Touring, 20 Jay St, #826, Brooklyn NY 11201 USA
**Cooke, Nicole D** — Cyclist
PO Box 38, Cowbridge CF71 7XU, England
**Cooke, Pamela D (Pam)** — Animator
1809 San Jacinto St, Los Angeles CA 90026, USA
**Cooke, Sasha** — Opera Singer
I M G Artists, Hogarth Business Park, Chiswick, London W4 2TH, England
**Cooke, Steven M (Steve)** — Baseball Player
20709 SW Trails End Dr, Sherwood OR 97140, USA
**Cooke, Victoria** — Model, Actress
Playboy Promotions, 2706 Media Center Dr, Los Angeles CA 90065 USA
**Cooks, Johnie E** — Football Player
1305 Meadow Creek Dr, #111, Irving TX 75038, USA
**Cool, Tre** — Drummer (Green Day)
P M C, 5900 Wilshire Blvd, #1720, Los Angeles CA 90036, USA
**Cooley, Chelsea** — Beauty Queen
Miss Universe Organization, 1370 Ave of Americas, #1600, New York NY 10019 USA
**Cooley, Cheryl** — Guitarist (Klymaxx)
R D M J Entertainment Mgmt, 3619 Rose Ave, Long Beach CA 90807 USA
**Cooley, Denton A** — Surgeon
3014 Del Monte Dr, Houston TX 77019, USA
**Coolidge, Charles H** — WW II Army Hero (CMH)
1054 Balmoral Dr, Signal Mountain TN 37377, USA

| | |
|---|---|
| **Coolidge, Harold J** | Conservationist |
| 38 Standley St, Beverly MA 01915, USA | |
| **Coolidge, Jennifer** | Actress, Comedienne |
| Mannic Productions, 1170 26th St, #600, New York NY 10001, USA | |
| **Coolidge, Martha** | Director |
| A P A Talent/Literary Agency, 405 S Beverly Dr, #300, Beverly Hills CA 90212 USA | |
| **Coolidge, Rita** | Singer, Actress |
| Axis Artist Mgmt, 9715 Belmar Ave, Northridge CA 91324, USA | |
| **Coolio** | Rap Artist, Actor |
| Haber Entertainment, 434 S Canon Dr, #204, Beverly Hills CA 90212, USA | |
| **Coombs, Daniel B (Danny)** | Baseball Player |
| 14130 Cleobrook Dr, Houston TX 77070, USA | |
| **Coombs, Stephen** | Concert Pianist |
| Wordplay, 35 Lisbon St, Blackheath, London SE3 8SS, England | |
| **Coombs-Mueller, Carol** | Actress |
| 772 Tyrol Court, Crestline CA 92325, USA | |
| **Coomer, Ronald B (Ron)** | Baseball Player |
| 7021 Howard Lane, Eden Prairie MN 55346, USA | |
| **Coon, Charles (Chuck), Sr** | Harness Racing Executive |
| 9433 E Shady Grove Court, White Lake MI 48386, USA | |
| **Cooney, Gerry** | Boxer |
| PO Box 525, Fanwood NJ 07023, USA | |
| **Cooney, Joan Ganz** | Educator, Businesswoman |
| Children's TV Workshop, 1 Lincoln Plaza, New York NY 10023, USA | |
| **Cooney, Thomas M** | Businessman |
| 854 Country Club Dr, Cincinnati OH 45245, USA | |
| **Coonts, Stephen** | Writer |
| 109 Marland Road S, Colorado Springs CO 80906, USA | |
| **Cooper, A Louis** | Football Player |
| 200 Gregg Ave, Marion SC 29571, USA | |
| **Cooper, A Wayne** | Basketball Player |
| 5013 Millstone Way, Granite Bay CA 95746, USA | |
| **Cooper, Abraham** | Religious Leader, Rabbi |
| Simon Wiesental Center, 1399 S Roxbury, #100, Los Angeles CA 90035, USA | |
| **Cooper, Adam** | Actor, Singer |
| Diamond Mgmt, 31 Percy St, London, England W1T 2DD, England | |
| **Cooper, Adrian** | Football Player |
| 3120 Saint Paul St, Denver CO 80205, USA | |
| **Cooper, Alice** | Singer, Songwriter |
| Bx2 Mgmt, 15304 Sunset Blvd, #202, Pacific Palisades CA 90272, USA | |
| **Cooper, Amy Levin** | Editor |
| 60 Sutton Place S, #16C, New York NY 10022, USA | |
| **Cooper, Anderson** | Commentator |
| CNN-TV, 190 Marietta Ave SW, Atlanta GA 30303 USA | |
| **Cooper, Bernadette** | Musician (Klymaxx) |
| R D M J Entertainment Mgmt, 3619 Rose Ave, Long Beach CA 90807 USA | |
| **Cooper, Bradley** | Actor, Comedian |
| Creative Artists Agency, 2000 Ave of Stars, #100, Los Angeles CA 90067 USA | |
| **Cooper, Brian J** | Baseball Player |
| 346 W Ada Ave, Glendora CA 91741, USA | |
| **Cooper, Camille** | Basketball Player |
| New York Liberty, Madison Square Garden, 2 Penn Plaza, New York NY 10121 USA | |
| **Cooper, Cecil C** | Baseball Player, Manager |
| 24802 Boulder Lakes Court, Katy TX 77494, USA | |
| **Cooper, Charles G** | Marine Corps General |
| 3410 Barger Dr, Falls Church VA 22044, USA | |
| **Cooper, Chris** | Actor |
| Untitled Entertainment, 350 S Beverly Dr, #200, Beverly Hills CA 90212 USA | |
| **Cooper, Christin** | Alpine Skier |
| 1001 E Hyman Ave, Aspen CO 81611, USA | |
| **Cooper, Daniel L** | Navy Admiral |
| 400 Willow Valley Square, #GA110, Lancaster PA 17602, USA | |
| **Cooper, Dominic** | Actor |
| Markham Froggatt Irwin, Julian House, 4 Windmill St, London W1P 1HF, England | |
| **Cooper, Eric R** | Baseball Umpire |
| 4330 NW 169th Court, Clive IA 50325, USA | |
| **Cooper, Helene** | Writer, Journalist |
| New York Times, Editorial Dept, 229 W 43rd St, New York NY 10036 USA | |
| **Cooper, Imogen** | Concert Pianist |
| Askonas Holt, Lincoln House, 300 High Holborn, London WC1V 7JH, England | |
| **Cooper, James A (Jim)** | Football Player |
| 12910 Low Meadow Court, Charlotte NC 28277, USA | |
| **Cooper, Jilly** | Writer |
| Curtis Brown Group, 28-29 Haymarket St, #500, London SW1Y 4SP, England | |
| **Cooper, John** | Football Coach |
| ESPN-TV, ESPN Plaza, 935 Middle St, Bristol CT 06010 USA | |
| **Cooper, John M** | Philosopher |
| 182 Western Way, Princeton NJ 08540, USA | |
| **Cooper, Leon N** | Nobel Physics Laureate |
| 49 Intervale Road, Providence RI 02906, USA | |
| **Cooper, Lester I** | Producer |
| 45 Morningside Dr S, Westport CT 06880, USA | |
| **Cooper, Lynn A** | Psychologist |
| Columbia University, Psychology Dept, 1190 Amsterdam Ave, New York NY 10027, USA | |
| **Cooper, M Earl** | Football Player |
| 2224 E Highway 21, Lincoln TX 78948, USA | |
| **Cooper, Martin** | Inventor (Cell Phone) |
| ArrayComm, 2480 N 1st St, #200, San Jose CA 95131, USA | |
| **Cooper, Matthew T** | Marine Corps General |
| 9326 Fairfax St, Alexandria VA 22309, USA | |
| **Cooper, Pat** | Actor, Comedian |
| 243 W 70th St, #8D, New York NY 10023, USA | |
| **Cooper, Richard N** | Economist |
| 33 Washington Ave, Cambridge MA 02140, USA | |
| **Cooper, Roxanne** | Singer |
| Freemantle Media, 2700 Colorado Ave, #450, Santa Monica CA 90404, USA | |

# C

**Cooper, Stuart** — Director, Actor
Creative Artists Agency, 2000 Ave of Stars, #100, Los Angeles CA 90067 USA
**Cooper, Susan M** — Writer
Simon & Schuster, 1230 Ave of Americas, Concourse 1, New York NY 10020 USA
**Cooper, Wayne** — Artist, Sculptor
PO Box 106, Depew OK 74028, USA
**Cooper, William A (Bill)** — Football Player
16056 Greenwood Road, Monte Sereno CA 95030, USA
**Cooper-Dyke, Cynthia** — Basketball Player, Coach
University of North Carolina, Athletic Dept, Wilmington NC 28403, USA
**Coor, Lattie F** — Educator
Arizona State University, Public Affairs School, Tempe AZ 85287, USA
**Coors, William K** — Businessman
Adolph Coors Co, 311 10th St, Golden CO 80401, USA
**Coote, Alice** — Opera Singer
I M G Artists, Hogarth Business Park, Chiswick, London W4 2TH, England
**Coover, Robert** — Writer
Brown University, Linden Press, 49 George St, Providence RI 02912, USA
**Cope, Derrike** — Auto Racing Driver
103 Turnerlair Court, Mooresville NC 28117, USA
**Cope, Jonathan** — Ballet Dancer
Royal Ballet, Covent Garden, Bow St, London WC2E 9DD, England
**Copeland, Horace C** — Football Player
4195 Blakemore Place, Spring Hill FL 34609, USA
**Copeland, Kenneth** — Evangelist
Kenneth Copeland Ministries, PO Box 2908, Fort Worth TX 76113, USA
**Copeland, Shemekia** — Singer
Alligator Records, PO Box 60234, Chicago IL 60660, USA
**Copeland, Stewart** — Drummer (Police, Oysterhead), Composer
2420 Arbutus Dr, Los Angeles CA 90049, USA
**Coples, Quinton** — Football Player
New York Jets, 1 Jets Dr, Florham Park NJ 07932 USA
**Copley, Teri** — Actress, Model
13351 Riverside Dr, #D513, Sherman Oaks CA 91423, USA
**Copley, William** — Artist
1 Frisbie Road, Roxbury CT 06783, USA
**Copon, Michael S** — Actor, Model, Singer
Don Buchwald, 6500 Wilshire Blvd, #2200, Los Angeles CA 90048 USA
**Copp, D Harold** — Physiologist
4755 Belmont Ave, Vancouver BC V6T 1A8, Canada
**Coppa, Giovanni** — Religious Leader
Apostolic Nuncio, Vorsilska Ul 12, 11000 Prague 1, Czech Republic
**Coppens, Yves** — Paleoanthropologist
4 Rue du Pont-aux-Choux, 75003 Paris, France
**Copperfield, David** — Illusionist
Magic Arts Entertainment, 10145 Philipp Parkway, #A, Streetsboro OH 44241, USA
**Copperwheat, Lee** — Fashion Designer
Copperwheat Blundell, 14 Cheshire St, London E2 6EH, England
**Coppinger, John T (Rocky)** — Baseball Player
7280 Alto Rey Ave, El Paso TX 79912, USA
**Coppo, Paul** — Ice Hockey Player
3458 Solitude Road, De Pere WI 54115, USA
**Coppola, Alicia** — Actress
A P A Talent/Literary Agency, 405 S Beverly Dr, #300, Beverly Hills CA 90212 USA
**Coppola, Francis Ford** — Director
Niebaum-Coppola Estate, 1991 Saint Helena Highway, Rutherford CA 94573, USA
**Coppola, Imani** — Singer, Songwriter
International Talent Booking, Ariel House, 74A Charlotte St, #100 London W1T 4QJ, England
**Coppola, Sofia** — Actress, Director, Writer
I C M Partners, 10250 Constellation Blvd, #900, Los Angeles CA 90067 USA
**Copps Michael J** — Government Official
Federal Communications Commission, 1919 M St NW, Washington DC 20036, USA
**Cora, Catherine (Cat)** — Chef
W M E Entertainment, 9601 Wilshire Blvd, #300, Beverly Hills CA 90210 USA
**Cora, J Alexander (Alex)** — Baseball Player
150 Brookline Ave, Boston MA 02215, USA
**Cora, Jose M (Joey)** — Baseball Player
17734 SW 47th St, Miramar FL 33029, USA
**Corabi, John** — Singer, Guitarist (Motley Crue)
Union Entertainment Group, 1323 Newbury Road, #104, Newbury Park CA 91320, USA
**Coraci, Frank** — Director
I C M Partners, 10250 Constellation Blvd, #900, Los Angeles CA 90067 USA
**Corbat, Michael L (Mike)** — Financier
Citigroup Inc, 55 E 52nd St, New York NY 10055, USA
**Corbato, Fernando J** — Computer Scientist
88 Temple St, West Newton MA 02465, USA
**Corbet, Brady** — Actor, Director
W M E Entertainment, 9601 Wilshire Blvd, #300, Beverly Hills CA 90210 USA
**Corbett, Douglas M (Doug)** — Baseball Player
75083 Edwards Road, Yulee FL 32097, USA
**Corbett, Gretchen** — Actress
S D B Partners, 1801 Ave of Stars, #902, Los Angeles CA 90067 USA
**Corbett, John** — Actor
Gersh Agency, 9465 Wilshire Blvd, #600, Beverly Hills CA 90212 USA
**Corbett, Mike** — Rock Climber
41828 Road 600, Ahwahnee CA 93601, USA
**Corbett, Ronnie** — Actor, Comedian
International Artistes, 235 Regent St, London W1R 8AX, England
**Corbijn, Anton** — Photographer, Cinematographer
Independent Talent Group, 40 Whitfield St, London W1T 2RH, England
**Corbin, A Ray** — Baseball Player
65 Moore St, Franklin NC 28734, USA
**Corbin, Barry** — Actor
Linda McAlister Talent, 530 S Lake Ave, #435, Pasadena CA 91101, USA
**Corbin, Tom** — Sculptor
201 Wyandotte St, #102, Kansas City MO 64105, USA

**Cooper - Corbin**

**Corbin, Tyrone K** — Basketball Player, Coach
652 Edgewood Dr, North Salt Lake UT 84054, USA
**Corbitt, Jerry** — Singer, Guitarist (Youngbloods)
First Rainbow, 1650 Barnes Mill Road, #1214, Marietta GA 30062, USA
**Corchiani, Christopher (Chris)** — Basketball Player
1106 Harvey St, Raleigh NC 27608, USA
**Corcoran, Barbara** — Writer
W M E Entertainment, 9601 Wilshire Blvd, #300, Beverly Hills CA 90210 USA
**Corcoran, Kevin** — Actor
8617 Balcom Ave, Northridge CA 91325, USA
**Corcoran, Norm** — Ice Hockey Player
20 Nickerson Ave, Saint Catherines ON L2N 3L4, Canada
**Corcoran, Timothy M (Tim)** — Baseball Player
4349 Friar Circle, La Verne CA 91750, USA
**Cord, Alex** — Actor
Cord Equestrian, 7639 FM 2071, Gainesville TX 76240, USA
**Corday, Barbara** — Businesswoman, Writer, Producer
317 N Van Ness Ave, Los Angeles CA 90004, USA
**Corday, Ken** — Producer
Corday Productions, 3400 W Olive Ave, #170, Burbank CA 91505, USA
**Corday, Mara** — Actress, Model
29532 Mendoze Dr, Valencia CA 91355, USA
**Corddry, Nathan (Nate)** — Actor
B/W/R, 9100 Wilshire Blvd, #500W, Beverly Hills CA 90212 USA
**Corddry, Rob** — Actor, Comedian
Principato-Young, 9465 Wilshire Blvd, #880, Beverly Hills CA 90212 USA
**Corden, James** — Actor
United Agents, 12-26 Lexington St, London W1F 0LE, England
**Cordero Lanza di Montezemolo, Andrea** — Religious Leader
Nunciature to Italy, Via Po 27-29, 00198 Rome, Italy
**Cordero, Angel T, Jr** — Thoroughbred Racing Jockey
4 Osborne Lane, Greenvale NY 11548, USA
**Cordero, Francisco J** — Baseball Player
4125 Oak Tree Court, Loveland OH 45140, USA
**Cordero, Sebastian** — Director, Writer
Creative Artists Agency, 2000 Ave of Stars, #100, Los Angeles CA 90067 USA
**Cordero, Wilfredo N (Wil)** — Baseball Player
25844 Kensington Dr, Westlake OH 44145, USA
**Cordes, Paul J Cardinal** — Religious Leader
Pontifical Council Cor Unum, Piazza S Calisto 16, 00153 Rome, Italy
**Cordes-Elliott, Gloria** — Baseball Player
86 Malone Ave, Staten Island NY 10306, USA
**Cordingly, Beth** — Actress
Hatton McEwan, 3 Chocolate Studios, 7 Shepherdess Place, London N1 7LJ, England
**Cordova, France A** — Educator
Purdue University, President's Office, West Lafayette IN 47907, USA
**Cordova, Martin K (Marty)** — Baseball Player
47 Club Vista Dr, Henderson NV 89052, USA
**Corduner, Allan** — Actor
Conway Van Gelder Grant, 8-12 Broadwick St, #300, London W1F 8HW, England
**Core, Ericson** — Director, Cinematographer
Gersh Agency, 9465 Wilshire Ave, #600, Beverly Hills CA 90212 USA
**Corea, Armando A (Chick)** — Jazz Pianist, Composer
Chick Corea Productions, 10400 Samoa Ave, Tujunga CA 91042, USA
**Corey, Bryan S** — Baseball Player
7829 E Riverdale Circle, Mesa AZ 85207, USA
**Corey, Clint** — Rodeo Rider
30635 W Mission Road, Powell Butte OR 97753, USA
**Corey, Elias J** — Nobel Chemistry Laureate
20 Avon Hill St, Cambridge MA 02140, USA
**Corey, Irwin (Professor)** — Actor, Comedian
Worlds Foremost Mgmt, 165 W 21st St, New York NY 10011, USA
**Corey, Jill** — Singer
64 Division Ave, Levittown NY 11756, USA
**Corey, Walter M (Walt)** — Football Player
26007 Timber Meadow Dr, Lees Summit MO 64086, USA
**Corfield, Kenneth G** — Businessman
10 Chapel Place, Rivington St, London EC2A 3DQ, England
**Corgan, William P (Billy), Jr** — Singer (Smashing Pumpkins), Songwriter
Evolution Music Partners, 1680 N Vine St, #500, Los Angeles CA 90028, USA
**Corigliano, John P** — Composer
365 W End Ave, New York NY 10024, USA
**Corinealdi, Emayatzy** — Actress
I C M Partners, 10250 Constellation Blvd, #900, Los Angeles CA 90067 USA
**Corkins, Michael P (Mike)** — Baseball Player
3760 Chemehuevi Blvd, Lake Havasu City AZ 86406, USA
**Corley, Al** — Actor
1177 Embury St, Pacific Palisades CA 90272, USA
**Corley, W Gene** — Structural Engineer
Construction Tech Laboratories, 5400 Old Orchard Road, Skokie IL 60077, USA
**Cormack, Danielle** — Actress
Johnson & Laird Mgmt, PO Box 78340, Grey Lynn, Auckland 1002, New Zealand
**Corman, Roger W** — Director, Producer
Concorde New Horizons, 11600 San Vicente Blvd, Los Angeles CA 90049, USA
**Cormier, Lance R** — Baseball Player
3630 Windy Ridge, Tuscaloosa AL 35406, USA
**Cormier, Rheal P** — Baseball Player
2640 Cody Circle, Park City UT 84098, USA
**Corn, Alfred** — Writer
350 W 14th St, #6A, New York NY 10014, USA
**Cornelison, Jerry G** — Football Player
12713 Cedar St, Leawood KS 66209, USA
**Cornelius** — Singer, Guitarist
Magnum Public Relations, 32 E 31st St, #900, New York NY 10016, USA
**Cornelius, Helen** — Singer, Songwriter
PO Box 12089, Nashville TN 37212, USA

# C

**Cornelius, James M** — Businessman
Bristol-Myers Squibb, 345 Park Ave, New York NY 10154, USA
**Cornelius, Kathy** — Golfer
5744 W Dek Rio St, Chandler AZ 85226, USA
**Cornell, Chris** — Singer, Drummer (Soundgarden)
W M E Entertainment, 9601 Wilshire Blvd, #300, Beverly Hills CA 90210 USA
**Cornell, Eric A** — Nobel Physics Laureate
University of Colorado, Physics Dept, PO Box 440, Boulder CO 80328, USA
**Cornell, Harry M, Jr** — Businessman
Leggett & Platt Inc, 1 Leggett Road, Carthage MO 64836, USA
**Cornell, Lydia** — Actress
J K A Talent, 12725 Ventura Blvd, #H, Studio City CA 91604, USA
**Cornell, Robert P (Bo)** — Football Player
2605 239th Ave SE, Sammamish WA 98075, USA
**Cornet, Alize** — Tennis Player
11 Ave Jean Medecin, 06000 Nice, France
**Cornette, Jim** — Wrestler
PO Box 436963, Louisville KY 40253, USA
**Cornforth, John W** — Nobel Chemistry Laureate
Saxon Down, Cuilfail, Lewes, East Sussex BN7 2BE, England
**Cornforth, Mark** — Ice Hockey Player
11 Indian Spring Road, Milton MA 02186, USA
**Cornish, Abbie** — Actress
W M E Entertainment, 9601 Wilshire Blvd, #300, Beverly Hills CA 90210 USA
**Cornish, Frank E, III** — Football Player
1024 Inca Dr, #A, Harvey LA 70058, USA
**Cornish, Nick** — Actor
James Levy Jacobson Mgmt, 3500 W Olive Ave, #900, Burbank CA 91505, USA
**Cornwell, Bernard** — Writer
Harper Collins Publishers, 10 E 53rd St, Cellar 1, New York NY 10022 USA
**Cornwell, Frederick K (Fred)** — Football Player
2107 Windward Lane, Newport Beach CA 92660, USA
**Cornwell, Hugh** — Singer, Guitarist (Stranglers)
Red Entertainment, 16 Penn Plaza, #824, New York NY 10001, USA
**Cornwell, Patricia D** — Writer
G P Putnam's Sons, 375 Hudson St, New York NY 10014 USA
**Cornwell, Peter** — Director, Producer, Writer
I C M Partners, 10250 Constellation Blvd, #900, Los Angeles CA 90067 USA
**Corona, Jose de Jesus** — Soccer Player
C D Cruz Azul, san Pablo 100, C La Nora Xochimilco, 16030 Ciudad de Mexico, Mexico
**Corr, Andrea** — Singer, Tin Whistle Player (Corrs)
John Hughes, 6 Martello Terrace, Sandycove, Dunlaoughaire, Dublin, Ireland
**Corr, Caroline** — Singer, Percussionist, Pianist (Corrs)
John Hughes, 6 Martello Terrace, Sandycove, Dunlaoughaire, Dublin, Ireland
**Corr, Jim** — Singer, Keyboardist, Guitarist (Corrs)
John Hughes, 6 Martello Terrace, Sandycove, Dunlaoughaire, Dublin, Ireland
**Corr, Sharon** — Singer, Violinist (Corrs)
John Hughes, 6 Martello Terrace, Sandycove, Dunlaoughaire, Dublin, Ireland
**Corraface, Georges** — Actor
Agents Associes, 201 Rue du Faubourg Saint Honore, 75008 Paris, France
**Corrales, Patrick (Pat)** — Baseball Player, Manager
2 W Wesley Road NW, #18, Atlanta GA 30305, USA
**Correa Delgado, Rafael V** — President, Ecuador
Palacio de Gobierno, Garcia Moreno 1043, Quito, Ecuador
**Correa, Charles M** — Architect
Sonmarg, Napean Sea Road, Mumbai 400006, India
**Correia, Amy** — Singer, Guitarist, Songwriter
Season of Mist Records, 111 Rt de la Valentinell, 13011 Marseille, France
**Correia, Kevin J** — Baseball Player
2081 Gatun St, Del Mar CA 92014, USA
**Corretja, Alex** — Tennis Player
Association of Tennis Professionals, 200 Tournament Road, Ponte Vedra Beach FL 32082 USA
**Corri, Adrienne** — Actress
Rolf & Rachel Kruger, 205 Chudleigh Road, London SE4 1EG, England
**Corrigan, E Gerald** — Government Official, Financier
Goldman Sachs Co, 85 Broad St, Building 85, New York NY 10004, USA
**Corrigan, Kevin** — Actor
Innovative Artists, 1505 10th St, Santa Monica CA 90401 USA
**Corrigan, Michale D (Mike)** — Ice Hockey Player
21 Birchwood Road, Enfield CT 06082, USA
**Corrigan, Patrick** — Editorial Cartoonist
Toronto Star, Editorial Dept, 1 Yonge St, Toronto ON M5E 1E5, Canada
**Corrigan-Maguire, Mairead** — Nobel Peace Laureate
Peace People, 224 Lisburn Road, Belfast BT9 6GE, Northern Ireland
**Corriveau, Yvon** — Ice Hockey Player
396 Willard Ave, #A2, Newington CT 06111, USA
**Corsaro, Frank A** — Director
33 Riverside Dr, New York NY 10023, USA
**Corsi, James B (Jim)** — Baseball Player
6 Edwards Circle, Bellingham MA 02019, USA
**Corso, John A** — Cinematographer
241 W 13th St, #21, New York NY 10011, USA
**Corso, Leland (Lee)** — Sportscaster
ESPN-TV, ESPN Plaza, 935 Middle St, Bristol CT 06010 USA
**Corson, Shayne** — Ice Hockey Player
Tappo Restaurant, 3-55 Mill St, Toronto ON M5A 3C4, Canada
**Cort, Bud** — Actor
2609 Lake View Ave, Los Angeles CA 90039, USA
**Cortazar, Esteban** — Fashion Designer
111 NE 1st St, #900, Miami FL 33132, USA
**Cortes Granados, Javier** — Soccer Player
Tigres U A N L, Estadio Universitario, 66451 San Nicolas de los Garza, Mexico
**Cortes, Joaquin** — Flamenco Dancer, Choreographer
W M E Entertainment, 9601 Wilshire Blvd, #300, Beverly Hills CA 90210 USA
**Cortes, Ron** — Journalist
Philadelphia Inquirer, Editorial Dept, 400 N Broad St, Philadelphia PA 19130, USA

**Cornelius - Cortes**

| | |
|---|---|
| **Cortese, Dan** | Actor |
| 3 Arts Entertainment, 9460 Wilshire Blvd, #700, Beverly Hills CA 90212 USA | |
| **Cortese, Federico** | Conductor |
| Boston Youth Symphony, 855 Commonwealth Ave, Boston MA 02215, USA | |
| **Cortese, Genevieve** | Actress |
| Innovative Artists, 1505 10th St, Santa Monica CA 90401 USA | |
| **Cortese, Joe** | Actor |
| 100 S Hayworth Ave, #201, Los Angeles CA 90048, USA | |
| **Cortese, Valentina** | Actress |
| Pretta S Erasmo 6, 20121 Milan, Italy | |
| **Cortez, Alfonso** | Actor, Producer |
| C E S D, 10635 Santa Monica Blvd, #130, Los Angeles CA 90025 USA | |
| **Cortright, Edgar M, Jr** | Aerospace Engineer |
| 9701 Calvin St, Northridge CA 91324, USA | |
| **Corvo, Joseph (Joe)** | Ice Hockey Player |
| 2004 Falls Forest Dr, Raleigh NC 27615, USA | |
| **Corwin, Jeff** | Actor |
| Jeff Corwin Experience, PO Box 2904, Toluca Lake CA 91610, USA | |
| **Corwin, Morena** | Model |
| Playboy Promotions, 2706 Media Center Dr, Los Angeles CA 90065 USA | |
| **Coryatt, Quentin J** | Football Player |
| 611 Cannon Lane, Sugar Land TX 77479, USA | |
| **Coryell, Larry** | Guitarist |
| Jazz-Map, Hans Bredow Str 32A, 65189 Weisbaden, Germany | |
| **Corzine, David J (Dave)** | Basketball Player |
| 1161 W Hunting Dr, Palatine IL 60067, USA | |
| **Cosbie, Douglas D (Doug)** | Football Player |
| 1503 Fordham Court, Mountain View CA 94040, USA | |
| **Cosby, Bill** | Actor, Comedian |
| PO Box 808, Bardwell Ferry Road, Greenfield MA 01302, USA | |
| **Coscina, Dennis** | Golfer |
| 211 Main St, East Windsor CT 06088, USA | |
| **Cosgrave, Liam** | Prime Minister, Ireland |
| Beech Park, Templeogue County, Dublin 6W, Ireland | |
| **Cosgriff, Kevin J** | Navy Admiral |
| Deputy Commander, Fleet Forces Command, Norfolk VA 23551, USA | |
| **Cosgrove, Daniel** | Actor |
| James/Levy Mgmt, 3500 W Olive Ave, #1470, Burbank CA 91505 USA | |
| **Cosgrove, Miranda** | Actress, Singer |
| W M E Entertainment, 9601 Wilshire Blvd, #300, Beverly Hills CA 90210 USA | |
| **Cosic, Dobrica** | President, Yugoslavia |
| Sciences & Arts Academy, Knez Mihailova 35, 11000 Belgrade, Serbia | |
| **Coslet, Bruce N** | Football Player, Coach |
| 1778 Ivy Pointe Court, Naples FL 34109, USA | |
| **Cosmo, James** | Actor |
| United Agents, 12-26 Lexington St, London W1F 0LE, England | |
| **Cosmos, Jean** | Writer |
| 57 Rue de Versailles, 92410 Ville d'Avray, France | |
| **Cosmovici, Cristiano B** | Astronaut, Italy |
| Instituto Fisica Spazio Interplanetario, CP 27, 00044 Frascati, Italy | |
| **Cosper, Kina** | Singer (Brownstone), Songwriter |
| Richard Walters, PO Box 2789, Toluca Lake CA 91610 USA | |
| **Cossack, Roger** | Attorney, Commentator |
| ESPN-TV, ESPN Plaza, 935 Middle St, Bristol CT 06010 USA | |
| **Cosso, Pierre** | Actor |
| Agents Associes, 201 Rue du Faubourg Saint Honore, 75008 Paris, France | |
| **Cossotto, Fiorenza** | Opera Singer |
| Via Ezio Biondi 1, 21 Milan, Italy | |
| **Costa, Manuel Rui** | Soccer Player |
| F C Milan, Via Filippo Turati 3, 20121 Milan, Italy | |
| **Costa, Mary** | Opera Singer |
| California Artists Mgmt, 41 Sutter St, #420, San Francisco CA 94104, USA | |
| **Costa, Nikka** | Singer, Songwriter |
| Front Line Mgmt, 1100 Glendon Ave, #2000, Los Angeles CA 90024 USA | |
| **Costa, S Paul** | Football Player |
| 8017 Kristina Lane, North Richland Hills TX 76182, USA | |
| **Costabile, David** | Actor |
| Innovative Artists, 1505 10th St, Santa Monica CA 90401 USA | |
| **Costa-Gavras, Konstaninos** | Director |
| Artmedia, 20 Ave Rapp, 75007 Paris, France | |
| **Costanzo, Paulo** | Actor |
| Principato-Young, 9465 Wilshire Blvd, #880, Beverly Hills CA 90212 USA | |
| **Costas, Robert Q (Bob)** | Sportscaster |
| W M E Entertainment, 9601 Wilshire Blvd, #300, Beverly Hills CA 90210 USA | |
| **Costello, Barry M** | Navy Admiral |
| A D S Ventures, 500 New Jersey Ave NW, #400, Washington DC 20001 20001, USA | |
| **Costello, Elvis** | Singer, Guitarist, Songwriter |
| I C M Partners, 10250 Constellation Blvd, #900, Los Angeles CA 90067 USA | |
| **Costello, Mariclare** | Actress |
| Borinstein Oreck Bogart, 3172 Dona Susana Dr, Studio City CA 91604 USA | |
| **Costello, Murray** | Ice Hockey Player, Executive |
| 105 Kenilworth St, Ottawa ON K1Y 3Y8, Canada | |
| **Costello, Vince** | Football Player |
| 12300 Perry Road, Overland Park KS 66213, USA | |
| **Costelloe, Paul** | Fashion Designer |
| 30 Westminster Palace Gardens, Artillery Row, London SW1P 1RR, England | |
| **Coster, Nicolas** | Actor |
| Momentum Talent, 9401 Wilshire Blvd, 501, Beverly Hills CA 90212, USA | |
| **Coster-Waldau, Nikolaj** | Actor |
| Lindberg Mgmt, Lavendelstr 5-7, Baghuset, 4 Sal, 1462 Copenhagen K, Denmark | |
| **Costigan, C C** | Actress |
| I C M Partners, 10250 Constellation Blvd, #900, Los Angeles CA 90067 USA | |
| **Costle, Douglas M** | Government Official, Educator |
| Harvard University, Public Health School, Cambridge MA 02138, USA | |
| **Costner, Kevin** | Actor, Director |
| Treehouse Films, 4450 Lakeside Dr, #225, Burbank CA 91505, USA | |

**Cota, Chad G** — Football Player
216 Island Pointe Dr, Medford OR 97504, USA

**Cotchery, Jerricho** — Football Player
79 Carriage Lane, Plainview NY 11803, USA

**Cote, Alain** — Ice Hockey Player
1352 Rue Gabrielle Roy, Quebec QC G1Y 3K3, Canada

**Cote, David M** — Businessman
Honeywell International, 61 Columbia Road, Morristown NJ 07960, USA

**Cote, Laurence** — Actress
Agents Associes, 201 Rue du Faubourg Saint Honore, 75008 Paris, France

**Cote, Sylvain** — Ice Hockey Player
1432 Wild Cranberry Court, Crownsville MD 21032, USA

**Cothran, Sherry** — Singer (EvinRudes)
Turner Management Group, 9200 W Sunset Blvd, #600, West Hollywood CA 90069, USA

**Cotillard, Marion** — Actress
Agence Artiste Adequet, 108 Rue Reaumur, 75002 Paris, France

**Cotroneo, Vince** — Sportscaster
4455 E Palmdale Lane, Gilbert AZ 85298, USA

**Cotrubas, Ileana** — Opera Singer
Royal Opera House, Covent Garden, Bow St, London WC2, England

**Cotte, Pascal** — Engineer
Lumiere Technology, 215 Bis Blvd Saint Germain, 75007 Paris, France

**Cottee, Kay** — Yachtswoman
Showboat Productions, 113 Willoughby Road, Crows Nest NSW 2065, Australia

**Cottencon, Fanny** — Actress, Producer
Agence Artiste Adequet, 108 Rue Reaumur, 75002 Paris, France

**Cotterill, Tim (Frogman)** — Sculptor
518 Victoria Ave, Venice CA 90291, USA

**Cotti, Flavio** — President, Switzerland
Christian Democratic Party, Klaraweg 6, 3001 Bern, Switzerland

**Cottier, Charles K (Chuck)** — Baseball Player, Manager
7129 Lake Ballinger Way, Edmonds WA 98026, USA

**Cottier, George Cardinal** — Religious Leader
Convento Santa Sabina, Piazza Pierro d'Illiria, 00193 Rome, Italy

**Cottingham, Robert** — Artist
PO Box 604, Blackman Road, Newtown CT 06470, USA

**Cottle, Tameka** — Singer (Xscape)
Richard Walters, PO Box 2789, Toluca Lake CA 91610 USA

**Cotto, Miguel** — Boxer
Top Rank Inc, 3908 Howard Hughes Parkway, #580, Las Vegas NV 89169 USA

**Cotton, Blaine** — Actor
Jack Scagnetti Talent, 5118 Vineland Ave, #102, North Hollywood CA 91601, USA

**Cotton, James** — Singer, Harmonica Player
Jacklyn Hairston Mgmt, PO Box 150402, Austin TX 78715, USA

**Cotton, John G** — Navy Admiral
Commander, Naval Reserve Force, HqUSN, Pentagon, Washington DC 20350 USA

**Cotton, John J (Jack)** — Basketball Player
11426 Country Road 4 S, Alamosa CO 81101, USA

**Cotton, Joseph F** — Test Pilot
20 Linda Vista Ave, Atherton CA 94027, USA

**Cotton, Maxwell Perry** — Actor
Greene Assoc, 1901 Ave of Stars, #130, Los Angeles CA 90067 USA

**Cottrell, Erin** — Actress
Talent Works, 3500 W Olive Ave, #1400, Burbank CA 91505 USA

**Cottrell, William H (Bill)** — Football Player
39675 Patterson Lane, Solon OH 44139, USA

**Couch, Chris** — Golfer
307 Johns Creek Parkway, Saint Augustine FL 32092, USA

**Couch, Timothy S (Tim)** — Football Player
3041 Brookmonte Lane, Lexington KY 40515, USA

**Couchepin, Pascal** — President, Switzerland
Federal Chancellery, Bundeshaus-W, Bundesgasse, 3033 Berne, Switzerland

**Couelle, Savin** — Architect
Localita Abbiadori CP 4, 07020 Porto Cervo, Italy

**Couffer, Jack** — Cinematographer
Original Artists, 9465 Wilshire Blvd, #324, Beverly Hills CA 90212, USA

**Coughlan, Marisa** — Actress
Mosaic Media Group, 9200 W Sunset Blvd, #1000, Los Angles CA 90069, USA

**Coughlin, Jeg (Jeggy), Jr** — Auto Racing Driver
Jeg's High Performance Racing, 751 E 11th Ave, Columbus OH 43211, USA

**Coughlin, Natalie** — Swimmer
4139 Coralee Lane, Lafayette CA 94549, USA

**Coughlin, Tom** — Football Coach
New York Giants, Meadowlands Stadium, 102 Route 120, East Rutherford NJ 07073 USA

**Coughran, John W** — Basketball Player
5476 Morningside Dr, San Jose CA 95138, USA

**Coulier, David** — Actor
Brillstein Entertainment Partners, 9150 Wilshire Blvd, #350, Beverly Hills CA 90212 USA

**Coulson, Catherine E** — Actress
1115 Terra Ave, Ashland OR 97520, USA

**Coulter, Ann H** — Commentator, Writer
Crown Publishing Group, 1745 Broadway, #1300, New York NY 10019 USA

**Coulter, Catherine** — Writer
PO Box 17, Mill Valley CA 94942, USA

**Coulter, Michael** — Cinematographer
35 Carlton Mansions, Randolph Ave, London W9 1NP, England

**Coulthard, David M** — Auto Racing Driver
Red Bull, Am Brunnen 1, 5330 Puschi am See, Austria

**Coulthard, Raymond** — Actor
United Agents, 12-26 Lexington St, London W1F 0LE, England

**Counsell, Craig J** — Baseball Player
992 E Circle Dr, Milwaukee WI 53217, USA

**Countryman, Michael** — Actor
Paradigm Agency, 360 N Crescent Dr, North Building, Beverly Hills CA 90210 USA

**Counts, Mel G** — Basketball Player
1581 Matheny Road, Gervais OR 97026, USA

**Coupe, Eliza** — Actress
Creative Artists Agency, 2000 Ave of Stars, #100, Los Angeles CA 90067 USA
**Coupland, Douglas** — Writer, Producer, Actor
United Talent Agency, U T A Plaza, 9336 Civic Center Dr, Beverly Hills CA 90210 USA
**Couples, Fredrerick S (Fred)** — Golfer
Players Group, 1851 Alexander Bell Dr, #410, Reston VA 20191, USA
**Courant, Ernest D** — Physicist
40 W 72nd St, #4I, New York NY 10023, USA
**Couric, Katherine (Katie)** — Commentator
1155 Park Ave, #2SW, New York NY 10128, USA
**Courier, James S (Jim), Jr** — Tennis Player
9533 Blandford Road, Orlando FL 32827, USA
**Cournoyer, Yvan S** — Ice Hockey Player
104 Boul Des Chateaux, Blainville QC J7B 1K6, Canada
**Courreges, Andre** — Fashion Designer
27 Rue Delabordere, 92 Neuilly-Sur-Seine, France
**Court, Charles** — Government Official, Australia
21 Lewanna Way, City Beach, Perth WA 9060, Australia
**Courtenay, Tom** — Actor
Jonathan Altaras Assoc, 11 Garrick St, London WC2E 9AR, England
**Courtnall, Geoffrey L (Geoff)** — Ice Hockey Player
2730 Queenswood Dr, Victoria BC V8N 1X5, Canada
**Courtnall, Russ** — Ice Hockey Player
398 W Stafford Road, Thousand Oaks CA 91361, USA
**Courtney, Joel** — Actor
676 W Pullman Road, #301, Moscow ID 83841, USA
**Courtney, Stephanie** — Actress
Greene Assoc, 1901 Ave of Stars, #130, Los Angeles CA 90067 USA
**Courtney, Thomas W (Tom)** — Track Athlete
336 Edgemere Way E, Naples FL 34105, USA
**Coury, Fred** — Singer, Drummer (Cinderella)
Union Entertainment Group, 1323 Newbury Road, #104, Thousand Oaks CA 91320, USA
**Cousin, Philip R** — Religious Leader
African Methodist Episcopal Church, 2625 Orange Picker Road, Jacksonville FL 32223, USA
**Cousin, Terry S** — Football Player
9213 Everwood Court, Tampa FL 33647, USA
**Cousineau, Tom** — Football Player
910 Eaton Ave, Akron OH 44303, USA
**Cousino, Tishara** — Model, Actress
T L C, 1602 Alton Road, Miami Beach FL 33139, USA
**Cousins, Christopher** — Actor
DiSante Frank, 10061 Riverside Dr, #377, Toluca Lake CA 91602, USA
**Cousins, Derryl** — Baseball Umpire
78136 Desert Mountain Circle, Bermuda Dunes CA 92203, USA
**Cousins, Robin** — Figure Skater
Billy Marsh, 174-8 N Gower St, London NW1 2NB, England
**Cousins, Rose** — Singer, Songwriter, Guitarist
Old Farm Pony Records, PO Box 36054, RPO Spring Garden Road, Halifax NS B3J 3S9, Canada
**Cousins, Tina** — Singer, Model
Tony Denton Promotions, Charter House, 157-159 High St, London N14 6BP, England
**Cousteau, Jean-Michel** — Oceanographer
Ocean Futures Society, 325 Chapala St, Santa Barbara CA 93101, USA
**Cousy, Robert J (Bob)** — Basketball Player
427 Salisbury St, Worcester MA 01609, USA
**Coutterand, Leslie** — Actress
Agence Elisabeth Simpson, 62 Boulevard Du Montparnasse, 75015 Paris, France , USA
**Couture, Barbara** — Educator
Association of Public & Land Grant Universities, 1307 New York Ave NW, #400, Washington DC 20005, USA
**Couture, Randy D (Natural)** — Martial Arts Fighter, Wrestler, Actor
Xtreme Couture, 4055 W Sunset Road, Las Vegas NV 89118, USA
**Covay, Don** — Singer, Songwriter
Rawstock, PO Box 110002, Cambria Heights NY 11411, USA
**Coventry, Kirsty** — Swimmer
Octagon Worldwide, 1751 Pinnacle Dr, #1500, McLean VA 22102 USA
**Coveny, John** — Producer, Writer
Creative Artists Agency, 2000 Ave of Stars, #100, Los Angeles CA 90067 USA
**Coverdale, David** — Singer (Whitesnake, Deep Purple)
Agency Group Ltd, 142 W 57th St, #600, New York NY 10019 USA
**Coverly, Dave** — Editorial Cartoonist (Speed Bump)
Bloomington Herald-Times, Editorial Dept, 1900 S Walnut, Bloomington IN 47401, USA
**Covert, Allen** — Actor
B/W/R, 9100 Wilshire Blvd, #500W, Beverly Hills CA 90212 USA
**Covert, James P (Jimbo)** — Football Player
2647 Nelson Court, Weston FL 33332, USA
**Covey, Richard O** — Astronaut
United Space Alliance, 1102 John Glenn Blvd, Titusville FL 32780, USA
**Covic, Nebojsa** — Prime Minister, Serbia & Montenegro
Prime Minister's Office, Nemanjina 11, 11000 Belgrade, Serbia
**Coville, Bruce** — Writer
Oddly Enough, PO Box 6110, Syracuse NY 13217, USA
**Covington, Bucky** — Singer
30141 Deercroft Dr, Wagram NC 28396, USA
**Covington, Warren** — Orchestra Leader
1627 Open Field Loop, Brandon FL 33510, USA
**Covino, William A** — Educator
California State University, President's Office, 5151 State University Dr, Los Angeles CA 90032, USA
**Cowan, Billy R** — Baseball Player
PO Box 1087, Palos Verdes Estates CA 90274, USA
**Cowan, John** — Singer, Bassist (John Cowan Band)
Squire Mgmt, 3960 Radio Road, #206, Naples FL 34104, USA
**Cowan, Ralph Wolfe** — Artist
243 29th St, West Palm Beach FL 33407, USA
**Cowart, Sam, III** — Football Player
11110 Fallgate Point Court, Jacksonville FL 32256, USA
**Cowell, Simon P** — Actor
J G M, 15 Lexham Mews, London W8 6JW, England

**Cowen, Robert E** — Judge
US Court of Appeals, Judicial Complex, 402 E State St, Trenton NJ 08608, USA
**Cowen, Scott S** — Educator
Tulane University, President's Office, New Orleans LA 70118, USA
**Cowens, David W (Dave)** — Basketball Player, Coach
132 Deep Cove, Raymond ME 04071, USA
**Cowher, William L (Bill)** — Football Player, Coach; Sportscaster
1225 Briar Patch Lane, Raleigh NC 27615, USA
**Cowhill, William J** — Navy Admiral
9428 Vernon Dr, Great Falls VA 22066, USA
**Cowie, Lennox L** — Astronomer
University of Hawaii, Astronomy Dept, 2600 Campus Road, Honolulu HI 96822, USA
**Cowin, Dana** — Editor
Food & Wine, Editor's Office, 1120 Ave of Americas, New York NY 10036, USA
**Cowley, Anthony (Tony)** — Art Director
Innovative Artists, 1505 10th St, Santa Monica CA 90401 USA
**Cowley, John M** — Physicist
Arizona State University, Physics & Astronomy Dept, Tempe AZ 85287, USA
**Cowley, Joseph A (Joe)** — Baseball Player
904 Andover Garden, Lexington KY 40509, USA
**Cowlings, Allen G (A C)** — Football Player
PO Box 1064, Pacific Palisades CA 90272, USA
**Cowper, Nicola** — Actress
Brunskill Mgmt, 169 Queens Gate, #A8, London SW7 5EH, England
**Cowper, Stephen C (Steve)** — Governor, AK
PO Box A, Juneau AK 99811, USA
**Cox, Archibald, Jr** — Financier
998 5th Ave, #6W, New York NY 10028, USA
**Cox, Brian** — Actor
I F A Talent Agency, 8730 W Sunset Blvd, #490, West Hollywood CA 90069 USA
**Cox, Brian E** — Physicist
Sue Rider Mgmt, PO Box 49175, London SW19 3WY, England
**Cox, Bryan K** — Football Player
1306 Preservation Way, Oldsmar FL 34677, USA
**Cox, C Christopher** — Government Official
4000 MacArthur Blvd, #430, Newport Beach CA 92660, USA
**Cox, Charlie** — Actor
United Agents, 12-26 Lexington St, London W1F 0LE, England
**Cox, Courteney** — Actress
W M E Entertainment, 9601 Wilshire Blvd, #300, Beverly Hills CA 90210 USA
**Cox, Craig** — Writer, Producer
Kaplan/Perrone Entertainment, 9744 Wilshire Blvd, #300, Beverly Hills CA 90212, USA
**Cox, Danny B** — Baseball Player, Manager
306 Feagin Mill Road, Warner Robins GA 31088, USA
**Cox, David R** — Geneticist
Stanford University, Human Genome Center, Stanford CA 94305, USA
**Cox, David R** — Statistician
Nuffield College, Statistics Dept, Oxford OX1 1NF, England
**Cox, DeAnna** — Singer
McFadden Artists, 818 18th Ave S, Nashville TN 37203, USA
**Cox, Deborah** — Singer, Songwriter
Abrams Artists, 275 7th Ave, #2600, New York NY 10001 USA
**Cox, Don** — Singer
Stellar Entertainment, 1019 17th Ave S, Nashville TN 37212, USA
**Cox, Emmett R** — Judge
US Court of Appeals, 113 Saint Joseph St, #433, Mobile AL 36602, USA
**Cox, Frederick W (Fred)** — Football Player
401 E River St, Monticello MN 55362, USA
**Cox, Gary W** — Political Scientist
University of California, Political Science Dept, La Jolla CA 92093, USA
**Cox, Gerald** — Respirologist
McMasters University Medical School, Respirology Division, Hamilton ON L85 4L8, Canada
**Cox, Harvey G, Jr** — Educator, Theologian
Harvard University, Divinity School, Cambridge MA 02140, USA
**Cox, J Casey** — Baseball Player
2840 La Concha Dr, Clearwater FL 33762, USA
**Cox, Jennifer Elise** — Actress
Don Buchwald, 6500 Wilshire Blvd, #2200, Los Angeles CA 90048 USA
**Cox, Johnny W** — Basketball Player, Coach
849 N Main St, Hazard KY 41701, USA
**Cox, Kris** — Golfer
2009 Lunenburg Dr, Allen TX 75013, USA
**Cox, Lynne** — Distance Swimmer
Martha Kaplan Agency, 115 W 29th St, #3, New York NY 10001, USA
**Cox, Paul** — Director, Producer, Writer
Illumination Films, 1 Victoria Ave, Albert Park VIC 3208, Australia
**Cox, Philip S** — Architect
Cox Richardson Architects, 204 Clarence St, Sydney NSW 2000, Australia
**Cox, Ralph** — Ice Hockey Player
8R Rolfes Lane, Newbury MA 01951, USA
**Cox, Robert J (Bobby)** — Baseball Manager, Executive
2190 Heathermoor Hill Dr, Marietta GA 30062, USA
**Cox, Ronny** — Actor
A P A Talent/Literary Agency, 405 S Beverly Dr, #300, Beverly Hills CA 90212 USA
**Cox, Stephanie R** — Soccer Player
Atlanta Beat, 1955 Vaughn Road, #209, Kennesaw GA 30144, USA
**Cox, Stephen J** — Artist
154 Barnsbury Road, Islington, London N1 0ER, England
**Cox, Steve** — Football Player
1001 E Lakeshore Dr, Jonesboro AR 72401, USA
**Cox, Tony** — Actor
New Wave Entertainment, 2660 W Olive Ave, Burbank CA 91505, USA
**Cox, Torrie T** — Football Player
42 NW 92nd St, Miami Shores FL 33150, USA
**Cox, W Ted** — Baseball Player
109 W Pratt Dr, Oklahoma City OK 73110, USA

| | |
|---|---|
| **Cox, Warren J**<br>3111 N St NW, Washington DC 20007, USA | Architect |
| **Coxe, Craig**<br>Teddy Griffin Arena, 3450M 119th, Harbor Springs MI 49740, USA | Ice Hockey Player |
| **Coxon, Graham L**<br>X-Ray Touring, 77-79 Great Eastern St, #A, London EC2A 3HU, England | Singer, Guitarist (Blur), Actor |
| **Coyle, Brendan**<br>Rights House, Drury House, 34-43 Russell St, London WC2B 5HA, England | Actor |
| **Coyle, Richard**<br>Troika, 74 Clerkenwell Road, #300, London EC1M 5QA, England | Actor |
| **Coyne, Colleen**<br>3 Baldwin Lane, North Reading MA 01864, USA | Ice Hockey Player |
| **Coyne, Jonny**<br>Belfield & Ward, 80-81 Saint Martin Lane, Top Level, London WC2N 4AA, England | Actor |
| **Coyne, Wayne M**<br>World's Fair Mgmt, 1208 Chowning Ave, Edmond OK 73034, USA | Singer, Guitarist (Flaming Lips) |
| **Coyote, Peter**<br>Untitled Entertainment, 350 S Beverly Dr, #200, Beverly Hills CA 90212 USA | Actor |
| **Coz, Steve**<br>National Enquirer, 1000 American Media Way, Boca Raton FL 33464, USA | Editor |
| **Cozier, Jimmy**<br>Padell Nadell Fine Wineberger, 59 Maiden Lane, #2700, New York NY 10038 USA | Singer, Songwriter |
| **Crabbe, Claude C**<br>49581 Wayne St, Indio CA 92201, USA | Football Player |
| **Crable, Robert E (Bob)**<br>564 Miami Trace Court, Loveland OH 45140, USA | Football Player |
| **Crabtree, Colleen**<br>A P A Talent/Literary Agency, 405 S Beverly Dr, #300, Beverly Hills CA 90212 USA | Actress |
| **Crabtree, Eric L**<br>3101 Walnut St, Denver CO 80205, USA | Football Player |
| **Crabtree, Michael**<br>San Francisco 49ers, 4949 Centennial Blvd, Santa Clara CA 95054 USA | Football Player |
| **Crabtree, Timothy L (Tim)**<br>1503 Kingswood Lane, Colleyville TX 76034, USA | Baseball Player |
| **Cracknell, James**<br>Headway, 190 Bagnall Road, Old Basford, Nottingham, Nottinghamshire NG6 8SF, England | Rowing Athlete |
| **Craddock, Bantz J**<br>Military Professional Resources, 1320 Braddock Place, Alexandria VA 22314, USA | Army General |
| **Craddock, Billy (Crash)**<br>3007 Old Martinsville Road, Greensboro NC 27455, USA | Singer, Songwriter |
| **Craft, Christine**<br>KRBK-TV, News Dept, 500 Media Place, Sacramento CA 95815, USA | Commentator |
| **Craft, Jason D A**<br>11688 Armistad Court, Jacksonville FL 32256, USA | Football Player |
| **Crafter, Jane**<br>317 W Almeria Road, Phoenix AZ 85003, USA | Golfer |
| **Cragg, Anthony D (Tony)**<br>Lise-Meitner-Str 33, 42119 Wuppertal, Germany | Sculptor |
| **Cragg, Stephen**<br>Thrive Entertainment, 1093 Broxton Ave, Ste 228, Los Angeles CA 90024, USA | Director |
| **Craggs, George**<br>6223 6th Ave NW, Seattle WA 98107, USA | Soccer Player |
| **Craig of Radley, David B**<br>House of Lords, Westminster, London SW1A 0PW, England | Air Force Marshal, England |
| **Craig, Adam Jamal**<br>Keyword Entertainment, 1015 Gayley Ave, #601, Los Angeles CA 90024, USA | Actor |
| **Craig, Cornelius (Neal), Jr**<br>2231 Crane Ave, Cincinnati OH 45207, USA | Football Player |
| **Craig, Daniel**<br>Independent Talent Group, 40 Whitfield St, London W1T 2RH, England | Actor |
| **Craig, Eli**<br>Creative Artists Agency, 2000 Ave of Stars, #100, Los Angeles CA 90067 USA | Director, Producer |
| **Craig, Elijah**<br>Gilbertson Entertainment, 1334 3rd Street Promenade, #201, Santa Monica CA 90401 USA | Actor |
| **Craig, James D (Jim)**<br>PO Box 1199, Mattapoisett MA 02739, USA | Ice Hockey Player |
| **Craig, Jenny**<br>5770 Fleet St, Carlsbad CA 92008, USA | Nutritionist |
| **Craig, Jonny**<br>Artery Foundation, 142 S St, Sacramento CA 95811, USA | Singer |
| **Craig, Judy**<br>Lustig Talent, PO Box 770850, Orlando FL 32877 USA | Singer (Chiffons) |
| **Craig, Keren**<br>Marquesa, 60 W 26th St, #1425, New York NY 10001, USA | Fashion Designer (Marchesa), Model |
| **Craig, Larry E**<br>PO Box 2271, Eagle ID 83616, USA | Senator, ID |
| **Craig, Michael**<br>Chatto & Linnit, 123A King's Road, London SW3 4PL, England | Actor |
| **Craig, Mike**<br>29907 County Road 3, Merrifield MN 56465, USA | Ice Hockey Player |
| **Craig, Richard**<br>Pacific Northwest National Laboratory, 902 Battelle Blvd, Richland WA 99354, USA | Inventor (Land-Mine Detector) |
| **Craig, Roger L**<br>16327 Bassett Court, Ramona CA 92065, USA | Baseball Player, Manager |
| **Craig, Roger T**<br>271 Vista Verde Way, Portola Valley CA 94028, USA | Football Player |
| **Craig, Ryan**<br>United Agents, 12-26 Lexington St, London W1F 0LE, England | Director, Writer |
| **Craig, Stuart**<br>Skouras Agency, 1149 3rd St, #300, Santa Monica CA 90403 USA | Production Designer |
| **Craig, William (Bill)**<br>PO Box 629, Newport Beach CA 92661, USA | Swimmer |
| **Craig, Yvonne**<br>Y C/M C Ltd, PO Box 827, Pacific Palisades CA 90272, USA | Actress |
| **Craighead, John J**<br>5125 Orchard Ave, Missoula MT 59803, USA | Ecologist |

**Crain, Jesse A** — Baseball Player
20702 Hartford Way, Lakeville MN 55044, USA
**Crain, William** — Director
Contemporary Artists, 610 Santa Monica Blvd, #202, Santa Monica CA 90401 USA
**Crais, Robert** — Writer
12829 Landale St, Studio City CA 91604, USA
**Cramer, Darrell** — Hero
708 E 150 N, Springville UT 84663, USA
**Cramer, Grant** — Actor
9911 W Pico Blvd, #1060, Los Angeles CA 90035, USA
**Cramer, Tom** — Artist
Mark Wooley Gallery, 120 NW 9th, Portland OR 97209, USA
**Crampton, Barbara** — Actress
Amsel Eisenstadt Frazier, 5055 Wilshire Blvd, #865, Los Angeles CA 90036 USA
**Crampton, Bruce** — Golfer
225 Winter Crest Lane, Severna Park MD 21146, USA
**Cramton, Roger C** — Attorney, Educator
475 Savage Farm Dr, Ithaca NY 14850, USA
**Crandall, Bruce P** — Vietnam War Air Force Hero (CMH)
PO Box 736, Manchester WA 98353, USA
**Crandall, Delmar W (Del)** — Baseball Player
807 Azalea Lane, Vero Beach FL 32963, USA
**Crandall, Stephen H** — Mechanical Engineer
80 Deaconess Road, #348, Concord MA 01742, USA
**Crane, Benjamin M (Ben)** — Golfer
2223 Cedar Elm Terrace, Westlake TX 76262, USA
**Crane, Brian** — Cartoonist (Pickles)
PO Box 51771, Sparks NV 89435, USA
**Crane, David** — Writer, Director, Producer
W M E Entertainment, 9601 Wilshire Blvd, #300, Beverly Hills CA 90210 USA
**Crane, Paul E** — Football Player
12 N Monterey St, Mobile AL 36604, USA
**Cranham, Kenneth** — Actor
Markham Froggatt Irwin, Julian House, 4 Windmill St, London W1P 1HF, England
**Cranston, Bryan** — Actor
United Talent Agency, U T A Plaza, 9336 Civic Center Dr, Beverly Hills CA 90210 USA
**Cranston, Toller** — Figure Skater
International Management Group, 1 Saint Clair Ave E, Toronto ON M4T 2V7, Canada
**Crary, Dan** — Singer, Guitarist
Rob Hall Acoustic Music, PO Box 2105, Ringwood North VIC 3134, Australia
**Crashley, Bart** — Ice Hockey Player
90 Goacher Road, Campbellford ON K0L 1L0, Canada
**Craven, Matt** — Actor
Paradigm Agency, 360 N Crescent Dr, North Building, Beverly Hills CA 90210 USA
**Craven, Murray** — Ice Hockey Player
2814 Rest Haven Dr, Whitefish MT 59937, USA
**Craven, Richard A (Ricky)** — Auto Racing Driver
3585 Boy Scout Camp Road, Kannapolis NC 28081, USA
**Craven, Wesley E (Wes)** — Director
2419 Solar Dr, Los Angeles CA 90046, USA
**Craver, Aaron L** — Football Player
821 W Maple St, Compton CA 90220, USA
**Crawford Stanley, Marianne** — Basketball Coach
Washington Mystics, Verizon Center, 401 9th St NW, #750, Washington DC 20004 USA
**Crawford, A Jamal** — Basketball Player
Los Angeles Clippers, Staples Center, 1111 S Figueroa St, Los Angeles CA 90015 USA
**Crawford, Billy J** — Singer
Concorde International, 101 Shepherds Bush Road, London W6 7LP, England
**Crawford, Bob** — Ice Hockey Player
6 Progress Dr, Cromwell CT 06416, USA
**Crawford, Brad** — Football Player
RR 2, Winamac IN 46996, USA
**Crawford, Carl D** — Baseball Player
15618 Bristol Lake Dr, Houston TX 77070, USA
**Crawford, Chace** — Actor
Podwall Entertainment, 710 N Orbach Ave, #203, West Hollywood CA 90069, USA
**Crawford, Christina** — Writer
Seven Springs Farm, Sanders Road, Tensed ID 83870, USA
**Crawford, Chuck** — Fiddler, Singer (Heartland)
Country Thunder Records, 1016 17th Ave S, Nashville TN 37212, USA
**Crawford, Cindy** — Model, Actress
Creative Artists Agency, 2000 Ave of Stars, #100, Los Angeles CA 90067 USA
**Crawford, Clayne** — Actor
A P A Talent/Literary Agency, 405 S Beverly Dr, #300, Beverly Hills CA 90212 USA
**Crawford, Eve** — Actress
Nobel Caplan Abrams, 1260 Younge St, #200, Toronto ON M4T 1W6, Canada
**Crawford, Frederick R (Fred)** — Basketball Player
24 W Lawn Dr, Teaneck NJ 07666, USA
**Crawford, Gerald J (Gerry)** — Baseball Umpire
111 9th St E, Saint Petersburg FL 33715, USA
**Crawford, Joan** — Basketball Player
4748 S Harvard Ave, #80, Tulsa OK 74135, USA
**Crawford, John E (Johnny)** — Actor, Singer
PO Box 1851, Los Angeles CA 90078, USA
**Crawford, Keith L** — Football Player
119 A N County Road 2203, Palestine TX 75803, USA
**Crawford, Kirsty** — Singer, Songwriter
All Terrain Music Rights, 53 Chandos Place, London WC2N 4HS, England
**Crawford, Lavell** — Actor, Comedian
Anonymous Content, 3532 Hayden Ave, Culver City CA 90232 USA
**Crawford, Mac** — Businessman
C V S/Caremark Corp, 1 C V S/Caremark Dr, Woonsocket RI 02895, USA
**Crawford, Michael** — Actor, Singer
W M E Entertainment, 9601 Wilshire Blvd, #300, Beverly Hills CA 90210 USA
**Crawford, Nancy** — Model, Actress
Playboy Promotions, 2706 Media Center Dr, Los Angeles CA 90065 USA

| | |
|---|---|
| **Crawford, Rachel** | Actress |
| Edna Talent Mgmt, 318 Dundas St W, Toronto ON M5T 1G5, Canada | |
| **Crawford, Randy** | Singer |
| Performers of the World, 5657 Wilshire Blvd, #280, Los Angeles CA 90036 USA | |
| **Crawford, Steve** | Singer (Annointed), Songwriter |
| 4011 Hillman Way, #100, Youngstown OH 44512, USA | |
| **Crawford, Steven R (Steve)** | Baseball Player |
| 6122 E 480, Salina OK 74365, USA | |
| **Crawley, Sylvia** | Basketball Player, Coach |
| Ohio University, Athletic Dept, Athens OH 45701, USA | |
| **Cray, Robert** | Singer, Guitarist |
| Conquero Public Relations, 11271 Ventura Blvd, #522, Studio City CA 91604, USA | |
| **Crazy Mohan** | Actor, Comedian |
| 5 Hokkalingam St, Mandavelli, Chennai TN 600028, India | |
| **Crea, Vivien S** | Coast Guard Admiral |
| Vice Commandant, US Coast Guard, 2100 2nd St SW, Washington DC 20593 USA | |
| **Creadon, Patrick** | Director |
| Paradigm Agency, 360 N Crescent Dr, North Building, Beverly Hills CA 90210 USA | |
| **Creager, Melora** | Singer, Cellist, Songwriter |
| Ken-Ran Entertainment, 418 S Barton St, Grapevine TX 76051, USA | |
| **Creamer, Paula** | Golfer |
| 4705 Joanna Garden Court, Windermere FL 34786, USA | |
| **Creamer, Roger W** | Sportswriter |
| 180 E Hartsdale Ave, #2E, Hartsdale NY 10530, USA | |
| **Creamer, Timothy J** | Astronaut |
| 5103 Carefree Dr, League City TX 77573, USA | |
| **Crean, Tom** | Basketball Coach |
| University of Indiana, Athletic Dept, Bloomington IN 47405, USA | |
| **Crear, Mark** | Track Athlete |
| 27023 McBean Parkway, Valencia CA 91355, USA | |
| **Crebassa, Marianne** | Opera Singer |
| I M G Artists, Hogarth Business Park, Chiswick, London W4 2TH, England | |
| **Crede, Joseph (Joe)** | Baseball Player |
| 42 Dry Creek Trail, Linn MO 65051, USA | |
| **Creech, Sharon** | Writer |
| Harper Collins Publishers, 10 E 53rd St, Cellar 1, New York NY 10022 USA | |
| **Creeggan, Jim** | Bassist (Barenaked Ladies) |
| Nettwerk Mgmt, 6525 W Sunset Blvd, #800, Los Angeles CA 90028 USA | |
| **Creek, P Douglas (Doug)** | Baseball Player |
| 17500 White Water Court, Punta Gorda FL 33982, USA | |
| **Creekmore, Nathaniel R (Nate)** | Cartoonist (Maintaining) |
| Universal Press Syndicate, 4520 Main St, #700, Kansas City MO 64111, USA | |
| **Creel, Gavin** | Actor, Singer |
| Bill Silva Mgmt, 8225 Santa Monica Blvd, West Hollywood CA 90046, USA | |
| **Creel, Monica** | Actress |
| Amsel Eisenstadt Frazier, 5055 Wilshire Blvd, #865, Los Angeles CA 90036 USA | |
| **Cregeen, Peter** | Director, Producer |
| Associated International Mgmt, 7 Hatton Garden, #400, London EC1N 8AD, England | |
| **Cregger, Zach** | Actor, Producer, Director, Writer |
| B/W/R, 9100 Wilshire Blvd, #500W, Beverly Hills CA 90212 USA | |
| **Creighton, Adam** | Ice Hockey Player |
| 5202 Spectacular Bid Dr, Wesley Chapel FL 33544, USA | |
| **Creighton, David T (Dave), Sr** | Ice Hockey Player, Coach |
| 5202 Spectacular Bid Dr, Wesley Chapel FL 33544, USA | |
| **Creighton, Jim** | Basketball Player |
| 5297 S Geneva St, Englewood CO 80111, USA | |
| **Creighton, Joanne V** | Educator |
| Mount Holyoke College, President's Office, South Hadley MA 01075, USA | |
| **Creighton, John O** | Astronaut |
| 2111 SW 174th St, Burien WA 98166, USA | |
| **Crennel, Romeo** | Football Coach |
| 411 W 46th Terrace, #701, Kansas City MO 64112, USA | |
| **Crensha, George** | Cartoonist (Belvedere) |
| 22 Morning State Way, Sequim WA 98382, USA | |
| **Crenshaw, Ben D** | Golfer |
| 2610 Kenmore Court, Austin TX 78703, USA | |
| **Crenshaw, Lewis W, Jr** | Navy Admiral |
| D C N O, Resource/Warfare Requirements, HqUSN, Pentagon, Washington DC 20350, USA | |
| **Crenshaw, Marshall** | Singer, Songwriter |
| Rascoff/Zysblat Organization, 250 W 57th St, New York NY 10107 USA | |
| **Crenshaw, Willis C** | Football Player |
| 21 Carly Dr, Woodstock NY 12498, USA | |
| **Creskoff, Rebecca** | Actress |
| Innovative Artists, 1505 10th St, Santa Monica CA 90401 USA | |
| **Crespo Claudio, Felipe J** | Baseball Player |
| PO Box 592363, Orlando FL 32859, USA | |
| **Crespo, Elvis** | Singer |
| A-P R Media, 8334 Lefferts Blvd, #3C, Kew Gardens NY 11415, USA | |
| **Crespo, Hernan** | Soccer Player |
| Chelsea F C, Stamford Bridge, Fulham Road, London SW6 1HS, England | |
| **Cressida, Kathryn** | Actress |
| W M E Entertainment, 9601 Wilshire Blvd, #300, Beverly Hills CA 90210 USA | |
| **Cresson, Edith** | Prime Minister, France |
| Mairie, 86018 Chatellerault Cedex, France | |
| **Cretier, Jean-Luc** | Alpine Skier |
| 153 Ave du Marechal Leclerc, BP 20, 73700 Bourg Saint Maurice, France | |
| **Crew, Amanda** | Actress |
| United Talent Agency, U T A Plaza, 9336 Civic Center Dr, Beverly Hills CA 90210 USA | |
| **Crewdson, Gregory** | Photographer |
| 247 16th St, Brooklyn NY 11215, USA | |
| **Crewe, Candida** | Writer |
| Bloomsbury Publishing, 50 Bedford Square, London WC1B 3DP, England | |
| **Crews, David P** | Psychobiologist |
| University of Texas, Biological Science Division, Zoology Dept, Austin TX 78712, USA | |
| **Crews, Frederick C** | Educator, Writer |
| 636 Vicente Ave, Berkeley CA 94707, USA | |

**C**

| | |
|---|---|
| **Crews, Phillip** | Chemist |
| University of California, Chemistry Dept, 1156 High St, Santa Cruz CA 99064, USA | |
| **Crews, Terry A** | Actor, Football Player |
| 3 Arts Entertainment, 9460 Wilshire Blvd, #700, Beverly Hills CA 90212 USA | |
| **Crewson, Wendy** | Actress |
| Oscars Abrams Zimel, 438 Queen St E, Toronto ON M5A 1T4, Canada | |
| **Crha, Jiri** | Ice Hockey Player |
| 16390 Braeburn Ridge Trail, Delray Beach FL 33446, USA | |
| **Cribbins, Bernard** | Actor |
| Gavin Barker Assoc, 2D Wimpole St, London W1G 0EB, England | |
| **Cribbs, Joe S** | Football Player |
| 5333 Creekside Loop, Birmingham AL 35244, USA | |
| **Crichlow, Lenora** | Actress |
| B W H Agency, 117 Shaftesbury Ave, London WC2H 8AD, England | |
| **Crickhowell of Pont Esgob, Nicholas E** | Government Leader, England |
| 4 Henning St, London SW11 3DR, England | |
| **Crider, Melissa (Missy)** | Actress |
| Mavrick Artists Agency, 6100 Wilshire Blvd, #550, Los Angeles CA 90048, USA | |
| **Crier, Catherine** | Commentator |
| Crier Communications, PO Box 627, Katonaj NY 10536, USA | |
| **Crile, Susan** | Artist |
| 168 W 86th St, New York NY 10024, USA | |
| **Crilley, Mark** | Writer |
| PO Box 103, Walled Lake MI 48390, USA | |
| **Crim, Charles R (Chuck)** | Baseball Player |
| 50039 Golden Horse Dr, Oakhurst CA 93644, USA | |
| **Crippen, Robert L** | Astronaut |
| 781 Harbour Isle Place, West Palm Beach FL 33410, USA | |
| **Crisostomo, Manny** | Photojournalist |
| Pacific Daily News, PO Box DN, Hagatna GU 96932, USA | |
| **Crisp, Terry A** | Ice Hockey Player, Coach |
| 805 Cherry Laurel Court, Nashville TN 37215, USA | |
| **Criss, Charles W (Charlie)** | Basketball Player |
| 4310 Melanie Lane, Atlanta GA 30349, USA | |
| **Criss, Darren** | Actor |
| C E S D, 10635 Santa Monica Blvd, #130, Los Angeles CA 90025 USA | |
| **Criss, Peter** | Singer, Drummer (Kiss) |
| 2111 Friar Court, Wall Township NJ 07719, USA | |
| **Crist, Charles T (Chuck)** | Football Player |
| PO Box 369, Greenhurst NY 14742, USA | |
| **Crist, George B** | Marine Corps General |
| 406 East St, Beaufort SC 29902, USA | |
| **Crist, Myndy** | Actress |
| Abrams Artists, 9200 W Sunset Blvd, #1125, West Hollywood CA 90069 USA | |
| **Crista, Heloise** | Sculptor |
| Taliesin West, PO Box 4430, Scottsdale AZ 85261, USA | |
| **Cristal, Linda** | Actress |
| 9129 Hazen Dr, Beverly Hills CA 90210, USA | |
| **Cristofer, Michael** | Writer, Director, Actor |
| I C M Partners, 10250 Constellation Blvd, #900, Los Angeles CA 90067 USA | |
| **Cristol, Stanley J** | Chemist |
| 1638 W 3rd Ave, Durango CO 81301, USA | |
| **Criswell, Jeffrey L (Jeff)** | Football Player |
| 811 Walnut St, Kansas City MO 64106, USA | |
| **Critelli, Michael** | Businessman |
| Pitney Bowes Inc, 1 Elmcroft Road, Stamford CT 06926, USA | |
| **Criter, Kenneth W (Ken)** | Football Player |
| PO Box 441343, Aurora CO 80044, USA | |
| **Crittenton, Javaris C** | Basketball Player |
| Washington Wizards, M C I Centre, 601 F St NW, Washington DC 20004 USA | |
| **Croasdell, Adam** | Actor |
| Ken McReddie Assoc, 101 Finsbury Pavement, London EC2A 1RS, England | |
| **Croce, Adrian J (A J)** | Singer |
| Railway Tour Consultants, 800 W 3rd St, #2308, Austin TX 78701, USA | |
| **Croce, Joseph** | Singer (Chimes) |
| Wolfman Jack Entertainment, 105 Rivershore Dr, Hertford NC 27944 USA | |
| **Crocicchia, Olivia** | Actress |
| United Talent Agency, U T A Plaza, 9336 Civic Center Dr, Beverly Hills CA 90210 USA | |
| **Crocker, Ian** | Swimmer |
| 8901 Ovalia Ave, Austin TX 78749, USA | |
| **Crocker, J Dillard** | Basketball Player |
| 5601 Holiday Park Blvd, North Port FL 34287, USA | |
| **Crocker, Mary Lou** | Golfer |
| 1403 Sutton Dr, Carrollton TX 75006, USA | |
| **Crocker, Ryan C** | Diplomat |
| State Department, 2201 C St NW, Washington DC 20520 USA | |
| **Crockett, Affion** | Actor |
| Lejan Entertainment, 11271 Ventura Blvd, #186, Studio City CA 91604, USA | |
| **Crockett, Billy** | Singer, Songwriter |
| McGuckin Entertainment Public Relations, 500 Riverside Dr, #160, Austin TX 78704, USA | |
| **Crockett, Zack** | Football Player |
| 3301 NE 183rd St, #604, Aventura FL 33160, USA | |
| **Croel, Mike** | Football Player |
| 8305 Lookout Mountain Ave, Los Angeles CA 90046, USA | |
| **Croft, Dwayne** | Opera Singer |
| I M G Artists, Carnegie Hall Tower, 152 W 57th St, #500, New York NY 10019 USA | |
| **Croft, Richard** | Opera Singer |
| I M G Artists, Hogarth Business Park, Chiswick, London W4 2TH, England | |
| **Crofts, Dash** | Singer, Songwriter (Seals & Crofts) |
| 4Star Entertainment, 1675 York Ave, #32C, New York NY 10128, USA | |
| **Croker, Stephen B (Steve)** | Air Force General |
| 2 Byford Court, Chestertown MD 21620, USA | |
| **Cromartie, Antonio** | Football Player |
| New York Jets, 1 Jets Dr, Florham Park NJ 07932 USA | |
| **Crombeen, Mike** | Ice Hockey Player |
| 817 Foxcroft Blvd, Newmarket ON L3X 1MB, Canada | |

**Crombey, Bernard** — Actor
Artmedia, 20 Ave Rapp, 75007 Paris, France
**Crombie, Jonathan** — Actor
Gage Group, 450 7th Ave, #1809, New York NY 10123 USA
**Cromer, Roy B (Tripp), III** — Baseball Player
32 W Tombee Lane, Columbia SC 29209, USA
**Cromme, Gerhard** — Businessman
Siemens AG, Wittelsbacherplatz 2, 80333 Munich, Germany
**Crompton, Alfred W** — Archaeologist, Ethnologist, Biologist
Harvard University, Museum of Comparative Zoology, Cambridge MA 02138, USA
**Crompton, Steven S** — Cartoonist (Demi the Demoness)
PO Box 2018, Scottsdale AZ 85252, USA
**Cromwell, James** — Actor
Koshari Films, 13251 Ventura Blvd, #1, Studio City CA 91604, USA
**Cronan, Peter J (Pete)** — Football Player
13 Saddle Hill Road, Hopkinton MA 01748, USA
**Cronbach, Lee J** — Psychologist
2614 Oregon St, Union City CA 94587, USA
**Crone, Raymond H (Ray)** — Baseball Player
508 Panarama, Waxahachie TX 75165, USA
**Cronenberg, David** — Director
Sentient Entertainment, 1617 Broadway, Mezzanine Suite, Santa Monica CA 90404, USA
**Cronenweth, Jeffrey S (Jeff)** — Cinematographer
2241 Corinth Ave, Los Angeles CA 90064, USA
**Cronin, Anthony** — Writer
30 Oakley Road, Dublin 6, Ireland
**Cronin, Eugene E (Gene)** — Football Player
2445 37th Ave, Sacramento CA 95822, USA
**Cronin, James W** — Nobel Physics Laureate
175 N Harbor Dr, #4902, Chicago IL 60601, USA
**Cronin, Shawn** — Ice Hockey Player
4163 SE Oakland St, Stuart FL 34997, USA
**Cronk, William F (Rick), III** — Businessman, Non-Profit Executive
Boy Scouts of America, National Council, PO Box 152079, Irving TX 75015, USA
**Crook, Mackenzie** — Actor, Comedian
Karushi Mgmt, 7 Wenlock Road, #10, London N1 7SL, England
**Croom, Sylvester** — Football Player, Coach
3909 12th St NE, Tuscaloosa AL 35404, USA
**Crosbie, Annette** — Actress
Independent Talent Group, 40 Whitfield St, London W1T 2RH, England
**Crosbie, John C** — Political Leader, Canada
Scotia Center, 235 Water St, Saint John's NF A1C 5L3, Canada
**Crosby, Alfred W** — Historian
2506 Bowman Ave, Austin TX 78703, USA
**Crosby, B J** — Actress, Singer
Gage Group, 14724 Ventura Blvd, #505, Sherman Oaks CA 91403 USA
**Crosby, Cathy Lee** — Actress
Epstein Wyckoff Corsa Ross, 11350 Ventura Blvd, #100, Studio City CA 91604, USA
**Crosby, David** — Singer (Byrds, Crosby Stills Nash)
Lookout Mgmt, 1460 4th St, #300, Santa Monica CA 90401 USA
**Crosby, Denise** — Actress, Model
Rebel Entertainment Partners, 5700 Wilshire Blvd, #456, Los Angeles CA 90036, USA
**Crosby, Edward C (Ed)** — Baseball Player
6952 Brightwood Lane, #9, Garden Grove CA 92845, USA
**Crosby, Elaine** — Golfer
2580 Meadowbrook Lane, Jackson MI 49201, USA
**Crosby, Kathryn Grant** — Actress
508 W 3rd St, Carson City NV 89703, USA
**Crosby, Mary** — Actress
2875 S Barrymore Dr, Malibu CA 90265, USA
**Crosby, Robert E (Bobby)** — Baseball Player
11463 Anticost Way, Cypress CA 90630, USA
**Crosby, Sidney P** — Ice Hockey Player
Pittsburgh Penguins, Consol Energy Center, 1001 5th Ave, Pittsburgh PA 15219 USA
**Croshere, Austin** — Basketball Player
11721 Sea Star Dr, Indianapolis IN 46256, USA
**Cross, Ben** — Actor
Shepherd & Ford, 13 Radnor Walk, London SW3 4BP, England
**Cross, Christopher** — Singer, Guitarist, Songwriter
Front Line Mgmt, 1100 Glendon Ave, #2000, Los Angeles CA 90024 USA
**Cross, Cory** — Ice Hockey Player
2963 Bayshore Pointe Dr, Tampa FL 33611, USA
**Cross, David** — Actor, Comedian
Brillstein Entertainment Partners, 9150 Wilshire Blvd, #350, Beverly Hills CA 90212 USA
**Cross, Donna Woolfolk** — Writer
Onondaga Community College, English Dept, Syracuse NY 13202, USA
**Cross, Helen** — Writer
Rogers Coleridge White, 20 Powis Mews, London W11 1JN, England
**Cross, Howard E** — Football Player
79 Poplar Dr, Paramus NJ 07652, USA
**Cross, Irv A** — Football Player, Sportscaster
2196 Marion Road, Roseville MN 55113, USA
**Cross, Jeffrey A (Jeff)** — Football Player
8045 SW 100th St, Miami FL 33156, USA
**Cross, Joseph** — Actor
United Talent Agency, U T A Plaza, 9336 Civic Center Dr, Beverly Hills CA 90210 USA
**Cross, Justin A** — Football Player
10 Longwood Dr, Hampton NH 03842, USA
**Cross, Marcia** — Actress
Gersh Agency, 9465 Wilshire Blvd, #600, Beverly Hills CA 90212 USA
**Cross, Mike** — Guitarist, Fiddler
Blade Agency, PO Box 1556, Gainesville FL 32602, USA
**Cross, Randall L (Randy)** — Football Player, Sportscaster
155 Travertine Trail, Alpharetta GA 30022, USA
**Cross, Shauna** — Writer
W K T Public Relations, 9350 Wilshire Blvd, #450, Beverly Hills CA 90212 USA

# C

**Crossan, David H (Dave)** — Football Player
3314 Emory Dr, Winston Salem NC 27103, USA
**Crosse, Clay** — Singer
Breen Agency, 110 30th Ave N, #3, Nashville TN 37203, USA
**Crosse, Liris** — Model, Actress
Britto Agency, 234 W 56th St, #PH, New York NY 10019, USA
**Crossett, Howard W** — Bobsled Athlete
US Bobsled & Skeleton Federation, 1631 Mesa Ave, #A, Colorado Springs CO 80906 USA
**Crossley, Paul C R** — Concert Pianist
Connaught Artists, 2 Molasses Row, London SW11 3UX, England
**Crossley-Mercer, Edwin** — Opera Singer
I M G Artists, Hogarth Business Park, Chiswick, London W4 2TH, England
**Crossman, Doug** — Ice Hockey Player
107 Franklin Road, Glassboro NJ 08028, USA
**Croteau, Gary P** — Ice Hockey Player
8380 E Hinsdale Ave, Centennial CO 80112, USA
**Crotty, John K** — Basketball Player
370 NE Edgewater Dr, #404, Stuart FL 34996, USA
**Crouch, Andrae** — Singer, Pianist, Songwriter
Universal Attractions, 135 W 26th St, #1200, New York NY 10001 USA
**Crouch, Eric E** — Football Player
19453 Walnut Circle, Omaha NE 68130, USA
**Crouch, Paul** — Evangelist
Trinity Broadcasting Network, PO Box A, Santa Ana CA 92711, USA
**Crouch, Roger K** — Astronaut
120 6th St NE, Washington DC 20002, USA
**Crouch, Sandra** — Drummer, Songwriter
Sparrow Communications Group, 101 Winners Circle, Brentwood TN 37027, USA
**Crouch, Stanley** — Writer, Columnist
Georges Borchardt Agency, 136 E 57th St, #1400, New York NY 10022, USA
**Crouch, William W (Bill)** — Army General
Isilon Systems, 3101 Western Ave, Seattle WA 98121, USA
**Croucier, Juan C** — Bassist (Dokken, Ratt)
45 Cayuse Lane, Rancho Palos Verdes CA 90275, USA
**Crouse, Lindsay** — Actress
263 Monte Grigio Dr, Pacific Palisades CA 90272, USA
**Crouther, Lance** — Actor
Circle of Confusion, 8548 Washington Blvd, Culver City CA 90232, USA
**Crow, Ashley** — Actress
Don Buchwald, 6500 Wilshire Blvd, #2200, Los Angeles CA 90048 USA
**Crow, Harlan R** — Businessman
Trammell Crow Co, Trammell Crow Center, 2001 Ross Ave, #325, Dallas TX 75201, USA
**Crow, John David** — Football Player, Coach
5004 Augusta Circle, College Station TX 77845, USA
**Crow, Kim** — Rowing Athlete
Melbourne University Boat Club, Boathouse Dr, Melbourne VIC 3004, Australia
**Crow, Lindon** — Football Player
6800 S Strand Ave, #481, Yuma AZ 85364, USA
**Crow, Mark H** — Basketball Player
501 W Bay St, Jacksonville FL 32202, USA
**Crow, Michael M** — Educator
Arizona State University, President's Office, Tempe AZ 85287, USA
**Crow, Sheryl** — Singer, Songwriter, Actress
W Mgmt, 75 E 4th St, Front 1, New York NY 10003, USA
**Crow, Thomas E** — Art Historian
New York University, Art History Institute, New York NY 10012, USA
**Crow, William R (Bill)** — Basketball Player
21300 River Road, #15, Perris CA 92570, USA
**Crowder, Bruce** — Ice Hockey Player
7 Kyle Dr, Nashua NH 03062, USA
**Crowder, David** — Singer, Guitarist, Pianist
Media Collective, PO Box 273, Franklin TN 37065, USA
**Crowder, J Corey** — Basketball Player
725 Ballard Bridge Road, Carrollton GA 30117, USA
**Crowder, Keith** — Ice Hockey Player
PO Box 95 Station Main, Essex ON N8M 2Y1, Canada
**Crowder, Randolph C (Randy)** — Football Player
803 Strawberry Lane, Brandon FL 33511, USA
**Crowder, Troy** — Ice Hockey Player
103 Panache North Shore Road, Whitefish ON P0M 3E0, Canada
**Crowder, William D** — Navy Admiral
Deputy CNO, Operations/Plans/Strategy, HqUSN, Pentagon, Washington DC 20350 USA
**Crowe, Cameron** — Director, Writer
1016 Amalfi Dr, Pacific Palisades CA 90272, USA
**Crowe, Martin D** — Cricketer
PO Box 109302, Newmarket, Auckland 1149, New Zealand
**Crowe, Mia** — Actress
C E S D, 10635 Santa Monica Blvd, #130, Los Angeles CA 90025 USA
**Crowe, Phil** — Ice Hockey Player
204 Duffield St, Willow Grove PA 19090, USA
**Crowe, Russell** — Actor
W M E Entertainment, 9601 Wilshire Blvd, #300, Beverly Hills CA 90210 USA
**Crowe, Tonya** — Actress, Writer
13030 Mindanao Way, #4, Marina del Rey CA 90292, USA
**Crowell, Angelo D** — Football Player
PO Box 38203, Tallahassee FL 32315, USA
**Crowell, Germane L** — Football Player
200 Luzelle Dr, Winston Salem NC 27103, USA
**Crowell, John C** — Geologist
300 Hot Springs Road, Santa Barbara CA 93108, USA
**Crowell, Rodney J** — Singer, Songwriter
Maine Road Mgmt, 195 Chrystie St, #901F, New York NY 10002, USA
**Crowley, Dermot** — Actor
United Agents, 12-26 Lexington St, London W1F 0LE, England
**Crowley, Mart** — Writer
I C M Partners, 10250 Constellation Blvd, #900, Los Angeles CA 90067 USA

| | |
|---|---|
| **Crowley, Michael** | Columnist, Writer |
| Three Rivers Press, 1745 Broadway, New York NY 10019, USA | |
| **Crowley, Patricia** | Actress |
| T M C E, 270 N Canon Dr, #1064, Beverly Hills CA 90210, USA | |
| **Crowley, Terrence M (Terry)** | Baseball Player |
| 18405 Ensor Farm Court, Parkton MD 21120, USA | |
| **Crowson, Richard** | Editorial Cartoonist |
| Wichita Eagle-Beacon, Editorial Dept, 825 E Douglas Ave, Wichita KS 67202, USA | |
| **Crowton, Gary** | Football Coach |
| Brigham Young University, Athletic Dept, Provo UT 84602, USA | |
| **Croyle, J Brodie** | Football Player |
| 105 Apple Blossom Dr, Brandon MS 39047, USA | |
| **Croze, Marie-Josee** | Actress |
| U B B A, 6 Rue de Braque, 75003 Paris, France | |
| **Crozier, Joseph R (Joe)** | Ice Hockey Player, Coach |
| 299 Randwood Dr, Buffalo NY 14221, USA | |
| **Crudup, Billy** | Actor |
| Creative Artists Agency, 2000 Ave of Stars, #100, Los Angeles CA 90067 USA | |
| **Cruickshank, John A** | WW II Air Force Hero (VC) |
| Victoria Cross Assn, Old Admiralty Building, London SW1A 2BL, England | |
| **Cruikshank, Thomas H** | Businessman |
| 5949 Sherry Lane, #1035, Dallas TX 75225, USA | |
| **Cruise, Tom** | Actor |
| 42 West, 220 W 42nd St, #1200, New York NY 10036 USA | |
| **Crum, E Denzel (Denny)** | Basketball Coach |
| 6901 Routt Road, Louisville KY 40299, USA | |
| **Crumb, George H** | Composer |
| 240 Kirk Lane, Media PA 19063, USA | |
| **Crumb, Robert (R)** | Cartoonist (Keep on Truckin') |
| 20 Rue du Pont Vieux, 30610 Sauve, France | |
| **Crump, Simon** | Writer |
| A M Heath Co, 79 Saint Martin's Lane, London WC2N 4RE, England | |
| **Crumpler, Algernon D (Alge)** | Football Player |
| 2155 Enclave Mill Dr, Dacula GA 30019, USA | |
| **Crusan, Douglas G (Doug), Jr** | Football Player |
| 6263 Hanover Court, Fishers IN 46038, USA | |
| **Crutcher, Chris** | Writer |
| 3405 E Marion Court, Spokane WA 99223, USA | |
| **Crutzen, Paul J** | Nobel Chemistry Laureate |
| Am Fort Gonsenheim 36, 55122 Mainz, Germany | |
| **Cruyff, Johan** | Soccer Player, Coach |
| Koninklijke Nederk Voetbalbod, Postbus 515, 3700 AM Zeist, Netherlands | |
| **Cruz Dilan, Jose L, Sr** | Baseball Player |
| 2309 Delta Bridge Dr, Pearland TX 77584, USA | |
| **Cruz Garcia, Deivi** | Baseball Player |
| 611 Woodward Ave, Detroit MI 48226, USA | |
| **Cruz Martinez, Nelson R** | Baseball Player |
| Texas Rangers, Ameriquest Field, 1000 Ballpark Way, #306, Arlington TX 76011 USA | |
| **Cruz Smith, Martin** | Writer |
| Simon & Schuster, 1230 Ave of Americas, Concourse 1, New York NY 10020 USA | |
| **Cruz, Alexis** | Actor |
| Defining Artists, 4370 Tujunga Ave, #120, Studio City CA 91604, USA | |
| **Cruz, Anthony** | Singer |
| Latin Artist Group, 11271 Ventura Blvd, #151, Studio City CA 91604, USA | |
| **Cruz, Brandon** | Actor, Musician |
| Taang Records & Retail, 706 Pismo Court, San Diego CA 92109, USA | |
| **Cruz, Jacob** | Baseball Player |
| 1582 W Commerce Ave, Gilbert AZ 85233, USA | |
| **Cruz, Jose L, Jr** | Baseball Player |
| 8475 SW 53rd Ave, Miami FL 33143, USA | |
| **Cruz, Nilo** | Writer |
| Paradigm Agency, 360 N Crescent Dr, North Building, Beverly Hills CA 90210 USA | |
| **Cruz, Penelope** | Actress, Model |
| Kuranda Mgmt, Santo Angel 84, 28043 Madrid, Spain | |
| **Cruz, Raymond** | Actor |
| Media Artists Group, 8222 Melrose Ave, #203, Los Angeles CA 90048 USA | |
| **Cruz, Taio** | Singer, Songwriter |
| Helter Skelter, 347-353 Chiswick High Road, London W4 4HS, England | |
| **Cruz, Valerie** | Actress |
| Innovative Artists, 1505 10th St, Santa Monica CA 90401 USA | |
| **Cruz, Victor M** | Football Player |
| New York Giants, Meadowlands Stadium, 102 Route 120, East Rutherford NJ 07073 USA | |
| **Cruzado, Waded** | Educator |
| Montana State University, President's Office, Bozeman MT 59717, USA | |
| **Cruz-Diez, Carlos** | Artist |
| 23 Rue Pierre Semard, 75009 Paris, France | |
| **Crvenkovski, Branko** | President, Macedonia |
| Bihacka 8, 1000 Skopje, Macedonia | |
| **Cryder, Robert J (Bob)** | Football Player |
| 17411 NE 129th St, Redmond WA 98052, USA | |
| **Cryer, Gretchen** | Writer, Lyricist, Actress |
| 885 W End Ave, New York NY 10025, USA | |
| **Cryer, Jon** | Actor |
| Forward Entertainment, 9255 Sunset Blvd, #805, Los Angeles CA 90069, USA | |
| **Cryer, Suzanne** | Actress |
| Essential Talent Mgmt, 3151 Cahuenga Blvd W, #220, Los Angeles CA 90068, USA | |
| **Crystal, Billy** | Actor, Comedian |
| M B S T Entertainment, 345 N Maple Dr, #200, Beverly Hills CA 90210 USA | |
| **Crystal, Ronald G** | Molecular Biologist |
| 435 E 70th St, #34B, New York NY 10021, USA | |
| **Csikszentmihalyi, Mihaly** | Psychologist |
| 700 Alamosa Dr, Claremont CA 91711, USA | |
| **Csokas, Marton** | Actor |
| Sue Barnett Assoc, 1/96 Albion St, Surry Hills NSW 2010, Australia | |
| **Csonka, Lawrence R (Larry)** | Football Player |
| 6940 Stella Place, Anchorage AK 99507, USA | |

# C

**Csupo, Gabor** — Director
Grand Allure Entertainment, 12835 Mulholland Drive, Beverly Hills CA 90210, USA
**Ctvrtlik, Robert (Bob)** — Volleyball Player
22 Leon Way, Rancho Mirage CA 92270, USA
**Cua, Rick** — Singer, Pianist
Greg Menza, 1086 Rip Steele Road, Columbia TN 38401, USA
**Cuaron Orozoco, Carlos J** — Director, Producer, Writer
United Talent Agency, U T A Plaza, 9336 Civic Center Dr, Beverly Hills CA 90210 USA
**Cuaron, Alfonso** — Director, Producer
United Talent Agency, U T A Plaza, 9336 Civic Center Dr, Beverly Hills CA 90210 USA
**Cuba, Alex** — Singer, Songwriter
Agency Group Ltd, 1880 Century Park E, #711, Los Angeles CA 90067 USA
**Cuban, Mark** — Basketball Executive, Businessman
Dallas Mavericks, Pavilion, 2909 Taylor St, Dallas TX 75226 USA
**Cubbage, Michael L (Mike)** — Baseball Player, Manager
3349 Carroll Creek Road, Keswick VA 22947, USA
**Cubitt, David** — Actor
Resolution, 1801 Century Park East, #2300, Los Angeles CA 90067 USA
**Cuccarini, Lorella** — Actress
Assoziazione Italia, CP 6323, 00100 Rome-Prati, Italy
**Cucchi, Enzo** — Artist
Galerie Bruno Bischofberger, Weissenrainstr 1, 8708 Mannedorf, Switzerland
**Cuccurullo, Warren** — Guitarist (Duran Duran)
D D Productions, 93A Westbourne Park Villas, London W2 5ED, England
**Cuche, Didier** — Alpine Skier
Bonne Auberge, 2058 Les Bugnenets, Switzerland
**Cucinotta, Maria Grazia** — Actress, Model
Class Mgmt, Pizza Cavour 66, 02100 Rieti, Italy
**Cudahy, Richard D** — Judge
US Court of Appeals, 219 S Dearborn St, #2302B, Chicago IL 60604, USA
**Cuddy, Jim** — Singer, Guitarist (Blue Rodeo)
Starfish Entertainment, 906A Logan Ave, Toronto ON M4K 3E4, Canada
**Cuddyer, Michael B** — Baseball Player
10240 Washington Palm Way, Malverne NY 11565, USA
**Cudlitz, Michael** — Actor
Gold Coast, 1023 1/2 Abbot Kinney Blvd, Venice CA 90291, USA
**Cudmore, Daniel** — Actor
Characters Talent Agency, 1505 W 2nd Ave, #200, Vancouver, BC V6H 3Y4, Canada
**Cuesta, Michael** — Director
W M E Entertainment, 9601 Wilshire Blvd, #300, Beverly Hills CA 90210 USA
**Cuevas, Beto** — Singer, Actor, Composer
Espada-Zimmatore, PO Box 6577, Burbank CA 91510, USA
**Cuevas, Jose Luis** — Artist
Galeana 109, San Angel Inn, Mexico City 20 DF, Mexico
**Culbertson, Brian** — Jazz Musician
Stiletto Entertainment, 8295 S La Cienega Blvd, Inglewood CA 90301, USA
**Culbertson, Frank L, Jr** — Astronaut
15500 Meherrin Dr, Centreville VA 20120, USA
**Culbreath, Joshua (Josh)** — Track Athlete
Central State University, Athletic Dept, Wilberforce OH 45384, USA
**Culbreth, Fieldin H, III** — Baseball Umpire
224 Claiborne Court, Spartanburg SC 29301, USA
**Culea, Melinda** — Actress
Blueline Productions, 212 26th St, #295, Santa Monica CA 90402, USA
**Culhane, Jim** — Ice Hockey Player
8547 Hathaway Road, Kalamazoo MI 49009, USA
**Culkin, Courtney Rachel** — Model
Playboy Promotions, 2706 Media Center Dr, Los Angeles CA 90065 USA
**Culkin, Kieran** — Actor
W K T Public Relations, 9350 Wilshire Blvd, #450, Beverly Hills CA 90212 USA
**Culkin, Macaulay** — Actor
Brookside Artist Mgmt, 250 W 57th St, #2303, New York NY 10107 USA
**Culkin, Rory** — Actor
Brookside Artists Mgmt, 450 N Roxbury Dr, #400, Beverly Hills CA 90210, USA
**Cullen, Barry** — Ice Hockey Player
Cullen Motors, 905 Woodlawn Road W, Guelph ON N1K 1B7, Canada
**Cullen, Brett** — Actor
Lovett Mgmt, 1327 Brinkley Ave, Los Angeles CA 90049, USA
**Cullen, John** — Ice Hockey Player
1002 Legacy Hills Dr, McDonough GA 30253, USA
**Cullen, Matthew (Matt)** — Ice Hockey Player
6008 Over Hadden Court, Raleigh NC 27614, USA
**Cullen, Ray** — Ice Hockey Player
20 Sydenham Dr, RR 2, Iderton ON N0M 2A0, Canada
**Cullen, Sean M** — Actor
Henderson Hogan Agency, 850 7th Ave, #1003, New York NY 10019, USA
**Cullen, Timothy L (Tim)** — Baseball Player
159 W G St, Benicia CA 94510, USA
**Culler, Glen** — Computer Scientist
Culler Scientific Systems Corp, 100 Burns Place, Goleta CA 93117, USA
**Culligan, Joe** — Private Investigator, Writer
Research Investigative Services, 650 NE 126th St, North Miami FL 33161, USA
**Cullimore, Jassen A** — Ice Hockey Player
8610 Dolce Vita Lane, Odessa FL 33556, USA
**Cullinan, Edward H** — Architect
Wharf, 1 Baldwin Terrace, London N1 7RU, England
**Cullum, Jamie** — Jazz Pianist, Singer, Songwriter
Direct Management Group, 947 La Cienega Blvd, #G, West Hollywood CA 90069, USA
**Cullum, John** — Actor, Singer
Stone Manners Salners, 9911 W Pico Blvd, #1400, Los Angeles CA 90035 USA
**Cullum, Mark E** — Editorial Cartoonist
5401 Forest Acres Dr, Nashville TN 37220, USA
**Culp, Joseph** — Actor, Director, Producer
Gage Group, 14724 Ventura Blvd, #505, Sherman Oaks CA 91403 USA
**Culp, Ray L** — Baseball Player
7400 Waterline Road, Austin TX 78731, USA

Culp, Steven — Actor
Miriam Milgrom Entertainment, 3614 Lankershim Blvd, Los Angeles CA 90068, USA
Culpepper, Daunte — Football Player
16730 Berkshire Court, Southwest Ranches FL 33331, USA
Culpepper, J Broward (Brad) — Football Player
60 Bahama Circle, Tampa FL 33606, USA
Culpepper, James — Drummer (Flyleaf)
W M E Entertainment, 9601 Wilshire Blvd, #300, Beverly Hills CA 90210 USA
Culpepper, R Edward (Ed) — Football Player
811 Bluewater Dr, Sun City Center FL 33573, USA
Culver, George R — Baseball Player
5409 Rustic Canyon St, Bakersfield CA 93306, USA
Culver, John C — Senator, IA
5409 Spangler Ave, Bethesda MD 20816, USA
Culver, Michael — Actor
Waring & McKenna, 22 Grafton St, London W1S 4EX, England
Culver, Molly — Actress
Jonas Public Relations, 240 26th St, #3, Santa Monica CA 90402, USA
Cumberbatch, Benedict — Actor
United Talent Agency, U T A Plaza, 9336 Civic Center Dr, Beverly Hills CA 90210 USA
Cumberland, John S — Baseball Player
19417 Golden Slipper Place, Lutz FL 33558, USA
Cumby, George E — Football Player
12090 Cross Fence Trail, Tyler TX 75706, USA
Cuming, Ry — Singer, Songwriter
Agency Group Ltd, 142 W 57th St, #600, New York NY 10019 USA
Cumming, Alan — Actor, Singer, Director
Troika, 74 Clerkenwell Road, #300, London EC1M 5QA, England
Cumming, Charles — Writer
Jankow & Nesbit, 33 Drayson Mews, London W8 4LY, England
Cumming, Ian M — Businessman
Leucadia National Corp, 315 Park Ave S, New York NY 10010, USA
Cummings, Burton — Singer (Guess Who), Songwriter
S L Feldman Mgmt, 1505 W 2nd Ave, #200, Vancouver BC V6H 3Y4, Canada
Cummings, Erin — Actress
Paradigm Agency, 360 N Crescent Dr, North Building, Beverly Hills CA 90210 USA
Cummings, James J (Jim) — Actor
Atlas Talent Agency, 15 E 32nd St, #600, New York NY 10016, USA
Cummings, Midre A — Baseball Player
19525 Morden Blush Dr, Lutz FL 33558, USA
Cummings, Quinn — Actress, Writer
HipHugger Inc, PO Box 93963, Pasadena CA 91109, USA
Cummings, Stephen P (Steve) — Cyclist
Barloworld, 1800 Katherine St, Sandton 2146, Scotland
Cummings, T Terrell (Terry) — Basketball Player
12820 W Golden Lane, San Antonio TX 78249, USA
Cummings, Whitney — Actress, Comedienne
Creative Artists Agency, 2000 Ave of Stars, #100, Los Angeles CA 90067 USA
Cummins, Barry — Ice Hockey Player
155 Marsden St, Kimberley BC V1A 1G8, Canada
Cummins, Corryn — Actress
Mitchell K Stubbs Assoc, 8695 W Washington Blvd, #204, Culver City CA 90232 USA
Cummins, Gregory Scott — Actor
Schiowitz Connor, 1680 N Vine St, #1016, Los Angeles CA 90028 USA
Cummins, Jim — Ice Hockey Player
15 W Quincy St, #B, Westmont IL 60559, USA
Cummins, Peggy — Actress
17 Brockley Road, Bexhill on Sea, Sussex TN39 4TT, England
Cumpsty, Michael — Actor
Innovative Artists, 1505 10th St, Santa Monica CA 90401 USA
Cundey, Dean R — Cinematographer
250 S De Lacey Ave, #207, Pasadena CA 91105, USA
Cundieff, Rusty — Actor, Director
Code Entertainment, 9229 Sunset Blvd, #615, Los Angeles CA 90069, USA
Cundiff, William A (Billy) — Football Player
Cleveland Browns, 76 Lou Groza Blvd, Berea OH 44017 USA
Cunnane, William J (Will) — Baseball Player
123 Sleepy Hollow Lane, Congers NY 10920, USA
Cunneyworth, Randy W — Ice Hockey Player, Coach
141 Caversham Woods, Pittsford NY 14534, USA
Cunningham, Bennie L — Football Player
Quincy Road, Seneca SC 29672, USA
Cunningham, Bill — Singer, Bassist, Pianist (Box Tops)
Horizon Mgmt, PO Box 8770, Endwell NY 13762, USA
Cunningham, Carl M — Football Player
4471 Saddleworth Circle, Orlando FL 32826, USA
Cunningham, Danny — Actor
United Agents, 12-26 Lexington St, London W1F 0LE, England
Cunningham, David L — Director
United Talent Agency, U T A Plaza, 9336 Civic Center Dr, Beverly Hills CA 90210 USA
Cunningham, J Douglas (Doug) — Football Player
5060 Harling Place, Jackson MS 39211, USA
Cunningham, Jared — Basketball Player
Dallas Mavericks, Pavilion, 2909 Taylor St, Dallas TX 75226 USA
Cunningham, John — Actor
Gage Group, 14724 Ventura Blvd, #505, Sherman Oaks CA 91403 USA
Cunningham, Joseph R (Joe) — Baseball Player
RR 1 Box 80A, Koshkonong MO 65692, USA
Cunningham, Liam — Actor
Management 360, 9111 Wilshire Blvd, Beverly Hills CA 90210 USA
Cunningham, Michael — Writer
Columbia University, Creative Writing Center, Lewisohn Hall, New York NY 10014, USA
Cunningham, R Walter (Walt) — Astronaut
5110 San Felipe, #162W, Houston TX 77056, USA
Cunningham, Randall — Football Player
380 E Robindale Road, Las Vegas NV 89123, USA

# C

**Cunningham, Richard A (Richie)** — Football Player
610 Cheyenne Dr, Houma LA 70360, USA
**Cunningham, Richard K (Dick)** — Football Player
100 Rosewood Court, Peachtree City GA 30269, USA
**Cunningham, Samuel L (Sam), Jr** — Football Player
9316 S 4th Ave, Inglewood CA 90305, USA
**Cunningham, Sean S** — Director, Producer
Crystal Lake Entertainment, 4420 Hayvenhurst Ave, Encino CA 91436, USA
**Cunningham, Wallace E** — Architect
PO Box 371493, San Diego CA 92137, USA
**Cunningham, William J (Billy)** — Basketball Player, Coach, Executive
Court Restaurant, 31 Front St, #33, Conshohocken PA 19428, USA
**Cuoco, Kaley** — Actress, Comedienne
S D B Partners, 1801 Ave of Stars, #902, Los Angeles CA 90067 USA
**Cuomo, Andrew M** — Governor, NY; Secretary, HUD
Governor's Office, State Capitol, Albany NY 12224 USA
**Cuomo, Christopher** — Commentator
ABC-TV, News Dept, 147 Columbus Ave, New York NY 10023, USA
**Cuomo, Jerome J** — Inventor (Read-Write Optical Storage)
I B M Watson Research Center, PO Box 218, Yorktown Heights NY 10598 USA
**Cuomo, Mario M** — Governor, NY
50 Sutton Place S, #11G, New York NY 10022, USA
**Cuomo, Rivers** — Singer, Guitarist (Weezer), Songwriter
W M E Entertainment, 1600 Division St, #300, Nashville TN 37203 USA
**Cuozzo, Gary S** — Football Player
4 Swimming River Road, #4, Lincroft NJ 07738, USA
**Cura, Jose** — Opera Singer
Columbia Artists Mgmt Inc, 1790 Broadway, #702, New York NY 10019 USA
**Curatola, Vincent** — Actor
Stone Manners Salners, 9911 W Pico Blvd, #1400, Los Angeles CA 90035 USA
**Curb, Michael (Mike)** — Composer, Businessman
3907 W Alameda Ave, #2, Burbank CA 91505, USA
**Curbeam, Robert L, Jr** — Astronaut
15806 Virginia Fern Way, Houston TX 77059, USA
**Curci, Francis (Fran)** — Football Player, Coach
14707 Croydon Place, Tampa FL 33618, USA
**Cureton, Earl** — Basketball Player
31190 Country Way, Farmington Hills MI 48331, USA
**Curfman, Shannon** — Singer, Guitarist
A R M Entertainment, 1257 Arcade St, Saint Paul MN 55106, USA
**Curl, Carolyn** — Speed Skier, Mountain Cyclist
Robert U Curl, 405 N Westridge Dr, Idaho Falls ID 83402, USA
**Curl, Robert F, Jr** — Nobel Chemistry Laureate
1824 Bolsover St, Houston TX 77005, USA
**Curlander, Paul J** — Businessman
Lexmark International, 740 W New Circle Road, Lexington KY 40550, USA
**Curless, Ann** — Singer (Expose), Songwriter
Richard Walters, PO Box 2789, Toluca Lake CA 91610 USA
**Curley, Cindy** — Ice Hockey Player
166 Barton Road, Stow MA 01775, USA
**Curley, Edwin M** — Philosopher
2645 Pin Oak Dr, Ann Arbor MI 48103, USA
**Curley, John** — Bassist (Afghan Whigs)
Rascoff/Zysblat Organization, 250 W 57th St, New York NY 10107 USA
**Curley, John J** — Publisher
Gannett Co, 1100 Wilson Blvd, Arlington VA 22209, USA
**Curley, William M (Bill)** — Basketball Player
377 Autumn Ave, Duxbury MA 02332, USA
**Curnen, Monique Gabriela** — Actress
Kritzer Levine Wilkins, 8840 Wilshire Blvd, #100, Beverly Hills CA 90211, USA
**Curran, Brian** — Ice Hockey Player
Kalamazoo Wings, 3600 Vanrick Dr, Kalamazoo MI 49001, USA
**Curran, Brittany** — Actress
Medavoy Mgmt, 10203 Santa Monica Blvd, #400, Los Angeles CA 90067 USA
**Curran, Charles E** — Theologian
Southern Methodist University, Theology Dept, Dallas Hall, Dallas TX 75275, USA
**Curran, John** — Director
H L A Mgmt, PO Box 1536, Strawberry Hills NSW 2012, Australia
**Curran, Kelly** — Actress
J K A Talent, 12725 Ventura Blvd, #H, Studio City CA 91604 91604, USA
**Curran, Michael V (Mike)** — Ice Hockey Player
7615 Lanewood Lane N, Osseo MN 55311, USA
**Curran, Patrick M (Pat)** — Football Player
3195 Avenida Magoria, Escondido CA 92029, USA
**Curran, Paul** — Director
National Opera, Millenium Centre, Bute Place, Cardiff CF10 5AL, Wales
**Curran, Sean** — Dancer
Sean Curran Co, 21 1st Ave, #18, New York NY 10003, USA
**Curran, Tony** — Actor
Paradigm Agency, 360 N Crescent Dr, North Building, Beverly Hills CA 90210 USA
**Curren, Thomas R (Tom)** — Surfer
Troubadour Entertainment, 3732 Gregory Way, #4, Santa Barbara CA 93105, USA
**Currentzis, Teodor** — Conductor
I M G Artists, Hogarth Business Park, Chiswick, London W4 2TH, England
**Curreri, Lee** — Composer
Gorfaine/Schwartz, 4111 W Alameda Ave, #509, Burbank CA 91505 USA
**Currey, Francis S** — WW II Army Hero (CMH)
PO Box 515, Selkirk NY 12158, USA
**Currie, Cherie** — Singer, Actress
Times Productions, 520 Washington Blvd, #199, Marina del Rey CA 90292, USA
**Currie, Daniel G (Dan)** — Football Player
6650 W Flamingo Road, #152, Las Vegas NV 89103, USA
**Currie, Gordon** — Actor
Characters Talent Agency, 8 Elm St, Toronto ON M5G 1G7, Canada
**Currie, Louise** — Actress
1317 Delresto Dr, Beverly Hills CA 90210, USA

**Cunningham - Currie**

**Currie, Monique** — Basketball Player
Washington Mystics, Verizon Center, 401 9th St NW, #750, Washington DC 20004 USA

**Currie, Nancy J** — Astronaut
1023 Knoll Bridge Lane, Friendswood TX 77546, USA

**Currie, Sondra** — Actress
Geddes Agency, 8430 Santa Monica Blvd, #201, West Hollywood CA 90069 USA

**Currier, William F (Bill)** — Football Player
8661 Monticello Road, Columbia SC 29203, USA

**Currington, William M (Billy)** — Singer, Songwriter
Parallel Entertainment, 209 10th Ave S, #506, Nashville TN 37203, USA

**Curry, Aaron** — Football Player
Seattle Seahawks, 12 Seahawks Way, Renton WA 98056 USA

**Curry, Adrianne** — Model, Actress
Wilhelmina Models, 300 Park Ave S, #200, New York NY 10010 USA

**Curry, Alana** — Actress
Sovereign Talent Group, 8421 Wilshire Blvd, #200, Beverly Hills CA 90211 USA

**Curry, Ann** — Commentator
NBC-TV, News Dept, 30 Rockefeller Plaza, #270E, New York NY 10112 USA

**Curry, Anne E** — Actress
Edna Talent Mgmt, 318 Dundas St West, Toronto ON M5T 1G5, Canada

**Curry, Christopher** — Actor
Darlene Kaplan, 4450 Balboa Ave, Encino CA 91316, USA

**Curry, Clifford** — Singer
Fat City Artists, 1906 Chet Atkins Place, #502, Nashville TN 37212 USA

**Curry, Denise** — Basketball Player, Coach
21 Maple Dr, Aliso Viejo CA 92656, USA

**Curry, Don (DC)** — Actor, Comedian
Rush Hour Productions, 6464 Sunset Blvd, #750, Los Angeles CA 90028, USA

**Curry, Donald (Don)** — Boxer
41 Woodland Ave, West Orange NJ 07052, USA

**Curry, Eddy, Jr** — Basketball Player
17 Magnolia Dr, Purchase NY 10577, USA

**Curry, John A H** — Tennis Executive
All England Lawn Tennis Club, Church Road, Wimbledon, London SW19 5AE, England

**Curry, Mark** — Actor
Nine Yards Entertainment, 8530 Wilshire Blvd, #500, Beverly Hills CA 90211 USA

**Curry, Michael E (Mike)** — Basketball Player, Coach
2880 Wells Dr, Augusta GA 30906, USA

**Curry, Stephen** — Actor, Comedian
R G M Assoc, 64076 Kippax St, #202, Surry Hills NSW 2010, Australia

**Curry, Tim** — Singer, Actor
Innovative Artists, 1505 10th St, Santa Monica CA 90401 USA

**Curry, Valorie** — Actress
I C M Partners, 10250 Constellation Blvd, #900, Los Angeles CA 90067 USA

**Curry, Wardell S (Dell)** — Basketball Player
1615 Rutledge Ave, Charlotte NC 28211, USA

**Curry, William A (Bill)** — Football Player, Coach
2660 Peachtree Road NW, #27H, Atlanta GA 30305, USA

**Curtin, David S** — Journalist
Colorado Springs Gazette Telegraph, 30 S Prospect, Colorado Springs CO 80903, USA

**Curtin, Jane T** — Actress
I C M Partners, 10250 Constellation Blvd, #900, Los Angeles CA 90067 USA

**Curtin, John J, Jr** — Attorney
Bingham Dana Gould, 100 High St, #1500, Boston MA 02110, USA

**Curtin, Phyllis** — Opera Singer
Boston University, Fine Arts College, 855 Commonwealth Ave, Boston MA 02215, USA

**Curtin, Valerie** — Actress
15622 Meadowgate Road, Encino CA 91436, USA

**Curtis, A Scott** — Football Player
31661 Prairie Dunes Court, Evergreen CO 80439, USA

**Curtis, Ben** — Golfer
8959 Bevington Lane, Orlando FL 32827, USA

**Curtis, Benjamin B (Ben)** — Actor
Hatton McEwan, PO Box 37385, London N1 7XF, England

**Curtis, Catie** — Singer, Guitarist, Songwriter
Deep Blue Arts, 4440 Morse Ave, Studio City CA 91604, USA

**Curtis, Chad D** — Baseball Player
1400 Buttrick Ave SE, Ada MI 49301, USA

**Curtis, Christopher Paul** — Writer
Random House, 1745 Broadway, #1800, New York NY 10019 USA

**Curtis, Cliff** — Actor
Abrams Artists, 9200 W Sunset Blvd, #1125, West Hollywood CA 90069 USA

**Curtis, Isaac C** — Football Player
711 Clinton Springs Ave, Cincinnati OH 45229, USA

**Curtis, J Michael (Mike)** — Football Player
5101 River Road, #1803, Bethesda MD 20816, USA

**Curtis, Jamie Lee** — Actress
Creative Artists Agency, 2000 Ave of Stars, #100, Los Angeles CA 90067 USA

**Curtis, John D, II** — Baseball Player
1800 Roundhill Road, #1207, Charleston WV 25314, USA

**Curtis, Kenneth M** — Governor, ME; Diplomat
1211 Southport Dr, Sarasota FL 34242, USA

**Curtis, Kevin D** — Football Player
Tennessee Titans, 460 Great Circle Road, Nashville TN 37228 USA

**Curtis, Paul E** — Ice Hockey Player
PO Box 6325, Abilene TX 79608, USA

**Curtis, Richard** — Director, Writer
United Agents, 12-26 Lexington St, London W1F 0LE, England

**Curtis, Simon** — Director
United Talent Agency, U T A Plaza, 9336 Civic Center Dr, Beverly Hills CA 90210 USA

**Curtis, Thomas N (Tom)** — Football Player
5433 NW 94th Doral Place, Doral FL 33178, USA

**Curtis-Hall, Vondie** — Actor, Director
Film Independent, 9911 W Pico Blvd, #1100, Los Angeles CA 90035, USA

**Curtiss, Shelley Smith** — Sculptor
PO Box 497, Joseph OR 97846, USA

# C

**Cusack, Ann** — Actress
Innovative Artists, 1505 10th St, Santa Monica CA 90401 USA
**Cusack, Joan** — Actress, Comedienne
W M E Entertainment, 9601 Wilshire Blvd, #300, Beverly Hills CA 90210 USA
**Cusack, John** — Actor
New Crime Productions, 1041 N Formosa Ave, Formosa Building, West Hollywood CA 90046, USA
**Cusack, Sinead M** — Actress
Curtis Brown Group, 28-29 Haymarket St, #500, London SW1Y 4SP, England
**Cuse, Carlton** — Writer, Producer
W M E Entertainment, 9601 Wilshire Blvd, #300, Beverly Hills CA 90210 USA
**Cushenan, Ian** — Ice Hockey Player
4014 Dryden Dr, North Olmsted OH 44070, USA
**Cushing, Matthew J (Matt)** — Football Player
5752 Lyman Ave, Downers Grove IL 60516, USA
**Cushman, Karen** — Writer
17804 Thorsen Road SW, Vashon WA 98070, USA
**Cusick, Henry Ian** — Actor
Ken McReddie Assoc, 101 Finsbury Pavement, London EC2A 1RS, England
**Cussler, Clive E** — Writer
13835 N Tatum Blvd, #9-421, Phoenix AZ 85032, USA
**Cust, John J (Jack), III** — Baseball Player
9 Club House Dr, Whitehouse Station NJ 08889, USA
**Custom** — Singer
ArtistDirect, 10900 Wilshire Blvd, #1400, Los Angeles CA 90024 USA
**Cut Chemist** — DJ, Rap Musician
Vision Entertainment Group, 1100 Glendon Ave, #1100, Los Angeles 90024, USA
**Cutcliffe, David** — Football Coach
Duke University, Athletic Dept, Durham NC 27708, USA
**Cutell, Lou** — Actor
Conan Carroll Assoc, 11350 Ventura Blvd, #200, Studio City CA 91604, USA
**Cuthbert, Elisha** — Actress
I C M Partners, 10250 Constellation Blvd, #900, Los Angeles CA 90067 USA
**Cuthbeth, Elizabeth (Betty)** — Track Athlete
4/7 Karara Close, Hall's Head, Mandurah WA 6210, Australia
**Cutler, Eric** — Opera Singer
I M G Artists, Hogarth Business Park, Chiswick, London W4 2TH, England
**Cutler, James** — Architect
Cutler Anderson Architects, 135 Parfitt Way, Bainbridge Island WA 98110, USA
**Cutler, Jay C** — Football Player
39 Bancroft Place, Nashville TN 37215, USA
**Cutler, Laurel** — Businesswoman
Foote Cone Belding, 767 5th Ave, New York NY 10153, USA
**Cutler, Walter L** — Diplomat
Meridian International Center, 1630 Crescent Place NW, Washington DC 20009, USA
**Cutrone, Angela** — Speed Skater
Speed Skating Canada, 2781 Lancaster Road, #402, Ottawa ON K1B 1A7, Canada
**Cutrufello, Mary** — Singer, Songwriter
Mercury Records, 11150 Santa Monica Blvd, #1000, Los Angeles CA 90025 USA
**Cutsinger, Gary L** — Football Player
600 Mountain Dew Road, Horseshoe Bay TX 78657, USA
**Cutter, Lise** — Actress
PO Box 2665, Sag Harbor NY 11963, USA
**Cuyler, Milton (Milt), Jr** — Baseball Player
962 Lamar Road, Macon GA 31210, USA
**Cuzin, Francois** — Cell Biologist
Instit Pasteur, 25 Rue du Docteur Roux, 75724 Paris Cedex 15, France
**Cuzzi, Philip (Phil)** — Baseball Umpire
32 Maples Ave, Nutley NJ 07110, USA
**Cvijanovic, Adam** — Artist
Bellwether Gallery, 134 10th St, Front A, New York NY 10011, USA
**Cwiklinski, Stanley** — Rowing Athlete
2840 Maple St, San Diego CA 92104, USA
**Cymphonique** — Singer, Songwriter, Actress
I C M Partners, 10250 Constellation Blvd, #900, Los Angeles CA 90067 USA
**Cypher, Jon** — Actor
PO Box 25040, Ventura CA 93002, USA
**Cyr, Denis** — Ice Hockey Player
9816 N Townsend Dr, Peoria IL 61615, USA
**Cyr, Myriam** — Actress
John DeHority Mgmt, 125 Christopher St, #6C, New York NY 10014, USA
**Cyrus, Billy Ray** — Singer, Guitarist, Songwriter
C E S D, 10635 Santa Monica Blvd, #130, Los Angeles CA 90025 USA
**Cyrus, Miley** — Actress, Singer
Creative Artists Agency, 2000 Ave of Stars, #100, Los Angeles CA 90067 USA
**Czapsky, Stefan** — Cinematographer
RR 3 Box 278, Unadilla NY 13849, USA
**Czerny, Henry** — Actor
Oscars Abrams Zimel, 438 Queen St E, Toronto ON M5A 1T4, Canada
**Czerwinska, Anna** — Mountaineer
Anamax-Import-Export, Ul Lomianska 10 m 4, 01 685 Warsaw, Poland
**Czisny, Alissa** — Figure Skater
Detroit Skating Club, 888 Denison Court, Bloomfield Hills MI 48302, USA
**Czuchry, Matt** — Actor
Gersh Agency, 9465 Wilshire Blvd, #600, Beverly Hills CA 90212 USA

**Cusack - Czuchry**

**Da Brat** — Rap Artist
Mauldin Brand Agency, 1280 W Peachtree St NW, #300, Atlanta GA 30309, USA

**Daal, Omar J** — Baseball Player
3859 E Bellerive Dr, Queen Creek AZ 85142, USA

**Daane, James D** — Financier, Government Official
102 Westhampton Place, Nashville TN 37205, USA

**D'Abaldo, Chris** — Guitarist (Saliva)
Helter Skelter, 347-353 Chiswick High Road, London W4 4HS, England

**Dabich, Mike** — Basketball Player
PO Box 236, Hudson WY 82515, USA

**D'Abo, Maryam** — Actress
Gage Group, 14724 Ventura Blvd, #505, Sherman Oaks CA 91403 USA

**D'Abo, Olivia** — Actress
Great Vision Artists Talent Agency, 8981 Sunset Blvd, #101, Los Angeles CA 90069, USA

**Dabul, Brian** — Tennis Player
Octagon Worldwide, 1751 Pinnacle Dr, #1500, McLean VA 22102 USA

**D'Accone, Frank A** — Music Educator
725 Fontana Way, Laguna Beach CA 92651, USA

**Dacic, Ivica** — Prime Minister, Serbia
Prime Minister's Office, Nemanjina 11, 11000 Belgrade, Serbia

**DaCosta, Rebecca** — Actress
Rogers & Cowan, 8687 Melrose Ave, #G700, West Hollywood CA 90069 USA

**DaCosta, Yaya** — Actress, Model
Gersh Agency, 41 Madison Ave, #3301, New York NY 10010 USA

**D'Acquisto, John F** — Baseball Player
32010 N 20th Lane, Phoenix AZ 85085, USA

**Daddario, Alexandra** — Actress
United Talent Agency, U T A Plaza, 9336 Civic Center Dr, Beverly Hills CA 90210 USA

**Daddo, Cameron** — Actor
Innovative Artists, 1505 10th St, Santa Monica CA 90401 USA

**Daddy Yankee** — Reggaeton Singer
Nevarez Communications, 6020 NW 99th Ave, #307, Doral FL 33178, USA

**Dade, L Paul** — Baseball Player
5212 66th Street Court W, University Place WA 98467, USA

**Daehlie, Bjorn** — Cross Country Skier
Cathinka Guldbergs Veg 64, 2034 Holter, Norway

**Dafoe, Bryon** — Ice Hockey Player
6620 Lakeshore Road, Kelowna BC V1W 4J5, Canada

**Dafoe, Willem** — Actor
I C M Partners, 10250 Constellation Blvd, #900, Los Angeles CA 90067 USA

**Daggett, Timothy (Tim)** — Gymnast
134 Country Club Dr, East Longmeadow MA 01028, USA

**Daghe, Noelle** — Golfer
1300 Tamarac St, Denver CO 80220, USA

**D'Agostino, James S, Jr** — Businessman
Encore Bank, 1220 Augusta Dr, Houston TX 77057, USA

**D'Agosto, Nicholas (Nick)** — Actor
Emerald Talent Group, 15260 Ventura Blvd, #1200, Sherman Oaks CA 91403, USA

**D'Aguanno, Emanuele** — Opera Singer
I M G Artists, Hogarth Business Park, Chiswick, London W4 2TH, England

**Dagworthy Prew, Wendy A** — Fashion Designer
Royal College of Art, Kensington Gore, London SW7 3EU, England

**Dahal, Pushpa Kamal (Prachanda)** — Prime Minister, Nepal
Premier's Office, Central Secretariat, Singha Durbar, Kathmandu, Nepal

**Dahan, Olivier** — Director, Writer
Agents Associes, 201 Rue du Faubourg Saint Honore, 75008 Paris, France

**Dahl, Arlene** — Actress
Dahlmark Productions, PO Box 116 Rockland Road, Sparkill NY 10976, USA

**Dahl, John** — Director, Writer
United Talent Agency, U T A Plaza, 9336 Civic Center Dr, Beverly Hills CA 90210 USA

**Dahl, Kevin C** — Ice Hockey Player
4000 Astoria Way, Avon OH 44011, USA

**Dahl, Lawrence F** — Chemist
4817 Woodburn Dr, Madison WI 53711, USA

**Dahl, Robert A** — Political Scientist
200 Leeder Hill Dr, Hamden CT 06517, USA

**Dahl, Sophie** — Model, Actress
Ed Victor, 6 Bayley St, London WC18 3HE, England

**Dahlberg, James E** — Biomolecular Chemist
University of Wisconsin, Biochemical Sciences Building, Madison WI 53706, USA

**Daigle, Alain** — Ice Hockey Player
3510 Rue Bordeaux, Trois-Rivieres-Ouest QC G8Y 3P7, Canada

**Daigle, Alexandre** — Ice Hockey Player
3510 Rue Bordeaux, Trois-Rivieres-Quest QC G8Y 3P7, Canada

**Daigle, Sylvie** — Speed Skater
Speed Skating Canada, 2781 Lancaster Road, #402, Ottawa ON K1B 1A7, Canada

**Daigneault, Jean-Jacques (J J)** — Ice Hockey Player
Hartford Wolf Pack, 196 Trumbull St, #300, Hartford CT 06103, USA

**Dailey, Benjamin P** — Chemist
440 Riverside Dr, New York NY 10027, USA

**Dailey, Janet** — Writer
HC 4 Box 2197, Branson MO 65616, USA

**Dailey, John R** — Marine Corps General
National Air & Space Museum, Director's Office, Independence Ave, Washington DC 20472, USA

**Dailor, Brann** — Drummer, Singer (Mastodon)
Pinnacle Entertainment, 30 Glenn St, White Plains NY 10603, USA

**Daily, Bill** — Actor
1331 Park Ave SW, #802, Albuquerque NM 87102, USA

**Daily, Bob** — Producer
Gersh Agency, 9465 Wilshire Blvd, #600, Beverly Hills CA 90212 USA

**Daily, E G** — Singer, Songwriter, Actress
369 Universal Artists, 468 N Camden Dr, #200, Beverly Hills CA 90210, USA

**Daish, Charles** — Actor
Gavin Barker Assoc, 2D Wimpole St, London W1G 0EB, England

**Dajani, Nadia** — Actress
Innovative Artists, 1505 10th St, Santa Monica CA 90401 USA

**D**

**Da Brat - Dajani**

**Dalai Lama** — Religious Leader; Nobel Peace Laureate
Thekchen Choeling, McLeod Ganj 176219, Dharamsal, Himachal Pradesh, India

**Daland, Peter** — Swimming Coach
14 Chris Court, Riverhead NY 11901, USA

**Dalberto, Michel** — Concert Pianist
13 Blvd Henri Plumhof, 1800 Vevey, Switzerland

**Daldry, Stephen** — Director
Creative Artists Agency, 2000 Ave of Stars, #100, Los Angeles CA 90067 USA

**Dale, Alan** — Actor
Management 360, 9111 Wilshire Blvd, Beverly Hills CA 90210 USA

**Dale, Bruce** — Photographer
National Geographic, Editorial Dept, 1145 17th St NW, Washington DC 20036 USA

**Dale, Carroll W** — Football Player
Clinch Valley College, Athletic Dept, 1 College Ave, Wise VA 24293, USA

**Dale, Dick** — Singer, Guitarist, Songwriter
Dick Dale Mgmt, PO Box 1713, Twentynine Palms CA 92277, USA

**Dale, James Badge** — Actor
M J Mgmt, 130 W 57th St, New York NY 10019, USA

**Dale, Jim** — Actor, Comedian
C E S D, 10635 Santa Monica Blvd, #130, Los Angeles CA 90025 USA

**Dalembert, Samuel D** — Basketball Player
899 NE Orchid Bay Dr, Boca Raton FL 33487, USA

**D'Alemberte, Talbot (Sandy)** — Educator
Florida State University, Law College, 425 W Jefferson, Tallahassee FL 32301, USA

**D'Aleo, Angelo** — Singer (Dion & the Belmonts)
Paramount Entertainment, PO Box 12, Far Hills NJ 07931 USA

**Dalesandro, Mark A** — Baseball Player
1908 Arbor Fields Dr, Plainfield IL 60586, USA

**Daley, Joe** — Golfer
10015 E Mountain View Road, #2126, Scottsdale AZ 85258, USA

**Daley, Joe** — Ice Hockey Player
Joe Daley's Cards, 666 Saint James St, Winnipeg MB R3G 3J6, Canada

**Daley, John Francis** — Actor
United Talent Agency, U T A Plaza, 9336 Civic Center Dr, Beverly Hills CA 90210 USA

**Daley, Leavitt L (Buddy)** — Baseball Player
922 Moose Dr, Riverton WY 82501, USA

**Daley, Patrick** — Ice Hockey Player
118 Mount Olive Dr, Toronto ON M9V 2E2, Canada

**Daley, Peter H (Pete)** — Baseball Player
4019 Calle Mira Monte, Newbury Park CA 91320, USA

**Daley, Richard M** — Mayor, Chicago
University of Chicago, Harris Public Policy School, Chicago IL 60637, USA

**Daley, Rosie** — Chef, Writer
Harpo Productions, 110 N Carpenter St, Chicago IL 60607, USA

**DalFabbro, Corrado** — Bobsled Athlete
Olympic Committee, Foro Italico, Largo Lauro de Bosis 15, 00135 Rome, Italy

**Dalgarno, Alexander** — Astronomer
27 Robinson St, Cambridge MA 02138, USA

**Dalgarno, Brad** — Ice Hockey Player
1146 Fairfield Place, Oakville ON L6M 2L9, Canada

**Dalglish, Kenneth M (Kenny)** — Soccer Player, Manager
Celtic FC, Celtic Park, Glasgow G4O 3RE, Scotland

**Dalhausser, Philip** — Volleyball Player
593 Citation Way, Newbury Park CA 91320, USA

**Dalheimer, Patrick** — Musician (Live)
Freedman & Smith, 350 W End Ave, #1, New York NY 10024, USA

**Dali, Tracy** — Actress, Model
PO Box 69541, West Hollywood CA 90069, USA

**Dalis, Irene** — Opera Singer, Executive
San Jose Opera, 2149 Paragon Dr, San Jose CA 95131, USA

**Dalkas, Nicole** — Golfer
288 Green Mountain Dr, Palm Desert CA 92211, USA

**Dall, Bobby** — Bassist (Poison)
Front Line Mgmt, 1100 Glendon Ave, #2000, Los Angeles CA 90024 USA

**Dallafior, Kenneth R (Ken)** — Football Player
188 Four Seasons Dr, Lake Orion MI 48360, USA

**Dallara, Charles H** — Government Official, Financier
International Finance Institute, 2000 Pennsylvania Ave NW, Washington DC 20006, USA

**Dalle, Beatrice** — Actress
Artmedia, 20 Ave Rapp, 75007 Paris, France

**Dallek, Robert** — Historian
2138 Cathedral Ave NW, Washington DC 20008, USA

**Dallenbach, Wally** — Auto Racing Executive
5315 Stowe Lane, Harrisburg NC 28075, USA

**Dallman, Marty** — Ice Hockey Player
3843 Main St, Niagara Falls ON L2G 6B4, Canada

**Dalrymple, Clayton E (Clay)** — Baseball Player
28248 Mateer Road, Gold Beach OR 97444, USA

**Dalrymple, Gary B** — Geologist
1847 NW Hillcrest Dr, Corvallis OR 97330, USA

**Dalton, Audrey** — Actress
2241 Labrusca, Mission Viejo CA 92692, USA

**Dalton, James E** — Air Force General
61 Misty Acres Road, Rolling Hills Estates CA 90274, USA

**Dalton, John H** — Government Official
3710 University Ave NW, Washington DC 20016, USA

**Dalton, Kristen** — Actress
Daniel Hoff Agency, 5455 Wilshire Blvd, #1100, Los Angeles CA 90036, USA

**Dalton, Lacy J** — Singer
Bobby Roberts, 3050 Business Park Circle, #303, Goodlettsville TN 37221 USA

**Dalton, Lional D** — Football Player
9858 Clint Moore Road, #128, Boca Raton FL 33496, USA

**Dalton, Nic** — Bassist (Lemonheads)
Agency Group Ltd, 142 W 57th St, #600, New York NY 10019 USA

**Dalton, Nicole** — Actress
Domain Talent, 9229 W Sunset Blvd, #710, West Hollywood CA 90069 USA

**Dalai Lama - Dalton**

| | |
|---|---|
| **Dalton, Suzy** | Singer |
| Gold Dust Talent, Route 78, Exit 19, Strausstown PA 19559, USA | |
| **Dalton, Timothy** | Actor |
| Independent Talent Group, 40 Whitfield St, London W1T 2RH, England | |
| **Daltrey, Roger** | Singer (Who), Actor |
| Talent Works, 3500 W Olive Ave, #1400, Burbank CA 91505 USA | |
| **Daluiso, Bradley W (Brad)** | Football Player |
| 13258 Glencliff Way, San Diego CA 92130, USA | |
| **Daly, Andrew (Andy)** | Actor, Comedian, Writer |
| Creative Artists Agency, 2000 Ave of Stars, #100, Los Angeles CA 90067 USA | |
| **Daly, Carson** | Actor, Entertainer |
| Dixon Talent, 375 Greenwich St, #500, New York NY 10013, USA | |
| **Daly, Herman** | Social Activist |
| 6934 Pineway, University Park MD 20782, USA | |
| **Daly, Jim** | Religious Leader |
| Focus on the Family, 8605 Explorer Drive, Colorado Springs CO 80920, USA | |
| **Daly, John P** | Golfer |
| 1009 Par St, Dardanelle AR 72834, USA | |
| **Daly, Lance** | Director, Writer |
| FastNet Films, 75-76 Camden St, Lower, Dublin 2, Ireland | |
| **Daly, Timothy (Tim)** | Actor |
| Gateway Mgmt, 860 Via de la Paz, #F10, Pacific Palisades CA 90272 90272, USA | |
| **Daly, Tyne** | Actress |
| 405 E 54th St, #12D, New York NY 10022, USA | |
| **Daly-Donofrio, Heather** | Golfer |
| 414 Long Cove Court, Ormond Beach FL 32174, USA | |
| **Dalziel, Ryan** | Auto Racing Driver |
| S A M A X Motorsports, 203 NW 16th St, Pompano Beach FL 33060, USA | |
| **Dam, Kenneth W** | Government Official |
| University of Chicago, Law School, 1111 E 60th St, #1, Chicago IL 60637, USA | |
| **Damadian, Raymond V** | Inventor (Cancer Tissue Detector-M R I) |
| F O N A R Corp, 110 Marcus Dr, Melville NY 11747, USA | |
| **Damas, Bertila** | Actress |
| Craig Wyckoff Assoc, 11350 Ventura Blvd, #100, Studio City CA 91604, USA | |
| **D'Amato, Alfonse M** | Senator, NY |
| Park Strategies, 101 Park Ave, #2506, New York NY 10178, USA | |
| **DaMatta, Cristiano M** | Auto Racing Driver |
| Newman-Haas Racing, 50 Tower Parkway, Lincolnshire IL 60069, USA | |
| **D'Amboise, Charlotte** | Actress, Dancer |
| Don Buchwald, 10 E 44th St, New York NY 10017 USA | |
| **D'Amboise, Jacques J** | Dancer, Choreographer |
| National Dance Institute, 594 Broadway, #805, New York NY 10012, USA | |
| **Dame Edna** | Actor, Comedian |
| P B J Mgmt, 22 Rathbone St, London W1T 1LA, England | |
| **Dameshek, David** | Actor, Writer |
| Creative Artists Agency, 2000 Ave of Stars, #100, Los Angeles CA 90067 USA | |
| **Damian, Michael** | Actor, Singer |
| United Talent Agency, U T A Plaza, 9336 Civic Center Dr, Beverly Hills CA 90210 USA | |
| **Damiano, Jennifer** | Actress |
| Innovative Artists, 1505 10th St, Santa Monica CA 90401 USA | |
| **Damiao, Leandro** | Soccer Player |
| Confederacion de Futebol, Rua Victor Civita 66, #1, Rio de Janeiro 22775 044, Brazil | |
| **D'Amico, Jeffrey C (Jeff)** | Baseball Player |
| 2223 Muirfield Way, Oldsmar FL 34677, USA | |
| **D'Amico, Marcus** | Actor |
| 26 Astwood Mews, London SW7 4DE, England | |
| **D'Amico, Mike** | Percussionist (Wondermints) |
| Paradise Artists, PO Box 1821, Ojai CA 93024 USA | |
| **Dam-Jensen, Inger** | Opera Singer |
| Hollaendervej 4A, 1855 Frederiksberg C, Denmark | |
| **Damon, Grey** | Actor |
| Paradigm Agency, 360 N Crescent Dr, North Building, Beverly Hills CA 90210 USA | |
| **Damon, Johnny D** | Baseball Player |
| 904 Main St, Windermere FL 34786, USA | |
| **Damon, Mark** | Actor, Producer |
| 2781 Benedict Canyon Dr, Beverly Hills CA 90210, USA | |
| **Damon, Matt** | Actor, Producer |
| Pearl Street Productions, 517 N Robertson, #200, West Hollywood CA 90048, USA | |
| **Damon, Una** | Actress, Director, Writer |
| DeWalt & Muzik Mgmt, 623 N Parish Place, Burbank CA 91506, USA | |
| **Damone, Vic** | Singer, Actor |
| International Ventures, 25864 Tournament Road, #L, Valencia CA 91355, USA | |
| **D'Amore, Caroline** | Actress |
| Element Talent Agency, 120 S Vignes, #202, Los Angeles CA 90012, USA | |
| **Damphousse, Vincent** | Ice Hockey Player |
| Le Scandinave Spa, 4280 Montee Ryan, Mont-Tremblant QC J8E 1S4, Canada | |
| **Dampier, Erick T** | Basketball Player |
| 18724 Wainsborough Lane, Dallas TX 75287, USA | |
| **Dampier, Louie (Lou)** | Basketball Player |
| Dampier Distributing, 2808 New Moody Lane, La Grange KY 40031, USA | |
| **Damson, Barrie M** | Businessman |
| 1720 Post Road E, #215, Westport CT 06880, USA | |
| **Damus, Mike** | Actor |
| Untitled Entertainment, 350 S Beverly Dr, #200, Beverly Hills CA 90212 USA | |
| **Dana, Bill** | Actor, Comedian |
| Amsel Eisenstadt Frazier, 5055 Wilshire Blvd, #865, Los Angeles CA 90036 USA | |
| **Dana, William H (Bill)** | Test Pilot |
| 15805 W Vale Dr, Goodyear AZ 85395, USA | |
| **Danby, Gordon T** | Inventor (Magnetic Levitation Train) |
| PO Box 12, Wading River NY 11792, USA | |
| **Dance, Charles** | Actor |
| Tavistock Wood Mgmt, 45 Conduit St, London W1S 2YN, England | |
| **Dancy, Hugh** | Actor, Model |
| United Agents, 12-26 Lexington St, London W1F 0LE, England | |
| **Dancy, John** | Commentator |
| Harvard University, Kennedy Government School, Cambridge MA 02138, USA | |

**D**

**Dalton - Dancy**

**Dando, Carolyn** — Actress
Red11 Mgmt, 441 Queen St, Auckland 1010, New Zealand
**Dando, Evan** — Singer (Lemonheads), Songwriter
Agency Group Ltd, 142 W 57th St, #600, New York NY 10019 USA
**Dandridge, Robert L (Bob)** — Basketball Player
1708 Saint Denis Ave, Norfolk VA 23509, USA
**Dandry, Evelyne** — Actress
Artmedia, 20 Ave Rapp, 75007 Paris, France
**Dane, Eric** — Actor
Management 360, 9111 Wilshire Blvd, Beverly Hills CA 90210 USA
**Dane, Paul** — Test Pilot
17105 Ambassador Dr, #515, Colorado Springs CO 80921, USA
**Dane, Shelton** — Actor
Innovative Artists, 235 Park Ave S, #1000, New York NY 10003 USA
**Danelli, Dino** — Drummer (Rascals)
Thomas Cassidy, PO Box 1311, Tucson AZ 85702 USA
**Danelo, Joseph P (Joe)** — Football Player
3601 Roxbury St, San Pedro CA 90731, USA
**Danes, Claire** — Actress
W M E Entertainment, 9601 Wilshire Blvd, #300, Beverly Hills CA 90210 USA
**Daneyko, Ken** — Ice Hockey Player
11 Combs Hollow Road, Mendham NJ 07945, USA
**Danforth, Douglas D** — Businessman, Baseball Executive
8787 Bay Colony Dr, #1002, Naples FL 34108, USA
**Danforth, Fred** — Artist
PO Box 828, Middlebury VT 05753, USA
**Danforth, John C (Jack)** — Senator, MO
Bryan Cave LLP, 211 N Broadway, #3600, Saint Louis MO 63102, USA
**D'Angelo** — Singer, Songwriter
W M E Entertainment, 9601 Wilshire Blvd, #300, Beverly Hills CA 90210 USA
**D'Angelo, Beverly** — Actress
I C M Partners, 10250 Constellation Blvd, #900, Los Angeles CA 90067 USA
**Danger Mouse** — Rap Artist (Gnarls Barkley)
Hall or Nothing, Poplar Mews, Uxbridge Road, London W12 7JS, England
**D'Angio, Giulio J** — Radiation Therapist
201 S 18th St, #1818, Philadelphia PA 19103, USA
**Daniel** — Prince, Sweden
Royal Palace, Kundg Slottet, Stottsbacken, 111 30 Stockholm, Sweden
**Daniel, Brittany** — Actress
A P A Talent/Literary Agency, 405 S Beverly Dr, #300, Beverly Hills CA 90212 USA
**Daniel, Elizabeth A (Beth)** — Golfer
219 Palm Trail, Delray Beach FL 33483, USA
**Daniel, Eugene, Jr** — Football Player
PO Box 80345, Baton Rouge LA 70898, USA
**Daniel, Jeffrey** — Singer (Shalamar)
Green Light Talent Agency, PO Box 3172, Beverly Hills CA 90212 USA
**Daniel, Paul W** — Conductor
Ingpen & Williams, 131 Putney Bridge Road, London SW15 2PA, England
**Daniel, William P (Willie)** — Football Player
1711 Oktoc Road, Starkville MS 39759, USA
**Daniele, Graciela** — Director, Choreographer
Abrams Artists, 9200 W Sunset Blvd, #1125, West Hollywood CA 90069 USA
**Danielpour, Richard** — Composer
Sony Classics Records, 2100 Colorado Ave, Santa Monica CA 90404, USA
**Daniels, Anthony** — Actor
Artists First International, 45 Monmouth St, London WC2H 9DG, England
**Daniels, Antonio** — Basketball Player
Philadelphia 76ers, 1st Union Center, 3601 S Broad St, Philadelphia PA 19148 USA
**Daniels, Ben** — Actor
Hamilton Hodell, 66-68 Margaret St, #500, London W1W 8SR, England
**Daniels, Bennie, Jr** — Baseball Player
938 W 156th St, Compton CA 90220, USA
**Daniels, Charlie** — Singer, Songwriter
C D B Inc, 17060 Central Pike, Lebanon TN 37090, USA
**Daniels, Cheryl** — Bowler
6574 Crest Top Dr, West Bloomfield MI 48322, USA
**Daniels, Clemon (Bo)** — Football Player
8683 Mountain Road, Oakland CA 94605, USA
**Daniels, David** — Opera Singer
Askonas Holt, Lincoln House, 300 High Holborn, London WC1V 7JH, England
**Daniels, Erin** — Actress, Director, Writer
Framework Entertainment, 9057 Nemo St, #C, West Hollywood CA 90069, USA
**Daniels, Faith** — Commentator
CBS-TV, News Dept, 51 W 52nd St, New York NY 10019 USA
**Daniels, Greg** — Actor, Director, Producer, Writer
W M E Entertainment, 9601 Wilshire Blvd, #300, Beverly Hills CA 90210 USA
**Daniels, Jeff** — Actor
701 Glazier Road, Chelsea MI 48118, USA
**Daniels, Jeff** — Ice Hockey Player
108 Delaplane Court, Morrisville NC 27560, USA
**Daniels, Kalvoski (Kal)** — Baseball Player
PO Box 9632, Warner Robins GA 31095, USA
**Daniels, Kevin** — Actor
Talent Works, 3500 W Olive Ave, #1400, Burbank CA 91505 USA
**Daniels, Lee** — Director, Producer
Lee Daniels Entertainment, 315 W 36th St, #1002 , New York NY 10037, USA
**Daniels, Marquis A** — Basketball Player
2501 Sutton Place Dr S, Carmel IN 46032, USA
**Daniels, Melvin J (Mel)** — Basketball Player
19789 Centennial Road, Sheridan IN 46069, USA
**Daniels, Mitchell E (Mitch), Jr** — Governor, IN
Purdue University, West Lafayette IN 47907 USA
**Daniels, Owen** — Football Player
5425 Inwood Dr, Houston TX 77056, USA
**Daniels, Quincey** — Boxer
112 Sunny Meadows Dr, Blackshear GA 31516, USA

| | |
|---|---|
| **Daniels, Scott** | Ice Hockey Player |
| 36 Deer Run, Southwick MA 01077, USA | |
| **Daniels, Travis A** | Football Player |
| 4665SW 75th Way, #104, Davie FL 33314, USA | |
| **Daniels, William** | Actor |
| Gage Group, 14724 Ventura Blvd, #505, Sherman Oaks CA 91403 USA | |
| **Daniels, William B** | Physicist |
| 1100 Lovering Ave, #1208, Wilmington DE 19806, USA | |
| **Danielsen, Egil** | Track Athlete |
| Roreks Gate 9, 2300 Hamar, Norway | |
| **Danielson, Gary D** | Football Player |
| 10112 Magnolia Bend, Bonita Springs FL 34135, USA | |
| **Danielsson, Bengt F** | Anthropologist |
| PO Box 558, Papette, Tahiti | |
| **Daniloff, Nicholas** | Journalist |
| PO Box 892, Chester VT 05143, USA | |
| **Danko, William D** | Writer |
| PO Box 9125, Niskayuna NY 12309, USA | |
| **Danks, John W** | Baseball Player |
| 702 Oaklands Dr, Round Rock TX 78681, USA | |
| **Danmeier, Richard C (Rick)** | Football Player |
| 4917 Ridge Road, Minneapolis MN 55436, USA | |
| **Danneels, Godfried Cardinal** | Religious Leader |
| Aartsbisdom, Wollemarkt 15, 2800 Mechelen, Belgium | |
| **Dannelly, Brian** | Director, Writer |
| Creative Artists Agency, 2000 Ave of Stars, #100, Los Angeles CA 90067 USA | |
| **Danner, Blythe** | Actress |
| Anonymous Content, 3532 Hayden Ave, Culver City CA 90232 USA | |
| **Danning, Sybil** | Actress, Model |
| 8491 W Sunset Blvd, #361, West Hollywood CA 90069, USA | |
| **Dano, Linda** | Actress |
| 70 Riverside Lane, Riverside CT 06878, USA | |
| **Dano, Paul F** | Actor |
| Anonymous Content, 3532 Hayden Ave, Culver City CA 90232 USA | |
| **Dansby, Karlos M** | Football Player |
| 2844 E Honeysuckle Place, Chandler AZ 85286, USA | |
| **Danson, Ted** | Actor |
| Creative Artists Agency, 2000 Ave of Stars, #100, Los Angeles CA 90067 USA | |
| **Dante, Joe** | Director |
| Renfield Productions, 1041 N Formosa Ave, Writers Building, West Hollywood CA 90046, USA | |
| **Dantley, Adrian D** | Basketball Player, Coach |
| 9 Barn Ridge Court, Silver Spring MD 20906, USA | |
| **D'Antoni, Mike** | Basketball Player, Coach |
| 9 Hunter Lane, Rye NY 10580, USA | |
| **D'Antoni, Philip** | Producer, Director |
| Saint Andrews, 10 Old Jackson Ave, Hastings on Hudson NY 10706, USA | |
| **Dantonio, Mark** | Football Coach |
| Michigan State University, Athletic Dept, East Lansing MI 48824, USA | |
| **Dantzscher, Jamie A** | Gymnast |
| Arizona State University, Athletic Dept, Tempe AZ 85287, USA | |
| **Danvers, Tasha** | Track Athlete |
| Shaftesbury Barnet, Greenlands Lane, Herndon, London NW 1RL, England | |
| **Danz, Ingeborg** | Opera Singer |
| Kunstler Sekretariat am Gasteig, Rosenheimer Str 52, 81669 Munich, Germany | |
| **Danz, Shirley** | Baseball Player |
| 330 Greystone Dr, Hendersonville NC 28792, USA | |
| **Danza, Tony** | Actor |
| Paradigm Agency, 360 N Crescent Dr, North Building, Beverly Hills CA 90210 USA | |
| **Danzenie, Billy** | Rap Artist (M O P) |
| Pyramid Entertainment Group, 377 Rector Place, #21A, New York NY 10280 USA | |
| **Danziger, Jeff** | Editorial Cartoonist |
| RFD, Plainfield VT 05667, USA | |
| **Danziger, Sheldon H** | Economist |
| University of Michigan, Public Policy School, Ann Arbor MI 48109, USA | |
| **Daoust, Dan** | Ice Hockey Player |
| 55 John Silver Crescent, Markham ON L3R 9B, Canada | |
| **Dapper, Marco** | Actor, Model |
| Himber Entertainment, PO Box 950, South Orange NJ 07079 USA | |
| **D'Aquino, Carl** | Interior Designer |
| D'Aquino Monaco Inc, 214 W 29th St, #1202, New York NY 10001, USA | |
| **D'Aquino, Rosca** | Actress |
| Carol Levi Mgmt, Via Giuseppe Pisanelli 2, 00196 Rome, Italy | |
| **Darabont, Frank** | Director, Writer |
| Darkwoods Productions, 301 E Colorado Blvd, #705, Pasadena CA 91101, USA | |
| **D'Arbanville-Quinn, Patti** | Actress |
| Hartig-Hilepo Agency, 54 W 21st St, #610, New York NY 10010 USA | |
| **Darbinyan, Armen R** | Prime Minister, Armenia |
| 19 Str Sayat Nova, 375001 Yerevan, Armenia | |
| **Darby, Chartric T** | Football Player |
| 14335 Simonds Road NE, Bothell WA 98011, USA | |
| **Darby, Craig** | Ice Hockey Player |
| 40 Vista Dr, Saratoga Springs NY 12866, USA | |
| **Darby, Kim** | Actress |
| C R Mgmt, 22337 Pacific Coast Highway, #627, Malibu CA 90265, USA | |
| **Darby, Matthew L (Matt)** | Football Player |
| 501 Sagecreek Court, Winter Springs FL 32708, USA | |
| **Darby, Rhys** | Actor |
| Creative Artists Agency, 2000 Ave of Stars, #100, Los Angeles CA 90067 USA | |
| **D'Arby, Terence Trent** | Singer |
| Agency Group Ltd, 142 W 57th St, #600, New York NY 10019 USA | |
| **Darc, Mireille** | Actress |
| Agents Associes, 201 Faubourg Saint Honore, 75008 Paris, France | |
| **D'Arcangelo, Ildebrando** | Opera Singer |
| I M G Artists, Hogarth Business Park, Chiswick, London W4 2TH, England | |
| **D'Arcevia, Bruno** | Artist, Sculptor |
| Via Luigi Angeloni 29, 00149 Rome, Italy | |

**D**

**Daniels - D'Arcevia**

**Darche, Jean-Philippe** — Football Player
9507 W 160th Terrace, Stilwell KS 66085, USA
**Darchinyan, Vic** — Boxer
Billy Hussein, 49 The Avenue, Yagoona NSW 2199, Australia
**Darcy, Dame** — Cartoonist, Artist
22 W Bryan St, #185, Savannah GA 31401, USA
**D'Arcy, James** — Actor
Creative Artists Agency, 2000 Ave of Stars, #100, Los Angeles CA 90067 USA
**Darden, Thomas V (Thom)** — Football Player
637 20th Ave SW, Cedar Rapids IA 52404, USA
**Darensbourg, Victor A (Vic)** — Baseball Player
4151 Abernethy Forest Place, Las Vegas NV 89141, USA
**Darin, Ricardo** — Actor
Media Art Mgmt, C/ Castelló 82, 2 Derecha, 28006 Madrid, Spain
**Darius, Donovin (Don)** — Football Player
12051 Scarsdale Dr, Jacksonville FL 32246, USA
**Dark, Alvin R (Al)** — Baseball Player, Manager
103 Cranberry Way, Easley SC 29642, USA
**Darlan, Eva** — Actress
Agents Associes, 201 Rue du Faubourg Saint Honore, 75008 Paris, France
**Darling, Alistair M** — Government Official, England
Chancellory of Exchequer, 1 Horse Guards Road, London SW1A 2HQ, England
**Darling, Charles (Chuck)** — Basketball Player
8066 S Kramerie Way, Centennial CO 80112, USA
**Darling, David** — Astronomer, Writer
John Wiley & Sons, 111 River St, Hoboken NJ 07030 USA
**Darling, Devard L** — Football Player
4234 NE Park Springs Dr, Lees Summit MO 64064, USA
**Darling, Gary R** — Baseball Umpire
16609 S 32nd Lane, Phoenix AZ 85045, USA
**Darling, Jennifer** — Actress
C E S D, 10635 Santa Monica Blvd, #130, Los Angeles CA 90025 USA
**Darling, Katrina** — Dancer, Model
Playboy Promotions, 2706 Media Center Dr, Los Angeles CA 90065 USA
**Darling, Ronald M (Ron)** — Baseball Player
10 Barclay St, #34C, New York NY 10007, USA
**Darlington, Jonathan** — Conductor
I M G Artists, Hogarth Business Park, Chiswick, London W4 2TH, England
**Darmaatmadja, Julius Riyadi Cardinal** — Religious Leader
Keuskupan Agung, J I Katedral 7, Jakarta 10710, Indonesia
**Darnell, August** — Singer (Kid Creole & the Coconuts)
Ron Rainey Mgmt, 315 S Beverly Dr, #407, Beverly Hills CA 90212, USA
**Darnell, Bruce** — Model
Fashion4Art, Ingendorfer Str 34, 50529 Pulheim, Germany
**Darnell, Daniel J** — Air Force General
Deputy Commander, Pacific Command, Camp H M Smith HI 96861, USA
**Darnell, Erik** — Truck Racing Driver
Darmer Motorsports, 3627 Washington St, Park City IL 60085, USA
**Darnell, James E, Jr** — Molecular Biologist
Rockefeller University Medical Center, 1230 York Ave, New York NY 10065 USA
**Darnton, John** — Journalist, Writer
New York Times, Editorial Dept, 229 W 43rd St, New York NY 10036 USA
**Darnton, Robert C** — Historian
985 Memorial Dr, #403, Cambridge MA 02138, USA
**Darr, Lisa** — Actress
Stone Manners Salners, 9911 W Pico Blvd, #1400, Los Angeles CA 90035 USA
**Darrell, Katrina** — Singer, Actress
Avo Talent, 8500 Melrose Ave, #212, West Hollywood CA 90069, USA
**Darren, James** — Singer, Actor
PO Box 1088, Beverly Hills CA 90213, USA
**Darrow, Henry** — Actor
Hervey/Grimes Talent, 10561 Missouri Ave, #2, Los Angeles CA 90025 USA
**Darvill, Arthur** — Actor
Independent Talent Group, 40 Whitfield St, London W1T 2RH, England
**Darvish, Yu** — Baseball Player
Texas Rangers, Ameriquest Field, 1000 Ballpark Way, #306, Arlington TX 76011 USA
**Darwin, Daniel W (Danny)** — Baseball Player
6489 Stags Leap Road, Sanger TX 76266, USA
**Darwin, Matthew W (Matt)** — Football Player
414 Love Bird Lane, Murphy TX 75094, USA
**Darwitz, Natalie** — Ice Hockey Player
4655 Pine Cone Circle, Saint Paul MN 55123, USA
**Dascascos, Mark** — Actor
Three-X Vision, 18850 Vista del Canon, #A, Newhall CA 91321, USA
**D'Ascoli, Bernard** — Concert Pianist
C L B Mgmt, 28 Earlswood Road, London NW10 5QB, England
**Dash, Damon** — Actor, Director, Producer
Dash Films, 825 8th Ave, #2900, New York NY 10019, USA
**Dash, Leon D, Jr** — Journalist
Washington Post, Editorial Dept, 1150 15th Ave NW, Washington DC 20071, USA
**Dash, Stacey** — Actress, Model
Bleecker Street Entertainment, 853 Broadway, #1214, New York NY 10003
**DaSilva, Danilo L** — Soccer Player
Confederacion de Futebol, Rua Victor Civita 66, #1, Rio de Janeiro 22775 044, Brazil
**DaSilva, Rafael Pereira** — Soccer Player
Manchester United, Busby Way, Old Trafford, Manchester M16 0RA, England
**Dassler, Uwe** — Swimmer
Stolze-Schrey-Str 6, 15745 Wilday, Germany
**Dastmalchian, David** — Actor
C E S D, 10635 Santa Monica Blvd, #130, Los Angeles CA 90025 USA
**Dater, Judy L** — Photographer
2430 5th St, #J, Berkeley CA 94710, USA
**Datsyuk, Pavel V** — Ice Hockey Player
3166 Rosedale St, Ann Arbor MI 48108, USA
**Daub, Matthew** — Artist
A C A Galleries, 529 W 20th St, #500, New York NY 10011, USA

**Daubach, Brian M** — Baseball Player
2709 Timberline Dr, Belleville IL 62226, USA
**Daubechies, Ingrid C** — Computer Mathematician, Physicist
Princeton University, Mathematics Dept, Princeton NJ 08544, USA
**Dauer, Richard F (Rich)** — Baseball Player
2510 Brook Haven Lane, Hinckley OH 44233, USA
**Daughaday, William H** — Endocrinologist
1840 N Prospect Ave, #322, Milwaukee WI 53202, USA
**Daugherty, Bradley L (Brad)** — Basketball Player, Sportscaster
10 Inspiration Way, Swananoa NC 28778, USA
**Daugherty, George** — Conductor
I M G Artists, Hogarth Business Park, Chiswick, London W4 2TH, England
**Daugherty, John M (Jack)** — Baseball Player
20360 N 95th Place, Scottsdale AZ 85255, USA
**Daugherty, Michael** — Composer
Argo London Records, 810 7th Ave, New York NY 10019, USA
**Daughtrey, Martha Craig** — Judge
US Court of Appeals, 701 Broadway, #207, Nashville TN 37203, USA
**Daughtry, Christopher (Chris)** — Singer, Guitarist, Songwriter
19 Music & Mgmt, 35-37 Parkgate Road, London SW11 4NP, England
**Daugman, John** — Inventor (Scan Security System)
Cambridge University, Computer Laboratory, Cambridge CB3 0FD, England
**Dauline, Marie** — Singer (Zap Mama)
Todo Mundo, PO Box 319, New York NY 10012, USA
**Daulton, Darren A** — Baseball Player
643 Woodbridge Dr, Melbourne FL 32940, USA
**Dauterive, Jim** — Producer, Writer
United Talent Agency, U T A Plaza, 9336 Civic Center Dr, Beverly Hills CA 90210 USA
**Davalillo Romero, Victor J (Vic)** — Baseball Player
Calle Trujillo 7, Mariperez QV, Caracas, Venezuela
**Davalos, Alexa** — Actress
Brillstein Entertainment Partners, 9150 Wilshire Blvd, #350, Beverly Hills CA 90212 USA
**Davalos, Richard** — Actor
23388 Mulholland Dr, #28, Woodland Hills CA 91364, USA
**Davanger, Flemming** — Curling Athlete
Curling Assn, Sognsveien 75, Serviceboks 1, 0840 Oslo, Norway
**Davanon, Jeffrey G (Jeff)** — Baseball Player
731 E Buena Vista Dr, Chandler AZ 85249, USA
**Davenport, Ian** — Artist
Paul Kasmin Gallery, 293 10th Ave, New York NY 10001, USA
**Davenport, Jack** — Actor
Hamilton Hodell, 66-68 Margaret St, #500, London W1W 8SR, England
**Davenport, James H (Jim)** — Baseball Player, Manager
1016 Hewitt Dr, San Carlos CA 94070, USA
**Davenport, Jeremy** — Trumpeter, Singer
Columbia Artists Mgmt Inc, 1790 Broadway, #702, New York NY 10019 USA
**Davenport, Jessica** — Basketball Player
Indiana Fever, Conseco Fieldhouse, 125 S Pennsylvania, Indianapolis IN 46204 USA
**Davenport, Lindsay** — Tennis Player
PO Box 10179, Newport Beach CA 92658, USA
**Davenport, Madison** — Actress
C E S D, 10635 Santa Monica Blvd, #130, Los Angeles CA 90025 USA
**Davenport, N'Dea** — Singer (Brand New Heavies), Songwriter
David Levin Business Mgmt, 200 W 57th St, #1101, New York NY 10019, USA
**Davenport, N'Dea** — Singer, Dancer
Sangfroid Music Group, 24 Caradoc St, Greenwich, London SE10 9AG, England
**Davenport, Wilbur B, Jr** — Electrical Engineer
1120 Skyline Dr, Medford OR 97504, USA
**Daves, Michael** — Singer
Paradigm Agency, 360 N Crescent Dr, North Building, Beverly Hills CA 90210 USA
**Davey, Donald V (Don)** — Football Player
1525 Beach Ave, Atlantic Beach FL 32233, USA
**Davi, Robert** — Actor
Chuck Binder Mgmt, 1465 Lindacrest Dr, Beverly Hills CA 90210 USA
**Daviau, Allen** — Cinematographer
2249 Bronson Hill Dr, Los Angeles CA 90068, USA
**Davich, Marty** — Composer
530 S Greenwood Lane, Pasadena CA 91107, USA
**David Mohato** — Crown Prince, Lesotho
Royal Palace, PO Box 524, Maseru, Lesotho
**David, Anna** — Columnist, Writer
8424 Santa Monica Blvd, #A754, West Hollywood CA 90069, USA
**David, Craig A** — Singer, Songwriter
Creative Artists Agency, 2000 Ave of Stars, #100, Los Angeles CA 90067 USA
**David, Edward E, Jr** — Underwater Sound, Electrical Engineer
E E D Inc, PO Box 435, Bedminster NJ 07921, USA
**David, George A L** — Businessman
United Technologies Corp, United Technologies Building, Hartford CT 06101, USA
**David, John R** — Internist
Harvard Public Health School, Tropical Health Dept, 665 Huntington Ave, Boston MA 02115, USA
**David, Keith** — Actor, Producer
Stone Manners Salners, 9911 W Pico Blvd, #1400, Los Angeles CA 90035 USA
**David, Larry** — Writer, Actor, Producer
L D Productions, 3000 Olympic Blvd, Santa Monica CA 90404, USA
**David, Michael Stahl** — Actor
Management 360, 9111 Wilshire Blvd, Beverly Hills CA 90210 USA
**David, Peter** — Actor
PO Box 239, Bayport NY 11705, USA
**Davidoff, Dov** — Actor, Comedian
United Talent Agency, U T A Plaza, 9336 Civic Center Dr, Beverly Hills CA 90210 USA
**Davidovich, Bella** — Concert Pianist
Agnes Bruneau Assoc, 155 W 68th St, #1010, New York NY 10023, USA
**Davidovich, Lolita** — Actress
Mavrick Artists Agency, 6100 Wilshire Blvd, #550, Los Angeles CA 90048, USA
**Davidovici, Brigette** — Actress
W M E Entertainment, 9601 Wilshire Blvd, #300, Beverly Hills CA 90210 USA

**Davidovsky, Mario** — Composer
490 W End Ave, New York NY 10024, USA

**Davids, Edgar** — Soccer Player
F C Juventus, Corso Galilo Ferraris 32, 10128 Turin, Italy

**Davidson, Adam** — Director
Creative Artists Agency, 2000 Ave of Stars, #100, Los Angeles CA 90067 USA

**Davidson, Amy** — Actress
Stone Manners Salners, 9911 W Pico Blvd, #1400, Los Angeles CA 90035 USA

**Davidson, Andrew** — Writer
Doubleday Press, 1745 Broadway, New York NY 10019 USA

**Davidson, Barbara** — Photographer
Los Angeles Times, Editorial Dept, 202 W 1st St, Los Angeles CA 90012 USA

**Davidson, Bruce O** — Equestrian
RR 842, Unionville PA 19375, USA

**Davidson, Diane Mott** — Writer
William Morrow Publishers, 1350 Ave of Americas, New York NY 10019 USA

**Davidson, Eileen** — Actress
Media Artists Group, 8222 Melrose Ave, #203, Los Angeles CA 90048 USA

**Davidson, Ernest R** — Chemist
5051 50th Ave NE, #22, Seattle WA 98105, USA

**Davidson, Francis M (Cotton)** — Football Player
435 Old Osage Road, Gatesville TX 76528, USA

**Davidson, Gordon** — Producer, Director
165 Mabery Rd, Santa Monica CA 90402, USA

**Davidson, J Mark** — Baseball Player
996 Old Mountain Road, Statesville NC 28677, USA

**Davidson, Jeff** — Motivational Speaker
Breathing Space Institute, 3202 Ruffin St, Raleigh NC 27607, USA

**Davidson, John** — Ice Hockey Player, Executive
6 Briarbrook Trail, Saint Louis MO 63131, USA

**Davidson, John** — Singer, Actor
8605 Santa Monica Blvd, West Hollywood CA 90069, USA

**Davidson, Justin** — Journalist
New York Newsday, Editorial Dept, 235 Pinelawn Road, Melville NY 11747 USA

**Davidson, Kenneth D (Kenny)** — Football Player
1922 Thompson Crossing Dr, Richmond TX 77406, USA

**Davidson, Owen** — Tennis Player
39 N Lakemist Harbour Place, Spring TX 77381, USA

**Davidson, Richard** — Neuroplastic Surgeon
University of Wisconsin, Keck Brain Imaging & Behavior Laboratory, Madison WI 53706, USA

**Davidson, Tommy** — Actor, Comedian
Glick Agency, 1321 7th St, #203, Santa Monica CA 90401 USA

**David-Weill, Michel** — Financier
Lazard, 121 Blvd Haussmann, 75008 Paris, France

**Davie, J Alan** — Artist
Gamels Studio, Rush Green, Hertfordshire SG13 7SB, England

**Davie, Karin** — Artist, Sculptor
James Harris Gallery, 309 3rd Ave S, #A, Seattle WA 98104, USA

**Davie, Robert (Bob)** — Football Coach, Sportscaster
University of New Mexico, Athletic Dept, Albuquerque NM , USA

**Davies, Alan** — Actor
Rights House, Drury House, 34-43 Russell St, London WC2B 5HA, England

**Davies, Caryn** — Rowing Athlete
Columbia University, Law School, New York NY 10027, USA

**Davies, Dave** — Singer, Guitarist (Kinks)
Talent Consultants International, 105 Shad Row, #B, Piermont NY 10968 USA

**Davies, David R** — Biophysicist
4224 Franklin St, Kensington MD 20895, USA

**Davies, Dennis Russell** — Conductor, Concert Pianist
Columbia Artists Mgmt Inc, 1790 Broadway, #702, New York NY 10019 USA

**Davies, Gail** — Singer, Guitarist, Songwriter
246 Cherokee Road, Nashville TN 37205, USA

**Davies, Geraint Wyn** — Actor
Oscars Abrams Zimel, 438 Queen St W, Toronto ON M5A 1T4, Canada

**Davies, H Kyle** — Baseball Player
1495 E Lake Road, McDonough GA 30252, USA

**Davies, Jeremy** — Actor
Untitled Entertainment, 350 S Beverly Dr, #200, Beverly Hills CA 90212 USA

**Davies, John G** — Judge, Swimmer
520 Madeline Dr, Pasadena CA 91105, USA

**Davies, Karle** — Actor
Curtis Brown Group, 28-29 Haymarket St, #500, London SW1Y 4SP, England

**Davies, Laura** — Golfer
Tytherington Club, Tytherington Macclesfield SK10 2JP, England

**Davies, Linda** — Writer
Calle Once 286, La Molona, Lima, Peru

**Davies, Matt** — Editorial Cartoonist
Journal News, Editorial Dept, 1 Gannett Dr, West Harrison NY 10604, USA

**Davies, Mike** — Architect
Rogers Partnership, Thames Wharf, Rainville Road, London N6 94A, England

**Davies, Paul C W** — Mathematical Physicist
PO Box 389, Burnside SA 5066, Australia

**Davies, Peter Maxwell** — Composer
Judy Arnold, 50 Hogarth Road, London SW5 OPU, England

**Davies, Raymond D (Ray)** — Singer, Guitarist (Kinks)
Agency Group Ltd, 1880 Century Park E, #711, Los Angeles CA 90067 USA

**Davies, Ryland** — Opera Singer
71 Fairmile Lane, Cobham, Surrey KT11 2DG, England

**Davies, S Howard** — Director
Royal National Theater, South Bank, London SE 19PX, England

**Davies, William** — Writer
United Talent Agency, U T A Plaza, 9336 Civic Center Dr, Beverly Hills CA 90210 USA

**Davila, Robert** — Educator
Gallaudet University, President's Office, 800 Florida NW, Washington DC 20002, USA

**Davis, Alia** — Singer (Allure)
Universal Attractions, 135 W 26th St, #1200, New York NY 10001 USA

| | |
|---|---|
| **Davis, Alvin G** | Baseball Player |
| 7983 Armagosa Dr, Riverside CA 92508, USA | |
| **Davis, Andre' N** | Football Player |
| 11407 Jutland Road, Houston TX 77048, USA | |
| **Davis, Andrew** | Director |
| Chicago Pacific Entertainment, 1475 Hillcrest Road, Santa Barbara CA 93103, USA | |
| **Davis, Andrew F** | Conductor |
| Columbia Artists Mgmt Inc, 1790 Broadway, #702, New York NY 10019 USA | |
| **Davis, Angela Y** | Political Activist, Educator |
| Speakout, PO Box 22748, Oakland CA 94609, USA | |
| **Davis, Ann B** | Actress |
| 23315 Eagle Gap Road, San Antonio TX 78255, USA | |
| **Davis, Anthony** | Jazz Pianist, Composer |
| Andriolo Communications, 115 E 9th St, New York NY 10003, USA | |
| **Davis, Anthony** | Football Player |
| 8011 Carter Ave, #2606, Overland Park KS 66204, USA | |
| **Davis, Anthony, Jr** | Basketball Player |
| New Orleans Pelicans, 1250 Poydras St, #101, New Orleans LA 70113 USA | |
| **Davis, Antone** | Football Player |
| 2252 Red Bud Road, Sevierville TN 37876, USA | |
| **Davis, Antonio L** | Basketball Player |
| 21 Buford Village Walk, Buford GA 30518, USA | |
| **Davis, Baron W L** | Basketball Player |
| PO Box 12109, Marina del Rey CA 90295, USA | |
| **Davis, Barry** | Freestyle Wrestler |
| 417 N High Point Road, Madison WI 53717, USA | |
| **Davis, Benjamin (Ben)** | Opera Singer |
| Encompass Arts, 119 W 72nd St, 371, New York NY 10023, USA | |
| **Davis, Benjamin F (Ben)** | Football Player |
| 1144 Brandon Road, Cleveland OH 44112, USA | |
| **Davis, Benjamin Jay** | Actor |
| Untitled Entertainment, 350 S Beverly Dr, #200, Beverly Hills CA 90212 USA | |
| **Davis, Bennie L** | Air Force General |
| 101 Golden Road, Georgetown TX 78633, USA | |
| **Davis, Bill** | Auto Racing Executive |
| Bill Davis Racing, 810 Newport Road, Batesville AR 72501, USA | |
| **Davis, Billy, Jr** | Singer (Fifth Dimension) |
| Brokaw Co, 9255 W Sunset Blvd, #804, West Hollywood CA 90069 USA | |
| **Davis, Bradley E (Brad)** | Basketball Player |
| 2703 Ridge Top Lane, Arlington TX 76006, USA | |
| **Davis, Bradley J (Brad)** | Soccer Player |
| Houston Dynamo, 1415 Louisiana, #3400, Houston TX 77002 USA | |
| **Davis, Brian W** | Football Player |
| 3847 E Hiddenview Dr, Phoenix AZ 85048, USA | |
| **Davis, Brianne** | Actress |
| Sager Mgmt, 260 S Beverly Dr, #205, Beverly Hills CA 90212, USA | |
| **Davis, Bryshear B (Brock)** | Baseball Player |
| 23759 Heliotrope Way, Moreno Valley CA 92557, USA | |
| **Davis, Charles A** | Jazz Saxophonist |
| 201 E 19th St, #9E, New York NY 10003, USA | |
| **Davis, Charles E (Charlie)** | Basketball Player |
| 615 Main St, Nashville TN 37206, USA | |
| **Davis, Charles F** | Sportscaster |
| N F L Network, 10950 Washington Blvd, #100, Culver City CA 90232 USA | |
| **Davis, Charles M (Charlie)** | Football Player |
| 2400 Bowler Road, Waller TX 77484, USA | |
| **Davis, Charles T (Chili)** | Baseball Player |
| 4625 Lake Washington Blvd SE, Bellevue WA 98006, USA | |
| **Davis, Clarence E** | Football Player |
| 171 Longleaf St, Pickerington OH 43147, USA | |
| **Davis, Clifton** | Actor |
| C E S D, 10635 Santa Monica Blvd, #130, Los Angeles CA 90025 USA | |
| **Davis, Clive J** | Businessman |
| R C A Records, 8750 Wilshire Blvd, Beverly Hills CA 90211 USA | |
| **Davis, Dana** | Actress |
| Marshak/Zachary Co, 8840 Wilshire Blvd, #100, Beverly Hills CA 90211 USA | |
| **Davis, Daniel** | Actor |
| Innovative Artists, 1505 10th St, Santa Monica CA 90401 USA | |
| **Davis, Daniel M** | Immunologist |
| Imperial College, Biological Sciences Dept, London SW7 2AZ, England | |
| **Davis, David (Dave)** | Bowler |
| DeStasio, 710 Shore Road, Spring Lake Heights NJ 07762, USA | |
| **Davis, David Brion** | Writer, Historian |
| 783 Lambert Road, Orange CT 06477, USA | |
| **Davis, Debbie** | Model |
| Playboy Promotions, 2706 Media Center Dr, Los Angeles CA 90065 USA | |
| **Davis, DeRay** | Actor |
| Principato-Young, 9465 Wilshire Blvd, #880, Beverly Hills CA 90212 USA | |
| **Davis, Destiny** | Model |
| 10624 S Eastern Ave, #A157, Henderson NV 89052, USA | |
| **Davis, Dexter W** | Football Player |
| 5054 Vermack Road, Atlanta GA 30338, USA | |
| **Davis, Diane** | Actress |
| Paradigm Agency, 360 N Crescent Dr, North Building, Beverly Hills CA 90210 USA | |
| **Davis, Don** | Golfer |
| 15910 FM 529, #219, Houston TX 77095, USA | |
| **Davis, Douglas N (Doug)** | Baseball Player |
| 26125 N 116th St, Scottsdale AZ 85255, USA | |
| **Davis, E Lydell (Dale)** | Basketball Player |
| 2000 Westwood Circle SE, Smyrna GA 30080, USA | |
| **Davis, Edgar** | Space Scientist |
| Jet Propulsion Laboratory, 4800 Oak Grove Dr, Pasadena CA 91109 USA | |
| **Davis, Elliot M** | Cinematographer |
| 1328 Arch St, Berkeley CA 94708, USA | |
| **Davis, Eric K** | Baseball Player |
| 6203 Variel Ave, #118, Woodland Hills CA 91367, USA | |

**D**

**Davis - Davis**

**Davis - Davis**

**Davis, Eric W** — Football Player
236 S Oakhurst Dr, Beverly Hills CA 90212, USA

**Davis, Essie** — Actress
United Agents, 12-26 Lexington St, London W1F 0LE, England

**Davis, Gary C** — Football Player
10750 San Marcus Road, Atascadero CA 93422, USA

**Davis, Geena** — Actress
Creative Artists Agency, 2000 Ave of Stars, #100, Los Angeles CA 90067 USA

**Davis, George E (Storm)** — Baseball Player
7931 Dawsons Creek Dr, Jacksonville FL 32222, USA

**Davis, Gregory B (Greg)** — Football Player
793 Vernon Road NE, Rome GA 30165, USA

**Davis, H Thomas (Tommy)** — Baseball Player
9767 Whirlaway St, Rancho Cucamonga CA 91737, USA

**Davis, Harry A** — Basketball Player
1966 E 75th St, Cleveland OH 44103, USA

**Davis, Harry R, Jr** — Chemist
Schering-Plough Research, 2000 Galloping Hill Road, Kenilworth NJ 07033, USA

**Davis, Hope** — Actress
United Talent Agency, U T A Plaza, 9336 Civic Center Dr, Beverly Hills CA 90210 USA

**Davis, Hubert I** — Basketball Player
204 Lancaster Dr, Chapel Hill NC 27517, USA

**Davis, J Graham (Gray), Jr** — Governor, CA
Loeb & Loeb, 10100 Santa Monica Blvd, #2200, Los Angeles CA 90067, USA

**Davis, James B** — Air Force General
3600 Wimber Blvd, Palm Harbor FL 34685, USA

**Davis, James O** — Physician
612 Maplewood Dr, Columbia MO 65203, USA

**Davis, James R (Jim)** — Cartoonist (Garfield)
Paws Inc, 5440 E Country Road 450 N, Albany IN 47320, USA

**Davis, James S** — Football Player
5701 S Saint Andrews Place, Los Angeles CA 90062, USA

**Davis, Jamie** — Actress
Curtis Brown Group, 28-29 Haymarket St, #500, London SW1Y 4SP, England

**Davis, Jason T** — Baseball Player
474 Leatha Lane NW, Cleveland TN 37312, USA

**Davis, Jay** — Golfer
2152 S State St, Springfield IL 62704, USA

**Davis, Jeff** — Producer, Writer
Magnet Mgmt, 11704 Wilshire Blvd, #210, Los Angeles CA 90025, USA

**Davis, Jeff (Stick)** — Bassist (Amazing Rhythm Aces)
Gen-X Entertainment, PO Box 128164, Nashville TN 37212, USA

**Davis, Jeff Bryan** — Actor, Comedian, Director
Domain Talent, 9229 W Sunset Blvd, #710, West Hollywood CA 90069 USA

**Davis, Jeffrey E (Jeff)** — Football Player
106 Sycamore Dr, Clemson SC 29631, USA

**Davis, Jesse** — Jazz Saxophonist
Concord Records, 100 N Crescent Dr, #275, Beverly Hills CA 90210 USA

**Davis, Jill A** — Writer
Random House, 1745 Broadway, #1800, New York NY 10019 USA

**Davis, Jody R** — Baseball Player
5631 N 79th St, #4, Scottsdale AZ 85250, USA

**Davis, John A** — Actor, Director, Producer, Writer
W M E Entertainment, 9601 Wilshire Blvd, #300, Beverly Hills CA 90210 USA

**Davis, John H** — Football Player
901 Forest Pond Dr, Marietta GA 30068, USA

**Davis, John K** — Marine Corps General
303 Calle Empalome, San Clemente CA 92672, USA

**Davis, Johnny R** — Basketball Player, Coach
135 W Market St, #2D, Indianapolis IN 46204, USA

**Davis, Jonathan H** — Singer (Korn), Bagpipe Player
Kraft-Engel Mgmt, 15233 Ventura Blvd, #200, Sherman Oaks CA 91403, USA

**Davis, Judy** — Actress
Shanahan Mgmt, PO Box 1509, Darlinghurst NSW 1300, Australia

**Davis, Julie** — Director, Writer
Felker Toczak Gellman, 10880 Wilshire Blvd, #2070, Los Angeles CA 90024 USA

**Davis, Kane** — Baseball Player
1558 Noble Ridge, Reedy WV 25270, USA

**Davis, Kenneth E** — Football Player
1224 Brooklawn Dr, Arlington TX 76018, USA

**Davis, Keno** — Basketball Coach
Providence College, Athletic Dept, Providence RI 02918, USA

**Davis, Kim** — Ice Hockey Player
14 Shorecrest Dr, Winnipeg MB R3P 1N2, Canada

**Davis, Kristin** — Actress, Model
Mosiac Media Group, 9200 W Sunset Blvd, #1000, Los Angeles CA 90069 USA

**Davis, Kyle** — Actor
Global Artists Agency, 6253 Hollywood Blvd, #508, Los Angeles CA 90028, USA

**Davis, Lance** — Baseball Player
5845 Old Berkley Road, Auburdale FL 33823, USA

**Davis, Lance E** — Economist
9717 Thistle Court, Fort Smith AR 72908, USA

**Davis, Lauren** — Tennis Player
2302 NE 5th Ave, Boca Raton FL 33431, USA

**Davis, Lee C** — Basketball Player
5024 Fieldgreen Crossing, #82, Stone Mountain GA 30088, USA

**Davis, Linda K** — Singer
Alkahest Artists, 1709 Verona Dr, Chattanooga TN 37421, USA

**Davis, Louis (Chip), Jr** — Musician
Sound Trak, 9120 Mormon Bridge Road, Omaha NE 68152, USA

**Davis, Lowell** — Artist, Sculptor
1070 3rd St, #E, Carthage MO 64836, USA

**Davis, Lucy** — Actress
Melanie Greene Mgmt, 425 N Robertson Blvd, West Hollywood CA 90048 USA

**Davis, Mac** — Singer, Songwriter, Actor
Abrams Artists, 9200 W Sunset Blvd, #1125, West Hollywood CA 90069 USA

**Davis, Mackenzie** — Actress
United Talent Agency, U T A Plaza, 9336 Civic Center Dr, Beverly Hills CA 90210 USA
**Davis, Mark A** — Basketball Player
108 Government Circle, #A, Thibodaux LA 70301, USA
**Davis, Mark C (Ben)** — Baseball Player
416 Homestead Dr, West Chester PA 19382, USA
**Davis, Mark M** — Microbiologist
Stanford University Medical Center, Microbiology Dept, Stanford CA 94305, USA
**Davis, Mark W** — Baseball Player
8867 E Sierra Pinta Dr, Scottsdale AZ 85255, USA
**Davis, Martha** — Singer (Motels)
Paradise Artists, PO Box 1821, Ojai CA 93024 USA
**Davis, Matthew (Matt)** — Actor
Brillstein Entertainment Partners, 9150 Wilshire Blvd, #350, Beverly Hills CA 90212 USA
**Davis, Melvyn J (Mel)** — Basketball Player
PO Box 29, Suffern NY 10901, USA
**Davis, Meryl** — Ice Dancer
Artic Edge Skating Club, 46615 Michigan Ave, Canton MI 48188, USA
**Davis, Michael** — Director, Producer, Writer
I C M Partners, 10250 Constellation Blvd, #900, Los Angeles CA 90067 USA
**Davis, Michael D (Mike)** — Baseball Player
2491 San Ramon Valley Blvd, #1407, San Ramon CA 94583, USA
**Davis, Michael L (Mike)** — Football Player
37039 N 109th St, Scottsdale AZ 85262, USA
**Davis, N Jan** — Astronaut
4105 Cumberland Pass, #814, Fort Worth TX 76116, USA
**Davis, Oliver J** — Football Player
1708 Fountain Court, #3702, Columbus GA 31904, USA
**Davis, Paige** — Actress, Entertainer
3 Arts Entertainment, 9460 Wilshire Blvd, #700, Beverly Hills CA 90212 USA
**Davis, Phyllis** — Actress
29330 SE Hillyard Dr, #D14, Boring OR 97009, USA
**Davis, Preston** — Actor
Vincent Cirrincione Assoc, 1516 N Fairfax Ave, Los Angeles CA 90046 USA
**Davis, R Glen (Big Baby)** — Basketball Player
Performance Sports Mgmt, PO Box 270715, Houston TX 77277, USA
**Davis, Rajal L** — Baseball Player
31 Pond Edge Dr, Waterford CT 06385, USA
**Davis, Reuben C** — Football Player
4424 Lystra Road, Chapel Hill NC 27517, USA
**Davis, Richard** — Jazz Bassist
S R O Artists, 6629 University Ave, #206, Middleton WI 53562, USA
**Davis, Richard D (Rick)** — Soccer Player
12501 Isis Ave, Hawthorne CA 90250, USA
**Davis, Richard E (Dick)** — Baseball Player
11091 Sultan St, Moreno Valley CA 92557, USA
**Davis, Richard K (Ted)** — Football Player
5401 Riverbend Dr, Knoxville TN 37919, USA
**Davis, Robert J E (Bob)** — Baseball Player
PO Box 198, Locust Grove OK 74352, USA
**Davis, Roger W** — Football Player
17522 Harvard Ave, Cleveland OH 44128, USA
**Davis, Ronald (Ron)** — Artist
PO Box 293, Arroyo Hondo NM 87513, USA
**Davis, Ronald G (Ron)** — Baseball Player
11748 N 90th Place, Scottsdale AZ 85260, USA
**Davis, Ronald H** — Basketball Player
5668 W Evergreen Road, Glendale AZ 85302, USA
**Davis, Russell M** — Football Player
605 Jones Ferry Road, Carrboro NC 27510, USA
**Davis, Russell S (Russ)** — Baseball Player
3351 Crescent Dr, Bessemer AL 35023, USA
**Davis, Sammy J, Jr** — Football Player
4020 Murphy Canyon Road, San Diego CA 92123, USA
**Davis, Sammy L** — Vietnam War Army Hero (CMH)
3376 N 100th St, Flat Rock IL 62427, USA
**Davis, Sampson** — Physician
Three Doctors Foundation, 65 Hazelwood Ave, Newark NJ 07106, USA
**Davis, Samuel R (Sam)** — Football Player
423 Edgemont St, Mount Washington PA 15211, USA
**Davis, Scott** — Figure Skater, Coach
5308 Worthington Dr, Bethesda MD 20816, USA
**Davis, Shani** — Speed Skater
7639 N Eastlake Terrace, #1A, Chicago IL 60626, USA
**Davis, Sharen** — Costume Designer
Sandra Marsh & Associates, 9150 Wilshire Blvd, #220, Beverly Hills CA 90212, USA
**Davis, Spencer** — Singer, Guitarist
Alan Cottam Agency, 19 Charles St, Lancashire, Wigan WN1 2BP, England
**Davis, Stephen H** — Mathematician, Engineer
2735 Simpson St, Evanston IL 60201, USA
**Davis, Stephen L** — Football Player
PO Box 31847, Saint Louis MO 63131, USA
**Davis, Steve** — Snooker Player
Matchroom Snooker, 10 Western Road, Romford, Essex RM1 3JT, England
**Davis, Tamra** — Director, Cinematographer
Paradigm Agency, 360 N Crescent Dr, North Building, Beverly Hills CA 90210 USA
**Davis, Tania** — Violist (Bond)
Mel Bush, Tanglewood, Arrowsmith Road, Wimborne, Dorset BH21 3BG, England
**Davis, Terrell L** — Football Player, Sportscaster
19750 E Geddes Place, Centennial CO 80016, USA
**Davis, Terry R** — Basketball Player
2933 Kenmore Road, Richmond VA 23225, USA
**Davis, Vernon** — Football Player
San Francisco 49ers, 4949 Centennial Blvd, Santa Clara CA 95054 USA
**Davis, Viola** — Actress
Principal Entertainment, 130 W 42nd St, #614, New York NY 10036, USA

**Davis, W Eugene** — Judge
US Court of Appeals, 800 Lafayette St, #2100, Lafayette LA 70501, USA
**Davis, Wallace M (Butch)** — Baseball Player
1108 Brucemont Dr, Garner NC 27529, USA
**Davis, Walter F (Buddy)** — Track Athlete, Basketball Player
5200 E Donald Ave, #A, Denver CO 80222, USA
**Davis, Walter P** — Basketball Player
5200 E Donald Ave, #A, Denver CO 80222, USA
**Davis, Warwick A** — Actor
Independent Talent Group, 40 Whitfield St, London W1T 2RH, England
**Davis, Wendy** — Actress
Pakula/King, 9229 W Sunset Blvd, #315, West Hollywood CA 90069 USA
**Davis, William D (Willie)** — Football Player
100 Corporate Pointe, #310, Culver City CA 90230, USA
**Davison, Bruce** — Actor
Innovative Artists, 1505 10th St, Santa Monica CA 90401 USA
**Davison, Fred C** — Foundation Executive, Educator
National Science Foundation, 1 7th St, #502, Augusta GA 30901, USA
**Davison, Peter** — Actor
Conway Van Gelder Grant, 8-12 Broadwick St, #300, London W1F 8HW, England
**Davison, Ronald K** — Governor General, New Zealand; Judge
11/217 Kupe St Orakei, Auckland 1071, New Zealand
**Davison, Rosana D** — Beauty Queen, Model
Storm Model Agency, 5 Jubilee Place, Chelsea, London SW3 3TD, England
**Davis-Wrightsil, Clarissa** — Basketball Player
Phoenix Mercury, American West Arena, 201 E Jefferson St, Phoenix AZ 85004 USA
**Davitian, Ken** — Actor
Luber Rocklin Entertainment, 8530 Wilshire Blvd, #555, Beverly Hills CA 90211 USA
**Davuluri, Nina** — Beauty Queen
Miss America Organization, 1370 Ave of Americas, #1600, New York NY 10019 USA
**Dawber, Pam** — Actress
Talent Works, 3500 W Olive Ave, #1400, Burbank CA 91505 USA
**Dawe, Jason** — Ice Hockey Player
9077 Drayton Lane, Fort Mill SC 29707, USA
**Dawes, Dominque M** — Gymnast
5484 Randolph Road, Rockville MD 20852, USA
**Dawes, Scott** — Construction Engineer
Dawes Construction Co, 1122 W 156th St, #100, Glenpool OK 74033, USA
**Dawid, Igor B** — Molecular Geneticist
Tufts Regenerative & Developmental Biology Center, 200 Boston Ave, #4600, Medford , MA 02155, USA
**Dawkins, Brian P** — Football Player
9874 Red Sumac Place, Parker CO 80138, USA
**Dawkins, C Richard** — Biologist, Ethologist, Writer
Oxford University, Museum, Parks Road, Oxford OX1 3PW, England
**Dawkins, Darryl** — Basketball Player
1708 Glacier Court, Allentown PA 18104, USA
**Dawkins, Johnny E** — Basketball Player, Coach
40 Sunkist Lane, Los Altos CA 94022, USA
**Dawkins, Peter M (Pete)** — Football Player, Businessman
80 W River Road, Rumson NJ 07760, USA
**Dawkins, Sean R** — Football Player
826 Weichert Dr, Morgan Hill CA 95037, USA
**Dawkins, Travis S (Gookie)** — Baseball Player
106 Hunter Ridge Court, Boiling Springs SC 29316, USA
**Dawley, Joseph W (Joe)** — Artist
13 Holly St, Cranford NJ 07016, USA
**Dawley, William C (Bill)** — Baseball Player
8127 Landau Park Lane, Spring TX 77379, USA
**Dawsey, Lawrence** — Football Player
4341 Cheval Blvd, Lutz FL 33558, USA
**Dawson, Andre N** — Baseball Player
10601 SW 74th Ave, Miami FL 33156, USA
**Dawson, Carol** — Writer
Simon & Schuster, 1230 Ave of Americas, Concourse 1, New York NY 10020 USA
**Dawson, Chad** — Boxer
Gary Shaw Productions, 555 Preakness Ave, #9, Totowa NJ 07502, USA
**Dawson, Dermontti F** — Football Player
PO Box 712481, San Diego CA 92171, USA
**Dawson, J Cutler, Jr** — Navy Admiral
Navy Federal Credit Union, PO Box 3000, Merrifield VA 22119, USA
**Dawson, James C (Jim)** — Basketball Player
61 Glendale Road, Rye NY 10580, USA
**Dawson, Leonard R (Lenny)** — Football Player, Sportscaster
1030 W 59th Terrace, Kansas City MO 64113, USA
**Dawson, Lynne** — Opera Singer
I M G Artists, Hogarth Business Park, Chiswick, London W4 2TH, England
**Dawson, Marco** — Golfer
3053 Shoal Creek Village Dr, Lakeland FL 33803, USA
**Dawson, Philip D (Phil)** — Football Player
4000 Dunning Lane, Austin TX 78746, USA
**Dawson, Rosario** — Actress, Singer
Creative Artists Agency, 2000 Ave of Stars, #100, Los Angeles CA 90067 USA
**Dawson, Roxann** — Actress, Director
Andrea Simon Entertainment, 4230 Woodman Ave, Sherman Oaks CA 91423, USA
**Dawson, Trent** — Actor
Innovative Artists, 1505 10th St, Santa Monica CA 90401 USA
**Day George, Lynda** — Actress
10310 Riverside Dr, #104, Toluca Lake CA 91602, USA
**Day, Bill** — Editorial Cartoonist
Cagle Cartoons, PO Box 22342, Santa Barbara CA 93121 USA
**Day, Charles F (Boots)** — Baseball Player
1154 Vespasian Way, Chesterfield MO 63017, USA
**Day, Charles P (Charlie)** — Actor, Producer
3 Arts Entertainment, 9460 Wilshire Blvd, #700, Beverly Hills CA 90212 USA
**Day, Doris** — Singer, Actress
C W P Public Relations, 901 Hancock Ave, #312, West Hollywood CA 90069, USA

**Day, Felicia** — Actress
W M E Entertainment, 9601 Wilshire Blvd, #300, Beverly Hills CA 90210 USA
**Day, Glen** — Golfer
6 Hickory Hills Circle, Little Rock AR 72212, USA
**Day, Joe** — Ice Hockey Player
805 Shoreline Road, Lake Barrington IL 60010, USA
**Day, Julian** — Businessman
Kmart, 3000 W 14 Mile Road, Royal Oak MI 48073, USA
**Day, Laura** — Writer
Harper Collins Publishers, 10 E 53rd St, Cellar 1, New York NY 10022 USA
**Day, Matt** — Actor
United Agents, 12-26 Lexington St, London W1F 0LE, England
**Day, Patrick (Pat)** — Thoroughbred Racing Jockey
14703 Isleworth Court, Louisville KY 40245, USA
**Day, Peter R** — Agricultural Scientist
8200 Tarsier Ave, New Port Richey FL 34653, USA
**Day, Robert** — Director
8832 Ferncliff Ave NE, Bainbridge Island WA 98110, USA
**Day, S Zachary (Zach)** — Baseball Player
9663 Lupine Dr, Cincinnati OH 45241, USA
**Day, Skyler** — Actress
I C M Partners, 10250 Constellation Blvd, #900, Los Angeles CA 90067 USA
**Daye, Darren K** — Basektball Player
17 Elderberry, Irvine CA 92603, USA
**Dayett, Brian K** — Baseball Player
276 Phillips Dr, Winchester TN 37398, USA
**Daykin, Anthony A (Tony)** — Football Player
5204 Cross Ridge Circle, Woodstock GA 30188, USA
**Day-Lewis, Daniel** — Actor
Julian Belfrage Assoc, 9 Argyll St, #300, London W1F 7TG, England
**Dayley, Kenneth G (Ken)** — Baseball Player
1300 Wingate Way Court, Chesterfield MO 63005, USA
**Dayne, Ron** — Football Player
2135 Regent St, Madison WI 53726, USA
**Dayne, Taylor** — Singer, Songwriter, Actress
Almond Talent Agency, 8217 Beverly Blvd, #8, West Hollywood CA 90048, USA
**Days, Drews S, III** — Government Official
Yale University, Law School, New Haven CT 06520, USA
**Dayton, Jonathan** — Director
United Talent Agency, U T A Plaza, 9336 Civic Center Dr, Beverly Hills CA 90210 USA
**Dea, Billy** — Ice Hockey Player
2636 W Bartlett Way, Queen Creek AZ 85142, USA
**Deacon, Max** — Actor
Julian Belfrage Assoc, 9 Argyll St, #300, London W1F 7TG, England
**Deacon, Richard** — Sculptor
Lisson Gallery, 67 Lisson St, London NW1 5DA, England
**Deadmarsh, Adam** — Ice Hockey Player
PO Box 3346, Coeur D'Alene ID 83816, USA
**DeAgostini-Rossetti, Doris** — Alpine Skier
Strada de Valle, 6780 Airolo, Switzerland
**Deakin, Julia** — Actress
Curtis Brown Group, 28-29 Haymarket St, #500, London SW1Y 4SP, England
**Deakin, Paul** — Drummer (Mavericks)
AristoMedia, 1620 16th Ave S, Nashville TN 37212, USA
**Deakins, Roger A** — Cinematographer
I C M Partners, 10250 Constellation Blvd, #900, Los Angeles CA 90067 USA
**Deal, Kimberly A (Kim)** — Singer, Bassist (Pixies, Breeders)
X-Ray Touring, 77-79 Great Eastern St, London EC2A 3HU, England
**Deal, Lance** — Track Athlete
845 Park Ave, Eugene OR 97404, USA
**DeAlmeida, Joaquim** — Actor
A P A Talent/Literary Agency, 405 S Beverly Dr, #300, Beverly Hills CA 90212 USA
**Dean, Barry** — Ice Hockey Player
315 Marsh St, Maple Creek SK S0N 1N0, Canada
**Dean, Billy** — Singer, Songwriter
Graham Brothers Entertainment, 6999 E Highway 80, Odessa TX 79762, USA
**Dean, Christopher** — Ice Dancer
4575 Governors Point, Colorado Springs CO 80906, USA
**Dean, David** — Football Coach
Valdosta State University, Athletic Dept, Valdosta GA 31698, USA
**Dean, Frederick G (Fred)** — Football Player, Coach
3911 Whitchurch Dr, Houston TX 77066, USA
**Dean, Fredrick R (Fred)** — Football Player
2411 Highway 3061, Ruston LA 71270, USA
**Dean, Graham** — Artist
Lacey Gallery, 1 Crawford Passage, Bay Street, London EC1R 3DP, England
**Dean, Hazell** — Singer, Songwriter
7 Kentish Town Road, London NW1 8N4, England
**Dean, Ira** — Singer (Trick Pony)
Warner Bros Records, 20 Music Square East, Nashville TN 37203 USA
**Dean, John G** — Diplomat
Chalet Crettaz, BP 1318, 1936 Verbier Valais, Switzerland
**Dean, John W, III** — Watergate Figure
9496 Rembert Lane, Beverly Hills CA 90210, USA
**Dean, Kevin** — Ice Hockey Player
1905 Wayzata Blvd, Wayzata MN 55391, USA
**Dean, Kiley** — Singer
Music World Entertainment, 1505 Hadley St, Houston TX 77002, USA
**Dean, Laura** — Choreographer, Composer
Dean Dance & Music Foundation, 552 Broadway, #400, New York NY 10012, USA
**Dean, Stafford R** — Opera Singer
I M G Artists, Burlington Lane, Chiswick, London W4 2TH, England
**Dean, Vernon D** — Football Player
2345 Hemlock St, Beaumont TX 77701, USA
**DeAnda, Paula** — Singer
I C M Partners, 10250 Constellation Blvd, #900, Los Angeles CA 90067 USA

# D

**DeAndrea, John** — Artist
2220 Suncrest Dr, Loveland CO 80537, USA

**Deane, William Patrick** — Governor General, Australia
PO Box 4168, Manu Ka 2603 ACT, Australia

**DeAngelis, Beverly** — Psychiatrist
505 S Beverly Dr, #1017, Beverly Hills CA 90212, USA

**DeAngelis, William R (Billy)** — Basketball Player
14 Pickering Dr, Trenton NJ 08691, USA

**DeAragon, Maria** — Actress
1159 10th Ave, San Diego CA 92101, USA

**Dearborn, Matthew (Matt)** — Producer, Writer
Original Artists, 9465 Wilshire Blvd, #324, Beverly Hills CA 90212

**Deardurff-Schmidt, Deena** — Swimmer
742 Murray Dr, El Cajon CA 92020, USA

**Dearman, John** — Guitarist (LAGQ)
California State University, Music Dept, 18111 Nordhoff St, Northridge CA 91330, USA

**DeArmond, Frank M** — Astronaut
3086 Ravencrest Circle, Prescott AZ 86303, USA

**Deas, Justin** — Actor
I C M Partners, 10250 Constellation Blvd, #900, Los Angeles CA 90067 USA

**D'Eath, Tom** — Boat Racing Driver
435 Bay Road, Mount Dora FL 32757, USA

**Deaton, Brady J** — Educator
University of Missouri, Chancellor's Office, Jesse Hall, Columbia MO 65211, USA

**Deaver, Jeffrey** — Writer
Simon & Schuster, 1230 Ave of Americas, Concourse 1, New York NY 10020 USA

**deAviz, Joao B Cardinal** — Religious Leader
Institutes of Consecrated Life, Piazza Pio XII 3, 00193 Rome, Italy

**DeBankole, Isaach** — Actor
Magrit Polak Mgmt, 1411 Carroll Ave, Los Angeles CA 90026, USA

**DeBarge, Chico** — Singer, Songwriter
Entertainment Artists, 2409 21st Ave S, #100, Nashville TN 10019 USA

**DeBarge, Eldra P (El)** — Singer, Pianist, Songwriter
Universal Attractions, 135 W 26th St, #1200, New York NY 10001 USA

**DeBarge, Kristina** — Singer, Songwriter
Soda Pop/Def Soul Records, 825 8th Ave, #2700, New York NY 10019, USA

**Debarr, Dennis L (Denny)** — Baseball Player
33843 Juliet Circle, Fremont CA 94555, USA

**Debbie Deb** — Singer
Harmony Artists, 6399 Wilshire Blvd, #914, Los Angeles CA 90048, USA

**Debbouze, Jamel** — Actor
Artmedia, 20 Ave Rapp, 75007 Paris, France

**DeBeaufort, India** — Actress, Singer
Safron Co, 2000 Ave of Stars, #600N, Los Angeles CA 90067, USA

**DeBellevue, Charles B** — Vietnam War Air Force Hero
916 Huntsman Road, Edmond OK 73003, USA

**Debello, James** — Actor
Full Circle Mgmt, 4932 Lankershim Blvd, #202, North Hollywood CA 91601, USA

**Debenedet, Nelson** — Ice Hockey Player
38142 N Vista Dr, Livonia MI 48152, USA

**DeBenning, Burr** — Actor
4235 Kingfisher Road, Calabasas CA 91302, USA

**DeBerg, Steve** — Football Player, Coach
17920 Simms Road, Odessa FL 33556, USA

**Debie, Benoit** — Cinematographer
I C M Partners, 10250 Constellation Blvd, #900, Los Angeles CA 90067 USA

**Debison, Aselin (Azi)** — Singer
S L Feldman Mgmt, 1505 W 2nd Ave, #200, Vancouver BC V6H 3Y4, Canada

**DeBlaeij, Merel** — Field Hockey Player
Larensche Mixed Hockey Club, Postbus 105, 1250 Laren AC, Netherlands

**DeBlois, Dean** — Director, Writer
W M E Entertainment, 9601 Wilshire Blvd, #300, Beverly Hills CA 90210 USA

**Deblois, Lucien** — Ice Hockey Player
407-350 Boul Graham, Mont Royal QC H3P 2C8, Canada

**Debney, John** — Composer
First Artists Mgmt, 4764 Park Granada, #210, Calabasas CA 91302 USA

**DeBoer, Nicole** — Actress
Kritzer Levine Wilkins Griffin, 11872 La Grange Ave, #100, Los Angeles CA 90025 USA

**DeBoer, Peter** — Ice Hockey Coach
New Jersey Devils, Arena, 50 State Route 120, East Rutherford NJ 07073 USA

**DeBont, Jan** — Cinematographer, Director
Blue Tulip Productions, 2202 Main St, Santa Monica CA 90405, USA

**DeBoor, Carl-Wilhelm R** — Mathematician
University of Wisconsin, Mathematics Dept, Madison WI 53706, USA

**Debre, Michel** — Prime Minister, France
20 Rue Jacob, 75006 Paris, France

**DeBruijn, Inge** — Swimmer
Alsemhof 6, 2991 Barendrecht HA, Netherlands

**DeBrunhoff, Laurent** — Writer, Illustrator (Babar)
Mary Ryan Gallery, 527 W 26th St, New York NY 10001, USA

**Debrusk, Louie** — Ice Hockey Player
27502 N 84th Dr, Peoria AZ 85383, USA

**DeBurgh, Chris** — Singer, Songwriter
Kenny Thomson Mgmt, 754 Fulham Road, London SW6 5SH, England

**Deby Itno, Idriss** — President, Chad; Army General
President's Office, Presidential Palace, BP 74, N'Djamena, Chad

**DeCaestecker, Iain** — Actor
W M E Entertainment, 9601 Wilshire Blvd, #300, Beverly Hills CA 90210 USA

**DeCamilli, Pietro V** — Biologist
Yale University Medical School, Cell Biology Dept, New Haven CT 06512, USA

**DeCarlo, Arthur A (Art), Jr** — Football Player
9030 Manordale Lane, Ellicott City MD 21042, USA

**DeCarlo, Mark** — Actor
3292 Carse Dr, Los Angeles CA 90068, USA

**Decarnin, Christophe** — Fashion Designer
Balmain, 44 Rue Francois, 75008 Paris, France

DeAndrea - Decarnin

**DeCaro, Frank** — Actor, Comedian
Sirius, 1221 Ave of Americas, #1900, New York NY 10020, USA
**DeCasabianca, Camille** — Actress
Artmedia, 20 Ave Rapp, 75007 Paris, France
**DeCastella, F Robert** — Track Athlete
Smart Start, PO Box 3808, Weston ACT 2611, Australia
**DeCastro, David** — Football Player
Pittsburgh Steelers, 3400 S Water St, Pittsburgh PA 15203 USA
**DeCastro, Manuel M Cardinal** — Religious Leader
Apostolic Penitentiary, Palazzo della Cancelleria 1, 00186 Rome, Italy
**DeCercio, Tom** — Director
Farah Films Mgmt, 11640 Mayfield, #208, Brentwood CA 90049, USA
**DeCinces, Douglas V (Doug)** — Baseball Player
124 Riviera Way, Laguna Beach CA 92651, USA
**Decker, Brooklyn** — Model, Actress
Place Model Mgmt, Am Felde 29, 22765 Hamburg, Germany
**Declan** — Singer, Guitarist, Pianist
PO Box 161, Market Rasen LN8 6EX, England
**Decoder** — Drum, Bass Producer (Kosheen)
Moskaha Mgmt, PO Box 102, London E15 2HH, England
**DeConcini, Dennis** — Senator, AZ
6014 Chesterbrook Road, McLean VA 22101, USA
**DeCosta, Sara** — Ice Hockey Player
200 Cowesett Green Dr, Warwick RI 02886, USA
**DeCoster, Roger** — Motorcycle Racing Rider
M C Sports, 1919 Torrance Blvd, Torrance CA 90501, USA
**DeCrane, Alfred C, Jr** — Businessman
30 Wax Myrtle Way, Vero Beach FL 32963, USA
**Decrem, Bart** — Educator, Social Activist
Tapulous, 854 High St, Palo Alto CA 94301, USA
**Decter, Midge** — Writer, Journalist
120 E 81st St, New York NY 10028, USA
**Dedes, Spero** — Sportscaster
N F L Network, 10950 Washington Blvd, #100, Culver City CA 90232 USA
**Dedkov, Anatoli I** — Cosmonaut
Cosmonaut Training Center, Star City, 141160 Zvezdny Gorodok, Moscow Oblast, Russia
**Dee, Donald M (Don)** — Basketball Player
7924 N Pennsylvania Ave, Kansas City MO 64118, USA
**Dee, Joey** — Singer
Universal Attractions, 135 W 26th St, #1200, New York NY 10001 USA
**Dee, Kiki** — Singer, Songwriter
Alan Cottam Agency, 19 Charles St, Lancashire Wigam WN1 2BP, England
**Dee, Ruby** — Actress
44 Cortland Ave, New Rochelle NY 10801, USA
**Dee, Sally** — Golfer
3508 W Barcelona St, Tampa FL 33629, USA
**Dee, Wanda** — Singer, Songwriter
Universal Attractions, 135 W 26th St, #1200, New York NY 10001 USA
**Deeb, Gary** — TV Critic
Chicago Sun-Times, Editorial Dept, 401 N Wabash Ave, Chicago IL 60611 USA
**Deeley, Catherine E (Cat)** — Actress, DJ, Model
Maydew & Golenberg, 8383 Wilshire Blvd, #1050, Beverly Hills CA 90211, USA
**Deeley, Justin** — Actor
Arlook Group, 205 S Beverly Dr, #209, Beverly Hills CA 90212, USA
**Deemer, Audrey** — Baseball Player
4401 Country Club Dr, #30, Steubenville OH 43953, USA
**Deen, Paula H** — Chef, Restaurateur, Writer
102 W Congress St, Savannah GA 31401, USA
**Deep Roy** — Actor
C E S D, 10635 Santa Monica Blvd, #130, Los Angeles CA 90025 USA
**Deer, Ada E** — Government Official
2537 Mutchler Road, Fitchburg WI 53711, USA
**Deer, Robert G (Rob)** — Baseball Player
22217 N 78th St, Scottsdale AZ 85255, USA
**Deering, John** — Editorial Cartoonist
6701 Westover Dr, Little Rock AR 72207, USA
**Deery, Tom** — Football Player
49 Yale Square, Morton PA 19070, USA
**Dees, Archie W** — Basketball Player
4405 N Hillview Dr, Bloomington IN 47408, USA
**Dees, Charles H (Charlie)** — Baseball Player
1064 Allison Woods Court, Lawrenceville GA 30043, USA
**Dees, Morris S, Jr** — Attorney, Civil Rights Activist
Southern Poverty Law Center, PO Box 548, Montgomery AL 36101, USA
**Dees, Rick** — Entertainer, Singer
Dees Entertainment, 3601 W Olive St, #675, Burbank CA 91505, USA
**Deese, Derrick** — Football Player
PO Box 3356, Cerritos CA 90703, USA
**Deezen, Eddie** — Actor
Coolwaters Productions, 10061 Riverside Dr, Box 531, Toluca Lake CA 91602 USA
**Deezer D** — Actor, Rap Artist
Acme Talent Agency, 4727 Wilshire Blvd, #333, Los Angeles CA 90010, USA
**Def Jef** — Rap Artist
Turner Accountancy, 13245 Riverside Dr, #330, Sherman Oaks CA 91423, USA
**DeFanti, Sylvia** — Actress
Fox & Gould Mgmt, Via Arenula 29, 00186 Rome, Italy
**DeFanti, Thomas A (Tom)** — Inventor (Cave Electronic Visualization)
University of Illinois, Electronic Visualization Laboratory, 842 W Taylor St, Chicago IL 60607, USA
**DeFelitta, Raymond** — Director, Writer
Paradigm Agency, 360 N Crescent Dr, North Building, Beverly Hills CA 90210 USA
**DeFer, Kaylee** — Actress
Innovative Artists, 1505 10th St, Santa Monica CA 90401 USA
**DeFerran, Gil** — Auto Racing Driver
524 Royal Plaza Dr, Fort Lauderdale FL 33301, USA
**DeFilippo, Jacy** — Actress
C E S D, 10635 Santa Monica Blvd, #130, Los Angeles CA 90025 USA

# D

DeFrance, Cecile                                         Actress
Margrit Polak Mgmt, 1920 Hillhurst, #405, Los Angeles CA 90027, USA
DeFranceschi, Alexandre          Editor
I C M Partners, 10250 Constellation Blvd, #900, Los Angeles CA 90067 USA
DeFrancisco, Joseph E (Joe)      Army General
1201 N Nash St, #203, Arlington VA 22209, USA
DeFranco, Buddy          Jazz Clarinetist
978 Colorado Ave, #A, Whitefish MT 59937, USA
DeFrank, Joe        Harness Racing Official
PO Box 655, Lake Pleasant NY 12108, USA
DeFreitas, Eric               Bowler
175 W 12th St, New York NY 10011, USA
DeGale, James                Boxer
Amateur Boxing Assn, National Sports Centre, London SE19 2B8, England
DeGarmo, Diana K    Singer, Actress, Songwriter
Mauldin Brand Agency, 1280 W Peachtree St, #300, Atlanta GA 30309, USA
DeGarmo, Todd    Architect, Interior Designer
Studios Architecture, 1625 M St NW, Washington DC 20036, USA
DeGeneres, Ellen      Actress, Comedienne
I C M Partners, 10250 Constellation Blvd, #900, Los Angeles CA 90067 USA
Degerick, Michael A (Mike)      Baseball Player
2702 Lake Osborne Dr, Lake Worth FL 33461, USA
DeGiorgi, Salvatore Cardinal      Religious Leader
Curia Archivescovile, Corso Vittorio Emanuele 461, 90134 Palermo, Italy
DeGivenchy, Hubert T      Fashion Designer
3 Ave George V, 75008 Paris, France
Degler, Carl N            Historian
907 Mears Court, Stanford CA 94305, USA
Degout, Stephane        Opera Singer
I M G Artists, Hogarth Business Park, Chiswick, London W4 2TH, England
DeGouw, Jessica           Actress
R G M Artist, 64-76 Kippax St, #202, Surry Hills NSW 2010, Australia
DeGraw, Gavin      Singer, Songwriter
C E S D, 257 Park Ave S, #950, New York NY 10010 USA
Degray, Dale      Ice Hockey Player
Owen Sound Attack, Box 1420 Station Main, Owen Sound ON N4K 6T5, Canada
DeHaan, Dane             Actor
Creative Artists Agency, 2000 Ave of Stars, #100, Los Angeles CA 90067 USA
Dehaene, Jean-Luc J M    Prime Minister, Belgium
Berkendallaan 52, 1800 Vilvoorde, Belgium
Dehart, Richard A (Rick)      Baseball Player
811 NE Wabash Ave, Topeka KS 66616, USA
DeHaven, Gloria          Actress
2223 W San Miguel Ave, North Las Vegas NV 89032, USA
DeHavilland, Olivia         Actress
BP 156-16, 75764 Paris Cedex 16, France
Dehmelt, Hans G    Nobel Physics Laureate
1600 43rd Ave E, #211, Seattle WA 98112, USA
Dehner, Dorothy           Artist
33 5th Ave, New York NY 10003, USA
DeHomem Christo, Guy-Manuel   Musician (Daft Punk)
Clintons, 55 Drury Lane, Covent Garden, London WC2B 5RZ, England
Deibert, Charles (Larry)    Vietnam War Army Hero
201 NE Saizman Road, Corbett OR 97019, USA
Deidel, James L (Jim)      Baseball Player
14312 Wright Way, Broomfield CO 80023, USA
Deighton, Leonard C (Len)        Writer
Fairymount, Blackrock, Dundalk, County Louth, Ireland
Deisenhofer, Johann    Nobel Chemistry Laureate
3860 Echo Brook Lane, Dallas TX 75229, USA
Deitch, Donna           Director
Paradigm Agency, 360 N Crescent Dr, North Building, Beverly Hills CA 90210 USA
Deja, Andreas          Animator
Disney Animation, PO Box 10200, Orlando FL 32830, USA
DeJager, Cornelis         Astronomer
Zonnenburg 1, 352 NL Utrecht, Netherlands
DeJesus, Ivan        Baseball Player
14608 Velleux Dr, Orlando FL 32837, USA
DeJesus, Wanda           Actress
McGowan Mgmt, 8733 W Sunset Blvd, #103, West Hollywood CA 90069, USA
DeJohnette, Jack    Jazz Drummer, Composer
Silver Hollow Road, Willow NY 12495, USA
DeJong, Bob          Speed Skater
Drechtlaan 131, 2451 Leimuiden CL, Netherlands
DeJong, Pierre          Geneticist
Lawrence Livermore Laboratory, 7000 East St, Livermore CA 94550, USA
DeJonge, Peter           Writer
Little Brown, 3 Center Plaza, #100, Boston MA 02108 USA
DeJongh, John P, Jr    Governor, Virgin Islands
Governor's Office, 21-2 Kongens Gade, Charlotte Amalie, Saint Thomas VI 00802 USA
DeJordy, Denis E      Ice Hockey Player
472 Chemin Des-Patriotes, Saint Charles QC J0L 2G0, Canada
DeJurnett, Charles R      Football Player
1355 Heritage Court, Escondido CA 92027, USA
Dekker, Thomas           Actor
Schiff Co, 9200 Sunset Blvd, #430, West Hollywood CA 90232 USA
DeKlerk, Albert    Concert Organist, Composer
Crayenesterlaan 22, 2012 Haarlem DK, Netherlands
DeKlerk, Frederik W   Nobel Laureate; President, South Africa
DeKlerk Foundation, PO Box 15785, Panorama, Cape Town 7506, South Africa
Deklin, Mark           Actor
Michael Black Mgmt, 9701 Wilshire Blvd, #1000, Beverly Hills CA 90212, USA
DeKnight, Steven S      Producer, Writer
Creative Artists Agency, 2000 Ave of Stars, #100, Los Angeles CA 90067 USA
DeLaBilliere, Peter    Army General, England
Naval & Military Club, 4 Saint James's Square, London SW1Y 4JU, England

DeFrance - DeLaBilliere

**Delacote, Jacques** — Conductor
Dr Hilbert Maximilianstr 22, 80539 Munich, Germany
**DeLaCruz, Rosie** — Model
Wilhelmina Models, 300 Park Ave S, #200, New York NY 10010 USA
**DeLaFuente, Cristian** — Actor
Abrams Artists, 9200 W Sunset Blvd, #1125, West Hollywood CA 90069 USA
**DeLaFuente, Marian** — Commentator
Latin World Entertainment, 2601 S Bayshore Dr, #235, Miami FL 33133, USA
**DelaGarza, Alana** — Actress
Brillstein Entertainment Partners, 9150 Wilshire Blvd, #350, Beverly Hills CA 90212 USA
**Delahoussay, Edward (Eddie)** — Thoroughbred Racing Jockey
1024 S 4th Ave, Arcadia CA 91006, USA
**Delahoussaye, Ryan** — Violinist (Blue October)
Rainmaker Artists, PO Box 551665, Dallas TX 75355, USA
**DeLaHoya, Oscar** — Boxer
Golden Boy Promotions, 626 Wilshire Blvd, #350, Los Angeles CA 90017, USA
**DeLaHoz, Miguel A (Mike)** — Baseball Player
PO Box 441233, Miami FL 33144, USA
**DeLaHuerta, Paz** — Actress
T C A/Jed Root, 9220 Sunset Blvd, #315, Los Angeles CA 90069, USA
**Delahunt, William D (Bill)** — Representative, MA
Prime Policy Group LLP, 1110 Vermont Ave NW, #1000, Washington DC 20005, USA
**Delainey, Gary** — Cartoonist (Bub Slug, Betty)
United Feature Syndicate, PO Box 5610, Cincinnati OH 45201 USA
**Delaire, Suzy** — Actress, Singer
46 Rue de Varenne, 75007 Paris, France
**DeLaMaza, Roland** — Baseball Player
28533 Silverking Trial, Santa Clarita CA 91390, USA
**DeLamielleure, Joseph M (Joe)** — Football Player
7818 Ridgeloch Place, Charlotte NC 28226, USA
**DeLancey, William J, III** — Businessman
200 Public Square, #1950, Cleveland OH 44114, USA
**DeLancie, John** — Actor
S D B Partners, 1801 Ave of Stars, #902, Los Angeles CA 90067 USA
**Delaney, Frank** — Writer
Random House, 1745 Broadway, #1800, New York NY 10019 USA
**Delaney, Jeffrey J (Jeff)** — Football Player
215 Village Green Dr, Canonsburg PA 15317, USA
**Delaney, Kim** — Actress, Model
Gersh Agency, 9465 Wilshire Blvd, #600, Beverly Hills CA 90212 USA
**Delaney, Simon** — Actor, Writer
Lorraine Brennan Mgmt, Greenmount Industrial Estate, #22, Harold's Cross, Dublin 6, Ireland
**Delano, Diane** — Actress
Abrams Artists, 9200 W Sunset Blvd, #1125, West Hollywood CA 90069 USA
**Delano, Robert B** — Association Executive
American Farm Bureau, 1501 E Woodfield Road, #300W, Schaumburg IL 60173, USA
**Delany, Dana** — Actress
United Talent Agency, U T A Plaza, 9336 Civic Center Dr, Beverly Hills CA 90210 USA
**Delany, Samuel R** — Writer
Vintage Books, 1745 Broadway, New York NY 10019 USA
**DeLap, Tony** — Artist, Sculptor
225 Jasmine St, Corona del Mar CA 92625, USA
**DeLaParra, Alondra** — Conductor
I M G Artists, Hogarth Business Park, Chiswick, London W4 2TH, England
**DeLaPena, Gemmenne** — Actress
Corsa Agency, 11704 Wilshire Blvd, #204, Los Angeles CA 90025 90025, USA
**DelArco, Jonathan** — Actor
S D B Partners, 1801 Ave of Stars, #902, Los Angeles CA 90067 USA
**Delarme, Julie** — Actress
Artmedia, 20 Ave Rapp, 75007 Paris, France
**DeLaRocha, Zack** — Singer (Rage Against the Machine)
Creative Artists Agency, 2000 Ave of Stars, #100, Los Angeles CA 90067 USA
**DeLaRosa, Evelyn** — Opera Singer
Dorothy Cone Artists, 150 W 55th St, New York NY 10019, USA
**DeLaRosa, Pedro M** — Auto Racing Driver
P D L R, Pedro de la Creu, 08017 Barcelona, Spain
**DeLaSalle, Lise** — Concert Pianist
Frank Salomon, 121 W 27th St, #703, New York NY 10001 USA
**Delasin, Dorothy** — Golfer
20 Longview Dr, Daly City CA 94015, USA
**DeLaTour, Frances** — Actress
Independent Talent Group, 40 Whitfield St, London W1T 2RH, England
**Delaughter, Tim** — Singer, Musician (Polyphonic Spree)
Gorfaine/Schwartz, 4111 W Alameda Ave, #509, Burbank CA 91505 USA
**DeLaurentiis, Giada** — Chef, Writer
W M E Entertainment, 9601 Wilshire Blvd, #300, Beverly Hills CA 90210 USA
**DeLautour, David** — Actor, Writer, Producer
Karen Kay Mgmt, 2/25 Sale St, Freemans Bay, Auckland 1010, New Zealand
**Delavan, Mark** — Opera Singer
Columbia Artists Mgmt Inc, 1790 Broadway, #702, New York NY 10019 USA
**Delbanco, Nicholas** — Writer
Warner Books, 1271 Ave of Americas, New York NY 10020 USA
**Delbonnel, Bruno** — Cinematographer
United Talent Agency, U T A Plaza, 9336 Civic Center Dr, Beverly Hills CA 90210 USA
**DelBuono, Brett** — Actor
C E S D, 10635 Santa Monica Blvd, #130, Los Angeles CA 90025 USA
**DelCarlo, John** — Singer
Opus 3 Artists, 470 Park Ave S, #900N, New York NY 10016 USA
**Delcarmen, Manny** — Baseball Player
68 Surrey Lane, East Bridgewater MA 02333, USA
**DelCastillo Galvez, Jorge A A** — Prime Minister, Peru
Premier's Office, Urb Corpac, Calle 1 Oeste, San Isidro, Lima 27, Peru
**DelCastillo, Kate** — Actress
Creative Artists Agency, 2000 Ave of Stars, #100, Los Angeles CA 90067 USA
**DeLeeuw, Ton** — Composer
Costeruslaan 4, 1217 Hilversum JT, Netherlands

**Delehanty, Hugh** — Editor
A A R P Publications, Editorial Dept, 601 E St NW, Washington DC 20049, USA

**DeLeo, Dean** — Guitarist (Stone Temple Pilots)
Q Prime, 729 7th Ave, #1600, New York NY 10019 USA

**DeLeo, Robert** — Bassist (Stone Temple Pilots), Composer
Q Prime, 729 7th Ave, #1600, New York NY 10019 USA

**Deleon, Luis A** — Baseball Player
120 Calle San Antonio, Bda Clausells, Ponce PR 00730, USA

**DeLeone, Thomas D (Tom)** — Football Player
PO Box 681472, Park City UT 84068, USA

**Delerm, Graziella** — Actress
Artmedia, 20 Ave Rapp, 75007 Paris, France

**Delfino, Carlos F** — Basketball Player
Milwaukee Bucks, Bradley Center, 1001 N 4th St, #2, Milwaukee WI 53203 USA

**Delgado, Alvaro** — Artist
Biarritz 5, Parque de las Avenidas, 28028 Madrid, Spain

**Delgado, Carlos J** — Baseball Player
9 Repto Ramos Bo Borinquen, Aguadilla PR 00603, USA

**Delgado, Emilio** — Actor
About Artists Agency, 1650 Broadway, #1406, New York NY 10019, USA

**Delgado, Isaac** — Singer, Orchestra Leader
Second Octave Talent, 720 South Point Blvd, #A200, Petaluma CA 94954, USA

**DelGreco, Albert L (Al), Jr** — Football Player
1012 Little Turtle Circle, Birmingham AL 35242, USA

**DelGreco, Robert G (Bobby)** — Baseball Player
625 Southview Dr, Pittsburgh PA 15226, USA

**Delhomme, Jake C** — Football Player
1459 Mills Highway, Breaux Bridge LA 70517, USA

**D'Elia, Bill** — Director, Producer, Writer
W M E Entertainment, 9601 Wilshire Blvd, #300, Beverly Hills CA 90210 USA

**D'Elia, Chris** — Actor, Writer
United Talent Agency, U T A Plaza, 9336 Civic Center Dr, Beverly Hills CA 90210 USA

**Deligne, Pierre R** — Mathematician
Institute for Advanced Study, Math School, Einstein Dr, Princeton NJ 08540, USA

**DeLillo, Don** — Writer
57 Rossmore Ave, Bronxville NY 10708, USA

**DeLint, Derek** — Actor
Features Creative Mgmt, Entrepotdok 76A, 101 Amsterdam AD, Netherlands

**DeLisle, Paul** — Bassist (Smash Mouth), Actor
Interscope Records, 2220 Colorado Ave, Santa Monica CA 90404 USA

**Delk, Denny** — Actor
Innovative Artists, 235 Park Ave S, #700, New York NY 10003, USA

**Delk, Joan** — Golfer
830 Forest Path Lane, Alpharetta GA 30022, USA

**Delk, Tony L** — Basketball Player
1843 Glenhill Dr, Lexington KY 40502, USA

**Dell, Charlie** — Actor
Scott Stander Assoc, 4533 Van Nuys Blvd, #401, Sherman Oaks CA 91403 USA

**Dell, Donald L** — Tennis Player, Attorney
Blue Entertainment, 333 E Main St, #200, Louisville KY 40202 USA

**Dell, Michael S** — Businessman
Dell Inc, 1 Dell Way, Round Rock TX 78682, USA

**Dellacqua, Casey** — Tennis Player
107 Alana Road, Gibson WA 6448, Australia

**Dellanos, Myrka** — Actress
United Talent Agency, U T A Plaza, 9336 Civic Center Dr, Beverly Hills CA 90210 USA

**DelleDonne, Elena** — Basketball Player
Chicago Sky, 20 W Kinzie St, #1010, Chicago IL 60654 USA

**Dellenbach, Jeffrey A (Jeff)** — Football Player
1002 Pine Branch Dr, Weston FL 33326, USA

**Dellinger, Walter** — Educator, Attorney
Duke University, Law School, Durham NC 27706, USA

**Dellinger, William (Bill)** — Track Athlete, Coach
1993 Fircrest Dr, Eugene OR 97403, USA

**Dell'Orefice, Carmen** — Model
Ford Models Inc, 111 5th Ave, #900, New York NY 10003 USA

**Dellucci, David M** — Baseball Player
5512 Summer Lake Dr, Baton Rouge LA 70817, USA

**Dellums, Ronald V (Ron)** — Representative, CA
658 Santa Ray Ave, Oakland,CA 94610, USA

**Delly, Emmanuel III Cardinal** — Religious Leader
Patriarat Chaldeen Catholique, PO Box 6112, Al-Mansouri, Baghdad, Iraq

**DelNegro, Vincent J (Vinny)** — Basketball Player, Coach
58 Bagnell Dr, Pembroke MA 02359, USA

**DeLoach, Nikki** — Singer (Innosense), Actress
R C A Records, 8750 Wilshire Blvd, Beverly Hills CA 90211 USA

**Delock, Ivan M (Ike)** — Baseball Player
433 Cypress Way E, Naples FL 34110, USA

**Delon, Alain** — Actor
Alain Delon Diffusion, 12 Rue Saint-Victor, 1206 Geneva, Switzerland

**Delon, Anthony** — Actor
Intertalent, 5 Rue Clement-Marot, 75008 Paris, France

**DeLong, Keith A** — Football Player
1850 Greywell Road, Knoxville TN 37922, USA

**DeLong, Michael P** — Marine Corps General
Deputy Commander, US Central Command, MacDill Air Force Base, Tampa FL 33621, USA

**Delong, Nathan J (Nate)** — Basketball Player
PO Box 485, Hayward WI 54843, USA

**DeLonge, Tom** — Singer, Guitarist, Songwriter
1665 Neptune Ave, Encinitas CA 92024, USA

**DeLorenzo, Michael** — Actor
Geddes Agency, 8430 Santa Monica Blvd, #201, West Hollywood CA 90069 USA

**Delorme, Daniele** — Actress
Gueville Productions, 16 Rue de Marignan, 75008 Paris, France

**Delorme, Ronald (Ron)** — Ice Hockey Player
94 Ravine Dr, Port Moody BC V3H 4T8, Canada

**Delors, Jacques L J** — Government Official, France
Notre Europe Assn, 41 Blvd des Capucines, 75002 Paris, France
**DeLosReyes, Kamar** — Actor
Talent Works, 3500 W Olive Ave, #1400, Burbank CA 91505 USA
**DeLosSantos, Becky** — Model
Playboy Promotions, 2706 Media Center Dr, Los Angeles CA 90065 USA
**DeLosSantos, Marisa** — Writer
Hudson Street Press, 375 Hudson St, Basement 3, New York NY 10014, USA
**DeLosSantos, Valerio L** — Baseball Player
9838 N 119th Place, Scottsdale AZ 85259, USA
**Delpeyrat, Scali** — Actor
U B B A, 6 Rue de Braque, 75003 Paris, France
**DelPiero, Alessandro** — Soccer Player
F C Juventus, Corso Galilo Ferrarisi 32, 10128 Turin, Italy
**Delpino, Robert L** — Football Player
9569 Calle Del Casa, Riverside CA 92503, USA
**DelPonte, Carla** — Attorney
War Crimes Tribunal, Churchilluplein 1, 2517 The Hague JW, Netherlands
**DelPorto, Juan Martin** — Tennis Player
Association of Tennis Professionals, Palliser Road, London W14 9EB, England
**Delpy, Julie** — Actress, Director
Markham Froggatt Irwin, Julian House, 4 Windmill St, London W1P 1HF, England
**DelRey, Lana** — Singer, Songwriter
Creative Artists Agency, 2000 Ave of Stars, #100, Los Angeles CA 90067 USA
**DelRio, David** — Actor
Paradigm Agency, 360 N Crescent Dr, North Building, Beverly Hills CA 90210 USA
**DelRio, Jack** — Football Player, Coach
2708 Coliseum St, New Orleans LA 70130, USA
**Delsing, Jay** — Golfer
14020 Woods Mill Cove Dr, Chesterfield MO 63017, USA
**Delson, Brad** — Guitarist (Linkin Park)
Artist Group International, 150 E 58th St, #1900, New York NY 10155, USA
**Delson, Rudolph** — Writer
Houghton Mifflin Harcourt, 215 Park Ave S, #1200, New York NY 10003 USA
**DelToro, Benicio** — Actor
Creative Artists Agency, 2000 Ave of Stars, #100, Los Angeles CA 90067 USA
**DelToro, Guillermo** — Director, Writer
W M E Entertainment, 9601 Wilshire Blvd, #300, Beverly Hills CA 90210 USA
**DelTredici, David** — Composer
463 West St, #G121, New York NY 10014, USA
**Deluc, Xavier** — Actor
A A C Agence Artistique, 10 Ave George V, 75009 Paris, France
**DeLuca, Fred** — Businessman
1924 Sunrise Key Blvd, Fort Lauderdale FL 33304, USA
**DeLuca, Rocco** — Singer, Dobro Player
Primary Talent International, 10-11 Jockey's Fields, London WC1R 4BN, England
**DeLucas, Lawrence J** — Astronaut
909 19th St S, Birmingham AL 35205, USA
**DeLucca, Gerald D (Jerry)** — Football Player
27 Pulaski St, Peabody MA 01960, USA
**DeLucchi, Michele** — Architect
Via Cenisio 40, 20154 Milan, Italy
**DeLucia, Paco** — Jazz Guitarist
Monterey International, 200 W Superior St, #202, Chicago IL 60654 USA
**Delugg, Milton** — Accordionist, Band Leader, Composer
2740 Claray Dr, Los Angeles CA 90077, USA
**DeLuise, Michael** — Actor, Director, Producer
Stone Manners Salners, 9911 W Pico Blvd, #1400, Los Angeles CA 90035 USA
**DelVecchi, Mauro** — Army General, Italy
Senato Della Repubblica, Piazza Madama, 00196 Rome, Italy
**Delvecchio, Alexander P (Alex)** — Ice Hockey Player
Pen Pro, 2602 Stoodleigh Dr, Rochester Hills MI 48309, USA
**Demaestri, Joseph P (Joe)** — Baseball Player
50 Fairway Dr, Novato CA 94949, USA
**DeMaistre, Xavier** — Concert Harpist
Konzertdirektion Schmid, Konigstra 36, 30175 Hannover, Germany
**DeMaizire, K E Thomas** — Government Official, Germany
Bundesministerium der Verteidigung, Hardthohe, 53125 Bonn, Germany
**DeMaiziere, Lothar** — Prime Minister, East Germany
Buro Berlin Mitte, Chausseestr 128A, 10115 Berlin, Germany
**Demarchelier, Patrick** — Photographer
162 W 21st St, New York NY 10011, USA
**DeMarco, Albert (Ab), Jr** — Ice Hockey Player
211 Regal Road, North Bay ON P1B 8G4, Canada
**DeMarco, Jean** — Sculptor
Cervaro 03044, Prov-Frosinore, Italy
**DeMarco, Robert A (Bob)** — Football Player
13055 Midfield Terrace, Saint Louis MO 63146, USA
**DeMarco, Tony** — Boxer
150 Staniford St, #709, Boston MA 02114, USA
**DeMarcus, Jay** — Singer, Bassist (Rascal Flatts)
Turner & Nichols, 49 Music Square W, #500, Nashville TN 37203, USA
**Demarest, Arthur A** — Archaeologist
Vanderbilt University, Anthropology Dept, Nashville TN 37235, USA
**Demarie, John E** — Football Player
416 Greenway St, Lake Charles LA 70605, USA
**Demars, Bruce** — Navy Admiral
41 Manters Point Road, Plymouth MA 02360, USA
**Demars, William L (Billy)** — Baseball Player
770 Island Way, #305, Clearwater Beach FL 33767, USA
**DeMartini, Warren J (Torch)** — Guitarist (Ratt)
2666 Carmar Dr, Los Angeles CA 90046, USA
**DeMartino, Jules** — Drummer (Ting Tings)
Paradigm Agency, 404 W Franklin St, Monterey CA 93940 USA
**DeMatteo, Drea** — Actress
Gersh Agency, 9465 Wilshire Blvd, #600, Beverly Hills CA 90212 USA

**Dembo, Fennis M** — Basketball Player
430 N Pine St, San Antonio TX 78202, USA
**DeMedeiros, Maria** — Actress
Alsira Garcia-Maroto Talent Agency, Calle de Los Invencibles 8, Bajo, Madrid 28019, Spain
**DeMenezes, Fradique B M** — President, Sao Tome & Principe
President's Office, Pargo do Povo, Sao Tome, Sao Tome & Principe
**DeMent, Iris** — Singer, Songwriter
Nick Ben-Meir, 652 N Doheny Dr, West Hollywood CA 90069, USA
**DeMent, Jack** — Chemist
Oregon Health Care Center, 11325 NE Weidler St, #44, Portland OR 97220, USA
**Dementieva, Elena V** — Tennis Player
Myasnitskaya Str, #6/7, 10100 Moscow, Russia
**DeMerit, Jay** — Soccer Player
Watford F C, Vicarage Stadium, Vicarage Road, Watford, Hertfordshire WD18 0ER, England
**DeMerit, John S** — Baseball Player
550 W Walters St, Port Washington WI 53074, USA
**Demery, Lawrence C (Larry)** — Baseball Player
10407 Pinnacle Ridge Ave, Bakersfield CA 93311, USA
**Demet-Barry, Dede** — Cyclist
2607 Thornbird Place, Boulder CO 80304, USA
**Demeter, Donald L (Don)** — Baseball Player
6240 S Country Club Dr, Oklahoma City OK 73159, USA
**Demetral, Christopher (Chris)** — Actor
J M G Mgmt, 18000 Coastline Dr, #8, Malibu CA 90265, USA
**Demetrios** — Religious Leader
Greek Orthodox Church, 89 E 79th St, #19, New York NY 10075, USA
**Demetrius, Duppy** — Writer
Creative Artists Agency, 2000 Ave of Stars, #100, Los Angeles CA 90067 USA
**Demetz, Peter** — Educator
Rutgers State University, German Dept, 172 College Ave, New Brunswick NJ 08901, USA
**Demeulmeester, Ann** — Fashion Designer
6 Rue Milne Edwards, 75017 Paris, France
**DeMeuron, Pierre** — Pritzker Architectural Laureate
Herzog & DeMeuron Architekten, Rheinschanze 6, 4056 Basel, Switzerland
**Demic, Lawrence C (Larry)** — Basketball Player
680 S Lassen Court, Anaheim CA 92804, USA
**DeMicco, Kirk** — Director, Writer
Gersh Agency, 9465 Wilshire Blvd, #600, Beverly Hills CA 90212 USA
**DeMille, Nelson** — Writer
61 Hilton Ave, #23, Garden City NY 11530, USA
**Demin, Lev S** — Cosmonaut
Cosmonaut Training Center, Star City, 141160 Zvezdny Gorodok, Moscow Oblast, Russia
**Deming, Peter** — Cinematographer
Sandra Marsh Assoc, 9150 Wilshire Blvd, #220, Beverly Hills CA 90212 USA
**DeMita, L Ciriaco** — Prime Minister, Italy
Partito Democrazia Cristiana, Piazza de Gesu 46, 00186 Rome, Italy
**Demme, Jonathan** — Director
Clinico Estetico, 319 Lafayette St, #144, New York NY 10012, USA
**DeMol, Johannes H H (John)** — Producer, Director
Talpa, Zevenend 45-IV, PO Box 154, Laren, Noord Holland 1250 AD, Netherlands
**Demola, Donald J (Don)** — Baseball Player
352 Village Dr, Hauppauge NY 11788, USA
**DeMonaco, James** — Writer, Producer, Director
United Talent Agency, U T A Plaza, 9336 Civic Center Dr, Beverly Hills CA 90210 USA
**Demong, Bill** — Nordic Combined Skier
N Y S E F, Route 86, PO Box 300, Wilmington NY 12997, USA
**Demongeot, Mylene** — Actress
Artmedia, 20 Ave Rapp, 75007 Paris, France
**DeMont, Rick** — Swimmer
84-596 Upena St, Waianae HI 96792, USA
**DeMontebello, Philippe L** — Museum Executive
40 E 94th St, #11G, New York NY 10128, USA
**DeMontreuil, Ricardo** — Director
3 Arts Entertainment, 9460 Wilshire Blvd, #700, Beverly Hills CA 90212 USA
**DeMoraes, Ronaldo (Ron)** — Producer
W M E Entertainment, 9601 Wilshire Blvd, #300, Beverly Hills CA 90210 USA
**DeMornay, Rebecca** — Actress
Binder & Assoc, 1465 Lindacrest Dr, Beverly Hills CA 90210, USA
**DeMoss, Harold R, Jr** — Judge
US Court of Appeals, 515 Rusk Ave, #12015, Houston TX 77002, USA
**Demps, Jeffery (Jeff)** — Track Athlete, Football Player
Tampa Bay Buccaneers, 1 W Buccaneer Place, Tampa FL 33607 USA
**Dempsey, Clint** — Soccer Player
Fulham F C, Craven Cottage, Stevenage Road, London SW6 6HH, England
**Dempsey, George P** — Basketball Player
6945 Cedar Ave, Pennsauken NJ 08109, USA
**Dempsey, J Rikard (Rick)** — Baseball Player
3081 Township Ave, Simi Valley CA 93063, USA
**Dempsey, M Clinton (Clint)** — Soccer Player
New England Revolution, 1 Patriot Place, Foxboro MA 02035 USA
**Dempsey, Martin E** — Army General
Chairman, Joint Chiefs of Staff, Pentagon, Washington DC 20318 USA
**Dempsey, Michael** — Bassist (Cure)
Primary Talent International, 10-11 Jockey's Fields, London WC1R 4BN, England
**Dempsey, Patrick** — Actor
Burstein Co, 15304 Sunset Blvd, #208, Pacific Palisades CA 90272, USA
**Dempsey, Thomas (Tom)** — Football Player
541 Julius Ave, New Orleans LA 70121, USA
**Dempsie, Joseph** — Actor
Troika, 74 Clerkenwell Road, #300, London EC1M 5QA, England
**Dempster, Ryan S** — Baseball Player
3537 N Greenview Ave, Chicago IL 60657, USA
**Demsetz, Harold** — Economist
University of California, Economics Dept, Los Angeles CA 90024, USA
**Demsey, Todd** — Golfer
Gaylord Sports Mgmt, 13845 N Northsight Blvd, #200, Scottsdale AZ 85260 USA

**DeMulder, Kim** — Cartoonist, Illustrator
76 Lafayette Ave, Coxsackie NY 12051, USA
**DeMunn, Jeffrey (Jeff)** — Actor
Davis Spylios Agency, 244 W 54th St, #707, New York NY 10019, USA
**Demuro, Francesco** — Opera Singer
I M G Artists, Hogarth Business Park, Chiswick, London W4 2TH, England
**Demus, Chaka** — Singer (Chaka Demus & Pliers)
Mission Control, City Business Center, Lower Road, London SE16 2XB, England
**Demus, Jorg** — Concert Pianist
Lyra Artists Mgmt, Doblinger Hauptstr 77A/10, 1190 Vienna, Austria
**Demuth, Richard H** — Attorney, Financier
7 Eliot Road, Lexington MA 02421, USA
**Denault, Jim** — Cinematographer
Gersh Agency, 9465 Wilshire Blvd, #600, Beverly Hills CA 90212 USA
**Denberg, Susan** — Model
Playboy Promotions, 2706 Media Center Dr, Los Angeles CA 90065 USA
**Dench, Judi** — Actress
Julian Belfrage, 9 Argyll St, London W1F 7TG, England
**Dencik, David** — Actor
A P A Talent/Literary Agency, 405 S Beverly Dr, #300, Beverly Hills CA 90212 USA
**Deneriaz, Antoine** — Alpine Skier
775 Ave de la Republique, 74300 Cluses, France
**Denes, Agnes C** — Artist
595 Broadway, New York NY 10012, USA
**Deneuve, Catherine** — Actress
Artmedia, 20 Ave Rapp, 75007 Paris, France
**Denevan, William M** — Geographer, Ecologist
University of Wisconsin, Geography Dept, Madison, WI 53706, USA
**Deneve, Stephane** — Conductor
I C M Artists, 40 W 57th St, #1800, New York NY 10019 USA
**Deng Yaping** — Table Tennis Player
International Olympic Committee, Chateau de Vidy, 1007 Lausanne, Switzerland
**Deng, Luol** — Basketball Player
3280 Sunset Trail, Northbrook IL 60062, USA
**Dengler, Carlos** — Bassist (Interpol)
Flowerbooking, 1532 N Milwaukee Ave, #201, Chicago IL 60622, USA
**Denham, Alice** — Model
Playboy Promotions, 2706 Media Center Dr, Los Angeles CA 90065 USA
**Denhardt, David T** — Biologist
Rutgers University, Nelson Biological Laboratories, Piscataway NJ 08855, USA
**DenHerder, Vern W** — Football Player
2342 Riviera Road, Sioux Center IA 51250, USA
**Denicourt, Marianne** — Actress
Artmedia, 20 Ave Rapp, 75007 Paris, France
**DeNiese, Danielle** — Opera Singer
I M G Artists, Hogarth Business Park, Chiswick, London W4 2TH, England
**DeNiro, Robert** — Actor
Stan Rosenfield Assoc, 2029 Century Park E, #1190, Los Angeles CA 90067, USA
**Denis, Catalina** — Actress
A C T 1, 83 Rue Saint Honore, 75001 Paris, France
**Denisof, Alexis** — Actor
A P A Talent/Literary Agency, 405 S Beverly Dr, #300, Beverly Hills CA 90212 USA
**Denisov, Edison V** — Composer
Studentcheskaia 44/28, #35, 121165 Moscow, Russia
**Denisse, Francois-Jean** — Astronomer
48 Rue Monsieur Le Prince, 75006 Paris, France
**Denisyuk, Yuri N** — Optical Engineer
Vavilov Optical Institute, 12 Burzhevaya, 199034 Saint Petersburg, Russia
**Denk, Jeremy** — Concert Pianist
Opus 3 Artists, 470 Park Ave S, #900N, New York NY 10016 USA
**Denman, David** — Actor
Hofflund/Polone, 9465 Wilshire Blvd, #420, Beverly Hills CA 90212 USA
**Dennard, Preston** — Football Player
4545 Greene Ave NW, Albuquerque NM 87114, USA
**Dennard, Robert H** — Inventor (Random Access Memory Cell)
2054 Quaker Ridge Road, Croton-on-Hudson NY 10520, USA
**Dennehy, Brian** — Actor
Susan Smith, 1344 N Wetherly Dr, Los Angeles CA 90069 USA
**Dennen, Brett** — Singer
Mick Mgmt, 35 Washington St, Brooklyn NY 11201, USA
**Dennerlein, Barbara** — Jazz Organist
Tsingtauer Str 66, 81827 Munich, Germany
**Dennett, Daniel C** — Philosopher
20 Ironwood Road, North Andover MA 01845, USA
**Denney, Kyle** — Baseball Player
PO Box 300, Prague OK 74864, USA
**Denney, Ryan C** — Football Player
351 Silver Circle, Alpine UT 84004, USA
**Denning, Blaine** — Basketball Player
1283 NW Bentley Circle, #A, Port Saint Lucie FL 34986, USA
**Dennings, Kat** — Actress
Management 360, 9111 Wilshire Blvd, Beverly Hills CA 90210 USA
**Dennis, Cathy** — Singer
19 Mgmt, Ransomes Dock, 35-37 Parkgate Road, London SW11 4NP, England
**Dennis, Clark** — Golfer
4117 Sarita Dr, Fort Worth TX 76109, USA
**Dennis, Donna F** — Sculptor, Artist
131 Duane St, New York NY 10013, USA
**Dennis, Gabrielle** — Actress
Pantheon Talent Group, 1900 Ave of the Stars, #2840, Los Angeles CA 90064, USA
**Dennis, Guy D** — Football Player
PO Box 2500, Hawthorne FL 32640, USA
**Dennis, James L** — Judge
US Court of Appeals, 600 Camp St, New Orleans LA 70130, USA
**Dennis, Jim** — Harness Racing Driver, Trainer
1810 Little Masters Corner Road, Harrington DE 19952, USA

**D**

| | |
|---|---|
| **Dennis, Mike**<br>American Promotions, 2011 Ferry Ave, #U19, Camden NJ 08104, USA | Singer (Dovells) |
| **Dennis, Norm**<br>1531 Highway 3B, Fruitvale BC V0G 1L0, Canada | Ice Hockey Player |
| **Dennis, Pamela**<br>10 McGuirk Lane, West Orange NJ 7052, USA | Fashion Designer |
| **Dennis, Rowly**<br>H R I Talent, 100 Universal City Plaza, #7152, Universal City CA 91608, USA | Actor |
| **Dennis, Wesley**<br>Mercury Records, 401 Commerce St, #1100, Nashville TN 37219 USA | Singer, Guitarist |
| **Dennison, George M**<br>International Heart Institute Foundation, 500 W Broadway, #350, Missoula MT 59802, USA | Educator |
| **Dennison, Rick S**<br>12322 Overcup Dr, Houston TX 77024, USA | Football Player |
| **Denny, Floyd W, Jr**<br>1 Carolina Meadows, #308, Chapel Hill NC 27517, USA | Pediatrician |
| **Denny, John A**<br>13750 W Colonial Dr, #350, Winter Garden FL 34787, USA | Baseball Player |
| **Denny, Robyn**<br>20/30 Wilds Rents, #4B, London SE1 4QG, England | Artist |
| **DeNooijer, Teun**<br>H C Bloemendaal, Aelbertsbergweg 3, 2061 Bloemendaal AA, Netherlands | Field Hockey Player |
| **Denorfia, Christopher A (Chris)**<br>3468 Longmeadow, Sarasota FL 34235, USA | Baseball Player |
| **Densmore, John**<br>Doors Music, 8899 Beverly Blvd, #812, Los Angeles CA 90048, USA | Drummer (Doors) |
| **Denson, Alfred F (Al)**<br>10838 Naples Court S, Jacksonville FL 32218, USA | Football Player |
| **Denson, Karl**<br>Madison House, 2060 Broadway, #225, Boulder CO 80302, USA | Musician, Singer |
| **Dent, Burnell J**<br>2904 Essex Ave, La Place LA 70068, USA | Football Player |
| **Dent, Catherine**<br>S D B Partners, 1801 Ave of Stars, #902, Los Angeles CA 90067 USA | Actress |
| **Dent, Frederick B**<br>221 Montgomery St, Spartanburg SC 29302, USA | Secretary, Commerce |
| **Dent, Kevin**<br>221 Brannan Ave, Byram MS 39272, USA | Football Player |
| **Dent, Richard L**<br>R L D Resources, 333 N Michigan Ave, #2800, Chicago IL 60601, USA | Football Player, Coach |
| **Dent, Russell E (Bucky)**<br>8895 Indian River Run, Boynton Beach FL 33472, USA | Baseball Player, Manager |
| **Denton, Derek A**<br>816 Irring Road, Toorak VIC 3142, Australia | Physiologist |
| **Denton, James**<br>Paradigm Agency, 360 N Crescent Dr, North Building, Beverly Hills CA 90210 USA | Actor |
| **Denton, Jeremiah A, Jr**<br>531 Thomas Bransby, Williamsburg VA 23185, USA | Senator, AL; WW II Navy Hero |
| **Denton, Randall D (Randy)**<br>515 Sunnybrook Road, Raleigh NC 27610, USA | Basketball Player |
| **Denton, Robert (Bob)**<br>6669 Embarcadero Dr, #7, Stockton CA 95219, USA | Football Player |
| **Denton, Sandi (Pepa)**<br>Richard Walters, PO Box 2789, Toluca Lake CA 91610 USA | Rap Artist (Salt'N'Pepa) |
| **Denton, Will**<br>Gersh Agency, 9465 Wilshire Blvd, #600, Beverly Hills CA 90212 USA | Actor |
| **Denzongapa, Danny**<br>29 Dzongrilla 11th Road, J V P D Scheme, Juhu, Mumbai MB 400049, India | Actor |
| **Deodato, Eumir**<br>Carlini Group, 445 Park Ave, #900, New York NY 10022, USA | Keyboardist, Composer, Producer |
| **Deol, Sunny**<br>Plot 22 11th Road, J V P D Scheme Juhu, Mumbai MS 400049, India | Actor, Director |
| **DeOliveira, Manoel**<br>Rua H Lopes Mendoca, 4010 Porto, Portugal | Director, Writer |
| **DeOre, Bill**<br>Dallas News, Editorial Dept, Communications Center, Dallas TX 75265, USA | Editorial Cartoonist |
| **DeOssie, Steven L (Steve)**<br>835 Chestnut St, North Andover MA 01845, USA | Football Player |
| **DePaiva, James**<br>PO Box 11152, Greenwich CT 06831, USA | Actor |
| **DePaiva, Kassie**<br>CornerStone Talent Agency, 37 W 20th St, #1108, New York NY 10011, USA | Actress, Singer |
| **DePalma, Brian R**<br>I C M Partners, 10250 Constellation Blvd, #900, Los Angeles CA 90067 USA | Director |
| **DePaolis, Luciano**<br>Olympic Committee, Foro Italico, Largo Lauro de Bosis 15, 00135 Rome, Italy | Bobsled Athlete |
| **Depardieu, Gerard X M**<br>Artmedia, 20 Ave Rapp, 75007 Paris, France | Actor |
| **Depardieu, Julie**<br>Cineart, 28 Rue Mogador, 78009 Paris, France | Actress |
| **Depardon, Raymond**<br>18 Bis Rue Henri Barbusse, 75005 Paris, France | Photographer |
| **DePaul, Lynsey**<br>21A Clifftown Road, Southend-on-Sea, Essex SS1 1AB, England | Singer, Songwriter |
| **Depaula, Sean M**<br>2 Thomas St, Derry NH 03038, USA | Baseball Player |
| **DePaulo, Lisa**<br>Tournament Treasures, 2 Muirfield Greens Lane, Lakeway TX 78738, USA | Golfer |
| **Depenbusch, Anna**<br>105 Music GmbH, Hopfensack 20, 20457 Hamburg, Germany | Singer |
| **DePencier, Miranda**<br>United Talent Agency, U T A Plaza, 9336 Civic Center Dr, Beverly Hills CA 90210 USA | Producer |
| **DePeyer, Gervase**<br>42 Tower Bridge Wharf, Saint Katherine's Way, London E1 9UR, England | Concert Clarinetist, Conductor |
| **DePortzamparc, Christian**<br>Architecte D P L G, 1 Rue de l'Aude, 75014 Paris, France | Pritzker Architectural Laureate |

**Dennis - DePortzamparc**

**Depp, John C (Johnny)** — Actor, Director
United Talent Agency, U T A Plaza, 9336 Civic Center Dr, Beverly Hills CA 90210 USA
**Depre, Joe** — Basketball Player
59 Oneida St, Rochester NY 14621, USA
**Depres, Cyril** — Motorcycle Racing Rider
Red Bull GmbH, Am Brunnen 1, 5330 Fuschl am See Austria
**DePriest, Tommy Lee** — Actor
Paceline Entertainment, 12444 Ventura Blvd, #103, Studio City CA 91604 USA
**Deptula, David A** — Air Force General
Deputy CofS, Intelligence & Survelliance, HqUSAF, Pentagon, Washington DC 20310, USA
**DeQuadros, Ciro** — Epidemiologist
Pan American Health Organization, 525 23rd St NW, Washington DC 20037, USA
**Dequenne, Emilie** — Actress
Cineart, 28 Rue Mogador, 78009 Paris, France
**Der, Lambert** — Editorial Cartoonist
Houston Post, Editorial Dept, 4888 Loop Central Dr, #390, Houston TX 77081, USA
**DeRakoff, Alex** — Director, Writer
W M E Entertainment, 9601 Wilshire Blvd, #300, Beverly Hills CA 90210 USA
**DeRavin, Emilie** — Actress
Gersh Agency, 41 Madison Ave, #3301, New York NY 10010 USA
**Derby, C Dean** — Football Player
1682 Corkrum Road, Walla Walla WA 99362, USA
**Derbyshire, Andrew G** — Architect
4 Sunnyfield, Hatfield, Hertsforshire AL9 5DX, England
**Dercho, Natalia** — Opera Singer
I M G Artists, Hogarth Business Park, Chiswick, London W4 2TH, England
**Derek, Bo** — Actress, Model
Guttman Assoc, 118 S Beverly Dr, #201, Beverly Hills CA 90212 USA
**DeRist, Joseph** — Molecular Biologist
University of California Medical Center, 505 Parnassus, San Francisco CA 94122 USA
**Dern, Bruce** — Actor
Pure Arts, 9925 Jefferson Blvd, Culver City CA 90232, USA
**Dern, Laura** — Actress
Creative Artists Agency, 2000 Ave of Stars, #100, Los Angeles CA 90067 USA
**Dernesch, Helga** — Opera Singer
Salztogasse 8/11, 1013 Vienna, Austria
**Dernier, Robert E (Bob)** — Baseball Player
1242 SW Arbormill Terrace, Lees Summit MO 64082, USA
**Deromedi, Herbert** — Football Coach
885 Hiawatha Dr, Mount Pleasant MI 48858, USA
**DeRoo, David C (Dave)** — Bassist (Adema)
Novi Entertainment, PO Box 17077, Beverly Hills CA 90209, USA
**Deroo, Romain** — Actor
Artmedia, 20 Ave Rapp, 75007 Paris, France
**DeRosa, Mark T** — Baseball Player
58 Avalon Way, Waretown NJ 08758, USA
**DeRosier, David** — Biophysicist
27 Chesterfield Road, West Newton MA 02465, USA
**Derosier, Michael** — Drummer (Heart)
Borman Entertainment, 1250 6th St, #401, Santa Monica CA 90401, USA
**DeRossi, Massimo** — Actor
Carol Levi Mgmt, Via Giuseppe Pisanelli 2, 00196 Rome, Italy
**DeRossi, Portia** — Actress, Model
I C M Partners, 10250 Constellation Blvd, #900, Los Angeles CA 90067 USA
**Derow, Peter A** — Publisher
PO Box 534, Bedford NY 10506, USA
**Deroyer, Jean** — Conductor
I M G Artists, Hogarth Business Park, Chiswick, London W4 2TH, England
**DeRozan, DeMar D** — Basketball Player
Toronto Raptors, Air Canada Center, 20 Bay St, Toronto ON M5J 2N8, Canada
**Derr, Kenneth T** — Businessman
Chevron Corp, 6001 Bollinger Canyon Road, San Ramon CA 94583, USA
**Derricks, Cleavant** — Actor
Kazarian/Measures/Ruskin, 11969 Ventura Blvd, #300, Studio City CA 91604 USA
**Derrickson, Scott** — Director, Writer
W M E Entertainment, 9601 Wilshire Blvd, #300, Beverly Hills CA 90210 USA
**D'Errico, Donna** — Model, Actress
Michael Forman Agency, 409 N Camden Drive, #205, Beverly Hills CA 90210, USA
**Derringer, Rick** — Singer, Guitarist
Lustig Talent, PO Box 770850, Orlando FL 32877 USA
**Derrington, C James (Jim)** — Baseball Player
107 Oliver St, West Columbia SC 29169, USA
**Derry, Kathy** — Physical Fitness Instructor
Co-Ed Trainers Club, PO Box 785, New York NY 10101, USA
**Dersch, Hans** — Swimmer
7217 E 55th Place, Tulsa OK 74145, USA
**Dershowitz, Alan M** — Attorney, Educator
1563 Massachusetts Ave, Cambridge MA 02138, USA
**Dervan, Peter B** — Chemist
California Institute of Technology, Chemistry Dept, Pasadena CA 91125, USA
**Derwin, Mark** — Actor
Innovative Artists, 1505 10th St, Santa Monica CA 90401 USA
**Desai, Anita** — Writer
Deborah Rogers Ltd, 20 Powis Mews, London W11 1JN, England
**Desailly, Marcel** — Soccer Player
Chelsea F C, Stamford Bridge, Fulham Road, London SW6 1HS, England
**DeSalvo, Anne** — Actress, Director
Don Buchwald, 6500 Wilshire Blvd, #2200, Los Angeles CA 90048 USA
**DeSalvo, Matthew T (Matt)** — Baseball Player
10 Village Gate Blvd, Delaware OH 43015, USA
**DeSanctis, Roman W** — Cardiologist
5 Thoreau Circle, Winchester MA 01890, USA
**DeSando, Anthony** — Actor
D2 Mgmt, 9255 Sunset Blvd, #600, West Hollywood CA 90069, USA
**DeSantis, Jaclyn** — Actress
Hess Entertainment, 195 S Beverly Dr, #401, Beverly Hills CA 90212, USA

**Depp - DeSantis**

**DeSanto, Greg** — Clown
Big Apple Circus, 505 8th Ave, #1900, New York NY 10018 USA
**DeSanto, Karen** — Clown
Big Apple Circus, 505 8th Ave, #1900, New York NY 10018 USA
**Desarthe, Gerard** — Actor
National Conservatory of Dramatic Art, 2 Bis Rue du Conservatoire, 75009 Paris, France
**Descas, Alex** — Actor
Artmedia, 20 Ave Rapp, 75007 Paris, France
**Deschamps, Didier C** — Soccer Player
Monaco Association Sportive, 7 Ave des Castelans, 98000 Monaco
**Deschanel, Caleb** — Cinematographer
Optimism Entertainment, 303 N La Peer Dr, #205, Beverly Hills CA 90211, USA
**Deschanel, Emily** — Actress
Management 360, 9111 Wilshire Blvd, Beverly Hills CA 90210 USA
**Deschanel, Zooey** — Actress, Model, Singer
United Talent Agency, U T A Plaza, 9336 Civic Center Dr, Beverly Hills CA 90210 USA
**Deser, Stanley** — Physicist
Brandeis University, Physics Dept, Waltham MA 02254, USA
**Desfor, Max** — Photojournalist
15115 Interlachen Dr, #1018, Silver Spring MD 20906, USA
**Desfosses, Erik** — Actor
Artmedia, 20 Ave Rapp, 75007 Paris, France
**Deshaies, James J (Jim)** — Baseball Player
151 N Taylor Point Dr, Spring TX 77382, USA
**Deshorties, Alexandra** — Singer
Opus 3 Artists, 470 Park Ave S, #900N, New York NY 10016 USA
**Desiderio, Robert** — Actor
1475 Sierra Vista Dr, Aspen CO 81611, USA
**DeSilva, John R** — Baseball Player
32750 Airport Road, Fort Bragg CA 95437, USA
**Desjardins, Eric** — Ice Hockey Player
9 Woodglen Lane, Voorhees NJ 08043, USA
**DesLauriers, Kit** — Free Skier
Teton Village, Jackson Hole WY 83001, USA
**Deslongchamps, Pierre** — Chemist
RR 1, 11 Church McFarland, North Hatley QC J0B 2C0, Canada
**Desormeaux, Kent** — Thoroughbred Racing Jockey
292 W Carter Ave, Sierra Madre CA 91024, USA
**DeSousa, Mauricio** — Cartoonist (Monica)
Mauricio de Sousa Producoes, Rua do Curtume 745, Sao Paulo SP, Brazil
**DeSousa, Melissa** — Actress
Stone Manners Salners, 9911 W Pico Blvd, #1400, Los Angeles CA 90035 USA
**Desplat, Alexandre** — Composer
B M I, 8730 W Sunset Blvd, #300, Los Angeles CA 90069 USA
**Des'ree** — Singer
Creative Artists Agency, 2000 Ave of Stars, #100, Los Angeles CA 90067 USA
**Desrosiers, David P** — Bassist (Simple Plan)
Depot Sainte-Dorothee, PO Box 223, Lavel QC H7X 2T4, Canada
**Dess, Darrell C** — Football Player
224 Summer Ave, New Castle PA 16105, USA
**Desselle, Natalie** — Actress
Innovative Artists, 1505 10th St, Santa Monica CA 90401 USA
**Dessens Jusaino, Elmer** — Baseball Player
5427 E Sheena Dr, Scottsdale AZ 85254, USA
**Dessner, Bryce** — Guitarist (National)
Brassland Records, PO Box 76, Prince Street Station, New York NY 10012, USA
**Destrade, Orestes** — Baseball Player
10653 Garda Dr, Trinity FL 34655, USA
**Destri, James (Jimmy)** — Keyboardist (Blondie)
Agency Group Ltd, 142 W 57th St, #600, New York NY 10019 USA
**Desurvive, Emmanuel** — Optical Fiber Engineer
Alcatel Submarine Networks, Villarceaux Centre, 91625 Nozay, France
**DeTar, Dean E** — Vietnam War Air Force Hero
7785 Portwood Road, Azle TX 76020, USA
**DeThe, Guy Blaudin** — Oncologist, Biologist
14 Rue Le Regrattier, 75004 Paris, France
**Detmer, Amanda** — Actress
John Carrabino Mgmt, 5900 Wilshire Blvd, #406, Los Angeles CA 90036 USA
**Detmer, Ty H** — Football Player
18449 Flagler Dr, Austin TX 78738, USA
**Detmers, Maruschka** — Actress
Agence Metropolitan Paris, 23 Blvd des Capucines, 75002 Paris, France
**Detorie, Rick** — Cartoonist (One Big Happy)
Creators Syndicate, 737 3rd St, Hermosa Beach CA 90254 USA
**Detroit, Marcella** — Singer, Songwriter, Guitarist
Dawson Breed Music, Spenser House, London SE24 0NR, England
**Dettlaff, Bill** — Golfer
133 Clearlake Dr, Ponte Vedra Beach FL 32082, USA
**DeTurck, Dennis** — Mathematician
University of Pennsylvania, Arts & Sciences College, Philadelphia PA 19104, USA
**Detwiler, Ross** — Baseball Player
359 Brown Swiss Circle, Duncansville PA 16635, USA
**Deukmejian, C George** — Governor, CA
Sidley & Austin, 555 W 5th St, #3900, Los Angeles CA 90013, USA
**Deutch, Howard** — Director, Producer, Writer
I C M Partners, 10250 Constellation Blvd, #900, Los Angeles CA 90067 USA
**Deutch, John M** — Government Official
51 Clifton St, Belmont MA 02478, USA
**Deutch, Zoey** — Actress
Innovative Artists, 1505 10th St, Santa Monica CA 90401 USA
**Deutekom, Cristina** — Opera Singer
Lancasterdreef 41, Dronten 8251 TG, Holland
**Deutsch, David (Dave)** — Basketball Player
315 Fairmount Road, Long Valley NJ 07853, USA
**Dev** — Singer, Rap Artist, Songwriter
Paradigm Agency, 360 N Crescent Dr, North Building, Beverly Hills CA 90210 USA

**Dev, Mukul** — Actor
Karan Apts, #500, Yari Road Versova, Mumbai MS 400061, India

**Deva, Prabhu** — Actor, Dancer, Director
68 T T K Road, Alwarpet, Chennai TN 600018, India

**DeValeria, Dennis** — Sportswriter
213 Hillendale Road, Pittsburgh PA 15237, USA

**Devane, William** — Actor
Shelter Entertainment, 9255 Sunset Blvd, #300, Los Angeles CA 90069 USA

**Devarez, Cesar S** — Baseball Player
35 Arden St, #B, New York NY 10040, USA

**DeVarona, Donna** — Swimmer, Sportscaster
3 Avon Lane, Greenwich CT 06830, USA

**DeVasquez, Devin** — Model, Actress
9903 Santa Monica Blvd, #169, Beverly Hills CA 90212, USA

**Devault, Calvin** — Actor
Amsel Eisenstadt Frazier, 5055 Wilshire Blvd, #865, Los Angeles CA 90036 USA

**Devayani** — Actress
51 Indira Gandhi St, Saligramam, Chennai TN 600093, India

**Devendorf, Bryan** — Drummer (National)
Brassland Records, PO Box 76, Prince Street Station, New York NY 10012, USA

**Devendorf, Scott** — Guitarist (National)
Brassland Records, PO Box 76, Prince Street Station, New York NY 10012, USA

**DeVenzio, Dick** — Basketball Player
1116 Home Place, Matthews NC 28105, USA

**Dever, Barbara** — Opera Singer
Wolf Artists Mgmt, 13 E 69th St, #3R, New York NY 10021, USA

**Dever, Kaitlyn** — Actress
United Talent Agency, U T A Plaza, 9336 Civic Center Dr, Beverly Hills CA 90210 USA

**Dever, Seamus** — Actor
A P A Talent/Literary Agency, 405 S Beverly Dr, #300, Beverly Hills CA 90212 USA

**Deveraux, Jude** — Writer
Atria/Simon & Schuster, 1230 Ave of Americas, Concourse 1, New York NY 10020, USA

**Devereaux, Michael (Mike)** — Baseball Player
2236 W Doublegrove St, West Covina CA 91790, USA

**Devers, Gail** — Track Athlete
G B M Mgmt, 4207 Corrales Dr, #100, Florissant MO 63034, USA

**DeVevo, Juan** — Guitarist (Casting Crowns)
Proper Mgmt, PO Box 150867, Nashville TN 37215, USA

**DeVevo, Melodee** — Violinist (Casting Crowns)
Proper Mgmt, PO Box 150867, Nashville TN 37215, USA

**Devgan, Ajay** — Actor, Director, Producer
5/6 Sheetak Apts, Opp Chandand Cinema, Juhu, Mumbai MS 400049, India

**DeVicenzo, Roberto** — Golfer
Noni Lann, 5025 Veloz Ave, Tarzana CA 91356, USA

**DeVilla, Alfredo** — Director
Underground Films & Mgmt, 447 S Highland Ave, Los Angeles CA 90036, USA

**DeVille, Cecil (C C)** — Guitarist (Poison)
Esterman.Com, PO Box 514, Riva MD 21140, USA

**Deville, Michel** — Director
36 Rue Reinhardt, 92100 Boulogne, France

**Devin, Anna** — Opera Singer
I M G Artists, Hogarth Business Park, Chiswick, London W4 2TH, England

**DeVine, Adam** — Actor, Writer
W M E Entertainment, 9601 Wilshire Blvd, #300, Beverly Hills CA 90210 USA

**Devine, Aidan** — Actor
S M S Talent, 8383 Wilshire Blvd, #230, Beverly Hills CA 90211 USA

**Devine, Elizabeth** — Writer, Producer
Creative Artists Agency, 2000 Ave of Stars, #100, Los Angeles CA 90067 USA

**Devine, Joseph N (Joey)** — Baseball Player
2616 Long Pointe, Roswell GA 30076, USA

**Devine, Loretta** — Actress
Essential Talent Mgmt, 3151 Cahuenga Blvd W, #220, Los Angeles CA 90068, USA

**Devine, P Adrian** — Baseball Player
271 Timber Laurel Lane, Lawrenceville GA 30043, USA

**DeVita, Vincent T, Jr** — Oncologist
Yale Comprehensive Cancer Center, 333 Cedar St, New Haven CT 06510, USA

**DeVito, Danny** — Actor, Comedian, Director
1028 Ridgedale Dr, Beverly Hills CA 90210, USA

**DeVito, Joe** — Actor, Comedian
OmniPop Talent Group, 4605 Lankershim Blvd, #201, Toluca Lake CA 91602 USA

**Devitt, John** — Swimmer
46 Beacon Ave, Beacon Hill NSW 2100, Australia

**Devlin, Bruce** — Golfer
3601 Foot Hills Dr, Weatherford TX 76087, USA

**Devlin, Christopher J (Chris)** — Football Player
100 Meadowlark Lane, Boalsburg PA 16827, USA

**Devlin, Dean** — Director, Producer, Actor
Electric Entertainment, 940 N Highland Ave, #A, Los Angeles CA 90038, USA

**Devlin, Joseph (Joe)** — Football Player
3815 Schintzius Road, Eden NY 14057, USA

**Devlin, Michael R (Mike)** — Football Player
48 Shore Road, Mount Sinai NY 11766, USA

**Devlin, Peter J** — Sound Mixer
Doug Apatow Agency, 12049 Jefferson Blvd, #200, Culver City CA 90230, USA

**Devlin, Ryan** — Actor
Michelle Grant Mgmt, 1158 26th St, #414, Santa Monica CA 90403, USA

**DeVoe, Ronald (Ronnie)** — Singer (New Edition, Bell Biv DeVoe)
Pyramid Entertainment Group, 377 Rector Place, #21A, New York NY 10280 USA

**Devoll, Hal** — Basketball Player
8928 Fox Ave, Allen Park MI 48101, USA

**DeVoogd, Bob** — Field Hockey Player
Oanje-Zwart M H C, Charles Roelslaan 13, 5644 Eindhoven NX, Netherlands

**Devor, Robinson** — Director, Writer
United Talent Agency, U T A Plaza, 9336 Civic Center Dr, Beverly Hills CA 90210 USA

**Devore, Doug** — Baseball Player
5247 Willow Grove Place S, Dublin OH 43017, USA

**DeVore, Irven** — Anthropologist, Evolutionary Biologist
Harvard University, Peabody Archeaology Museum, Cambridge MA 02138, USA

**DeVorzon, Barry** — Songwriter
MasterWriter, 70 State St, Santa Barbara CA 93101, USA

**Devos, Emmanuelle** — Actress
Zelig, 57 Rue Reaumur, 75002 Paris, France

**DeVos, Richard M** — Businessman, Philanthropist
6565 Otis Lane, Harbor Springs MI 49740, USA

**DeVries, Greg** — Ice Hockey Player
25 Colonel Winstead Dr, Brentwood TN 37027, USA

**Devries, Jared** — Football Player
15342 Lambert Dr, Clear Lake IA 50428, USA

**DeVries, Jill** — Model
Playboy Promotions, 2706 Media Center Dr, Los Angeles CA 90065 USA

**DeVries, Marius** — Composer
Gorfaine/Schwartz, 4111 W Alameda Ave, #509, Burbank CA 91505 USA

**DeVries, William C** — Surgeon
Hardin Memorial Hospital, 913 N Dixie Ave, Elizabethtown KY 42701, USA

**DeWaal, Frans** — Primatologist
Emory University, Primate Behavior Dept, Atlanta GA 30322, USA

**DeWaart, Edo** — Conductor
Milwaukee Symphony, 700 N Water St, #700, Milwaukee, WI 53202, USA

**DeWaele, Ellen** — Producer, Production Manager
Serendipity Films, Huigeveldstraat 37, 9550 Saint-Antelinks, Belgium

**Dewan-Tatum, Jenna** — Actress, Producer
Sanders/Armstrong/Caserta Mgmt, 2120 Colorado Ave, #120, Santa Monica CA 90404 USA

**Dewar, Susan** — Cartoonist (Us & Them)
Universal Press Syndicate, 4520 Main St, #700, Kansas City MO 64111 USA

**DeWarren, Patrick** — Photographer
153 Roebling St, #100, Brooklyn NY 11211, USA

**Dewdney, Christopher** — Writer
Bloomsbury Publishing, 50 Bedford Square, London WC1B 3DP, England

**DeWet, Shaun** — Model
Elite Model Mgmt, 404 Park Ave S, #900, New York NY 10016 USA

**Dewey, Duane E** — Korean War Marine Corps Hero (CMH)
10550 N Forman Road, Irons MI 49644, USA

**Dewey, Mark A** — Baseball Player
28150 Rivermont Dr, Meadowview VA 24361, USA

**DeWijn, Sander** — Field Hockey Player
S V Kampong Hockey, Postbus 85219, 3508 Utrecht AE, Netherlands

**DeWilde, Edy** — Museum Executive
Stedelijk Museum, Oosterdokskade 5, 1011 Amsterdam AD, Netherlands

**DeWillis, Jeffrey A (Jeff)** — Baseball Player
8918 Wind Side Dr, Richmond Hill ON L4C 1T4, Canada

**DeWinne, Frank** — Cosmonaut, Belgium
349th Squadron, Vliegbasis 10W T A C Kleine Brogel, 3990 Peer, Belgium

**DeWit, Peter** — Cartoonist
Galerie Lambiek, Kerkstaat 78, 1017 GP Amsterdam, Netherlands

**DeWit, William T (Willie)** — Boxer
Wolch Hursh DeWit, 1500-633 6th Ave SW, Calgary AB T2P 2Y5, Canada

**DeWitt, Doug** — Boxer
176 Garth Road, #TM, Scarsdale NY 10583, USA

**DeWitt, Joyce** — Actress, Model
PO Box 7309, Santa Monica CA 90406, USA

**DeWitt, Rosemarie** — Actress
I C M Partners, 10250 Constellation Blvd, #900, Los Angeles CA 90067 USA

**Dewitt, Willie** — Boxer
605 N Water St, Burnet TX 78611, USA

**DeWitt-Morette, Cecile** — Physicist
2411 Vista Lane, Austin TX 78703, USA

**Dews, Peter B** — Psychiatrist
99 Norumbega Road, #231, Weston MA 02493, USA

**DeWulf, Noureen** — Actress
Evolution Entertainment, 901 N Highland Ave, Los Angeles CA 90038 USA

**DeWyze, Lee** — Singer, Songwriter
Sony Records, 2100 Colorado Ave, Santa Monica CA 90404 USA

**Dexter, Mary** — Director
Hank Tani, 14542 Delaware Dr, Moorpark CA 93021, USA

**Dexter, N Colin** — Writer
456 Banbury Road, Oxford 0X2 7RG, England

**Dexter, Peter W** — Writer, Columnist
Sacramento Bee, Editorial Dept, 21st & Q Sts, Sacramento CA 95852, USA

**Dey, Charles** — Association Executive
Start on Success, 910 16th Ave NW, Washington DC 20006, USA

**Dey, Susan** — Actress
I C M Partners, 10250 Constellation Blvd, #900, Los Angeles CA 90067 USA

**Dey, Tom** — Director
W M E Entertainment, 9601 Wilshire Blvd, #300, Beverly Hills CA 90210 USA

**DeYoung, Cliff** — Actor
Geddes Agency, 8430 Santa Monica Blvd, #201, West Hollywood CA 90069 USA

**DeYoung, Michelle** — Singer
Opus 3 Artists, 470 Park Ave S, #900N, New York NY 10016 USA

**DeZarn, Tim** — Actor
C E S D, 10635 Santa Monica Blvd, #130, Los Angeles CA 90025 USA

**Dezhurov, Vladimir N** — Cosmonaut
Cosmonaut Training Center, Star City, 141160 Zvezdny Gorodok, Moscow Oblast, Russia

**DeZordo, Nevio** — Bobsled Athlete
Olympic Committee, Foro Italico, Largo Lauro de Bosis 15, 00135 Rome, Italy

**Dhabhara, Firdaus S** — Neuroscientist
Rockefeller University, Neurology Dept, 1230 York Ave, New York NY 10065, USA

**Dhalia, Heitor** — Director
W M E Entertainment, 9601 Wilshire Blvd, #300, Beverly Hills CA 90210 USA

**Dhaliwal, Daljit** — Commentator
Knight Ayton Mgmt, 114 Saint Martin's Lane, London WC2N 4BE, England

**Dhanapala, Jayantha C P** — Government Official, Sri Lanka
United Nations, Sri Lanka Delegation, United Nations Plaza, New York NY 10007, USA

**Dhanoa, Guddu** — Director
8A My Little Home, 10th Road J V P D Scheme, Mumbai MS 400049, India
**Dharker, Ayesha** — Actress
Independent Talent Group, 40 Whitfield St, London W1T 2RH, England
**Dharma Master Cheng Yen** — Religious Leader
Tzu Chi Foundation, 701 Zhongyang Road, Hualien 97004, Taiwan
**Dhavernas, Caroline** — Actress
Gersh Agency, 41 Madison Ave, #3301, New York NY 10010 USA
**Dhawan, Sacha** — Actress
Troika, 74 Clerkenwell Road, #300, London EC1M 5QA, England
**Dhoinine, Iklilou** — President, Comores
President's Office, Palais de Beit Salam, BP 421, Moroni, Grand Comoro, Comoros
**Dhoni, Mahendra Singh** — Cricket Player
Chennai Super Kings, Gummidipundi, Tamil Nadu 132400 India
**Diadkova, Larissa** — Opera Singer
I M G Artists, Hogarth Business Park, Chiswick, London W4 2TH, England
**Diamantopoulos, Chris** — Actor
Untitled Entertainment, 350 S Beverly Dr, #200, Beverly Hills CA 90212 USA
**Diamond of Gloucester, John** — Government Official, England
Aynhoe, Doggetts Wood Lane, Chalfont Saint Giles, Buckinghamshire HP8 4TH, England
**Diamond, Abel J** — Architect
Diamond Schmitt Co, 2 Berkeley St, #600, Toronto ON M5A 2W3, Canada
**Diamond, Jared M** — Biologist
University of California Medical School, Physiology Dept, Los Angeles CA 90024, USA
**Diamond, Marian C** — Neuroanatomist
100 Bay Place, #804, Oakland CA 94610, USA
**Diamond, Michael (Mike D)** — Rap Artist (Beastie Boys)
Nasty Little Man, 110 Greene St, #605, New York NY 10012, USA
**Diamond, Neil L** — Singer, Songwriter
Richard De La Font Agency, 4845 S Sheridan Road, #505, Tulsa OK 74145 USA
**Diamond, Peter A** — Nobel Economics Laureate
Massachusetts Institute of Technology, Economics Dept, Cambridge MA 02139, USA
**Diamond, Reed** — Actor
Paradigm Agency, 360 N Crescent Dr, North Building, Beverly Hills CA 90210 USA
**Diamond, Seymour** — Physician
Diamond Headache Clinic, 467 W Deming Place, #500, Chicago IL 60614, USA
**Diamond, William** — Financier
28 Preakness Court, Owings Mills MD 21117, USA
**Diamont, Anita** — Writer
Charles Scribner's Sons, 866 3rd Ave, New York NY 10022 USA
**Diamont, Don** — Actor, Model
Craig Mgmt, 2240 Miramonte Circle E, #C, Palm Springs CA 92264 USA
**Dias, Ivan Cardinal** — Religious Leader
Archbishop's House, 21 Nathalal Parekh Marg, Mumbai 400001, India
**DiasDosSantos, Fernando da Piedade** — Prime Minister, Angola
Prime Minister's Office, Avda 4 de Fevereiro, Luanda CP 2723, Angola
**Diaw, Boris** — Basketball Player
10430 N 108th Place, Scottsdale AZ 85259, USA
**Diaz, Alex** — Photojournalist
Associated Press, Editorial Dept, 450 W 33rd St, #1500, New York NY 10001 USA
**Diaz, Cameron** — Actress, Model
Creative Artists Agency, 2000 Ave of Stars, #100, Los Angeles CA 90067 USA
**Diaz, Carlos A** — Baseball Player
45-236 Ka Hanahou Circle, Kaneohe HI 96744, USA
**Diaz, David** — Boxer
1524 N Avers Ave, Chicago IL 60651, USA
**Diaz, Einar A** — Baseball Player
4315 70th Ave E, Ellenton FL 34222, USA
**Diaz, Gloria M A** — Beauty Queen, Actress
Miss Universe Organization, 1370 Ave of Americas, #1600, New York NY 10019 USA
**Diaz, Guillermo** — Actor
Innovative Artists, 1505 10th St, Santa Monica CA 90401 USA
**Diaz, Jorge A** — Football Player
10801 Starkey Road, Seminole FL 33777, USA
**Diaz, Juan** — Boxer
13616 Monarch Road, Houston TX 77047, USA
**Diaz, Julio** — Boxer
PO Box 1812, Indio CA 92202, USA
**Diaz, Junot** — Writer
Riverhead/Penguin Books, 375 Hudson St, Basement 1, New York NY 10014, USA
**Diaz, Laura** — Golfer
Ladies Pro Golf Assn, 100 International Golf Dr, Daytona Beach FL 32124 USA
**Diaz, Manuel A (Manny)** — Mayor, Miami
Mayor's Office, 3500 Pan American Dr, Miami FL 33133, USA
**Diaz, Matthew E (Matt)** — Baseball Player
1124 Afton St, Lakeland FL 33803, USA
**Diaz, Melonie** — Actress
Gersh Agency, 9465 Wilshire Blvd, #600, Beverly Hills CA 90212 USA
**Diaz, Michael A (Mike)** — Baseball Player
1113 Everglades Dr, Pacifica CA 94044, USA
**Diaz-Balart, Jose** — Commentator
Telmundo, 2470 W 8th Ave, Hialeah FL 33010, USA
**Diaz-Infante, G David M** — Football Player
24723 E Park Crescent Dr, Aurora CO 80016, USA
**Diaz-Rahi, Yamila** — Model
Next Model Mgmt, 9 Boul de la Madeleine, 75001 Paris, France
**Dibaba, Tirunesh** — Track Athlete
Global Athletics & Marketing, 437 Boylston St, #400, Boston MA 02116, USA
**Dibb, Sam** — Director
Casorotto Ramsay, Waverley House, 7-12 Noel St, London W1F 8GQ, England
**Dibble, Dorne A** — Football Player
18601 Jamestown Circle, Northville MI 48168, USA
**Dibble, Robert K (Rob)** — Baseball Player
30020 Trail Creek Dr, Agoura Hills CA 91301, USA
**DiBeligiojoso, Lodovico B** — Architect
8 Via Perugia, 20121 Milan, Italy

**D**

**DiBenedetto, Kaitlyn** — Instrumentalist (Just Kait)
Transfer Media Group, 5200 Lankershim Blvd, #400, North Hollywood CA 91601, USA
**DiBlasio, Raul** — Singer
World Entertainment Assoc, 8815 Conroy Windermere Road, #407, Orlando FL 32835, USA
**DiBona, Craig** — Cinematographer
333 E 66th St, #7-O, New York NY 10065, USA
**DiBonaventura, Lorenzo** — Producer
Rogers & Cowan, 8687 Melrose Ave, #G700, West Hollywood CA 90069 USA
**Dibos, Alicia** — Golfer
1465 E Putnam Ave, #112E, Old Greenwich, T 06870, USA
**Dibowski, Andreas** — Equestrian
Waldwinkel 2, 21272 Egestorf, Germany
**Dibra, Bash** — Dog Trainer
3476 Bailey Ave, Bronx NY 10463, USA
**DiCamillo, Gary T** — Businessman
1001 Saint Georges Road, Baltimore MD 21210, USA
**DiCamillo, Katrice E (Kate)** — Writer
Candlewick Press, 99 Dover St, Somerville MA 02144, USA
**DiCaprio, Leonardo** — Actor
L B I Entertainment, 2000 Avenue of Stars, Century City CA 90067 90067, USA
**DiCenta, Giorgio** — Cross Country Skier
33020 Treppo Carnico (UD), Italy
**Dichter, Misha** — Concert Pianist
Columbia Artists Mgmt Inc, 1790 Broadway, #702, New York NY 10019 USA
**Dick, Andrew R (Andy)** — Actor, Comedian
A P A Talent/Literary Agency, 405 S Beverly Dr, #300, Beverly Hills CA 90212 USA
**Dick, Bryan** — Actor
Markham Froggatt Irwin, Julian House, 4 Windmill St, London W1P 1HF, England
**Dickau, Daniel D (Dan)** — Basketball Player
190 Marietta St SW, Atlanta GA 30303, USA
**Dickel, Daniel L (Dan)** — Football Player
970 Maplewood Dr, Coralville IA 52241, USA
**Dicken, Paul** — Baseball Player
4421 NW Blitchton Road, Ocala FL 34482, USA
**Dickens, Chris** — Editor
United Agents, 12-26 Lexington St, London W1F 0LE, England
**Dickens, Kim** — Actress
Gersh Agency, 41 Madison Ave, #3301, New York NY 10010 USA
**Dickens, Little Jimmy** — Singer
5010 W Concord Road, Brentwood TN 37027, USA
**Dickenson, Gary** — Bowler
501 Wade Martin Dr, Edmond OK 73034, USA
**Dickenson, Herb** — Ice Hockey Player
240 Jerseyville Road, RR 8 Station Main, Brantford ON N3T 5M1, Canada
**Dickerson, Christopher C (Chris)** — Baseball Player
Milwaukee Brewers, Miller Park, 1 Brewers Way, Milwaukee WI 53214 USA
**Dickerson, Eric D** — Football Player, Sportscaster
516 Dickerson St, Sealy TX 77474, USA
**Dickerson, Ernest R** — Director
Untitled Entertainment, 350 S Beverly Dr, #200, Beverly Hills CA 90212 USA
**Dickerson, Marty** — Golfer
4225 Luzon Way, Sarasota FL 34241, USA
**Dickerson, Sandra** — Actress
Howes & Prior, Berkeley House, Hay Hill, London W1X 7LH, England
**Dickey, Boh A** — Businessman
Safeco Corp, Safeco Plaza, 1001 4th Ave, #800, Seattle WA 98154, USA
**Dickey, C Lynn** — Football Player
9220 Pawnee Lane, Leawood KS 66206, USA
**Dickey, Doug** — Football Coach
11677 Thornapple Dr, Jacksonville FL 32223, USA
**Dickey, Robert A (R A)** — Baseball Player
1015 Lynnwood Blvd, Nashville TN 37215, USA
**Dickinson, Amy** — Columnist
Tribune Media Services, 435 N Michigan Ave, #1500, Chicago IL 60611 USA
**Dickinson, Angie** — Actress
1715 Carla Ridge, Beverly Hills CA 90210, USA
**Dickinson, Bruce** — Singer (Iron Maiden)
Chipster, 100 Village Square Crossing, Palm Beach Gardens FL 33410 USA
**Dickinson, Gary** — Bowler
501 Wade Martin Road, Edmond OK 73034, USA
**Dickinson, Janice** — Model, Actress, Photographer
Total Talent Mgmt, 11005 Morrison St, #105, North Hollywood CA 91601, USA
**Dickinson, Judy** — Golfer
18277 SE Heritage Dr, Jupiter FL 33469, USA
**Dickinson, Peter** — Writer
Mysterious Press, Warner Books, 1271 Ave of Americas, New York NY 10020 USA
**Dickinson, Richard L (Bo)** — Football Player
PO Box 166, New Augusta MS 39462, USA
**Dickinson, Rob** — Singer, Guitarist (Catherine Wheel)
Paradigm Agency, 360 Park Ave, #1600, New York NY 10022 USA
**Dickinson, Sandra** — Actress
Associated International Mgmt, 7 Hatton Garden, #400, London EC1N 8AD, England
**Dickinson, Steve** — Cartoonist (Tar Pit)
King Features Syndicate, 300 W 57th St, #1500, New York NY 10019 USA
**Dickman, James B (Jay)** — Photographer
3176 S Vine St, Englewood CO 80113, USA
**Dickson, Billy** — Director, Cinematographer
Global Artists Agency, 6253 Hollywood Blvd, #508, Los Angeles CA 90028 USA
**Dickson, Chris** — Yachtsman
International Mangement Group, 1 Erieview Plaza, 1360 E 9th St, Cleveland OH 44114 USA
**Dickson, Jason R** — Baseball Player
15 Edison St, Sainte Margarets NB E1N 5B4, Canada
**Dickson, Jennifer** — Artist, Photographer
20 Osborne St, Ottawa ON K1S 4Z9, Canada
**Dickson, Neil** — Actor
Clear Talent Group, 10950 Ventura Blvd, Studio City CA 91604, USA

| | |
|---|---|
| **Dickson, Ngila**<br>Weta Workshop, PO Box 15208, Miramar, Wellington, New Zealand | Costume Designer |
| **DiCorcia, Philip-Lorca**<br>55 Hudson St, #8D, New York NY 10013, USA | Photographer |
| **Dicus, Charles W (Chuck)**<br>852 N Mansfield Ave, Los Angeles CA 90038, USA | Football Player |
| **Dicus, John C**<br>Capitol Federal Savings & Loan, 700 S Kansas Ave, #100, Topeka KS 66603, USA | Financier |
| **Diczfalusy, Egon R**<br>Ronninger 21, 144 61 Ronninge, Sweden | Endocrinologist |
| **Didier, Clint**<br>8770 N Glade Road, Pasco WA 99301, USA | Football Player |
| **Didier, Robert D (Bob)**<br>1819 N Lynch, Mesa AZ 85207, USA | Baseball Player |
| **Didion, Joan**<br>Creative Artists Agency, 2000 Ave of Stars, #100, Los Angeles CA 90067 USA | Writer |
| **Didion, John L**<br>48 Elk Ridge Lane, Naselle WA 98638, USA | Football Player |
| **Dido**<br>Paradigm Agency, 360 N Crescent Dr, North Building, Beverly Hills CA 90210 USA | Singer, Songwriter |
| **Diebel, John C**<br>Meade Instruments Corp, 27 Hubble, #100, Irvine CA 92618, USA | Businessman |
| **Diebel, Nelson**<br>401 Webb Road, Newark DE 19711, USA | Swimmer |
| **Diegel, Adam**<br>I M G Artists, Hogarth Business Park, Chiswick, London W4 2TH, England | Opera Singer |
| **Diego Florez, Juan**<br>Opera et Concert, 37 Rue de la Chaussee d'Antin, 75009 Paris, France | Opera Singer |
| **Diehl, David M**<br>116 Liberty Ridge Trail, Totowa NJ 07512, USA | Football Player |
| **Diehl, Digby R**<br>788 S Lake Ave, Pasadena CA 91106, USA | Journalist |
| **Diehl, John**<br>Don Buchwald, 6500 Wilshire Blvd, #2200, Los Angeles CA 90048 USA | Actor |
| **Dieken, Doug H**<br>29876 Lake Road, Bay Village OH 44140, USA | Football Player |
| **Diemberger, Kurt**<br>Via Amola 23/1, 40050 Calderino (BO), Italy | Mountaineer |
| **Diemecke, Enrique Arturo**<br>Herbert Barrett, 266 W 37th St, #2000, New York NY 10018 USA | Conductor |
| **Diemer, Brian**<br>Calvin College, Athletic Dept, Grand Rapids MI 49506, USA | Track Athlete |
| **Diener, Theodor O**<br>PO Box 272, 11711 Battersea Dr, Beltsville MD 20704, USA | Plant Virologist |
| **Dieng, Gorgui**<br>Utah Jazz, Energy Solutions Arena, 301 W South Temple, Salt Lake City UT 84101 USA | Basketball Player |
| **Dier, Brett**<br>Gersh Agency, 9465 Wilshire Blvd, #600, Beverly Hills CA 90212 USA | Actor |
| **Dierdorf, Daniel L (Dan)**<br>13302 Buckland Hall Road, Saint Louis MO 63131, USA | Football Player, Sportscaster |
| **Dierker, Lawrence E (Larry)**<br>8318 N Tahoe Dr, Houston TX 77040, USA | Baseball Player, Manager |
| **Dierking, Conrad W (Connie)**<br>5730 Windridge View, Cincinnati OH 45243, USA | Basketball Player |
| **Dierking, Scott E**<br>1862 Wingate Lane, Wheaton IL 60189, USA | Football Player |
| **Dierkop, Charles R**<br>10 Town Plaza, #428, Durango CO 81301, USA | Actor |
| **Diesel, Vin**<br>One Race Productions, 9100 Wilshire Blvd, 535 East Tower, Beverly Hills CA 90212, USA | Director, Actor |
| **Dieterich, Christian J (Chris)**<br>804 Edisto River Road, Myrtle Beach SC 29588, USA | Football Player |
| **Dietrich, Don**<br>310 Finlay Avenue E, Deloraine MB R0M 0M0, Canada | Ice Hockey Player |
| **Dietrich, William A (Bill)**<br>Seattle Times, Editorial Dept, 1000 Denny Way, Seattle WA 98109 USA | Journalist |
| **Dietrick, Coby J**<br>644 Patterson Ave, San Antonio TX 78209, USA | Basketball Player |
| **Dietz, Michael**<br>Michael Bruno Group, 13576 Cheltenham Dr, Sherman Oaks CA 91423, USA | Actor |
| **Difelice, Michael W (Mike)**<br>3980 Mimosa Place, Palm Harbor FL 34685, USA | Baseball Player |
| **Diffie, Joe**<br>Bobby Roberts, 3050 Business Park Circle, #303, Goodlettsville TN 37221 USA | Singer, Songwriter |
| **Diffie, Whitfield**<br>Sun Microsystems, 4150 Network Circle, Santa Clara CA 95054, USA | Inventor (Public Key Cryptology) |
| **DiFiore, Vince**<br>Umbrella Group, 1 West St, #3506, New York NY 10004, USA | Trumpeter, Keyboardist (Bush) |
| **DiFranco, Ani**<br>Scot Fisher PO Box 95, Ellicott Station, Buffalo NY 14205, USA | Singer, Songwriter, Musician |
| **Digby, Marie**<br>Hollywood Records, 1851 Ivar, #500, Los Angeles CA 90028, USA | Singer, Guitarist |
| **DiGenova, Joseph E**<br>DiGenova & Toensing, 1776 K St NW, #700, Washington DC 20006, USA | Attorney |
| **Diggins, Skylar K**<br>Tulsa Shock, B O K Center, 200 S Denver, Tulsa OK 74103 USA | Basketball Player |
| **Diggle, Steve**<br>Free Trade Agency, Chapel Place, Rivington St, London EC2A 3DQ, England | Guitarist, Bassist (Buzzcocks) |
| **Diggs, Na'il R**<br>2006 Connonade Dr, Waxhaw NC 28173, USA | Football Player |
| **Diggs, Taye**<br>O'Taye Productions, 12001 Ventura Place, #340, Studio City CA 91604, USA | Actor, Singer |
| **DiGiallonardo, Rick**<br>Pacific Talent Agency, PO Box 19145, Portland OR 97280, USA | Keyboardist (Quarterflash) |
| **DiGiovanni, Janine**<br>David Godwin Assoc, 55 Monmouth St, London WC2H 9DG, England | Journalist, Writer |

**D**

Dickson - DiGiovanni

**DiGregorio, Ernest (Ernie)** — Basketball Player
60 Chestnut Ave, Narragansett RI 02882, USA
**Dijkstra, Rineke** — Photographer
Marian Goodman Gallery, 24 W 57th St, New York NY 10019, USA
**Dilba** — Singer, Musician, Songwriter
United Stage Production, PO Box 11029, 100 61 Stockholm, Sweden
**Dildarian, Steve** — Producer, Writer, Actor
W M E Entertainment, 9601 Wilshire Blvd, #300, Beverly Hills CA 90210 USA
**Dileita, Dileita Mohamed** — Prime Minister, Djibouti
Prime Minister's Office, BP 2086, Djibouti City, Djibouti
**Dilfer, Trent F** — Football Player, Sportscaster
15288 Quito Road, Saratoga CA 95070, USA
**Dilger, Kennth R (Ken)** — Football Player
10403 Windemere, Carmel IN 46032, USA
**Dill, Craig H** — Basketball Player
10200 Thomas Woods Road, Saginaw MI 48609, USA
**Dill, Guy** — Artist, Sculptor
13215 Innes Place, Venice CA 90291, USA
**Dill, Laddie John** — Artist
1625 Electric Ave, Venice CA 90291, USA
**Dillahunt, Garret** — Actor
United Talent Agency, U T A Plaza, 9336 Civic Center Dr, Beverly Hills CA 90210 USA
**Dillane, Stephen** — Actor
W M E Entertainment, 9601 Wilshire Blvd, #300, Beverly Hills CA 90210 USA
**Dillard, Alex** — Businessman
Dillard's Inc, 1600 Cantrell Road, Little Rock AR 72201, USA
**Dillard, Annie** — Writer
Russell Volkering, 50 W 29th St, New York NY 10001, USA
**Dillard, Stephen B (Steve)** — Baseball Player
154 Drive 841, Saltillo MS 38866, USA
**Dillard, Victoria** — Actress
Alliance Talent, 2734 E Oakland Park Blvd, #101, Fort Lauderdale FL 33306 USA
**Dillard, W Harrison** — Track Athlete
3449 Glencairn Road, Shaker Heights OH 44122, USA
**Dillard, William T, Jr** — Businessman
Dillard's Inc, 1600 Cantrell Road, Little Rock AR 72201, USA
**Dillehay, Thomas (Tom)** — Anthropologist
University of Kentucky, Anthropology Dept, Lexington KY 40506, USA
**Diller, Barry** — Businessman
I A C/InterActive Corp, 152 W 57th St, #4200, New York NY 10019, USA
**Diller, Elizabeth** — Architect, Designer
Diller Scofidio & Renfro, 601 W 26th St, #1815, New York NY 10001, USA
**Dillman, Bradford** — Actor
770 Hot Springs Road, Santa Barbara CA 93108, USA
**Dillon, Corey** — Football Player
31 Marlboro Road, Woburn MA 01801, USA
**Dillon, Joseph W (Joe)** — Baseball Player
2360 Water Way, Rockwall TX 75087, USA
**Dillon, Kevin** — Actor
I C M Partners, 10250 Constellation Blvd, #900, Los Angeles CA 90067 USA
**Dillon, Matt** — Actor, Director
Untitled Entertainment, 350 S Beverly Dr, #200, Beverly Hills CA 90212 USA
**Dillon, Melinda** — Actress
Innovative Artists, 1505 10th St, Santa Monica CA 90401 USA
**Dillon, Shawn** — Model
Playboy Promotions, 2706 Media Center Dr, Los Angeles CA 90065 USA
**Dillon, Wayne** — Ice Hockey Player
Hockey Development, 301-1185 Eglinton E, North York ON M3C 3C6, Canada
**Dilly, Erin** — Actress, Singer
Paradigm Agency, 360 N Crescent Dr, North Building, Beverly Hills CA 90210 USA
**Dilone, Miguel A** — Baseball Player
Calle El Sol, #190, Santiago, Dominican Republic
**DiLoreto, Dante** — Producer
Creative Artists Agency, 2000 Ave of Stars, #100, Los Angeles CA 90067 USA
**Dils, Stephen W (Steve)** — Football Player
10285 Midway Ave, Alpharetta GA 30022, USA
**DiMaggio, John** — Actor
Gersh Agency, 9465 Wilshire Blvd, #600, Beverly Hills CA 90212 USA
**Dimaio, Robert (Rob)** — Ice Hockey Player
Saint Louis Blues, Scott Trade Center, 1401 Clark Ave, Saint Louis MO 63103 USA
**DiMarco, Chris** — Golfer
3545 Rice Lake Loop, Longwood FL 32779, USA
**Dimas, Trent** — Gymnast
Gold Cup Gymnastics School, 6009 Carmel Ave NE, Albuquerque NM 87113, USA
**Dimbleby, David** — Journalist, Commentator
14 King St, Richmond, Surrey TW9 1NF, England
**DiMeco, Allie** — Singer (Naked Brothers Band)
Untitled Entertainment, 350 S Beverly Dr, #200, Beverly Hills CA 90212 USA
**DiMeola, Al** — Jazz Guitarist
Georg Leitner Productions, Huetteldorfer Str 259, 1140 Vienna, Austria
**Dimitrakos, Niko** — Ice Hockey Player
71 Pennsylvania Ave, Somerville MA 02145, USA
**Dimmel, Michael W (Mike)** — Baseball Player
526 Country Lane, Coppell TX 75019, USA
**Dimon, James (Jamie)** — Businessman
J P Morgan Chase, 270 Park Ave, #1200, New York NY 10017, USA
**Dimry, Charles L, III** — Football Player
PO Box 461266, Escondido CA 92046, USA
**DiNardo, Daniel N Cardinal** — Religious Leader
Chancery Office, PO Box 907, 1700 San Jacinto St, Houston TX 77002, USA
**Dinardo, Lenny** — Baseball Player
10000 SW 52nd Ave, #164, Gainesville FL 32608, USA
**Dindal, Mark** — Animator, Director
I C M Partners, 10250 Constellation Blvd, #900, Los Angeles CA 90067 USA
**Dine, James (Jim)** — Artist, Sculptor, Photographer
Pace Wildenstein Gallery, 32 E 57th St, #400, New York NY 10022, USA

**Dineen, Gord**
51 Fitzgerald Road, Queensbury NY 12804, USA — Ice Hockey Player

**Dineen, Kevin**
149 Birdsall Road, Queensbury NY 12804, USA — Ice Hockey Player, Coach

**Dineen, William P (Bill)**
18 Fairwood Dr, Queensbury NY 12804, USA — Ice Hockey Player, Executive

**Dinello, Paul**
United Talent Agency, U T A Plaza, 9336 Civic Center Dr, Beverly Hills CA 90210 USA — Director, Actor, Writer

**Dinerstein, James**
Salander-O'Reilly Gallery, 22 E 71st St, New York NY 10021, USA — Sculptor

**Dingle, Adrian K**
3228 W Canyon Ave, San Diego CA 92123, USA — Football Player

**Dingman, Christopher R (Chris)**
9220 Pine Island Court, Tampa FL 33647, USA — Ice Hockey Player

**Dingman, Craig**
3573 W Del Sienno St, Wichita KS 67203, USA — Baseball Player

**Dinicol, Joe**
I C M Partners, 10250 Constellation Blvd, #900, Los Angeles CA 90067 USA — Actor

**Dinkel, Thomas (Tom)**
877 Squire Lake Court, Villa Hills KY 41017, USA — Football Player

**Dinkeloo, John**
Roche & Dinkeloo, 20 Davis St, Hamden CT 06517, USA — Architect

**Dinkins, Byron**
10326 Tallent Lane, Huntersville NC 28078, USA — Basketball Player

**Dinkins, Darnell J**
9006 Pembroke Court, Pittsburgh PA 15237, USA — Football Player

**Dinklage, Peter**
Arcieri Assoc, 305 Madison Ave, #2315, New York NY 10165 USA — Actor

**Dinnel, Harry**
1427 El Nido Dr, Fallbrook CA 92028, USA — Basketball Player

**Dinner, Michael**
Creative Artists Agency, 2000 Ave of Stars, #100, Los Angeles CA 90067 USA — Director

**Dinnerstein, Simone**
I M G Artists, Hogarth Business Park, Chiswick, London W4 2TH, England — Concert Pianist

**Dinnigan, Collette**
22-24 Hutchinson St, Surry Hills, Sydney NSW 2010, Australia — Fashion Designer

**Diogu, Ikechukwa S (Ike)**
2052 W Lagoon Road, Pleasanton CA 94566, USA — Basketball Player

**DioGuardi, Kara**
Arthouse Entertainment, PO Box 3900, Los Angeles CA 90078, USA — Songwriter, Producer, Entertainer

**Dion**
Lustig Talent, PO Box 770850, Orlando FL 32877 USA — Singer

**Dion, Celine**
Feeling Productions, 2540 Blvd Daniel-Johnson, #755, Lavel QC H7T 2S3, Canada — Singer

**Dion, Michel**
33 Mulrain Way, Bluffton SC 29910, USA — Ice Hockey Player

**Dionisi, Stefano**
Media Art Mgmt, C/ Castelló 82, 2 Derecha, 28006 Madrid, Spain — Actor

**Dionne, Marcel E**
4424 Montrose Road, Niagara Falls ON L2H 1K2, Canada — Ice Hockey Player

**Diop, Bineta**
Femmes Africa Solidarite, 8 Rue du Vieux-Billard, Box 5037, 1211 Geneva 11, Switzerland — Human Rights Activist

**Diop, DeSagana N**
4300 Haddonfield Road, #309, Pennsauken NJ 8109, USA — Basketball Player

**DiOrio, Nicholas (Nick)**
273 Clark St, Lemoyne PA 17043, USA — Soccer Player

**DiPasquale, James**
Gorfaine/Schwartz, 4111 W Alameda Ave, #509, Burbank CA 91505 USA — Composer

**Dipino, Frank M**
5479 Pebble Beach Dr, Camillus NY 13031, USA — Baseball Player

**Dipoto, Gerald P (Jerry)**
15130 E Camelview Dr, Fountain Hills AZ 85268, USA — Baseball Player

**DiPrete, Edward D**
555 Wilbur Ave, Cranston RI 02921, USA — Governor, RI

**Dirda, Michael**
Washington Post, Editorial Dept, 1150 15th St NW, Washington DC 20071 USA — Journalist

**Dirie, Waris**
Media Pros Handels, Ungargasse 24/6, 1030 Vienna, Austria — Model, Human Rights Activist, Actress

**Dirk, Robert**
4441 Lee Ave, Groves TX 77619, USA — Ice Hockey Player

**Dirnt, Mike**
P M C, 5900 Wilshire Blvd, #1720, Los Angeles CA 90036, USA — Bassist (Green Day)

**Disarcina, Gary T**
141 Martingale Lane, Plymouth MA 2360, USA — Baseball Player

**Dischinger, Terry G**
1739 Oak Ave, Northbrook IL 60062, USA — Basketball Player

**Dishman, Cris E**
5019 Mariposa Circle, Fresno TX 77545, USA — Football Player

**Dishman, Gleneig E (Glenn)**
5400 Fairway Dr, San Jose CA 95127, USA — Baseball Player

**Diskin, Ben**
C E S D, 10635 Santa Monica Blvd, #130, Los Angeles CA 90025 USA — Actor

**Disl, Ursula (Uschi)**
Powerplay Mgmt, Seepromenade 53, 14467 Gross Glienicke, Germany — Biathlete, Cross Country Skier

**Disney, Anthea**
News America Corp, 1211 Ave of Americas, #700, New York NY 10036, USA — Editor

**Disney, William**
1610 Kirk Dr, Lake Havasu City AZ 86404, USA — Speed Skater

**DiSpirito, Rocco**
Linda Lisco Mgmt, 360 E Randolph St, #3203, Chicago IL 60601, USA — Chef, Restauranteur

**DiStefano, Andrea**
W M E Entertainment, 9601 Wilshire Blvd, #300, Beverly Hills CA 90210 USA — Actor

**DiStefano, Philip P**
University of Colorado, Chancellor's Office, 914 Broadway St, Boulder CO 80309, USA — Educator

**Disterheft, Brandi**
Agency Group Ltd, 1880 Century Park E, #711, Los Angeles CA 90067 USA — Bassist, Composer

# D

| | |
|---|---|
| **Distler, Natalie** <br> A P A Talent/Literary Agency, 405 S Beverly Dr, #300, Beverly Hills CA 90212 USA | Actress |
| **DiSuvero, Mark** <br> PO Box 2218, Astoria NY 11102, USA | Sculptor |
| **Ditka, Michael K (Mike)** <br> 161 E Chicago Ave, #39F, Chicago IL 60611, USA | Football Player, Coach, Sportscaster |
| **Ditmar, Arthur J (Art)** <br> 6687 Wisteria Dr, Myrtle Beach SC 29588, USA | Baseball Player |
| **Dittl, Ursula** <br> 216 Munsel Creek Road, Florence OR 97439, USA | Sculptor |
| **Dittmer, Andreas** <br> Fischerbank 5, 17033 Neubrandenburg, Germany | Canoeing Athlete |
| **Dittmer, Edward C** <br> 702 Old Mescalero Road, Tularosa NM 88352, USA | Space Scientist |
| **Dittmer, John D (Jack)** <br> 200 S Main St, Elkader IA 52043, USA | Baseball Player |
| **Ditz, Nancy** <br> 524 Moore Road, Woodside CA 94062, USA | Track Athlete |
| **Divac, Vlade** <br> 811 Haverford Ave, Pacific Palisades CA 90272, USA | Basketball Player |
| **Divakaruni, Chitra Banerjee** <br> Doubleday Press, 1745 Broadway, New York NY 10019 USA | Writer |
| **Divoff, Andrew** <br> Marshak/Zachary Co, 8840 Wilshire Blvd, #100, Beverly Hills CA 90211 USA | Actor |
| **Dix, Drew D** <br> HC 68, Box 70, Mimbres NM 88049, USA | Vietnam War Army Hero (CMH) |
| **Dixit, Avinash K** <br> 36 Gordon Way, Princeton NJ 08540, USA | Economist |
| **Dixit, Madhuri** <br> Vijaydeep, #300, Iris Park, Juhu, Mumbai MS 400049, India | Actress |
| **Dixon, Alan J** <br> 7606 Foley Dr, Belleville IL 62223, USA | Senator, IL |
| **Dixon, Alesha** <br> Independent Talent Group, 40 Whitfield St, London W1T 2RH, England | Singer (Mis-Teeq) |
| **Dixon, Becky** <br> ABC-TV, Sports Dept, 77 W 66th St, New York NY 10023 USA | Sportscaster |
| **Dixon, Blake** <br> Virgin Records, 338 N Foothill Road, Beverly Hills CA 90210 USA | Drummer (Saving Abel) |
| **Dixon, Calvert R (Cal)** <br> 179 Las Palmas, Merritt Island FL 32953, USA | Football Player |
| **Dixon, Craig** <br> 10630 Wellworth Ave, Los Angeles CA 90024, USA | Track Athlete |
| **Dixon, D Jeremy** <br> 44 Gloucester Ave, #6C, London NW1 8JD, England | Architect |
| **Dixon, David T** <br> 4795 W 131 1/2 St, Savage MN 55378, USA | Football Player |
| **Dixon, Donna** <br> Applied Action Research, 859 N Hollywood Way, #497, Burbank CA 91505, USA | Actress |
| **Dixon, Hanford** <br> 2034 Acadia Trace, Westlake OH 44145, USA | Football Player |
| **Dixon, Jack E** <br> Howard Hughes Medical Institute, 4000 Jones Bridge Road, Chevy Chase MD 20815, USA | Biochemist |
| **Dixon, Jamie** <br> University of Pittsburgh, Athletic Dept, Pittsburgh PA 15260, USA | Basketball Coach |
| **Dixon, Kenneth J (Ken)** <br> 4317 Highview Ave, Baltimore MD 21229, USA | Baseball Player |
| **Dixon, Larry** <br> Willow Oak Court, Avon IN 46123, USA | Drag Racing Driver |
| **Dixon, Leslie** <br> Creative Artists Agency, 2000 Ave of Stars, #100, Los Angeles CA 90067 USA | Writer, Producer, Director |
| **Dixon, Mark K** <br> 4016 Ivy Lane, Kitty Hawk NC 27949, USA | Football Player |
| **Dixon, Michael** <br> Markham Froggatt Irwin, Julian House, 4 Windmill St, London W1P 1HF, England | Actor |
| **Dixon, Randolph C (Randy)** <br> 9910 Summerlakes Dr, Carmel IN 46032, USA | Football Player |
| **Dixon, Rodney P (Rod)** <br> 22 Entrican Ave, Remuera, Auckland 1050, New Zealand | Track Athlete |
| **Dixon, Ronnie C** <br> 1440 W Kemper Road, #510, Cincinnati OH 45240, USA | Football Player |
| **Dixon, Scott R** <br> 7161 Zionville Road, Indianapolis IN 45250, USA | Auto Racing Driver |
| **Dixon, Thomas F** <br> 1761 Cuba Island Lane, Hayes VA 23072, USA | Aerospace Engineer |
| **Dixon, Zachary** <br> 19365 Hottinger Circle, Germantown MD 20874, USA | Football Player |
| **Dizon, Jesse** <br> PO Box 572105, Tarzana CA 91357, USA | Actor |
| **DJ Babu** <br> W M E Entertainment, 9601 Wilshire Blvd, #300, Beverly Hills CA 90210 USA | Rap Artist (Dilated Peoples) |
| **DJ Champion** <br> Agency Group Ltd, 142 W 57th St, #600, New York NY 10019 USA | DJ Musician |
| **DJ Diesel** <br> International Talent Booking, Ariel House, 74A Charlotte St, #100 London W1T 4QJ, England | DJ Musician (X-Press 2) |
| **DJ Green Lantern** <br> Central Entertainment Group, 166 5th Ave, #400, New York NY 10010, USA | DJ Musician |
| **DJ Jazzy Jeff** <br> Coast to Coast Entertainment, 8671 Wilshire Blvd, Beverly Hills, CA, 90211, USA | Rap Artist |
| **DJ Kool** <br> 2 Bala Plaza, #300, Bala Cynwyd PA 19004, USA | DJ Musician, Rap Artist |
| **DJ Kool Herc** <br> Kool Herc Productions, PO Box 20472, Huntington Station NY 11746, USA | Rap Artist |
| **DJ Magic Mike** <br> Entertainment Artists, 2409 21st Ave S, #100, Nashville TN 10019 USA | DJ Musician |
| **DJ Muggs** <br> Regime Mgmt, 150 W Alameda, #230, Burbank CA 91502, USA | Rap Artist (Cypress Hill) |

*Distler - DJ Muggs*

**DJ Pam** — DJ Musician (Coup)
Windish Agency, 1658 N Milwaukee Ave, #211, Chicago IL 60647, USA
**DJ Quik** — Rap Artist, Record Producer
A P A Talent/Literary Agency, 405 S Beverly Dr, #300, Beverly Hills CA 90212 USA
**DJ Rocky** — DJ Musician (X-Press 2)
International Talent Booking, Ariel House, 74A Charlotte St, #100 London W1T 4QJ, England
**DJ Shadow** — Rap Artist
Universal/Island Records, 1755 Broadway, #600, New York NY 10019, USA
**DJ Spooky** — Electronica Musician
Music & Art Mgmt, 9 W Walnut St, #2D, Asheville NC 28801, USA
**DJ Total K-Oss** — Rap Artist (Above the Law)
Green Light Talent Agency, PO Box 3172, Beverly Hills CA 90212 USA
**DJ Virman** — Singer (Far East Movement)
Stampede Mgmt, 12530 Beatrice St, Los Angeles CA 90066, USA
**Djalili, Omid** — Actor
Independent Talent Group, 40 Whitfield St, London W1T 2RH, England
**Djawadi, Ramin** — Composer
Gorfaine/Schwartz, 4111 W Alameda Ave, #509, Burbank CA 91505 USA
**Djebar, Assia** — Writer
13 University Place, #621, New York, New York NY 1003, USA
**Djerassi, Carl** — Inventor (Oral Contraceptive)
2325 Bear Gulch Road, Redwood City CA 94062, USA
**Djerassi, Isaac** — Physician
2034 Delancey Place, Philadelphia PA 19103, USA
**Djokovic, Novak** — Tennis Player
Novak Tennis Academy, 63A Tadeusa Koscucka, 11000 Belgrade, Serbia
**Djou, Charles K** — Representative, HI
Majority Group LLP, 1701 Pennsylvania Ave NW, #300, Washington DC 20006, USA
**Dlamini, A Themba** — Prime Minister, Swaziland
Prime Minister's Office, PO Box 395, Mbabane, Swaziland
**D'Lyn, Shae** — Actress
Talent House,3000 Olympic Blvd, #2226, Santa Monica CA 90404, USA
**Dmitriev, Artur** — Figure Skater
Russian Skating Federation, Luchneksaia Nab 8, 119871 Moscow, Russia
**DMX** — Rap Artist (Ruff Ryders), Actor
Media Artists Group, 8222 Melrose Ave, #203, Los Angeles CA 90048 USA
**Do Amaral, Diogo F** — Government Official, Portugal
Ave Fontes Pereira de Melo 35, #13A, 1050 Lisbon, Portugal
**Do Carma Silveira, Maria** — Prime Minister, Sao Tome & Principe
Prime Minister's Office, CP 38, Sao Tome, Sao Tome & Principe
**Do Muoi** — Secretary General, Vietnam
Communist Party, 1 Hoang Van Thu, Hanoi, Vietnam
**Do Nascimento, Alexandre Cardinal** — Religious Leader
Arcebispado, CP 87, 1230C Luanda, Angola
**Doak, Gary W** — Ice Hockey Player
47 Highland Ave, Lynnfield MA 1940, USA
**Doan, Shane A** — Ice Hockey Player
9820 E Thompson Peak Parkway, #725, Scottsdale AZ 85255, USA
**Doane, Melanie** — Singer, Songwriter
Live Tour Artists, 1451 White Oak Blvd, Oakville ON L6H 4R9, Canada
**Dobbek, Daniel J (Dan)** — Baseball Player
4042 SE Yamhill St, Portland OR 97214, USA
**Dobbin, Brian** — Ice Hockey Player
5075 Shiloh Line, Petrolia ON N0N 1R0, Canada
**Dobbs, Greg S** — Baseball Player
2255 Richey Dr, La Canada Flintridge CA 91011, USA
**Dobbs, Louis C (Lou)** — Commentator
Fox-TV, News Dept, 205 E 67th St, New York NY 10065 USA
**Dobbs, Mattiwilda** — Opera Singer
1101 S Arlington Ridge Road, #301, Arlington VA 22202, USA
**Dobek, Michelle** — Golfer
292 Chicopee St, Chicopee MA 01013, USA
**Dobey, James K** — Financier
26611 Carmel Center Place, Carmel CA 93923, USA
**Dobie, Alan** — Actor
Pontus Molash, Kent CT4 8HW, England
**Dobkins, Carl, Jr** — Singer
5618 Harbourside Dr, Mason OH 45040, USA
**Dobler, Conrad F** — Football Player
6227 W 126th Terrace, Leawood KS 66209, USA
**Dobrev, Nina** — Actress
Noble Caplan Abrams, 1260 Yonge St, #200, Toronto ON M4T 1W6, Canada
**Dobrin, Tory** — Choreographer, Dance Executive
Les Ballets Trockadero de Monte Carlo, Box 46 Cathedral Station, New York City, NY 10025, USA
**Dobroshi, Arta** — Actress
U B B A, 6 Rue de Braque, 75003 Paris, France
**Dobslow, Bill** — Singer (Rivieras)
945 Handlebar Road, Mishawaka IN 46544, USA
**Dobson, Anita** — Actress
I T G, 1 Stedham Place, London W1CA 1HU, England
**Dobson, Charles T (Chuck)** — Baseball Player
4208 Locust St, Kansas City MO 64110, USA
**Dobson, Dominic** — Auto Racing Executive
PacWest Racing Group, PO Box 1717, Bellevue WA 98009, USA
**Dobson, FeFe** — Singer, Songwriter
Chris Smith Mgmt, 21 Camden St, #500, Toronto ON M5V 1V2, Canada
**Dobson, Helen** — Golfer
7638 Eagle Creek Dr, Sarasota FL 34243, USA
**Dobson, James C** — Religious Leader
Focus on the Family, 8605 Explorer Dr, Colorado Springs CO 80920, USA
**Dobson, Kevin** — Actor
Rothman/Patino/Andrés Entertainment, 4370 Tujunga Ave, #120, Studio City CA 91604, USA
**Dockery, Derrick D** — Football Player
21522 Wild Timber Court, Broadlands VA 20148, USA
**Dockery, Michelle** — Actress
Hamilton Hodell, 66-68 Margaret St, #500, London W1W 8SR, England

# D

**Dockett, Darnell**
2197 E Teakwood Place, Chandler AZ 85249, USA — Football Player
**Dockser, Amy**
Wall Street Journal, Editorial Dept, 1 World Financial Center, New York NY 10281, USA — Journalist
**Dockson, Robert R**
1301 Collingwood Place, Los Angeles CA 90069, USA — Financier
**Dockstader, Frederick J**
165 W 66th St, New York NY 10023, USA — Museum Executive
**Doctorow, Edgar Lawrence (E L)**
333 E 57th St, #118, New York NY 10022, USA — Writer
**Doda, Carol**
PO Box 387, Fremont CA 94537, USA — Exotic Dancer, Actress
**Dodd, Christina**
Pocket Books, 1230 Ave of Americas, New York NY 10020 USA — Writer
**Dodd, Deryl**
Ken-Ran Entertainment, 418 S Barton St, Grapevine TX 76051, USA — Singer, Songwriter
**Dodd, Kenneth A**
Michael O'Mara Books, 9 Lion Yard, Tremadoc Road, London SW4 7NQ, England — Actor, Comedian
**Dodd, Lois**
30 E 2nd St, New York NY 10003, USA — Artist
**Dodd, Michael T (Mike)**
1017 Manhattan Ave, Manhattan Beach CA 90266, USA — Volleyball Player
**Dodd, Patty Orozco**
1017 Manhattan Ave, Manhattan Beach CA 90266, USA — Volleyball Player
**Dodds, Megan**
Independent Talent Group, 40 Whitfield St, London W1T 2RH, England — Actress
**Dodds, Trevor**
13103 Beaver Dam Road, Saint Louis MO 63131, USA — Golfer
**Dodge, Brooks**
PO Box C, Jackson NH 03846, USA — Skier
**Dodge, Charles M**
Brooklyn College, Center for Computer Music, Brooklyn NY 11210, USA — Composer
**Dodge, Dedrick A**
1109 Bowlin Dr, Locust Grove GA 30248, USA — Football Player
**Dodge, Geoffrey A**
Business Week, Publisher's Office, 1221 Ave of Americas, New York NY 10020, USA — Publisher
**Dodge, Marcia Milgrom**
Abrams Artists, 275 7th Ave, #2600, New York NY 10001, USA — Director, Choreographer
**Dodik, Milorad**
Prime Minister's Office, Nemanjina 11, 11000 Belgrade, Serbia — Prime Minister, Serb Republic
**Dodrill, Dale F**
2579 S Independence St, Lakewood CO 80227, USA — Football Player
**Dods, Walter A, Jr**
Banc West Corp, PO Box 3200, Honolulu HI 96847, USA — Financier
**Dodson, Patrick N (Pat)**
4104 Holly Hill Road, Mebane NC 27302, USA — Baseball Player
**Doe, John**
Talent Works, 3500 W Olive Ave, #1400, Burbank CA 91505 USA — Actor
**Doering, Christopher P (Chris)**
3723 SW 20th St, Gainesville FL 32608, USA — Football Player
**Doering-Powell, Mark**
Paradigm Agency, 360 N Crescent Dr, North Building, Beverly Hills CA 90210 USA — Cinematographer
**Doerr, Robert P (Bobby)**
94449 Territorial Highway, Junction City OR 97448, USA — Baseball Player
**Doherty, John H**
202 Alpine Place, Tuckahoe NY 10707, USA — Baseball Player
**Doherty, Matt**
Southern Methodist University, Athletic Dept, Dallas TX 75275, USA — Basketball Player, Coach
**Doherty, Pete**
Primary Talent International, 10-11 Jockey's Fields, London C1R 4BN, England , USA — Singer (Libertines, Babyshambles)
**Doherty, Peter C**
67 Madison Ave, #417, Memphis TN 38103, USA — Nobel Medicine Laureate
**Doherty, Shannen**
Rebel Entertainment Partners, 5700 Wilshire Blvd, #456, Los Angeles CA 90036, USA — Actress, Model
**Dohle, Markus**
Random House, 1745 Broadway, #1800, New York NY 10019 USA — Businessman, Publisher
**Dohmann, Scott**
3222 W Paxton Ave, Tampa FL 33611, USA — Baseball Player
**Dohring, Jason**
Innovative Artists, 1505 10th St, Santa Monica CA 90401 USA — Actor
**Dohrmann, Angela**
Innovative Artists, 235 Park Ave S, #1000, New York NY 10003 USA — Actress
**Dohrmann, George**
Saint Paul Pioneer Press, Editorial Dept, 345 Cedar St, Saint Paul MN 55101, USA — Journalist
**Doi, Takako**
Socialist Democratic Party, 1-8-1 Nagatacho, Chiyodaku, Tokyo 100 8910, Japan — Government Official, Japan
**Doi, Takao**
Japanese Aerospace Exploration Agency, 2-1-1 Sengen, Tsukuba-shi, Ibaraki 305 8505, Japan — Astronaut, Japan
**Doig, Ivan**
University of Washington, English Dept, Seattle WA 98195, USA — Writer
**Doig, Jason**
2153 Broderick Ave, Duarte CA 91010, USA — Ice Hockey Player
**Doig, Lexa**
Talent Works, 3500 W Olive Ave, #1400, Burbank CA 91505 USA — Actress
**Doig, Stephen G (Steve)**
PO Box 206, North Reading MA 01864, USA — Football Player
**Doillon, Lou**
Gersh Agency, 41 Madison Ave, #3301, New York NY 10010 USA — Actress, Model
**Dokic, Jelena**
Octagon Worldwide, 800 Connecticut Ave, #200, Norwalk CT 06854 USA — Tennis Player
**Dokish, Wanita**
2480 S Grande Blvd, Greensburg PA 15601, USA — Baseball Player
**Dokiwari, Duncan**
Thell Torrence Enterprises, 5449 S Eastern Ave, #3, Las Vegas NV 89119, USA — Boxer
**Dokovic, Novak (Nole)**
Studio Magnet, Milan Marijanac, Sime Solaje 55A, 21410 Futog, Serbia , USA — Tennis Player

**Doky, Niels Lan** — Jazz Pianist, Composer
P D H Dansk Musikformidling, Dag Hammerskjolds Alle 42G, 2100 Copenhagen, Denmark
**Dolan, Charles F** — Businessman
Cablevision Systems Corp, 1111 Stewart Ave, Bethpage NY 11714, USA
**Dolan, James** — Businessman
Cablevision Systems Corp, 1111 Stewart Ave, Bethpage NY 11714, USA
**Dolan, Julie** — Actress
Laura Lichen Mgmt, PO Box 33051, Granada Hills CA 91394, USA
**Dolan, Louise A** — Physicist
University of North Carolina, Physics Dept, Chapel Hill NC 27599, USA
**Dolan, Mary Anne** — Editor
M A D Inc, 1033 Gayley Ave, #205, Los Angeles CA 90024, USA
**Dolan, Michael P** — Government Official
Internal Revenue Service, 1111 Constitution Ave NW, Washington DC 20224, USA
**Dolan, Timothy M Cardinal** — Religious Leader
Archdiocese of New York, 1011 First St, New York NY 10022, USA
**Dolan, Tom** — Swimmer
610 Poplar Dr, Falls Church VA 22046, USA
**Dolan, Xavier** — Actor
W M E Entertainment, 9601 Wilshire Blvd, #300, Beverly Hills CA 90210 USA
**Dolbin, John T (Jack)** — Football Player
1775 Howard Ave, Pottsville PA 17901, USA
**Dolby, Thomas** — Singer, Songwriter
International Talent Group, 729 7th Ave, #1600, New York NY 10019 USA
**Dolce, Domenico** — Fashion Designer
Dolce & Gabbana, Via Santa Cecilia 7, 20122 Milan, Italy
**Dold, R Bruce** — Journalist
501 N Park Road, #HSE, La Grange Park IL 60526, USA
**Dole, Elizabeth H** — Secretary, Transportation & Labor
Wings of Hope, 18370 Wings of Hope Blvd, Saint Louis MO 63005, USA
**Dole, Kathryn** — Landscape Architect
512 Brinkerhoff Ave, Santa Barbara CA 93101, USA
**Dole, Robert J** — Senator, KS
Verner Liipfert Berhard, 1200 19th St NW, Washington DC 20036, USA
**Doleac, Michael S** — Basketball Player
1155 Old Rail Lane, Park City UT 84098, USA
**Doleman, Christopher J (Chris)** — Football Player
1025 Leadenhall St, Alpharetta GA 30022, USA
**Dolenz, Ami** — Actress
K C Talent, 2408 W 8th Ave, Vancouver BC V6K 2B1, Canada
**Dolenz, Micky** — Actor, Singer, Drummer (Monkees)
Amsel Eisenstadt Frazier, 5055 Wilshire Blvd, #865, Los Angeles CA 90036 USA
**Dolgen, Jonathan L** — Businessman
Viacom Inc, 1515 Broadway, New York NY 10036, USA
**D'Oliveira, Damon** — Actor, Film Producer
LeFeaver Talent Agency, 2 College St, #202, Toronto ON M5G 1K5, Canada
**Doll, W Richard S** — Epidemiologist
12 Rawlinson Road, Oxford OX2 6UE, England
**Dollar, Linda** — Volleyball Coach
Southwest Missouri State University, Athletic Dept, Springfield MO 65804, USA
**Dolman, Bob** — Director, Writer, Actor
United Talent Agency, U T A Plaza, 9336 Civic Center Dr, Beverly Hills CA 90210 USA
**Dolmayan, John** — Drummer (System of a Down)
Velvet Hammer Music, 9014 Melrose Ave, West Hollywood CA 90069, USA
**Dombasle, Arielle** — Actress
Agence Intertalent, 5 Rue Clement Marot, 75008 Paris, France
**Dombroski, Paul M** — Football Player
19122 Beckett Dr, Odessa FL 33556, USA
**Dombrovskis, Vladis** — Prime Minister, Latvia
Prime Minister's Office, Brivibus Bulv 36, 22617 Riga PDP, Latvia
**Dombrowski, James M (Jim)** — Football Player
220 Evangeline Dr, Mandeville LA 70471, USA
**Domenichelli, Hnat A** — Ice Hockey Player
H C Lugano, Casella Postale 4226, 6904 Lugano, Switzerland
**Domi, Tie** — Ice Hockey Player
1-7357 Woodbine Ave, #415, Markham ON L3R 6L3, Canada
**Dominczyk, Dagmara** — Actress
Paradigm Agency, 360 N Crescent Dr, North Building, Beverly Hills CA 90210 USA
**Dominczyk, Marika** — Actress
I C M Partners, 10250 Constellation Blvd, #900, Los Angeles CA 90067 USA
**Domingo, Colman** — Actor
Wolf Talent Group, 165 West 46, #1104, New York NY 10036, USA
**Domingo, Placido** — Opera Singer
2728 Thomson Ave, #712, Long Island City NY 11101, USA
**Dominguez, Adolfo** — Fashion Designer
Polingono Industrial Calle 4, 32901 San Ciprian de Vinas, Ourense, Spain
**Dominguez, Mario** — Auto Racing Driver
Herdez Competition, 57 Gasoline Alley, #A, Indianapolis IN 46222, USA
**Dominik, Andrew** — Director
Creative Artists Agency, 2000 Ave of Stars, #100, Los Angeles CA 90067 USA
**Dominis, John** — Photographer
252 W 102nd St, #4, New York NY 10025, USA
**Domino, Antoine (Fats)** — Singer, Pianist
9 Wedgwood Court, Harvey LA 70058, USA
**Dominy, Charles E (Chuck)** — Army General
300 Fox Mill Road, Oakton VA 22124, USA
**Domracheva, Darya** — Biathlete
Biathlon Federation, Karl Marx Ul 10, 1220020 Minsk, Belarus
**Domres, Martin F (Marty)** — Football Player
Deutsche Bank, 1 South St, #2400, Baltimore MD 21202, USA
**Donahoe, John** — Businessman
eBay, 2125 Hamilton Ave, San Jose CA 95125, USA
**Donahue, Ann M** — Producer, Writer
W M E Entertainment, 9601 Wilshire Blvd, #300, Beverly Hills CA 90210 USA
**Donahue, Kenneth** — Museum Executive
245 S Westgate Ave, Los Angeles CA 90049, USA

Doky - Donahue

**D**

| | |
|---|---|
| **Donahue, Phil**<br>244 Madison Ave, #707, New York NY 10016, USA | Entertainer |
| **Donahue, Terry**<br>707 N Bayfront, Newport Beach CA 92662, USA | Football Coach, Sportscaster |
| **Donahue, Thomas R**<br>2425 L St NW, #326, Washington DC 20037, USA | Labor Leader |
| **Donaire, Nonito**<br>Golden Boy Promotions, 626 Wilshire Blvd, #350, Los Angeles CA 90017 USA | Boxer |
| **Donald, Jason T**<br>Cleveland Indians, Jacobs Field, 2401 Ontario St, Cleveland OH 44115 USA | Baseball Player |
| **Donald, Kirkland H**<br>Commander, Nuclear Propulsion, Washington Navy Yard, Washington DC 20374, USA | Navy Admiral |
| **Donald, Luke**<br>8 Bristol Road, Northfield IL 60093, USA | Golfer |
| **Donaldson, James L, III**<br>2843 34th Ave W, Seattle WA 98199, USA | Basketball Player |
| **Donaldson, Jeffery M (Jeff)**<br>PO Box 270634, Fort Collins CO 80527, USA | Football Player |
| **Donaldson, Lily**<br>I M G Models, 304 Park Ave S, #PH N, New York NY 10010 USA | Model |
| **Donaldson, Mark G**<br>Victoria Cross Assn, Old Admiralty Building, London SW1A 2BL, England | Afghanistan War R A F Hero (VC) |
| **Donaldson, Roger**<br>Cameron Creswell, 61 Marlborough St, #700, Surry Hills NSW 2010, Australia | Director |
| **Donaldson, Samuel A (Sam)**<br>1125 Crest Lane, McLean VA 22101, USA | Commentator |
| **Donaldson, Simon K**<br>Imperial College, 180 Queen's Gate, London SW7 2BZ, England | Mathematician |
| **Donan, Holland R (Hollie)**<br>213 Southwinds, Tinton Falls NJ 7753, USA | Football Player |
| **Donat, Peter**<br>Gersh Agency, 9465 Wilshire Blvd, #600, Beverly Hills CA 90212 USA | Actor |
| **Donatelli, Clark**<br>1101 Curtis Corner Road, Wakefield RI 02879, USA | Ice Hockey Player |
| **Donath, Helen**<br>Hannagret Bueker Agentur, Fuhsestr 2, 30419 Hannover, Germany | Opera Singer |
| **Donato, Marc**<br>C E S D, 10635 Santa Monica Blvd, #130, Los Angeles CA 90025 USA | Actor |
| **Donato, Ted**<br>34 Whitcomb Road, Scituate MA 02066, USA | Ice Hockey Player |
| **Done, Kenneth S (Ken)**<br>17 Thurlow St, Redfern NSW 2016, Australia | Graphic Artist |
| **Donegan, Dan**<br>Agency Group Ltd, 142 W 57th St, #600, New York NY 10019 USA | Guitarist (Disturbed) |
| **Donella, Chad E**<br>Talent Works, 3500 W Olive Ave, #1400, Burbank CA 91505 USA | Actor |
| **Donelly, Tanya**<br>Helter Skelter, 347-353 Chiswick High Road, London W4 4HS, England | Singer, Songwriter |
| **Donen, Stanley**<br>30 W 63rd St, #25, New York NY 10023, USA | Director |
| **Doniger, Wendy**<br>1319 E 55th St, Chicago IL 60615, USA | Theologian, Historian |
| **Donlan, Yolande**<br>11 Mellina Place, Belgravia, London NW8 9SA, England | Actress |
| **Donleavy, James Patrick (J P)**<br>Levington Park, Mullingar, County Westmeath, Ireland | Writer |
| **Donlon, Roger H C**<br>2101 Wilson Ave, Leavenworth KS 66048, USA | Vietnam War Army Hero (CMH) |
| **Donnalley, Kevin E**<br>8910 Dove Stand Lane, Charlotte NC 28226, USA | Football Player |
| **Donnellan, Declan**<br>Cheek by Jowl Theatre Co, Aveline St, London SW11 5DQ, England | Director |
| **Donnelly, Brendan K**<br>2815 E Arrowhead Trail, Gilbert AZ 85297, USA | Baseball Player |
| **Donnelly, Declan**<br>B/W/R, 9100 Wilshire Blvd, #500W, Beverly Hills CA 90212 USA | Actor |
| **Donnelly, Gord**<br>110 Ave Claude, Dorval QC H9S 3A7, Canada | Ice Hockey Player |
| **Donnelly, John J**<br>Commander, Submarine Command Atlantic, 7958 Blandy Road, Norfolk VA 23511 USA | Navy Admiral |
| **Donnelly, Rick**<br>1796 Danforth Dr, Marietta GA 30062, USA | Football Player |
| **Donnelly, Russell J**<br>2175 Olive St, Eugene OR 97405, USA | Physicist |
| **Donnelly, Tanya**<br>High Road Touring, 751 Bridgeway, #200, Sausalito CA 94965 USA | Singer, Guitarist |
| **Donnels, Chris B**<br>5 Stone Pine, Aliso Viejo CA 92656, USA | Baseball Player |
| **Donner, Jorn J**<br>Pohjoisranta 12, 00170 Helsinki 17, Finland | Director |
| **D'Onofrio, Vincent**<br>Maydew & Golenberg, 8383 Wilshire Blvd, #1050, Beverly Hills CA 90211, USA | Actor |
| **Donoghue, Denis**<br>Gaybrook, North Ave, Mount Merrion, County Dublin, Ireland | Writer |
| **Donoghue, Mary Agnes**<br>Gersh Agency, 9465 Wilshire Blvd, #600, Beverly Hills CA 90212 USA | Writer |
| **Donoghue, Paul**<br>Sony Music, 9 Derry St, London W8 5HY, England | Singer, Bassist (Glasvegas) |
| **Donohoe, Amanda**<br>Artist Rights Group, 4 Great Portland St, London W1W 8PA, England | Actress |
| **Donohoe, Michael P (Mike)**<br>1110 E Acacia Circle, Litchfield Park AZ 85340, USA | Football Player |
| **Donohoe, Peter H**<br>82 Hampton Lane, Solihull, West Midlands B91 2RS, England | Concert Pianist |
| **Donohue, James T (Jim)**<br>16 Huntleigh Downs, Saint Louis MO 63131, USA | Baseball Player |

Donohue, Leon — Football Player
1904 Bechelli Lane, Redding CA 96002, USA
Donohue, Peter M — Educator
Villanova University, President's Office, 800 Lancaster Ave, Villanova PA 19085, USA
Donohue, Thomas J (Tom) — Baseball Player
249 Liberty Ave, Westbury NY 11590, USA
Donohue, Timothy — Businessman
Nextel Communications, 2001 Edmund Halley Dr, Reston VA 20191, USA
Donose, Ruxandra — Opera Singer
Columbia Artists Mgmt Inc, 1790 Broadway, #702, New York NY 10019 USA
Donovan — Singer, Songwriter, Actor
PO Box 1119, London SW9 9JW, England
Donovan, Anne — Basketball Player, Coach
138 Ridge Road, Nutley NJ 7110, USA
Donovan, Brian — Journalist
Newsday, Editorial Dept, 235 Pinelawn Road, Melville NY 11747, USA
Donovan, Francis R (Frank) — Navy Admiral
9216 Dellwood Dr, Vienna VA 22180, USA
Donovan, H Harry — Basketball Player
8303 Bayonet Point Court, #C, Gainesville FL 32608, USA
Donovan, Jason S — Singer, Actor
United Agents, 12-26 Lexington St, London W1F 0LE, England
Donovan, Jeffrey — Actor
Paradigm Agency, 360 Park Ave S, #1600, New York NY 10010 USA
Donovan, Landon — Soccer Player
Los Angeles Galaxy, Home Depot Center, 18400 Avalon Blvd, Carson CA 90746 USA
Donovan, Martin — Actor
Parseghian/Planco, 388 2nd Ave, #506, New York, NY 10010 USA
Donovan, Patrick E (Pat) — Football Player
113 S Prairiesmoke Circle, Whitefish MT 59937, USA
Donovan, Raymond J — Secretary, Labor
1600 Paterson Park Road, Secaucus NJ 07094, USA
Donovan, Shaun L S — Secretary, Housing & Urban Development
Housing & Urban Development Department, 451 7th SW, Washington DC 20410 USA
Donovan, Tate — Actor
Gersh Agency, 9465 Wilshire Blvd, #600, Beverly Hills CA 90212 USA
Donovan, William J (Billy) — Basketball Player, Coach
8515 SW 31st Ave, Gainesville FL 32608, USA
Donowho, Ryan — Actor, Producer
Schiff Co, 9200 Sunset Blvd, #430, West Hollywood CA 90232 USA
Donzelli, Valerie — Director
U B B A, 6 Rue de Braque, 75003 Paris, France
Doo Ri Chung — Fashion Designer
Doo Ri Fashions, 831 Madison Ave, New York NY 10021, USA
Doody, Alison — Actress
Commercial Agency, 16 Harcourt Terrace, London SW1W 9JR, England
Doolan, Wendy — Golfer
3353 Turnberry Dr, Lakeland FL 33803, USA
Dooley, David M — Educator
University of Rhode Island, President's Office, 6 Rhodney Ram Way, Kingston RI 02881, USA
Dooley, James M (Jim) — Composer
Gorfaine/Schwartz, 4111 W Alameda Ave, #509, Burbank CA 91505 USA
Dooley, Paul — Actor
Innovative Artists, 1505 10th St, Santa Monica CA 90401 USA
Dooley, Taylor M — Actress
Evolution Entertainment, 901 N Highland Ave, Los Angeles CA 90038 USA
Dooley, Vincent J (Vince) — Football Player, Coach, Administrator
University of Georgia, Athletic Dept, PO Box 1472, Athens GA 30603, USA
Dooling, Keyon L — Basketball Player
2016 NW 3rd Court, Fort Lauderdale FL 33311, USA
Doolittle, Eliza — Singer, Songwriter
Insanity Artists, 5 Little Portland St, London W1W 7JD, England
Doolittle, Melinda — Singer
1524 Braden Circle, Franklin TN 37067, USA
Doorman, Dana — Golfer
David Binkley, 201 W Big Beaver Road, #500, Troy MI 48084, USA
Doornink, Daniel E (Dan) — Football Player
401 S 12th Ave, Yakima WA 98902, USA
Dopson, John R — Baseball Player
3337 Old Gambler Road, Finksburg MD 21048, USA
Dor, Karin — Actress
Nordliche Munchner Str 43, 82031 Grunwald, Germany
Doran, William P (Bill) — Baseball Player
5720 Grand Legacy Dr, Maineville OH 45039, USA
Dore, Andre — Ice Hockey Player
73 Betsys Lane, Kingston ON K7M 7B6, Canada
Dore, Jon — Actor, Comedian
Gersh Agency, 9465 Wilshire Blvd, #600, Beverly Hills CA 90212 USA
Dore, Ronald Philip — Sociologist
157 Surrenden Road, Brighton, East Sussex BN1 6ZA, England
Dorensky, Sergey L — Concert Pianist
Bryusov Per 8/10, #75, Moscow 103009, Russia
Dorey, Jim — Ice Hockey Player
105 Aaron Place, Amherstview ON K7N 2A1, Canada
Dorff, Stephen — Actor
I C M Partners, 10250 Constellation Blvd, #900, Los Angeles CA 90067 USA
Dorfman, Ariel — Writer
Duke University, International Studies Center, 2122 Campus Dr, Durham NC 27708, USA
Dorfman, David — Actor
Abrams Artists, 9200 W Sunset Blvd, #1125, West Hollywood CA 90069 USA
Dorfmeister, Michaela — Alpine Skier
Quellenstr 12, 2763 Neusiedl, Austria
Dorgan, Byron L — Senator, ND
Arent Fox LLP, 1050 Connecticut Ave NW, Washington DC 20036, USA
Dorian, Antonia — Actress
3940 Laurel Canyon Blvd, PO Box 342, Studio City CA 91604, USA

# D

| | |
|---|---|
| **Dorin, Marie** | Biathlete |
| Le Ruisseay, 38190 Laval, France | |
| **Dorin-Ballard, Carolyn** | Bowler |
| Del Ballard, Ebonite International, PO Box 746, Hopkinsville KY 42241, USA | |
| **Dorion, Dan** | Ice Hockey Player |
| 3910 28th St, Long Island City NY 11101, USA | |
| **Dority, Douglas H** | Labor Leader |
| United Food/Commercial Workers Union, 1775 K St NW, Washington DC 20006, USA | |
| **Dorman, Dave** | Illustrator |
| Rolling Thunder, 405 Windham Trail, Carpentersville IL 60110, USA | |
| **Dormann, Dana** | Golfer |
| 4887 Arlene Place, Pleasanton CA 94566, USA | |
| **Dormer, Natalie** | Actress |
| United Agents, 12-26 Lexington St, London W1F 0LE, England | |
| **Dorn, Michael** | Actor |
| Innovative Artists, 1505 10th St, Santa Monica CA 90401 USA | |
| **Dornan, Jamie** | Actor, Model |
| United Agents, 12-26 Lexington St, London W1F 0LE, England | |
| **Dorney, Keith R** | Football Player |
| 2450 Blucher Valley Road, Sebastopol CA 95472, USA | |
| **Dornhelm, Robert** | Actor |
| Paradigm Agency, 360 N Crescent Dr, North Building, Beverly Hills CA 90210 USA | |
| **Dornhoefer, Gary** | Ice Hockey Player |
| 267 Chestnut Neck Road, Port Republic NJ 08241, USA | |
| **Doronina, Tatyana V** | Actress |
| Gorky Arts Theater, 22 Tverskoi Blvd, 119146 Moscow, Russia | |
| **Dorough, Howie** | Singer (Backstreet Boys) |
| World Concerts, Hamburger Str 273a, 38114 Braunschweig, Germany | |
| **Dorris, Andrew M (Andy)** | Football Player |
| 12391 Ike White Road, Conroe TX 77303, USA | |
| **Dorroh, Jefferson D** | WW II Marine Corps Air Force Hero |
| 10032 136th Ave NE, Kirkland WA 98033, USA | |
| **Dorrough, Holley Ann** | Model |
| D G I Mgmt, 609 Greenwich St, #600, New York NY 10014, USA | |
| **D'Orsay, Brooke** | Actress |
| M B S T Entertainment, 345 N Maple Dr, #200, Beverly Hills CA 90210, USA | |
| **Dorsaz, Damien** | Actor |
| Artmedia, 20 Ave Rapp, 75007 Paris, France | |
| **Dorsen, Norman** | Attorney |
| 146 Central Park W, New York NY 10023, USA | |
| **Dorsett, Anthony D (Tony)** | Football Player |
| Tony Dorsett Foods, 321 High St, Burlington NJ 08016, USA | |
| **Dorsett, Anthony, Jr** | Football Player |
| 3817 Bowser Ave, #C, Dallas TX 75219, USA | |
| **Dorsett, Brian R** | Baseball Player |
| 700 Dobbs Glen St, Terre Haute IN 47803, USA | |
| **Dorsey, Eric H** | Football Player |
| 5 London Court, Teaneck NJ 07666, USA | |
| **Dorsey, Glenn** | Football Player |
| 4242 NE Edmonson Court, Lees Summit MO 64064, USA | |
| **Dorsey, Jack** | Businessman |
| Twitter Inc, 795 Folsom St, #600, San Francisco CA 94107, USA | |
| **Dorsey, Jacky** | Basketball Player |
| 1231 S Teal Estates Circle, Fresno TX 77545, USA | |
| **Dorsey, James E (Jim)** | Baseball Player |
| 335 Elm St, Seekonk MA 02771, USA | |
| **Dorsey, Kenneth S (Ken)** | Football Player |
| 7108 Presidio Glen, Lakewood Ranch FL 34202, USA | |
| **Dorsey, Kerris Lilla** | Actress |
| W M E Entertainment, 9601 Wilshire Blvd, #300, Beverly Hills CA 90210 USA | |
| **Dorsey, Richard E (Joey)** | Basketball Player |
| Houston Rockets, 1730 Jefferson St, Houston TX 77003 USA | |
| **Dorta, Melvin** | Baseball Player |
| 1351 Cambridge Court, Palmyra PA 17078, USA | |
| **Doshi, Balkkrishna V** | Architect |
| 14 Shree Sadma Society, Navrangpura, Ahmedabad 380009, India | |
| **Dosoretz, Daniel E** | Physician, Businessman |
| 1120 Lee Blvd, Lehigh Acres FL 33936, USA | |
| **DosSantos Ramirez, Giovani** | Soccer Player |
| Federacion de Futbol, Colima 373 Colonia Roma, Delegacion Cuauhtemoc, Mexico City DF 06700, Mexico | |
| **DosSantos, Alexandre J M Cardinal** | Religious Leader |
| Paco Arquiepiscopal, Avenida Eduardo Mondlane 1448, CP Maputo, Mozambique | |
| **DosSantos, Jose Eduardo** | President, Angola |
| President's Office, Palacio do Povo, Luanda, Angola | |
| **Dost, Andrew P** | Musician (Fun), Songwriter |
| Nettwerk Management Group, 1650 W 2nd Ave, Vancouver BC V6J 4R3, Canada , USA | |
| **Dostal, Josef** | Canoeing Athlete |
| A S O Dukla Prague, Cisarska Iouka 1, 15500 Prague, Czech Republic | |
| **Dotel, Octavio E** | Baseball Player |
| 382 Oakland Road, Lawrenceville GA 30044, USA | |
| **Dotrice, Roy** | Actor |
| Lord, 6 Meadow Lane, Leasingham, Sleaford, Lincolnshire NG34 8LL, England | |
| **Dotson, Earl C** | Football Player |
| 1112 Azalea Dr, Longview TX 75601, USA | |
| **Dotson, Richard E (Rich)** | Baseball Player |
| 7 Colonel Watson Dr, New Richmond OH 45157, USA | |
| **Dotson, Santana N** | Football Player |
| PO Box 79134, Houston TX 77279, USA | |
| **Dotter, Bobby** | Auto, Truck Racing Driver |
| 3630 N Pacific Ave, Chicago IL 60634, USA | |
| **Dotter, Gary R** | Baseball Player |
| 7413 Ravenswood Road, Granbury TX 76049, USA | |
| **Dottley, Jason** | Actor |
| B/W/R, 9100 Wilshire Blvd, #500W, Beverly Hills CA 90212 USA | |
| **Doty, Mark** | Writer |
| Rutgers State University, English Dept, New Brunswick NJ 08903, USA | |

**Dorin - Doty**

| | |
|---|---|
| **Douaihy, Saliba** | Artist |
| Vining Road, Windham NY 12496, USA | |
| **Doucet, David** | Singer, Guitarist (BeauSoleil) |
| Rosebud Agency, PO Box 170429, San Francisco CA 94117 USA | |
| **Doucet, Michael** | Singer, Fiddler (BeauSoleil) |
| Rosebud Agency, PO Box 170429, San Francisco CA 94117 USA | |
| **Doucett, Linda** | Actress, Model |
| Michael Slessinger, 8730 W Sunset Blvd, #220W, West Hollywood CA 90069 USA | |
| **Doucette, Jeff** | Actor |
| C E S D, 10635 Santa Monica Blvd, #130, Los Angeles CA 90025 USA | |
| **Doufexis, Stella** | Opera Singer |
| Kunstler Sekretariat am Gasteig, Rosenheimer Str 52, 81669 Munich, Germany | |
| **Doug, Doug E** | Actor, Comedian |
| Brillstein Entertainment, 375 Greenwich St, New York NY 10013, USA | |
| **Dougherty, Dennis A** | Chemist |
| 1817 Bushnell Ave, South Pasadena CA 91030, USA | |
| **Dougherty, Ed** | Golfer |
| 448 SW Fairway Vista, Port Saint Lucie FL 34986, USA | |
| **Dougherty, James E (Jim)** | Baseball Player |
| 102 Pinnacle Court, Kitty Hawk NC 27949, USA | |
| **Dougherty, Joseph** | Producer, Director, Writer |
| Katz Golden Sullivan Rosenman, 2001 Wilshire Blvd, #400, Santa Monica CA 90403, USA | |
| **Dougherty, Mike** | Guitarist, Songwriter |
| High Road Touring, 751 Bridgeway, #200, Sausalito CA 94965 USA | |
| **Dougherty, Tom** | Clown |
| Ringling Bros Barnum & Bailey, 8607 Westwood Circle Dr, Vienna VA 22182 USA | |
| **Dougherty, William A, Jr** | Navy Admiral |
| 1505 Colonial Court, Arlington VA 22209, USA | |
| **Doughty, Glenn** | Football Player |
| 8808 Saint Charles Rock Road, Saint Louis MO 63114, USA | |
| **Doughty, Kenny** | Actor |
| United Agents, 12-26 Lexington St, London W1F 0LE, England | |
| **Doughty, Neal** | Keyboardist (REO Speedwagon) |
| Front Line Mgmt, 1100 Glendon Ave, #2000, Los Angeles CA 90024 USA | |
| **Doughty, Reed** | Football Player |
| Washington Redskins, 21300 Redskin Park Dr, Ashburn VA 20147 USA | |
| **Douglas, Andrew** | Director |
| W M E Entertainment, 9601 Wilshire Blvd, #300, Beverly Hills CA 90210 USA | |
| **Douglas, Anslem** | Composer, Entertainer |
| J W Records, 2833 Church Ave, Brooklyn NY 11226, USA | |
| **Douglas, Barry** | Concert Pianist |
| I M G Artists, Hogarth Business Park, Chiswick, London W4 2TH, England | |
| **Douglas, Bobby** | Wrestler, Coach |
| Bobby Douglas Wrestling Camps, 5520 Hickory Hills Dr, Ames IA 50014, USA | |
| **Douglas, Brandon** | Actor |
| 1546 Caitlyn Circle, Westlake Village CA 91361, USA | |
| **Douglas, Cameron** | Actor |
| Creative Management Group, 8522 National Blvd, #108, Culver City CA 90232 USA | |
| **Douglas, Charles W (Whammy)** | Baseball Player |
| 1711 Caterine Lake Road, Jacksonville NC 28540, USA | |
| **Douglas, Cullen** | Actor |
| Greene Assoc, 1901 Ave of Stars, #130, Los Angeles CA 90067 USA | |
| **Douglas, David A (Dave)** | Drummer (Relient K, Attack Cat) |
| Janlyn Public Relations, 106 Cabrini Blvd, #4-I, New York NY 10033, USA | |
| **Douglas, David G** | Football Player |
| 605 Snowshill Way, Maryville TN 37803, USA | |
| **Douglas, Denzil L** | Prime Minister, Saint Kitts & Nevis |
| Prime Minister's Office, Government Building, Waterfront, Basseterre, Saint Kitts & Nevis | |
| **Douglas, Donna** | Actress |
| B G A Music, PO Box 1038, Lincolnton NC 28093, USA | |
| **Douglas, Gabriel C V (Gabby)** | Gymnast |
| Chow's Gymnastics/Dance Institute, 2210 Park Dr, West Des Moines IA 50265, USA | |
| **Douglas, Illeana** | Actress |
| Eleven Minutes Entertainment, 11812 San Vicente Blvd, Los Angeles CA 90049, USA | |
| **Douglas, James (Buster)** | Boxer |
| 545 Towne Court N, Gahanna OH 43230, USA | |
| **Douglas, Jerry** | Actor |
| Stone Manners Salners, 9911 W Pico Blvd, #1400, Los Angeles CA 90035 USA | |
| **Douglas, Jordy** | Ice Hockey Player |
| Courts Financial Group, 5-2727 Portage Ave, Winnipeg MB R3J 0R2, Canada | |
| **Douglas, Kirk** | Actor |
| 805 N Rexford Dr, Beverly Hills CA 90210, USA | |
| **Douglas, Kyan** | Actor |
| Creative Artists Agency, 2000 Ave of Stars, #100, Los Angeles CA 90067 USA | |
| **Douglas, Leon** | Basketball Player |
| 6265 Sun Blvd, #402G, Saint Petersburg FL 33715, USA | |
| **Douglas, Merrill G** | Football Player |
| 2185 E 3970 S, Salt Lake City UT 84124, USA | |
| **Douglas, Michael K** | Actor, Director, Producer |
| Furthur Films, 250 W 57th St, #808, New York NY 10107, USA | |
| **Douglas, Sarah** | Actress |
| R D F Mgmt, 3-6 Kenrick Place, London W1U 6HD, England | |
| **Douglas, Sherman** | Basketball Player |
| 10401 Stapleford Hall Dr, Potomac MD 20854, USA | |
| **Douglass, Dale** | Golfer |
| 6601 E San Miguel Ave, Paradise Valley AZ 85253, USA | |
| **Douglass, Maurice G** | Football Player |
| 1021 Sunset Dr, Englewood OH 45322, USA | |
| **Douglass, Robert G (Bobby)** | Football Player |
| 151 E Laurel Ave, #203, Lake Forest IL 60045, USA | |
| **Doumbia, Mariam** | Singer (Amadou & Mariam) |
| Partisan Arts, PO Box 5085, Larkspur CA 94977, USA | |
| **Doumit, Ryan M** | Baseball Player |
| 5232 Ridgeview Dr Loop NE, Moses Lake WA 98837, USA | |
| **Doumit, Sam** | Actress |
| B/W/R, 9100 Wilshire Blvd, #500W, Beverly Hills CA 90212 USA | |

**D**

Douaihy - Doumit

**Dourdan, Gary** — Actor
Talent Works, 3500 W Olive Ave, #1400, Burbank CA 91505 USA
**Dourif, Bradford C (Brad)** — Actor
Innovative Artists, 1505 10th St, Santa Monica CA 90401 USA
**Dove, Dennis** — Baseball Player
144 Kirk Lane, Ocilla GA 31774, USA
**Dove, Edward E (Eddie)** — Football Player
1750 Poppy Ave, Menlo Park CA 94025, USA
**Dove, Rita F** — Writer
1757 Lambs Road, Charlottesville VA 22901, USA
**Dove, Ronnie** — Singer
Ken Keene Artists, PO Box 1875, Gretna LA 70054, USA
**Dovolani, Driton (Tony)** — Dancer
Abrams Artists, 9200 W Sunset Blvd, #1125, West Hollywood CA 90069 USA
**Dow, Ellen Albertini** — Actress
Greene Assoc, 1901 Ave of Stars, #130, Los Angeles CA 90067 USA
**Dow, Tony** — Actor
Imperium 7 Artists, 5455 Wilshire Blvd, #1706, Los Angeles CA 90036 USA
**Dowd, Ann** — Actress
Innovative Artists, 1505 10th St, Santa Monica CA 90401 USA
**Dowd, James T (Jim)** — Ice Hockey Player
708 New Jersey Ave, Point Pleasant Beach NJ 08742, USA
**Dowd, Maureen** — Columnist
New York Times, Editorial Dept, 229 W 43rd St, New York NY 10036 USA
**Dowding, Leilani** — Model, Actress
A C Talent Agency, 9595 Wilshire Blvd, #900, Beverly Hills CA 90212, USA
**Dowell, Anthony J** — Ballet Dancer
Royal Ballet, Covent Garden, Bow St, London WC2E 9DD, England
**Dowell, Kenneth A (Ken)** — Baseball Player
5221 Helen Way, Sacramento CA 95822, USA
**Dower, John W** — Writer
Massachusetts Institute of Technology, History Dept, Cambridge MA 02139, USA
**Dowle, David** — Drummer (Whitesnake)
International Talent Booking, Ariel House, 74A Charlotte St, #100 London W1T 4QJ, England
**Dowler, Boyd H** — Football Player
5309 Creek Heights Dr, Midlothian VA 23112, USA
**Dowling, David B (Dave)** — Baseball Player
173 Whelan Way, Manteca CA 95336, USA
**Dowling, John E** — Biologist, Neurobiologist
135 Charles St, Boston MA 02114, USA
**Dowling, Timothy (Tim)** — Actor, Writer
Mosiac Media Group, 9200 W Sunset Blvd, #1000, Los Angeles CA 90069 USA
**Down, Lesley-Anne** — Actress
6252 Paseo Canyon Dr, Malibu CA 90265, USA
**Down, Sarah** — Cartoonist (Betsey's Buddies)
Playboy, Reader Services, 680 N Lake Shore Dr, Chicago IL 60611, USA
**Downes, Lorraine E** — Beauty Queen
Miss Universe NZ, PO Box 39624, Howick, Auckland 2145, New Zealand
**Downes, Terry** — Boxer
Oaklea, 29 Meadowsbank, Watford WD19 4NP, England
**Downey, Chris** — Producer, Writer
Creative Artists Agency, 2000 Ave of Stars, #100, Los Angeles CA 90067 USA
**Downey, Raymond** — Boxer
Boxing Canada, 888 Belfast Road, Ottawa ON K1G 0Z6, Canada
**Downey, Robert J** — Director
I C M Partners, 10250 Constellation Blvd, #900, Los Angeles CA 90067 USA
**Downey, Robert, Jr** — Actor, Singer, Songwriter
McDaniel Entertainment, 1311 Broadway, Santa Monica CA 90404, USA
**Downey, Roma** — Actress
Abrams Artists, 9200 W Sunset Blvd, #1125, West Hollywood CA 90069 USA
**Downey, William K (Bill)** — Basketball Player
1035 S Moorings Dr, Arlington Heights IL 60005, USA
**Downie, Gordon** — Singer, Guitarist (Tragically Hip)
Bobby Breen Mgmt, 13 Blackburn St, #300, Toronto ON M4M 2B3, Canada
**Downing, Alphonso E (Al)** — Baseball Player
25343 Silver Aspen Way, #735, Valencia CA 91381, USA
**Downing, Brian J** — Baseball Player
8095 County Road 135, Celina TX 75009, USA
**Downing, George** — Surfer, Surfing Executive
Get Wet!, 3021 Waialae Ave, Honolulu HI 96816, USA
**Downing, James (Jim)** — Auto Racing Driver
5096 Peachtree Road, Atlanta GA 30341, USA
**Downing, Kenneth K (K K), Jr** — Guitarist (Judas Priest)
Trinifold Mgmt, 12 Oval Road, #300, Camden, London NW1 7D4, England
**Downing, Sara** — Actress
Amsel Eisenstadt Frazier, 5055 Wilshire Blvd, #865, Los Angeles CA 90036 USA
**Downing, Vern** — Bowler
523 Napa St, Rodeo CA 94572, USA
**Downing, Walter T (Walt)** — Football Player
1141 Durham Circle NW, Massillon OH 44646, USA
**Downs, Anthony** — Political Scientist
Brookings Institute, 1775 Massachusetts Ave NW, Washington DC 20036 USA
**Downs, David R (Dave)** — Baseball Player
925 E 1050 N, Bountiful UT 84010, USA
**Downs, Gary M** — Football Player
3953 Balleycastle Dr, Duluth GA 30097, USA
**Downs, Hugh M** — Commentator
7993 N Ridgeview Dr, Paradise Valley AZ 85253, USA
**Downs, Kelly R** — Baseball Player
6459 Willow Creek Road, Morgan UT 84050, USA
**Downs, Michael (Mike)** — Football Player
1405 Knob Hill Dr, DeSoto TX 75115, USA
**Downs, Scott** — Baseball Player
6814 Barbrook Road, Louisville KY 40258, USA
**Dowse, Michael** — Director
United Talent Agency, U T A Plaza, 9336 Civic Center Dr, Beverly Hills CA 90210 USA

**Dowson, Philip M** — Architect
Royal Academy of Arts, Piccadilly, London W1V 0DS, England
**Doyle, Allan** — Singer (Great Big Sea)
Fleming Assoc, 167 Little Lake Dr, Ann Arbor MI 48103, USA
**Doyle, Allen** — Golfer
512 Riverside Dr, LaGrange GA 30240, USA
**Doyle, Brian R** — Baseball Player
1310 Meadown Circle NE, Winter Haven FL 33881, USA
**Doyle, Christopher** — Cinematographer
I C M Partners, Marlborough House, 10 Earlham St, #300, London WC2H 9LNP, England
**Doyle, J Patrick** — Businessman
Domino's Pizza, PO Box 997, Ann Arbor MI 48106, USA
**Doyle, James H, Jr** — Navy Admiral
6200 Oregon Ave NW, #420, Washington DC 20015, USA
**Doyle, Jeffrey D (Jeff)** — Baseball Player
830 SE Bayshore Circle, Corvallis OR 97333, USA
**Doyle, Patrick** — Composer
Air Edel, 9100 Wilshire Blvd, #350E, Beverly Hills CA 90212 USA
**Doyle, R Dennis (Denny)** — Baseball Player
PO Box 9156, Winter Haven FL 33883, USA
**Doyle, Roddy** — Writer
Random House, 1745 Broadway, #1800, New York NY 10019 USA
**Doyle, Shawn** — Actor
Paul Kohner, 9300 Wilshire Blvd, #555, Beverly Hills CA 90212 USA
**Doyle-Murray, Brian** — Actor, Comedian
Abrams Artists, 9200 Sunset Blvd, #625, Los Angeles CA 90069, USA
**Doyne, Cory** — Baseball Player
20229 County Line Road, Lutz FL 33558, USA
**Dozier, James L** — Army General
1387 Wales Dr, Fort Myers FL 33901, USA
**Dozier, Lamont** — Singer, Songwriter
320 E Charleston Blvd, #205-130, Las Vegas NV 89104, USA
**Dozier, Terry** — Basketball Player
1037 Congress Road, Arlington Heights IL 60005, USA
**Dozier, Thomas D (Tom)** — Baseball Player
1231 Willow Ave, #D7, Hercules CA 94547, USA
**Dozier, William H (D J)** — Football, Baseball Player
PO Box 2722, Norfolk VA 23501, USA
**Dozy** — Bassist (Dave Dee Dozy Beaky Mick Tich)
Gerd Kehren Mgmt, Postfach 1408, 41804 Erkelenz, Germany
**Dr Demento** — Entertainer
Skyline Music, 48 Prospect St, Whitefield NH 03598, USA
**Dr Dre** — Rap Artist, Record Producer, Actor
Aftermath Entertainment, 2220 Colorado Ave, Santa Monica CA 90404, USA
**Dr John** — Jazz Pianist, Singer, Songwriter
Impact Artists Mgmt, 356 W 123rd St, New York NY 10027, USA
**Drabble, Margaret** — Writer
Penguin Books, 375 Hudson St, Basement 1, New York NY 10014 USA
**Drabek, Douglas D (Doug)** — Baseball Player
2 Peony Springs Court, Spring TX 77382, USA
**Drabinsky, Garth H** — Producer
Livent Inc, 165 Avenue Road, #600, Toronto ON M5R 3S4, Canada
**Draffen, Willis** — Singer (Bloodstone)
16103 Vista Del Mar Dr, Houston TX 77083, USA
**Draft, Christopher M (Chris)** — Football Player
970 E Oak St, Anaheim CA 92805, USA
**Dragic, Goran** — Basketball Player
Phoenix Suns, 201 E Jefferson St, Phoenix AZ 85004 USA
**Draglia, Stacy** — Track Athlete
PO Box 30931, Phoenix AZ 85046, USA
**Drago, Billy** — Actor
Deborah Miller, 9454 Wilshire Blvd, #715, Beverly Hills CA 90212, USA
**Drago, Richard A (Dick)** — Baseball Player
4703 Belle Chase Circle, Tampa FL 33634, USA
**Dragon, Daryl** — Musician (Captain & Tennille)
Greenlaw, 1251 S Cimarron Road, #22, Las Vegas NV 89117, USA
**Dragoti, Stan** — Director
1800 Ave of Stars, #430, Los Angeles CA 90067, USA
**Drahman, Brian S** — Baseball Player
46 Mariner Green Dr, Corte Madera CA 94925, USA
**Drahos, Nicholas (Nick)** — Football Player
3158 State Route 90, Aurora NY 13026, USA
**Draiman, Dave** — Singer (Disturbed)
Agency Group Ltd, 142 W 57th St, #600, New York NY 10019 USA
**Drake** — Singer, Rap Artist, Actor
Bryant Mgmt, 800 Brickell Ave, #550, Miami FL 33131, USA
**Drake, Bebe** — Actress
Ashby/Rojo Entertainment, 1485 S Beverly Dr, Los Angeles CA 90035, USA
**Drake, Dallas** — Ice Hockey Player
11472 E Cedar Bay Trail, Traverse City MI 49684, USA
**Drake, Frank D** — Astronomer
Search for ExtraTerrestrial Intelligence Institute, 515 N Whisman Road, Mountain View CA 94043, USA
**Drake, Jamie** — Interior Designer
Drake Design Assoc, 315 E 62nd St, #500, New York NY 10065, USA
**Drake, Jeremy** — Astronomer
Harvard University, Smithsonian Center for Astrophysics, Cambridge MA 02138, USA
**Drake, Judith** — Actress
Schiowitz Connor, 1680 N Vine St, #1016, Los Angeles CA 90028 USA
**Drake, Julius** — Concert Pianist
I M G Artists, Hogarth Business Park, Chiswick, London W4 2TH, England
**Drake, Kenneth** — Artist, Sculptor
Carrer D'es Port 2, #6, 07720 Es Castell, Minorca, Balearic Islands, Spain
**Drake, Larry** — Actor
Amsel Eisenstadt Frazier, 5055 Wilshire Blvd, #865, Los Angeles CA 90036 USA
**Drake, Michael V** — Educator
University of California, Chancellor's Office, Irvine CA 92697, USA

**Drake, Solomon L (Solly)** — Baseball Player
1732 S Corning St, Los Angeles CA 90035, USA
**Drake, Thomas** — Basketball Coach
Drake University, Athletic Dept, Des Moines IA 50311, USA
**Drakeford, Tyronne J** — Football Player
2311 Baron DeKalb Road, Camden SC 29020, USA
**Draper, Courtnee** — Actress
C E S D, 10635 Santa Monica Blvd, #130, Los Angeles CA 90025 USA
**Draper, Dave** — Body Builder
837 California St, Santa Cruz CA 95060, USA
**Draper, Kris** — Ice Hockey Player
3418 Westchester Road, Bloomfield Hills MI 48304, USA
**Draper, Michael H (Mike)** — Baseball Player
18317 Manor Church Road, Boonsboro MD 21713, USA
**Draper, Polly** — Actress
Innovative Artists, 1505 10th St, Santa Monica CA 90401 USA
**Draper, Timothy C** — Financier
Draper Fisher Jurvetson, 2802 Sand Hill Road, Menlo Park CA 94025, USA
**Draper, Tom** — Ice Hockey Player
76 Blackstone Ave, Binghamton NY 13903, USA
**Draper, William H, III** — Financier
91 Tallwood Court, Atherton CA 94027, USA
**Dratch, Rachel** — Actress, Comedienne
Paradigm Agency, 360 N Crescent Dr, North Building, Beverly Hills CA 90210 USA
**Dravecky, David F (Dave)** — Baseball Player
475 W 12th Ave, #8F, Denver CO 80204, USA
**Draxl, Tim** — Actor
Management 360, 9111 Wilshire Blvd, Beverly Hills CA 90210 USA
**Dray, Albert** — Actor
Artmedia, 20 Ave Rapp, 75007 Paris, France
**Drayton, Kia** — Model
Playboy Promotions, 2706 Media Center Dr, Los Angeles CA 90065 USA
**Drayton, T Anthony (Troy)** — Football Player
31 Oak St, #1, Patchogue NY 11772, USA
**Drechsler, Heike** — Track Athlete
Ans Sport GmbH, An der Eickesmuhle 31, 41238 Monohengladbach, Germany
**Drecker, Anneli M** — Singer (Bel Canto)
Kjell Kalleklev Mgmt, Georgernes Verft 12N, 5011 Bergen, Norway
**Drees, Thomas K (Tom)** — Baseball Player
18638 Bearpath Trail, Eden Prairie MN 55347, USA
**Dreesen, Tom** — Actor, Comedian
14538 Benefit St, #301, Sherman Oaks CA 91403, USA
**Dreier, R Chad** — Businessman
Ryland Group, 6300 Canoga Ave, Woodland Hills CA 91367, USA
**Dreifort, Darren J** — Baseball Player
463 Wynola St, Pacific Palisades CA 90272, USA
**Dreiling, Gregory A (Greg)** — Basketball Player
5952 Willowross Way, Plano TX 75093, USA
**Drell, Persis** — Physicist
Stanford University, Linear Accelerator Center, Stanford CA 94305, USA
**Drell, Sidney D** — Physicist
620 Sand Hill Road, #420D, Palo Alto CA 94304, USA
**Drescher, Fran** — Actress
Manatt Phelps Phillips, 11355 W Olympic Blvd, #20, Los Angeles CA 90064 USA
**Drese, Ryan T** — Baseball Player
2201 Bear Lake Dr, Euless TX 76039, USA
**Dressel, Chris** — Football Player
410 Whiskey Hill Road, Woodside CA 94062, USA
**Dresselhaus, Mildred S** — Physicist, Electrical Engineer
Energy Department, 1000 Independence Ave SW, Washington DC 20585, USA
**Dressendorfer, Kirk R** — Baseball Player
1004 Oaklands Dr, Round Rock TX 78681, USA
**Dressler, Alan M** — Astronomer
Carnegie Observatories, 813 Santa Barbara St, Pasadena CA 91101, USA
**Dressler, Douglas J (Doug)** — Football Player
118 Frostwood Dr, Westwood CA 96137, USA
**Dressler, Robert A (Rob)** — Baseball Player
2037 17th Ave, Forest Grove OR 97116, USA
**Dretske, Frederick I** — Philosopher
212 Selkirk St, Durham NC 27707, USA
**Drew, B Alvin, Jr** — Astronaut
2814 Lighthouse Dr, Houston TX 77058, USA
**Drew, David J (J D)** — Baseball Player
5006 Old US Highway 41 N, Hahira GA 31632, USA
**Drew, Griffin** — Actress, Model
9066 Cambridge Circle, Vallejo CA 94591, USA
**Drew, Heather** — Golfer
76160 Desert Mountain Circle, Indio CA 92203, USA
**Drew, John E** — Basketball Player
2303 W Tidwell Road, #3404, Houston TX 77091, USA
**Drew, Larry D** — Basketball Player, Coach
4942 Densmore Ave, Encino CA 91436, USA
**Drew, Sarah** — Actress
Innovative Artists, 1505 10th St, Santa Monica CA 90401 USA
**Drew, Tim** — Baseball Player
5006 Old US Highway 41N, Hahira GA 31632, USA
**Drewrey, Willie J** — Football Player
2714 Cheryl Court, Missouri City TX 77459, USA
**Drexler Prada, Jorge A** — Singer, Songwriter
Morgan Britos Mgmt, Calle Princesa 3, Depdo Ofic 1331, 28008 Madrid, Spain
**Drexler, Clyde A** — Basketball Player, Coach
4045 Piping Rock Lane, Houston TX 77027, USA
**Drexler, Millard S (Mickey)** — Businessman
J Crew, 770 Broadway, #1200, New York NY 10003, USA
**Dreyer, Steven W (Steve)** — Baseball Player
6018 Greywood Circle, Johnston IA 50131, USA

**Dreyfus, George** — Composer
3 Grace St, Camberwell VIC 3124, Australia
**Dreyfus, Hubert L** — Philosopher
University of California, Industrial Engineering Dept, Berkeley CA 94720, USA
**Dreyfuss, Richard S** — Actor
A P A Talent/Literary Agency, 405 S Beverly Dr, #300, Beverly Hills CA 90212 USA
**Drickamer, Harry G** — Chemical Engineer
1174 Old Racebrook Road, Woodbridge CT 06525, USA
**Driessen, Daniel (Dan)** — Baseball Player
208 Mitchellville Road, Hilton Head Island SC 29926, USA
**Drinfeld, Vladimir** — Mathematician
Steklov Mathematics Institute, 42 Vavilova, 117966 ESP-1 Moscow, Russia
**Drinkwater, Carol** — Actress
Ken McReddie Assoc, 101 Finsbury Pavement, London EC2A 1RS, England
**Driscoll, Edward C (Terry)** — Basketball Player
101 Taylor Circle, Williamsburg VA 23185, USA
**Driscoll, James B (Jim)** — Baseball Player
18 Coyne Road, Waban MA 02468, USA
**Driscoll, Jean** — Track Athlete
Pat Fettig, 8142 Traverse Court, Cincinnati OH 45242, USA
**Driskill, Travis** — Baseball Player
800 Blue Spring Circle, Round Rock TX 78681, USA
**Driver, Adam** — Actor
Gersh Agency, 9465 Wilshire Blvd, #600, Beverly Hills CA 90212 USA
**Driver, Bruce** — Ice Hockey Player
21A Crest Terrace, Montville NJ 07045, USA
**Driver, Donald J** — Football Player
1501 Noble Way, Flower Mound TX 75022, USA
**Driver, Minnie** — Actress, Singer
Untitled Entertainment, 350 S Beverly Dr, #200, Beverly Hills CA 90212 USA
**D'Rivera, Paquito** — Jazz, Concert Saxophonist
Charismic Productions, 2604 Mozart Place NW, Washington DC 20009, USA
**Drmanac, Radoje (Rade)** — Research Scientist
Complete Genomics, 2071 Stierlin Court, Mountain View CA 94043, USA
**Droge, Pete** — Singer, Songwriter
1423 34th Ave, Seattle WA 98122, USA
**Drolet, Francois L** — Speed Skater
Speed Skating Canada, 2781 Lancaster Road, #402, Ottawa ON K1B 1A7, Canada
**Drolet, Marie-Eve** — Speed Skater
Skate Canada, 865 Shefford Road, Ottawa ON K1J 1H9, Canada
**Drollinger, Ralph K** — Basketball Player
22831 Market St, Newhall CA 91321, USA
**Drosdick, John G** — Businessman
Sunoco Inc, 10 Penn Center, 1801 Market St, Philadelphia PA 19103, USA
**Drougas, Thomas C (Tom)** — Football Player
PO Box 1596, Sun Valley ID 83353, USA
**Droughns, Reuben** — Football Player
5955 S Elkhart Court, Centennial CO 80016, USA
**Drouin, Jude** — Ice Hockey Player
44479 Maltese Falcon Square, Ashburn VA 20147, USA
**Drozd, Steven G** — Drummer, Guitarist (Flaming Lips)
World's Fair Mgmt, 1208 Chowning Ave, Edmond OK 73034, USA
**Drozdova, Margarita S** — Ballerina
Stanislavsky Musical Theater, Pushkinskaya Str 17, 143900 Moscow, Russia
**Druce, John** — Ice Hockey Player
Freedom 55 Financial, 405-360 George St N, Peterborough ON K9H 7E7, Canada
**Drucker, Eugene** — Violinist (Emerson String Quartet)
I M G Artists, Burlington Lane, Chiswick, London W4 2TH, England
**Drukarova, Dinara** — Actress
Voyez Mon Agent, 20 Ave Rapp, 75007 Paris, France
**Druken, Harold** — Ice Hockey Player
16 Shaw Dr, Wayland MA 01778, USA
**Druker, Brian J** — Oncologist, Hematologist
Oregon Health Science University, Cancer Research Center, Portland OR 97201, USA
**Drulia, Stan** — Ice Hockey Player
3939 Essex Place, Fort Gratiot MI 48059, USA
**Drummond, Alice** — Actress
351 E 50th St, New York NY 10022, USA
**Drummond, Andre** — Basketball Player
Detroit Pistons, Palace, 4 Championship Dr, Auburn Hills MI 48326 USA
**Drummond, Jonathan (Jon)** — Track Athlete
PO Box 982, Arlington TX 76004, USA
**Drummond, Lauren** — Actress
Independent Talent Group, 40 Whitfield St, London W1T 2RH, England
**Drummond, Ryan** — Actor
Artists Management Agency, 835 5th Ave, #411, San Diego CA 92101, USA
**Drummond, Timothy D (Tim)** — Baseball Player
102 Haldane Court, La Plata MD 20646, USA
**Drummond, Tom** — Singer, Bassist (Better Than Ezra)
Uppercut Mgmt, 805 N Milwaukee Ave, #401, Chicago IL 60642, USA
**Drummond, William E (Bill)** — Guitarist (KLF), Record Producer
Nene Musik Productions, 1460 SW Santiago Ave, Port Saint Lucie FL 34953 USA
**Drury, Chris** — Ice Hockey Player
145 Parsonage Road, Greenwich CT 06830, USA
**Drury, James** — Actor
100 Spring Lake Dr, Montgomery TX 77356, USA
**Drury, Theodore E (Ted)** — Ice Hockey Player
305 Hibbard Road, Wilmette IL 60091, USA
**Drut, Guy J** — Track Athlete
Mairie, 77120 Coulommiers, France
**Dryburgh, Stuart** — Cinematographer
Gersh Agency, 9465 Wilshire Blvd, #600, Beverly Hills CA 90212 USA
**Dryden, Dave** — Ice Hockey Player
2257 All Saints Crescent, Oakville ON L6J 5N1, Canada
**Dryden, Kenneth W (Ken)** — Ice Hockey Player
58 Poplar Plains Road, Toronto ON M4V 2M8, Canada

**D**

| | |
|---|---|
| **Dryer, J Frederick (Fred)** | Football Player, Actor |
| Fred Dryer Productions, 2934 Beverly Glen Circle, #703, Los Angeles CA 90077, USA | |
| **Dryke, Matthew (Matt)** | Marksman |
| 292 Dryke Road, Sequim WA 98382, USA | |
| **Drysdale, Cliff** | Tennis Player, Sportscaster |
| A T Y, 4725 N Lois Ave, Tampa FL 33614, USA | |
| **Duany, Andres** | Architect |
| Duany & Plater-Zyberk Architects, 1023 SW 25th Ave, Miami FL 33135, USA | |
| **Duarte, Chris** | Musician |
| Intrepid Artists, Midtown Plaza, 1300 Baxter St, #405, Charlotte NC 28204, USA | |
| **Duato, Nacho** | Ballet Dancer, Choreographer |
| Compania Nacional de Danza, Paseo de la Chopera 4, 28045 Madrid, Spain | |
| **Dubberley, Emily** | Writer, Journalist |
| Fox & Howard Literary Agency, 39 Eland Road, London SW11 5JX, England | |
| **Dube, Desmond** | Actor |
| Mahogany, PO Box 3085, Saxonwold, Johannesburg 2132, South Africa | |
| **Dubenion, Elbert (Duby)** | Football Player |
| 610 E Walnut St, Westerville OH 43081, USA | |
| **Duberman, Justin** | Ice Hockey Player |
| 4004 Avalon Pointe Dr, Boca Raton FL 33496, USA | |
| **Dubia, John A** | Army General |
| 10095 Cover Place, Fairfax VA 22030, USA | |
| **Dubinbaum, Gail** | Opera Singer |
| Metropolitan Opera Assn, Lincoln Center Plaza, New York NY 10023 USA | |
| **Dubinin, Yuri V** | Government Official, Russia |
| Boslhoy Palashevsky Per 3, #34, 102104 Moscow, Russia | |
| **Dubinsky, Steve** | Ice Hockey Player |
| 939 Central Ave, Highland Park IL 60035, USA | |
| **Dublinski, Thomas E (Tom), Jr** | Football Player |
| 15918 El Lago Blvd, Fountain Hills AZ 85268, USA | |
| **Dubner, Stephen J** | Economist, Writer |
| William Morrow Publishers, 1350 Ave of Americas, New York NY 10019 USA | |
| **Dubois, Brian A** | Baseball Player |
| 3 Spartan Place, Springfield IL 62703, USA | |
| **DuBois, G Macy** | Architect |
| 175 Carlton St, Toronto ON M5A 2K3, Canada | |
| **DuBois, Ja'Net** | Actress |
| C E S D, 10635 Santa Monica Blvd, #130, Los Angeles CA 90025 USA | |
| **Dubois, Jason** | Baseball Player |
| 2204 Lord Seaton Circle, Virginia Beach VA 23454, USA | |
| **Dubois, Marie** | Actress |
| Artmedia, 20 Ave Rapp, 75007 Paris, France | |
| **DuBois, Marta** | Actress |
| Orange Grove Group, 12178 Ventura Blvd, #205, Studio City CA 91604, USA | |
| **Dubose, Eric** | Baseball Player |
| 326 County Road 8, Gilbertown AL 36908, USA | |
| **Dubreuil, Maroussia** | Actress |
| Agence Artistique Sophie Lemaitre, 9 Rue de Mubeuge, 75009 Paris, France | |
| **Dubus, Andre, III** | Writer |
| Penguin Group, 375 Hudson St, Basement 1, New York NY 10014, USA | |
| **Ducasse, Alain** | Chef |
| Groupe Alain Ducasse, 25 Ave Montaigne, 75008 Paris, France | |
| **Ducey, Robert T (Rob)** | Baseball Player |
| 699 Richmond Close, Tarpon Springs FL 34688, USA | |
| **Duchesnay, Isabelle** | Ice Dancer |
| Im Steinach 30, 87561 Oberstdorf, Germany | |
| **Duchesnay, Paul** | Ice Dancer |
| Bundesleistungszentrum, Rossbichstr 2-6, 87561 Oberstdorf, Germany | |
| **Duchesne, Steve** | Ice Hockey Player |
| 2104 Cedar Elm Terrace, Westlake TX 76262, USA | |
| **Duchin, Peter** | Jazz Pianist, Orchestra Leader |
| Peter Duchin Music, 244 Madison Ave, #333, New York NY 10016, USA | |
| **Duchovny, David** | Actor, Director |
| Affirmative Entertainment, 425 N Robertson Blvd, Los Angeles CA 90048 USA | |
| **DuCille, Michel** | Photojournalist |
| 9571 Pine Meadow Lane, Burke VA 22015, USA | |
| **Duckett, Todd J (T J)** | Football Player |
| Seattle Seahawks, 12 Seahawks Way, Renton WA 98056 USA | |
| **Duckworth, Charles** | Actor |
| Landis-Simon Productions, 3625 E Thousand Oaks Blvd, #279, Thousand Oaks CA 91362, USA | |
| **Duckworth, Marilyn** | Writer |
| 41 Queen St, Mount Victoria, Wellington 6001, New Zealand | |
| **Ducsmal Jaroszewska, Agnieszka** | Conductor |
| Polish Radio Orchestra, Al Marchinkowskiego 3, 61745 Pozna, Poland | |
| **Dudek, Anne** | Actress |
| Innovative Artists, 1505 10th St, Santa Monica CA 90401 USA | |
| **Dudek, Joseph A (Joe)** | Football Player |
| 31 Ryan Road, Auburn NH 03032, USA | |
| **Duden, H Richard (Dick), Jr** | Football Player |
| 11 Old Station Road, Severna Park MD 21146, USA | |
| **Duderstadt, James J** | Educator, Government Official |
| National Science Foundation, 1800 G St NW, Washington DC 20006, USA | |
| **Dudikoff, Michael** | Actor |
| 4341 Birch St, #201, Newport Beach CA 92660, USA | |
| **Dudley, Anne** | Keyboardist (Art of Noise), Composer |
| Cool Music, 1-A Fishers Lane, Chiswick London W4 1RX, England | |
| **Dudley, Charles** | Basketball Player |
| 4032 42nd Ave S, Seattle WA 98118, USA | |
| **Dudley, Christen G (Chris)** | Basketball Player |
| PO Box 703, Rancho Santa Fe CA 92067, USA | |
| **Dudley, Jaquelin** | Microbiologist |
| University of Texas, Microbiology Dept, Austin TX 78712, USA | |
| **Dudley, Jared A** | Basketball Player |
| Los Angeles Clippers, Staples Center, 1111 S Figueroa St, Los Angeles CA 90015 USA | |
| **Dudley, Rick** | Ice Hockey Player, Coach |
| 5150 Oakhill Dr, Lewiston NY 14092, USA | |

*Dryer - Dudley*

**Dudley, Rickey D** — Football Player
4529 Mahogany Lane, Lewisville TX 75077, USA
**Dudman, Nick** — Makeup Artist
Pigs Might Fly, Gawithfield Barn, Arrad Foot, Ulverston, Cumbria LA12 7SL, England
**Duenkel Fuldner, Virginia (Ginny)** — Swimmer
2132 NE 17th Terrace, #500, Wilton Manors FL 33305, USA
**Duensing, Brian** — Baseball Player
524 S 198th St, Elkhorn NE 68022, USA
**Duerod, Terry** — Basketball Player
6542 Chirrewa St, Westland MI 48185, USA
**Duesenberry, James S** — Economist
514 Harvard St, #3B, Brookline MA 02446, USA
**Dufay, Rick** — Guitarist (Aerosmith)
H K Mgmt, 9200 W Sunset Blvd, #530, West Hollywood CA 90069 USA
**Dufek, Donald P (don)** — Football Player
570 S Maple Road, Ann Arbor MI 48103, USA
**Duff, Anne-Marie** — Actress
Gordon & French, 12-13 Poland St, London W1F 8QB, England
**Duff, Haylie** — Actress, Singer, Songwriter
Curtis Talent Mgmt, 9607 Arby Dr, Beverly Hills CA 90210, USA
**Duff, Hilary** — Actress, Singer, Model
Creative Artists Agency, 2000 Ave of Stars, #100, Los Angeles CA 90067 USA
**Duff, John E** — Sculptor
5 Doyers St, New York NY 10013, USA
**Duff, T Richard (Dick)** — Ice Hockey Player
4-7 Elmwood Ave S, Mississauga ON L5G 3J6, Canada
**Duffalo, James F (Jim)** — Baseball Player
1505 Savannah St, Mesquite TX 75149, USA
**Duffey, Joseph D** — Educator
2891 New Mexico Ave NW, #311, Washington DC 20007, USA
**Duffie, John B** — Baseball Player
177 Lakeside Circle, Douglas GA 31535, USA
**Duffield, Burkely** — Actor
United Talent Agency, U T A Plaza, 9336 Civic Center Dr, Beverly Hills CA 90210 USA
**Duffner, Christof** — Ski Jumper
Am Sagebauer 1, 78141 Schonwald, Germany
**Duffner, Mark** — Football Coach
University of Maryland, Athletic Dept, College Park MD 20740, USA
**Duffus, Parris** — Ice Hockey Player
8609 Timbermill Place, Fort Wayne IN 46804, USA
**Duffy** — Singer, Songwriter
13 Artists, 11-14 Kensington St, Brighton BN1 4AJ, England
**Duffy, Brian** — Editorial Cartoonist
Des Moines Register, Editorial Dept, PO Box 957, Des Moines IA 50306, USA
**Duffy, Brian** — Astronaut
16410 Heather Bend Court, Houston TX 77059, USA
**Duffy, Carol Ann** — Writer
Manchester Metropolitan University, English Dept, All Saints, Manchester M15 6BH, England
**Duffy, Francis (Frank)** — Architect
Three Ways, Street, Walberswick near Southwold, Suffolk IP18 6UE, England
**Duffy, Frank T** — Baseball Player
1740 E Silver St, Tucson AZ 85719, USA
**Duffy, J C** — Cartoonist (Fusco Brothers)
Universal Press Syndicate, 4520 Main St, #700, Kansas City MO 64111 USA
**Duffy, John** — Composer
Meet the Composer, 2112 Broadway, New York NY 10023, USA
**Duffy, Julia** — Actress
C E S D, 10635 Santa Monica Blvd, #130, Los Angeles CA 90025 USA
**Duffy, Keith** — Singer (Boyzone)
Carol/War Mgmt, Bushy Park Road, 57 Meadowgate, Dublin 6, Ireland
**Duffy, Maureen P** — Writer
18 Fabian Road, London SW6 7TZ, England
**Duffy, Patrick** — Actor
PO Box 749, Eagle Point OR 97524, USA
**Duffy, Roger T** — Football Player
6509 Lutz Ave NW, Massillon OH 44646, USA
**Duffy, Troy** — Actor, Director, Writer
Original Artists, 9465 Wilshire Blvd, #324, Beverly Hills CA 90212, USA
**Duffy, William H (Billy)** — Guitarist (Cult)
Tom Vitorino Mgmt, 11606 Viny Road, Granada Hills CA 91344, USA
**Duflo, Esther** — Economist
Massachusetts Institute of Technology, Economics Dept, Cambridge MA 02139, USA
**Dufner, Jason** — Golfer
2002 Saint Patrick Court, Auburn AL 36830, USA
**Dufresne, John** — Writer
W W Norton, 500 5th Ave, #600, New York NY 10110 USA
**Dufresne, Mark** — Drummer (Confederate Railroad)
Bobby Roberts, 3050 Business Park Circle, #303, Goodlettsville TN 37221 USA
**Dugan, Dennis** — Actor, Director
United Talent Agency, U T A Plaza, 9336 Civic Center Dr, Beverly Hills CA 90210 USA
**Dugan, J Fred** — Football Player
1827 Tamiami Trail N, Nokomia FL 34275, USA
**Dugan, Michael J** — Air Force General, Association Executive
36 James Court, Dillon CO 80435, USA
**Duggan, James S (Hacksaw Jim)** — Professional Wrestler, Football Player
1328 Hornsby Circle, Lugoff SC 29078, USA
**Dugger, John Scott** — Artist
410 Evelyn Ave, #201, Albany CA 94706, USA
**Dugoni, Robert** — Writer
Warner Books, 1271 Ave of Americas, New York NY 10020 USA
**Duguay, Christian** — Director
Gersh Agency, 9465 Wilshire Blvd, #600, Beverly Hills CA 90212 USA
**Duguay, Ron** — Ice Hockey Player
982 Porte Vedra Blvd, Ponte Vedra Beach FL 32082, USA
**Duhamel, Josh** — Actor
John Carrabino Mgmt, 5900 Wilshire Blvd, #406, Los Angeles CA 90036 USA

# D

| | |
|---|---|
| **Duhe, Adam J (A J), Jr** | Football Player |
| 379 Coconut Circle, Weston FL 33326, USA | |
| **Duhe, John M, Jr** | Judge |
| US Court of Appeals, 556 Jefferson St, Lafayette LA 70501, USA | |
| **Duigan, John** | Director |
| 54A Tite St, London SW3 4JA, England | |
| **Dujardin, Jean** | Actor, Comedian |
| W M E Entertainment, 9601 Wilshire Blvd, #300, Beverly Hills CA 90210 USA | |
| **Duk Kim, Randall** | Actor |
| Charles Bright, 135 Houpe Road, Great Meadows NJ 07838, USA | |
| **Duka, Dominik J Cardinal** | Religious Leader |
| Archdiocese, Hradcanske nam 16, 11902 Prague 1, Czech Republic | |
| **Dukakis, Michael S** | Governor, MA |
| 85 Perry St, Brookline MA 02446, USA | |
| **Dukakis, Olympia** | Actress |
| Innovative Artists, 235 Park Ave S, #1000, New York NY 10003 USA | |
| **Duke, Annie** | Poker Player |
| Federated Sports & Gaming, Palms Casino & Resort, 4301 W Flamingo Road, Las Vegas NV 89103, USA | |
| **Duke, Bill** | Director |
| Duke Media, 7510 Sunset Blvd, #523, Los Angeles CA 90046, USA | |
| **Duke, Charles M, Jr** | Astronaut, Air Force General |
| Duke Ministry for Christ, PO Box 310345, New Braunfels TX 78131, USA | |
| **Duke, Clark** | Actor, Director, Writer |
| W M E Entertainment, 9601 Wilshire Blvd, #300, Beverly Hills CA 90210 USA | |
| **Duke, Elizabeth** | Government Official, Financier |
| Federal Reserve System, 20th St & Constitution Ave NW, Washington DC 20551, USA | |
| **Duke, Kenneth W (Ken)** | Golfer |
| 3612 SW Rivers End Way, Palm City FL 34990, USA | |
| **Duke, Michael** | Businessman |
| Wal-Mart Stores, 702 SW 8th St, Bentonville AR 72716, USA | |
| **Duke, Norm** | Bowler |
| 719 2nd Ave, #701, Seattle WA 98104, USA | |
| **Duke, Patty** | Actress |
| Mitchell K Stubbs Assoc, 8695 W Washington Blvd, #204, Culver City CA 90232 USA | |
| **Duke, Robin Chandler** | Association Executive, Diplomat |
| 435 E 52nd St, New York NY 10022, USA | |
| **Duke, Zachary T (Zach)** | Baseball Player |
| 2517 County Road 4240, Clifton TX 76634, USA | |
| **Dukes, Jamie D** | Football Player, Sportscaster |
| 2553 Northern Oak Dr, Braselton GA 30517, USA | |
| **Dukes, Thomas E (Tom)** | Baseball Player |
| 325 Monte Vista Road, Arcadia CA 91007, USA | |
| **Dukuchitz, Jonathan** | Actor, Singer |
| Innovative Artists, 235 Park Ave S, #1000, New York NY 10003 USA | |
| **Dulany, Caitlin** | Actress |
| Talent Works, 3500 W Olive Ave, #1400, Burbank CA 91505 USA | |
| **Dulery, Antoine** | Actor |
| Artmedia, 20 Ave Rapp, 75007 Paris, France | |
| **Dulfer, Candy** | Musician, Actress |
| Sun Music, PO Box 130, 3235 Erlach, Switzerland | |
| **Duliba, Robert J (Bob)** | Baseball Player |
| 327 Philadelphia Ave, West Pittston PA 18643, USA | |
| **Dullea, Keir** | Actor |
| Bret Adams Agency, 448 W 44th St, New York NY 10036, USA | |
| **Dulli, Gregory (Greg)** | Singer, Guitarist (Twilight Singers) |
| Rascoff/Zysblat Organization, 250 W 57th St, New York NY 10107 USA | |
| **Dumais, Troy M** | Diver |
| US Olympic Committee, 1 Olympic Plaza, Building 6, Colorado Springs CO 80909 USA | |
| **Dumars, Joe, III** | Basketball Player |
| 3499 Franklin Road, Bloomfield Hills MI 48302, USA | |
| **Dumaux, Christophe** | Opera Singer |
| I M G Artists, Hogarth Business Park, Chiswick, London W4 2TH, England | |
| **Dumervil, Elvis K** | Football Player |
| 6115 Trailhead Road, Littleton CO 80130, USA | |
| **Dumont, J P** | Ice Hockey Player |
| 1512 Kimberleigh Court, Franklin TN 37069, USA | |
| **DuMont, James** | Actor |
| House of Representatives, 1434 6th St, #1, Santa Monica CA 90401 USA | |
| **Dumoulin, Daniel L (Dan)** | Baseball Player |
| 202 Nancy Dr, Kokomo IN 46901, USA | |
| **Dunaev, Andrej** | Opera Singer |
| I M G Artists, Hogarth Business Park, Chiswick, London W4 2TH, England | |
| **Dunagin, Ralph** | Cartoonist (Dunagin's People) |
| North American Syndicate, 235 E 45th St, New York NY 10017 USA | |
| **Dunaway, Faye** | Actress |
| Mavrick Artists Agency, 6100 Wilshire Blvd, #550, Los Angeles CA 90048, USA | |
| **Dunaway, James E (Jim)** | Football Player |
| 170 Mount Carmel Church Road, Sandy Hook MS 39478, USA | |
| **Dunbar, Bonnie J** | Astronaut |
| 2200 Todville Road, Seabrook TX 77586, USA | |
| **Dunbar, Dale** | Ice Hockey Player |
| 41 Nahant Ave, Winthrop MA 02152, USA | |
| **Dunbar, Gavin** | Bassist (Camera Obscura) |
| Ground Control Touring, 20 Jay St, #826, Brooklyn NY 11201 USA | |
| **Dunbar, Jo-Lonn D** | Football Player |
| Saint Louis Rams, 901 N Broadway, Saint Louis MO 63101 USA | |
| **Dunbar, Matt** | Baseball Player |
| 6328 County Donegal Court, Charlotte NC 28277, USA | |
| **Dunbar, Rockmond** | Actor |
| Untitled Entertainment, 350 S Beverly Dr, #200, Beverly Hills CA 90212 USA | |
| **Duncan Nalasco, Mariano** | Baseball Player |
| Ingenio Angelina #137, San Pedro de Macoris, Dominican Republic | |
| **Duncan, Arne** | Secretary, Education |
| Education Department, 400 Maryland Ave SW, Washington DC 20202 USA | |
| **Duncan, Charles W, Jr** | Secretary, Energy |
| 9 Briarwood Court, Houston TX 77019, USA | |

**Duncan, Curtis E**  Football Player
4915 Glen Hollow St, Sugar Land TX 77479, USA
**Duncan, David Douglas**  Photojournalist
Castellaras Mouans-Sartoux 06370, France
**Duncan, Glen**  Writer
Knopf Publishers, 1745 Broadway, New York NY 10019 USA
**Duncan, Ian**  Actor
Ken McReddie Assoc, 101 Finsbury Pavement, London EC2A 1RS, England
**Duncan, Jamie R**  Football Player
217 Remi Dr, New Castle DE 19720, USA
**Duncan, Jeff**  Baseball Player
825 Lincoln Lane, Frankfort IL 60423, USA
**Duncan, Leslie H (Speedy)**  Football Player
1607 Porter Way, Stockton CA 95207, USA
**Duncan, Lindsay V**  Actress
Dalzell & Beresford, 26 Astwood Mews, London SW7 4DE, England
**Duncan, Melvin L (Buck)**  Baseball Player
470 Bedford St, PO Box 980407, Ypsilanti MI 48198, USA
**Duncan, Peter**  Director
Cameron Creswell, 61 Marlborough St, #700, Surry Hills NSW 2010, Australia
**Duncan, Robert**  Actor
Ken McReddie Assoc, 101 Finsbury Pavement, London EC2A 1RS, England
**Duncan, Robert C**  Astrophysicist
University of Texas, Astronomy Dept, Austin TX 78712, USA
**Duncan, Robert W**  WW II Navy Air Force Hero
1511 Ryder Cup Blvd, Marion IL 62959, USA
**Duncan, Sandy**  Actress, Comedienne
Douglas Gorman Rothacker Wilhelm, 1501 Broadway, #703, New York NY 10036, USA
**Duncan, Shelley**  Baseball Player
6421 N Foothills Dr, Tucson AZ 85718, USA
**Duncan, Timothy T (Tim)**  Basketball Player
13215 Vista del Mundo, San Antonio TX 78216, USA
**Duncan, Whitney**  Singer, Songwriter
W B R Nashville, 20 Music Square E, Nashville TN 37203, USA
**Duncanson, Craig**  Ice Hockey Player
Laurentian University, Athletic Dept, Sudbury ON P3E 2C6, Canada
**Dundas, Jennifer**  Actress
Paradigm Agency, 360 N Crescent Dr, North Building, Beverly Hills CA 90210 USA
**Dundas, Peter H**  Fashion Designer
Palazzo Pucci, 6 Via de Pucci, 50122 Florence, Italy
**Dundas, Rocky**  Ice Hockey Player
14 Nantucket Dr, Richmond Hill ON L4E 3V1, Canada
**Dunegan, James W (Jim)**  Baseball Player
20246 180th St, New London IA 52645, USA
**Dunford, Joseph F, Jr**  Marine Corps General
I S A Force/US Forces, N A T O Headquarters, Blvd Leopold III, Brussels 1110, Belgium
**Dungey, Lon**  Actor
Auckland Actors, PO Box 56460, Auckland 1030, New Zealand
**Dungey, Merrin**  Actress
Gersh Agency, 9465 Wilshire Blvd, #600, Beverly Hills CA 90212 USA
**Dungy, Tony**  Football Coach
16604 Villalenda de Avila, Tampa FL 33613, USA
**Dunham, Archie W**  Businessman
ConocoPhillips Inc, 600 N Dairy Ashford, Houston TX 77079, USA
**Dunham, Chip**  Cartoonist (Overboard)
Universal Press Syndicate, 4520 Main St, #700, Kansas City MO 64111 USA
**Dunham, Lena**  Writer, Film Director, Actress
United Talent Agency, U T A Plaza, 9336 Civic Center Dr, Beverly Hills CA 90210 USA
**Dunham, Michael (Mike)**  Ice Hockey Player
39 Garfield Road, Concord MA 01742, USA
**Dunigan, Tim**  Actor
Hervey/Grimes Talent, 10561 Missouri Ave, #2, Los Angeles CA 90025 USA
**Dunitz, Jack D**  Chemist
Obere Heslibachstr 77, 8700 Kusnacht, Switzerland
**Dunkle, Nancy**  Basketball Player
1350 Lorawood St, La Habra CA 90631, USA
**Dunlap, Alexander W**  Astronaut
N A S A, Johnson Space Center, 2101 NASA Road, Houston TX 77058 USA
**Dunlap, Grant L**  Baseball Player
1431 Alga Court, Vista CA 92081, USA
**Dunleavy, Mary**  Opera Singer
Fletcher Artist Mgmt, 809 W 181st St, #274, New York NY 10033, USA
**Dunleavy, Michael J (Mike), Jr**  Basketball Player
Chicago Bulls, United Center, 1901 W Madison St, Chicago IL 60612 USA
**Dunleavy, Michael J (Mike), Sr**  Basketball Player, Coach
127 S Carmelina Ave, Los Angeles CA 90049, USA
**Dunlop, Andy**  Guitarist (Travis)
Wildlife Entertainment, 21 Heathmans Road, London SW6 4TJ, England
**Dunlop, Blake**  Ice Hockey Player
8112 Maryland Ave, Saint Louis MO 63105, USA
**Dunmore, Laurence**  Director
Independent Talent Group, 40 Whitfield St, London W1T 2RH, England
**Dunn, Adam T**  Baseball Player
533 Tusculum Ave, Cincinnati OH 45226, USA
**Dunn, Andrew W**  Cinematographer
525 Broadway, #250, Santa Monica CA 90401, USA
**Dunn, Colton**  Actor
Paradigm Agency, 360 N Crescent Dr, North Building, Beverly Hills CA 90210 USA
**Dunn, Dave**  Ice Hockey Player
1433 Hamilton St, Regina SK S4H 7V4, Canada
**Dunn, Gary E**  Football Player
243 Navajo St, Tavernier FL 33070, USA
**Dunn, Holly**  Singer, Songwriter
8624 Poplar Creek Road, Nashville TN 37221, USA
**Dunn, John M**  Educator
Western Michigan University, President's Office, Kalamazoo MI 49008, USA

# D

| | |
|---|---|
| **Dunn, Jourdan**<br>Storm Model Agency, 5 Jubilee Place, Chelsea, London SW3 3TD, England | Model |
| **Dunn, Keldrick D (K D)**<br>1640 Township Terrace, McDonough GA 30252, USA | Football Player |
| **Dunn, Kevin**<br>Gersh Agency, 9465 Wilshire Blvd, #600, Beverly Hills CA 90212 USA | Actor |
| **Dunn, Larry**<br>Spirit Media, PO Box 43591, Phoenix AZ 85080, USA | Pianist (Earth Wind & Fire), Songwriter |
| **Dunn, Lin**<br>Indiana Fever, Conseco Fieldhouse, 125 S Pennsylvania, Indianapolis IN 46204 USA | Basketball Coach |
| **Dunn, Mignon**<br>Bloch Artists Mgmt, 360 W 28th St, #6B, New York NY 10001, USA | Opera Singer |
| **Dunn, Mike**<br>PO Box 128, Wrightsville PA 17368, USA | Drag Racing Driver |
| **Dunn, Moira**<br>15803 Bridgewater Lane, Tampa FL 33624, USA | Golfer |
| **Dunn, Nora**<br>Stone Manners Salners, 9911 W Pico Blvd, #1400, Los Angeles CA 90035 USA | Actress, Comedienne |
| **Dunn, Perry L**<br>64 Glenway Place, Brandon MS 39042, USA | Football Player |
| **Dunn, Richard (Richie)**<br>12229 Clarence Center Road, Akron NY 14001, USA | Ice Hockey Player |
| **Dunn, Robert F**<br>Lexington Institute, 1600 Wilson Blvd, #900, Arlington VA 22209 USA | Navy Admiral |
| **Dunn, Ronald R (Ron)**<br>1161 Husted Ave, San Jose CA 95125, USA | Baseball Player |
| **Dunn, Ronnie**<br>Spalding Entertainment, 54 Music Square E, #200, Nashville TN 37203, USA | Singer (Brooks & Dunn), Songwriter |
| **Dunn, Scott**<br>1331 Arizona Ash St, San Antonio TX 78232, USA | Baseball Player |
| **Dunn, Stephen**<br>Stockton State College, Humanities & Fine Arts Dept, Pomona NJ 08240, USA | Writer |
| **Dunn, Steven R (Steve)**<br>484 Broadmoor Dr, Maryville TN 37803, USA | Baseball Player |
| **Dunn, Susan**<br>Herbert Breslin, 119 W 57th St, #1505, New York NY 10019, USA | Opera Singer |
| **Dunn, Teala**<br>Abrams Artists, 275 7th Ave, #2600, New York NY 10001 USA | Actress, Singer |
| **Dunn, Theodore R (T R)**<br>1014 19th St SW, Birmingham AL 35211, USA | Basketball Player |
| **Dunn, Todd K**<br>12030 London Lake Dr W, Jacksonville FL 32258, USA | Baseball Player |
| **Dunn, Warrick D**<br>6016 Beacon Shores St, Tampa FL 33616, USA | Football Player |
| **Dunne, Colin**<br>I M G Artists, Hogarth Business Park, Chiswick, London W4 2TH, England | Dancer |
| **Dunne, Griffin**<br>Arcieri Assoc, 305 Madison Ave, #2315, New York NY 10165 USA | Actor, Director |
| **Dunne, Michael D (Mike)**<br>5115 W Ancient Oak Dr, Peoria IL 61615, USA | Baseball Player |
| **Dunne, Robin**<br>Empera Southpaw Productions, #317 1275 W 6th Ave, Vancouver BC BC V6H 1A6, Canada | Actor, Writer, Producer |
| **Dunning, Debbe**<br>1373 Crest Road, Del Mar CA 92014, USA | Actress, Model |
| **Dunning, Jeanne**<br>2438 N Bernard St, Chicago IL 60647, USA | Artist, Photographer |
| **Dunning, John**<br>Pocket Books, 1230 Ave of Americas, New York NY 10020 USA | Writer |
| **Dunning, Steven J (Steve)**<br>35 Prairie, Irvine CA 92618, USA | Baseball Player |
| **Dunn-Luoma, Tricia**<br>4 Huson Ave, Derry NH 03038, USA | Ice Hockey Player |
| **Duno, Milka**<br>S A M A X Motorsports, 203 NW 16th St, Pompano Beach FL 33060, USA | Auto Racing Driver |
| **Dunphy, Marv**<br>33370 Decker School Road, Malibu CA 90265, USA | Volleyball Coach |
| **Dunsky, Evan**<br>Creative Artists Agency, 2000 Ave of Stars, #100, Los Angeles CA 90067 USA | Director |
| **Dunsmore, Barrie**<br>ABC-TV, News Dept, 5010 Creston St, Hyattsville MD 20781 USA | Commentator |
| **Dunst, Kirsten**<br>United Talent Agency, U T A Plaza, 9336 Civic Center Dr, Beverly Hills CA 90210 USA | Actress |
| **Dunstan, A H Bernard**<br>10 High Park Road, Kew, Richmond, Surrey TW9 4BH, England | Artist |
| **Dunstan, William E (Bill)**<br>PO Box 514, Rancho Mirage CA 92270, USA | Football Player |
| **Dunston, Shawon D**<br>957 Corte del Sol, Fremont CA 94539, USA | Baseball Player |
| **Dunwoody, Ann E**<br>Commanding General, Army Material Command, Alexandria VA 22333, USA | Army General |
| **Dunwoody, T Richard**<br>Sports Marketing, Litten, Newtown Road, Newbury, Berkshire RG14 7BB, England | Thoroughbred Racing Jockey |
| **Dunwoody, Todd F**<br>1704 King Eider Dr, West Lafayette IN 47906, USA | Baseball Player |
| **DuPage, Julie**<br>Artmedia, 20 Ave Rapp, 75007 Paris, France | Actress |
| **Duper, Mark K**<br>1905 Banks Road, Margate FL 33063, USA | Football Player |
| **Dupere, Denis**<br>26 Lorraine Ave, Kitchener ON N2B 2M8, Canada | Ice Hockey Player |
| **Duperey, Anny**<br>Agents Associes, 201 Rue du Faubourg Saint Honore, 75008 Paris, France | Actress |
| **Duplaix, Daphnee Lynn**<br>Greene Assoc, 1901 Ave of Stars, #130, Los Angeles CA 90067 USA | Actress, Model |
| **Duplass, Jay**<br>I C M Partners, 10250 Constellation Blvd, #900, Los Angeles CA 90067 USA | Writer, Director, Actor |

**Dunn - Duplass**

**Duplass, Mark D** — Writer, Director, Actor
Brigade Marketing, 548 W 28th St, #670, New York NY 10001, USA
**Dupont, Andre (Moose)** — Ice Hockey Player
905 Rue Gilbert, Trois-Rivieres QC G8T 5V5, Canada
**DuPont, Pierre S, IV** — Governor, DE
Richards Layton Finger, 1 Rodney Square, PO Box 551, Wilmington DE 19899, USA
**Dupont, Tiffany** — Actress
Paradigm Agency, 360 N Crescent Dr, North Building, Beverly Hills CA 90210 USA
**Dupre, John** — Philosopher
University of Exeter, Genomics Center, Exeter, Devon EX4 4QJ, England
**DuPree, Billy Joe** — Football Player
3621 Llano River Trail, McKinney TX 75070, USA
**Dupree, Candice** — Basketball Player
Phoenix Mercury, American West Arena, 201 E Jefferson St, Phoenix AZ 85004 USA
**Dupree, Mike** — Baseball Player
2358 E Richmond Ave, Fresno CA 93720, USA
**DuPrez, John** — Composer
Air Edel, 18 Rodmarton St, London W1U 8BJ, England
**Dupri, Jermaine** — Rap Artist, Singer
Three Rings Projects, 111 Westwood Place, #101, Brentwood TN 37027, USA
**Dupuis, Bob** — Ice Hockey Player
446 Algonquin Ave, North Bay ON P1B 4W5, Canada
**Dupuis, Roy** — Actor
Agence Premier Role, 3451 Hotel de Ville, Montreal QC H2X 3B5, Canada
**Duque, Pedro** — Astronaut, Spain
European Space Center, Linder Hohe, Box 906096, 51127 Cologne, Germany
**Durack, David T** — Physician
815 W Knox St, Durham NC 27701, USA
**Duran, Daniel J (Dan)** — Baseball Player
493 Maxine Court, Sunnyvale CA 94086, USA
**Duran, Elise** — Producer, Director, Writer
Creative Artists Agency, 2000 Ave of Stars, #100, Los Angeles CA 90067 USA
**Duran, Roberto** — Boxer
Calle F El Cangrejo, Casa 33, Panama City, Panama
**Durance, Erica** — Actress
Gersh Agency, 9465 Wilshire Blvd, #600, Beverly Hills CA 90212 USA
**Durand, Kevin** — Actor
Alchemy Entertainment, 7024 Melrose Ave, #420, Los Angeles CA 90038 USA
**Durang, Christopher** — Writer
I C M Partners, 730 5th Ave, New York NY 10019 USA
**Durant, Graham J** — Inventor (Antiulcer Compound)
Cambridge NeuroScience, 333 Boston Providence Turnpike, Norwood MA 02062, USA
**Durant, Joseph S (Joe)** — Golfer
PO Box 910, Gulf Breeze FL 32562, USA
**Durant, Kevin** — Basketball Player
Oklahoma City Thunder, 211 N Robinson Ave, #300, Oklahoma City OK 73102 USA
**Durant, Michael J (Mike)** — Baseball Player
7520 Marston Lane, Dublin OH 43016, USA
**Durante, Viviana P** — Ballerina
20 Bristol Gardens, Little Venice, London W9, England
**Durbin, Chad G** — Baseball Player
17918 Jefferson Ridge Dr, Baton Rouge LA 70817, USA
**Durbin, Michael W (Mike)** — Bowler
1042 Wilshire Dr, Roanoke TX 76262, USA
**Duren, Clarence E** — Football Player
201 W 54th St, Los Angeles CA 90037, USA
**Duren, John T** — Basketball Player
1107 1st St NW, Washington DC 20001, USA
**Durham, Joseph V (Joe)** — Baseball Player
9715 Mendoza Road, Randallstown MD 21133, USA
**Durham, Ray (Sugar Ray)** — Baseball Player
199 Lake Road, Stanley NC 28164, USA
**Duris, Romain** — Actor
Agents Associes, 201 Rue du Faubourg Saint Honore, 75008 Paris, France
**Duritz, Adam** — Singer (Counting Crowes), Lyricist
Interscope/Geffen Records, 2220 Colorado Ave, #300, Santa Monica CA 90404, USA
**Durjan'narc, Ogan** — Conductor, Composer
Moscow Symphony Orchestra, Gorky Park, 9 Krymsky Val, 119049 Moscow, Russia
**Durkin, Clare** — Model
Models 1, 12 Macklin St, Covent Garden, London WC2B 5SZ, England
**Durr Browning, Francoise** — Tennis Player
195 Rue de Lourmel, 75015 Paris, France
**Durr, Jason** — Actor
S D B Partners, 1801 Ave of Stars, #902, Los Angeles CA 90067 USA
**Durrance, Samuel T** — Astronaut, Astronomer
770 Kerry Downs Circle, Melbourne FL 32940, USA
**Durrant, Jennifer A** — Artist
9-10 Holly Grove, London SE15 5DF, England
**Durrett, Richard T** — Mathematician
Duke University, Mathematics Dept, Durham NC 27708, USA
**Durrington, Trent J** — Baseball Player
499 N Canon Dr, #400, Beverly Hills CA 90210, USA
**Durst, W Frederick (Fred)** — Musician (Limp Bizkit), Director
KillerMoxie Mgmt, 5890 W Jefferson Blvd, #J, Los Angeles CA 90016, USA
**Durst, Will** — Actor, Comedian
Entertainment Alliance, PO Box 1544, Mendocino CA 95460, USA
**Dusard, Jay** — Photographer
5261 N Stewart Ranch Road, Douglas AZ 85607, USA
**Dusay, Marj** — Actress
1964 Westwood Blvd, #6F, New York NY 10025, USA
**Dusek, J Bradley (Brad)** — Football Player
4th Quarter Ranch, 8311 FM 2086, Temple TX 76501, USA
**Dusenberg, Walter** — Sculptor
Stone Mill Hall, 109 Cemetery Road, Fly Creek NY 13337, USA
**Dusenberry, Ann** — Actress
1615 San Leandro Lane, Santa Barbara CA 93108, USA

| | | |
|---|---|---|
| **Duser, Carl R** | | Baseball Player |
| 3021 Cornwall Road, Bethlehem PA 18017, USA | | |
| **Dushku, Eliza** | | Actress, Producer, Director |
| United Talent Agency, U T A Plaza, 9336 Civic Center Dr, Beverly Hills CA 90210 USA | | |
| **Dussault, Jean H** | | Endocrinologist |
| Laval Medical Center, 2705 Blvd Laurier, Sainte Foy QC G1V 4G2, Canada | | |
| **Dussault, Nancy** | | Actress, Singer |
| 4406 Moorpark Way, Toluca Lake CA 91602, USA | | |
| **Dussollier, Andre** | | Actor |
| Artmedia, 20 Ave Rapp, 75007 Paris, France | | |
| **Dustal, Robert A (Bob)** | | Baseball Player |
| 625 Marian Lane, Lakeland FL 33813, USA | | |
| **Dutch, Deborah** | | Actress |
| William Carroll Agency, 12811 Garden Grove Blvd, #209, Garden Grove CA 92843 USA | | |
| **Dutoit, Charles E** | | Conductor |
| Montreal Symphony, 260 Blvd Maisonneuve W, Montreal QC H2X 1Y9, Canada | | |
| **DuToit, Élize** | | Actress |
| Special Artists Agency, 9200 Sunset Blvd, #410, West Hollywood CA 90069 USA | | |
| **Dutronc, Jacques** | | Actor |
| Voyez Mon Agent, 20 Ave Rapp, 75007 Paris, France | | |
| **Dutrow, Richard E (Rick), Jr** | | Thoroughbred Racing Trainer |
| 2 The Howl W, East Norwich NY 11732, USA | | |
| **Dutt, Hank** | | Concert Violist (Kronos Quartet) |
| Kronos Quartet, 1235 9th Ave, San Francisco CA 94122, USA | | |
| **Dutt, Sanjay** | | Actor |
| 58 Smt Nargis Dutt Road, Pali Hill Bandra (W), Mumbai MS 400050, India | | |
| **Dutta Bhupathi, Lara** | | Beauty Queen, Actress, Model |
| 401 Merry Ville, 25 Saint Andrews Road, Bandra (W), Mumbai 400050, India | | |
| **Dutton, Charles S** | | Actor, Director |
| Marsh Entertainment, 12444 Ventura Blvd, #203, Studio City CA 91604, USA | | |
| **Dutton, James P (Jim), Jr** | | Astronaut |
| 1604 Mossy Stone Dr, Friendswood TX 77546, USA | | |
| **Dutton, John O** | | Football Player |
| 5706 Moss Creek Trail, Dallas TX 75252, USA | | |
| **Dutton, Lawrence** | | Violist (Emerson String Quartet) |
| I M G Artists, Burlington Lane, Chiswick, London W4 2TH, England | | |
| **Dutton, Simon** | | Actor |
| Marmont Mgmt, Langham House, 302/8 Regent St, London W1R 5AL, England | | |
| **Duty, Kenton** | | Actor |
| Osbrink Talent Agency, 4343 Lankershim Blvd, #100, North Hollywood CA 91602 USA | | |
| **Duva, Louis (Lou)** | | Boxing Promoter, Trainer, Manager |
| Main Events, 811 Totowa Road, #100, Totowa NJ 07512, USA | | |
| **Duval, David R** | | Golfer |
| 11 Parkway Dr, Englewood CO 80113, USA | | |
| **Duval, Dennis** | | Basketball Player |
| 8105 Verbeck Dr, Manlius NY 13104, USA | | |
| **Duval, Helen** | | Bowler |
| PO Box 2071, Oakland CA 94604, USA | | |
| **Duval, James** | | Actor |
| Artistry Mgmt, 340 N Camden Dr, #302, Beverly Hills CA 90210, USA | | |
| **Duval, Michael A (Mike)** | | Baseball Player |
| 2743 Nature Pointe Loop, Fort Myers FL 33905, USA | | |
| **DuVall, Clea** | | Actress |
| Framework Entertainment, 9057 Nemo St, #C, West Hollywood CA 90069 USA | | |
| **Duvall, Jed** | | Commentator |
| ABC-TV, News Dept, 5010 Creston St, Hyattsville MD 20781 USA | | |
| **Duvall, Robert** | | Actor |
| I C M Partners, 10250 Constellation Blvd, #900, Los Angeles CA 90067 USA | | |
| **Duvall, Sammy** | | Water Skier |
| PO Box 871, Windermere FL 34786, USA | | |
| **Duvauchelle, Nicolas** | | Actor |
| U B B A, 6 Rue de Braque, 75003 Paris, France | | |
| **DuVernay, Ava** | | Director |
| Paradigm Agency, 360 N Crescent Dr, North Building, Beverly Hills CA 90210 USA | | |
| **Duvert, Michael** | | Actor |
| Liebman Entertainment, 25 E 21st St, #PH, New York NY 10010, USA | | |
| **Duvillard, Henri** | | Alpine Skier |
| Le Mont d'Arbois, 74120 Megere, France | | |
| **Duwelius, Rich** | | Volleyball Player |
| 266 Stoddards Wharf Road, Gales Ferry CT 06335, USA | | |
| **Dvorak, Radek** | | Ice Hockey Player |
| 10342 Lexington Estates Blvd, Boca Raton FL 33428, USA | | |
| **Dvorak, Tomas** | | Track Athlete |
| Stadium Juliska, 16000 Prague 6, Czech Republic | | |
| **Dvorak, Wayne C** | | Actor |
| 2204 Stanley Hills Dr, Los Angeles CA 90046, USA | | |
| **Dvorsky, Peter** | | Opera Singer |
| J Hronca 1A, 84102 Bratislava, Slovakia | | |
| **Dwight, Edward, Jr** | | Astronaut |
| 4022 Montview Blvd, Denver CO 80207, USA | | |
| **Dwight, Timothy J (Tim), Jr** | | Football Player |
| 26164 Indigo Dr, Park Rapids MN 56470, USA | | |
| **Dworaczyk, Hope** | | Model |
| Playboy Promotions, 2706 Media Center Dr, Los Angeles CA 90065 USA | | |
| **Dwork, Melvin** | | Interior Designer |
| Melvin Dwork Inc, 50 Murray St, #1710, New York NY 10007, USA | | |
| **Dworkin, Martin** | | Microbiologist |
| 2123 Hoyt Ave W, Saint Paul MN 55108, USA | | |
| **Dworkins, Lenny** | | Cartoonist (Buck Rogers) |
| 2906 Wilmette Ave, Wilmette IL 60091, USA | | |
| **Dworsky, Daniel L (Dan)** | | Football Player, Architect |
| 9225 Nightingale Dr, Los Angeles CA 90069, USA | | |
| **Dwurnik, Edward** | | Artist |
| Ul Podgorska 5, 02 921 Warsaw, Poland | | |
| **Dwyer, James E (Jim)** | | Baseball Player |
| 826 Hancock Bridge Parkway, Cape Coral FL 33990, USA | | |

**D**

**Duser - Dwyer**

| | |
|---|---|
| **Dwyer, Jim**<br>New York Times, Editorial Dept, 229 W 43rd St, New York NY 10036 USA | Journalist |
| **Dwyer, Karyn**<br>Oscars Abrams Zimel, 438 Queen St E, Toronto ON M5A 1T4, Canada | Actress |
| **Dyas, Guy Hendrix**<br>United Talent Agency, U T A Plaza, 9336 Civic Center Dr, Beverly Hills CA 90210 USA | Production Designer |
| **Dybzinski, Jerome M (Jerry)**<br>1626 Haywood Place, Fort Collins CO 80526, USA | Baseball Player |
| **Dychtwald, Ken**<br>Age Wave Inc, 1900 Powell St, Emeryville CA 94608, USA | Psychologist |
| **Dye, Ernest T**<br>580 Bienville Court, Alpharetta GA 30004, USA | Football Player |
| **Dye, Ian**<br>Gorfaine/Schwartz, 4111 W Alameda Ave, #509, Burbank CA 91505, USA | Composer |
| **Dye, Lee**<br>Dye Designs, 5500 E Yale Ave, #300, Denver CO 80222, USA | Golf Course Architect |
| **Dye, Melissa Dori**<br>Dye Productions, 5403 Everhart Road, #140, Corpus Christi TX 78411, USA | Singer, Songwriter |
| **Dye, Paul B (Pete)**<br>3247 Polo Dr, Delray Beach FL 33483, USA | Golf Course Architect |
| **Dyer, Danny**<br>Independent Talent Group, 40 Whitfield St, London W1T 2RH, England | Actor |
| **Dyer, Donald R (Duffy)**<br>742 W Las Palmaritas Dr, Phoenix AZ 85021, USA | Baseball Player |
| **Dyk, Timothy B**<br>US Court of Appeals, 717 Madison Place NW, Washington DC 20439, USA | Judge |
| **Dyka, Oksana**<br>I M G Artists, Hogarth Business Park, Chiswick, London W4 2TH, England | Opera Singer |
| **Dyke, Charles W**<br>International Technical/Trade Assoc, 1330 Connecticut NW, Washington DC 20036, USA | Army General, Association Executive |
| **Dykema, Craig**<br>10525 Destino St, Bellflower CA 90706, USA | Basketball Player |
| **Dykers, Craig**<br>Snohetta, Skur 39, Vippetangen, 0150 Oslo, Norway | Architect |
| **Dykes Bower, John**<br>4Z Artillery Mansions, Westminster, London SW1P 1RR, England | Concert Organist |
| **Dykinga, Jack**<br>1519 E Tascal Loop, Tucson AZ 85737, USA | Photojournalist |
| **Dykstra, John**<br>15060 Encanto Dr, Sherman Oaks CA 91403, USA | Artist, Animator, Cinematographer |
| **Dykstra, Leonard K (Lenny)**<br>10550 Wilshire Blvd, #1203, Los Angeles CA 90024, USA | Baseball Player |
| **Dylan, Bob**<br>Creative Artists Agency, 2000 Ave of Stars, #100, Los Angeles CA 90067 USA | Singer, Songwriter |
| **Dylan, Jakob**<br>Paradigm Agency, 360 N Crescent Dr, North Building, Beverly Hills CA 90210 USA | Singer, Guitarist (Wallflowers) |
| **Dylan, Jesse**<br>Creative Artists Agency, 2000 Ave of Stars, #100, Los Angeles CA 90067 USA | Director |
| **Dymott, Adiam**<br>Agency Group Ltd, 361-373 City Road, London EC1V 1PQ, England | Singer |
| **Dyrdek, Robert D (Rob)**<br>I C M Partners, Marlborough House, 10 Earlham St, #300, London WC2H 9LNP, England | Skateboarder, Actor |
| **Dyroen-Lancer, Rebekah (Becky)**<br>31101 Via Madera, San Juan Capistrano CA 92675, USA | Sychronized Swimmer |
| **Dysart, Richard**<br>654 Copeland Court, Santa Monica CA 90405, USA | Actor |
| **Dyson, Andre**<br>3367 N Shoreline Circle, Layton UT 84040, USA | Football Player |
| **Dyson, Esther**<br>Edventure Holdings, 104 5th Ave, #2000, New York NY 10011, USA | Businesswoman, Writer |
| **Dyson, Freeman J**<br>105 Battle Road Circle, Princeton NJ 08540, USA | Physicist, Templeton Religion Laureate |
| **Dyson, James**<br>Dyson Appliances, Tetbury Hill, Malmesbury Wiltshire SN16 0RP, England | Industrial Designer |
| **Dyson, Kevin T**<br>3109 Chase Point Dr, Franklin TN 37067, USA | Football Player |
| **Dyson, Michael Eric**<br>DePaul University, English Dept, Chicago IL 60604, USA | Writer |
| **Dzau, Victor J**<br>Duke University Health System, Chancellor's Office, Durham NC 27708, USA | Molecular Biologist |
| **Dzhanibekov, Vladimir A**<br>Cosmonaut Training Center, Star City, 141160 Zvezdny Gorodok, Moscow Oblast, Russia | Cosmonaut, Air Force General |
| **Dziedzic, Joe**<br>2195 Marion Road, Saint Paul MN 55113, USA | Ice Hockey Player |
| **Dziedzic, Stanley**<br>835 Hedgegate Court, Roswell GA 30075, USA | Freestyle Wrestler |
| **Dziena, Alexis**<br>Paradigm Agency, 360 N Crescent Dr, North Building, Beverly Hills CA 90210 USA | Actress |
| **Dziewonski, Adam M**<br>Harvard University, Seismology Dept, Cambridge MA 02138, USA | Seismologist, Geophysicist |
| **Dziubinska, Anulka**<br>Playboy Promotions, 2706 Media Center Dr, Los Angeles CA 90065 USA | Model, Actress |
| **Dziwisz, Stanislaw Cardinal**<br>Archdiocese of Cracow, Ul Franciszkanska 3, 31 004 Cracow, Poland | Religious Leader |
| **Dzundza, George**<br>PO Box 133, Netarts OR 97143, USA | Actor |
| **Dzyaloshinskii, Igor E**<br>University of California, Physics Dept, Irvine CA 92697, USA | Physicist |

**Eackles, Ledell** — Basketball Player
9134 Elmgrove Garden Dr, Baton Rouge LA 70807, USA
**Eade, George J** — Air Force General
1131 Sunnyside Dr, Healdsburg CA 95448, USA
**Eads, George** — Actor
Innovative Artists, 1505 10th St, Santa Monica CA 90401 USA
**Eagle, Ian** — Sportscaster
CBS-TV, Sports Dept, 51 W 52nd St, New York NY 10019 USA
**Eagles, Mike** — Ice Hockey Player
59 Abbott Court, Fredericton NB E3B 5V8, Canada
**Eagling, Wayne J** — Ballet Dancer, Choreographer
Postbus 16486, 1001 RN Amsterdam, Netherlands
**Eakes, Bobbie** — Actress, Singer
Bauman Redanty Shaul Agency, 5757 Wilshire Blvd, #473, Los Angeles CA 90036 USA
**Eakin, Thomas C** — Businessman
245 Sandover Dr, Aurora OH 44202, USA
**Eakins, Dallas F** — Ice Hockey Player, Coach
19705 N 84th Way, Scottsdale AZ 85255, USA
**Eakins, James S (Jim)** — Basketball Player
2575 Little Cottonwood Road, Sandy UT 84092, USA
**Ealy, Michael** — Actor
Epidemic Pictures, 1635 N Cahuenga Blvd, #500, Los Angeles CA 90028, USA
**Eanes, Antonio dos Santos Ramalho** — President, Portugal; Army General
Partido Renovador Democratico, Travessa do Falo 9, 1200 Lisbon, Portugal
**Earl, Anthony S** — Governor, WI
Quarles & Brady, 1st Wisconsin Plaza, 1 S Pinckney St, Madison WI 53703, USA
**Earl, Roger** — Drummer (Foghat)
Lustig Talent, PO Box 770850, Orlando FL 32877 USA
**Earle Mead, Sylvia A** — Oceanographer
12812 Skyline Blvd, Oakland CA 94619, USA
**Earle, Acie B** — Basketball Player
2301 14th Ave, Moline IL 61265, USA
**Earle, Steve** — Singer, Guitarist, Songwriter
Gold Village Entertainment, 72 Madison Ave, #800, New York NY 10016, USA
**Earles, Jason** — Actor
C E S D, 10635 Santa Monica Blvd, #130, Los Angeles CA 90025 USA
**Earley, Liz** — Golfer
24 Morton Dr, Buffalo NY 14226, USA
**Early, Gerald L** — Writer, Educator
Washington University, English Dept, McMillan Hall, Saint Louis MO 63130, USA
**Early, Quinn R** — Football Player
PO Box 675752, Rancho Santa Fe CA 92067, USA
**Earnhardt, R Dale, Jr** — Auto Racing Driver
955 Shinnville Road, Mooresville NC 28115, USA
**Earp, Mildred** — Baseball Player
217 Dolly, West Fork AR 72774, USA
**Easler, Michael A (Mike)** — Baseball Player
2824 White Peaks Ave, North Las Vegas NV 89081, USA
**Easley, Bill** — Jazz Saxophonist, Clarinetist, Flutist
Hot Jazz Mgmt, 116 E 27th St, New York NY 10016, USA
**Easley, J Damion** — Baseball Player
6420 W Line Dr, Glendale AZ 85310, USA
**Easley, Kenny M (Ken)** — Football Player
3906 Kegagie Dr, Norfolk VA 23518, USA
**Eason, Bo** — Football Player, Actor, Writer
Creative Artists Agency, 2000 Ave of Stars, #100, Los Angeles CA 90067 USA
**Eason, Charles C (Tony), IV** — Football Player
PO Box 340, Walnut Grove CA 95690, USA
**East, Clyde B** — WW II Army Air Corps Hero
6643 Maplegrove St, Oak Park CA 91377, USA
**East, Jeff** — Actor
99 Spindrift Dr, Rancho Palos Verdes CA 90275, USA
**East, Ronald A (Ron)** — Football Player
PO Box 3442, Redmond WA 98073, USA
**Easter, Robert A** — Educator
University of Illinois, President's Office, 506 S Wright St, Urbana IL 61801, USA
**Easterbrook, Frank H** — Judge
US Court of Appeals, 219 S Dearborn St, #2302B, Chicago IL 60604, USA
**Easterbrook, Leslie** — Actress, Singer
Tufield Entertainment, 19521 Rosita St, Tarzana CA 91356, USA
**Easterlin, Richard A** — Economist
329 Patrician Way, Pasadena CA 91105, USA
**Easterly, James M (Jamie)** — Baseball Player
1306 Plantation Dr, Crockett TX 75835, USA
**Eastin, Jeff** — Producer, Writer
Creative Artists Agency, 2000 Ave of Stars, #100, Los Angeles CA 90067 USA
**Eastman, Dean E** — Physicist
336 Coonley Road, Riverside IL 60546, USA
**Eastman, John** — Attorney
Eastman & Eastman, 39 W 54th St, #200, New York NY 10019, USA
**Eastman, Kevin** — Cartoonist (Ninja Turtles)
1527 N Wickiup Road, Apache Junction AZ 85119, USA
**Eastman, Marilyn** — Actress
Greater Talent Network, 437 5th Ave, #700, New York NY 10016, USA
**Easton, David Anthony** — Interior Designer
72 Spring St, #700, New York NY 10012, USA
**Easton, Earnest Lee** — Educator
3040 E Charleston Blvd, #1046, Las Vegas NV 89104, USA
**Easton, Michael** — Actor
2810 Baseline Trail, Los Angeles CA 90068, USA
**Easton, Sheena** — Singer, Actress
Emmis Mgmt, 18136 Califa St, Tarzana CA 91356, USA
**Eastwick, Rawlins J (Rawly)** — Baseball Player
10 River Meadow Dr, West Newbury MA 01985, USA
**Eastwood, Clint** — Director, Actor
Hogs Breath Inn, Carlos St, PO Box 4366, Carmel by the Sea CA 93921, USA

**Eastwood, Robert F (Bob)** — Golfer
PO Box 14769, Haltom City TX 76117, USA
**Eathorne, A J** — Golfer
23023 N 25th Place, Phoenix AZ 85024, USA
**Eaton, Adam T** — Baseball Player
17404 NE 126th Place, Redmond WA 98052, USA
**Eaton, John C** — Composer
4585 N Hartstrait Road, Bloomington IN 47404, USA
**Eaton, Mark A** — Ice Hockey Player
3 Fieldstone Circle, Greenville RI 02828, USA
**Eaton, Mark E** — Basketball Player
2104 Dayton Ave NE, Renton WA 98056, USA
**Eaton, Meredith** — Actress
Amsel Eisenstadt Frazier, 5055 Wilshire Blvd, #865, Los Angeles CA 90036 USA
**Eaton, Rebecca** — Producer
Masterpiece Theater, WGBH-TV, 1 Guest St, Brighton MA 02135, USA
**Eaton, Shirley** — Actress
Diamond Mgmt, 31 Percy St, London W1T 2DD, England
**Eaton, T Scott** — Football Player
3950 W Lake Sammamish Parkway SE, Bellevue WA 98008, USA
**Eaton, Tracey B** — Football Player
PO Box 881, Preston WA 98050, USA
**Eatough, Jeff** — Ice Hockey Player
2050 Insley Road, Mississauga ON L4Y 1P9, Canada
**Eaves, Jerry L** — Basketball Player
10 Perch Place, Greensboro NC 27455, USA
**Eaves, Michael G (Mike)** — Ice Hockey Player, Coach
3615 Culver Trail, Faribault MN 55021, USA
**Eaves, Murray J** — Ice Hockey Player
Shattuck-Saint Mary's School, 1000 Shumway Ave, Faribault MN 55021, USA
**Eaves, Patrick C** — Ice Hockey Player
3693 Chappuis Trail, Faribault MN 55021, USA
**Ebadi, Shirin** — Nobel Peace Laureate
University of Tehran, Enghelab Ave & 16 Azar St, 14174 Tehran, Iran
**Ebanks, Selita** — Model
Women Model Mgmt, 199 Lafayette St, #700, New York NY 10012 USA
**Ebashi, Setsuro** — Biophysicist, Pharmacologist
17-503 Nagaizumi Myodaiji, Okazaki 444 0864, Japan
**Ebel, David M** — Judge
US Court of Appeals, US Courthouse, 1929 Stout St, Denver CO 80294, USA
**Eberhart, Ralph E (Ed)** — Air Force General
Armed Forces Benefit Assn, 909 N Washington St, #767, Alexandria VA 22314, USA
**Eberharter, Stephan (Steff)** — Alpine Skier
Dorfstr 21, 6272 Stumm, Austria
**Eberle, Markus** — Alpine Skier
Unterwestweg 27, 87567 Riezlern, Germany
**Ebersol, Dick** — Businessman
174 West St, #54, Litchfield CT 06759, USA
**Ebersole, Christine** — Actress, Singer
A P A Talent/Literary Agency, 405 S Beverly Dr, #300, Beverly Hills CA 90212 USA
**Ebersole, John J** — Football Player
1470 Village Square, Mount Pleasant SC 29464, USA
**Ebert, Peter** — Opera Director
Col di Mura, 06010 Lippiano, Italy
**Ebnoether, Luzia** — Curling Athlete
Curling Assn, PO Box 606, 3000 Bern, Switzerland
**Ebron, Roy** — Basketball Player
7100 Virgilian St, New Orleans LA 70126, USA
**Ebsen, Bonnie** — Actress
PO Box 356, Agoura CA 91376, USA
**Eby, Betsy** — Artist
Winston Wachter Fine Art, 39 E 78th St, New York NY 10075, USA
**Eccles, Spencer F** — Financier
Wells Fargo Bank, 299 S Main St, #400, Salt Lake City UT 84111, USA
**Eccleston, Christopher** — Actor
Independent Talent Group, 40 Whitfield St, London W1T 2RH, England
**Ecclestone, Bernie** — Auto Racing Executive
Formula One Ltd, 6 Prince's Gate, London SW7 1QJ, England
**Ecclestone, Tamara** — Actress, Model
Lucy Hibbard, 6 Princes Gate, London SW7 1QJ, England
**Ecclestone, Timothy J (Tim)** — Ice Hockey Player
10095 Fairway Village Dr, Roswell GA 30076, USA
**Echevarria, Angel S** — Baseball Player
23830 231st Place SE, Maple Valley WA 98038, USA
**Echeverria Alvarez, Luis** — President, Mexico
Magnolia 131, San Jeronimo Lidice, Magdalena Contreras CP 10200, Mexico
**Echikunwoke, Megalyn** — Actress
United Talent Agency, U T A Plaza, 9336 Civic Center Dr, Beverly Hills CA 90210 USA
**Ecker, Haylie** — Violinist
Mel Bush, Tanglewood, Arrowsmith Road, Wimborne, Dorset BH21 2BS, England
**Eckersley, Dennis L** — Baseball Player
6 Macy Lane, Ipswich MA 01938, USA
**Eckert, Shari** — Actress, Model
PO Box 5761, Sherman Oaks CA 91413, USA
**Eckhart, Aaron** — Actor
Creative Artists Agency, 2000 Ave of Stars, #100, Los Angeles CA 90067 USA
**Eckholdt, Steven** — Actor
Innovative Artists, 1505 10th St, Santa Monica CA 90401 USA
**Eckstein, David M** — Baseball Player
6969 Sylvan Woods Dr, Sanford FL 32771, USA
**Eco, Umberto** — Writer, Educator
Piazza Castello 13, 20121 Milan, Italy
**Edberg, Rolf** — Ice Hockey Player
Helmerdaisv 4, 12 352 Farst, Sweden
**Edberg, Stefan** — Tennis Player
Swedish Tennis Assn, Box 27915, 115 95 Stockholm, Sweden

V.I.P. Address Book

# E

**Eddery, Patrick J**  Thoroughbred Racing Jockey
Musk Hill Farm, Nether Winchendon, Aylesbury, Bucks HP18 0DT, England
**Eddings, Douglas L (Doug)**  Baseball Umpire
8072 Constitution Road, Las Cruces NM 88007, USA
**Eddington, Roderick I (Rod)**  Businessman
British Airways, Waterside, PO Box 365, Harmondsworth UB7 0GB, England
**Eddy, Duane**  Singer, Songwriter, Guitarist
1906 Chet Atkins Blvd, #502, Nashville TN 37212, USA
**Edel, Uli**  Director
Gersh Agency, 9465 Wilshire Blvd, #600, Beverly Hills CA 90212 USA
**Edell, Marc Z**  Attorney
Budd Larner Gross, 150 John F Kennedy Parkway, #301, Short Hills NJ 07078, USA
**Edelman, Brad M**  Football Player
828 Royal St, #410, New Orleans LA 70116, USA
**Edelman, Elazer R**  Cardiologist
Harvard-MIT Biomedical Center, 77 Massachusetts Ave, Cambridge MA 02139, USA
**Edelman, Gerald M**  Nobel Medicine Laureate
Scripps Research Institute, Neurobiology Dept, La Jolla CA 92037, USA
**Edelman, Ian**  Producer, Writer
United Talent Agency, U T A Plaza, 9336 Civic Center Dr, Beverly Hills CA 90210 USA
**Edelman, Marian Wright**  Association Executive
Children's Defense Fund, 25 E St NW, Washington DC 20001, USA
**Edelman, Pawel**  Cinematographer
I C M Partners, 10250 Constellation Blvd, #900, Los Angeles CA 90067 USA
**Edelman, Randy**  Composer
Gorfaine/Schwartz, 4111 W Alameda Ave, #509, Burbank CA 91505 USA
**Edelstein, Jean**  Artist
48 Brooks Ave, Venice CA 90291, USA
**Edelstein, Lisa**  Actress
Water Street Anthem Entertainment, 5225 Wilshire Blvd, #615, Los Angeles CA 90036 USA
**Edelstein, Victor A**  Fashion Designer, Artist
3 Stanhope Mews West, London SW7 5RB, England
**Eden, Barbara**  Actress
9816 Denbigh Dr, Beverly Hills CA 90210, USA
**Eden, Harry**  Actor
Independent Talent Group, 40 Whitfield St, London W1T 2RH, England
**Eden, Richard**  Actor
Abrams Artists, 9200 W Sunset Blvd, #1125, West Hollywood CA 90069 USA
**Edens, Thomas P (Tom)**  Baseball Player
2033 Quailridge Court, Clarkston WA 99403, USA
**Eder, Richard G**  Journalist
Los Angeles Times, Editorial Dept, 202 W 1st St, Los Angeles CA 90012 USA
**Eder, Simon**  Biathlete
Taxauweg 18, 5760 Saalfelden, Austria
**Edestrand, Darryl**  Ice Hockey Player
391 Beechwood Ave, London ON N6J 3J9, Canada
**Edgar, David**  Writer
Alan Brodie Representation, 211 Piccadilly, London W1V 9LD, England
**Edgar, David (Dave)**  Swimmer
2633 Middle River Dr, #3, Fort Lauderdale FL 33306, USA
**Edgar, James (Jim)**  Governor, IL
University of Illinois, Public Affairs Institute, Urbana IL 61801, USA
**Edgar, Ross**  Cyclist
Ashwood Laboratories, Brockhall Village, Blackburn, Lancashire BB6 8BB, England
**Edge**  Guitarist (U-2), Singer
Regine Moylet, 9 Ivebury Court, 325 Latimer Road, London W10 6RA, England
**Edge, Graeme**  Drummer (Moody Blues)
Insight Mgmt, 1222 16th Ave S, #300, Nashville TN 37212, USA
**Edge, Mitzi**  Golfer
118 Kings Chapel Road, Augusta GA 30907, USA
**Edgerson, Booker T**  Football Player
68 Union Common, Buffalo NY 14221, USA
**Edgerton, Joel**  Actor
Shanahan Mgmt, PO Box 1509, Darlinghurst NSW 1300, Australia
**Edgley, Gigi**  Actress, Singer
Soverign Talent Group, 8421 Wilshire Blvd, #200, Beverly Hills CA 90211, USA
**Edinger, Paul E, IV**  Football Player
2313 York Place, Lakeland FL 33810, USA
**Edlund, Ben**  Comic Book Artist, Animator
United Talent Agency, U T A Plaza, 9336 Civic Center Dr, Beverly Hills CA 90210 USA
**Edlund, Richard P**  Cinematographer
2710 Wilshire Blvd, Santa Monica CA 90403, USA
**Edmonds, Albert J (Al)**  Air Force General
Military Officers Assn, 201 N Washington St, Alexandria VA 22314, USA
**Edmonds, Jacque**  Producer, Writer
Collective, 8383 Wilshire Blvd, #1050, Beverly Hills CA 90211 USA
**Edmonds, James P (Jim)**  Baseball Player
25 Boulder View, Irvine CA 92603, USA
**Edmonds, Kenneth (Babyface)**  Singer, Keyboardist, Songwriter
Creative Artists Agency, 2000 Ave of Stars, #100, Los Angeles CA 90067 USA
**Edmonds, Tracey E**  Actress, Producer
Our Stories Films, 1635 N Cahuenga Blvd, Los Angeles CA 90028, USA
**Edmondson, Adrian**  Actor, Writer, Director
Jonathan Altaras Assoc, 11 Garrick St, London WC2E 9AR, England
**Edmondson, Jaime Faith**  Model
Playboy Promotions, 2706 Media Center Dr, Los Angeles CA 90065 USA
**Edmondson, James L (J L)**  Judge
US Court of Appeals, 56 Forsyth St NW, Atlanta GA 30303, USA
**Edmondson, Sarah**  Actress
Characters Talent Mgmt, 8 Elm St, Toronto ON M5G 1G7, Canada
**Edmunds, Dave**  Singer, Guitarist, Songwriter
A B S Agency, PO Box 932A, Sirbiton KT1 9QR, England
**Edmunds, Ferrell, Jr**  Football Player
PO Box 414, Blairs VA 24527, USA
**Edmundson, Gary**  Ice Hockey Player
Silvercrest Western Homes, 299 N Smith Ave, Corona CA 92880, USA

**Edner, Ashley** — Actress
10061 Riverside Dr, #341, North Hollywood CA 91602, USA
**Edney, Leon A (Bud)** — Navy Admiral
1037 Encino Row, Coronado CA 92118, USA
**Edney, Tyus D** — Basketball Player
1800 S Floyd Court, La Habra CA 90631, USA
**Edsall, Randy D** — Football Coach
University of Maryland, Athletic Dept, College Park MD 20742, USA
**Eduardo dos Santos, Jose** — President, Angola
President's Office, Palacio do Povo, Luanda, Angola
**Edur, Tom** — Ice Hockey Player
Puhanzu 77, 10316 Talinn, Estonia
**Edward** — Prince, England
Bagshot, Bagshot Park, Surrey GU19 5PN, England
**Edward, John** — Psychic
Berkley Publishing Group, 375 Hudson St, Basement 1, New York NY 10014 USA
**Edwards, Anthony** — Actor
Creative Artists Agency, 2000 Ave of Stars, #100, Los Angeles CA 90067 USA
**Edwards, Antuan M** — Football Player
8108 Connestee Dr, McKinney TX 75070, USA
**Edwards, Barbara** — Model, Actress
Hansen, 7767 Hollywood Blvd, #202, Los Angeles CA 90046, USA
**Edwards, Braylon J** — Football Player
32388 Legacy Pointe Parkway, Avon Lake OH 44012, USA
**Edwards, Carl M** — Auto, Truck Racing Driver
3910 Trinity Church Road, Concord NC 28027, USA
**Edwards, Chris** — Bassist (Kasabian)
Independent Talent Group, 40 Whitfield St, London W1T 2RH, England
**Edwards, Cleophus (Cid)** — Football Player
5343 Adobe Fall Road, San Diego CA 92120, USA
**Edwards, David** — Golfer
5 Champion Place, Stillwater OK 74074, USA
**Edwards, David L (Dave)** — Baseball Player
5059 Quail Run Road, #75, Riverside CA 92507, USA
**Edwards, Dennis** — Singer (Temptations)
Paradise Artists, PO Box 1821, Ojai CA 93024 USA
**Edwards, Don** — Singer
Scott O'Malley Assoc, PO Box 9188, Colorado Springs CO 80932, USA
**Edwards, Don** — Ice Hockey Player
530 Saint Andrews Road, #4, Saginaw MI 48638, USA
**Edwards, Earl** — Football Player
1534 W Saint Thomas Dr, Gilbert AZ 85233, USA
**Edwards, Eric** — Cinematographer
3404 SW Water Ave, Portland OR 97239, USA
**Edwards, Gareth** — Writer
W M E Entertainment, 9601 Wilshire Blvd, #300, Beverly Hills CA 90210 USA
**Edwards, Gareth O** — Rugby Player
Hamdden Ltd, Plas y Ffynnon, Cambrian Way, Brecon Powys LD3 7HP, Wales
**Edwards, Gary** — Ice Hockey Player
6818 Pecan Ave, Moorpark CA 93021, USA
**Edwards, Glen** — Football Player
4115 31st St S, Saint Petersbug FL 33712, USA
**Edwards, Harry** — Educator, Social Activist
University of California, Sociology Dept, Berkeley CA 94720, USA
**Edwards, Harry T** — Judge
US Court of Appeals, 333 Constitution Ave NW, #4400, Washington DC 20001, USA
**Edwards, Herman L (Herm)** — Football Player, Coach, Sportscaster
433 Ward Parkway, #1, Kansas City MO 64112, USA
**Edwards, Howard R (Doc)** — Baseball Player, Manager
3706 Driftwood Dr, San Angelo TX 76904, USA
**Edwards, James B** — Secretary, Energy; Governor, SC
100 Venning St, Mount Pleasant SC 29464, USA
**Edwards, Jay C** — Basketball Player
121 N Washington St, #506, MARION IN 46952, USA
**Edwards, Jennifer** — Actress
I C M Partners, 10250 Constellation Blvd, #900, Los Angeles CA 90067 USA
**Edwards, Joe F, Jr** — Astronaut
National Sciences Center, 1 7th St, #502, Augusta GA 30901, USA
**Edwards, Joel** — Golfer
5809 Shoreside Bend, Irving TX 75039, USA
**Edwards, John** — Singer (Spinners)
Buddy Allen Mgmt, 3750 Hudson Manor Terrace, #3AE, Bronx NY 10463, USA
**Edwards, John A (Johnny)** — Baseball Player
2511 E Blue Lake Dr, Magnolia TX 77354, USA
**Edwards, John R** — Senator, NC
North Carolina University, Work Poverty Center, Chapel Hill NC 27599, USA
**Edwards, Jonathan** — Track Athlete
Jonathan Marks, 20 York St, London W1U 6PU, England
**Edwards, Jonathan** — Singer, Songwriter
Northern Lights, 437 Live Oak Loop NE, Albuquerque NM 87122, USA
**Edwards, Kalimba** — Football Player
6140 Sibling Pine Dr, Durham NC 27705, USA
**Edwards, Kathleen** — Singer, Songwriter
Potty Mouth, 13 Blackburn St, #300, Toronto ON M4M 2B3, Canada
**Edwards, Kevin** — Basketball Player
821 Reilly Lane, Lake Forest IL 60045, USA
**Edwards, Kim** — Writer
Penguin Books, 375 Hudson St, Basement 1, New York NY 10014 USA
**Edwards, Luke** — Actor, Producer, Writer
Abrams Artists, 9200 W Sunset Blvd, #1125, West Hollywood CA 90069 USA
**Edwards, Mario L** — Football Player
PO Box 216, Prosper TX 75078, USA
**Edwards, Mark J** — Navy Admiral
Deputy CNO, Communications Networks, HqUSN, Pentagon, Washington DC 20350, USA
**Edwards, R LaVell** — Football Player, Coach
Brigham Young University, Athletic Dept, Provo UT 84602, USA

**Edwards, Robert** — Director, Producer, Writer
Creative Artists Agency, 2000 Ave of Stars, #100, Los Angeles CA 90067 USA
**Edwards, Robert A (Bob)** — Commentator
Sirius XM Satellite Radio, 1500 Eckington Place NE, Washington DC 20002, USA
**Edwards, Sandra** — Model, Actress
Playboy Promotions, 2706 Media Center Dr, Los Angeles CA 90065 USA
**Edwards, Sian** — Conductor
70 Twisden Road, London NW5 1DN, England
**Edwards, Stacy** — Actress
Talent Works, 3500 W Olive Ave, #1400, Burbank CA 91505 USA
**Edwards, Stephen (Steve)** — Composer
3980 Royal Oak Place, Encino CA 91436, USA
**Edwards, Teresa** — Basketball Player, Coach
600 1st Ave N, #Sky, Minneapolis MN 55403, USA
**Edwards, Theodore (Blue)** — Basketball Player
11945 Maria Ester Court, Charlotte NC 28277, USA
**Edwards, Tommy Lee** — Illustrator
D C Comics, 1700 Broadway, #400, New York NY 10019 USA
**Edwards, Trent** — Football Player
Chicago Bears, 1000 Football Dr, Lake Forest IL 60045 USA
**Edwards, Troy** — Football Player
6835 Foghorn Lane, Grand Prairie TX 75054, USA
**Edwards, Wayne** — Guitarist
PO Box 153, 2441Q Old Fort Parkway, Murfreesboro TN 37133, USA
**Edwin, Colin** — Bassist (Porcupine Tree)
Agency Group Ltd, 361-373 City Road, London EC1V 1PQ, England
**Efremova, Svetlana** — Actress
Greene Assoc, 1901 Ave of Stars, #130, Los Angeles CA 90067 USA
**Efron, Zac** — Actor
Ninjas Runnin' Wild Productions, 7024 Melrose Ave, #420, Los Angeles CA 90038, USA
**Egan, Christopher (Chris)** — Actor
Troika, 74 Clerkenwell Road, #300, London EC1M 5QA, England
**Egan, Edward M Cardinal** — Religious Leader
Archdiocese of New York, 1011 1st St, New York NY 10022, USA
**Egan, Jennifer** — Writer
Knopf Publishers, 1745 Broadway, New York NY 10019 USA
**Egan, John F (Johnny)** — Basketball Player, Coach
2124 Nantucket Dr, #B, Houston TX 77057, USA
**Egan, John L** — Businessman
Inchape PLC, 33 Cavendish Square, London W1M 9HF, England
**Egan, Melissa Claire** — Actress
Don Buchwald, 6500 Wilshire Blvd, #2200, Los Angeles CA 90048 USA
**Egan, Richard W (Dick)** — Baseball Player
709 Carnoustie Court, Garland TX 75044, USA
**Egan, Susan** — Actress, Singer, Dancer
13801 Ventura Blvd, Sherman Oaks CA 91423, USA
**Egan, Thomas P (Tom)** — Baseball Player
184 E Myrna Lane, Tempe AZ 85284, USA
**Egers, Jack** — Ice Hockey Player
24 Zinkann Crescent Gardens, Wellesley ON 0B 2T0, Canada
**Egerszegi, Krisztina** — Swimmer
Budapest Spartacus, Koer Utca 1/A, 1103 Budapest, Hungary
**Egerton, Tamsin** — Actress
Independent Talent Group, 40 Whitfield St, London W1T 2RH, England
**Eggar, Samantha** — Actress
5005 Varna Ave, Sherman Oaks CA 91423, USA
**Eggby, David** — Cinematographer
4344 Promenade Way, #209, Marina del Rey CA 90292, USA
**Eggeling, Dale** — Golfer
8918 Magnolia Chase Circle, Tampa FL 33647, USA
**Eggers, Dave** — Writer
Simon & Schuster 1230 Ave of Americas, New York NY 10020, USA
**Eggers, Douglas B (Doug)** — Football Player
12803 Cedarbrook Lane, Laurel MD 20708, USA
**Eggert, Nicole** — Actress
Global Artists Agency, 6253 Hollywood Blvd, #508, Los Angeles CA 90028, USA
**Eggert, Robert J** — Economist
Eggert Economic Enterprises, 1195 S Bates Road, Cottonwood AZ 86326, USA
**Eggler, Markus** — Curling Athlete
Bruckfeldstr 2, 4142 Munchenstein BL, Switzerland
**Egglesfield, Colin** — Actor
United Talent Agency, U T A Plaza, 9336 Civic Center Dr, Beverly Hills CA 90210 USA
**Eggleston, William** — Photographer, Artist
Robert Miller Gallery, 526 W 26th St, #10A, New York NY 10001, USA
**Eggleton, Arthur C** — Government Official, Canada
National Defense Ministry, 101 Colonel By Dr, Ottawa ON K1A 0K2, Canada
**Eggold, Ryan J** — Actor
Gersh Agency, 9465 Wilshire Blvd, #600, Beverly Hills CA 90212 USA
**Egielski, Richard** — Illustrator
525 B St, #1900, San Diego CA 92101, USA
**Egington, Richard P** — Rowing Athlete
Leander Club, Henley-on-Thames, Oxfordshire, Leander RG9 2LP, England
**Egloff, Bruce E** — Baseball Player
3136 S Emporia Court, Denver CO 80231, USA
**Egon, Nicholas** — Artist
Villa Aetos, Katakali, Corinthia 20100, Greece
**Ehart, Phil** — Drummer (Kansas)
Lustig Talent, PO Box 770850, Orlando FL 32877 USA
**Eheart, Brenda Krause** — Social Activist
Hope Meadows, 1530 Fairway Dr, Rantoul IL 61866, USA
**Ehle, Jennifer** — Actress
I C M Partners, 10250 Constellation Blvd, #900, Los Angeles CA 90067 USA
**Ehlers, Walter D** — WW II Army Hero (CMH)
8382 Valley View, Buena Park CA 90620, USA
**Ehlert, Lois** — Writer
Scholastic Press, 555 Broadway, New York NY 10012 USA

**Ehlo, J Craig** — Basketball Player
3323 E 77th Ave, Spokane WA 99223, USA
**Ehrenfeld, Rachel** — Writer
American Center for Democracy, 330 W 56th St, #24E, New York NY 10019, USA
**Ehrenkrantz, Dan** — Religious Leader, Rabbi, Educator
Reconstructionist Rabbinical College, 1299 Church Road, Wyncote PA 19095, USA
**Ehrenreich, Alden** — Actor
Creative Artists Agency, 2000 Ave of Stars, #100, Los Angeles CA 90067 USA
**Ehrenreich, Barbara** — Women's Activist, Writer
I C M Partners, 10250 Constellation Blvd, #900, Los Angeles CA 90067 USA
**Ehret, Gloria** — Golfer
3335 Royal Lane, Dallas TX 75229, USA
**Ehrhoff, Christian** — Ice Hockey Player
4517 Carlyle Court, Santa Clara CA 95054, USA
**Ehrlich, Paul R** — Population Biologist
Stanford University, Biological Sciences Dept, Stanford CA 94305, USA
**Ehrlich, Thomas** — Educator
Carnegie Teaching Foundation, 51 Vista Lane, Stanford CA 94305, USA
**Ehrmann, Joseph C (Joe)** — Football Player
5 Elmhurst Road, Baltimore MD 21210, USA
**Eichelberger, Charles B** — Army General
California Microwave, 124 Sweetwater Oaks, Peachtree City GA 30269, USA
**Eichelberger, David** — Golfer
1947 Judd Hillside Road, Honolulu HI 96822, USA
**Eichelberger, Juan T** — Baseball Player
14674 Silverset St, Poway CA 92064, USA
**Eichhorn, Lisa** — Actress
1919 W 44th St, #1000, New York NY 10036, USA
**Eichhorn, Mark A** — Baseball Player
147 Norma Court, Aptos CA 95003, USA
**Eichhorst, Richard A (Dick)** — Basketball Player
2701 Sheridan Road, Saint Louis MO 63125, USA
**Eigen, Manfred** — Nobel Chemistry Laureate
Georg-Dehio-Weg 4, 37075 Gottingen, Germany
**Eigenberg, David** — Actor
Paul Kohner, 9300 Wilshire Blvd, #555, Beverly Hills CA 90212 USA
**Eijk, Willem J (Wim) Cardinal** — Religious Leader
Archdiocese, Post Bus 14019, 3508 Utrech SB, Netherlands
**Eikenberry, Jill** — Actress
PO Box 843, Santa Ynez CA 93460, USA
**Eikenberry, Karl W** — Army General
State Department, 2201 C St NW, Washington DC 20520 USA
**Eiland, David W (Dave)** — Baseball Player
2824 Blue Springs Place, Wesley Chapel FL 33544, USA
**Eilbacher, Lisa** — Actress
Metropolitan Talent Agency, 5405 Wilshire Blvd, #218, Los Angeles CA 90036 USA
**Eilber, Janet** — Actress
Irv Schechter, 9460 Wilshire Blvd, #300, Beverly Hills CA 90212 USA
**Eilers, David L (Dave)** — Baseball Player
602 Perkins Lane, Brenham TX 77833, USA
**Eilers, Patrick C (Pat)** — Football Player
177 De Windt Road, Winnetka IL 60093, USA
**Eine, Simon** — Actor
Anne Alvares Correa, 34 Rue Jouffroy d'Abbans, 75017 Paris, France
**Einhorn, Lawrence** — Oncologist
Indiana University Medical School, Oncology Dept, Bloomington IN 47405, USA
**Einhorn, Richard** — Composer
320 Riverside Dr, #15C, New York NY 10025, USA
**Einstein, Bob (Super Dave Osbourne)** — Actor, Comedian
9842 Cardigan Place, Beverly Hills CA 90210, USA
**Einziger, Mike** — Guitarist (Incubus), Songwriter
Variety Artists, 1924 Spring St, Paso Robles CA 93446 USA
**Eischeid, Michael D (Mike)** — Football Player
306 Auburn St, West Union IA 52175, USA
**Eischen, Joseph R (Joey)** — Baseball Player
3678 E Thornton Ave, Gilbert AZ 85297, USA
**Eisen, Herman N** — Immunologist
75 Cambridge Parkway, #E806, Cambridge MA 02142, USA
**Eisen, Rich** — Sportscaster
N F L Network, 10950 Washington Blvd, #100, Culver City CA 90232 USA
**Eisen, Tripp** — Guitarist (Static-X)
United Talent Agency, U T A Plaza, 9336 Civic Center Dr, Beverly Hills CA 90210 USA
**Eisenach, Kathleen** — Pathologist
University of Arkansas Medical Sciences, 4301 W Markham, Little Rock AR 72205, USA
**Eisenberg, David S** — Chemist
University of California, Chemisty & Biochemistry Dept, Los Angeles CA 90024, USA
**Eisenberg, Hallie Kate** — Actress
Abrams Artists, 9200 W Sunset Blvd, #1125, West Hollywood CA 90069 USA
**Eisenberg, Jesse A** — Actor
Creative Artists Agency, 2000 Ave of Stars, #100, Los Angeles CA 90067 USA
**Eisenberg, Lee** — Actor, Comedian, Writer
W M E Entertainment, 9601 Wilshire Blvd, #300, Beverly Hills CA 90210 USA
**Eisenberg, Melvin A** — Attorney, Educator
1197 Keeler Ave, Berkeley CA 94708, USA
**Eisenhauer, Lawrence C (Larry)** — Football Player
19 Hobart Lane, Cohasset MA 02025, USA
**Eisenhauer, Stephen S (Steve)** — Football Player
105 Abbey Road, Winchester VA 22602, USA
**Eisenman, Peter D** — Architect
Eisenman Architects, 40 W 25th St, New York NY 10010, USA
**Eisenreich, James M (Jim)** — Baseball Player
11 Emerald Shore Dr, Blue Springs MO 64015, USA
**Eisenstein, Michael** — Guitarist (Letters to Cleo)
Little Big Man, 155 Ave of Americas, #700, New York NY 10013, USA
**Eisinger, Jesse** — Journalist
ProPublica, Editorial Dept, 1 Exchange Plaza, 55 Broadway, #2300, New York NY 10006, USA

Ehlo - Eisinger

# E

**Eisler, Barry** — Writer
Penguin Group, 375 Hudson St, Basement 1, New York NY 10014, USA

**Eisler, Lloyd E** — Figure Skater
Los Angeles Kings Valley Ice Center, 8750 Van Nuys Blvd, Panorama City CA 91402, USA

**Eisley, Howard J** — Basketball Player
20250 Rodeo Court, Southfield MI 48075, USA

**Eisley, India** — Actress
I C M Partners, 10250 Constellation Blvd, #900, Los Angeles CA 90067 USA

**Eisman, Hy** — Cartoonist (Katzenjammer Kids)
99 Boulevard, Glen Rock NJ 07452, USA

**Eisner, Breck** — Director
Creative Artists Agency, 2000 Ave of Stars, #100, Los Angeles CA 90067 USA

**Eisner, Michael D** — Businessman
Tornante Co, 233 S Beverly Dr, #200, Beverly Hills CA 90212, USA

**Eitner, Lorenz E A** — Art Historian
684 Mirada Ave, Stanford CA 94305, USA

**Eitzel, Mark** — Singer, Songwriter
Gearbox Agency, Halmtonvet 29, Bygning 12A, 1799 Copenhagen, Denmark

**Eizenstat, Stuart E** — Government Official, Diplomat
5610 Wisconsin Ave, #603, Chevy Chase MD 20815, USA

**Ejiofor, Chiwetel** — Actor
B/W/R, 9100 Wilshire Blvd, #500W, Beverly Hills CA 90212 USA

**Ejogo, Carmen** — Actress
I F A Talent Agency, 8730 W Sunset Blvd, #490, West Hollywood CA 90069 USA

**Ek, Klara** — Opera Singer
Harrison/Parrott, 5-6 Albion Court, London W6 0QT, England

**Ekberg, Anita** — Actress, Model
Via Aspro N 1, 00045 Genzano di Rome, Italy

**Ekberg, Niclas** — Handball Player
T H W Kiel Handball, Herzog-Friedrich-Str 52, 24103 Kiel, Germany

**Ekberg, Ulf** — Singer (Ace of Base)
United Stage Artists, Asogatan 142, Box 11029, 100 61 Stockholm, Sweden

**Ekimov, Viatcheslav V** — Cyclist
TeamRadio Shack, Capital Sports & Mgmt, 98 San Jacinto Blvd, #430, Austin, TX 78701, USA

**Eklund, Greg** — Drummer (Everclear)
Pinnacle Entertainment, 30 Glenn St, White Plains NY 10603, USA

**Eklund, Per-Erik (Pelle)** — Ice Hockey Player
Sunnanangyttervagen 67, 793 90 Leksand, Sweden

**Ekman, Paul** — Psychologist
University of California Medical Center, 505 Parnassus, San Francisco CA 94122 USA

**Ekstrom, Michael** — Baseball Player
1616 SE 282nd Ave, Gresham OR 97080, USA

**Ekuban, Ebenezer, Jr** — Football Player
5391 Moonlight Way, Parker CO 80134, USA

**El DeBarge** — Singer
205 Hill St, Santa Monica CA 90405, USA

**El Fadil, Siddig** — Actor
Paramount, 5555 Melose Ave, Los Angeles CA 90038, USA

**El Fassi, Abbas** — Prime Minister, Morocco
Prime Minister's Office, Palais Royal, Le Mechouar, Rabat, Morocco

**Elam, Jason** — Football Player
PO Box 1425, Soldotna AK 99669, USA

**Elam, Katrina** — Singer
PO Box 209, Marlow OK 73055, USA

**Elarton, V Scott** — Baseball Player
52922 Raines Road, Limon CO 80828, USA

**Elba, Idris** — Actor
W M E Entertainment, 9601 Wilshire Blvd, #300, Beverly Hills CA 90210 USA

**ElBaradei, Mohamed M** — Nobel Peace Laureate
Constitution Party, Abdin, Qasr El-Nile St, Cairo 002, Egypt

**Eldard, Ron** — Actor
United Talent Agency, U T A Plaza, 9336 Civic Center Dr, Beverly Hills CA 90210 USA

**Elder, Larry** — Actor
C E S D, 10635 Santa Monica Blvd, #130, Los Angeles CA 90025 USA

**Elder, Lee E** — Golfer
PO Box 667200, Pompano Beach FL 33066, USA

**Elder, Mark P** — Conductor
Ingpen & Williams, 131 Putney Bridge Road, London SW15 2PA, England

**Elders, M Jocelyn** — Pediatrician, Government Official
810 Marcia Cove, Little Rock AR 72206, USA

**Eldon, Kevin** — Actor
R D F Mgmt, 3-6 Kendrick Place, London W1U 6HD, England

**Eldred, Bradley R (Brad)** — Baseball Player
4182 SW Saint Lucie Lane, Palm City FL 34990, USA

**Eldred, Calvin J (Cal)** — Baseball Player
1893 Horn Road, Mount Vernon IA 52314, USA

**Eldredge, Todd** — Figure Skater
2463 N Lake Angelus Road W, Auburn Hills MI 48326, USA

**Electra, Carmen** — Actress, Singer, Model
E M C Bowery, 5971 W 3rd St, Los Angeles CA 90036, USA

**Eleniak, Erika** — Model, Actress
Kirk Talent Agencies, 196 W 3rd Ave, #102, Vancouver BC V5Y 1E9, Canada

**Elephant Man** — Singer
Bad Boy Entertainment, 1440 Broadway, #16, New York NY 10018 USA

**Elfman, Bodhi** — Actor
Lewis & Beal Talent Agency, 15303 Ventura Blvd, #900, Sherman Oaks CA 91403, USA

**Elfman, Danny** — Singer, Composer
Musica de la Muerte, 1901 Ave of Stars, #1450, Los Angeles CA 90067, USA

**Elfman, Jenna** — Actress, Model
Brillstein Entertainment Partners, 9150 Wilshire Blvd, #350, Beverly Hills CA 90212 USA

**Elg, Taina** — Actress
789 W End Ave, New York NY 10025, USA

**Elgart, Larry J** — Orchestra Leader
2065 Gulf of Mexico Dr, Longboat Key FL 34228, USA

**Eli, Mike** — Singer, Guitarist (Eli Youn Band)
Triple 8 Mgmt, 1611 6th St, Austin TX 78703, USA

Eisler - Eli

|  |  |
|---|---|
| **Elia, Lee C**<br>11613 Innfields Dr, Odessa FL 33556, USA | Baseball Player, Manager |
| **Elia, Nicolas**<br>Paceline Entertainment, 12444 Ventura Blvd, #103, Studio City CA 91604 USA | Actor |
| **Eliane, Elias**<br>RR 376 Box 1282, Wappingers FL 12590, USA | Singer, Pianist, Composer |
| **Elias, Antonio L**<br>Orbital Sciences Corp, 21839 Atlantic Blvd, Dulles VA 20166, USA | Space Scientist |
| **Elias, Eliane**<br>Axis Artists Mgmt, 9715 Belmar Ave, Northridge CA 91324, USA | Jazz Pianist, Singer, Composer |
| **Elias, Hector**<br>C E S D, 10635 Santa Monica Blvd, #130, Los Angeles CA 90025 USA | Actor |
| **Elias, Jonathan**<br>Elias Arts, 2219 Main St, Santa Monica CA 90405, USA | Composer |
| **Elias, Keith H**<br>4507 Norma Place, Toms River NJ 08755, USA | Football Player |
| **Elias, Patrik**<br>1005 Smith Manor Blvd, #98, West Orange NJ 07052, USA | Ice Hockey Player |
| **Elias, Rosalind**<br>Robert Lombardo Assoc, Harkness Plaza, 61 W 62nd St, #6F, New York NY 10023 USA | Opera Singer |
| **Elice, Rick**<br>I C M Partners, 10250 Constellation Blvd, #900, Los Angeles CA 90067 USA | Writer |
| **Elie, Mario A**<br>1 Mott Lane, Houston TX 77024, USA | Basketball Player |
| **Elinson, Jack**<br>655 Pomander Walk, #210, Teaneck NJ 07666, USA | Sociomedical Scientist |
| **Eliot, Darren J**<br>1100 Grayton St, Grosse Pointe Park MI 48230, USA | Ice Hockey Player |
| **Eliot, Jan**<br>PO Box 50032, Eugene OR 97405, USA | Cartoonist (Stone Soup) |
| **Elise, Christine**<br>Luber Rocklin Entertainment, 8530 Wilshire Blvd, #555, Beverly Hills CA 90211 USA | Actress |
| **Elise, Kimberly**<br>Untitled Entertainment, 350 S Beverly Dr, #200, Beverly Hills CA 90212 USA | Actress |
| **Eliuk, Dallas**<br>Portland LumberJax, Rose Garden Arena, 1 N Center Court, Portland OR 97227, USA | Lacrosse Player |
| **Elizabeth II**<br>Buckingham Palace, London SW1A 1AA, England | Queen, England |
| **Elizabeth, Sarah**<br>Playboy Promotions, 2706 Media Center Dr, Los Angeles CA 90065 USA | Model |
| **Elizabeth, Shannon**<br>Fortitude, 9595 Wilshire Blvd, Beverly Hills CA 90212 USA | Actress, Model |
| **Elizabeth, Shannon**<br>Mavrick Artists Agency, 6100 Wilshire Blvd, #550, Los Angeles CA 90048, USA | Actress, Model |
| **Elizondo, Hector**<br>Gersh Agency, 9465 Wilshire Blvd, #600, Beverly Hills CA 90212 USA | Actor |
| **Elkaim, Jeremie**<br>Artmedia, 20 Ave Rapp, 75007 Paris, France | Actor |
| **Elkes, Joel**<br>University of Louisville, Psychiatry & Behavioral Science Dept, Louisville KY 40292, USA | Psychiatrist |
| **Elkind, Mortimer M**<br>10234 Rue Chamonix, San Diego CA 92131, USA | Biophysicist |
| **Elkington, Steve**<br>7010 Kelsey Rae Court, Houston TX 77069, USA | Golfer |
| **Elkins, Lawrence C (Larry)**<br>1 Keats Ave, Norden, Rochdale, Lancashire OL12 7PZ, England | Football Player |
| **Ellard, Henry A**<br>5800 Airline Dr, Metairie LA 70003, USA | Football Player |
| **Ellena, Jack D**<br>73164 Monterra Circle N, Palm Desert CA 92260, USA | Football Player |
| **Ellenshaw, Harrison**<br>2060 Avenida de los Arboles, #D317, Thousand Oaks CA 91362, USA | Special Effects Artist |
| **Ellenson, David**<br>Hebrew Union College, Jewish Religious Institute, 1 W 4th St, New York NY 10012, USA | Religious Leader, Rabbi, Educator |
| **Eller, Carl**<br>1035 Washburn Ave N, Minneapolis MN 55411, USA | Football Player, Executive |
| **Eller, Claudia**<br>Variety, 5900 Wilshire Blvd, #3100, Los Angeles CA 90036, USA | Editor |
| **Eller, Walter (Glenn), III**<br>US Army Marksmanship Unit, Fort Benning GA 31905, USA | Marksman |
| **Ellerbee, Linda**<br>Lucky Duck Productions, 96 Morton St, #400, New York NY 10014, USA | Commentator |
| **Ellerson, Rich**<br>US Military Academy, Athletic Dept, West Point NY 10996, USA | Football Coach |
| **Ellett, Dave**<br>36611 N 51st St, Cave Creek AZ 85331, USA | Ice Hockey Player |
| **Ellickson, Robert C**<br>Yale University, Law School, 127 Wall St, New Haven CT 06511, USA | Attorney, Educator |
| **Elliman, Yvonne**<br>Talent Consultants International, 105 Shad Row, #B, Piermont NY 10968 USA | Singer |
| **Ellin, Doug**<br>Leverage Mgmt, 3030 Pennsylvania Ave, Santa Monica CA 90404, USA | Director, Producer |
| **Elling, Kurt**<br>Jazz Tree, 648 Broadway, #303, New York NY 10012, USA | Singer |
| **Ellingsen, H Bruce**<br>5873 Daneland St, Lakewood CA 90713, USA | Baseball Player |
| **Ellingson, Evan**<br>Innovative Artists, 1505 10th St, Santa Monica CA 90401 USA | Actor |
| **Elliot, Janet**<br>Kirkwood Stables, 21 Mount Eden Road, Kirkwood PA 17536, USA | Steeplechase Racing Trainer |
| **Elliot, Lawrence L (Larry)**<br>13010 Caminito Bracho, San Diego CA 92128, USA | Baseball Player |
| **Elliott, Abby**<br>Creative Artists Agency, 2000 Ave of Stars, #100, Los Angeles CA 90067 USA | Actress, Comedienne |
| **Elliott, Alecia**<br>Creative Artists Agency, 2000 Ave of Stars, #100, Los Angeles CA 90067 USA | Singer, Actress |

## E

**Elliott, Alison** — Actress
Innovative Artists, 1505 10th St, Santa Monica CA 90401 USA
**Elliott, Andrea** — Journalist
New York Times, Editorial Dept, 229 W 43rd St, New York NY 10036 USA
**Elliott, Brennan** — Actor
Red Management, Box 3, 415 W Esplanade, North Vancouver, BC V7M, Canada
**Elliott, Brooke** — Actress, Singer
Innovative Artists, 1505 10th St, Santa Monica CA 90401 USA
**Elliott, Chalmers (Bump)** — Football Player, Coach
1 Oaknoll Court, Iowa City IA 52246, USA
**Elliott, Chris** — Actor, Comedian
Mosiac Media Group, 9200 W Sunset Blvd, #1000, Los Angeles CA 90069 USA
**Elliott, David James** — Actor
Paradigm Agency, 360 N Crescent Dr, North Building, Beverly Hills CA 90210 USA
**Elliott, Dennis** — Drummer (Foreigner)
Hard to Handle Mgmt, 16501 Ventura Blvd, #602, Encino CA 91436, USA
**Elliott, Donald G (Donnie)** — Baseball Player
1206 Bayou Vista Dr, Deer Park TX 77536, USA
**Elliott, E Matthew (Matt)** — Football Player
7453 Coventry Woods Dr, Dublin OH 43017, USA
**Elliott, Gordon** — Chef
Food Network, 1180 Ave of Americas, #1200, New York NY 10036 USA
**Elliott, Harry L** — Baseball Player
9608 Los Coches Road, Lakeside CA 92040, USA
**Elliott, Herbert (Herb)** — Track Athlete
Fortescue Metals Group, 87 Adelaide Terrace, East Perth WA 6004, Australia
**Elliott, Ira S** — Drummer (Fuzztones, Nada Surf)
M-Squared Mgmt, 201 W 72nd St, #12G, New York NY 10023, USA
**Elliott, Joe** — Singer, Musician (Def Leppard)
Front Line Mgmt, 1100 Glendon Ave, #2000, Los Angeles CA 90024 USA
**Elliott, John H** — Historian
122 Church Way, Iffley, Oxford OX4 4EG, England
**Elliott, John S (Jumbo)** — Football Player
17 Fieldstone Lane, Oyster Bay NY 11771, USA
**Elliott, Missy** — Singer, Songwriter, Actress
Monami Entertainment, 220 12th Ave, #300, New York NY 10001, USA
**Elliott, Paul H** — Cinematographer
Sandra Marsh Assoc, 9150 Wilshire Blvd, #220, Beverly Hills CA 90212 USA
**Elliott, Ralph E** — WW II Navy Air Force Hero
5150 Damascus Road S, Jacksonville FL 32207, USA
**Elliott, Ramblin' Jack** — Singer, Songwriter, Guitarist
Keith Case Assoc, 1025 17th Ave S, #200, Nashville TN 37212 USA
**Elliott, Rand** — Architect
Elliott Assoc, 35 Harrison Ave, Oklahoma City OK 73104, USA
**Elliott, Randy L** — Baseball Player
1002 Steuben St, Wausau WI 54403, USA
**Elliott, Robert A (Bob)** — Basketball Player
6760 E Fieldstone Lane, Tucson AZ 85750, USA
**Elliott, Sam** — Actor
33050 Pacific Coast Highway, Malibu CA 90265, USA
**Elliott, Sean M** — Basketball Player
1726 Greystone Ridge, San Antonio TX 78258, USA
**Elliott, Steve** — Harness Racing Driver, Trainer
36 Brookwood Road, Mount Laurel NJ 8054, USA
**Elliott, Ted A** — Writer, Producer
Creative Artists Agency, 2000 Ave of Stars, #100, Los Angeles CA 90067 USA
**Elliott, William C (Bill)** — Auto Racing Driver
Bill Elliott Racing, 200 Woodhaven Lane, Ball Ground GA 30107, USA
**Ellis Bextor, Sophie** — Singer
Primary Talent International, 10-11 Jockey's Fields, London WC1R 4BN, England
**Ellis, Alex** — Basketball Player
10121 Lone Wolf Dr, Indianapolis IN 46235, USA
**Ellis, Anita** — Jazz Singer
130 E End Ave, New York NY 10028, USA
**Ellis, Aunjanue** — Actress
I C M Partners, 10250 Constellation Blvd, #900, Los Angeles CA 90067 USA
**Ellis, Bret Easton** — Writer
Vintage Books, 1745 Broadway, New York NY 10019 USA
**Ellis, Caroline** — Actress
8060 Saint Clair Ave, North Hollywood CA 91605, USA
**Ellis, Chris** — Actor
Bauman Redanty Shaul Agency, 5757 Wilshire Blvd, #473, Los Angeles CA 90036 USA
**Ellis, Cliff** — Basketball Coach
Auburn University, Athletic Dept, Auburn AL 36831, USA
**Ellis, Dale** — Basketball Player
3564 W Hampton Dr NW, Marietta GA 30064, USA
**Ellis, Danny** — Golfer
1543 Cherry Lake Way, Lake Mary FL 32746, USA
**Ellis, Don** — Bowler
34 Crestwood Circle, Sugar Land TX 77478, USA
**Ellis, Elmer** — Historian, Educator
3300 New Haven Ave, #223, Columbia MO 65201, USA
**Ellis, F (Cot)** — Baseball Player
9505 N Silver Lake Dr, Oklahoma City OK 73162, USA
**Ellis, George F R** — Mathematician, Templeton Laureate
3 Marlowe Road, Capetown 7700, South Africa
**Ellis, Gerry L** — Football Player
250 Cavil Way, De Pere WI 54115, USA
**Ellis, Greg** — Actor
Kritzer Levine Wilkins Griffin, 11872 La Grange Ave, #100, Los Angeles CA 90025 USA
**Ellis, Gregory L (Greg)** — Football Player
PO Box 96075, Southlake TX 76092, USA
**Ellis, Harold** — Basketball Player
9420 Parkwood Ave, Douglasville GA 30135, USA
**Ellis, Hunter** — Actor
Ideal Mgmt, 5780 W Centennial Ave, #313, Los Angeles CA 90045, USA

**Elliott - Ellis**

| | |
|---|---|
| **Ellis, James R**<br>4213 Swann Ave, Tampa FL 33609, USA | Army General |
| **Ellis, James R (Jim)**<br>13608 Ave 24, Tulare CA 93274, USA | Baseball Player |
| **Ellis, Janet**<br>Arlington Entertainments, 1/3 Charlotte St, London W1P 1HD, England | Actress |
| **Ellis, Jimmy**<br>5218 Saint Gabriel Lane, Louisville KY 40291, USA | Boxer |
| **Ellis, John C**<br>14 Marina Point Dr, Old Saybrook CT 06475, USA | Baseball Player |
| **Ellis, Joseph J**<br>Mount Holyoke College, History Dept, South Hadley MA 01075, USA | Writer |
| **Ellis, K Ray**<br>4666 E Olney Ave, Gilbert AZ 85234, USA | Football Player |
| **Ellis, Kenneth A (Ken)**<br>2700 Gulf Freeway, #2111, Texas City TX 77591, USA | Football Player |
| **Ellis, LaPhonso**<br>51215 Shannon Brook Court, Granger IN 46530, USA | Basketball Player |
| **Ellis, Larry R**<br>3425 SW 2nd Ave, Gainesville FL 32607, USA | Army General |
| **Ellis, Mary Elizabeth**<br>Flutie Entertainment, 9320 Wilshire Blvd, #202, Beverly Hills CA 90212 USA | Actress |
| **Ellis, MeShaunda P (Shaun)**<br>26 Green St, Newbury MA 01951, USA | Football Player |
| **Ellis, Monta**<br>Dallas Mavericks, Pavilion, 2909 Taylor St, Dallas TX 75226 USA | Basketball Player |
| **Ellis, Nelsan**<br>I C M Partners, 10250 Constellation Blvd, #900, Los Angeles CA 90067 USA | Actor |
| **Ellis, Osian G**<br>90 Chandos Ave, London N20 9DZ, England | Concert Harpist |
| **Ellis, Richard S**<br>California Institute of Technology, Astronomy Dept, Pasadena CA 91125, USA | Astronomer |
| **Ellis, Robin**<br>Ken McReddie Assoc, 101 Finsbury Pavement, London EC2A 1RS, England | Actor |
| **Ellis, Romallis**<br>2062 San Marco Dr, Ellenwood GA 30294, USA | Boxer |
| **Ellis, Ronald J E (Ron)**<br>B C E Place, 30 Yonge St, Toronto ON M5E 1X8, Canada | Ice Hockey Player |
| **Ellis, Rosemary**<br>Good Housekeeping, Editor's Office, 300 W 57th St, New York NY 10019, USA | Editor |
| **Ellis, Samuel J (Sam)**<br>12511 Forest Highlands Dr, Dade City FL 33525, USA | Baseball Player |
| **Ellis, Scott**<br>301 W 118th St, #10-I, New York NY 10026, USA | Director |
| **Ellis, Sean**<br>I C M Partners, 10250 Constellation Blvd, #900, Los Angeles CA 90067 USA | Director, Producer, Writer |
| **Ellis, Terry**<br>Green Light Talent Agency, PO Box 3172, Beverly Hills CA 90212 USA | Singer (En Vogue) |
| **Ellison, Brooke**<br>Hyperion Books, 114 5th Ave, New York NY 10011 USA | Writer |
| **Ellison, Harlan J**<br>Kilimanjaro Group, PO Box 55540, Sherman Oaks CA 91413, USA | Writer |
| **Ellison, Jason J**<br>3745 248th Ave SE, Issaquah WA 98029, USA | Baseball Player |
| **Ellison, Jennifer**<br>C A M, 55-59 Shaftsbury Ave, London W1D 6LD, England | Actress |
| **Ellison, Keith**<br>Buffalo Bills, 1 Bills Dr, Orchard Park NY 14127 USA | Football Player |
| **Ellison, Lawrence J**<br>Oracle Systems, 500 Oracle Parkway, Redwood Shores CA 94065, USA | Businessman, Yachtsman |
| **Ellison, Pervis**<br>4602 Kettering Dr NE, Roswell GA 30075, USA | Basketball Player |
| **Ellison, William H (Willie)**<br>3503 Mosley Court, Houston TX 77004, USA | Football Player |
| **Elliss, Luther J**<br>118 E 3200 N, Kamas UT 84036, USA | Football Player |
| **Ellmann, Lucy**<br>David Godwin Assoc, 55 Monmouth St, London WC2H 9DG, England | Writer |
| **Ellroy, James**<br>Sobel Weber Assoc, 146 E 19th St, New York NY 10003, USA | Writer |
| **Ellsberg, Daniel**<br>90 Norwood Ave, Kensington CA 94707, USA | Political Activist |
| **Ellsbury, Jacoby M**<br>1204 Suncast Lane, #2, El Dorado Hills CA 95762, USA | Baseball Player |
| **Ellsworth, Kiko**<br>Stone Manners Salners, 9911 W Pico Blvd, #1400, Los Angeles CA 90035 USA | Actor |
| **Ellsworth, Percy D**<br>11261 Fortsville Road, Capron VA 23829, USA | Football Player |
| **Ellsworth, Richard C (Dick)**<br>1099 W Morris Ave, Fresno CA 93711, USA | Baseball Player |
| **Ellwood, Paul M, Jr**<br>68 Dell Creek Road, Bondurant WY 82922, USA | Physician |
| **Ellyson, Erica**<br>9850 S Maryland Parkway, #A5-446, Las Vegas NV 89183, USA | Model |
| **Elmaleh, Gad**<br>Thruline Entertainment, 9250 Wilshire Blvd, #100, Beverly Hills CA 90212 USA | Actor, Comedian |
| **Elmendorf, David C (Dave)**<br>17990 FM 1452 W, Normangee TX 77871, USA | Football Player |
| **Elmes, Fredrick**<br>Mirisch Agency, 8840 Wilshire Blvd, #100, Beverly Hills CA 90211 USA | Cinematographer |
| **Elmore, Leonard J (Len)**<br>PO Box 22, Highland MD 20777, USA | Basketball Player, Sportscaster |
| **Elrod, Jack**<br>7240 Hunter's Branch Dr NE, Atlanta GA 30328, USA | Cartoonist (Mark Trail) |
| **Elrod, Scott**<br>Independent Group, 8444 Wilshire Blvd, #500, Beverly Hills CA 90211, USA | Actor |

**Els, T Ernest (Ernie)** — Golfer
Ernie Els Design, PO Box 73, Virginia Water GU25 4ZS, England

**Elshire, Neil J** — Football Player
2441 NW Torsway St, Bend OR 97701, USA

**Elsley, Bryan** — Producer
The Agency, 24 Pottery Lane, London W11 4LZ, England , USA

**Elsna, Hebe** — Writer
Curtis Brown Group, 28-29 Haymarket St, #500, London SW1Y 4SP, England

**Elsner, Christian** — Opera Singer
Kunstler Sekretariat am Gasteig, Rosenheimer Str 52, 81669 Munich, Germany

**Elson, Francisco** — Basketball Player
92 Foxton Dr, San Antonio TX 78258, USA

**Elson, Karen** — Model
Elite Model Mgmt, 404 Park Ave S, #900, New York NY 10016 USA

**Elster, Jennifer** — Director
P M K-B N C, 622 3rd Ave, #800, New York NY 10017 USA

**Elswit, Richard (Rik)** — Singer, Guitarist (Dr Hook)
Artists International Mgmt, 9850 Sandalwood Blvd, #458, Boca Raton FL 33428, USA

**Elswit, Robert** — Cinematographer
United Talent Agency, U T A Plaza, 9336 Civic Center Dr, Beverly Hills CA 90210 USA

**Elton, Ben** — Actor, Comedian
Phil McIntyre Mgmt, 35 Soho Square, London W1D 3QX, England

**Elts, Olari** — Conductor
Van Walsum Mgmt, Tower Building, 11 York Road, London SE1 7NX, England

**Elvin, Violetta** — Ballerina
Marina di Equa, 80066 Seiano, Bay of Naples, Italy

**Elvin-Lewis, Memory** — Ethnobotanist
7915 Park Dr, Saint Louis MO 63117, USA

**Elvira, (Cassandra Peterson)** — Actress
Queen B Productions, PO Box 38246, Los Angeles CA 90038, USA

**Elway, John A** — Football Player
13644 E Dole Valley, Englewood CO 80112, USA

**Elwes, Cary** — Actor
Kritzer Levine Wilkins Griffin, 11872 La Grange Ave, #100, Los Angeles CA 90025 USA

**Elwood, Hugh M** — WW II Marine Corps Air Force Hero
1 Fleet Landing Blvd, Atlantic Beach FL 32233, USA

**Ely, Alexandre (Alex)** — Soccer Player
5526 N 2nd St, Philadelphia PA 19120, USA

**Ely, Jack** — Singer, Guitarist
Rolling Highway Mgmt, PO Box 1176, Marfa TX 79843, USA

**Ely, Joe** — Singer, Guitarist, Songwriter
L C Media, PO Box 965, Antioch TN 37011, USA

**Ely, Ron** — Actor
4161 Mariposa Dr, Santa Barbara CA 93110, USA

**Ely, Shyra** — Basketball Player
Indiana Fever, Conseco Fieldhouse, 125 S Pennsylvania, Indianapolis IN 46204 USA

**Elynuik, Patrick G (Pat)** — Ice Hockey Player
143 Aspen Green, Calgary AB T3Z 3B9, Canada

**Emanuel, Alphonsia** — Actress
Marina Martin, 12/13 Poland St, London W1V 3DE, England

**Emanuel, Bert T** — Football Player
15 Bees Creek Court, Missouri City TX 77459, USA

**Emanuel, David** — Fashion Designer
David Emanuel Couture, Lanesborough Hotel, London SW1X 7TA, England

**Emanuel, Elizabeth F** — Fashion Designer
Sew Forth Productions, 26 Chiltern St, London W1M 1PF, England

**Emanuel, Kerry A** — Meteorologist
Massachusetts Institute of Technology, Atmospheric Science Center, Cambridge MA 02139, USA

**Emanuel, Rahm** — Mayor, Chicago; Government Official
Mayor's Office, 121 N La Salle St, #507, Chicago IL 60602, USA

**Emanuel, T Frank** — Football Player
10211 Deercliff Dr, Tampa FL 33647, USA

**Embach, Carsten** — Bobsled Athlete
B S R Rennsteig e V, Grafenrodaer Str 2, 98559 Oberhof, Germany

**Emberg, Kelly** — Actress, Model
PO Box 675401, Rancho Santa Fe CA 92067, USA

**Embery, Joan** — Animal Activist
American Zoo Keepers Assn, 3601 SW 29th St, #133, Topeka KS 66614, USA

**Embree, Ainslie T** — Historian
PO Box 433, Centerville MA 02632, USA

**Embree, Alan D** — Baseball Player
61971 Kildonan Court, Bend OR 97702, USA

**Embree, Jon W** — Football Player, Coach
9450 Owl Lane, Boulder CO 80301, USA

**Embry, Ethan** — Actor
A P A Talent/Literary Agency, 405 S Beverly Dr, #300, Beverly Hills CA 90212 USA

**Embry, Wayne R** — Basketball Player, Executive
1101-211 Queens Quay W, Toronto ON M5J 2M6, Canada

**Emburey, John E** — Cricketer
Middlesex Cricket Club, Lord's Cricket Ground, London NW8 8QN, England

**Emerick, Kate** — Actress
Matt Sherman Mgmt, 9107 Wilshire Blvd, #225, Beverly Hills CA 90210, USA

**Emerick, Scotty** — Singer, Songwriter
Paradise Artists, PO Box 1821, Ojai CA 93024 USA

**Emerson, Claudia** — Writer
Mary Washington University, English Dept, 1301 College, Frederickburg VA 22401, USA

**Emerson, David F** — Navy Admiral
211 E 18th St, #5O, New York NY 10003, USA

**Emerson, Keith** — Keyboardist (Emerson Lake & Palmer)
Asia, 9 Hillgate St, London W8 7SP, England

**Emerson, Michael** — Actor
Innovative Artists, 1505 10th St, Santa Monica CA 90401 USA

**Emerson, Nelson** — Ice Hockey Player
717 33rd St, Manhattan Beach CA 90266, USA

**Emerson, Roy** — Tennis Player
2221 Alta Vista Dr, Newport Beach CA 92660, USA

**Emery, Gideon**  
Greene Assoc, 1901 Ave of Stars, #130, Los Angeles CA 90067 USA — Actor  
**Emery, John**  
Bobsled Canada, 140 Canada Olympic Road SW, Calgary AB T3B 5R5, Canada — Bobsled Athlete  
**Emery, Julie Ann**  
Principal Entertainment, 9255 Sunset Blvd, #500, Los Angeles CA 90069 USA — Actress  
**Emery, Lin**  
7520 Dominican St, New Orleans LA 70118, USA — Artist, Sculptor  
**Emery, R Lee**  
Bill Rogin Mgmt, 427 N Canon Dr, #215, Beverly Hills CA 90210, USA — Actor  
**Emery, Ralph**  
RFD-TV, Rural Media Group, 1 Valmont Plaza, #400, Omaha NE 68154, USA — Entertainer  
**Emery, Ray**  
1723 Haldimand Road 20, Cayuga ON N0A 1E0, Canada — Ice Hockey Player  
**Emery, Victor (Vic)**  
Bobsled Canada, 140 Canada Olympic Road SW, Calgary AB T3B 5R5, Canada — Bobsled Athlete  
**Emick, Jarrod**  
Douglas Gorman Rothacker Wilhelm, 1501 Broadway, #703, New York NY 10036 USA — Actor  
**Emilio**  
Refugee Mgmt, 209 10th Ave S, #347 Cummins Station, Nashville TN 37203, USA — Singer  
**Eminem**  
W M E Entertainment, 9601 Wilshire Blvd, #300, Beverly Hills CA 90210 USA — Rap Artist, Actor  
**Emma, David**  
193 Eugenia Dr, Naples FL 34108, USA — Ice Hockey Player  
**Emmanuel**  
Sendyk Leonard, 532 Colorado Ave, Santa Monica CA 90401, USA — Singer  
**Emmanuel, Tommy**  
Gina Mendello, C P R Entertainment, PO Box 121983, Nashville TN 37212, USA — Guitarist  
**Emme**  
EmmeNation, PO Box 546, Closter NJ 07624, USA — Model  
**Emmerich, Noah J**  
Gersh Agency, 9465 Wilshire Blvd, #600, Beverly Hills CA 90212 USA — Actor  
**Emmerich, Roland**  
Creative Artists Agency, 2000 Ave of Stars, #100, Los Angeles CA 90067 USA — Director, Producer  
**Emmerich, Toby**  
New Line Cinema, 888 7th Ave, #1900, New York NY 10106, USA — Producer, Writer  
**Emmert, Mark A**  
National Collegiate Athletic Assn, President's Office, 700 W Washington St, Indianapolis IN 46204, USA — Association Executive, Educator  
**Emmett, John C**  
Oak House, Hatfield Broad Oak, Bishop's Stortford, Hertfordshire CM22 7HG, England — Inventor (Antiulcer Compound)  
**Emmett, Rik**  
Agency Group Ltd, 142 W 57th St, #600, New York NY 10019 USA — Singer, Guitar Player  
**Emory, Sonny**  
Great Scott Productions, 4750 Lincoln Blvd, #229, Marina del Rey CA 90292, USA — Drummer (Earth Wind & Fire)  
**Emtman, Steven C (Steve)**  
19601 S Cheney Spangle Road, Cheney WA 99004, USA — Football Player  
**Enberg, Dick**  
1275 Virginia Way, La Jolla CA 92037, USA — Sportscaster  
**Encarnacion, Juan D**  
Toronto Blue Jays, Skydome, 1 Blue Jay Way, Toronto ON M5V 1J1, Canada — Baseball Player  
**Endelman, Stephen**  
First Artists Mgmt, 4764 Park Granada, #210, Calabasas CA 91302 USA — Composer  
**Ender Grummt, Kornelia**  
D S V, Postfach 420140, 34070 Kassel, Germany — Swimmer  
**Enders, Anthony T**  
Brown Brothers Harriman, 59 Wall St, New York NY 10005, USA — Financier  
**Enders, Thomas**  
Airbus Industrie, Ronde Point Maurice Bellont 1, 31707 Blagnac, France — Businessman  
**Endicott, Lori**  
351 Dogwood Ridge, Rogersville MO 65742, USA — Volleyball Player  
**Endicott, Sam**  
+1 Mgmt, 242 Wythe Ave, #6, Brooklyn NY 11211, USA — Singer, Guitarist (Bravery)  
**Endicott, William F (Bill)**  
14219 Oak Knoll Road, Sonora CA 95370, USA — Baseball Player  
**Enevoldsen, Einar**  
103 City Limits Circle, Emeryville CA 94608, USA — Test Pilot  
**Enfeldt, Monique Gabrecht**  
Rosenthaler Str 40-41, Hackesche Hofe, 10178 Berlin, Germany — Speedskater  
**Engberg, Lotta**  
Gallviksvagen 20, 44163 Alingsas, Sweden — Singer  
**Engblom, Brian**  
824 Ridgemont Circle, Littleton CO 80126, USA — Ice Hockey Player  
**Engel, Albert J, Jr**  
5497 Forest Bend Dr SE, Ada MI 49301, USA — Judge  
**Engel, Georgia**  
C E S D, 10635 Santa Monica Blvd, #130, Los Angeles CA 90025 USA — Actress  
**Engelberger, John A**  
8176 Cliffview Ave, Springfield VA 22153, USA — Football Player  
**Engelberger, Joseph F**  
HelpMate Robotics, Shelter Rock Lane, Danbury CT 06810, USA — Robotics Engineer  
**Engelhardt, Thomas A (Tom)**  
Saint Louis Post-Dispatch, Editorial Dept, 900 N Tucker, Saint Louis MO 63101, USA — Editorial Cartoonist  
**Engen, D Travis**  
I T T Industries, 4 W Red Oak Lane, #200, West Harrison NY 10604, USA — Businessman  
**Enger, Leif**  
Grove/Atlantic Monthly Press, 841 Broadway, New York NY 10003, USA — Writer  
**Engerman, Stanley L**  
181 Warrington Dr, Rochester NY 14618, USA — Economist, Historian  
**Engh, Michael E**  
Santa Clara University, President's Office, 500 El Camino Real, Santa Clara CA 95053, USA — Educator  
**Engibous, Thomas J**  
Texas Instruments, 8505 Forest Lane, PO Box 660199, Dallas TX 75266, USA — Businessman  
**England, Anthony W**  
7949 Ridgeway Court, Dexter MI 48130, USA — Astronaut, Geophysicist  
**England, Richard**  
The Gardens, 8 Oleander St, Saint Julians SJ 12, Malta — Architect

**England, Tyler (Ty)** — Singer, Guitarist, Songwriter
Harmony Artists, 6399 Wilshire Blvd, #914, Los Angeles CA 90048, USA
**England, Yan** — Actor, Director, Writer
Arlook Group, 205 S Beverly Dr, #209, Beverly Hills CA 90212, USA
**Englander, Harold R** — Public Health Dentist
625 Baldwin Ave, Charlotte NC 28204, USA
**Engle, Joe H** — Astronaut, Air Force General
PO Box 58386, Houston TX 77258, USA
**Engle, Robert F** — Nobel Economics Laureate
New York University, Stern Business School, 44 W 4th St, New York NY 10012, USA
**Englehart, Robert W (Bob), Jr** — Editorial Cartoonist
Hartford Courant, Editorial Dept, 280 Broad St, Hartford CT 06105, USA
**Englehorn, Shirley** — Golfer
849 Shrine View, Colorado Springs CO 80906, USA
**Engler, Erich** — Space Scientist
80 Valley Way Circle SE, Huntsville AL 35802, USA
**Engler, Michael** — Director
United Talent Agency, U T A Plaza, 9336 Civic Center Dr, Beverly Hills CA 90210 USA
**Englert, Alice** — Actress
Creative Artists Agency, 2000 Ave of Stars, #100, Los Angeles CA 90067 USA
**Englert, Francois** — Nobel Physics Laureate
Physique Theorique Service, CP225, Blvd du Triomphe, 1050 Bruxelles, Belgium
**English, Alexander (Alex)** — Basketball Player
596 Rimer Pond Road, Blythewood SC 29016, USA
**English, Bill** — Actor
Innovative Artists, 1505 10th St, Santa Monica CA 90401 USA
**English, CariDee** — Model
Elite Model Mgmt, 404 Park Ave S, #900, New York NY 10016 USA
**English, Diane** — Writer
Shukovsky-English Entertainment, 4024 Radford Ave, Studio City CA 91604, USA
**English, James F, Jr** — Educator
31 Potter St, Groton CT 06340, USA
**English, Joseph T** — Psychiatrist
Saint Vincent's Hospital, 203 W 12th St, New York NY 10011, USA
**English, Kim** — Singer
Universal Attractions, 135 W 26th St, #1200, New York NY 10001 USA
**English, L Douglas (Doug)** — Football Player
Lone Star Paralysis, 1215 Red River St, Austin TX 78701, USA
**English, Michael** — Singer
Trifecta Entertainment, 209 10th Ave S, #302, Nashville TN 37203, USA
**English, Mitch** — Actor, Writer, Producer
Abrams Artists, 9200 W Sunset Blvd, #1125, West Hollywood CA 90069 USA
**Englund, Robert** — Actor
1278 Glenneyre, #73, Laguna Beach CA 92651, USA
**Engram, Simon J (Bobby), III** — Football Player
2009 High Pointe Court, Murrysville PA 15668, USA
**Engstrom, Erik** — Businessman
General Atlantic Partners, 3 Pickwick Plaza, #8, Greenwich CT 06830, USA
**Engstrom, Molly** — Ice Hockey Player
7582 Southshore Dr, Siren WI 54872, USA
**Engstrom, Royce C** — Educator
University of Montana, President's Office, 32 Campus Dr, Missoula MT 59812, USA
**Engvall, Bill** — Actor, Comedian
Paradigm Agency, 360 N Crescent Dr, North Building, Beverly Hills CA 90210 USA
**Enke, Frederick W (Fred), Jr** — Football Player
206 E McMurray Road, Casa Grande AZ 85122, USA
**Enkhsaikhan, Mendsaikhany** — Prime Minister, Mongolia
Pease Ave 11A, Ulan Bator 210648, Mongolia
**Ennis, Garth** — Cartoonist, Writer
Avatar Press, 515 N Century Blvd, Rantoul IL 61866, USA
**Ennis, Jessica** — Track Athlete
J C C M Ltd, Matrix Studios, 91 Peterborough Road, London SW6 3BU, England
**Ennis, John** — Baseball Player
14255 Dearborn St, Panorama City CA 91402, USA
**Ennis, Ralph** — Singer, Guitarist
2 Kirklake Bank, Formby, Liverpool L37 2Y5, England
**Ennis, Raymond V (Ray)** — Singer, Guitarist
2 Kirklake Bank, Formby, Liverpool L37 2Y5, England
**Ennis,Victor Ray** — Sound Editor
Soundelux, 7080 Hollywood Blvd, #1100, Los Angeles CA 90028, USA
**Eno, Brian** — Composer, Keyboardist
Creative Artists Agency, 2000 Ave of Stars, #100, Los Angeles CA 90067 USA
**Enoch, Ed** — Singer (Stamps Quartet)
PO Box 1471, Brentwood TN 37024, USA
**Enos, Clay** — Photographer
96 5th Ave, #2, New York NY 10011, USA
**Enos, John, III** — Actor
I C M Partners, 10250 Constellation Blvd, #900, Los Angeles CA 90067 USA
**Enos, Mark** — Interior Designer
Enos Co, 705 N Alfred St, West Hollywood CA 90069, USA
**Enos, Mireille** — Actress
Gartner / Green Entertainment, 5225 Wilshire Blvd, #1200, Los Angeles CA 90036, USA
**Enos, Randall** — Cartoonist, Illustrator
402 N Park Ave, Easton CT 06612, USA
**Enrico, Roger A** — Businessman
PepsiCo Inc, 700 Anderson Hill Road, Purchase NY 10577, USA
**Enright, Agnes Leahy** — Singer, Keyboardist (Leahy)
PO Box 716, Lakefield ON K0L 2H0, Canada
**Enright, Anne** — Writer
Jonathan Cape Ltd, 20 Vauxhall Bridge Road, London SW1V 2SA, England
**Enright, Barbara** — Poker Player
All American Speakers, 437 5th Ave, New York NY 10016, USA
**Enright, George A** — Baseball Player
3075 Strawflower Way, Lake Worth FL 33467, USA
**Enriquez Garcia, Jorge** — Soccer Player
Club Deportivo Guadalajara, Av Aviacion 3800, #20, Col De Ocot, Zapopan Jalisco 45018, Mexico

**Enriquez, Jocelyn** — Singer
Nene Musik Productions, 1460 SW Santiago Ave, Port Saint Lucie FL 34953 USA
**Enroth-Cugell, Christina A E** — Neurophysiologist
Northwestern University, Engineering School, 2145 Sheridan, Evanston IL 60208, USA
**Ensberg, Morgan P** — Baseball Player
5535 Memorial Dr, #F114, Houston TX 77007, USA
**Ensher, Jason R** — Physicist
University of Colorado, Physics Dept, Boulder CO 80309, USA
**Ensign, Michael** — Actor
Abrams Artists, 9200 W Sunset Blvd, #1125, West Hollywood CA 90069 USA
**Ensler, Eve** — Actress, Comedienne, Writer
Grand Central Publishing, 237 Park Ave, New York NY 10017, USA
**Ensler, Jason** — Director
Pitt Group, 9465 Wilshire Blvd, #420, Beverly Hills CA 90212, USA
**Enthoven, Alain C** — Economist
1 McCormick Lane, Atherton CA 94027, USA
**Entner, Warren** — Singer, Guitarist (Grass Roots)
Thomas Cassidy, PO Box 1311, Tucson AZ 85702 USA
**Entremont, Philippe** — Conductor, Concert Pianist
Columbia Artists Mgmt Inc, 1790 Broadway, #702, New York NY 10019 USA
**Enya** — Singer, Composer
Manderley, Victoria Road, Killiney, County Dublin, Ireland
**Enyart, William (Bill)** — Football Player
61070 Parrell Road, Bend OR 97702, USA
**Enzensberger, Hans M** — Writer
Lindenstr 29, 60325 Frankfurt am Maim, Germany
**Eotvos, Peter** — Composer, Conductor
Naardeweg 56, 1261 BV Blaircum, Netherlands
**Ephron, Hallie** — Writer
William Morrow Publishers, 1350 Ave of Americas, New York NY 10019 USA
**Epic** — Rap Artist (Crazy Town)
Wyze Mgmt, 34 Maple St, London W1 5GD, England
**Epley, John M** — Otologist, Inventor
Portland Otologic Clinic, 52657 NE 2nd St, Scappoose OR 97056, USA
**Eppard, James G (Jim)** — Baseball Player
23115 153rd Ave, Rapid City SD 57703, USA
**Epperson-Doumani, Brenda** — Actress
Kazarian/Measures/Ruskin, 11969 Ventura Blvd, #300, Studio City CA 91604 USA
**Eppinger, Dale L** — Vietnam War Air Force Hero
4100 Colina Cove, Round Rock TX 78681, USA
**Epple, Maria** — Alpine Skier
Gunzesried 3, 87544 Blaicach, Germany
**Epps, Mike** — Actor, Comedian
Creative Artists Agency, 2000 Ave of Stars, #100, Los Angeles CA 90067 USA
**Epps, Omar** — Actor
Anonymous Content, 3532 Hayden Ave, Culver City CA 90232 USA
**Epps, Phillip E (Phil)** — Football Player
212 Boulder Creek Dr, DeSoto TX 75115, USA
**Epps, Raymond E (Ray)** — Basketball Player
4030 Old Warwick Road, Richmond VA 23234, USA
**Epstein, Daniel M** — Writer
843 W University Parkway, Baltimore MD 21210, USA
**Epstein, Emmanuel** — Plant Nutritionist, Microbiologist
University of California, Land Air Water Resources Dept, Davis CA 95616, USA
**Epstein, Jason** — Editor
PO Box 1143, Sag Harbor NY 11963, USA
**Epstein, Joseph** — Writer, Educator
522 Church St, #6B, Evanston IL 60201, USA
**Epstein, Michael P (Mike)** — Baseball Player
6384 S Blackhawk Way, Aurora CO 80016, USA
**Erat, Martin** — Ice Hockey Player
4 Crooked Stick Lane, Brentwood TN 37027, USA
**Erautt, Edward L S (Eddie)** — Baseball Player
7252 Waite Dr, La Mesa CA 91941, USA
**Erb, Fred** — Lyricist
I C M Partners, 10250 Constellation Blvd, #900, Los Angeles CA 90067 USA
**Erb, Richard D** — Government Official
University of Montana, Business School, Missoula MT 59807, USA
**Erbe, Kathryn** — Actress
Innovative Artists, 1505 10th St, Santa Monica CA 90401 USA
**Ercegan, Milan** — Wrestling Executive
F I L A, Rue du Chateau 6, 1804 Corsier-sur-Vevey, Switzerland
**Erdman, Dennis** — Actor, Director, Producer
Creative Artists Agency, 2000 Ave of Stars, #100, Los Angeles CA 90067 USA
**Erdman, Richard** — Sculptor
3188 S Brownell Road, Williston VT 05495, USA
**Erdman, Richard** — Actor
5655 Greenbush Ave, Van Nuys CA 91401, USA
**Erdmann, Susi-Lisa** — Bobsled Athlete
Karwendelstr 8A, 81369 Munich, Germany
**Erdo, Peter Cardinal** — Religious Leader
Mindszenty Hercegprimas Ter 2, 2501 Esztergom Magyarirszay, Hungary
**Erdogan, Recep Tayyip** — Prime Minister, Turkey
Premier's Office, Eski Basbakanlik Binasi, Bakanliklar, 06573 Ankara, Turkey
**Erdos, Todd M** — Baseball Player
118 Windsor Court, Cranberry Township PA 16066, USA
**Erdrich, K Louise** — Writer
Andrew Wylie Agency, 250 W 57th St, #2114, New York NY 10107, USA
**Ergen, Charles W** — Businessman
EchoStar Corporation, 100 Inverness Terrace E, Englewood CO 80112, USA
**Eric B** — Rap Artist (Eric B & Rakim)
Richard Walters, PO Box 2789, Toluca Lake CA 91610 USA
**Ericks, John E** — Baseball Player
17000 Oketo Ave, Tinley Park IL 60477, USA
**Erickson, Bryan L** — Ice Hockey Player
114 3rd St NW, #A, Roseau MN 56751, USA

**E**

**Enriquez - Erickson**

**Erickson, Dennis** — Football Coach
911 W Kidd Island Road, Coeur D'Alene ID 83814, USA
**Erickson, Ethan** — Actor
Greater Visions Artists Talent Agency, 8981 W Sunset Blvd, #101, West Hollywood CA 90069 USA
**Erickson, Grant** — Ice Hockey Player
222 Parks St, Whitewood SK S0G 5C0, Canada
**Erickson, Keith R** — Basketball, Volleyball Player
333 23rd St, Santa Monica CA 90402, USA
**Erickson, Matt** — Baseball Player
1408 S Fidelis St, Appleton WI 54915, USA
**Erickson, Roger F** — Baseball Player
PO Box 235, Sautee Nacoochee GA 30571, USA
**Erickson, Roger K (Roky)** — Singer, Guitarist, Songwriter
Ten Pin Mgmt, 176 Park Ave, Warwick RI 02889, USA
**Erickson, Roky** — Singer, Songwriter
Agency Group Ltd, 142 W 57th St, #600, New York NY 10019 USA
**Erickson, Scott** — Actor
I C M Partners, 10250 Constellation Blvd, #900, Los Angeles CA 90067 USA
**Erickson, Scott G** — Baseball Player
1183 Corral Ave, Sunnyvale CA 94086, USA
**Ericson, John** — Actor
7 Avenida Vista Grande, #310, Santa Fe NM 87508, USA
**Erika Jo** — Singer
Universal South Artists, 2303 21st Ave S, #400, Nashville TN 37212, USA
**Eriksen, Stein** — Skier
7700 Stein Way, Park City UT 84060, USA
**Erikson, Duke** — Bassist, Keyboardist (Garbage)
Borman Entertainment, 1250 6th St, #401, Santa Monica CA 90401, USA
**Erikson, Raymond L** — Medical Researcher
Harvard University Medical School, Biology Dept, 25 Shattuck St, Boston MA 02115, USA
**Eriksson, Aleksandra** — Model
Elite Model Mgmt, 404 Park Ave S, #900, New York NY 10016 USA
**Eriksson, Anders** — Ice Hockey Player
2259 Arlington Ave, Columbus OH 43221, USA
**Eriksson, Per-Olaf** — Businessman
Hedasvagen 57, 81 161 Sandviken, Sweden
**Eriksson, Peter K** — Ice Hockey Player
Vastra Storgatan 10, 55 315 Jonokoping, Sweden
**Erland, Jonathan** — Visual Effects Artist
Composite Components Co, 134 N Ave 61, #102-103, Los Angeles CA 90042, USA
**Erlandson, Eric** — Guitarist (Hole), Songwriter
Artist Group International, 9560 Wilshire Blvd, #400, Beverly Hills CA 90212 USA
**Erlandson, Thomas D (Tom), Sr** — Football Player
1045 E Possee Road, Castle Rock CO 80108, USA
**Erman, John** — Director
Creative Artists Agency, 2000 Ave of Stars, #100, Los Angeles CA 90067 USA
**Ermey, R Lee** — Actor
Bill Rogin Mgmt, 427 N Canon Dr, #215, Beverly Hills CA 90210, USA
**Erna, Salvatore P (Sully)** — Singer, Guitarist (Godsmack); Songwriter
Front Line Mgmt, 1100 Glendon Ave, #2000, Los Angeles CA 90024 USA
**Ernaga, Frank J** — Baseball Player
50 N Roop St, Susanville CA 96130, USA
**Ernst, Bret** — Actor, Comedian
United Talent Agency, U T A Plaza, 9336 Civic Center Dr, Beverly Hills CA 90210 USA
**Ernst, Richard R** — Nobel Chemistry Laureate
Kurlistr 24, 8404 Winterthur, Switzerland
**Ernst, Wallace Gary** — Geologist
Stanford University, Earth & Environment Sciences Dept, Stanford CA 94305, USA
**Eroglu, Dervis** — President, Turkish Northern Cyprus
President's Office, Via Mersin 10, Lefkosa, Turkish Northern Cyprus, Turkey
**Errazuriz Ossa, Francisco J Cardinal** — Religious Leader
Casilla 30D, Erasmo Escala 1894, Santiago, Chile
**Errey, Bob** — Ice Hockey Player
156 Hickory Heights Dr, Bridgeville PA 15017, USA
**Errico, Melissa** — Actress, Singer
Right Side Mgmt, PO Box 250806, New York NY 10025, USA
**Erskine, Carl D** — Baseball Player
4031 Fallbrook Lane, Anderson IN 46011, USA
**Erskine, Peter** — Jazz Drummer, Composer
1727 Hill St, Santa Monica CA 90405, USA
**Erstad, Darin C** — Baseball Player
6230 Doe Creek Circle, Lincoln NE 68516, USA
**Ertegun, Mica** — Interior Designer
M A C II, 125 E 81st St, New York NY 10028, USA
**Ertl, Gerhard L** — Nobel Chemistry Laureate
Garystr 18, 14195 Berlin, Germany
**Ertl, Martina** — Alpine Skier
Ertlrenz, Broenner Str 13, 80333 Munich, Germany
**Ertl, Sue** — Golfer
4707 Sabal Key Dr, Bradenton FL 34203, USA
**Eruzione, Michael (Mike)** — Ice Hockey Player
40 Floyd St, Winthrop MA 02152, USA
**Erving, Julius W (Dr J)** — Basketball Player
108 Windrush Road, Winston-Salem NC 27106, USA
**Ervins, Ricky** — Football Player
20984 Nightshade Place, Ashburn VA 20147, USA
**Erwin, Mike** — Actor
Leverage Mgmt, 3030 Pennsylvania Ave, Santa Monica CA 90404 USA
**Erwitt, Elliott R** — Photographer
88 Central Park West, #1S, New York NY 10023, USA
**Esaki, Reona (Leo)** — Nobel Physics Laureate
12-6 Sanbancho, Chiyodaku, Tokyo 102 0075, Japan
**Esasky, Nicholas A (Nick)** — Baseball Player
1779 Starlight Dr, Marietta GA 30062, USA
**Escalera, Alfredo, Jr** — Boxer
Star Boxing, 991 Morris Park Ave, Bronx NY 10462, USA

**Escamilla, Michael Ray** — Actor, Director
Bauman Redanty Shaul Agency, 5757 Wilshire Blvd, #473, Los Angeles CA 90036 USA

**Esche, Robert** — Ice Hockey Player
6750 W Carter Road, Rome NY 13440, USA

**Eschenbach, Christoph** — Conductor, Concert Pianist
National Symphony Orchestra, Kennedy Performing Arts Center, 2700 F St NW, Washington, DC 20566, USA

**Eschenmoser, Albert J** — Chemist
Bergstra 9, 8700 Kusnacht ZH, Switzerland

**Eschert, Jurgen** — Canoeing Athlete
Tornowstr 8, 14473 Potsdam, Germany

**Escobar, Kelvin J B** — Baseball Player
12296 Circula Panorama, Santa Ana CA 92705, USA

**Escobar, Yunel** — Baseball Player
15763 SW 43rd St, Miami FL 33185, USA

**Escovedo, Alejandro** — Singer, Songwriter
MongrelMusic, 746 Center Blvd, Fairfax CA 94930, USA

**Escovedo, Peter (Pete)** — Percussionist
Universal Attractions, 135 W 26th St, #1200, New York NY 10001 USA

**Eselin, Caroline** — Costume Designer
United Talent Agency, U T A Plaza, 9336 Civic Center Dr, Beverly Hills CA 90210 USA

**Esfahani, Mahan** — Concert Harpsichordist
Borletti-Buitoni Trust, 20 Leythe Road, London W3 8AW, England

**Eshelman, Vaughn M** — Baseball Player
30106 Falher Dr, Spring TX 77386, USA

**Esiason, Norman J (Boomer)** — Football Player, Sportscaster
25 Heights Road, Manhasset NY 11030, USA

**Esipovich, Alla** — Photographer
Maya Polsky Gallery, 215 W Superior St, Chicago IL 60654, USA

**Eskew, Michael L** — Businessman
United Parcel Service, 55 Glenlake Parkway NE, Atlanta GA 30328, USA

**Eskridge, William N, Jr** — Attorney, Educator
Yale University, Law School, 127 Wall St, New Haven CT 06511, USA

**Esler-Smith, Frank** — Keyboardist (Air Supply)
PO Box 3367, Beverly Hills CA 90212, USA

**Esparza, Raul** — Actor, Singer
Elin Flack Mgmt, 435 W 57th St, #3M, New York NY 10019, USA

**Esper, Michael** — Actor
Gersh Agency, 9465 Wilshire Blvd, #600, Beverly Hills CA 90212 USA

**Esperian, Kallen R** — Opera Singer
514 Lindseywood Cove, Memphis TN 38117, USA

**Espineli, Geno** — Baseball Player
1222 Park Lane, Katy TX 77450, USA

**Espinosa, Daniel** — Director
United Talent Agency, U T A Plaza, 9336 Civic Center Dr, Beverly Hills CA 90210 USA

**Espinosa, Eden** — Actress, Singer
Gersh Agency, 41 Madison Ave, #3301, New York NY 10010 USA

**Esposito, Anthony J (Tony)** — Ice Hockey Player
418 55th Ave, Saint Pete Beach FL 33706, USA

**Esposito, Frank** — Bowling Executive
200 N State Route 17, Paramus NJ 07652, USA

**Esposito, Jennifer** — Actress
Washington Square Arts, 1041 N Formosa Ave, Formosa Building, West Hollywood CA 90046, USA

**Esposito, Philip A (Phil)** — Ice Hockey Player, Coach
4003 W Tacon St, Tampa FL 33629, USA

**Esposito, Samuel (Sammy)** — Baseball Player
PO Box 1826, Banner Elk NC 28604, USA

**Espy, A Michael (Mike)** — Secretary, Agriculture
Commodity Credit Corp, PO Box 2415, Washington DC 20013, USA

**Espy, Cecil E** — Baseball Player
5480 Encina Dr, San Diego CA 92114, USA

**Esquivel, Manuel** — Prime Minister, Belize
United Democratic Party, 19 King St, PO Box 1143, Belize City, Belize

**Essandoh, Ato** — Actor
S M S Talent, 8383 Wilshire Blvd, #230, Beverly Hills CA 90211 USA

**Essegian, Charles A (Chuck)** — Baseball Player
15639 Bronco Dr, Canyon Country CA 91387, USA

**Essensa, Bob** — Ice Hockey Player
1130 Iroquois Trail, Oxford MI 48371, USA

**Esser, Mark G** — Baseball Player
717 S US Highway 1, #708, Jupiter FL 33477, USA

**Essex, David** — Singer, Actor, Composer
Stratford Saye, 20 Wellington Road, Bournemouth, Dorset BG8 8JN, England

**Essex, Myron E** — Microbiologist
Harvard School of Public Health, 665 Huntington Ave, Boston MA 02115, USA

**Essian, James S (Jim)** — Baseball Player, Manager
134 Eckford Dr, Troy MI 48085, USA

**Essick, Todd** — Photographer
PO Box 2376, West Palm Beach FL 33402, USA

**Essink, Ronald A** — Football Player
PO Box 265, Hamilton MI 49419, USA

**Esslinger, Hartmut** — Industrial Designer
FrogDesign, 3460 Hillview Ave, Palo Alto CA 94304, USA

**Essman, Susan (Susie)** — Actress, Comedienne
Paradigm Agency, 360 N Crescent Dr, North Building, Beverly Hills CA 90210 USA

**Esswood, Paul L V** — Opera Singer
Jasmine Cottage, 42 Ferring Lane, Ferring, West Sussex BN12 6QT, England

**Estabrook, Christine** — Actress
Don Buchwald, 6500 Wilshire Blvd, #2200, Los Angeles CA 90048 USA

**Estalella, Robert M (Bobby)** — Baseball Player
3612 Churchill Downs Dr, Davie FL 33328, USA

**Esteban, Manuel A** — Educator
California State University, O'Connell Hall, Chico CA 95929, USA

**Estefan, Emilio, Jr** — Musician, Producer
Estefan Enterprises, 420 Jefferson Ave, Miami Beach FL 33139, USA

**Estefan, Gloria** — Singer, Songwriter
39 Star Island Dr, Miami Beach FL 33139, USA

# E

**Estefan, Lili** — Actress
T G A Voice, 100 Lincoln Road, #928, Miami Beach FL 33178, USA
**Estelle** — Singer
I C M Partners, 10250 Constellation Blvd, #900, Los Angeles CA 90067 USA
**Esten, Charles (Chip)** — Actor, Comedian
Stone Manners Salners, 9911 W Pico Blvd, #1400, Los Angeles CA 90035 USA
**Estern, Neil** — Sculptor
432 Cream Hill Road, West Cornwall CT 06796, USA
**Estes, A Shawn** — Baseball Player
9694 E Legacy Lane, Scottsdale AZ 85255, USA
**Estes, Bob** — Golfer
4408 Long Champ Dr, #21, Austin TX 78746, USA
**Estes, Clarissa Pinkola** — Psychologist, Writer
Knopf Publishers, 201 E 50th St, New York NY 10022, USA
**Estes, Jacob Aaron** — Director, Writer
Management 360, 9111 Wilshire Blvd, Beverly Hills CA 90210 USA
**Estes, James** — Cartoonist
1103 Callahan St, Amarillo TX 79106, USA
**Estes, Lawrence G (Larry)** — Football Player
115 Alida St, Hammond LA 70403, USA
**Estes, Richard** — Artist
PO Box 685, Northeast Harbour ME 04662, USA
**Estes, Robert (Rob)** — Actor
Thruline Entertainment, 9250 Wilshire Blvd, #100, Beverly Hills CA 90212 USA
**Estes, Simon L** — Opera Singer
Hochstr 43, 8706 Feldmeilen, Switzerland
**Estes, Will** — Actor
Paradigm Agency, 360 N Crescent Dr, North Building, Beverly Hills CA 90210 USA
**Estes, William K** — Psychologist
65 Gaston Road, Morristown NJ 07960, USA
**Esteve-Coll, Elizabeth** — Museum Executive
27 Ursula St, London SW11 3DW, England
**Estevez, Emilio** — Actor, Director
Alchemy Entertainment, 7024 Melrose Ave, #420, Los Angeles CA 90038 USA
**Estevez, Luis** — Fashion Designer
122 E 7th St, Los Angeles CA 90014, USA
**Estevez, Ramon L** — Actor
Special Artists Agency, 9200 Sunset Blvd, #410, West Hollywood CA 90069 USA
**Estevez, Renee** — Actress
House of Representatives, 1434 6th St, #1, Santa Monica CA 90401 USA
**Esthero** — Singer
ArtistDirect, 10900 Wilshire Blvd, #1400, Los Angeles CA 90024 USA
**Estil, Frode** — Cross Country Skier
7530 Meraker, Norway
**Estleman, Loren Daniel** — Writer
5552 Walsh Road, Whitmore Lake MI 48189, USA
**Estrada, Charles L (Chuck)** — Baseball Player
1289 Manzanita Way, San Luis Obispo CA 93401, USA
**Estrada, Erik** — Actor, Producer
Creative Talent Group, 1900 Ave of Stars, #2475, Los Angeles CA 90067, USA
**Estrada, Erik-Michael** — Singer (O-Town)
Trans Continental Records, 127 W Church St, #350, Orlando FL 32801, USA
**Estrada, Johnny P** — Baseball Player
20 Winged Foot Ridge, Newnan GA 30265, USA
**Estrich, Susan R** — Attorney
947 Berkeley St, Santa Monica CA 90403, USA
**Estrin, Zack** — Producer, Writer
W M E Entertainment, 9601 Wilshire Blvd, #300, Beverly Hills CA 90210 USA
**Eswaran, Vijay** — Businessman
Q I Group, Bank of China Tower, #5500, Hong Kong Central, China
**E-Swift** — Rap Artist
Likwit Entertainment, PO Box 360713, Los Angeles CA 90036, USA
**Eszterhas, Joseph A** — Writer
Baumgarten Mgmt, 406 Wilshire Blvd, Santa Monica CA 90401, USA
**Etaix, Pierre** — Director, Actor
Editions du Seuil, 27 Rue Jacob, 75261 Paris Cedex 06, France
**Etchebarren, Andrew A (Andy)** — Baseball Player
1488 Vermeer Dr, Nokomis FL 34275, USA
**Etchegaray, Roger Cardinal** — Religious Leader
Piazza San Calisto, 00120 Vatican City
**Etcheverry, Marco** — Soccer Player
D C United, R F K Stadium, 2400 E Capitol St SE, Washington DC 20003 USA
**Etcoff, Nancy** — Psychologist
Harvard Medical School, Mind Brain Behavior Initiative, 25 Shattuck St, Boston MA 02115, USA
**Etebari, Eric** — Actor
Mystic Warrior Productions, 12400 Ventura Blvd, #237, Studio City CA 91604, USA
**Etel, Alex** — Actor
Independent Talent Group, 40 Whitfield St, London W1T 2RH, England
**Etheridge, Melissa L** — Singer, Songwriter, Guitarist
Creative Artists Agency, 2000 Ave of Stars, #100, Los Angeles CA 90067 USA
**Ethier, Andre E** — Baseball Player
21423 S 147th St, Gilbert AZ 85298, USA
**Ethier, Linda** — Artist
2846 NE Glissan St, Portland OR 97232, USA
**Ethridge, Mark F, III** — Editor
5516 Gorham Dr, Charlotte NC 28226, USA
**Etienne, Jean-Louis** — Explorer
Musee Oceanographique de Monaco, Ave Saint-Martin, 98000 Monaco
**Etienne, Pauline** — Actress
A C T 1, 83 Rue Saint Honore, 75001 Paris, France
**Etrog, Sorel** — Artist
PO Box 67034, 2300 Yonge St, Toronto ON M4P 1E0, Canada
**Etsel, Edward (Ed)** — Marksman
University of Virginia, Athletic Dept, Charlottesville VA 22906, USA
**Ettinger, Cynthia** — Actress
Thruline Entertainment, 9250 Wilshire Blvd, #100, Beverly Hills CA 90212 USA

Estefan - Ettinger

**Ettinger, Dan** — Conductor
Mannheim Opera House, Mozartstr 9, 68161 Mannheim, Germany

**Ettles, Mark** — Baseball Player
3-10 Rose Ave, Perth WA 6151, Australia

**Ettlin, Lukas** — Cinematographer
Mirisch Agency, 8840 Wilshire Blvd, #100, Beverly Hills CA 90211 USA

**Etura, Marta** — Actress
Kuranda Mgmt, Santo Angel 84, 28043 Madrid, Spain

**Etzel, Gregory A M** — Vietnam War Air Force Hero
7822 Wonder St, Citrus Heights CA 95610, USA

**Etzioni, Amitai W** — Sociologist
George Washington University, Sociology Dept, Washington DC 20052, USA

**Etzwiler, Donnell D** — Pediatrician
International Diabetes Center, 5000 W 39th St, Minneapolis MN 55416, USA

**Eubank, Chris** — Boxer
3 Vallensdean Cottages, Hangleton Lane, Portslade, Sussex BN41 2FQ, England

**Eubanks, Kevin** — Jazz Guitarist
Blue Note Records, 6920 W Sunset Blvd, Los Angeles CA 90028 USA

**Eubanks, Robert L (Bob)** — Actor, Producer
Cheryl Kagan Public Relations, 4422 E 103rd St, Tulsa OK 74137, USA

**Eubesio, R Antonio (Tony)** — Baseball Player
2078 Shannon Lakes Blvd, Kissimmee FL 34743, USA

**Euge Groove** — Jazz Saxophonist
Variety Artists, 1924 Spring St, Paso Robles CA 93446 USA

**Eugenides, Jeffrey** — Writer
Janklow & Nesbit Assoc, 445 Park Ave, #1300, New York NY 10022 USA

**Eustis, Joshua** — Musician (Telefon Tel Aviv)
Aero Booking, 8008 Greenwood Ave N, #3, Seattle WA 98103, USA

**Evancho, Jackie** — Singer
W M E Entertainment, 9601 Wilshire Blvd, #300, Beverly Hills CA 90210 USA

**Evangelista, Christine** — Actress
M J Management, 130 W 57th St, #11A, New York NY 10019, USA

**Evangelista, Linda** — Model
D N A Model Mgmt, 520 Broadway, #1100, New York NY 10012, USA

**Evanovich, Janet** — Writer
PO Box 2889, Naples FL 34106, USA

**Evans, Alice** — Actress
Domain Talent, 9229 W Sunset Blvd, #710, West Hollywood CA 90069 USA

**Evans, Barry S** — Baseball Player
128 Russell Dr, McDonough GA 30252, USA

**Evans, Bill** — Jazz Saxophonist, Keyboardist, Composer
Sony Records, 2100 Colorado Ave, Santa Monica CA 90404 USA

**Evans, Byron N** — Football Player
1763 E Carter Road, Phoenix AZ 85042, USA

**Evans, Cadell** — Cyclist
B M C Racing Team, Sportstr 49, 2540 Grenchen, Switzerland

**Evans, Christine** — Singer, Songwriter
Jane Harbury Publicity, 1290 Dundas St E, Toronto ON M4M 1S6, Canada

**Evans, Christopher R (Chris)** — Actor
3 Arts Entertainment, 9460 Wilshire Blvd, #700, Beverly Hills CA 90212 USA

**Evans, Daniel** — Actor, Singer
Hamilton Hodell, 66-68 Margaret St, #500, London W1W 8SR, England

**Evans, Daniel E** — Businessman
Bob Evans Farms, 3776 S High St, Columbus OH 43207, USA

**Evans, Daniel J** — Governor, Senator, WA; Educator
Daniel J Evans Assoc, 1111 3rd Ave, #3400, Seattle WA 98101, USA

**Evans, Danielle** — Model
Click Model Mgmt, 881 7th Ave, New York NY 10019 USA

**Evans, Darrell W** — Baseball Player
1400 E Tahquitz Canyon Way, Palm Springs CA 92262, USA

**Evans, Daryl** — Ice Hockey Player
22403 Marjorie Ave, Torrance CA 90505, USA

**Evans, David A** — Chemist
Harvard University, Chemistry & Chemical Biology Dept, Cambridge MA 02138, USA

**Evans, Demetric U** — Football Player
PO Box 2256, Allen TX 75013, USA

**Evans, Dick** — Bowling Columnist
121 Morning Dove Court, Daytona Beach FL 32119, USA

**Evans, Donald L** — Secretary, Commerce
Financial Services Forum, 601 13th Street NW, #750 South, Washington DC 20005, USA

**Evans, Donald L** — Football Player
12407 Beauvoir St, Raleigh NC 27614, USA

**Evans, Douglas E (Doug)** — Football Player
8099 Highway 534, Haynesville LA 71038, USA

**Evans, Dwight M** — Baseball Player
123 Johnson Woods Dr, Reading MA 01867, USA

**Evans, Evans** — Actress
3114 Abington Dr, Beverly Hills CA 90210, USA

**Evans, Faith** — Singer, Songwriter
Padell Nadell Fine, 59 Maiden Lane, #2700, New York NY 10038, USA

**Evans, Frederick H (Fred)** — Football Player
Minnesota Vikings, 9520 Viking Dr, Eden Prairie MN 55344 USA

**Evans, Gareth** — Director
Management 360, 9111 Wilshire Blvd, Beverly Hills CA 90210 USA

**Evans, George** — Cartoonist (Anna & Corrigan)
King Features Syndicate, 300 W 57th St, #1500, New York NY 10019 USA

**Evans, Glen** — Molecular Biologist
Salk Institute, 10100 N Torrey Pines Road, La Jolla CA 92037 USA

**Evans, Greg** — Cartoonist (Luann)
216 Country Garden Lane, San Marcos CA 92069, USA

**Evans, Harold J** — Plant Physiologist
17360 Holy Names Dr, #2037, Lake Oswego OR 97034, USA

**Evans, J Thomas** — Freestyle Wrestler
607 S Fir Court, Broken Arrow OK 74012, USA

**Evans, Jahri** — Football Player
New Orleans Saints, 5800 Airline Highway, Metairie LA 70003 USA

| | |
|---|---|
| **Evans, James B (Jim)** | Baseball Umpire |
| 1801 Rogge Lane, Austin TX 78723, USA | |
| **Evans, Janet** | Swimmer |
| 8 Barneburg, Trabuco Canyon CA 92679, USA | |
| **Evans, John R** | Foundation Executive |
| Rockefeller Foundation, 1133 Ave of Americas, New York NY 10036, USA | |
| **Evans, John V** | Governor, ID |
| D L Evans Bank, 397 N Overland, Burley ID 83318, USA | |
| **Evans, Jonathan** | Law Enforcement Official |
| Security Service (MI-5), Thames House, 11 Millbank, London SW1P AQJ, England | |
| **Evans, Lee** | Actor |
| Off the Kerb Productions, Hammer House, 113-117 Wardour St, #300, London W1F 0UN, England | |
| **Evans, Lee E** | Track Athlete |
| 250 S Sage Ave, Mobile AL 36606, USA | |
| **Evans, Linda** | Actress |
| PO Box 29, Rainier WA 98576, USA | |
| **Evans, Lindsey Gayle** | Model |
| Playboy Promotions, 2706 Media Center Dr, Los Angeles CA 90065 USA | |
| **Evans, Luke** | Actor |
| United Agents, 12-26 Lexington St, London W1F 0LE, England | |
| **Evans, Lynn** | Singer (Chordettes) |
| Richard Paul Assoc, 16207 Mott Dr, Macomb Township MI 48044, USA | |
| **Evans, M Terry** | Baseball Player |
| 1049 Dunedin Trail, Woodstock GA 30188, USA | |
| **Evans, Marc** | Director |
| Tessa Sayle Agency, 11 Jubilee Place, London SW3 3TE, England | |
| **Evans, Martin J** | Nobel Medicine Laureate |
| Cardiff University Museum, PO Box 911, Cardiff CF10 3US, Wales | |
| **Evans, Martina** | Writer |
| Sayle Literary Agency, 25-27 Bickerton Road, London N19 5JT, England | |
| **Evans, Mary Beth** | Actress |
| Michael Bruno Group, 13576 Cheltenham Dr, Sherman Oaks CA 91423, USA | |
| **Evans, Michael L (Mike)** | Basketball Player |
| 9931 Cottoncreek Dr, Littleton CO 80130, USA | |
| **Evans, Mijoshki A (Josh)** | Football Player |
| PO Box 273309, Boca Raton FL 33427, USA | |
| **Evans, Nicholas (Nick)** | Writer |
| Signet Books, 375 Hudson St, New York NY 10014 USA | |
| **Evans, Nicky** | Actor |
| Associated International Mgmt, 7 Hatton Garden, #400, London EC1N 8AD, England | |
| **Evans, Norm E** | Football Player |
| 360 NW Boulder Place, Issaquah WA 98027, USA | |
| **Evans, Richard** | Sports Executive |
| Madison Square Garden, 4 Pennsylvania Plaza, New York NY 10001, USA | |
| **Evans, Richard Paul** | Writer |
| PO Box 712137, Salt Lake City UT 84171, USA | |
| **Evans, Robert J (Bob)** | Producer |
| Robert Evans Productions, Paramount Pictures, 5555 Melrose, Los Angeles, CA 90038, USA | |
| **Evans, Robert S** | Businessman |
| Crane Co, 100 Stamford Plaza, Stamford CT 06902, USA | |
| **Evans, Ronald M** | Geneticist |
| Salk Institute, 10100 N Torrey Pines Road, La Jolla CA 92037 USA | |
| **Evans, Roy** | WW II Army Air Corps Hero |
| 15221 Lime St, Hesperia CA 92345, USA | |
| **Evans, Rupert** | Actor |
| Curtis Brown Group, 28-29 Haymarket St, #500, London SW1Y 4SP, England | |
| **Evans, Sara E** | Singer, Songwriter |
| Gersh Agency, 9465 Wilshire Blvd, #600, Beverly Hills CA 90212 USA | |
| **Evans, Shaun** | Actor |
| Hamilton Hodell, 66-68 Margaret St, #500, London W1W 8SR, England | |
| **Evans, Sian** | Singer, Songwriter (Kosheen) |
| Moksha Mgmt, PO Box 102, London E15 2HH, England | |
| **Evans, Terence T** | Judge |
| US Court of Appeals, 517 E Wisconsin Ave, Milwaukee WI 53202, USA | |
| **Evans, Tiffany** | Singer, Actress |
| W M E Entertainment, 9601 Wilshire Blvd, #300, Beverly Hills CA 90210 USA | |
| **Evans, Troy** | Actor |
| Stone Manners Salners, 9911 W Pico Blvd, #1400, Los Angeles CA 90035 USA | |
| **Evans, Tyreke** | Basketball Player |
| New Orleans Pelicans, 1250 Poydras St, #101, New Orleans LA 70113 USA | |
| **Evans, Vincent T (Vince)** | Football Player |
| 14084 Bronte Dr, Whittier CA 90602, USA | |
| **Evans, Walker** | Truck, Off-Road Racing Driver |
| Walker Evans Racing, PO Box 2469, Riverside CA 92516, USA | |
| **Evans, William (Billy)** | Basketball Player |
| 24369 Sandpiper Isle Way, #105, Bonita Springs FL 34134, USA | |
| **Evason, Dean C** | Ice Hockey Player |
| Washington Capitals, 627 N Glebe Road, #850, Arlington VA 22203 USA | |
| **Evatt, Christopher** | Motivational Speaker |
| P O Box 294, 06101 Porvoo, Finland | |
| **Eve** | Rap Artist (Ruff Ryders), Actress |
| 1438 N Gower St, #115, Los Angeles CA 90028, USA | |
| **Eve, Alice** | Actress |
| Artist Rights Group, 4 Great Portland St, London W1W 8PA, England | |
| **Eve, Trevor J** | Actor |
| Insight Entertainment, 1134 S Cloverdale Ave, Los Angeles CA 90019, USA | |
| **Evensen, Johan Remen** | Ski Jumper |
| Molde og Omega I F, PB 2326, 6402 Molde, Norway | |
| **Everett, Carl E** | Baseball Player |
| 19108 Harborbridge Lane, Lutz FL 33558, USA | |
| **Everett, Danny** | Track Athlete |
| Santa Monica Track Club, 1801 Ocean Park Ave, #112, Santa Monica CA 90405, USA | |
| **Everett, J Adam** | Baseball Player |
| 4374 Oglethorpe Loop NW, Acworth GA 30101, USA | |
| **Everett, James S (Jim)** | Football Player |
| 555 N El Camino Real, #A445, San Clemente CA 92672, USA | |

| | |
|---|---|
| **Everett, Mark Oliver (E, Eels)**<br>International Talent Booking, Ariel House, 74A Charlotte St, #100 London W1T 4QJ, England | Singer, Guitarist, Songwriter |
| **Everett, Rupert**<br>Rights House, Drury House, 34-43 Russell St, London WC2B 5HA, England | Actor |
| **Everett, Thomas G**<br>PO Box 795337, Dallas TX 75379, USA | Football Player |
| **Everhard, Nancy**<br>Talent Management Group, 339 E 3900 S, #200, Salt Lake City UT 84107, USA | Actress |
| **Everhart, Thomas E**<br>705 Poinsettia Way, Santa Barbara CA 93111, USA | Educator |
| **Everitt, Steven M (Steve)**<br>17252 Snapper Lane, Summerland Key FL 33042, USA | Football Player |
| **Everlast**<br>A A Music Mgmt, 1100 Glendon Ave, #2000, Los Angeles CA 90024, USA | Rap Artist, Actor, Songwriter |
| **Everly, Donald (Don)**<br>401 W 9th St, Columbia TN 38401, USA | Singer (Everly Brothers) |
| **Everly, Phil**<br>401 W 9th St, Columbia TN 38401, USA | Singer (Everly Brothers) |
| **Evers, Charles**<br>1018 Pecan Park Dr, Jackson MS 39209, USA | Civil Rights Activist |
| **Eversgerd, Bryan D**<br>9212 Huey Road, Centralia IL 62801, USA | Baseball Player |
| **Eversley, Frederick J**<br>1110 W Abbot Kinney Blvd, Venice CA 90291, USA | Sculptor |
| **Eversman, Nick**<br>Medavoy Mgmt, 10203 Santa Monica Blvd, #400, Los Angeles CA 90067 USA | Actor |
| **Everson, Corinna (Cory)**<br>23705 Van Owen St, West Hills CA 91307, USA | Body Builder |
| **Evers-Williams, Myrlie**<br>15 SW Colorado Ave, #310, Bend OR 97702, USA | Association Executive |
| **Evert, Ray F**<br>810 Woodward Dr, Madison WI 53704, USA | Botanist |
| **Evert-Mill, Christine M (Chris)**<br>8563 Horseshoe Lane, Boca Raton FL 33496, USA | Tennis Player |
| **Evidence**<br>W M E Entertainment, 9601 Wilshire Blvd, #300, Beverly Hills CA 90210 USA | Rap Artist (Dilated Peoples) |
| **Evigan, Briana**<br>Gersh Agency, 9465 Wilshire Blvd, #600, Beverly Hills CA 90212 USA | Actress |
| **Evigan, Greg**<br>Stone Manners Salners, 9911 W Pico Blvd, #1400, Los Angeles CA 90035 USA | Actor, Singer |
| **Evren, Kenan**<br>Beyaz Ev Sokak 21, Armutalan, 48700 Marmaris, Turkey | President, Turkey; Army General |
| **Ewald, Elwyn**<br>Free Lutheran Congregations, 12015 Manchester Road, Saint Louis MO 63131, USA | Religious Leader |
| **Ewald, Reinhold**<br>D L R Astronauterburo WT/AN, Linder Hohe, 51140 Cologne, Germany | Cosmonaut, Germany |
| **Ewell, Kayla**<br>Innovative Artists, 1505 10th St, Santa Monica CA 90401 USA | Actress |
| **Ewen, Harold I**<br>60 Hillcrest Dr, South Deerfield MA 01373, USA | Astronomer, Physicist |
| **Ewen, Paterson**<br>1015 Wellington St, London ON N6A 3T5, Canada | Artist |
| **Ewen, Todd**<br>420 Thunderhead Canyon Dr, Ballwin MO 63011, USA | Ice Hockey Player |
| **Ewing, Barbara**<br>1 Candover St, #4, London W1W 7DG, England | Actress |
| **Ewing, Donald Ralph (Skip)**<br>Sussman Assoc, 1222 16th Ave S, #300, Nashville TN 37212, USA | Singer, Songwriter |
| **Ewing, Maria L**<br>Mitchell-Godfrey Mgmt, 48 Gary's Inn Road, London WC1X 8LT, England | Opera Singer |
| **Ewing, Patrick A**<br>Orlando Magic, 8701 Maitland Summit Blvd, Orlando FL 32810 USA | Basketball Player |
| **Ewing, Reid**<br>United Talent Agency, U T A Plaza, 9336 Civic Center Dr, Beverly Hills CA 90210 USA | Actor |
| **Exelby, Garnet**<br>1182 Saint Louis Place NE, Atlanta GA 30306, USA | Ice Hockey Player |
| **Eyharts, Leopold**<br>49 Rue Desnouttes, 75015 Paris, France | Spatinaut, France |
| **Eyoghe Ndong, Jean**<br>Prime Minister's Office, BP 91, Immeuble du 2 Decembre, Libreville, Gabon | Prime Minister, Gabon |
| **Eyre, Chris**<br>Critical Mass Mgmt, 1158 26th St, #414, Santa Monica CA 90403, USA | Actor, Director, Producer |
| **Eyre, Ivan**<br>1098 Des Trappistes St, Winnipeg MB R3V 1B8, Canada | Artist |
| **Eyre, Richard**<br>Judy Daish Assoc, 2 Saint Charles Place, London W10 6EG, England | Director, Writer |
| **Eyre, Scott A**<br>7010 190th St E, Bradenton FL 34211, USA | Baseball Player |
| **Eyring, Henry B**<br>Church of Latter Day Saints, 50 E North Temple, Salt Lake City UT 84150, USA | Religious Leader |
| **Eyskens, Mark M F**<br>Graaf de Grunnelaan 17, 3001 Heverlee-Leuven, Belgium | Prime Minister, Belgium |
| **Eytchison, Ronald M**<br>11 Prentice Lane, Signal Mountain TN 37377, USA | Navy Admiral |
| **Ezeli, I Festus**<br>Golden State Warriors, 1011 Broadway, Oakland CA 94605 USA | Basketball Player |
| **Ezersky, John J (Johnny)**<br>2564 Walnut Blvd, #103, Walnut Creek CA 94596, USA | Basketball Player |
| **Ezra, Derek**<br>2 Salisbury Road, Wimbledon, London SW19 4EZ, England | Government Official, Businessman |

**Fabares, Shelley** — Actress, Singer
Innovative Artists, 1505 10th St, Santa Monica CA 90401 USA
**Fabbricini, Tiziana** — Opera Singer
Gianni Testa, Via Wrenteggio 31/6, 20146 Milan, Italy
**Faber, Michel** — Writer
Canongate Books, 14 High St, Edinburgh EH1 1TE, Scotland
**Faber, Sandra M** — Astronomer
16321 Ridgecrest Ave, Monte Sereno CA 95030, USA
**Faber, Steve** — Writer, Producer
McKuin Frankel Whitehead, 141 El Camino Drive, #100, Beverly Hills CA 90212 USA
**Fabian** — Singer
Universal Attractions, 135 W 26th St, #1200, New York NY 10001 USA
**Fabian DeLa Mora, Marco J** — Soccer Player
Club Deportivo Guadalajara, Av Aviacion 3800, Col De Ocot, Zapopan Jalisco 45019, Mexico
**Fabian, Ava** — Actress, Model
Playboy Enterprises, 680 N Lake Shore Dr, Chicago IL 60611 USA
**Fabian, John M** — Astronaut
100 Shine Road, Port Ludlow WA 98365, USA
**Fabian, Lara** — Singer, Songwriter
Productions Clandestines, 1 Place du Commerce, #400, Ile des Soeurs QC H3E 1A2, Canada
**Fabio** — Model, Actor
Premier Talent Group, 4370 Tujunga Ave, #110, Studio City CA 91604, USA
**Fabiola Mora y Aragon, Dona** — Queen Mother, Belgium
Royal Palace of Laeken, Avenue du Parc, 1020 Laeken-Brussels, Belgium
**Fabius, Laurent** — Premier, France
National Assembly, Casier de la Poste, Paris Bourbon, 75355 Paris, France
**Fabolous** — Rap Artist, Actor
Artist Representation Group, 9701 Wilshire Blvd, #1000, Beverly Hills CA 90212, USA
**Fabray, Nanette** — Singer, Actress
13834 Magnolia Blvd, Sherman Oaks CA 91423, USA
**Fabre, Jan** — Artist
Pastorihstaat 23, 2060 Antwerp, Belgium
**Face, Elroy L (Roy)** — Baseball Player
608 Della Dr, #5F, North Versailles PA 15137, USA
**Fachinetti, Alessandra** — Fashion Designer
Gucci Group, 1 Amstelplein, 10966 Amsterdam HA, Netherlands
**Facinelli, Peter** — Actor
A P A Talent/Literary Agency, 405 S Beverly Dr, #300, Beverly Hills CA 90212 USA
**Fadden, Jimmie** — Musician (Nitty Gritty Dirt Band)
W M E Entertainment, 9601 Wilshire Blvd, #300, Beverly Hills CA 90210 USA
**Faddeyev, Ludwig D** — Mathematician, Physicist
Steklov Mathematics Institute, Gubkina Str 8, 119991 Moscow, Russia
**Faddis, Jonathan (Jon)** — Jazz Trumpeter, Flugelhorn Player
Carolyn McClair, PO Box 55, Radio Station, New York NY 10101, USA
**Fadek, Timothy** — Photographer
Polaris Images, 259 W 30th St, #1300, New York NY 10001, USA
**Fadem, Josh** — Actor
United Talent Agency, U T A Plaza, 9336 Civic Center Dr, Beverly Hills CA 90210 USA
**Fadeyechev, Alexei** — Ballet Dancer
Karenty Ryad Str 5/10, #20, 103006 Moscow Russia
**Fadeyechev, Nicolai B** — Ballet Dancer
Bolshoi Theater, Teatralnaya Pl 1, 103009 Moscow, Russia
**Fadiman, Anne** — Editor, Writer
Farrar Straus Giroux, 18 W 18th St, #700, New York NY 10011 USA
**Faedo, Leonardo L (Lenny)** — Baseball Player
2920 W Collins St, Tampa FL 33607, USA
**Faerch, Daeg** — Actor
Stone Manners Salners, 9911 W Pico Blvd, #1400, Los Angeles CA 90035 USA
**Fagan, Garth** — Choreographer
Garth Fagan Dance, 50 Chestnut Plaza, #1, Rochester NY 14604, USA
**Fagan, Giles** — Actor
Ken McReddie Assoc, 101 Finsbury Pavement, London EC2A 1RS, England
**Fagan, Kevin** — Cartoonist (Drabble)
26771 Ashford, Mission Viejo CA 92692, USA
**Fagen, Donald** — Singer (Steely Dan); Songwriter
Creative Artists Agency, 2000 Ave of Stars, #100, Los Angeles CA 90067 USA
**Fagenson, Anthony E (Tony)** — Drummer (Eve 6)
Agency Group Ltd, 1880 Century Park E, #711, Los Angeles CA 90067 USA
**Fagerbakke, Bill** — Actor
Main Title Mgmt, 8383 Wilshire Blvd, #408, Beverly Hills CA 90211 USA
**Fagg, George G** — Judge
US Court of Appeals, US Courthouse, 110 E Court Ave, Des Moines IA 50309, USA
**Faggin, Federico** — Co-Inventor (Microprocessor)
27910 Roble Blanco Dr, Los Altos Hills CA 94022, USA
**Faggins, DeMarcus** — Football Player
3002 Southworth Lane, Manvel TX 77578, USA
**Fagin, Claire M** — Educator
200 Central Park S, #12E, New York NY 10019, USA
**Fahey, Jeff** — Actor
Jeff Goldberg Mgmt, 817 Monte Leon Dr, Beverly Hills CA 90210, USA
**Fahey, John M, Jr** — Association Executive
National Geographic, President's Office, 1145 17th St NW, Washington DC 20036, USA
**Fahey, William R (Bill)** — Baseball Player
5740 Mona Lane, Dallas TX 75236, USA
**Fahl, Mary** — Singer
Invasion Group, 133 W 25th St, #500, New York NY 10001, USA
**Fahn, Stanley** — Neurologist
155 Edgars Lane, Hastings on Hudson NY 10706, USA
**Fahnhorst, Keith V** — Football Player
12216 Chadwick Lane, Eden Prairie MN 55344, USA
**Faibisovich, Semyon** — Artist, Photographer
Regina Gallery, 1, 4 Syromyatnichesky Pereulok, 105120 Moscow, Russia
**Fainaru, Steve** — Journalist
Washington Post, Editorial Dept, 1150 15th St NW, Washington DC 20071 USA
**Fair, Lorrie** — Soccer Player
300 3rd St, #1515, San Francisco CA 94107, USA

**Fair, Terrtance D (Terry)** — Football Player
12910 W Monte Vista Road, Avondale AZ 85392, USA
**Fairbairn, Bruce** — Actor
975 N Vendome St Apt 214, Los Angeles CA 90026, USA
**Fairbank, Richard D** — Financier
Capital One Financial, 1680 Capital One Dr, #1, McLean VA 22102, USA
**Fairbrass, Craig** — Actor
Screen 360, 145-157 Saint John St, London EC1V 4PW, England
**Fairchild, John B** — Publisher
Chalet Bianchina, Talstr GR, 7250 Klosters, Switzerland
**Fairchild, Morgan** — Actress
McGowan Mgmt, 8733 W Sunset Blvd, #103, West Hollywood CA 90069 USA
**Fairchild, Paul J** — Football Player
PO Box 25442, Overland Park KS 66225, USA
**Fairchild, Shelly** — Singer
Creative Artists Agency, 2000 Ave of Stars, #100, Los Angeles CA 90067 USA
**Faircloth, D McLauchlin (Lauch)** — Senator, NC
PO Box 496, Clinton NC 28329, USA
**Fairley, Michelle** — Actress
C A M, 111 Shoreditch High St, #400, London E1 6JN, England
**Fairley, Nick** — Football Player
Detroit Lions, 222 Republic Dr, Allen Park MI 48101 USA
**Fairly, Ronald R (Ron)** — Baseball Player, Sportscaster
75369 Spyglass Dr, Indian Wells CA 92210, USA
**Fairs, Eric J** — Football Player
32707 Wales Circle, Fulshear TX 77441, USA
**Fairstein, Linda** — Writer, Attorney
I C M Partners, 10250 Constellation Blvd, #900, Los Angeles CA 90067 USA
**Faison, Donald** — Actor
A P A Talent/Literary Agency, 405 S Beverly Dr, #300, Beverly Hills CA 90212 USA
**Faison, W Earl** — Football Player
2279 N Sequoia Dr, Prescott AZ 86301, USA
**Faithfull, Marianne** — Singer, Songwriter, Actress
Republic Media, Westbourne Studios, 242 Acklam Road, #202, London W10 5JJ, England
**Fakhri, Nargis** — Actress
Ford Models Inc, 111 5th Ave, #900, New York NY 10003 USA
**Fakir, Abdul (Duke)** — Singer (Four Tops)
I C M Partners, 730 5th Ave, New York NY 10019 USA
**Falana, Lola** — Singer, Dancer
Capital Entertainment, 217 Seaton Place NE, Washington DC 20002, USA
**Falardeau, Philippe** — Director
United Talent Agency, U T A Plaza, 9336 Civic Center Dr, Beverly Hills CA 90210 USA
**Falcao, Jose Freire Cardinal** — Religious Leader
QL 12-CJ 12, Lote 1, Lago Sul, Brasilia DF 71660 325, Brazil
**Falchuk, Brad** — Producer, Director, Writer
W M E Entertainment, 9601 Wilshire Blvd, #300, Beverly Hills CA 90210 USA
**Falco, Ed** — Writer
Virginia Polytechnic Institute, English Dept, Blacksburg VA 24060, USA
**Falco, Edie** — Actress
I C M Partners, 10250 Constellation Blvd, #900, Los Angeles CA 90067 USA
**Falcon, Rose** — Singer, Songwriter
Show Dog/Universal Records, 70 Universal City Plaza, Universal City CA 91608, USA
**Falcone, Ben** — Actor
Creative Artists Agency, 2000 Ave of Stars, #100, Los Angeles CA 90067 USA
**Falcone, Peter F (Pete)** — Baseball Player
2232 Thornton Court, Alexandria LA 71301, USA
**Falconer, Eric** — Producer, Writer, Actor
United Talent Agency, U T A Plaza, 9336 Civic Center Dr, Beverly Hills CA 90210 USA
**Falconer, Ian W** — Writer, Illustrator
Simon & Schuster, 1230 Ave of Americas, Concourse 1, New York NY 10020 USA
**Faldo, Nicholas A (Nick)** — Golfer, Sportscaster
Elizabeth House, 18-20 Sheet St, Windsor Berkshire SL4 1BG, England
**Falk, Adam F** — Educator
Williams College, President's Office, 880 Main St, Williamstown MA 01267, USA
**Falk, David B** — Sports Attorney
Falk Assoc, 5335 Wisconsin Ave NW, #850, Washington DC 20015, USA
**Falk, Dean** — Anthropologist
Florida State University, Anthropology Dept, Tallahassee FL 32306, USA
**Falk, Ingrid** — Photographer, Artist
FA+, Drottninggatan 71A, 111 36 Stockholm, Sweden
**Falk, Lisanne** — Actress
9255 W Sunset Blvd, #515, West Hollywood CA 90069, USA
**Falk, Paul** — Figure Skater
Sybelstr 21, 40239 Dusseldorf, Germany
**Falk, Thomas J** — Businessman
Kimberly-Clark Corp, 351 Phelps Dr, Irving TX 75038, USA
**Falkenborg, Brian T** — Baseball Player
30223 N 125th Dr, Peoria AZ 85383, USA
**Falkow, Stanley** — Microbiologist
Stanford University Medical School, Microbiology Dept, Stanford CA 94305, USA
**Fall, Timothy** — Actor
Greenberg Glusker, 1900 Ave of Stars, #2100, Los Angeles CA 90067 USA
**Falldin, N O Thorbjorn** — Prime Minister, Sweden
As, 870 16 Ramvik, Sweden
**Fallon, Brian** — Singer, Guitarist (Gaslight Anthem)
Esther Creative Group, 27 W 24th St, #404, New York NY 10010, USA
**Fallon, James T (Jimmy), Jr** — Actor, Comedian
Creative Artists Agency, 2000 Ave of Stars, #100, Los Angeles CA 90067 USA
**Fallon, Robert J (Bob)** — Baseball Player
801 Somerset Circle, Hanover Park IL 60133, USA
**Fallon, Tiffany** — Model, Actress
Enter Talking Client Relations, 645 W 9th St, #110, Los Angeles CA 90010, USA
**Falloon, Pat** — Ice Hockey Player
112-155 10th St, Birtle MB R0M 0C0, Canada
**Falls, Kevin** — Producer, Writer
W M E Entertainment, 9601 Wilshire Blvd, #300, Beverly Hills CA 90210 USA

F

Fair - Falls

**F**

**Falls, Robert A** — Director
Creative Artists Agency, 2000 Ave of Stars, #100, Los Angeles CA 90067 USA
**Faloona, Christopher J** — Cinematographer
Paradigm Agency, 360 N Crescent Dr, North Building, Beverly Hills CA 90210 USA
**Falsani, Cathleen** — Columnist
Chicago Sun-Times, Editorial Dept, 401 N Wabash Ave, Chicago IL 60611 USA
**Faltings, Gerd** — Mathematician
Princeton University, Mathematics Dept, Princeton NJ 08544, USA
**Faltskog, Agnetha (Anna)** — Singer (ABBA)
Sodra Brobanken 41A, 111 49 Stockholm, Sweden
**Faludi, Susan C** — Writer, Journalist
Sandra Dijkstra Literary Agency, 1155 Camino del Mar, #515, Del Mar CA 92014, USA
**Fama, Eugene F** — Nobel Economics Laureate
University of Chicago, Booth Business School, 5807 S Woodlawn Ave, Chicago IL 60637, USA
**Fama, Eugene F** — Economist
University of Chicago, Booth Business School, Chicago IL 60637, USA
**Fambrough, Henry** — Singer (Spinners)
Buddy Allen Mgmt, 3750 Hudson Manor Terrace, #3AG, Bronx NY 10463, USA
**Famechon, Johnny** — Boxer
9 Wandana Court, Frankston VIC 3199, Australia
**Famie, Keith** — Chef, Director, Producer
W M E Entertainment, 9601 Wilshire Blvd, #300, Beverly Hills CA 90210 USA
**Famiglietti, Mark** — Actor
Hofflund/Polone, 9465 Wilshire Blvd, #420, Beverly Hills CA 90212 USA
**Fanaro, Barry** — Writer, Producer
I C M Partners, 10250 Constellation Blvd, #900, Los Angeles CA 90067 USA
**Fancher, Hampton** — Director, Writer, Actor
Earthbourne Films, 1810 14th St, #214, Santa Monica CA 90404, USA
**Faneca, Alan J, Jr** — Football Player
3800 S Clubhouse Dr, #6, Chandler AZ 85248, USA
**Fang Lijun** — Artist
Max Protetch Gallery, 511 W 22nd St, New York NY 10011, USA
**Fankhauser, Merrell** — Guitarist, Composer
Franklyn Agency, 1010 Hammond St, #312, West Hollywood CA 90069, USA
**Fankhouser, Scott** — Ice Hockey Player
2043 Crippled Oak Trail, Jasper GA 30143, USA
**Fann, Al** — Actor
6051 Hollywood Blvd, #207, Los Angeles CA 90028, USA
**Fanning, Bernard** — Singer (Powderfinger)
Secret Service, PO Box 401, Fortitude Valley QLD 4006, Australia
**Fanning, Dakota** — Actress
W M E Entertainment, 9601 Wilshire Blvd, #300, Beverly Hills CA 90210 USA
**Fanning, Elle** — Actress
W M E Entertainment, 9601 Wilshire Blvd, #300, Beverly Hills CA 90210 USA
**Fanning, Michael L (Mike)** — Football Player
28808 S 4190 Road, Inola OK 74036, USA
**Fanning, W James (Jim)** — Baseball Player, Manager
154 Tiner Ave, Dorchester ON N0L 1G2, Canada
**Fantoni, Sergio** — Actor
Via del Cappellari 35, 00186 Rome, Italy
**Fanzone, Carmen R** — Baseball Player
5114 Ranchito Ave, Sherman Oaks CA 91423, USA
**Faraci, John V, Jr** — Businessman
International Paper Corp, 2 Manhattanville Road, Purchase NY 10577, USA
**Faracy, Stephanie** — Actress
Michael Slessinger, 8730 W Sunset Blvd, #220W, West Hollywood CA 90069 USA
**Faragalli, Lindy** — Bowler
113 N 5th Ave, Manville NJ 08835, USA
**Farah** — Queen, Iran
Hellen Medien Projekte, Kornweg 1G, 44805 Bochum, Germany
**Farah, Mohammed (Mo)** — Track Athlete
Pace Sports Mgmt, 6 Causeway, Teddington, Middlesex TW11 0HE, England
**Farar, Hassan Abshir** — Prime Minister, Somalia
Prime Minister's Office, People's Palace, Mogadishu, Somalia
**Farenthold, Frances T** — Women's Activist, Educator
2929 Buffalo Speedway, #18B, Houston TX 77098, USA
**Farentino, Debrah** — Actress
Innovative Artists, 1505 10th St, Santa Monica CA 90401 USA
**Fares, Muhammad Ahmed Al** — Cosmonaut, Syria
PO Box 1272, Aleppo, Syria
**Fargis, Joseph H (Joe), IV** — Equestrian
25 Hampton Road, Southampton NY 11968, USA
**Fargo, Donna** — Singer, Guitarist
Prima Donna Entertainment, PO Box 150527, Nashville TN 37215, USA
**Fargo, Thomas B** — Navy Admiral
Trex Enterprises, 10455 Pacific Center Court, San Diego CA 92121, USA
**Farha, Ihsam (Sam)** — Poker Player
14027 Memorial Dr, #234, Houston TX 77079, USA
**Farhadi, Asghar** — Director, Producer, Writer
United Talent Agency, U T A Plaza, 9336 Civic Center Dr, Beverly Hills CA 90210 USA
**Farham, John P** — Singer
Gotham/B M G Records, 69-79 Fulham High St, London SW6 3JW, England
**Farhi, Nicole** — Fashion Designer
16 Foubert's Place, London W1F 7PJ, England
**Farina, Johnny** — Guitarist (Santo & Johnny)
Bellrose Music, 308 E 6th St, #13, New York NY 10003, USA
**Farina, Raffaele Cardinal** — Religious Leader
Vatican Library, 00120 Vatican City
**Farino, Julian** — Director
Independent Talent Group, 40 Whitfield St, London W1T 2RH, England
**Faris, Al** — Actor
Chaotik, 6446 Santa Monica Blvd, Los Angeles CA 90038, USA
**Faris, Anna** — Actress
Anonymous Content, 3532 Hayden Ave, Culver City CA 90232 USA
**Faris, Sean H** — Actor
Gersh Agency, 9465 Wilshire Blvd, #600, Beverly Hills CA 90212 USA

Falls - Faris

**Faris, Valerie** — Director
United Talent Agency, U T A Plaza, 9336 Civic Center Dr, Beverly Hills CA 90210 USA
**Farish, William S** — Diplomat
W S Farish Co, 1100 Louisiana St, #2200, Houston TX 77002, USA
**Fariss, Monty T** — Baseball Player
PO Box 249, Leedey OK 73654, USA
**Farkas, Bertalan** — Cosmonaut, Hungary
A Magyar Koztarsasag, Kutato Urhajosa, Pf 25, 1885 Budapest, Hungary
**Farkas, Ferenc** — Composer
Nagyatai Utca 12, 1026 Budapest, Hungary
**Farkas, Jeff** — Ice Hockey Player
284 Patrice Terrace, Buffalo NY 14221, USA
**Farley, Carole** — Opera, Concert Singer
270 Riverside Dr, New York NY 10025, USA
**Farley, Kevin P** — Actor
Brillstein Entertainment Partners, 9150 Wilshire Blvd, #350, Beverly Hills CA 90212 USA
**Farley, Terrence M** — Financier
Brown Brothers Harriman, 59 Wall St, New York NY 10005, USA
**Farmar, Jordan R** — Basketball Player
2625 Zinfandel Dr, Rancho Cordova CA 95670, USA
**Farmer, Charles (Red)** — Auto Racing Driver
Talladega Walk of Fame, PO Drawer 1179, Talladega AL 35161, USA
**Farmer, D Michael (Mike)** — Basketball Player, Coach
2520 Lakeview Dr, Santa Rosa CA 95405, USA
**Farmer, Edward J (Ed)** — Baseball Player
4581 Camino del Sol, Calabasas CA 91302, USA
**Farmer, Gary** — Actor
Gonzo Drive Records, PO Box 31096, Santa Fe NM 87594, USA
**Farmer, George T** — Football Player
332 Lorraine Blvd, Los Angeles CA 90020, USA
**Farmer, James H (Jim)** — Basketball Player
214 Ashborough Circle, Dothan AL 36301, USA
**Farmer, John, Jr** — Governor, NJ
Attorney General's Office, Hughes Justice Complex, Trenton NJ 08625, USA
**Farmer, Paul** — Physician, Anthropologist
Partners in Health, 641 Huntington Ave, #100, Boston MA 02115, USA
**Farmiga, Vera A** — Actress, Director
Creative Artists Agency, 2000 Ave of Stars, #100, Los Angeles CA 90067 USA
**Farner, Mark** — Singer, Guitarist
Bobby Roberts, 3050 Business Park Circle, #303, Goodlettsville TN 37221 USA
**Farnham, John P** — Singer, Actor
Talentworks, PO Box 246, South Yarra VIC 3141, Australia
**Farnon, Shannon** — Actress
12743 Milbank St, Studio City CA 91604, USA
**Farnsworth, Kyle L** — Baseball Player
1163 Wilde Dr, Kissimmee FL 34747, USA
**Farquhar, John W** — Physician
Stanford University Medical School, Disease Prevention Center, Stanford CA 94305, USA
**Farquhar, Kurt** — Composer
First Artists Mgmt, 4764 Park Granada, #210, Calabasas CA 91302 USA
**Farquhar, Marilyn G** — Cell Biologist, Pathologist
12894 Via Latina, Del Mar CA 92014, USA
**Farr, David N** — Businessman
Emerson Electric, 800 S Florissant Ave, Saint Louis MO 63135, USA
**Farr, Diane** — Actress
United Talent Agency, U T A Plaza, 9336 Civic Center Dr, Beverly Hills CA 90210 USA
**Farr, James A (Jimmy)** — Baseball Player
3 Tyndal Court, Williamsburg VA 23188, USA
**Farr, Jamie** — Actor
51 Ranchero Road, Bell Canyon CA 91307, USA
**Farr, Melvin (Mel), Sr** — Football Player
5000 Town Center, #2803, Southfield MI 48075, USA
**Farr, Norman (Rocky)** — Ice Hockey Player
3850 Overton Park Dr W, Fort Worth TX 76109, USA
**Farr, Shonda** — Actress
Creative Artists Agency, 2000 Ave of Stars, #100, Los Angeles CA 90067 USA
**Farr, Steven M (Steve)** — Baseball Player
126 Chicahauk Trail, Kitty Hawk NC 27949, USA
**Farrakhan, Louis** — Religious Leader
Nation of Islam, 734 W 79th St, Chicago IL 60620, USA
**Farrar, Frank L** — Governor, SD
PO Box 1029, Britton SD 57430, USA
**Farrar, Jay** — Singer (Uncle Tupelo, Son Volt)
Steel Toe Artist Mgmt, PO Box 3165, Jersey City NJ 07303, USA
**Farrell, Colin** — Actor
Creative Artists Agency, 2000 Ave of Stars, #100, Los Angeles CA 90067 USA
**Farrell, Gemma Lee** — Model
Playboy Promotions, 2706 Media Center Dr, Los Angeles CA 90065 USA
**Farrell, John E** — Baseball Player, Manager
PO Box 3519, Clearwater Beach FL 33767, USA
**Farrell, Mike** — Actor
Innovative Artists, 1505 10th St, Santa Monica CA 90401 USA
**Farrell, Perry** — Singer (Jane's Addiction)
Paradigm Agency, 360 N Crescent Dr, North Building, Beverly Hills CA 90210 USA
**Farrell, Sean W** — Football Player
PO Box 21426, Tampa FL 33622, USA
**Farrell, Sharon** — Actress
Wallis Agency, 210 Pass Ave, Burbank CA 91505, USA
**Farrell, Suzanne** — Ballet Dancer
Kennedy Center for Performing Arts, 2700 F St NW, Washington DC 20566, USA
**Farrell, Terence (Terry)** — Architect
Terry Farrell Partners, 7 Hatton St, London NW8 8PL, England
**Farrell, Terry** — Actress
Don Buchwald, 6500 Wilshire Blvd, #2200, Los Angeles CA 90048 USA
**Farrelly, Bernard (Midget)** — Surfer
Parkes Australia, PO Box 505, Byron Bay NSW 2481, Australia

**Farrelly, Bobby** — Director
Conundrum Entertainment, 325 Wilshire Blvd, #201, Santa Monica CA 90401, USA
**Farrelly, Peter J** — Director
Conundrum Entertainment, 325 Wilshire Blvd, #201, Santa Monica CA 90401, USA
**Farrimond, Richard A** — Astronaut, England
Metra Marconi Center, Gunnels Wood Road, Stevenage, Hertsfordshire SG1 2AS, England
**Farrington, Robert G (Bob)** — Harness Racing Driver
105 Country Place, Sanford FL 32771, USA
**Farrior, James A** — Football Player
5925 Almeda Road, #11115, Houston TX 77004, USA
**Farris, Dionne** — Singer (Arrested Development)
Creative Artists Agency, 2000 Ave of Stars, #100, Los Angeles CA 90067 USA
**Farris, Isaac Newton, Jr** — Religious Leader
Southern Christian Leadership Conference, 320 Auburn Ave NE, Atlanta GA 30303, USA
**Farris, J Jerome** — Judge
US Court of Appeals, US Courthouse, 1010 5th Ave, Seattle WA 98104, USA
**Farris, Joseph** — Cartoonist
Long Meadow Lane, Bethel CT 06801, USA
**Farris, Roy Wayne** — Professional Wrestler
H T M Enterprises, 4655 E Harwell St, Gilbert AZ 85234, USA
**Farriss, Andrew** — Keyboardist (INXS)
8 Hayes St, #1, Neutral Bay 20891 NSW, Australia
**Farriss, Jon** — Drummer, Singer (INXS)
8 Hayes St, #1, Neutral Bay 20891 NSW, Australia
**Farrow, Mallory** — Actress
Hervey/Grimes Talent, 10561 Missouri Ave, #2, Los Angeles CA 90025 USA
**Farrow, Mia V** — Actress, Social Activist
Hofflund/Polone, 9465 Wilshire Blvd, #420, Beverly Hills CA 90212 USA
**Faryniarz, Brett A** — Football Player
1021 S Patrick Way, Anaheim CA 92808, USA
**Fasano, Salvatore F (Sal)** — Baseball Player
905 Catherine Glenn, Minooka IL 60447, USA
**Fasman, Gerald D** — Biochemist
180 Wells Ave, #106, Newton Center MA 02459, USA
**Fassbaender, Brigitte** — Opera Singer
Sekretariat, Haiming 2, 83119 Obing, Germany
**Fassbender, Michael** — Actor
Troika, 74 Clerkenwell Road, #300, London EC1M 5QA, England
**Fassell, James E (Jim)** — Football Player, Coach
56 Jacquelin Ave, Ho Ho Kus NJ 07423, USA
**Fassero, Jeffrey J (Jeff)** — Baseball Player
9841 N 56th St, Paradise Valley AZ 85253, USA
**Fast, Alexia** — Actress
Sanders/Armstrong/Caserta Mgmt, 2120 Colorado Ave, #120, Santa Monica CA 90404 USA
**Fat Joe** — Rap Artist (Terror Squad), Actor
Universal Media Artists, 8222 Melrose Ave, #203, Los Angeles CA 90048, USA
**Fatmi, Mourir** — Artist
Galerie Hussenot, 5 bis Rue des Haudriettes, 75003 Paris, France
**Fatone, Joseph (Joey), Jr** — Singer ('N Sync)
P M K-B N C, 8687 Melrose Ave, #800, Los Angeles CA 90069 USA
**Fauci, Anthony S** — Immunologist
3012 43rd St NW, Washington DC 20016, USA
**Faucon, Bernard** — Photographer
6 Rue Barbanegre, 75019 Paris, France
**Faulk, Kevin T** — Football Player
190 Summer St, South Wapole MA 02071, USA
**Faulk, Marshall** — Football Player, Sportscaster
6340 Clayton Road, #305, Saint Louis MO 63117, USA
**Faulkner, Frank** — Artist
Arden Gallery, 129 Newbury St, Mezzanine 2, Boston MA 02116, USA
**Faulkner, Newton** — Singer, Guitarist, Songwriter
Sony-BMG Records, 69-79 Fulham High St, London SW8 3JW, England
**Faulkner, Shannon** — Educational Activist
Woodmont High School, 2831 W Georgia Road, Piedmont SC 29673, USA
**Faure, Maurice H** — Government Official, France
28 Blvd Raspail, 75007 Paris, France
**Fauria, Christian** — Football Player
51 Jeffrey Dr, North Attleboro MA 02760, USA
**Fauser, Mark** — Actor
United Talent Agency, U T A Plaza, 9336 Civic Center Dr, Beverly Hills CA 90210 USA
**Faussart, Helene** — Singer
Evolution Talent Agency, 1501 Broadway, #1301, New York NY 10036, USA
**Faust, Chad** — Actor
Untitled Entertainment, 350 S Beverly Dr, #200, Beverly Hills CA 90212 USA
**Faust, Chris** — Photographer
308 Prince St, Saint Paul MN 55101, USA
**Faust, Drew Gilpin** — Educator
Harvard University, President's Office, 33 Elmwood Ave, Cambridge MA 02138, USA
**Faustino, David** — Actor
Abrams Artists, 9200 W Sunset Blvd, #1125, West Hollywood CA 90069 USA
**Fauza, Dario O** — Surgeon
Harvard Medical School, Surgery Dept, 25 Shattuck St, Boston MA 02115, USA
**Favier, Jean-Jacques** — Spatinaut, France
Technologies Avances, 17 Ave des Martys, 38054 Grenoble Cedex, France
**Favor, Mike** — Football Player
Robinsdale Cooper High School, 8230 47th Ave N, New Hope MN 55428, USA
**Favors, Derrick B** — Basketball Player
Utah Jazz, Energy Solutions Arena, 301 W South Temple, Salt Lake City UT 84101 USA
**Favre, Brett L** — Football Player
7698 US Highway 98W, Sumrall MS 39482, USA
**Favreau, Jon** — Actor, Writer, Director
Creative Artists Agency, 2000 Ave of Stars, #100, Los Angeles CA 90067 USA
**Fawcett, Don W** — Anatomist
3710 American Way, #325, Missoula MT 59808, USA
**Fawcett, Joy** — Soccer Player
11 Calle Marta, Rancho Santa Margarita CA 92688, USA

**Fawcett, Sherwood L**	Physicist
1800 Riverside Dr, #2314, Columbus OH 43212, USA
**Faxon, Brad**	Golfer
85 Nayatt Road, Barrington RI 02806, USA
**Faxon, Nat**	Actor, Writer
Creative Artists Agency, 2000 Ave of Stars, #100, Los Angeles CA 90067 USA
**Fay, Johnny**	Drummer (Tragically Hip)
Bobby Breen Mgmt, 13 Blackburn St, #300, Toronto ON M4M 2B3, Canada
**Fay, Meagen**	Actress
Main Title Mgmt, 8383 Wilshire Blvd, #408, Beverly Hills CA 90211 USA
**Fay, Peter T**	Judge
US Court of Appeals, 36 NE 1st St, #300, Miami FL 33132, USA
**Faydoedeelay**	Rap Artist, Bassist (Crazy Town)
Q Prime, 729 7th Ave, #1600, New York NY 10019, USA
**Fayed, Mohamed al-**	Businessman
Craven Cottage, Stevenage Road, Fulham, London SW6 6HH, England
**Fazio, Ernest J (Ernie)**	Baseball Player
2310 Royal Oaks Dr, Alamo CA 94507, USA
**Fazio, Tom**	Golf Course Architect
Fazio Golf Course Designers, 401 N Main St, #400, Hendersonville NV 28792, USA
**Fazzini, Enrico**	Neurologist
New York University Medical Center, Neurology Dept, 353 Lexington Ave, #101, New York NY 10016, USA
**Fazzino, Charles**	Artist
32 Relyea Place, #2, New Rochelle NY 10801, USA
**Feachem, Richard**	Foundation Executive
Global Fund, Chemin de Blandonnet 8, 1214 Vernier, Switzerland
**Feagles, Jeffrey A (Jeff)**	Football Player
326 W End Ave, Ridgewood NJ 07450, USA
**Fearnley, James**	Accordianist (Pogues)
Agency Group Ltd, 361-373 City Road, London EC1V 1PQ, England
**Fearnley-Whittingstall, Hugh**	Writer, Chef
Bloomsbury Publishing, 50 Bedford Square, London WC1B 3DP, England
**Featherstone, Glen**	Ice Hockey Player
8 Larrabee Ave, Danvers MA 01923, USA
**Fedak, Chris**	Producer, Writer
W M E Entertainment, 9601 Wilshire Blvd, #300, Beverly Hills CA 90210 USA
**Federer, Michelle**	Actress, Singer
Gotham Talent Agency, 570 7th Ave, New York NY 10018, USA
**Federer, Roger**	Tennis Player
Postfach, 4103 Bottmingen, Switzerland
**Federighi, Christine M**	Sculptor
1315 Obispo Ave, Coral Gables FL 33134, USA
**Federko, Bernie**	Ice Hockey Player
2219 Devonsbrook Dr, Chesterfield MO 63005, USA
**Federspiel, Joseph M (Joe)**	Football Player
2016 Lakeside Dr, Lexington KY 40502, USA
**Fedewa, Tim**	Auto Racing Driver
1737 Onondaga Road, Holt MI 48842, USA
**Fedorov, Sergei V**	Ice Hockey Player
Metallurg Magnitogorsk, Pr Lenin 105, 455000, Magnitogorsk, Chelysbinsk Oblast, Russia
**Fedoseyev, Vladimir I**	Conductor
Recording/Broadcasting House, Malaya Nikitskaya 24, 121069 Moscow, Russia
**Fedotenko, Ruslan V**	Ice Hockey Player
130 S 18th St, #1402, Philadelphia PA 19103, USA
**Fedotov, Maxim V**	Concert Violinist
Tolbukhin Str 8, Korp 1, #6, 121596 Moscow, Russia
**Feehan, Christine**	Writer
Penguin Books, 375 Hudson St, Basement 1, New York NY 10014 USA
**Feehery, Gerald (Gerry)**	Football Player
5 Sharpless Lane, Media PA 19063, USA
**Feehily, Mark**	Singer (Westlife)
Solo Agency, 53-55 Fulham High St, #200, London SW6 3JJ, England
**Feeley, Adam J (A J)**	Football Player
19062 Park Ridge St, Weston FL 33332, USA
**Feely, T James (Jay)**	Football Player
15923 Noting Hill Dr, Lutz FL 33548, USA
**Feeney, Mark**	Journalist
Boston Globe, Editorial Dept, 135 William Morrissey Blvd, Dorchester MA 02125 USA
**Fegan, Roshon B**	Actor
W M E Entertainment, 9601 Wilshire Blvd, #300, Beverly Hills CA 90210 USA
**Feher, George**	Physicist
University of California, Physics Dept, 9500 Gilman Dr, La Jolla CA 92093, USA
**Feher, Raymond**	Basketball Player
62 Cool Springs Road, Signal Mountain TN 37377, USA
**Feherty, David**	Golfer
6422 Prestonshire Lane, Dallas TX 75225, USA
**Fehr, Brendan**	Actor
Roar Mgmt, 9701 Wilshire Blvd, #800, Beverly Hills CA 90212 USA
**Fehr, Richard E (Rick)**	Golfer
2869 W Haley Dr, Anthem AZ 85086, USA
**Fehr, Steve**	Bowler
1329 Castlebridge Court, Cincinnati OH 45233, USA
**Fei Junlong**	Taikonaut
Japanese Aerospace Exploration Agency, 2-1-1 Sengen, Tsukuba-shi, Ibaraki 305 8505, Japan
**Feiffer, Halley**	Actress
Gersh Agency, 9465 Wilshire Blvd, #600, Beverly Hills CA 90212 USA
**Feiffer, Jules**	Cartoonist
PO Box 373, Southampton NY 11969, USA
**Feig, Paul S**	Actor, Director, Writer
Creative Artists Agency, 2000 Ave of Stars, #100, Los Angeles CA 90067 USA
**Feigenbaum, Armand V**	Businessman, Systems Engineer
General Systems, 23 South St, #250, Pittsfield MA 01201, USA
**Feigenbaum, Edward A**	Computer Scientist
1017 Cathcart Way, Stanford CA 94305, USA
**Feign, Larry**	Cartoonist (World of Lily Wong)
Heineman Educational Books, GPO Box 6086, Tsim Sha Tsui Post Office, Kowloon, Hong Kong, China

# F

| | |
|---|---|
| **Feigum, Christopher**<br>I M G Artists, Hogarth Business Park, Chiswick, London W4 2TH, England | Opera Singer |
| **Feild, J J**<br>Ken McReddie Assoc, 101 Finsbury Pavement, London EC2A 1RS, England | Actor |
| **Feilden, Richard J R**<br>Bradley Architects, Bath Brewery, Toll Bridge Road, Bath BA1 7DE, England | Architect |
| **Feinberg, Alan**<br>C M Artists, 127 W 96th St, #13B, New York NY 10025 USA | Concert Pianist |
| **Feinberg, Wilfred**<br>US Court of Appeals, Moynihan Courthouse, 500 Pearl St, New York NY 10007, USA | Judge |
| **Feiner, Edward F**<br>General Services Administration, 1800 F St NW, #3341, Washington DC 20405, USA | Architect |
| **Feinstein, A Richard**<br>1760 2nd Ave, #32C, New York NY 10128, USA | Epidemiologist |
| **Feinstein, Alan**<br>Connor Ankrum & Associates, 1680 Vine St, #1016, Los Angeles CA 90028, USA | Actor |
| **Feinstein, John**<br>Little Brown, 1271 Ave of Americas, New York NY 10020, USA | Sportswriter, Commentator |
| **Feinstein, Michael**<br>Paradigm Agency, 360 N Crescent Dr, North Building, Beverly Hills CA 90210 USA | Singer, Pianist |
| **Feist, Leslie**<br>Interscope Records, 2220 Colorado Ave, Santa Monica CA 90404 USA | Singer, Songwriter |
| **Feitl, Dave S**<br>12255 Highway 62 E, Harrison AR 72601, USA | Basketball Player |
| **Felber, Dean**<br>FishCo Mgmt, 2519 Devine Street  Columbia SC 29205, USA | Bassist (Hootie & the Blowfish) |
| **Felch, William C**<br>8545 Carmel Valley Road, Carmel CA 93923, USA | Physician |
| **Feld, Eliot**<br>Feld Ballet, 890 Broadway, #800, New York NY 10003, USA | Dancer, Choreographer |
| **Feld, Steven**<br>New Mexico University, Anthropology Dept, Albuquerque NM 87131, USA | Ethnomusicologist, Anthropologist |
| **Felder, Donald W (Don)**<br>Renaissance Literary & Talent, PO Box 17379, Beverly Hills CA 90209, USA | Singer, Guitarist (Eagles) |
| **Felder, Michael O (Mike)**<br>322 S 17th St, Richmond CA 94804, USA | Baseball Player |
| **Felder, Raoul Lionel**<br>437 Madison Ave, #3000, New York NY 10022, USA | Attorney |
| **Feldman, Bella**<br>12 Summit Lane, Berkeley CA 94708, USA | Artist |
| **Feldman, Corey**<br>Scott Carlson Entertainment, 5739 Bucknell Ave, Valley Village CA 91607, USA | Actor |
| **Feldman, Donna**<br>Across the Board Talent, 22543 Ventura Blvd, #225, Woodland Hills CA 91364, USA | Actress, Model |
| **Feldman, Ed**<br>Gersh Agency, 9465 Wilshire Blvd, #600, Beverly Hills CA 90212 USA | Actor |
| **Feldman, Jerome M**<br>2744 Sevier St, Durham NC 27705, USA | Physician |
| **Feldman, Jon H**<br>Gersh Agency, 9465 Wilshire Blvd, #600, Beverly Hills CA 90212 USA | Producer, Writer |
| **Feldman, Kurt**<br>Slumberland Records, PO Box 19029, Oakland CA 94619, USA | Drummer (Pains of Being Pure at Heart) |
| **Feldman, Marcus W**<br>Stanford University, Biological Sciences Dept, Stanford CA 94305, USA | Biological Scientist |
| **Feldman, Michael**<br>Inphenate, 9701 Wilshire Blvd, #1000, Beverly Hills CA 90212 USA | Producer, Writer |
| **Feldman, Michelle**<br>Gary Feldman, PO Box 713, Skaneateles NY 13152, USA | Bowler |
| **Feldman, Scott W**<br>1021 Balboa Ave, Burlingame CA 94010, USA | Baseball Player |
| **Feldman, Susie**<br>Scott Carlson Entertainment, 5739 Bucknell Ave, Valley Village CA 91607, USA | Actress |
| **Feldmann, Marc**<br>Charing Cross Hospital, Saint Dunstan's Road, London W6 8RP, England | Rheumatologist |
| **Feldmann, Sabine**<br>Shape, Publisher's Office, 1 Park Ave, New York NY 10016, USA | Publisher |
| **Feldon, Barbara**<br>Creative Artists Agency, 2000 Ave of Stars, #100, Los Angeles CA 90067 USA | Actress, Model |
| **Feldshuh, Tovah S**<br>Gage Group, 450 7th Ave, #1809, New York NY 10123 USA | Actress |
| **Feldstein, Martin S**<br>147 Clifton St, Belmont MA 02478, USA | Government Official, Economist |
| **Feliciano, Jose**<br>Feliciano Enterprises, 606 Boston Post Road E, #880, Westport CT 06880, USA | Singer, Guitarist |
| **Felipe**<br>Palacio de la Zarzuela, Carretera del Pardo S/N, 28071 Madrid, Spain | Crown Prince, Spain |
| **Felke, Petra**<br>S C Motor Jena, Wollnitzevstr 42, 07749 Jena, Germany | Track Athlete |
| **Fellag, Mohamed**<br>Agence Artiste Adequet, 108 Rue Reaumur, 75002 Paris, France | Actor |
| **Feller, Anke**<br>Heinrich-Claes Str 11, 51373 Leverkusen, Germany | Track Athlete, Model |
| **Fellmeth, Catherine**<br>Professional Bowlers Assn, 719 2nd Ave, #701, Seattle WA 98104 USA | Bowler |
| **Fellner, Eric**<br>Working Title Films, 26 Aybrook St, London W1U 4AN, England | Producer |
| **Fellner, Till**<br>Ingpen & Williams, 131 Putney Bridge Road, London SW15 2PA, England | Concert Pianist |
| **Fellowes, Julian**<br>Independent Talent Group, 40 Whitfield St, London W1T 2RH, England | Director, Writer |
| **Fellows, Ron**<br>PO Box 564, RPO Turtle Creek, Mississauga ON L5J 4S6, Canada | Auto Racing Driver |
| **Fellows, Ronald L (Ron)**<br>202 Creekview Dr, Wylie TX 75098, USA | Football Player |
| **Fellows, Simon**<br>United Agents, 12-26 Lexington St, London W1F 0LE, England | Director |

**Feigum - Fellows**

|  |  |
|---|---|
| **Felmy, Hansjorg**<br>Berghofen, 84174 Eching, Germany | Actor |
| **Felsenfeld, Gary**<br>National Institutes of Health, Physical Chemistry Section, 5 Memorial Dr, Bethesda MD 20892, USA | Molecular Biologist |
| **Felsenstein, Lee**<br>1479 Regent St, Redwood City CA 94061, USA | Inventor (Portable Computer) |
| **Felske, John F**<br>3804 Ridge Road, Spring Grove IL 60081, USA | Baseball Player, Manager |
| **Felton, Dennis**<br>University of Georgia, Athletic Dept, Athens GA 30602, USA | Basketball Coach |
| **Felton, John**<br>G M S, PO Box 1031, Montrose CA 91021, USA | Singer (Diamonds) |
| **Felton, Lindsay**<br>Geddes Agency, 8430 Santa Monica Blvd, #201, West Hollywood CA 90069 USA | Actress |
| **Felton, Raymond B**<br>15814 Sullivan Ridge Road, Charlotte NC 28277, USA | Basketball Player |
| **Felton, Tom**<br>Troika, 74 Clerkenwell Road, #300, London EC1M 5QA, England | Actor |
| **Felts, Narvel**<br>Joe Taylor Artist Agency, 2802 Columbine Place, Nashville TN 37204 USA | Singer, Songwriter |
| **Feltus, Alan E**<br>Porziano 68, 06081 Assisi, Italy | Artist |
| **Fencik, J Gary**<br>1134 W Schubert Ave, Chicago IL 60614, USA | Football Player |
| **Fendrich, Rainhard J**<br>Management Agnes Rehling, Kirchenstras 17C, 82110 Germering, Germany | Singer, Actor, Composer |
| **Fenech Adami, Edward (Eddie)**<br>176 Main St, Birkikara, Malta | President, Malta |
| **Fenech, Edwige**<br>Carol Levi Mgmt, Via G Pisanelli 2, 00196 Rome, Italy | Actress, Producer |
| **Fenech, Jeff**<br>Team Fenech, PO Box 66, Millers Point NSW 2000, Australia | Boxer, Trainer |
| **Feng Ying**<br>Central Ballet of China, 3 Taiping St, Beijing 100050, China | Ballerina |
| **Feng Zhengjie**<br>Primo Marella Gallery, Viale Stelvio 66, 20159 Milan, Italy | Artist |
| **Feng-Hsiung Hsu**<br>I B M Watson Research Center, PO Box 218, Yorktown Heights NY 10598 USA | Computer Engineer |
| **Fenical, William**<br>Scripps Institution of Oceanography, Organic Chemistry Dept, La Jolla CA 92093, USA | Organic Chemist |
| **Fenn, Sherilyn**<br>Water Street Anthem Entertainment, 5225 Wilshire Blvd, #615, Los Angeles CA 90036 USA | Actress |
| **Fenner, Derrick S**<br>7533 33rd Ave NW, Seattle. WA 98117, USA | Football Player |
| **Fenson, Pete**<br>3760 Crest Court NE, Bemidji MN 56601, USA | Curling Athlete |
| **Fenton, George**<br>Gorfaine/Schwartz, 4111 W Alameda Ave, #509, Burbank CA 91505 USA | Composer |
| **Fenton, James**<br>Farrar Straus Giroux, 18 W 18th St, #700, New York NY 10011 USA | Writer |
| **Fenton, Paul**<br>16 Bridle Path Road, Brewster MA 02631, USA | Ice Hockey Player |
| **Fentress, Curtis W**<br>Fentress Bradburn Assoc, 421 Broadway, Denver CO 80203, USA | Architect |
| **Fenty, Adrian**<br>Mayor's Office, 1 Judiciary Square, 414 4th St NW, Washington DC 20001, USA | Mayor, Washington DC |
| **Fenwick, Robert R (Bobby)**<br>51201 Hutchinson Road, Three Rivers MI 49093, USA | Baseball Player |
| **Fenyves, Dave**<br>940 Parish Place, Hummelstown PA 17036, USA | Ice Hockey Player |
| **Feore, Colm**<br>Coronel Group, 1100 Glendon Ave, #1700, Los Angeles CA 90046, USA | Actor |
| **Feranec, Peter**<br>Bolshoi Theater, Teatralnaya Pl 1, 103009 Moscow, Russia | Conductor |
| **Feraud, Gianfranco**<br>25 Rue Saint Honore, 75001 Paris, France | Fashion Designer |
| **Ferdinand, Ron**<br>PO Box 1997, Monterey CA 93942, USA | Inventor (Portable Computer) |
| **Ferdinand-Harris, Marie**<br>Los Angeles Sparks, 888 S Figueroa St, #2010, Los Angeles CA 90017 USA | Basketball Player |
| **Ference, Andrew**<br>220 Commercial St, Boston MA 02109, USA | Ice Hockey Player |
| **Ferentz, Kirk J**<br>University of Iowa, Athletic Dept, Iowa City IA 52242, USA | Football Coach |
| **Fergie**<br>13701 Ventura Blvd, #800, Sherman Oaks CA 91423, USA | Rap Artist |
| **Fergon, Vicki**<br>44 Partridge Lane, Aliso Viejo CA 92656, USA | Golfer |
| **Fergus, Keith C**<br>11515 Noblewood Crest Lane, Houston TX 77082, USA | Golfer |
| **Fergus, Tom**<br>Blue Leaf Ltd, 2134 Speers Road, Oakville ON L6L 2X8, Canada | Ice Hockey Player |
| **Ferguson Cullum, Cathy**<br>515 Amanda Dr, Bear DE 19701, USA | Swimmer |
| **Ferguson, Alexander C (Alex)**<br>Manchester United, Busby Way, Old Trafford, Manchester M16 0RA, England | Soccer Player, Manager |
| **Ferguson, Charles A**<br>123 Walnut St, #801, New Orleans LA 70118, USA | Editor |
| **Ferguson, Charles E (Charley)**<br>81 Stonecroft Lane, Buffalo NY 14226, USA | Football Player |
| **Ferguson, Charles H**<br>Representational Pictures, 75 E 4th St, #83, New York NY 10003, USA | Director |
| **Ferguson, Christopher J**<br>2405 Airline Dr, Friendswood TX 77546, USA | Astronaut |
| **Ferguson, Colin**<br>United Talent Agency, U T A Plaza, 9336 Civic Center Dr, Beverly Hills CA 90210 USA | Actor, Comedian |

**F**

**Felmy - Ferguson**

**Ferguson, Craig**
Green Mountain Werst, 7800 Beverly Blvd, Los Angeles CA 90036, USA — Actor, Comedian
**Ferguson, D'Brickashaw M**
New York Jets, 1 Jets Dr, Florham Park NJ 07932 USA — Football Player
**Ferguson, Frederick E**
5420 E Lincoln Dr, Paradise Valley AZ 85253, USA — Vietnam War Army Hero (CMH)
**Ferguson, James (Jim)**
2404 Stonybrook Road, Opelika AL 36804, USA — Water Polo Player
**Ferguson, James L**
General Foods Corp, 800 Westchester Ave, Rye Brook NY 10573, USA — Businessman
**Ferguson, Jesse Tyler**
I C M Partners, 10250 Constellation Blvd, #900, Los Angeles CA 90067 USA — Actor
**Ferguson, Joe C, Jr**
12 Mason Lane, Bella Vista AR 72715, USA — Football Player, Coach
**Ferguson, Joseph V (Joe)**
11322 River Run Lane, Berlin MO 21811, USA — Baseball Player
**Ferguson, Keith T**
PO Box 19006, Sugar Land TX 77496, USA — Football Player
**Ferguson, Kent**
199 Tiffany Ave, #407, San Francisco CA 94110, USA — Diver, Model
**Ferguson, Lynnda**
606 N Larchmont Blvd, #309, Los Angeles CA 90004, USA — Actress
**Ferguson, M Paul**
Agency Group, 9348 Civic Center Dr, #200, Beverly Hills CA 90210 USA — Drummer (Killing Joke)
**Ferguson, Mark E, III**
Chief, Naval Personnel, 2 Navy St, Washington DC 20380 USA — Navy Admiral
**Ferguson, Megan**
Don Buchwald, 6500 Wilshire Blvd, #2200, Los Angeles CA 90048 USA — Actress
**Ferguson, Nick**
114 Arlington Ave SW, Atlanta GA 30310, USA — Football Player
**Ferguson, Rebecca L**
Tavistock Wood Mgmt, 45 Conduit St, London W1S 2YN, England — Actress
**Ferguson, Robert A**
Columbia University, Jerome Green Hall, New York NY 10027, USA — Educator, Attorney
**Ferguson, Robert C**
15102 Oldtown Bridge Court, Sugar Land TX 77498, USA — Football Player
**Ferguson, Sarah**
Birchhall, Windlesham, Surrey GU20 6BN, England — Duchess of York, England
**Ferguson, Stacy**
Paradigm Agency, 360 N Crescent Dr, North Building, Beverly Hills CA 90210 USA — Actress
**Ferguson, Thomas A, Jr**
Newell Rubbermaid Inc, Newell Center, 29 E Stephenson St, Freeport IL 61032, USA — Businessman
**Ferguson, Tom**
General Delivery, Miami OK 74354, USA — Rodeo Rider
**Fergus-Thompson, Gordon**
12 Audley Road, Hendon, London NW4 3EY, England — Concert Pianist
**Ferilli, Sabrina**
Camelia Srl, Via Giorgio Vasari 4, 00196 Rome, Italy — Actress
**Feringa, Ben L**
University of Groningen, Chemistry Dept, Nijenborgh 4, 9747 Groningen AG, Netherlands — Chemist
**Ferland, E James**
Public Service Enterprise, 80 Park Plaza, PO Box 1171, Newark NJ 07101, USA — Businessman
**Ferland, Guy V**
W M E Entertainment, 9601 Wilshire Blvd, #300, Beverly Hills CA 90210 USA — Director
**Ferland, Jodelle**
Play Mgmt, 807 Powell St, #220, Vancouver BC V6A 1H7, Canada — Actress
**Ferlinghetti, Lawrence**
City Lights Booksellers, 261 Columbus Ave, San Francisco CA 94133, USA — Writer, Publisher
**Ferlito, Vanessa**
Alchemy Entertainment, 7024 Melrose Ave, #420, Los Angeles CA 90038 USA — Actress
**Fermin, Felix J**
Akron Aeros, 300 S Main St, Akron OH 44308, USA — Baseball Player
**Fernandez de Kirchner, Cristina E**
Casa de Gobierno, Balcarce 50, Buenos Aires 1064, Argentina — President, Argentina
**Fernandez Krupij, Stefania**
Miss Universe Organization, 1370 Ave of Americas, #1600, New York NY 10019 USA — Beauty Queen
**Fernandez Molinos, Begona**
R K Zajecar, Dositejeva 11, 19000 Zajecar, Serbia — Handball Player
**Fernandez, Adrian**
Fernandez Racing, PO Box 68828, Indianapolis IN 46268, USA — Auto Racing Driver
**Fernandez, Alejandro**
Creative Artists Agency, 2000 Ave of Stars, #100, Los Angeles CA 90067 USA — Singer, Actor
**Fernandez, Alexander (Alex)**
12323 SW 55th St, #1007, Cooper City FL 33330, USA — Baseball Player
**Fernandez, C Sidney (Sid)**
25 Aulike St, #218, Kailua HI 96734, USA — Baseball Player
**Fernandez, Emmanuel (Manny)**
Boston Bruins, 100 Legends Way, #250, Boston MA 02114 USA — Ice Hockey Player
**Fernandez, Ferdinand F**
US Court of Appeals, 125 S Grand Ave, Pasadena CA 91105, USA — Judge
**Fernandez, Frank**
37 Couglan Ave, Staten Island NY 10310, USA — Baseball Player
**Fernandez, Gigi**
US Lawn Tennis Assn, 1212 Ave of Americas, New York NY 10036, USA — Tennis Player
**Fernandez, Karina**
United Agents, 12-26 Lexington St, London W1F 0LE, England — Actress
**Fernandez, Lisa**
1460 Homewood Road, #95B, Seal Beach CA 90740, USA — Softball Player
**Fernandez, Lujan**
Fashion Model Mgmt, 40 Ang Via Monte Rosa, 20149 Milan, Italy — Model, Actress
**Fernandez, Manuel J (Manny)**
5805 SW 120th St, Cooper City FL 33330, USA — Football Player
**Fernandez, Mariestela**
Sandra Marsh Assoc, 9150 Wilshire Blvd, #220, Beverly Hills CA 90212 USA — Costume Designer
**Fernandez, Mary Joe**
1121 Crandon Blvd, #D606, Key Biscayne FL 33149, USA — Tennis Player

| | |
|---|---|
| **Fernandez, Mervyn**<br>2477 Briarwood Dr, San Jose CA 95125, USA | Football Player |
| **Fernandez, O Antonio (Tony)**<br>Tony Fernandez Foundation, 19232 N Gardenia Ave, Weston FL 33332, USA | Baseball Player |
| **Fernandez, Pedro**<br>S D L Productions, PO Box 65948, Los Angeles CA 90065, USA | Singer, Songwriter |
| **Fernandez, Raul**<br>F C Dallas, 9200 World Cup Way, #202, Frisco TX 75034 USA | Soccer Player |
| **Fernandez, Shiloh**<br>W M E Entertainment, 9601 Wilshire Blvd, #300, Beverly Hills CA 90210 USA | Actor |
| **Fernandez, Vicente**<br>Hauser Entertainment, 3703 San Gabriel River Parkway, Pico Rivera CA 90660, USA | Singer |
| **Ferneyhough, Brian J P**<br>848 Allardice Way, Stanford CA 94305, USA | Composer |
| **Ferns, Alex**<br>Ken McReddie Assoc, 101 Finsbury Pavement, London EC2A 1RS, England | Actor |
| **Fernsten, Eric R**<br>5634 Linden St, Dublin CA 94568, USA | Basketball Player |
| **Ferragamo, Vince A**<br>Touchdown Real Estate, 6200 E Canyon Rim Road, #204, Anaheim CA 92807, USA | Football Player |
| **Ferrara, Abel**<br>I C M Partners, 10250 Constellation Blvd, #900, Los Angeles CA 90067 USA | Director |
| **Ferrara, Adam**<br>Gersh Agency, 9465 Wilshire Blvd, #600, Beverly Hills CA 90212 USA | Actor, Comedian |
| **Ferrara, Alfred J (Al)**<br>4901 Whitsett Ave, #207, Valley Village CA 91607, USA | Baseball Player |
| **Ferrara, Jerry**<br>W M E Entertainment, 9601 Wilshire Blvd, #300, Beverly Hills CA 90210 USA | Actor |
| **Ferrara, Stephane**<br>Artmedia, 20 Ave Rapp, 75007 Paris, France | Actress |
| **Ferrare, Cristina**<br>10727 Wilshire Blvd, #1602, Los Angeles CA 90024, USA | Model, Entertainer |
| **Ferrarese, Donald H (Don)**<br>15290 Myalon Road, Apple Valley CA 92307, USA | Baseball Player |
| **Ferrari, Albert R (Al)**<br>5911 Bristlecone Court, Saint Louis MO 63129, USA | Basketball Player |
| **Ferrari, Gillian**<br>Team Canada, 2424 University Dr NW, Calgary AB T2N 3Y9, Canada | Ice Hockey Player |
| **Ferrari, Michael R, Jr**<br>570 Greenway Dr, Lake Forest IL 60045, USA | Educator |
| **Ferrari, Tina**<br>2901 S Las Vegas Blvd, Las Vegas NV 89109, USA | Dancer, Wrestler |
| **Ferraro, Dave**<br>672 E Chester St, Kingston NY 12401, USA | Bowler |
| **Ferraro, Michael D (Mike)**<br>5201 Rim View Lane, Las Vegas NV 89130, USA | Baseball Player, Manager |
| **Ferraro, Raymond (Ray)**<br>Team 1040 Sports Radio, 30-380 W 2nd Ave, Vancouver BC V5Y 1C8, Canada | Ice Hockey Player, Sportscaster |
| **Ferrarone, Jessica**<br>Evolution Entertainment, 901 N Highland Ave, Los Angeles CA 90038 USA | Actress |
| **Ferratti, Rebecca M**<br>10061 Riverside Dr, #721, Toluca Lake CA 91602, USA | Model, Actress |
| **Ferrazzi, Pierpaolo**<br>EuroGrafica, Via del Progresso, 36035 Marano Vicenza, Italy | Canoeing Athlete |
| **Ferree, Jim**<br>12 Kings Tree Road, Hilton Head Island SC 29928, USA | Golfer |
| **Ferreira, Gabriel Vasconcellos**<br>Confederacion de Futebol, Rua Victor Civita 66, #1, Rio de Janeiro 22775 044, Brazil | Soccer Player |
| **Ferreira, Wayne**<br>International Mangement Group, 1 Erieview Plaza, 1360 E 9th St, Cleveland OH 44114 USA | Tennis Player |
| **Ferrell Edmonson, Barbara A**<br>University of Nevada, Athletic Dept, Las Vegas NV 89154, USA | Track Athlete |
| **Ferrell, Conchata**<br>Gage Group, 14724 Ventura Blvd, #505, Sherman Oaks CA 91403 USA | Actress |
| **Ferrell, Earl T**<br>107 E Forest Trail, South Boston VA 24592, USA | Football Player |
| **Ferrell, Perry**<br>DeMann Entertainment, 1017 N La Cienega Blvd, #103, West Hollywood CA 90069, USA | Singer (Porno for Pyros) |
| **Ferrell, Rachelle**<br>Wenig-LaMonica Associates, 580 White Plains Road, #130, Tarrytown NY 10591 USA | Singer |
| **Ferrell, Robert S (Bobby)**<br>1090 N Shooting Star Dr, Beaumont CA 92223, USA | Football Player |
| **Ferrell, Tyra**<br>Gersh Agency, 9465 Wilshire Blvd, #600, Beverly Hills CA 90212 USA | Actress |
| **Ferrell, Will**<br>Mosiac Media Group, 9200 W Sunset Blvd, #1000, Los Angeles CA 90069 USA | Actor, Comedian |
| **Ferreol, Andrea**<br>Artmedia, 20 Ave Rapp, 75007 Paris, France | Actress |
| **Ferrer Ern, David**<br>Association of Tennis Professionals, 200 Tournament Road, Ponte Vedra Beach FL 32082 USA | Tennis Player |
| **Ferrer, Danay**<br>R C A Records, 8750 Wilshire Blvd, Beverly Hills CA 90211 USA | Singer (Innosense) |
| **Ferrer, Miguel**<br>Danis Panaro Nist, 9201 W Olympic Blvd, Beverly Hills CA 90212, USA | Actor |
| **Ferrer, Tessa**<br>A P A Talent/Literary Agency, 405 S Beverly Dr, #300, Beverly Hills CA 90212 USA | Actress |
| **Ferrera, America**<br>I C M Partners, 10250 Constellation Blvd, #900, Los Angeles CA 90067 USA | Actress |
| **Ferreras, Francisco (Pipin)**<br>7548 W Treasure Dr, North Bay Village FL 33141, USA | Free Diver |
| **Ferrero, Juan Carlos**<br>Echegaray 2, 468 70 Ontynent, Spain | Tennis Player |
| **Ferretti, Alberta**<br>Via delle Querce 51, 47842 San Giovanni in Marignano, Italy | Fashion Designer |
| **Ferretti, Dante**<br>Sandra Marsh & Associates, 9150 Wilshire Blvd, #220, Beverly Hills CA 90212, USA | Art Director |

**Ferrick, Melissa** — Singer, Songwriter
Agency Group Ltd, 142 W 57th St, #600, New York NY 10019 USA
**Ferrigno, Lou** — Actor, Body Builder
Lou Ferrigno Enterprises, PO Box 1671, Santa Monica CA 90406, USA
**Ferrigno, Robert** — Writer
Charles Scribner's Sons, 866 3rd Ave, New York NY 10022 USA
**Ferrin, Arnold (Arnie)** — Basketball Player
2104 S Barona Road, Palm Springs CA 92264, USA
**Ferrin, Jennifer** — Actress
Gersh Agency, 9465 Wilshire Blvd, #600, Beverly Hills CA 90212 USA
**Ferris, Charles D** — Government Official
Mintz Levin Ferris Assoc, 701 Pennsylvania Ave NW, Washington DC 20004, USA
**Ferris, John** — Swimmer
1961 Klamath River Dr, Rancho Cordova CA 95670, USA
**Ferris, Michael (Mike)** — Writer, Producer, Actor
United Talent Agency, U T A Plaza, 9336 Civic Center Dr, Beverly Hills CA 90210 USA
**Ferriss, David M (Boo)** — Baseball Player
510 Robinson Dr, Cleveland MS 38732, USA
**Ferro, Cindy** — Golfer
1901 Brookside Dr, Scotch Plains NJ 07076, USA
**Ferro, Tiziano** — Singer, Songwriter
EMI Italiana, Via Bergamo 315, 21402 Coronno Pertusella, Italy
**Ferron** — Singer, Synthesizer Player, Songwriter
Silverleaf Booking, 589 W 1st St, Bolling Springs PA 17007, USA
**Ferry, April** — Costume Designer
United Talent Agency, U T A Plaza, 9336 Civic Center Dr, Beverly Hills CA 90210 USA
**Ferry, Bjorn** — Biathlete
Hojdvagen 24G, 923 31 Storuman, Sweden
**Ferry, Bryan** — Singer, Songwriter
Agency Group Ltd, 142 W 57th St, #600, New York NY 10019 USA
**Ferry, Daniel J W (Danny)** — Basketball Player, Executive
145 Blackland Road NW, Atlanta GA 30342, USA
**Ferry, David R** — Writer
Wellesley College, English Dept, Wellesley MA 02181, USA
**Ferry, Robert D (Bob)** — Basketball Player
2129 Beach Haven Road, Annapolis MD 21409, USA
**Fersht, Alan R** — Organic Chemist
2 Barrow Close, Cambridge CB2 2AT, England
**Fert, Albert** — Nobel Physics Laureate
C N R S/Thales, Domaine de Corbeville, 91404 Orsay Cedex, France
**Fery, John B** — Businessman
PO Box 15407, Boise ID 83715, USA
**Ferzetti, Gabriele** — Actor
NCE Italiana, Viale Bruno Buozzi 53, 00197 Rome, Italy
**Fessel, Craig** — Cartoonist (Sandman)
40 El Camino Alto, #2306, Mill Valley CA 94941, USA
**Fessenden, Larry** — Director, Writer
Glass Eye Pix, 18 Bridge St, #2G, Brooklyn NY 11201, USA
**Fest, Howard A** — Football Player
133 Forest Circle, Bandera TX 78003, USA
**Feste, Shana** — Writer, Director
Creative Artists Agency, 2000 Ave of Stars, #100, Los Angeles CA 90067 USA
**Festinger, Leon** — Psychologist
37 W 12th St, New York NY 10011, USA
**Fetisov, Vyacheslav A (Slava)** — Ice Hockey Player
196 Rensselaer Road, Essex Falls NJ 07021, USA
**Fetter, Laurie** — Model
Playboy Promotions, 2706 Media Center Dr, Los Angeles CA 90065 USA
**Fetterman, John H (Jack), Jr** — Navy Admiral
Naval Aviation Museum Foundation, 1750 Radford Blvd, Pensacola FL 32508, USA
**Fetters, Michael L (Mike)** — Baseball Player
2411 E Cedar Place, Chandler AZ 85249, USA
**Fettig, Jeff M** — Businessman
Whirlpool Corp, 2000 N State St, RR 63, Benton Harbor MI 49022, USA
**Fetting, Katie** — Actress, Writer
United Talent Agency, U T A Plaza, 9336 Civic Center Dr, Beverly Hills CA 90210 USA
**Fetting, Rainer** — Artist, Sculptor
Andino Fine Arts, 2450 Virginia Ave NW, Washington DC 20037, USA
**Fettman, Martin J** — Astronaut, Veterinarian
1572 N Saguaro Cliffs Court, Tucson AZ 85745, USA
**Feuer, Debra** — Actress
United Talent Agency, U T A Plaza, 9336 Civic Center Dr, Beverly Hills CA 90210 USA
**Feuerman, Carole A** — Sculptor
200 Mercer St, #1F, New York NY 10012, USA
**Feuerstein, Mark** — Actor
United Talent Agency, U T A Plaza, 9336 Civic Center Dr, Beverly Hills CA 90210 USA
**Feuerwerker, Albert** — Historian
827 Asa Gray Dr, #356, Ann Arbor MI 48105, USA
**Feuerzeig, Jeff** — Director, Writer
W M E Entertainment, 9601 Wilshire Blvd, #300, Beverly Hills CA 90210 USA
**Feustel, Andrew J (Drew)** — Astronaut
4003 Elm Crest Trail, Houston TX 77059, USA
**Feuti, Norm** — Cartoonist (Gil)
King Features Syndicate, 300 W 57th St, #1500, New York NY 10019 USA
**Fewx, Gene** — Sculptor
666 15th St NE, Salem OR 97301, USA
**Fexler, Forrest O** — Golfer
6270 Old Water Oak Road, Tallahassee FL 32312, USA
**Fey** — Singer
R A C, Paseo Palmas 1005, Chapultepec Lomas, Mexico City DF 11000, Mexico
**Fey, Michael** — Cartoonist (Committed)
United Feature Syndicate, PO Box 5610, Cincinnati OH 45201 USA
**Fey, Tina** — Actress, Comedienne, Producer
3 Arts Entertainment, 9460 Wilshire Blvd, #700, Beverly Hills CA 90212 USA
**Fezler, Forrest O** — Golfer
1523 Pine St, Tallahassee FL 32303, USA

**Fforde, Jasper** — Writer
Viking Press, 375 Hudson St, New York NY 10014, USA

**Fiala, John C** — Football Player
12113 268th Dr NE, Duvall WA 98019, USA

**Fialkowska, Janina** — Concert Pianist
Ingpen & Williams, 131 Putney Bridge Road, London SW15 2PA, England

**Fiasco, Lupe** — Rap Artist, Songwriter
1st & 15th Records, 437 Brookwood Dr, Olympia Fields IL 60461, USA

**Ficarra, Glenn** — Writer, Director
W M E Entertainment, 9601 Wilshire Blvd, #300, Beverly Hills CA 90210 USA

**Ficatier, Carol** — Model, Actress
Playboy Promotions, 2706 Media Center Dr, Los Angeles CA 90065 USA

**Ficca, Billy** — Drummer (Television, Waitresses)
Primary Talent International, 10-11 Jockey's Fields, London WC1R 4BN, England

**Ficca, Daniel R (Dan)** — Football Player
151 Kansas Lane, Kulpmont PA 17834, USA

**Fichaud, Eric** — Ice Hockey Player
191 Rue Charron, Lemoyne QC J4R 2K6, Canada

**Fichtel-Mauritz, Anja** — Fencer
Stauferring 104, 97941 Taunerbischofsheim, Germany

**Fichter, Michael (Mike)** — Baseball Umpire
2942 192nd Place, Lansing IL 60438, USA

**Fichter, Rick T** — Cinematographer
3630 Cabrillo St, San Francisco CA 94121, USA

**Fichtner, Hans J** — Space Scientist
612 Cleermont Dr SE, Huntsville AL 35801, USA

**Fichtner, Ross W** — Football Player
46833 Danbridge St, Plymouth MI 48170, USA

**Fichtner, William (Bill)** — Actor
Paradigm Agency, 360 N Crescent Dr, North Building, Beverly Hills CA 90210 USA

**Fick, Robert C** — Baseball Player
164 Brodia Way, Walnut Creek CA 94598, USA

**Fickman, Andy** — Director
W M E Entertainment, 9601 Wilshire Blvd, #300, Beverly Hills CA 90210 USA

**Fico, Robert** — Prime Minister, Slovakia
Prime Minister's Office, Nam Slobody, 81370 Bratislava 1, Slovakia

**Fiddler, Vernon (Vern)** — Ice Hockey Player
3659 Hickory Grove Lane, Frisco TX 75033, USA

**Fiedler, Jay B** — Football Player
25 Russell Road, Garden City NY 11530, USA

**Fieger, Geoffrey** — Attorney
Fieger Fieger Schwartz, 19390 W Ten Mile Road, Southfield MI 48075, USA

**Field, Arabella** — Actress
S M S Talent, 8383 Wilshire Blvd, #230, Beverly Hills CA 90211 USA

**Field, Ayda** — Actress, Comedienne
Paradigm Agency, 360 N Crescent Dr, North Building, Beverly Hills CA 90210 USA

**Field, Chelsea** — Actress
Allegory Creative Mgmt, 13261 Moorpark St, #103, Sherman Oaks CA 91423, USA

**Field, David** — Actor
Sue Barnett & Associates, 1/96 Albion St, Surry Hills NSW 2010, Australia , USA

**Field, George B** — Theoretical Astrophysicist
Harvard University Observatory, 60 Garden St, Cambridge MA 02138, USA

**Field, Helen** — Opera Singer
Athole Still, Foresters Hall, 25-27 Weston St, London SE19 3RV, England

**Field, John J (J J)** — Actor
Ken McReddie Assoc, 101 Finsbury Pavement, London EC2A 1RS, England

**Field, Nathan P (Nate)** — Baseball Player
1040 W Ridge Road, Littleton CO 80120, USA

**Field, Sally** — Actress
Hofflund/Polone, 9465 Wilshire Blvd, #420, Beverly Hills CA 90212 USA

**Field, Shirley Ann** — Actress
Roger Carey Assoc, Old House, Shepperton Film Studios, Shepperton, Middlesex TW17 0QD, England

**Field, Todd** — Actor, Director, Writer
Smuggler, 38 W 21st St, #1200, New York NY 10010, USA

**Fielder, Cecil G** — Baseball Player
6907 Smokey Brook Lane, Katy TX 77494, USA

**Fielder, Harry** — Actor
Guild House, Upper Saint Martins, London WC2H 9EG, England

**Fielder, Prince S** — Baseball Player
Detroit Tigers, Comerica Park, 2100 Woodward Ave, Detroit MI 48201 USA

**Fielding, Fred F** — Attorney, Government Official
Wiley Rein Fielding, 1776 K St NW, #300, Washington DC 20006, USA

**Fielding, Helen** — Writer
Creative Artists Agency, 2000 Ave of Stars, #100, Los Angeles CA 90067 USA

**Fielding, Joy** — Writer
Atria Books, 1230 Ave of Americas, New York NY 10020, USA

**Fields, Alexis** — Actress
Rookery, 8200 Wilshire Blvd, #100, Beverly Hills CA 90212, USA

**Fields, Edgar E** — Football Player
435 Musket Entry, Roswell GA 30076, USA

**Fields, Harold T, Jr** — Army General
126 Deer Run Strut, Enterprise AL 36330, USA

**Fields, Johnny** — Singer (Blind Boys of Alabama)
Blind Ambition Mgmt, 6 Courthouse Way, Jonesboro GA 30236, USA

**Fields, Joseph C (Joe), Jr** — Football Player
Widener University, Alumni Association, 1 University Place, Chester PA 19013, USA

**Fields, Kenny** — Basketball Player
1050 E Ramon Road, #81, Palm Springs CA 92264, USA

**Fields, Kim** — Actress
Rookery, 8200 Wilshire Blvd, #100, Beverly Hills CA 90212, USA

**Fields, Mark L** — Football Player
887 W Palo Brea Dr, Litchfield Park AZ 85340, USA

**Fields, Stanley** — Microbiologist
University of Washington Medical School, Microbiology Dept, Seattle WA 98195, USA

**Fiennes, Joseph** — Actor
Ken McReddie Assoc, 101 Finsbury Pavement, London EC2A 1RS, England

F

Fforde - Fiennes

**Fiennes, Ralph N** — Actor
Dalzell & Beresford, 26 Astwood Mews, London SW7 4DE, England

**Fiennes, Ranulph T-W** — Transglobal Explorer
Greenlands, Exford, Minehead, West Sussex TA24 7NU, England

**Fierek, Wolfgang** — Singer, Actor
Scenario Agentur, Rambergstr 5, 80799 Munich, Germany

**Fierstein, Harvey F** — Actor, Singer, Writer
10106 Empyrean Way, #101, Los Angeles CA 90067, USA

**Fieser, Louis** — Inventor (Napalm)
58 Medford St, Arlington MA 02474, USA

**Fifty Cent** — Rap Artist, Actor
Shady Records, 151 Lafayette St, #6, New York NY 10013, USA

**Figaro, Cedric N** — Football Player
205 Staten St, Lafayette LA 70501, USA

**Figga, Mike** — Baseball Player
16434 Turnbury Oak Dr, Odessa FL 33556, USA

**Figg-Currier, Cindy** — Golfer
109 Blue Jay Dr, Lakeway TX 78734, USA

**Figgins, D'DeChone (Chone)** — Baseball Player
16 San Sovino, Newport Coast CA 92657, USA

**Figgis, Michael (Mike)** — Director
Red Mullet, Waterside, 44-48 Wharf Road, #22, London N1 7UX, England

**Figo, Luis** — Soccer Player
F C Real Madrid, Avda Concha Espana 1, 28036 Madrid, Spain

**Figueroa, Eduardo (Ed)** — Baseball Player
Calle 41, #AN15, Santa Juanita PR 00619, USA

**Fike, Dan C, Jr** — Football Player
23479 Wingedfoot Dr, Westlake OH 44145, USA

**Fikrig, Erol** — Immunologist
Yale University Medical Center, Infectious Disease Dept, New Haven CT 06510, USA

**Filali, Yasmina** — Actress
Agency GmbH, Under Krahnenbaeumer 9, 50688 Cologne, Germany

**Filat, Vladimir (Vlad)** — Prime Minister, Moldova
Prime Minister's Office, Piata Marii Adunari Nacional, 227033 Chishinev, Moldova

**Filer, Thomas C (Tom)** — Baseball Player
425 Fox Hollow Dr, Feasterville Terrace PA 19053, USA

**Filicia, Thom** — Actor, Interior Designer
Artist & Brand Management, 9320 Wilshire Blvd, #212, Beverly Hills CA 90212, USA

**Filigno, Jonelle** — Soccer Player
Canadian Soccer, Place Soccer Canada, 237 Metcalfe St, Ottawa ON K2P 1R2, Canada

**Filion, Herve** — Harness Racing Driver
18 Evans Ave, Albertson NY 11507, USA

**Filipacchi, Daniel** — Publisher
Hachette Filipacchi, 149-51 Rue Anatole-France, 92534 Levallois, France

**Filipchenko, Anatoli N** — Cosmonaut; Air Force General
Cosmonaut Training Center, Star City, 141160 Zvezdny Gorodok, Moscow Oblast, Russia

**Filippini, Andre** — Bobsled Athlete
Olympic Committee, Foro Italico, Largo Lauro de Bosis 15, 00135 Rome, Italy

**Fillion, Nathan** — Actor
I C M Partners, 10250 Constellation Blvd, #900, Los Angeles CA 90067 USA

**Fillmore, Charles J** — Linguist
University of California, Linguistics Dept, Berkeley CA 94720, USA

**Fillon, Francois-Charles A** — Prime Minister, France
Premier's Office, Hotel Matignon, 57 Rue de Varenne, 75700 Paris, France

**Filo, David** — Businessman, Computer Scientist
Yahoo!, 701 1st Ave, Sunnyvale CA 94089, USA

**Filson, W Peter (Pete)** — Baseball Player
1034 10th Ave, Folsom PA 19033, USA

**Fimbres, Andrea** — Singer (Danity Kane)
Bad Boy Entertainment, 1440 Broadway, #16, New York NY 10018 USA

**Fimmel, Travis** — Model, Actor
Paradigm Agency, 360 N Crescent Dr, North Building, Beverly Hills CA 90210 USA

**Fina, John J** — Football Player
5180 E Fort Lowell Road, Tucson AZ 85712, USA

**Finch, Jennie** — Softball Player, Model
3265 W Bird Haven Place, Tucson AZ 85745, USA

**Finch, Joel D** — Baseball Player
68571 Oak Spring Road, Edwardsburg MI 49112, USA

**Finch, Jon N** — Actor
London Mgmt, 2-4 Noel St, London W1V 3RB, England

**Finch, Linda** — Aviatrix
World Flight, 211 Switch Oak, Shavano Park TX 78230, USA

**Finchem, Timothy W** — Golf Executive
Professional Golfer's Assn, Sawgrass, Ponte Vedra Beach FL 32082, USA

**Finck, George C** — Vietnam War Air Force Hero
143 Beaver Lane, Benton LA 71006, USA

**Fincke, E Michael (Mike)** — Astronaut
15819 El Dorado Oaks Dr, Houston TX 77059, USA

**Finckel, David** — Cellist (Emerson String Quartet)
I M G Artists, Burlington Lane, Chiswick, London W4 2TH, England

**Finder, Joseph** — Writer
United Talent Agency, U T A Plaza, 9336 Civic Center Dr, Beverly Hills CA 90210 USA

**Findlay, Conn F** — Rowing Athlete, Yachtsman
1920 Oak Knoll, Belmont CA 94002, USA

**Findlay, Jessica Brown** — Actress
Troika, 74 Clerkenwell Road, #300, London EC1M 5QA, England

**Findley, Vern M (Rusty), II** — Air Force General
Vice Commander, Air Mobility Command, Scott Air Force Base IL 62225 USA

**Fine, Jud** — Sculptor
1366 Appleton Way, Venice CA 90291, USA

**Fine, Russell Lee** — Cinematographer
Creative Artists Agency, 2000 Ave of Stars, #100, Los Angeles CA 90067 USA

**Finer, Jeremy (Jem)** — Banjoist (Pogues)
Agency Group Ltd, 361-373 City Road, London EC1V 1PQ, England

**Finer, Lawrence** — Sociologist
Guttmacher Institute, 120 Wall St, #2100, New York NY 10005, USA

**Fingaz, Sticky** — Rap Artist, Actor
Major Independents, 22425 Ventura Blvd, #106, Woodland Hills CA 91364, USA
**Fingers, Roland G (Rollie)** — Baseball Player
PO Box 230729, Las Vegas NV 89105, USA
**Fink, Kenneth** — Director, Producer, Writer
United Talent Agency, U T A Plaza, 9336 Civic Center Dr, Beverly Hills CA 90210 USA
**Fink, Michael** — Visual Effects Editor
B U F, 7720 W Sunset Blvd, Los Angeles CA 90046, USA
**Fink, Natascha** — Golfer
Golfclub Murhof, Adriach 54, 8130 Irohnleiten, Austria
**Finkel, David** — Journalist
Washington Post, Editorial Dept, 1150 15th St NW, Washington DC 20071 USA
**Finkel, Fyvush** — Actor
C E S D, 10635 Santa Monica Blvd, #130, Los Angeles CA 90025 USA
**Finkel, Henry J (Hank)** — Basketball Player
2 Pocahontas Way, Lynnfield MA 01940, USA
**Finkel, Sheldon (Shelly)** — Boxing Promoter, Manager
Shelly Finkel Mgmt, 110 Greene St, #403, New York NY 10012, USA
**Finkelstein, Joel S** — Endocrinologist
Masssachusetts General Hospital, Endocrinology Dept, 55 Fruit St, Boston MA 02114, USA
**Finlay, Frank** — Actor
Ken McReddie Assoc, 101 Finsbury Pavement, London EC2A 1RS, England
**Finley, Charles E (Chuck)** — Baseball Player
500 Mccormick Road, West Monroe LA 71291, USA
**Finley, David** — Astronaut, Astronomer
1642 Milvia St, #3S, Berkeley CA 94709, USA
**Finley, Gerard H** — Opera Singer
I M G Artists, Hogarth Business Park, Chiswick, London W4 2TH, England
**Finley, Greg** — Actor
Paul Kohner, 9300 Wilshire Blvd, #555, Beverly Hills CA 90212 USA
**Finley, Karen** — Conceptual Artist
Creative Time, 59 E 4th St, #6E, New York NY 10003, USA
**Finley, Michael H** — Basketball Player
5934 Walnut Hill Lane, Dallas TX 75230, USA
**Finley, Steven A (Steve)** — Baseball Player
PO Box 2101, Rancho Santa Fe CA 92067, USA
**Finn, Charlie** — Actor
Brillstein Entertainment Partners, 9150 Wilshire Blvd, #350, Beverly Hills CA 90212 USA
**Finn, James (Jim)** — Football Player
12-14 Western Dr, Fair Lawn NJ 07410, USA
**Finn, John** — Actor, Director, Writer
Domain Talent, 9229 W Sunset Blvd, #710, West Hollywood CA 90069 USA
**Finn, Neil** — Singer (Split Enz, Crowded House)
Ignition Mgmt, 54 Linhope St, London NW1 7JQ, England
**Finn, Patrick** — Actor
Brillstein Entertainment Partners, 9150 Wilshire Blvd, #350, Beverly Hills CA 90212 USA
**Finn, Tim** — Singer (Split Enz, Crowded House)
Harbour Agency, 135 Forbes St, Woolloomoloo NSW 2011, Australia
**Finn, Veronica** — Singer (Innosense)
R C A Records, 8750 Wilshire Blvd, Beverly Hills CA 90211 USA
**Finn, William** — Composer, Lyricist
New York University, Music Dept, New York NY 10012, USA
**Finn-Burrell, Michelle** — Track Athlete
1801 Ocean Park Blvd, #112, Santa Monica CA 90405, USA
**Finneran, Brian** — Football Player
1905 Sugarloaf Club Dr, Duluth GA 30097, USA
**Finneran, John G** — Navy Admiral
2904 N Leisure World Blvd, #404, Silver Spring MD 20906, USA
**Finneran, Katie** — Actress
Innovative Artists, 1505 10th St, Santa Monica CA 90401 USA
**Finneran, Siobhan** — Actress
Shane Collins Assoc, 11-15 Betterton St, Covent Garden, London WC2H 9BP, England
**Finnerty, Dan** — Actor, Comedian, Musician
Gersh Agency, 9465 Wilshire Blvd, #600, Beverly Hills CA 90212 USA
**Finney, Albert** — Actor
Simpkins Partnership, 45/51 Whitfield St, London W1P 4HB, England
**Finney, Allison** — Golfer
78160 Desert Mountain Circle, Bermuda Dunes CA 92203, USA
**Finney, Tom** — Soccer Player, Executive
4 Newgate, Fulwood, Preston PR2 8LR, England
**Finnie, Linda A** — Concert Singer
16 Golf Course, Girvan, Ayrshire KA26 9HW, England
**Finnie, Roger L** — Football Player
937 NW 58th St, Miami FL 33127, USA
**Finnigan, Jennifer** — Actress
I C M Partners, 10250 Constellation Blvd, #900, Los Angeles CA 90067 USA
**Finsterwald, Dow** — Golfer
2772 Fawn Grove Court, Colorado Springs CO 80906, USA
**Fiona, Melanie** — Singer
Creative Artists Agency, 2000 Ave of Stars, #100, Los Angeles CA 90067 USA
**Fionda, Andrew** — Fashion Designer
Pearce Fionda, Loft, 27 Horsell Road, Highbury, London N5 1XL, England
**Fiordaliso, Marina** — Singer
Mithos Agency, Via Koristka 8, 20154 Milan, Italy
**Fiore, David A (Dave)** — Football Player
868 Southampton Dr, Palo Alto CA 94303, USA
**Fiore, Kathryn** — Actress
Talent Works, 3500 W Olive Ave, #1400, Burbank CA 91505 USA
**Fiore, Mark** — Editorial Cartoonist
265 Frisco St, San Francisco CA 94133, USA
**Fiore, Michael G J (Mike)** — Baseball Player
17 Silver St, Malverne NY 11565, USA
**Fiore, William J (Bill)** — Actor
Access Talent Mgmt, 171 Madison Ave, #910, New York NY 10016, USA
**Fiori, Ed** — Golfer
50 Burwick St, Sugar Land TX 77479, USA

| | |
|---|---|
| **Fiorillo, Elisbetta**<br>I U M A Mgmt, Via E Filiberto 125, 00185 Rome, Italy | Opera Singer |
| **Fire, Andrew Z**<br>Stanford University Medical School, Pathology Dept, 3000 Pasteur Dr, Stanford CA 94305, USA | Nobel Medicine Laureate |
| **Firek, Marc**<br>United Talent Agency, U T A Plaza, 9336 Civic Center Dr, Beverly Hills CA 90210 USA | Producer, Writer |
| **Fireman, Paul B**<br>Reebok International, 1895 J W Foster Blvd, Canton MA 02021, USA | Businessman |
| **Fires, Earlie S**<br>2603 Arlingdale Dr, Palatine IL 60067, USA | Thoroughbred Racing Jockey |
| **Firestone, Andrew**<br>Paradigm Agency, 360 N Crescent Dr, North Building, Beverly Hills CA 90210 USA | Actor |
| **Firestone, Roy**<br>Fat City Sports, 1906 Chet Atkins Place, #502, Nashville TN 37212, USA | Sportscaster, Actor |
| **First, Neal L**<br>9437 W Garnette Dr, Sun City AZ 85373, USA | Geneticist |
| **Firth, Colin**<br>Independent Talent Group, 40 Whitfield St, London W1T 2RH, England | Actor |
| **Firth, Peter**<br>Lou Coulson Assoc, 37 Berwick St, London W1V 8RS, England | Actor |
| **Fisch, Asher**<br>Opus 3 Artists, 470 Park Ave S, #900N, New York NY 10016 USA | Conductor |
| **Fisch, Jonas**<br>Joel Stevens Entertainment, 750 Fairmont Ave, #100, Glendale CA 91203, USA | Actor, Comedian |
| **Fischbacher, Andrea**<br>5531 Eben im Pongau, Salzburg, Austria | Alpine Skier |
| **Fischer Schmidt, Birgit**<br>Kuckuckswald 11, 14532 Kleinmachnow, Germany | Canoeing Athlete |
| **Fischer, Adam**<br>Askonas Holt, Lincoln House, 300 High Holborn, London WC1V 7JH, England | Conductor |
| **Fischer, Alain**<br>Hospitalier Necker-Enfants-Malades, 149 Rue Sevres, 75015 Paris, France | Pediatric Immunologist |
| **Fischer, Edmond H**<br>5540 N Windermere Road, Seattle WA 98105, USA | Nobel Medicine Laureate |
| **Fischer, Fanny**<br>Kanu Club Potsdam, Am Luftschiffhafen 2, 14471 Potsdam, Germany | Canoeing Athlete |
| **Fischer, Gotthilf**<br>Buro Gotthilf Fischer, Postfach 45, 71715 Berlin, Germany | Composer |
| **Fischer, Heinz**<br>Prasidentschaftskanzlei, Hofburg, Alderstiege, 1010 Vienna, Austria | President, Austria |
| **Fischer, Henry W (Hank)**<br>10367 Big Canoe, Big Canoe GA 30143, USA | Baseball Player |
| **Fischer, Ivan**<br>1 Andrassy Utca 27, 1061 Budapest, Hungary | Conductor |
| **Fischer, Jenna**<br>Odenkirk Provissiero Entertainment, 1936 N Bronson Ave, Los Angeles CA 90069 USA | Actress |
| **Fischer, Joschka**<br>Princeton University, Liechtenstein Institute, Princeton NJ 08544, USA | Government Official, Germany |
| **Fischer, Julia**<br>Kunstler Sekretariat am Gasteig, Rosenheimer Str 52, 81669 Munich, Germany | Concert Violinist |
| **Fischer, Lisa**<br>Alive Enterprises, 3264 S Kihei Road, Kihei HI 96753, USA | Singer |
| **Fischer, Patrick (Pat)**<br>PO Box 4289, Leesburg VA 20177, USA | Football Player |
| **Fischer, Stanley**<br>Bank of Israel, PO Box 780, 91007 Jerusalem, Israel | Economist |
| **Fischer, Sven (Fritz)**<br>Schillerhoehe 7, 98574 Schmalkalden, Germany | Biathlete |
| **Fischer, Todd**<br>7347 Linwood Court, Pleasanton CA 94588, USA | Golfer |
| **Fischer, Urs**<br>Gavin Brown Gallery, 620 Greenwich St, New York NY 10014, USA | Sculptor |
| **Fischer, William A (Moose)**<br>23191 Shady Oak Lane, Estero FL 33928, USA | Football Player |
| **Fischer, William C (Bill)**<br>139 Upland Dr, Council Bluffs IA 51503, USA | Baseball Player |
| **Fischer-Nielsen, Joachim**<br>Heslegardsvej 8-2, 2900 Hellerup, Denmark | Badminton Player |
| **Fischetti, Brad**<br>Evolution Talent Agency, 1501 Broadway, #1301, New York NY 10036 USA | Singer, Rap Artist |
| **Fischetti, Vincent A**<br>Rockefeller University Medical Center, 1230 York Ave, New York NY 10065 USA | Microbiologist |
| **Fischl, Eric**<br>Mary Boone Gallery, 745 5th Ave, #405, New York NY 10151, USA | Artist |
| **Fischlin, Michael T (Mike)**<br>1010 Curtright Place, Greensboro GA 30642, USA | Baseball Player |
| **Fish, Ginger**<br>Interscope Records, 2220 Colorado Ave, Santa Monica CA 90404 USA | Drummer (Marilyn Manson) |
| **Fish, Howard M**<br>15797 Dockside Court, Tyler TX 75703, USA | Air Force General |
| **Fish, Mardy**<br>S F X Sports, 846 Lincoln Road, #500, Miami Beach Fl 33139 USA | Tennis Player |
| **Fishburne, Laurence**<br>Paradigm Agency, 360 N Crescent Dr, North Building, Beverly Hills CA 90210 USA | Actor |
| **Fishburne, Rodes**<br>Delacorte Press, 1540 Broadway, New York NY 10036 USA | Writer |
| **Fishel, Danielle**<br>Levity Entertainment Group, 6701 Center Dr W, #1111, Los Angeles CA 90045, USA | Actress |
| **Fisher Hartman, Sarah**<br>Sarah Fisher Racing, 1255 Main St, Indianapolis IN 46224, USA | Auto Racing Driver |
| **Fisher, Allison**<br>Bailey's Sports Bar, 8500 Pineville-Mathew Road, Charlotte NC 28226, USA | Billiards Player |
| **Fisher, Anna L**<br>1912 Elmen St, Houston TX 77019, USA | Astronaut |
| **Fisher, Bernard**<br>5636 Aylesboro Ave, Pittsburgh PA 15217, USA | Surgeon |

**Fisher, Bernard F** — Vietnam War Air Force Hero (CMH)
4200 W King Road, Kuna ID 83634, USA
**Fisher, Brian K** — Baseball Player
3660 S Uravan St, Aurora CO 80013, USA
**Fisher, Carrie** — Actress, Writer
1700 Coldwater Canyon Road, Beverly Hills CA 90210, USA
**Fisher, Debra Mae** — Artist
2150 NW Hill St, #2, Bend OR 97701, USA
**Fisher, Derek L** — Basketball Player
25515 Prado de Azul, Calabasas CA 91302, USA
**Fisher, Eddie G** — Baseball Player
408 Cardinal Circle S, Altus OK 73521, USA
**Fisher, Edwin L (Ed)** — Football Player
4734 E Redfield Road, Phoenix AZ 85032, USA
**Fisher, Elder A (Bud)** — Bowling Executive
7551 Brackenwood Circle N, Indianapolis IN 46260, USA
**Fisher, Evan** — Singer (Diamonds)
G E M S, PO Box 1031, Montrose CA 91021, USA
**Fisher, Frances** — Actress
Greene Assoc, 1901 Ave of Stars, #130, Los Angeles CA 90067 USA
**Fisher, Frederick** — Interior Designer, Architect
Frederick Fisher Partners, 12248 Santa Monica Blvd, Los Angeles CA 90025, USA
**Fisher, Isla** — Actress
Creative Artists Agency, 2000 Ave of Stars, #100, Los Angeles CA 90067 USA
**Fisher, Jeffrey M (Jeff)** — Football Player, Coach
Saint Louis Rams, 901 N Broadway, Saint Louis MO 63101 USA
**Fisher, Jeremy** — Singer, Songwriter
Agency Group Ltd, 142 W 57th St, #600, New York NY 10019 USA
**Fisher, Joel** — Sculptor
PO Box 65, Palisades NY 10964, USA
**Fisher, Joely** — Actress
John Carrabino Mgmt, 5900 Wilshire Blvd, #406, Los Angeles CA 90036 USA
**Fisher, John H (Jack)** — Baseball Player
4407 Nicholas St, Easton PA 18045, USA
**Fisher, John Norwood** — Bassist (Fishbone)
Silverback Mgmt, 9469 Jefferson Blvd, #101, Culver City CA 90232, USA
**Fisher, Kimberly** — Model, Actress
PO Box 69330, #436, West Hollywood CA 90069, USA
**Fisher, Mary** — AIDS Activist
Charles Scribner's Sons, 866 3rd Ave, New York NY 10022 USA
**Fisher, Matthew** — Organist (Procol Harum), Songwriter
39 Croham Road, South Croydon CR2 7HD, England
**Fisher, Noel** — Actor
United Talent Agency, U T A Plaza, 9336 Civic Center Dr, Beverly Hills CA 90210 USA
**Fisher, Raymond C** — Judge
US Court of Appeals, 125 S Grand Ave, Pasadena CA 91105, USA
**Fisher, Red** — Sportswriter
Montreal Gazette, 250 Saint Antoine W, Montreal QC H2Y 3R7, Canada
**Fisher, Richard W** — Financier, Government Official
Dallas Federal Reserve Bank, 2200 N Pearl St, Dallas TX 75201, USA
**Fisher, Rob** — Conductor
I M G Artists, Carnegie Hall Tower, 152 W 57th St, #500, New York NY 10019 USA
**Fisher, Robert J** — Businessman
Gap Inc, 2 Folsom St, San Francisco CA 94105, USA
**Fisher, Roger** — Guitarist (Heart)
PO Box 1162, Woodinville WA 98072, USA
**Fisher, Scott** — Astronomer
Gemini Observatory, Mauna Kea, Hilo HI 96720, USA
**Fisher, Steve** — Basketball Coach
San Diego State University, Athletic Dept, San Diego CA 92182, USA
**Fisher, Todd** — Producer
Paradigm Agency, 360 N Crescent Dr, North Building, Beverly Hills CA 90210 USA
**Fisher, William F** — Astronaut
1119 Woodbank Dr, Seabrook TX 77586, USA
**Fishman, Alan F** — Financier
Columbia Financial Partners, 195 Montague St, Brooklyn NY 11201, USA
**Fishman, Bill** — Director
Fallout Entertainment, 3100 Airport Ave, Santa Monica CA 90405, USA
**Fishman, James H (Jim)** — Publisher
A A R P Magazine, Publisher's Office, 601 E St NW, Washington DC 20049, USA
**Fishman, Jay S** — Businessman
Saint Paul Travelers, 388 Greenwich St, #3900, New York NY 10013, USA
**Fishman, Jon** — Drummer (Phish)
Dionysian Productions, 431 Pine St, Burlington VT 05401, USA
**Fishman, Michael** — Actor
4141 Ball Road, Cypress CA 90630, USA
**Fisichella, Giancarlo** — Auto Racing Driver
Movie & Sport Mgmt, Finsgate, 5-7 Cranwood St, London EC1V 9EE, England
**Fisk, Carlton E** — Baseball Player
18705 63rd Ave E, Bradenton FL 34211, USA
**Fisk, Jason** — Football Player
2619 Regatta Lane, Davis CA 95618, USA
**Fisk, Sari K** — Ice Hockey Player
Ice Hockey Assn, Makelankatu 91, 00610 Helsinki, Finland
**Fisk, Schuyler** — Actress, Singer
Innovative Artists, 1505 10th St, Santa Monica CA 90401 USA
**Fiske, James (Jim)** — Electrical Engineer
Launchpoint Technologies, 5735 Hollister Ave, #B, Goleta CA 93117, USA
**Fiske, Robert B, Jr** — Attorney
19 Juniper Road, Darien CT 06820, USA
**Fister, Bruce L** — Air Force General
400 Regatta Dr, Niceville FL 32578, USA
**Fistric, Mark** — Ice Hockey Player
Anaheim Ducks, 2695 E Katella Ave, Anaheim CA 92806 USA
**Fitch, Janet** — Writer
Little Brown, 3 Center Plaza, #100, Boston MA 02108 USA

# F

**Fitch, Val L** — Nobel Physics Laureate
292 Hartley Ave, Princeton NJ 08540, USA
**Fitch, William C (Bill)** — Basketball Coach
627 Nerita St, #A, Sanibel FL 33957, USA
**Fites, Donald V** — Businessman
Caterpillar Inc, 100 NE Adams St, Peoria IL 61629, USA
**Fitial, Benigno R** — Governor, Northern Mariana Islands
Governor's Office, Caller Box 10007, Saipan MP 96950 USA
**Fittipaldi, Christian** — Auto Racing Driver
282 Alphaville Barueri, Sao Paulo 0640 500, Brazil
**Fittipaldi, Emerson** — Auto Racing Driver
Ave Reboucas 3551, Jardim Paulistano, Sao Paulo 05401 400, Brazil
**Fittipaldi, Lisa** — Artist
Mind's Eye Foundation, 215 Beauregard, San Antonio TX 78204, USA
**Fitts, Rick** — Actor
Gage Group, 14724 Ventura Blvd, #505, Sherman Oaks CA 91403 USA
**Fitzgerald, Annie** — Actress
Stone Manners Salners, 9911 W Pico Blvd, #1400, Los Angeles CA 90035 USA
**Fitzgerald, Caitlin** — Actress, Model
I C M Partners, 730 5th Ave, New York NY 10019 USA
**Fitzgerald, Christopher** — Actor
United Talent Agency, U T A Plaza, 9336 Civic Center Dr, Beverly Hills CA 90210 USA
**FitzGerald, Edward R (Ed)** — Baseball Player
431 Christopher St, Folsom CA 95630, USA
**Fitzgerald, Fern** — Actress
7409 Leescott Ave, Van Nuys CA 91406, USA
**FitzGerald, Frances** — Writer
Simon & Schuster, 1230 Ave of Americas, Concourse 1, New York NY 10020, USA
**Fitzgerald, Frankie** — Actor
Creative Artists Agency, 2000 Ave of Stars, #100, Los Angeles CA 90067 USA
**FitzGerald, Helen** — Actress
Paul Kohner, 9300 Wilshire Blvd, #555, Beverly Hills CA 90212 USA
**Fitzgerald, Jack** — Actor
William Kerwin Agency, 1605 N Cahuenga, #202, Los Angeles CA 90028, USA
**Fitzgerald, Larry D, Jr** — Football Player
15832 S 22nd St, Phoenix AZ 85048, USA
**Fitzgerald, Mark P** — Navy Admiral
Commander, Naval Forces Africa, PSC 809, Box 70, FPO AE 09626 USA
**Fitzgerald, Michael R (Mike)** — Baseball Player
502 Flint Ave, Long Beach CA 90814, USA
**FitzGerald, Niall W A** — Businessman
Hakluyt Co, 34 Upper Brook St, London W1K 7QS, England
**Fitzgerald, Pat** — Football Player, Coach
Northwestern University, Athletic Dept, Evanston IN 60208, USA
**Fitzgerald, Patrick J** — Attorney, Government Official
Justice Dept, Dirksen Building, 219 S Dearborn St, #500, Chicago IL 60604, USA
**Fitzgerald, Tara** — Actress
United Agents, 12-26 Lexington St, London W1F 0LE, England
**FitzGerald, Thomas** — Environmentalist
Kentucky Resources Council, 213 Saint Clair St, Frankfort KY 40601, USA
**Fitzgerald, Tom** — Ice Hockey Player
3 Samuel Phelps Way, North Reading MA 01864, USA
**Fitzgerald-Brown, Benita** — Track Athlete
Women in Cable/Telecommunications, 14555 Avion Parkway, Chantilly VA 20151, USA
**Fitzmaurice, David J** — Labor Leader
Electrical Radio & Machinists Union, 11256 156th St NW, Washington DC 20005, USA
**Fitzmaurice, Deanne** — Photojournalist
San Francisco Chronicle, Editorial Dept, 925 Mission, San Francisco CA 94103 USA
**Fitzmaurice, Michael J** — Vietnam War Army Hero (CMH)
PO Box 178, Hartford SD 57033, USA
**Fitzmorris, Alan J (Al)** — Baseball Player
17512 W 159th Terrace, Olathe KS 66062, USA
**Fitzpatrick, Leo** — Actor
Don Buchwald, 6500 Wilshire Blvd, #2200, Los Angeles CA 90048 USA
**Fitzpatrick, Stephen** — Guitarist (Veruca Salt, Ashtar Command)
S T C Entertainment, 5627 Sepulveda Blvd, #230, Van Nuys CA 91411, USA
**FitzRandolph, Casey** — Speed Skater
Janey Miller Mgmt, 1435 Cherryvale Dr, Boulder CO 80303, USA
**Fitzsimmons, Greg** — Actor, Comedian
United Talent Agency, U T A Plaza, 9336 Civic Center Dr, Beverly Hills CA 90210 USA
**Fitzsimonds, Roger L** — Financier
Firstar Corp, 777 E Wisconsin Ave, Milwaukee WI 53202, USA
**FitzSimons, Dennis J** — Publisher
Tribune Co, 435 N Michigan Ave, Chicago IL 60611, USA
**Fitzwater, Marlin** — Government Official
851 Cedar Dr, Deale MD 20751, USA
**Fitzwilliam, Wendy M** — Beauty Queen
Evolving TecKnologies, Don Miguel Road Extension, El Socorro, Trinidad
**Fix, Oliver** — Canoeing Athlete
Ringstr 6, 86391 Stadtbergen, Germany
**Fixman, Marshall** — Chemist
Colorado State University, Chemistry Dept, Fort Collins CO 80523, USA
**Fjuioka, Sachio** — Conductor
I M G Artists, Hogarth Business Park, Chiswick, London W4 2TH, England
**Flacco, Joe V** — Football Player
Baltimore Ravens, Ravens Stadium, 1 Winning Dr, Baltimore MD 21230 USA
**Flach, Ken** — Tennis Player, Coach
Vanderbilt University, Athletic Dept, Nashville TN 37240, USA
**Flach, Thomas** — Yachtsman
Johanna-Resch-Str 13, 12439 Berlin, Germany
**Flack, Roberta** — Singer, Songwriter
Red Entertainment Agency, 505 8th Ave, #1004, New York NY 10018, USA
**Flade, H Klaus-Dietrich** — Cosmonaut, Germany
Airbus Industries, 1 Rond Point M Bellonte, 31707 Blagnac Cedex, France
**Flagg, Fannie** — Actress, Comedienne
Creative Artists Agency, 2000 Ave of Stars, #100, Los Angeles CA 90067 USA

**Fitch - Flagg**

| | |
|---|---|
| **Flaherty, Joe** <br> S M S Talent, 8383 Wilshire Blvd, #230, Beverly Hills CA 90211 USA | Actor, Comedian |
| **Flaherty, John T** <br> 17 Joseph Bow Court, Pearl River NY 10965, USA | Baseball Player |
| **Flaherty, Stephen** <br> W M E Entertainment, 9601 Wilshire Blvd, #300, Beverly Hills CA 90210 USA | Composer |
| **Flaim, Eric J** <br> 52 East St, Rutland VA 05701, USA | Speed Skater |
| **Flair, Ric** <br> 5701 Providence Country Club Dr, Charlotte NC 28277, USA | Professional Wrestler |
| **Flamand, Didier** <br> U B B A, 6 Rue de Braque, 75003 Paris, France | Actor |
| **Flanagan, Crista** <br> Liberman-Zerman Mgmt, 252 N Larchmont Blvd, #200, Los Angeles CA 90004 USA | Actress |
| **Flanagan, Edward J (Ed)** <br> 10981 Clayton St, Northglenn CO 80233, USA | Football Player |
| **Flanagan, Edward M, Jr** <br> Parade Rest, 12 Oyster Catcher Road, Beaufort SC 29907, USA | Army General |
| **Flanagan, Fionnula** <br> Lisa Richards Agency, 108 Upper Leeson St, Dublin 4, Ireland | Actress |
| **Flanagan, Michael C (Mike)** <br> 5 Moss Springs Court, Henderson NV 89052, USA | Football Player |
| **Flanery, Sean Patrick** <br> A P A Talent/Literary Agency, 405 S Beverly Dr, #300, Beverly Hills CA 90212 USA | Actor |
| **Flanigan, James M (Jim)** <br> 3820 Sand Point Road, Sturgeon Bay WI 54235, USA | Football Player |
| **Flanigan, James M (Jim), Jr** <br> 4511 Wyandot Trail, Green Bay WI 54313, USA | Football Player |
| **Flanigan, Joe** <br> C E S D, 10635 Santa Monica Blvd, #130, Los Angeles CA 90025 USA | Actor, Writer |
| **Flanigan, Lauren** <br> Robert Lombardo Assoc, Harkness Plaza, 61 W 62nd St, #6F, New York NY 10023 USA | Opera Singer |
| **Flannery, John M** <br> 9002 Scottish Pastures Dr, Austin TX 78750, USA | Baseball Player |
| **Flannery, Susan** <br> Bell-Phillip Television Productions, 7800 Beverly Blvd, #3371, Los Angeles CA 90036, USA | Actress |
| **Flannery, Thomas** <br> 911 Dartmouth Glen Way, Baltimore MD 21212, USA | Editorial Cartoonist |
| **Flannery, Timothy E (Tim)** <br> 715 Hymettus Ave, Encinitas CA 92024, USA | Baseball Player |
| **Flannigan, Maureen** <br> Don Buchwald, 10 E 44th St, New York NY 10017 USA | Actress |
| **Flansburgh, John C** <br> Hornblow Group, PO Box 176, Palisades NY 10964, USA | Singer, Guitarist (They Might Be Giants) |
| **Flathman, Richard E** <br> 112 Rafael Dr, San Rafael CA 94901, USA | Political Scientist |
| **Flatley, Michael** <br> Creative Artists Agency, 2000 Ave of Stars, #100, Los Angeles CA 90067 USA | Dancer |
| **Flatley, Paul R** <br> 795 Woods Road, Richmond IN 47374, USA | Football Player |
| **Flaum, Joel M** <br> US District Court, 219 S Dearborn St,, #2302B, Chicago IL 60604, USA | Judge |
| **Flavell, Richard A** <br> Yale University Medical Center, Immunology Dept, New Haven CT 06520, USA | Immunologist |
| **Flavin, Jennifer** <br> 30 Beverly Park, Beverly Hills CA 90210, USA | Model |
| **Flavor Flav** <br> Media Artists Group, 8222 Melrose Ave, #203, Los Angeles CA 90048 USA | Rap Artist, Actor, Comedian |
| **Flay, Bobby** <br> Bold Food, PO Box 1102, New York NY 10159, USA | Restauranteur, Chef |
| **Flea** <br> Innovative Artists, 1505 10th St, Santa Monica CA 90401 USA | Bassist (Red Hot Chili Peppers) |
| **Fleck, Bela** <br> Shore Fire Media, 32 Court St, #1600, Brooklyn NY 11201 USA | Guitarist, Banjoist, Composer |
| **Fleck, Jack** <br> 12006 Edgewater Road, Fort Smith AR 72903, USA | Golfer |
| **Fleck, John** <br> Greater Vision Artists Talent, 8981 Sunset Blvd, #101, Los Angeles CA 90069, USA | Performance Artist, Actor |
| **Fleck, Ryan** <br> Management 360, 9111 Wilshire Blvd, Beverly Hills CA 90210 USA | Director, Writer |
| **Fleder, Gary R** <br> Mojo Films, Animation Building, 500 S Buena Vista St, Burbank CA 91521, USA | Director |
| **Fleeshman, Richard** <br> Independent Talent Group, 40 Whitfield St, London W1T 2RH, England | Actor |
| **Fleetwood, Mick J K** <br> Sabre Entertainment, 5737 Kanan Road, #237, Agoura Hills CA 91301, USA | Drummer (Fleetwood Mac) |
| **Fleischer, Ari** <br> Harper Collins Publishers, 10 E 53rd St, Cellar 1, New York NY 10022 USA | Government Official, Journalist |
| **Fleischer, Ruben** <br> United Talent Agency, U T A Plaza, 9336 Civic Center Dr, Beverly Hills CA 90210 USA | Director, Writer |
| **Fleischman, Paul** <br> PO Box 646, Aromas CA 95004, USA | Writer |
| **Fleischmann, Peter** <br> Filmzentrum Babelsberg, August-Bebel-Str 26-53, 14482 Potsdam, Germany | Director, Producer |
| **Fleisher, Bruce** <br> 301 Grand Key Terrace, Palm Beach Gardens FL 33418, USA | Golfer |
| **Fleisher, Leon** <br> 20 Merrymount Road, Baltimore MD 21210, USA | Concert Pianist, Conductor |
| **Fleiss, Michael** <br> Creative Artists Agency, 2000 Ave of Stars, #100, Los Angeles CA 90067 USA | Producer, Writer |
| **Fleming Jenkins, Peggy** <br> 16387 Aztec Ridge Dr, Los Gatos CA 95030, USA | Figure Skater |
| **Fleming, Andrew M (Andy)** <br> I/D Public Relations, 7060 Hollywood Blvd, #800, Los Angeles CA 90028 USA | Director |
| **Fleming, Anne Taylor** <br> Janklow & Nesbit Assoc, 445 Park Ave, #1300, New York NY 10022 USA | Journalist, Writer |

| | |
|---|---|
| **Fleming, David A**<br>PO Box 692, Lincolndale NY 10540, USA | Baseball Player |
| **Fleming, Eric**<br>A P A Talent/Literary Agency, 405 S Beverly Dr, #300, Beverly Hills CA 90212 USA | Actor |
| **Fleming, Jacky**<br>Bloomsbury Publishing, 50 Bedford Square, London WC1B 3DP, England | Writer |
| **Fleming, James P**<br>PO Box 487, Manvel TX 77578, USA | Vietnam War Air Force Hero (CMH) |
| **Fleming, Marvin (Marv)**<br>909 Howard St, Marina del Rey CA 90292, USA | Football Player |
| **Fleming, Renee**<br>Gorfaine/Schwartz, 4111 W Alameda Ave, #509, Burbank CA 91505 USA | Opera Singer |
| **Fleming, Rhonda**<br>10281 Century Woods Dr, Los Angeles CA 90067, USA | Actress |
| **Fleming, Scott**<br>2425 Elendil Lane, Davis CA 95616, USA | Government Official |
| **Fleming, Valerie**<br>Q Sports Marketing, 534 W Evergreen St, Wheaton IL 60187 USA | Bobsled Athlete |
| **Fleming, Vern**<br>10713 Brixton Lane, Fishers IN 46037, USA | Basketball Player |
| **Flemings, Merton C**<br>975 Memorial Dr, #608, Cambridge MA 02138, USA | Materials Engineer |
| **Flemming, John**<br>1409 Cambronne St, New Orleans LA 70118, USA | Artist |
| **Flemyng, Jason**<br>Conway Van Gelder Grant, 8-12 Broadwick St, #300, London W1F 8HW, England | Actor |
| **Flender, Rodman**<br>Apostle Mgmt, 9696 Culver Blvd, #110, Culver City CA 90232, USA | Director, Producer, Actor |
| **Flesch, Steve**<br>PO Box 440, Union KY 41091, USA | Golfer |
| **Fletcher, Andrew J (Andy)**<br>Reach Media, 295 Greenwich St. #109, New York NY 10007, USA | Synthesizer Musician (Depeche Mode) |
| **Fletcher, Anne**<br>United Talent Agency, U T A Plaza, 9336 Civic Center Dr, Beverly Hills CA 90210 USA | Director, Choreographer |
| **Fletcher, Christopher C (Chris)**<br>4818 La Cruz Dr, La Mesa CA 91941, USA | Football Player |
| **Fletcher, Cliff**<br>19980 N 94th Way, Scottsdale AZ 85255, USA | Ice Hockey Executive |
| **Fletcher, Darrin G**<br>9146 E 2100 North Road, Oakwood IL 61858, USA | Baseball Player |
| **Fletcher, Dexter**<br>Independent Talent Group, 40 Whitfield St, London W1T 2RH, England | Actor |
| **Fletcher, E Paul**<br>548 Mockingbird Way, Warrington PA 18976, USA | Baseball Player |
| **Fletcher, Guy**<br>Air Edel, 9100 Wilshire Blvd, #350E, Beverly Hills CA 90212 USA | Keyboardist (Dire Straits) |
| **Fletcher, Jamar M**<br>11063 Worchester Dr, Saint Louis MO 63136, USA | Football Player |
| **Fletcher, London L**<br>300 Oakmont Lane, Waxhaw NC 28173, USA | Football Player |
| **Fletcher, Louise**<br>1520 Camden Ave, #105, Los Angeles CA 90025, USA | Actress |
| **Fletcher, Martin**<br>NBC-TV, News Dept, 4001 Nebraska Ave NW, Washington DC 20016 USA | Commentator |
| **Fletcher, Scott B**<br>300 Birkdale Dr, Fayetteville GA 30215, USA | Baseball Player |
| **Fletcher, Simon R**<br>1722 N Avenue U, Freeport TX 77541, USA | Football Player |
| **Fletcher, Terrell A**<br>13889 Etude Road, San Diego CA 92128, USA | Football Player |
| **Fletcher, Thomas M (Tom)**<br>Helter Skelter, 347-353 Chiswick High Road, London W4 4HS, England | Singer, Guitarist (McFly); Songwriter |
| **Fletcher, Thomas W (Tom)**<br>9287 E 2085 North Road, Oakwood IL 61858, USA | Baseball Player |
| **Fletcher, William A**<br>US Court of Appeals, Court Building, 95 7th St, San Francisco CA 94103, USA | Judge |
| **Fleury, Marc-Andre**<br>1123 Castletown Court, Sewickley PA 15143, USA | Ice Hockey Player |
| **Fleury, Theoren W (Theo)**<br>Concrete Coatings, 4519 Manhattan Road SE, Calgary AB T2G 4B3, Canada | Ice Hockey Player |
| **Flick, Bob**<br>Bob Flick Productions, 300 Vine St, #14, Seattle WA 98121, USA | Singer, Fiddle Player (Brothers Four) |
| **Flicker, John**<br>National Audubon Society, 225 Varick St, #700, New York NY 10014, USA | Association Executive |
| **Flindt, George H**<br>PO Box 2486, Prescott AZ 86302, USA | Football Player |
| **Flint, Jill**<br>Innovative Artists, 1505 10th St, Santa Monica CA 90401 USA | Actress |
| **Flint, Keith**<br>Maverick Records, 3300 Warner Blvd, Burbank CA 91505, USA | Dancer, Singer (Prodigy) |
| **Flipkens, Kirsten**<br>Autohandel Marino Flipkens, Saint Janstraat 22, 2400 Moi, Belgium | Tennis Player |
| **Flippin, Lucy Lee**<br>713 Eagle Road, Fleetwood PA 19522, USA | Actress |
| **Fliter, Ingrid**<br>C M Artists, 127 W 96th St, #13B, New York NY 10025 USA | Concert Pianist |
| **Flitter, Josh**<br>Abrams Artists, 9200 W Sunset Blvd, #1125, West Hollywood CA 90069 USA | Actor |
| **Float, Jeffrey (Jeff)**<br>1906 University Park Dr, Sacramento CA 95825, USA | Swimmer |
| **Flockhart, Calista**<br>Industry Entertainment, 955 Carillo Dr, #300, Los Angeles CA 90048 USA | Actress |
| **Flood, Debbie**<br>Leander Club, Henley on Thames, Leander RG9 2LP, England | Rowing Athlete |
| **Flor, Claus Peter**<br>I M G Artists, Hogarth Business Park, Chiswick, London W4 2TH, England | Conductor |

| | |
|---|---|
| **Florance, Sheila** | Actress |
| Melbourne Artists, 643 Saint Kikla Road, Melbourne VIC 3004, Australia | |
| **Florek, Dann** | Actor |
| Access Talent Mgmt, 171 Madison Ave, #910, New York NY 10016, USA | |
| **Florence, David** | Canoeing Athlete |
| Frasser Florence, 160 Wilford Grove, Nottingham, Nottinghamshire NG2 2DW, England | |
| **Flores, Gene** | Artist |
| Portland Community College, Art Dept, 1200 SW 49th Ave, Portland OR 97219, USA | |
| **Flores, Rosie** | Singer, Guitarist |
| Rounder Records, 1 Rounder Way, Burlington MA 01803 USA | |
| **Flores, Thomas R (Tom)** | Football Player, Coach, Executive |
| 77741 Cove Point Circle, Indian Wells CA 92210, USA | |
| **Floria, Holly** | Actress |
| Epstein-Wyckoff, 280 S Beverly Dr, #400, Beverly Hills CA 90212 USA | |
| **Florie, Bryce B** | Baseball Player |
| 1118 Lands End Dr, Hanahan SC 29410, USA | |
| **Florin, Susan** | Golfer |
| 10342 Pontofino Circle, Trinity FL 34655, USA | |
| **Florio, James J (Jim)** | Governor, NJ |
| Mudge Rose Guthrie, Corporate Center 2, 1673 E 16th St, #16, Brooklyn NY 11229, USA | |
| **Florio, Thomas A** | Publisher |
| New Yorker, Publisher's Office, 4 Times Square, New York NY 10036, USA | |
| **Florschuetz, Thomas** | Photographer |
| Gary Tatintsian Gallery, 526 W 26th St, New York NY 10001, USA | |
| **Flory, Med** | Actor |
| 6044 Ensign Ave, North Hollywood CA 91606, USA | |
| **Flowers, Brandon** | Singer, Pianist (Killers) |
| W M E Entertainment, 9601 Wilshire Blvd, #300, Beverly Hills CA 90210 USA | |
| **Flowers, Bruce** | Basketball Player |
| 276 W Grantley Ave, Elmhurst IL 60126, USA | |
| **Flowers, Charles (Charlie)** | Football Player |
| 6170 Mountain Brook Way NW, Atlanta GA 30328, USA | |
| **Flowers, Frank E** | Director, Writer |
| Brillstein Entertainment Partners, 9150 Wilshire Blvd, #350, Beverly Hills CA 90212 USA | |
| **Flowers, Richmond M, Jr** | Football Player |
| 3434 Indian Lake Dr, Pelham AL 35124, USA | |
| **Floyd, C Clifford (Cliff), Jr** | Baseball Player |
| 3283 Birch Terrace, Davie FL 33330, USA | |
| **Floyd, Carlisle** | Composer |
| 3552 Trillium Court, Tallahassee FL 32312, USA | |
| **Floyd, Eddie** | Singer, Songwriter |
| J W Entertainment, PO Box 78904, Atlanta GA 30357 USA | |
| **Floyd, Elson S** | Educator |
| Washington State University, President's Office, Pullman WA 99164, USA | |
| **Floyd, Eric A (Sleepy)** | Basketball Player |
| 3191 Ivy Creek Road, Gastonia NC 28056, USA | |
| **Floyd, Eric C** | Football Player |
| 18047 Sailfish Dr, Lutz FL 33558, USA | |
| **Floyd, Gavin C** | Baseball Player |
| 9809 Milano Dr, Trinity FL 34655, USA | |
| **Floyd, George, Jr** | Football Player |
| 8621 Heritage Dr, Florence KY 41042, USA | |
| **Floyd, Heather** | Singer (Point of Grace) |
| W M E Entertainment, 1600 Division St, #300, Nashville TN 37203 USA | |
| **Floyd, Marlene** | Golfer |
| Marlene Floyd Golf School, 5370 Club House Lane, Hope Mills NC 28348, USA | |
| **Floyd, Michael** | Football Player |
| Arizona Cardinals, PO Box 888, Phoenix AZ 85001 USA | |
| **Floyd, Raymond (Ray)** | Golfer |
| 505 S Flagler Dr, #910, West Palm Beach FL 33401, USA | |
| **Floyd, Robert** | Actor |
| C E S D, 10635 Santa Monica Blvd, #130, Los Angeles CA 90025 USA | |
| **Floyd, Robert N (Bobby)** | Baseball Player |
| 1757 SE Dominic Ave, Port Saint Lucie FL 34952, USA | |
| **Floyd, Susan** | Actress |
| Untitled Entertainment, 350 S Beverly Dr, #200, Beverly Hills CA 90212 USA | |
| **Floyd, Tim** | Basketball Coach |
| University of Texas, Athletic Dept, El Paso TX 79968, USA | |
| **Floyd, William A** | Football Player |
| 7827 Glen Echo Road, Jacksonville FL 32211, USA | |
| **Fluckey, Tim** | Guitarist, Pianist (Adema) |
| Novi Entertainment, PO Box 17077, Beverly Hills CA 90209, USA | |
| **Fluegel, Darlanne** | Actress |
| Shelter Entertainment, 9255 Sunset Blvd, #300, Los Angeles CA 90069 USA | |
| **Flueger, Patrick John** | Actor |
| United Talent Agency, U T A Plaza, 9336 Civic Center Dr, Beverly Hills CA 90210 USA | |
| **Flutie, Douglas R (Doug)** | Football Player, Sportscaster |
| 22 Chieftain Lane, Natick MA 01760, USA | |
| **Flynn, George W** | Chemist |
| 382 Summit Ave, Leonia NJ 07605, USA | |
| **Flynn, Jackie** | Actress, Comedienne |
| Don Buchwald, 6500 Wilshire Blvd, #2200, Los Angeles CA 90048 USA | |
| **Flynn, Jerome** | Actor |
| Rights House, Drury House, 34-43 Russell St, London WC2B 5HA, England | |
| **Flynn, Johnny** | Singer, Musician |
| Agency Group Ltd, 1880 Century Park, #711, Los Angeles CA 90067 USA | |
| **Flynn, Jonny F** | Basketball Player |
| Portland Trail Blazers, Rose Garden, 1 N Center Court St, Portland OR 97227 USA | |
| **Flynn, Matt** | Drummer (Maroon 5) |
| J Records, 745 5th Ave, #600, New York NY 10151 USA | |
| **Flynn, Michael D (Mike)** | Basketball Player |
| 3934 E Battala Ave, Gilbert AZ 85297, USA | |
| **Flynn, Michael P (Mike)** | Football Player |
| 1922 Clifden Road, Catonsville MD 21228, USA | |
| **Flynn, R Douglas (Doug), Jr** | Baseball Player |
| 2465 Vale Dr, Lexington KY 40514, USA | |

**Flynn, Raymond L** — Mayor, Boston; Diplomat
Catholic Alliance, Via Catholic City, PO Box 1872, Chesapeake VA 23327, USA
**Flynn, Sean** — Actor
Innovative Artists, 1505 10th St, Santa Monica CA 90401 USA
**Flynn, Thomas J (Tom)** — Football Player
4008 Holiday Park Dr, Murrysville PA 15668, USA
**Flynt, Larry** — Publisher
Larry Flynt Publications Inc, 8484 Wilshire Blvd, #900, Beverly Hills CA 90211, USA
**Fo, Dario** — Nobel Literature Laureate
C T F R, Corso di Porta Romana 132, 20122 Milan, Italy
**Foa, Barrett** — Actor
Jackoway Tyerman Wertheimer, 1925 Century Park E, #2200, Los Angeles CA 90067 USA
**Foad, James** — Rowing Athlete
Molesey Boat Club, Barge Walk, East Molesey KT8 9AJ, England
**Foale, C Michael (Mike)** — Astronaut
2101 Todville Road, #11, Seabrook TX 77586, USA
**Foale, Marion A** — Fashion Designer
Foale Ltd, 133A Long St, Atherstone, Warwicks CV9 1AD, England
**Fobbs, Brandon** — Actor
Stone Manners Salners, 9911 W Pico Blvd, #1400, Los Angeles CA 90035 USA
**Foege, William H** — Public Health Executive
PO Box 450989, Atlanta GA 31145, USA
**Foeger, Luggi** — Skier
Christopher Foeger, 230 S Balsamina Way, Portola Valley CA 94028, USA
**Foer, Jonathan Safran** — Writer
Little Brown, 237 Park Ave, #1300, New York NY 10017, USA
**Foerster, Paul** — Yachtsman
126 Dunford Dr, Rockwall TX 75032, USA
**Fofana, Mohamed Said** — Prime Minister, Guinea
Prime Minister's Office, PO Box 5141, Cite des Nations, Conakry, Guinea
**Fogarty, Thomas J** — Inventor (Embolectomy Catheter)
Thomas Fogarty Winery, 3270 Alpine Road, Portola Valley CA 94028, USA
**Fogel, Daniel M** — Educator
University of Vermont, President's Office, Burlington VT 05405, USA
**Fogerty, John** — Singer, Guitarist, Songwriter
Paradigm Agency, 360 N Crescent Dr, North Building, Beverly Hills CA 90210 USA
**Fogg, Joshua S (Josh)** — Baseball Player
4910 S Quincy St, Tampa FL 33611, USA
**Fogle, Larry** — Basketball Player
72 Beechwood St, Rochester NY 14609, USA
**Fogleman, Ronald R (Ron)** — Air Force General
406 Snowshoe Lane, Durango CO 81301, USA
**Fogler, Dan** — Actor
W M E Entertainment, 9601 Wilshire Blvd, #300, Beverly Hills CA 90210 USA
**Fogler, Eddie** — Basketball Coach
University of South Carolina, Athletic Dept, Columbia SC 33233, USA
**Foglesong, Robert H (Doc)** — Air Force General, Educator
Council on Foreign Relations, 58 E 68th St, New York NY 10065, USA
**Fohrer, Alan J** — Businessman
Edison International, 2244 Walnut Grove Ave, Rosemead CA 91770, USA
**Foiles, Henry L (Hank), Jr** — Baseball Player
4333 Silverleaf Court, Virginia Beach VA 23462, USA
**Fois, Marina** — Actress
U B B A - Cecile Feisenberg, 6 Rue de Braque, 75003 Paris, France
**Fok, Clarence** — Director
Becsey Wisdom Kalajian, 849 S Wooster St, #7, Los Angeles CA 90035, USA
**Fokin, Vitold P** — Prime Minister, Ukraine
Vezkhovna Rada, M Hrushevskoho Rul 5, 252019 Kiev, Ukraine
**Folau, Spencer S** — Football Player
14003 Woodens Lane, Reisterstown MD 21136, USA
**Folds, Ben** — Singer, Pianist, Songwriter
Primary Talent International, 10-11 Jockey's Fields, London WC1R 4BN, England
**Foley, Alina** — Actress
Seven Summits Mgmt, 8906 W Olympic Blvd, Beverly Hills CA 90211 USA
**Foley, Dave** — Football Player
4500 Redmond Road, Springfield OH 45505, USA
**Foley, David S (Dave)** — Actor, Comedian
A P A Talent/Literary Agency, 405 S Beverly Dr, #300, Beverly Hills CA 90212 USA
**Foley, Gerry** — Ice Hockey Player
352 Skead Road, Garson ON P3L 1N4, Canada
**Foley, James** — Director
W M E Entertainment, 9601 Wilshire Blvd, #300, Beverly Hills CA 90210 USA
**Foley, Kathleen** — Neurologist
Memorial Sloan Kettering Cancer Center, 1275 York Ave, New York NY 10065 USA
**Foley, Mark A** — Representative, FL; Commentator
WSVU-FM, News Dept, 8895 N Military Trail, West Palm Beach FL 33410, USA
**Foley, Marvis E (Marv)** — Baseball Player
10166 Glenmore Ave, Bradenton FL 34202, USA
**Foley, Maurice B** — Judge
US Tax Court, 400 2nd St NW, Washington DC 20217, USA
**Foley, Robert F** — Vietnam War Army Hero (CMH), General
2121 Jamieson Ave, #606, Alexandria VA 22314, USA
**Foley, Scott** — Actor
I C M Partners, 10250 Constellation Blvd, #900, Los Angeles CA 90067 USA
**Foley, Stephen J (Steve)** — Football Player
6321 S Newport Circle, Centennial CO 80111, USA
**Foley, Sue** — Singer, Guitarist, Songwriter
Agency Group, 2 Berkeley St, #202, Toronto ON M5A 4J5, Canada
**Foley, Sylvester R, Jr** — Navy Admiral
50 Apple Hill Dr, Tewksbury MA 01876, USA
**Foley, Thomas D (Tim)** — Football Player
3029 Isola Bella Blvd, Mount Dora FL 32757, USA
**Foley, Thomas M (Tom)** — Baseball Player
5237 Karlsburg Place, Palm Harbor FL 34685, USA
**Folger, Franklin** — Cartoonist
King Features Syndicate, 300 W 57th St, #1500, New York NY 10019 USA

**Folguera, Ruy** — Composer
Gorfaine/Schwartz, 4111 W Alameda Ave, #509, Burbank CA 91505 USA
**Foli, Timothy J (Tim)** — Baseball Player
525 Timberline Dr, Lenoir City TN 37772, USA
**Folk, Nicholas A (Nick)** — Football Player
New York Jets, 1 Jets Dr, Florham Park NJ 07932 USA
**Folk, Robert** — Composer
A S C A P, 7920 Sunset Blvd, #300, Los Angeles CA 90046, USA
**Folkenberg, Robert S** — Religious Leader
Seventh-Day Adventists, 12501 Old Columbia Pike, Silver Spring MD 20904, USA
**Folkers, Richard N (Rich)** — Baseball Player
7100 3rd Ave N, Saint Petersburg FL 33710, USA
**Folkins, L Leroy (Lee)** — Football Player
8749 The Esplanade, #13, Orlando FL 32836, USA
**Folkson, Sheree** — Director
Casorotto Ramsay, Waverley House, 7-12 Noel St, London W1F 8GQ, England
**Follesdal, Dagfinn K** — Philosopher
Staverhagen 7, 1312 Slepemdem, Norway
**Follett, Ken** — Writer
Follett House, Primett Road, Stevenage, Hertfordshire Sg1 3EE, England
**Followill, Caleb** — Singer (Kings of Leon)
Vector Mgmt, 1100 Glendon Ave, #2000, Los Angeles CA 90024, USA
**Followill, Jared** — Bassist (Kings of Leon)
Vector Mgmt, 1100 Glendon Ave, #2000, Los Angeles CA 90024, USA
**Followill, Matthew** — Guitarist (Kings of Leon)
Vector Mgmt, 1100 Glendon Ave, #2000, Los Angeles CA 90024, USA
**Followill, Nathan** — Drummer (Kings of Leon)
Vector Mgmt, 1100 Glendon Ave, #2000, Los Angeles CA 90024, USA
**Follows, Megan** — Actress
Greene Assoc, 1901 Ave of Stars, #130, Los Angeles CA 90067 USA
**Folman, Ari** — Director, Writer
Creative Artists Agency, 2000 Ave of Stars, #100, Los Angeles CA 90067 USA
**Folsom, Allan R** — Writer
Marion Rosenberg, PO Box 69826, West Hollywood CA 90069 USA
**Folsom, James E (Jim), Jr** — Governor, AL
1482 Orchard Dr NE, Cullman AL 35055, USA
**Folsome, Claire** — Microbiologist
University of Hawaii, Microbiology Dept, 2600 Campus Road, Honolulu HI 96822, USA
**Folta, Danelle M** — Model
537 S Highland Ave, Winter Garden FL 34787, USA
**Fonda, Bridget** — Actress
I F A Talent Agency, 8730 W Sunset Blvd, #490, West Hollywood CA 90069 USA
**Fonda, Jane** — Actress
Fonda Foundation, PO Box 5840, Atlanta GA 31107, USA
**Fonda, Peter** — Actor
Indian Hills Ranch, RR 38G, Box 2024, Livingston MT 59047, USA
**Foner, Eric** — Historian
606 W 116th St, New York NY 10027, USA
**Fong, Bobby** — Educator
Ursinus College, President's Office, 601 E Main St, Collegeville PA 19426, USA
**Fonseca, Caio** — Artist
Charles Cowles, 210 11th Ave, #500, New York NY 10001, USA
**Fonseca, Lyndsy** — Actress
I C M Partners, 10250 Constellation Blvd, #900, Los Angeles CA 90067 USA
**Fonsi, Luis** — Singer, Songwriter
Tony Mojena Entertainment, 463 Sergio Cuevas Bustamante, San Juan PR 00198, USA
**Fontaine, Joan** — Actress
PO Box 222600, Carmel CA 93922, USA
**Fontaine, Levi** — Basketball Player
25 11th Ave, San Mateo CA 94401, USA
**Fontaine, Lucien** — Thoroughbred Racing Jockey
1680 Riverwood Lane, Coral Springs FL 33071, USA
**Fontaine, Maurice A** — Physiologist
25 Rue Pierre Nicole, 75005 Paris, France
**Fontana, Arianna** — Speed Skater
23010 Berbenno di Valtellina (SO), Italy
**Fontana, Isabeli** — Model
Women Model Mgmt, 199 Lafayette St, #700, New York NY 10012 USA
**Fontana, Wayne** — Singer
Brian Gannon Mgmt, PO Box 106, Rochdale OL16 4HW, England
**Fontas, Jon** — Ice Hockey Player
38a Worthen Road, #1, Lexington MA 02421, USA
**Fontenot, Jerry P** — Football Player
938 Bristol Dr, Deerfield IL 60015, USA
**Fontenot, S Ray** — Baseball Player
1674 N Crestview Dr, Lake Charles LA 70605, USA
**Fontes, Wayne H** — Football Player, Coach
2043 Harbour Watch Circle, Tarpon Springs FL 34689, USA
**Fonteyne, Valere R (Val)** — Ice Hockey Player
5403 52nd Ave, Wetaskiwin AB T9A 0X8, Canada
**Fonville, Chad E** — Baseball Player
2338 Piney Green Road, Midway Park NC 28544, USA
**Fonville, Charles** — Track Athlete
1845 Wintergreen Court, Ann Arbor MI 48103, USA
**Foo, Sharin** — Singer, Guitarist, Bassist (Raveonettes)
Orchard, 100 Park Ave, #200, New York NY 10017, USA
**Foor, James E (Jim)** — Baseball Player
2018 Bolsover St, Houston TX 77005, USA
**Foote, Adam D V** — Ice Hockey Player
4656 S Ogden St, Englewood CO 80113, USA
**Foote, Barry C** — Baseball Player
2588 High Hammock Road, Johns Island SC 29455, USA
**Foote, Dan** — Editorial Cartoonist
Dallas Times Herald, Editorial Dept, Herald Square, Dallas TX 75202, USA
**Foppert, Jesse** — Baseball Player
PO Box 150682, San Rafael CA 94915, USA

**Foray, June** — Actress
22745 Erwin St, Woodland Hills CA 91367, USA
**Forbert, Steve** — Singer, Guitarist, Songwriter
W N S Group, 6 Rolyn Hills Dr, Orangeburg NY 10962, USA
**Forbes, James A, Jr** — Religious Leader
Riverside Church, Senior Minister Office, 490 Riverside Dr, New York NY 10027, USA
**Forbes, Malcolm S (Steve), Jr** — Editor
Forbes, President's Office, 60 5th Ave, New York NY 10011, USA
**Forbes, Maya** — Producer, Writer
I C M Partners, 10250 Constellation Blvd, #900, Los Angeles CA 90067 USA
**Forbes, Michelle R** — Actress
Hofflund/Polone, 9465 Wilshire Blvd, #420, Beverly Hills CA 90212 USA
**Forbes, West** — Singer (Five Satins)
Paramount Entertainment, PO Box 12, Far Hills NJ 07931 USA
**Forbes-Robinson, Elliott** — Auto Racing Driver
7118 Vinewood Road, Sherrills Ford NC 28673, USA
**Forbis, Clifton** — Opera Singer
Columbia Artists Mgmt Inc, 1790 Broadway, #702, New York NY 10019 USA
**Force, John** — Drag Racing Driver
John Force Racing, 22722 Old Canal Road, Yorba Linda CA 92887, USA
**Forciniti, Rosalba** — Judo Athlete
Federazione Judo Lotta Karate, Via dei Sandolini 79, 00122 Rome, Italy
**Ford, Alissa** — Actress
Innovative Artists, 1505 10th St, Santa Monica CA 90401 USA
**Ford, Atina** — Curling Athlete
Curling Assn, 1660 Vimont Court, Cumberland ON K4A 4J4, Canada
**Ford, Benjamin C (Ben)** — Baseball Player
1717 Applewood Place NE, Cedar Rapids IA 52402, USA
**Ford, Bette** — Actress
Innovative Artists, 1505 10th St, Santa Monica CA 90401 USA
**Ford, Bruce** — Opera Singer
Athole Still, Foresters Hall, 25-27 Wistrow St, London SE19 3BY, England
**Ford, Candy** — Actress
C E S D, 10635 Santa Monica Blvd, #130, Los Angeles CA 90025 USA
**Ford, Charles G (Charlie)** — Football Player
2995 South St, Beaumont TX 77702, USA
**Ford, Cheryl** — Basketball Player
New York Liberty, Madison Square Garden, 2 Penn Plaza, New York NY 10121 USA
**Ford, Christopher J (Chris)** — Basketball Player, Coach
424 N Vendome Ave, Margate City NJ 08402, USA
**Ford, Colin** — Actor
Management 360, 9111 Wilshire Blvd, Beverly Hills CA 90210 USA
**Ford, Courtney** — Actress
Main Title Mgmt, 8383 Wilshire Blvd, #408, Beverly Hills CA 90211 USA
**Ford, Darnell G (Dan)** — Baseball Player
1271 Linton Road, Benton LA 71006, USA
**Ford, Donald (Don)** — Basketball Player
519 W Quinto St, #B, Santa Barbara CA 93105, USA
**Ford, Douglas (Doug)** — Golfer
3737 Gulfstream Road, Delray Beach FL 33483, USA
**Ford, Edward C (Whitey)** — Baseball Player
PO Box 160, Sea Cliff NY 11579, USA
**Ford, Eileen O** — Businesswoman
Ford Models Inc, 111 5th Ave, #900, New York NY 10003 USA
**Ford, Faith** — Actress
Hofflund/Polone, 9465 Wilshire Blvd, #420, Beverly Hills CA 90212 USA
**Ford, Frankie** — Singer, Songwriter
Sea Cruise Productions, PO Box 1875, Gretna LA 70054, USA
**Ford, Gilbert (Gib)** — Basketball Player, Coach
264 Edgemere Way E, Naples FL 34105, USA
**Ford, Harrison** — Actor
3555 N Moose Wilson Road, Jackson Hole WY 83001, USA
**Ford, Henry** — Football Player
7222 Shannon Road, Verona PA 15147, USA
**Ford, J Lewis (Lew)** — Baseball Player
2201 Lady Cornwall Dr, Lewisville TX 75056, USA
**Ford, Jack** — Commentator
CBS-TV, News Dept, 51 W 52nd St, New York NY 10019 USA
**Ford, Katie** — Businesswoman
Ford Models Inc, 111 5th Ave, #900, New York NY 10003 USA
**Ford, Kevin A** — Astronaut
3526 E 200 N, Hartford City IN 47348, USA
**Ford, Lita** — Singer, Guitarist (Runaways)
Monterey International, 200 W Superior St, #202, Chicago IL 60654 USA
**Ford, Luke** — Actor
W K T Public Relations, 9350 Wilshire Blvd, #450, Beverly Hills CA 90212 USA
**Ford, Maria** — Actress
Momentum Talent, 9401 Wilshire Blvd, #501, Beverly Hills CA 90212, USA
**Ford, Mark** — Publisher
Time Inc Sports Group, Publisher's Office, Time-Life Building, New York NY 10020, USA
**Ford, Melyssa** — Model, Actress
Don Buchwald, 6500 Wilshire Blvd, #2200, Los Angeles CA 90048 USA
**Ford, Phil J, Jr** — Basketball Player
2928 Cone Manor Lane, Raleigh NC 27613, USA
**Ford, Ray** — Actor
Rectangle Entertainment, 357 S Fairfax Ave, #414, Los Angeles CA 90036, USA
**Ford, Richard** — Writer
Ecco/Harper Collins Publishers, 10 E 53rd St, Cellar 1, New York NY 10022, USA
**Ford, Robben** — Jazz Guitarist (Yellowjackets)
Maria Matias Music, 316 Mid Valley Center, #203, Carmel CA 93922, USA
**Ford, Robert A (Bob)** — Basketball Player
202 Pathway Lane, West Lafayette IN 47906, USA
**Ford, Scott** — Businessman
Alltel Corp, PO Box 94255, Palatine IL 60094, USA
**Ford, Thomas Mikal** — Actor
Talent Works, 3500 W Olive Ave, #1400, Burbank CA 91505 USA

**Ford, Tom** — Fashion Designer, Director
Creative Artists Agency, 2000 Ave of Stars, #100, Los Angeles CA 90067 USA
**Ford, Trent** — Actor
Talent Works, 3500 W Olive Ave, #1400, Burbank CA 91505 USA
**Ford, Wendell H** — Governor, Senator, KY
423 Frederica St, #314, Owensboro KY 42301, USA
**Ford, Willa** — Singer, Model, Actress
A P A Talent/Literary Agency, 405 S Beverly Dr, #300, Beverly Hills CA 90212 USA
**Ford, William Clay, Jr** — Businessman
Ford Motor Co, American Road, Dearborn MI 48121, USA
**Fordham, Julia** — Singer, Songwriter
Lori Levee Mgmt, 1366 Miller Dr, West Hollywood CA 90069, USA
**Fordyce, Brook A** — Baseball Player
5 River Crest, Stuart FL 34996, USA
**Foreman, Amanda** — Actress
Abrams Artists, 9200 W Sunset Blvd, #1125, West Hollywood CA 90069 USA
**Foreman, Carol L T** — Government Official
5600 Wisconsin Ave, #502, Chevy Chase MD 20815, USA
**Foreman, Chris (Chrissie Boy)** — Guitarist (Madness)
I T F, Ariel House, 74A Charlotte St, London W1T 4QJ, England
**Foreman, George** — Boxer
PO Box 1405, Huffman TX 77336, USA
**Foreman, Michael J** — Astronaut
N A S A, Johnson Space Center, 2101 NASA Road, Houston TX 77058 USA
**Foreman, Walter E (Chuck)** — Football Player
9716 Mill Creek Dr, Eden Prairie MN 55347, USA
**Foremsky, Fred (Skee)** — Bowler
914 Manchester Dr, Conroe TX 77304, USA
**Forest, Michael** — Actor
1327 N Vista, #203, Los Angeles CA 90046, USA
**Forester, Nicole** — Actress
Thruline Entertainment, 9250 Wilshire Blvd, #100, Beverly Hills CA 90212 USA
**Foret, Mickey P** — Businessman
7829 Brookhollow Blvd, Frisco TX 75034, USA
**Foret, Sarah** — Actress
B/W/R, 9100 Wilshire Blvd, #500W, Beverly Hills CA 90212 USA
**Forgeard, Noel** — Businessman
85 Ave de Wagram, 75017 Paris, France
**Forget, Guy** — Tennis Player
Rue des Pacs 2, 2000 Neuchatel, Switzerland
**Forke, Farrah** — Actress
Pop Art Mgmt, 9615 Brighton Way, #426, Beverly Hills CA 90210, USA
**Forlani, Arnaldo** — Prime Minister, Italy
Piazzale Schumann 15, 00187 Rome, Italy
**Forlani, Claire** — Actress
Independent Talent Group, 40 Whitfield St, London W1T 2RH, England
**Forman, Donald J (Donnie)** — Basketball Player
1532 Gormican Lane, Naples FL 34110, USA
**Forman, Milos** — Director
Aspland Mgmt, 245 W 55th St, #1102, New York NY 10019, USA
**Forman, Stanley** — Photojournalist
17 Cherry Road, Beverly MA 01915, USA
**Forman, Tom** — Cartoonist (Motley's Crew)
10544 James Road, Celina TX 75009, USA
**Formia, Osvaldo** — Harness Racing Trainer
6501 Winfield Blvd, #A10, Margate FL 33063, USA
**Forney, G David, Jr** — Computer Scientist
6 Coolidge Hill Road, Cambridge MA 02138, USA
**Forney, Kynan L** — Football Player
2046 Skybrooke Lane, Hoschton GA 30548, USA
**Fornos, Werner H** — Association Executive
Population Institute, 107 2nd St NE, Washington DC 20002, USA
**Foronjy, Richard** — Actor
House of Representatives, 1434 6th St, #1, Santa Monica CA 90401 USA
**Forrest, Bayard** — Basketball Player
300A Squaw Valley Place, Pagosa Springs CO 81147, USA
**Forrest, Emma** — Writer
Lutyens & Rubinstein, 231 Westbourne Park Road, London W11 1EB, England
**Forrest, Frederic** — Actor
11300 W Olympic Blvd, #610, Los Angeles CA 90064, USA
**Forrest, Sally** — Actress
1125 Angelo Dr, Beverly Hills CA 90210, USA
**Forrest, Steve** — Drummer (Placebo)
Riverman Records, George House, Brecon Road, London W6 8PY, England
**Forrestal, Robert P** — Government Official, Financier
1200 Brookhaven Park Place NE, Atlanta GA 30319, USA
**Forrester, Jay W** — Inventor (Digital Storage Device)
Massachusetts Institute of Technology, Management School, Cambridge MA 02139, USA
**Forrester, Patrick G** — Astronaut
3923 Park Circle Way, Houston TX 77059, USA
**Forsberg, Fred C** — Football Player
1727 223rd Ave SE, Sammamish WA 98075, USA
**Forsberg, Peter M** — Ice Hockey Player
1155 Sherman St, Denver CO 80203, USA
**Forsch, Kenneth R (Ken)** — Baseball Player
881 S Country Glen Way, Anaheim CA 92808, USA
**Forsee, Gary D** — Businessman, Educator
University of Missouri System, President's Office, University Hall, Columbia MO 65211, USA
**Forslund, Constance** — Actress
165 W 46th St, #1109, New York NY 10036, USA
**Forsman, Dan** — Golfer
88 W 4500 N, Provo UT 84604, USA
**Forsse, Ken** — Inventor (Teddy Ruxpin), Animator
Alchemy II, 9207 Eton Ave, Chatsworth CA 91311, USA
**Forst, Bill** — Cartoonist
2320 Byer Road, Santa Cruz CA 95062, USA

| | |
|---|---|
| **Forstemann, Robert** <br> SSV Gera 1990 e V, Vollersdorfer Str 32, 07548 Gera, Germany | Cyclist |
| **Forster, Marc** <br> Management 360, 9111 Wilshire Blvd, Beverly Hills CA 90210 USA | Director, Producer |
| **Forster, Robert** <br> Don Buchwald, 6500 Wilshire Blvd, #2200, Los Angeles CA 90048 USA | Actor |
| **Forster, Terry J** <br> PO Box 711658, Santee CA 92072, USA | Baseball Player |
| **Forster, William H** <br> 10245 Fairfax Dr, Fort Belvoir VA 22060, USA | Army General |
| **Forsyth, Bill** <br> 20 Winton Dr, Glasgow G12 0QA, Scotland | Director |
| **Forsyth, Bruce** <br> Straidarran, Wentworth Dr, Virginia Water, Surrey GU25 4NY, England | Actor, Comedian |
| **Forsyth, David** <br> C E S D, 10635 Santa Monica Blvd, #130, Los Angeles CA 90025 USA | Actor |
| **Forsyth, Frederick** <br> Trans World Publishers, 61-63 Oxbridge Road, Ealing, London W5 5SA, England | Writer |
| **Forsyth, Rosemary** <br> 1591 Benedict Canyon, Beverly Hills CA 90210, USA | Actress |
| **Forsythe, Gerald (Gary)** <br> Forsythe Racing, 7231 Georgetown Road, Indianapolis IN 46268, USA | Auto Racing Executive |
| **Forsythe, William** <br> Innovative Artists, 1505 10th St, Santa Monica CA 90401 USA | Actor |
| **Forsythe, William** <br> Frankfurt Ballet, Untermainanlage 11, 60311 Frankfurt, Germany | Choreographer |
| **Fort-Brescia, Bernardo** <br> Arquitectonica International, 801 Brickell Ave, #1100, Miami FL 33131, USA | Architect |
| **Forte, Allen** <br> Columbia University, Music Dept, New York NY 10027, USA | Musicologist |
| **Forte, Donald R (Ike)** <br> 5811 Winchester Dr, Texarkana TX 75503, USA | Football Player |
| **Forte, Marlene** <br> Greater Visions Artists Talent Agency, 8981 W Sunset Blvd, #101, West Hollywood CA 90069 USA | Actress, Producer, Director |
| **Forte, Matthew G (Matt)** <br> 2067 N Laurel Valley Dr, Vernon Hills IL 60061, USA | Football Player |
| **Forte, Will** <br> Mosiac Media Group, 9200 W Sunset Blvd, #1000, Los Angeles CA 90069 USA | Actor, Comedian |
| **Fortier, David E (Dave)** <br> 150 Kingsmount Blvd, Sudbury ON P3E 1K9, Canada | Ice Hockey Player |
| **Fortier, Laurie** <br> Vincent Cirrincione Assoc, 1516 N Fairfax Ave, Los Angeles CA 90046 USA | Actress |
| **Fortin, Roman B** <br> 10741 Bell Road, Duluth GA 30097, USA | Football Player |
| **Fortner, Nell** <br> Auburn University, Athletic Dept, Auburn AL 36849, USA | Basketball Coach |
| **Fortson, Daniel A (Danny)** <br> 3447 W Blaine St, Seattle WA 98199, USA | Basketball Player |
| **Fortunato, Joseph F (Joe)** <br> PO Box 934, Natchez MS 39121, USA | Football Player |
| **Fortunato, Ron** <br> 1 Columbus Place, #N5G, New York NY 10019, USA | Cinematographer |
| **Fortune, Jimmy** <br> American Major Talent, 8747 Highway 304, Hernando MS 38632, USA | Singer (Statler Brothers) |
| **Fortuno Burset, Luis G** <br> Governor's Office, La Fortaleza, PO Box 9020082, San Juan PR 00902 USA | Governor, Representative, PR |
| **Fosbury, Richard D (Dick)** <br> 708 Canyon Run Blvd, Ketchum ID 83340, USA | Track Athlete |
| **Foss, Anita** <br> 452 S Highland Ave, Los Angeles CA 90036, USA | Baseball Player |
| **Foss, Eric** <br> Pepsi Bottling Group, 1 Pepsi Way, #1, Somers NY 10589, USA | Businessman |
| **Foss, John W, II** <br> 16 Hampton Key, Williamsburg VA 23185, USA | Army General |
| **Fosse, Raymond E (Ray)** <br> PO Box 567, Diablo CA 94528, USA | Baseball Player |
| **Fossey, Brigitte** <br> Anne Alvares Correa, 34 Rue Jouffroy d'Abbans, 75017 Paris, France | Actress |
| **Fossum, Casey P** <br> 1087 White Bluff Dr, Whitney TX 76692, USA | Baseball Player |
| **Fossum, Michael E** <br> 822 Rolling Run Court, Houston TX 77062, USA | Astronaut |
| **Foster of Thames Bank, Norman R** <br> Foster Assoc, Riverside 3, 22 Hester Road, London SW11 4AN, England | Architect |
| **Foster, Alan B** <br> 10330 Grandview Dr, La Mesa CA 91941, USA | Baseball Player |
| **Foster, Alan Dean** <br> Thranx Inc, PO Box 12757, Prescott AZ 86304, USA | Writer |
| **Foster, Barry** <br> PO Box 750, Colleyville TX 76034, USA | Football Player |
| **Foster, Ben** <br> W M E Entertainment, 9601 Wilshire Blvd, #300, Beverly Hills CA 90210 USA | Actor |
| **Foster, Catherine** <br> 19689 7th Ave NE, #351, Poulsbo WA 98370, USA | Artist |
| **Foster, Corey J** <br> 71 Pine Ridge Dr, Arnprior ON K7S 3G8, Canada | Ice Hockey Player |
| **Foster, Coy** <br> 5486 Glen Lakes Dr, Dallas TX 75231, USA | Balloonist |
| **Foster, David** <br> Paradigm Agency, 360 N Crescent Dr, North Building, Beverly Hills CA 90210 USA | Producer |
| **Foster, David** <br> 3903 Carbon Canyon Road, Malibu CA 90265, USA | Songwriter, Musician |
| **Foster, George** <br> 4057 Meadowbrook Dr, Macon GA 31204, USA | Football Player |
| **Foster, George A** <br> 15 E Putnam Ave, #320, Greenwich CT 06830, USA | Baseball Player |

**Foster, Hunter** — Actor, Singer
Gersh Agency, 41 Madison Ave, #3301, New York NY 10010 USA
**Foster, Jeffrey D (Jeff)** — Basketball Player
333 Pickwick Court, Noblesville IN 46062, USA
**Foster, Jodie** — Actress, Director
I C M Partners, 10250 Constellation Blvd, #900, Los Angeles CA 90067 USA
**Foster, Jon** — Actor
Gersh Agency, 9465 Wilshire Blvd, #600, Beverly Hills CA 90212 USA
**Foster, Karen** — Model, Actress
Playboy Promotions, 2706 Media Center Dr, Los Angeles CA 90065 USA
**Foster, Lawrence T** — Conductor
Opus 3 Artists, 470 Park Ave S, #900N, New York NY 10016 USA
**Foster, Leonard N (Leo)** — Baseball Player
699 Glensprings Dr, Cincinnati OH 45246, USA
**Foster, Meg** — Actress
741 Fort Ebey Road, Coupeville WA 98239, USA
**Foster, Robert W (Bob)** — Boxer
913 Valencia Dr NE, Albuquerque NM 87108, USA
**Foster, Roderick A (Rod)** — Basketball Player
1246 Armacost Ave, #105, Los Angeles CA 90025, USA
**Foster, Roy A** — Football Player
12110 Salem Dr, Granada Hills CA 91344, USA
**Foster, Ruthie** — Singer, Songwriter
Blind Ambition Mgmt, 6 Courthouse Way, Jonesboro GA 30236, USA
**Foster, Sara** — Actress
Innovative Artists, 1505 10th St, Santa Monica CA 90401 USA
**Foster, Scott Michael** — Actor
United Talent Agency, U T A Plaza, 9336 Civic Center Dr, Beverly Hills CA 90210 USA
**Foster, Stan** — Actor, Writer, Producer, Director
I C M Partners, 10250 Constellation Blvd, #900, Los Angeles CA 90067 USA
**Foster, Sutton** — Actress, Singer
Creative Artists Agency, 2000 Ave of Stars, #100, Los Angeles CA 90067 USA
**Foster, Todd (Kid)** — Boxer
303 13th St NW, Great Falls MT 59404, USA
**Foster, William E (Bill)** — Basketball Coach
152 Hollywood Dr, Coppell TX 75019, USA
**Fosterling, Karsten** — Rowing Athlete
13 Elder Corners, Nowra NSW 2541, Australia
**Fotiu, Nicholas E (Nick)** — Ice Hockey Player
16 Backus River Road, East Falmouth MA 02536, USA
**Foucault, Steven R (Steve)** — Baseball Player
24353 Rolling View Court, Lutz FL 33559, USA
**Foudy Sawyers, Judy (Julie)** — Soccer Player, Model, Sportscaster
6208 Colina Pacifica, San Clemente CA 92673, USA
**Fought, John, III** — Golfer
5010 E Shea Blvd, #A217, Scottsdale AZ 85254, USA
**Foules, Elbert** — Football Player
633 E Ohea St, Greenville MS 38701, USA
**Foulke, Keith C** — Baseball Player
4844 W Electra Lane, Glendale AZ 85310, USA
**Foulkes, Arthur A** — Governor General, Bahamas
Governor General's Office, Government House, PO Box N8301, Nassau NP, Bahamas
**Foulkes, Llyn** — Artist
6010 Eucalyptus Lane, Los Angeles CA 90042, USA
**Fountain, Clarence** — Singer (Blind Boys of Alabama)
Blind Ambition Mgmt, 6 Courthouse Way, Jonesboro GA 30236, USA
**Fountain, Peter D (Pete), Jr** — Jazz Clarinetist
Kuoni Destination Mgmt, 650 Poydras St, #2050, New Orleans LA 70130, USA
**Fourcade, Martin** — Biathlete
Ski Federation, 50 Rue des Marquisats, BP 2451, 74011 Annecy Cedex, France
**Fournier, Evan** — Basketball Player
Denver Nuggets, Pepsi Center, 1000 Chopper Circle, Denver CO 80204 USA
**Foust, Nina** — Golfer
901 East Dr, Morehead City NC 28557, USA
**Fouts, Daniel F (Dan)** — Football Player, Sportscaster
16820 Varco Road, Bend OR 97701, USA
**Fowke, Philip F** — Concert Pianist
Patrick Garvey, 59 Lansdowne Place, Hove, East Sussex BN3 1FL, England
**Fowler, Beth** — Actress, Singer
Gage Group, 450 7th Ave, #1809, New York NY 10123 USA
**Fowler, Calvin B (Cal)** — Basketball Player
10121 Godspeed Dr, Ocean City MD 21842, USA
**Fowler, E Michael C** — Architect
Branches, Giffords Road, RD 3, Blenheim, New Zealand
**Fowler, Mark S** — Government Official
Latham & Watkins, 555 11th St NW, #1000, Washington DC 20004, USA
**Fowler, Rick Y (Rickie)** — Golfer
Professional Golfer's Assn, PO Box 109601, Palm Beach Gardens FL 33410 USA
**Fowler, Ryan O** — Football Player
1713 Montclair Blvd, Brentwood TN 37027, USA
**Fowler, W Wyche, Jr** — Senator, GA; Diplomat
701 A St NE, Washington DC 20002, USA
**Fowles, Sylvia** — Basketball Player
2116 NW 96th Terrace, Miami FL 33147, USA
**Fowlkes, Curtis** — Trombonist (Jazz Passengers)
Cross Road Mgmt, 45 W 11th St, #7B, New York NY 10011, USA
**Fox Quesada, Vicente** — President, Mexico
San Francisco del Rincon, San Cristobal, Guanajuato 36440 CP, Mexico
**Fox, Andy** — Baseball Player
9087 Tarmac Court, Fair Oaks CA 95628, USA
**Fox, Bernard** — Actor
6601 Burnet Ave, Van Nuys CA 91405, USA
**Fox, Chad D** — Baseball Player
6007 Windrose Hollow Lane, Spring TX 77379, USA
**Fox, Charles I** — Composer, Conductor
American International Artists, 356 Pine Valley Road, Hoosick Falls NY 12090, USA

| | |
|---|---|
| **Fox, Edward** | Actor |
| 25 Maida Ave, London W2 1ST, England | |
| **Fox, Emilia** | Actress |
| Tavistock Wood Management, 45 Conduit St, London W1S 2YN, England , USA | |
| **Fox, George** | Singer, Songwriter |
| Agency Group, 2 Berkeley St, #202, Toronto ON M5A 4J5, Canada | |
| **Fox, Greg** | Ice Hockey Player |
| 323 Resource Parkway # 6A, Winder GA 30680, USA | |
| **Fox, Harold** | Basketball Player |
| 6511 Wilburn D, Capitol Heights MD 20743, USA | |
| **Fox, James** | Actor |
| Dalzell & Beresford, 26 Astwood Mews, London SW7 4DE, England | |
| **Fox, James L (Jim)** | Basketball Player |
| 4136 N 52nd St, Phoenix AZ 85018, USA | |
| **Fox, Jessica** | Actress |
| Associated International Mgmt, 7 Hatton Garden, #400, London EC1N 8AD, England | |
| **Fox, Jessica** | Canoeing Athlete |
| Penrith Valley Canoeing, PO Box 92, Penrith NSW 2751, Australia | |
| **Fox, John** | Football Coach |
| 7512 Baltusrol Lane, Charlotte NC 28210, USA | |
| **Fox, Jorja** | Actress |
| Framework Entertainment, 9057 Nemo St, #C, West Hollywood CA 90069 USA | |
| **Fox, Marye Anne P** | Educator, Organic Chemist |
| 5926 Sagebrush Road, La Jolla CA 92037, USA | |
| **Fox, Matthew** | Actor |
| Management 360, 9111 Wilshire Blvd, Beverly Hills CA 90210 USA | |
| **Fox, Megan** | Actress |
| I C M Partners, 10250 Constellation Blvd, #900, Los Angeles CA 90067 USA | |
| **Fox, Michael J** | Actor |
| B/W/R, 9100 Wilshire Blvd, #500W, Beverly Hills CA 90212 USA | |
| **Fox, Neil** | Actor, Entertainer |
| Magic 105.4, Mappin House, 4 Winsley St, London W1W 8HF, England | |
| **Fox, Paula** | Writer |
| Robert Lescher, 47 E 19th St, New York NY 10003, USA | |
| **Fox, Rachel G** | Actress |
| Paradigm Agency, 360 N Crescent Dr, North Building, Beverly Hills CA 90210 USA | |
| **Fox, Samantha K** | Singer, Model |
| Global Entertainments, PO Box 6945, Beeston, Nottingham NG9 4WA, England | |
| **Fox, Terrence E (Terry)** | Baseball Player |
| 2312 Sugar Mill Road, New Iberia LA 70563, USA | |
| **Fox, Timothy R (Tim)** | Football Player |
| 11 Glover Ave, Hull MA 02045, USA | |
| **Fox, Tom** | Opera Singer |
| Columbia Artists Mgmt Inc, 1790 Broadway, #702, New York NY 10019 USA | |
| **Fox, Ulrich A (Rick)** | Basketball Player, Actor |
| 17530 Ventura Blvd, #201, Encino CA 91316, USA | |
| **Fox, Vernon L, III** | Football Player |
| 6704 Willow Run Court, Las Vegas NV 89108, USA | |
| **Fox, Vivica A** | Actress |
| Foxy Brown Productions, PO Box 6305, Woodland Hills CA 91365, USA | |
| **Fox, Wesley L** | Vietnam War Marine Corps Hero (CMH) |
| 855 Deercraft Dr, Blacksburg VA 24060, USA | |
| **Fox-Pitt, William S** | Equestrian |
| Barled Farmhouse, Hinton-Sainte-Mary/Sturminster Newton, Dorset DT10 1NA, England | |
| **Foxworth, Robert** | Actor |
| C E S D, 10635 Santa Monica Blvd, #130, Los Angeles CA 90025 USA | |
| **Foxworthy, Jeff** | Actor, Comedian |
| Parallel Entertainment, 9420 Wilshire Blvd, #250, Beverly Hills CA 90212 USA | |
| **Foxx, Anthony R** | Secretary, Transportation |
| Transportation Department, 400 7th St SW, Washington DC 20590 USA | |
| **Foxx, Jamie** | Actor, Comedian, Singer |
| 4477 Sherman Oaks Circle, Sherman Oaks CA 91403, USA | |
| **Foyle, Adonal D** | Basketball Player |
| 174 Crestview Dr, Orinda CA 94563, USA | |
| **Foyt, Anthony J (A J), Jr** | Auto Racing Driver |
| Foyt Racing, 19480 Stokes Road, Waller TX 77484, USA | |
| **Foytack, Paul E** | Baseball Player |
| 1910 Portview Dr, Spring Hill TN 37174, USA | |
| **Frabotta, Don** | Actor |
| PO Box 962, Douglas MA 01516, USA | |
| **Fraccaro, Walter** | Opera Singer |
| Opera et Concert, 37 Rue de la Chaussee d'Antin, 75009 Paris, France | |
| **Fradon, Dana** | Cartoonist |
| 2 Brushy Hill Road, Newtown CT 06470, USA | |
| **Fradon, Ramona** | Cartoonist (Brenda Starr) |
| Tribune Media Services, 435 N Michigan Ave, #1500, Chicago IL 60611 USA | |
| **Frailing, Kenneth D (Ken)** | Baseball Player |
| 2150 Shadow Oaks Road, Sarasota FL 34240, USA | |
| **Frain, James** | Actor |
| A P A Talent/Literary Agency, 405 S Beverly Dr, #300, Beverly Hills CA 90212 USA | |
| **Fraisse, Robert** | Cinematographer |
| Paradigm Agency, 360 N Crescent Dr, North Building, Beverly Hills CA 90210 USA | |
| **Fraiture, Nikolai** | Bassist (Strokes) |
| M V O Ltd, 370 7th Ave, #807, New York NY 10001, USA | |
| **Frakes, Jonathan** | Actor, Director |
| Paradigm Agency, 360 N Crescent Dr, North Building, Beverly Hills CA 90210 USA | |
| **Fraley, Mark** | Football Coach |
| Northern Iowa University, Athletic Dept, Cedar Falls IA 50614, USA | |
| **Fralic, William (Bill)** | Football Player |
| 280 Galsworthy Court, Roswell GA 30075, USA | |
| **Frampton, Peter** | Singer, Guitarist, Songwriter |
| W M E Entertainment, 1325 Ave of Americas, New York NY 10019 USA | |
| **France, Brian** | Auto Racing Executive |
| 1151 N Halifax Ave, Daytona Beach FL 32118, USA | |
| **France, David** | Producer, Director, Writer |
| W M E Entertainment, 9601 Wilshire Blvd, #300, Beverly Hills CA 90210 USA | |

|  |  |
|---|---|
| **France, F Douglas (Doug), Jr**<br>6056 Great Falls Ave, Las Vegas NV 89110, USA | Football Player |
| **Francella, Meaghan**<br>16 Maywood Ave, Port Chester NY 10573, USA | Golfer |
| **Franchitti, G Dario M**<br>G P Sports Mgmt, 299 Milwaukee St, #329, Denver CO 80020, USA | Auto Racing Driver |
| **Francia, Susan**<br>1022 Kipling Road, Jenkintown PA 19046, USA | Rowing Athlete |
| **Francis**<br>Apostolic Palace, Vatican Square, 00120 Vatican City | Pope of Catholic Church |
| **Francis, Clarence (Bevo)**<br>18340 Steubenville Pike Road, Salineville OH 43945, USA | Basketball Player |
| **Francis, Connie**<br>6413 NW 102nd, Pompano Beach FL 33076, USA | Singer, Actress |
| **Francis, Emile P**<br>7220 Crystal Lake Dr, West Palm Beach FL 33411, USA | Ice Hockey Player, Coach |
| **Francis, Genie**<br>Glick Agency, 1321 7th St, #203, Santa Monica CA 90401 USA | Actress |
| **Francis, Hubert**<br>I M G Artists, Hogarth Business Park, Chiswick, London W4 2TH, England | Opera Singer |
| **Francis, James**<br>2727 Crossview Dr, Houston TX 77063, USA | Football Player |
| **Francis, Jeffrey W (Jeff)**<br>3191 Quitman St, Denver CO 80212, USA | Baseball Player |
| **Francis, Mark**<br>Maureen Paley Gallery, 21 Herald St, London E2 6JT, England | Artist |
| **Francis, Norman C**<br>Xavier University, President's Office, New Orleans LA 70125, USA | Educator |
| **Francis, Robert**<br>Aeronaut Records, PO Box 361432, Los Angeles CA 90036, USA | Singer |
| **Francis, Robert E (Bob)**<br>23725 N 75th Place, Scottsdale AZ 85255, USA | Ice Hockey Player, Coach |
| **Francis, Ron**<br>12312 Birchfalls Dr, Raleigh NC 27614, USA | Ice Hockey Player |
| **Francis, Russell R (Russ)**<br>800 Putney Road, Brattleboro VT 05301, USA | Football Player |
| **Francis, Steve D**<br>632 Pifer Road, Houston TX 77024, USA | Basketball Player |
| **Francis, Wallace D (Wally)**<br>2452 Wilshire Way, Douglasville GA 30135, USA | Football Player |
| **Francis, William (Bill)**<br>Artists International, 9850 Sandalwood Blvd, #458, Boca Raton FL 33428, USA | Keyboardist, Singer |
| **Francisco, Aaron**<br>5064 W Geronimo St, Chandler AZ 85226, USA | Football Player |
| **Francisco, Don**<br>Univision, 605 3rd Ave, #1200, New York NY 10158, USA | Entertainer |
| **Francisco, Franklin (Frank)**<br>Texas Rangers, Ameriquest Field, 1000 Ballpark Way, #306, Arlington TX 76011 USA | Baseball Player |
| **Francks, Rainbow Sun**<br>Characters Talent Mgmt, 8 Elm St, Toronto ON M5G 1G7, Canada | Actor |
| **Franco Gomez, L Frederico**<br>Palacio de Gobinerno, Ave Mariscal Lopez, 1807 Asuncion, Paraguay | President, Paraguay |
| **Franco, Carlos**<br>10561 NW 51st St, Doral FL 33178, USA | Golfer |
| **Franco, Dave**<br>Paradigm Agency, 360 N Crescent Dr, North Building, Beverly Hills CA 90210 USA | Actor |
| **Franco, David**<br>Global Artists Agency, 6253 Hollywood Blvd, #508, Los Angeles CA 90028 USA | Cinematographer |
| **Franco, James**<br>Creative Artists Agency, 2000 Ave of Stars, #100, Los Angeles CA 90067 USA | Actor, Director |
| **Franco, John A**<br>111 Helena Road, Staten Island NY 10309, USA | Baseball Player |
| **Franco, Julio C**<br>651 NE 23rd Court, Pompano Beach FL 33064, USA | Baseball Player |
| **Franco, L Federico**<br>Palacio de Gobinerno, Ave Mariscal Lopez, 1807 Asuncion, Paraguay | President, Paraguay |
| **Franco, Matthew N (Matt)**<br>1008 Clear Sky Place, Simi Valley CA 93065, USA | Baseball Player |
| **Franco, Ramon**<br>Greene Assoc, 1901 Ave of Stars, #130, Los Angeles CA 90067 USA | Actor |
| **Francoeur, Jeffrey B (Jeff)**<br>3111 Willowstone Dr, Duluth GA 30096, USA | Baseball Player |
| **Francois, Jacques**<br>Artmedia, 20 Ave Rapp, 75007 Paris, France | Actor |
| **Francois, Mike**<br>PO Box 3184, Westerville OH 43086, USA | Body Builder |
| **Francona, John P (Tito)**<br>1109 Penn Ave, New Brighton PA 15066, USA | Baseball Player |
| **Francona, Terry J (Tito)**<br>750 Newton St, Chestnut Hill MA 02467, USA | Baseball Player, Manager |
| **Frandsen, Kevin V**<br>2521 Coffee Ave, San Jose CA 95125, USA | Baseball Player |
| **Frangilli, Michele**<br>Frangilli Vittorio, Via Filzi F45, 21013 Gallarate (VA), Italy | Archery Athlete |
| **Frank Chang ting Hsieh**<br>Premier's Office, 1 Chunghsiao East Road, Section 1, Taipei, Taiwan | Prime Minister, Taiwan |
| **Frank, Anthony A**<br>Colorado State University, President's Office, Fort Collins CO 80523, USA | Educator |
| **Frank, Anthony M**<br>Independent Bancorp, 3800 N Central, Phoenix AZ 85012, USA | Government Official, Financier |
| **Frank, Charles**<br>S D B Partners, 1801 Ave of Stars, #902, Los Angeles CA 90067 USA | Actor |
| **Frank, Claude**<br>Columbia Artists Mgmt Inc, 1790 Broadway, #702, New York NY 10019 USA | Concert Pianist |
| **Frank, David Michael**<br>Soundtrack Music, 229 Cloverfield Blvd, Santa Monica CA 90405, USA | Composer |

**F**

| | |
|---|---|
| **Frank, Diana** | Actress |
| The Agency, 3711 Ocean Front Walk, #1, Marina del Rey CA 90292 USA | |
| **Frank, Donald L** | Football Player |
| 2039 Weston Green Loop, Cary NC 27513, USA | |
| **Frank, Gary** | Actor |
| 861 S Bundy Dr, Los Angeles CA 90049, USA | |
| **Frank, Joanna** | Actress |
| 1274 Capri Dr, Pacific Palisades CA 90272, USA | |
| **Frank, Joe** | Actor |
| I C M Partners, 10250 Constellation Blvd, #900, Los Angeles CA 90067 USA | |
| **Frank, John E** | Football Player |
| Medical Hair Restoration, 150 Central Park S, #299, New York NY 10019, USA | |
| **Frank, Louis A** | Astronomer |
| University of Iowa, Astronomy Dept, Iowa City IA 52242, USA | |
| **Frank, Pamela** | Concert Violinist |
| Opus 3 Artists, 470 Park Ave S, #900N, New York NY 10016 USA | |
| **Frank, Scott** | Director, Writer |
| Creative Artists Agency, 2000 Ave of Stars, #100, Los Angeles CA 90067 USA | |
| **Frank, Tellis S** | Basketball Player |
| 4936 Van Noord Ave, Sherman Oaks CA 91423, USA | |
| **Franke, William A (Bill)** | Businessman |
| Spirit Airlines, 2800 Executive Way, Miramar FL 33025, USA | |
| **Frankee** | Singer |
| Levine Communication Office, 10333 Ashton Ave, Los Angeles CA 90024, USA | |
| **Frankel, Bethenny** | Chef, Entertainer, Writer |
| Creative Artists Agency, 2000 Ave of Stars, #100, Los Angeles CA 90067 USA | |
| **Frankel, Max** | Editor |
| New York Times, Editorial Dept, 229 W 43rd St, New York NY 10036, USA | |
| **Frankel, Neil** | Interior Designer |
| Frankel & Coleman, 727 S Dearborn St, #412, Chicago IL 60605, USA | |
| **Franken, Al** | Senator, Actor, Comedian, Writer |
| US Senate, Hart Office Building, Washington DC 20510 USA | |
| **Frankfort, Lew** | Businessman |
| Coach Inc, 516 W 34th St, Basement 5, New York NY 10001, USA | |
| **Frankie J** | Singer, Songwriter |
| Esterman Entertainment, PO Box 514, Riva MD 21140, USA | |
| **Franklin, Anthony R (Tony)** | Football Player |
| 117 Shady Trail St, San Antonio TX 78232, USA | |
| **Franklin, Aretha** | Singer |
| 2948 Turtle Pond Court, Bloomfield Hills MI 48302, USA | |
| **Franklin, Aubrayo R** | Football Player |
| 1 Castleton Court, Johnson City TN 37615, USA | |
| **Franklin, Barbara Hackman** | Secretary, Commerce |
| 1875 Perkins St, Bristol CT 06010, USA | |
| **Franklin, Bobby R** | Football Player |
| 384 Country Club Dr, Senatobia MS 38668, USA | |
| **Franklin, Carl M** | Director, Writer |
| I C M Partners, 10250 Constellation Blvd, #900, Los Angeles CA 90067 USA | |
| **Franklin, Diane** | Actress |
| Third Hill Entertainment, 195 S Beverly Dr, #400, Beverly Hills CA 90212, USA | |
| **Franklin, G Wayne** | Baseball Player |
| PO Box 679, North East MD 21901, USA | |
| **Franklin, Howard** | Director, Writer |
| W M E Entertainment, 9601 Wilshire Blvd, #300, Beverly Hills CA 90210 USA | |
| **Franklin, John** | Actor |
| Gilla Roos, 9744 Wilshire Blvd, #203, Beverly Hills CA 90212 USA | |
| **Franklin, Jon D** | Journalist |
| 9650 Strickland Road, Raleigh NC 27615, USA | |
| **Franklin, Kirk** | Singer, Songwriter |
| Paradigm Agency, 360 N Crescent Dr, North Building, Beverly Hills CA 90210 USA | |
| **Franklin, Marcus Carl** | Actor, Singer |
| Don Buchwald, 10 E 44th St, New York NY 10017 USA | |
| **Franklin, Melissa** | Physicist |
| Harvard University, Physics Dept, Cambridge MA 02138, USA | |
| **Franklin, Melissa J (Missy)** | Swimmer |
| Colorado Stars Swim Club, 6400 S Lewiston Way, Aurora CO 80016, USA | |
| **Franklin, Micah I** | Baseball Player |
| 3948 E Lafayette Ave, Gilbert AZ 85298, USA | |
| **Franklin, Nelson** | Actor |
| W M E Entertainment, 9601 Wilshire Blvd, #300, Beverly Hills CA 90210 USA | |
| **Franklin, Robert M, Jr** | Educator |
| Morehouse College, President's Office, 830 Westview Dr SW, Atlanta GA 30314, USA | |
| **Franklin, Ronnie** | Thoroughbred Racing Jockey |
| Max Bauer's Cabinet Shop, 12811 Folly Quarter Road, Ellicott City MD 21042, USA | |
| **Franklin, Roshawn** | Actor |
| B/W/R, 9100 Wilshire Blvd, #500W, Beverly Hills CA 90212 USA | |
| **Franklin, Ryan R** | Baseball Player |
| PO Box 723, Shawnee OK 74802, USA | |
| **Franklin, Scott** | Producer |
| Protozoa Films, 104 N 7th St, Brooklyn NY 11211, USA | |
| **Franklin, Shirley** | Mayor, Atlanta |
| Mayor's Office, City Hall, 55 Trinity Ave S, Atlanta GA 30303, USA | |
| **Franklin, William** | Bowling Executive |
| 920 La Sombra Dr, San Marcos CA 92078, USA | |
| **Franklyn, Sabina** | Actress |
| C C A Mgmt, 4 Court Lodge, 48 Sloane Square, London SW1W 8AT, England | |
| **Franks, Daniel L (Bubba)** | Football Player |
| 108 Solomon Lane, Midland TX 79705, USA | |
| **Franks, Frederick M, Jr** | Army General |
| 5016 Kensington High St, Naples FL 34105, USA | |
| **Franks, Lucinda L** | Journalist |
| 64 E 86th St, New York NY 10028, USA | |
| **Franks, Michael** | Singer, Songwriter, Guitarist |
| A P A Talent/Literary Agency, 405 S Beverly Dr, #300, Beverly Hills CA 90212 USA | |
| **Franks, Tommy R (Tom)** | Army General |
| Franks Assoc, 15273 N 2280 Road, Roosevelt OK 73564, USA | |

**Frank - Franks**

**Frankston, Robert M (Bob)** — Computer Software Designer (VisiCalc)
Software Arts Inc, 675 Massachusetts Ave, Boston MA 02118, USA
**Franquin, Andre** — Cartoonist
21 Ave Belelaere, 1170 Brussels, Belgium
**Fransioli, Thomas A** — Artist
55 Dodges Row, Wenham MA 01984, USA
**Franti, Michael** — Singer (Spearhead)
Guerilla Mangement Collective, 2180 Bryant St, #206, San Francisco CA 94110, USA
**Frantz, Adrienne** — Actress
Innovative Artists, 1505 10th St, Santa Monica CA 90401 USA
**Frantz, Chris** — Drummer (Talking Heads, Tom Tom Club)
Premier Talent, 3 E 54th St, #1100, New York NY 10022 USA
**Frantz, Justus** — Concert Pianist
Osterbekstr 90B, 22083 Hamburg, Germany
**Franz, Dennis** — Actor
PO Box 5370, Santa Barbara CA 93150, USA
**Franz, Judy R** — Physicist
American Physical Society, 1 Physics Eclipse, College Park MD 20740, USA
**Franz, Ron** — Basketball Player
8590 Beaverwood Dr, Germantown TN 38138, USA
**Franz, S Todd** — Football Player
5629 N Classen Blvd, Oklahoma City OK 73118, USA
**Franzen, Jonathan** — Writer
Farrar Straus Giroux, 18 W 18th St, #700, New York NY 10011 USA
**Frasca, Robert J** — Architect
Zimmer Gunsul Frasca, 1223 SW Washington St, #200, Portland OR 97205, USA
**Frascatore, John V** — Baseball Player
PO Box 1411, Brooksville FL 34605, USA
**Frase, Paul M** — Football Player
124 Crossroad Lakes Dr, Ponte Vedra FL 32082, USA
**Fraser, Antonia** — Writer
Orion Publishing Group, Orion House, 5 Upper Saint Martin's Lane, London WC2H 9EA, England
**Fraser, Brendan** — Actor
Brillstein Entertainment Partners, 9150 Wilshire Blvd, #350, Beverly Hills CA 90212 USA
**Fraser, Curt** — Ice Hockey Player, Coach
2205 Whitney Pointe Dr, Chesterfield MO 63005, USA
**Fraser, Dawn** — Swimmer
87 Birchgrove Road, Balmain NSW 2041, Australia
**Fraser, Elisabeth** — Singer (Cocteau Twins)
International Talent Booking, Ariel House, 74A Charlotte St, #100 London W1T 4QJ, England
**Fraser, Honor** — Model
Select Model Mgmt, Archer House, 43 King St, London WC2E 8RJ, England
**Fraser, Hugh** — Actor
3 Gate Apartments, 2 Chepstow Road, London W2 5BH, England
**Fraser, J Malcolm** — Prime Minister, Australia
101 Collins St, Level 2, Melbourne VIC 3000, Australia
**Fraser, Laura** — Actress
Emptage Hallett, 14 Rathbone Place, London W1T 1HT, England
**Fraser, Neale A** — Tennis Player
21 Bolton Ave, Hampton VIC 3188, Australia
**Fraser, Toa** — Director
I C M Partners, 10250 Constellation Blvd, #900, Los Angeles CA 90067 USA
**Fraser, William M, III** — Air Force General
Commander, Air Combat Command, Langley Air Force Base VA 23665 USA
**Frasor, Jason A** — Baseball Player
15043 Landings Lane, Oak Forest IL 60452, USA
**Frassinelli, Adriano** — Bobsled Athlete
Olympic Committee, Foro Italico, Largo Lauro de Bosis 15, 00135 Rome, Italy
**Fratello, Michael R (Mike)** — Basketball Coach, Sportscaster
7642 Fisher Island Dr, Miami Beach FL 33109, USA
**Fratianne Maricich, Linda S** — Figure Skater
3352 Whispering Glen Court, Simi Valley CA 93065, USA
**Frayn, Michael** — Writer
Greene & Heaton, 37A Goldhawk Road, London W12 8QQ, England
**Frazar, Harrison** — Golfer
3208 Villanova St, Dallas TX 75225, USA
**Frazier, Amy** — Tennis Player
Octagon Worldwide, 1751 Pinnacle Dr, #1500, McLean VA 22102 USA
**Frazier, Andre** — Football Player
9650 Fallshill Circle, Cincinnati OH 45231, USA
**Frazier, Charles** — Writer
I C M Partners, 10250 Constellation Blvd, #900, Los Angeles CA 90067 USA
**Frazier, Charles D (Charlie0** — Football Player
4018 Brookston St, Houston TX 77045, USA
**Frazier, Dallas** — Singer, Songwriter
RR 5 Box 133, Longhollow Pike, Gallatin TN 37066, USA
**Frazier, George A** — Baseball Player
6886 S Evanston Ave, Tulsa OK 74136, USA
**Frazier, Guy S** — Football Player
3944 Dickson Ave, Cincinnati OH 45229, USA
**Frazier, Herman** — Track Athlete
1024 E Frye Road, #1011, Phoenix AZ 85048, USA
**Frazier, Ian** — Writer
Farrar Straus Giroux, 18 W 18th St, #700, New York NY 10011 USA
**Frazier, Kevin** — Actor
250 President St, #201, Baltimore MD 21202, USA
**Frazier, Leslie A** — Football Player, Coach
17559 Bearpath Trail, Eden Prairie MN 55347, USA
**Frazier, Owsley B** — Businessman
Brown-Forman Corp, 850 Dixie Highway, Louisville KY 40210, USA
**Frazier, Sheila** — Actress
J K A Talent Agency, 12725 Ventura Blvd, #H, Studio City CA 91604, USA
**Frazier, Stan** — Drummer (Sugar Ray)
Lava/Atlantic Records, 9229 W Sunset Blvd, #900, West Hollywood CA 90069, USA
**Frazier, Walter (Clyde), II** — Basketball Player
200 E 82nd St, New York NY 10028, USA

## F

| | |
|---|---|
| **Frazier, Willie**<br>6203 Bankside Dr, Houston TX 77096, USA | Football Player |
| **Frears, Stephen A**<br>Casorotto Ramsay, Waverley House, 7-12 Noel St, London W1F 8GQ, England | Director |
| **Freberg, Stanley V (Stan)**<br>Radio Spirits, PO Box 3107, Wallingford CT 06494, USA | Actor, Comedian |
| **Frechette, Sylvie**<br>Cirque du Soleil, 8400 2nd Ave, Montreal QC H1Z 4M6, Canada | Synchronized Swimmer |
| **Frecheville, James**<br>United Talent Agency, U T A Plaza, 9336 Civic Center Dr, Beverly Hills CA 90210 USA | Actor |
| **Frederick, Andrew B (Andy)**<br>7247 Alexander Dr, Dallas TX 75214, USA | Football Player |
| **Frederick, Kevin**<br>5701 Foxlake Dr, #A, North Fort Myers FL 33917, USA | Baseball Player |
| **Frederick-Blanchette, Marcia**<br>105 High St, Assonet MA 02702, USA | Gymnast |
| **Fredericks, Frank (Frankie)**<br>4497 Wimbledon Dr, Provo UT 84604, USA | Track Athlete |
| **Fredericks, Fred**<br>PO Box 475, Eastham MA 02642, USA | Cartoonist (Mandrake the Magician) |
| **Frederickson, Ivan C (Tucker)**<br>12414 Indian Road, North Palm Beach FL 33408, USA | Football Player |
| **Frederickson, Scott E**<br>20703 Turning Leaf Lake Court, Cypress TX 77433, USA | Baseball Player |
| **Frederik**<br>Amalienborg Palace, 1257 Copenhagen K, Denmark | Prince, Denmark |
| **Fredette, James T (Jimmer)**<br>Sacramento Kings, Arco Arena, 1 Sports Parkway, Sacramento CA 95834 USA | Basketball Player |
| **Fredrickson, Robert J (Rob)**<br>8312 N 50th St, Paradise Valley AZ 85253, USA | Football Player |
| **Fredriksson, Marie**<br>D & D Mgmt, Drottninggatan 55, 111 21 Stockholm, Sweden | Singer, Songwriter (Roxette) |
| **Free, Helen M**<br>3752 E Jackson Blvd, Elkhart IN 46516, USA | Chemist, Inventor (Glucose Detector) |
| **Free, Lloyd B (World)**<br>1131 E County Lane Road, Lakewood NJ 08701, USA | Basketball Player, Coach, Executive |
| **Freed, Jack H**<br>108 Homestead Circle, Ithaca NY 14850, USA | Chemist |
| **Freedman, Alix M**<br>Wall Street Journal, Editorial Dept, 1 World Financial Center, New York NY 10281 USA | Journalist |
| **Freedman, Eric**<br>Detroit News, Editorial Dept, 615 W Lafayette Blvd, Detroit MI 48226, USA | Journalist |
| **Freedman, Ronald**<br>1200 Earhart Road, #228, Ann Arbor MI 48105, USA | Sociologist |
| **Freeh, Louis J**<br>Saint Martin's Press, 175 5th Ave, #400, New York NY 10010 USA | Law Enforcement Official |
| **Freehan, William A (Bill)**<br>6999 Indian Garden Road, Petoskey MI 49770, USA | Baseball Player |
| **Freelon, Nnenna**<br>Ed Keene Assoc, 573 Pleasant St, Winthrop MA 02152, USA | Singer |
| **Freeman, Antonio M**<br>PO Box 450718, Fort Lauderdale FL 33345, USA | Football Player |
| **Freeman, Bobby**<br>First Class Entertainment, 483 Ridgewood Road, Maplewood NJ 07040, USA | Singer |
| **Freeman, Cassidy**<br>Paul Kohner, 9300 Wilshire Blvd, #555, Beverly Hills CA 90212 USA | Actress |
| **Freeman, Catherine A (Cathy)**<br>Jane Cowmeadow, Bron Madigan, PO Box 5138, Ringwood VIC 3134, Australia | Track Athlete |
| **Freeman, Charles W, Jr**<br>Project International, 1800 K St NW, #1010, Washington DC 20006, USA | Diplomat |
| **Freeman, Gary C**<br>PO Box 1399, Albany OR 97321, USA | Basketball Player |
| **Freeman, Gregory A**<br>PO Box 680922, Marietta GA 30068, USA | Writer |
| **Freeman, Harold P**<br>Lauren Cancer Prevention Center, 1919 Madison Ave, New York NY 10035, USA | Oncologist |
| **Freeman, Isaac**<br>Keith Case Assoc, 1025 17th Ave S, #200, Nashville TN 37212 USA | Singer |
| **Freeman, J E**<br>Opus Entertainment, 5225 Wilshire Blvd, #905, Los Angeles CA 90036, USA | Actor |
| **Freeman, Jennifer**<br>Pakula/King, 9229 W Sunset Blvd, #315, West Hollywood CA 90069 USA | Actress, Model |
| **Freeman, Jimmy L**<br>4716 E 106th St, Tulsa OK 74137, USA | Baseball Player |
| **Freeman, Jonathan**<br>Bauman Redanty Shaul Agency, 5757 Wilshire Blvd, #473, Los Angeles CA 90036 USA | Actor |
| **Freeman, LaVel M**<br>8941 Laguna Place Way, Elk Grove CA 95758, USA | Baseball Player |
| **Freeman, Martin**<br>United Talent Agency, U T A Plaza, 9336 Civic Center Dr, Beverly Hills CA 90210 USA | Actor |
| **Freeman, Marvin**<br>20135 Mohawk Trail, Olympia Fields IL 60461, USA | Baseball Player |
| **Freeman, Morgan**<br>Creative Artists Agency, 2000 Ave of Stars, #100, Los Angeles CA 90067 USA | Actor |
| **Freeman, R Matthew (Matt)**<br>Leave Home Booking, 10 W Broadway, #608, Salt Lake City UT 84101, USA | Singer, Bassist (Rancid) |
| **Freeman, Rich**<br>Paramount Entertainment, PO Box 12, Far Hills NJ 07931 USA | Singer (Five Satins) |
| **Freeman, Richard**<br>Economic Research Bureau, 1050 Massachusetts Ave, Cambridge MA 02138, USA | Economist |
| **Freeman, Rodney L (Rod)**<br>6308 Murray Lane, Brentwood TN 37027, USA | Basketball Player |
| **Freeman, Yvette**<br>Stone Manners Salners, 9911 W Pico Blvd, #1400, Los Angeles CA 90035 USA | Actress, Singer |
| **Freeney, Dwight J**<br>11021 Hintocks Circle, Carmel IN 46032, USA | Football Player |

Frazier - Freeney

**Freese, David R** — Baseball Player
Saint Louis Cardinals, Busch Stadium, 250 Stadium Plaza, Saint Louis MO 63102 USA

**Freeway** — Rap Artist
Agency Group Ltd, 142 W 57th St, #600, New York NY 10019 USA

**Freeze, Hugh** — Football Coach
University of Mississippi, Athletic Dept, University MS 38677, USA

**Fregosi, James L (Jim)** — Baseball Player, Manager
1092 Copeland Court, Tarpon Springs FL 34688, USA

**Frehley, Paul D (Ace)** — Singer, Guitarist (Kiss)
Creative Artists Agency, 2000 Ave of Stars, #100, Los Angeles CA 90067 USA

**Frei Ruiz-Tagle, Eduardo** — President, Chile
Christian Democratic Party, O'Higgins 1460, #20, Santiago, Chile

**Frei, Tanya** — Curling Athlete
Curling Assn, PO Box 606, 3000 Bern, Switzerland

**Freiberger, Marcus** — Basketball Player
985 US Highway 64 W, Mocksville NC 27028, USA

**Freidheim, Cyrus** — Businessman
Chiquita Brands International, 250 E 5th St, #2600, Cincinnati OH 45202, USA

**Freilicher, Jane** — Artist
51 5th Ave, New York NY 10003, USA

**Freire, Nelson** — Concert Pianist
Columbia Artists Mgmt Inc, 1790 Broadway, #702, New York NY 10019 USA

**Freireich, Emil J** — Physician
M D Anderson Medical Center, 1515 Holcombe Blvd, #207, Houston TX 77030 USA

**Freisleben, David J (Dave)** — Baseball Player
1326 Diamante Dr, Pasadena TX 77504, USA

**Freitas, Acelino (Popo)** — Boxer
Banner Promotions, 1231 Bainbridge St, Philadelphia PA 19147, USA

**Freitas, Rockne C (Rocky)** — Football Player
2667 E Manoa Road, Honolulu HI 96822, USA

**Frelich, Phyllis** — Actress
Artists Group, 3345 Wilshire Blvd, #915, Los Angeles CA 90010, USA

**Fremaux, Louis J F** — Conductor
25 Edencroft, Wheeley's Road, Birmingham B15 2LW, England

**French, Dawn** — Actress, Comedienne
United Agents, 12-26 Lexington St, London W1F 0LE, England

**French, Heather R** — Beauty Queen
567 Circle Dr, Maysville KY 41056, USA

**French, Jay Jay** — Singer, Guitarist (Twisted Sister)
Rebellion Entertainment, 2440 Broadway, #111, New York NY 10024, USA

**French, Kate** — Actress
Caliber Media, 9229 W Sunset Blvd, #705, West Hollywood CA 90069, USA

**French, Nicola S (Niki)** — Singer
Energise Records, 347 Caspian Way, Purfleet, Essex RM19 1LB, England

**French, Paige** — Actress
Collier Talent Agency, 2313 Lake Austin Blvd, #103, Austin TX 78703, USA

**French, R James (Jim)** — Baseball Player
PO Box 6452, Chicago IL 60680, USA

**French, Tara** — Writer
Viking Press, 375 Hudson St, New York NY 10014 USA

**Frenette, Matt** — Drummer (Loverboy)
Loverboy Touring Offices, 425 Carrall St, Vancouver BC V6A 6E3, Canada

**Freni, Mirella** — Opera Singer
I M G Artists, Hogarth Business Park, Chiswick, London W4 2TH, England

**Frenkel, Jacob A** — Economist
J P MorganChase Co, 270 Park Ave, New York NY 10017, USA

**Frenkiel, Richard H** — Systems Engineer, Inventor
Rutgers University, WinLab, PO Box 909, Piscataway NJ 08855, USA

**Frentzen, Heinz-Harald** — Auto Racing Driver
Jordan Grand Prix, Silverstone Circuit, Towcester Northhamptonshire NN12 8TN, England

**Frenzel, Eric** — Nordic Combined Skier
Wiesenstr 11, 09468 Geyer, Germany

**Frerotte, Gustave J (Gus)** — Football Player
10040 Litzsinger Road, Saint Louis MO 63124, USA

**Fresco, Michael** — Director
I C M Partners, 10250 Constellation Blvd, #900, Los Angeles CA 90067 USA

**Fresco, Paolo** — Businessman
Fiat SpA, Corso Marconi 10/20, 10125 Turin, Italy

**Fresco, Victor** — Writer, Producer
I C M Partners, 10250 Constellation Blvd, #900, Los Angeles CA 90067 USA

**Fresh, Doug E** — Rap Artist
Pyramid Entertainment Group, 377 Rector Place, #21A, New York NY 10280 USA

**Fresnadillo, Juan Carlos** — Director
United Talent Agency, U T A Plaza, 9336 Civic Center Dr, Beverly Hills CA 90210 USA

**Fretton, Anthony (Tony)** — Architect
49-59 Old St, London EC1V 9XH, England

**Freud, Bella L** — Fashion Designer
21 Saint Charles Square, London W10 6EF, England

**Freudenberger, Nell** — Writer
Harper Collins Publishers, 10 E 53rd St, Cellar 1, New York NY 10022 USA

**Freund, Lambert B** — Mechanical Engineer
3 Palisade Lane, Barrington RI 02806, USA

**Freundlich, Bart** — Director
Creative Artists Agency, 2000 Ave of Stars, #100, Los Angeles CA 90067 USA

**Frewer, Matt** — Actor
Gilbertson Entertainment, 1334 3rd Street Promenade, #201, Santa Monica CA 90401 USA

**Frey, Glenn** — Singer (Eagles), Songwriter, Actor
I C M Partners, 10250 Constellation Blvd, #900, Los Angeles CA 90067 USA

**Frey, James G (Jim)** — Baseball Manager
12101 Tullamore Court, #406, Lutherville Timonium MD 21093, USA

**Frey, Sami** — Actor
Les Visiteurs du Soir, 40 Rue de la Folie Regnault, 75011 Paris, France

**Frey, Steven F (Steve)** — Baseball Player
1414 2nd Street Pike, Southampton PA 18966, USA

**Freytag, Arny** — Photographer
22735 MacFarlane Dr, Woodland Hills CA 91364, USA

**Frias, Arturo** — Boxer
12418 Penn St, Whittier CA 90602, USA
**Frick, Stephen N** — Astronaut
27998 Mercurio Road, Carmel CA 93923, USA
**Fricke, Janie** — Singer, Guitarist
Janie Fricke Concerts, PO Box 798, Lancaster TX 75146, USA
**Fricker, Brenda** — Actress
Aegis Entertainment Group, 7510 Sunset Blvd, #275, Los Angeles CA 90046, USA
**Frickman, Andrew J (Andy)** — Director, Producer
W M E Entertainment, 9601 Wilshire Blvd, #300, Beverly Hills CA 90210 USA
**Friday, Gavin** — Singer, Composer, Artist
Bloomsbury Publishing, 50 Bedford Square, London WC1B 3DP, England
**Friday, Nancy** — Writer
Harper Collins Publishers, 10 E 53rd St, Cellar 1, New York NY 10022 USA
**Fridell, Squire** — Actor
Stars Agency, 23 Grant Ave, #400, San Francisco CA 94108, USA
**Fridovich, David P** — Army General
Special Operations Center, 7701 Tampa Point Blvd, McDill Air Force Base FL 33621, USA
**Fried, Charles** — Government Official, Judge, Educator
Harvard University, Law School, Cambridge MA 02138, USA
**Fried, Miriam** — Concert Violinist
Opus 3 Artists, 470 Park Ave S, #900N, New York NY 10016 USA
**Friedberg, Rick** — Director
A P A Talent/Literary Agency, 405 S Beverly Dr, #300, Beverly Hills CA 90212 USA
**Friedberger, Eleanor** — Singer (Fiery Furnaces)
High Road Touring, 751 Bridgeway, #200, Sausalito CA 94965 USA
**Friedberger, Matthew** — Singer, Drummer (Fiery Furnaces)
High Road Touring, 751 Bridgeway, #200, Sausalito CA 94965 USA
**Frieden, Tanja** — Snowboard Athlete
Kari Frieden, Freisestr 29A, 3604 Thun, Switzerland
**Frieden, Thomas R** — Government Official, Physician
Centers for Disease Control, 1600 Clifton Road NE, Atlanta GA 30329 USA
**Friedericy, Bonita** — Actress
Amsel Eisenstadt Frazier, 5055 Wilshire Blvd, #865, Los Angeles CA 90036 USA
**Friedkin, William** — Director
10741 Levico Way, Los Angeles CA 90077, USA
**Friedlaender, Jonathan** — Biological Anthropologist
3401 N Broad St, Philadelphia PA 19140, USA
**Friedlander, Judah** — Actor, Comedian
Cohen & Gardner, 345 N Maple Drive, #181, Beverly Hills CA 90210, USA
**Friedlander, Lee** — Artist, Photographer
Janet Borden, 560 Broadway, #601, New York NY 10012, USA
**Friedlander, Liz** — Director
Gersh Agency, 9465 Wilshire Blvd, #600, Beverly Hills CA 90212 USA
**Friedlander, Saul** — Writer
University of California, History Dept, Los Angeles CA 90024, USA
**Friedle, Will** — Actor
Innovative Artists, 1505 10th St, Santa Monica CA 90401 USA
**Friedman, Bruce Jay** — Writer
Biblioasis, PO Box 92, Emeryville ON N0R 1C0, Canada
**Friedman, Caitlin** — Writer
Y C Media, 145 W 28th St, #1200, New York NY 10001, USA
**Friedman, Emanuel A** — Obstetrician
Beth-Israel Hospital, 330 Brookline Ave, Boston MA 02215, USA
**Friedman, Jeffrey M** — Molecular Geneticist
Rockefeller University Hughes Medical Institute, Molecular Genetics Laboratory, New York NY 10021, USA
**Friedman, Jeremiah** — Writer
United Talent Agency, U T A Plaza, 9336 Civic Center Dr, Beverly Hills CA 90210 USA
**Friedman, Jerome I** — Nobel Physics Laureate
75 Greenough St, Brookline MA 02445, USA
**Friedman, Kinky** — Singer, Songwriter, Writer
1101 Crown Ridge Path, Austin TX 78753, USA
**Friedman, Leonard L (Lennie)** — Football Player
1000 Cross Clay Court, Raleigh NC 27614, USA
**Friedman, Maggie** — Producer
Ensemble Entertainment, 280 S Beverly Dr, #402, Beverly Hills CA 90212, USA
**Friedman, Mal** — Actor
J E Talent, 323 Geary St, #302, San Francisco CA 94102, USA
**Friedman, Mark** — Writer, Producer
United Talent Agency, U T A Plaza, 9336 Civic Center Dr, Beverly Hills CA 90210 USA
**Friedman, Michael** — Composer, Lyricist
I C M Partners, 10250 Constellation Blvd, #900, Los Angeles CA 90067 USA
**Friedman, Peter** — Actor, Singer
J Michael Bloom, 233 Park Ave S, #1000, New York NY 10003 USA
**Friedman, Philip** — Writer
Ivy Books/Random House, 1745 Broadway, #B1, New York NY 10019, USA
**Friedman, Sonya** — Psychologist, Entertainer
111 S Old Woodward Ave, #212B, Birmingham MI 48009, USA
**Friedman, Thomas L** — Journalist
New York Times, Editorial Dept, 229 W 43rd St, New York NY 10036 USA
**Friedman, Tom** — Sculptor
Luhring Augustine Gallery, 531 W 24th St, New York NY 10011, USA
**Friedrich, Hans-Peter** — Government Official, Germany
Bundestag, Platz der Republik 1, 10557 Berlin, Germany , USA
**Friel, Anna** — Actress
Ken McReddie Assoc, 101 Finsbury Pavement, London EC2A 1RS, England
**Friel, Brian** — Writer
Drumaweir House, Greencastle, County Donegal, Ireland
**Friels, Colin** — Actor
129 Brooke St, Woollomooloo, Sydney NSW 2011, Australia
**Friend, Robert B (Bob)** — Baseball Player
4 Salem Circle, Pittsburgh PA 15238, USA
**Friend, Rupert** — Actor
Creative Artists Agency, 2000 Ave of Stars, #100, Los Angeles CA 90067 USA
**Friesinger-Postma, Anna (Anni)** — Speed Skater
Am Bichi 4, 83334 Inzell, Germany

**Friesz, John M** — Football Player
1454 E W Pebblestone Court, Hayden ID 83835, USA
**Frigo, Francesco** — Model, Actress
Playboy Promotions, 2706 Media Center Dr, Los Angeles CA 90065 USA
**Friis, Morten** — Percussion Musician (Safri Duo)
P D H Music, Dag Hammarskjold Alle 42 G, 2100 Copenhagen 0, Denmark
**Frimout, Dirk D** — Astronaut, Belgium
Flanders Language Foundation, Merghelynckstraat 4, 8900 Iper, Belgium
**Fripp, Robert** — Guitarist (King Crimson), Songwriter
Agency Group Ltd, 361-373 City Road, London EC1V 1PQ, England
**Frischmann, Justine** — Singer (Elastica)
C M O Mgmt, Studio 2.6, Shepherds East, Richmond Way, London W14 0DQ, England
**Frisell, Sonja** — Director
Columbia Artists Mgmt Inc, 1790 Broadway, #702, New York NY 10019 USA
**Frisell, William R (Bill)** — Jazz Guitarist
Rosebud Agency, PO Box 170429, San Francisco CA 94117 USA
**Frishberg, David L** — Jazz Singer, Pianist, Composer
Irvin Arthur Assoc, 350 E 79th St, #18C, New York NY 10075 USA
**Frist, William H (Bill), Sr** — Senator, TN
V O L P A C, PO Box 15852, Nashville TN 37215, USA
**Fristsche, Jim** — Basketball Player
470 Emerson Ave W, Saint Paul MN 55118, USA
**Fritsch, Theodore E (Ted), Jr** — Football Player
5014 Odins Way, Marietta GA 30068, USA
**Fritsche, Dan** — Ice Hockey Player
116 Olentangy Point, Columbus OH 43202, USA
**Fritts, Debra** — Artist
Chase Gallery, 129 Newbury St, Mezzanine, Boston MA 02116, USA
**Fritz, Harold A** — Vietnam War Army Hero (CMH)
1017 W Scottwood Dr, Peoria IL 61615, USA
**Fritz, Laurence J (Larry)** — Baseball Player
2632 Schrage Ave, Whiting IN 46394, USA
**Fritz, Nikki** — Actress
1158 28th St, #683, Santa Monica CA 90403, USA
**Frizza, Riccardo** — Conductor
I M G Artists, Hogarth Business Park, Chiswick, London W4 2TH, England
**Frizzell, David** — Singer
Symons Adams Myers Promotions, PO Box 30, Fostoria OH 44830, USA
**Frizzell, John** — Composer
First Artists Mgmt, 4764 Park Granada, #210, Calabasas CA 91302 USA
**Frizzelle, William J** — Football Player
8001 Tylerton Dr, Raleigh NC 27613, USA
**Frobel, Douglas S (Doug)** — Baseball Player
169 Springwater Dr, Kanata ON K2K 1Z8, Canada
**Froboess, Cornelia** — Singer, Actress
Rinkhof Kleinholzhausen, 83064 Raubling, Germany
**Froch, Carl** — Boxer
Gedling Road, Carlton, Nottingham NG4 3FG, England
**Froemming, Bruce N** — Baseball Umpire
702 W Haddonstone Place, Thiensville WI 53092, USA
**Froese, Bob** — Ice Hockey Player
11701 Clarence Center Road, Akron NY 14001, USA
**Froggatt, Joanne** — Actress
Conway Van Gelder Grant, 8-12 Broadwick St, #300, London W1F 8HW, England
**Frohnmayer, John E** — Government Official
38511 Kelly Road, Jefferson OR 97352, USA
**Frohwirth, Todd G** — Baseball Player
S66W24360 Skyline Ave, Waukesha WI 53189, USA
**Froines, John R** — Social Activist, Educator
University of California Public Health School, Environmental Health Science Dept, Los Angeles CA 90024, USA
**Frolov, Alexander** — Ice Hockey Player
1467 3rd St, Manhattan Beach CA 90266, USA
**Fromm, Fritz** — Handball Player
An der Bismarckschule 64, 30173 Hannover, Germany
**Frongillo, John R** — Football Player
10230 Elmhurst Dr NW, Albuquerque NM 87114, USA
**Fronius, Hans** — Artist
Guggenberggasse 18, 2380 Perchtoldadorf bei Vienna, Austria
**Froome, Chris** — Cyclist
Team Sky, National Cycling Centre, Stuart St, Great Manchester M11 4DQ, England
**Frosch, Robert A** — Government Official, Space Scientist
18 Heritage Hills Dr, Somers NY 10589, USA
**Frost, Alex** — Actor
Industry Entertainment, 955 Carillo Dr, #300, Los Angeles CA 90048 USA
**Frost, C David (Dave)** — Baseball Player
2206 Ocana Ave, Long Beach CA 90815, USA
**Frost, David L** — Golfer
5836 Royal Lane, Dallas TX 75230, USA
**Frost, Lindsay** — Actress
Glick Agency, 1321 7th St, #203, Santa Monica CA 90401 USA
**Frost, Mark** — Writer
Mark Frost Productions, PO Box 1723, Studio City CA 91614, USA
**Frost, Martin** — Concert Clarinetist
Kunstlermanagement Till Doench, Roegergasse 24-26/G2, 1090 Vienna, Austria
**Frost, Nick** — Actor, Comedian, Writer
Hamilton Hodell, 66-68 Margaret St, #500, London W1W 8SR, England
**Frost, Sadie** — Actress
Money Mgmt, 22 Noel St, London W1F 8GS, England
**Frost, Scott A** — Football Player
99 Thomas Lake, Ashland NE 68003, USA
**Fruchtman, Lisa** — Film Editor
United Talent Agency, U T A Plaza, 9336 Civic Center Dr, Beverly Hills CA 90210 USA
**Fruhbeck de Burgos, Rafael** — Conductor
Avenida del Mediterraneo 21, 28007 Madrid, Spain
**Fruhwirth, Amy** — Golfer
26431 N 44th Way, Phoenix AZ 85050, USA

| | |
|---|---|
| **Frusciante, John A** | Guitarist (Red Hot Chili Peppers) |
| Q Prime, 729 7th Ave, #1600, New York NY 10019 USA | |
| **Fry Irvin, Shirley** | Tennis Player |
| 1970 Asylum Ave, West Hartford CT 06117, USA | |
| **Fry, Jerry R** | Baseball Player |
| 3300 Stanton St, Springfield IL 62703, USA | |
| **Fry, John A** | Educator |
| Drexel University, President's Office, 3141 Chestnut St, #103, Philadelphia PA 19104, USA | |
| **Fry, Michael** | Cartoonist (Committed, Over the Hedge) |
| United Feature Syndicate, PO Box 5610, Cincinnati OH 45201 USA | |
| **Fry, Robert N (Bob)** | Football Player |
| 1604 Bexley Dr, Wilmington NC 28412, USA | |
| **Fry, Stephen J** | Actor, Comedian, Director |
| Hamilton Hodell, 66-68 Margaret St, #500, London W1W 8SR, England | |
| **Fryar, Chris** | Drummer (Zac Brown Band) |
| Roar, 9701 Wilshire Blvd, #800, Beverly Hills CA 90212, USA | |
| **Fryar, Irving D** | Football Player, Sportscaster |
| 51 Applegate Road, Jobstown NJ 08041, USA | |
| **Frye, Channing T** | Basketball Player |
| Phoenix Suns, 201 E Jefferson St, Phoenix AZ 85004 USA | |
| **Frye, Jeffrey A (Jeff)** | Baseball Player |
| 6833 Lahontan Dr, Fort Worth TX 76132, USA | |
| **Frye, Soliel Moon** | Actress |
| Herb Tannen, 10801 National Blvd, #101, Los Angeles CA 90064 USA | |
| **Fryling, Victor J** | Businessman |
| C M S Energy, Fairlane Plaza South, 330 Town Center Dr, Dearborn MI 48126, USA | |
| **Fryman, D Travis** | Baseball Player |
| 2600 Highway 196, Molino FL 32577, USA | |
| **Ftorek, Robert B (Robbie)** | Ice Hockey Player, Coach |
| 79 Sunset Point Road, Wolfeboro NH 03894, USA | |
| **Fu Mingxia** | Diver |
| General Physical Culture Bureau, 9 Tiyuguan Road, Dongcheng District, Beijing 100061, China | |
| **Fu, Haijing** | Opera Singer |
| I M G Artists, Hogarth Business Park, Chiswick, London W4 2TH, England | |
| **Fucarino, Frank A** | Basketball Player |
| 21 Heathcote Court, Shirley NY 11967, USA | |
| **Fuchs, Florian** | Field Hockey Player |
| U H C Hamburg, Wesselblek 8, 22339 Hamburg, Germany | |
| **Fuchs, Victor R** | Economist |
| 796 Cedro Way, Stanford CA 94305, USA | |
| **Fuente, David I** | Businessman |
| Office Depot Inc, 6600 N Military Trail, Boca Raton FL 33496, USA | |
| **Fuentes Fache, Andrea** | Synchronized Swimmer |
| Club Natcio Sincronizada Kallipolis, Calle dels Esports S/N, 08017 Barcelona, Spain | |
| **Fuentes, Brian C** | Baseball Player |
| 1342 El Portal Dr, Merced CA 95340, USA | |
| **Fuentes, Daisy** | Actress, Model |
| Shelter Entertainment, 9255 Sunset Blvd, #300, Los Angeles CA 90069 USA | |
| **Fuentes, Julio M** | Judge |
| US Court of Appeals, US Courthouse, 50 Walnut St, #5032, Newark NJ 07102, USA | |
| **Fuentes, Rigoberto B (Tito)** | Baseball Player |
| 61 S Maddux Dr, Reno NV 89512, USA | |
| **Fuentes, Val** | Drummer (It's a Beautiful Day) |
| Tabletop Productions, PO Box 698, Carson City NV 89702, USA | |
| **Fugard, Athol H** | Writer |
| PO Box 5090, Walmer, Port Elizabeth 6065, South Africa | |
| **Fugate, Katherine** | Producer, Writer |
| Stakevich-Gothman, 9777 Wilshire Blvd, #550, Beverly Hills CA 90212, USA | |
| **Fugelsang, John** | Actor, Comedian |
| Brillstein Entertainment Partners, 9150 Wilshire Blvd, #350, Beverly Hills CA 90212 USA | |
| **Fugere, Joseph (Joe)** | Baseball Umpire |
| 415 Cinnamon Ridge, Rutherfordton NC 28139, USA | |
| **Fugett, Jean S, Jr** | Football Player |
| 4801 Westparkway, Baltimore MD 21229, USA | |
| **Fugit, Patrick** | Actor |
| Levin/Brown Mgmt, M M Productions, 1351 4th St, #201, Santa Monica CA 90401, USA | |
| **Fuglesang, A Christer** | Astronaut, Sweden |
| PO Box 555, Bellaire TX 77402, USA | |
| **Fuhrman, Isabelle** | Actress |
| Trilogy Talent, 13425 Ventura Blvd, #200, Sherman Oaks CA 91423, USA | |
| **Fujita, Hiroyuki** | Microbiotics Engineer |
| Fujita Laboratory, 4-6-1 Komaba, Meguroku, Tokyo 153 8505, Japan | |
| **Fuksas, Massimiliano** | Architect |
| Piazzi del Monte di Pieta 30, 00186 Rome, Italy | |
| **Fukuda, Yasuo** | Prime Minister, Japan |
| 4-20-7 Nazawa, Setagayaku, Tokyo 154 0003, Japan | |
| **Fukui, Takeo** | Businessman |
| Honda Motor Co, 2-1-1 Minami-Aoyama, Minatoku, Tokyo 107 8556, Japan | |
| **Fukumoto, Miho** | Soccer Player |
| Football Assn, 3-10-15 Hongo, Bunkyoku, Tokyo 113 0033 Japan | |
| **Fukuyama, Francis** | Social Scientist |
| George Mason University, Public Policy Dept, Fairfax VA 22030, USA | |
| **Fulcher, David D** | Football Player |
| All Pro Sports, PO Box 378, Mason OH 45040, USA | |
| **Fulcher, Rich** | Actor |
| United Talent Agency, U T A Plaza, 9336 Civic Center Dr, Beverly Hills CA 90210 USA | |
| **Fuld, Samuel B (Sam)** | Baseball Player |
| 8 Meadow Road, Durham NH 03824, USA | |
| **Fulghum, Robert** | Writer, Religious Leader |
| Random House, 1745 Broadway, #1800, New York NY 10019 USA | |
| **Fulgoni, Sara** | Opera Singer |
| I M G Artists, Hogarth Business Park, Chiswick, London W4 2TH, England | |
| **Fulhage, Scott A** | Football Player |
| 2430 N Road, Beloit KS 67420, USA | |
| **Fulks, Robbie** | Singer, Songwriter |
| Mongrel Music, 743 Center Blvd, Fairfax CA 94930, USA | |

**Fuller, Anthony I (Tony)** — Basketball Player
4222 Lost Springs Dr, Agoura Hills CA 91301, USA
**Fuller, Carl** — Basketball Player
8302 Kirkville Dr, Houston TX 77089, USA
**Fuller, Charles** — Writer
Creative Artists Agency, 2000 Ave of Stars, #100, Los Angeles CA 90067 USA
**Fuller, Cindy** — Model
Playboy Promotions, 2706 Media Center Dr, Los Angeles CA 90065 USA
**Fuller, Corey** — Football Player
626 Raspberry Way, Tallahassee FL 32312, USA
**Fuller, Delores** — Actress, Songwriter
3628 Ottawa Circle, Las Vegas NV 89169, USA
**Fuller, Drew** — Actor
Gersh Agency, 9465 Wilshire Blvd, #600, Beverly Hills CA 90212 USA
**Fuller, James H (Jim)** — Baseball Player
5107 Bur Oak Dr, Pasadena TX 77505, USA
**Fuller, John C (Johnny)** — Football Player
1925 Highland Dr, Salado TX 76571, USA
**Fuller, John E** — Baseball Player
31912 Paseo Terraza, San Juan Capistrano CA 92675, USA
**Fuller, Kathryn S** — Association Executive
World Wildlife Fund, 1250 24th St NW, #600, Washington DC 20037, USA
**Fuller, Linda** — Association Executive, Social Activist
Habitat for Humanity, 121 Habitat St, Americus GA 31709, USA
**Fuller, Mark** — Sculptor
Wet Design, 90 Universal City Plaza, Universal City CA 91608, USA
**Fuller, Marvin D** — Army General
6799 Patton Dr, Fort Hood TX 76544, USA
**Fuller, Michael D (Mike)** — Football Player
4241 Abingdon Trail, Birmingham AL 35243, USA
**Fuller, Penny** — Actress
Paradigm Agency, 360 N Crescent Dr, North Building, Beverly Hills CA 90210 USA
**Fuller, Randy L** — Football Player
2257 Patsy Lane, Columbus GA 31903, USA
**Fuller, Robert (Bob)** — Actor
5012 Auckland Ave, North Hollywood CA 91601, USA
**Fuller, Rod** — Drag Racing Driver
David Powers Motorsports, 10205 Westheimer Road, Houston TX 77042, USA
**Fuller, Simon** — Producer, Writer
Creative Artists Agency, 2000 Ave of Stars, #100, Los Angeles CA 90067 USA
**Fuller, Stephen R (Steve)** — Football Player
81 Oak Tree Lane, Bluffton SC 29910, USA
**Fuller, Todd D** — Basketball Player
Miami Heat, American Airlines Arena, 601 Biscayne Blvd, Miami FL 33132 USA
**Fuller, Vernon G (Vern)** — Baseball Player
155 Ironwood Circle, Aurora OH 44202, USA
**Fuller, Victoria** — Model, Actress
PO Box 6010-513, Sherman Oaks CA 91453, USA
**Fuller, William H, Jr** — Football Player
4025 Church Point Road, Virginia Beach VA 23455, USA
**Fullerton, Larry** — Inventor (Low Power Pulses for Messages)
Time Domain, 6700 Odyssey Dr NW, Huntsville AL 35806, USA
**Fullington, Darrell** — Football Player
1023 W Patrick Circle, Daytona Beach FL 32117, USA
**Fullmer, Bradley R (Brad)** — Baseball Player
400 S Barrington Ave, #202, Los Angeles CA 90049, USA
**Fulmer, Phillip** — Football Coach, Sportscaster
CBS-TV, Sports Dept, 51 W 52nd St, New York NY 10019 USA
**Fulton, Christina** — Actress
Innovative Artists, 1505 10th St, Santa Monica CA 90401 USA
**Fulton, Eileen** — Actress, Singer
60 E 42nd St, #305, New York NY 10165, USA
**Fulton, Fitzhugh L, Jr** — Test Pilot
1023 E Ave J, #5, Lancaster CA 93535, USA
**Fulton, Hamish** — Artist
John Weber Gallery, 529 W 20th St, New York NY 10011, USA
**Fulton, Keith** — Director
Sloss Law Office, 555 W 25th St, #400, New York NY 10001, USA
**Fulton, Robert D** — Governor, IA
PO Box 2634, Waterloo IA 50704, USA
**Fulton, Soren** — Actor
Paradigm Agency, 360 N Crescent Dr, North Building, Beverly Hills CA 90210 USA
**Fulton, William D (Bill)** — Baseball Player
3001 Lexington Dr, Export PA 15632, USA
**Fultz, Jeff** — Auto Racing Driver
J C R 3 Racing, PO Box 561001, Charlotte NC 28256, USA
**Fultz, Michael D (Mike)** — Football Player
1900 W Foothills Road, Lincolon NE 68523, USA
**Fumusa, Dominic** — Actor
Gersh Agency, 9465 Wilshire Blvd, #600, Beverly Hills CA 90212 USA
**Funaro, Frank** — Drummer (Cracker)
Back Bay Mgmt, 397 Little Neck Road, #305, Virginia Beach VA 23452 USA
**Funchess, Thomas (Tom)** — Football Player
1015 Funchess St, Crystal Springs MS 39059, USA
**Funderburk, Leonard J** — Vietnam War Air Force Hero
2311 Lathan Road, Monroe NC 28112, USA
**Funderburke, Lawrence** — Basketball Player
1688 Meadoway Court, Blacklick OH 43004, USA
**Funes Cartagena, C Mauricio** — President, El Salvador
Casa Presidencial, Calle Dario Gonzales 806, San Salvador, El Salvador
**Funk, Eric** — Composer
PO Box 1073, Helena MT 59624, USA
**Funk, Fred** — Golfer
24729 Harbour View Dr, Ponte Vedra FL 32082, USA
**Funk, Mary Wallace (Wally)** — Astronaut Candidate
243 Oak Hill Dr, Roanoke TX 76262, USA

# F

**Funk, Thomas J (Tom)** — Baseball Player
6952 N Olive St, Kansas City MO 64118, USA
**Funke, Alex** — Cinematographer
1176 Fiske St, Pacific Palisades CA 90272, USA
**Fuqua, Antoine** — Director
Steve Callas Assoc, 12424 Wilshire Blvd, Los Angeles CA 90025, USA
**Fuqua, Johnny W Frenchy)** — Football Player
13983 Glastonbury Ave, Detroit MI 48223, USA
**Furay, Richie** — Singer (Buffalo Springfield, Poco)
Agency Group, 9348 Civic Center Dr, #200, Beverly Hills CA 90210, USA
**Furcal, Rafael A** — Baseball Player
397 Sweet Bay Ave, Plantation FL 33324, USA
**Furie, Sidney J** — Director
I C M Partners, 10250 Constellation Blvd, #900, Los Angeles CA 90067 USA
**Furlan, Mira** — Actress
Imperium 7 Artists, 5455 Wilshire Blvd, #1706, Los Angeles CA 90036 USA
**Furler, Sia** — Singer, Songwriter
Paradigm Agency, 360 N Crescent Dr, North Building, Beverly Hills CA 90210 USA
**Furlong, Shirley** — Golfer
6251 S Kimberlee Way, Chandler AZ 85249, USA
**Furman, Brad** — Director, Producer, Writer
Atlas Entertainment, 9200 W Sunset Blvd, Los Angeles CA 90069, USA
**Furmaniak, Jason J (J J)** — Baseball Player
184 Nottingham Dr, Bolingbrook IL 60440, USA
**Furmann, Benno** — Actor
Gersh Agency, 41 Madison Ave, #3301, New York NY 10010 USA
**Furnas, Barnaby** — Artist
Marianne Boesky Gallery, 509 W 24th St, New York NY 10011, USA
**Furness, Deborra-Lee** — Actress
Lou Coulson Assoc, 37 Berwick St, London W1V 8RS, England
**Furniss, Bruce M** — Swimmer
1 Segada, Rancho Santa Margarita CA 92688, USA
**Furniss, Steve** — Swimmer
6478 Frampton Circle, Huntington Beach CA 92648, USA
**Furno, Carlo Cardinal** — Religious Leader
Piazza Della Citta Leonina, 00193 Rome, Italy
**Furrey, Michael T (Mike)** — Football Player
12397 Steeplechase Lane, Strongsville OH 44149, USA
**Furshpan, Edwin J** — Neurobiologist
27 Stonewall Lane, Falmouth MA 02540, USA
**Furst, Alan** — Writer
Random House, 1745 Broadway, #1800, New York NY 10019 USA
**Furst, Stephen** — Actor, Comedian
Marshak/Zachary Co, 8840 Wilshire Blvd, #100, Beverly Hills CA 90211 USA
**Furste, Moritz** — Field Hockey Player
U H C Hamburg, Wesselblek 8, 22339 Hamburg, Germany
**Furstenberg, Frank F, Jr** — Sociologist
University of Pennsylvania, Population Studies Center, Phildelphia PA 19104, USA
**Furstenfeld, Jeremy** — Drummer (Blue October)
Rainmaker Artists, PO Box 551665, Dallas TX 75355, USA
**Furstenfeld, Justin** — Singer, Guitarist (Blue October)
Rainmaker Artists, PO Box 551665, Dallas TX 75355, USA
**Furtado, Nelly** — Singer, Songwriter
Chris Smith Mgmt, 21 Camden St, #500, Toronto ON M5V 1V2, Canada
**Furtsch Ojeda, Evelyn** — Track Athlete
841 Clemenson Ave, Santa Ana CA 92705, USA
**Furuholmen, Magne** — Singer, Keyboardist (A-Ha)
Agency Group Ltd, 361-373 City Road, London EC1V 1PQ, England
**Furukawa, Satoshi** — Astronaut
Japanese Aerospace Exploration Agency, 2-1-1 Sengen, Tsukuba-shi, Ibaraki 305 8505, Japan
**Furuseth, Ole Christian** — Alpine Skier
John Colletts Alle 74, 0854 Oslo, Norway
**Furyk, James M (Jim)** — Golfer
240 Deer Haven Dr, Ponte Vedra FL 32082, USA
**Fusco, Mark E** — Ice Hockey Player
155 Grove St, Westwood MA 02090, USA
**Fusco, Scott M** — Ice Hockey Player
25083 Pioneer Way NW, Poulsbo WA 98370, USA
**Fusco, Simona** — Actress, Model
Scott Stander Assoc, 4533 Van Nuys Blvd, #401, Sherman Oaks CA 91403 USA
**Fusina, Charles A (Chuck)** — Football Player
1548 King James St, Pittsburgh PA 15237, USA
**Fuss, Adam** — Photographer
151 Ave B, New York NY 10009, USA
**Futey, Bohdan A** — Judge
US Claims Court, 717 Madison Place NW, Washington DC 20439, USA
**Futia, Leo R** — Businessman
18 Interlaken Road, Greenwich CT 06830, USA
**Futral, Elizabeth** — Opera Singer
Neil Funkhouser Mgmt, 105 Arden St, #5G, New York NY 10040, USA
**Futterman, Daniel (Dan)** — Actor, Writer
Principal Entertainment, 9255 Sunset Blvd, #500, Los Angeles CA 90069 USA
**Fyfe, William S** — Geochemist, Geologist
1 Joanna Dr, Sainte Catherines ON L2N 1V1, Canada
**Fyhie, Michael E (Mike)** — Baseball Player
4 Wellesley Court, Trabuco Canyon CA 92679, USA
**Fylstra, Daniel** — Computer Software Designer
Frontline Systems, PO Box 4288, Incline Village CA 89450, USA
**Fywell, Tim** — Director
I C M Partners, 10250 Constellation Blvd, #900, Los Angeles CA 90067 USA

**Funk - Fywell**

| | |
|---|---|
| **G Z A** | Rap Artist (Wu-Tang Clan) |
| A&E Entertainment, 13280 NE Freeway, #F328, Houston TX 77040, USA | |
| **Gaarder, Jostein** | Philosopher, Writer |
| Gullkroken 22A, 0377 Oslo, Norway | |
| **Gabaldon, Diana** | Writer |
| PO Box 584, Scottsdale AZ 85252, USA | |
| **Gabarra, Carin L** | Soccer Player, Coach |
| 305 Rosslare Dr, Arnold MD 21012, USA | |
| **Gabbana, Stefano** | Fashion Designer |
| Dolce & Gabbana, Via Santa Cecilia 7, 20122 Milan, Italy | |
| **Gabbert, Blaine** | Football Player |
| Jacksonville Jaguars, 1 AllTel Stadium Place, Jacksonville FL 32202 USA | |
| **Gabel, Seth** | Actor |
| Management 360, 9111 Wilshire Blvd, Beverly Hills CA 90210 USA | |
| **Gabel, Shainee** | Director |
| Creative Artists Agency, 2000 Ave of Stars, #100, Los Angeles CA 90067 USA | |
| **Gabelli, Mario J** | Financier |
| Gabelli Asset Mgmt, 1 Corporate Center, Rye NY 10580, USA | |
| **Gabellini, Michael** | Interior Designer |
| Gabellini-Sheppard Assoc, 665 Broadway, #706, New York NY 10012, USA | |
| **Gabetta, Sol** | Concert Cellist |
| Harrison/Parrott, Lucile-Grahn-Str 37, 81675 Munich, Germany | |
| **Gable, Daniel M (Danny)** | Freestyle Wrestler, Coach |
| 4343 Treefarm Lane NE, Iowa City IA 52240, USA | |
| **Gabor, William A (Billy)** | Basketball Player |
| 101 Ocean Bluffs Blvd, #501, Jupiter FL 33477, USA | |
| **Gabor, Zsa Zsa** | Actress |
| 1001 Bel Air Road, Los Angeles CA 90077, USA | |
| **Gabriel, Ana B** | Singer, Composer, Actress |
| A G Musicales, Peten 117 Col Narvarte, Mexico City DF 03020, Mexico | |
| **Gabriel, Andrea** | Actress |
| Global Artists Agency, 6253 Hollywood Blvd, #508, Los Angeles CA 90028 USA | |
| **Gabriel, Jani** | Model |
| Premier Model Mgmt, 40-42 Parker St, London WC2B 5PQ, England | |
| **Gabriel, John** | Actor |
| Access Talent Voice Overs, 171 Madison Ave, #910, New York NY 10016, USA | |
| **Gabriel, Juan** | Singer, Songwriter |
| J E P Entertainment Group, 16027 Ventura Blvd, #510, Encino CA 91436, USA | |
| **Gabriel, Mike** | Director, Animator |
| I C M Partners, 10250 Constellation Blvd, #900, Los Angeles CA 90067 USA | |
| **Gabriel, Peter** | Singer, Keyboardist, Songwriter |
| Box Mill, Mill Lane, Corsham SN13 8PL, England | |
| **Gabriel, Roman I, Jr** | Football Player |
| PO Box 4173, Calabash NC 28467, USA | |
| **Gabriela** | Circus Trapeze Artist |
| Ringling Bros Barnum & Bailey, 8607 Westwood Circle Dr, Vienna VA 22182 USA | |
| **Gabrielle, Monique** | Model, Actress |
| Purrfect Productions, 1231 NE 28th Ave, Pompano Beach FL 33062 USA | |
| **Gabrielson, Leonard G (Len)** | Baseball Player |
| 24230 Hillview Road, Los Altos Hills CA 94024, USA | |
| **Gaddis, John L** | Historian |
| Ohio University, Contemporary History Institute, Brown House, Athens OH 45701, USA | |
| **Gade, Ariel** | Actress |
| Paradigm Agency, 360 N Crescent Dr, North Building, Beverly Hills CA 90210 USA | |
| **Gadjo** | DJ Musician |
| Mission Control, City Business Center, Lower Road, London SE16 2XB, England | |
| **Gadon, Sarah** | Actress |
| Creative Drive Artists, 166 King St E, #400, Toronto ON M5A 1J3, Canada | |
| **Gadot, Gal** | Actress, Model |
| I C M Partners, 10250 Constellation Blvd, #900, Los Angeles CA 90067 USA | |
| **Gadsby, William A (Bill)** | Ice Hockey Player |
| 28765 E Kalong Circle, Southfield MI 48034, USA | |
| **Gadsden, Oronde B** | Football Player |
| 11241 NW 15th St, Plantation FL 33323, USA | |
| **Gadzuric, Dan** | Basketball Player |
| 1312 Villa Barolo Ave, Henderson NV 89052, USA | |
| **Gaebel, Tom** | Singer |
| Telemedia Music, Distlerstr 39, 70184 Stuttgart, Germany | |
| **Gaechter, Michael T (Mike)** | Football Player |
| 13 Horizon Point, Frisco TX 75034, USA | |
| **Gaeta, Alexander L** | Optical Engineer |
| Cornell University, Applied & Engineering Physics Dept, Clark Hall, Ithaca NY 14853, USA | |
| **Gaeta, John** | Special Effects Designer |
| Creative Artists Agency, 2000 Ave of Stars, #100, Los Angeles CA 90067 USA | |
| **Gaetti, Gary J** | Baseball Player |
| 7819 Silent Forest Dr, Sugar Land TX 77479, USA | |
| **Gaffigan, James** | Conductor |
| C M Artists, 127 W 96th St, #13B, New York NY 10025 USA | |
| **Gaffigan, Jim** | Actor, Comedian |
| Creative Artists Agency, 2000 Ave of Stars, #100, Los Angeles CA 90067 USA | |
| **Gaffney, D Jabar** | Football Player |
| 11750 Cherry Bark Dr E, Jacksonville FL 32218, USA | |
| **Gaffney, Derrick T** | Football Player |
| 11750 Cherry Bark Dr E, Jacksonville FL 32218, USA | |
| **Gaffney, F Andrew (Drew)** | Astronaut |
| 2311 Pierce Ave, Nashville TN 37232, USA | |
| **Gaffney, Mo** | Actor |
| Stone Manners Salners, 9911 W Pico Blvd, #1400, Los Angeles CA 90035 USA | |
| **Gage, Fred H** | Neurobiologist |
| Salk Biological Study Institute, 10110 N Torrey Pines Road, La Jolla CA 92037, USA | |
| **Gage, John** | Labor Leader |
| American Government Employees Federation, 80 F St NW, #700, Washington DC 20001, USA | |
| **Gage, Nathaniel L** | Educator |
| 6033 45th Ave NE, Seattle WA 98115, USA | |
| **Gage, Nicholas** | Columnist, Writer |
| 37 Nelson St, North Grafton MA 01536, USA | |

**G**

**G Z A - Gage**

**Gage, Paul** — Computer Scientist
Crag Research, Highway 178 N, Chippewa Falls WI 55402, USA

**Gaghan, Stephen** — Director, Writer
Unsupervised, 10201 W Pico Blvd, #75, Los Angeles CA 90035, USA

**Gagliano, Philip J (Phil)** — Baseball Player
1095 Crescent Dr, Hollister MO 65672, USA

**Gagliano, Robert F (Bob)** — Football Player
1064 Dover Lane, Ventura CA 93001, USA

**Gagne, Eric S** — Baseball Player
Los Angeles Dodgers, Stadium, 1000 Elysian Park Ave, Los Angeles CA 90090 USA

**Gagne, Greg C** — Baseball Player
746 Whetstone Hill Road, Somerset MA 02726, USA

**Gagne, Paul L** — Ice Hockey Player
Gagne Hockey, 2100 Airport Road, RR 2, Timmons ON P4N 7C3, Canada

**Gagne, Simon** — Ice Hockey Player
601 Laurel Oak Road, Voorhees NJ 08043, USA

**Gagner, Larry J** — Football Player
205 W Curtis St, Tampa FL 33603, USA

**Gagnier, Holly** — Actress
Commercial Talent, 9255 Sunset Blvd, #505, Los Angeles CA 90069, USA

**Gagnon, Andre-Philippe** — Actor, Comedian, Impressionist
89 Rue Alexandra, Ganby QC J2C 2P4, Canada

**Gagnon, Marc** — Speed Skater
Speed Skating Canada, 2781 Lancaster Road, #402, Ottawa ON K1B 1A7, Canada

**Gago, Jenny** — Actress
Paul Kohner, 9300 Wilshire Blvd, #555, Beverly Hills CA 90212 USA

**Gahan, David** — Singer (Depeche Mode)
Mute Records, 429 Harrow Road, London W10 4RE, England

**Gail, Max** — Actor
28198 Rey de Copas Lane, Malibu CA 90265, USA

**Gailes, Jason** — Rowing Athlete
17 Mark Vincent Dr, Westford MA 01886, USA

**Gailey, T Chandler (Chan)** — Football Player, Coach
176 Rocky Branch Road, Clarkesville GA 30523, USA

**Gaillard, Bob** — Basketball Coach
Lewis & Clark University, Athletic Dept, Pamplin Sports Center, Portland OR 97219, USA

**Gaillard, J Edward (Eddie)** — Baseball Player
134 Sweet Bay Circle, Jupiter FL 33458, USA

**Gaillard, Mary Katharine** — Physicist
University of California, Physics Dept, Berkeley CA 94720, USA

**Gaiman, Neil R** — Cartoonist, Writer
Creative Artists Agency, 2000 Ave of Stars, #100, Los Angeles CA 90067 USA

**Gain, Robert (Bob)** — Football Player
11 Nokomis Dr, Eastlake OH 44095, USA

**Gainer, Derrick** — Boxer
420 Elcino Dr, Pensacola FL 32526, USA

**Gaines Miller, Chryste** — Track Athlete
5408 E Saddleridge Lane, Lithonia GA 30038, USA

**Gaines, A Joe** — Baseball Player
77 Anair Way, Oakland CA 94605, USA

**Gaines, Ambrose (Rowdy), IV** — Swimmer
6800 Hawaii Kai Dr, Honolulu HI 96825, USA

**Gaines, Boyd P** — Actor, Singer
9220 Sunset Blvd, #625, West Hollywood CA 90069, USA

**Gaines, C Reece** — Basketball Player
Milwaukee Bucks, Bradley Center, 1001 N 4th St, #2, Milwaukee WI 53203 USA

**Gaines, Clark** — Football Player
21364 Scara Place, Broadlands VA 20148, USA

**Gaines, Corey Y** — Basketball Player, Coach
3968 Windansea St, Las Vegas NV 89147, USA

**Gaines, Davis** — Actor, Singer
Bobby Roberts, 3050 Business Park Circle, #303, Goodlettsville TN 37221 USA

**Gaines, Ernest J** — Writer
PO Box 81, Oscar LA 70762, USA

**Gaines, William C** — Journalist
Chicago Tribune, Editorial Dept, 435 N Michigan Ave, #1, Chicago IL 60611, USA

**Gainey, Kathleen** — Army General
Director, Defense Logistics Agency, Joint Staff, Pentagon, Washington DC 20318 USA

**Gainey, M C** — Actor
Miriam Milgrom Mgmt, 3614 Lankershim Blvd, Los Angeles CA 90068, USA

**Gainey, Robert M (Bob)** — Ice Hockey Player, Coach
PO Box 829, Coppell TX 75019, USA

**Gainsbourg, Charlotte** — Actress, Singer
U B B A, 6 Rue de Braque, 75003 Paris, France

**Gait, Gary** — Lacrosse Player, Coach
Colorado Mammouth, Pepsi Center, 1000 Chopper Circle, Denver CO 80204, USA

**Gaiter, Dorothy J** — Writer
I C M Partners, 10250 Constellation Blvd, #900, Los Angeles CA 90067 USA

**Gaither, Gloria S** — Singer, Songwriter
Gaither Music Co, PO Box 737, Alexandria IN 46001, USA

**Gaither, Israel L** — Religious Leader
Salvation Army USA, 615 Slaters Lane, Alexandria VA 22314, USA

**Gaither, Jared** — Football Player
San Diego Chargers, 4020 Murphy Canyon Road, San Diego CA 92123 USA

**Gaither, William J (Bill)** — Singer, Songwriter
Gaither Concerts, PO Box 178, Alexandria IN 46001, USA

**Gaitskill, Mary** — Writer
Pantheon/Random House, 1745 Broadway, New York NY 10019, USA

**Gajarsa, Arthur J** — Judge
US Court of Appeals, 717 Madison Place NW, Washington DC 20439, USA

**Gal, Edward** — Equestrian
Maatschap Dressuurstall Werner/Gal, Laarweg 15, 6732 Harskamp DG, Netherlands

**Galan, Nely** — Actress, Writer
Galan Entertainment, 523 Victoria Ave, Venice CA 90291, USA

**Galanos, James** — Fashion Designer
1316 Sunset Plaza Dr, Los Angeles CA 90069, USA

Galanos, Mike — Commentator
CNN-TV, 190 Marietta Ave SW, Atlanta GA 30303 USA
Galanter, Marc S — Attorney, Educator
University of Wisconsin, Law School, Madison WI 53706, USA
Galarraga, Andres J P — Baseball Player
1639 Enclave Circle, West Palm Beach FL 33411, USA
Galbraith, A Scott — Football Player
4440 Plato Court, Stockton CA 95207, USA
Galbraith, Clint — Harness Racing Driver
PO Box 902, Edwardsville IL 62025, USA
Galbreath, Anthony D (Tony) — Football Player
411 W 9th St, Fulton MO 65251, USA
Galdikas, Birute M F — Anthropologist
Orangutan Foundation International, 822 Wellesley Ave, Los Angeles CA 90049, USA
Gale, M Robert (Bob) — Writer, Producer, Director
A P A Talent/Literary Agency, 405 S Beverly Dr, #300, Beverly Hills CA 90212 USA
Gale, Michael E (Mike) — Basketball Player
18003 4th Ave S, Burien WA 98148, USA
Gale, Richard B (Rich) — Baseball Player
869 Center Park St, Daniel Island SC 29492, USA
Gale, Robert P — Physician, Medical Researcher
11808 Dorothy St, #304, Los Angeles CA 90049, USA
Gale, Tristan — Skeleton Athlete
Ego Sports Mgmt, PO Box 680051, Park City UT 84068, USA
Galecki, John M (Johnny) — Actor, Comedian
W M E Entertainment, 9601 Wilshire Blvd, #300, Beverly Hills CA 90210 USA
Galella, Ronald E (Ron) — Photographer
Ron Galella Ltd, 12 Nelson Lane, Montville NJ 07045, USA
Galeotti, Bethany Joy — Actress
Gersh Agency, 9465 Wilshire Blvd, #600, Beverly Hills CA 90212 USA
Galfione, Jean — Track Athlete
Athletes du Monde, 2 Passage de Melun, 75019 Paris, France
Galiazzo, Marco — Archery Athlete
Via Sorio 80/B, 35141 Padua (PD), Italy
Galiena, Anna — Actress
Media Art Mgmt, C/ Castelló 82, 2 Derecha, 28006 Madrid, Spain
Galifianakis, Zachary K (Zach) — Actor, Comedian, Pianist
Brillstein Entertainment Partners, 9150 Wilshire Blvd, #350, Beverly Hills CA 90212 USA
Galigher, Edward A (Ed) — Football Player
1025 Prospect St, #150, La Jolla CA 92037, USA
Galina, Stacy — Actress
11400 Cashmere St, Los Angeles CA 90049, USA
Galindo, Rudy — Figure Skater
1115 E Haley St, Santa Barbara CA 93103, USA
Gall, Hugues R — Opera Executive
Opera National de Paris, 120 Rue de Lyon, 75012 Paris, France
Gall, John C — Baseball Player
20 Corte del Sol, Millbrae CA 94030, USA
Gall, Joseph G — Biologist
5702 Ainsley Garth, Baltimore MD 21212, USA
Gallacher, Kevin — Soccer Player
Blackburn Rovers, Ewood Park, Blackburn, Lancashire BB2 4JF, England
Gallagher — Actor, Writer, Producer
14984 Roan Court, Wellington FL 33414, USA
Gallagher, Alan M E G P H (Al) — Baseball Player
1810 N Parkwood Dr, Harlingen TX 78550, USA
Gallagher, Brian — Association Executive
United Way of America, 701 N Fairfax Ave, Lobby, Alexandria VA 22314, USA
Gallagher, Bronagh — Actor
Hamilton Hodell, 66-68 Margaret St, #500, London W1W 8SR, England
Gallagher, Chad A — Basketball Player
482 Wynstone Way, Rockton IL 61072, USA
Gallagher, David — Actor
Innovative Artists, 1505 10th St, Santa Monica CA 90401 USA
Gallagher, David D (Dave) — Football Player
6105 Horizon Dr, Columbus IN 47201, USA
Gallagher, David T (Dave) — Baseball Player
29 Carrs Tavern Road, Millstone Township NJ 08510, USA
Gallagher, Ellen — Artist
Mario Diacono Gallery, 207 South St, Boston MA 02111, USA
Gallagher, Frank J — Football Player
6572 Enclave Dr, Clarkston MI 48348, USA
Gallagher, Gus — Actor
Ken McReddie Assoc, 101 Finsbury Pavement, London EC2A 1RS, England
Gallagher, Helen — Singer, Actress
260 W End Ave, New York NY 10023, USA
Gallagher, Jim, Jr — Golfer
PO Box 507, Greenwood MS 38935, USA
Gallagher, John, Jr — Actor, Singer
Gersh Agency, 9465 Wilshire Blvd, #600, Beverly Hills CA 90212 USA
Gallagher, Kathleen — Journalist
Milwaukee Journal Sentinel, Editorial Dept, PO Box 371, Milwaukee WI 53201 USA
Gallagher, Liam — Singer (Oasis)
Beady Eye Records, PO Box 14877, London NW1 62X, England
Gallagher, Megan — Actress
Shelter Entertainment, 9454 Wilshire Blvd, #715, Beverly Hills CA 90212, USA
Gallagher, Noel T D — Singer, Guitarist (Oasis), Songwriter
Ignition Mgmt, 54 Linhope St, London NW1 6HL, England
Gallagher, Peter — Actor, Singer
Gersh Agency, 9465 Wilshire Blvd, #600, Beverly Hills CA 90212 USA
Gallagher, Richard K — Navy Admiral
US Representative, NATO Military Committee, PSC 80, Box 300, APO AE 09724 USA
Gallagher, Robert C (Bob) — Baseball Player
315 Fair Ave, Santa Cruz CA 95060, USA
Gallagher, Tim — Ornithologist
Cornell University, Ornithology Laboratory, Ithaca NY 14853, USA

Galanos - Gallagher

**G**

| | |
|---|---|
| **Gallagher-Smith, Jackie** | Golfer |
| 193 Paradise Circle, Jupiter FL 33458, USA | |
| **Gallant, Gerard** | Ice Hockey Player, Coach |
| Montreal Canadiens, 1275 Saint Antoine St W, Montreal QC H3C 5L2, Canada | |
| **Gallant, Mavis L** | Writer |
| 14 Rue Jean Ferrandi, 75006 Paris, France | |
| **Gallardo, Yovani** | Baseball Player |
| Milwaukee Brewers, Miller Park, 1 Brewers Way, Milwaukee WI 53214 USA | |
| **Gallatin, Harry J** | Basketball Player, Coach |
| 2010 Madison Ave, Edwardsville IL 62025, USA | |
| **Gallego, Gina** | Actress |
| Ellis Talent Group, 4705 Laurel Canyon Blvd, #300, Valley Village CA 91607, USA | |
| **Gallego, Michael A (Mike)** | Baseball Player |
| 20205 Chandler Dr, Yorba Linda CA 92887, USA | |
| **Gallegos, Reynaldo** | Actor |
| Greater Vision Talent Agency, 8981 Sunset Blvd, #101, Los Angeles CA 90069, USA | |
| **Gallena, Anna** | Actress |
| Artmedia, 20 Ave Rapp, 75007 Paris, France | |
| **Gallery, Robert J** | Football Player |
| 3163 210th St, Masonville IA 50654, USA | |
| **Galles, Rick** | Auto Racing Executive |
| Galles Racing, PO Box 2507, Albuquerque NM 87165, USA | |
| **Galley, Garry M** | Ice Hockey Player |
| CBC-TV, PO Box 500, Station A, Toronto ON M5W 1E6, Canada | |
| **Galli, Joseph, Jr** | Businessman |
| Newell Rubbermaid Co, Newell Center, 29 E Stephenson St, Freeport IL 61032, USA | |
| **Gallico, Gregory, III** | Surgeon, Inventor (Synthetic Skin) |
| Massachusetts General Hospital, 275 Cambridge St, Boston MA 02114, USA | |
| **Galligan, Zach** | Actor |
| Innovative Artists, 1505 10th St, Santa Monica CA 90401 USA | |
| **Gallinari, Danilo** | Basketball Player |
| Denver Nuggets, Pepsi Center, 1000 Chopper Circle, Denver CO 80204 USA | |
| **Gallison, Joseph** | Actor |
| PO Box 10187, Wilmington NC 28404, USA | |
| **Gallo, Frank** | Sculptor |
| T R A Art Group, 1700 Stutz Dr, #15, Troy MI 48084, USA | |
| **Gallo, Richard L** | Dermatologist |
| University of California Medical Center, Dermatology Dept, 200 W Arbor Dr, San Diego CA 92103, USA | |
| **Gallo, Robert C** | Research Scientist |
| University of Maryland, Study of Viruses Institute, Baltimore MD 21228, USA | |
| **Gallo, Valentino** | Water Polo Player |
| Circolo Nautico Posillipo, Via Posillipo 5, 80123 Naples, Italy | |
| **Gallo, Vincent** | Actor, Director, Producer |
| Gray Daisy Films, 8033 W Sunset Blvd, #833, Los Angeles CA 90046, USA | |
| **Gallois, Louis** | Businessman |
| Airbus E A D S, Ronde Point Maurice Bellont 1, 31207 Blagnac, France | |
| **Gallop, Tom** | Actor |
| A P A Talent/Literary Agency, 405 S Beverly Dr, #300, Beverly Hills CA 90212 USA | |
| **Galloway, David L** | Football Player |
| 5441 NW 184th St, Miami Gardens FL 33055, USA | |
| **Galloway, George** | Government Official, England |
| Talk Sport Radio, 18 Hatfields, London SE1 8DJ, England | |
| **Galloway, Joseph S (Joey)** | Football Player |
| 1611 Cherokee Trail, Plano TX 75023, USA | |
| **Gallucci, Robert L** | Foundation Executive |
| MacArthur Foundation, 140 S Dearborn St, Chicago IL 60603, USA | |
| **Galvez, Balvino** | Baseball Player |
| 3986 SW 190th St, Miramar FL 33029, USA | |
| **Galvin, James** | Writer |
| University of Iowa, Writers' Workshop, Iowa City IA 52242, USA | |
| **Galvin, John R** | Army General |
| 2714 Lake Jodeco Dr, Jonesboro GA 30236, USA | |
| **Galway, James** | Concert Flutist, Conductor |
| Benseholzstr 11, 6045 Meggan, Switzerland | |
| **Galyon, Scott** | Football Player |
| 4631 Horseshoe Trail, Morristown TN 37814, USA | |
| **Gam, Rita** | Actress |
| 180 W 58th St, #8B, New York NY 10019, USA | |
| **Gamache, Joey** | Boxer |
| 60 Pettingill St, #2, Lewiston ME 4240, USA | |
| **Gamba, Rumon** | Conductor |
| NorrlandsOperan, Operaplan 5, 901 08 Umea, Sweden | |
| **Gamba, Veronica** | Actress, Model |
| 32230 Alvarado Blvd, #128, Union City CA 94587, USA | |
| **Gambee, David P (Dave)** | Basketball Player |
| 6175 SW Arrow Wood Lane, Portland OR 97223, USA | |
| **Gambino, Richard J** | Inventor (Read-Write Optical Storage) |
| State University of New York, Materials Science Dept, Stony Brook NY 11794, USA | |
| **Gamble, Ed** | Editorial Cartoonist |
| Florida Times-Union, Editorial Dept, 1 Riverside Ave, Jacksonville FL 32202, USA | |
| **Gamble, John R** | Baseball Player |
| 369 Caliente St, Reno NV 89509, USA | |
| **Gamble, Kenneth (Kenny)** | Songwriter |
| W M E Entertainment, 9601 Wilshire Blvd, #300, Beverly Hills CA 90210 USA | |
| **Gamble, Kenneth P (Kenny)** | Football Player |
| 4 Algonquin Dr, Wilbraham MA 01095, USA | |
| **Gamble, Mason** | Actor |
| Bresler Kelly Assoc, 11500 W Olympic Blvd, #400, Los Angeles CA 90064 USA | |
| **Gamble, Nathan** | Actor |
| Paradigm Agency, 360 N Crescent Dr, North Building, Beverly Hills CA 90210 USA | |
| **Gamble, Oscar C** | Baseball Player |
| 9705 Bent Brook Dr, Montgomery AL 36117, USA | |
| **Gamble, Patrick K** | Air Force General, Educator |
| PO Box 107500, Anchorage AK 99510, USA | |
| **Gamble, Richard F (Dick)** | Ice Hockey Player |
| 1 Vantage Dr, Pittsford NY 14534, USA | |

**Gamblin, Jacques** — Actor
Agence Artiste Adequet, 108 Rue Reaumur, 75002 Paris, France
**Gambon, Michael J** — Actor
Independent Talent Group, 40 Whitfield St, London W1T 2RH, England
**Gambrell, David H** — Senator, GA
3205 Arden Road NW, Atlanta GA 30305, USA
**Gambrell, William E (Billy)** — Football Player
341 Osceola Ave, Bogart GA 30622, USA
**Gambril, Don** — Swimming Coach
4409 Spring Row, Northport AL 35473, USA
**Gambucci, Andre P (Andy)** — Ice Hockey Player, Coach
9241 Yukon Ave S, Minneapolis MN 55438, USA
**Gambucci, Gary A** — Ice Hockey Player
9241 Yukon Ave S, Minneapolis MN 55438, USA
**Gambucci, Sergio (Serge)** — Ice Hockey Coach
14098 W Roanoke Ave, Goodyear AZ 85395, USA
**Game** — Rap Artist
I C M Partners, 10250 Constellation Blvd, #900, Los Angeles CA 90067 USA
**Gamez, Robert** — Golfer
Team Gamez Foundation, PO Box 690362, Orlando FL 32869, USA
**Gammon, Kendall R** — Football Player
14429 Maple St, Overland Park KS 66223, USA
**Gammons, Peter** — Sportswriter
Boston Globe, Editorial Dept, 135 William Morrissey Blvd, Dorchester MA 02125 USA
**Ganassi, Floyd (Chip)** — Auto Racing Driver, Executive
Chip Ganassi Racing, 8500 Westmoreland Dr, Concord NC 28027, USA
**Ganassi, Sonia** — Opera Singer
Columbia Artists Mgmt Inc, 1790 Broadway, #702, New York NY 10019 USA
**Ganatra, Nitin C** — Actor
United Agents, 12-26 Lexington St, London W1F 0LE, England
**Ganchar, Perry** — Ice Hockey Player
8043 Summerhouse Dr W, Dublin OH 43016, USA
**Gand, Gayle** — Chef
674 N Saint Clair St, Chicago IL 60611, USA
**Gandee, Sherman H (Sonny)** — Football Player
1525 Hinton St, Port Charlotte FL 33952, USA
**Gandhi, Sonia** — Government Official, India
All India Congress Party, 24 Akbar Road, New Delhi 110011, India
**Gandy, Mike J** — Football Player
8508 E Sweetwater Ave, Scottsdale AZ 85260, USA
**Gandy, Wayne L** — Football Player
6 Pinecrest Road NE, Atlanta GA 30342, USA
**Ganellin, C Robin** — Inventor (Antiulcer Compound)
University College, Chemistry Dept, 20 Gordon, London WC1H 0AJ, England
**Gangel, Geraldine (Gig)** — Model, Actress
Playboy Promotions, 2706 Media Center Dr, Los Angeles CA 90065 USA
**Gangloff, Mark** — Swimmer
5318 Camden Dr, Stow OH 44224, USA
**Gann, Jason W** — Actor, Writer
W M E Entertainment, 9601 Wilshire Blvd, #300, Beverly Hills CA 90210 USA
**Gann, Mike A** — Football Player
1479 Ashford Place NE, Atlanta GA 30319, USA
**Gann, Pamela B** — Educator
Claremont McKenna College, President's Office, 500 E 9th, Claremont CA 91711, USA
**Gannascoli, Joseph R** — Actor, Writer
Acme Talent Agency, 4727 Wilshire Blvd, #333, Los Angeles CA 90010 USA
**Gannaway, Preston** — Photojournalist
Concord Monitor, Editorial Dept, 1 Monitor Dr, Concord NH 03301, USA
**Gannon, Richard J (Rich)** — Football Player, Sportscaster
6472 Smithtown Road, Atlanta GA 30319, USA
**Ganso, Paulo Henrique** — Soccer Player
Confederacion de Futebol, Rua Victor Civita 66, #1, Rio de Janeiro 22775 044, Brazil
**Gant, Harry P** — Auto Racing Driver
7531 Millersville Road, Taylorsville NC 28681, USA
**Gant, Kenneth D (Kenny)** — Football Player
1820 W 10th St, Lakeland FL 33805, USA
**Gant, Reuben C** — Football Player
PO Box 3051, Tulsa OK 74101, USA
**Gant, Richard** — Actor
Pakula/King, 9229 W Sunset Blvd, #315, West Hollywood CA 90069 USA
**Gant, Robert** — Actor
Mythgarden, 960 N Ridgewood Place, Los Angeles CA 90038, USA
**Gant, Ronald E (Ron)** — Baseball Player
1027 Wellesley Crest Dr, Woodstock GA 30189, USA
**Gantz, Robert J** — Cinematographer
20 Kettle Creek Road, Weston CT 06883, USA
**Ganz, Bruno** — Actor
Braumbauer Actors, Hanfelderstr 32, 82319 Starnberg, Germany
**Ganzel, Teresa** — Actress
I C M Partners, 10250 Constellation Blvd, #900, Los Angeles CA 90067 USA
**Gao Min** — Diver
Olympic Committee, 9 Tiyuguan Road, Chongwen District, Beijing 100763, China
**Gao Xingjian** — Nobel Literature Laureate
Editions l'Aube, Le Moulin de Chateau, 84240 Le Tour d'Aigues, France
**Gao, Xiang** — Concert Violinist
Columbia Artists Mgmt Inc, 1790 Broadway, #702, New York NY 10019 USA
**Gaona, Tito** — Circus Trapeze Artist
432 Spadora Dr, Venice FL 34285, USA
**Gara, Jeremy** — Musician (Arcade Fire)
Billions Corp, 3522 W Armitage Ave, Chicago IL 60647 USA
**Garabaldi, Robert R (Bob)** — Baseball Player
2143 Oregon Ave, Stockton CA 95204, USA
**Garagiola, Joseph H (Joe)** — Sportscaster, Baseball Player
4555 E Mayo Blvd, #3331, Phoenix AZ 85050, USA
**Garagozzo, Keith J** — Baseball Player
16 Foxcroft Way, Mount Laurel NJ 08054, USA

# G

| | |
|---|---|
| **Garai, Romola** | Actress |
| Artist Rights Group, 4 Great Portland St, London W1W 8PA, England | |
| **Garan, Ronald J, Jr** | Astronaut |
| 2002 Sea Cove Court, Houston TX 77058, USA | |
| **Garant, Robert Ben** | Actor |
| Creative Artists Agency, 2000 Ave of Stars, #100, Los Angeles CA 90067 USA | |
| **Garant, Sylvie** | Model, Actress |
| Playboy Promotions, 2706 Media Center Dr, Los Angeles CA 90065 USA | |
| **Garas, Kaz** | Actor |
| 400 W 43rd St, #42L, New York NY 10036, USA | |
| **Garavito, R Michael** | Biochemist |
| Michigan State University, Biochemistry Dept, East Lansing MI 48824, USA | |
| **Garbacz, Lori** | Golfer |
| 777 Albany Post Road, Briarcliff Manor NY 10510, USA | |
| **Garber, H Eugene (Gene)** | Baseball Player |
| 771 Stonemill Dr, Elizabethtown PA 17022, USA | |
| **Garber, Terri** | Actress |
| 38 E 1st St, #2B, New York NY 10003, USA | |
| **Garber, Victor** | Actor |
| United Talent Agency, U T A Plaza, 9336 Civic Center Dr, Beverly Hills CA 90210 USA | |
| **Garces, Paula** | Actress |
| B/W/R, 9100 Wilshire Blvd, #500W, Beverly Hills CA 90212 USA | |
| **Garces, Richard A (Rich)** | Baseball Player |
| 605 Swigert St, Kerrville TX 78028, USA | |
| **Garci, Jose Luis** | Director, Producer, Writer |
| Direccion General del Libro, Paseo de la Castellana 109, 20846 Madrid, Spain | |
| **Garcia Bernal, Gael** | Actor, Director, Producer |
| Canana Films, San Luis Potosi, #211 Piso 8, Colonia Roma, Mexico City  DF 06700, Mexico | |
| **Garcia Marquez, Gabriel** | Nobel Literature Laureate |
| Fuego 144, Pedregal de San Angel, Mexico City DF 01000, Mexico | |
| **Garcia Swisher, Joanna** | Actress |
| John Carrabino Mgmt, 5900 Wilshire Blvd, #406, Los Angeles CA 90036 USA | |
| **Garcia, Adam G** | Actor |
| I C M Partners, 10250 Constellation Blvd, #900, Los Angeles CA 90067 USA | |
| **Garcia, Aimee** | Actress |
| Paradigm Agency, 360 N Crescent Dr, North Building, Beverly Hills CA 90210 USA | |
| **Garcia, Alfonso R (Kiko)** | Baseball Player |
| 526 Trailview Circle, Martinez CA 94553, USA | |
| **Garcia, Andy** | Actor |
| CineSon Entertainment, 4519 Varna Ave, Sherman Oaks CA 91423, USA | |
| **Garcia, Carlos J** | Baseball Player |
| 5208 William St, Lancaster NY 14086, USA | |
| **Garcia, Danna** | Actress, Singer, Model |
| Innovative Artists, 1505 10th St, Santa Monica CA 90401 USA | |
| **Garcia, Danny (Swift)** | Boxer |
| Golden Boy Promotions, 626 Wilshire Blvd, #350, Los Angeles CA 90017 USA | |
| **Garcia, David (Dave)** | Baseball Manager |
| 17842 Avenida Cordillera, #28, San Diego CA 92128, USA | |
| **Garcia, Eric** | Writer |
| W M E Entertainment, 9601 Wilshire Blvd, #300, Beverly Hills CA 90210 USA | |
| **Garcia, Freddy A** | Baseball Player |
| Quisquella Gta Etapa M22, #52, La Ramana, Dominican Republic | |
| **Garcia, G Karim** | Baseball Player |
| 38 Agnew Farm Road, Armonk NY 10504, USA | |
| **Garcia, Gina** | Artist |
| Garcia Art Glass, 123 Losoya St, #5, San Antonio TX 78205, USA | |
| **Garcia, Gregory Thomas** | Producer, Writer |
| Creative Artists Agency, 2000 Ave of Stars, #100, Los Angeles CA 90067 USA | |
| **Garcia, Guillermo A** | Baseball Player |
| 3806 Shoma Dr, West Palm Beach FL 33414, USA | |
| **Garcia, Jeffrey J (Jeff)** | Football Player |
| PO Box 8977, Rancho Santa Fe CA 92067, USA | |
| **Garcia, Jesus** | Singer |
| Columbia Artists Mgmt Inc, 1790 Broadway, #702, New York NY 10019 USA | |
| **Garcia, Jorge** | Actor |
| Kritzer Levine Wilkins Griffin, 11872 La Grange Ave, #100, Los Angeles CA 90025 USA | |
| **Garcia, Juan Carlos** | Actor |
| Gabriel Blanco, Rio Balsas 35-32, Colonia Cuauhtemoc DF 6500, Mexico | |
| **Garcia, Lucrezia** | Opera Singer |
| I M G Artists, Hogarth Business Park, Chiswick, London W4 2TH, England | |
| **Garcia, Mayte** | Actress |
| C E S D, 10635 Santa Monica Blvd, #130, Los Angeles CA 90025 USA | |
| **Garcia, Miguel A (Mike)** | Baseball Player |
| 28428 Eagle St, Moreno Valley CA 92555, USA | |
| **Garcia, Nicole** | Actress |
| Voyez Mon Agent, 20 Ave Rapp, 75007 Paris, France | |
| **Garcia, Pedro M** | Baseball Player |
| Parque del Condado L4, Urb Bairoa Park, Caguas PR 00725, USA | |
| **Garcia, Richard R (Rich)** | Baseball Umpire |
| 769 Harbor Isle, Clearwater FL 33767, USA | |
| **Garcia, Rodrigo** | Director, Producer |
| Kuranda Mgmt, Santo Angel 84, 28043 Madrid, Spain | |
| **Garcia, Rupert** | Artist |
| Aurobora Press, 370 Brannan St, #100, San Francisco CA 94107, USA | |
| **Garcia, Sergio** | Golfer |
| International Mangement Group, 1 Erieview Plaza, 1360 E 9th St, Cleveland OH 44114 USA | |
| **Garciaparra, A Nomar** | Baseball Player |
| 613 15th St, Manhattan Beach CA 90266, USA | |
| **Garcon, Pierre** | Football Player |
| Washington Redskins, 21300 Redskin Park Dr, Ashburn VA 20147 USA | |
| **Gard, Robert G, Jr** | Army General |
| Center for Arms Control, 322 4th St NE, Washington DC 20002, USA | |
| **Gard, Toby** | Video Games Designer (Lara Croft) |
| SCi Entertainment Group, 1 Hartfield Road, London SW19 3RU, England | |
| **Gardell, Billy** | Actor, Comedian |
| Creative Artists Agency, 2000 Ave of Stars, #100, Los Angeles CA 90067 USA | |

Garai - Gardell

**Gardener, Daryl R** — Football Player
8925 Legacy Court, #106, Kissimmee FL 34747, USA
**Gardener, Jason** — Track Athlete
Athletics World Mgmt, 7097 Alvern St, #308, Los Angeles CA 90045 USA
**Gardenhire, Ronald C (Ron)** — Baseball Player, Manager
585 County Road B2 E, Saint Paul MN 55117, USA
**Gardiner, Greg** — Cinematographer
Paradigm Agency, 360 N Crescent Dr, North Building, Beverly Hills CA 90210 USA
**Gardiner, John Eliot** — Conductor
Monteverdi Choir & Orchestra, 25 Cabot Square, Canary Wharf, London E14 4QA, England
**Gardiner, Margaret** — Beauty Queen
Andre Nel, 200 UCLA Medical Plaza, Los Angeles CA 90095, USA
**Gardiner, Michael J (Mike)** — Baseball Player
26 Read Dr, Hanover MA 02339, USA
**Gardner, Ashley** — Actress
S M S Talent, 8383 Wilshire Blvd, #230, Beverly Hills CA 90211 USA
**Gardner, Barry A** — Football Player
24964 S Willow Brook Trail, Crete IL 60417, USA
**Gardner, Brett M** — Baseball Player
117 Drake St, Charleston SC 29403, USA
**Gardner, Carwell E** — Football Player
9603 Galene Dr, Louisville KY 40299, USA
**Gardner, Dale A** — Astronaut
60 Blue Mesa Circle, Divide CO 80814, USA
**Gardner, David P** — Educator, Foundation Executive
2989 American Saddler Dr, Park City UT 84060, USA
**Gardner, Emerson N, Jr** — Marine Corps General
Deputy CofS, Programs/Resources, HqUSMC, 2 Navy St, Washington DC 20380 USA
**Gardner, Guy S** — Astronaut
N A S A, Johnson Space Center, 2101 NASA Road, Houston TX 77058 USA
**Gardner, Howard E** — Psychologist, Neurobiologist
Harvard University, Graduate Education School, Cambridge MA 02138, USA
**Gardner, James** — Director
Shapiro-Lichtman, 8827 Beverly Blvd, Los Angeles CA 90048 USA
**Gardner, Jeffrey S (Jeff)** — Baseball Player
1906 Port Weybridge Place, Newport Beach CA 92660, USA
**Gardner, John** — Ballet Dancer
American Ballet Theatre, 890 Broadway, #300, New York NY 10003 USA
**Gardner, Lisa** — Writer
Jane Rotrosen Agency, 318 E 51st St, New York NY 10022, USA
**Gardner, Mark A** — Baseball Player
15216 Mesa View Ave, Friant CA 93626, USA
**Gardner, Randy** — Figure Skater
4640 Glencoe Ave, #6, Marina del Rey CA 90292, USA
**Gardner, Robert G** — Educator
Harvard University, Visual & Environmental Studies Dept, Cambridge MA 02138, USA
**Gardner, Roderick F (Rod)** — Football Player
1883 Executive Dr, Duluth GA 30096, USA
**Gardner, Rulon** — Greco-Roman Wrestler
Elite Training Center, 981 S Main St, #130, Logan UT 84321, USA
**Gardner, Tom** — Editor
124 N Pitt St, Alexandria VA 22314, USA
**Gardner, Wesley B (Wes)** — Baseball Player
305 Ruth, Benton AR 72019, USA
**Gardner, Wilford R** — Physicist
University of California, Natural Resources College, Berkeley CA 94720, USA
**Gardner, William F (Billy)** — Baseball Player, Manager
35 Dayton Road, Waterford CT 06385, USA
**Gardocki, Christopher A (Chris)** — Football Player
63 Yorkshire Dr, Hilton Head Island SC 29928, USA
**Gardot, Melody** — Singer, Pianist, Guitarist
W M E Entertainment, 9601 Wilshire Blvd, #300, Beverly Hills CA 90210 USA
**Gare, Danny** — Ice Hockey Player
950 Hopkins Road, #F, Buffalo NY 14221, USA
**Garelick, Jeremy** — Producer, Writer
United Talent Agency, U T A Plaza, 9336 Civic Center Dr, Beverly Hills CA 90210 USA
**Garfat, Jance** — Bassist, Singer (Dr Hook)
Artists Int'l Mgmt, 9850 Sandalwood Blvd, #458, Boca Raton FL 33428, USA
**Garfield, Allen** — Actor
8271 Melrose Ave, #203, Los Angeles CA 90046, USA
**Garfield, Andrew** — Actor
Gordon & French, 12-13 Poland St, London W1F 8QB, England
**Garfunkel, Art** — Singer, Actor
Metropolitan Talent Agency, 5405 Wilshire Blvd, #218, Los Angeles CA 90036 USA
**Garibaldi, Bob R** — Baseball Player
2143 Oregon Ave, Stockton CA 95204, USA
**Garity, Troy** — Actor
Untitled Entertainment, 350 S Beverly Dr, #200, Beverly Hills CA 90212 USA
**Garland, Alex** — Writer
Creative Artists Agency, 2000 Ave of Stars, #100, Los Angeles CA 90067 USA
**Garland, George D** — Geophysicist
5 Mawhiney Court, Huntsville ON P0A 1K0, Canada
**Garland, Jon S** — Baseball Player
2924 Summerwood Dr, Springfield IL 62712, USA
**Garland, Nicholas** — Editorial Cartoonist
Daily Telegraph, 111 Buckingham Palace Road, London SW1W 0DT, England
**Garland, R Wayne** — Baseball Player
7556 Mossback St, Las Vegas NV 89123, USA
**Garland, Winston K** — Basketball Player
1512 Southoak Dr, Nashville TN 37211, USA
**Garlin, Jeff** — Actor, Producer
I C M Partners, 10250 Constellation Blvd, #900, Los Angeles CA 90067 USA
**Garlits, Donald G (Big Daddy)** — Drag Racing Driver
Garlits Racing Museum, 13700 SW 16th Ave, Ocala FL 34473, USA
**Garmaker, Richard E (Dick)** — Basketball Player
5824 E 111th St, Tulsa OK 74137, USA

**Garman, Michael D (Mike)**
15144 Kings Row Road, Caldwell ID 83607, USA — Baseball Player

**Garn, E Jacob (Jake)**
1267 Chalder Circle, Salt Lake City UT 84103, USA — Senator, UT; Astronaut

**Garn, Stanley M**
1200 Earhart Road, #223, Ann Arbor MI 48105, USA — Anthropologist

**Garneau, Marc**
Space Agency, 6767 Route de Aeroport, Sainte-Hubert QC J3Y 8Y9, Canada — Astronaut, Canada

**Garner, Charlie, III**
12944 Royal George Ave, Odessa FL 33556, USA — Football Player

**Garner, James**
2515 Fountain Hill Loop, Lincoln CA 95648, USA — Actor

**Garner, Jennifer**
Vandalia Films, 9100 Wilshire Blvd, #1000W, Beverly Hills CA 90212, USA — Actress

**Garner, Julia**
W M E Entertainment, 9601 Wilshire Blvd, #300, Beverly Hills CA 90210 USA — Actress

**Garner, Kelli**
John Carrabino Mgmt, 5900 Wilshire Blvd, #406, Los Angeles CA 90036 USA — Actress

**Garner, Philip M (Phil)**
2 Sapling Place, Spring TX 77382, USA — Baseball Player, Manager

**Garner, Wendell R**
105 Northcreek Circle, Walnut Creek CA 94598, USA — Psychologist

**Garner, William S**
Memphis Commercial Appeal, Editorial Dept, 495 Union Ave, Memphis TN 38103, USA — Editorial Cartoonist

**Garnes, Sam A**
7322 S Valdai Circle, Aurora CO 80016, USA — Football Player

**Garnett, Kevin M**
75 Buttricks Hill Dr, Concord MA 01742, USA — Basketball Player

**Garofalo, Janeane**
I C M Partners, 10250 Constellation Blvd, #900, Los Angeles CA 90067 USA — Actress, Comedienne

**Garouste, Gerard**
La Mesangere, 27810 Marcilly-sur-Eure, France — Artist

**Garr, Ralph A**
22314 Auburn Canyon Lane, Richmond TX 77469, USA — Baseball Player

**Garr, Teri**
Paradigm Agency, 360 N Crescent Dr, North Building, Beverly Hills CA 90210 USA — Actress

**Garrard, David D**
4372 Hunterston Lane, Jacksonville FL 32224, USA — Football Player

**Garrard, Rose**
105 Carpenters Road, #21, London E18, England — Artist, Sculptor

**Garre, Gregory G**
George Washington University, Law Center, Washington DC 20052, USA — Government Official, Attorney

**Garrelts, Scott W**
11070 Ashland Way, Shreveport LA 71106, USA — Baseball Player

**Garrett, Brad**
United Talent Agency, U T A Plaza, 9336 Civic Center Dr, Beverly Hills CA 90210 USA — Actor, Comedian

**Garrett, Carl L**
203 S Crawford St, Denton TX 76205, USA — Football Player

**Garrett, David**
Music & Media Partnership, 126-129 Power Road, London W4 5PY, England — Concert Violinist

**Garrett, Eldo (Dick)**
7100 N Park Manor Dr, Milwaukee WI 53224, USA — Basketball Player

**Garrett, H Adrian (Ade)**
PO Box 201, Manchaca TX 78652, USA — Baseball Player

**Garrett, H Lawrence, III**
RR 1 Box 136-18, Boyce VA 22620, USA — Government Official

**Garrett, Jason C**
3656 Maplewood Ave, Dallas TX 75205, USA — Football Player, Coach

**Garrett, Jeremy**
W M E Entertainment, 9601 Wilshire Blvd, #300, Beverly Hills CA 90210 USA — Actor

**Garrett, John M**
Rogers Sportsnet, 181 Keefer Place, #221, Vancouver BC V6B 6C1, Canada — Ice Hockey Player

**Garrett, Kathleen**
Don Buchwald, 10 E 44th St, New York NY 10017 USA — Actress

**Garrett, Kenneth**
National Geographic, Editorial Dept, 1145 17th St NW, Washington DC 20036 USA — Photographer

**Garrett, Kenny**
Management Ark, 116 Village Blvd, #200, Princeton NJ 08540, USA — Jazz Saxophonist, Flutist

**Garrett, LaMonica**
Elevate Entertainment, 1925 Century Park E, #2320 Los Angeles CA 90067, USA — Actor

**Garrett, Leif**
Barbara Papageorge, 790 Amsterdam Ave, #4E, New York NY 10025, USA — Actor, Singer

**Garrett, Leonard N (Len)**
9413 W Tampa Dr, Baton Rouge LA 70815, USA — Football Player

**Garrett, Lesley**
Music Partnership, 41 Aldebert Terrace, London SW8 1BH, England — Opera Singer

**Garrett, Maureen**
Paradigm Agency, 360 N Crescent Dr, North Building, Beverly Hills CA 90210 USA — Actress

**Garrett, Megan**
Proper Mgmt, PO Box 150867, Nashville TN 37215, USA — Keyboardist (Casting Crowns)

**Garrett, Pat**
Gold Dust Talent/Records, RR 78, Exit 19, Strausstown PA 19559, USA — Singer, Guitarist, Songwriter

**Garrett, Peter R**
806-812 Anzac Parade, #600, PO Box 249, Maroubra NSW 2035, Australia — Singer, Government Official

**Garrett, R Wayne**
4331 Linwood St, Sarasota FL 34232, USA — Baseball Player

**Garrett, Siedah**
McClure & Associates Public Relations, 5225 Wilshire Blvd, #909, Los Angeles CA 90036, USA — Singer (Brand New Heavies), Songwriter

**Garrett, Spencer**
Stone Manners Salners, 9911 W Pico Blvd, #1400, Los Angeles CA 90035 USA — Actor

**Garrett, Wilbur E (Bill)**
209 Seneca Road, Great Falls VA 22066, USA — Editor

**Garrick, Barbara**
CornerStone Talent, 37 W 20th St, #1108, New York NY 10011, USA — Actress

**Garrick, Thomas S (Tom)**
235 Providence St, West Warwick RI 02893, USA — Basketball Player

| | |
|---|---|
| **Garrido Davidds, Norberto, Jr**<br>15633 Briarbank St, La Puente CA 91744, USA | Football Player |
| **Garrido, Gil G**<br>11311 SW 200th St, #110D, Miami FL 33157, USA | Baseball Player |
| **Garrigus, Thomas**<br>PO Box 681, Plains MT 59859, USA | Marksman |
| **Garriott, Owen K**<br>111 Lost Tree Dr SW, Huntsville AL 35824, USA | Astronaut |
| **Garriott, Richard A**<br>NCsoft, 6801 N Capital of Texas Highway, #1-102, Austin TX 78731, USA | Tourist Cosmonaut |
| **Garris, Mick**<br>Paradigm Agency, 360 N Crescent Dr, North Building, Beverly Hills CA 90210 USA | Director |
| **Garrison, David**<br>S M S Talent, 8383 Wilshire Blvd, #230, Beverly Hills CA 90211 USA | Actor |
| **Garrison, Gary L**<br>7757 Caminito Encanto Lane, #102, Carlsbad CA 92009, USA | Football Player |
| **Garrison, Lane**<br>Untitled Entertainment, 350 S Beverly Dr, #200, Beverly Hills CA 90212 USA | Actor, Writer |
| **Garrison, Walter B (Walt)**<br>3475 E Hickory Hill Road, Argyle TX 76226, USA | Football Player |
| **Garrison, Webster L**<br>2038 Rue Racine, Marrero LA 70072, USA | Baseball Player |
| **Garrison, Zina**<br>All Court Tennis Foundation, 12335 Kingsride, #106, Houston TX 77024, USA | Tennis Player |
| **Garrity, Gregg D**<br>86 Seldom Seen Road, Bradfordwoods PA 15015, USA | Football Player |
| **Garrity, John (Jack)**<br>1530 Beacon St, #1201, Brookline MA 02446, USA | Ice Hockey Player |
| **Garrity, Patrick J (Pat)**<br>6126 Ches Court, Orlando FL 32819, USA | Basketball Player |
| **Garro, Julia**<br>Innovative Artists, 1505 10th St, Santa Monica CA 90401 USA | Actress |
| **Garron, Lawrence (Larry), Jr**<br>3 Debra Lane, Framingham MA 01701, USA | Football Player |
| **Garrone, Matteo**<br>Archimede, Via Tiburtina 521, 00159 Rome, Italy | Director |
| **Garson, Willie**<br>John Carrabino Mgmt, 5900 Wilshire Blvd, #406, Los Angeles CA 90036 USA | Actor |
| **Garten, Ina**<br>46 Newton Ave, #3, East Hampton NY 11937, USA | Food Expert |
| **Garth, Jennie**<br>W M E Entertainment, 9601 Wilshire Blvd, #300, Beverly Hills CA 90210 USA | Actress |
| **Garth, Leonard I**<br>US Court of Appeals, US Courthouse, 50 Walnut St, #5040, Newark NJ 07102, USA | Judge |
| **Gartner, Claus-Theo**<br>Postfach 230313, 45071 Essen, Germany | Actor |
| **Gartner, James**<br>I C M Partners, 10250 Constellation Blvd, #900, Los Angeles CA 90067 USA | Director |
| **Gartner, Michael A (Mike)**<br>N H L Players Assn, 1700-20 Bay St, Toronto ON M5J 2N8, Canada | Ice Hockey Player |
| **Gartner, Michael G**<br>100 Market St, #515, Des Moines IA 50309, USA | Publisher, Editor, Businessman |
| **Gartner, Stephen**<br>Gartner & Blade, 4-1354 Kuhio Highway, Kapaa HI 96746, USA | Artist |
| **Garver, Kathy**<br>PO Box 117345, Burlingame CA 94011, USA | Actress |
| **Garver, Ned F**<br>1121 Town Line Road, #164, Bryan OH 43506, USA | Baseball Player |
| **Garvey, Steven P (Steve)**<br>Athlete Promotions, 2247 Rickover Place, Winter Garden FL 34787, USA | Baseball Player |
| **Garwin, Richard L**<br>1 Christie Place, #402W, Scarsdale NY 10583, USA | Physicist |
| **Gary, Keith J**<br>450 Massachusetts Ave NW, #903, Washington DC 20001, USA | Football Player |
| **Gary, Lorraine**<br>1158 Tower Dr, Beverly Hills CA 90210, USA | Actress |
| **Garza, David**<br>Partisan Arts, PO Box 5085, Larkspur CA 94977, USA | Singer |
| **Garza, Emilio M**<br>US Court of Appeals, US Courthouse, 8200 I-10 W, San Antonio TX 78230, USA | Judge |
| **Garza, Henry**<br>Loophole Entertainment, PO Box 162045, Austin TX 78716, USA | Guitarist (Los Lonely Boys) |
| **Garza, JoJo**<br>Loophole Entertainment, PO Box 162045, Austin TX 78716, USA | Bassist (Los Lonely Boys) |
| **Garza, Loreto**<br>6 Napa Place, Woodland CA 95695, USA | Boxer |
| **Garza, Nicole**<br>Kritzer Levine Wilkins Griffin, 11872 La Grange Ave, #100, Los Angeles CA 90025 USA | Actress, Model |
| **Garza, Ringo**<br>Loophole Entertainment, PO Box 162045, Austin TX 78716, USA | Drummer (Los Lonely Boys) |
| **Garzon, Baltasar**<br>Audiencia Nacional, Garcia Gutierrez 1, 28004 Madrid, Spain | Judge |
| **Gascoigne, Paul J**<br>Robertson Craig Co, Clairmont Gardens, Glasgow G3 7LW, Scotland | Soccer Player |
| **Gascoine, Jill**<br>Marina Martin, 12/13 Poland St, London W1V 3DE, England | Actress |
| **Gash, Samuel L (Sam)**<br>18549 Steep Hollow Court, Northville MI 48168, USA | Football Player |
| **Gaskell, Anna**<br>Albright-Kerr Gallery, 1285 Elmwood Ave, Buffalo NY 14222, USA | Photographer |
| **Gaskin, F Neal, Jr**<br>Gaskin Architectural, 2900 S Rancho Drive, #101, Las Vegas NV 89102, USA | Architect |
| **Gaskins, Reggie**<br>I C M Partners, 10250 Constellation Blvd, #900, Los Angeles CA 90067 USA | Actor, Director, Writer |
| **Gasol I Saez, Pau**<br>Los Angeles Lakers, Staples Center, 1111 S Figueroa St, Los Angeles CA 90015 USA | Basketball Player |

# G

|  |  |
|---|---|
| **Gasol I Sasez, Marc** <br> Memphis Grizzlies, 191 Beale St, Memphis TN 38103 USA | Basketball Player |
| **Gaspar, Rodney E (Rod)** <br> 28771 Peach Blossom, Mission Viejo CA 92692, USA | Baseball Player |
| **Gasparovic, Ivan** <br> President's Office, Hodzova Namestie 2978/1, 81006 Bratislava, Slovakia | President, Slovakia |
| **Gasquet, Richard** <br> 49 Rue Gaite, 92140 Clamart, France | Tennis Player |
| **Gass, Kyle R** <br> Greene Assoc, 1901 Ave of Stars, #130, Los Angeles CA 90067 USA | Actor, Singer, Guitarist |
| **Gass, William H** <br> 6304 Westminster Place, Saint Louis MO 63130, USA | Philosopher, Writer |
| **Gass-Donnelly, Ed** <br> I C M Partners, 10250 Constellation Blvd, #900, Los Angeles CA 90067 USA | Director |
| **Gassiyev, Nikolai T** <br> Mariinsky Theater, Teatralnaya Square 1, 190000 Saint Petersburg, Russia | Opera Singer |
| **Gassner, Dave** <br> N1376 Woodland Dr, Greenville WI 54942, USA | Baseball Player |
| **Gast, Alice P** <br> Lehigh University, President's Office, 27 Memorial Dr W, Bethlehem PA 18015, USA | Educator |
| **Gasteyer, Ana K** <br> Gersh Agency, 9465 Wilshire Blvd, #600, Beverly Hills CA 90212 USA | Actress, Comedienne |
| **Gastineau, Marcus D (Mark)** <br> 22202 N 48th St, Phoenix AZ 85054, USA | Football Player |
| **Gaston, Clarence E (Cito)** <br> 1454 Woodstream Dr, Oldsmar FL 34677, USA | Baseball Player, Manager |
| **Gaston, Marilyn H** <br> Gaston-Porter Health Improvement Center, 8612 Timber Hill, Potomac MD 20854, USA | Physician, Administrator |
| **Gaston, Michael** <br> A P A Talent/Literary Agency, 405 S Beverly Dr, #300, Beverly Hills CA 90212 USA | Actor |
| **Gate, Aaron** <br> 6 Kipling Ave, Epsom Auckland 1023, New Zealand | Cyclist |
| **Gates, Antonio M** <br> PO Box 11369, Charlotte NC 28220, USA | Football Player |
| **Gates, Brent R** <br> 4229 Haralson Court SE, Grand Rapids MI 49546, USA | Baseball Player |
| **Gates, David** <br> Icon Performing Arts, 1557 Westwood Blvd, #242, Los Angeles CA 90024, USA | Singer, Keyboardist (Bread), Songwriter |
| **Gates, Gareth P** <br> 19 Music & Mgmt, 35-37 Parkgate Road, London SW11 4NP, England | Singer |
| **Gates, Henry Lewis, Jr** <br> Harvard University, Afro-American Studies Dept, Cambridge MA 02138, USA | Educator |
| **Gates, Marshall D, Jr** <br> 41 W Brook Road, Pittsford PA 14534, USA | Chemist |
| **Gates, Tucker** <br> United Talent Agency, U T A Plaza, 9336 Civic Center Dr, Beverly Hills CA 90210 USA | Director, Producer |
| **Gates, William H (Bill), III** <br> Microsoft Corp, 1 Microsoft Way, Redmond WA 98052, USA | Computer Software Designer, Businessman |
| **Gatewood, Mark** <br> Gatewood Studio, 211 SE Morrison St, Portland OR 97214, USA | Artist |
| **Gathegi, Edi** <br> Framework Entertainment, 9057 Nemo St, #C, West Hollywood CA 90069 USA | Actor |
| **Gathright, Joey R** <br> 9100 Dr Martin Luther King Jr St N, #902, Saint Petersburg FL 33702, USA | Baseball Player |
| **Gatien, Elise** <br> Carrie Wheeler Mgmt, 101-1001 W Broadway, #338, Vancouver BC V6H 4E4, Canada | Actress |
| **Gatins, John** <br> United Talent Agency, U T A Plaza, 9336 Civic Center Dr, Beverly Hills CA 90210 USA | Actor, Writer |
| **Gatlin, Justin** <br> 6979 Raborn Road, Pensacola FL 32526, USA | Track Athlete |
| **Gatlin, Larry W** <br> Press Office, 1009 16th Ave S, Nashville TN 37212, USA | Singer, Songwriter (Gatlin Brothers) |
| **Gatling, Chris R** <br> 175 Canon Dr, Orinda CA 94563, USA | Basketball Player |
| **Gatos, Harry C** <br> 20 Indian Hill Road, Weston MA 02493, USA | Electrical Engineer |
| **Gatti, Daniele** <br> Via Scaglia Est 134, 41100 Modena, Italy | Conductor |
| **Gatti, Jennifer** <br> S D B Partners, 1801 Ave of Stars, #902, Los Angeles CA 90067 USA | Actress |
| **Gatting, Michael W** <br> Middlesex Cricket Club, Saint John's Wood Road, London NW8 8QN, England | Cricketer |
| **Gattison, Kenneth A (Kenny)** <br> 1115 I St NE, Washington DC 20002, USA | Basketball Player |
| **Gaubatz, Dennis E** <br> 1250 County Road 943, West Columbia TX 77486, USA | Football Player |
| **Gauci, Miriam** <br> Kunstleragentur Raab & Bohm, Plankengasse 7, 1010 Vienna, Austria | Opera Singer |
| **Gauck, Joachim** <br> Bundespraesidialamt, Spreeweg 1, 10557 Berlin, Germany | President, Germany; Political Activist |
| **Gaudin, Chad E** <br> 108 Cirtus Road, New Orleans LA 70123, USA | Baseball Player |
| **Gaudio, Robert J (Bob)** <br> I C M Partners, 10250 Constellation Blvd, #900, Los Angeles CA 90067 USA | Singer, Organist (Four Seasons) |
| **Gaughan, Brendan** <br> Germain Racing, 218 Raceway Drive, Mooresville NC 28117, USA | Truck Racing Driver |
| **Gault, Scott** <br> Roger A Gault, 615 Park Way, Piedmont CA 94611, USA | Rowing Athlete |
| **Gault, William Campbell** <br> 481 Mountain Dr, Santa Barbara CA 93103, USA | Writer |
| **Gault, Willie J** <br> 15460 La Maida St, Sherman Oaks CA 91403, USA | Football Player |
| **Gaultier, Jean-Paul** <br> 30 Rue Saint Martin, 75003 Paris, France | Fashion Designer |
| **Gauthier, Dan** <br> Michael Einfeld Mgmt, 10630 Moorpark Ave, #101, Toluca Lake CA 91602, USA | Actor |

**Gauthier, Daniel** — Circus Executive
Cirque du Soleil, 8400 2nd Ave, Montreal QC H1Z 4M6, Canada

**Gauthier, Denis, Jr** — Ice Hockey Player
1658 9th St, Manhattan Beach CA 90266, USA

**Gauthier, Jean P** — Ice Hockey Player
415 Vinet Ave, Dorval QC H9S 2M7, Canada

**Gauthier, Mary** — Singer, Songwriter
Mark Spector Co, 100 5th Ave, #1100, New York NY 10011

**Gautier, Dick** — Actor
11333 Moorpark St, #59, North Hollywood CA 91602, USA

**Gava, Cassandra** — Actress
1745 Camino Palmero St, #210, Los Angeles CA 90046, USA

**Gavanelli, Paolo** — Opera Singer
I M G Artists, Hogarth Business Park, Chiswick, London W4 2TH, England

**Gavankar, Janina** — Actress
Talent Works, 3500 W Olive Ave, #1400, Burbank CA 91505 USA

**Gavaskar, Sunil M** — Cricketer
Nirlon Synthetics, Annie Besant Road, #254B, Worli, Mumbai 400025, India

**Gavey, Aaron** — Ice Hockey Player
84 Park Place Dr, Sault Sainte Marie ON P6B 6L3, Canada

**Gavin, John** — Actor, Diplomat
606 N Larchmont Blvd, #210, Los Angeles CA 90004, USA

**Gaviria Trujillo, Cesar** — President, Colombia
Club de Madrid, C/Goya 5-7, Pasaje 2, 28001 Madrid, Spain

**Gavrilov, Andrei V** — Concert Pianist
Konzertdirektion Schlote, Danreitergasse 4, 5020 Salzburg, Austria

**Gavron, Rafi** — Actor
Affirmative Entertainment, 425 N Robertson Blvd, Los Angeles CA 90048 USA

**Gay, Don** — Rodeo Rider
1818 Rodeo Dr, Mesquite TX 75149, USA

**Gay, Gerald H (Jerry)** — Photojournalist
2121 Madison St, #C, Everett WA 98203, USA

**Gay, J Brian** — Golfer
Professional Golfer's Assn, PO Box 109601, Palm Beach Gardens FL 33410 USA

**Gay, Peter J** — Historian
270 Riverside Dr, #8C, New York NY 10025, USA

**Gay, Randall J, Jr** — Football Player
6706 Joyce Dr, #3C, Addis LA 70710, USA

**Gay, Rudy C, Jr** — Basketball Player
91 W Galloway Dr, Memphis TN 38111, USA

**Gay, Tyson** — Track Athlete
Global Athletics & Marketing, 437 Boylston St, #400, Boston MA 02116, USA

**Gay, William H (Bill)** — Football Player
8200 E Jefferson Ave, #804, Detroit MI 48214, USA

**Gaydukov, Sergei N** — Cosmonaut
Cosmonaut Training Center, Star City, 141160 Zvezdny Gorodok, Moscow Oblast, Russia

**Gaye, Nona** — Singer, Model, Actress
Kritzer Levine Wilkins Griffin, 11872 La Grange Ave, #100, Los Angeles CA 90025 USA

**Gayheart, Rebecca** — Actress, Model
Gersh Agency, 9465 Wilshire Blvd, #600, Beverly Hills CA 90212 USA

**Gayl, Franz** — Military Activist
5823 Crowfoot Dr, Burke VA 22015, USA

**Gayle, Crystal** — Singer
Gayle Enterprises, 51 Music Square E, Nashville TN 37203, USA

**Gayle, Michelle P** — Singer, Actress
Mission Control, City Business Center, Lower Road, London SE16 2XB, England

**Gayle, Robyn K** — Soccer Player
Canadian Soccer, Place Soccer Canada, 237 Metcalfe St, Ottawa ON K2P 1R2, Canada

**Gayle, Shaun L** — Football Player
1530 N Elk Grove Ave, #1, Chicago IL 60622, USA

**Gaylor, Christopher J (Chris)** — Drummer (All-American Rejects)
Creative Artists Agency, 2000 Ave of Stars, #100, Los Angeles CA 90067 USA

**Gaylord, Frank** — Sculptor
2844 Vermont Route 14, Williamstown VT 05679, USA

**Gaylord, Mitchell J (Mitch)** — Gymnast, Actor
9601 Bowman Dr, Fort Worth TX 76244, USA

**Gaynes, George** — Actor
Innovative Artists, 1505 10th St, Santa Monica CA 90401 USA

**Gaynor, Gloria** — Singer
Red Entertainment Agency, 505 8th Ave, #1004, New York NY 10018, USA

**Gaynor, Mitzi** — Actress, Dancer, Singer
610 N Arden Dr, Beverly Hills CA 90210, USA

**Gayoom, Maumoon Abdul** — President, Maldives
Ma Ki'nbigasdhoshuge, Male 20229, Maldives

**Gayson, Eunice** — Actress
Spotlight, 7 Leicester Place, London WC2H 7BP, England

**Gayton, Joe** — Producer, Writer
United Talent Agency, U T A Plaza, 9336 Civic Center Dr, Beverly Hills CA 90210 USA

**Gayton, Tony** — Producer, Writer
United Talent Agency, U T A Plaza, 9336 Civic Center Dr, Beverly Hills CA 90210 USA

**Gazarek, Sara** — Singer, Guitarist
Stiletto Entertainment, 5200 W 83rd St, #G, Los Angeles CA 90045, USA

**Gaze, Andrew** — Basketball Player
Basketball Resources, PO Box 2222, Ivanhoe East VIC 3029, Australia

**Gazit, Doron** — Artist
Air Dimensional Inc, 14141 Covello St, Building 1, Van Nuys CA 91405, USA

**Gazzaniga, Michael S** — Psychologist
University of California, Study of Mind Center, Santa Barbara CA 93106, USA

**Gbaja-Biamila, Akbar O** — Football Player
1050 Armitage Ave, Alameda CA 94502, USA

**Gbowee, Leymah R** — Nobel Peace Activist
Women's Peace & Security Network, 68 Onyankle St, Abelempke, Accra, Ghana

**Geale, Daniel** — Boxer
Team Fenech, PO Box 66, Millers Point NSW 2000, Australia

**Gearhart, G David** — Educator
University of Arkansas, Chancellor's Office, Administration Building, Fayetteville AR 72701, USA

**G**

| | |
|---|---|
| **Gearhart, John P** <br> Johns Hopkins University Medical Center, Baltimore MD 21218 USA | Neurologist, Biologist |
| **Gearing, Ashley** <br> W M E Entertainment, 1600 Division St, #300, Nashville TN 37203 USA | Singer |
| **Geary, Anthony (Tony)** <br> 7010 Pacific View Dr, Los Angeles CA 90068, USA | Actor |
| **Geary, Cynthia** <br> Baumgarten/Prophet, 1041 N Formosa Ave, #200, West Hollywood CA 90046, USA | Actress |
| **Geary, Geoffrey M (Geoff)** <br> 175 Maple Ave, #2, Carlsbad CA 92008, USA | Baseball Player |
| **Geary, Nancy** <br> Nicholas Ellison, 55 5th Ave, #1500, New York NY 10003, USA | Writer |
| **Geathers, James A (Jumpy)** <br> 200 Tony Dr, Cape Elizabeth ME 04107, USA | Football Player |
| **Geathers, Robert L, Jr** <br> 1 Dab Dr, Georgetown SC 29440, USA | Football Player |
| **Gebhard, Robert H (Bob)** <br> 5242 E Otero Place, Littleton CO 80122, USA | Baseball Player, Executive |
| **Gebo, Daniel** <br> Northern Illinois University, Paleontology Dept, DeKalb IL 60115, USA | Paleontologist |
| **Gebrselassie, Haile** <br> Waterdelweg 14, 5427 LS Boehel 98007, Monaco | Track Athlete |
| **Gedda, Nicolai** <br> Valhavagen 128, 114 41 Stockholm, Sweden | Opera Singer |
| **Geddes, Anne** <br> K Geddes Mgmt, 2 York St, Parnell 1001, Auckland, New Zealand | Photographer |
| **Geddes, James L (Jim)** <br> 6738 Harrisburg London Road, Orient OH 43146, USA | Baseball Player |
| **Geddes, Jane** <br> 33 Fairview Ave, Darien CT 06820, USA | Golfer |
| **Geddes, Kenneth L (Ken)** <br> 7702 147th Ave NE, Redmond WA 98052, USA | Football Player |
| **Geddis, Peter** <br> Brown & Simcocks, 109 Blackfriars Road, London SE1 8HW, England | Actor |
| **Gedeck, Martina** <br> Postfach 370521, 14135 Berlin, Germany | Actress |
| **Gedman, Richard L (Rich)** <br> 10 Parmenter Road, Framingham MA 01701, USA | Baseball Player |
| **Gedney, Christopher J (Chris)** <br> 4881 Excalibur Dr, Syracuse NY 13215, USA | Football Player |
| **Gedrick, Jason** <br> I F A Talent Agency, 8730 W Sunset Blvd, #490, West Hollywood CA 90069 USA | Actor |
| **Gee, E Gordon** <br> Ohio State University, President's Office, Columbus OH 43210, USA | Educator |
| **Gee, Prunella** <br> Michael Ladkin Mgmt, 1 Duchess St, #1, London W1N 3DE, England | Actress |
| **Geer, Charlotte** <br> PO Box 324, Hinesburg VT 05461, USA | Rowing Athlete |
| **Geer, Ellen** <br> Kyle Fritz Mgmt, 6325 Heather Dr, Los Angeles CA 90068 USA | Actress |
| **Geer, Josh** <br> 10836 Peach Circle, Forney. TX 75126, USA | Baseball Player |
| **Geesaman, Lynn** <br> Thomas Barry Fine Arts, 530 N 3rd St, #B10, Minneapolis MN 55401, USA | Photographer |
| **Geesen, Masha** <br> Bloomsbury Publishing, 50 Bedford Square, London WC1B 3DP, England | Writer |
| **Geeson, Judy** <br> Bauman Redanty Shaul Agency, 5757 Wilshire Blvd, #473, Los Angeles CA 90036 USA | Actress |
| **Geffen, David** <br> 22108 Pacific Coast Highway, Malibu CA 90265, USA | Producer, Businessman |
| **Gehring, Frederick W** <br> 1200 Earhart Road, Ann Arbor MI 48105, USA | Mathematician |
| **Gehring, Lana** <br> US Speedskating, 5662 S Cougar Lane, Salt Lake City UT 84118 USA | Speed Skater |
| **Gehring, Walter J** <br> Hochfeldstr 32, 4106 Therwil, Switzerland | Geneticist |
| **Gehry, Frank O** <br> Gehry Partners, 12541 Beatrice St, Los Angeles CA 90066, USA | Pritzker Architectural Laureate |
| **Geiberger, Al** <br> 80555 Tangelo Court, Indio CA 92201, USA | Golfer |
| **Geiduschek, E Peter** <br> University of California, Biology Dept, 9500 Gilman Dr, La Jolla CA 92093, USA | Biologist |
| **Geier, Philip H, Jr** <br> Geier Group, Heron Tower, 70 E 55th St, #1500, New York NY 10022, USA | Businessman |
| **Geiger, Ken** <br> National Geographic Magazine, Editorial Dept, PO Box 98199, Washington DC 20090, USA | Photojournalist |
| **Geiger, Matthew A (Matt)** <br> 3385 Old Keystone Road, Tarpon Springs FL 34688, USA | Basketball Player |
| **Geiger, Teddy** <br> I C M Partners, 10250 Constellation Blvd, #900, Los Angeles CA 90067 USA | Singer, Songwriter, Actor |
| **Geisel, J David (Dave)** <br> 4 Blacksmith Lane, Media PA 19063, USA | Baseball Player |
| **Geisenberger, Natalie** <br> On the Green 35, 83714 Miesbach, Germany | Luge Athlete |
| **Geismar, Thomas H** <br> Chermayeff & Geismar, 15 E 26th St, #1200, New York NY 10010, USA | Architect |
| **Geiss, Johannes** <br> International Space Science Institute, Hallestr 6, 3012 Berne, Switzerland | Physicist |
| **Geist, William (Willie)** <br> NBC-TV, News Dept, 30 Rockefeller Plaza, #270E, New York NY 10112 USA | Sports Commentator |
| **Geithner, Timothy** <br> Treasury Department, 1500 Pennsylvania Ave NW, Washington DC 20220 USA | Secretary, Treasury |
| **Gelana, E Tiki** <br> Global Sports Communication, Snelliustraat 10, 6533 Nijmegen NV, Netherlands | Track Athlete |
| **Gelb, Leslie H** <br> Council on Foreign Relations, 58 E 68th St, New York NY 10065, USA | Educator |

**Gelb, Peter** — Opera Executive
Metropolitan Opera Assn, Lincoln Center Plaza, New York NY 10023 USA
**Gelbaugh, Stanley M (Stan)** — Football Player
10819 Hob Nail Court, Potomac MD 20854, USA
**Geldof, Bob** — Singer, Songwriter
Red Entertainment, 505 8th Ave, #1004, New York NY 10018, USA
**Gellar, Sarah Michelle** — Actress
I C M Partners, 10250 Constellation Blvd, #900, Los Angeles CA 90067 USA
**Geller, Margaret J** — Astronomer
Harvard University, Astronomy Dept, 60 Garden St, Cambridge MA 02138, USA
**Geller, Uri** — Psychic, Illusionist
Celeb Agents, 77 Oxford St, London W1D 2ES, England
**Gellman, Marc** — Religious Leader, Rabbi, Commentator
Temple Beth Torah, 35 Bagatelle Road, Melville NY 11747, USA
**Gell-Mann, Murray** — Nobel Physics Laureate
Santa Fe Institute, 1399 Hyde Park Road, Santa Fe NM 87501, USA
**Gelman, Barton** — Journalist
Washington Post, Editorial Dept, 1150 15th St NW, Washington DC 20071 USA
**Gelman, Larry** — Actor
5121 Greenbush Ave, Sherman Oaks CA 91423, USA
**Gelman, Michael S** — Producer
7 W 63rd St, #500, New York NY 10023, USA
**Gelnar, John R** — Baseball Player
300 N Hitchcock St, Hobart OK 73651, USA
**Gemar, Charles D** — Astronaut
7660 N 159th St Court E, Benton KS 67017, USA
**Gemignani, Alexander** — Actor, Singer
Innovative Artists, 1505 10th St, Santa Monica CA 90401 USA
**Gemma** — Model
I M G Models, 304 Park Ave S, #PH N, New York NY 10010 USA
**Gemmell, Ruth** — Actress
Hamilton Hodell, 66-68 Margaret St, #500, London W1W 8SR, England
**Genaux, Vivica** — Opera Singer
K K N Enterprises, 277 W End Ave, #11A, New York NY 10023, USA
**Gendron, George M** — Editor, Educator
Clark University, Graduate Management School, 950 Main St, Worcester MA 01610, USA
**Genest, Veronique** — Actress
Artmedia, 20 Ave Rapp, 75007 Paris, France
**Genova, Lisa** — Writer
Pocket Books, 1230 Ave of Americas, New York NY 10020 USA
**Genovese, George M** — Baseball Player
11474 Erwin St, North Hollywood CA 91606, USA
**Genscher, Hans-Dietrich** — Government Official, Germany
Am Kottenforst 16, 53343 Wachtberg-Pech, Germany
**Genser, Eli Morgan** — Actor
Innovative Artists, 1505 10th St, Santa Monica CA 90401 USA
**Genshaft, Judy L** — Educator
University of South Florida, President's Office, Tampa FL 33620, USA
**Gensler, M Arthur, Jr** — Architect
Gensler & Assoc Architects, 550 Kearny St, San Francisco CA 94108, USA
**Genthe, Eva Z** — Photographer
C A 1 Photography, Scholdstr 1, 76227 Karlsruhe-Durlach, Germany
**Gentile, James E (Jim)** — Baseball Player
1016 W Neptune Road, Edmond OK 73003, USA
**Gentry, Alvin** — Basketball Coach, Executive
Los Angeles Clippers, Staples Center, 1111 S Figueroa St, Los Angeles CA 90015 USA
**Gentry, Dennis L** — Football Player
916 Queen Elizabeth Dr, McGregor TX 76657, USA
**Gentry, Gary E** — Baseball Player
301 W Lawrence Lane, Phoenix AZ 85021, USA
**Gentry, Teddy W** — Singer, Guitarist (Alabama)
Alabama Band Promotions, PO Box 680529, Fort Payne AL 35968, USA
**Gentry, Troy** — Singer (Montgomery Gentry)
Parallel Entertainment, 209 10th Ave S, #506, Nashville TN 37203, USA
**Genzel, Carrie** — Actress
Pakula/King, 9229 W Sunset Blvd, #315, West Hollywood CA 90069 USA
**Genzel, Reinhard** — Astrophysicist
Extraterrestrial Institute, Schwarzschild Str 1, 85741 Garchung, Germany
**Geoffroy, Gregory** — Educator
Iowa State University, President's Office, Ames IA 50011, USA
**George, Anton H (Tony)** — Auto Racing Executive
Vision Racing, 6803 Coffman Road, Indianapolis IN 46268, USA
**George, Christopher S (Chris)** — Baseball Player
7703 Goldengrove Dr, Spring TX 77379, USA
**George, Devean J** — Basketball Player
14001 53rd Ave N, Minneapolis MN 55446, USA
**George, Edward N (Eddie)** — Football Player, Actor
9538 Sanctuary Place, Brentwood TN 37027, USA
**George, Elizabeth** — Writer
Byron's Mgmt, 76 Saint James Lane, London N10 3DF, England
**George, Eric** — Actor
Lasher McManus Robinson, 1964 Westwood Blvd, #400, Los Angeles CA 90025, USA
**George, Francis E Cardinal** — Religious Leader
Chicago Pastoral Center, PO Box 1979, Chicago IL 60690, USA
**George, Helen** — Actress
D A A Management, Welbeck House, 66-67 Wells St, London WIT 3PY, England
**George, Inara** — Singer, Guitarist (Bird & the Bee)
Blue Note Records, 6920 W Sunset Blvd, Los Angeles CA 90028 USA
**George, James (Jim)** — Weightlifter
4319 Regal Dr, Akron OH 44321, USA
**George, Jason Winston** — Actor
Management 360, 9111 Wilshire Blvd, Beverly Hills CA 90210 USA
**George, Jeffrey S (Jeff)** — Football Player
1980 Schwier Court, Indianapolis IN 46229, USA
**George, Maximillian A (Max)** — Singer (Wanted)
Industry Music Group, 128 Regent Road, Hanley Stoke, Trent ST1 3AY, England

**G**

| | |
|---|---|
| **George, Melissa**<br>I C M Partners, 10250 Constellation Blvd, #900, Los Angeles CA 90067 USA | Actress |
| **George, Oorlagh**<br>Northwood Productions, 2901 Ocean Park Blvd, #217, Santa Monica CA 90405, USA | Producer |
| **George, Phyllis**<br>C E S D, 10635 Santa Monica Blvd, #130, Los Angeles CA 90025 USA | Entertainer, Beauty Queen |
| **George, Rocky**<br>Silverback Mgmt, 9469 Jefferson Blvd, #101, Culver City CA 90232, USA | Guitarist (Fishbone) |
| **George, Ronald L (Ron)**<br>13720 Piedmont Vista Dr, Haymarket VA 20169, USA | Football Player |
| **George, Susan**<br>McKorkindale & Holton, 1-2 Langham Place, London W1A 3DD, England | Actress |
| **George, Tate**<br>55 Georgetown Road, Bristol CT 06010, USA | Basketball Player |
| **George, Terry**<br>Independent Talent Group, 40 Whitfield St, London W1T 2RH, England | Director, Writer |
| **George, William W**<br>Harvard University, Business School, Cambridge MA 02138, USA | Businessman, Educator |
| **Georgel, Pierre**<br>41 Blvd Saint-Germain, 75005 Paris, France | Museum Official |
| **Georgi, Howard**<br>Harvard University, Physics Dept, Lyman Laboratory, Cambridge MA 02138, USA | Physicist |
| **Georgian, Theodore J**<br>Orthodox Presbyterian Church, PO Box P, Willow Grove PA 19090, USA | Religious Leader |
| **Georgije, Bishop**<br>Serbian Orthodox Church, Sava Monastery, PO Box 519, Libertyville IL 60048, USA | Religious Leader |
| **Georgis, William T**<br>233 E 72nd St, New York NY 10021, USA | Architect |
| **Geraci, Sonny**<br>Precious Time Productions, 30799 Pine Tree Road, #135, Pepper Pike OH 44124, USA | Singer (Outsiders, Climax) |
| **Geraghty, Brian T**<br>United Talent Agency, U T A Plaza, 9336 Civic Center Dr, Beverly Hills CA 90210 USA | Actor |
| **Geragos, Mark J**<br>Geragos & Geragos, 2 California Plaza, 350 S Grand Ave, Los Angeles CA 90071, USA | Attorney |
| **Gerard, Cindy**<br>Pocket/Star Books, 1230 Ave of Americas, New York NY 10020, USA | Writer |
| **Gerard, Daniel J (Gus)**<br>614 Cypresswood Dr, Spring TX 77388, USA | Basketball Player |
| **Gerard, Gil**<br>Michael Einfeld Mgmt, 10630 Moorpark Ave, #101, Toluca Lake CA 91602, USA | Actor, Producer, Director |
| **Gerard, Leo W**<br>United Steel Workers of America, 5 Gateway Center, Pittsburgh PA 15222, USA | Labor Leader |
| **Gerardo**<br>Nene Musik Productions, 1460 SW Santiago Ave, Port Saint Lucie FL 34953 USA | Rap Artist |
| **Gerber, Craig S**<br>4297 N Pershing Ave, San Bernardino CA 92407, USA | Baseball Player |
| **Gerber, H Joseph**<br>Gerber Scientific Inc, 83 Gerber Road W, South Windsor CT 06074, USA | Businessman |
| **Gerber, Joel**<br>US Tax Court, 400 2nd St NW, Washington DC 20217, USA | Judge |
| **Gerberding, Julie L**<br>Emory University Medical School, Infectious Disease Dept, Atlanta GA 30322, USA | Government Official, Physician |
| **Gere, Richard**<br>Hirsch Wallerstein, 10100 Santa Monica Blvd, #1700, Los Angeles CA 90067, USA | Actor |
| **Gerela, Roy**<br>3933 Ramrod Forge, Las Cruces NM 88012, USA | Football Player |
| **Geren, Robert P (Bob)**<br>2710 Bay Canyon Court, San Diego CA 92117, USA | Baseball Player, Manager |
| **Gerety, Tom, Jr**<br>Amherst College, President's Office, Amherst MA 01002, USA | Educator |
| **Gerg, Hilde**<br>Richard-Voss-Str 63, 83471 Schonau am Konigssee, Germany | Alpine Skier |
| **Gergen, David R**<br>31 Ash St, Cambridge MA 02138, USA | Editor |
| **Gergiev, Valery A**<br>Kirov Ballet Theater, 1 Pl Iskusstr, 190000 Saint Petersburg, Russia | Conductor |
| **Gergov, Rossen**<br>Harrison/Parrott, 5-6 Albion Court, London W6 0QT, England | Conductor |
| **Gerhaher, Christian**<br>Kunstler Sekretariat am Gasteig, Rosenheimer Str 52, 81669 Munich, Germany | Opera Singer |
| **Gering, Jenna**<br>Paradigm Agency, 360 N Crescent Dr, North Building, Beverly Hills CA 90210 USA | Actress |
| **Germann, Greg**<br>Innovative Artists, 1505 10th St, Santa Monica CA 90401 USA | Actor |
| **Germano, Lisa**<br>Artists & Audience Entertainment, PO Box 35, Pawling NY 12564 USA | Singer, Violinist, Songwriter |
| **Germany, Willie**<br>4401 Pratt St, Omaha NE 68111, USA | Football Player |
| **Germeshausen, Bernhard**<br>Hinter Dem Salon 39, 99195 Schwansee, Germany | Bobsled Athlete |
| **Gernert, Richard E (Dick)**<br>1801 Cambridge Ave, #C12, Reading PA 19610, USA | Baseball Player |
| **Gernhardt, Michael L**<br>2705 Lighthouse Dr, Houston TX 77058, USA | Astronaut |
| **Gero, Gary D**<br>2 McLaren, #A, Irvine CA 92618, USA | Cinematographer |
| **Gerring, Cathy**<br>3328 Tarrant Springs Trail, Fort Wayne IN 46804, USA | Golfer |
| **Gerrish, Brian A**<br>9142 Sycamore Hill Place, Mechanicsville VA 23116, USA | Theologian |
| **Gerritsen, Tess**<br>11 Pleasant Ridge Dr, Camden ME 04843, USA | Writer |
| **Gersbach, Carl R**<br>PO Box 433, Devon PA 19333, USA | Football Player |
| **Gershon, Gina**<br>Apostle Management, 9696 Culver Blvd, #108, Culver City CA 90232, USA | Actress |

**George - Gershon**

**Gerson, Mark** — Photographer
3 Regal Lane, Regent's Park, London NW1 7TH, England
**Gerstein, Kirill** — Concert Pianist
I M G Artists, Hogarth Business Park, Chiswick, London W4 2TH, England
**Gerstell, A Frederick** — Businessman
CalMat Co, 3200 San Fernando Road, Los Angeles CA 90065, USA
**Gerth, Jeff** — Journalist
New York Times, Editorial Dept, 229 W 43rd St, New York NY 10036 USA
**Gertz, Jami** — Actress
Innovative Artists, 1505 10th St, Santa Monica CA 90401 USA
**Gerut, Joseph D (Jody)** — Baseball Player
623 Rochdale Circle, Lombard IL 60148, USA
**Gervais, Ricky** — Actor, Comedian, Producer, Director
United Agents, 12-26 Lexington St, London W1F 0LE, England
**Gervin, George** — Basketball Player, Coach
44 Gervin Pass, Spring Branch TX 78070, USA
**Gerwick, Ben C, Jr** — Construction Engineer
5727 Country Club Dr, Oakland CA 94618, USA
**Gerwig, Greta** — Actress
United Talent Agency, U T A Plaza, 9336 Civic Center Dr, Beverly Hills CA 90210 USA
**Gerzmava, Hibla** — Opera Singer
Elena Kharakidzyan Art-Brand Artists, 6/66 Klimentovsky Per, 115184 Moscow, Russia
**Geschke, Charles** — Businessman
Adobe Systems, 375 Park Ave, San Jose CA 95110, USA
**Gesek, John C, Jr** — Football Player
105 Sand Point Court, Coppell TX 75019, USA
**Gesinger, Michael** — Photographer
1136 Umatilla Ave, Port Townsend WA 98368, USA
**Gesner, Zen** — Actor
Jenny Delaney Mgmt, 3238 Fond Dr, Encino CA 91436, USA
**Gessendorf, Mechthild** — Opera Singer
Columbia Artists Mgmt Inc, 1790 Broadway, #702, New York NY 10019 USA
**Gessle, Per** — Singer, Guitarist (Roxette)
D & D Mgmt, Drottninggatan 55, 111 21 Stockholm, Sweden
**Gethard, Chris** — Actor
Creative Artists Agency, 2000 Ave of Stars, #100, Los Angeles CA 90067 USA
**Gets, Malcolm** — Actor, Singer
Viking Entertainment, 445 W 23rd St, #1A, New York NY 10011, USA
**Gettelfinger, Ron** — Labor Leader
United Auto Workers Union, 800 E Jefferson Ave, Detroit MI 48214, USA
**Gettis, Byron** — Baseball Player
6313 Whalen Ave, East Saint Louis IL 62207, USA
**Getty, Balthazar** — Actor
Patricola Public Relations, 9171 Wilshire Blvd, #441, Beverly Hills CA 90210 USA
**Getty, Charles M (Charlie)** — Football Player
3736 W Morningside St, Springfield MO 65807, USA
**Getz, John** — Actor
Beddingfield Co, 13600 Ventura Blvd, #B, Sherman Oaks CA 91423, USA
**Getzenberg, Robert** — Urologist
Johns Hopkins University Medical Center, Urological Institute, Baltimore MD 21218, USA
**Geyer, Hugh** — Singer (Vogues)
2218 Ridge Road, McKeesport PA 15135, USA
**Ghaffari, Matt** — Greco-Roman Wrestler
32834 Fox Chappel Lane, Avon Lake OH 44012, USA
**Ghai, Subhash** — Director, Producer
Mount Saint Mary Church Road, #12, Bandra (W), Mumbai MS 400050, India
**Ghauri, Yasmeen** — Model
Next Model Mgmt, 23 Watts St, New York NY 10013 USA
**Ghedi, Ali Muhammad** — Prime Minister, Somalia
Prime Minister's Office, People's Palace, Mogadishu, Somalia
**Ghelfi, Anthony P (Tony)** — Baseball Player
3414 Geneva Lane, La Crosse WI 54601, USA
**Gheorghiu, Angela** — Opera Singer
Askonas Holt, Lincoln House, 300 High Holborn, London WC1V 7JH, England
**Gheorghiu, Ion A** — Artist
6 Aviator Petre Cretu St, 012151 Bucharest, Romania
**Gheorghiu, Teo** — Concert Pianist
Harrison/Parrott, 5-6 Albion Court, London W6 0QT, England
**Ghesquiere, Nicolas** — Fashion Designer
Angie Rubioni, 40 Rue du Cherche-Midi, 75006 Paris, France
**Ghez, Andrea M** — Physicist, Astronomer
University of California, Physics & Astronomy Dept, Los Angeles CA 90024, USA
**Ghiardi, John F L** — Government Official, Economist
12 Park Overlook Court, Bethesda MD 20817, USA
**Ghiuselev, Nicola** — Opera Singer
Villa della Pisana 370/B2, 00163 Rome, Italy
**Ghomeshi, Jian** — Broadcaster, Writer, Musician
Agency Group Lts, 2 Berkeley St, #202, Toronto ON M5A 4J5, Canada
**Ghormley, Antony** — Sculptor
European Graduate School, Alter Kehr 20, 3953 Leuk-Stadt, Switzerland.
**Ghosh, Amitrav** — Writer
Farrar Straus Giroux, 18 W 18th St, #700, New York NY 10011 USA
**Ghosh, Gautam** — Director
28/1A Gariahat Road, Block 5, #50, Mumbai WB 700029, India
**Ghosn, Carlos** — Businessman
Nissan Motor Co, 1-1-1 Takashima, Nishi-ku, Yokohamashi, Kanagawa 220 8686, Japan
**Ghostface Killa** — Rap Artist (Wu-Tang Clan)
Agency Group Ltd, 142 W 57th St, #600, New York NY 10019 USA
**Ghribi, Habiba** — Track Athlete
Demadonnathletics, Via Jacopina 4, 38100 Trento, Italy
**Ghuman, J B, Jr** — Actor, Director
W M E Entertainment, 9601 Wilshire Blvd, #300, Beverly Hills CA 90210 USA
**Giacchino, Michael** — Composer
Gorfaine/Schwartz, 4111 W Alameda Ave, #509, Burbank CA 91505 USA
**Giacconi, Riccardo** — Nobel Physics Laureate
5630 Wisconsin Ave, #604, Chevy Chase MD 20815, USA

**G**

| | |
|---|---|
| **Giacomin, Edward (Ed)** | Ice Hockey Player |
| 6575 Red Maple Lane, Bloomfield MI 48301, USA | |
| **Giacoppo, Massimo** | Water Polo Player |
| A S D Pro Recco, Via Biagio Assereto 10/A, 16036 Recco (GE), Italy | |
| **Giaever, Ivar** | Nobel Physics Laureate |
| 2080 Van Antwerp Road, Schenectady NY 12309, USA | |
| **Giamatti, Paul** | Actor |
| United Talent Agency, U T A Plaza, 9336 Civic Center Dr, Beverly Hills CA 90210 USA | |
| **Giambi, Jason G** | Baseball Player |
| 34 Iselworth Dr, Henderson NV 89052, USA | |
| **Giambi, Jeremy D** | Baseball Player |
| 23360 S Power Road, Gilbert AZ 85298, USA | |
| **Giambra, Joey** | Boxer |
| 4673 Ashington St, Las Vegas NV 89147, USA | |
| **Giammarese, Carl** | Guitarist (Buckinghams) |
| Thomas Cassidy, PO Box 1311, Tucson AZ 85702 USA | |
| **Gianelli, John A** | Basketball Player |
| 28241 Pine Ave, Pinecrest CA 95364, USA | |
| **Giannelli, Raymond J (Ray)** | Baseball Player |
| 56 E Saltaire Road, Lindenhurst NY 11757, USA | |
| **Giannini, Adriano** | Actor |
| Media Art Mgmt, C/ Castelló 82, 2 Derecha, 28006 Madrid, Spain | |
| **Giannini, Alfreda** | Fashion Designer |
| Gucci Group, 1 Amstelplein, 1096 Amsterdam HA, Netherlands | |
| **Giannini, Giancarlo** | Actor |
| Via Salaria 292, 00199 Rome, Italy | |
| **Giannoni, Giovani** | Co-Regent, San Marino |
| Co-Regent's Office, Government Palace, 47031 San Marino | |
| **Giannulli, Mossimo** | Fashion Designer |
| Mossimo Supply, 2450 White Road, #200, Irvine CA 92614, USA | |
| **Gianopulos, Mimi** | Actress |
| I C M Partners, 10250 Constellation Blvd, #900, Los Angeles CA 90067 USA | |
| **Gianotti, Fabiola** | Physicist |
| C E R N, Large Hadron Collider, 1211 Geneva 23, Switzerland | |
| **Gibara, Samir** | Businessman |
| Goodyear Tire & Rubber, 1144 E Market St, Akron OH 44316, USA | |
| **Gibb, Barry** | Singer (Bee Gees), Songwriter |
| Rhino Entertainment, 3400 Olive Ave, #400, Burbank CA 91505, USA | |
| **Gibb, Cynthia** | Actress |
| Scott Hart Mgmt, 14622 Ventura Blvd, #746, Sherman Oaks CA 91403, USA | |
| **Gibb, Donald** | Actor |
| Ashby/Rojo Entertainment, 1485 S Beverly Dr, Los Angeles CA 90035, USA | |
| **Gibbard, Allan F** | Philosopher |
| University of Michigan, Philosophy Dept, Ann Arbor MI 48109, USA | |
| **Gibbard, Benjamin (Ben)** | Singer (Death Cab for Cutie) |
| Zeitgeist Artist Mgmt, 660 York St, #216, San Francisco CA 94110, USA | |
| **Gibbon, Joseph C (Joe)** | Baseball Player |
| 26 County Road 24142, Newton MS 39345, USA | |
| **Gibbons, Beth** | Singer (Portishead), Songwriter |
| High Road Touring, 751 Bridgeway, #200, Sausalito CA 94965 USA | |
| **Gibbons, Billy** | Singer, Guitarist (ZZ Top) |
| Sanctuary Mgmt, 15301 Ventura Blvd, Building B, Sherman Oaks CA 91403, USA | |
| **Gibbons, Gail** | Writer, Illustrator |
| 1 Goose Green St, Corinth VT 05039, USA | |
| **Gibbons, Gemma J** | Judo Athlete |
| Metro Judo Club, Mycenae House, 90 Mycenae Road, London SE3 7SE, England | |
| **Gibbons, James E (Jim)** | Football Player |
| 9 Sagewood Court, Basalt CO 81621, USA | |
| **Gibbons, James F** | Electrical Engineer |
| 15 Red Berry Ridge, Portola Valley CA 94028, USA | |
| **Gibbons, Jay J** | Baseball Player |
| 758 Donnington Court, Simi Valley CA 93065, USA | |
| **Gibbons, John D** | Prime Minister, Bermuda |
| Leeward, 5 Leeside Dr, Pembroke HM 05, Bermuda | |
| **Gibbons, John M (Gibby)** | Baseball Player, Manager |
| 3602 Hunters Quail, San Antonio TX 78230, USA | |
| **Gibbons, Julia Smith** | Judge |
| US Court of Appeals, 167 N Main St, #970, Memphis TN 38103, USA | |
| **Gibbons, Kaye** | Writer |
| Houghton Mifflin Harcourt, 215 Park Ave S, #1200, New York NY 10003 USA | |
| **Gibbons, Leeza** | Actress, Producer |
| 9025 Ashcroft Ave, West Hollywood CA 90048, USA | |
| **Gibbs, Freddie** | Rap Artist |
| Agency Group Ltd, 1880 Century Park E, #711, Los Angeles CA 90067 USA | |
| **Gibbs, Jerry D (Jake)** | Football, Baseball Player |
| 223 Saint Andres Circle, Oxford MS 38655, USA | |
| **Gibbs, Joe J** | Football Coach, Auto Racing Executive |
| 19133 Penisula Point Dr, Cornelius NC 28031, USA | |
| **Gibbs, L Richard (Lance)** | Cricketer |
| 276 Republic Park, Peter's Hall EBD, Guyana | |
| **Gibbs, Marla** | Actress, Singer |
| Momentum Talent, 9401 Wilshire Blvd, #501, Beverly Hills CA 90212, USA | |
| **Gibbs, Martin** | Biologist |
| 5 Arbor Court, Burlington MA 01803, USA | |
| **Gibbs, Terri** | Singer, Songwriter |
| P O Box 2100, Thomson GA 30824, USA | |
| **Gibbs, Terry** | Jazz Vibist, Drummer |
| Thomas Cassidy, PO Box 1311, Tucson AZ 85702 USA | |
| **Gibbs, Timothy B** | Actor |
| Jefferson Rilke Cooper, 50 Lexington Ave, #23D, New York NY 10010, USA | |
| **Gibgot, Jennifer** | Producer |
| Offspring Entertainment, 8755 Colgate Ave, Los Angeles CA 90048, USA | |
| **Giblett, Eloise R** | Hematologist |
| 2518 3rd Ave W, Seattle WA 98119, USA | |
| **Giblin, Vincent J** | Labor Leader |
| Internationall Union of Operating Engineers, 1125 17th St NW, Washington DC 20036, USA | |

**Giacomin - Giblin**

| | |
|---|---|
| **Gibney, Alex** <br> I C M Partners, 10250 Constellation Blvd, #900, Los Angeles CA 90067 USA | Director |
| **Gibney, Rebecca** <br> Robyn Gardiner Mgmt, PO Box 128, Surrey Hills NSW 2010, Australia | Actress |
| **Gibney, Susan** <br> Insight Mgmt, 11245 Cloverdale Ave, Los Angeles CA 90019, USA | Actress |
| **Gibran, Kahlil G** <br> 160 W Canton St, Boston MA 02118, USA | Sculptor |
| **Gibson, Aaron** <br> PO Box 637, Roanoke IN 46783, USA | Football Player |
| **Gibson, Antonio M** <br> 2320 Jaguar Dr, #502, Bryan TX 77807, USA | Football Player |
| **Gibson, Beau** <br> I M G Artists, Hogarth Business Park, Chiswick, London W4 2TH, England | Opera Singer |
| **Gibson, Charles D** <br> ABC-TV, News Dept, 47 W 66th St, New York NY 10023, USA | Commentator |
| **Gibson, Claude** <br> 47 Gladstone Road, Asheville NC 28805, USA | Football Player |
| **Gibson, Deborah** <br> David Shapira Assoc, 193 N Robertson Blvd, Beverly Hills CA 90211 USA | Singer, Actress, Model |
| **Gibson, Dennis M** <br> 6900 NE 11th Court, Ankeny IA 50023, USA | Football Player |
| **Gibson, Derrick A** <br> 303 Ave O NW, Winter Haven FL 33881, USA | Baseball Player |
| **Gibson, Ernest G** <br> 6518 Paradise Point Road, Flowery Branch GA 30542, USA | Football Player |
| **Gibson, Fred** <br> 2006 Avenel St, Orlando FL 32828, USA | Golfer |
| **Gibson, John R** <br> US Court of Appeals, US Courthouse, 811 Grand Ave, Kansas City MO 64106, USA | Judge |
| **Gibson, Kelly** <br> 13 Wisteria Lane, Covington LA 70433, USA | Golfer |
| **Gibson, Kirk H** <br> 15135 Charlevoix St, Grosse Pointe Park MI 48230, USA | Baseball, Football Player |
| **Gibson, Mel** <br> Icon Productions, 808 Wilshire Blvd, #400, Santa Monica CA 90401, USA | Actor, Director |
| **Gibson, Oliver D** <br> 1448 E 52nd St, #406, Chicago IL 60615, USA | Football Player |
| **Gibson, Paul M** <br> 23421 Water Circle, Boca Raton FL 33486, USA | Baseball Player |
| **Gibson, Quentin H** <br> 5 Carrot Hill Road, Woods Hole MA 02543, USA | Biochemist |
| **Gibson, Ralph H** <br> 331 W Broadway, #400, New York NY 10013, USA | Photographer |
| **Gibson, Raquel** <br> Playboy Promotions, 2706 Media Center Dr, Los Angeles CA 90065 USA | Model |
| **Gibson, Reginald W** <br> US Claims Court, 717 Madison Place NW, Washington DC 20439, USA | Judge |
| **Gibson, Robert (Bob)** <br> 215 Bellevue Blvd S, Bellevue NE 68005, USA | Baseball Player |
| **Gibson, Robert L (Bob)** <br> 751 W Rolling Road, Springfield PA 19064, USA | Baseball Player |
| **Gibson, Robert L (Hoot)** <br> 1709 Shagbark Trail, Murfreesboro TN 37130, USA | Astronaut |
| **Gibson, Thomas** <br> Paradigm Agency, 360 N Crescent Dr, North Building, Beverly Hills CA 90210 USA | Actor |
| **Gibson, Thomas A (Tom)** <br> 5940 E Sandra Terrace, Scottsdale AZ 85254, USA | Football Player |
| **Gibson, Tyrese D** <br> H Q Pictures, 15260 Ventura Blvd, #2100, Sherman Oaks CA 91403, USA | Singer, Songwriter, Actor, Producer |
| **Gibson, William Ford** <br> G P Putnam's Sons, 375 Hudson St, New York NY 10014 USA | Writer, Photographer |
| **Giddins, Gary** <br> Oxford University Press, 198 Madison Ave, #800, New York NY 10016 USA | Writer, Columnist |
| **Giddish, Kelli** <br> Paradigm Agency, 360 N Crescent Dr, North Building, Beverly Hills CA 90210 USA | Actress |
| **Gideon, Raynold** <br> 3524 Multiview Dr, Los Angeles CA 90068, USA | Actor, Writer |
| **Gidley, Pamela** <br> 32 Cliff Ave, Hampton NH 03842, USA | Actress |
| **Gidzenko, Yuri P** <br> Cosmonaut Training Center, Star City, 141160 Zvezdny Gorodok, Moscow Oblast, Russia | Cosmonaut |
| **Gielen, Michael A** <br> Ingpen & Williams, 131 Putney Bridge Road, London SW15 2PA, England | Conductor, Composer |
| **Giella, Joseph** <br> 191 Morris Dr, East Meadow NY 11554, USA | Cartoonist (Mary Worth) |
| **Gien, Pamela** <br> I C M Partners, 10250 Constellation Blvd, #900, Los Angeles CA 90067 USA | Actress |
| **Gierasch, Adam** <br> Gersh Agency, 9465 Wilshire Blvd, #600, Beverly Hills CA 90212 USA | Director, Writer |
| **Gierer, Vincent A, Jr** <br> U S T Inc, 100 W Putnam Ave, Greenwich CT 06830, USA | Businessman |
| **Gierowski, Stefan** <br> Ul Gagarina 15 m 97, 00 753 Warsaw, Poland | Artist |
| **Giesler, Jon W** <br> 141 Via Isabela, Jupiter FL 33458, USA | Football Player |
| **Gietz, Gordon** <br> I M G Artists, Hogarth Business Park, Chiswick, London W4 2TH, England | Opera Singer |
| **Giff, Patricia Reilly** <br> Bantam Books, 1745 Broadway, New York NY 10019 USA | Writer |
| **Gifford, Barry** <br> Creative Artists Agency, 2000 Ave of Stars, #100, Los Angeles CA 90067 USA | Writer |
| **Gifford, Frank N** <br> I C M Partners, 10250 Constellation Blvd, #900, Los Angeles CA 90067 USA | Football Player, Sportscaster |
| **Gifford, Gloria** <br> Gloria Gifford Theater, 6468 Santa Monica Blvd, Los Angeles CA 90038, USA | Actress |

**G**

Gifford, Kathie Lee — Entertainer
Artist Brand Alliance, 11 E 86th St, #900, New York NY 10028, USA
Gift, Roland — Singer (Fine Young Cannibals), Actor
Primary Talent International, 10-11 Jockey's Fields, London WC1R 4BN, England
Gigandet, Cam — Actor
Luber Rocklin Entertainment, 8530 Wilshire Blvd, #555, Beverly Hills CA 90211 USA
Giggie, Robert T (Bob) — Baseball Player
89 McAndrew Road, Braintree MA 02184, USA
Gigli, Romeo — Fashion Designer
37 W 57th St, #900, New York NY 10019, USA
Gigon, Norman P (Norm) — Baseball Player
2503 Rio Vista Dr, Mahwah NJ 07430, USA
Gigot, Paul A — Journalist
Wall Street Journal, Editorial Dept, 1 World Financial Center, New York NY 10281, USA
Giguere, Jean-Sebastien — Ice Hockey Player
Colorado Avalanche, Pepsi Center, 1000 Chopper Circle, Denver CO 80204 USA
Giguere, Russ — Singer, Guitarist (Association)
Variety Artists, 1924 Spring St, Paso Robles CA 93446 USA
Gil, Gilberto — Singer, Songwriter, Guitarist
M G Ltd, 520 8th Ave, #2205, New York NY 10010, USA
Gil, Maria Luisa — Model
Playboy Promotions, 2706 Media Center Dr, Los Angeles CA 90065 USA
Gil, R Benjamin (Benji) — Baseball Player
1654 Paseo Aurora, San Diego CA 92154, USA
Gilbert, Bradley (Brad) — Tennis Player
ProServe, 1101 Woodrow Wilson Blvd, #1800, Arlington VA 22209 USA
Gilbert, Chris — Football Player
Greenbriar Mgmt, 4422 FM 1960 Road W, Houston TX 77068, USA
Gilbert, David — Cartoonist (Buckles)
King Features Syndicate, 300 W 57th St, #1500, New York NY 10019 USA
Gilbert, Drew E (Buddy) — Baseball Player
1913 Belcaro Dr, Knoxville TN 37918, USA
Gilbert, Elizabeth — Writer
Penguin Books, 375 Hudson St, Basement 1, New York NY 10014 USA
Gilbert, Greg — Ice Hockey Player, Coach
Toronto Marlies, 100 Princess Blvd, Toronto ON M6K 3C3, Canada
Gilbert, J Freeman — Geophysicist
780 Kalamath Dr, Del Mar CA 92014, USA
Gilbert, Joe D — Baseball Player
512 W Martin Luther King Blvd, Jasper TX 75951, USA
Gilbert, Jonathan — Actor
PO Box 15583, Newport Beach CA 92659, USA
Gilbert, Kenneth A — Concert Harpsichordist
11 Rue Ernest-Psichari, 75007 Paris, France
Gilbert, Lawrence I — Biologist
857 Fearrington Post, Pittsboro NC 27312, USA
Gilbert, Lewis — Director, Producer
19 Blvd de Suisse, 98000 Monte Carlo, Monaco
Gilbert, Martin J — Historian
Merton College, History Dept, Oxford OX1 4JD, England
Gilbert, Melissa — Actress, Labor Leader
Innovative Artists, 1505 10th St, Santa Monica CA 90401 USA
Gilbert, Rodrique G (Rod) — Ice Hockey Player
52 E End Ave, #33A, New York NY 10028, USA
Gilbert, Ronnie — Singer
Donna Korones Mgmt, 1031 Merced St, Berkeley CA 94707, USA
Gilbert, S J, Sr — Religious Leader
Baptist Convention of America, 6717 Centennial Blvd, Nashville TN 37209, USA
Gilbert, Sara — Actress
Framework Entertainment, 9057 Nemo St, #C, West Hollywood CA 90069 USA
Gilbert, Sean — Football Player
7912 N Baltusrol Lane, Charlotte NC 28210, USA
Gilbert, Simon — Drummer (Suede)
Interceptor Enterprises, 98 White Lion St, London N1 9PF, England
Gilbert, Walter — Nobel Chemistry Laureate
15 Gray Gardens W, Cambridge MA 02138, USA
Gilberto, Astrud — Singer
Absolute Artists, 530 Howard Ave, #200, San Francisco CA 94105, USA
Gilberto, Bebel — Singer
Umbrella Group, 20 West St, #30E, New York NY 10002, USA
Gilbertson, Bob — Drag Racing Driver, Owner
Terminator Motorsports, 2250 Toomey Ave, Charlotte NC 28203, USA
Gilbreath, Rodney J (Rod) — Baseball Player
1438 Ridgeland Way SW, Lilburn GA 30047, USA
Gilbride, Kevin — Football Player, Coach
New York Giants, Meadowlands Stadium, 102 Route 120, East Rutherford NJ 07073 USA
Gilburg, Thomas D (Tom) — Football Player
29 Valley Road, Warminster PA 18974, USA
Gilchrist, Brent — Ice Hockey Player
Bank of Montreal, 200-3200 30th Ave, Vernon BC V1T 2C5, Canada
Gilchrist, Guy — Cartoonist (Nancy, Mudpie)
20 Bristol Dr, Canton CT 06019, USA
Gilchrist, Keir — Actor
I C M Partners, 10250 Constellation Blvd, #900, Los Angeles CA 90067 USA
Gilchrist, Lara — Actress
Lauren Levitt Assoc, 1525 W 8th Ave, #300, Vancouver BC V6J 1T5, Canada
Gilchrist, Paul R — Religious Leader
Presbyterian Church in America, 1862 Century Place, Atlanta GA 30345, USA
Gilder, Bob — Golfer
1977 NW Bonney Dr, Corvallis OR 97330, USA
Gilder, George F — Economist
Gilder Publishing, 291A Main St, Great Barrington MA 01230, USA
Gildon, Jason L — Football Player
1562 Barrington Dr, Wexford PA 15090, USA
Giles, Brian J — Baseball Player
136 Coronation Ave, Las Vegas NV 89123, USA

**Giles, Brian S** — Baseball Player
4130 Rancho Las Brisas Trail, San Diego CA 92130, USA
**Giles, Curtis J (Curt)** — Ice Hockey Player
5225 Grandview Square, #402, Minneapolis MN 55436, USA
**Giles, Jimmie, Jr** — Football Player
10429 Greenmont Dr, Tampa FL 33626, USA
**Giles, Marcus W** — Baseball Player
1434 Marshall Road, #40, Alpine CA 91901, USA
**Giles, Nancy** — Actress
12047 178th St, Jamaica NY 11434, USA
**Giletti, Alain** — Figure Skater
103 Place de L'Eglise, 74400 Chamonix, France
**Gilfillan, Jason** — Baseball Player
153 Gilfillan Road, Blacksburg SC 29702, USA
**Gilford, Zach** — Actor
W M E Entertainment, 9601 Wilshire Blvd, #300, Beverly Hills CA 90210 USA
**Gilfry, Rodney** — Opera Singer
Askonas Holt, Lincoln House, 300 High Holborn, London WC1V 7JH, England
**Gilham, David R** — Writer
Berkley/Penguin Group, 375 Hudson St, New York NY 10014, USA
**Gilhousen, Klein** — Inventor
Qualcomm, 5775 Morehouse Dr, San Diego CA 92121, USA
**Gilkey, O Bernard** — Baseball Player
11463 Patty Ann Dr, Saint Louis MO 63146, USA
**Gill, Harold P (Hal)** — Ice Hockey Player
1 Fairfield Place, #4, Boston MA 02109, USA
**Gill, Janis** — Singer (Sweethearts of the Rodeo)
2803 Bransford Ave, Nashville TN 37204, USA
**Gill, Johnny** — Singer, Songwriter
Universal Attractions, 135 W 26th St, #1200, New York NY 10001 USA
**Gill, Kendall C** — Basketball Player
3133 S Calumet Ave, Chicago IL 60616, USA
**Gill, Tim** — Computer Software Designer (Quark)
Gill Foundation, 2215 Market St, Denver CO 80205, USA
**Gill, Tonya** — Golfer
3655 Habersham Road NE, #B229, Atlanta GA 30305, USA
**Gill, Turner H** — Football Player, Coach
University of Kansas, Athletic Dept, Lawrence KS 66045, USA
**Gill, Vince** — Singer, Songwriter, Guitarist
Fitzgerald Hartley Co, 1908 Wedgewood Ave, Nashville TN 37212, USA
**Gill, William A, Jr** — Labor Leader, Government Official
15975 Cove Lane, Dumfries VA 22025, USA
**Gillan, Ian** — Singer, Musician (Deep Purple)
Coda Agency, 229 Shoreditch High St, London E1 6PJ, England
**Gillan, Karen S** — Actress
United Talent Agency, U T A Plaza, 9336 Civic Center Dr, Beverly Hills CA 90210 USA
**Gillanders, J David** — Swimmer
1617 Briarwood Dr, Jonesboro AR 72401, USA
**Gille, Bertrand** — Handball Player
Chambery Savoie H B, 688 Ave des Follaz, 73000 Chambery, France
**Gille, Guillaume A** — Handball Player
Chambery Savoie H B, 688 Ave des Follaz, 73000 Chambery, France
**Gillen, Aidan** — Actor
Independent Talent Group, 40 Whitfield St, London W1T 2RH, England
**Gilles, Frederic** — Actor
Martinez Creative Mgmt, 6856 Saint-Laurent Blvd, #205, Montreal QC H2S 3C7, Canada
**Gilles, Thomas B (Tom)** — Baseball Player
14615 W Southern St, Princeville IL 61559, USA
**Gillespie, Aaron R** — Singer, Drummer (Underoath)
Force Media Mgmt, 135 Voorhis Ave, Rockville Centre NY 11570, USA
**Gillespie, Jack A** — Basketball Player
1104 37th Ave NE, Great Falls MT 59404, USA
**Gillespie, Jim** — Director
Creative Artists Agency, 2000 Ave of Stars, #100, Los Angeles CA 90067 USA
**Gillespie, Rhondda M** — Concert Pianist
2 Princess Road, Saint Leonards on Sea, East Sussex TN37 6EL, England
**Gillespie, Robert W** — Financier
KeyCorp, 127 Public Square, Cleveland OH 44114, USA
**Gillespie, Ronald J** — Chemist
150 Wilson St W, Ancaster ON L9G 4E7, Canada
**Gillette, Anita** — Actress
Harden-Curtis Assoc, 214 W 29th St, #1203, New York NY 10001, USA
**Gillette, Gabby** — Actress
Amsel Eisenstadt Frazier, 5055 Wilshire Blvd, #865, Los Angeles CA 90036 USA
**Gillette, James (Jim)** — Singer (Tuff, Nitro)
Nene Musik Productions, 1460 SW Santiago Ave, Port Saint Lucie FL 34953 USA
**Gillette, Walker A** — Football Player
401 N College Dr, Franklin VA 23851, USA
**Gilley, J Wade** — Educator
University of Tennessee, President's Office, Knoxville TN 37996, USA
**Gilley, Mickey L** — Singer, Pianist, Songwriter
Mickey Gilley Interests, PO Box 1242, Pasadena TX 77501, USA
**Gilliam, Elijah** — Baseball Player
1617 5th Ave N, Birmingham AL 35203, USA
**Gilliam, John R** — Football Player
4045 Moheb St SW, Atlanta GA 30331, USA
**Gilliam, Jon R** — Football Player
440 S Walnut Grove Road, Midlothian TX 76065, USA
**Gilliam, Sam** — Artist
Lou Stovall Workshop, 3145 Newark St NW, Washington DC 20008, USA
**Gilliam, Terry V** — Actor, Animator, Writer (Monty Python)
Old Hall, South Grove, Highgate, London N6 6BP, England
**Gilliard, Lawrence (Larry), Jr** — Actor
Innovative Artists, 1505 10th St, Santa Monica CA 90401 USA
**Gillick, L Patrick D (Pat)** — Baseball Executive
Philadelphia Phillies, 1 Citizens Bank Way, Philadelphia PA 19148 USA

# G

**Gillies, Ben** — Drummer (Silverchair)
John Watson Mgmt, PO Box 281, Sunny Hills NSW 2010, Australia
**Gillies, Clark (Jethro)** — Ice Hockey Player
17 Pinta Court, Greenlawn NY 11740, USA
**Gillies, Daniel** — Actor
A P A Talent/Literary Agency, 405 S Beverly Dr, #300, Beverly Hills CA 90212 USA
**Gillies, Isabel** — Actress, Writer
Charles Scribner's Sons, 866 3rd Ave, New York NY 10022 USA
**Gilliford, Paul G** — Baseball Player
7 Woodland Dr, Malvern PA 19355, USA
**Gilligan, Carol** — Educator
Harvard University, Gender Studies Dept, Cambridge MA 02138, USA
**Gilligan, Paul** — Cartoonist
160 Baldwin St, #607, Toronto ON M5T 1L8, Canada
**Gilligan, Vince** — Producer
I C M Partners, 10250 Constellation Blvd, #900, Los Angeles CA 90067 USA
**Gillilan, William J, III** — Businessman
Centex Corp, PO Box 199000, Dallas TX 75219, USA
**Gilliland, David** — Auto Racing Driver
8556 Dog Leg Road, Sherrills Ford NC 28673, USA
**Gilliland, Richard** — Actor
9145 W Sunset Blvd, #228, West Hollywood CA 90069, USA
**Gilliland, Robert J (Bob)** — Test Pilot
PO Box 84, Palm Desert CA 92261, USA
**Gillingham, Charles T (Charlie)** — Musician (Counting Crowes)
Geffen Records, 10900 Wilshire Blvd, #1000, Los Angeles CA 90024 USA
**Gillispie, Billy C** — Basketball Coach
Texas Tech University, Athletic Dept, Lubbock TX 79409, USA
**Gillom, Jennifer** — Basketball Player
Washington Mystics, Verizon Center, 401 9th St NW, #750, Washington DC 20004 USA
**Gilman, Alfred G** — Nobel Medicine Laureate
10996 Crooked Creek Dr, Dallas TX 75229, USA
**Gilman, Jared** — Actor
D-mand Talent Agency, 85 S Broadway, #4, Nyack NY 10960, USA
**Gilman, Richard C** — Educator
131 Annandale Road, Pasadena CA 91105, USA
**Gilman, Richard H** — Publisher
Boston Globe, Publisher's Office, 135 Morrissey Blvd, Dorchester MA 02125, USA
**Gilman, Ronald Lee** — Judge
US Court of Appeals, 167 N Main St, #1176, Memphis TN 38103, USA
**Gilman, Sid** — Neurologist
3441 Geddes Road, Ann Arbor MI 48105, USA
**Gilmartin, Paul** — Actor, Comedian, Producer, Writer
Gersh Agency, 9465 Wilshire Blvd, #600, Beverly Hills CA 90212 USA
**Gilmer, Harry V** — Football Player
7467 Highway N, O'Fallon MO 63368, USA
**Gilmore, Alexie** — Actress
Paradigm Agency, 360 N Crescent Dr, North Building, Beverly Hills CA 90210 USA
**Gilmore, Artis** — Basketball Player
11043 Turnbridge Dr, Jacksonville FL 32256, USA
**Gilmore, Bryan** — Football Player
PO Box 815, Prosper TX 75078, USA
**Gilmore, Jimmie Dale** — Singer, Songwriter
Maine Road Mgmt, 195 Chrystie St, #901F, New York NY 10002, USA
**Gilmore, Stephone** — Football Player
Buffalo Bills, 1 Bills Dr, Orchard Park NY 14127 USA
**Gilmore, Thea** — Singer, Songwriter
Mongrel Music, 743 Center Blvd, Fairfax CA 94930, USA
**Gilmore, Walt** — Basketball Player
257 Benjamin Blvd, Bear DE 19701, USA
**Gilmour, Buddy** — Harness Racing Driver
50 Merrick Ave, #410, East Meadow NY 11554, USA
**Gilmour, David** — Singer, Guitarist (Pink Floyd)
One Fifteen, 1 Globe House, Middle Lane Mews, London 8N 8PN, England
**Gilmour, Doug** — Ice Hockey Player
Octagon Worldwide, 1751 Pinnacle Dr, #1500, McLean VA 22102 USA
**Gilmur, Charles E (Chuck)** — Basketball Player
230 Farallone Ave, Fircrest WA 98466, USA
**Gilot, Fabien** — Swimmer
C N Marseille, Extremite Blvd Charles Livon, 13007 Marseille, France
**Gilpin, Peri** — Actress
Burstein Co, 15304 W Sunset Blvd, #208, Pacific Palisades CA 90272 USA
**Gilpin, Robert G, Jr** — Political Scientist
133 Covington Lane, Shelburne VT 05482, USA
**Gilroy, Frank D** — Writer
8 Mangin Road, Monroe NY 10950, USA
**Gilroy, Tom** — Actor, Director, Producer, Writer
Sweet 180, 141 W 28th St, #300, New York NY 10001, USA
**Gilroy, Tony** — Writer, Director, Producer
Creative Artists Agency, 2000 Ave of Stars, #100, Los Angeles CA 90067 USA
**Gilsean, Matthew** — Singer (Celtic Tenors)
PO Box 32, Kells, County Meath, Ireland
**Gilsig, Jessalyn** — Actress
Paradigm Agency, 360 N Crescent Dr, North Building, Beverly Hills CA 90210 USA
**Gilyard, Clarence, Jr** — Actor, Director, Producer
Dick Delson Assoc, 4520 Bakman Ave, Studio City CA 91602, USA
**Gimble, Johnny** — Fiddle Player
Nancy Fly Agency, 6618 Wolfcreek Pall, Austin TX 78749, USA
**Gimbrone, Michael A, Jr** — Pathologist
Brigham & Women's Hospital, Vascular Pathology Dept, Boston MA 02115, USA
**Gimeno, Andres** — Tennis Player
Paseo de la Bonanova 38, Barcelona 6, Spain
**Gimpel, Erica** — Actress
Innovative Artists, 1505 10th St, Santa Monica CA 90401 USA
**Gina G** — Singer
What Mgmt, PO Box 1463, Culver City CA 90232, USA

Gillies - Gina G

| | |
|---|---|
| **Ginepri, Robby** | Tennis Player |
| Olde Towne Athletic Club, 4950 Olde Towne Parkway, Marietta GA 30068, USA | |
| **Ging, Jack** | Actor |
| 48701 San Pedro St, La Quinta CA 92253, USA | |
| **Ginger Fish** | Drummer (Marilyn Manson) |
| Coast II Coast Entertainment, 8671 Wilshire Blvd, Beverly Hills, CA 90211, USA | |
| **Gingrich, Newton L (Newt)** | Representative, GA; Speaker |
| 7410 Windy Hill Court, McLean VA 22102, USA | |
| **Ginibre, Jean-Louis** | Editor |
| Hachette Filipacchi, Editorial Dept, 1633 Broadway, #4001, New York NY 10019, USA | |
| **Ginn, Chad** | Golfer |
| Signature Sports Group, 4150 Olson Memorial Highway, #110, Minneapolis, MN 55422, USA | |
| **Ginn, Drew C** | Rowing Athlete |
| Mercantile Rowing Club, 5 Boathouse Dr, Melbourne VIC 3000, Australia | |
| **Ginn, Hubert (Hubie)** | Football Player |
| 16 Egrets Nest Dr, Savannah GA 31406, USA | |
| **Ginn, Theodore (Ted), Jr** | Football Player |
| 18289 SW 54th St, Savannah GA 31406, USA | |
| **Ginobili, Emmanuel (Manny)** | Basketball Player |
| 10 Queens Hill, San Antonio TX 78257, USA | |
| **Ginsburg, Ruth Bader** | Supreme Court Justice |
| US Supreme Court, 1 1st St NE, Washington DC 20543 USA | |
| **Ginter, Keith** | Baseball Player |
| 2907 Maple Ave, Fullerton CA 92835, USA | |
| **Ginter, Matthew S (Matt)** | Baseball Player |
| 3320 Boonesboro Road, Winchester KY 40391, USA | |
| **Ginuwine** | Singer |
| Universal Attractions, 135 W 26th St, #1200, New York NY 10001 USA | |
| **Giocante, Vahina** | Actress |
| Artmedia, 20 Ave Rapp, 75007 Paris, France | |
| **Giola, Dana** | Government Official, Writer |
| National Endowment for Arts, 1100 Pennsylvania Ave NW, Washington DC 20004, USA | |
| **Gionta, Brian** | Ice Hockey Player |
| PO Box 16499, Rochester NY 14616, USA | |
| **Giordano, Thomas A (Tommy)** | Baseball Player |
| 176 Riverside Ave, Amityville NY 11701, USA | |
| **Giorgetti, Alex** | Water Polo Player |
| A S D Pro Recco, Via Biagio Assereto 10/A, 16036 Recco, Italy | |
| **Giovanelli, Gordon** | Rowing Athlete |
| 332 Ouci de la Loma, Escondido CA 92029, USA | |
| **Giovanni, Joseph** | Architect |
| Giovanni Assoc, 140 E 40th St, New York NY 10016, USA | |
| **Giovanni, Nikki E** | Writer |
| Virginia Polytechnic Institute, English Dept, Blacksburg VA 24061, USA | |
| **Giovanola, Edward T (Ed)** | Baseball Player |
| 1741 Nomark Court, San Jose CA 95125, USA | |
| **Giovi, Andrea** | Volleyball Player |
| Sir Safety Perugio, Viale Giontella 1, 06083 Bastia Umbra, Italy | |
| **Giovinazzo, Carmine** | Actor |
| Paradigm Agency, 360 N Crescent Dr, North Building, Beverly Hills CA 90210 USA | |
| **Gipson, Charles W** | Baseball Player |
| 632 S Earlham St, Orange CA 92869, USA | |
| **Gipson, Dre** | Singer, Keyboardist (Fishbone) |
| Silverback Mgmt, 9469 Jefferson Blvd, #101, Culver City CA 90232, USA | |
| **Giradelli, Marc** | Alpine Skier |
| Marc Giradelli Sport AG, Wiesentalstr 6, 9445 Reibstein, Switzerland | |
| **Giraldo, Neil** | Producer, Composer |
| Bel Chiasso Entertainment, 7956 Glade Ave, Canoga Park CA 91304, USA | |
| **Girard, Christine** | Weightlifter |
| British Columbia Weightlifting Assn, 1449 Hornby St, Vancouver BC V6Z 1W8, Canada | |
| **Girard, Ken** | Ice Hockey Player |
| 6-519 Riverside Dr, London ON N6H 5J3, Canada | |
| **Girardi, Joseph E (Joe)** | Baseball Player, Manager |
| 7320 Wisteria Ave, Parkland FL 33076, USA | |
| **Girardin, Ray** | Actor |
| Academy of Performing Arts, PO Box 1843, Orleans MA 02653, USA | |
| **Girardot, Hippolyte** | Actor |
| Artmedia, 20 Ave Rapp, 75007 Paris, France | |
| **Giraud, Joyce** | Actress |
| C E S D, 10635 Santa Monica Blvd, #130, Los Angeles CA 90025 USA | |
| **Giri, Tulsi** | Prime Minister, Nepal |
| Jawakpurdham, District Dhanuka, Nepal | |
| **Girone, Remo** | Actor |
| Cristiano Cucchino Mgmt, Lungotevere dei Mellini 10, 00193 Rome, Italy | |
| **Giscard d'Estaing, Valery M R** | President, France |
| 11 Rue Benouville, 75116 Paris, France | |
| **Gisele** | Model |
| I M G Models, 304 Park Ave S, #PH N, New York NY 10010 USA | |
| **Gish, Annabeth** | Actress |
| Innovative Artists, 1505 10th St, Santa Monica CA 90401 USA | |
| **Gisler, Michael (Mike)** | Football Player |
| 407 Tampa Dr, Victoria TX 77904, USA | |
| **Gisondo, Skyler** | Actor |
| Paradigm Agency, 360 N Crescent Dr, North Building, Beverly Hills CA 90210 USA | |
| **Gitlin, Todd** | Historian |
| New York University, Culture & Communications Dept, New York NY 10012, USA | |
| **Gittins, Calum** | Actor |
| Wing Nut Films, PO Box 15 208, Miramar, Wellington, New Zealand | |
| **Gittins, Jeremy** | Actor |
| Associated International Mgmt, 7 Hatton Garden, #400, London EC1N 8AD, England | |
| **Gitto, Niccolo** | Water Polo Player |
| A S D Pro Recco, Via Biagio Assereto 10/A, 16036 Recco (GE), Italy | |
| **Giuliani, Rudolph W** | Mayor, New York City |
| Giuliani Partners, 5 Times Square, Converse Level 1, New York NY 10036, USA | |
| **Giuliano, Louis J** | Businessman |
| I T T Industries, 4 W Red Oak Lane, #200, West Harrison NY 10604, USA | |

**G**

**Ginepri - Giuliano**

| | |
|---|---|
| **Giuliano, Tom** | Singer (Happenings) |
| 6929 N Hayden Road, Scottsdale AZ 85250, USA | |
| **Giuranna, Bruno** | Concert Violist |
| Via Bembo 96, 31011 Asolo TV, Italy | |
| **Giurescu, Dino** | Historian |
| 3033 32nd St, Astoria NY 11102, USA | |
| **Giusti, David J (Dave)** | Baseball Player |
| 524 Clair Dr, Pittsburgh PA 15241, USA | |
| **Giusti, Katy** | Foundation Executive |
| Multiple Myeloma Research Consortium, 383 Main Ave, #500, Norwalk CT 06851, USA | |
| **Givens, Adele** | Actress, Comedienne |
| Artistry Mgmt, 340 N Camden Dr, #302, Beverly Hills CA 90210, USA | |
| **Givens, David L** | Football Player |
| 1117 Lochland Dr, Galllatin TN 37066, USA | |
| **Givens, Robin** | Actress, Model |
| Marshak/Zachary Co, 8840 Wilshire Blvd, #100, Beverly Hills CA 90211 USA | |
| **Givhan, Robin** | Journalist |
| Washington Post, Editorial Dept, 1150 15th St NW, Washington DC 20071 USA | |
| **Givins, Brian A** | Baseball Player |
| 719 Stonemont Court, Castle Rock CO 80108, USA | |
| **Givins, Ernest P, Jr** | Football Player |
| 3115 48th Ave S, Saint Petersburg FL 33712, USA | |
| **Gizenga, Antoine** | Premier, Congo Democratic Republic |
| Palais de la Primature, BP 1354, Brazzaville, Congo Republic | |
| **Gizyn, Louie** | Artist |
| 1161 NW Taylor Ave, Corvallis OR 97330, USA | |
| **Gjertsen, Douglas (Doug)** | Swimmer |
| 7130 Havenridge Way, McDonough GA 30253, USA | |
| **Gjokaj, Enver** | Actor |
| Suskin Mgmt, 2 Charlton St, #5K, New York NY 10014, USA | |
| **Gladden, C Daniel (Dan)** | Baseball Player |
| 6543 Pinnacle Dr, Eden Prairie MN 55346, USA | |
| **Gladding, Fred E** | Baseball Player |
| 436 Marsh Pointe Dr, Columbia SC 29229, USA | |
| **Gladis, Michael** | Actor |
| Stone Manners Salners, 9911 W Pico Blvd, #1400, Los Angeles CA 90035 USA | |
| **Gladwell, Malcolm** | Writer |
| Black Bay/Little Brown, 3 Center Plaza, Boston MA 02108, USA | |
| **Glaesser, Jasmin** | Cyclist |
| National Cycling Assn, 2197 Riverside Dr, #203, Ottawa ON K1H 7X3, Canada | |
| **Glaister, Lesley** | Writer |
| A M Heath Co, 79 Saint Martin's Lane, London WC2N 4RE, England | |
| **Glance, Harvey** | Track Athlete |
| 2408 Old Creek Road, Montgomery AL 36117, USA | |
| **Glanfield, Joe** | Yachtsman |
| W N W Design, 24A Upper Church St, Exmouth, Devon EX8 2TA, England | |
| **Glanville, Brian L** | Writer |
| 160 Holland Park Ave, London W11 4UH, England | |
| **Glanville, Douglas M (Doug)** | Baseball Player |
| 2043 W McLean Ave, Chicago IL 60647, USA | |
| **Glanville, Jerry** | Football Coach, Auto Racing Driver |
| Jerry Glanville Motorsports, 550 Twinflower Court, Roswell GA 30075, USA | |
| **Glasbergen, Randy** | Cartoonist (Better Half) |
| King Features Syndicate, 300 W 57th St, #1500, New York NY 10019 USA | |
| **Glaser, Daniel** | Sociologist |
| 63 Walk Hill St, Jamaica Plain MA 02130, USA | |
| **Glaser, Jim** | Singer |
| Joe Taylor Artist Agency, 2802 Columbine Place, Nashville TN 37204 USA | |
| **Glaser, Jon** | Actor, Writer |
| Creative Artists Agency, 2000 Ave of Stars, #100, Los Angeles CA 90067 USA | |
| **Glaser, Milton** | Graphic Artist |
| Milton Glaser Assoc, 207 E 32nd St, New York NY 10016, USA | |
| **Glaser, Paul Michael** | Actor, Director |
| 508 San Juan Ave, Venice CA 90291, USA | |
| **Glaser, Rob** | Businessman, Inventor |
| Real Networks, 2601 Elliott Ave, Seattle WA 98121, USA | |
| **Glaser, Robert J** | Foundation Executive |
| 868 Boyce Ave, Palo Alto CA 94301, USA | |
| **Glaser, Rose Mary** | Baseball Player |
| 8929 Long Lane, Cincinnati OH 45231, USA | |
| **Glasgow, Nesby L** | Football Player |
| 8402 165th Ave NE, #106, Redmond WA 98052, USA | |
| **Glasgow, Walter** | Yachtsman |
| 781 Silver Spur Dr, Weatherford TX 76087, USA | |
| **Glashow, Jonathan L** | Sports Medicine Surgeon |
| 737 Park Ave, New York NY 10021, USA | |
| **Glashow, Sheldon Lee** | Nobel Physics Laureate |
| 30 Prescott St, Brookline MA 02446, USA | |
| **Glasper, Robert** | Jazz Pianist |
| Second Son Productions, 5500 Prytania St, #142, New Orleans LA 70115, USA | |
| **Glaspie, April** | Diplomat |
| State Department, 2201 C St NW, Washington DC 20520 USA | |
| **Glass, Charles (Chip)** | Football Player |
| 23704 Lake Dr E, Bothell WA 98021, USA | |
| **Glass, David D** | Businessman |
| Wal-Mart Stores, 702 SW 8th St, Bentonville AK 72712, USA | |
| **Glass, Gerald** | Basketball Player |
| 1123 Tillman Road, Port Gibson MS 39150, USA | |
| **Glass, Glenn M** | Football Player |
| 301 Portsmouth Road, Knoxville TN 37909, USA | |
| **Glass, Leland S** | Football Player |
| 9 Bayou Court, Sacramento CA 95831, USA | |
| **Glass, Mona** | Actress |
| Agentur Eberstein, Mullenhoffstr 2, 10967 Berlin, Germany | |
| **Glass, Philip** | Composer |
| 48 E 3rd St, #2, New York NY 10003, USA | |

**Glass, Ron** — Actor
Mitchell K Stubbs Assoc, 8695 W Washington Blvd, #204, Culver City CA 90232 USA
**Glass, William S (Bill)** — Football Player
Bill Glass Ministries, PO Box 761101, Dallas TX 75376, USA
**Glasser, Ira S** — Attorney
American Civil Liberties Union, 132 W 43rd St, New York NY 10036, USA
**Glassic, Thomas J (Tom)** — Football Player
1030 S Pine Dr, Bailey CO 80421, USA
**Glassner, Barry** — Educator, Sociologist
Lewis & Clark College, President's Office, 0615 SW Palatine Hill Road, Portland OR 97219, USA
**Glasson, Bill** — Golfer
5819 W Villas Court, Stillwater OK 74074, USA
**Glasson, Stephanie** — Model
Playboy Promotions, 2706 Media Center Dr, Los Angeles CA 90065 USA
**Glatter, Lesli Linka** — Director, Producer
Anonymous Content, 3532 Hayden Ave, Culver City CA 90232 USA
**Glau, Summer L** — Actress
Schiff Co, 9200 Sunset Blvd, #430, West Hollywood CA 90232 USA
**Glauber, Keith H** — Baseball Player
20 Highland Court, Freehold NJ 07728, USA
**Glauber, Robert R** — Businessman
National Assn of Securities Dealers, 33 Whitehall St, New York NY 10004, USA
**Glauber, Roy J** — Nobel Physics Laureate
221 Pleasant St, Arlington MA 02476, USA
**Glaudini, Lola** — Actress
Paul Kohner, 9300 Wilshire Blvd, #555, Beverly Hills CA 90212 USA
**Glaus, Troy E** — Baseball Player
4300 Bibleway Court, Holly Springs NC 27540, USA
**Glave, Matthew** — Actor
Sanders/Armstrong/Caserta Mgmt, 2120 Colorado Ave, #120, Santa Monica CA 90404 USA
**Glaviano, Marco** — Photographer
150 W 56th St, New York NY 10019, USA
**Glavine, Thomas M (Tom)** — Baseball Player
920 Hurleston Lane, Alpharetta GA 30022, USA
**Glazer, Eugene Robert** — Actor
20058 Ventura Blvd, #61, Woodland Hills CA 91364, USA
**Glazer, Jay** — Sportscaster
Fox-TV, Sports Dept, 205 W 67th St, New York NY 10065 USA
**Glazer, Jonathan** — Director
Independent Talent Group, 40 Whitfield St, London W1T 2RH, England
**Glazer, Nathan** — Sociologist
12 Scott St, Cambridge MA 02138, USA
**Glazunov, Ilya S** — Artist
Academy of Painting, Myasnitskaya Str 21, 101000 Moscow, Russia
**Gleason, Joanna** — Actress
Innovative Artists, 1505 10th St, Santa Monica CA 90401 USA
**Gleason, Timothy (Tim)** — Ice Hockey Player
2908 Spaldwick Court, Raleigh NC 27613, USA
**Gleason, Vanessa** — Model, Actress
4821 Lankershim Blvd, #F, North Hollywood CA 91601, USA
**Gleaton, Jerry Don** — Baseball Player
3008 Ave K, Brownwood TX 76801, USA
**Glebova, Natalie** — Beauty Queen
Miss Universe Organization, 1370 Ave of Americas, #1600, New York NY 10019 USA
**Gleeson, Brendan** — Actor, Director, Writer
The Agency, 9 Upper Fitzwilliam St, Dublin 2, Ireland
**Gleeson, Domhnall** — Actor, Writer, Director
The Agency, 9 Upper Fitzwilliam St, Dubln 2, Ireland
**Glen, Iain** — Actor
Independent Talent Group, 40 Whitfield St, London W1T 2RH, England
**Glen, John** — Director
Skouras Agency, 1149 3rd St, #300, Santa Monica CA 90403 USA
**Glen, Marla** — Singer
Mom Productions, 20 Rue de la Providence, 75013 Paris, France
**Glendon, Mary Ann** — Attorney, Educator
Harvard University, Law School, Cambridge MA 02138, USA
**Glenesk, Dean** — Modern Pentathlete
1705 Ben Crenshaw Way, Austin TX 78746, USA
**Glenister, Philip** — Actor
Ken McReddie Assoc, 101 Finsbury Pavement, London EC2A 1RS, England
**Glenn, Aaron D** — Football Player
30 Commanders Cove, Missouri City TX 77459, USA
**Glenn, Devon** — Drummer (Buckcherry)
10th Street Mgmt, 700 N San Vicente Blvd, #G410, West Hollywood CA 90069, USA
**Glenn, Jason** — Football Player
15530 Ella Blvd, #501, Houston TX 77090, USA
**Glenn, John** — Baseball Player
32 Edgewater Ave, Beverly NJ 08010, USA
**Glenn, John** — Director, Writer
Brian Lutz Mgmt, 6565 Sunset Blvd, #416, Los Angeles CA 90028, USA
**Glenn, John H, Jr** — Senator, OH; Astronaut
Ohio State University, Stillman Hall, 1810 S College Road, Columbus OH 43210, USA
**Glenn, Mike T** — Basketball Player
3571 Kilpatrick Lane, Snellville GA 30039, USA
**Glenn, Scott** — Actor
Innovative Artists, 1505 10th St, Santa Monica CA 90401 USA
**Glenn, Tarik** — Football Player
5216 N Delaware St, Indianapolis IN 46220, USA
**Glenn, Terrance T (Terry)** — Football Player
Dallas Cowboys, 1 Cowboys Parkway, Irving TX 75063 USA
**Glenn, Wendy** — Actress
Paradigm Agency, 360 N Crescent Dr, North Building, Beverly Hills CA 90210 USA
**Glennie, Brian A** — Ice Hockey Player
4 Curling Road, Bracebridge ON P1L 1M6, Canada
**Glennie, Evelyn E A** — Concert Percussionist
PO Box 6, Sawtry, Huntingdon, Cambridgeshire PE17 5WE, England

**Glennie-Smith, Nick** — Composer
First Artists Mgmt, 4764 Park Granada, #210, Calabasas CA 91302 USA

**Gless, Sharon** — Actress
Domain Talent, 9229 W Sunset Blvd, #710, West Hollywood CA 90069 USA

**Glick, Frederick C (Freddy)** — Football Player
4226 Antlers Court, Fort Collins CO 80526, USA

**Glick, Gary G** — Football Player
2801 Middlesborough Court, Fort Collins CO 80525, USA

**Glicker, Daniel (Danny)** — Costume Designer
I C M Partners, 10250 Constellation Blvd, #900, Los Angeles CA 90067 USA

**Glickman, Andrew Z** — Photographer
4903 Newport Ave, Bethesda MD 20816, USA

**Glickman, Daniel R** — Secretary, Agriculture
Motion Picture Assn, 4635 Ashby St NW, Washington DC 20007, USA

**Glidden, Bob** — Auto Racing Driver
Route 1, Box 236, Whiteland IN 46184, USA

**Glidewell, Iain** — Judge
Rough Heys Farm, Macclesfield, Cheshire SK11 9PF, England

**Glier, Seth** — Singer, Songwriter
Mpress Records, 200 E 10th St, #106, New York NY 10003, USA

**Glimcher, Arnold O (Arne)** — Director, Producer, Composer
Paradigm Agency, 360 N Crescent Dr, North Building, Beverly Hills CA 90210 USA

**Glimm, James G** — Mathematician
State University of New York, Applied Math Dept, Stony Brook NY 11794, USA

**Glinatsis, George** — Baseball Player
13742 W 59th Ave, Arvada CO 80004, USA

**Glisson, Henry T (Tom)** — Army General
V T Services, 40 E 52nd St, #1400, New York NY 10022, USA

**Glitter, Gary** — Singer, Songwriter
Jef Hanlon Mgmt, 1 York St, London W1H 1PZ, England

**Glitter, Lesli Linka** — Director
Anonymous Content, 3532 Hayden Ave, Culver City CA 90232 USA

**Gload, Ross P** — Baseball Player
23 Harrison Ave, East Hampton NY 11937, USA

**Globus, Yoram** — Producer
Pathe International, 8670 Wilshire Blvd, Beverly Hills CA 90211, USA

**Glocer, Tom** — Businessman
Reuters Group PLC, Canary Wharf, South Colonnade, London E14 5EP, England

**Glockner, Michael** — Cyclist
Kaiserslautener Str 54, 66123 Saarbrucken, Germany

**Gloor, Olga** — Bowler
Professional Bowlers Assn, 719 2nd Ave, #701, Seattle WA 98104 USA

**Glouberman, Michael** — Producer, Writer
Creative Artists Agency, 2000 Ave of Stars, #100, Los Angeles CA 90067 USA

**Glover, Andrew L** — Football Player
33226 Magnolia Circle, Magnolia TX 77354, USA

**Glover, Bloc** — Motorcycle Racing Rider
American Motorcycle Assn, 13515 Yarmouth Dr, Pickerington OH 43147 USA

**Glover, Bruce** — Actor
11449 Woodbine St, Los Angeles CA 90066, USA

**Glover, Clarence** — Basketball Player
811 Lake Forest Parkway, Louisville KY 40245, USA

**Glover, Corey** — Singer (Living Colour), Actor
Entertainment Artists, 2409 21st Ave S, #100, Nashville TN 10019 USA

**Glover, Crispin** — Actor
A P A Talent/Literary Agency, 405 S Beverly Dr, #300, Beverly Hills CA 90212 USA

**Glover, Danny** — Actor
Carrie Productions, 3200 College Ave, Berkeley CA 94705, USA

**Glover, Dion** — Basketball Player
3691 Seton Hall Way, Decatur GA 30034, USA

**Glover, Donald** — Actor
Creative Artists Agency, 2000 Ave of Stars, #100, Los Angeles CA 90067 USA

**Glover, Helen** — Rowing Athlete
Minerva Bath Rowing Club, 11 Bathwick St, #5, Bath BA2 6NX, England

**Glover, Jane A** — Conductor
Askonas Holt, Lincoln House, 300 High Holborn, London WC1V 7JH, England

**Glover, John** — Actor
Innovative Artists, 1505 10th St, Santa Monica CA 90401 USA

**Glover, Julian** — Actor
Conway Van Gelder Grant, 8-12 Broadwick St, #300, London W1F 8HW, England

**Glover, Kevin B** — Football Player
11553 Manorstone Lane, Columbia MD 21044, USA

**Glover, La'Roi D** — Football Player
PO Box 410589, Saint Louis MO 63141, USA

**Glover, Lucas** — Golfer
105 Annas Place, Simpsonville SC 29681, USA

**Glover, M Dionae (Dion)** — Basketball Player
2052 Channing Dr, Conyers GA 30094, USA

**Glover, Martin (Youth)** — Bassist (Killing Joke)
Agency Group, 9348 Civic Center Dr, #200, Beverly Hills CA 90210 USA

**Glover, Richard E (Rich)** — Football Player
215 Claremont Ave, Jersey City NJ 07305, USA

**Glover, Roger D** — Bassist (Deep Purple)
Thames Talent, 1720 Post Road E, #101, Westport CT 06880, USA

**Glover, Savion** — Dancer, Choreographer, Actor
Savion Glover Productions, 131 Brunswick St, Newark NJ 07114, USA

**Glover, Stephen (Steve-O)** — Actor, Writer
I C M Partners, 10250 Constellation Blvd, #900, Los Angeles CA 90067 USA

**Glowacki, Janusz** — Writer
845 W End Ave, #4B, New York NY 10025, USA

**Glowinski, Jacques** — Neuropharmacologist
Unite INSERM College de France, 111 Pl M Berthelot, 75005 Paris, France

**Gluck, Carol** — Historian
440 Riverside Dr, New York NY 10027, USA

**Gluck, Louise E** — Writer
14 Ellsworth Park, Cambridge MA 02139, USA

**Gluck, Will**  —  Director
United Talent Agency, U T A Plaza, 9336 Civic Center Dr, Beverly Hills CA 90210 USA
**Gluckman, Richard**  —  Architect
Gluckman Mayer Architects, 250 Hudson Ave, New York NY 10013, USA
**Glueck, Lawrence D (Larry)**  —  Football Player
10 Cooper Road, East Falmouth MA 02536, USA
**Glushchenko, Fedor I**  —  Conductor
1st Pryadilnaya Str 11, #5, 105037 Moscow, Russia
**Glushenko, Yevgenia K**  —  Actress
1905 Goda Str 3, #91, 123100 Moscow, Russia
**Glynn, Brian**  —  Ice Hockey Player
Prince Albert Police Dept, 1084 Central, Prince Albert SK S6V 7P3, Canada
**Glynn, Carlin**  —  Actress
1165 5th Ave, New York NY 10029, USA
**Glynn, Edward P (Ed)**  —  Baseball Player
157 San Carlos St, Toms River NJ 08757, USA
**Glynn, Ian M**  —  Physiologist
Daylesford, Conduit Head Road, Cambridge CB3 0EY, England
**Glynn, Ryan D**  —  Baseball Player
1226 Melaleuca Lane, Fort Myers FL 33901, USA
**Gminski, Michael T (Mike)**  —  Basketball Player, Sportscaster
1309 Canterbury Hill Circle, Charlotte NC 28211, USA
**Gnedovsky, Yuri P**  —  Architect
Union of Architects, Granatny Per 22, 103001 Moscow, Russia
**Goad, Jim**  —  Journalist, Writer
Simon & Schuster Books, 1230 Ave of Americas, Concourse 1, New York NY 10020, USA
**Goad, Timothy R (Tim)**  —  Football Player
138 Birchwood Dr, Pittsboro NC 27312, USA
**Goalby, Bob**  —  Golfer
904 Briar Hill Road, Belleville IL 62223, USA
**Goapele**  —  Singer
I C M Partners, 10250 Constellation Blvd, #900, Los Angeles CA 90067 USA
**Gobble, B James (Jimmy)**  —  Baseball Player
150 Lake View Estates Dr, Bristol TN 37620, USA
**Gober, Robert**  —  Sculptor
Matthew Marks Gallery, 523 W 24 St, New York NY 10011, USA
**Gobert, Rudy**  —  Basketball Player
Utah Jazz, Energy Solutions Arena, 301 W South Temple, Salt Lake City UT 84101 USA
**Goberville, Celine**  —  Markswoman
Federation de Tir, 38 Rue Brunel, 75017 Paris, France
**Goc, Marcel**  —  Ice Hockey Player
12348 NW 69th Court, Parkland FL 33076, USA
**Gocong, Christopher A (Chris)**  —  Football Player
PO Box 93, Berea OH 44017, USA
**Godal, Tore**  —  Physician
World Health Organization, 20 Ave Appia, 1211 Geneva 27, Switzerland
**Godard, Jean-Luc**  —  Director
26 Ave Pierre 1er de Serbie, 75116 Paris, France
**Godber, John**  —  Writer
Alan Brodie, Fairgate House, 78 New Oxford St, London WC1A 1HB, England
**Godby, Danny R**  —  Baseball Player
RR 2 Box 17A, Chapmanville WV 25508, USA
**Godchaux, Stephen**  —  Producer
Paradigm Agency, 360 N Crescent Dr, North Building, Beverly Hills CA 90210 USA
**Goddard, Joseph H (Joe)**  —  Baseball Player
304 Ridgepark Dr, Beckley WV 25801, USA
**Goddet, Michelle**  —  Actress
Artmedia, 20 Ave Rapp, 75007 Paris, France
**Goderie, Maartje**  —  Field Hockey Player
H C Den Bosch, Oosterplasweg 35, 5215 'S-Hertpgebosch HT, Netherlands
**Godfread, Dan**  —  Basketball Player
622 Michigan St, Eagle River WI 54521, USA
**Godfrey**  —  Actor, Comedian
Paradigm Agency, 360 N Crescent Dr, North Building, Beverly Hills CA 90210 USA
**Godfrey, Christopher J (Chris)**  —  Football Player
52383 Swanson Dr, South Bend IN 46635, USA
**Godfrey, Paul V**  —  Businessman
Postmedia Network, 1450 Don Mills Road, Don Mills ON M3B 3R5, Canada
**Godfrey, Randall E**  —  Football Player
4102 Mount Zion Church Road, South Bend IN 46635, USA
**Godin, Elodie**  —  Basketball Player
Familia Basket Schio, Viale Dell'Industria, 36025 Schio, France
**Godley, Georgina**  —  Fashion Designer
42 Bassett Road, London W10 6UL, England
**Godmanis, Ivars**  —  Prime Minister, Latvia
Palasta St 1, 1954 Riga, Latvia
**Godovsky, Yan**  —  Ballet Dancer, Executive
Bolshoi Theater, Teatralnaya Pl 1, 103009 Moscow, Russia
**Godwin, Gail K**  —  Writer
PO Box 946, Woodstock NY 12498, USA
**Godwin, Linda M**  —  Astronaut, Physicist
3801 Eagle View Court, Columbia MO 65203, USA
**Godynyuk, Alexander**  —  Ice Hockey Player
217 Follen Road, Lexington MA 02421, USA
**Goeas, Leo D**  —  Football Player
95-104 Hiilei Place, Mililani HI 96789, USA
**Goebel, Timothy**  —  Figure Skater
Lee Marshall Mgmt, 199 E Garfield Road, Aurora OH 44202, USA
**Goeddeke, George A**  —  Football Player
1227 Pinecrest Dr, White Lake MI 48386, USA
**Goeddel, David V N**  —  Biochemist
Tularik Inc, 270 Grand Ave, San Francisco CA 94108, USA
**Goedgedrag, Frits M D L S**  —  Governor, Netherlands Antilles
Governor's Office, Fort Amsterdam 2, Willemstad, Netherlands Antilles
**Goehr, P Alexander**  —  Composer
University of Cambridge, Music Faculty, 11 West Road, Cambridge, England

**G**

**Gluck - Goehr**

**Goellner, Marc-Kevin** — Tennis Athlete
Blau-Weiss Neuss, Tennishall Jahnstra, 41464 Neuss, Germany
**Goelz, Dave (Gonzo)** — Puppeteer
Jim Henson Productions, 117 E 69th St, New York NY 10021, USA
**Goen, Robert K (Bob)** — Entertainer
Rebel Entertainment Partners, 5700 Wilshire Blvd, #456, Los Angeles CA 90036, USA
**Goerke, Christine** — Opera Singer
I M G Artists, Hogarth Business Park, Chiswick, London W4 2TH, England
**Goerke, Glenn A** — Educator
University of Houston, President's Office, Houston TX 77204, USA
**Goerne, Matthias** — Opera Singer
I M G Artists, Hogarth Business Park, Chiswick, London W4 2TH, England
**Goertz, LeRoy** — Sculptor, Jewelry Designer, Composer
Refiner's Fire, PO Box 66612, Portland OR 97290, USA
**Goestschi, Renate** — Alpine Skier
Schwarzenbach 3, 8742 Obdach, Austria
**Goetz, Dick** — Golfer
4301 Fillbrook Lane, Tyler TX 75707, USA
**Goetz, Eric** — Yacht Builder
Eric Goetz Marine & Technology, 15 Broad Common Road, Bristol RI 02809, USA
**Goetz-Ackerman, Vicki** — Golfer
3621 Sally Parrish Trail, Valrico FL 33596, USA
**Goetzman, Gary M** — Producer
Playtone Productions, PO Box 7340, Santa Monica CA 90406, USA
**Goff, Michael J (Mike)** — Football Player
2225 5th St, Peru IL 61354, USA
**Goffin, Gerry** — Lyricist
9171 Hazen Dr, Beverly Hills CA 90210, USA
**Goffin, Louise L** — Singer, Songwriter
Evolution Music, 1680 N Vine St, #500, Los Angeles CA 90028, USA
**Gogan, Kevin P** — Football Player
4643 286th Ave E, Fall City MA 98024, USA
**Goganious, Keith L** — Football Player
4173 Cheswick Lane, Virginia Beach VA 23455, USA
**Gogel, Matt** — Golfer
3509 W 68th St, Mission Hills KS 66208, USA
**Goggin, Charles F (Chuck)** — Baseball Player
1224 Roundhouse Lane, Alexandria VA 22314, USA
**Goggins, Walton** — Actor
A P A Talent/Literary Agency, 405 S Beverly Dr, #300, Beverly Hills CA 90212 USA
**Gogo, David** — Guitarist
Cordova Bay Entertainment, 2750 Quadra St, #209, Victoria BC V8T 4EB, Canada
**Gogolak, Charles P (Charlie)** — Football Player
PO Box 361, Northeast Harbor ME 04662, USA
**Gogolak, Peter (Pete)** — Football Player
24 Arrowhead Way, Darien CT 06820, USA
**Gogolewski, William J (Bill)** — Baseball Player
1522 Graham Ave, Oshkosh WI 54902, USA
**Gogue, Jay** — Educator
Auburn University, President's Office, Auburn AL 36849, USA
**Goh Chok Tong** — Prime Minister, Singapore
Senior Minister's Office, Istana Annexe, 238823 Singapore, Singapore
**Goh, Rex** — Guitarist (Air Supply)
PO Box 3367, Beverly Hills CA 90212, USA
**Gohl, Matthias** — Composer
I C M Artists, 40 W 57th St, #1800, New York NY 10019 USA
**Gohlke, Frank** — Photographer
Howard Greenberg Gallery, 41 E 57th St, #1406, New York NY 10022, USA
**Gohr, Gregory J (Greg)** — Baseball Player
77 Scotland Road, Reading MA 01867, USA
**Goich, Daniel J (Dan)** — Football Player
PO Box 19068, Las Vegas NV 89132, USA
**Goicolea, Anthony** — Photographer
149-151 Grand St, #1, Brooklyn NY 11211, USA
**Goin, Suzanne** — Restauranteur
Lucques, 8484 Melrose Ave, West Hollywood CA 90069, USA
**Goines, Siena** — Actress
Don Buchwald, 6500 Wilshire Blvd, #2200, Los Angeles CA 90048 USA
**Going, Joanna** — Actress
Vanguard Management Group, 8060 Melrose Ave, #400, Los Angeles CA 90046, USA
**Goings, E V** — Businessman
Tupperware Corp, PO Box 2353, Orlando FL 32802, USA
**Goings, Nick A** — Football Player
660 Caicos Court, Wilmington NC 28405, USA
**Goitschel-Beranger, Marielle** — Alpine Skier
Val Thorens, 73440 Saint-Martin de Belleville, France
**Gojun, Jakov** — Handball Player
Club Balonmano Athletico, Paseo del Pintor Rosales 26, 28008 Madrid, Spain
**Gola, Thomas J (Tom)** — Basketball Player, Coach
15 Kings Oak Lane, Philadelphia PA 19115, USA
**Golay, Jeanne** — Cyclist
1125 Red Mountain Dr, Glenwood Springs CO 81601, USA
**Gold, Christina A** — Businesswoman
Western Union, 12500 Belford Ave, Englewood CO 80112, USA
**Gold, Elon** — Actor, Comedian
Gersh Agency, 9465 Wilshire Blvd, #600, Beverly Hills CA 90212 USA
**Gold, Herbert** — Writer
1051 Broadway, #A, San Francisco CA 94133, USA
**Gold, Ian M** — Football Player
10275 Tradition Place, Lone Tree CO 80124, USA
**Gold, Jack** — Director
The Agency, 24 Pottery Lane, Holland Park,London W11 4LZ, England , USA
**Gold, Jonathan** — Journalist
L A Weekly, Editorial Dept, 6715 Sunset Blvd, Los Angeles CA 90028, USA
**Gold, Louise** — Actress
Gavin Barker Assoc, 2D Wimpole St, London W1G 0EB, England

**Gold, Tracey** — Actress
Talent Works, 3500 W Olive Ave, #1400, Burbank CA 91505 USA

**Goldberg, Adam C** — Actor
Luber Rocklin Entertainment, 8530 Wilshire Blvd, #555, Beverly Hills CA 90211 USA

**Goldberg, Bernard R** — Commentator
CBS-TV, News Dept, 51 W 52nd St, New York NY 10019 USA

**Goldberg, Bill** — Actor
Kritzer Levine Wilkins Griffin, 11872 La Grange Ave, #100, Los Angeles CA 90025 USA

**Goldberg, Daryl** — Director, Producer
Pipeline Entertainment, 305 2nd Ave, #302, New York NY 10003, USA

**Goldberg, Eric** — Animator
Walt Disney Studios, Animation Dept, 500 S Buena Vista St, Burbank CA 91521, USA

**Goldberg, Evan** — Producer
United Talent Agency, U T A Plaza, 9336 Civic Center Dr, Beverly Hills CA 90210 USA

**Goldberg, Fred T, Jr** — Government Official
Skadden Arps Slate, 1440 New York Ave NW, #600, Washington DC 20005, USA

**Goldberg, Harris** — Director, Writer
Key Creatives, 1800 N Highland Ave, Los Angeles CA 90028, USA

**Goldberg, Iddo** — Actor
Gordon & French, 12-13 Poland St, London W1F 8QB, England

**Goldberg, Jim** — Photographer
California College of Arts, Fine Arts Dept, San Francisco CA 94107, USA

**Goldberg, Leonard** — Producer
Spectradyne Inc, 1198 Commerce Dr, Richardson TX 75081, USA

**Goldberg, Lucianne S** — Publisher
4 Oak St, Weehawken NJ 7086, USA

**Goldberg, Luella G** — Educator
7019 Tupa Dr, Minneapolis MN 55439, USA

**Goldberg, Myla** — Writer
Doubleday Press, 1745 Broadway, New York NY 10019, USA

**Goldberg, Richard W** — Judge
US International Trade Court, 1 Federal Plaza, New York NY 10278, USA

**Goldberg, Stan** — Cartoonist (Archie)
8 White Birch Lane, Scarsdale NY 10583, USA

**Goldberg, Whoopi** — Actress, Comedienne, Writer, Producer
Whoop/One Ho Productions, 333 W 52nd St, #602, New York NY 10019, USA

**Goldberg, William S (Bill)** — Professional Wrestler, Football Player
Vox Inc, 6420 Wilshire Blvd, #1080, Los Angeles CA 90048 USA

**Goldberger, Andreas** — Ski Jumper
Bleckenwegen 4, 4924 Waldzell, Austria

**Goldberger, Marvin L** — Physicist, Educator
5205 Pacifica Dr, San Diego CA 92109, USA

**Goldberger, Paul J** — Journalist, Architectural Critic
New York Times, Editorial Dept, 229 W 43rd St, New York NY 10036, USA

**Goldblatt, David** — Photographer
South Picture Portal, Box 91776, Auckland Park, 2006 Gauteng, South Africa

**Goldblatt, Stephen L** — Cinematographer
Skouras Agency, 1149 3rd St, #300, Santa Monica CA 90403 USA

**Goldblum, Jeff** — Actor
Creative Artists Agency, 2000 Ave of Stars, #100, Los Angeles CA 90067 USA

**Golden, Alfred J (Al)** — Football Player, Coach
University of Miami, Athletic Dept, Coral Gables FL 33124, USA

**Golden, Arthur** — Writer
Vintage Books, 1745 Broadway, New York NY 10019 USA

**Golden, Daniel** — Journalist
Wall Street Journal, Editorial Dept, 1 World Financial Center, New York NY 10281, USA

**Golden, Harry** — Bowling Executive
Professional Bowlers Assn, 719 2nd Ave, #701, Seattle WA 98104 USA

**Golden, James E (Jim)** — Baseball Player
8630 SW 10th Ave, Topeka KS 66615, USA

**Golden, Kate** — Golfer
969 Hunterwood Dr, Jasper TX 75951, USA

**Golden, William Lee** — Singer (Oak Ridge Boys); Songwriter
329 Rockland Road, Hendersonville TN 37075, USA

**Goldenhersh, Heather** — Actress
Gersh Agency, 9465 Wilshire Blvd, #600, Beverly Hills CA 90212 USA

**Goldenthal, Elliot** — Composer
Gorfaine/Schwartz, 4111 W Alameda Ave, #509, Burbank CA 91505 USA

**Goldfaden, Benjamin P (Ben)** — Basketball Player
5819 Bounty Circle, Tavares FL 32778, USA

**Goldfinger, June** — Interior Designer
June Goldfinger Designs, 109 Katonah Ave, Katonah NY 10536, USA

**Goldfinger, Myron** — Architect
PO Box 53, Waccabuc NY 10597, USA

**Goldfinger, Sarah** — Actress, Producer
Creative Artists Agency, 2000 Ave of Stars, #100, Los Angeles CA 90067 USA

**Goldhor, David** — Director
Eagle Eye, 4013 Topanga Ave, Studio City CA 91604, USA

**Goldin, Claudia D** — Economist
Harvard University, Economics Dept, Cambridge MA 02138, USA

**Goldin, Judah** — Educator
3300 Darby Road, Haverford PA 19041, USA

**Goldin, Nan** — Photographer
334 Bowery, New York NY 10012, USA

**Goldin, Ricky Paull** — Actor
Stone Manners Salners, 9911 W Pico Blvd, #1400, Los Angeles CA 90035 USA

**Golding, Anders** — Marksman
Skytte Union, Idraettens Hus, Broendby Stadion 20, 2605 Brondby, Denmark

**Golding, Meta** — Actress
I F A Talent Agency, 8730 W Sunset Blvd, #490, West Hollywood CA 90069 USA

**Golding, O Bruce** — Prime Minister, Jamaica
Prime Minister's Office, 1 Devon Road, PO Box 272, Kingston 6, Jamaica

**Goldman, Bo** — Writer
Creative Artists Agency, 2000 Ave of Stars, #100, Los Angeles CA 90067 USA

**Goldman, Dan** — Writer
I C M Partners, 10250 Constellation Blvd, #900, Los Angeles CA 90067 USA

**Goldman, Jean-Jacques** — Singer, Guitarist, Songwriter
J S M Music, 73 Ave de la Republique, 92120 Montrouge, France

**Goldman, Julie** — Actress, Comedienne
427 Union St, #3, Brooklyn NY 11231, USA

**Goldman, Matt** — Entertainer (Blue Man Group)
Blue Man Group Productions, 411 Lafayette St, #300, New York NY 10003, USA

**Goldman, William** — Writer
Janklow & Nesbit Assoc, 445 Park Ave, #1300, New York NY 10022 USA

**Goldreich, Peter M** — Astronomer
471 S Catalina Ave, Pasadena CA 91106, USA

**Goldsboro, Bobby** — Singer, Songwriter
Jim Stephany Mgmt, 1021 Preston Dr, Nashville TN 37206, USA

**Goldschmidt, Neil E** — Secretary, Transportation; Governor, OR
1150 SW King Ave, Portland OR 97205, USA

**Goldsman, Akiva** — Director, Writer
Weed Road Pictures, 4000 Warner Blvd, Building 81, Burbank CA 91522, USA

**Goldsmith, Barbara** — Writer
Janklow Nesbit Assocs, 445 Park Ave, #1300, New York NY 10022, USA

**Goldsmith, Clio** — Actress
Elephant Family, 81 Gower St, London WC1E 6HJ, England

**Goldsmith, Judy** — Social Activist
National Organization for Women, 425 13th St NW, Washington DC 20002, USA

**Goldsmith, Myron** — Architect
Skidmore Owings Merrill, 224 S Michigan Ave, #1000, Chicago IL 60604, USA

**Goldsmith, Paul** — Auto Racing Driver, Motorcycle Rider
1705 E Main St, Griffith IN 46319, USA

**Goldsmith, Timothy H** — Biologist
Yale University, Biology Dept, New Haven CT 06520, USA

**Goldson, Dashon H** — Football Player
Tampa Bay Buccaneers, 1 W Buccaneer Place, Tampa FL 33607 USA

**Goldstein, Allan A** — Director
6488 Mary Ellen Ave, Van Nuys CA 91401, USA

**Goldstein, Allan L** — Biochemist, Immunologist
PO Box 296, Reedville VA 22539, USA

**Goldstein, Alon** — Concert Pianist
Frank Salomon, 121 W 27th St, #703, New York NY 10001 USA

**Goldstein, Avram** — Pharmacologist
355 S Grand Ave, #2600, Los Angeles CA 90071, USA

**Goldstein, Joseph L** — Nobel Medicine Laureate
3831 Turtle Creek Blvd, #22B, Dallas TX 75219, USA

**Goldstein, Lisa** — Actress
Harrison Stokes, 8730 W Sunset Blvd, #270, West Hollywood CA 90069, USA

**Goldstein, Murray** — Physician, Association Executive
United Cerebral Palsy Foundation, 1660 L St NW, #700, Washington DC 20036, USA

**Goldstein, Rebecca** — Writer, Philosopher
2 Payamel Lane, Truro MA 02666, USA

**Goldstone, Jeffrey** — Physicist
77 Massachusetts Ave, #6-313, Cambridge MA 02139, USA

**Goldstone, Richard J** — Judge
Constitutional Court, Private Bag X32, Braamfontein 2017, South Africa

**Goldsworthy, Andrew C (Andy)** — Artist, Photographer
Hue-Williams Fine Art, 21 Cork St, London W1X 1HB, England

**Goldthwait, Bob (Bobcat)** — Actor, Comedian, Director
Gersh Agency, 9465 Wilshire Blvd, #600, Beverly Hills CA 90212 USA

**Goldwyn, Samuel J, Jr** — Producer
Samuel Goldwyn Co, 9570 W Pico Blvd, #400, Los Angeles CA 90035, USA

**Goldwyn, Tony** — Actor, Director
Creative Artists Agency, 2000 Ave of Stars, #100, Los Angeles CA 90067 USA

**Golic, Mike** — Football Player
108 Westland Road, Avon CT 06001, USA

**Golic, Robert P (Bob)** — Football Player, Sportscaster
6130 Loch Lomond Court, Solon OH 44139, USA

**Golijov, Osvaldo** — Composer
Opus 3 Artists, 470 Park Ave S, #900N, New York NY 10016, USA

**Golimowski, David A** — Astronomer
515 Holden Road, Towson MD 21286, USA

**Golino, Valeria** — Actress
Cineart, 28 Rue Mogador, 78009 Paris, France

**Golisano, B Thomas** — Businessman
Paychex Inc, 911 Panorama Trail S, Rochester NY 14625, USA

**Golonka, Arlene** — Actress
David Moss Company, 733 N Seward St, #PH, Hollywood CA 90038 90038, USA

**Golota, Andrzej** — Boxer
26852 W Apple Tree Lane, Barrington IL 60010, USA

**Golovkin, Gennady G** — Boxer
Spotlight Boxing, Am Stadtrand 27, 22047 Hamburg, Germany

**Golson, Benny** — Jazz Saxophonist, Composer
Bridge Agency, 35 Clark St, #A5, Brooklyn Heights NY 11201, USA

**Golsteyn, Jerry M** — Football Player
243 Tadcaster Court, Raeford NC 28376, USA

**Goltz, David A (Dave)** — Baseball Player
1009 Stonybrook Manor, Fergus Falls MN 56537, USA

**Golub, Jeff** — Jazz Guitarist
Chapman & Co Mgmt, 14011 Ventura Blvd, #405, Sherman Oaks CA 91423, USA

**Golubeva, Yekatarina** — Actress
Artmedia, 20 Ave Rapp, 75007 Paris, France

**Goluboff, Bryan** — Writer, Director
Paradigm Agency, 360 N Crescent Dr, North Building, Beverly Hills CA 90210 USA

**Golzari, Sam** — Actor
Innovative Artists, 1505 10th St, Santa Monica CA 90401 USA

**Gomes Junior, Carlos D** — Prime Minister, Guinea-Bissau
Premier's Office, Ave Unidad Africana, CP 137, Bissau, Guinea-Bissau

**Gomes, Jessica** — Model
Vivien's Model Mgmt, 43 Bay St, Double Bay, Sydney NSW 2028, Australia

**Gomes, Jonathan J (Jonny)** — Baseball Player
7901 Garden Dr N, Saint Petersburg FL 33710, USA

**Gomes, Wayne M** — Baseball Player
5104 W Creek Court, Suffolk VA 23435, USA
**Gomez Noya, Francisco Javier** — Triathlete
Mourente 9, 36164 Mourente, Spain
**Gomez, Andres** — Tennis Player
ProServe, 1101 Woodrow Wilson Blvd, #1800, Arlington VA 22209 USA
**Gomez, Carlos** — Actor
Stone Manners Salners, 9911 W Pico Blvd, #1400, Los Angeles CA 90035 USA
**Gomez, Chris C** — Baseball Player
8 Vernal Spring, Irvine CA 92603, USA
**Gomez, Christian** — Soccer Player
D C United, R F K Stadium, 2400 E Capitol St SE, Washington DC 20003 USA
**Gomez, Ian** — Actor
A P A Talent/Literary Agency, 405 S Beverly Dr, #300, Beverly Hills CA 90212 USA
**Gomez, Jaime P** — Actor
Susan Nathe Assoc, 8281 Melrose Ave, #200, Los Angeles CA 90046, USA
**Gomez, Jeff** — Cartoonist
Starlight Runner Entertainment, 5 Union Square, #400, New York NY 10003, USA
**Gomez, Jesus R Salazar** — Religious Leader
Arzobispado, Carrera 7A, #10-20, Bogota DC 1, Colombia
**Gomez, Jill** — Opera Singer
16 Milton Park, London N6 5QA, England
**Gomez, Joshua E** — Actor
Progressive Artists Agency, 9696 Culver Blvd, #110, Culver City CA 90232 USA
**Gomez, Leonardo (Leo)** — Baseball Player
273 Portofino Dr, North Venice FL 34275, USA
**Gomez, Luis J** — Baseball Player
676 Chesterfield Dr, Lawrenceville CA 30044, USA
**Gomez, Mariette Himes** — Interior Designer
504 E 74th St, #300, New York NY 10021, USA
**Gomez, Randall S (Rocky)** — Baseball Player
50 Oak St, San Martin CA 95046, USA
**Gomez, Rick** — Actor, Writer, Producer
A P A Talent/Literary Agency, 405 S Beverly Dr, #300, Beverly Hills CA 90212 USA
**Gomez, Scott** — Ice Hockey Player
14121 Thunder Road, Anchorage AK 99516, USA
**Gomez, Selena M** — Actress, Singer
July Moon Productions, 10100 Santa Monica Blvd, #1300, Los Angeles CA 90067, USA
**Gomez, Wilfredo** — Boxer
U E C A, Edificio 54 Apt 01, Trujillo Alto PR 00976, USA
**Gomez-Preston, Reagan** — Actress
Innovative Artists, 1505 10th St, Santa Monica CA 90401 USA
**Gomis, Emilie** — Basketball Player
Federation de Basketball, Rue du Chateau des Rentiers 117, 75013 Paris, France
**Gomory, Ralph E** — Foundation Executive, Mathematician
Alfred P Sloan Foundation, President's Office, 630 5th Ave, New York NY 10111, USA
**Gompf, Thomas (Tom)** — Diver
2716 Barret Ave, Plant City FL 33566, USA
**Gomyo, Karen** — Concert Violinist
Seldy Cramer Artists, 3439 Springhill Road, Lafayette CA 94549, USA
**Gonchar, Sergei V** — Ice Hockey Player
7 Kevin Dr, Sewickley PA 15143, USA
**Gonchor, Jess** — Art Director
Murtha Agency, 4240 Promenade Way, #232, Marina del Rey CA 90292, USA
**Gondoline, Michel** — Actor
Alais Agence Artisqaue, 13 Rue Chevreul, 75011 Paris, France
**Gondrezick, Grant** — Basketball Player
5906 Etiwanda Ave, #19, Tarzana CA 91356, USA
**Gondry, Michel** — Director
Creative Artists Agency, 2000 Ave of Stars, #100, Los Angeles CA 90067 USA
**Gonet, Stella** — Actress
Markham Froggatt Irwin, Julian House, 4 Windmill St, London W1P 1HF, England
**Gong Li** — Actress, Model
I C M Partners, 10250 Constellation Blvd, #900, Los Angeles CA 90067 USA
**Gongora, Omar** — Drummer (Kinky)
Marcella C Public Relations, 646 S Barrington Ave, #206, Brentwood CA 90049, USA
**Gonick, Larry** — Cartoonist (Prehistoric Animals)
247 Missouri St, San Francisco CA 94107, USA
**Gonnenwein, Wolfgang** — Conductor
Buro Beate Gienger, Im Boblinger 2, 71636 Ludwigsburg, Germany
**Gonsalves, Ralph E** — Premier, Saint Vincent & Grenadines
Prime Minister's Office, Administration Centre, Kingstown, Saint Vincent & Grenadines
**Gonshaw, Francesca** — Actress
Greg Mellard, 12 D'Arblay St, #200, London W1V 3FP, England
**Gonsoulin, Austin W Goose)** — Football Player
7720 Summer Wind Dr, Beaumont TX 77713, USA
**Gonzales, Carlos** — Cinematographer
3850 Tracy St, Los Angeles CA 90027, USA
**Gonzales, Chilly** — Singer, Songwriter
Agency Group Ltd, 1880 Century Park E, #711, Los Angeles CA 90067 USA
**Gonzales, Rene A** — Baseball Player
755 E Orangewood Dr, Covina CA 91723, USA
**Gonzalez Echevarria, Roberto** — Educator
Yale University, Hispanic/Comparative Literature Dept, New Haven CT 06520, USA
**Gonzalez Gonzalez, Clifton** — Actor
Paradigm Agency, 360 N Crescent Dr, North Building, Beverly Hills CA 90210 USA
**Gonzalez Inarritu, Alejandro** — Director
Creative Artists Agency, 2000 Ave of Stars, #100, Los Angeles CA 90067 USA
**Gonzalez Marquez, Felipe** — Prime Minister, Spain
Fundacion Socialismo XXI, Gobelas 31, 28023 Madrid, Spain
**Gonzalez Zumarraga, Antonio J Cardinal** — Religious Leader
Arzobispado, Apartado 17-01-00106, Called Chile 1140, Quito, Ecuador
**Gonzalez, A Antonio (Tony)** — Baseball Player
8011 SW 196th Terrace, Cutler Bay FL 33189, USA
**Gonzalez, Adrian** — Baseball Player
Los Angeles Dodgers, Stadium, 1000 Elysian Park Ave, Los Angeles CA 90090 USA

# G

**Gonzalez, Alex** — Actor
Kuranda Mgmt, Santo Angel 84, 28043 Madrid, Spain
**Gonzalez, Alexander S (Alex)** — Baseball Player
7743 SW 119th Court, Miami FL 33183, USA
**Gonzalez, Anthony D (Tony)** — Football Player
18935 Evening Breeze Circle, Huntington Beach CA 92648, USA
**Gonzalez, Arthur** — Judge
US Bankruptcy Court, 1 Bowling Green, #534, New York NY 10004, USA
**Gonzalez, Ashie** — Bowler
Professional Bowlers Assn, 719 2nd Ave, #701, Seattle WA 98104 USA
**Gonzalez, Carlos A** — Baseball Player
Colorado Rockies, Coors Field, 2001 Blake St, #A, Denver CO 80205 USA
**Gonzalez, Fredi J** — Baseball Manager
2768 Pete Shaw Road, Marietta GA 30066, USA
**Gonzalez, Giovanny A (Gio)** — Baseball Player
Oakland Athletics, McAfee Coliseum, 7000 Coliseum Way, #3, Oakland CA 94621 USA
**Gonzalez, Hector** — Religious Leader
Baptist Churches USA, PO Box 851, Valley Forge PA 19482, USA
**Gonzalez, Jaslene** — Model
Elite Model Mgmt, 404 Park Ave S, #900, New York NY 10016 USA
**Gonzalez, Juan A** — Baseball Player
Ext Catoni A9, Vega Baja PR 00693, USA
**Gonzalez, Lissette** — Commentator, Model
CBS4-TV, 8900 NW 18th Terrace, Doral FL 33172, USA
**Gonzalez, Luis E** — Baseball Player
6026 E Jenan Dr, Scottsdale AZ 85254, USA
**Gonzalez, Michael V (Mike)** — Baseball Player
2414 Pine Brook Court, Deer Park TX 77536, USA
**Gonzalez, Nicholas** — Actor
Pakula/King, 9229 W Sunset Blvd, #315, West Hollywood CA 90069 USA
**Gonzalez, Omar** — Soccer Player
Los Angeles Galaxy, Home Depot Center, 18400 Avalon Blvd, Carson CA 90746 USA
**Gonzalez, Pedro O** — Baseball Player
104 Gen Cabral, San Pedro de Macoris, Dominican Republic
**Gonzalez, Raul** — Soccer Player
F C Real Madrid, Avda Concha Espana 1, 28036 Madrid, Spain
**Gonzalez, Rick** — Actor
Framework Entertainment, 9057 Nemo St, #C, West Hollywood CA 90069 USA
**Gonzalo, Julie** — Actress
United Talent Agency, U T A Plaza, 9336 Civic Center Dr, Beverly Hills CA 90210 USA
**Gonzi, Lawrence** — Prime Minister, Malta
Prime Minister's Office, Auberge de Castille, 13 Saint Paul's St, Valletta VLT 1210, Malta
**Gooch, Jeffrey L (Jeff)** — Football Player
12709 Seronera Valley Court, Spring Hill FL 34610, USA
**Gooch, Rich** — Bassist (Quarterflash)
Pacific Talent Agency, PO Box 19145, Portland OR 97280, USA
**Good, Andrew R** — Baseball Player
1433 S Belcher Road, #G4, Clearwater FL 33764, USA
**Good, Hugh W** — Religious Leader
Primitive Advent Christian Church, 6403 Frame Road, Elkview WV 25071, USA
**Good, Meagan** — Actress
Untitled Entertainment, 350 S Beverly Dr, #200, Beverly Hills CA 90212 USA
**Good, Michael T** — Astronaut
2617 Broussard Court, Seabrook TX 77586, USA
**Goodacre Connick, Jill** — Model
Harry Connick, Wilkins Mgmt, 323 Broadway, Cambridge MA 02139, USA
**Goodacre, Glenna** — Sculptor
1202 Ojo Verde, Santa Fe NM 87501, USA
**Goodall, Caroline** — Actress
United Agents, 12-26 Lexington St, London W1F 0LE, England
**Goodall, V Jane** — Ethologist, Primatologist
Jane Goodall Institute, 4245 Fairfax Dr, #600, Arlington VA 22203, USA
**Goodburn, Kelly J** — Football Player
3710 W 52nd Place, Mission KS 66205, USA
**Goode, Chris K** — Football Player
1428 Egret Lane, Birmingham AL 35214, USA
**Goode, David R** — Businessman
Norfolk Southern Corp, 3 Commercial Place, #100, Norfolk VA 23510, USA
**Goode, Donald R (Don)** — Football Player
30177 Tattersall Way, Menifee CA 92584, USA
**Goode, Irvin L (Irv)** — Football Player
1030 Schnucks Woodsmill Plaza, Chesterfield MO 63017, USA
**Goode, Joe** — Artist
PO Box 10372, Playa del Rey CA 90291, USA
**Goode, Matthew** — Actor
Dazwell & Beresford, 26 Astwood Mews, London SW7 4DE, England
**Goode, Richard S** — Concert Pianist
Frank Salomon, 121 W 27th St, #703, New York NY 10001 USA
**Goode, W Wilson** — Mayor, Philadelphia; Social Activist
Amachi, 2000 Market St, #600, Philadelphia PA 19103, USA
**Goodell, Brian S** — Swimmer
27040 S Ridge Dr, Mission Viejo CA 92692, USA
**Goodell, Roger** — Football Executive
National Football League, 280 Park Ave, #12W, New York NY 10017, USA
**Gooden, Dwight E** — Baseball Player
20114 Nob Oak Ave, Tampa FL 33647, USA
**Goodenough, Ward H** — Anthropologist
3300 Darby Road, #5306, Haverford PA 19041, USA
**Goodfellow, Peter N** — Geneticist
Cancer Research Fund, Lincoln Inn Fields, London WC2A 3PX, England
**Goodfriend, Lynda** — Actress
338 S Beachwood Dr, Burbank CA 91506, USA
**Gooding, Cuba, Sr** — Singer (Main Ingredient)
Universal Attractions, 135 W 26th St, #1200, New York NY 10001 USA
**Gooding, Omar** — Actor
Innovative Artists, 1505 10th St, Santa Monica CA 90401 USA

**Gonzalez - Gooding**

| | |
|---|---|
| **Goodison, Paul** <br> Utley Sailing Club, Pleasley Road, Aughton, Sheffield S26 3XL, England | Yachtsman |
| **Goodkind, Terry** <br> G P Putnam's Sons, 375 Hudson St, New York NY 10014 USA | Writer |
| **Goodman, Alfred** <br> Bodenstedtstr 31, 81241 Munich, Germany | Composer |
| **Goodman, Allegra** <br> Dial Press, 375 Hudson St, New York NY 10014, USA | Writer |
| **Goodman, Brian** <br> Nine Yards Entertainment, 8530 Wilshire Blvd, #500, Beverly Hills CA 90211 USA | Actor |
| **Goodman, Corey S** <br> Howard Hughes Medical Institute, Molecular/Cell Biology Dept, Berkeley CA 94720, USA | Neurobiologist |
| **Goodman, Eli** <br> Maverick Artists Agency, 1680 N Vine St, #802, Los Angeles CA 90028, USA | Actor |
| **Goodman, Ellen H** <br> Boston Globe, Editorial Dept, 135 William Morrissey Blvd, Dorchester MA 02125 USA | Columnist |
| **Goodman, Hazelle** <br> C E S D, 10635 Santa Monica Blvd, #130, Los Angeles CA 90025 USA | Actress |
| **Goodman, John** <br> Gersh Agency, 9465 Wilshire Blvd, #600, Beverly Hills CA 90212 USA | Actor |
| **Goodman, John F** <br> Commander, Marine Forces Pacific, Camp H M Smith HI 96861 USA | Marine Corps General |
| **Goodman, John R** <br> 800 E 9th St, Edmond OK 73034, USA | Football Player |
| **Goodman, Joseph W** <br> 570 University Terrace, Los Altos CA 94022, USA | Electrical Engineer |
| **Goodman, Katy (La Sera)** <br> Agency Group Ltd, 1880 Century Park E, #711, Los Angeles CA 90067 USA | Singer, Songwriter |
| **Goodman, Len** <br> Strictly Come Dancing, BBC Television, Wood Lane, London W12 7RJ, England | Dance Judge |
| **Goodman, Oscar** <br> 520 S 4th St, Las Vegas NV 89101, USA | Attorney |
| **Goodrem, Delta** <br> Harbour Agency, 135 Forbes St, Woolloomooloo NSW 2011, Australia | Singer, Pianist |
| **Goodrich, Gail C, Jr** <br> PO Box 4969, Greenwich CT 06831, USA | Basketball Player |
| **Goodridge, Robin J** <br> Front Line Mgmt, 1100 Glendon Ave, #2000, Los Angeles CA 90024 USA | Drummer (Bush) |
| **Goodrum, Charles L (Charlie)** <br> 117 Pico Road, East Palatka FL 32131, USA | Football Player |
| **Goodson, J Edward (Ed)** <br> PO Box 1655, Palatka FL 32178, USA | Baseball Player |
| **Goodson, James A** <br> 37 Carolina Trail, Marshfield MA 02050, USA | WW II Army Air Corps Hero |
| **Goodwin, Carly** <br> 3624 Westbrook Ave, Nashville TN 37205, USA | Singer |
| **Goodwin, Curtis L** <br> 14939 Western Ave, San Leandro CA 94578, USA | Baseball Player |
| **Goodwin, Danny K** <br> 1555 Linksview Close, Stone Mountain GA 30088, USA | Baseball Player |
| **Goodwin, Doris Kearns** <br> 1649 Monument Lane, Concord MA 01742, USA | Historian, Commentator |
| **Goodwin, Frederick Tutu** <br> Queen's Representative's Office, Avarua, Rarotonga, Cook Islands | Queen's Representative, Cook Islands |
| **Goodwin, Ginnifer** <br> John Carrabino Mgmt, 5900 Wilshire Blvd, #406, Los Angeles CA 90036 USA | Actress |
| **Goodwin, Gordon** <br> Randex Communications, 906 Jonathan Lane, Marlton NJ 08053, USA | Jazz Orchestra Leader |
| **Goodwin, Malcolm J** <br> I F A Talent Agency, 8730 W Sunset Blvd, #490, West Hollywood CA 90069 USA | Actor |
| **Goodwin, Michael** <br> Office & Professional Employees, 1660 L St NW, #801, Washington DC 20036, USA | Labor Leader |
| **Goodwin, Michael** <br> Dulcina Eisen Assoc, 154 E 61st St, New York NY 10065, USA | Actor |
| **Goodwin, R Hunter** <br> 1011 Lyceum Court, College Station TX 77840, USA | Football Player |
| **Goodwin, Raven** <br> C E S D, 10635 Santa Monica Blvd, #130, Los Angeles CA 90025 USA | Actress |
| **Goodwin, Ronald R (Ronnie)** <br> 3702 Sul Ross St, San Angelo TX 76904, USA | Football Player |
| **Goodwin, Thomas J (Tom)** <br> 8 Maple St, Massapequa NY 11758, USA | Baseball Player |
| **Goodwin, Trudie** <br> Bosun House, 1 Deer Park Road, Merton, London SW19 3TL, England | Actress |
| **Goodwyn, Myles** <br> S L Feldman Mgmt, 1505 W 2nd Ave, #200, Vancouver BC V6H 3Y4, Canada | Singer, Guitarist (April Wine) |
| **Goody, Joan E** <br> Goody Clancy Assoc, 334 Boylston St, Boston MA 02116, USA | Architect |
| **Goodyear, Scott** <br> Scott Goodyear Racing, PO Box 589, Carmel IN 46082, USA | Auto Racing Driver |
| **Goodyear, Stewart** <br> Columbia Artists Mgmt Inc, 1790 Broadway, #702, New York NY 10019 USA | Concert Pianist |
| **Goolagong Cawley, Yvonne F** <br> PO Box 1347, Noosa Heads QLD 4567, Australia | Tennis Player |
| **Goolrick, Robert** <br> Algonquin Books, PO Box 27515, Chapel Hill NC 27515 USA | Writer |
| **Goolsby, Austan D** <br> White House, 1600 Pennsylvania Ave NW, Washington DC 20500 USA | Government Official, Economist |
| **Goorjian, Michael** <br> Lyceum Entertainment, 4221 Hollis St, Emeryville CA 94608, USA | Actor |
| **Goose, Claire** <br> C A M, 55-59 Shaftesbury Ave, London W1D 6LD, England | Actress |
| **Goosen, Don** <br> 1315 N Riverview Ave, Reedley CA 93654, USA | Boxing Promoter, Manager |
| **Goosen, Retief** <br> 9228 Sloane St, Orlando FL 32827, USA | Golfer |

**G**

**Goodison - Goosen**

| | |
|---|---|
| **Goossen, Jeananne** | Actress |
| Characters Talent Agency, 8 Elm St, Toronto, ON M5G 1G7, Canada | |
| **Gopnik, Adam** | Writer |
| New Yorker, Editorial Dept, 4 Times Square, Basement C1B, New York NY 10036 USA | |
| **Gora, Jo Ann M** | Educator |
| Ball State University, President's Office, A D Building, Muncie IN 47306, USA | |
| **Goranson, Alicia** | Actress |
| Paradigm Agency, 360 Park Ave S, #1600, New York NY 10010 USA | |
| **Gorbachev, Mikhail S** | Nobel Peace Laureate; Gen Sec, USSR |
| Leningradsky Prospekt 39, 125167 Moscow, Russia | |
| **Gorbachev, Yuri** | Artist |
| Adrienne Editions, 377 Geary St, San Francisco CA 94102, USA | |
| **Gorbatko, Viktor V** | Cosmonaut; Air Force General |
| Cosmonaut Training Center, Star City, 141160 Zvezdny Gorodok, Moscow Oblast, Russia | |
| **Gorchakova, Galina** | Opera Singer |
| Kirov Opera, Mariinsky Theater, Teatralnaya Pl 1, 190000 Saint Petersburg, Russia | |
| **Gordeeva, Ekaterina** | Figure Skater, Model |
| Anaheim Ice, 300 W Lincoln Ave, Anaheim CA 92805, USA | |
| **Gordeyev, Vyacheslav M** | Ballet Dancer, Choreographer |
| Tverskaya Str 9, #78, 103009 Moscow, Russia | |
| **Gordimer, Nadine** | Nobel Literature Laureate |
| 7 Frere Road, Parktown, Johannesburg 2193, South Africa | |
| **Gordley, James R** | Attorney, Educator |
| University of California, Law School, Boalt Hall, Berkeley CA 94720, USA | |
| **Gordon, Barry** | Actor, Singer |
| 1912 Kaweah Dr, Pasadena CA 91105, USA | |
| **Gordon, Benjamin (Ben)** | Basketball Player |
| 4300 Sharon Road, #418, Charlotte NC 28211, USA | |
| **Gordon, Bert I** | Director |
| 9640 Arby Dr, Beverly Hills CA 90210, USA | |
| **Gordon, Bridgette** | Basketball Player |
| Pattonville High School, 2497 Creve Coeur Mill Road, Maryland Heights MO 63043, USA | |
| **Gordon, Bryan** | Director, Producer, Writer |
| Creative Artists Agency, 2000 Ave of Stars, #100, Los Angeles CA 90067 USA | |
| **Gordon, Christopher** | Composer |
| I C M Partners, 10250 Constellation Blvd, #900, Los Angeles CA 90067 USA | |
| **Gordon, Cornell K** | Football Player |
| 4029 Spring Meadow Crescent, Chesapeake VA 23321, USA | |
| **Gordon, Dan** | Director, Producer, Writer |
| I C M Partners, 10250 Constellation Blvd, #900, Los Angeles CA 90067 USA | |
| **Gordon, Danso** | Actor |
| Evolution Entertainment, 901 N Highland Ave, Los Angeles CA 90038 USA | |
| **Gordon, Darrien X J** | Football Player |
| 1500 Pecos Dr, Southlake TX 76092, USA | |
| **Gordon, David** | Choreographer |
| 47 Great Jones St, #2, New York NY 10012, USA | |
| **Gordon, Dennie** | Director, Producer, Actress |
| Creative Artists Agency, 2000 Ave of Stars, #100, Los Angeles CA 90067 USA | |
| **Gordon, Don** | Actor |
| 10576 Rocca Way, Los Angeles CA 90077, USA | |
| **Gordon, Donald T (Don)** | Baseball Player |
| 711 Sunset Mountain Dr, Chattanooga TN 37421, USA | |
| **Gordon, Douglas** | Artist |
| Gagosian Gallery, 6-24 Britannia St, London WC1X 9JD, England | |
| **Gordon, Ed** | Commentator |
| NBC-TV, News Dept, 30 Rockefeller Plaza, #270E, New York NY 10112 USA | |
| **Gordon, Eric, Jr** | Basketball Player |
| Los Angeles Clippers, Staples Center, 1111 S Figueroa St, Los Angeles CA 90015 USA | |
| **Gordon, Eve** | Actress |
| Talent Works, 3500 W Olive Ave, #1400, Burbank CA 91505 USA | |
| **Gordon, Hannah Taylor** | Actress |
| Olivia Bell Mgmt, 193 Wardour St, London W1F 8ZF, England | |
| **Gordon, Harold P** | Businessman |
| Hasbro Inc, 1027 Newport Ave, Pawtucket RI 02861, USA | |
| **Gordon, Howard** | Writer, Producer |
| W M E Entertainment, 9601 Wilshire Blvd, #300, Beverly Hills CA 90210 USA | |
| **Gordon, Josh** | Director, Producer, Writer |
| Creative Artists Agency, 2000 Ave of Stars, #100, Los Angeles CA 90067 USA | |
| **Gordon, Keith** | Director |
| Arlook Group, 205 S Beverly Dr, #209, Beverly Hills CA 90212, USA | |
| **Gordon, Keith B** | Baseball Player |
| 4601 Thornhurst St, Olney MD 20832, USA | |
| **Gordon, Kim** | Singer, Bassist (Sonic Youth) |
| Silva Artist Mgmt, 722 Seward St, Los Angeles CA 90038, USA | |
| **Gordon, Kiowa** | Actor |
| A P A Talent/Literary Agency, 405 S Beverly Dr, #300, Beverly Hills CA 90212 USA | |
| **Gordon, Lalonde** | Track Athlete |
| National Athletics, PO Box 605, Port-of-Spain, Trinidad & Tobago | |
| **Gordon, Lamar D** | Football Player |
| 5428 N 19th St, Milwaukee WI 53209, USA | |
| **Gordon, Lancaster** | Basketball Player |
| 550 Robinhood Road, Jackson MS 39206, USA | |
| **Gordon, Lawrence** | Businessman |
| Largo Entertainment, 20th Century Fox, 10201 W Pico Blvd, Los Angeles CA 90064, USA | |
| **Gordon, Mark** | Producer |
| Mark Gordon Productions, 12200 W Olympic Blvd, #250, Los Angeles CA 90064, USA | |
| **Gordon, Mary C** | Writer |
| Viking Penguin Press, 375 Hudson St, New York NY 10014, USA | |
| **Gordon, Matt** | Actor |
| Edna Talent Mgmt, 318 Dundas St W, Toronto, ON M5T 1G5, Canada | |
| **Gordon, Michael E (Mike)** | Bassist (Phish) |
| PO Box 4400, Burlington VT 05404, USA | |
| **Gordon, Michael W (Mike)** | Baseball Player |
| 17 Highland Court, Needham MA 02492, USA | |
| **Gordon, Milton A** | Educator |
| California State University, President's Office, Fullerton CA 99264, USA | |

| | |
|---|---|
| **Gordon, Nina** | Singer, Guitarist, Songwriter |
| Paradigm Agency, 360 Park Ave S, #1600, New York NY 10010 USA | |
| **Gordon, Pamela F** | Prime Minister, Bermuda |
| United Bermuda Party, Chancery Lane, Box HM715, Hamilton HM CX, Bermuda | |
| **Gordon, Phil** | Actor |
| Alexandria Alvarez, 3145 Geary Blvd, #744, San Francisco CA 94118, USA | |
| **Gordon, Richard** | Writer, Anesthetist |
| 1 Craven Hill, London W2 3EN, England | |
| **Gordon, Richard F (Dick)** | Football Player |
| 7119 Sandy Springs Road, Maumee OH 43537, USA | |
| **Gordon, Richard F, Jr** | Astronaut |
| 65 Woodside Dr, Prescott AZ 86305, USA | |
| **Gordon, Robert W (Robby)** | Auto Racing Driver |
| 19525 Mary Ardrey Circle, Cornelius NC 28031, USA | |
| **Gordon, Seth** | Director |
| W M E Entertainment, 9601 Wilshire Blvd, #300, Beverly Hills CA 90210 USA | |
| **Gordon, Stuart** | Director |
| Red Hen Productions, 3607 W Magnolia, #L, Burbank CA 91505, USA | |
| **Gordon, Thomas (Tom)** | Baseball Player |
| 2006 Lake Lotela Dr, Avon Park FL 33825, USA | |
| **Gordon, Zachary** | Actor |
| Industry Entertainment, 955 Carillo Dr, #300, Los Angeles CA 90048 USA | |
| **Gordon-Levitt, Joseph** | Actor |
| W M E Entertainment, 9601 Wilshire Blvd, #300, Beverly Hills CA 90210 USA | |
| **Gordon-Reed, Annette** | Writer, Educator |
| New York University, Law School, 57 Worth St, New York NY 10013, USA | |
| **Gordy, Berry, Jr** | Businessman, Composer |
| 878 Stradella Road, Los Angeles CA 90077, USA | |
| **Gordy, Walter** | Physicist |
| 2521 Perkins Road, Durham NC 27705, USA | |
| **Gore, Albert A, Jr** | Nobel Peace Laureate, Vice President |
| 312 Lynnwood Blvd, Nashville TN 37205, USA | |
| **Gore, Frank** | Football Player |
| 6641 SW 159th Place, Miami FL 33193, USA | |
| **Gore, Lesley** | Singer, Songwriter, Actress |
| 228 W 71st St, #1E, New York NY 10023, USA | |
| **Gore, Michael** | Composer |
| Soundtrack Music Assoc, 1460 4th St, #308, Santa Monica CA 90401 USA | |
| **Gore, Robert W** | Inventor (Gore-Tex) |
| W L Gore Assoc, 555 Paper Mill Road, Newark DE 19711, USA | |
| **Gorenstein, Mark B** | Conductor |
| Rublevskoye Shosse 28, #25, 121609 Moscow, Russia | |
| **Gorfinkel, Jordan (Gorf)** | Cartoonist |
| 2427 White Road, Cleveland OH 44118, USA | |
| **Gorgal, Kenneth R (Ken)** | Football Player |
| 4 The Court of Harborside, Northbrook IL 60062, USA | |
| **Gorgl, Elisabeth** | Alpine Skier |
| Helmut Zangerl, Innrain 15/4/32, 6020 Innsbruck, Austria | |
| **Gorham, Christopher** | Actor |
| Creative Artists Agency, 2000 Ave of Stars, #100, Los Angeles CA 90067 USA | |
| **Gorham, Mel** | Actress |
| Gage Group, 450 7th Ave, #1809, New York NY 10123 USA | |
| **Gorie, Dominic L** | Astronaut |
| 13656 Hidden Valley Lane, Salida CO 81201, USA | |
| **Gorilla Zoe** | Rap Artist |
| Multi Entertainment Group, 4044 W Lake Mary Blvd, #104-324, Lake Mary FL 32746, USA | |
| **Gorin, Brandon M** | Football Player |
| 11031 Mirador Lane, Fishers IN 46037, USA | |
| **Goring, Robert T (Butch)** | Ice Hockey Player, Coach |
| 245 W 5th Ave, #108, Anchorage AK 99501, USA | |
| **Gorinski, Robert J (Bob)** | Baseball Player |
| PO Box 133, Calumet PA 15621, USA | |
| **Goris, Eva** | Actress |
| I C M Partners, 10250 Constellation Blvd, #900, Los Angeles CA 90067 USA | |
| **Gorka, John** | Singer, Songwriter |
| Roots Agency, 177 Woodland Ave, Westwood NJ 07675, USA | |
| **Gorlin, Alexander** | Architect |
| Alexander Gorlin Architect, 137 Varick St, #500, New York NY 10013, USA | |
| **Gorman, Bryan** | Golfer |
| Auld Course, 525 Hunte Parkway, Chula Vista CA 91914, USA | |
| **Gorman, E J** | Writer |
| PO Box 669, Cedar Rapids IA 52406, USA | |
| **Gorman, John G** | Pathologist |
| Mediware Information Systems, 11711 W 79th St, Lenexa KS 66214, USA | |
| **Gorman, Joseph T** | Businessman |
| T R W Inc, 1900 Richmond Road, Cleveland OH 44124, USA | |
| **Gorman, Leigh** | Bassist (Bow Wow Wow) |
| M O B Agency, 6404 Wilshire Blvd, #505, Los Angeles CA 90048 USA | |
| **Gorman, Patrick** | Actor |
| Circle Talent Assoc, 520 Broadway, #350, Santa Monica CA 90401, USA | |
| **Gorman, Paul F, Jr** | Army General |
| 9175 Batesville Road, Afton VA 22920, USA | |
| **Gorman, Steve** | Drummer (Black Crowes) |
| Angeles Entertainment, 16000 Ventura Blvd, #600, Encino CA 91436, USA | |
| **Gorman, Thomas P (Tom)** | Baseball Player |
| 1615 SW 5th Ave, Portland OR 97201, USA | |
| **Gorman, Tom** | Tennis Player |
| ProServe, 1101 Woodrow Wilson Blvd, #1800, Arlington VA 22209 USA | |
| **Gormley, Antony** | Sculptor |
| 13 South Villas, London NW1 9BS, England | |
| **Gorneault, Nick** | Baseball Player |
| 94 Seymour Ave, Springfield MA 01109, USA | |
| **Gorney, Karen Lynn** | Actress, Model |
| Karen Company, PO Box 231060, New York NY 10023, USA | |
| **Gorouuch, Edward Lee** | Educator |
| University of Alaska, President's Office, Anchorage AK 99508, USA | |

**Gorrell, Bob** — Editorial Cartoonist
Creators Syndicate, 737 3rd St, Hermosa Beach CA 90254 USA

**Gorrell, Fred** — Balloonist
501 E Port au Prince Lane, Phoenix AZ 85022, USA

**Gorris, Marleen** — Director
Gersh Agency, 9465 Wilshire Blvd, #600, Beverly Hills CA 90212 USA

**Gorshkov, Aleksandr G** — Ice Dancer
Skating Federation, Luchnesksaia Nab 8, 119871 Moscow, Russia

**Gorsky, Alex** — Businessman
Johnson & Johnson, 1 Johnson & Johnson Plaza, New Bruswick NJ 08993, USA

**Gortat, Marcin** — Basketball Player
Washington Wizards, M C I Centre, 601 F St NW, Washington DC 20004 USA

**Goryl, John A** — Baseball Player, Manager
528 Dry Run Road, Monongahela PA 15063, USA

**Gorzelanny, Thomas A (Tom)** — Baseball Player
208 Shadow Creek, Cranberry Township PA 16066, USA

**Gosger, James C (Jim)** — Baseball Player
1823 7th St, Port Huron MI 48060, USA

**Gosling, James** — Computer Software Designer (Java)
Sun Microsystems, 2550 Garcia Ave, Mountain View CA 94043, USA

**Gosling, Ryan T** — Actor
I F A Talent Agency, 8730 W Sunset Blvd, #490, West Hollywood CA 90069 USA

**Gosnell, Raja** — Director
Creative Artists Agency, 2000 Ave of Stars, #100, Los Angeles CA 90067 USA

**Goss, Fred** — Actor, Director
A P A Talent/Literary Agency, 405 S Beverly Dr, #300, Beverly Hills CA 90212 USA

**Goss, Luke** — Actor
Luber Rocklin Entertainment, 8530 Wilshire Blvd, #555, Beverly Hills CA 90211 USA

**Gossage, John** — Photographer
Light Work, 316 Waverly Ave, Syracuse NY 13210, USA

**Gossage, Richard M (Goose)** — Baseball Player
35 Marland Dr, Colorado Springs CO 80906, USA

**Gossard, Stone** — Guitarist (Green River, Pearl Jam)
Curtis Mgmt, 1900 S Corgiat Dr, Seattle WA 98108, USA

**Gosselaar, Mark-Paul** — Actor
Paradigm Agency, 360 N Crescent Dr, North Building, Beverly Hills CA 90210 USA

**Gosselin, Katie I (Kate)** — Actress
The Alexander, 201 W 72nd St, New York NY 10023, USA

**Gosselin, Mario** — Ice Hockey Player
Energie Ecole, 70 Rue Favvettes, Saint Basile Grand QC J3N 1P4, Canada

**Gossett, D Bruce** — Football Player
6109 Puerto Dr, Rancho Murieta CA 95683, USA

**Gossett, David** — Golfer
4501 Spanish Oaks Club Blvd, #9, Austin TX 78738, USA

**Gossett, Jeffery A (Jeff)** — Football Player
6 Lake Forest Court, Roanoke TX 76262, USA

**Gossett, Louis, Jr** — Actor
Logo Entertainment, PO Box 6187, Malibu CA 90265, USA

**Gossett, Robert** — Actor
Stone Manners Salners, 9911 W Pico Blvd, #1400, Los Angeles CA 90035 USA

**Gossick Crockatt, Sue** — Diver
11738 Villageview Court, Moorpark CA 93021, USA

**Gossner, Miriam** — Cross Country Skier
Rheinstalstr 3, 82467 Garmisch-Partenkirchen, Germany

**Gostowski, Stephen C (Steve)** — Football Player
18 Rhodes Dr, Wrentham MA 02093, USA

**Gotschlich, Emil C** — Internist
1435 Lexington Ave, New York NY 10128, USA

**Gotshalk, Leonard W (Len)** — Football Player
1200 Butler Creek Road, Ashland OR 97520, USA

**Gott, James W (Jim)** — Baseball Player
860 La Vina Lane, Altadena CA 91001, USA

**Gott, Karel** — Singer
Goja Spol, Pod Prusekem 3, 10200 Prague 10, Czech Republic

**Gottfried, Brian** — Tennis Player
10671 NW 51st St, Coral Springs FL 33076, USA

**Gottfried, Gilbert** — Actor, Comedian
W M E Entertainment, 1325 Ave of Americas, New York NY 10019 USA

**Gotti, Yo** — Rap Artist
J Records, 745 5th Ave, #600, New York NY 10151 USA

**Gottlieb, Lisa** — Director
Stone Manners Salners, 9911 W Pico Blvd, #1400, Los Angeles CA 90035 USA

**Gottschalk, Thomas** — Actor
Agenehme Unterhaultungs, Von-Simolin-Str 1, 82402 Seeshaupt, Germany

**Gottwald, Felix** — Nordic Combined Skier
Rosengasse 12, 5700 Zell am See, Austria

**Gotye** — Singer, Musician, Songwriter
Agency Group Ltd, 361-373 City Road, London EC1V 1PQ, England

**Gotz, George** — Actor
Terrassenstr 32, 14129 Berlin, Germany

**Gough, Alfred, III** — Producer, Writer
Millar Gough Ink, 500 S Buena Vista St, Animations 1E17, Burbank CA 91521, USA

**Gough, Darren** — Cricketer
Octagon, 81-83 Fulham High St, London SW6 3JW, England

**Goulart, Izabel** — Model
Women Model Mgmt, 199 Lafayette St, #700, New York NY 10012 USA

**Goulart, Ron** — Writer, Cartoonist (Star Hawks)
232 Georgetown Road, Weston CT 06883, USA

**Gould, Alexander** — Actor
Coast to Coast Talent, 3350 Barham Blvd, Los Angeles CA 90068 USA

**Gould, Dana** — Actor, Writer, Producer
United Talent Agency, U T A Plaza, 9336 Civic Center Dr, Beverly Hills CA 90210 USA

**Gould, Elliott** — Actor
A P A Talent/Literary Agency, 405 S Beverly Dr, #300, Beverly Hills CA 90212 USA

**Gould, Georgia** — Cyclist
240 N McKinley Ave, Fort Collins CO 80521, USA

**Gould, Nolan** — Actor
Stone Manners Salners, 9911 W Pico Blvd, #1400, Los Angeles CA 90035 USA
**Gould, Peter** — Writer
Larchmont Literary Agency, 444 N Larchmont Blvd, #200, Los Angeles CA 90004, USA
**Gould, Robert P (Robbie)** — Football Player
544 Cliffwood Lane, Gurnee IL 60031, USA
**Gould, Ronald M** — Judge
US Court of Appeals, US Courthouse, 1010 5th Ave, Seattle WA 98104, USA
**Gould, Tony** — Writer
Rogers Coleridge White, 20 Powis Court, London W11 1JN, England
**Goulding, Ellie** — Singer, Songwriter
Polydor Records, 364-366 Kensington High St, London W14 8NS, England
**Goulet, Michel** — Ice Hockey Player
PO Box 656, Sedalia CO 80135, USA
**Goulet-Nadon, Amelie** — Speed Skater
Speed Skating Canada, 2781 Lancaster Road, #402, Ottawa ON K1B 1A7, Canada
**Goulian, Mehran K** — Physician, Biochemist
8433 Prestwick Dr, La Jolla CA 92037, USA
**Goulston, Mark** — Psychiatrist, Commentator
1150 Yale St, #3, Santa Monica CA 90403, USA
**Gourley, Roark** — Artist
Roark Gourley Art Gallery, 33151 Paso Dr, South Laguna Beach CA 92677, USA
**Gourmet, Olivier** — Actor
Artmedia, 20 Ave Rapp, 75007 Paris, France
**Gouveia, Kurt K** — Football Player
138 Seagrove Lane, Mooresville NC 28117, USA
**Govan, Gerald** — Basketball Player
30 Newport Parkway, #2112, Jersey City NJ 07310, USA
**Govich, Milena** — Actress
A P A Talent/Literary Agency, 405 S Beverly Dr, #300, Beverly Hills CA 90212 USA
**Govinda** — Actor
105 Jal Darshan, A Wing Ruia Park, Juhu, Mumbai MS 400049, India
**Gowan, Caroline** — Golfer
209 Crescent Ave, Greenville SC 29605, USA
**Gowan, James** — Architect
2 Linden Gardens, London W2 4ES, England
**Gowariker, Ashutosh** — Director
I C M Partners, 10250 Constellation Blvd, #900, Los Angeles CA 90067 USA
**Gowda, H D Deve** — Prime Minister, India
5 Safdarjung Lane, New Delhi 110011, India
**Gower, David I** — Cricketer
David Gower Promotions, 6 George St, Nottingham NG1 3BE, England
**Gowers, W Timothy** — Mathematician
Math Services Centre, Wilberforce Road, Cambridge CB3 0WB, England
**Gowin, Toby** — Football Player
1605 Oak Creek Circle, Tyler TX 75703, USA
**Gowon, Yakub** — President, Nigeria; Army General
National Oil & Chemical Marketing Co, 38-39 Marina, 2052 Lagos, Nigeria
**Gowrie, Earl of** — Government Official, England
Government Securities, Stag Place, London SW1E 5DS, England
**Goycoechea, Sergio J** — Soccer Player
Football Assn, Via Monte 1366-76, Buenos Aires 1053, Argentina
**Goydos, Paul** — Golfer
1864 Stearnlee Ave, Long Beach CA 90815, USA
**Goyer, David S** — Director, Writer
Holmes Defender of the Faith, PO Box 6873, Malibu CA 90265, USA
**Goyette, Danielle** — Ice Hockey Player
Team Canada, 2424 University Dr NW, Calgary AB T2N 3Y9, Canada
**Goyette, Philippe J G (Phil)** — Ice Hockey Player
815 38 E Ave, Lachine QC H8T 2C4, Canada
**Goyo, Dakota** — Actor
W M E Entertainment, 9601 Wilshire Blvd, #300, Beverly Hills CA 90210 USA
**Gozlan, Yann** — Writer, Director
Gersh Agency, 9465 Wilshire Blvd, #600, Beverly Hills CA 90212 USA
**Gozney, Richard H T** — Governor General, Bermuda
Governor General's Office, 11 Langton Hill, Pembroke HM 13, Bermuda
**Gozzo, Mauro P** — Baseball Player
156 Newton St, Berlin CT 06037, USA
**Grabarkewitz, Billy C** — Baseball Player
2162 Estes Park Road, Southlake TX 76092, USA
**Grabarz, Robert K** — Track Athlete
Athletics House, Central Blvd, Blythe Valley Park, Solihull B9O 8AJ, England
**Grabe, Ronald J** — Astronaut
3380 S Price Road, Chandler AZ 85248, USA
**Grabeel, Lucas** — Actor, Singer
Paradigm Agency, 360 N Crescent Dr, North Building, Beverly Hills CA 90210 USA
**Graber, Rodney B (Rod)** — Baseball Player
4674 Mount Armet Dr, San Diego CA 92117, USA
**Graber, Susan P** — Judge
US Court of Appeals, Pioneer Courthouse, 555 SW Yamhill St, Portland OR 97204, USA
**Grabois, Neil R** — Educator
Colgate University, President's Office, Hamilton NY 13346, USA
**Grabow, John W** — Baseball Player
6810 S Amethyst Dr, Chandler AZ 85249, USA
**Grabowski, James S (Jim)** — Football Player
1523 Withorn Lane, Inverness IL 60067, USA
**Grace, Alana** — Actress, Singer, Songwriter
Creative Artists Agency, 2000 Ave of Stars, #100, Los Angeles CA 90067 USA
**Grace, April** — Actress
Innovative Artists, 1505 10th St, Santa Monica CA 90401 USA
**Grace, Bud** — Cartoonist (Ernie, Piranha Club)
King Features Syndicate, 300 W 57th St, #1500, New York NY 10019 USA
**Grace, Dick** — Businessman, Social Activist
Grace Vineyards, 1210 Rockland Dr, Saint Helena CA 94574, USA
**Grace, Emily** — Actress
Bad Girl Productions, 14 Parkside Court, Brooklyn NY 11225, USA

| | |
|---|---|
| **Grace, Helen**<br>Gavin Barker Assoc, 2D Wimpole St, London W1G 0EB, England | Actress |
| **Grace, Jillian**<br>Playboy Promotions, 2706 Media Center Dr, Los Angeles CA 90065 USA | Model, Actress |
| **Grace, Maggie**<br>United Talent Agency, U T A Plaza, 9336 Civic Center Dr, Beverly Hills CA 90210 USA | Actress |
| **Grace, Mark E**<br>5624 E Via Buena Vista, Paradise Valley AZ 85253, USA | Baseball Player |
| **Grace, Michael J (Mike)**<br>1156 Buell Ave, Joliet IL 60435, USA | Baseball Player |
| **Grace, Nancy**<br>Breaking News Public Relations, 9601 Wilshire Blvd, #1106, Beverly Hills CA 90210, USA | Commentator |
| **Grace, Topher**<br>I C M Partners, 10250 Constellation Blvd, #900, Los Angeles CA 90067 USA | Actor |
| **Gracen, Elizabeth**<br>James Levy Mgmt, 3500 W Olive Ave, #920, Burbank CA 91505, USA | Actress, Beauty Queen, Model |
| **Gracey, James S**<br>1 Westin Center, 2445 M St NW, #260, Washington DC 20037, USA | Coast Guard Admiral, Businessman |
| **Grach, Eduard D**<br>1st Smolensky Per 9, #98, 121099 Moscow, Russia | Concert Violinist |
| **Gracheva, Nadezhda A**<br>1st Truzhennikov Per 17, #49, 119121 Moscow, Russia | Ballerina |
| **Gracias, Oswald Cardinal**<br>Archbishop's House, 1 Nathalal Parekh Marg, Mumbai 40001, India | Religious Leader |
| **Gracie, Charlie**<br>Joe Taylor Artist Agency, 2802 Columbine Place, Nashville TN 37204 USA | Singer, Guitarist |
| **Gracin, Joshua M (Josh)**<br>Buddy Lee Attractions, 38 Music Square E, #300, Nashville TN 37203 USA | Singer |
| **Grad, Harold**<br>248 Overlook Road, New Rochelle NY 10804, USA | Mathematician |
| **Graddy, Sam**<br>4792 Brasac Dr, Stone Mountain GA 30083, USA | Football Player, Track Athlete |
| **Gradishar, Randy C**<br>7628 Pineridge Terrace, Castle Rock CO 80108, USA | Football Player |
| **Grady, Michael**<br>I C M Partners, 10250 Constellation Blvd, #900, Los Angeles CA 90067 USA | Actor |
| **Grady, Wayne**<br>PO Box 78, Coolum Beach QLD 4573, Australia | Golfer |
| **Graebner, Clark**<br>411 Harbor Road, Fairfield CT 06431, USA | Tennis Player |
| **Graebner, Norman A**<br>University of Virginia, History Dept, Charlottesville VA 22903, USA | Historian |
| **Graef, Jed**<br>PO Box 880, Shelburne VT 05482, USA | Swimmer |
| **Graells, Francisco (Pancho)**<br>Le Monde, Editorial Dept, 21 Bis Rue Claude Bernard, 75005 Paris, France | Editorial Cartoonist |
| **Graf, David F (Dave)**<br>1825 Bel Air Ave, Pompano Beach FL 33062, USA | Football Player |
| **Graf, Hans**<br>Konzertdirektion Schmid, Konigstra 36, 30175 Hannover, Germany | Conductor |
| **Graf, Jim**<br>Jet Propulsion Laboratory, 4800 Oak Grove Dr, Pasadena CA 91109 USA | Space Scientist |
| **Graf, Richard G (Rick)**<br>6609 Biscayne Blvd, Minneapolis MN 55436, USA | Football Player |
| **Graf, Stefanie M (Steffi)**<br>9804 Camden Hills Ave, Las Vegas NV 89145, USA | Tennis Player |
| **Graff, Ilene**<br>Sovereign Talent Group,, 8421 Wilshire Blvd, #200, Beverly Hills CA 90211, USA | Actress |
| **Graff, Randy**<br>Lava Entertainment, 1560 Broadway, #1001, New York NY 10036, USA | Actress |
| **Graff, Todd**<br>United Talent Agency, U T A Plaza, 9336 Civic Center Dr, Beverly Hills CA 90210 USA | Director, Writer, Actor |
| **Graffanino, Anthony J (Tony)**<br>16 Amberfield Lane, Hockessin DE 19707, USA | Baseball Player |
| **Graffe, Anne-Caroline**<br>Aix Universite Club Taekwondo, 33 Chemin des Infirmeries, 13100 Aix-en-Provence, France | Taekwondo Athlete |
| **Graffin, Gregory W (Greg)**<br>Goldstar Public Relations, PO Box 130, Ross on Wye HR9 6WY, England | Singer (Bad Religion), Songwriter |
| **Graffin, Guillaume**<br>American Ballet Theatre, 890 Broadway, #300, New York NY 10003, USA | Ballet Dancer |
| **Graffman, Gary**<br>Curtis Institute of Music, 1726 Locust St, Philadelphia PA 19103, USA | Concert Pianist |
| **Grafstein, Bernice**<br>Weill Medical College, Physiology Dept, 1300 York Ave, New York NY 10065, USA | Neurologist, Physiologist |
| **Grafton, Anthony T**<br>Princeton University, History Dept, Dickinson Hall, Princeton NJ 08544, USA | Historian |
| **Grafton, Sue**<br>PO Box 41446, Santa Barbara CA 93140, USA | Writer |
| **Gragg, Scott**<br>583 Cash Nichols Road, Stevensville MT 59870, USA | Football Player |
| **Graham, Alex**<br>Tribune Media Services, 435 N Michigan Ave, #1500, Chicago IL 60611 USA | Cartoonist (Fred Basset) |
| **Graham, Arthur W (Art), III**<br>PO Box 785, South Orleans MA 02662, USA | Football Player |
| **Graham, Charles P**<br>134 Warbler Way, Georgetown TX 78633, USA | Army General |
| **Graham, Currie**<br>Paradigm Agency, 360 N Crescent Dr, North Building, Beverly Hills CA 90210 USA | Actor |
| **Graham, David**<br>4201 Lomo Alto Dr, #305, Dallas TX 75219, USA | Golfer |
| **Graham, Detrice A (Derrick)**<br>203 Pine Hill Road, West End NC 27376, USA | Football Player |
| **Graham, Dirk M**<br>17001 S Blackfoot Dr, Lockport IL 60441, USA | Ice Hockey Player |
| **Graham, Donald E**<br>Washington Post Co, 1150 15th St NW, Washington DC 20071, USA | Publisher |

**G**

Grace - Graham

**Graham, Franklin**
Samaritan's Purse, PO Box 3000, Boone NC 28607, USA — Religious Leader

**Graham, Gary**
Amsel Eisenstadt Frazier, 5055 Wilshire Blvd, #865, Los Angeles CA 90036 USA — Actor

**Graham, Gerrit**
S M S Talent, 8383 Wilshire Blvd, #230, Beverly Hills CA 90211 USA — Actor

**Graham, Glen**
Shapiro Co, 9229 W Sunset Blvd, #607, West Hollywood CA 90069 USA — Drummer (Blind Melon)

**Graham, Heather**
Gersh Agency, 9465 Wilshire Blvd, #600, Beverly Hills CA 90212 USA — Actress

**Graham, Jack**
Prestonwood Baptist Church, 6801 W Park Blvd, Plano TX 75093, USA — Religious Leader

**Graham, Jeffrey T (Jeff)**
1849 Infirmary Road, Dayton OH 45417, USA — Football Player

**Graham, Joey J**
Cleveland Cavaliers, Gund Arena, 1 Center Court, Cleveland OH 44115 USA — Basketball Player

**Graham, Jorie**
12 Quincy St, Cambridge MA 02138, USA — Writer

**Graham, Julie**
Troika, 74 Clerkenwell Road, #300, London EC1M 5QA, England — Actress

**Graham, Kate**
Gavin Barker Assoc, 2D Wimpole St, London W1G 0EB, England — Actress

**Graham, Katerina**
Simmon & Scott, 7942 Mulholland Dr, Los Angeles CA 90046, USA — Actress

**Graham, Kenneth J (Kenny)**
PO Box 7402, Santa Monica CA 90406, USA — Football Player

**Graham, Kent D**
1001 N Washington St, Wheaton IL 60187, USA — Football Player

**Graham, Larry**
Groove Entertainment, 1005 N Alfred St, #2, West Hollywood CA 90069, USA — Guitarist (Sly & Family Stone), Singer

**Graham, Lauren**
John Carrabino Mgmt, 5900 Wilshire Blvd, #406, Los Angeles CA 90036 USA — Actress

**Graham, Lee W**
481 Richmond Road, Cleveland OH 44143, USA — Baseball Player

**Graham, Linda**
4147 E Seneca Ave, Des Moines IA 50317, USA — Bowler

**Graham, Loren R**
7 Francis Ave, Cambridge MA 02138, USA — Historian

**Graham, Louis K (Lou)**
85 Concord Park W, Nashville TN 37205, USA — Golfer

**Graham, Marcus**
Shanahan Mgmt, Berman House, 91 Campbell St, #300, Surry Hills NSW 2010, Australia — Actor

**Graham, Mary Lou**
Professional Bowlers Assn, 719 2nd Ave, #701, Seattle WA 98104 USA — Bowler

**Graham, Michael J**
Xavier University, President's Office, 3800 Victory Parkway, Cincinnati OH 45207, USA — Educator

**Graham, Mikey**
J C Music, 84A Strand-on-the-Green, London W43 PU, England — Singer (Boyzone)

**Graham, Nancy Perry**
A A R P Magazine, Editorial Dept, 601 E St NW, Washington DC 20049, USA — Editor

**Graham, Norma V**
Columbia University, Psychology Dept, New York NY 10027, USA — Psychologist

**Graham, Patricia A**
Harvard University, Graduate School of Education, Cambridge MA 02138, USA — Educator

**Graham, Patrick**
Jack Rutberg Fine Arts, 357 N La Brea Ave, Los Angeles CA 90036, USA — Artist, Writer

**Graham, Rodney**
Hauser & Wirth Limmatstr 270, 8005 Zurich, Switzerland — Artist

**Graham, Ronald L**
University of California, Computer & Information Science Dept, La Jolla CA 92093, USA — Mathematician

**Graham, Stephen**
Independent Talent Group, 40 Whitfield St, London W1T 2RH, England — Actor

**Graham, Susan**
I M G Artists, Hogarth Business Park, Chiswick, London W4 2TH, England — Opera Singer

**Graham, Susan L**
University of California, Computer Science Dept, Soda Hall, Berkeley CA 94720, USA — Computer Scientist

**Graham, Thomas L (Tom)**
4084 S Wisteria Way, Denver CO 80237, USA — Football Player

**Graham, Wayne L**
2017 Dryden Road, Houston TX 77030, USA — Baseball Player

**Graham, William F (Billy)**
Billy Graham Evangelistic Assn, 1 Billy Graham Parkway, Charlotte NC 28201, USA — Evangelist

**Graham, William R (Bill)**
11013 Sierra Verde Trail, Austin TX 78759, USA — Football Player

**Grahame, Ron**
9000 E Jewell Circle, Denver CO 80231, USA — Ice Hockey Player

**Grahe, Joseph M (Joe)**
2317 N Wallen Dr, West Palm Beach FL 33410, USA — Baseball Player

**Grahn, Nancy Lee**
Innovative Artists, 1505 10th St, Santa Monica CA 90401 USA — Actress

**Grainger, Holliday**
Troika, 74 Clerkenwell Road, #300, London EC1M 5QA, England — Actress

**Grainger, Katherine**
Saint Andrews Boat Club, Meggetland, 60F Colinton Road, Edinburgh EH14 1AS, Scotland — Rowing Athlete

**Grainger, Sebastien A**
Biz 3 Publicity, 1321 N Milwaukee Ave, #452, Chicago IL 60622, USA — Singer, Drummer (Death from Above 1979)

**Grais, Michael**
Metropolitan Talent Agency, 5405 Wilshire Blvd, #218, Los Angeles CA 90036, USA — Writer

**Gralish, Tom**
203 E Cottage Ave, Haddonfield NJ 08033, USA — Photojournalist

**Graman, Alex**
450 E Sunset Dr, Huntingburg IN 47542, USA — Baseball Player

**Gramatica, Martin**
3912 Northampton Way, Tampa FL 33618, USA — Football Player

**Gramly, B Thomas (Tommy)**
16485 Red Wood Circle W, McKinney TX 75071, USA — Baseball Player

**Gramm, Lou** — Singer (Foreigner)
Elite Talent Agency, 1208 17th Ave S, Nashville TN 37212, USA
**Gramm, W Philip (Phil)** — Senator, TX
U B S Securities, 299 Park Ave, New York NY 10171, USA
**Gramm, Wendy L** — Government Official, Economist
George Mason University, 3301 N Fairfax Dr, #450, Arlington VA 22201, USA
**Grammas, Alexander P (Alex)** — Baseball Player, Manager
4030 Vestview Dr, Vestavia AL 35242, USA
**Grammer, Kathy** — Actress
Artists Agency, 9430 Olympic Blvd, Beverly Hills CA 90212 USA
**Grammer, Kelsey** — Actor
Grammnet Productions, 2461 Santa Monica Blvd, #521, Santa Monica CA 90404, USA
**Grammer, Spencer** — Actress
United Talent Agency, U T A Plaza, 9336 Civic Center Dr, Beverly Hills CA 90210 USA
**Granada, Julieta** — Golfer
Ladies Pro Golf Assn, 100 International Golf Dr, Daytona Beach FL 32124 USA
**Granatelli, Anthony (Andy)** — Auto Racing Executive
1469 Edgecliff Lane, Santa Barbara CA 93108, USA
**Granato, Anthony L (Tony)** — Ice Hockey Player, Coach
1481 Hollow Tree Dr, Pittsburgh PA 15241, USA
**Granby, John E, Jr** — Football Player
8905 Melwood Oak Dr, Arlington TN 38002, USA
**Grandage, Michael** — Director
Donmar Warehouse, 41 Earlham St, Seven Dials, London WC2H 9LX, England
**Grande, Ariana** — Actress, Singer
Creative Artists Agency, 2000 Ave of Stars, #100, Los Angeles CA 90067 USA
**Granderson, Curtis** — Baseball Player
1450 S Emerald St, Chicago IL 60607, USA
**Grandholm, Jim** — Basketball Player
211 Spring Park Ave, Sawyer MI 49125, USA
**Grandin, Temple** — Animal Scientist
2918 Silver Plume Dr, #C3, Fort Collins CO 80526, USA
**Grandison, Ronnie** — Basketball Player
6151 Chappellfield Dr, West Chester OH 45069, USA
**Grandmaster Flash** — Rap Artist
K L B Production, 302A W 12th St, #296, New York NY 10014, USA
**Grandmaster Mele-Mel** — Rap Artist
Groove Entertainment, 1005 N Alfred St, #2, West Hollywood CA 90069 USA
**Grandmaster Roc Raida** — Rap Artist (X-Ecutioners)
Agency Group Ltd, 142 W 57th St, #600, New York NY 10019 USA
**Grandmont, Jean-Michel** — Economist
55 Blvd de Charonne, Les Doukas 23, 75011 Paris, France
**Grandpa Pike** — Singer
PO Box 3008, Hillsborough NB E4H 4W5, Canada
**GrandPre, Mary** — Illustrator
Scholastic Press, 555 Broadway, New York NY 10012 USA
**Grandy, Fred** — Actor; Representative, IA
9417 Spruce Tree Circle, Bethesda MD 20814, USA
**Granger, Danny** — Basketball Player
141 S Meridian St, #602, Indianapolis IN 46225, USA
**Granger, Hoyle J** — Football Player
13427 Paradise Valley Dr, Houston TX 77069, USA
**Granger, Jeffrey A (Jeff)** — Baseball Player
2905 Glasgow Dr, Arlington TX 76015, USA
**Granger, Stewart F** — Basketball Player
552 E 53rd St, Brooklyn NY 11203, USA
**Granger, Wayne A** — Baseball Player
133 Redtail Place, Winter Springs FL 32708, USA
**Granholm, Jennifer M** — Governor, MI
University of California, Law & Public Policy Dept, Berkeley CA 94720, USA
**Granier-Deferre, Celia** — Actress
Artmedia, 20 Ave Rapp, 75007 Paris, France
**Granik, Debra** — Director, Writer, Cinematographer
Gersh Agency, 9465 Wilshire Blvd, #600, Beverly Hills CA 90212 USA
**Grannis, Kina** — Singer, Songwriter
Agency Group Ltd, 142 W 57th St, #600, New York NY 10019 USA
**Grannis, Paul D** — Physicist
Fermi National Accelerator Laboratory, C D F Collaboration, PO Box 500, Batavia IL 60510, USA
**Grant Walsh, Margo** — Interior Designer
Gensler & Associates/Architects, 1 Rockefeller Plaza, #500, New York NY 10020, USA
**Grant, Alan** — Football Player
148 Cisco Road, Asheville NC 28805, USA
**Grant, Allie** — Actress
Sweeney Entertainment, 6253 Hollywood Blvd, #201, Los Angeles CA 90028, USA
**Grant, Amy L** — Singer, Songwriter
Creative Artists Agency, 3310 W End Ave, #500, Nashville TN 37203 USA
**Grant, B Rosemary** — Evolutionary Biologist
Princeton University, Ecology & Evolution Biology Dept, Princeton NJ 08544, USA
**Grant, Beth** — Actress
Don Buchwald, 6500 Wilshire Blvd, #2200, Los Angeles CA 90048 USA
**Grant, Boyd** — Basketball Coach
Colorado State University, Athletic Dept, Fort Collins CO 80523, USA
**Grant, Brea** — Actress
B/W/R, 9100 Wilshire Blvd, #500W, Beverly Hills CA 90212 USA
**Grant, Brian W, III** — Basketball Player
24152 SW Petes Mountain Road, West Linn OR 97068, USA
**Grant, Charles** — Actor
Spotlight, 7 Leicester Place, London WC2H 7RJ, England
**Grant, Daniel F (Danny)** — Ice Hockey Player
1163 Route 101 Highway, Nasonworth NB E3C 2C3, Canada
**Grant, Darryl** — Football Player
6931 Compton Lane, Centreville VA 20121, USA
**Grant, David Marshall** — Actor, Writer
Creative Artists Agency, 2000 Ave of Stars, #100, Los Angeles CA 90067 USA
**Grant, Deon D** — Football Player
4465 Cape Cod Dr, Evans GA 30809, USA

**Grant, Edmond (Eddy)** — Singer, Songwriter
Paradigm Agency, 360 N Crescent Dr, North Building, Beverly Hills CA 90210 USA
**Grant, Faye** — Actress
S M S Talent, 8383 Wilshire Blvd, #230, Beverly Hills CA 90211 USA
**Grant, Frank** — Football Player
10713 Heatherleigh Dr, Cheltenham MD 20623, USA
**Grant, Gil** — Producer, Writer
Paradigm Agency, 360 N Crescent Dr, North Building, Beverly Hills CA 90210 USA
**Grant, Gogi** — Singer
10323 Alamo Ave, #202, Los Angeles CA 90064, USA
**Grant, Harold P (Bud)** — Football, Basketball Player, Coach
8134 Oakmere Road, Minneapolis MN 55438, USA
**Grant, Harvey** — Basketball Player
15604 Marathon Circle, #401, Gaithersburg MD 20878, USA
**Grant, Horace J** — Basketball Player
195 Michael Lane, Arroyo Grande CA 93420, USA
**Grant, Hugh** — Actor
42 West, 220 W 42nd St, #1200, New York NY 10036 USA
**Grant, Hugh, Jr** — Harness Racing Executive
35 E 84th St, #8B, New York NY 10028, USA
**Grant, James T (Mudcat)** — Baseball Player
1020 S Dunsmuir Ave, Los Angeles CA 90019, USA
**Grant, Jennifer** — Actress
Teitelbaum Artists, 8840 Wilshire Blvd, Beverly Hills CA 90212, USA
**Grant, John D** — Football Player
6365 S Harrison Court, Centennial CO 80121, USA
**Grant, Joshua D (Josh)** — Basketball Player
3191 S Davis Blvd, Bountiful UT 84010, USA
**Grant, Kate Jennings** — Actress
Melanie Greene Mgmt, 425 N Robertson Blvd, West Hollywood CA 90048 USA
**Grant, Lee** — Actress, Director
Fleury/Grant Entertainment, 610 W End Ave, #7B, New York NY 10024, USA
**Grant, Mark A** — Baseball Player
2837 Via Dieguenos, Alpine CA 91901, USA
**Grant, Mickie** — Actress
250 W 94th St, #6G, New York NY 10025, USA
**Grant, Natalie** — Singer, Songwriter
Maximum Artist Mgmt, 1305 Clinton St, #200A, Nashville TN 37203, USA
**Grant, Peter R** — Evolutionary Biologist
Princeton University, Ecology & Evolutionary Biology Dept, Princeton NJ 08544, USA
**Grant, Quiana** — Model
Traffic Models, Pasaje Sert, 2, 08010 Barcelona, Spain
**Grant, Richard E** — Actor, Director
Artist Rights Group, 4 Great Portland St, London W1W 8PA, England
**Grant, Rodney A** — Actor
Omar, 526 N Larchmont Blvd, Los Angeles CA 90004, USA
**Grant, Stephen M (Steve)** — Football Player
20134 SW 123rd Dr, Miami FL 33177, USA
**Grant, Susannah** — Writer, Director
Creative Artists Agency, 2000 Ave of Stars, #100, Los Angeles CA 90067 USA
**Grant, Thomas R (Tom)** — Baseball Player
36 Millville Road, Mendon MA 01756, USA
**Grant, Tom** — Jazz Musician
Brad Simon Organization, 445 E 80th St, #4C, New York NY 10075 USA
**Grant, Toni** — Radio Psychologist
610 S Ardmore Ave, Los Angeles CA 90005, USA
**Grant, Travis** — Basketball Player
3314 Pointe Bleue Court, Decatur GA 30034, USA
**Grant, Wally** — Ice Hockey Player
4853 Lone Oak Court, Ann Arbor MI 48108, USA
**Grantham, George** — Singer, Drummer (Poco)
Rick Alter Mgmt, 1018 17th Ave S, #12, Nashville TN 37212, USA
**Grantham, J Larry** — Football Player
312 Wicklow Cove, Brandon MS 39047, USA
**Grantham, Victoria** — Fashion Designer
VGrantham, Via Morimondo 2/3, 20143 Milan, Italy
**Grapenthin, Richard R (Dick)** — Baseball Player
5040 170th Ave, Linn Grove IA 51033, USA
**Grapey, Marc** — Actor
Talent Works, 3500 W Olive Ave, #1400, Burbank CA 91505 USA
**Grasmanis, Paul R** — Football Player
1073 Watkins Creek Dr, Franklin TN 37067, USA
**Grasmick, Louis J (Lou)** — Baseball Player
6715 Quad Ave, Rosedale MD 21237, USA
**Grass, Gunter** — Nobel Literature Laureate
G Kiepenheuer Buhnenvertrieb, Schweinfurthstr 60, 14195 Berlin, Germany
**Grassle, Karen** — Actress, Writer
J E Talent, 323 Geary St, #302, San Francisco CA 94102, USA
**Grata, Enrique** — Actor
Univision, 605 3rd Ave, #1200, New York NY 10158, USA
**Grate, Donald (Don)** — Baseball, Basketball Player
1245 NW 203rd St, Miami FL 33169, USA
**Grater, Mark A** — Baseball Player
1136 Indiana Ave, Monaca PA 15061, USA
**Grattard, Adeline** — Chef
Yam'Tacha Restaurant, 4 Rue Sauval, 75001 Paris, France
**Grau, Shirley Ann** — Writer
12 Nassau Dr, Metairie LA 70005, USA
**Grauer, Ona** — Actress
Performers Mgmt, 258 E 3rd St, #B, Vancouver BC V7W 1E7, Canada
**Grausman, Phillip** — Sculptor
21 Barnes Road, Washington CT 06793, USA
**Gravel, Maurice R (Mike)** — Senator, AK
1600 N Oak St, #1412, Arlington VA 22209, USA
**Graveline, Duane E** — Astronaut
PO Box 92, Underhill Center VT 05490, USA

G

Grant - Graveline

# G

|  |  |
|---|---|
| **Gravelle, Gordon C**<br>186 Kuss Road, Danville CA 94526, USA | Football Player |
| **Graves, Adam**<br>574 Lis Crescent, Windsor ON N9G 2M5, Canada | Ice Hockey Player |
| **Graves, Alex**<br>Creative Artists Agency, 2000 Ave of Stars, #100, Los Angeles CA 90067 USA | Director, Producer, Writer |
| **Graves, Daniel P (Danny)**<br>5041 Rishley Run Way, Mount Dora FL 32757, USA | Baseball Player |
| **Graves, Denyce A**<br>I M G Artists, Carnegie Hall Tower, 152 W 57th St, #500, New York NY 10019 USA | Opera Singer |
| **Graves, Earl G (Butch), Jr**<br>123 Random Farms Dr, Chappaqua NY 10514, USA | Basketball Player |
| **Graves, Ernest, Jr**<br>2328 S Nash St, Arlington VA 22202, USA | Army General |
| **Graves, Harold N, Jr**<br>PO Box 8390, Gaithersburg MD 20898, USA | Journalist, Government Official |
| **Graves, Liza**<br>The Kirby Organization, 9200 Sunset Blvd, #600, Los Angeles CA 90069, USA | Singer (Civet) |
| **Graves, Michael**<br>Michael Graves Assoc, 341 Nassau St, Princeton NJ 08540, USA | Architect |
| **Graves, Ray**<br>420 Bay Ave, #821, Clearwater FL 33756, USA | Football Coach |
| **Graves, Richard G**<br>43 Villa Verde, San Antonio TX 78230, USA | Army General |
| **Graves, Rupert**<br>A P A Talent/Literary Agency, 405 S Beverly Dr, #300, Beverly Hills CA 90212 USA | Actor |
| **Graves, Thomas E (Tom)**<br>1902 Montclair Ave, Norfolk VA 23523, USA | Football Player |
| **Gravett, Michael G**<br>University of Washington Medical Center, Obstetrics Dept, PO Box 356460, Seattle WA 98195, USA | Obstetrician |
| **Gravitte, Beau**<br>Gage Group, 450 7th Ave, #1809, New York NY 10123 USA | Actor |
| **Gray, Aaron M**<br>Toronto Raptors, Air Canada Center, 20 Bay St, Toronto ON M5J 2N8, Canada | Basketball Player |
| **Gray, Alasdair J**<br>Rogers Coleridge White, 20 Powis Mews, London W11 1JN, England | Writer |
| **Gray, Alfred M, Jr**<br>6317 Chaucer View Circle, Alexandria VA 22304, USA | Marine Corps General |
| **Gray, Billy**<br>19612 Grandview Dr, Topanga Canyon CA 90290, USA | Actor |
| **Gray, C Boyden**<br>Wilmer Cutler Pickering, 1875 Pennsylvania Ave NW, Washington DC 20006, USA | Government Official |
| **Gray, Carleton P**<br>11981 Kenn Road, Cincinnati OH 45240, USA | Football Player |
| **Gray, Chad (Kud)**<br>Agency Group Ltd, 142 W 57th St, #600, New York NY 10019 USA | Singer (Mudvayne) |
| **Gray, Cleve**<br>102 Melius Road, Warren CT 06754, USA | Artist, Sculptor |
| **Gray, Coleen**<br>2841 Roscomare Road, Los Angeles CA 90077, USA | Actress |
| **Gray, David**<br>Mondo Mgmt, Clatham Nove Art Centre, 26-32 Voltaire Road, London SW4 6DH, England | Singer, Songwriter |
| **Gray, Del**<br>Splash Public Relations, 1520 16th Ave S, #2, Nashville TN 37212, USA | Drummer (Little Texas) |
| **Gray, Doug**<br>Ron Rainey Mgmt, 315 S Beverly Dr, #407, Beverly Hills CA 90212, USA | Singer (Marshall Tucker Band) |
| **Gray, D'Wayne**<br>3423 Barger Dr, Falls Church VA 22044, USA | Marine Corps General |
| **Gray, Earnest**<br>6746 Kirby Oaks Lane, Memphis TN 38119, USA | Football Player |
| **Gray, Edward (Ed)**<br>Houston Rockets, 1730 Jefferson St, Houston TX 77003 USA | Basketball Player |
| **Gray, Erin**<br>10921 Alta View Dr, Studio City CA 91604, USA | Actress, Model |
| **Gray, F Gary**<br>United Talent Agency, U T A Plaza, 9336 Civic Center Dr, Beverly Hills CA 90210 USA | Director |
| **Gray, Fred, Sr**<br>1005 Lakeshore Dr, Tuskegee AL 36083, USA | Attorney |
| **Gray, Gary G**<br>PO Box 98, La Place LA 70069, USA | Baseball Player |
| **Gray, George W**<br>Juniper House, Furzehill, Wimborne, Dorset BH21 4HD, England | Organic Chemist |
| **Gray, Harry B**<br>1415 E California Blvd, Pasadena CA 91106, USA | Chemist |
| **Gray, James**<br>Creative Artists Agency, 2000 Ave of Stars, #100, Los Angeles CA 90067 USA | Director, Writer |
| **Gray, Jamie Lynn B**<br>3522 Bridgewater Road, Columbus GA 31909, USA | Markswoman |
| **Gray, Jerry**<br>27 Birdsong Parkway, Orchard Park NY 14127, USA | Football Player |
| **Gray, John**<br>John Gray's Mars Venus, 20 Sunnyside Ave, #A130, Mill Valley CA 94941, USA | Director, Writer |
| **Gray, John E**<br>4115 Bloomdale Dr, #16, Charlotte NC 28211, USA | WW II, Korean & Vietnam Army Hero |
| **Gray, John L (Johnny)**<br>10645 Greenbriar Court, Boca Raton FL 33498, USA | Baseball Player |
| **Gray, Johnnie L**<br>535 Brule Road, #13, De Pere WI 54115, USA | Football Player |
| **Gray, Kenneth D (Ken)**<br>356 Campa Pajama Lane, Kingsland TX 78639, USA | Football Player |
| **Gray, Linda**<br>PO Box 5064, Sherman Oaks CA 91413, USA | Actress |
| **Gray, Lorenzo**<br>2680 E 19th St, #1, Signal Hill CA 90755, USA | Baseball Player |
| **Gray, Macy**<br>Vox Inc, 6420 Wilshire Blvd, #1080, Los Angeles CA 90048 USA | Singer, Songwriter, Actress |

**Gravelle - Gray**

**Gray, Melvin D (Mel)** — Football Player
4507 Skyline Dr, Rockford IL 61107, USA
**Gray, Melvin J (Mel)** — Football Player
137 Winterset Pass, Williamsburg VA 23188, USA
**Gray, Shan R** — Sculptor
The American, 3600 E 32nd St, Edmond OK 73013, USA
**Gray, Stuart A** — Basketball Player
909 Andover Green, Lexington KY 40509, USA
**Gray, Tamyra M** — Singer, Actress
19 Music & Mgmt, 35-37 Parkgate Road, London SW11 4NP, England
**Gray, Timothy (Tim)** — Football Player
6109 Crane St, Houston TX 77026, USA
**Gray, Tom** — Guitarist, Keyboardist (Gomez)
Red Light Mgmt, 44 Wall St, #2200, New York NY 10005, USA
**Graybiel, Ann M** — Anatomist
Massachusetts Institute of Technology, Cognitive Science Dept, Cambridge MA 02139, USA
**Gray-Cabey, Noah** — Actor
Kritzer Levine Wilkins Griffin, 11872 La Grange Ave, #100, Los Angeles CA 90025 USA
**Grayden, Sprague** — Actress
Untitled Entertainment, 350 S Beverly Dr, #200, Beverly Hills CA 90212 USA
**Graydon, Michael J** — Air Force Marshal, England
Lloyds Bank, Cox & King's Branch, 7 Pall Mall, London SW1Y 5NA, England
**Grayer, Jeffrey (Jeff)** — Basketball Player
1617 Barbara Dr, Flint MI 48504, USA
**Gray-Garcia, Lisa (Tiny)** — Social Activist
City Lights Books, 261 Columbus Ave, San Francisco CA 94133, USA
**Grayling, A C** — Philosopher, Writer
Bloomsbury Publishing, 50 Bedford Square, London WC1B 3DP, England
**Graynor, Ari** — Actress
United Talent Agency, U T A Plaza, 9336 Civic Center Dr, Beverly Hills CA 90210 USA
**Graysmith, Robert** — Editorial Cartoonist, Writer
Berkley Publishing Group, 375 Hudson St, Basement 1, New York NY 10014 USA
**Grayson, C Jackson, Jr** — Government Official, Educator
123 N Post Oak Lane, Houston TX 77024, USA
**Grayson, David L (Dave), Jr** — Football Player
5962 Rancho Mission Road, #218, San Diego CA 92108, USA
**Grayson, David L (Dave), Sr** — Football Player
PO Box 601292, San Diego CA 92160, USA
**Gray-Stanford, Jason** — Actor
Headline Talent Agency, 138 W 25th St, #1000, New York NY 10001, USA
**Grazer, Brian** — Producer
Imagine Entertainment, 9465 Wilshire Blvd, #700, Beverly Hills CA 90212, USA
**Grazia, Eugene (Gene)** — Ice Hockey Player
2344 NE 12th St, #10, Pompano Beach FL 33062, USA
**Graziadei, Michael** — Actor
Main Title Mgmt, 8383 Wilshire Blvd, #408, Beverly Hills CA 90211 USA
**Grazzola, Kenneth E** — Publisher
Aviation Week, Publisher's Office, 1221 Ave of Americas, New York NY 10020, USA
**Grba, Eli** — Baseball Player
106 Fox Run, Florence AL 35633, USA
**Grbac, Elvis** — Football Player
17361 Coldwater Trail, Chagrin Falls OH 44023, USA
**Greason, William H (Bill)** — Baseball Player
4536 Hillman Dr NW, Birmingham AL 35221, USA
**Grebeck, Craig A** — Baseball Player
27856 Homestead Road, Laguna Nigel CA 92677, USA
**Grebenshchikov, Boris** — Singer, Guitarist (Akvarium)
2 Marata St, #3, 191025 Saint Petersburg, Russia
**Greceanii, Zinaida** — Prime Minister, Moldova
Prime Minister's Office, Piata Marii Adunari Nacional, 227033 Chishinev, Moldova
**Grech, Prospero (Stanley) Cardinal** — Religious Leader
Order of Saint Augustine, Via Paolo VI, 25, 00193 Rome, Italy
**Grechko, Georgi M** — Cosmonaut
Cosmonaut Training Center, Star City, 141160 Zvezdny Gorodok, Moscow Oblast, Russia
**Greco, Buddy** — Singer, Pianist
Fast Forward Communications, PO Box 1655, Troy NY 12181, USA
**Greco, Emilio** — Sculptor
Viale Cortina d'Ampezzo 132, 00135 Rome, Italy
**Greco, Juliette** — Actress, Singer
Productions Gerald Meys, 110 Rue Saint Florentin, 75001 Paris, France
**Greco, Marco** — Auto Racing Driver
11717 W Rockville Road, Indianapolis IN 46232, USA
**Greco, Michael** — Actor
Greg Millard Mgmt, 38 Barton House, Sable St, London N1 2AF, England
**Greczyn, Alice** — Actress
A P A Talent/Literary Agency, 405 S Beverly Dr, #300, Beverly Hills CA 90212 USA
**Greehey, William E** — Businessman
Valero Energy Corp, 530 McCullough Ave, San Antonio TX 78215, USA
**Green, A C** — Basketball Player
904 Silver Spur Road, Rolling Hills Estates CA 90274, USA
**Green, Adam** — Director, Writer
ArieScope Pictures, 10750 Cumpston St, North Hollywood CA 91601, USA
**Green, Ahman R** — Football Player
1750 Limestone Trail, De Pere WI 54115, USA
**Green, Al** — Singer, Songwriter
Al Green Music, PO Box 456, Millington TN 38083, USA
**Green, Andy D** — Land Speed Racing Driver
London Speaker Bureau, Elsinore House, 77 Fulham Palace Road, London W6 8JA, England
**Green, Anthony W (Bubba)** — Football Player
9611 Wesland Circle, Randallstown MD 21133, USA
**Green, Art** — Religious Leader, Rabbi, Educator
Hebrew College, Rabbinical School, 160 Herrick Road, Newton Centre MA 02459, USA
**Green, B Eric** — Football Player
13131 Luntz Point Lane, Windermere FL 34786, USA
**Green, Barrett** — Football Player
1004 Green Pine Blvd, #D1, West Palm Beach FL 33409, USA

**G**

| | |
|---|---|
| **Green, Barry** | Auto Racing Executive |
| Team Green, 7615 Zionsville Road, Indianapolis IN 46268, USA | |
| **Green, Belina R** | Beauty Queen |
| Wildlife Information Rescue & Education Service, PO Box 260, Forestville NSW 2087, Australia | |
| **Green, Benny** | Jazz Pianist |
| Thomas Cassidy, PO Box 1311, Tucson AZ 85702 USA | |
| **Green, Boyce K** | Football Player |
| 18812 Parting Oaks Lane, Davidson NC 28036, USA | |
| **Green, Brian Austin** | Actor, Producer, Director |
| I C M Partners, 10250 Constellation Blvd, #900, Los Angeles CA 90067 USA | |
| **Green, Brunson** | Producer |
| Slate Public Relations, 9000 Sunset Blvd, #915, West Hollywood CA 90069 USA | |
| **Green, Charles H (Charlie)** | Football Player |
| 255 S Kyrene Road, #214, Chandler AZ 85226, USA | |
| **Green, Chris A** | Football Player |
| 331 Patio Village Terrace, Weston FL 33326, USA | |
| **Green, Cornell D** | Football Player |
| 2106 Trinidad Dr, Dallas TX 75232, USA | |
| **Green, D Jacquez** | Football Player |
| 5102 Madison Lakes Circle W, Davie FL 33328, USA | |
| **Green, Dallas** | Singer, Songwriter |
| Agency Group Ltd, 142 W 57th St, #600, New York NY 10019 USA | |
| **Green, Darrell R** | Football Player |
| 20998 Rostormel Court, Ashburn VA 20147, USA | |
| **Green, David** | Director |
| September Films, Glen House, 22 Glenthorne Road, London W6 0NG, England | |
| **Green, David A** | Auto Racing Driver |
| 118 Reel Brook Lane, Mooresville NC 28117, USA | |
| **Green, David A** | Baseball Player |
| Colinia Managua Grupo H407, Managua, Nicaragua | |
| **Green, David E** | Chemist |
| 5339 Brody Dr, Madison WI 53705, USA | |
| **Green, David E** | Football Player |
| 8311 Pat Blvd, Tampa FL 33615, USA | |
| **Green, David Gordon** | Director, Writer |
| Rough House, 1722 Whitley Ave, Los Angeles CA 90028, USA | |
| **Green, David T** | Inventor (Surgical Instruments) |
| 401 Black Rock Turnpike, Easton CT 06612, USA | |
| **Green, Debbie** | Volleyball Player |
| 239 5th St, Seal Beach CA 90740, USA | |
| **Green, Dennis** | Football Coach |
| 3930 Torrey Hill Lane, San Diego CA 92130, USA | |
| **Green, Donnie G** | Football Player |
| PO Box 685, Hagerstown MD 21741, USA | |
| **Green, Donte D** | Basketball Player |
| Houston Rockets, 1730 Jefferson St, Houston TX 77003 USA | |
| **Green, Douglas B (Ranger Doug)** | Singer (Riders in the Sky), Songwriter |
| New Frontier Mgmt, 1921 Broadway, Nashville TN 37203, USA | |
| **Green, Eric** | Medical Administrator |
| National Institutes of Health, 50 South Dr, Bethesda MD 20892, USA | |
| **Green, Ernest (Ernie)** | Football Player |
| 424 Rue Marseille, Dayton OH 45429, USA | |
| **Green, Eva** | Actress |
| 8 Bis Blvd de Courcelles, 75017 Paris, France | |
| **Green, G Dallas** | Baseball Player, Manager, Executive |
| 846 Conowingo Road, Conowingo MD 21918, USA | |
| **Green, Gary A** | Baseball Player |
| 939 Kennebec St, Pittsburgh PA 15217, USA | |
| **Green, Gary F** | Football Player |
| 16330 Walnut Creek Dr, San Antonio TX 78247, USA | |
| **Green, Gaston A, III** | Football Player |
| 13524 Stanford Ave, Los Angeles CA 90059, USA | |
| **Green, Gerald, Jr** | Basketball Player |
| Phoenix Suns, 201 E Jefferson St, Phoenix AZ 85004 USA | |
| **Green, Hamilton** | Prime Minister, Guyana |
| Plot D Lodge, Georgetown, Guyana | |
| **Green, Harold, Jr** | Football Player |
| 145 Folk Road, Blythewood SC 29016, USA | |
| **Green, Howard** | Cellular Physiologist |
| Harvard Medical School, Physiology & Biophysics Dept, Boston MA 02115, USA | |
| **Green, Hubert (Hubie)** | Golfer |
| Assured Management Co, 1901 W 47th Place, #200, Mission KS 66205, USA | |
| **Green, Hugh D** | Football Player |
| 4758 Highway 61, Fayette MS 39069, USA | |
| **Green, Jacob C** | Football Player |
| 4921 Whistling Straits Loop, College Station TX 77845, USA | |
| **Green, Janine** | Actress |
| Don Buchwald, 6500 Wilshire Blvd, #2200, Los Angeles CA 90048 USA | |
| **Green, Jarvis P** | Football Player |
| 21717 Turkey Creek Dr, Baton Rouge LA 70817, USA | |
| **Green, Jeffrey (Jeff)** | Auto Racing Driver |
| Haas C N C Racing, 6001 Haas Way, Kanapolis NC 28081, USA | |
| **Green, Jeffrey L (Jeff)** | Basketball Player |
| Boston Celtics, 226 Causeway St, #4, Boston MA 02114 USA | |
| **Green, John M (Johnny)** | Basketball Player |
| 9 Susan Lane, Dix Hills NY 11746, USA | |
| **Green, John N (Jack), Jr** | Cinematographer |
| 516 Esplanade, #E, Redondo Beach CA 90277, USA | |
| **Green, Lamar** | Basketball Player |
| PO Box 490208, Chicago IL 60649, USA | |
| **Green, Leonard C (Lenny)** | Baseball Player |
| 18693 Sunset St, Detroit MI 48234, USA | |
| **Green, Leonard I** | Businessman |
| Rite Aid Corp, 30 Hunter Lane, Camp Hill PA 17011, USA | |
| **Green, Litterial** | Basketball Player |
| 1500 N Opdyke Road, Auburn Hills MI 48326, USA | |

**Green, Mark J** — Activist, Attorney, Writer
Democracy Project, 43 E 19th St, #300, New York NY 10003, USA
**Green, Michael** — Cinematographer
11 Stevenson Lane, Upper Saddle River NJ 07458, USA
**Green, Pat** — Singer, Songwriter
Spaulding Entertainment, 54 Music Square E, #200, Nashville TN 37203, USA
**Green, Richard D (Rick)** — Ice Hockey Player
RR 1, Peterborough ON K9J 6X2, Canada
**Green, Richard L (Dick)** — Baseball Player
3924 Ridemoor Dr, Rapid City SD 57702, USA
**Green, Rickey** — Basketball Player
20584 Tyler Dr, Lynwood IL 60411, USA
**Green, Robson** — Actor
Creative Artists Agency, 2000 Ave of Stars, #100, Los Angeles CA 90067 USA
**Green, Seth** — Actor, Comedian
United Talent Agency, U T A Plaza, 9336 Civic Center Dr, Beverly Hills CA 90210 USA
**Green, Shawn D** — Baseball Player
1430 Village Way, Santa Ana CA 92705, USA
**Green, Tammie** — Golfer
4990 Township Road 147 NE, Somerset OH 43783, USA
**Green, Timothy J (Tim)** — Football Player, Sportscaster, Writer
1194 Greenfield Lane, Skaneateles NY 13152, USA
**Green, Tom** — Actor, Comedian
I C M Partners, 10250 Constellation Blvd, #900, Los Angeles CA 90067 USA
**Green, Travis** — Ice Hockey Player
2 Riverside, Irvine CA 92602, USA
**Green, Trent J** — Football Player
12109 Alhambra St, Leawood KS 66209, USA
**Green, Victor B** — Football Player
10 Dover Cliff Way, Alpharetta GA 30022, USA
**Green, Vivian** — Singer, Songwriter, Actress
I C M Partners, 10250 Constellation Blvd, #900, Los Angeles CA 90067 USA
**Green, William D** — Businessman
Accenture, 50 W San Fernando St, #1200, San Jose CA 95113, USA
**Green, Willie A** — Football Player
152 Farmington Road, Shelby NC 28150, USA
**Green, Willie J** — Basketball Player
Los Angeles Clippers, Staples Center, 1111 S Figueroa St, Los Angeles CA 90015 USA
**Greenawalt, Kent** — Attorney, Educator
Columbia University, Law School, 435 W 116th St, New York NY 10027, USA
**Greenaway, Peter** — Director
V U E, Gabriel Metsu Straat 34, #100, 1071 Amsterdam EC, Netherlands
**Greenbaum, Michael** — Religious Leader, Rabbi, Educator
Jewish Theological Seminary, 3080 Broadway, New York NY 10027, USA
**Greenbaum, Norman** — Singer, Songwriter
Greenbaum Music, 2513 Saddleback Court, Santa Rosa CA 95401, USA
**Greenberg, Adam** — Cinematographer
Gersh Agency, 9465 Wilshire Blvd, #600, Beverly Hills CA 90212 USA
**Greenberg, Adam D** — Baseball Player
79 Fernwood Dr, Guilford CT 06437, USA
**Greenberg, Alan C** — Financier
Bear Stearns Co, 383 Madison Ave, New York NY 10179, USA
**Greenberg, Bernard** — Biological Scientist, Entomologist
1463 E 55th Place, Chicago IL 60637, USA
**Greenberg, Bryan** — Actor
Gersh Agency, 9465 Wilshire Blvd, #600, Beverly Hills CA 90212 USA
**Greenberg, Carl** — Journalist
6001 Canterbury Dr, Culver City CA 90230, USA
**Greenberg, Evan** — Businessman
American International Group, 70 Pine St, New York NY 10270, USA
**Greenberg, Jack** — Attorney, Educator
118 Riverside Dr, New York NY 10024, USA
**Greenberg, Jay** — Composer
I M G Artists, Carnegie Hall Tower, 152 W 57th St, #500, New York NY 10019 USA
**Greenberg, Kathy** — Writer, Producer
Kaplan/Perrone Entertainment, 9744 Wilshire Blvd, #300, Beverly Hills CA 90212, USA
**Greenberg, Morton I** — Judge
US Court of Appeals, Judicial Complex, 402 E State St, Trenton NJ 08608, USA
**Greenberg, Peter S** — Travel Commentator, Producer, Actor
CBS-TV, News Dept, 51 W 52nd St, New York NY 10019 USA
**Greenberg, Robbie S** — Cinematographer
11 Reef St, Marina del Rey CA 90292, USA
**Greenblatt, Stephen J** — Writer
Harvard University, English Dept, Cambridge MA 02138, USA
**Greenburg, Dan** — Writer
323 E 50th St, New York NY 10022, USA
**Greenburg, Paul** — Journalist
5900 Scenic Dr, Little Rock AR 72207, USA
**Greenbush, Rachel Lindsay** — Actress
Inmotion Management, 5200 Kanan Road, Agoura Hills CA 91377, USA
**Greenbush, Sidney Robin** — Actress
Inmotion Management, 5200 Kanan Road, Agoura Hills CA 91377, USA
**Greene, Anthony (Tony)** — Football Player
1890 Briarcliff Circle NE, #D, Atlanta GA 30329, USA
**Greene, Ashley** — Actress
McKeon-Myrones Mgmt, 3500 Olive Ave, #770, Burbank CA 91505 USA
**Greene, Bob** — Exercise Physiologist, Writer
Simon & Schuster Books, 1230 Ave of Americas, Concourse 1, New York NY 10020, USA
**Greene, Brian** — Physicist, Mathematician
Columbia University, Physics Dept, New York NY 10027, USA
**Greene, Charles E (Charlie)** — Track Athlete
PO Box 6938, Lincoln NE 68506, USA
**Greene, Charles P (Charlie)** — Baseball Player
1449 Oldfield Dr, Tallahassee FL 32308, USA
**Greene, Daniel** — Actor
Michael Slessinger, 8730 W Sunset Blvd, #220W, West Hollywood CA 90069 USA

Greene, Ellen — Actress, Singer
Innovative Artists, 1505 10th St, Santa Monica CA 90401 USA
Greene, Graham — Actor
Greene Assoc, 1901 Ave of Stars, #130, Los Angeles CA 90067 USA
Greene, Herb — Photographer
PO Box 1141, Vineyard Haven MA 02568, USA
Greene, I Thomas (Tommy) — Baseball Player
PO Box 10, Warrington PA 18976, USA
Greene, Jack P — Historian
1974 Division Road, East Greenwich RI 02818, USA
Greene, James — Actor
Talent Works, 3500 W Olive Ave, #1400, Burbank CA 91505 USA
Greene, Joseph E (Mean Joe) — Football Player, Coach
PO Box 270953, Flower Mound TX 75027, USA
Greene, Kenneth E (Ken) — Football Player
5569 Nevil Point, Brentwood TN 37027, USA
Greene, Kevin D — Football Player
3448 Amber Lane, Green Bay WI 54311, USA
Greene, Khalil T — Baseball Player
10 Green Hill Dr, Simpsonville SC 29681, USA
Greene, Kim Morgan — Actress
Kazarian/Measures/Ruskin, 11969 Ventura Blvd, #300, Studio City CA 91604 USA
Greene, Maurice — Track Athlete
H S I Sports Mgmt, 9871 Irvine Center Dr, Irvine CA 92618, USA
Greene, Michele — Actress, Singer, Writer
PO Box 382, Skyforest CA 92385, USA
Greene, Robert B (Bob), Jr — Columnist
Chicago Tribune, Editorial Dept, 435 N Michigan Ave, #1, Chicago IL 60611, USA
Greene, Shecky — Actor, Comedian
Charles Rapp Enterprises, 55 Broad St, #2600, New York NY 10004, USA
Greene, Todd A — Baseball Player
725 Pine Leaf Court, Alpharetta GA 30022, USA
Greene, William L (Willie) — Baseball Player
1044 Georgia Highway 22 E, Haddock GA 31033, USA
Green-Ellis, BenJarvus — Football Player
Cincinnati Bengals, 1 Paul Brown Stadium, Cincinnati OH 45202 USA
Greenert, Jonathan W — Navy Admiral
Vice Chief of Naval Operations, HqUSN, Pentagon, Washington DC 20350 USA
Greenfield, James L — Journalist
470 Park Ave, #9A, New York NY 10022, USA
Greenfield, Jeff — Commentator
CNN-TV, News Dept, 820 1st St NE, #1000, Washington DC 20002 USA
Greenfield, Luke — Director
Creative Artists Agency, 2000 Ave of Stars, #100, Los Angeles CA 90067 USA
Greenfield, Max — Actor
W M E Entertainment, 9601 Wilshire Blvd, #300, Beverly Hills CA 90210 USA
Greengard, Paul — Nobel Medicine Laureate
450 E 63rd St, #11J, New York NY 10065, USA
Greengrass, James R (Jim) — Baseball Player
232 Rock Creek Road, Chatsworth CA 30705, USA
Greengrass, Paul — Director
Creative Artists Agency, 2000 Ave of Stars, #100, Los Angeles CA 90067 USA
Greenhouse, Linda — Journalist
New York Times, Editorial Dept, 229 W 43rd St, New York NY 10036, USA
Greenland, Seth — Writer
R W S H Agency, 1107 1/2 Glendon Ave, Los Angeles CA 90024, USA
Greenough, George — Filmmaker, Surfer
PO Box 611, Byron Bay NSW 2481, Australia
Greenquist, Brad — Actor
Gage Group, 14724 Ventura Blvd, #505, Sherman Oaks CA 91403 USA
Greenspan, Alan — Producer
International Arts Entertainment, 8899 Beverly Blvd, #800, Los Angeles CA 90048, USA
Greenspan, Alan — Government Official, Financier
Greenspan Assoc, 1133 Connecticut Ave NW, Washington DC 20036, USA
Greenspan, Gerald (Jerry) — Basketball Player
291 County Line Road, Riegelsville PA 18077, USA
Greenspoon, Jimmy — Organist (Three Dog Night)
McKenzie Accountancy, 5171 Caliente St, #134, Las Vegas NV 89119, USA
Greenstein, Barry — Poker Player, Writer
3303 Palos Verdes Dr, Rancho Palos Verdes CA 90272, USA
Greenstein, Fred I — Political Scientist
1 Conifer Court, Princeton NJ 08540, USA
Greenstein, Jeff — Producer
I C M Partners, 10250 Constellation Blvd, #900, Los Angeles CA 90067 USA
Greenville, Georgina — Model
Next Model Mgmt, 188 Rue de Rivoli, 75001 Paris, France
Greenwald, Alex — Actor, Model, Singer (Phantom Planet)
C A M, 10635 Santa Monica Blvd W, #340, Los Angeles CA 90025, USA
Greenwald, Milton — Paleontologist
University of California, Museum of Paleontology, Berkeley CA 94720, USA
Greenwald, Robert — Director
Brave New Films, 10510 Culver Blvd, Culver City CA 90232, USA
Greenwald, Todd J — Producer, Writer
Creative Artists Agency, 2000 Ave of Stars, #100, Los Angeles CA 90067 USA
Greenway, Chad — Football Player
39448 250th St, Mount Vernon SD 57363, USA
Greenwell, Michael L (Mike) — Baseball Player, Auto Racing Driver
20150 S River Road, Alva FL 33920, USA
Greenwood, Bruce — Actor
Chuck Binder Mgmt, 1465 Lindacrest Dr, Beverly Hills CA 90210 USA
Greenwood, Colin C — Bassist (Radiohead)
Courtyard, 21 Nursery, Sutton Courtenay, Abingdon, Oxfordshire OX14 4UA, England
Greenwood, David K — Basketball Player
4991 Glenview St, Chino Hills CA 91709, USA
Greenwood, James C (Jim) — Representative, PA
Biotechnology Industry, 1201 Maryland Ave SW, Washington DC 20024, USA

| | |
|---|---|
| **Greenwood, Jonathan R G (Jonny)** | Guitarist (Radiohead) |
| Courtyard, 21 Nursery, Sutton Courtenay, Abingdon, Oxfordshire OX14 4UA, England | |
| **Greenwood, Kerry** | Writer |
| Allen & Unwin, 83 Alexander St, Crows Nest NSW 2065, Australia | |
| **Greenwood, Lee** | Singer, Songwriter |
| Umberger Agency, 1562 Steele Drive NW, Atlanta GA 30309, USA | |
| **Greenwood, Morlon O** | Football Player |
| 2772 Drummossie Dr, Henderson NV 89044, USA | |
| **Greenwood, Norman** | Chemist |
| University of Leeds, Chemistry Dept, Leeds LS2 9JT, England | |
| **Greer, Brian** | Baseball Player |
| 307 Bagnall Ave, Placentia CA 92870, USA | |
| **Greer, David S** | Internist |
| Brown University, PO Box G, Providence RI 02901, USA | |
| **Greer, Donovan O** | Football Player |
| 3423 Shadowside Court, Houston TX 77082, USA | |
| **Greer, Germaine** | Social Activist, Writer |
| University of Warwick, English Literature Dept, Coventry CV4 7AL, England | |
| **Greer, Harold E (Hal)** | Basketball Player |
| 7900 E Princess Dr, #1021, Scottsdale AZ 85255, USA | |
| **Greer, Howard E (Howie)** | Navy Admiral |
| 2845 Granada Blvd Apt 2C, Coral Gables FL 33134, USA | |
| **Greer, Judy** | Actress |
| Creative Artists Agency, 2000 Ave of Stars, #100, Los Angeles CA 90067 USA | |
| **Greer, Kenneth W (Kenny)** | Baseball Player |
| 17 Hill St, Cohasset MA 02025, USA | |
| **Greer, Thurman C (Rusty), III** | Baseball Player |
| 4793 Patterson Lane, Colleyville TX 76034, USA | |
| **Gregg, A Forrest** | Football Player, Coach, Administrator |
| 926 Summer Spring View, Colorado Springs CO 80906, USA | |
| **Gregg, Clark** | Actor |
| United Talent Agency, U T A Plaza, 9336 Civic Center Dr, Beverly Hills CA 90210 USA | |
| **Gregg, John** | Actor |
| International Casting Service, 2/218 Crown St, Darlinghurst NSW 2010, Australia | |
| **Gregg, Kelly M** | Football Player |
| 13800 Hollow Glen Road, Edmond OK 73013, USA | |
| **Gregg, Kevin M** | Baseball Player |
| 1907 SW Brooklane Dr, Corvallis OR 97333, USA | |
| **Gregg, Ricky Lynn** | Singer |
| E R Rimes Mgmt, 1103 Bell Grimes Lane, Nashville TN 37207, USA | |
| **Gregg, Stephen** | Writer |
| Creative Artists Agency, 2000 Ave of Stars, #100, Los Angeles CA 90067 USA | |
| **Gregg, W Thomas (Tommy)** | Baseball Player |
| 16 Cottage Dr, Newnan GA 30265, USA | |
| **Gregga, Bruce** | Interior Designer |
| Gregga Jordan Smieszny, 1255 N State Parkway, Chicago IL 60610, USA | |
| **Gregor, Gary W** | Basketball Player |
| 444 Dove Ridge Road, Columbia SC 29223, USA | |
| **Gregorian, Vartan** | Educator |
| Carnegie Corp, President's Office, 437 Madison Ave, New York NY 10022, USA | |
| **Gregorio, Rose** | Actress |
| Bauman Redanty Shaul Agency, 5757 Wilshire Blvd, #473, Los Angeles CA 90036 USA | |
| **Gregorio, Tom** | Baseball Player |
| 66 McArthur Ave, Staten Island NY 10312, USA | |
| **Gregorios, Metropolitan Paulos M** | Religious Leader |
| Orthodox Seminary, PO Box 98, Kottayam, Kerala 686001, India | |
| **Gregory, Alex** | Rowing Athlete |
| Leander Rowing Club, Henley-on-Thames Oxfordshire RG9 2LP, England | |
| **Gregory, Bettina L** | Commentator |
| ABC-TV, News Dept, 3361 75th Ave, #X, Hyattsville MD 20785, USA | |
| **Gregory, Claude** | Basketball Player |
| 14621 Blackburn Road, Burtonsville MD 20866, USA | |
| **Gregory, Cynthia** | Ballet Dancer |
| American Ballet Theatre, 890 Broadway, #300, New York NY 10003 USA | |
| **Gregory, David** | Commentator |
| NBC-TV, News Dept, 4001 Nebraska Ave NW, Washington DC 20016 USA | |
| **Gregory, Dick** | Actor, Comedian, Social Activist |
| Dick Gregory Health Enterprises, PO Box 3270, Plymouth MA 02361, USA | |
| **Gregory, E Jackson (Jack), Jr** | Football Player |
| 108 Robertson St, Okolona MS 38860, USA | |
| **Gregory, Frederick D** | Astronaut |
| 506 Tulip Road, Annapolis MD 21403, USA | |
| **Gregory, G Leroy (Lee)** | Baseball Player |
| 6456 N Teilman Ave, Fresno CA 93711, USA | |
| **Gregory, James M (Jim)** | Ice Hockey Executive |
| National Hockey League, 75 International Blvd, Rexdale ON M9W 6L9, Canada | |
| **Gregory, Kathy** | Cartoonist |
| Playboy, Reader Services, 680 N Lake Shore Dr, Chicago IL 60611, USA | |
| **Gregory, Leo** | Actor |
| Ken McReddie Assoc, 101 Finsbury Pavement, London EC2A 1RS, England | |
| **Gregory, Philippa** | Writer, Historian |
| Simon & Schuster, 222 Gray's Inn Road, London WC1X 8HE, England | |
| **Gregory, Richard** | Religious Leader |
| Independent Fundamental Churches, 2684 Meadow Ridge, Byron Center MI 49315, USA | |
| **Gregory, Sebastian** | Actor |
| Active Artists Mgmt, 43/38 Manchester Lane, Melbourne VIC 3000, Australia | |
| **Gregory, William G** | Astronaut |
| 2027 E Freeport Lane, Gilbert AZ 85234, USA | |
| **Gregory, William P (Bill), Jr** | Football Player |
| 4317 Cityview Dr, Plano TX 75093, USA | |
| **Gregory, Wilton D** | Religious Leader |
| Illinois Diocese, Chancery Office, 222 S 3rd St, Belleville IL 62220, USA | |
| **Gregson Wagner, Natasha** | Actress |
| 1014 N Doheny Dr, #8, West Hollywood CA 90069, USA | |
| **Gregson, Wallace C** | Marine Corps General |
| Commander, Marine Forces Pacific, Camp H M Smith HI 96861 USA | |

Gregson-Williams, Harry — Composer
Gorfaine/Schwartz, 4111 W Alameda Ave, #509, Burbank CA 91505 USA
Grehl, Michael — Editor
Memphis Commercial Appeal, Editorial Dept, 495 Union Ave, Memphis TN 38103, USA
Greider, Carolyn W (Carol) — Nobel Medicine Laureate
Johns Hopkins University Medical Center, Greider Laboratory, 725 N Wolfe Ave, Baltimore MD 21205, USA
Greif, Matthew — Guitarist (LAGQ)
Jana Jae Enterprises, PO Box 35726, Tulsa OK 74153, USA
Greif, Michael — Director
I C M Partners, 730 5th Ave, New York NY 10019 USA
Greif, William B (Bill) — Baseball Player
807 E 31st St, Austin TX 78705, USA
Greifeld, Robert A — Financier
NASDAQ OMX Group, 1 Liberty Plaza, 165 Broadway, New York NY 10006, USA
Greig, John W — Basketball Player
2031 218th Place NE, Sammamish WA 98074, USA
Greilsammer, David — Conductor, Concert Pianist
I M G Artists, The Light Box, 111 Power Road, London W4 5PY, England
Greiner, William R — Educator
80 Aspenwood Dr, East Amherst NY 14051, USA
Greinke, D Zackary (Zack) — Baseball Player
8629 Vista Pine Court, Orlando FL 32836, USA
Greis, Michael — Biathlete
Postfach 1120, 83318 Ruhpolding, Germany
Greisinger, Seth A — Baseball Player
6460 Overbrook St, Falls Church VA 22043, USA
Greist, Kim — Actress
Jeffrey Leavitt Agency, 11500 W Olympic Blvd, #400, Los Angeles CA 90064, USA
Grenier, Adrian — Actor
Leverage Mgmt, 3030 Pennsylvania Ave, Santa Monica CA 90404 USA
Grenier, Sylvain — Professional Wrestler
World Wrestling Entertainment, Titan Towers, 1241 E Main St, Stamford CT 06902 USA
Grenier, Zach — Actor
Stone Meyer Genow, 9665 Wilshire Blvd, #510, Beverly Hills CA 90212 USA
Grentz, Theresa Shank — Basketball Coach
University of Illinois, Athletic Dept, Champaign IL 61820, USA
Greschner, Ron — Ice Hockey Player
PO Box 4513, Greenwich CT 6831, USA
Gresham, Robert C (Bob) — Football Player
2428 Portstewart Lane, Charlotte NC 28270, USA
Gretsch, Joel J — Actor
A P A Talent/Literary Agency, 405 S Beverly Dr, #300, Beverly Hills CA 90212 USA
Gretzky, Wayne D — Ice Hockey Player, Coach
6436 E Gainsborough Road, Scottsdale AZ 85251, USA
Greutert, Kevin — Director, Editor
Paradigm Agency, 360 N Crescent Dr, North Building, Beverly Hills CA 90210 USA
Grevelius, Anna — Opera Singer
I M G Artists, Hogarth Business Park, Chiswick, London W4 2TH, England
Grevers, Matthew (Matt) — Swimmer
821 N Waukegan Road, Lake Forest IL 60045, USA
Grevey, Kevin M — Basketball Player
528 River Bend Road, Great Falls VA 22066, USA
Grevill, Laurent — Actor
Artmedia, 20 Ave Rapp, 75007 Paris, France
Grewal, Alexi — Cyclist
US Cycling Federation, 1750 E Boulder, Colorado Springs CO 80909, USA
Grey, Beryl E — Ballerina
Fernhill, Priory Road, Forest Row, East Sussex RH18 5JE, England
Grey, Brad — Businessman, Producer, Agent
Paramount Pictures, 5555 Melrose Ave, Los Angeles CA 90038, USA
Grey, Jennifer — Actress
United Talent Agency, U T A Plaza, 9336 Civic Center Dr, Beverly Hills CA 90210 USA
Grey, Joel — Actor
Innovative Artists, 1505 10th St, Santa Monica CA 90401 USA
Grey, Sasha — Actress, Model
A P A Talent/Literary Agency, 405 S Beverly Dr, #300, Beverly Hills CA 90212 USA
Grey, Skylar — Singer, Songwriter
W M E Entertainment, 9601 Wilshire Blvd, #300, Beverly Hills CA 90210 USA
Greyeyes, Michael — Actor
Talent Works, 3500 W Olive Ave, #1400, Burbank CA 91505 USA
Gribble, David — Cinematographer
Sheldon Prosnit Agency, 800 S Robertson Blvd, Los Angeles CA 90035, USA
Grich, Robert A (Bobby) — Baseball Player
31 Madison Lane, Trabuco Canyon CA 92679, USA
Grichting, Damian — Curling Athlete
Curling Assn, PO Box 606, 3000 Bern, Switzerland
Grider, Robbin — Keyboardist (Klymaxx)
R D M J Entertainment Mgmt, 3619 Rose Ave, Long Beach CA 90807 USA
Grieco, Richard — Actor
Independent Artists, 9601 Wilshire Blvd, #750, Beverly Hills CA 90210 USA
Grieder, William — Journalist
Simon & Schuster, 1230 Ave of Americas, Concourse 1, New York NY 10020, USA
Grier, David Alan — Actor, Comedian
Innovative Artists, 1505 10th St, Santa Monica CA 90401 USA
Grier, J A D — Businessman
Cincinnati Milacron Inc, 4701 Marbury Ave, Cincinnati OH 45209, USA
Grier, Mike — Ice Hockey Player
72 Stonecrest Dr, Needham MA 2492, USA
Grier, Pam — Actress
Talent Works, 3500 W Olive Ave, #1400, Burbank CA 91505 USA
Grier, Roosevelt (Rosey) — Football Player, Actor
1250 4th St, #600, Santa Monica CA 90401, USA
Griese, Brian D — Football Player
17 Polo Club Dr, Denver CO 80209, USA
Griese, Robert A (Bob) — Football Player, Sportscaster
3195 Ponce de Leon Blvd, #412, Coral Gables FL 33134, USA

**Griesemer, John N** — Government Official
RR 2 Box 204B, Springfield MO 65802, USA
**Grieve, Benjamin (Ben)** — Baseball Player
6906 Fairway Road, La Jolla CA 92037, USA
**Grieve, Pierson M** — Businessman
Ecolab Inc, Ecolab Center, 370 Wabasha St N, Saint Paul MN 55102, USA
**Griffey, G Kenneth (Ken)** — Baseball Player
1102 Portmoor Way, Winter Garden FL 34787, USA
**Griffey, G Kenneth (Ken), Jr** — Baseball Player
8815 Conroy Windermere Road, Orlando FL 32835, USA
**Griffin, Adrian D** — Basketball Player
2909 Taylor St, Dallas TX 75226, USA
**Griffin, Alfredo C** — Baseball Player
9731 NW 41st St, Doral FL 33178, USA
**Griffin, Archie M** — Football Player
6845 Temperance Point Place, Westerville OH 43082, USA
**Griffin, Blake A** — Basketball Player
Los Angeles Clippers, Staples Center, 1111 S Figueroa St, Los Angeles CA 90015 USA
**Griffin, Cedric L** — Football Player
3015 Garwood St, Austin TX 78702, USA
**Griffin, Cornelius** — Football Player
224 Countryside Dr, Troy AL 36079, USA
**Griffin, Douglas L (Doug)** — Baseball Player
15811 El Soneto Dr, Whittier CA 90603, USA
**Griffin, Eddie** — Actor, Comedian
Front Of The Bus, 7400 Hollywood Blvd, #626, Los Angeles CA 90046, USA
**Griffin, Greg** — Basketball Player
12051 Bayport St, #1-208, Garden Grove CA 92840, USA
**Griffin, John** — Actor, Writer, Producer
David Shapira Assoc, 193 N Robertson Blvd, Beverly Hills CA 90211 USA
**Griffin, John-Ford** — Baseball Player
PO Box 1359, Sarasota FL 34230, USA
**Griffin, Kathleeen (Kathy)** — Actress, Comedienne
W M E Entertainment, 9601 Wilshire Blvd, #300, Beverly Hills CA 90210 USA
**Griffin, Keith** — Football Player
4330 Canada Hills Court, Waldorf MD 20602, USA
**Griffin, Kevin** — Singer, Guitarist (Better Than Ezra)
Uppercut Mgmt, 805 N Milwaukee Ave, #401, Chicago IL 60642, USA
**Griffin, Khamani** — Actor
Commercial Talent, 9255 Sunset Blvd, #505, West Hollywood CA 90069, USA
**Griffin, Larry A** — Football Player
5617 Silchester Lane, Charlotte NC 28215, USA
**Griffin, Leonard J, Jr** — Football Player
PO Box 480, Calhoun LA 71225, USA
**Griffin, Michael D (Mike)** — Government Official
University of Alabama, Mechanical & Aerospace Engineering Dept, Huntsville AL 35805, USA
**Griffin, Michael L (Mike)** — Baseball Player
1620 Grove Ave, Woodland CA 95695, USA
**Griffin, Nikki** — Actress
Corsa Agency, 11704 Wilshire Blvd, #204, Los Angeles CA 90025, USA
**Griffin, Patty** — Singer, Songwriter, Guitarist
High Road Touring, 751 Bridgeway, #200, Sausalito CA 94965 USA
**Griffin, Paul A** — Basketball Player
903 Great Tree Dr, San Antonio TX 78260, USA
**Griffin, Raymond (Ray)** — Football Player
5395 Anacala Court, Westerville OH 43082, USA
**Griffin, Robert L, III** — Football Player
Washington Redskins, 21300 Redskin Park Dr, Ashburn VA 20147 USA
**Griffin, Robert P** — Senator, MI; Judge
Michigan Supreme Court, PO Box 30052, Lansing MI 48909, USA
**Griffin, Thomas J (Tom)** — Baseball Player
13147 Avenida La Valencia, Poway CA 92064, USA
**Griffin, Thomas N, Jr** — Army General
9749 S Park Circle, Fairfax Station VA 22039, USA
**Griffin, Tim** — Actor
Untitled Entertainment, 350 S Beverly Dr, #200, Beverly Hills CA 90212 USA
**Griffin, W E B** — Writer
Penguin Books, 375 Hudson St, Basement 1, New York NY 10014 USA
**Griffin, Wade H, Jr** — Football Player
2937 Highway 72, Holly Springs MS 38635, USA
**Griffith, Anastasia** — Actress
Paradigm Agency, 360 Park Ave S, #1600, New York NY 10010 USA
**Griffith, Anthony** — Actor
Spivak Sobol Entertainment, 11845 W Olympic Blvd, #1125, Los Angeles CA 90064, USA
**Griffith, Bill** — Cartoonist (Zippy the Pinhead)
Pinhead Productions, PO Box 88, Hadlyme CT 06439, USA
**Griffith, Darrell S** — Basketball Player
PO Box 24841, Louisville KY 40224, USA
**Griffith, Howard T** — Football Player
9152 S Clyde Ave, Chicago IL 60617, USA
**Griffith, James** — Businessman
eBay, 2145 Hamilton Ave, San Jose CA 95125, USA
**Griffith, James** — Businessman
Timken Co, 1835 Dueber Ave SW, Canton OH 44706, USA
**Griffith, Melanie** — Actress, Model
Green Moon Productions, Paseo Maritimo, Cludad de Melilla 23, 29016 Malaga, Spain
**Griffith, Nanci** — Singer, Songwriter
Gold Mountain, 11 Music Square E, #103, Nashville TN 37203, USA
**Griffith, R Derrell** — Baseball Player
201 E Central Blvd, Anadarko OK 73005, USA
**Griffith, Richard P (Rich)** — Football Player
9368 Stoneglen Dr, Colorado Springs CO 80920, USA
**Griffith, Robert O** — Football Player
3525 Del Mar Heights Road, #331, San Diego CA 92130, USA
**Griffith, Ronald H (Ron)** — Army General
Military Professional Resources, 1320 Braddock Place, Alexandria VA 22314, USA

| | |
|---|---|
| **Griffith, Thomas B** <br> US Court of Appeals, 333 Constitution Ave NW, #4400, Washington DC 20001, USA | Judge |
| **Griffith, Thomas Ian** <br> Pitt Group, 9465 Wilshire Blvd, #420, Beverly Hills CA 90212, USA | Actor |
| **Griffith, Tom W** <br> Rural Letter Carriers Assn, 1448 Duke St, #100, Alexandria VA 22314, USA | Labor Leader |
| **Griffith, Tracy** <br> Rodriguez Mgmt, 223 S Beverly Dr, #207, Beverly Hills CA 90212, USA | Actress |
| **Griffiths, Jeremy** <br> 120 Beachdale Dr, Avon Lake OH 44012, USA | Baseball Player |
| **Griffiths, Phillip A** <br> Advanced Study Institute, Director's Office, Olden Lane, Princeton NJ 08540, USA | Mathematician, Educator |
| **Griffiths, Rachel** <br> W M E Entertainment, 9601 Wilshire Blvd, #300, Beverly Hills CA 90210 USA | Actress |
| **Griggs, Andrew T (Andy)** <br> Splash Public Relations, 1520 16th Ave S, #2, Nashville TN 37212, USA | Singer |
| **Griggs, William E (Bill), III** <br> 18 Summerhill Lane, Medford NJ 08055, USA | Football Player |
| **Grijalva, Lucy** <br> PO Box 1634, Benicia CA 94510, USA | Writer |
| **Grijalva, Victor E** <br> Schlumberger Ltd, 277 Park Ave, New York NY 10172, USA | Businessman |
| **Grilli, Jason** <br> 9037 Point Cypress Dr, Orlando FL 32836, USA | Baseball Player |
| **Grillo, Frank** <br> Creative Artists Agency, 2000 Ave of Stars, #100, Los Angeles CA 90067 USA | Actor |
| **Grim, Robert L (Bob)** <br> 18 NW Saginaw Ave, Bend OR 97701, USA | Football Player |
| **Grimaldi, Dan** <br> Kingsborough Community College, Mathematics Dept, Brooklyn NY 11235, USA | Actor |
| **Grimaldi, James V** <br> Washington Post, Editorial Dept, 1150 15th St NW, Washington DC 20071 USA | Journalist |
| **Grimaldi, Martina** <br> Swimming Federation, Stadio Olimpico, Curve Nord, 00194 Rome, Italy | Swimmer |
| **Grimaud, Helene** <br> Harm's Way Mgmt, Fritschestr 27/28, Fabrik 2, Aufgang C, 10585 Berlin, Germany | Concert Pianist |
| **Grimes, Brent O** <br> Miami Dolphins, 7500 SW 30th St, Davie FL 33314 USA | Football Player |
| **Grimes, Kareem** <br> Coast to Coast Talent, 3350 Barham Blvd, Los Angeles CA 90068 USA | Actor |
| **Grimes, Karolyn** <br> PO Box 432, Manchester WA 98353, USA | Actress |
| **Grimes, Luke** <br> Global Creative, 1051 N Cole Ave, #B, Los Angeles CA 90038, USA | Actor |
| **Grimes, Martha** <br> 115 D St SE, #G6, Washington DC 20003, USA | Writer |
| **Grimes, Randall C (Randy)** <br> 13214 Halifax St, Houston TX 77015, USA | Football Player |
| **Grimes, Scott** <br> Abrams Artists, 9200 W Sunset Blvd, #1125, West Hollywood CA 90069 USA | Actor |
| **Grimes, Shenae** <br> Gersh Agency, 9465 Wilshire Blvd, #600, Beverly Hills CA 90212 USA | Actress |
| **Grimes, Tammy** <br> Don Buchwald, 10 E 44th St, New York NY 10017 USA | Actress, Singer |
| **Grimes, Tinsely** <br> Innovative Artists, 1505 10th St, Santa Monica CA 90401 USA | Actress |
| **Grimm, Alexander** <br> Wallgauer Weg 7A, 86163 Augsburg, Germany | Canoeing Athlete |
| **Grimm, Daniel J (Dan)** <br> 2514 Smith Harbour Dr, Denver NC 28037, USA | Football Player |
| **Grimm, Oliver** <br> Kronberger Str 15, 94086 Bad-Griesbach, Germany | Actor |
| **Grimm, Russ** <br> 2654 E Mead Place, Chandler AZ 85249, USA | Football Player, Coach |
| **Grimm, Tim** <br> Abrams Artists, 9200 W Sunset Blvd, #1125, West Hollywood CA 90069 USA | Actor, Singer |
| **Grimmette, Mark** <br> 21 Snowberry Lane, Lake Placid NY 12946, USA | Luge Athlete |
| **Grimsbo, Kari Aalvik** <br> Klaebuveien 157, 7037 Trondheim, Norway | Handball Player |
| **Grimshaw, Nicholas T** <br> Fitzroy Square, 1 Conway St, London W1P 5HA, England | Architect |
| **Grimsley, Jason A** <br> 13315 Timberwild Court, Tomball TX 77375, USA | Baseball Player |
| **Grimsley, Ross A** <br> 92 Conewago Court, Owings Mill MD 21117, USA | Baseball Player |
| **Grimsmo, Anthon** <br> Curling Assn, Sognsveien 75, Serviceboks 1, 0840 Oslo, Norway | Curling Athlete |
| **Grimson, A Stuart (Stu)** <br> 999 Jones Parkway, Brentwood TN 37027, USA | Ice Hockey Player |
| **Grimsson, Olafur Ragnar** <br> President's Office, Stadastadur, Soleyjargata 1, 150 Reykjavik, Iceland | President, Iceland |
| **Grinberg, Anouk** <br> Voyez Mon Agent, 20 Ave Rapp, 75007 Paris, France | Actress |
| **Grindenko, Tatyana T** <br> Moscow State Philharmonic, Tverskaya Str 31, 103050 Moscow, Russia | Concert Violinist |
| **Griner, Brittney** <br> Phoenix Mercury, American West Arena, 201 E Jefferson St, Phoenix AZ 85004 USA | Basketball Player |
| **Griner, Paul** <br> Random House, 1745 Broadway, #1800, New York NY 10019 USA | Writer |
| **Grinham Rawley, Judy** <br> 103 Green Lane, Northwood, Middx HA6 1AP, England | Swimmer |
| **Grinnage, Jack** <br> Discover Mgmt, 11624 Moorpark St, Studio City CA 91602, USA | Actor |
| **Grinnell, Alan D** <br> University of California Medical School, Lewis Center, Los Angeles CA 90024, USA | Physiologist |

**Grinnell, Todd A** — Actor
Gersh Agency, 9465 Wilshire Blvd, #600, Beverly Hills CA 90212 USA
**Grinney, Jay** — Businessman
Healthsouth Corp, 3660 Grandview Parkway, #200, Birmingham AL 35243, USA
**Grinstead, Irish** — Singer (702)
Richard Walters, PO Box 2789, Toluca Lake CA 91610, USA
**Grinstead, LeMisha** — Singer (702)
Richard Walters, PO Box 2789, Toluca Lake CA 91610 USA
**Grint, Rupert** — Actor
Gersh Agency, 9465 Wilshire Blvd, #600, Beverly Hills CA 90212 USA
**Grinville, Patrick** — Writer
Academie Goncourt, 38 Rue du Faubourg Saint Jacques, 75014 Paris, France
**Grione, Remo** — Actor
Cristiano Cucchino Mgmt, Lungotevere dei Mellini 10, 00193 Rome, Italy
**Grippe, Peter** — Artist, Sculptor
1190 Boylston St, Newton Upper Falls MA 02464, USA
**Grisanti, Eugene P** — Businessman
International Flavors, 521 W 57th St, New York NY 10019, USA
**Grisdale, John R** — Ice Hockey Player
A-455 Bromley St, Coquitlam BC V3K 6N7, Canada
**Grisez, Germain** — Theologian
Mount Saint Mary's College, Christian Ethics Dept, Emmitsburg MD 21727, USA
**Grisham, John** — Writer
Gernert Co, 136 E 57th St, New York NY 10022, USA
**Grishin, Aleksei** — Freestyle Aerials Skier
Olympic Committee, Ul Ya Kolas 2, 220005 Minsk, Belarus
**Grishuk, Oksana (Pasha)** — Ice Dancer, Actress
PO Box 420, Beverly Hills CA 90213, USA
**Grisman, David** — Singer, Mandolin Player, Composer
C M Mgmt, 5749 Larryan Dr, Woodland Hills CA 91367, USA
**Grissom, Marquis D** — Baseball Player
694 Highway 279, Fayetteville GA 30214, USA
**Grissom, Steve** — Auto Racing Driver
5901 Orr Road, Charlotte NC 28211, USA
**Groat, Richard M (Dick)** — Baseball, Basketball Player
320 Beech St, Pittsburgh PA 15218, USA
**Grob, Mike** — Golfer
3611 Quimet Circle, Billings MT 59106, USA
**Groban, Joshua W (Josh)** — Singer, Actor, Songwriter
W M E Entertainment, 9601 Wilshire Blvd, #300, Beverly Hills CA 90210 USA
**Grobe, Jim** — Football Coach
Wake Forest University, Athletic Dept, Winston-Salem NC 27109, USA
**Grobert, Xavier Perez** — Cinematographer
Dattner Dispoto, 10635 Santa Monica Blvd, #165, Los Angeles CA 90025, USA
**Groce, Clifton A (Clif)** — Football Player
1632 Park Place, College Station TX 77840, USA
**Grocholewski, Zenon Cardinal** — Religious Leader
Palazzo della Congregazioni, Piazzo Pio XII, #3, 00193 Rome, Italy
**Grodin, Charles** — Actor
187 Chestnut Hill Road, Wilton CT 06897, USA
**Grodnikaite, Liora** — Opera Singer
I M G Artists, Hogarth Business Park, Chiswick, London W4 2TH, England
**Groening, Matthew (Matt)** — Cartoonist (Life in Hell, Simpsons)
1650 21st St, Santa Monica CA 90404, USA
**Groetzinger, Jon, Jr** — Businessman
American Greetings Corp, 1 American Road, Cleveland OH 44144, USA
**Groff, Jonathan** — Actor, Singer
W M E Entertainment, 9601 Wilshire Blvd, #300, Beverly Hills CA 90210 USA
**Grogan, Clare** — Actress
United Agents, 12-26 Lexington St, London W1F 0LE, England
**Grogan, John** — Writer
Harper Collins Publishers, 10 E 53rd St, Cellar 1, New York NY 10022 USA
**Grogan, Steven J (Steve)** — Football Player
PO Box 530, Foxboro MA 02035, USA
**Groh, Gary** — Golfer
331 Signe Court, Lake Bluff IL 60044, USA
**Grohl, David E (Dave)** — Singer, Songwriter, Drummer
S A M, 722 Seward St, Los Angeles CA 90038, USA
**Grohmann, Tim** — Rowing Athlete
Dresden Rowing Club, Hamburger Str 74, 01157 Dresden, Germany
**Grol, Hindrik H A (Henk)** — Judo Athlete
Junoplantsoen 15, 2024 Haarlem RL, Netherlands
**Gromada, John** — Sound Designer, Composer
I C M Partners, 10250 Constellation Blvd, #900, Los Angeles CA 90067 USA
**Groman, William F (Bill)** — Football Player
7906 Scherzo Lane, Houston TX 77040, USA
**Gromov, Mikhael L** — Abel Mathematics Laureate
91 Rue de la Sante, 75013 Paris, France
**Grondin, Marc-Andre** — Actor
United Talent Agency, U T A Plaza, 9336 Civic Center Dr, Beverly Hills CA 90210 USA
**Gronk** — Artist
Daniel Saxon Gallery, 7000 Romaine St, #211, West Hollywood CA 90038, USA
**Gronkowski, Rob** — Football Player
New England Patriots, 1 Patriot Place, Foxboro MA 02035 USA
**Gronman, Tuomas O** — Ice Hockey Player
Pittsburgh Penguins, Consol Energy Center, 1001 5th Ave, Pittsburgh PA 15219 USA
**Gronvole, Audun** — Freestyle Cross Skier
Ski Federation, Ulleval Stadion, 0840 Oslo, Norway
**Groom, Sam** — Actor
8730 W Sunset Blvd, #440, West Hollywood CA 90069, USA
**Groom, Wedsel G (Buddy)** — Baseball Player
1991 Saint Andrews Dr, Red Oak TX 75154, USA
**Grooms, Charles R (Red)** — Artist
85 Walker St, New York NY 10013, USA
**Groop, Monica** — Opera Singer
I M G Artists, Hogarth Business Park, Chiswick, London W4 2TH, England

**Groopman, Jerome** — Hematologist
Beth Israel Deaconess Medical Center, 330 Brookline Ave, Boston MA 02215, USA

**Gropper, Steven L (Steve)** — Guitarist (Mar-Keys), Songwriter
Insomnia Studios, 119 17th Ave S, Nashville TN 37203, USA

**Gros, Earl R** — Football Player
17424 Airline Highway, #12, Prairieville LA 70769, USA

**Grosek, Michal** — Ice Hockey Player
5 Samba Circle, Sandwich MA 02563, USA

**Gross, Alfred E (Al), Jr** — Football Player
8227 Grandstaff Dr, Sacramento CA 95823, USA

**Gross, Arye** — Actor
S D B Partners, 1801 Ave of Stars, #902, Los Angeles CA 90067 USA

**Gross, Brian** — Actor
Amsel Eisenstadt Frazier, 5055 Wilshire Blvd, #865, Los Angeles CA 90036 USA

**Gross, Charles G** — Psychologist
18 E Shore Dr, Princeton NJ 08540, USA

**Gross, Clayton K** — WW II Army Air Corps Hero
2306 SE Spyglass Dr, Vancouver WA 98683, USA

**Gross, David** — Actor, Comedian, Writer
Creative Artists Agency, 2000 Ave of Stars, #100, Los Angeles CA 90067 USA

**Gross, David J** — Nobel Physics Laureate
30 Pueblo Vista Road, Santa Barbara CA 93103, USA

**Gross, Gabriel J (Gabe)** — Baseball Player
1756 Raymer Place, Auburn AL 36830, USA

**Gross, Gregory E (Greg)** — Baseball Player
802 Hallowell Dr, West Chester PA 19382, USA

**Gross, Henry** — Singer, Guitarist (Sha Na Na)
Zelda Mgmt, PO Box 150163, Nashville TN 37215, USA

**Gross, Jordan A** — Football Player
12725 Ninebark Trail, Charlotte NC 28278, USA

**Gross, Kevin F** — Baseball Player
117 Principia Court, Claremont CA 91711, USA

**Gross, Kip L** — Baseball Player
2015 Ridgeview Court, Redlands CA 92373, USA

**Gross, Lance** — Actor
Schiff Co, 9200 Sunset Blvd, #430, West Hollywood CA 90232 USA

**Gross, Mary** — Actress, Comedienne
Danis Panaro Nist Mgmt, 9201 W Olympic Blvd, Beverly Hills CA 90212, USA

**Gross, Michael** — Actor
Stone Manners Salners, 9911 W Pico Blvd, #1400, Los Angeles CA 90035 USA

**Gross, Michael** — Swimmer
Paul-Ehrlich-Str 6, 60596 Frankfurt/Main, Germany

**Gross, Paul** — Actor
Bresler Kelly Assoc, 11500 W Olympic Blvd, #400, Los Angeles CA 90064 USA

**Gross, Ricco** — Biathlete
Waldbahnstr 34A, 83324 Ruhpolding, Germany

**Gross, Robert A** — Physicist
14 Sunnyside Way, New Rochelle NY 10804, USA

**Gross, Robert E (Bob)** — Basketball Player
13466 SE Red Rose Lane, Happy Valley OR 97086, USA

**Gross, Sam** — Cartoonist
New Yorker, Editorial Dept, 4 Times Square, Basement C1B, New York NY 10036 USA

**Gross, Terry R** — Commentator
WHYY-Radio, News Dept, Independence Mall W, Philadelphia PA 19104, USA

**Gross, Wayne D** — Baseball Player
45 Leonard Court, Danville CA 94526, USA

**Grossfeld, Stanley** — Photojournalist
Boston Globe, Editorial Dept, 135 William Morrissey Blvd, Dorchester MA 02125 USA

**Grossheusch, Leroy (Lee)** — WW II Army Air Corps Hero
1239 Kupau St, Kailua HI 96734, USA

**Grossman, Allen R** — Writer
113 Richdale Ave, #25, Cambridge MA 02140, USA

**Grossman, Austin** — Writer
Pantheon/Random House, 1745 Broadway, New York NY 10019, USA

**Grossman, Ben** — Visual Effects Designer
Syndicate, 100 Universal City Plaza, #6148, Universal City CA 91608, USA

**Grossman, C Randy** — Football Player
204 Ridge Road, Pittsburgh PA 15238, USA

**Grossman, David** — Director, Producer
United Talent Agency, U T A Plaza, 9336 Civic Center Dr, Beverly Hills CA 90210 USA

**Grossman, David** — Writer
Bloomsbury Publishing, 50 Bedford Square, London WC1B 3DP, England

**Grossman, Eric** — Bassist (K's Choice)
Sharpe Entertainment Services, 683 Palmera Ave, Pacific Palisades CA 90272, USA

**Grossman, Gene M** — Economist
Princeton University, Economics Dept, Princeton NJ 08544, USA

**Grossman, Judith** — Writer
Warren Wilson College, English Dept, Swannanoa NC 28778, USA

**Grossman, Leslie** — Actress
Marsh Entertainment, 12444 Ventura Blvd, #203, Sherman Oaks CA 91604, USA

**Grossman, Rex D** — Football Player
17230 Crawley Road, Odessa FL 33556, USA

**Grossman, Robert** — Illustrator
19 Crosby St, New York NY 10013, USA

**Grosvenor, Benjamin** — Concert Pianist
Hazard Chase, 25 City Road, Cambridge CB1 1DP, England

**Grosvenor, Gilbert M** — Foundation Executive, Publisher
National Geographic, Editorial Dept, 1145 17th St NW, Washington DC 20036 USA

**Grote, Gerald W (Jerry)** — Baseball Player
2608 N Main St, #B, Belton TX 76513, USA

**Grotenfelt, Georg E J** — Architect
Kapteeninkatu 20D, 00140 Helsinki, Finland

**Groth, Jacob** — Composer
Air Edel, 18 Rodmarton St, London W1U 8BJ, England

**Groth, Jeffrey E (Jeff)** — Football Player
13824 Driftwood Dr, Carmel IN 46033, USA

**Groth, John T (Johnny)** — Baseball Player
170 N Ocean Blvd, #307, Palm Beach FL 33480, USA
**Grotjahn, Mark** — Artist
Blum & Poe Gallery, 2727 S La Cienega Blvd, Los Angeles CA 90034, USA
**Grott, Matthew A (Matt)** — Baseball Player
19431 N Concho Circle, Sun City AZ 85373, USA
**Grouch, Roger K** — Astronaut
Life/Microgravity Sciences Office, NASA Headquarters, Washington DC 20546, USA
**Grove, Andrew S** — Businessman
Intel Corp, 2200 Mission College Blvd, Santa Clara CA 95054, USA
**Grove, Jill** — Opera Singer
I M G Artists, Hogarth Business Park, Chiswick, London W4 2TH, England
**Groves, Kristina** — Speed Skater
Agenda Sport Marketing, 119-9A St NE, Calgary AB T2E 9C5, Canada
**Groves, Richard H** — Army General
9110 Belvoir Woods Parkway, #216, Fort Belvoir VA 22060, USA
**Groves, Robert M** — Government Official, Statistician
Georgetown University, Provost's Office, Washington DC 20057, USA
**Groves, S Russell** — Architect
210 11th Ave, New York NY 10001, USA
**Growney, Robert L** — Businessman
Motorola Inc, 1303 E Algonquin Road, Schaumburg IL 60196, USA
**Grubb, John M** — Baseball Player
6618 Bel Lac Dr, Chester VA 23831, USA
**Grubbs, Benjamin R (Ben)** — Football Player
New Orleans Saints, 5800 Airline Highway, Metairie LA 70003 USA
**Grubbs, Gary** — Actor
Talent Works, 3500 W Olive Ave, #1400, Burbank CA 91505 USA
**Grubbs, Robert H** — Nobel Chemistry Laureate
1700 Spruce St, South Pasadena CA 91030, USA
**Gruber, J Mackye** — Director
New Wave Entertainment, 2660 W Olive Ave, Burbank CA 91505, USA
**Gruber, Kelly W** — Baseball Player
4317 Canyon Glen Circle, Austin TX 78732, USA
**Gruber, Michael** — Writer
William Morrow Publishers, 1350 Ave of Americas, New York NY 10019 USA
**Gruber, Paul B** — Football Player
PO Box 4239, Edwards CO 81632, USA
**Gruberova, Edita** — Opera Singer
Theateragentur Hilbert, Maximilianstr 22, 80539 Munich, Germany
**Grubinger, Martin** — Concert Percussionist
Harrison/Parrott, 5-6 Albion Court, London W6 0QT, England
**Grubman, Allen J** — Attorney
Grubman Indursky Schindler Goldstein, 152 W 57th St, New York NY 10019, USA
**Grubnic, Dave** — Drag Racing Driver
Kalitta Motorsports, 1010 James L Hart Parkway, Ypsilanti MI 48197, USA
**Gruden, Jon** — Football Coach, Sportscaster
709 Guisando de Avila, Tampa FL 33613, USA
**Grudt, Mona** — Beauty Queen
Ditt Bryllup, Editor's Office, PO Box 24, 1485 Hakadal, Norway
**Grudzielanek, Mark J** — Baseball Player
833 Aspen Peak Loop, #1113, Henderson NV 89011, USA
**Gruenberg, Erich** — Concert Violinist
80 Northway, Hampstead Garden Suburb, London NW11 6PA, England
**Gruenberg, Peter** — Nobel Physics Laureate
Solid State Research Institute, Wilhelm-Johnen-Str, 52425 Juelich, Germany
**Gruevski, Nikola** — Prime Minister, Macedonia
Prime Minister's Office, Ilindenska BB, 1000 Skopje, Macedonia
**Gruffudd, Ioan** — Actor
Framework Entertainment, 9057 Nemo St, #C, West Hollywood CA 90069 USA
**Grum, Clifford J** — Businessman
Temple-Inland Inc, 303 S Temple Dr, Diboll TX 75941, USA
**Grumman, Cornelia** — Journalist
Chicago Tribune, Editorial Dept, 350 N Orleans St, Chicago IL 60654 USA
**Grummer, Elisabeth** — Opera Singer
Am Schlachtensee 104, 14163 Berlin, Germany
**Grunberg-Manago, Marianne** — Biochemist
80 Boulevard Pasteur, 75015 Paris, France
**Grundfest, Joseph A** — Government Official
Stanford University, Law School, Stanford CA 94305, USA
**Grundhofer, Jerry A** — Financier
US Bancorp, 601 2nd Ave S, Minneapolis MN 55402, USA
**Grundhofer, John F** — Financier
Donaldson Co, 1400 W 94th St, Minneapolis MN 55431, USA
**Grundman, Bernie** — Music Executive
Bernie Grundman Mastering, 1640 N Gower St, Los Angeles CA 90028, USA
**Grundt, Kenneth A (Ken)** — Baseball Player
4814 W Parker Ave, Chicago IL 60639, USA
**Grundy, Hugh** — Drummer (Zombies)
Lustig Talent, PO Box 770850, Orlando FL 32877 USA
**Grune, George V** — Publisher, Foundation Executive
PO Box 2348, Ponte Vedra Beach FL 32004, USA
**Gruneisen, Samuel K (Sam)** — Football Player
569 Finsbay Court, Ocoee FL 34761, USA
**Grunfeld, Ernest (Ernie)** — Basketball Player, Executive
10121 Counselman Road, Potomac MD 20854, USA
**Grunhard, Timothy G (Tim)** — Football Player
2005 Arno Road, Mission Hills KS 66208, USA
**Grunsfeld, John M** — Astronaut
PO Box 279, Highland MD 20777, USA
**Grunstein, Michael** — Biological Chemist
University of California, Biological Chemistry Dept, Los Angeles CA 90024, USA
**Grunwald, Ernie** — Actor
Stone Manners Salners, 9911 W Pico Blvd, #1400, Los Angeles CA 90035 USA
**Grupp, Robert W (Bob)** — Football Player
305 Hill Ave, Langhorne PA 19047, USA

**G**

Groth - Grupp

# G

**Grushecky, Joe** — Singer (Iron City Houserockers)
Brothers Management Assoc, 141 Dunbar Ave, Fords NJ 08863 USA
**Grusin, Dave** — Composer, Pianist
Kraft-Engel Mgmt, 15233 Ventura Blvd, #200, Sherman Oaks CA 91403 USA
**Grutman, N Roy** — Attorney
Grutman Miller Greenspoon Hendler, 505 Park Ave, New York NY 10022, USA
**Gruttadauria, Michael J (Mike)** — Football Player
4250 Swift Road, Sarasota FL 34231, USA
**Grybauskaite, Dalia** — President, Lithuania
President's Office, Gediminas 53, 232026 Vilnius, Lithuania
**Gryboski, Kevin** — Baseball Player
127 Castlebrooke Dr, Venetia PA 15367, USA
**Grylls, Edward M (Bear)** — Entertainer, Writer, Mountaineer
Second Assn, Gilwell Park, Chingford, London E4 7QW, England
**Grzanich, Michael E (Mike)** — Baseball Player
176 Holliday Trace, Raymond MS 39154, USA
**Guang Yang** — Opera Singer
Columbia Artists Mgmt Inc, 1790 Broadway, #702, New York NY 10019 USA
**Guanlao, Christopher** — Drummer (Silversun Pickps)
Ink Tank Public Relations, 1824 W Sunset Blvd, #102, Los Angeles CA 90026, USA
**Guard, Christopher** — Actor
76 Oxford St, London W1N 0AX, England
**Guardado, Edward A (Eddie)** — Baseball Player
11268 Overlook Point, Tustin CA 92782, USA
**Guare, John** — Writer
R Andrew Boose, 1 Dag Hammarskjold Plaza, New York NY 10017, USA
**Guarini, Justin** — Singer
Axis Artist Management, 9715 Belmar Ave, Northridge CA 91324, USA
**Guaty, Camille** — Actress
B/W/R, 9100 Wilshire Blvd, #500W, Beverly Hills CA 90212 USA
**Guay, Paul F** — Ice Hockey Player
34 Kirkbrae Dr, Lincoln RI 02865, USA
**Gubaidulina, Sofia A** — Composer
2D Pugachevskaya 8, Korp 5, #130, 107061 Moscow, Russia
**Gubanich, Creighton W** — Baseball Player
10 Galicia Dr, Phoenixville PA 19460, USA
**Gubanova, Ekaterina** — Opera Singer
Mariinsky Theater, Theater Square, 1 Pl Iskusstr, 190000 Saint Petersburg, Russia
**Gubarev, Aleksei A** — Cosmonaut; Air Force General
Cosmonaut Training Center, Star City, 141160 Zvezdny Gorodok, Moscow Oblast, Russia
**Guber, Peter** — Producer
Mandalay Entertainment, 10202 W Washington Blvd, #1070, Culver City CA 90232, USA
**Gubicza, Mark S** — Baseball Player
11808 Macoda Lane, Chatsworth CA 91311, USA
**Gubler, Matthew Gray** — Actor
Creative Artists Agency, 2000 Ave of Stars, #100, Los Angeles CA 90067 USA
**Guccione, Christopher (Chris)** — Baseball Umpire
15362 W Iliff Dr, Denver CO 80228, USA
**Guckel, Henry** — Microbiotics Engineer
University of Wisconsin, Engineering Dept, Madison WI 53706, USA
**Gudereit, Marcia** — Curling Athlete
Curling Assn, 1660 Vimont Court, Cumberland ON K4A 4J4, Canada
**Gudgeon, Simon** — Sculptor
Halcyon Gallery, 144-146 New Bond St, London W1S 2PF, England
**Gudmundsson, Petur** — Basketball Player
2423 Vibrant Oak, San Antonio TX 78232, USA
**Guebuza, Armando** — President, Mozambique
President's Office, Avenida Julius Nyerere 1780, Maputo, Mozambique
**Guelleh, Ismail Omar** — President, Djibouti
President's Office, 8-10 Ahmed Nessim St, BP 109, Djibouti City, Djibouti
**Guennel, Joe** — Soccer
835 Front Range Road, Littleton CO 80120, USA
**Gueno, James A (Jim)** — Football Player
6939 General Haig St, New Orleans LA 70124, USA
**Guenot, Steeve** — Greco-Roman Wrestler
Federation de Lutte, 2 Rue Louis Pergaud, 94706 Maisons Alfort Cedex, France
**Guenther, Johnny** — Bowler
23826 115th Place W, Woodway WA 98020, USA
**Guerard, Michel E** — Chef
Les Pres d'Eugenie, 40320 Eugenie les Bains, France
**Guerdat, Steve** — Equestrian
Rutihof 1560, 8704 Herrliberg, Switzerland
**Guerin, Richard V (Richie)** — Basketball Player
1355 Bear Island Dr, West Palm Beach FL 33409, USA
**Guerin, Wiliam R (Bill)** — Ice Hockey Player
12 North Road, Oyster Bay NY 11771, USA
**Guerra, Andrea** — Composer
First Artists, 4764 Park Granada, #210, Calabasas CA 91302 USA
**Guerra, Eddie** — Actor
Creative Artists Agency, 2000 Ave of Stars, #100, Los Angeles CA 90067 USA
**Guerra, Juan Luis** — Singer, Songwriter
Joyce Agency Entertainment, 370 Harrison Ave, Harrison NY 10528, USA
**Guerra, Vida** — Actress, Model, Singer
It Girl Public Relations, 225 1/2 Howland Canal, Venice CA 90291, USA
**Guerrero Coles, Lisa** — Sportscaster, Actress, Model
Lorraine Berglund Mgmt, 11537 Hesby St, North Hollywood CA 91601, USA
**Guerrero, Giancarlo** — Conductor
Opus 3 Artists, 470 Park Ave S, #900N, New York NY 10016 USA
**Guerrero, Julen** — Soccer Player
A C Bilbao, Alameda Mazarredo 23, 48009 Bilbao, Spain
**Guerrero, Mario M** — Baseball Player
Calle Duarte 450, 10211 Santo Domingo, Dominican Republic
**Guerrero, Pedro** — Baseball Player
10720 NW 66th St, #408, Doral FL 33178, USA
**Guerrero, Robert J (Ghost)** — Boxer
14810 Delano St, Van Nuys CA 91411, USA

Grushecky - Guerrero

Guerrero, Roberto J — Auto Racing Driver
31642 Via Cervantes, San Juan Capistrano CA 92675, USA
Guerrero, Vladimir A — Baseball Player
5160 E Copa de Oro Dr, Anaheim CA 92807, USA
Guerrier, Matthew O (Matt) — Baseball Player
200 Highland View Dr, Birmingham AL 35242, USA
Guers, Paul — Actor
40 Rue de Buci, 75006 Paris, France
Guesmi, Samir — Actor
Artmedia, 20 Ave Rapp, 75007 Paris, France
Guest, Christopher H — Director, Actor, Comedian
United Talent Agency, U T A Plaza, 9336 Civic Center Dr, Beverly Hills CA 90210 USA
Guest, Cornelia — Actress, Model, Socialite
Brillstein Entertainment Partners, 9150 Wilshire Blvd, #350, Beverly Hills CA 90212 USA
Guest, Lance — Actor
116 Pinehurst Ave, #G23, New York NY 10033, USA
Guetary, Francois — Actor
Paola Bonelli Consuelenza Cinematografica, 50, Viale Parioli, 00197 Rome, Italy
Guetta, David — DJ Musician, Songwriter
Creative Artists Agency, 2000 Ave of Stars, #100, Los Angeles CA 90067 USA
Guettel, Adam — Composer, Lyricist
Gersh Agency, 9465 Wilshire Blvd, #600, Beverly Hills CA 90212 USA
Guetterman, A Lee — Baseball Player
108 1/2 E Broadway St, Lenoir City TN 37771, USA
Guffey, John W, Jr — Businessman
Coltec Industries, 2550 W Tyvola Road, Charlotte NC 28217, USA
Gugelmin, Mauricio — Auto Racing Driver
Ave 7 de Septembre 4476-60-62, Cuiriba PR 80250210, Brazil
Guggenheim, Alan — Inventor (Hydrogen Energy Processor)
Northwest Power Systems, PO Box 5339, Bend OR 97708, USA
Guggenheim, Davis — Director
Electric Kinney Films, 1661 Lincoln Blvd, #101, Santa Monica CA 90404, USA
Gugino, Carla — Actress
Untitled Entertainment, 350 S Beverly Dr, #200, Beverly Hills CA 90212 USA
Guglielmi, Ralph V — Football Player
159 Red Berry Dr, Wallace NC 28466, USA
Gugliotta, Thomas J (Tom) — Basketball Player
1267 Francis St NW, Atlanta GA 30318, USA
Guice, Jackson — Cartoonist (Resurrection Man)
D C Comics, 1700 Broadway, #400, New York NY 10019 USA
Guida, Gloria — Actress
C D A Studio di Nardo, Via Cavour 171, 00184 Rome, Italy
Guida, Louis P (Lou) — Harness Racing Driver, Trainer
173 San Remo Dr, Jupiter FL 33458, USA
Guidarini, Marco — Conductor
I M G Artists, Hogarth Business Park, Chiswick, London W4 2TH, England
Guidinger, Jay P — Basketball Player
N39W22702 Grandview Dr, Pewaukee WI 53072, USA
Guidolin, Aldo — Ice Hockey Player
34 Blair Dr, Guelph ON N1L 1N7, Canada
Guidoni, Umberto — Astronaut, Italy
European Space Center, Linder Hohe, Box 906096, 51127 Cologne, Germany
Guidry, Mark — Thoroughbred Racing Jockey
102 S William Dr, Lafayette LA 70506, USA
Guidry, N T — Aeronautical Engineer
23971 Coral Springs Lane, Tehachapi CA 93561, USA
Guidry, Paul M — Football Player
880 Noel Dr, Mount Juliet TN 37122, USA
Guidry, Ronald A (Ron) — Baseball Player
PO Box 278, Scott LA 70583, USA
Guiel, Aaron — Baseball Player
18944 69th Ave, Surrey BC V4N 5K1, Canada
Guigou, Michael — Handball Player
Montpellier Agglomeration H B, 1000 Ave du Val de Montferrand, 34090 Montpellier, France
Guilbert, Ann — Actress
550 Erskine Dr, Pacific Palisades CA 90272, USA
Guilfoyle, Paul — Actor
S M S Talent, 8383 Wilshire Blvd, #230, Beverly Hills CA 90211 USA
Guill, Julianna — Actress
Luber Rocklin Entertainment, 8530 Wilshire Blvd, #555, Beverly Hills CA 90211 USA
Guillaume — Hereditary Grand Duke, Luxembourg
Palais Grand-Ducal, 17 Rue du Marche-aux-Herbes, 1728 Luxembourg-Ville, Luxembourg
Guillaume, Robert — Actor
Alan David Mgmt, 8840 Wilshire Blvd, #200, Beverly Hills CA 90211, USA
Guillem, Sylvie — Ballerina
Royal Ballet, Covent Garden, Bow St, London WC2E 9DD, England
Guillemin, Roger C L — Nobel Medicine Laureate
7316 Encelia Ave, La Jolla CA 92037, USA
Guillen, Oswaldo J (Ozzie) — Baseball Player, Manager
19462 38th Court, Golden Beach FL 33160, USA
Guillerman, John — Director
309 S Rockingham Ave, Los Angeles CA 90049, USA
Guillo, Dominque — Actor
Agence Artiste Adequet, 108 Rue Reaumur, 75002 Paris, France
Guillory, Sienna — Actress
United Talent Agency, U T A Plaza, 9336 Civic Center Dr, Beverly Hills CA 90210 USA
Guilmette, Jonathan — Speed Skater
Speed Skating Canada, 2781 Lancaster Road, #402, Ottawa ON K1B 1A7, Canada
Guindon, Richard G — Cartoonist (Guindon)
321 W Lafayette Blvd, Detroit MI 48226, USA
Guindon, Robert J (Bob) — Baseball Player
437 Marsh Creek Road, Venice FL 34292, USA
Guinee, Tim — Actor
Innovative Artists, 1505 10th St, Santa Monica CA 90401 USA
Guinier, Lani — Attorney, Educator
University of Pennsylvania, Law School, 3400 Chestnut, Philadelphia PA 19104, USA

**Guinn, Drannon E (Skip)** — Baseball Player
PO Box 911, Stilwell OK 74960, USA
**Guirgis, Stephen Adly** — Actor, Comedian
Anonymous Content, 3532 Hayden Ave, Culver City CA 90232 USA
**Guiry, Tom** — Actor
Gersh Agency, 9465 Wilshire Blvd, #600, Beverly Hills CA 90212 USA
**Guisewite, Cathy L** — Cartoonist (Cathy)
4039 Camilla Ave, Studio City CA 91604, USA
**Guiter, Sophie** — Actress
Artmedia, 20 Ave Rapp, 75007 Paris, France
**Gul, Abdullah** — President, Turkey
President's Office, Cumhurbaskanlgl Kosku, Cankaya, 06689 Ankara, Turkey
**Gulan, Michael W (Mike)** — Baseball Player
4409 Fairway Dr, Steubenville OH 43953, USA
**Gulbinowicx, Henryk Roman Cardinal** — Religious Leader
Metropolita Wroclawski, Ul Katedraina 11, 50 328 Wroclaw, Poland
**Gulbis, Natalie** — Golfer, Model
7733 Glenn Ave, Citrus Heights CA 95610, USA
**Gulden, Bradford L (Brad)** — Baseball Player
15820 Lundstead Road, Carver MN 55315, USA
**Guleghina, Maria** — Opera Singer
I M G Artists, Carnegie Hall Tower, 152 W 57th St, #500, New York NY 10019 USA
**Gullett, Donald E (Don)** — Baseball Player
194 Kingsway Dr, South Shore KY 41175, USA
**Gullickson, William L (Bill)** — Baseball Player
3 Banchory Court, Palm Beach Gardens FL 33418, USA
**Gulliver, Harold** — Editor
Atlanta Constitution, 223 Perimeter Center Parkway NE, Atlanta GA 30346, USA
**Gullotta, Leo** — Actor
Carol Levi Mgmt, Via Giuseppe Pisanelli 2, 00196 Rome, Italy
**Guloien, Krista** — Rowing Athlete
Rowing Canada Aviron, 100-4636 Elk Lake Dr, Victoria V8Z 5M1, Canada
**Gulyas, Denes** — Opera Singer
Hungarian State Opera, Andrassy Utca 22, 1061 Budapest, Hungary
**Gulzar** — Director, Songwriter
Boskiyana Pali Hill, Bandra (W), Mumbai MS 400050, India
**Guman, Michael D (Mike)** — Football Player
3913 Pleasant Ave, Allentown PA 18103, USA
**Gumbel, Bryant C** — Commentator
Home Box Office, 1100 Ave of Americas, Front 300, New York NY 10036 USA
**Gumbel, Greg** — Sportscaster
10372 N Lake Vista Circle, Davie FL 33328, USA
**Gummer, Grace** — Actress
Creative Artists Agency, 2000 Ave of Stars, #100, Los Angeles CA 90067 USA
**Gummer, Mamie** — Actress
Creative Artists Agency, 2000 Ave of Stars, #100, Los Angeles CA 90067 USA
**Gummersall, Devon** — Actor
A P A Talent/Literary Agency, 405 S Beverly Dr, #300, Beverly Hills CA 90212 USA
**Gumpert, David L (Dave)** — Baseball Player
68371 Fleetwood Dr, South Haven MI 49090, USA
**Gund, Graham** — Architect
47 Thorndike St, #1, Cambridge MA 02141, USA
**Gunderson, Eric A** — Baseball Player
19809 SE 10th St, Camas WA 98607, USA
**Gundi** — Artist
RR 1, Roseneath ON K0K 2X0, Canada
**Gunesekera, Romesh** — Writer
A M Heath Co, 79 Saint Martin's Lane, London WC2N 4RE, England
**Gunn, Anna** — Actress
United Talent Agency, U T A Plaza, 9336 Civic Center Dr, Beverly Hills CA 90210 USA
**Gunn, Chanda L** — Ice Hockey Player
74 Rockcroft Road, Weymouth MA 02188, USA
**Gunn, James E** — Astrophysicist
Princeton University, Astrophysics Dept, Princeton NJ 08544, USA
**Gunn, Janet** — Actress
David Shapira Assoc, 193 N Robertson Blvd, Beverly Hills CA 90211 USA
**Gunn, Lee F** — Navy Admiral
Public Research Institute, CNA Corp, 4825 Mark Center Dr, Alexandria VA 22311, USA
**Gunn, Nathan** — Concert, Opera Singer
Opus 3 Artists, 470 Park Ave S, #900N, New York NY 10016 USA
**Gunnarsson, Martin** — Marksman
3536 Saint Marys Road, #D24, Columbus GA 31906, USA
**Gunnell, Owen** — Concert Percussionist (O Duo)
Sony/BMI Records, 550 Madison Ave, #600, New York NY 10022, USA
**Gunnell, Sally** — Track Athlete
Old School Cottage, School Lane, Pycombe, West Sussex BN45 7FQ, England
**Gunnels, J Riley** — Football Player
606 Wesley Ave, Ocean City NJ 08226, USA
**Gunnestad, Stig-Arne** — Curling Athlete
Curling Assn, Sognsveien 75, Serviceboks 1, 0840 Oslo, Norway
**Gunnlaugsson, Sigmundur David** — Prime Minister, Iceland
Prime Minister's Office, Stornarroshusino v/Laekjartou, 150 Reykjavik, Iceland
**Gunther, Dan** — Actor
Century Artists, PO Box 59747, Santa Barbara CA 93150 USA
**Gunther, David C (Dave)** — Basketball Player
4510 Cherry St, Grand Forks ND 58201, USA
**Gunton, Bob** — Actor
Abrams Artists, 275 7th Ave, #2600, New York NY 10001 USA
**Guokas, Matthew G (Matt), Jr** — Basketball Player, Coach, Executive
2410 S 19th St, Philadelphia PA 19145, USA
**Guolla, Steve** — Ice Hockey Player
733 Spartan Dr, Rochester Hills MI 48309, USA
**Gupta, Amit** — Director
United Agents, 12-26 Lexington St, London W1F 0LE, England
**Gupta, Modadugu V** — Aquaculturist
Jalan Batu Maung, Batu Maung 11960 Bayan Lepas, Penang, Malaysia

**Gupta, Raj** — Businessman
Rohm & Haas Co, 100 S Independence Mall W, #1A, Philadelphia PA 19106, USA
**Gupta, Subodh** — Artist
Hauser & Wirth Art Gallery, 32 E 69th St, New York NY 10021, USA
**Gupta, Sudhir** — Immunologist
University of California, Medicine Dept, Irvine CA 92717, USA
**Gupton, Damon** — Actor
Harden-Curtis Associates, 850 7th Ave, #903, New York NY 10019, USA
**Gur, Mordechai** — Army General, Israel
25 Mishmeret St, Afeka, Tel-Aviv 69694, Israel
**Gura, Larry C** — Baseball Player
PO Box 94, Litchfield Park AZ 85340, USA
**Gurdon, John B** — Nobel Medicine Laureate
Whittlesford Grove, Whittlesford, Cambridge CB2 4W2, England
**Guren, Peter** — Cartoonist (Ask Shagg, Committed)
Creators Syndicate, 737 3rd St, Hermosa Beach CA 90254 USA
**Gurewitz, Brett W** — Guitarist (Bad Religion)
Goldstar Public Relations, PO Box 130, Ross on Wye HR9 6WY, England
**Gurian, Michael** — Psychotherapist, Social Philosopher
417 W 32nd Ave, Spokane WA 99203, USA
**Gurira, Danai Jekesai** — Actress
United Talent Agency, U T A Plaza, 9336 Civic Center Dr, Beverly Hills CA 90210 USA
**Gurnah, Abdulrazak** — Writer
Roger Coleridge White, 20 Powis Mews, London W11 1KN, England
**Gurnett, Jane** — Actress
Hamilton Hodell, 66-68 Margaret St, #500, London W1W 8SR, England
**Gurney, Albert R (A R), Jr** — Writer
Gersh Agency, 9465 Wilshire Blvd, #600, Beverly Hills CA 90212 USA
**Gurney, Daniel S (Dan)** — Auto Racing Driver, Executive
All-American Racers Inc, 2334 S Broadway, Santa Ana CA 92707, USA
**Gurney, Hilda** — Equestrian
8430 Waters Road, Moorpark CA 93021, USA
**Gurney, James** — Writer, Illustrator
PO Box 693, Rhinebeck NY 12572, USA
**Gurraggchaa, Jugderdemidijn** — Cosmonaut, Mongolia; Air Force General
Lyotchik Kosmonavt, MNR, Central Post Office Box 378, Ulan Bator, Mongolia
**Gursky, Andreas** — Photographer
Matthew Marks Gallery, 523 W 24th St, New York NY 10011, USA
**Gurung, Prabal** — Fashion Designer
247 W 37th St, #1501, New York NY 10018, USA
**Gurwitch, Annabelle** — Actress
Global Artists Agency, 6253 Hollywood Blvd, #508, Los Angeles CA 90028 USA
**Guryakova, Olga** — Opera Singer
I M G Artists, Hogarth Business Park, Chiswick, London W4 2TH, England
**Gusarov, Alexei** — Ice Hockey Player
1168 Yankee Creek Road, Evergreen CO 80439, USA
**Gusella, James** — Biologist
Harvard Medical School, 25 Shattuck St, Boston MA 02115, USA
**Gusenbauer, Alfred** — Chancellor, Austria
Chancellor's Office, Ballhausplatz 2, 1014, Vienna, Austria
**Gushue, Brad** — Curling Athlete
Curling Assn, 1660 Vimont Court, Cumberland ON K4A 4J4, Canada
**Gusmao, Jose Alexandre (Xanana)** — Prime Minister, Timor-Leste
Prime Minister's Office, Government Palace, President Nicolau Lobato Ave, Dili, Timor-Leste
**Gustafson, Elisabet** — Curling Athlete
Curling Assn, Idrottshuser, Marbackagatan 19, 123 43 Farsta, Sweden
**Gustafson, Kathryn** — Landscape Architect
Gustafson Guthrie Nichol, Pier 55, #31101, Alaskan Way, Seattle WA 98101, USA
**Gustafson, Steven** — Bassist (10000 Maniacs)
Geffen Records, 10900 Wilshire Blvd, #1000, Los Angeles CA 90024 USA
**Gustafsson, Jan-Ake** — Biologist
University of Houston, Biosciences Dept, 4800 Calhoun Road, Houston TX 77004, USA
**Gustafsson, Mattias** — Handball Player
TuS Nettelstedt-Lubbecke, Gerichtsstr 1A, 31312 Lubbecke, Germany
**Gustafsson, Per** — Ice Hockey Player
5605 NE 3rd Ave, Fort Lauderdale FL 33334, USA
**Gustin, Grant** — Actor
C E S D, 10635 Santa Monica Blvd, #130, Los Angeles CA 90025 USA
**Guterres, Antonio Manuel de Oliveira** — Prime Minister, Portugal
U N High Commission for Refugees, CP 2500, 1211 Geneva 2, Switzerland
**Guterson, David** — Writer
Georges Borchardt, 136 E 57th St, #1400, New York NY 10022, USA
**Guth, Alan H** — Physicist
Massachusetts Institute of Technology, Physics Dept, Cambridge MA 02139, USA
**Guthe, Manfred** — Cinematographer
122 Collier St, Toronto ON M4W 1M3, Canada
**Guthe, Nick** — Writer, Director, Producer
Artist International Mgmt, 9107 Wilshire Blvd, #600, Beverly Hills CA 90210, USA
**Guthrie, Arlo** — Singer, Guitarist, Songwriter
Rising Son Records, 218 Beach Road, Washington MA 01223, USA
**Guthrie, Janet** — Auto Racing Driver
PO Box 505, Aspen CO 81612, USA
**Guthrie, Jeremy S** — Baseball Player
1004 Clay St, Ashland OR 97520, USA
**Guthrie, Mark A** — Baseball Player
3129 Donald Rosse Road E, Sarasota FL 34240, USA
**Guthrie, Savannah C** — Commentator
NBC-TV, News Dept, 30 Rockefeller Plaza, #270E, New York NY 10112 USA
**Guthy, Jackson** — Singer
Creative Artists Agency, 2000 Ave of Stars, #100, Los Angeles CA 90067 USA
**Gutierrez, Brock** — Football Player
1040 Pueblo Pass, Weidman MI 48893, USA
**Gutierrez, Carlos M** — Businessman
Woodrow Wilson Center, 1300 Pennsylvania Ave NW, #300, Washington DC 20004, USA
**Gutierrez, Diego** — Producer, Writer
Creative Artists Agency, 2000 Ave of Stars, #100, Los Angeles CA 90067 USA

**G**

**Gupta - Gutierrez**

**Gutierrez, F Javier** — Director
Paradigm Agency, 360 N Crescent Dr, North Building, Beverly Hills CA 90210 USA

**Gutierrez, Franklin R** — Baseball Player
5130 Preferred Place, Hilliard OH 43026, USA

**Gutierrez, Gustavo** — Theologian
Instituto Bartolome Las Casas-Rimac, Apartado 3090, Lima 100, Peru

**Gutierrez, Horacio** — Concert Pianist
C M Artists, 127 W 96th St, #13B, New York NY 10025 USA

**Gutierrez, Joaquin F (Jackie)** — Baseball Player
10631 SW 126th Ave, Miami FL 33186, USA

**Gutierrez, Ricardo (Ricky)** — Baseball Player
13803 NW 10th Court, Pembroke Pines FL 33028, USA

**Gutierrez, Sidney M** — Astronaut
324 Sarah Lane NW, Albuquerque NM 87114, USA

**Gutman, Natalia G** — Concert Cellist
Augstein & Hahn, Tal 28, 80331 Munich, Germany

**Gutman, Roy W** — Journalist
1349 Windy Hill Road, McLean VA 22102, USA

**Gutmann, Amy** — Educator
University of Pennsylvania, President's Office, 3451 Walnut St, Philadelphia PA 19104, USA

**Gutsche, Torsten** — Canoeing Athlete
Hans-Marchwitza-Ring 51, 14473 Potsdam, Germany

**Guttenberg, Steve** — Actor
Chuck Binder Mgmt, 1465 Lindacrest Dr, Beverly Hills CA 90210 USA

**Guttentag, Bill** — Director, Writer
W M E Entertainment, 9601 Wilshire Blvd, #300, Beverly Hills CA 90210 USA

**Guttman, Ronald** — Actor
Don Buchwald, 6500 Wilshire Blvd, #2200, Los Angeles CA 90048 USA

**Guy, Buddy** — Singer, Guitarist
Buddy Guy's Legends, 754 S Wabash Ave, Chicago IL 60605, USA

**Guy, Francois-Frederic** — Concert Pianist
Van Walsum Mgmt, Tower Building, 11 York Road, London SE1 7NX, England

**Guy, Jasmine** — Actress
Kass Management, 501 Santa Monica Blvd, #604, Los Angeles CA 90401, USA

**Guy, Ralph B, Jr** — Judge
US Court of Appeals, PO Box 7910, Ann Arbor MI 48107, USA

**Guy, W Ray** — Football Player
936 Central Road SW, Thomson GA 30824, USA

**Guyer, Cindy** — Model, Producer
2 Lincoln Square, New York NY 10023, USA

**Guyer, David B** — Foundation Executive
Save the Children Foundation, 514 2nd St, Owyhee NV 89832, USA

**Guyot, Paul** — Actor, Writer
Gersh Agency, 9465 Wilshire Blvd, #600, Beverly Hills CA 90212 USA

**Guyton, Myron M** — Football Player
PO Box 3481, Thomasville GA 31799, USA

**Guzman Pinal, Alejandra G** — Singer, Actress
O C E S A Seitrack Mgmt, Av Industria Militar S/N Col, Mexico City 11200, Mexico

**Guzman, Andrea** — Actress
Fox TeleColombia, Cra 50, #17-77, 4174200 Bogota, Colombia

**Guzman, Jose A** — Baseball Player
4401 Shadycreek Lane, Colleyville TX 76034, USA

**Guzman, Juan A** — Baseball Player
176 Dockside Circle, Weston FL 33327, USA

**Guzman, Luis** — Actor
PO Box 21, Peacham VT 05862, USA

**Guzman, Ryan** — Actor
Luber Rocklin Entertainment, 8530 Wilshire Blvd, #555, Beverly Hills CA 90211 USA

**Guzman, Santiago D** — Baseball Player
1712 N Douty St, Hanford CA 93230, USA

**Guzy, Carol** — Photojournalist
2412 Fort Scott Dr, Arlington VA 22202, USA

**Gwinn, Mary Ann** — Journalist
Seattle Times, Editorial Dept, 1000 Denny Way, Seattle WA 98109 USA

**Gwynn, Anthony K (Tony)** — Baseball Player, Coach
San Diego State University, Athletic Dept, San Diego CA 92182, USA

**Gwynn, Christopher K (Chris)** — Baseball Player
10975 Hillside Road, Rancho Cucamonga. CA 91737, USA

**Gwynn, Darrell** — Drag Racing Driver
Darrell Gwynn Ventures, 4850 SW 52nd St, Davie FL 33314, USA

**Gyanendra** — King, Nepal
Royal Palace, Narayanhiti, Durbag Marg, Kathmandu, Nepal

**Gyll, J Soren** — Businessman
Volvo AB, Torslanda, 405 08 Gothenborg, Sweden

**Gyllenhaal, Jake** — Actor
W M E Entertainment, 9601 Wilshire Blvd, #300, Beverly Hills CA 90210 USA

**Gyllenhaal, Maggie** — Actress
Schiff Co, 9200 Sunset Blvd, #430, West Hollywood CA 90232 USA

**Gyllenhaal, Stephen** — Director, Writer, Actor
Gersh Agency, 9465 Wilshire Blvd, #600, Beverly Hills CA 90212 USA

**Gyllenhammar, Pehr G** — Businessman
C G U, Saint Helen's, 1 Undershaft, London EC3P 3DQ, England

**Gysi, Gregor** — General Secretary, East Germany
Fraktion Die Linke, Platz der Repubik 1, 11011 Berlin, Germany

**Gyurcsany, Ferenc** — Prime Minister, Hungary
Prime Minister's Office, Kossuth Lajos Ter 1-3, 1055 Budapest, Hungary

**Gyurta, Daniel** — Swimmer
Jovo SC Veolia, Hangyalepcso Utca 6, 1121 Budapest, Hungary

| | |
|---|---|
| **Ha Jin**<br>Emory University, English Dept, Atlanta GA 30332, USA | Writer |
| **Haack, Susan**<br>University of Miami, Philosophy Dept, Coral Gables FL 33124, USA | Philosopher |
| **Haacke, Hans C**<br>Paula Cooper Gallery, 534 W 21st St, New York NY 10011, USA | Artist |
| **Haag, Anna M**<br>Ski Federation, Riksskidstadion, 791 19 Falun, Sweden | Cross Country Skier |
| **Haag, Rudolf**<br>Waldschmidt Str 4B, 83727 Schliersee-Neuhaus, Germany | Theoretical Physicist |
| **Haakon**<br>Royal Palace, Det Kongelige Slott, Drammensveien 1, 0010 Oslo, Norway | Crown Prince, Norway |
| **Haarhuis, Paul**<br>Octagon Worldwide, 1751 Pinnacle Dr, #1500, McLean VA 22102 USA | Tennis Player |
| **Haas, Bryan E (Moose)**<br>4351 E Lariat Lane, Phoenix AZ 85050, USA | Baseball Player |
| **Haas, Carl**<br>Newman-Haas Racing, 500 Tower Parkway, Lincolnshire IL 60069, USA | Auto Racing Executive |
| **Haas, Ed**<br>180 W End Ave, #11C, New York NY 10023, USA | Photographer |
| **Haas, G Edwin (Eddie)**<br>8314 Alpena Way, Louisville KY 40242, USA | Baseball Player, Manager |
| **Haas, Hunter J**<br>6424 Barkwood Lane, Dallas TX 75248, USA | Golfer |
| **Haas, Jay D**<br>4 Tuscany Court, Greer SC 29650, USA | Golfer |
| **Haas, Lukas**<br>Innovative Artists, 1505 10th St, Santa Monica CA 90401 USA | Actor |
| **Haas, R David (Dave)**<br>160 E 6th Place, Mesa AZ 85201, USA | Baseball Player |
| **Haas, Richard J**<br>361 W 36th St, #5A, New York NY 10018, USA | Artist |
| **Haas, Robert D**<br>Levi Strauss Assoc, 1155 Battery St, San Francisco CA 94111, USA | Businessman |
| **Haas, Thomas M (Tommy)**<br>4715 67th Ave Terrace W, Bradenton FL 34210, USA | Tennis Player |
| **Haas, William H**<br>Professional Golfer's Assn, PO Box 109601, Palm Beach Gardens FL 33410 USA | Golfer |
| **Haataja, Samuli (J J)**<br>Welldone Agency, Hameentie 15, 00500 Helsinki, Finland | Singer, Bassist (Crash) |
| **Haavisto, Nina**<br>Aleksanterinkatu 29 B 29, 15040 Lahti, Finland | Body Builder |
| **Habek, Janine**<br>Playboy Promotions, 2706 Media Center Dr, Los Angeles CA 90065 USA | Model |
| **Habel, Karl**<br>Reading Institute of Rehabilitation, RR 1 Box 252, Reading PA 19607, USA | Medical Researcher |
| **Habeler, Peter**<br>Apinschule Mount Everest, Haupstra 458, 6290 Mayrhofen Zillertal, Austria | Mountaineer |
| **Haber, Karen**<br>2270 N Beachwood Terrace, Los Angeles CA 90068, USA | Writer |
| **Haber, Norman**<br>Haber Inc, 470 Main Road, Towaco NJ 07082, USA | Inventor (Electromolecular Propulsion) |
| **Haberlandt, Fritzi**<br>Die Agenten, Ackerstr 11B, 10115 Berlin, Germany | Actress |
| **Habib, Brian R**<br>17235 Sangallo Lane, San Diego CA 92127, USA | Football Player |
| **Habib, Hasan**<br>World Poker Tour Enterprises, 5700 Wilshire Blvd, #350, Los Angeles CA 90036 USA | Poker Player |
| **Habib, Munir**<br>Cosmonaut Training Center, Star City, 141160 Zvezdny Gorodok, Moscow Oblast, Russia | Cosmonaut, Syria |
| **Habibie, Baharuddin Jusuf**<br>Bina Craha, Istana Negana, Jarkata 10110, Indonesia | President, Indonesia |
| **Habiger, Eugene E (Gene)**<br>University of Georgia, International Trade & Security Center, Athens GA 30602, USA | Air Force General |
| **Habumuremyi, Pierre Damien**<br>Prime Minister's Office, Kigali, Rwanda | Prime Minister, Rwanda |
| **Habyan, John G**<br>4 Dorfer Lane, Nesconset NY 11767, USA | Baseball Player |
| **Hachette, Jean-Louis**<br>Hachette Livre, 83 Ave Marceau, 75116 Paris, France | Publisher |
| **Hack, Shelley**<br>Deborah Miller, 9454 Wilshire Blvd, #715, Beverly Hills CA 90212, USA | Actress, Model |
| **Hackbart, Dale L**<br>2541 Cowley Dr, Lafayette CO 80026, USA | Football Player |
| **Hacke, Axel**<br>Bloomsbury Publishing, 50 Bedford Square, London WC1B 3DP, England | Writer |
| **Hacker, Alan**<br>Royal Academy of Music, Marylebone Road, London NW1 5HT, England | Concert Clarinetist, Composer |
| **Hacker, Joseph**<br>University of Southern California, Theater School, Los Angeles CA 90089, USA | Actor |
| **Hackett, B Dean (Dino)**<br>1152 Kearns Hackett Road, Pleasant Garden NC 27313, USA | Football Player |
| **Hackett, Grant**<br>Swimming Australia, PO Box 3286, Belconnen ACT 2617, Australia | Swimmer |
| **Hackett, James T**<br>Anadarko Petroleum, 1201 Lake Robbins Dr, Spring TX 77380, USA | Businessman |
| **Hackett, Jeff**<br>Colorado Avalanche, Pepsi Center, 1000 Chopper Circle, Denver CO 80204 USA | Ice Hockey Player |
| **Hackett, Steve**<br>Publicity Connection, Haversham Lodge, Melrose Ave, London NW2 4JS, England | Guitarist (Genesis) |
| **Hackford, Taylor**<br>2003 La Brea Terrace, Los Angeles CA 90046, USA | Director, Producer |
| **Hackl, Georg**<br>Caftehaus Soamatl, Ramsauerstr 100, 83470 Berchtesgaden-Engedey, Germany | Luge Athlete |
| **Hackman, Gene**<br>Guttman Assoc, 118 S Beverly Dr, #201, Beverly Hills CA 90212 USA | Actor |

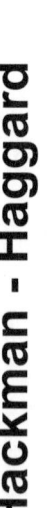

**Hackman, Luther G** — Baseball Player
1406 12th Ave N, #16G, Columbus MS 39701, USA

**Hackney, F Sheldon** — Educator
University of Pennsylvania, History Dept, Philadelphia PA 19104, USA

**Hadas, Rachel C** — Writer, Educator
838 W End Ave, #3A, New York NY 10025, USA

**Haddix, Michael M** — Football Player
465 Tanners Bridge Road NW, Monroe GA 30656, USA

**Haddock, Laura** — Actress
Independent Talent Group, 40 Whitfield St, London W1T 2RH, England

**Haddock, Marcus** — Opera Singer
Columbia Artists Mgmt Inc, 1790 Broadway, #702, New York NY 10019 USA

**Haddon, Dayle** — Actress, Model
Hyperion Books, 114 5th Ave, New York NY 10011 USA

**Hadek, Krystof** — Actor
Markham Froggatt Irwin, Julian House, 4 Windmill St, London W1P 1HF, England

**Haden, Charles E (Charlie)** — Jazz Bassist, Composer
Michael Kline Artists, PO Box 312, Cape May Point NJ 08212, USA

**Haden, Patrick C (Pat)** — Football Player, Sportscaster
1525 Wilson Ave, San Marino CA 91108, USA

**Hader, Bill** — Actor, Comedian
Odenkirk Provissiero Entertainment, 1936 N Bronson Ave, Los Angeles CA 90069 USA

**Hadfield, Chris A** — Astronaut, Canada
N A S A, Johnson Space Center, 2101 NASA Road, Houston TX 77058 USA

**Hadid, Zaha** — Pritzker Architectural Laureate
Studio 9, 10 Bowling Green Lane, London WC1R 0BD, England

**Hadjii** — Director, Writer
Paradigm Agency, 360 N Crescent Dr, North Building, Beverly Hills CA 90210 USA

**Hadl, John W** — Football Player
3700 Quail Creek Court, Lawrence KS 66047, USA

**Hadlee, Richard J** — Cricketer
PO Box 29186, Fendalton, Christchurch 8540, New Zealand

**Hadley, Stephen** — Government Official
White House, 1600 Pennsylvania Ave NW, Washington DC 20500, USA

**Hadley, Tony** — Singer (Spandau Ballet)
Tony Denton Promotions, Charter House, 157-159 High St, London N14 6BP, England

**Hadnot, J Rex, Jr** — Football Player
2677 Center Court Dr, Weston FL 33332, USA

**Hadnott, Joy** — Actress
M P G Mgmt, 1136 Roxbury Drive, Los Angeles CA 90035, USA

**Haebler, Ingrid** — Concert Pianist
5412 Saint Jakob am Thurn, Post Puch Bei Hallein, 5020 Land Salzburg, Austria

**Haefliger, Andrea** — Concert Pianist
Opus 3 Artists, 470 Park Ave S, #900N, New York NY 10016 USA

**Haegele, Patricia** — Publisher
Good Housekeeping, Publisher's Office, 300 W 57th St, New York NY 10019, USA

**Haenchen, Hartmut** — Conductor
Van Walsum Mgmt, Tower Building, 11 York Road, London SE1 7NX, England

**Haensch, Theodor W** — Nobel Physics Laureate
Ludwig-Maximilian University, Geschwister-Scholl, 80539 Munich, Germany

**Hafer, Fred D** — Businessman
G P U Inc, 300 Madison Ave, Morristown NJ 07960, USA

**Haffner, Scott R** — Basketball Player
5062 Sweetwater Dr, Noblesville IN 46062, USA

**Hafner, Dudley H** — Foundation Executive
140 Estrada Maya, Santa Fe NM 87506, USA

**Hafner, Travis L** — Baseball Player
32696 Lake Road, Avon Lake OH 44012, USA

**Hagan, Clifford O (Cliff)** — Basketball Player, Coach
8839 Lakeside Circle, Vero Beach FL 32963, USA

**Hagan, Derek S, Jr** — Football Player
14611 SW 7th St, Pembroke Pines FL 33027, USA

**Hagan, Glenn** — Basketball Player
34 Roth St, Rochester NY 14621, USA

**Hagan, Molly** — Actress
Paul Kohner, 9300 Wilshire Blvd, #555, Beverly Hills CA 90212 USA

**Hagan, Victoria** — Interior Designer
Victoria Hagan Interiors, 654 Madison Ave, #2201, New York NY 10065, USA

**Hagar, Sammy** — Singer, Songwriter, Guitarist
Front Line Mgmt, 1100 Glendon Ave, #2000, Los Angeles CA 90024 USA

**Hagee, Michael W** — Marine Corps General
Rackable Systems, 46600 Landing Parkway, Fremont CA 94538, USA

**Hagegard, Hakan** — Opera Singer
Gunnarsbyn, 670 30 Edane, Sweden

**Hageman, Fred J** — Football Player
4608 Merion Court, Lawrence KS 66047, USA

**Hagemeister, Charles C** — Vietnam War Army Hero (CMH)
1908 Canterbury Court, Leavenworth KS 66048, USA

**Hagen, Nina** — Singer
Hanns Wolters International, 501 5th Ave, #2112A, New York NY 10017, USA

**Hagen, Reinhard** — Opera Singer
I M G Artists, Hogarth Business Park, Chiswick, London W4 2TH, England

**Hagenbeck, Franklin L** — Army General, Educator
Superintendent's Office, US Military Academy, West Point NY 10996 USA

**Hager, Britt H** — Football Player
6200 Indian Canyon Dr, Austin TX 78746, USA

**Hager, Kristen** — Actress
Paul Kohner, 9300 Wilshire Blvd, #555, Beverly Hills CA 90212 USA

**Hagerman, Jamie** — Ice Hockey Player
USA Hockey, 1775 Bob Johnson Dr, Colorado Springs CO 80906 USA

**Hagerty, Julie** — Actress
Framework Entertainment, 9057 Nemo St, #C, West Hollywood CA 90069 USA

**Hagerty, Michael (Mike)** — Actor
Mark Holder Mgmt, 5225 Wilshire Blvd, #600, Los Angeles CA 90036, USA

**Haggard, Merle** — Singer, Songwriter
Department 56, 22410 Collins St, Woodland Hills CA 91367, USA

**Haggard, Piers** — Director
Casorotto Ramsay, Waverley House, 7-12 Noel St, London W1F 8GQ, England
**Hagge, Marlene Bauer** — Golfer
PO Box 570, La Quinta CA 92247, USA
**Haggerty, Dan** — Actor
Blind Squirrel Entertainment, 155 Bent Oak, Palm Beach FL 33411, USA
**Haggerty, Dylan** — Actor, Writer, Director
KillerMoxie Mgmt, 5890 W Jefferson Blvd, #J, Los Angeles CA 90016, USA
**Haggerty, Tim** — Cartoonist (Ground Zero)
PO Box 4203, New York NY 10163, USA
**Haggis, Paul E** — Director, Writer
Hwy61, 1660 Euclid, Santa Monica CA 90404, USA
**Hagins, Isaac B (Ike)** — Football Player
9008 Tudor Dr, #105, Tampa FL 33615, USA
**Hagler, Marvin** — Boxer
Valerie Sweet, 1 Design Center Place, #600, Boston MA 02210, USA
**Haglund, Kirsten** — Beauty Queen
Miss America Organization, 1370 Ave of Americas, #1600, New York NY 10019 USA
**Hagman, Niklas O** — Ice Hockey Player
48 Crimson Rose, Irvine CA 92603, USA
**Hagn, Johanna** — Judo Athlete
A S G Elsdorf, Behrgasse 6, 50198 Elsdorf, Germany
**Hagner, Meredith** — Actress
Abrams Artists, 9200 W Sunset Blvd, #1125, West Hollywood CA 90069 USA
**Hagner, Viviane** — Concert Violinist
Kirshbaum Demler, 711 W End Ave, #5KN, New York NY 10025, USA
**Hagon, Garrick** — Actor
Castaway Voice Overs, 15 Broad Court, #3, London WC2B 5QN, England
**Hague, William J** — Government Official, England
House of Commons, Westminster, London SW1A 0AA, England
**Hahn, Beatrice H** — Microbiologist
University of Alabama Medical School, Microbiology Dept, Birmingham AL 35294, USA
**Hahn, Donald A (Don)** — Baseball Player
1046 Boise Dr, Campbell CA 95008, USA
**Hahn, Erwin L** — Physicist
69 Stevenson Ave, Berkeley CA 94708, USA
**Hahn, Frank H** — Economist
16 Adams Road, Cambridge CB3 9AD, England
**Hahn, Hilary** — Concert Violinist
Lovell House, 616 Chiswick High Road, London W4 5RX, England
**Hahn, Jessica** — Model, Actress
6345 Balboa Blvd, #375, Encino CA 91316, USA
**Hahn, Joseph** — DJ Musician (Linkin Park)
United Talent Agency, U T A Plaza, 9336 Civic Center Dr, Beverly Hills CA 90210 USA
**Hahn, Kathryn** — Actress
Gersh Agency, 41 Madison Ave, #3301, New York NY 10010 USA
**Haid, Charles** — Actor, Director
4376 Forman Ave, Toluca Lake CA 91602, USA
**Haiduk, Stacy** — Actress
Stone Manners Salners, 9911 W Pico Blvd, #1400, Los Angeles CA 90035 USA
**Haig, Matt** — Writer
A P Watt, 20 John St, London WC1N 2DR, England , USA
**Haig, Sid** — Actor
Don Buchwald, 6500 Wilshire Blvd, #2200, Los Angeles CA 90048 USA
**Haigh, Juliette** — Rowing Athlete
West End Rowing Club, 26 Saunders Place, Avondale, Auckland 1026, New Zealand
**Haight, Michael (Mike)** — Football Player
2401 Biltmore Lane, Coralville IA 52241, USA
**Haignere, Jean-Pierre** — Spatinaut, France
C N E S, 2 Place Maurice Quentin, 75039 Paris Cedeux, France
**Hailemaria-Mariam Desalegn** — Prime Minister, Ethiopia
Prime Minister's Office, PO Box 1031, Addis Ababa, Ethiopia
**Hailey, Cedric (K-Ci)** — Singer (Jodeci, Ki-Ci & JoJo)
Red Entertainment Agency, 505 8th Ave, #1004, New York NY 10018, USA
**Hailey, Joel L (JoJo)** — Singer (Jodeci, K-Ci & JoJo)
Creative Artists Agency, 2000 Ave of Stars, #100, Los Angeles CA 90067 USA
**Hailey, Leisha** — Singer (Murmurs), Songwriter, Actress
Innovative Artists, 1505 10th St, Santa Monica CA 90401 USA
**Hailston, Earl B** — Marine Corps General
Commanding General, Marine Force Central Asia, HqUSMC, Washington DC 20380, USA
**Haines, Randa** — Director
1429 Avon Park Terrace, Los Angeles CA 90026, USA
**Hairston, Carl B** — Football Player, Coach
9023 Gleneagle Dr, Blaine WA 98230, USA
**Hairston, Jerry W, Jr** — Baseball Player
6 Austringer Court, Pikesville MD 21208, USA
**Hairston, Jerry W, Sr** — Baseball Player
7831 W Peace Pipe Road, Tucson AZ 85743, USA
**Hairston, Scott A** — Baseball Player
4658 S Banning Dr, Gilbert AZ 85297, USA
**Haise, Fred W, Jr** — Astronaut, Test Pilot
PO Box 5765, Pasadena TX 77508, USA
**Haislett, Nicole** — Swimmer
275 N Poplar St, Massapequa NY 11758, USA
**Haislip, Marcus L** — Basketball Player
Milwaukee Bucks, Bradley Center, 1001 N 4th St, #2, Milwaukee WI 53203 USA
**Haith, Frank** — Basketball Coach
University of Missouri, Athletic Dept, Columbia MO 65211, USA
**Haitink, Bernard J H** — Conductor
Askonas Holt, Lincoln House, 300 High Holborn, London WC1V 7JH, England
**Haje, Khrystyne** — Actress
C E S D, 10635 Santa Monica Blvd, #130, Los Angeles CA 90025 USA
**Hajek, Andreas** — Rowing Athlete
Weissbundenweg 18, 06128 Halle/Saale, Germany
**Haji-Sheikh, Ali** — Football Player
550 S Spinningwheel Lane, Bloomfield Township MI 48304, USA

| | |
|---|---|
| **Hakkinen, Henri**<br>Joensuun Ampujat Ry, Sepankatu 18A B15, 80110 Joensuu, Finland | Marksman |
| **Hakkinen, Mika P**<br>Le Scguylkill, Blvd de Suisse 8, 98000 Monte Carlo, Monaco | Auto Racing Driver |
| **Halama, John T**<br>7615 Fort Hamilton Parkway, Brooklyn NY 11228, USA | Baseball Player |
| **Halas, John**<br>Educational Film Center, 5-7 Kean St, London WC2B 4AT, England | Animator |
| **Halbert, Charles P (Chuck)**<br>100 E Whidbey Ave, #35, Oak Harbor WA 98277, USA | Basketball Player |
| **Haldeman, Charles (Ed), Jr**<br>McGraw-Hill, 1221 Avenue of Americas, #4700, New York NY 10020, USA | Financier, Government Official |
| **Haldorson, Burdette (Burdie)**<br>2868 Stonewall Heights, Colorado Springs CO 80909, USA | Basketball Player |
| **Hale, Alan**<br>Southwest Space Research Institute, 15 E Spur Road, Cloudcraft NM 88317, USA | Astronomer |
| **Hale, Amanda**<br>Gordon & French, 12-13 Poland St, London W1F 8QB, England | Actress |
| **Hale, Barbara**<br>PO Box 6061-261, Sherman Oaks CA 91413, USA | Actress |
| **Hale, David**<br>3470 Cortina Dr, Colorado Springs CO 80918, USA | Ice Hockey Player |
| **Hale, David R (Dave)**<br>1204 S Maple St, #B, Ottawa KS 66067, USA | Football Player |
| **Hale, Georgina**<br>74A Saint John's Wood, High St, London NW8, England | Actress |
| **Hale, John S**<br>2200 Pine St, Bakersfield CA 93301, USA | Baseball Player |
| **Hale, Lucy K**<br>W M E Entertainment, 9601 Wilshire Blvd, #300, Beverly Hills CA 90210 USA | Actress |
| **Hale, Robert H (Bob)**<br>616 Overhill Ave, Park Ridge IL 60068, USA | Baseball Player |
| **Hale, Tony**<br>United Talent Agency, U T A Plaza, 9336 Civic Center Dr, Beverly Hills CA 90210 USA | Actor |
| **Hale, Walter W (Chip)**<br>190 Driftwood Court, Aptos CA 95003, USA | Baseball Player |
| **Haley, Charles L**<br>3787 Royal Cove Dr, Dallas TX 75229, USA | Football Player |
| **Haley, G Richard (Dick), Jr**<br>5248 Shoreline Circle, Sanford FL 32771, USA | Football Player |
| **Haley, Jackie Earle**<br>Leslie Allan-Rice Mgmt, 1007 Maybrooke Dr, Beverly Hills CA 90210, USA | Actor |
| **Haley, Jermaine**<br>16806 Heather Knolls Place, Hamilton VA 20158, USA | Football Player |
| **Haley, Shay**<br>Virgin Records, 338 N Foothill Road, Beverly Hills CA 90210 USA | Singer, Rap Artist (NERD) |
| **Haley, Todd**<br>Pittsburgh Steelers, 3400 S Water St, Pittsburgh PA 15203 USA | Football Coach |
| **Halford, Robert J A (Rob)**<br>Trinifold Mgmt, 12 Oval Road, Camden, London NW1 7DH, England | Singer (Judas Priest) |
| **Halfpenny, Jill**<br>Ken McReddie Assoc, 101 Finsbury Pavement, London EC2A 1RS, England | Actress |
| **Halfvarson, Eric F**<br>1264 Harwood Road, #100, Bedford, TX 76021, USA | Opera Singer |
| **Hali, Tamba B**<br>13227 Outlook Dr, Leawood KS 66209, USA | Football Player |
| **Halicki, Edward L (Ed)**<br>19605 Paddlewheel Lane, Reno NV 89521, USA | Baseball Player |
| **Halimon, Shaler**<br>9535 SW Millen Dr, Portland OR 97224, USA | Basketball Player |
| **Hall Greff, Kaye**<br>906 3rd St, Mukilteo WA 98275, USA | Swimmer |
| **Hall, Albert**<br>1628 Spaulding Ishkooda Road, Birmingham AL 35211, USA | Baseball Player |
| **Hall, Albert**<br>Stone Manners Salners, 9911 W Pico Blvd, #1400, Los Angeles CA 90035 USA | Actor |
| **Hall, Andrew C (Drew)**<br>4107 Spreading Oaks Court, Waxhaw NC 28173, USA | Baseball Player |
| **Hall, Anthony Michael**<br>I C M Partners, 10250 Constellation Blvd, #900, Los Angeles CA 90067 USA | Actor, Comedian |
| **Hall, Arsenio**<br>Career Mgmt, 9229 Sunset Blvd, #720, West Hollywood CA 90069, USA | Actor, Producer, Writer |
| **Hall, Brad, II**<br>W M E Entertainment, 9601 Wilshire Blvd, #300, Beverly Hills CA 90210 USA | Actor, Comedian |
| **Hall, Bridget**<br>I M G Models, 304 Park Ave S, #PH N, New York NY 10010 USA | Model |
| **Hall, Bruce**<br>Front Line Mgmt, 1100 Glendon Ave, #2000, Los Angeles CA 90024 USA | Guitarist (REO Speedwagon) |
| **Hall, Bug**<br>Glick Agency, 1321 7th St, #203, Santa Monica CA 90401 USA | Actor |
| **Hall, Charles**<br>Basic Designs, 5815 Bennett Valley Road, Santa Rosa CA 95404, USA | Inventor (Waterbed) |
| **Hall, Charles L (Charlie)**<br>602 Lavaca St, Yaokum TX 77995, USA | Football Player |
| **Hall, Daryl F**<br>Doyle-Kos Entertainment, 1 Penn Plaza, 2107, New York, NY 10119, USA | Singer (Hall & Oates), Songwriter |
| **Hall, DeAngelo E**<br>5553 Legends Dr, Braselton GA 30517, USA | Football Player |
| **Hall, Deidre**<br>PO Box 715, 11041 Santa Monica Blvd, Los Angeles CA 90078, USA | Actress |
| **Hall, Delton D**<br>9 Mystic Court, Greensboro NC 27406, USA | Football Player |
| **Hall, Donald**<br>Eagle Point Farm, Wilmot NH 03287, USA | Writer |
| **Hall, Donald J**<br>Hallmark Cards, 2501 McGee St, Kansas City MO 64108, USA | Businessman |

**Hall, Donald R (Dino)** — Football Player
355 Chestnut Neck Road, Port Republic NJ 08241, USA
**Hall, Esther** — Actress
United Agents, 12-26 Lexington St, London W1F 0LE, England
**Hall, Fawn** — Government Secretary
9008 Norma Place, West Hollywood CA 90069, USA
**Hall, Galen** — Football Player, Coach
Pennsylvania State University, Athletic Dept, Greenberg Complex, University Park PA 16802, USA
**Hall, Gary** — Swimmer
151 Kahiki Dr, Tavernier FL 33070, USA
**Hall, Gary, Jr** — Swimmer
2409 E Luke Ave, Phoenix AZ 85016, USA
**Hall, Glenn H** — Ice Hockey Player
PO Box 2483, Main Station, Stony Plain AB T7Z 1X, Canada
**Hall, Hanna** — Actress
Glick Agency, 1321 7th St, #203, Santa Monica CA 90401, USA
**Hall, James E (Jim)** — Auto Racing Driver, Executive
Jim Hall Kart Racing School, 1555 Morse Ave, #G, Ventura CA 93003, USA
**Hall, James S (Jim)** — Jazz Guitarist
Jazz Tree, 211 Thompson St, #LD, New York NY 10012, USA
**Hall, Jerry** — Model, Actress
Ford Models, 9200 Sunset Blvd, #805, West Hollywood CA 90069, USA
**Hall, Jimmie R** — Baseball Player
8622 Carter Grove Dr, Elm City NC 27822, USA
**Hall, Joe B** — Basketball Coach
Central Bank & Trust Co, 300 W Vine St, #3, Lexington KY 40507, USA
**Hall, John L** — Nobel Physics Laureate
3748 Davidson Place, Boulder CO 80305, USA
**Hall, Joseph G (Joe)** — Baseball Player
961 Preachers Mill Road, Clarksville TN 37042, USA
**Hall, Kevan** — Fashion Designer
Kevan Hall Studio, 756 S Spring St, #11E, Los Angeles CA 90014, USA
**Hall, Kristen** — Singer, Guitarist (Sugarland)
Gail Gelman Mgmt, 23852 Pacific Coast Highway, #920, Malibu CA 90265, USA
**Hall, Lani** — Singer
31930 Pacific Coast Highway, Malibu CA 90265, USA
**Hall, Lawrence** — Physicist
University of California, Physics Dept, Berkeley CA 94720, USA
**Hall, Lemanski S** — Football Player
171 Hillhaven Lane, Franklin TN 37064, USA
**Hall, Leon L L** — Football Player
2343 Clydes Crossing, Cincinnati OH 45244, USA
**Hall, Lloyd M, Jr** — Religious Leader
Congregation Christian Church Assn, PO Box 1620, Oak Creek MI 53154, USA
**Hall, M Darren** — Baseball Player
5008 Townsend Dr, Flower Mound TX 75028, USA
**Hall, Mark** — Singer (Casting Crowns)
Proper Mgmt, PO Box 150867, Nashville TN 37215, USA
**Hall, Michael C** — Actor
Hamilton Hodell, 66-68 Margaret St, #500, London W1W 8SR, England
**Hall, Nigel J** — Artist
11 Kensington Park Gardens, London W11 3HD, England
**Hall, Peter R F** — Director
68 Lamont Road, London SW10 0HX, England
**Hall, Philip Baker** — Actor
Paradigm Agency, 360 N Crescent Dr, North Building, Beverly Hills CA 90210 USA
**Hall, Reamy** — Actress
Amsel Eisenstadt Frazier, 5055 Wilshire Blvd, #865, Los Angeles CA 90036 USA
**Hall, Rebecca M** — Actress
Julian Belfrage Assoc, 9 Argyll St, #300, London W1F 7TG, England
**Hall, Regina** — Actress
I C M Partners, 10250 Constellation Blvd, #900, Los Angeles CA 90067 USA
**Hall, Richard W (Dick)** — Baseball Player
403 Plumbridge Court, #202, Lutherville Timonium MD 21093, USA
**Hall, Robert David** — Actor
Gage Group, 14724 Ventura Blvd, #505, Sherman Oaks CA 91403 USA
**Hall, Robert E (Bob)** — Economist
Stanford University, Hoover Institution, Stanford CA 94305, USA
**Hall, Robert N** — Inventor (Semiconductor Injection Laser)
325 Kings Road, #8, Schenectady NY 12304, USA
**Hall, Ronald G (Ronnie)** — Football Player
14008 NE 162nd St, Kearney MO 64060, USA
**Hall, Samuel (Sam)** — Diver
5759 Wilcke Way, Dayton OH 45459, USA
**Hall, Sonny** — Labor Leader
AFL-CIO, 815 16th St, NW, Washington DC 20006, USA
**Hall, Thomas E (Tom)** — Baseball Player
3592 Lillian St, Riverside CA 92504, USA
**Hall, Thomas F (Tom)** — Football Player
PO Box 60441, Longmeadow MA 01116, USA
**Hall, Toby J** — Baseball Player
3814 Evergreen Oaks Dr, Lutz FL 33558, USA
**Hall, Tom T** — Singer, Guitarist, Songwriter
John D Lentz, PO Box 198888, Nashville TN 37219, USA
**Hall, Trevor** — Singer, Guitarist, Songwriter
Monterey International, 200 W Superior St, #202, Chicago IL 60654 USA
**Hall, Willie C** — Football Player
717 S Hacienda St, Anaheim CA 92804, USA
**Hall, Windlan E** — Football Player
13609 Pleasant Lane, Burnsville MN 55337, USA
**Halla, Brian L** — Businessman
National Semiconductor, 2900 Semiconductor Dr, Santa Clara CA 95051, USA
**Halladay, H Leroy (Roy), III** — Baseball Player
18509 Council Crest Dr, Odessa FL 33556, USA
**Halldorson, Daniel A (Dan)** — Golfer
209 South Road, Cambridge IL 61238, USA

**H**

**Hallen, Robert J (Bob)** — Football Player
7052 Rushmore Way, Painesville OH 44077, USA
**Haller, Fritz** — Furniture Designer, Architect
U S M Berlin, Franzosische Str 48, 10117 Berlin, Germany
**Haller, Gordon** — Triathlete
16 Thetford Dr, Bella Vista AR 72715, USA
**Haller, Kevin** — Ice Hockey Player
Hockey Ministries, 1100 Dela Gauchetiere W, Montreal QC H3B 2S2, Canada
**Hallett, Bob** — Singer (Great Big Sea)
Fleming Assoc, 167 Little Lake Dr, Ann Arbor MI 48103, USA
**Hallinan, Joseph T (Joe)** — Journalist, Writer
Random House, 1745 Broadway, #1800, New York NY 10019 USA
**Halliwell, Geri** — Singer (Spice Girls)
19 Entertainment, 35-37 Parkgate Road, #32/33, London SW11 4NP, England
**Hallman, Tom, Jr** — Journalist
Portland Oregonian, Editorial Dept, 1320 SW Broadway, Portland OR 97201, USA
**Hallock, Bob** — Auto Racing Driver
2185 Santa Ana Ave, Costa Mesa CA 92627, USA
**Hallock, Ty E** — Football Player
3676 Hunters Way Dr SE, Ada MI 49301, USA
**Hallstrom, Lasse** — Director
LaHa Films, 137 W 57th St, #700, New York NY 10019, USA
**Hallstrom, Ronald D (Ron)** — Football Player
Hallstrom's Marina, PO Box 379, Woodruff WI 54568, USA
**Hallyday, Estelle** — Model
I M G Models, 304 Park Ave S, #PH N, New York NY 10010 USA
**Hallyday, Johnny** — Singer, Actor
Voyez Mon Agent, 20 Ave Rapp, 75007 Paris, France
**Halmich, Regina** — Boxer
Gunter Halmich, Inselstr 3, 76189 Karlsruhe, Germany
**Halperin, Bertrand I** — Physicist
Harvard University, Lyman Physics Laboratory, Cambridge MA 02138, USA
**Halpern, Daniel** — Writer
57 Mountain Ave, Princeton NJ 08540, USA
**Halpern, Jack** — Chemist
5801 S Dorchester Ave, #4A, Chicago IL 60637, USA
**Halpern, James S** — Judge
US Tax Court, 400 2nd St NW, Washington DC 20217, USA
**Halpern, Jeff** — Ice Hockey Player
9212 Sprinklewood Lane, Potomac MD 20854, USA
**Halsell, James D, Jr** — Astronaut
257 River Cove Road, Huntsville AL 35811, USA
**Halsey, Darcy** — Actress
Arts & Letters Mgmt, 7715 W Sunset Blvd, #208, Los Angeles CA 90046, USA
**Halton, Thomas L** — Nutritionist
Harvard Public Health School, Nutrition Dept, 655 Huntington, Boston MA 02115, USA
**Halver, John E** — Biochemist, Nutritionist
16502 41st Ave NE, Lake Forest Park WA 98155, USA
**Halverson, R Dean** — Football Player
45971 State Highway 74, Palm Desert CA 92260, USA
**Halvorsen, Gail** — Berlin Airlift Air Force Hero
1525 W Dove Way, Amado AZ 85645, USA
**Ham, Carter F** — Army General
Commander, US Africa Command, APO AE 09751 USA
**Ham, Jack R** — Football Player
Ham Enterprises, 540 Lindbergh Dr, Coraopolis PA 15108, USA
**Ham, Kenneth T** — Astronaut
32 Upshur Road, Annapolis MD 21402, USA
**Hamada, Hiroshi** — Businessman
Ricoh Co, 1-15-5 Minami-Aoyama, Minatoku, Tokyo 107 8544, Japan
**Hamari, Julia** — Opera Singer
Max Brodweg 14, 70437 Stuttgart, Germany
**Hambling, Maggi** — Artist
Morley College, Westminster Bridge Road, London SE1 7HT, England
**Hambright, Roger D** — Baseball Player
8709 NE 37th Ave, Vancouver WA 98665, USA
**Hambrock, John** — Cartoonist
King Features Syndicate, 300 W 57th St, #1500, New York NY 10019 USA
**Hambuchen, Fabian** — Gymnast
Pfaffenrain 35, 35585 Wetzlar, Germany
**Hamburg, John** — Director, Producer, Writer
W M E Entertainment, 9601 Wilshire Blvd, #300, Beverly Hills CA 90210 USA
**Hamburg, Margaret (Peggy)** — Government Official
Food & Drug Administration, 10903 New Hampshire Ave, Silver Spring MD 20903, USA
**Hamburger, Cao** — Director
Anonymous Content, 3532 Hayden Ave, Culver City CA 90232 USA
**Hamdallah, Rami** — Prime Minister, Palestine
Prime Minister's Office, Gaza City, Gaza Strip, Palestine, Israel
**Hamed, Naseem (Prince)** — Boxer
Ciaralinn, Woodlands Road W, Virginia Water, Surrey GU25 4PL, England
**Hamel, Dean** — Football Player
1007 Hawthorne Dr NE, Lenoir NC 28645, USA
**Hamel, Peter Michael** — Composer
Bergsedter Markt 12, 22395 Hamburg, Germany
**Hamel, Veronica** — Actress, Model
12305 Fifth Helen Dr, Brentwood CA 94513, USA
**Hamelin, Charles** — Speed Skater
Club Montreal, 930 Av Roland-Beaudin, Quebec QC G1V 4H8, Canada
**Hamelin, Francois** — Speed Skater
Speed Skating Canada, 2781 Lancaster Road, #402, Ottawa ON K1B 1A7, Canada
**Hamelin, Robert J (Bob)** — Baseball Player
51 Patton Court SE, Concord NC 28025, USA
**Hamhuis, Dan** — Ice Hockey Player
9553 Hampton Reserve Dr, Brentwood TN 37027, USA
**Hamill, Dorothy S** — Figure Skater
10045 Red Run Blvd, #250, Owings Mills MD 21117, USA

**Hamill, Mark**
Danis Panaro Nist Talent, 9201 W Olympic Blvd, Beverly Hills CA 90212, USA — Actor

**Hamill, W Pete**
8 Whiskey Hill Road, Wallkill NY 12589, USA — Writer, Editor

**Hamilton**
Agency Group Ltd, 361-373 City Road, London EC1V 1PQ, England — Guitarist (British Sea Power)

**Hamilton, Allan G (Al)**
2452 115th St, Edmonton AB T6J 3S1, Canada — Ice Hockey Player

**Hamilton, Ann**
64 Smith Place, Columbus OH 43201, USA — Sculptor

**Hamilton, Anthony**
Special Assignment Operations, 269 S Beverly Drive, #1173, Beverly Hills CA 90212, USA — Singer, Rap Artist

**Hamilton, Ashley G**
Mavrick Artists Agency, 6100 Wilshire Blvd, #550, Los Angeles CA 90048, USA — Actor

**Hamilton, Benjamin T (Ben)**
5240 Golden Ridge Court, Parker CO 80134, USA — Football Player

**Hamilton, C Robert (Bobby), Jr**
Motorsports Decisions, 1435 W Morehead St, #190, Charlotte NC 28208, USA — Auto Racing Driver

**Hamilton, Clyde H**
US Appeals Court, Federal Courthouse, 1100 Laurel St, Columbia SC 29201, USA — Judge

**Hamilton, Conrad**
19619 N 35th Place, Phoenix AZ 85050, USA — Football Player

**Hamilton, Darryl Q**
4721 Southwind Dr, Baton Rouge LA 70816, USA — Baseball Player

**Hamilton, David**
41 Blvd du Montparnasse, 75006 Paris, France — Photographer

**Hamilton, David E (Dave)**
9464 Cherry Hills Lane, San Ramon CA 94583, USA — Baseball Player

**Hamilton, De'Marr**
One Moment Mgmt, PO Box 55156, Sherman Oaks CA 91413 USA — Drummer (Plain White T's), Songwriter

**Hamilton, Foreststorn (Chico)**
Chico Hamilton Productions, 321 E 45th St, #PH A, New York NY 10017, USA — Jazz Drummer

**Hamilton, George**
Talent Works, 3500 W Olive Ave, #1400, Burbank CA 91505 USA — Actor

**Hamilton, George, IV**
Joe Taylor Artist Agency, 2802 Columbine Place, Nashville TN 37204 USA — Singer, Songwriter, Guitarist

**Hamilton, Guy**
Palma de Mallorca, Apartado III, 01753 Andratz, Baleric Islands, Spain — Director

**Hamilton, Harry E**
PO Box 986, Lemont PA 16851, USA — Football Player

**Hamilton, Hugo**
Harper Collins Publishers, 10 E 53rd St, Cellar 1, New York NY 10022 USA — Writer

**Hamilton, J Joseph (Joey)**
4035 Wellington Mist Point, Duluth GA 30097, USA — Baseball Player

**Hamilton, Jane**
Doubleday Press, 1540 Broadway, New York NY 10036, USA — Writer

**Hamilton, Jeffrey R (Jeff)**
2485 Golfview Circle, Fenton MI 48430, USA — Baseball Player

**Hamilton, Josh**
Paradigm Agency, 360 N Crescent Dr, North Building, Beverly Hills CA 90210 USA — Actor

**Hamilton, Joshua H (Josh)**
4317 Willowdale Court, Apex NC 27539, USA — Baseball Player

**Hamilton, Keith L**
6 Bonnieview Lane, Towaco NJ 07082, USA — Football Player

**Hamilton, Laird J**
Ziffren Brittenham Branca, 1801 Century Park W, #700, Los Angeles CA 90067 USA — Surfer

**Hamilton, Laurell K**
PO Box 190306, Saint Louis MO 63119, USA — Writer

**Hamilton, Leonard**
Florida State University, Athletic Dept, Tallahassee FL 32306, USA — Basketball Coach

**Hamilton, Lewis C D**
Lewis Hamilton Motorsports, 32 Saint James's St, London SW1A 1HD, England — Auto Racing Driver

**Hamilton, Linda**
Innovative Artists, 1505 10th St, Santa Monica CA 90401 USA — Actress

**Hamilton, Lisa Gay**
Paradigm Agency, 360 N Crescent Dr, North Building, Beverly Hills CA 90210 USA — Actress

**Hamilton, Marcus**
12225 Ranburne Road, Charlotte NC 28227, USA — Cartoonist (Dennis the Menace)

**Hamilton, Melinda Page**
Don Buchwald, 6500 Wilshire Blvd, #2200, Los Angeles CA 90048 USA — Actress

**Hamilton, Michael**
2012 N 19th St, Boise ID 83702, USA — Artist

**Hamilton, Milo**
2001 Holcombe Blvd, #901, Houston TX 77030, USA — Sportscaster

**Hamilton, Page**
Maine Road Mgmt, 195 Chrystie St, #901F, New York NY 10002, USA — Guitarist (Band of Susans, Helmet)

**Hamilton, Richard C**
2301 W Big Beaver Road, #535, Troy MI 48084, USA — Basketball Player

**Hamilton, Roy Lee**
1644 Del Mar Road, Oceanside CA 92057, USA — Basketball Player

**Hamilton, Ruffin, III**
236 Sumac Trail, Woodstock GA 30188, USA — Football Player

**Hamilton, Scott S**
2451 Hidden River Lane, Franklin TN 37069, USA — Figure Skater

**Hamilton, Suzanna**
Julian Belfrage Assoc, 9 Argyll St, #300, London W1F 7TG, England — Actress

**Hamilton, Thomas W (Tom)**
Front Line Mgmt, 1100 Glendon Ave, #2000, Los Angeles CA 90024 USA — Bassist (Aerosmith)

**Hamilton, Todd**
2004 Rock Dove Court, Westlake TX 76262, USA — Golfer

**Hamilton, Tom**
31704 Sailors Cove, Avon Lake OH 44012, USA — Sportscaster

**Hamilton, Tyler**
32 Russell St, Marblehead MA 01945, USA — Cyclist

**Hamilton, Victoria**
Paradigm Agency, 360 Park Ave S, #1600, New York NY 10010 USA — Actress

# H

**Hamill - Hamilton**

| | |
|---|---|
| **Hamilton, Wendy**<br>Playboy Promotions, 2706 Media Center Dr, Los Angeles CA 90065 USA | Model, Actress |
| **Hamilton, William**<br>17 E 95th St, #3F, New York NY 10128, USA | Cartoonist, Writer |
| **Hamlett, Denis**<br>Chicago Fire, 700 S Harlem Ave, Bridgeview IL 60455 USA | Soccer Coach |
| **Hamlin, Catherine**<br>Addis Adaba Fistula Hospital, PO Box 5066 Turramurra NSW 2074, Australia | Obstetrician, Gynaecologist |
| **Hamlin, Harry**<br>Paradigm Agency, 360 N Crescent Dr, North Building, Beverly Hills CA 90210 USA | Actor |
| **Hamlin, J Dennis A (Denny)**<br>19135 Pennsylvanis Point Dr, Cornelius NC 29031, USA | Auto Racing Driver |
| **Hamlin, Kenneth L (Ken)**<br>5242 County Road 413, McMillan MI 49853, USA | Baseball Player |
| **Hamlin, Shelley**<br>4311 W Ardmore Road, Laveen AZ 85339, USA | Golfer |
| **Hamm, Jon**<br>Creative Artists Agency, 2000 Ave of Stars, #100, Los Angeles CA 90067 USA | Actor |
| **Hamm, Mia**<br>613 15th St, Manhattan Beach CA 90266, USA | Soccer Player, Model |
| **Hamm, Morgan**<br>Sandy Hamm, W230S3827 Milky Way Road, Waukesha WI 53189, USA | Gymnast |
| **Hamm, Nick**<br>I C M Partners, 10250 Constellation Blvd, #900, Los Angeles CA 90067 USA | Director |
| **Hamm, Paul**<br>Sandy Hamm, W230S3827 Milky Way Road, Waukesha WI 53189, USA | Gymnast |
| **Hammaker, C Atlee**<br>12740 Manning Lane, Knoxville TN 37932, USA | Baseball Player |
| **Hammel, Eugene A**<br>2332 Piedmont Ave, Berkeley CA 94720, USA | Anthropologist |
| **Hammell, Penny**<br>4786 Orchard Lane, Delray Beach FL 33445, USA | Golfer |
| **Hammer**<br>Media Artists Group, 8222 Melrose Ave, #203, Los Angeles CA 90048 USA | Rap Artist |
| **Hammer, A J**<br>CNN-TV, 190 Marietta Ave SW, Atlanta GA 30303 USA | Commentator |
| **Hammer, Armie**<br>W M E Entertainment, 9601 Wilshire Blvd, #300, Beverly Hills CA 90210 USA | Actor |
| **Hammer, Jan, Jr**<br>2 W 45th St, #1102, New York NY 10036, USA | Jazz Keyboardist, Composer |
| **Hammer, Sarah K**<br>1960 Knoxville Ave, Long Beach CA 90815, USA | Cyclist |
| **Hammer, Victor S**<br>Gersh Agency, 9465 Wilshire Blvd, #600, Beverly Hills CA 90212 USA | Cinematographer |
| **Hammergren, John H**<br>McKesson Inc, 1 Post St, #1800, San Francisco CA 94104, USA | Businessman |
| **Hammes, Gordon G**<br>11 Staley Place, Durham NC 27705, USA | Chemist |
| **Hammett, Kirk**<br>2505 Divisadero St, San Francisco CA 94115, USA | Guitarist (Metallica) |
| **Hammock, Robert W (Robby)**<br>8644 S 21st Place, Phoenix AZ 85042, USA | Baseball Player |
| **Hammon, Becky**<br>San Antonio Silver Stars, 1 AT&T Center, San Antonio TX 78219 USA | Basketball Player |
| **Hammond, Albert, Jr**<br>Albert Hammond Music, 10100 Santa Moncia Blvd, #1050, Los Angeles CA 90067, USA | Guitarist (Strokes) |
| **Hammond, Christopher A (Chris)**<br>116144 Palomino Valley Road, San Diego CA 92127, USA | Baseball Player |
| **Hammond, Darrell**<br>W M E Entertainment, 1325 Ave of Americas, New York NY 10019 USA | Actor, Comedian |
| **Hammond, Donnie**<br>1642 Bridgewater Dr, Lake Mary FL 32746, USA | Golfer |
| **Hammond, Fred**<br>Face to Face Ministries, 21421 Hilltop St, #20, Southfield MI 48033, USA | Singer, Bassist (Radical for Christ) |
| **Hammond, Gary A**<br>5321 Seascape Lane, Plano TX 75093, USA | Football Player |
| **Hammond, George S**<br>27 Timber Lane, Painted Post NY 14870, USA | Chemist |
| **Hammond, Joan H**<br>Private Bag 101, Geelong Mail Center VIC 3221, Australia | Opera Singer |
| **Hammond, John P**<br>Rosebud Agency, PO Box 170429, San Francisco CA 94117 USA | Singer, Guitarist |
| **Hammond, Josh**<br>Hines & Hurt Entertainment, 1213 W Magnolia Blvd, Burbank CA 91506, USA | Actor, Producer |
| **Hammond, Julian H (Julie)**<br>2943 S Ulster St, Denver CO 80231, USA | Basketball Player |
| **Hammond, L Blaine, Jr**<br>Gulfstream Aircraft, 4150 E Donald Douglas Dr, #926, Long Beach CA 90808, USA | Astronaut |
| **Hammond, Richard**<br>Independent Talent Group, 40 Whitfield St, London W1T 2RH, England | Actor, Producer |
| **Hammond, Robert D**<br>219 Del Mesa Carmel, Carmel CA 93923, USA | Army General |
| **Hammond, Robert L (Bobby)**<br>2535 Butler St, East Elmhurst NY 11369, USA | Football Player |
| **Hammond, Steven B (Steve)**<br>11104 Lake Butler Road, Windermere FL 34786, USA | Baseball Player |
| **Hammond, Tom**<br>NBC-TV, Sports Dept, 30 Rockefeller Plaza, #270E, New York NY 10112 USA | Sportscaster |
| **Hammonds, Bruce**<br>M B N A Corp, 1100 N King St, Wilmington DE 19884, USA | Businessman |
| **Hammonds, Jeffrey B (Jeff)**<br>2950 Meadow Lane, Weston FL 33331, USA | Baseball Player |
| **Hammonds, Tom E**<br>122 Windsor Dr, Crestview FL 32539, USA | Basketball Player |
| **Hammons, David**<br>Studio Museum in Harlem, 144 W 125th St, #200, New York NY 10027, USA | Sculptor |

Hamilton - Hammons

**Hamner, Earl, Jr** — Producer, Writer
11575 Amanda Dr, Studio City CA 91604, USA
**Hamnett, Katharine** — Fashion Designer
Aberdeen Studios, 22-24 Highbury Grove, #3D, London N5 2EA, England
**Hamon, Gwendoline** — Actress
Artmedia, 20 Ave Rapp, 75007 Paris, France
**Hamon, Lucienne** — Actress
Agents Associes, 201 Rue du Faubourg Saint Honore, 75008 Paris, France
**Hamp, Eric P** — Language Educator
1190 Railroad Trail, Beulah MI 49617, USA
**Hampe, Michael** — Director
Tiergartenstr 36, 01219 Dresden, Germany
**Hampshire, Susan** — Actress
Rob Groves Personal Management, 33 Glasshouse St, Soho London W1B 5DG, England
**Hampson, Edward G (Ted)** — Ice Hockey Player
4436 Claremore Dr, Minneapolis MN 55435, USA
**Hampson, Justin M** — Baseball Player
7018 Richmond Dr, Glen Carbon IL 62034, USA
**Hampson, Thomas** — Opera Singer
Starkfriedgasse 53, 1180 Vienna, Austria
**Hampton, Brenda** — Producer
Paradigm Agency, 360 N Crescent Dr, North Building, Beverly Hills CA 90210 USA
**Hampton, Casey, Jr** — Football Player
105 Conover Road, Pittsburgh PA 15208, USA
**Hampton, Christopher J** — Writer
Casorotto Ramsay, Waverley House, 7-12 Noel St, London W1F 8GQ, England
**Hampton, Daniel O (Dan)** — Football Player
9191 Falling Waters Dr E, Burr Ridge IL 60527, USA
**Hampton, Isaac B (Ike)** — Baseball Player
4415 E Ridge Gate Road, Anaheim CA 92807, USA
**Hampton, James** — Actor
102 Forest Hill Dr, Roanoke TX 76262, USA
**Hampton, Locksley W (Slide)** — Jazz Trombonist
Thomas Cassidy, PO Box 1311, Tucson AZ 85702 USA
**Hampton, Lorenzo T** — Football Player
16231 NW 77th Place, Hialeah FL 33016, USA
**Hampton, Mark G** — Architect
Mark Hampton Architect, 3900 Loquat Ave, Miami FL 33133, USA
**Hampton, Michael W (Mike)** — Baseball Player
8601 N 59th Place, Paradise Valley AZ 85253, USA
**Hampton, Millard** — Track Athlete
201 W Mission St, San Jose CA 95110, USA
**Hampton, Ralph C, Jr** — Religious Leader
Free Will Baptist Bible College, 3606 W End Ave, Nashville TN 37205, USA
**Hampton, Rodney C** — Football Player
5603 Grand Floral Blvd, Houston TX 77041, USA
**Hamra, Khalil** — Photojournalist
Associated Press, Editorial Dept, 450 W 33rd St, #1500, New York NY 10001 USA
**Hamri, Sanaa** — Director
Creative Artists Agency, 2000 Ave of Stars, #100, Los Angeles CA 90067 USA
**Hamrlik, Roman** — Ice Hockey Player
56 Alhambra Dr, Oceanside NY 11572, USA
**Hamulack, Tim** — Baseball Player
530 Campbell Road, York PA 17402, USA
**Han Seung-Soo** — Prime Minister, South Korea
Prime Minister's Office, 77 Sejong-no, Chongnogu, Seoul 110 760, South Korea
**Han, Jefferson Y (Jeff)** — Computer Scientist
New York University, Courant Math Sciences Institute, New York NY 10012, USA
**Hanafusa, Hidesaburo** — Microbiologist
500 E 63rd St, New York NY 10065, USA
**Hanauer, Lee E (Chip)** — Boat Racing Driver
Hanauer Enterprises, 2702 NE 88th St, Seattle WA 98115, USA
**Hanburger, Christian (Chris), Jr** — Football Player
125 Wyandot St, Darlington SC 29532, USA
**Hancock, Anthony D** — Football Player
8233 Corteland Dr, Knoxville TN 37909, USA
**Hancock, Herbert J (Herbie)** — Jazz Pianist, Composer
Red Light Mgmt, PO Box 1467, Charlottesville VA 22902, USA
**Hancock, John** — Opera Singer
Columbia Artists Mgmt Inc, 1790 Broadway, #702, New York NY 10019 USA
**Hancock, John D** — Director, Producer, Writer
7355 N Fail Road, La Porte IN 46350, USA
**Hancock, John Lee** — Director
Creative Artists Agency, 2000 Ave of Stars, #100, Los Angeles CA 90067 USA
**Hancock, Lee** — Baseball Player
8338 Brentwood Blvd, Brentwood CA 94513, USA
**Hancock, Phillip** — Golfer
3339 Handy Road, #728, Tampa FL 33618, USA
**Hancock, R Garry** — Baseball Player
2217 Greenhills Dr, Valrico FL 33596, USA
**Hancock, Sheila** — Actress, Writer
Independent Talent Group, 40 Whitfield St, London W1T 2RH, England
**Hancock, Vincent** — Marksman
168 Lee Road, #2181, Phenix City AL 36780, USA
**Hand, Elizabeth** — Writer
Editions Denoel, 9 Rue du Cherche-Midi, 75278 Paris Cedex 06, France
**Hand, Joey** — Auto Racing Driver
Joey Hand Racing, 5877 Power Inn Road, Sacramento CA 95824, USA
**Hand, Jon T** — Football Player
PO Box 40296, Indianapolis IN 46240, USA
**Hand, Richard A (Rich)** — Baseball Player
3824 Bay Court, Fort Worth TX 76179, USA
**Handelsman, Walt** — Editorial Cartoonist
Newsday, Editorial Dept, 235 Pinelawn Road, Melville NY 11747, USA
**Handford, Martin** — Cartoonist (Where's Waldo)
Walker Books, 87 Vauxhall Walk, London SE11 5HU, England

Hamner - Handford

**Handke, Peter** — Writer
Farrar Straus Giroux, 18 W 18th St, #700, New York NY 10011 USA
**Handler, Chelsea** — Actress, Comedienne
Borderline Amazing Productions, 12312 W Olympic Blvd, Los Angeles CA 90064, USA
**Handler, Daniel** — Writer
Harper Collins Publishers, 10 E 53rd St, Cellar 1, New York NY 10022 USA
**Handley, Robert R (Ray)** — Football Coach
PO Box 275, Glenbrook NV 89413, USA
**Handley, Taylor** — Actor
Paradigm Agency, 360 N Crescent Dr, North Building, Beverly Hills CA 90210 USA
**Hands, Guy** — Businessman
Terra Firma Capital, 2 More London Riverside, London SE1 2AP, England
**Hands, Terence D** — Director
Clwyd Theater Cymru, Mold, Flintshire CH7 1YA, North Wales
**Hands, William A (Bill)** — Baseball Player
PO Box 334, Orient NY 11957, USA
**Handy, James** — Actor
C E S D, 10635 Santa Monica Blvd, #130, Los Angeles CA 90025 USA
**Handy, John** — Jazz Saxophonist
Integrity Talent, 1 Westcroft Court, Cockeysville MD 21030 USA
**Haneef-Park, Tayyiba M** — Volleyball Player
USA Volleyball, 4065 Sinton Road, #200, Colorado Springs CO 80907, USA
**Haneke, Michael** — Director, Writer
Filmakademie Vienna, Metternichgasse 12, 1030 Vienna, Austria
**Haner, Martin** — Field Hockey Player
Berlin Hockey Club, Wilskistr 70, 14163 Berlin, Germany
**Hanevold, Halvard** — Biathlete
Barlindbakken 23, 1388 Borgen, Norway
**Haney, Cecil D** — Navy Admiral
Commander, Pacific Command, 250 Makalapa Dr, Pearl Harbor HI 96860 USA
**Haney, Christopher D (Chris)** — Baseball Player
PO Box 135, Barboursville VA 22923, USA
**Haney, Lee** — Body Builder
Lee Haney Enterprises, 105 Trail Point Circle, Fayetteville GA 30214, USA
**Haney, Todd M** — Baseball Player
5404 Pointwood Circle, Waco TX 76710, USA
**Hanft, Ruth S** — Medical Researcher
606 Rainier Road, Charlottesville VA 22903, USA
**Hangartner, Geoffrey T (Geoff)** — Football Player
805 Park Slope Dr, Charlotte NC 28209, USA
**Hanggi, Kristin** — Director
Wonderfalls Entertainment, 1041 N Formosa Ave, Formosa Building, Los Angeles CA 90067, USA
**Hanifan, James M (Jim)** — Football Coach
1217 Grey Fox Run, Weldon Spring MO 63304, USA
**Hanigan, Ryan M** — Baseball Player
55 Bailey Road, Andover MA 01810, USA
**Hanisch, Cornelia** — Fencer
Rosemarie Hanisch, Via San Rocco 25, 18017 Lingueglietta/Imperia, Italy
**Hankin, Larry** — Actor, Writer, Producer
Stephen James Entertainmet, 5101 Lankershim Blvd, #203, Los Angeles CA 91601, USA
**Hankinson, Tim** — Soccer Coach
Columbus Crew, 1 Black & Gold Blvd, Columbus OH 43211 USA
**Hankowsky, William** — Financier
Liberty Property Trust, 7201 Wayne Ave, Philadelphia PA 19119, USA
**Hanks, Colin** — Actor
United Talent Agency, U T A Plaza, 9336 Civic Center Dr, Beverly Hills CA 90210 USA
**Hanks, Merton E** — Football Player
62 Oakland Ave, Bloomfield NJ 07003, USA
**Hanks, Tom** — Actor, Director, Producer
Playtone Productions, PO Box 7340, Santa Monica CA 90406, USA
**Hanley, Charles** — Journalist
Associated Press, Editorial Dept, 450 W 33rd St, #1500, New York NY 10001 USA
**Hanley, Dan** — Editor
I C M Partners, 10250 Constellation Blvd, #900, Los Angeles CA 90067 USA
**Hanley, Frank** — Labor Leader
International Union of Operating Engineers, 1125 17th St NW, Washington DC 20036, USA
**Hanley, Jenny** — Actress
M G A, Southbank House, Black Prince Road, London SE1 7SJ, England
**Hanley, Kay** — Singer (Letters to Cleo)
Creamer Mgmt, 32 Oak Square Ave, Brighton MA 02135, USA
**Hanley, Richard (Dick)** — Swimmer
266 Lake Road, Hurley WI 54534, USA
**Hanlon, Edward, Jr** — Marine Corps General
US Representative NATO Military Committee, PSC 80, Box 300, APO AE 09724, USA
**Hanlon, Glenn A** — Ice Hockey Player, Coach
8781 Piney Orchard Parkway, Odenton MD 21113, USA
**Hanna, Preston L** — Baseball Player
5555 Mayfair Dr, Pensacola FL 32506, USA
**Hannah, Bob** — Baseball Coach
University of Delaware, Athletic Dept, Newark DE 19716, USA
**Hannah, Charles A (Charley)** — Football Player
PO Box 2671, Lutz FL 33548, USA
**Hannah, Daryl** — Actress, Model
Chuck Binder Mgmt, 1465 Lindacrest Dr, Beverly Hills CA 90210 USA
**Hannah, John** — Actor
Artist Rights Group, 4 Great Portland St, London W1W 8PA, England
**Hannah, John A** — Football Player
2407 Hideaway Place SE, Decatur AL 35603, USA
**Hannah, Kristin** — Writer
Saint Martin's Press, 175 5th Ave, #400, New York NY 10010 USA
**Hannah, Robert (Bob)** — Motorcycle Racing Rider
Bob Hannah Aviation, 22499 Channel Road, Caldwell ID 83607, USA
**Hannahan, John J (Jack), IV** — Baseball Player
1995 Bayard Ave, Saint Paul MN 55116, USA
**Hannan, David P (Dave)** — Ice Hockey Player
408 Timberlake Dr, Venetia PA 15367, USA

Handke - Hannan

Hannan, James J (Jim)                                                                              Baseball Player
3907 Cherry Hill Way, Annandale VA 22003, USA
Hannan, K Scott                                                                                    Ice Hockey Player
35 S Bellaire St, Denver CO 80246, USA
Hannan, Mary Claire                                                                                Costume Designer
Dattner Dispoto, 10635 Santa Monica Blvd, #165, Los Angeles CA 90025, USA
Hannawald, Sven                                                                                    Ski Jumper
W H Sport International GmbH, Im Sabel 4, 54294 Trier, Germany
Hanneman, Craig L                                                                                  Football Player
4350 Gibson Road NW, Salem OR 97304, USA
Hannibal, Lars                                                                                     Concert Guitarist
Nordskraenten 3, 2980 Kokkedal, Denmark
Hannigan, Alyson                                                                                   Actress
A P A Talent/Literary Agency, 405 S Beverly Dr, #300, Beverly Hills CA 90212 USA
Hannigan, Barbara                                                                                  Opera Singer, Conductor
Harrison/Parrott, 5-6 Albion Court, London W6 0QT, England
Hanning, Rob                                                                                       Producer, Writer
Ziffren Brittenham Branca, 1801 Century Park W, #700, Los Angeles CA 90067 USA
Hannity, Sean                                                                                      Commentator
Hannity & Colmes, Fox-TV, News Dept, 1211 Ave of Americas, New York NY 10036, USA
Hannon, Thomas E (Tom)                                                                             Football Player
17398 Roxbury Ave, Southfield MI 48075, USA
Hannula, Dick                                                                                      Swimming Coach
1021 Westley Dr, Tacoma WA 98465, USA
Hannum, Taimie                                                                                     Actress, Model
7095 Hollywood Blvd, #762, Los Angeles CA 90028, USA
Hano, Gregg R                                                                                      Publisher
Popular Science, Publisher's Office, 2 Park Ave, #900, New York NY 10016, USA
Hanold, Marilyn                                                                                    Model, Actress
Playboy Promotions, 2706 Media Center Dr, Los Angeles CA 90065 USA
Hanover, Donna                                                                                     Commentator
Helen Brezinsky, 1301 Ave of Americas, New York NY 10019, USA
Hanrahan, Joel R                                                                                   Baseball Player
2026 Cashen Wood Dr, Fernandina Beach FL 32034, USA
Hanratty, Samantha (Sammi)                                                                         Actress
Paradigm Agency, 360 N Crescent Dr, North Building, Beverly Hills CA 90210 USA
Hanratty, Terrance R (Terry)                                                                       Football Player
31 Gower Road, New Canaan CT 06840, USA
Hans-Adam II                                                                                       Prince, Liechtenstein
Prince's Residence, Schloss Vaduz, 9490 Vaduz, Liechtenstein
Hansard, Glen                                                                                      Actor, Singer, Songwriter
Frames, PO Box 67 Gorey, County Wexford, Ireland
Hansbrough, A Tyler                                                                                Basketball Player
Indiana Pacers, Conseco Fieldhouse, 125 S Pennsylvania, Indianapolis IN 46204 USA
Hansch, Theodor W                                                                                  Nobel Physics Laureate
Max Plack Institut, Hans-Kopermann-Str 1, 85748 Garching, Germany
Hansen, Alfred G                                                                                   Air Force General, Businessman
Lockheed Aero Systems, 86 S Cobb Dr, Marietta GA 30063, USA
Hansen, Barbara C                                                                                  Neuroscientist
University of Maryland, Obesity/Diabetes Research Center, Baltimore MD 21201, USA
Hansen, Brendan J                                                                                  Swimmer
8704 Framdale Cove, Austin TX 78749, USA
Hansen, Brian                                                                                      Speed Skater
US Speedskating, 5662 S Cougar Lane, Salt Lake City UT 84118 USA
Hansen, Brian D                                                                                    Football Player
101 W Hazletine Lane, Sioux Falls SD 57108, USA
Hansen, Chris                                                                                      Commentator
NBC-TV, News Dept, 30 Rockefeller Plaza, #270E, New York NY 10112 USA
Hansen, David A (Dave)                                                                             Baseball Player
9852 Orchard Lane, Villa Park CA 92861, USA
Hansen, Donald R (Don)                                                                             Football Player
3390 Spain Road, Snellville GA 30039, USA
Hansen, Frederick M (Fred)                                                                         Track Athlete
201 Vanderpool Lane, #12, Houston TX 77024, USA
Hansen, Gunnar                                                                                     Actor
Amsel Eisenstadt Frazier, 5055 Wilshire Blvd, #865, Los Angeles CA 90036 USA
Hansen, J Stanley (Stan)                                                                           Professional Wrestler
233 Fannin Dr, Hewitt TX 76643, USA
Hansen, James Lee                                                                                  Sculptor
28219 NE 63rd Ave, Battle Ground WA 98604, USA
Hansen, Joseph T                                                                                   Labor Leader
United Food/Commercial Workers Union, 1775 K St NW, Washington DC 20006, USA
Hansen, Lars P                                                                                     Economist
University of Chicago, Economics Dept, Chicago IL 60637, USA
Hansen, Lars Peter                                                                                 Nobel Economics Laureate
University of Chicago, Economics Dept, 1126 E 59th St, Chicago IL 60637, USA
Hansen, Lasse Norman                                                                               Cyclist
Team Concordia-Himmerland, Vestergade 20, 9620 Aalestrup, Denmark
Hansen, Mark Victor                                                                                Motivational Speaker, Writer
PO Box 7665, Newport Beach CA 92658, USA
Hansen, Monica                                                                                     Model
Playboy Promotions, 2706 Media Center Dr, Los Angeles CA 90065 USA
Hansen, Patti                                                                                      Model, Actress
Redlands, West Wittering, Chichester, Sussex PO20 8QE, England
Hansen, Peter                                                                                      Actor
Stone Manners Salners, 9911 W Pico Blvd, #1400, Los Angeles CA 90035 USA
Hansen, Phillip A (Phil)                                                                           Football Player
24921 N Melissa Dr, Detroit Lakes MN 56501, USA
Hansen, Robert L (Bob)                                                                             Basketball Player
710 36th St, West Des Moines IA 50265, USA
Hansen, Ronald L (Ron)                                                                             Baseball Player
13602 Alliston Dr, Baldwin MD 21013, USA
Hansen, Ryan                                                                                       Actor
Gersh Agency, 9465 Wilshire Blvd, #600, Beverly Hills CA 90212 USA
Hanshaw, Anthony L                                                                                 Boxer
Gary Shaw Productions, 555 Preakness Ave, #9, Totowa NJ 07502, USA

**Hanson, Carl T** — Navy Admiral
3377 E Arroyo Chico, Tucson AZ 85716, USA
**Hanson, Curtis** — Director, Writer
United Talent Agency, U T A Plaza, 9336 Civic Center Dr, Beverly Hills CA 90210 USA
**Hanson, Erik B** — Baseball Player
20333 N 83rd Place, Scottsdale AZ 85255, USA
**Hanson, Hart** — Producer, Writer
W M E Entertainment, 9601 Wilshire Blvd, #300, Beverly Hills CA 90210 USA
**Hanson, Isaac** — Singer, Guitarist (Hanson); Songwriter
10th Street Entertainment, 700 San Vicente Blvd, #G410, West Hollywood CA 90069, USA
**Hanson, J Taylor** — Singer, Keyboardist (Hanson); Songwriter
10th Street Entertainment, 700 San Vicente Blvd, #G410, West Hollywood CA 90069, USA
**Hanson, Janine** — Rowing Athlete
Winnipeg Rowing Club, 20 Lyndale Dr, Saint Boniface MB R2H 3H2, Canada
**Hanson, Jason D** — Football Player
27272 Ovid Court, Franklin MI 48025, USA
**Hanson, Jennifer K** — Singer
Mission Mgmt, 24 Middleton St, Nashville TN 37210, USA
**Hanson, Joselio B** — Football Player
2531 Hudspeth St, Inglewood CA 90303, USA
**Hanson, Marcy** — Model, Actress
8721 W Sunset Blvd, #101, West Hollywood CA 90069, USA
**Hanson, Scott** — Sportscaster
N F L Network, 10950 Washington Blvd, #100, Culver City CA 90232 USA
**Hanson, Zachary** — Singer, Drummer (Hanson); Songwriter
10th Street Entertainment, 700 San Vicente Blvd, #G410, West Hollywood CA 90069, USA
**Hanson-Sfingi, Beverly** — Golfer
79915 Horseshoe Road, La Quinta CA 92253, USA
**Hanus, Tomas** — Conductor
I M G Artists, Hogarth Business Park, Chiswick, London W4 2TH, England
**Hanway, H Edward** — Businessman
C I G N A Corp, 1 Liberty Place, 1650 Market St, Philadelphia PA 19103, USA
**Hanzlik, William H (Bill)** — Basketball Player, Coach
5701 Green Oaks Dr, Greenwood Village CO 80121, USA
**Hape, Patrick S** — Football Player
105 Sutton Circle, Birmingham AL 35242, USA
**Happ, James A (J A)** — Baseball Player
902 14th St, Peru IL 61354, USA
**Harad, George J** — Businessman
Boise Cascade Corp, 1111 W Jefferson St, Boise ID 83728, USA
**Harada, Ann** — Actress
Davis Spylios Management, 244 W 54th St, #707, New York NY 10019, USA
**Harada, Masahiko (Fighting)** — Boxer
Boxing Commission, Tokyo Dome, 1-3-61, Koraku, Bunkyoku, Tokyo 112 8562 , Japan
**Harald V** — King, Norway
Royal Palace, Henrik Ibsens Gate 1, 0010 Oslo, Norway
**Harang, Aaron M** — Baseball Player
7828 Sendero Angelica, San Diego CA 92127, USA
**Harangody, Luke C** — Basketball Player
Cleveland Cavaliers, Gund Arena, 1 Center Court, Cleveland OH 44115 USA
**Harareet, Haya** — Actress
Herons Flight, Marlow, Buckinghamshire SL7 2LE, England
**Harbaugh, Gregory J** — Astronaut
1936 Thornwood Ave, Wilmette IL 60091, USA
**Harbaugh, James J (Jim)** — Football Player, Coach
San Francisco 49ers, 4949 Centennial Blvd, Santa Clara CA 95054 USA
**Harbaugh, John** — Football Coach
Baltimore Ravens, Ravens Stadium, 1 Winning Dr, Baltimore MD 21230 USA
**Harbison, John H** — Composer
479 Franklin St, Cambridge MA 02139, USA
**Harbour, David** — Actor
Lou Coulson Assoc, 37 Berwick St, London W1V 8RS, England
**Hard, Darlene R** — Tennis Player
22924 Erwin St, Woodland Hills CA 91367, USA
**Hardaway, Anfernee D (Penny)** — Basketball Player
3217 Point Hill Cove, Memphis TN 38125, USA
**Hardaway, Timothy D (Tim)** — Basketball Player
10050 SW 62nd Ave, Miami FL 33156, USA
**Hardaway, Timothy D (Tim), Jr** — Basketball Player
New York Knicks, Madison Square Garden, 2 Penn Plaza, New York, NY 10121 USA
**Hardee, James E (Trey), III** — Decathlete
2409 E 9th St, Austin TX 78702, USA
**Hardeman, Donald R (Don)** — Football Player
901 S Valley Mills Dr, #207B, Waco TX 76711, USA
**Harden, J Richard (Rich)** — Baseball Player
Texas Rangers, Ameriquest Field, 1000 Ballpark Way, #306, Arlington TX 76011 USA
**Harden, James** — Basketball Player
Houston Rockets, 1730 Jefferson St, Houston TX 77003 USA
**Harden, Marcia Gay** — Actress
Framework Entertainment, 9057 Nemo St, #C, West Hollywood CA 90069 USA
**Harden, Michael (Mike)** — Football Player
21512 E Portland Place, Aurora CO 80016, USA
**Hardesty, Brandon A** — Actor
Strong Mgmt, 9350 Wilshire Blvd, #224, Beverly Hills CA 90212, USA
**Hardin, Melora** — Actress, Singer, Director
Paul Kohner, 9300 Wilshire Blvd, #555, Beverly Hills CA 90212, USA
**Harding, Daniel** — Conductor
Columbia Artists Mgmt Inc, 1790 Broadway, #702, New York NY 10019 USA
**Harding, Ian** — Actor
Gersh Agency, 9465 Wilshire Blvd, #600, Beverly Hills CA 90212 USA
**Harding, John Wesley** — Singer, Guitarist, Songwriter, Writer
Concerted Efforts, PO Box 440326, Somerville MA 02144, USA
**Harding, Josh** — Ice Hockey Player
1415 Brown St, Regina SK S4N 5C9, Canada
**Harding, Lindsey M** — Basketball Player
Minnesota Lynx, Target Center, 600 1st Ave N, Minneapolis MN 55403 USA

Harding, Peter R    Air Force Marshal, England
Avalon House, Marnhull, Dorset DT10 1PT, England
Harding, Sarah N    Actress, Singer (Girls Aloud)
Concorde International, 101 Shepherds Bush Road, London W6 7LP, England
Harding, Tonya M    Figure Skater, Actress
11805 Bastrop St, Manor TX 78653, USA
Hardis, Stephen R    Businessman
Eaton Corp, Eaton Center, 1111 Superior Ave, #1900, Cleveland OH 44114, USA
Hardison, Bethann    Producer
Bethann Entertainment, 388 2nd Ave, #223, New York NY 10010, USA
Hardison, Kadeem    Actor
Peter Strain, 5455 Wilshire Blvd, #1812, Los Angeles CA 90036 USA
Hardison, W David (Dee)    Football Player
756 Belvin Maynard Road, Harrells NC 28444, USA
Hardman, Cedrick W    Football Player
364 Myrtle St, Laguna Beach CA 92651, USA
Hardnett, Charles (Charlie)    Basketball Player, Coach
1906 Swainsboro Dr, Louisville KY 40218, USA
Hardrict, Cory    Actor
A P A Talent/Literary Agency, 405 S Beverly Dr, #300, Beverly Hills CA 90212 USA
Hardt, Michael    Educator
Duke University, English Dept, Durham NC 27708, USA
Hardwick, Catherine    Director
Creative Artists Agency, 2000 Ave of Stars, #100, Los Angeles CA 90067 USA
Hardwick, Chris    Actor, Comedian (Hard n Phirm)
Brillstein Entertainment Partners, 9150 Wilshire Blvd, #350, Beverly Hills CA 90212 USA
Hardwick, Gary C    Director, Writer
Gersh Agency, 9465 Wilshire Blvd, #600, Beverly Hills CA 90212 USA
Hardwick, Johnny    Writer
Creative Artists Agency, 2000 Ave of Stars, #100, Los Angeles CA 90067 USA
Hardwick, Nicholas A (Nick)    Football Player
San Diego Chargers, 4020 Murphy Canyon Road, San Diego CA 92123 USA
Hardwick, Omari    Actor
3 Arts Entertainment, 9460 Wilshire Blvd, #700, Beverly Hills CA 90212 USA
Hardwicke, Catherine    Director, Writer
Creative Artists Agency, 2000 Ave of Stars, #100, Los Angeles CA 90067 USA
Hardy, Bruce A    Football Player
252 W 325 N, Ivins UT 84738, USA
Hardy, Carroll W    Football, Baseball Player
1514 Whitehall Dr, Longmont CO 80504, USA
Hardy, Francoise    Singer, Songwriter
Voyez Mon Agent, 20 Ave Rapp, 75007 Paris, France
Hardy, Hagood    Vibrist, Composer
S O C A N, 41 Valleybrook Dr, Don Mills ON M3B 2S6, Canada
Hardy, Hugh    Architect
Hardy Holzman Pfeiffer, 902 Broadway, #1900, New York NY 10010, USA
Hardy, James F (Jim)    Football Player
48490 San Vicente St, La Quinta CA 92253, USA
Hardy, James J (J J)    Baseball Player
5070 S Roosevelt St, Tempe AZ 85282, USA
Hardy, Jessica A    Swimmer
218 Rivo Alto Canal, Long Beach CA 90803, USA
Hardy, Kevin L    Football Player
1228 Windsor Harbor Dr, Jacksonville FL 32225, USA
Hardy, Kevin T    Football Player
298 Paraiso Dr, Danville CA 94526, USA
Hardy, Robert    Actor
Chatto & Linnit, 123A King's Road, London SW3 4PL, England
Hardy, Robert B (Bob)    Bassist (Franz Ferdinand)
M A M A Group, 57-65 Worship Ave, London EC2A 2DU, London, England
Hardy, Thomas A (Tom)    Sculptor
1530 SW Harrison, #203, Portland OR 97201, USA
Hardy, Tom    Actor
United Agents, 12-26 Lexington St, London W1F 0LE, England
Hare, David    Writer, Director
Casorotto Ramsay, Waverley House, 7-12 Noel St, London W1F 8GQ, England
Haren, Daniel J (Dan)    Baseball Player
7724 E Santa Catalina Dr, Scottsdale AZ 85255, USA
Harewood, David    Actor
A P A Talent/Literary Agency, 405 S Beverly Dr, #300, Beverly Hills CA 90212 USA
Harewood, Dorian    Actor
S M S Talent, 8383 Wilshire Blvd, #230, Beverly Hills CA 90211 USA
Hargan, Steven L (Steve)    Baseball Player
2502 E Morongo Trail, Palm Springs CA 92264, USA
Harge, Ira L    Basketball Player
328 Yucca Dr NW, Albuquerque NM 87105, USA
Hargett, Edward E (Edd)    Football Player
379 County Road 222, Nacogdoches TX 75965, USA
Hargis, V Burns    Educator
Oklahoma State University, President's Office, Stillwater OK 74078, USA
Hargitay, Mariska    Actress
Creative Artists Agency, 2000 Ave of Stars, #100, Los Angeles CA 90067 USA
Hargreaves, Brad    Drummer (Third Eye Blind)
Eric Godtland Mgmt, 1040 Mariposa St, #200, San Francisco CA 94107, USA
Hargrove, Brian    Director
Broder Webb Chervin Silberman, 9242 Beverly Blvd, Beverly Hills CA 90210 USA
Hargrove, D Michael (Mike)    Baseball Player, Manager
3925 Ramblewood Dr, Richfield OH 44286, USA
Harikkala, Timothy A (Tim)    Baseball Player
W6132 Everglade Road, Greenville WI 54942, USA
Haring, Robert W    Editor
Tulsa World, Editorial Dept, 315 S Boulder Ave, Tulsa OK 74103, USA
Harington, Kit    Actor
Creative Artists Agency, 2000 Ave of Stars, #100, Los Angeles CA 90067 USA
Hariri, Gisue    Architect
Hariri & Hariri, 39 W 29th St, #1200, New York NY 10001, USA

**H**

**Harding - Hariri**

**Hariri, Mojgan** — Architect
Hariri & Hariri, 39 W 29th St, #1200, New York NY 10001, USA
**Harker, Patrick T** — Educator
University of Delaware, President's Office, Newark DE 19716, USA
**Harker, Susannah** — Actress
55 Ashburnham Grove, Greenwich, London SW10 8UL, England
**Harket, Morten** — Singer (A-Ha)
Agency Group Ltd, 361-373 City Road, London EC1V 1PQ, England
**Harkey, Michael A (Mike)** — Baseball Player
2344 Eaglewood Dr, Chino Hills CA 91709, USA
**Harkleroad, Ashley** — Tennis Player, Model
Women's Tennis Assn, 1 Progress Plaza, #1500, Saint Petersburg FL 33701 USA
**Harkness, Jerald B (Jerry)** — Basketball Player
8340 Misty Dr, Indianapolis IN 46236, USA
**Harlan, Jack R** — Plant Geneticist
University of Illinois, Agronomy Dept, Urbana IL 61801, USA
**Harlan, Kevin** — Sportscaster
CBS-TV, Sports Dept, 51 W 52nd St, New York NY 10019 USA
**Harley, Carol** — Singer, Guitarist (Misty River)
1111B NW 131st Way, Vancouver WA 98685, USA
**Harley, Steve** — Singer (Steve Harley & Cockney Rebel)
Work Hard, 19D Pinfold Road, London SW16 2SL, England
**Harlin, Renny** — Director, Producer
Midnight Sun Pictures, 10960 Wilshire Blvd, #700, Los Angeles CA 90024, USA
**Harlock, David A** — Ice Hockey Player
3234 Chamberlain Circle, Ann Arbor MI 48103, USA
**Harlow, Bill** — Writer
Charles Scribner's Sons, 866 3rd Ave, New York NY 10022 USA
**Harlow, Larry D** — Baseball Player
26348 W Burnett Road, Buckeye AZ 85396, USA
**Harlow, Patrick C (Pat)** — Football Player
230 W Avenida San Antonio, San Clemente CA 92672, USA
**Harlow, Shalom** — Model, Actress
United Talent Agency, 9560 Wilshire Blvd, #500, Beverly Hills CA 90212, USA
**Harman, Jennifer** — Poker Player
Prince Marketing Group, 18 Carillon Circle, Livingston NJ 07039 USA
**Harman, Katie** — Beauty Queen, Singer
3631 NW 1st Court, Gresham OR 97030, USA
**Harmel, Pierre C J M** — Prime Minister, Belgium
8 Ave de l'Horizon, 1150 Brussels, Belgium
**Harmer, Nicholas (Nick)** — Bassist (Death Cab for Cutie)
Zeitgeist Artist Mgmt, 660 York St, #216, San Francisco CA 94110, USA
**Harmer, Sarah** — Singer, Songwriter
Agency Group Ltd, 2 Berkeley St, #202, Toronto ON M5A 4J5, Canada
**Harmon, Amy** — Journalist
New York Times, Editorial Dept, 229 W 43rd St, New York NY 10036 USA
**Harmon, Andrew P (Andy)** — Football Player
1258 Waters Edge Dr, Dayton OH 45458, USA
**Harmon, Angie** — Actress, Model
John Carrabino Mgmt, 5900 Wilshire Blvd, #406, Los Angeles CA 90036 USA
**Harmon, Charles B (Chuck)** — Baseball Player
6035 Ridgeacres Dr, #A, Cincinnati OH 45237, USA
**Harmon, Clarence, Jr** — Football Player
PO Box 571, Verona MS 38879, USA
**Harmon, Curtis** — Drummer (Pieces of a Dream)
23309 Commerce Park Road, Cleveland OH 44122, USA
**Harmon, Dan** — Producer, Writer, Actor
United Talent Agency, U T A Plaza, 9336 Civic Center Dr, Beverly Hills CA 90210 USA
**Harmon, Joy** — Actress
9901 Poole Ave, Sunland CA 91040, USA
**Harmon, Mark** — Actor
Wings Inc, 2236 Encinitas Blvd, #A, Encinitas CA 92024, USA
**Harmon, Noah** — Bassist (Airborne Toxic Event)
Island Def Jam Records, 8920 W Sunset Blvd, #200, West Hollywood CA 90069 USA
**Harmon, Robert** — Director
Paradigm Agency, 360 N Crescent Dr, North Building, Beverly Hills CA 90210 USA
**Harmon, Ronnie K** — Football Player
13022 218th St, Springfield Gardens NY 11413, USA
**Harmotta, Christa D** — Volleyball Player
Universal Volley Modena, Viale dello Sport 25, 41122 Modena, Italy
**Harms, Alfred G, Jr** — Navy Admiral
Commander, Education/Training Command, Naval Air Station, Pensacola FL 32508 USA
**Harms, Joni** — Singer, Songwriter
PO Box 272, Canby OR 97013, USA
**Harner, Jason Butler** — Actor
I C M Partners, 10250 Constellation Blvd, #900, Los Angeles CA 90067 USA
**Harner, Levi** — Harness Racing Driver
RR 1, Millville PA 17846, USA
**Harney, Corinna** — Model, Actress
Playboy Promotions, 2706 Media Center Dr, Los Angeles CA 90065 USA
**Harnick, Sheldon M** — Writer, Lyricist
Deutsch Deutsch & Blasband, 800 3rd Ave, New York NY 10022, USA
**Harnisch, Peter T (Pete)** — Baseball Player
35 Brentwood Dr S, Colts Neck NJ 07722, USA
**Harnois, Elisabeth R** — Actress
Schachter Entertainment, 1157 S Beverly Dr, #200, Los Angeles CA 90035 USA
**Harnois, Marlene** — Taekwondo Athlete
INSEP, 11 Ave du Tremblay, 75012 Paris, France
**Harnoncourt, Nikolaus** — Conductor
38 Piaristangasse, 1080 Vienna, Austria
**Harnoy, Ofra** — Concert Cellist
437 Spadina Road, PO Box 23046, Toronto ON M5P 2W0, Canada
**Haro, Melissa** — Model, Actress
Elite Model Mgmt, 119 Washington Ave, #501, Miami Beach FL 33139, USA
**Harold, Gale** — Actor
Gersh Agency, 9465 Wilshire Blvd, #600, Beverly Hills CA 90212 USA

**Harouche, Serge** — Nobel Physics Laureate
College de France, 11 Place Marcelin Berthelot, 75231 Paris Cedex 05, France
**Harout, Magda** — Actress
13452 Vose St, Van Nuys CA 91405, USA
**Harp, Everette** — Jazz Saxophonist
Universal Attractions, 135 W 26th St, #1200, New York NY 10001 USA
**Harper, Alvin C** — Football Player
501 Harry S Truman Dr, #109, Upper Marlboro MD 20774, USA
**Harper, Ben** — Singer, Guitarist, Songwriter
Red Light Mgmt, 44 Wall St, #2200, New York NY 10005, USA
**Harper, Billy** — Jazz Saxophonist
Joel Chriss Co, 300 Mercer St, #3J, New York NY 10003 USA
**Harper, Bob** — Physical Fitness Instructor, Actor
Entertainment Fusion Group, 8899 Beverly Blvd, #412, West Hollywood CA 90046, USA
**Harper, Brian D** — Baseball Player
8319 E Shetland Trail, Scottsdale AZ 85258, USA
**Harper, Bruce S** — Football Player
311 Lindbergh Ave, Closter NJ 07624, USA
**Harper, Charles L (Charlie)** — Football Player
2115 Augusta, McKinney TX 75070, USA
**Harper, Charles M** — Businessman
6625 State St, Omaha NE 68152, USA
**Harper, Conrad K** — Attorney, Government Official
US State Department, 2201 C St NW, Washington DC 20520, USA
**Harper, Dawn** — Track Athlete
USA Track & Field, RCA Dome, PO Box 140, Indianapolis IN 46225 USA
**Harper, Derek R** — Basketball Player
5665 Arapaho Road, #1223, Dallas TX 75248, USA
**Harper, Deveron A** — Football Player
2749 Huntsville St, Kenner LA 70062, USA
**Harper, Donald D W (Don)** — Diver
1765 Lynnhaven Dr, Columbus OH 43221, USA
**Harper, Dwayne A** — Football Player
104 Cue St, Orangeburg SC 29115, USA
**Harper, Heather M** — Opera Singer
Royal Academy of Music/Drama, 100 Renfrew St, Glasgow G2 3DB, England
**Harper, Helen** — Actress
Gavin Barker Assoc, 2D Wimpole St, London W1G 0EB, England
**Harper, Hill** — Actor
Innovative Artists, 1505 10th St, Santa Monica CA 90401 USA
**Harper, Jessica** — Actress, Singer
2337 Roscomare Road, #2-244, Los Angeles CA 90077, USA
**Harper, Judson M** — Chemical Engineer
1818 Westview Road, Fort Collins CO 80524, USA
**Harper, Mark** — Football Player
2162 Albany Ave, Memphis TN 38108, USA
**Harper, Michael S** — Writer
Brown University, English Dept, Providence RI 02912, USA
**Harper, Nicholas N (Nick)** — Football Player
9549 Sanctuary Place, Brentwood TN 37027, USA
**Harper, Roland** — Football Player
1391 Westbourne Parkway, Algonquin IL 60102, USA
**Harper, Ron** — Actor
13317 Ventura Blvd, #1, Sherman Oaks CA 91423, USA
**Harper, Ronald (Ron)** — Basketball Player
8934 Brecksville Road, #417, Brecksville OH 44141, USA
**Harper, Stephen J** — Prime Minister, Canada
Prime Minister's Office, Langevin Block, Ottawa ON K1A 0A1, Canada
**Harper, Terry J** — Baseball Player
4225 Jailette Road, Atlanta GA 30349, USA
**Harper, Tess** — Actress
Bauman Redanty Shaul Agency, 5757 Wilshire Blvd, #473, Los Angeles CA 90036 USA
**Harper, Thomas (Tommy)** — Baseball Player
5 Cow Hill Road, Sharon MA 02067, USA
**Harper, Tom** — Actor
Ken McReddie Assoc, 101 Finsbury Pavement, London EC2A 1RS, England
**Harper, Valerie** — Actress
David Shapira Assoc, 193 N Robertson Blvd, Beverly Hills CA 90211 USA
**Harpring, Matthew H (Matt)** — Basketball Player
4550 Stella Dr NW, Atlanta GA 30327, USA
**Harrah, Colbert D (Toby)** — Baseball Player, Manager
316 Leewood Circle, Azle TX 76020, USA
**Harrah, Dennis W** — Football Player
925 Rockin One Way, Paso Robles CA 93446, USA
**Harrell, James C, Jr** — Football Player
17826 Crystal Preserve Dr, Lutz FL 33548, USA
**Harrell, Lynn M** — Concert Cellist, Conductor
Opus 3 Artists, 470 Park Ave S, #900N, New York NY 10016 USA
**Harrell, Maestro** — Actor
C E S D, 10635 Santa Monica Blvd, #130, Los Angeles CA 90025 USA
**Harrell, Willard R** — Football Player
8 Scarlet Oak Court, Lake Saint Louis MO 63367, USA
**Harrell, William (Billy)** — Baseball Player
253 Mount Hope Court, Albany NY 12202, USA
**Harrelson, Derrell M (Bud)** — Baseball Player, Manager
357 Ridgefield Road, Hauppauge NY 11788, USA
**Harrelson, Kenneth S (Ken)** — Baseball Player
90006 Shawn Park Place, Orlando FL 32819, USA
**Harrelson, Woody** — Actor
Creative Artists Agency, 2000 Ave of Stars, #100, Los Angeles CA 90067 USA
**Harries, Kathryn** — Opera Singer
Ingpen & Williams, 131 Putney Bridge Road, London SW15 2PA, England
**Harrigan, Lori** — Softball Player
828 Rainbow Rock St, Las Vegas NV 89123, USA
**Harring, Laura E** — Actress, Beauty Queen
Brillstein Entertainment Partners, 9150 Wilshire Blvd, #350, Beverly Hills CA 90212 USA

**H**

Harouche - Harring

**Harrington, Albert F (Al)** — Basketball Player
16124 Chancellors Ridge Way, Noblesville IN 46062, USA
**Harrington, Dan** — Poker Player, Writer
Poker Gives, Nevada Community Foundation, 1635 Village Center Circle, #160, Las Vegas NV 89134, USA
**Harrington, Desmond** — Actor
Untitled Entertainment, 350 S Beverly Dr, #200, Beverly Hills CA 90212 USA
**Harrington, Donald J** — Educator
Saint John's University, President's Office, 8000 Utopia Parkway, Queens NY 11439, USA
**Harrington, Jay** — Actor
A Mgmt, 12001 Ventura Place, #340, Studio City CA 91604 USA
**Harrington, John** — Ice Hockey Player, Coach
8138 Golden Valley Road, Minneapolis MN 55427, USA
**Harrington, Laura** — Actress
Creative Artists Agency, 2000 Ave of Stars, #100, Los Angeles CA 90067 USA
**Harrington, Othella F** — Basketball Player
1602 Rika Point, Houston TX 77077, USA
**Harrington, Padraig** — Golfer
International Mgmt Group, Pier House, Strand on the Green, London W4 3NN, England
**Harrington, Pat** — Actor
730 Marzella Ave, Los Angeles CA 90049, USA
**Harrington, Pat, Jr** — Actor
C E S D, 10635 Santa Monica Blvd, #130, Los Angeles CA 90025 USA
**Harrington, Perry D** — Football Player
1302 Roxbury Court, Jackson MS 39211, USA
**Harris, Alfred C (Al)** — Football Player
12 Stone Ridge Dr, South Barrington IL 60010, USA
**Harris, Barbara C** — Religious Leader, Social Activist
Episcopal Diocese of Massachusetts, 138 Tremont St, Boston MA 02111, USA
**Harris, Barry** — Jazz Pianist
Thomas Cassidy, PO Box 1311, Tucson AZ 85702 USA
**Harris, Bernard A, Jr** — Astronaut
1330 Post Oak Blvd, #2550, Houston TX 77056, USA
**Harris, Brendon M** — Baseball Player
30 Fox Hollow Lane, Queensbury NY 12804, USA
**Harris, Callard** — Actor
United Talent Agency, U T A Plaza, 9336 Civic Center Dr, Beverly Hills CA 90210 USA
**Harris, Carter** — Producer, Director, Writer
W M E Entertainment, 9601 Wilshire Blvd, #300, Beverly Hills CA 90210 USA
**Harris, Charlaine** — Writer
PO Box 354, Magnolia AR 71754, USA
**Harris, Clifford A (Cliff)** — Football Player
722 Kentwood Dr, Rockwall TX 75032, USA
**Harris, Clint L (Bo)** — Football Player
PO Box 52539, Shreveport LA 71135, USA
**Harris, Corey** — Guitarist
Blue Mountain Artists, 810 Tyvola Road, #114, Charlotte NC 28217, USA
**Harris, Corey L** — Football Player
933 N Tremont St, Indianapolis IN 46222, USA
**Harris, Cristi Ellen** — Actress
House of Representatives, 1434 6th St, #1, Santa Monica CA 90401 USA
**Harris, Cynthia** — Actress
Paradigm Agency, 360 N Crescent Dr, North Building, Beverly Hills CA 90210 USA
**Harris, Damian** — Director
I C M Partners, 10250 Constellation Blvd, #900, Los Angeles CA 90067 USA
**Harris, Daniel P (Dan)** — Director, Writer
Chasen Agency, 8899 Beverly Blvd, #405, Los Angeles CA 90048 USA
**Harris, Danielle** — Actress
Sager Mgmt, 260 S Beverly Dr, #205, Beverly Hills CA 90212, USA
**Harris, Danneel** — Actress
Untitled Entertainment, 350 S Beverly Dr, #200, Beverly Hills CA 90212 USA
**Harris, Delmar (Del)** — Basketball Coach
1229 Ducks Landing, Frisco TX 75034, USA
**Harris, Duriel L, Jr** — Football Player
3875 San Pablo Road S, #1212, Jacksonville FL 32224, USA
**Harris, Ed** — Actor
Special Artists Agency, 9200 Sunset Blvd, #410, West Hollywood CA 90069 USA
**Harris, Emmylou** — Singer, Songwriter
Vector Mgmt, PO Box 120479, Nashville TN 37212 USA
**Harris, Estelle** — Actress
Danis Panaro Nist, 9201 W Olympic Blvd, Beverly Hills CA 90212, USA
**Harris, Franco** — Football Player
200 Chaucer Court S, Sewickley PA 15143, USA
**Harris, Gail** — Actress
Don Gerler, 3349 Cahuenga Blvd W, #1, Los Angeles CA 90068 USA
**Harris, Greg A** — Baseball Player
10262 Mardel Dr, Cypress CA 90630, USA
**Harris, Gregory W (Greg)** — Baseball Player
6708 Green Hollow Court, Wake Forest NC 27587, USA
**Harris, Henry** — Cell Biologist
William Dunn Pathology School, South Parks Road, Oxford OX1 3RE, England
**Harris, Hollis L** — Businessman
200 Horseshoe Circle, Fayetteville GA 30215, USA
**Harris, Hugh** — Ice Hockey Player
150 Sycamore Dr, Carmel IN 46033, USA
**Harris, Jackie B** — Football Player
7905 Haydenberry Court, Nashville TN 37221, USA
**Harris, James L** — Football Player
9838 Old Baymeadows Road, Jacksonville FL 32256, USA
**Harris, Jamie** — Actor
Innovative Artists, 1505 10th St, Santa Monica CA 90401 USA
**Harris, Jared** — Actor
Paradigm Agency, 360 N Crescent Dr, North Building, Beverly Hills CA 90210 USA
**Harris, Jay** — Cartoonist (Better Half)
King Features Syndicate, 300 W 57th St, #1500, New York NY 10019 USA
**Harris, Joanne** — Writer
Knopf Publishers, 1745 Broadway, New York NY 10019 USA

| | |
|---|---|
| **Harris, Joe Frank**<br>712 West Ave, Cartersville GA 30120, USA | Governor, GA |
| **Harris, John E**<br>270 NW 120th St, Miami FL 33168, USA | Football Player |
| **Harris, John R**<br>24 Devonshire Place, London W1N 2BX, England | Architect |
| **Harris, John R**<br>4316 Fremont Ave S, Minneapolis MN 55409, USA | Golfer |
| **Harris, Joseph A (Joe)**<br>4747 River Road, Ellenwood GA 30294, USA | Football Player |
| **Harris, Joshua**<br>Talent Works, 3500 W Olive Ave, #1400, Burbank CA 91505 USA | Actor |
| **Harris, Lara**<br>Arlook Group, 205 S Beverly Dr, #209, Beverly Hills CA 90212, USA | Actress |
| **Harris, Lee**<br>Pilobolus Dance Theater, PO Box 388, Washington Depot CT 06794, USA | Dance Executive |
| **Harris, Leon**<br>CNN-TV, 190 Marietta Ave SW, Atlanta GA 30303 USA | Commentator |
| **Harris, Leonard A (Lenny)**<br>7435 N Augusta Dr, Hialeah FL 33015, USA | Baseball Player |
| **Harris, Leroy**<br>1919 Live Oak St, Savannah GA 31404, USA | Football Player |
| **Harris, Leroy, Jr**<br>890 Arlington Heights Dr, Brentwood TN 37027, USA | Football Player |
| **Harris, Louis**<br>200 E 66th St, #2004, New York NY 10065, USA | Statistician |
| **Harris, Lucious H**<br>1149 W 62nd St, Los Angeles CA 90044, USA | Basketball Player |
| **Harris, Mark Jonathan**<br>Principato-Young, 9465 Wilshire Blvd, #880, Beverly Hills CA 90212 USA | Director |
| **Harris, Mark Yale**<br>Artwork, 170 Lena St, #A, Santa Fe NM 87505, USA | Sculptor |
| **Harris, Mel**<br>Abrams Artists, 9200 W Sunset Blvd, #1125, West Hollywood CA 90069 USA | Actress |
| **Harris, Michael L (M L)**<br>M L Harris Outreach, 15589 Apple Valley Road, Apple Valley CA 92307, USA | Football Player |
| **Harris, Mike**<br>Curling Assn, 1660 Vimont Court, Cumberland ON K4A 4J4, Canada | Curling Athlete |
| **Harris, Naomie M**<br>United Talent Agency, U T A Plaza, 9336 Civic Center Dr, Beverly Hills CA 90210 USA | Actress |
| **Harris, Napoleon B**<br>Napoleon Harris Foundation, 15774 S LaGrange Road, #214, Orland Park IL 60462, USA | Football Player |
| **Harris, Neil**<br>5555 S Everett Ave, Chicago IL 60637, USA | Historian |
| **Harris, Neil Patrick**<br>Creative Artists Agency, 2000 Ave of Stars, #100, Los Angeles CA 90067 USA | Actor |
| **Harris, Nicholas J (Nick)**<br>2035 Kingsway Dr, Troy MI 48098, USA | Football Player |
| **Harris, Quentin H**<br>3013 W Glass Lane, Phoenix AZ 85041, USA | Football Player |
| **Harris, Rachael E**<br>United Talent Agency, U T A Plaza, 9336 Civic Center Dr, Beverly Hills CA 90210 USA | Actress, Comedienne |
| **Harris, Raymont L**<br>1144 Aroya Court, New Albany OH 43054, USA | Football Player |
| **Harris, Reginald A (Reggie)**<br>133 Paige St, Waynesboro VA 22980, USA | Baseball Player |
| **Harris, Richard**<br>Paramount Entertainment, PO Box 12, Far Hills NJ 07931 USA | Singer (Jive Five) |
| **Harris, Rickie C**<br>613 Q St NW, Washington DC 20001, USA | Football Player |
| **Harris, Robert D**<br>Inkwell Mgmt, 521 5th Ave, New York NY 10175, USA | Writer |
| **Harris, Robert L**<br>2711 13th St SW, Lehigh Acres FL 33976, USA | Football Player |
| **Harris, Rolf**<br>Billy Marsh, 76A Grove End Road, Saint John's Wood, London NW8 9ND, England | Actor |
| **Harris, Rosemary**<br>Independent Talent Group, 40 Whitfield St, London W1T 2RH, England | Actress |
| **Harris, Sam**<br>Bauman Redanty Shaul Agency, 5757 Wilshire Blvd, #473, Los Angeles CA 90036 USA | Singer, Actor |
| **Harris, Samantha**<br>E! Network, 5750 Wilshire Blvd, Los Angeles CA 90036, USA | Actress, Model |
| **Harris, Sean**<br>Troika, 74 Clerkenwell Road, #300, London EC1M 5QA, England | Actor |
| **Harris, Sidney**<br>302 W 86th St, #9A, New York NY 10024, USA | Cartoonist |
| **Harris, Stefon**<br>Unlimited Myles, 6 Imaginary Place, Aberdeen NJ 07747, USA | Jazz Vibraphone Player |
| **Harris, Stephen E**<br>Stanford University, Ginzton Laboratory, 450 Via Palou, Stanford CA 94305, USA | Electrical Engineer, Physicist |
| **Harris, Steve**<br>Brillstein Entertainment Partners, 9150 Wilshire Blvd, #350, Beverly Hills CA 90212 USA | Actor |
| **Harris, Steve**<br>Sanctuary Music Mgmt, 82 Bishop's Bridge Road, London W2 6BB, England | Bassist (Iron Maiden) |
| **Harris, Steven D (Steve)**<br>3005 W Fort Worth St, Broken Arrow OK 74012, USA | Basketball Player |
| **Harris, T Eugene (Gene)**<br>1267 NE 16th Ave, Okeechobee FL 34972, USA | Baseball Player |
| **Harris, Ted**<br>1 Stonegate Court, Blackwood NJ 08012, USA | Ice Hockey Player |
| **Harris, Thomas**<br>Creative Artists Agency, 2000 Ave of Stars, #100, Los Angeles CA 90067 USA | Writer |
| **Harris, Timothy D (Tim)**<br>843 N N St, Livermore CA 94551, USA | Football Player |
| **Harris, Tommie, Jr**<br>San Diego Chargers, 4020 Murphy Canyon Road, San Diego CA 92123 USA | Football Player |

# H

Harris - Harris

**Harris, Victor L (Vic)**                                    Baseball Player
5420 S Garth Ave, Los Angeles CA 90056, USA
**Harris, Walt**                                              Football Coach
Akron University, Athletic Dept, Akron OH 44325, USA
**Harris, Walter F (Buddy)**                                  Baseball Player
2305 Carol Lane, Norristown PA 19401, USA
**Harris, Walter L (Walt)**                                   Football Player
4103 Shinault Lane, Olive Branch MS 38654, USA
**Harris, William C (Willie)**                                Baseball Player
1176 Willie C Harris Dr, Cairo GA 39828, USA
**Harris, William E (Billy)**                                 Ice Hockey Player
Muskoka Candle Co, PO Box 233, Rosseau ON P0C 1J0, Canada
**Harris, Wood**                                              Actor
Gersh Agency, 9465 Wilshire Blvd, #600, Beverly Hills CA 90212 USA
**Harrison Breetzke, Joan**                                   Swimmer
16 Clevedon Road, East London 5201, South Africa
**Harrison, Alvin**                                           Track Athlete
Octagon Worldwide, 800 Connecticut Ave, #200, Norwalk CT 06854 USA
**Harrison, Audley**                                          Boxer
Thell Torrence, 5449 S Eastern Ave, #3, Las Vegas NV 89119, USA
**Harrison, Bret**                                            Actor
United Talent Agency, U T A Plaza, 9336 Civic Center Dr, Beverly Hills CA 90210 USA
**Harrison, C Richard**                                       Businessman
Parametric Technology, 140 Kendrick St, #C120, Needham Heights MA 02494, USA
**Harrison, Charles (Tex)**                                   Basketball Player, Coach
Harlem Globetrotters, 400 E Van Buren St, #300, Phoenix AZ 85004, USA
**Harrison, Charles W (Chuck)**                               Baseball Player
222 Buckskin Road, Abilene TX 79602, USA
**Harrison, Christopher (Chris)**                             Actor
Allure Model & Talent, 5556 S Centinela Ave, Los Angeles CA 90066, USA
**Harrison, Colin**                                           Writer
Farrar Straus Giroux, 18 W 18th St, #700, New York NY 10011 USA
**Harrison, Dennis**                                          Football Player
1048 Hickory Hollow Road, Nashville TN 37221, USA
**Harrison, Donald (Duck)**                                   Jazz Saxophonist
Carolyn McClair, PO Box 55, Radio City Station, New York NY 10101, USA
**Harrison, Dwight W**                                        Football Player
2265 Buchanan St, Beaumont TX 77703, USA
**Harrison, Fiona**                                           Physicist
California Institute of Technology, Physics Dept, Pasadena CA 91125, USA
**Harrison, Gregory**                                         Actor
Himber Entertainment, PO Box 950, South Orange NJ 07079 USA
**Harrison, James D (Jim)**                                   Ice Hockey Player
102-645 Barrera Road, Kelowna BC V1W 3C9, Canada
**Harrison, James, Jr**                                       Football Player
2525 Matterhorn Dr, Wexford PA 15090, USA
**Harrison, Jenilee**                                         Actress
J Lee Corp, 19528 Ventura Blvd, #365, Tarzana CA 91356, USA
**Harrison, Jim**                                             Writer
Grove Press, 841 Broadway, New York NY 10003 USA
**Harrison, Kathryn**                                         Writer
Random House, 1745 Broadway, #1800, New York NY 10019 USA
**Harrison, Kayla**                                           Judo Athlete
9 Summer St, Wakefield MA 01880, USA
**Harrison, Linda**                                           Actress
10370 Ashton Ave, Los Angeles CA 90024, USA
**Harrison, Marcus**                                          Football Player
New England Patriots, 1 Patriot Place, Foxboro MA 02035 USA
**Harrison, Marvin D**                                        Football Player
928 Morgan Road, Jenkintown PA 19046, USA
**Harrison, Matthew**                                         Director
Trisko Talent Management, 209 Carrall St, #240, Vancouver, BC V6B 2J2, Canada
**Harrison, Michael Allen**                                   Pianist, Composer
M A H Records, 828 NE Prescott St, Portland OR 97211, USA
**Harrison, Nolan**                                           Football Player
2121 N Westmoreland St, #543, Arlington VA 22213, USA
**Harrison, Paul D**                                          Ice Hockey Player
5-215 Royale St, Timmins ON P4N 8S7, Canada
**Harrison, Randy**                                           Actor
Paradigm Agency, 360 N Crescent Dr, North Building, Beverly Hills CA 90210 USA
**Harrison, Robert L (Bob)**                                  Baseball Player
1104 N Meridian St, Lebanon IN 46052, USA
**Harrison, Robert L (Bob), Jr**                              Football Player
3 Westwind Circle, Stamford TX 79553, USA
**Harrison, Robert W (Bob)**                                  Basketball Player
Harbour Ridge, 13405 NW Wax Myrtle Trail, Palm City FL 34990, USA
**Harrison, Rodney**                                          Football Player, Sportscaster
24 Country Club Dr, Olympia Fields IL 60461, USA
**Harrison, Roric E**                                         Baseball Player
2932 Channing Way, Los Alamitos CA 90720, USA
**Harrison, Sabrina Ward**                                    Writer
Chronicle Books, 680 2nd St, San Francisco CA 94107 USA
**Harrison, Teri Marie**                                      Model, Actress
2973 Harbor Blvd, #350, Costa Mesa CA 92626, USA
**Harrison, Thomas J (Tom)**                                  Baseball Player
2932 Channing Way, Los Alamitos CA 90720, USA
**Harrison, Tony**                                            Writer
Gordon Dickinson, 2 Crescent Grove, London SW4 7AH, England
**Harrison, William B, Jr**                                   Financier
J P Morgan Chase Corp, 270 Park Ave, #1200, New York NY 10017, USA
**Harrison, William H**                                       Army General
7302 Amber Lane SW, Lakewood WA 98498, USA
**Harris-Stewart, Lusia M (Lucy)**                            Basketball Player
1002 Cherry St, Greenwood MS 38930, USA
**Harrold, Kathryn**                                          Actress
9255 W Sunset Blvd, #901, West Hollywood CA 90069, USA

Harris - Harrold

|  | |  |
|---|---|---|
| **Harron, Mary** | Circle of Confusion, 315 S Beverly Dr, #201, Beverly Hills CA 90212, USA | Director |
| **Harrowyn, Danni** | The Kirby Organization, 9200 Sunset Blvd, #600, Los Angeles CA 90069, USA | Drummer (Civet) |
| **Harry** | Clarence House, Stable Yard Gate, London SW1A 1BA, England | Prince, England |
| **Harry, Deborah A (Debbie)** | Tavistock Wood Mgmt, 45 Conduit St, London W1S 2YN, England | Singer, Songwriter, Actress |
| **Harry, Emile M** | 34 Villa Vista Dr, Brownsville TX 78520, USA | Football Player |
| **Harsch, Eddie** | Mitch Schneider Organization, 14724 Ventura Blvd, #500, Sherman Oaks CA 91403 USA | Keyboardist (Black Crowes) |
| **Harshman, John E (Jack)** | 1010 Baywood Circle, #E, Chula Vista CA 91915, USA | Baseball Player |
| **Harshman, Margo** | A P A Talent/Literary Agency, 405 S Beverly Dr, #300, Beverly Hills CA 90212 USA | Actress |
| **Hart, Anita** | Joni's Stunt People, 8147 Tunney Ave, Reseda CA 91335, USA | Stuntwoman |
| **Hart, Ann Weaver** | Temple University, President's Office, 1801 N Broad St, Philadelphia PA 19122, USA | Educator |
| **Hart, Beth** | W M E Entertainment, 1600 Division St, #300, Nashville TN 37203 USA | Singer, Songwriter |
| **Hart, Bob** | 5740 Laurel Oak Dr, Suwanee GA 30024, USA | Bowler |
| **Hart, Bobby** | 1422 LaMar Ave, #613, Memphis TN 38104, USA | Singer, Composer |
| **Hart, Bodhi J (Bo)** | 1815 Portola Dr, #A, Santa Cruz CA 95062, USA | Baseball Player |
| **Hart, Bret (Hitman)** | 435 Patina Place SW, Calgary AB T3H 2P5, Canada | Professional Wrestler |
| **Hart, Carolyn G** | 1705 Drakestone Ave, Nichols Hills OK 73120, USA | Writer |
| **Hart, Charles** | London Mgmt, 2-4 Noel St, London W1V 3RB, England | Lyricist |
| **Hart, Clinton G** | 2894 County Road 730, Webster FL 33597, USA | Football Player |
| **Hart, Corey M** | PO Box 1100, Station A, Montreal QC H3C 2X6, Canada | Singer, Songwriter |
| **Hart, Dolores (Mother Dolores)** | Regina Laudis Abbey, 275 Flanders Road, Bethlehem CT 06751, USA | Actress |
| **Hart, Doris** | 600 Biltmore Way, #306, Coral Gables FL 33134, USA | Tennis Player |
| **Hart, Douglas W (Doug)** | 2192 Medina Road, Long Lake MN 55356, USA | Football Player |
| **Hart, Dru** | Playboy Promotions, 2706 Media Center Dr, Los Angeles CA 90065 USA | Model |
| **Hart, Dudley** | 5130 Rockledge Dr, Clarence NY 14031, USA | Golfer |
| **Hart, Emerson** | Sanctuary Artist Mgmt, 54 Music Square E, #300, Nashville TN 37203, USA | Singer, Guitarist (Tonic), Songwriter |
| **Hart, Freddie** | 317 N Kenwood St, Burbank CA 91505, USA | Singer, Songwriter, Guitarist |
| **Hart, Gary W** | 730 17th St, #300, Denver CO 80202, USA | Senator, CO |
| **Hart, Harold J** | 2004 E Caracas St, Tampa FL 33610, USA | Football Player |
| **Hart, Ian** | A P A Talent/Literary Agency, 405 S Beverly Dr, #300, Beverly Hills CA 90212 USA | Actor |
| **Hart, J Corey** | 808 Oakwood Dr, Waukesha WI 53186, USA | Baseball Player |
| **Hart, James V** | Creative Artists Agency, 2000 Ave of Stars, #100, Los Angeles CA 90067 USA | Writer, Director, Producer |
| **Hart, James W (Jim)** | 3141 Dominica Way, Naples FL 34119, USA | Football Player, Sports Administrator |
| **Hart, Jason W** | 3202 S Westwood Ave, Springfield MO 65807, USA | Baseball Player |
| **Hart, Jeff** | 105 Guanajuato Court, Solana Beach CA 92075, USA | Golfer |
| **Hart, Jeffery A (Jeff)** | 1307 SE 14th Ave, Canby OR 97013, USA | Football Player |
| **Hart, John R** | I C M Partners, 730 5th Ave, New York NY 10019 USA | Commentator |
| **Hart, Kevin** | United Talent Agency, U T A Plaza, 9336 Civic Center Dr, Beverly Hills CA 90210 USA | Actor, Comedian |
| **Hart, Kevin** | 5605 Plantation Circle, Plano TX 75093, USA | Baseball Player |
| **Hart, Mary** | Brokaw Co, 9255 W Sunset Blvd, #804, West Hollywood CA 90069 USA | Entertainer |
| **Hart, Melissa Joan** | Hartbreak Productions, 14622 Ventura Blvd, #102, Sherman Oaks CA 91403, USA | Actress |
| **Hart, Mickey** | Pinnacle Entertainment, 30 Glenn St, White Plains NY 10603, USA | Drummer (Grateful Dead) |
| **Hart, Roxanne** | Abrams Artists, 9200 W Sunset Blvd, #1125, West Hollywood CA 90069 USA | Actress |
| **Hart, Stanley R** | PO Box 625, Green Valley AZ 85622, USA | Geologist |
| **Hart, Terry J** | PO Box V, Hellertown PA 18055, USA | Astronaut |
| **Hart, Tommy L** | 3503 Highland Ave, Redwood City CA 94062, USA | Football Player |
| **Harte, Houston H** | Harte-Hanks Communications, 200 Concord Plaza Dr, San Antonio TX 78216, USA | Publisher |
| **Hartenstein, Charles O (Chuck)** | 10735 Cassia Dr, Austin TX 78759, USA | Baseball Player |
| **Hartenstine, Michael A (Mike)** | 322 Winchester Court, Lake Bluff IL 60044, USA | Football Player |

**H**

Harron - Hartenstine

| | |
|---|---|
| **Hartings, Jeffrey A (Jeff)**<br>171 Manchester Circle, Pittsburgh PA 15237, USA | Football Player |
| **Hartley, Hal**<br>True Fiction Pictures, 39 W 14th St, #406, New York NY 10011, USA | Director |
| **Hartley, Harry J**<br>University of Connecticut, President's Office, Storrs CT 06269, USA | Educator |
| **Hartley, Justin S**<br>Innovative Artists, 1505 10th St, Santa Monica CA 90401 USA | Actor, Director, Writer |
| **Hartley, Mariette**<br>J Michael Bloom, 9255 W Sunset Blvd, #710, West Hollywood CA 90069 USA | Actress |
| **Hartley, Michael E (Mike)**<br>9845 Quail Canyon Road, El Cajon CA 92021, USA | Baseball Player |
| **Hartley, Robert (Bob)**<br>2713 Bonar Hall Path, Duluth GA 30097, USA | Ice Hockey Coach |
| **Hartman Black, Lisa**<br>Innovative Artists, 1505 10th St, Santa Monica CA 90401 USA | Actress |
| **Hartman, Arthur A**<br>A P C O Consulting Group, 1615 L St NW, Washington DC 20036, USA | Diplomat |
| **Hartman, David**<br>3215 Stoneybrook Dr, Durham NC 27705, USA | Actor, Commentator |
| **Hartman, Elmer E (Butch), IV**<br>Gotham Group, 9255 Sunset Blvd, #515, Los Angeles CA 90069, USA | Animator, Composer, Director |
| **Hartman, Geoffrey H**<br>200 Leeder Hill Dr, #2401, Hamden CT 6517, USA | Language Educator |
| **Hartman, George E**<br>1657 31st St, Washington DC 20007, USA | Architect |
| **Hartman, J C**<br>3425 Rosedale St, Houston TX 77004, USA | Baseball Player |
| **Hartman, Kevin**<br>Sporting Kansas City, 210 W 19th Terrace, #200, Kansas City MO 64108 USA | Soccer Player |
| **Hartman, William K (Bill)**<br>Planetary Science Institute, 1700 E Fort Lowell Road, #106, Tucson AZ 85719, USA | Astrophysicist |
| **Hartmanis, Juris**<br>43 Janivar Dr, Ithaca NY 14850, USA | Computer Scientist |
| **Hartman-Smith, Rhonda**<br>Hart Enterprises, 5611 Highway 81 N, Williamston SC 29697, USA | Auto Racing Driver |
| **Hartner, Rona**<br>Artmedia, 20 Ave Rapp, 75007 Paris, France | Actress |
| **Hartnett, Josh**<br>Management 360, 9111 Wilshire Blvd, Beverly Hills CA 90210 USA | Actor |
| **Harto, Joshua**<br>Madhouse Entertainment, 8484 Wilshire Blvd, #640, Beverly Hills CA 90211, USA | Actor |
| **Harts, Gregory R (Greg)**<br>829 Humphries St SW, Atlanta GA 30310, USA | Baseball Player |
| **Hartsburg, Craig W**<br>Columbus Blue Jackets, Arena, 200 W Nationwide Blvd, #1, Columbus OH 43215 USA | Ice Hockey Player, Coach |
| **Hartsfield, Henry W (Hank), Jr**<br>422 Willow Vista Dr, Seabrook TX 77586, USA | Astronaut |
| **Hartsock, Jeffrey R (Jeff)**<br>1720 Swannanoa Dr, Greensboro NC 27410, USA | Baseball Player |
| **Hartung, James**<br>6426 Tanglewood Lane, Lincoln NE 68516, USA | Gymnast |
| **Hartwell, Edgerton (Ed), II**<br>3830 Galendo Dr, N Las Vegas NV 89032, USA | Football Player |
| **Hartwell, Leland H (Lee)**<br>Hutchinson Cancer Research Center, PO Box 19024, Seattle WA 98109, USA | Nobel Medicine Laureate |
| **Hartwig, Carter**<br>5539 FM 762 Road, Richmond TX 77469, USA | Football Player |
| **Hartwig, Justin J**<br>2250 Mary St, #117, Pittsburgh PA 15203, USA | Football Player |
| **Hartzell, Paul F**<br>1 Hays Mews, London W1J 5PU, England | Baseball Player |
| **Haruf, Kent**<br>Southern Illinois University, English Dept, Carbondale IL 62901, USA | Writer |
| **Harutyunyan, Arayik**<br>Premier's Office, Nagorno-Karabakh, Stepanarket, Nagornyi, Azerbaijan | Prime Minister, Nagorno-Karabakh |
| **Harvey, Adam Paul**<br>Associated International Mgmt, 7 Hatton Garden, #400, London EC1N 8AD, England | Actor |
| **Harvey, Anthony**<br>Arthur Greene, 101 Park Ave, #2607, New York NY 10178, USA | Director |
| **Harvey, Antonio**<br>5906 Yaupon Ave, Moss Point MS 39563, USA | Basketball Player |
| **Harvey, Brian**<br>National Geographic, Editorial Dept, 1145 17th St NW, Washington DC 20036 USA | Photographer, Explorer |
| **Harvey, Bryan S**<br>1224 Astoria Parkway, Catawba NC 28609, USA | Baseball Player |
| **Harvey, Cynthia T**<br>American Ballet Theater, 890 Broadway, #300, New York NY 10003, USA | Ballerina |
| **Harvey, H Douglas (Doug)**<br>32398 River Island Dr, Springville CA 93265, USA | Baseball Umpire |
| **Harvey, Harry**<br>34 Deep Hollow Lane N, Columbus NJ 08022, USA | Harness Racing Driver, Trainer |
| **Harvey, James B (Jim), Jr**<br>3685 Clarice Cove, Memphis TN 38133, USA | Football Player |
| **Harvey, James Michael**<br>Papal Household Prefecture, Roman Curia, 00120 Vatican City | Religious Leader |
| **Harvey, John C, Jr**<br>Commander, Fleet Forces Command, 1562 Mitscher Ave, Norfolk VA 23551 USA | Navy Admiral |
| **Harvey, Kenneth E (Ken)**<br>5012 Grand Ave, #C, Kansas City MO 64112, USA | Baseball Player |
| **Harvey, Kenneth R (Ken)**<br>11600 Great Falls Way, Great Falls VA 22066, USA | Football Player |
| **Harvey, Nancy**<br>7006 E Jensen St, #62, Mesa AZ 85207, USA | Golfer |
| **Harvey, Polly Jean (P J)**<br>Creative Artists Agency, 2000 Ave of Stars, #100, Los Angeles CA 90067 USA | Singer, Guitarist, Songwriter |

**Harvey, Richard C** — Football Player
3414 Baltimore Ave, Pascagoula MS 39581, USA

**Harvey, Stephen P** — Archaeologist
University of Chicago, Oriental Institute, 1155 E 58th St, Chicago IL 60637, USA

**Harvey, Steve** — Actor, Comedian
W M E Entertainment, 9601 Wilshire Blvd, #300, Beverly Hills CA 90210 USA

**Harvick, Kerry** — Singer
L G B Media, 861 High Point Ridge Road, Franklin TN 37069, USA

**Harvick, Kevin M** — Auto Racing Driver
703 Park Lawn Court, Kernersville NC 27284, USA

**Harville, Chad A** — Baseball Player
261 Farmington Road, Savannah TN 38372, USA

**Harvin, W Percy, III** — Football Player
Seattle Seahawks, 12 Seahawks Way, Renton WA 98056 USA

**Harwell, Steve** — Singer (Smash Mouth)
Creative Artists Agency, 2000 Ave of Stars, #100, Los Angeles CA 90067 USA

**Harwood, Ronald** — Writer
Judy Daish Assoc, 2 Saint Charles Place, London W10 6EG, England

**Hase, Dagmar** — Swimmer
Niederndodeleber Str 14, 29110 Magdeburg, Germany

**Hasegawa, Shigetoshi** — Baseball Player
110 Newport Center Dr, #200, Newport Beach CA 92660, USA

**Haselkorn, Robert** — Virologist
5834 S Stony Island Ave, Chicago IL 60637, USA

**Haselman, William J (Bill)** — Baseball Player
14501 SE 85th St, Newcastle WA 98059, USA

**Haselrig, Carlton L** — Football Player, Wrestler
386 William Penn Ave, Johnstown PA 15901, USA

**Haseltine, Daniel P (Dan)** — Singer (Jars of Clay)
Nettwerk Mgmt, 1650 W 2nd Ave, Vancouver BC V6J 4R3, Canada

**Haseltine, William A** — Molecular Biologist
Human Genome Sciences, 14200 Shady Grove Road, Rockville MD 20850, USA

**Hasen, Irvin H** — Cartoonist (Goldbergs, Dondi)
68 E 79th St, #E, New York NY 10075, USA

**Hasenmayer, Donald I (Don)** — Baseball Player
721 Golf Dr, Warrington PA 18976, USA

**Hasina Wajed, Sheikh** — Prime Minister, Bangladesh
Sere-e Bangla Nagar, Gono, Bhaban, Sher-e-Banglanagar, Dhakar 1207, Bangladesh

**Haskins, Clem S** — Basketball Player, Coach
2632 Roberts Road, Campbellsville KY 42718, USA

**Haskins, Dennis** — Actor
Maverick Artists Agency, 1680 N Vine St, #802, Los Angeles CA 90028, USA

**Haslem, Udonis J** — Basketball Player
3489 Gulfstream Way, Davie FL 33328, USA

**Haslett, James D (Jim)** — Football Player, Coach
118 Crandon Dr, Saint Louis MO 63105, USA

**Hass, Robert** — Writer
University of California, English Dept, Berkeley CA 94720, USA

**Hassan Ibn Talal** — Crown Prince, Jordan
Deputy King's Office, Royal Palace, Amman, Jordan

**Hassan, Fred** — Businessman
Schering-Plough Corp, 2000 Galloping Hill Road, Kenilworth NJ 07033, USA

**Hassan, Kamal** — Actor, Director
63 Lutz Church Road, Chennai TN 600004, India

**Hassan, Mohammed Waheed** — President, Maldives
Presidential Palace, Orchid Magu, Male 20208, Maldives

**Hassanal Bolkiah** — Sultan, Brunei
Istana Darul Hana, Bandar Seri Begawan, BA 1000 Brunei

**Hassel, Gerald L** — Financier
Bank of New York, 1 Wall St, #200, New York NY 10286, USA

**Hasselbeck, Donald W (Don)** — Football Player
38 Noon Hill Ave, Norfolk VA 02056, USA

**Hasselbeck, Mattthew M (Matt)** — Football Player
9027 NE 1st St, Bellevue WA 98004, USA

**Hasselbeck, Timothy T (Tim)** — Football Player, Sportscaster
38 Noon Hill Ave, Norfolk VA 02056, USA

**Hasselhoff, David** — Actor, Singer, Producer
Panacea Entertainment, 13587 Andalusia Dr E, Santa Rosa Valley CA 93012, USA

**Hasselmo, Nils** — Educator
Association of American Universities, 1200 New York Ave, #550, Washington DC 20005, USA

**Hassenfeld, Alan G** — Businessman
Hasbro Inc, 1027 Newport Ave, Pawtucket RI 02861, USA

**Hassett, Joseph P (Joey)** — Basketball Player
28 Marigold Circle, Providence RI 02904, USA

**Hassett, Marilyn** — Actress
8905 Rosewood Ave, West Hollywood CA 90048, USA

**Hassey, Ronald W (Ron)** — Baseball Player
6330 N Calle Tregua Serena, Tucson AZ 85750, USA

**Hassler, Andrew E (Andy)** — Baseball Player
PO Box 15932, Phoenix AZ 85060, USA

**Hasson, Maddie** — Actress
Coast to Coast Talent, 3350 Barham Blvd, Los Angeles CA 90068 USA

**Hasson, Maurice** — Concert Violinist
18 West Heath Court, North End Road, London NW11, England

**Hastings, Andre O** — Football Player
700 N Dobson Road, #17, Chandler AZ 85224, USA

**Hastings, Barry G** — Financier
Northern Trust Corp, 50 S La Salle St, #1, Chicago IL 60603, USA

**Hastings, Don** — Actor
524 W 57th St, #5330, New York NY 10019, USA

**Hastings, Reed** — Businessman
Netflix Inc, 100 Winchester Circle, Los Gatos CA 95032, USA

**Hastings, Scott A** — Basketball Player
10210 Ridgegate Circle, Lone Tree CO 80124, USA

**Hasty, James E** — Football Player
8212 127th Ave SE, Newcastle WA 98056, USA

**Hatch, Annia P** — Gymnast
1800 Sans Souci Blvd, #239, North Miami FL 33181, USA
**Hatch, Harold A** — Marine Corps General
8655 White Beach Way, Vienna VA 22182, USA
**Hatch, Henry J** — Army General
2715 Silkwood Court, Oakton VA 22124, USA
**Hatch, Monroe W, Jr** — Air Force General
8210 Thomas Ashleigh Lane, Clifton VA 20124, USA
**Hatch, Richard** — Actor
Omniquest Media, 1416 N La Brea Ave, Hollywood CA 90028, USA
**Hatchell, Sylvia** — Basketball Coach
University of North Carolina, Athletic Dept, Chapel Hill NC 27515, USA
**Hatcher, Derian** — Ice Hockey Player
567 Chews Landing Road, Haddonfield NJ 08033, USA
**Hatcher, Kevin J** — Ice Hockey Player
1225 S Water St, Marine City MI 48039, USA
**Hatcher, Michael V (Mickey)** — Baseball Player
1179 N Williams Dr, Queen Valley AZ 85118, USA
**Hatcher, R Dale** — Football Player
906 White Plains Road, Gaffney SC 29340, USA
**Hatcher, Teri** — Actress
United Talent Agency, U T A Plaza, 9336 Civic Center Dr, Beverly Hills CA 90210 USA
**Hatcher, William A (Billy)** — Baseball Player
7079 Shawnee Run Road, Cincinnati OH 45243, USA
**Hatchett, Joseph W** — Judge
9119 Shoal Creek Dr, Tallahassee FL 32312, USA
**Hatchette, Matthew (Matt)** — Football Player, Actor
3222 Winding Pine Trail, Longwood FL 32779, USA
**Hatfield, Juliana** — Singer, Songwriter
Ye Olde Records, PO Box 398110, Cambridge MA 02139, USA
**Hathaway, Amy** — Actress
Peter Strain, 5455 Wilshire Blvd, #1812, Los Angeles CA 90036 USA
**Hathaway, Anne** — Actress
Management 360, 9111 Wilshire Blvd, Beverly Hills CA 90210 USA
**Hathaway, Lalah** — Singer
Agency Group Ltd, 1880 Century Park E, #711, Los Angeles CA 90067 USA
**Hatori, Miho** — Singer (Cibo Matto)
Billions Corp, 3522 W Armitage Ave, Chicago IL 60647, USA
**Hatosy, Shawn** — Actor
Vox Inc, 6420 Wilshire Blvd, #1080, Los Angeles CA 90048 USA
**Hatoum, Milton** — Writer
Rogers Coleridge White, 20 Powis Mews, London W11 1JN, England
**Hatsopoulos, George N** — Businessman, Mechanical Engineer
Thermo Electron Corp, 81 Wyman St, PO Box 9046, Waltham MA 02454, USA
**Hatteberg, Scott A** — Baseball Player
802 Berg Court NW, Gig Harbor WA 98335, USA
**Hatten, Tom** — Actor
1759 Sunset Plaza Dr, Los Angeles CA 90069, USA
**Hattersley, Roy S G** — Government Official, England
House of Lords, Westminster, London SW1A 0PW, England
**Hattestad, Stine Lise** — Moguls Skier
Sundlia 1B, 1315 Nesoya, Norway
**Hatton, Ricky** — Boxer
Heart Break Hotel, 47 Rock St, Hyde, Cheshire SK14 5JH, England
**Hatton, W Vernon (Vern)** — Basketball Player
PO Box 8405, Lexington KY 40533, USA
**Hatzigiannis, Mihalis** — Singer
Universal Records, 70 Universal City Plaza, Universal City CA 91608 USA
**Hau, Lene Vestergaard** — Physicist
Harvard University, Applied Physics Dept, Cambridge MA 02138, USA
**Hauck, Frederick H (Rick)** — Astronaut
2 Redwood Lane, Falmouth ME 04105, USA
**Hauck, Timothy C (Tim)** — Football Player
2410 42nd St, Missoula MT 59803, USA
**Hauer, Brett** — Ice Hockey Player
2921 Branch St, Duluth MN 55812, USA
**Hauer, Rutger** — Actor
Glick Agency, 1260 6th St, #100, Santa Monica CA 90401, USA
**Hauerwas, Stanley** — Theologian
Duke University, Divinity School, Durham NC 27706, USA
**Haug, Ian** — Guitarist (Powderfinger)
Secret Service, PO Box 401, Fortitude Valley QLD 4006, Australia
**Haug, Norbert F** — Auto Racing Executive
Mercedes-Benz Motorsport, Brackley, Northantshire UNN 13 7BD, England
**Haugedal, Majken** — Model
Playboy Promotions, 2706 Media Center Dr, Los Angeles CA 90065 USA
**Haugen, Greg** — Boxer
PO Box 155, 1802 A St SE, Auburn WA 98002, USA
**Haukohl, Guenter** — Space Scientist
714 Watts Dr SE, Huntsville AL 35801, USA
**Haun, Lindsey** — Actress
Talent Works, 3500 W Olive Ave, #1400, Burbank CA 91505 USA
**Hauptman, Micah A** — Actor
Chaiotek, 6446 Santa Monica Blvd, Los Angeles CA 90038, USA
**Haus, Hermann A** — Electrical Engineer, Computer Scientist
38 Jeffrey Terrace, Lexington MA 02420, USA
**Hauser, Arthur A (Art)** — Football Player
2816 Walsh Road, Cincinnati OH 45208, USA
**Hauser, Cole** — Actor
A P A Talent/Literary Agency, 405 S Beverly Dr, #300, Beverly Hills CA 90212 USA
**Hauser, Erich** — Sculptor
Saline 36, 78628 Rottweil, Germany
**Hauser, Marc D** — Ethnologist, Neurologist
Harvard University, Cognitive Evolution Laboratory, 33 Kirkland, Cambridge MA 02138, USA
**Hauser, Tim** — Singer (Manhattan Transfer)
Merlin Co, 16574 Bosque Dr, Encino CA 91436, USA

Hauser, Wings — Actor
David Shapira Assoc, 193 N Robertson Blvd, Beverly Hills CA 90211 USA
Hausman, Jerry A — Economist
Massachusetts Institute of Technology, Economics Dept, Cambridge MA 02139, USA
Hausman, Thomas M (Tom) — Baseball Player
3165 Westfield Circle, Las Vegas NV 89121, USA
Hauss, Lenard M (Len) — Football Player
110 Portmere Dr, Jesup GA 31546, USA
Hauswald, Simone H — Biathlete
Robert-Schumannstr 15, 78141 Schoenwald, Germany
Hauver, Charles D — Hero
6250 S Commerce Court, #1118, Tucson AZ 85746, USA
Havelid, A Niclas — Ice Hockey Player
PO Box 129, Point Roberts WA 98281, USA
Havens, Bradley D (Brad) — Baseball Player
3227 Eden Trail, Brighton MI 48114, USA
Havens, Frank B — Canoeing Athlete
PO Box 55, Harborton VA 23389, USA
Havergal, Giles — Actor, Director
Gavin Barker Assoc, 2D Wimpole St, London W1G 0EB, England
Havig, Dennis E — Football Player
5964 Old Stilesboro Road NW, Acworth GA 30101, USA
Havlicek, John J — Basketball Player
Naismith Basketball Hall of Fame, 1150 W Columbus Ave, Springfield MA 01105 USA
Havlish, Jean — Bowler, Baseball Player
PO Box 122, Rockville MN 56369, USA
Havnevik, Kate — Singer, Songwriter
Continentica Records, 1/710 Fulham Road, London SW6 5SB, England
Havok, Davey — Singer (AFI)
S A M, 722 Seward St, Los Angeles CA 90038, USA
Havrilak, Samuel C (Sam) — Football Player
1 Trojan Horse Dr, Phoenix MD 21131, USA
Hawerchuk, Dale — Ice Hockey Player
Grande Farms, RR 5 LCD Main, Orangeville ON L9W 2Z2, Canada
Hawes, Keeley — Actress
Troika, 74 Clerkenwell Road, #300, London EC1M 5QA, England
Hawes, Roy L — Baseball Player
PO Box 854, Ringgold GA 30736, USA
Hawes, Spencer — Basketball Player
Philadelphia 76ers, 1st Union Center, 3601 S Broad St, Philadelphia PA 19148 USA
Hawes, Steven S (Steve) — Basketball Player
400 W Highland Dr, Seattle WA 98119, USA
Hawk, Aaron James (A J) — Football Player
460 B Olden Glen, De Pere WI 54115, USA
Hawk, Kali — Actress
Intellectual Artists Management, 10585 Santa Monica Blvd, #135, Los Angeles CA 90025
Hawk, Tony — Skateboarder, Actor
900 Films, 1203 Activity Dr, Vista CA 92081, USA
Hawke, Ethan — Actor, Writer
I/D Public Relations, 7060 Hollywood Blvd, #800, Los Angeles CA 90028 USA
Hawke, Robert J L (Bob) — Prime Minister, Australia
Westfield Towers, 100 William St, Level 13, Sydney NSW 2001, Australia
Hawkes, John — Actor
Innovative Artists, 1505 10th St, Santa Monica CA 90401 USA
Hawkes, Rechelle M — Field Hockey Player
I C M I, PO Box 2311, Praham VIC 3181, Australia
Hawking, Stephen W — Theoretical Physicist
University of Cambridge, Applied Math Dept, Cambridge CB3 9EW, England
Hawkins, Artrell — Football Player
12166 Peak Dr, Cincinnati OH 45246, USA
Hawkins, Barbara — Singer (Dixie Cups)
Superstars Unlimited, PO Box 371371, Las Vegas NV 89137, USA
Hawkins, Benjamin C (Ben) — Football Player
104 Deforest St, Roslindale MA 02131, USA
Hawkins, C Alexander (Alex) — Football Player
215 Bonanza Road, Denmark SC 29042, USA
Hawkins, Cornelius L (Connie) — Basketball Player, Executive
33 W Missouri Ave, #27, Phoenix AZ 85013, USA
Hawkins, Courtney T, Jr — Football Player
8305 Gale Road, Goodrich MI 48438, USA
Hawkins, Dan — Guitarist (Darkness)
Whitehouse Mgmt, PO Box 43829, London NW6 3PJ, England
Hawkins, Edwin — Gospel Musician
Sierra Mgmt, 1035 Bates Court, Hendersonville TN 37075, USA
Hawkins, Frank — Football Player
2300 Alta Dr, Las Vegas NV 89107, USA
Hawkins, Hersey R, Jr — Basketball Player
2687 Beacon Hill Dr, West Linn OR 97068, USA
Hawkins, Jennifer — Beauty Queen, Model, Actress
22 Mgmt, 34 Darling St, #B, Balmain NSW 2041, Australia
Hawkins, Justin — Singer (Darkness)
Whitehouse Mgmt, PO Box 43829, London NW6 3PJ, England
Hawkins, LaTroy (Roy) — Baseball Player
3521 Amberwood Lane, Prosper TX 75078, USA
Hawkins, M Andrew (Andy) — Baseball Player
PO Box 1595, Bruceville TX 76630, USA
Hawkins, Michael Daly — Judge
US Court of Appeals, 230 N 1st St, Phoenix AZ 85004, USA
Hawkins, Ronnie — Singer
Live Tour Artists, 1454 White Oaks Blvd, Oakville ON L6H 4R9, Canada
Hawkins, Rosa — Singer (Dixie Cups)
Superstars Unlimited, PO Box 371371, Las Vegas NV 89137, USA
Hawkins, Ross C (Rip) — Football Player
100 Tower Road, Devils Tower WY 82714, USA
Hawkins, Sally — Actress
Conway Van Gelder Grant, 8-12 Broadwick St, #300, London W1F 8HW, England

**Hawkins, Sophie B**
Trumpet Swan Productions, 520 Washington Blvd, #337, Marina del Rey CA 90292, USA — Singer, Songwriter

**Hawkins, Taylor**
Silva Artist Mgmt, 722 Seward St, Los Angeles CA 90038, USA — Drummer (Foo Fighters), Actor

**Hawkins, Thomas J (Tommy)**
1745 Manzanita Park Ave, Malibu CA 90265, USA — Basketball Player, Sportscaster

**Hawkins, Wayne A**
1 Dogwood Court, San Ramon CA 94583, USA — Football Player

**Hawkins, Wynn F**
5326 Cottage Dr, Cortland OH 44410, USA — Baseball Player

**Hawkinson, Tim**
Ace Gallery, 5514 Wilshire Blvd, #200, Los Angeles CA 90036, USA — Artist

**Hawlata, Franz**
Columbia Artists Mgmt Inc, 1790 Broadway, #702, New York NY 10019 USA — Opera Singer

**Hawley, D Sanford (Sandy)**
9625 Merrill Road, Silverwood MI 48760, USA — Thoroughbred Racing Jockey

**Hawley, Frank**
Frank Hawley Racing School, 3300 Hamilton Mill Road, #102, Buford, GA 30519, USA — Auto Racing Driver

**Hawley, Noah**
26 Keys Productions, 500 S Buena Vista St, Old Animation Building, Burbank CA 91521, USA — Producer, Writer

**Hawley, Steven A**
3303 Calvin Dr, Lawrence KS 66049, USA — Astronaut

**Hawn, Goldie**
Renaissance Literary & Talent, PO Box 17379, Beverly Hills CA 90209, USA — Actress

**Haworth, Alan**
845 112E Ave, Drummondville QC J2B 4K5, Canada — Ice Hockey Player

**Hawpe, David V**
507 Penwood Road, Louisville KY 40206, USA — Editor

**Hawthorne, Chris**
Hawthorne Gallery, 517 Jefferson St, Port Orford OR 97465, USA — Artist

**Hawthorne, Gregory D (Greg)**
1428 E Jefferson Ave, Fort Worth TX 76104, USA — Football Player

**Hawthorne, Julie**
Hawthorne Gallery, 517 Jefferson St, Port Orford OR 97465, USA — Artist

**Hawthorne, Mayer**
Creative Artists Agency, 2000 Ave of Stars, #100, Los Angeles CA 90067 USA — Singer, Songwriter

**Hax, Carolyn**
Washington Post, Editorial Dept, 1150 15th St NW, Washington DC 20071 USA — Columnist

**Hay, Colin**
Fleming Artists, 543 N Main St, Ann Arbor MI 48104, USA — Singer (Men at Work)

**Hay, Louise L**
Hay House, PO Box 5100, Carlsbad CA 92018, USA — Writer

**Haya Rashed Al Khalifa, Sheikha**
General Assembly, United Nations, United Nations Plaza, New York NY 10017, USA — Government Official, Bahrain

**Hayaishi, Osamu**
1-29 Izumigawacho, Shimogamo Sakyoku, Kyoto 606 0807, Japan — Biochemist

**Hayashi, Izuo**
OptoElectrics Research Laboratory, 5-5 Tohkodai, Tsukuba, Ibaraki 300 26, Japan — Engineer

**Hayashida, Erika**
1470 NW 107th St, Doral FL 33172, USA — Golfer

**Haydee, Marcia**
Stuttgart Ballet, Oberer Schlossgarten 6, 70173 Stuttgart, Germany — Ballerina

**Haydel, J Harold (Hal)**
304 Lynwood Dr, Houma LA 70360, USA — Baseball Player

**Hayden**
Fat Possum Records, PO Box 1923, Oxford MS 38655, USA — Singer

**Hayden, Dennis**
Susan J Talent Agency, 13273 Ventura Blvd, #104, Sherman Oaks CA 91604, USA — Actor, Producer

**Hayden, J Michael (Mike)**
5809 Sagamore Court, Lawrence KS 66047, USA — Governor, KS

**Hayden, Jim**
Philadelphia Inquirer, 400 N Broad St, Philadelphia PA 19130, USA — Publisher

**Hayden, Linda**
Michael Ladkin Mgmt, 1 Duchess St, #1, London W1N 3DE, England — Actress

**Hayden, Michael**
H W A Talent, 3500 W Olive Ave, #1400, Burbank CA 91505 USA — Actor

**Hayden, Neil Steven**
1755 York Ave, #19A, New York NY 10128, USA — Publisher

**Hayden, Pamela**
W M E Entertainment, 9601 Wilshire Blvd, #300, Beverly Hills CA 90210 USA — Actress

**Hayden, Tom**
152 Wadsworth Ave, Santa Monica CA 90405, USA — Political Activist

**Hayden, William George**
GPO Box 7829, Waterfront Place, Brisbane QLD 4001, Australia — Governor General, Australia

**Haydon Jones, Ann**
85 Westerfield Road, Edge Aston, Birmingham, West Midlands B15 3JF, England — Tennis Player

**Haye, David D**
Golden Boy Promotions, 626 Wilshire Blvd, #350, Los Angeles CA 90017 USA — Boxer

**Hayek, Salma**
Management 360, 9111 Wilshire Blvd, Beverly Hills CA 90210 USA — Actress, Model

**Hayers, Sidney A**
John Redway, 5 Denmark St, London WC2H 8LP, England — Director

**Hayes, Amy**
PO Box 717, Burgin KY 40310, USA — Model, Sportscaster

**Hayes, Anthony**
Lou Coulson Assoc, 37 Berwick St, London W1V 8RS, England — Actor

**Hayes, Ben J**
3501 10th St NE, Saint Petersburg FL 33704, USA — Baseball Player

**Hayes, Bill**
4528 Beck Ave, North Hollywood CA 91602, USA — Singer, Actor

**Hayes, Cathy Lind**
Talent Agency, 6310 San Vicente Blvd, #200, Los Angeles CA 90048, USA — Actress

**Hayes, Charles D (Charlie)**
22503 Holy Creek Trail, Tomball TX 77377, USA — Baseball Player

**Hayes, Charles E (Chuck), Jr**
Houston Rockets, 1730 Jefferson St, Houston TX 77003 USA — Basketball Player

**Hayes, Darren** — Singer (Savage Garden)
Harbour Agency, 135 Forbes St, Woolloomooloo NSW 2011, Australia
**Hayes, Denis A** — Environmentalist
Bullitt Foundation, 1212 Minor Ave, Seattle WA 98101, USA
**Hayes, Dennis C** — Engineer, Co-Inventor (Modem)
Hayes Microcomputer Products, 945 E Paces Ferry Road NE, Atlanta GA 30326, USA
**Hayes, Elvin E** — Basketball Player
14 Canaveral Creek Lane, Sugar Land TX 77479, USA
**Hayes, Erinn** — Actress
United Talent Agency, U T A Plaza, 9336 Civic Center Dr, Beverly Hills CA 90210 USA
**Hayes, Gemma** — Singer, Songwriter
Paradigm Agency, 360 N Crescent Dr, North Building, Beverly Hills CA 90210 USA
**Hayes, Gerald B** — Football Player
3841 E Windsong Dr, Phoenix AZ 85048, USA
**Hayes, Jarvis J** — Basketball Player
4495 Greycliff Pointe, Douglasville GA 30135, USA
**Hayes, Joanna D** — Track Athlete
Brentwood School, 100 S Barrington Place, Los Angeles CA 90049, USA
**Hayes, John** — Geologist, Geophysicist
Oceanographic Institution, 266 Woods Hole Road, Woods Hole MA 02543, USA
**Hayes, John P (J P)** — Golfer
740 Camino Real Ave, El Paso TX 79922, USA
**Hayes, Jonathan M** — Football Player
9632 W 116th Place, Overland Park KS 66210, USA
**Hayes, Julia** — Actress, Model
Carolina Moon Enterprises, PO Box 2571, Columbia SC 29202, USA
**Hayes, Laura** — Actress
Performance Artists Agency, 137 Goswell Road, London EC1V 7ET, England
**Hayes, Louis S** — Jazz Drummer
Abby Hoffer Enterprises, 223 1/2 E 48th St, New York NY 10017 USA
**Hayes, Mark S** — Golfer
1014 Saint Andrews Dr, Edmond OK 73025, USA
**Hayes, Patty** — Golfer
3436 Sipsey St, Villages FL 32162, USA
**Hayes, Peter** — Guitarist (Black Rebel Motorcycle Club)
Paradigm Agency, 360 Park Ave, #1600, New York NY 10022 USA
**Hayes, Reginald C (Reggie)** — Actor
Amsel Eisenstadt Frazier, 5055 Wilshire Blvd, #865, Los Angeles CA 90036 USA
**Hayes, Robert M** — Social Activist
National Coalition for the Homeless, 105 E 22nd St, New York NY 10010, USA
**Hayes, Sean P** — Actor
Hazy Mills Productions, 4024 Radford Ave, Studio City CA 91604, USA
**Hayes, Steven L (Steve)** — Basketball Player
1630 Mercoal Dr, Spring TX 77386, USA
**Hayes, Von F** — Baseball Player
435 E Illinois Road, Lake Forest IL 60045, USA
**Hayes, Wade** — Singer
Morris Management Group, 818 19th Ave S, Nashville TN 37203, USA
**Hayes, Wendell** — Football Player
1935 E 30th St, #23, Oakland CA 94606, USA
**Hayhoe, William (Bill), II** — Football Player
5146 Santa Anita Dr, Sparks NV 89436, USA
**Hayhurst, Dirk V** — Baseball Player
570 Harvey St, Kent OH 44240, USA
**Hayhurst, John O** — Inventor (Bone Tissue Reattachment)
14741 SE Wanda Dr, Portland OR 97267, USA
**Hayman, Conway** — Football Player
6811 Stiller Dr, Missouri City TX 77489, USA
**Hayman, David T** — Actor, Director
Markham Froggatt Irwin, Julian House, 4 Windmill St, London W1P 1HF, England
**Hayman, Fred** — Fashion Designer
6946 Wildlife Road, Malibu CA 90265, USA
**Hayman, Gordon I** — Cinematographer
54 Lakes Lane, Beaconsfield, Buckinghamshire HP9 2LB, England
**Hayman, James** — Producer, Director
Paradigm Agency, 360 N Crescent Dr, North Building, Beverly Hills CA 90210 USA
**Haymond, Alvin H (Juggie)** — Football Player
2857 Mantis Dr, San Jose CA 95148, USA
**Haynes, Abner** — Football Player
1950 FM 489, Oakwood TX 75855, USA
**Haynes, Al** — Airline Pilot Hero
4410 S 182nd St, Seatac WA 98188, USA
**Haynes, Colton** — Actor
I C M Partners, 10250 Constellation Blvd, #900, Los Angeles CA 90067 USA
**Haynes, Gibson J (Gibby)** — Singer, Guitarist (Butthole Surfers)
Agency Group Ltd, 142 W 57th St, #600, New York NY 10019 USA
**Haynes, Jimmy W** — Baseball Player
2601 N John B Dennis Highway, #1108, Kingsport TN 37660, USA
**Haynes, Mark** — Football Player
220 S Oneida St, Denver CO 80230, USA
**Haynes, Marques O** — Basketball Player, Coach
954 Taylor Dr, Winnsboro TX 75494, USA
**Haynes, Michael D** — Football Player
2375 Saddlesprings Dr, Alpharetta GA 30004, USA
**Haynes, Michael J (Mike)** — Football Player
7931 Entrada Lazanja, San Diego CA 92127, USA
**Haynes, Richard** — Attorney
2701 Fannin St, Houston TX 77002, USA
**Haynes, Roy O** — Jazz Drummer
Ted Kurland, 173 Brighton Ave, Boston MA 02134 USA
**Haynes, Todd** — Director
Creative Artists Agency, 2000 Ave of Stars, #100, Los Angeles CA 90067 USA
**Haynes, Verron U** — Football Player
2500 Northwinds Parkway, #275, Alpharetta GA 30009, USA
**Haynes, Warren** — Singer, Guitarist, Songwriter
Hard Head Productions, PO Box 651, New York NY 10014, USA

**Haynesworth, Albert (Al), III** — Football Player
5060 Abington Ridge Lane, Franklin TN 37067, USA

**Haynie, Jim** — Actor
2721 Reynier Ave, Los Angeles CA 90034, USA

**Haynie, Kristin** — Basketball Player
Sacramento Monarchs, Arco Arena, 1 Sports Parkway, Sacramento CA 95834 USA

**Haynie, Sandra J** — Golfer
301 Stockade Lane, Denton TX 76205, USA

**Hays, Kathryn** — Actress
Look Talent Agency, 166 Geary St, San Francisco CA 94108, USA

**Hays, L Harold** — Football Player
10410 Ravenswood Road, Granbury TX 76049, USA

**Hays, Robert** — Actor
Fran Saperstein Organization, 919 Victoria Ave, Venice CA 90291, USA

**Hays, Ronald J** — Navy Admiral
869 Kamoi Place, Honolulu HI 96825, USA

**Hays, Todd** — Bobsled Athlete
US Bobsled & Skeleton Federation, 1631 Mesa Ave, #A, Colorado Springs CO 80906 USA

**Haysbert, Dennis** — Actor
G S Mgmt, 861 S Windsor Blvd, #105, Los Angeles CA 90005, USA

**Hayter, David** — Director, Writer, Actor
United Talent Agency, U T A Plaza, 9336 Civic Center Dr, Beverly Hills CA 90210 USA

**Haythe, Justin** — Writer
Creative Artists Agency, 2000 Ave of Stars, #100, Los Angeles CA 90067 USA

**Hayward, Jimmy** — Animator, Director, Actor
United Talent Agency, U T A Plaza, 9336 Civic Center Dr, Beverly Hills CA 90210 USA

**Hayward, Justin** — Singer, Guitarist (Moody Blues)
Threshold Records, 54 High St, Cobham, Surrey KT11 3DP, England

**Hayward, Kara** — Actress
I C M Partners, 10250 Constellation Blvd, #900, Los Angeles CA 90067 USA

**Hayward, Matt** — Drummer (Band of Skulls)
Pias Entertainment Group, Trading Centre, 101 Farm Lane, #24, London SW6 1QJ, England

**Hayward, Reginald J (Reggie), Jr** — Football Player
4651 Swilcan Bridge Lane S, Jacksonville FL 32224, USA

**Hayward, Thomas B** — Navy Admiral
2200 Ross Ave, #3800, Dallas TX 75201, USA

**Haywood, Brendan T** — Basketball Player
4514 Lawndale Dr, #E, Greensboro NC 27455, USA

**Haywood, Dave** — Singer, Musician (Lady Antebellum)
Capitol Records, 3322 West End Ave, #1100, Nashville TN 37203 USA

**Haywood, Hurley** — Auto Racing Driver
1445 Ponte Vedra Blvd, Ponte Vedra Beach FL 32082, USA

**Haywood, Spencer** — Basketball Player
49447 Plymouth Way, Plymouth MI 48170, USA

**Hayworth, Tracy K** — Football Player
528 Knights Church Road, Decherd TN 37324, USA

**Hazanavicius, Michel** — Director, Editor, Writer
Creative Artists Agency, 2000 Ave of Stars, #100, Los Angeles CA 90067 USA

**Hazard, Geoffrey C, Jr** — Attorney, Educator
200 W Willow Grove Ave, Philadelphia PA 19118, USA

**Hazell, Keeley R** — Model, Singer
98 De Beauvoir Road, London N1 4EN, England

**Hazelwood, Rebecca** — Actress
Don Buchwald, 6500 Wilshire Blvd, #2200, Los Angeles CA 90048 USA

**Hazen, Maya** — Actress, Model
K Dash, 2-7-10-5F, Higashi, Shibuya Tokyo 150 0011, Japan

**Haziza, Shlomi** — Artist
H Studio, 8421 Lankershim Blvd, Sun Valley CA 91352, USA

**Hazzard, Shirley** — Writer
200 E 66th St, New York NY 10065, USA

**Head, Anthony Stewart** — Actor
Gordon & French, 12-13 Poland St, London W1F 8QB, England

**Head, Dena** — Basketball Player
Central Connecticut State University, Athletic Dept, New Britain CT 06050, USA

**Head, Donald C (Don)** — Ice Hockey Player
15240 NE Knott St, Portland OR 97230, USA

**Head, Emily** — Actress
United Talent Agency, U T A Plaza, 9336 Civic Center Dr, Beverly Hills CA 90210 USA

**Head, Glenn O** — Financier
First Investors Corp, 95 Wall St, #2200, New York NY 10005, USA

**Head, Luther D** — Basketball Player
3952 Feagan St, Houston TX 77007, USA

**Head, Roy** — Singer
Texas Sounds Entertainment, 2317 Pecan, Dickinson TX 77539, USA

**Head, Tim D** — Artist
271 Eversholt St, London NW1 1BA, England

**Headden, Susan M** — Journalist
US News & World Report, 2400 N St NW, Washington DC 20037, USA

**Headen, Andrew R (Andy)** — Football Player
PO Box 821, Liberty NC 27298, USA

**Headey, Lena** — Actress
Troika, 74 Clerkenwell Road, #300, London EC1M 5QA, England

**Headley, Chase J** — Baseball Player
3221 Baker Lane, Franklin TN 37064, USA

**Headley, Heather** — Singer, Actress
Creative Artists Agency, 2000 Ave of Stars, #100, Los Angeles CA 90067 USA

**Headly, Glenne** — Actress
I C M Partners, 10250 Constellation Blvd, #900, Los Angeles CA 90067 USA

**Headon, Nicky (Topper)** — Drummer (Clash)
Clash, 268 Camden Road, London NW1 9AB, England

**Heald, Anthony** — Actor
Abrams Artists, 9200 W Sunset Blvd, #1125, West Hollywood CA 90069 USA

**Healey, Denis W** — Government Official, England
Pingles Place, Alfriston, East Sussex BN26 5TT, England

**Healey, Derek E** — Composer
29 Stafford Road, Ruislip Gardens, Middlesex H4A 6PB, England

**Healey, John G**
Amnesty International USA, 322 8th Ave, New York NY 10001, USA — Association Executive

**Healy, Cornelius T**
Plate Die Engravers Union, 228 S Swarthmore Ave, Ridley Park PA 19078, USA — Labor Leader

**Healy, Fran**
Wildlife Entertainment, 21 Heathmans Road, London SW6 4TJ, England — Singer (Travis)

**Healy, Francis X (Fran)**
1 Primrose Lane, Holyoke MA 01040, USA — Baseball Player, Sportscaster

**Healy, Jane E**
Orlando Sentinel, Editorial Dept, 633 N Orange Ave, Lobby, Orlando FL 32801, USA — Journalist

**Healy, Jeremiah**
625 Oaks Dr, #703, Pompano Beach FL 33069, USA — Writer

**Healy, M Donald (Don)**
3427 Boca Ciega Dr, Naples FL 34112, USA — Football Player

**Healy, Patricia**
McCabe Group, 3211 Cahuenga Blvd W, #104, Los Angeles CA 90068, USA — Actress

**Healy, Timothy M (Tim)**
Ken McReddie Assoc, 101 Finsbury Pavement, London EC2A 1RS, England — Actor

**Heap, Imogen**
Primary Talent International, 10-11 Jockey's Fields, London WC1R 4BN, England — Singer (Frou Frou)

**Heap, Mark**
Curtis Brown Group, 28-29 Haymarket St, #500, London SW1Y 4SP, England — Actor, Comedian

**Heard, Amber**
W M E Entertainment, 9601 Wilshire Blvd, #300, Beverly Hills CA 90210 USA — Actress

**Heard, Garfield (Gar)**
185 Saddle Ridge Way, Fayetteville GA 30215, USA — Basketball Player, Coach

**Heard, Herman W, Jr**
PO Box 938, Broomfield CO 80038, USA — Football Player

**Heard, Jerry**
PO Box 429, Central Lake MI 49622, USA — Golfer

**Heard, John**
Forster Entertainment, 12533 Woodgreen St, Building B, Los Angeles CA 90066, USA — Actor

**Hearn, Edward J (Ed)**
5737 Theden St, Shawnee KS 66218, USA — Baseball Player

**Hearn, George**
Paradigm Agency, 360 Park Ave S, #1600, New York NY 10010 USA — Actor, Singer

**Hearn, Kevin**
Shore Fire Media, 32 Court St, #1600, Brooklyn NY 11201 USA — Musician (Barenaked Ladies)

**Hearne, Bill**
Class Act Entertainment, PO Box 160236, Nashville TN 37216, USA — Singer, Guitarist

**Hearney, Richard D**
Armed Forces Y M C A, PO Box 555028, Building 16144, Camp Pendleton CA 92055, USA — Marine Corps General

**Hearns, Thomas (Tommy)**
20551 S Norwood St, Southfield MI 48075, USA — Boxer

**Hearron, Jeffrey V (Jeff)**
5820 Hill Road, Powder Springs GA 30127, USA — Baseball Player

**Hearst Shaw, Patricia C (Patty)**
110 5th St, San Francisco CA 94103, USA — Writer

**Hearst, G Garrison**
3753 Augusta Highway, Lincolnton GA 30817, USA — Football Player

**Hearst, Richard C (Rick)**
Debbie O'Connor, PO Box 16212, Irvine CA 92623, USA — Actor

**Heat, Reverend Horton**
Atomic Music Group, 9836 Gloucester Dr, Beverly Hills CA 90210, USA — Singer, Guitarist, Songwriter

**Heath, Albert (Tootie)**
Ted Kurland, 173 Brighton Ave, Boston MA 02134 USA — Jazz Drummer (Modern Jazz Quarter)

**Heath, James E (Jimmy)**
Ted Kurland, 173 Brighton Ave, Boston MA 02134 USA — Jazz Saxophonist, Composer

**Heath, Michael T (Mike)**
2107 Timothy Terrace, Valrico FL 33594, USA — Baseball Player

**Heath, Stanley (Stan), III**
University of South Florida, Athletic Dept, Tampa FL 33620, USA — Basketball Player, Coach

**Heath, Tobin P**
US Soccer Federation, 1801 S Prairie Ave, Chicago IL 60616 USA — Soccer Player

**Heath, William C (Bill)**
1626 Lake Charlotte Lane, Richmond TX 77406, USA — Baseball Player

**Heathcock, Clayton H**
5235 Alhambra Valley Road, Martinez CA 94553, USA — Chemist

**Heathcock, R Jeffrey (Jeff)**
24962 Calle Vecindad, Lake Forest CA 92630, USA — Baseball Player

**Heathcote, Alastair**
Amateur Rowing Assn, 6 Lower Mall, London W6 9DJ, England — Rowing Athlete

**Heathcote, Jud**
5418 S Quail Ridge Circle, Spokane WA 99223, USA — Basketball Coach

**Heatherly, Eric**
A P A Talent/Literary Agency, 405 S Beverly Dr, #300, Beverly Hills CA 90212 USA — Singer

**Heatley, Daniel J (Dany)**
686 Leguime Road, #306, Kelowna BC V1W 1A4, Canada — Ice Hockey Player

**Heaton, Neal**
3 Nursery Court, East Patchogue NY 11772, USA — Baseball Player

**Heaton, Patricia**
Creative Artists Agency, 2000 Ave of Stars, #100, Los Angeles CA 90067 USA — Actress

**Heaverlo, David W (Dave)**
3720 W Lakeshore Dr, Moses Lake WA 98837, USA — Baseball Player

**Hebert, Bobby J, Jr**
855 Walker St, New Orleans LA 70124, USA — Football Player

**Hebert, Doug**
1443 E Gastib St, Lincolnton NC 28092, USA — Auto Racing Driver

**Hebert, Guy**
8 Gleneagles Dr, Newport Beach CA 92660, USA — Ice Hockey Player

**Hebert, Johnny**
Team Lotus, Kettering Hamm Hall, Wymondham, Norfolk NR18 7HW, England — Auto Racing Driver

**Hebner, Richard J (Richie)**
6 Tetreault Dr, Walpole MA 02081, USA — Baseball Player

**Hebron, Vaughn H**
800 Summit Trace Road, Langhorne PA 19047, USA — Football Player

**Hebson, Bryan** — Baseball Player
1151 Fairmont Lane, Auburn AL 36830, USA
**Heche, Anne** — Actress
United Talent Agency, U T A Plaza, 9336 Civic Center Dr, Beverly Hills CA 90210 USA
**Hecht, Duvall** — Rower
2910 W Garry Ave, Santa Ana CA 92704, USA
**Hecht, Gina** — Actress
5930 Foothill Dr, Los Angeles CA 90068, USA
**Hecht, Jessica** — Actress
Innovative Artists, 1505 10th St, Santa Monica CA 90401 USA
**Hecht, William F** — Businessman
P P & L Resources, 2 N 9th St, Allentown PA 18101, USA
**Heck, Andrew R (Andy)** — Football Player
1 Bullrush Court, Stafford VA 22554, USA
**Heck, Ralph A** — Football Player
1906 Wicks Ridge Lane, Marietta GA 30062, USA
**Hecke, Christina** — Actress
Agentur Scenario, Rambergstr 5, 80799 Munich, Germany
**Hecker, Zvi** — Architect
19 Elzar St, Tel Aviv 65157, Israel
**Heckerling, Amy** — Director, Producer
1330 Schuyler Road, Beverly Hills CA 90210, USA
**Heckler, Margaret M** — Secretary, Health & Human Services
1401 N Oak St, Arlington VA 22209, USA
**Heckman, James J** — Nobel Economics Laureate
4807 S Greenwood Ave, Chicago IL 60615, USA
**Heckscher, August** — Writer
333 E 68th St, New York NY 10065, USA
**Hector, Jamie** — Actor
T C A/Jed Root, 9220 Sunset Blvd, #315, Los Angeles CA 90069, USA
**Hector, Johnny L** — Football Player
525 Caroline St, New Iberia LA 70560, USA
**Hedaya, Dan** — Actor
Gersh Agency, 9465 Wilshire Blvd, #600, Beverly Hills CA 90212 USA
**Hedeman, Richard (Tuff)** — Rodeo Bull Rider
PO Box 224, Morgan Mill TX 76465, USA
**Heder, Jon** — Actor
B/W/R, 9100 Wilshire Blvd, #500W, Beverly Hills CA 90212 USA
**Hedford, Eric** — Singer, Drummer (Dandy Warhols)
Monqui Mgmt, PO Box 5908, Portland OR 97228, USA
**Hedgepeth, Whitney** — Swimmer
9801 Westward Dr, Austin TX 78733, USA
**Hedges, Peter** — Director, Writer
Creative Artists Agency, 2000 Ave of Stars, #100, Los Angeles CA 90067 USA
**Hedican, Bret** — Ice Hockey Player
290 Las Quebradas Lane, Alamo CA 94507, USA
**Hedison, David** — Actor
Ambrosio/Mortimer, 165 W 46th St, New York NY 10036 USA
**Hedlund, Garrett** — Actor, Singer
Brillstein Entertainment Partners, 9150 Wilshire Blvd, #350, Beverly Hills CA 90212 USA
**Hedlund, Michael D (Mike)** — Baseball Player
2412 Klinger Road, Arlington TX 76016, USA
**Hedren, Tippi** — Actress
PO Box 189, Acton CA 93510, USA
**Hedrick, Chad** — Speed Skater
5504 Fellowship Lane, Spring TX 77379, USA
**Hedrick, Joan D** — Writer
Trinity College, Women's Studies Program, 300 Summit St, Hartford CT 06106, USA
**Heeger, Alan J** — Nobel Chemistry Laureate
1042 Las Alturas Road, Santa Barbara CA 93103, USA
**Heelan, Briga** — Actress
Gersh Agency, 9465 Wilshire Blvd, #600, Beverly Hills CA 90212 USA
**Heep, Daniel W (Dan)** — Baseball Player
18610 Crosstimber, San Antonio TX 78258, USA
**Heeschen, David S** — Radio Astronomer
702 Copa de Oro, Marathon FL 33050, USA
**Heeter, Carrie** — Inventor (Sign-Language Software)
Michigan State University, Communication Technology Laboratory, East Lansing MI 48824, USA
**Heffernan, Bertram A (Bert)** — Baseball Player
130 Eagle Court, Locust Grove VA 22508, USA
**Heffernan, John** — Actor
Ken McReddie Assoc, 101 Finsbury Pavement, London EC2A 1RS, England
**Heffernan, Kevin** — Actor, Comedian
Broken Lizard Industries, PO Box 642809, Los Angeles CA 90064, USA
**Heffner, Robert F (Bob)** — Baseball Player
910 N 12th St, Allentown PA 18102, USA
**Heffron, John** — Actor, Comedian
Conversation Co, 1044 Northern Blvd, #304, Roslyn NY 11576, USA
**Heflin, Vincent G (Vince)** — Football Player
5603 Regency Park Court, #3, Suitland MD 20746, USA
**Hefner, Hugh M** — Publisher, Editor
10236 Charing Cross Road, Los Angeles CA 90024, USA
**Hegamin, George R** — Football Player
1409 S Lamar St, #512, Dallas TX 75215, USA
**Hegan, J Michael (Mike)** — Baseball Player
7 Wild Turkey Run, Hilton Head Island SC 29926, USA
**Hegarty, John F** — Labor Leader
National Postal Mail Handlers Union, 1101 Connecticut Ave NW, #500, Washington DC 20036, USA
**Hegman, Michael W (Mike)** — Football Player
2958 Suesand Dr, Memphis TN 38128, USA
**Hegman, Robert H (Bob)** — Baseball Player
3529 NW Winding Woods Dr, Lees Summit MO 64064, USA
**Hegre, Petter** — Photographer
Ocinum, Rua das Hortas, 9050-024 Funchal Madeira, Portugal
**Heidemann, Jack S** — Baseball Player
1816 S Salida del Sol Circle, Mesa AZ 85202, USA

**Heiden, Elizabeth L (Beth)** — Speed Skater
915 Swarthmore Court, Madison WI 53705, USA
**Heiden, Eric A** — Speed Skater, Cyclist
1219 Cottonwood Lane, Park City UT 84098, USA
**Heiden, Steve A** — Football Player
12047 Tivoli Park Row, #3, San Diego CA 92128, USA
**Heigl, Katherine** — Actress, Model
Jason Heigl Foundation, 3450 Cahuenga Blvd W, #905, Los Angeles CA 90068, USA
**Heil, Jennifer** — Freestyle Moguls Skier
Newport Sports Mgmt, 201 City Centre Dr, #400, Missisauga ON L5B 2T4, Canada
**Heil, Reinhold** — Composer
First Artists, 4764 Park Granada, #210, Calabasas CA 91302 USA
**Heilman, Aaron M** — Baseball Player
39W814 Kellar Square, Geneva IL 60134, USA
**Heilmeier, George H** — Inventor (Liquid Crystal Display)
Telecordia Technologies, 1 Telecordia Dr, Piscataway NJ 08854, USA
**Heimbold, Charles A, Jr** — Businessman
Bristol-Myers Squibb, 345 Park Ave, Basement LC3, New York NY 10154, USA
**Heimlich, Henry J** — Physician
3939 Erie Ave, #4060, Cincinnati OH 45208, USA
**Heimueller, Gorman J** — Baseball Player
2148 Glen Ave, Riverton UT 84065, USA
**Hein, Jeppe** — Artist
Karriere Bar, Bacon Square 57-67, 1711 Copenhagen V, Denmark
**Heine, Jutta** — Track Athlete
Blaue Muhle, 57614 Burglahr, Germany
**Heineman, Kenneth R (Ken)** — Football Player
300 Innis Free Circle, #C4, Rogers AR 72758, USA
**Heinen, Mike** — Golfer
4518 E Meadow Lane, Lake Charles LA 70605, USA
**Heinkel, Donald E (Don)** — Baseball Player
508 Covington Ave, Birmingham AL 35206, USA
**Heinle, Amelia** — Actress
Don Buchwald, 6500 Wilshire Blvd, #2200, Los Angeles CA 90048 USA
**Heinrich, Stephanie** — Model
294 S Beverly Dr, Beverly Hills CA 90212, USA
**Heinrichs, Albert M** — Philologist
Harvard University, Classics Dept, Cambridge MA 02138, USA
**Heinrichs, Rick** — Art Director, Production Designer
Sandra Marsh & Associates, 9150 Wilshire Blvd, #220, Beverly Hills CA 90212, USA
**Heins, Thorsten** — Businessman
BlackBerry, Research in Motion, 295 Phillip St, Waterloo ON N2L 3W8, Canada
**Heins, Trevor** — Actor
Abrams Artists, 275 7th Ave, #2600, New York NY 10001 USA
**Heinsohn, Thomas W (Tom)** — Basketball Player, Coach
15 Hunters Way, Needham Heights MA 02494, USA
**Heintz, Christopher J (Chris)** — Baseball Player
6002 Laketree Lane, #N, Tampa FL 33617, USA
**Heinz, Andras** — Writer
Luber Rocklin Entertainment, 8530 Wilshire Blvd, #555, Beverly Hills CA 90211 USA
**Heinz, Robert K (Bob)** — Football Player
516 Mansion Court, #502, Santa Clara CA 95054, USA
**Heinzmann, Stefanie** — Singer
Universal Music Group, 401 Commerce St, #1100, Nashville TN 37219 USA
**Heise, Robert L (Bob)** — Baseball Player
537 Live Oak Dr, Angels Camp CA 95222, USA
**Heiser, Rolland V** — Army General
4721 Ocean Blvd, #W7, Sarasota FL 34242, USA
**Heisler, Eileen** — Producer
United Talent Agency, U T A Plaza, 9336 Civic Center Dr, Beverly Hills CA 90210 USA
**Heisler, Gregory** — Photographer
Hallmark Institute of Photography, 241 Millers Falls Road, Turners Falls MA 01376, USA
**Heisler, Todd** — Photojournalist
Rocky Mountain News, Editorial Dept, 101 W Colfax Ave, Denver CO 80202, USA
**Heiss Jenkins, Carol** — Figure Skater
3183 Regency Place, Westlake OH 44145, USA
**Heist, Ari** — Singer, Songwriter
Agency Group Ltd, 142 W 57th St, #600, New York NY 10019 USA
**Heist, Hans-Joachim** — Actor
H B Mgmt, Marsiliusstr 36, 50937 Cologne, Germany
**Heitman, Dana C** — Trumpeter (Cherry Poppin' Daddies)
Paradise Artists, PO Box 1821, Ojai CA 93024 USA
**Hejda, Jan** — Ice Hockey Player
9929 Sara Gulch Circle, Parker CO 80138, USA
**Hejduk, Milan** — Ice Hockey Player
7895 Forest Keep Circle, Parker CO 80134, USA
**Hejlik, Dennis J** — Marine Corps General
Commander, Marine Forces Command, 1468 Ingram St, Norfolk VA 23511 USA
**Hekman, Peter M, Jr** — Navy Admiral
5021 Via Papel, San Diego CA 92122, USA
**Helberg, Simon** — Actor, Comedian
Brillstein Entertainment Partners, 9150 Wilshire Blvd, #350, Beverly Hills CA 90212 USA
**Held, Alan** — Opera Singer
Opus3 Artists, 470 Park Ave S, #900, New York NY 10016, USA
**Held, Archie** — Sculptor
A New Leaf Garden, 1286 Gilman St, Albany CA 94706, USA
**Held, Franklin (Bud)** — Track Athlete
13367 Caminito Mar Villa, Del Mar CA 92014, USA
**Held, Ingrid** — Actress
Agents Associes, 201 Rue du Faubourg Saint Honore, 75008 Paris, France
**Held, Mara** — Artist
Garth Greenan Gallery, 529 W 20th St, #1000, New York NY 10011, USA
**Held, Richard M** — Psychologist
Massachusetts Institute of Technology, Psychology Dept, Cambridge MA 02139, USA
**Helders, Matthew (Matt)** — Drummer (Arctic Monkeys)
Wildlife Entertainment, 21 Heathmans Road, London SW6 4TJ, England

**Helfand, Eric J** — Baseball Player
7314 Jackson Dr, San Diego CA 92119, USA
**Helfer, Ricki Tigert** — Government Official, Financier
Federal Deposit Insurance, 550 17th St NW, Washington DC 20429, USA
**Helfer, Tricia** — Model, Actress
Gilbertson Entertainment, 1334 3rd Street Promenade, #201, Santa Monica CA 90401 USA
**Helfgott, David** — Concert Pianist
PO Box 264, Vellengen NSW 2454, Australia
**Helford, Bruce** — Producer, Writer
United Talent Agency, U T A Plaza, 9336 Civic Center Dr, Beverly Hills CA 90210 USA
**Helgeland, Brian** — Director, Writer
Brillstein Entertainment Partners, 9150 Wilshire Blvd, #350, Beverly Hills CA 90212 USA
**Helgen, Kristofer M** — Vertebrate Zoologist
Smithsonian Institution, PO Box 37012, MRC 108, Washington DC 20013, USA
**Helgenberger, Marg** — Actress
Sanders/Armstrong/Caserta Mgmt, 2120 Colorado Ave, #120, Santa Monica CA 90404 USA
**Heline, DeAnn** — Producer, Writer
United Talent Agency, U T A Plaza, 9336 Civic Center Dr, Beverly Hills CA 90210 USA
**Helland, J Roy** — Make-Up Artist
Crew Co, 3941 E Chandler Blvd, #106-259, Phoenix AZ 85048, USA
**Hellawell, Keith** — Law Enforcment Official
Government Offices, Great George St, London SW1A 2AL, England
**Hellberg, Nisse** — Singer, Guitarist (Wilmer X)
United Stage Artists, Asogatan 142, Box 11029, 100 61 Stockholm, Sweden
**Hellekant, Charlotte** — Opera Singer
Harrison/Parrott, 5-6 Albion Court, London W6 0QT, England
**Heller, Andre** — Actor, Entertainer, Writer
Singerstr 8, 1010 Vienna, Austria
**Heller, Bruno** — Producer/Screenwriter
W M E Entertainment, 9601 Wilshire Blvd, #300, Beverly Hills CA 90210 USA
**Heller, Jane** — Writer
1014 Ladera Lane, Santa Barbara CA 93108, USA
**Heller, Jeffrey M** — Businessman
Electronic Data Systems, 5400 Legacy Dr, Plano TX 75024, USA
**Heller, Joe** — Editorial Cartoonist
Green Bay Press-Gazette, Editorial Dept, 435 E Walnut St, Green Bay WI 54301, USA
**Heller, John H** — Physician, Research Scientist
74 Horseshoe Road, Wilton CT 06897, USA
**Heller, Ronald J (Ron)** — Football Player
3894 Nathan Road, Santa Barbara CA 93110, USA
**Heller, Ronald R (Ron)** — Football Player
538 Stillwater River Road, Absarokee MT 59001, USA
**Hellerman, Fred** — Singer (Weavers), Songwriter
83 Good Hill Road, Weston CT 06883, USA
**Hellestrae, Dale R** — Football Player
4960 E Fellars Dr, Scottsdale AZ 85254, USA
**Hellickson, Russell (Russ)** — Freestyle Wrestler
6893 Lauren Place, Columbus OH 43235, USA
**Helliker, Kevin** — Journalist
Wall Street Journal, Editorial Dept, 1 World Financial Center, New York NY 10281, USA
**Helling, Ricky A (Rick)** — Baseball Player
3672 Landings Dr, Excelsior MN 55331, USA
**Hellman, Bonnie** — Actress
C E S D, 257 Park Ave S, #950, New York NY 10010 USA
**Hellman, Martin E** — Inventor (Public Key Cryptology)
855 Serra St, Stanford CA 94305, USA
**Hellman, Monte** — Director
8588 Appian Way, Los Angeles CA 90046, USA
**Hellmuth, Phil** — Poker Player
World Poker Tour, 1041 N Formosa, Building 99, West Hollywood CA 90046, USA
**Hellner, Marcus** — Cross Country Skier
Swedish Ski Federation, Riksskidstadion, 791 19 Falun, Sweden
**Hellstrand, Kristoffer** — Microbiologist
Goteborg University, Vice Dean's Office, 405 03 Goteborg, Sweden
**Helluin, F Jerome (Jerry)** — Football Player
3930 Southdown Mandalay Road, Houma LA 70360, USA
**Hellyer, Paul T** — Government Official, Canada
65 Harbour Square, #506, Toronto ON M5J 2L4, Canada
**Helm, Amy** — Singer (Ollabelle)
Columbia Records, 9830 Wilshire Blvd, Beverly Hills CA 90212 USA
**Helm, Zach** — Director, Writer
Gang of Two Productions, 8750 Wilshire Blvd, Beverly Hills CA 90211, USA
**Helmberger, Don V** — Seismologist
California Institute of Technology, Seismology Dept, Pasadena CA 91125, USA
**Helmer, Thomas** — Soccer Player
Rosenthaler Str 40-41, Hackesche Hofe, 10178 Berlin, Germany
**Helmerich, Hans C** — Businessman
Helmerich & Payne Inc, 1437 S Boulder Ave, #1400, Tulsa OK 74119, USA
**Helmerich, Walter H, III** — Businessman
Helmerich & Payne Inc, 1437 S Boulder Ave, #1400, Tulsa OK 74119, USA
**Helmick, Frank** — Army General
Multi-National Security Transition Command, Bagdad Iraq, APO AE 09348, USA
**Helminen, Raimo I** — Ice Hockey Player
269 N Regent St, Port Chester NY 10573, USA
**Helmond, Katherine** — Actress
14170 Montecito Place, Victorville CA 92395, USA
**Helmreich, Ernst J M** — Chemist
University of Wurzburg Biozentrum, Am Hubland, 97074 Wurzburg, Germany
**Helms, Cory** — Writer
Writers Guild of America, 700 W 3rd St, Los Angeles CA 90071, USA
**Helms, Edward P (Ed)** — Actor, Comedian
Creative Artists Agency, 2000 Ave of Stars, #100, Los Angeles CA 90067 USA
**Helms, Susan J** — Astronaut, Air Force General
Commander, 14th Air Force, Vandenberg Air Force Base CA 93437 USA
**Helms, Tommy V** — Baseball Player, Manager
5427 Blue Sky Dr, Cincinnati OH 45247, USA

**Helms, Wesley R (Wes)** — Baseball Player
9314 Bear Creek Road, Sterrett AL 35147, USA

**Helnwein, Gottfried** — Artist
Auf der Burg 2, 56659 Burgbrohl, Germany

**Heloise, (Cruse Evans)** — Columnist, Writer
PO Box 795000, San Antonio TX 78279, USA

**Helpern, Joan G** — Fashion Designer
Joan & David Helpern Inc, 46 W 55th St, #200, New York NY 10019, USA

**Helseth, Tine Ting** — Concert Trumpeter
I M G Artists, Hogarth Business Park, Chiswick, London W4 2TH, England

**Helton, Michael (Mike)** — Auto Racing Executive
National Assn of Stock Car Racing, 1801 Speedway Blvd, Daytona Beach FL 32114 USA

**Helton, Todd L** — Baseball Player
8720 E 127th Court, Brighton CO 80602, USA

**Helvin, Marie** — Model
I M G Models, 131-151 Great Titchfield St, London W1W 5BB, England

**Helwig, David G** — Writer
General Delivery, Belfast PE C0A 1A0, Canada

**Hely, Steve** — Actor
W M E Entertainment, 9601 Wilshire Blvd, #300, Beverly Hills CA 90210 USA

**Heman, Russell F (Russ)** — Baseball Player
5555 Canyon Crest Dr, #30, Riverside CA 92507, USA

**Hemingway, Gerardine** — Fashion Designer
Red or Dead Ltd, Courtney Road, Bldg 201, Wembley, Middlesex HA9 7PP, England

**Hemingway, Mariel** — Model, Actress
21300 Victory Blvd, Woodland Hills CA 91367, USA

**Hemingway, Toby** — Actor
United Talent Agency, U T A Plaza, 9336 Civic Center Dr, Beverly Hills CA 90210 USA

**Hemingway, Wayne** — Fashion Designer
15 Wembley Park Dr, Wembley, Middlesex HA9 8HD, England

**Hemme, Christy (Sunni)** — Wrestler, Model, Actress
Strachota Insurance Agency, 43500 Ridge Park Dr, #203, Temecula CA 92590, USA

**Hemmens, Heather** — Actress
Untitled Entertainment, 350 S Beverly Dr, #200, Beverly Hills CA 90212 USA

**Hemmer, Bill** — Commentator
Fox-TV, News Dept, 205 E 67th St, New York NY 10065 USA

**Hemmi, Heini** — Alpine Skier
Chalet Bel-Lia, 7077 Valbella, Switzerland

**Hemming, Lindy** — Costume Designer
Independent Talent Group, 40 Whitfield St, London W1T 2RH, England

**Hemmings, Fred, Jr** — Surfer, Surfing Executive
45-075 Auloa Road, Kaneohe HI 96744, USA

**Hemmis, Paige** — Actress
Tuff Chix, 22817 Ventura Blvd, #317, Woodland Hills CA 91364, USA

**Hemond, Scott M** — Baseball Player
263 Florida Ave, Dunedin FL 34698, USA

**Hempel, Amy** — Writer
Charles Scribner's Sons, 866 3rd Ave, New York NY 10022 USA

**Hemphill, Joel** — Singer, Songwriter
PO Box 656, Joelton TN 37080, USA

**Hemphill, Labreeska** — Singer
PO Box 656, Joelton TN 37080, USA

**Hemric, N Dixon (Dick)** — Basketball Player
1220 7th St NE, North Canton OH 44720, USA

**Hemse, Rebecka** — Actress
A I S Agency, Bergmansgatan 20, 00150 Helsinfors, Finland

**Hemsley, Stephen J** — Businessman
United HealthCare Corp, Opus Center, 9900 Bren Road E, Hopkins MN 55343, USA

**Hemsworth, Chris** — Actor
Roar Mgmt, 9701 Wilshire Blvd, #800, Beverly Hills CA 90212 USA

**Hemsworth, Liam** — Actor
Roar Mgmt, 9701 Wilshire Blvd, #800, Beverly Hills CA 90212 USA

**Hemsworth, Martin C** — Mechanical Engineer
11200 Springfield Pike, Cincinnati OH 45246, USA

**Hemus, Solomon J (Solly)** — Baseball Player, Manager
5100 San Felipe St, #194E, Houston TX 77056, USA

**Henao, Zulay** — Actress
Creative Artists Agency, 2000 Ave of Stars, #100, Los Angeles CA 90067 USA

**Henchy, Chris** — Actor, Producer, Writer
Mosiac Media Group, 9200 W Sunset Blvd, #1000, Los Angeles CA 90069 USA

**Hencken, John F** — Swimmer
PO Box 2540, Weaverville NC 28787, USA

**Henderson, Alan L** — Basketball Player
8080 N Pennsylvania St, Indianapolis IN 46260, USA

**Henderson, Bruce** — Singer, Songwriter
Fitch Thomas Mgmt, 75 E End Ave, #4C, New York NY 10028, USA

**Henderson, Cathy** — Guitarist (Antigone Rising)
W Mgmt, 266 Elizabeth St, #1A, New York NY 10012, USA

**Henderson, Cedric** — Basketball Player
PO Box 148, Smyrna GA 30081, USA

**Henderson, Craig** — Actor
Lee Morgan Management, 4 Bloomsbury Square, London WC1A 2RP, England

**Henderson, David L (Dave)** — Baseball Player
6004 142nd Court SE, Bellevue WA 98006, USA

**Henderson, David M (Dave)** — Basketball Player
805 Sweet Hollow Court, Middletown DE 19709, USA

**Henderson, Devery W, Jr** — Football Player
835 E Bellevue St, Opelousas LA 70570, USA

**Henderson, Eric N (E J), Jr** — Football Player
Minnesota Vikings, 9520 Viking Dr, Eden Prairie MN 55344 USA

**Henderson, Felicia D** — Producer, Director, Writer
Paradigm Agency, 360 N Crescent Dr, North Building, Beverly Hills CA 90210 USA

**Henderson, Fergus** — Chef, Writer
Lutyens & Rubinstein, 231 Westbourne Park Road, London W11 1EB, England

**Henderson, Florence** — Actress, Singer
F H B Productions, PO Box 11295, Marina del Rey CA 90295, USA

**Henderson, Gordon** — Fashion Designer
World Hong Kong, 80 W 40th St, New York NY 10018, USA

**Henderson, James A** — Businessman
Cummins Engine Co, PO Box 3005, 500 Jackson St, Columbus IN 47201, USA

**Henderson, Jerome M (Gerald)** — Basketball Player
185 Birkdale Dr, Blue Bell PA 19422, USA

**Henderson, Jerome M (Gerald), Jr** — Basketball Player
Charlotte Bobcats, 333 E Trade St, #A, Charlotte NC 28202 USA

**Henderson, John W** — Football Player
11667 Blackstone River Dr, Jacksonville FL 32256, USA

**Henderson, Joseph L (Jose)** — Baseball Player
525 Agua Clara St, El Paso TX 79928, USA

**Henderson, Josh** — Actor
Impression Entertainment, 9229 W Sunset Blvd, #700, Los Angeles CA 90069, USA

**Henderson, Kara** — Sportscaster
N F L Network, 10950 Washington Blvd, #100, Culver City CA 90232 USA

**Henderson, Karen LeCraft** — Judge
US Court of Appeals, 333 Constitution Ave NW, #4400, Washington DC 20001, USA

**Henderson, Kenneth J (Ken)** — Baseball Player
182 La Montagne Court, Los Gatos CA 95032, USA

**Henderson, Kristen** — Guitarist (Antigone Rising)
W Mgmt, 266 Elizabeth St, #1A, New York. NY 10012, USA

**Henderson, Martin** — Actor
Management 360, 9111 Wilshire Blvd, Beverly Hills CA 90210 USA

**Henderson, Melissa** — Soccer Player
Sky Blue F C, 80 Cottontail Lane, #400, Somerset NJ 08873 USA

**Henderson, Michael (Mike)** — Singer, Guitarist, Songwriter
Press Network, PO Box 176, Pleasant Shade TN 37145, USA

**Henderson, Paul, III** — Journalist
Seattle Times, Editorial Dept, 1000 Denny Way, Seattle WA 98109 USA

**Henderson, Pete** — Comedian (Skiles & Henderson)
Jack Grenier Productions, 32630 Concord Dr, Madison Heights MI 48071 USA

**Henderson, Rickey H** — Baseball Player
10561 Englewood Dr, Oakland CA 94605, USA

**Henderson, Shirley** — Actress
Hamilton Hodell, 66-68 Margaret St, #500, London W1W 8SR, England

**Henderson, Stephen C (Steve)** — Baseball Player
10509 Gretna Green Dr, Tampa FL 33626, USA

**Henderson, Tareva** — Singer
PO Box 17678, Nashville TN 37217, USA

**Henderson, Thomas E (Hollywood)** — Football Player
3106 E 13th St, Austin TX 78702, USA

**Henderson, Thomas E (Tom)** — Basketball Player
6822 Baron Gate Court, Spring TX 77379, USA

**Henderson, Wayne (Trombone)** — Jazz Trombonist
I C M Partners, 10250 Constellation Blvd, #900, Los Angeles CA 90067 USA

**Henderson, Wymon** — Football Player
634 Braidwood Dr NW, Acworth GA 30101, USA

**Hendley, C Robert (Bob)** — Baseball Player
645 Wimbish Road, Macon GA 31210, USA

**Hendrick, George A, Jr** — Baseball Player
72 Wildwing Court, Las Vegas NV 89135, USA

**Hendricks, Barbara** — Opera Singer
Ingpen & Williams, 131 Putney Bridge Road, London SW15 2PA, England

**Hendricks, Barkley L** — Artist
Connecticut College, Art Dept, 270 Mohegan Ave, New London CT 06320, USA

**Hendricks, Christina** — Actress
Kritzer Levine Wilkins Griffin, 11872 La Grange Ave, #100, Los Angeles CA 90025 USA

**Hendricks, Jon** — Singer
7437 Savanna Dr, Temperance MI 48182, USA

**Hendricks, Theodore P (Ted)** — Football Player
PO Box 7470, Buffalo Grove IL 60089, USA

**Hendrickson, Darby J** — Ice Hockey Player
3939 Huntingdon Dr, Hopkins MN 55305, USA

**Hendrickson, Elizabeth** — Actress
Talent Works, 3500 W Olive Ave, #1400, Burbank CA 91505 USA

**Hendrickson, Mark A** — Baseball, Basketball Player
1585 Wyndham Dr, York PA 17403, USA

**Hendrickson, Steven D (Steve)** — Football Player
2558 Miller Ave, Escondido CA 92029, USA

**Hendrie, Phil** — Actor
I C M Partners, 10250 Constellation Blvd, #900, Los Angeles CA 90067 USA

**Hendrix, Elaine** — Actress
Innovative Artists, 1505 10th St, Santa Monica CA 90401 USA

**Hendrix, John W** — Army General
Military Officers Assn, 201 N Washington St, Alexandria VA 22314, USA

**Hendry, Gloria** — Actress
H David Moss, 733 Seward St, #PH, Los Angeles CA 90038 USA

**Hendryx, Nona** — Singer, Songwriter
Take Out Productions, 630 9th Ave, #603, New York NY 10036, USA

**Henenlotter, Frank** — Director
81 Bedford St, #6E, New York NY 10014, USA

**Hengel, David L (Dave)** — Baseball Player
2642 Kingfisher Lane, Lincoln CA 95648, USA

**Henin, Justine** — Tennis Player
Blue Entertainment, 333 E Main St, #200, Louisville KY 40202 USA

**Henke, Brad William** — Actor
I F A Talent Agency, 8730 W Sunset Blvd, #490, West Hollywood CA 90069 USA

**Henke, Edgar E (Ed)** — Football Player
769 Lisa Lane, Ashland OR 97520, USA

**Henke, Nolan** — Golfer
1323 Florida Ave, Fort Myers FL 33901, USA

**Henke, Thomas A (Tom)** — Baseball Player
6200 Saint Francis Dr, Jefferson City MO 65101, USA

**Henkel, Andrea** — Biathlete
Friedensstr 37, 98701 Grossbreitenbach, Germany

**Henkel, Heike** — Track Athlete
Tannenbergstr 57, 51373 Leverkusen, Germany

**Henkel, Herbert L** — Businessman
Ingersoll-Rand Co, PO Box 6820, Piscataway NJ 08855, USA

**Henle, Gertrude** — Virologist
533 Ott Road, Bala Cynwyd PA 19004, USA

**Henley, Don** — Singer (Eagles), Songwriter
Front Line Mgmt, 1100 Glendon Ave, #2000, Los Angeles CA 90024 USA

**Henley, Drewe** — Actor
1 Granary Cottages, Combpyne, Axminster, Devon EX13 8SX, England

**Henley, Elizabeth B (Beth)** — Writer
W M E Entertainment, 9601 Wilshire Blvd, #300, Beverly Hills CA 90210 USA

**Henley, Gail C** — Baseball Player
7338 Alta Vista, La Verne CA 91750, USA

**Henley, Georgie** — Actress
Hamilton Hodell, 66-68 Margaret St, #500, London W1W 8SR, England

**Henley, Jeff** — Businessman
Oracle Systems, 500 Oriole Parkway, Redwood Shores CA 94065, USA

**Henley, Larry** — Composer
Creative Directions, PO Box 335, Brentwood TN 37024, USA

**Henley, Robert C (Bob)** — Baseball Player
11050 Moreland Dr E, Grand Bay AL 36541, USA

**Henley, Virginia** — Writer
Penguin Putnam Press, 375 Hudson St, New York NY 10014, USA

**Henn, Mark** — Animator (Little Mermaid)
Walt Disney Animation, PO Box 10200, Orlando FL 32830, USA

**Henn, Sean M** — Baseball Player
4747 Kelly Road, Aledo TX 76008, USA

**Hennagan, Monique** — Track Athlete
505 Winter View Way, Stockbridge GA 30281, USA

**Henne, Chad S** — Football Player
Jacksonville Jaguars, 1 AllTel Stadium Place, Jacksonville FL 32202 USA

**Henneman, Brian** — Singer, Guitarist (Bottle Rockets)
Undertow, 2307 Milan Court, Champaign IL 61822, USA

**Henneman, Michael A (Mike)** — Baseball Player
806 Lake Creek Dr, McKinney TX 75070, USA

**Hennen, Thomas J** — Astronaut
16315 Cascade Caverns Lane, Houston TX 77044, USA

**Henner, Marilu** — Actress
Gutmann Assoc, 188 S Bevery Dr, Beverly Hills CA 90212, USA

**Hennessey, Brad** — Baseball Player
6657 Brentridge Lane, Lambertville MI 48144, USA

**Hennessey, Debbie** — Singer, Songwriter
Rustic Music, 10736 Jefferson Blvd, #777, Culver City CA 90230, USA

**Hennessey, Walter (Wally)** — Harness Racing Driver
4141 NW 9th Court, Coconut Creek FL 33066, USA

**Hennessy, Jill** — Actress, Model
Paradigm Agency, 360 N Crescent Dr, North Building, Beverly Hills CA 90210 USA

**Hennessy, John L** — Educator
Stanford University, President's Office, Stanford CA 94305, USA

**Henney, Daniel** — Actor
Creative Artists Agency, 2000 Ave of Stars, #100, Los Angeles CA 90067 USA

**Hennig, Larry** — Wrestler
7426 43rd Ave SE, Saint Cloud MN 56304, USA

**Hennigan, Charles T (Charley)** — Football Player
3875 Line Ave, #108, Shreveport LA 71106, USA

**Hennigan, Phillip W (Phil)** — Baseball Player
PO Box 1212, Cookeville TN 38503, USA

**Hennigan, T Michael (Mike)** — Football Player, Coach
542 N Washington Ave, Cookeville TN 38501, USA

**Henning, Cameron** — Swimmer
Swimming Canada, 2197 Riverside Dr, #700, Ottawa ON K1H 7X3, Canada

**Henning, Dan** — Football Player, Coach
116 Meeting Way, Ponte Vedra Beach FL 32082, USA

**Henning, Linda** — Actress
Trinkets & Treasures, 4342 Tujunga Ave, Studio City CA 91604, USA

**Henning, Lorne E** — Ice Hockey Player, Coach
18 Coldbrook, Irvine CA 92604, USA

**Henning, Megan** — Actress
Greene Assoc, 1901 Ave of Stars, #130, Los Angeles CA 90067 USA

**Henninger, Brian** — Golfer
25481 SW Newland Road, Wilsonville OR 97070, USA

**Hennings, Chad W** — Football Player
6101 Bay Valley Court, Flower Mound TX 75022, USA

**Hennings, Sam** — Actor
S M S Talent, 8383 Wilshire Blvd, #230, Beverly Hills CA 90211 USA

**Henning-Walker, Anne** — Speed Skater
12359 E LaSalle Place, Aurora CO 80014, USA

**Hennis, Randall P (Randy)** — Baseball Player
1747 Sienna Dr, Melbourne FL 32934, USA

**Henri** — Grand Duke, Luxembourg
Palais Grand-Ducal, 17 Rue du Marche-aux-Herbes, 1728 Luxembourg-Ville, Luxembourg

**Henrich, Robert E (Bobby)** — Baseball Player
1531 Via Los Coyotes, La Habra CA 90631, USA

**Henrichs, April** — Soccer Player, Coach
US Olympic Committee, 1 Olympic Plaza, Building 6, Colorado Springs CO 80909 USA

**Henricks, Jon N** — Swimmer
254 Laurel Ave, Des Plaines IL 60016, USA

**Henricks, Terence T (Tom)** — Astronaut
Aviation Week, President's Office, 1200 G St NW, #922, Washington DC 20005, USA

**Henrie, David** — Actor
Untitled Entertainment, 350 S Beverly Dr, #200, Beverly Hills CA 90212 USA

**Henrik** — Prince Consort, Denmark
Amalienborg Palace, 1257 Copenhagen K, Denmark

**Henriksen, Donald A (Don)** — Basketball Player
18160 Cottonwood Road, Bend OR 97707, USA

**H**

| | |
|---|---|
| **Henriksen, Lance** | Actor |
| Henriksen Talent Management, 13024 Hesby St, Sherman Oaks CA 91423, USA | |
| **Henriquez, Ron** | Actor |
| PO Box 38027, Los Angeles CA 90038, USA | |
| **Henry, Albert J (Al)** | Basketball Player |
| 2410 N 52nd St, Philadelphia PA 19131, USA | |
| **Henry, Alex** | Ice Hockey Player |
| Montreal Canadiens, 1275 Saint Antoine St W, Montreal QC H3C 5L2, Canada | |
| **Henry, Boris** | Track Athlete |
| Semperstr 18, 66123 Saarbrucken, Germany | |
| **Henry, Buck** | Actor, Writer |
| 117 E 57th St, New York NY 10022, USA | |
| **Henry, Clarence (Frogman)** | Singer, Pianist, Songwriter |
| 3309 Lawrence St, New Orleans LA 70114, USA | |
| **Henry, Dale (Hank)** | Ice Hockey Player |
| 8611 Datapoint Dr, #43, San Antonio TX 78229, USA | |
| **Henry, David** | Actor |
| Rights House, Drury House, 34-43 Russell St, London WC2B 5HA, England | |
| **Henry, Dwayne A** | Baseball Player |
| 407 E Hampstead Court, Middletown DE 19709, USA | |
| **Henry, F Buford (Butch), III** | Baseball Player |
| 12072 Paseo de Amor Lane, El Paso TX 79936, USA | |
| **Henry, Gloria** | Actress |
| 849 N Harper Ave, Los Angeles CA 90046, USA | |
| **Henry, Gregg** | Actor |
| Framework Entertainment, 9057 Nemo St, #C, West Hollywood CA 90069 USA | |
| **Henry, J J** | Golfer |
| 6901 Sanctuary Lane, Fort Worth TX 76132, USA | |
| **Henry, Joe** | Singer, Guitarist, Songwriter |
| Maine Road Mgmt, 195 Chrystie St, #901F, New York NY 10002, USA | |
| **Henry, Joseph L** | Dentist |
| 60 Marinita Ave, San Rafael CA 94901, USA | |
| **Henry, Justin** | Actor |
| Metropolitan Talent Agency, 5405 Wilshire Blvd, #218, Los Angeles CA 90036 USA | |
| **Henry, Kevin L** | Football Player |
| 2408 Sardis Chase Court, Buford GA 30519, USA | |
| **Henry, Lenny** | Actor, Comedian |
| P B J Management Ltd, 5 Soho St, London W1D 3QA, England | |
| **Henry, Michael (Mike)** | Producer, Writer, Actor |
| United Talent Agency, U T A Plaza, 9336 Civic Center Dr, Beverly Hills CA 90210 USA | |
| **Henry, Michael D (Mike)** | Football Player, Actor |
| 10803 Blix St, #3, North Hollywood CA 91602, USA | |
| **Henry, Nicole** | Singer |
| NikiSings, PO Box 192011, Miami Beach FL 33119, USA | |
| **Henry, R Douglas (Doug)** | Baseball Player |
| 1804 Burries Road, Hartland WI 53029, USA | |
| **Henry, Robert H** | Judge |
| US Court of Appeals, PO Box 1767, Oklahoma City OK 73101, USA | |
| **Henry, Steve A** | Football Player |
| 1907 Darlene Way, Emporia KS 66801, USA | |
| **Henry, Thierry D (Titi)** | Soccer Player |
| Red Bulls New York, 600 Cape May St, Harrison, NJ 07029 USA | |
| **Henry, Travis D** | Football Player |
| 6698 S Shawnee Court, Aurora CO 80016, USA | |
| **Henry, Wallace (Wally)** | Football Player |
| 3444 Bernadette Court, #A, West Covina CA 91792, USA | |
| **Henry, William R (Bill)** | Baseball Player |
| 2313 Kilkenny Lane, Deer Park TX 77536, USA | |
| **Henshall, Douglas** | Actor |
| Ken McReddie Assoc, 101 Finsbury Pavement, London EC2A 1RS, England | |
| **Henshall, Ruthie** | Singer, Dancer, Actress |
| Roar Global Entertainment, 34-35 Eastcastle St, Oxford Circle, London W1W 8DW, England | |
| **Hensilwood, Christopher** | Anthropologist |
| Iziko Museum, 25 Queen Victoria St, Cape Town, South Africa | |
| **Henske, Judy** | Singer |
| Fair Star Music, PO Box 326, Plaza Station, Pasadena CA 91102, USA | |
| **Hensley, Charles F (Chuck)** | Baseball Player |
| 259 Bonanza Dr, Erie CO 80516, USA | |
| **Hensley, Clayton A (Clay)** | Baseball Player |
| 3601 Dogwood Blossom Court, Pearland TX 77581, USA | |
| **Hensley, Jimmy** | Auto, Truck Racing Driver |
| 2570 Horsepasture Price Road, Ridgeway VA 24148, USA | |
| **Hensley, John C** | Actor |
| A P A Talent/Literary Agency, 405 S Beverly Dr, #300, Beverly Hills CA 90212 USA | |
| **Hensley, Pamela** | Actress |
| Overlook Press, 141 Wooster St, #4B, New York NY 10012, USA | |
| **Hensley, Shuler** | Actor, Singer |
| Paradigm Agency, 360 N Crescent Dr, North Building, Beverly Hills CA 90210 USA | |
| **Henson, Darrin Dewitt** | Actor, Choreographer |
| Darrin's Dance Group, PO Box 3383, Memorial Station, Montclair NJ 07042, USA | |
| **Henson, John** | Actor, Comedian |
| 6347 Ivarene Ave, Los Angeles CA 90068, USA | |
| **Henson, Robby** | Director, Writer |
| New Wave Entertainment, 2660 W Olive Ave, Burbank CA 91505, USA | |
| **Henson, Samuel (Sammy)** | Freestyle Wrestler |
| U S Military Academy, Athletic Dept, West Point NY 10996, USA | |
| **Henson, Taraji P** | Actress, Singer |
| Vincent Cirrincione Assoc, 1516 N Fairfax Ave, Los Angeles CA 90046 USA | |
| **Henstridge, Elizabeth** | Actress |
| Evolution Entertainment, 901 N Highland Ave, Los Angeles CA 90038 USA | |
| **Henstridge, Natasha** | Actress, Model |
| Mosiac Media Group, 9200 W Sunset Blvd, #1000, Los Angeles CA 90069 USA | |
| **Hentgen, Patrick G (Pat)** | Baseball Player |
| 14451 Knightsbridge Dr, Shelby Township MI 48315, USA | |
| **Hentoff, Nathan I (Nat)** | Jazz Critic |
| Village Voice, Editorial Dept, 36 Cooper Square, Front 1, New York NY 10003, USA | |

**Henriksen - Hentoff**

| | |
|---|---|
| **Hentrich, Craig A** | Football Player |
| 9130 Old Smyrna Road, Brentwood TN 37027, USA | |
| **Hephner, Jeff** | Actor |
| W M E Entertainment, 9601 Wilshire Blvd, #300, Beverly Hills CA 90210 USA | |
| **Hepler, William L (Bill)** | Baseball Player |
| 12518 Fort King Road, Dade City FL 33525, USA | |
| **Heppel, Leon A** | Biochemist |
| Cornell University, Biochemistry Dept, Ithaca NY 14850, USA | |
| **Heppner, Ben** | Opera Singer |
| Columbia Artists Mgmt Inc, 1790 Broadway, #702, New York NY 10019 USA | |
| **Heras-Casado, Pablo** | Conductor |
| 21C Media Group, 162 W 56th Street, #506, New York NY 10019, USA | |
| **Herbers, Ian** | Ice Hockey Player |
| 1135 Ridgeway Road, Brookfield WI 53045, USA | |
| **Herbert of Hemingford, D Nicholas** | Publisher |
| Old Rectory, Hemingford Abbots, Huntington Cambridgeshire PE18 9AN, England | |
| **Herbert, Bob** | Columnist |
| New York Times, Editorial Dept, 229 W 43rd St, New York NY 10036 USA | |
| **Herbert, Doug** | Drag Racing Driver |
| Herbert Performance Parts, 4030 Concord Parkway S, Concord NC 28027, USA | |
| **Herbert, Johnny** | Auto Racing Driver |
| P P Sayber AG, Wildbachstr 9, 8340 Hinwil, Switzerland | |
| **Herbert, Michael K** | Editor |
| 990 Grove St, Evanston IL 60201, USA | |
| **Herbert, Raymond E (Ray)** | Baseball Player |
| 9360 Taylors Turn, Gadsden AL 35901, USA | |
| **Herbig, Gunther** | Conductor |
| Toronto Symphony, 60 Simcoe St, #C116, Toronto ON MJ5 2H5, Canada | |
| **Herbig, Michael (Bully)** | Actor, Comedian, Director |
| HerbX Medienproduktions, Sudliche Munchner Str 35A, 82031 Gruenwald, Germany | |
| **Herbst, Jeffrey** | Educator |
| Colgate University, President's Office, 13 Oak Dr, Hamilton NY 13346, USA | |
| **Herbst, Susan** | Educator |
| University of Connecticut, President's Office, Storrs CT 06269, USA | |
| **Herbst, William** | Astronomer |
| Wesleyan University, Astronomy Dept, Middletown CT 06459, USA | |
| **Herbstreit, Kirk** | Sportscaster |
| ESPN-TV, ESPN Plaza, 935 Middle St, Bristol CT 06010, USA | |
| **Herczegh, Gezar G** | Judge |
| International Justice Court, Carnegieplein 2, 2517 KJ Hague, Netherlands | |
| **Herd, Richard** | Actor |
| PO Box 56297, Sherman Oaks CA 91413, USA | |
| **Herda, Frank A** | Vietnam War Army Hero (CMH) |
| PO Box 30967, Cleveland OH 44130, USA | |
| **Heredia, Felix P** | Baseball Player |
| PO Box 4842, Hialeah FL 33014, USA | |
| **Heredia, Gilbert (Gil)** | Baseball Player |
| 4233 E Pontatoc Dr, Tucson AZ 85718, USA | |
| **Heredia, Wilson Jermaine** | Actor, Singer |
| Shadow, 10 Universal City Plaza, #2000, Universal City CA 91608, USA | |
| **Herek, Stephen R** | Director |
| Hughes Capital Entertainment, 22817 Ventura Blvd, #471, Woodland Hills CA 91364, USA | |
| **Herforth, Ralph** | Actor |
| Agentur Velvet, Dieffenbachstr 33, Hof Aufgang C, 10967 Berlin, Germany | |
| **Herges, Matthew T (Matt)** | Baseball Player |
| 21029 N 79th Place, Scottsdale AZ 85255, USA | |
| **Herheim, Stefan** | Opera Director |
| Berlin Opera, Behrenstra 55-57, 10117 Berlin, Germany | |
| **Herincx, Raimund** | Opera Singer |
| Monks' Vineyard, Larkbarrow, Shepton Mallet, Somerset BA4 4NR, England | |
| **Herkenhoff, Matthew B (Matt)** | Football Player |
| 16000 Baywood Lane, Eden Prairie MN 55346, USA | |
| **Herlihy, Tim** | Writer, Actor |
| W M E Entertainment, 9601 Wilshire Blvd, #300, Beverly Hills CA 90210 USA | |
| **Herman, Bill** | Basketball Player |
| 200 Laurel Lake Dr, #305, Hudson OH 44236, USA | |
| **Herman, David** | Actor |
| Gersh Agency, 9465 Wilshire Blvd, #600, Beverly Hills CA 90212 USA | |
| **Herman, David J (Dave)** | Football Player |
| 19 Stephens Lane, Valhalla NY 10595, USA | |
| **Herman, Jerry** | Composer, Lyricist |
| 5801 Collins Ave, #1400, Miami Beach FL 33140, USA | |
| **Herman, Mark** | Director |
| United Agents, 12-26 Lexington St, London W1F 0LE, England | |
| **Herman, Pee Wee, (Paul Reubens)** | Actor, Comedian |
| PO Box 29373, Los Angeles CA 90029, USA | |
| **Herman, Susan** | Social Activist |
| American Civil Liberties Union, 125 Broad St, #1800, New York NY 10004, USA | |
| **Hermann, Allen M** | Physicist |
| 2704 Lookout View Dr, Golden CO 80401, USA | |
| **Hermann, Peter** | Actor |
| Gersh Agency, 41 Madison Ave, #3301, New York NY 10010 USA | |
| **Hermansen, Chad B** | Baseball Player |
| 2104 Rhonda Terrace, Henderson NV 89074, USA | |
| **Hermanson, Dustin M** | Baseball Player |
| 9002 E Rimrock Dr, Scottsdale AZ 85255, USA | |
| **Herman-Wurmfeld, Charles** | Director |
| A P A Talent/Literary Agency, 405 S Beverly Dr, #300, Beverly Hills CA 90212 USA | |
| **Hermaszewski, Miroslav** | Cosmonaut, Poland; Air Force General |
| Ul Zwirki Wigury 105A, 00912 Warsaw, Poland | |
| **Hermeling, Terry A** | Football Player |
| PO Box 7321, Bend OR 97708, USA | |
| **Hermesh, Michael** | Sculptor |
| 104-800 Macleod Trail SE, Calgary AB T2G 5E6, Canada | |
| **Hermida, Jeremy R** | Baseball Player |
| 3728 Paces Park Circle SE, Smyrna GA 30080, USA | |

**Herms, George** — Artist, Sculptor
Tobey Moss Gallery, 7321 Beverly Blvd, Los Angeles CA 90036, USA
**Hernandez Colon, Rafael** — Governor, PR
Puerta de Tierra, PO Box 5788, San Juan PR 00906, USA
**Hernandez Navarro, Agustin** — Architect, Sculptor
Bosque de Acacias 61, Bosques de las Lomas, Mexico City DF 11700, Mexico
**Hernandez, Carlos** — Boxer
2038 Milan, San Antonio TX 78258, USA
**Hernandez, David** — Singer
Jeff Ballard Public Relations, 4814 N Lemona Ave, Sherman Oaks CA 91403, USA
**Hernandez, E Livan** — Baseball Player
560 Gate Lane, Miami FL 33137, USA
**Hernandez, F Xavier** — Baseball Player
3002 E Autumn Run Circle, Sugar Land TX 77479, USA
**Hernandez, Gerard** — Actor
Artmedia, 20 Ave Rapp, 75007 Paris, France
**Hernandez, Guillermo (Willie)** — Baseball Player
Calle C Buzon, PO Box 125, Bo Espina, Aguada PR 00602, USA
**Hernandez, Jay** — Actor
Alchemy Entertainment, 7024 Melrose Ave, #420, Los Angeles CA 90038 USA
**Hernandez, Jose A** — Baseball Player
22 Calle Sur, Vega Alta PR 00692, USA
**Hernandez, Jose M** — Astronaut
N A S A, Johnson Space Center, 2101 NASA Road, Houston TX 77058 USA
**Hernandez, Keith** — Baseball Player
14 Woodland Court, Southampton NY 11968, USA
**Hernandez, Lazaro** — Fashion Designer
Proenza Schouler, 120 Walker St, #1600, New York NY 10013, USA
**Hernandez, Orlando (El Duque)** — Baseball Player
1001 Brickell Bay Dr, #1710, Miami FL 33131, USA
**Hernandez, Robert J** — Businessman
U S X Corp, 600 Grant St, #450, Pittsburgh PA 15219, USA
**Hernandez, Roberto M** — Baseball Player
5969 Bayview Circle S, Saint Petersburg FL 33707, USA
**Hernandez, Rodolfo P** — Korean War Army Hero (CMH)
5328 Bluewater Place, College Lakes, Fayetteville NC 28311, USA
**Hernandez, Runelvys A** — Baseball Player
18717 E 24th Street Court S, Independence MO 64057, USA
**Herndon, Junior** — Baseball Player
1477 Sequoia Ave, Craig CO 81625, USA
**Herndon, Larry D** — Baseball Player
6149 Brunswick Road, Arlington TN 38002, USA
**Herndon, Mark J** — Singer, Drummer (Alabama)
Alabama Band Promotions, PO Box 680529, Fort Payne AL 35968, USA
**Herndon, Ty** — Singer
Cody Entertainment Group, PO Box 456, Winchester VA 22604, USA
**Herold, Catherine** — Actress
Agence Peggy Fischer, 11 Rue Du Bouloi, 75001 Paris, France
**Herr, Matt** — Ice Hockey Player
1951 Holly Creek Place, Concord CA 94521, USA
**Herr, Michael** — Writer
I C M Partners, 730 5th Ave, New York NY 10019 USA
**Herr, Thomas M (Tommy)** — Baseball Player
1077 Olde Forge Crossing, Lancaster PA 17601, USA
**Herranz Casado, Julian Cardinal** — Religious Leader
Legislative Texts Curia, Piazza Pio XII, #10, 00193 Rome, Italy
**Herremans, Todd** — Football Player
Philadelphia Eagles, 1 Novacare Way, Philadelphia PA 19145 USA
**Herrera Lopez, Hector M** — Soccer Player
Federacion de Futbol, Colima 373 Colonia Roma, Delegacion Cuauhtemoc, Mexico City DF 06700, Mexico
**Herrera, Carl V** — Basketball Player
1201 Dulles Ave, #6305, Stafford TX 77477, USA
**Herrera, Carolina** — Fashion Designer
Carolina Herrera Ltd, 501 Fashion Ave, #1700, New York NY 10018, USA
**Herrera, Efren** — Football Player
861 Atlanta Court, Claremont CA 91711, USA
**Herrera, Kristin** — Actress
Innovative Artists, 1505 10th St, Santa Monica CA 90401 USA
**Herrera, Michael A (Mike)** — Singer, Guitarist (MxPx)
W M E Entertainment, 9601 Wilshire Blvd, #300, Beverly Hills CA 90210 USA
**Herrera, Paloma** — Ballerina
American Ballet Theatre, 890 Broadway, #300, New York NY 10003 USA
**Herriage, W Troy** — Baseball Player
238 California Ave, Oakdale CA 95361, USA
**Herriman, Damon** — Actor
Lisa Mann Creative Mgmt, 99 Spring St, Bondi Junction, NSW 2022, Australia
**Herring, Hayim** — Religious Leader, Rabbi
S T A R, 1660 S Highway 100, #344, Saint Louis Park MO 55416, USA
**Herring, Kimani M (Kim)** — Football Player
6503 Cartmel Lane, Windermere FL 34786, USA
**Herring, Lynn** — Actress
Cynthia Snyder Public Relations, 5739 Colfax Ave, North Hollywood CA 91601, USA
**Herrington, John B** — Astronaut
University of Colorado, Space Studies Center, Colorado Springs CO 80918, USA
**Herrington, John S** — Secretary, Energy; Businessman
Vic Stewart's Steakhouse, 850 S Broadway Walnut Creek, CA 94596
**Herrmann, Donald B (Don)** — Football Player
PO Box 318, Brookside NJ 07926, USA
**Herrmann, Edward** — Actor
Paul Kohner, 9300 Wilshire Blvd, #555, Beverly Hills CA 90212 USA
**Herrmann, Edward M (Ed)** — Baseball Player
13153 Tobiasson Road, Poway CA 92064, USA
**Herrmann, Mark D** — Football Player
8525 Tidewater Dr W, Indianapolis IN 46236, USA
**Herrod, Jeff S** — Football Player
7645 Ballinshire N, Indianapolis IN 46254, USA

Herron, Bruce W — Football Player
8504 S Calumet Ave, Chicago IL 60619, USA
Herron, Denis — Ice Hockey Player
12841 Marsh Pointe Way, West Palm Beach FL 33418, USA
Herron, Keith O — Basketball Player
5374 Chew Ave, #G2, Philadelphia PA 19138, USA
Herron, Robert J — Architect
Herron Assoc, 28-30 Rivington St, London EC2A 3DU, England
Herron, Tim (Lumpy) — Golfer
20440 Linden Road, Excelsior MN 55331, USA
Herron-Braggs, Cindy — Singer (En Vogue)
28396 Falcon Crest Dr, Canyon Country CA 91351, USA
Herrscher, Richard F (Rick) — Baseball Player
7714 Marquette St, Dallas TX 75225, USA
Hersch, Fred — Jazz Pianist
Bennett Morgan, 1022 RR 376, #3, Wappinger Falls NY 12590 USA
Hersch, Michael — Composer
21C Music Publishing, 30 W 63rd St, #15S, New York NY 10023, USA
Herschbach, Dudley R — Nobel Chemistry Laureate
116 Conanat Road, Lincoln MA 01773, USA
Herschberger, Gary — Actor
Goodloe Law, 2029 Century Park E, #1400, Los Angeles CA 90067, USA
Herscher, Uri D — Religious Leader, Rabbi
Skirball Cultural Center, 2701 N Sepulveda Blvd, Los Angeles CA 90049, USA
Herschler, E David — Artist
New Horizon Gallery, PO Box 5859, Santa Barbara CA 93150, USA
Herschman, Adam — Actor
Kazarian/Measures/Ruskin, 11969 Ventura Blvd, #300, Studio City CA 91604 USA
Hersh, Kristin — Singer, Guitarist (Throwing Muses)
Throwing Mgmt, PO Box 248, Batesville VA 22924, USA
Hersh, Seymour M — Writer, Journalist
1211 Connecticut Ave NW, #320, Washington DC 20036, USA
Hershey, Barbara — Actress
Independent Artists, 9601 Wilshire Blvd, #750, Beverly Hills CA 90210 USA
Hershiser, Orel L Q — Baseball Player, Sportscaster
2167 Orchard Mist St, Las Vegas NV 89135, USA
Hershko, Avram — Nobel Chemistry Laureate
Technion-Israel Institute, Medical Faculty, 1 Efron St, Haifa 31096, Israel
Herskovitz, Marshall — Director
Bedford Falls Co, 409 Santa Monica Blvd, #PH, Santa Monica CA 90401, USA
Herta, Bryan J — Auto Racing Driver
24803 Los Altos Dr, Santa Clarita CA 91355, USA
Hertford, Brighton — Actor
C E S D, 10635 Santa Monica Blvd, #130, Los Angeles CA 90025 USA
Herthum, Louis — Actor
Ransack Films, 10000 Celtic Drive, #504, Baton Rouge LA 70809, USA
Hertling, Mark P — Army General
Deputy Commanding General, Initial Military Training, TraDoc, Fort Monroe VA 23651, USA
Hertweck, Neal C — Baseball Player
111 Leesburg Lane, Troutman NC 28166, USA
Hertz, C Hellmuth — Physicist
Lund Institute of Technology, Physics School, 221 00 Lund, Sweden
Hertz, Stephen A (Steve) — Baseball Player
10211 SW 96th Terrace, Miami FL 33176, USA
Hertz, Tom — Producer, Writer
W M E Entertainment, 9601 Wilshire Blvd, #300, Beverly Hills CA 90210 USA
Hertzberg, Daniel — Journalist
Wall Street Journal, Editorial Dept, 1 World Financial Center, #900, New York NY 10281, USA
Hervey, Jason — Actor
Hervey/Grimes Talent, 10561 Missouri Ave, #2, Los Angeles CA 90025 USA
Herzfeld, John M — Director
New Redemption Pictures, 3000 W Olympic Blvd, Building 3, Santa Monica CA
Herzigova, Eva — Model
One Model Mgmt, 424 W Broadway, #200, New York NY 10012 USA
Herzog, Dorrel N E (Whitey) — Baseball Player, Manager, Executive
9426 Sappington Estates Dr, Saint Louis MO 63127, USA
Herzog, Jacques — Pritzker Architectural Laureate
Herzog & De Meuron Architekten, Rheinschanze 6, 4056 Basel, Switzerland
Herzog, Roman — President, Germany
Roman Herzog Institut, Max-Joseph Str 5, 80333 Munich, Germany
Herzog, Werner — Director
Werner Herzog Film, Spiegelgasse 9, 1010 Vienna, Austria
Hesburgh, Theodore M — Educator
University of Notre Dame, 1301 Hesburgh Library, Notre Dame IN 46556, USA
Heseltine, Michael R D — Government Official, England
Thenford House, Banbury, Oxon OX17 2BX, England
Hesketh, Joseph T (Joe) — Baseball Player
202 Glenridge Road, East Aurora NY 14052, USA
Heskett, Myles — Drummer (Wolfmother)
John Watson Mgmt, PO Box 281, Surry Hills NSW 2010, Australia
Heskin, Kam — Actress
Thruline Entertainment, 9250 Wilshire Blvd, #100, Beverly Hills CA 90212 USA
Heslov, Grant A — Actor, Producer, Writer
Abrams Artists, 9200 W Sunset Blvd, #1125, West Hollywood CA 90069 USA
Hesme, Clotilde — Actress
Artmedia, 20 Ave Rapp, 75007 Paris, France
Hess, Erika — Alpine Skier
Aeschi, 6388 Gratenort, Switzerland
Hess, Jared — Director, Writer, Actor
United Talent Agency, U T A Plaza, 9336 Civic Center Dr, Beverly Hills CA 90210 USA
Hess, John B — Businessman
Amerada Hess Corp, 1185 Ave of Americas, #3900, New York NY 10036, USA
Hess, Robert — Sculptor
2661 Dorfs Ave NE, Salem OR 97301, USA
Hess, Robert G (Bob) — Ice Hockey Player
PO Box 598, Chesterfield MO 63006, USA

**Hesse, Dan** — Businessman
Sprint Nextel Corp, 2001 Edmund Halley Dr, Reston VA 20191, USA
**Hesse, Jonathan A (Jon)** — Football Player
3401 S 30th St, Lincoln NE 68502, USA
**Hesseman, Howard** — Actor
Kass Management, 501 Santa Monica Blvd, #604, Los Angeles CA 90401, USA
**Hessler, Gordon** — Director
8910 Holly Place, Los Angeles CA 90046, USA
**Hessler, Robert R** — Oceanographer
Scripps Institute of Oceanography, Biodiversity Dept, La Jolla CA 92037, USA
**Hester, Dan** — Basketball Player
13846 N Sunset Dr, Fountain Hills AZ 85268, USA
**Hester, Devin** — Football Player
2600 Lyndale Lane, Riverwoods IL 60015, USA
**Hester, Jessie L** — Football Player
12813 Pineacre Court, Wellington FL 33414, USA
**Hester, Phil** — Businessman
Advanced Micro Devices, 1 A M D Place, PO Box 3453, Sunnyvale CA 94088, USA
**Hetfield, James** — Singer, Guitarist (Metallica)
Q Prime Inc, 729 7th Ave, #1400, New York NY 10019, USA
**Hetki, John E (Johnny)** — Baseball Player
4004 Stary Dr, Cleveland OH 44134, USA
**Hetland, Tor Arne** — Cross Country Skier
Leirbruveien 24, 7026 Trondheim, Norway
**Hetrick, Jennifer** — Actress
A K A Talent, 6310 San Vicente Blvd, #200, Los Angeles CA 90048, USA
**Hetson, Greg** — Guitarist (Red Kross, Circle Jerks)
Goldstar Public Relations, PO Box 130, Ross on Wye HR9 6WY, England
**Hettich, Georg** — Nordic Combined Skier
Albert-Schweitzer-Str 1, 78136 Schonach, Germany
**Hetzel, Eric P** — Baseball Player
2271 Hetzel Road, Crowley LA 70526, USA
**Hetzel, Fred** — Basketball Player
40290 Iron Liege Court, Leesburg VA 20176, USA
**Heuer, Rolf** — Physicist
C E R N, Large Hadron Collider, 1211 Geneva 23, Switzerland
**Heughan, Sam** — Actor
United Talent Agency, U T A Plaza, 9336 Civic Center Dr, Beverly Hills CA 90210 USA
**Heuring, Lori** — Actress
B/W/R, 9100 Wilshire Blvd, #500W, Beverly Hills CA 90212 USA
**Heusinger, Patrick** — Actor
Group Entertainment, 115 W 29th St, #1102, New York NY 10001, USA
**Heward, Jamie** — Ice Hockey Player
159 Bentley Dr, Regina SK S4N 4S7, Canada
**Hewer, Mitch** — Actor
United Agents, 12-26 Lexington St, London W1F 0LE, England
**Hewett, Howard** — Singer (Shalamar)
Wenig-LaMonica Associates, 580 White Plains Road, #130, Tarrytown NY 10591 USA
**Hewish, Anthony** — Nobel Physics Laureate
Pryor's Cottage, Kingston, Cambridge CB3 7NQ, England
**Hewitt, Angela** — Concert Pianist
Opus 3 Artists, 470 Park Ave S, #900N, New York NY 10016 USA
**Hewitt, Jennifer Love** — Actress, Singer
11601 Wilshire Blvd, #1840, Los Angeles CA 90025, USA
**Hewitt, Lleyton** — Tennis Player
PO Box 1235, North Sydney NSW 2059, Australia
**Hewitt, Martin** — Actor
1147 Horn Ave, #3, West Hollywood CA 90069, USA
**Hewitt, Paul** — Basketball Coach
Georgia Institute of Technology, Athletic Dept, Atlanta GA 30332, USA
**Hewitt, Peter** — Director
Casorotto Ramsay, Waverley House, 7-12 Noel St, London W1F 8GQ, England
**Hewlett, David** — Actor
Northern Exposure Talent, 2888 Birch St, Vancouver BC V6H 2T6, Canada
**Hewlett, Jamie C** — Cartoonist (Tank Girl)
Nasty Little Man, 110 Greene St, #605, New York NY 10012 USA
**Hewson, John** — Government Official, Australia
A B N Amro Australia, 10 Spring St, #14, Sydney NSW 2000, Australia
**Hewson, John G (Jack)** — Basketball Player
114 Tahlequah Lane, Loudon TN 37774, USA
**Hextall, Dennis H** — Ice Hockey Player
2631 Harvest Hill Dr, Brighton MI 48114, USA
**Hextall, Ronald (Ron)** — Ice Hockey Player
570 29th St, Manhattan Beach CA 90266, USA
**Hexum, Nicholas L (Nick)** — Singer, Songwriter (311)
311 Hive, 8904 Florence Dr, Omaha NE 68147, USA
**Hey, Virginia** — Actress
Anthony Williams Mgmt, 50 Oxford St, Paddington NSW 2021, Australia
**Heydeman, Gregory G (Greg)** — Baseball Player
702 Ramona Ave, Monterey CA 93940, USA
**Heyer, Ingeburg** — Astronomer
PO Box 143, Burtonsville MD 20866, USA
**Heyerdahl, Christopher** — Actor
Kirk Talent Agencies, 196 W 3rd Ave, #102, Vancouver BC V5Y 1E9, Canada
**Heyland, Rob** — Actor
United Agents, 12-26 Lexington St, London W1F 0LE, England
**Heyman, David** — Producer
Bloom Hergott Diemer, 150 S Rodeo Dr, #300, Beverly Hills CA 90212 USA
**Heyman, Mark** — Writer
Protozoa Pictures, 104 N 7th St, Brooklyn NY 11211, USA
**Heyman, Richard** — Geneticist
Ligand Pharmaceuticals, 9393 Town Center Dr, #100, San Diego CA 92121, USA
**Heynert, Josef** — Actor
Agentur Gottschalk & Behrens, Sillemstr 60A, 20257 Hamburg, Germany
**Heywood, Anne** — Actress
9966 Liebe Dr, Beverly Hills CA 90210, USA

**Hiassen, Carl** — Writer
Knopf Publishers, 1745 Broadway, New York NY 10019 USA
**Hiatt, Andrew** — Molecular Biologist
Scripps Research Foundation, 10666 N Torrey Pines Road, La Jolla CA 92037, USA
**Hiatt, Fred** — Journalist
Washington Post, Editorial Dept, 1150 15th St NW, Washington DC 20071 USA
**Hiatt, John** — Singer, Guitarist, Songwriter
United Talent Agency, U T A Plaza, 9336 Civic Center Dr, Beverly Hills CA 90210 USA
**Hiatt, Philip A (Phil)** — Baseball Player
30 Littleton St, Cantonment FL 32533, USA
**Hiatt, Shana** — Model
Shandrew Public Relations, 1050 S Stanley Ave, Los Angeles CA 90019 USA
**Hibbard, J Gregory (Greg)** — Baseball Player
5287 Conifer View Lane, Lakeland TN 38002, USA
**Hibbert, Edward** — Actor
A K A Talent, 6310 San Vicente Blvd, #200, Los Angeles CA 90048 USA
**Hibbert, Frederick N (Toots)** — Singer, Orchestra Leader
Keep on Kicking Music, 330 84th St, #9, Miami Beach FL 33141, USA
**Hibbert, Roy D** — Basketball Player
Indiana Pacers, Conseco Fieldhouse, 125 S Pennsylvania, Indianapolis IN 46204 USA
**Hibbs, James K (Jim)** — Baseball Player
4659 Foothill Road, Ventura CA 93003, USA
**Hibel, Edna** — Artist
1530 53rd St, West Palm Beach FL 33407, USA
**Hick, Graeme A** — Cricketer
Worcestershire County Cricket Club, New Road, Worcester WR2 4QQ, England
**Hickam, Homer H, Jr** — Writer
9532 Hemlock Dr SE, Huntsville AL 35803, USA
**Hicke, Ernie** — Ice Hockey Player
5287 S Sugarberry Court, Gilbert AZ 85298, USA
**Hickerson, Bryan D** — Baseball Player
275 S Hunters Ridge, Warsaw IN 46582, USA
**Hickey, David L** — Labor Leader
Security Police Fire Professional Union, 25510 Kelly Road, Roseville MI 48066, USA
**Hickey, John Benjamin** — Actor
Paradigm Agency, 360 N Crescent Dr, North Building, Beverly Hills CA 90210 USA
**Hickey, Thomas H (Bo)** — Football Player
94 Field Crest Road, New Canaan CT 06840, USA
**Hickey, Thomas J** — Air Force General
2127 Bobbyber Dr, Vienna VA 22182, USA
**Hickey, William V** — Businessman
Sealed Air Corp, Park 80 E, Saddle Brook NJ 07663, USA
**Hickland, Catherine** — Actress
255 W 84th St, #2A, New York NY 10024, USA
**Hickman, Ana** — Model
I D Model Mgmt, 137 Varick St, New York NY 10013, USA
**Hickman, Dallas M** — Football Player
6521 E Dreyfus Dr, Scottsdale AZ 85254, USA
**Hickman, Darryl** — Actor
171 Hermosillo Road, Santa Barbara CA 93108, USA
**Hickman, Dwayne** — Actor
PO Box 17226, Encino CA 91416, USA
**Hickman, Fred** — Sportscaster
Atlanta Braves, Turner Field, 755 Hank Aaron Dr, Atlanta GA 30315 USA
**Hickman, James L (Jim)** — Baseball Player
PO Box 455, Henning TN 38041, USA
**Hickman, Johnny** — Singer, Guitarist (Cracker)
Back Bay Mgmt, 397 Little Neck Road, #305, Virginia Beach VA 23452 USA
**Hickman, Sara** — Singer, Songwriter
Roots Agency, 177 Woodland Ave, Westwood NJ 07675, USA
**Hickox, Anthony** — Director
United Agents, 12-26 Lexington St, London W1F 0LE, England
**Hickox, Marc** — Actor
Creative Drive Artists, 166 King St E, #400, Toronto ON M5A 1J3, Canada
**Hicks, Artis** — Football Player
1804 Woods Edge Dr NE, Leesburg VA 20176, USA
**Hicks, Bill** — Fiddler (Red Clay Ramblers)
Keith Case Assoc, 1025 17th Ave S, #200, Nashville TN 37212 USA
**Hicks, Catherine** — Actress
Margrit Polak Mgmt, 1411 Carroll Ave, Los Angeles CA 90026, USA
**Hicks, Clifford W (Cliff), Jr** — Football Player
8967 Windham Court, Spring Valley CA 91977, USA
**Hicks, Dan** — Sportscaster
NBC-TV, Sports Dept, 30 Rockefeller Plaza, #270E, New York NY 10112 USA
**Hicks, Daniel I (Dan)** — Singer
Dave Kaplan Mgmt, 1126 S Coast Highway, #101, Encinitas CA 92024, USA
**Hicks, Dwight** — Football Player
PO Box 342, Sierra Madre CA 91025, USA
**Hicks, Elizabeth (Betty)** — Golfer
669 Canyon View Dr, Laguna Beach CA 92651, USA
**Hicks, Eric D** — Football Player
6714 W 148th Terrace, Overland Park KS 66223, USA
**Hicks, India A C** — Model, Interior Designer
Storm Model Agency, 5 Jubilee Place, Chelsea, London SW3 3TD, England
**Hicks, J Stephen** — Photographer
2445 Kanan Road, Agoura Hills CA 91301, USA
**Hicks, James E (Jim)** — Baseball Player
9331 Portal Dr, Houston TX 77031, USA
**Hicks, John C, Jr** — Football Player
3287 Green Cook Road, Johnstown OH 43031, USA
**Hicks, Michelle** — Actress, Model
Domain Talent, 9229 W Sunset Blvd, #710, West Hollywood CA 90069 USA
**Hicks, Robert** — Writer
Warner Books, 1271 Ave of Americas, New York NY 10020 USA
**Hicks, Scott** — Director, Writer
PO Box 824, Kent Town 5071, South Africa

**H**

**Hicks, Taylor** — Singer
19 Entertainment, 8560 W Sunset Blvd, #900, West Hollywood CA 90069, USA
**Hicks, Thomas L (Tom)** — Football Player
207 Rivershire Lane, #106, Lincolnshire IL 60069, USA
**Hicks, W Joseph (Joe)** — Baseball Player
2707 Brookmere Road, Charlottesville VA 22901, USA
**Hicks, Wayne W** — Ice Hockey Player
7726 E Buteo Dr, Scottsdale AZ 85255, USA
**Hicks, Wilmer Kenzie (W K)** — Football Player
10149 Kemp Forest Dr, Houston TX 77080, USA
**Hickson, James E (J J), Jr** — Basketball Player
Denver Nuggets, Pepsi Center, 1000 Chopper Circle, Denver CO 80204 USA
**Hidalgo, David** — Singer (Los Lobos), Songwriter
Gold Mountain, 3940 Laurel Canyon Blvd, #444, Studio City CA 91604 USA
**Hidalgo, John** — Government Official
Mays Valentine Davenport Moore, 1899 L St NW, Washington DC 20036, USA
**Hiddleston, Thomas W (Tom)** — Actor
W M E Entertainment, 9601 Wilshire Blvd, #300, Beverly Hills CA 90210 USA
**Hide, Herbie** — Boxer
Lionheart Boxing, 415 Argyle Road, #5M, Brooklyn NY 11218, USA
**Hide, Raymond** — Geophysicist
17 Clinton Ave, East Molesey, Surrey KT8 0HS, England
**Hieb, Richard J** — Astronaut
N A S A, Johnson Space Center, 2101 NASA Road, Houston TX 77058 USA
**Hiebert, Erwin N** — Historian
40 Payson Road, Belmont MA 02478, USA
**Hiegel, Catherine** — Actress
Artmedia, 20 Ave Rapp, 75007 Paris, France
**Hier, Marvin** — Religious Leader, Rabbi, Social Activist
Simon Wiesenthal Holocaust Center, 9766 W Pico Blvd, Los Angeles CA 90035, USA
**Hieronymus, Clara W** — Journalist
50 Spring St, Savannah TN 38372, USA
**Hietpas, Joe** — Baseball Player
611 E Timberline Dr, Appleton WI 54913, USA
**Higareda, Martha** — Actress
I C M Partners, 10250 Constellation Blvd, #900, Los Angeles CA 90067 USA
**Higdon, Bruce** — Cartoonist
210 Canvasback Court, Murfreesboro TN 37130, USA
**Higgenson, Tom** — Singer, Songwriter (Plain White T's)
One Moment Mgmt, PO Box 55156, Sherman Oaks CA 91413 USA
**Higginbotham, Joan E** — Astronaut
1409 Mija Lane, Seabrook TX 77586, USA
**Higginbotham, Patrick E** — Judge
US Court of Appeals, US Courthouse, 1100 Commerce St, Dallas TX 75242, USA
**Higgins, Alan J** — Producer
Creative Artists Agency, 2000 Ave of Stars, #100, Los Angeles CA 90067 USA
**Higgins, Anthony** — Actor
I C M Partners, 10250 Constellation Blvd, #900, Los Angeles CA 90067 USA
**Higgins, Bertie** — Singer, Songwriter
J-Bird Entertainment, 248 W Park Ave, #180, Long Beach NY 11561 USA
**Higgins, Chester, Jr** — Photographer
New York Times, Editorial Dept, 229 W 43rd St, New York NY 10036, USA
**Higgins, David Anthony** — Actor, Writer, Producer
Stone Manners Salners, 9911 W Pico Blvd, #1400, Los Angeles CA 90035 USA
**Higgins, Dennis D** — Baseball Player
1123 Boonville Road, Jefferson Cty MO 65109, USA
**Higgins, J Kenneth** — Test Pilot
Boeing Commercial Airplane Group, PO Box 3707, Seattle WA 98124, USA
**Higgins, Jack** — Editorial Cartoonist
59 Waverly Ave, Clarendon Hills IL 60514, USA
**Higgins, Jack** — Writer
September Tide, Mont de la Roque, Jersey, Channel Islands JE3 8BQ, England
**Higgins, Joel** — Actor, Singer
Gage Group, 450 7th Ave, #1809, New York NY 10123 USA
**Higgins, John** — Swimmer, Swimming Coach
40 Williams Dr, Annapolis MD 21401, USA
**Higgins, John Michael** — Actor
Magnolia Entertainment, 9595 Wilshire Blvd, #601, Beverly Hills CA 90212, USA
**Higgins, Melissa (Missy)** — Singer, Songwriter
John Watson Mgmt, PO Box 281 Surry Hills NSW 2010, Australia
**Higgins, Michael D** — President, Ireland
President's Office, 'Aras an Uachtarain, Phoenix Park, Dublin 8, Ireland
**Higgins, Michael S (Mike)** — Basketball Player
137 48th Ave, Greeley CO 80634, USA
**Higgins, Robert** — Businessman
Fleet Boston Corp, PO Box 55850, Boston MA 02205, USA
**Higgins, Roderick D (Rod)** — Basketball Player
743 Mendenhall Court, Fort Mill SC 29715, USA
**Higgins, Rosalyn** — Judge
International Court of Justice, Peace Palace, 2517 The Hague KJ, Netherlands
**Higgins, Steve** — Actor
Creative Artists Agency, 2000 Ave of Stars, #100, Los Angeles CA 90067 USA
**Higginson, John** — Pathologist
16 Sundew Road, Savannah GA 31411, USA
**Higginson, Torri** — Actress
Don Buchwald, 6500 Wilshire Blvd, #2200, Los Angeles CA 90048 USA
**Higgs, Kenny** — Basketball Player
746 Sargent Dr, Owensboro KY 42301, USA
**Higgs, Peter W** — Nobel Physics Laureate
2 Darnaway St, Edinburgh EH3 6BG, Scotland
**Higham, Scott** — Journalist
Washington Post, Editorial Dept, 1150 15th St NW, Washington DC 20071 USA
**Highmore, Freddie** — Actor
Artist Rights Group, 4 Great Portland St, London W1W 8PA, England
**Highsmith, Alonzo W** — Football Player
3703 E Valley Dr, Missouri City TX 77459, USA

**Hicks - Highsmith**

**Hightower, Chelsie K** — Dancer
Abrams Artists, 9200 W Sunset Blvd, #1125, West Hollywood CA 90069 USA

**Hightower, Dont'a** — Football Player
New England Patriots, 1 Patriot Place, Foxboro MA 02035 USA

**Hightower, Rosetta** — Singer (Orlons)
Lustig Talent, PO Box 770850, Orlando FL 32877 USA

**Higuera, Joel** — Singer (Los Tucanes de Tijuana)
Tucanes Inc, 6055 E Washington Blvd, #455, Commerce CA 90040, USA

**Higuera, Teodoro V** — Baseball Player
1567 S Sycamore Place, Chandler AZ 85286, USA

**Hilario, Maybyner R (Nene)** — Basketball Player
300 W 11th Ave, #18C, Denver CO 80204, USA

**Hilbert, Andy** — Ice Hockey Player
419 N Michigan Ave, Howell MI 48843, USA

**Hildebrand, Roger H** — Astronomer, Astrophysicist
University of Chicago, Fermi Institute, 5640 S Ellis Ave, Chicago IL 60637, USA

**Hildebrandt, Greg** — Cartoonist (Terry & the Pirates)
Spiderweb Art, 5 Waterloo Road, Hopatcong NJ 07843, USA

**Hildreth, Eugene A** — Physician
2000 Cambridge Ave, #129, Reading PA 19610, USA

**Hildreth, Mark** — Actor
Characters Talent Agency, 8 Elm St, Toronto ON M5G 1G7, Canada

**Hilfiger, Tommy** — Fashion Designer
Tommy Hilfiger USA, 601 W 26th St, #500, New York NY 10001, USA

**Hilgenberg, Jay W** — Football Player
1296 Kimmer Court, Lake Forest IL 60045, USA

**Hilgenberg, Joel** — Football Player
2027 Ridgeway Dr, Iowa City IA 52245, USA

**Hilgenbrinck, Tad** — Actor
Innovative Artists, 1505 10th St, Santa Monica CA 90401 USA

**Hilgendorf, Thomas E (Tom)** — Baseball Player
PO Box 124, Camanche IA 52730, USA

**Hilger, Russell T (Rusty)** — Football Player
2625 SW 67th St, Oklahoma City OK 73159, USA

**Hiljus, Eric K** — Baseball Player
2253 Demaray Dr, Grants Pass OR 97527, USA

**Hill Smith, Marilyn** — Opera Singer
Music International, 13 Ardilaun Road, Highbury, London N5 2QR, England

**Hill, Aaron W** — Baseball Player
4741 W Addisyn Court, Visalia CA 93291, USA

**Hill, Achim** — Rowing Athlete
Dahmestr 94, 12526 Berlin, Germany

**Hill, Al D** — Ice Hockey Player
4807 Margaret Lane, Harrisburg PA 17110, USA

**Hill, Amy** — Actress
J G M, 15 Lexham Mews, London W8 6JW, England

**Hill, Anita** — Educator
Brandeis University, Heller Law School, Waltham MA 02254, USA

**Hill, Armond G** — Basketball Player
1626 Laurens Way SW, Atlanta GA 30311, USA

**Hill, Bernard** — Actor
Optimism Entertainment, 3383 Robertson Place, #2, Los Angeles CA 90034, USA

**Hill, Bob** — Basketball Coach
205 Rio Cordillera, Boerne TX 78006, USA

**Hill, Brendan C C** — Drummer (Blues Traveler)
C3 Presents, 98 San Jacinto Blvd, #400, Austin TX 78701, USA

**Hill, Brian** — Basketball Coach
Detroit Pistons, Palace, 4 Championship Dr, Auburn Hills MI 48326 USA

**Hill, Bruce E** — Football Player
1919 E Citation Lane, Tempe AZ 85284, USA

**Hill, Calvin** — Football Player, Executive
10300 Walker Lake Dr, Great Falls VA 22066, USA

**Hill, Carolyn** — Golfer
5906 Summer Point Blvd S, Gulfport FL 33707, USA

**Hill, Damon G D** — Auto Racing Driver
B R D C, Silverstone, Towcester, Northamptonshire NN12 8TN, England

**Hill, Dan** — Singer, Songwriter
Paquin Entertainment, 1067 Sherwin Road, Winnipeg MB R3H 1C1, Canada

**Hill, Dave** — Actor, Comedian
C E S D, 10635 Santa Monica Blvd, #130, Los Angeles CA 90025 USA

**Hill, David** — Football Player
13844 Buckhart St, Corona CA 92880, USA

**Hill, David B (Dave)** — Baseball Player
125 Jenny Lind Dr, Hendersonville NC 28791, USA

**Hill, David H (Dave)** — Football Player
402 Le Grand Dr, Panama City Beach FL 32413, USA

**Hill, Donald E (Donnie)** — Baseball Player
6 Knob Hill, Laguna Niguel CA 92677, USA

**Hill, Draper** — Editorial Cartoonist
1818 Northbrook Dr, Lancaster PA 17601, USA

**Hill, Dule** — Actor
I C M Partners, 10250 Constellation Blvd, #900, Los Angeles CA 90067 USA

**Hill, Dusty** — Singer, Bassist (ZZ Top)
Sanctuary Mgmt, 15301 Ventura Blvd, Building B, Sherman Oaks CA 91403, USA

**Hill, Eddie** — Drag Racing Driver
Eddie Hill's Fun Cycles, 401 N Scott Ave, Wichita Falls TX 76306, USA

**Hill, Edwin D** — Labor Leader
International Brotherhood of Electrical Workers, 1125 15th St NW, Washington DC 20005, USA

**Hill, Eric D** — Football Player
PO Box 870637, New Orleans LA 70187, USA

**Hill, Erica R** — Commentator
CNN-TV, 190 Marietta Ave SW, Atlanta GA 30303 USA

**Hill, Faith** — Singer, Actress
Creative Artists Agency, 2000 Ave of Stars, #100, Los Angeles CA 90067 USA

**Hill, Frederick G (Fred)** — Football Player
31441 Paseo Riobo, San Juan Capistrano CA 92675, USA

**Hill, Garry A** — Baseball Player
9602 Willowglen Trail, Charlotte NC 28215, USA
**Hill, Gary** — Artist
Donald Young Gallery, 224 S Michigan Ave, #266, Chicago IL 60604, USA
**Hill, Geoffrey W** — Writer
Boston University, University Professors, 745 Commonwealth St, Boston MA 02215, USA
**Hill, George J, Jr** — Basketball Player
Indiana Pacers, Conseco Fieldhouse, 125 S Pennsylvania, Indianapolis IN 46204 USA
**Hill, Gerald A (Jerry)** — Football Player
300 Hudson St, #202, Denver CO 80220, USA
**Hill, Glenallen** — Baseball Player
2913 Cortez Court, College Station TX 77845, USA
**Hill, Grant H** — Basketball Player
9600 McCormick Place, Windermere FL 34786, USA
**Hill, Gregory M (Greg)** — Football Player
8014 Downington Court, Spring TX 77379, USA
**Hill, Harry** — Hero
4225 Shore Dr, #147, Virginia Beach VA 23455, USA
**Hill, Ian** — Bassist (Judist Priest)
Trinifold Mgmt, 12 Oval Road, #300, Camden, London NW1 7DH, England
**Hill, J D** — Football Player
2375 W Comstock Dr, Chandler AZ 85224, USA
**Hill, Jack** — Director, Producer, Writer
5310 Clear Run Dr, Wilmington NC 28403, USA
**Hill, James C** — Judge
US Court of Appeals, PO Box 52598, Jacksonville FL 32201, USA
**Hill, Jane H** — Language Educator
University of Arizona, Language Dept, Tucson AZ 85721, USA
**Hill, Jeremy D** — Baseball Player
10050 Gooding Dr, Dallas TX 75229, USA
**Hill, Jim** — Football Player, Sportscaster
4120 Parva Ave, Los Angeles CA 90027, USA
**Hill, Jody** — Actor, Producer, Director
Rough House, 1722 Whitley Ave, Los Angeles CA 90028, USA
**Hill, John S** — Football Player
2005 Boyce Bridge Road, Creedmoor NC 27522, USA
**Hill, Jon Michael** — Actor
CornerStone Talent Agency, 37 West 20th St, #1108, New York NY 10011, USA
**Hill, Jonah** — Actor
W M E Entertainment, 9601 Wilshire Blvd, #300, Beverly Hills CA 90210 USA
**Hill, Jordan** — Basketball Player
Los Angeles Lakers, Staples Center, 1111 S Figueroa St, Los Angeles CA 90015 USA
**Hill, Jordan** — Singer, Songwriter
143/Atlantic Records, 9229 W Sunset Blvd, #900, West Hollywood CA 90069, USA
**Hill, Julia Butterfly** — Environmentalist
Circle of Life Foundation, PO Box 6747, Albany CA 94706, USA
**Hill, Kenneth W (Ken)** — Baseball Player
1360 Shady Oaks Dr, Southlake TX 76092, USA
**Hill, Kenneth W (Kenny)** — Football Player
121 Hawkins Place, Boonton NJ 07005, USA
**Hill, Kent A** — Football Player
630 Hawthorne Place, Fayetteville GA 30214, USA
**Hill, Kim** — Singer, Guitarist
Breen Agency, 110 30th Ave, #3, Nashville TN 37203, USA
**Hill, Koyie D** — Baseball Player
1704 NW 146th St, Edmond OK 73013, USA
**Hill, Lauren Michelle** — Model, Actress
Playboy Promotions, 2706 Media Center Dr, Los Angeles CA 90065 USA
**Hill, Lauryn** — Rap Artist (Fugees), Actress
Press Here, 138 W 25th St, #700, New York NY 10001, USA
**Hill, Marc K** — Baseball Player
203 Maple St, Elsberry MO 63343, USA
**Hill, Michael J (Mike)** — Golfer
6750 Jefferson Road, Brooklyn MI 49230, USA
**Hill, Mike** — Editor
Paradigm Agency, 360 N Crescent Dr, North Building, Beverly Hills CA 90210 USA
**Hill, Pat** — Football Coach
California State University, Athletic Dept, Fresno CA 93740, USA
**Hill, Richard J (Rich)** — Baseball Player
17 Spafford Road, Milton MA 02186, USA
**Hill, Ron** — Track Athlete
PO Box 11, Hyde, Cheshire SK14 1RD, England
**Hill, Sean** — Ice Hockey Player
2735 E Carob Dr, Chandler AZ 85286, USA
**Hill, Shaun** — Football Player
4956 Shorewood Dr, Osage Beach MO 65065, USA
**Hill, Solomon** — Basketball Player
Indiana Pacers, Conseco Fieldhouse, 125 S Pennsylvania, Indianapolis IN 46204 USA
**Hill, Steven** — Actor
18 Jill Lane, Monsey NY 10952, USA
**Hill, Susan E** — Writer
Longmoor Farmhouse, Ebrington, Chipping Campden, Gloucestershire GL55 6NW, England
**Hill, Talmadga L (Ike)** — Football Player
412 Randolph St, Oak Park IL 60302, USA
**Hill, Terence** — Actor
Iniziative Promozioni Cinematografiche, Via Francesco Siacci 38, 00197 Rome, Italy
**Hill, Terrell L** — Biophysicist, Chemist
5320 Fox Hollow Road, Eugene OR 97405, USA
**Hill, Thomas (Tom)** — Track Athlete
428 Elmcrest Dr, Norman OK 73071, USA
**Hill, Tim** — Director, Producer, Writer
Gersh Agency, 9465 Wilshire Blvd, #600, Beverly Hills CA 90212 USA
**Hill, Tyrone** — Basketball Player
Atlanta Hawks, Centennial Tower, 101 Marietta St NW, #1900, Atlanta GA 30303 USA
**Hill, Virgil** — Boxer
Timothy Downey, PO Box 442, Oceanville NJ 08231, USA

**Hill, Virgil L, Jr** — Navy Admiral, Educator
1000 Glendevon Court, Ambler PA 19002, USA
**Hill, W Robert (Bobby)** — Baseball Player
1874 Dry Creek Road, San Jose CA 95124, USA
**Hill, Walter** — Director
836 Greenway Dr, Beverly Hills CA 90210, USA
**Hill, Warren** — Jazz Saxophonist
Air Tight Mgmt, PO Box 113, Winchester Center MA 01748, USA
**Hill, Winston C** — Football Player
1900 E Girard Place, #605, Englewood CO 80113, USA
**Hillaby, John** — Writer
Constable Co, Lanchesters, 102 Fulham Palace Road, London W6 9ER, England
**Hillary, Barbara** — Model
Playboy Promotions, 2706 Media Center Dr, Los Angeles CA 90065 USA
**Hillcoat, John** — Director
Creative Artists Agency, 2000 Ave of Stars, #100, Los Angeles CA 90067 USA
**Hille, Bertil** — Physiologist
10630 Lakeside Ave NE, Seattle WA 98125, USA
**Hille, Einar** — Mathematician
8862 La Jolla Scenic Dr N, La Jolla CA 92037, USA
**Hillebrand, Gerald J (Jerry)** — Football Player
23 Madison Circle, Davenport IA 52806, USA
**Hillegas, Shawn P** — Baseball Player
870 Rockville Road, South Fork PA 15956, USA
**Hillel, Shlomo** — Government Official, Israel
14 Gelber St, Jerusalem 96755, Israel
**Hillen, Bobby, Jr** — Auto Racing Driver
Donleavy Racing, 5011 Midlothian Turnpike, Richmond VA 23225, USA
**Hillenbrand, Daniel A** — Businessman
Hillenbrand Industries, 700 State RR 46 E, Batesville IN 47006, USA
**Hillenbrand, Laura** — Writer
Jankow & Nesbitt, 445 Park Ave, New York NY 10022, USA
**Hiller, Arthur** — Director
1218 Benedict Canyon, Beverly Hills CA 90210, USA
**Hiller, David D** — Publisher
Chicago Tribune, Publisher's Office, 435 N Michigan Ave, Chicago IL 60611, USA
**Hiller, John F** — Baseball Player
W8085 Becker Dr, Iron Mountain MI 49801, USA
**Hillerman, John** — Actor
Prager & Hillerman, 12424 Wilshire Blvd, #1000, Los Angeles CA 90025, USA
**Hilliard, Dalton** — Football Player
23 Hermitage Dr, Destrehan LA 70047, USA
**Hilliard, Isaac J (Ike)** — Football Player
17020 SW 74th Ave, Palmetto Bay FL 33157, USA
**Hillier, Bevis** — Writer
Maggie Noach Literary Agency, 21 Redan St, London W14 0AB, England
**Hillier, Paul D** — Concert Singer, Music Director
Hazard Chase, 25 City Road, Cambridge CB1 1DP, England
**Hillier, Steve** — Keyboardist (Dubstar)
Primary Talent, 2-12 Petonville Road, London N1 9PL, England
**Hillis, Ali** — Actress
Luber Rocklin Entertainment, 8530 Wilshire Blvd, #555, Beverly Hills CA 90211 USA
**Hillis, David M** — Integrative Biologist
University of Texas, Computational Biology Center, Austin TX 78712, USA
**Hillis, Peyton** — Football Player
New York Giants, Meadowlands Stadium, 102 Route 120, East Rutherford NJ 07073 USA
**Hillis, W Daniel (Danny)** — Computer Scientist
Applied Minds, 1209 Grand Central Ave, Glendale CA 91201, USA
**Hillman, Chris** — Singer, Bassist (Byrds)
New Frontier Touring, 1503 17th Ave S, Nashville TN 37212, USA
**Hillman, Darius D (Dave)** — Baseball Player
849 Mimosa Dr, Kingsport TN 37660, USA
**Hillman, Darnell** — Basketball Player
6011 Medora Dr, Indianapolis IN 46228, USA
**Hillman, J Eric** — Baseball Player
157 Bellaire St, Denver CO 80220, USA
**Hillman, Larry M** — Ice Hockey Player
57 Westland St, Sainte Catharine's ON L2S 3W8, Canada
**Hills, Anthony T (Tony)** — Football Player
Buffalo Bills, 1 Bills Dr, Orchard Park NY 14127 USA
**Hills, Carla A** — Secretary, Housing & Urban Development
3125 Chain Bridge Road NW, Washington DC 20016, USA
**Hills, Douglas** — Architect
Douglas Hills Assoc, 920 S Waukegan Road, #300, Lake Forest IL 60045, USA
**Hills, Hollis H** — WW II Navy Air Force Hero
570 Marnie Circle, Melbourne FL 32904, USA
**Hills, Roderick M** — Businessman, Government Official
Mudge Rose Guthrie Alexander Ferdon, 1200 19th St NW, Washington DC 20036, USA
**Hilmers, David C** — Astronaut
2846 Bellefontaine St, Houston TX 77025, USA
**Hilmes, Jerome B** — Army General
4900 Windsor Park, Sarasota FL 34235, USA
**Hilson, Keri** — Singer, Songwriter
I C M Partners, 10250 Constellation Blvd, #900, Los Angeles CA 90067 USA
**Hilton, Barron** — Businessman
Hilton Hotels Corp, 7930 Jones Branch Dr, #100, McLean VA 22102, USA
**Hilton, J David (Dave)** — Baseball Player
4910 E Sunnyside Dr, Scottsdale AZ 85254, USA
**Hilton, John J** — Football Player
3911 S Fairway Dr, Powhatan VA 23139, USA
**Hilton, Paris** — Model, Actress
Paris Hilton Entertainment, 250 N Canon Dr, #100, Beverly Hills CA 90210 USA
**Hilton, Roy L** — Football Player
8332 Merrymount Dr, Windsor Mill MD 21244, USA
**Hilton, Tyler** — Actor, Singer
Emblem Mgmt, 22315 Mulholland Highway, Calabasas CA 91302, USA

**Hilty, Megan** — Actress, Singer
Gersh Agency, 9465 Wilshire Blvd, #600, Beverly Hills CA 90212 USA
**Hiltz, Nichole** — Actress
Sanders/Armstrong/Caserta Mgmt, 2120 Colorado Ave, #120, Santa Monica CA 90404 USA
**Hiltzik, Michael A** — Journalist
Los Angeles Times, Editorial Dept, 202 W 1st St, Los Angeles CA 90012 USA
**Himelstein, Aaron** — Actor
Innovative Artists, 1505 10th St, Santa Monica CA 90401 USA
**Himes Gomez, Margaret** — Interior Designer
Gomez Assoc, 504 E 74th St, #300, New York NY 10021, USA
**Himes, Richard D (Dick)** — Football Player
431 Prairie Lane, Luxemburg WI 54217, USA
**Hinault, Bernard** — Cyclist
Quest Levure, 7 Rue de la Sauvaie, 21 Sud-Est, 35000 Rennes, France
**Hinchcliffe, James** — Auto Racing Driver
Andretti Audiosport, 7615 Zionsville Road, Indianapolis IN 46268, USA
**Hinchliffe, Dickon** — Composer
First Artists Mgmt, 4764 Park Granada, #210, Calabasas CA 91302 USA
**Hindle, Art** — Actor
Independent Artists, 9601 Wilshire Blvd, #750, Beverly Hills CA 90210 USA
**Hindman, Stanley C (Stan)** — Football Player
824 Creed Road, Oakland CA 94610, USA
**Hindmarch, Anya** — Fashion Designer
Plough Brewery, 516 Wandsworth Road, London SW8 3JX, England
**Hinds, Aisha** — Actress
Greene Assoc, 1901 Ave of Stars, #130, Los Angeles CA 90067 USA
**Hinds, Brent** — Guitarist, Singer (Mastodon)
Pinnacle Entertainment, 30 Glenn St, White Plains NY 10603, USA
**Hinds, Ciaran** — Actor
Dalzell & Beresford, 26 Astwood Mews, London SW7 4DE, England
**Hinds, David** — Singer, Guitarist (Steel Pulse)
Steel Pulse Ltd, 33 Kersley Road, London N16 0NT, England
**Hinds, Samuel A A** — Prime Minister, Guyana
Prime Minister's Office, Wights Lane, Georgetown, Guyana
**Hinds, Samuel R (Sam)** — Baseball Player
320 S 56th Terrace, Hollywood FL 33023, USA
**Hinds, William E (Bill)** — Cartoonist (Tank McNamara)
1301 Spring Oaks Circle, Houston TX 77055, USA
**Hine, Maynard K** — Dentist
1121 W Michigan St, Indianapolis IN 46202, USA
**Hine, Patrick** — Air Force Marshal, England
Lloyd's Bank, Cox's & Kings, 7 Pall Mall, London SW1 5NA, England
**Hiner, Glen H, Jr** — Businessman
Owens-Corning, 1 Owens Corning Parkway, Toledo OH 43659, USA
**Hines, Brendan** — Actor
Talent Works, 3500 W Olive Ave, #1400, Burbank CA 91505 USA
**Hines, Cheryl** — Actress, Comedienne
W M E Entertainment, 9601 Wilshire Blvd, #300, Beverly Hills CA 90210 USA
**Hines, Deni** — Singer
Entertainment Consulting, 15 Alice St, Padstow NSW 2211, Australia
**Hines, Garrett** — Bobsled Athlete
US Bobsled & Skeleton Federation, 1631 Mesa Ave, #A, Colorado Springs CO 80906 USA
**Hines, Glen R** — Football Player
861 N Queen Annes Lace Dr, Fayetteville AR 72704, USA
**Hines, Mimi** — Actress, Comedienne
Scott Stander Assoc, 4533 Van Nuys Blvd, #401, Sherman Oaks CA 91403 USA
**Hingis, Martina** — Tennis Player
Inselweg 28, 8640 Hurden, Switzerland
**Hingorani, Narain G** — Electrical Engineer
835 W Big Sand Place, Oro Valley AZ 85755, USA
**Hingsen, Jurgen** — Track Athlete
655 Circle Dr, Santa Barbara CA 93108, USA
**Hinkle, Bryan E** — Football Player
1402 Missouri Ave, Bridgeville PA 15017, USA
**Hinkle, George A** — Football Player
4998 Willowford Road, Robertsville MO 63072, USA
**Hinkle, Lon** — Golfer
PO Box 1347, Bigfork MT 59911, USA
**Hinkle, Marin** — Actress
Innovative Artists, 1505 10th St, Santa Monica CA 90401 USA
**Hinnant, Michael W (Mike)** — Football Player
43 Ashford Way, Schwenksville PA 19473, USA
**Hinners, Noel** — Government Official
7 Greyswood Court, Potomac MD 20854, USA
**Hino, Kazuyoshi** — Fashion Designer
Hino & Malee Inc, 3701 N Ravenswood Ave, Chicago IL 60613, USA
**Hinojosa, Ricardo H** — Judge
US District Court, PO Box 5007, McAllen TX 78502, USA
**Hinojosa, Tish** — Singer, Songwriter
PO Box 3304, Austin TX 78764, USA
**Hinote, Daniel C (Dan)** — Ice Hockey Player
4323 Forest Park Ave, Saint Louis MO 63108, USA
**Hinrich, Kirk J** — Basketball Player
1886 Hilltop Lane, Bannockburn IL 60015, USA
**Hinrichs, Fabian** — Actor
Heppeler Agency, Steinstr 54, 81667 Munich, Germany
**Hinse, Andre** — Ice Hockey Player
PO Box 237, Fort Cobb OK 73038, USA
**Hinske, Eric S** — Baseball Player
10222 E Southwind Lane, #1041, Scottsdale AZ 85262, USA
**Hinson, Jordan D** — Actress
Inphenate, 9701 Wilshire Blvd, #1000, Beverly Hills CA 90212 USA
**Hinson, Larry** — Golfer
3179 Highway 32 E, Douglas GA 31533, USA
**Hinson, Roy M** — Basketball Player
8167 Quail Meadow Way, West Palm Beach FL 33412, USA

| | |
|---|---|
| **Hinterseer, Ernst** | Alpine Skier |
| Hahnenkammstr, 6370 Kitzbuhel, Austria | |
| **Hinton, Christopher J (Chris)** | Football Player |
| 374 Citadella Court, Alpharetta GA 30022, USA | |
| **Hinton, Eddie** | Football Player |
| 34 Auburn Ridge, Spring Branch TX 78070, USA | |
| **Hinton, Jerrika** | Actress |
| Greene Assoc, 1901 Ave of Stars, #130, Los Angeles CA 90067 USA | |
| **Hinton, Jessa** | Model |
| Playboy Promotions, 2706 Media Center Dr, Los Angeles CA 90065 USA | |
| **Hinton, Richard M (Rich)** | Baseball Player |
| 7447 Hawkins Road, Sarasota FL 34241, USA | |
| **Hinton, Susan Eloise (S E)** | Writer |
| Delacorte Press, 1540 Broadway, New York NY 10036, USA | |
| **Hintz, Donald C** | Businessman |
| Entergy Corp, 10055 Grogans Mill Road, #150, Spring TX 77380, USA | |
| **Hinze, Kristy** | Model, Actress |
| Ford Models Inc, 111 5th Ave, #900, New York NY 10003 USA | |
| **Hinzo, Thomas L (Tommy)** | Baseball Player |
| 635 Imperial Beach Blvd, Imperial Beach CA 91932, USA | |
| **Hiort, Esbjorn** | Architect |
| Bel Colles Farm, Parkvej 6, 2960 Rungsted Kyst, Denmark | |
| **Hipp, Paul** | Actor |
| Stone Manners Salners, 9911 W Pico Blvd, #1400, Los Angeles CA 90035 USA | |
| **Hipple, Eric E** | Football Player |
| 7155 Driftwood Dr, Fenton MI 48430, USA | |
| **Hire, Kathryn P (Kay)** | Astronaut |
| PO Box 580146, Houston TX 77258, USA | |
| **Hirsch, Corey** | Ice Hockey Player |
| Saint Louis Blues, Scott Trade Center, 1401 Clark Ave, Saint Louis MO 63103 USA | |
| **Hirsch, E D, Jr** | Educator |
| University of Virginia, Education Dept, Charlottesville VA 22906, USA | |
| **Hirsch, Emile** | Actor |
| Maydew & Golenberg, 8383 Wilshire Blvd, #1050, Beverly Hills CA 90211, USA | |
| **Hirsch, Hallee** | Actress |
| B/W/R, 9100 Wilshire Blvd, #500W, Beverly Hills CA 90212 USA | |
| **Hirsch, Howard** | Interior Designer |
| Hirsch/Bedner Assoc, 3216 Nebraska Ave, Santa Monica CA 90404, USA | |
| **Hirsch, Janis** | Writer, Producer |
| Creative Artists Agency, 2000 Ave of Stars, #100, Los Angeles CA 90067 USA | |
| **Hirsch, Judd** | Actor |
| Joan Sittenfield Mgmt, 1064 S Ogden Dr, Los Angeles CA 90019, USA | |
| **Hirsch, Laurence E** | Businessman |
| Centex Corp, 2728 N Harwood, #200, Dallas TX 75201, USA | |
| **Hirsch, Leon C** | Inventor (Surgical Stapler) |
| 150 Glover Ave, Norwalk CT 06850, USA | |
| **Hirsch, Paul** | Editor |
| Innovative Artists, 1505 10th St, Santa Monica CA 90401 USA | |
| **Hirsch, Robert P** | Actor |
| 1 Place du Palais Bourbon, 75007 Paris, France | |
| **Hirsch, Sherre** | Writer, Religious Leader, Rabbi |
| Canyon Ranch, 8600 E Rockcliffe Road, Tucson AZ 85750, USA | |
| **Hirschbeck, Mark** | Baseball Umpire |
| 12 Isinglass Terrace, Trumbull CT 06611, USA | |
| **Hirschbiegel, Oliver** | Director, Actor |
| United Talent Agency, U T A Plaza, 9336 Civic Center Dr, Beverly Hills CA 90210 USA | |
| **Hirschfeld, Gerald J** | Cinematographer |
| 826 Pavilion Place, Ashland OR 97520, USA | |
| **Hirschfield, Alan J** | Businessman |
| PO Box 7443, Jackson WY 83002, USA | |
| **Hirschfield, Bradley** | Religious Leader, Rabbi |
| Center for Learning & Leadership, 440 Park Ave S, #400, New York NY 10016, USA | |
| **Hirst, Damien** | Sculptor |
| White Cube Gallery, Saint James's, 44 Duke St, London SW1Y 6DD, England | |
| **Hirtz, Dagmar** | Director |
| Jollystr 45, 81545 Munich, Germany | |
| **Hiscock, Norm** | Producer |
| Vanguarde Artists Mgmt, 119 Spadina Ave, #501, Toronto ON M5V 2L1, Canada | |
| **Hiser, Gene T** | Baseball Player |
| 1450 Caldwell Lane, Hoffman Estates IL 60169, USA | |
| **Hiskey, Bryant (Babe)** | Golfer |
| 4046 Pirates Beach, Galveston TX 77554, USA | |
| **Hisle, Larry E** | Baseball Player |
| 10603 N Hidden Reserve Circle, Mequon WI 53092, USA | |
| **Hitchcock, Ken** | Ice Hockey Coach |
| 11118 Valleydale Dr, #C, Dallas TX 75230, USA | |
| **Hitchcock, Robyn** | Singer (Soft Boys), Songwriter |
| High Road Touring, 751 Bridgeway, #200, Sausalito CA 94965 USA | |
| **Hitchcock, Russell C** | Singer (Air Supply) |
| PO Box 3367, Beverly Hills CA 90212, USA | |
| **Hitchcock, Sterling A** | Baseball Player |
| 255 Yucca Road, Naples FL 34102, USA | |
| **Hitchcock, Sylvia L** | Beauty Queen |
| Miss Universe Organization, 1370 Ave of Americas, #1600, New York NY 10019 USA | |
| **Hite, Robert L** | WW II Army Air Corps Hero |
| 112 Elaine Ave, Camden AR 71701, USA | |
| **Hite, Shere D** | Writer |
| 75 Haywood St, #312, Asheville NC 28801, USA | |
| **Hite, William P** | Labor Leader |
| United Plumbing/Pipefitters Assn, 3 Park Place, Annapolis MD 21401, USA | |
| **Hitsujia, Shirotama** | Director |
| Yubiwa Hotel, 4-41-15-701, Yoyogi Shibuyaku, Tokyo 151 0053, Japan | |
| **Hitt, John C** | Educator |
| University of Central Florida, President's Office, Orlando FL 32816, USA | |
| **Hix, Charles** | Fashion Expert, Writer |
| Simon & Schuster, 1230 Ave of Americas, Concourse 1, New York NY 10020, USA | |

| | |
|---|---|
| **Hjalmarsson, Niklas** | Ice Hockey Player |
| Chicago Blackhawks, United Center, 1901 W Madison St, Chicago IL 60612 USA | |
| **Hjejle, Iben** | Actress |
| Tavistock Wood, 45 Conduit St, London W1S 2YN, England , USA | |
| **Hjorth, Maria A (Mimmi)** | Golfer |
| 608 Henley Circle, Davenport FL 33896, USA | |
| **Hlavackova, Andrea** | Tennis Player |
| Na Zahonech 1303/45, 14100 Prague, Czech Republic | |
| **Hlinka, Nichol** | Ballerina |
| New York City Ballet, Lincoln Center Plaza, New York NY 10023 USA | |
| **Hnatiuk, Glen** | Golfer |
| 8746 Mississippi Run, Weeki Wachee FL 34613, USA | |
| **Hnidy, Shane** | Ice Hockey Player |
| 1704 Silvermere Court, Duluth GA 30097, USA | |
| **Ho, David** | Medical Researcher |
| Aaron Diamond AIDS Research Center, 455 1st Ave, New York NY 10016, USA | |
| **Ho, Derek K** | Surfer |
| Association of Surfing Professionals, PO Box 309, Huntington Beach CA 92648, USA | |
| **Ho, Josie** | Actress |
| I C M Partners, 10250 Constellation Blvd, #900, Los Angeles CA 90067 USA | |
| **Ho, Tao** | Architect |
| 499 King's Road, #8/B, North Point, Hong Kong Special Region, China | |
| **Hoag, Jan** | Actress |
| Amsel Eisenstadt Frazier, 5055 Wilshire Blvd, #865, Los Angeles CA 90036 USA | |
| **Hoag, Judith W** | Actress |
| Bauman Redanty Shaul Agency, 5757 Wilshire Blvd, #473, Los Angeles CA 90036 USA | |
| **Hoag, Peter C** | Test Pilot |
| 3655 Little Rock Dr, Provo UT 84604, USA | |
| **Hoag, Tami** | Writer |
| Bantam/Dell Books, 1745 Broadway, New York NY 10019, USA | |
| **Hoage, Terrell L (Terry)** | Football Player |
| 870 Arbor Road, Paso Robles CA 93446, USA | |
| **Hoagland, Edward** | Writer |
| PO Box 51, Barton VT 05822, USA | |
| **Hoagland, Jimmie L (Jim)** | Journalist |
| Washington Post, Editorial Dept, 1150 15th St NW, Washington DC 20071, USA | |
| **Hoaglin, G Frederick (Fred)** | Football Player, Coach |
| 7 Governors Road, Hilton Head SC 29928, USA | |
| **Hoak, Richard j (Dick)** | Football Player |
| 162 Crest View Dr, Greensburg PA 15601, USA | |
| **Hoar, Joseph P** | Marine Corps General |
| 386 13th St, Del Mar CA 92014, USA | |
| **Hoard, Leroy** | Football Player |
| 13141 NW 8th Court, Sunrise FL 33325, USA | |
| **Hoare, C Antony R** | Computer Engineer |
| Oxford University, Computing Laboratory, Parks Road, Oxford OX1 3QD, England | |
| **Hobaugh, Charles O** | Astronaut |
| N A S A, Johnson Space Center, 2101 NASA Road, Houston TX 77058 USA | |
| **Hobault, John** | Space Scientist |
| 15 Piper Road, #K319, Scarborough ME 04074, USA | |
| **Hobbie, Glen F** | Baseball Player |
| RR 2 Box 234A, Ramsey IL 62080, USA | |
| **Hobbs, Becky** | Singer, Pianist |
| Entertainment Artists, 2409 21st Ave S, #100, Nashville TN 10019 USA | |
| **Hobbs, Chelsea** | Actress |
| Paradigm Agency, 360 N Crescent Dr, North Building, Beverly Hills CA 90210 USA | |
| **Hobbs, David** | Auto Racing Driver, Sportscaster |
| David Hobbs Honda, 6100 N Green Bay Ave, Glendale WI 53209, USA | |
| **Hobbs, Ellis, III** | Football Player |
| 8885 Old Southwick Pass, Alpharetta GA 30022, USA | |
| **Hobbs, Jeff** | Writer |
| Simon & Schuster, 1230 Ave of Americas, Concourse 1, New York NY 10020 USA | |
| **Hobbs, John D (Jack)** | Baseball Player |
| 3 Wade Dr, Cherry Hill NJ 08034, USA | |
| **Hoberman, David** | Producer |
| Mandeville Films, 500 S Buena Vista St, Animation Building 2G, Burbank CA 91521, USA | |
| **Hobert, Billy J** | Football Player |
| 255 Portofino Way, Redondo Beach CA 90277, USA | |
| **Hoblit, Gregory (Greg)** | Director |
| W M E Entertainment, 9601 Wilshire Blvd, #300, Beverly Hills CA 90210 USA | |
| **Hobolt, John C** | Space Scientist |
| 15 Piper Road, #K319, Scarborough ME 04074, USA | |
| **Hobson, Clell L (Butch)** | Baseball Player, Manager |
| 6302 Catarata St, Bakersfield CA 93311, USA | |
| **Hobson, Helen** | Actress |
| Gavin Barker Assoc, 2D Wimpole St, London W1G 0EB, England | |
| **Hobson, Jeff** | Illusionist |
| Jack Grenier Productions, 32630 Concord Dr, Madison Heights MI 48071 USA | |
| **Hobson, Victor B** | Football Player |
| 505 Gracelyn Court SW, Atlanta GA 30331, USA | |
| **Hoch, Carin** | Golfer |
| International Mangement Group, 1 Erieview Plaza, 1360 E 9th St, Cleveland OH 44114 USA | |
| **Hoch, Danny** | Performance Artist, Actor |
| Gersh Agency, 9465 Wilshire Blvd, #600, Beverly Hills CA 90212 USA | |
| **Hoch, Scott** | Golfer |
| 9239 Cypress Cove Dr, Orlando FL 32819, USA | |
| **Hochevar, Luke A** | Baseball Player |
| 2452 Glen Meadow Road, Knoxville TN 37909, USA | |
| **Hochhuth, Rolf** | Writer |
| PO Box 661, 4002 Basel, Switzerland | |
| **Hochschorner, Pavol** | Canoeing Athlete |
| Lesna 8, 81104 Bratislava, Slovakia | |
| **Hochstein, Russ** | Football Player |
| 10 Sidney St, Plainville MA 2762, USA | |
| **Hochwald, Bari** | Actress |
| Herb Tannen, 10801 National Blvd, #101, Los Angeles CA 90064 USA | |

**Hock, Dee Ward** — Businessman
Visa International, 900 Metro Center Blvd, Foster City CA 94404, USA

**Hocke, Stefan** — Ski Jumper
Sportgymnasium, Am Harzwald 3, 98558 Oberhof, Germany

**Hockenbery, Charles M (Chuck)** — Baseball Player
1546 Birka Lane, Onalaska WI 54650, USA

**Hockfield, Susan** — Educator
Massachusetts Institute of Technology, President's Office, Cambridge MA 02139, USA

**Hocking, Amanda** — Writer
Saint Martin's Press, 175 5th Ave, #400, New York NY 10010 USA

**Hocking, Dennis L (Denny)** — Baseball Player
7384 E Villanueva Dr, Orange CA 92867, USA

**Hockney, David** — Artist, Photographer
Tradhart Ltd, 19B Buckingham Ave, Slough SL1 4QB, England

**Hodder, Kane W** — Actor, Stuntman
Amsel Eisenstadt Frazier, 5055 Wilshire Blvd, #865, Los Angeles CA 90036 USA

**Hoddle, Glenn** — Soccer Player, Manager
Football Assn, 16 Lancaster Gate, London W2 3LW, England

**Hodel, Donald P** — Secretary, Energy; Labor
1801 Sara Dr, #L, Chesapeake VA 23320, USA

**Hodel, Nathan W** — Football Player
2411 Goldenrod Way, Wauconda IL 60084, USA

**Hodge, Aldis** — Actor
Paradigm Agency, 360 N Crescent Dr, North Building, Beverly Hills CA 90210 USA

**Hodge, Chad** — Writer, Producer
W M E Entertainment, 9601 Wilshire Blvd, #300, Beverly Hills CA 90210 USA

**Hodge, Charles E (Charlie)** — Ice Hockey Player
27111 25A Ave, Aldergrove BC V4W 3N4, Canada

**Hodge, Daniel A (Dan)** — Freestyle Wrestler
914 Jackson St, Perry OK 73077, USA

**Hodge, Douglas** — Actor
United Agents, 12-26 Lexington St, London W1F 0LE, England

**Hodge, Ed O** — Baseball Player
127 Jedwell St, Johnson City TN 37601, USA

**Hodge, Edwin** — Actor
Luber Rocklin Entertainment, 8530 Wilshire Blvd, #555, Beverly Hills CA 90211 USA

**Hodge, John** — Producer
United Agents, 12-26 Lexington St, London W1F 0LE, England

**Hodge, Kenneth R (Ken), Sr** — Ice Hockey Player
13 Longfellow Dr, Newburyport MA 01950, USA

**Hodge, Patricia** — Actress
I C M Partners, Marlborough House, 10 Earlham St, #300, London WC2H 9LNP, England

**Hodge, Sedrick J** — Football Player
120 Victoria Place, Fayetteville GA 30214, USA

**Hodges, Bill** — Basketball Coach
Georgia College, Athletic Dept, Milledgeville GA 31061, USA

**Hodges, Craig A** — Basketball Player
67 Elm St, Park Forest IL 60466, USA

**Hodges, J T** — Singer, Songwriter
Show Dog-Universal Music, 2303 21st Ave S, #400, Nashville TN 37212 USA

**Hodges, Mike** — Director
Wesley Farm, Durweston, Blanford Forum, Dorset DT11 0QG, England

**Hodges, Robert H, Jr** — Judge
US Claims Court, 717 Madison Place NW, Washington DC 20439, USA

**Hodges, Ronald W (Ron)** — Baseball Player
110 Hajo Lane, Rocky Mount VA 24151, USA

**Hodges, Roneeka** — Basketball Player
Indiana Fever, Conseco Fieldhouse, 125 S Pennsylvania, Indianapolis IN 46204 USA

**Hodges, Trey** — Baseball Player
19506 Kuykendahl Road, Spring TX 77379, USA

**Hodgins, William** — Interior Designer
232 Clarendon St, Boston MA 02116, USA

**Hodgman, John** — Actor, Writer
United Talent Agency, U T A Plaza, 9336 Civic Center Dr, Beverly Hills CA 90210 USA

**Hodgson, Nicholas J D (Nick)** — Singer, Drummer (Kaiser Chiefs)
Red Light Mgmt, 8439 Sunset Blvd, West Hollywood CA 90069, USA

**Hodgson, Roger** — Guitarist (Supertramp)
Agency Group Ltd, 142 W 57th St, #600, New York NY 10019 USA

**Hoechlin, Tyler** — Actor
United Talent Agency, U T A Plaza, 9336 Civic Center Dr, Beverly Hills CA 90210 USA

**Hoeg, Peter** — Writer
Farrar Straus Giroux, 18 W 18th St, #700, New York NY 10011 USA

**Hoeks, Sylvia** — Actress
Copper En Co, Wamondstraat 73-1, 1058 Amsterdam KR, Netherlands

**Hoelsher, Vanessa** — Model
Playboy Promotions, 2706 Media Center Dr, Los Angeles CA 90065 USA

**Hoelzer, Margaret** — Swimmer
535 N Coast Highway, Laguna Beach CA 92651, USA

**Hoenig, Heinz** — Actor
Society Relations, Mundsburger Damm 2, 22087 Hamburg, Germany

**Hoenig, Thomas M** — Government Official, Financier
615 W Meyer Blvd, Kansas City MO 64113, USA

**Hoest, Bunny** — Cartoonist (Lockhorns)
William Hoest Enterprises, 27 Watch Way, Lloyd Neck, Huntington NY 11743, USA

**Hoewing, Gerald L** — Navy Admiral
Navy Mutual Aid Assn, 29 Carpenter Road, Arlington VA 22214, USA

**Hoey, George W** — Football Player
13635 Clermont Court, Thornton CO 80602, USA

**Hofer, Paul D** — Football Player
981 June Road, Memphis TN 38119, USA

**Hoff, Kathryn (Katie)** — Swimmer
106 Kenilworth Park, #4D, Towson MD 21204, USA

**Hoff, Lawrence C** — Businessman
8720 Cypress Club Dr, Raleigh NC 27615, USA

**Hoff, Marcian E (Ted), Jr** — Inventor (Microprocessor)
26541 Taafe Road, Los Altos Hills CA 94022, USA

**Hoff, Michael** — Art Historian
University of Nebraska, Art & Art History Dept, 120 Richards Hall, Lincoln NE 68588, USA
**Hoff, Philip H** — Governor, VT
Hoff Wilson Powell Lang, PO Box 123, Essex Junction VT 05453, USA
**Hoffa, James P** — Labor Leader
2593 Hounds Chase Dr, Troy MI 48098, USA
**Hoffman, Alan J** — Mathematician
I B M Research Center, PO Box 218, Yorktown Heights NY 10598, USA
**Hoffman, Alice** — Writer
32 Lowell Road, Concord MA 1742, USA
**Hoffman, Basil** — Actor
26 Aller Court, Glendale CA 91206, USA
**Hoffman, Charley** — Golfer
Professional Golfer's Assn, PO Box 109601, Palm Beach Gardens FL 33410 USA
**Hoffman, Darleane C** — Nuclear Physicist
Lawrence Berkeley Laboratory, 1 Cyclotron Road, Berkeley CA 94720, USA
**Hoffman, David** — Actor
Mavrick Artists Agency, 6100 Wilshire Blvd, #550, Los Angeles CA 90048, USA
**Hoffman, Dustin L** — Actor
Punch Productions, 11661 San Vicente Blvd, #222, Los Angeles CA 90049, USA
**Hoffman, Gaby** — Actress
Innovative Artists, 235 Park Ave S, #1000, New York NY 10003 USA
**Hoffman, Glenn E** — Baseball Player, Manager
201 S Old Bridge Road, Anaheim CA 92808, USA
**Hoffman, Guy A** — Baseball Player
313 Fairway Dr, #S, Bloomington IL 61701, USA
**Hoffman, Jackie** — Actress
Don Buchwald, 6500 Wilshire Blvd, #2200, Los Angeles CA 90048 USA
**Hoffman, Jeffrey A** — Astronaut
US Embassy, 2 Ave Gabriel, PSC 116/NASA, 75382 Paris Cedex, France
**Hoffman, John Robert** — Director, Writer
Creative Artists Agency, 2000 Ave of Stars, #100, Los Angeles CA 90067 USA
**Hoffman, Matt** — Actor
D D K Talent, 16255 Ventura Blvd, #525, Encino CA 91436, USA
**Hoffman, Michael** — Director, Writer
United Talent Agency, U T A Plaza, 9336 Civic Center Dr, Beverly Hills CA 90210 USA
**Hoffman, Philip Seymour** — Actor
Cooper's Town Productions, 302A W 12th St, #214, New York NY 10014, USA
**Hoffman, Reid G** — Businessman
LinkedIn, 2029 Stierlin Court, #200, Mountain Valley CA 94043, USA
**Hoffman, Rick** — Actor
Framework Entertainment, 9057 Nemo St, #C, West Hollywood CA 90069 USA
**Hoffman, Robert James, III** — Actor
Impression Entertainment, 9229 W Sunset Blvd, #700, Los Angeles CA 90069, USA
**Hoffman, Ted, Jr** — Bowling Executive
1568 Partarian Way, San Jose CA 95129, USA
**Hoffman, Thom** — Actor
Anne Alvares Correa, 34 Rue Jouffroy d'Abbans, 75017 Paris, France
**Hoffman, William M** — Lyricist, Writer
190 Prince St, New York NY 10012, USA
**Hoffmann, Ambrosi** — Alpine Skier
Talstrasse 63, 7250 Davos Dorf, Switzerland
**Hoffmann, Christian** — Cross Country Skier
Frunwald 7, 4160 Aigen, Austria
**Hoffmann, Gaby** — Actress
I C M Partners, 10250 Constellation Blvd, #900, Los Angeles CA 90067 USA
**Hoffmann, Jan** — Figure Skater
Ice Skating Union, Menzinger Str 68, 80992 Munich, Germany
**Hoffmann, Jules A** — Nobel Medicine Laureate
Biologie Moléculaire & Cellulaire Institut, 15 Rue Descartes, 67084 Strasbourg Cedex, France
**Hoffmann, Roald** — Nobel Chemistry Laureate
4 Sugarbush Lane, Ithaca NY 14850, USA
**Hoffmann, Robert** — Actor
Agentur Rehling, Mommsenstr 47, 10629 Berlin, Germany
**Hoffmann, Stanley H** — Political Scientist
Harvard University, Government Dept, Cambridge MA 02138, USA
**Hoffpauir, Jarrett L** — Baseball Player
2043 Viking St, Vidalia LA 71373, USA
**Hoffs, Susanna** — Singer, Guitarist (Bangles)
Creative Artists Agency, 2000 Ave of Stars, #100, Los Angeles CA 90067 USA
**Hofheimer, Charlie** — Actor
Innovative Artists, 1505 10th St, Santa Monica CA 90401 USA
**Hoflehner, Rudolf** — Artist
Ottensteinstr 62, 2344 Maria Enzersdorf, Austria
**Hofmann, Detlef** — Canoeing Athlete
Saarlandstr 164, 76187 Karlsruhe, Germany
**Hofmann, Douglas W** — Artist
15 W Mount Vernon Place, Baltimore MD 21201, USA
**Hofmann, Isabella** — Actress
Artistry Mgmt, 340 N Camden Dr, #302, Beverly Hills CA 90210, USA
**Hofmeister, John** — Businessman
Shell Oil Co, PO Box 2463, Houston TX 77252, USA
**Hofschneider, Marco** — Actor
Agent U Nicolai, Schorlemerallee 16, 14195 Berlin, Germany
**Hogan, Brooke** — Singer, Actress
Sovereign Talent Group, 8421 Wilshire Blvd, #200, Beverly Hills CA 90211, USA
**Hogan, Darrell** — Football Player
14988 Scenic Loop Road, Helotes TX 78023, USA
**Hogan, Hulk** — Professional Wrestler, Actor
756 Eldorado Ave, Clearwater Beach FL 33767, USA
**Hogan, Jack** — Actor
22 Altura Road, Santa Fe NM 87508, USA
**Hogan, Linda** — Writer
University of Colorado, English Dept, Boulder CO 80309, USA
**Hogan, Paul** — Actor
18 Marshall Crescent, Beacon Hill NSW 2060, Australia

**Hogan, Paul J (P J)** — Director, Writer
Creative Artists Agency, 2000 Ave of Stars, #100, Los Angeles CA 90067 USA
**Hoge, Merril D** — Football Player, Sportscaster
155 W Maple Ave, Fort Mitchell KY 41011, USA
**Hogeboom, Gary K** — Football Player
13635 Hofma Court, Grand Haven MI 49417, USA
**Hogestyn, Drake** — Actor
6080 Cavalleri Road, Malibu CA 90265, USA
**Hogg, Christopher A** — Businessman
Financial Reporting Council, 71-91 Aldwych, London  WC2B 4HN, England
**Hogg, James R** — Navy Admiral
Prescott Farm, 2556 W Main Road, Portsmouth RI 02871, USA
**Hoggard, Jay** — Jazz Vibraphonist
Wesleyan University, Music Dept, Middletown CT 06459, USA
**Hogland, M Douglas (Doug)** — Football Player
1514 4th St, Tillamook OR 97141, USA
**Hogue, Benoit** — Ice Hockey Player
488 Village Oaks Lane, Babylon NY 11702, USA
**Hogwood, Christopher J H** — Concert Harpsichordist, Conductor
10 Brookside, Cambridge CB2 1JE, England
**Hohlmayer, Alice (Lefty)** — Baseball Player
5155 Cedarwood Road #47, Bonita CA 91902, USA
**Hoiberg, Frederick K (Fred)** — Basketball Player, Coach
2129 Quail Ridge Road, Ames IA 50010, USA
**Hoiles, Christopher A (Chris)** — Baseball Player
8688 Jersey City Road, Wayne OH 43466, USA
**Hoke, Brady** — Football Coach
University of Michigan, Athletic Dept, Ann Arbor MI 48109, USA
**Hoke, Christopher L (Chris)** — Football Player
121 Cardinal Circle, Pittsburgh PA 15237, USA
**Holbert, Jerry** — Editorial Cartoonist
Boston Herald, Editorial Dept, 1 Herald St, Boston MA 02118, USA
**Holbert, Ray A, III** — Baseball Player
13981 W Desert Cove Road, Surprise AZ 85379, USA
**Holbrook, Bill** — Cartoonist (Safe Havens)
King Features Syndicate, 300 W 57th St, #1500, New York NY 10019 USA
**Holbrook, Boyd** — Actor
Creative Artists Agency, 2000 Ave of Stars, #100, Los Angeles CA 90067 USA
**Holbrook, Hal** — Actor
Abrams Artists, 9200 W Sunset Blvd, #1125, West Hollywood CA 90069 USA
**Holbrook, Karen A** — Educator
University of South Florida, Research & Innovation Dept, 42-2 E Fowler Ave, Tampa FL 33620, USA
**Holcomb, B Kelly** — Football Player
114 Spence Creek Lane, Murfreesboro TN 37128, USA
**Holcomb, Steven** — Bobsled Athlete
Team Holcomb, PO Box 118, Oakley UT 84055, USA
**Holcombe, Robert W** — Football Player
2611 Hardy St, Houston TX 77009, USA
**Holden, Alexandra** — Actress
Abrams Artists, 9200 W Sunset Blvd, #1125, West Hollywood CA 90069 USA
**Holden, Amanda** — Actress
Artist Rights Group, 4 Great Portland St, London W1W 8PA, England
**Holden, Laurie** — Actress
A P A Talent/Literary Agency, 405 S Beverly Dr, #300, Beverly Hills CA 90212 USA
**Holden, Mari K** — Cyclist
11160 Vista Sorrento Parkway, #302, San Diego CA 92130, USA
**Holden, Marjean** — Actress
Defining Artists, 10 Universal City Plaza, #2000, Universal City CA 91608 USA
**Holden, Rebecca** — Actress, Singer, Model
Box Office, 5207 Rustic Way, Old Hickory TN 37138, USA
**Holden, Robert L (Bob)** — Governor, MO
Webster University, Political Science Dept, 470 E Lockwood Ave, Saint Louis MO 63119, USA
**Holden, Steven A (Steve)** — Football Player
1202 N Nevada Way, Mesa AZ 85203, USA
**Holden, Warrick D** — Football Player
17202 Stratford Green Dr, Sugar Land TX 77498, USA
**Holden-Reid, Kris** — Actress
Oscars Abrams Zimel, 438 Queen St E, Toronto ON M5A 1T4, Canada
**Holder, Eric** — Attorney General
Justice Department, 10th St & Constitution Ave NW, Washington DC 20530 USA
**Holder, Geoffrey** — Actor, Dancer
Innovative Artists, 235 Park Ave S, #1000, New York NY 10003 USA
**Holdsclaw, Chamique** — Basketball Player
San Antonio Silver Stars, 1 AT&T Center, San Antonio TX 78219 USA
**Holdsworth, Frederick W (Fred)** — Baseball Player
578 Upland Hills Dr, Chelsea MI 48118, USA
**Holecek, John F** — Football Player
1828 Prairie St, Glenview IL 60025, USA
**Holiday, Phillip** — Boxer
Pacific Boxing Club, 14 Channel St, Cleveland QLD, Australia
**Holl, Steven M** — Architect
Steven Holl Architects, 435 Hudson St, #400, New York NY 10014, USA
**Holladay, Wilhelmina Cole** — Museum Executive
National Museum of Women in Arts, 1250 New York NW, Washington DC 20005, USA
**Holland, Agnieszka** — Director, Writer
Field Entertainment, 1240 N Wetherly Dr, Los Angeles CA 90069, USA
**Holland, Alfred W (Al)** — Baseball Player
443 Lewiston St NW, Roanoke VA 24017, USA
**Holland, Brian** — Songwriter
9912 Cozy Glen Circle, Las Vegas NV 89117, USA
**Holland, Darius J** — Football Player
13972 Meadowbrook Dr, Broomfield CO 80020, USA
**Holland, Dexter** — Singer (Offspring)
Rebel Waltz, 31652 2nd Ave, Laguna Beach CA 92651, USA
**Holland, Edward (Eddie), Jr** — Songwriter
555 S Burlingame Ave, Los Angeles CA 90049, USA

Hogan - Holland

**Holland, James F** — Oncologist
Mount Sinai Medical Center, Oncology Dept, 1190 5th Ave, New York NY 10029, USA

**Holland, Jamie L** — Football Player
4025 Jonesville Road, Wake Forest NC 27587, USA

**Holland, Jolie** — Singer (Be Good Tanyas), Songwriter
525 Worldwide Music Co, PO Box 957, Salem MA 01945, USA

**Holland, Julian M (Jools)** — Pianist (Squeeze, The The)
One Fifteen, Globe House, Middle Lane Mews, London N8 8PN, England

**Holland, Kimberly** — Model
Playboy Promotions, 2706 Media Center Dr, Los Angeles CA 90065 USA

**Holland, Montrae R** — Football Player
1096 Sendero Dr, Keller TX 76248, USA

**Holland, Richard J** — Art Director
Screen Talent Agency, Rich Mix Building, 35-47 Bethnal Green Road, London E1 6LA, England

**Holland, Tara Dawn** — Beauty Queen
9050 Carothers Parkway, #104, Franklin TN 37067, USA

**Holland, Terry** — Basketball Player, Coach, Administrator
East Carolina University, Athletic Dept, Greenville NC 27858, USA

**Holland, Todd** — Director, Producer
W M E Entertainment, 9601 Wilshire Blvd, #300, Beverly Hills CA 90210 USA

**Holland, Tom** — Director
Dead Rabbit Films, 215 Zelley Ave, Moorestown NJ 08057 08057, USA

**Holland, Wilbur** — Basketball Player
538 Georgia Dr, Columbus GA 31907, USA

**Holland, Willa** — Actress, Model
Gersh Agency, 9465 Wilshire Blvd, #600, Beverly Hills CA 90212 USA

**Holland, Willard R, Jr** — Businessman
FirstEnergy Corp, 76 S Main St, Akron OH 44308, USA

**Hollande, Francois G G** — President, France
Palais de l'Elysee, 55 Rue Faubourg Saint Honore, 75008 Paris, France

**Hollander, Edmund D** — Landscape Architect
Hollander Landscape Design, 200 Park Ave S, New York NY 10003, USA

**Hollander, Lorin** — Concert Pianist
I C M Artists, 40 W 57th St, #1800, New York NY 10019 USA

**Hollander, Nicole** — Cartoonist (Sylvia)
Sylvia Syndicate, 1440 N Dayton St, Chicago IL 60642, USA

**Hollander, Tom** — Actor, Producer, Writer
Independent Talent Group, 40 Whitfield St, London W1T 2RH, England

**Hollandsworth, Todd M** — Baseball Player
1310 MacAlpin Court, Inverness IL 60010, USA

**Hollas, Donald W** — Football Player
1811 Mayweather Lane, Richmond TX 77406, USA

**Holldobler, Berthold K** — Writer, Biologist, Zoologist
University of Wurzburg, Zoology Dept, Am Nubland, 97074 Wurzburg, Germany

**Hollein, Hans** — Pritzker Architectural Laureate
Eiskellerstr 1, 40213 Dusseldorf, Germany

**Holler, J Edward (Ed)** — Football Player
4500 Ivy Hall Dr, Columbia SC 29206, USA

**Hollerer, Walter F** — Writer
Heerstr 99, 14055 Berlin, Germany

**Holliday, Cheryl** — Writer, Producer
W M E Entertainment, 9601 Wilshire Blvd, #300, Beverly Hills CA 90210 USA

**Holliday, D Giovonni (Vonnie)** — Football Player
1060 Canter Road NE, Atlanta GA 30324, USA

**Holliday, Jennifer Y** — Singer, Actress
Holliday 6 Entertainment, 3330 Cumberland Blvd, #500, Atlanta GA 30339, USA

**Holliday, Matthew T (Matt)** — Baseball Player
4 Ravenswood Road, Englewood CO 80113, USA

**Holliday, Polly D** — Actress, Singer
Blake Agency, 23441 Malibu Colony Road, Malibu CA 90265 USA

**Hollier, Dwight L** — Football Player
5012 Woodview Lane, Matthews NC 28104, USA

**Holliger, Heinz** — Concert Oboist, Composer
Konzertgellschaft, Hochstr 51, 4002 Basel, Switzerland

**Holliman, Earl** — Actor
PO Box 1969, Studio City CA 91614, USA

**Hollimon, Mike** — Baseball Player
9922 Glenn Canyon Dr, Dallas TX 75243, USA

**Hollings, Michael R** — Religious Leader
Saint Mary of Angels, Moorhouse Road, Bayswater, London W2 5DJ, England

**Hollingsworth, David S** — Space Scientist
Orbital Sciences Corp, 21839 Atlantic Blvd, Dulles VA 20166, USA

**Hollinquest, Lamont** — Football Player
13709 S San Pedro St, Los Angeles CA 90061, USA

**Hollins, David M (Dave)** — Baseball Player
3221 Southwestern Blvd, Orchard Park NY 14127, USA

**Hollins, Lionel E** — Basketball Player, Coach
7594 Tagg Dr, Germantown TN 38138, USA

**Hollis, Michael S (Mike)** — Football Player
124 Sawbill Palm Dr, Ponte Vedra Beach FL 32082, USA

**Hollister, Dave** — Singer, Actor
I C M Partners, 10250 Constellation Blvd, #900, Los Angeles CA 90067 USA

**Holloman, Gus M** — Football Player
2489 County Road 139, Cameron TX 76520, USA

**Holloman, Laurel** — Actress
Sanders/Armstrong/Caserta Mgmt, 2120 Colorado Ave, #120, Santa Monica CA 90404 USA

**Holloway, Brenda** — Singer
Universal Attractions, 135 W 26th St, #1200, New York NY 10001 USA

**Holloway, Brian D** — Football Player
4110 Heritage Lake Court, Lutz FL 33558, USA

**Holloway, Glen L** — Football Player
2737 N Columbus Blvd, #6, Tucson AZ 85712, USA

**Holloway, James L, III** — Navy Admiral
4800 Fillmore Ave, #1058, Alexandria VA 22311, USA

**Holloway, Jennifer** — Opera Singer
I M G Artists, Carnegie Hall Tower, 152 W 57th St, #500, New York NY 10019 USA

**Holloway, Joshua L (Josh)** — Actor, Model
W M E Entertainment, 9601 Wilshire Blvd, #300, Beverly Hills CA 90210 USA

**Holloway, Ken** — Singer
World Class/Berry Mgmt, 1848 Tyne Blvd, Nashville TN 37215, USA

**Holloway, Matt** — Writer
Creative Artists Agency, 2000 Ave of Stars, #100, Los Angeles CA 90067 USA

**Holloway, Robin G** — Composer
Gonville & Caius College, Music Dept, Cambridge CB2 1TA, England

**Holloway, William J, Jr** — Judge
US Court of Appeals, PO Box 1767, Oklahoma City OK 73101, USA

**Hollweg, Ryan** — Ice Hockey Player
190 John Olds Dr, #212, Manchester CT 06042, USA

**Holly, Lauren** — Actress
Gilbertson Entertainment, 1334 3rd St Promenade, #207, Santa Monica CA 90401, USA

**Hollyday, Christopher** — Jazz Saxophonist
Ted Kurland, 173 Brighton Ave, Boston MA 02134 USA

**Holm, Anders** — Actor, Writer
United Talent Agency, U T A Plaza, 9336 Civic Center Dr, Beverly Hills CA 90210 USA

**Holm, Dorthe Elisabeth** — Curling Athlete
Curling Assn, Idraettens Hus, 2605 Brondby, Denmark

**Holm, Ian** — Actor
Markham Froggatt Irwin, Julian House, 4 Windmill St, London W1P 1HF, England

**Holm, Joan** — Bowler
3639 S 61st Court, Cicero IL 60804, USA

**Holm, Peter** — Singer
1 Rue de Fer Achevel Port Grimaud, 83310 Cogolin, France

**Holman, Brian S** — Baseball Player
23595 W 223rd St, Spring Hill KS 66083, USA

**Holman, C Ray** — Businessman
Mallinckrodt Inc, 675 McDonnell Blvd, Saint Louis MO 63134, USA

**Holman, Clare** — Actress
United Agents, 12-26 Lexington St, London W1F 0LE, England

**Holman, Marshall** — Bowler
288 Island Pointe Dr, Medford OR 97504, USA

**Holman, Ralph T** — Biochemist
3900 Bethel Dr, Saint Paul MN 55112, USA

**Holman, Rodney A** — Football Player
41460 Herwig Bluff Road, Slidell LA 70461, USA

**Holman, Shawn L** — Baseball Player
105 Edgewood Road, Sewickley PA 15143, USA

**Holmberg, Jonas** — Drummer (Komeda)
M O B Agency, 6404 Wilshire Blvd, #505, Los Angeles CA 90048 USA

**Holmberg, Marcus** — Bassist (Komeda)
M O B Agency, 6404 Wilshire Blvd, #505, Los Angeles CA 90048 USA

**Holmberg, Robert A (Rob)** — Football Player
611 Richfield Court, Greensburg PA 15601, USA

**Holmes, Amy M (A M)** — Writer
Princeton University, Creative Writing Program, Princeton NJ 08544, USA

**Holmes, Andre (PaDre)** — Musician (Fishbone)
Silverback Mgmt, 9469 Jefferson Blvd, #101, Culver City CA 90232, USA

**Holmes, Ashton** — Actor
B/W/R, 9100 Wilshire Blvd, #500W, Beverly Hills CA 90212 USA

**Holmes, Clint** — Singer
Conversation Co, 1044 Northern Blvd, #304, Roslyn NY 11576 USA

**Holmes, Darren L** — Baseball Player
1 Emerald Court, Arden NC 28704, USA

**Holmes, David** — Music Producer, Composer
First Artists Mgmt, 4764 Park Granada, #210, Calabasas CA 91302 USA

**Holmes, Earl L** — Football Player
2978 Stonybrook Court, Tallahassee FL 32309, USA

**Holmes, J B** — Golfer
5175 Latrobe Dr, Windermere FL 34786, USA

**Holmes, J Patrick (Pat)** — Football Player
221 Mack Hollimon Dr, Kerrville TX 78028, USA

**Holmes, Jennifer** — Actress
PO Box 6303, Carmel CA 93921, USA

**Holmes, Jerry** — Football Player
107 Chatham Terrace, Hampton VA 23666, USA

**Holmes, Katie** — Actress
I C M Partners, 10250 Constellation Blvd, #900, Los Angeles CA 90067 USA

**Holmes, Kelly** — Track Athlete
Talk Mgmt, 26/28 Hammersmith Grove, London W6 7BA, England

**Holmes, Kenneth (Kenny)** — Football Player
6103 Aqua Ave, #PH #, Miami Beach FL 33141, USA

**Holmes, Larry** — Boxer
228 W Canal St, Easton PA 18042, USA

**Holmes, Lester** — Football Player
3760 Motor Ave, Los Angeles CA 90034, USA

**Holmes, Pete** — Actor
W M E Entertainment, 9601 Wilshire Blvd, #300, Beverly Hills CA 90210 USA

**Holmes, Priest A** — Football Player
9937 Spring Beauty, San Antonio TX 78254, USA

**Holmes, Robert** — Sculptor
PO Box 244, Sheep Ranch CA 95246, USA

**Holmes, Rupert** — Singer, Songwriter, Writer
Creative Artists Agency, 2000 Ave of Stars, #100, Los Angeles CA 90067 USA

**Holmes, Santonio, Jr** — Football Player
PO Box 1959, Burleson TX 76097, USA

**Holmes, Tina** — Actress
Abrams Artists, 9200 W Sunset Blvd, #1125, West Hollywood CA 90069 USA

**Holmgren, Michael G (Mike)** — Football Coach, Executive
905 Lake St S, #101, Kirkland WA 98033, USA

**Holmgren, Paul H** — Ice Hockey Player, Coach
724 Southwick Circle, Somerdale NJ 08083, USA

**Holmquest, Donald L** — Astronaut
205 Princeton Road, Menlo Park CA 94025, USA

**H**

**Holmstrom, B Tomas** — Ice Hockey Player
43479 McLean Court, Novi MI 48375, USA
**Holmstrom, Bengt R** — Economist
Massachusetts Institute of Technology, Economics Dept, Cambridge MA 02139, USA
**Holofcener, Nicole** — Director
United Talent Agency, U T A Plaza, 9336 Civic Center Dr, Beverly Hills CA 90210 USA
**Holohan, Peter J (Pete)** — Football Player
2945 Curie St, San Diego CA 92122, USA
**Holonyak, Nick, Jr** — Inventor (Light Emitting Diode)
101 W Windsor Road, Urbana IL 61802, USA
**Holroyd, Michael D** — Writer
85 Saint Marks Road, London W10 6JS England
**Holroyd, Scott** — Actor
Stone Manners Salners, 9911 W Pico Blvd, #1400, Los Angeles CA 90035 USA
**Holscher, Mark** — Attorney
O'Melveny & Meyers, 400 S Hope St, Los Angeles CA 90071, USA
**Holsinger, James W, Jr** — Physician
University of Kentucky Medical School, Public Health College, Lexington KY 40506, USA
**Holst, Per** — Producer
Per Holst Film A/S, Rentemestervej 69A, 2400 Copenhagen NV, Denmark
**Holt, Christopher M (Chris)** — Baseball Player
152 Hollywood Dr, Coppell TX 75019, USA
**Holt, David Lee** — Guitarist (Mavericks)
AristoMedia, 1620 16th Ave S, Nashville TN 37212, USA
**Holt, Issiac, III** — Football Player
4028 Fairmont Place, Birmingham AL 35207, USA
**Holt, James W (Jim)** — Baseball Player
150 Judge Sharpe Road, Graham NC 27253, USA
**Holt, Lester** — Commentator
NBC-TV, News Dept, 30 Rockefeller Plaza, #270E, New York NY 10112 USA
**Holt, Pierce** — Football Player
5101 County Road 430, San Angelo TX 76901, USA
**Holt, Sandrine** — Actress
A P A Talent/Literary Agency, 405 S Beverly Dr, #300, Beverly Hills CA 90212 USA
**Holt, Terrence** — Football Player
9924 Thoughtful Spot Way, Raleigh NC 27614, USA
**Holt, Torrance J (Torry)** — Football Player
2604 Prosser Court, Raleigh NC 27614, USA
**Holten, Kasper** — Director
Royal Danish Theatre, Postbox 2185, 1017 Copenhagen K, Denmark
**Holtermann, E Louis, Jr** — Publisher
Glamour, Publisher's Office, 350 Madison Ave, New York NY 10017, USA
**Holton, A Linwood, Jr** — Governor, VA
3883 Black Stump Road, Weems VA 22576, USA
**Holton, Gerald** — Physicist
64 Francis Ave, Cambridge MA 02138, USA
**Holton, Michael D** — Basketball Player, Coach
5822 NW Redfox Dr, Portland OR 97229, USA
**Holtz, Louis L (Lou)** — Football Coach, Sportscaster
9201 Cromwell Park Place, Orlando FL 32827, USA
**Holtz, Michael J (Mike)** — Baseball Player
243 Goodridge Road, Northern Cambria PA 15714, USA
**Holtzman, David** — Neurologist
Washington University Medical Center, 660 S Euclid Ave, Saint Louis MO 63110, USA
**Holtzman, Kenneth D (Ken)** — Baseball Player
256 Waterside Dr, Grover MO 63040, USA
**Holub, Emil Joe (E J)** — Football Player
2311 S County Road 1120, Midland TX 79706, USA
**Holub, Robert C** — Educator
University of Massachusetts, Chancellor's Office, Whitmore Building, Amherst MA 01003, USA
**Holum, Dianne** — Speed Skater
2835 W 32nd Ave, #89, Denver CO 80211, USA
**Holum, Kristin** — Speed Skater
2835 W 32nd Ave, #89, Denver CO 80211, USA
**Holway, Jerome F** — Cinematographer
448 Spruce Dr, Exton PA 19341, USA
**Holyfield, Evander** — Boxer
PO Box 143420, Fayetteville GA 30214, USA
**Holz, Gordon F (Gordy)** — Football Player
730 S Plaza Dr, #222, Saint Paul MN 55120, USA
**Holzemer, Mark H** — Baseball Player
10044 S MacAlister Trail, Littleton CO 80129, USA
**Holzer, Helmut** — Space Scientist
2403 Little Cove Road, Owens Crossroads AL 35763, USA
**Holzer, Jenny** — Artist
80 Hewitt Road, Hoosick Falls NY 12090, USA
**Holzinger, Brian A** — Ice Hockey Player
1005 Ledgemont Dr, Broadview Heights OH 44147, USA
**Holzl, Kathrin (Katy)** — Alpine Skier
Urbanweg 25A, 83483 Bischofswiesen, Germany
**Holzmair, Wolfgang** — Opera Singer
Augstein & Hahn, Tal 28, 80331 Munich, Germany
**Holzman, Malcolm** — Architect
Hardy Holzman Pfeiffer, 902 Broadway, #1900, New York NY 10010, USA
**Homan, Dennis** — Football Player
1950 Charlotte Court, Florence AL 35630, USA
**Homewrecker, Suzi** — Singer, Guitarist (Civet)
The Kirby Organization, 9200 Sunset Blvd, #600, Los Angeles CA 90069, USA
**Homfeld, Conrad** — Equestrian
Sandron, 11744 Marblestone Court, Wellington FL 33414, USA
**Hon, John T Cardinal** — Religious Leader
Catholic Diocese Center, 12F, 16 Caine Road, Hong Kong, China
**Honda, Yuka** — Singer (Cibo Matto)
Billions Corp, 3522 W Armitage Ave, Chicago IL 60647, USA
**Honeck, Manfred** — Conductor
Pittsburgh Symphony, Heinz Hall, 600 Penn Ave, Pittsburgh PA 15222, USA

| | |
|---|---|
| **Honeycutt, Frederick W (Rick)** | Baseball Player |
| 207 Forrest Road, Fort Oglethorpe GA 30742, USA | |
| **Honeycutt, Van B** | Businessman |
| Computer Sciences Corp, 2100 E Grand Ave, El Segundo CA 90245, USA | |
| **Honeyghan, Lloyd** | Boxer |
| 50 Barnfield Wood Road, Park Langley, Beckenham, Kent BR3 6SZ, England | |
| **Hong Chih Kuo** | Baseball Player |
| Seattle Mariners, Safeco Field, PO Box 4100, Seattle WA 98194 USA | |
| **Hong, James** | Actor, Producer, Director |
| Stage 9 Talent 1249 N Lodi Place, Hollywood CA 90038, USA | |
| **Hongsakula, Apasra (Pook)** | Beauty Queen |
| Slimming Spa, 95 Ladprao Soi 23, Chatuchak, Bangkok 10900, Thailand | |
| **Honore, Russel L** | Army General |
| Keppler Speakers, 4350 N Fairfax Dr, #700, Arlington VA 22203, USA | |
| **Honrubia, Samuel** | Handball Player |
| Montpellier Agglomeration H B, 1000 Ave du val de Montferrand, 34090 Montpellier, France | |
| **Honti, Zolton** | Cinematographer |
| Gersh Agency, 9465 Wilshire Blvd, #600, Beverly Hills CA 90212 USA | |
| **Hood, Donald H (Don)** | Baseball Player |
| 20753 Charing Cross Circle, Estero FL 33928, USA | |
| **Hood, Estus, III** | Football Player |
| 2105 W Grace St, Kankakee IL 60901, USA | |
| **Hood, Gavin** | Director |
| Anonymous Content, 3532 Hayden Ave, Culver City CA 90232 USA | |
| **Hood, Kenneth** | Religious Leader |
| 5799 Bloomfield Ave, Verona NJ 07044, USA | |
| **Hood, Leroy E** | Inventor (DNA Sequencer), Geneticist |
| Institutions for Systems Biology, 1441 N 34th St, Seattle WA 98103, USA | |
| **Hood, Robin** | Golfer |
| 6705 Shoal Creek Dr, Arlington TX 76001, USA | |
| **Hood, Walter** | Landscape Designer |
| Hood Studio, 3016 Filbert St, Oakland CA 94608, USA | |
| **Hood, Winford D** | Football Player |
| 79 Anderson Ave NW, Atlanta GA 30314, USA | |
| **Hook, James W (Jay)** | Baseball Player |
| PO Box 90, Maple City MI 49664, USA | |
| **Hooker, Charles R** | Artist |
| 28 Whippingham Road, Brighton, Sussex BN2 3PG, England | |
| **Hooker, Fair, Jr** | Football Player |
| 3728 Rutherford Court, Inglewood CA 90305, USA | |
| **Hooker, Jake** | Journalist |
| New York Times, Editorial Dept, 229 W 43rd St, New York NY 10036 USA | |
| **Hooks, Bell** | Writer |
| 291 W 12th St, New York NY 10014, USA | |
| **Hooks, Brian** | Actor |
| Don Buchwald, 6500 Wilshire Blvd, #2200, Los Angeles CA 90048 USA | |
| **Hooks, Jan** | Actress, Comedienne |
| Innovative Artists, 1505 10th St, Santa Monica CA 90401 USA | |
| **Hooks, Kevin** | Director, Producer |
| Gyre Entertainment, 4119 W Burbank Blvd, Burbank CA 91505, USA | |
| **Hooks, Robert** | Actor |
| 145 N Valley St, Burbank CA 91505, USA | |
| **Hooks, Roland** | Football Player |
| 3724 Calgary Dr, Reno NV 89511, USA | |
| **Hookstratten, Edward G** | Attorney |
| Ed Hookstratten Mgmt, 9536 Wilshire Blvd, #500, Beverly Hills CA 90212, USA | |
| **Hooper, Bobby Joe** | Basketball Player |
| 825 Ivywood St, #4, Dayton OH 45420, USA | |
| **Hooper, Brandon** | Actor, Writer, Producer |
| United Talent Agency, U T A Plaza, 9336 Civic Center Dr, Beverly Hills CA 90210 USA | |
| **Hooper, C Darrow** | Track Athlete |
| 6 Braemore Place, Dallas TX 75230, USA | |
| **Hooper, Ella** | Singer (Killing Heidi) |
| Harbour Agency, 135 Forbes St, Woolloomooloo NSW 2011, Australia | |
| **Hooper, Kay** | Writer |
| Bantam/Dell Books, 1745 Broadway, New York NY 10019, USA | |
| **Hooper, Thomas G (Tom)** | Director |
| I C M Partners, 10250 Constellation Blvd, #900, Los Angeles CA 90067 USA | |
| **Hooper, Tobe** | Director |
| Gersh Agency, 9465 Wilshire Blvd, #600, Beverly Hills CA 90212 USA | |
| **Hoopes, Chad** | Concert Violinist |
| I M G Artists, Carnegie Hall Tower, 152 W 57th St, #500, New York NY 10019 USA | |
| **Hooser, Carroll L** | Basketball Player |
| 925 Edgefield Trail, Flower Mound TX 75028, USA | |
| **Hooton, Burt C** | Baseball Player |
| 3619 Granby Court, San Antonio TX 78217, USA | |
| **Hoover, Alice** | Baseball Player |
| 340 Roosevelt Ave, Reading PA 19605, USA | |
| **Hoover, Bradley R (Brad)** | Football Player |
| 2130 Climbing Rose Lane, Matthews NC 28104, USA | |
| **Hoover, Houston R** | Football Player |
| 1216 Mareed Ave, Yazoo City MS 39194, USA | |
| **Hoover, Paul C** | Baseball Player |
| 2320 Anderson Road, Cuyahoga Falls OH 44221, USA | |
| **Hoover, Richard** | Scenic Designer |
| I C M Partners, 10250 Constellation Blvd, #900, Los Angeles CA 90067 USA | |
| **Hoover, Robert A (Bob)** | Test Pilot |
| Bob Hoover Airshows, 1100 E Imperial Ave, El Segundo CA 90245, USA | |
| **Hoover, Thomas L (Tom)** | Basketball Player |
| 9 Apple Manor Lane, East Brunswick NJ 08816, USA | |
| **Hopcroft, John E** | Computer Scientist |
| Cornell University, Engineering College, Carpenter Hall, Ithaca NY 14853, USA | |
| **Hope, Alec D** | Writer |
| PO Box 7949, Alice Springs NT 0871, Australia | |
| **Hope, Amanda** | Model |
| Playboy Promotions, 2706 Media Center Dr, Los Angeles CA 90065 USA | |

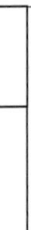

**Hope, David (Dave)** — Bassist (Kansas)
Immanuel Angelican Church, 250 Indian Bayou Trail, Destin FL 32541, USA
**Hope, Jim** — Producer, Writer
A P A Talent/Literary Agency, 405 S Beverly Dr, #300, Beverly Hills CA 90212 USA
**Hope, Leslie** — Actress
Oscars Abrams Zimel, 438 Queen St E, Toronto ON M5A 1T4, Canada
**Hope, William (Bill)** — Actor
Ken McReddie Assoc, 101 Finsbury Pavement, London EC2A 1RS, England
**Hopkins, Anthony** — Actor
United Talent Agency, U T A Plaza, 9336 Civic Center Dr, Beverly Hills CA 90210 USA
**Hopkins, Antony** — Composer, Writer
Woodyard Cottage, Ashridge Park, Little Gaddesden, Berkhamsted HP4 1PS, England
**Hopkins, Bo** — Actor
6628 Ethel Ave, North Hollywood CA 91606, USA
**Hopkins, Bradley D (Brad)** — Football Player
95 Timberline Dr, Nashville TN 37221, USA
**Hopkins, Donald (Don)** — Baseball Player
PO Box 8817, Benton Harbor MI 49023, USA
**Hopkins, Gail E** — Baseball Player
120 Canterbury Dr, Parkersburg WV 26104, USA
**Hopkins, Godfrey T** — Photographer
Wilmington Cottage, Wilmington Road, Seaford, East Sussex BN25 2EH, England
**Hopkins, James** — Artist, Sculptor
Saatchi Gallery, Duke Of York's HQ, King's Road, London SW3 4RY, England
**Hopkins, Jan** — Commentator
CNN-TV, 190 Marietta Ave SW, Atlanta GA 30303 USA
**Hopkins, Jennifer** — Tennis Player
4312 W 110 St, Leawood KS 66211, USA
**Hopkins, Jerry W** — Football Player
1025 Burberry, Woodway TX 76712, USA
**Hopkins, John** — Bassist (Zac Brown Band)
Shore Fire Media, 32 Court St, #1600, Brooklyn NY 11201 USA
**Hopkins, Josh** — Actor
Gersh Agency, 9465 Wilshire Blvd, #600, Beverly Hills CA 90212 USA
**Hopkins, Joshua** — Opera Singer
I M G Artists, Hogarth Business Park, Chiswick, London W4 2TH, England
**Hopkins, Kaitlin** — Actress
Gage Group, 450 7th Ave, #1809, New York NY 10123 USA
**Hopkins, Linda** — Singer, Actress
Scott Stander Assoc, 4533 Van Nuys Blvd, #401, Sherman Oaks CA 91403 USA
**Hopkins, Michael J** — Architect
27 Broadley Terrace, London NW1 6LG, England
**Hopkins, Paul** — Actor
Edna Talent Mgmt, 318 Dundas St W, Toronto ON M5T 1G5, Canada
**Hopkins, Robert M (Bob)** — Basketball Player
8421 SE 71st St, Mercer Island WA 98040, USA
**Hopkins, Stephen J** — Director
Creative Artists Agency, 2000 Ave of Stars, #100, Los Angeles CA 90067 USA
**Hopkins, Sy** — Singer (Five Satins)
Paramount Entertainment, PO Box 12, Far Hills NJ 07931 USA
**Hopkins, Telma** — Actress, Singer
Innovative Artists, 1505 10th St, Santa Monica CA 90401 USA
**Hopkins, Tom** — Writer
7531 E 2nd St, Scottsdale AZ 85251, USA
**Hopkins, Wesley (Wes)** — Football Player
7412 White Oak Road, Fairfield AL 35064, USA
**Hoppe, Fred** — Sculptor
PO Box 42, Milford NE 68405, USA
**Hoppe, Wolfgang** — Bobsled Athlete
Dieterstedter Str 11, 99510 Apolda, Germany
**Hoppen, David D (Dave)** — Basketbal Player
16341 Webster St, Omaha NE 68118, USA
**Hopper, Heather** — Actress
Baron Entertainment, 13848 Ventura Blvd, #A, Sherman Oaks CA 91423, USA
**Hopper, Norris S** — Baseball Player
902 Hampton St, Shelby NC 28152, USA
**Hopperdeitz, Anna** — Actress
Agentur Fuhrmann, Lindenstr 8A, 84424 Isen-Pemmering, Germany
**Hoppus, Mark** — Bassist (Blink-182, +44)
14015 Chestnut Hill Lane, San Diego CA 92128, USA
**Hopson, Dennis** — Basketball Player
7229 Donnybrook Dr, Dublin OH 43017, USA
**Hora, Jeremy** — Guitarist (Default)
Union Entertainment, 1323 Newbury Road, #104, Newbury Park CA 91320, USA
**Horan, Dennis, Jr** — Bowler
32458 Galatina St, Temecula CA 92592, USA
**Horan, James** — Actor
Angel City Talent, 8318 Kirkwood Dr, Los Angeles CA 90046, USA
**Horan, Michael W (Mike)** — Football Player
7235 E La Cumbre Dr, Orange CA 92869, USA
**Horan, Monica** — Actress
Creative Artists Agency, 2000 Ave of Stars, #100, Los Angeles CA 90067 USA
**Horbiger, Christiane** — Actress
Agentur Alexander, Lamontstr 9, 81679 Munich, Germany
**Hordges, Cedrick T** — Basketball Player
237 W 127th St, #28, New York NY 10027, USA
**Horford Reynoso, Alfred J (Al)** — Basketball Player
Atlanta Hawks, Centennial Tower, 101 Marietta St NW, #1900, Atlanta GA 30303 USA
**Horgan, Joe** — Baseball Player
2039 Kellogg Way, Rancho Cordova CA 95670, USA
**Horgan, Patrick** — Actor
I C M Partners, 10250 Constellation Blvd, #900, Los Angeles CA 90067 USA
**Horgan, Sharon** — Actress, Comedienne
United Agents, 12-26 Lexington St, London W1F 0LE, England
**Horinek, Ramon A** — Vietnam War Air Force Hero
184 National Blvd, Universal City TX 78148, USA

**Horlen, Joel E (Joe)**
3718 Chartwell Dr, San Antonio TX 78230, USA — Baseball Player

**Horlock, John H**
2 The Avenue, Ampthill, Bedford MK45 2NR, England — Mechanical Engineer, Educator

**Horn, Donald G (Don)**
2229 Wynterbrook Dr, Littleton CO 80126, USA — Football Player

**Horn, Joseph (Joe)**
316 Grenier Terrace, Lawrenceville GA 30045, USA — Football Player

**Horn, Marian Blank**
US Claims Court, 717 Madison Place NW, Washington DC 20439, USA — Judge

**Horn, Paul J**
Thomas Cassidy, PO Box 1311, Tucson AZ 85702 USA — Jazz Flutist, Saxophonist

**Horn, Samuel L (Sam)**
1305 Narragansett Blvd, Cranston RI 02905, USA — Baseball Player

**Hornacek, Jeffrey J (Jeff)**
5821 N 37th St, Paradise Valley AZ 85253, USA — Basketball Player, Coach

**Hornaday, Jeffrey**
I C M Partners, 10250 Constellation Blvd, #900, Los Angeles CA 90067 USA — Choreographer

**Hornaday, Ronald (Ron), Jr**
116 Courtney Lane, Mooresville NC 28117, USA — Truck, Auto Racing Driver

**Hornbacher, Scott**
United Talent Agency, U T A Plaza, 9336 Civic Center Dr, Beverly Hills CA 90210 USA — Producer

**Hornbuckle, Linda**
Pacific Talent, PO Box 19145, Portland OR 97280, USA — Singer

**Hornby, Nick**
Penguin Books, 80 Stand, London WC2R 0RL, England — Writer

**Horne, Jimmy Bo**
Talent Consultants International, 105 Shad Row, #B, Piermont NY 10968 USA — Singer, Dancer

**Horne, John R**
Navistar International, PO Box 1488, Warrenville IL 60555, USA — Businessman

**Horne, Marilyn**
Marilyn Home Foundation, 315 W 86th St, #2D, New York NY 10024, USA — Opera Singer

**Horne, Steve**
Tasman Motor Sports Group, 4192 Weaver Court, Hilliard OH 43026, USA — Auto Racing Executive

**Horneber, Petra**
Ringstr 77, 85402 Kranzberg, Germany — Markswoman

**Horneff, Will**
Abrams Artists, 9200 W Sunset Blvd, #1125, West Hollywood CA 90069 USA — Actor

**Horner, Alex Kapp**
Innovative Artists, 1505 10th St, Santa Monica CA 90401 USA — Actress

**Horner, Charles A (Chuck)**
2824 Jack Nicklaus Way, Shalimar FL 32579, USA — Air Force General

**Horner, Craig**
Marquee Mgmt, 188 Oxford St, Paddington NSW 2021, Australia — Actor

**Horner, J Robert (Bob)**
209 Steeplechase Dr, Irving TX 75062, USA — Baseball Player

**Horner, James**
Gorfaine/Schwartz, 4111 W Alameda Ave, #509, Burbank CA 91505 USA — Composer

**Horner, John R (Jack)**
70 Cougar Dr, Bozeman MT 59718, USA — Paleontologist

**Horner, Martina S**
T I A A-C R E F, 730 3rd Ave, New York NY 10017, USA — Educator, Businesswoman

**Hornish, Samuel J (Sam), Jr**
Penske Championship Racing, 220 Penske Way, Mooresville NC 28115, USA — Auto Racing Driver

**Hornlein, Horst**
Tambascherstr 13, 98559 Oberhoff, Germany — Luge Athlete

**Hornsby, Bruce**
Red Light Mgmt, PO Box 1467, Charlottesville VA 22902, USA — Singer, Pianist, Actor

**Hornsby, David**
Schachter Entertainment, 1157 S Beverly Dr, #200, Los Angeles CA 90035 USA — Actor

**Hornsby, Russell**
Paradigm Agency, 360 N Crescent Dr, North Building, Beverly Hills CA 90210 USA — Actor

**Hornung, Paul V**
3115 Arden Road, Louisville KY 40222, USA — Football Player

**Horovitz, Adam (King Ad-Rock)**
Capitol Records, 810 7th Ave, New York NY 10019 USA — Rap Artist (Beastie Boys)

**Horovitz, Israel A**
Washington Square Arts, 310 Bowery, #200, New York NY 10012, USA — Writer

**Horovitz, Joseph**
Royal College of Music, Prince Consort Road, London SW7 2BS, England — Composer

**Horovitz, Rachael**
Creative Artists Agency, 2000 Ave of Stars, #100, Los Angeles CA 90067 USA — Producer, Actress

**Horowitz, Ben**
Esther Creative Group, 27 W 24th St, #404, New York NY 10010, USA — Drummer (Gaslight Anthem)

**Horowitz, David C**
Fight Back Productions, 139 S Beverly Dr, #233, Beverly Hills CA 90210, USA — Commentator

**Horowitz, Jerome P**
Wayne State University Medical School, 540 E Canfield Ave, Detroit MI 48201, USA — Internist

**Horowitz, Paul**
111 Chilton St, Cambridge MA 02138, USA — Physicist, Electrical Engineer

**Horowitz, Sari**
Washington Post, Editorial Dept, 1150 15th St NW, Washington DC 20071 USA — Journalist

**Horowitz, Scott J**
5491 Freestyle Way, Park City UT 84098, USA — Astronaut

**Horrigan, Sam**
Prestige Talent Agency, 9250 Wilshire Blvd, #208, Beverly Hills CA 90212, USA — Actor, Producer

**Horrocks, Jane**
United Agents, 12-26 Lexington St, London W1F 0LE, England — Actress, Singer

**Horry, Robert K**
2126 Countryshire Ln, Richmond TX 77406, USA — Basketball Player

**Horsey, David**
King Features Syndicate, 300 W 57th St, #1500, New York NY 10019 USA — Editorial Cartoonist

**Horsford, Anna Maria**
Innovative Artists, 1505 10th St, Santa Monica CA 90401 USA — Actress

**Horsley, Jack**
608 N Sampson St, Ellensburg WA 98926, USA — Swimmer

V.I.P. Address Book

**Horsley, Lee A**
Central Artists, 3310 W Burbank Blvd, Burbank CA 91505, USA
Actor

**Horsman, Vincent S J (Vince)**
1941 Pinehurst Dr, Clearwater FL 33763, USA
Baseball Player

**Horton, Anthony D (Tony)**
17001 Livorno Dr, Pacific Palisades CA 90272, USA
Baseball Player

**Horton, Ethan S**
4602 Fairvista Dr, Charlotte NC 28269, USA
Football Player

**Horton, Frank E**
288 River Ranch Circle, Bayfield CO 81122, USA
Educator

**Horton, Gregory K (Greg)**
1053 Lytle St, Redlands CA 92374, USA
Football Player

**Horton, Peter**
W M E Entertainment, 9601 Wilshire Blvd, #300, Beverly Hills CA 90210 USA
Actor

**Horton, Raymond A (Ray)**
3400 S Water St, Pittsburgh PA 15203, USA
Football Player

**Horton, Ricky N**
16026 Aston Court, Chesterfield MO 63005, USA
Baseball Player

**Horton, Robert**
5317 Andasol Ave, Encino CA 91316, USA
Actor

**Horton, William W (Willie)**
5655 Woodland Pass, Bloomfield Hills MI 48301, USA
Baseball Player

**Horvath, Bronco J**
27 Oliver St, South Yarmouth MA 02664, USA
Ice Hockey Player

**Horvitz, H Robert**
34 Pilgrim Road, Wellesley Hills MA 02481, USA
Nobel Medicine Laureate

**Horvitz, Louis J**
Gersh Agency, 9465 Wilshire Blvd, #600, Beverly Hills CA 90212 USA
Director

**Horwitz, Dominique**
Agentur Patricia Horwitz, Erdmannstra 10, 22765 Hamburg, Germany
Actress, Singer

**Horwitz, Morton J**
Harvard University, Law School, Cambridge MA 02138, USA
Attorney, Educator

**Horwitz, Tony**
PO Box 5056, Vineyard Haven MA 02568, USA
Journalist, Writer

**Hosey, Dwayne S**
164 N Plum Ave, Ontario CA 91764, USA
Baseball Player

**Hoshide, Akihiko (Aki)**
J A X A, Tsukuba Space Center, 2-1-1 Sengen, Tsukubashi, Ibaraki 305 8505, Japan
Astronaut, Japan

**Hosket, Wilmer F (Bill)**
4721 Bayford Court, Columbus OH 43220, USA
Basketball Player

**Hoskins, Bob**
United Agents, 12-26 Lexington St, London W1F 0LE, England
Actor

**Hoskins, Derrick**
10491 Road 842, Philadelphia MS 39350, USA
Football Player

**Hosley, Timothy K (Tim)**
112 Elena Dr, Moore SC 29369, USA
Baseball Player

**Hosmer, Bradley C (Brad)**
PO Box 1128, Cedar Crest NM 87008, USA
Air Force General

**Hospodar, Edward D (Ed)**
217 Orchard Way, Wayne PA 19087, USA
Ice Hockey Player

**Hossa, Marian**
270 E Pearson St, #1402, Chicago IL 60611, USA
Ice Hockey Player

**Hossack, Allison**
Characters Talent Mgmt, 8 Elm St, Toronto ON M5G 1G7, Canada
Actress

**Hossein, Robert**
Ghislaine de Wing, 10 Rue du Docteur Roux, 75015 Paris, France
Actor, Director

**Hosseini, Khaled**
Riverhead/Penguin Group, 375 Hudson St, Basement 1, New York NY 10014, USA
Writer

**Hostak, Martin**
Ceska Televize, Kavci Hory, 14070 Prague 4, Czech Republic
Ice Hockey Player

**Hostetler, David A (Dave)**
3404 Steeplechase Trail, Arlington TX 76016, USA
Baseball Player

**Hostetler, David L**
PO Box 989, Athens OH 45701, USA
Sculptor

**Hostetler, Jeff W**
2032 Magnolia Dr, Morgantown WV 26508, USA
Football Player

**Hostetter, G Richard**
Presbyterian Church in America, 1852 Century Place NE, #201, Atlanta GA 30345, USA
Religious Leader

**Hotani, Hirokazu**
Teikyo University, Biosciences Dept, Toyosatodai, Utsunomiya 320 0003, Japan
Microbiotics Engineer

**Hotchkiss, Rob**
Jon Landau, 150 Rowayton Ave, Norwalk CT 06853, USA
Guitarist (Train)

**Hotez, Peter**
Sabin Vaccine Institute, 2000 Pennsylvania Ave NW, #7100, Washington DC 20006, USA
Microbiologist, Immunologist

**Hottelet, Richard C**
120 Chestnut Hill Road, Wilton CT 06897, USA
Commentator

**Hotten, Terry**
Eli Lilly Wood Laboratory, Windlesham, Surrey GO20 6PH, England
Chemist

**Hottman, Kenneth (Ken)**
9537 2nd Ave, Elk Grove CA 95624, USA
Baseball Player

**Hoty, Dee**
Gage Group, 450 7th Ave, #1809, New York NY 10123 USA
Actress, Singer

**Hotz, Kenneth J (Kenny)**
Paradigm Agency, 360 N Crescent Dr, North Building, Beverly Hills CA 90210 USA
Actor, Director, Writer

**Hou, Ya-Ming**
Massachusetts Institute of Technology, Biology Dept, Cambridge MA 02139, USA
Biologist

**Houbregs, Robert J (Bob)**
1949 Arena Court SE, Olympia WA 98501, USA
Basketball Player

**Houcke, Sara**
Ringling Bros Barnum & Bailey, 8607 Westwood Circle Dr, Vienna VA 22182 USA
Circus Animal Trainer

**Houellebecq, Michel**
Green Ufos, Parque Pisa, C/Exposicion, 1 Izq, 41927 Mairena del Aljarafe, Spain
Writer, Director

**Hough, Charles O (Charlie)**
2266 Shade Tree Circle, Brea CA 92821, USA
Baseball Player

**Hough, Derek**
Brillstein Entertainment Partners, 9150 Wilshire Blvd, #350, Beverly Hills CA 90212 USA
Dancer, Choreographer

**Hough, James H (Jim)**
2440 Christian Dr, Chaska MN 55318, USA — Football Player
**Hough, Joseph C, Jr**
Union Theological Seminary, President's Office, New York NY 10027, USA — Educator
**Hough, Julianne M**
Creative Artists Agency, 2000 Ave of Stars, #100, Los Angeles CA 90067 USA — Dancer, Singer, Actress
**Hough, Stephen A G**
C M Artists, 127 W 96th St, #13B, New York NY 10025 USA — Concert Pianist
**Houghton, Frances**
Tyrian Club, 6 Lower Mall, Hammersmith W6 9DJ, England — Rowing Athlete
**Houghton, Israel**
Integrity Music, 1000 Cody Road, Mobile AL 36695, USA — Singer, Songwriter, Guitarist
**Houghton, James R**
36 Spencer Hill Road, Corning NY 14830, USA — Businessman
**Houghton, John T**
Hadley Center, London Broad, Bracknell, Berkshire RG12 2SZ, England — Physicist, Climatologist
**Houghton, Katharine**
Ambrosio/Mortimer, 165 W 46th St, New York NY 10036 USA — Actress
**Houghton, Michael**
Chiron Corp, 4560 Horton St, Emeryville CA 94608, USA — Geneticist
**Hougland, William (Bill)**
PO Box 2629, Edwards CO 81632, USA — Basketball Player
**Houle, Rejean**
7941 Boul Lasalle, Lasalle QC H8P 3R1, Canada — Ice Hockey Player
**Hoult, Nicholas**
United Talent Agency, U T A Plaza, 9336 Civic Center Dr, Beverly Hills CA 90210 USA — Actor
**Houlton, D J**
2357 N Campus Ave, Upland CA 91784, USA — Baseball Player
**Houngbo, Gilbert**
Prime Minister's Office, BP 5618, Lome, Togo — Prime Minister, Togo
**Hounsou, Djimon**
Creative Artists Agency, 2000 Ave of Stars, #100, Los Angeles CA 90067 USA — Actor, Model
**House, David (Dave)**
Nortel Networks Corp, 8200 Dixie Road, Brampton ON L6T 5P6, Canada — Businessman
**House, Edward L (Eddie)**
Miami Heat, American Airlines Arena, 601 Biscayne Blvd, Miami FL 33132 USA — Basketball Player
**House, James R (J R)**
34 River Ridge Trail, Ormond Beach FL 32174, USA — Baseball Player
**House, James S**
University of Michigan, Social Research Institute, Ann Arbor MI 48106, USA — Psychologist
**House, Karen Eliot**
58 Cleveland Lane, Princeton NJ 08540, USA — Journalist
**House, Thomas R (Tom)**
12794 Via Felino, Del Mar CA 92014, USA — Baseball Player
**House, Yoanna**
I M G Models, 304 Park Ave S, #PH N, New York NY 10010 USA — Model
**Householder, Paul W**
521 N Swinton Ave, Delray Beach FL 33444, USA — Baseball Player
**Houser, John W, Jr**
2197 Creekside Dr, Solvang CA 93463, USA — Football Player
**Houser, Kevin J**
941 Montclair Circle, Westlake OH 44145, USA — Football Player
**Houser, Randy**
Fitzgerald Hartley, 1964 Wedgewood Ave, Nashville TN 37212 USA — Singer, Songwriter
**Houshmandzadeh, Touraj (T J), Jr**
16703 Greenbrook Circle, Cerritos CA 90703, USA — Football Player
**Housley, Phil**
2877 Itasca Ave S, Lakeland MN 55043, USA — Ice Hockey Player
**Houston, Allan W**
Allan Houston Foundation, 350 5th Ave, #5900, New York NY 10118, USA — Basketball Player
**Houston, Bobby**
4640 Vendue Range Dr, Raleigh NC 27604, USA — Football Player
**Houston, Byron D**
3108 Birch Land, Edmond OK 73034, USA — Basketball Player
**Houston, Cissy**
Nippy Inc, 60 Park Place, #1800, Newark NJ 07102, USA — Singer
**Houston, James E (Jim)**
925 Trimble Place, Northfield OH 44067, USA — Football Player
**Houston, Kenneth R (Ken)**
3603 Forest Village Dr, Kingwood TX 77339, USA — Football Player
**Houston, Marques B**
Pyramid Entertainment Group, 377 Rector Place, #21A, New York NY 10280 USA — Singer, Actor
**Houston, Penelope**
Absolute Artists, 8490 W Sunset Blvd, #403, West Hollywood CA 90069, USA — Singer
**Houston, Russell**
General Delivery, Eagar AZ 85925, USA — Artist
**Houston, Stephen D**
Brown University, Anthropology Dept, Providence RI 02912, USA — Anthropologist, Social Scientist
**Houston, Thelma**
Diva Central, 7510 W Sunset Blvd, #1445, Los Angeles CA 90046, USA — Singer
**Houston, Tyler S**
325 Pleasant Summit Dr, Henderson NV 89012, USA — Baseball Player
**Houston, Wade**
University of Tennessee, Athletic Dept, Knoxville TN 37901, USA — Basketball Coach
**Hout, Michael**
University of California, Demography Center, 2538 Channing, Berkeley CA 94720, USA — Demographer
**Hovan, Christopher J (Chris)**
17301 Ladera Estates Blvd, Lutz FL 33548, USA — Football Player
**Hove, Andrew C (Skip), Jr**
Promontory Financial Group, 1201 Pennsylvania NW, #617, Washington DC 20004, USA — Government Official, Financier
**Hovind, David J**
Paccar Inc, 777 106th Ave NE, Bellevue WA 98004, USA — Businessman
**Hovland, Tim**
Association of Volleyball Professionals, 960 Knox St, #A, Torrance CA 90502 USA — Volleyball Player
**Hovsepian, Vatche**
Armenian Church of America West, 1201 N Vine St, Los Angeles CA 90038, USA — Religious Leader

**Howard, Adina** — Singer
A&M Entertainment, 13280 NW Freeway, #F328, Houston TX 77040, USA

**Howard, Alan M** — Actor
Julian Belfrage Assoc, 9 Argyll St, #300, London W1F 7TG, England

**Howard, Andrew** — Actor
Julian Belfrage Assoc, 9 Argyll St, #300, London W1F 7TG, England

**Howard, Ann** — Opera Singer
Stafford Law Assoc, 6 Barham Close, Weybridge, Surrey KT13 9PR, England

**Howard, Arliss** — Actor, Director
Innovative Artists, 235 Park Ave S, #1000, New York NY 10003 USA

**Howard, Barbara** — Actress
PO Box 459, Chelsea MI 48118, USA

**Howard, Bruce E** — Baseball Player
8705 Misty Creek Dr, Sarasota FL 34241, USA

**Howard, Bryce Dallas** — Actress
Management 360, 9111 Wilshire Blvd, Beverly Hills CA 90210 USA

**Howard, Christian (Chris)** — Baseball Player
11 Hawser Lane, Swampscott MA 01907, USA

**Howard, Christopher H (Chris)** — Baseball Player
8655 Jones Road, #301, Houston TX 77065, USA

**Howard, Clark** — Entertainer
WSB-AM, 1601 West Peachtree St, Atlanta GA 30309, USA

**Howard, Clint** — Actor
4286 Clybourn Ave, Burbank CA 91505, USA

**Howard, David** — Football Player
5516 E Rosedale St, Fort Worth TX 76112, USA

**Howard, David W** — Baseball Player
22846 Chesterview Loop, #111, Land O Lakes FL 34639, USA

**Howard, Desmond K** — Football Player
Prince Promotions, 9663 Santa Monica Blvd, #324, Beverly Hills CA 90210, USA

**Howard, Douglas L (Doug)** — Baseball Player
8038 Deer Creek Road, Salt Lake City UT 84121, USA

**Howard, Dwight D** — Basketball Player
3565 Rice Lake Loop, Longwood FL 32779, USA

**Howard, Eugene (Gene)** — Football Player
11051 Lavender Ave, Fountain Valley CA 92708, USA

**Howard, Frank O** — Baseball Player
24178 Lenah Woods Place, Aldie VA 20105, USA

**Howard, George** — Jazz Saxophonist
David Rubinson, PO Box 411197, San Francisco CA 94141, USA

**Howard, George** — Bowler
8415 Brookwood Dr, Portage MI 49024, USA

**Howard, Greg** — Basketball Player
4517 W 16th Place, #2, Los Angeles CA 90019, USA

**Howard, Greg** — Cartoonist (Sally Forth)
3403 W 28th St, Minneapolis MN 55416, USA

**Howard, Harry N** — Historian
6508 Greentree Road, Bradley Hills Grove, Bethesda MD 20817, USA

**Howard, Hobie** — Singer (Sawyer Brown)
O-Seven Artist Mgmt, PO Box 210586, Nashville TN 37221, USA

**Howard, James J, III** — Businessman
Northern States Power, 414 Nicollett Mall, Minneapolis MN 55401, USA

**Howard, James Newton** — Composer
Gorfaine/Schwartz, 4111 W Alameda Ave, #509, Burbank CA 91505 USA

**Howard, Jan** — Singer, Songwriter
Tessier-Marsh Talent, 2825 Blue Brick Dr, Nashville TN 37214, USA

**Howard, Jason** — Opera Singer
I M G Artists, Hogarth Business Park, Chiswick, London W4 2TH, England

**Howard, Jeffrey R** — Judge
US Court of Appeals, US Courthouse, 55 Pleasant St, Concord NH 03301, USA

**Howard, Jeremy** — Actor
Stone Manners Salners, 9911 W Pico Blvd, #1400, Los Angeles CA 90035 USA

**Howard, John W** — Prime Minister, Australia
GPO Box 59, Sydney NSW 2001, Australia

**Howard, Joshua J (Josh)** — Basketball Player
6306 Linden Lane, Dallas TX 75230, USA

**Howard, Juwan A** — Basketball Player
11714 Bistro Lane, Houston TX 77082, USA

**Howard, Ken** — Actor, Labor Leader
Screen Actors Guild, 5757 Wilshire Blvd, Los Angeles CA 90036, USA

**Howard, Kyle** — Actor, Writer, Director
United Talent Agency, U T A Plaza, 9336 Civic Center Dr, Beverly Hills CA 90210 USA

**Howard, Linda** — Writer
Ballatine Books, 1745 Broadway, New York NY 10019 USA

**Howard, Michael** — Government Official, England
House of Lords, Westminster, London SW1A 0PW, England

**Howard, Michelle J** — Navy Admiral
Deputy Commander, Fleet Forces Command, 1562 Mitscher Ave, Norfolk VA 23551 USA

**Howard, Miki** — Singer, Actress
Majestic Entertainment Group, 3645 Marketplace Blvd, #130-40, East Point GA 30344, USA

**Howard, Otis** — Basketball Player
231 Manhattan Ave, Oak Ridge TN 37830, USA

**Howard, Paul G** — Football Player
10859 W 85th Place, Arvada CO 80005, USA

**Howard, Rance** — Actor
4286 Clybourn Ave, Burbank CA 91505, USA

**Howard, Rebecca Lynn** — Singer
W M E Entertainment, 1600 Division St, #300, Nashville TN 37203 USA

**Howard, Reginald C (Reggie)** — Football Player
PO Box 382666, Germantown TN 38183, USA

**Howard, Richard** — Writer
23 Waverly Place, #5X, New York NY 10003, USA

**Howard, Robert E** — Cartoonist (Conan)
Dark House Publishing, 10956 SE Main St, Portland OR 97222, USA

**Howard, Ronald F (Ron)** — Football Player
14701 NE 61st Court, Redmond WA 98052, USA

**Howard, Ronald W (Ron)** — Actor, Director
Imagine Entertainment, 9465 Wilshire Blvd, #700, Beverly Hills CA 90212, USA

**Howard, Russ** — Curling Athlete
Curling Assn, 1660 Vimont Court, Cumberland ON K4A 4J4, Canada

**Howard, Ryan J** — Baseball Player
1630 Bentshire Court, Ballwin MO 63011, USA

**Howard, Sherri** — Track Athlete
14059 Bridle Ridge Road, Sylmar CA 91342, USA

**Howard, Sophie** — Model
International Model Mgmt, Elysium Gate, 126-128 New Kings Road, London SW6 4LZ, England

**Howard, Steven B (Steve)** — Baseball Player
4712 Shetland Ave, Oakland CA 94605, USA

**Howard, Susan** — Actress
PO Box 1456, Boerne TX 78006, USA

**Howard, Terrence D** — Actor
Creative Artists Agency, 2000 Ave of Stars, #100, Los Angeles CA 90067 USA

**Howard, Thomas S** — Baseball Player
822 8th Ave, Middletown OH 45044, USA

**Howard, Tish** — Model
Playboy Promotions, 2706 Media Center Dr, Los Angeles CA 90065 USA

**Howard, Traylor** — Actress
John Carrabino Mgmt, 5900 Wilshire Blvd, #406, Los Angeles CA 90036 USA

**Howard, Walker** — Actor
Stone Manners Salners, 9911 W Pico Blvd, #1400, Los Angeles CA 90035 USA

**Howard, Walter I (Todd)** — Football Player
1300 Bienville Ave, Ruston LA 71270, USA

**Howard, Wilbur L** — Baseball Player
643 Walston Lane, Houston TX 77060, USA

**Howard, William W, Jr** — Association Executive
National Wildlife Federation, 11100 Wildlife Center Dr, Reston VA 20190, USA

**Howarth, Elgar** — Composer
27 Cromwell Ave, London N6 5HN, England

**Howarth, James E (Jim)** — Baseball Player
PO Box 401, 1 Hancock Plaza, Gulfport MS 39502, USA

**Howarth, Roger** — Actor
K & H, 1212 Ave of Americas, #3, New York NY 10036, USA

**Howarth, Thomas** — Architect
University of Toronto, 230 College St, Toronto ON M5S 1R1, Canada

**Howatch, Susan** — Writer
Aitken & Stone, 29 Fernshaw Road, London SW10 0TG, England

**Howatt, Glenn** — Journalist
Minneapolis Star Tribune, Editorial Dept, 425 Portland Ave S, Minneapolis MN 55488 USA

**Howe of Aberavon, R E Geoffrey** — Government Official, England
Barclays Bank, Cavendish Square Branch, 4 Vere St, London W1, England

**Howe, Arthur** — Journalist
Philadelphia Inquirer, Editorial Dept, 400 N Broad St, Philadelphia PA 19130, USA

**Howe, Arthur H (Art), Jr** — Baseball Player, Manager
17214 Calico Peak Way, Cypress TX 77433, USA

**Howe, Brian** — Singer (Bad Company)
Artists International Mgmt, 9850 Sandalfoot Blvd, #458, Boca Raton FL 33428 USA

**Howe, Daniel Walker** — Writer
Oxford University Press, 198 Madison Ave, #800, New York NY 10016 USA

**Howe, Gordon (Gordie)** — Ice Hockey Player
Power Play International, 1119 Rochester Road, Troy MI 48083, USA

**Howe, Jonathan T** — Navy Admiral
Arthur Vining Davis Foundation, 225 Water St, #1510, Jacksonville FL 32202, USA

**Howe, Mark S** — Ice Hockey Player
106 Barrington Road, Bloomfield Hills MI 48302, USA

**Howe, Oscar** — Artist
5900 S Prairie View Court, Sioux Falls SD 57108, USA

**Howe, Tina** — Writer
333 W End Ave, New York NY 10023, USA

**Howell, Alex** — Cartoonist (Butch & Dougie)
King Features Syndicate, 300 W 57th St, #1500, New York NY 10019 USA

**Howell, Anthony** — Actor
Ken McReddie Assoc, 101 Finsbury Pavement, London EC2A 1RS, England

**Howell, Bailey E** — Basketball Player
1989 S Montgomery St, Starkville MS 39759, USA

**Howell, C Thomas** — Actor
Glick Agency, 1321 7th St, #203, Santa Monica CA 90401 USA

**Howell, Charles, III** — Golfer
5187 Vardon Dr, Windermere FL 34786, USA

**Howell, Delles R** — Football Player
1907 Crescent Dr, Monroe LA 71202, USA

**Howell, Henry V (Harry)** — Ice Hockey Player
401-49 Robinson St, Hamilton ON L8P 1Y7, Canada

**Howell, Jack R** — Baseball Player
822 S Lehigh Dr, Tucson AZ 85710, USA

**Howell, James P (J P)** — Baseball Player
808 46th St, Sacramento CA 95819, USA

**Howell, Jay C** — Baseball Player
4560 Colony Point, Suwanee GA 30024, USA

**Howell, Jefferson D, Jr** — Marine Corps General
2207 Villa Rose Dr, Houston TX 77062, USA

**Howell, John T** — Football Player
8276 San Dollar Dr, Windsor CO 80528, USA

**Howell, Kathleen** — Aeronautical Engineer
Purdue University, Aeronautical Engineering Dept, West Lafayette IN 47907, USA

**Howell, Kenneth (Ken), Jr** — Baseball Player
29512 Bradmoor Court, Farmington Hills MI 48334, USA

**Howell, Margaret** — Actress
Chateau/Billings Agency, 8489 W 3rd St, #1032, Los Angeles CA 90048, USA

**Howell, Margaret** — Fashion Designer
5 Garden House, 8 Battersea Park Road, London SW8 4BG, England

**Howell, Michael L (Mike)** — Football Player
200 Charlotte St, Monroe LA 71202, USA

**Howell, Pat G** — Football Player
7692 N Kincaid Ave, Fresno CA 93711, USA

**Howell, Porter** — Guitarist (Little Texas)
Splash Public Relations, 1520 16th Ave S, #2, Nashville TN 37212, USA

**Howell, William R** — Businessman
J C Penney Co, PO Box 10001, Dallas TX 75301, USA

**Howells, Anne E** — Opera Singer
Milestone, Broom Close, Esher, Surrey KT10 9NP, England

**Howerton, Glenn** — Producer, Writer, Actor
W M E Entertainment, 9601 Wilshire Blvd, #300, Beverly Hills CA 90210 USA

**Howes, Sally Ann** — Actress, Singer
Palm Beach Theater Guild, PO Box 667, Palm Beach FL 33480, USA

**Howey, Steve** — Actor
United Talent Agency, U T A Plaza, 9336 Civic Center Dr, Beverly Hills CA 90210 USA

**Howfield, Robert (Bobby)** — Football Player
5529 S Lowell Blvd, Littleton CO 80123, USA

**Howison, Ryan** — Golfer
245 Barbados Dr, Jupiter FL 33458, USA

**Howitt, Dann P J** — Baseball Player
PO Box 565, Douglas MI 49406, USA

**Howitt, Peter** — Director
Industry Entertainment, 955 Carillo Dr, #300, Los Angeles CA 90048 USA

**Howland, Beth** — Actress, Singer
Access Talent Voice Overs, 171 Madison Ave, #910, New York NY 10016, USA

**Howland, Rick** — Actor
Oscars Abrams Zimel, 438 Queen St E, Toronto ON M5A 1T4, Canada

**Howle, Paul** — Cartoonist (In Their Own Words)
United Feature Syndicate, PO Box 5610, Cincinnati OH 45201 USA

**Howlett, Liam P** — Musician (Prodigy), Composer
Midi Mgmt, Jenkins Lane, Great Hallinsbury, Essex CM22 7QL, England

**Howley, Charles L (Chuck)** — Football Player
Happy Hollow Ranch, 26875 FM 47, Wills Point TX 75169, USA

**Howley, Peter M** — Pathologist
Harvard Medical School, 200 Longwood Ave, Boston MA 02115, USA

**Howry, Bobby D (Bob)** — Baseball Player
24108 N 73rd Lane, Peroia AZ 85383, USA

**Howson, Peter** — Artist
Flowers East, 82 Kingsland Road, London E2 8DP, England

**Howton, William H (Bill)** — Football Player
1796 County Road 10, Plainview TX 79072, USA

**Howze, Leonard Earl** — Actor
Kritzer Levine Wilkins Griffin, 11872 La Grange Ave, #100, Los Angeles CA 90025 USA

**Hoy, Christopher A (Chris)** — Cyclist
British Cycling Centre, Stuart St, Manchester M11 4DQ, England

**Hoy, Peter A** — Baseball Player
26 Woods Dr, Canton NY 13617, USA

**Hoying, Robert C (Bobby)** — Football Player
Crawford Hoying Real Estate, 555 Metro Place N, #600, Dublin OH 43017, USA

**Hoyle, Dan** — Actor, Comedian
Gersh Agency, 41 Madison Ave, #3301, New York NY 10010 USA

**Hoyt, D LaMarr** — Baseball Player
1594 Lost Creek Dr, Columbia SC 29212, USA

**Hozumi, Masako** — Speed Skater
Skating Federation, 1-1-1 Jinnan, #414, Shibuyaku, Tokyo 150 8050, Japan

**HR** — Singer (Bad Brains)
Agency Group Ltd, 142 W 57th St, #600, New York NY 10019 USA

**Hrabosky, Alan T (Al)** — Baseball Player, Sportscaster
9 Frontenac Estates Dr, Saint Louis MO 63131, USA

**Hrabowski, Freeman A, III** — Educator
University of Maryland Baltimore County, President's Office, 1000 Hilltop Circle, Baltimore MD 21250, USA

**Hradecka, Lucie** — Tennis Player
C T L K Prague, Stvanice 38, 17000 Prague 7, Czech Republic

**Hrbaty, Dominik** — Tennis Player
Octagon Worldwide, 800 Connecticut Ave, #200, Norwalk CT 06854 USA

**Hrbek, Kent A** — Baseball Player
Hrbek Outdoors, 5500 Lincoln Dr, #150, Edina MN 55436, USA

**Hrdy, Sarah Blaffer** — Anthropologist
University of California, Anthropology Dept, Davis CA 95616, USA

**Hriniak, Walter J (Walt)** — Baseball Player
18 Stacy Dr, North Andover MA 01845, USA

**Hristov, Momchil** — Photographer
Hristo Vakavelski Str Bl 5, #3, 1700 Sofia, Bulgaria

**Hrkac, Anthony J (Tony)** — Ice Hockey Player
6818 Kasota Court, Mequon WI 53092, USA

**Hrudey, Kelly** — Ice Hockey Player
CBC-TV, PO Box 500, Station A, Toronto ON M5W 1E6, Canada

**Hrusa, Jakub** — Conductor
I M G Artists, Hogarth Business Park, Chiswick, London W4 2TH, England

**Hruska, Carrie B** — Biomedical Engineer
Mayo Clinic, Biomedical Engineering Dept, 200 1st St SW, Rochester MN 55905, USA

**Hsiang, Wu-chung** — Mathematician
Princeton University, Mathematics Dept, Princeton NJ 08544, USA

**Hsiao, Rita** — Writer
W M E Entertainment, 9601 Wilshire Blvd, #300, Beverly Hills CA 90210 USA

**Hsuan Yu Chen** — Oncologist
Taiwan University Medical Center, Roosevelt Road, Taipei 10517, Taiwan

**Hu Jintao** — President, China
Chairman's Office, Zhongnanhai, Beijing 100017, China

**Hu Qili** — Government Official, China
Consultative Conference, 23 Taipingqiao St, Beijing 100283, China

**Hu Shuli** — Editor
Caijing Media, Winterless Center, 1 Xidawanglu, Chaoyang District, Beijing 100026 PR, China

**Hu, Ann** — Director, Writer
C E S D, 10635 Santa Monica Blvd, #130, Los Angeles CA 90025 USA

**Hu, Kelly** — Actress
Paul Kohner, 9300 Wilshire Blvd, #555, Beverly Hills CA 90212 USA

**Huan, Zhang** — Artist/Sculptor
Pace Gallery, 32 E 57th St, New York NY 10022 USA
**Huang Qun** — Gymnast
Global Athletics & Marketing, 611 Tremont St, #400, Boston MA 02118, USA
**Huang, Helen** — Concert Pianist
I C M Artists, 40 W 57th St, #1800, New York NY 10019 USA
**Huang, Henry** — Inventor (DNA Sequencer), Biologist
Washington University, McDonnell Pediatrics Dept, Saint Louis MO 63110, USA
**Huang, James** — Actor, Producer
Kazarian/Measures/Ruskin, 11969 Ventura Blvd, #300, Studio City CA 91604 USA
**Huang, Kerson** — Physicist
Massachusetts Institute of Technology, Physics Dept, 77 Massachusetts, #6309, Cambridge MA 02139, USA
**Huang, Ying** — Opera Singer
Columbia Artists Mgmt Inc, 1790 Broadway, #702, New York NY 10019 USA
**Huard, Damon P** — Football Player
9508 NE 18th St, Clyde Hill WA 98004, USA
**Huarte, John G** — Football Player
14959 La Cumbre Dr, Pacific Palisades CA 90272, USA
**Hub** — Bassist (Roots)
W M E Entertainment, 1325 Ave of Americas, New York NY 10019 USA
**Hubbard, Elizabeth (Liz)** — Actress
Liebman Entertainment, 25 E 21st St, #PH, New York NY 10010, USA
**Hubbard, Erica** — Actress
Pantheon Talent, 1801 Century Park E, #1910, Los Angeles CA 90067, USA
**Hubbard, Glenn D** — Baseball Player
1515 Kings Crossing, Stone Mountain GA 30087, USA
**Hubbard, Gregg (Hobie)** — Singer, Keyboardist (Sawyer Brown)
O-Seven Artist Mgmt, PO Box 210586, Nashville TN 37221, USA
**Hubbard, John** — Artist
Chilcombe House, Chilcombe near Bridport, Dorset DT6 4PN, England
**Hubbard, Marvin R (Marv)** — Football Player
5804 Dawn View Court, Castro Valley CA 94552, USA
**Hubbard, Michael W (Mike)** — Baseball Player
2552 Brookstone Lane, Richmond VA 23233, USA
**Hubbard, Phillip G (Phil)** — Basketball Player, Coach
5130 Pleasant Forest Dr, Centreville VA 20120, USA
**Hubbard, R Glenn** — Government Official, Economist
Columbia University, Graduate Management School, New York NY 10027, USA
**Hubbard, Robert** — Basketball Player
353 Piper Road, West Springfield MA 01089, USA
**Hubbard, Trenidad A (Trent)** — Baseball Player
4206 Clearwater Court, Missouri City TX 77459, USA
**Hubbard, William N, Jr** — Businessman
3634 Woodcliff Dr, Kalamazoo MI 49008, USA
**Hubby, Sandra** — Model
Playboy Promotions, 2706 Media Center Dr, Los Angeles CA 90065 USA
**Huber, Anja** — Skeleton Athlete
Loslerstr 48, 83471 Schonau am Konigssee, Germany
**Huber, Anke** — Tennis Player
Dieselstr 10, 76689 Karlsdorf-Neuthard, Germany
**Huber, Gunther** — Bobsled Athlete
Olympic Committee, Foro Italico, Largo Lauro de Bosis 15, 00135 Rome, Italy
**Huber, Jon** — Baseball Player
4409 S Angeline St, Seattle WA 98118, USA
**Huber, Liezel** — Tennis Player
14423 Middle Bluff Trail, Cypress TX 77429, USA
**Huber, Robert** — Nobel Chemistry Laureate
Planck Biochemie Institut, Am Klopferspitz, 82152 Martinsried, Germany
**Hubert, Janet L** — Actress
Michael Slessinger, 8730 W Sunset Blvd, #220W, West Hollywood CA 90069 USA
**Hubley, Season** — Actress
47 Pleasant St, Essex Junction VT 05452, USA
**Hubley, Whip** — Actor
Geddes Agency, 8430 Santa Monica Blvd, #201, West Hollywood CA 90069 USA
**Huck, A Francis (Fran)** — Ice Hockey Player
313-2505 11th Ave, Regina SK S4P 0K6, Canada
**Huck, John Lloyd** — Businessman
233 Lion's Hill Road, State College PA 16803, USA
**Huckabee, Cooper** — Actor
Kazarian/Measures/Ruskin, 11969 Ventura Blvd, #300, Studio City CA 91604 USA
**Huckabee, Michael (Mike)** — Governor, AR
Fox-TV, News Dept, 5151 Wisconsin Ave NW, #100, Washington DC 20016 USA
**Huckaby, Ken** — Baseball Player
4490 S Rio Dr, Chandler AZ 85249, USA
**Hucknall, Michael J (Mick)** — Singer (Simply Red)
Sideways Mgmt, Junction Mews, Paddington, London WC1E 7EA, England
**Huckstep, Ronald L** — Orthopedic Surgeon
108 Sugarloaf Crescent, Castlecrag, Syndey NSW 2068, Australia
**Hucles, Angela** — Soccer Player
8 Worcester Square, #1, Boston MA 02118, USA
**Hucul, Fred** — Ice Hockey Player
4550 N Flowing Wells Road, #226, Tucson AZ 85705, USA
**Hudd, Roy** — Actor
Associated International Mgmt, 7 Hatton Garden, #400, London EC1N 8AD, England
**Huddleston, David** — Actor
9200 W Sunset Blvd, #612, West Hollywood CA 90069, USA
**Huddleston, Mark W** — Educator
University of New Hampshire, President's Office, Durham NH 03824, USA
**Huddy, Charlie** — Ice Hockey Player
9114 100 A Ave, Edmonton AB T5H 4N7, Canada
**Hudecek, Vaclav** — Concert Violinist
Londynska 25, 12000 Prague 2, Czech Republic
**Hudek, John R** — Baseball Player
7603 Shady Way Dr, Sugar Land TX 77479, USA
**Hudepohl, Joe** — Swimmer
10437 Greendale Dr, Tampa FL 33626, USA

# H

| | |
|---|---|
| **Hudgens, David M (Dave)**<br>5802 E Windsor Ave, Scottsdale AZ 85257, USA | Baseball Player |
| **Hudgens, Vanessa A**<br>Untitled Entertainment, 350 S Beverly Dr, #200, Beverly Hills CA 90212 USA | Singer, Actress, Model |
| **Hudler, Jiri**<br>555 S Old Woodward Ave, Birmingham MI 48009, USA | Ice Hockey Player |
| **Hudler, Rex A**<br>9430 W 157th Court, Overland Park KS 66221, USA | Baseball Player |
| **Hudlin, Reginald**<br>3 Arts Entertainment, 9460 Wilshire Blvd, #700, Beverly Hills CA 90212 USA | Actor, Director, Writer |
| **Hudner, Thomas J, Jr**<br>31 Allen Farm Lane, Concord MA 01742, USA | Korean War Navy Hero (CMH) |
| **Hudson, C B, Jr**<br>Torchmark Corp, 2001 3rd Ave S, Birmingham AL 35233, USA | Businessman |
| **Hudson, Cary**<br>Michelle Roche Media Relations, 360 University Circle, Athens GA 30605, USA | Singer, Songwriter |
| **Hudson, Charles (Charlie)**<br>32 W Hooker Ave, Coalgate OK 74538, USA | Baseball Player |
| **Hudson, Charles L**<br>PO Box 368, Oakwood TX 75855, USA | Baseball Player |
| **Hudson, Clifford G**<br>Securities Investor Protection, 805 15th St NW, #800, Washington DC 20005, USA | Financier |
| **Hudson, Ernie**<br>Talent Works, 3500 W Olive Ave, #1400, Burbank CA 91505 USA | Actor |
| **Hudson, Garth**<br>Skyline Music, 32 Clayton St, Portland ME 04103, USA | Organist (Band) |
| **Hudson, Gordon L**<br>5350 Edgewood Circle, Salt Lake City UT 84117, USA | Football Player |
| **Hudson, Hugh**<br>Jenks & Partners, 37 W 28th St, #7, New York NY 10001, USA | Director |
| **Hudson, James**<br>Harvard Medical School, Psychiatry Dept, 25 Shattuck St, Boston MA 02115, USA | Psychiatrist |
| **Hudson, Jennifer**<br>Creative Artists Agency, 2000 Ave of Stars, #100, Los Angeles CA 90067 USA | Actress, Singer |
| **Hudson, Jessie J (Jesse)**<br>341 Albert Lewis Way, Mansfield LA 71052, USA | Baseball Player |
| **Hudson, John L**<br>3320 Highway 77, Paris TN 38242, USA | Football Player |
| **Hudson, Joseph P (Joe)**<br>109 Pine Valley Dr, Medford NJ 08055, USA | Baseball Player |
| **Hudson, Kate**<br>Creative Artists Agency, 2000 Ave of Stars, #100, Los Angeles CA 90067 USA | Actress |
| **Hudson, Louis C (Lou)**<br>2002 Lakeview Dr, Park City UT 84060, USA | Basketball Player |
| **Hudson, Luke**<br>9912 Aster Circle, Fountain Valley CA 92708, USA | Baseball Player |
| **Hudson, Oliver**<br>Management 360, 9111 Wilshire Blvd, Beverly Hills CA 90210 USA | Actor |
| **Hudson, Orlando T**<br>PO Box 1888, Darlington SC 29540, USA | Baseball Player |
| **Hudson, Ray**<br>D C United, R F K Stadium, 2400 E Capitol St SE, Washington DC 20003 USA | Soccer Player, Coach |
| **Hudson, Richard S (Dick)**<br>3320 Highway 77, Paris TN 38242, USA | Football Player |
| **Hudson, Robert W (Bob)**<br>3408 Dalrock Road, Rowlett TX 75088, USA | Football Player |
| **Hudson, Sally**<br>PO Box 2343, Olympic Valley CA 96146, USA | Skier |
| **Hudson, Timothy A (Tim)**<br>600 Graystone Court, Peachtree City GA 30269, USA | Baseball Player |
| **Hudson, Troy**<br>6040 Earle Brown Dr, #450, Minneapolis MN 55430, USA | Basketball Player |
| **Hudspeth, Mark**<br>University of Louisiana, Athletic Dept, 104 University Circle, Lafayette LA 70504, USA | Football Coach |
| **Huebel, Rob**<br>Creative Artists Agency, 2000 Ave of Stars, #100, Los Angeles CA 90067 USA | Actor |
| **Huefner, Tatjana**<br>Welfenstr 32, 38889 Blankenburg/Harz, Germany | Luge Athlete |
| **Huerta, Dolores**<br>United Farm Workers, 29700 Woodford Tehachapi Road, Keene CA 93531, USA | Labor Activist |
| **Huertas, Jon**<br>Innovative Artists, 1505 10th St, Santa Monica CA 90401 USA | Actor |
| **Huett, Zane**<br>Coast to Coast Talent, 3350 Barham Blvd, Los Angeles CA 90068 USA | Actor |
| **Huey**<br>Multi Entertainment Group, 4044 W Lake Mary Blvd, #104-324, Lake Mary FL 32746, USA | Rap Artist |
| **Huff, Aubrey L, III**<br>471 H C R 3121, Hillsboro TX 76645, USA | Baseball Player |
| **Huff, Brent**<br>Vox Inc, 6420 Wilshire Blvd, #1080, Los Angeles CA 90048 USA | Actor |
| **Huff, Gary E**<br>3175 Hawks Landing Dr, Tallahassee FL 32309, USA | Football Player |
| **Huff, Kenneth W (Ken)**<br>74003 Harvey, Chapel Hill NC 27517, USA | Football Player |
| **Huff, Leon A**<br>W M E Entertainment, 9601 Wilshire Blvd, #300, Beverly Hills CA 90210 USA | Songwriter, Pianist, Businessman |
| **Huff, Michael K (Mike)**<br>PO Box 6176, Woodridge IL 60517, USA | Baseball Player |
| **Huff, Robert L (Sam)**<br>8 N Jay St, Middleburg VA 20117, USA | Football Player |
| **Huffington, Arianna S**<br>3299 K St NW, #402, Washington DC 20007, USA | Writer |
| **Huffins, Chris**<br>1319 Wildcliff Parkway NE, Atlanta GA 30329, USA | Track Athlete |
| **Huffman, Cady**<br>Don Buchwald, 6500 Wilshire Blvd, #2200, Los Angeles CA 90048 USA | Actress, Singer |

Hudgens - Huffman

**Huffman, Chris** — Bassist (Casting Crowns)
Proper Mgmt, PO Box 150867, Nashville TN 37215, USA

**Huffman, Felicity K** — Actress
Creative Artists Agency, 2000 Ave of Stars, #100, Los Angeles CA 90067 USA

**Huffman, Kerry** — Ice Hockey Player
5557 Sea Forest Dr, #215, New Port Richey FL 34652, USA

**Huffman, Logan** — Actor
Gersh Agency, 9465 Wilshire Blvd, #600, Beverly Hills CA 90212 USA

**Huffman, Phillip L (Phil)** — Baseball Player
194 Paxton Road, Rochester NY 14617, USA

**Huffman, Timothy P (Tim)** — Football Player
3365 Jubilee Trail, Dallas TX 75229, USA

**Hufner, Tatjana** — Luge Athlete
Welfenstr 32, 38889 Blankenburg/Harz, Germany

**Hufsey, Billy** — Actor
7585 Blue Copper Court, Las Vegas NV 89113, USA

**Hufstedler, Shirley M** — Secretary, Education; Judge
720 Iverness Dr, La Canada Flintridge CA 91011, USA

**Hug, Procter R, Jr** — Judge
US Court of Appeals, Courthouse, 400 S Virginia St, Reno NV 89501, USA

**Huggins, Bob** — Basketball Coach
West Virginia University, Athletic Dept, Morgantown WV 26506, USA

**Hughes, Albert** — Director, Producer, Writer
W M E Entertainment, 9601 Wilshire Blvd, #300, Beverly Hills CA 90210 USA

**Hughes, Alfredrick (Alfred)** — Basketball Player
5024 S Kildare Ave, Chicago IL 60632, USA

**Hughes, Allen** — Director, Producer, Writer
W M E Entertainment, 9601 Wilshire Blvd, #300, Beverly Hills CA 90210 USA

**Hughes, Bradley** — Golfer
204 Easton Court, Simpsonville SC 29680, USA

**Hughes, Bronwen** — Director
Gersh Agency, 9465 Wilshire Blvd, #600, Beverly Hills CA 90212 USA

**Hughes, Chris** — Businessman, Publisher, Editor
New Republic, 1400 K St NW, #1200, Washington DC 20005, USA

**Hughes, Clara** — Speed Skater, Cyclist
Speed Skating Canada, 2781 Lancaster Road, #402, Ottawa ON K1B 1A7, Canada

**Hughes, Dan** — Basketball Coach, Executive
San Antonio Silver Stars, 1 AT&T Center, San Antonio TX 78219 USA

**Hughes, David A** — Football Player
5307 240th Ave NE, Redmond WA 98053, USA

**Hughes, Eddie** — Basketball Player
4253 Deerfield Hills Road, Colorado Springs CO 80916, USA

**Hughes, Ernest L (Ernie)** — Football Player
2116 Camino Brazos, Pleasanton CA 94566, USA

**Hughes, Finola** — Actress
Harrison Stokes, 8730 W Sunset Blvd, #270, West Hollywood CA 90069, USA

**Hughes, Frank John** — Actor
A P A Talent/Literary Agency, 405 S Beverly Dr, #300, Beverly Hills CA 90212 USA

**Hughes, H Richard** — Architect
47 Chiswick Quay, London W4 3UR, England

**Hughes, Harold R (Harry)** — Governor, MD
Patton Boggs Blow, 2550 M St NW, #500, Washington DC 20037, USA

**Hughes, J Randell (Randy)** — Football Player
17608 Cedar Creek Canyon Dr, Dallas TX 75252, USA

**Hughes, James M (Jim)** — Baseball Player
7526 El Manor Ave, Los Angeles CA 90045, USA

**Hughes, John** — Ice Hockey Player
317 Laudholm Farm Road, Wells ME 04090, USA

**Hughes, Karen** — Government Official
Harper Collins Publishers, 10 E 53rd St, Cellar 1, New York NY 10022 USA

**Hughes, Kathleen** — Actress
8818 Rising Glen Place, Los Angeles CA 90069, USA

**Hughes, Larry D** — Basketball Player
3 Hanna Court, Cleveland OH 44108, USA

**Hughes, Mervyn G** — Cricketer
Australian Cricket Board, 90 Jollimant St, Melbourne VIC 3002, Australia

**Hughes, Miko** — Actor
Jamieson Assoc, 53 Sunrise Road, Superior MT 59872, USA

**Hughes, Nicola** — Actress
Gavin Barker Assoc, 2D Wimpole St, London W1G 0EB, England

**Hughes, Pat** — Ice Hockey Player
8388 Webster Hills Road, Dexter MI 48130, USA

**Hughes, Phil** — Baseball Player
275 Bayshore Blvd, #501, Tampa FL 33606, USA

**Hughes, Richard D** — Drummer (Keane)
Agency Group Ltd, 361-373 City Road, London EC1V 1PQ, England

**Hughes, Richard H (Dick)** — Baseball Player
PO Box 598, Stephens AR 71764, USA

**Hughes, Sally** — Actress
Associated International Mgmt, 7 Hatton Garden, #400, London EC1N 8AD, England

**Hughes, Sarah E** — Figure Skater
John Hughes, 12 Channel Dr, Great Neck NY 11024, USA

**Hughes, Terry** — Director
Creative Artists Agency, 2000 Ave of Stars, #100, Los Angeles CA 90067 USA

**Hughes, Terry W** — Baseball Player
532 Pierpoint Avenue Extension, Spartanburg SC 29303, USA

**Hughes, Thomas E (Tom)** — Baseball Player
610 Kimswick Court, Deer Park TX 77536, USA

**Hughes, Thomas J, Jr** — Navy Admiral
400 Mar Vista Dr, #4, Monterey CA 93940, USA

**Hughes, Tom** — Actor
C E S D, 10635 Santa Monica Blvd, #130, Los Angeles CA 90025 USA

**Hughes, Tyrone C** — Football Player
5812 W Deer Park Blvd, New Orleans LA 70127, USA

**Hughes, W Patrick (Pat)** — Football Player
4 Woodside Dr, Stratham NH 03885, USA

**Hughes, Wendy**
I C M Partners, 10250 Constellation Blvd, #900, Los Angeles CA 90067 USA — Actress

**Hughes-Fulford, Millie**
Veterans Affairs Dept, Medical Center, 4150 Clement St, San Francisco CA 94121, USA — Astronaut

**Hughey, Gary H**
Deputy CinC, US Transportation Command, Scott Air Force Base IL 62225 USA — Marine Corps General

**Hughley, D L**
I C M Partners, 10250 Constellation Blvd, #900, Los Angeles CA 90067 USA — Actor, Comedian

**Hugo, Chad**
Virgin Records, 338 N Foothill Road, Beverly Hills CA 90210 USA — Singer, Rap Artist (NERD)

**Huguenin, G Richard**
Millitech Corp, 5 North St, South Deerfield MA 01373, USA — Inventor (Portable Gun Detector Camera)

**Huh, John**
Professional Golfer's Assn, PO Box 109601, Palm Beach Gardens FL 33410 USA — Golfer

**Huisgen, Rolf**
Kaulbachstr 10, 80539 Munich, Germany — Chemist

**Huish, Justin**
3475 Indian Mesa Dr, Thousand Oaks CA 91360, USA — Archer

**Huisman, Justin R**
8713 Forest Glen Court, Saint John IN 46373, USA — Baseball Player

**Huisman, Michiel**
Conway Van Gelder Grant, 8-12 Broadwick St, #300, London W1F 8HW, England — Actor

**Huisman, Richard A (Rick)**
17W25 Oak Lane, Bensenville IL 60106, USA — Baseball Player

**Huismann, Mark L**
5751 NW Plantation Lane, Lees Summit MO 64064, USA — Baseball Player

**Huizenga, H Wayne**
1575 Ponce del Leon Dr, Fort Lauderdale FL 33316, USA — Businessman

**Huizenga, John R**
354 Gravilla St, La Jolla CA 92037, USA — Nuclear Chemist

**Hulbert, Mike**
7770 Apple Tree Circle, Orlando FL 32819, USA — Golfer

**Hulce, Tom**
Anonymous Content, 3532 Hayden Ave, Culver City CA 90232 USA — Actor

**Hulk**
Confederacion de Futebol, Rua Victor Civita 66, #1, Rio de Janeiro 22775 044, Brazil — Soccer Player

**Hull, Brett A**
3826 Maplewood Ave, Dallas TX 75205, USA — Ice Hockey Player

**Hull, Dennis W**
11642 County Road 29, Roseneath ON K0K 2X0, Canada — Ice Hockey Player

**Hull, Eric**
803 N 4th St, Selah WA 98942, USA — Baseball Player

**Hull, Frank M**
US Court of Appeals, 56 Forsyth St NW, Atlanta GA 30303, USA — Judge

**Hull, Gina**
479 Arricola Ave, Saint Augustine FL 32080, USA — Golfer

**Hull, Mike**
3809 Vista Azul, San Clemente CA 92672, USA — Football Player

**Hull, Robert M (Bobby)**
6916 Lennox Place, University Park FL 34201, USA — Ice Hockey Player

**Hull, Roger H**
Union College, Chancellor's Office, Schenectady NY 12308, USA — Educator

**Hullar, Theodore L**
3 Lowell Place, Ithaca NY 14850, USA — Educator

**Hulme, Etta**
Fort Worth Star-Telegram, Editorial Dept, 808 Throckmorton St, Fort Worth TX 76102 USA — Editorial Cartoonist

**Hulme, Keri**
PO Box 1, Whataroa, South Westland, Aotearoa 7587, New Zealand — Writer

**Hulse, Cale**
9290 E Thompson Peak Parkway, #107, Scottsdale AZ 85255, USA — Ice Hockey Player

**Hulse, David L**
1301 Kenwood Dr, San Angelo TX 76903, USA — Baseball Player

**Hulse, Russell A**
PO Box 451, Princeton NJ 08542, USA — Nobel Physics Laureate

**Hulsey, Corey S**
178 Pine Needle Trail, Villa Rica GA 30180, USA — Football Player

**Hulten, Jens**
T C G Artists Mgmt, 14A Goodwin's Court, Covent Garden, London WC2N 4LL, England — Actor

**Hultqvist, Bengt K G**
Gronstensv 2, 98 140 Kiruna, Sweden — Space Physicist

**Hultz, W Donald (Don)**
5078 Pleasant Ridge Road, Millington TN 38053, USA — Football Player

**Huly, Jan C**
M B O Partners, 13454 Sunrise Valley Dr, #550, Herndon VA 20171, USA — Marine Corps General

**Humala, Ollanta**
Palacio de Gobierno S/N, Plaza de Armas S/N, Lima 1, Peru — President, Peru

**Humann, L Phillip**
SunTrust Banks, 303 Peachtree St NE, Atlanta GA 30308, USA — Financier

**Humayan, Mark S**
University of Southern California, Doheny Eye Institute, Los Angeles CA 90033, USA — Ophthalmologist

**Humber, Philip**
PO Box 130788, Tyler TX 75713, USA — Baseball Player

**Humbert, John O**
Christian Church Disciples of Christ, 130 E Washington, Indianapolis IN 46204, USA — Religious Leader

**Hume, A Britton (Brit)**
1401 N Oak St, #608, Arlington VA 22209, USA — Commentator

**Hume, Gary**
Kentmere Photographic Ltd, Staveley, Kendal LA8 9PB, England — Artist

**Hume, John**
Constituency, 5 Bayview Terrace, Derry BT48 7EE, Northern Ireland — Nobel Peace Laureate

**Hume, Kirsty**
Elite Model Mgmt, 404 Park Ave S, #900, New York NY 10016 USA — Model

**Hume, Thomas H (Tom)**
3810 Redfish Court, Palmetto FL 34221, USA — Baseball Player

**Humenik, Ed**
4746 SW Hammock Creek Dr, Palm City FL 34990, USA — Golfer

**Humes, Edward** — Journalist
Simon & Schuster, 1230 Ave of Americas, Concourse 1, New York NY 10020, USA
**Humes, H David** — Surgeon, Nephrologist
University of Michigan Medical Center, 1500 E Medical Center Dr, Ann Arbor MI 48109, USA
**Humes, Mary-Margaret** — Actress, Model
Stone Manners Salners, 9911 W Pico Blvd, #1400, Los Angeles CA 90035 USA
**Humes, Steven** — Opera Singer
Opera et Concert, 37 Rue de la Chaussee d'Antin, 75009 Paris, France
**Humm, David H** — Football Player
4301 Via Olivero Ave, Las Vegas NV 89102, USA
**Hummel, Tim** — Baseball Player
1550 Kerr Road, Whiteford MD 21160, USA
**Hummer, John R** — Basketball Player
2640 Baker St, San Francisco CA 94123, USA
**Hummes, Claudio Cardinal** — Religious Leader
Avenida Higienopolis 890, CP 1670, 01238 908 Sao Paulo, Brazil
**Humperdinck, Engelbert** — Singer
10642 Santa Monica Blvd, #105, Los Angeles CA 90025, USA
**Humphrey, Claude B** — Football Player
3399 Lord Dunmore Cove, Memphis TN 38134, USA
**Humphrey, Gordon J** — Senator, NH
78 Garvin Hill Road, Chichester NH 03258, USA
**Humphrey, Jackie** — Track Athlete
616 Powder Horn Road, Richmond KY 40475, USA
**Humphrey, Neil D** — Educator
963 Ridgeview Dr, Reno NV 89511, USA
**Humphrey, Terryal G (Terry)** — Baseball Player
7 Oakmont, Trabuco Canyon CA 92679, USA
**Humphreys, Matthew** — Actor
Don Buchwald, 6500 Wilshire Blvd, #2200, Los Angeles CA 90048 USA
**Humphreys, Michael B (Mike)** — Baseball Player
1402 Lost Creek Dr, De Soto TX 75115, USA
**Humphreys, Robert W (Bob)** — Baseball Player
1803 Oakwood St, Bedford VA 24523, USA
**Humphries, J Jay** — Basketball Player
22107 N 37th Terrace, Phoenix AZ 85050, USA
**Humphries, Kaillie** — Bobsled Athlete
Alberta Bobsled, Niven Center, 140 Canada Olympic Road, Calgary AB T3B 5RS, Canada
**Humphries, Stefan G** — Football Player
8708 E Redwood Lane, Spokane WA 99217, USA
**Humphry, Derek** — Social Activist
Euthanasia Research & Guidance Organization, 24828 Norris Lane, Junction City OR 97448, USA
**Hun Sen, Samdech** — Prime Minister, Cambodia
Prime Minister's Office, Supreme National Council, Phnom Penh, Cambodia
**Hundley, C Randolph (Randy)** — Baseball Player
122 E Forest Lane, Palatine IL 60067, USA
**Hundley, Rodney C (Hot Rod)** — Basketball Player, Sportscaster
29769 N 130th Dr, Peoria AZ 85383, USA
**Hundley, Todd R** — Baseball Player
105 Open Parkway S, Hawthorn Woods IL 60047, USA
**Hundt, Reed E** — Government Official
6416 Brookside Dr, Chevy Chase MD 20815, USA
**Hung, Sammo** — Actor
Blue Stone Entertainment, 9000 Sunset Blvd, #515, Los Angeles CA 90069, USA
**Hunger, Daniela** — Swimmer
S V Preussen, Hansastr 190, 13088 Berlin, Germany
**Hunger, Sophie** — Singer
Agency Group Ltd, 142 W 57th St, #600, New York NY 10019 USA
**Huniford, James** — Interior Designer, Architect
Huniford Design Studio, 210 11th Ave, #601, New York NY 10001, USA
**Hunkapiller, Michael** — Inventor (DNA Sequencer), Biochemist
Applied Biosystems, 850 Lincoln Centre Dr, Foster City CA 94404, USA
**Hunley, Leann** — Actress
Mitchell K Stubbs Assoc, 8695 W Washington Blvd, #204, Culver City CA 90232 USA
**Hunley, Rickard C (Ricky)** — Football Player
4435 Circle View Blvd, Los Angeles CA 90043, USA
**Hunnam, Charlie** — Actor
Creative Artists Agency, 2000 Ave of Stars, #100, Los Angeles CA 90067 USA
**Hunnicutt, Gayle** — Actress
174 Regents Park Road, London NW1 8XP, England
**Hunold, Joachim** — Businessman
Air Berlin PLC, Saatwinkler Damm 42-43, 13627 Berlin, Germany
**Hunt, Bonnie** — Actress, Director
W M E Entertainment, 9601 Wilshire Blvd, #300, Beverly Hills CA 90210 USA
**Hunt, Bruce** — Director
I C M Partners, 10250 Constellation Blvd, #900, Los Angeles CA 90067 USA
**Hunt, Bryan** — Artist, Sculptor
9 White St, New York NY 10013, USA
**Hunt, Byron R** — Football Player
PO Box 281, Rutherford NJ 07070, USA
**Hunt, Caroline R** — Businesswoman
100 Crescent Court, #1700, Dallas TX 75201, USA
**Hunt, Courtney** — Writer
W M E Entertainment, 9601 Wilshire Blvd, #300, Beverly Hills CA 90210 USA
**Hunt, Crystal** — Actress
Don Buchwald, 6500 Wilshire Blvd, #2200, Los Angeles CA 90048 USA
**Hunt, Darlene** — Producer, Writer, Actress
United Talent Agency, U T A Plaza, 9336 Civic Center Dr, Beverly Hills CA 90210 USA
**Hunt, David** — Actor, Director
Ken McReddie Assoc, 101 Finsbury Pavement, London EC2A 1RS, England
**Hunt, Helen** — Actress
Creative Artists Agency, 2000 Ave of Stars, #100, Los Angeles CA 90067 USA
**Hunt, J Randall (Randy)** — Baseball Player
324 Holly Ridge Dr, Montgomery AL 36109, USA
**Hunt, James B, Jr** — Governor, NC
Womble Carlyle Sandridge Rice, 150 Fayetteville St Mall, Raleigh NC 27601, USA

# H

| | |
|---|---|
| **Hunt, Johnny M**<br>First Baptist Church, 11905 Highway 92, Woodstock GA 30188, USA | Religious Leader |
| **Hunt, Joseph (Joe)**<br>Iron Workers Union, 1750 New York Ave NW, #400, Washington DC 20006, USA | Labor Leader |
| **Hunt, Linda**<br>W M E Entertainment, 9601 Wilshire Blvd, #300, Beverly Hills CA 90210 USA | Actress |
| **Hunt, Nelson Bunker**<br>Hunt Resources Corp, Fountain Place, 1445 Ross at Field, Dallas TX 75202, USA | Businessman |
| **Hunt, R Kevin**<br>11 Royal Lane, Londonderry NH 03053, USA | Football Player |
| **Hunt, R Timothy**<br>Rose Cottage, Ridge, Hertfordshire EN6 3LH, England | Nobel Medicine Laureate |
| **Hunt, Rameck**<br>Three Doctors Foundation, 65 Hazelwood Ave, Newark NJ 07106, USA | Physician |
| **Hunt, Richard H**<br>1017 W Lill Ave, Chicago IL 60614, USA | Sculptor |
| **Hunt, Robert K (Bobby)**<br>5928 Bentway Dr, Charlotte NC 28226, USA | Football Player |
| **Hunt, Ronald K (Ron)**<br>2806 Jackson Road, Wentzville MO 63385, USA | Baseball Player |
| **Hunt, Samuel K (Sam)**<br>1708 Eliza St, Nacogdoches TX 75961, USA | Football Player |
| **Hunt, Stephanie**<br>Innovative Artists, 1505 10th St, Santa Monica CA 90401 USA | Actress |
| **Hunten, Donald M**<br>1828 E Barn Swallow Lane, Green Valley AZ 85614, USA | Astronomer |
| **Hunter, Anthony R (Tony)**<br>4578 Vista de la Patria, Del Mar CA 92014, USA | Molecular Biologist |
| **Hunter, Brian L**<br>8349 S Aberdeen St, Chicago IL 60620, USA | Baseball Player |
| **Hunter, Brian R**<br>12141 Centralia St, #219, Lakewood CA 90715, USA | Baseball Player |
| **Hunter, Charlie**<br>Mongrel Music. 743 Center Blvd, Fairfax CA 94930, USA | Jazz Guitarist (Charlie Hunter Quartet) |
| **Hunter, Daniel L**<br>210 N Lakeview Dr, Farmerville LA 71241, USA | Football Player |
| **Hunter, Dave**<br>53350 Range Road 220, Androssan AB T8E 2B5, Canada | Ice Hockey Player |
| **Hunter, G William (Billy)**<br>104 E Seminary Ave, Lutherville MD 21093, USA | Baseball Player, Manager |
| **Hunter, Harold J (Buddy)**<br>14616 Fir Circle, Plattsmouth, NE 68048, USA | Baseball Player |
| **Hunter, Holly**<br>Special Artists Agency, 9200 Sunset Blvd, #410, West Hollywood CA 90069 USA | Actress |
| **Hunter, Ian**<br>High Road Touring, 751 Bridgeway, #200, Sausalito CA 94965 USA | Singer, Songwriter (Mott the People) |
| **Hunter, J Scott**<br>6386 Dolive Court, Daphne AL 36526, USA | Football Player |
| **Hunter, James**<br>Large Public Relations, 1 Brickfield Cottages High Road, Tharnwood, London CM 16TH, England | Singer, Guitarist |
| **Hunter, James M (Jim)**<br>12939 Penshurst Lane, Windermere FL 34786, USA | Baseball Player |
| **Hunter, Jeffrey O (Jeff)**<br>2004 Barton Court, Augusta GA 30906, USA | Football Player |
| **Hunter, Jesse**<br>Friedman & LaRosa, 1334 Lexington Ave, New York NY 10128, USA | Singer, Guitarist |
| **Hunter, Jim**<br>Jungle Jim Hunter Mgmt, 864 Woodpark Way SW, Calgary AB T2W 2V8, Canada | Skier |
| **Hunter, John**<br>Lawrence Livermore Laboratory, 7000 East St, Livermore CA 94550, USA | Rocket Engineer |
| **Hunter, Leslie (Les)**<br>8712 W 92nd St, Overland Park KS 66212, USA | Basketball Player |
| **Hunter, Lindsey B**<br>4355 Hickory Ridge Court, Plymouth MI 48170, USA | Basketball Player, Coach |
| **Hunter, Mark**<br>London Knights, 99 Dundas St, London ON N6A 6K1, Canada | Ice Hockey Player |
| **Hunter, Patrick E**<br>8901 S 10th Dr, Phoenix AZ 85041, USA | Football Player |
| **Hunter, Rachel**<br>23 Beverly Park Terrace, Beverly Hills CA 90210, USA | Model, Actress |
| **Hunter, Robert**<br>Agency Group Ltd, 1880 Century Park E, #711, Los Angeles CA 90067 USA | Songwriter (Grateful Dead) |
| **Hunter, Simon**<br>United Talent Agency, U T A Plaza, 9336 Civic Center Dr, Beverly Hills CA 90210 USA | Director |
| **Hunter, Stephen**<br>Washington Post, Editorial Dept, 1150 15th St NW, Washington DC 20071 USA | Writer |
| **Hunter, T Othello**<br>Atlanta Hawks, Centennial Tower, 101 Marietta St NW, #1900, Atlanta GA 30303 USA | Basketball Player |
| **Hunter, Tab**<br>PO Box 50308, Santa Barbara CA 93150, USA | Actor, Singer |
| **Hunter, Tim**<br>Toronto Maple Leafs, AirCanada Center, 40 Bay St, Toronto ON M5J 2K2, Canada | Ice Hockey Player |
| **Hunter, Tim**<br>A P A Talent/Literary Agency, 250 W 57th St, #1701, New York NY 10107 USA | Director |
| **Hunter, Torii K**<br>7164 Richmond Dr, Frisco TX 75035, USA | Baseball Player |
| **Hunter, Willard M**<br>2562 Poppleton Ave, Omaha NE 68105, USA | Baseball Player |
| **Hunter-Gault, Charlayne**<br>News Hour Show, 2700 S Quincy St, #250, Arlington VA 22206, USA | Commentator, Writer |
| **Hunthausen, Raymond G**<br>Catholic Archdiocese of Seattle, 710 9th Ave, Seattle WA 98104, USA | Religious Leader |
| **Huntington, Sam**<br>United Talent Agency, U T A Plaza, 9336 Civic Center Dr, Beverly Hills CA 90210 USA | Actor |
| **Huntington-Whiteley, Rosie**<br>Women Model Mgmt, 199 Lafayette St, #700, New York NY 10012 USA | Model, Actress |

**Huntley, Joni** — Track Athlete
7148 SW 4th Ave, Portland OR 97219, USA
**Huntley, Richard E** — Football Player
7123 Rumple Road, Charlotte NC 28262, USA
**Huntsman, Jon M, Jr** — Diplomat; Governor, UT
Brookings Institute, 1775 Massachusetts Ave NW, Washington DC 20036 USA
**Huntsman, Stanley H** — Track Coach
5532 Timbercrest Trail, Knoxville TN 37909, USA
**Huntz, Stephen M (Steve)** — Baseball Player
3303 Linden Road, #405, Rocky River OH 44116, USA
**Hunyadfi, Steven** — Swimming Coach
838 Ridgewood Dr, #12, Fort Wayne IN 46805, USA
**Hunyady, Emese** — Speed Skater
Beim Spitzriegel 1/2/9, 2500 Baden, Austria
**Hunziker, Terry** — Interior Designer
208 3rd Ave S, Seattle WA 98104, USA
**Hupp, Jana Marie** — Actress
A P A Talent/Literary Agency, 405 S Beverly Dr, #300, Beverly Hills CA 90212 USA
**Huppert, David B (Dave)** — Baseball Player
6732 Stephens Path, Zephyrhills FL 33542, USA
**Huppert, Isabelle** — Actress
Voyez Mon Agent, 20 Ave Rapp, 75007 Paris, France
**Hurd of Westwell, Douglas R** — Government Official, England
Hawkpoint, Crosby Court, 4 Great Saint Helens, London EC3A 6HA, England
**Hurd, Gale Anne** — Producer
Valhalla Motion Pictures, 3201 Cahuenga Blvd W, Los Angeles CA 90068, USA
**Hurd, Michelle** — Actress
T M T Entertainment, 648 Broadway, #1002, New York NY 10012, USA
**Hurdle, Clinton M (Clint)** — Baseball Player, Manager
9068 Sturbridge Place, Littleton CO 80129, USA
**Hurd-Wood, Rachel C** — Actress
Troika, 74 Clerkenwell Road, #300, London EC1M 5QA, England
**Hurford, Peter J** — Concert Organist
Broom House, Saint Bernard's Road, Saint Albans, Hertfordshire AL3 5RA, England
**Hurlbert, Jacquline (Jackie)** — Artist
Studio Ten XIII, 16396 SW Kimball Ave, Lake Oswego OR 97035, USA
**Hurlbut, Laura** — Golfer
6609 Jamieson Ave, Reseda CA 91335, USA
**Hurley, Alfred F** — Educator, Historian
3505 Turtle Creek Blvd, #6A, Dallas TX 75219, USA
**Hurley, Andrew (Andy)** — Drummer (Fall Out Boy)
PO Box 219, 1187 Wilmette Ave, Wilmette IL 60091, USA
**Hurley, Bob** — Surfing Executive
Hurley International, 1945 Placentia Ave, Costa Mesa CA 92627, USA
**Hurley, Bob** — Basketball Coach
Saint Anthony High School, Athletic Dept, 175 8th St, Jersey City NJ 07302, USA
**Hurley, Chad** — Businessman
YouTube, 1000 Cherry Ave, #200, San Bruno CA 94066, USA
**Hurley, Craig** — Actor
Avo Talent, 8500 Melrose Ave, #212, West Hollywood CA 90069, USA
**Hurley, Douglas G** — Astronaut
1848 Lake Landing Dr, League City TX 77573, USA
**Hurley, Elizabeth** — Model, Actress
United Talent Agency, U T A Plaza, 9336 Civic Center Dr, Beverly Hills CA 90210 USA
**Hurley, Robert M (Bobby)** — Basketball Player, Coach
State University of New York, Athletic Dept, Buffalo NY 14260, USA
**Hurn, David** — Photographer
Prospect Cottage, Tintern, Chepstow, Gwent NP16 6SG, Wales
**Hurran, Nick** — Director
Independent Talent Group, 40 Whitfield St, London W1T 2RH, England
**Hurst, Bruce V** — Baseball Player
1080 N Riata St, Gilbert AZ 85234, USA
**Hurst, Geoff** — Soccer Player
Dragonwyck, Saint George's Hill, Weybridge, Surrey KT13 0PY, England
**Hurst, Maurice R** — Football Player
3520 Leonidas St, New Orleans LA 70118, USA
**Hurst, Michael** — Actor, Director, Producer
Johnson & Laird Mgmt, PO Box 78340, Grey Lynn, Auckland 1245, New Zealand
**Hurst, Pat** — Golfer
730 Camino Amigo, Danville CA 94526, USA
**Hurst, Rick** — Actor
1230 N Horn Road, West Hollywood CA 90069, USA
**Hurst, Ryan D** — Actor
Piper Kaniecki Mgmt, 13273 Ventura Blvd, #104, Studio City CA 91604, USA
**Hurst, William H (Bill)** — Baseball Player
9331 SW 192nd Dr, Cutler Bay FL 33157, USA
**Hurston, Charles F (Chuck)** — Football Player
9360 Prestwick Club Dr, Duluth GA 30097, USA
**Hurt, John** — Actor
Independent Talent Group, 40 Whitfield St, London W1T 2RH, England
**Hurt, Mary Beth** — Actress
I C M Partners, 10250 Constellation Blvd, #900, Los Angeles CA 90067 USA
**Hurt, Weston** — Opera Singer
Opus 3 Artists, 470 Park Ave S, #900N, New York NY 10016 USA
**Hurt, William** — Actor
I C M Partners, 10250 Constellation Blvd, #900, Los Angeles CA 90067 USA
**Hurtado Larrea, Oswaldo** — President, Ecuador
Suecia 277 y Av Los Shyris, Quito, Ecuador
**Hurtado, Edwin A** — Baseball Player
1202 15th Ave N, Lake Worth FL 33460, USA
**Hurvich, Leo M** — Psychologist
276 5th Ave, #306, New York NY 10001, USA
**Hurwitz, Charles E** — Businessman
Maxxam Inc, 1330 Post Oak Blvd, #2000, Houston TX 77056, USA
**Hurwitz, Jerard** — Molecular Biologist
Memorial Sloan Kettering Cancer Center, 1275 York Ave, New York NY 10065, USA

**Hurwitz, Jon** — Director, Producer, Writer
Creative Artists Agency, 2000 Ave of Stars, #100, Los Angeles CA 90067 USA
**Hurwitz, Mitchell (Mitch)** — Producer, Writer
Creative Artists Agency, 2000 Ave of Stars, #100, Los Angeles CA 90067 USA
**Husa, Karel J** — Composer, Conductor
3417 Foy Glen Court, Apex NC 27539, USA
**Husar, Lubomyr Cardinal** — Religious Leader
Ploscha Sviatoho Jura 5, 290000 Lviv, Ukraine
**Huscroft, Jamie** — Ice Hockey Player
3024 38th St SE, Puyallup WA 98374, USA
**Huselius, Kristian** — Ice Hockey Player
Columbus Blue Jackets, Arena, 200 W Nationwide Blvd, #1, Columbus OH 43215 USA
**Husen, Torsten** — Educator
Armfeltsgatan 10, 115 34 Stockholm, Sweden
**Husmann, Edward E (Ed)** — Football Player
27266 Orth Lane, Conroe TX 77385, USA
**Huson, Jeffrey K (Jeff)** — Baseball Player
10349 Rowlock Way, Parker CO 80134, USA
**Hussain, Mamnoon** — President, Pakistan
President's Office, Aiwan-e-Sadr, Mall & Mayo Roads, Islamabad, Pakistan
**Hussey, Olivia** — Actress
Frozen Frame Entertainment, 3115 Foothill Blvd, #247, La Crescenta CA 91214, USA
**Husted, Wayne D** — Artist
Keep Homestead Museum, Ely Road, Monson MA 01057, USA
**Huster, Marc** — Weightlifter
Grundstr 111, 0132 Dresden, Germany
**Huston, Anjelica** — Actress, Director
57 Windward Ave, Venice CA 90291, USA
**Huston, Daniel (Danny)** — Director, Actor
Julian Belfrage Assoc, 9 Argyll St, #300, London W1F 7TG, England
**Huston, Geoff A** — Basketball Player
1960 Ellis Ave, Bronx NY 10472, USA
**Huston, Jack** — Actor
United Talent Agency, U T A Plaza, 9336 Civic Center Dr, Beverly Hills CA 90210 USA
**Huston, John** — Golfer
1134 Skye Lane, Palm Harbor FL 34683, USA
**Hutcherson, Josh** — Actor
I C M Partners, 10250 Constellation Blvd, #900, Los Angeles CA 90067 USA
**Hutcherson, Robert (Bobby)** — Jazz Vibraphonist
Blue Note Records, 6920 W Sunset Blvd, Los Angeles CA 90028 USA
**Hutchins, Melvin R (Mel)** — Basketball Player
160 Sherri Lane, Oceanside CA 92054, USA
**Hutchins, Will** — Actor
PO Box 371, Glen Head NY 11545, USA
**Hutchinson, Barbara** — Labor Leader
American Federation of Labor, 815 15th St NW, Washington DC 20005, USA
**Hutchinson, Chad M** — Football, Baseball Player
1388 Elder Ave, Menlo Park CA 94025, USA
**Hutchinson, Eric** — Singer, Pianist, Songwriter
W F Leopold Mgmt, 4425 Riverside Dr, #102, Burbank CA 91505, USA
**Hutchinson, Frederick E** — Educator
University of Maine, President's Office, Orono ME 04469, USA
**Hutchinson, J Maxwell** — Architect
58 Hatton Garden, London EC1N 8LX, England
**Hutchinson, Scott R** — Football Player
1223 Northern Way, Winter Springs FL 32708, USA
**Hutchinson, Steven J (Steve)** — Football Player
16119 Crosby Cove Road, Wayzata MN 55391, USA
**Hutchison, Dave** — Ice Hockey Player
Re/Max Realty, 3922 Hamilton Road, Dorchester ON N0L 1G2, Canada
**Hutchison, Fiona** — Actress
Don Buchwald, 6500 Wilshire Blvd, #2200, Los Angeles CA 90048 USA
**Huth, Edward J** — Editor, Physician
1124 Morris Ave, Bryn Mawr PA 19010, USA
**Huther, Bruce A** — Football Player
1156 N Bonnie Brae St, Denton TX 76201, USA
**Hutman, Jon** — Production Designer
Gersh Agency, 9465 Wilshire Blvd, #600, Beverly Hills CA 90212 USA
**Hutsell, Melanie** — Actress, Comedienne
Greene Assoc, 1901 Ave of Stars, #130, Los Angeles CA 90067 USA
**Hutshing, Joe** — Editor
Gersh Agency, 9465 Wilshire Blvd, #600, Beverly Hills CA 90212 USA
**Hutson, G Herbert (Herb)** — Baseball Player
7203 W Sugar Tree Court, Savannah GA 31410, USA
**Hutson, Martin** — Actor
Ken McReddie Assoc, 101 Finsbury Pavement, London EC2A 1RS, England
**Hutt, Peter B** — Attorney
124 S Fairfax St, Alexandria VA 22314, USA
**Hutter, Mark** — Actor
Judy Fox Mgmt, 1525 1/2 S Beverly Dr, Los Angeles, CA 90035, USA
**Hutter, Sidney** — Artist
Sidney Hutter Glass & Light, 225 Riverside Ave, Auburndale MA 02466, USA
**Hutto, James N (Jim)** — Baseball Player
1317 John Carroll Dr, Pensacola FL 32504, USA
**Hutton, Danny** — Singer (Three Dog Night)
2437 Horseshoe Canyon Road, Los Angeles CA 90046, USA
**Hutton, Lauren** — Model, Actress
Untitled Entertainment, 350 S Beverly Dr, #200, Beverly Hills CA 90212 USA
**Hutton, Mark S** — Baseball Player
6 Corfu Court, Westlakes, Adelaide SA 5021, Australia
**Hutton, Thomas G (Tommy)** — Baseball Player, Sportscaster
18 Huntly Dr, Palm Beach Gardens FL 33418, USA
**Hutton, Timothy** — Actor
W M E Entertainment, 9601 Wilshire Blvd, #300, Beverly Hills CA 90210 USA
**Hutton, W Thomas (Tom)** — Football Player
85 Pinehurst St, Memphis TN 38117, USA

**Huxhold, Kenneth W (Ken)** — Football Player
5007 Prairie Rose Court, Middleton WI 53562, USA
**Huxley, Hugh E** — Biologist
349 Nashawtuc Road, Concord MA 01742, USA
**Huyck, Willard** — Director, Writer
39 Oakmont Dr, Los Angeles CA 90049, USA
**Hvorostovsky, Dmitri** — Opera Singer
Askonas Holt, Lincoln House, 300 High Holborn, London WC1V 7JH, England
**Hwang Seok-Ho** — Soccer Player
Football Assn, 1-131 Sinmunno, 2-Ga Jongno-Gu, Seoul 110 062, South Korea
**Hwang, David Henry** — Writer
Bobbi Thompson Mgmt, 870 Galloway St, Pacific Palisades CA 90272, USA
**Hyams, Peter** — Director
627 San Lorenzo St, Santa Monica CA 90402, USA
**Hyatt, Fred P (Freddie)** — Football Player
19350 SE 52nd Place, Morriston FL 32668, USA
**Hyatt, Joel Z** — Attorney, Businessman
Hyatt Legal Services, 1215 Superior Ave E, Cleveland OH 44114, USA
**Hybl, William J** — Foundation, Sports Executive
El Pomar Foundation, 10 Lake Circle, Colorado Springs CO 80906, USA
**Hyche, Heath** — Actor, Comedian
Brillstein Entertainment Partners, 9150 Wilshire Blvd, #350, Beverly Hills CA 90212 USA
**Hyde, Christopher** — Writer
Onyx Penguin Putnam, 375 Hudson St, New York NY 10014, USA
**Hyde, Glenn T** — Football Player
955 Eudora St, #201, Denver CO 80220, USA
**Hyde, James** — Actor
Innovative Artists, 1505 10th St, Santa Monica CA 90401 USA
**Hyde, Jonathan** — Actor
Artist Rights Group, 4 Great Portland St, London W1W 8PA, England
**Hyde, Richard E (Dick)** — Baseball Player
1506 Cambridge Dr, Champaign IL 61821, USA
**Hyder, Greg** — Basketball Player
16228 Wato Road, #A, Apple Valley CA 92307, USA
**Hyde-White, Alex** — Actor
Amsel Eisenstadt Frazier, 5055 Wilshire Blvd, #865, Los Angeles CA 90036 USA
**Hyers, Timothy J (Tim)** — Baseball Player
241 Ridge Road, Covington GA 30016, USA
**Hyland, Brian** — Singer
Stone Buffalo, PO Box 101, Silver Lakes CA 92342, USA
**Hyland, Robert J (Bob)** — Football Player
30 Colonial Road, White Plains NY 10605, USA
**Hyland, Sarah** — Actress
R K M, 400 N Mansfield Ave, Los Angeles CA 90036, USA
**Hylton, James** — Auto Racing Driver
15 Avalon Road, Martin GA 30557, USA
**Hylton, Thomas J** — Journalist
Pottstown Mercury, Editorial Dept, Hanover & King Sts, Pottstown PA 19464, USA
**Hyman, B D** — Evangelist, Writer
PO Box 7107, Charlottesville VA 22906, USA
**Hyman, Earle** — Actor
Henderson/Hogan, 850 7th Ave, #1003, New York NY 10019 USA
**Hyman, Misty** — Swimmer
3826 E Lupine Ave, Phoenix AZ 85028, USA
**Hyman, Richard R (Dick)** — Jazz Pianist, Composer
Abby Hoffer Enterprises, 223 1/2 E 48th St, New York NY 10017 USA
**Hyman, Timothy** — Artist
62 Muddelton Square, London EC1, England
**Hymes, Dell H** — Anthropologist
20 Mountvue Dr, Charlottesville VA 22901, USA
**Hynd, Noel** — Writer
I C M Partners, 10250 Constellation Blvd, #900, Los Angeles CA 90067 USA
**Hynd, Ronald** — Ballet Dancer, Choreographer
Fern Cottage, U Somerton, Bury Saint Edmonds, Suffolk IP29 4ND, England
**Hynde, Christine E (Chrissie)** — Singer, Guitarist, Songwriter
Gailforce Mgmt, 91 Peterborough Road, London SW6 3BU, England
**Hynes, Garry** — Director
Druid Theater Co, Druid Lane & Flood St, North County Galway, Ireland
**Hynes, Jessica** — Actress, Comedienne, Writer
Independent Talent Group, 40 Whitfield St, London W1T 2RH, England
**Hynes, Richard O** — Biologist
Massachusetts Institute of Technology, Cancer Research Center, Cambridge MA 02139, USA
**Hynes, Samuel** — Writer
130 Moore St, Princeton NJ 08540, USA
**Hynes, Tyler** — Actor
Butler Ruston Bell, 10 Sainte Mary St, #310, Toronto ON M4Y 1P9, Canada
**Hynoski, Henry, Jr** — Football Player
New York Giants, Meadowlands Stadium, 102 Route 120, East Rutherford NJ 07073 USA
**Hysong, Nick** — Track Athlete
10424 N 38th St, Phoenix AZ 85028, USA
**Hytner, Nicholas R** — Director
United Agents, 12-26 Lexington St, London W1F 0LE, England
**Hyzdu, Adam** — Baseball Player
7823 E Red Hawk Circle, Mesa AZ 85207, USA

**I Coco Blame** — Singer, Songwriter
Universal Music, 364-366 Kensington High St, London W14 8NS, England

**Iacavazzi, Cosmo J** — Football Player
90 Vine St, Taylor PA 18517, USA

**Iacobellis, Sam F** — Businessman, Aeronautical Engineer
Rockwell International, PO Box 5090, Costa Mesa CA 92628, USA

**Iacocca, Lido A (Lee)** — Businessman
75252 Pepperwood Dr, Indian Wells CA 92210, USA

**Iaconio, Frank** — Auto Racing Driver
250 US Highway 206, Flanders NJ 07836, USA

**Iafrate, Al A** — Ice Hockey Player
17320 Fairfield St, Livonia MI 48152, USA

**Ian, Janis** — Singer, Songwriter
S R O Artists, 6629 University Ave, #206, Middleton WI 53562, USA

**Iannetta, Christopher D (Chris)** — Baseball Player
7422 E 7th Ave, #14, Denver CO 80230, USA

**Iassonga, Daniel (Dan)** — Baseball Umpire
1501 Bailey Farm Court SW, Marietta GA 30064, USA

**Iavarone, Michael** — Thoroughbred Racing Executive
I E A H Stables, 595 Stewart Ave, #450, Garden City NY 11530, USA

**Iavaroni, Marcus J (Marc)** — Basketball Player, Coach
8129 N Via de Lago, Scottsdale AZ 85258, USA

**Ibaka, Serge J** — Basketball Player
Oklahoma City Thunder, 211 N Robinson Ave, #300, Oklahoma City OK 73102 USA

**Ibanez, Raul J** — Baseball Player
26004 SE 23rd Place, Sammamish WA 98075, USA

**Ibbetson, Bruce** — Rowing Athlete
424 San Bernardino Ave, Newport Beach CA 92663, USA

**Ibragimov, Sultan** — Boxer
Warrior's Boxing Promotions, 5397 Orange Dr, #202, Davie FL 33314, USA

**Ibrahim, Abdullah, (Dollar Brand)** — Jazz Pianist, Composer
Brad Simon Organization, 445 E 80th St, #4C, New York NY 10075 USA

**Icahn, Carl C** — Businessman
Icahn Co, 445 Hamilton Ave, #1210, White Plains NY 10601, USA

**Ice Cube** — Rap Artist, Actor, Director
Cube Vision, 9000 W Sunset Blvd, West Hollywood CA 90069, USA

**Ice T** — Rap Artist, Actor
Jorge Hinojosa Mgmt, 6606 Maryland Dr, Los Angeles CA 90048, USA

**Ickx, Jacques B (Jacky)** — Auto Racing Driver
171 Chaussee de la Hulpe, 1170 Brussels, Belgium

**Idle, Eric** — Actor, Comedian (Monty Python)
Mayday Mgmt, 68A Delancey St, Camden Town, London NW1 7RY, England

**Idol, Billy** — Singer, Songwriter
East End Mgmt, 13721 Ventura Blvd, #200, Sherman Oaks CA 91423, USA

**Idowu, Phillips** — Track Athlete
Belgrave Harriers, Denmark Road, London SW19 4PG, England

**Idziak, Slawomir** — Cinematographer
Ul Wazow 1-Z, Warsaw 01-986, Poland

**Ielemia, Apisai** — Prime Minister, Tuvalu
Prime Minister's Office, Vaiaku, Funafuti, Tuvalu

**Ifans, Rhys** — Actor
Brillstein Entertainment Partners, 9150 Wilshire Blvd, #350, Beverly Hills CA 90212 USA

**Ifill, Gwen** — Commentator
Public Broadcasting System, 1320 Braddock Place, Alexandria VA 22314 USA

**Iger, Robert A** — Businessman
Walt Disney Co, 500 S Buena Vista St, Burbank CA 91521, USA

**Iginla, Jarome A A** — Ice Hockey Player
Pittsburgh Penguins, Consol Energy Center, 1001 5th Ave, Pittsburgh PA 15219 USA

**Iglesias, Enrique** — Singer
2345 Lake Ave, Sunset Isle 3, Miami Beach FL 33140, USA

**Iglesias, Gabriel** — Comedian, Actor
Creative Artists Agency, 2000 Ave of Stars, #100, Los Angeles CA 90067 USA

**Iglesias, Julio** — Singer
901 Surfside Blvd, Surfside FL 33154, USA

**Iglesias, Julio** — Singer
Doyle-Kos Entertainment, Penn Plaza, #2107, New York NY 10119, USA

**Iglesias, Julio, Jr** — Singer, Songwriter
A R Entertainment, 3400 Coral Way, #404, Miami FL 33145, USA

**Ignarro, Louis J** — Nobel Medicine Laureate
C H A, 10833 La Conte Ave, Los Angeles CA 90095, USA

**Ignasiak, Michael J (Mike)** — Baseball Player
8473 Dixie Highway, Ira MI 48023, USA

**Ignatius Zakka I Iwas, Patriarch** — Religious Leader
Syrian Orthodox Patriarchate, Bab Touma, BP 914, Damascus, Syria

**Ignatius, David** — Writer, Columnist
W W Norton, 500 5th Ave, #600, New York NY 10110 USA

**Ignatius, Paul R** — Government Official
2700 Calvert St NW, #416, Washington DC 20008, USA

**Ignizo, Mildred** — Bowler
241 Shore Acres Dr, Rochester NY 14612, USA

**Iguodala, Andre T** — Basketball Player
1111 Riverview Lane, West Conshohocken PA 19428, USA

**Igwebuike, Donald A** — Football Player
1118 Tumlin Court, Lawrenceville GA 30045, USA

**Iha, James Y** — Guitarist (Smashing Pumpkins)
Spivak Sobol Entertainment, 11845 W Olympic Blvd, #1125, Los Angeles CA 90064, USA

**Ihara, Michio** — Sculptor
63 Wood St, Concord MA 01742, USA

**Ihle, Andreas** — Canoeing Athlete
Wiesenweg 5, 39114 Magedburg, Germany

**Ikeda, Daisaku** — Religious Leader, Philosopher
Soka Gakkai, 32 Shinanomachi, Shinjuku, Tokyo 160 8583, Japan

**Ikenberry, Stanley O** — Educator
University of Illinois, Education Dept, 1310 S 6th St, Champaign IL 61820, USA

**Ikola, Willard** — Ice Hockey Player, Coach
5697 Green Circle Drive, #316, Hopkins MN 55343, USA

| | |
|---|---|
| **Iler, Robert**<br>B/W/R, 9100 Wilshire Blvd, #500W, Beverly Hills CA 90212 USA | Actor |
| **Iles, Greg**<br>Creative Artists Agency, 2000 Ave of Stars, #100, Los Angeles CA 90067 USA | Writer |
| **Ilg, Raymond P**<br>1830 Fountain Dr, #1505, Reston VA 20190, USA | Navy Admiral |
| **Ilgauskas, Zydrunas**<br>32654 Lake Road, Avon Lake OH 44012, USA | Basketball Player |
| **Iliff, W Peter**<br>Mavrick Artists Agency, 6100 Wilshire Blvd, #550, Los Angeles CA 90048, USA | Director, Writer |
| **Iliff, W Peter**<br>Hard Noir Films, 660 Iliff St, Pacific Palisades CA 90272, USA | Director, Writer |
| **Ilitch, Michael (Mike)**<br>23670 Woodlyne Dr, Bingham Farms MI 48025, USA | Ice Hockey, Baseball Executive |
| **Ilken, Tunch A**<br>1105 Grandview Ave, #3A, Pittsburgh PA 15211, USA | Football Player |
| **Ilonzeh, Annie**<br>Vincent Cirrincione Assoc, 1516 N Fairfax Ave, Los Angeles CA 90046 USA | Actress |
| **Ilunga-Mbenga, Didier (D J)**<br>Los Angeles Lakers, Staples Center, 1111 S Figueroa St, Los Angeles CA 90015 USA | Basketball Player |
| **Ilves, Toomas Hendrik**<br>President's Office, 39 Av Weizenbergi, 15050 Tallinn, Estonia | President, Estonia |
| **Imada, Ryuji**<br>16204 Sierra de Avila, Tampa FL 33613, USA | Golfer |
| **Iman**<br>Essex House, 160 Central Park S, New York NY 10019, USA | Model, Actress |
| **Imants, Marcis**<br>Bamberger Symphony Orchestra, Postfach 110146, 96029 Bamberger, Germany | Conductor |
| **Imbruglia, Natalie**<br>Untitled Entertainment, 350 S Beverly Dr, #200, Beverly Hills CA 90212 USA | Singer, Songwriter, Actress |
| **Imhoff, Darrall T**<br>3637 Sterling Woods Dr, Eugene OR 97408, USA | Basketball Player |
| **Imhoff, Gary**<br>Samantha Group, 300 S Raymond Ave, Pasadena CA 91105, USA | Actor |
| **Immelman, Trevor J**<br>5174 Vardon Dr, Windermere FL 34786, USA | Golfer |
| **Immelt, Jeffrey (Jeff)**<br>General Electric Co, 3135 Easton Turnpike, Fairfield CT 06828, USA | Businessman |
| **Imperioli, Michael**<br>T M T Entertainment Group, 648 Broadway, #1002, New York NY 10012, USA | Actor |
| **Imrie, Celia**<br>Rights House, Drury House, 34-43 Russell St, London WC2B 5HA, England | Actress |
| **Imus, Don**<br>I C M Partners, 10250 Constellation Blvd, #900, Los Angeles CA 90067 USA | Actor |
| **In Kyung Kim**<br>Ladies Pro Golf Assn, 100 International Golf Dr, Daytona Beach FL 32124 USA | Golfer |
| **Inaba, Carrie Ann**<br>EnterMediArts, 800 S Main St, #200, Burbank CA 91506, USA | Dancer, Choreographer, Singer |
| **Inamori, Kazuo**<br>R D D I Corp, 3-22 Nishi-Shinjuku, Shinjuku, Tokyo 163 8003, Japan | Businessman |
| **Inarritu, Alejandro Gonzalez**<br>Gang Tyrer Ramer, 132 S Rodeo Dr, #306, Beverly Hills CA 90212 USA | Director |
| **Inbal, Eliahu**<br>Askonas Holt, Lincoln House, 300 High Holborn, London WC1V 7JH, England | Conductor |
| **Incandela, Joseph (Joe)**<br>University of California, Physics Dept, Broida Hall, Santa Barbara CA 93106, USA | Particle Physicist |
| **Incaviglia, Peter J (Pete)**<br>PO Box 1047, Argyle TX 76226, USA | Baseball Player |
| **Incognito, Richard D (Richie)**<br>3231 NW 125th Ave, Sunrise FL 33323, USA | Football Player |
| **Indelicato, Mark**<br>Station3, 300 W 55th St, #5L, New York NY 10019, USA | Actor |
| **India**<br>Granada Entertainment, 480 NE 30th St, #101, Miami FL 33137, USA | Singer |
| **India.Arie**<br>Creative Artists Agency, 2000 Ave of Stars, #100, Los Angeles CA 90067 USA | Singer, Guitarist, Songwriter |
| **Indiana, Robert**<br>Star of Hop, Press Box 464, Vinalhaven ME 04863, USA | Artist |
| **Indovina, Lorenza**<br>Carol Levi Mgmt, Via Giuseppe Pisanelli 2, 00196 Rome, Italy | Actress |
| **Indurain, Miguel**<br>Avenida Villava, 31013 Pamplona, Navarra, Spain | Cyclist |
| **Infante, Lindy**<br>6780 A1A S, Saint Augustine FL 32080, USA | Football Coach |
| **Infante, Omar R**<br>Detroit Tigers, Comerica Park, 2100 Woodward Ave, Detroit MI 48201 USA | Baseball Player |
| **Ingarfield, Earl, Sr**<br>1715 Lakehill Crescent S, Lethbridge AB T1K 3R2, Canada | Ice Hockey Player |
| **Inge, C Brandon**<br>5003 Windsong Trail, Salem SC 29676, USA | Baseball Player |
| **Ingels, Marty**<br>4531 Noeline Way, Encino CA 91436, USA | Actor, Comedian |
| **Ingelsby, Tom**<br>1507 Canterbury Lane, Berwyn PA 19312, USA | Basketball Player |
| **Ingersoll, Andrew P**<br>California Institute of Technology, Geological/Planetary Sciences Division, Pasadena CA 91125, USA | Meteorologist, Climatologist |
| **Inghram, Mark G**<br>PO Box 771721, Eagle River AK 99577, USA | Physicist |
| **Ingle, Doug**<br>Entertainment Services International, 6400 Pleasant Park Dr, Chanhassen MN 55317 USA | Singer, Keyboardist (Iron Butterfly) |
| **Ingman, Einar H, Jr**<br>W4053 N Silver Lake Road, Irma WI 54442, USA | Korean War Army Hero (CMH) |
| **Ingraham, Laura**<br>Sirius XM Radio, 1221 Ave of Americas, New York NY 10020, USA | Commentator |
| **Ingram, Alfred**<br>983 Oakland Dr, Atlanta GA 30315, USA | Baseball Player |

**Ingram, Jack** — Auto Racing Driver
699 Brevard Road, Asheville NC 28806, USA

**Ingram, James** — Singer, Songwriter
867 S Muirfield Road, Los Angeles CA 90005, USA

**Ingram, Marv** — Singer (Four Preps)
4339 Ensenada Dr, Woodland Hills CA 91364, USA

**Ingram, Melvin** — Football Player
San Diego Chargers, 4020 Murphy Canyon Road, San Diego CA 92123 USA

**Ingram, Preston** — Baseball Player
174 Douglas St SE, Atlanta GA 30317, USA

**Ingrassia, Paul J** — Journalist
111 Division Ave, New Providence NJ 07974, USA

**Inkeles, Alex** — Sociologist
32 Plaza Dr, Berkeley CA 94705, USA

**Inkster, Juli Simpson** — Golfer
23140 Mora Glen Dr, Los Altos Hills CA 94024, USA

**Inman, Bobby Ray** — Navy Admiral, Government Official
Arboretum Plaza, 9442 N Capital of Texas Highway, #685, Austin TX 78759, USA

**Inman, John S** — Golfer
2210 Chase St, Durham NC 27707, USA

**Inman, Joseph C (Joe), Jr** — Golfer
3599 Tuckers Farm SE, Marietta GA 30067, USA

**Innauer, Anton (Toni)** — Ski Jumper, Coach
Steinbruckstr 8/II, 6024 Innsbruck, Austria

**Innaurato, Albert F** — Writer
325 W 22nd St, New York NY 10011, USA

**Innes, Laura** — Actress
Creative Artists Agency, 2000 Ave of Stars, #100, Los Angeles CA 90067 USA

**Innis, Jeffrey D (Jeff)** — Baseball Player
4920 Woodlong Lane, Cumming GA 30040, USA

**Innis, Roy E A** — Civil Rights Activist
817 Broadway, New York NY 10003, USA

**Inogradov, Pavel** — Cosmonaut
Cosmonaut Training Center, Star City, 141160 Zvezdny Gorodok, Moscow Oblast, Russia

**Inoni, Ephraim** — Prime Minister, Cameroon Republic
Palais de L'Unite, Rue de l'Exploratour, Yaounde, Cameroon

**Inoue, Rena** — Figure Skater
Lee Marshall Mgmt, 199 E Garfield Road, Aurora OH 44202, USA

**Inoue, Shinya** — Biologist, Photographer
Marine Biological Laboratory, 167 Water St, Woods Hole MA 02543, USA

**Inouye, Lisa** — Actress
Media Artists Group, 8222 Melrose Ave, #203, Los Angeles CA 90048 USA

**Insalaco, Kim** — Ice Hockey Player
USA Hockey, 1775 Bob Johnson Dr, Colorado Springs CO 80906 USA

**Insko, Delmer M (Del)** — Harness Racing Driver
2360 Fischer Road, South Beloit IL 61080, USA

**Insley, Will** — Artist
231 Bowery, New York NY 10002, USA

**Inspectah Deck** — Rap Artist (Wu-Tang Clan)
A&E Entertainment, 13280 NE Freeway, #F328, Houston TX 77040, USA

**Insulza, Jose Miguel** — Government Official, Chile
Organization of American States, 17th St & Constitution Ave, Washington DC 20006, USA

**Intriligator, Michael D** — Economist
140 Foxtail Dr, Santa Monica CA 90402, USA

**Inui, Kumiko** — Architect
Showa Women's University, 1-7 Taishide, Satagayaku, Tokyo 154 8533, Japan

**Inzaghi, Filippo (Pippo)** — Soccer Player
F C Milan, Via Filippo Turati 3, 20121 Milan, Italy

**Inzko, Valentin** — High Representative, Bosnia-Herzegovia
Emerika Bluma 1, 71000 Sarajevo, Bosnia-Herzegovina

**Iommi, F Anthony (Tony)** — Guitarist (Black Sabbath), Songwriter
Sharon Osborne Mgmt, 8899 Beverly Blvd, #905, West Hollywood CA 90048, USA

**Iooss, Walter** — Photographer
152 DeForest Road, Montauk NY 11954, USA

**Iorg, Dane C** — Baseball Player
5358 W Evergreen Circle, American Fork UT 84003, USA

**Iorg, Garth R** — Baseball Player
10635 Alameda Dr, Knoxville TN 37932, USA

**Iovine, Vicki** — Writer, Columnist, Model
Trident Media Group, 41 Madison Ave, #3600, New York NY 10010, USA

**Ipcar, Dahlov** — Illustrator, Artist, Writer
Thomas Crotty Frost Gully Gallery, 1159 US Route 1, Freeport ME 04032, USA

**Iraheta, Allison** — Singer
Jive Records, 137-39 W 25th St, #1100, New York NY 10001 USA

**Irani, Ray R** — Businessman
Occidental Petroleum, 10889 Wilshire Blvd, #1000, Los Angeles CA 90024, USA

**Irbe, Arturs** — Ice Hockey Player
10733 Trego Trail, Raleigh NC 27614, USA

**Irby, Michael C** — Actor
Greene Assoc, 1901 Ave of Stars, #130, Los Angeles CA 90067 USA

**Iredale, Randle W** — Architect
1151 W 8th Ave, Vancouver BC V6H 1C5, Canada

**Ireland, Dan** — Director, Producer, Writer
Gersh Agency, 9465 Wilshire Blvd, #600, Beverly Hills CA 90212 USA

**Ireland, Julius W (Buck)** — WW II Marine Corps Hero
4389 Malaai St, #324, Honolulu HI 96818, USA

**Ireland, Kathy** — Model, Actress
Guttman Assoc, 118 S Beverly Dr, #201, Beverly Hills CA 90212 USA

**Ireland, Marin** — Actress
I C M Partners, 10250 Constellation Blvd, #900, Los Angeles CA 90067 USA

**Ireland, Patricia** — Association Executive
Katz Kutter Haigler Assoc, 801 Pennsylvania Ave NW, #750, Washington DC 20004, USA

**Irglova, Marketa** — Actress, Pianist, Songwriter
Billions Corp, 3522 W Armitage Ave, Chicago IL 60647 USA

**Irigoyen, Adam** — Actor
Amatruda Benson, 433 N Camden Drive, #400, Beverly Hills CA 90210, USA

|  |  |
|------|-----------|
| **Irimia, Gabriela**<br>Concorde International, 101 Shepherds Bush Road, London W6 7LP, England | Singer (Cheeky Girls) |
| **Irimia, Monica**<br>Concorde International, 101 Shepherds Bush Road, London W6 7LP, England | Singer (Cheeky Girls) |
| **Irina**<br>Marilyn Model Agency, 32 Union Square E, #PH, New York NY 10003 USA | Model |
| **Iris, Donnie**<br>807 Darlington Road, Beaver Falls PA 15010, USA | Singer, Songwriter |
| **Iron & Wine**<br>Sub Pop Records, 2013 4th Ave, #300, Seattle WA 98121, USA | Singer, Guitarist, Songwriter |
| **Irons, Gerald D**<br>30010 E Legends Trail Court, Spring TX 77386, USA | Football Player |
| **Irons, Jeremy**<br>Ken McReddie Assoc, 101 Finsbury Pavement, London EC2A 1RS, England | Actor |
| **Irons, Max**<br>United Talent Agency, U T A Plaza, 9336 Civic Center Dr, Beverly Hills CA 90210 USA | Actor, Model |
| **Ironside, Michael**<br>Abrams Artists, 9200 W Sunset Blvd, #1125, West Hollywood CA 90069 USA | Actor |
| **Irrera, Domenick J (Dom)**<br>Metropolitan Talent Agency, 5405 Wilshire Blvd, #218, Los Angeles CA 90036 USA | Actor, Comedian, Writer, Producer |
| **Irvan, V Earnest (Ernie)**<br>9939 Troutman Road, Midland NC 28107, USA | Auto Racing Driver |
| **Irvin, Cal**<br>1311 Julian St, Greensboro NC 27406, USA | Baseball Player, Basketball Coach |
| **Irvin, John**<br>6 Lower Common South, London SW15 1BP, England | Director |
| **Irvin, Kenneth P (Ken)**<br>8151 Nesbit Ferry Road, Atlanta GA 30350, USA | Football Player |
| **Irvin, LeRoy, Jr**<br>2905 Ruby Dr, #C, Fullerton CA 92831, USA | Football Player |
| **Irvin, Michael J**<br>2339 Aberdeen Bend, Carrolton TX 75007, USA | Football Player, Sportscaster |
| **Irvin, Monford M (Monte)**<br>1815 Enclave Parkway, #6203, Houston TX 77077, USA | Baseball Player |
| **Irvin, Sandora**<br>San Antonio Silver Stars, 1 AT&T Center, San Antonio TX 78219 USA | Basketball Player |
| **Irvine, Edmund (Eddie), Jr**<br>Jaguar Racing, Browns Lane, Allesley Coventry CV5 9DR, England | Auto Racing Driver |
| **Irvine, Edward A (Ted)**<br>5-2727 Portage Ave, Winnipeg MB R3J 0R2, Canada | Ice Hockey Player |
| **Irvine, Jeremy**<br>Hatton McEwan, 3 Chocolate Studios, 7 Shepherdess Place, London N1 7LJ, England | Actor |
| **Irving, Amy**<br>Talent Works, 3500 W Olive Ave, #1400, Burbank CA 91505 USA | Actress, Producer |
| **Irving, John W**<br>Turnbull Agency, PO Box 757, Dorset VT 05251, USA | Writer |
| **Irving, K Stuart (Stu)**<br>93 Hart St, Beverly MA 01915, USA | Ice Hockey Player |
| **Irving, Kyrie A**<br>Cleveland Cavaliers, Gund Arena, 1 Center Court, Cleveland OH 44115 USA | Basketball Player |
| **Irving, Paul H**<br>Manatt Phelps Phillips, 11355 W Olympic Blvd, #20, Los Angeles CA 90064, USA | Attorney |
| **Irwin, Elaine**<br>Innovative Artists, 1505 10th St, Santa Monica CA 90401 USA | Model |
| **Irwin, Hale S**<br>5720 N Saguaro Road, Paradise Valley AZ 85253, USA | Golfer |
| **Irwin, Jay**<br>Artists Agency, 9430 Olympic Blvd, Beverly Hills CA 90212 USA | Actor, Writer |
| **Irwin, Jennifer**<br>Gersh Agency, 9465 Wilshire Blvd, #600, Beverly Hills CA 90212 USA | Actress |
| **Irwin, Mark**<br>1260 Coast Village Circle, Santa Barbara CA 93108, USA | Cinematographer |
| **Irwin, Paul G**<br>Humane Society of the United States, PO Box 9100, League City TX 77574, USA | Association Executive |
| **Irwin, Robert W**<br>501 S Beverly Dr, Beverly Hills CA 90212, USA | Artist |
| **Irwin, Terence H**<br>University of California, Philosophy Dept, Irvine CA 92697, USA | Philosopher |
| **Irwin, Timothy E (Tim)**<br>5512 River Point Cove Road, Knoxville TN 37919, USA | Football Player |
| **Irwin, Tom, II**<br>Framework Entertainment, 9057 Nemo St, #C, West Hollywood CA 90069 USA | Actor |
| **Isaac, Oscar**<br>United Talent Agency, U T A Plaza, 9336 Civic Center Dr, Beverly Hills CA 90210 USA | Actor |
| **Isaacks, Levie C**<br>6634 Sunnyslope Ave, Van Nuys CA 91401, USA | Cinematographer |
| **Isaacs, Jason**<br>Gersh Agency, 9465 Wilshire Blvd, #600, Beverly Hills CA 90212 USA | Actor |
| **Isaacs, Jeremy I**<br>Royal Opera House, Covent Garden, Bow St, London WC2E 9DD, England | Director |
| **Isaacs, Levie**<br>Innovative Artists, 1505 10th St, Santa Monica CA 90401 USA | Cinematographer |
| **Isaacs, Susan**<br>Harper Collins Publishers, 10 E 53rd St, Cellar 2, New York NY 10022, USA | Writer |
| **Isaacson, Walter S**<br>I C M Partners, 10250 Constellation Blvd, #900, Los Angeles CA 90067 USA | Journalist |
| **Isaak, Chris**<br>W M E Entertainment, 9601 Wilshire Blvd, #300, Beverly Hills CA 90210 USA | Singer, Songwriter, Actor |
| **Isacco, Jennifer**<br>Olympic Committee, Foro Italico, Largo Lauro de Bosis 15, 00135 Rome, Italy | Bobsled Athlete |
| **Isacksen, Peter**<br>Sutton-Barth Vennari, 5900 Wilshire Blvd, #700, Los Angeles CA 90036 USA | Actor |
| **Isaksson, Irma Sara**<br>United Stage Artists, PO Box 11029, 100 61, Stockholm, Sweden | Singer, Songwriter |
| **Isbell, Jason**<br>Ground Control Touring, 20 Jay St, #826, Brooklyn NY 11201 USA | Singer, Guitarist, Songwriter |

**Isbell, Stewart** — Photographer
Retna, 24 W 25th St, #1200, New York NY 10010, USA
**Isbin, Sharon** — Concert Guitarist
Columbia Artists Mgmt Inc, 1790 Broadway, #702, New York NY 10019 USA
**Isbister, Brad** — Ice Hockey Player
1818 Lakeview Dr, Fort Wayne IN 46808, USA
**Iscove, Robert (Rob)** — Director
Course Mgmt, 15159 Greenleaf St, Sherman Oaks CA 91403, USA
**Isdell, E Neville** — Businessman
International Business Leaders Forum, 15 Cornwall Terrace, London NW1 4QP, England
**Isham, Mark** — Composer
23679 Calabasas Road, #522, Calabasas CA 91302, USA
**Ishibashi, Brittany** — Actress
Abrams Artists, 9200 W Sunset Blvd, #1125, West Hollywood CA 90069 USA
**Ishida, Jim** — Actor
871 N Vail Ave, Montebello CA 90640, USA
**Ishida, Nobuhiro** — Boxer
Golden Boy Promotions, 626 Wilshire Blvd, #350, Los Angeles CA 90017 USA
**Ishiguro, Kazuo** — Writer
Rogers Coleridge White, 20 Powis Mews, London W11 1JN, England
**Ishii, Ken** — Composer
3-5-12 Yakumo, Meguroku, Tokyo 152 0023, Japan
**Ishikawa, Shigeru** — Economist
19-8-4 Chome Kugayama, Suginamiku, Tokyo 168 0082, Japan
**Ishimaru, Akira** — Electrical Engineer
2913 165th Place NE, Bellevue WA 98008, USA
**Ishizaka, Kimishige** — Allergist
Allergy/Immunology Institute, 11149 N Torrey Pines Road, La Jolla CA 92037, USA
**Ishizaka, Teruko** — Allergist
Good Samaritan Hospital, 5601 Loch Raven Blvd, Baltimore MD 21239, USA
**Isikoff, Michael** — Writer, Journalist
6209 Meadowbrook Lane, Chevy Chase MD 20815, USA
**Isinbayeva, Yelena G** — Track Athlete
Podium Group, 3 Ave de Grande Bretagne, 98000 Monte Carlo, Monaco
**Iskander, Fazil A** — Writer
Leningradski Prosp Korp 2, #67, 125040 Moscow, Russia
**Isler, Jennifer (J J)** — Yachtswoman
6828 Country Club Dr, La Jolla CA 92037, USA
**Isley, Ronald (Ron)** — Singer (Isley Brothers)
Walt Reeder Productions, 93 Old York Road, #I-604, Jenkintown PA 19046, USA
**Ismael, Gerard** — Actor
Agents Associes, 201 Rue du Faubourg Saint Honore, 75008 Paris, France
**Ismail, Qadry R** — Football Player
1506 Sunningdale Way, Bel Air MD 21015, USA
**Ismail, Raghib R (Rocket)** — Football Player
7423 Marigold Dr, Irving TX 75063, USA
**Isner, John R** — Tennis Player
5700 Saddlebrook Way, Wesley Chapel FL 33543, USA
**Ison, Christopher J** — Journalist
Minneapolis-Saint Paul Star Tribune, 425 Portland Ave, Minneapolis MN 55488, USA
**Isozaki, Arata** — Architect
5-12-9 Akasaka, Minatoku, Tokyo 107 0052, Japan
**Israel, Steven D (Steve)** — Football Player
14039 Lissadell Circle, Charlotte NC 28277, USA
**Israel, Werner** — Physicist
2323 Hamiota St, #401, Victoria BC V8R 2N1, Canada
**Isringhausen, Jason D** — Baseball Player
550 E Lake Dr, Tarpon Springs FL 34688, USA
**Issel, Daniel P (Dan)** — Basketball Player, Coach, Executive
325 E Palace Ave, Santa Fe NM 87501, USA
**Isserlis, Steven** — Concert Cellist
I M G Artists, Hogarth Business Park, Chiswick, London W4 2TH, England
**Isso, Lorenza** — Actress
A P A Talent/Literary Agency, 405 S Beverly Dr, #300, Beverly Hills CA 90212 USA
**Italeli, Iakoba T** — Governor General, Tuvalu
Governor General's Office, Government House, Vaiaku, Funafuti, Tuvalu
**Itin, Ilya** — Concert Pianist
Jonathan Wentworth Assoc, 10 Fiske Place, #530, Mount Vernon NY 10550 USA
**Ito, Lance** — Judge
Los Angeles Superior Court, 210 W Temple St, #M6, Los Angeles CA 90012, USA
**Ito, Midori** — Figure Skater
Prince Hotel Skate Club, 3-4 Shin Yokohama, Kanagawa 222 8533, Japan
**Ito, Robert** — Actor
843 N Sycamore Ave, Los Angeles CA 90038, USA
**Ito, Takenobu** — Businessman
Honda Motor Co, 2-1-1 Minami-Aoyama, Minatoku, Tokyo 107 8556, Japan
**Itzin, Gregory** — Actor
S M S Talent, 8383 Wilshire Blvd, #230, Beverly Hills CA 90211 USA
**Iu, Carolyn** — Interior Designer
Iu & Bibliowicz, 57 E 11th St, #700, New York NY 10003, USA
**Ivanchenkov, Aleksandr S** — Cosmonaut
Cosmonaut Training Center, Star City, 141160 Zvezdny Gorodok, Moscow Oblast, Russia
**Ivanek, Zeljko** — Actor
Leading Artists, 145 W 45th St, #1000, New York NY 10036, USA
**Ivanisevic, Goran** — Tennis Player
Alijnoviceva 28, 58000 Split, Serbia
**Ivanishvili, Bidzina** — President, Georgia
Prime Minister's Office, Government House, Ingorokva 7, 380034 Tbilisi, Georgia
**Ivanov, Georgi I** — Cosmonaut, Bulgaria
Air Sofia Ltd, Sofia Airport, 1 Brussels Blvd, 1540 Sofia, Bulgaria
**Ivanov, Gjorge** — President, Macedonia
President's Office, Villa Vodno, Aco Karamanov BB, 1000 Skopje, Macedonia
**Ivanov, Igor S** — Government Official, Russia
Moscow State Institute, Vernadskogo Prospekt 76, 119454 Moscow, Russia
**Ivanov, Kalina** — Actress, Designer, Art Director
Marsh-Best Assoc, 9150 Wilshire Blvd, #220, Beverly Hills CA 90212 USA

| | |
|---|---|
| **Ivanov, Vyacheslav V** | Philologist, Linguist |
| University of California, Slavic Languages Dept, Los Angeles CA 90024, USA | |
| **Ivanovic, Ana** | Tennis Player |
| D H Mgmt, Holeestra 86, 4054 Basel, Switzerland | |
| **Ivar, Stan** | Actor |
| Borinstein Oreck Bogart, 3172 Dona Susana Dr, Studio City CA 91604 USA | |
| **Ivens, Terri** | Actress |
| Paul Kohner, 9300 Wilshire Blvd, #555, Beverly Hills CA 90212 USA | |
| **Iveri, Tamar** | Opera Singer |
| I M G Artists, Hogarth Business Park, Chiswick, London W4 2TH, England | |
| **Ivers, Eileen** | Fiddler |
| Roots Agency, 177 Woodland Ave, Westwood NJ 07675, USA | |
| **Iversen, Leslie M** | Pharmacologist |
| Oxford University, Pharmacology Dept, Oxford OX1 3QT, England | |
| **Iverson, Allen** | Basketball Player |
| 308 Harper Dr, #210, Moorestown NJ 8057, USA | |
| **Iverson, Becky** | Golfer |
| 4723 Poplar Creek Dr, Madison WI 53718, USA | |
| **Ivery, Eddie Lee** | Football Player |
| 1080 Wrightsboro Road, Thomson GA 30824, USA | |
| **Ivey, Dana** | Actress |
| Paradigm Agency, 360 N Crescent Dr, North Building, Beverly Hills CA 90210 USA | |
| **Ivey, James B (Jim)** | Editorial Cartoonist |
| 5840 Dahlia Dr, #7, Orlando FL 32807, USA | |
| **Ivey, Judith** | Actress |
| Abrams Artists, 9200 W Sunset Blvd, #1125, West Hollywood CA 90069 USA | |
| **Ivey, Royal T** | Basketball Player |
| 6080 Indian Wood Circle SE, Mableton GA 30126, USA | |
| **Ivey, Susan** | Businesswoman |
| Reynolds American, PO Box 2990, Winston-Salem NC 27102, USA | |
| **Ivie, Michael W (Mike)** | Baseball Player |
| PO Box 1565, Loganville GA 30052, USA | |
| **Ivins, Marsha S** | Astronaut |
| 2811 Timber Briar Circle, Houston TX 77059, USA | |
| **Ivins, Michael L** | Bassist, Keyboardist (Flaming Lips) |
| World's Fair Mgmt, 1208 Chowning Ave, Edmond OK 73034, USA | |
| **Ivory, Horace O** | Football Player |
| 5321 Diaz Ave, Fort Worth TX 76107, USA | |
| **Ivory, James (Sap)** | Baseball Player |
| 3026 Wenonah Park Road SW, Birmingham AL 35211, USA | |
| **Ivory, James F** | Director, Producer |
| 18 Patroon St, Claverack NY 12513, USA | |
| **Ivosev, Aleksandra** | Markswoman |
| Sluzbeni put Zavoda 5, Careva Cuprija, 11030 Belgrade, Serbia | |
| **Ivy Queen** | Reggaeton, Rap Artist, Songwriter |
| I C M Partners, 10250 Constellation Blvd, #900, Los Angeles CA 90067 USA | |
| **Ivy, Corey T** | Football Player |
| 8412 Seven Coves Court, Tampa FL 33634, USA | |
| **Iwabuchi, Mana** | Soccer Player |
| Football Assn, 3-10-15 Hongo, Bunkyoku, Tokyo 113 0033 Japan | |
| **Iwamura, Akinori** | Baseball Player |
| 623 Saxony Road, Saint Petersburg FL 33716, USA | |
| **Iwan, Dafydd** | Singer, Songwriter |
| Carrog, Rhos-Bach, Caeathro, Caernarfon, Gwynedd LL55 2TF, Wales | |
| **Iwaniec, Henryk** | Mathematician |
| Rutgers State University, Mathematics Dept, New Brunswick NJ 08903, USA | |
| **Iwashimizu, Azusa** | Soccer Player |
| Football Assn, 3-10-15 Hongo, Bunkyoku, Tokyo 113 0033 Japan | |
| **Iwata, Satoru** | Businessman |
| Nintendo, 11-1 Kamitoba Hokotatecho, Minamiku, Kyoto 601 8501, Japan | |
| **Iwatani, Toru** | Computer Game Inventor |
| Tokyo Polytechnic University, 1583 Iiyama, Atsugi Kanagawa 243 0297, Japan | |
| **Iwerks, Donald W** | Businessman |
| Iwerks Entertainment, 4520 W Valerio St, Burbank CA 91505, USA | |
| **Iwuoma, Chidi** | Football Player |
| 4616 Benton St, Antioch CA 94531, USA | |
| **Izambard, Sebastien** | Singer (Il Divo) |
| Octagon, 81-83 Fulham High St, London SW6 3JW, England | |
| **Izo, George W** | Football Player |
| PO Box 325, Alexandria VA 22313, USA | |
| **Izon, David** | Boxer |
| Stanley Levin, 226 Palafox Place, Pensacola FL 32502, USA | |
| **Izturis, Cesar D** | Baseball Player |
| 375 Douglas Ave, Clearwater FL 33755, USA | |
| **Izzard, Eddie** | Actor, Comedian |
| A P A Talent/Literary Agency, 405 S Beverly Dr, #300, Beverly Hills CA 90212 USA | |
| **Izzo, Lawrence A (Larry)** | Football Player |
| 1 Snowbird Place, Spring TX 77381, USA | |
| **Izzo, Tom** | Basketball Coach |
| Michigan State University, Athletic Dept, Breslin Center, East Lansing MI 48824, USA | |

**J Splif** — Singer (Far East Movement)
Stampede Mgmt, 12530 Beatrice St, Los Angeles CA 90066, USA

**Ja Rule** — Pop, Rap Artist; Actor
Universal Media Artists, 8222 Melrose Ave, #203, Los Angeles CA 90048, USA

**Jaafari, Ibrahim al-** — Prime Minister, Iraq
Parliament, Karradat Mariam, Baghdad, Iraq

**Jaar, Alfredo** — Photographer, Sculptor, Filmmaker
252 Lafayette St, #3G, New York NY 10012, USA

**Jablonski, Joseph** — Concert Pianist
Carlscrona Chamber Music Festival, Verstorp Skarfva, 371 91 Karlskrona, Sweden

**Jablonski, Patrick D (Pat)** — Ice Hockey Player
18814 Wimbledon Circle, Lutz FL 33558, USA

**Jabs, Matthias** — Guitarist
M J Guitars, Pariser Str 32, 81667 Munich, Germany

**Jace, Michael** — Actor
Blueprint Mgmt, 5670 Wilshire Blvd, #2525, Los Angeles CA 90036, USA

**Jack, Jarrett M** — Basketball Player
Golden State Warriors, 1011 Broadway, Oakland CA 94605 USA

**Jacke, Christopher L (Chris)** — Football Player
1158 S Taylor St, #C, Green Bay WI 54304, USA

**Jackee** — Actress
Metropolitan Talent Agency, 5405 Wilshire Blvd, #218, Los Angeles CA 90036 USA

**Jackendoff, Ray S** — Language Educator
Brandies University, Linguistics & Cognitive Dept, Waltham MA 02254, USA

**Jackiw, Roman W** — Physicist
Massachusetts Institute of Technology, Physics Dept, Cambridge MA 02139, USA

**Jackiw, Stefan** — Concert Violinist
Opus 3 Artists, 470 Park Ave S, #900N, New York NY 10016 USA

**Jacklin, Bill** — Artist
62 Bank St, New York NY 10014, USA

**Jacklin, Tony** — Golfer, Sportscaster
1175 51st St W, Bradenton FL 34209, USA

**Jackman, Hugh** — Actor, Singer, Dancer
W M E Entertainment, 9601 Wilshire Blvd, #300, Beverly Hills CA 90210 USA

**Jackson Hoye, Rose** — Actress
Haldeman Business Mgmt, 1137 2nd St, #119, Santa Monica CA 90403, USA

**Jackson Nelson, Marjorie** — Track Athlete
Athletics Australia, 431 Saint Kilda Road, Melbourne VIC 3004, Australia

**Jackson, Ed, Jr** — Architect
ArchD Consulting, PO Box 1345, Fairfax VA 22038

**Jackson, Alan** — Singer, Guitarist, Songwriter
Co-Op, 1510 16th Ave S, Nashville TN 37212, USA

**Jackson, Alfred** — Football Player
1811 Kirby Dr, Houston TX 77019, USA

**Jackson, Alvin N (Al)** — Baseball Player
3221 SE Morningside Blvd, Port Saint Lucie FL 34952, USA

**Jackson, Anne** — Actress
Talent Works, 3500 W Olive Ave, #1400, Burbank CA 91505 USA

**Jackson, Arthur J** — WW II Marine Corps Hero (CMH)
1290 E Spring Court, Boise ID 83712, USA

**Jackson, Barry** — Actor
Angel & Frances, 12 D'Arblay St, London W1F 8DU, England

**Jackson, Betty** — Fashion Designer
Betty Jackson Ltd, 1 Netherwood Place, London W14 0BW, England

**Jackson, Bobby** — Basketball Player
Houston Rockets, 1730 Jefferson St, Houston TX 77003 USA

**Jackson, Brandon T** — Actor
Class Clown Entertainment, 14622 Ventura Blvd, #1002, Sherman Oaks CA 91403, USA

**Jackson, Charles M** — Football Player
PO Box 888285, Atlanta GA 30356, USA

**Jackson, Cheyenne** — Actor
Schiff Co, 9200 Sunset Blvd, #430, West Hollywood CA 90232 USA

**Jackson, Chuck** — Singer
Universal Attractions, 135 W 26th St, #1200, New York NY 10001 USA

**Jackson, Colin R** — Track Athlete
4 Jackson Close, Rhoose, Vale of Glamorgan CF62 3DQ, England

**Jackson, Danny L** — Baseball Player
16332 Larsen St, Overland Park KS 66062, USA

**Jackson, Darrell L** — Football Player
Darrell Jackson Family Foundation, 720 E Fletcher Ave, #202, Tampa FL 33612, USA

**Jackson, Darrell P** — Baseball Player
PO Box 4424, Downey CA 90241, USA

**Jackson, Darrin J** — Baseball Player
432 E Mead Dr, Chandler AZ 85249, USA

**Jackson, DeSean** — Football Player
Philadelphia Eagles, 1 Novacare Way, Philadelphia PA 19145 USA

**Jackson, Earnest (Ernie)** — Football Player
938 Pisgah N, Eads TN 38028, USA

**Jackson, Eddie** — Bowler
3961 Glenmore Ave, Cincinnati OH 45211, USA

**Jackson, Edwin** — Baseball Player
6955 Setter Dr, Columbus GA 31909, USA

**Jackson, Elly** — Singer, Keyboardist (La Roux)
Beatnik Public Relations, 5 Little Portland St, London W1W 7JD, England

**Jackson, Eric (E J)** — Canoeing Athlete
Jackson Kayak, 325 Iris Dr, Sparta TN 38583, USA

**Jackson, Francis A** — Concert Organist, Composer
Nether Garth, East Acklam, Malton, North Yorkshire YO17 9RG, England

**Jackson, Frank H** — Football Player
2812 Boll St, Dallas TX 7504, USA

**Jackson, Freddie** — Singer, Songwriter
Orpheus, 630 9th Ave, #1101, New York NY 10036, USA

**Jackson, Gildart** — Actor
Ellis Talent Agency, 4705 Laurel Canyon Blvd, #300, Valley Village CA 91607, USA

**Jackson, Glenda** — Actress
Agents Associes, 201 Rue du Faubourg Saint Honore, 75008 Paris, France

Jackson, Grady O     Football Player
PO Box 841, Braselton GA 30517, USA
Jackson, Grant D     Baseball Player
212 Mesa Circle, Pittsburgh PA 15241, USA
Jackson, Harold     Journalist
57 Fox Hollow Lane, Sewell NJ 08080, USA
Jackson, Harold L     Football Player, Coach
6144 Flight Ave, Los Angeles CA 90056, USA
Jackson, James A (Jim)     Basketball Player
17827 Windflower Way, Dallas TX 75252, USA
Jackson, Janet     Singer, Actress, Dancer
Guttman Assoc, 118 S Beverly Dr, #201, Beverly Hills CA 90212 USA
Jackson, Jaren     Basketball Player
7728 Solana Dr, Indianapolis IN 46240, USA
Jackson, Javon     Jazz Saxophonist
Palmetto Records, 67 Hill Road, Redding CT 06896, USA
Jackson, Jeff     Ice Hockey Player
1119 Parkview Dr, Griffin GA 30224, USA
Jackson, Jeff     Basketball Coach
Furman University, Athletic Dept, Greenville SC 29613, USA
Jackson, Jeremy     Actor
Mary Grady Agency, 269 S Beverly Dr, #1088, Beverly Hills CA 90212 USA
Jackson, Jermaine     Singer, Guitarist, Songwriter
Entertainment Artists, 2409 21st Ave S, #100, Nashville TN 10019 USA
Jackson, Jesse L     Civil Rights Activist, Evangelist
Operation Push, 930 E 50th St, Chicago IL 60615, USA
Jackson, Joanne     Swimmer
Nova Centurion S C, Beechdale Road, Bilborough, Nottingham NG8 3LL, England
Jackson, Joe     Singer, Pianist, Songwriter
Big Hassle, 44 Wall St, #2200, New York NY 10005, USA
Jackson, Joe M     Vietnam War Air Force Hero (CMH)
25320 38th Ave S, Kent WA 98032, USA
Jackson, John     Baseball Player
PO Box 898, Hodge LA 71247, USA
Jackson, John     Football Player
8183 Alpine Aster Court, Liberty Township OH 45044, USA
Jackson, John David     Boxer
1022 S State St, Tacoma WA 98405, USA
Jackson, Jonathan     Actor
Echo Lake Management, 421 S Beverly Dr, #800, Beverly Hills CA 90212, USA
Jackson, Joshua     Actor
Creative Artists Agency, 2000 Ave of Stars, #100, Los Angeles CA 90067 USA
Jackson, Julian     Boxer
Sugar Estate Branc, PO Box 10246, Charlotte Amalie VI 00801, USA
Jackson, Kate     Actress
Greater Talent Network, 437 5th Ave, #700, New York NY 10016, USA
Jackson, Keith J     Football Player
PO Box 241695, Little Rock AR 72223, USA
Jackson, Keith M     Sportscaster
ABC-TV, Sports Dept, 77 W 66th St, New York NY 10023 USA
Jackson, Kenneth B (Ken)     Baseball Player
PO Box 613, Waskom TX 75692, USA
Jackson, Kevin     Freestyle Wrestler
7215 Montarbor Dr, Colorado Springs CO 80918, USA
Jackson, Kirby     Football Player
3575 Candytuft Run, Auburn GA 30011, USA
Jackson, Larry R     Labor Leader
Grain Millers Federation, 14115 Lincoln St NE, #200, Andover MN 55304, USA
Jackson, LaToya     Singer, Model
Chuck Jones Public Relations, 150 W 51st, #802, New York NY 10019, USA
Jackson, Lauren     Basketball Player
Seattle Storm, Key Arena, 351 Elliott Ave W, #500, Seattle WA 98119 USA
Jackson, Lillian     Baseball Player
1050 W Camino Velesquez, Green Valley AZ 85622, USA
Jackson, Lisa     Writer
Signet Books, 375 Hudson St, New York NY 10014 USA
Jackson, Lucious B (Luke)     Basketball Player
4580 Cartwright St, Beaumont TX 77707, USA
Jackson, Mannie     Basketball Player, Executive
Harlem Globetrotters, 400 E Van Buren, #300, Phoenix AZ 85004, USA
Jackson, Mark A     Football Player
4351 Flandes St, Las Vegas NV 89121, USA
Jackson, Mark A     Basketball Player, Coach
25548 Kingston Court, Calabassas CA 91302, USA
Jackson, Mary Ann     Actress
30108 Village 30, #30, Camarillo CA 93012, USA
Jackson, Matthew Day     Artist
Hauser & Wirth, 32 E 69th St, New York NY 10021, USA
Jackson, Mel     Actor
101 E 119th St, #2D, New York NY 10035, USA
Jackson, Melvin (Mel), Jr     Football Player
4345 Enoro Dr, Los Angeles CA 90008, USA
Jackson, Mervin P (Merv)     Basketball Player
16638 Kildare Court, Tinley Park IL 60477, USA
Jackson, Michael A     Football Player
PO Box 473, Tangiaphoa LA 70465, USA
Jackson, Michael R (Mike)     Baseball Player
17214 Oak Dale Dr, Spring TX 77379, USA
Jackson, Mick     Director
1349 Berea Place, Pacific Palisades CA 90272, USA
Jackson, Millie     Singer, Songwriter, Actress
Associated Booking Corp, 501 Madison Ave, #501, New York NY 10022 USA
Jackson, Monte C     Football Player
7646 Westbrook Ave, San Diego CA 92139, USA
Jackson, Noah D     Football Player
1640 Milburne Road, Lake Forest IL 60045, USA

**Jackson, Peter** — Director, Producer
Wing Nut Films, PO Box 15208, Miramar, Wellington 6003, New Zealand
**Jackson, Philip** — Actor
Markham Froggatt Irwin, Julian House, 4 Windmill St, London W1P 1HF, England
**Jackson, Philip D (Phil)** — Basketball Player, Coach
18942 Medicine Rock Lane, Lakeside MT 59922, USA
**Jackson, Quinton (Rampage)** — Ultimate Fighter, Actor
Roar Mgmt, 9701 Wilshire Blvd, #800, Beverly Hills CA 90212 USA
**Jackson, R Graham** — Architect
Calhoun Tungate Jackson Dill Architects, 6200 Savoy Dr, Houston TX 77036, USA
**Jackson, Ralph A** — Basketball Player
3235 W 11th Place, Inglewood CA 90303, USA
**Jackson, Randall B (Randy)** — Football Player
747 Musago Run, Lake Mary FL 32746, USA
**Jackson, Randall D (Randy)** — Bassist, Entertainer
Dream Merchant 21 Entertainment, 1416 N La Brea Ave, Hollywood CA 90028, USA
**Jackson, Ransom J (Randy)** — Baseball Player
250 Hunnicutt Dr, Athens GA 30606, USA
**Jackson, Rebbie** — Singer, Songwriter
Groove Entertainment, 1005 N Alfred St, #2, West Hollywood CA 90069, USA
**Jackson, Reginald M (Reggie)** — Baseball Player
305 Amador Ave, Seaside CA 93955, USA
**Jackson, Richard Lee** — Actor
1815 Butler Ave, #120, Los Angeles CA 90025, USA
**Jackson, Rickey A** — Football Player
2744 Hyde Park Ave N, Harvey LA 70058, USA
**Jackson, Roland T (Sonny)** — Baseball Player
117 Palm Bay Dr, #B, Palm Beach Gardens FL 33418, USA
**Jackson, Ronnie D (Ron)** — Baseball Player
515 White Road, Fayetteville GA 30214, USA
**Jackson, Roy Lee** — Baseball Player
8269 Lee Road 54, Auburn AL 36830, USA
**Jackson, S Randall (Randy)** — Singer
Big J Productions, 854 Florida Blvd, New Orleans LA 70124 USA
**Jackson, Samuel L** — Actor
Anonymous Content, 3532 Hayden Ave, Culver City CA 90232 USA
**Jackson, Sharisse (Shar)** — Actress, Singer
Sovereign Talent Group, 8421 Wilshire Blvd, #200, Beverly Hills CA 90211, USA
**Jackson, Sherry** — Actress
13082 Mindanao Way, #54, Marina Del Rey CA 90292, USA
**Jackson, Shirley Ann** — Educator, Theoretical Physicist
Rensselaer Polytechnic Institute, President's Office, Troy NY 12180, USA
**Jackson, Stephen J** — Basketball Player
10541 Titan Run, Carmel IN 46032, USA
**Jackson, Steven W (Steve)** — Football Player
43752 Lees Mill Square, Leesburg VA 20176, USA
**Jackson, Stonewall** — Singer, Guitarist, Songwriter
6007 Cloverland Dr, Brentwood TN 37027, USA
**Jackson, Stoney** — Actor
1602 N Fuller Ave, #102, Los Angeles CA 90046, USA
**Jackson, Stu** — Basketball Coach, Executive
National Basketball Assn, 645 5th Ave, #1900, New York NY 10022, USA
**Jackson, Tarvaris F** — Football Player
11171 Sun Center Dr, #290, Rancho Cordova CA 95670, USA
**Jackson, Terence L (Terry)** — Football Player
2269 Glenmore Terrace, Rockville MD 20850, USA
**Jackson, Thomas (Tom)** — Football Player, Sportscaster
7475 Brill Road, Cincinnati OH 45243, USA
**Jackson, Tiffany** — Basketball Player
Tulsa Shock, B O K Center, 200 S Denver, Tulsa OK 74103 USA
**Jackson, Tito** — Singer (Jackson Five)
2467 Taylor Ave, Corona CA 92882, USA
**Jackson, Tony** — Basketball Player
1009 Trevey Point, Lexington KY 40515, USA
**Jackson, Tracey** — Writer
Arlook Group, 205 S Beverly Drive, #209, Beverly Hills CA 90212, USA
**Jackson, Trina** — Swimmer
9271 Saltwater Way, Jacksonville FL 32256, USA
**Jackson, Tyoka** — Football Player
16312 Birkdale Dr, Odessa FL 33556, USA
**Jackson, Vestee, II** — Football Player
2800 S Eastern Ave, #410, Las Vegas NV 89169, USA
**Jackson, Victoria** — Actress, Comedienne
Breen Agency, 25 Music Square W, Nashville TN 37203, USA
**Jackson, Vincent** — Football Player
Tampa Bay Buccaneers, 1 W Buccaneer Place, Tampa FL 33607 USA
**Jackson, Vincent E (Bo)** — Football, Baseball Player
100 Oak Ridge Dr, Burr Ridge IL 60527, USA
**Jackson, Wanda** — Singer
Wanda Jackson Enterprises, 11700 S Western Ave, Oklahoma City OK 73170, USA
**Jackson, Wardell** — Basketball Player
PO Box 164142, Columbus OH 43216, USA
**Jackson, Wilbur** — Football Player
PO Box 1571, Ozark AL 36361, USA
**Jackson, Willie B, Jr** — Football Player
PO Box 12643, Gainesville FL 32604, USA
**Jackson, Zachary T (Zach)** — Baseball Player
7630 Menler Dr, Austin TX 78735, USA
**Jaco, Charles** — Commentator, Writer
PO Box 220182, Saint Louis MO 63122, USA
**Jacob, Irene** — Actress
Paradigm Agency, 360 N Crescent Dr, North Building, Beverly Hills CA 90210 USA
**Jacob, Jacob-Farj-Rafael (J F R)** — Indian Army General
Roli Press, M-75 Greater Kailash 2 Market, New Delhi 110048, India
**Jacob, John E** — Civil Rights Activist
Anheuser-Busch, 1 Busch Place, Saint Louis MO 63118, USA

| | |
|---|---|
| **Jacob, Stanley W**<br>1055 SW Westwood Court, Portland OR 97239, USA | Surgeon |
| **Jacobellis, Lindsey**<br>30648 E Ski Bowl Way, Government Camp OR 97028, USA | Snowboard Athlete |
| **Jacobi, Derek G**<br>Independent Talent Group, 40 Whitfield St, London W1T 2RH, England | Actor |
| **Jacobi, Doreen**<br>Agentur Breilmann, Toppenstedter Kirchweg 11, 21376 Salzhausen, Germany | Actress |
| **Jacobi, Walter**<br>2004 Max Luther Dr NW, #419, Huntsville AL 35810, USA | Space Scientist |
| **Jacobs, Allen W**<br>3050 Tolcate Lane, Salt Lake City UT 84121, USA | Football Player |
| **Jacobs, Arnold S (A J), Jr**<br>Simon & Schuster, 1230 Ave of Americas, Concourse 1, New York NY 10020 USA | Writer |
| **Jacobs, Brandon**<br>New York Giants, Meadowlands Stadium, 102 Route 120, East Rutherford NJ 07073 USA | Football Player |
| **Jacobs, David J (Dave)**<br>8388 Glen Eagle Dr, Manlius NY 13104, USA | Football Player |
| **Jacobs, Debbie**<br>T-Best Talent Agency, 508 Honey Lake Court, Danville CA 94506 USA | Singer |
| **Jacobs, Dennis G**<br>US Appeals Court, Moynihan Courthouse, 500 Pearl St, New York NY 10007, USA | Judge |
| **Jacobs, Gillian**<br>United Talent Agency, U T A Plaza, 9336 Civic Center Dr, Beverly Hills CA 90210 USA | Actress |
| **Jacobs, Glenn**<br>World Wrestling Entertainment, Titan Towers, 1241 E Main St, Stamford CT 06902 USA | Professional Wrestler |
| **Jacobs, Harry E**<br>108 Lenora Dr, Hamburg NY 14075, USA | Football Player |
| **Jacobs, Howard L**<br>Forgie Jacobs Leonard, 4165 E Thousand Oaks Blvd, Westlake Village CA 91362, USA | Attorney |
| **Jacobs, Irwin M**<br>Qualcomm Inc, 5775 Morehouse Dr, San Diego CA 92121, USA | Businessman |
| **Jacobs, Jack H**<br>Bankers Trust Co, 1 Appold St, London EC2A 2HE, England | Vietnam War Army Hero (CMH) |
| **Jacobs, Jeremy M**<br>1300 N Davis Road, East Aurora NY 14052, USA | Businessman, Hockey Executive |
| **Jacobs, Jim**<br>Ronald Taft, 18 W 55th St, New York NY 10019, USA | Writer, Composer, Actor |
| **Jacobs, Julien I**<br>US Tax Court, 400 2nd St NW, Washington DC 20217, USA | Judge |
| **Jacobs, Kate**<br>East Central One, All Saints Road, Suffolk 1P6 8PR, England | Singer, Guitarist, Songwriter |
| **Jacobs, Katie**<br>Heel & Toe Films, 2058 Broadway, Santa Monica CA 90404, USA | Writer, Producer |
| **Jacobs, Lawrence-Hilton**<br>PO Box 67905, Los Angeles CA 90067, USA | Actor |
| **Jacobs, Lloyd A**<br>University of Toledo, President's Office, 2801 W Bancroft, Toledo OH 43606, USA | Educator |
| **Jacobs, Marc**<br>72 Spring St, New York NY 10012, USA | Fashion Designer |
| **Jacobs, Michael J (Mike)**<br>1583 Hikers Trail Dr, Chula Vista CA 91915, USA | Baseball Player |
| **Jacobs, Paul E**<br>Qualcomm, 5775 Morehouse Dr, San Diego CA 92121, USA | Businessman |
| **Jacobs, Proverb G**<br>4369 Detroit Ave, Oakland CA 94619, USA | Football Player |
| **Jacobs, Robert Nathan**<br>Gersh Agency, 9465 Wilshire Blvd, #600, Beverly Hills CA 90212 USA | Writer |
| **Jacobs, Taylor H**<br>8083 Longmeadow Dr, Tallahassee FL 32312, USA | Football Player |
| **Jacobsen, Anders**<br>Ringkollen Skilubb, Owrensgt 28, 3510 Honefoss, Norway | Ski Jumper |
| **Jacobsen, Casey G**<br>24622 Cresta Court, Laguna Hills CA 92653, USA | Basketball Player |
| **Jacobsen, Hugh Newell**<br>Hugh Newell Jacobsen Architect, 2529 P St NW, Washington DC 20007, USA | Architect |
| **Jacobsen, Peter**<br>27771 Marina Pointe Dr, Bonita Springs FL 34134, USA | Golfer |
| **Jacobsen, Stephanie**<br>1 Mgmt, 9000 W Sunset Blvd, #1550, Los Angeles CA 90069 USA | Actress |
| **Jacobs-Lorena, Marcelo**<br>Johns Hopkins University, Malaria Research Institute, Baltimore MD 21218, USA | Molecular Microbiologist |
| **Jacobson, D D**<br>8261 Rees St, Playa del Rey CA 90293, USA | Bowler |
| **Jacobson, Danny**<br>Brillstein Entertainment Partners, 9150 Wilshire Blvd, #350, Beverly Hills CA 90212 USA | Writer |
| **Jacobson, Herbert L**<br>Apartado 160, Escazu, Costa Rica | Diplomat, Journalist |
| **Jacobson, Nina**<br>Color Force, 1524 Cloverfield Blvd, #C, Santa Monica CA 90404, USA | Producer |
| **Jacobson, Peter**<br>Innovative Artists, 235 Park Ave S, #1000, New York NY 10003 USA | Actor |
| **Jacoby, Brook W**<br>21825 N Dobson Road, Scottsdale AZ 85255, USA | Baseball Player |
| **Jacoby, Joe**<br>Jacoby Jeep/Eagle/Chrysler, 7308 Cedar Run Dr, Warrenton VA 20187, USA | Football Player |
| **Jacoby, Mark**<br>Talent Works, 3500 W Olive Ave, #1400, Burbank CA 91505 USA | Actor, Singer |
| **Jacoby, Scott**<br>PO Box 5569, Sherman Oaks CA 91413, USA | Actor, Director, Writer |
| **Jacome, Jason J**<br>5115 N Camino Esplendora, Tucson AZ 85718, USA | Baseball Player |
| **Jacot, Christopher**<br>Characters Talent Mgmt, 8 Elm St, Toronto ON M5G 1G7, Canada | Actor |
| **Jacot, Michele**<br>Residence du Brevent, 74 Chamonix, France | Alpine Skier |

**Jacott, Carlos** — Actor
Thruline Entertainment, 9250 Wilshire Blvd, #100, Beverly Hills CA 90212 USA
**Jacox, Kendyl L** — Football Player
50 Schubach Dr, Sugar Land, TX 77479, USA
**Jacquemard, Simonne** — Writer
Le Verdier, 24520 Sireuil, France
**Jacques, Russell K** — Sculptor
38 Drake St, Newport Beach CA 92663, USA
**Jacquot, Benoit** — Director
Voyez Mon Agent, 20 Ave Rapp, 75007 Paris, France
**Jaczko, Gregory B** — Government Official
US Nuclear Regulatory Commission, Mail Stop 0-16G4, Washington DC 20555, USA
**Jadakiss** — Rap Artist (Ruff Ryders)
J Erving Group, 154 Krog St, #130, Atlanta GA 30307, USA
**Jaeckin, Just** — Director, Writer
Galerie Anne et Just Jaeckin, 19 Rue Guenegaud, 75006 Paris, France
**Jaeger, Aaron** — Actor
Allegory Creative Management, 13261 Moorpark St, #103, Sherman Oaks CA 91423, USA
**Jaeger, Andrea** — Tennis Player
Kids Stuff Foundation, Silver Lining Ranch, 1490 S Ute Ave, Aspen CO 81611, USA
**Jaeger, Jeff T** — Football Player
3026 Sahalee Dr W, Sammamish WA 98074, USA
**Jaeger, Sam** — Actor
Greene Assoc, 1901 Ave of Stars, #130, Los Angeles CA 90067 USA
**Jaeggi, Andreas** — Opera Singer
I M G Artists, Hogarth Business Park, Chiswick, London W4 2TH, England
**Jaenicke, Hannes** — Actor
Rough Diamond Mgmt, 1424 N Kings Road, Los Angeles CA 90069, USA
**Jaenisch, Rudolf** — Biologist
Massachusetts Institute of Technology, Biology Dept, 9 Cambridge Center, Cambridge MA 02142, USA
**Jaffe, Arthur M** — Mathematical Physicist
27 Lancaster St, Cambridge MA 02140, USA
**Jaffe, Harold W** — Epidemiologist
Centers for Disease Control, 1600 Clifton Road NE, Atlanta GA 30329 USA
**Jaffe, Robert L** — Theoretical Physicist
Massachusetts Institute of Technology, Physics Dept, Cambridge MA 02139, USA
**Jaffe, Stanley R** — Producer, Director
152 W 57th St, #5200F, New York NY 10019, USA
**Jaffe, Susan** — Ballerina
American Ballet Theatre, 890 Broadway, #300, New York NY 10003 USA
**Jaffrey, Raza** — Actor
United Agents, 12-26 Lexington St, London W1F 0LE, England
**Jaffrey, Saeed** — Actor, Comedian
503 Sejal New Link Road, Andheri, Mumbai MS 400058, India
**Jagendorf, Andre T** — Plant Physiologist
455 Savage Farm Dr, Ithaca NY 14850, USA
**Jager, Thomas (Tom)** — Swimmer
1416 Chinook St, Moscow ID 83843, USA
**Jagge, Finn Christian** — Alpine Skier
Michelets Vei 108, 1320 Stabekk, Norway
**Jagger, Bianca** — Actress, Model
Bianca Jagger Human Rights Foundation, 272 Kensington High St, #246, London, W8 6ND, England
**Jagger, Elizabeth (Lizzy)** — Model
Tess Mgmt, 9-10 Market Place, #400, London W1W 8AQ, England
**Jagger, Michael (Mick)** — Singer (Rolling Stones)
Jagged Films, 1041 N Formosa Ave, West Hollywood CA 90046, USA
**Jagland, Thorbjoern** — Prime Minister, Norway
Stortinget, Karl Johans Gate 22, 0026 Oslo, Norway
**Jaglom, Henry** — Director
9165 W Sunset Blvd, #300, West Hollywood CA 90069, USA
**Jagr, Jaromir** — Ice Hockey Player
New Jersey Devils, Arena, 50 State Route 120, East Rutherford NJ 07073 USA
**Jaha, John E** — Baseball Player
9494 SE Chatfield Court, Happy Valley OR 97086, USA
**Jahan, Marine** — Actress, Dancer
Media Artists Group, 8222 Melrose Ave, #203, Los Angeles CA 90048 USA
**Jaheim** — Singer
Universal Attractions, 135 W 26th St, #1200, New York NY 10001 USA
**Jahn, Helmut** — Architect
Murphy/Jahn, 33 E Wacker Dr, #300, Chicago IL 60601, USA
**Jahn, Robert G** — Aeronautical Engineer
Princeton University, Aerospace Sciences Dept, Princeton NJ 08544, USA
**Jahn, Sigmund** — Cosmonaut, East Germany; General
Fontanestr 35, 15344 Strausberg, Germany
**Jaidah, Ali Mohammed** — Government Official, Qatar
Qatar Petroleum Corp, PO Box 3212, Doha, Qatar
**Jakel, Bernd** — Yachtsman
Salvador-Allende-Str 48, 12559 Berlin, Germany
**Jakes, John** — Writer
445 Meadow Lark Dr, Sarasota FL 34236, USA
**Jakes, T D** — Religious Leader
T D Jakes Ministries, PO Box 763518, Dallas TX 75376, USA
**Jakes, Van K** — Football Player
305 Worthing Lane, McDonough GA 30253, USA
**Jakobs, Marco** — Bobsled Athlete
Oststr 1B, 59427 Unna, Germany
**Jakobsson, Johan M** — Handball Player
Aalborg Handbold, Willy Brandts Vej 31, 9220 Aalborg Ost, Denmark
**Jakopin, John** — Ice Hockey Player
57 Samana Dr, Miami FL 33133, USA
**Jakosits, Michael** — Marksman
Karlsbergstr 140, 66424 Homburg/Saar, Germany
**Jakub, Lisa** — Actress
Lafeaver Talent, 785 Carlaw Ave, #101, Toronto ON M4K 3L1, Canada
**Jakubowicz, Jonathan** — Director, Producer, Writer
Creative Artists Agency, 2000 Ave of Stars, #100, Los Angeles CA 90067 USA

| | |
|---|---|
| **Jalal, Farida** | Actress |
| 3B Nandini Unik Housing Society, Andheri, Mumbai MS 400058, India | |
| **Jalali, Bahram** | Electrical Engineer |
| University of California, Electrical Engineering Dept, Los Angeles CA 90024, USA | |
| **Jamail, Joseph D, Jr** | Attorney |
| Jamail & Kolius, 500 Dallas St, #3434, Houston TX 77002, USA | |
| **Jamal, Ahmad** | Jazz Pianist |
| Ellora Mgmt, PO Box 755, 11 Brook St, Lakeville CT 06039, USA | |
| **Jamelia** | Singer, Songwriter |
| Roar Global Entertainment, 34-35 Eastcastle St, Oxford Circus, London W1W 8DW, England | |
| **James, Aaron (A J)** | Basketball Player |
| 3057 Orrin Ave, Youngstown OH 44505, USA | |
| **James, Anthony** | Actor |
| C N A Assoc, 1875 Century Park East, #2250, Los Angeles CA 90067 USA | |
| **James, Arthur (Art)** | Baseball Player |
| 6935 Brown Dr S, Fairburn GA 30213, USA | |
| **James, Boney** | Saxophonist, Songwriter |
| Direct Management Group, 947 N La Cienega Blvd, #G, West Hollywood CA 90069, USA | |
| **James, Bradie D** | Football Player |
| 2509 Silver Table Dr, Lewisville TX 75056, USA | |
| **James, Brett** | Singer, Guitarist, Songwriter |
| Starstruck Entertainment, 40 Music Square W, Nashville TN 37203, USA | |
| **James, Brian D'Arcy** | Actor |
| Thruline Entertainment, 9250 Wilshire Blvd, #100, Beverly Hills CA 90212 USA | |
| **James, Charity** | Actress |
| C E S D, 10635 Santa Monica Blvd, #130, Los Angeles CA 90025 USA | |
| **James, Charmayne** | Rodeo Rider |
| Gold Buckle Ranch, 2100 N Highway 360, #1207, Grand Prairie TX 75050, USA | |
| **James, Cheryl (Salt)** | Rap Artist (Salt'N'Pepa) |
| Entertainment Artists, 2409 21st Ave S, #100, Nashville TN 10019 USA | |
| **James, Clifton** | Actor |
| 500 W 43rd St, #26J, New York NY 10036, USA | |
| **James, Colton** | Actor |
| James/Levy Mgmt, 3500 W Olive Ave, #1470, Burbank CA 91505 USA | |
| **James, D Christopher (Chris)** | Baseball Player |
| 1040 County Road 2707, Alto TX 75925, USA | |
| **James, D Clayton** | Historian |
| 106 Wagon Wheel Trail, Moneta VA 24121, USA | |
| **James, Daniel J, III** | Air Force General |
| Director, Air National Guard, HqUSAF, Pentagon, Washington DC 20330, USA | |
| **James, Dion** | Baseball Player |
| 5 Shelter Point Court, Sacramento CA 95831, USA | |
| **James, Donald M** | Businessman |
| Vulcan Materials Co, 1200 Urban Center Dr, Birmingham AL 35242, USA | |
| **James, E L** | Writer |
| Vintage Books, 1745 Broadway, New York NY 10019 USA | |
| **James, Edgerrin T** | Football Player |
| 709 Hendry St, Immokalee FL 34142, USA | |
| **James, Elgin** | Director, Writer, Actor |
| W M E Entertainment, 9601 Wilshire Blvd, #300, Beverly Hills CA 90210 USA | |
| **James, Eloisa** | Writer |
| Mary Bly, Fordham University, English Dept, Lincoln Center Campus, New York NY 10023, USA | |
| **James, Forrest H (Fob), Jr** | Governor, AL |
| 39 Alabama Road, Lehigh Acres FL 33936, USA | |
| **James, Frances C** | Biologist |
| Florida State University, Biological Sciences Dept, Tallahassee FL 32306, USA | |
| **James, G William (Bill)** | Baseball Writer, Statistician |
| 625 Ohio St, Lawrence KS 66044, USA | |
| **James, Geraldine** | Actress |
| Denville Hall, 62 Ducks Hill Road, Northwood, Middlesex HA6 2SB, England | |
| **James, Godfrey** | Actor |
| Shack, Western Road, Pevensey Bay, East Sussex BN23 6HG, England | |
| **James, Henry C** | Basketball Player |
| 527 E Leith St, Fort Wayne IN 46806, USA | |
| **James, J Craig** | Football Player, Sportscaster |
| 12714 W FM 455, Celina TX 75009, USA | |
| **James, James (Boney)** | Jazz Saxophonist |
| Direct Mgmt Group, 947 N La Cienega Blvd, #G, West Hollywood CA 90069, USA | |
| **James, Jenorris (Jeno)** | Football Player |
| 1620 NW 117th Ave, Plantation FL 33323, USA | |
| **James, Jesse** | Actor |
| Dino May Mgmt, 6362 Hollywood Blvd, #PH 422, Los Angeles CA 90028, USA | |
| **James, Jesse G** | Producer |
| West Coast Choppers, 718 W Anaheim St, Long Beach CA 90813, USA | |
| **James, Jessica R (Jessie)** | Singer, Songwriter |
| Show Dog/Universal Music, 2303 21st Ave S, #400, Nashville TN 37212, USA | |
| **James, Jimmy** | Singer (Jimmy James & the Vagabonds) |
| Barry Collings Entertainments, PO Box 2112, Essex Hockley SS5 4WD, England | |
| **James, John** | Actor |
| PO Box 9, Cambridge NY 12816, USA | |
| **James, John P (Johnny)** | Baseball Player |
| 6037 E Larkspur Dr, Scottsdale AZ 85254, USA | |
| **James, John W, Jr** | Football Player |
| 23108 NE 69th Ave, Melrose FL 32666, USA | |
| **James, Joni** | Singer |
| Silent Angels Productions, 439 E 74th St, #5FW, New York NY 10021, USA | |
| **James, Kate** | Model |
| Men/Women Model Inc, 199 Lafayette St, New York NY 10012, USA | |
| **James, Kevin, III** | Illusionist, Actor |
| Jeff Sussman Mgmt, 603 W 115th St, #282, New York NY 10025, USA | |
| **James, LeBron R** | Basketball Player |
| Miami Heat, American Airlines Arena, 601 Biscayne Blvd, Miami FL 33132 USA | |
| **James, Leela** | Singer, Songwriter |
| R K D Music Mgmt, PO Box 11611, Beverly Hills CA 90213, USA | |
| **James, Lennie** | Actor |
| Principal Entertainment, 130 W 42nd St, #614, New York NY 10036, USA | |

**J**

**Jalal - James**

**James, Liam** — Actor
Gersh Agency, 9465 Wilshire Blvd, #600, Beverly Hills CA 90212 USA
**James, Lionel** — Football Player
199 Woodbury Dr, Sterret AL 35147, USA
**James, M William (Billy)** — Basketball Player
12 S Sunset Dr, Lexington IN 47138, USA
**James, Marco** — Actor
Don Buchwald, 6500 Wilshire Blvd, #2200, Los Angeles CA 90048 USA
**James, Marianne** — Jazz Guitarist, Composer
89 Ave Charles de Gaulle, 92575 Neuilly-sur-Seine Cedex, France
**James, Michael E (Mike)** — Baseball Player
115 Austin Court, Mary Esther FL 32569, USA
**James, Oliver** — Actor
Independent Talent Group, 40 Whitfield St, London W1T 2RH, England
**James, Oliver** — Psychologist, Writer
Gillon Aitken Assoc, 18-21 Cavaye Place, London SW10 9PT, England
**James, P D** — Writer
Greene & Heaton Ltd, 37A Goldhawk Road, London W12 8QQ, England
**James, Pell** — Actress
I C M Partners, 730 5th Ave, New York NY 10019 USA
**James, Robert (Bob)** — Jazz Keyboardist (Bob James Trio)
Monterey International, 200 W Superior St, #202, Chicago IL 60654 USA
**James, Robert D** — Football Player
1511 N Highland Ave, Murfreesboro TN 37130, USA
**James, Robert H (Bob)** — Baseball Player
15844 Cindy Court, Canyon Country CA 91387, USA
**James, Roland O** — Football Player
19 Spring Lane, Sharon MA 02067, USA
**James, Shannon** — Model
Playboy Promotions, 2706 Media Center Dr, Los Angeles CA 90065 USA
**James, Sheryl** — Journalist
Saint Petersburg Times, Editorial Dept, 490 1st Ave, Saint Petersburg FL 33701, USA
**James, Sonny** — Singer, Guitarist, Songwriter
W M E Entertainment, 1600 Division St, #300, Nashville TN 37203 USA
**James, Thomas (Tom)** — Rowing Athlete
Molesey Boat Club, Barge Walk, East Molesey, Surrey KT8 9AJ, England
**James, Tommy** — Singer (Shondells)
Paradise Artists, PO Box 1821, Ojai CA 93024 USA
**James, Tory S** — Football Player
70 N Gary Glen Circle, Spring TX 77382, USA
**James-Collier, Rob** — Actor
Rights House, Drury House, 34-43 Russell St, London WC2B 5HA, England
**James-Kuehl, Sheila** — Actress
3201 Pearl St, Santa Monica CA 90405, USA
**Jameson, Keith** — Opera Singer
Columbia Artists Mgmt Inc, 1790 Broadway, #702, New York NY 10019 USA
**Jameson, Nick** — Actor
Danis Panaro Nist, 9201 W Olympic Blvd, Beverly Hills CA 90212, USA
**James-Rodman, Charmayne** — Rodeo Rider
General Delivery, Clayton NM 88415, USA
**Jamieson, Janet** — Baseball Player
6324 212th St SW, #3, Lynnwood WA 98036, USA
**Jamieson, John K** — Businessman
10313 Stanley Circle, Minneapolis MN 55437, USA
**Jamison, Antawn C** — Basketball Player
6041 Providence Country Club Dr, Charlotte NC 28277, USA
**Jamison, George R, Jr** — Football Player
3430 Vineyard Hill Dr, Rochester MI 48306, USA
**Jamison, Judith** — Dancer, Choreographer
Alvin Ailey American Dance Foundation, 405 W 55th St, New York NY 10019, USA
**Jammeh, Yahya A J J** — Head of State, Gambia; Army Officer
President's Office, Private Mail Bag, State House, Banjul, Gambia
**Jammer, Quentin T** — Football Player
7815 Sendero Angelica, San Diego CA 92127, USA
**Jampolsky, Gerald** — Writer
Celestial Arts, 6001 Shellmound St, #400, Emeryville CA 94608, USA
**Janas, Elizabeth** — Actress
Don Buchwald, 6500 Wilshire Blvd, #2200, Los Angeles CA 90048 USA
**Janaszak, Steve** — Ice Hockey Player
42 Montrose Ave, Babylon NY 11702, USA
**Jance, J A** — Writer
William Morrow, 1350 Ave of Americas, New York NY 10019, USA
**Jancso, Miklos** — Director
Eszter Utca 17, 1022 Budapest, Hungary
**Janda, Krystyna** — Actress
Teatr Powszechny, Ul Zamoyskiego 20, 03801 Warsaw, Poland
**Jane, Thomas** — Actor
Creative Artists Agency, 2000 Ave of Stars, #100, Los Angeles CA 90067 USA
**Janes, Dominic** — Actor
Rising Talent Mgmt, 137 S Spalding Drive, #406, Beverly Hills CA 90212, USA
**Janetti, Gary** — Producer, Writer
W M E Entertainment, 9601 Wilshire Blvd, #300, Beverly Hills CA 90210 USA
**Janeway, Michael C** — Editor, Educator, Writer
Columbia University, Graduate Journalism School, New York NY 10027, USA
**Janeway, Richard** — Physician
PO Box 188, Blowing Rock NC 28605, USA
**Jang, Jeong (J J)** — Golfer
8749 The Esplanade, #33, Orlando FL 32836, USA
**Janic, Adrienne** — Actress
Bleu Entertainment, 5225 Wilshire Blvd, #401, Los Angeles CA 90036, USA
**Janics, Natasa Dusev-** — Canoeing Athlete
E D F Demas Szeged, PF 199, 6701 Szeged, Hungary
**Janikowski, Sebastian** — Football Player
11958 Brady Road, Jacksonville FL 32223, USA
**Janis, Byron** — Concert Pianist
Phillips Records, 810 7th Ave, New York NY 10019 USA

**Janis, Conrad** — Actor, Jazz Trombonist
Feminine Touch, 300 N Swall Dr, #251, Beverly Hills CA 90211, USA
**Janish, Paul R** — Baseball Player
11926 Deep Woods Dr, Cypress TX 77429, USA
**Janitz, John A** — Businessman
Textron Inc, 40 Westminster St, #500, Providence RI 02903, USA
**Janka, Carlo** — Alpine Skier
Miraniga, 7134 Obersaxen, Switzerland
**Jankovic, Jelena** — Tennis Player
Octagon Worldwide, 1751 Pinnacle Dr, #1500, McLean VA 22102 USA
**Jankovic, Joseph** — Neurologist
Baylor College of Medicine, Neurology Dept, Baylor Plaza, Houston TX 77030, USA
**Jankowska-Cieslak, Jadwiga** — Actress
Film Polski, Ul Mazewiecka 6/8, 00950 Warsaw, Poland
**Jankowski, Gene F** — Businessman
American Film Institute, 901 15th St NW, #700, Washington DC 20005, USA
**Jankowski, Peter** — Producer
United Talent Agency, U T A Plaza, 9336 Civic Center Dr, Beverly Hills CA 90210 USA
**Jann, Michael Patrick** — Director, Producer, Actor
Creative Artists Agency, 2000 Ave of Stars, #100, Los Angeles CA 90067 USA
**Jannazzo, Izzy** — Boxer
6924 62nd Ave, Middle Village NY 11379, USA
**Janney, Allison** — Actress
W M E Entertainment, 9601 Wilshire Blvd, #300, Beverly Hills CA 90210 USA
**Janney, Craig H** — Ice Hockey Player
198 Hawley Lane, Geneva IL 60134, USA
**Jannot, Mark** — Editor
Popular Science, Editorial Dept, 2 Park Ave, #900, New York NY 10016, USA
**Janotta, Howard (Howie)** — Basketball Player
18118 Brookwood Forest, San Antonio TX 78258, USA
**Janov, Arthur** — Psychologist, Psychotherapist
1205 Abbot Kinney Blvd, Venice CA 90291, USA
**Janovitz, Bill** — Singer, Guitarist (Buffalo Tom)
Agency Group Ltd, 142 W 57th St, #600, New York NY 10019 USA
**Janowicz, Josh** — Actor
1 Mgmt, 9000 W Sunset Blvd, #1550, Los Angeles CA 90069 USA
**Janowitz, Gundula** — Opera Singer
3072 Kasten 75, Austria
**Janowitz, Tama** — Writer
Random House, 1745 Broadway, #1800, New York NY 10019 USA
**Janowski, Marek** — Conductor
Columbia Artists Mgmt Inc, 1790 Broadway, #702, New York NY 10019 USA
**Jansa, Janez** — Prime Minister, Slovenia
Prime Minister's Office, Gregorcicova St 20, 61000 Ljublijana, Slovenia
**Jansch, Heather** — Artist
Knowle, Rundlerohy, Newton Abbot, Devon TQ12 2PJ, England
**Jansen, Daniel E (Dan)** — Speed Skater
PO Box 3354, Mooresville NC 28117, USA
**Jansen, Janine** — Concert Violinist
Harrison/Parrott, 5-6 Albion Court, London W6 0QT, England
**Janson, Karin Stahre** — Cruise Ship Captain
Royal Carribean Int'l, 1111 S Arroyo Parkway, #450, Pasadena CA 91105, USA
**Jansons, Mariss** — Conductor
Opus 3 Artists, 470 Park Ave S, #900N, New York NY 10016 USA
**Jansrud, Kjetil** — Alpine Skier
Vinstra, 2640 Gudbrandsdalen, Norway
**Janssen, Daniel** — Businessman
La Ronciere, 108 Ave Ernest Solvay, 1310 La Hulpe, Belgium
**Janssen, Famke** — Actress, Model
Brookside Artist Mgmt, 250 W 57th St, #2303, New York NY 10107 USA
**Janssen, Marlene** — Model, Actress
Playboy Promotions, 2706 Media Center Dr, Los Angeles CA 90065 USA
**Janssen, Tom** — Editorial Cartoonist
Prinsengract 304, 1016 Amsterdam HW, Netherlands
**Janssens, Mark** — Ice Hockey Player
115 Central Park W, #17A, New York NY 10023, USA
**Jantz, Richard** — Anthropologist
University of Tennessee, Anthropology Dept, Knoxville TN 37996, USA
**January, Briann J** — Basketball Player
Indiana Fever, Conseco Fieldhouse, 125 S Pennsylvania, Indianapolis IN 46204 USA
**January, Donald R (Don)** — Golfer
5006 Village Place, Dallas TX 75248, USA
**Jany, Alexandre (Alex)** — Swimmer
104 Blvd Livon, 13007 Marseille, France
**Janzen, Daniel H** — Biologist
Parque Nacional Santa Rosa, #169, Liberia, Guanacaste Province, Costa Rica
**Janzen, Edmund** — Religious Leader
General Conference of Mennonite Brethren, 8000 W 21st St, Wichita KS 67205, USA
**Janzen, Lee M** — Golfer
9088 Point Cypress Dr, Orlando FL 32836, USA
**Janzen, Rhoda** — Writer
Hope College, English Dept, Holland MI 49422, USA
**Jaquess, Lindel G (Pete)** — Football Player
631 Cunningham Lane, El Cajon CA 92019, USA
**Jaquiss, Nigel** — Journalist
Willamette Week, Editorial Dept, 822 SW 10th Ave, Portland OR 97205, USA
**Jaramillo. Jason C** — Baseball Player
6111 Madeline Lane, Caledonia WI 53108, USA
**Jardine, Alan C (Al)** — Singer, Guitarist (Beach Boys)
Edge Mgmt, 10850 Wilshire Blve, #380, Los Angeles CA 90024, USA
**Jardine, Ray** — Mountaineer, Hiker, Cyclist, Rower
Ray-Way Products, PO Box 2153, Arizona City AZ 85123, USA
**Jarecki, Andrew** — Director
Creative Artists Agency, 2000 Ave of Stars, #100, Los Angeles CA 90067 USA
**Jarecki, Nicholas** — Director, Writer
W M E Entertainment, 9601 Wilshire Blvd, #300, Beverly Hills CA 90210 USA

**Jarman, Claude, Jr** — Actor
16 Tamal Vista Lane, Axminster, Kentfield CA 94904, USA
**Jarmusch, Jim** — Director
Cinetic Mgmt, 555 W 25th St, #400, New York NY 10001, USA
**Jarosz, Sarah** — Singer, Songwriter, Musician
D S Artists Mgmt, PO Box 121499, Nashville TN 37212, USA
**Jarre, Jean M A** — Composer
Creme-Creative Mgmt, 8 Rue de Levis, 75017 Paris, France
**Jarreau, Alwyn L (Al)** — Singer
Tsunami Entertainment, 2525 Hyperion Ave, Los Angeles CA 90027, USA
**Jarrell, Jessica** — Singer
Island Def Jam Records, 8920 W Sunset Blvd, #200, West Hollywood CA 90069 USA
**Jarrett, Dale A** — Auto Racing Driver
1510 46th Ave NE, Hickory NC 28601, USA
**Jarrett, Douglas W (Doug)** — Ice Hockey Player
3486 Maisonneuve Ave, Windsor ON N9E 1Y8, Canada
**Jarrett, Gabriel** — Actor
Hervey/Grimes Talent, 10561 Missouri Ave, #2, Los Angeles CA 90025 USA
**Jarrett, Gary W** — Ice Hockey Player
9662 E Peak View Road, Scottsdale AZ 85262, USA
**Jarrett, Keith** — Jazz Pianist, Composer
Stephen Cloud Presentation, PO Box 578, Santa Ynez CA 93460, USA
**Jarrett, Ned M** — Auto Racing Driver
3182 Ninth Tee Dr, Newton NC 28658, USA
**Jarriel, Thomas E (Tom)** — Commentator
ABC-TV, News Dept, 77 W 66th St, New York NY 10023 USA
**Jarrin, Jaime** — Sportscaster
Los Angeles Dodgers, Stadium, 1000 Elysian Park Ave, Los Angeles CA 90090 USA
**Jarrold, Julian** — Director, Producer, Actor
W M E Entertainment, 9601 Wilshire Blvd, #300, Beverly Hills CA 90210 USA
**Jarryd, Anders** — Tennis Player
Maaneskoldsgatan 37, 531 00 Lidkoping, Sweden
**Jaruzelski, Wojciech** — President, Poland; Army General
Biuro Bylego, Al Jerozolimskie 91, 02001 Warsaw, Poland
**Jarvi, Kristjan** — Conductor
I M G Artists, Hogarth Business Park, Chiswick, London W4 2TH, England
**Jarvi, Neeme** — Conductor
Harrison/Parrott, 5-6 Albion Court, London W6 0QT, England
**Jarvi, Paavo** — Conductor
Orchestre de Paris, Salle Pleyel, 252 Rue du Faubourg Saint-Honore, 75008 Paris, France
**Jarvik, Robert K** — Surgeon, Inventor (Artificial Heart)
Jarvick Heart Inc, 333 W 52nd St, New York NY 10019, USA
**Jarvis, Doug** — Ice Hockey Player
Montreal Canadiens, 1275 Saint Antoine St W, Montreal QC H3C 5L2, Canada
**Jarvis, James C (Jim)** — Basketball Player
PO Box 154, Asotin WA 99402, USA
**Jarvis, Katie** — Actress
Artist Rights Group, 4 Great Portland St, London W1W 8PA, England
**Jarvis, Kevin T** — Baseball Player
1613 Whispering Hills Dr, Franklin TN 37069, USA
**Jarvis, L Raeminton (Ray)** — Football Player
19155 Hi View Dr, Brookfield WI 53045, USA
**Jarvis, R Patrick (Pat)** — Baseball Player
4201 Providence Lane, Tucker GA 30084, USA
**Jarvis, Wes** — Ice Hockey Player
National Training Rinks, 1115 Stellar Dr, Newmarket ON L3Y 7B8, Canada
**Jason, David** — Actor, Comedian
Richard Stone Partnership, De Walden Court, 85 New Cavendish St, London W1W 6XD, England
**Jasontek, Rebecca** — Synchronized Swimmer
1201 Retswood Dr, Loveland OH 45140, USA
**Jasper, Edward V (Ed)** — Football Player
113 N Price St, Troup TX 75789, USA
**Jaster, Larry E** — Baseball Player
1105 Mill Creek Dr, Saint Johns FL 32259, USA
**Jastremski, Chester A (Chet)** — Swimmer
5064 W September Dr, Bloomington IN 47404, USA
**Jastrow, Kenneth M, II** — Businessman
Temple-Inland Inc, 303 S Temple Dr, Diboll TX 75941, USA
**Jastrow, Terry L** — Director
13201 Old Oak Lane, Los Angeles CA 90049, USA
**Jata, Paul** — Baseball Player
117 Hidden Ridge Court, Highland Heights KY 41076, USA
**Jaugstetter, Robert** — Rowing Athlete
619 Mandeville St, #3, New Orleans LA 70117, USA
**Jaumotte, Andre** — Mechanical Engineer
33 Ave Jeanne, Bte 17, 1050 Brussels, Belgium
**Jauron, Dick M** — Football Player, Coach
Cleveland Browns, 76 Lou Groza Blvd, Berea OH 44017 USA
**Javan, Ali** — Physicist, Inventor
12 Hawthorne St, Cambridge MA 02138, USA
**Javed Miandad Khan** — Cricketer
Cricket Control Board, Gaddafi Stadium, Lahore, Pakistan
**Javerbaum, David** — Writer
3 Arts Entertainment, 9460 Wilshire Blvd, #700, Beverly Hills CA 90212 USA
**Javier Liranzo, M Julian** — Baseball Player
PO Box 71, San Francisco de Marcoris, Dominican Republic
**Javier, Stanley J A (Stan)** — Baseball Player
5798 Hammock Isles Dr, Naples FL 34119, USA
**Jawara, Dawda K** — President, Gambia
15 Birchen Lane, Haywards Heath, West Sussex RH16 1RY, England
**Jaworski, Marian Cardinal** — Religious Leader
Lviv Archdiocese Curia, Katedralna Square, 79008 Lviv, Ukraine
**Jaworski, Ronald V (Ron)** — Football Player, Sportscaster
18 Brookwood Dr, Medford NJ 08055, USA
**Jax, J Garth** — Football Player
12014 E Lake Circle, Greenwood Village CO 80111, USA

**Jay, Anjali** — Actress
Independent Talent Group, 40 Whitfield St, London W1T 2RH, England
**Jay, Joseph R (Joey)** — Baseball Player
7209 Battenwood Court, Tampa FL 33615, USA
**Jay, Ken** — Drummer (Static-X)
Warner Bros Records, 3300 Warner Blvd, Burbank CA 91505 USA
**Jay, Martin E** — Historian
University of California, History Dept, Berkeley CA 94720, USA
**Jay, Peter** — Government Official, England
Hensington Farmhouse, Woodstock, Oxfordshire OX20 1LH, England
**Jay, Ricky** — Illusionist, Actor
W M E Entertainment, 9601 Wilshire Blvd, #300, Beverly Hills CA 90210 USA
**Jay, Vincent** — Biathlete
Ski Federation, 50 Rue des Marquisats, BP 2451, 74011 Annecy Cedex, France
**Jayner, Travis** — Speed Skater
US Speed Skating, PO Box 18370, Kearns UT 84118, USA
**Jayston, Michael** — Actor
Michael Whitehall, 125 Gloucester Road, London SW7 4TE, England
**Jean, B C** — Singer, Songwriter
Intellectual Artists Mgmt, 10585 Santa Monica Blvd, #135, Los Angeles CA 90025, USA
**Jean, Christiane** — Actress
C D A Studio Di Nardo, Via Cavour 171, 00184 Rome, Italy
**Jean, Kenneth** — Conductor
Columbia Artists Mgmt Inc, 1790 Broadway, #702, New York NY 10019 USA
**Jean, Michaelle** — Governor General, Canada
Governor General's Office, 1 Sussex Dr, Ottawa ON K1A 0A2, Canada
**Jean, Nikki** — Singer, Songwriter
Creative Artists Agency, 2000 Ave of Stars, #100, Los Angeles CA 90067 USA
**Jean, Olivier** — Speed Skater
Speed Skating Canada, 2781 Lancaster Road, #402, Ottawa ON K1B 1A7, Canada
**Jean, Vadim** — Director
United Agents, 12-26 Lexington St, London W1F 0LE, England
**Jean, Wyclef** — Rap Artist, Actor
W M E Entertainment, 1325 Ave of Americas, New York NY 10019, USA
**Jean-Baptiste, Marianne R** — Actress
A P A Talent/Literary Agency, 405 S Beverly Dr, #300, Beverly Hills CA 90212 USA
**Jean-Charles, Livio** — Basketball Player
San Antonio Spurs, Alamodome, 1 AT&T Center Parkway, San Antonio TX 78219 USA
**Jeangerard, Robert E (Bob)** — Basketball Player
1930 Belmont Ave, San Carlos CA 94070, USA
**Jean-Gilles, Max** — Football Player
Philadelphia Eagles, 1 Novacare Way, Philadelphia PA 19145 USA
**Jean-Louis, Jimmy** — Actor
Ken McReddie Assoc, 101 Finsbury Pavement, London EC2A 1RS, England
**Jeanmaire, Zizi** — Ballerina, Actress
Ballets Roland Petit, 20 Blvd Gabes, 13008 Marseille, France
**Jeanrenaud, Joan** — Concert Cellist (Kronos Quartet)
Kronos Quartet, 1235 9th Ave, San Francisco CA 94122, USA
**Jeantot, Philippe** — Yachtsman, Explorer
Jeantot Organization, BP 01, 85100 Les Sables D'Olonne, France
**Jee, Elizabeth** — Actress
Actors Creative Team, Panther House, 38 Mount Pleasant, London WC1X 0AN, England
**Jee, M James** — Astronomer
Johns Hopkins University, Astronomy Dept, Baltimore MD 21218, USA
**Jeelani, Abdul Q** — Basketball Player
W515 State Road 59, Palmyra WI 53156, USA
**Jeetendra** — Actor
26 Gulmohar Cross Road 5, JVPD Scheme, Mumbai MS 400049, India
**Jeezy** — Rap Artist
Def Jam Records, 828 8th Ave, New York NY 10019 USA
**Jeffcoat, Donald L (Donnie)** — Actor
Antrim Street Entertainment, 5225 Wilshire Blvd, #424, Los Angeles CA 90036, USA
**Jeffcoat, J Michael (Mike)** — Baseball Player
4224 Oak Springs Dr, Arlington TX 76016, USA
**Jeffcoat, James W (Jim)** — Football Player
5135 Summit Hill Dr, Dallas TX 75287, USA
**Jefferies, Gregory S (Greg)** — Baseball Player
7806 Bernal Ave, Pleasanton CA 94588, USA
**Jeffers, Eve** — Actress
I C M Partners, 10250 Constellation Blvd, #900, Los Angeles CA 90067 USA
**Jeffers, Patrick C** — Football Player
5810 Buckpasser Cove, Austin TX 78746, USA
**Jefferson, Al** — Basketball Player
Charlotte Bobcats, 333 E Trade St, #A, Charlotte NC 28202 USA
**Jefferson, Herb, Jr** — Actor
California Paralyzed Veterans, 5901 E 7th St, Building 150, Long Beach CA 90822, USA
**Jefferson, James A, III** — Football Player
11220 NE 53rd St, Kirkland WA 98033, USA
**Jefferson, John L** — Football Player
43590 Merchant Mill Terrace, Leesburg VA 20176, USA
**Jefferson, Margo** — Journalist
New York Times, Editorial Dept, 229 W 43rd St, New York NY 10036, USA
**Jefferson, Reginal J (Reggie)** — Baseball Player
1881 Raymond Tucker Road, Tallahassee FL 32311, USA
**Jefferson, Richard A** — Basketball Player
Utah Jazz, Energy Solutions Arena, 301 W South Temple, Salt Lake City UT 84101 USA
**Jefferson, Roy L** — Football Player
8813 Queen Elizabeth Blvd, Annandale VA 22003, USA
**Jefferson, Stanley (Stan)** — Baseball Player
2420 Hunter Ave, #3E, Bronx NY 10475, USA
**Jefferts Schori, Katharine** — Religious Leader
Espicopal Church Center, 815 2nd Ave, New York NY 10017, USA
**Jeffires, Haywood F** — Football Player
2601 Courtyard Lane, Pearland TX 77584, USA
**Jeffre, Justin P** — Singer (98 Degrees)
D A S Communications, 83 Riverside Dr, New York NY 10024, USA

**Jeffrey, Arthur F** — WW II Army Air Corps Hero
7305 Englewood Hill Place, Yakima WA 98908, USA
**Jeffrey, P Michael** — Governor General, Australia
Governor General's Office, Government House, Canberra ACT 2600, Australia
**Jeffrey, Richard C** — Philosopher
55 Patton Ave, Princeton NJ 08540, USA
**Jeffreys, Alec J** — Inventor (Genetic Fingerprinting)
Leicester University, Biochemistry Dept, University Road, Leicester LE1 7RH, England
**Jeffreys, Anne** — Actress
Don Gibble Assoc, 8945 Canby Ave, Northridge CA 91325, USA
**Jeffries, Edward (Dean)** — Custom Car Painter, Stuntman
Jeffries Studio of Style, 3077 Cahuenga Blvd, Los Angeles CA 90028, USA
**Jeffries, Fran** — Singer, Actress, Model
Terry M Hill, 41910 Boardwalk, #A2, Palm Desert CA 92211 USA
**Jeffries, Herbert (Herb)** — Singer, Actor
Terry M Hill, 41910 Boardwalk, #A2, Palm Desert CA 92211 USA
**Jeffries, John T** — Astronomer
1652 E Camino Cielo, Tucson AZ 85718, USA
**Jeffries, Sabrina** — Writer
Pocket Star Books, 1230 Ave of Americas, New York NY 10020, USA
**Jeffries, Tony** — Boxer
Amateur Boxing Assn, National Sports Centre, London SE19 2B8, England
**Jeffs, Christine** — Director, Writer
United Talent Agency, U T A Plaza, 9336 Civic Center Dr, Beverly Hills CA 90210 USA
**Jeinsen, Elke E W** — Model
Playboy Promotions, 2706 Media Center Dr, Los Angeles CA 90065 USA
**Jelen, Ben** — Singer, Musician, Songwriter, Actor
555 W 53rd St, #1252, New York NY 10019, USA
**Jelic, Christopher J (Chris)** — Baseball Player
33 Allegheny Ave, #5, Cuddy PA 15031, USA
**Jelinek, Elfriede** — Nobel Literature Laureate
Jupiterweg 40, 1140 Vienna, Austria
**Jellis, Paul** — Actor
Ken McReddie Assoc, 101 Finsbury Pavement, London EC2A 1RS, England
**Jeltz, L Steven (Steve)** — Baseball Player
608 W 28th Place, Lawrence KS 66046, USA
**Jemison, Eddie** — Actor
Don Buchwald, 6500 Wilshire Blvd, #2200, Los Angeles CA 90048 USA
**Jemison, Mae C** — Astronaut
Dartmouth College, Environmental Studies Dept, Hanover NH 03755, USA
**Jencks, William P** — Biochemist
11 Revere St, Lexington MA 02420, USA
**Jendresen, Erik** — Writer
W M E Entertainment, 9601 Wilshire Blvd, #300, Beverly Hills CA 90210 USA
**Jenes, Theodore G, Jr** — Army General
809 169th Place SW, Lynnwood WA 98037, USA
**Jenkin of Roding, Patrick F** — Government Official, England
703 Howard House, Dolphin Square, London SW1V 3PQ, England
**Jenkin, Warren** — Bassist (Killing Heidi)
Harbour Agency, 135 Forbes St, Woolloomooloo NSW 2011, Australia
**Jenkins, Alfred D** — Football Player
4267 Janice Dr, Atlanta GA 30337, USA
**Jenkins, Carter** — Actor
InMomentum Mgmt, 14622 Ventura Blvd, #778, Sherman Oaks CA 91403, USA
**Jenkins, Charles H, Jr** — Businessman
Publix Super Markets, PO Box 407, Lakeland FL 33802, USA
**Jenkins, Charles L (Charlie)** — Track Athlete, Coach
12826 Forest Creek Court, Sykesville MD 21784, USA
**Jenkins, Cullen D** — Football Player
49124 Peninsular Dr, Belleville MI 48111, USA
**Jenkins, Daniel** — Actor
S M S Talent, 8383 Wilshire Blvd, #230, Beverly Hills CA 90211 USA
**Jenkins, David W** — Figure Skater
5947 S Atlanta Ave, Tulsa OK 74105, USA
**Jenkins, Don J** — Vietnam War Army Hero (CMH)
3783 Bowling Green Road, Morgantown KY 42261, USA
**Jenkins, Eddie J (Ed)** — Football Player
PO Box 190278, Boston MA 02119, USA
**Jenkins, Ferguson A (Fergie), Jr** — Baseball Player
3655 W Anthem Way, #A109, Anthem AZ 85086, USA
**Jenkins, Geoffrey S (Geoff)** — Baseball Player
6683 E Judson Road, Paradise Valley AZ 85253, USA
**Jenkins, George** — Physician
Three Doctors Foundation, 65 Hazelwood Ave, Newark NJ 07106, USA
**Jenkins, Hayes Alan** — Figure Skater
3183 Regency Place, Westlake OH 44145, USA
**Jenkins, Izel, Jr** — Football Player
5106 Masters Lane N, Wilson NC 27896, USA
**Jenkins, Jerry B** — Writer
Tyndale House Publishers, 351 Executive Dr, PO Box 80, Wheaton IL 60187, USA
**Jenkins, John L** — Basketball Player
Atlanta Hawks, Centennial Tower, 101 Marietta St NW, #1900, Atlanta GA 30303 USA
**Jenkins, Katherine** — Singer
247 Worldwide Mgmt, 500 Chiswick High Road, #25, London W4 5RG, England
**Jenkins, Ken** — Actor
Paradigm Agency, 360 N Crescent Dr, North Building, Beverly Hills CA 90210 USA
**Jenkins, Kerry C** — Football Player
5492 Scout Trace Lane, Birmingham AL 35244, USA
**Jenkins, Kristopher R-C (Kris)** — Football Player
9525 Sweetleaf Place, Charlotte NC 28278, USA
**Jenkins, Larry Flash** — Actor
B/W/R, 9100 Wilshire Blvd, #500W, Beverly Hills CA 90212 USA
**Jenkins, Loren** — Journalist
Washington Post, Editorial Dept, 1150 15th St NW, Washington DC 20071, USA
**Jenkins, Michael G** — Football Player
4817 Basingstoke Dr, Suwanee GA 30024, USA

**Jenkins, Mike P** — Football Player
Oakland Raiders, 1220 Harbor Bay Parkway, Alameda CA 94502 USA
**Jenkins, Noam** — Actor
Glick Agency, 1321 7th St, #203, Santa Monica CA 90401 USA
**Jenkins, Patricia L (Patty)** — Director, Writer
Creative Artists Agency, 2000 Ave of Stars, #100, Los Angeles CA 90067 USA
**Jenkins, Richard** — Actor
Gersh Agency, 9465 Wilshire Blvd, #600, Beverly Hills CA 90212 USA
**Jenkins, Robert L** — Football Player
2878 Fieldview Terrace, San Ramon CA 94583, USA
**Jenkins, Sandra** — Curling Athlete
Curling Assn, 1660 Vimont Court, Cumberland ON K4A 4J4, Canada
**Jenkins, Stephan D** — Singer, Guitarist (Third Eye Blind)
Eric Godtland Mgmt, 1040 Mariposa St, #200, San Francisco CA 94107, USA
**Jenkins, Tamara** — Director
Cinetic Mgmt, 555 W 25th St, #400, New York NY 10001 USA
**Jenkins, Thomas (Tomi)** — Singer (Cameo)
Reprise Records, 3300 Warner Blvd, Burbank CA 91505 USA
**Jenks, Downing B** — Businessman
1 McKnight Place, #115, Saint Louis MO 63124, USA
**Jenks, Robert S (Bobby)** — Baseball Player
8383 Wilshire Blvd, #500, Beverly Hills CA 90211, USA
**Jenner, Brody** — Entertainer, Model
I C M Partners, 10250 Constellation Blvd, #900, Los Angeles CA 90067 USA
**Jenner, Bruce** — Track Athlete, Actor
Commercial Talent, 9255 Sunset Blvd, #505, West Hollywood CA 90069, USA
**Jenness, James** — Businessman
Kellogg Co, 1 Kellogg Square, PO Box 3599, Battle Creek MI 49016, USA
**Jennings, Alex** — Actor
Royal National Theater, South Park, London SE1 9PX, England
**Jennings, Brandon** — Basketball Player
Detroit Pistons, Palace, 4 Championship Dr, Auburn Hills MI 48326 USA
**Jennings, Brian L** — Football Player
San Francisco 49ers, 4949 Centennial Blvd, Santa Clara CA 95054 USA
**Jennings, Byron** — Actor
Bauman Redanty Shaul Agency, 5757 Wilshire Blvd, #473, Los Angeles CA 90036 USA
**Jennings, Garth** — Director
Hammer & Tongs, Holborn Studios, 49-50 Eagle Wharf Road, London N1 7ED, England
**Jennings, Gregory (Greg), Jr** — Football Player
4115 Oakharbor St, Kalamazoo MI 49009, USA
**Jennings, J Douglas (Doug)** — Baseball Player
PO Box 812692, Boca Raton FL 33481, USA
**Jennings, Jason R** — Baseball Player
5647 Buena Vista Dr, Frisco TX 75034, USA
**Jennings, Jim** — Architect
Jim Jennings Architect, 49 Rodgers Alley, San Francisco CA 94103, USA
**Jennings, Jonas D** — Football Player
123 Davis Road, Fayetteville GA 30215, USA
**Jennings, Keith O** — Football Player
119 Axtell Dr, Summerville SC 29485, USA
**Jennings, Keith R** — Basketball Player
808 Lakeland Court, Culpeper VA 22701, USA
**Jennings, Paul** — Writer
PO Box 1459, Warrnambool VIC 3280, Australia
**Jennings, Paul C** — Civil Engineer
640 S Grand Ave, Pasadena CA 91105, USA
**Jennings, Robert B** — Pathologist
Duke University Medical Center, Pathology Dept, Durham NC 27710, USA
**Jennings, Stanford J** — Football Player
215 Jasmine Way, Alpharetta GA 30004, USA
**Jennings, Waylon A (Shooter)** — Singer, Songwriter
208 Bibb St, Campbellsville KY 42718, USA
**Jennings, Wilbur (Will)** — Composer, Songwriter
B M I, 8730 W Sunset Blvd, #300, Los Angeles CA 90069 USA
**Jenrette, Richard H** — Businessman
67 E 93rd St, New York NY 10128, USA
**Jens, Salome** — Actress
C E S D, 10635 Santa Monica Blvd, #130, Los Angeles CA 90025 USA
**Jensen, Ashley** — Actress, Comedienne
Hamilton Hodell, 66-68 Margaret St, #500, London W1W 8SR, England
**Jensen, David** — Entertainer
Capital Gold, 30 Leicester Square, London WC2H 7LA, England
**Jensen, Debra** — Model
31441 Santa Margarita Parkway, #322, Rancho Santa Margarita CA 92688, USA
**Jensen, Derrick** — Football Player
147 Downing St, Panama City FL 32413, USA
**Jensen, Eivind Gullberg** — Conductor
Ophelias Public Relations for Culture, Lucile-Grahn-Str 37, 81675 Munich, Germany
**Jensen, Jacob** — Industrial Designer
Bang Olufsen, Peter Bangs Vej 15, PO Box 40, DK 7600 Struer, Denmark
**Jensen, James** — Geologist
Brigham Young University, Geology Dept, Provo UT 84602, USA
**Jensen, James C (Jim)** — Football Player
9811 N Oak Knoll Circle, Davie FL 33324, USA
**Jensen, James D (Jim)** — Football Player
1972 Cayman Dr, Windsor CO 80550, USA
**Jensen, James W, Jr** — Cinematographer
28853 Garnet Hill Court, Agoura Hills CA 91301, USA
**Jensen, Jonathan W (Jon)** — Football Player
36771 Allder School Road, Purcellville VA 20132, USA
**Jensen, Liz** — Writer
Gillon Aitken Assoc, 18-21 Cavaye Place, London SW10 9PT, England
**Jensen, Marcus C** — Baseball Player
19550 N Grayhawk Dr, #1134, Scottsdale AZ 85255, USA
**Jenson, Victoria (Vicky)** — Director, Animator
Creative Artists Agency, 2000 Ave of Stars, #100, Los Angeles CA 90067 USA

J

Jenkins - Jenson

**Jenssen, Amanda** — Singer
Sony Music Sweden, Box 3187, 103 63 Stockholm, Sweden , USA
**Jent, Chris** — Basketball Player
445 Retreat Lane W, Powell OH 43065, USA
**Jentsch, Julia** — Actress
Agentur Vogel, Katzbachstr 8, 10965 Berlin, Germany
**Jeon Da-Hye** — Speed Skater
Skating Union, 88 Bangyee-Dong, Songpaku, Seoul 138 749, South Korea
**Jeong, Ken** — Actor, Comedian
United Talent Agency, U T A Plaza, 9336 Civic Center Dr, Beverly Hills CA 90210 USA
**Jepsen, Carly Rae** — Singer, Songwriter
W M E Entertainment, 9601 Wilshire Blvd, #300, Beverly Hills CA 90210 USA
**Jepsen, Kevin M** — Baseball Player
425 Cannon Green Dr, #H, Goleta CA 93117, USA
**Jepsen, Les** — Basketball Player
8075 9th Street Way N, Saint Paul MN 55128, USA
**Jepsen, Roger W** — Senator, IA
3799 Cadbury Circle, #400, Venice FL 34293, USA
**Jepson, Mary Lou** — Computer Scientist, Social Activist
Massachusetts Institute of Technology, Media Laboratory, Cambridge MA 02139, USA
**Jepson, Mikael** — Guitarist (The Ark)
Live Nation, Linnegatan 89, Box 21451, 104 51 Stockholm, Sweden
**Jeremih** — Singer, Rap Artist, Songwriter
Def Jam Records, 828 8th Ave, New York NY 10019 USA
**Jeremy** — Singer, Guitarist (Chad & Jeremy)
Icon Performing Arts, 1557 Westwood Blvd, #242, Los Angeles CA 90024, USA
**Jerins, Ruby** — Actress
Management 360, 9111 Wilshire Blvd, Beverly Hills CA 90210 USA
**Jerkens, H Allen** — Thoroughbred Racing Trainer
9509 242nd St, Floral Park NY 11001, USA
**Jerkins, Rodney (Darkchild)** — Music Producer
Paradigm Agency, 360 N Crescent Dr, North Building, Beverly Hills CA 90210 USA
**Jernigan, Tamara E (Tammy)** — Astronaut
4268 Brindisi Place, Pleasanton CA 94566, USA
**Jeru the Damaja** — Rap Artist
W M E Entertainment, 1325 Ave of Americas, New York NY 10019 USA
**Jerusalem, Siegfried** — Opera Singer
Sudring 9, 90542 Eckental, Germany
**Jervey, Travis R** — Football Player
22 Sand Dolalr Dr, Isle of Palms SC 29451, USA
**Jerzak, Stephen** — Singer, Songwriter
Agency Group Ltd, 142 W 57th St, #600, New York NY 10019 USA
**Jerzembeck, Michael J (Mike)** — Baseball Player
10625 S Hall Dr, Charlotte NC 28270, USA
**Jeselnik, Anthony** — Actor, Comedian
Mosiac Media Group, 9200 W Sunset Blvd, #1000, Los Angeles CA 90069 USA
**Jessee, Michael A** — Government Official, Financier
Federal Home Loan Bank, 1 Financial Center, #2000, Boston MA 02111, USA
**Jessen, Gene Nora** — Astronaut Candidate
630 S Tiburon Ave, Meridian ID 83642, USA
**Jessie J** — Singer, Songwriter
Crown Music, Matrix Complex, 91 Peterborough Road, London SW6 3BU, England
**Jessup, Bill (Billy0** — Football Player
13341 Saint Andrews Dr, #137D, Seal Beach CA 90740, USA
**Jesus, Juan** — Soccer Player
Confederacion de Futebol, Rua Victor Civita 66, #1, Rio de Janeiro 22775 044, Brazil
**Jet Li** — Actor
Current Entertainment, 9378 Wilshire Blvd, #210, Beverly Hills CA 90212, USA
**Jeter, Derek S** — Baseball Player
845 United Nations Plaza, #888, New York NY 10017, USA
**Jeter, Gary M** — Football Player
3612 Quail Ridge Dr, Plainsboro NJ 8536, USA
**Jeter, John (Johnny)** — Baseball Player
1012 N 5th St, Monroe LA 71201, USA
**Jetsun Pema** — Queen, Bhutan
Royal Palace, Tashichhodzong, Thimphu, Bhutan
**Jett, Brent W, Jr** — Astronaut
2529 Goldsmith St, Houston TX 77030, USA
**Jett, James** — Football Player, Track Athlete
PO Box 430, Kearneysville WV 25430, USA
**Jett, Joan** — Singer, Guitarist, Songwriter
Blackheart Records, 636 Broadway, #1210, New York NY 10012, USA
**Jett, John** — Football Player
177 Crowder Point Dr, Reedville VA 22539, USA
**Jeunet, Jean-Pierre** — Director
I C M Partners, 10250 Constellation Blvd, #900, Los Angeles CA 90067 USA
**Jevanord, Oystein** — Drummer (A-Ha)
Bandana Mgmt, 11 Elvaston Place, #300, London SW7 5QC, England
**Jewel** — Singer, Songwriter, Actress
Front Line Mgmt, 1100 Glendon Ave, #2000, Los Angeles CA 90024 USA
**Jewell, Buddy, Jr** — Singer, Songwriter
Third Coast Talent, PO Box 334, Kingston Springs TN 37082, USA
**Jewison, Norman F** — Director, Producer
Yorktown Productions, 300 W Olympic Blvd, #1314, Santa Monica CA 90401, USA
**Ji Dong-Won** — Soccer Player
Football Assn, 1-131 Sinmunno, 2-Ga Jongno-Gu, Seoul 110 062, South Korea
**Ji Yai-Shin** — Golfer
Ladies Pro Golf Assn, 100 International Golf Dr, Daytona Beach FL 32124 USA
**Ji Young Oh** — Golfer
Ladies Pro Golf Assn, 100 International Golf Dr, Daytona Beach FL 32124 USA
**Jia, Li** — Hematologist
Duke University Medical Center, Hematology Dept, Durham NC 27708, USA
**Jia, Ran** — Concert Pianist
I M G Artists, Hogarth Business Park, Chiswick, London W4 2TH, England
**Jiang Tiefeng** — Artist
Jiang Publishing, 1329 San Carlos Road, Arcadia CA 91006, USA

**Jiear, Alison** — Singer, Actress
United Agents, 12-26 Lexington St, London W1F 0LE, England

**Jiggets, Daniel M (Dan)** — Football Player
4751 RFD, Long Grove IL 60047, USA

**Jiles, Dwayne** — Football Player
3712 Churchill Court, Plano TX 75075, USA

**Jillian, Ann** — Actress
PO Box 57739, Sherman Oaks CA 91413, USA

**Jim Yong Kim** — Physician
Partners in Health, 641 Huntington Ave, #100, Boston MA 02115, USA

**Jimenez Rodriguez, Raul A** — Soccer Player
Federacion de Futbol, Colima 373 Colonia Roma, Delegacion Cuauhtemoc, Mexico City DF 06700, Mexico

**Jimenez, Carlos** — Architect
Jimenez Architectural Design Studio, 1116 Willard St, Houston TX 77006, USA

**Jimenez, Flaco** — Singer/Accordionist (Texas Tornados)
Management Plus, PO Box 132, Sequin TX 78155, USA

**Jimenez, Gladys** — Actress
Stone Manners Salners, 9911 W Pico Blvd, #1400, Los Angeles CA 90035 USA

**Jimenez, Jessica** — Actress
A P A Talent/Literary Agency, 405 S Beverly Dr, #300, Beverly Hills CA 90212 USA

**Jimenez, Miguel Angel** — Golfer
Advantage International, 1025 Thomas Jefferson NW, #450, Washington DC 20007 USA

**Jimenez, Nicario** — Artist
5531 Teak Wood Dr NW, Naples FL 34119, USA

**Jimenez, Penelope** — Model
Playboy Promotions, 2706 Media Center Dr, Los Angeles CA 90065 USA

**Jimenez, Santiago, Jr** — Singer, Accordian Player
Folklore Productions, PO Box 7003, Santa Monica CA 90406, USA

**Jimerson, Charlton** — Baseball Player
22048 Betlen Way, Castro Valley CA 94546, USA

**Jiminez, Joe** — Golfer
29243 Enchanted Glen, Boerne TX 78015, USA

**Jiminez, Miguel A** — Baseball Player
16 Shelley Court, Middletown NY 10941, USA

**Jimmy Jam** — Businessman, Producer, Composer
Universal Attractions, 135 W 26th St, #1200, New York NY 10001 USA

**Jimoh, Ade** — Football Player
41782 Bristow Manor Dr, Ashburn VA 20148, USA

**Jin** — Rap Artist, Actor
Great Co, 1234 Wilshire Blvd, #422, Los Angeles CA 90017, USA

**Jin Sun-Yu** — Speed Skater
Skating Union, 88 Bangyee-Dong, Songpaku, Seoul 138 749, South Korea

**Jing Haipeng** — Taikonaut
Satellite Launch Center, Jiuquan, Guangzhou Province, China

**Jinks, Dan** — Producer
Dan Jinks Co, 4024 Radford Ave, Bungalow 9, Studio City CA 91604, USA

**Jiricna, Eva M** — Architect
Jiricna Architects, 38 Warren St, #300, London W1T 6AE, England

**Jiro Ono** — Chef, Restauranteur
Sukiyabashi Jiro, Tsukamoto Sogyo Building, 2-15-4 Ginza, Chuoku, Tokyo 104 0061, Japan

**Jirov, Vassili** — Boxer
Thell Torrence, 5449 S Eastern Ave, #3, Las Vegas NV 89119, USA

**Jirtle, Randy L** — Geneticist
Duke University Medical Center, Radiation Oncology Dept, Durham NC 27708, USA

**J-Kwon** — Rap Artist
Universal Attractions, 135 W 26th St, #1200, New York NY 10001 USA

**Jo, Sumi** — Opera Singer
Askonas Holt, Lincoln House, 300 High Holborn, London WC1V 7JH, England

**Jo, Timothy W (Tim)** — Actor
Innovative Artists, 1505 10th St, Santa Monica CA 90401 USA

**Joannou, Chris** — Bassist (Silverchair)
John Watson Mgmt, PO Box 281, Sunny Hills NSW 2010, Australia

**Joanou, Phil** — Director
Todd Smith Assoc, 11835 W Olympic Blvd, #640, Los Angeles CA 90064, USA

**Job, Brian G** — Swimmer
PO Box 213, Palo Alto CA 94302, USA

**Jobe, Emmett** — Auto Racing Executive
Phoenix International Raceway, 125 S Avondale Blvd, #200, Avondale AZ 85323, USA

**Jobe, Frank W** — Sports Orthopedic Surgeon
Kerlan-Jobe Orthopedic Clinic, 501 E Hardy St, #200, Inglewood CA 90301, USA

**Jobert, Marlene** — Actress
8-10 Blvd de Courcelles, 75008 Paris, France

**Jobrani, Maz** — Actor
Levity Entertainment, 6701 Center Drive W, #1111, Los Angeles CA 90045 USA

**Jobson, Richard** — Director, Producer, Writer
Curtis Brown Group, 28-29 Haymarket St, #500, London SW1Y 4SP, England

**Jodat, James S (Jim)** — Football Player
25032 Mammoth Circle, Lake Forest CA 92630, USA

**Jodie, Brett** — Baseball Player
1359 Corley Mill Road, Lexington SC 29072, USA

**Jodorowsky, Alejandro** — Director, Producer, Composer
Agence Josiane Stroh, 3 Allee Marie Laurent, 75020 Paris, France

**Jodzio, Rick** — Ice Hockey Player
23731 Perth Bay, Dana Point CA 92629, USA

**Joe** — Singer, Songwriter, Record Producer
Kedar Entertainment, 21 W 39th St, #600, New York NY 10018, USA

**Joe, Leon M** — Football Player
7917 Woodyard Road, Clinton MD 20735, USA

**Joe, William (Billy)** — Football Player, Coach
3964 Butler Springs Way, Birmingham AL 35226, USA

**Joel, Billy** — Singer, Songwriter
Maritime Inc, 34 Audrey Ave, #4, Oyster Bay NY 11771, USA

**Joel, Richard M** — Educator
Yeshiva University, President's Office, 500 W 185th St, New York NY 10033, USA

**Joerger, David (Dave)** — Basketball Coach
Memphis Grizzlies, 191 Beale St, Memphis TN 38103 USA

**J**

**Joerres, Jeffrey** — Businessman
Manpower Inc, 600 A B Data Dr, Milwaukee WI 53217, USA
**Joey Z** — Guitarist (Life of Agony, Stereomud)
Agency Group Ltd, 142 W 57th St, #600, New York NY 10019 USA
**Joffe, Roland V** — Director, Producer
Baumgartan Mgmt, 406 Wilshire Blvd, Santa Monica CA 90401, USA
**Joffin, Jon** — Cinematographer
Dattner Dispoto, 10635 Santa Monica Blvd, #165, Los Angeles CA 90025, USA
**Jofre, Eder** — Boxer
Alamo de Ministero Rocha, Azevedo 373, C Cesar 21-15, Sao Paulo, Brazil
**Jogia, Avan** — Actor
United Talent Agency, U T A Plaza, 9336 Civic Center Dr, Beverly Hills CA 90210 USA
**Johannesen, Lena** — Body Builder, Model
PO Box 325, Culver City CA 90232, USA
**Johannsen, Jake** — Actor
Paradigm Agency, 360 N Crescent Dr, North Building, Beverly Hills CA 90210 USA
**Jóhannsson, Jóhann** — Composer
Agency Group Ltd, 142 W 57th St, #600, New York NY 10019 USA
**Johannsson, Kristjan** — Opera Singer
Herbert Breslin, 119 W 57th St, #1505, New York NY 10019 USA
**Johansen, Iris** — Writer
Jane Rotrosen Agency, 318 E 51st St, New York NY 10022, USA
**Johansen, Roy** — Writer
Saint Martin's Press, 175 5th Ave, #400, New York NY 10010 USA
**Johanson, Chris** — Artist
Jack Hanley Gallery, 327 Broome St, New York NY 10002, USA
**Johanson, Donald C** — Anthropologist
Arizona State University, Human Origins Institute, Tempe AZ 85287, USA
**Johanson, Jai Johnny (Jaimoe)** — Drummer (Allman Brothers Band)
Allman Brothers Band Inc, 18 Tamworth Road, Waban MA 02468, USA
**Johanson, Sue** — Educator, Writer, Commentator
Sunday Night Sex Show, 42 Pardee Ave, Toronto ON M6K 3H5, Canada
**Johansson, Calle** — Ice Hockey Player
1708 Mayfair Place, Crofton MD 21114, USA
**Johansson, Kathy** — Model, Body Builder
PO Box 43351, Tucson AZ 85733, USA
**Johansson, Lars-Olof** — Guitarist, Keyboardist (Cardigans)
Talent Trust, Kungsgatan 9C, 411 19 Gothenburg, Sweden
**Johansson, Paul** — Actor
Innovative Artists, 1505 10th St, Santa Monica CA 90401 USA
**Johansson, Per-Ulik** — Golfer
18710 SE Pineneedle Lane, Jupiter FL 33469, USA
**Johansson, Scarlett** — Actress, Model, Singer
Creative Artists Agency, 2000 Ave of Stars, #100, Los Angeles CA 90067 USA
**Johansson, Stefan** — Auto Racing Driver
3546 Crownridge Dr, Sherman Oaks CA 91403, USA
**Johaug, Therese** — Cross Country Skier
Nansen I L Ski, Toini Berg Brynhildsvoll, Dalsbygda, 2550 Os I Osterdalen, Norway
**Johjima, Kenji** — Baseball Player
2412 109th Ave SE, Bellevue WA 98004, USA
**John, Chris** — Boxer
Harry's Gym, 14 Cressall Road, Balcatta, Perth WA 6021, Australia
**John, David D** — Museum Executive, Explorer
7 Cyncoed Ave, Cardiff CF2 6ST, Wales
**John, Elton** — Singer, Songwriter
Rogers & Cowan, 8687 Melrose Ave, #G700, West Hollywood CA 90069 USA
**John, Thomas E (Tommy)** — Baseball Player
6202 Seton House Lane, Charlotte NC 28277, USA
**John, Tylyn** — Model, Actress
813 Harbor Blvd, #133, West Sacramento CA 95691, USA
**Johnagin, Tommy** — Actor, Comedian
Avalon Mgmt, 4a Exmoor St, London W10 6BD, England
**Johncock, Gordon** — Auto Racing Driver
649 S Fall River Dr, Coldwater MI 49036, USA
**John-Jules, Danny** — Actor
Jonathan Altaras Assoc, 11 Garrick St, London WC2E 9AR, England
**Johnny A** — Guitarist, Songwriter
Ralph Jaccodine Mgmt, PO Box 381982, Cambridge MA 02238, USA
**Johnny O** — Singer
Universal Attractions, 135 W 26th St, #1200, New York NY 10001 USA
**Johnova, Andriena** — Artist
Nad Kralovskou Oborou 278/15, 17000 Prague 7, Czech Republic
**John-Roger** — Religious Leader
Movement of Spiritual InnerAwareness, PO Box 513935, Los Angeles CA 90051, USA
**Johns, Chris** — Editor
National Geographic, Editorial Dept, 1145 17th St NW, Washington DC 20036 USA
**Johns, Daniel** — Singer, Guitarist (Silverchair)
John Watson Mgmt, PO Box 281, Sunny Hills NSW 2010, Australia
**Johns, Douglas A (Doug)** — Baseball Player
1131 SW 72nd Ave, Plantation FL 33317, USA
**Johns, Glynis** — Actress
2051 N Highland Ave, Los Angeles CA 90068, USA
**Johns, Jasper** — Artist
97 Low Road, #642, Sharon CT 06069, USA
**Johns, Lori** — Drag Racing Driver
PO Box 3667, Corpus Christi TX 78463, USA
**Johns, R Keith** — Baseball Player
1525 Suzanne Ridge Court, Glencoe MO 63038, USA
**Johns, Raymond E, Jr** — Air Force General
Commander, Air Mobility Command, Scott Air Force Base IL 62225 USA
**Johns, Simon** — Bassist (Stereolab)
Duophonic Records, PO Box 3787, London SE22 9DZ, England
**Johnson Pucci, Gail** — Synchronized Swimmer
2132 Ward Dr, Walnut Creek CA 94596, USA
**Johnson, Aaron** — Actor
Hamilton Hodell, 66-68 Margaret St, #500, London W1W 8SR, England

**Johnson, Aaron** — Ice Hockey Player
3810 Gabrielle Dr, Dublin OH 43016, USA
**Johnson, Adam** — Writer
Stanford University, English Dept, Stanford CA 94305, USA
**Johnson, Addison** — Cartoonist (Bringing Up Father)
King Features Syndicate, 300 W 57th St, #1500, New York NY 10019 USA
**Johnson, Alexander (Alex)** — Baseball Player
18425 Bretton Dr, Detroit MI 48223, USA
**Johnson, Alexzander S (Alexz)** — Actress
W M E Entertainment, 9601 Wilshire Blvd, #300, Beverly Hills CA 90210 USA
**Johnson, Allen** — Track Athlete
Octagon Worldwide, 800 Connecticut Ave, #200, Norwalk CT 06854 USA
**Johnson, Amy Jo** — Actress, Singer, Songwriter
Burstein Co, 15304 Sunset Blvd, #208, Pacific Palisades CA 90272, USA
**Johnson, Anderson J (Andy)** — Football Player
PO Box 6828, Athens GA 30604, USA
**Johnson, Andre L** — Football Player
Houston Texans, 2 Reliant Park, Houston TX 77054 USA
**Johnson, Andreas** — Singer, Songwriter
International Talent Booking, Ariel House, 74A Charlotte St, #100 London W1T 4QJ, England
**Johnson, Anne-Marie** — Actress
Diverse Talent Group, 9911 Pico Blvd, #350W, Los Angeles CA 90035 USA
**Johnson, Anthony C (Tony)** — Baseball Player
4446 Janssen Dr, Memphis TN 38128, USA
**Johnson, Anthony M** — Basketball Player
5162 Inwood Place, Mableton GA 30126, USA
**Johnson, Anthony S** — Football Player
752 Peppervine Ave, Saint Johns FL 32259, USA
**Johnson, Arte** — Actor, Comedian
2725 Bottlebrush Dr, Los Angeles CA 90077, USA
**Johnson, Arthur** — Hero
5735 E Waltann Lane, Scottsdale AZ 85254, USA
**Johnson, Ashley** — Actress
Anonymous Content, 3532 Hayden Ave, Culver City CA 90232 USA
**Johnson, Avery** — Basketball Player, Coach
Legacy Agency, 230 Park Ave, #851, New York NY 10169 USA
**Johnson, Bart** — Actor
B/W/R, 9100 Wilshire Blvd, #500W, Beverly Hills CA 90212 USA
**Johnson, Ben** — Artist
4 Saint Peter's Wharf, Hammersmith Terrace, London W6 9UD, England
**Johnson, Benjamin F (Ben)** — Baseball Player
112 Locksley Dr, Greenwood SC 29649, USA
**Johnson, Benjamin S (Ben), Jr** — Track Athlete
Ed Futerman, 2 Saint Clair Ave E, #1500, Toronto ON M4T 2R1, Canada
**Johnson, Bernie** — Ice Hockey Player
15 Carriage Way, Scarborough ME 04074, USA
**Johnson, Betsey L** — Fashion Designer
Betsey Johnson Co, 498 Fashion Ave, #2103, New York NY 10018, USA
**Johnson, Beverly** — Model, Actress
PO Box 1474, Rancho Mirage CA 92270, USA
**Johnson, Bjorn** — Actor, Director
Talent Works, 3500 W Olive Ave, #1400, Burbank CA 91505 USA
**Johnson, Bob** — Monster Truck Executive
Bigfoot 4X4, 6311 N Lindbergh Blvd, Hazelwood MO 63042, USA
**Johnson, Brad** — Model, Actor
Metropolitan Talent Agency, 5405 Wilshire Blvd, #218, Los Angeles CA 90036 USA
**Johnson, Brandon H** — Football Player
1541 W Coquina Dr, Gilbert AZ 85233, USA
**Johnson, Brent** — Ice Hockey Player
808 N Florida St, Arlington VA 22205, USA
**Johnson, Brian** — Singer (AC/DC)
Alberts Music, 9 Rangers Road, Neutral Bay, Sydney NSW 2089, Australia
**Johnson, Brian D** — Baseball Player
1405 Balmoral Dr, Detroit MI 48203, USA
**Johnson, Bryant A** — Football Player
5749 Legends Club Circle, Braselton GA 30517, USA
**Johnson, Bryce** — Actor
Untitled Entertainment, 350 S Beverly Dr, #200, Beverly Hills CA 90212 USA
**Johnson, Buck** — Basketball Player
701 Pine Grove Road, Harvest AL 35749, USA
**Johnson, C Barth (Bart)** — Baseball Player
1929 N Newland Ave, Chicago IL 60707, USA
**Johnson, C Stephen (Steve)** — Basketball Player
9715 SW Quail Post Road, Portland OR 97219, USA
**Johnson, Calvin, Jr** — Football Player
185 Roscommon Court, Tyrone GA 30290, USA
**Johnson, Carolyn Dawn** — Singer, Songwriter
Paquin Entertainment, 468 Stradbrook Ave, Winnipeg MB R3L 0J9, Canada
**Johnson, Chad J J** — Football Player
Miami Dolphins, 7500 SW 30th St, Davie FL 33314 USA
**Johnson, Charles** — Football Player
Carolina Panthers, Ericsson Stadium, 800 S Mint St, Charlotte NC 28202 USA
**Johnson, Charles E** — Baseball Player
12301 NW 7th St, Plantation FL 33325, USA
**Johnson, Charles E** — Football Player
6549 Wakefalls Dr, Wake Forest NC 27587, USA
**Johnson, Charles L (Charley)** — Football Player
PO Box 1312, Mesilla NM 88046, USA
**Johnson, Charles R** — Writer
University of Washington, English Dept, Seattle WA 98105, USA
**Johnson, Cheryl L** — Labor Leader
United American Nurses, 8515 Georgia Ave, Silver Spring MD 20910, USA
**Johnson, Chris J** — Actor
A P A Talent/Literary Agency, 405 S Beverly Dr, #300, Beverly Hills CA 90212 USA
**Johnson, Christa** — Golfer
6210 W Sunset Road, Tucson AZ 85743, USA

**Johnson, Clark** — Actor, Director
United Talent Agency, U T A Plaza, 9336 Civic Center Dr, Beverly Hills CA 90210 USA
**Johnson, Clemon** — Basketball Player
835 N Waukeenah St, Monticello FL 32344, USA
**Johnson, Clifford (Cliff)** — Baseball Player
9618 Mediator Pass, Converse TX 78109, USA
**Johnson, Corey** — Actor
Another Tongue, 10-11 D'Arblay St, London W1F 8DS, England
**Johnson, Cornelius O** — Football Player
603 Dale St, Highland Springs VA 23075, USA
**Johnson, Courtney** — Water Polo Player
408 Tharp Dr, Moraga CA 94556, USA
**Johnson, Craig** — Ice Hockey Player
812 Island Dr, #A, Alameda CA 94502, USA
**Johnson, Craig A** — Writer
Penguin Books, 375 Hudson St, Basement 1, New York NY 10014 USA
**Johnson, Curtis W** — Football Player
PO Box 70608, Toledo OH 43607, USA
**Johnson, Curtis, Jr** — Football Coach
Tulane University, Athletic Dept, New Orleans LA 70118, USA
**Johnson, Daniel R (Dan)** — Baseball Player
3355 134th Ave NE, Andover MN 55304, USA
**Johnson, Darren** — Chemist
University of Oregon, Chemistry Dept, Eugene OR 97403, USA
**Johnson, Darrius D** — Football Player
402 Thomas St, Terrell TX 75160, USA
**Johnson, Dave** — Labor Leader
United Garment Workers, 4207 Lebanon Road, Hermitage TN 37076, USA
**Johnson, David A (Davey)** — Baseball Player, Manager
1064 Howell Branch Road, Winter Park FL 32789, USA
**Johnson, David Allen (D J)** — Football Player
500 Tripoli St, Pittsburgh PA 15212, USA
**Johnson, David C (Dave)** — Baseball Player
3202 Woodhollow Circle, Abilene TX 79606, USA
**Johnson, David Cay** — Journalist
New York Times, Editorial Dept, 229 W 43rd St, New York NY 10036 USA
**Johnson, David G** — Economist
5500 S Shore Dr, #1406, Chicago IL 60637, USA
**Johnson, David W** — Businessman
Campbell Soup Co, 1 Campbell Place, Camden NJ 08103, USA
**Johnson, David W (Dave)** — Baseball Player
7101 Mount Vista Road, Kingsville MD 21087, USA
**Johnson, Demetrios** — Football Player
840 Garonne Dr, Ballwin MO 63021, USA
**Johnson, DerMarr M** — Basketball Player
14610 Man O War Dr, Bowie MD 20721, USA
**Johnson, Derrick O** — Football Player
524 Private Road 4450, Uvalde TX 78801, USA
**Johnson, Diane** — Writer
Creative Artists Agency, 2000 Ave of Stars, #100, Los Angeles CA 90067 USA
**Johnson, Don** — Actor
Don Johnson Productions, 9663 Santa Monica Blvd, #278, Beverly Hills CA 90210, USA
**Johnson, Donald (Groundhog)** — Baseball Player
3935 King Place, Cincinnati OH 45223, USA
**Johnson, Donald R (Don)** — Baseball Player
1529 NE 21st Ave, #205, Portland OR 97232, USA
**Johnson, Dwayne D (The Rock)** — Actor, Professional Wrestler
White Buffalo Entertainment, One State Street Plaza, #2400, New York NY 10004, USA
**Johnson, Dwight O** — Football Player
1812 King Cole Dr, Waco TX 76705, USA
**Johnson, Earvin (Magic), Jr** — Basketball Player, Coach
Magic Johnson Foundation, 9100 Wilshire Blvd, #700E, Beverly Hills CA 90212, USA
**Johnson, Echo L** — Model
2402 Jarratt Ave, #B, Austin TX 78703, USA
**Johnson, Edward (Eddie)** — Soccer Player
Seattle Sounders, 12 Seahawks Way, Renton WA 98056 USA
**Johnson, Edward A (Eddie)** — Basketball Player
6133 N 61st Place, Paradise Valley AZ 85253, USA
**Johnson, Edward L (Eddie), Jr** — Basketball Player
PO Box 542, Weirsdale FL 32195, USA
**Johnson, Edward S (Tre), III** — Football Player
680 Harrison Ave, Peekskill NY 10566, USA
**Johnson, Emma** — Concert Clarinetist
Columbia Artists Mgmt Inc, 1790 Broadway, #702, New York NY 10019 USA
**Johnson, Eric** — Golfer
893 Chateau Meadows Dr, Eugene OR 97401, USA
**Johnson, Eric** — Writer
Verve Talent/Literary Agency, 9696 Culver Blvd, #301, Culver City CA 90232 USA
**Johnson, Eric** — Actor
A P A Talent/Literary Agency, 405 S Beverly Dr, #300, Beverly Hills CA 90212 USA
**Johnson, Eric** — Guitarist
Joe Priesnitz Artist Mgmt, PO Box 5249, Austin TX 78763, USA
**Johnson, Erik** — Ice Hockey Player
Colorado Avalanche, Pepsi Center, 1000 Chopper Circle, Denver CO 80204 USA
**Johnson, Ernest T (Ernie), Jr** — Sportscaster
TNT-TV, Sports Dept, 1050 Techwood Dr, Atlanta GA 30318 USA
**Johnson, Ervin** — Basketball Player
Minnesota Timberwolves, Target Center, 600 1st Ave N, Minneapolis MN 55403 USA
**Johnson, Essex L** — Football Player
1633 E Dimondale Dr, Carson CA 90746, USA
**Johnson, Ezra R** — Football Player
330 Millhaven Landing, Fayetteville GA 30215, USA
**Johnson, Frank** — Cartoonist (Bringing Up Father)
King Features Syndicate, 300 W 57th St, #1500, New York NY 10019 USA
**Johnson, Frank A** — Baseball Player
1151 Cypress Hill Lane, Stockton CA 95206, USA

| | |
|---|---|
| **Johnson, Franklin L (Frank)** | Basketball Player, Coach |
| 4320 N 40th St, Phoenix AZ 85018, USA | |
| **Johnson, Fred** | Singer (Marcels) |
| 5501 Camelia St, Pittsburgh PA 15201, USA | |
| **Johnson, Gary** | Baseball Player |
| 50 Tallwood Court, Atherton CA 94027, USA | |
| **Johnson, Gene** | Guitarist, Mandolin Player (Diamond Rio) |
| Modern Mgmt, 1625 Broadway, #600, Nashville TN 37203, USA | |
| **Johnson, Georgann** | Actress |
| 218 Glenroy Place, Los Angeles CA 90049, USA | |
| **Johnson, George** | Singer, Guitarist (Brothers Johnson) |
| Green Light Talent Agency, PO Box 3172, Beverly Hills CA 90212 USA | |
| **Johnson, George** | Golfer |
| 2860 Brookford Lane SW, Atlanta GA 30331, USA | |
| **Johnson, George T** | Basketball Player |
| 630 Highland Overlook, Atlanta GA 30349, USA | |
| **Johnson, George W** | Educator |
| George Mason University, President's Office, Fairfax VA 22030, USA | |
| **Johnson, Glen** | Boxer |
| DiBella Entertainment, 350 7th Ave, #800, New York NY 10001, USA | |
| **Johnson, Gregory C** | Astronaut |
| N A S A, Johnson Space Center, 2101 NASA Road, Houston TX 77058 USA | |
| **Johnson, Gregory C (Greg)** | Ice Hockey Player |
| 1058 Runyon Road, Rochester Hills MI 48306, USA | |
| **Johnson, Gregory H** | Astronaut |
| N A S A, Johnson Space Center, 2101 NASA Road, Houston TX 77058 USA | |
| **Johnson, Hansford T** | Air Force General |
| U S A A Capital Corp, 9800 Fredericksburg Road, San Antonio TX 78240, USA | |
| **Johnson, Harold** | Boxer |
| 2964 N Bambrey St, Philadelphia PA 19132, USA | |
| **Johnson, Holly** | Singer (Frankie Goes to Hollywood) |
| Wolfgang Kuhle Artist Mgmt, PO Box 425, London SW6 3TX, England | |
| **Johnson, Howard M (Hojo)** | Baseball Player |
| 8597 SE Coconut St, Hobe Sound FL 33455, USA | |
| **Johnson, Hugh T** | Director, Cinematographer |
| Mirisch Agency, 8840 Wilshire Blvd, #100, Beverly Hills CA 90211 USA | |
| **Johnson, Ian** | Journalist |
| Wall Street Journal, Editorial Dept, 1 World Financial Center, New York NY 10281, USA | |
| **Johnson, J Bradley (Brad)** | Football Player |
| 1911 Nellie Gray Court, Athens GA 30606, USA | |
| **Johnson, J Curley** | Football Player |
| 5512 Wedgefield Road, Granbury TX 76049, USA | |
| **Johnson, J Seward, II** | Sculptor |
| Grounds for Sculpture, 18 Fairgrounds Road, Hamilton NJ 08619, USA | |
| **Johnson, Jack** | Singer, Guitarist, Songwriter |
| Universal Republic Records, 1755 Broadway, #800, New York NY 10019 USA | |
| **Johnson, James A** | Government Official, Financier |
| Perseus LLC, 1325 Ave of Americas, #2500, New York NY 10019, USA | |
| **Johnson, James E (Jimmy)** | Football Player |
| 656 Amaranth Blvd, Mill Valley CA 94941, USA | |
| **Johnson, James W (Jimmy)** | Football Coach, Sportscaster |
| Fox-TV, Sports Dept, 205 W 67th St, New York NY 10065 USA | |
| **Johnson, Jamey** | Singer, Songwriter |
| Vector Mgmt, PO Box 120479, Nashville TN 37212 USA | |
| **Johnson, Jarret W** | Football Player |
| 437 Evans Road, Niceville FL 32578, USA | |
| **Johnson, Jason M** | Baseball Player |
| 18122 Emerald Bay St, Tampa FL 33647, USA | |
| **Johnson, Jay** | Actor, Comedian, Ventriloquist |
| Comedians USA, 1308 Sumac Drive, Knoxville TN 37919, USA | |
| **Johnson, Jay Kenneth** | Actor |
| A P A Talent/Literary Agency, 405 S Beverly Dr, #300, Beverly Hills CA 90212 USA | |
| **Johnson, Jay L** | Navy Admiral, Businessman |
| General Dynamics, 2941 Fairview Park Dr, #100, Falls Church VA 22042, USA | |
| **Johnson, Jenna** | Swimmer, Coach |
| University of Tennessee, Athletic Dept, PO Box 15016, Knoxville TN 37901, USA | |
| **Johnson, Jennifer** | Producer, Writer |
| W M E Entertainment, 9601 Wilshire Blvd, #300, Beverly Hills CA 90210 USA | |
| **Johnson, Jerome L** | Navy Admiral |
| Navy-Marine Corps Relief Society, 801 N Randolph St, Arlington VA 22203, USA | |
| **Johnson, Jerry M** | Baseball Player |
| 16670 Espola Road, Poway CA 92064, USA | |
| **Johnson, Jesse** | Football Player |
| 102 Rosegill Road, Richmond VA 23236, USA | |
| **Johnson, Jimmie K** | Auto Racing Driver |
| PO Box 4283, Mooresville NC 28117, USA | |
| **Johnson, Jimmy** | Cartoonist (Arlo & Janis) |
| United Media Syndicate, PO Box 5610, Cincinnati OH 45201 USA | |
| **Johnson, Joe M** | Basketball Player |
| 2365 Rugby Lane, Atlanta GA 30337, USA | |
| **Johnson, Johari** | Actress |
| H W A Talent, 3500 W Olive Ave, #1400, Burbank CA 91505 USA | |
| **Johnson, John H** | Basketball Player |
| 4751 N 18th St, Milwaukee WI 53209, USA | |
| **Johnson, John Henry** | Baseball Player |
| 3345 Delna, Sparks NV 89431, USA | |
| **Johnson, John J L (Jack), III** | Ice Hockey Player |
| Los Angeles Kings, Staples Center, 1111 S Figueroa St, Los Angeles CA 90015 USA | |
| **Johnson, Johnnie, Jr** | Football Player |
| 3540 W Sahara Ave, #780, Las Vegas NV 89102, USA | |
| **Johnson, Joseph E, III** | Physician |
| 187 Sea Hammock Way, Ponte Vedra Beach FL 32082, USA | |
| **Johnson, Joshua M (Josh)** | Baseball Player |
| 10855 S 94th East Place, Tulsa OK 74133, USA | |
| **Johnson, K Lance** | Baseball Player |
| 5712 Foxfire Road, Mobile AL 36618, USA | |

**Johnson, Kate Lang** — Actress
Innovative Artists, 1505 10th St, Santa Monica CA 90401 USA
**Johnson, Kathy** — Gymnast
2102 Clubside D, Longwood FL 32779, USA
**Johnson, Keith** — Labor Leader
Woodworkers of America Union, 1622 N Lombard St, Portland OR 97217, USA
**Johnson, Kenneth A (Kenny)** — Actor
Paradigm Agency, 360 N Crescent Dr, North Building, Beverly Hills CA 90210 USA
**Johnson, Kenneth H (Ken)** — Basketball Player
1401 N Wheeler Ave, Portland OR 97227, USA
**Johnson, Kenneth T (Ken)** — Baseball Player
121 Myrtlewood Dr, Pineville LA 71360, USA
**Johnson, Kevin M** — Basketball Player, Sportscaster, Mayor
Mayor's Office, City Hall, 915 I St, #500, Sacramento CA 95814, USA
**Johnson, Keyshawn** — Football Player, Sportscaster
19232 Northfleet Way, Tarzana CA 91356, USA
**Johnson, Kylie** — Model
Playboy Promotions, 2706 Media Center Dr, Los Angeles CA 90065 USA
**Johnson, Kym** — Dancer, Model
Rothman Patino Andres Entertainment, 4370 Tujunga Ave, #120, Studio City CA 91604, USA
**Johnson, Lamar** — Baseball Player
4105 Sangre Trail, Arlington TX 76016, USA
**Johnson, Landon T** — Football Player
7556 Fox Chase Dr, West Chester OH 45069, USA
**Johnson, Larry A, Jr** — Football Player
340 Glengarry Lane, State College PA 16801, USA
**Johnson, Larry D** — Basketball Player
Larry Johnson's R W A C, 15303 Dallas Parkway, #970, Addison TX 75001, USA
**Johnson, Laura** — Actress
Geddes Agency, 8430 Santa Monica Blvd, #201, West Hollywood CA 90069 USA
**Johnson, Laurie** — Composer
Priority House, Camp Hill, Stanmore, Middlesex HA7 3JQ, England
**Johnson, LeShon E** — Football Player
15102 Beverly St, Overland Park KS 66223, USA
**Johnson, Levi** — Football Player
1202 Craig Dr, Westland MI 48186, USA
**Johnson, Linda** — Poker Player
Poker Gives, PO Box 434, Conyers NY 10920, USA
**Johnson, Lonnie D** — Football Player
8500 Amber Ridge Court, Sanford FL 32771, USA
**Johnson, Louis** — Singer, Bassist (Brothers Johnson)
Green Light Talent Agency, PO Box 3172, Beverly Hills CA 90212 USA
**Johnson, Louis B (Lou)** — Baseball Player
4532 Valley Ridge Ave, Los Angeles CA 90008, USA
**Johnson, Lynn-Holly** — Actress
2109 S Wilbur Ave, Walla Walla WA 99362, USA
**Johnson, Manuel H, Jr** — Government Official, Economist
Johnson Smick Int'l, 2099 Pennsylvania Ave NW, #950, Washington DC 20006, USA
**Johnson, Marc** — Jazz Bassist, Composer
Word of Mouth Music, 235 E 22nd St, #9F, New York NY 10010, USA
**Johnson, Marcia Thornton** — Writer
Scholastic Press, 555 Broadway, New York NY 10012 USA
**Johnson, Mark** — Producer
Gran Via Productions, 1888 Century Park E, #1400, Los Angeles CA 90067, USA
**Johnson, Mark** — Journalist
Milwaukee Journal Sentinel, Editorial Dept, PO Box 371, Milwaukee WI 53201 USA
**Johnson, Mark** — Boxer
1204 Howison Place SW, Washington DC 20081, USA
**Johnson, Mark E** — Ice Hockey Player
1609 Hidden Hill Dr, Verona WI 53593, USA
**Johnson, Mark P** — Baseball Player
40 Helen Ave, Rye NY 10580, USA
**Johnson, Mark Steven** — Director, Writer
Creative Artists Agency, 2000 Ave of Stars, #100, Los Angeles CA 90067 USA
**Johnson, Marques K** — Basketball Player
5133 Dawn View Place, Los Angeles CA 90043, USA
**Johnson, Marvin** — Boxer
5452 Turfway Circle, Indianapolis IN 46228, USA
**Johnson, Marvin M** — Chemical Engineer
3055 SE Bison Road, Bartlesville OK 74006, USA
**Johnson, Matt** — Singer, Guitarist (The The); Songwriter
Free Trade Agency, Chapel Place, Rivington St, London EC2A 3DQ, England
**Johnson, Michael** — Singer, Guitarist, Songwriter
A R T R A-Artists Mgmt, 130 S Canal St, #211, Chicago IL 60606, USA
**Johnson, Michael D** — Track Athlete
Baylor University, Athletic Dept, 150 Bear Run, Waco TX 76711, USA
**Johnson, Michael K (Mike)** — Baseball Player
446 23rd Place, Manhattan Beach CA 90266, USA
**Johnson, Michael M (Butch)** — Football Player
9719 S Red Oakes Dr, Littleton CO 80126, USA
**Johnson, Michelle** — Actress, Model
Angel City Talent, 4741 Laurel Canyon Blvd, Valley Village CA 91607, USA
**Johnson, Mike** — Animator, Director
Paradigm Agency, 360 N Crescent Dr, North Building, Beverly Hills CA 90210 USA
**Johnson, Monte C** — Football Player
2349 Hurst Dr NE, Atlanta GA 30305, USA
**Johnson, N James (Jim)** — Ice Hockey Player
Interactive Coaching, 34522 N Scottsdale Road, #D8, Scottsdale AZ 85266, USA
**Johnson, Neil A** — Basketball Player
821 Plymouth Lane, Virginia Beach VA 23451, USA
**Johnson, Nicholas R (Nick)** — Baseball Player
8008 Sacramento St, Fair Oaks CA 95628, USA
**Johnson, Nicole Randall** — Actress
Greene Assoc, 1901 Ave of Stars, #130, Los Angeles CA 90067 USA
**Johnson, Norman D (Norm)** — Football Player
8523 NW Anderson Hill Road, Silverdale WA 98383, USA

| | |
|---|---|
| **Johnson, Ollie**<br>1700 Spring Garden St, Philadelphia PA 19130, USA | Basketball Player |
| **Johnson, Ora J**<br>General Baptists Ministries, 100 Stinson Dr, Poplar Bluff MO 63901, USA | Religious Leader |
| **Johnson, Paatricia M (Trish)**<br>Encompass, 121 Hook Road, Epsom, Surrey KT19 8TU, England | Golfer |
| **Johnson, Patricia (Tish)**<br>Professional Bowlers Assn, 719 2nd Ave, #701, Seattle WA 98104 USA | Bowler |
| **Johnson, Patrick**<br>A P A Talent/Literary Agency, 405 S Beverly Dr, #300, Beverly Hills CA 90212 USA | Actor |
| **Johnson, Paul**<br>Georgia Institute of Technology, Athletic Dept, Atlanta GA 30332, USA | Football Coach |
| **Johnson, Paul B**<br>29 Newton Road, London W2 5JR, England | Historian |
| **Johnson, Paul H**<br>1719 Yale Ave, Burley ID 83318, USA | Ice Hockey Player |
| **Johnson, Penny**<br>Mitchell K Stubbs Assoc, 8695 W Washington Blvd, #204, Culver City CA 90232 USA | Actress |
| **Johnson, Pete**<br>6304 Misty Cove Lane, Columbus OH 43231, USA | Football Player |
| **Johnson, R E**<br>Train Dispatchers Assn, 4239 W 150th St, #1, Cleveland OH 44135, USA | Labor Leader |
| **Johnson, R Keith**<br>PO Box 4122, Park City UT 84060, USA | Baseball Player |
| **Johnson, Rafer L**<br>4217 Woodcliff Road, Sherman Oaks CA 91403, USA | Track Athlete, Actor |
| **Johnson, Randall D (Randy)**<br>8404 N El Maro Circle, Paradise Valley AZ 85253, USA | Baseball Player |
| **Johnson, Raylee T**<br>2010 Black Fox Dr NE, Atlanta GA 30345, USA | Football Player |
| **Johnson, Rebecca**<br>United Agents, 12-26 Lexington St, London W1F 0LE, England | Actress |
| **Johnson, Reed C**<br>10008 Mirada Dr, Las Vegas NV 89144, USA | Baseball Player |
| **Johnson, Reggie D (Sweet)**<br>Puglistic Drama, 1029 Highway 6 N, #650-150, Houston TX 77079, USA | Boxer |
| **Johnson, Reginald R (Reggie)**<br>17907 Souter Lane, Land O'Lakes FL 34638, USA | Football Player |
| **Johnson, Richard**<br>234 Route 197, Woodstock CT 06281, USA | Archer |
| **Johnson, Richard A (Dick)**<br>5001 E Main St, #762, Mesa AZ 85205, USA | Baseball Player |
| **Johnson, Richard J**<br>926 Peachwood Bend Dr, Houston TX 77077, USA | Football Player |
| **Johnson, Richard K**<br>Conway Van Gelder Grant, 8-12 Broadwick St, #300, London W1F 8HW, England | Actor |
| **Johnson, Richard S**<br>Professional Golfer's Assn, PO Box 109601, Palm Beach Gardens FL 33410 USA | Golfer |
| **Johnson, Rob C**<br>26635 Aracena Dr, Mission Viejo CA 92691, USA | Football Player |
| **Johnson, Robert D (Bob)**<br>650 Caves Highway, Cave Junction OR 97523, USA | Baseball Player |
| **Johnson, Robert D (Bob)**<br>165 Magnolia Ave, Cincinnati OH 45246, USA | Football Player |
| **Johnson, Robert G (Junior), Jr**<br>3200 Seven Eagles Road, Charlotte NC 28210, USA | Auto Racing Driver, Executive |
| **Johnson, Robert L**<br>Black Entertainment TV, 1900 W Place NE, Washington DC 20018, USA | Businessman, Basketball Executive |
| **Johnson, Robert Sherlaw**<br>Omnibus Press, 14/15 Berners St, London W1T 3LJ, England | Composer, Concert Pianist |
| **Johnson, Robert W (Bob)**<br>1474 Barclay St, Saint Paul MN 55106, USA | Baseball Player |
| **Johnson, Romina**<br>Mission Control, City Business Center, Lower Road, London SE16 2XB, England | Singer |
| **Johnson, Ron, Sr**<br>1080 Stafford Place, Detroit MI 48207, USA | Football Player |
| **Johnson, Ronald A (Ron)**<br>226 Summit Ave, Summit NJ 07901, USA | Football Player |
| **Johnson, Roy**<br>Roofers & Waterproofers Union, 1125 17th St NW, Washington DC 20036, USA | Labor Leader |
| **Johnson, Rudi A**<br>5177 Rollman Estates Dr, Cincinnati OH 45236, USA | Football Player |
| **Johnson, Rupert**<br>Franklin Resources, 277 Mariners Island Blvd, San Mateo CA 94404, USA | Financier |
| **Johnson, Russell**<br>Amsel Eisenstadt Frazier, 6310 San Vicente Blvd, #401, Los Angeles CA 90048, USA | Actor |
| **Johnson, Samuel L (Sammy)**<br>142 Old Mill Road, #B, High Point NC 27265, USA | Football Player |
| **Johnson, Sandy**<br>Playboy Promotions, 2706 Media Center Dr, Los Angeles CA 90065 USA | Model, Actress |
| **Johnson, Sankey Anton (S A)**<br>PO Box 976, Trabuco Canyon CA 92678, USA | Businessman |
| **Johnson, Scott**<br>Tzadik Records, 200 E 10th St, Box 126, New York, NY 10003, USA | Composer |
| **Johnson, Scott**<br>W M E Entertainment, 1600 Division St, #300, Nashville TN 37203 USA | Guitarist (Gin Blossoms/Low Watts) |
| **Johnson, Scott**<br>PO Box 195222, Winter Springs FL 32719, USA | Gymnast |
| **Johnson, Seleena**<br>Shanachie Records, 37 E Clinton St, #1, Newton NJ 07860 USA | Singer, Songwriter |
| **Johnson, Shawn**<br>5910 Ashworth Road, PO Box 227, West Des Moines IA 50266, USA | Gymnast |
| **Johnson, Sonia**<br>3318 2nd St S, Arlington VA 22204, USA | Women's, Religious Activist |
| **Johnson, Spencer**<br>G P Putnam's Sons, 375 Hudson St, New York NY 10014 USA | Writer |

**Johnson, Stanley L (Stan)** — Baseball Player
56 Moringside Dr, Daly City CA 94015, USA
**Johnson, Steffond** — Basketball Player
10525 Marsh Lane, Dallas TX 75229, USA
**Johnson, Syleena** — Singer, Songwriter
Rodgers Redding, PO Box 4603, Macon GA 31208 USA
**Johnson, Ted C** — Football Player
10 Appletree Lane, Wayland MA 01778, USA
**Johnson, Temeko** — Basketball Player
Phoenix Mercury, American West Arena, 201 E Jefferson St, Phoenix AZ 85004 USA
**Johnson, Terry** — Ice Hockey Player
Endev Energy, 200-207 9th Ave SW, Calgary AB T2P 1K3, Canada
**Johnson, Terry (Buzzy)** — Singer (Flamingos)
Resort Attractions, 2375 E Tropicana Ave, #304, Las Vegas NV 89119, USA
**Johnson, Thomas (Pepper)** — Football Player
New England Patriots, 1 Patriot Place, Foxboro MA 02035 USA
**Johnson, Thomas F** — Baseball Player
1611 Constitution Blvd, Rock Hill SC 29732, USA
**Johnson, Thomas R (Tom)** — Baseball Player
2700 Knox Ave N, Minneapolis MN 55411, USA
**Johnson, Timothy (Tim)** — Football Player
2839 Dorell Ave, Orlando FL 32814, USA
**Johnson, Timothy E (Tim)** — Baseball Player, Manager
2550 E River Road, #3205, Tucson AZ 85718, USA
**Johnson, Tom** — Sound Editor
Ardmore Sound, Ardmore Studios, Herbert Road, Bray, County Wicklow, Ireland
**Johnson, Tommy** — Musician (Brothers Johnson)
Green Light Talent Agency, PO Box 3172, Beverly Hills CA 90212 USA
**Johnson, Torrence V** — Astronomer, Space Scientist
Jet Propulsion Laboratory, 4800 Oak Grove Dr, Pasadena CA 91109 USA
**Johnson, Trent** — Basketball Coach
Stanford University, Athletic Dept, Stanford CA 94305, USA
**Johnson, Vance E** — Football Player
PO Box 606, Parachute CO 81635, USA
**Johnson, Vaughan M** — Football Player
4915 Arendell St, #253, Morehead City NC 28557, USA
**Johnson, Victoria** — Physical Fitness Instructor
V J International, PO Box 1744, Lake Oswego OR 97035, USA
**Johnson, Vincent (Vinnie)** — Basketball Player
5236 Elmsgate Dr, Orchard Lake MI 48324, USA
**Johnson, Virginia** — Ballerina
Dance Theatre of Harlem, 466 W 152nd St, New York NY 10031, USA
**Johnson, W Bruce** — Businessman
Sears Holdings, 3333 Beverly Road, Hoffman Estates IL 60179, USA
**Johnson, W Leon** — Football Player
813 Vine Arden Road, Morganton NC 28655, USA
**Johnson, W Russell (Russ)** — Baseball Player
3542 Russell Road, Green Cove Springs FL 32043, USA
**Johnson, Wallace D** — Baseball Player
5210 S Campbell Ave, Chicago IL 60632, USA
**Johnson, Wallace E (Mickey)** — Basketball Player
3642 W Grenshaw St, Chicago IL 60624, USA
**Johnson, Warren** — Auto Racing Driver
Warren Johnson Enterprises, 700 N Price Road, Sugar Hill GA 30518, USA
**Johnson, Warren C** — Chemist
946 Bellclair Road SE, Grand Rapids MI 49506, USA
**Johnson, Wendy** — Auto Racing Driver
126 Red Brook Lane, Mooresville NC 28117, USA
**Johnson, William A (Billy White Shoes)** — Football Player
3701 Whitney Place, Duluth GA 30096, USA
**Johnson, William B** — Businessman
Ritz-Carlton Hotels, 4445 Willard Ave, #800, Chevy Chase MD 20815, USA
**Johnson, William E (Bill)** — Football Player
3399 Hartwood Road, Cleveland Heights OH 44112, USA
**Johnson, William Merritt** — Writer
Creative Artists Agency, 2000 Ave of Stars, #100, Los Angeles CA 90067 USA
**Johnson, William R** — Businessman
H J Heinz Co, PO Box 57, Pittsburgh PA 15230, USA
**Johnson, Zach** — Golfer
267 Saint Andrews, Saint Simons Island GA 31522, USA
**Johnson-Scharpf, Brandy** — Gymnast
Brandy Johnson's Global Gymnastics, 1945 Don Wickham Dr, Clermont FL 34711, USA
**Johnsson, Kim** — Ice Hockey Player
5308 Oaklawn Ave, Minneapolis MN 55424, USA
**Johnstad, Kurt** — Writer
W M E Entertainment, 9601 Wilshire Blvd, #300, Beverly Hills CA 90210 USA
**Johnston McKay, Mary H** — Astronaut
University of Tennessee, Space Institute, Tullahoma TN 37388, USA
**Johnston, Allen H** — Religious Leader
Bishop's House, 3 Wymer Terrace, PO Box 21, Chartwell, Hamilton 3210, New Zealand
**Johnston, Bruce** — Singer (Beach Boys)
I C M Partners, 10250 Constellation Blvd, #900, Los Angeles CA 90067 USA
**Johnston, Daniel D** — Singer, Songwriter
Dog Day Press, Finsbury Centre, 40 Bowling Green Lane, London EC1R 0NE, England
**Johnston, Daryl P (Moose)** — Football Player
4414 Woodfin Dr, Dallas TX 75220, USA
**Johnston, Freedy** — Singer, Songwriter
High Road Touring, 751 Bridgeway, #200, Sausalito CA 94965 USA
**Johnston, Gerald A** — Businessman
McDonnell Douglas Corp, PO Box 516, Saint Louis MO 63166, USA
**Johnston, Gerald E** — Businessman
Clorox Co, 1221 Broadway, Oakland CA 94612, USA
**Johnston, Harold S** — Chemist
285 Franklin St, Harrisonburg VA 22801, USA
**Johnston, J Bennett, Jr** — Senator, LA
Johnston Assoc, 900 19th St NW, #800, Washington DC 20006, USA

| | |
|---|---|
| **Johnston, Jimmy** | Golfer |
| Pro's Inc, 9 S 12th St, #300, Richmond VA 23219, USA | |
| **Johnston, Joanna** | Costume Designer |
| Independent Talent Group, 40 Whitfield St, London W1T 2RH, England | |
| **Johnston, Joel R** | Baseball Player |
| 1318 Meadowview Dr, #M, Pottstown PA 19464, USA | |
| **Johnston, John Dennis** | Actor |
| S D B Partners, 1801 Ave of Stars, #902, Los Angeles CA 90067 USA | |
| **Johnston, Joseph E (Joe)** | Director |
| Resolution, 1801 Century Park East, #2300, Los Angeles CA 90067 USA | |
| **Johnston, Kristen** | Actress |
| Paradigm Agency, 360 N Crescent Dr, North Building, Beverly Hills CA 90210 USA | |
| **Johnston, L Marshall** | Ice Hockey Player |
| 3933 Waville Road NE, Bemidji MN 56601, USA | |
| **Johnston, Lynn** | Cartoonist (For Better or For Worse) |
| Universal Press Syndicate, 4520 Main St, #700, Kansas City MO 64111 USA | |
| **Johnston, Mark R** | Football Player |
| 609 Carolyn Ave, Austin TX 78705, USA | |
| **Johnston, Nate** | Basketball Player |
| 8870 Fontainbleau Blvd, #301, Miami FL 33172, USA | |
| **Johnston, Rebecca** | Ice Hockey Player |
| Cornell University, Athletic Dept, Ithaca NY 14853, USA | |
| **Johnston, Rex D** | Football, Baseball Player |
| 15117 Illinois Ave, Paramount CA 90723, USA | |
| **Johnston, S K, Jr** | Businessman |
| Coca-Cola Enterprises, 2500 Windy Ridge Parkway, #700, Atlanta GA 30339, USA | |
| **Johnston, Steven E (Stevie)** | Boxer |
| Silverhawk Boxing, 10120 S Eastern Ave, #200, Henderson NV 89052, USA | |
| **Johnstone, John W** | Baseball Player |
| 9330 Clubside Circle, #3305, Sarasota FL 34238, USA | |
| **Johnstone, John W (Jay), Jr** | Baseball Player |
| 853 Chapea Road, Pasadena CA 91107, USA | |
| **Johnstone, John W, Jr** | Businessman |
| 467 Carter St, New Canaan CT 06840, USA | |
| **Johnstone, Parker, III** | Auto Racing Driver |
| Parker Johnstone Honda, 30600 SW Parkway Ave, Wilsonville OR 97070, USA | |
| **Johnston-Forbes, Cathy** | Golfer |
| 5104 Lunar Dr, Kitty Hawk NC 27949, USA | |
| **Johnston-Ulrich, Kim** | Actress |
| S D B Partners, 1801 Ave of Stars, #902, Los Angeles CA 90067 USA | |
| **Joiner, Charles (Charlie), Jr** | Football Player, Coach |
| 16935 W Bernardo Dr, #107, San Diego CA 92127, USA | |
| **Joiner, J Russell (Rusty)** | Actor, Model |
| Talent Works, 3500 W Olive Ave, #1400, Burbank CA 91505 USA | |
| **JoJo** | Singer, Songwriter, Actress |
| Universal Records, 70 Universal City Plaza, Universal City CA 91608 USA | |
| **Jokinen, Jussi** | Ice Hockey Player |
| Pittsburgh Penguins, Consol Energy Center, 1001 5th Ave, Pittsburgh PA 15219 USA | |
| **Jokinen, Olli** | Ice Hockey Player |
| 6501 N Federal Highway, #2, Boca Raton FL 33487, USA | |
| **Jokubonis, Gediminas** | Sculptor |
| V Kudirkos 4-3, 2009 Vilnius, Lithuania | |
| **Jolas, Betsy M** | Composer |
| Nat Superieur Musique Conservatoire, 209 Ave Jaures, 75019 Paris, France | |
| **Joli, France** | Singer |
| Brothers Management Assoc, 141 Dunbar Ave, Fords NJ 08863 USA | |
| **Jolicoeur, David** | Rap Artist (DeLaSoul) |
| Entertainment Artists, 2409 21st Ave S, #100, Nashville TN 10019 USA | |
| **Jolie, Angelina** | Actress, Model, Director |
| Media Talent Group, 9200 W Sunset Blvd, #550, West Hollywood CA 90069 USA | |
| **Joliff, Howard (Howie)** | Basketball Player |
| 2346 Fallen Oak Circle NE, Massillon OH 44646, USA | |
| **Joliot, Pierre A** | Biologist |
| 16 Rue de la Glaciere, 75013 Paris, France | |
| **Jollett, Mikel** | Singer, Guitarist (Airborne Toxic Event) |
| Island Def Jam Records, 8920 W Sunset Blvd, #200, West Hollywood CA 90069 USA | |
| **Jolley, Gordon H** | Football Player |
| 1459 Navajo Dr, Saint George UT 84790, USA | |
| **Jolly, Allison** | Yachtswoman |
| 27122 Benidorm, Mission Viejo CA 92692, USA | |
| **Jolly, E Grady** | Judge |
| US Court of Appeals, Eastland Courthouse, 245 E Capitol St, Jackson MS 39201, USA | |
| **Jolovitz, Jenna** | Actress, Writer |
| Creative Artists Agency, 2000 Ave of Stars, #100, Los Angeles CA 90067 USA | |
| **Joltz, Joachim** | Electrical Engineer |
| A M Forsthof 16, 42119 Wuppertal, Germany | |
| **Jon B** | Singer, Songwriter |
| Entertainment Artists, 2409 21st Ave S, #100, Nashville TN 10019 USA | |
| **Jonas, Joseph A (Joe)** | Singer, Guitarist (Jonas Brothers) |
| Philymack Inc, 11661 San Vicente Blvd, #609, Los Angeles CA 90049, USA | |
| **Jonas, Nicholas J (Nick)** | Singer, Guitarist (Jonas Brothers) |
| Jonas Group, 6725 W Sunset Blvd, #350, Los Angeles CA 90028, USA | |
| **Jonas, P Kevin** | Singer, Guitarist (Jonas Brothers) |
| Philymack Inc, 11661 San Vicente Blvd, #609, Los Angeles CA 90049, USA | |
| **Jonathan, Wesley** | Actor |
| Marsh Entertainment, 12444 Ventura Blvd, #203, Studio City CA 91604, USA | |
| **Jones Gillian** | Actress |
| Shanahan Mgmt, Berman House, 91 Campbell St, #300, Surry Hills NSW 2010, Australia | |
| **Jones, Aaron D, II** | Football Player |
| 7677 Torino Court, Orlando FL 32835, USA | |
| **Jones, Adam B (Pacman)** | Football Player |
| 4282 N Chapel Road, Franklin TN 37067, USA | |
| **Jones, Adam L** | Baseball Player |
| Baltimore Orioles, Oriole Park, 333 W Camden St, Baltimore MD 21201 USA | |
| **Jones, Adam T** | Guitarist (Tool) |
| Volcano Records, 3575 Cahuenga Blvd W, #590, Los Angeles CA 90068, USA | |

# J

**Jones, Aled** — Singer
Agency Group Ltd, 361-373 City Road, London EC1V 1PQ, England

**Jones, Alex S** — Journalist
1 Waterhouse St, #61, Cambridge MA 02138, USA

**Jones, Alfred** — Boxer
19610 Northbrook Dr, Southfield MI 48076, USA

**Jones, Allen C** — Artist
41 Charterhouse Square, London EC1M 6EA, England

**Jones, Andruw R** — Baseball Player
2931 Grey Moss Pass, Duluth GA 30097, USA

**Jones, Angus T** — Actor
Paradigm Agency, 360 N Crescent Dr, North Building, Beverly Hills CA 90210 USA

**Jones, Anthony H** — Basketball Player
44 Hempstead Dr, Newark DE 19702, USA

**Jones, Antonia** — Actress
Baron Entertainment, 13848 Ventura Blvd, #A, Sherman Oaks CA 91423, USA

**Jones, Asjha T** — Basketball Player
Connecticut Sun, 1 Mohegan Sun Blvd, Uncasville CT 06382 USA

**Jones, Barry L** — Baseball Player
411 S Morton Ave, Centerville IN 47330, USA

**Jones, Ben** — Representative, GA; Actor
Cooter's Place, 157 Parkway, Gatlinburg TN 37738, USA

**Jones, Bertram H (Bert)** — Football Player
1492 Madera Sr, Ruston LA 71270, USA

**Jones, Bill T** — Choreographer
219 W 19th St, New York NY 10011, USA

**Jones, Booker T** — Singer, Guitarist (Booker T & the MG's)
Wenig-LaMonica Associates, 580 White Plains Road, #130, Tarrytown NY 10591 USA

**Jones, Brad** — Bassist (Jazz Passengers)
Cross Road Mgmt, 45 W 11th St, #7B, New York NY 10011, USA

**Jones, Brad** — Ice Hockey Player
International Hockey League, PO Box 175, Bedford MI 49020, USA

**Jones, Brandon V** — Football Player
1070 Randall Road, Texarkana TX 75501, USA

**Jones, Brent M** — Football Player, Sportscaster
756 El Pintado Road, Danville CA 94526, USA

**Jones, Caldwell** — Basketball Player
625 Edgecombe, Stockbridge GA 30281, USA

**Jones, Caleb Landry** — Actor
Paradigm Agency, 360 N Crescent Dr, North Building, Beverly Hills CA 90210 USA

**Jones, Calvin (Fuzz)** — Singer, Musician (Legendary Blues Band)
J W Entertainment, PO Box 78904, Atlanta GA 30357 USA

**Jones, Carnetta** — Actress
C E S D, 10635 Santa Monica Blvd, #130, Los Angeles CA 90025 USA

**Jones, Cedric D** — Football Player
804 Hawkesbury Park, Norman OK 73072, USA

**Jones, Charles A** — Basketball Player
304 Chestnut St, Elizabethtown KY 42701, USA

**Jones, Cherry** — Actress
W M E Entertainment, 9601 Wilshire Blvd, #300, Beverly Hills CA 90210 USA

**Jones, Christine** — Scenic Designer
Abrams Artists, 275 7th Ave, #2600, New York NY 10001 USA

**Jones, Cleon J** — Baseball Player
751 Edwards St, Mobile AL 36610, USA

**Jones, Cleve** — Social Activist
Names Project Foundation, 637 Hope St, Atlanta GA 30310, USA

**Jones, Clinton (Clint)** — Football Player
16555 Sherman Way, #C, Lake Balboa CA 91406, USA

**Jones, Cobi** — Soccer Player, Coach
501 N Edinburgh Ave, Los Angeles CA 90048, USA

**Jones, Courtney J L** — Figure Skating Executive
National Skating Assn, 15-27 Gee St, London EC1V 3RE, England

**Jones, Cullen A** — Swimmer
Premier Management Group, 115 Crescent Commons, Cary, NC 27518 USA

**Jones, Dahntay L** — Basketball Player
PO Box 9984, Trenton NJ 8650, USA

**Jones, Damon** — Football Player
12690 Copper Springs Road, Jacksonville Fl 32246, USA

**Jones, Damon** — Basketball Player
10703 Karter Court, Houston TX 77064, USA

**Jones, Daniel A D (Danny)** — Singer, Guitarist (McFly), Songwriter
Helter Skelter, 347-353 Chiswick High Road, London W4 4HS, England

**Jones, Daniel W** — Educator
University of Mississippi, Chancellor's Office, 1848 University Circle, Oxford MS 38677, USA

**Jones, Dante D** — Football Player
328 Partridge Run Dr, Duncanville TX 75137, USA

**Jones, Darryl** — Bassist (Rolling Stones)
Rascoff/Zysblat Organization, 250 W 57th St, New York NY 10107 USA

**Jones, Darryl L** — Baseball Player
15628 King Dr, Meadville PA 16335, USA

**Jones, David** — Conductor
Owen White Mgmt, 22 Brunswick Terrace, Hove, East Sussex BN3 1HJ, England

**Jones, David A** — Businessman
Humana Corp, 500 W Main St, Louisville KY 40202, USA

**Jones, Davy** — Auto Racing Driver
T R W Racing, 2000 Jaguar Dr, Valparaiso IN 46383, USA

**Jones, Dean** — Actor, Singer
Dean Jones Productions, PO Box 570276, Tarzana CA 91357, USA

**Jones, Denise R M** — Singer (Point of Grace)
Blanton Harrell Cooke Corzine, 1014 Cross Bow Court, Hendersonville TN 37075 USA

**Jones, Dhani M** — Football Player
10300 Gary Road, Potomac MD 20854, USA

**Jones, Dick (Dickie)** — Actor
17744 Romar St, Northridge CA 91325, USA

**Jones, Donell** — Singer, Songwriter
Universal Attractions, 135 W 26th St, #1200, New York NY 10001 USA

**Jones - Jones**

| | |
|---|---|
| **Jones, Dot-Marie** <br> Levin Agency, 8484 Wilshire Blvd, #750, Beverly Hills CA 90211, USA | Actress |
| **Jones, Doug** <br> Coolwaters Productions, 10061 Riverside Dr, Box 531, Toluca Lake CA 91602 USA | Actor |
| **Jones, Douglas R (Doug)** <br> 129 E Navilla Place, Covina CA 91723, USA | Baseball Player |
| **Jones, Dwight E** <br> 28926 Enchanted Dr, Shenandoah TX 77381, USA | Basketball Player |
| **Jones, Eddie** <br> Gage Group, 14724 Ventura Blvd, #505, Sherman Oaks CA 91403 USA | Actor |
| **Jones, Eddie** <br> Jones Studio, 4450 N 12th St, Phoenix AZ 85014, USA | Architect |
| **Jones, Eddie C** <br> 3400 Paddock Road, Weston FL 33331, USA | Basketball Player |
| **Jones, Edith H** <br> US Court of Appeals, US Courthouse, 515 Rusk Ave, #12015, Houston TX 77002, USA | Judge |
| **Jones, Edward L (Too Tall)** <br> 1 Lost Valley Dr, Dallas TX 75234, USA | Football Player |
| **Jones, Edward M** <br> Jones Studios, 4450 N 12th St, Phoenix AZ 85014, USA | Architect |
| **Jones, Edward P** <br> Amistad/Harper Collins Publishers, 10 E 53rd St, New York NY 10022, USA | Writer |
| **Jones, Ernest L (Ernie)** <br> 17410 SW 109th Ave, Miami FL 33157, USA | Football Player |
| **Jones, Evan** <br> A P A Talent/Literary Agency, 405 S Beverly Dr, #300, Beverly Hills CA 90212 USA | Actor |
| **Jones, Fay** <br> Grover Thurston Gallery, 309 Occidental Ave S, Seattle WA 98104, USA | Artist |
| **Jones, Felicity** <br> Independent Talent Group, 40 Whitfield St, London W1T 2RH, England | Actress |
| **Jones, Freddie** <br> Diamond Mgmt, 31 Percy St, London W1T 2DD, England | Actor |
| **Jones, Freddie R, Jr** <br> 151 S 111th Place, Mesa AZ 85208, USA | Football Player |
| **Jones, Gary D** <br> 3510 Rosedale St, Houston TX 77004, USA | Football Player |
| **Jones, Gemma** <br> Conway Van Gelder Grant, 8-12 Broadwick St, #300, London W1F 8HW, England | Actress |
| **Jones, Glenn** <br> Andi Howard Entertainment, 30765 Pacific Coast Highway, #134, Malibu CA 90265, USA | Singer |
| **Jones, Gordon** <br> 18919 Fishermans Bend Dr, Lutz FL 33558, USA | Football Player |
| **Jones, Grace** <br> Society Management, 156 Fifth Ave, #800, New York NY 10010 10010, USA | Model, Actress, Singer |
| **Jones, Greg** <br> PO Box 500, Tahoe City CA 96145, USA | Skier |
| **Jones, Greg P** <br> 2331 S Fenton Dr, Lakewood CO 80227, USA | Football Player |
| **Jones, Grover W (Deacon)** <br> 1015 Goldfinch Ave, Sugar Land TX 77478, USA | Baseball Player |
| **Jones, Gwyneth** <br> Opera et Concert, 37 Rue de la Chaussee d'Antin, 75009 Paris, France | Opera Singer |
| **Jones, Hassan A** <br> 1010 Eldridge St, Clearwater FL 33755, USA | Football Player |
| **Jones, Hayes W** <br> 408 Stonewood Dr, Peachtree City GA 30269, USA | Track Athlete |
| **Jones, Homer C** <br> 408 S Texas St, Pittsburg TX 75686, USA | Football Player |
| **Jones, Horace A** <br> 7925 Hobart Ave, Pensacola FL 32534, USA | Football Player |
| **Jones, Howard** <br> F M L, 33 Alexander Road, Aylesbury, Buckinghamshire HP20 2NR, England | Singer, Songwriter |
| **Jones, J Dalton** <br> 4688 S Dixon Lane, Liberty MS 39645, USA | Baseball Player |
| **Jones, Jack** <br> 6 Exeter Court, Rancho Mirage CA 92270, USA | Singer |
| **Jones, Jacque D** <br> 347 Saint Rita Court, San Diego CA 92113, USA | Baseball Player |
| **Jones, James (Jimmy)** <br> 319 Salinas Dr, Henderson NV 89014, USA | Basketball Player |
| **Jones, James A (J J)** <br> PO Box 16, Bettendorf IA 52722, USA | Football Player |
| **Jones, James C (Jimmy)** <br> 3054 Newcastle Dr, Dallas TX 75220, USA | Baseball Player |
| **Jones, James C (Jimmy)** <br> 2 Odyssey Dr, Tinley Park IL 60477, USA | Football Player |
| **Jones, James D** <br> Green Bay Packers, 1265 Lombardi Ave, Green Bay WI 54304 USA | Football Player |
| **Jones, James Earl** <br> Paradigm Agency, 360 N Crescent Dr, North Building, Beverly Hills CA 90210 USA | Actor |
| **Jones, James R** <br> 18130 Palm Breeze Dr, Tampa FL 33647, USA | Football Player |
| **Jones, Jamie** <br> Big Machine Media, 575 Lexington Ave, #400, New York NY 10022, USA | Singer (All-4-One) |
| **Jones, Jamison** <br> Jay D Schwartz, 3151 Cahuenga Blvd W, #220, Los Angeles CA 90068 USA | Actor |
| **Jones, Janet** <br> 9100 Wilshire Blvd, #1000W, Beverly Hills CA 90212, USA | Actress, Producer |
| **Jones, January** <br> Mosiac Media Group, 9200 W Sunset Blvd, #1000, Los Angeles CA 90069, USA | Actress |
| **Jones, Jason** <br> United Talent Agency, U T A Plaza, 9336 Civic Center Dr, Beverly Hills CA 90210 USA | Actor, Writer |
| **Jones, Jason D** <br> Detroit Lions, 222 Republic Dr, Allen Park MI 48101 USA | Football Player |
| **Jones, Jeffrey A (Jeff)** <br> 2200 Ready Road, Carleton MI 48117, USA | Baseball Player |

| | |
|---|---|
| **Jones, Jeffrey D**<br>S M S Talent, 8383 Wilshire Blvd, #230, Beverly Hills CA 90211 USA | Actor |
| **Jones, Jenny**<br>600 Plum Tree Road, Barrington IL 60010, USA | Entertainer, Comedienne |
| **Jones, Jerrauld C (Jerry)**<br>4400 Preston Road, Dallas TX 75205, USA | Football Executive |
| **Jones, Jill Marie**<br>Global Artists Agency, 6253 Hollywood Blvd, #508, Los Angeles CA 90028 USA | Actress |
| **Jones, Jim**<br>A&M Entertainment, 13280 NW Freeway, #F328, Houston TX 77040, USA | Rap Artist |
| **Jones, Jimmie**<br>2658 Unicorn Court, Herndon VA 20171, USA | Football Player |
| **Jones, Jimmie S**<br>204 Moss Dr, Cedar Hill TX 75104, USA | Football Player |
| **Jones, John E, III**<br>US District Court, Federal Building, 240 W 3rd St, Williamsport PA 17701, USA | Judge |
| **Jones, John Paul**<br>Opium Arts, 49 Portland Road, London W11 4LJ, England | Bassist, Keyboardist (Led Zeppelin) |
| **Jones, Johnny (Lam)**<br>1903 Pachea Trail, Round Rock TX 78665, USA | Football Player, Track Athlete |
| **Jones, Julia**<br>Mavrick Artists Agency, 6100 Wilshire Blvd, #550, Los Angeles CA 90048, USA | Actress |
| **Jones, Julius A M**<br>517 Northwood Trail, Southlake TX 76092, USA | Football Player |
| **Jones, June S, III**<br>Southern Methodist University, Athletic Dept, Dallas TX 75275, USA | Football Player, Coach |
| **Jones, Junior**<br>Golden Boy Promotions, 626 Wilshire Blvd, #350, Los Angeles CA 90017, USA | Boxer |
| **Jones, Kelly**<br>Marsupial Mgmt, Home Farm, Welfor, Newbury, Berkshire RG20 8HR, England | Singer, Guitarist (Stereophonics) |
| **Jones, Ken**<br>4455 Porter Road, Niagara Falls NY 14305, USA | Football Player |
| **Jones, Kenneth V**<br>P R S, 29/33 Berners St, London W1P 4AA, England | Actor |
| **Jones, Kim R**<br>1396 Madison Ave, #150, Loveland CO 80537, USA | Football Player |
| **Jones, Kimberly**<br>YES Network, 405 Lexington Ave, #3600, New York NY 10174, USA | Sportscaster |
| **Jones, Kirk**<br>Creative Artists Agency, 2000 Ave of Stars, #100, Los Angeles CA 90067 USA | Director, Writer |
| **Jones, L Q**<br>Sovereign Talent Group, 8421 Wilshire Blvd, #200, Beverly Hills CA 90211, USA | Actor |
| **Jones, Larry**<br>1442 Cottingham Court, Columbus OH 43209, USA | Basketball Player |
| **Jones, Larry W (Chipper)**<br>5015 Heatherwood Court, Roswell GA 30075, USA | Baseball Player |
| **Jones, LeRoy**<br>347 Kantor Blvd, Casselberry FL 32707, USA | Football Player |
| **Jones, Leslie**<br>I C M Partners, 10250 Constellation Blvd, #900, Los Angeles CA 90067 USA | Actress |
| **Jones, Levi J**<br>1448 W Bahia Court, Gilbert AZ 85233, USA | Football Player |
| **Jones, Luka**<br>3 Arts Entertainment, 9460 Wilshire Blvd, #700, Beverly Hills CA 90212 USA | Actor, Comedian |
| **Jones, Lupita**<br>Miss Universe Organization, 1370 Ave of Americas, #1600, New York NY 10019 USA | Beauty Queen |
| **Jones, Lynn M**<br>9959 Dicksonburg Road, Conneautville PA 16406, USA | Baseball Player |
| **Jones, M Donta'**<br>4495 Jimmy Greens Place, La Plata MD 20646, USA | Football Player |
| **Jones, Major J B**<br>2475 Brandy Mill Road, Houston TX 77067, USA | Basketball Player |
| **Jones, Marcus E**<br>18701 Pepper Pike, Lutz FL 33558, USA | Football Player |
| **Jones, Marilyn**<br>Kaplan-Stahler Agency, 8383 Wilshire Blvd, #923, Beverly Hills CA 90211, USA | Actress |
| **Jones, Marion L**<br>PO Box 3065, Cary NC 27519, USA | Track Athlete, Basketball Player |
| **Jones, Marvin M**<br>8891 Brighton Lane, #114, Bonita Springs FL 34135, USA | Football Player |
| **Jones, Matt**<br>Paradigm Agency, 360 N Crescent Dr, North Building, Beverly Hills CA 90210 USA | Actor |
| **Jones, Matthew (Matt)**<br>13838 Bella Riva Lane, Jacksonville FL 32225, USA | Football Player |
| **Jones, Maxine**<br>East West Records, 75 Rockefeller Plaza, #1200, New York NY 10019, USA | Singer (En Vogue) |
| **Jones, Michael D (Mike)**<br>Lincoln University, Athletic Dept, Jefferson MO 65101, USA | Football Player |
| **Jones, Michael G (Mick)**<br>Function, 8330 W 3rd St, Los Angeles CA 90048, USA | Singer, Guitarist (Clash, Foreigner) |
| **Jones, Mickey**<br>Hervey/Grimes Talent, 10561 Missouri Ave, #2, Los Angeles CA 90025 USA | Actor, Musician |
| **Jones, Nate**<br>7801 South Shore Dr, Chicago IL 60649, USA | Boxer |
| **Jones, Nathaniel R**<br>201 E 5th St, #1700, Cincinnati OH 45202, USA | Judge |
| **Jones, Newton B**<br>International Brotherhood of Boilermakers, 753 State Ave, #570, Kansas City KS 66101, USA | Labor Leader |
| **Jones, Norah**<br>Creative Artists Agency, 2000 Ave of Stars, #100, Los Angeles CA 90067 USA | Singer, Pianist; Songwriter |
| **Jones, Odell**<br>5831 Opal Ave, Palmdale CA 93552, USA | Baseball Player |
| **Jones, Orlando**<br>Paradigm Agency, 360 N Crescent Dr, North Building, Beverly Hills CA 90210 USA | Actor |
| **Jones, P J**<br>Gurney Racing, 2334 S Broadway, #2186, Santa Ana CA 92707, USA | Auto Racing Driver |

| | |
|---|---|
| **Jones, Parnelli** | Auto Racing Driver, Executive |
| 20550 Earl St, Torrance CA 90503, USA | |
| **Jones, Paul** | Guitarist (Elastica) |
| Chatto & Linnit, 123A King's Road, London SW3 4PL, England | |
| **Jones, Perry J, III** | Basketball Player |
| Oklahoma City Thunder, 211 N Robinson Ave, #300, Oklahoma City OK 73102 USA | |
| **Jones, Pete** | Director, Writer |
| Creative Artists Agency, 2000 Ave of Stars, #100, Los Angeles CA 90067 USA | |
| **Jones, Quincy D, Jr** | Composer, Conductor |
| Quincy Jones Productions, 6671 W Sunset Blvd, #1574A, Los Angeles CA 90028, USA | |
| **Jones, Quintorris L (Julio)** | Football Player |
| Atlanta Falcons, 4400 Falcon Parkway, Flowery Branch GA 30542 USA | |
| **Jones, Randall L (Randy)** | Baseball Player |
| 2638 Cranston Dr, Escondido CA 92025, USA | |
| **Jones, Randy** | Bobsled Athlete |
| US Bobsled & Skeleton Federation, 1631 Mesa Ave, #A, Colorado Springs CO 80906 USA | |
| **Jones, Rashida** | Actress, Writer |
| United Talent Agency, U T A Plaza, 9336 Civic Center Dr, Beverly Hills CA 90210 USA | |
| **Jones, Renee** | Actress |
| 256 S Robertson Blvd, #700, Beverly Hills CA 90211, USA | |
| **Jones, Rhydian** | Actor |
| Associated International Mgmt, 7 Hatton Garden, #400, London EC1N 8AD, England | |
| **Jones, Richard T** | Actor |
| Mavrick Artists Agency, 6100 Wilshire Blvd, #550, Los Angeles CA 90048, USA | |
| **Jones, Richard W (Rich)** | Basketball Player |
| 101 Luna Way, #232, Las Vegas NV 89145, USA | |
| **Jones, Rickie Lee** | Singer, Songwriter |
| Esther Creative Group, 27 W 24th St, #404, New York NY 10010, USA | |
| **Jones, Robbie** | Actor |
| Untitled Entertainment, 350 S Beverly Dr, #200, Beverly Hills CA 90212 USA | |
| **Jones, Robert (K C)** | Basketball Player, Coach |
| 13405 NW Spirit Court W, Silverdale WA 98383, USA | |
| **Jones, Robert C (Bobby)** | Basketball Player |
| 7413 Valleybrook Road, Charlotte NC 28270, USA | |
| **Jones, Robert E (Bobby)** | Football Player |
| 6824 Stewart Sharon Road, Brookfield OH 44403, USA | |
| **Jones, Robert J (Bobby)** | Baseball Player |
| 10222 N Whitney Ave, Fresno CA 93730, USA | |
| **Jones, Robert L** | Football Player |
| 728 Barton Creek Blvd, Austin TX 78746, USA | |
| **Jones, Robert M (Bobby)** | Baseball Player |
| 32 Elm St, Rutherford NJ 07070, USA | |
| **Jones, Robert O (Bobby)** | Baseball Player |
| 7809 S Oxford Ave, Tulsa OK 74136, USA | |
| **Jones, Rod** | Guitarist (Idlewild) |
| Agency Group Ltd, 361-373 City Road, London EC1V 1PQ, England | |
| **Jones, Roderick W (Rod)** | Football Player |
| 517 Tealridge Lane, De Soto TX 75115, USA | |
| **Jones, Roger C** | Football Player |
| 712 Trebor Dr, Goodlettsville TN 37072, USA | |
| **Jones, Ronald J (Popeye)** | Basketball Player |
| 29 Bass Pond Dr, Frisco TX 75034, USA | |
| **Jones, Rondell T** | Football Player |
| 423 Competition Road, Raleigh NC 27603, USA | |
| **Jones, Rosie** | Model |
| Samantha Bond Mgmt, Elysium Gate, 126-128 New Kings Road, London SW6 4LZ, England | |
| **Jones, Rosie** | Golfer |
| 4895 High Point Road, Atlanta GA 30342, USA | |
| **Jones, Ross A** | Baseball Player |
| 4135 Eastridge Circle, Pompano Beach FL 33064, USA | |
| **Jones, Roy, Jr** | Boxer |
| 4590 Isbella Ingram Dr, Pensacola FL 32504, USA | |
| **Jones, Rulon K** | Football Player |
| 4003 N 3775 E, Eden UT 84310, USA | |
| **Jones, Rupert Penry** | Actor |
| Artist Rights Group, 4 Great Portland St, London W1W 8PA, England | |
| **Jones, Ruppert S** | Baseball Player |
| 17925 Valle de Lobo Dr, Poway CA 92064, USA | |
| **Jones, Sam, III** | Actor |
| Pantheon Talent, 1801 Century Park E, #1910, Los Angeles CA 90067, USA | |
| **Jones, Samuel (Sam)** | Basketball Player |
| 338 S Hampton Club Way, Saint Augustine FL 32092, USA | |
| **Jones, Sarah** | Actress |
| Management 360, 9111 Wilshire Blvd, Beverly Hills CA 90210 USA | |
| **Jones, Scott A** | Inventor (LED Video Animation) |
| Dittoe Public Relations, 2815 E 62nd St, #300, Indianapolis IN 46220, USA | |
| **Jones, Sean** | Football Player |
| 4602 McKeever Lane, Missouri City TX 77459, USA | |
| **Jones, Serene** | Educator |
| Union Theological Seminary, President's Office, 3041 Broadway, New York NY 10027, USA | |
| **Jones, Sharon** | Singer |
| Motormouth Media, 2525 Hyperion Ave, #1, Los Angeles CA 90027, USA | |
| **Jones, Shirley** | Actress, Singer |
| Suchin Co, 16501 Ventura Blvd, #504, Encino CA 91436, USA | |
| **Jones, Simon** | Actor |
| Innovative Artists, 1505 10th St, Santa Monica CA 90401 USA | |
| **Jones, Stacy** | Singer, Guitarist, Songwriter |
| Crush Music, 584 Broadway, #1102, New York NY 10012, USA | |
| **Jones, Stephen** | Attorney |
| Jones & Wyatt, PO Box 472, Enid OK 73702, USA | |
| **Jones, Stephen H (Steve)** | Basketball Player |
| 26 Kingwood Greens Dr, Kingwood TX 77339, USA | |
| **Jones, Stephen J M** | Fashion Designer |
| Steve Jones Millinery, 36 Great Queen St, London WC1E 6BT, England | |
| **Jones, Steve** | Golfer |
| Whirlwind Golf Club, 5200 Grand Del Mar Way, San Diego CA 92130, USA | |

**Jones, Steve** — Guitarist (Sex Pistols)
Solo Agency, 53-55 Fulham High St, #200, London SW6 3JJ, England

**Jones, Steve H** — Football Player
12774 Fee Fee Road, Saint Louis MO 63146, USA

**Jones, Steven** — Physicist
Brigham Young University, Physics Dept, Provo UT 84602, USA

**Jones, Steven H (Steve)** — Baseball Player
8116 Kingsdale Dr, Knoxville TN 37919, USA

**Jones, Stewart** — Architect
Meyer/Gifford/Jones, 270 Lafayette St, New York NY 10012, USA

**Jones, T Frederick (Rick)** — Baseball Player
6319 Nancy Dr, Jacksonville FL 32244, USA

**Jones, Tamala** — Actress
A P A Talent/Literary Agency, 405 S Beverly Dr, #300, Beverly Hills CA 90212 USA

**Jones, Taylor** — Editorial Cartoonist
Cagle Cartoons, PO Box 22342, Santa Barbara CA 93121 USA

**Jones, Tebucky S** — Football Player
11 Salisbury Way, Farmington CT 6032, USA

**Jones, Terrence** — Basketball Player
Houston Rockets, 1730 Jefferson St, Houston TX 77003 USA

**Jones, Terry** — Animator, Director (Monty Python)
Python Pictures, 34 Thistlewaite Road, London E5 QQQ, England

**Jones, Thomas D** — Astronaut
N A S A, Johnson Space Center, 2101 NASA Road, Houston TX 77058 USA

**Jones, Thomas Q** — Football Player
2742 Clinch Haven Road, Big Stone Gap VA 24219, USA

**Jones, Thomas V** — Businessman
1050 Moraga Dr, Los Angeles CA 90049, USA

**Jones, Timothy B (Tim)** — Baseball Player
6049 Roloff Way, Orangevale CA 95662, USA

**Jones, Toby** — Actor
United Talent Agency, U T A Plaza, 9336 Civic Center Dr, Beverly Hills CA 90210 USA

**Jones, Todd B G** — Baseball Player
421 Eagle Point Dr, Pell City AL 35128, USA

**Jones, Tom** — Singer
W M E Entertainment, 9601 Wilshire Blvd, #300, Beverly Hills CA 90210 USA

**Jones, Tommy Lee** — Actor, Director
Creative Artists Agency, 2000 Ave of Stars, #100, Los Angeles CA 90067 USA

**Jones, Tracy D** — Baseball Player
101 Harbor Green Dr, #602, Bellevue KY 41073, USA

**Jones, Trevor** — Composer
46 Ave Road, Highgate, London N6 5DR, England

**Jones, Tyler Patrick** — Actor
House of Representatives, 1434 6th St, #1, Santa Monica CA 90401 USA

**Jones, Vaughan F R** — Mathematician
University of California, Mathematics Dept, Berkeley CA 94720, USA

**Jones, Victor P** — Football Player
17727 Sedona Way, Cornelius NC 28031, USA

**Jones, Victor T** — Football Player
PO Box 132241, Dallas TX 75313, USA

**Jones, Vinnie** — Actor
Cole Kitchenn Personal Mgmt, 212 Strand, London WC2R 1AP, England

**Jones, W Timothy (Tim)** — Baseball Player
30 Chicot Dr, Maumelle AR 72113, USA

**Jones, Wallace C (Wah-Wah)** — Basketball Player
512 Chinoe Road, Lexington KY 40502, USA

**Jones, Walter (Wali)** — Basketball Player
3160 SW 132nd Ave, Miramar FL 33027, USA

**Jones, Walter J** — Football Player
520 Raymond Place NW, Renton WA 98057, USA

**Jones, Wesley** — Architect
Holt Hinshaw Jones, 320 Florida St, San Francisco CA 94110, USA

**Jones, Wilbert (Wil)** — Basketball Player
3360 Idlecreek Way, Decatur GA 30034, USA

**Jones, William A (Dub)** — Football Player
904 Glendale Dr, Ruston LA 71270, USA

**Jones, Zoe Lister** — Actress, Writer
W M E Entertainment, 9601 Wilshire Blvd, #300, Beverly Hills CA 90210 USA

**Jones-Doxey, Marilyn C** — Baseball Player
320 15th Street Court W, Bradenton FL 34205, USA

**Jong, Erica M** — Writer
PO Box 1434, New York NY 10021, USA

**Jongh, John P** — Governor, VI
Governor's Office, 21-2 Kongens Gade, Charlotte Amalie, Saint Thomas VI 00802 USA

**Jonrowe, Dee Dee** — Dog Sled Racer
PO Box 272, Willow AK 99688, USA

**Jonsen, Albert R** — Physician
1383 Jones St, #502, San Francisco CA 94109, USA

**Jonsson, U P Jorgen** — Ice Hockey Player
Anaheim Ducks, 2695 E Katella Ave, Anaheim CA 92806 USA

**Jonze, Spike** — Director, Actor
Creative Artists Agency, 2000 Ave of Stars, #100, Los Angeles CA 90067 USA

**Joo Min-Jin** — Speed Skater
Skating Union, 88 Bangyee-Dong, Songpaku, Seoul 138 749, South Korea

**Joop, Jette** — Fashion Designer
Jette Design Group, Parkallee 53, 20144 Hamburg, Germany

**Joop, Wolfgang** — Fashion Designer
Seestr 35-37, 14467 Potsdam, Germany

**Jopling of Alnderby Quernhow, T Michael** — Government Official, England
Ainderby Hall, Thirsk, North Yorkshire YO7 4HZ, England

**Joppy, William T** — Boxer
5107 Cansing Dr, Camp Springs MD 20748, USA

**Jorda, Claude J C** — Judge
International Criminal Tribunal, PO Box 13888, 2501 The Hague EW, Netherlands

**Jordan, Alex** — Interior Designer
Gregga Jordan Smieszny, 1225 N State Parkway, Chicago IL 60610, USA

| | |
|---|---|
| **Jordan, Alexis** <br> Roc Nation, 1411 Broadway, #3800, New York NY 10018, USA | Singer |
| **Jordan, Brian O** <br> 2631 Trailing Ivy Way, Buford GA 30519, USA | Football, Baseball Player |
| **Jordan, Claudia** <br> C E S D, 10635 Santa Monica Blvd, #130, Los Angeles CA 90025 USA | Model, Entertainer |
| **Jordan, Curtis W** <br> 629 Surfside Ave, Virginia Beach VA 23451, USA | Football Player |
| **Jordan, Darin G** <br> 44 Connell Dr, Stoughton MA 02072, USA | Football Player |
| **Jordan, Dion** <br> Miami Dolphins, 7500 SW 30th St, Davie FL 33314 USA | Football Player |
| **Jordan, Don D** <br> Reliant Energy, 1111 Louisiana Ave, Houston TX 77002, USA | Businessman |
| **Jordan, Edward M (Eddie)** <br> 158 Monroe Ave, Belle Mead NJ 08502, USA | Basketball Player, Coach |
| **Jordan, Glenn** <br> 9401 Wilshire Blvd, #700, Beverly Hills CA 90212, USA | Director |
| **Jordan, Gregor** <br> H L A Mgmt, PO Box 1536, Strawberry Hills, Sydney NSW 2012, Australia | Director |
| **Jordan, H DeAndre, Jr** <br> Los Angeles Clippers, Staples Center, 1111 S Figueroa St, Los Angeles CA 90015 USA | Basketball Player |
| **Jordan, Jeremy** <br> Lacam Management, 283 W Montecito Ave, Sierra Madre CA 91024, USA | Actor, Singer |
| **Jordan, Jeremy** <br> I C M Partners, 10250 Constellation Blvd, #900, Los Angeles CA 90067 USA | Actor |
| **Jordan, Kathy** <br> 114 Walter Hays Dr, Palo Alto CA 94303, USA | Tennis Player |
| **Jordan, Kevin W** <br> 127 Ney St, San Francisco CA 94112, USA | Baseball Player |
| **Jordan, LaMont D** <br> 1407 Alberta Dr, District Heights MD 20747, USA | Football Player |
| **Jordan, Lee Roy** <br> 7710 Caruth Blvd, Dallas TX 75225, USA | Football Player |
| **Jordan, Leslie** <br> Michael Slessinger, 8730 W Sunset Blvd, #220W, West Hollywood CA 90069 USA | Actor |
| **Jordan, Marc** <br> Live Tour Artists, 1451 White Oaks Blvd, Oakville ON L6H 4R9, Canada | Singer, Songwriter |
| **Jordan, Mary** <br> Washington Post, Editorial Dept, 1150 15th St NW, Washington DC 20071 USA | Journalist |
| **Jordan, Michael B** <br> United Talent Agency, U T A Plaza, 9336 Civic Center Dr, Beverly Hills CA 90210 USA | Actor |
| **Jordan, Michael J** <br> David Falk Mgmt, 5335 Wisconsin Ave, #850, Washington DC 20015, USA | Basketball Player |
| **Jordan, Montell** <br> Red Entertainment Agency, 505 8th Ave, #1004, New York NY 10018, USA | Singer, Songwriter |
| **Jordan, Neil P** <br> 2 Martello Terrace, Strand Road, Bray, County Wicklow, Ireland | Director |
| **Jordan, P Buford** <br> 11 Acadia St, Kenner LA 70065, USA | Football Player |
| **Jordan, Paul S (Ricky)** <br> 5691 Power Inn Road, #A, Sacramento CA 95824, USA | Baseball Player |
| **Jordan, Philippe** <br> I M G Artists, Hogarth Business Park, Chiswick, London W4 2TH, England | Conductor |
| **Jordan, Randy L** <br> 514 Mountain Laurel, Chapel Hill NC 27517, USA | Football Player |
| **Jordan, Ronny** <br> Universal Attractions, 135 W 26th St, #1200, New York NY 10001 USA | Jazz Guitarist |
| **Jordan, Sass** <br> Management Trust, 411 Queen St W, #300, Toronto ON M5V 2A5, Canada | Singer, Songwriter |
| **Jordan, Sheila J** <br> F A M, 4102 Rue Saint Urbain, Montreal QC H2W 1V3, Canada | Singer, Songwriter |
| **Jordan, Shelby L** <br> 29208 Posey Way, Rancho Palos Verdes CA 90275, USA | Football Player |
| **Jordan, Steven R (Steve)** <br> 581 W San Marcos Dr, Chandler AZ 85225, USA | Football Player |
| **Jordan, Thomas J (Tom)** <br> 2909 S Wyoming Ave, Roswell NM 88203, USA | Baseball Player |
| **Jordan, Tina Marie** <br> Playboy Promotions, 2706 Media Center Dr, Los Angeles CA 90065 USA | Model |
| **Jordan, Vernon E, Jr** <br> 2940 Benton Place NW, Washington DC 20008, USA | Civil Rights Activist |
| **Jordanova, Vera** <br> Special Artists Agency, 9200 Sunset Blvd, #410, West Hollywood CA 90069 USA | Actress, Model |
| **Jorge, Seu** <br> Windish Agency, 1658 N Milwaukee Ave, #211, Chicago IL 60647, USA | Singer, Songwriter, Actor |
| **Jorgensen, Anker** <br> Borgbjergvej 1, 2450 SV Copenhagen, Denmark | Prime Minister, Denmark |
| **Jorgensen, Michael (Mike)** <br> 1820 Harbor Mill Dr, Fenton MO 63026, USA | Baseball Player, Manager |
| **Jorgensen, Roger K** <br> 642 Woodcrest Dr, Pittsburgh PA 15205, USA | Basketball Player |
| **Jorgenson, Dale W** <br> 1010 Memorial Dr, #14C, Cambridge MA 02138, USA | Economist |
| **Jorgenson, John** <br> T G Squared Artist Representation, 201 Rainbow Dr, Carrboro NC 27510, USA | Guitarist (Desert Rose Band) |
| **Jorginho de Amorim Campos** <br> Rua Levi Carneiro 420, Barra dd Tijuca 22630 150, Brazil | Soccer Player |
| **Jorndt, L Daniel** <br> Walgreen Co, 200 Wilmot Road, Deerfield IL 60015, USA | Businessman |
| **Jose, D Felix A** <br> 9825 Equus Circle, Boynton Beach FL 33472, USA | Baseball Player |
| **Jose, Jose** <br> Joyce Agency Entertainment Services, 370 Harrison Ave, Harrison NY 10528, USA | Singer |
| **Josefowicz, Leila** <br> C M Artists, 127 W 96th St, #13B, New York NY 10025 USA | Concert Violinist |

**J**

| | |
|---|---|
| **Joseph Wenzel**<br>Prince's Residence, Schloss Vaduz, 9490 Vaduz, Liechtenstein | Prince, Liechtenstein |
| **Joseph, Amin**<br>Jay Schachter Entertainment, 28994 Sam Place, Canyon Country CA 91387, USA | Actor |
| **Joseph, Curtis S**<br>Newport Sports Mgmt, 601-201 City Centre, Mississauga ON L5B 2T4, Canada | Ice Hockey Player |
| **Joseph, Daryl J**<br>615 Peachtree Court, Campbell CA 95008, USA | Astronaut |
| **Joseph, James**<br>8942 Stoneridge Place, Montgomery AL 36117, USA | Football Player |
| **Joseph, Johnathan**<br>Houston Texans, 2 Reliant Park, Houston TX 77054 USA | Football Player |
| **Joseph, Joseph E, III**<br>University of Michigan, Taubman Center, Ann Arbor MI 48109, USA | Physician |
| **Joseph, Kimberly**<br>Creative Representation, 1/44 Derby St, Collingwood VIC 3065, Australia | Actress, Director, Writer |
| **Joseph, R Christopher (Chris)**<br>17 L'Hirondelle Court, Saint Albert AB T8N 5X9, Canada | Ice Hockey Player |
| **Joseph, Shalrie**<br>New England Revolution, 1 Patriot Place, Foxboro MA 02035 USA | Soccer Player |
| **Joseph, Stephen**<br>New York City Health Department, 125 Worth St, New York NY 10013, USA | Physician |
| **Joseph, William**<br>1071 NE 107th St, Miami FL 33161, USA | Football Player |
| **Josephson, Brian D**<br>Cavendish Laboratory, Madingley Road, Cambridge CB3 0HE, England | Nobel Physics Laureate |
| **Josephson, Karen**<br>1923 Junction Dr, Concord CA 94518, USA | Synchronized Swimmer |
| **Josephson, Lester J (Josey)**<br>5388 N Genematas Dr, Tucson AZ 85704, USA | Football Player |
| **Josephson, Sarah**<br>1923 Junction Dr, Concord CA 94518, USA | Synchronized Swimmer |
| **Joshi, Indira**<br>B B C Artist Mail, PO Box 116, Belfast BT2 7AJ, Northern Ireland | Singer |
| **Joshi, Pallavi**<br>23 Veer Savarkar Road, Mahim, Mumbai MS 400016, India | Actress, Entertainer |
| **Joshua, Von E**<br>20922 E Glen Haven Circle, Northville MI 48167, USA | Baseball Player |
| **Josipovic, Ivo**<br>Presidential Palace, Banski Dvori, Zagreb 10000, Croatia | President, Croatia |
| **Jospin, Lionel R**<br>Parti Socialiste, 10 Rue de Solfarino, 75333 Paris Cedex 07, France | Prime Minister, France |
| **Josserand, Marion**<br>Ski Federation, 50 Rue des Marquisats, BP 2451 , 74011 Annecy Cedex, France | Freestyle Cross Skier |
| **Joubert, Beverly**<br>National Geographic, Editorial Dept, 1145 17th St NW, Washington DC 20036 USA | Photographer |
| **Joubert, Dereck**<br>National Geographic, Editorial Dept, 1145 17th St NW, Washington DC 20036 USA | Photographer |
| **Joulwan, George A**<br>1348 S 19th St, Arlington VA 22202, USA | Army General |
| **Jourdain, Michel, Jr**<br>Team Rahal, 4601 Lyman Dr, Hilliard OH 43026, USA | Auto Racing Driver |
| **Jourdan, Louis**<br>1139 Maybrook Dr, Beverly Hills CA 90210, USA | Actor |
| **Jourgensen, Al**<br>First Row Talent, 6220 Lemona Ave, #8, Van Nuys CA 91411, USA | Singer, Guitarist (Ministry) |
| **Journell, Jimmy**<br>1511 Eastgate Road, Springfield OH 45503, USA | Baseball Player |
| **Jousset, Anne**<br>Artmedia, 20 Ave Rapp, 75007 Paris, France | Actress |
| **Jovanotti**<br>Trident Mgmt, Corso Europa 13, 20122 Milan, Italy | Singer, Rap Artist, Songwriter, Actor |
| **Jovanovich, Brandon**<br>I M G Artists, Hogarth Business Park, Chiswick, London W4 2TH, England | Opera Singer |
| **Jovanovich, Peter W**<br>Pearson Education, 1 Lake St, Upper Saddle River NJ 07458, USA | Publisher |
| **Jovanovski, Edward (Ed)**<br>5224 NW 27th Court, Margate FL 33063, USA | Ice Hockey Player |
| **Jovich, John B**<br>1342 Rosepointe Dr, York PA 17404, USA | Historian |
| **Jovovich, Milla**<br>Untitled Entertainment, 350 S Beverly Dr, #200, Beverly Hills CA 90212 USA | Actress, Model, Singer |
| **Joy, Mike**<br>111 Mystic Lake Loop, Mooresville NC 28117, USA | Sportscaster |
| **Joyal, Edward A (Eddie)**<br>6469 Wandermere Dr, San Diego CA 92120, USA | Ice Hockey Player |
| **Joyce, Andrea**<br>Arts & Entertainment, 235 E 45th St, #200, New York NY 10017, USA | Sportscaster, Commentator |
| **Joyce, James A**<br>9785 SW 167th Place, Beaverton OR 97007, USA | Baseball Umpire |
| **Joyce, Joan**<br>20024 Back Nine Dr, Boca Raton FL 33498, USA | Softball Player, Golfer |
| **Joyce, John T (Jack)**<br>Bricklayers & Allied Craftsmen, 815 15th St NW, Washington DC 20005, USA | Labor Leader |
| **Joyce, Kara Lynn**<br>5973 Cedar Ridge Dr, Ann Arbor MI 48103, USA | Swimmer |
| **Joyce, Kevin F**<br>420 W Olive St, #9, Long Beach NY 11561, USA | Basketball Player |
| **Joyce, Matt**<br>6330 E Wilshire Dr, Scottsdale AZ 85257, USA | Football Player |
| **Joyce, Matthew R (Matt)**<br>Tampa Bay Rays, 1 Tropicana Dr, Saint Petersburg FL 33705 USA | Baseball Player |
| **Joyce, Tom**<br>21 Likely Road, Santa Fe NM 87508, USA | Sculptor |
| **Joyce, William**<br>2911 Centenary Blvd, PO Box 4188, Shreveport LA 71104, USA | Artist, Writer |

**Joseph Wenzel - Joyce**

**Joyce, William H** — Businessman
Union Carbide, 39 Old Ridgebury Road, #1, Danbury CT 06810, USA

**Joyeux, Odette** — Actress
Agents Associes, 201 Rue du Faubourg Saint Honore, 75008 Paris, France

**Joyner, Alrederick (Al)** — Track Athlete
10500 Crosspoint Blvd, Indianapolis IN 46256, USA

**Joyner, Michelle** — Actress
Kritzer Levine Wilkins Griffin, 11872 La Grange Ave, #100, Los Angeles CA 90025 USA

**Joyner, Seth** — Football Player, Sportscaster
502 E Bishop Dr, Tempe AZ 85282, USA

**Joyner, Wallace K (Wally)** — Baseball Player
516 E 2800 S, Mapleton UT 84664, USA

**Joyner-Kersee, Jacqueline (Jackie)** — Track Athlete
1049 Bristol Manor Dr, Ballwin MO 63011, USA

**Jozwiak, Brian J** — Football Player, Coach
203 Ruby Lake Lane, Winter Haven FL 33884, USA

**J-Ro** — Rap Artist
Likwit Entertainment, PO Box 360713, Los Angeles CA 90036, USA

**Ju Ming** — Sculptor
208 No 2 She-shi-hu, Chin-shan, Taipei, Taiwan

**Juan Carlos I** — King, Spain
Palacio de la Zarzuela, 28671 Madrid, Spain

**Juanes** — Singer, Guitarist
Fernan Martinez Mgmt, 4141 NE 2nd Ave, #106C, Miami FL 33137, USA

**Juantorena Danger, Alberto** — Track Athlete
National Institute for Sports, Sports City, Havana, Cuba

**Juarez, Ricardo (Rocky)** — Boxer
3916 Weems St, Houston TX 77009, USA

**Juby, Marcus L** — Religious Leader
Reformed Church of Latter-Day Saints, 801 E 23rd St, Independence MO 64055, USA

**Juchhelm, Alwin M, Jr** — WW II Army Air Corps Hero
939 Ave of Pines, Grenada MS 38901, USA

**Judah, Zab** — Boxer
Prize Fight Boxing, 7160 Tchulahoma Road, #A1, Southhaven MS 38671, USA

**Judd, Ashley** — Actress, Model
PO Box 1569, Franklin TN 37065, USA

**Judd, Bob** — Writer
Harper Collins Publishers, 10 E 53rd St, Cellar 1, New York NY 10022 USA

**Judd, Harry M C** — Drummer (McFly)
Helter Skelter, 347-353 Chiswick High Road, London W4 4HS, England

**Judd, Jackie** — Commentator
ABC-TV, News Dept, 77 W 66th St, New York NY 10023 USA

**Judd, Michael G (Mike)** — Baseball Player
9805 Shadow Road, La Mesa CA 91941, USA

**Judd, Naomi** — Singer (Judds), Songwriter
Gary Good Entertainment, 2614 NW 62nd St, Oklahoma City OK 73112, USA

**Judd, Wynonna** — Singer, Guitarist
Big Enterprises, PO Box 682708, Franklin TN 37068, USA

**Juden, Jeffrey D (Jeff)** — Baseball Player
85 Proctor St, Salem MA 01970, USA

**Judge, George** — Economist
University of California, Economics Dept, Berkeley CA 94720, USA

**Judge, Mike** — Animator (Beavis & Butt-Head), Actor
3 Arts Entertainment, 9460 Wilshire Blvd, #700, Beverly Hills CA 90212 USA

**Judkins, Jeffrey R (Jeff)** — Basketball Player, Coach
3471 S 3570 E, Salt Lake City UT 84109, USA

**Judson, Howard K (Howie)** — Baseball Player
239 Fairway Circle NE, Winter Haven FL 33881, USA

**Judson, William T** — Football Player
652 Sinclair Way, Jonesboro GA 30238, USA

**Jue, Blawoh P** — Football Player
4514 Billingham St, Fairfax VA 22030, USA

**Jugnauth, Anerood** — President, Mauritius
President's Office, Government Centre, Port Louis, Mauritius

**Jugnot, Gerard** — Director, Actor
J G P M, 11 Rue Chavez, 75016 Paris, France

**Ju-Ju** — Rap Artist (Beatnuts)
Agency Group Ltd, 142 W 57th St, #600, New York NY 10019 USA

**Julavits, Heidi** — Writer
G P Putnam's Sons, 375 Hudson St, New York NY 10014 USA

**Julian, Alexander, II** — Fashion Designer
323 Florida Hill Road, Ridgefield CT 6877, USA

**Julien, Claire** — Actress
Creative Artists Agency, 2000 Ave of Stars, #100, Los Angeles CA 90067 USA

**Julien, Claude** — Ice Hockey Player, Coach
3 Myrna Road, Lexington MA 02420, USA

**Julius, DeAnne** — Economist
Bank of England, Threadneedle St, London EC2R 8AH, England

**July, Miranda** — Actor, Director, Writer
United Talent Agency, U T A Plaza, 9336 Civic Center Dr, Beverly Hills CA 90210 USA

**Jumaliyev, Kubanychbek M** — Prime Minister, Kyrgyzstan
Transport Ministry, Isanova Str 42, 720017 Bishkek, Kyrgyzstan

**Junck, Mary E** — Businesswoman
Lee Enterprises, 201 N Harrison St, #600, Davenport IA 52801, USA

**Juncker, Jean-Claude** — Prime Minister, Luxembourg
Prime Minister's Office, 33 Boul Roosevelt, 1728 Luxembourg-Ville, Luxembourg

**June, Carl H** — Pathologist
University of Pennsylvania Medical School, 421 Curie Blvd, Philadelphia PA 19104, USA

**June, Cato N** — Football Player
13500 Van Brady Road, Upper Marlboro MD 20772, USA

**June, Valerie** — Singer, Songwriter
Billions Corp, 3522 W Armitage Ave, Chicago IL 60647 USA

**Juneau, Joseph (Joe)** — Ice Hockey Player
Harlem Technologies, 100-2 Rue du Jardin, Pont Rouge QC G3H 3R7, Canada

**Jung Sung-Ryong** — Soccer Player
Football Assn, 1-131 Sinmunno, 2-Ga Jongno-Gu, Seoul 110 062, South Korea

Joyce - Jung Sung-Ryong

**Jung Woo-Young** — Soccer Player
Football Assn, 1-131 Sinmunno, 2-Ga Jongno-Gu, Seoul 110 062, South Korea

**Jung, Andrea** — Businesswoman
Avon Products, 1345 Ave of Americas Basement Concourse 9, New York NY 10105, USA

**Jung, Ernst** — Writer
88515 Lagenensligen/Wiltlingen, Germany

**Jung, Richard** — Neurologist
Waldhofstr 42, 71691 Freiburg, Germany

**Junge, Daniel** — Director
Milkhaus/Jungefilm, 3059 Vine St, Denver Co 80205, USA

**Junger, Sebastian** — Writer, Director
United Talent Agency, U T A Plaza, 9336 Civic Center Dr, Beverly Hills CA 90210 USA

**Junior, Ester J (E J)** — Football Player
911 W Summit St, Bolivar MO 65613, USA

**Junker, Steve N** — Football Player
5660 Julmar Dr, Cincinnati OH 45238, USA

**Junkie XL** — Keyboardist, Guitarist, Drummer
Primary Talent International, 10-11 Jockey's Fields, London WC1R 4BN, England

**Junkin, Abner K (Trey)** — Football Player
5 Lakeside Lane, Newport AR 72112, USA

**Junkin, Michael W (Mike)** — Football Player
1002 Whitehall Dr, Doylestown PA 18901, USA

**Junqueira, Bruno** — Auto Racing Driver
3669 Royal Palm Ave, Miami FL 33133, USA

**Juntunen, Helena** — Opera Singer
Harrison/Parrott, 5-6 Albion Court, London W6 0QT, England

**Juppe, Alain M** — Prime Minister, France
Mairie, Place Pey-Berland, 33077 Bordeaux Cedex, France

**Jur, Jeffrey** — Cinematographer
4438 Wortser Ave, Studio City CA 91604, USA

**Jurado, Jeanette L** — Singer (Expose), Songwriter
Richard Walters, PO Box 2789, Toluca Lake CA 91610 USA

**Jurak, Edward J (Ed)** — Baseball Player
3650 S Walker Ave, San Pedro CA 90731, USA

**Jurasik, Peter** — Actor
2109 S Wilbur Ave, Walla Walla WA 99362, USA

**Jurevicius, Joseph M (Joe)** — Football Player
3310 Brainard Road, Pepper Pike OH 44142, USA

**Jurgens, Udo** — Singer, Pianist, Songwriter
Freddy Burger Mgmt, Carmentstr 12, 8030 Zurich, Switzerland

**Jurgensen, Christian A (Sonny), III** — Football Player
6963 Greentree Dr, Naples FL 34108, USA

**Jurgensmeier-Carroll, Margaret** — Baseball Player
5245 Rowena Dr, Roscoe IL 61073, USA

**Jurin, Michael** — Guitarist (Stellarstar)
+1 Management/Public Relations, 242 Wythe Ave, #6, Brooklyn NY 11211, USA

**Jurkovic, John I** — Football Player
2212 June Dr, Schereville IN 46375, USA

**Jurowski, Michail** — Conductor
Amalienhof 20, 13581 Berlin, Germany

**Jurowski, Vladimir** — Conductor
I M G Artists, Hogarth Business Park, Chiswick, London W4 2TH, England

**Jurrjens, Jair F** — Baseball Player
Atlanta Braves, Turner Field, 755 Hank Aaron Dr, Atlanta GA 30315 USA

**Just, Ward S** — Writer
Janklow & Nesbit Assoc, 445 Park Ave, #1300, New York NY 10022 USA

**Juster, Norton** — Writer, Architect
55 Kellogg Ave, Amherst MA 01002, USA

**Justice, David C** — Baseball Player
18570 Old Coach Way, Poway CA 92064, USA

**Justice, Victoria** — Actress, Singer
United Talent Agency, U T A Plaza, 9336 Civic Center Dr, Beverly Hills CA 90210 USA

**Justin, Kerry J** — Football Player
13331 W Marlette Court, Litchfield Park AZ 85340, USA

**Justman, Seth** — Singer, Keyboardist (J Geils Band)
Nick Ben-Meir, 652 N Doheny Dr, West Hollywood CA 90069, USA

**Jutze, Alfred H (Skip)** — Baseball Player
3395 Zephry Court, Wheat Ridge CO 80033, USA

**Juvenile** — Rap Artist
Pretty Special, 200 W 72nd St, #64, New York NY 10023, USA

**K7**
AM/PM Entertainment Concepts, 415 63rd St, #200, Brooklyn NY 11220, USA — Rap Artist

**Kaake, Jeff** — Actor
2533 N Carson St, #3105, Carson City NV 89706, USA

**Kaas, Carmen** — Model
Men/Women Model Inc, 199 Lafayette St, #700, New York NY 10012 USA

**Kaas, Patricia** — Singer
Attitude, 71 Rue Robespierre, 93100 Montreuil, France

**Kaat, James L (Jim)** — Baseball Player
PO Box 1130, Port Salerno FL 34992, USA

**Kabakov, Ilya** — Artist
Gladstone Gallery, 515 W 52nd St, New York NY 10019, USA

**Kaberle, Frantisek** — Ice Hockey Player
3105 Briar Stream Run, Raleigh NC 27612, USA

**Kaberle, Tomas** — Ice Hockey Player
Montreal Canadiens, 1275 Saint Antoine St W, Montreal QC H3C 5L2, Canada

**Kabila, Joseph** — President, Congo; Army General
President's Office, Mont Ngaliema, Kinshasa, Congo Democratic Republic

**Kabui, Frank** — Governor General, Soloman Islands
Governor General's House, Box 252, Honiara, Guadacanal, Solomon Islands

**Kac, Eduardo** — Artist
Chicago Art Institute, 112 S Michigan Ave, #400, Chicago IL 60603, USA

**Kaci** — Singer, Songwriter, Dancer
Spectrum Talent Agency, 1650 Broadway, #1105, New York NY 10019, USA

**Kacyvenski, Isaiah J** — Football Player
1081 Beacon St, #8, Brookline MA 02446, USA

**Kaczmarek, Jane** — Actress
Greenlight Mgmt, 13848 Valleyheart Drive, Sherman Oaks CA 91423, USA

**Kaczur, Nick** — Football Player
17K Marie Dr, Attleboro MA 02703, USA

**Kad** — Actor, Writer, Director
1 Mgmt, 9000 W Sunset Blvd, #1550, Los Angeles CA 90069 USA

**Kadanoff, Leo P** — Physicist
5421 S Cornell Ave, Chicago IL 60615, USA

**Kadare, Ismail** — Writer
40 Rue Violet, 75015 Paris, France

**Kadenyuk, Leonid K** — Cosmonaut
Cosmonaut Training Center, Star City, 141160 Zvezdny Gorodok, Moscow Oblast, Russia

**Kadish, Michael S (Mike)** — Football Player
7941 Sudbury Lane SE, Ada MI 49301, USA

**Kadison, Joshua** — Singer, Songwriter, Pianist
Nick Bode, 1265 Electric Ave, Venice CA 90291, USA

**Kaeding, Nathaniel J (Nate)** — Football Player
1528 1st Ave, #A, Coralville IA 52241, USA

**Kaestle, Carl F** — Historian
35 Charlesfield St, Providence RI 02906, USA

**Kaesviharn, Kevin R** — Football Player
6334 Merrimac Lane N, Osseo MN 55311, USA

**Kafatos, Fotis C** — Biologist
Imperial College, Cell/Molecular Biology Dept, London SW7 2AZ, England

**Kafelnikov, Yevgeny A** — Tennis Player
International Mgmt Group, 26 Riverside Dr, Rumson NJ 07760, USA

**Kaftan, George A** — Basketball Player
2591 Lantern Light Way, Manasquan NJ 08736, USA

**Kagan, Daryn** — Commentator
CNN-TV, 190 Marietta Ave SW, Atlanta GA 30303 USA

**Kagan, Elaine** — Actress, Writer
Greene Assoc, 1901 Ave of Stars, #130, Los Angeles CA 90067 USA

**Kagan, Elena** — Supreme Court Justice
US Supreme Court, 1 1st St NE, Washington DC 20543 USA

**Kagan, Henri Boris** — Chemist
Universite Paris-Sud, Institut de Chimie Moleculaire, 91405 Orsay, France

**Kagan, Jeremy Paul** — Director
2024 N Curson Ave, Los Angeles CA 90046, USA

**Kagan, Robert A** — Attorney, Educator
University of California, Law School, Boalt Hall, Berkeley CA 94720, USA

**Kagasoff, Daren** — Actor
Anderson Group Public Relations, 8060 Melrose Ave, #400, Los Angeles CA 90046, USA

**Kagge, Erling** — Polar Skier
Munkedamsveien 86, 0270 Oslo, Norway

**Kahane, Gabriel** — Composer
I M G Artists, Hogarth Business Park, Chiswick, London W4 2TH, England

**Kahane, Jeffrey** — Concert Pianist, Conductor
C M Artists, 127 W 96th St, #13B, New York NY 10025 USA

**Kahin, Brian** — Educator
Harvard University, Information Infrastructure Project, Cambridge MA 02138, USA

**Kahin, Dahir Riyale** — President, Somaliland Republic
President's Office, Hargiesa, Somaliland Republic

**Kahler, Eric** — Educator
University of Minnesota, President's Office, 176 N Mississippi River Blvd, Saint Paul MN 55104, USA

**Kahn, David R** — Publisher
New Yorker, Publisher's Office, 4 Times Square, New York NY 10036, USA

**Kahn, Harold** — Businessman
Wet Seal Inc, 26972 Burbank, Foothill Ranch CA 92610, USA

**Kahn, Joseph** — Director
I C M Partners, 10250 Constellation Blvd, #900, Los Angeles CA 90067 USA

**Kahn, Joseph** — Journalist
New York Times, Editorial Dept, 229 W 43rd St, New York NY 10036 USA

**Kahn, Michael** — Editor
Motion Picture Editors Guild, 7715 Sunset Blvd, #200, Hollywood CA 90046, USA

**Kahn, Nikki** — Photographer
Washington Post, Editorial Dept, 1150 15th St NW, Washington DC 20071 USA

**Kahn, Oliver** — Soccer Player
Playce AG, Osterwaldstr 10, 80805 Munich, Germany

**Kahn, Robert E** — Inventor (Internet Protocol)
909 Lynton Place, McLean VA 22102, USA

**Kahn, Roger** — Writer
PO Box 556, Stone Ridge NY 12484, USA
**Kahn, Si** — Singer, Musician, Songwriter
Real People's Music, 520 S Clinton Ave, Oak Park IL 60304, USA
**Kahne, Kasey K** — Auto Racing Driver
265 Cayuga Dr, Mooresville NC 28117, USA
**Kahneman, Daniel** — Nobel Economics Laureate
70 E 10th St, #HD, New York NY 10003, USA
**Kaifu, Toshiki** — Prime Minister, Japan
House of Representatives, Diet, Tokyo 100 0014, Japan
**Kaihori, Ayumi** — Soccer Player
Football Assn, 3-10-15 Hongo, Bunkyoku, Tokyo 113 0033 Japan
**Kain, Karin A** — Ballet Dancer
National Ballet of Canada, 470 Queens Quay, Toronto ON M5V 3K4, Canada
**Kain, Khalil** — Actor
Envision Entertainment, 8840 Wilshire Blvd, Beverly Hills CA 90211 USA
**Kaine, Whitney** — Model
Playboy Promotions, 2706 Media Center Dr, Los Angeles CA 90065 USA
**Kaipanen, Aume H** — Writer
Sinebrychffinkatu 11B 17, Helsinki 12, Finland
**Kaiser, A Dale** — Biochemist
832 Santa Fe Ave, Stanford CA 94305, USA
**Kaiser, George B** — Financier
Bank of Oklahoma, Bank of Oklahoma Tower, PO Box 2300, Tulsa OK 74102, USA
**Kaiser, Jeffrey P (Jeff)** — Baseball Player
26227 James Dr, Grosse Isle MI 48138, USA
**Kaiser, Joseph** — Opera Singer, Actor
I M G Artists, Carnegie Hall Tower, 152 W 57th St, #500, New York NY 10019 USA
**Kaiser, Michael M** — Concert Executive
Kennedy Center for Performing Arts, 2700 F St NW, Washington DC 20566, USA
**Kaiser, R Thomas (Tom)** — Baseball Player
8 Independence Way, Southampton NJ 08088, USA
**Kaiser, Raf** — Physical Chemist
University of Hawaii, Physical Chemistry Dept, Honolulu HI 96822, USA
**Kaiser, Suki** — Actress
Greene Assoc, 1901 Ave of Stars, #130, Los Angeles CA 90067 USA
**Kaiser, Tim** — Producer
Vision Art Mgmt, 530 N Larchmont Blvd, #2, Los Angeles CA 90004, USA
**Kaiser-Brown, Natasha** — Track Athlete
2601 Hickman Road, Des Moines IA 50310, USA
**Kaiserman, William** — Fashion Designer
29 W 56th St, New York NY 10019, USA
**Kaji, Gautam S** — Government Official, Financier
World Bank Group, 1818 H St NW, Washington DC 20433, USA
**Kajlich, Bianca** — Model, Actress
United Talent Agency, U T A Plaza, 9336 Civic Center Dr, Beverly Hills CA 90210 USA
**Kajol** — Actress
Craving Dreams, 304 Oberoi Chambers II, B Wing off New Link Road, Andheri W, Mumbai 400053, India
**Kaka, Ricardo** — Soccer Player
F C Milan, Via Filippo Turati 3, 20121 Milan, Italy
**Kakhidze, Djansug I** — Conductor
Leselidze St 18, 380005 Tbilisi, Georgia
**Kaku, Michio** — Theoretical Physicist
City University of New York, Physics Dept, New York NY 10031, USA
**Kakutani, Michiko** — Journalist
New York Times, Editorial Dept, 229 W 43rd St, New York NY 10036, USA
**Kalainov, Samuel C** — Businessman
American Mutual Life, 611 5th Ave, Des Moines IA 50309, USA
**Kalashnikov, Mikhail T** — Weapon Designer (AK-47), Army General
Sovietskaya Ul 21A, #KV 46, 426076 Izhevsk, Russia
**Kalb, Marvin** — Commentator, Educator
1717 Massachusetts Ave NW, #610, Washington DC 20036, USA
**Kaldor, Connie** — Singer, Songwriter
Fleming Artists, 543 N Main St, Ann Arbor MI 48104, USA
**Kalem, Toni** — Actress
Creative Artists Agency, 2000 Ave of Stars, #100, Los Angeles CA 90067 USA
**Kalember, Patricia** — Actress
Innovative Artists, 1505 10th St, Santa Monica CA 90401 USA
**Kalen, Herbert D** — Vietnam War Air Force Hero
General Delivery, Angel Fire NM 87710, USA
**Kaler, Jamie** — Actor, Comedian
Paradigm Agency, 360 N Crescent Dr, North Building, Beverly Hills CA 90210 USA
**Kaleri, Aleksandr Y (Sasha)** — Cosmonaut
141 160 Svyosdny Gorodok, Moskovskoi Oblasti, Potchta Kosmonavtor, Russia
**Kalesniko, Michael** — Director, Writer
Creative Artists Agency, 2000 Ave of Stars, #100, Los Angeles CA 90067 USA
**Kalichstein, Joseph** — Concert Pianist
Opus 3 Artists, 470 Park Ave S, #900N, New York NY 10016 USA
**Kalikow, Peter S** — Publisher
H J Kalikow Co, 101 Park Ave, #2500, New York NY 10178, USA
**Kalil, Matt** — Football Player
Minnesota Vikings, 9520 Viking Dr, Eden Prairie MN 55344 USA
**Kalin, Tom** — Director, Writer
Creative Artists Agency, 2000 Ave of Stars, #100, Los Angeles CA 90067 USA
**Kalina, Mike** — Chef
Travelin' Gourmet Show, PBS-TV, 1320 Braddock Place, Alexandria VA 22314, USA
**Kalina, Richard** — Artist
44 King St, New York NY 10014, USA
**Kaline, Albert W (Al)** — Baseball Player
3613 York Court, Bloomfield Hills MI 48301, USA
**Kaling, Mindy** — Actress, Comedienne, Writer
United Talent Agency, U T A Plaza, 9336 Civic Center Dr, Beverly Hills CA 90210 USA
**Kalinin, Dmitri** — Ice Hockey Player
555 Pleasantville Road, #210N, Briarcliff NY 10510, USA
**Kalis, Todd A** — Football Player
900 Bayview Court, Cranberry Township PA 16066, USA

| | |
|---|---|
| **Kalish, Martin** | Labor Leader |
| School Administrators Federation, 853 Broadway, New York NY 10003, USA | |
| **Kalish, Robert P** | Government Official, Financier |
| Government National Mortgage Assn, 451 7th St SW, Washington DC 20410, USA | |
| **Kalitta, Connie** | Auto Racing Driver |
| Kalitta Motorsports, 1010 James L Hart Parkway, Ypsilanti MI 48197, USA | |
| **Kaljuste, Tonu** | Conductor |
| Konzertdirektion Hortnagel, Oranienburgen Str 50D, 10117 Berlin, Germany | |
| **Kalla, Charlotte** | Cross Country Skier |
| Swedish Ski Federation, Riksskidstadion, 791 19 Falun, Sweden | |
| **Kallaugher, Kevin (Kall)** | Editorial Cartoonist |
| Baltimore Sun, Editorial Dept, 501 N Calvert St, Baltimore MD 21278, USA | |
| **Kallen, Jackie** | Boxing Manager |
| Trident Media, 41 Madison Ave, #3600, New York NY 10010, USA | |
| **Kallen, Kitty** | Singer, Actress |
| 35 Winthrop Place, Englewood NJ 07631, USA | |
| **Kallin, Catherine** | Physicist |
| 224 Hillcrest Ave, Hamilton ON L8P 2X5, Canada | |
| **Kallisch, Cornelia** | Opera Singer |
| Kunstler Sekretariat am Gasteig, Rosenheimer Str 52, 81669 Munich, Germany | |
| **Kallita, Doug** | Auto Racing Driver |
| Kalitta Motorsports, 1010 James L Hart Parkway, Ypsilanti MI 48197, USA | |
| **Kallosh, Renata** | Physicist |
| Stanford University, Physics Dept, Stanford CA 94305, USA | |
| **Kallur, Anders** | Ice Hockey Player |
| Utsiktsvagen 14, 791 31 Falun, Sweden | |
| **Kalman, Rudolf E** | Mathematician |
| E T H Zentrum, 8092 Zurich, Switzerland | |
| **Kalonji, Sizzla** | Singer |
| Agency Group Ltd, 142 W 57th St, #600, New York NY 10019 USA | |
| **Kalpokas, Donald M** | Prime Minister, Vanuatu |
| Vanuaaku Pati, PO Box 472, Port Vila, Vanuatu | |
| **Kalu, Ndukwe D (N D)** | Football Player |
| 3719 Popular Springs Dr, Missouri City TX 77459, USA | |
| **Kalule, Ayub** | Boxer |
| Palie, Skjulet, Bagsvaert 12, Copenhagen 2880, Denmark | |
| **Kalyan, Adhir** | Actor |
| Abrams Artists, 9200 W Sunset Blvd, #1125, West Hollywood CA 90069 USA | |
| **Kamal, Gray** | Keyboardist (Roots) |
| Helter Skelter, 347-353 Chiswick High Road, London W4 4HS, England | |
| **Kamali, Norma** | Fashion Designer |
| O M O Norma Kamali, 11 W 56th St, New York NY 10019, USA | |
| **Kaman, Christopher Z (Chris)** | Basketball Player |
| 300 N Dianthus St, Manhattan Beach CA 90266, USA | |
| **Kamano, Stacy** | Actress, Model |
| Vision Mgmt, 8500 Steller Dr, Building 8, Culver City CA 90232, USA | |
| **Kamarck, Andrew M** | Financier, Diplomat |
| PO Box 1267, Brewster MA 02631, USA | |
| **Kamarck, Martin A** | Government Official, Financier |
| Export-Import Bank, 811 Vermont Ave NW, Washington DC 20571, USA | |
| **Kamb, Alexander** | Geneticist |
| 300 Alberta Way, Hillsborough CA 94010, USA | |
| **Kamen, Dean** | Inventor (Portable Dialysis Machine) |
| D E K A Research & Development, 340 Commercial St, Manchester NH 03101, USA | |
| **Kamen, Robert Mark** | Writer |
| Paradigm Agency, 360 N Crescent Dr, North Building, Beverly Hills CA 90210 USA | |
| **Kamensky, Valeri** | Ice Hockey Player |
| 4 Stonehedge Dr S, Greenwich CT 06831, USA | |
| **Kamieniecki, Scott A** | Baseball Player |
| 7800 Somerhill Lane, Clarkston MI 48348, USA | |
| **Kamin, Aaron K** | Guitarist (Calling), Songwriter |
| Prince Promotions, 9663 Santa Monica Blvd, #324, Beverly Hills CA 90210, USA | |
| **Kamin, Blair** | Architectural Critic |
| Chicago Tribune, Editorial Dept, 350 N Orleans St, Chicago IL 60654 USA | |
| **Kaminir, Lisa** | Actress |
| Ellis Talent Group, 4705 Laurel Canyon Blvd, #300, Valley Village CA 91607, USA | |
| **Kaminski, Janusz Z** | Cinematographer |
| 23801 Calabasas Road, #2004, Calabasas CA 91302, USA | |
| **Kaminski, Larry M** | Football Player |
| 31423 State Highway 3 NE, Poulsbo WA 98370, USA | |
| **Kaminski, Marek** | Explorer |
| Ul Dickmana 14/15, 80339 Gdansk, Poland | |
| **Kaminsky, Arthur C** | Sports Attorney |
| Athletes & Artists, 888 7th Ave, #3700, New York NY 10106, USA | |
| **Kaminsky, James** | Editor |
| Maxim, Dennis Publishing, 1040 Ave of Americas, #1500, New York NY 10018, USA | |
| **Kaminsky, Kevin S** | Ice Hockey Player |
| 162 Dryad Woods Road, Raymond ME 04071, USA | |
| **Kaminsky, Walter** | Chemist |
| Hamburg University, Chemistry Dept, Martin-Luther-King Platz 6, 20146 Hamburg, Germany | |
| **Kamisar, Yale** | Attorney, Educator |
| 2910 Daleview Dr, Ann Arbor MI 48105, USA | |
| **Kamm, Henry** | Journalist |
| New York Times, Editorial Dept, 229 W 43rd St, New York NY 10036, USA | |
| **Kammen, Michael G** | Historian |
| Cornell University, History Dept, McGraw Hall, Ithaca NY 14853, USA | |
| **Kammer, Jerry** | Journalist |
| San Diego Union-Tribune, Editorial Dept, 350 Camino Reina, San Diego CA 92108 USA | |
| **Kammerer, Carlton C (Carl)** | Football Player |
| 6941 Brooks Road, Highland MD 20777, USA | |
| **Kammerlander, Hansjorg (Hans)** | Mountaineer |
| Hotel Kammerlander, #69A, 6274 Aschau im Zillertal (T), Austria | |
| **Kamp, Alexandra** | Actress, Model |
| Agentur Aziel, Pfarrstr 94, 10317 Berlin, Germany | |
| **Kampman, Aaron A** | Football Player |
| PO Box 246, Solon IA 52333, USA | |

**Kampmeier, Deborah** — Director, Writer
I C M Partners, 10250 Constellation Blvd, #900, Los Angeles CA 90067 USA

**Kamu, Okko T** — Conductor
Calle Mozart 7, Rancho Domingo, 29639 Benalmedina Pueblo, Spain

**Kan, Yuet Wai** — Geneticist
20 Yerba Buena Ave, San Francisco CA 94127, USA

**Kanakaredes, Melina** — Actress
W M E Entertainment, 9601 Wilshire Blvd, #300, Beverly Hills CA 90210 USA

**Kanal, Tony** — Bassist, Songwriter (No Doubt)
Rebel Waltz, 31652 2nd Ave, Laguna Beach CA 92651, USA

**Kanaly, Steve** — Actor
C E S D, 10635 Santa Monica Blvd, #130, Los Angeles CA 90025 USA

**Kanamori, Hiroo** — Geophysicist
California Institute of Technology, Geophysics Dept, Pasadena CA 91125, USA

**Kanan, Sean** — Actor
Stone Manners Salners, 9911 W Pico Blvd, #1400, Los Angeles CA 90035 USA

**Kananin, Roman G** — Architect
Joint-Stock Mosprojekt, 13/14 1 Brestkaya Str, 125190 Moscow, Russia

**Kancheli, Giya A (Georgy)** — Composer
Tovstonogov Str 6, 380064 Tbilisi, Georgia

**Kandel, Eric R** — Nobel Medicine Laureate
9 Sigma Place, Bronx NY 10471, USA

**Kander, John H** — Composer
146 Central Park W, #14D, New York NY 10023, USA

**Kandil, Hesham** — Prime Minister, Egypt
Prime Minister's Office, PO Box 191, 1 Majlis El-Shaab St, Cairo CA104, Egypt

**Kane Elson, Marion** — Synchronized Swimmer
4669 Badger Road, Santa Rosa CA 95409, USA

**Kane, Carol** — Actress
Glick Agency, 1321 7th St, #203, Santa Monica CA 90401 USA

**Kane, Chelsea** — Actress, Singer
United Talent Agency, U T A Plaza, 9336 Civic Center Dr, Beverly Hills CA 90210 USA

**Kane, Christian** — Actor, Singer, Songwriter
Sutton-Barth Vennari, 5900 Wilshire Blvd, #700, Los Angeles CA 90036 USA

**Kane, Howie** — Singer (Jay & the Americans)
T C I, 105 Shad Row, #D, Piermont NY 10968, USA

**Kane, John C** — Businessman
Cardinal Health, 7000 Cardinal Place, Dublin OH 43017, USA

**Kane, Kelly** — Actress
D H Talent, 1800 N Highland Ave, #300, Los Angeles CA 90028 USA

**Kane, Lorie** — Golfer
101-5397 Eglinton Ave W, Etobicoke ON M9C 5K6, Canada

**Kane, Matt** — Actor
United Talent Agency, U T A Plaza, 9336 Civic Center Dr, Beverly Hills CA 90210 USA

**Kane, Nick** — Singer (Mavericks)
AstroMedia, 1620 16th Ave S, Nashville TN 37212, USA

**Kane, Patrick T** — Ice Hockey Player
213 McKinley Parkway, Buffalo NY 14220, USA

**Kane, Robert H** — Philosopher
University of Texas, Philosophy Dept, Austin TX 78712, USA

**Kanell, Daniel P (Danny)** — Football Player
4631 NE 25th Ave, Fort Lauderdale FL 33308, USA

**Kanellis, Maria** — Professional Wrestler, Model
World Wrestling Entertainment, Titan Towers, 1241 E Main St, Stamford CT 06902 USA

**Kanengiser, William** — Guitarist (LAGQ)
Besen Arts, 77 Park Ave, #128, Hoboken NJ 07030, USA

**Kaneswaren, Siva** — Singer (Wanted), Model
Industry Music Group, 128 Regent Road, Hanley Stoke, Trent ST1 3AY, England

**Kang, Dong-Suk** — Concert Violinist
Clarion/Seven Muses, 47 Whitehall Park, London N19 3TW, England

**Kang, Jimin** — Golfer
8539 E Cactus Wren Circle, Scottsdale AZ 85266, USA

**Kang, Tim** — Actor
Vincent Cirrincione Assoc, 1516 N Fairfax Ave, Los Angeles CA 90046 USA

**Kanicki, James H (Jim)** — Football Player
Tackle Hill Farm, 4590 Schramling Road, Pierpont OH 44082, USA

**Kanievska, Marek** — Director
I C M Partners, 10250 Constellation Blvd, #900, Los Angeles CA 90067 USA

**Kann Valar, Paula** — Alpine Skier
34 Hubertus Ring, Franconia NH 03580, USA

**Kann, Peter R** — Businessman, Publisher, Journalist
Dow Jones Co, 1 World Financial Center, #900, New York NY 10281, USA

**Kanne, Michael S** — Judge
US Court of Appeals, PO Box 1340, Lafayette IN 47902, USA

**Kannenberg, Bernd** — Track Athlete
Sportschule, 87527 Sonthofen/Allgau, Germany

**Kanouse, Lyle** — Actor
Avalon Artists Group, 5455 Wilshire Blvd, #900, Los Angeles CA 90036, USA

**Kantner, Paul L** — Guitarist (Jefferson Airplane, Starship)
Mission Control, 15030 Ventura Blvd, #300, Sherman Oaks CA 91403, USA

**Kantor, Michael (Mickey)** — Secretary, Commerce
2709 Olive Ave NW, Washington DC 20007, USA

**Kao, Archie** — Actor
C E S D, 10635 Santa Monica Blvd, #130, Los Angeles CA 90025 USA

**Kao, Charles K** — Nobel Physics Laureate
Yee Foundation, 1 Harbour Road, #1708, Wan Chai, Hong Kong, China

**Kao, Min H** — Businessman
Garmin International, 1200 E 151st St, Olathe KS 66062, USA

**Kapadia, Asif** — Actor, Writer, Director
Independent Talent Group, 40 Whitfield St, London W1T 2RH, England

**Kapadia, Dimple** — Actress
201A Vastu Building, Military Road Juhu, Mumbai MS 400049, India

**Kapanen, Niko K P** — Ice Hockey Player
Ak Bars Kazan, Tatneff Arena, Kazan, Tatarstan, Russia

**Kapanen, Sami H K** — Ice Hockey Player
Kalpa Hockey, Sairaalakatu 15, 70110 Kuopio, Finland

**Kapches, Ko** — Singer, Songwriter
Agency Group Ltd, 142 W 57th St, #600, New York NY 10019 USA
**Kapelos, John** — Actor
Axiom Mgmt, 10701 Wilshire Blvd, #1202, Los Angeles CA 90024, USA
**Kapilow, Robert (Rob)** — Conductor, Composer
I M G Artists, Hogarth Business Park, Chiswick, London W4 2TH, England
**Kapinos, Tom** — Producer, Writer
Creative Artists Agency, 2000 Ave of Stars, #100, Los Angeles CA 90067 USA
**Kapioitas, John** — Businessman
I T T Sheraton Corp, 1111 Westchester Ave, West Harrison NY 10604, USA
**Kaplan, Gabe** — Actor, Comedian
9551 Hidden Valley Road, Beverly Hills CA 90210, USA
**Kaplan, Jonathan S** — Director
4323 Ben Ave, Studio City CA 91604, USA
**Kaplan, Justin** — Writer
PO Box 219, Truro MA 02666, USA
**Kaplan, Nathan O** — Biochemist
8587 La Jolla Scenic Dr, La Jolla CA 92037, USA
**Kaplan, Paul** — Singer, Songwriter
Old Coat Music, 203 Heatherstone Road, Amherst MA 01002, USA
**Kaplansky, Lucy** — Singer, Guitarist, Songwriter
Fleming Artists, 543 N Main St, Ann Arbor MI 48104, USA
**Kapler, Gabriel S (Gabe)** — Baseball Player
18316 Palomar Place, Tarzana CA 91356, USA
**Kaplin, Marvin** — Actor, Writer, Producer
Stage 9 Talent, 1249 N Lodi Place, Los Angeles CA 90038, USA
**Kapnek, Emily** — Producer, Wrtiter
Gotham Group, 9255 Sunset Blvd, #515, Los Angeles CA 90069, USA
**Kapoor, Anil** — Actor
I C M Partners, 10250 Constellation Blvd, #900, Los Angeles CA 90067 USA
**Kapoor, Anish** — Sculptor
33 Coleherne Road, London SW10, England
**Kapoor, Kareena** — Actress
2B/110/1201 Excellency 4th Cross Road, Mumbai MS 400058, India
**Kapoor, Karisma** — Actress
1101/1201 4th Cross Road, Andheri W, Mumbai MS 400048, India
**Kapoor, Rishi** — Actor
27 Krishna Raj, Pali Hill Bandra, Mumbai MS 400058, India
**Kapoor, Shashi** — Actor
112 Atlas Apartments, Mumbai 400006, India
**Kapor, Mitchell D** — Computer Programmer
Open Source Application Foundation, 177 Post St, #900, San Francisco CA 94108, USA
**Kapp, Joseph (Joe)** — Football Player, Coach
PO Box 1973, Los Gatos CA 95031, USA
**Kappe, Ron** — Architect
715 Brooktree Road, Pacific Palisades CA 90272, USA
**Kapranos, Alexander P (Alex)** — Singer, Guitarist (Franz Ferdinand)
M A M A Group, 59-65 Worship St, London EC2A 2DU, England
**Kaprisky, Valerie** — Actress
Artmedia, 20 Ave Rapp, 75007 Paris, France
**Kapture, Mitzi** — Actress
Lovett Mgmt, 1327 Brinkley Ave, Los Angeles CA 90049 USA
**Kapur, Shekhar** — Director
Sentient Entertainment, 1617 Broadway, Mezzanine, Santa Monica CA 90404, USA
**Karabits, Kirill** — Conductor
Bournemouth Symphony Orchestra, 2 Seldown Lane, Poole, Dorset BH15 1UF, England
**Karadaglic, Milos** — Concert Guitarist
I M G Artists, Hogarth Business Park, Chiswick, London W4 2TH, England
**Karaev, Anatol** — Concert Violinist
I M G Artists, Hogarth Business Park, Chiswick, London W4 2TH, England
**Karageorghis, Vassos** — Archaeologist
Foundation Anastasios Leventis, 28 Sofoulis St, Nicosia, Cyprus
**Karagias, Evan** — Professional Wrestler
2009 Tomshire Dr, Gastonia NC 28056, USA
**Karamanov, Alemdar S** — Composer
Voykova Str 2, #4, Simferopol, Crimea, Ukraine
**Karamesines, Chris** — Drag Racing Driver
7444 S Claremont Ave, Chicago IL 60636, USA
**Karan, Amara** — Actress
Curtis Brown Group, 28-29 Haymarket St, #500, London SW1Y 4SP, England
**Karan, Donna** — Fashion Designer
Donna Karan Co, 361 Newbury St, Boston MA 02115, USA
**Karasev, Sergey V** — Basketball Player
Cleveland Cavaliers, Gund Arena, 1 Center Court, Cleveland OH 44115 USA
**Karathanasis, Sotirios K** — Physiologist
AstraZeneca, Bioscience Dept, Pepparedsleden 1, 431 83 Molndal, Sweden
**Karchner, Matthew D (Matt)** — Baseball Player
401 E 2nd St, Berwick PA 18603, USA
**Kardashian, Khloe A** — Actress, Producer
W M E Entertainment, 9601 Wilshire Blvd, #300, Beverly Hills CA 90210 USA
**Kardashian, Kimberly (Kim)** — Actress, Model
W M E Entertainment, 9601 Wilshire Blvd, #300, Beverly Hills CA 90210 USA
**Kardashian, Kourtney** — Actress
W M E Entertainment, 9601 Wilshire Blvd, #300, Beverly Hills CA 90210 USA
**Kardashian, Robert A (Rob), Jr** — Actor
A P A Talent/Literary Agency, 405 S Beverly Dr, #300, Beverly Hills CA 90212 USA
**Karelin, Alesander A** — Greco-Roman Wrestler
State Duma, Yedinstvo Faction, Okhotny Ryad 1, 103265 Moscow, Russia
**Karelskaya, Rimma K** — Ballerina
Bolshoi Theater, Teatralnaya Pl 1, 103009 Moscow, Russia
**Karen, James** — Actor
Amsel Eisenstadt Frazier, 5055 Wilshire Blvd, #865, Los Angeles CA 90036 USA
**Karieva, Bernara** — Ballerina
National Ballet Theater, 28 MK Otaturk St, 700029 Tashkent, Uzbekistan
**Karim, Jawed** — Businessman
YouTube, 1000 Cherry Ave, #200, San Bruno CA 94066, USA

**K**

| | |
|---|---|
| **Karim-Lamrani, Mohammed**<br>Rue du Mont Saint Michel, Anfa Superieur, Casablanca 21300, Morocco | Prime Minister, Morocco |
| **Karimov, Islom M**<br>President's Office, Uzbekistansky Prosp 45, 700163 Tashkent, Uzbekistan | President, Uzbekistan |
| **Karina, Anna**<br>Artmedia, 20 Ave Rapp, 75007 Paris, France | Actress |
| **Kariya, Paul T**<br>2493 Aquasanta, Tustin CA 92782, USA | Ice Hockey Player |
| **Karkovice, Ronald J (Ron)**<br>3201 Oakstand Lane, Orlando FL 32812, USA | Baseball Player |
| **Karl, Benjamin M**<br>Snowboard Federation, Olympic St 10, 6010 Innsbruck, Austria | Snowboarding Athlete |
| **Karl, George M**<br>145 Kearney St, Denver CO 80220, USA | Basketball Coach, Executive |
| **Karl, R Scott**<br>11765 Costa Blanca Ave, Las Vegas NV 89138, USA | Baseball Player |
| **Karle, Isabella**<br>6304 Lakeview Dr, Falls Church VA 22041, USA | Chemist |
| **Karlen, John**<br>Gersh Agency, 9465 Wilshire Blvd, #600, Beverly Hills CA 90212 USA | Actor |
| **Karlic, Estanislao E Cardinal**<br>Monte Caseris 77, 3100 Parana (Entre Rios), Argentina | Religious Leader |
| **Karlin, Ben**<br>United Talent Agency, U T A Plaza, 9336 Civic Center Dr, Beverly Hills CA 90210 USA | Writer, Producer |
| **Karlis, Richard J (Rich)**<br>13807 E Greenwood Dr, Aurora CO 80014, USA | Football Player |
| **Karlsson, Erik**<br>Ottawa Senators, Scotia Bank Place, Kanata ON K2V 1A5, Canada | Ice Hockey Player |
| **Karlsson, Lena**<br>M O B Agency, 6404 Wilshire Blvd, #505, Los Angeles CA 90048 USA | Singer (Komeda) |
| **Karlstad, Geir**<br>Hamarveien 5A, 1472 Fjellhamar, Norway | Speed Skater |
| **Karlzen, Mary**<br>Little Big Man, 155 Ave of Americas, #700, New York NY 10013, USA | Singer, Songwriter |
| **Karman, Tawakul**<br>Al-Islah Party, Parliament Building, Sana's, Yemen | Nobel Peace Laureate |
| **Karmann, Sam**<br>Les Films A4, 41 Rue Vivienne 75002 Paris, France | Actor |
| **Karmanos, Peter, Jr**<br>Compuware Corp, 1 Campus Martius, Detroit MI 48226, USA | Businessman, Hockey Executive |
| **Karmazin, Mel**<br>Sirius Satelite Radio, 1221 Avenue of Americas, #3600, New York NY 10020, USA | Businessman |
| **Karmi-Melamede, Ada**<br>Karmi Architects, 17 Kaplan St, Tel Aviv 64734, Israel | Architect |
| **Karn, Richard**<br>Stone Manners Salners, 9911 W Pico Blvd, #1400, Los Angeles CA 90035 USA | Actor |
| **Karnes, David K**<br>9639 Oak Circle, Omaha NE 68124, USA | Senator, NE |
| **Karnes, Jay**<br>Innovative Artists, 1505 10th St, Santa Monica CA 90401 USA | Actor |
| **Karneus, Katarina**<br>Ingpen & Williams, 131 Putney Bridge Road, London SW15 2PA, England | Opera Singer |
| **Karolyi, Bela**<br>454 Forest Service 200 Road, Huntsville TX 77340, USA | Gymnastics Coach |
| **Karolyi, Marta**<br>World Gymnastics Academy, 1937 W Parker Road, Plano TX 75023, USA | Gymnastics Coach |
| **Karon, Jan**<br>7060 Esmont Farm, Esmont VA 22937, USA | Writer |
| **Karp, Peter**<br>Road Dawg Touring, PO Box 2835, Evergreen CO 80437, USA | Singer, Songwriter |
| **Karp, Richard M**<br>University of Washington, Computer Science Dept, Seattle WA 98195, USA | Computer Scientist, Engineer |
| **Karpati, Gyorgy**<br>Il Liva Utca 1, 1025 Budapest, Hungary | Water Polo Player |
| **Karpluk, Erin**<br>Play Mgmt, 807 Powell St, #220, Vancouver BC V6A 1H7, Canada | Actress |
| **Karplus, Martin**<br>Harvard University, Chemistry Dept, Cambridge MA 02138, USA | Nobel Chemistry Laureate |
| **Karponosov, Gennadiy**<br>146 Dallam Road, Newark DE 19711, USA | Ice Dancer, Coach |
| **Karpovsky, Alex**<br>Mosiac Media Group, 9200 W Sunset Blvd, #1000, Los Angeles CA 90069 USA | Actor, Director |
| **Karr, Mary**<br>Syracuse University, English Dept, Syracuse NY 13244, USA | Writer |
| **Karrass, Chester L**<br>1633 Stanford St, Santa Monica CA 90404, USA | Writer |
| **Karros, Eric P**<br>1170 Longfellow Dr, Manhattan Beach CA 90266, USA | Baseball Player |
| **Karrys, George**<br>Curling Assn, 1660 Vimont Court, Cumberland ON K4A 4J4, Canada | Curling Athlete |
| **Karsay, Stefan A (Steve)**<br>20244 N 102nd Place, Scottsdale AZ 85255, USA | Baseball Player |
| **Karsenty, Gerard**<br>Columbia University Medical Center, 701 W 168th St, #1602A, New York NY 10032, USA | Geneticist |
| **Karsh, Jonathan**<br>Relativity Real, 1040 N Las Palmas Ave, Los Angeles CA 90038, USA | Producer, Director |
| **Karst, Kenneth L**<br>University of California, Law School, PO Box 951476, Los Angeles CA 90095, USA | Attorney, Educator |
| **Karstens, Jeffrey W (Jeff)**<br>212 S Moody Ave, #3, Tampa FL 33609, USA | Baseball Player |
| **Kartheiser, Vincent P**<br>Paradigm Agency, 360 N Crescent Dr, North Building, Beverly Hills CA 90210 USA | Actor |
| **Kartz, Keith L**<br>19232 E Hinsdale Lane, Centennial CO 80016, USA | Football Player |
| **Karume, Amani Abeid**<br>President's Office, State House, PO Box 776, Zanzibar, Tanzania | President, Zanzibar |

**Karim-Lamrani - Karume**

| | |
|---|---|
| **Karyo, Tcheky** | Actor |
| Artmedia, 20 Ave Rapp, 75007 Paris, France | |
| **Karzai, Hamid** | President, Afghanistan |
| President's Office, Shar Rahi Sedarat, Kabul, Afghanistan | |
| **Kasaks, Sally Frame** | Businesswoman |
| AnnTaylor Stores, 7 Times Square, #4, New York NY 10036, USA | |
| **Kasarova, Vesselina** | Opera Singer |
| Opera et Concert, 37 Rue de la Chaussee d'Antin, 75009 Paris, France | |
| **Kasatkina, Natalya K** | Ballerina, Choreographer |
| Karietny Riad, H 5/10, #37, 103006 Moscow, Russia | |
| **Kasatonov, Alexei V** | Ice Hockey Player |
| 153 Eagle Rock Way, Montclair NJ 07042, USA | |
| **Kasay, John D** | Football Player |
| 8812 Covey Rise Court, Charlotte NC 28226, USA | |
| **Kasch, Cody** | Actor |
| Talent Works, 3500 W Olive Ave, #1400, Burbank CA 91505 USA | |
| **Kasch, Max** | Actor |
| Abrams Artists, 9200 W Sunset Blvd, #1125, West Hollywood CA 90069 USA | |
| **Kasdan, Jacob (Jake)** | Director, Actor |
| W M E Entertainment, 9601 Wilshire Blvd, #300, Beverly Hills CA 90210 USA | |
| **Kasdan, Lawrence E** | Director, Writer |
| Kasdan Pictures, PO Box 17578, Beverly Hills CA 90209, USA | |
| **Kaselawski, Bradley R (Brad)** | Auto Racing Driver |
| K Auto Motorsports, 2790 Auburn Road, Auburn Hills MI 48326, USA | |
| **Kasem, Casey** | Entertainer, Actor |
| 138 N Mapleton Dr, Los Angeles CA 90077, USA | |
| **Kasem, Jean** | Actress |
| 138 N Mapleton Dr, Los Angeles CA 90077, USA | |
| **Kaseman, Keith** | Architect |
| Kaseman Beckman Advanced Strategies, 408 Vine St, #2B, Philadelphia PA 19106, USA | |
| **Kaser, Helmut A** | Soccer Executive |
| Hitzigweg 11, 8032 Zurich, Switzerland | |
| **Kasha, Al** | Composer, Lyricist |
| 458 N Oakhurst Dr, #102, Beverly Hills CA 90210, USA | |
| **Kasher, Tim** | Singer, Guitarist (Cursive) |
| Ground Control Touring, 20 Jay St, #826, Brooklyn NY 11201 USA | |
| **Kashiwara, Masaki** | Mathematician |
| Mathematical Science Institute, Kyoto University, Kyoto 606 8502, Japan | |
| **Kashkari, Neel** | Financier, Government Official |
| Treasury Department, 1500 Pennsylvania Ave NW, Washington DC 20220 USA | |
| **Kashkashian, Kim** | Concert Violist |
| Musicians Corporate Mgmt, PO Box 825, Highland NY 12528, USA | |
| **Kaskey, Raymond J** | Sculptor, Architect |
| 2221 Hiatt Place NW, Washington DC 20007, USA | |
| **Kasko, Edward M (Eddie)** | Baseball Player, Manager |
| 32 Major Ginter Court, Richmond VA 23227, USA | |
| **Kasler, James H** | Korean War Air Force Hero |
| 8993 E 1500N Road, Momence IL 60954, USA | |
| **Kasling, Dagmar Luhenschloss** | Track Athlete |
| Hollehocjstr 27E, 39110 Magdeburg, Germany | |
| **Kasman, Yakov** | Concert Pianist |
| Jonathan Wentworth Assoc, 10 Fiske Place, #530, Mount Vernon NY 10550 USA | |
| **Kasparov, Garry K** | Chess Player |
| Kasparov Agency, 3114 45th St, #8, West Palm Beach FL 33407, USA | |
| **Kasper, Kevin J** | Football Player |
| 3119 Landore Dr, Naperville IL 60564, USA | |
| **Kasper, Steve** | Ice Hockey Player, Coach |
| 6 Swan Lane, Andover MA 01810, USA | |
| **Kasper, Walter Cardinal** | Religious Leader |
| Consiglio per L'Unita dei Crostoamo, Via dell'Erba 1, 00193 Rome, Italy | |
| **Kaspszyk, Jacek** | Conductor |
| Teatr Wielki, Pl Teatralny 1, 00077 Warsaw, Poland | |
| **Kasrashvili, Makvala** | Opera Singer |
| Bolshoi Theater, Teatralnaya Pl 1, 103009 Moscow, Russia | |
| **Kass, Carmen** | Model, Actress |
| Women Model Mgmt, 199 Lafayette St, #700, New York NY 10012 USA | |
| **Kass, Daniel (Danny)** | Snowboard Skier |
| 4315 NE Laurelhurst Place, Portland OR 97213, USA | |
| **Kass, Leon R** | Bioethicist |
| 1150 17th St NW, #AE1, Washington DC 20036, USA | |
| **Kassay, Jacob** | Artist |
| Eleven Rivington, 11 Rivington St & 195 Chrystie St, New York NY 10002, USA | |
| **Kassebaum, Nancy Landon** | Senator, KS |
| Robert Wood Johnson Foundation, College Road E, Princeton NJ 08543, USA | |
| **Kassell, Brad** | Football Player |
| 20117 Rancho Cielo Court, Lago Vista TX 78645, USA | |
| **Kassell, Carl** | Commentator |
| National Public Radio, 635 Massachusetts Ave NW, #1, Washington DC 20001, USA | |
| **Kassell, Nicole** | Director, Writer |
| Washington Square Arts, 1041 N Formosa Ave, Formosa Building, West Hollywood CA 90046, USA | |
| **Kassir, John** | Actor, Producer |
| Vincent Cirrincione Assoc, 1516 N Fairfax Ave, Los Angeles CA 90046 USA | |
| **Kassoma, A Paulo** | Prime Minister, Angola |
| National Assemby, Rua do 1 Confresso do M P L A, CP 1204 Luanda, Angola | |
| **Kassorla, Irene C** | Psychologist |
| 908 N Roxbury Dr, Beverly Hills CA 90210, USA | |
| **Kassovitz, Mathieu** | Actor, Director |
| M N P Enterprise, 18 Rue Du Fabourge du Temple, 75011 Paris, France | |
| **Kasten, Robert W, Jr** | Senator, WI |
| Kasten Co, 888 16th St NW, #700, Washington DC 20006, USA | |
| **Kastor, Deena** | Track Athlete |
| 1208 Majestic Pines Dr, Mammoth Lakes CA 93546, USA | |
| **Kasulke, Benjamin** | Cinematographer |
| United Talent Agency, U T A Plaza, 9336 Civic Center Dr, Beverly Hills CA 90210 USA | |
| **Kasyanov, Mikhail M** | Prime Minister, Russia |
| House of Government, Krasnopresneskaya Nab 2, 103274 Moscow, Russia | |

**K**

| | |
|---|---|
| **Katainen, Jyrki T** | Prime Minister, Finland |
| Prime Minister's Office, Snellmaninkatu 1A, 00170, Helsinki, Finland | |
| **Katchor, Ben** | Cartoonist (Julius Knipl) |
| Wylie Agency, 250 W 57th St, #2114, New York NY 10107 USA | |
| **Kate** | Duchess of Cambridge |
| Clarence House, Stable Yard Gate, London SW1A 1BA, England | |
| **Katehi, Linda P B** | Educator |
| University of California, Chancellor's Office, 1 Shields Ave, Davis CA 95616, USA | |
| **Kates, Kimberley** | Actress |
| David Talent, 116 S Gardner St, Los Angeles CA 90036, USA | |
| **Kates, Robert W** | Geographer |
| 1081 Bar Harbor Road, Trenton ME 04605, USA | |
| **Kathpalia, Rajeev** | Architect |
| Vastu Shilpa Consultants, Sangath, Thaltej Road, Ahmedabad 380054, India | |
| **Katic, Stana J** | Actress |
| Third Hill Entertainment, 195 S Beverly Dr, #400, Beverly Hills CA 90212, USA | |
| **Katims, Jason** | Producer |
| Creative Artists Agency, 2000 Ave of Stars, #100, Los Angeles CA 90067 USA | |
| **Katin, Peter R** | Concert Pianist |
| 4 Clarence Road, Croydon, Surrrey CR0 2EN, England | |
| **Katleman, Michael** | Director |
| United Talent Agency, U T A Plaza, 9336 Civic Center Dr, Beverly Hills CA 90210 USA | |
| **Kato, Masaya** | Actor |
| Paceline Entertainment, 12444 Ventura Blvd, #103, Studio City CA 91604 USA | |
| **Katon, Rosanne** | Actress, Model |
| 407 Ocean Front Walk, #5, Venice CA 90291, USA | |
| **Katona, Kerry J E** | Entertainer, Singer |
| Flood Bumstead McCready McCarthy, 1700 Hayes St, #304, Nashville TN 37203 USA | |
| **Katritzky, Alan R** | Chemist |
| 1221 SW 21st Ave, Gainesville FL 32601, USA | |
| **Katsoudas, Stella** | Singer (Sister Soleil), Songwriter |
| Ashley Talent, 2002 Hogback Road, #20, Ann Arbor MI 48105 USA | |
| **Katt, William** | Actor, Writer, Director |
| Horne Agency, 4420 W Lovers Lane, Dallas TX 75209, USA | |
| **Kattan, Chris** | Actor, Comedian |
| A P A Talent/Literary Agency, 405 S Beverly Dr, #300, Beverly Hills CA 90212 USA | |
| **Kattan, Mohammed Imad** | Architect |
| PO Box 950846, Amman 11195, Jordan | |
| **Kattus, J Eric** | Football Player |
| 854 Adams Road, Loveland OH 45140, USA | |
| **Katz, Abraham** | Diplomat |
| US Council for International Business, 1212 Ave of Americas, New York NY 10036, USA | |
| **Katz, Alex** | Artist |
| 435 W Broadway, New York NY 10012, USA | |
| **Katz, Bernard** | Sculptor |
| PO Box 41064, Philadelphia PA 19127, USA | |
| **Katz, Donald L** | Petroleum Engineer |
| 2011 Washtenaw Ave, Ann Arbor MI 48104, USA | |
| **Katz, Douglas J (Doug)** | Navy Admiral |
| 1530 Gordon Cove Dr, Annapolis MD 21403, USA | |
| **Katz, Harold** | Basketball Executive |
| Philadelphia 76ers, 1st Union Center, 3601 S Broad St, Philadelphia PA 19148 USA | |
| **Katz, Hilda** | Artist |
| 915 W End Ave, #5D, New York NY 10025, USA | |
| **Katz, Jonathan** | Actor, Comedian, Animator |
| Creative Artists Agency, 2000 Ave of Stars, #100, Los Angeles CA 90067 USA | |
| **Katz, Michael** | Pediatrician |
| 200 E 57th St, #11K, New York NY 10022, USA | |
| **Katz, Omri** | Actor |
| J H Productions, 23679 Calabasas Road, #333, Calabasas CA 91302, USA | |
| **Katz, Ross** | Producer, Director, Writer |
| Ross Katz Films, 200 Park Ave S, #800, New York NY 10003, USA | |
| **Katz, Samuel L** | Pediatrician |
| 1917 Wildcat Creek Road, Chapel Hill NC 27516, USA | |
| **Katz, Stanley N** | Attorney, Educator |
| American Council on Learned Societies, 228 E 45th St, New York NY 10017, USA | |
| **Katz, Stephen M** | Cinematographer |
| C E S D, 10635 Santa Monica Blvd, #130, Los Angeles CA 90025 USA | |
| **Katzenberg, David** | Producer, Writer |
| Katz/Smith Productions, 8447 Wilshire Blvd, #210, Beverly Hills CA 90211, USA | |
| **Katzenberg, Jeffrey** | Businessman, Philanthropist |
| DreamWorks SKG, 100 Flower St, Glendale CA 91201, USA | |
| **Katzenmoyer, Andrew W (Andy)** | Football Player |
| 5764 Salem Dr, Westerville OH 43082, USA | |
| **Katzmann, Robert A** | Judge |
| US Court of Appeals, Moynihan Courthouse, 500 Pearl St, New York NY 10007, USA | |
| **Katzur, Klaus** | Swimmer |
| Robert-Siewart-Str 76, 0912 Chemnitz, Germany | |
| **Kauffman, Marta** | Writer, Producer |
| W M E Entertainment, 9601 Wilshire Blvd, #300, Beverly Hills CA 90210 USA | |
| **Kauffman, Stuart A A** | Biologist |
| Biocomplexity Institute, 2500 University NW, Calgary AB T2N 1N4, Canada | |
| **Kaufman, Adam** | Actor |
| S D B Partners, 1801 Ave of Stars, #902, Los Angeles CA 90067 USA | |
| **Kaufman, Bel** | Writer |
| 1020 Park Ave, New York NY 10028, USA | |
| **Kaufman, Charles S (Charlie)** | Director, Producer, Writer |
| W M E Entertainment, 9601 Wilshire Blvd, #300, Beverly Hills CA 90210 USA | |
| **Kaufman, Dan S** | Hematologist |
| University of Wisconsin Medical School, Hematology Dept, Madison WI 53706, USA | |
| **Kaufman, Donald** | Writer |
| United Talent Agency, U T A Plaza, 9336 Civic Center Dr, Beverly Hills CA 90210 USA | |
| **Kaufman, Henry** | Financier |
| Henry Kaufman Co, 65 E 55th St, New York NY 10022, USA | |
| **Kaufman, Moises** | Director, Writer |
| Gersh Agency, 41 Madison Ave, #3301, New York NY 10010 USA | |

Kaufman, Napoleon — Football Player
1913 Via Di Salerno, Pleasanton CA 94566, USA
Kaufman, Philip — Director, Writer
I C M Partners, 10250 Constellation Blvd, #900, Los Angeles CA 90067 USA
Kaufman, Thomas C (Thom) — Biologist
Indiana University, Biology Dept, Bloomington IN 47405, USA
Kaufmann, Christine — Actress
Zentralburo, Kleiner Griechenmarkt 81, 50676 Cologne, Germany
Kaufmann, Robert (Bob) — Basketball Player
1677 Rivermist Dr SW, Lilburn GA 30047, USA
Kaukonen, Jorma L, Jr — Guitarist (Jefferson Airplane, Hot Tuna)
Moneypenny Agency, Westwood House, Main St, Driffield, East Yorkshire YO25 9XA, England
Kaunda, Kenneth D — President, Zambia
21A Serval Road, Private Bag E501, Lusaka, Zambia
Kaurismaki, Aki — Director, Producer, Writer
Sputnik, Museokato 13A, 00100 Helsinki, Finland
Kausalya — Actress
15A-2 Akshar, Palace Road, Bangalore JA 52, India
Kaushal, Kamini — Actress, Dancer
B2 Anita Mount Pleasant Road, Malabar Hill, Mumbai MS 400006, India
Kauth, Kathleen — Ice Hockey Player
13 Hillcrest Lane, Saratoga Springs NY 12866, USA
Kava, Caroline — Actress
Talent Works, 3500 W Olive Ave, #1400, Burbank CA 91505 USA
Kavanaugh, Brett M — Judge
US Appellate Court, 333 Constitution Ave NW, #4400, Washington DC 20001, USA
Kavanaugh, John — Actor
The Agency, 9 Upper Fitzwilliam St, 2 Dublin, Ireland
Kavandi, Janet L — Astronaut
3907 Park Circle Way, Houston TX 77059, USA
Kavrakos, Dimitri — Opera Singer
Columbia Artists Mgmt Inc, 1790 Broadway, #702, New York NY 10019 USA
Kawakubo, Rei — Fashion Designer
Comme des Garcons, 16 Place Vendome, 75001 Paris, France
Kawasumi, Nahomi — Soccer Player
Football Assn, 3-10-15 Hongo, Bunkyoku, Tokyo 113 0033 Japan
Kay, Alan C — Computer Scientist
Viewpoints Research Institute, 1209 Grand Capital Ave, Glendale CA 91201, USA
Kay, Clarence H — Football Player
1648 Lansing St, Aurora CO 80010, USA
Kay, Dianne — Actress
1565 Calle Del Estribo, Pacific Palisades CA 90272, USA
Kay, Dominic Scott — Actor
Paradigm Agency, 360 N Crescent Dr, North Building, Beverly Hills CA 90210 USA
Kay, Herma H — Attorney, Educator
University of California, Law School, Boalt Hall, Berkeley CA 94720, USA
Kay, Jason (Jay) — Singer (Jamiroquai)
Nettwerk Mgmt, 6525 W Sunset Blvd, #800, Los Angeles CA 90028 USA
Kay, John — Singer, Guitarist (Steppenwolf)
Paradise Artists, PO Box 1821, Ojai CA 93024 USA
Kay, Lesli — Actress
Innovative Artists, 1505 10th St, Santa Monica CA 90401 USA
Kay, Stephen T — Actor
I C M Partners, 10250 Constellation Blvd, #900, Los Angeles CA 90067 USA
Kaye, Carol — Guitarist, Bassist
25852 McBean Parkway, #200, Valencia CA 91355, USA
Kaye, Jonathan — Golfer
328 W El Camino, Phoenix AZ 85021, USA
Kaye, Paul — Actor, Writer, Composer
Richard Stone Partnership, De Walden Court, 85 New Cavendish St, London W1W 6XD, England
Kaye, Thorsten — Actor
I C M Partners, 10250 Constellation Blvd, #900, Los Angeles CA 90067 USA
Kayne — Singer, Songwriter
Agency Group Ltd, 142 W 57th St, #600, New York NY 10019 USA
Kays, Roland W — Zoologist
Nature Research Center, 121 W Jones St, Raleigh NC 27603, USA
Kayser, Manfred — Molecular Biologist
Erasmus University Medical Center, 3013 Rotterdam GE, Netherlands
Kazan, Lainie — Singer, Actress
Irvin Arthur Assoc, 350 E 79th St, #18C, New York NY 10075 USA
Kazan, Zoe — Actress
United Talent Agency, U T A Plaza, 9336 Civic Center Dr, Beverly Hills CA 90210 USA
Kazankina, Tatyana — Track Athlete
Hoshimina St, 111211 Saint Petersburg, Russia
Kazanski, Theodore S (Ted) — Baseball Player
1544 Dormie Dr, Gladwin MI 48624, USA
Kazee, Steve — Actor
Innovative Artists, 1505 10th St, Santa Monica CA 90401 USA
Kazer, Beau — Actor
139A N San Fernando Blvd, Burbank CA 91502, USA
Kazmir, Scott E — Baseball Player
16619 Rose Bay Trail, Cypress TX 77429, USA
Kazurinsky, Tim — Actor, Comedian
Geddes Agency, 1633 N Halsted St, #300, Chicago IL 60614, USA
Ke$ha — Singer, Songwriter
Creative Artists Agency, 2000 Ave of Stars, #100, Los Angeles CA 90067 USA
Keach, James — Actor
Catfish Productions, 22631 Pacific Coast Highway, #313, Malibu CA 90265, USA
Keach, Stacy — Actor
Lionel Larner, 119 West 57th St New York NY 10019 10019, USA
Keady, L Eugene (Gene) — Basketball Coach
Saint John's University, Athletic Dept, 8000 Utopia Parkway, Queens NY 11439, USA
Keaggy, Phil — Guitarist
Ray Ware Artist Mgmt, 3108 Saint Stephens Way, Franklin TN 37064, USA
Kealey, Steven W (Steve) — Baseball Player
1080 1700 Ave, Abilene KS 67410, USA

Kaufman - Kealey

# K

| | |
|---|---|
| **Kean, Jane**<br>Sutton-Barth Vennari, 5900 Wilshire Blvd, #700, Los Angeles CA 90036 USA | Actress |
| **Kean, Laurel**<br>11831 Forest Mere Dr, Bonita Springs FL 34135, USA | Golfer |
| **Kean, Thomas H**<br>PO Box 332, Far Hills NJ 07931, USA | Governor, NJ; Educator |
| **Keanan, Staci**<br>Vox Inc, 6420 Wilshire Blvd, #1080, Los Angeles CA 90048 USA | Actress |
| **Keane, Dolores**<br>Kieren Cavanaugh Promotions, PO Box 5639, Dublin 4, Ireland | Singer, Musician |
| **Keane, Glen**<br>Walt Disney Studios, Animation Dept, 500 S Buena Vista St, Burbank CA 91521, USA | Animator |
| **Keane, John**<br>Bloomsbury Publishing, 50 Bedford Square, London WC1B 3DP, England | Writer |
| **Keane, John M**<br>United Talent Agency, U T A Plaza, 9336 Civic Center Dr, Beverly Hills CA 90210 USA | Film Composer |
| **Keane, John M (Jack)**<br>General Dynamics, 2941 Fairview Park Dr, #100, Falls Church VA 22042, USA | Army General |
| **Keane, Kerrie**<br>S D B Partners, 1801 Ave of Stars, #902, Los Angeles CA 90067 USA | Actress |
| **Keane, Louis M (Dillie)**<br>Gavin Barker Assoc, 2D Wimpole St, London W1G 0EB, England | Actress, Singer, Comedienne |
| **Keane, Roy M**<br>Manchester United, Busby Way, Old Trafford, Manchester M16 0RA, England | Soccer Player |
| **Keane, Sean**<br>Macklam/Feldman Mgmt, 1505 W 2nd Ave, #200, Vancouver BC V6H 3Y4, Canada | Fiddler (Chieftains) |
| **Keane, William**<br>C E S D, 10635 Santa Monica Blvd, #130, Los Angeles CA 90025 USA | Actor |
| **Kear, David**<br>34 W End, Ohope 3121, New Zealand | Geologist |
| **Kearney, Hannah**<br>Waterville Valley B B T S, Box 277, Waterville Valley NH 03215, USA | Moguls Skier |
| **Kearney, James L (Jim)**<br>1817 E 59th St, Kansas City MO 64130, USA | Football Player |
| **Kearney, Mat**<br>A2 Mgmt, 1316 Sherman Ave, #215, Evanston IL 60201, USA | Singer, Songwriter |
| **Kearney, Robert H (Bob)**<br>4155 Elizabeth Dr, Stevensville MI 49127, USA | Baseball Player |
| **Kearney, Timothy E (Tim)**<br>2144 Dartmouth Gate Court, Ballwin MO 63011, USA | Football Player |
| **Kearns, Austin R**<br>719 Haverhill Dr, Lexington KY 40503, USA | Baseball Player |
| **Kearns, Dennis M**<br>1292 Esquimalt Ave, West Vancouver BC V7T 1K3, Canada | Ice Hockey Player |
| **Kearse, Amalya L**<br>US Court of Appeals, Moynihan Courthouse, 500 Pearl St, New York NY 10007, USA | Judge |
| **Kearse, Jevon**<br>61 Whitworth Blvd, Nashville TN 37205, USA | Football Player |
| **Kearse, NaShawn**<br>Leverage Mgmt, 3030 Pennsylvania Ave, Santa Monica CA 90404 USA | Actor |
| **Keaser, Lloyd (Butch)**<br>43960 Tavern Dr, Ashburn VA 20147, USA | Freestyle Wrestler |
| **Keating, Charles**<br>Don Buchwald, 10 E 44th St, New York NY 10017 USA | Actor |
| **Keating, Christopher P (Chris)**<br>741 Canton Ave, Milton MA 02186, USA | Football Player |
| **Keating, Dominic**<br>Talent Works, 3500 W Olive Ave, #1400, Burbank CA 91505 USA | Actor |
| **Keating, Francis A (Frank), II**<br>American Life Insurers, 101 Constitution Ave NW, #700W, Washington DC 20001, USA | Governor, OK |
| **Keating, Paul J**<br>GPO Box 1265, Potts Point NSW 1335, Australia | Prime Minister, Australia |
| **Keating, Ronan**<br>Outside Organization, 177-178 Tottenham Court Road, London W1T 7NY, England | Singer (Boyzone) |
| **Keating, Thomas A (Tom)**<br>3725 W St NW, Washington DC 20007, USA | Football Player |
| **Keating, Timothy J**<br>7443 Collins Meade Way, Alexandria VA 22315, USA | Navy Admiral |
| **Keaton, Danielle**<br>Paceline Entertainment, 12444 Ventura Blvd, #103, Studio City CA 91604 USA | Actress |
| **Keaton, Diane**<br>15260 Ventura Blvd, #1040, Sherman Oaks CA 91403, USA | Actress, Director |
| **Keaton, Michael**<br>I C M Partners, 10250 Constellation Blvd, #900, Los Angeles CA 90067 USA | Actor |
| **Keats, Donald H**<br>University of Denver, Music School, Denver CO 80208, USA | Composer |
| **Keb' Mo'**<br>J B Mgmt, PO Box 25703, Chicago IL 60625, USA | Singer, Songwriter |
| **K'eba, Miftah Muhammed**<br>General Secretary's Office, Bab el Asiziya Barracks, Tripoli, Libya | General Secretary, Libya |
| **Kebbel, Arielle**<br>Paradigm Agency, 360 N Crescent Dr, North Building, Beverly Hills CA 90210 USA | Actress |
| **Kebbell, Toby**<br>Independent Talent Group, 40 Whitfield St, London W1T 2RH, England | Actor |
| **Kebede, Liya**<br>I M G Models, 304 Park Ave S, #PH N, New York NY 10010 USA | Model, Actress |
| **Kebich, Vyacheslav F**<br>National Assembly, K Marksa Str 38, Dom Urada, 220016 Minsk, Belarus | Prime Minister, Belarus |
| **Keck, Donald B**<br>2877 Chequers Circle, Big Flats NY 14814, USA | Inventor (Silica Optical Waveguide) |
| **Keck, Howard B**<br>600 Wilshire Blvd, #17, Los Angeles CA 90017, USA | Philanthropist |
| **Keczmer, Daniel L (Dan)**<br>9533 Sanctuary Place, Brentwood TN 37027, USA | Ice Hockey Player |
| **Kedah**<br>Istana Anak Bukit, Alor Setar, Kedah, Darul Aman, Malaysia | Sultan, Kedah |

**Kee, John P** — Singer
A&M Entertainment, 13280 NW Freeway, #328, Houston,TX 77040, USA

**Keefe, Adam T** — Basketball Player
15933 Alcima Ave, Pacific Palisades CA 90272, USA

**Keefe, Mike** — Editorial Cartoonist
Denver Post, Editorial Dept, PO Box 1709, Denver CO 80201, USA

**Keefer, Don** — Actor
4146 Allott Ave, Sherman Oaks CA 91423, USA

**Keeffe, Bernard** — Conductor
153 Honor Oak Road, London SE23 3RN, England

**Keegan, Andrew** — Actor
C E S D, 10635 Santa Monica Blvd, #130, Los Angeles CA 90025, USA

**Keegan, Kevin J** — Soccer Player, Executive
Manchester City F C, Maine Road, Moss Side, Manchester M14 7WN, England

**Keegan, Robert J** — Businessman
Goodyear Tire & Rubber, 1144 E Market St, Akron OH 44316, USA

**Keegan, Scarlett** — Model
C E S D, 10635 Santa Monica Blvd, #130, Los Angeles CA 90025 USA

**Keehne, Virginya** — Actress
Craig Mgmt, 2240 Miramonte Circle E, #C, Palm Springs CA 92264 USA

**Keel, Alton G, Jr** — Diplomat, Businessman
Atlantic Partners, 2891 S River Road, Stanardsville VA 22973, USA

**Keelaghan, James** — Singer, Songwriter
Jensen Music International, PO Box 3445, Charlottetown PE C1A 8W5, Canada

**Keeler, Jesse F** — Electronic Musician (Mstrkrft)
Biz 3 Publicity, 1321 N Milwaukee Ave, #452, Chicago IL 60622, USA

**Keeler, William H Cardinal** — Religious Leader
National Conference of Catholic Bishops, 3211 4th St, Washington DC 20017, USA

**Keeley, Edmund L** — Writer
140 Littlebrook Road, Princeton NJ 08540, USA

**Keeley, Robert V** — Diplomat
3814 Livingston St NW, Washington DC 20015, USA

**Keeley, Sam** — Actor
Paradigm Agency, 360 N Crescent Dr, North Building, Beverly Hills CA 90210 USA

**Keelor, Greg** — Singer, Guitarist (Blue Rodeo)
Starfish Entertainment, 906A Logan Ave, Toronto ON M4K 3E4, Canada

**Keen, Robert Earl** — Singer, Songwriter
C3 Presents, 98 San Jacinto Blvd, #400, Austin TX 78701, USA

**Keen, Sam** — Writer, Philosopher
16331 Norrbom Road, Sonoma CA 95476, USA

**Keena, Monica** — Actress
Greater Vision Agency, 8981 Sunset Blvd, #101, Los Angeles CA 90069, USA

**Keenan, Edward L** — Historian
Harvard University, History Dept, Robinson Hall, Cambridge MA 02138, USA

**Keenan, Joseph D** — Labor Leader
2727 29th St NW, Washington DC 20008, USA

**Keenan, Larry** — Ice Hockey Player
132 Gordon Dr, North Bay ON P1B 8B2, Canada

**Keenan, Maynard James** — Singer (Tool, Perfect Circle)
Spivak Sobol Entertainment, 11845 W Olympic Blvd, #1125, Los Angeles CA 90064, USA

**Keenan, Michael E (Mike)** — Ice Hockey Coach
PO Box 175, 1975 Duval St, Key West FL 33041, USA

**Keene Cherot, Kyera** — Producer, Writer
C C A, 7 Saint Georges Square, London SW1V 2HX, England

**Keene, Donald L** — Language Educator
Columbia University, Language Dept, Kent Hall, New York NY 10027, USA

**Keene, Phillip P** — Actor
A K A Talent, 6310 San Vicente Blvd, #200, Los Angeles CA 90048 USA

**Keene, Tommy** — Singer, Guitarist, Songwriter
Black Park Mgmt, PO Box 107, Sunbury NC 27979, USA

**Keener, Catherine** — Actress
Gersh Agency, 9465 Wilshire Blvd, #600, Beverly Hills CA 90212 USA

**Keenlyside, Simon** — Opera Singer
Askonas Holt, Lincoln House, 300 High Holborn, London WC1V 7JH, England

**Keenum, Mark E** — Educator
Mississippi State University, President's Office, Allen Hall, Mississippi State MS 39762, USA

**Keeny, Spurgeon M, Jr** — Association Executive
3600 Albemarle St NW, Washington DC 20008, USA

**Keeslar, Matt** — Actor
Martin Berneman Mgmt, 5820 Wilshire Blvd, #200, Los Angeles CA 90036 USA

**Keezer, Geoff** — Jazz Pianist
D L Media, 124 N Highland Ave, Bala Cynwyd PA 19004, USA

**Keflezighi, Mebrahtom (Meb)** — Track Athlete
Mammoth Track Club, PO Box 7552, Mammoth Lakes CA 93546, USA

**Kegel, Oliver** — Canoeing Athlete
Am Bogen 23, 13589 Berlin, Germany

**Kegeles, Gerson** — Chemist
RR 1 Box 156, Groveton NH 03582, USA

**Keggi, Caroline** — Golfer
807 Westlake Dr, Ormond Beach FL 32174, USA

**Kehler, C Robert (Bob)** — Air Force General
Commander, US Strategic Command, Offutt Air Force Base NE 68113 USA

**Kehoe, Rick** — Ice Hockey Player, Coach
1027 Highland Dr, Cincinnati OH 45211, USA

**Kehoe, Robert (Bob)** — Soccer Player, Coach
4848 Towne South Road, Saint Louis MO 63128, USA

**Keibler, Stacy** — Actress, Model, Wrestler
W M E Entertainment, 9601 Wilshire Blvd, #300, Beverly Hills CA 90210 USA

**Keifer, C Tom** — Singer, Guitarist (Cinderella)
Union Entertainment Group, 1323 Newbury Road, #104, Thousand Oaks CA 91320, USA

**Keifer, Elizabeth** — Actress
Stone Manners Salners, 9911 W Pico Blvd, #1400, Los Angeles CA 90035 USA

**Keightley, David N** — Historian
University of California, History Dept, Berkeley CA 94720, USA

**Keil, Val** — Model
Playboy Promotions, 2706 Media Center Dr, Los Angeles CA 90065 USA

**K**

| | |
|---|---|
| **Keillor, Garrison E** | Actor, Writer, Producer |
| Prairie Home Productions, 480 Cedar St, Saint Paul MN 55101, USA | |
| **Keineg, Katell** | Singer |
| Headline Agency, 39 Churchfields, Milltown, Dublin 14, Ireland | |
| **Keisel, Brett** | Football Player |
| 2015 W Grove Dr, Gibsonia PA 15044, USA | |
| **Keisler, Randy** | Baseball Player |
| 6842 Durango Creek Dr, Magnolia TX 77354, USA | |
| **Keita, Ibrahim Boubacar** | Prime Minister, Mali |
| Alliance pour la Demoractie au Mali, BP 1791, Bamako-Coura, Mali | |
| **Keita, Salif** | Singer, Composer |
| Mad Minute Music, 5-7 Rue Paul Bert, 93400 Saint Ouen, France | |
| **Keitel, Harvey** | Actor |
| Finch & Partners, 35 Heddon St, #PH, London W1B 4BR, England | |
| **Keith, Damon J** | Judge |
| US Court of Appeals, US Courthouse, 231 W Lafayette Blvd, Detroit MI 48226, USA | |
| **Keith, David** | Actor |
| Kritzer Levine Wilkins Griffin, 11872 La Grange Ave, #100, Los Angeles CA 90025 USA | |
| **Keith, Louis** | Physician |
| 333 E Superior St, #476, Chicago IL 60611, USA | |
| **Keith, Toby** | Singer, Actor |
| T K O Artist Mgmt, 2303 21st Ave S, #300, Nashville TN 37212, USA | |
| **Kekalainen, Jarmo** | Ice Hockey Player, Executive |
| Jokerit H C, Areenankuja 1, 00240 Helsinki, Finland | |
| **Keker, John** | Attorney |
| 710 Sansome St, San Francisco CA 94111, USA | |
| **Kekich, Michael D (Mike)** | Baseball Player |
| 4942 Kolopelli Dr, Rio Rancho NM 87144, USA | |
| **Kekilli, Sibel** | Actress |
| Wasted Mgmt, Diffenbachstr 33, 10967 Berlin, Germany | |
| **Kelcher, J Louie** | Football Player |
| 10204 Carlotta Cove, Austin TX 78733, USA | |
| **Kele** | Singer, Musician |
| Agency Group Ltd, 142 W 57th St, #600, New York NY 10019 USA | |
| **Keleti, Agnes** | Gymnast |
| Wingate Institute for Physical Education & Sport, Netanya 42902, Israel | |
| **Kelif, Atmen** | Actor |
| Artmedia, 20 Ave Rapp, 75007 Paris, France | |
| **Kelis** | Singer |
| Creative Artists Agency, 2000 Ave of Stars, #100, Los Angeles CA 90067 USA | |
| **Kell, Ayla** | Actress |
| Savage Agency, 6212 Banner Ave, Los Angeles CA 90038 USA | |
| **Kell, Everett L (Skeeter)** | Baseball Player |
| PO Box 10113, Conway AR 72034, USA | |
| **Kellar-Duke, Rebecca D (Becky)** | Ice Hockey Player |
| Team Canada, 2424 University Dr NW, Calgary AB T2N 3Y9, Canada | |
| **Kellaway, Roger** | Composer, Jazz Pianist |
| Joel Chriss Co, 300 Mercer St, #3J, New York NY 10003 USA | |
| **Kelleher, Herbert D** | Businessman |
| 144 Thelma Dr, San Antonio TX 78212, USA | |
| **Kelleher, Michael D (Mick)** | Baseball Player |
| 1451 Alamo Pintado Road, Solvang CA 93463, USA | |
| **Kelleher, Tim** | Actor |
| Paradigm Agency, 360 N Crescent Dr, North Building, Beverly Hills CA 90210 USA | |
| **Keller, Bill** | Journalist |
| New York Times, Editorial Dept, 229 W 43rd St, New York NY 10036, USA | |
| **Keller, Erhard** | Speed Skater |
| Sudliche Munchneustr 6A, 82031 Grunwald, Germany | |
| **Keller, Jason** | Auto Racing Driver |
| Progressive Motorsports, 177 Knob Hill Road, Mooresville NC 28117, USA | |
| **Keller, Joseph B** | Mathematician |
| 820 Sonoma Terrace, Stanford CA 94305, USA | |
| **Keller, Julia** | Journalist |
| Chicago Tribune, Editorial Dept, 350 N Orleans St, Chicago IL 60654 USA | |
| **Keller, Kasey** | Soccer Player |
| Seattle Sounders, 12 Seahawks Way, Renton WA 98056 USA | |
| **Keller, Klete** | Swimmer |
| 3015 N Hozoni Road, Prescott AZ 86305, USA | |
| **Keller, Marthe** | Actress |
| Lemonstr 9, 81679 Munich, Germany | |
| **Keller, Mary Page** | Actress |
| S M S Talent, 8383 Wilshire Blvd, #230, Beverly Hills CA 90211 USA | |
| **Keller, Nino** | Drummer (Caesars) |
| Paradigm Agency, 360 Park Ave, #1600, New York NY 10022 USA | |
| **Keller, Robert P** | Marine Corps General |
| 6367 Kirby Oaks Dr, Memphis TN 38119, USA | |
| **Keller, Shawn** | Animator |
| C A A T Studios, 36 King Eider Lane, Aliso Viejo CA 92656, USA | |
| **Keller, Thomas** | Chef, Restauranteur |
| French Laundry, 6640 Washington St, Yountville CA 94599, USA | |
| **Kellerman, Ernie J** | Football Player |
| 522 Spice Bush Lane, Chagrin Falls OH 44023, USA | |
| **Kellerman, Faye** | Writer |
| Karpfinger Agency, 357 W 20th St, #A, New York NY 10011, USA | |
| **Kellerman, Jonathan S** | Writer |
| Karpfinger Agency, 357 W 20th St, #A, New York NY 10011, USA | |
| **Kellerman, Martin** | Cartoonist (Rocky) |
| Krukmakargatan 29, 118 51 Stockhom, Sweden | |
| **Kellerman, Max** | Sportscaster, Commentator |
| Fox-TV, Sports Dept, PO Box 900, Beverly Hills CA 90213 USA | |
| **Kellerman, Sally** | Actress |
| Polimedia Communications, 1010 Wilshire Blvd, Los Angeles CA 90017, USA | |
| **Kelley, Brian L** | Football Player |
| 98 Constitution Way, Basking Ridge NJ 07920, USA | |
| **Kelley, David E** | Producer, Writer |
| David E Kelley Productions, 2900 Olympic Blvd, Santa Monica CA 90404, USA | |

Keillor - Kelley

**Kelley, Dean** — Basketball Player
5900 Longleaf Dr, Lawrence KS 66049, USA
**Kelley, Donald R** — Historian
45 Jefferson Ave, New Brunswick NJ 08901, USA
**Kelley, E Allen (Al)** — Basketball Player
5900 Longleaf Dr, Lawrence KS 66049, USA
**Kelley, Elijah** — Actor, Singer
Schiff Co, 9200 Sunset Blvd, #430, West Hollywood CA 90232 USA
**Kelley, Gaynor N** — Businessman
Perkin-Elmer Corp, 710 Bridgeport Ave, Shelton CT 06484, USA
**Kelley, Harold H** — Psychologist
21634 Rambla Vista St, Malibu CA 90265, USA
**Kelley, Josh** — Singer, Songwriter
Wilspro Mgmt, 1335 Martin Ave, Point Pleasant NJ 08742, USA
**Kelley, Kitty** — Writer
1228 Eton Court NW, Washington DC 20007, USA
**Kelley, Malcolm David** — Actor
Amsel Eisenstadt Frazier, 5055 Wilshire Blvd, #865, Los Angeles CA 90036 USA
**Kelley, Nathalie** — Actress
Innovative Artists, 1505 10th St, Santa Monica CA 90401 USA
**Kelley, Paul X** — Marine Corps General
1600 N Oak St, #1619, Arlington VA 22209, USA
**Kelley, Richard R (Rich)** — Basketball Player
314 Raymundo Dr, Woodside CA 94062, USA
**Kelley, Robert O** — Educator
University of North Dakota, President's Office, Grand Forks ND 58202, USA
**Kelley, Ryan J** — Actor
A P A Talent/Literary Agency, 405 S Beverly Dr, #300, Beverly Hills CA 90212 USA
**Kelley, S R** — Sculptor
PO Box 682, Mendocino CA 95460, USA
**Kelley, Sheila** — Actress
I F A Talent Agency, 8730 W Sunset Blvd, #490, West Hollywood CA 90069 USA
**Kelley, Steve** — Editorial Cartoonist
Creators Syndicate, 737 3rd St, Hermosa Beach CA 90254 USA
**Kelley, Thomas G** — Vietnam War Navy Hero (CMH)
600 Washington St, #1100, Boston MA 02111, USA
**Kelley, Thomas H (Tom)** — Baseball Player
710 11th Ave S, North Myrtle Beach SC 29582, USA
**Kelley, William G** — Businessman
Consolidated Stores, 1105 N Market St, Wilmington DE 19801, USA
**Kelliher, Bill** — Guitarist, Singer (Mastodon)
Pinnacle Entertainment, 30 Glenn St, White Plains NY 10603, USA
**Kellis, Manolis** — Electrical Engineer
Massachusetts Institute of Technology, Engineering Dept, Cambridge MA 02139, USA
**Kellman, Barnet** — Director
Paradigm Agency, 360 N Crescent Dr, North Building, Beverly Hills CA 90210 USA
**Kellmeyer, Fern L (Peachy)** — Tennis Executive
Women's Tennis Assn, 1 Progress Plaza, #1500, Saint Petersburg FL 33701 USA
**Kellner, Lawrence (Larry)** — Businessman
Continental Airlines, PO Box 4607, Houston TX 77210, USA
**Kellogg, Allan J, Jr** — Vietnam War Marine Air Hero (CMH)
250 Ilihau St, Kailua HI 96734, USA
**Kellogg, Clark C** — Basketball Player, Sportscaster
5423 Medallion Dr E, Westerville OH 43082, USA
**Kellogg, David** — Director
I C M Partners, 10250 Constellation Blvd, #900, Los Angeles CA 90067 USA
**Kellogg, William S** — Businessman
Kohl's Corp, N56W17000 Ridgewood Dr, Menomonee Falls WI 53051, USA
**Kellum, Marvin L (Marv)** — Football Player
235 Jamaica Ave, Pittsburgh PA 15229, USA
**Kelly, Annese** — Bowler
3812 Bach Way, North Las Vegas NV 89032, USA
**Kelly, Arvesta** — Basketball Player
1040 Oxford St N, Saint Paul MN 55103, USA
**Kelly, Brendan** — Actor
Allman/Rea Mgmt, 141 Barrington Walk, #E, Los Angeles CA 90049, USA
**Kelly, Brian K** — Football Coach
University of Notre Dame, Athletic Dept, Notre Dame IN 46556, USA
**Kelly, Charles (Chip)** — Football Coach
Philadelphia Eagles, 1 Novacare Way, Philadelphia PA 19145 USA
**Kelly, Daniel Hugh** — Actor
Innovative Artists, 1505 10th St, Santa Monica CA 90401 USA
**Kelly, David Patrick** — Actor
Paradigm Agency, 360 N Crescent Dr, North Building, Beverly Hills CA 90210 USA
**Kelly, Eamon M** — Educator
123 Walnut St, #804, New Orleans LA 70118, USA
**Kelly, Ellsworth** — Artist
PO Box 151, Spencertown NY 12165, USA
**Kelly, Gary C** — Businessman
Southwest Airlines, PO Box 36647, Dallas TX 75235, USA
**Kelly, J Thomas (Tom)** — Baseball Player, Manager
1643 Currie St N, Saint Paul MN 55119, USA
**Kelly, James E (Jim)** — Football Player
6 Woodcrest Dr, Orchard Park NY 14127, USA
**Kelly, James M (Jim)** — Astronaut
403 S Northfield St, Mediapolis IA 52637, USA
**Kelly, Jean Louisa** — Actress
Levine/Okwu/Erickson, 6363 Wilshire Blvd, #300, Los Angeles CA 90048, USA
**Kelly, Jerry** — Golfer
531 Farwell Dr, Madison WI 53704, USA
**Kelly, Joanne** — Actress
Domain Talent, 9229 W Sunset Blvd, #710, West Hollywood CA 90069 USA
**Kelly, John** — Singer (Kelly Family)
E M I America Records, 6920 W Sunset Blvd, Los Angeles CA 90028 USA
**Kelly, John H** — Diplomat
John Kelly Consulting, 1808 Over Lake Dr SE, #D, Conyers GA 30013, USA

| | |
|---|---|
| **Kelly, Joseph W (Joe)** | Football Player |
| PO Box 6335, Cincinnati OH 45206, USA | |
| **Kelly, Krista** | Model |
| Playboy Promotions, 2706 Media Center Dr, Los Angeles CA 90065 USA | |
| **Kelly, Laura Michelle** | Actress |
| Dalzell & Beresford, 26 Astwood Mews, London SW7 4DE, England | |
| **Kelly, Leonard P (Red)** | Ice Hockey Player, Coach |
| 30 Dunvegan, Toronto ON M4V 2P6, Canada | |
| **Kelly, Leroy** | Football Player |
| 91 Club House Dr, Willingboro NJ 8046, USA | |
| **Kelly, Lisa** | Singer (Celtic Woman) |
| W M E Entertainment, 9601 Wilshire Blvd, #300, Beverly Hills CA 90210 USA | |
| **Kelly, Mark E** | Astronaut |
| 2121 Barrington Dr, League City TX 77573, USA | |
| **Kelly, Michael J** | Actor |
| Liebman Entertainment, 35 E 21st St, #PH, New York NY 10010, USA | |
| **Kelly, Michael R (Mike)** | Baseball Player |
| 5072 S Serpentine Road, Flagstaff AZ 86001, USA | |
| **Kelly, Minka** | Actress |
| Creative Artists Agency, 2000 Ave of Stars, #100, Los Angeles CA 90067 USA | |
| **Kelly, Moira** | Actress |
| Gersh Agency, 9465 Wilshire Blvd, #600, Beverly Hills CA 90212 USA | |
| **Kelly, Patrick F (Pat)** | Baseball Player |
| 3519 Capri Court, Philadelphia PA 19145, USA | |
| **Kelly, Paul** | Singer, Guitarist, Songwriter |
| One Louder Entertainment, PO Box 989, Darlinghurst NSW 1300, Australia | |
| **Kelly, Paul J, Jr** | Judge |
| US Appeals Court, 120 S Federal Plaza, Santa Fe NM 87501, USA | |
| **Kelly, R** | Rap Artist, Singer, Songwriter |
| Creative Artists Agency, 2000 Ave of Stars, #100, Los Angeles CA 90067 USA | |
| **Kelly, Raymond** | Law Enforcement Official |
| Police Commissioner's Office, 1 Police Plaza, New York NY 10038, USA | |
| **Kelly, Richard** | Director, Writer |
| Darko Entertainment, 1041 N Formosa Ave, West Hollywood CA 90046, USA | |
| **Kelly, Robert** | Financier |
| Bank of New York Mellon Corp, 1 Wall St, New York NY 10005, USA | |
| **Kelly, Robert J (Bob)** | Ice Hockey Player |
| 10 Peyton Court, Marlton NJ 08053, USA | |
| **Kelly, Roberto C (Bobby)** | Baseball Player |
| 510 Franklin Dr, Arlington TX 76011, USA | |
| **Kelly, Sam** | Actor |
| Richard Stone Partnership, De Walden Court, 85 New Cavendish St, London W1W 6XD, England | |
| **Kelly, Sarah** | Singer |
| Creative Artists Agency, 2000 Ave of Stars, #100, Los Angeles CA 90067 USA | |
| **Kelly, Scott J** | Astronaut |
| 315 N Abrego Dr, Green Valley AZ 85614, USA | |
| **Kelly, Shane J** | Cyclist |
| Fairsy Consultancy, 25 Kerran Crescent, Lanceston TAS 7249, Australia | |
| **Kelly, T Ross** | Chemist |
| Boston College, Chemistry Dept, 140 Commonwealth Ave, Chestnut Hill MA 02467, USA | |
| **Kelly, Thomas J (Tom), III** | Photojournalist |
| PO Box 2208, Sanatoga Branch, Pottstown PA 19464, USA | |
| **Kelly, Thomas J, Jr** | Molecular Biologist |
| Memorial Sloan Kettering Cancer Center, 1275 York Ave, New York NY 10065, USA | |
| **Kelly, Thomas P** | Sculptor |
| 1518 Thurber Road, Corning NY 14830, USA | |
| **Kelly, Van H** | Baseball Player |
| 11 Beauregard Dr, Spencer NC 28159, USA | |
| **Kelm, Larry D** | Football Player |
| 67 Driftoak Circle, Spring TX 77381, USA | |
| **Kelman, Arthur** | Plant Pathologist |
| 1406 Springmoor Circle, Raleigh NC 27615, USA | |
| **Kelman, James** | Writer |
| Weidenfeld-Nicolson, Upper Saint Martin's Lane, London WC2H 9EA, England | |
| **Kelser, Gregory (Greg)** | Basketball Player |
| 30400 Forest Dr, Franklin MI 48025, USA | |
| **Kelsey, Linda** | Actress |
| 500 S Sepulveda Blvd, #500, Los Angeles CA 90049, USA | |
| **Kelsey, Quinn** | Opera Singer |
| Columbia Artists Mgmt Inc, 1790 Broadway, #702, New York NY 10019 USA | |
| **Kelso, Ben** | Basketball Player |
| 1877 Midchester Dr, West Bloomfield MI 48324, USA | |
| **Kelso, Mark A** | Football Player |
| 897 Luther Road, East Aurora NY 14052, USA | |
| **Kelso, Megan** | Cartoonist, Writer |
| 4416 S Othello St, Seattle WA 98118, USA | |
| **Kem** | Singer, Keyboardist, Songwriter |
| Project Producers, 16500 N Park Dr, #101, Southfield MI 48075, USA | |
| **Kemal, Yashar** | Writer |
| P K 14 Basinkoy, 34360 Istanbul, Turkey | |
| **Kemme, Thomas** | Labor Leader |
| Stove Furnace & Appliance Union, 2929 S Jefferson Ave, Saint Louis MO 63118, USA | |
| **Kemmer, Heike** | Equestrian |
| Am Amselhof 4, 47495 Rheinberg, Germany | |
| **Kemmerer, Russell P (Russ)** | Baseball Player |
| 6335 Colebrook Dr, Indianapolis IN 46220, USA | |
| **Kemner, Caren** | Volleyball Player |
| 2045 Elm St, Quincy IL 62301, USA | |
| **Kemoeatu, Ma'ake T** | Football Player |
| 8 Pellinore Court, Pikesville MD 21208, USA | |
| **Kemp, Charlotte** | Model |
| Playboy Promotions, 2706 Media Center Dr, Los Angeles CA 90065 USA | |
| **Kemp, Gary** | Guitarist (Spandau Ballet) |
| International Talent Group, 729 7th Ave, #1600, New York NY 10019 USA | |
| **Kemp, Jeffrey A (Jeff)** | Football Player |
| 22101 NE 66th Place, Redmond WA 98053, USA | |

**Kemp, Jeremy** — Actor
Marina Martin, 12/13 Poland St, London W1V 3DE, England
**Kemp, Perry C** — Football Player
PO Box 78, Westland PA 15378, USA
**Kemp, Ross** — Actor, Producer
Brillstein Entertainment Partners, 9150 Wilshire Blvd, #350, Beverly Hills CA 90212 USA
**Kemp, Shawn T** — Basketball Player
Oskar's Kitchen, 621 1/2 Queen Anne Ave, Seattle WA 98109, USA
**Kemp, Steven (Steve) F** — Baseball Player
1428 Colony Plaza, Newport Beach CA 92660, USA
**Kemp, Will** — Actor, Dancer, Model
United Agents, 12-26 Lexington St, London W1F 0LE, England
**Kemper, David W, II** — Financier
Commerce Bancshares, 1000 Walnut St, Kansas City MO 64106, USA
**Kemper, Ellie** — Actress
Mosiac Media Group, 9200 W Sunset Blvd, #1000, Los Angeles CA 90069 USA
**Kemper, Hunter C** — Triathlete
1700 Piedmont Place, Lake Mary FL 32746, USA
**Kemper, J Mariner, Jr** — Financier
U M B Financial Corp, 1010 Grand Ave, Kansas City MO 64106, USA
**Kemper, Randolph E (Randy)** — Fashion Designer
Randy Kemper Corp, 530 Fashion Ave, #1400, New York NY 10018, USA
**Kemper, Victor J** — Cinematographer
Mirisch Agency, 8840 Wilshire Blvd, #100, Beverly Hills CA 90211 USA
**Kempf, Cecil J** — Navy Admiral
831 Olive Ave, Coronado CA 92118, USA
**Kempf, Freddy** — Concert Pianist
I M G Artists, Hogarth Business Park, Chiswick, London W4 2TH, England
**Kempner, Patty** — Swimmer
1605 Harris Dr, Fort Collins CO 80524, USA
**Kempner, Walter** — Nutritionist
1505 Virginia Ave, Durham NC 27705, USA
**Kempthorne, Dirk A** — Secretary, Interior; Governor, Senator
2081 S White Pine Lane, Boise ID 83706, USA
**Kempton, Timothy J (Tim)** — Basketball Player
4131 N 43rd St, Phoenix AZ 85018, USA
**Kenan, Gil** — Director, Animator
W M E Entertainment, 9601 Wilshire Blvd, #300, Beverly Hills CA 90210 USA
**Kendal, Felicity** — Actress
Chatto & Linnit, 123A King's Road, London SW3 4PL, England
**Kendall, A Bruce** — Yachtsman
6 Pedersen Place, Bucklands Beach, Auckland 2012, New Zealand
**Kendall, Barbara** — Yachtswoman
Kendall Distributing, 26 Great South Road, Otahuhu 1062, New Zealand
**Kendall, David** — Producer
Rothman Brecher Agency, 9465 Wilshire Blvd, #840, Beverly Hills CA 90212 USA
**Kendall, Donald M** — Businessman
PepsiCo Inc, Anderson Hill Road, Purchase NY 10577, USA
**Kendall, Fred L** — Baseball Player
57575 Johnston Road, Anza CA 92539, USA
**Kendall, Jeannie** — Singer (Kendalls)
Joe Taylor Artist Agency, 2802 Columbine Place, Nashville TN 37204 USA
**Kendall, Kerri** — Model
4128 Catalina Place, San Diego CA 92107, USA
**Kendall, Skip** — Golfer
8406 Kemper Lane, Windermere FL 34786, USA
**Kendall, Tom** — Auto Racing Driver
International Motor Sports Assn, 1394 Broadway Ave, Braselton GA 30517, USA
**Kendler, Bob** — Handball, Raquetball Player
US Handball Assn, 4101 Dempster St, Skokie IL 60076, USA
**Kendrick, Alex** — Religious Leader, Filmmaker, Writer
Sherwood Baptist Church, 2201 Whispering Pines Road, Albany GA 31707, USA
**Kendrick, Anna** — Actress, Singer
Creative Artists Agency, 2000 Ave of Stars, #100, Los Angeles CA 90067 USA
**Kendrick, Howard J (Howie)** — Baseball Player
4030 E Anderson Dr, Phoenix AZ 85032, USA
**Kendrick, Rodney** — Singer, Jazz Pianist, Composer
Carolyn McClair, 410 W 53rd St, #128C, New York NY 10019, USA
**Kendrick, Stephen** — Religious Leader, Writer
Sherwood Baptist Church, 2201 Whispering Pines Road, Albany GA 31707, USA
**Keneally, Thomas M** — Writer
24 Serpentine, Bilgola Beach NSW 2107, Australia
**Kenilorea, Peter** — Prime Minister, Solomon Islands
Kalala House, PO Box 535, Honiara, Guadacanal, Solomon Islands
**Kenn, Michael L (Mike)** — Football Player
360 Bardolier, Alpharetta GA 30022, USA
**Kenna, E Douglas (Doug)** — Businessman, Football Player
Carlisle Companies, 250 S Clinton Square, Syracuse NY 13202, USA
**Kennard, Derek C** — Football Player
15849 S 35th Way, Phoenix AZ 85048, USA
**Kennard, William E (Bill)** — Government Official
Carlyle Group, 1001 Pennsylvania Ave NW, #220S, Washington DC 20004, USA
**Kennedy, Adam T** — Baseball Player
5025 Windhill Dr, Riverside CA 92507, USA
**Kennedy, Adrienne** — Writer
I C M Partners, 10250 Constellation Blvd, #900, Los Angeles CA 90067 USA
**Kennedy, Alan D** — Businessman
Tupperware Corp, PO Box 2353, Orlando FL 32802, USA
**Kennedy, Anthony M** — Supreme Court Justice
US Supreme Court, 1 1st St NE, Washington DC 20543 USA
**Kennedy, Cam** — Cartoonist
Dark Horse Publishing, 10956 SE Main St, Portland OR 97222 USA
**Kennedy, Caroline B** — Diplomat, Writer, Attorney
State Department, 2201 C St NW, Washington DC 20520 USA
**Kennedy, Cornelia G** — Judge
US Court of Appeals, US Courthouse, 231 W Lafayette Blvd, Detroit MI 48226, USA

V.I.P. Address Book

499

**Kennedy, Cortez** — Football Player
121 Gary Lynn Dr, Osceola AR 72370, USA
**Kennedy, Courtney** — Ice Hockey Player
13 Whispering Hill Road, Woburn MA 01801, USA
**Kennedy, David** — Actor
Ken McReddie Assoc, 101 Finsbury Pavement, London EC2A 1RS, England
**Kennedy, David M** — Historian
Stanford University, History Dept, Stanford CA 94305, USA
**Kennedy, Dean** — Ice Hockey Player
General Delivery, Pincher Creek AB T0K 1W0, Canada
**Kennedy, Delicious** — Singer (All-4-One)
Universal Attractions, 135 W 26th St, #1200, New York NY 10001 USA
**Kennedy, Diana S** — Chef, Writer
Clarkson Potter/Crown Publishing Group, 1745 Broadway, New York NY 10019, USA
**Kennedy, Donald** — Educator
Stanford University, International Studies Institute, Stanford CA 94305, USA
**Kennedy, Ethel** — Wife of Robert Kennedy
PO Box 328, Hyannis Port MA 02647, USA
**Kennedy, Eugene (Gene)** — Basketball Player
8218 Westrock Dr, Dallas TX 75243, USA
**Kennedy, Forbes T** — Ice Hockey Player
20 Oakland Dr, Charlottetown  PE C1C 1P4, Canada
**Kennedy, George** — Actor
719 N Cactus Creek Ave, Eagle ID 83616, USA
**Kennedy, Ian P** — Baseball Player
1204 Suncast Lane, #2, El Dorado Hills CA 95762, USA
**Kennedy, James C** — Businessman
1601 W Peachtree St NE, Atlanta GA 30309, USA
**Kennedy, James E (Jim)** — Baseball Player
13940 SW Lisa Lane, Beaverton OR 97005, USA
**Kennedy, Jamie** — Actor, Comedian
3 Arts Entertainment, 9460 Wilshire Blvd, #700, Beverly Hills CA 90212 USA
**Kennedy, Jason** — Actor
United Talent Agency, U T A Plaza, 9336 Civic Center Dr, Beverly Hills CA 90210 USA
**Kennedy, Jimmy W** — Football Player
New York Giants, Meadowlands Stadium, 102 Route 120, East Rutherford NJ 07073 USA
**Kennedy, Joey D (Joe), Jr** — Journalist
1635 11th Place S, Birmingham AL 35205, USA
**Kennedy, John E** — Baseball Player
2 Rodney Road, Peabody MA 01960, USA
**Kennedy, John Milton** — Actor
5711 Reseda Blvd, #204, Tarzana CA 91356, USA
**Kennedy, Junior R** — Baseball Player
6001 Eucalyptus Dr, #215, Bakersfield CA 93306, USA
**Kennedy, Kathleen** — Producer
Lucasfilm, 5858 Lucas Valley Road, Nicasio CA 94946, USA
**Kennedy, Kevin** — Producer, Writer
R W S H Agency, 1107 1/2 Glendon Ave, Los Angeles CA 90024, USA
**Kennedy, Kevin C** — Baseball Player, Manager
Fox-TV, Sports Dept, 205 W 67th St, New York NY 10065 USA
**Kennedy, Lee** — Businessman
Equifax Inc, 1550 Peachtree St NE, Atlanta GA 30309, USA
**Kennedy, Leon Isaac** — Actor
859 N Hollywood Way, #384, Burbank CA 91505, USA
**Kennedy, M Peter** — Figure Skater
7650 SE 41st, Mercer Island WA 98040, USA
**Kennedy, Maria Doyle** — Actress, Singer
United Agents, 12-26 Lexington St, London W1F 0LE, England
**Kennedy, Maura** — Singer (Kennedys)
PO Box 1298, New York NY 10276, USA
**Kennedy, Mimi** — Actress
Justice & Ponder, PO Box 480033, Los Angeles CA 90048, USA
**Kennedy, Myles R** — Singer, Guitarist
Wind-Up Records, 72 Madison Ave, #800, New York NY 10016 USA
**Kennedy, Nigel** — Concert Violinist
George Leitner Productions, Huetteldurfer St 259, 1140 Vienna, Austria
**Kennedy, Paul M** — Historian
409 Humphrey St, New Haven CT 06511, USA
**Kennedy, Pete** — Singer (Kennedys)
PO Box 1298, New York NY 10276, USA
**Kennedy, Randall L** — Attorney, Educator
Harvard University, Law School, Cambridge MA 02138, USA
**Kennedy, Ray F** — Businessman
Masco Corp, 21001 Van Born Road, Taylor MI 48180, USA
**Kennedy, Robert A** — Educator
University of Maine, President's Office, 5703 Alumni Hall, Orono ME 04469, USA
**Kennedy, Rory** — Director, Producer
Moxie Firecracker Films, 232 3rd St, #B403, Brooklyn NY 11215, USA
**Kennedy, T Lincoln, Jr** — Football Player
3555 E Jasmine Circle, Mesa AZ 85213, USA
**Kennedy, Terrence E (Terry)** — Baseball Player
333 N Pennington Dr, #23, Chandler AZ 85224, USA
**Kennedy, William J** — Writer
New York State Writers Institute, 1400 Washington Ave, Albany NY 12222, USA
**Kennedy, William R (Pickles)** — Basketball Player
9927 Galleon Dr, West Palm Beach FL 33411, USA
**Kennedy, X Joseph (X J)** — Writer
22 Revere St, Lexington MA 02420, USA
**Kennedy-Powell, Kathleen** — Judge
Los Angeles Municipal Court, 110 N Grand Ave, Los Angeles CA 90012, USA
**Kennerly, David Hume** — Photojournalist
1015 18th St, Santa Monica CA 90403, USA
**Kennerty, Michael B (Mike)** — Singer, Guitarist (All-American Rejects)
Interscope Records, 2220 Colorado Ave, Santa Monica CA 90404 USA
**Kenney, Emma** — Actress
Innovative Artists, 1505 10th St, Santa Monica CA 90401 USA

| | |
|---|---|
| **Kenney, Gerald T (Jerry)** | Baseball Player |
| 1980 Harrison Ave, Beloit WI 53511, USA | |
| **Kenney, William P (Bill)** | Football Player |
| 2808 SW Arthur Dr, Lees Summit MO 64082, USA | |
| **Kennicott, Philip** | Architectural Critic, Journalist |
| Washington Post, Editorial Dept, 1150 15th St NW, Washington DC 20071 USA | |
| **Kenniebrew, Dolores (Dee Dee)** | Singer (Crystals) |
| Superstars Unlimited, PO Box 371371, Las Vegas NV 89137, USA | |
| **Kennison, Eddie J, III** | Football Player |
| 14813 Sherwood Road, Overland Park KS 66224, USA | |
| **Kenny G** | Saxophonist |
| Front Line Mgmt, 1100 Glendon Ave, #2000, Los Angeles CA 90024 USA | |
| **Kenny, Andrew** | Singer (American Analog Set), Songwriter |
| Flower Booking, 1532 N Milwaukee Ave, #201, Chicago IL 60622, USA | |
| **Kenny, Enda** | Prime Minister, Ireland |
| Taoiseach's Office, Government Buildings, Upper Merrion St, Dublin 2, Ireland | |
| **Kenny, Jason** | Cyclist |
| Ashwood Laboratories, Brockhall Village, Blackburn, Lancashire BB6 8BB, England | |
| **Kenny, Shirley Strum** | Educator |
| State University of New York, President's Office, Stony Brook NY 11794, USA | |
| **Kenny, Tom** | Actor, Comedian |
| Innovative Artists, 1505 10th St, Santa Monica CA 90401 USA | |
| **Kenny, Yvonne** | Opera Singer |
| I M G Artists, Burlington Lane, Chiswick, London W4 2TH, England | |
| **Kenon, Larry J** | Basketball Player |
| 25057 Toutant Beauregard Road, San Antonio TX 78255, USA | |
| **Kenseth, Matthew R (Matt)** | Auto Racing Driver |
| 111 Stonewall Beach Lane, Mooresville NC 28117, USA | |
| **Kensing, Logan F** | Baseball Player |
| 450 Rodalyn Dr, Boerne TX 78006, USA | |
| **Kensit, Patsy** | Actress, Singer |
| A P A Talent/Literary Agency, 405 S Beverly Dr, #300, Beverly Hills CA 90212 USA | |
| **Kent** | Duke, England |
| York House, Saint James's Palace, London SW1A 1BQ, England | |
| **Kent, Allegra** | Ballerina |
| New York City Ballet, Lincoln Center Plaza, New York NY 10023 USA | |
| **Kent, Arthur** | Commentator |
| 2184 Torringford St, Torrington CT 06790, USA | |
| **Kent, Jean** | Actress |
| London Mgmt, 2-4 Noel St, London W1V 3RB, England | |
| **Kent, Jeffrey A (Jeff)** | Baseball Player |
| 550 Chaparral Court, Altadena CA 91001, USA | |
| **Kent, Jonathan** | Director |
| International Talent Booking, Ariel House, 74A Charlotte St, #100 London W1T 4QJ, England | |
| **Kent, Julie** | Ballerina |
| American Ballet Theatre, 890 Broadway, #300, New York NY 10003 USA | |
| **Kent, Muhtar** | Businessman |
| Coca-Cola Co, 1 Coca-Cola Plaza, 310 North Ave NW, Atlanta GA 30313, USA | |
| **Kent, Stacey** | Singer |
| John Boddy Agency, 10 Southfield Gardens, Twickenham TW1 4SZ, England | |
| **Kentridge, William** | Artist |
| David Krut Projects, Box 892, Houghton, 2041 Johannesburg, South Africa | |
| **Kenty, Hilmer** | Boxer |
| Escot Boxing, 19260 Bretton Dr, Detroit MI 48223, USA | |
| **Kenville, William M (Bill)** | Basketball Player |
| 59 Crary Ave, Binghamton NY 13905, USA | |
| **Keny-Guyer, Neal L** | Association Executive |
| Mercy Corps, 45 SW Ankeny St, Portland OR 97204, USA | |
| **Kenyon, Melvin E (Mel)** | Auto Racing Driver |
| 2645 S 25th West, Lebanon IN 46052, USA | |
| **Kenyon, Sherrilyn** | Writer |
| Pocket Books, 1230 Ave of Americas, New York NY 10020 USA | |
| **Kenzo** | Fashion Designer |
| 54 Rue Etienne Marcel, 75002 Paris, France | |
| **Keogh, Lainey** | Fashion Designer |
| 42 Dawson St, Dublin 2, Ireland | |
| **Keoghan, Phil** | Entertainer |
| I C M Partners, 10250 Constellation Blvd, #900, Los Angeles CA 90067 USA | |
| **Keon, David M (Dave)** | Ice Hockey Player |
| 115 Brackenwood Road, Palm Beach Gardens FL 33418, USA | |
| **Keough, Donald R (Don)** | Financier |
| 200 Galleria Parkway, #970, Atlanta GA 30339, USA | |
| **Keough, Matthew L (Matt)** | Baseball Player |
| 12 Shire, Trabuco Canyon CA 92679, USA | |
| **Keough, Riley** | Model, Actress |
| W M E Entertainment, 9601 Wilshire Blvd, #300, Beverly Hills CA 90210 USA | |
| **Keppinger, Jeffrey S (Jeff)** | Baseball Player |
| 1578 Cordillo Court, Dacula GA 30019, USA | |
| **Kerber, Angelique** | Tennis Player |
| Postfach 2846, 24027 Kiel, Germany | |
| **Kercheval, Ken** | Actor |
| PO Box 3371, Granada Hills CA 91634, USA | |
| **Kerdyk, Tracy L** | Golfer |
| 935 S Alhambra Circle, Coral Gables FL 33146, USA | |
| **Keresztes, K Sandor** | Architect |
| Fo Utca 44/50, 1011 Budapest, Hungary | |
| **Kerfeld, Charles P (Charlie)** | Baseball Player |
| PO Box 1666, Gig Harbor WA 98335, USA | |
| **Kerger, Paula** | Government Official |
| Public Broadcasting System, 1320 Braddock Dr, Alexandria VA 22314, USA | |
| **Kerim, Srgjan** | Government Official, Macedonia |
| United Nations, General Assembly, New York NY 10017, USA | |
| **Kerkeling, Hape** | Actor |
| Postfach 200257, 13512 Berlin, Germany | |
| **Kerkorian, Kirk** | Businessman |
| M G M/U A Communications, 2500 Broadway St, Santa Monica CA 90404, USA | |

**K**

**Kenney - Kerkorian**

**Kerkovich, Rob** — Actor
I C M Partners, 10250 Constellation Blvd, #900, Los Angeles CA 90067 USA

**Kerlikowske, R Gil** — Government, Law Enforcement Official
National Drug Control Policy Office, White House, Washington DC 20500, USA

**Kern, Geof** — Photographer
1355 Conant St, Dallas TX 75207, USA

**Kern, James L (Jim)** — Baseball Player
6009 Amberwood Court, Arlington TX 76016, USA

**Kern, Joey** — Actor
Abrams Artists, 9200 W Sunset Blvd, #1125, West Hollywood CA 90069 USA

**Kern, Olga** — Concert Pianist
Agence de Concerts Caecilia, 29 Rue de la Coulouvreniere, 1204 Geneva, Switzerland

**Kern, Otto** — Fashion Designer
Augustastr 1, 67655 Kaiserslautern, Germany

**Kern, Paul J** — Army General
A M Industries, 105 N Niles Ave, South Bend IN 46617, USA

**Kern, Rex W** — Football Player
2816 Avenida de Autlan, Camarillo CA 93010, USA

**Kernan, William F (Buck)** — Army General
30 Pinewild Dr, Pinehurst NC 28374, USA

**Kernek, George B** — Baseball Player
16423 Cotton Gin Ave, Wayne OK 73095, USA

**Kernen, Joe** — Commentator
CNBC-TV, 2200 Fletcher Ave, #600, Fort Lee NJ 07024, USA

**Kernis, Aaron Jay** — Composer
Yale University, Music Dept, New Haven CT 06520, USA

**Kernochan, Sarah** — Writer, Director, Producer
Mange-Ment, 1103 1/2 Glendon Ave, Los Angeles CA 90024, USA

**Kerns, David V, Jr** — Microbiotics Engineer
Vanderbilt University, Electrical Engineering Dept, Nashville TN 37235, USA

**Kerns, Joanna** — Actress
Paradigm Agency, 360 N Crescent Dr, North Building, Beverly Hills CA 90210 USA

**Keropian, Michael** — Sculptor
Keropian Sculpture LLC, 392 Gipsy Trail Road, Carmel NY 10512, USA

**Kerr, Allen** — Plant Pathologist
419 Carrington St, Adelaide SA 5000, Australia

**Kerr, Anita** — Singer
235 W 36th St, #321M, New York NY 10018, USA

**Kerr, Brook** — Actress
Precision Entertainment, 6338 Wilshire Blvd, Los Angeles CA 90048, USA

**Kerr, Cristie** — Golfer
10810 E Addy Way, Scottsdale AZ 85262, USA

**Kerr, Donald M, Jr** — Physicist
Science Applications International, 1241 Cave St, La Jolla CA 92037, USA

**Kerr, Edward** — Actor
A K A Talent, 6310 San Vicente Blvd, #200, Los Angeles CA 90048 USA

**Kerr, Graham** — Food Expert, Writer
Kerr Corp, 1020 N Sunset Dr, Camano Island WA 98282, USA

**Kerr, Miranda** — Model
I M G Models, 179-191 New South Head Road, Edgecliff NSW 2027, Australia

**Kerr, Pat** — Fashion Designer
Pat Kerr Inc, 200 Wagner Place, Memphis TN 38103, USA

**Kerr, Philip** — Writer
Independent Talent Group, 40 Whitfield St, London W1T 2RH, England

**Kerr, Tim** — Ice Hockey Player
335 Tom Brown Road, Moorestown NJ 08057, USA

**Kerr, William T** — Businessman
Meredith Corp, 1716 Locust St, Des Moines IA 50309, USA

**Kerrey, J Robert (Bob)** — Governor, Senator; Vietnam Hero (CMH)
278 W 4th St, New York NY 10014, USA

**Kerrigan, Joseph T (Joe)** — Baseball Player, Manager
450 Forest Lane, North Wales PA 19454, USA

**Kerrigan, Nancy A** — Figure Skater
40 Salem St, #101, Lynnfield MA 01940, USA

**Kerrigan, Pamela** — Golfer
3205 Truckers Lane, Hingham MA 02043, USA

**Kerry, Alexandra** — Actress, Producer, Director
Tar Art Media, 304 Hudson St, #600, New York NY 10013, USA

**Kerry, James** — Astronaut
N A S A, Johnson Space Center, 2101 NASA Road, Houston TX 77058 USA

**Kersee, Bob** — Track Coach
University of California, Athletic Dept, Los Angeles CA 90024, USA

**Kersey, Jerome** — Basketball Player
24140 SW Peters Mountain Road, West Linn OR 97068, USA

**Kersey, Paul** — Actor
Talent Works, 3500 W Olive Ave, #1400, Burbank CA 91505 USA

**Kersh, David** — Singer
Mark Hybner Entertainment, 50 Music Square W, #802, Nashville TN 37203, USA

**Kershaw, Clayton E** — Baseball Player
Los Angeles Dodgers, Stadium, 1000 Elysian Park Ave, Los Angeles CA 90090 USA

**Kershaw, Douglas J (Doug)** — Singer, Fiddler, Songwriter
Cooking Vinyl, 10 Allied Way, London W3 0RQ, England

**Kershaw, Sammy** — Singer
Sammy Kershaw Mgmt, 38 Music Square E, #111, Nashville TN 37203, USA

**Kertesz, Imre** — Nobel Literature Laureate
Rowohit Verlage, Hamburger Str 17, 21465 Reinbeck, Germany

**Kerwin, Brian** — Actor
Paradigm Agency, 360 Park Ave S, #1600, New York NY 10010 USA

**Kerwin, Cornelius** — Educator
American University, President's Office, Washington DC 20006, USA

**Kerwin, Joseph P** — Astronaut
10411 River Road, College Station TX 77845, USA

**Kerwin, Lance** — Actor
26331 Osborne Lane, Homeland CA 92548, USA

**Kerwin, Larkin** — Physicist
2166 Bourboniere Park, Sillery QC G1T 1B4, Canada

| | |
|---|---|
| **Kerwin, Thomas V (Tom)** | Basktball Player |
| 283 Salter Path Road, #114, Atlantic Beach NC 28512, USA | |
| **Keselowski, Bradley R (Brad)** | Auto Racing Driver |
| Penske Racing, 200 Penske Way, Mooresville, NC 28115 28115, USA | |
| **Keshen, Christine** | Curling Athlete |
| Curling Assn, 1660 Vimont Court, Cumberland ON K4A 4J4, Canada | |
| **Keshishian, Alek** | Director |
| Creative Artists Agency, 2000 Ave of Stars, #100, Los Angeles CA 90067 USA | |
| **Kesler, Ryan** | Ice Hockey Player |
| Vancouver Canucks, 800 Griffiths Way, Vancouver BC V6B 6G1, Canada | |
| **Kessel, Philip J (Phil), Jr** | Ice Hockey Player |
| 500 Atlantic Ave, #198, Boston MA 02210, USA | |
| **Kessinger, Donald E (Don)** | Baseball Player, Manager |
| 1306 Pelican Loop, Oxford MS 38655, USA | |
| **Kessler, David A** | Physician, Government Official |
| University of California Medical School, Dean's Office, San Francisco CA 94143, USA | |
| **Kessler, Glenn D** | Producer, Writer |
| Creative Artists Agency, 2000 Ave of Stars, #100, Los Angeles CA 90067 USA | |
| **Kessler, Jeffrey L** | Attorney |
| Dewey Ballantine, 1301 Ave of Americas, Basement 3, New York NY 10019, USA | |
| **Kessler, Mikkel** | Boxer |
| Bettina Palle, Frederiksberg Alle 76, 1820 Frederiksberg C, Denmark | |
| **Kessler, Ron** | Writer |
| Newsman.com, PO Box 20989, West Palm Beach FL 33416, USA | |
| **Kessler, Stephen** | Director |
| Nikki Weiss Co, 754 N La Jolla Ave, Los Angeles CA 90046, USA | |
| **Kessler, Todd A** | Producer, Writer |
| Creative Artists Agency, 2000 Ave of Stars, #100, Los Angeles CA 90067 USA | |
| **Kester, Richard L (Rick)** | Baseball Player |
| PO Box 623, Gardnerville NV 89410, USA | |
| **Kestner, Boyd** | Actor |
| Mirisch Agency, 8840 Wilshire Blvd, #100, Beverly Hills CA 90211 USA | |
| **Ketchum, Hal** | Singer, Songwriter |
| 602 Wayside Dr, Wimberley TX 78676, USA | |
| **Ketchum, Howard** | Color Engineer |
| 3800 Washington Road, West Palm Beach FL 33405, USA | |
| **Ketchum, Robert Glenn** | Photographer |
| Art Source, 11901 Santa Monica Blvd, Los Angeles CA 90025, USA | |
| **Ketelsen, Kyle** | Opera Singer |
| I M G Artists, Carnegie Hall Tower, 152 W 57th St, #500, New York NY 10019 USA | |
| **Ketterle, Wolfgang** | Nobel Physics Laureate |
| 25 Bellingham Dr, Brookline MA 02446, USA | |
| **Kettle, Roger** | Cartoonist (Man Called Horse) |
| King Features Syndicate, 300 W 57th St, #1500, New York NY 10019 USA | |
| **Kettner, Carla** | Producer, Writer |
| W M E Entertainment, 9601 Wilshire Blvd, #300, Beverly Hills CA 90210 USA | |
| **Kev Nish** | Singer (Far East Movement) |
| Stampede Mgmt, 12530 Beatrice St, Los Angeles CA 90066, USA | |
| **Keves, Gyorgy** | Architect |
| Keves es Epitesztarsai Rt, Melinda Utca 21, 1121 Budapest, Hungary | |
| **Key, A Wade** | Football Player |
| PO Box 857, Hondo TX 78861, USA | |
| **Key, James E (Jimmy)** | Baseball Player |
| 128 Talavera Place, Palm Beach Gardens FL 33418, USA | |
| **Key, John** | Prime Minister, New Zealand |
| Prime Minister's Office, Parliament Buildings, Wellington 6160, New Zealand | |
| **Key, Keegan-Michael** | Actor |
| United Talent Agency, U T A Plaza, 9336 Civic Center Dr, Beverly Hills CA 90210 USA | |
| **Keyes, Daniel** | Writer |
| 7491 N Federal Highway, #C5-110, Boca Raton FL 33487, USA | |
| **Keyes, Irwin** | Actor |
| Studio Talent Group, 1328 12th St, Santa Monica CA 90401, USA | |
| **Keyes, James W** | Businessman |
| Blockbuster Inc, 3704 Stratford Ave, Dallas TX 75205, USA | |
| **Keyes, Leroy** | Football Player |
| 3935 Glen Eagles Place, West Lafayette IN 47906, USA | |
| **Keyes, Nathan** | Actor |
| Creative Artists Agency, 2000 Ave of Stars, #100, Los Angeles CA 90067 USA | |
| **Keyes, Robert W** | Physicist, Engineer |
| I B M Research Division, PO Box 218, Yorktown Heights NY 10598, USA | |
| **Keyfitz, Nathan** | Statistician |
| 1580 Massachusetts Ave, #7C, Cambridge MA 02138, USA | |
| **Keynes, Skander** | Actor |
| Hamilton Hodell, 66-68 Margaret St, #500, London W1W 8SR, England | |
| **Keys, Alicia** | Singer, Songwriter, Pianist |
| Big Pita Little Pita Productions, Walt Disney Co, 500 S Buena Vista St, Burbank CA 91521, USA | |
| **Keys, Brady, Jr** | Football Player |
| 2931 Banchory Road, Winter Park FL 32792, USA | |
| **Keys, Donald** | Educator |
| Planetary Citizens, 777 United Nations Plaza, New York NY 10017, USA | |
| **Keys, Tyrone P** | Football Player |
| 5708 Clouds Peak Dr, Lutz FL 33558, USA | |
| **Keyser, F Ray, Jr** | Governor, VT |
| 64 Warner Ave, Proctor VT 05765, USA | |
| **Keyser, Richard L** | Businessman |
| W W Grainger Inc, 14441 W Illinois Route 60, Lake Forest IL 60045, USA | |
| **Keyworth, Jonathan K (Jon)** | Football Player |
| 1722 E Ridgefield Road, Spanish Fork UT 84660, USA | |
| **Khabibulin, Nikolai I** | Ice Hockey Player |
| 6451 E El Maro Circle, Paradise Valley AZ 85253, USA | |
| **Khajag Barsamian** | Religious Leader |
| Armenian Church of America, Eastern Diocese, 630 2nd Ave, New York NY 10016, USA | |
| **Khaled** | Singer |
| George Leitner Productions, Huetteldorfer Str 259, 1140 Vienna, Austria | |
| **Khalfoun, Franck** | Actor, Director |
| United Talent Agency, U T A Plaza, 9336 Civic Center Dr, Beverly Hills CA 90210 USA | |

# K

|  |  |
|---|---|
| **Khali, Simbi**<br>I C M Partners, 10250 Constellation Blvd, #900, Los Angeles CA 90067 USA | Actress |
| **Khalifa, Sheikh Hamad bin Isa al-**<br>Rifa's Palace, PO Box 555, Manama, Bahrain | Emir, Bahrain |
| **Khalifa, Sheikh Khalifa bin Sulman, al-**<br>Prime Minister's Office, Government House, PO Box 1000, Manama, Bahrain | Prime Minister, Bahrain |
| **Khalifa, Sheikh Salman bin Hamad al-**<br>Defense Ministry, PO Box 245, West Rif'a, Bahrain | Crown Prince, Bahrain |
| **Khalifa, Wiz**<br>Atlantic Records, 9229 W Sunset Blvd, #900, West Hollywood CA 90069 USA | Rap Artist |
| **Khama, K lan**<br>President's Office, State House, Private Bag 001, Gaborone, Botswana | President, Botswana; Army General |
| **Khamenei, Hojatolislam Sayyed Ali**<br>President's Office, Pastor Ave, Teheran, Iran | President, Iran |
| **Khan, Aamir**<br>Aamir Khan Productions, Kuber Niwas, #2, Meera Baug Road, Santacruz (W), Mumbai 400054, India | Actor |
| **Khan, Amir I**<br>Golden Boy Promotions, 626 Wilshire Blvd, #350, Los Angeles CA 90017 USA | Boxer |
| **Khan, Amjad Ali**<br>Eye for Talent, 1139 San Carlos Abe, #310, San Carlos CA 94070, USA | Sarod Player, Composer |
| **Khan, Chaka**<br>Management for Advancement of Artists, 9100 Wilshire Blvd, #450E, Beverly Hills CA 90212, USA | Singer, Actress |
| **Khan, Irrfan**<br>Paradigm Agency, 360 N Crescent Dr, North Building, Beverly Hills CA 90210 USA | Actor |
| **Khan, Nareem**<br>Deborah Hughes, 311 W 43rd St, #1102, New York NY 10036, USA | Fashion Designer |
| **Khan, Niazi Imran**<br>Pakistan Tehreek-e-Insaf, Street #84, Ho 2, Sector G-6/4, Islamabad, Pakistan | Cricketer |
| **Khan, Salman**<br>3 Galaxy Apartments, B J Road, Band Stand Bandra, Mumbai MS 400050, India | Actor |
| **Khan, Salman A (Sal)**<br>Khan Academy Discovery Laboratory, 151 Laura Lane, Palo Alto CA 94303, USA | Educator |
| **Khan, Shahrukh**<br>Amrit Apartments, #700, 15th Carter Road Bandra, Mumbai MS 400050, India | Actor |
| **Khan, Ustad Sultan**<br>Agency Group Ltd, 1880 Century Park E, #711, Los Angeles CA 90067, USA | Sarangi Musician |
| **Khanh, Emmanuelle**<br>Emmanuelle Khanh International, 39 Ave Victor Hugo, 75116 Paris, France | Fashion Designer |
| **Khanna, Akshay**<br>13/C Elplaza, Little Gibs Road, Malabar Hill, Mumbai MS 400026, India | Actor |
| **Khanna, Rinke**<br>201A Vastu Building, Military Road Juhu, Mumbai MS 400049, India | Actress |
| **Khanna, Vinod**<br>11 Palazo, #1300, Malabar Hill, Mumbai MS 400006, India | Actor |
| **Khanzadian, Vahan**<br>PO Box 137, Jewett NY 12444, USA | Opera Singer |
| **Kharbanda, Kulbhushan**<br>501 Silver Cascade, Mount Mary Road, Bandra, Mumbai MS 400050, India | Actor |
| **Khashoggi, Adnan M**<br>La Baraka, 29604 Marbella, Spain | Businessman |
| **Khavin, Vladimir Y**<br>Glavmosarchitectura, Triumfalnaya Square 1, 103001 Moscow, Russia | Architect |
| **Khayat, Edward (Eddie)**<br>7813 Haydenberry Cove, Nashville TN 37221, USA | Football Player, Coach |
| **Khayat, Robert C (Bob)**<br>PO Box 677, Oxford MS 38655, USA | Educator, Football Player |
| **Kher, Anupam**<br>402 Marina, Juhu Tara Road Juhu Beach, Mumbai MS 400049, India | Actor |
| **Khmylev, Yuri A**<br>8236 Oakway Lane, Buffalo NY 14221, USA | Ice Hockey Player |
| **Khokhlov, Boris**<br>Myaskovsky St 11-13, #102, 121019 Moscow, Russia | Ballet Dancer |
| **Khondji, Darius**<br>Independent Talent Group, 40 Whitfield St, London W1T 2RH, England | Cinematographer |
| **Khorkina, Svetlana**<br>Gymnastics Federation, Lujnetskaya Nabererynaya 8, 119270 Moscow, Russia | Gymnast |
| **Khosla, Vinod**<br>Khosla Ventures, 3000 Sand Hill Road, Building 3, Menlo Park CA 94025, USA | Businessman |
| **Khouri, Callie**<br>Creative Artists Agency, 2000 Ave of Stars, #100, Los Angeles CA 90067 USA | Director, Writer |
| **Khoury, Raymond**<br>Penguin Books, 375 Hudson St, Basement 1, New York NY 10014 USA | Writer |
| **Khristenko, Viktor**<br>Prime Minister's Office, Krasnopresneskaya Nab 2, 103274 Moscow, Russia | Prime Minister, Russia |
| **Khristich, Dmitri**<br>5002 N Convent Lane, #E, Philadelphia PA 19114, USA | Ice Hockey Player |
| **Khrushchev, Sergei**<br>3 Laurelhurst Road, Cranston RI 02920, USA | Writer |
| **Khush, Gurdev S**<br>International Rice Institute, Box 3127, Makati City 1271, Philippines | Agricultural Researcher |
| **Ki Sung-Yueng**<br>Football Assn, 1-131 Sinmunno, 2-Ga Jongno-Gu, Seoul 110 062, South Korea | Soccer Player |
| **Kiarostami, Abbas**<br>Zeitgeist Films, 247 Center St, #203, New York NY 10013, USA | Director |
| **Kibaki, Mwai**<br>President's Office, Harambee House, Harambee Ave, Nairobi, Kenya | President, Kenya |
| **Kiberlain, Sandrine**<br>Voyez Mon Agent, 20 Ave Rapp, 75007 Paris, France | Actress, Singer |
| **Kibrick, Anne**<br>381 Seminary Ave, #221, Auburndale MA 02466, USA | Medical Educator |
| **Kid Capri**<br>Asti Artist Mgmt, 66 Irving Place, New York NY 10003, USA | DJ Musician, Actor |
| **Kid Frost**<br>Green Light Talent Agency, PO Box 3172, Beverly Hills CA 90212 USA | Rap Artist |
| **Kid Rock**<br>Creative Artists Agency, 2000 Ave of Stars, #100, Los Angeles CA 90067 USA | Rap Artist |

**Khali - Kid Rock**

# K

**Kidd, Jason F**  
367 Cottonwood Way, Mahwah NJ 07430, USA — Basketball Player, Coach

**Kidd, Jodie**  
I M G Models, 131-151 Great Titchfield St, London W1W 5BB, England — Model

**Kidd, M John**  
4204 Moorland Dr, Midland MI 48640, USA — Football Player

**Kidd, Warren L**  
313 River Road, Harpersville AL 35078, USA — Basketball Player

**Kidd, William W (Billy)**  
Billy Kidd Racing, 2305 Mount Werner Circle, Steamboat Springs CO 80487, USA — Alpine Skier

**Kidder Lee, Barbara**  
1308 W Highland, Phoenix AZ 85013, USA — Alpine Skier

**Kidder, Margot**  
Muse Mgmt, 1541 Ocean Ave, #200, Santa Monica CA 90401, USA — Actress

**Kidder, Tracy**  
Random House, 1745 Broadway, #1800, New York NY 10019 USA — Writer

**Kidd-Gilchrist, Michael**  
Charlotte Bobcats, 333 E Trade St, #A, Charlotte NC 28202 USA — Basketball Player

**Kidjo, Angelique**  
Vector Mgmt, PO Box 120479, Nashville TN 37212 USA — Singer, Songwriter

**Kidron, Beeban**  
Independent Talent Group, 40 Whitfield St, London W1T 2RH, England — Director, Producer, Writer

**Kieber, Walter**  
Landstra 22, 9494 Schaan, Liechtenstein — Head of Government, Liechtenstein

**Kiechel, Walter, III**  
929 Washington St, Hoboken NJ 07030, USA — Editor

**Kiecker, Dana E**  
4104 Prairie Ridge Road, Saint Paul MN 55123, USA — Baseball Player

**Kiedis, Anthony**  
Untitled Entertainment, 350 S Beverly Dr, #200, Beverly Hills CA 90212 USA — Singer (Red Hot Chili Peppers)

**Kiefel, Ronald**  
3893 Field Dr, Wheat Ridge CO 80033, USA — Cyclist

**Kiefer, Adolph G**  
42125 N Hunt Club Road, Wadsworth IL 60083, USA — Swimmer, Coach

**Kiefer, Anselm**  
Gagosian Gallery, 980 Madison Ave, New York NY 10075 USA — Artist

**Kiefer, Mark A**  
11832 Old Fashion Way, Garden Grove CA 92840, USA — Baseball Player

**Kiefer, Nicolas**  
B L A Z, Bonner Str 12A, 30173 Hanover, Germany — Tennis Player

**Kiefer, Steven G (Steve)**  
12389 Cloudburst Trail, Moreno Valley CA 92555, USA — Baseball Player

**Kieffer, James M**  
422 Stoutenburgh Lane, Pittsford NY 14534, USA — Businessman

**Kiehl, Marina**  
Hermie-Bland Str 11, 81545 Munich, Germany — Alpine Skier

**Kiehl, Stuart**  
4193 Concord Ave, Santa Rosa CA 95407, USA — Cinematographer

**Kiel, Richard**  
1056 Loyola Ave, Clovis CA 93619, USA — Actor

**Kielty, Robert M (Bobby)**  
21504 Appaloosa Court, Canyon Lake CA 92587, USA — Baseball Player

**Kier, Udo**  
Richard Schwartz Mgmt, 2934 N Beverly Glen Circle, #107, Los Angeles CA 90077 USA — Actor

**Kiermayer, Susanne**  
Amthofplatz 5, 94259 Kirchberg, Germany — Markswoman

**Kieschnick, M Brooks**  
210 Joliet Ave, #A, San Antonio TX 78209, USA — Baseball Player

**Kiesel, Theresia**  
Stifterstr 24, 4050 Truan, Austria — Track Athlete

**Kiffin, Irv**  
1441 Trellis Lane, Pembroke Pines FL 33026, USA — Basketball Player

**Kigeli V Ndagindurwa**  
Kigeli Foundation, Fairfax Towers, 9941 Oak Creek Place, Oakton VA 22124, USA — King, Rwanda

**Kightlinger, Laura**  
Avalon Mgmt, 8332 Melrose Ave, #200, Los Angeles CA 90069, USA — Actress, Comedienne

**Kihlstedt, Rya**  
Brookside Mgmt, 250 W 57th St, #2303, New York NY 10107, USA — Actress

**Kihn, Greg**  
Riot Mgmt, PO Box 8553, Berkeley CA 94707, USA — Singer, Guitarist (Greg Kihn Band)

**Kihune, Robert K U**  
1428 Aunauna St, Kailua HI 96734, USA — Navy Admiral

**Kiick, James F (Jim)**  
2900 S University Dr, #9112, Davie FL 33328, USA — Football Player

**Kiir Mayardit, Salva**  
President Office, Juba, Southern Sudan — President, South Sudan

**Kiiskinen, Kalle**  
Curling Assn, Kalatorppa 2A62, 02230 Espoo, Finland — Curling Athlete

**Kikuchi, Rinko**  
Anore, 6-17-15-9F Jingumae, Shibuya, Tokyo 150 0001, Japan — Actress

**Kikuchi, Rioko**  
Japanese Aerospace Exploration Agency, 2-1-1 Sengen, Tsukuba-shi, Ibaraki 305 8505, Japan — Astronaut, Japan; Photographer

**Kikwete, Jakaya Mrisho**  
President's Office, State House, PO Box 9120, Dar es Salaam, Tanzania — President, Tanzania

**Kilar, Jason**  
Hulu, 12312 W Olympic Blvd, Los Angeles CA 90064, USA — Businessman

**Kilar, Wojciech**  
Ul Kosciuszki 165, 40 524 Katowice, Poland — Composer

**Kilbane, Pat**  
Amsel Eisenstadt Frazier, 5055 Wilshire Blvd, #865, Los Angeles CA 90036 USA — Actor

**Kilbey, Steven J**  
M O B Agency, 6404 Wilshire Blvd, #505, Los Angeles CA 90048 USA — Singer, Guitarist (Church); Songwriter

**Kilborn, Craig**  
Apostle Management, 9696 Culver Blvd, #108, Culver City CA 90232, USA — Actor, Comedian, Writer, Producer

**Kilbourne, Wendy**  
9200 W Sunset Blvd, #612, West Hollywood CA 90069, USA — Actress

# K

**Kilburn, Terry** — Actor
Oakland University, Meadowbrook Theatre, Walton & Squirrel, Rochester MI 48063, USA
**Kilcline, Thomas J (Tom), Jr** — Navy Admiral
Commander, Naval Air Force Pacific, NAS North Island, San Diego CA 92135 USA
**Kilcullen, Robert B (Bob)** — Football Player
400 E Division St, Pilot Point TX 76258, USA
**Kildea, Bobby** — Guitarist, Bassist (Belle & Sebastian)
Ground Control Touring, 20 Jay St, #826, Brooklyn NY 11201 USA
**Kiley, Ariel** — Actress
Untitled Entertainment, 350 S Beverly Dr, #200, Beverly Hills CA 90212 USA
**Kilgallon, Robert D** — Environmental Researcher
662 Park Ave, Meadville PA 16335, USA
**Kilgore, Jerry** — Singer, Songwriter
T B A Artist Mgmt, 300 10th Ave S, Nashville TN 37203, USA
**Kilgore, Jon** — Football Player
2422 Glen Oaks Court NE, Atlanta GA 30345, USA
**Kilgus, Paul N** — Baseball Player
968 Threewood Circle, Bowling Green KY 42103, USA
**Kilius, Marika** — Figure Skater
Postfach 201151, 63271 Dreieich, Germany
**Kill, Jerry** — Football Coach
Legacy Agency, 230 Park Ave, #851, New York NY 10169 USA
**Killam, Taran** — Actor
Principato-Young, 9465 Wilshire Blvd, #880, Beverly Hills CA 90212 USA
**Killar, Wojciech** — Composer
Ul Ksciuszki 165, 40 524 Katowice, Poland
**Killeen, Denise** — Golfer
803 Golden Wood Trace, Canton GA 30114, USA
**Killen, Kyle** — Producer, Writer
W M E Entertainment, 9601 Wilshire Blvd, #300, Beverly Hills CA 90210 USA
**Killens, Terry D** — Football Player
5665 Water Spring Way, Mason OH 45040, USA
**Killer Mike** — Rap Artist
J L Entertainment, 18653 Ventura Blvd, #340, Los Angeles CA 91356 USA
**Killing, Laure** — Actress
Agence Christine Parat, 9 Rue de Maubeuge, 75009 Paris, France
**Killip, Christopher D** — Photographer
Harvard University, Visual Studies Dept, 24 Quincy St, Cambridge MA 02138, USA
**Killy, Jean-Claude** — Alpine Skier
Villa Les Oiseaux 13 Chemin Bellefontaine, 1223 Cologny GE, Switzerland
**Kilman, Sato** — Prime Minister, Vanuatu
Prime Minister's Office, PO Box 053, Port Vila, Vanuatu
**Kilmer, Val** — Actor
PO Box 364, Rowe NM 87562, USA
**Kilmer, William O (Billy)** — Football Player
1853 Monte Carlo Way, #36, Coral Springs FL 33071, USA
**Kilmore, Chris** — DJ Musician, Keyboardist (Incubus)
Variety Artists, 1924 Spring St, Paso Robles CA 93446 USA
**Kilner, Clare** — Director, Writer
Gersh Agency, 9465 Wilshire Blvd, #600, Beverly Hills CA 90212 USA
**Kilner, Kevin** — Actor
Innovative Artists, 1505 10th St, Santa Monica CA 90401 USA
**Kilpatrick, Carl** — Basketball Player
10517 23rd Street Court E, Edgewood WA 98372, USA
**Kilrain, Susan L** — Astronaut
2168 Lords Landing, Virginia Beach VA 23454, USA
**Kilrea, Brian** — Ice Hockey Player, Coach
2192 Saunderson Dr, Ottawa ON K1G 2G4, Canada
**Kilts, James M** — Businessman
Centerview Partners, 31 W 52nd St, #2200, New York NY 10019, USA
**Kilzer, Louis C (Lon)** — Journalist
Minneapolis-Saint Paul Star-Tribune, 425 Portland Ave, Minneapolis MN 55488, USA
**Kim Bo-Kyung** — Soccer Player
Football Assn, 1-131 Sinmunno, 2-Ga Jongno-Gu, Seoul 110 062, South Korea
**Kim Chang-Soo** — Soccer Player
Football Assn, 1-131 Sinmunno, 2-Ga Jongno-Gu, Seoul 110 062, South Korea
**Kim Dong-Sung** — Speed Skater
Skating Union, 88 Bangyee-Dong, Songpaku, Seoul 138 749, South Korea
**Kim Hyun-Sung** — Soccer Player
Football Assn, 1-131 Sinmunno, 2-Ga Jongno-Gu, Seoul 110 062, South Korea
**Kim Jong-Pil** — Prime Minister, South Korea; General
340-38, Sindang 4-Dongku, Seoul, South Korea
**Kim Jong-Un** — President Designate, North Korea
President's Office, Pyongyang, North Korea
**Kim Kee-Hee** — Soccer Player
Football Assn, 1-131 Sinmunno, 2-Ga Jongno-Gu, Seoul 110 062, South Korea
**Kim Ki-Hoon** — Speed Skater
Skating Union, 88 Bangyee-Dong, Songpaku, Seoul 138 749, South Korea
**Kim Seoung Il** — Speed Skater
Skating Union, 88 Bangyee-Dong, Songpaku, Seoul 138 749, South Korea
**Kim So-Hui** — Speed Skater
Skating Union, 88 Bangyee-Dong, Songpaku, Seoul 138 749, South Korea
**Kim Young-Gwon** — Soccer Player
Football Assn, 1-131 Sinmunno, 2-Ga Jongno-Gu, Seoul 110 062, South Korea
**Kim Young-Sam** — President, South Korea
7-6-1 Sangdo, Dongjakku, Seoul 156 743, South Korea
**Kim Yu-Na** — Figure Skater
Toronto C S C C, 141 Wilson Ave, Toronto ON M5M 3A3, Canada
**Kim Yun-Mi** — Speed Skater
Skating Union, 88 Bangyee-Dong, Songpaku, Seoul 138 749, South Korea
**Kim, Anthony** — Golfer
Professional Golfer's Assn, PO Box 109601, Palm Beach Gardens FL 33410 USA
**Kim, Byung Hyun** — Baseball Player
4601 E Skyline Dr, #1302, Tucson AZ 85718, USA
**Kim, Christina** — Golfer
Ladies Pro Golf Assn, 100 International Golf Dr, Daytona Beach FL 32124 USA

**Kim, Daniel Dae** — Actor
A P A Talent/Literary Agency, 405 S Beverly Dr, #300, Beverly Hills CA 90212 USA
**Kim, Grace** — Model
Playboy Promotions, 2706 Media Center Dr, Los Angeles CA 90065 USA
**Kim, Jacqueline** — Actress
Innovative Artists, 1505 10th St, Santa Monica CA 90401 USA
**Kim, Jaegwon** — Philosopher
Brown University, Philosophy Dept, Providence RI 02912, USA
**Kim, Jim Yong** — Financier, Educator
World Bank Group, 1818 H St NW, Washington DC 20433, USA
**Kim, John J** — Journalist
Chicago Sun-Times, Editorial Dept, 401 N Wabash Ave, Chicago IL 60611 USA
**Kim, Kathleen** — Opera Singer
Harrison/Parrott, 5-6 Albion Court, London W6 0QT, England
**Kim, Kwang Soo** — Neuroscientist, Psychiatrist
McLean Hospital, Molecular Neurobiology Laboratory, 115 Mill St, Belmont MA 02478, USA
**Kim, Nelli V** — Gymnast
2480 Cobblehill, #A, Alcove, Woodbury MN 55125, USA
**Kim, Peter S** — Biochemist, Geneticist
Whitehead Institute, 9 Cambridge Center, Cambridge MA 02142, USA
**Kim, Yunjin** — Actress
Ace Mgmt, 210 5th Ave, Venice CA 90291, USA
**Kimball, Bobby** — Singer (Toto)
World Entertainment Assoc, 8815 Conroy Windermere Road, #407, Orlando FL 32835, USA
**Kimball, Charlie** — Auto Racing Driver
Chip Ganassi Racing, 8500 Westmoreland Dr, Concord NC 28027, USA
**Kimball, Cheyenne** — Singer, Songwriter, Actress
Creative Artists Agency, 2000 Ave of Stars, #100, Los Angeles CA 90067 USA
**Kimball, Christopher** — Chef
Public Broadcasting System, 1320 Braddock Place, Alexandria VA 22314 USA
**Kimball, Dick** — Diver, Diving Coach
1540 Waltham Dr, Ann Arbor MI 48103, USA
**Kimball, Jeffrey** — Cinematographer
Paradigm Agency, 360 N Crescent Dr, North Building, Beverly Hills CA 90210 USA
**Kimball, Lynnda** — Model
Playboy Promotions, 2706 Media Center Dr, Los Angeles CA 90065 USA
**Kimball, Thomas (Toby)** — Basketball Player
6859 Avenida Andorra, La Jolla CA 92037, USA
**Kimball, Warren F** — Historian
2540 Otter Lane, Johns Island SC 29455, USA
**Kimble, Avis** — Model
Playboy Promotions, 2706 Media Center Dr, Los Angeles CA 90065 USA
**Kimble, Gregory K (Bo)** — Basketball Player
100 Poe Court, North Wales PA 19454, USA
**Kimble, Warren** — Artist
RR 3 Box 1038, Brandon VT 05733, USA
**Kimbrough, Charles** — Actor, Singer
255 Amalfi Dr, Santa Monica CA 90402, USA
**Kimbrough, Elbert L** — Football Player
886 W 2nd St, Galesburg IL 61401, USA
**Kimbrough, R Shane** — Astronaut
N A S A, Johnson Space Center, 2101 NASA Road, Houston TX 77058 USA
**Kimbrough, Stan** — Basketball Player
3922 Elm Ave, Cincinnati OH 45236, USA
**Kimery, James L** — Association Executive
Veterans of Foreign Wars, 405 W 34th St, Kansas City MO 64111, USA
**Kimm, Bruce E** — Baseball Player, Manager
3168 121st St, Amana IA 52203, USA
**Kimmel, Jimmy** — Actor, Comedian
Jackhole Industries, 6834 Hollywood Blvd, Los Angeles CA 90028, USA
**Kimmelman, Michael** — Art Critic
New York Times, Editorial Dept, 229 W 43rd St, New York NY 10036 USA
**Kimura, Doreen** — Psychologist
211 Madison Ave, Toronto ON M5R 2S6, Canada
**Kimura, Kazuo** — Industrial Designer
Japan Design Foundation, 2-2 Cenba Chuo, Higashiku, Osaka 541 0046, Japan
**Kinard, A Terance (Terry)** — Football Player
18 Safe Harbor Ave, Pawleys Island SC 29585, USA
**Kinard, William R (Billy)** — Football Player
PO Box 680944, Fort Payne AL 35968, USA
**Kincaid, Jamaica** — Writer
College Road, North Bennington VT 05257, USA
**Kinchen, Arif S** — Actor
Xpose Talent Agency, 1055 E Colorado Blvd, #5, Pasadena CA 91106, USA
**Kinchen, Brian D** — Football Player
19502 E Pinnacle Circle, Baton Rouge LA 70810, USA
**Kinchla, Chandler (Chan)** — Guitarist (Blues Traveler)
C3 Presents, 98 San Jacinto Blvd, #400, Austin TX 78701, USA
**Kinchla, Thaddeus A (Tad)** — Bassist (Blues Traveler)
C3 Presents, 98 San Jacinto Blvd, #400, Austin TX 78701, USA
**Kincses, Veronika** — Opera Singer
Hungarian State Opera, Andrassy Utca 22, 1061 Budapest, Hungary
**Kind, Richard** — Actor
Foster Entertainment, 12533 Woodgreen St, Building B, Los Angeles CA 90066, USA
**Kind, Roslyn** — Actress, Singer
Randy Johnson Co, PO Box 69A18, West Hollywood CA 90069, USA
**Kindall, Gerald D (Jerry)** — Baseball Player
7220 E Grey Fox Lane, Tucson AZ 85750, USA
**Kinder, Donald R** — Political Scientist
University of Michigan, Political Science Dept, Ann Arbor MI 48109, USA
**Kinder, Melvyn** — Psychologist, Writer
1951 San Ysidro Dr, Beverly Hills CA 90210, USA
**Kinder, Richard D** — Businessman
Kinder-Morgan Inc, 500 Dallas St, #1000, Houston TX 77002, USA
**Kindig, Howard W, Jr** — Football Player
8740 Bayside Ave, Baton Rouge LA 70806, USA

**Kindler, Damian** — Producer, Writer
H2F Entertainment, 644 N Cherokee Ave, Los Angeles CA 90004, USA
**Kindler, Jeffrey B** — Businessman
Pfizer Inc, 235 E 42nd St, New York NY 10017, USA
**Kindrachuk, Orest** — Ice Hockey Player
106 Meeshaway Trail, Medford Lakes NJ 08055, USA
**Kindred, David A** — Sportswriter
Atlanta Constitution, 223 Perimeter Center Parkway NE, Atlanta GA 30346, USA
**Kiner, Kevin** — Composer
First Artists Mgmt, 4764 Park Granada, #210, Calabasas CA 91302 USA
**Kiner, Ralph M** — Baseball Player, Sportscaster
19 Doubling Road, Greenwich CT 06830, USA
**Kiner, Steven A (Steve)** — Football Player
112 N Ole Hickory Trail, Carrollton GA 30117, USA
**King Hogue, Maxine (Micki)** — Diver
3509 Colt Neck Lane, Lexington KY 40502, USA
**King Tee** — Rap Artist
Likwit Entertainment, PO Box 360713, Los Angeles CA 90036, USA
**King, Albert** — Basketball Player
88 Sturbridge Circle, Wayne NJ 07470, USA
**King, Angelo T** — Football Player
2922 W Royal Lane, #2090, Irving TX 75063, USA
**King, Anthony S** — Political Scientist
Mill House, Middle Green, Wakes Colne, Colchester, Essex CP6 2BP, England
**King, B B** — Singer, Guitarist
W M E Entertainment, 9601 Wilshire Blvd, #300, Beverly Hills CA 90210 USA
**King, Ben E** — Singer
Randy Irwin, PO Box 11862, Naples FL 34101, USA
**King, Bernard** — Basketball Player
307 Jupiter Hills Dr, Duluth GA 30097, USA
**King, Billie Jean** — Tennis Player
World Team Tennis, 1776 Broadway, #600, New York NY 10019, USA
**King, Brent** — Actor
Malaky International, 205 S Beverly Dr, #211, Beverly Hills CA 90212, USA
**King, Carole** — Composer, Singer, Pianist
Carole King Productions, 11684 Ventura Blvd, #273, Studio City CA 91604, USA
**King, Carolyn Dineen** — Judge
US Court of Appeals, US Courthouse, 515 Rusk Ave, #12015, Houston TX 77002, USA
**King, Charles G (Chick)** — Baseball Player
4036 Highway 54, Paris TN 38242, USA
**King, Cheryl** — Actress
CLInc Talent, 843 N Sycamore Ave, Los Angeles CA 90038, USA
**King, Colbert** — Journalist
Washington Post, Editorial Dept, 1150 15th St NW, Washington DC 20071 USA
**King, Curtis E** — Baseball Player
2538 Beechwood Dr, Vineland NJ 08361, USA
**King, Dana** — Commentator
CBS-TV, News Dept, 524 W 57th St, New York NY 10019, USA
**King, David A** — Chemist
20 Glisson Road, Cambridge CB1 2EW, England
**King, Dennis** — Artist
108 Andrew Court, Mount Shasta CA 96067, USA
**King, Derek** — Ice Hockey Player
8184 E Wingspan Way, Scottsdale AZ 85255, USA
**King, Dexter Scott** — Association Executive
Martin Luther King Nonviolent Social Change Center, 449 Auburn Ave NE, Atlanta GA 30312, USA
**King, Diana** — Singer, Songwriter
Wenig-LaMonica Associates, 580 White Plains Road, #130, Tarrytown NY 10591 USA
**King, Don** — Boxing Promoter
Don King Productions, 501 Fairway Dr, Deerfield Beach FL 33441, USA
**King, Edward E (Ed)** — Football Player
9903 North Blvd, Cleveland OH 44108, USA
**King, Elizabeth (Betsy)** — Golfer
7418 E Alta Sierra Dr, Scottsdale AZ 85266, USA
**King, Emanuel** — Football Player
Hollywood Christian High School, 1708 N 60th Ave, Hollywood FL 33021, USA
**King, Eric S** — Baseball Player
1063 Stanford Dr, Simi Valley CA 93065, USA
**King, Erik** — Actor
Burstein Co, 15304 W Sunset Blvd, #208, Pacific Palisades CA 90272 USA
**King, Evelyn (Champagne)** — Singer
T-Best Talent Agency, 508 Honey Lake Court, Danville CA 94506 USA
**King, Fallon** — Singer (Cherish)
Capitol Records, 810 7th Ave, New York NY 10019 USA
**King, Farrah** — Singer (Cherish)
Capitol Records, 810 7th Ave, New York NY 10019 USA
**King, Felisha** — Singer (Cherish)
Capitol Records, 810 7th Ave, New York NY 10019 USA
**King, G Stephen (Steve)** — Football Player
45 Chipping Stone Road, North Attleboro MA 02760, USA
**King, Gary** — Political Scientist
Harvard University, Quantitative Social Science Institute, Cambridge MA 02138, USA
**King, Georgia** — Actress
Paradigm Agency, 360 N Crescent Dr, North Building, Beverly Hills CA 90210 USA
**King, Gilbert** — Writer
Chase Literary Agency, 220 E 23rd St, #1100 New York NY 10011, USA
**King, Gordon D** — Football Player
2641 Highwood Dr, Roseville CA 95661, USA
**King, Graham** — Writer, Producer
G K Films, 1540 2nd St, #200, Santa Monica CA 90401, USA
**King, Harold (Hal)** — Baseball Player
828 Geneva Dr, Oviedo FL 32765, USA
**King, Horace E** — Football Player
884 Fairburn Road NW, Atlanta GA 30331, USA
**King, Jaime** — Actress, Model
Gersh Agency, 9465 Wilshire Blvd, #600, Beverly Hills CA 90212 USA

| | |
|---|---|
| **King, James** | Singer |
| Rounder Records, 1 Rounder Way, Burlington MA 01803 USA | |
| **King, James H (Jim)** | Baseball Player |
| 720 Stokenbury Road, Elkins AR 72727, USA | |
| **King, Jamie Thomas** | Actor |
| 3 Arts Entertainment, 9460 Wilshire Blvd, #700, Beverly Hills CA 90212 USA | |
| **King, Jeff** | Dog Sled Racer |
| PO Box 48, Denali National Park AK 99755, USA | |
| **King, Jeffrey F (Jeff)** | Producer, Director, Writer |
| Creative Artists Agency, 2000 Ave of Stars, #100, Los Angeles CA 90067 USA | |
| **King, Jeffrey W (Jeff)** | Baseball Player |
| 50401 Highway 278, Wisdom MT 59761, USA | |
| **King, Joanne** | Actress |
| T N Enterprises, 14 Beach Grove, Blackrock County, Dublin, Ireland | |
| **King, Joe** | Singer, Guitarist (Fray) |
| A2 Mgmt, 624 Davis St, #200, Evanston IL 60201, USA | |
| **King, Joey** | Actress |
| Coast to Coast Talent, 3350 Barham Blvd, Los Angeles CA 90068 USA | |
| **King, Jon** | Singer (Gang of Four) |
| Story Worldwide, Primrose Hill, 15B Saint George's Mews, London NW1 8XC, England | |
| **King, Kaki** | Singer, Guitarist |
| Big Hasssle, 44 Wall St, #2200, New York NY 10005, USA | |
| **King, Kathryn (Katie)** | Ice Hockey Player |
| 3 Birchwood Road, Salem NH 3079, USA | |
| **King, Kris** | Ice Hockey Player |
| National Hockey League, 50 Bay St, #1100, Toronto ON M5J 2X8, Canada | |
| **King, Kristin** | Ice Hockey Player |
| USA Hockey, 1775 Bob Johnson Dr, Colorado Springs CO 80906 USA | |
| **King, Lamar** | Football Player |
| 5082 Springhouse Circle, Rosedale MD 21237, USA | |
| **King, Larry** | Commentator, Columnist |
| Media Talent Group, 9200 Sunset Blvd, #550, West Hollywood CA 90069, USA | |
| **King, Linden K** | Football Player |
| 1130 S Flower St, #418, Los Angeles CA 90015, USA | |
| **King, Loyd** | Basketball Player |
| 118 Wilde Brook Dr, Asheville NC 28806, USA | |
| **King, Mark** | Artist |
| King Griffin Inc, 8665 Miralani Dr, #100, San Diego CA 92126, USA | |
| **King, Mark** | Singer, Bassist (Level 42) |
| Level 42, PO Box 23, Sandown P036 0QL, Canada | |
| **King, Mary E** | Equestrian |
| Matford Park Farm, Exminster, Exeter, Devon EX6 8AT, England | |
| **King, Mary-Claire** | Geneticist |
| University of Washington Medical School, Genetics Dept, Seattle WA 98195, USA | |
| **King, Michael Patrick** | Director, Writer |
| Creative Artists Agency, 2000 Ave of Stars, #100, Los Angeles CA 90067 USA | |
| **King, Michelle** | Producer, Writer |
| Paradigm Agency, 360 N Crescent Dr, North Building, Beverly Hills CA 90210 USA | |
| **King, Morgana** | Singer, Actress |
| 13327 Cheltenham Dr, Sherman Oaks CA 91423, USA | |
| **King, Neosha** | Singer (Cherish) |
| Capitol Records, 810 7th Ave, New York NY 10019 USA | |
| **King, Perry** | Actor |
| 3647 Wrightwood Dr, Studio City CA 91604, USA | |
| **King, Peter** | Sportscaster, Sportswriter |
| NBC-TV, Sports Dept, 30 Rockefeller Plaza, #270E, New York NY 10112 USA | |
| **King, Phillip** | Sculptor |
| Royal College of Arts, Kensington Gore, London SW7 2EU, England | |
| **King, Raymond K (Ray)** | Baseball Player |
| 4220 N 161st Ave, Goodyear AZ 85395, USA | |
| **King, Regina** | Actress |
| I C M Partners, 10250 Constellation Blvd, #900, Los Angeles CA 90067 USA | |
| **King, Reginald B (Reggie)** | Basketball Player |
| 4716 Chouteau St, Shawnee KS 66226, USA | |
| **King, Richard L** | Businessman |
| Albertson's Inc, 250 E Parkcenter Blvd, Boise ID 83706, USA | |
| **King, Robert** | Producer, Writer |
| Paradigm Agency, 360 N Crescent Dr, North Building, Beverly Hills CA 90210 USA | |
| **King, Robert B** | Judge |
| US Court of Appeals, 300 Virginia St E, #2630, Charleston WV 25301, USA | |
| **King, Ronette** | Interior Designer |
| Gensler Assoc, 600 California St, #1000, San Francisco CA 94108, USA | |
| **King, Shaun E** | Football Player, Sportscaster |
| 10116 Caraway Spice Ave, Riverview FL 33578, USA | |
| **King, Stephen E** | Writer |
| 1380 Hammond St, Bangor ME 04401, USA | |
| **King, Stephenson T** | Prime Minister, Saint Lucia |
| Prime Minister's Office, Greaham Louisy Building, #500, Waterfront, Castries, Saint Lucia | |
| **King, Theodore W (Ted)** | Actor |
| Brady Brannon Rich, 5670 Wilshire Blvd, #820, Los Angeles CA 90036, USA | |
| **King, Thomas J (Tom)** | Government Official, England |
| House of Commons, Westminster, London SW1A 0AA, England | |
| **King, Thomas V (Tom)** | Basketball Player |
| 4930 Sea Witch Dr, Fernandina Beach FL 32034, USA | |
| **King, Vania** | Tennis Player |
| 380 Forsyth St, Boca Raton FL 33487, USA | |
| **King, W David (Dave)** | Ice Hockey Coach |
| Phoenix Coyotes, 6751 N Sunset Blvd, #200, Glendale AZ 85305 USA | |
| **King, William (Bill)** | Trumpeter (Commodores) |
| Management Assoc, 1920 Benson Ave, Saint Paul MN 55116, USA | |
| **King, Woodie, Jr** | Producer |
| 417 Convent Ave, New York NY 10031, USA | |
| **Kinga, Yukari** | Soccer Player |
| Football Assn, 3-10-15 Hongo, Bunkyoku, Tokyo 113 0033 Japan | |
| **Kingdom, Roger** | Track Athlete |
| 146 S Fairmont St, #1, Pittsburgh PA 15206, USA | |

# K

**Kingery, Michael S (Mike)**
51923 298th St, Grove City MN 56243, USA — Baseball Player

**King-Hele, Desmond G** — Writer
7 Hilltops Court, 65 North Lane, Buriton, Hampshire GU31 5RS, England

**Kingman, David A (Dave)** — Baseball Player
PO Box 209, Glenbrook NV 89413, USA

**Kingrea, Richard O (Rick)** — Football Player
102 N Bayview St, Fairhope AL 36532, USA

**Kingsale, Eugene H (Gene)** — Baseball Player
105 Angelfish Lane, Jupiter FL 33477, USA

**Kingsbury, Gina** — Ice Hockey Player
Team Canada, 2424 University Dr NW, Calgary AB T2N 3Y9, Canada

**Kingsbury, Tim** — Musician (Arcade Fire)
Billions Corp, 3522 W Armitage Ave, Chicago IL 60647 USA

**Kingsley, Ben** — Actor
New Penworth House, Stratford upon Avon, Warwickshire 0V3 7QX, England

**Kingsolver, Barbara E** — Writer
PO Box 160, Meadowview VA 24361, USA

**Kingston, Alex** — Actress
Principal Entertainment, 9255 Sunset Blvd, #500, Los Angeles CA 90069 USA

**Kingston, George** — Ice Hockey Coach
235 W Camino Descanso, Palm Springs CA 92264, USA

**Kingston, Kenny** — Astrologer
C E S D, 10635 Santa Monica Blvd, #130, Los Angeles CA 90025 USA

**Kingston, Maxine Hong** — Writer
University of California, English Dept, Berkeley CA 94720, USA

**Kingston, Sean** — Rap Artist, Songwriter, Actor
I C M Partners, 10250 Constellation Blvd, #900, Los Angeles CA 90067 USA

**Kinkade, Mike** — Baseball Player
3005 SE Spyglass Dr, Vancouver WA 98683, USA

**Kinkel, Klaus** — Government Official, Germany
Auswartigen Amt, Adenauerallee 101, 53113 Bonn, Germany

**Kinley, Heather** — Singer (Kinleys)
PO Box 128501, Nashville TN 37212, USA

**Kinley, Jennifer** — Singer (Kinleys)
Sony Records, 2100 Colorado Ave, Santa Monica CA 90404 USA

**Kinmont, Kathleen** — Actress
9929 Sunset Blvd, #310, Los Angeles CA 90069, USA

**Kinnally, Jon** — Writer, Producer
W M E Entertainment, 9601 Wilshire Blvd, #300, Beverly Hills CA 90210 USA

**Kinnaman, Joel** — Actor
Creative Artists Agency, 2000 Ave of Stars, #100, Los Angeles CA 90067 USA

**Kinnear, Dominic** — Soccer Coach
Houston Dynamo, 1415 Louisiana, #3400, Houston TX 77002 USA

**Kinnear, Greg** — Actor, Comedian
Creative Artists Agency, 2000 Ave of Stars, #100, Los Angeles CA 90067 USA

**Kinnear, James W, III** — Businessman
149 Taconic Road, Greenwich CT 06831, USA

**Kinnear, Rory** — Actor
Markham Froggatt Irwin, Julian House, 4 Windmill St, London W1P 1HF, England

**Kinnebrew, Larry D** — Football Player
216 Kingston Ave NE, Rome GA 30161, USA

**Kinnell, Galway** — Writer
110 Bleecker St, #6D, New York NY 10012, USA

**Kinney, Dallas** — Photojournalist
13010 Silver Sands Dr, Fort Myers FL 33913, USA

**Kinney, Dennis P** — Baseball Player
1981 Arundel Road, Myrtle Beach SC 29577, USA

**Kinney, Emily** — Actress
Abrams Artists, 9200 W Sunset Blvd, #1125, West Hollywood CA 90069 USA

**Kinney, Erron Q** — Football Player
1103 State Blvd, Franklin TN 37064, USA

**Kinney, Jeff** — Writer, Cartoonist
Harry N Abrams/Amulet Publishers, 115 W 18th St, New York NY 10011, USA

**Kinney, Jeffrey B (Jeff)** — Football Player
2720 W 161st Terrace, Stilwell KS 66085, USA

**Kinney, Kathy** — Actress
Truhett/Garcia Mgmt, 12031 Ventura Blvd, #4, Studio City CA 91604, USA

**Kinney, Matt** — Baseball Player
12 Owens Way, Hermon ME 04401, USA

**Kinney, Sean H** — Drummer (Alice in Chains)
Atmosphere Artists Mgmt, 6523 California Ave SW, #348, Seattle WA 98136, USA

**Kinney, Taylor** — Actor
Gersh Agency, 9465 Wilshire Blvd, #600, Beverly Hills CA 90212 USA

**Kinnock, Neil G** — Government Official, England
European Communities Commission, 200 Rue de Loi, 1049 Brussels, Belgium

**Kinsella, John P** — Swimmer
PO Box 3067, Sumas WA 98295, USA

**Kinsella, Thomas** — Writer
639 Addison St, Philadelphia PA 19147, USA

**Kinsella, William Patrick (W P)** — Writer
9442 Nowell, Chilliwack BC V2P 4X7, Canada

**Kinser, Steve** — Auto Racing Driver
Kinser Racing, 280 E Smithville Road, Bloomington IN 47401, USA

**Kinsey, Angela** — Actress
United Talent Agency, U T A Plaza, 9336 Civic Center Dr, Beverly Hills CA 90210 USA

**Kinsey, Donald** — Singer, Guitarist (Kinsey Report)
Jay Reil Assoc, 3490 Bayberry Dr, Northbrook IL 60062, USA

**Kinsey, James L** — Chemist
Rice University, Natural Sciences School, Houston TX 77005, USA

**Kinsey, Kenneth** — Bassist (Kinsey Report)
Jay Reil Assoc, 3490 Bayberry Dr, Northbrook IL 60062, USA

**Kinsey, Ralph (Woody)** — Drummer (Kinsey Report)
Jay Reil Assoc, 3490 Bayberry Dr, Northbrook IL 60062, USA

**Kinshofer-Guthlein, Christa** — Alpine Skier
Munchnerstr 44, 83026 Rosenheim, Germany

*(side text)* Kingery - Kinshofer-Guthlein

| | |
|---|---|
| **Kinski, Nastassja** | Actress, Model |
| 1000 Bel Air Place, Los Angeles CA 90077, USA | |
| **Kinsler, Ian M** | Baseball Player |
| 4029 Westmont Court, Bedford TX 76021, USA | |
| **Kinsley, Michael E** | Editor, Commentator |
| 14150 NE 20th St, #527, Bellevue WA 98007, USA | |
| **Kinsman, Brent** | Actor |
| Coast to Coast Talent, 3350 Barham Blvd, Los Angeles CA 90068 USA | |
| **Kinsman, Shane** | Actor |
| Coast to Coast Talent, 3350 Barham Blvd, Los Angeles CA 90068 USA | |
| **Kinsman, T James (Jim)** | Vietnam War Army Hero (CMH) |
| 111 Howe Road E, Toledo WA 98591, USA | |
| **Kiper, Mel, Jr** | Sportscaster |
| ESPN-TV, ESPN Plaza, 935 Middle St, Bristol CT 06010 USA | |
| **Kipketer, Wilson** | Track Athlete |
| Atletik Forbund, Idraettens Hus, Brondby Stadion 20, 2605 Brondby, Denmark | |
| **Kiplinger, Austin H** | Publisher |
| Montevideo, 1680 River Road, Poolesville MD 20837, USA | |
| **Kipnis, David M** | Physician |
| 710 S Hanley Road, #15A, Saint Louis MO 63105, USA | |
| **Kipniss, Robert** | Artist |
| Hudson House, PO Box 112, Ardsley on Hudson NY 10503, USA | |
| **Kipper, Robert W (Bob)** | Baseball Player |
| 117 Tuscany Way, Greer SC 29650, USA | |
| **Kiprusoff, Miikka S** | Ice Hockey Player |
| Calgary Flames, PO Box 1540, Station M, Calgary AB T2P 3B9, Canada | |
| **Kiraly, Charles F (Karch)** | Volleyball Player, Coach |
| 307 Boca del Canon, San Clemente CA 92672, USA | |
| **Kiraly, John** | Artist |
| Lynn Roberts, 2410 Avenue A, Bradenton Beach FL 34217, USA | |
| **Kirby, Luke** | Actor |
| Parseghian/Planco, 388 2nd Ave, #506, New York, NY 10010 USA | |
| **Kirby, Peter** | Bobsled Athlete |
| Bobsled Canada, 140 Canada Olympic Road SW, Calgary AB T3B 5R5, Canada | |
| **Kirby, Ronald H** | Architect |
| PO Box 337, Melville, 2109 Johannesburg, South Africa | |
| **Kirby, Terry G** | Football Player |
| 744 Michelle Dr, Newport News VA 23601, USA | |
| **Kirby, Wayne L** | Baseball Player |
| 320 Kenya Road, Las Vegas NV 89123, USA | |
| **Kirch, Patrick V** | Archaeologist |
| University of California, Anthropology Dept, Kroeber Hall, Berkeley CA 94720, USA | |
| **Kirchbach, Gunar** | Canoeing Athlete |
| Georgi-Dobrowolski-Str 10, 15517 Furstenwalde, Germany | |
| **Kirchberger, Sonja** | Actress |
| Calle C'An Sanc 14, 07001 Palma de Mallorca, Baleares, Spain | |
| **Kircheisen, Bjorn** | Nordic Combined Skier |
| Georg-Baumgarten-Str 4, 08349 Johanngeorgenstadt, Germany | |
| **Kirchen, Bill** | Guitarist (Twangbangers) |
| 6935 Chinook Dr, Austin TX 78736, USA | |
| **Kirchhoff, Ulrich** | Equestrian |
| Hoven 258, 48720 Rosendahl, Germany | |
| **Kirchner, Cristina F** | President, Agentina |
| Casa de Gobierno, Balcarce 50, Buenos Aires 1064, Argentina | |
| **Kirchner, Jamie Lee** | Actress |
| Gersh Agency, 41 Madison Ave, #3301, New York NY 10010 USA | |
| **Kirchner, Mark** | Biathlete |
| Hauptstr 74A, 98749 Scheibe-Alsbach, Germany | |
| **Kirchschlager, Angelika** | Opera Singer |
| Mastrioanni Assoc, 161 W 61st St, #32B, New York NY 10023, USA | |
| **Kiriasis, Sandra Prokoff** | Bobsled Athlete |
| Bonifatiusweg 6, 59955 Winterberg, Germany | |
| **Kirilenko, Andrei G** | Basketball Player |
| 1406 Perrys Hollow Road, Salt Lake City UT 84103, USA | |
| **Kirilenko, Maria Y** | Tennis Player, Model |
| Women's Tennis Assn, 1 Progress Plaza, #1500, Saint Petersburg FL 33701 USA | |
| **Kirk, Justin** | Actor |
| Management 360, 9111 Wilshire Blvd, Beverly Hills CA 90210 USA | |
| **Kirk, Rahsaan Roland** | Jazz Musician |
| Atlantic Records, 9229 W Sunset Blvd, #900, West Hollywood CA 90069 USA | |
| **Kirk, Tammy Joe** | Motorcyle Racing Rider, Auto Driver |
| 732 Peek Road, Dalton GA 30721, USA | |
| **Kirk, Thomas B** | Physicist |
| Brookhaven National Laboratory, Physics Dept, 2 Center St, Upton NY 11973, USA | |
| **Kirk, Tommy** | Actor |
| 833 Beacon Ave, Los Angeles CA 90017, USA | |
| **Kirkby, Emma** | Opera, Concert Singer |
| Consort of Music, 54A Leamington Road Villas, London W11 1HT, England | |
| **Kirkcaldy, Robert** | Epidemiologist |
| Centers for Disease Control, S T D Prevention Center, 1600 Clifton Road NE, Atlanta GA 30329, USA | |
| **Kirke, Jemima** | Actress |
| Creative Artists Agency, 2000 Ave of Stars, #100, Los Angeles CA 90067 USA | |
| **Kirke, Simon** | Drummer (Free, Bad Company) |
| Tabletop Productions, PO Box 698, Carson City NV 89702, USA | |
| **Kirkeby, Per** | Artist |
| Margarete Roeder Gallery, 545 Broadway, New York NY 10012, USA | |
| **Kirkland, Douglas** | Photographer |
| 9060 Wonderland Park Ave, Los Angeles CA 90046, USA | |
| **Kirkland, Gelsey** | Ballerina |
| Dube Zakin Mgmt, 67 Riverside Dr, #3B, New York NY 10024, USA | |
| **Kirkland, L Levon** | Football Player |
| 3255 Whitman Way, Tallahassee FL 32311, USA | |
| **Kirkland, Mike** | Singer, Banjo Player (Brothers Four) |
| Bob Flick Productions, 300 Vine St, #14, Seattle WA 98121, USA | |
| **Kirkland, Ric** | Editor |
| Fortune Magazine, Time & Life Building, Rockefeller Center, New York NY 10020, USA | |

# K

**Kirkland, Sally** — Actress
Greene Assoc., 1901 Ave of Stars, #130, Los Angeles CA 90067 USA
**Kirkland, Willie C** — Baseball Player
19374 Northrup St, Detroit MI 48219, USA
**Kirkman, Rick** — Cartoonist (Baby Blues)
King Features Syndicate, 300 W 57th St, #1500, New York NY 10019 USA
**Kirkpatrick, Chris** — Singer ('N Sync)
Wright Entertainment, PO Box 590009, Orlando FL 32859 USA
**Kirkpatrick, D/Andre L (Dre)** — Football Player
Cincinnati Bengals, 1 Paul Brown Stadium, Cincinnati OH 45202 USA
**Kirkpatrick, Kevin** — Actor
Stone Manners Salners, 9911 W Pico Blvd, #1400, Los Angeles CA 90035 USA
**Kirkpatrick, Maggie** — Actress
Karen Kay Mgmt, PO Box 446, Auckland 1140, New Zealand
**Kirkwood, Curt** — Singer (Meat Puppets)
High Road Touring, 751 Bridgeway, #200, Sausalito CA 94965 USA
**Kirla, John A** — WW II Army Air Corps Hero
447 Main St, PO Box 396, Deep River CT 06417, USA
**Kirn, Walter** — Writer
Creative Artists Agency, 2000 Ave of Stars, #100, Los Angeles CA 90067 USA
**Kirner, Gary B** — Football Player
3507 Senasac Ave, Long Beach CA 90808, USA
**Kirrane, John J (Jack), Jr** — Ice Hockey Player
3 Country Road, Chestnut MA 02467, USA
**Kirrene, Joseph J (Joe)** — Baseball Player
2557 Kilpatrick Court, San Ramon CA 94583, USA
**Kirsch, Russell** — Inventor (Square Pixels)
4610 SW Greenhills Way, Portland OR 97221, USA
**Kirsch, Stan** — Actor
Stan Kirsch Studios, 6671 Sunset Blvd, #1584-A, Los Angeles CA 90028, USA
**Kirschke, Travis** — Football Player
10196 Crooked Stick Trail, Lone Tree CO 80124, USA
**Kirschner, Carl** — Educator
Rutgers State University College, President's Office, New Brunswick NJ 08093, USA
**Kirschner, David M** — Animator, Producer
David Kirschner Productions, 400 S June St, Los Angeles CA 90020, USA
**Kirschner, Marc W** — Cell Biologist
Harvard Medical School, Cell Biology Dept, 25 Shattuck St, Boston MA 02115, USA
**Kirschstein, Ruth L** — Physician
6 West Dr, Bethesda MD 20814, USA
**Kirshbaum, Laurence J** — Publisher
Warner Books, Time-Life Building, Rockefeller Center, New York NY 10020, USA
**Kirshbaum, Ralph** — Concert Cellist
Ingpen & Williams, 131 Putney Bridge Road, London SW15 2PA, England
**Kirshner, Mia** — Actress
Gersh Agency, 9465 Wilshire Blvd, #600, Beverly Hills CA 90212 USA
**Kirst, Michael W** — Educator
Stanford University, Education School, Stanford CA 94305, USA
**Kirstein, Peter T** — Computer Scientist
University College, Computer Science Dept, London WC1E 6BT, England
**Kirszenstein Szewinska, Irena** — Track Athlete
Ul Bagno 5 m 80, 00112 Warsaw, Poland
**Kirtadze, Nino** — Actress
GoDigital Media Group, 233 Wilshire Blvd, #100, Santa Monica CA 90401, USA
**Kirton, Mark R** — Ice Hockey Player
251 N Service Road W, Oakville ON L6M 3E7, Canada
**Kirvesniemi, Harri** — Cross Country Skier
Karhu Ski, Henrikinkatu 2, 21100 Naantali, Finland
**Kirwan, Larry** — Singer, Guitarist (Black 47)
Skyline Music, 28 Union St, Whitefield NH 03598, USA
**Kirwan, William E, II** — Educator
3112 Old Court Road, Pikesville MD 21208, USA
**Kisabaka, Lisa** — Track Athlete
Franz-Hitze-Str 22, 51372 Leverkusen, Germany
**Kiser, Garland R** — Baseball Player
267 Carr Dr, Blountville TN 37617, USA
**Kiser, Terry** — Actor
Innovative Artists, 1505 10th St, Santa Monica CA 90401 USA
**Kishida, Shuzo** — Chef, Restauranteur
Restaurant Quintessence, 6-7-29 Garden City Shinagawa Gotenyama, Tokyo 141 0001, Japan
**Kishlansky, Mark A** — Historian
Harvard University, History Dept, Cambridge MA 02138, USA
**Kisio, Kelly W** — Ice Hockey Player
Calgary Hitmen, PO Box 1420 Station Main, Calgary AB T2P 3B9, Canada
**Kisner, Jacob** — Writer
245 Park Ave S, #PH F, New York NY 10003, USA
**Kison, Bruce E** — Baseball Player
1403 Riverview Circle, Bradenton FL 34209, USA
**Kissane, James J (Jim)** — Basketball Player
6 Mellen Lane, Wayland MA 01778, USA
**Kissin, Evgeni I** — Concert Pianist
I M G Artists, Carnegie Hall Tower, 152 W 57th St, #500, New York NY 10019 USA
**Kissinger, Henry A** — Secretary, State; Nobel Peace Laureate
PO Box 38, South Kent CT 06785, USA
**Kissling, Conny** — Freestyle Skier
Hubel, 3254 Messen, Switzerland
**Kistler, Darci** — Ballerina
New York City Ballet, Lincoln Center Plaza, New York NY 10023 USA
**Kita, Toshiyuki** — Industrial Designer
TS Bild 2F, 3-1-2 Tenma, Kitauku, Osaka 530 0043, Japan
**Kitaen, Tawny** — Actress
Brady Brannon Rich, 5670 Wilshire Blvd, #820, Los Angeles CA 90036 USA
**Kitamura, Ryuhei** — Director
Capitol Motion Pictures, 610 Brazos, #300D, Austin TX 78701, USA
**Kitano, Takeshi** — Actor, Director, Writer
Office Kitano, 5-4-14 Akasaka Minataku, 107 0052 Tokyo, Japan

**Kitaro** — Musician, Composer
Hands On Public Relations, 9800-D Topanga Canyon Blvd, #117, Chatsworth CA 91311, USA
**Kitayenko, Dmitri G** — Conductor
Chalet Kalimor, 1652 Botterens, Switzerland
**Kitbunchu, M Michai Cardinal** — Religious Leader
122 Soi Naaksuwan, Thanon Nonsi, Yannawa, Bangkok 10120, Thailand
**Kitchell, Sonya** — Singer, Songwriter
Monterey International, 200 W Superior St, #202, Chicago IL 60654 USA
**Kitchen, Curtis** — Basketball Player
343 19th Ave, Seattle WA 98122, USA
**Kitchen, Michael** — Actor
Rights House, Drury House, 34-43 Russell St, London WC2B 5HA, England
**Kitchen, Mike** — Ice Hockey Player, Coach
5570 NE Trieste Way, Boca Raton FL 33487, USA
**Kite, Gregory F (Greg)** — Basketball Player
3060 Seigneury Dr, Windermere FL 34786, USA
**Kite, Jonathan** — Actor
Full Circle Mgmt, 4932 Lankershim Blvd, #202, North Hollywood CA 91601, USA
**Kite, Thomas O (Tom), Jr** — Golfer
907 Terrace Mountain Dr, West Lake Hills TX 78746, USA
**Kitsch, Taylor** — Actor
Rogers & Cowan, 8687 Melrose Ave, #G700, West Hollywood CA 90069 USA
**Kitson, Linda F** — Artist
1 Argyll Mansions, Kings Road, London SW3 5ER, England
**Kitsopoulos, Constantine** — Conductor
I M G Artists, Hogarth Business Park, Chiswick, London W4 2TH, England
**Kitt, A J** — Alpine Skier
Colt Realty Group, 509 Cascade Ave, #A, Hood River OR 97031, USA
**Kittel, Charles** — Physicist
University of California, Physics Dept, Berkeley CA 94720, USA
**Kittinger, Joseph W (Joe), Jr** — Parachutist, Balloonist
608 Mariner Way, Altamonte Springs FL 32701, USA
**Kittle, Ronald D (Ron)** — Baseball Player
1840 Tour Trace, Chesterton IN 46304, USA
**Kittles, Tory** — Actor
Paradigm Agency, 360 N Crescent Dr, North Building, Beverly Hills CA 90210 USA
**Kittredge, William A** — Writer
42 Brookside Way, Missoula MT 59802, USA
**Kivelson, Margaret Galland** — Physicist
University of California, Earth & Space Sciences Dept, Los Angeles CA 90024, USA
**Kiwanuka, Mathias K** — Football Player
456 9th St, #13, Hoboken NJ 07030, USA
**Kiyosaki, Robert T** — Writer
Cashflow Technologies, 4330 N Civic Center Plaza, #100, Scottsdale AZ 85251, USA
**Kizer, Carolyn A** — Writer
University of Arizona, English Dept, Tucson AZ 85721, USA
**Kjus, Lasse** — Alpine Skier
Rugdeveien 2C, 1404 Siggerud, Norway
**Klabunde, Charles S** — Artist
68 W 3rd St, New York NY 10012, USA
**Klammer, Franz** — Alpine Skier
Mooswald 22, 9712 Friesach, Austria
**Klaplisch, Cedric** — Director, Writer
Ce Qui Me Meut Motion Pictures, 23 Passage de la Main d'Or, 75011 Paris, France
**Klapman, Lia** — Sculptor
2581 Mission St, Santa Cruz CA 95060, USA
**Klarik, Jeffrey** — Producer, Writer
W M E Entertainment, 9601 Wilshire Blvd, #300, Beverly Hills CA 90210 USA
**Klas, Eri** — Conductor
C M Artists, 127 W 96th St, #13B, New York NY 10025 USA
**Klassen, Daniel V (Danny)** — Baseball Player
28925 N 111th Place, Scottsdale AZ 85262, USA
**Klatt, Trent T** — Ice Hockey Player
21704 Shallow Lake Road, Warba MN 55793, USA
**Klattenhoff, Diego** — Actor
A P A Talent/Literary Agency, 405 S Beverly Dr, #300, Beverly Hills CA 90212 USA
**Klausing, Chuck** — Football Coach
2115 Lazor St, Indiana PA 15701, USA
**Klausner, Julie** — Actress, Writer
Avalon Mgmt, 8332 Melrose Ave, #200, Los Angeles CA 90069, USA
**Klausner, Richard D** — Cell Biologist
Column Group, 1700 Owens Street, #500, San Francisco CA 94158, USA
**Klavan, Andrew** — Writer
Gersh Agency, 9465 Wilshire Blvd, #600, Beverly Hills CA 90212 USA
**Klaveno, Mariana** — Actress
A P A Talent/Literary Agency, 405 S Beverly Dr, #300, Beverly Hills CA 90212 USA
**Klawe, Maria** — Educator
Harvey Mudd College, President's Office, Claremont CA 91711, USA
**Klawitter, Thomas C (Tom)** — Baseball Player
605 Foxglove Lane, Whitewater WI 53190, USA
**Klaws, Alexander** — Singer, Actor
19 Music & Mgmt, 35-37 Parkgate Road, London SW11 4NP, England
**Klecko, Daniel R (Dan)** — Football Player
234 Cedar Road, Mullica Hill NJ 08062, USA
**Klecko, Joseph E (Joe)** — Football Player
6 Victorian Way, Colts Neck NJ 07722, USA
**Klee, Ken** — Ice Hockey Player
78 W Ranch Trail, Morrison CO 80465, USA
**Klees, Christian** — Marksman
Eutiner Sportschutzen, Schutzenweg 26, 23701 Eutin, Germany
**Kleibrink, Shannon** — Curling Athlete
Curling Assn, 1660 Vimont Court, Cumberland ON K4A 4J4, Canada
**Klein, Abigail** — Actress
Brillstein Entertainment Partners, 9150 Wilshire Blvd, #350, Beverly Hills CA 90212 USA
**Klein, Calvin R** — Fashion Designer
650 Meadow Lane, Southampton NY 11968, USA

## K

**Klein, Chris** — Actor
I C M Partners, 10250 Constellation Blvd, #900, Los Angeles CA 90067 USA
**Klein, Dale E** — Government Official
US Nuclear Regulatory Commission, 11555 Rockville Pike, Rockville MD 20852, USA
**Klein, Danny** — Bassist (J Geils Band)
Nick Ben-Meir, 652 N Doheny Dr, West Hollywood CA 90069, USA
**Klein, David** — Geneticist
National Child Health Institute, 49 Convent Dr, Bethesda MD 20892, USA
**Klein, Edward** — Writer
Random House, 1745 Broadway, #1800, New York NY 10019 USA
**Klein, Emilee** — Golfer
5350 E Deer Valley Dr, #1431, Phoenix AZ 85054, USA
**Klein, George** — Tumor Biologist
Kottlavagen 10, 181 61 Lidingo, Sweden
**Klein, Jess** — Singer, Guitarist, Songwriter
Invasion Group, 133 W 25th St, #500, New York NY 10001, USA
**Klein, Joe** — Journalist, Writer
Time, Editorial Dept, Time-Life Building, 1271 Ave of Americas, New York NY 10020, USA
**Klein, Joel** — Attorney, Government Official, Educator
New York City Schools, Chancellor's Office, 110 Livingston, Brooklyn NY 11201, USA
**Klein, Lester A** — Urologist
Scripps Clinic, Urology Dept, 10666 N Torrey Pines Road, La Jolla CA 92037, USA
**Klein, Marci** — Producer
Slate Public Relations, 9000 Sunset Blvd, #915, West Hollywood CA 90069 USA
**Klein, Richard G** — Paleoanthropologist
Stanford University, Anthropologist Services Dept, Stanford CA 94305, USA
**Klein, Robert** — Actor, Comedian
67 Ridgecrest Road, Briarcliff Manor NY 10510, USA
**Klein, Robert O (Bob)** — Football Player
15263 Friends St, Pacific Palisades CA 90272, USA
**Kleine, Joseph W (Joe)** — Basketball Player
53 Hickory Hills Circle, Little Rock AR 72212, USA
**Kleinert, Harold E** — Microsurgeon
225 Abraham Flexner Way, #700, Louisville KY 40202, USA
**Kleinfeld, Andrew J** — Judge
US Court of Appeals, Courthouse Square, 250 Cushman St, Fairbanks AK 99701, USA
**Kleinman, Arthur M** — Anthropologist, Psychiatrist
Harvard University, Anthropology Dept, Cambridge MA 02138, USA
**Kleinrock, Leonard** — Computer Scientist, Engineer
318 N Rockingham Ave, Los Angeles CA 90049, USA
**Kleinsasser, Jimmy C (Jim)** — Football Player
6835 Cardinal Cove Dr, Mound MN 55364, USA
**Kleinsmith, Bruce** — Cartoonist
PO Box 1083, San Juan Bautista CA 95045, USA
**Kleintank, Luke** — Actor
Robert Stein Management, 345 N Maple Dr, #317, Beverly Hills CA 90210, USA
**Kleiser, Randal** — Director
3050 Runyan Canyon Road, Los Angeles CA 90046, USA
**Kleiza, Linas** — Basketball Player
Toronto Raptors, Air Canada Center, 20 Bay St, Toronto ON M5J 2N8, Canada
**Klembaum, Sharon** — Religious Leader, Rabbi
Congregation Beth Simchat Torah, 57 Bethune St, New York NY 10014, USA
**Klemm, Adrian W** — Football Player
14944 Otsego St, Sherman Oaks CA 91403, USA
**Klemm, Jon** — Ice Hockey Player
400 61st St, Willowbrook IL 60527, USA
**Klemmer, John** — Jazz Saxophonist
Boardman, 10548 Clearwood Court, Los Angeles CA 90077, USA
**Klemperer, William** — Chemist
53 Shattuck Road, Watertown MA 02472, USA
**Klemt, Becky** — Attorney
Pence & MacMillan, PO Box 1285, Laramie WY 82073, USA
**Klesko, Ryan A** — Baseball Player
735 Henderson Mill Road, Covington GA 30014, USA
**Klesla, Rotislav** — Ice Hockey Player
6751 N Sunset Blvd, #200, Glendale AZ 85305, USA
**Klett, Peter** — Guitarist (Candlebox)
Novi Entertainment, 201 N Robertson Blvd, #201, Beverly Hills CA 90211, USA
**Klever, Victor K (Rocky)** — Football Player
3829 W 42nd St, Anchorage AK 99517, USA
**Kley, Chaney** — Actor
Paradigm Agency, 360 N Crescent Dr, North Building, Beverly Hills CA 90210 USA
**Klibanoff, Hank** — Journalist, Historian
Emory University, Journalism Dept, 201 Dowman Drive, Atlanta GA 30322, USA
**Klim, Michael** — Swimmer
177 Bridge Road, Richmond VIC 3121, Australia
**Klima, Petr** — Ice Hockey Player
1000 Forest Lane, Bloomfield Hills MI 48301, USA
**Klimchock, Louis S (Lou)** — Baseball Player
8876 S Myrtle Ave, Tempe AZ 85284, USA
**Klimisch, Dick** — Inventor (Auto Catalytic Converter)
43 Fairfold Road, Grosse Pointe Shores MI 48236, USA
**Klimke, Ingrid** — Equestrian
Kanalstr 340, 48159 Munster, Germany
**Klimke, Reiner** — Equestrian
Krumme Str 3, 48143 Munster, Germany
**Klimova, Marina V** — Ice Dancer
Sharks Ice, 1500 S 10th St, San Jose CA 95112, USA
**Klimuk, Pyotr I** — Cosmonaut, Air Force General
Cosmonaut Training Center, Star City, 141160 Zvezdny Gorodok, Moscow Oblast, Russia
**Kline, J Robert (Bobby)** — Baseball Player
6656 31st Way S, Saint Petersburg FL 33712, USA
**Kline, Jeff** — Writer, Producer
Creative Artists Agency, 2000 Ave of Stars, #100, Los Angeles CA 90067 USA
**Kline, Kevin D** — Actor
1636 3rd Ave, #309, New York NY 10128, USA

Klein - Kline

**Kline, Richard H** — Cinematographer
1015 Manning Ave, Los Angeles CA 90024, USA
**Kline, Steven J (Steve)** — Baseball Player
PO Box 1525, Chelan WA 98816, USA
**Kline-Randall, Maxine** — Baseball Player
105 Nottingham Road, Bloomsberg PA 17815, USA
**Kling, Anja** — Actress
Agentur Margarita Kling, Amselweg 6, 14557 Wilhelmhorst, Germany
**Kling, Gerit** — Actress
Z A V Kunstiervermittlung, Friedrichstr 39, 10969 Berlin, Germany
**Klingbeil, Charles (Chuck)** — Football Player
47921 US Highway 41, Houghton MI 49931, USA
**Klingenbeck, Scott E** — Baseball Player
6230 Kincora Court, Cincinnati OH 45233, USA
**Klingensmith, Michael J** — Publisher
Entertainment Weekly, Rockefeller Center, New York NY 10020, USA
**Klingler, David R** — Football Player
Dallas Theological Seminary, 6000 Dale Carnegie Lane, Houston TX 77036, USA
**Klinsmann, Jurgen** — Soccer Player, Coach
F C Bayern Munich, Postfach 900451, 81504 Munich, Germany
**Klitschko, Vitali V** — Boxer
Klitschko Management Group, Borselstr 28, Haus 1, 22765 Hamburg, Germany
**Klitschko, Wladimir** — Boxer
Klitschko Management Group, Borselstr 28, Haus 1, 22765 Hamburg, Germany
**Klooparens, Beth** — Architect
Klooparens Inc, 250 5th Ave, New York NY 10001, USA
**Klop, Cody** — Actor
Curtis Talent Management, 9607 Arby Dr, Beverly Hills CA 90210, USA
**Klose, Miroslav** — Soccer Player
A S B W Sports Marketing, Ubierring 7, 50678 Colgone, Germany
**Kloser, Harald** — Composer
Gorfaine/Schwartz, 4111 W Alameda Ave, #509, Burbank CA 91505 USA
**Kloss, Karlie E** — Model
Next Model Mgmt, 23 Watts St, New York NY 10013 USA
**Klotz, Frank G** — Air Force General
Commander, Air Global Strike Force Command, Barksdale Air Force Base LA 71110, USA
**Klotz, H Louis (Red)** — Basketball Player, Coach
114 S Osbourne Ave, Margate City NJ 08402, USA
**Klotz, Irving M** — Chemist, Biochemist
1500 Sheridan Road, #7D, Wilmette IL 60091, USA
**Klotz, John S (Jack)** — Football Player
729 E 25th St, Chester PA 19013, USA
**Klous, Patricia** — Actress
2539 Benedict Canyon Dr, Beverly Hills CA 90210, USA
**Kloves, Steve** — Director, Writer
Creative Artists Agency, 2000 Ave of Stars, #100, Los Angeles CA 90067 USA
**Klueh, Duane** — Basketball Player, Coach
252 Francis Avenue Court, Terre Haute IN 47804, USA
**Klug, Aaron** — Nobel Chemistry Laureate
70 Cavendish Ave, Cambridge CB1 4OT, England
**Klug, Chris** — Snowboard Skier
Chris Klug Foundation, 182 Riverdown Dr, Aspen CO 81611, USA
**Kluger, Richard** — Writer
Random House, 1745 Broadway, #1800, New York NY 10019 USA
**Klugh, Earl** — Jazz Guitarist
I C M Partners, 10250 Constellation Blvd, #900, Los Angeles CA 90067 USA
**Klum, Heidi** — Model, Actress
W M E Entertainment, 9601 Wilshire Blvd, #300, Beverly Hills CA 90210 USA
**Klum, Mattias** — Photographer
Svanliden, Hammarskog, 755 91 Uppsala, Sweden
**Klunk, William E** — Neurologist
Alzheimer's Disease Laboratory, 200 Lothrop St, Pittsburgh PA 15213, USA
**Klutts, Gene E (Mickey)** — Baseball Player
6136 Maple Ave, Lake Isabella CA 93240, USA
**Kluttz, Lonnie** — Basketball Player
183 Greenwing Lane, Saint Matthews SC 29135, USA
**Kluwe, Christopher J (Chris)** — Football Player
13026 Ottawa Dr, Savage MN 55378, USA
**K'Maro** — Singer, Rap Artist, Songwriter
Warner Music, Alter Wandrahm 14, 20457 Hamburg, Germany
**KMG the Illustrator** — Rap Artist (Above the Law)
Green Light Talent Agency, PO Box 3172, Beverly Hills CA 90212 USA
**K'Naan** — Rap Artist, Singer, Guitarist
Paquin Entertainment, 206B-219 Dufferin St, Toronto ON M6K 3J1, Canada
**Knackert, Brent B** — Baseball Player
16802 Leafwood Circle, Huntington Beach CA 92647, USA
**Knafelc, Gary** — Football Player
2147 Burley Ave, Clermont FL 34711, USA
**Knaifel, Alexander A** — Composer
Skobelevski Pr 5, #130, 194214 Saint Petersburg, Russia
**Knape Lindberg, Ulrike** — Diver
Drostvagen 7, 691 33 Karlskoga, Sweden
**Knapp, Alexis** — Actress
Creative Artists Agency, 2000 Ave of Stars, #100, Los Angeles CA 90067 USA
**Knapp, Charles B** — Educator
120 Brookview Circle N, Atlanta GA 30339, USA
**Knapp, Cleon T** — Publisher
Talewood Corp, 8939 S Sepulveda Blvd, #110, Los Angeles CA 90045, USA
**Knapp, Jennifer L** — Singer
Maximum Artist Mgmt, 1305 Clinton St, #200-A, Nashville TN 37203, USA
**Knapp, John W** — Educator, Army General
Virginia Military Institute, Superintendent's Office, Lexington VA 24450, USA
**Knapp, R Christian (Chris)** — Baseball Player
788 Rich Dr, Oviedo FL 32765, USA
**Knapp, Steven** — Educator
George Washington University, President's Office, Washington DC 20052, USA

# K

| | |
|---|---|
| **Knaus, Chad A** <br> 149 Pin Oak Lane, Mooresville NC 28117, USA | Auto Racing Crew Chief |
| **Knaus, William A** <br> University of Virginia Medical School, Public Health Service Dept, Charlottesville VA 22908, USA | Physician, Medical Activist |
| **Knauss, Hans** <br> Fastenberg 60, 8970 Schladming, Austria | Alpine Skier |
| **Knauss, Melania** <br> T Mgmt, 91 5th Ave, #300, New York NY 10003 USA | Model |
| **Kneale, R Bryan C** <br> 10A Muswell Road, London N10 2BG, England | Sculptor |
| **Knebel, John A** <br> 1418 Laburnum St, McLean VA 22101, USA | Secretary, Agriculture |
| **Knepper, Robert** <br> Innovative Artists, 1505 10th St, Santa Monica CA 90401 USA | Actor |
| **Knepper, Robert W (Bob)** <br> 5704 Callcott Way, #E, Alexandria VA 22312, USA | Baseball Player |
| **Kness, Richard M** <br> 240 Central Park South, #16M, New York NY 10019, USA | Opera Singer |
| **Kneuer, Cameo** <br> Starshape by Cameo, 2554 Lincoln Blvd, #640, Venice CA 90291, USA | Physical Fitness Expert |
| **Knibb, Sean** <br> Knibb Design, 141 S Barrington Ave, Los Angeles CA 90049, USA | Landscape Architect |
| **Knicely, Alan L** <br> PO Box 433, Dayton VA 22821, USA | Baseball Player |
| **Knickman, Roy** <br> 436 Fallbrook Ave, Newbury Park CA 91320, USA | Cyclist |
| **Knight, Beverly** <br> D W L, 53 Goodge St, #200, London W1T 1TG, England | Singer, Songwriter |
| **Knight, Brandon M** <br> 191 S Pacific Ave, #B, Ventura CA 93001, USA | Baseball Player |
| **Knight, Brevin** <br> 3226 Bedford Lane, Germantown TN 38139, USA | Basketball Player |
| **Knight, C Ray** <br> PO Box 129, Auburn AL 36831, USA | Baseball Player, Manager |
| **Knight, Charles F** <br> Emerson Electric Co, 8000 W Florissant Ave, Box 41000, Saint Louis MO 63136, USA | Businessman |
| **Knight, Chris** <br> Rick Alter Mgmt, 1018 17th Ave S, #12, Nashville TN 37212, USA | Singer, Songwriter |
| **Knight, Christopher** <br> Identity Talent Agency, 9107 Wilshire Blvd, #450, Beverly Hills CA 90210 USA | Actor |
| **Knight, David R** <br> 2600 Farm Road, Alexandria VA 22302, USA | Football Player |
| **Knight, Gladys** <br> Shakeji, 3221 La Mirada Ave, Las Vegas NV 89120, USA | Singer |
| **Knight, Hilary** <br> USA Hockey, 1775 Bob Johnson Dr, Colorado Springs CO 80906 USA | Ice Hockey Player |
| **Knight, Jean** <br> Acts Nashville, 1103 Bell Grimes Lane, Nashville TN 37207, USA | Singer |
| **Knight, Jonathan** <br> 90 Apple St, Essex MA 01929, USA | Singer (New Kids on the Block) |
| **Knight, Jordan** <br> Supreme Entertainment Artists, PO Box 15601, Boston MA 02115, USA | Singer (New Kids on the Block) |
| **Knight, Keith** <br> PO Box 341862, Los Angeles CA 90034, USA | Cartoonist (K Chronicles) |
| **Knight, L Curtis (Curt), Jr** <br> 7230 Rio Flora Place, Downey CA 90241, USA | Football Player |
| **Knight, Negele** <br> 18624 N 4th Ave, Phoenix AZ 85027, USA | Basketball Player |
| **Knight, Philip H** <br> Nike Inc, 1 SW Bowerman Dr, Beaverton OR 97005, USA | Businessman |
| **Knight, Robert M (Bobby)** <br> 8003 County Road 6910, Lubbock TX 79407, USA | Basketball Coach |
| **Knight, Shirley** <br> Diamond Mgmt, 31 Percy St, London W1T 2DD, England | Actress |
| **Knight, Sterling** <br> Greene Assoc, 1901 Ave of Stars, #130, Los Angeles CA 90067 USA | Actor |
| **Knight, Steven** <br> Creative Artists Agency, 2000 Ave of Stars, #100, Los Angeles CA 90067 USA | Writer |
| **Knight, T R** <br> Innovative Artists, 1505 10th St, Santa Monica CA 90401 USA | Actor |
| **Knight, Thomas L (Tommy)** <br> 70 Overington Ave, Marlton NJ 08053, USA | Football Player |
| **Knight, Travis J** <br> 3159 Millcreek Road, Pleasant Grove UT 84062, USA | Basketball Player |
| **Knight, Tuesday** <br> Stephany Hurkos Mgmt, 11935 Kling St, #10, Valley Village CA 91607 USA | Actress |
| **Knight, Wayne** <br> Brillstein Entertainment Partners, 9150 Wilshire Blvd, #350, Beverly Hills CA 90212 USA | Actor, Comedian |
| **Knight, William R (Billy)** <br> 1051 Bluffhaven Way NE, Atlanta GA 30319, USA | Basketball Player, Executive |
| **Knightley, Keira** <br> United Agents, 12-26 Lexington St, London W1F 0LE, England | Actress |
| **Knighton, Zachary** <br> 3 Arts Entertainment, 9460 Wilshire Blvd, #700, Beverly Hills CA 90212 USA | Actor |
| **Knight-Pulliam, Keshia** <br> PO Box 866, Teaneck NJ 07666, USA | Actress |
| **Knights, Dave** <br> 195 Sandycombe Road, Kew TW9 2EW, England | Bassist (Procol Harum) |
| **Knisley, Sam** <br> 14808 Hanover Pike, Upperco MD 21155, USA | Basketball Player |
| **Knizka, Roman** <br> Girke Mgmt, Nymphenburgerstr 4, 10825 Berlin, Germany | Actor |
| **Knoblauch, E Charles (Chuck)** <br> 11702 Forest Glen St, Houston TX 77024, USA | Baseball Player |
| **Knoff, Kurt** <br> 11121 Bluestem Lane, Eden Prairie MN 55347, USA | Football Player |

Knaus - Knoff

**Knol, Monique**
Draarlier 6, 3766 Soest ET, Netherlands — Cyclist

**Knoll, Andrew H**
Harvard University, Botanical Museum, 26 Oxford St, Cambridge MA 02138, USA — Paleontologist

**Knoll, Jozsef**
Semmelweis Medical University, Pharmacology Dept, 1445 Budapest, Hungary — Pharmacologist

**Knoop, Robert F (Bobby)**
2543 E Mountain Sky Ave, Phoenix AZ 85048, USA — Baseball Player

**Knopf, Sascha**
Stone Manners Salners, 9911 W Pico Blvd, #1400, Los Angeles CA 90035 USA — Actress, Model

**Knopfler, David**
Damage Mgmt, 16 Lambton Place, London W11 2SH, England — Guitarist (Dire Straits)

**Knopfler, Mark**
Paul Crockford Mgmt, 272 Latimer Road, London W10 6QY, England — Singer, Guitarist (Dire Straits)

**Knorr, Randy D**
3200 Arville St, #279, Las Vegas NV 89102, USA — Baseball Player

**Knowles, Beyonce**
Music World Entertainment, 1505 Hadley St, Houston TX 77002, USA — Singer, Actress, Model

**Knowles, Darold D**
1515 Whisper Wind Lane, Oldsmar FL 34677, USA — Baseball Player

**Knowles, Michael R**
University of North Carolina Medical School, Pulmonary & Critical Care Dept, Chapel Hill NC 27599, USA — Medical Researcher

**Knowles, Rodney**
3592 Island Dr, North Topsail Beach NC 28460, USA — Basketball Player

**Knowles, Sabrina**
3824 SW Morgan St, Seattle WA 98126, USA — Artist

**Knowles, Solange**
I C M Partners, 10250 Constellation Blvd, #900, Los Angeles CA 90067 USA — Actress, Singer

**Knowlson, Elizabeth**
Bloomsbury Publishing, 50 Bedford Square, London WC1B 3DP, England — Writer

**Knowlson, James R**
Bloomsbury Publishing, 50 Bedford Square, London WC1B 3DP, England — Writer

**Knowlton, Steve R**
Palmer Yeager Assoc, 6600 E Hampden Ave, #210, Denver CO 80224, USA — Skier

**Knox, Charles R (Chuck)**
48711 San Vicente St, La Quinta CA 92253, USA — Football Coach

**Knox, Deborah**
Curling Assn, 14 Donnelly Dr, Bedford, Bedfordshire MK4 9TU, England — Curling Athlete

**Knox, Heather**
Playboy Promotions, 2706 Media Center Dr, Los Angeles CA 90065 USA — Model

**Knox, Kenny**
3813 Dills Road, Monticello FL 32344, USA — Golfer

**Knox, Ruth A**
Wesleyan College, President's Office, 4760 Forsyth Road, Macon GA 31210, USA — Educator

**Knox, Taylor**
Pro Surfing Mgmt, 320 High Tide Dr, #101, Saint Augustine FL 32080 USA — Surfer

**Knox, Terence**
House of Representatives, 1434 6th St, #1, Santa Monica CA 90401 USA — Actor

**Knox-Johnston, W R P (Robin)**
26 Sefton St, Putney, London SW15, England — Yachtsman

**Knoxville, Johnny**
Creative Artists Agency, 2000 Ave of Stars, #100, Los Angeles CA 90067 USA — Actor, Comedian

**Knuble, Michael (Mike)**
2107 San Lu Rae Dr SE, Grand Rapids MI 49506, USA — Ice Hockey Player

**Knudsen, Erik**
Fountainhead Talent, 131 Davenport Road, Toronto ON M5R 1H8, Canada — Actor

**Knudsen, Lars**
United Talent Agency, U T A Plaza, 9336 Civic Center Dr, Beverly Hills CA 90210 USA — Producer

**Knudson, Alfred G, Jr**
Institute for Cancer Research, 7701 Burholme Ave, Philadelphia PA 19111, USA — Geneticist

**Knudson, Mark R**
881 W 100th Ave, Northglenn CO 80260, USA — Baseball Player

**Knudson, Thomas J**
Sacramento Bee, Editorial Dept, 21st & Q Sts, Sacramento CA 95852, USA — Journalist

**Knuppe, Franziska**
Model Mgmt, Hartungstr 5, 20146 Hamburg, Germany — Model

**Knussen, S Oliver**
BBC Symphony Orchestra, BBC Maida Vale Studios, Delaware Road, London W9 2LG, England — Conductor, Composer

**Knuth, Donald E**
Stanford University, Computer Science Dept, Gates Building, Stanford CA 94305, USA — Computer Scientist; Kyoto Laureate

**Knuth, Shay**
Playboy Promotions, 2706 Media Center Dr, Los Angeles CA 90065 USA — Model

**Ko Gi-Hyun**
Skating Union, 88 Bangyee-Dong, Songpaku, Seoul 138 749, South Korea — Speed Skater

**Ko Un**
Anseong, Gyeonggi-do 456 600, South Korea — Writer

**Ko, Lydia**
Pinehurst School, 75 Bush Road, Albany North Shore, Aukland 0632, New Zealand — Golfer

**Koback, Nicholas N (Nick)**
71 Hopmeadow St, #9A-1, Weatogue CT 06089, USA — Baseball Player

**Kobayashi, Makoto**
High Energy Accelerator Research, 1-1 Oho, Tsukuba 305 0801, Japan — Nobel Physics Laureate

**Kobel, Kevin R**
7650 E Williams Dr, #1072, Scottsdale AZ 85255, USA — Baseball Player

**Kober, Amelie**
Meet Success, Heilmannstr 19, 81479 Munich, Germany — Snowboard Athlete

**Kober, Jeff**
4544 Ethel Ave, Studio City CA 91604, USA — Actor

**Kobilka, Brian K**
Stanford University Medical School, 450 Serra Mall, 300 Pasteur Drive, Palo Alto CA 94305, USA — Nobel Chemistry Laureate

**Koblik, Steven**
Huntington Library & Art Gallery, 1151 Oxford Road, San Marino CA 91108, USA — Museum Executive, Educator

**Kobrin, Alex**
I M G Artists, Hogarth Business Park, Chiswick, London W4 2TH, England — Concert Pianist

**Kobylt, John**
248 Oceano Dr, Los Angeles CA 90049, USA — Entertainer

K

Knol - Kobylt

# K

**Koch, Alan G** — Baseball Player
1714 Pebble Creek Dr, Prattville AL 36066, USA
**Koch, Carin** — Golfer
2000 Auburn Dr, #330, Beachwood OH 44122, USA
**Koch, Charles G** — Businessman
Koch Industries, PO Box 2256, Wichita KS 67201, USA
**Koch, Christopher (Chris)** — Director
United Talent Agency, U T A Plaza, 9336 Civic Center Dr, Beverly Hills CA 90210 USA
**Koch, David H** — Businessman
Koch Industries, PO Box 2256, Wichita KS 67201, USA
**Koch, Edwin** — Artist
1211 NW Ogden Ave, Bend OR 97701, USA
**Koch, Gary** — Golfer
2934 W Lawn Ave, Tampa FL 33611, USA
**Koch, Gregory M (Greg)** — Football Player
34 Valley Oaks Circle, Spring TX 77382, USA
**Koch, James V** — Educator, Economist
Old Dominion University, Economics Dept, Norfolk VA 23529, USA
**Koch, Peter A (Pete)** — Football Player
866 W 16th St, Newport Beach CA 92663, USA
**Koch, Sebastian** — Actor
Die Agenten Beate Wolgast, Ackerstra 11B, 10115 Berlin, Germany
**Koch, Sophie** — Opera Singer
I M G Artists, Hogarth Business Park, Chiswick, London W4 2TH, England
**Koch, William (Bill)** — Nordic Skier
PO Box 115, Ashland OR 97520, USA
**Koch, William C (Billy)** — Baseball Player
3160 Tusket Ave, North Port FL 34286, USA
**Koch, William I (Bill)** — Yachtsman, Businessman
Oxbow Corp, 1601 Forum Place, West Palm Beach FL 33401, USA
**Kocherga, Anatoli I** — Opera Singer
Gogolevskaho 37 Korp 2, #47, 254053 Kiev, Ukraine
**Kocherry, Thomas** — Social Activist
Kerala Swatantra Matsyathozhilali Federation, Kerala 69508, India
**Kochi, Jay K** — Chemist
4372 Faculty Lane, Houston TX 77004, USA
**Kocsis, Zoltan** — Concert Pianist, Composer
Ringlo Utica 60/A, 1116 Budapest, Hungary
**Kocur, Joey** — Ice Hockey Player
2830 Vero Dr, Highland MI 48356, USA
**Kodes, Jan** — Tennis Player
I C L T K Tennis Club, Ostrov Stvanice, 17000 Prague 7, Czech Republic
**Kodjoe, Boris** — Model, Actor
Untitled Entertainment, 350 S Beverly Dr, #200, Beverly Hills CA 90212 USA
**Koechner, David** — Actor
Creative Artists Agency, 2000 Ave of Stars, #100, Los Angeles CA 90067 USA
**Koelle, George B** — Pharmacologist
3300 Darby Road, #3310, Haverford PA 19041, USA
**Koelling, Brian W** — Baseball Player
20230 Augusta Dr, Lawrenceburg IN 47025, USA
**Koen, Karleen** — Writer
Random House, 1745 Broadway, #1800, New York NY 10019 USA
**Koenekamp, Fred** — Cinematographer
9222 Corbin Ave, #402, Northridge CA 91324, USA
**Koenig, Ezra** — Singer, Guitarist (Vampire Weekend)
Monotone Inc, 820 Seward St, Los Angeles CA 90038, USA
**Koenig, Walter** — Actor
PO Box 4395, Valley Village CA 91617, USA
**Koepp, David** — Director, Writer
Creative Artists Agency, 2000 Ave of Stars, #100, Los Angeles CA 90067 USA
**Koester, Helmut H K E** — Theologian
12 Flintlock Road, Lexington MA 02420, USA
**Koffigoh, Joseph Kokou** — Prime Minister, Togo
Regional Integration Ministry, Lome, Togo
**Kofler, Andreas** — Ski Jumper
A-Sponsoring, Spengergasse 37/3, 1050 Vienna, Austria
**Kofoed, Bart** — Basketball Player
10161 Foxhall Dr, Charlotte NC 28210, USA
**Kofoed, Seana** — Actress
Greene Assoc, 1901 Ave of Stars, #130, Los Angeles CA 90067 USA
**Kogan, Pavel L** — Concert Violinist, Conductor
Bryusov Per 8/10, #19, 103009 Moscow, Russia
**Kogan, Theo** — Singer (Lunachicks), Actress
Wilhelmina Creative Mgmt, 300 Park Ave S, #200, New York NY 10010, USA
**Kogen, Jay K** — Producer, Writer, Actor
Paradigm Agency, 360 N Crescent Dr, North Building, Beverly Hills CA 90210 USA
**Koh, Terence** — Artist
Galerie Thaddaeus Ropac, 7 Rue Debelleyme, 75003 Paris, France
**Kohan, David** — Producer
Vision Art Mgmt, 530 N Larchmont Blvd, #2, Los Angeles CA 90004, USA
**Kohde-Kilsch, Claudia** — Tennis Player
Elsa-Brandstrom-Str 22, 66119 Saarbrucken, Germany
**Kohl, Ernest** — Singer
Nene Musik Productions, 1460 SW Santiago Ave, Port Saint Lucie FL 34953 USA
**Kohl, Helmut** — Chancellor, Germany
Marbacherstr 11, 67071 Ludwigshafen/Rhein-Obbersheim, Germany
**Kohlberg, Jerome, Jr** — Financier
155 Crow Hill Road, Mount Kisco NY 10549, USA
**Kohlbrand, Joseph (Joe)** — Football Player
480 Greenview Road, Merritt Island FL 32952, USA
**Kohler, Juliane** — Actress
Agentur Jarzyk-Holter, Sophienstr 21, 10178 Berlin, Germany
**Kohler, Jurgen** — Soccer Player
V f R Aalen, Gmunder Str 16, 73430 Aalen, Germany
**Kohler, Sheila** — Writer
Margaret Hanbury, 27 Walcott Square, London SE11 4UB, England

**Koch - Kohler**

| | |
|---|---|
| **Kohlmeier, Ryan** | Baseball Player |
| 301 Vine St, Cottonwood Falls KS 66845, USA | |
| **Kohls, Kris** | Drummer (Adema) |
| Novi Entertainment, PO Box 17077, Beverly Hills CA 90209, USA | |
| **Kohlsaat, Peter** | Cartoonist (Single Slices) |
| 420 N 5th St, #707, Minneapolis MN 55401, USA | |
| **Kohn, A Eugene** | Architect |
| Kohn Pedersen Fox Assoc, 111 W 57th St, #300, New York NY 10019, USA | |
| **Kohn, Joseph J** | Mathematician |
| 32 Sturges Way, Princeton NJ 08540, USA | |
| **Kohn, Mike** | Bobsled Athlete |
| US Bobsled & Skeleton Federation, 1631 Mesa Ave, #A, Colorado Springs CO 80906 USA | |
| **Kohn, Walter** | Nobel Chemistry Laureate |
| 236 La Vista Grande, Santa Barbara CA 93103, USA | |
| **Kohner, Susan** | Actress |
| John Weitz Inc, 3 E 66th St, #2C, New York NY 10065, USA | |
| **Kohoutek, Lubos** | Astronomer |
| Corthumstr 5, 21029 Hamburg, Germany | |
| **Kohrs, Robert H (Bob)** | Football Player |
| 2910 E Nance St, Mesa AZ 85213, USA | |
| **Koirala, Manisha** | Actress, Producer |
| 302 Beachwood Towers, Yari Road, Versova, Andheri (W), Mumbai 400061, India | |
| **Koivu, Mikko S** | Ice Hockey Player |
| Minnesota Wild, XCel Energy Arena, 1275 Saint Antoine W, Saint Paul MN 55104 USA | |
| **Koivu, Saku A** | Ice Hockey Player |
| 2200-201 Portage Ave, Winnipeg MB R3B 3L3, Canada | |
| **Kojac, George** | Swimmer |
| 33 Arboles del Norte, Fort Pierce FL 34951, USA | |
| **Kojima, Ariko** | Beauty Queen |
| Miss Universe Organization, 1370 Ave of Americas, #1600, New York NY 10019 USA | |
| **Kojis, Donald R (Don)** | Basketball Player |
| 8186 Commercial St, La Mesa CA 91942, USA | |
| **Kojovic, Lora** | Actress |
| Craig Wyckoff Assoc, 11350 Ventura Blvd, #100, Studio City CA 91604, USA | |
| **Kok Oudegeest, Mary** | Swimmer |
| Escuela Nacional de Natacion, Izarra, Alava, Spain | |
| **Kok, Willem (Wim)** | Prime Minister, Netherlands |
| Dijsselhofplantsoen 12, 1077, Amersterdam BL, Netherlands | |
| **Kokesh, Chris** | Singer, Fiddle Player (Misty River) |
| 1111B NW 131st Way, Vancouver WA 98685, USA | |
| **Kokonin, Vladimir** | Opera, Ballet Executive |
| Bolshoi Theater, Teatralnaya Pl 1, 103009 Moscow, Russia | |
| **Kolander, Steve** | Singer, Guitarist, Songwriter |
| Sussman Assoc, 1222 16th Ave S, #300, Nashville TN 37212, USA | |
| **Kolb Thomas, Claudia A** | Swimmer, Coach |
| Stanford University, Athletic Dept, Stanford CA 94305, USA | |
| **Kolb, Brandon** | Baseball Player |
| 2043 Pine Oak Place, Danville CA 94506, USA | |
| **Kolb, Edward W (Rocky)** | Cosmologist |
| Fermi National Accelerator Laboratory, PO Box 500, Batavia IL 60510 USA | |
| **Kolb, Gary A** | Baseball Player |
| 5143 Hopewell Dr, Charleston WV 25313, USA | |
| **Kolb, Jon P** | Football Player |
| 1775 McDowell St, Sharon PA 16146, USA | |
| **Kolbe, James T (Jim)** | Representative, AZ |
| German Marshall Fund, 1744 R St NW, Washington DC 20009, USA | |
| **Kolber, Suzy** | Sportscaster |
| ESPN-TV, ESPN Plaza, 935 Middle St, Bristol CT 06010 USA | |
| **Kolbert, Kathryn** | Attorney |
| Center for Reproductive Law & Policy, 120 Wall St, New York NY 10005, USA | |
| **Kolden, Scott C** | Actor |
| 1515 E Trenton Ave, Orange CA 92867, USA | |
| **Kole, Kelly** | Actress, Model |
| PO Box 226, Hartsdale NY 10530, USA | |
| **Kole, Warren** | Actor |
| Paul Kohner, 9300 Wilshire Blvd, #555, Beverly Hills CA 90212 USA | |
| **Kolehmaisen, Mikko** | Canoeing Athlete |
| Poppelitie 18, 50130 Mikkeli, Finland | |
| **Kolen, J Michael (Mike)** | Football Player |
| 1613 Manchester Lane, Birmingham AL 35243, USA | |
| **Kolirin, Eran** | Director |
| I C M Partners, 10250 Constellation Blvd, #900, Los Angeles CA 90067 USA | |
| **Kolius, John** | Yachtsman |
| PO Box 2113, Pearland TX 77588, USA | |
| **Kollar, Trudi Eberle** | Gymnast |
| Pozsar's Gymnastics Academy, 2709 El Camino Ave, Sacramento CA 95821, USA | |
| **Koller, Arnold** | President, Switzerland |
| Steinegg, Gschwendes 8, 9050 Appenzell, Switzerland | |
| **Kollhoff, Hans** | Architect |
| Kurfursendamm 178-179, 10707 Berlin, Germany | |
| **Kollner, Eberhard** | Cosmonaut, East Germany |
| An der Trainierbahn 7, 11536 Neuenhagen, Germany | |
| **Kollo, Rene** | Opera Singer |
| Pran Event Gmbh, Ralf Sellelberg, An der Brucke 18, 26180 Rastede, Germany | |
| **Kolm, Henry V** | Electrical Engineer (Magnetic Train) |
| Weir Meadow Road, Wayland MA 01778, USA | |
| **Kolodner, Richard D** | Biochemist, Cancer Researcher |
| Dana-Farber Cancer Institute, 44 Binney St, Boston MA 02115, USA | |
| **Kolodziej, Ross A** | Football Player |
| 1123 Sandalwood Dr, Lawrenceville GA 30043, USA | |
| **Koloskov, Alex** | Photographer |
| 2320 Rose Walk Dr, Alpharetta GA 30005, USA | |
| **Kolpakova, Irina A** | Ballerina |
| American Ballet Theatre, 890 Broadway, #300, New York NY 10003 USA | |
| **Kolstad, Dean** | Ice Hockey Player |
| 15492 Brooklodge Road, Hickory Corners MI 49060, USA | |

**K**

| | |
|---|---|
| **Kolstad, Harold E (Hal)**<br>15149 Bel Escou Dr, San Jose CA 95124, USA | Baseball Player |
| **Kolsti, Paul**<br>Dallas News, Editorial Dept, Communications Center, Dallas TX 75265, USA | Editorial Cartoonist |
| **Koltai, Lajos**<br>Gersh Agency, 9465 Wilshire Blvd, #600, Beverly Hills CA 90212 USA | Cinematographer, Director |
| **Kolvenbach, Peter-Hans**<br>Borgo Santo Spirito 5, CP 6139, 00195 Rome, Italy | Religious Leader |
| **Kolzig, Olaf**<br>400 Beach Dr NE, #903, Saint Petersburg FL 33701, USA | Ice Hockey Player |
| **Koman, Jacek**<br>R G M Artist, 64-76 Kippax St, #202, Surry Hills NSW 2010, Australia | Actor |
| **Koman, William J (Bill)**<br>5 Upper Ladue Road, Saint Louis MO 63124, USA | Football Player |
| **Komar, Vitaly**<br>55 Lisspenard St, New York NY 10013, USA | Artist |
| **Komenich, Kim**<br>111 Cornelia Ave, Mill Valley CA 94941, USA | Photojournalist |
| **Kometani, Pam**<br>4342 Kilauea Ave, Honolulu HI 96816, USA | Golfer |
| **Komleva, Gabriela T**<br>Fontanka Nab 116, #34, 198005 Saint Petersburg, Russia | Ballerina |
| **Komlos, Peter**<br>Sport-U 6, 2083 Solymar, Hungary | Concert Violinist |
| **Komminski, Brad L**<br>688 Fallside Lane, Westerville OH 43081, USA | Baseball Player |
| **Komorowski, Bronislaw M**<br>Palac Prezydencki, Ul Krakowskie Przedmiescie 48, 00071 Warsaw, Poland | President, Poland |
| **Komsic, Zeljko**<br>President's Office, Marsala Titz 7, 71000 Sarajevo, Bosnia & Herzegovina | President, Bosnia & Herzegovina |
| **Komunyakaa, Yusef**<br>900 W State St, Trenton NY 08618, USA | Writer |
| **Kon Artis**<br>Coast to Coast Talent, 3350 Barham Blvd, Los Angeles CA 90068 USA | Rap Artist (D-12) |
| **Koncak, Jon**<br>PO Box 10040, Jackson WY 83002, USA | Basketball Player |
| **Koncar, Mark**<br>447 N Alpine Blvd, Alpine UT 84004, USA | Football Player |
| **Konchalovsky, Andrei**<br>Weissmann Wolff Bergman, 9665 Wilshire Blvd, #900, Beverly Hills CA 90212, USA | Director |
| **Kondakova, Elena V**<br>Scientific Industrial Assn, Utica Lenina 4A, 141070 Kaliningrad, Russia | Cosmonaut |
| **Kondla, Thomas A (Tom)**<br>3517 Cleveland Ave, Brookfield IL 60513, USA | Basketball Player |
| **Kondo, Jun**<br>A I S T, Tsukuba Central 2, Tsukuba, Ibaraki 305 8568, Japan | Theoretical Physicist |
| **Kondrattyeva, Marina V**<br>Bolshoi Theater, Teatralnaya Pl 1, 103009 Moscow, Russia | Ballerina |
| **Kondratyev, Dmitri Y**<br>Cosmonaut Training Center, Star City, 141160 Zvezdny Gorodok, Moscow Oblast, Russia | Cosmonaut |
| **Konerko, Paul H**<br>8053 E Leaning Rock Road, Scottsdale AZ 85266, USA | Baseball Player |
| **Kong, Venice**<br>Playboy Promotions, 2706 Media Center Dr, Los Angeles CA 90065 USA | Model, Actress |
| **Konieczny, Douglas J (Doug)**<br>9503 Dundalk St, Spring TX 77379, USA | Baseball Player |
| **Konik, George**<br>1027 Savannah Road, Saint Paul MN 55123, USA | Ice Hockey Player |
| **Konitz, Lee**<br>Bennett Morgan, 1022 RR 376, #3, Wappinger Falls NY 12590 USA | Jazz Saxophonist |
| **Konkol, Mark**<br>Chicago Sun-Times, Editorial Dept, 401 N Wabash Ave, Chicago IL 60611 USA | Journalist |
| **Konner, Jennifer (Jenni)**<br>United Talent Agency, U T A Plaza, 9336 Civic Center Dr, Beverly Hills CA 90210 USA | Producer |
| **Kono, Tamio (Tommy)**<br>98-2025 Hapaki St, Aiea HI 96701, USA | Weightlifter |
| **Kononenko, Oleg D**<br>Cosmonaut Training Center, Star City, 141160 Zvezdny Gorodok, Moscow Oblast, Russia | Cosmonaut |
| **Konrad, Cathy**<br>Tree Line Films, 1708 Berkeley St, Santa Monica CA 90404, USA | Producer |
| **Konrad, Robert L (Rob), Jr**<br>11884 Windmill Lake Dr, Boynton Beach FL 33473, USA | Football Player |
| **Konroyd, Steve**<br>317 S Park Ave, Hinsdale IL 60521, USA | Ice Hockey Player |
| **Konstantinov, Vladimir**<br>6782 Enclave, West Bloomfield MI 48322, USA | Ice Hockey Player |
| **Kont, Paul**<br>Doblinger Music, Dorotheergasse 10, 1011 Vienna, Austria | Composer |
| **Kontos, Christopher (Chris)**<br>40 Beck Blvd, Penetanguishene ON L9M 1E1, Canada | Hockey Player |
| **Konyukhov, Fedor F**<br>Tourism/Sports Union, Studeniy Proyezd 7, 129282 Moscow, Russia | Explorer |
| **Kool Moe Dee**<br>Universal Attractions, 135 W 26th St, #1200, New York NY 10001 USA | Rap Artist |
| **Koolhaas, Rem**<br>Metropolitan Architecture, Heer Bokelweg 149, 3032 Rotterdam AD, Netherlands | Architect |
| **Koolman, Olindo**<br>Governor's Office, L G Smith Blvd 76, Oranjestad, Aruba | Governor, Aruba |
| **Koonce, George E, Jr**<br>925 E Wells St, #217, Milwaukee WI 53202, USA | Football Player |
| **Koonce, Graham**<br>2474 Pimlico Place, Alpine CA 91901, USA | Baseball Player |
| **Koones, Charles C**<br>Rockmore Media, 16026 Royal Oak Road, Encino CA 91436, USA | Publisher |
| **Koons, Jeff**<br>Jeff Koons Productions, 601 W 29th St, New York NY 10001, USA | Artist, Sculptor |

**Koontz, Dean R** — Writer
PO Box 9529, Newport Beach CA 92658, USA
**Kooper, Al** — Singer, Guitarist
Second Octave Talent, 720 S Pointe Blvd, #A200, Petaluma CA 94954, USA
**Koopman, A Ton G M** — Conductor, Concert Keyboardist
Meerweg 23, 1405 Bussu BC, Netherlands
**Koopmans-Kint, Cor** — Swimmer
Pacific Sands C'Van Park, Nambucca Heads NSW 2448, Australia
**Kooser, Ted** — Writer
1820 Branched Oak Road, Garland NE 68360, USA
**Koosman, Jerry M** — Baseball Player
2483 State Road 35, Osceola WI 54020, USA
**Kopacz, George F** — Baseball Player
14150 Somerset Court, Orland Park IL 60467, USA
**Kopatchinskaja, Patricia** — Concert Violinist
Maren Borchers, Schlüterstrasse 36, 10629 Berlin, Germany
**Kopay, David M (Dave)** — Football Player
100 W Highland Dr, #102, Seattle WA 98119, USA
**Kopecky, Tomas** — Ice Hockey Player
4401 N Federal Highway, #201, Boca Raton FL 33431, USA
**Kopell, Bernard M (Bernie)** — Actor
Amsel Eisenstadt Frazier, 5055 Wilshire Blvd, #865, Los Angeles CA 90036 USA
**Kopeloff, Eric** — Producer
I C M Partners, 10250 Constellation Blvd, #900, Los Angeles CA 90067 USA
**Kopelson, Arnold** — Producer
Kopelson Entertainment, 8560 Sunset Blvd, West Hollywood CA 90069, USA
**Koper, Herbert L (Bud)** — Basketball Player
1225 Lakeshore Dr, #118, Edmond OK 73013, USA
**Kopervas, Gary** — Cartoonist (Out on a Limb)
King Features Syndicate, 300 W 57th St, #1500, New York NY 10019 USA
**Kopicki, Joseph G (Joe)** — Basketball Player
47608 Cheryl Court, Shelby Township MI 48315, USA
**Kopins, Karen** — Actress
Sutton-Barth Vennari, 5900 Wilshire Blvd, #700, Los Angeles CA 90036 USA
**Kopit, Arthur** — Writer
207 W 106th St, #7D, New York NY 10025, USA
**Koplan, Jeffrey** — Medical Administrator
Emory University, Academic Health Affairs Dept, Atlanta GA 30322, USA
**Koplitz, Howard D (Howie)** — Baseball Player
623 Boyd St, Oshkosh WI 54901, USA
**Koplitz, Lynne** — Actress
Paradigm Agency, 360 N Crescent Dr, North Building, Beverly Hills CA 90210 USA
**Koplove, Michael P (Mike)** — Baseball Player
3235 Chaucer St, Philadelphia PA 19145, USA
**Kopp, Jeffrey B (Jeff)** — Football Player
13752 Deer Chase Place, Jacksonville FL 32224, USA
**Kopp, Wendy** — Association Executive
Teach for America Foundation, 315 W 36th St, #700, New York NY 10018, USA
**Koppel, Ted** — Commentator
3505 Belfont Dr, Elliot City MD 21043, USA
**Koppelman, Brian** — Director, Writer
Creative Artists Agency, 2000 Ave of Stars, #100, Los Angeles CA 90067 USA
**Koppelman, Chaim** — Artist
141 Wooster St, #6C, New York NY 10012, USA
**Koppen, Daniel (Dan)** — Football Player
1807 Old Bridge Lane, Bellingham MA 02019, USA
**Kopper, Hilmar** — Financier
DaimlerChrysler AG, Mercedestr 137, 70237 Stuttgart, Germany
**Kopperud, Gunnar** — Writer
Bloomsbury Publishing, 50 Bedford Square, London WC1B 3DP, England
**Koppes, Peter** — Guitarist (Church)
M O B Agency, 6404 Wilshire Blvd, #505, Los Angeles CA 90048 USA
**Kopple, Barbara J** — Director
Inphenate, 9701 Wilshire Blvd, #1000, Beverly Hills CA 90212 USA
**Kopra, Timothy L** — Astronaut
4912 Cross Creek Lane, League City TX 77573, USA
**Koptchak, Sergei** — Opera Singer
Robert Lombardo Assoc, Harkness Plaza, 61 W 62nd St, #6F, New York NY 10023 USA
**Korab, Jamie** — Curling Athlete
Curling Assn, 1660 Vimont Court, Cumberland ON K4A 4J4, Canada
**Korab, Jerry** — Ice Hockey Player
Korab Inc, 960 N Weigel Ave, Elmhurst IL 60126, USA
**Koralek, Paul G** — Architect
7 Chalcot Road, #1, London NW1 8LH, England
**Korbut, Olga V** — Gymnast
16356 N Thompson Peak Parkway, #2024, Scottsdale AZ 85260, USA
**Korcheck, Stephen J (Steve)** — Baseball Player
6424 98th St E, Bradenton FL 34202, USA
**Korcia, Laurent** — Concert Violinist
E M I Records, 18 Rue de la Convention, 75-15 Paris, France
**Kord, Kazimierz** — Conductor
Ul Nadarzynska 37A, 05 805 Kanie-Otrebusy, Poland
**Korda, Jessica** — Golfer
Ladies Pro Golf Assn, 100 International Golf Dr, Daytona Beach FL 32124 USA
**Korda, Michael V** — Writer
Simon & Schuster, 1230 Ave of Americas, Concourse 1, New York NY 10020, USA
**Korda, Petr** — Tennis Player
4909 61st Ave Dr W, Bradenton FL 34210, USA
**Korder, Howard** — Writer
I C M Partners, 10250 Constellation Blvd, #900, Los Angeles CA 90067 USA
**Korec, Jan Chryzostom Cardinal** — Religious Leader
Biskupstvo Nitra, PP 46A, 95050 Nitra, Slovakia
**Korecky, Robert J (Bobby)** — Baseball Player
209 Culver Road, Monmouth Junction NJ 08852, USA
**Koreeda, Hirokazu** — Director, Producer
TV Man Union, 5-53-67 Jingumae, Shibuya, Tokyo 150 0001, Japan

**K**

**Koontz - Koreeda**

**K**

**Koren - Kostelecki**

| | |
|---|---|
| **Koren, Christine (Chris)** <br> Playboy Promotions, 2706 Media Center Dr, Los Angeles CA 90065 USA | Model |
| **Koren, Edward B** <br> PO Box 464, Brookfield VT 05036, USA | Cartoonist |
| **Koren, Steve** <br> Creative Artists Agency, 2000 Ave of Stars, #100, Los Angeles CA 90067 USA | Writer, Producer |
| **Koretsky, Kenny** <br> K P K Development Corp, 149 Newbold Road, Fairless Hills PA 19030, USA | Drag Racing Driver, Builder |
| **Korf, Mia** <br> Fran Saperstein Organization, 919 Victoria Ave, Venice CA 90291, USA | Actress |
| **Korie, Michael** <br> I C M Partners, 10250 Constellation Blvd, #900, Los Angeles CA 90067 USA | Librettist |
| **Korine, Harmony** <br> Creative Artists Agency, 2000 Ave of Stars, #100, Los Angeles CA 90067 USA | Director, Writer, Actor |
| **Kormakur, Baltasar** <br> Blueeyes Productions, Seljaveg 2, 101 Reykjavik, Iceland | Director, Producer, Actor |
| **Korman, Maxime Carlot** <br> PO Box 698, Port Vila, Vanuatu | Prime Minister, Vanuatu |
| **Kormann, Manuela** <br> Curling Assn, PO Box 606, 3000 Bern, Switzerland | Curling Athlete |
| **Korn, Jim** <br> 19679 Sweetwater Curve, Excelsior MN 55331, USA | Ice Hockey Player |
| **Korn, Lester B** <br> 466 Lexington Ave, #237, New York NY 10017, USA | Businessman |
| **Kornberg, Roger D** <br> 345 Walsh Road, Atherton CA 94027, USA | Nobel Chemistry Laureate |
| **Kornfeld, Stuart A** <br> Washington University Medical School, Clinical Science Dept, Saint Louis MO 63110, USA | Hematologist |
| **Kornheiser, Anthony I (Tony)** <br> ESPN-TV, ESPN Plaza, 935 Middle St, Bristol CT 06010 USA | Sportswriter, Sportscaster |
| **Koroll, Cliff** <br> 23W569 Glendale Terrace, Roselle IL 60172, USA | Ice Hockey Player |
| **Koroma, Ernest Bai** <br> President's Office, State House, Independence Ave, Freetown, Sierra Leone | President, Sierra Leone |
| **Koronka, John** <br> 1403 10th St, Clermont FL 34711, USA | Baseball Player |
| **Korot, Alla** <br> Stone Manners Salners, 9911 W Pico Blvd, #1400, Los Angeles CA 90035 USA | Actress |
| **Kors, Michael** <br> 11 W 42nd St, #2000, New York NY 10036, USA | Fashion Designer |
| **Korte, Steven J (Steve)** <br> 137 Dunleith Lane, Mandeville LA 70471, USA | Football Player |
| **Korver, Kyle E** <br> 1483 Wesleys Run, Gladwyne PA 19035, USA | Basketball Player |
| **Korver, Paul** <br> Gersh Agency, 9465 Wilshire Blvd, #600, Beverly Hills CA 90212 USA | Actor |
| **Korzeniowski, Abel** <br> Evolution Music Partners, 1680 N Vine St, #500, Los Angeles CA 90028 90028, USA | Composer |
| **Korzun, Valery G** <br> Cosmonaut Training Center, Star City, 141160 Zvezdny Gorodok, Moscow Oblast, Russia | Cosmonaut |
| **K-OS** <br> Agency Group Ltd, 142 W 57th St, #600, New York NY 10019 USA | Rap Artist, Songwriter |
| **Kosar, Bernie J, Jr** <br> PO Box 8, Nashport OH 43830, USA | Football Player |
| **Kosar, Scott** <br> Gotham Group, 9255 Sunset Blvd, #515. Los Angeles, CA 90069, USA | Writer |
| **Kosco, Andrew J (Andy)** <br> 10324 Springfield Road, Youngstown OH 44514, USA | Baseball Player |
| **Koshalek, Richard** <br> Museum of Contemporary Art, 250 S Grand Ave, Los Angeles CA 90012, USA | Museum Executive |
| **Koshansky, Joseph S (Joe)** <br> 13314 Point Pleasant Dr, Fairfax VA 22033, USA | Baseball Player |
| **Koshiba, Masatoshi** <br> University of Tokyo, 7-3-1 Hongo, Nunkyoku, Tokyo 113 8654, Japan | Nobel Physics Laureate |
| **Koshiro, Matsumoto, IV** <br> Kabukiza Theatre, 12-15-4 Ginza, Chuoku, Tokyo 104 0061, Japan | Kabuki Actor, Dancer |
| **Koshlyakov, Valery N** <br> Kolodzei Art Foundation, 123 S Adelaide Ave, #1N, Highland Park NJ 08904, USA | Artist |
| **Kosier, Kyle B** <br> 8943 E Calle del Palo Verde, Scottsdale AZ 85255, USA | Football Player |
| **Kosinski, Joseph** <br> Verve Talent/Literary Agency, 9696 Culver Blvd, #301, Culver City CA 90232 USA | Director |
| **Koskie, Cordel L (Corey)** <br> 161 Primrose Lane, Hamel MN 55340, USA | Baseball Player |
| **Koskinen, John A** <br> Internal Revenue Service, Commissioner's Office, 12th St & Pennsylvania Ave NW, Washington DC 20004, USA | Government Official |
| **Koskoff, Sarah** <br> Anonymous Content, 3532 Hayden Ave, Culver City CA 90232 USA | Actress |
| **Koslow, Lauren** <br> Michael Bruno, 13576 Cheltenham Dr, Sherman Oaks CA 91423, USA | Actress |
| **Kosmalski, Lenonard J (Len)** <br> 404 Washington Ave, #PH 8, Miami Beach FL 33139, USA | Basketball Player |
| **Kosminsky, Peter** <br> United Agents, 12-26 Lexington St, London W1F 0LE, England | Director |
| **Koss, Alan** <br> I C M Partners, 10250 Constellation Blvd, #900, Los Angeles CA 90067 USA | Actor |
| **Koss, Johann Olav** <br> Dagaliveien 21, 0387 Oslo, Norway | Speed Skater |
| **Koss, John C** <br> Koss Corp, 4129 N Port Washington Ave, Milwaukee WI 53212, USA | Inventor |
| **Kostabi, Mark** <br> Kostabi World, 514 W 24th St, New York NY 10011, USA | Artist, Sculptor, Composer |
| **Kostadinova, Stefka** <br> Rue Anghel Kantchev 4, 1000 Sofia, Bulgaria | Track Athlete |
| **Kostelecki, David** <br> Palackeho 127, 66461 Holasice, Czech Republic | Marksman |

| | |
|---|---|
| **Kostelic, Ivica** | Alpine Skier |
| Skiing Federation, Trg Sportova 11, 10000 Zagreb, Croatia | |
| **Kostelic, Janica** | Alpine Skier |
| Medvedgradsken 45A, 10000 Zagreb, Croatia | |
| **Koster, Steven J** | Cinematographer |
| 26881 Goya Circle, Mission Viejo CA 92691, USA | |
| **Kostic, Goran** | Actor |
| Agence Christine Parat 9 Rue de Maubeuge 75009 Paris France | |
| **Kostomarov, Roman** | Ice Dancer |
| Skating Federation, Luchnesksaia Nab 8, 119871 Moscow, Russia | |
| **Kostov, Ivan** | Prime Minister, Bulgaria |
| Blvd Rakovski 134, 1000 Sofia, Bulgaria | |
| **Kostova, Elizabeth J** | Writer |
| Little Brown, 3 Center Plaza, #100, Boston MA 02108 USA | |
| **Kostro, Frederick C (Frank)** | Baseball Player |
| 3161 S Jasmine Way, Denver CO 80222, USA | |
| **Kostroff, Michael** | Actor |
| Don Buchwald, 10 E 44th St, New York NY 10017 USA | |
| **Kosugi, Kane** | Actor |
| Sun Music, 4-28 Yotsuya, Shinjuku, Tokyo 160 8501, Japan | |
| **Kosuth, Joseph** | Artist |
| Spruth Magers Gallery, Oranienburger Stra 18, 10178 Berlin, Germany | |
| **Koszelak, Stanley N** | Biochemist |
| 1125 Mendocino Way, Redlands CA 92374, USA | |
| **Kotalik, Ales** | Ice Hockey Player |
| 17681 Hackberry Court, Eden Prairie MN 55347, USA | |
| **Kotb, Hoda** | Commentator |
| NBC-TV, News Dept, 30 Rockefeller Plaza, #270E, New York NY 10112 USA | |
| **Kotcheff, W Theodore (Ted)** | Director |
| Baumgarten Management & Productions, 406 Wilshire Blvd, Santa Monica CA 90401, USA | |
| **Kotchman, Casey J** | Baseball Player |
| 8442 125th Court, Seminole FL 33776, USA | |
| **Koteas, Elias** | Actor |
| United Talent Agency, U T A Plaza, 9336 Civic Center Dr, Beverly Hills CA 90210 USA | |
| **Kotelnik, Andreas** | Boxer |
| Universum Boxing Promotion, Am Stadtrand 27, 22047 Hamburg, Germany | |
| **Koterba, Jeff** | Sports, Editorial Cartoonist |
| Omaha World Herald, Editorial Dept, 14th & Dodge St, Omaha NE 68102, USA | |
| **Kotite, Richard E (Rich)** | Football Player, Coach |
| 241 Fanning St, Staten Island NY 10314, USA | |
| **Kotlarek, Gene** | Skier |
| 4910 Walking Horse Point, Colorado Springs CO 80923, USA | |
| **Kotlayakov, Vladimir M** | Geographer, Glacierologist |
| Profsoyuznaya St 43-1-80, 117420 Moscow, Russia | |
| **Kotov, Oleg V** | Cosmonaut |
| Cosmonaut Training Center, Star City, 141160 Zvezdny Gorodok, Moscow Oblast, Russia | |
| **Kotova, Nina** | Concert Cellist |
| I M G Artists, Hogarth Business Park, Chiswick, London W4 2TH, England | |
| **Kotsay, Mark S** | Baseball Player |
| 6659 Calle Ponte Bella, Rancho Santa Fe CA 92091, USA | |
| **Kottaras, George** | Baseball Player |
| 167 Cartmel Dr, Markham ON L3S 1W6, Canada | |
| **Kottke, Leo** | Singer, Songwriter, Guitarist |
| A E G Live, 930 W 7th Ave, Denver CO 80204, USA | |
| **Kotto, Yaphet F** | Actor |
| Rival Agency, 9157 Sunset Blvd, #212, West Hollywood CA 90069, USA | |
| **Kotulak, Ronald** | Editor |
| Chicago Tribune, Editorial Dept, 435 N Michigan Ave, #1, Chicago IL 60611, USA | |
| **Kotzky, Alex S** | Cartoonist (Apartment 3-G) |
| 25 Highfield Road, Glen Cove NY 11542, USA | |
| **Kouchner, Bernard** | Physician; Government Official, France |
| L'Action d'Humanitaire, 8 Ave de Segur, 75350 Paris, France | |
| **Koudelka, Josef** | Photographer |
| Magnum Photos, 19 Rue Hegesippe Moneau, 75018 Paris, France | |
| **Koufax, Sanford (Sandy)** | Baseball Player |
| Los Angeles Dodgers, Stadium, 1000 Elysian Park Ave, Los Angeles CA 90090 USA | |
| **Koufos, Konstantine D (Kosta)** | Basketball Player |
| Denver Nuggets, Pepsi Center, 1000 Chopper Circle, Denver CO 80204 USA | |
| **Kounrouzan, Karen** | Model |
| Playboy Promotions, 2706 Media Center Dr, Los Angeles CA 90065 USA | |
| **Kournikova, Anna** | Tennis Player, Model |
| 2345 Lake Ave, Sunset Isle 3, Miami Beach FL 33140, USA | |
| **Koutouvides, Niko S** | Football Player |
| 129 9th Lane, Kirkland WA 98033, USA | |
| **Kouwenhoven, Leo P** | Physicist |
| University of Delft, Van Leeuwenhoek Laboratory,Van der Waalsweg 14, 2628 Delft CH, Netherlands | |
| **Kouzmanoff, Kevin** | Baseball Player |
| 28606 Evergreen Manor Dr, Evergreen CO 80439, USA | |
| **Kovacevich, Stephen** | Concert Pianist, Conductor |
| C M Artists, 127 W 96th St, #13B, New York NY 10025 USA | |
| **Kovach, Bill** | Editor, Foundation Executive |
| Harvard University, Nieman Fellows Program, Cambridge MA 02138, USA | |
| **Kovacic, Ernst** | Concert Violinist |
| Im Muehlfeld 3, 2102 Bisamberg, Austria | |
| **Kovacs, Andras** | Director |
| Magyar Jakobinusok Ter 2/3, 1122 Budapest, Hungary | |
| **Kovacs, Denes** | Concert Violinist |
| Iranyi Utca 12, 1053 Budapest V, Hungary | |
| **Kovacs, Istvan (Koko)** | Boxer |
| Box Utca, Bajcsy Zs, Ut 21, 1065 Budapest, Hungary | |
| **Kovalainen, Heikki J** | Auto Racing Driver |
| Caterham Motorsport Kennet Road Dartford Kent DA1 4QN, England | |
| **Kovalchuk, Ilja V** | Ice Hockey Player |
| S K A Saint Petersburg, Dobrolyubov Prospekt 16, 197198 Saint Petersburg, Russia | |
| **Kovalenko, Andrei** | Ice Hockey Player |
| Kontinental Hockey League, 20/2 Ovchinnikovskaya, 115035 Moscow, Russia | |

**K**

| | |
|---|---|
| **Kovalenok, Vladimir S**<br>3 Hovanskaya St, #22, 129515 Moscow, Russia | Cosmonaut, Air Force General |
| **Kovalev, Alexei V**<br>676 Riversville Road, Greenwich CT 6831, USA | Ice Hockey Player |
| **Kovalevsky, Jean**<br>Villa La Padovane, 8 Rue Saint Michel, Saint-Antoine, 06130 Grasse, France | Astronomer |
| **Kovatchev, Julian**<br>I M G Artists, Hogarth Business Park, Chiswick, London W4 2TH, England | Conductor |
| **Kove, Martin**<br>Rogues Gallery, 9107 Wilshire Blvd, #450, Beverly Hills CA 90210, USA | Actor |
| **Kowal, Charles T**<br>Space Telescope Science Institute, Homewood Campus, Baltimore MD 21218, USA | Astronomer |
| **Kowal, Kristian A (Kristy)**<br>128 Laurel Court, #128B, Reading PA 19610, USA | Swimmer |
| **Kowalczyk, Ed**<br>Monterey Peninsula Artists, 404 W Franklin St, Monterey CA 93940 USA | Singer, Guitarist (Live) |
| **Kowalczyk, Jozef**<br>Metropolitan Curia, Ul Kanclerza Jana Laskiego 7, 62200 Gniezno, Poland | Religious Leader |
| **Kowalczyk, Justyna**<br>Budynek Poiskiego Radia, Ul Karkonoska 10, 53015 Wroclaw, Poland | Cross Country Skier |
| **Kowalczyk, Walter J (Walt)**<br>144 W Maryknoll Road, Rochester Hills CA 48309, USA | Football Player |
| **Kowalewicz, Ben**<br>Big Machine Media, 579 Lexington Ave, #400, New York NY 10022, USA | Singer (Billy Talent) |
| **Kowalik, Trent**<br>Gersh Agency, 41 Madison Ave, #3301, New York NY 10010 USA | Actor |
| **Kowalkowski, Scott T**<br>3995 Kelsey Road, Lake Orion MI 48360, USA | Football Player |
| **Kowalski, James M**<br>Commander, Air Force Global Strike Command, Barksdale Air Force Base LA 71110 USA | Air Force General |
| **Kowitz, Brian M**<br>1657 Bullock Circle, Owings Mills MD 21117, USA | Baseball Player |
| **Koy, Ernest M (Ernie), Jr**<br>PO Box 6, Kenney TX 77452, USA | Football Player |
| **Koy, Jo**<br>Creative Artists Agency, 2000 Ave of Stars, #100, Los Angeles CA 90067 USA | Actor, Comedian, Writer |
| **Koyagialo, Louis Alphonse**<br>Prime Minister's Office, Kinshasa, Congo Democratic Republic | Premier, Congo Democratic Republic |
| **Koyama, Debbie**<br>118 Tranquila Dr, Camarillo CA 93012, USA | Golfer |
| **Koyamada, Shin**<br>Shannon Murphy, 8224A Santa Monica Blvd, #721, West Hollywood CA 90046, USA | Actor |
| **Koz, Dave**<br>W F Leopold Mgmt, 4425 Riverside Dr, #102, Burbank CA 91505, USA | Jazz Saxophonist, Flutist, Actor |
| **Kozak, Donald (Don)**<br>1028 N Columbus Dr, Gilbert AZ 85234, USA | Ice Hockey Player |
| **Kozak, Harley Jane**<br>Talent Works, 3500 W Olive Ave, #1400, Burbank CA 91505 USA | Actress |
| **Kozak, Scott A**<br>18617 S Grasle Road, Oregon City OR 97045, USA | Football Player |
| **Kozar, Heather**<br>C E S D, 10635 Santa Monica Blvd, #130, Los Angeles CA 90025 USA | Model, Actress |
| **Kozeev, Konstantin M**<br>Cosmonaut Training Center, Star City, 141160 Zvezdny Gorodok, Moscow Oblast, Russia | Cosmonaut |
| **Kozelko, Thomas W (Tom)**<br>6200 Peninsula Dr, Traverse City MI 49686, USA | Basketball Player |
| **Kozena, Magdalena**<br>Narodni Divadlo, Dvorakova 11, 60000 Brno, Czech Republic | Opera Singer |
| **Kozerski, Bruce**<br>3088 Waterbury Court, Edgewood KY 41017, USA | Football Player |
| **Kozinski, Alex**<br>US Court of Appeals, 125 S Grand Ave, Pasadena CA 91105, USA | Judge |
| **Koziol, John C**<br>Deputy CinC, Intelligence & Surveillance, HgUSAF, Pentagon, Washington DC 20330 USA | Air Force General |
| **Kozlicki, Ronald F (Ron)**<br>5002 Hidden Branches Dr, Atlanta GA 30338, USA | Basketball Player |
| **Kozlov, Akexey S**<br>Shchepkin Str 25, #28, 129090 Moscow, Russia | Jazz Saxophonist, Band Leader, Composer |
| **Kozlov, Viktor N**<br>363 Merlin Way, Plantation FL 33324, USA | Ice Hockey Player |
| **Kozlov, Vyacheslav A**<br>4934 Powers Ferry Road, Atlanta GA 30327, USA | Ice Hockey Player |
| **Kozlova, Valentina**<br>New York City Ballet, Lincoln Center Plaza, New York NY 10023 USA | Ballerina |
| **Kozlowski, Brian S**<br>61 E Shore Dr, Niantic CT 06357, USA | Football Player |
| **Kozlowski, Glen A**<br>455 Belmont Place, #262, Provo UT 84606, USA | Football Player |
| **Kozlowski, Linda**<br>Bedford & Pearce, 19 Abbotsford Road, Katoomba NSW 2780, Australia | Actress |
| **Kozlowski, Michael J (Mike)**<br>932 NW 110th Ave, Plantation FL 33324, USA | Football Player |
| **Koznick, Kristina**<br>PO Box 85, Wolcott CO 81655, USA | Alpine Skier |
| **Kozol, Jonathan**<br>PO Box 145, Byfield MA 01922, USA | Writer |
| **Kraatz, Victor**<br>Connecticut Skating Center, 300 Alumni Road, Newington CT 06111, USA | Figure Skater |
| **Kraayeveld, Cathrine H**<br>Atlanta Dream, 83 Walton St NW, #400, Atlanta, GA 30303 USA | Basketball Player |
| **Krabbe, Jeroen**<br>Conway Van Gelder Grant, 8-12 Broadwick St, #300, London W1F 8HW, England | Actor |
| **Krabbe, Tim**<br>Bloomsbury Publishing, 50 Bedford Square, London WC1B 3DP, England | Writer |
| **Krabbe-Zimmermann, Katrin**<br>Dorfstr 9, 17091 Pinnow, Germany | Track Athlete |

Kovalenok - Krabbe-Zimmermann

Krackow, Jurgen — Businessman
Schumannstr 100, 40237 Dusseldorf, Germany
Kraemer, Harry J — Businessman
Baxter International, 1 Baxter Parkway, Deerfield IL 60015, USA
Kraemer, Joseph W (Joe) — Baseball Player
3212 NE 401st Circle, La Center WA 98629, USA
Kraft, Christopher C (Chris), Jr — Space Administrator
14919 Village Elm St, Houston TX 77062, USA
Kraft, Craig A — Artist, Sculptor
931 R St NW, Washington DC 20001, USA
Kraft, Greg — Golfer
14820 Rue de Bayonne, #302, Clearwater FL 33762, USA
Kraft, Leo A — Composer
45 Hill Park Ave, #3E, Great Neck NY 11021, USA
Kraft, Robert — Composer
4722 Noeline Ave, Encino CA 91436, USA
Kraft, Robert P — Astrophysicist
University of California, Lick Observatory, Santa Cruz CA 95064, USA
Kragen, Greg — Football Player
1447 Boulevard Way, Walnut Creek CA 94595, USA
Kraggerud, Henning — Concert Violinist
I M G Artists, Hogarth Business Park, Chiswick, London W4 2TH, England
Kragthorpe, Steve — Football Coach
University of Louisville, Athletic Dept, Louisville KY 40292, USA
Kraguly, Radovan — Artist
Llwyngarth Fawr, Comin Coch, Builth Wells, Powys LD2 3PP, Wales
Krajicek, Richard — Tennis Player
Krajicek Foundation, Olympisch Stadion 3, 1076 Amsterdam DE, Netherlands
Krakau, Mervin F (Merv) — Football Player
706 Prairie St, Guthrie Center IA 50115, USA
Krakoff, Reed — Fashion Designer
831 Madison Ave, New York NY 10021, USA
Krakoski, Joseph A (Joe) — Football Player
560 Village Blvd, #37, Incline Village NV 89451, USA
Krakowski, Jane — Actress, Singer
United Talent Agency, U T A Plaza, 9336 Civic Center Dr, Beverly Hills CA 90210 USA
Krall, Diana — Singer, Pianist, Songwriter
S L Feldman Mgmt, 1505 W 2nd Ave, #200, Vancouver BC V6H 3Y4, Canada
Kraly, Steven C (Steve) — Baseball Player
12 Davis Ave, Johnson City NY 13790, USA
Kramarsky, David — Director
1630 Berkeley St, #1, Santa Monica CA 90404, USA
Kramek, Robert E — Coast Guard Admiral
43 Firefall Court, Spring TX 77380, USA
Kramer, Barry D — Basketball Player
101 Deanna Court, Schenectady NY 12309, USA
Kramer, Billy J — Singer (Billy J Kramer & the Dakotas)
Lustig Talent, PO Box 770850, Orlando FL 32877 USA
Kramer, Chris — Actor
Lucas Talent, 100 W Pender St, #700, Vancouver BC V6B 1RB, Canada
Kramer, Clare — Actress
S M S Talent, 8383 Wilshire Blvd, #230, Beverly Hills CA 90211 USA
Kramer, Eric Allen — Actor
Stone Manners Salners, 9911 W Pico Blvd, #1400, Los Angeles CA 90035 USA
Kramer, Gerald L (Jerry) — Football Player
11768 W Chinden Blvd, Garden City ID 83714, USA
Kramer, Jeffrey — Director, Writer
Innovative Artists, 1505 10th St, Santa Monica CA 90401 USA
Kramer, Jim — Writer
I C M Partners, 10250 Constellation Blvd, #900, Los Angeles CA 90067 USA
Kramer, Joel B — Basketball Player
3817 E Highland Ave, Phoenix AZ 85018, USA
Kramer, Joseph M (Joey) — Drummer (Aerosmith)
Front Line Mgmt, 1100 Glendon Ave, #2000, Los Angeles CA 90024 USA
Kramer, Kent D — Football Player
200 Troon Road, McKinney TX 75070, USA
Kramer, Larry — Social Activist, Writer
Gay Men's Health Crisis, 119 W 24th St, Lobby 1, New York NY 10011, USA
Kramer, Randall J (Randy) — Baseball Player
143 Camino Pacifico, Aptos CA 95003, USA
Kramer, Stepfanie — Actress
Teitelbaum Artists Group, 8840 Wilshire Blvd, #200, Beverly Hills CA 90211, USA
Kramer, Thomas F (Tommy) — Football Player
806 Emerald Bay, San Antonio TX 78260, USA
Kramer, Thomas J (Tom) — Baseball Player
10665 Hamilton Ave, Cincinnati OH 45231, USA
Kramer, W Erik — Football Player
5950 Kingham Court, Agoura Hills CA 91301, USA
Kramer, Wayne — Jazz Guitarist (Was Not Was, MC5)
I C M Partners, 730 5th Ave, New York NY 10019 USA
Kramer, Wayne — Director
W M E Entertainment, 9601 Wilshire Blvd, #300, Beverly Hills CA 90210 USA
Kramlich, Richard S — Marine Corps General
Deputy CofS, Installations/Logistics, HqUSMC, Navy St, Washington DC 20380 USA
Kramnik, Vladimir — Chess Player
Russian Chess Federation, Luchnetskaya 8, 119270 Moscow, Russia
Kranepool, Edward E (Ed) — Baseball Player
M E Promotions, 177 High Pond Dr, Jericho NY 11753, USA
Krantz, Judith T — Writer
166 Groverton Place, Los Angeles CA 90077, USA
Kranz, Eugene (Gene) — Space Scientist
1108 Shady Oak Lane, Dickinson TX 77539, USA
Kranz, Fran — Actor
United Talent Agency, U T A Plaza, 9336 Civic Center Dr, Beverly Hills CA 90210 USA
Krapek, Karl — Businessman
United Technologies Corp, United Technologies Building, Hartford CT 06101, USA

Krackow - Krapek

**K**

| | |
|---|---|
| **Krasinski, John**<br>W M E Entertainment, 9601 Wilshire Blvd, #300, Beverly Hills CA 90210 USA | Actor, Comedian |
| **Krasniqi, Luan**<br>Oschleweg 10, 78628 Rottweil, Germany | Boxer |
| **Krasnoff, Eric**<br>Pall Corp, 25 Harbor Park Dr, Port Washington NY 11050, USA | Businessman |
| **Krasny, Yuri**<br>Sloane Gallery, Oxford Office Building, 1612 17th St, Denver CO 80202, USA | Artist |
| **Kratch, Robert A (Bob)**<br>10685 County Road 24, Watertown MN 55388, USA | Football Player |
| **Kratochvilova, Jarmila**<br>Pod Vysehradem 207, 58282 Golcuv Jenikov, Czech Republic | Track Athlete |
| **Kratzert, William A (Bill)**<br>8130 Merganser Dr, Ponte Vedra Beach FL 32082, USA | Golfer |
| **Kraulis, Andrew**<br>Rosenthal Agency, 204-14 Prince Arthur Ave, Toronto ON M5R 1A9, Canada | Actor |
| **Kraus, Alanna**<br>Speed Skating Canada, 2781 Lancaster Road, #402, Ottawa ON K1B 1A7, Canada | Speed Skater |
| **Kraus, Daniel J (Dan)**<br>10101 Governor Warfield Parkway, #222, Columbia MD 21044, USA | Basketball Player |
| **Kraus, Nicola**<br>Atria Books, 1230 Ave of Americas, New York NY 10020 USA | Writer |
| **Krause, Brian**<br>Glick Agency, 1321 7th St, #203, Santa Monica CA 90401 USA | Actor, Director, Producer |
| **Krause, Chester L**<br>Krause Publications, 700 E State St, Iola WI 54990, USA | Publisher |
| **Krause, Paul J**<br>Pinewood Golf Course, Real Estate Dept, 18150 Waco St NW, Elk River MN 55330, USA | Football Player |
| **Krause, Peter**<br>Creative Artists Agency, 2000 Ave of Stars, #100, Los Angeles CA 90067 USA | Actor |
| **Krause, Richard M**<br>4000 Cathedral Ave NW, #134B, Washington DC 20016, USA | Immunologist |
| **Kraushaar-Pielach, Silke**<br>Gorkistr 22, 96515 Sonneberg, Germany | Luge Athlete |
| **Krauss, Alison**<br>Arcieri Assoc, 305 Madison Ave, #2315, New York NY 10165 USA | Singer, Fiddler |
| **Krauss, Barry**<br>5346 Creekbend Dr, Carmel IN 46033, USA | Football Player |
| **Krauss, Lawrence M (Larry)**<br>Case Western Reserve University, Physics Dept, Cleveland OH 44106, USA | Astrophysicist |
| **Krauss, Nicole**<br>W W Norton, 500 5th Ave, #600, New York NY 10110 USA | Writer |
| **Krauss, Robert M**<br>Columbia University, Psychology Dept, Schermerhorn Hall, New York NY 10027, USA | Psychologist |
| **Krausse, Lewis B (Lew), Jr**<br>12811 NE 186th St, Holt MO 64048, USA | Baseball Player |
| **Krausse, Stefan**<br>Karl-Zink-Str 2, 96883 Ilmenau, Germany | Luge Athlete |
| **Krauthammer, Charles**<br>Washington Post Writers Group, 1150 15th St NW, Washington DC 20071, USA | Columnist |
| **Kravchuk, Igor A**<br>Harrington College, Athletic Dept, 300 Riviere Rouge, Harrington QC J8G 2S7, Canada | Ice Hockey Player |
| **Kravchuk, Leonid M**<br>Verkhovna Rada, M Hruspevskoho 5, 252019 Kiev, Ukraine | President, Ukraine |
| **Kravec, Kenneth P (Ken)**<br>6752 Taeda Dr, Sarasota FL 34241, USA | Baseball Player |
| **Kravitz, Lee**<br>Parade, Editorial Dept, 711 3rd Ave, New York NY 10017, USA | Editor |
| **Kravitz, Lenny**<br>Creative Artists Agency, 2000 Ave of Stars, #100, Los Angeles CA 90067 USA | Singer, Songwriter, Musician |
| **Krawczyk, Raymond A (Ray)**<br>67 Cloudcrest, Aliso Viejo CA 92656, USA | Baseball Player |
| **Krayer, Otto H**<br>4140 E Cooper St, Tucson AZ 85711, USA | Pharmacologist |
| **Krayzelburg, Lenny**<br>55 Oceana Dr E, #5H, Brooklyn NY 11235, USA | Swimmer |
| **Krayzie Bone**<br>Life Entertainment, 15441 Red Hill Ave, #G, Tustin CA 92780, USA | Rap Artist (Bone Thugs-N-Harmony) |
| **Kreamer, Ann**<br>W M E Entertainment, 9601 Wilshire Blvd, #300, Beverly Hills CA 90210 USA | Writer |
| **Krebbs, John**<br>Diamond Ridge, 3232 Amoruso Way, Roseville CA 95747, USA | Auto Racing Driver |
| **Krebs, Robert D**<br>Burlington North/Santa Fe, 2650 Lou Menk Dr, Fort Worth TX 76131, USA | Businessman |
| **Krebs, Susan**<br>6019 Buffalo Ave, #A, Van Nuys CA 91401, USA | Actress |
| **Kredel, Elmar Maria**<br>Obere Karolinenstra 5, 96033 Bamber, Germany | Religious Leader |
| **Kregel, Kevin R**<br>2601 Bay Shore Dr, Seabrook TX 77586, USA | Astronaut |
| **Kreider, Dan**<br>1069 Iron Bridge Road, Mount Joy PA 17552, USA | Football Player |
| **Kreider, Steve K**<br>350 Harrow Lane, Blue Bell PA 19422, USA | Football Player |
| **Kreis, Jason**<br>Real Salt Lake, 9256 S State St, Sandy UT 84070 USA | Soccer Player, Coach |
| **Kreitling, Richard A (Rich)**<br>24017 Trout Lake Road, Bovey MN 55709, USA | Football Player |
| **Kreklow, Wayne**<br>4001 S Old Mill Creek Road, Columbia MO 65203, USA | Basketball Player |
| **Krementz, Jill**<br>620 Sagaponack Main St, Southampton NY 11968, USA | Photographer |
| **Kremer, Andrea**<br>NBC-TV, Sports Dept, 30 Rockefeller Plaza, #270E, New York NY 10112 USA | Sportscaster |
| **Kremer, Arthur**<br>+1 Management/Public Relations, 242 Wythe Ave, #6, Brooklyn NY 11211, USA | Drummer (Stellarstarr*) |

| | |
|---|---|
| **Kremer, Gidon**<br>Opus 3 Artists, 470 Park Ave S, #900N, New York NY 10016 USA | Concert Violinist |
| **Kremer, J Kendall (Ken)**<br>6116 Double Eagle Court, Kansas City MO 64152, USA | Football Player |
| **Kremers, James E (Jimmy)**<br>6209 W Orlando St, Broken Arrow OK 74011, USA | Baseball Player |
| **Kremmel, James L (Jim)**<br>524 W 18th Ave, Spokane WA 99203, USA | Baseball Player |
| **Krens, Thomas**<br>Solomon R Guggenheim Museum, 1071 5th Ave, New York NY 10128, USA | Museum Executive |
| **Krentz, Jayne Ann (Amanda Quick)**<br>Axelrod Agency, 66 Church St, Lenox MA 01240, USA | Writer |
| **Krenz, Jan**<br>Al J Ch Szucha 16, 00 582 Warsaw, Poland | Conductor, Composer |
| **Kreps, David M**<br>Stanford University, Graduate Business School, Stanford CA 94305, USA | Economist |
| **Kresa, Kent**<br>General Motors Corp, 100 Renaissance Center, Detroit MI 48243, USA | Businessman |
| **Kresge, Chris**<br>834 Trailwood Dr, Apopka FL 32712, USA | Golfer |
| **Kreskin**<br>444 2nd St, Pitcairn PA 15140, USA | Illusionist |
| **Kress, Charles S (Charlie)**<br>1705 Pine St, #104, Sandpoint ID 83864, USA | Baseball Player |
| **Kress, Nathan**<br>A P A Talent/Literary Agency, 405 S Beverly Dr, #300, Beverly Hills CA 90212 USA | Actor |
| **Kressley, Carson**<br>Untitled Entertainment, 350 S Beverly Dr, #200, Beverly Hills CA 90212 USA | Entertainer |
| **Kretchmer, Arthur**<br>Playboy, Editorial Dept, 680 N Lake Shore Dr, Chicago IL 60611, USA | Editor |
| **Kretschmann, Thomas**<br>Hoestermann Mgmt, Gneisenaustr 94, 10961 Berlin, Germany | Actor |
| **Kreuger, Richard A (Rick)**<br>4664 Sheldon Court, Hudsonville MI 49426, USA | Baseball Player |
| **Kreuk, Kristin L**<br>Gersh Agency, 9465 Wilshire Blvd, #600, Beverly Hills CA 90212 USA | Actress |
| **Kreuter, Chadden M (Chad)**<br>6737 SW 77th Terrace, South Miami FL 33143, USA | Baseball Player |
| **Kreutz, Olin G**<br>750 S Southmeadow Lane, Lake Forest IL 60045, USA | Football Player |
| **Kreutzberger, Mario**<br>W M E Entertainment, 9601 Wilshire Blvd, #300, Beverly Hills CA 90210 USA | Actor, Comedian, Writer, Producer |
| **Kreutzer, Franklin J (Frank)**<br>921 Windwhisper Lane, Annapolis MD 21403, USA | Baseball Player |
| **Kreutzmann, Bill**<br>Oliver & Sabec, 50 Balmy Alley, San Francisco CA 94110, USA | Drummer (Grateful Dead) |
| **Kreviazuk, Chantal**<br>Characters Talent Mgmt, 8 Elm St, Toronto ON M5G 1G7, Canada | Singer, Pianist, Songwriter |
| **Kribel, Joel**<br>26254 N 46th St, Phoenix AZ 85050, USA | Golfer |
| **Krick, Jaynie**<br>1522 Azalea Dr, Arlington TX 76013, USA | Baseball Player |
| **Krickstein, Aaron**<br>7559 Fairmont Court, Boca Raton FL 33496, USA | Tennis Player |
| **Krieg, Arthur M**<br>University of Iowa Medical College, Immunology Dept, Iowa City IA 52242, USA | Immunologist |
| **Krieg, David M (Dave)**<br>2439 E Desert Willow Dr, Phoenix AZ 85048, USA | Football Player |
| **Krieger, Ellie**<br>Flutie Entertainment, 9320 Wilshire Blvd, #202, Beverly Hills CA 90212, USA | Dietician, Entertainer |
| **Krieger, Lee Toland**<br>72nd Street Productions, 1041 N Formosa Ave, West Hollywood CA 90046, USA | Director |
| **Krieger, Robby**<br>Doors Music, 8899 Beverly Blvd, #812, Los Angeles CA 90048, USA | Guitarist (Doors), Songwriter |
| **Krier, Leon**<br>8 Rue des Chapeliers, 83830 Claviers, France | Architect |
| **Kriewaldt, Clint**<br>W3189 Center Valley Road, Freedom WI 54165, USA | Football Player |
| **Krige, Alice**<br>Diamond Mgmt, 31 Percy St, London W1T 2DD, England | Actress |
| **Krikalev, Sergei K**<br>Cosmonaut Training Center, Star City, 141160 Zvezdny Gorodok, Moscow Oblast, Russia | Cosmonaut |
| **Krim, Mathilde**<br>AmfAR Foundation for AIDS Research, 5900 Wilshire Blvd, Los Angeles CA 90036, USA | Philanthropist, Medical Activist |
| **Kring, Tim**<br>W M E Entertainment, 9601 Wilshire Blvd, #300, Beverly Hills CA 90210 USA | Writer, Producer |
| **Krinsky, Yehuda**<br>Chabad-Lubavitch, 841 Ocean Parkway, Brooklyn NY 11230, USA | Religious Leader, Rabbi |
| **Kripke, Eric**<br>Principato-Young, 9465 Wilshire Blvd, #880, Beverly Hills CA 90212 USA | Writer, Director, Producer |
| **Kripke, Saul A**<br>Princeton University, Philosophy Dept, Princeton NJ 08544, USA | Philosopher |
| **Krislov, Marvin**<br>Oberlin College, President's Office, 70 N Professor St, Oberlin OH 44074, USA | Educator |
| **Kriss, Gerard A**<br>Johns Hopkins University, Astronomy Dept, Baltimore MD 21218, USA | Astronomer |
| **Kristen, Marta**<br>475 Mesa Dr, Santa Monica CA 90402, USA | Actress |
| **Kristensen, Tom**<br>Autosport International, Broom Road, Teddington Middlesex TW11 9BE, England | Auto Racing Driver |
| **Kristiansen, Ingrid**<br>Nils Collett Vogts Vei 51B, 0765 Oslo, Norway | Track Athlete |
| **Kristiansen, Kjeld Kirk**<br>Lego Group, 7190 Billund, Denmark | Businessman, Educator |
| **Kristine W**<br>Spectrum Talent, 1650 Broadway, #1105, New York NY 10019, USA | Singer |

# K

| | |
|---|---|
| **Kristjansson, Thor** | Actor |
| Creative Artists Agency, 2000 Ave of Stars, #100, Los Angeles CA 90067 USA | |
| **Kristmanson, Kyrie** | Singer, Songwriter |
| Agency Group Ltd, 142 W 57th St, #600, New York NY 10019 USA | |
| **Kristof, Emory** | Photographer |
| National Geographic, Editorial Dept, 1145 17th St NW, Washington DC 20036 USA | |
| **Kristof, Joe** | Bowler |
| 4290 Meadowview Court, Columbus OH 43224, USA | |
| **Kristof, Kathy M** | Columnist |
| Los Angeles Times, Editorial Dept, 202 W 1st St, Los Angeles CA 90012 USA | |
| **Kristof, Nicholas D** | Journalist |
| New York Times, Editorial Dept, 229 W 43rd St, New York NY 10036, USA | |
| **Kristofferson, Kris** | Singer, Songwriter, Actor |
| I C M Partners, 10250 Constellation Blvd, #900, Los Angeles CA 90067 USA | |
| **Krivda, Rick M** | Baseball Player |
| 112 Dolores Dr, Irwin PA 15642, USA | |
| **Krivokrasov, Sergei V** | Ice Hockey Player |
| 16500 Collins Ave, #1556, Sunny Island Beach FL 33160, USA | |
| **Kriwet, Heinz** | Businessman |
| Thyssen AG, August-Thyssen-Str 1, 40211 Dusseldorf, Germany | |
| **Krmpotich, David** | Rowing Athlete |
| 128 Archbishop Dr, Conshocken PA 19428, USA | |
| **Kroeger, Chad R** | Singer, Guitarist (Nickelback) |
| Union Entertainment Group, 1323 Newbury Road, #104, Newbury Park CA 91320, USA | |
| **Kroeger, Gary** | Actor, Comedian |
| 10474 Santa Monica Blvd, #380, Los Angeles CA 90025, USA | |
| **Kroeger, Josh** | Baseball Player |
| 1007 Wildlife Road, San Diego CA 92131, USA | |
| **Kroeger, Michael D H (Mike)** | Bassist (Nickelback) |
| Union Entertainment Group, 1323 Newbury Road, #104, Newbury Park CA 91320, USA | |
| **Kroemer, Herbert** | Nobel Physics Laureate |
| University of California, Electrical Engineering Dept, Santa Barbara CA 93106, USA | |
| **Kroenig, Brad** | Model |
| Ford Models Inc, 111 5th Ave, #900, New York NY 10003 USA | |
| **Kroes, Doutzen** | Model |
| D N A Model Mgmt, 555 W 25th St, #600, New York NY 10001, USA | |
| **Kroes, Neelie** | Government Official, Netherlands |
| European Commission, 200 Rue de la Loi, 1049 Brussels, Belgium | |
| **Krofft, Marty** | Puppeteer |
| 700 Greentree Road, Pacific Palisades CA 90272, USA | |
| **Krofft, Sid** | Puppeteer |
| 7710 Woodrow Wilson Dr, Los Angeles CA 90046, USA | |
| **Kroft, Steve** | Commentator |
| CBS-TV, News Dept, 51 W 52nd St, New York NY 10019 USA | |
| **Krokidas, John** | Director |
| United Talent Agency, U T A Plaza, 9336 Civic Center Dr, Beverly Hills CA 90210 USA | |
| **Krol, Joachim** | Actor |
| Barbarella Entertainment, Aachener Str 26, 50674 Cologne, Germany | |
| **Kroll, Alexander S (Alex)** | Football Player, Businessman |
| 581 Whalley Road, Charlotte VT 05445, USA | |
| **Kroll, Lucien** | Architect |
| Ave Louis Berlaimont 20, Boite 9, 1160 Brussels, Belgium | |
| **Kroll, Nick** | Actor, Comedian |
| Mosiac Media Group, 9200 W Sunset Blvd, #1000, Los Angeles CA 90069 USA | |
| **Kromm, Richard (Rich)** | Ice Hockey Player |
| 1935 Cheyenne Dr, Evansville IN 47715, USA | |
| **Kron, Elizabeth S (Lisa)** | Actress |
| I C M Partners, 10250 Constellation Blvd, #900, Los Angeles CA 90067 USA | |
| **Kronberger, Petra** | Alpine Skier |
| Ellmautal 37, 5452 Pfarrwerfen, Austria | |
| **Krone, Julie** | Thoroughbred Racing Jockey |
| 7305 Marine Place, Carlsbad CA 92011, USA | |
| **Kronwall, H Niklas** | Ice Hockey Player |
| 22235 Picadilly Circle, Novi MI 48375, USA | |
| **Kropf, Susan** | Businesswoman |
| Avon Products, 1251 Ave of Americas, #C2-63, New York NY 10020, USA | |
| **Kropfeld, Jim** | Boat Racing Driver |
| Hydroplanes Inc, 9117 Zoellner Dr, Cincinnati OH 45251, USA | |
| **Kropfelder, Nicholas** | Soccer Player |
| 13803 Lighthouse Ave, Ocean City MD 21842, USA | |
| **Kropp, Tom** | Basketball Player |
| 1811 W 41st St, Kearney NE 68845, USA | |
| **Kross, David** | Actor |
| Julian Belfrage Assoc, 9 Argyll St, #300, London W1F 7TG, England | |
| **Kross, Kayden** | Actress |
| Media Artists Group, 8222 Melrose Ave, #203, Los Angeles CA 90048 USA | |
| **Kroszner, Randall** | Government Official, Economist |
| Federal Reserve Board, 20th St & Constitution Ave NW, Washington DC 20551, USA | |
| **Krot, Alexander N** | Astrobiologist, Cosmochemist |
| University of Hawaii-Manoa, Geophysics Institute, 1680 East-West Road, #602, Honolulu HI 96822, USA | |
| **Kroto, Harold W** | Nobel Chemistry Laureate |
| Sussex University, Chemistry Dept, Falmer, Brighton BN1 9QJ, England | |
| **Krsnich, Rocco P (Rocky)** | Baseball Player |
| 5701 W 92nd St, Overland Park KS 66207, USA | |
| **KRS-One** | Rap Artist |
| Richard Walters, PO Box 2789, Toluca Lake CA 91610 USA | |
| **Krstic, Nenad** | Basketball Player |
| Boston Celtics, 226 Causeway St, #4, Boston MA 02114 USA | |
| **Kruczek, Michael (Mike)** | Football Player |
| 4028 Gilder Rose Place, Winter Park FL 32792, USA | |
| **Krueck, Ronald** | Architect |
| Krueck & Sexton Architects, 221 W Erie, Chicago IL 60654, USA | |
| **Krueger, Alan B** | Government Official, Economist |
| White House, 1600 Pennsylvania Ave NW, Washington DC 20500 USA | |
| **Krueger, Anne O** | Economist |
| Stanford University, Economics Dept, Stanford CA 94305, USA | |

Kristjansson - Krueger

| | |
|---|---|
| **Krueger, Charles A (Charlie)** | Football Player |
| 44 Regency Dr, Clayton CA 94517, USA | |
| **Krueger, James G** | Dermatologist |
| Rockefeller University Medical Center, 1230 York Ave, New York NY 10065 USA | |
| **Krueger, Ralph** | Ice Hockey Coach |
| Edmonton Oilers, 11230 110th St, Edmonton AB T5G 3H7, Canada | |
| **Krueger, Robert C (Bob)** | Senator, TX; Diplomat |
| PO Box 311717, New Braunfels TX 78131, USA | |
| **Krueger, Rolf F** | Football Player |
| 6502 Lake Circle, Wallis TX 77485, USA | |
| **Krueger, William C (Bill)** | Baseball Player |
| 30132 SE Redmond Fall City Road, Fall City WA 98024, USA | |
| **Kruger, Barbara** | Artist |
| Mary Boone Gallery, 745 5th Ave New York NY 10151, USA | |
| **Kruger, Diane** | Actress, Model |
| U B B A, 6 Rue de Braque, 75003 Paris, France | |
| **Kruger, Hardy** | Actor |
| Agence Elizabeth Simpson, 62 Blvd du Montparnasse, 75015 Paris, France | |
| **Kruger, Kelly** | Actress |
| Glick Agency, 1321 7th St, #203, Santa Monica CA 90401 USA | |
| **Kruger, Lon** | Basketball Coach |
| University of Oklahoma, Athletic Dept, Norman OK 73019, USA | |
| **Kruger, Mike** | Actor, Comedian, Singer |
| Management Tone Stallmeyer, Pleister-Muhlenweg 194, 48157 Munster, Germany | |
| **Krugman, Paul R** | Nobel Economics Laureate |
| 70 Lambert Dr, Princeton NJ 08540, USA | |
| **Kruk, John M** | Baseball Player, Sportscaster |
| PO Box 7847, Naples FL 34101, USA | |
| **Krukow, Michael E (Mike)** | Baseball Player |
| 6094 Madbury Court, San Luis Obispo CA 93401, USA | |
| **Krulak, Charles C** | Marine Corps General |
| 4801 Bonita Bay Blvd, Bonita Springs FL 34134, USA | |
| **Krulwich, Robert** | Commentator |
| CBS-TV, News Dept, 524 W 57th St, New York NY 10019, USA | |
| **Krumholtz, David** | Actor |
| Maydew & Golenberg, 8383 Wilshire Blvd, #1050, Beverly Hills CA 90211, USA | |
| **Krumrie, Timothy A (Tim)** | Football Player |
| 21215 Bucking Way, Oak Creek CO 80467, USA | |
| **Krupa, Joanna** | Model, Actress |
| Major Model Mgmt, 419 Park Ave, #1201, New York NY 10016, USA | |
| **Krupp, Uwe** | Ice Hockey Player |
| 3716 Strand, Manhattan Beach CA 90266, USA | |
| **Krushelnyski, Mike** | Ice Hockey Player |
| 7080 Holiday Dr, Bloomfield Hills MI 48301, USA | |
| **Kruspe, Richard Z** | Guitarist (Rammstein) |
| Pilgrim Mgmt, PO Box 540101, 10042 Berlin, Germany | |
| **Krylova, Angelika** | Ice Dancer |
| Skating Assn, Luchnesksaia Nab 8, 119871 Moscow, Russia | |
| **Krynzel, Dave** | Baseball Player |
| 951 Derringer Lane, Henderson NV 89014, USA | |
| **Krypreos, Nick** | Ice Hockey Player |
| 9209 Copenhaven Dr, Potomac MD 20854, USA | |
| **Krystkowiak, Larry B** | Basketball Player, Coach |
| 2343 S Dallin St, Salt Lake City UT 84109, USA | |
| **Krzyzewski, Michael W (Mike)** | Basketball Coach |
| 4406 W Cornwallis Road, Durham NC 27705, USA | |
| **K's Choice** | Rock Musical Group |
| Sharpe's Entertainment Services, 683 Palmera Ave, Pacific Palisades CA 90272, USA | |
| **Kuba, Filip** | Ice Hockey Player |
| 17216 Emerald Chase Dr, Tampa FL 33647, USA | |
| **Kuban, Bob** | Singer, Drummer |
| 17626 Lasiandra Dr, Chesterfield MO 63005, USA | |
| **Kubasov, Valeri N** | Cosmonaut |
| Cosmonaut Training Center, Star City, 141160 Zvezdny Gorodok, Moscow Oblast, Russia | |
| **Kubek, Anthony C (Tony)** | Baseball Player, Sportscaster |
| 121 E Water St, #120, Appleton WI 54911, USA | |
| **Kubel, Jason J** | Baseball Player |
| 21031 Ventura Blvd, #1000, Woodland Hills CA 91364, USA | |
| **Kube-McDowell, Michael P** | Writer |
| 4403 Cherry Hill Dr, Okemos MI 48864, USA | |
| **Kubenka, Jeffrey S (Jeff)** | Baseball Player |
| 6935 FM 957, Schulenburg TX 78956, USA | |
| **Kuberski, Robert K (Bob), Jr** | Football Player |
| 13 Forwood Dr, Garnet Valley PA 19060, USA | |
| **Kuberski, Stephen P (Steve)** | Basketball Player |
| 91 Lawson Road, Winchester MA 01890, USA | |
| **Kubiak, Gary** | Football Player, Coach |
| 14 Woods Edge Lane, Houston TX 77024, USA | |
| **Kubiak, Leo** | Basketball Player |
| 2638 N Prestwick Way, Lecanto FL 34461, USA | |
| **Kubiak, Teresa M** | Opera Singer |
| Indiana University, Jacobs Music School, Bloomington IN 47405, USA | |
| **Kubiak, Theodore R (Ted)** | Baseball Player |
| 11956 Bernando Plaza Dr, San Diego CA 92128, USA | |
| **Kubilius, Andrius** | Prime Minister, Lithuania |
| Prime Minister's Office, Tumo-Vaizganto 2, 01511 Vilnius, Lithuania | |
| **Kubina, Pavel** | Ice Hockey Player |
| 1145 81st St S, Saint Petersburg FL 33707, USA | |
| **Kubski, Gilbert T (Gil)** | Baseball Player |
| 4542 Scenario Dr, Huntington Beach CA 92649, USA | |
| **Kucek, John A C (Jack)** | Baseball Player |
| 8220 Blue Heron Lane, Canfield OH 44406, USA | |
| **Kucera, Frantisek** | Ice Hockey Player |
| Sportovni, Tupolevova Ul 669, 19900 Prague Letnany 9, Czech Republic | |
| **Kuchar, Matthew G (Matt)** | Golfer |
| 1909 Dixon Lann, Saint Simons Island GA 31522, USA | |

# K

**Kucinich, Dennis J** — Representative, OH; Mayor, Cleveland
14518 Drake Road, Strongsville OH 44136, USA

**Kuczenski, Bruce J** — Basketball Player
135 Southshire Dr, Southington CT 06489, USA

**Kuczynski Godard, Pedro-Pablo** — Prime Minister, Peru
Premier's Office, Urb Corpac, Calle 1 Oeste, San Isidro, Lima 27, Peru

**Kuczynski, Betty** — Bowler
4515 Prescott Ave, Lyons IL 60534, USA

**Kudelka, James A** — Ballet Choreographer, Dancer
National Ballet of Canada, 470 Queens Quay W, Toronto ON M5V 3K4, Canada

**Kudelski, Bob** — Ice Hockey Player
93 Copperleaf Dr, Cody WY 82414, USA

**Kuder, Mary** — Artist
Kuder Art Studio, 539 Navahopi Road, Sedona AZ 86336, USA

**Kudlow, Lawrence A** — Government Official, Economist
Kudlow Co, 301 Tahmore Dr, Fairfield CT 06825, USA

**Kudrna, Julius** — Canoeing Athlete
Sekaninova 36, 12000 Prague 2, Czech Republic

**Kudrow, Lisa** — Actress
Is or Isn't Entertainment, 8391 Beverly Blvd, #125, Los Angeles CA 90048, USA

**Kuebler, David** — Opera Singer
Haydn Rawstron, 36 Station Road, London SE20 7BQ, England

**Kuechenberg, Robert J (Bob)** — Football Player
2519 Arbor Dr, Fort Lauderdale FL 33312, USA

**Kuechenberg, Rudolph B (Rudy)** — Football Player
2928 SE 20th Ave, Cape Coral FL 33904, USA

**Kuechly, Luke A** — Football Player
Carolina Panthers, Ericsson Stadium, 800 S Mint St, Charlotte NC 28202 USA

**Kuehn, Enrico** — Bobsled Athlete
B S D, An der Schiessstatte 4, 83471 Berchtesgaden, Germany

**Kuehne, Hank** — Golfer
11117 Green Bayberry Dr, Palm Beach Gardens FL 33418, USA

**Kuehne, Kelli** — Golfer
245 Kings Peak Court, Heber City UT 84032, USA

**Kuerten, Gustavo** — Tennis Player
Octagon Worldwide, 1751 Pinnacle Dr, #1500, McLean VA 22102 USA

**Kuerti, Julian** — Conductor
I M G Artists, Hogarth Business Park, Chiswick, London W4 2TH, England

**Kuester, John D, Jr** — Basketball Player, Coach
105 Carnoustie Way, Media PA 19063, USA

**Kufeldt, James** — Businessman
Winn-Dixie Stores, 5050 Edgewood Court, Jacksonville FL 32254, USA

**Kufuor, John Agyekum** — President, Ghana
President's Office, Golden Jubilee House, PO Box 1627, Accra, Ghana

**Kugler, Pete D** — Football Player
33 Peach Court, Marco Island FL 34145, USA

**Kuhaulua, Jesse** — Sumo Wrestler
Azumazeki Stable, 4-6-4 Higashi Komagata, Ryogoku, Tokyo 130 0005, Japan

**Kuhl, Patrick** — Swimmer
Sudring 2, 76532 Baden-Baden, Germany

**Kuhlman, Arkadi** — Financier
I N G Direct, PO Box 80, Saint Cloud MN 56302, USA

**Kuhlman, Ron** — Actor
5738 Willis Ave, Van Nuys CA 91411, USA

**Kuhlmann, Kathleen M** — Opera Singer
International Management Group, 54 Ave Marceau, 75008 Paris, France

**Kuhlmann-Wilsdorf, Doris** — Physicist
University of Virginia, Materials Science Dept, Charlottesville VA 22901, USA

**Kuhn, David E** — Animator
Plum TV, 419 Lafayette St, #700, New York NY 10003, USA

**Kuhn, Gustav** — Conductor
Winkel 25, 6343 Ere, Austria

**Kuhn, Stephen L (Steve)** — Jazz Pianist, Composer
Berkeley Agency, 2608 9th St, #301, Berkeley CA 94710 USA

**Kuhne-Schiemann, Rita** — Track Athlete
Rosenweg 8, 14542 Werder/Havel, Germany

**Kuiper, Duane E** — Baseball Player
3665 Deer Trail Dr, Danville CA 94506, USA

**Kuipers, Andre** — Astronaut, Netherlands
European Space Centre, 8-10 Rue Mario Nikis, 75738 Paris Cedex, France

**Kuisma, Antti** — Nordic Combined Skier
Olympic Committee, Radiokatu 20, 00240 Helsinki, Finland

**Kukoc, Toni** — Basketball Player
1850 Hybernia Dr, Highland Park IL 60035, USA

**Kula, Irwin** — Religious Leader, Rabbi, Writer
Center for Learning & Leadership, 440 Park Ave S, #400, New York NY 10016, USA

**Kuleshov, Valery** — Concert Pianist
Musicians Corporate Mgmt, PO Box 825, Highland NY 12528, USA

**Kulich, Vladimir** — Actor
Jeff Goldberg Mgmt, 817 Monte Leon Dr, Beverly Hills CA 90210, USA

**Kulick, Kelly** — Bowler
Professional Bowlers Assn, 719 2nd Ave, #701, Seattle WA 98104 USA

**Kulik, Ilia A** — Figure Skater
Celebrity Consultants, 3340 Ocean Park Blvd, #1005, Santa Monica CA 90405 USA

**Kulka, Konstanty A** — Concert Violinist
Filharmonia Narodowa, Ul Jasna 5, 00007 Warsaw, Poland

**Kulkarni, Shrinivas R** — Astronomer
California Institute of Technology, Astronomy Dept, Pasadena CA 91125, USA

**Kullberg, Duane R** — Businessman
6444 N 79th St, Scottsdale AZ 85250, USA

**Kullman, Ellen** — Businesswoman
E I DuPont de Nemours, 1007 Market St, Wilmington DE 19895, USA

**Kulov, Feliks S** — Prime Minister, Kyrgyzstan
Prime Minister's Office, Ul Perromayskaya 57, 720003 Bishkek, Kyrgyzstan

**Kuma, Kengo** — Architect
Kengo Kuma Assoc, 2-12-12, Minamiaoyama, Minatoku, Tokyo 107 0062, Japan

**Kumagai, Saki** — Soccer Player
Football Assn, 3-10-15 Hongo, Bunkyoku, Tokyo 113 0033 Japan
**Kumanyika, Shiriki K** — Nutritionist
University of Illinois, Nutrition & Dietetics Dept, Chicago IL 60607, USA
**Kumar, Akshay** — Actor
Benzer Lokhandwala Complex Andheri (W), 203A Wing, Mumbai MS 400053, India
**Kumar, Dilip** — Actor
34/B Palli Hill, Nargis Dutt Road Bndra (W), Mumbai MS 400050, India
**Kumar, Manoj** — Actor, Director, Producer
Lakshmi Villa Grount, Tagore Road Santacruz (W), Mumbai MS 400050, India
**Kumbernuss, Astrid** — Track Athlete
Max Adrian Str 1, 17034 Neubrandenburg, Germany
**Kumble, Roger** — Director, Actor, Writer
United Talent Agency, U T A Plaza, 9336 Civic Center Dr, Beverly Hills CA 90210 USA
**Kume, John M** — Baseball Player
6810 Woodard Road, Andover OH 44003, USA
**Kumin, Maxine W** — Writer
30 W Joppa Road, Warner NH 03278, USA
**Kummer, Glenn F** — Businessman
Fleetwood Enterprises, 3125 Myers St, Riverside CA 92503, USA
**Kundera, Milan** — Writer
Gallimard, 5 Rue Sebastien-Bottin, 75007 Paris, France
**Kundla, John A** — Basketball Coach
909 Main St NE, #208, Minneapolis MN 55413, USA
**Kunerth, Mark J** — Writer, Producer
Broder Webb Chervin Silbermann, 9242 Beverly Blvd, Beverly Hills CA 90210 USA
**Kunes, Ellen** — Editor
Oprah Magazine, Editor's Office, 224 W 57th St, #900, New York NY 10019, USA
**Kung, Candie** — Golfer
Ladies Pro Golf Assn, 100 International Golf Dr, Daytona Beach FL 32124 USA
**Kung, Hans** — Theologian
Waldhauserstr 23, 72076 Tubingen, Germany
**Kung, Patrick C** — Pharmacologist
T Cell Sciences, 119 4th Ave, Needham MA 02494, USA
**Kunin, Madeline M** — Governor, VT
60 Southwind Dr, Burlington VT 05401, USA
**Kunis, Mila** — Actress
Creative Artists Agency, 2000 Ave of Stars, #100, Los Angeles CA 90067 USA
**Kunitz, Matt** — Producer
Endemol Entertainment, 9255 W Sunset Blvd, #1100, Los Angeles CA 90069, USA
**Kunkel, Jeffrey W (Jeff)** — Baseball Player
4921 County Road 605, Burleson TX 76028, USA
**Kunkel, Louis M** — Pediatrician
Children's Hospital, 300 Longwood Ave, Boston MA 02115, USA
**Kunkle, John F** — Religious Leader
Evangelical Methodist Church, 3000 W Kellogg Dr, Wichita KS 67213, USA
**Kunnert, Kevin R** — Basketball Player
8286 SW Wilderland Court, Portland OR 97224, USA
**Kunstler, Morton** — Artist, Illustrator
137 Cove Neck Road, Oyster Bay NY 11771, USA
**Kuntz, Russell J (Rusty)** — Baseball Player
10102 W 152nd Terrace, Overland Park KS 66221, USA
**Kunz, George J** — Football Player
8215 S Bermuda Road, Las Vegas NV 89123, USA
**Kunze, Terry D** — Basketball Player
6931 Halifax Ave N, Minneapolis MN 55429, USA
**Kunzru, Hari** — Writer
E P Dutton, 375 Hudson St, New York NY 10014 USA
**Kupchak, Mitchell (Mitch)** — Basketball Player
361 Fordyce Road, Los Angeles CA 90049, USA
**Kupcinet, Kari** — Actress
1660 Mill Trail, Highland Park IL 60035, USA
**Kupec, Charles J** — Basketball Player
6448 River Run, Columbia MD 21044, USA
**Kupets, Courtney** — Gymnast
133 Falling Shoals Dr, Athens GA 30605, USA
**Kupfer, Abraham (Avi)** — Immunologist
Johns Hopkins University Medical School, Immunobiology Dept, 733 N Broadway, Baltimore MD 21205, USA
**Kupfer, Carl** — Ophthalmologist
National Institutes of Health, 10 Center Dr, Bethesda MD 20892, USA
**Kupfer, Harry** — Director
Komische Oper, Behrenstr 55-57, 10117 Berlin, Germany
**Kupferberg, Sabine** — Ballerina
Dans Theater 3, Scheldoldoekshaven 60, 2511 Gravenhage EN, Netherlands
**Kupp, Jacob R (Jake)** — Football Player
4801 Snowmountain Road, Yakima WA 98908, USA
**Kupperman, Joel J** — Philosopher
115 E 9th St, #15E, New York NY 10003, USA
**Kurant, Willy** — Cinematographer
Lyons Sheldon Agency, 800 S Robertson Blvd, #6, Los Angeles CA 90035, USA
**Kuras, Ellen M** — Cinematographer
54 Summit St, Nyack NY 10960, USA
**Kureishi, Hanif** — Writer
Rogers Coleridge White, 20 Powis Mews, London W11 1JN, England
**Kurek, Ralph E** — Football Player
1311 Lime Pond Road, South Royalton VT 05068, USA
**Kurita, Toyomichi** — Cinematographer
Sandra Marsh Assoc, 9150 Wilshire Blvd, #220, Beverly Hills CA 90212 USA
**Kurkova Emmons, Katerina** — Markswoman
US Olympic Committee, 1 Olympic Plaza, Building 6, Colorado Springs CO 80909 USA
**Kurkova, Karolina I** — Model, Actress
Storm Model Agency, 5 Jubilee Place, Chelsea, London SW3 3TD, England
**Kurlander, Tom** — Actor
Independent Artists Agency, 9601 Wilshire Blvd, #750, Beverly Hills CA 90210, USA
**Kuroda, Emily** — Actress
Stone Manners Salners, 9911 W Pico Blvd, #1400, Los Angeles CA 90035 USA

# K

**Kuroda, Hiroki** — Baseball Player
New York Yankees, Yankee Stadium, E 161st St & River Ave, Bronx NY 10451 USA
**Kurosaki, Ryan Y** — Baseball Player
3324 Huelani Dr, Honolulu HI 96822, USA
**Kurrat, Klaus-Dieter** — Track Athlete
Am Hochwald 30, 28460, 14532 Kleinmachnow, Germany
**Kurri, Jari P** — Ice Hockey Player
Hockey Hall of Fame, B C E Place, 30 Yonge St, Toronto ON M5E 1X8, Canada
**Kursinski, Anne** — Equestrian
107 Spring Hill Road, Frenchtown NJ 08825, USA
**Kurstin, Gregory A (Greg)** — Keyboardist (Bird & the Bee)
Blue Note Records, 6920 W Sunset Blvd, Los Angeles CA 90028 USA
**Kurtag, Gyorgy** — Composer
Lihego V3, 2621 Veroce, Hungary
**Kurtenbach, Orland J** — Ice Hockey Player
14066 29A Ave, Surrey BC V4P 2J8, Canada
**Kurth, Wallace (Wally)** — Actor, Singer
C E S D, 10635 Santa Monica Blvd, #130, Los Angeles CA 90025 USA
**Kurtha, Akbar** — Actor
United Agents, 12-26 Lexington St, London W1F 0LE, England
**Kurtis, Bill** — Commentator
Kurtis Productions, 400 W Erie St, #500, Chicago IL 60654, USA
**Kurtis, Darlene** — Model, Actress
Playboy Promotions, 2706 Media Center Dr, Los Angeles CA 90065 USA
**Kurtova, Karolina** — Model
D N A Model Mgmt, 555 W 25th St, #600, New York NY 10001 USA
**Kurtz, Harold J (Hal)** — Baseball Player
511 Flat Iron Square Road, Church Hill MD 21623, USA
**Kurtz, Swoosie** — Actress, Singer
Innovative Artists, 1505 10th St, Santa Monica CA 90401 USA
**Kurtze, Andrew** — Businessman
Sprint P C S Group, 6391 Sprint Parkway, Overland Park KS 66251, USA
**Kurtzig, Sandra L** — Businesswoman
E-Benefits, 2420 Sand Hill Road, #201, Menlo Park CA 94025, USA
**Kurtzman, Alex** — Writer, Producer
Kurtzman Orci Paper Products, 100 Universal Plaza, Building 5171, Universal City CA 91608, USA
**Kurupt** — Rap Artist, Songwriter, Actor
Likwit Entertainment, PO Box 360713, Los Angeles CA 90036, USA
**Kurvers, Tom** — Ice Hockey Player
10146 Birch Grove Road, Brainerd MN 56401, USA
**Kurylenko, Olga** — Actress, Model
Tavistock Wood Mgmt, 45 Conduit St, London W1S 2YN, England
**Kurzak, Aleksandra** — Opera Singer
I M G Artists, Hogarth Business Park, Chiswick, London W4 2TH, England
**Kurzel, Justin** — Director
H L A Management, PO Box 1536, Strawberry Hills, NSW 2012, Australia , USA
**Kurzweil, Raymond** — Inventor (Computer-Generated Voice)
Capel & Land, 29 Wardour St, London W1D 6PS, England
**Kusama, Karyn** — Director
I C M Partners, 10250 Constellation Blvd, #900, Los Angeles CA 90067 USA
**Kusama, Yayoi** — Artist
Gagosian Gallery, 980 Madison Ave, New York NY 10075 USA
**Kusatsu, Clyde** — Actor
Stone Manners Salners, 9911 W Pico Blvd, #1400, Los Angeles CA 90035 USA
**Kuschak, Metropolitan Andrei** — Religious Leader
Ukranian Orthodox Church in America, 3 Davenport Ave, New Rochelle NY 10805, USA
**Kush, Rod R** — Football Player
45 Willow Point Dr, Ashland NE 68003, USA
**Kushboo** — Actress
20/1 Arch Bishop, Mathiyas Ave, Boat Club Road, Chennai TN 600028, India
**Kushell, Lisa** — Actress
Abrams Artists, 9200 W Sunset Blvd, #1125, West Hollywood CA 90069 USA
**Kushner, Harold S** — Religious Leader, Rabbi, Writer
Temple Israel, 145 Hartford St, Natick MA 01760, USA
**Kushner, Robert E** — Artist
D C Moore Gallery, 724 5th Ave, #800, New York NY 10019, USA
**Kushner, Tony** — Writer
Steve Barclay Agency, 12 Western Ave, Petaluma CA 94952, USA
**Kuske, Kevin** — Bobsled Athlete
K-Solution, Lindstedter Str 13B, 14469 Potsdam, Germany
**Kusnyer, Arthur W (Art)** — Baseball Player
6598 Taeda Dr, Sarasota FL 34241, USA
**Kustra, Robert W** — Educator
Boise State University, President's Office, Boise ID 83725, USA
**Kusturica, Emir** — Director, Writer, Actor
Fondazione Cultural Edison, Largo VIII Marzo 9, 43100 Parma, Italy
**Kutcher, Ashton** — Actor
Katalyst Films, 6806 Lexington Ave, Los Angeles CA 90038, USA
**Kutcher, Randy S** — Baseball Player
3016 Purple Sage Lane, Palmdale CA 93550, USA
**Kuttner, Stephan G** — Historian
2270 Le Conte Ave, #601, Berkeley CA 94709, USA
**Kutyna, Donald J** — Air Force General, Businessman
4818 Kenyon Court, Colorado Springs CO 80917, USA
**Kutyna, Marion J (Marty)** — Baseball Player
2255 NW 14th St, Delray Beach FL 33445, USA
**Kutzler, Jerry S** — Baseball Player
9500 81st St, #311, Pleasant Prairie WI 53158, USA
**Kuusela, Armi H** — Beauty Queen
6241 Waverly Ave, La Jolla CA 92037, USA
**Kuykendall, Fulton G** — Football Player
1497 Rucker Circle, Woodstock GA 30188, USA
**Kuzava, Robert L (Bob)** — Baseball Player
1118 Vinewood St, Wyandotte MI 48192, USA
**Kuziel, Robert C (Bob)** — Football Player
3375 Walnut Dr, Ellicott City MD 21043, USA

| | |
|---|---|
| **Kuzmina, Anastasiya V** | Biathlete |
| Biathlon Assn, Partizánska Cesta 71, 974 01 Banska Bystrica, Slovakia | |
| **Kuznetsoff, Alexei** | Concert Pianist |
| Columbia Artists Mgmt Inc, 1790 Broadway, #702, New York NY 10019 USA | |
| **Kuznetsova, Svetlana A** | Tennis Player |
| Women's Tennis Assn, 1 Progress Plaza, #1500, Saint Petersburg FL 33701 USA | |
| **Kuznetsoya, Dina** | Opera Singer |
| Harrison/Parrott, 5-6 Albion Court, London W6 0QT, England | |
| **Kuzyk, Mimi** | Actress |
| Characters Talent Mgmt, 8 Elm St, Toronto ON M5G 1G7, Canada | |
| **Kvapil, Radoslav** | Concert Pianist |
| Hradecka 5, 13000 Prague 3, Czech Republic | |
| **Kvapil, Travis** | Auto, Truck Racing Driver |
| 141 Silverleaf Lane, Mooresville NC 28115, USA | |
| **Kvasha, Oleg V** | Ice Hockey Player |
| 22 Bluff Road, Glen Cove NY 11542, USA | |
| **Kvitova, Petra** | Tennis Player |
| T K Agrofert Prostejev, Za Kestleckou 51, 79640 Prostejov, Czech Republic | |
| **Kwak Yoon-Gy** | Speed Skater |
| Skating Union, 88 Bangyee-Dong, Songpaku, Seoul 138 749, South Korea | |
| **Kwalick, Thaddeus J (Ted)** | Football Player |
| 755 Purdue Court, Santa Clara CA 95051, USA | |
| **Kwan, Jennie** | Actress |
| Innovative Artists, 1505 10th St, Santa Monica CA 90401 USA | |
| **Kwan, Michelle W** | Figure Skater |
| Tufts University, Fletcher Law & Diplomacy School, Medford MA 02155, USA | |
| **Kwan, Nancy** | Actress |
| Marlin, 252 7th Ave, #9P, New York NY 10001, USA | |
| **Kwanten, Ryan** | Actor |
| Orly Adelson Productions, 2900 Olympic Blvd, Los Angeles CA 90404, USA | |
| **Kwapis, Ken** | Director, Producer, Actor |
| United Talent Agency, U T A Plaza, 9336 Civic Center Dr, Beverly Hills CA 90210 USA | |
| **Kwasniewski, Aleksander** | President, Poland |
| Kancelaria Prezydenta RP, Ul Wiejska 4/8, 00 902 Warsaw, Poland | |
| **Kweli, Talib** | Rap Artist (Black Star), Songwriter |
| Creative Artists Agency, 2000 Ave of Stars, #100, Los Angeles CA 90067 USA | |
| **Kweller, Ben** | Singer, Songwriter |
| Big Hassle, 44 Wall St, #2200, New York NY 10005, USA | |
| **Kwiatkowski, Joel** | Ice Hockey Player |
| 2020 Tall Pines Dr SE, Grand Rapids MI 49546, USA | |
| **Kwoh, Yik San** | Electrical Engineer, Inventor |
| Hi-Tech Medical Systems, 17155 Newhope St, Fountain Valley CA 92708, USA | |
| **Kwolek, Stephanie L** | Inventor (Kevlar) |
| 312 Spalding Road, Wilmington DE 19803, USA | |
| **Kwouk, Burt** | Actor |
| QVoice, Holborn Hall, 193-197 High Holborn, London WC1V 7BD, England | |
| **Kyd, Gerald** | Actor |
| Ken McReddie Assoc, 101 Finsbury Pavement, London EC2A 1RS, England | |
| **Kydland, Finn E** | Nobel Economics Laureate |
| 169 Noble Lane, Worthington PA 16262, USA | |
| **Kyle, Aaron D** | Football Player |
| 14420 Ballantyne Lake Road, #313, Charlotte NC 28277, USA | |
| **Kyle, David L** | Businessman |
| O N E O K Inc, 100 W 5th St, PO Box 871, Tulsa OK 74102, USA | |
| **Kyle, Jason C** | Football Player |
| 19109 W Catawba Ave, #200, Cornelius NC 28031, USA | |
| **Kyle, Kaylyn** | Soccer Player |
| Canadian Soccer, Place Soccer Canada, 237 Metcalfe St, Ottawa ON K2P 1R2, Canada | |
| **Kylian, Jiri** | Ballet Dancer |
| Netherlands Dance Theater, Schedeldoekshaven 60, 2501 The Haag CH, Netherlands | |
| **Kynaston, Nicholas** | Concert Organist |
| 25 High Park Road, Richmond-upon-Thames, Surrey TW9 4BH, England | |
| **Kyo, Machiko** | Actress |
| Olimpia Copu, 6-35 Jingumae, Shibuyaku, Tokyo 151 0001, Japan | |
| **Kyrillos, Jean-Paul** | Publisher |
| Food & Wine, Publisher's Office, 1120 Ave of Americas, New York NY 10036, USA | |
| **Kyson Lee, James** | Actor |
| Prestige Talent Agency, 9250 Wilshire Blvd, #208, Beverly Hills CA 90212 90212, USA | |
| **Kyte, Jim** | Ice Hockey Player |
| 226 Sherwood Dr, Ottawa ON K1Y 3V8, Canada | |

# L

| | |
|---|---|
| **Laage, Gerhart**<br>Schulterblatt 36, 20357 Hamburg, Germany | Architect |
| **Laaksonen, Antti**<br>9225 Red Oak Dr, Victoria MN 55386, USA | Ice Hockey Player |
| **Laarayedh, Ali**<br>Prime Minister's Office, Place du Gouvernement, Tunis, Tunisia | Prime Minister, Tunisia |
| **Laaveg, Paul M**<br>PO Box 406, Berryville VA 22611, USA | Football Player |
| **LaBar, Jeffrey P (Jeff)**<br>Union Entertainment Group, 1323 Newbury Road, #104, Thousand Oaks CA 91320, USA | Singer, Guitarist (Cinderella) |
| **Labarthe, Samuel**<br>Cineart, 28 Rue Mogador, 78009 Paris, France | Actor |
| **LaBelle, Patti**<br>Resolution, 1801 Century Park East, #2300, Los Angeles CA 90067 USA | Singer |
| **Labelle, Rob**<br>Foundation Features, 88 E Pender St, #515, Vancouver BC V6A 3X3, Canada | Actor, Producer, Director |
| **LaBeouf, Shia S**<br>John Crosby Mgmt, 1310 N Spaulding Ave, Los Angeles CA 90046 USA | Actor |
| **Labeque, Katia**<br>Askonas Holt, Lincoln House, 300 High Holborn, London WC1V 7JH, England | Concert Pianist |
| **Labeque, Marielle**<br>Askonas Holt, Lincoln House, 300 High Holborn, London WC1V 7JH, England | Concert Pianist |
| **Labine, Tyler**<br>Creative Artists Agency, 2000 Ave of Stars, #100, Los Angeles CA 90067 USA | Actor |
| **Labis, Attilo**<br>13 Ave Rubens, 78400 Chateau, France | Ballet Dancer, Choreographer |
| **Labonte, Justin**<br>PO Box 843, Trinity NC 27370, USA | Auto Racing Driver |
| **Labonte, Robert A (Bobby)**<br>Bobby Labonte Racing, PO Box 358, Trinity NC 27370, USA | Auto Racing Driver |
| **Labonte, Terrance L (Terry)**<br>PO Box 370, Trinity NC 27370, USA | Auto, Truck Racing Driver |
| **Laborde, Alden J**<br>63 Oriole St, New Orleans LA 70124, USA | Businessman |
| **Labounty, Matthew J (Matt)**<br>360 W 17th Ave, Eugene OR 97401, USA | Football Player |
| **LaBour, Fred (Too Slim)**<br>New Frontier Mgmt, 1921 Broadway, Nashville TN 37203, USA | Singer, Bassist (Riders in the Sky) |
| **Labourier, Dominique**<br>Agence Elisabeth Simpson, 62 Blvd du Montparnasse, 75015 Paris, France | Actress |
| **LaBoy, Travis J**<br>6207 Radcliffe Dr, San Diego CA 92122, USA | Football Player |
| **Labre, Yvon**<br>7812 Tilmont Ave, Parkville MD 21234, USA | Ice Hockey Player |
| **LaBute, Neil**<br>Contemptible Entertainment, 1202 Poinsettia Drive, West Hollywood CA 90046, USA | Director, Writer |
| **Labyorteaux, Matthew**<br>167 W 72nd St, #3R, New York NY 10023, USA | Actor |
| **Labyorteaux, Patrick**<br>C E S D, 10635 Santa Monica Blvd, #130, Los Angeles CA 90025 USA | Actor |
| **Lace, Jerry E**<br>10214 Pine Glade Dr, Colorado Springs CO 80920, USA | Figure Skating Executive |
| **Lacey, Deborah**<br>A K A Talent, 6310 San Vicente Blvd, #200, Los Angeles CA 90048 USA | Actress |
| **Lacey, Jesse T**<br>Stunt Company Media, 20 Jay St, #208, Brooklyn NY 11201, USA | Singer (Taking Back Sunday, Brand New) |
| **Lacey, Robert J (Bob)**<br>1717 20th St NW, #308, Washington DC 20009, USA | Baseball Player |
| **Lach, Elmer J**<br>89 Bayview Ave, Pointe Claire QC H9S 5C4, Canada | Ice Hockey Player |
| **Lachance, Michel (Mike)**<br>183 Sweetmans Lane, Millstone Township NJ 08535, USA | Harness Racing Driver |
| **LaChance, Scott**<br>15 Meadow View Lane, Andover MA 01810, USA | Ice Hockey Player |
| **LaChapelle, David**<br>Creative Exchange Agency, 45 W 25th St, #1900, New York NY 10001, USA | Photographer |
| **Lachemann, Marcel E**<br>PO Box 1967, Nipomo CA 93444, USA | Baseball Player, Manager |
| **Lachemann, Rene G**<br>7500 E Boulders Parkway, #68, Scottsdale AZ 85266, USA | Baseball Player, Manager |
| **Lacher, Blaine**<br>29 Shannon Crescent SE, Medicine Hat AB T1B 4C2, Canada | Ice Hockey Player |
| **Lachey, Andrew J (Drew)**<br>Core Entertainment, 14742 Ventura Blvd, #PH, Sherman Oaks CA 91403, USA | Singer (98 Degrees), Actor |
| **Lachey, James M (Jim)**<br>1445 Roxbury Road, Columbus OH 43212, USA | Football Player |
| **Lachey, Nicholas S (Nick)**<br>I C M Partners, 10250 Constellation Blvd, #900, Los Angeles CA 90067 USA | Singer (98 Degrees) |
| **LaChiusa, Michael John**<br>Abrams Artists, 9200 W Sunset Blvd, #1125, West Hollywood CA 90069 USA | Composer, Librettist |
| **Lachman, Dichen**<br>Gersh Agency, 9465 Wilshire Blvd, #600, Beverly Hills CA 90212 USA | Actress |
| **Lachman, Gary Valentine**<br>Tarcher/Penguin Books, 375 Hudson St, Basement 1, New York NY 10014, USA | Writer, Musician |
| **Lacina, Corbin**<br>1550 Skyline Court, Saint Paul MN 55121, USA | Football Player |
| **Lack, Andrew**<br>Sony/BMG Music Entertainment, 550 Madison Ave, #600, New York NY 10022, USA | Businessman |
| **Lackberg, Camilla**<br>Nordin Agency, Gotgatan 58, 102 61 Stockholm, Sweden | Writer |
| **Lacke, Elizabeth (Beth)**<br>Aria Model & Talent Mgmt, 1017 W Washington, #2C, Chicago IL 60607, USA | Actress |
| **Lacker, Jeffrey**<br>Federal Reserve Board, 701 E Byrd St, #200, Richmond VA 23219, USA | Financier, Government Official |
| **Lackey, Elizabeth (Lisa)**<br>Marquee Mgmt, Gate House, 188 Oxford St, Paddington NSW 2021, Australia | Actress |

**Laage - Lackey**

**Lackey, John D** — Baseball Player
15176 NW 100th Avenue Road, Reddick FL 32686, USA
**Laclavere, Georges** — Geophysicist
53 Ave de Breteuil, 70075 Paris, France
**Laclotte, Michel R** — Museum Executive
10 Bis Rue du Pre-aux-Clerc, 75007 Paris, France
**Lacock, R Pierre (Pete)** — Baseball Player
10019 Mackey Circle, Overland Park KS 66212, USA
**Lacombe, Francois** — Ice Hockey Player
Webster Hockey Academy, 22 Hampton Gardens, Point Claire QC H9S 5B8, Canada
**Lacombe, Henri** — Oceanographer
20 Bis Ave de Lattre de Tassigny, 92340 Bourg la Reine, France
**Lacorte, Frank J** — Baseball Player
1667 El Dorado Dr, Gilroy CA 95020, USA
**Lacoste, Catherine** — Golfer
Calle B6, #4, El Soto de la Moraleja Alcobendas, Madrid, Spain
**Lacroix, Andre J** — Ice Hockey Player
115 S Franklin St, Chagrin Falls OH 44022, USA
**Lacroix, Christian M M** — Fashion Designer
73 Rue du Faubourg Saint Honore, 75008 Paris, France
**Lacroix, Eric** — Ice Hockey Player
10463 Meadowleaf Way, Highlands Ranch CO 80126, USA
**Lacy, Alan** — Businessman
Sears Roebuck Co, 3333 Beverly Blvd, Hoffman Estates IL 60179, USA
**Lacy, Edgar E** — Basketball Player
215 6th St, #D, West Sacramento CA 95605, USA
**Lacy, Jake** — Actor
Creative Artists Agency, 2000 Ave of Stars, #100, Los Angeles CA 90067 USA
**Lacy, Jeffrey S (Jeff)** — Boxer
5718 Eaglemount Dr, Lithia FL 33547, USA
**Lacy, Jerry** — Actor
Sutton-Barth Vennari, 5900 Wilshire Blvd, #700, Los Angeles CA 90036 USA
**Lacy, Leondaus (Lee)** — Baseball Player
6130 Nevada Ave, #E420, Woodland Hills CA 91367, USA
**Ladd, Alan W, Jr** — Producer
706 N Arden Dr, Beverly Hills CA 90210, USA
**Ladd, Andrew** — Ice Hockey Player
550 N Saint Clair St, #2403, Chicago IL 60611, USA
**Ladd, Cheryl** — Actress
Don Buchwald, 6500 Wilshire Blvd, #2200, Los Angeles CA 90048 USA
**Ladd, David** — Actor, Producer
David Ladd Films, 9465 Wilshire Blvd, Beverly Hills CA 90212, USA
**Ladd, Diane** — Actress
Scott Hart Mgmt, 14622 Ventura Blvd, #746, Sherman Oaks CA 91403, USA
**Ladd, Peter L (Pete)** — Baseball Player
239 Town Farm Road, New Gloucester ME 04260, USA
**Laderman, Ezra** — Composer
Yale University, Music School, New Haven CT 06520, USA
**Ladin, Eric** — Actor
Innovative Artists, 1505 10th St, Santa Monica CA 90401 USA
**Ladner, Benjamin** — Educator
American University, President's Office, Washington DC 20016, USA
**Ladouceur, Randy** — Ice Hockey Player
8700 Brittdale Lane, #203, Raleigh NC 27617, USA
**Lady Gaga** — Singer, Songwriter
135 W 70th St, #1A, New York NY 10023, USA
**Lady Sovereign** — Rap Artist
Paradigm Agency, 360 N Crescent Dr, North Building, Beverly Hills CA 90210 USA
**Laemmle, Carla** — Actress
645 N Serrano Blvd, Los Angeles CA 90004, USA
**Laettner, Christian D** — Basketball Player
1041 Ponte Vedra Blvd, Ponte Vedra Beach FL 32082, USA
**Lafayette, John** — Actor
Greene Assoc, 1901 Ave of Stars, #130, Los Angeles CA 90067 USA
**Lafayette, Nathan** — Ice Hockey Player
Travel Guard Canada, 145 Welligton St W, Toronto ON M5J 1H8, Canada
**Laffer, Arthur B** — Economist
24255 Pacific Coast Highway, Malibu CA 90263, USA
**Lafferty, James** — Actor, Director, Producer
United Talent Agency, U T A Plaza, 9336 Civic Center Dr, Beverly Hills CA 90210 USA
**Lafferty, Stuart** — Actor
Paceline Entertainment, 12444 Ventura Blvd, #103, Studio City CA 91604 USA
**Lafforgue, Laurent** — Mathematician
I H E S, Mathematics Dept, 91440 Bures sur Yvette, France
**LaFlamme, David** — Violinist (It's a Beautiful Day)
Tabletop Productions, PO Box 698, Carson City NV 89702, USA
**Lafleur, Gregory L (Greg)** — Football Player
PO Box 612, Baton Rouge LA 70821, USA
**Lafleur, Guy D** — Ice Hockey Player
14 Place du Moulin, L'Ile Bizard QC H9E 1N2, Canada
**Lafley, Alan G** — Businessman
Procter & Gamble Co, 1 Procter & Gamble Plaza, Cincinnati OH 45202, USA
**Laflin, Bonnie-Jill** — Model, Entertainer
C E S D, 10635 Santa Monica Blvd, #130, Los Angeles CA 90025 USA
**LaFontaine, Patrick (Pat)** — Ice Hockey Player
3 Beach Dr, Lloyd Harbor NY 11743, USA
**Laforet, Marie** — Actress
Agents Associes, 201 Rue du Faubourg Saint Honore, 75008 Paris, France
**Lafrance, Noemie** — Choreographer
148 Classon Ave, Brooklyn NY 11205, USA
**Lafreniere, Roger** — Ice Hockey Player
110 Eugene Road, North Bay ON P1B 8B7, Canada
**LaFrentz, Raef A** — Basketball Player
PO Box 88, Decorah IA 52101, USA
**Laga, Michael R (Mike)** — Baseball Player
148 Maple Ridge Road, Florence MA 01062, USA

## L

**Lagarde, Christine** — Financier
International Monetary Fund, 700 19th Ave NW, Washington DC 20431, USA

**LaGarde, Thomas J (Tom)** — Basketball Player
3809 E Greensboro Chapel Hill Road, Snow Camp NC 27349, USA

**Lagardere, Arnaud** — Businessman
Airbus Industrie, Ronde Point Maucie Bellont 1, 31707 Blagnac, France

**Lagasse, Emeril** — Chef, Restauranteur
829 Saint Charles Ave, New Orleans LA 70130, USA

**Lagat, Bernard** — Track Athlete
9121 E Cottonwood Court, Tucson AZ 85749, USA

**Lagattuta, Bill** — Commentator
CBS-TV, News Dept, 7800 Beverly Blvd, Los Angeles CA 90036, USA

**Lageman, Jeffrey D (Jeff)** — Football Player
PO Box 364, Basye VA 22810, USA

**Lagerberg, Bengt F A** — Drummer (Cardigans)
Talent Tust, Kungsgaten 9C, 411 19 Gothenburg, Sweden

**Lagerfeld, Karl** — Fashion Designer, Photographer
31 Blvd de la Maubourg, 75007 Paris, France

**Lago, Clara** — Actress
Kuranda Mgmt, Santo Angel 84, 28043 Madrid, Spain

**Lagoo, Shreeram** — Actor
3 Gold Mist, 36 Carter Road, Bandra, Mumbai MS 400050, India

**Lagos Escobar, Ricardo** — President, Chile
Club de Madrid, C/Goya 5-7, Pasaje 2, 28001 Madrid, Spain

**LaGravenese, Richard** — Director, Writer
Creative Artists Agency, 2000 Ave of Stars, #100, Los Angeles CA 90067 USA

**LaGrossa, Stephanie** — Actress
42 Caldwell Dr, Toms River NJ 08757, USA

**Lagrow, Lerrin H** — Baseball Player
12271 E Turquoise Ave, Scottsdale AZ 85259, USA

**Laguna, Frederica de** — Anthropologist
10 S Bryn Mawr Ave, Bryn Mawr PA 19010, USA

**LaHaie, Dick** — Drag Racing Driver
Kalitta Motorsports, 1010 James L Hart Parkway, Ypsilanti MI 48197, USA

**LaHaye, Tim** — Writer
Tyndale House Publishers, 351 Executive Dr, PO Box 80, Wheaton IL 60187, USA

**Lahbib, Simone** — Actress, Producer
Ken McReddie Assoc, 101 Finsbury Pavement, London EC2A 1RS, England

**Lahiri, Jhumpa** — Writer
Knopf Publishers, 1745 Broadway, New York NY 10019 USA

**Lahm, Philipp** — Soccer Player
Rinab Grill, Rathausstr 39, 83734 Hausham, Germany

**LaHood, Ray** — Secretary, Transporation
Transportation Department, 400 7th St SW, Washington DC 20590 USA

**Lahoud, Joseph M (Joe)** — Baseball Player
90 Tinker Hill Road, New Preston Marble Dale CT 06777, USA

**Lahti, Christine** — Actress, Director
Management 360, 9111 Wilshire Blvd, Beverly Hills CA 90210 USA

**Lahti, Christine** — Actress, Director
126 Wadsworth Ave, Santa Monica CA 90405, USA

**Lahti, Jeffrey A (Jeff)** — Baseball Player
4632 Tyler Dr, Hood River OR 97031, USA

**Lai, Francis** — Composer
23 Rue Franklin, 75016 Paris, France

**Laidlaw, R Scott** — Football Player
2286 Franklin Pike, Lewisburg TN 37091, USA

**Laidlaw, Tom** — Ice Hockey Player
Laidlaw Sports Mgmt, 32 Ridge Blvd, Port Chester NY 10573, USA

**Laimbeer, William (Bill)** — Basketball Player
470 Gray Court, Marco Island FL 34145, USA

**Laine, Cleo** — Singer
Old Rectory, Wavendon, Milton Keynes MK17 8LT, England

**Laine, Denny** — Singer, Guitarist (Moody Blues)
I C M Partners, 10250 Constellation Blvd, #900, Los Angeles CA 90067 USA

**Laing, Richard** — Actor
Ken McReddie Assoc, 101 Finsbury Pavement, London EC2A 1RS, England

**Laingen, L Bruce** — Diplomat
9707 Old Georgetown Road, #2112, Bethesda MD 20814, USA

**Lair, Michael J** — Actor
Hyco Kid, 87 Oyster Cove Landing, Hartfield VA 23071, USA

**Laird, Bruce A** — Football Player
1405 Margarette Ave, Towson MD 21286, USA

**Laird, Gerald L, III** — Baseball Player
13735 E Yucca St, Scottsdale AZ 85259, USA

**Laird, Martin** — Golfer
Professional Golfer's Assn, PO Box 109601, Palm Beach Gardens FL 33410 USA

**Laird, Melvin R** — Secretary, Defense; Businessman
1730 Rhode Island Ave NW, #406, Washington DC 20036, USA

**Laird, Peter** — Cartoonist (Ninja Turtles)
PO Box 417, Haydenville MA 01039, USA

**Laird, Ronald (Ron)** — Track Athlete
4706 Diane Dr, Ashtabula OH 44004, USA

**Laitman, Jeffrey** — Anatomist
Mount Sinai Medical Center, Anatomy Dept, 1 Levy Place, New York NY 10029, USA

**Lajoie, Jonathan** — Actor, Writer
United Talent Agency, U T A Plaza, 9336 Civic Center Dr, Beverly Hills CA 90210 USA

**LaJoie, Randall (Randy)** — Auto Racing Driver
PO Box 3478, Westport CT 06880, USA

**Lajolo, Giovanni Cardinal** — Religious Leader
Pontifical Commission for Vatican City State, 00120 Vatican City

**Lake, Carnell A** — Football Player
PO Box 55048, Irvine CA 92619, USA

**Lake, Don** — Actor, Writer
Divine Mgmt, 3822 Latrobe Ave, Los Angeles CA 90031, USA

**Lake, Gregory (Greg)** — Singer, Bassist (Emerson Lake Palmer)
Bruce Pilato Mgmt, PO Box 17775, Rochester NY 14617, USA

| | |
|---|---|
| **Lake, James A**<br>University of California, Molecular Biology Institute, Los Angeles CA 90024, USA | Molecular Biologist |
| **Lake, Oliver E**<br>D L Media, 124 N Highland Ave, Bala Cynwyd PA 19004, USA | Jazz Saxophonist, Synthesizer Player |
| **Lake, Ricki**<br>W M E Entertainment, 9601 Wilshire Blvd, #300, Beverly Hills CA 90210 USA | Actress |
| **Lake, Stephen M (Steve)**<br>7402 N 177th Ave, Waddel AZ 85355, USA | Baseball Player |
| **Laker, Jim**<br>Oak End, 9 Portinscale Road, Putney, London SW15, England | Cricketer |
| **Laker, Timothy J (Tim)**<br>673 Azure Hills Dr, Simi Valley CA 93065, USA | Baseball Player |
| **Lakes, Gary**<br>I C M Artists, 40 W 57th St, #1800, New York NY 10019 USA | Opera Singer |
| **Lake-Tack, Louise A**<br>Governor General's Office, Government House, Saint John's, Antigua & Barbuda | Governor General, Antigua & Barbuda |
| **Lakin, Christine**<br>Don Buchwald, 6500 Wilshire Blvd, #2200, Los Angeles CA 90048 USA | Actress |
| **Lakner, Yehoshua**<br>Postfach 7851, 6000 Lucerne 7, Switzerland | Composer |
| **Lakshmi, Padma**<br>B/W/R, 9100 Wilshire Blvd, #500W, Beverly Hills CA 90212 USA | Actress, Model, Writer |
| **Lal, Devendra**<br>4445 Via Precipicio, San Diego CA 92122, USA | Oceanographer |
| **Lala, Joe**<br>I C M Partners, 10250 Constellation Blvd, #900, Los Angeles CA 90067 USA | Singer, Percussionist (Blues Image) |
| **LaLande, Hector (Hec)**<br>848 McIntyre St E, North Bay ON P1B 1G1, Canada | Ice Hockey Player |
| **Lalas, Alexi**<br>1007 Maybrook Dr, Beverly Hills CA 90210, USA | Soccer Player, Executive, Sportscaster |
| **Laliberte, Guy**<br>Cirque du Soleil, 8400 2nd Ave, Montreal QC H1Z 4M6, Canada | Businessman, Circus Executive, Astronaut |
| **LaLiberte, Nicole**<br>Click Model Mgmt, 881 7th Ave, New York NY 10019 USA | Model |
| **Laliberte-Bourque, Andree**<br>Musee du Quebec, 1 Ave Wolfe-Montcalm, Quebec QC G1R 5H3, Canada | Museum Executive |
| **Lalime, Patrick**<br>70 Rive du Golf, Grand Mere QC G9T 5K4, Canada | Ice Hockey Player |
| **Lalla Salma**<br>Palais Royal, Le Mechouar, Rabat, Morocco | Princess Consort, Morocco |
| **Lalonde, R Lawrence (Larry)**<br>Creative Artists Agency, 2000 Ave of Stars, #100, Los Angeles CA 90067 USA | Guitarist (Primus) |
| **Lalonde, Robert P (Bobby)**<br>523 Broadgreen St, Pickering ON L1W 3E8, Canada | Ice Hockey Player |
| **Lam, Derek**<br>Jeffrey Lam Co, 446 W 13th St, New York NY 10014, USA | Fashion Designer |
| **Lam, Mei-Ling**<br>Playboy Promotions, 2706 Media Center Dr, Los Angeles CA 90065 USA | Model |
| **Lam, Sal Kit**<br>Malaysia University, Microbiolgy Dept, 50603 Kuala Lumpur, Malaysia | Virologist |
| **Lamar, Dwight (Bo)**<br>103 Claire St, Lafayette LA 70507, USA | Basketball Player |
| **LaMarr, Phil**<br>Talent Works, 3500 W Olive Ave, #1400, Burbank CA 91505 USA | Actor, Comedian |
| **Lamas, Lorenzo**<br>Mavrick Artists Agency, 6100 Wilshire Blvd, #550, Los Angeles CA 90048, USA | Actor |
| **Lamb, Allan J**<br>Lamb Assoc, 4 Saint Giles St, #400, Northampton NN1 1JB, England | Cricketer |
| **Lamb, Brian P**<br>C-Span Network, 400 N Capitol St NW, #650, Washington DC 20001, USA | Businessman |
| **Lamb, Dennis**<br>19 Rue de Franqueville, 75016 Paris, France | Diplomat |
| **Lamb, Jeremy**<br>Oklahoma City Thunder, 211 N Robinson Ave, #300, Oklahoma City OK 73102 USA | Basketball Player |
| **Lamb, Larry**<br>MacFarlane Chard Assoc, 33 Percy St, London W1T 2DF, England | Actor |
| **Lamb, Michael**<br>Bobby Roberts, 3050 Business Park Circle, #303, Goodlettsville TN 37221 USA | Guitarist (Confederate Railroad) |
| **Lamb, Michael R (Mike)**<br>17 Meadow Wood Dr, Trabuco Canyon CA 92679, USA | Baseball Player |
| **Lamberg, Adam M**<br>Innovative Artists, 1505 10th St, Santa Monica CA 90401 USA | Actor |
| **Lambert, Adam M**<br>19 Music & Mgmt, 35-37 Parkgate Road, London SW11 4NP, England | Singer, Songwriter |
| **Lambert, Chloe**<br>Artmedia, 20 Ave Rapp, 75007 Paris, France | Actress |
| **Lambert, Christopher**<br>A P A Talent/Literary Agency, 405 S Beverly Dr, #300, Beverly Hills CA 90212 USA | Actor |
| **Lambert, John E**<br>884 Dolphin Dr, Danville CA 94526, USA | Basketball Player |
| **Lambert, John H (Jack)**<br>PO Box 512, Worthington PA 16262, USA | Football Player |
| **Lambert, Lane**<br>258 E Washington St, Jefferson WI 53549, USA | Ice Hockey Player, Coach |
| **Lambert, Mary M**<br>Don Buchwald, 6500 Wilshire Blvd, #2200, Los Angeles CA 90048 USA | Director |
| **Lambert, Miranda**<br>W M E Entertainment, 1600 Division St, #300, Nashville TN 37203 USA | Singer, Guitarist, Songwriter |
| **Lambert, Nathalie**<br>Speed Skating Canada, 2781 Lancaster Road, #402, Ottawa ON K1B 1A7, Canada | Speed Skater |
| **Lambert, Phyllis**<br>Centre d'Architecture, 1920 Rue Baile, Montreal QC H3H 2S6, Canada | Architect |
| **Lambiel, Stephane**<br>Route de Praz Berard 3A, 1844 Villeneuve, Switzerland | Figure Skater |
| **Lambo, T Adeoye**<br>Lambo Foundation, 11 Olatunsbosun St, Ikeja, Lagos State, Nigeria | Psychiatrist |

**Lambrecht, Dietrich R** — Electrical Engineer
Rathenaustr 11, 45470 Mulheim an der Ruhr, Germany
**Lambrecht, Yves** — Actor
Artmedia, 20 Ave Rapp, 75007 Paris, France
**Lambro, Phillip** — Composer, Pianist
Trigram Music, 1888 Century Park East, #10, Los Angeles CA 90067, USA
**Lamm, Norman** — Educator, Religious Leader, Rabbi
Eicharen Theological Seminary, 2540 Amsterdam Ave, New York NY 10033, USA
**Lamm, Richard D** — Governor, CO
University of Denver, Public Policy Center, Denver CO 80208, USA
**Lamm, Robert W** — Singer, Keyboardist (Chicago)
Front Line Mgmt, 1100 Glendon Ave, #2000, Los Angeles CA 90024 USA
**Lamm, Tonya** — Singer (Tres Chicas)
Conqueroo, 11271 Ventura Blvd, #522, Studio City CA 91604 USA
**Lammers, Esmee** — Director, Writer
Features Creative Mgmt, Entrepotdok 76A, 101 AD Amsterdam, Netherlands
**Lamonica, Daryle P** — Football Player
All Star Warehouse, 2860 S East Ave, Fresno CA 93725, USA
**Lamont, Gene W** — Baseball Player, Manager
5194 Siesta Woods Dr, Sarasota FL 34242, USA
**Lamont, Norman S H** — Government Official, England
Balli Group PLC, 5 Stanhope Gate, London W1Y 5LA, England
**Lamontagne, Ray** — Singer, Songwriter
Mick Mgmt, 35 Washington St, Brooklyn NY 11201 USA
**Lamoriello, Louis (Lou)** — Ice Hockey Executive, Coach
New Jersey Devils, Arena, 50 State Route 120, East Rutherford NJ 07073 USA
**Lamott, Anne** — Writer
Wylie Agency, 250 W 57th St, #2114, New York NY 10107 USA
**LaMotta, Jake** — Boxer
3598 Yacht Club Dr, #503, Miami FL 33180, USA
**Lamp, Dennis P** — Baseball Player
30824 La Miranda, #228, Rancho Santa Margarita CA 92688, USA
**Lamp, Jeffrey A (Jeff)** — Basketball Player
4971 Credit River Dr, Savage MN 55378, USA
**Lampanelli, Lisa** — Actress, Comedienne
Parallel Artists Mgmt, 9420 Wilshire Blvd, #250, Beverly Hills CA 90212, USA
**Lampard, C Keith** — Baseball Player
6124 Highway 6 N, Houston TX 77084, USA
**Lamparski, Richard** — Writer
4202 Calle Real, #245, Santa Barbara CA 93110, USA
**Lampert, Edward S (Eddie)** — Businessman
E S L Investments, 1170 Kane Concourse, #200, Bay Harbour FL 33154, USA
**Lampert, Zohra** — Actress
Don Buchwald, 6500 Wilshire Blvd, #2200, Los Angeles CA 90048 USA
**Lampkin, Thomas M (Tom)** — Baseball Player
3810 SE 153rd Court, Vancouver WA 98683, USA
**Lampley, James (Jim)** — Sportscaster
3325 Caminito Daniella, Del Mar CA 92014, USA
**Lamprey, Zane** — Actor, Comedian
W M E Entertainment, 9601 Wilshire Blvd, #300, Beverly Hills CA 90210 USA
**Lampson, Butler W** — Computer Engineer
Microsoft Corp, 1 Microsoft Way, Redmond WA 98052, USA
**Lampton, Michael** — Astronaut
University of California, Space Science Laboratory, Berkeley CA 94720, USA
**Lamsma, Simone** — Concert Violinist
I M G Artists, Hogarth Business Park, Chiswick, London W4 2TH, England
**Lamy, Pascal L F** — Government Official, France
World Trade Organization, Rue Lausanne 154, 1211 Geneva 21, Switzerland
**LaNasa, Katherine** — Actress
Anderson Group Public Relations, 8060 Melrose Ave, #400, Los Angeles CA 90046, USA
**Lancaster, Lester W (Les)** — Baseball Player
PO Box 1105, Dothan AL 36302, USA
**Lancaster, Mark** — Artist
Cunningham Dance Foundation, 55 Bethune St, New York NY 10014, USA
**Lancaster, Neal** — Golfer
6 Quail Run, Smithfield NC 27577, USA
**Lance, Dirk** — Bassist (Incubus)
Variety Artists, 1924 Spring St, Paso Robles CA 93446 USA
**Lancelotti, Richard A (Rick)** — Baseball Player
5190 Thompson Road, Clarence NY 14031, USA
**Landau, Juliet** — Actress
Miss Juliet Productions, PO Box 2792, Los Angeles CA 90078, USA
**Landau, Martin** — Actor
PO Box 10959, Beverly Hills CA 90213, USA
**Landau, Russ** — Composer
Evolution Music Partners, 1680 Vine St, #500, Los Angeles CA 90028 USA
**Landau, Tina** — Director
I C M Partners, 10250 Constellation Blvd, #900, Los Angeles CA 90067 USA
**Lander, David L** — Actor
918 S Tremaine Ave, Los Angeles CA 90019, USA
**Lander, Eric S** — Mathematician, Biologist
Broad Institute, 9 Cambridge Circle, Cambridge MA 02142, USA
**Landers, Andy** — Basketball Coach
University of Georgia, Athletic Dept, Athens GA 30602, USA
**Landers, Audrey** — Actress, Singer
Landers Productions, 4048 Las Palmas Dr, Sarasota FL 34238, USA
**Landers, Judy** — Actress
Landers Productions, 4048 Las Palmas Dr, Sarasota FL 34238, USA
**Landers, Larry** — Golfer
PO Box 497, Azle TX 76098, USA
**Landers, Paul H** — Guitarist (Rammstein)
Pilgrim Mgmt, PO Box 540101, 10042 Berlin, Germany
**Landes, Michael** — Actor
Creative Artists Agency, 2000 Ave of Stars, #100, Los Angeles CA 90067 USA
**Landeskog, Gabriel I J** — Ice Hockey Player
Colorado Avalanche, Pepsi Center, 1000 Chopper Circle, Denver CO 80204 USA

Lambrecht - Landeskog

**Landestoy, Rafael** — Baseball Player
PO Box 940755, Miami FL 33194, USA
**Landeta, Sean E** — Football Player
137 Powerhouse Road, #7W, Roslyn Heights NY 11577, USA
**Landis, Floyd** — Cyclist
4632 Felton St, #2, San Diego CA 92116, USA
**Landis, James H (Jim)** — Baseball Player
203 Alchemy Way, Napa CA 94558, USA
**Landis, John D** — Director
Resolution, 1801 Century Park East, #2300, Los Angeles CA 90067 USA
**Landis, William H (Bill)** — Baseball Player
525 E Sycamore Dr, Hanford CA 93230, USA
**Lando, Joe** — Actor
Jay D Schwartz & Assoc, 6767 Forest Lawn Dr, #211, Los Angeles CA 90068, USA
**Landon, Michael, Jr** — Director
Believe Pictures, 2 Saint Elias, Dove Canyon CA 92679, USA
**Landreaux, Kenneth F (Ken)** — Baseball Player
1510 N Siesta Ave, La Puente CA 91746, USA
**Landress, Ilene S** — Producer
Creative Artists Agency, 2000 Ave of Stars, #100, Los Angeles CA 90067 USA
**Landrieu, Moon** — Secretary, Housing & Urban Development
4301 S Prieur St, New Orleans LA 70125, USA
**Landrum, Terry L (Tito)** — Baseball Player
428 E 50th St, Garden, New York NY 10022, USA
**Landry, Carl C** — Basketball Player
Sacramento Kings, Arco Arena, 1 Sports Parkway, Sacramento CA 95834 USA
**Landry, Dawan F** — Football Player
309 Kennedy St, Ama LA 70031, USA
**Landry, Gregory P (Greg)** — Football Player, Coach
133 Melanie Lane, Troy MI 48098, USA
**Landry, Karen** — Actress
Don Buchwald, 6500 Wilshire Blvd, #2200, Los Angeles CA 90048 USA
**Landry, LaRon L** — Football Player
New York Jets, 1 Jets Dr, Florham Park NJ 07932 USA
**Landsberger, Mark W** — Basketball Player
1702 8th Ave SE, Saint Cloud MN 56304, USA
**Landsbergis, Vytautas** — President, Lithuania
European Parliament, Bat Altiero Spinelli, Wiertzstraat 60, 1047 Brussels, Belgium
**Landsburg, Valerie** — Actress
PO Box 1617, Topanga CA 90290, USA
**Landshamer, Christina** — Opera Singer
Kunstler Sekretariat am Gasteig, Rosenheimer Str 52, 81669 Munich, Germany
**Landsman, Mark** — Producer, Director
Hirsch Wallerstein Hayum, 10100 Santa Monica Blvd, #1700, Los Angeles CA 90067 USA
**Landy, Bernard** — Government Official, Canada
Gouvement du Quebec, 885 Grand Allee Est, Quebec QC GLA 1A2, Canada
**Lane, Abbe** — Singer, Actress
500 Bel Air Road, Los Angeles CA 90077, USA
**Lane, Akira** — Model
PO Box 8052, Laguna Hills CA 92654, USA
**Lane, Cristy** — Singer
L S Records, PO Box 654, Madison TN 37116, USA
**Lane, David P** — Oncologist
Dundee Medical Center, Molecular Research Dept, Dundee DD1 9SY, Scotland
**Lane, Diane** — Actress
W M E Entertainment, 9601 Wilshire Blvd, #300, Beverly Hills CA 90210 USA
**Lane, Gord** — Ice Hockey Player
8 Magnolia Dr, Brandon MB R7A 0Y9, Canada
**Lane, John R (Jack)** — Museum Executive
San Francisco Museum of Modern Art, 151 3rd St, San Francisco CA 94103, USA
**Lane, Kenneth Jay** — Fashion Designer
Kenneth Jay Lane Inc, 20 W 37th St, #900, New York NY 10018, USA
**Lane, Lilas** — Actress
Talent Works, 3500 W Olive Ave, #1400, Burbank CA 91505 USA
**Lane, MacArthur** — Football Player
3238 Knowland Ave, Oakland CA 94619, USA
**Lane, Malcolm D** — Biological Chemist
717 Maiden Choice Lane, #525, Catonsville MD 21228, USA
**Lane, Marvin (Marv)** — Baseball Player
40164 Gulliver Dr, Sterling Heights MI 48310, USA
**Lane, Matthew** — Golfer
Links Mgmt, 5068 W Plano Parkway, #256, Plano TX 75093, USA
**Lane, Max A** — Football Player
16 Strong St, Newburyport MA 1950, USA
**Lane, Mike** — Editorial Cartoonist
Baltimore Sun, Editorial Dept, 501 N Calvert St, Baltimore MD 21278, USA
**Lane, Nathan** — Actor, Singer
I C M Partners, 10250 Constellation Blvd, #900, Los Angeles CA 90067 USA
**Lane, Richard H (Dick)** — Baseball Player
2717 Legend Dr, Las Vegas NV 89134, USA
**Lane, Robert W** — Businessman
Deere Co, 1 John Deere Place, Moline IL 61265, USA
**Lane, Robin** — Dancer, Choreographer
Do Jump Co, Echo Theater, 1515 SE 37th Ave, Portland OR 97214, USA
**Lanegan, Mark** — Singer, Guitarist (Queens of Stone Age)
Steve Stewart Mgmt, 10 Universal City Plaza, 2000, Universal City CA 91608, USA
**Laneuville, Eric** — Actor, Director
5138 W Slauson Ave, Los Angeles CA 90056, USA
**Laney, James T** — Educator, Diplomat
2015 Grand Prix Dr NE, Atlanta GA 30345, USA
**Laney, Sandra E** — Businesswoman
201 E 5th St, #1800, Cincinnati OH 45202, USA
**Lang Lang** — Concert Pianist
Bedlam Mgmt, PO Box 34449, London W6 0RT, England
**Lang, Andrew C** — Basketball Player
1048 Woodruff Plantation Parkway SE, Marietta GA 30067, USA

# L

**Lang, Antonio M** — Basketball Player
2255 Barretts Lane, Mobile AL 36617, USA
**Lang, Belinda** — Actress
Rabbit Vocal Mgmt, 94 Strand on the Green, London W4 3NN, England
**Lang, Brittany** — Golfer
Gaylord Sports Mgmt, 13845 N Northsight Blvd, #200, Scottsdale AZ 85260 USA
**Lang, David** — Composer
Red Poppy Music, 66 Greene St, #500, New York NY 10012, USA
**Lang, Gene E** — Football Player
11526 Azalea Trace, Gulfport MS 39503, USA
**Lang, Helmut** — Fashion Designer
Michele Morgan, 184 Rue Saint-Maur, 75010 Paris, France
**Lang, Jack M E** — Government Official, France
Mairie, 41000 Blois, France
**Lang, Jonny** — Singer, Guitarist
A B C Public Relations, 4570 Van Nuys Blvd, #320, Sherman Oaks CA 91403, USA
**lang, k d** — Singer, Actress
Paradigm Agency, 360 N Crescent Dr, North Building, Beverly Hills CA 90210 USA
**Lang, Katherine Kelly** — Actress, Model
Edmonds Entertainment Group, 1635 N Cahuenga Blvd, Los Angeles CA 90028, USA
**Lang, Kenard D** — Football Player
1781 Oakbrook Dr, Longwood FL 32779, USA
**Lang, Michelle** — Actress
Paceline Entertainment, 12444 Ventura Blvd, #103, Studio City CA 91604 USA
**Lang, Perry** — Actor
A P A Talent/Literary Agency, 405 S Beverly Dr, #300, Beverly Hills CA 90212 USA
**Lang, Robert** — Ice Hockey Player
PO Box 633, Diablo CA 94528, USA
**Lang, Stephen** — Actor, Director, Writer
Innovative Artists, 1505 10th St, Santa Monica CA 90401 USA
**Langan, Kevin** — Opera Singer
Columbia Artists Mgmt Inc, 1790 Broadway, #702, New York NY 10019 USA
**Langbein, John H** — Attorney, Educator
Yale University, Law School, 127 Wall St, New Haven CT 06511, USA
**Langbo, Arnold G** — Businessman
Kellogg Co, 1 Kellogg Square, PO Box 3599, Battle Creek MI 49016, USA
**Langdon, Darren** — Ice Hockey Player
1 Oake's Road, Deer Lake NF A8K 1X5, Canada
**Langdon, Harry** — Photographer
501 Center St, #6, El Segundo CA 90245, USA
**Lange, Andre** — Bobsled Athlete
Team Andre Lange, Robert-Schumann-Str 14B, 98529 Suhl, Germany
**Lange, Artie** — Actor, Comedian
3 Arts Entertainment, 9460 Wilshire Blvd, #700, Beverly Hills CA 90212 USA
**Lange, Eric** — Actor
Domain Talent, 9229 W Sunset Blvd, #710, West Hollywood CA 90069 USA
**Lange, Jessica** — Actress
Untitled Entertainment, 350 S Beverly Dr, #200, Beverly Hills CA 90212 USA
**Lange, Niklaus** — Actor
A P A Talent/Literary Agency, 405 S Beverly Dr, #300, Beverly Hills CA 90212 USA
**Lange, Otto L** — Botanist
Leitengraben 37, 97084 Wuerzburg, Germany
**Lange, Richard O (Dick)** — Baseball Player
39744 Salvatore Dr, Sterling Heights MI 48313, USA
**Lange, Ted** — Actor
House of Representatives, 1434 6th St, #1, Santa Monica CA 90401 USA
**Lange, Thomas** — Rowing Athlete
Ratzeburger Ruderclub, Domhof 57, 23909 Ratzburg, Germany
**Langella, Frank** — Actor
I C M Partners, 10250 Constellation Blvd, #900, Los Angeles CA 90067 USA
**Langen, Christoph** — Bobsled Athlete
B C Unterhaching, Ottobrunner Str 16, 82008 Unterhaching, Germany
**Langenbrunner, Jaime** — Ice Hockey Player
94096 Warloe Shore Lane, Moose Lake MN 55767, USA
**Langer, A J** — Actress
Valeo Entertainment, 8265 Sunset Blvd, #103, Los Angeles CA 90046, USA
**Langer, Alois A** — Inventor (Implantable Defibrillator)
111 Saddlebrook Dr, Harrison City PA 15636, USA
**Langer, Bernhard** — Golfer
3667 Princeton Place, Boca Raton FL 33496, USA
**Langer, James J (Jim)** — Football Player
14280 Wolfram St NW, Anoka MN 55303, USA
**Langer, James S** — Physicist
1130 Las Canoas Lane, Santa Barbara CA 93105, USA
**Langer, Robert S, Jr** — Inventor (Controlled Drug Delivery)
Massachusetts Institute of Technolgy, Langer Laboratory, Cambridge MA 02139, USA
**Langerhans, Ryan D** — Baseball Player
PO Box 1026, Round Rock TX 78680, USA
**Langevin, David (Dave)** — Ice Hockey Player
1090 W Circle Court, Saint Paul MN 55118, USA
**Langfield, Camille** — Actress
PO Box 254, Carmel by the Sea CA 93921, USA
**Langford, J Rick** — Baseball Player
8330 9th Avenue Terrace NW, Bradenton FL 34209, USA
**Langham, C Antonio** — Football Player
PO Box 232, Town Creek AL 35672, USA
**Langham, Franklin** — Golfer
PO Box 3428, Peachtree City GA 30269, USA
**Langham, Wallace** — Actor
Imperium 7 Talent, 5455 Wilshire Blvd, #1706, Los Angeles CA 90036, USA
**Langhorne, Reginald D (Reggie)** — Football Player
12260 Smiths Neck Road, Carrollton VA 23314, USA
**Langkow, Daymond R** — Ice Hockey Player
11549 E Cochise Dr, Scottsdale AZ 85259, USA
**Langlands, Robert P** — Mathematician
60 Battle Road, Princeton NJ 08540, USA

**Lang - Langlands**

**Lang-Lessing, Sebastian** — Conductor
I M G Artists, Hogarth Business Park, Chiswick, London W4 2TH, England
**Langlois, Albert, Jr** — Ice Hockey Player
2473 Crest View Dr, Los Angeles CA 90046, USA
**Langlois, Paul** — Guitarist (Tragically Hip)
Bobby Breen Mgmt, 13 Blackburn St, #300, Toronto ON M4M 2B3, Canada
**Langmaid, Ben** — Singer, Songwriter (La Roux)
Beatnik Public Relations, 5 Little Portland St, London W1W 7JD, England
**Langmann, Thomas** — Producer, Actor
La Petite Reine, 20 Rue de Saint-Petersbourg, 75008 Paris, France
**Langridge, Matthew** — Rowing Athlete
Leander Club, Henley on Thames, Leander RG9 2LP, England
**Langston, J William** — Neurologist
Parkinson's Foundation, 2444 Moorpark Ave, San Jose CA 95128, USA
**Langston, Mark E** — Baseball Player
56 Golden Eagle, Irvine CA 92603, USA
**Langston, Murray** — Actor, Comedian
Entertainment Alliance, PO Box 4734, Santa Rosa CA 95402, USA
**Langton, Brooke** — Actress
Gersh Agency, 9465 Wilshire Blvd, #600, Beverly Hills CA 90212 USA
**Langway, Rod C** — Ice Hockey Player
8260 Powhickery Dr, Mechanicsville VA 23116, USA
**Lanier, Cathy L** — Law Enforcement Official
Metropolitan Police Dept, 300 Indiana Ave NW, Washington DC 20001, USA
**Lanier, Harold C (Hal)** — Baseball Player, Manager
3270 Countryside View Dr, Saint Cloud FL 34772, USA
**Lanier, Jaron Z** — Computer Engineer (Virtual Reality)
University of Southern California, Annenberg Center, Los Angeles CA 90089, USA
**Lanier, Kenneth W (Ken)** — Football Player
21923 E Ridge Trail Circle, Aurora CO 80016, USA
**Lanier, Robert J (Bob), Jr** — Basketball Player, Coach
13027 E Saddlehorn Trail, Scottsdale AZ 85259, USA
**Lanier, Willie E** — Football Player
2911 E Brigstock Road, Midlothian VA 23113, USA
**Lanig, Hans-Peter** — Alpine Skier
Omachstr 11, 87541 Hindelang, Germany
**Lankford, Frank G** — Baseball Player
104 Lakeview Ave NE, Atlanta GA 30305, USA
**Lankford, Kim** — Actress
House of Representatives, 1434 6th St, #1, Santa Monica CA 90401 USA
**Lankford, Paul J** — Football Player
3838 Biggin Church Road W, Jacksonville FL 32224, USA
**Lankford, Raymond L (Ray)** — Baseball Player
1520 Lake Whitney Dr, Windermere FL 34786, USA
**Lanners, Bouli** — Actor
Voyez Mon Agent, 20 Ave Rapp, 75007 Paris, France
**Lanois, Daniel** — Singer, Musician, Songwriter
Monterey Peninsula Artists, 404 W Franklin St, Monterey CA 93940 USA
**Lanoue, Virginie** — Actress
Artmedia, 20 Ave Rapp, 75007 Paris, France
**Lansbury, Angela** — Actress, Singer
Mavrick Artists Agency, 6100 Wilshire Blvd, #550, Los Angeles CA 90048, USA
**Lansbury, David** — Actor
Don Buchwald, 6500 Wilshire Blvd, #2200, Los Angeles CA 90048 USA
**Lansdale, Joe R** — Writer
199 County Road 508, Nacogdoches TX 75961, USA
**Lansford, Alex J (Buck)** — Football Player
PO Box 905, Lampasas TX 76550, USA
**Lansford, Carney R** — Baseball Player
43736 Pocahontas Road, Baker City OR 97814, USA
**Lansford, Michael J (Mike)** — Football Player
6200 E Canyon Rim Road, #205, Grants Pass OR 97526, USA
**Lansing, Michael T (Mike)** — Baseball Player
9691 S Sun Meadow St, Littleton CO 80129, USA
**Lansing, P J** — Model
Playboy Promotions, 2706 Media Center Dr, Los Angeles CA 90065 USA
**Lansing, Sherry L** — Producer
10741 Levico Way, Los Angeles CA 90077, USA
**Lanter, Matt** — Actor
Emerald Talent Group, 15260 Ventura Blvd, #1200, Sherman Oaks CA 91403
**Lantz, Stuart B (Stu)** — Basketball Player
5270 Mount Burnham Dr, San Diego CA 92111, USA
**Lanvin, Bernard** — Fashion Designer
22 Rue du Faubourg Saint Honore, 70008 Paris, France
**Lanvin, Gerard** — Actor, Writer
Voyez Mon Agent, 20 Ave Rapp, 75007 Paris, France
**Lanz, Rick** — Ice Hockey Player
18962 20th Ave, Surrey BC V3S 9V2, Canada
**Lanza, Manuel** — Opera Singer
I C M Artists, 40 W 57th St, #1800, New York NY 10019 USA
**Lanza, Suzanne** — Model, Actress
Greater Visions Artists Talent Agency, 8981 W Sunset Blvd, #101, West Hollywood CA 90069 USA
**Laoretti, Larry** — Golfer
10567 SW Whooping Crane Way, Palm City FL 34990, USA
**LaPaglia, Anthony** — Actor
400 N Bristol Ave, Los Angeles CA 90049, USA
**LaPaglia, Jonathan** — Actor
Untitled Entertainment, 350 S Beverly Dr, #200, Beverly Hills CA 90212 USA
**Laperriere, Ian** — Ice Hockey Player
415 Washington Ave, Haddonfield NJ 8033, USA
**Laperriere, J Jacques H** — Ice Hockey Player
1490 Rue Bergeron, Quebec QC G3E 1G5, Canada
**Lapham, David A (Dave)** — Football Player
8254 Sunfish Lane, Maineville OH 45039, USA
**Lapham, Lewis H** — Editor
Harper's, Editorial Dept, 666 Broadway, New York NY 10012, USA

# L

**LaPier, Darcy L** — Actress, Model
Double R Mgmt, 5424 Crebs Ave, Tarzana CA 91356, USA
**Lapierre, Dominique** — Historian
Les Bignoles, 83350 Ramatuelle, France
**LaPierre, Wayne** — Association Executive
National Rifle Assn, 11250 Waples Mill Road, Fairfax VA 22030, USA
**Lapine, James E** — Writer, Director
85 Mill River Road, South Salem NY 10590, USA
**Lapira, Liza** — Actress
Paradigm Agency, 360 N Crescent Dr, North Building, Beverly Hills CA 90210 USA
**LaPlanche, Rosemary** — Actress, Beauty Queen
13914 Hartsook St, Sherman Oaks CA 91423, USA
**LaPlant, Rob** — Producer
Lighthearted Entertainment, 4111 W Alameda Ave, #409, Burbank CA 91505, USA
**LaPlante, Lynda** — Writer, Actress
LaPlante Productions, 162-170 Wardour St, London W1V 3AT, England
**Lapoint, David J (Dave)** — Baseball Player
11704 Stonewood Gate Dr, Riverview FL 33579, USA
**Lapointe, Guy G** — Ice Hockey Player
Minnesota Wild, XCel Energy Arena, 1275 Saint Antoine W, Saint Paul MN 55104 USA
**LaPorte, Danny** — Motorcycle Racing Rider
18033 S Santa Fe Ave, Compton CA 90221, USA
**LaPorte, Juan** — Boxer, Trainer
77 Front St, Brooklyn NY 11201, USA
**Laposata, Joseph S** — Army General
Battle Monuments Commission, 20 Massachusetts, Washington DC 20314, USA
**Lapotaire, Jane** — Actress
92 Oxford Gardens, #C, London W10, England
**Lappalainen, Markku** — Bassist (Hoobastank)
Island Def Jam Records, 8920 W Sunset Blvd, #200, West Hollywood CA 90069 USA
**Lappas, Steve** — Basketball Coach
Villanova University, Athletic Dept, Villanova PA 19085, USA
**Laprade, Edgar** — Ice Hockey Player
12 Shuniah St, Thunder Bay ON P7A 2Y8, Canada
**LaPraed, Ronald (Ron)** — Bassist, Trumpeter (Commodores)
Management Assoc, 1920 Benson Ave, Saint Paul MN 55116, USA
**Laqueur, Walter** — Historian
Journal of Contemporary History, 4 Devonshire St, London W1N 2BH, England
**Lara, Alexandra Maria** — Actress
Players Agentur Mgmt, Sophienstra 21, 10178 Berlin-Mitte, Germany
**Lara, Brian C** — Cricketer
West Indies Cricket Club, PO Box 616, Saint John's, Antigua
**Lara, Joanne** — Actress
Abraxas Talent, 4260 Troost Ave, #1, Studio City CA 91604, USA
**Laragh, John H** — Physician
435 E 70th St, New York NY 10021, USA
**Lardner, George, Jr** — Journalist
Washington Post, Editorial Dept, 1150 15th St NW, Washington DC 20071, USA
**Lardo, Vincent** — Writer
G P Putnam's Sons, 375 Hudson St, New York NY 10014 USA
**Laresca, Vincent** — Actor
Talent Works, 3500 W Olive Ave, #1400, Burbank CA 91505 USA
**Larese, York B** — Basketball Player, Coach
22 Grove Place, #15, Winchester MA 01890, USA
**Largent, Steve M** — Football Player; Representative, OK
3835 N Randolph Court, Arlington VA 22207, USA
**Larholm, Jonas** — Handball Player
Aalborg Handbold, Willy Brandts Vej 31, 9220 Aalborg Ost, Denmark
**Larionov, Igor N** — Ice Hockey Player
2363 Tilbury Place, Bloomfield Hills MI 48301, USA
**Lariviere, Richard W** — Museum Executive, Educator
Field Museum of Natural History, 1400 S Lake Shore Dr, Chicago IL 60605, USA
**Lark, Maria** — Actress
Coast to Coast Talent, 3350 Barham Blvd, Los Angeles CA 90068 USA
**Larkin, Barry L** — Baseball Player
5410 Osprey Isle Lane, Orlando FL 32819, USA
**Larkin, Christopher (Chris)** — Actor
Ken McReddie Assoc, 101 Finsbury Pavement, London EC2A 1RS, England
**Larkin, DeShane (Shane)** — Basketball Player
Dallas Mavericks, Pavilion, 2909 Taylor St, Dallas TX 75226 USA
**Larkin, Eugene T (Gene)** — Baseball Player
9496 Abbott Court, Eden Prairie MN 55347, USA
**Larmer, Steve** — Ice Hockey Player
1664 Poplar Point Road, RR 4, Peterborough ON K9J 6X5, Canada
**Larmore, Jennifer** — Opera Singer
I M G Artists, Carnegie Hall Tower, 152 W 57th St, #500, New York NY 10019 USA
**Laro, David** — Judge
US Tax Court, 400 2nd St NW, Washington DC 20217, USA
**LaRoche, Andrews C (Andy)** — Baseball Player
842 195th St, Fort Scott KS 66701, USA
**LaRoche, David E (Dave)** — Baseball Player
815 W 18th St, Fort Scott KS 66701, USA
**LaRocque, Gene R** — Government Official, Navy Admiral
5015 Macomb St NW, Washington DC 20016, USA
**Laroque, Michele** — Actress
Agents Associes, 201 Faubourg Saint Honore, 75008 Paris, France
**LaRosa, Julius** — Singer
67 Sycamore Lane, Irvington NY 10533, USA
**LaRosa, Paul** — Opera Singer
I M G Artists, Hogarth Business Park, Chiswick, London W4 2TH, England
**Larose, Claude D** — Ice Hockey Player
5060 NW 54th St, Coconut Creek FL 33073, USA
**LaRose, M Daniel (Danny)** — Football Player
4873 N Raymond Road, Luther MI 49656, USA
**LaRouche, Lyndon H, Jr** — Political Activist
18520 Round Top Lane, Round Hill VA 20141, USA

*LaPier - LaRouche*

**Larouche, Pierre R** — Ice Hockey Player
1005 Cherry Hill Dr, Presto PA 15142, USA
**Larrabee, Martin G** — Biophysicist
11630 Glen Arm Road, #V54, Glen Arm MD 21057, USA
**Larrain, Pablo** — Director, Producer, Writer
Fabula, Holanda 3017, in Nunoa, Santiago 7770057, Chile
**Larrieux, Amel** — Singer
Blisslife Records, 725 River Road, #32-215, Edgewater NJ 07020, USA
**Larroquette, John** — Actor
Brillstein Entertainment Partners, 9150 Wilshire Blvd, #350, Beverly Hills CA 90212 USA
**Larry the Cable Guy** — Actor, Comedian
Parallel Entertainment, 9420 Wilshire Blvd, #250, Beverly Hills CA 90212 USA
**Larry, Wendy** — Basketball Coach
Old Dominion University, Institutional Advancement Office, Norfolk VA 23529, USA
**Larsen, Blaine** — Singer, Songwriter
Morris Management Group, 818 19th Ave S, Nashville TN 37203, USA
**Larsen, Don J** — Baseball Player
C M G Worldwide, 10500 Crosspoint Blvd, Indianapolis IN 46256, USA
**Larsen, Gary L** — Football Player
4317 San Juan St NE, Olympia WA 98516, USA
**Larsen, Jack Lenor** — Textile Designer
LongHouse Reserve, 133 Hands Creek Road, East Hampton NY 11937, USA
**Larsen, Libby** — Composer
2205 Kenwood Parkway, Minneapolis MN 55405, USA
**Larsen, Marit** — Singer, Songwriter (M-2-M)
United Stage, Box 11029, 100 61 Stockholm, Sweden
**Larsen, Ralph S** — Businessman
100 Albany St, #200, New Brunswick NJ 08901, USA
**Larsen, Terrance A** — Financier
75 Bryn Mawr Ave, Lansdowne PA 19050, USA
**Larson, Brie** — Actress
Gersh Agency, 9465 Wilshire Blvd, #600, Beverly Hills CA 90212 USA
**Larson, Charles R (Chuck)** — Navy Admiral
591 Coover Road, Annapolis MD 21401, USA
**Larson, Daniel J (Dan)** — Baseball Player
797 Oxen St, Paso Robles CA 93446, USA
**Larson, Edward J (Ed)** — Historian
24346 Baxter Dr, Malibu CA 90265, USA
**Larson, Erik** — Writer
Crown Publishing Group, 1745 Broadway, #1300, New York NY 10019 USA
**Larson, Gary** — Cartoonist (Far Side)
FarWorks, 601 Union St, #620, Seattle WA 98101, USA
**Larson, Glen A** — Producer, Writer, Singer
5125 Kelvin Ave, Woodland Hills CA 91364, USA
**Larson, Gregory K (Greg)** — Football Player
PO Box 393, Nisswa MN 56468, USA
**Larson, Jack E** — Actor
449 N Skyewiay Road, Los Angeles CA 90049, USA
**Larson, Jill** — Actress
Innovative Artists, 1505 10th St, Santa Monica CA 90401 USA
**Larson, Lance** — Swimmer
1131 La Limonar Road, Santa Ana CA 92705, USA
**Larson, Peter N** — Businessman
Brunswick Corp, 1 N Field Court, Lake Forest IL 60045, USA
**Larson, Reed** — Ice Hockey Player
14334 Fairway Dr, Eden Prairie MN 55344, USA
**Larson, Wolf** — Actor, Producer, Writer
Kazarian/Measures/Ruskin, 11969 Ventura Blvd, #300, Studio City CA 91604 USA
**Larsson, Dean** — Golfer
Advantage International, 1025 Thomas Jefferson NW, #450, Washington DC 20007 USA
**Larter, Ali** — Actress, Model
Water Street Mgmt, 5225 Wilshire Blvd, #615, Los Angeles CA 90036, USA
**LaRue, Eva** — Actress
A P A Talent/Literary Agency, 405 S Beverly Dr, #300, Beverly Hills CA 90212 USA
**LaRue, Florence** — Singer (Fifth Dimension), Actress
W M E Entertainment, 1325 Ave of Americas, New York NY 10019 USA
**Larue, M Jason** — Baseball Player
30020 Twin Ridge Dr, Bulverde TX 78163, USA
**LaRussa, Anthony (Tony), Jr** — Baseball Player, Manager
338 Golden Meadow Place, Alamo CA 94507, USA
**LaRusso, Vincent** — Actor
419 Park Ave S, #1009, New York NY 10016, USA
**Lary, Frank S** — Baseball Player
11813 Baseball Dr, Northport AL 35475, USA
**Lary, R Yale** — Football Player
6366 Lansdale Road, Fort Worth TX 76116, USA
**LaSala, James** — Labor Leader
Amalgamated Transit Union, 5025 Wisconsin Ave NW, Washington DC 20016, USA
**LaSalle, Eriq** — Actor, Director
Principato-Young, 9465 Wilshire Blvd, #880, Beverly Hills CA 90212 USA
**Lascarro, Juanita** — Opera Singer
Harrison/Parrott, 5-6 Albion Court, London W6 0QT, England
**Lascher, David** — Actor
Amatruda Benson Assoc, 9107 Wilshire Blvd, #500, Beverly Hills CA 90210, USA
**Lash, Bill** — Skier
17438 Bothell Way NE, #C305, Bothell WA 98011, USA
**Laskey, William A (Bill)** — Baseball Player
PO Box 1556, Burlingame CA 94011, USA
**Laskey, William G (Bill)** — Football Player
PO Box 734, 3257 N Manitou Trail, Leland MS 49654, USA
**Laskin, Larissa** — Actress
Marshak/Zachary, 8840 Wilshire Blvd, #100, Beverly Hills CA 90211, USA
**Laslavic, James E (Jim)** — Football Player
648 A Ave, Coronado CA 92118, USA
**LaSorda, Thomas** — Businessman
Daimler-Chrysler Group, 100 Chrysler Dr, Auburn Hills MI 48326, USA

# L

**Lasorda, Thomas C (Tommy)**      Baseball Player, Manager, Executive
1473 W Maxzim Ave, Fullerton CA 92833, USA
**Lassally, Walter**      Cinematographer
6 Ladbroke Gardens, London W11 2PT, England
**Lasse, Richard S (Dick)**      Football Player
111 Windcrest Court, Beaver Falls PA 15010, USA
**Lasser, Louise**      Actress, Comedienne
200 E 71st St, #20C, New York NY 10021, USA
**Lasseter, John**      Director, Animator
Pixar Animation, 1200 Park Ave, Emeryville CA 94608, USA
**Lassetter, Donald O (Don)**      Baseball Player
379 Old Carrollton Road, Newnan GA 30263, USA
**Lassez, Sarah**      Actress
Untitled Entertainment, 350 S Beverly Dr, #200, Beverly Hills CA 90212 USA
**Lassiter, Isaac T (Ike)**      Football Player
2812 Rawson St, Oakland CA 94619, USA
**Lassiter, Kwamie**      Football Player
122 W Sunrise Place, Chandler AZ 85248, USA
**Last, James**      Orchestra Leader
Schone Aussicht 16, 22085 Hamburg, Germany
**Laster, Danny B**      Animal Research Scientist
Hruska Meat Animal Research Center, PO Box 166, Clay Center NE 68933, USA
**Lastra, Pilar**      Model, Actress
Playboy Promotions, 2706 Media Center Dr, Los Angeles CA 90065 USA
**Latana, Valerie**      Editor
Shape, Editorial Dept, 1 Park Ave, New York NY 10016, USA
**Lateef, Yusef**      Jazz Saxophonist, Flutist, Composer
BookArts, 6404 Wilshire Blvd, #1750, Los Angeles CA 90048, USA
**Latham, Louise**      Actress
300 Hot Springs Road, Santa Barbara CA 93108, USA
**Lathan, Sanaa**      Actress
John Carrabino Mgmt, 5900 Wilshire Blvd, #406, Los Angeles CA 90036 USA
**Lathan, Stan**      Director, Producer, Writer
Simmons Latham Media Group, 6100 Wilshire Blvd, #1111, Los Angeles CA 90048, USA
**Lathrop, Kit D**      Football Player
16634 S 36th Place, Phoenix AZ 85048, USA
**Latimer, Don B**      Football Player
562 S Kalispell Way, Aurora CO 80017, USA
**Latimore**      Singer, Keyboardist
Rodgers Redding, PO Box 4603, Macon GA 31208 USA
**Latimore, Jacob**      Actor
Creative Artists Agency, 2000 Ave of Stars, #100, Los Angeles CA 90067 USA
**Latman, A Barry**      Baseball Player
2726 Shelter Island Dr, PO Box 519, San Diego CA 92106, USA
**Lattimore, Kenny**      Singer
Mauldin Brand Agency, 1280 W Peachtree St, #300, Atlanta GA 30309, USA
**Lattin, David (Big Daddy)**      Basketball Player
8230 Twin Tree Lane, Houston TX 77071, USA
**Lattisaw, Stacy**      Singer
Walt Reeder Productions, 93 Old York Road, #1-604, Jenkintown PA 19046, USA
**Lattner, John J (Johnny)**      Football Player
1700 Riverwoods Dr, #503, Melrose Park IL 60160, USA
**Laub, Larry**      Bowler
5380 W Eaglestone Loop, Tucson AZ 85742, USA
**Lauby, Chantal**      Actress
Voyez Mon Agent, 20 Ave Rapp, 75007 Paris, France
**Lauda, Andreas-Nikolaus (Niki)**      Auto Racing Driver
San Costa de Baix, Santa Eulalia del Rio, 07840 Ibiza, Spain
**Lauder, Leonard A**      Businessman
Estee Lauder Companies, 767 5th Ave, Basement 1, New York NY 10153, USA
**Lauder, Ronald S**      Businessman, Diplomat
Estee Lauder Companies, 767 5th Ave, Basement 1, New York NY 10153, USA
**Lauderdale, Jim**      Singer, Songwriter
Rosebud Agency, PO Box 170429, San Francisco CA 94117 USA
**Laudner, Timothy J (Tim)**      Baseball Player
PO Box 10, Hamel MN 55340, USA
**Laudrup, Brian**      Soccer Player
2960 Rungsted Kyst, Denmark
**Lauer, Andrew**      Actor
Motive Entertainment, 1149 3rd St, Santa Monica CA 90403, USA
**Lauer, Bonnie**      Golfer
525 Via Laguna Vista, San Luis Obispo CA 93405, USA
**Lauer, Martin**      Track Athlete
D L V, Alsfeder Str 17, 64289 Darmstadt, Germany
**Lauer, Matt**      Commentator
2301 Deerfield Road, Sag Harbor NY 11963, USA
**Lauer, Tod R**      Astronomer
6471 N Tierra de Las Catalina, Tucson AZ 85718, USA
**Laughlin, John**      Actor
Laughlin Enterprises, 13116 Albers St, Sherman Oaks CA 91401, USA
**Laughlin, Robert B**      Nobel Physics Laureate
960 Mears Court, Stanford CA 94305, USA
**Laughlin, Thomas R (Tom)**      Actor, Director
PO Box 840, Moorpark CA 93020, USA
**Laukkanen, Janne K**      Ice Hockey Player
Tampa Bay Lightning, 401 Channelside Dr, Tampa FL 33602 USA
**Lauper, Cyndi**      Singer, Songwriter
So What Mgmt, 890 W End Ave, #1A, New York NY 10025, USA
**Laurance, Dale R**      Businessman
Occidental Petroleum, 10889 Wilshire Blvd, #1000, Los Angeles CA 90024, USA
**Laurance, Matthew W**      Actor
1951 Hillcrest Road, Los Angeles CA 90068, USA
**Laure, Carole**      Singer, Actress
Voyez Mon Agent, 20 Ave Rapp, 75007 Paris, France
**Laurel, Richard (Rich)**      Basketball Player
706 Antelope Way, Kissimmee FL 34759, USA

**Lasorda - Laurel**

**Lauren, Joy** — Actress
Paradigm Agency, 360 N Crescent Dr, North Building, Beverly Hills CA 90210 USA
**Lauren, Ralph** — Fashion Designer
867 Madison Ave, New York NY 10021, USA
**Lauren, Tammy** — Actress
Glick Agency, 1321 7th St, #203, Santa Monica CA 90401 USA
**Laurens, Camille** — Writer
Bloomsbury Publishing, 50 Bedford Square, London WC1B 3DP, England
**Laurent, Melanie** — Actress
U B B A, 6 Rue de Braque, 75003 Paris, France
**Laurer, Joanie (Chyna)** — Professional Wrestler, Model
Esterman Entertainment, 12333 Pretoria Dr, Silver Spring MD 20904 USA
**Lauria, Dan** — Actor
Marshak/Zachary Co, 8840 Wilshire Blvd, #100, Beverly Hills CA 90211 USA
**Lauricella, Francis E (Hank)** — Football Player
1200 S Clearview Parkway, #1166, New Orleans LA 70123, USA
**Lauridsen, Morten** — Composer, Musician
University of Southern California, Music Dept, Los Angeles CA 90089, USA
**Laurie, Harry** — Basketball Player
540 Bramhall Ave, #3, Jersey City NJ 07304, USA
**Laurie, Hugh** — Actor, Comedian, Writer
Hamilton Hodell, 66-68 Margaret St, #500, London W1W 8SR, England
**Laurie, Piper** — Actress
Susan Smith, 1344 N Wetherly Dr, Los Angeles CA 90069 USA
**Laurinaitis, James R** — Football Player
Saint Louis Rams, 901 N Broadway, Saint Louis MO 63101 USA
**Laursen, Jeppe (Senior)** — Singer, Keyboardist (Junior Senior)
Festival Network Mgmt, 30 Irving Place, #600, New York NY 10003, USA
**Lauterbach, Robert E** — Businessman
118 Dowling Dr, Pittsburgh PA 15215, USA
**Lautner, Georges C** — Director
9 Chemin des Basses Ribes, 06130 Grasse, France
**Lautner, Taylor D** — Actor
Management 360, 9111 Wilshire Blvd, Beverly Hills CA 90210 USA
**Lavadour, James** — Artist
Umatilla Indian Reservation Confederated Tribles, Pendleton OR 97801, USA
**Lavalliere, Michael E (Mike)** — Baseball Player
216 81st St W, Bradenton FL 34209, USA
**Lavanant, Dominique** — Actress
Voyez Mon Agent, 20 Ave Rapp, 75007 Paris, France
**Lavant, Denis** — Actor
U B B A, 6 Rue de Braque, 75003 Paris, France
**Lave, Lester B** — Economist
1008 Devonshire Road, Pittsburgh PA 15213, USA
**Laveikin, Aleksandr I** — Cosmonaut
Cosmonaut Training Center, Star City, 141160 Zvezdny Gorodok, Moscow Oblast, Russia
**Lavelle, Gary R** — Baseball Player
1100 Worthington Court, Virginia Beach VA 23464, USA
**Lavender, Jay** — Producer, Director, Writer
Verve Talent, 9696 Culver Blvd, #301, Culver City CA 90232, USA
**Lavender, Joseph (Joe)** — Football Player
1929 W Erie Ave, Philadelphia PA 19140, USA
**Laventhol, Henry L (Hank)** — Artist
445 Heritage Hills, #F, Somers NY 10589, USA
**Laver, Rodney G (Rod)** — Tennis Player
3009 Via Conquistador, Carlsbad CA 92009, USA
**Lavergne, Didier** — Makeup Artist
Mirisch Agency, 8840 Wilshire Blvd, #100, Beverly Hills CA 90211 USA
**Laverick, Elise** — Rowing Athlete
Thames Rowing Club, Putney Embankment, London SW15 1LB, England
**Lavery, Sean** — Ballet Dancer, Choreographer
New York City Ballet, Lincoln Center Plaza, New York NY 10023 USA
**LaVette, Bettye** — Singer
Rosebud Agency, PO Box 170420, San Francisco CA 94117 USA
**Lavi, Daliah** — Actress
134 W Wainman Ave, Asheboro NC 27203, USA
**Lavia, Gabriele** — Actor
Carol Levi Mgmt, Via Giuseppe Pisanelli 2, 00196 Rome, Italy
**Lavigne, Avril** — Singer, Songwriter
Azoff Music Mgmt, 1100 Glendon Ave, #2000, Los Angeles CA 90024, USA
**Lavin, Leonard H** — Businessman
Alberto-Culver, 2525 Armitage Ave, Melrose Park IL 60160, USA
**Lavin, Linda** — Actress, Singer
Innovative Artists, 1505 10th St, Santa Monica CA 90401 USA
**Laviolette, Peter** — Ice Hockey Player, Coach
7000 Firehouse Road, Longboat Key FL 34228, USA
**LaVorgna, Adam** — Actor
Hartig-Hilepo Agency, 54 W 21st St, #610, New York NY 10010 USA
**Lavoy, Robert W (Bob)** — Basketball Player
4902 Bayshore Blvd, #605, Tampa FL 33611, USA
**Lavrosky, Mikhail L** — Ballet Dancer
Voznesesenky Per 16/4, #7, 103009 Moscow, Russia
**Lavrsen, Helena Blach** — Curling Athlete
Curling Assn, Idraettens Hus, 2605 Brondby, Denmark
**Law, Bernard F Cardinal** — Religious Leader
Saint Mary Major Basilica, 00120 Vatican City
**Law, Bob** — Artist, Sculptor
Warehouse, 18 Bread St, Penzance, Cornwall TR18 2EG, England
**Law, Jude** — Actor
Julian Belfrage Assoc, 9 Argyll St, #300, London W1F 7TG, England
**Law, Kelley** — Curling Athlete
Curling Assn, 1660 Vimont Court, Cumberland ON K4A 4J4, Canada
**Law, Tajuan E (Ty)** — Football Player
10862 Hawks Vista St, Plantation FL 33324, USA
**Law, Vance A** — Baseball Player
1682 N 1950 W, Provo UT 84604, USA

L

Lauren - Law

**Law, Vernon S (Vern)** — Baseball Player
Bace Sports, 5699 Kanan Road, #157, Agoura Hills CA 91301, USA

**Lawanson, Ruth** — Volleyball Player
2050 Dickerson Road, Reno NV 89503, USA

**Lawler, Jerry** — Professional Wrestler, Sportscaster
415 Saint Nick Dr, Memphis TN 38117, USA

**Lawler, John (King)** — Professional Wrestler
415 Saint Nick Dr, Memphis TN 38117, USA

**Lawless, Blackie** — Singer, Guitarist (WASP)
Chipster, 100 Village Square Crossing, Palm Beach Gardens FL 33410 USA

**Lawless, Lucy** — Actress
Valeo Entertainment, 8265 Sunset Blvd, #103, Los Angeles CA 90046, USA

**Lawless, Paul** — Ice Hockey Player
4231 N Winfield Scott Plaza, #1, Scottsdale AZ 85251, USA

**Lawless, R Burton** — Football Player
2035 Oak Glen Dr, McGregor TX 76657, USA

**Lawless, Robert W** — Educator
University of Tulsa, President's Office, Tulsa OK 74104, USA

**Lawless, Thomas J (Tom)** — Baseball Player
1238 Laura St, Casselberry FL 32707, USA

**Lawrence, Andrew (Andy)** — Actor
Rebel Entertainment Partners, 5700 Wilshire Blvd, #456, Los Angeles CA 90036, USA

**Lawrence, Bill** — Producer, Director
I C M Partners, 10250 Constellation Blvd, #900, Los Angeles CA 90067 USA

**Lawrence, Carol** — Actress, Singer
Unified Mgmt, 4231 National Ave, Burbank CA 91505, USA

**Lawrence, Carolyn** — Actress
W M E Entertainment, 9601 Wilshire Blvd, #300, Beverly Hills CA 90210 USA

**Lawrence, Francis** — Director
3 Arts Entertainment, 9460 Wilshire Blvd, #700, Beverly Hills CA 90212 USA

**Lawrence, Henry** — Football Player
401 17th St W, Palmetto FL 34221, USA

**Lawrence, James (Loz)** — Guitarist (Strawberry Blondes)
PO Box 33, Pontypool, Gwent NP4 6YU, England

**Lawrence, James R (Jim)** — Baseball Player
225 Haddington St, Caledonia ON N3W 1G1, Canada

**Lawrence, Jennifer** — Actress
Creative Artists Agency, 2000 Ave of Stars, #100, Los Angeles CA 90067 USA

**Lawrence, Joseph (Joey)** — Actor
United Talent Agency, U T A Plaza, 9336 Civic Center Dr, Beverly Hills CA 90210 USA

**Lawrence, Josie** — Actress
International Artists, 193-97 High Holborn, London WC1V 7BD, England

**Lawrence, Marc** — Director, Producer, Writer
United Talent Agency, U T A Plaza, 9336 Civic Center Dr, Beverly Hills CA 90210 USA

**Lawrence, Martin F** — Actor, Comedian
Collective, 8383 Wilshire Blvd, #1050, Beverly Hills CA 90211 USA

**Lawrence, Matthew W** — Actor
Talent Works, 3500 W Olive Ave, #1400, Burbank CA 91505 USA

**Lawrence, Nina** — Publisher
W Magazine, Publisher's Office, 3500 Piedmont Road, #505, Atlanta GA 30305, USA

**Lawrence, Rebecca** — Actress
I C M Partners, 10250 Constellation Blvd, #900, Los Angeles CA 90067 USA

**Lawrence, Richard D** — Army General
7301 Valburn Dr, Austin TX 78731, USA

**Lawrence, Robert S** — Physician
Highfield House, 4000 N Charles St, #1112, Baltimore MD 21218, USA

**Lawrence, Robert Z** — Government Official, Economist
Harvard University, Kennedy Government School, Cambridge MA

**Lawrence, Rolland D** — Football Player
317 Sugarcreek Dr, Franklin PA 16323, USA

**Lawrence, Scott** — Actor
Ellis Talent Gorup, 4705 Laurel Canyon Blvd, #300, Valley Village CA 91607, USA

**Lawrence, Sean C** — Baseball Player
336 S Poplar Ave, Elmhurst IL 60126, USA

**Lawrence, Sharon** — Actress
A P A Talent/Literary Agency, 405 S Beverly Dr, #300, Beverly Hills CA 90212 USA

**Lawrence, Steve** — Singer
944 Pinehurst Dr, Las Vegas NV 89109, USA

**Lawrence, Steven Anthony** — Actor
Axiom Mgmt, 10701 Wilshire Blvd, #1202, Los Angeles CA 90024, USA

**Lawrence, Vicki** — Actress, Comedienne, Singer
6000 Lido Ave, Long Beach CA 90803, USA

**Lawrence, Wendy B** — Astronaut
National Reconnaissance Office, 14675 Lee Road, Chantilly VA 20151, USA

**Lawrie, Nathan E (Nate)** — Football Player
1157 Melville Ave, Fairfield CT 06825, USA

**Lawrie, Paul S** — Golfer
Code:4 Sports Ltd, Milton Gate, 60 Chiswell St, London EC1Y 4AG, England

**Lawson of Blaby, Nigel** — Government Official, England
32 Sutherland Walk, London SE17, England

**Lawson, Ben** — Actor
Untitled Entertainment, 350 S Beverly Dr, #200, Beverly Hills CA 90212 USA

**Lawson, Bianca** — Actress
Don Buchwald, 6500 Wilshire Blvd, #2200, Los Angeles CA 90048 USA

**Lawson, Denis** — Actor
Independent Talent Group, 40 Whitfield St, London W1T 2RH, England

**Lawson, Doyle** — Mandolinist
Sugar Hill Records, 3322 West End Ave, #1100, Nashville TN 37203 USA

**Lawson, Joshua (Josh)** — Actor
Management 360, 9111 Wilshire Blvd, Beverly Hills CA 90210 USA

**Lawson, Kara M** — Basketball Player
Wasserman Media Group, 10960 Wilshire Blvd, #2200, Los Angeles CA 90024, USA

**Lawson, Leigh** — Actor
CornerStone Talent Agency, 37 W 20th St, #1107, New York NY 10011, USA

**Lawson, Maggie** — Actress
Gersh Agency, 9465 Wilshire Blvd, #600, Beverly Hills CA 90212 USA

| | |
|---|---|
| **Lawson, Manny**<br>Buffalo Bills, 1 Bills Dr, Orchard Park NY 14127 USA | Football Player |
| **Lawson, Michael**<br>C E S D, 10635 Santa Monica Blvd, #130, Los Angeles CA 90025 USA | Writer |
| **Lawson, Nigella**<br>Creative Artists Agency, 2000 Ave of Stars, #100, Los Angeles CA 90067 USA | Chef, Writer |
| **Lawson, Richard**<br>Gage Group, 14724 Ventura Blvd, #505, Sherman Oaks CA 91403 USA | Actor |
| **Lawson, Richard L**<br>6910 Clifton Road, Clifton VA 20124, USA | Air Force General |
| **Lawson, Sonia**<br>Royal Academy, Burlington House, Piccadilly, London W1V 0DS, England | Artist |
| **Lawson, Tywon R (Ty)**<br>Denver Nuggets, Pepsi Center, 1000 Chopper Circle, Denver CO 80204 USA | Basketball Player |
| **Lawton, Brian R**<br>5012 Oak Bend Lane, Minneapolis MN 55436, USA | Ice Hockey Player |
| **Lawton, Mary**<br>Chronicle Features, 901 Mission St, San Francisco CA 94103, USA | Cartoonist (Nowhere to Hide) |
| **Lawton, Matthew (Matt), III**<br>27264 Highway 67, Saucier MS 39574, USA | Baseball Player |
| **Lax, Benjamin**<br>Massachusetts Institute of Technology, Physics Dept, Cambridge MA 02139, USA | Physicist |
| **Lax, Peter D**<br>Courant Math Institute, 251 Mercer St, #910, New York NY 10012, USA | Abel Mathematics Laureate |
| **Laxalt, Paul D**<br>Paul Laxalt Group, 245 E Liberty St, #510, Reno NV 89501, USA | Governor, Senator, NV |
| **Laybourne, Geraldine (Gerry)**<br>Oxygen Media, 75 9th Ave, #700, New York NY 10011, USA | Businessman |
| **Layer, Friedemann**<br>I M G Artists, Hogarth Business Park, Chiswick, London W4 2TH, England | Conductor |
| **Layton, Dennis (Mo)**<br>872 S 14th St, Newark NJ 07108, USA | Basketball Player |
| **Layton, Donald H**<br>Federal Home Loan Mortgage Corp, 8100 Jones Branch Dr, McLean VA 22102, USA | Financier |
| **Layton, Lester K (Les)**<br>8780 E McKellips Road, #27, Scottsdale AZ 85257, USA | Baseball Player |
| **Layton, Peter**<br>London Glassblowing, 7 Leather Market, Weston St, London SE1 3ER, England | Artist |
| **Layzie Bone**<br>Green Light Talent Agency, PO Box 3172, Beverly Hills CA 90212 USA | Rap Artist (Bone Thugs-N-Harmony) |
| **Lazar, Aaron**<br>Abrams Artists, 9200 W Sunset Blvd, #1125, West Hollywood CA 90069 USA | Actor |
| **Lazar, J Dan (Danny)**<br>8444 Oakwood Ave, Munster IN 46321, USA | Baseball Player |
| **Lazarev, Alexander N**<br>Christopher Tennant Artists, 39 Tadema Road, #2, London SW10 0PY, England | Conductor |
| **Lazarus, Mell**<br>Creators Syndicate, 737 3rd St, Hermosa Beach CA 90254 USA | Cartoonist (Miss Peach, Momma) |
| **Lazarus, Rochelle B (Shelly)**<br>106 E 78th St, New York NY 10075, USA | Businesswoman |
| **Lazear, Edward P**<br>277 Old Spanish Trail, Portola Valley CA 94028, USA | Government Official, Economist |
| **Lazenby, George**<br>Hervey/Grimes Talent, 10561 Missouri Ave, #2, Los Angeles CA 90025 USA | Actor |
| **Lazetich, Peter G (Pete)**<br>185 Martin St, Reno NV 89509, USA | Football Player |
| **Lazier, Robert (Buddy)**<br>386 Hanson Ranch Road, Vail CO 81657, USA | Auto Racing Driver |
| **Lazlo, Viktor**<br>56 Rue de Lisbonne, 75008 Paris, France | Actress, Singer |
| **Lazorko, Jack T**<br>1360 Meandering Way, Rockwall TX 75087, USA | Baseball Player |
| **Lazuktin, Alexander I**<br>Cosmonaut Training Center, Star City, 141160 Zvezdny Gorodok, Moscow Oblast, Russia | Cosmonaut |
| **Lazure, Gabrielle**<br>A C T 1, 83 Rue Saint Honore, 75001 Paris, France | Actress |
| **Le Toya**<br>Creative Artists Agency, 2000 Ave of Stars, #100, Los Angeles CA 90067 USA | Singer (Destiny's Child) |
| **Lea, Nicholas**<br>Global Artists Agency, 6253 Hollywood Blvd, #508, Los Angeles CA 90028 USA | Actor |
| **Leach, Jalal**<br>3718 Phillip Island Road, West Sacramento CA 95691, USA | Baseball Player |
| **Leach, Michael C (Mike)**<br>Washington State University, Athletic Dept, Pullman WA 99164, USA | Football Coach |
| **Leach, Penelope**<br>3 Tanza Lane, London NW3 2UA, England | Child Psychologist |
| **Leach, Reginald J (Reggie)**<br>263 Thomas Jefferson Terrace, Elkton MD 21921, USA | Ice Hockey Player |
| **Leach, Richard M (Rick)**<br>593 Layman Creek Circle, Grand Blanc MI 48439, USA | Baseball Player |
| **Leach, Robin**<br>Media Artists Group, 8222 Melrose Ave, #200, Los Angeles CA 90046, USA | Producer, Entertainer |
| **Leach, Rosemary**<br>Felix de Wolfe, 51 Maida Vale, London W9 1SD, England | Actress |
| **Leach, Sheryl**<br>Lyons Group, 300 E Bethany Road, Allen TX 75002, USA | Animator (Barney) |
| **Leach, Stephen (Steve)**<br>197 South St, Reading MA 01867, USA | Ice Hockey Player |
| **Leach, T Vonta**<br>5409 White Oak Dr, Lumberton NC 28358, USA | Football Player |
| **Leach, Terry H**<br>2135 SW Locks Road, Stuart FL 34997, USA | Baseball Player |
| **Leachman, Cloris**<br>410 S Barrington Ave, #307, Los Angeles CA 90049, USA | Actress |
| **Leader, Tom**<br>537 Golden Gate Ave, Richmond CA 94801, USA | Architect |

**L**

**Lawson - Leader**

**Leadon, Bernie** — Singer, Guitarist (Eagles)
Northstar Entertainment, 501 S Reino Road, #1-380, Thousand Oaks CA 91320, USA

**League, Brandon P** — Baseball Player
2385 Lake Heather Heights Court, Dunedin FL 34698, USA

**Leah, Rachelle** — Model, Actress
W M E Entertainment, 9601 Wilshire Blvd, #300, Beverly Hills CA 90210 USA

**Leahy, Patrick J (Pat)** — Football Player
717 Chamblee Lane, Saint Louis MO 63141, USA

**Leak, Jennifer** — Actress
James D'Auria Assoc, PO Box 2219, Amagansett NY 11930, USA

**Leak, Justice** — Actor
S M S Talent, 8383 Wilshire Blvd, #230, Beverly Hills CA 90211 USA

**Leakes, Nene** — Actress
Guttman Assoc, 118 S Beverly Dr, #201, Beverly Hills CA 90212 USA

**Leakey, Meave G** — Paleontologist
PO Box 24926, Nairobi 00502, Kenya

**Leakey, Richard E F** — Paleonotolgist
PO Box 24926, Nairobi 00502, Kenya

**Leaks, Emanuel (Manny), Jr** — Basketball Player
9912 North Blvd, Cleveland OH 44108, USA

**Leaks, Roosevelt, Jr** — Football Player
Roosevelt Leaks Properties, 11525 Glen Falloch Court, Austin TX 78754, USA

**Leal, Sharon** — Actress, Singer
I F A Talent Agency, 8730 W Sunset Blvd, #490, West Hollywood CA 90069 USA

**Leali, Richard L, Sr** — Financier
1761 W Hillsboro Blvd, #104, Deerfield Beach FL 33442, USA

**Leanderson, Matthew** — Rowing Athlete
1301 N Highlands Parkway, #110, Tacoma WA 98406, USA

**Leandro Alfonso de Borbon** — Infante, Spain
Ediciones Martinez Rocca, Paseo de Recoletos 4, 28001 Madrid, Spain

**Lear, Amanda** — Singer
Tony Denton Promotions, Charter House, 157-159 High St, London N14 6BP, England

**Lear, Harold C (Hal)** — Basketball Player
11321 E Sunnyside Dr, Scottsdale AZ 85259, USA

**Lear, Norman M** — Producer, Director
Act III Communications, 100 N Crescent Dr, #250, Beverly Hills CA 90210, USA

**Learned, Michael** — Actress
Gage Group, 14724 Ventura Blvd, #505, Sherman Oaks CA 91403 USA

**Leary, Denis** — Actor, Comedian, Producer
Apostle, 568 Broadway, #301, New York NY 10012, USA

**Leary, Paul** — Guitarist, Singer (Butthole Surfers)
Kork Agency, 1880 Century Park E, #711, Los Angeles CA 90067, USA

**Leary, Timothy J (Tim)** — Baseball Player
2461 Santa Monica Blvd, Santa Monica CA 90404, USA

**Leaud, Jean-Pierre** — Actor
Artmedia, 20 Ave Rapp, 75007 Paris, France

**Leavell, Alan F** — Basketball Player
7007 Windy Pines Dr, Spring TX 77379, USA

**Leavenworth, Scott** — Actor
Curtis Talent Mgmt, 9607 Arby Dr, Beverly Hills CA 90210, USA

**Leavitt, Judith W** — Historian
University of Wisconsin, Medical History Dept, Madison WI 53706, USA

**Leavitt, Phil** — Singer (Diamonds)
Lustig Talent, PO Box 770850, Orlando FL 32877 USA

**Leavy, Edward** — Judge
US Court of Appeals, Pioneer Courthouse, 555 SW Yamhill St, Portland OR 97204, USA

**Lebadang** — Artist
Circle Gallery, 303 E Wacker Dr, Chicago IL 60601, USA

**LeBar, Joshua** — Actor, Director, Writer
Glick Agency, 1321 7th St, #203, Santa Monica CA 90401 USA

**LeBaron, Edward W (Eddie), Jr** — Football Player
7524 Pineridge Lane, Fair Oaks CA 95628, USA

**LeBeau, C Richard (Dick)** — Football Player, Coach
10405 Stone Court, Cincinnati OH 45242, USA

**LeBeau, Patrick-Michael** — Ice Hockey Player
610 Vanier, Saint Jerome QC J7Z 6B4, Canada

**LeBeauf, Sabrina** — Actress
11 Asbury Road, Asheville NC 28804, USA

**Lebedev, Valentin V** — Cosmonaut
Cosmonaut Training Center, Star City, 141160 Zvezdny Gorodok, Moscow Oblast, Russia

**LeBel, B Harper** — Football Player
3379 Scadlock Lane, Sherman Oaks CA 91403, USA

**Leber, Ben** — Football Player
4457 35th Ave S, Minneapolis MN 55406, USA

**LeBlanc, Christian** — Actor
Glick Agency, 1250 6th St, #100, Santa Monica CA 90401, USA

**Leblanc, Jean-Paul (J P)** — Ice Hockey Player
120 Gadwall Lane, Manlius NY 13104, USA

**LeBlanc, Karina** — Soccer Player
Canadian Soccer, Place Soccer Canada, 237 Metcalfe St, Ottawa ON K2P 1R2, Canada

**LeBlanc, Matt** — Actor
W M E Entertainment, 9601 Wilshire Blvd, #300, Beverly Hills CA 90210 USA

**LeBlanc, Sherri** — Ballerina
New York City Ballet, Lincoln Center Plaza, New York NY 10023 USA

**LeBlanc-Boucher, Anouk** — Speed Skater
Speed Skating Canada, 2781 Lancaster Road, #402, Ottawa ON K1B 1A7, Canada

**Lebo, Jeffrey B (Jeff)** — Basketball Player, Coach
500 Hidden Lake Way, Santa Rosa Beach FL 32459, USA

**Leboeuf, Laurence** — Actress
K L Benzakein Talent, 1155 Rene-Levesque Blvd W, #2500, Montreal QC H3B 2K4, Canada

**LeBoeuf, Raymond W** — Businessman
P P G Industries, 1 P P G Place, Pittsburgh PA 15272, USA

**LeBon, Simon** — Singer, Songwriter (Duran Duran)
D D Productions, 93A Westbourne Park Villas, London W2 5ED, England

**LeBon, Yasmin** — Model
Place Model Mgmt, Am Feld 29, 22765 Hamburg, Germany

| | |
|---|---|
| **LeBor, Adam** | Journalist, Writer |
| Bloomsbury Publishing, 50 Bedford Square, London WC1B 3DP, England | |
| **Lebovitz, Nolan** | Director, Writer |
| Paradigm Agency, 360 N Crescent Dr, North Building, Beverly Hills CA 90210 USA | |
| **Lebowitz, Fran** | Actress, Producer, Writer |
| Random House, 1745 Broadway, #1800, New York NY 10019 USA | |
| **Lebowitz, Joel L** | Mathematician |
| Rutgers University, Math Sciences Center, New Brunswick NJ 08903, USA | |
| **Leboyer, Frederick** | Physician |
| Georges Borchardt, 136 E 57th St, #1400, New York NY 10022, USA | |
| **LeBrock, Kelly** | Actress, Model |
| Kaplan-Stahler Agency, 8383 Wilshire Blvd, #923, Beverly Hills CA 90211, USA | |
| **LeBrun, Christopher M** | Artist |
| Marlborough Fine Art, 6 Albermarle St, London W1X 4BY, England | |
| **LeBrun, Denis** | Cartoonist (Blondie) |
| King Features Syndicate, 300 W 57th St, #1500, New York NY 10019 USA | |
| **LeCarre, John** | Writer |
| 9 Gainsborough Gardens, London NW3 1BJ, England | |
| **LeCause, Carl D** | Harness Racing Driver, Owner |
| 124 Ashbury Ave, Freehold NJ 07728, USA | |
| **Lecavalier, Vincent** | Ice Hockey Player |
| 401 Channelside Dr, Tampa FL 33602, USA | |
| **Lechleiter, John** | Businessman |
| Eli Lilly Co, Lilly Corporate Center, Indianapolis IN 46285, USA | |
| **Lechler, E Shane** | Football Player |
| 4608 Sandyford Court, Dublin CA 94568, USA | |
| **Lechter, Sharon L** | Writer |
| Cashflow Technologies, 4330 N Civic Center Plaza, #100, Scottsdale AZ 85251, USA | |
| **Lechtman, Heather N** | Historian |
| Massachusetts Institute of Technology, History Dept, Cambridge MA 02139, USA | |
| **Leckey, Nicholas N (Nick)** | Football Player |
| 1056 E Windsor Dr, Gilbert AZ 85296, USA | |
| **Leckie, Mike** | Sculptor |
| PO Box 5718, Eugene OR 97405, USA | |
| **Leckner, Eric** | Basketball Player |
| 608 27th St, Manhattan Beach CA 90266, USA | |
| **LeClair, James M (Jim)** | Football Player |
| 32 4th Ave NE, Mayville ND 58257, USA | |
| **LeClair, John C** | Ice Hockey Player |
| 108 Tunbridge Circle, Haverford PA 19041, USA | |
| **LeClerc, Jean** | Actor |
| 19 W 44th St, #1500, New York NY 10036, USA | |
| **LeClerc, Mike** | Ice Hockey Player |
| 473 Abbie Way, Costa Mesa CA 92627, USA | |
| **LeClerc, Paul** | Librarian |
| New York Public Library, 5th Ave & 42nd St, New York NY 10018, USA | |
| **Leclerc, Roger A** | Football Player |
| 257 Elm St, Agawam MA 01001, USA | |
| **LeClezio, Jean-Marie Gustave** | Nobel Literature Laureate |
| Editions Gallimard, 5 Rue Sebastien-Bottin, 75007 Paris, France | |
| **Lecomte, Benoit** | Swimmer |
| Cross Atlantic Swimming Challenge, 3005 S Lamar, #D109-353, Austin TX 78704, USA | |
| **Leconte, Henri** | Tennis Player |
| International Mangement Group, Pier House, Chiswick, London W4M 3NN, England | |
| **Leconte, Patrice** | Director |
| Artmedia, 20 Ave Rapp, 75007 Paris, France | |
| **Lecount, Terry J** | Football Player |
| 1288 Branchfield Court, Riverdale GA 30296, USA | |
| **LeCroy, Matt** | Baseball Player |
| 11314 Cedar Pointe Dr N, Hopkins MN 55305, USA | |
| **L'Ecuyer, John** | Director |
| Paradigm Agency, 360 N Crescent Dr, North Building, Beverly Hills CA 90210 USA | |
| **Ledbetter, Lilly** | Social Activist |
| PO Box 72, Jacksonville AL 36265, USA | |
| **Ledee, Ricardo  A (Ricky)** | Baseball Player |
| D29 Calle Antonio Ledee Rivera, Extension Carmen, Salinas PR 00751, USA | |
| **Leder, Mimi** | Director |
| Creative Artists Agency, 2000 Ave of Stars, #100, Los Angeles CA 90067 USA | |
| **Leder, Philip** | Geneticist |
| Harvard Medical School, Genetics Dept, 77 Ave Louis Pasteur, Boston MA 02115, USA | |
| **Leder, Steven** | Religious Leader, Rabbi |
| Wilshire Boulevard Temple, 3663 Wilshire Blvd, Los Angeles CA 90010, USA | |
| **Lederman, Leon M** | Nobel Physics Laureate |
| 2163 Mount Davidson Dr, Driggs ID 83422, USA | |
| **Ledesma, Aaron D** | Baseball Player |
| 247 Los Prados Dr, Safety Harbor FL 34695, USA | |
| **Ledford, Brandy** | Actress, Model |
| Ellis Talent Group, 4705 Laurel Canyon Blvd, #300, Valley Village CA 91607, USA | |
| **Ledford, Frank F, Jr** | Army General, Physician |
| Southwest Biomed Research Foundation, PO Box 760549, San Antonio TX 78245, USA | |
| **Ledisi** | Singer, Songwriter |
| I C M Partners, 10250 Constellation Blvd, #900, Los Angeles CA 90067 USA | |
| **Ledoyen, Virginie** | Actress, Model |
| 80 Ave Gen Charles de Gaulle, 92200 Neuilly, France | |
| **Ledyard, Grant** | Ice Hockey Player |
| 5072 Old Goodrich Road, Clarence NY 14031, USA | |
| **Lee Beom-Young** | Soccer Player |
| Football Assn, 1-131 Sinmunno, 2-Ga Jongno-Gu, Seoul 110 062, South Korea | |
| **Lee Bo-Kyung** | Soccer Player |
| Football Assn, 1-131 Sinmunno, 2-Ga Jongno-Gu, Seoul 110 062, South Korea | |
| **Lee Byung-Chun** | Veternarian |
| National University, San 56-1, Shillim-Dong, Seoul 151 742, South Korea | |
| **Lee Hong-Koo** | Prime Minister, South Korea |
| Club de Madrid, C/Goya 5-7, Pasaje 2, 28001 Madrid, Spain | |
| **Lee Ho-Suk** | Speed Skater |
| Skating Union, 88 Bangyeo-Dong, Songpaku, Seoul 138 749, South Korea | |

**L**

**LeBor - Lee Ho-Suk**

**Lee Hsien Loong** — Prime Minister, Singapore
Premier's Office, Istana Annexe, Istana, 238823 Singapore, Singapore
**Lee Sang-Hwa** — Speed Skater
Skating Union, 88 Bangyee-Dong, Songpaku, Seoul 138 749, South Korea
**Lee Seung-Hoon** — Speed Skater
Skating Union, 88 Bangyee-Dong, Songpaku, Seoul 138 749, South Korea
**Lee Ufan** — Artist, Sculptor
Pace Gallery, 32 E 57th St, New York NY 10022, USA
**Lee, Alexondra** — Actress
Sanders/Armstrong/Caserta Mgmt, 2120 Colorado Ave, #120, Santa Monica CA 90404 USA
**Lee, Amos** — Singer, Songwriter
Red Light Mgmt, 44 Wall St, #2200, New York NY 10005, USA
**Lee, Amy** — Singer, Musician (Evanescence)
Dennis Rider Mgmt, 931 Hilldale Ave, West Hollywood CA 90069, USA
**Lee, Andrew P (Andy)** — Football Player
San Francisco 49ers, 4949 Centennial Blvd, Santa Clara CA 95054 USA
**Lee, Ang** — Director
Creative Artists Agency, 2000 Ave of Stars, #100, Los Angeles CA 90067 USA
**Lee, Anthonia W (Amp)** — Football Player
990 Brickyard Road, Chipley FL 32428, USA
**Lee, Ben** — Singer (Luna), Songwriter
Gold Village Entertainment, 72 Madison Ave, #800, New York NY 90016, USA
**Lee, Beverly** — Singer (Shirelles)
Bevi Corp, PO Box 100, Clifton NJ 07015, USA
**Lee, Bobby** — Actor
Creative Artists Agency, 2000 Ave of Stars, #100, Los Angeles CA 90067 USA
**Lee, Brenda** — Singer
Brenda Lee Productions, 2175 Carson St, Nashville TN 37211, USA
**Lee, Brook A M** — Beauty Queen, Actress
A K A Talent, 6310 San Vicente Blvd, #200, Los Angeles CA 90048 USA
**Lee, Carl, III** — Football Player
1 Stonegate Dr, Hurricane WV 25526, USA
**Lee, Carlos N** — Baseball Player
1400 N 11th Ave, Melrose Park IL 60160, USA
**Lee, Change Rae** — Writer
Princeton University, English Dept, Princeton NJ 08544, USA
**Lee, Charles R** — Businessman
Marathon Petroleum Corp, 539 S Main St, Findlay OH 45840, USA
**Lee, Charles S (C S)** — Actor
Peter Strain, 5455 Wilshire Blvd, #1812, Los Angeles CA 90036 USA
**Lee, Christopher F C** — Actor
5 Sandown House, Wheat Field Terrace, London W4, England
**Lee, Clifton P (Cliff)** — Baseball Player
5706 Riviera Dr, Benton AR 72019, USA
**Lee, Clyde W** — Basketball Player
1118 Crater Hill Dr, Nashville TN 37215, USA
**Lee, Corey W** — Baseball Player
278 Lancashire Run, Smithfield NC 27577, USA
**Lee, Courtney** — Basketball Player
Boston Celtics, 226 Causeway St, #4, Boston MA 02114 USA
**Lee, David** — Basketball Player
Golden State Warriors, 1011 Broadway, Oakland CA 94605 USA
**Lee, David** — Director, Writer
Grub Street Productions, 5555 Melrose Ave, #101, Los Angeles CA 90038, USA
**Lee, David A** — Football Player
2518 N Waverly Dr, Bossier City LA 71111, USA
**Lee, David E** — Baseball Player
56 Terrace Dr, Pittsburgh PA 15205, USA
**Lee, David G (Dave)** — Basketball Player
2580 Rampart Terrace, Reno NV 89519, USA
**Lee, David H** — Astronomer
Plenum Publishing Group, 233 Spring St, #600, New York NY 10013, USA
**Lee, David L** — Businessman
Global Crossing Ltd, Wessex House, 45 Reid St, Hamilton HM 12, Bermuda
**Lee, David M** — Nobel Physics Laureate
Cornell University, Physics Dept, Clark Hall, Ithaca NY 14853, USA
**Lee, Dennis** — Director
I C M Partners, 10250 Constellation Blvd, #900, Los Angeles CA 90067 USA
**Lee, Derrek L** — Baseball Player
3576 Brittany Way, El Dorado Hills CA 95762, USA
**Lee, Dickey** — Singer
Cape Entertainment, 4799 Coconut Creek Parkway, Coconut Grove FL 33063, USA
**Lee, Don** — Writer
Ploughshares, Emerson College, 120 Boylston St, #414, Boston MA 02116, USA
**Lee, Donald E (Don)** — Baseball Player
9101 E Palm Tree Dr, Tucson AZ 85710, USA
**Lee, Doug** — Basketball Player
10770 Procyon St, Las Vegas NV 89141, USA
**Lee, Gary L** — Interior Designer
Gary Lee Partners, 360 W Superior, #1, Chicago IL 60654, USA
**Lee, Geddy** — Singer, Bassist (Rush)
S L Feldman Mgmt, 1505 W 2nd Ave, #200, Vancouver BC V6H 3Y4, Canada
**Lee, Grandma** — Actress, Comedienne
Lee Strong, 626 Staffordshire Dr, Jacksonville FL 32225, USA
**Lee, Gregory S (Greg)** — Basketball Player
8077 Wild Flower Way, San Diego CA 92120, USA
**Lee, Harper** — Writer
PO Box 278, Monroeville AL 36461, USA
**Lee, Ho Wang** — Virologist
Life Sciences Institute, 388 Poongnap-Dong, Seoul 138 736, South Korea
**Lee, Howard V** — Vietnam War Marine Corps Hero (CMH)
529 King Arthur Dr, Virginia Beach VA 23464, USA
**Lee, Jack R (Jacky)** — Football Player
6306 Mid Pines Dr, Houston TX 77069, USA
**Lee, Janice Y K** — Writer
Park Literary Group, 270 Lafayette St, #1504, New York NY 10012, USA

**Lee, Jared B** — Cartoonist
Jared B Lee Studio, 2942 Hamilton Road, Lebanon OH 45036, USA

**Lee, Jason** — Actor
Ribisi Entertainment Group, 3278 Wilshire Blvd, #702, Los Angeles CA 90010, USA

**Lee, Jason Scott** — Actor
Untitled Entertainment, 350 S Beverly Dr, #200, Beverly Hills CA 90212 USA

**Lee, Jeanette** — Billards Player
Octagon Worldwide, 1751 Pinnacle Dr, #1500, McLean VA 22102 USA

**Lee, Jenny** — Golfer
1705 Canyon Edge Dr, Austin TX 78733, USA

**Lee, Jieho** — Director, Writer
United Talent Agency, U T A Plaza, 9336 Civic Center Dr, Beverly Hills CA 90210 USA

**Lee, Jim** — Cartoonist
Wildstorm Productions, 888 Prospect St, #240, La Jolla CA 92037, USA

**Lee, Joe** — Businessman
Darden Restaurants, 1000 Darden Center Dr, Orlando FL 32837, USA

**Lee, Johnny** — Singer, Guitarist, Songwriter
Red 11 Music, 2110 S Lamar Blvd, Austin TX 78704, USA

**Lee, Jonathan (Jon)** — Actor, Singer (S Club 7)
Elinor Hilton Assoc, 1 Goodwins Court, London WC2N 4LL, England

**Lee, Jonna** — Actress
8721 W Sunset Blvd, #103, West Hollywood CA 90069, USA

**Lee, Keith D** — Basketball Player
11653 Metz Place, Eads TN 38028, USA

**Lee, Kristin** — Concert Violinist
I C M Artists, 40 W 57th St, #1800, New York NY 10019 USA

**Lee, Kurk** — Basketball Player
2745 Scarborough Circle, Windsor Mill MD 21244, USA

**Lee, Larry D** — Football Player
PO Box 3889, Highland Park MI 48203, USA

**Lee, Laura** — Singer
Lee Magid, 15414 Ridgewood Dr, Sonora CA 95370, USA

**Lee, Lela** — Actress
S M S Talent, 8383 Wilshire Blvd, #230, Beverly Hills CA 90211 USA

**Lee, Leron** — Baseball Player
8150 Warren Court, Granite Bay CA 95746, USA

**Lee, Luanne** — Actress, Model
Playboy Promotions, 2706 Media Center Dr, Los Angeles CA 90065 USA

**Lee, Malcolm D** — Director
Creative Artists Agency, 2000 Ave of Stars, #100, Los Angeles CA 90067 USA

**Lee, Manuel L (Manny)** — Baseball Player
321 NW 31st St, Miami FL 33127, USA

**Lee, Mark D** — Guitarist (Third Day), Songwriter
Creative Trust, 5141 Virginia Way, #320, Brentwood TN 37027, USA

**Lee, Mark A** — Football Player
3610 208th St SE, Bothell WA 98021, USA

**Lee, Mark C** — Astronaut
79 S Player Crest Circle, Spring TX 77382, USA

**Lee, Michele** — Actress, Singer
Michele Lee Productions, 10866 Wilshire Blvd, #1100, Los Angeles CA 90024, USA

**Lee, Minkyu** — Animator, Director, Writer
United Talent Agency, U T A Plaza, 9336 Civic Center Dr, Beverly Hills CA 90210 USA

**Lee, Nikki S** — Photographer
Sikkema Jenkins Co, 530 W 22nd St, New York NY 10011, USA

**Lee, Nina** — Concert Cellist
David Rowe Artists, 24 Beesom St, #2, Marblehead MA 01945, USA

**Lee, Patrick** — Golfer
Links Mgmt, 5068 W Plano Parkway, #256, Plano TX 75093, USA

**Lee, Rachel** — Concert Violinist
I M G Artists, Carnegie Hall Tower, 152 W 57th St, #500, New York NY 10019 USA

**Lee, Rex** — Actor
A P A Talent/Literary Agency, 405 S Beverly Dr, #300, Beverly Hills CA 90212 USA

**Lee, Robert D (Bob)** — Baseball Player
PO Box 1589, Lake Havasu City AZ 86405, USA

**Lee, Robert M (Bob)** — Football Player
363 Parker Ave, San Francisco CA 94118, USA

**Lee, Robinne** — Actress
Abrams Artists, 9200 W Sunset Blvd, #1125, West Hollywood CA 90069 USA

**Lee, Rock A** — Basketball Player
4616 Blackfoot Ave, San Diego CA 92117, USA

**Lee, Ronald V (Ronnie)** — Football Player
139 Shady Trail, McGregor TX 76657, USA

**Lee, RonReaco** — Actor
Principato-Young, 9465 Wilshire Blvd, #880, Beverly Hills CA 90212 USA

**Lee, Russell E** — Basketball Player
1457 Smokehouse Lane, Stone Mountain GA 30088, USA

**Lee, Ruta** — Actress
2623 Laurel Canyon Road, Los Angeles CA 90046, USA

**Lee, Samuel (Sammy)** — Diver, Coach
16537 Harbour Lane, Huntington Beach CA 92649, USA

**Lee, Sandra** — Style Expert
W M E Entertainment, 9601 Wilshire Blvd, #300, Beverly Hills CA 90210 USA

**Lee, Sandra** — Chef, Writer
Food Network, 1180 Ave of Americas, #1200, New York NY 10036 USA

**Lee, Shannon E** — Actress
Innovative Artists, 1505 10th St, Santa Monica CA 90401 USA

**Lee, Sheryl** — Actress
Brillstein Entertainment Partners, 9150 Wilshire Blvd, #350, Beverly Hills CA 90212 USA

**Lee, Spike** — Director
Forty Acres & A Mule Filmworks, 75 S Elliott Place, Brooklyn NY 11217, USA

**Lee, Stan** — Publisher, Cartoonist
Pow Entertainment, 9440 Santa Monica Blvd, #620, Beverly Hills CA 90210, USA

**Lee, Sung Hi** — Actress, Model
Marshak/Zachary Co, 8840 Wilshire Blvd, #100, Beverly Hills CA 90211 USA

**Lee, Terry J** — Baseball Player
4650 Wendover St, Eugene OR 97404, USA

**Lee, Tommy** — Drummer, Singer (Motley Crue)
David Weise Assoc, 16000 Ventura Blvd, #600, Encino CA 91436, USA
**Lee, Travis R** — Baseball Player
PO Box 231081, Encinitas CA 92023, USA
**Lee, Tsung-Dao** — Nobel Physics Laureate
512 Clinton St, Brooklyn NY 11231, USA
**Lee, Wayne** — Space Engineer
Jet Propulsion Laboratory, 4800 Oak Grove Dr, Pasadena CA 91109 USA
**Lee, Will Yun** — Actor
A P A Talent/Literary Agency, 405 S Beverly Dr, #300, Beverly Hills CA 90212 USA
**Lee, William F (Bill)** — Baseball Player
305 Common View Dr, Craftsbury VT 05826, USA
**Lee, William Gregory** — Actor
Berneman Mgmt, 5820 Wilshire Blvd, #200, Los Angeles CA 90036, USA
**Lee, Yuan T** — Nobel Chemistry Laureate
19 Las Piedras, Orinda CA 94563, USA
**Leebron, David W** — Educator
Rice University, President's Office, Houston TX 77005, USA
**Leech, Allen** — Actor
Troika, 74 Clerkenwell Road, #300, London EC1M 5QA, England
**Leech, Beverly** — Actress
House of Representatives, 1434 6th St, #1, Santa Monica CA 90401 USA
**Leech, Kenneth** — Theologian, Social Activist
Centrepoint, Central House, 25 Camperdown St, London E1 8DZ, England
**Leech, Richard** — Opera Singer
Thea Dispeker Artists, 59 E 54th St, New York NY 10022 USA
**Leede, Ed** — Basketball Player
307 Roca Place, Castle Rock CO 80108, USA
**Leek, Eugene H (Gene)** — Baseball Player
2722 E Parker Court, Visalia CA 93292, USA
**Leeman, Gary** — Ice Hockey Player
15 Willow Fern Dr, Barrie ON L4N 0Z9, Canada
**Leemans, Kimberly** — Model, Actress
New Wave Entertainment, 2660 W Olive Ave, Burbank CA 91505, USA
**Leen, Bill** — Bassist (Gin Blossoms)
W M E Entertainment, 1600 Division St, #300, Nashville TN 37203 USA
**Leeper, David D (Dave)** — Baseball Player
23997 Kaleb Dr, Corona CA 92883, USA
**Leerhuber, Brian** — Opera Singer
I M G Artists, Hogarth Business Park, Chiswick, London W4 2TH, England
**Leese, Howard** — Guitarist, Keyboardist (Heart)
1770 N Highland Ave, #H-482, Los Angeles CA 90028, USA
**Leestma, David C** — Astronaut
4314 Lake Grove Dr, Seabrook TX 77586, USA
**Leetch, Brian J** — Ice Hockey Player
40 Battery St, #PH 12, Boston MA 02109, USA
**Leeuwenburg, Jay R** — Football Player
6268 S Coventry Lane W, Littleton CO 80123, USA
**Leeves, Jane** — Actress
23501 Malibu Colony Road, Malibu CA 90265, USA
**Lefcourt, Gerald** — Attorney
211 Central Park W, New York NY 10024, USA
**Lefcourt, Peter** — Actor
Creative Artists Agency, 2000 Ave of Stars, #100, Los Angeles CA 90067 USA
**LeFebure, Estelle** — Model, Actress
Cineart, 28 Rue Mogador, 78009 Paris, France
**Lefebvre, James K (Jim)** — Baseball Player, Manager
10160 E Whispering Wind Dr, Scottsdale AZ 85255, USA
**Lefebvre, Joseph H (Joe)** — Baseball Player
PO Box 16658, Hooksett NH 03106, USA
**Lefebvre, Sylvain** — Ice Hockey Player
Colorado Avalanche, Pepsi Center, 1000 Chopper Circle, Denver CO 80204 USA
**Lefevre, Rachelle** — Actress
W M E Entertainment, 9601 Wilshire Blvd, #300, Beverly Hills CA 90210 USA
**Lefferts, Craig L** — Baseball Player
40820 N Laurel Valley Way, Anthem AZ 85086, USA
**Lefkofsky, Eric** — Businessman
Groupon Inc, 600 W Chicago Ave, #620, Chicago IL 60654, USA
**Lefkovitz, Keili** — Actress
Metropolitan Talent Agency, 5405 Wilshire Blvd, #218, Los Angeles CA 90036 USA
**Lefkowitz, Robert J** — Nobel Chemistry Laureate
Duke University Medical Center, Chemistry Dept, PO Box 3821, Durham NC 27710, USA
**Lefley, Chuck** — Ice Hockey Player
PO Box 65, Grosses Isle MB R0C 1G0, Canada
**Leflore, Ronald (Ron)** — Baseball Player
6263 93rd Terrace, #4206, Pinellas Park FL 33782, USA
**Leftwich, Byron A** — Football Player
1322 Charter Court E, Jacksonville FL 32225, USA
**Leftwich, Phillip D (Phil)** — Baseball Player
15819 S 31st St, Phoenix AZ 85048, USA
**Legace, Emmanuel F (Manny)** — Ice Hockey Player
40708 Village Oaks, Novi MI 48375, USA
**Legace, Jean-Guy** — Ice Hockey Player
126 Casa Grande Lane, Santa Rosa Beach FL 32459, USA
**Legato, Robert (Rob)** — Visual Effects Artist
W M E Entertainment, 9601 Wilshire Blvd, #300, Beverly Hills CA 90210 USA
**Legend, John** — Singer, Pianist, Songwriter, Actor
Creative Artists Agency, 2000 Ave of Stars, #100, Los Angeles CA 90067 USA
**Legette, Tyrone C** — Football Player
1304 Hancock St, Columbia SC 29205, USA
**Leggero, Natasha** — Actress, Comedienne, Writer
Brillstein Entertainment Partners, 9150 Wilshire Blvd, #350, Beverly Hills CA 90212 USA
**Leggett, Anthony J** — Nobel Physics Laureate
607 W Pennsylvania Ave, Urbana IL 61801, USA
**Legien, Waldemar** — Judo Athlete
Ul Grottgera 10, 41902 Bytom, Poland

**Legler, Timothy E (Tim)** — Basketball Player
20 W Woodland Ave, Cape May Court House NJ 08210, USA
**Legrand, Michel** — Composer, Conductor, Concert Pianist
Kraft-Engel Mgmt, 15233 Ventura Blvd, #200, Sherman Oaks CA 91403 USA
**Legrande, Larry E, Sr** — Baseball Player
1331 Leon St NW, Roanoke VA 24017, USA
**Legree, Lance** — Football Player
25 Ardmore Ave, Clifton NJ 07012, USA
**Legris, Manuel C** — Ballet Dancer
National Theater of Paris Opera, 8 Rue Scribe, 75009 Paris, France
**LeGros, James** — Actor
I F A Talent Agency, 8730 W Sunset Blvd, #490, West Hollywood CA 90069 USA
**LeGuin, Ursula K** — Writer
3321 NW Thurman St, Portland OR 97210, USA
**Leguizamo, John** — Actor, Comedian
United Talent Agency, U T A Plaza, 9336 Civic Center Dr, Beverly Hills CA 90210 USA
**Lehan, Michael** — Football Player
418 Madison Ave S, Hopkins MN 55343, USA
**Lehane, Dennis** — Writer
341 Kerrville South Dr, Kerrville TX 78028, USA
**Lehew, James A (Jim)** — Baseball Player
3086 Fairview Road, Grantsville MD 21536, USA
**Lehman, I Robert** — Biochemist
895 Cedro Way, Stanford CA 94305, USA
**Lehman, Kristin** — Actress, Dancer
Oscars Abrams Zimel, 438 Queen St E, Toronto ON M5A 1T4, Canada
**Lehman, Thomas E L (Tom)** — Golfer
9820 E Thompson Peak Parkway, #704, Scottsdale AZ 85255, USA
**Lehmann, Edie** — Actress
24844 Malibu Road, Malibu CA 90265, USA
**Lehmann, Jens** — Cyclist
V f B Stuttgart, Mercedesstr 109, 70372 Stuttgart, Germany
**Lehmann, Jens** — Soccer Player
Rosenthaler Str 40-41, Hackesche Hofe, 10179 Berlin, Germany
**Lehmann, Karl Cardinal** — Religious Leader
Bischofliches Ordinariat, PF 1560, Bischofsplatz 2A, 55116 Mainz, Germany
**Lehmann, Michael** — Director
Industry Entertainment, 955 Carillo Dr, #300, Los Angeles CA 90048 USA
**Lehman-Smith, Debra** — Interior Designer
Lehman-Smith & McLeish, 1212 Banks St NW, Washington DC 20007, USA
**Lehmberg, Stanford E** — Historian
1005 Calle Largo, Santa Fe NM 87501, USA
**Lehn, Jean-Marie P** — Nobel Chemistry Laureate
6 Rue des Pontonniers, 67000 Strasbourg, France
**Lehne, Fredric** — Actor
Bauman Assoc, 250 W 57th St, #2223, New York NY 10107 USA
**Lehninger, Albert L** — Biochemist
15020 Tanyard Road, Sparks MD 21152, USA
**Lehr, Charles L (Justin)** — Baseball Player
6015 Nagel St, La Mesa CA 91942, USA
**Lehr, John** — Actor, Writer
Grade A Entertainment, 149 S Barrington Ave, #719, Los Angeles CA 90049, USA
**Lehrer, James C (Jim)** — Commentator, Writer
News Hour Show, 2700 S Quincy St, #250, Arlington VA 22206, USA
**Lehrer, Scott** — Sound Designer
I C M Partners, 10250 Constellation Blvd, #900, Los Angeles CA 90067 USA
**Lehrer, Thomas A (Tom)** — Pianist, Comedian
11 Sparks St, Cambridge MA 02138, USA
**Lehtinen, Dexter** — Attorney, Government Official
US Attorney's Office, Justice Dept, 155 S Miami Ave, Miami FL 33130, USA
**Lehtinen, Jere K** — Ice Hockey Player
622 Stratford Lane, Coppell TX 75019, USA
**Lehtonen, Kari** — Ice Hockey Player
6331 Deloache Ave, Dallas TX 75225, USA
**Leibman, Ron** — Actor
27 W 87th St, #2, New York NY 10024, USA
**Leibovitz, Annie** — Photographer
68 River Road, Rhinebeck NY 12572, USA
**Leibovitz, Mitchell G** — Businessman
Pep Boys-Manny Moe & Jack, 3111 W Allegheny Ave, Philadelphia PA 19132, USA
**Leibrandt, Charles L (Charlie), Jr** — Baseball Player
1235 Stuart Ridge, Alpharetta GA 30022, USA
**Leick, Hudson** — Actress
Glick Agency, 1321 7th St, #203, Santa Monica CA 90401 USA
**Leifer, Carol** — Actress, Comedienne
A P A Talent/Literary Agency, 405 S Beverly Dr, #300, Beverly Hills CA 90212 USA
**Leifer, Neil** — Photographer
235 W 56th St, #21B, New York NY 10019, USA
**Leiferkus, Sergei P** — Opera Singer
5 The Paddocks, Abberbury Road, Iffley, Oxford OX4 4ET, England
**Leifheit, Sylvia** — Model, Actress
L A P Services, Erika Mann Str 21, 80636 Munich, Germany
**Leigh, Chyler** — Actress
N2N Entertainment, 1230 Montana Ave, #303, Santa Monica CA 90403 USA
**Leigh, Danni** — Singer
Cramden Coach Corp, PO Box 463, Austin TX 78767, USA
**Leigh, Doug** — Figure Skating Coach
Mariposa Skating School, PO Box 444, Barrie ON L4M 4T7, Canada
**Leigh, Jennifer Jason** — Actress
Untitled Entertainment, 350 S Beverly Dr, #200, Beverly Hills CA 90212 USA
**Leigh, Mike** — Director
37 Marylebone Lane, London W1U 2NW, England
**Leigh, Mitch** — Composer
29 W 57th St, #1000, New York NY 10019, USA
**Leigh, Monica** — Model
Playboy Promotions, 2706 Media Center Dr, Los Angeles CA 90065 USA

**Leigh, Nikki** — Model
Playboy Promotions, 2706 Media Center Dr, Los Angeles CA 90065 USA
**Leigh, Regina** — Singer (Regina Regina)
Buddy Lee Attractions, 38 Music Square E, #300, Nashville TN 37203 USA
**Leigh, Vince** — Actor
Ken McReddie Assoc, 101 Finsbury Pavement, London EC2A 1RS, England
**Leighton, Laura** — Actress
A P A Talent/Literary Agency, 405 S Beverly Dr, #300, Beverly Hills CA 90212 USA
**Leija, James (Jesse)** — Boxer
116 Cas Hills Dr, San Antonio TX 78213, USA
**Leiker, Anthony W (Tony)** — Football Player
411 E 21st St, Hays KS 67601, USA
**Leimkuehler, Paul** — Amputee Skier, Businessman
351 Darbys Run, Bay Village OH 44140, USA
**Leinart, Matthew S (Matt)** — Football Player
22 E Oakwood Hills Dr, Chandler AZ 85248, USA
**Leiner, Danny** — Director, Producer, Writer
Creative Artists Agency, 2000 Ave of Stars, #100, Los Angeles CA 90067 USA
**Leiper, David P (Dave)** — Baseball Player
3312 E Glenrosa Ave, Phoenix AZ 85018, USA
**Leipheimer, Levi** — Cyclist
1755 Crystal Springs Court, Santa Rosa CA 95404, USA
**Leishman, Marc** — Golfer
Professional Golfer's Assn, PO Box 109601, Palm Beach Gardens FL 33410 USA
**Leister, John W** — Baseball Player
304 Devon Dr, Saint Louis MI 48880, USA
**Leisure, David** — Actor
Talent Works, 3500 W Olive Ave, #1400, Burbank CA 91505 USA
**Leiter, Alois T (Al)** — Baseball Player
181 E 90th St, #9B, New York NY 10128, USA
**Leiter, Mark E** — Baseball Player
121 Carriage Way, Forked River NJ 8731, USA
**Leiter, Michael E** — Government Official
National Counterterrorism Center, 1505 Tysons McLean Blvd, McLean VA 22102, USA
**Leiter, Robert E (Bob)** — Ice Hockey Player
1921 Shorepoint Village, Gimli BC R0C 1B0, Canada
**Leith, Prudence M** — Food Expert
94 Kensington Park Road, London W11 2PN, England
**Leithauser, Hamilton** — Singer, Guitarist (Walkmen)
Mick Mgmt, 35 Washington St, Brooklyn NY 11201 USA
**Leitner, Patric-Fritz** — Luge Athlete
Gesprachsstoff Marketing, Scholssstr 9B, 82140 Olching, Germany
**Leitso, Tyron** — Actor
Lucas Talent, 6-1238 Homer St, Vancouver BC V6B 2YB, Canada
**Leitzel, Joan** — Educator
University of Nebraska, President's Office, Lincoln NE 68588, USA
**Leius, Scott T** — Baseball Player
12620 42nd Place N, Minneapolis MN 55442, USA
**Lekang, Anton** — Ski Jumper
47 Pratt St, Winsted CT 06098, USA
**Lekman, Jens** — Singer, Songwriter
Agency Group Ltd, 142 W 57th St, #600, New York NY 10019 USA
**Leland, David** — Director
Creative Artists Agency, 2000 Ave of Stars, #100, Los Angeles CA 90067 USA
**Lelie, Ashley J** — Football Player
501 Hahaione St, #13H, Honolulu HI 96825, USA
**Lelliott, Jeremy** — Actor
Joan Green Mgmt, 1836 Courtney Terrace, Los Angeles CA 90046, USA
**Lellouche, Gilles** — Actor
U B B A, 6 Rue de Braque, 75003 Paris, France
**Lelong, Pierre J** — Mathematician
9 Place de Rungis, 75013 Paris, France
**Lelouch, Claude** — Director
15 Ave Hoche, 75008 Paris, France
**Lelouch, Salome** — Actress
Artmedia, 20 Ave Rapp, 75007 Paris, France
**Lelyveld, Joseph** — Editor
Wylie Agency, 250 W 57th St, #2114, New York NY 10107 USA
**LeMaho, Yvon** — Ecologist
Centre for Ecological & Evolutionary Synthesis, PO Box 1066 Blindern, 0316 Oslo, Norway
**Lemaire, Jacques G** — Ice Hockey Player, Coach
PO Box 1207, Palmetto FL 34220, USA
**Lemanczyk, David L (Dave)** — Baseball Player
24 Lehigh Court, Rockville Centre NY 11570, USA
**LeMarche, Maurice** — Actor
Danis Panaro Nist, 9201 W Olympic Blvd, Beverly Hills CA 90212 USA
**Lemaster, Denver C (Denny)** — Baseball Player
4833 Carlene Way SE, Lilburn GA 30047, USA
**LeMaster, Frank P** — Football Player
PO Box 159, Birchrunville PA 19421, USA
**Lemaster, Johnnie L** — Baseball Player
PO Box 943, Paintsville KY 41240, USA
**LeMat, Paul** — Actor
6300 Wilshire Blvd, #1460, Los Angeles CA 90048, USA
**Lematta, Wes** — Auto Racing Executive
PacWest Racing Group, PO Box 1717, Bellevue WA 98009, USA
**Lemay, Richard P (Dick)** — Baseball Player
1741 Holland Lane, Wichita KS 67212, USA
**LeMay-Doan, Catriona A** — Speed Skater
Landmark Sport Group, 277 Richmond St W, Toronto ON M54 1X1, Canada
**Lembeck, Michael** — Director, Actor
Principato-Young, 9465 Wilshire Blvd, #880, Beverly Hills CA 90212 USA
**Lembo, Joseph** — Interior Designer
220 Riverside Blvd, #16V, New York NY 10069, USA
**Leme, Sebasitao Carvalho** — Photographer
Av Pedro de Toledo 1114, Banzato Marilia, Sao Paulo 17509 021, Brazil

| | |
|---|---|
| **Lemelin, Reggie** | Ice Hockey Player |
| 10 Benevenuto Circle, Peabody MA 01960, USA | |
| **Lemelin, Stephanie** | Actress |
| Paradigm Agency, 360 N Crescent Dr, North Building, Beverly Hills CA 90210 USA | |
| **Lemercier, Valerie** | Actress |
| Artmedia, 20 Ave Rapp, 75007 Paris, France | |
| **Lemieux, Claude P** | Ice Hockey Player |
| 6008 N Saguaro Road, Paradise Valley AZ 85253, USA | |
| **LeMieux, George S** | Senator, FL |
| Gunster Yoakley, 450 E Las Olas Blvd, Fort Lauderdale FL 30301, USA | |
| **Lemieux, Jocelyn** | Ice Hockey Player |
| 2004 E Glenn Dr, Phoenix AZ 85020, USA | |
| **Lemieux, Joseph H** | Businessman |
| Owens-Illinois Inc, 1 Sea Gate, Toledo OH 43666, USA | |
| **Lemieux, Laurence** | Dancer |
| Coleman Lemieux Compagnie, 304 Parliament St, Toronto ON M5A 3A4, Canada | |
| **Lemieux, Mario** | Ice Hockey Player |
| 630 Academy St, Sewickley PA 15143, USA | |
| **Lemieux, Raymond U** | Chemist |
| 7602 119th St, Edmonton AB T6G 1W3, Canada | |
| **Lemke, Mark A** | Baseball Player |
| 3 Olena Dr, Whitesboro NY 13492, USA | |
| **Lemme, Steve** | Actor, Comedian, Writer, Producer |
| United Talent Agency, U T A Plaza, 9336 Civic Center Dr, Beverly Hills CA 90210 USA | |
| **Lemmon, Chris** | Actor |
| 80 Murray St, South Glastonbury CT 06073, USA | |
| **Lemmons, Kasi** | Director, Writer, Actress |
| Gersh Agency, 9465 Wilshire Blvd, #600, Beverly Hills CA 90212 USA | |
| **Lemon, Chester E (Chet)** | Baseball Player |
| 38150 Timberlane Dr, Umatilla FL 32784, USA | |
| **Lemon, George (Meadowlark), III** | Basketball Player |
| 6501 E Greenway Parkway, #1206, Scottsdale AZ 85254, USA | |
| **Lemon, Peter C** | Vietnam War Army Hero (CMH) |
| Lemco Enterprises, PO Box 49025, Colorado Springs CO 80949, USA | |
| **LeMond, Gregory J (Greg)** | Cyclist |
| 3000 Willow Dr, Hamel MN 55340, USA | |
| **Lemonds, David L (Dave)** | Baseball Player |
| 1501 Aringill Lane, Matthews NC 28104, USA | |
| **Lemper, Ute** | Singer, Actress, Dancer |
| Columbia Artists Mgmt Inc, 1790 Broadway, #702, New York NY 10019 USA | |
| **Lenahan, Edward P** | Publisher |
| Fortune, Publisher's Office, Rockefeller Center, New York NY 10020, USA | |
| **Lenard, Michael B** | Olympics Executive |
| US Olympic Committee, 1 Olympic Plaza, Building 6, Colorado Springs CO 80909 USA | |
| **Lenard, Voshon K** | Basketball Player |
| 22694 Nottingham Lane, Southfield MI 48033, USA | |
| **Lenchewski, Andrew** | Producer, Writer |
| Creative Artists Agency, 2000 Ave of Stars, #100, Los Angeles CA 90067 USA | |
| **Lendl, Ivan** | Tennis Player |
| 400 5 1/2 Mile Road, Goshen CT 06756, USA | |
| **Lenehan, Nancy** | Actress |
| Meghan Schumacher Mgmt, 12551D Riverside Dr, #387, Sherman Oaks CA 91423, USA | |
| **Lenfant, Claude J M** | Physician |
| PO Box 65278, Vancouver WA 98665, USA | |
| **Lengies, Vanessa** | Actress |
| Gersh Agency, 9465 Wilshire Blvd, #600, Beverly Hills CA 90212 USA | |
| **Lenhardt, Donald E (Don)** | Baseball Player |
| 1513 Timberlake Manor Parkway, Chesterfield MO 63017, USA | |
| **Lenk, Hans** | Rowing Athlete, Philosopher |
| Neubrunnenschlag 15, 76337 Waldbronn, Germany | |
| **Lenk, Thomas** | Sculptor |
| Gemeinde Braunsbach, 74542 Schloss Tierberg, Germany | |
| **Lenk, Tom** | Actor, Writer, Producer |
| Vanguard Management Group, 8060 Melrose Ave, #400, Los Angeles CA 90046, USA | |
| **Lenka** | Singer, Songwriter |
| Eon Shapiro Mgmt, 56 W 22nd St, #600, New York NY 10010, USA | |
| **Lenkaitis, William E (Bill)** | Football Player |
| 26 Rose Court Way, East Walpole MA 02032, USA | |
| **Lenkov, Peter M** | Producer, Writer |
| Creative Artists Agency, 2000 Ave of Stars, #100, Los Angeles CA 90067 USA | |
| **Lenkus, Linnea** | Photographer |
| 820 Gladys Ave, Long Beach CA 90804, USA | |
| **Lennertz, Christopher** | Composer |
| Kraft-Engel Mgmt, 15233 Ventura Blvd, #200, Sherman Oaks CA 91403 USA | |
| **Lennix, Harry J** | Actor |
| Brookside Artist Mgmt, 250 W 57th St, #2303, New York NY 10107, USA | |
| **Lennon, Diane** | Singer (Lennon Sisters) |
| 1984 State Highway 165, Branson MO 65616, USA | |
| **Lennon, Janet** | Singer (Lennon Sisters) |
| 1984 State Highway 165, Branson MO 65616, USA | |
| **Lennon, Julian** | Singer, Songwriter |
| Man from Another Room, 20 Bulstrode St, London W1M 5FR, England | |
| **Lennon, Kathy** | Singer (Lennon Sisters) |
| Overlook Dr, #10, Branson MO 65616, USA | |
| **Lennon, Patrick O** | Baseball Player |
| 60 Meister Blvd, Freeport NY 11520, USA | |
| **Lennon, Peggy** | Singer (Lennon Sisters) |
| 1984 State Highway 165, Branson MO 65616, USA | |
| **Lennon, Richard G** | Religious Leader |
| Archdiocese of Boston, 66 Brooks Dr, Braintree MA 02184, USA | |
| **Lennon, Sean** | Singer, Actor |
| KillerMoxie Mgmt, 5890 W Jefferson Blvd, #J, Los Angeles CA 90016, USA | |
| **Lennon, Thomas (Tom)** | Actor, Comedian |
| Creative Artists Agency, 2000 Ave of Stars, #100, Los Angeles CA 90067 USA | |
| **Lennox, Annie** | Singer (Eurythmics), Songwriter |
| 19 Music & Mgmt, 35-37 Parkgate Road, London SW11 4NP, England | |

**L**

Lemelin - Lennox

| | |
|---|---|
| **Lennox, Kai** | Actor |
| Talent Works, 3500 W Olive Ave, #1400, Burbank CA 91505 USA | |
| **Lennox, William J, Jr** | Army General, Educator |
| University of Nevada, President's Office, Las Vegas NV 89154, USA | |
| **Leno, Jay** | Actor, Comedian |
| I C M Partners, 10250 Constellation Blvd, #900, Los Angeles CA 90067 USA | |
| **Lenoir, Noemie** | Model |
| U B B A, 6 Rue de Braque, 75003 Paris, France | |
| **Lenon, Paris M** | Football Player |
| 1505 Taylor St, Lynchburg VA 24504, USA | |
| **Lenormand, Marie** | Opera Singer |
| Columbia Artists Mgmt Inc, 1790 Broadway, #702, New York NY 10019 USA | |
| **Lenox, Jack, Jr** | WW II Army Air Corps Hero |
| 1550 Killingsworth Way, #309, The Villages FL 32162, USA | |
| **Lenska, Rula** | Model, Actress |
| David Daley Assoc, 586A Kings Road, London SW6 2DX, England | |
| **Lentine, James M (Jim)** | Baseball Player |
| 1066 Calle del Cerro, #1411, San Clemente CA 92672, USA | |
| **Lentz, Larry L (Leary)** | Basketball Player |
| 1309 Whispering Pines Dr, Houston TX 77055, USA | |
| **Lenz, Kay** | Actress |
| Kritzer Levine Wilkins, 8840 Wilshire Blvd, #100, Beverly Hills CA 90211, USA | |
| **Lenz, Kim** | Singer, Songwriter |
| Mark Pucia Media, 5000 Oak Bluff Court, Atlanta GA 30350, USA | |
| **Lenz, Rick** | Actor |
| 12955 Calvert St, Van Nuys CA 91401, USA | |
| **Leo, Melissa C** | Actress |
| Creative Artists Agency, 2000 Ave of Stars, #100, Los Angeles CA 90067 USA | |
| **Leon** | Actor, Singer (Young Lions) |
| Stone Manners Salners, 9911 W Pico Blvd, #1400, Los Angeles CA 90035 USA | |
| **Leon, Adam** | Director |
| United Talent Agency, U T A Plaza, 9336 Civic Center Dr, Beverly Hills CA 90210 USA | |
| **Leon, Eduardo A (Eddie)** | Baseball Player |
| 5285 N Strada de Rubino, Tucson AZ 85750, USA | |
| **Leon, Kenny** | Director |
| W M E Entertainment, 1325 Ave of Americas, New York NY 10019 USA | |
| **Leon, Valerie** | Actress |
| Essanay Ltd, 2 Conduit St, London W1R 9TG, England | |
| **Leonard, Isabel** | Opera Singer |
| I M G Artists, Hogarth Business Park, Chiswick, London W4 2TH, England | |
| **Leonard, Bob** | Basketball Player |
| 1241 Hillcrest Dr, Carmel IN 46033, USA | |
| **Leonard, Brett** | Director, Producer, Writer |
| Quattro Media, 171 Pier Ave, #328, Santa Monica CA 90405, USA | |
| **Leonard, Brian** | Football Player |
| 20 Countryside Court Dr, Gouverneur NY 13642, USA | |
| **Leonard, Dennis P** | Baseball Player |
| 4102 SW Evergreen Lane, Blue Springs MO 64015, USA | |
| **Leonard, Gary** | Basketball Player |
| 2406 Ridgefield Road, Columbia MO 65203, USA | |
| **Leonard, J Wayne** | Businessman |
| Entergy Corp, 10055 Grogans Mill Road, #150, Spring TX 77380, USA | |
| **Leonard, James F (Jim)** | Football Player |
| 119 Cress Road, Santa Cruz CA 95060, USA | |
| **Leonard, Joanne** | Photographer |
| University of Michigan, Art Dept, Ann Arbor MI 48109, USA | |
| **Leonard, Joe** | Motorcycle Racing Rider, Auto Driver |
| PO Box 194, Gasoline Alley, Indianapolis IN 46222, USA | |
| **Leonard, Joshua** | Actor |
| Silver Lining Entertainment, 421 S Beverly Drive, #700, Beverly Hills CA 90212 USA | |
| **Leonard, Justin** | Golfer |
| 3700 Euclid Ave, Dallas TX 75205, USA | |
| **Leonard, Kawhi** | Basketball Player |
| San Antonio Spurs, Alamodome, 1 AT&T Center Parkway, San Antonio TX 78219 USA | |
| **Leonard, Mark D** | Baseball Player |
| 22042 Hibiscus Dr, Cupertino CA 95014, USA | |
| **Leonard, Myers** | Basketball Player |
| Portland Trail Blazers, Rose Garden, 1 N Center Court St, Portland OR 97227 USA | |
| **Leonard, Ray C (Sugar Ray)** | Boxer |
| PO Box 1433, Pacific Palisades CA 90272, USA | |
| **Leonard, Robert Sean** | Actor |
| W M E Entertainment, 9601 Wilshire Blvd, #300, Beverly Hills CA 90210 USA | |
| **Leonard, William R (Slick)** | Basketball Player, Coach |
| 5398 Baltimore Court, Carmel IN 46033, USA | |
| **Leonard, Zoe** | Photographer |
| Paula Cooper Gallery, 534 W 21st St, New York NY 10011, USA | |
| **Leonardini, Jean-Pierre** | Actor |
| U B B A, 6 Rue de Braque, 75003 Paris, France | |
| **Leonardis, Tom** | Producer |
| Whoop/One Ho Productions, 333 W 52nd St, #600, New York NY 10019, USA | |
| **Leone, Justin** | Baseball Player |
| 5605 Dawnbreak Dr, Las Vegas NV 89149, USA | |
| **Leone, Marianne** | Actress |
| Paradigm Agency, 360 N Crescent Dr, North Building, Beverly Hills CA 90210 USA | |
| **Leonetti, John R** | Cinematographer |
| Montana Artists Agency, 9150 Wilshire Blvd, #100, Beverly Hills CA 0212, USA | |
| **Leonetti, Matthew F, Jr** | Cinematographer |
| 1362 Bella Oceana Vista, Pacific Palisades CA 90272, USA | |
| **Leong, Page** | Actress |
| C N A Assoc, 1875 Century Park East, #2250, Los Angeles CA 90067 USA | |
| **Leonhard, David P (Dave)** | Baseball Player |
| 87 Corning St, Beverly MA 01915, USA | |
| **Leonhardt, David** | Journalist |
| New York Times, Editorial Dept, 229 W 43rd St, New York NY 10036 USA | |
| **Leonhardt, Ulf** | Theoretical Physicist |
| Saint Andrews University, Physics Dept, Fife KY16 9AJ, Scotland | |

|  |  |
|---|---|
| **Leonhart, William**<br>119 Oak Terrace, Lake Bluff IL 60044, USA | Diplomat |
| **Leoni, Tea**<br>United Talent Agency, U T A Plaza, 9336 Civic Center Dr, Beverly Hills CA 90210 USA | Actress |
| **Leonov, Aleksei A**<br>Alfa Capital, Masha Porivaeva Ul 11, 107078 Moscow, Russia | Cosmonaut, Air Force General |
| **Leonskaja, Elisabeth**<br>I M G Artists, Hogarth Business Park, Chiswick, London W4 2TH, England | Concert Pianist |
| **Leonti, Nikki**<br>W M E Entertainment, 9601 Wilshire Blvd, #300, Beverly Hills CA 90210 USA | Singer |
| **Leopardi, Chauncey**<br>Abrams Artists, 9200 W Sunset Blvd, #1125, West Hollywood CA 90069 USA | Actor |
| **Leopold, Jordan**<br>10988 Mississippi Dr N, Champlin MN 55316, USA | Ice Hockey Player |
| **Leopold, Leroy J (Bobby)**<br>4221 W Spruce St, #1404, Tampa FL 33607, USA | Football Player |
| **Leopold, Tom**<br>Gersh Agency, 9465 Wilshire Blvd, #600, Beverly Hills CA 90212 USA | Actor, Comedian, Producer |
| **Lepage, Robert**<br>103 Dalhousie, Quebec City QC G1K 4B9, Canada | Actor, Director |
| **Lepcio, Thaddeus S (Ted)**<br>263 Greenlodge St, Dedham MA 02026, USA | Baseball Player |
| **LePelley, Guernsey**<br>35 Saint Germain St, Boston MA 02115, USA | Editorial Cartoonist |
| **LePen, Marine**<br>National Front, 76-78 Rue des Suisses, 92000 Nanterre, France | Government Official, France |
| **LePichon, Xavier**<br>Ecole Normale Superieure, 24 Rue Lhomond, 75005 Paris Cedex 05, France | Geologist |
| **Lepore, Nanette**<br>225 W 35th St, #1700, New York NY 10001, USA | Fashion Designer |
| **Lepore, Tatiana**<br>Carol Levi Mgmt, Via Giuseppe Pisanelli 2, 00196 Rome, Italy | Actress |
| **Leppard, Raymond J**<br>Indianapolis Symphony, 32 E Washington St, #600, Indianapolis IN 46204, USA | Conductor |
| **LePrevost, Nicholas**<br>Ken McReddie Assoc, 101 Finsbury Pavement, London EC2A 1RS, England | Actor |
| **Lepsis, Matthew S (Matt)**<br>1833 Broken Bend Dr, Westlake TX 76262, USA | Football Player |
| **Lerach, William (Bill)**<br>Milberg Weiss Hynes Lerach, 1600 W Broadway, #1800, San Diego CA 92101, USA | Attorney |
| **Lerch, Randy L**<br>19490 Monterey St, Morgan Hill CA 95037, USA | Baseball Player |
| **Lerche, Sondre**<br>Zeitgeist Artist Mgmt, 660 York Ave, #216, San Francisco CA 94110, USA | Singer, Guitarist, Songwriter |
| **Lerman, Logan**<br>Creative Artists Agency, 2000 Ave of Stars, #100, Los Angeles CA 90067 USA | Actor |
| **Lerner, Dan**<br>Paradigm Agency, 360 N Crescent Dr, North Building, Beverly Hills CA 90210 USA | Director |
| **Lerner, Michael**<br>Tikkun, 2342 Shattuck Ave, #1200, Berkeley CA 94704, USA | Religious Leader, Rabbi |
| **Lerner, Michael**<br>Abrams Artists, 9200 W Sunset Blvd, #1125, West Hollywood CA 90069 USA | Actor |
| **Leroux, Francois**<br>507 Hickory Grade Road, Bridgeville PA 15017, USA | Ice Hockey Player |
| **LeRoux, Francois**<br>I M G Artists, Burlington Lane, Chiswick, London W4 2TH, England | Opera Singer |
| **Leroux, Sydney R**<br>Atlanta Beat, 1955 Vaughn Road, #209, Kennesaw GA 30144 USA | Soccer Player |
| **LeRoy, Gloria**<br>Talent Works, 3500 W Olive Ave, #1400, Burbank CA 91505 USA | Actress |
| **Les, James A (Jim)**<br>4030 Shadybrook Court, Granite Bay CA 95746, USA | Basketball Player, Coach |
| **Lesar, David**<br>Halliburton Co, Lincoln Plaza, 500 N Akard St, Dallas TX 75201, USA | Businessman |
| **LeSaunier, Jacqueline**<br>Angentur Retzlaff, Kurfuerstenstra 34, 10785 Berlin, Germany | Actress |
| **Lesch, James R**<br>15840 Malibu E, Willis TX 77318, USA | Businessman |
| **Leschin, Luisa**<br>W M E Entertainment, 9601 Wilshire Blvd, #300, Beverly Hills CA 90210 USA | Actress, Writer, Producer |
| **Leschyshyn, Curtis**<br>40 Laurel Mountain Dr, Littleton CO 80127, USA | Ice Hockey Player |
| **Lescroart, John T**<br>Penguin Books, 375 Hudson St, Basement 1, New York NY 10014 USA | Writer |
| **Lesh, Phil**<br>Paradigm Agency, 360 N Crescent Dr, North Building, Beverly Hills CA 90210 USA | Bassist (Grateful Dead) |
| **LeShana, David C**<br>8246 E Hoverland Road, Scottsdale AZ 85255, USA | Educator |
| **Lesher, Brian H**<br>217 Vassar Dr, Newark DE 19711, USA | Baseball Player |
| **LeSieur, Michael**<br>Kaplan/Perrone Entertainment, 9744 Wilshire Blvd, #300, Beverly Hills CA 90212, USA | Producer, Writer |
| **Leskanic, Curtis J (Curt)**<br>2032 Alaqua Dr, Longwood FL 32779, USA | Baseball Player |
| **Leskanich, Katrina**<br>Barry Collins, PO Box 2112, Hockley, Essex SS4 4WD, England | Singer (Katrina & the Waves) |
| **Leslie, A Ryan**<br>Laine Mgmt, 131 Victoria Road, Salford M6 8LF, England | Singer, Songwriter, Producer |
| **Leslie, Fred W**<br>2038 Springhouse Road SE, Huntsville AL 35802, USA | Astronaut |
| **Leslie, Joan**<br>2228 N Catalina St, Los Angeles CA 90027, USA | Actress |
| **Leslie, Lisa**<br>PO Box 452447, Los Angeles CA 90045, USA | Basketball Player, Model |
| **Leslie, Rose**<br>United Talent Agency, U T A Plaza, 9336 Civic Center Dr, Beverly Hills CA 90210 USA | Actress |

L

**Leonhart - Leslie**

**Leslie, Ryan** — Rap Artist
W M E Entertainment, 9601 Wilshire Blvd, #300, Beverly Hills CA 90210 USA

**Lesnie, Andrew** — Cinematographer
United Talent Agency, U T A Plaza, 9336 Civic Center Dr, Beverly Hills CA 90210 USA

**Lespert, Jalil** — Actor
Artmedia, 20 Ave Rapp, 75007 Paris, France

**Lessac, Michael** — Director
Creative Artists Agency, 2000 Ave of Stars, #100, Los Angeles CA 90067 USA

**Lessard, Stefan** — Bassist (Dave Matthews Band), Songwriter
Red Light Mgmt, PO Box 520, Crozet VA 22932, USA

**Lessin, Robert H** — Financier
Smith Barney Inc, 590 Madison Ave, #1100, New York NY 10022, USA

**Lester of Herne Hill, Anthony P** — Attorney
Blackstone Chambers, Blackstone House, Temple, London EC4Y 9BW, England

**Lester, Adrian** — Actor
Medavoy Mgmt, 10203 Santa Monica Blvd, #400, Los Angeles CA 90067 USA

**Lester, Jonathan T (Jon)** — Baseball Player
Boston Red Sox, Fenway Park, 4 Yawkey Way, Boston MA 02215 USA

**Lester, Joseph (Joe)** — Keyboardist (Silversun Pickups)
Ink Tank Public Relations, 1824 W Sunset Blvd, #102, Los Angeles CA 90026, USA

**Lester, Ketty** — Actress, Singer
5931 Comey Ave, Los Angeles CA 90034, USA

**Lester, Mark L** — Director
American World Pictures, 21700 Oxnard St, #1770, Woodland Hills CA 91367, USA

**Lester, Richard (Dick)** — Director
Petersham Lodge, River Lane, Richmond Surrey TW10 7AG, England

**Lester, Ronnie** — Basketball Player, Executive
4841 NW 16th Terrace, Boca Raton FL 33431, USA

**Lester, Timothy L (Tim)** — Football Player
1160 Bream Dr, Alpharetta GA 30004, USA

**Lester, Tom** — Actor
PO Box 363, Laurel MS 39441, USA

**Lesuk, Bill** — Ice Hockey Player
40 Bracken Ave, East Saint Paul MB R2E 0K2, Canada

**Lesure, James** — Actor
Wolman Wealth Mgmt, 10640 Rochester Ave, Los Angeles CA 90024, USA

**Letarte, Pierre** — Cinematographer
551 W Pinacle, Abercorn QC J0E 1B0, Canada

**Letarte, Steve** — Auto Racing Mechanic
18420 Nantz Road, Cornelius NC 28031, USA

**Letbetter, R Steve** — Businessman
Reliant Energy, 1111 Louisiana, Houston TX 77002, USA

**Leterrier, Louis** — Director
Management 360, 9111 Wilshire Blvd, Beverly Hills CA 90210 USA

**Lethem, Jonathan** — Writer
McSweeney's Books, 372 5th Ave, Brooklyn NY 11215, USA

**Letheren, Mark** — Actor
Ken McReddie Assoc, 101 Finsbury Pavement, London EC2A 1RS, England

**Letherman, Lindze L** — Actress
Lovett Mgmt, 1327 Brinkley Ave, Los Angeles CA 90049, USA

**Letizia** — Crown Princess, Spain
Palacio de la Zarzuela, 28080 Madrid, Spain

**Leto, Jared** — Actor
Untitled Entertainment, 350 S Beverly Dr, #200, Beverly Hills CA 90212 USA

**Letowski, Trevor** — Ice Hockey Player
3612 Lion Ridge Court, Raleigh NC 27612, USA

**Letscher, Matthew (Matt)** — Actor
Sanders/Armstrong/Caserta Mgmt, 2120 Colorado Ave, #120, Santa Monica CA 90404 USA

**Letsie III** — King, Lesotho
Royal Palace, PO Box 524, Maseru, Lesotho

**Letsinger, Robert L** — Chemist
8711 25th Ave NE, Seattle WA 98115, USA

**Lett, Clifford** — Basketball Player
7067 Rampart Way, Pensacola FL 32505, USA

**Lett, Leon, Jr** — Football Player
2 Longleaf Circle, Fairhope AL 36532, USA

**Letteri, Joseph (Joe)** — Special Effects Designer
Weta Digital, 9-11 Manuka St, Miramar, Wellington 6022, New Zealand

**Letterman, David** — Entertainer, Comedian
Worldwide Pants, 1697 Broadway, #3000, New York NY 10019, USA

**Letts, Tracy** — Writer, Actor
1756 W School St, Chicago IL 60657, USA

**Leung Chiu Wai, Tony** — Actor
W M E Entertainment, 9601 Wilshire Blvd, #300, Beverly Hills CA 90210 USA

**Leung, Ken** — Actor
Hartig-Hilepo Agency, 54 W 21st St, #610, New York NY 10010 USA

**Leuthard, Doris** — President, Switzerland
Federal Chancellery, Bundeshaus-W, Bundesgasse, 3033 Berne, Switzerland

**Levada, William J Cardinal** — Religious Leader
Doctrine of Faith Congregation, Palazzo del Uffizio 11, 00193 Rome, Italy

**Leval, Pierre N** — Judge
US Court of Appeals, Moynihan Courthouse, 500 Pearl St, New York NY 10007, USA

**Levane, Andrew J** — Basketball Player, Coach
14 Northstone Court, Irmo SC 29063, USA

**Levant, Brian** — Director
W M E Entertainment, 9601 Wilshire Blvd, #300, Beverly Hills CA 90210 USA

**LeVay, Simon** — Neuroscientist
970 Palm Ave, West Hollywood CA 90069, USA

**Leveaux, David** — Director
Simpson Fox Assoc, 52 Shaftesbury Ave, London W1V 7DE, England

**Leven, Jeremy** — Director, Writer
Paradigm Agency, 360 N Crescent Dr, North Building, Beverly Hills CA 90210 USA

**Levene, Ben** — Artist
Royal Academy of Arts, Piccadilly, London W1V 0DS, England

**Levens, H Dorsey** — Football Player
4249 Olde Mille Lane NE, Atlanta GA 30342, USA

**Leveque, Michel** — Minister of State, Monaco
57 Rue de l'Universite, 75007 Paris, France
**Lever, Don** — Ice Hockey Player
247 Quail Hollow Lane, East Amherst NY 14051, USA
**Lever, Lafayette (Fat)** — Basketball Player
50 Regency Park Circle, #12107, Sacramento CA 95835, USA
**Levering, Kate** — Actress
Paradigm Agency, 360 N Crescent Dr, North Building, Beverly Hills CA 90210 USA
**LeVert, Edward (Eddie)** — Singer (O'Jays)
Pyramid Entertainment Group, 377 Rector Place, #21A, New York NY 10280 USA
**Leverton, Irene** — Astronaut Candidate
1100 Willow Park Road, Prescott AZ 86301, USA
**Levesque, Joanna (JoJo)** — Singer, Actress
I C M Partners, 10250 Constellation Blvd, #900, Los Angeles CA 90067 USA
**Levi, Wayne** — Golfer
17 Ironwood Road, New Hartford NY 13413, USA
**Levi, Zachary** — Actor
Creative Artists Agency, 2000 Ave of Stars, #100, Los Angeles CA 90067 USA
**LeVias, Jerry** — Football Player
1626 Park St, Houston TX 77019, USA
**Levien, David** — Director, Writer
Creative Artists Agency, 2000 Ave of Stars, #100, Los Angeles CA 90067 USA
**Levieva, Margarita** — Actress
United Talent Agency, U T A Plaza, 9336 Civic Center Dr, Beverly Hills CA 90210 USA
**Levin, A Leo** — Attorney, Educator
University of Pennsylvania, Law School, 3400 Chestnut, Philadelphia PA 19104, USA
**Levin, Andres** — Composer, Musician
First Artists Mgmt, 4764 Park Granada, #210, Calabasas CA 91302 USA
**Levin, Jerry W** — Businessman
1 Central Park W, New York NY 10023, USA
**Levin, Marc** — Director, Producer
Blowback Productions, 601 W 26 St, #1776, New York NY 10001, USA
**Levin, Mark** — Entertainer, Writer
WPLJ-FM Radio, 2 Pennsylvania Plaza, #1700, New York NY 10121, USA
**Levin, Richard C** — Educator
Yale University, President's Office, New Haven CT 06520, USA
**Levin, Robert D** — Musicologist, Pianist, Composer
Harvard University, Music Dept, Cambridge MA 02138, USA
**Levine, Adam** — Singer (Maroon 5), Actor
Career Artists Mgmt, 203-207 W Hastings St, Vancouver BC V6B 1H7, Canada
**Levine, Alan B (Al)** — Baseball Player
10916 E Paradise Dr, Scottsdale AZ 85259, USA
**Levine, Alex** — Bassist (Gaslight Anthem)
Esther Creative Group, 27 W 24th St, #404, New York NY 10010, USA
**Levine, Arnold** — Molecular Biologist, Educator
Rockefeller University, President's Office, 1230 York Ave, New York NY 10065, USA
**Levine, James** — Conductor
Boston Symphony Orchestra, 301 Massachusetts Ave, Boston MA 02115, USA
**Levine, Jerry** — Actor, Director
Rain Mgmt, 1801 Stanford St, Santa Monica CA 90404, USA
**Levine, Jonathan** — Director, Writer
Creative Artists Agency, 2000 Ave of Stars, #100, Los Angeles CA 90067 USA
**Levine, Philip** — Writer
4549 N Van Ness Blvd, Fresno CA 93704, USA
**Levine, Rachmiel** — Endocrinologist
614 Walnut St, Newton MA 02460, USA
**Levine, S Robert** — Businessman
Cabletron Systems, 50 Minuteman Road, Andover MA 01810, USA
**Levine, Samm** — Actor
A P A Talent/Literary Agency, 405 S Beverly Dr, #300, Beverly Hills CA 90212 USA
**Levine, Seymour** — Psychobiologist
1515 Shasta Dr, #3103, Davis CA 95616, USA
**Levine, Ted** — Actor
Kass Management, 501 Santa Monica Blvd, #604, Los Angeles CA 90401, USA
**Levingstone, Ken** — Government Official, England
House of Commons, Westminster, London SW1A 0AA, England
**Levinsohn, Gary** — Producer
Mutual Film Co, 150 S Rodeo Dr, #120, Beverly Hills CA 90212, USA
**Levinson, Arthur D** — Businessman
Genentech Inc, 400 Point San Bruno Blvd S, South San Francisco CA 94080, USA
**Levinson, Barry L** — Director
Baltimore Pictures, 8306 Wilshire Blvd, PMB 1012, Beverly Hills CA 90211, USA
**Levinson, Chris** — Producer, Writer
W M E Entertainment, 9601 Wilshire Blvd, #300, Beverly Hills CA 90210 USA
**Levinson, Sanford V** — Attorney, Educator
3410 Windsor Road, Austin TX 78703, USA
**Levinson, Stephen** — Producer
Leverage Mgmt, 3030 Pennsylvania Ave, Santa Monica CA 90404 USA
**Levinthal, David L** — Photographer
32 W 20th St, New York NY 10011, USA
**Levis, Jesse** — Baseball Player
1219 Highland Ave, Fort Washington PA 19034, USA
**Levis, Patrick** — Actor, Singer
Least of Three, PO Box 902652, Sylmar CA 91392, USA
**Levit, Igor** — Concert Pianist
Harrison/Parrott, 5-6 Albion Court, London W6 0QT, England
**Levitan, Steven (Steve)** — Director, Producer
United Talent Agency, U T A Plaza, 9336 Civic Center Dr, Beverly Hills CA 90210 USA
**Levitas, Andrew** — Actor
Creative Artists Agency, 2000 Ave of Stars, #100, Los Angeles CA 90067 USA
**Levitin, Daniel J** — Psychologist, Neuroscientist
McGill University, Psychology Dept, Montreal QC H3A 2T5, Canada
**Levitt, Arthur, Jr** — Government Official, Financier
Carlyle Group, 1001 Pennsylvania Ave NW, #220S, Washington DC 20004, USA
**Levitt, George** — Chemist
82 Via Del Corso, Palm Beach Gardens FL 33418, USA

**Levitt, Michael** — Nobel Chemistry Laureate
Stanford University Medical School, Structural Biology Dept, Stanford CA 94305, USA

**Levitt, Steven D** — Economist, Writer
University of Chicago, Economics Dept, Chicago IL 60637, USA

**LeVox, Gary** — Singer (Rascal Flatts)
Turner & Nichols, 49 Music Square W, #500, Nashville TN 37203, USA

**Levrault, Allen** — Baseball Player
5 Granada Dr, Westport MA 02790, USA

**Levrone, Kevin** — Body Builder, Actor
Beacon Talent, 170 Apple Ridge Road, Woodcliff Lake NJ 07677, USA

**Levy, Barrington A** — Singer
Solid Agency, 7 Dumbarton Ave, Kingston 10, Jamaica

**Levy, Bernard-Henri** — Philosopher
Editions Grasset/Fasquelle, 61 Rue des Saint-Peres, 75006 Paris, France

**Levy, Clifford J** — Journalist
New York Times, Editorial Dept, 229 W 43rd St, New York NY 10036 USA

**Levy, Dan** — Actor, Comedian
Great North Artists Mgmt, 350 Dupont St, Toronto ON M5R 1V9, Canada

**Levy, David H** — Astronomer
Mount Palomar Observatory, 35899 Canfield Road, Palomar Mountain CA 92060, USA

**Levy, Eugene** — Actor, Comedian, Director
Anonymous Content, 3532 Hayden Ave, Culver City CA 90232 USA

**Levy, Jane** — Actress
Suskin Management, 2 Charlton St, #5K, New York NY 10014, USA

**Levy, Jean-Bernard** — Businessman
Vivendi, 42 Ave de Friedland, 75380 Paris Cedex 08, France

**Levy, Marvin D (Marv)** — Football Coach
National Pro Athletes Organization, 1806 Watermere Lane, Windermere FL 34786, USA

**Levy, Marvin David** — Composer
Sheldon Sofer Mgmt, 130 W 56th St, New York NY 10019, USA

**Levy, Naomi** — Religious Leader, Rabbi
Academy of Jewish Religion, 574 Hilgard Ave, Los Angeles CA 90024, USA

**Levy, Peter** — Cinematographer
I C M Partners, 10250 Constellation Blvd, #900, Los Angeles CA 90067 USA

**Levy, William** — Actor
Creative Artists Agency, 2000 Ave of Stars, #100, Los Angeles CA 90067 USA

**Lew, Jacob J (Jack)** — Government Official
White House, 1600 Pennsylvania Ave NW, Washington DC 20500 USA

**Lew, Scott** — Director
Principato-Young, 9465 Wilshire Blvd, #880, Beverly Hills CA 90212 USA

**Lewin, Gene** — Drummer, Singer (GrooveLily)
GrooveLily, PO Box 11570, Glendale CA 91226, USA

**Lewin, Josh** — Sportscaster
1081 W Winding Creek Dr, Grapevine TX 76051, USA

**Lewis, Albert R** — Football Player
3532 Macedonia Road, Centreville MS 39631, USA

**Lewis, Ananda** — Actress
Britto Agency, 234 W 56th St, #PH, New York NY 10019, USA

**Lewis, Andrew L (Drew)** — Secretary, Transportation; Businessman
PO Box 70, Lederach PA 19450, USA

**Lewis, Barbara** — Singer
American Mgmt, 19948 Mayall St, Chatsworth CA 91311, USA

**Lewis, Bernard** — Historian
Princeton University, Near Eastern Studies Dept, Princeton NJ 08544, USA

**Lewis, Blake C** — Singer, Songwriter
PO Box 806, Lynnwood WA 98046, USA

**Lewis, Bob** — Basketball Player
63910 E Squash Blossom Lane, Tucson AZ 85739, USA

**Lewis, Bobby** — Singer
Lustig Talent, PO Box 770850, Orlando FL 32877 USA

**Lewis, Charlotte** — Basketball Player
2814 N Sheridan Road, Peoria IL 61604, USA

**Lewis, Clea** — Actress
Innovative Artists, 1505 10th St, Santa Monica CA 90401 USA

**Lewis, Colby P** — Baseball Player
14800 Orchard Crest Ave, Bakersfield CA 93314, USA

**Lewis, Crystal** — Singer, Rap Artist
Creative Artists Agency, 2000 Ave of Stars, #100, Los Angeles CA 90067 USA

**Lewis, Cynthia R** — Publisher
Harper's Bazaar, Publisher's Office, 1770 Broadway, New York NY 10019, USA

**Lewis, Damaris** — Model
Elite Model Mgmt, 404 Park Ave S, #900, New York NY 10016 USA

**Lewis, Damian** — Actor
Markham Froggatt Irwin, Julian House, 4 Windmill St, London W1P 1HF, England

**Lewis, Damione R** — Football Player
9601 Gato del Sol Court, Waxhaw NC 28173, USA

**Lewis, Daniel N (Dan)** — Football Player
460 S Park St, Detroit MI 48215, USA

**Lewis, Darren J** — Baseball Player
2212 Rosemount Lane, San Ramon CA 94582, USA

**Lewis, Dave** — Ice Hockey Player, Coach
2040 Ranch Road, Holly MI 48442, USA

**Lewis, David** — Industrial Designer
Bang & Olufsen A/S, Peter Bangs Vej 15, PO Box 40, 7600 Stuer, Denmark

**Lewis, David Levering** — Writer
Rutgers University, History Dept, East Rutherford NJ 07073, USA

**Lewis, David R (Dave)** — Football Player
406 142nd St, Ocean City MD 21842, USA

**Lewis, Dawnn** — Actress
Stone Manners Salners, 9911 W Pico Blvd, #1400, Los Angeles CA 90035 USA

**Lewis, De'Andre D (D D)** — Football Player
10230 125th Ave NE, Kirkland WA 98033, USA

**Lewis, Denise** — Heptathlete
Outside Organization, 177-8 Tottenham Court Road, London W1T 7NY, England

**Lewis, Dwight D (D D)** — Football Player
P C S Sales, 1624 Northcrest Dr, Plano TX 75075, USA

**Lewis, Emmanuel** — Actor
Orange Grove Group, 12178 Ventura Blvd, #205, Studio City CA 91604, USA
**Lewis, F Carlton (Carl)** — Track Athlete
528 Palisades Dr, Pacific Palisades CA 90272, USA
**Lewis, Frank D** — Football Player
118 Presque Isle Dr, Houma LA 70363, USA
**Lewis, Frederick L (Fritz)** — Basketball Player
4122 Illinois Ave NW, Washington DC 20011, USA
**Lewis, Gary** — Singer (Gary Lewis & the Playboys)
701 Balin Court, Nashville TN 37221, USA
**Lewis, Geoffrey** — Actor
5210 Collier Place, Woodland Hills CA 91364, USA
**Lewis, Herschell Gordon** — Director
Lewis Enterprises, 451 Heritage Dr, #215, Pompano Beach FL 33060, USA
**Lewis, Huey** — Singer, Actor
Hulex Corp, PO Box 819, Mill Valley CA 94942, USA
**Lewis, J L** — Golfer
2504 Orleans Dr, Cedar Park TX 78613, USA
**Lewis, Jamal L** — Football Player
10614 Lee Ave, Cleveland OH 44106, USA
**Lewis, Jasmine** — Actress
Evolution Entertainment, 901 N Highland Ave, Los Angeles CA 90038 USA
**Lewis, Jason** — Actor
Untitled Entertainment, 350 S Beverly Dr, #200, Beverly Hills CA 90212 USA
**Lewis, Jenifer** — Actress, Singer
Innovative Artists, 1505 10th St, Santa Monica CA 90401 USA
**Lewis, Jermaine E** — Football Player
4919 Pleasant Grove Road, Reisterstown MD 21136, USA
**Lewis, Jerry** — Actor, Comedian, Director
Jerry Lewis Films, 3160 W Sahara Ave, #C16, Las Vegas NV 89102, USA
**Lewis, Jerry Lee** — Singer, Pianist, Composer
PO Box 206, Old Hickory TN 37138, USA
**Lewis, Jim** — Composer
I C M Partners, 10250 Constellation Blvd, #900, Los Angeles CA 90067 USA
**Lewis, Jonathan Guy** — Actor
Ken McReddie Assoc, 101 Finsbury Pavement, London EC2A 1RS, England
**Lewis, Juliette** — Actress
Don Buchwald, 6500 Wilshire Blvd, #2200, Los Angeles CA 90048 USA
**Lewis, Karen** — Writer
Sarnoff Co, 10 Universal City Plaza, #2000, Universal City CA 91608, USA
**Lewis, Kevin** — Football Player
4417 Roy St, Orlando FL 32812, USA
**Lewis, Lennox** — Boxer
Gainsborough House, 81 Oxford St, #206, London W1D 2EU, England
**Lewis, Leo, III** — Football Player
10116 Ivywood Court, Eden Prairie MN 55347, USA
**Lewis, Lisa** — Boxer
7242 N Wheeler Ave, Fresno CA 93722, USA
**Lewis, Marcedes A** — Football Player
3725 Bouton Dr, Lakewood CA 90712, USA
**Lewis, Mark D** — Baseball Player
1246 Cleveland Ave, Hamilton OH 45013, USA
**Lewis, Marvin** — Football Coach
Cincinnati Bengals, 1 Paul Brown Stadium, Cincinnati OH 45202 USA
**Lewis, Michael** — Writer
Creative Artists Agency, 2000 Ave of Stars, #100, Los Angeles CA 90067 USA
**Lewis, Michael H (Mike)** — Football Player
3350 Blodgett St, Houston TX 77004, USA
**Lewis, Mike** — Basketball Player
490 Windsor Park Road, Kernersville NC 27284, USA
**Lewis, Monica** — Singer, Actress
Lang, 1100 Alta Loma Road, #16A, West Hollywood CA 90069, USA
**Lewis, Morris C (Mo)** — Football Player
22012 Gardner Dr, Alpharetta GA 30009, USA
**Lewis, Neville** — Interior Designer
Ted Moudis Assoc, 79 Madison Ave, #1000, New York NY 10016, USA
**Lewis, Phill** — Actor
Kritzer Levine Wilkins Griffin, 11872 La Grange Ave, #100, Los Angeles CA 90025 USA
**Lewis, Ramsey E, Jr** — Jazz Pianist, Composer
7655 N Sheridan Road, Chicago IL 60626, USA
**Lewis, Rashard Q** — Basketball Player
9 E Rivercrest Dr, Houston TX 77042, USA
**Lewis, Ray A** — Football Player
2401 Tufton Ave, Reisterstown MD 21136, USA
**Lewis, Richard** — Actor, Comedian
Bauman Redanty Shaul Agency, 5757 Wilshire Blvd, #473, Los Angeles CA 90036 USA
**Lewis, Richie T** — Baseball Player
13209 E Country Road 700 S, Losantville IN 47354, USA
**Lewis, Robert Lloyd** — Producer
Gersh Agency, 9465 Wilshire Blvd, #600, Beverly Hills CA 90212 USA
**Lewis, Russell T** — Businessman, Publisher
New York Times Co, Publisher's Office, 229 W 43rd St, New York NY 10036, USA
**Lewis, Sally Sirkin** — Interior Designer
502 N Oak St, Inglewood CA 90302, USA
**Lewis, Sherman** — Football Player, Coach
45822 Bristol Circle, Novi MI 48377, USA
**Lewis, Stacy** — Golfer
Sterling Sports Mgmt, 7650 Rivers Edge Dr, Columbus OH 43235, USA
**Lewis, Stephani** — Costume Deisgner
Sheldon Prosnit Agency, 800 S Robertson Blvd, #6, Los Angeles CA 90035, USA
**Lewis, T** — Cartoonist (Over the Hedge)
United Feature Syndicate, PO Box 5610, Cincinnati OH 45201 USA
**Lewis, Tom** — Singer
I C M Partners, 10250 Constellation Blvd, #900, Los Angeles CA 90067 USA
**Lewis, Vaughan A** — Prime Minister, Saint Lucia
West Indies University, International Relations Institute, Saint Augustine, Trinidad & Tobago

**Lewis, Vicki** — Actress, Comedienne
Stone Manners Salners, 9911 W Pico Blvd, #1400, Los Angeles CA 90035 USA
**Lewis, Victor** — Jazz Drummer
Joanne Klein, 130 W 28th St, New York NY 10001, USA
**Lewis, Walter** — Ethnobotanist
7915 Park Dr, Saint Louis MO 63117, USA
**Lewis, William J (Bill)** — Football Coach
University of Notre Dame, Athletic Dept, Notre Dame IN 46556, USA
**Lewiston, Denis C** — Cinematographer
13700 Tahiti Way, #24, Marina del Rey CA 90292, USA
**Leyden, Paul** — Actor
Paradigm Agency, 360 N Crescent Dr, North Building, Beverly Hills CA 90210 USA
**Leygue, Louis Georges** — Sculptor
6 Rue de Docteur Blanche, 75016 Paris, France
**Leyla** — Model, Actress
Model Management Group, 1024 6th Ave, #201, New York NY 10018, USA
**Leyland, James R (Jim)** — Baseball Manager
261 Tech Road, Pittsburgh PA 15205, USA
**Leyritz, James J (Jim)** — Baseball Player
11060 Cameron Court, #304, Davie FL 33324, USA
**Leyton, John** — Actor, Singer
53 Keyes House, Dolphin Square, London SW1V 3NA, England
**Leyva, Nicholas T (Nick)** — Baseball Manager
1098 Tilghman Road, Chesterbrook PA 19087, USA
**Lezak, Jason E** — Swimmer
3 Galena, Irvine CA 92602, USA
**Lezcano, Sixto J** — Baseball Player
7828 Bardmoor Chill Circle, Orlando FL 32835, USA
**Lhuillier, Monique** — Fashion Designer
1201 S Grand Ave, #300, Los Angeles CA 90015, USA
**Li Hongzhi** — Religious Leader
Universe Publishing, PO Box 193, Gillette NJ 07933, USA
**Li Jiajun** — Speed Skater
Skating Assn, 56 Zhongguancun South St, Haidian, Beijing 100044, China
**Li Ka Shing** — Businessman
70/F Cheung Kong Center, 2 Queen's Road, Cental Region, Hong Kong, China
**Li Keyu** — Fashion Designer
21 Gong-Jian Hutong, Di An-Men, Beijing 100009, China
**Li Lanqing** — Government Official, China
Communist Party Central Committee, Zhonganahai, Beijing 100017, China
**Li Na** — Tennis Player
Women's Tennis Assn, 1 Progress Plaza, #1500, Saint Petersburg FL 33701 USA
**Li Peng** — Premier, China
Communist Party Central Committee, Zhonganahai, Beijing 100017, China
**Li, Frederick** — Molecular Biologist
Dana-Farber Cancer Institute, 44 Binney St, Boston MA 02115, USA
**Liagigre, Christian** — Interior Designer
122 Rue de Grenelle, 75007 Paris, France
**Liakhovich, Sergei** — Boxer
Central Boxing Gym, 1755 W Van Buren St, Phoenix AZ 85007, USA
**Liano, Jennifer** — Model
Playboy Promotions, 2706 Media Center Dr, Los Angeles CA 90065 USA
**Liao, Sheri Xiaoyi** — Environmental Activist
Global Village, 86 Bei Yuan Road, Jiaming District, Beijing 100101, China
**Libano Christo, Carlos A** — Social Activist, Writer
Escola Dominicana de Teologia, Rua Atibaia 420, Sao Paulo SP 01235 010, Brazil
**Libatique, Matthew J** — Cinematographer
4524 Ambrose Ave, Los Angeles CA 90027, USA
**Libby, Wendy B** — Educator
Stetson University, President's Office, 421 N Woodland Blvd, DeLand FL 32723, USA
**Liberato, Liana** — Actress
Creative Artists Agency, 2000 Ave of Stars, #100, Los Angeles CA 90067 USA
**Liberman, Avigdor** — Government Official, Israel
Knesset, Kiryat Ben Gurion, Israel 91950, Israel
**Libertini, Richard** — Actor
2313 McKinley Ave, Venice CA 90291, USA
**Libeskind, Daniel** — Architect
Studio Daniel Libeskund, Windscheidstr 18, 10627 Berlin, Germany
**Libett, Nick** — Ice Hockey Player
4272 N McNay Court, West Bloomfield MI 48323, USA
**Libman, Leslie** — Director, Writer
I C M Partners, 10250 Constellation Blvd, #900, Los Angeles CA 90067 USA
**Liboiron, Landon** — Actor
Characters Talent Mgmt, 8 Elm St, Toronto ON M5G 1G7, Canada
**Libor, Christiane** — Opera Singer
I M G Artists, Hogarth Business Park, Chiswick, London W4 2TH, England
**Libutti, Frank** — Marine Corps General, Police Official
New York City Deputy Commissioner's Office, 1 Police Plaza, New York NY 10038, USA
**Licht, Jeremy** — Actor
4355 Clybourn Ave, Toluca Lake CA 91602, USA
**Licht, Louis** — Environmental Scientist
Ecoltree, 3017 Valley View Lane NE, North Liberty IA 52317, USA
**Lichtblau, Eric** — Journalist
New York Times, Editorial Dept, 229 W 43rd St, New York NY 10036 USA
**Lichtenberg, Byron K** — Astronaut
5701 Impala South Road, Athens TX 75752, USA
**Lichtenberger, H W** — Businessman
Praxair Inc, 39 Old Ridgebury Road, #7, Danbury CT 06810, USA
**Lichtenstein, Harvey** — Music Executive
Brooklyn Academy of Music, 30 Lafayette Ave, Brooklyn NY 11217, USA
**Lichti, Todd S** — Basketball Player
2331 Holly View Dr, Martinez CA 94553, USA
**Lick, Dale W** — Mathematician, Computer Scientist
348 Remington Run Loop, Tallahassee FL 32312, USA
**Lick, Dennis A** — Football Player
6140 S Knox Ave, Chicago IL 60629, USA

| | |
|---|---|
| **Lickliter, Frank, II** | Golfer |
| 846 S Main St, Franklin OH 45005, USA | |
| **Lickliter, Todd** | Basketball Coach |
| Marian University, Athletic Dept, 3200 Cold Spring Road, Indianapolis IN 46222, USA | |
| **Licon, Jeffrey (Jeff)** | Director, Actor |
| Innovative Artists, 1505 10th St, Santa Monica CA 90401 USA | |
| **Lidback, Jenny** | Golfer |
| 1130 Graystone Crossing, Alpharetta GA 30005, USA | |
| **Liddell, Chuck** | Wrestler, Mixed Martial Athlete |
| Zinkin Entertainment, 5 E River Park Place W, #203, Fresno CA 93720, USA | |
| **Liddy, G Gordon** | Watergate Figure, Actor |
| 9112 Riverside Dr, Fort Washington MD 20744, USA | |
| **Lidell, Jamie** | Singer |
| Windish Agency, 1658 N Milwaukee Ave, #211, Chicago IL 60647 USA | |
| **Lidge, Bradley T (Brad)** | Baseball Player |
| 4833 Front St, Castle Rock CO 80104, USA | |
| **Lidov, Arthur** | Artist |
| Pleasant Ridge Road, Poughquag NY 12570, USA | |
| **Lidstrom, Nicklas E** | Ice Hockey Player |
| 47725 Bellagio Dr, Northville MI 48167, USA | |
| **Lieber, Charles M** | Chemist |
| Harvard University, Chemistry Dept, Cambridge MA 02138, USA | |
| **Lieber, Jonathan R (Jon)** | Baseball Player |
| 3060 Isle of Palms Dr W, Mobile AL 36695, USA | |
| **Lieber, Larry** | Cartoonist (Amazing Spider-Man) |
| King Features Syndicate, 300 W 57th St, #1500, New York NY 10019 USA | |
| **Lieber, Mimi** | Actress |
| Talent Works, 3500 W Olive Ave, #1400, Burbank CA 91505 USA | |
| **Lieber, Rob** | Writer, Actor |
| Anonymous Content, 3532 Hayden Ave, Culver City CA 90232 USA | |
| **Lieberman, Myron** | Educator |
| 910 17th St NW, #800, Washington DC 20006, USA | |
| **Lieberman, Robert** | Director |
| A P A Talent/Literary Agency, 405 S Beverly Dr, #300, Beverly Hills CA 90212 USA | |
| **Lieberman, Todd** | Producer |
| Mandeville Films, 500 S Buena Vista St, Animation Building 2G, Burbank CA 91521, USA | |
| **Lieberman, Wendy** | Actress, Comedienne |
| Art/Work Entertainment, 5900 Wilshire Blvd, #1720, Los Angeles CA 9003, USA | |
| **Lieberman-Cline, Nancy** | Basketball Player |
| 2636 Creekway Dr, Carrollton TX 75010, USA | |
| **Lieberstein, Paul B** | Actor, Comedian, Writer, Producer |
| Creative Artists Agency, 2000 Ave of Stars, #100, Los Angeles CA 90067 USA | |
| **Liebert, Ottmar** | Guitarist, Composer |
| Segue Entertainment, PO Box A12, Santa Rosa CA 95403, USA | |
| **Lieberthal, Michael S (Mike)** | Baseball Player |
| 1740 Larkfield Ave, Westlake Village CA 91362, USA | |
| **Liebeskind, John** | Brain Surgeon, Psychologist |
| University of California Medical Center, Surgery Dept, Los Angeles CA 90024, USA | |
| **Liebesman, Jonathan** | Director |
| Principato-Young, 9465 Wilshire Blvd, #880, Beverly Hills CA 90212 USA | |
| **Liebman, David** | Jazz Saxophonist |
| 2206 Brislin Road, Stroudsberg PA 18360, USA | |
| **Liebowitz, Ronald D, Jr** | Educator |
| Middlebury College, President's Office, 9 Old Chapel Road, Middlebury VT 05753, USA | |
| **Liefeld, Rob** | Cartoonist (Youngblood) |
| 1440 N Harbor Blvd, #305, Fullerton CA 92835, USA | |
| **Liefer, Jeff** | Baseball Player |
| 1116 W Bay Ave, Newport Beach CA 92661, USA | |
| **Liekens, Koen** | Drummer (K's Choice) |
| Sharpe Entertainment Services. 683 Palmera Ave, Pacific Palisades CA 90272, USA | |
| **Lien, Jennifer** | Actress |
| Abrams Artists, 9200 W Sunset Blvd, #1125, West Hollywood CA 90069 USA | |
| **Lienhard, William (Bill)** | Basketball Player |
| 1320 Lawrence Ave, Lawrence KS 66049, USA | |
| **Liepa, Andris** | Ballet Dancer |
| Bryusov Per 17, #13, 103009 Moscow, Russia | |
| **Liepa, Ilsa** | Ballerina |
| Bryusov Per 17, #12, 103009 Moscow, Russia | |
| **Liepmann, Hans W** | Aeronautical Engineer, Physicist |
| 55 Haverstock Road, La Canada Flintridge CA 91011, USA | |
| **Lietzke, Bruce** | Golfer |
| PO Box 177, Larue TX 75770, USA | |
| **Lifeson, Alex** | Guitarist (Rush) |
| S L Feldman Mgmt, 1505 W 2nd Ave, #200, Vancouver BC V6H 3Y4, Canada | |
| **Ligety, Ted** | Alpine Skier |
| Park City Ski Resort, Ski Director's Office, 1345 Lowell Ave, Park City UT 84060, USA | |
| **Light, John** | Actor |
| Markham Froggatt Irwin, Julian House, 4 Windmill St, London W1P 1HF, England | |
| **Light, Judith** | Actress |
| Gersh Agency, 9465 Wilshire Blvd, #600, Beverly Hills CA 90212 USA | |
| **Light, Matthew C (Matt)** | Football Player |
| 261 East St, Foxboro MA 02035, USA | |
| **Lightbody, Gary** | Singer, Songwriter (Snow Patrol) |
| Big Life Mgmt, 67-69 Charlton St, London NW1 1HY, England | |
| **Lightfoot, Edwin N** | Chemical, Biological Engineer |
| University of Wisconsin, Chemical Engineering Dept, 1415 Engineering Dr, Madison WI 53706, USA | |
| **Lightfoot, Gordon** | Singer, Guitarist, Songwriter |
| ICON Performing Arts, 1557 Westwood Blvd, #242, Los Angeles CA 90024, USA | |
| **Lightman, Alan P** | Physicist, Writer |
| Harvard University, Humanities Dept, Cambridge MA 02138, USA | |
| **Lightman, Toby** | Singer, Songwriter |
| Creative Artists Agency, 2000 Ave of Stars, #100, Los Angeles CA 90067 USA | |
| **Lightner, Candance L (Candy)** | Social Activist |
| 1216 Portner Road, Alexandria VA 22314, USA | |
| **Ligon, Bill** | Basketball Player |
| PO Box 1432, Gallatin TN 37066, USA | |

**L**

**Lickliter - Ligon**

**Ligouri, James A** — Educator
Iona College, President's Office, New Rochelle NY 10801, USA

**Ligtenberg, Kerry** — Baseball Player
9274 Albright Court, Inver Grove Heights MN 55077, USA

**Lijn, Liliane** — Sculptor
99 Camden Mews, London NW1 9BU, England

**Likens, Gene E** — Ecologist, Biologist
Ecosystem Studies Institute, PO Box AB, Millbrook NY 12545, USA

**Lil Bow Wow** — Rap Artist
Central Entertainment Group, 251 W 39st, #700, New York NY 10018, USA

**Lil' Fame** — Rap Artist (MOP)
Pyramid Entertainment Group, 377 Rector Place, #21A, New York NY 10280 USA

**Lil' J** — Rap Artist
Thruline Entertainment, 9250 Wilshire Blvd, #100, Beverly Hills CA 90212 USA

**Lil' JJ** — Actor, Comedian
W M E Entertainment, 9601 Wilshire Blvd, #300, Beverly Hills CA 90210 USA

**Lil' Jon** — Rap Artist, Songwriter
FilmEngine, 345 Maple Dr, #222, Beverly Hills CA 90210, USA

**Lil' Kim** — Rap Artist
Universal Media Artists, 8222 Melrose Ave, #203, Los Angeles CA 90048, USA

**Lil Mama** — Rap Artist
F Y I Public Relations, 45 E 20th St, #5B, New York NY 10003, USA

**Lil' Wayne** — Rap Artist (Hot Boys), Actor
Bryant Mgmt, 800 Brickell Ave, #550, Miami FL 33131, USA

**Liles, John-Michael** — Ice Hockey Player
1540 E Shore Dr, Culver IN 46511, USA

**Liles, Robert L** — WW II Army Air Corps Hero
19520 Tiber Court, Montgomery Village MD 20886, USA

**Lilienfeld, Abraham M** — Epidemiologist
3203 Old Post Dr, Pikesville MD 21208, USA

**Lilja, Andreas** — Ice Hockey Player
6501 N Federal Highway, #2, Boca Raton FL 33487, USA

**Lilja, George V** — Football Player
8 Driftwood Dr, Warren PA 16365, USA

**Lill, Dennis** — Actor
Ken McReddie Assoc, 101 Finsbury Pavement, London EC2A 1RS, England

**Lillard, Bill** — Bowler
5418 Imogene St, Houston TX 77096, USA

**Lillard, Damian** — Basketball Player
Portland Trail Blazers, Rose Garden, 1 N Center Court St, Portland OR 97227 USA

**Lillard, Matthew** — Actor
Paradigm Agency, 360 N Crescent Dr, North Building, Beverly Hills CA 90210 USA

**Lillee, Dennis K** — Cricketer
Swan Sport, PO Box 158, Byron Bay NSW 2481, Australia

**Lilley, Chris** — Producer, Writer, Actor
Princess Pictures, 11 Princes St, Saint Kilda VIC 3182, Australia

**Lilley, James R** — Diplomat
2801 New Mexico Ave NW, #407, Washington DC 20007, USA

**Lilley, John M** — Educator
Baylor University, President's Office, 1 Bear Place, Waco TX 76798, USA

**Lillibridge, Brent S** — Baseball Player
22714 43rd Dr SE, Bothell WA 98021, USA

**Lilliquist, Derek J** — Baseball Player
226 10th Ave, Vero Beach FL 32962, USA

**Lillis, Robert P (Bob)** — Baseball Player, Manager
5107 Cherry Tree Lane, Orlando FL 32819, USA

**Lilly, Evangeline** — Actress, Model
Maydew & Golenberg, 8383 Wilshire Blvd, #1050, Beverly Hills CA 90211, USA

**Lilly, Kristine** — Soccer Player
10 Bradford Terrace, #2, Brookline MA 02446, USA

**Lilly, Robert L (Bob)** — Football Player
3310 Drexel Dr, Dallas TX 75205, USA

**Lilly, Theodore R (Ted), III** — Baseball Player
1305 W Waveland Ave, Chicago IL 60613, USA

**Lim Chwen Jeng** — Architect
Bartlett Architecture School, 22 Gordon St, London WC1H 0QB, England

**Lim Siew Al** — Golfer
304 Morning Sun Dr, Birmingham AL 35242, USA

**Lim, H J** — Concert Pianist
Harrison/Parrott, 5-6 Albion Court, London W6 0QT, England

**Lima, Adriana** — Model
Marilyn Agency, 4 Rue de la Paix, 75002 Paris, France

**Lima, Devin** — Singer, Rap Artist (Lyte Funky Ones)
LFO/BMG Records, 8750 Wilshire Blvd, Beverly Hills CA 90211, USA

**Lima, Kevin** — Director, Producer
W M E Entertainment, 9601 Wilshire Blvd, #300, Beverly Hills CA 90210 USA

**Liman, Doug** — Director
Dutch Oven, 12233 W Olympic Blvd, #256, Los Angeles CA 90064, USA

**Limbaugh, Rush** — Entertainer
PO Box 2795, Palm Beach FL 33480, USA

**Limbert, Deborah (Deb)** — Explorer, Speleologist
British Cave Research Assn, Old Methodist Chapel, Great Hucklow, Buxton SK17 8RG, England

**Limbert, Howard** — Explorer, Speleologist
British Cave Research Assn, Old Methodist Chapel, Great Hucklow, Buxton SK17 8RG, England

**Lime-Fedderson, Yvonne** — Actress
15757 N 78th St, Scottsdale AZ 85260, USA

**Lin, Cho-Liang** — Concert Violinist
Julliard School, 60 Lincoln Center Plaza, New York NY 10023, USA

**Lin, Jeremy S** — Basketball Player
Houston Rockets, 1730 Jefferson St, Houston TX 77003 USA

**Lin, Justin** — Director
Trailing Johnson Productions, 2100 Sawtell Blvd, Los Angeles CA 90025, USA

**Lin, Maya Ying** — Architect, Sculptor
Sidney Janis Gallery, 120 E 75th St, #6A, New York NY 10021, USA

**Lin, Yu Ping** — Golfer
Jerry Wong, 1450 Subtropic Dr, La Habra Heights CA 90631, USA

|  |  |
|---|---|
| **Lincecum, Timothy L (Tim)**<br>16062 SE 4th St, Belluvue WA 98008, USA | Baseball Player |
| **Lincicome, Brittany G**<br>7971 Idlewild Lane, Seminole FL 33777, USA | Golfer |
| **Lincoln, Andrew**<br>Markham Froggatt Irwin, Julian House, 4 Windmill St, London W1P 1HF, England | Actor |
| **Lincoln, Craig**<br>20930 Almazan Road, Woodland Hills CA 91364, USA | Diver |
| **Lincoln, Jeremy A**<br>3411 W Lincolnshire Blvd, Toledo OH 43606, USA | Football Player |
| **Lincoln, Keith P**<br>550 SE Crestview St, Pullman WA 99163, USA | Football Player |
| **Lincoln, Lar Park**<br>Premiere Artists Agency, 1875 Century Park E, #2250, Los Angeles CA 90067 USA | Actress |
| **Lincoln, Michael G (Mike)**<br>8269 Moss Oak Ave, Citrus Heights CA 95610, USA | Baseball Player |
| **Lincoln, Todd**<br>Creative Artists Agency, 2000 Ave of Stars, #100, Los Angeles CA 90067 USA | Director, Writer |
| **Lind, Adam A**<br>6520 Turf Way, Anderson IN 46013, USA | Baseball Player |
| **Lind, Don L**<br>51 N 376 E, Smithfield UT 84335, USA | Astronaut |
| **Lind, Heather**<br>I C M Partners, 10250 Constellation Blvd, #900, Los Angeles CA 90067 USA | Actress |
| **Lind, Jackson H (Jack)**<br>6132 E Redmont Dr, Mesa AZ 85215, USA | Baseball Player |
| **Lind, Joan**<br>240 Euclid Ave, Long Beach CA 90803, USA | Rowing Athlete |
| **Lind, Jose**<br>18 Brisas del Plata, Dorado PR 00646, USA | Baseball Player |
| **Lind, Juha P**<br>Montreal Canadiens, 1275 Saint Antoine St W, Montreal QC H3C 5L2, Canada | Ice Hockey Player |
| **Lind, Marshall L**<br>University of Alaska, Chancellor's Office, Fairbanks AK 99775, USA | Educator |
| **Lind, Zach**<br>S A M, 722 Seward St, Los Angeles CA 90038, USA | Drummer (Jimmy Eat World) |
| **Lindahl, Cathrine**<br>Curling Assn, Idrottshuser, Marbackagatan 19, 123 43 Farsta, Sweden | Curling Athlete |
| **Lindahl, George, III**<br>Anadarko Petroleum Corp, 1201 Lake Robbins Dr, Spring TX 77380, USA | Businessman |
| **Lindahl, Margaretha**<br>Curling Assn, Idrottshuser, Marbackagatan 19, 123 43 Farsta, Sweden | Curling Athlete |
| **Lindbeck, Assar**<br>50 Ostermalmsgatan, 114 26 Stockholm, Sweden | Economist |
| **Lindbeck, George A**<br>Yale University, Divinity School, New Haven CT 06520, USA | Theologian |
| **Lindberg, Athena**<br>Playboy Promotions, 2706 Media Center Dr, Los Angeles CA 90065 USA | Model |
| **Lindberg, Chad**<br>Creative Partners Group, 1522 2nd St, Santa Monica CA 90401, USA | Actor |
| **Lindbergh, Peter**<br>Camerawork AG, Kantstr 149, 10623 Berlin, Germany | Photographer |
| **Lindelind, Liv**<br>PO Box 1029, Frazier Park CA 93225, USA | Model |
| **Lindell, Rian D**<br>45 Stoughton Lane, Orchard Park NY 14127, USA | Football Player |
| **Lindeman, James W (Jim)**<br>2278 S Scott St, Des Plaines IL 60018, USA | Baseball Player |
| **Lindemann, Til**<br>Pilgrim Mgmt, PO Box 540101, 10042 Berlin, Germany | Singer (Rammstein) |
| **Linden, Eugene**<br>Penguin Books, 375 Hudson St, Basement 1, New York NY 10014 USA | Writer |
| **Linden, Hal**<br>Stone Manners Salners, 9911 W Pico Blvd, #1400, Los Angeles CA 90035 USA | Actor |
| **Linden, Jamie**<br>Paradigm Agency, 360 N Crescent Dr, North Building, Beverly Hills CA 90210 USA | Director, Writer |
| **Linden, Trevor**<br>1362 23rd St SE, Medicine Hat AB T1A 2C9, Canada | Ice Hockey Player |
| **Lindenlaub, Karl W**<br>3021 Nichols Canyon Road, Los Angeles CA 90046, USA | Cinematographer |
| **Linder, Kate**<br>Siegal Co, 9025 Wilshire Blvd, #400, Beverly Hills CA 90211, USA | Actress |
| **Linderman, Earl W**<br>5005 E Camelback Road, Phoenix AZ 85018, USA | Artist |
| **Lindes, Hal**<br>Damage Mgmt, 16 Lambton Place, London W11 2SH, England | Guitarist (Dire Straits) |
| **Lindh, Hilary**<br>PO Box 33036, Juneau AK 99803, USA | Alpine Skier |
| **Lindholm, Ingvar N**<br>Hringe Hages Vag 33, 144 00 Ronninge, Sweden | Composer |
| **Lindholm, Tobias**<br>W M E Entertainment, 9601 Wilshire Blvd, #300, Beverly Hills CA 90210 USA | Director |
| **Lindhome, Riki**<br>Principato-Young, 9465 Wilshire Blvd, #880, Beverly Hills CA 90212 USA | Actress |
| **Lindig, Bill M**<br>Sysco Corp, 1390 Enclave Parkway, Houston TX 77077, USA | Businessman |
| **Lindley, Christina**<br>Esterman Entertainment, 12333 Pretoria Dr, Silver Spring MD 20904, USA | Model, Actress |
| **Lindley, David**<br>Rosebud Agency, PO Box 170429, San Francisco CA 94117 USA | Guitarist |
| **Lindley, John W**<br>PO Box 351, 15332 Antioch St, Pacific Palisades CA 90272, USA | Cinematographer |
| **Lindman, Karl**<br>Wilhelmina Models, 300 Park Ave S, #200, New York NY 10010 USA | Model |
| **Lindner, William G**<br>Transport Workers Union, 80 W End Ave, New York NY 10023, USA | Labor Leader |

**Lindo, Delroy** — Actor
Innovative Artists, 1505 10th St, Santa Monica CA 90401 USA
**Lindquist, Barbara M (Barb)** — Triathlete
215 Targhee Towne Road, Alta WY 83414, USA
**Lindquist, Susan L** — Biologist
Whitehead Institute, 9 Cambridge Circle, Cambridge MA 02142, USA
**Lindqvist, David** — Bassist (Caesars)
Paradigm Agency, 360 Park Ave, #1600, New York NY 10022 USA
**Lindros, Eric B** — Ice Hockey Player
1 Morton Square, #6BE, New York NY 10014, USA
**Lindroth, Eric** — Water Polo Player
13151 Dufresne Place, San Diego CA 92129, USA
**Lindsay, Bill** — Ice Hockey Player
700 NW 7th Ave, Boca Raton FL 33486, USA
**Lindsay, Elvin (Lin)** — WW II Navy Air Force Hero
6220 E Broadway Road, #347, Mesa AZ 85206, USA
**Lindsay, Everett E** — Football Player
5191 Bald Eagle Ave, Saint Paul MN 55110, USA
**Lindsay, James J** — Army General
676 Azalea Dr, Vass NC 28394, USA
**Lindsay, Mark** — Singer, Songwriter
Lustig Talent, PO Box 770850, Orlando FL 32877 USA
**Lindsay, R B Theodore (Ted)** — Ice Hockey Player
2598 Invitational Dr, Oakland MI 48363, USA
**Lindsay, Robert** — Actor, Singer
Hamilton Hodell, 66-68 Margaret St, #500, London W1W 8SR, England
**Lindsay-Abaire, David** — Writer
W M E Entertainment, 9601 Wilshire Blvd, #300, Beverly Hills CA 90210 USA
**Lindsey, James E (Jim)** — Football Player
1165 E Joyce Blvd, Fayetteville AR 72703, USA
**Lindsey, P Dale** — Football Player
4020 Murphy Canyon Road, San Diego CA 92123, USA
**Lindsey, Steven W** — Astronaut
3217 W Yarrow Circle, Superior CO 80027, USA
**Lindsey, Tracy** — Actress
651B N Kilkea Dr, Los Angeles CA 90048, USA
**Lindskog, Par** — Opera Singer
Maxine Robertson Mgmt, 14 Forge Dr, Claygate KT10 0HR, England
**Lindsley, Blake** — Actress
Shelter Entertainment, 9255 Sunset Blvd, #300, Los Angeles CA 90069 USA
**Lindsley, Donald B** — Psychologist, Physiologist
517 11th St, Santa Monica CA 90402, USA
**Lindstrand, Per** — Balloonist
Thunder & Colt, Maesbury Road, Oswestry, Shropshire SY10 8HA, England
**Lindstrom Breer, Murle** — Golfer
7008 Sand Road, Savannah GA 31410, USA
**Lindstrom, David A (Dave)** — Football Player
11562 Hardy St, Overland Park KS 66210, USA
**Lindstrom, Jack** — Cartoonist (Executive Suite)
United Feature Syndicate, PO Box 5610, Cincinnati OH 45201 USA
**Lindstrom, Jon** — Actor, Writer, Producer
Jailbreak Films, 4341 Birch St, Newport Beach CA 92660, USA
**Lindstrom, Matthew J (Matt)** — Baseball Player
316 Mohawk Ave, Rexburg ID 83440, USA
**Lindvall, Angela** — Model, Actress
Rogue Entertainment, 10900 Wilshire Blvd, #1400, Los Angeles CA 90024, USA
**Lineback, Richard** — Actor
S M S Talent, 8383 Wilshire Blvd, #230, Beverly Hills CA 90211 USA
**Linebrink, Scott** — Baseball Player
2100 County Road 156, Granger TX 76530, USA
**Linehan, Marsha M** — Psychologist
University of Washington, Behavioral Research & Therapy Clinic, Seattle WA 98195, USA
**Linehan, Scott** — Football Coach
Detroit Lions, 222 Republic Dr, Allen Park MI 48101 USA
**Lineker, Gary W** — Soccer Player
Markee UK, 6 Saint George St, Nottingham NG1 3BE, England
**Linenger, Jerry M** — Astronaut
550 S Stoney Point Road, Suttons Bay MI 49682, USA
**Lines, Aaron** — Singer
Mark Jones Mgmt, 54 Music Square E, #200, Nashville TN 37203, USA
**Lines, Richard G (Dick)** — Baseball Player
1716 Pebble Beach Lane, Lady Lake FL 32159, USA
**Ling** — Model
I M G Models, 304 Park Ave S, #PH N, New York NY 10010 USA
**Ling, Jahja** — Conductor
Opus 3 Artists, 470 Park Ave S, #900N, New York NY 10016 USA
**Ling, Lisa** — Commentator
W M E Entertainment, 1325 Ave of Americas, New York NY 10019 USA
**Ling, Sergei S** — Prime Minister, Belarus
Belarus Mission, United Nations, 136 E 67th St, New York NY 10065, USA
**Ling, Victor** — Biophysicist
5671 Trafalgar St, Vancouver BC V6N 1C2, Canada
**Lingenfelter, Steven R (Steve)** — Basketball Player
17378 Ithaca Court, Lakeville MN 55044, USA
**Linger, Andreas** — Luge Athlete
Bettelwurfsiedlung 9, 6067 Absam, Austria
**Linger, Wolfgang** — Luge Athlete
Bettelwurfsiedlung 9, 6067 Absam, Austria
**Lingner, Adam J** — Football Player
8395 Norwood Lane N, Maple Grove MN 55369, USA
**Linhart, Carl J** — Baseball Player
2647 Delmar Ave, Granite City IL 62040, USA
**Lini, Ham** — Prime Minister, Vanuatu
Prime Minister's Office, PO Box 053, Port Vila, Vanuatu
**Liniak, Cole E** — Baseball Player
PO Box 235625, Encinitas CA 92023, USA

| | |
|---|---|
| **Linichuk, Natalia** | Ice Dancer, Coach |
| 146 Dallam Road, Newark DE 19711, USA | |
| **Link, Caroline** | Director |
| Just Publicity, Erhardstr 8, 80469 Munich, Germany | |
| **Linker, Amy** | Actress |
| Lemack Co, 508 Gerona Ave, San Gabriel CA 91775, USA | |
| **Linklater, Hamish** | Actor, Writer |
| I C M Partners, 10250 Constellation Blvd, #900, Los Angeles CA 90067 USA | |
| **Linklater, Richard** | Director, Writer |
| Creative Artists Agency, 2000 Ave of Stars, #100, Los Angeles CA 90067 USA | |
| **Linkletter, Nicole** | Model |
| Elite Model Mgmt, 404 Park Ave S, #900, New York NY 10016 USA | |
| **Linley, Cody** | Actor |
| C E S D, 10635 Santa Monica Blvd, #130, Los Angeles CA 90025 USA | |
| **Linn, Rex** | Actor |
| Vox Inc, 6420 Wilshire Blvd, #1080, Los Angeles CA 90048 USA | |
| **Linn, Richard** | Judge |
| US Court of Appeals, 717 Madison Place NW, Washington DC 20439, USA | |
| **Linn, Teri Ann** | Actress |
| Sutton-Barth Vennari, 5900 Wilshire Blvd, #700, Los Angeles CA 90036 USA | |
| **Linn-Baker, Mark** | Actor |
| 27702 Fairweather St, Canyon Country CA 91351, USA | |
| **Linnehan, Richard M** | Astronaut |
| 16802 Hartwood Way, Houston TX 77058, USA | |
| **Linney, Laura** | Actress |
| Brillstein Entertainment Partners, 9150 Wilshire Blvd, #350, Beverly Hills CA 90212 USA | |
| **Linseman, Ken** | Ice Hockey Player |
| 1070 Ocean Blvd, Hampton NH 03842, USA | |
| **Linson, Art** | Director, Producer |
| I C M Partners, 10250 Constellation Blvd, #900, Los Angeles CA 90067 USA | |
| **Lintel, Michelle** | Actress |
| Kazarian/Measures/Ruskin, 11969 Ventura Blvd, #300, Studio City CA 91604 USA | |
| **Linteris, Gregory T** | Astronaut |
| US Commerce Dept, Fire Science Division, Gaithersburg MD 20899, USA | |
| **Linton, Douglas W (Doug)** | Baseball Player |
| 201 Ellison St, Rochester NY 14609, USA | |
| **Linton, Tom** | Guitarist (Jimmy Eat World) |
| S A M, 722 Seward St, Los Angeles CA 90038, USA | |
| **Lintu, Hannu** | Conductor |
| Tampere Philharmonic Orchestra, PL 16, 33101 Tampere, Finland | |
| **Lintz, Larry** | Baseball Player |
| 8529 Sun Sprite Way, Elk Grove CA 95624, USA | |
| **Linville, Joanne** | Actress |
| Special Artists Agency, 9200 Sunset Blvd, #410, West Hollywood CA 90069 USA | |
| **Linz, Philip F (Phil)** | Baseball Player |
| 20 Rocky Rapids Road, Stamford CT 06903, USA | |
| **Linzy, Frank A** | Baseball Player |
| 38947 E 151st St S, Coweta OK 74429, USA | |
| **Lioeanjie, Rene** | Labor Leader |
| National Maritime Union, 1150 17th St NW, Washington DC 20036, USA | |
| **Lionetti, Donald M** | Army General |
| 4517 W Rosemere Road, Tampa FL 33609, USA | |
| **Lions, Pierre-Louis** | Mathematician |
| Paris University, Mathematics Dept, Place Marechal Lattre-de-Tessigny, 75775 Paris, France | |
| **Liotta, Ray** | Actor |
| United Talent Agency, U T A Plaza, 9336 Civic Center Dr, Beverly Hills CA 90210 USA | |
| **Lipa, Elisabeta** | Rowing Athlete |
| Str Reconstructiei 1, #78, Bucharest, Romania | |
| **Lipes, Jody Lee** | Cinematographer |
| Sheldon Prosnit Agency, 800 S Robertson Blvd, Los Angeles CA 90035, USA | |
| **Lipetri, N Angelo** | Baseball Player |
| 150 Yoakum Ave, Farmingdale NY 11735, USA | |
| **Lipez, Kermit V** | Judge |
| US Court of Appeals, 537 Congress St, Portland ME 04101, USA | |
| **Lipinski, Ann Marie** | Journalist |
| Chicago Tribune, Editorial Dept, 435 N Michigan Ave, #1, Chicago IL 60611, USA | |
| **Lipinski, Tara** | Figure Skater, Actress |
| Thumbs Up Enterprises, PO Box 1487, Sugar Land TX 77487, USA | |
| **Lipman, Elinor** | Writer |
| Houghton Mifflin Harcourt, 215 Park Ave S, #1200, New York NY 10003 USA | |
| **Lipman, Maureen** | Actress |
| Talking Concepts, 19 Bird St, Lichfield, Straffordshire WS13 6PW, England | |
| **Lipnicki, Jonathan** | Actor |
| Greene Assoc, 1901 Ave of Stars, #130, Los Angeles CA 90067 USA | |
| **Lipovsek, Marjana** | Opera Singer |
| Kunstleragentur Raab & Bohm, Plankengasse 7, 1010 Vienna, Austria | |
| **Lippard, Stephen J** | Chemist |
| 975 Memorial Dr, #602, Cambridge MA 02138, USA | |
| **Lippett, Ronald G (Ronnie)** | Football Player |
| 610 Foundry St, South Easton MA 02375, USA | |
| **Lippincott, Philip E** | Businessman |
| Campbell Soup Co, Campbell Place, Camden NJ 08103, USA | |
| **Lipps, Louis A** | Football Player |
| 17 Brilliant Ave, #100, Pittsburgh PA 15215, USA | |
| **Lipscomb, Steve** | Poker Executive |
| World Poker Tour Enterprises, 5700 Wilshire Blvd, #350, Los Angeles CA 90036 USA | |
| **Lipski, Robert P (Bob)** | Baseball Player |
| 1 Snook St, Scranton PA 18505, USA | |
| **Lipton, Martin** | Attorney |
| Wachtell Lipton Rosen Katz, 51 W 52nd St, New York NY 10019, USA | |
| **Lipton, Peggy** | Actress |
| Saint Martin's Press, 175 5th Ave, #400, New York NY 10010 USA | |
| **Liquori, Martin (Marty)** | Track Athlete, Sportscaster |
| 2915 NW 58th Blvd, Gainesville FL 32606, USA | |
| **Liriano, Nelson A** | Baseball Player |
| Burlington Royals, PO Box 1143, Burlington NC 27216, USA | |

**L**

Linichuk - Liriano

**Lisa Lisa** — Singer (Lisa Lisa & Cult Jam)
Green Light Talent Agency, PO Box 3172, Beverly Hills CA 90212 USA
**LisaRaye** — Actress
C E S D, 10635 Santa Monica Blvd, #130, Los Angeles CA 90025 USA
**Lisbe, Mike** — Writer, Producer
I C M Partners, 10250 Constellation Blvd, #900, Los Angeles CA 90067 USA
**Liscio, Anthony F (Tony)** — Football Player
10348 Trailcliff Dr, Dallas TX 75238, USA
**Lisi, Ricardo P E (Rick)** — Baseball Player
1207 N Wren Dr, Rogers AR 72756, USA
**Lisi, Virna** — Actress
Voyez Mon Agent, 20 Ave Rapp, 75007 Paris, France
**Lisicki, Sabine** — Tennis Player
5500 34th St W, Bradenton FL 34210, USA
**Lisiecki, Jan** — Concert Pianist
I M G Artists, Hogarth Business Park, Chiswick, London W4 2TH, England
**Lisitsa, Valentina** — Concert Pianist
Columbia Artists Mgmt Inc, 1790 Broadway, #702, New York NY 10019 USA
**Liske, Peter A (Pete)** — Football Player
116 E Mountain Brook Lane, Wenatchee WA 98801, USA
**Liskevych, Taras** — Volleyball Player, Coach
Oregon State University, Athletic Dept, Corvallis OR 97331, USA
**Liskov, Barbara H** — Computer Engineer
Massachusetts Institute of Technology, Computer Science Laboratory, Cambridge MA 02139, USA
**Lissack, Russell D** — Guitarist (Bloc Party)
Coalition Mgmt, 12 Barley Mow Passage, London W4 4PH, England
**Lissner, Stephane M** — Director
Theatre du Chatelet, 2 Rue Eduouard Colonne, 75001 Paris, France
**Lissoni, Piero** — Interior Designer
Lissoni Assoc, Via Goito 9, 20121 Milan, Italy
**List, Peyton** — Actress
United Talent Agency, U T A Plaza, 9336 Civic Center Dr, Beverly Hills CA 90210 USA
**List, Peyton R** — Actress, Model
United Talent Agency, U T A Plaza, 9336 Civic Center Dr, Beverly Hills CA 90210 USA
**List, Robert F** — Governor, NV
1660 Catalpa Lane, Reno NV 89511, USA
**List, Spencer** — Actor
Untitled Entertainment, 350 S Beverly Dr, #200, Beverly Hills CA 90212 USA
**Listach, Patrick A (Pat)** — Baseball Player
6030 Durande Dr, Baton Rouge LA 70820, USA
**Lister, Alton L** — Basketball Player
5413 Kirkridge Place, Garland TX 75044, USA
**Lister, Tommy (Tiny)** — Actor, Wrestler
Abrams Artists, 9200 W Sunset Blvd, #1125, West Hollywood CA 90069 USA
**Liteky, Angelo J (Charles)** — Vietnam War Army Chaplain (CMH)
Medal of Honor Society, 40 Patriots Point Road, Mount Pleasant SC 29464, USA
**Lithgow, John** — Actor, Singer
W M E Entertainment, 9601 Wilshire Blvd, #300, Beverly Hills CA 90210 USA
**Litsch, Jesse A** — Baseball Player
6948 80th Terrace, Pinellas Park FL 33781, USA
**Littell, Jonathan** — Writer
Harper Collins Publishers, 10 E 53rd St, Cellar 1, New York NY 10022 USA
**Littell, Mark A** — Baseball Player
21001 N Tatum Blvd, #1630511, Phoenix AZ 85050, USA
**Littell, Robert** — Writer
Simon & Schuster, 1230 Ave of Americas, Concourse 1, New York NY 10020 USA
**Littenberg, Barbara** — Architect
Peterson/Littenberg Architecture, 13 E 66th St, New York NY 10065, USA
**Little Anthony** — Singer
Dassinger Creative, 172 2nd Ave, Little Falls NJ 07424, USA
**Little Richard** — Singer
Hyatt Sunset Hotel, 8401 W Sunset Blvd, West Hollywood CA 90069, USA
**Little Steven** — Singer, Musician, Actor
Premier Talent, 3 E 54th St, #1100, New York NY 10022 USA
**Little, Carole** — Fashion Designer
Carole Little Inc, PO Box 77917, Los Angeles CA 90007, USA
**Little, Chad** — Auto Racing Driver
8718 Statesville Road, Charlotte NC 28269, USA
**Little, Charles L** — Labor Leader
United Transportation Union, 24950 Country Club Blvd, North Olmsted OH 44070, USA
**Little, D Jeffrey (Jeff)** — Baseball Player
5711 W Camper Road, Genoa OH 43430, USA
**Little, Dwight H** — Director
A P A Talent/Literary Agency, 405 S Beverly Dr, #300, Beverly Hills CA 90212 USA
**Little, Floyd D** — Football Player
34505 5th Place SW, Federal Way WA 98023, USA
**Little, Larry C** — Football Player, Coach
14761 SW 169th Lane, Miami FL 33187, USA
**Little, Leonard A** — Football Player
4 Rainier Pointe Court, Saint Charles MO 63301, USA
**Little, Natasha** — Actress
Hamilton Hodell, 66-68 Margaret St, #500, London W1W 8SR, England
**Little, Rich** — Actor, Comedian
C E S D, 10635 Santa Monica Blvd, #130, Los Angeles CA 90025 USA
**Little, Robert A** — Chef
49 Firth St, London W1V 5TE, England
**Little, Sally** — Golfer
3210 S Ocean Blvd, #702, Highland Beach FL 33487, USA
**Little, Steve** — Actor
Odenkirk Provissiero Entertainment, 650 N Bronson Ave, #B145, Los Angeles, CA 90004, USA
**Little, Tasmin E** — Concert Violinist
Chamber Music Society, 70 Lincoln Center Plaza, Front 2, New York NY 10023, USA
**Little, Tawny Godin** — Entertainer, Beauty Queen
17941 Sky Park Circle, #F, Irvine CA 92614, USA
**Little, W Grady** — Baseball Manager
13115 Odell Heights Dr, Mint Hill NC 28227, USA

| | |
|---|---|
| **Littlefield, John A**<br>1935 Ramar Road, Bullhead City AZ 86442, USA | Baseball Player |
| **Littlefield, Warren**<br>Littlefield Co, 500 S Buena Vista St, #1835, Burbank CA 91521, USA | Businessman, Producer |
| **Littleford, Beth**<br>Domain Talent, 9229 W Sunset Blvd, #710, West Hollywood CA 90069 USA | Actress, Comedienne |
| **Littlejohn, Dennis G**<br>6813 Klamath Way, #D, Bakersfield CA 93309, USA | Baseball Player |
| **Littler, Gene A**<br>PO Box 1949, Rancho Santa Fe CA 92067, USA | Golfer |
| **Littles, Eugene S (Gene)**<br>6421 E Beck Lane, Scottsdale AZ 85254, USA | Basketball Player, Coach |
| **Littleton, Cynthia**<br>Variety, 5900 Wilshire Blvd, #3100, Los Angeles CA 90036, USA | Editor |
| **Littleton, Harvey K**<br>232 E Ridge Dr, Spruce Pine NC 28777, USA | Sculptor |
| **Littman, Jonathan**<br>Jerry Bruckheimer Films, 1631 10th St, Santa Monica CA 90404, USA | Producer |
| **Litton, Andrew**<br>I M G Artists, Burlington Lane, Chiswick, London W4 2TH, England | Conductor |
| **Litton, Bruce**<br>10184 E US Highway 136, Clermont IN 46234, USA | Auto Racing Driver |
| **Litton, Drew**<br>Rocky Mountain News, Editorial Dept, 101 W Colfax Ave, #500, Denver CO 80202, USA | Editorial Cartoonist |
| **Litton, J Gregory (Greg)**<br>22 Hillbrook Way, Pensacola FL 32503, USA | Baseball Player |
| **Littrell, Brian T**<br>Wright Entertainment Group, PO Box 590009, Orlando FL 32859, USA | Singer (Backstreet Boys) |
| **Littrell, Gary L**<br>4302 Belle Vista Dr, Saint Pete Beach FL 33706, USA | Vietnam War Army Hero (CMH) |
| **Litwack, Leon F**<br>University of California, History Dept, Berkeley CA 94720, USA | Historian |
| **Liu Boming**<br>Satellite Launch Center, Jiuquan, Guangzhou Province, China | Taikonaut |
| **Liu Chao Shiuan**<br>Premier's Office, 1 Chunghsiao East Road, Section 1, Taipei, Taiwan | Prime Minister, Taiwan |
| **Liu Chunhong**<br>9 Tiyuguan Road, Beijing 100763, China | Weightlifter |
| **Liu Yang**<br>Satellite Launch Center, Jiuquan, Guangzhou Province, China | Taikonaut |
| **Liu, Lucy**<br>United Talent Agency, U T A Plaza, 9336 Civic Center Dr, Beverly Hills CA 90210 USA | Actress, Model |
| **Liukin, Nastia**<br>World Olympic Gymnastics Academy, 1937 W Parker Road, Plano TX 75023, USA | Gymnast |
| **Liukin, Valeri**<br>World Olympic Gymnastics Academy, 1937 W Parker Road, Plano TX 75023, USA | Gymnast, Coach |
| **Liut, Michael D (Mike)**<br>26011 German Mill Road, Franklin MI 48025, USA | Ice Hockey Player |
| **Livadiotti, Massimo**<br>Piazza Vittorio Emanuele II, #31, 00185 Rome, Italy | Artist |
| **Livage, Jacques**<br>College de France, 11 Place M Berthelot, 75231 Paris Cedex 05, France | Chemist |
| **Lively, Blake**<br>Untitled Entertainment, 350 S Beverly Dr, #200, Beverly Hills CA 90212 USA | Actress |
| **Lively, Everett A (Bud)**<br>8605 Esslinger Court SE, Huntsville AL 35802, USA | Baseball Player |
| **Lively, Penelope M**<br>Duck End, Great Rollright, Chipping, Northern Oxfordshire OX7 5SB, England | Writer |
| **Lively, Pierce**<br>US Court of Appeals, PO Box 1226, Danville KY 40423, USA | Judge |
| **Lively, Robyn**<br>Mavrick Artists Agency, 6100 Wilshire Blvd, #550, Los Angeles CA 90048, USA | Actress |
| **Livengood, Ed**<br>Vamp Music Source, 902 W Franklin Ave, #15, Minneapolis MN 55405, USA | Drummer (Jucifer) |
| **Liveris, Andrew N**<br>Dow Chemical, 2030 Dow Center, Midland MI 48674, USA | Businessman |
| **Livermore, Ann**<br>Hewlett-Packard Co, 300 Hanover St, Palo Alto CA 94304, USA | Businesswoman |
| **Livermore, Brooks**<br>Associated International Mgmt, 7 Hatton Garden, #400, London EC1N 8AD, England | Actor |
| **Liverpool, Nicholas J O**<br>President's Office, Morne Bruce, Victoria St, Rouseau, Dominica | President, Dominica |
| **Livers, Virgil C, Jr**<br>313 Clearview Ave, Bowling Green KY 42101, USA | Football Player |
| **Livier, Ruth**<br>C E S D, 10635 Santa Monica Blvd, #130, Los Angeles CA 90025 USA | Actress |
| **Livingston, Andrew L (Andy)**<br>650 E Century Ave, Gilbert AZ 85296, USA | Football Player |
| **Livingston, Barry**<br>T G M D Agency, 6267 Forest Lawn Dr, #101, Los Angeles CA 90068, USA | Actor |
| **Livingston, David M**<br>Dana-Farber Cancer Institute, 44 Binney St, Boston MA 02115 USA | Internist |
| **Livingston, James E**<br>365 Cooper River Dr, Mount Pleasant SC 29464, USA | Vietnam Marine Hero (CMH), General |
| **Livingston, John**<br>Defining Artists, 10 Universal City Plaza, #2000, Universal City CA 91608, USA | Actor |
| **Livingston, Michael P (Mike)**<br>8181 Monrovia St, Lenexa KS 66215, USA | Football Player |
| **Livingston, Robert L, Jr**<br>Livingston Group, 499 S Capitol St SW, #600, Washington DC 20003, USA | Representative, LA |
| **Livingston, Ron**<br>United Talent Agency, U T A Plaza, 9336 Civic Center Dr, Beverly Hills CA 90210 USA | Actor |
| **Livingston, Shaun P**<br>7334 Trask Ave, Playa del Rey CA 90293, USA | Basketball Player |
| **Livingston, Stanley**<br>PO Box 1782, Studio City CA 91614, USA | Actor |

# L

**Livingston, Warren** — Football Player
308 E Malibu Dr, Tempe AZ 85282, USA
**Livingstone, Scott L** — Baseball Player
3504 Sunrise Ranch Road, Southlake TX 76092, USA
**Livio, Mario** — Astrophysicist
Hubble Space Technology Institute, 3700 San Martin Dr, Baltimore MD 21218, USA
**Livni, Tzipi** — Acting Prime Minister, Israel
Foreign Ministry, 9 Yitzhak Rubin Road, Jerusalem 91035, Israel
**Livsey, William J** — Army General
230 Carriage Chase, Fayetteville GA 30214, USA
**Liwienski, Chris** — Football Player
6721 Pointe Lake Lucy, Chanhassen MN 55317, USA
**Lizer, Kari** — Actress, Producer
Jackoway Tyerman Wertheimer, 1925 Century Park E, #2200, Los Angeles CA 90067 USA
**Ljungberg, K Fredrik (Freddie)** — Model, Soccer Player
Seattle Sounders, 12 Seahawks Way, Renton WA 98056 USA
**Ljungberg, Lasse 'Leari'** — Bassist (The Ark)
Live Nation, Linnegatan 89, Box 21451, 104 51 Stockholm, Sweden
**Ljungqvist, Ida** — Model
Playboy Promotions, 2706 Media Center Dr, Los Angeles CA 90065 USA
**LL Cool J** — Rap Artist, Actor
Alchemy Entertainment, 7024 Melrose Ave, #420, Los Angeles CA 90038 USA
**Llamosa, Carlos** — Soccer Player
13803 Via Lido, #300, Newport Beach CA 92663, USA
**Llewellyn, John A** — Astronaut
University of South Florida, Chemical & Biomedical Engineering Dept, 4202 E Fowler Ave, Tampa FL 33620, USA
**Llewellyn, Robert** — Actor, Writer
United Agents, 12-26 Lexington St, London W1F 0LE, England
**Llewelyn, Doug** — Actor
Rebel Entertainment Partners, 5700 Wilshire Blvd, #456, Los Angeles CA 90036, USA
**Llorenna, Kelly** — Singer
Mission Control, City Business Center, Lower Road, London SE16 2XB, England
**Lloyd** — Singer, Songwriter
Island Records, 925 8th St, New York NY 10019 USA
**Lloyd Webber, Andrew** — Composer
Really Useful Group, 19/22 Tower St, London WC2H 9TW, England
**Lloyd Webber, Julian** — Concert Cellist
I M G Artists, Burlington Lane, Chiswick, London W4 2TH, England
**Lloyd, Brandon M** — Football Player
5112 NW Downing St, Blue Springs MO 64015, USA
**Lloyd, Carli** — Soccer Player
Atlanta Beat, 1955 Vaughn Road, #209, Kennesaw GA 30144, USA
**Lloyd, Charles** — Jazz Saxophonist, Composer
Joel Chriss Co, 300 Mercer St, #3J, New York NY 10003 USA
**Lloyd, Cher** — Singer, Songwriter
Syco Music, Bedford House, 69-79 Fulham High St, London SW6 3JW, England
**Lloyd, Clive H** — Cricketer
Harefield, Harefield Dr, Wilmslow, Cheshire SK9 1NJ, England
**Lloyd, David A (Dave)** — Football Player
24432 County Road 3107, Gladewater TX 75647, USA
**Lloyd, Earl F** — Basketball Player, Coach
15 Pineridge Court, Crossville TN 38558, USA
**Lloyd, Emily** — Actress
Rights House, Drury House, 34-43 Russell St, London WC2B 5HA, England
**Lloyd, Eric** — Actor
Osbrink Talent Agency, 4343 Lankershim Blvd, #100, North Hollywood CA 91602 USA
**Lloyd, Geoffrey E R** — Philosopher
2 Prospect Row, Cambridge CB1 1DU, England
**Lloyd, Georgina** — Writer
Bantam Books, 1745 Broadway, New York NY 10019 USA
**Lloyd, Graeme J** — Baseball Player
455 Oceanview Ave, Palm Harbor FL 34683, USA
**Lloyd, Gregory L (Greg)** — Football Player
805 Glynn St, #127, Box 305, Fayetteville GA 30214, USA
**Lloyd, Jake** — Actor
Osbrink Talent, 4343 Lankershim Blvd, #100, North Hollywood CA 91602, USA
**Lloyd, James** — Keyboardist (Pieces of a Dream)
23309 Commerce Park Road, Cleveland OH 44122, USA
**Lloyd, Kathleen** — Actress
House of Representatives, 1434 6th St, #1, Santa Monica CA 90401 USA
**Lloyd, Lewis K** — Basketball Player
1038 N Pallas St, Philadelphia PA 19104, USA
**Lloyd, Madison** — Actress
Osbrink Talent Agency, 4343 Lankershim Blvd, #100, North Hollywood CA 91602, USA
**Lloyd, Norman** — Actor
1813 Old Ranch Road, Los Angeles CA 90049, USA
**Lloyd, Phyllida** — Director
Annette Stone Assoc, 97 Mortimer St, London W1W 7SU, England
**Lloyd, Robert A** — Opera Singer
67B Fortis Green, London SE1 9HL, England
**Lloyd, Sabrina** — Actress
Don Buchwald, 6500 Wilshire Blvd, #2200, Los Angeles CA 90048 USA
**Lloyd, Sam** — Actor
Sloat Entertainment, 27631 Belmonte, Mission Viejo CA 92692, USA
**Lloyd, Scott G** — Basketball Player
6838 Alexander Dr, Dallas TX 75214, USA
**Lloyd, Walt** — Cinematographer
22287 Mulholland Highway, #393, Calabasas CA 91302, USA
**Lloyd-Jones, David M** — Conductor
94 Whitelands House, Cheltenham Terrace, London SW3 4RA, England
**Lo, Ismael** — Singer, Composer
Mad Minute Music, 5-7 Rue Paul Bert, 93400 Saint Ouen, France
**Loach, Kenneth (Ken)** — Director
Sixteen Films, 187 Wardour St, #200, London W1F 8ZB, England
**Loach, Lonnie** — Ice Hockey Player
1263 Colby Dr, Saint Peters MO 63376, USA

**Loader, Danyon J** — Swimmer
9 Prince Albert Road, Saint Kilda, Dunedin 9012, New Zealand

**Loaiza Veyna, Esteban A** — Baseball Player
2871 Gate Three Place, Chula Vista CA 91914, USA

**Lobacheva, Irina** — Ice Dancer
Skating Federation, Luchnesksaia Nab 8, 119871 Moscow, Russia

**Lobdell, Frank** — Artist
2754 Octavia, San Francisco CA 94123, USA

**Lobel, Anita** — Writer
Greenwillow/William Morrow, 1350 Ave of Americas, New York NY 10019, USA

**LoBianco, Tony** — Actor
David Shapira Assoc, 193 N Robertson Blvd, Beverly Hills CA 90211 USA

**Lobkowicz, Nicholas** — Philosopher
Am Kirchberg 6, 91804 Mornsheim, Germany

**Lobo** — Singer, Songwriter
14432 Clubhouse Dr, Bokeelia FL 33922, USA

**Lobo Sosa, Porfirio** — President, Honduras
Casa Presidencial, Blvd Juan Pablo II, Tegucigalpa MDC, Honduras

**Lobo, Rebecca** — Basketball Player
PO Box 734, Granby CT 06035, USA

**Loca, Jean-Louie** — Actor
Jean-François Pignard de Marthod, 11 Rue Chanez, 75781 Paris Cedex 16, France

**Locane, Amy** — Actress
McCabe Group, 3211 Cahuenga Blvd W, #104, Los Angeles CA 90068, USA

**LoCascio, Luigi** — Actor
Media Art Mgmt, C/ Castelló 82, 2 Derecha, 28006 Madrid, Spain

**Loceff, Michael** — Producer
Paradigm Agency, 360 N Crescent Dr, North Building, Beverly Hills CA 90210 USA

**Loch, Felix** — Luge Athlete
Am Bergheim 1, 83471 Schonau am Konigssee, Germany

**Locher, Richard (Dick)** — Editorial Cartoonist
Chicago Tribune, Editorial Dept, 435 N Michigan Ave, #1, Chicago IL 60611, USA

**Lochner, Philip R, Jr** — Government Official, Businessman
Time Warner Inc, 1 Time Warner Center, New York NY 10019, USA

**Lochner, Rudolf (Rudi)** — Bobsled Athlete
Hofreiterstr 15, 83471 Schonau/Konigsee, Germany

**Lochte, Ryan** — Swimmer
1852 NW 34th St, Gainesville FL 32605, USA

**Lock, Donald W (Don)** — Baseball Player
11725 W Alderny Court, #42, Wichita KS 67212, USA

**Lockbaum, Gordon C (Gordie)** — Football Player
35 Brookshire Road, Worcester MA 01609, USA

**Locke, Bruce** — Actor
Vox Inc, 6420 Wilshire Blvd, #1080, Los Angeles CA 90048 USA

**Locke, Charles E (Chuck)** — Baseball Player
1560 Haven Hills Road, Poplar Bluff MO 63901, USA

**Locke, Gary F** — Secretary, Commerce; Governor, WA
Commerce Department, 14th St & Constitution Ave NW, Washington DC 20230 USA

**Locke, Lawrence D (Bobby)** — Baseball Player
194 Eight 80 Acres Road, Dunbar PA 15431, USA

**Locke, Sondra** — Actress, Director
7465 Hillside Ave, Los Angeles CA 90046, USA

**Locke, Spencer** — Actress
A P A Talent/Literary Agency, 405 S Beverly Dr, #300, Beverly Hills CA 90212 USA

**Locker, Jacob C (Jake)** — Football Player
Tennessee Titans, 460 Great Circle Road, Nashville TN 37228 USA

**Locker, Robert A (Bob)** — Baseball Player
1561 Rancho View Road, Lafayette CA 94549, USA

**Lockett, Kevin E** — Football Player
1319 W Xyler St, Tulsa OK 74127, USA

**Lockhart, Anne** — Actress
Linda McAlister Talent, 530 S Lake Ave, #435, Pasadena CA 91101, USA

**Lockhart, Dennis** — Government Official, Financier
Federal Reserve Bank, 1000 Peachtree St NE, Atlanta GA 30309, USA

**Lockhart, Eugene, Jr** — Football Player
2215 High Country Dr, Carrollton TX 75007, USA

**Lockhart, Ian** — Basketball Player
Q25 Calle Excelsa Villas del Cafetal II, Yauco PR 00698, USA

**Lockhart, James** — Conductor
105 Woodcock Hill, Harrow, Middx HA3 0JJ, England

**Lockhart, June** — Actress
PO Box 3207, Will Rogers Unit 261, Santa Monica CA 90408, USA

**Lockhart, Keith** — Conductor
Boston Pops Orchestra, Symphony Hall, 301 Massachusetts Ave, Boston MA 02115, USA

**Lockhart, Keith V** — Baseball Player
3330 McKinley Point Dr, Dacula GA 30019, USA

**Lockhart, Paul S** — Astronaut
8605 Cross View, Fairfax Station VA 22039, USA

**Lockhart, Sharon** — Photographer, Filmmaker
Barbara Gladstone Gallery, 515 W 24th St, New York NY 10011, USA

**Lockington, David** — Conductor
C M Artists, 127 W 96th St, #13B, New York NY 10025 USA

**Locklear, Heather** — Actress, Model
Gersh Agency, 9465 Wilshire Blvd, #600, Beverly Hills CA 90212 USA

**Locklear, Samuel J, III** — Navy Admiral
Commander, 3rd Fleet San Diego, FPO AP 96601 USA

**Locklear, Sean H** — Football Player
New York Giants, Meadowlands Stadium, 102 Route 120, East Rutherford NJ 07073 USA

**Lockwood, Claude E (Skip), Jr** — Baseball Player
47 John Druce Lane, Wrentham MA 02093, USA

**Lockwood, Gary** — Actor
3083 1/2 Rambla Pacifica, Malibu CA 90265, USA

**Locorriere, Dennis** — Singer, Guitarist (Dr Hook)
John Taylor Mgmt, PO Box 272, London N2O O2Y, England

**Loder, Kevin** — Basketball Player
505 W 4th St, Mishawaka IN 46544, USA

L

**Loader - Loder**

**Lodge, David J** — Writer
University of Birmingham, English Dept, Birmingham B15 2TT, England

**Lodge, Roger** — Entertainer
Paradigm Agency, 360 N Crescent Dr, North Building, Beverly Hills CA 90210 USA

**Lodish, Harvey F** — Biologist
195 Fisher Ave, Brookline MA 02445, USA

**Lodish, Michael T (Mike)** — Football Player
171 E Lincoln St, Birmingham MI 48009, USA

**LoDuca, Joseph** — Composer
1117 Isabel St, Burbank CA 91506, USA

**LoDuca, Paul** — Baseball Player
3227 Medaris Lane, San Antonio TX 78258, USA

**Lodwick, Todd** — Nordic Combined Skier
Winter Sports Club, 845 Howelsen Hill Parkway, Steamboat Springs CO 84077, USA

**Loe, Harald A** — Dentist
National Dental Research Institute, 9000 Rockville Pike, Bethesda MD 20892, USA

**Loe, Kameron D** — Baseball Player
2323 N Houston St, #312, Dallas TX 75219, USA

**Loeb, Abraham (Avi)** — Theoretical Physicist
Harvard University, Theory & Computation Institute, Cambridge MA 02138, USA

**Loeb, Allan** — Writer
Scarlet Fire Entertainment, 561 28th Ave, Venice CA 90291, USA

**Loeb, Caroline** — Actress
A A C Agence Artistique, 10 Ave George V, 75009 Paris, France

**Loeb, Damian** — Artist
49 Lispenard St, New York NY 10013, USA

**Loeb, Jerome T** — Businessman
May Department Stores, 611 Olive St, #2076, Saint Louis MO 63101, USA

**Loeb, John L, Jr** — Diplomat, Financier
John L Loeb Jr Assoc, 50 Broad St, #1137, New York NY 10004, USA

**Loeb, Lisa** — Singer, Songwriter, Actress
Atlas Talent Agency, 15 E 32nd St, #600, New York NY 10016, USA

**Loeb, Marshall R** — Editor, Writer, Columnist
41 E 72nd St, New York NY 10021, USA

**Loeb, Sebastien** — Auto Racing Driver
I S C, 6 Saint Catherine's Mews, Milner St, London SW3 2PX, England

**Loeffler, Pete** — Singer, Guitarist (Chevelle)
In De Goot Entertainment, 119 W 23rd St, #609, New York NY 10011, USA

**Loeffler, Sam** — Drummer (Chevelle)
In De Goot Entertainment, 119 W 23rd St, #609, New York NY 10011, USA

**Loeillet, Sylvie** — Actress
Agence Laurence Bagoe, 11 Rue Delambre, 75014 Paris, France

**Loengard, John** — Photographer
20 W 86th St, New York NY 10024, USA

**Loescher, Peter** — Businessman
Siemens AG, Wittelsbacherplatz 2, 80333 Munich, Germany

**Loewen, James W** — Historian
Catholic University, History Dept, Washington DC 20064, USA

**Loewer, Carlton E** — Baseball Player
PO Box 3590, Alpine WY 83128, USA

**Lofgren, Nils** — Singer, Guitarist, Songwriter
7422 E Berridge Lane, Scottsdale AZ 85250, USA

**Loftin, R Bowen** — Educator
Texas A&M University, President's Office, College Station TX 77843, USA

**Lofton, Curtis T** — Football Player
New Orleans Saints, 5800 Airline Highway, Metairie LA 70003 USA

**Lofton, Fred C** — Religious Leader
Progressive National Baptist Convention, 601 50th St NE, Washington DC 20019, USA

**Lofton, James** — Baseball Player
14103 Cerise Ave, #18, Hawthorne CA 90250, USA

**Lofton, James D** — Football Player
13177 Via Mesa Dr, San Diego CA 92129, USA

**Lofton, Kenneth (Kenny)** — Baseball Player
PO Box 68473, Tucson AZ 85737, USA

**Loftus, Aisling** — Actress
W M E Entertainment, 1325 Ave of Americas, New York NY 10019 USA

**Logan, David R** — Football Player
5875 S Dry Creek Court, Greenwood Village CO 80121, USA

**Logan, Ernest E (Ernie)** — Football Player
609 Francis Court, Spring Lake NC 28390, USA

**Logan, Exavier (Nook)** — Baseball Player
19410 Creek Bend Dr, Spring TX 77388, USA

**Logan, Jack** — Singer
W M E Entertainment, 1325 Ave of Americas, New York NY 10019 USA

**Logan, James K** — Judge
US Court of Appeals, PO Box 790, 1 Patrons Plaza, Olathe KS 66061, USA

**Logan, Jerry D** — Football Player
1624 Hillcrest Dr, Graham TX 76450, USA

**Logan, John** — Writer, Producer
Creative Artists Agency, 2000 Ave of Stars, #100, Los Angeles CA 90067 USA

**Logan, Lara** — Commentator
CBS-TV, News Dept, 51 W 52nd St, New York NY 10019, USA

**Logan, Marc A** — Football Player
2501 Glascow Lane, Lexington KY 40511, USA

**Logan, Melissa** — Singer (Chicks in Speed)
K Records, 924 Jefferson St SE, #101, Olympia WA 98501, USA

**Logan, Phyllis** — Actress
47 Courtfield Road, #9, London SW7 4DB, England

**Logan, Randolph (Randy)** — Football Player
330 W Fornance St, Norristown PA 19401, USA

**Logan, Samuel, Jr** — Relgious Leader
World Reformed Fellowship, 430 Montier Road, Glenside PA 19038, USA

**Logano, Joseph T (Joey)** — Auto Racing Driver
Joe Gibbs Racing, 13415 Reese Blvd W, Huntersville NC 28078, USA

**Loges, Stephan** — Opera Singer
Hazard Chase, 72 Charlotte St, London W1T 4QQ, England

**Logevall, Fredrik**
Cornell University, Einaudi International Studies Center, Ithaca NY 14853, USA — Historian

**Logg, Charles P, Jr**
3634 Shady Oak Trail, Gainesville GA 30506, USA — Rowing Athlete

**Loggia, Robert**
323 W Grand Ave, El Segundo CA 90245, USA — Actor

**Logue, Antonia**
Bloomsbury Publishing, 50 Bedford Square, London WC1B 3DP, England — Writer

**Logue, Donal**
Kipperman Mgmt, 420 W End Ave, #1G, New York NY 10024 USA — Actor

**Logunov, Anatoly A**
High Energy Research Center, 142281 Protvino, Moscow Region, Russia — Physicist

**Loh, John M (Mike)**
125 Captain Graves, Williamsburg VA 23185, USA — Air Force General

**Loh, Sandra Tsing**
Crown Publishing Group, 1745 Broadway, #1300, New York NY 10019 USA — Entertainer, Writer, Activist

**Loh, Wallace D**
University of Maryland, President's Office, College Park MD 20742, USA — Educator

**Lohan, Aliana D (Ali)**
B/W/R, 9100 Wilshire Blvd, #500W, Beverly Hills CA 90212 USA — Singer

**Lohan, Lindsay**
Untitled Entertainment, 350 S Beverly Dr, #200, Beverly Hills CA 90212 USA — Actress, Singer, Model

**Lohan, Sinead**
Pat Egan Sound, Merchant's Court, 24 Merchant's Quay, Dublin 8, Ireland — Singer, Songwriter

**Lohas, Brad A**
55 Tartan Dr, North Liberty IA 52317, USA — Basketball Player

**Lohman, Alison**
Principato-Young, 9465 Wilshire Blvd, #880, Beverly Hills CA 90212 USA — Actress

**Lohmiller, John M (Chip)**
PO Box 810, Crosslake MN 56442, USA — Football Player

**Lohr, Bob**
8225 Breeze Cove Lane, Orlando FL 32819, USA — Golfer

**Lohse, Kyle M**
8613 E Artisan Pass, Scottsdale AZ 85266, USA — Baseball Player

**Loiola, Jose G**
1141 2nd St, Manhattan Beach CA 90266, USA — Volleyball Player

**Loiret, Anne**
Agence Artiste Adequet, 108 Rue Reaumur, 75002 Paris, France — Actress

**Loiseau, Sebastien**
Cineart, 28 Rue Mogador, 78009 Paris, France — Actor

**Loiselle, Claude**
3 Warren St, Hudson Falls NY 12839, USA — Ice Hockey Player

**Loiselle, Richard F (Rich)**
560 Timber Dr, Harvard IL 60033, USA — Baseball Player

**Loken, James B**
US Court of Appeals, 300 S 4th St, Minneapolis MN 55415, USA — Judge

**Loken, Kristanna**
Levity Entertainment Group, 6701 Center Drive W, #1111, Los Angeles CA 90045, USA — Actress, Model

**Lolene**
Red Light Mgmt, 44 Wall St, #2200, New York NY 10005, USA — Singer, Songwriter

**Lolich, Michael S (Mickey)**
6252 Robin Hill, Washington MI 48094, USA — Baseball Player

**Lollobrigida, Gina**
Via Appia Antica 223, 00178 Rome, Italy — Actress

**Lomas, Barbara Joyce**
Star-Vest Mgmt, 102 Ryders Lane, East Brunswick NJ 08816, USA — Singer (BT Express)

**Lomas, Mark A**
PO Box 17781, Irvine CA 92623, USA — Football Player

**Lomax, Michael**
United Negro Fund, 500 E 62nd St, New York NY 10065, USA — Foundation Executive, Educator

**Lomax, Neil V**
2140 Windham Oaks Court, West Linn OR 97068, USA — Football Player

**Lomax, Noah**
Amsel Eisenstadt Frazier, 5055 Wilshire Blvd, #865, Los Angeles CA 90036 USA — Actor

**Lombard, George P**
2275 Rhinehill Road NE, Atlanta GA 30315, USA — Baseball Player

**Lombard, Karina**
Genesis Entertainment Partners, 4145 Garden Ave, Los Angeles CA 90039, USA — Actress, Model

**Lombard, Louise**
Paradigm Agency, 360 N Crescent Dr, North Building, Beverly Hills CA 90210 USA — Actress

**Lombardi, Louis**
Stone Manners Salners, 9911 W Pico Blvd, #1400, Los Angeles CA 90035 USA — Actor, Director, Writer

**Lombardi, Michael (Mike)**
Paul Kohner Agency, 9300 Wilshire Blvd, #555, Beverly Hills CA 90212 USA — Actor

**Lombardozzi, Domenick**
Gersh Agency, 9465 Wilshire Blvd, #600, Beverly Hills CA 90212 USA — Actor

**Lombardozzi, Stephen P (Steve)**
12404 Hall Shop Road, Fulton MD 20759, USA — Baseball Player

**Lombreglio, Ralph**
Doubleday Press, 1540 Broadway, New York NY 10036, USA — Writer

**Lomonaco, Michael**
Porter House, Time Warner Center, 10 Columbus Circle, #400, New York NY 10019, USA — Restauranteur, Chef

**Lomotey, Lofi**
Southern University, Chancellor's Office, Baton Rouge LA 70813, USA — Educator

**Lonard, Peter**
Links Sports, PO Box 6111, Lake Munmorah NSW 2259, Australia — Golfer

**Lonborg, James R (Jim)**
498 First Parish Road, Scituate MA 02066, USA — Baseball Player

**Loncar, Amanda**
Gersh Agency, 9465 Wilshire Blvd, #600, Beverly Hills CA 90212 USA — Actress

**Lonchakov, Yuri V**
Cosmonaut Training Center, Star City, 141160 Zvezdny Gorodok, Moscow Oblast, Russia — Cosmonaut

**Loncraine, Richard**
Casorotto Ramsay, Waverley House, 7-12 Noel St, London W1F 8GQ, England — Director

**London, Alexandra**
Artmedia, 20 Ave Rapp, 75007 Paris, France — Actress

**London, Antonio M** — Football Player
404 SW Atlantic St, Tullahoma TN 37388, USA
**London, Daniel** — Actor
Paradigm Agency, 360 N Crescent Dr, North Building, Beverly Hills CA 90210 USA
**London, Irving M** — Physician
Harvard-M I T Health Sciences, 77 Massachusetts Ave, Cambridge MA 02139, USA
**London, Jason** — Actor
A K A Talent, 6310 San Vicente Blvd, #200, Los Angeles CA 90048 USA
**London, Jeremy** — Actor
Media Artists Group, 8222 Melrose Ave, #203, Los Angeles CA 90048 USA
**London, Jonathan** — Writer
Chronicle Books, 680 2nd St, San Francisco CA 94107 USA
**London, Lauren** — Actress
John Carrabino Mgmt, 5900 Wilshire Blvd, #406, Los Angeles CA 90036 USA
**London, Lisa** — Actress, Model
Brooke Dunn Oliver, 9169 W Sunset Blvd, #202, West Hollywood CA 90069 USA
**London, Rick** — Cartoonist
Artistic Licensing Agency, 126 Oriole St, #516, Hot Springs AR 71901, USA
**Lone, John** — Actor
Sussman Assoc, 1222 16th Ave S, #300, Nashville TN 37212, USA
**Lonergan, Kenneth** — Director, Writer, Actor
Creative Artists Agency, 2000 Ave of Stars, #100, Los Angeles CA 90067 USA
**Loney, James A** — Baseball Player
4926 Birdsong Lane, Missouri City TX 77459, USA
**Loney, Troy** — Ice Hockey Player
4245 Glasgow Road, Valencia PA 16059, USA
**Long, Anthony A** — Educator
1088 Telvin St, Albany CA 94706, USA
**Long, Barry** — Ice Hockey Player
San Jose Sharks, San Jose Arena, 525 W Santa Clara St, San Jose CA 95113 USA
**Long, Charles F (Chuck), II** — Football Player, Coach
2504 Walnut Road, Norman OK 73072, USA
**Long, Dallas** — Track Athlete
PO Box 355, Whitefish MT 59937, USA
**Long, David F (Dave)** — Football Player
177 E Kaibab Way, Cochise AZ 85606, USA
**Long, Grant A** — Basketball Player
8501 Morton Taylor Road, Belleville MI 48111, USA
**Long, Howie** — Football Player, Sportscaster, Actor
I C M Partners, 10250 Constellation Blvd, #900, Los Angeles CA 90067 USA
**Long, Jodi** — Actress
Innovative Artists, 1505 10th St, Santa Monica CA 90401 USA
**Long, John E (Johnny)** — Basketball Player
11976 Hunt St, Romulus MI 48174, USA
**Long, Justin** — Actor
Creative Artists Agency, 2000 Ave of Stars, #100, Los Angeles CA 90067 USA
**Long, Kathy** — Actress
Cavaleri Assoc, 3500 W Olive Ave, #300, Burbank CA 91505, USA
**Long, Matthew (Matt)** — Actor
United Talent Agency, U T A Plaza, 9336 Civic Center Dr, Beverly Hills CA 90210 USA
**Long, Melvin (Mel), Sr** — Football Player
837 Imani Circle, Toledo OH 43604, USA
**Long, Nia** — Actress
Global Artists Agency, 6253 Hollywood Blvd, #508, Los Angeles CA 90028 USA
**Long, Robert A J (Bob)** — Football Player
3695 Stonebrook Court, Brookfield WI 53005, USA
**Long, Robert E (Bob)** — Baseball Player
3648 Willow Lake Circle, Chattanooga TN 37419, USA
**Long, Robert M** — Businessman
Longs Drug Stores, 1 C V S Dr, Woonsocket RI 02895, USA
**Long, Robert W (Bob)** — Football Player
1413 W Via de la Gloria, Green Valley AZ 85622, USA
**Long, Shelley** — Actress, Comedienne
Stone Manners Salners, 9911 W Pico Blvd, #1400, Los Angeles CA 90035 USA
**Long, Terrence D** — Baseball Player
4208 Abrams Dr, Millbrook AL 36054, USA
**Long, William D (Bill)** — Baseball Player
7699 Dimmick Road, Cincinnati OH 45241, USA
**Long, William Ivey** — Costume Designer
I C M Partners, 730 5th Ave, New York NY 10019 USA
**Longet, Claudine** — Actress
Ronald D Austin, 6000 E Hopkins, Aspen CO 81611, USA
**Longley, Lucien J (Luc)** — Basketball Player
500 Marquette Ave NW, #400, Albuquerque NM 87102, USA
**Longo, Jeannie Ciprelli-** — Cyclist
Federation de Cyclisme, 5 Rue de Rome, 93561 Rosny-sous-Bois, France
**Longo, Lenny** — Singer (Box Tops)
Texas Sounds, PO Box 1644, Dickinson TX 77539, USA
**Longo, Robert** — Artist, Sculptor
Longo Studio, 224 Center St, New York NY 10013, USA
**Longo, Tony** — Actor
310 Tahiti Way, #209, Marina del Rey CA 90292, USA
**Longoria, Eva** — Actress, Model, Producer
UnbeliEVAble Entertainment, 7095 Hollywood Blvd, #797, Hollywood CA 90028, USA
**Longoria, Evan M** — Baseball Player
1211 E Cumberland Ave, #1403, Tampa FL 33602, USA
**Longwell, Ryan W** — Football Player
9748 Green Island Cove, Windermere FL 34786, USA
**Lonich, Yogi** — Guitarist (Buckcherry)
10th Street Mgmt, 700 N San Vicente Blvd, #G410, West Hollywood CA 90069, USA
**Lonnett, Joseph D (Joe)** — Baseball Player
126 Duncan Circle, Beaver PA 15009, USA
**Lonow, Claudia** — Actress, Comedienne, Producer
W M E Entertainment, 9601 Wilshire Blvd, #300, Beverly Hills CA 90210 USA
**Lonsdale, Gordon C** — Cinematographer
4513 W 10600 N, Highland UT 84003, USA

**Lonsdale, Michael**
France Degand, 25 Rue du General Foy, 75008 Paris, France — Actor
**Loob, P Hakan**
Farjestads BK, Box 318, 65108 Karlstad, Sweden — Ice Hockey Player
**Look, Dean Z**
80 Victorian Hills Dr, Okemos MI 48864, USA — Baseball, Football Player
**Looker, Dane A**
7213 41st Avenue Court E, Tacoma WA 98443, USA — Football Player
**Lookinland, Mike**
PO Box 9968, Salt Lake City UT 84109, USA — Actor
**Lookstein, Haskel**
Congregation Kehilath Jeshurun, Ramaz School, 60 E 78th St, New York NY 10075, USA — Religious Leader, Rabbi
**Loomer, Lisa**
Abrams Artists, 9200 W Sunset Blvd, #1125, West Hollywood CA 90069 USA — Writer
**Loomis, Rick**
Los Angeles Times, Editorial Dept, 202 W 1st St, Los Angeles CA 90012 USA — Journalist
**Looney, Brian J**
188 Romulus Road, Cheshire CT 06410, USA — Baseball Player
**Looney, Shelley**
31 Beaman Lane, North Falmouth MA 02556, USA — Ice Hockey Player
**Looper, Braden L**
16253 Wynncrest Ridge Court, Chesterfield MO 63005, USA — Baseball Player
**Loose, Michael K**
Deputy CNO, Fleet Readiness/Logistics, HqUSN, Pentagon, Washington DC 20350 USA — Navy Admiral
**Lopardo, Frank**
7 Suzanne B Court, Massapequa NY 11758, USA — Opera Singer
**Lopata, Stanley E (Stan)**
2239 Leisure World, Mesa AZ 85206, USA — Baseball Player
**Loper, Daniel R**
1115 Stillwater Trail, Hendersonville TN 37075, USA — Football Player
**Lopert, Tanya**
Cineart, 28 Rue Mogador, 78009 Paris, France — Actress
**Lopes, David E (Davey)**
309 San Elijo St, San Diego CA 92106, USA — Baseball Player, Manager
**Lopes, Leila**
Miss Universe Organization, 1370 Ave of Americas, #1600, New York NY 10019 USA — Beauty Queen
**Lopez de Ayala, Pilar**
Media Art Mgmt, C/ Castelló 82, 2 Derecha, 28006 Madrid, Spain — Actress
**Lopez Lujan, Leonardo**
Museo del Templo Mayor, 8 Seminario Ave, Mexico City DF 06060, Mexico — Archaeologist
**Lopez Rodriguez, Nicolas de J Cardinal**
Archdiocese of Santo Domingo, Santo Domingo, AP 186, Dominican Republic — Religious Leader
**Lopez, Albert A (Albie)**
2887 E Palo Verde Court, Gilbert AZ 85296, USA — Baseball Player
**Lopez, Brook R**
Brooklyn Nets, 15 Metro Tech Center, #1100, Brooklyn NY 11201 USA — Basketball Player
**Lopez, Danny (Little Red)**
16531 Aquamarine Court, Chino Hills CA 91709, USA — Boxer
**Lopez, Felipe**
2414 Hassonite St, Kissimmee FL 34744, USA — Baseball Player
**Lopez, George**
Creative Artists Agency, 2000 Ave of Stars, #100, Los Angeles CA 90067 USA — Actor, Comedian
**Lopez, Gerry**
PO Box 1202, Bend OR 97709, USA — Surfer, Executive
**Lopez, Javier A**
4824 Quaker Lane, Golden CO 80403, USA — Baseball Player
**Lopez, Jennifer**
Nuyorican Productions, 1100 Glendon Ave, #920, Los Angeles CA 90024, USA — Actress, Singer, Model
**Lopez, Juan Manuel**
P R Best Promotions, Cond Santa Juanita L58, Bayamon PR 00956, USA — Boxer
**Lopez, Lourdes**
Miami City Ballet, Roca Center, 2200 Liberty Ave, Miami Beach FL 33139, USA — Ballerina, Ballet Executive
**Lopez, Luis S**
1701 Pleasant Run Road, Carrollton TX 75006, USA — Baseball Player
**Lopez, Mario**
Talent Works, 3500 W Olive Ave, #1400, Burbank CA 91505 USA — Actor
**Lopez, Mickey**
17430 SW 117th Ave, Miami FL 33177, USA — Baseball Player
**Lopez, Nancy**
2308 Tara Dr, Albany GA 31721, USA — Golfer
**Lopez, Nano**
96 Frontage Road, Walla Walla WA 99362, USA — Sculptor
**Lopez, Óscar**
Agency Group Ltd, 1880 Century Park E, #711, Los Angeles CA 90067 USA — Guitar Player
**Lopez, Priscilla**
Stone Manners Salners, 9911 W Pico Blvd, #1400, Los Angeles CA 90035 USA — Actress
**Lopez, Raul**
Memphis Grizzlies, 191 Beale St, Memphis TN 38103 USA — Basketball Player
**Lopez, Robert S**
41 Richmond Ave, New Haven CT 06515, USA — Historian
**Lopez, Robin B**
Portland Trail Blazers, Rose Garden, 1 N Center Court St, Portland OR 97227 USA — Basketball Player
**Lopez, Sal**
DePaz Mgmt, 2011 N Vermont Ave, Los Angeles CA 90027, USA — Actor
**Lopez, Sandra**
Columbia Artists Mgmt Inc, 1790 Broadway, #702, New York NY 10019 USA — Opera Singer
**Lopez, Sergi**
Artmedia, 20 Ave Rapp, 75007 Paris, France — Actor
**Lopez, Steve**
G P Putnam's Sons, 375 Hudson St, New York NY 10014 USA — Writer
**Lopez, Steven**
Elite Taekwondo Center, 9707 S Highway 6, Sugar Land TX 77498, USA — Taekwondo Athlete
**Lopez, T Joseph**
Lexington Institute, 1600 Wilson Blvd, #900, Arlington VA 22209 USA — Navy Admiral
**Lopez, Tim G**
One Moment Mgmt, PO Box 55156, Sherman Oaks CA 91413 USA — Bassist (Plain White T's)

## L

**Lopez, Tony (Tiger)** — Boxer
3221 Sweet Maple Way, Sacramento CA 95833, USA
**Lopez, Trini** — Singer, Actor, Orchestra Leader
1139 Abrigo Road, Palm Springs CA 92262, USA
**Lopez-Alegria, Michael E** — Astronaut
1919 Tangle Press Court, Houston TX 77062, USA
**Lopez-Cobos, Jesus** — Conductor
8 Chemin de Bellerive, 1007 Lausanne, Switzerland
**Lopez-Gallego, Gonzalo** — Director
I C M Partners, 10250 Constellation Blvd, #900, Los Angeles CA 90067 USA
**Lopez-Garcia, Antonio** — Artist
Galeria Marlborough, Orfila 5, 28010 Madrid, Spain
**Loquasto, Santo** — Lighting, Costume Designer
Paradigm Agency, 360 N Crescent Dr, North Building, Beverly Hills CA 90210 USA
**Lorca, Daniel** — Bassist (Nada Surf)
M-Square Mgmt, 201 W 72nd St, #12G, New York NY 10023, USA
**Lorch, George A** — Businessman
Armstrong World, 313 W Liberty St, Lancaster PA 17603, USA
**Lorch, Karl P, Jr** — Football Player
92-861 Palailai St, Kapolei HI 96707, USA
**Lorcy, Julian** — Boxer
BoBoxe, 68 Blvd Henri Barbusse, 78800 Houilles, France
**Lord, Albert L** — Businessman
S L M Corp, 12061 Bluemont Dr, Reston VA 20190, USA
**Lord, M G** — Editorial Cartoonist
Janklow & Nesbit Assoc, 445 Park Ave, #1300, New York NY 10022 USA
**Lord, Marjorie** — Actress
1110 Maytor Place, Beverly Hills CA 90210, USA
**Lord, Mary Lou** — Singer, Guitarist
Combat Jack Mgmt, 110-120 Brookline St, Cambridge MA 02139, USA
**Lord, Peter** — Animator, Director
Aardman Animations, Gas Ferry Road, Bristol BS1 6UN, England
**Lord, Winston** — Diplomat
740 Park Ave, New York NY 10021, USA
**Lordi, Mr** — Singer (Lordi)
Le Kepi Rouge, PL 285, 02601 Espoo, Finland
**Lords, Traci** — Actress
Innovative Artists, 1505 10th St, Santa Monica CA 90401 USA
**Loren, Josie** — Actress
Ellen Meyer Mgmt, 8899 Beverly Blvd, #612, West Hollywood CA 90048, USA
**Loren, Natalie** — DJ Musician, Model
Leni's Model Mgmt, 55E Hatton Garden, London EC1N 8HP, England
**Loren, Sophia** — Actress
Casa Postale 430, 1211 Geneva 12, Switzerland
**Lorensson, Jalle** — Harmonica Player (Wilmer X)
United Stage Artists, Asogatan 142, Box 11029, 100 61 Stockholm, Sweden
**Lorentz, Jim** — Ice Hockey Player
2555 Staley Road, Grand Island NY 14072, USA
**Lorenz, Christian (Flake)** — Keyboardist (Rammstein)
Pilgrim Mgmt, PO Box 540101, 10042 Berlin, Germany
**Lorenz, Ericka** — Water Polo Player
2604 Fulton St, Berkeley CA 94704, USA
**Lorenz, Lee** — Cartoonist
PO Box 131, Easton CT 06612, USA
**Lorenzen, Fred** — Auto Racing Driver
64 E Elm St, #4, Chicago IL 60611, USA
**Lorenzo, Blas** — Actor
PO Box 2127, Los Angeles CA 90078, USA
**Lorenzoni, Andrea** — Astronaut, Italy
Via B Vergine del Carmelo 168, 00144 Rome, Italy
**Loretta, Mark D** — Baseball Player
7844 Sendora Angelica, San Diego CA 92127, USA
**Loria, Christopher J (Gus)** — Astronaut
102 Sea Mist Dr, League City TX 77573, USA
**Lorick, W Anthony (Tony)** — Football Player
349 Burney Lane, Kerrville TX 78028, USA
**Lorimer, Bob** — Ice Hockey Player
24 Cranberry Lane, Aurora ON L4G 5Y3, Canada
**Loring, Gloria** — Singer, Songwriter, Actress
R M C Mgmt, PO Box 1308, Pacific Palisades CA 90272, USA
**Loring, John R** — Artist
621 Avon Road, West Palm Beach FL 33401, USA
**Loring, Lynn** — Actress, Producer
Lynn Loring Assoc, 2313 Canyonback Road, Los Angeles CA 90049, USA
**Lorius, Claude** — Glaciologist
Glaciologies Laboratoire, Rue Moliere, 38402 Saint-Martin d'Heres, France
**Lorraine, Andrew J** — Baseball Player
14609 N 103rd Way, Scottsdale AZ 85255, USA
**Lorre, Chuck** — Producer
I C M Partners, 10250 Constellation Blvd, #900, Los Angeles CA 90067 USA
**Lortie, Louis** — Concert Pianist
Seldy Cramer Artists, 3436 Springhill Road, Lafayette CA 94549, USA
**Lortkipanidze, Vazha G** — Minister of State, Georgia
Government House, Ingorokva 7, 380034 Tbilsi, Georgia
**Losada, Isabel** — Writer
Curtis Brown Group, 28-29 Haymarket St, #500, London SW1Y 4SP, England
**LoSchiavo, Francesca** — Set Decorator
Via delle Querce 51, 47842 San Giovanni in Marignano, Italy
**Loscutoff, James (Jim)** — Basketball Player, Coach
166 Jenkins Road, Andover MA 01810, USA
**Losick, Richard M** — Molecular Biologist
Harvard Medical School, 25 Shattuck St, Boston MA 02115, USA
**Losier, Michele** — Opera Singer
I M G Artists, Hogarth Business Park, Chiswick, London W4 2TH, England
**Losman, Jonathan P (J P)** — Football Player
70 Oakland Place, Buffalo NY 14222, USA

**L**

| | |
|---|---|
| **Loss, Harold**<br>Temple Israel, 5725 Walnut Lake Road, West Bloomfield MI 48323, USA | Religious Leader, Rabbi |
| **Lotan, Jonah**<br>Gersh Agency, 9465 Wilshire Blvd, #600, Beverly Hills CA 90212 USA | Actor |
| **Lothamer, Edward D (Ed)**<br>14545 W 183rd St, Olathe KS 66062, USA | Football Player |
| **LoTruglio, Joe**<br>United Talent Agency, U T A Plaza, 9336 Civic Center Dr, Beverly Hills CA 90210 USA | Actor |
| **Lott, Felicity A**<br>Augstein & Hahn, Tal 28, 80331 Munich, Germany | Opera Singer |
| **Lott, Ronald M (Ronnie)**<br>2965 Woodside Road, Woodside CA 94062, USA | Football Player, Sportscaster |
| **Lotti, Helmut**<br>Bevrijdinstraat 39, 2300 Turnhout, Belgium | Singer, Songwriter |
| **Lotton, Gerald**<br>Lotton Glass, 24760 Country Lane, Crete IL 60417, USA | Artist |
| **Lotz, Anne Graham**<br>AnGeL Ministries, 515 Hollyridge Dr, Raleigh NC 27612, USA | Religious Leader |
| **Lotz, Dick**<br>2058 Riesling Way, Shingle Springs CA 95682, USA | Golfer |
| **Louboutin, Christian**<br>19 Rue Jean-Jacques Rousseau, 75001 Paris, France | Footwear Designer |
| **Loucks, Scott G**<br>1801 Viola Dr, Sierra Vista AZ 85635, USA | Baseball Player |
| **Loucks, Vernon R, Jr**<br>Baxter Healthcare Corp, 1450 Waukegan Road, Waukegan IL 60085, USA | Businessman |
| **Louderback, Thomas F (Tom)**<br>15 Leopard Road, #1G, Berwyn PA 19312, USA | Football Player |
| **Loudon, Aarnout A**<br>Rembrandt Kaan 16, 6881 Velp CS, Netherlands | Businessman |
| **Loudon, Rodney**<br>3 Gaston St, East Bergholt, Colchester, Essex CO7 6SD, England | Theoretical Physicist |
| **Loueke, Lionel**<br>Blue Note Records, 6920 W Sunset Blvd, Los Angeles CA 90028 USA | Jazz Guitarist |
| **Louganis, Gregory E (Greg)**<br>Premier Management Group, 115 Crescent Commons, Cary, NC 27518 USA | Diver |
| **Loughery, Kevin M (Murph)**<br>4474 Club Dr NE, Atlanta GA 30319, USA | Basketball Player, Coach, Executive |
| **Loughlin, Lori**<br>United Talent Agency, U T A Plaza, 9336 Civic Center Dr, Beverly Hills CA 90210 USA | Actress, Singer |
| **Loughlin, Mary Anne**<br>WTBS-TV, News Dept, 1050 Techwood Dr NW, Atlanta GA 30318, USA | Commentator |
| **Loughnane, Lee David**<br>Front Line Mgmt, 1100 Glendon Ave, #2000, Los Angeles CA 90024 USA | Trumpeter (Chicago), Songwriter |
| **Loughran, James**<br>34 Cleveden Dr, Glasgow G12 0RX, Scotland | Conductor |
| **Louis C K**<br>3 Arts Entertainment, 9460 Wilshire Blvd, #700, Beverly Hills CA 90212 USA | Director, Writer, Actor |
| **Louis, Justin**<br>Lucas Talent, 1238 Homer St, #6, Vancouver BC V6B 2Y5, Canada | Actor |
| **Louis, Murray**<br>Nikolais/Louis Foundation, 375 W Broadway, New York NY 10012, USA | Dancer, Choreographer |
| **Louisa, Maria**<br>Next Model Mgmt, 23 Watts St, New York NY 10013 USA | Model |
| **Louisa-Godett, Mima**<br>Premier's Office, Fort Amsterdam 17, Willemstad, Netherlands Antilles | Premier, Netherlands Antilles |
| **Louis-Dreyfus, Julia**<br>Hofflund/Polone, 9465 Wilshire Blvd, #420, Beverly Hills CA 90212 USA | Actress, Comedienne |
| **Louise, Tina**<br>310 E 46th St, #24G, New York NY 10017, USA | Actress, Singer |
| **Louiso, Todd**<br>Anonymous Content, 3532 Hayden Ave, Culver City CA 90232 USA | Actor, Director, Writer |
| **Louisy, C Pearlette**<br>Governor General's Office, Government House, Box 216, Morne Fortune, Castries, Saint Lucia | Governor General, Saint Lucia |
| **Loukos, Yorgos**<br>Lyon Opera Ballet, Place de la Comédie, 69001 Lyon, France | Ballet Executive |
| **Loun, Donald N (Don)**<br>9095 Wexford Dr, Vienna VA 22182, USA | Baseball Player |
| **Lourdusamy, D Simon Cardinal**<br>Palazzo dei Convertendi, 64 Via della Conciliazione, 00193 Rome, Italy | Religious Leader |
| **Lourie, Alan D**<br>US Court of Appeals, 717 Madison Place NW, Washington DC 20439, USA | Judge |
| **Louris, Gary**<br>Sussman Assoc, 1222 16th Ave S, #300, Nashville TN 37212, USA | Singer, Songwriter (Jayhawks) |
| **Lousma, Jack R**<br>2722 Roseland St, Ann Arbor MI 48103, USA | Astronaut |
| **Loutfi, Ali Mahmoud**<br>29 Ahmed Heshmat St, Zamalek, Cairo, Egypt | Prime Minister, Egypt |
| **Louvier, Alain**<br>53 Ave Victor Hugo, 92100 Boulogne-Billancourt, France | Composer |
| **Louwerse, Mirusia**<br>PO Box 3169, Birkdale QLD 4159, Australia | Opera, Concert Singer |
| **Loux, Shane A**<br>4134 E Cherrywood Place, Chandler AZ 85249, USA | Baseball Player |
| **Lovano, Joe**<br>66 Beaver Brook Road, New Windsor NY 12553, USA | Jazz Saxophonist, Composer |
| **Lovato, Demi**<br>Creative Artists Agency, 2000 Ave of Stars, #100, Los Angeles CA 90067 USA | Actress, Singer |
| **Love, Courtney**<br>Anderson Group Public Relations, 8060 Melrose Ave, #400, Los Angeles CA 90046, USA | Singer (Hole), Actress, Songwriter |
| **Love, Darlene**<br>Rainbow High Entertainment, 3500 W Olive Ave, #300, Burbank CA 91505 91505, USA | Singer, Actress |
| **Love, Darris**<br>H G Entertainment, 1734 N Frederic St, Burbank CA 91505, USA | Actor |
| **Love, Davis, III**<br>Love Golf Design, 100 Brunswick Ave, Saint Simons Island GA 31522, USA | Golfer |

**Love, Duval L** — Football Player
8985 Yuba River Ave, Fountain Valley CA 92708, USA

**Love, Faizon** — Actor, Comedian, Writer, Director
Resolution, 1801 Century Park East, #2300, Los Angeles CA 90067 USA

**Love, Gerald** — Bassist (Teenage Fanclub)
High Road Touring, 751 Bridgeway, #200, Sausalito CA 94965 USA

**Love, Kevin W** — Basketball Player
Minnesota Timberwolves, Target Center, 600 1st Ave N, Minneapolis MN 55403 USA

**Love, Loni** — Actress, Comedienne
United Talent Agency, U T A Plaza, 9336 Civic Center Dr, Beverly Hills CA 90210 USA

**Love, Michael D (Mike)** — Singer (Beach Boys)
24563 Ebelden Ave, Newhall CA 91321, USA

**Love, Randy** — Football Player
2202 Fairlands Dr, Garland TX 75040, USA

**Love, Stanley G** — Astronaut
4315 Indian Sunrise Court, Houston TX 77059, USA

**Love, Stanley S (Stan)** — Basketball Player
1950 Egan Way, Lake Oswego OR 97034, USA

**Love, Terence P** — Educator
Curtin University, Design Dept, GPO Box U1987, Perth WA 6845, Australia

**Lovelace, James L** — Army General
Deputy Chief of Staff, Operations Plans, HqUSA, Pentagon, Washington DC 20310 USA

**Lovelace, Vance O** — Baseball Player
5608 12th Ave S, Tampa FL 33619, USA

**Loveless, Patty** — Singer, Songwriter
Flood Bumstead McCready McCarthy, 16 W 22nd St, #200, New York NY 10010 USA

**Lovell, Jacqueline** — Actress, Model
8707 Shirley Ave, Northridge CA 91324, USA

**Lovell, James A (Jim), Jr** — Astronaut
Lovell Communications, PO Box 49, Lake Forest IL 60045, USA

**Lovell, Robert R** — Space Scientist
Orbital Sciences Corp, 21839 Atlantic Blvd, Dulles VA 20166, USA

**Lovellette, Clyde E** — Basketball Player
8 Woodspoint Circle, North Manchester IN 46962, USA

**Lovelock, James E** — Chemist, Inventor
Coombe Mill, Saint Giles on Heath, Launceston, Cornwall PL15 9RY, England

**Lovely, Randy** — Editor
Arizona Republic, Editorial Dept, 200 E Van Buren St, Phoenix AZ 85004 USA

**Lover, Seth** — Inventor, Engineer (Humbucking Pickup)
4 Village Dr, Saint Louis MO 63146, USA

**Lovering, David** — Singer, Drummer (Pixies)
X-Ray Touring, 77-79 Great Eastern St, #A, London EC2A 3HU, England

**Loverne, David** — Football Player
2307 Amber Falls Dr, Rocklin CA 95765, USA

**LoVetere, John M** — Football Player
PO Box 2901, Lebanon TN 37088, USA

**Lovett, Lyle** — Singer, Songwriter
Vector Mgmt, 1100 Glendon Ave, #2000, Los Angeles CA 90024, USA

**Lovett, Ruby** — Singer
Myers Media, PO Box 378, Canton NY 13617, USA

**Loviglio, John P (Jay)** — Baseball Player
23 3rd Ave, East Islip NY 11730, USA

**Loville, Derek K** — Football Player
D B L Financial, 3020 E Camelback Road, #301, Phoenix AZ 85016, USA

**Loving, Candy** — Model, Actress
8560 W Sunset Blvd, #600, West Hollywood CA 90069, USA

**Lovins, Amory B** — Physicist
Hypercar Inc, 3768 Highway 82, #204, Glenwood Springs CO 81601, USA

**Lovitz, Jon** — Actor, Comedian
Chuck Binder Mgmt, 1465 Lindacrest Dr, Beverly Hills CA 90210 USA

**Lovland, Rolf** — Pianist (Secret Garden), Composer
Thranesgate 2B, 0175 Oslo, Norway

**Lovretta, Michelle A** — Producer, Writer
Alpern Group, 15645 Royal Oak Road, Encino CA 91436, USA

**Lovrich, Peter (Pete)** — Baseball Player
19626 Beechnut Dr, Mokena IL 60448, USA

**Lovullo, Salvatore A (Torey)** — Baseball Player
32108 Sailview Lane, Westlake Village CA 91361, USA

**Low, Francis E** — Physicist
7102 Plantation Lane, Rockville MD 20852, USA

**Lowder, Kyle** — Actor
Kazarian/Measures/Ruskin, 11969 Ventura Blvd, #300, Studio City CA 91604 USA

**Lowdermilk, R Kirk** — Football Player
9475 Apollo Road NE, Kensington OH 44427, USA

**Lowe, Barry** — Writer
315 Audley St, London W1K 2PJ, England

**Lowe, Chad** — Actor
Anonymous Content, 3532 Hayden Ave, Culver City CA 90232 USA

**Lowe, Chan** — Editorial Cartoonist
Fort Lauderdale Sun-Sentinel, Editorial Dept, 200 E Las Olas Blvd, Fort Lauderdale FL 33301, USA

**Lowe, Christopher S (Chris)** — Keyboardist (Pet Shop Boys)
W M E Entertainment, 9601 Wilshire Blvd, #300, Beverly Hills CA 90210 USA

**Lowe, Derek C** — Baseball Player
12711 Terabella Way, Fort Myers FL 33912, USA

**Lowe, Gary R** — Football Player
16940 Lauderdale Ave, Beverly Hills MI 48025, USA

**Lowe, J Sean** — Baseball Player
802 Oak Dr, Mesquite TX 75149, USA

**Lowe, Kevin** — Ice Hockey Player, Coach, Executive
Edmonton Oilers, 11230 110th St, Edmonton AB T5G 3H7, Canada

**Lowe, Nicholas D (Nick)** — Singer, Songwriter, Guitarist
High Road Touring, 751 Bridgeway, #200, Sausalito CA 94965 USA

**Lowe, Paul E** — Football Player
5134 Logan Ave, San Diego CA 92114, USA

**Lowe, Rebecca** — Sportscaster
NBC-TV, Sports Dept, 30 Rockefeller Plaza, #270E, New York NY 10112 USA

|  | |
|---|---|
| **Lowe, Rob** | Actor |
| W M E Entertainment, 9601 Wilshire Blvd, #300, Beverly Hills CA 90210 USA | |
| **Lowe, Sidney R** | Basketball Player, Coach |
| 2631 Wallingford Road, Winston-Salem NC 27101, USA | |
| **Lowe, Stephanie** | Golfer |
| 2004 Delancey Dr, Norman OK 73071, USA | |
| **Lowe, Woodrow** | Football Player, Coach |
| PO Box 988, Alabaster AL 35007, USA | |
| **Lowell, Abbe D** | Attorney |
| Chadbourne & Parke, 30 Rockefeller Plaza, New York NY 10112, USA | |
| **Lowell, Charles D (Charlie)** | Keyboardist (Jars of Clay) |
| Nettwerk Mgmt, 1650 W 2nd Ave, Vancouver BC V6J 4R3, Canada | |
| **Lowell, Chris** | Actor |
| Thruline Entertainment, 9250 Wilshire Blvd, #100, Beverly Hills CA 90212 USA | |
| **Lowell, Elizabeth** | Writer |
| Avon Books, 1350 Ave of Americas, New York NY 10019 USA | |
| **Lowell, Michael A (Mike)** | Baseball Player |
| 620 Santurce Ave, Coral Gables FL 33143, USA | |
| **Lowell, Scott** | Actor |
| Evolution Entertainment, 901 N Highland Ave, Los Angeles CA 90038 USA | |
| **Lowenstein, John L** | Baseball Player |
| 7017 Via Locanda Ave, Las Vegas NV 89131, USA | |
| **Lowery, Corey** | Bassist (Stereo Mud) |
| Agency Group Ltd, 142 W 57th St, #600, New York NY 10019 USA | |
| **Lowery, David** | Director |
| W M E Entertainment, 9601 Wilshire Blvd, #300, Beverly Hills CA 90210 USA | |
| **Lowery, David** | Singer, Guitarist (Cracker), Songwriter |
| Back Bay Mgmt, 397 Little Neck Road, #305, Virginia Beach VA 23452 USA | |
| **Lowery, Dominic G (Nick)** | Football Player |
| 8416 E Via de Jardin, Scottsdale AZ 85258, USA | |
| **Lowery, Steve** | Golfer |
| 1073 Royal Mile, Birmingham AL 35242, USA | |
| **Lowes, Katie** | Actress |
| Innovative Artists, 1505 10th St, Santa Monica CA 90401 USA | |
| **Lowman, Nate** | Artist |
| Carlson Gallery, 55 S Audley St, London W1K 2QH, England | |
| **Lown, Bernard** | Cardiologist |
| Lown Cardiovascular Group, 21 Longwood Ave, Brookline MA 02446, USA | |
| **Lown, Omar J (Turk)** | Baseball Player |
| 1106 Van Buren St, Pueblo CO 81004, USA | |
| **Lowndes, Jessica** | Actress |
| Creative Artists Agency, 2000 Ave of Stars, #100, Los Angeles CA 90067 USA | |
| **Lowrie, Jed C** | Baseball Player |
| 1895 Evergreen Ave NE, Salem OR 97301, USA | |
| **Lowry, Glenn D** | Museum Executive |
| Museum of Modern Art, Director's Office, 11 W 53rd St, New York NY 10019, USA | |
| **Lowry, Kyle** | Basketball Player |
| Toronto Raptors, Air Canada Center, 20 Bay St, Toronto ON M5J 2N8, Canada | |
| **Lowry, Lois** | Writer |
| 9 Whipple Farm Lane, Falmouth ME 04105, USA | |
| **Lowry, Noah** | Baseball Player |
| 2621 Matera Lane, San Diego CA 92108, USA | |
| **Lowry, Shanti** | Actress |
| Don Buchwald, 6500 Wilshire Blvd, #2200, Los Angeles CA 90048 USA | |
| **Loy, James M** | Coast Guard Admiral, Government Official |
| L-1 Identity Solutions, 177 Broad St, #1200, Stamford CT 06901, USA | |
| **Loy, Rory J** | Soccer Player |
| Rangers F C, Ibrox Stadium, 150 Edmiston Dr, Glasgow G51 2XD, Scotland | |
| **Loynd, Michael W (Mike)** | Baseball Player |
| 19 Randall Dr, Short Hills NJ 07078, USA | |
| **Lozano Barragan, Javier Cardinal** | Religious Leader |
| Health Care Workers Assistance, Via Conciliazione 3, 00193 Rome, Italy | |
| **Lozano, Conrad** | Singer, Bassist (Los Lobos) |
| Gold Mountain, 3940 Laurel Canyon Blvd, #444, Studio City CA 91604 USA | |
| **Lozano, Florencia** | Actress |
| Paradigm Agency, 360 N Crescent Dr, North Building, Beverly Hills CA 90210 USA | |
| **Lozano, Silvia** | Choreographer |
| Ballet Folklorico, 31 Esq Con Riva Palacio, Col Guerrero, Mexico DF CP 06300, Mexico | |
| **Lu Qihui** | Sculptor |
| 100-301, 398 Xin-Pei Road, Xin-Zuan, Shanghai, China | |
| **Lu, Edward T (Ed)** | Astronaut |
| 18222 Bal Harbour Dr, Houston TX 77058, USA | |
| **Lu, Marie** | Writer |
| Nelson Literary Agency, 1732 Wazee St, #207, Denver CO 80202, USA | |
| **Luan Jujie** | Fencer |
| 146 Shuang-Le Yuan, #301, Qin-Huai Region, Nanjing 210009, China | |
| **Lubanski, Ed** | Bowler |
| 5326 Christi Dr, Warren MI 48091, USA | |
| **Lubatti, Henri** | Actor |
| S D B Partners, 1801 Ave of Stars, #902, Los Angeles CA 90067 USA | |
| **Lubbers, Rudolphus F M (Ruud)** | Prime Minister, Netherlands |
| Lambertweg 4, 3062 Rotterdam RA, Netherlands | |
| **Lubchenco, Jane** | Marine Biologist, Zoologist |
| Oregon State University, Marine Biology Dept, Corvallis OR 97331, USA | |
| **Lubezki, Emmanuel** | Cinematographer |
| I C M Partners, 10250 Constellation Blvd, #900, Los Angeles CA 90067 USA | |
| **Lubich, Bronko** | Professional Wrestler |
| 3146 Whitemarsh Circle, Dallas TX 75234, USA | |
| **Lubin, Barry (Grandma)** | Clown |
| Big Apple Circus, 505 8th Ave, #1900, New York NY 10018 USA | |
| **Lubin, Gilson** | Actor, Comedian |
| Law Talent Agency, 5 Ambleside Ave, Toronto ON M8Z 2H5, Canada | |
| **Lubin, Steven** | Concert Pianist |
| State University of New York, School of Arts, Purchase NY 10577, USA | |
| **Lubotsky, Mark** | Concert Violinist |
| Overtoom 329 III, 1054 Amsterdam JM, Netherlands | |

**L**

**Lubovitch - Luckinbill**

| | |
|---|---|
| **Lubovitch, Lar** | Dancer, Choreographer |
| Lar Lubovitch Dance Co, 229 W 42nd St, #8, New York NY 10036, USA | |
| **Lubratich, Steven G (Steve)** | Baseball Player |
| 24 Sackett Road, Lee NH 03861, USA | |
| **Lubs, Herbert A** | Geneticist |
| 5133 SW 71st Place, Miami FL 33155, USA | |
| **Luby, Thia** | Writer, Yoga Instructor |
| 2918 Marion Dr, Colorado Springs CO 80909, USA | |
| **Luc, Tone** | Rap Artist, Actor |
| Headline Talent, 1650 Broadway, #401, New York NY 10313 USA | |
| **Lucado, Max** | Writer |
| Oak Hills Church of Christ, 6929 Camp Bullis Road, San Antonio TX 78256, USA | |
| **Lucas, Adetokunbo Oulmide** | Physician |
| 25 Adebajo St, Kongi, PO Box 30917, Sec Bo, Ibadan, Nigeria | |
| **Lucas, Ben C** | Director, Producer, Writer |
| Creative Artists Agency, 2000 Ave of Stars, #100, Los Angeles CA 90067 USA | |
| **Lucas, Craig** | Lyricist, Writer |
| Peikoff Law Office, 173 E Broadway, #C1, New York NY 10002 USA | |
| **Lucas, Gary P** | Baseball Player |
| 1511 High St, Rice Lake WI 54868, USA | |
| **Lucas, George** | Director, Producer |
| LucasFilm, 5858 Lucas Valley Road, Nicasio CA 94946, USA | |
| **Lucas, Isabel** | Actress |
| United Talent Agency, U T A Plaza, 9336 Civic Center Dr, Beverly Hills CA 90210 USA | |
| **Lucas, Jerry R** | Basketball Player |
| Dr Memorabilia, 231 E 2nd St, Chillicothe OH 45601, USA | |
| **Lucas, Jessica** | Actress |
| Thruline Entertainment, 9250 Wilshire Blvd, #100, Beverly Hills CA 90212 USA | |
| **Lucas, John H, Jr** | Basketball Player, Coach, Executive |
| 21 Pin Oak Estates, Bellaire TX 77401, USA | |
| **Lucas, Jon** | Director, Writer |
| Creative Artists Agency, 2000 Ave of Stars, #100, Los Angeles CA 90067 USA | |
| **Lucas, Josh** | Actor |
| Principato-Young, 9465 Wilshire Blvd, #880, Beverly Hills CA 90212 USA | |
| **Lucas, Kenneth C (Ken)** | Football Player |
| 404 Oakmont Lane, Waxhaw NC 28173, USA | |
| **Lucas, Marne** | Photographer |
| Aalto Lounge, 3356 SE Belmont St, Portland OR 97214, USA | |
| **Lucas, Matthew R (Matt)** | Actor |
| Troika, 74 Clerkenwell Road, #300, London EC1M 5QA, England | |
| **Lucas, Richard J (Richie)** | Football Player |
| 1269 Estate Dr, West Chester PA 19380, USA | |
| **Lucas, Robert E, Jr** | Nobel Economics Laureate |
| 5448 S East View Park, #3, Chicago IL 60615, USA | |
| **Lucas, Sarah** | Artist |
| Sadie Coles, 35 Heddon St, London W1B 4BP, England | |
| **Lucas, Timothy B (Tim)** | Football Player |
| 5081 S Florence Dr, Greenwood Village CO 80111, USA | |
| **Lucchesi, Bruno** | Sculptor |
| 30 5th Ave, New York NY 10011, USA | |
| **Lucchesi, Frank J** | Baseball Player, Manager |
| 4703 Mill Creek Dr, Colleyville TX 76034, USA | |
| **Lucchesini, Andrea** | Concert Pianist |
| Arts Manangement Group, 1133 Broadway, #1025, New York NY 10010, USA | |
| **Lucci, Michael G (Mike)** | Football Player |
| 3184 Middlebelt Road, West Bloomfield MI 48323, USA | |
| **Lucci, Susan** | Actress |
| Rogers & Cowan, 8687 Melrose Ave, #G700, West Hollywood CA 90069 USA | |
| **Luce, Derrel J** | Football Player |
| 4112 Green Oak Dr, Waco TX 76710, USA | |
| **Luce, Don** | Ice Hockey Player |
| 67 Tartan Lane, Buffalo NY 14221, USA | |
| **Luce, Richard N** | Governor, Gibraltar |
| House of Lords, Westminster, London SW1A 0PW, England | |
| **Luce, William (Bill)** | Writer |
| PO Box 370, Depoe Bay OR 97341, USA | |
| **Lucero, Carlos F** | Judge |
| US Court of Appeals, 1929 Stout St, Denver CO 80294, USA | |
| **Luchini, Fabrice** | Actor |
| Voyez Mon Agent, 20 Ave Rapp, 75007 Paris, France | |
| **Luchko, Klara S** | Actress |
| Kotelmicheskaya Nab 1/15 Korp B, #308, 109240 Moscow, Russia | |
| **Luchsinger, Susie** | Singer |
| Psalm Ministries, 406 W 10th St, Atoka OK 74525, USA | |
| **Lucic, Zeljko** | Opera Singer |
| Barrett Vantage Artists, 505 8th Ave, #12A00, New York NY 10018 10018, USA | |
| **Lucid, Shannon W** | Astronaut, Biophysicist |
| 1622 Gunwale Road, Houston TX 77062, USA | |
| **Lucier, Louis J (Lou)** | Baseball Player |
| 7 Jaclyn Rae Dr, Millbury MA 01527, USA | |
| **Lucio, Shannon** | Actress |
| Filament Pictures, 2104 N Cahuenga Blvd, #303, Los Angeles CA 90068, USA | |
| **Luck, Andrew A** | Football Player |
| Indianapolis Colts, 7001 W 56th St, Indianapolis IN 46254 USA | |
| **Luck, Frank** | Biathlete |
| Lerchenweg 9, 98587 Springstille, Germany | |
| **Luck, Gary E** | Army General |
| S A A H Foundation, 1147 N Clark St, #2044, West Hollywood CA 90069, USA | |
| **Luckett, LeToya** | Singer |
| Resolution, 1801 Century Park E, #2300, Los Angeles CA 90067, USA | |
| **Luckey, Ken** | Actor |
| Greene Assoc, 1901 Ave of Stars, #130, Los Angeles CA 90067 USA | |
| **Luckhurst, Michael C W (Mick)** | Football Player |
| 2757 Dawsons Chase, Duluth GA 30097, USA | |
| **Luckinbill, Lawrence** | Actor |
| PO Box 330, Georgetown CT 06829, USA | |

**Luckovich, Mike** — Editorial Cartoonist
Atlanta Constitution, 223 Perimeter Center Parkway NE, Atlanta GA 30346, USA

**Lucy, Donny** — Baseball Player
3674 Oakcliff Dr, Fallbrook CA 92028, USA

**Lucy, Tom** — Rowing Athlete
Leander Club, Henley on Thames, Leander RG9 2LP, England

**Luczo, Stephen J** — Businessman
Seagate Technology, 920 Disc Dr, Scotts Valley CA 95066, USA

**Ludacris** — Rap Artist, Actor
Creative Artists Agency, 2000 Ave of Stars, #100, Los Angeles CA 90067 USA

**Luddington, Camilla** — Actress
United Talent Agency, U T A Plaza, 9336 Civic Center Dr, Beverly Hills CA 90210 USA

**Luder, Owen H** — Architect
Communication in Construction, 2 Smith Square, London SW1P 3HS, England

**Ludes, John T** — Businessman
Fortune Brands Inc, 300 Tower Parkway, Lincolnshire IL 60069, USA

**Luding-Rothenburger, Christa** — Speed Skater, Cyclist
Dresdener Eisspot-Club, Pieschener Allee 1, 01067 Dresden, Germany

**Ludington, Ronald (Ron)** — Figure Skater
611 Thompson Station Road, Newark DE 19711, USA

**Ludwick, Ryan A** — Baseball Player
115 Roberts Circle, Georgetown TX 78633, USA

**Ludwig, Alexander** — Actor
B/W/R, 9100 Wilshire Blvd, #500W, Beverly Hills CA 90212 USA

**Ludwig, Christa** — Opera Singer
1458 Ter, Chemin des Colles, 06740 Chateauneuf de Grasse, France

**Ludwig, Craig** — Ice Hockey Player
421 River St, Eagle River WI 54521, USA

**Ludwig, George H** — Physicist
University of Iowa, Physics & Astronomy Dept, Iowa City IA 52242, USA

**Ludwig, Ken** — Writer
Gersh Agency, 9465 Wilshire Blvd, #600, Beverly Hills CA 90212 USA

**Lue, Tyronn J** — Basketball Player
2926 Montessouri St, Las Vegas NV 89117, USA

**Luebber, Stephen L (Steve)** — Baseball Player
3302 Moorehead Dr, Joplin MO 64804, USA

**Lueck, William M (Bill)** — Football Player
409 E Bird Lane, Litchfield Park AZ 85340, USA

**Luecken, Richard F (Rick)** — Baseball Player
2902 Fontana Dr, East Providence RI 02915, USA

**Lueders, Pierre** — Bobsled Athlete
Bobsled Canada, 140 Canada Olympic Road SW, Calgary AB T3B 5R5, Canada

**Luft, Lorna** — Actress, Singer
Stiletto Entertainment, 8295 S La Cienega Blvd, Inglewood CA 90301, USA

**Lugansky, Nicolai** — Concert Pianist
Harrison/Parrott, 5-6 Albion Court, London W6 0QT, England

**Lugbill, Jon** — Canoeing Athlete
8810 Wishart Road, Richmond VA 23229, USA

**Luger, Gery** — Photographer
Hinterfeld 598, 6861 Alberschwende, Austria

**Lugo, Julio** — Baseball Player
1555 Gants Circle, Kissimmee FL 34744, USA

**Luhrmann, Baz** — Director
Bazmark Inq, PO Box 430, Kings Cross NSW 2011, Australia

**Luisi, Fabio** — Conductor
Zurich Opera House, Falkenstr 1, 8008 Zurich, Switzerland

**Luisotti, Nicola** — Conductor
I M G Artists, Hogarth Business Park, Chiswick, London W4 2TH, England

**Lujack, John C (Johnny)** — Football Player
6321 Crow Valley Dr, Bettendorf IA 52722, USA

**Lujan, Manuel, Jr** — Secretary, Interior
Manuel Lujan Agencies, PO Box 3727, Albuquerque NM 87190, USA

**Lukachyk, Robert J** — Baseball Player
100 High St, Woodbridge NJ 07095, USA

**Lukas, D Wayne** — Thoroughbred Racing Trainer
1034 Oak Canyon Lane, Glendora CA 91741, USA

**Lukashenko, Aleksandr** — President, Belarus
President's Office, Karl Marx Str 38, 220016 Minsk, Belarus

**Lukasiewicz, Mark** — Baseball Player
8035 Fir Dr, Clay NY 13041, USA

**Lukather, Steve (Luke)** — Musician (Toto)
Monterey International, 200 W Superior St, #202, Chicago IL 60654 USA

**Luke, Derek** — Actor
W M E Entertainment, 9601 Wilshire Blvd, #300, Beverly Hills CA 90210 USA

**Luke, John A, Jr** — Businessman
Westvaco Corp, 299 Park Ave, #1300, New York NY 10171, USA

**Luke, Mathew C (Matt)** — Baseball Player
5262 Eucalyptus Hill Road, Yorba Linda CA 92886, USA

**Lukeba, Merveille** — Actor
Independent Talent Group, 40 Whitfield St, London W1T 2RH, England

**Luken, Thomas J (Tom)** — Football Player
8036 Cast A Way, Mason OH 45040, USA

**Lukens, Max L** — Businessman
Baker Hughes Inc, PO Box 4740, Houston TX 77210, USA

**Luketic, Robert** — Director
Mosiac Media Group, 9200 W Sunset Blvd, #1000, Los Angeles CA 90069 USA

**Lukin, Matt** — Bassist (Mudhoney)
Legends of 21st Century, 7 Trinity Row, Florence MA 01062, USA

**Lukin, Valery** — Oceanographer
Arctic/Antarctic Research Institute, 38 Bering Str, 199397 Saint Petersburg, Russia

**Lukis, Adrian** — Actor
Ken McReddie Assoc, 101 Finsbury Pavement, London EC2A 1RS, England

**Lukowich, Brad** — Ice Hockey Player
3400 Craig Dr, #721, McKinney TX 75070, USA

**Luksic, Igor** — Prime Minister, Montenegro
Prime Minister's Office, Jovana Tomasevica BB, Podgorica, Montenegro

**Luckovich - Luksic**

**L**

| | |
|---|---|
| **Lulu**<br>Concorde International, 101 Shepherds Bush Road, London W6 7LP, England | Singer, Actress |
| **Lum, Michael K (Mike)**<br>3476 Cochise Dr SE, Atlanta GA 30339, USA | Baseball Player |
| **Lumbly, Carl W**<br>Brady Brannon Talent, 204 N Rossmore Ave, Los Angeles CA 90004, USA | Actor |
| **Lumenti, Raphael A (Ralph)**<br>9 Tomaso Road, Milford MA 01757, USA | Baseball Player |
| **Lumidee**<br>Central Entertainment Group, 166 5th Ave, #400, New York NY 10010, USA | Singer |
| **Lumley, Dave**<br>PO Box 610, Murfreesboro AR 71958, USA | Ice Hockey Player |
| **Lumley, Joanna**<br>Independent Talent Group, 40 Whitfield St, London W1T 2RH, England | Actress |
| **Lumley, John L**<br>743 Snyder Hill Road, Ithaca NY 14850, USA | Physicist |
| **Lumme, Jyrki O**<br>9646 E Laurel Lane, Scottsdale AZ 85260, USA | Ice Hockey Player |
| **Lumpe, Jerry D**<br>732 S Pearson Dr, Springfield MO 65809, USA | Baseball Player |
| **Lumpkin, Sean F**<br>4708 Virginia Lane, Minneapolis MN 55424, USA | Football Player |
| **Lumpp, Raymond G (Ray)**<br>21 Hewlett Dr, East Williston NY 11596, USA | Basketball Player |
| **Lumsden, David J**<br>Melton House, Soham, Cambridgeshire CB7 5DB, England | Conductor, Concert Organist |
| **Luna, Barbara**<br>18026 Rodarte Way, Encino CA 91316, USA | Actress |
| **Luna, Diego**<br>Canana Films, Zacatecas 142-A, Colonia Roma, Mexico City DF 06700, Mexico | Actor |
| **Lunar, Fernando**<br>3125 Zuni Place, Alamogordo NM 88310, USA | Baseball Player |
| **Lund, Corb**<br>R G K Entertainment Group, 2B Minto St, #6, Toronto ON M4L 1B6, Canada | Singer, Songwriter |
| **Lund, Deanna**<br>Fred Eichelman, 545 Howard Dr, Salem VA 24153, USA | Actress |
| **Lund, Donald A (Don)**<br>1299 Laurel View Dr, Ann Arbor MI 48105, USA | Baseball Player |
| **Lund, Eva**<br>Curling Assn, Idrottshuser, Marbackagatan 19, 123 43 Farsta, Sweden | Curling Athlete |
| **Lund, Gordon T**<br>1602 S Harvard Ave, Arlington Heights IL 60005, USA | Baseball Player |
| **Lund, Katia**<br>Gersh Agency, 9465 Wilshire Blvd, #600, Beverly Hills CA 90212 USA | Director |
| **Lundaas, Terje**<br>Glass Art & Design, 7003 N Waterway Dr, #201, Miami FL 33133, USA | Artist, Sculptor |
| **Lundberg, Anders**<br>Goteberg University, Physiology Dept, Box 33031, 40 033 Goteborg, Sweden | Physiologist |
| **Lundberg, Athena**<br>Playboy Promotions, 2706 Media Center Dr, Los Angeles CA 90065 USA | Model |
| **Lundberg, Fred Borre**<br>Skogbrynet 11, 9250 Bardu, Norway | Nordic Combined Skier |
| **Lunden, Joan**<br>Celebrity Consultants, 3340 Ocean Park Blvd, #1005, Santa Monica CA 90405 USA | Commentator |
| **Lundgren, Dolph**<br>Baumgarten Mgmt, 11925 Wilshire Blvd, #310, Los Angeles CA 90025, USA | Actor |
| **Lundgren, Terry**<br>Federated Department Stores, 151 W 34th St, New York NY 10001, USA | Businessman |
| **Lundholm, Johan (Bengt)**<br>Torsgatan 16, 113 62 Stockholm, Sweden | Ice Hockey Player |
| **Lundi, Monika**<br>Ortlindestr 2, 81927 Munich, Germany | Actress |
| **Lundquist, M Laverne (Verne), Jr**<br>1710 Natches Way, Steamboat Springs CO 80487, USA | Sportscaster |
| **Lundquist, Stephen (Steve)**<br>246 Northwest Dr, Stockbridge GA 30281, USA | Swimmer |
| **Lundqvist, Alex**<br>Wilhelmina Models, 300 Park Ave S, #200, New York NY 10010 USA | Model |
| **Lundqvist, B Henrik**<br>310 W 52nd St, #PHD, New York NY 10019, USA | Ice Hockey Player |
| **Lundstedt, Thomas R (Tom)**<br>9813 Brookside Lane, Ephraim WI 54211, USA | Baseball Player |
| **Lundstrom, Tord G**<br>Brynas Byggnads AB, 801 33 Gavle, Sweden | Ice Hockey Player |
| **Lundy, Carmen**<br>Abby Hoffer Enterprises, 223 1/2 E 48th St, New York NY 10017 USA | Singer |
| **Lundy, Jessica**<br>Metropolitan Talent Agency, 5405 Wilshire Blvd, #218, Los Angeles CA 90036 USA | Actress |
| **Lundy, Victor A**<br>Victor A Lundy Assoc, 701 Mulberry Lane, Bellaire TX 77401, USA | Architect |
| **Lunenfeld, Bruno**<br>7 Rav Ashi St, Tel Aviv 69395, Israel | Endocrinologist |
| **Luner, Jaime**<br>Berneman Mgmt, 5820 Wilshire Blvd, #200, Los Angeles CA 90036, USA | Actress |
| **Lunghi, Cherie**<br>C A M, 111 Shoreditch High St, #400, London E1 6JN, England | Actress |
| **Lunka, Zoltan**<br>Weinheimer Str 2, 69198 Schriesheim, Germany | Boxer |
| **Lunke, Hilary**<br>11701 Broad Oaks Dr, Austin TX 78759, USA | Golfer |
| **Lunn, Bob**<br>PO Box 1495, Woodbridge CA 95258, USA | Golfer |
| **Lunney, Glenn**<br>United Space Alliance, 1150 Gemini Dr, Houston TX 77058, USA | Space Scientist |
| **Lunsford, Trey**<br>3955 Nail Road, Southaven MS 38672, USA | Baseball Player |

**Luongo, Aldo**
883 Westbourne Ave, West Hollywood CA 90069, USA
*Artist*

**Luongo, Christopher J (Chris)**
103 Arabian Dr, Madison AL 35758, USA
*Ice Hockey Player*

**Luongo, Roberto**
7280 Lemon Grass Dr, Parkland FL 33076, USA
*Ice Hockey Player*

**Lupberger, Edwin A**
Nesher Investments, 2010 NE 164th St, North Miami Beach FL 33162, USA
*Businessman*

**Lupica, Mike**
87 Bald Hill Road, New Canaan CT 06840, USA
*Sportswriter*

**Lupien, Gilles**
Sports Prospects, 77 Rue de Bleury, Rosemere QC J7A 4L9, Canada
*Ice Hockey Player*

**Luplow, Alvin D (Al)**
4250 Lakecress Dr E, Saginaw MI 48603, USA
*Baseball Player*

**Lupo, Janet P**
PO Box 6232, Hoboken NJ 07030, USA
*Model*

**LuPone, Patti**
235 Park Ave S, #700, New York NY 10003, USA
*Singer, Actress*

**Lupu, Radu**
Opus 3 Artists, 470 Park Ave S, #900N, New York NY 10016 USA
*Concert Pianist*

**Lupus, Peter**
Greene Assoc, 1901 Ave of Stars, #130, Los Angeles CA 90067 USA
*Actor, Bodybuilder, Model*

**Lurie, Alison**
Cornell University, English Dept, Ithaca NY 14850, USA
*Writer*

**Lurie, Jeffrey**
312 Llanfair Road, Wynnewood PA 19096, USA
*Football Executive*

**Lurie, Ranan R**
Cartoonnews International, 375 Park Ave, #1301, New York NY 10152, USA
*Editorial Cartoonist*

**Lurie, Rod**
Battleplan Productions, 1041 N Formosa Ave, Santa Monica W Building, West Hollywood CA 90046, USA
*Director, Producer*

**Lurtsema, Robert R (Bob)**
16920 Judicial Road, Lakeville MN 55044, USA
*Football Player*

**Lurz, Dagmar**
International Skating Union, Chemin du Primerose 2, 1007 Lausanne, Switzerland
*Figure Skater*

**Lusader, Scott E**
4169 Bold Meadows, Oakland Township MI 48306, USA
*Baseball Player*

**Lusardi, Linda**
E3 Artists, 56 Shorts Gardens, London WC2H 9AN, England
*Model*

**Lush, Billy**
Mary Erickson Entertainment, 2122 Hillhurst Ave, #A, Los Angeles CA 90027, USA
*Actor*

**Lusis, Janis**
Vesetas 8-3, 1013 Riga, Latvia
*Track Athlete*

**Lussier, Patrick**
Paradigm Agency, 360 N Crescent Dr, North Building, Beverly Hills CA 90210 USA
*Director*

**Lussier, Sheila**
Wilson Assoc, 5418 Wilshire Blvd, #510, Los Angeles CA 90036, USA
*Actress*

**Lust, Reimar**
Bellevue 49, 22301 Hamburg, Germany
*Physicist*

**Lusteg, G Booth**
1100 SW 111th Way, Davie FL 33324, USA
*Football Player*

**Lustig, M Bruce**
Washington Hebrew Congregation, 3935 Macomb St NW, Washington DC 20016, USA
*Religious Leader, Rabbi*

**Lustig, William**
15016 Marble Dr, Sherman Oaks CA 91403, USA
*Producer, Director, Actor*

**Lusztig, George**
106 Grant Ave, Newton MA 02459, USA
*Mathematician*

**Lute, Douglas E**
White House, 1600 Pennsylvania Ave NW, Washington DC 20500 USA
*Army General*

**Luter, Fred, Jr**
Franklin Avenue Baptist Church, 2515 Franklin Ave, New Orleans LA 70117, USA
*Religious Leader*

**Lutes, Eric**
Special Artists Agency, 9200 Sunset Blvd, #410, West Hollywood CA 90069 USA
*Actor*

**Luther, Edward A (Ed)**
30486 Le Port, Laguna Niguel CA 92677, USA
*Football Player*

**Luttrell, Rachel**
S M S Talent, 8383 Wilshire Blvd, #230, Beverly Hills CA 90211 USA
*Actress*

**Lutz, Bob**
101 Via Ensueno, San Clemente CA 92672, USA
*Tennis Player*

**Lutz, Joleen**
H David Moss, 733 Seward St, #PH, Los Angeles CA 90038 USA
*Actress*

**Lutz, Kellan**
B/W/R, 9100 Wilshire Blvd, #500W, Beverly Hills CA 90212 USA
*Actor*

**Lutz, Lisa**
Levine Greenberg Literary Agency, 307 7th Ave, #2407, New York NY 10001, USA
*Writer*

**Lutz, Robert A**
3966 Pleasant Lake Road, Ann Arbor MI 48103, USA
*Businessman*

**Lux, Danny**
I C M Partners, 10250 Constellation Blvd, #900, Los Angeles CA 90067 USA
*Composer*

**Lux, Loretta**
Yossi Milo Gallery, 555 W 24th St, New York NY 10011, USA
*Photographer*

**Luxon, Benjamin M**
Mazet, Relubbus Lane, Saint Hilary, Penzance, Cornwall TR20 9DS, England
*Opera Singer*

**Luyendyk, Arie**
9915 N Copper Ridge Trail, Fountain Hills AZ 85268, USA
*Auto Racing Driver*

**Luyties, Ricci**
2215 Hartford St, San Diego CA 92110, USA
*Volleyball Player*

**Luzinski, Gregory M (Greg)**
25680 Streamlet Court, Bonita Springs FL 34135, USA
*Baseball Player*

**Luzuriaga, Katherine**
University of Massachusetts Medical Center, Immunology Dept, 55 Lake Ave N, Worcester MA 01655, USA
*Immunologist*

**Lwin, Annabella**
M O B Agency, 6404 Wilshire Blvd, #505, Los Angeles CA 90048 USA
*Singer (Bow Wow Wow)*

**Lyakhov, Vladimir A**
Cosmonaut Training Center, Star City, 141160 Zvezdny Gorodok, Moscow Oblast, Russia
*Cosmonaut*

**Lyall, John A**
John Lyall Architects, 13-19 Curtain Road, London EC2A 3LT, England
*Architect*

**Lyden, Mitchell S (Mitch)** — Baseball Player
227 Shore Court, Lauderdale by the Sea FL 33308, USA
**Lydman, Toni** — Ice Hockey Player
6035 Corinne Lane, Clarence Center NY 14032, USA
**Lydon, Alexa** — Actress
Silver Lining Entertainment, 421 S Beverly Drive, #700, Beverly Hills CA 90212 USA
**Lydon, James (Jimmy)** — Actor
3538 Lomacitas Lane, Bonita CA 91902, USA
**Lydon, John (Johnny Rotten)** — Singer, Musician (Sex Pistols)
31962 Pacific Coast Highway, Malibu CA 90265, USA
**Lydon, Malcolm** — Astronaut
1429 Jaudon Road, Dover FL 33527, USA
**Lydy, D Scott** — Baseball Player
4278 S Leoma Lane, Chandler AZ 85249, USA
**Lyght, Todd W** — Football Player
912 Camino Ibiza, San Clemente CA 92672, USA
**Lyle, Gary T** — Football Player
222 Beach Dr NE, Saint Petersburg FL 33701, USA
**Lyle, Kami** — Singer, Trumpeter, Songwriter
D S Mgmt, 2814 12th Ave S, #202, Nashville TN 37204, USA
**Lyle, Keith A** — Football Player
9615 Maypan Place, Seminole FL 33777, USA
**Lyle, Sandy** — Golfer
4904 Duck Creek Lane, #450, Ponte Vedra Beach FL 32082, USA
**Lyles, Lester E** — Football Player
6315 14th St NW, Washington DC 20011, USA
**Lyles, Lester L (Les)** — Air Force General
United Services Automobile Assn, U S A A Building, 9800 Fredericksburg Road, San Antonio TX 78288, USA
**Lyles, Robert D** — Football Player
1012 Merritt Road, #C, West Point NY 10996, USA
**Lyman, Dorothy** — Actress
Stone Manners Salners, 9911 W Pico Blvd, #1400, Los Angeles CA 90035 USA
**Lyman, Dustin S** — Football Player
501 W Spruce St, Louisville CO 80027, USA
**Lyn, Nicole** — Actress
McGowan Mgmt, 8733 W Sunset Blvd, #103, West Hollywood CA 90069, USA
**Lynam, Jim** — Basketball Coach, Executive
Philadelphia 76ers, 1st Union Center, 3601 S Broad St, Philadelphia PA 19148 USA
**Lynch, Allen J** — Vietnam War Army Hero (CMH)
438 Belle Plaine Ave, Gurnee IL 60031, USA
**Lynch, Charles A** — Businessman
24 Susan Gale Court, Menlo Park CA 94025, USA
**Lynch, Claire** — Singer
369 Gillette Road, Nashville TN 37211, USA
**Lynch, Dan** — Editorial Cartoonist
Fort Wayne Journal-Gazette, Editorial Dept, 600 W Main St, Fort Wayne IN 46802, USA
**Lynch, David K** — Director
David Lynch Foundation, PO Box 93158,Los Angeles CA 90093, USA
**Lynch, Edele** — Singer (B*Witched)
Clintons, 55 Drury Lane, Covent Garden, London WC2B 5SQ, England
**Lynch, Edward F (Ed)** — Baseball Player
7832 E Parkview Lane, Scottsdale AZ 85255, USA
**Lynch, Francis X (Fran)** — Football Player
2553 Lake Vista Dr, Broomfield CO 80023, USA
**Lynch, George D, III** — Basketball Player
1000 Phils Creek Road, Chapel Hill NC 27516, USA
**Lynch, Jair** — Gymnast
9207 Three Oaks Dr, Silver Spring MD 20901, USA
**Lynch, James E (Jim)** — Football Player
1717 W 91st Place, Kansas City MO 64114, USA
**Lynch, Jane** — Actress, Comedienne
Domain Talent, 9229 W Sunset Blvd, #710, West Hollywood CA 90069 USA
**Lynch, Jennifer Chambers** — Writer, Director
Water Street Anthem Entertainment, 5225 Wilshire Blvd, #615, Los Angeles CA 90036 USA
**Lynch, Jessica** — Iraqi War Army Hero
Gregory Lynch, RR 1, Palestine WV 26160, USA
**Lynch, John** — Actor
Markham Froggatt Irwin, Julian House, 4 Windmill St, London W1P 1HF, England
**Lynch, John Carroll** — Actor
Abrams Artists, 9200 W Sunset Blvd, #1125, West Hollywood CA 90069 USA
**Lynch, John T, Jr** — Football Player
13 Sandy Lake Road, Englewood CO 80113, USA
**Lynch, Keavy** — Singer (B*Witched)
Clintons, 55 Drury Lane, Covent Garden, London WC2B 5SQ, England
**Lynch, Kelly** — Model, Actress
Talent Works, 3500 W Olive Ave, #1400, Burbank CA 91505 USA
**Lynch, Lorenzo** — Football Player
864 Bentwater Parkway, Cedar Hill TX 75104, USA
**Lynch, Marshawn T** — Football Player
2100 Lake Washington Blvd N, #C101, Renton WA 98056, USA
**Lynch, Peter S** — Financier
27 State St, Boston MA 02109, USA
**Lynch, Sandra L** — Judge
US Court of Appeals, 1 Courthouse Way, Boston MA 02210, USA
**Lynch, Shane** — Singer (Boyzone), Actor
Associated International Mgmt, 7 Hatton Garden, #400, London EC1N 8AD, England
**Lynch, Susan** — Actress
Troika, 74 Clerkenwell Road, #300, London EC1M 5QA, England
**Lynch, Thomas C** — Navy Admiral
751 Eagle Farm Road, Villanova PA 19085, USA
**Lynch, Thomas W (Tom)** — Producer
Tom Lynch Co, 1801 Ave of Stars, #710, Los Angeles CA 90067, USA
**Lynde, Janice** — Actress
Stage 9 Talent, 1249 Lodi Place, Los Angeles CA 90038, USA
**Lynden-Bell, Donald** — Astronomer
Institute of Astronomy, Madingley Road, Cambridge CB3 0HA, England

| | |
|---|---|
| **Lyndon, Frank**<br>Paramount Entertainment, PO Box 12, Far Hills NJ 07931 USA | Singer (Belmonts) |
| **Lynds, Roger**<br>Kitt Peak National Observatory, Tucson AZ 85726, USA | Astronomer |
| **Lyne, Adrian**<br>W M E Entertainment, 9601 Wilshire Blvd, #300, Beverly Hills CA 90210 USA | Director |
| **Lyngstad, Anni-Frida**<br>Mono Music, Sodra Brobaeken 41A, 111 49 Stockholm, Sweden | Singer (ABBA), Songwriter |
| **Lynn Salomon, Janet**<br>PO Box 1026, Haymarket VA 20168, USA | Figure Skater |
| **Lynn, Cheryl**<br>PO Box 667, Smithtown NY 11787, USA | Singer, Actress |
| **Lynn, Frederic M (Fred)**<br>7336 El Fuerte St, Carlsbad CA 92009, USA | Baseball Player |
| **Lynn, Greg**<br>University of California, Architecture School, Los Angeles CA 90024, USA | Architect |
| **Lynn, Johnny R**<br>1031 Fair Oaks Ave, Alameda CA 94501, USA | Football Player |
| **Lynn, Jonathan**<br>United Agents, 12-26 Lexington St, London W1F 0LE, England | Director |
| **Lynn, Loretta**<br>44 Hurricane Mills Road, Hurricane Mills TN 37078, USA | Singer, Guitarist, Songwriter |
| **Lynn, Meredith Scott**<br>Bauman Redanty Shaul Agency, 5757 Wilshire Blvd, #473, Los Angeles CA 90036 USA | Actress |
| **Lynn, Theresa**<br>1435 Winter Ave, Louisville KY 40204, USA | Actress |
| **Lynn, Vera**<br>Hampers Croft, Common Lane, Ditchling, East Sussex BN6 8TJ, England | Actress, Singer |
| **Lynne, Gillian**<br>Lean-2 Productions, 18 Rutland St, Knightsbridge, London SW7 1EF, England | Dance Director, Choreographer |
| **Lynne, Jeff**<br>Front Line Mgmt, 1100 Glendon Ave, #2000, Los Angeles CA 90024 USA | Singer, Guitarist, Songwriter |
| **Lynne, Rockie**<br>Music Works, PO Box 447, Center City MN 55012, USA | Singer, Songwriter |
| **Lynne, Shelby**<br>High Road, 751 Bridgeway, #200, Sausalito CA 94965, USA | Singer, Fiddle Player, Songwriter |
| **Lynskey, Melanie**<br>Susan Smith, 1344 N Wetherly Dr, Los Angeles CA 90069 USA | Actress |
| **Lyon, Brandon J**<br>4291 S Iowa St, Chandler AZ 85248, USA | Baseball Player |
| **Lyon, Sue**<br>Rudman, 1317 N Whitnall Highway, Burbank CA 91505, USA | Actress |
| **Lyonne, Natasha**<br>A P A Talent/Literary Agency, 405 S Beverly Dr, #300, Beverly Hills CA 90212 USA | Actress |
| **Lyons, Barry S**<br>527 Front Beach Dr, #71, Ocean Springs MS 39564, USA | Baseball Player |
| **Lyons, Ben**<br>W M E Entertainment, 9601 Wilshire Blvd, #300, Beverly Hills CA 90210 USA | Film Critic, Columnist |
| **Lyons, Curt R**<br>124 Virginia Dr, Richmond KY 40475, USA | Baseball Player |
| **Lyons, David**<br>Anonymous Content, 3532 Hayden Ave, Culver City CA 90232 USA | Actor |
| **Lyons, Elena**<br>Innovative Artists, 1505 10th St, Santa Monica CA 90401 USA | Actress |
| **Lyons, James A, Jr**<br>9481 Piney Mountain Road, Warrenton VA 20186, USA | Navy Admiral |
| **Lyons, Martin A (Marty)**<br>8 White Pine Court, Smithtown NY 11787, USA | Football Player |
| **Lyons, Mitchell W (Mitch)**<br>8344 Woodcrest Dr NE, Rockford MI 49341, USA | Football Player |
| **Lyons, Phyllis**<br>Bauman Redanty Shaul Agency, 5757 Wilshire Blvd, #473, Los Angeles CA 90036 USA | Actress |
| **Lyons, Robert F**<br>3810 Magnolia Blvd, PO Box 1292, Burbank CA 91507, USA | Actor |
| **Lyons, Stephen K (Steve)**<br>8196 E Del Platino Dr, Scottsdale AZ 85258, USA | Baseball Player |
| **Lyons, Thomas L (Tommy)**<br>2814 Drummond Point SE, Atlanta GA 30339, USA | Football Player |
| **Lysacek, Evan F**<br>Toyota Sports Center, 555 N Nash St, El Segundo CA 90245, USA | Figure Skater |
| **Lysenko, Tatiana**<br>Harris Agency, 17814 Lillian St, Omaha NE 68136, USA | Gymnast |
| **Lysiak, Thomas J (Tom)**<br>1050 Cedar Grove Road, Buckhead GA 30625, USA | Ice Hockey Player |
| **Lyst, John H**<br>Indianapolis Newspapers Inc, PO Box 145, Indianapolis IN 46206, USA | Editor |
| **Lythgoe, Nigel**<br>Nigel Lythgoe Productions, 8560 W Sunset Blvd, #900, West Hollywood CA 90069, USA | Producer, Director, Writer |
| **Lyttle, James L (Jim)**<br>751 Camino Lakes Circle, Boca Raton FL 33486, USA | Baseball Player |
| **Lyttle, Kevin**<br>Nene Musik Productions, 1460 SW Santiago Ave, Port Saint Lucie FL 34953 USA | Singer |
| **Lyttle, Sancho**<br>Atlanta Dream, 83 Walton St NW, #400, Atlanta, GA 30303 USA | Basketball Player |
| **Lyubimov, Yuri P**<br>M Nikitskaya Str 16-21, 121069 Moscow, Russia | Director, Actor |
| **Lyubshin, Stanislav A**<br>Vernadskogo Prosp 123, #171, 117571 Moscow, Russia | Actor |

**M I A** — Rap Artist
2:30 Publicity, 304 Hudson St, #700, New York NY 10013, USA

**M J G** — Rap Artist (8Ball & M J G)
J L Entertainment, 18653 Ventura Blvd, #340, Los Angeles CA 91356 USA

**Ma Ying Jeou** — President, Taiwan
President's Office, Chieshshou Hall, Chongcing S Road, Taipei 100, Taiwan

**Ma, Tzi** — Actor
A P A Talent/Literary Agency, 405 S Beverly Dr, #300, Beverly Hills CA 90212 USA

**Ma, Yo-Yo** — Concert Cellist, Composer
Musichall Ltd, Vicarage Way, Ringmer BN8 5LA, England

**Maas, Kevin C** — Baseball Player
PO Box 21019, Castro Valley CA 94546, USA

**Maas, William T (Bill)** — Football Player, Sportscaster
653 N Shoreline Dr, Lees Summit MO 64064, USA

**Maazel, Lorin V** — Conductor, Concert Violinist
Z des Aubris, Tal 15 5th Floor, 80331 Munich, Germany

**Mabbs, Edward C** — Businessman
21 Stonehedge Road, Lincoln MA 01773, USA

**Mabe, Ricky** — Actor
K L Benzakein Talent, 1155 Rene-Levesque Blvd W, #2500, Montreal QC H3B 2K4, Canada

**Mabeus, Chris** — Baseball Player
151 Shady Lane, Soldotna AK 99669, USA

**Mabius, Eric** — Actor
I C M Partners, 10250 Constellation Blvd, #900, Los Angeles CA 90067 USA

**Mabrey, Sunny** — Actress
Paradigm Agency, 360 N Crescent Dr, North Building, Beverly Hills CA 90210 USA

**Mabry, John S** — Baseball Player
715 Bellerive Manor Dr, Saint Louis MO 63141, USA

**Mabus, Raymond E, Jr** — Governor, MS
Secretary of Navy, HqUSN, Pentagon, Washington DC 20350, USA

**MacAdam, Al** — Ice Hockey Player
PO Box 232, Morrell PE C0A 1S0, Canada

**MacAfee, Kenneth A (Ken), II** — Football Player
154 South St, Needham MA 02492, USA

**Macal, Zdenek** — Conductor
Opus 3 Artists, 470 Park Ave S, #900N, New York NY 10016 USA

**Macarron Jaime, Ricardo** — Artist
Agustin de Bethencourt 7, 28003 Madrid, Spain

**MacArthur, Ellen** — Yachtswoman
Whitegates, Arctic Road, Cowes, Isle of Wight PO31 7PG, England

**MacArthur, Hayes** — Actor
Creative Artists Agency, 2000 Ave of Stars, #100, Los Angeles CA 90067 USA

**Macat, Julio G** — Cinematographer
Paradigm Agency, 360 N Crescent Dr, North Building, Beverly Hills CA 90210 USA

**Macaulay, Stewart** — Attorney, Educator
University of Wisconsin, Law School, 975 Bascom Mall, #6107, Madison WI 53706, USA

**MacAvoy, Paul W** — Economist
920 Indian Beach Dr, Sarasota FL 34234, USA

**Maccarinelli, Enzo** — Boxer
13 Hengoed Hall Dr, Cefn, Hengoed, Mid Glamorgan CF8 7JW, Wales

**Macchio, Ralph** — Actor
Don Buchwald, 6500 Wilshire Blvd, #2200, Los Angeles CA 90048 USA

**Maccioni, Sirio** — Restauranteur, Chef
Le Cirque 200, 151 E 58th St, Front 1, New York NY 10022, USA

**MacDermid, Paul** — Ice Hockey Player
81 Lakeland Dr, Sauble Beach ON N0H 2G0, Canada

**MacDermot, Galt** — Composer
MacDermot Assoc, 12 Silver Lake Road, Staten Island NY 10301, USA

**Macdissi, Peter** — Actor
United Talent Agency, U T A Plaza, 9336 Civic Center Dr, Beverly Hills CA 90210 USA

**MacDonald, Amy** — Singer, Songwriter
Melodramatic Records, PO Box 623, Weybridge KT13 3DE, England

**MacDonald, C Parker** — Ice Hockey Player
3 Miller Road, Northford CT 06472, USA

**MacDonald, Danielle** — Actress
Justice & Ponder, PO Box 480033, Los Angeles CA 90048, USA

**Macdonald, Hettie** — Director
Independent Talent Group, 40 Whitfield St, London W1T 2RH, England

**MacDonald, Julien** — Fashion Designer
Haydens Place, 447A Portobello Road, London W11 1LT, England

**Macdonald, Kelly** — Actress
Independent Talent Group, 40 Whitfield St, London W1T 2RH, England

**Macdonald, Kevin** — Director
United Agents, 12-26 Lexington St, London W1F 0LE, England

**Macdonald, Norm** — Actor, Comedian
Gersh Agency, 9465 Wilshire Blvd, #600, Beverly Hills CA 90212 USA

**MacDonald, Parker** — Ice Hockey Player
3 Miller Road, Northford CT 06472, USA

**MacDonald, Richard** — Sculptor
213 Galisteo St, Santa Fe NM 87501, USA

**Macdonald, Robert (Bob)** — Baseball Player
522 Harbor Grove Circle, Safety Harbor FL 34695, USA

**Macdonald, Shauna** — Actress
United Agents, 12-26 Lexington St, London W1F 0LE, England

**Macdougal, R Meiklejohn (Mike)** — Baseball Player
2429 N Travis St, Mesa AZ 85207, USA

**MacDowell, Andie** — Model, Actress
Schiff Co, 9200 Sunset Blvd, #430, West Hollywood CA 90232 USA

**MacEachern, David** — Bobsled Athlete
Bobsled Canada, 140 Canada Olympic Road SW, Calgary AB T3B 5R5, Canada

**Macek, Donald M (Don)** — Football Player
3615 Monte Real, Escondido CA 92029, USA

**Macer, Sterling, Jr** — Actor, Director, Writer
Gage Group, 14724 Ventura Blvd, #505, Sherman Oaks CA 91403 USA

**MacFadyen, Angus** — Actor
Alchemy Entertainment, 7024 Melrose Ave, #420, Los Angeles CA 90038 USA

**MacFadyen, Matthew** — Actor
Hamilton Hodell, 66-68 Margaret St, #500, London W1W 8SR, England
**MacFarlane, Michael A (Mike)** — Baseball Player
7421 Woodside Ave, Stockton CA 95207, USA
**MacFarlane, Seth** — Animator, Producer, Writer, Composer
Fuzzy Door Productions, 5700 Wilshire Blvd, #325, Los Angeles CA 90036, USA
**MacGraw, Ali** — Actress
Relatively Mgmt, 8899 Beverly Blvd, #509, Los Angeles CA 90048, USA
**MacGregor, Bruce** — Ice Hockey Player
8112 NW 133rd St, Edmonton AB T5R 0B1, Canada
**MacGregor, Jeff** — Writer
ESPN-TV, ESPN Plaza, 935 Middle St, Bristol CT 06010 USA
**MacGregor, Joanna C** — Concert, Jazz Pianist
SoundCircus Records, PO Box 57, Reading, Berkshire BG1 5TX, England
**MacGregor, Katherine** — Actress
23388 Mulholland Dr, #205, Woodland Hills CA 91364, USA
**Mach, David S** — Sculptor
64 Canonbie Road, Forest Hill, London SE23 3AG, England
**Macha, Kenneth E (Ken)** — Baseball Player, Manager
1118 Winnie Way, Latrobe PA 15650, USA
**Machada, Lesley Ann** — Actress
Principato-Young, 9465 Wilshire Blvd, #880, Beverly Hills CA 90212 USA
**Machado Fajardo, Alicia** — Beauty Queen, Actress, Model
Miss Universe Organization, 1370 Ave of Americas, #1600, New York NY 10019 USA
**Machado Ventura, Jose Ramon** — Vice President, Cuba
Palacio de Gobierno, Cibsejo de la Ravolucion, Havana, Cuba
**Machado, China** — Model
I M G Models, 304 Park Ave S, #PH N, New York NY 10010 USA
**Machado, Justina** — Actress
Allman/Rhea Mgmt, 141 S Barrington Ave, #E, Los Angeles CA 90049, USA
**Machado, Rodolfo** — Architect
Machado & Silvetti, 500 Harrison Ave, Boston MA 02118, USA
**Macharski, Franciszak Cardinal** — Religious Leader
Metropolita Krakowski, Ul Franciszkanska 3, 31004 Krakow, Poland
**Machen, J Bernard** — Educator
University of Florida, President's Office, Tigert Hall, Gainesville FL 32611, USA
**Machlis, Gail** — Cartoonist (Quality Time)
Gail Machlis Illustrations, 1 Arcade Ave, Berkeley CA 94708, USA
**Machover, Tod** — Composer
Massachusetts Institute of Technology, Media Laboratory, Cambridge MA 02139, USA
**Macht, Gabriel S** — Actor
I C M Partners, 10250 Constellation Blvd, #900, Los Angeles CA 90067 USA
**Machungo, Mario F de Graca** — Prime Minister, Mozambique
Banco International, Avda Zedequias, Mananhela 478, Maputo, Mozambique
**Maclellan, Brian** — Ice Hockey Player
Washington Capitals, 627 N Glebe Road, #850, Arlington VA 22203 USA
**MacInnis, Allan (Al)** — Ice Hockey Player, Executive
1132 Highland Point Dr, Saint Louis MO 63131, USA
**MacInnis, Frank T** — Businessman
E M C O R Group, 301 Merritt Seven, #600, Norwalk CT 06851, USA
**MacIntosh, Craig** — Cartoonist (Sally Forth)
3403 W 28th St, Minneapolis MN 55416, USA
**Macintyre, Carter** — Actor
United Talent Agency, U T A Plaza, 9336 Civic Center Dr, Beverly Hills CA 90210 USA
**MacIsaac, Martha** — Actress
A M I Artists Mgmt, 464 King St E, Toronto ON M5A 1L7, Canada
**MacIver, Norm** — Ice Hockey Player
2119 Ponderosa Circle, Duluth MN 55811, USA
**MacIvor, Daniel** — Actor
I C M Partners, 10250 Constellation Blvd, #900, Los Angeles CA 90067 USA
**Mack, Allison** — Actress
Industry Entertainment, 955 Carillo Dr, #300, Los Angeles CA 90048 USA
**Mack, Bill** — Sculptor
Erin Taylor Editions, 5222 W 78th St, Minneapolis MN 55435, USA
**Mack, Cedric M** — Football Player
116 Chestnut St, Lake Jackson TX 77566, USA
**Mack, Consuelo** — Commentator
WealthTrack, PO Box 20485, Dag Hammarskjold Convenience Center, New York NY 10017, USA
**Mack, J Kevin** — Football Player
29359 Hummingbird Circle, Westlake OH 44145, USA
**Mack, John J** — Financier
Morgan Stanley Co, 1585 Broadway, Lower B, New York NY 10036, USA
**Mack, Lonnie** — Singer, Guitarist
Concerted Efforts, PO Box 440326, Somerville MA 02144 USA
**Mack, Shane L** — Baseball Player
35324 Marsh Lane, Wildomar CA 92595, USA
**Mack, Thomas I (Tom)** — Football Player
52 Grand Miramar Dr, Henderson NV 89011, USA
**Mackall, Michelle** — Golfer
2057 Oxford Ave, Cardiff CA 92007, USA
**Mackanin, Peter (Pete), Jr** — Baseball Player, Manager
11563 E Bronco Trail, Scottsdale AZ 85255, USA
**Mackay, David** — Director, Producer
Gersh Agency, 9465 Wilshire Blvd, #600, Beverly Hills CA 90212 USA
**Mackay, Harvey** — Writer
Mackay Envelope Corp, 2100 Elm St SE, Minneapolis MN 55414, USA
**MacKay-Lyons, Brian** — Architect
MacKay-Lyons Architect Inc, 2188 Gottingen St, Halifax NS B3K 3B4, Canada
**Macke, Richard C** — Navy Admiral
1887 Alaweo St, Honolulu HI 96821, USA
**Macken, Eoin** — Actor
I C M Partners, 10250 Constellation Blvd, #900, Los Angeles CA 90067 USA
**Mackenzie, Alastair** — Actor
Ken McReddie Assoc, 101 Finsbury Pavement, London EC2A 1RS, England
**MacKenzie, David** — Director
United Agents, 12-26 Lexington St, London W1F 0LE, England

# M

**MacKenzie, J Barry** — Ice Hockey Player
Minnesota Wild, XCel Energy Arena, 1275 Saint Antoine W, Saint Paul MN 55104 USA
**MacKenzie, Kenneth P (Ken)** — Baseball Player
15 Fair St, Guilford CT 06437, USA
**MacKenzie, Peter** — Actor
Precision Entertainment, 6338 Wilshire Blvd, Los Angeles CA 90048, USA
**Mackey, Cindy** — Golfer
1190 Millstone Run, Bogart GA 30622, USA
**Mackey, Lance** — Dog Sled Racer
PO Box 75015, Fairbanks AK 99707, USA
**Mackey, Malcolm M** — Basketball Player
504 Hemphill Ave, Chattanooga TN 37411, USA
**Mackey, Rick** — Dog Sled Racer
5938 Four Mile Road, Nenana AK 99760, USA
**Mackie, Allison** — Actress
A P A Talent/Literary Agency, 405 S Beverly Dr, #300, Beverly Hills CA 90212 USA
**Mackie, Anthony** — Actor
Inspire Entertainment, 1517 S Bentley Ave, #202, Los Angeles CA 90025, USA
**Mackie, Robert G (Bob)** — Fashion Designer
Bob Mackie Ltd, 530 Fashion Ave, New York NY 10018, USA
**Mackin, Sean** — Violinist (Yellowcard)
Capitol Records, 1750 N Vine St, Los Angeles CA 90028 USA
**MacKinnon, Catherine** — Attorney, Social Activist
University of Michigan, Law School, 625 S State St, Ann Arbor MI 48109, USA
**MacKinnon, Roderick** — Nobel Chemistry Laureate
53 Winchester St, #2, Brookline MA 2446, USA
**MacKinnon, Simmone J** — Actress
Mark Morrissey Assoc, 45 Oxford St, Bondi Junction NSW 2022, Australia
**Mackintosh, Cameron A** — Producer
Cameron Mackintosh Ltd, 1 Bedford Square, London WC1B 3RA, England
**Macklin, David** — Actor
Wilson, 5410 Wilshire Blvd, #510, Los Angeles CA 90036, USA
**Macknowski, John A** — Basketball Player
1902 Garnet Lane, Dandridge, TN 37225, USA
**Macknowski, Stephen** — Canoeing Athlete
462 Kimball Ave, Yonkers NY 10704, USA
**Mackowiak, Robert W (Rob)** — Baseball Player
2414 W Superior St, Chicago IL 60612, USA
**Mackrides, William (Bill)** — Football Player
1060 Beverly Lane, Newtown Square PA 19073, USA
**MacLachlan, Kyle** — Actor
Gersh Agency, 9465 Wilshire Blvd, #600, Beverly Hills CA 90212 USA
**Maclachlan, Patricia** — Writer
21 Unquomonk Road, Williamsburg MA 01096, USA
**MacLaine, Shirley** — Actress
MacLaine Enterprise, PO Box 25962, Munds Park AZ 86017, USA
**MacLean, Donald J (Don)** — Basketball Player
216 Los Padres Dr, Thousand Oaks CA 91361, USA
**MacLean, Doug** — Ice Hockey Coach
466 Notre Dame St, Summerside PE C1N 1T3, Canada
**MacLean, John** — Ice Hockey Player, Coach
44 Old Farm Road, Basking Ridge NJ 7920, USA
**MacLean, Paul A** — Ice Hockey Player, Coach
41544 Glade Road, Canton MI 48187, USA
**MacLean, Steven G** — Astronaut, Canada
N A S A, Johnson Space Center, 2101 NASA Road, Houston TX 77058 USA
**Macleod, Carla** — Ice Hockey Player
Team Canada, 2424 University Dr NW, Calgary AB T2N 3Y9, Canada
**MacLeod, Gavin** — Actor
70070 Frank Sinatra Dr, #7, Rancho Mirage CA 92270, USA
**MacLeod, John M** — Basketball Coach
4610 E Fanfol Dr, Phoenix AZ 85028, USA
**Macleod, Thomas W (Tom)** — Football Player
15412 N Hazard Road, Spokane WA 99208, USA
**MacMaster, Natalie** — Fiddler
Columbia Artists Mgmt Inc, 1790 Broadway, #702, New York NY 10019 USA
**MacMillan, John S** — Ice Hockey Player
2672 W Conifer Dr, Eagle ID 83616, USA
**MacMillan, William S (Billy)** — Ice Hockey Player
Upper Meadowbank Road, RR 2, Cornwall PE C0A 1H0, Canada
**MacMurray, William** — Electrical Engineer
200 Deer Run Road, Schaghticoke NY 12154, USA
**Macnee, Patrick** — Actor
7 Mount Holyoke, Rancho Mirage CA 92270, USA
**MacNeil, Allister W (Al)** — Ice Hockey Player, Coach
151 Parkview Way SE, Calgary AB T2J 4N3, Canada
**MacNeil, Robert B W** — Commentator
2700 S Quincy St, Arlington VA 22206, USA
**MacNeille, Tress** — Actress
Sutton-Barth Vennari, 5900 Wilshire Blvd, #700, Los Angeles CA 90036 USA
**MacNicol, Peter** — Actor
Principato-Young, 9465 Wilshire Blvd, #880, Beverly Hills CA 90212 USA
**Macomber, Debbie** — Writer
PO Box 1458, Port Orchard WA 98366, USA
**Macomber, Dick** — Thoroughbred Racing Jockey
6720 NW 28th Terrace, Fort Lauderdale FL 33309, USA
**Macomber, George B N** — Skier
1 Design Center Place, #600, Boston MA 02210, USA
**Macoun, Jamie** — Ice Hockey Player
J M A C Drilling, 1313 10th St, Misku AB T3E 2X3, Canada
**MacPherson, Duncan I** — Editorial Cartoonist
Toronto Star, Editorial Dept, 1 Yonge St, Toronto ON M5E 1E6, Canada
**Macpherson, Elle** — Model
Mavrick Artists Agency, 6100 Wilshire Blvd, #550, Los Angeles CA 90048, USA
**Macpherson, Wendy** — Bowler
PO Box 93433, Henderson NV 89009, USA

**MacQuitty, Jonathan** — Inventor (Immunodeficient Mouse)
Abingworth Mgmt Inc, 3000 Sand Hill Road, #4-135, Menlo Park CA 94025, USA
**MacRae, Sheila** — Actress, Singer
666 W End Ave, #10H, New York NY 10025, USA
**MacTavish, Craig** — Ice Hockey Player, Coach
3 Quail Hollow Court, Voorhees NJ 08043, USA
**Macurdy, John** — Opera Singer
Columbia Artists Mgmt Inc, 1790 Broadway, #702, New York NY 10019 USA
**MacWhorter, Keith** — Baseball Player
75 Martin St, Rehoboth MA 02769, USA
**Macy, Geoffrey W** — Astronomer
University of California, Integrative Planetary Center, Berkeley CA 94720, USA
**Macy, Kyle R** — Basketball Player, Coach
3320 Overbrook Dr, Lexington KY 40502, USA
**Macy, William H (Bill)** — Actor
W M E Entertainment, 9601 Wilshire Blvd, #300, Beverly Hills CA 90210 USA
**Madden, Beezie** — Equestrian
3908 Stone Bridge Road, Cazenovia NY 13035, USA
**Madden, Benji L** — Singer, Guitarist (Good Charlotte)
A Fein Martini, 37 W 20th St, #1008, New York NY 10011, USA
**Madden, Dave** — Actor, Comedian
1564 Summerdown Way, Saint Johns FL 32259, USA
**Madden, Joel R** — Singer (Good Charlotte)
Girlie Action, 59 W 19th St, #4B, New York NY 10011, USA
**Madden, John** — Ice Hockey Player
6 Briarcliff Road, Montville NJ 07045, USA
**Madden, John E** — Football Player, Coach, Sportscaster
5095 Coronado Blvd, Pleasanton CA 94588, USA
**Madden, John P** — Director
Casorotto Ramsay, Waverley House, 7-12 Noel St, London W1F 8GQ, England
**Madden, Michael A (Mike)** — Baseball Player
4733 Frankfort Way, Denver CO 80239, USA
**Madden, Mickey** — Bassist (Maroon 5)
J Records, 745 5th Ave, #600, New York NY 10151 USA
**Madden, Morris D** — Baseball Player
105 Jennings St, Laurens SC 29360, USA
**Madden, Richard** — Actor
Troika, 74 Clerkenwell Road, #300, London EC1M 5QA, England
**Maddin, Guy** — Director
Loeb & Loeb, 10100 Santa Monica Blvd, #2200, Los Angeles CA 90067, USA
**Maddon, Joseph J (Joe)** — Baseball Manager
2560 N Lindsay Road, #32, Mesa AZ 85213, USA
**Maddow, Rachel A** — Commentator
Napoli Mgmt, 8844 W Olympic Blvd, #100, Beverly Hills CA 90211, USA
**Maddox, David M** — Army General
2301 Fort Scott Dr, Arlington VA 22202, USA
**Maddox, Elliott** — Baseball Player
980 Coral Ridge Dr, #104, Coral Springs FL 33071, USA
**Maddox, Eva** — Interior Designer
Eva Maddox Assoc, 333 N Wabash Ave, #3600, Chicago IL 60611, USA
**Maddox, Jerry G** — Baseball Player
20647 Thundersky Circle, Riverside CA 92508, USA
**Maddox, Mark A** — Football Player
100 W Washington St, #1900, Phoenix AZ 85003, USA
**Maddox, Rachel** — Commentator
MSNBC, News Dept, 22 Fletcher Ave, Fort Lee NJ 07024, USA
**Maddox, Thomas A (Tommy)** — Football Player
210 Ridge View Lane, Roanoke TX 76262, USA
**Maddux, Gregory A (Greg)** — Baseball Player
36 Innisbrook Ave, Las Vegas NV 89113, USA
**Madekwe, Ashley** — Actress
Maydew & Golenberg, 8383 Wilshire Blvd, #1050, Beverly Hills CA 90211, USA
**Madeley, Anna** — Actress
Independent Talent Group, 40 Whitfield St, London W1T 2RH, England
**Madfai, Kahtan al** — Architect
22 Vassileos Constantinou, 11635 Athens, Greece
**Madi, Hamada (Bolero)** — Prime Minister, Comoros
Prime Minister's Office, BP 421, Moroni, Comoros
**Madigan, Amy** — Actress
Industry Entertainment, 955 Carillo Dr, #300, Los Angeles CA 90048 USA
**Madigan, Kathleen** — Actress, Comedienne, Writer, Producer
Creative Artists Agency, 2000 Ave of Stars, #100, Los Angeles CA 90067 USA
**Madigan, Martha** — Photographer
730 Carpenter Lane, Philadelphia PA 19119, USA
**Madinier, Bruno** — Actor
Agence Artiste Adequat, 108 Rue Reaumur, 75002 Paris, France
**Madison, C Scott (Scotty)** — Baseball Player
5397 Thornapple Lane NW, Acworth GA 30101, USA
**Madison, Holly** — Model, Actress
Entertainment Fusion Group, 8899 Beverly Blvd, #412, West Hollywood CA 90046, USA
**Madison, Samuel A (Sam)** — Football Player
13153 SW 25th Place, Davie FL 33325, USA
**Madkins, Gerald** — Basketball Player
528 W 8th St, Merced CA 95341, USA
**Madlock, Bill, Jr** — Baseball Player
1565 Calle del Estribo, Pacific Palisades CA 90272, USA
**Madobe, Sheikh Adeb Mohamed Nor** — President, Somalia
President's Office, People's Palace, Mogadishu, Somalia
**Madonna** — Singer, Actress
Untitled Entertainment, 350 S Beverly Dr, #200, Beverly Hills CA 90212 USA
**Madrigal, Al** — Actor
Creative Artists Agency, 2000 Ave of Stars, #100, Los Angeles CA 90067 USA
**Madrigali, Jeff** — Yachtsman
6212 Greenblower Lane, Clinton WA 98236, USA
**Madritsch, Bobby** — Baseball Player
8628 Linder Ave, Burbank IL 60459, USA

**Madsen, Loren W** — Sculptor
428 Broome St, New York NY 10013, USA
**Madsen, Mark E** — Basketball Player
10132 Gristmill Ridge, Eden Prairie MN 55347, USA
**Madsen, Michael** — Actor
Madsen International Mgmt, 9000 Sunset Blvd, Los Angeles CA 90069, USA
**Madsen, Ole Christian** — Director
Nimbus Film Productions, Hauchsvej 17, 1825 Frederiksberg, Denmark
**Madsen, Virginia** — Actress
Untitled Entertainment, 350 S Beverly Dr, #200, Beverly Hills CA 90212 USA
**Madson, Ryan M** — Baseball Player
1204 Suncast Lane, #2, El Dorado Hills CA 95762, USA
**Mae, Audra** — Singer, Songwriter
The Mgmt Co, 4220 Lankershim Blvd, North Hollywood CA 91602, USA
**Maedizossian, Prelate Moushegh** — Religious Leader
Armenian Apostolic Church, 4401 Russell Ave, Los Angeles CA 90027, USA
**Maese, Joseph M (Joe)** — Football Player
4738 W Krystal Way, Glendale AZ 85308, USA
**Maestri, Hector A** — Baseball Player
581 SW 89th Court, Miami FL 33174, USA
**Maestro, Mia** — Actress
I C M Partners, Marlborough House, 10 Earlham St, #300, London WC2H 9LNP, England
**Maffei, Lamberto** — Neurobiologist
National Research Council, Piazzale Aldo Moro 7, 00185 Rome, Italy
**Maffett, Debra Sue (Debbie)** — Beauty Queen
1525 McGavock St, Nashville TN 37203, USA
**Maffia, Roma** — Actress
S M S Talent, 8383 Wilshire Blvd, #230, Beverly Hills CA 90211 USA
**Magadan, David J (Dave)** — Baseball Player
3733 Johnathon Ave, Palm Harbor FL 34685, USA
**Magaw, John W** — Law Enforcement Official
Transportation Security Administration, 400 7th St SW, Washington DC 20590, USA
**Magee, Dave** — Harness Racing Driver
5S350 Deer Ridge Path, Big Rock IL 60511, USA
**Magee, David** — Writer
Creative Artists Agency, 2000 Ave of Stars, #100, Los Angeles CA 90067 USA
**Magee, Herb** — Basketball Coach
PO Box 67, Southeastern PA 19399, USA
**Magee, Kenneth** — Actor
11491 Riverside Dr, Los Angeles CA 91602, USA
**Magee, Wendell E, Jr** — Baseball Player
6500 Muskogee Cove, Leeds AL 35094, USA
**Maggard, Dave** — Track Athlete, Sports Executive
University of Houston, Athletic Dept, Houston TX 77204, USA
**Maggenti, Maria** — Director
Paradigm Agency, 360 N Crescent Dr, North Building, Beverly Hills CA 90210 USA
**Maggert, Jeff** — Golfer
62 W Bracebridge Circle, Spring TX 77382, USA
**Maggs, Donald J (Don)** — Football Player
26525 Amhearst Circle, #106, Beachwood OH 44122, USA
**Magic Dick (Salwitz)** — Harmonica Player (J Geils Band)
Nick Ben-Meir, 652 N Doheny Dr, West Hollywood CA 90069, USA
**Magilton, Gerard E (Jerry)** — Astronaut
Martin Marietta Astro Space, 100 Campus Dr, Newtown PA 18940, USA
**Magimel, Benoit** — Actor
Intertalent, 48 Rue Gay-Lussac, 75005 Paris, France
**Maginn, Matt** — Bassist (Cursive)
Ground Control Touring, 20 Jay St, #826, Brooklyn NY 11201 USA
**Maginnes, John** — Golfer
612 Topwater Lane, Greensboro NC 27455, USA
**Magloire, Jamaal D** — Basketball Player
Toronto Raptors, Air Canada Center, 20 Bay St, Toronto ON M5J 2N8, Canada
**Magnani, Olivia** — Actress
Agents Associes, 201 Rue du Faubourg Saint Honore, 75008 Paris, France
**Magnante, Michael A (Mike)** — Baseball Player
5305 Via Quinto, Newbury Park CA 91320, USA
**Magnanti, Brooke** — Writer, Epidemiologist
Orion Publishing, 5 Upper Saint Martin's Lane, London WC2H 9EA, England
**Magni, James** — Architect, Interior Designer
Magni Design, Pacific Design Center, 8687 Melrose Ave, West Hollywood CA 90069, USA
**Magnus, Edie** — Commentator
NBC-TV, News Dept, 30 Rockefeller Plaza, #270E, New York NY 10112 USA
**Magnus, Sandra H (Sandy)** — Astronaut
3477 Vinings North Trail SE, Smyrna GA 30080, USA
**Magnuson, Ann** — Actress
1317 Maltman Ave, Los Angeles CA 90026, USA
**Magnussen-Ceila, Karen D** — Figure Skater
2852 Thorndiff Dr, North Vancouver BC V7R 285, Canada
**Magowan, Kate** — Actress
United Agents, 12-26 Lexington St, London W1F 0LE, England
**Magrane, Joseph D (Joe)** — Baseball Player
705 Guisando de Avila, Tampa FL 33613, USA
**Magri, Charles G (Charlie)** — Boxer
345 Bethnal Green Road, Bethnal Green, London E2 6LG, England
**Magris, Claudio** — Writer, Journalist
Via Carpaccio 2, 34127 Trieste, Italy
**Magruder, Christopher J (Chris)** — Baseball Player
1740 Leisure Lane, Yakima WA 98908, USA
**Magsamen, Sandra** — Writer, Artist
Orchard Books/Scholastic, 557 Broadway, New York NY 10012, USA
**Maguire, Adrian E** — Thoroughbred Racing Jockey
17 Willes Close, Faringdon, Oxfordshire SN7 7DU, England
**Maguire, Albert M** — Surgeon
Children's Hospital, 34th St & Civic Center Blvd, Philadelphia PA 19104, USA
**Maguire, Joseph** — Navy Admiral
National Counterterrorism Center, 1505 Tysons McLean Blvd, McLean VA 22102, USA

**Maguire, Les** — Pianist (Gerry & the Pacemakers)
Barry Collins, 21A Cliftown Road, Southend-on-Sea, Essex SS1 1AB, England
**Maguire, Michael** — Actor, Singer
Epstein-Wyckoff, 280 S Beverly Dr, #400, Beverly Hills CA 90212 USA
**Maguire, Paul L** — Sportscaster, Football Player
707 Ocean Blvd, Isle of Palms SC 29451, USA
**Maguire, Richard W** — Cinematographer
605 Summer Mesa Dr, Las Vegas NV 89144, USA
**Maguire, Sean** — Actor
Paul Kohner, 9300 Wilshire Blvd, #555, Beverly Hills CA 90212 USA
**Maguire, Sharon** — Director, Producer, Writer
United Talent Agency, U T A Plaza, 9336 Civic Center Dr, Beverly Hills CA 90210 USA
**Maguire, Tobey** — Actor
W M E Entertainment, 9601 Wilshire Blvd, #300, Beverly Hills CA 90210 USA
**Mahaffey, John D, Jr** — Golfer
594 Sawdust Road, #229, Spring TX 77380, USA
**Mahaffey, Randolph (Randy)** — Basketball Player
25 Berkeley Road, Avondale Estates GA 30002, USA
**Mahaffey, Valerie** — Actress
Innovative Artists, 1505 10th St, Santa Monica CA 90401 USA
**Mahaffrey, Arthur (Art)** — Baseball Player
PO Box 1212, Allentown PA 18105, USA
**Mahal, Taj** — Singer, Musician, Songwriter
Red Light Mgmt, 44 Wall St, #2200, New York NY 10005, USA
**Mahalanabis, Dilip** — Physician
Applied Studies Society, 108 Manicktata Main Road, Kolkata 700054, India
**Mahalic, Drew A** — Football Player
2114 W Sunset Dr, Portland OR 97239, USA
**Mahama, John D** — President, Ghana
President's Office, Golden Jubilee House, PO Box 1627, Accra, Ghana
**Mahan, Hunter** — Golfer
3316 Snowmass Lane, McKinney TX 75070, USA
**Mahan, Lawrence (Larry)** — Rodeo Rider
PO Box 119, Sunset TX 76270, USA
**Mahan, Sean C** — Football Player
4202 E 116th Place, Tulsa OK 74137, USA
**Mahanthappa, Rudresh** — Jazz Saxophonist, Composer
48 S Park St, #210, Montclair NJ 07042, USA
**Mahar, Kevin** — Baseball Player
2506 E Wheeler St, Midland MI 48642, USA
**Maharidge, Dale D** — Writer
Stanford University, Communications Dept, Stanford CA 94305, USA
**Mahay, Ronald M (Ron)** — Baseball Player
13177 E Cochise Road, Scottsdale AZ 85259, USA
**Mahendru, Annet** — Actress
I C M Partners, 10250 Constellation Blvd, #900, Los Angeles CA 90067 USA
**Maher, Bill** — Commentator, Comedian
Creative Artists Agency, 2000 Ave of Stars, #100, Los Angeles CA 90067 USA
**Maher, Chris** — Photographer
PO Box 5, Lambertville MI 48144, USA
**Maher, Sean** — Actor
S D B Partners, 1801 Ave of Stars, #902, Los Angeles CA 90067 USA
**Mahinmi, Ian** — Basketball Player
Indiana Pacers, Conseco Fieldhouse, 125 S Pennsylvania, Indianapolis IN 46204 USA
**Mahler, Michael J (Mickey)** — Baseball Player
7911 Quirt St, San Antonio TX 78227, USA
**Mahohato Mohato Seeiso** — Queen, Lesotho
Royal Palace, PO Box 524, Maseru 100, Lesotho
**Mahomes, Patrick L (Pat)** — Baseball Player
1834 Ridgeline Road, Tyler TX 75703, USA
**Mahon, Sean** — Actor
Principal Entertainment, 9255 Sunset Blvd, #500, Los Angeles CA 90069 USA
**Mahone, Ed** — Boxer
Marvin Millett, 6548 Whitney Ave, Saint Louis MO 63133, USA
**Mahoney, Brian C** — Basketball Player
96 Greystone Road, Rockville Center NY 11570, USA
**Mahoney, James T (Jim)** — Baseball Player
345 Hawthorne Ave, #2, Hawthorne NJ 07506, USA
**Mahoney, John** — Actor
I C M Partners, 10250 Constellation Blvd, #900, Los Angeles CA 90067 USA
**Mahoney, Margaret E** — Foundation Executive
M E H Assoc, 421 5th Ave, #2010, New York NY 10016, USA
**Mahoney, Maureen** — Attorney
Latham & Watkins, 555 7th St NW, Washington DC 20004, USA
**Mahoney, Mike** — Baseball Player
4412 98th St, Urbandale IA 50322, USA
**Mahoney, Roger** — Cartoonist (Millie)
2 Sussex Cottages, Emsworth Common Road, Emsworth, Hampshire, England
**Mahoney, Tim** — Guitarist (311), Songwriter
College Agency, 7907 Stafford Trail, Savage MN 55376, USA
**Mahony, Roger Cardinal** — Religious Leader
Archdiocese of Los Angeles, 3424 Wilshire Blvd, Los Angeles CA 90010, USA
**Mahorn, Derrick A (Rick)** — Basketball Player, Coach
44 Gordon Lane, East Hartford CT 06118, USA
**Mahovlich, Francis W (Frank)** — Ice Hockey Player
2-954 Ave Road, Toronto ON M5P 2K8, Canada
**Mahovlich, Peter J (Pete)** — Ice Hockey Player
116 Farr Lane, Queensbury NY 12804, USA
**Mahr, Joe** — Journalist
Toledo Blade, Editorial Dept, 541 N Superior St, Toledo OH 43660, USA
**Mahre, Phillip (Phil)** — Alpine Skier
Mahre Training Center, Deer Valley Resort, PO Box 739, Park City UT 84060, USA
**Mahre, Steve** — Alpine Skier
Mahre Training Center, Deer Valley Resort, PO Box 739, Park City UT 84060, USA
**Mahumdi, Baghadadi al-** — General Secretary, Libya
General Secretary's Office, Bab el Asiziya Barracks, Tripoli, Libya

**Maida, Adam J Cardinal** — Religious Leader
Archdiocese of Detroit, 1234 Washington Blvd, #1, Detroit MI 48226, USA
**Maiden-Naccarato, Jeanne** — Bowler
1 N Stadium Way, #4, Tacoma WA 98403, USA
**Maier, Hermann** — Alpine Skier
Im 8 ErJet, Unterbergasse, 5542 Flachau, Austria
**Maier, Mitchell W (Mitch)** — Baseball Player
435 Amelia Circle, South Lyon MI 48178, USA
**Maier, Sepp** — Soccer Player
Lindenstra 12, 85664 Hohenlinden, Germany
**Maiga, Hamchetou** — Basketball Player
Sacramento Monarchs, Arco Arena, 1 Sports Parkway, Sacramento CA 95834 USA
**Maiga, Ousmane Issoufi** — Prime Minister, Mali
Prime Minister's Office, BP 97, Bamako, Mali
**Maikki, Susanna** — Conductor
Ensemble Intercontemporain, 223 Ave Jean-Jaurès 75019 Paris, France
**Mailhouse, Robert** — Actor
Stone Manners Salners, 9911 W Pico Blvd, #1400, Los Angeles CA 90035 USA
**Maillard, Carol** — Singer (Sweet Honey in the Rock)
I C M Partners, 10250 Constellation Blvd, #900, Los Angeles CA 90067 USA
**Main, Frank** — Journalist
Chicago Sun-Times, Editorial Dept, 401 N Wabash Ave, Chicago IL 60611 USA
**Main, Ravinder** — Rheumatologist
Charing Cross Hospital, Saint Dunstan's Road, London W6 8RP, England
**Maine, John K** — Baseball Player
129 Richards Ferry Road, Fredericksburg VA 22406, USA
**Maines, Natalie** — Singer (Dixie Chicks)
Strategic Artist Mgmt, 1100 Glendon Ave, #1000, Los Angeles CA 90024, USA
**Maino** — Rap Artist
Hustle Hard Records, 1290 Ave of Americas, Concourse 3, New York NY 10104, USA
**Mair, Adam** — Ice Hockey Player
25 San Fernando Lane, East Amherst NY 14051, USA
**Mairena, Oswaldo** — Baseball Player
160 E 6th Place, Mesa AZ 85201, USA
**Maisel, Harvey** — Educator
University of Nebraska, Chancellor's Office, Lincoln NE 68588, USA
**Maisel, Jay** — Photographer
190 Bowery, New York NY 10012, USA
**Maisenberg, Olega** — Concert Pianist
In Der Gugl 9, 3400 Klosterneuburg, Austria
**Maisky, Mischa M** — Concert Cellist
138 Meerlaan, 1900 Overijse, Belgium
**Maisuradze, Badri** — Opera Singer
I M G Artists, Hogarth Business Park, Chiswick, London W4 2TH, England
**Maitland, Beth** — Actress
Epstein-Wyckoff, 280 S Beverly Dr, #400, Beverly Hills CA 90212 USA
**Maiwenn** — Actress, Director, Writer
Agence Artiste Adequet, 108 Rue Reaumur, 75002 Paris, France
**Majdarzavyn Ganzorig** — Cosmonaut, Mongolia
Academy of Sciences, Peace Ave 54B, Ulan Bator 51, Mongolia
**Majerle, Daniel L (Dan)** — Basketball Player
4534 E Oregon Ave, Phoenix AZ 85018, USA
**Majewski, Gary W** — Baseball Player
1103 Chamboard Lane, Houston TX 77018, USA
**Majewski, Janusz** — Director, Writer
Ul Forteczna 1A, 01540 Warsaw, Poland
**Majkowski, Donald V (Don)** — Football Player
1593 Bayhill Dr, Duluth GA 30097, USA
**Majoli, Iva** — Tennis Player
International Mangement Group, 1 Erieview Plaza, 1360 E 9th St, Cleveland OH 44114 USA
**Major, Clarence L** — Writer
University of California, English Dept, Voorhies Hall, Davis CA 95616, USA
**Major, Jason** — Actor, Writer
Principato-Young, 9465 Wilshire Blvd, #880, Beverly Hills CA 90212 USA
**Major, John** — Prime Minister, England
8 Stukeley Road, Huntingdon,  Cambridgeshire PE29 6HQ, England
**Major, Malvina L** — Opera Singer
PO Box 11-175, Manners St, Te Aero, Wellington 6011, New Zealand
**Major, Reema** — Singer
Agency Group Ltd, 142 W 57th St, #600, New York NY 10019 USA
**Majorino, Tina** — Actress
Leverage Mgmt, 3030 Pennsylvania Ave, Santa Monica CA 90404 USA
**Majors, John T (Johnny)** — Football Player, Coach
4207 Beechwood Road, Knoxville TN 37920, USA
**Majors, Lee** — Actor
1831 Rocking Horse Dr, Simi Valley CA 93065, USA
**Makarov, Askold A** — Ballet Dancer
Plutalova Str 18-4, 197136 Saint Petersburg, Russia
**Makarov, Sergei M** — Ice Hockey Player
4072 Teale Ave, San Jose CA 95117, USA
**Makarova, Natalia R** — Ballerina
Herbert Breslin, 119 W 57th St, #1505, New York NY 10019 USA
**Makela, P Helena** — Immunologist
National Public Health Service, Mannerheimintie 166, Helsinki, Finland
**Makela, Wille** — Curling Athlete
Curling Assn, Kalatorppa 2A62, 02230 Espoo, Finland
**Makela-Nummela, Satu** — Markswoman
Radiokatu 20, 00240 Helsinki, Finland
**Makerov, Julie** — Opera Singer
Columbia Artists Mgmt Inc, 1790 Broadway, #702, New York NY 10019 USA
**Makhalina, Yulia V** — Ballerina
Kirov Ballet Theater, 1 Pl Iskusstr, 190000 Saint Petersburg, Russia
**Maki, Chico** — Ice Hockey Player
Norfolk County Sports Hall of Fame, 95 Culver, Simcoe ON N3Y 2V5, Canada
**Maki, Fumihiko** — Pritzker Architectural Laureate
5-16-22 Higashi-Gotanda, Shinagawaku, Tokyo 141 0022, Japan

**Makings, Elizabeth** — Golfer
1500 N Markdale, #12, Mesa AZ 85201, USA

**Makkena, Wendy** — Actress
Schumachr Mgmt, 10323 Santa Monica Blvd, #101, Los Angeles CA 90025, USA

**Makoare, Lawrence** — Actor
Robert Bruce Agency, 218 Richmond Road, Grey Lynn, Auckland, New Zealand

**Maksimova, Yekaterina S** — Ballerina
Smolenskaya Naberezhnaya 5/13-62, 121099 Moscow, Russia

**Maksudian, Michael B (Mike)** — Baseball Player
12148 E San Simeon Dr, Scottsdale AZ 85259, USA

**Maksymiuk, Jerzy** — Conductor
Gdanska 2 m 14, 01633 Warsaw, Poland

**Maktoum, Mohammed bin Rashid Al** — Prime Minister, United Arab Emirates
Prime Minister's Office, Manhal Palace, Abu Dhabi, United Arab Emirates

**Malachi, Carolyn** — Singer
Clarke & Assoc, 2020 Pennsylvania Ave NW, #271, Washington DC 20006, USA

**Malahide, Patrick** — Actor
I C M Partners, Marlborough House, 10 Earlham St, #300, London WC2H 9LNP, England

**Malakhov, Vladimir I** — Ice Hockey Player
PO Box 420536, Kissimmee FL 34742, USA

**Malakian, Daron V** — Singer, Guitarist (System of a Down)
Velvet Hammer Music, 9014 Melrose Ave, West Hollywood CA 90069, USA

**Malamala, Siupeli** — Football Player
122 110th Ave SE, Bellevue WA 98004, USA

**Malandrino, Catherine** — Fashion Designer
468 Bromme St, New York NY 10013, USA

**Malarchuk, Clint** — Ice Hockey Player
1308 Myers Dr, Gardnerville NV 89410, USA

**Malaret Contreras, Marisol** — Beauty Queen, Actress
Miss Universe Organization, 1370 Ave of Americas, #1600, New York NY 10019 USA

**Malarkey, Donald G** — WW II Army Hero
2233 Juneau Court S, Salem OR 97302, USA

**Malaska, Mark** — Baseball Player
3823 Cumberland Dr, Youngstown OH 44515, USA

**Malchow, Tom** — Swimmer
10220 NW Edgewood Dr, Portland OR 97229, USA

**Malco, Romany** — Actor
Principato-Young, 9465 Wilshire Blvd, #880, Beverly Hills CA 90212 USA

**Malcom, Shirley M** — Association Executive
Science Advancement Assn, 1200 New York Ave NW, Washington DC 20005, USA

**Malcomson, Paula** — Actress
United Talent Agency, U T A Plaza, 9336 Civic Center Dr, Beverly Hills CA 90210 USA

**Maldacena, Juan** — Physicist
Harvard University, Physics Dept, Cambridge MA 02138, USA

**Maldini, Paolo** — Soccer Player
F C Milan, Via Filippo Turati 3, 20121 Milan, Italy

**Maldonado, Candido (Candy)** — Baseball Player
HC 2 Box 16800, Arecibo PR 00612, USA

**Malee, Chompoo** — Fashion Designer
Hino & Malee Inc, 3701 N Ravenswood Ave, Chicago IL 60613, USA

**Maleeva, Katerina** — Tennis Player
Mladostr 1, #45, NH 14, Sofia 1174, Bulgaria

**Maleeva-Fragniere, Manuela** — Tennis Player
Bourg-Dessous 28, 1814 La Tour de Peitz, Switzerland

**Malek, Rami** — Actor
W M E Entertainment, 9601 Wilshire Blvd, #300, Beverly Hills CA 90210 USA

**Malenchenko, Yuri I** — Cosmonaut
Cosmonaut Training Center, Star City, 141160 Zvezdny Gorodok, Moscow Oblast, Russia

**Maler, James M (Jim)** — Baseball Player
1758 NE 177th St, North Miami Beach FL 33162, USA

**Malerba, Franco E** — Astronaut
Italian Space Agency, Viale Liegi 26, 00198 Rome, Italy

**Malfitano, Catherine** — Opera Singer
I M G Artists, Burlington Lane, Chiswick, London W4 2TH, England

**Malgarini, Ryan** — Actor
Savage Agency, 6212 Banner Ave, Los Angeles CA 90038 USA

**Malhotra, Manny** — Ice Hockey Player
1210 Oakland Ave, Columbus OH 43212, USA

**Malice** — Rap Artist (Clipse)
American Talent Agency, 26 Finney Farm Road, Croton on Hudson NY 10520, USA

**Malick, Terrence F** — Director, Writer
Creative Artists Agency, 2000 Ave of Stars, #100, Los Angeles CA 90067 USA

**Malick, Wendie** — Actress, Model
Innovative Artists, 1505 10th St, Santa Monica CA 90401 USA

**Malicki-Sanchez, Keram** — Actor
Talent Works, 3500 W Olive Ave, #1400, Burbank CA 91505 USA

**Malielegaoi, Tuila'epa L Sa'ilele** — Prime Minister, Samoa
Prime Minister's Office, PO Box L1861, Vailima, Apia, Samoa

**Malignaggi, Paulie** — Boxer
1620 80th St, Brooklyn NY 11214, USA

**Malik, Art** — Actor
18 Sydney Mews, London SW3 6HL, England

**Malik, Marek** — Ice Hockey Player
919 Anchorage Road, Tampa FL 33602, USA

**Maliki, Nouri al-** — Prime Minister, Iraq
Prime Minister's Office, Karradat Mariam, Baghdad, Iraq

**Malina, Joshua** — Actor
I F A Talent Agency, 8730 W Sunset Blvd, #490, West Hollywood CA 90069 USA

**Malinchak, William J (Bill)** — Football Player
6422 NW 65th Way, Parkland FL 33067, USA

**Malini, Hema** — Actress
17 Jai Hind Society, 12th Road Juhu Scheme, Mumbai MS 400049, India

**Malinvaud, Edmond** — Economist
42 Ave de Saxe, 75007 Paris, France

**Maliponte, Adrianna** — Opera Singer
Gorlinsky Promotions, 35 Darer, London W1, England

**M**

Makings - Maliponte

# M

**Malizia, Mike** — Golfer
570 SE Southwood Trail, Stuart FL 34997, USA
**Malkin, Evgeni** — Ice Hockey Player
Pittsburgh Penguins, Consol Energy Center, 1001 5th Ave, Pittsburgh PA 15219 USA
**Malkin, Max** — Cinematographer
Skouras Agency, 1149 3rd St, #300, Santa Monica CA 90403, USA
**Malkmus, Robert E (Bobby)** — Baseball Player
400 Wallingford Terrace, Union NJ 07083, USA
**Malkovich, John** — Actor
Mr Mudd, 137 N Larchmont, Box 113, Los Angeles CA 90004, USA
**Mallary, Robert** — Sculptor
PO Box 97, Conway MA 01341, USA
**Mallette, Alfred J** — Army General
7040 Quail Hill Road, Charlotte NC 28210, USA
**Malley, Kenneth C** — Navy Admiral
136 Riverside Road, Edgewater MD 21037, USA
**Malley, M Matthew (Matt)** — Bassist (Counting Crowes), Songwriter
Direct Mgmt, 947 N La Cienega Blvd, #G, West Hollywood CA 90069, USA
**Mallick, Don** — Test Pilot
42045 N Tilton Dr, Lancaster CA 93536, USA
**Mallicoat, Robbin D (Rob)** — Baseball Player
2050 SE Larson Court, Hillsboro OR 97123, USA
**Mallon, Meg** — Golfer
5105 N Ocean Blvd, #C, Boynton Beach FL 33435, USA
**Mallon, Thomas** — Writer
801 25th St NW, Washington DC 20037, USA
**Mallory, Brenda** — Artist
Julie Nelson Gallery, 1280 Iron Horse Dr, Park City UT 84060, USA
**Mallory, Carole** — Actress
Pocket Books, 1230 Ave of Americas, New York NY 10020 USA
**Mallory, Glynn C, Jr** — Army General
19221 Heather Forest, San Antonio TX 78258, USA
**Malloy, Edward A** — Educator
University of Notre Dame, President's Office, Notre Dame IN 46556, USA
**Malloy, Tom** — Actor, Writer
Stone Manners Salners, 9911 W Pico Blvd, #1400, Los Angeles CA 90035 USA
**Malo, Raul** — Singer (Mavericks), Songwriter
Conqueroo, 11271 Ventura Blvd, #522, Studio City CA 91604 USA
**Malone, Ben (Benny)** — Football Player
49 E Broadway Road, Tempe AZ 85282, USA
**Malone, Charles R (Chuck)** — Baseball Player
310 Liberty St, Marked Tree AR 72365, USA
**Malone, James W** — Religious Leader
Catholic Bishops Conference, 1312 Massachusetts Ave NW, Washington DC 20005, USA
**Malone, Jeffrey N (Jeff)** — Basketball Player
415 Lee Road 313, Smiths Station AL 36877, USA
**Malone, Jena** — Actress
Gersh Agency, 9465 Wilshire Blvd, #600, Beverly Hills CA 90212 USA
**Malone, John C** — Businessman
Liberty Media Corp, 12300 Liberty Blvd, Englewood CO 80112, USA
**Malone, Karl** — Basketball Player
105 W Charter St, Farmerville LA 71241, USA
**Malone, Kype** — Singer (TV on the Radio)
D G C/Interscope Records, 2220 Colorado Ave, Santa Monica CA 90404, USA
**Malone, Maicel** — Track Athlete
4064 Bothwell Terrace, Tallahassee FL 32317, USA
**Malone, Mark M** — Football Player
15095 N Thompson Peak Parkway, #1052, Scottsdale AZ 85260, USA
**Malone, Moses E** — Basketball Player
310 S Keswick Court, Sugar Land TX 77478, USA
**Malone, Nancy** — Actress
8857 W Olympic Blvd, #201, Beverly Hills CA 90211, USA
**Malone, Patricia** — Businesswoman
Bruno Magli USA, 75 Triangle Blvd, Carlstadt NJ 07072, USA
**Malone, Ryan** — Ice Hockey Player
4908 Yacht Club Dr, Tampa FL 33616, USA
**Malone, Wallace D, Jr** — Financier
SouthTrust Corp, 420 20th St N, Birmingham AL 35203, USA
**Malone, William** — Director
A P A Talent/Literary Agency, 405 S Beverly Dr, #300, Beverly Hills CA 90212 USA
**Maloney, Dan** — Ice Hockey Player, Coach, Executive
Sutton Group Realty, 241 Minet's Point Road, Barrie ON L4N 4C4, Canada
**Maloney, David W (Dave)** — Ice Hockey Player
122 Dolphin Cove Quay, Stamford CT 06902, USA
**Maloney, Donald M (Don)** — Ice Hockey Player, Executive
21 Guilford Lane, Greenwich CT 06831, USA
**Maloney, James W (Jim)** — Baseball Player
7027 N Teilman Ave, #102, Fresno CA 93711, USA
**Maloney, Michael** — Actor
Markham Froggatt Irwin, Julian House, 4 Windmill St, London W1P 1HF, England
**Maloney, William R** — Marine Corps General
Navy Mutual Aid Assn, Henderson Hall, 29 Carpenter Road, Arlington VA 22214, USA
**Malouf, David G J** — Writer
Mobbs, 35A Sutherland Crescent, Darling Point, Sydney NSW 2027, Australia
**Malsby, Lynn** — Keyboardist (Klymaxx)
R D M J Entertainment Mgmt, 3619 Rose Ave, Long Beach CA 90807 USA
**Maltbie, Roger** — Golfer, Sportscaster
179 Longmeadow Dr, Los Gatos CA 95032, USA
**Maltby, Kirk** — Ice Hockey Player
58 Putnam Place, Grosse Pointe Shores MI 48236, USA
**Maltby, Richard E, Jr** — Lyricist, Director
200 E 89th St, #16B, New York NY 10128, USA
**Malter, Arnold S** — Attorney
301 N Lake Ave, #810, Pasadena CA 91101, USA
**Malthouse, Matthew** — Actor
Gavin Barker Assoc, 2D Wimpole St, London W1G 0EB, England

**Malizia - Malthouse**

**Maltin, Leonard** — Film, TV Critic, Producer
10424 Whipple St, Toluca Lake CA 91602, USA

**Maltzan, Michael** — Architect
2801 Hyperion Ave, Los Angeles CA 90027, USA

**Malyshev, Yuri V** — Cosmonaut
Cosmonaut Training Center, Star City, 141160 Zvezdny Gorodok, Moscow Oblast, Russia

**Malysz, Adam H** — Ski Jumper
K S Wisla Ustronianka, Ul Wyzwolenia 67, 43460 Wisla, Poland

**Malzone, Frank J** — Baseball Player
16 Aletha Road, Needham MA 02492, USA

**Mamby, Saoul** — Boxer
20 W Mosholu Parkway S, #17, Bronx NY 10468, USA

**Mamet, David A** — Writer, Director
2 Northfield Plaza, #200, Northfield IL 60093, USA

**Mamet, Zosia** — Actress
United Talent Agency, U T A Plaza, 9336 Civic Center Dr, Beverly Hills CA 90210 USA

**Mamula, Michael B (Mike)** — Football Player
4 Ithan Woods Lane, Villanova PA 19085, USA

**Manabe, Syukuro** — Meteorologist
Princeton University, Atmospheric Sciences Dept, Princeton NJ 08540, USA

**Manahan, George** — Conductor
Columbia Artists Mgmt Inc, 1790 Broadway, #702, New York NY 10019 USA

**Manakov, Gennadi M** — Cosmonaut
Cosmonaut Training Center, Star City, 141160 Zvezdny Gorodok, Moscow Oblast, Russia

**Manarov, Musa C** — Cosmonaut
Khovanskeya 3, 129515 Moscow, Russia

**Mancham, James R M** — President, Seychelles
PO Box 29, Mahe, Seychelles

**Manchester, Melissa** — Singer, Songwriter
A V O Talent Agency, 5670 Wilshire Blvd, #1930, Los Angeles CA 90036, USA

**Manchevski, Milcho** — Director
A P A Talent/Literary Agency, 405 S Beverly Dr, #300, Beverly Hills CA 90212 USA

**Mancina, Mark** — Composer
Gorfaine/Schwartz, 4111 W Alameda Ave, #509, Burbank CA 91505 USA

**Mancini, Ray (Boom Boom)** — Boxer, Actor
12524 Indianapolis St, Los Angeles CA 90066, USA

**Mancuso, Frank G** — Businessman
201 N Canon Dr, #328, Beverly Hills CA 90210, USA

**Mancuso, Julia** — Alpine Skier
US Ski Team, 1500 Kearns Blvd, #100, Park City UT 84060 USA

**Mancuso, Nick** — Actor
Law Talent Agency, 5 Ambleside Ave, Toronto ON M8Z 2H5, Canada

**Mandabach, Caryn** — Producer
Oxygen Media, 75 9th Ave, New York NY 10011, USA

**Mandarich, Ante J (Tony)** — Football Player
12767 E Altadena Dr, Scottsdale AZ 85259, USA

**Mandel, Howie** — Actor
Alevy Productions, 23679 Calabasas Road, #180, Calabasas CA 91302, USA

**Mandel, Johnny** — Composer
2401 Main St, Santa Monica CA 90405, USA

**Mandel, Robert C** — Director
I C M Partners, 10250 Constellation Blvd, #900, Los Angeles CA 90067 USA

**Mandela, N Winnie Madikizela-** — Social Activist
Orlando West, Soweto, Johannesburg 1804, South Africa

**Mandela, Nelson R** — President, South Africa; Nobel Laureate
Private Bag X70000, Houghton 2041, South Africa

**Mandella, Richard E** — Thoroughbred Racing Trainer
285 W Huntington Dr, Arcadia CA 91007, USA

**Mandelstam, Stanley** — Physicist
1800 Spruce St, Berkeley CA 94709, USA

**Manderino, Joey** — Actor, Comedian, Writer
Creative Artists Agency, 2000 Ave of Stars, #100, Los Angeles CA 90067 USA

**Manders, David F (Dave)** — Football Player
1504 Silverlake Road, McKinney TX 75070, USA

**Mandler, George** — Psychologist
1406 La Jolla Knoll, La Jolla CA 92037, USA

**Mandler, Jean M** — Psychologist
1406 La Jolla Knoll, La Jolla CA 92037, USA

**Mandley, William H (Pete)** — Football Player
103 E Smoke Tree Road, Gilbert AZ 85296, USA

**Mandlikova, Hana** — Tennis Player
Octagon Worldwide, 1751 Pinnacle Dr, #1500, McLean VA 22102 USA

**Mandoki, Luis** — Director
Paradigm Agency, 360 N Crescent Dr, North Building, Beverly Hills CA 90210 USA

**Mandrell, Barbara** — Singer, Actress
2020 Fieldstone Parkway, Franklin TN 37069, USA

**Mandrell, Erline** — Singer
544 W Main St, Gallatin TN 37066, USA

**Mandrell, Louise** — Singer
Mandrell Inc, 1101 Hunters Lane, Ashland City TN 37015, USA

**Mandvi, Aasif** — Actor, Writer
I C M Partners, 10250 Constellation Blvd, #900, Los Angeles CA 90067 USA

**Mandylor, Costas** — Actor
Kritzer Levine Wilkins Griffin, 11872 La Grange Ave, #100, Los Angeles CA 90025 USA

**Mane, Gucci** — Rap Artist
Susan Blond Inc, 50 W 57th St, #1400, New York NY 10019 USA

**Manea, Marius** — Opera Singer
I M G Artists, Hogarth Business Park, Chiswick, London W4 2TH, England

**Manea, Norman** — Writer
201 W 70th St, #101, New York NY 10023, USA

**Manery, Randy N** — Ice Hockey Player
14418 John Beck Dr, Charlotte NC 28273, USA

**Manetti, Larry** — Actor
Epstein-Wyckoff, 280 S Beverly Dr, #400, Beverly Hills CA 90212 USA

**Manfredi, Michael** — Architect, Sculpter
Weiss/Manfredi, 130 W 29th St, #1200, New York NY 10001, USA

**Manfredini, Harry** — Composer
Soundtrack Music, 2229 Cloverfield Blvd, Santa Monica CA 90405, USA

**Manganiello, Joe** — Actor
Creative Artists Agency, 2000 Ave of Stars, #100, Los Angeles CA 90067 USA

**Mangels, Andy** — Writer
PO Box 3226, Portland OR 97208, USA

**Mangelsdorf, David** — Geneticist
Salk Institute, 10100 N Torrey Pines Road, La Jolla CA 92037 USA

**Mangieri, Dino M** — Football Player
108 Lamport Blvd, #3C, Staten Island NY 10305, USA

**Mangione, Chuck** — Jazz Trumpeter, Composer
Gates Music, 99 Park Ave, New York NY 10019, USA

**Mangold, James** — Director, Producer, Writer
Tree Line Films, 1708 Berkeley St, Santa Monica CA 90404, USA

**Mangold, Nick** — Football Player
361 Shunpike Road, Chatham NJ 07928, USA

**Mangold, Sylvia P** — Artist
1 Bull Road, Washingtonville NY 10992, USA

**Mangrum, James L (Jim Dandy)** — Singer (Black Oak Arkansas)
Lustig Talent, PO Box 770850, Orlando FL 32877 USA

**Mangual, Jose M (Pepe)** — Baseball Player
2325 Calle Tabonuco, Ponce PR 00716, USA

**Mangue Gonzalez, Marta** — Handball Player
Z R K Zajecar, Dositejeva 11, 19000 Zajecar, Serbia

**Mangum, John W, Jr** — Football Player
150 Summerwood Dr, Pearl MS 39208, USA

**Manh, Nong Duc** — General Secretary, Vietnam
General's Secretary Office, Hoang Hoa Tham St, Hanoi, Vietnam

**Manheim, Camryn** — Actress
United Talent Agency, U T A Plaza, 9336 Civic Center Dr, Beverly Hills CA 90210 USA

**Maniago, Cesare** — Ice Hockey Player
19-788 Citadel Dr, Port Coquitlam BC V3C 6G9, Canada

**Maniatis, Thomas P** — Genetics Engineer, Molecular Biologist
Harvard University, Biochemistry Dept, 7 Divinity St, Cambridge MA 02138, USA

**Manigault-Stallworth, Omarosa** — Actress
Don Buchwald, 6500 Wilshire Blvd, #2200, Los Angeles CA 90048 USA

**Manilow, Barry** — Singer, Songwriter
Stilleto Entertainment, 8295 S La Cienega Blvd, Inglewood CA 90301, USA

**Manion, Daniel A** — Judge
US Court of Appeals, 204 S Main St, South Bend IN 46601, USA

**Maniscalco, Sebastian** — Actor, Comedian
Levity Entertainment Group, 6701 Center Drive W, #1111, Los Angeles CA 90045, USA

**Manji, Rizwan** — Actor
Don Buchwald, 6500 Wilshire Blvd, #2200, Los Angeles CA 90048 USA

**Mankell, Henning** — Writer
Leopard Forlag AB, Paulsgatan 11, 118 46 Stockholm, Sweden

**Mankins, Logan L** — Football Player
1 Jeffrey Dr, North Attleboro MA 02760, USA

**Mankiw, N Gregory** — Government Official, Economist
45 Chestnut St, Wellesley MA 02481, USA

**Mankoff, Robert** — Cartoonist
New Yorker, Editorial Dept, 4 Times Square, Basement C1B, New York NY 10036 USA

**Mankowski, Philip A (Phil)** — Baseball Player
2280 Southwestern Blvd, Buffalo NY 14224, USA

**Manley, Christopher** — Cinematographer
Sheldon Prosnit Agency, 800 S Robertson Blvd, Los Angeles CA 90035, USA

**Manley, Dexter** — Football Player
2350 Atascocita Road, Humble TX 77396, USA

**Manley, Elizabeth** — Figure Skater
Marco Enterprises, 74830 Velie Dr, #A, Palm Desert CA 92260, USA

**Manlove, William B (Bill), Jr** — Football Coach
Delaware Valley College, Athletic Dept, 700 E Butler Ave, Doylestown PA 18901, USA

**Mann, Aimee** — Singer ('Til Tuesday); Songwriter
Michael Hausman Mgmt, 511 Ave of Americas, #197, New York NY 10011, USA

**Mann, Barry** — Composer
1010 Laurel Way, Beverly Hills CA 90210, USA

**Mann, Byron** — Actor
Metropolitan Talent Agency, 5405 Wilshire Blvd, #218, Los Angeles CA 90036 USA

**Mann, Carol A** — Golfer
6 Cape Chestnut Dr, Spring TX 77381, USA

**Mann, Charles A** — Football Player
40741 Carry Back Lane, Leesburg VA 20176, USA

**Mann, Claude** — Actor
Artmedia, 20 Ave Rapp, 75007 Paris, France

**Mann, Cuonzo** — Basketball Player
111 Wiggins St, #8, West Lafayette IN 47906, USA

**Mann, Danny** — Actor
Danis Panaro Nist, 9201 W Olympic Blvd, Beverly Hills CA 90212 USA

**Mann, David W** — Religious Leader
10550 S 200 W, Columbia City IN 46725, USA

**Mann, Dick** — Motorcycle Racing Rider
American Motorcycle Assn, 13515 Yarmouth Dr, Pickerington OH 43147 USA

**Mann, Errol D** — Football Player
5521 Bonanza Place, Missoula MT 59808, USA

**Mann, Gabriel** — Actor, Model
A P A Talent/Literary Agency, 405 S Beverly Dr, #300, Beverly Hills CA 90212 USA

**Mann, H Thompson** — Swimmer
34 Titcomb St, #2, Newburyport MA 1950, USA

**Mann, James (Jim)** — Baseball Player
197 N Franklin St, Holbrook MA 02343, USA

**Mann, John W** — Actor
Mosiac Media Group, 9200 W Sunset Blvd, #1000, Los Angeles CA 90069 USA

**Mann, Kelly J** — Baseball Player
1335 Franklin St, #4, Santa Monica CA 90404, USA

**Mann, Kristen C** — Basketball Player
Washington Mystics, Verizon Center, 401 9th St NW, #750, Washington DC 20004 USA

**Mann, Leslie** — Actress
Creative Artists Agency, 2000 Ave of Stars, #100, Los Angeles CA 90067 USA
**Mann, Manfred** — Keyboardist
E M I Records, 43 Brook Green, London W6 7EF, England
**Mann, Michael K** — Producer, Director
Forward Pass, 12233 W Olympic Blvd, #340, Los Angeles CA 90064, USA
**Mann, Nieko** — Actress
C E S D, 10635 Santa Monica Blvd, #130, Los Angeles CA 90025 USA
**Mann, Shelley I** — Swimmer
1301 S Scott St, #638S, Arlington VA 22204, USA
**Mann, Terrance V** — Actor, Director
138 W 118th St, #2, New York NY 10026, USA
**Mann, Thomas E** — Political Scientist
Brookings Institute, 1775 Massachusetts Ave NW, Washington DC 20036 USA
**Mannelly, J Patrick** — Football Player
1128 Kildare Ave, Libertyville IL 60048, USA
**Manning Mims, Madeline** — Track Athlete
7477 E 48th St, #83-4, Tulsa OK 74145, USA
**Manning, Daniel R (Danny)** — Basketball Player
205 Running Ridge Road, Lawrence KS 66049, USA
**Manning, Dennis J** — Businessman
Guardian Life Insurance, 7 Hanover Square, New York NY 10004, USA
**Manning, Donald** — Singer (Abyssinians)
Fast Lane International, 4856 Haygood Road, #200, Virginia Beach VA 23455, USA
**Manning, E Archie, III** — Football Player, Sportscaster
1420 1st St, New Orleans LA 70130, USA
**Manning, Elisha N (Eli)** — Football Player
New York Giants, Meadowlands Stadium, 102 Route 120, East Rutherford NJ 07073 USA
**Manning, James B (Jim)** — Baseball Player
41 Fox Run Dr, Weaverville NC 28787, USA
**Manning, Jane** — Opera Singer
2 Wilton Square, London N1 3DL, England
**Manning, Linford** — Singer (Abyssinians)
Fast Lane International, 4856 Haygood Road, #200, Virginia Beach VA 23455, USA
**Manning, Paul C** — Cyclist
British Cycling Centre, Stuart St, Manchester M11 4DQ, England
**Manning, Peyton W** — Football Player
Denver Broncos, 13655 E Broncos Parkway, Englewood CO 80112 USA
**Manning, Richard E (Rick)** — Baseball Player
22447 N 49th Place, Phoenix AZ 85054, USA
**Manning, Rob** — Space Engineer
Jet Propulsion Laboratory, 4800 Oak Grove Dr, Pasadena CA 91109 USA
**Manning, Taryn** — Singer (Boomkat), Actress
A P A Talent/Literary Agency, 405 S Beverly Dr, #300, Beverly Hills CA 90212 USA
**Manningham, Mario C** — Football Player
San Francisco 49ers, 4949 Centennial Blvd, Santa Clara CA 95054 USA
**Mannion, Pace S** — Basketball Player
4190 Achilles Dr, Salt Lake City UT 84124, USA
**Manoff, Dinah** — Actress
Talent Works, 3500 W Olive Ave, #1400, Burbank CA 91505 USA
**Manojlovic, Miki** — Actor
Artmedia, 20 Ave Rapp, 75007 Paris, France
**Manon, Julio** — Baseball Player
4726 15th Ave S, Saint Petersburg FL 33711, USA
**Manor, Brison** — Football Player
3 Campden Hill Road, Sherwood AR 72120, USA
**Manos, James, Jr** — Producer, Director, Writer
James Manos Jr Productions, 215 W 6th St, #PH-15, Los Angeles CA 90014, USA
**Manoux, J P** — Actor
Bauman Redanty Shaul Agency, 5757 Wilshire Blvd, #473, Los Angeles CA 90036 USA
**Mansell, Clinton D (Clint)** — Composer
First Artists, 4764 Park Granada, #210, Calabasas CA 91302 USA
**Mansell, Kevin** — Businessman
Kohl's Corp, N56W17000 Ridgewood Dr, Menomonee Falls WI 53051, USA
**Mansell, Nigel** — Auto Racing Driver
Old House Farm, North Dean, High Wycombe, Buckshire HP14 4NL, England
**Manser, Michael J** — Architect
Manser Practice, Hammersmith Bridge, London W6 9DA, England
**Mansfield, E Von** — Football Player
1711 Lynwood Court, Flossmoor IL 60422, USA
**Mansfield, Peter** — Nobel Medicine Laureate
Nottingham University, Physics Dept, Nottingham NG7 2RD, England
**Manson, Dave** — Ice Hockey Player
Dallas Stars, 2601 Ave of Stars, #100, Frisco TX 75034 USA
**Manson, Marilyn** — Singer (Marilyn Manson)
Creative Artists Agency, 2000 Ave of Stars, #100, Los Angeles CA 90067 USA
**Manson, Shirley** — Singer (Garbage), Actress
Untitled Entertainment, 350 S Beverly Dr, #200, Beverly Hills CA 90212 USA
**Mansour, Adly** — President, Egypt
Presidential Palace, Abdin, Qasr El-Nile St, Cairo CA002, Egypt
**Mantalis, George** — Singer (Four Coins)
309 Winners Circle, Canonsburg PA 15317, USA
**Mantegna, Joe** — Actor
I C M Partners, 10250 Constellation Blvd, #900, Los Angeles CA 90067 USA
**Mantei, Matthew B (Matt)** — Baseball Player
4709 Chicago Path, Stevensville MI 49127, USA
**Mantel, Hilary M** — Writer
A M Heath, 79 Saint Martin's Lane, London WC2N 4AA, England
**Mantello, Joe** — Director
Creative Artists Agency, 2000 Ave of Stars, #100, Los Angeles CA 90067 USA
**Mantha, Moe** — Ice Hockey Player
1538 Scio Ridge Road, Ann Arbor MI 48103, USA
**Mantilla, Felix** — Baseball Player
6973 N Tacoma St, Milwaukee WI 53224, USA
**Mantis, Nick** — Basketball Player
1344 Autumn Dr, Crown Point IN 46307, USA

**Mantle, Anthony Dod** — Cinematographer
Independent Talent Group, 40 Whitfield St, London W1T 2RH, England
**Manto, Jeffrey P (Jeff)** — Baseball Player
725 Radcliffe St, Bristol PA 19007, USA
**Mantooth, Randolph** — Actor
6210 Rodgerton Dr, Los Angeles CA 90068, USA
**Mantreola, Patricia** — Singer, Model, Actress
B M G, 1540 Broadway, #9E, New York NY 10036, USA
**Mantz, Michael** — Astronaut
1940 Elanita Dr, San Pedro CA 90732, USA
**Mantzoukas, Jason** — Actor, Writer
United Talent Agency, U T A Plaza, 9336 Civic Center Dr, Beverly Hills CA 90210 USA
**Manuel, Barry P** — Baseball Player
805 Oak St, Mamou LA 70554, USA
**Manuel, Charles F (Chuck)** — Baseball Player, Manager
1496 Mira Vista Circle, Weston FL 33327, USA
**Manuel, Jerry** — Baseball Player, Manager
5556 Ridge Park Dr, Loomis CA 95650, USA
**Manuel, Lionel** — Football Player
827 E Cedar Dr, Chandler AZ 85249, USA
**Manuelidis, Laura** — Neuropathologist
Yale University Medical School, Neuropathology Dept, New Haven CT 06520, USA
**Manuelle, Victor** — Singer, Songwriter
Latin Artists Group, 11271 Ventura Blvd, #151, Studio City CA 91604, USA
**Manumaleuna, Brandon M** — Football Player
335 E Albertoni St, #200, Carson CA 90746, USA
**Manusky, Gregory (Greg)** — Football Player
11537 Willow Springs Dr, Zionsville IN 46077, USA
**Manwaring, Kurt D** — Baseball Player
20 Prospect Ridge, Horseheads NY 14845, USA
**Manx, Harry** — Singer, Guitar Player
Roots Agency, 177 Woodland Ave, Westwood NJ 07675, USA
**Manz, Wolfgang** — Concert Pianist
Pasteuralle 55, 30655 Hanover, Germany
**Manzanero, Armando** — Singer, Composer
Pro Art, Av El Rosario 165, #201, Lima 27, Peru
**Manzanillo, Josias (Jose)** — Baseball Player
274 Kennebec St, Mattapan MA 02126, USA
**Manzano, Leonel (Leo)** — Track Athlete
Lenihan Group, 3915 Rockledge Dr, Austin TX 78731, USA
**Manzano, Sonia** — Actress, Writer
American Program Bureau, 313 Washington St, #225, Newton MA 02458, USA
**Manzi, Catello** — Harness Racing Driver
1 Hickory Lane, Freehold NJ 07728, USA
**Manzi, Rocco** — Harness Racing Executive
112 Willow Meadow Way, Oneida NY 13421, USA
**Manzie, Jim** — Composer
649 Platt Circle, El Dorado Hills CA 95762, USA
**Manziel, Johnathan P (Johnny)** — Football Player
Texas A&M University, Athletic Dept, College Station TX 77843, USA
**Manzini, Antonio** — Actor
Carol Levi Mgmt, Via Giuseppe Pisanelli 2, 00196 Rome, Italy
**Manzoni, Giacomo** — Composer
Viale Papiniano 31, 20123 Milan, Italy
**Maple, Edward R (Eddie)** — Thoroughbred Racing Jockey
Rose Hill Plantation Boarding Center, 1 Rose Hill Dr, Bluffton SC 29910, USA
**Maples, David** — Producer, Writer
Manage-Ment, 1103 1/2 Glendon Ave, Los Angeles CA 90024, USA
**Mara, Kate** — Actress
United Talent Agency, U T A Plaza, 9336 Civic Center Dr, Beverly Hills CA 90210 USA
**Mara, Paul** — Ice Hockey Player
500 Commercial St, #D, Boston MA 02109, USA
**Mara, Rooney** — Actress
W M E Entertainment, 9601 Wilshire Blvd, #300, Beverly Hills CA 90210 USA
**Marak, Paul P** — Baseball Player
1211 Comanche Trail, Alamogordo NM 88310, USA
**Maramorosch, Karl** — Entomologist
1050 George St, New Brunswick NJ 08901, USA
**Maran, Josie** — Model, Actress
Global Creative, 1051 N Cole Ave, #B, Los Angeles CA 90038, USA
**Maraniss, David** — Journalist
Washington Post, Editorial Dept, 1150 15th St NW, Washington DC 20071, USA
**Maratos-Flier, Elfetheria** — Geneticist
Joslin Diabetes Center, 1 Joslin Place, Boston MA 02215, USA
**Marber, Patrick** — Writer
Judy Daish Assoc, 2 Saint Charles Place, London W10 6EG, England
**Marbley, Harlan** — Boxer
6113 Parkview Lane, Clinton MD 20735, USA
**Marboeuf, Julie** — Actress
Intertalent, 16 Rue Henri Barbusse, 75005 Paris, France
**Marbury, Stephon X** — Basketball Player
4 Sycamore Court, Purchase NY 10577, USA
**Marc 7** — Rap Artist
Vision Entertainment Group, 1100 Glendon Ave, #1100, Los Angeles CA 90024, USA
**Marc, Alessandra** — Opera Singer
Clarisse B Kampel Foundation, 330 E 63rd St, New York NY 10065, USA
**Marceau, Sophie** — Actress
Special Artists Agency, 9200 Sunset Blvd, #410, West Hollywood CA 90069 USA
**Marcello, Vince** — Director, Writer, Actor
Gersh Agency, 9465 Wilshire Blvd, #600, Beverly Hills CA 90212 USA
**March, Forbes** — Actor
Kirk Talent Agencies, 196 W 3rd Ave, #102, Vancouver BC V5Y 1E9, Canada
**March, Jane** — Actress, Model
International Talent Mgmt, 31 Harley St, London W1G 9QS, England
**March, Little Peggy** — Singer
Cape Entertainment, 8432 NW 31st Court, Sunrise FL 33351, USA

**March, Stephanie** — Actress
Gersh Agency, 9465 Wilshire Blvd, #600, Beverly Hills CA 90212 USA
**Marchal, Olivier** — Actor, Director
Artmedia, 20 Ave Rapp, 75007 Paris, France
**Marchand, Guy** — Actor
Voyez Mon Agent, 20 Ave Rapp, 75007 Paris, France
**Marchant, Todd** — Ice Hockey Player
10448 Caribou Way, Tustin CA 92782, USA
**Marchetti, Gino J** — Football Player
324 Devon Way, West Chester PA 19380, USA
**Marchibroda, Theodore J (Ted)** — Football Player, Coach, Executive
90 Orchard Point Dr, Weems VA 22576, USA
**Marchionne, Sergio** — Businessman
Fiat SpA, Via Nizza 250, 10126 Turin, Italy
**Marchisano, Francesco Cardinal** — Religious Leader
Cancelleria Apostolica Palazzo, Piazza Cancelleria 1, 00186 Rome, Italy
**Marchlewski, Frank C** — Football Player
428 Toledo Dr, New Kensington PA 15068, USA
**Marchment, Bryan** — Ice Hockey Player
San Jose Sharks, San Jose Arena, 525 W Santa Clara St, San Jose CA 95113 USA
**Marchuk, Guri I** — Applied Mathematician
Numerical Mathematics Institute, Gubkin Str 8, 117333 Moscow, Russia
**Marchuk, Yevhen K** — Prime Minister, Ukraine; General
Verkovna Rada, M Hrushevskoho Str 5, 252008 Kiev, Ukraine
**Marciano, David** — Actor
Don Buchwald, 6500 Wilshire Blvd, #2200, Los Angeles CA 90048 USA
**Marcikic, Ivan** — Physicist, Inventor (Unbreakable Codes)
Geneva University, 24 Rue du General Dufour, 1211 Geneva 4, Switzerland
**Marcil, Vanessa** — Actress
Paradigm Agency, 360 N Crescent Dr, North Building, Beverly Hills CA 90210 USA
**Marcinkiewicz, Kazimierz** — Prime Minister, Poland
European Bank for Reconstruction/Development, 1 Exchange Square, London EC2A 2JN, England
**Marcis, Dave** — Auto Racing Driver
Marcis Auto Racing, PO Box 645, Skyland NC 28776, USA
**Marciulionis, R Sarunas** — Basketball Player
Hotel Sarunas, Raitininku St 4, 2051 Vilnius, Lithuania
**Marcol, Czeslaw C (Chester)** — Football Player
PO Box 94, Dollar Bay MI 49922, USA
**Marcon, Andre** — Actor
Artmedia, 20 Ave Rapp, 75007 Paris, France
**Marcos, Imelda R** — First Lady, Philippines
Leyte Providencia Dept, Tolosa Leyte, Philippines
**Marcotte, Don** — Ice Hockey Player
12 Cote St, Amesbury MA 01913, USA
**Marcovicci, Andrea** — Actress, Singer
Michael Mann Mgmt, 8838 Saturn St, Los Angeles CA 90035, USA
**Marcum, Art** — Writer
Creative Artists Agency, 2000 Ave of Stars, #100, Los Angeles CA 90067 USA
**Marcum, Joseph L** — Financier
609 Lake Dr, Vero Beach FL 32963, USA
**Marcum, Shaun M** — Baseball Player
1413 Jill Lane, Excelsior Springs MO 64024, USA
**Marcus Schaffer, Jackie** — Producer, Director, Writer
United Talent Agency, U T A Plaza, 9336 Civic Center Dr, Beverly Hills CA 90210 USA
**Marcus, Bernard** — Businessman
Home Depot Inc, 2455 Paces Ferry Road SE, Atlanta GA 30339, USA
**Marcus, Egerton** — Boxer
Atlas Boxing Centre, 849 Saint Clair Ave W, Toronto ON M6C 1C1, Canada
**Marcus, Jurgen** — Singer
Pestalozzistr 23A, 80469 Munich, Germany
**Marcus, Ken** — Photographer
Ken Marcus Studio, 6916 Melrose Ave, Los Angeles CA 90038, USA
**Marcus, Rudolph A** — Nobel Chemistry Laureate
331 S Hill Ave, Pasadena CA 91106, USA
**Marcus, Stanley** — Judge
US Court of Appeals, 36 NE 1st St, #300, Miami FL 33132, USA
**Marcus, Trula M** — Actress
Artists Agency, 9430 Olympic Blvd, Beverly Hills CA 90212 USA
**Marcy, Geoffrey W (Geoff)** — Astronomer
University of California, Astronomy Dept, Berkeley CA 94720, USA
**Mardall, Cyril L** — Architect
5 Boyne Terrace Mews, London W11 3LR, England
**Marden, Brice** — Artist
6 Saint Lukes Place, New York NY 10014, USA
**Marden, Matthew** — Actor
Mosiac Media Group, 9200 W Sunset Blvd, #1000, Los Angeles CA 90069 USA
**Mardones, Benny** — Singer
Tony Cee Assoc, PO Box 410, Utica NY 13503, USA
**Mare, Olindo F** — Football Player
106 Wescoe Dr, Mooresville NC 28117, USA
**Maree, Sydney** — Track Athlete
2 Braxton Road, Bryn Mawr PA 19010, USA
**Maren, Jerry** — Actor
PO Box 90010, San Diego CA 92169, USA
**Marentette, Leo J** — Baseball Player
33606 Beechwood St, Westland MI 48185, USA
**Maretska, Maria** — Sculptor
730 W 14th St, Medford OR 97501, USA
**Margaglio, Maurizio** — Ice Dancer
Ice Sports Federation, Via Piransi 44B, 20137 Milan, Italy
**Margarito Montiel, Antonio** — Boxer
Top Rank Inc, 3908 Howard Hughes Parkway, #580, Las Vegas NV 89169 USA
**Margera, Brandon C (Bam)** — Actor, Skateboarder
PO Box 671, Westtown PA 19395, USA
**Margerum, Kenneth (Ken)** — Football Player
494 Riverview Dr, Capitola CA 95010, USA

**Margiela, Martin** — Fashion Designer
Maison Martin Margiela, 163 Rue Saint Maur, 75011 Paris, France
**Margison, Richard** — Opera Singer
George Martynuk, 352 7th Ave, New York NY 10001, USA
**Margo, Philip** — Singer, Pianist, Drummer (Tokens)
American Mgmt, 19948 Mayall St, Chatsworth CA 91311, USA
**Margolin, Phillip M** — Writer, Actor
United Talent Agency, U T A Plaza, 9336 Civic Center Dr, Beverly Hills CA 90210 USA
**Margolin, Stuart** — Actor, Director, Writer
Great North Artists Mgmt, 350 Dupont St, Toronto ON M5R 1V9, Canada
**Margolis, Cindy** — Model, Actress
12711 Ventura Blvd, #400, Studio City CA 91604, USA
**Margolis, Laura** — Actress
Artists Mgmt, 1119 Colorado Ave, #12, Santa Monica CA 90401, USA
**Margolis, Lawrence S** — Judge
US Claims Court, 717 Madison Place NW, Washington DC 20439, USA
**Margolis, Mark** — Actor
Abrams Artists, 9200 W Sunset Blvd, #1125, West Hollywood CA 90069 USA
**Margolyes, Miriam** — Actress
United Agents, 12-26 Lexington St, London W1F 0LE, England
**Margon, Bruce H** — Astronomer
University of Washington, Astronomy Dept, PO Box 351580, Seattle WA 98195, USA
**Margoneri, Joseph E (Joe)** — Baseball Player
341 Turkeytown Road, West Newton PA 15089, USA
**Margoyles, Miriam** — Actress
Innovative Artists, 1505 10th St, Santa Monica CA 90401 USA
**Margrave, John L** — Chemist
4511 Vrone, Bellaire TX 77401, USA
**Margrethe II** — Queen, Denmark
Amalienborg Palace, 1257 Copenhagen K, Denmark
**Margulies, Donald** — Writer
Yale University, English Dept, New Haven CT 06520, USA
**Margulies, James H (Jimmy)** — Editorial Cartoonist
Hackensack Record, Editorial Dept, 150 River St, Hackensack NJ 07601, USA
**Margulies, Julianna L** — Actress
W M E Entertainment, 9601 Wilshire Blvd, #300, Beverly Hills CA 90210 USA
**Maria Teresa** — Grand Duchess Consort, Luxembourg
Palais Grand-Ducal, 17 Rue du Marche-aux-Herbes, 1728 Luxembourg-Ville, Luxembourg
**Mariam, Mengistu Haile** — President, Ethiopia; Army General
PO Box 1536, Gunhill Enclave, Harare, Zimbabwe
**Marianelli, Dario** — Composer
Air Edel, 18 Rodmarton St, London W1U 8BJ, England
**Mariani, Carlo M** — Artist
117 W 171st St, #12E, New York NY 10023, USA
**Mariano, Jarah** — Model
I M G Models, 304 Park Ave S, #PH N, New York NY 10010 USA
**Marichal, Juan A S** — Baseball Player
9458 NW 54th Doral Circle Lane, Doral FL 33178, USA
**Marie** — Princess, Liechtenstein
Schloss Vaduz, 9490 Vaduz, Liechtenstein
**Marie, Constance** — Actress
Innovative Artists, 1505 10th St, Santa Monica CA 90401 USA
**Marimow, William K** — Journalist
440 S Broad St, #1602, Philadelphia PA 19146, USA
**Marin, Carlos** — Singer (Il Divo)
Octagon, 81-83 Fulham High St, London SW6 3JW, England
**Marin, John W (Jack)** — Basketball Player
3909 Regent Road, Durham NC 27707, USA
**Marin, Maguy** — Choreographer
10 Blvd de Lattre de Tassigny, 69143 Rillieux-la-Pape Cedex, France
**Marin, Richard A (Cheech)** — Actor, Comedian (Cheech & Chong)
Chicano Collection, 923 E 3rd St, #203, Los Angeles CA 90013, USA
**Marinaro, Edward F (Ed)** — Actor, Football Player
Amsel Eisenstadt Frazier, 5055 Wilshire Blvd, #865, Los Angeles CA 90036 USA
**Marinca, Anamaria** — Actress
Conway Van Gelder Grant, 8-12 Broadwick St, #300, London W1F 8HW, England
**Marinelli, Rod** — Football Coach
Chicago Bears, 1000 Football Dr, Lake Forest IL 60045 USA
**Marini, Gilles** — Actor, Model
A P A Talent/Literary Agency, 405 S Beverly Dr, #300, Beverly Hills CA 90212 USA
**Marinin, Maxim V** — Figure Skater
Skating Federation, Luznetskaya Nabererhnya 8, 119871 Moscow, Russia
**Marino, Cathy** — Golfer
6313 Willowdale Dr, Plano TX 75093, USA
**Marino, Daniel C (Dan), Jr** — Football Player, Sportscaster
3415 Stallion Lane, Weston FL 33331, USA
**Marino, Ken** — Actor
Paradigm Agency, 360 N Crescent Dr, North Building, Beverly Hills CA 90210 USA
**Marino, Peter** — Architect
150 E 58th St, #3600, New York NY 10155, USA
**Mario** — Singer, Actor
Creative Artists Agency, 2000 Ave of Stars, #100, Los Angeles CA 90067 USA
**Mario, Ernest** — Businessman, Pharmacist
20 Greenhouse Dr, Princeton NJ 08540, USA
**Marion, Brock E** — Football Player
10 NW 42nd St, Ocala FL 34475, USA
**Marion, Fred D** — Football Player
10032 Oak Quarry Dr, Orlando FL 32832, USA
**Marion, Shawn D** — Basketball Player
5434 E Cannon Dr, Paradise Valley AZ 85253, USA
**Marisol** — Sculptor
427 Washington St, #700, New York NY 10013, USA
**Mariucci, Steve** — Football Coach, Sportscaster
15940 Romita Court, Monte Sereno CA 95030, USA
**Mariye, Lily** — Actress
C E S D, 10635 Santa Monica Blvd, #130, Los Angeles CA 90025 USA

**Mariza** — Singer
Mad Minute Music, 5-7 Rue Paul Bert, Saint Ouen 93400, France
**Marjanovic, Zana** — Actress
Troika, 74 Clerkenwell Road, #300, London EC1M 5QA, England
**Mark, Hans M** — Government Official, Physicist, Educator
1715 Scenic Dr, Austin TX 78703, USA
**Mark, Heidi** — Actress, Model
8730 W Sunset Blvd, #270, West Hollywood CA 90069, USA
**Mark, Mary Ellen** — Photographer
Mary Ellen Mark Library, 134 Spring St, #502, New York NY 10012, USA
**Markakis, Nicholas W (Nick)** — Baseball Player
949 E Piney Hill Road, Monkton MD 21111, USA
**Markarian, Andranik N** — Prime Minister, Armenia
Prime Minister's Office, Ul Nalbandyyrna 32, 375010 Yerevan, Armenia
**Marker, Laurie** — Animal Activist, Biologist
Cheetah Conservation Fund, PO Box 1380, Ojai CA 93024, USA
**Marker, Steve** — Guitarist (Garbage)
Borman Entertainment, 1250 6th St, #401, Santa Monica CA 90401, USA
**Markey, Edward J** — Senator, Representative, MA
7 Townsend St, Malden MA 02148, USA
**Markey, James A** — Guitarist (Concrete Blonde)
Agency Group Ltd, 142 W 57th St, #600, New York NY 10019 USA
**Markey, Lucille P** — Thoroughbred Racing Breeder
18 La Gorce Circle Lane, La Gorce Island, Miami Beach FL 33141, USA
**Markey, Mary Jo** — Editor
Paradigm Agency, 360 N Crescent Dr, North Building, Beverly Hills CA 90210 USA
**Markgraf, Kate** — Soccer Player
Octagon Worldwide, 1751 Pinnacle Dr, #1500, McLean VA 22102 USA
**Markham, Monte** — Actor, Producer, Director
C R Mgmt, 22337 Pacific Coast Highway, #627, Malibu CA 90265, USA
**Markle, C Wilson** — Film Engineer
Colorization Inc, 26 Soho St, Toronto ON M5T 1Z7, Canada
**Markle, Peter F** — Director
Blue Line Productions, 212 26th St, #295, Santa Monica CA 90402, USA
**Marklund, E Elisabeth (Liza)** — Writer
Piratforlaget AB, Kaptensgatan 6, 114 57 Stockholm, Sweden
**Markov, Alexey** — Opera Singer
I M G Artists, Hogarth Business Park, Chiswick, London W4 2TH, England
**Markov, Daniil (Danny)** — Ice Hockey Player
17875 Collins Ave, Sunny Isles Beach FL 33160, USA
**Markowitz, Barry** — Cinematographer
Paradigm Agency, 360 N Crescent Dr, North Building, Beverly Hills CA 90210 USA
**Markowitz, Harry M** — Nobel Economics Laureate
1010 Turquoise St, #245, San Diego CA 92109, USA
**Markowitz, Robert** — Director, Producer
Paradigm Agency, 360 N Crescent Dr, North Building, Beverly Hills CA 90210 USA
**Marks, Albert J** — Beauty Pageant Executive
Miss America Organization, 1370 Ave of Americas, #1600, New York NY 10019 USA
**Marks, Bruce** — Ballet Dancer, Artistic Director
Boston Ballet Co, 19 Clarendon St, Boston MA 02116, USA
**Marks, David J** — Architect
Marks Barfield Architects, 50 Bromells Road, London SW4 0BG, England
**Marks, John G** — Ice Hockey Player
2733 47th St S, #205, Fargo ND 58104, USA
**Marks, Michael E** — Businessman
Flextronics International, 2090 Fortune St, San Jose CA 95131, USA
**Marks, Miko** — Singer, Guitarist
Mirrome Records, 2923 Verde Vista Dr, #C, Santa Barbara CA 93105, USA
**Marks, Paul A** — Oncologist, Cell Biologist
25680 Military Road, Watertown NY 13601, USA
**Marks, Sean A** — Basketball Player
2702 Circle Dr, Newport Beach CA 92663, USA
**Markstein, Gary** — Editorial Cartoonist
Milwaukee Journal, Editorial Dept, 333 W State St, Milwaukee WI 53203, USA
**Marleau, Patrick D** — Ice Hockey Player
12021 Magnolia Court, Saratoga CA 95070, USA
**Marley, Damian (Jr Gong)** — Singer, Songwriter
Headline Entertainment, 8 Haughton Ave, Kingston 10, Jamaica
**Marley, Ziggy** — Singer, Songwriter
Ziggy Marley Mgmt, 269 S Beverly Dr, #175, Beverly Hills CA 90212, USA
**Marlin, Sterling** — Auto Racing Driver
Phoenix Racing, 195 Jones Road, Spartanburg SC 29307, USA
**Marlind, Mans** — Director
Zero Gravity Mgmt, 9255 Sunset Blvd, #1010, Los Angeles CA 90069 USA
**Marling, Brit** — Actress, Writer
Creative Artists Agency, 2000 Ave of Stars, #100, Los Angeles CA 90067 USA
**Marlohe, Berenice** — Actress
I C M Partners, 10250 Constellation Blvd, #900, Los Angeles CA 90067 USA
**Marlowe, Andrew W** — Producer, Screenwriter
Creative Artists Agency, 2000 Ave of Stars, #100, Los Angeles CA 90067 USA
**Marm, Walter J, Jr** — Vietnam War Army Hero (CMH)
PO Box 2017, Fremont NC 27830, USA
**Marmel, Steve** — Producer, Writer
Gersh Agency, 9465 Wilshire Blvd, #600, Beverly Hills CA 90212 USA
**Marmol, Carlos A** — Baseball Player
1500 Robin Circle, #218, Hoffman Estates IL 60169, USA
**Marmont, Louise** — Curling Athlete
Curling Assn, Idrottshuser, Marbackagatan 19, 123 43 Farsta, Sweden
**Marnell, Anthony M, III** — Architect
Marnell Properties, 222 Via Marnell Way, Las Vegas NV 89119, USA
**Marohn, William D** — Businessman
Whirlpool Corp, 2000 N State St, RR 63, Benton Harbor MI 49022, USA
**Marois, Mario** — Ice Hockey Player
Chicago Blackhawks, United Center, 1901 W Madison St, Chicago IL 60612 USA
**Maron, Marc** — Actor
W M E Entertainment, 9601 Wilshire Blvd, #300, Beverly Hills CA 90210 USA

| | |
|---|---|
| **Maroney, Laurence** | Football Player |
| 12560 Grandview Forest Dr, Saint Louis MO 63127, USA | |
| **Maroon, Paul** | Guitarist, Pianist (Walkmen) |
| Mick Mgmt, 35 Washington St, Brooklyn NY 11201 USA | |
| **Marosz, Tom** | Artist |
| Botanical Enclosures, 606 Concepion Ave, La Mesa CA 91941, USA | |
| **Maroth, Michael W (Mike)** | Baseball Player |
| 909 Johns Pointe Dr, Oakland FL 34787, USA | |
| **Maroulis, Constantine** | Actor, Singer |
| Abrams Artists, 275 7th Ave, #2600, New York NY 10001 USA | |
| **Marozsan, Erika** | Actress |
| Scenario Agentur, Rambergstr 5, 80799 Munich, Germany | |
| **Marquette, Sean** | Actor |
| A K A Talent, 6310 San Vicente Blvd, #200, Los Angeles CA 90048 USA | |
| **Marquez, Alfonso** | Baseball Umpire |
| 4103 S Skyline Court, Gilbert AZ 85297, USA | |
| **Marquez, Juan Manuel** | Boxer |
| 961 Everett St, Los Angeles CA 90026, USA | |
| **Marquez, Martin** | Actor |
| United Agents, 12-26 Lexington St, London W1F 0LE, England | |
| **Marquez, Rafael** | Boxer |
| Romanza Gym, Regina St 252, Deligacion, Colonia Iztacalco, Mexico City DF 07300, Mexico | |
| **Marquez, Raul** | Boxer |
| 729 Evanston St, Houston TX 77015, USA | |
| **Marquis, Jason S** | Baseball Player |
| 300 Vogel Ave, Staten Island NY 10309, USA | |
| **Marrero, Elieser (Eli)** | Baseball Player |
| 10230 SW 64th St, Miami FL 33173, USA | |
| **Marriner, Neville** | Conductor |
| Academy Saint Martin in Fields, Raine St, London E1 9RG, England | |
| **Marriott, J Willard, Jr** | Businessman |
| Marriott International, 10400 Fernwood Road, Bethesda MD 20817, USA | |
| **Marriott, Richard E** | Businessman |
| Host Marriott Corp, 10400 Fernwood Road, Bethesda MD 20817, USA | |
| **Marron, Donald B** | Financier |
| U B S PaineWebber, 1285 6th Ave, New York NY 10019, USA | |
| **Marrone, Douglas C (Doug)** | Football Player, Coach |
| 6100 Waitsfield Dr S, Jamesville NY 13078, USA | |
| **Marrs, Audrey M** | Producer |
| Representational Pictures, 75 E 4th St, #83, New York NY 10003, USA | |
| **Mars, Bruno** | Singer, Songwriter |
| W M E Entertainment, 9601 Wilshire Blvd, #300, Beverly Hills CA 90210 USA | |
| **Mars, Chris** | Drummer (Replacements) |
| PO Box 24631, Minneapolis MN 55424, USA | |
| **Mars, Susannah** | Singer, Actress |
| L M L Music Records, PO Box 48081, Los Angeles CA 90048, USA | |
| **Marsalis, Branford** | Jazz Saxophonist, Composer |
| Wilkins Mgmt, 323 Broadway, Cambridge MA 02139, USA | |
| **Marsalis, Delfeayo** | Jazz Trombonist |
| Ted Kurland, 173 Brighton Ave, Boston MA 02134 USA | |
| **Marsalis, Ellis** | Jazz Pianist |
| Management Ark, 116 Village Blvd, #200, Princeton NJ 08540, USA | |
| **Marsalis, James (Jim)** | Football Player |
| 101 Royal Oak Lane, Kathleen GA 31047, USA | |
| **Marsalis, Wynton** | Jazz Trumpeter, Composer |
| Management Ark, 116 Village Blvd, #200, Princeton NJ 08540, USA | |
| **Marsan, Eddie** | Actor |
| Paradigm Agency, 360 N Crescent Dr, North Building, Beverly Hills CA 90210 USA | |
| **Marsden, Gerard (Gerry)** | Singer, Guitarist (Gerry & Pacemakers) |
| Chimes International Entertainment, PO Box 26312, Glasgow G76 7WX, Scotland | |
| **Marsden, James P** | Actor |
| W M E Entertainment, 9601 Wilshire Blvd, #300, Beverly Hills CA 90210 USA | |
| **Marsden, Roy** | Actor |
| Ken McReddie Assoc, 101 Finsbury Pavement, London EC2A 1RS, England | |
| **Marsden, Russell** | Singer, Guitarist (Band of Skulls) |
| Pias Entertainment Group, Trading Centre, 101 Farm Lane, #24, London SW6 1QJ, England | |
| **Marsh of Mannington, Richard W** | Government Official, England |
| House of Lords, Westminster, London SW1A 0PW, England | |
| **Marsh, Brad** | Ice Hockey Player |
| Ottawa Senators, Scotia Bank Place, Kanata ON K2V 1A5, Canada | |
| **Marsh, Doug** | Football Player |
| 629 Forest Ave, Saint Louis MO 63135, USA | |
| **Marsh, Graham** | Golfer |
| Marsh Golf Design, 29 Commerce Dr, Box 300, Robina QED 4226, Australia | |
| **Marsh, James** | Documentary Producer, Director |
| Independent Talent Group, 40 Whitfield St, London W1T 2RH, England | |
| **Marsh, Jean** | Actress |
| 52 Shaftesbury Ave, London W1V 7DE, England | |
| **Marsh, Jeff (Swampy)** | Producer, Animator |
| Disney Channel, Phineas & Ferb Show, 500 S Buena Vista St, Burbank, CA 91521, USA | |
| **Marsh, Jodie** | Model |
| News International, Editorial Dept, 1 Virginia St, London E98 1XY, England | |
| **Marsh, Kym** | Singer (Hear'say) |
| Safe Mgmt, 111 Guildford Road, Lightwater, Surrey GU18 5RA, England | |
| **Marsh, Linda** | Actress |
| 170 W End Ave, #22P, New York NY 10023, USA | |
| **Marsh, Michael (Mike)** | Track Athlete |
| 2425 Holly Hall St, #152, Houston TX 77054, USA | |
| **Marsh, Michelle** | Model |
| Neon Mgmt, 34 Clare Lane, London N1 3DB, England | |
| **Marsh, Miles L** | Businessman |
| Fort James Corp, 1919 S Broadway, Green Bay WI 54304, USA | |
| **Marsh, Robert T** | Air Force General, Businessman |
| 20550 Falcons Landing Circle, #5106, Sterling VA 20165, USA | |
| **Marsh, Terry** | Boxer |
| 69 Ingaway, Langdon Hills, Basildon SS16 5QJ, England | |

**Marsh, Thomas O (Tom)** — Baseball Player
9140 Summerfield Road, Temperance MI 48182, USA
**Marshal, Lyndsey** — Actress
Troika, 74 Clerkenwell Road, #300, London EC1M 5QA, England
**Marshall, Albert L (Bert)** — Ice Hockey Player
Calgary Flames, PO Box 1540, Station M, Calgary AB T2P 3B9, Canada
**Marshall, Amanda L** — Singer, Actress
Creative Artists Agency, 2000 Ave of Stars, #100, Los Angeles CA 90067 USA
**Marshall, Arthur J** — Football Player
4821 Rocky Shoals Circle, Evans GA 30809, USA
**Marshall, Barry J** — Nobel Medicine Laureate
Charles Gairdner Hospital, Verdun St, Nedlands WA 6009, Australia
**Marshall, Brian A** — Bassist (Creed, Alter Bridge)
Agency Group Ltd, 142 W 57th St, #600, New York NY 10019 USA
**Marshall, David L (Dave)** — Baseball Player
4802 E Centralia St, Long Beach CA 90808, USA
**Marshall, Donald (Don)** — Ice Hockey Player
5887 SE Riverboat Dr, Stuart FL 34997, USA
**Marshall, Donny E** — Basketball Player
410 N 63rd St, Seattle WA 98103, USA
**Marshall, Donyell L** — Basketball Player
55 Ridgecreek Trail, Chagrin Falls OH 44022, USA
**Marshall, F Ray** — Secretary, Labor
PO Box Y, Austin TX 78713, USA
**Marshall, Frank W** — Producer
Kennedy/Marshall Co, 619 Arizona Ave, Santa Monica CA 90401, USA
**Marshall, Garry K** — Director, Actor
Rogers & Cowan, 8687 Melrose Ave, #G700, West Hollywood CA 90069, USA
**Marshall, Grant** — Ice Hockey Player
General Delivery, North Rustico PE C0A 1X0, Canada
**Marshall, Henry H** — Football Player
68-1745 Waikoloa Road, #101, Waikoloa HI 96738, USA
**Marshall, James** — Actor
Susan J Talent Agency, 12501 Riverside Dr, #211, Studio City CA 91607, USA
**Marshall, James L (Jim)** — Football Player
4241 Basswood Road, Minneapolis MN 55416, USA
**Marshall, Jason** — Ice Hockey Player
438 Begonia Ave, Corona del Mar CA 92625, USA
**Marshall, John** — Geologist
S E T I Institute, 515 N Whitman Road, Mountain View CA 94043, USA
**Marshall, Kris** — Actor
Independent Talent Group, 40 Whitfield St, London W1T 2RH, England
**Marshall, Lawrence E (Larry)** — Football Player
1044 Washington St, Kansas City MO 64105, USA
**Marshall, Leonard A** — Football Player
PO Box 272016, Boca Raton FL 33427, USA
**Marshall, Margaret A** — Opera Singer
Woodside, Main St, Gargunnock, Stirling FK5 3BP, Scotland
**Marshall, Michael A (Mike)** — Baseball Player
1280 W Desert Sun Dr, Yuma AZ 85365, USA
**Marshall, Michael G (Mike)** — Baseball Player
38324 Jendral Ave, Zephyrhills FL 33542, USA
**Marshall, Neil** — Director
I C M Partners, 10250 Constellation Blvd, #900, Los Angeles CA 90067 USA
**Marshall, Paula** — Actress
Innovative Artists, 1505 10th St, Santa Monica CA 90401 USA
**Marshall, Penny** — Actress, Director, Producer
Shelter Entertainment, 9454 Wilshire Blvd, #715, Beverly Hills CA 90212, USA
**Marshall, Peter** — Actor
Kazarian/Measures/Ruskin, 11969 Ventura Blvd, #300, Studio City CA 91604 USA
**Marshall, R James (Jim)** — Baseball Player, Manager
19700 N 76th St, #1091, Scottsdale AZ 85255, USA
**Marshall, Ray** — Economist
University of Texas, L B Johnson Public Affairs School, Dallas TX 78713, USA
**Marshall, Richard** — Football Player
11232 Colonial Country Lane, Charlotte NC 28277, USA
**Marshall, Rob** — Director; Choreographer
Creative Artists Agency, 2000 Ave of Stars, #100, Los Angeles CA 90067 USA
**Marshall, Tom** — Publisher
Sunset, Publisher's Office, 80 Willow Road, Menlo Park CA 94025, USA
**Marshall, Tonie** — Director
Artmedia, 20 Ave Rapp, 75007 Paris, France
**Marshall, W W (Bones)** — Air Force General, Hero
4389 Malia St, #429, Honolulu HI 96821, USA
**Marshall, Wilber B** — Football Player
3016 E Main St, Mims FL 32754, USA
**Marshall, Willie** — Ice Hockey Player
2110 Acorn Court, Lebanon PA 17042, USA
**Marshall-Green, Logan** — Actor
Creative Artists Agency, 2000 Ave of Stars, #100, Los Angeles CA 90067 USA
**Marshburn, Thomas H (Tom)** — Astronaut
N A S A, Johnson Space Center, 2101 NASA Road, Houston TX 77058 USA
**Marson, Louis G (Lou)** — Baseball Player
6631 E Wilshire Dr, Scottsdale AZ 85257, USA
**Marsters, James** — Actor
Amanda Howard, 74 Clerkenwell Road, London EC1M 5QA, England
**Marston, Joshua M** — Director, Writer
W M E Entertainment, 9601 Wilshire Blvd, #300, Beverly Hills CA 90210 USA
**Marta** — Soccer Player
Dois Riachas, Alagoas, Brazil
**Martel, Arlene** — Actress
2109 S Wilbur Ave, Walla Walla WA 99362, USA
**Martel, Christiane** — Beauty Queen, Actress
Miss Universe Organization, 1370 Ave of Americas, #1600, New York NY 10019 USA
**Martel, Yann** — Writer
Houghton Mifflin Harcourt, 215 Park Ave S, #1200, New York NY 10003 USA

**Martell, Arthur E** — Chemist
4047 Martinshire Dr, Houston TX 77025, USA
**Martell, Donna** — Actress
PO Box 3335, Granada Hills CA 91394, USA
**Martella, Vincent** — Actor
C E S D, 10635 Santa Monica Blvd, #130, Los Angeles CA 90025 USA
**Martelly, J Michel (Sweet Micky)** — President, Haiti
President's Office, Palais Nacional, Champ de Mars, Port-au-Prince, Haiti
**Martha, J Paul** — Football Player
7471 University Ave, #207, La Mesa CA 91942, USA
**Marthouret, Francois** — Actor
Artmedia, 20 Ave Rapp, 75007 Paris, France
**Martika** — Singer
Entertainment Artists, 2409 21st Ave S, #100, Nashville TN 10019 USA
**Martikan, Michal** — Canoeing Athlete
K T K Dukla Liptovsky, Nabrezie J Krala 8, Liptovsky Mikulas, Slovakia
**Martin Chase, Deborah (Debra)** — Producer
Martin Chase Productions, 500 S Buena Vista St, Burbank CA 91521, USA
**Martin, Aaron B** — Football Player
3605 Seth Court, Springdale MD 20774, USA
**Martin, Albert S (Al)** — Baseball Player
400N Cornado St, #1062, Chandler AZ 85224, USA
**Martin, Andrea** — Actress, Comedienne
Innovative Artists, 1505 10th St, Santa Monica CA 90401 USA
**Martin, Ann M** — Writer
Chronicle Books, 85 2nd St, San Francisco CA 94105, USA
**Martin, Anne-Marie** — Actress
Creative Artists Agency, 2000 Ave of Stars, #100, Los Angeles CA 90067 USA
**Martin, Anthony I (Amos)** — Football Player
11824 Duane Point Circle, #201, Louisville KY 40243, USA
**Martin, Billy** — Jazz Percussionist, Composer
Creative Artists Agency, 2000 Ave of Stars, #100, Los Angeles CA 90067 USA
**Martin, Boyce F, Jr** — Judge
US Court of Appeals, US Courthouse, 601 W Broadway, Louisville KY 40202, USA
**Martin, Brad** — Singer
I C M Partners, 10250 Constellation Blvd, #900, Los Angeles CA 90067 USA
**Martin, Brian** — Luge Athlete
1123 66th St, Emeryville CA 94608, USA
**Martin, Carolyn (Biddy)** — Educator
University of Wisconsin, Chancellor's Office, 500 Lincoln Dr, Madison WI 53706, USA
**Martin, Casey** — Golfer
University of Oregon, Athletic Dept, 2727 Harris Parkway, Eugene OR 97405, USA
**Martin, Catherine** — Scenic, Costume Designer
Bazmark Films, PO Box 430, Kings Cross NSW 1340, Australia
**Martin, Cedric** — Singer, Bassist (Con Funk Shun)
Thrill Entertainment Group, 9530 Hageman St, #B278, Bakersfield CA 93312 USA
**Martin, Chris William** — Actor
A P A Talent/Literary Agency, 405 S Beverly Dr, #300, Beverly Hills CA 90212 USA
**Martin, Christoper A J (Chris)** — Singer (Coldplay)
Paradigm Agency, 360 N Crescent Dr, North Building, Beverly Hills CA 90210 USA
**Martin, Christopher (Chris)** — Football Player
15760 Horton Court, Overland Park KS 66223, USA
**Martin, Christy** — Boxer
2015 University Heights Lane, Charlotte NC 28213, USA
**Martin, Cuonzo L** — Basketball Player
4315 Thistlewood Way, Knoxville TN 37919, USA
**Martin, Curtis** — Football Player
100 Hilton Ave, #PH 1, Garden City NY 11530, USA
**Martin, D Renie** — Baseball Player
509 Little Eagle Court, Valrico FL 33594, USA
**Martin, Darnell** — Director, Producer, Writer
Paradigm Agency, 360 N Crescent Dr, North Building, Beverly Hills CA 90210 USA
**Martin, David** — Commentator
CBS-TV, News Dept, 2020 M St NW, Washington DC 20036 USA
**Martin, Demetri E** — Actor, Comedian, Producer
Creative Artists Agency, 2000 Ave of Stars, #100, Los Angeles CA 90067 USA
**Martin, Dewey** — Actor
1371 East Ave de los Arboles, Thousand Oaks CA 91360, USA
**Martin, Doug** — Football Player
17115 NE 183rd Place, Woodinville WA 98072, USA
**Martin, Doug** — Football Player
Tampa Bay Buccaneers, 1 W Buccaneer Place, Tampa FL 33607 USA
**Martin, Doug** — Golfer
Golf Ranch, 5390 Limaburg Road, Burlington KY 41005, USA
**Martin, Duane** — Actor, Producer, Writer
Paul Kohner, 9300 Wilshire Blvd, #555, Beverly Hills CA 90212 USA
**Martin, Edward H** — Navy Admiral
729 Guadalupe Ave, Coronado CA 92118, USA
**Martin, Eric W** — Football Player
111 Windfall Place, Clinton MS 39056, USA
**Martin, G Steven** — Biochemist, Biologist
University of California, Biological Sciences Dept, Barker Hall, Berkeley CA 94720, USA
**Martin, G Wayne** — Football Player
408 Rue de la Rivere, Kenner LA 70065, USA
**Martin, George C** — Aeronautical Engineer
900 University St, #5P, Seattle WA 98101, USA
**Martin, George D** — Football Player
50 Cheshire Lane, Ringwood NJ 07456, USA
**Martin, George H** — Businessman, Lyricist
Lynhurst Road, Hampstead, London NW3 5NG, England
**Martin, George R R** — Writer
103 San Salvador, Santa Fe NM 87501, USA
**Martin, Gerald W** — Football Player
New Orleans Saints, 5800 Airline Highway, Metairie LA 70003 USA
**Martin, Graham Patrick** — Actor
Talent Works, 3500 W Olive Ave, #1400, Burbank CA 91505 USA

| | |
|---|---|
| **Martin, Greg** | Singer, Musician (Kentucky Headhunters) |
| Bobby Roberts, 3050 Business Park Circle, #303, Goodlettsville TN 37221 USA | |
| **Martin, Harold** | President, New Caledonia |
| President's Office, Artillerie 8 Rt des Artfices, BP M2, 98849 Noumea Cedex, New Caledonia | |
| **Martin, Henry R** | Cartoonist (Good News Bad News) |
| 1382 Newtown Langhorne Road, #G206, Newtown PA 18940, USA | |
| **Martin, J Michael (Mike)** | Baseball Player |
| 7904 Waterfalls Ave, Las Vegas NV 89128, USA | |
| **Martin, J William (Billy)** | Football Player |
| PO Box 2969, Cumming GA 30028, USA | |
| **Martin, Jacques** | Ice Hockey Coach |
| Jacques Martin Hockey School, 198 Daventry Crescent, Nepean ON K2J 4N1, Canada | |
| **Martin, James G** | Governor, NC |
| Carolinas Medical Center, PO Box 32861, Charlotte NC 28232, USA | |
| **Martin, Jerry L** | Baseball Player |
| 109 Chelton Court, Columbia SC 29212, USA | |
| **Martin, Jesse L** | Actor, Singer |
| I C M Partners, 730 5th Ave, New York NY 10019 USA | |
| **Martin, Joe** | Cartoonist (Mister Boffo) |
| King Features Syndicate, 300 W 57th St, #1500, New York NY 10019 USA | |
| **Martin, John H** | Educator |
| J H M Corp, 3930 RCA Blvd, #3240, Palm Beach Gardens FL 33410, USA | |
| **Martin, Joseph C (J C)** | Baseball Player |
| 112 Oakmont Court, Advance NC 27006, USA | |
| **Martin, Judith (Miss Manners)** | Journalist |
| 1651 Harvard St NW, Washington DC 20009, USA | |
| **Martin, Kellie** | Actress, Producer |
| Thruline Entertainment, 9250 Wilshire Blvd, #100, Beverly Hills CA 90212 USA | |
| **Martin, Kelvin B** | Football Player |
| 608 Guadalupe Road, Keller TX 76248, USA | |
| **Martin, Kenyon L** | Basketball Player |
| 23104 Dolorosa St, Woodland Hills CA 91367, USA | |
| **Martin, Kevin** | Curling Athlete |
| Curling Assn, 1660 Vimont Court, Cumberland ON K4A 4J4, Canada | |
| **Martin, Kevin** | Singer, Guitarist (Candlebox) |
| Novi Entertainment, PO Box 17077, Beverly Hills CA 90209, USA | |
| **Martin, Kevin D, Jr** | Basketball Player |
| Minnesota Timberwolves, Target Center, 600 1st Ave N, Minneapolis MN 55403 USA | |
| **Martin, Luci** | Singer (Chic) |
| Lustig Talent, PO Box 770850, Orlando FL 32877 USA | |
| **Martin, Lynn M** | Secretary, Labor |
| Harry Walker Agency, 355 Lexington Ave, #2100, New York NY 10017, USA | |
| **Martin, Madeleine** | Actress |
| I C M Partners, 10250 Constellation Blvd, #900, Los Angeles CA 90067 USA | |
| **Martin, Marilyn** | Singer |
| Atlantic Records, 9229 W Sunset Blvd, #900, West Hollywood CA 90069 USA | |
| **Martin, Mark A** | Auto Racing Driver |
| D E I, 1675 Coddle Creek Highway, Mooresville NC 28115, USA | |
| **Martin, Marsha P** | Government Official, Financier |
| Farm Credit Administration, 1501 Farm Credit Dr, #3600, McLean VA 22102, USA | |
| **Martin, Millicent** | Actress, Singer |
| London Mgmt, 2-4 Noel St, London W1V 3RB, England | |
| **Martin, Nicholas** | Director |
| United Agents, 12-26 Lexington St, London W1F 0LE, England | |
| **Martin, Norberto E (Paco)** | Baseball Player |
| 5905 Ricker Road, Raleigh NC 27610, USA | |
| **Martin, Pamela Sue** | Actress |
| PO Box 2278, Hailey ID 83333, USA | |
| **Martin, Paul** | Ice Hockey Player |
| 3401 Annandale Dr, Presto PA 15142, USA | |
| **Martin, Paul C (Jake)** | Baseball Player |
| 1529 33rd St, San Diego CA 92102, USA | |
| **Martin, Phillip R (Phil)** | Basketball Player |
| 6937 Vineridge Dr, Dallas TX 75248, USA | |
| **Martin, R Bruce** | Chemist |
| University of Virginia, Chemistry Dept, Charlottesville VA 22903, USA | |
| **Martin, Ray** | Billiards Player |
| 11-05 Cadmus Place, Fair Lawn NJ 07410, USA | |
| **Martin, Raymond J (Ray)** | Baseball Player |
| 383 Adams St, Quincy MA 02169, USA | |
| **Martin, Rhona** | Curling Athlete |
| Curling Assn, 14 Donnelly Dr, Bedford, Bedfordshire MK4 9TU, England | |
| **Martin, Ricky** | Actor, Singer |
| Creative Artists Agency, 2000 Ave of Stars, #100, Los Angeles CA 90067 USA | |
| **Martin, Roderick D (Rod)** | Football Player |
| PO Box 23, Manhattan Beach CA 90267, USA | |
| **Martin, Rudolf** | Actor |
| Mary Erickson Management, 2126 N Commonwealth Ave, Los Angeles CA 90027, USA | |
| **Martin, Sandy** | Actress |
| Talent Works, 3500 W Olive Ave, #1400, Burbank CA 91505 USA | |
| **Martin, Sarah** | Singer, Violinist (Belle & Sebastian) |
| Ground Control Touring, 20 Jay St, #826, Brooklyn NY 11201 USA | |
| **Martin, Seth** | Ice Hockey Player |
| 1200 Heather Place, Trail BC V1R 4Y2, Canada | |
| **Martin, Steve** | Actor, Comedian, Writer |
| Martin/Stein Co, 1528 N Curson Ave, Los Angeles CA 90046, USA | |
| **Martin, Sylvia Wene** | Bowler |
| 2701 Clark Towers Court, #125, Las Vegas NV 89102, USA | |
| **Martin, T J** | Producer |
| Principato-Young, 9465 Wilshire Blvd, #880, Beverly Hills CA 90212 USA | |
| **Martin, Terry G** | Ice Hockey Player |
| 184 Hampton Hill Dr, Buffalo NY 14221, USA | |
| **Martin, Thomas E (Tom)** | Baseball Player |
| 8001 Surf Dr, Panama City FL 32408, USA | |
| **Martin, Todd C** | Tennis Player |
| 156 Coach Lamp Way, Ponte Vedra FL 32082, USA | |

**M**

Martin - Martin

**M**

**Martin, Tony D** — Football Player
1198 B Green Road, Boston GA 31626, USA
**Martin, Walter** — Organist, Bassist (Walkmen)
Mick Mgmt, 35 Washington St, Brooklyn NY 11201 USA
**Martina, Mia** — Singer
C P Records, 3341 Bloor St W, #77, Toronto ON M8X 1E9, Canada , USA
**Martindale, Margo** — Actress
Gersh Agency, 41 Madison Ave, #3301, New York NY 10010 USA
**Martindale, Wink** — Entertainer, Singer
5744 Newcastle Lane, Calabasas CA 91302, USA
**Martinelli Berrocal, Ricardo A** — President, Panama
Palacio Presidencial, Valija 50, Panama City 1, Panama
**Martines, Alessandra** — Actress
Artmedia, 20 Ave Rapp, 75007 Paris, France
**Martinez Sistach, Lluis Cardinal** — Religious Leader
Arzobispado, Carrer del Bisbe 5, 08002 Barcelona, Spain
**Martinez Somalo, Eduardo Cardinal** — Religious Leader
Palazzo delle Congregazioni, Piazza Pio XII 3, 00193 Rome, Italy
**Martinez, A** — Actor
David Shapira Assoc, 193 N Robertson Blvd, Beverly Hills CA 90211 USA
**Martinez, Alfredo (Fred)** — Baseball Player
2346 Thomas St, Los Angeles CA 90031, USA
**Martinez, Ana Maria** — Opera Singer
J F Mastroianni, 161 W 61st St, #17E, New York NY 10023, USA
**Martinez, Angela** — Actress
Abrams Artists, 9200 W Sunset Blvd, #1125, West Hollywood CA 90069 USA
**Martinez, Benito** — Actor
Platform Public Relations, 2666 N Beachwood Dr, Los Angeles CA 90068, USA
**Martinez, Carmelo** — Baseball Player
32 Brisas del Plata, Dorado PR 00646, USA
**Martinez, Conchita** — Tennis Player
511 Westminster Dr, Cardiff by the Sea CA 92007, USA
**Martinez, Constantino (Tino)** — Baseball Player
2705 W Kathleen St, Tampa FL 33607, USA
**Martinez, Daniel J** — Artist
Robert Berman/B1 Gallery, 2525 Michigan Ave, Santa Monica CA 90404, USA
**Martinez, David (Dave)** — Baseball Player
3315 Enterprise Road E, Safety Harbor FL 34695, USA
**Martinez, Douglas V (S A)** — Singer, DJ Musician (311), Songwriter
311 Hive, 8904 Florence Dr, Omaha NE 68147, USA
**Martinez, Edgar** — Baseball Player
3036 249th Ave SE, Sammamish WA 98075, USA
**Martinez, Felix A (Tippy)** — Baseball Player
1524 Dellsway Road, Towson MD 21286, USA
**Martinez, J Dennis** — Baseball Player
9400 SW 63rd Court, Miami FL 33156, USA
**Martinez, John A (Buck)** — Baseball Player, Manager
10315 Long Beach Blvd, Long Beach Township NJ 08008, USA
**Martinez, Melquiades R (Mel)** — Secretary, Housing & Urban Development
D L A Piper, 500 8th St NW, Washington DC 20004, USA
**Martinez, Natalie** — Actress, Model
W M E Entertainment, 9601 Wilshire Blvd, #300, Beverly Hills CA 90210 USA
**Martinez, Olivier** — Actor
Gersh Agency, 9465 Wilshire Blvd, #600, Beverly Hills CA 90212 USA
**Martinez, Pedro J** — Baseball Player
3029 Birkdale Dr, Weston FL 33332, USA
**Martinez, Ramon E** — Baseball Player
3029 Birkdale Lane, Weston FL 33332, USA
**Martinez, Ramon J** — Baseball Player
3029 Birkdale Dr, Weston FL 33332, USA
**Martinez, Rene O** — Drummer (Intocable)
Serca Music, 2020 W Houston Ave, McAllen TX 78501, USA
**Martinez, Robert (Bob)** — Government Official; Governor, FL
4647 W San Jose St, Tampa FL 33629, USA
**Martinez, Vincent** — Actor
Artmedia, 20 Ave Rapp, 75007 Paris, France
**Martin-Green, Sonequa** — Actress
Gersh Agency, 9465 Wilshire Blvd, #600, Beverly Hills CA 90212 USA
**Martini, Steve** — Writer
Plume/GP Putnam's Sons, 375 Hudson St, New York NY 10014, USA
**Martinie, Ryan** — Bassist (Mudvayne)
Agency Group Ltd, 142 W 57th St, #600, New York NY 10019 USA
**Martinkovic, John G** — Football Player
1001 Ernst Dr, Green Bay WI 54304, USA
**Martino, Pat** — Jazz Guitarist, Composer
Donofrio Productions, 607 W Shore Road, Brigatine NJ 08203, USA
**Martino, Renato R Cardinal** — Religious Leader
Justice & Peace Curia, Piazzo S Calisto 16, 00120 Vatican City
**Martins, Jean-Pierre** — Actor
Sophie Lemaitre, 22 Rue Nollet, 75017 Paris, France
**Martins, Peter** — Ballet Dancer, Artistic Director
New York City Ballet, Lincoln Center Plaza, New York NY 10023 USA
**Martinson, Leslie H** — Director
2288 Coldwater Canyon Dr, Beverly Hills CA 90210, USA
**Marton, Eva** — Opera Singer
International Artists Group, 201 E 87th St, #21E, New York NY 10128 USA
**Martorella, Mildred (Millie)** — Bowler
Professional Bowlers Assn, 719 2nd Ave, #701, Seattle WA 98104 USA
**Marts, Lonnie** — Football Player
13650 Bromley Point Dr, Jacksonville FL 32225, USA
**Marty, Martin E** — Theologian
175 E Delaware Place, #8508, Chicago IL 60611, USA
**Martzke, Rudy** — Sportswriter
USA Today, Editorial Dept, 1000 Wilson Blvd, Arlington VA 22209, USA
**Maruk, Dennis** — Ice Hockey Player
2624 Garfield Ave, Minneapolis MN 55408, USA

**Martin - Maruk**

| | |
|---|---|
| **Marusha** | Techno Musician |
| Kaiser-Friedrich-Str 41, 10627 Berlin, Germany | |
| **Maruyama, Karen** | Actress |
| Rooster Films, 5225 Wilshire Blvd, #406, Los Angeles CA 90036, USA | |
| **Maruyama, Karina** | Soccer Player |
| Football Assn, 3-10-15 Hongo, Bunkyoku, Tokyo 113 0033 Japan | |
| **Maruyama, Shigeki** | Golfer |
| 15210 Antelo Place, Los Angeles CA 90077, USA | |
| **Marve, Eugene R** | Football Player |
| 4510 S Cameron Ave, Tampa FL 33611, USA | |
| **Marvel, Jonathan** | Architect |
| Rogers Marvel Architects, 145 Hudson St, #304, New York NY 10013, USA | |
| **Marvin, Gisele** | Ice Hockey Player |
| USA Hockey, 1775 Bob Johnson Dr, Colorado Springs CO 80906 USA | |
| **Marvin, Hank B** | Guitarist (Shadows) |
| Universal Music, 364-366 Kensington High St, London W14 8NS, England | |
| **Marx, Gilda** | Fashion Designer |
| Gilda Marx Industries, 11755 Exposition Blvd, Los Angeles CA 90064, USA | |
| **Marx, Jeffrey A** | Journalist |
| Lexington Herald-Leader, Editorial Dept, Main & Midland, Lexington KY 40507, USA | |
| **Marx, Michael** | Fencer |
| Northwest Fencing Center, 4950 SW Western Ave, Beaverton OR 97005, USA | |
| **Marx, Richard** | Singer, Songwriter |
| Union Entertainment Group, 1323 Newbury Road, #102, Thousand Oaks CA 91329, USA | |
| **Marzich, Andy** | Bowler |
| 25141 Whitespring, Mission Viejo CA 92692, USA | |
| **Marzoli, Andrea** | Geologist |
| Berkeley Geochronolgy Center, 2455 Ridge Road, Berkeley CA 94709, USA | |
| **Marzouki, Moncef** | President, Tunisia |
| Palais Presidentiel, Tunis, Tunisia | |
| **Masak, Ron** | Actor, Writer, Producer |
| Neal Public Relations, 3117 Hollycrest Dr, Los Angeles CA 90068, USA | |
| **Masakayan, Liz** | Volleyball Player |
| 2864 Palomino Circle, La Jolla CA 92037, USA | |
| **Masako** | Crown Princess, Japan |
| Imperial Palace, 1-1 Chiyoda, Chiyodaku, Tokyo 100, Japan | |
| **Masaoka, Onan K S** | Baseball Player |
| 1323 Auwae Road, Hilo HI 96720, USA | |
| **Mascarenas, Andi** | Sculptor |
| 1984 Nova Road, Pine CO 80470, USA | |
| **Maschio, Robert** | Actor |
| Stone Manners Salners, 9911 W Pico Blvd, #1400, Los Angeles CA 90035 USA | |
| **Masco, Judit** | Model |
| S S & M Model Mgmt, C/Provenca 286-88, 08008 Barcelona, Spain | |
| **Masekela, Hugh R** | Jazz Trumpeter, Singer |
| Ritmo Artists, PO Box 684705, Austin TX 78768, USA | |
| **Mashburn, Jamal** | Basketball Player |
| 5625 Pine Tree Dr, Miami Beach FL 33140, USA | |
| **Mashburn, Jesse** | Track Athlete |
| 8520 S Pennsylvania Ave, Oklahoma City OK 73159, USA | |
| **Masire, Quett K J** | President, Botswana |
| PO Box 70, Gaborone, Botswana | |
| **Masius, John** | Producer, Writer |
| 11948 Saltair Terrace, Los Angeles CA 90049, USA | |
| **Maskaev, Oleg** | Boxer |
| Gleason's Boxing Gym, 75 Front St, New York NY 10005, USA | |
| **Maskawa, Toshihide** | Nobel Physics Laureate |
| Koyoto Sangyo University, Kamigamo, Kitaku, Kyoto City 603 8553, Japan | |
| **Maske, Henry** | Boxer |
| Tocardo, Neuer Wamdrahm 1, Speicherstadt, 20457 Hamburg, Germany | |
| **Maskin, Eric S** | Nobel Economics Laureate |
| 232 Washington St, Belmont MA 02478, USA | |
| **Maslansky, Paul** | Producer, Director |
| Bamberger Business, 10850 Wilshire Blvd, #575, Los Angeles CA 90024, USA | |
| **Maslany, Tatiana** | Actress |
| Resolution, 1801 Century Park East, #2300, Los Angeles CA 90067 USA | |
| **Maslin, Janet** | Writer, Journalist |
| New York Times, Editorial Dept, 229 W 43rd St, New York NY 10036 USA | |
| **Maslow, James** | Actor |
| Creative Artists Agency, 2000 Ave of Stars, #100, Los Angeles CA 90067 USA | |
| **Masohn, Mercedes** | Actress |
| Greene Assoc, 1901 Ave of Stars, #130, Los Angeles CA 90067 USA | |
| **Mason of Barnsley, Roy** | Government Official, England |
| 12 Victoria Ave, Barnsley, South Yorks S7O 2BH, England | |
| **Mason, Anthony G D** | Basketball Player |
| 9 Brownstone Way, #308, Englewood NJ 07631, USA | |
| **Mason, B John** | Meteorologist |
| 64 Christchurch Road, East Sheen, London SW14, England | |
| **Mason, Birny, Jr** | Chemical Engineer |
| 2208 Theall Road, Rye NY 10580, USA | |
| **Mason, Bob** | Ice Hockey Player |
| 9549 Yukon Ave S, Minneapolis MN 55438, USA | |
| **Mason, Bobbie Ann** | Writer |
| PO Box 518, Lawrenceburg KY 40342, USA | |
| **Mason, Brent** | Singer |
| Mercury Records, 401 Commerce St, #1100, Nashville TN 37219 USA | |
| **Mason, Chris** | Ice Hockey Player |
| PO Box 12465, Saint Louis MO 63132, USA | |
| **Mason, Connie** | Model, Actress |
| Playboy Promotions, 2706 Media Center Dr, Los Angeles CA 90065 USA | |
| **Mason, Connie** | Writer |
| 1954 Juanita Way, Tarpon Springs FL 34689, USA | |
| **Mason, Dave** | Singer, Guitarist (Traffic); Songwriter |
| Jensen Communications, 709 E Colorado Blvd, #220, Pasadena CA 91101, USA | |
| **Mason, Derrick J** | Football Player |
| 9640 Portofino Dr, Brentwood TN 37027, USA | |

**Mason, Desmond T** — Basketball Player
6440 N Lake Dr, Milwaukee WI 53217, USA
**Mason, Henry (Hank)** — Baseball Player
5004 W Leyburn Court, #102, Henrico VA 23228, USA
**Mason, Jackie** — Actor, Comedian, Writer
W M E Entertainment, 1325 Ave of Americas, New York NY 10019, USA
**Mason, James P (Jim)** — Baseball Player
11410 Queens Way, Theodore AL 36582, USA
**Mason, Larry B** — Vietnam War Air Force Hero
826 Cinebar Road, Cinebar WA 98533, USA
**Mason, Lawrence** — Actor
Kazarian/Measures/Ruskin, 11969 Ventura Blvd, #300, Studio City CA 91604 USA
**Mason, Lindsey M** — Football Player
8665 Ritchboro Road, District Heights MD 20747, USA
**Mason, Marlyn** — Actress, Singer
27 Glen Oak Court, Medford OR 97504, USA
**Mason, Marsha** — Actress
1444 S Saint Francis Dr, #A, Santa Fe NM 87505, USA
**Mason, Michael P (Mike)** — Baseball Player
2711 Piper Ridge Lane, Excelsior MN 55331, USA
**Mason, Mila** — Singer
Fat City Artists, 1906 Chet Atkins Place, #502, Nashville TN 37212 USA
**Mason, Molly** — Fiddler (Blue Rose, Mammals)
Mike Greene Assoc, 339 E Liberty St, #220, Ann Arbor MI 48104, USA
**Mason, Monica** — Ballerina, Ballet Director
Royal Opera House, Convent Garden, Bow St, London WC2, England
**Mason, Nick** — Drummer (Pink Floyd)
One Fifteen, Globe House, Middle Lane Mews, London N8 8PN, England
**Mason, Roger L** — Baseball Player
322 Park St, Bellaire MI 49615, USA
**Mason, Sally** — Educator
University of Iowa, President's Office, Iowa City IA 52242, USA
**Mason, Thomas C (Tommy)** — Football Player
240 S Orange Acres Dr, Anaheim CA 92807, USA
**Mason, Tom** — Actor
Hartig-Hilepo Agency, 54 W 21st St, #610, New York NY 10010 USA
**Mason, Valerie Denise** — Model
Playboy Promotions, 2706 Media Center Dr, Los Angeles CA 90065 USA
**Mason, Vince** — Rap Artist (De La Soul)
Richard Walters, PO Box 2789, Toluca Lake CA 91610 USA
**Masopust, Josef** — Soccer Player
Koulova 11, 16000 Prague 6, Czech Republic
**Masri, Tahir Nashat al-** — Prime Minister, Jordan
PO Box 5550, Amman 11183, Jordan
**Mass, Chris** — Writer, Producer, Actor
Untitled Entertainment, 350 S Beverly Dr, #200, Beverly Hills CA 90212 USA
**Mass, Wayne** — Football Player
71 Eagle View, Durango CO 81303, USA
**Massa, Felipe** — Auto Racing Driver
Caixa Postal 19091, Sao Paulo SP 04505 970, Brazil
**Massard, Didier** — Photographer
Julie Saul Gallery, 535 W 22nd St, #6F, New York NY 10011, USA
**Massari, Lea** — Actress
Viale Parioli 59, 00197 Rome, Italy
**Massenburg, Tony A** — Basketball Player
1817 Brentridge St, Vienna VA 22182, USA
**Massenburg, Walter B** — Navy Admiral
Commander, Naval Air Systems Command, Patuxent River MD 20670 USA
**Masset, Andrew** — Actor
People Store Talent Agency, 645 Lambert Dr, Atlanta GA 30324, USA
**Masset, Nicholas A (Nick)** — Baseball Player
14575 W Mountain View Blvd, #11107, Surprise AZ 85374, USA
**Massevitch, Alla G** — Astronomer
6 Pushkurev Per, #4, 103045 Moscow, Russia
**Massey, Chandler** — Actor
Ferrantino Entertainment, 139 S Beverly Dr, #312, Beverly Hills CA 90212, USA
**Massey, Debbie** — Golfer
PO Box 116, Cheboygan MI 49721, USA
**Massey, Kent** — Yachtsman
4085 Foothill Road, Carpinteria CA 93013, USA
**Massey, Robert L** — Football Player
9617 Worley Dr, Charlotte NC 28215, USA
**Massey, Walter E** — Educator, Physicist, Financier
Bank of America Corp, 100 N Tryon St, #220, Charlotte NC 28202, USA
**Massie, Robert K** — Writer
52 W Clinton Ave, Irvington NY 10533, USA
**Massimino, Michael J** — Astronaut
15814 Elk Park Lane, Houston TX 77062, USA
**Massimino, Rolland V (Rollie)** — Basketball Coach
18578 SE Ferland Court, Jupiter FL 33469, USA
**Massimov, Karim K** — Prime Minister, Kazakhstan
Dom Pravieelstva, Plaza im VI Lenina, 148008 Astana, Kazakhstan
**Massof, Robert W** — Inventor (Seeing Eye Apparatus)
Wilmer Ophthalmological Institute, 550 N Broadway, #600, Baltimore MD 21205, USA
**Massoglia, Chris** — Actor
Zero Gravity Mgmt, 1531 14th St, Santa Monica CA 90404, USA
**Massu, Nicolas A** — Tennis Player
Association of Tennis Professionals, 200 Tournament Road, Ponte Vedra Beach FL 32082 USA
**Mast, Richard K (Rick)** — Auto Racing Driver
390 E Midland Trail, Lexington VA 24450, USA
**Masta Killa** — Rap Artist (Wu-Tang Clan)
A&M Entertainment, 13280 NE Freeway, #F328, Houston TX 77040, USA
**Mastalli, Chiara** — Actress
Agenzie Fabrizia Mancuso, Piazza Benedetto Cairoli 6, 00186 Rome, Italy
**Master P** — Rap Artist, Actor, Producer
Silverstone Entertainment USA, 10 Universal City Plaza, #2400, Universal City CA 91608, USA

**Masters, Blake**  Writer, Producer, Director
Brant Rose Agency, 6671 Sunset Blvd, #1584B, Los Angeles CA 90028, USA
**Masters, William J (Billy)**  Football Player
501 SW Silver Spur Circle, Lees Summit MO 64081, USA
**Masterson, Chase**  Actress
Masterson Entertainment, 12400 Ventura Blvd, #1200, Studio City CA 91604, USA
**Masterson, Danny**  Actor
Masterson Mgmt, 1566 Hillcrest Ave, Glendale CA 91202, USA
**Masterson, Mary Stuart**  Actress
Don Buchwald, 10 E 44th St, New York NY 10017 USA
**Masterson, Peter**  Writer, Director, Producer
1165 5th Ave, #15A, New York NY 10029, USA
**Masterson, Valerie**  Opera Singer
Music International, 13 Ardilaun Road, London N5 2QR, England
**Maston, Le'Shai E**  Football Player
7856 Overridge Dr, Dallas TX 75232, USA
**Mastracchio, Richard A (Rick)**  Astronaut
1910 Hillside Oak Lane, Houston TX 77062, USA
**Mastrangelo, Carlo**  Singer (Dion & the Belmonts)
Paramount Entertainment, PO Box 12, Far Hills NJ 07931 USA
**Mastrantonio, Mary Elizabeth**  Actress, Singer
Lou Coulson Assoc, 37 Berwick St, London W1V 8RS, England
**Mastrogiacomo, Gina**  Actress
Pakula/King, 9229 W Sunset Blvd, #315, West Hollywood CA 90069 USA
**Mastroianni, Armand**  Director
Creative Artists Agency, 2000 Ave of Stars, #100, Los Angeles CA 90067 USA
**Mastroianni, Chiara**  Actress
Zelig Films, 57 Rue Reaumur, 75002 Paris, France
**Masui, Yoshio**  Zoologist
32 Overton Crescent, Don Mills, North York ON M3B 2V2, Canada
**Masur, Kurt**  Conductor
Masur Music, Ansonia, 790 Riverside Dr, #6N, New York NY 10032, USA
**Masur, Richard**  Actor
Susan Smith, 1344 N Wetherly Dr, Los Angeles CA 90069 USA
**Masvidal, Paul A**  Singer, Guitarist (Cynic, Aeon Spoke)
Season of Mist Records, 111 Route de Valentinell, 13011 Marseille, France
**Mata, Victor J**  Baseball Player
New York Yankees, Yankee Stadium, E 161st St & River Ave, Bronx NY 10451 USA
**Matalin, Mary**  Political Consultant
325 Fishers Road, Maureltown VA 22644, USA
**Matalon, J Rolando (Roly)**  Religious Leader, Rabbi
Congregation B'nai Jeshurun, 2109 Broadway, #2034, New York NY 10023, USA
**Matane, Paulius N**  Governor General, Papua New Guinea
Governor General's Office, PO Box 79, Port Moresby 121, Papua New Guinea
**Matarazzo, Heather**  Actress
Don Buchwald, 10 E 44th St, New York NY 10017 USA
**Matarazzo, Leonard (Len)**  Baseball Player
2715 Carlisle St, New Castle. PA 16105, USA
**Mataskelekele, Kalkot**  President, Vanuata; Judge
President's Office, Port Vila, Vanuatu
**Matchefts, John**  Ice Hockey Player
2415 Chelton Road, Colorado Springs CO 80909, USA
**Matchett, Kari**  Actress
Paradigm Agency, 360 N Crescent Dr, North Building, Beverly Hills CA 90210 USA
**Matchick, J Thomas (Tom)**  Baseball Player
7700 Pillod Road, Holland OH 43528, USA
**Mateparae, Jeremiah (Jerry)**  Governor General, New Zealand
Governor General's Office, Government House, Private Bag 39995, Wellington 5045, New Zealand
**Matheny, Eric**  Actor
Don Buchwald, 6500 Wilshire Blvd, #2200, Los Angeles CA 90048 USA
**Matheny, Logan**  Drummer (Roman Candle)
Russell Carter Artist Mgmt, 567 Ralph Magill Blvd, Atlanta GA 30312 USA
**Matheny, Skip**  Singer, Guitarist (Roman Candle)
Russell Carter Artist Mgmt, 567 Ralph Magill Blvd, Atlanta GA 30312 USA
**Matheny, Timshel**  Organist (Roman Candle)
Russell Carter Artist Mgmt, 567 Ralph Magill Blvd, Atlanta GA 30312 USA
**Mather, John C**  Nobel Physics Laureate
3400 Rosemary Lane, Hyattsville MD 20782, USA
**Mathers, Jerry**  Actor
McInerney Business Mgmt, 26372 Calle Lucana, San Juan Capistrano CA 92675, USA
**Matheson, Diana**  Soccer Player
Canadian Soccer, Place Soccer Canada, 237 Metcalfe St, Ottawa ON K2P 1R2, Canada
**Matheson, Hans**  Actor
Lou Coulson Assoc, 37 Berwick St, London W1V 8RS, England
**Matheson, Tim**  Actor, Director
Generate Mgmt, 1545 26th St, #200, Santa Monica CA 90404, USA
**Mathew, Suleka (Sue)**  Actress
S D B Partners, 1801 Ave of Stars, #902, Los Angeles CA 90067 USA
**Mathews, F David**  Secretary, Health Education & Welfare
6050 Mad River Road, Dayton OH 45459, USA
**Mathews, Gregory I (Greg)**  Baseball Player
11721 Old Ballas Road, #107, Saint Louis MO 63141, USA
**Mathews, Harlan**  Senator, TN
420 Hunt Club Road, Nashville TN 37221, USA
**Mathews, Jessica T**  Foundation Executive
Carnegie Int'l Peace Endowment, 1779 Massachusetts NW, Washington DC 20036, USA
**Mathews, Raymond D (Ray)**  Football Player
PO Box 108, Harrisville PA 16038, USA
**Mathews, Timothy J (T J)**  Baseball Player
839 Autumn Rise Lane, Columbia IL 62236, USA
**Mathieson, John**  Cinematographer
Independent Talent Group, 40 Whitfield St, London W1T 2RH, England
**Mathieu, Marquis**  Ice Hockey Player
113 W Lake Shore Dr, Hallandale FL 33009, USA
**Mathieu, Philip**  Concert Guitarist
Lindy S Martin Mgmt, 1007 Lakewater Dr, Henrico VA 23229, USA

**Mathilde** — Queen, Belgium
Koninklijk Palace, Rue de Brederode, 1000 Brussels, Belgium
**Mathis, Rashean** — Football Player
26200 Marsh Landing Parkway, Ponte Vedra FL 32082, USA
**Mathis, Buster, Jr** — Boxer
4409 Carol Ave SW, Wyoming MI 49519, USA
**Mathis, Chester A** — Radiologist
University of Pittsburgh Medical Center, P E T Facility, Radiology Dept, Pittsburgh PA 15213, USA
**Mathis, Clint** — Soccer Player
Los Angeles Galaxy, Home Depot Center, 18400 Avalon Blvd, Carson CA 90746 USA
**Mathis, Evan B** — Football Player
11938 N 113th Place, Scottsdale AZ 85259, USA
**Mathis, Jeffrey S (Jeff)** — Baseball Player
4420 Spring Valley Dr, Marianna FL 32448, USA
**Mathis, Johnny** — Singer
1469 Stebbins Terrace, Los Angeles CA 90069, USA
**Mathis, Samantha** — Actress
Paradigm Agency, 360 N Crescent Dr, North Building, Beverly Hills CA 90210 USA
**Mathis, Terance** — Football Player
3415 Camellia Lane, Suwanee GA 30024, USA
**Mathis-Eddy, Darlene** — Writer
1409 W Cardinal St, Muncie IN 47303, USA
**Mathison, Cameron** — Actor
Innovative Artists, 1505 10th St, Santa Monica CA 90401 USA
**Matisi, John R** — Baseball Player
98-1616 Hoolauae St, Aiea HI 96701, USA
**Matisyahu** — Singer
Agency Group Ltd, 142 W 57th St, #600, New York NY 10019 USA
**Matkevich, Mark** — Actor
Talent Works, 3500 W Olive Ave, #1400, Burbank CA 91505 USA
**Matlack, Jonathan T (Jon)** — Baseball Player
2495 Sawdust Road, #1101, Spring TX 77380, USA
**Matlin, Marlee** — Actress
Solo Productions, 8205 Santa Monica Blvd, #1279, West Hollywood CA 90046, USA
**Matlock, Glen** — Bassist (Sex Pistols)
Bruce Pilato Mgmt, PO Box 17775, Rochester NY 14617, USA
**Matlock, Jack F, Jr** — Diplomat
940 Princeton-Kingston Road, Princeton NJ 08540, USA
**Matlock, John J** — Football Player
127 Seagrape Dr, #102, Jupiter FL 33458, USA
**Matola, Sharon** — Zoo Director, Conservationist
Belize Zoo & Tropical Education Center, PO Box 1787, Belize City, Belize
**Matorin, Vladimir A** — Opera Singer
Ulansky Per 21, Korp 1, #53, 103045 Moscow, Russia
**Matos, Eddie** — Actor
Schumacher Mgmt, 10323 Santa Monica Blvd, #101, Los Angeles CA 90024, USA
**Matos, Elisabete** — Opera Singer
Opera et Concert, 37 Rue de la Chaussee d'Antin, 75009 Paris, France
**Matranga, Jonah** — Singer, Songwriter
Agency Group Ltd, 142 W 57th St, #600, New York NY 10019 USA
**Matronic, Ana** — Singer (Scissors Sisters), Songwriter
Girlie Action, 59 W 19th St, #4B, New York NY 10011 USA
**Matshikiza, Pumeza** — Opera Singer
I M G Artists, Hogarth Business Park, Chiswick, London W4 2TH, England
**Matson, J Randel (Randy)** — Track Athlete
1002 Park Place, College Station TX 77840, USA
**Matsos, Emil G (Archie)** — Football Player
1410 Coventry Close St, East Lansing MI 48823, USA
**Matsui, Hideki** — Baseball Player
119 W 72nd St, #306, New York NY 10023, USA
**Matsui, Keiko** — Jazz Pianist
M P I Talent Agency, 9255 Sunset Blvd, #407, West Hollywood CA 90069, USA
**Matsuzaka, Daisuke** — Baseball Player
Cleveland Indians, Jacobs Field, 2401 Ontario St, Cleveland OH 44115 USA
**Matsuzaki, Yuki** — Actor
Williams-Michael Relations, 3940 Laurel Canyon, #785, Studio City CA 91604, USA
**Matt, Mike** — Rodeo Rider
111 S 24th St W, #9125, Billings MT 59102, USA
**Matta, Thad** — Basketball Coach
Ohio State University, Athletic Dept, Columbus OH 43210, USA
**Matte, Thomas R (Tom)** — Football Player
11309 Old Carriage Road, Glen Arm MD 21057, USA
**Mattea, Kathy** — Singer, Guitarist
International Music Network, 278 Main St, #400, Gloucester MA 01930 USA
**Mattei, Frank** — Singer (Danny & the Juniors)
Joe Taylor Mgmt, PO Box 1017, Blackwood NJ 08012, USA
**Mattek-Sands, Bethany** — Tennis Player
1146 W MacKenzie Dr, Phoenix AZ 85013, USA
**Mattes, Eva** — Actress
Agentur Carola Studlar, Agnesstr 47, 80798 Munich, Germany
**Mattes, Ronald A (Ron)** — Football Player
1718 Moreland Wood Trail NW, Concord NC 28027, USA
**Matteson, John** — Writer
W W Norton, 500 5th Ave, #600, New York NY 10110 USA
**Matteson, Troy** — Golfer
6518 Old Shadburn Ferry Road, Buford GA 30518, USA
**Matthes, Roland** — Swimmer
Luitpoldstr 35A, 97828 Marktheidenfeld, Germany
**Matthes, Ulrich** — Actor
Bleibtreustr 8, 10623 Berlin, Germany
**Matthew, Catriona I** — Golfer
I M G, Pier House, Strand-on-Green, Chiswick, London W4 3NN, England
**Matthews, Alvin L (Al)** — Football Player
19451 Diablo Dr, Pflugerville TX 78660, USA
**Matthews, Bruce R** — Football Player
1565 Lost Hollow Dr, Brentwood TN 37027, USA

Matthews, Casey C — Football Player
Philadelphia Eagles, 1 Novacare Way, Philadelphia PA 19145 USA
Matthews, Cerys — Singer (Catatonia)
Rough Trade Mgmt, 66 Golborne Road, London W10 5PS, England
Matthews, Chris — Commentator
9 E Kirke St, Chevy Chase MD 20815, USA
Matthews, Dakin — Actor
Geddes Agency, 8430 Santa Monica Blvd, #201, West Hollywood CA 90069 USA
Matthews, Dave — Singer, Guitarist (Dave Matthews Band)
Red Light Mgmt, PO Box 1467, Charlottesville VA 22902, USA
Matthews, DeLane — Actress
Don Buchwald, 6500 Wilshire Blvd, #2200, Los Angeles CA 90048 USA
Matthews, Eric — Singer, Songwriter
Chords of Fame, 3030 Glenmanor Place, Los Angeles CA 90039, USA
Matthews, Francis — Actor
Scott Marshall Partners, 15 Little Portland, #200, London W1W 8BW, England
Matthews, Gary N, Jr — Baseball Player
Cincinnati Reds, Great American Ball Park, 100 Main St, Cincinnati OH 45202 USA
Matthews, Gary N, Sr — Baseball Player
1542 W Jackson Blvd, Chicago IL 60607, USA
Matthews, Ian — Singer, Guitarist
Geoffrey Blumenauer Artists, PO Box 343, Burbank CA 91503 USA
Matthews, Keith — Astronomer
California Institute of Technology, Astronomy Dept, Pasadena CA 91125, USA
Matthews, Liesel — Actress
Creative Artists Agency, 2000 Ave of Stars, #100, Los Angeles CA 90067 USA
Matthews, Lisa — Model, Actress
Playboy Promotions, 2706 Media Center Dr, Los Angeles CA 90065 USA
Matthews, Mike — Baseball Player
14326 Bakerwood Place, Haymarket VA 20169, USA
Matthews, Pat Stanley — Actress
210 Stanton St, Walla Walla WA 99362, USA
Matthews, Robert C O — Economist
Clare College, Economics Dept, Cambridge CB2 1TL, England
Matthews, Sally — Opera Singer
Maxine Robertson Mgmt, 14 Forge Dr, Claygate KT1O 0HR, England
Matthews, Shane — Football Player
848 NW 136th St, Agoura Hills CA 91301, USA
Matthews, Vincent (Vince) — Track Athlete
6755 193rd Lane, Fresh Meadows NY 11365, USA
Matthews, W Clay, III — Football Player
Green Bay Packers, 1265 Lombardi Ave, Green Bay WI 54304 USA
Matthews, W Clay, Jr — Football Player
6068 Canterbury Dr, Agoura Hills CA 91301, USA
Matthies, Nina — Volleyball Player, Coach
Pepperdine University, Athletic Dept, Malibu CA 90265, USA
Matthiesen, Mads — Director, Writer
Paradigm Agency, 360 N Crescent Dr, North Building, Beverly Hills CA 90210 USA
Matthiessen, Peter — Writer, Naturalist
527 Bridge Lane, Sagaponack NY 11962, USA
Mattiace, Len — Golfer
12802 Hunt Club Road N, Jacksonville FL 32224, USA
Mattila, Karita M — Opera Singer
45B Croxley Road, London W9 3HJ, England
Mattingly, Ashley — Model
Playboy Promotions, 2706 Media Center Dr, Los Angeles CA 90065 USA
Mattingly, Donald A (Don) — Baseball Player, Manager
7601 Newburgh Road, Evansville IN 47715, USA
Mattingly, Mack F — Senator, GA; Diplomat
4315 10th St, East Beach, Saint Simons Island GA 31522, USA
Mattingly, Thomas K, II — Astronaut, Navy Admiral
Systems Planning & Analysis, 2001 N Beauregard St, Alexandria VA 22311, USA
Mattis, James N — Marine Corps General
Commander, Central Command, 7115 S Boundary, MacDill Air Force Base FL 33621 USA
Mattscherodt, Katrin — Speed Skater
Sportclub Berlin, Weissenseer Weg 53, 13053 Berlin, Germany
Mattson, Robin — Actress
Stan Kamens Mgmt, 7772 Torreyson Dr, Los Angeles CA 90046, USA
Matuszek, Leonard J (Len) — Baseball Player
10326 Deerfield Road, Cincinnati OH 45242, USA
Matvichuk, Richard — Ice Hockey Player
PO Box 96225, Southlake TX 76092, USA
Matz, Michael R — Equestrian, Thoroughbred Racing Trainer
2953 Hurlinham Dr, Wellington FL 33414, USA
Matzdorf, Pat — Track Athlete
1252 Bainbridge Dr, Naperville IL 60563, USA
Matzner, Jason — Director
Paradigm Agency, 360 N Crescent Dr, North Building, Beverly Hills CA 90210 USA
Mau, Bruce — Multimedia Designer
197 Spadina Ave, #501, Toronto ON M5T 2C8, Canada
Maualuga, Rey — Football Player
Cincinnati Bengals, 1 Paul Brown Stadium, Cincinnati OH 45202 USA
Mauboy, Jessica — Actress
R G M Artist, 64-76 Kippax St, #202, Surry Hills NSW 2010, Australia
Mauceri, John — Conductor
I C M Artists, 40 W 57th St, #1800, New York NY 10019 USA
Mauck, Carl F — Football Player
2129 Winthrop Hill Road, Argyle TX 76226, USA
Maudsley, Tony — Actor
United Agents, 12-26 Lexington St, London W1F 0LE, England
Mauer, Joseph P (Joe) — Baseball Player
671 Lexington Parkway N, Saint Paul MN 55104, USA
Maultsby, Nancy — Opera Singer
I M G Artists, Hogarth Business Park, Chiswick, London W4 2TH, England
Mauney, Carl V — Navy Admiral
Deputy Commander, US Strategic Command, Offutt Air Force Base NE 68113, USA

# M

**Maupin, Armistead J, Jr** — Writer
Literary Bent, PO Box 4109990, #528, San Francisco CA 94141, USA
**Maura, Carmen** — Actress
Ramon Pilaces, C/Hortaleza 20, #1 Izqda, 28004 Madrid, Spain
**Maurel, Julien** — Actor
J F P M, 11 Rue Chanez, 75781 Paris Cedex 16, France
**Maurer, Andrew L (Andy)** — Football Player
30 Perrydale Ave, Medford OR 97501, USA
**Maurer, Ingo** — Inventor, Lighting Designer
Team Ingo Maurer, Kaiserstr 47, 80801 Munich, Germany
**Maurer, Robert D** — Inventor (Silica Optical Waveguide)
2572 W 28th Ave, Eugene OR 97405, USA
**Maurer, Robert J (Rob)** — Baseball Player
3114 E Gum St, Evansville IN 47714, USA
**Mauresmo, Amelie** — Tennis Player
Athleteline, 2 Rue du Chemin Vert, 92110 Clichy, France
**Maurice, Paul** — Ice Hockey Coach
Carolina Hurricanes, R B C Center, 1400 Edwards Mills Road, Raleigh NC 27607 USA
**Mauriello, Tammy** — Boxer
1148 E 81st St, Brooklyn NY 11236, USA
**Maurier, Claire** — Actress
Anne Alvares Correa, 34 Rue Jouffroy d'Abbans, 75017 Paris, France
**Maurstad, Toralv** — Director, Actor
Thorleif, Hangsvei 20, 0712 Voksenkollen, Norway
**Mauser, Timothy E (Tim)** — Baseball Player
114 Shadow Creek Lane, Aledo TX 76008, USA
**Mauz, Henry H (Hank), Jr** — Navy Admiral
1608 Viscaine Road, Pebble Beach CA 93953, USA
**Maven, Max** — Illusionist
PO Box 1298, La Mesa CA 91944, USA
**Mawae, Kevin J** — Football Player, Labor Leader
19414 Old Perkins Road E, Baton Rouge LA 70810, USA
**Mawby, Russell G** — Foundation Executive
W K Kellogg Foundation, 1 Michigan Ave E, Battle Creek MI 49017, USA
**Max, Kevin** — Singer, Songwriter
Pitch Music, PO Box 235185, Encinitas CA 92023, USA
**Max, Peter** — Artist
118 Riverside Dr, New York NY 10024, USA
**Maxcy, D Brian** — Baseball Player
982 Cobble Creek Dr, Birmingham AL 35226, USA
**Maxi Jazz** — Rap Artist (Faithless)
Helter Skelter, 347-353 Chiswick High Road, London W4 4HS, England
**Maxie, Brett D** — Football Player
1702 Richbourg Park Dr, Brentwood TN 37027, USA
**Maximova, Elena** — Opera Singer
I M G Artists, Hogarth Business Park, Chiswick, London W4 2TH, England
**Maxsom, Alvin E** — Football Player
3215 S Danube St, Aurora CO 80013, USA
**Maxvill, C Dalian (Dal)** — Baseball Player
1115 Eagle Creek Road, Chesterfield MO 63005, USA
**Maxwell** — Singer
W M E Entertainment, 9601 Wilshire Blvd, #300, Beverly Hills CA 90210 USA
**Maxwell, Arthur E** — Oceanographer
8200 Neely Dr, #260, Austin TX 78759, USA
**Maxwell, Brad** — Ice Hockey Player
27285 Natchez Ave, Elko MN 55020, USA
**Maxwell, Cedric B (Cornbread)** — Basketball Player
151 Tremont St, #25H, Boston MA 02111, USA
**Maxwell, Charles R (Charlie)** — Baseball Player
730 Mapleview Ave, Paw Paw MI 49079, USA
**Maxwell, Kevin F H** — Publisher
Moulsford Manor, Moulsford, Oxfordshire OX10 9HO, England
**Maxwell, Robert D** — WW II Army Hero (CMH)
1001 SE 15th St, #44, Bend OR 97702, USA
**Maxwell, Ronald F (Ron)** — Director, Writer
Weissmann Wolff Bergman, 9665 Wilshire Blvd, #900, Beverly Hills CA 90212, USA
**Maxwell, Thomas M (Tommy)** — Football Player
1634 Rockview Dr, Granbury TX 76049, USA
**Maxwell, Vernon** — Basketball Player
2601 NW 23rd Blvd, #170, Gainesville FL 32605, USA
**Maxwell, Vernon L** — Football Player
1955 E Citation Lane, Tempe AZ 85284, USA
**May of Oxford, Robert M M** — Biologist
Royal Society, 6 Carlton House Terrace, London SW1Y 5AG, England
**May, Antoinette** — Writer
William Morrow Publishers, 1350 Ave of Americas, New York NY 10019 USA
**May, Arthur** — Architect
Kohn Pedersen Fox Assoc, 111 W 57th St, #300, New York NY 10019, USA
**May, B Deems** — Football Player
3922 Ayscough Road, Charlotte NC 28211, USA
**May, Bob** — Golfer
420 Grand Augusta Lane, Las Vegas NV 89144, USA
**May, Brad** — Ice Hockey Player
9167 E Mountain Spring Road, Scottsdale AZ 85255, USA
**May, Brian** — Guitarist (Queen), Songwriter
Old Bakehouse, 16A High St, Barnes, London SW13, England
**May, Darrell K** — Baseball Player
747 Minthorne Road, Rogue River OR 97537, USA
**May, Deborah** — Actress
Artists Agency, 9430 Olympic Blvd, Beverly Hills CA 90212 USA
**May, Derrick B** — Baseball Player
2 Jaymar Road, Newark DE 19702, USA
**May, Donald J (Don)** — Basketball Player
1128 Colwick Dr, Dayton OH 45420, USA
**May, Elaine** — Actress, Comedienne, Director
146 Central Park West, #5D, New York NY 10023, USA

**Maupin - May**

**May, Imelda** — Singer, Guitarist, Songwriter
Neil O'Brien Entertainment, 26 Eastcastle St, #300, London W1W 8DQ, England
**May, James** — Actor
Arlington Enterprises, 1-3 Charlotte St, London W1T 1RD, England
**May, Lee A** — Baseball Player
2200 Manatee Ave W, Bradenton FL 34205, USA
**May, Mark E** — Football Player, Sportscaster
3557 E Minton St, Mesa AZ 85213, USA
**May, Mathilda** — Actress
Voyez Mon Agent, 20 Ave Rapp, 75007 Paris, France
**May, Milton S (Milt)** — Baseball Player
2200 Manatee Ave W, Bradenton FL 34205, USA
**May, Phillip (Phil)** — Singer (Pretty Things)
Talent Consultants International, 105 Shad Row, #B, Piermont NY 10968 USA
**May, Ralphie** — Actor, Comedian, Producer
United Talent Agency, U T A Plaza, 9336 Civic Center Dr, Beverly Hills CA 90210 USA
**May, Ray** — Football Player
1921 Wellington Road, Los Angeles CA 90016, USA
**May, Richard H** — WW II Navy Air Hero
3732 E Pasadena Ave, Phoenix AZ 85018, USA
**May, Rudolph (Rudy), Jr** — Baseball Player
8090 N Augusta St, Fresno CA 93720, USA
**May, Scott G** — Basketball Player
2001 E Hillside Dr, Bloomington IN 47401, USA
**May, Torsten** — Boxer
Frankfurt Boxing Ring, Kieler Str 9, 15234 Frankfurt/Oder, Germany
**Mayall, John** — Singer, Keyboardist, Composer
30844 Grenoble Court, Westlake Village CA 91362, USA
**Mayall, Rik** — Actor, Comedian
Brunskill Mgmt, 169 Queen's Gate, London SW7 5HE, England
**Mayasich, John E** — Ice Hockey Player
77 E Missouri Ave Unit 45, Phoenix AZ 85012, USA
**Maybank, Anthuan** — Track Athlete
171 N Porter St, Elgin IL 60120, USA
**Mayberry, E Anthony (Tony)** — Football Player
15704 Cochester Road, Tampa FL 33647, USA
**Mayberry, Jermane T** — Football Player
2208 Court del Rey, Round Rock TX 78681, USA
**Mayberry, John C** — Baseball Player
11115 W 121st Terrace, Overland Park KS 66213, USA
**Mayberry, O Lee** — Basketball Player
4115 E 36th St N, Tulsa OK 74115, USA
**Maybin, Cameron K** — Baseball Player
85 Brompton Road, Arden NC 28704, USA
**Maybury, John** — Director
Independent Talent Group, 40 Whitfield St, London W1T 2RH, England
**Mayer H, Jurgen** — Architect
Bleibtreystr 54, 10623 Berlin, Germany
**Mayer, Christian** — Alpine Skier
Siedlerweg 18, 9584 Finkelstein, Austria
**Mayer, Edwin D (Ed)** — Baseball Player
440 Oakdale Ave, Corte Madera CA 94925, USA
**Mayer, Gene** — Tennis Player
115 South St, Glenn Dale MD 20769, USA
**Mayer, H Robert** — Judge
US Court of Appeals, 717 Madison Place NW, Washington DC 20439, USA
**Mayer, John** — Singer, Songwriter
Mick Mgmt, 35 Washington St, Brooklyn NY 11201, USA
**Mayer, Joseph E** — Chemical Physicist
2345 Via Siena, La Jolla CA 92037, USA
**Mayer, Marissa** — Businesswoman
Yahoo Inc, 701 1st Ave, Sunnyvale CA 94089, USA
**Mayer, Michael** — Director
Creative Artists Agency, 2000 Ave of Stars, #100, Los Angeles CA 90067 USA
**Mayer, Travis** — Freestyle Skier
37050 Williams St, Steamboat Springs CO 80487, USA
**Mayers, Jamal** — Ice Hockey Player
9 Terrace Gardens, Saint Louis MO 63131, USA
**Mayes, Rueben** — Football Player
2953 Lord Byron Place, Eugene OR 97408, USA
**Mayfair, Billy** — Golfer
PO Box 25490, Scottsdale AZ 85255, USA
**Mayfield, Jeremy A** — Auto Racing Driver
Mayfield Motorsports, 2220 Highway 49 N, Harrisburg NC 28075, USA
**Mayfield, Les** — Director, Producer
Creative Artists Agency, 2000 Ave of Stars, #100, Los Angeles CA 90067 USA
**Mayhew of Twysden, Patrick B B** — Government Official, England
House of Lords, Westminster, London SW1A 0PW, England
**Mayhew, Lauren C** — Singer, Actress
Abrams Artists, 9200 W Sunset Blvd, #1125, West Hollywood CA 90069 USA
**Mayhew, Martin** — Football Player
4035 Sonnet Dr, Tallahassee FL 32303, USA
**Mayle, Peter** — Writer
Knopf Publishers, 201 E 50th St, New York NY 10022, USA
**Maynard, Bradley A (Brad)** — Football Player
4915 Sage Lane, Long Grove IL 60047, USA
**Maynard, Mimi** — Actress
Schiowitz Connor, 1680 N Vine St, #1016, Los Angeles CA 90028 USA
**Mayne, Brent D** — Baseball Player
1863 Parkglen Circle, Costa Mesa CA 92627, USA
**Mayne, D Roger** — Photographer
Colway Manor, Colway Lane, Lyme Regis, Dorset DT7 3HD, England
**Mayne, Kenny** — Sportscaster
ESPN-TV, ESPN Plaza, 935 Middle St, Bristol CT 06010 USA
**Mayne, Thomas** — Pritzker Architectual Laureate
Morphosis Architects, 3444 Wesley St, Culver City CA 90232, USA

**M**

May - Mayne

**Maynor, Asa** — Actress
PO Box 1469, Beverly Hills CA 90213, USA
**Maynor, Eric** — Basketball Player
Washington Wizards, M C I Centre, 601 F St NW, Washington DC 20004 USA
**Maynor, Stephanie** — Golfer
5205 Bordeaux Cove, Ellicott City MD 21043, USA
**Mayo, John L (Jackie)** — Baseball Player
450 Boardman Poland Road, Youngstown OH 44512, USA
**Mayo, O J** — Basketball Player
3576 Golf Walk Circle, Memphis TN 38125, USA
**Mayock, Michael F (Mike)** — Sportscaster
607 Georges Lane, Ardmore PA 19003, USA
**Mayopoulos, Timothy J** — Businessman, Government Official
Federal National Mortgage Association, 3900 Wisconsin Ave NW, Washington DC 20016, USA
**Mayor Zaragoza, Federico** — Government Official, Spain
Ma Caribe 15, Interland, Majadahonda, 28220 Madrid, Spain
**Mayor, Michel G E** — Astronomer
University of Geneva, Geneva Observatory, 1211 Geneva 4, Switzerland
**Mayotte, Timothy S (Tim)** — Tennis Player
266 W 115th St, #4A, New York NY 10026, USA
**Mayron, Melanie** — Actress, Director
1435 N Ogden Dr, Los Angeles CA 90046, USA
**Mays, Alvoid** — Football Player
3903 Cape Vista Dr, Bradenton FL 34209, USA
**Mays, Daniel** — Actor
Curtis Brown Group, 28-29 Haymarket St, #500, London SW1Y 4SP, England
**Mays, Jayma** — Actress
United Talent Agency, U T A Plaza, 9336 Civic Center Dr, Beverly Hills CA 90210 USA
**Mays, Joseph E (Joe)** — Baseball Player
10314 Riverbank Terrace, Bradenton FL 34212, USA
**Mays, Lyle** — Jazz Pianist
Ted Kurland, 173 Brighton Ave, Boston MA 02134 USA
**Mays, Melinda** — Model
2221 Peachtree Road NE, #D440, Atlanta GA 30309, USA
**Mays, Willie H** — Baseball Player
51 Mount Vernon Lane, Atherton CA 94027, USA
**May-Treanor, Misty** — Volleyball Player
460 NW 115th Way, Coral Springs FL 33071, USA
**Mayweather, Floyd, Jr** — Boxer
4720 Laguna Vista St, Las Vegas NV 89147, USA
**Mayweather, Roger** — Boxer, Trainer
2784 Trotwood Lane, Las Vegas NV 89108, USA
**Mazach, John J** — Navy Admiral
1137 Quail Roost Court, Virginia Beach VA 23451, USA
**Mazar, Debi** — Actress
Framework Entertainment, 9057 Nemo St, #C, West Hollywood CA 90069 USA
**Mazelle, Kym** — Singer
Tony Denton Promotions, Charter House, 157-159 High St, London N14 6BP, England
**Mazer, Dan** — Writer
United Agents, 12-26 Lexington St, London W1F 0LE, England
**Mazeroski, William S (Bill)** — Baseball Player
281 Walton Tea Room Road, Greensburg PA 15601, USA
**Mazor, Stanley (Stan)** — Inventor (Microprocessor)
F T I/Teklicon, 3031 Tisch Way, San Jose CA 95128, USA
**Mazur, Jay J** — Labor Leader
Industrial Textile Employees Needletrades, 1710 Broadway, New York NY 10019, USA
**Mazur, Monet** — Actress
Innovative Artists, 1505 10th St, Santa Monica CA 90401 USA
**Mazurok, Yuri A** — Opera Singer
Bolshoi State Theater, Teatralnaya Pl 1, 103009 Moscow, Russia
**Mazursky, Paul** — Director
614 26th St, Santa Monica CA 90402, USA
**Mazza, Marc** — Actor
S N Bellefaye, 30 Rue Saint Marc, 75002 Paris, France
**Mazza, Valeria** — Model
Riccardo Ga, 8/10 Via Revere, 20123 Milan, Italy
**Mazzante, Kelly** — Basketball Player
New York Liberty, Madison Square Garden, 2 Penn Plaza, New York NY 10121 USA
**Mazzanti, Jerry E** — Football Player
1712 S Lakeshore Dr, Lake Village AR 71653, USA
**Mazzara, Glen** — Producer, Writer
Creative Artists Agency, 2000 Ave of Stars, #100, Los Angeles CA 90067 USA
**Mazzello, Joseph** — Actor
J J M Productions, 9560 Wilshire Blvd, #500, Beverly Hills CA 90212, USA
**Mazzie, Marin** — Actress, Singer
Mitchell K Stubbs Assoc, 8695 W Washington Blvd, #204, Culver City CA 90232 USA
**Mazzilli, Lee L** — Baseball Player, Manager
67 Stonehedge Dr S, Greenwich CT 06831, USA
**Mazzo, Kay** — Ballerina
School of American Ballet, 70 Lincoln Center Plaza, New York NY 10012, USA
**Mazzucco, Raphael** — Photographer
Micon, 270 W 17th St, #6D, New York NY 10011, USA
**Mbah a Moute, Luc** — Basketball Player
Sacramento Kings, Arco Arena, 1 Sports Parkway, Sacramento CA 95834 USA
**Mbatha-Raw, Gugu** — Actress
Curtis Brown Group, 28-29 Haymarket St, #500, London SW1Y 4SP, England
**Mbaye, Abdoul** — Prime Minister, Senegal
Prime Minister's Office, Ave Leopold Sedar Senghor, Dakar, Senegal
**Mbeki, Thabo M** — President, South Africa
Postal Box X1000, Pretoria 0001, South Africa
**Mbenga, D J** — Basketball Player
6112 Winton St, Dallas TX 75214, USA
**Mbete, Baleka M** — President, South Africa
PO Box 15, Cape Town, South Africa
**M'Bow, Amadou-Mahtar** — Government Official, Senegal
BP 5276, Dakar-Fann, Senegal

**MC Lyte** — Rap Artist
C E S D, 10635 Santa Monica Blvd, #130, Los Angeles CA 90025 USA
**McAdam, Gary** — Ice Hockey Player
34 Meadow Lane, Portland ME 04103, USA
**McAdams, Rachel** — Actress
Magnolia Entertainment, 9595 Wilshire Blvd, #601, Beverly Hills CA 90212, USA
**McAdoo, Robert A (Bob)** — Basketball Player, Coach
16710 SW 82nd Ave, Village of Palmetto Bay FL 33157, USA
**McAfee, Stephanie** — Writer
New American Library, 1633 Broadway, New York NY 10019 USA
**McAlear, Nancy** — Actress
Fountainhead Talent, 121 Davenport Road, Toronto ON M5R 1HZ, Canada
**McAlister, Christopher J (Chris)** — Football Player
8206 Pumpkin Hill Court, Pikesville MD 21208, USA
**McAlister, Dulumus J (Deuce)** — Football Player
2177 Doc Webb Road, Lena MS 39094, USA
**McAlpine, Christopher W (Chris)** — Ice Hockey Player
4390 Reiland Lane, Saint Paul MN 55126, USA
**McAlpine, Donald M** — Cinematographer
377 Placer Creek Lane, Henderson NV 89014, USA
**McAnally, Mac** — Singer, Songwriter
T K O Artist Mgmt, 2302 21st Ave S, #300, Nashville TN 37212, USA
**McAnally, Ron** — Thoroughbred Racing Trainer
18653 Paso Nuevo Dr, Tarzana CA 91356, USA
**McAndrew, James C (Jim)** — Baseball Player
17917 N 93rd St, Scottsdale AZ 85255, USA
**McAndrew, Nell** — Model
1 The Stabling, Barnet Lane, Elstree, Borehamwood WD6 3HJ, England
**McAnuff, Des** — Director
W M E Entertainment, 9601 Wilshire Blvd, #300, Beverly Hills CA 90210 USA
**McAnulty, Paul** — Baseball Player
921 Palomar Way, Oxnard CA 93033, USA
**McArdle, Aidan** — Actor
42 Agency, 8 Flitcroft St, London WC2H 8DL, England
**McArdle, Andrea** — Actress, Singer
37 Wall St, #23P, New York NY 10005, USA
**McArthur, Alex** — Actor
9443 Hillrose St, Sunland CA 91040, USA
**McArthur, Derek** — Photographer
73 Strathaven Road, Kirkmuirhill, Lanark ML11 9RW, Scotland
**McArthur, James D, Jr** — Navy Admiral
Commander, Network Warfare Command, 2465 Guadalcanal, Norfolk VA 23521, USA
**McArthur, John H** — Educator
8 Kettle Lane, Weston MA 2493, USA
**McArthur, K Megan** — Astronaut
N A S A, Johnson Space Center, 2101 NASA Road, Houston TX 77058 USA
**McArthur, William S (Bill), Jr** — Astronaut
2512 Mountain Falls Court, Friendswood TX 77546, USA
**McAslan, John R** — Architect
McAslan Partners, 202 Kensington Church St, London W8 4DP, England
**McAuliffe, Callan** — Actor
R G M Artist, 64-76 Kippax St, #202, Surry Hills NSW 2010, Australia
**McAuliffe, Dennis P** — Army General
9160 Belvoir Woods Parkway, Fort Belvoir VA 22060, USA
**McAuliffe, Richard J (Dick)** — Baseball Player
32 Worthington Dr, Farmington CT 06032, USA
**McAvoy, James** — Actor
United Agents, 12-26 Lexington St, London W1F 0LE, England
**McAvoy, Thomas J (Tom)** — Baseball Player
2 Clinton Court, Stillwater NY 12170, USA
**McBain, Andrew** — Ice Hockey Player
87 Balsam Ave, Toronto ON M4E 3B8, Canada
**McBain, Fiona** — Singer, Guitarist, Songwriter
High Road Touring, 751 Bridgeway, #200, Sausalito CA 94965 USA
**McBain, Nicko** — Drummer (Iron Maiden)
Sanctuary Music Mgmt, 82 Bishop's Bridge Road, London W2 6BB, England
**McBath, Michael S (Mike)** — Football Player
5044 Sailwind Circle, Orlando FL 32810, USA
**McBean, Alvin O (Al)** — Baseball Player
PO Box 4475, Saint Thomas VI 00801, USA
**McBee, Rives** — Golfer
1504 Canyon Oaks Dr, Irving TX 75061, USA
**McBeth, Marcus A** — Baseball Player
42052 W Sunland Dr, Maricopa AZ 85138, USA
**McBrayer, Jack** — Actor, Comedian
United Talent Agency, U T A Plaza, 9336 Civic Center Dr, Beverly Hills CA 90210 USA
**McBriar, Mat** — Football Player
4020 Buena Vista St, Dallas TX 75204, USA
**McBride, Arnold R (Bake)** — Baseball Player
4077 Reliant Circle, Owensboro KY 42301, USA
**McBride, Brian** — Soccer Player
Chicago Fire, 700 S Harlem Ave, Bridgeview IL 60455 USA
**McBride, Chi** — Actor
United Talent Agency, U T A Plaza, 9336 Civic Center Dr, Beverly Hills CA 90210 USA
**McBride, Christian** — Jazz Bassist
Ted Kurland, 173 Brighton Ave, Boston MA 02134 USA
**McBride, Daniel F (Danny)** — Actor, Comedian
Rough House, 1722 Whitley Ave, Los Angeles CA 90028, USA
**McBride, Jeff** — Illusionist
Innovative Artists, 1505 10th St, Santa Monica CA 90401 USA
**McBride, Joe** — Singer, Keyboardist
Universal Attractions, 135 W 26th St, #1200, New York NY 10001 USA
**McBride, Jon A** — Astronaut
Image Development Group, 1018 Kanawha Blvd, #901, Charleston WV 25301, USA
**McBride, Justin T** — Rodeo Rider
1714 Revard Ave, Pawhuska OK 74056, USA

**McBride, Kenneth F (Ken)** — Baseball Player
3446 Cypress Ave, Cleveland OH 44109, USA
**McBride, Martina** — Singer
Creative Artists Agency, 2000 Ave of Stars, #100, Los Angeles CA 90067 USA
**McBride, Patricia** — Ballerina
Sharon Wagner Artists, 150 W End Ave, New York NY 10023, USA
**McBride, Will** — Photographer
Neuve Schonhauser Str 10, 10178 Berlin, Germany
**McBridge, Macay** — Baseball Player
Detroit Tigers, Comerica Park, 2100 Woodward Ave, Detroit MI 48201 USA
**McBroom, Amanda** — Singer, Songwriter
Kazarian/Measures/Ruskin, 11969 Ventura Blvd, #300, Studio City CA 91604 USA
**McBurney, Simon** — Director, Writer, Actor
Troika, 74 Clerkenwell Road, #300, London EC1M 5QA, England
**McCabe, Bryan** — Ice Hockey Player
6120 Via Venetia S, Delray Beach FL 33484, USA
**McCabe, Eamonn P** — Photographer
Guardian, 119 Farrington Road, London EC1R 3ER, England
**McCabe, Frank** — Basketball Player
6712 N White Fir Dr, Edwards IL 61528, USA
**McCabe, Joe R** — Baseball Player
3932 E 79th St, Indianapolis IN 46240, USA
**McCabe, John** — Composer, Concert Pianist
Novello Co, 8/9 Firth St, London W1V 5TZ, England
**McCabe, Patrick** — Writer
Picador, Macmillan Books, 25 Eccleston Place, London SW1W 9NF, England
**McCabe, Zia** — Singer, Guitarist (Dandy Warhols)
Monqui Mgmt, PO Box 5908, Portland OR 97228, USA
**McCafferty, Donald F (Don), Jr** — Football Coach
167 E Shore Road, Halesite NY 11743, USA
**McCaffrey, Barry R** — Army General, Government Official
McCaffrey Assoc, 1800 Diagonal Road, #600, Alexandria VA 22314, USA
**McCaffrey, Edward T (Ed)** — Football Player
321 Paragon Way, Castle Rock CO 80108, USA
**McCahill, Crystal** — Model
Playboy Promotions, 2706 Media Center Dr, Los Angeles CA 90065 USA
**McCain, Edwin** — Singer, Songwriter
Harrington Mgmt, PO Box 1267, Decatur GA 30031, USA
**McCain, Frances Lee** — Actress
8075 W 3rd St, #303, Los Angeles CA 90048, USA
**McCain, Howard** — Director, Writer
Circle of Confusion, 10723 71st Road, #300, Forest Hills NY 11375, USA
**McCall, Brian A** — Baseball Player
550 Tremont Ave, #200, London NW1 8HH, England
**McCall, C W** — Singer, Songwriter
PO Box E, Ouray CO 81427, USA
**McCall, Darrell** — Singer, Songwriter
Texas Sounds Entertainment, 957 NASA Parkway, #542, Houston TX 77058, USA
**McCall, John W (Windy)** — Baseball Player
8043 E Ragweed Dr, Tucson AZ 85710, USA
**McCall, Mitzi** — Actress
C E S D, 10635 Santa Monica Blvd, #130, Los Angeles CA 90025 USA
**McCall, Oliver** — Boxer
Warrior's Boxing Promotions, 5397 Orange Dr, #202, Davie FL 33314, USA
**McCall, Reese** — Football Player
1311 1st Ave N, Bessemer AL 35020, USA
**McCallany, Holt** — Actor
Mosiac Media Group, 9200 W Sunset Blvd, #1000, Los Angeles CA 90069 USA
**McCallister, Blaine** — Golfer
1878 Epping Forest Way S, Jacksonville FL 32217, USA
**McCallum, David** — Actor
Abrams Artists, 275 7th Ave, #2600, New York NY 10001, USA
**McCallum, Napoleon A** — Football Player
314 Doe Run Circle, Henderson NV 89012, USA
**McCament, L Randall (Randy)** — Baseball Player
17338 N Del Webb Blvd, Sun City AZ 85373, USA
**McCamus, Tom** — Actor
Gary Goddard Agency, 10 Sainte Mary St, #305, Toronto ON M4Y 1P9, Canada
**McCandless, Bruce, II** — Astronaut
210932 Pleasant Park Dr, Conifer CO 80433, USA
**McCanlies, Tim** — Director, Producer, Writer
Gotham Group, 9255 W Sunset Blvd, #515, Los Angeles CA 90069, USA
**McCann, Brendan M** — Basketball Player
599 Shinnecock Lane, Green Cove Springs FL 32043, USA
**McCann, Brian M** — Baseball Player
869 Big Horn Hollow, Sun City AZ 85373, USA
**McCann, Leslie C (Les)** — Jazz Singer, Pianist, Composer
De Leon Artists, PO Box 21329, Piedmont CA 94620 USA
**McCann, Lila** — Singer
W M E Entertainment, 1600 Division St, #300, Nashville TN 37203 USA
**McCann, Martin** — Actor
Markham Froggatt Irwin, Julian House, 4 Windmill St, London W1P 1HF, England
**McCann, Renetta E** — Businesswoman
Starcom MediaVest Group, 35 W Wacker Dr, Chicago IL 60601, USA
**McCann, Sean** — Singer (Great Big Sea)
Fleming Assoc, 167 Little Lake Dr, Ann Arbor MI 48103, USA
**McCardell, Keenan W** — Football Player
4918 Newpoint Dr, Fresno TX 77545, USA
**McCareins, Justin** — Football Player
7707 Andes Lane, Parkland FL 33067, USA
**McCarley, Erin** — Singer, Guitarist, Songwriter
Mick Mgmt, 35 Washington St, Brooklyn NY 11201, USA
**McCarney, P Daniel (Dan)** — Football Coach
North Texas University, Athletic Dept, 1155 Union Circle, Denton TX 76203, USA
**McCarren, Laurence A (Larry)** — Football Player
520 W Chickadee Lane, Green Bay WI 54313, USA

| | |
|---|---|
| **McCarrick, Theodore E Cardinal** | Religious Leader |
| Archdiocesan Pastoral Center, 5001 Eastern Ave, Washington DC 20017, USA | |
| **McCarron, Christopher (Chris)** | Thoroughbred Racing Jockey |
| 4158 Paris Pike, Georgetown KY 40324, USA | |
| **McCarron, Douglas J** | Labor Leader |
| Carpenters/Joiners Brotherhood, 101 Connecticut Ave NW, Washington DC 20001, USA | |
| **McCarron, Scott M** | Golfer |
| PO Box 1894, La Quinta CA 92247, USA | |
| **McCarry, Charles** | Writer |
| Random House, 1745 Broadway, #1800, New York NY 10019 USA | |
| **McCartan, John W (Jack)** | Ice Hockey Player |
| 15504 Almond Lane, Eden Prairie MN 55347, USA | |
| **McCarter, Andre E** | Basketball Player |
| 3257 Kibbe Court, Lawrenceville GA 30044, USA | |
| **McCarthy, Andrew** | Actor |
| 4708 Vesper Ave, Sherman Oaks CA 91403, USA | |
| **McCarthy, Cormac** | Writer |
| 1101 N Mesa, El Paso TX 79002, USA | |
| **McCarthy, Dennis** | Composer |
| First Artists Mgmt, 4764 Park Granada, #210, Calabasas CA 91302 USA | |
| **McCarthy, Jenny** | Model, Actress |
| Untitled Entertainment, 350 S Beverly Dr, #200, Beverly Hills CA 90212 USA | |
| **McCarthy, John J (Johnny)** | Basketball Player |
| 1350 Union Road, #2F, West Seneca NY 14224, USA | |
| **McCarthy, Julianna** | Actress |
| Stone Manners Salners, 9911 W Pico Blvd, #1400, Los Angeles CA 90035 USA | |
| **McCarthy, Justin D** | Navy Admiral |
| Director, Material Readiness/Logistics, HqUSN, Pentagon, Washington DC 20350, USA | |
| **McCarthy, Kevin** | Ice Hockey Player, Coach |
| 1139 Warf Road, Lexington NC 27292, USA | |
| **McCarthy, Laurie** | Producer |
| United Talent Agency, U T A Plaza, 9336 Civic Center Dr, Beverly Hills CA 90210 USA | |
| **McCarthy, Melissa** | Actress |
| Creative Artists Agency, 2000 Ave of Stars, #100, Los Angeles CA 90067 USA | |
| **McCarthy, Mike** | Football Coach |
| Green Bay Packers, 1265 Lombardi Ave, Green Bay WI 54304 USA | |
| **McCarthy, Nicholas A (Nick)** | Singer, Guitarist (Franz Ferdinand) |
| M A M A Group, 57-65 Worship Ave, London EC2A 2DU, England | |
| **McCarthy, Paul** | Artist |
| Hauser & Wirth Gallery, 196A Piccadilly, London W1J 9DY, England | |
| **McCarthy, Steve** | Ice Hockey Player |
| 1019 W Jackson Blvd, #3F, Chicago IL 60607, USA | |
| **McCarthy, Thomas J (Tom)** | Actor, Director |
| Gersh Agency, 9465 Wilshire Blvd, #600, Beverly Hills CA 90212 USA | |
| **McCarthy, Thomas M (Tom)** | Baseball Player |
| PO Box 38, Limington ME 04049, USA | |
| **McCarthy-Miller, Beth** | Director |
| Creative Artists Agency, 2000 Ave of Stars, #100, Los Angeles CA 90067 USA | |
| **McCartney, James L** | Singer, Guitarist, Songwriter |
| Engine Company Records, 334 Bleeker St, #K144, New York NY 10014, USA | |
| **McCartney, Jesse** | Actor, Singer |
| C E S D, 10635 Santa Monica Blvd, #130, Los Angeles CA 90025 USA | |
| **McCartney, Paul** | Singer (Beatles); Songwriter |
| Quest Mgmt, 36 Marple Way, #1D, London W3 0RG, England | |
| **McCartney, Stella** | Fashion Designer |
| 34-36 Perrymount Road, Haywards Heath, West Sussex RH16 3DN, England | |
| **McCarty, Darren** | Ice Hockey Player |
| McCarthy Cancer Foundation, PO Box 1874, Royal Oak MI 48066, USA | |
| **McCarty, David A** | Baseball Player |
| 110 Waldo Ave, Piedmont CA 94611, USA | |
| **McCarty, Walter L** | Basketball Player |
| 237 Rice Road, Wayland MA 01778, USA | |
| **McCarver, J Timothy (Tim)** | Baseball Player, Sportscaster |
| 5825 Riegels Harbor Road, Sarasota FL 34242, USA | |
| **McCary, Michael** | Singer (Boyz II Men) |
| Spectrum Talent, 9107 Wilshire Blvd, #450, Beverly Hills CA 90210, USA | |
| **McCashin, Constance** | Actress |
| 66 Fountain St, West Newton MA 02465, USA | |
| **McCaskill, Kirk E** | Baseball Player |
| 33985 Cape Cove, Dana Point CA 92629, USA | |
| **McCaslin, Donny** | Jazz Saxophonist |
| Greenleaf Records, PO Box 477364, Chicago IL 60647 USA | |
| **McCatty, Steven E (Steve)** | Baseball |
| 1075 Woodbriar Dr, Oxford MI 48371, USA | |
| **McCauley, Barry** | Opera Singer |
| 598 Ridgewood Road, Oradell NJ 07649, USA | |
| **McCauley, Donald F (Don), Jr** | Football Player |
| Rams Club, PO Box 2446, Chapel Hill NC 27515, USA | |
| **McCauley, James Michael** | Actor, Composer, Director |
| Stone Manners Salners, 9911 W Pico Blvd, #1400, Los Angeles CA 90035 USA | |
| **McCauley, William F** | Navy Admiral |
| 670 Margarita Ave, Coronado CA 92118, USA | |
| **McCaw, Bruce** | Auto Racing Executive |
| PacWest Racing Group, PO Box 1717, Bellevue WA 98009, USA | |
| **McCay, Peggy** | Actress |
| 2714 Carmar Dr, Los Angeles CA 90046, USA | |
| **McClain Johnson, Katrina** | Basketball Player |
| 1907 Carlton St, North Charleston SC 29405, USA | |
| **McClain, Cady** | Actress, Producer |
| Jey Assoc, 1507 7th St, #210, Santa Monica CA 90401, USA | |
| **McClain, Charly** | Singer |
| John D Lentz, PO Box 198888, Nashville TN 37219, USA | |
| **McClain, China Anne** | Actress |
| Paradigm Agency, 360 N Crescent Dr, North Building, Beverly Hills CA 90210 USA | |
| **McClain, Dewey L** | Football Player |
| 1032 Flagg Way, Lawrenceville GA 30044, USA | |

**M**

**McClain - McConkey**

**McClain, Johnathan** — Actor
Innovative Artists, 1505 10th St, Santa Monica CA 90401 USA

**McClain, Scott M** — Baseball Player
660 Golden Gate Point, #61, Sarasota FL 34236, USA

**McClain, Theodore (Ted)** — Basketball Player
104 Eaton Court, Nashville TN 37218, USA

**McClairen, Jack (Cy)** — Football Player, Basketball Coach
1337 Idlewild Dr, Daytona Beach FL 32114, USA

**McClamon, Zahn** — Actor
Amsel Eisenstadt Frazier, 5055 Wilshire Blvd, #865, Los Angeles CA 90036 USA

**McClanahan, Randall D (Randy)** — Football Player
8107 W Via del Sol, Peoria AZ 85383, USA

**McClanahan, Robert B (Rob)** — Ice Hockey Player
3310 Watertown Road, Long Lake MN 55356, USA

**McClary, Thomas (Tom)** — Guitarist, Singer (Commodores)
Management Assoc, 1920 Benson Ave, Saint Paul MN 55116, USA

**McClatchy, J D** — Writer, Editor
15 Grand St, Stonington CT 06378, USA

**McClean, Lalisha** — Singer (Allure)
Universal Attractions, 135 W 26th St, #1200, New York NY 10001 USA

**McClelland, Kevin** — Ice Hockey Player
2886 Keeley Cove, Southaven MS 38671, USA

**McClellin, Sheamus L (Shea)** — Football Player
Chicago Bears, 1000 Football Dr, Lake Forest IL 60045 USA

**McClements, Robert, Jr** — Businessman
31 Cardinal Lane, Key Largo FL 33037, USA

**McClenathan, Cory** — Drag Racing Driver
1681 E Northfield Dr, Brownsburg IN 46112, USA

**McClendon, Lloyd G** — Baseball Player, Manager
1082 Mission Hills Court, Chesterton IN 46304, USA

**McClendon, Reiley** — Actor
Innovative Artists, 1505 10th St, Santa Monica CA 90401 USA

**McCleon, Dexter K** — Football Player
1901 Post Oak Blvd, #509, Houston TX 77056, USA

**McClintock, Eddie** — Actor
I C M Partners, 10250 Constellation Blvd, #900, Los Angeles CA 90067 USA

**McClintock, William** — Space Scientist
University of Colorado, Atmospheric/Space Physics Dept, Boulder CO 80309, USA

**McClinton, Curtis R** — Football Player
McClinton Development, 11714 Jefferson St, Kansas City MO 64114, USA

**McClinton, Delbert** — Singer, Musician, Songwriter
PO Box 159008, Nashville TN 37215, USA

**McCloskey, Jim** — Social Activist
221 Witherspoon St, Princeton NJ 08542, USA

**McCloskey, Paul N (Pete), Jr** — Representative, CA
580 Mountain Home Road, Woodside CA 94062, USA

**McCloskey, Robert J** — Diplomat
84 Old Black Point Road, Niantic CT 06357, USA

**McClover, Darrell A, II** — Football Player
6120 SW 19th St, Pompano Beach FL 33068, USA

**McClure, Larry** — Auto Racing Executive
Morgan-McClure Motorsports, 26502 Newbanks Road, Abingdon VA 24210, USA

**McClure, Marc** — Actor
Amsel Eisenstadt Frazier, 5055 Wilshire Blvd, #865, Los Angeles CA 90036 USA

**McClure, Robert C (Bob)** — Baseball Player
3834 SE Fairway E, Stuart FL 34997, USA

**McClure, Tane** — Actress
Don Gerler, 3349 Cahuenga Blvd W, #1, Los Angeles CA 90068 USA

**McClure, Wilbert (Skeeter)** — Boxer
57 Broadlawn Park, #26, Newton MA 02467, USA

**McClurg, Edie** — Actress
Peyrot Lagnese Mucci, 5750 Wilshire Blve, #580, Los Angeles CA 90036, USA

**McClurkin, Donnie** — Singer
Sierra Mgmt, 1035 Bates Court, Hendersonvlle TN 37075, USA

**McColgan, Elizabeth (Liz)** — Track Athlete
Marquee UK, 6 George St, Nottingham NG1 3BE, England

**McColl, William F (Bill), Jr** — Football Player
5166 Chelsea St, La Jolla CA 92037, USA

**McCollough, Jack** — Fashion Designer
Proenza Schouler, 120 Walker St, #1600, New York NY 10013, USA

**McColluh, Thayne M** — Educator
Gonzaga University, President's Office, 502 E Boone Ave, Spokane WA 99258, USA

**McCollum, Andrew J (Andy)** — Football Player
3933 Autumn Farms Dr, Pacific MO 63069, USA

**McCollum, Rick** — Guitarist (Afghan Whigs)
Rascoff/Zysblat Organization, 250 W 57th St, New York NY 10107 USA

**McColm, Matt** — Actor
ReBar Mgmt, 10061 Riverside Dr, #722, Toluca Lake CA 91602, USA

**McComas, Brian** — Singer, Songwriter
Liz Gregory Talent, 9 Music Sqaure S, #357, Nashville TN 37203, USA

**McComb, Heather** — Actress
1 Mgmt, 9000 W Sunset Blvd, #1550, Los Angeles CA 90069 USA

**McComb, Jeremy** — Singer, Songwriter
Parallel Entertainment, 209th Ave S, #506, Nashville TN 37203, USA

**McComb, Joanne (Jo)** — Baseball Player
105 Nottingham Road, Bloomsburg PA 17815, USA

**McComb, William (Bill)** — Businessman
Liz Clairborne Inc, 1441 Broadway, New York NY 10018, USA

**McCombs, Davis** — Writer
University of Arkansas, Creative Writing Program, Fayetteville AR 72701, USA

**McConathy, John R** — Basketball Player
2320 Belmont Blvd, Bossier City LA 71111, USA

**McConaughey, Matthew** — Actor
Creative Artists Agency, 2000 Ave of Stars, #100, Los Angeles CA 90067 USA

**McConkey, Jim C** — Cinematographer
505 W 54th St, #PH 12, New York NY 10019, USA

**McConkey, Philip J (Phil)** — Football Player
1856 Viking Way, La Jolla CA 92037, USA
**McConnell, Denise** — Model
Playboy Promotions, 2706 Media Center Dr, Los Angeles CA 90065 USA
**McConnell, Harden M** — Chemist
Stanford University, Chemistry Dept, Stanford CA 94305, USA
**McConnell, Michael W** — Judge
US Court of Appeals, 2480 Cowper St, Palo Alto CA 94301, USA
**McConnell, Page** — Keyboardist (Phish)
Paradigm Agency, 360 N Crescent Dr, North Building, Beverly Hills CA 90210 USA
**McConnell-Serio, Suzanne (Suzie)** — Basketball Player, Coach
2590 Rossmoore Dr, Pittsburgh PA 15241, USA
**McCoo, Marilyn** — Singer (Fifth Dimension), Actress
Brokaw Co, 9255 W Sunset Blvd, #804, West Hollywood CA 90069 USA
**McCook, John** — Actor
Abrams Artists, 9200 W Sunset Blvd, #1125, West Hollywood CA 90069 USA
**McCool, William J (Billy)** — Baseball Player
9250 SE 121st Loop, Summerfield FL 34491, USA
**McCord, AnnaLynne** — Actress
Innovative Artists, 1505 10th St, Santa Monica CA 90401 USA
**McCord, Bob** — Ice Hockey Player
11540 N Donley Dr, Parker CO 80138, USA
**McCord, Gary D** — Golfer, Sportscaster
PO Box 1964, Edwards CO 81632, USA
**McCord, Joe Milton** — Biochemist
University of Colorado, Waring Institute, 4200 E 9th Ave, Denver CO 80262, USA
**McCord, Keith R** — Basketball Player
1609 Five Acre Road, Dolomite AL 35061, USA
**McCord, Kent** — Actor
1738 N Orange Grove Ave, Los Angeles CA 90046, USA
**McCormack, Catherine** — Actress
120 Riverside Dr, #7G, New York NY 10024, USA
**McCormack, Donald R (Don)** — Baseball Player
866 Glenfield Dr, Palm Harbor FL 34684, USA
**McCormack, Eric** — Actor
I C M Partners, 10250 Constellation Blvd, #900, Los Angeles CA 90067 USA
**McCormack, Mary** — Actress
Gersh Agency, 9465 Wilshire Blvd, #600, Beverly Hills CA 90212 USA
**McCormack, Patty** — Actress, Model
Rothman Patino Andres, 4360 Tujunga Ave, Studio City CA 91604, USA
**McCormack, Will** — Actor, Writer
United Talent Agency, U T A Plaza, 9336 Civic Center Dr, Beverly Hills CA 90210 USA
**McCormick, Maureen** — Actress, Singer
Rebel Entertainment Partners, 5700 Wilshire Blvd, #456, Los Angeles CA 90036, USA
**McCormick, Michael F (Mike)** — Baseball Player
1600 Morganton Road, #U9, Pinehurst NC 28374, USA
**McCormick, Patricia J (Pat)** — Diver
92 Riversea Road, Seal Beach CA 90740, USA
**McCormick, Timothy D (Tim)** — Basketball Player
2500 Leroy Lane, West Bloomfield MI 48324, USA
**McCorvey, Bill** — Singer (Pirates of the Mississippi)
Third Coast Talent, PO Box 110225, Nashville TN 37222, USA
**McCorvey, Norma** — Litigant
11343 Cactus Lane, Dallas TX 75238, USA
**McCouch, Grayson** — Actor
A P A Talent/Literary Agency, 405 S Beverly Dr, #300, Beverly Hills CA 90212 USA
**McCoughtry, Angel** — Basketball Player
Atlanta Dream, 83 Walton St NW, #400, Atlanta, GA 30303 USA
**McCourt, Frank** — Baseball Executive
22426 Pacific Coast Highway, Malibu CA 90265, USA
**McCoury, Del** — Singer, Guitarist (Del McCoury Band)
W M E Entertainment, 1600 Division St, #300, Nashville TN 37203 USA
**McCoury, Robbie** — Banjo Player (Del McCoury Band)
W M E Entertainment, 9601 Wilshire Blvd, #300, Beverly Hills CA 90210 USA
**McCoury, Ronnie** — Mandolin Player (Del McCoury Band)
Media Artists Group, 8222 Melrose Ave, #203, Los Angeles CA 90048 USA
**McCovey, Willie L** — Baseball Player
PO Box 620342, Redwood City CA 94062, USA
**McCowen, Alec** — Actor
Conway Van Gelder Grant, 8-12 Broadwick St, #300, London W1F 8HW, England
**McCown, Joshusa T (Josh)** — Football Player
1312 Lookout Circle, Waxhaw NC 28173, USA
**McCown, Lucas P (Luke)** — Football Player
30963 US Highway 69 N, Rusk TX 75785, USA
**McCoy, Glenn** — Editorial Cartoonist
Belleville News-Democrat, Editorial Dept, 120 S Illinois, Bellville IL 62220, USA
**McCoy, Jason** — Singer, Songwriter
Agency Group Ltd, 142 W 57th St, #600, New York NY 10019 USA
**McCoy, Jennifer** — Photographer, Artist
Postmasters Gallery, 459 W 19th St, New York NY 10011, USA
**McCoy, Jordan** — Singer
Bad Boy Entertainment, 1440 Broadway, #16, New York NY 10018 USA
**McCoy, Kevin** — Photographer, Artist
New York University, Steinhardt Art School, New York NY 10003, USA
**McCoy, Larry S** — Baseball Umpire
5758 Highway 139, Greenway AR 72430, USA
**McCoy, Michael P (Mike)** — Football Player
2224 Cotton Gin Row, Jefferson GA 30549, USA
**McCoy, Mike (Mouse)** — Director
Bandito Brothers, 3115 S La Cienega Blvd, Los Angeles CA 10016, USA
**McCoy, Neal** — Singer
Webster Assoc, PO Box 23015, Nashville TN 37202, USA
**McCoy, Sandra** — Actress
Main Title Mgmt, 8383 Wilshire Blvd, #408, Beverly Hills CA 90211 USA
**McCoy, Sherilyn S** — Businesswoman
Avon Products, 1345 Ave of Americas, Basement Concourse 9, New York NY 10105, USA

M

McConkey - McCoy

# M

**McCracken - McCutchen**

**McCracken, Quinton A** — Baseball Player
20802 Piercton Court, Katy TX 77494, USA
**McCrackin, Daisy** — Actress
Stone Manners Salners, 9911 W Pico Blvd, #1400, Los Angeles CA 90035 USA
**McCrae, George** — Singer
International Artists Holland, PO Box 32, 5360 Grave AA, Netherlands
**McCrane, Paul** — Actor
United Talent Agency, U T A Plaza, 9336 Civic Center Dr, Beverly Hills CA 90210 USA
**McCraney, Tarell Alvin** — Writer
I C M Partners, 10250 Constellation Blvd, #900, Los Angeles CA 90067 USA
**McCrary, Darius** — Actor
Diverse Talent Group, 9911 W Pico Blvd, #350W, Los Angeles CA 90035, USA
**McCrary, Fred D** — Football Player
134 Grandmar Chase, Clermont FL 34711, USA
**McCrary, Joel** — Actor
C E S D, 10635 Santa Monica Blvd, #130, Los Angeles CA 90025 USA
**McCrary, Michael C** — Football Player
9907 Chase Hill Court, Vienna VA 22182, USA
**McCraw, Tommy L (Tom)** — Baseball Player
3142 SE Monte Vista Court, Port Saint Lucie FL 34952, USA
**McCray, Bobby L, Jr** — Football Player
14907 SW 52nd St, Miramar FL 33027, USA
**McCray, Nikki** — Basketball Player
4278 Fox Hills Dr, Louisville TN 37777, USA
**McCray, Prentice** — Football Player
2109 N Argonaut St, Stockton CA 95204, USA
**McCray, Rodney E** — Basketball Player
33 Bonita Vista Road, Mount Vernon NY 10552, USA
**McCrea, John** — Singer (Cake), Songwriter
Umbrella Group, 1 West St, #3506, New York NY 10004, USA
**McCready, Mike** — Guitarist (Pearl Jam)
Curtis Mgmt, 1900 S Corgiat Dr, Seattle WA 98108, USA
**McCreary, Bear** — Composer
3622 Clarington Ave, #5, Los Angeles CA 90034, USA
**McCreary, William (Bill), Sr** — Ice Hockey Player, Coach
4318 Highcrest Dr, #1, Brighton MI 48116, USA
**McCree, Marlon T** — Football Player
2109 N Argonaut St, Windermere FL 34786, USA
**McCrory, Glenn** — Boxer
Yetholm Place, Newiggin Hall, Newcastle upon Tyne NE5 4EB, England
**McCrory, Helen** — Actress
Independent Talent Group, 40 Whitfield St, London W1T 2RH, England
**McCrory, Milton (Milt)** — Boxer
Escot Boxing Enterprises, 19244 Bretton Dr, Detroit MI 48223, USA
**McCrory, Robert (Bob)** — Baseball Player
30 Rebecca Lane, Hattiesburg MS 39402, USA
**McCue, Anne** — Singer, Guitarist, Songwriter
Conqueroo, 11271 Ventura Blvd, #522, Studio City CA 91604 USA
**McCuigan, Paul** — Director
Fallout Entertainment, 3100 Airport Ave, Santa Monica CA 90405, USA
**McCullagh, Peter** — Mathematician, Statistician
University of Chicago, Statistics Dept, 5734 University Ave, Chicago IL 60637, USA
**McCullers, Lance G** — Baseball Player
3309 Hoedt Road, Tampa FL 33618, USA
**McCulley, Michael J** — Astronaut
365 Private Road 652, Bay City TX 77414, USA
**McCullin, Donald (Don)** — Photographer
Hamiltons Gallery, 13 Carlos Place, London W1, England
**McCulloch, Bruce** — Actor, Writer, Producer
United Talent Agency, U T A Plaza, 9336 Civic Center Dr, Beverly Hills CA 90210 USA
**McCulloch, Earl** — Football Player, Track Athlete
2108 Santa Fe Ave, #15, Long Beach CA 90810, USA
**McCulloch, Ed (Ace)** — Auto Racing Driver
1397 Cherry Tree Road, Avon IN 46123, USA
**McCullough, Bernard J (Barry), III** — Navy Admiral
Commander, Cyber Command & 10th Fleet, Fort George C Meade MD 20755, USA
**McCullough, Colleen** — Writer
PO Box 333, Norfolk Island NSW 2899, Australia
**McCullough, David** — Writer, Entertainer
Creative Artists Agency, 2000 Ave of Stars, #100, Los Angeles CA 90067 USA
**McCullough, Kimberly** — Actress, Singer, Dancer
Brillstein Entertainment Partners, 9150 Wilshire Blvd, #350, Beverly Hills CA 90212 USA
**McCullough, Wayne** — Boxer
Sky Sports, Grants Way, Isleworth, Middlesex TW7 5QD, England
**McCullum, Samuel C (Sam)** — Football Player
7701 88th Place SE, Mercer Island WA 98040, USA
**McCumber, Mark** — Golfer, Sportscaster
527 Le Master Dr, Ponte Vedra Beach FL 32082, USA
**McCune, Don** — Bowler
3551 Coventry Gardens Dr, Las Vegas NV 89135, USA
**McCurdy, Jennette** — Actress, Singer
Management 360, 9111 Wilshire Blvd, Beverly Hills CA 90210 USA
**McCurry, Jeffrey D (Jeff)** — Baseball Player
9015 Linkmeadow Lane, Houston TX 77025, USA
**McCurry, Margaret** — Architect
Tigerman McCurry Architects, 444 N Wells St, #206, Chicago IL 60654, USA
**McCurry, Mike** — Government Official, Journalist
CNN-TV, 190 Marietta Ave SW, Atlanta GA 30303 USA
**McCurry, Steve** — Photographer
2 5th Ave, New York NY 10011, USA
**McCusker, James B (Jim)** — Football Player
209 N Main St, Jamestown NY 14701, USA
**McCusker, Joan** — Curling Athlete
Curling Assn, 1660 Vimont Court, Cumberland ON K4A 4J4, Canada
**McCutchen, Andrew S** — Baseball Player
Pittsburgh Pirates, P N C Park, 115 Federal St, #115B, Pittsburgh PA 15212 USA

**McCutcheon, Daylon**
4393 Hiwassee, Claremont CA 91711, USA — Football Player
**McCutcheon, Hugh**
US Olympic Committee, 1 Olympia Plaza, Building 6, Colorado Springs CO 80909, USA — Volleyball Coach
**McCutcheon, Lawrence**
19981 Weems Lane, Huntington Beach CA 92646, USA — Football Player
**McCutcheon, Linda**
A A R P Publications, Director's Office, 601 E St NW, Washington DC 20049, USA — Publisher
**McCutcheon, Martine**
Amanda Howard, 74 Clerkenwell Road, London EC1M 5QA, England — Actress, Singer
**McDaniel, Chris**
Bobby Roberts, 3050 Business Park Circle, #303, Goodlettsville TN 37221 USA — Keyboardist (Confederate Railroad)
**McDaniel, Edward (Ed)**
13111 Brenwood Trail, Hopkins MN 55343, USA — Football Player
**McDaniel, James**
Innovative Artists, 1505 10th St, Santa Monica CA 90401 USA — Actor
**McDaniel, John (Johnny)**
608 Andalusia Trail, De Soto TX 75115, USA — Football Player
**McDaniel, Lyndall D (Lindy)**
16641 E 1550 Road, Hollis OK 73550, USA — Baseball Player
**McDaniel, Randall C**
20405 Manor Road, Excelsior MN 55331, USA — Football Player
**McDaniel, Terence L (Terry)**
730 Shenandoah, Cedar Hill TX 75104, USA — Football Player
**McDaniel, Xavier M**
2 Oakmist Court, Blythewood SC 29016, USA — Basketball Player
**McDaniels, Darryl (Darryl M)**
Tracy Miller Assoc, 2610 Fire Road, Egg Harbor Township NJ 08234, USA — Rap Artist (Run-DMC)
**McDaniels, James R (Jim)**
2549 Smallhouse Road, Bowling Green KY 42104, USA — Basketball Player
**McDaniels, Josh**
Saint Louis Rams, 901 N Broadway, Saint Louis MO 63101 USA — Football Coach
**McDaniels, Pellom**
105 Sycamore Place, #419A, Decatur GA 30030, USA — Football Player
**McDavid, Ray D**
1245 Market St, #1348, San Diego CA 92101, USA — Baseball Player
**McDavis, Roderick J**
Ohio University, President's Office, Athens OH 45701, USA — Educator
**McDermott, Anne-Marie**
Opus 3 Artists, 470 Park Ave S, #900N, New York NY 10016 USA — Concert Pianist
**McDermott, Charlie**
Kritzer Levine Wilkins, 8840 Wilshire Blvd, #100, Beverly Hills CA 90211, USA — Actor
**McDermott, Colleen**
C E S D, 10635 Santa Monica Blvd, #130, Los Angeles CA 90025 USA — Actress
**McDermott, Dean**
United Talent Agency, U T A Plaza, 9336 Civic Center Dr, Beverly Hills CA 90210 USA — Actor, Writer, Producer
**McDermott, Dylan**
Schiff Co, 9200 Sunset Blvd, #430, West Hollywood CA 90232 USA — Actor
**McDermott, John**
McDermott Entertainment, 30 Rowes Wharf, #470, Boston MA 02110, USA — Singer, Songwriter
**McDermott, R Terrance (Terry)**
5078 Chainbridge Dr, Bloomfield Hills MI 48304, USA — Speed Skater
**McDermott, Terence K (Terry)**
7205 Sunlight Peak Dr NE, Rio Rancho NM 87144, USA — Baseball Player
**McDiarmid, Ian**
Independent Talent Group, 40 Whitfield St, London W1T 2RH, England — Actor
**McDill, Alan**
244 Richwoods Road, Arkadelphia AR 71923, USA — Baseball Player
**McDivitt, James A (Jim)**
3530 E Calle Puerta de Acero, Tucson AZ 85718, USA — Astronaut, Air Force General
**McDole, Roland O (Ron)**
2083 Lockes Mill Road, Berryville VA 22611, USA — Football Player
**McDonagh, John Michael**
United Talent Agency, U T A Plaza, 9336 Civic Center Dr, Beverly Hills CA 90210 USA — Director, Producer, Writer
**McDonagh, Martin**
Creative Artists Agency, 2000 Ave of Stars, #100, Los Angeles CA 90067 USA — Writer, Director
**McDonald, Alvin B (Ab)**
419 Thompson Dr, Winnipeg MB R3J 3E7, Canada — Ice Hockey Player
**McDonald, Arthur B**
Queen's University, Physics Dept, Kingston ON K7L 3N6, Canada — Physicist
**McDonald, Audra**
W M E Entertainment, 1325 Ave of Americas, New York NY 10019 USA — Actress, Singer
**McDonald, Ben**
8780 Henderson Road, Denham Springs LA 70726, USA — Baseball Player
**McDonald, Christopher**
Gersh Agency, 9465 Wilshire Blvd, #600, Beverly Hills CA 90212 USA — Actor
**McDonald, Country Joe**
Savoy Music, 1844 SW Troy St, Portland OR 97219, USA — Singer, Guitarist
**McDonald, James L (Jim)**
PO Box 995, Brea CA 92822, USA — Baseball Player
**McDonald, James Z**
Los Angeles Dodgers, Stadium, 1000 Elysian Park Ave, Los Angeles CA 90090 USA — Baseball Player
**McDonald, Jiggs**
8331 Arborfield Court, Fort Myers FL 33912, USA — Sportscaster
**McDonald, John J**
3546 Michigan Ave, Cincinnati OH 45208, USA — Baseball Player
**McDonald, L Benard (Ben)**
8780 Henderson Road, Denham Springs LA 70726, USA — Baseball Player
**McDonald, Lanny**
23 Springside St, Calgary AB T3Z 3M1, Canada — Ice Hockey Player
**McDonald, Mackey J**
V F Corp, 628 Green Valley Road, Greensboro NC 27408, USA — Businessman
**McDonald, Michael**
Vector Mgmt, 1607 17th Ave S, Nashville TN 37212, USA — Singer, Songwriter
**McDonald, Miriam**
Innovative Artists, 1505 10th St, Santa Monica CA 90401 USA — Actress

**McDonald, Paul B** — Football Player
1815 Tradewinds Lane, Newport Beach CA 92660, USA
**McDonald, Richie** — Singer (Lonestar)
W M E Entertainment, 9601 Wilshire Blvd, #300, Beverly Hills CA 90210 USA
**McDonald, Thomas F (Tommy)** — Football Player
537 W Valley Forge Road, King of Prussia PA 19406, USA
**McDonald, Timothy (Tim)** — Football Player
208 Stone Creek Court, Whippany NJ 07981, USA
**McDonell, Thomas** — Actor
W M E Entertainment, 9601 Wilshire Blvd, #300, Beverly Hills CA 90210 USA
**McDonnell, Dirk** — Photographer
Throckmorton Fine Art, 145 E 57th St, #300, New York NY 10022, USA
**McDonnell, John F** — Businessman
McDonnell Douglas Corp, PO Box 516, Saint Louis MO 63166, USA
**McDonnell, Mary** — Actress
Innovative Artists, 1505 10th St, Santa Monica CA 90401 USA
**McDonnell, Patrick** — Cartoonist (Mutts)
King Features Syndicate, 300 W 57th St, #1500, New York NY 10019 USA
**McDonough, Mary** — Actress
6858 Canteloupe Ave, Van Nuys CA 91405, USA
**McDonough, Matthew (Spag)** — Drummer (Mudvayne)
Agency Group Ltd, 142 W 57th St, #600, New York NY 10019 USA
**McDonough, Michael** — Cinematographer
Sheldon Prosnit Agency, 800 S Robertson Blvd, Los Angeles CA 90035, USA
**McDonough, Neal** — Actor
Paradigm Agency, 360 N Crescent Dr, North Building, Beverly Hills CA 90210 USA
**McDonough, Sean** — Sportscaster
ABC-TV, Sports Dept, 77 W 66th St, New York NY 10023 USA
**McDonough, William** — Architect
700 E Jefferson St, Charlottesville VA 22902, USA
**McDonough, William J** — Government Official, Financier
Public Company Accounting Oversight Board, 1666 K NW, Washington DC 20006, USA
**McDorman, Jake** — Actor
United Talent Agency, U T A Plaza, 9336 Civic Center Dr, Beverly Hills CA 90210 USA
**McDormand, Frances** — Actress
W M E Entertainment, 9601 Wilshire Blvd, #300, Beverly Hills CA 90210 USA
**McDougal, R Meiklejohn (Mike)** — Baseball Player
Kansas City Royals, Kauffman Stadium, 1 Royal Way, Kansas City MO 64129 USA
**McDougall, Charles** — Director, Writer
United Agents, 12-26 Lexington St, London W1F 0LE, England
**McDougall, Walter A** — Historian
University of Pennsylvania, History Dept, Philadelphia PA 19104, USA
**McDowell, Jack B** — Baseball Player
3104 Del Rey Ave, Carlsbad CA 92009, USA
**McDowell, Leonard (Bubba)** — Football Player
6353 Richmond Ave, Houston TX 77057, USA
**McDowell, Oddibe** — Baseball Player
5240 SW 18th St, West Park FL 33023, USA
**McDowell, Roger A** — Baseball Player
2690 Pete Shaw Road, Marietta GA 30066, USA
**McDowell, Ronnie** — Singer, Guitarist
PO Box 53, Portland TN 37148, USA
**McDowell, Samuel E (Sam)** — Baseball Player
City of Legends, 1925 Don Wickham Dr, Clermont FL 34711, USA
**McDuffie, Matthew** — Writer
Paradigm Agency, 360 N Crescent Dr, North Building, Beverly Hills CA 90210 USA
**McDuffie, Otis J (O J)** — Football Player
1333 NW 121st Ave, Plantation FL 33323, USA
**McDuffie, Robert** — Concert Violinist, Conductor
Columbia Artists Mgmt Inc, 1790 Broadway, #702, New York NY 10019 USA
**McDyess, Antonio K** — Basketball Player
30 Cranbrook Road, Bloomfield Hills MI 48304, USA
**McEachern, Shawn** — Ice Hockey Player
71 Beach St, Marblehead MA 01945, USA
**McEldowney, Brooke** — Cartoonist (9 Chickwood Lane, Pobgorn)
Pib Press, PO Box 942, Kennebunk ME 04043, USA
**McElhenney, Rob** — Producer, Writer, Actor
3 Arts Entertainment, 9460 Wilshire Blvd, #700, Beverly Hills CA 90212 USA
**McElhenny, Hugh E** — Football Player
3013 Via Venezia, Henderson NV 89052, USA
**McElhone, Natascha** — Actress
Paradigm Agency, 360 N Crescent Dr, North Building, Beverly Hills CA 90210 USA
**McElligott, Dominique** — Actress
Creative Artists Agency, 2000 Ave of Stars, #100, Los Angeles CA 90067 USA
**McElmury, James D (Jim)** — Ice Hockey Player
9122 78th Street S, Cottage Grove MN 55016, USA
**McElroy, Charles D (Chuck)** — Baseball Player
1049 Nederland Ave, Port Arthur TX 77640, USA
**McElroy, Reginald L (Reggie)** — Football Player
RR 1 Box 109A, Preston MO 65732, USA
**McElroy, Vann W** — Football Player
524 Private Road 4450, Uvalde TX 78801, USA
**McEnaney, William H (Will)** — Baseball Player
1055 SW 3rd St, Boca Raton FL 33486, USA
**McEnery, Peter R** — Actor
Richard Stone Partnership, De Walden Court, 85 New Cavendish St, London W1W 6XD, England
**McEnroe, John P, Jr** — Tennis Player, Sportscaster
1080 5th Ave, New York NY 10128, USA
**McEntire, Reba** — Singer, Actress
Starstruck Entertainment, 40 Music Square W, Nashville TN 37203, USA
**McEuen, John** — Musician (Nitty Gritty Dirt Band)
New Frontier Touring, 1503 17th Ave S, Nashville TN 37212, USA
**McEwan, Geraldine** — Actress
Independent Talent Group, 40 Whitfield St, London W1T 2RH, England
**McEwan, Ian R** — Writer
15 Park Town, Oxford OX2 6SN, England

**McEwen, Mark** — Commentator
CBS-TV, News Dept, 51 W 52nd St, New York NY 10019 USA

**McEwen, Mike** — Ice Hockey Player
3712 N Peniel Ave, Bethany OK 73008, USA

**McEwen, Tom** — Drag Racing Driver
17368 Buttonwood St, Fountain Valley CA 92708, USA

**McEwing, Joseph E (Joe)** — Baseball Player
630 Deerbrook Dr, Yardley PA 19067, USA

**McFadden, Bryan N** — Singer, Pianist, Songwriter, Actor
Creative Artists Agency, 2000 Ave of Stars, #100, Los Angeles CA 90067 USA

**McFadden, Cynthia** — Commentator
ABC-TV, News Dept, 77 W 66th St, New York NY 10023 USA

**McFadden, Daniel L** — Nobel Economics Laureate
41 Southampton Ave, Berkeley CA 94707, USA

**McFadden, Darren** — Football Player
Oakland Raiders, 1220 Harbor Bay Parkway, Alameda CA 94502 USA

**McFadden, Davenia** — Actress
Don Buchwald, 6500 Wilshire Blvd, #2200, Los Angeles CA 90048 USA

**McFadden, Gates** — Actress
Innovative Artists, 1505 10th St, Santa Monica CA 90401 USA

**McFadden, Katy** — Sculptor, Ceramist
313 SW Maricara St, Portland OR 97219, USA

**McFadden, Leon** — Baseball Player
8617 S 10th Ave, Inglewood CA 90305, USA

**McFadden, Mary J** — Fashion Designer
525 E 72nd St, #2A, New York NY 10021, USA

**McFadden, Paul** — Football Player
7395 Christopher Dr, Youngstown OH 44514, USA

**McFadden, Robert D** — Journalist
New York Times, Editorial Dept, 229 W 43rd St, New York NY 10036, USA

**McFadden-Rusynyk, Betty Jean** — Baseball Player
7267 W 130th St, Cleveland OH 44130, USA

**McFadyen, Jack** — Artist
284 Globe Road, London E2 0NS, England

**McFarland, Anthony D** — Football Player
7733 Still Lakes Dr, Odessa FL 33556, USA

**McFarland, Dennis** — Writer
Henry Holt, 175 5th Ave, #400, New York NY 10010 USA

**McFarland, James D (Jim)** — Football Player
5102 S 90th St, Lincoln NE 68526, USA

**McFarland, Michael C** — Educator
Holy Cross University, President's Office, 1 College St, Worcester MA 01610, USA

**McFarland, R Kay** — Football Player
7394 Monaco St, Centennial CO 80112, USA

**McFarlane, Robert C** — Government Official
2010 Prospect St NW, Washington DC 20037, USA

**McFarlane, Todd** — Cartoonist (Spawn)
Todd McFarlane Entertainment, 1711 W Greentree Dr, Tempe AZ 85284, USA

**McFarling, Ursula Lee** — Journalist
Los Angeles Times, Editorial Dept, 202 W 1st St, Los Angeles CA 90012 USA

**McFaull, David** — Yachtsman
109 Poloke Place, Honolulu HI 96822, USA

**McFeely, William S** — Historian, Writer
35 Mill Hill Road, Wellfleet MA 02667, USA

**McFerrin, Bobby** — Singer, Songwriter
Original Artists, 826 Broadway, #400, New York NY 10003, USA

**McG** — Director
W M E Entertainment, 9601 Wilshire Blvd, #300, Beverly Hills CA 90210 USA

**McGaffigan, Andrew J (Andy)** — Baseball Player
6243 Forestwood Dr E, Lakeland FL 33811, USA

**McGahee, Willis A, III** — Football Player
225 NE Mizner Blvd, #685, Boca Raton FL 33432, USA

**McGahey Heinzler, Kathleen** — Field Hockey Player
7427 W 81st St, Los Angeles CA 90045, USA

**McGann, Michelle** — Golfer
1200 Singer Dr, West Palm Beach FL 33404, USA

**McGann, Stephen** — Actor
Associated International Mgmt, 7 Hatton Garden, #400, London EC1N 8AD, England

**McGarrahan, J Scott** — Football Player
4704 Monte Carmelo Place, Austin TX 78738, USA

**McGarrigle, Anna** — Singer, Songwriter
Moneypenny Agency, Stables, Main St, North Dalton, Fiffield, East Yorkshire YO25 9XA, England

**McGarry, Steve** — Cartoonist (Pop Culture)
United Feature Syndicate, PO Box 5610, Cincinnati OH 45201 USA

**McGaughey, Claude R (Shug), III** — Thoroughbred Racing Trainer
1927 Keene Road, Nicholasville KY 40356, USA

**McGee, Benjamin (Ben)** — Football Player
35 Castle Cove, Jackson MS 39212, USA

**McGee, Jack** — Actor
Semler Entertainment, 13636 Ventura Blvd, #510, Sherman Oaks CA 91423, USA

**McGee, Michael B (Mike)** — Football Player
22710 Uncompahgre Road, Montrose CO 81403, USA

**McGee, Pat** — Singer, Guitarist, Songwriter
Elevation Group, 1408 Encinal Ave, #A, Alameda CA 94501, USA

**McGee, Willie D** — Baseball Player
2081 Lupine Road, Hercules CA 94547, USA

**Mcgee-Davis, Trina** — Actress
Framework Entertainment, 9057 Nemo St, #C, West Hollywood CA 90069 USA

**McGegan, Nicholas** — Conductor
Schwalbe Partners, 170 E 61st St, #500, New York NY 10065, USA

**McGehee, Scott** — Director, Producer
Oasis Media Group, 8730 W Sunset Blvd, #700, West Hollywood CA 90069, USA

**McGeorge, Missie** — Golfer
1836 Willow Springs Court, Haslet TX 76052, USA

**McGeorge, Richard E (Rich)** — Football Player
2200 Trail Wood Dr, Durham NC 27705, USA

**McGerr, Jason** — Drummer (Death Cab for Cutie)
Zeitgeist Artist Mgmt, 660 York St, #216, San Francisco CA 94110, USA

**McGhee, Carla** — Basketball Player
103 Indigo Chase, Columbia SC 29229, USA

**McGhee, Kanavis** — Football Player
Challenge Earl College High School, 5601 West Loop S, Houston TX 77081, USA

**McGhee-Anderson, Kathleen** — Writer, Producer
A P A Talent/Literary Agency, 405 S Beverly Dr, #300, Beverly Hills CA 90212 USA

**McGilberry, Randall K (Randy)** — Baseball Player
2110 Foxford St, Cantonment FL 32533, USA

**McGill, Anthony** — Concert Clarinetist
Metropolitan Opera Orchestra, Lincoln Center Plaza, New York NY 10023, USA

**McGill, Bill (Billy)** — Basketball Player
5129 W 58th Place, Los Angeles CA 90056, USA

**McGill, Bob** — Ice Hockey Player
116 Oriole Dr, Holland Landing ON L9N 1H1, Canada

**McGill, Bruce** — Actor
Stone Manners Salners, 9911 W Pico Blvd, #1400, Los Angeles CA 90035 USA

**McGill, C Leonard (Lenny)** — Football Player
3516 W 125th Circle, Broomfield CO 80020, USA

**McGill, Don** — Producer, Writer
W M E Entertainment, 9601 Wilshire Blvd, #300, Beverly Hills CA 90210 USA

**McGill, Jill** — Golfer
3765 Carmel View Road, #3, San Diego CA 92130, USA

**McGill, Michael (Mickey)** — Singer (Dells)
Associated Booking Corp, 501 Madison Ave, #501, New York NY 10022 USA

**McGill, Michael Patrick** — Actor, Comedian
C E S D, 10635 Santa Monica Blvd, #130, Los Angeles CA 90025 USA

**McGill, Michael R (Mike)** — Football Player
8930 Louis Court, Saint John IN 46373, USA

**McGillion, Paul** — Actor
Amanda Howard, 74 Clerkenwell Road, London EC1M 5QA, England

**McGillis, Dan** — Ice Hockey Player
9 Country Club Dr, Chatham NJ 07928, USA

**McGillis, Kelly** — Actress
David Williams Mgmt, 9614 Olympic Blvd, #F, Beverly Hills CA 90212, USA

**McGinest, William L (Willie)** — Football Player
20382 Tramore Lane, Strongsville OH 44149, USA

**McGinley, John C** — Actor
W M E Entertainment, 9601 Wilshire Blvd, #300, Beverly Hills CA 90210 USA

**McGinley, Raymond** — Guitarist (Teenage Fanclub)
High Road Touring, 751 Bridgeway, #200, Sausalito CA 94965 USA

**McGinley, Ted** — Actor
Innovative Artists, 1505 10th St, Santa Monica CA 90401 USA

**McGinn, Bernard J** — Theologian
5702 Kenwood Ave, Chicago IL 60637, USA

**McGinn, Colin** — Philosopher
4779 Collins Ave, #4302, Miami Beach FL 33140, USA

**McGinn, Daniel M (Dan)** — Baseball Player
1309 S 189th Court, Omaha NE 68130, USA

**McGinnis, Dave** — Football Coach
3526 E Equestrian Trail, Phoenix AZ 85044, USA

**McGinnis, George F** — Basketball Player
11245 Marlin Road, Indianapolis IN 46239, USA

**McGinnis, Joe** — Writer
Janklow & Nesbit, 445 Park Ave, #1300, New York NY 10022, USA

**McGinnis, Joe, Jr** — Writer
I C M Partners, 10250 Constellation Blvd, #900, Los Angeles CA 90067 USA

**McGirt, James (Buddy), Jr** — Boxer, Manager
Elite Youth Program, 104 Day Dr, Sebastian FL 32958, USA

**McGiver, Boris** — Actor
Harden-Curtis Associates, 850 7th Ave, #903, New York NY 10019, USA

**McGlocklin, Jon P** — Basketball Player
5281 State Road, #83, Hartland WI 53029, USA

**McGlone, Mike** — Actor
Don Buchwald, 6500 Wilshire Blvd, #2200, Los Angeles CA 90048 USA

**McGlothin, Ezra M (Pat)** — Baseball Player
1454 Kenesaw Ave, Knoxville TN 37919, USA

**McGlynn, Richard A (Dick)** — Ice Hockey Player
38 Rock Glen Road, Medford MA 02155, USA

**McGonagle, Marta** — Actress
Charles Sherman, 8306 Wilshire Blvd, #2017, Beverly Hills CA 90211, USA

**McGoon, Dwight C** — Surgeon
840 9th Ave SW, Rochester MN 55902, USA

**McGovern, Elizabeth** — Actress
Rights House, Drury House, 34-43 Russell St, London WC2B 5HA, England

**McGovern, James D (Jim)** — Golfer
900 Amaryllis Ave, Oradell NJ 07649, USA

**McGovern, Maureen** — Singer
Judy Katz, 250 W 57th St, #1818, New York NY 10107, USA

**McGowan, Patrick R (Pat)** — Golfer
PO Box 88, Southern Pines NC 28388, USA

**McGowan, Zach** — Actor
Innovative Artists, 1505 10th St, Santa Monica CA 90401 USA

**McGrady, Charles** — Environmentalist
Sierra Club, 85 2nd St, #200 San Francisco CA 94105, USA

**McGrady, Tracy L, Jr** — Basketball Player
23 Beacon Hill, Sugar Land TX 77479, USA

**McGrain, Peter** — Artist
207 Maple St, White Salmon WA 98672, USA

**McGrath, C Peter** — Educator
State University of New York, President's Office, 4400 Vestal Parkway E, Binghamton NY 13902, USA

**McGrath, Douglas** — Director, Actor, Writer
Creative Artists Agency, 2000 Ave of Stars, #100, Los Angeles CA 90067 USA

**McGrath, James** — Geneticist
Yale University, Genetics Dept, New Haven CT 06520, USA

| | |
|---|---|
| **McGrath, Jeremy** | Motorcycle Racing Rider |
| J R Motorsports 801 SW Ordnance Road, Ankeny IA 50023, USA | |
| **McGrath, Judy** | Businesswoman |
| MTV Networks, 1515 Broadway, New York NY 10036, USA | |
| **McGrath, Mark** | Singer (Sugar Ray), Entertainer |
| Pinnacle Entertainment, 30 Glenn St, White Plains NY 10603, USA | |
| **McGrath, Mike** | Bowler |
| 63 W Napa Dr, Petaluma CA 94954, USA | |
| **McGrath, Robert E (Bob)** | Actor, Writer |
| Bob McGrath Productions, 295 Frances St, Teaneck NJ 07666, USA | |
| **McGraw, Joseph** | WW II Navy Air Hero |
| 416 Alissa Lane, Burlington WA 98233, USA | |
| **McGraw, Melinda** | Actress |
| Domain Talent, 9229 W Sunset Blvd, #710, West Hollywood CA 90069 USA | |
| **McGraw, Michael S (Mike)** | Football Player |
| PO Box 529, Medicine Bow WY 82329, USA | |
| **McGraw, Muffet** | Basketball Coach |
| University of Notre Dame, Athletic Dept, Notre Dame IN 46556, USA | |
| **McGraw, Phillip C (Dr Phil)** | Entertainer, Psychologist |
| 1008 Lexington Road, Beverly Hills CA 90210, USA | |
| **McGraw, Tim** | Singer |
| Red Light Mgmt, PO Box 1467, Charlottesville VA 22902, USA | |
| **McGregor, Ewan** | Actor |
| United Agents, 12-26 Lexington St, London W1F 0LE, England | |
| **McGregor, Freddie** | Singer |
| Solid Agency, 7 Dumbarton Ave, Kingston 10, Jamaica | |
| **McGregor, Katherine Ann** | Actress, Producer |
| Iconoblast Talent Mgmt, 1335 N La Brea, #2148, Los Angeles CA 90028, USA | |
| **McGregor, Scott H** | Baseball Player |
| 1514 Providence Road, #A, Towson MD 21286, USA | |
| **McGriff, Frederick S (Fred)** | Baseball Player |
| 16314 Millan de Avila, Tampa FL 33613, USA | |
| **McGriff, Hershel** | Auto Racing Driver |
| General Delivery, Green Valley AZ 85622, USA | |
| **McGriff, Terence R (Terry)** | Baseball Player |
| 2905 Langston Dr, Fort Pierce FL 34946, USA | |
| **McGruder, Aaron** | Cartoonist (Boondocks) |
| Universal Press Syndicate, 4520 Main St, #700, Kansas City MO 64111 USA | |
| **McGuane, Thomas F, III** | Writer |
| 410 S 3rd Ave, Bozeman MT 59715, USA | |
| **McGuckin, Aislin** | Actress |
| Ken McReddie Assoc, 101 Finsbury Pavement, London EC2A 1RS, England | |
| **McGuigan, Paul** | Bassist (Oasis) |
| Ignition Mgmt, 54 Linhope St, London NW1 6HL, England | |
| **McGuigan, Paul** | Director |
| Fallout Entertainment Group, 3100 Airport Ave, Santa Monica CA 90405, USA | |
| **McGuinn, Roger** | Singer, Guitarist (Byrds), Songwriter |
| Miracle Artists, 26 Dorset St, London W1U 8AP, England | |
| **McGuinness, James (Jay)** | Singer (Wanted) |
| Industry Music Group, 128 Regent Road, Hanley Stoke, Trent ST1 3AY, England | |
| **McGuinness, Martin** | Government Official, Northern Ireland |
| Sinn Fein, 170 Falls Road, Belfast BT12 4PD, Northern Ireland | |
| **McGuire, Betty** | Actress |
| H David Moss, 733 Seward St, #PH, Los Angeles CA 90038 USA | |
| **McGuire, Christine** | Singer (McGuire Sisters) |
| 100 Rancho Circle, Las Vegas NV 89107, USA | |
| **McGuire, Jack** | Association Executive |
| American Red Cross, 431 18th St NW, Washington DC 20006, USA | |
| **McGuire, M C Adolfus (Mickey)** | Baseball Player |
| 1521 Middle Park Dr, Dayton OH 45414, USA | |
| **McGuire, Patti** | Model |
| 1962 E Valley Road, Santa Barbara CA 93108, USA | |
| **McGuire, Phyllis** | Singer (McGuire Sisters) |
| 100 Rancho Circle, Las Vegas NV 89107, USA | |
| **McGuire, Ryan B** | Baseball Player |
| 171 Great Lawn, Irvine CA 92620, USA | |
| **McGuire, W Eugene (Gene)** | Football Player |
| 3229 Country Club Dr, Lynn Haven FL 32444, USA | |
| **McGuire, Willard H** | Labor Leader |
| National Education Assn, 1201 16th St NW, Washington DC 20036, USA | |
| **McGuire, William Biff** | Actor |
| Gage Group, 14724 Ventura Blvd, #505, Sherman Oaks CA 91403 USA | |
| **McGwire, Mark D** | Baseball Player |
| PO Box 165, 4521 Campus Dr, East Irvine CA 92650, USA | |
| **McHaffie Vidal, Deborah** | Golfer |
| Tony Criscuolo, 8425 NW 222nd Ave, Alachua FL 32615, USA | |
| **McHale, Joel** | Actor, Comedian |
| W M E Entertainment, 9601 Wilshire Blvd, #300, Beverly Hills CA 90210 USA | |
| **McHale, Kevin** | Actor |
| Greene Assoc, 1901 Ave of Stars, #130, Los Angeles CA 90067 USA | |
| **McHale, Kevin E** | Basketball Player, Executive, Coach |
| 20 Blue Jay Lane, Saint Paul MN 55127, USA | |
| **McHattie, Stephen** | Actor |
| Christopher Wright Mgmt, 3207 Winnie Dr, Los Angeles CA 90068, USA | |
| **McHenry, Donald F** | Diplomat |
| Georgetown University, Foreign Service School, Washington DC 20057, USA | |
| **McHenry, Vance L** | Baseball Player |
| 2396 Brown St, Durham CA 95938, USA | |
| **McHugh, Heather** | Writer |
| University of Washington, English Dept, PO Box 354330, Seattle WA 98195, USA | |
| **McHugh, John M** | Secretary, Army; Representative, NY |
| Secretary's Office, HqUSA, Pentagon, Washington DC 20310, USA | |
| **McIlhenny, Donald B (Don)** | Football Player |
| 8505 Edgemere Road, #101, Dallas TX 75225, USA | |
| **McIlrath, Tim** | Singer, Guitarist (Rise Against) |
| Agency Group Ltd, 142 W 57th St, #600, New York NY 10019 USA | |

McGrath - McIlrath

**McIlravy, Lincoln** — Freestyle Wrestler
4220 210th St NE, Solon IA 52333, USA

**McIlroy, Rory** — Golfer
Holywood Golf Club, Nuns Walk, Demesne Road, Holywood, County Down BT18 9LE, Northern Ireland

**McIlvaine, James M (Jim)** — Basketball Player
Camp Anokijig, W5639 Anokijig Lane, Plymouth WI 53073, USA

**McInally, Patrick J (Pat)** — Football Player
19321 Ocean Heights Lane, Huntington Beach CA 92648, USA

**McInerney, John B (Jay), Jr** — Writer
I C M Partners, 10250 Constellation Blvd, #900, Los Angeles CA 90067 USA

**McInnis, Jeff L** — Basketball Player
3404 Lazy Day Lane, Charlotte NC 28269, USA

**McInnis, Marty** — Ice Hockey Player
21 Peter Hobart Dr, Hingham MA 02043, USA

**McIntosh, Damion A** — Football Player
1221 SW Summit Crossing Dr, Lees Summit MO 64081, USA

**McIntosh, Timothy A (Tim)** — Baseball Player
1815 S Talbott Place, Waynesboro VA 22980, USA

**McIntyre, Guy M** — Football Player
257 Arrowhead Way, Hayward CA 94544, USA

**McIntyre, Joey** — Singer (New Kids on the Block)
Spectrum Talent, 1650 Broadway, #1105, New York NY 10019, USA

**McIntyre, Liam** — Actor
Progressive Artists Agency, 9696 Culver Blvd, #110, Culver City CA 90232 USA

**McIver, Everett A** — Football Player
1205 Avignon Dr SW, Conyers GA 30094, USA

**McKagan, Duff** — Bassist (Guns N' Roses)
Sanctuary Artist Mgmt, 15301 Ventura Blvd, Building B, Sherman Oaks CA 91403, USA

**McKart, Bronco** — Boxer
Scott Beard, 11343 Telegraph Road, #A, Erie PA 48133, USA

**McKay, Adam** — Actor, Director, Writer
Gary Sanchez Productions, 729 Seward St, #200, Los Angeles CA 90038, USA

**McKay, Al** — Guitarist (Earth Wind Fire), Songwriter
Spirit Media, PO Box 43591, Phoenix AZ 85080, USA

**McKay, Ami** — Writer
PO Box 146, Canning NS B0P 1H0, Canada

**McKay, Caroline** — Drummer (Glasvegas)
Sony Music, 9 Derry St, London W8 5HY, England

**McKay, Christian** — Actor
Independent Talent Group, 40 Whitfield St, London W1T 2RH, England

**McKay, David L (Dave)** — Baseball Player
9702 W La Posada Circle, Scottsdale AZ 85255, USA

**McKay, Heather** — Squash, Racquetball Player
48 Nesbitt Dr, Toronto ON M4W 2G3, Canada

**McKay, Mhairi** — Golfer
898 W Ashbourne Dr, Eagle ID 83616, USA

**McKay, Monroe G** — Judge
US Court of Appeals, Federal Building, 125 S State St, Salt Lake City UT 84138, USA

**McKay, Nellie** — Singer, Pianist, Songwriter
Creative Artists Agency, 2000 Ave of Stars, #100, Los Angeles CA 90067 USA

**McKay, Peggy** — Actress
8811 Wonderland Ave, Los Angeles CA 90046, USA

**McKay, Randy** — Ice Hockey Player
44640 US Highway 41, Chassell MI 49916, USA

**McKay, Ritchie** — Basketball Coach
Liberty University, Athletic Dept, Lynchburg VA 24502, USA

**McKay, Robert C (Bob)** — Football Player
4110 Bluffridge Dr, Austin TX 78759, USA

**McKeague, David W** — Judge
US Appellate Court, 315 W Allegan St, Lansing MI 48933, USA

**McKean, James G (Jim)** — Baseball Umpire
740 Sand Pine Dr NE, Saint Petersburg FL 33703, USA

**McKean, Michael J** — Actor, Comedian
A P A Talent/Literary Agency, 405 S Beverly Dr, #300, Beverly Hills CA 90212 USA

**McKechnie, Walt** — Ice Hockey Player
McKeck's Place, PO Box 752, Haliburton ON K0M 1S0, Canada

**McKee, Frank S** — Labor Leader
United Steelworkers Union, 60 Blvd of Allies, #5, Pittsburgh PA 15222, USA

**McKee, Gina** — Actress
United Agents, 12-26 Lexington St, London W1F 0LE, England

**McKee, Jay** — Ice Hockey Player
1423 Topping Road, Saint Louis MO 63131, USA

**McKee, Kinnaird R** — Navy Admiral
7100 Wheeler Park Circle, Easton MD 21601, USA

**McKee, Maria** — Singer, Songwriter
Concerted Efforts, PO Box 440326, Somerville MA 02144 USA

**McKee, Theodore A** — Judge
US Appeals Court, US Courthouse, 601 Market St, #20614, Philadelphia PA 19106, USA

**McKee, Todd** — Actor
316 N Flores St, Los Angeles CA 90048, USA

**McKellar, Danica** — Actress
C E S D, 10635 Santa Monica Blvd, #130, Los Angeles CA 90025 USA

**McKellen, Ian** — Actor
2act, Mirza Co, 826 Garratt Lane, London SW17 0LZ, England

**McKeller, T Keith** — Football Player
1972 Waccamaw Path, Winston Salem NC 27127, USA

**McKelvey, Rob** — Golfer
1814 Duke Road, Atlanta GA 30341, USA

**McKenna, Alex** — Actress
Innovative Artists, 1505 10th St, Santa Monica CA 90401 USA

**McKenna, Bruce C** — Writer, Journalist, Producer
Flashpoint Entertainment, 9150 Wilshire Blvd, #247, Beverly Hills CA 90212, USA

**McKenna, Chris** — Actor
Stone Manners Salners, 9911 W Pico Blvd, #1400, Los Angeles CA 90035 USA

**McKenna, Kevin R** — Basketball Player
15387 Nicholas St, Omaha NE 68154, USA

**McKenna, Lori** — Singer, Songwriter
Rolling Thunder Artist Mgmt, 174 Allen Ave, Waban MA 02468, USA

**McKenna, Stephen F** — Artist
Crocknafeola, Killybegs, County Donegal, Ireland

**McKenna, Virginia** — Actress
Brunskill Management, 169 Queens Gate, #8A, London SW7 5HE, England

**McKenney, Donald H (Don)** — Ice Hockey Player
16 Edgewater Dr, Norton MA 02766, USA

**McKennitt, Loreena** — Singer, Songwriter
High Road Touring, 751 Bridgeway, #200, Sausalito CA 94965 USA

**McKenny, James C (Jim)** — Ice Hockey Player
City-TV, 299 Queen St W, Toronto ON M5V 2Z5, Canada

**McKenzie Smith, Ian** — Artist
70 Hamilton Place, Aberdeen AB15 5BA, Scotland

**McKenzie, Benjamin (Ben)** — Actor
Management 360, 9111 Wilshire Blvd, Beverly Hills CA 90210 USA

**McKenzie, Bret** — Singer (Flight of the Conchords), Actor
Creative Artists Agency, 2000 Ave of Stars, #100, Los Angeles CA 90067 USA

**McKenzie, Dan P** — Geologist
Bullard Labs, Madingley Rise, Madingley Road, Cambridge CB3 0EZ, England

**McKenzie, Derrick** — Drummer (Jamiroquai)
Nettwerk Mgmt, 6525 W Sunset Blvd, #800, Los Angeles CA 90028 USA

**McKenzie, Forrest D W** — Basketball Player
2516 S Laurelwood, Santa Ana CA 92704, USA

**McKenzie, Jacqueline** — Actress, Director, Writer
S M S Talent, 8383 Wilshire Blvd, #230, Beverly Hills CA 90211 USA

**McKenzie, James P (Jim)** — Ice Hockey Player
9266 Chevoit Dr, Brentwood TN 37027, USA

**McKenzie, John** — Ice Hockey Player
10 Clearview Road, Stoneham MA 02180, USA

**McKenzie, Julia** — Actress
Ken McReddie Assoc, 101 Finsbury Pavement, London EC2A 1RS, England

**McKenzie, Kevin** — Ballet Dancer
American Ballet Theatre, 890 Broadway, #300, New York NY 10003 USA

**McKenzie, Raleigh** — Football Player
715 Huntsman Place, Herndon VA 20170, USA

**McKenzie, Reggie** — Football Player, Executive
411 Carta Road, Knoxville TN 37914, USA

**McKenzie, Reginald (Reggie)** — Football Player
13853 Trumbull St, Highland Park MI 48203, USA

**McKenzie, Stanley (Stan)** — Basketball Player
8316 Governor Grayson Way, Ellicott City MD 21043, USA

**McKeon, Doug** — Actor
4644 Arriba Dr, Tarzana CA 91356, USA

**McKeon, Joel J** — Baseball Player
1901 Pierce St, Hollywood FL 33020, USA

**McKeon, John A (Jack)** — Baseball Player, Manager
1529 Charleigh Court, Elon NC 27244, USA

**McKeon, Nancy** — Actress
Stone Manners Salners, 9911 W Pico Blvd, #1400, Los Angeles CA 90035 USA

**McKeown, Bob** — Commentator
CBS-TV, News Dept, 51 W 52nd St, New York NY 10019 USA

**McKeown, M Margaret** — Judge
2447 Ardath Road, La Jolla CA 92037, USA

**McKernan, John R, Jr** — Governor, ME
77 Sanderson Road, Cumberland Foreside ME 04110, USA

**McKey, Derrick W** — Basketball Player
8 Woodard Place, Zionsville IN 46077, USA

**McKidd, Kevin** — Actor
W K T Public Relations, 9350 Wilshire Blvd, #450, Beverly Hills CA 90212 USA

**McKie, Aaron F** — Basketball Player
1400 Youngs Ford Road, Gladwyne PA 19035, USA

**McKie, Jason A** — Football Player
4431 W Lawn Ave, Waukegan IL 60085, USA

**McKinley, Alvin J** — Football Player
45274 W Miraflores St, Maricopa AZ 85139, USA

**McKinley, Craig R** — Air Force General
Chief, National Guard Bureau, HqUSAF, Pentagon, Washington DC 20330 USA

**McKinley, John** — Rowing Athlete
952 Bloomfield Village, Auburn Hills MI 48326, USA

**McKinley, John K** — Businessman
1 Canterbury Green, #800, Stamford CT 06901, USA

**McKinley, Robin** — Writer
Writer's House, 21 W 26th St, New York NY 10010, USA

**McKinley-Uselmann, Therese** — Baseball Player
1644 N Greenwood Ave, Park Ridge IL 60068, USA

**McKinnely, Philip B (Phil)** — Football Player
585 Edgehill Place, Alpharetta GA 30022, USA

**McKinney, C Richard (Rich)** — Baseball Player
2495 E Peterson Road, Troy OH 45373, USA

**McKinney, DeMetria** — Actress
Don Buchwald, 6500 Wilshire Blvd, #2200, Los Angeles CA 90048 USA

**McKinney, Kennedy** — Boxer
187 B & R Lane, Golden Meadow LA 70357, USA

**McKinney, Kurt** — Actor
5003 Tilden Ave, #206, Sherman Oaks CA 91423, USA

**McKinney, Mark** — Actor, Comedian, Writer
Oscars Abrams Zimel, 438 Queen St E, Toronto ON M5A 1T4, Canada

**McKinney, Odis, Jr** — Football Player
23126 Collins St, Woodland Hills CA 91367, USA

**McKinney, Richard (Rick)** — Archery Athlete
549 E Silver Creek Road, Gilbert AZ 85296, USA

**McKinney, Stephen M (Steve)** — Football Player
335 County Road 201, Centerville TX 75833, USA

**McKinney, Tamara** — Alpine Skier
4395 Parkers Mill Road, Lexington KY 40513, USA

**McKinnie, Bryant D** — Football Player
12535 Stoneway Court, Davie FL 33330, USA

**McKinnon, Bruce** — Editorial Cartoonist
Halifax Chronicle Herald, 1650 Argyle St, Halifax NS B3J 2T2, Canada

**McKinnon, Daniel D (Dan)** — Ice Hockey Player
610 Riverdale Dr NE, Warroad MN 56763, USA

**McKinnon, Dennis L** — Football Player
1016 Adams St, North Chicago IL 60064, USA

**McKinnon, Ray** — Actor
Creative Artists Agency, 2000 Ave of Stars, #100, Los Angeles CA 90067 USA

**McKinnon, Ronald (Ron)** — Football Player
1063 Grand Oaks Dr, Bessemer AL 35022, USA

**McKissack, Patricia** — Writer
Scholastic Press, 555 Broadway, New York NY 10012 USA

**McKissick, John** — Football Coach
Summerville High School, Athletic Dept, Summerville SC 29484, USA

**McKittrick, Rob** — Director, Writer
Creative Artists Agency, 2000 Ave of Stars, #100, Los Angeles CA 90067 USA

**McKnight, Anthony (Tony)** — Baseball Player
406 Dundee Road, Texarkana AR 71854, USA

**McKnight, Brian** — Singer, Songwriter
Universal Attractions, 135 W 26th St, #1200, New York NY 10001 USA

**McKnight, Clarence E, Jr** — Army General
1624 Linway Park Dr, McLean VA 22101, USA

**McKnight, Ira** — Baseball Player
608 S Summit Dr, #1, South Bend IN 46619, USA

**McKnight, James** — Football Player
16705 Berkshire Court, Southwest Ranches FL 33331, USA

**McKnight, Jefferson A (Jeff)** — Baseball Player
3296 Highway 92 W, Bee Branch AR 72013, USA

**McKnight, John** — Singer, Musician (Fishbone)
Silverback Mgmt, 9469 Jefferson Blvd, #101, Culver City CA 90232, USA

**McKnight, Steven L** — Molecular Biologist
8513 Swananoah Road, Dallas TX 75209, USA

**McKnight, Theodore R (Ted)** — Football Player
10236 Cedarbrooke Lane, Kansas City MO 64131, USA

**McKnight, Thomas F** — Artist
30 Peck Road, #2201, Torrington CT 06790, USA

**Mckown, Zack** — Interior Designer
Tsao-McKorn Design, 20 Vandam St, #1000, New York NY 10013, USA

**McKuen, Rod** — Singer, Songwiter, Writer
C E S D, 10635 Santa Monica Blvd, #130, Los Angeles CA 90025 USA

**McKyer, Timothy B (Tim)** — Football Player
11201 Golden Dr, Charlotte NC 28216, USA

**McLachlan, Craig D** — Actor, Singer
Neil Clugston Organisation, 11A Wigham Road, Glebe NSW 2037, Australia

**McLachlan, Sarah** — Singer, Songwriter
Sarah McLachlan School of Music, 138 E 7th Ave, #200, Vancouver, BC V5T 1M6, Canada

**McLafferty, Fred W** — Chemist
103 Needham Place, Ithaca NY 14850, USA

**McLaglen, Andrew V** — Director
Stanmore Productions, PO Box 1056, Friday Harbor WA 98250, USA

**McLain, Dennis D (Denny)** — Baseball Player
4432 Golf View Dr, Brighton MI 48116, USA

**McLane, James P (Jimmy), Jr** — Swimmer
97 Mount Vernon St, #1, Boston MA 02108, USA

**McLaren, Brandon Jay** — Actor
Pakula/King, 9229 W Sunset Blvd, #315, West Hollywood CA 90069 USA

**McLaren, John L** — Baseball Manager
Washington Nationals, 1500 S Capitol St SE, Washington DC 20003 USA

**McLaren, Kyle E** — Ice Hockey Player
6582 Skyfarm Dr, San Jose CA 95120, USA

**McLaughlin, Ann Dore** — Secretary, Labor
Rand Corp, 1200 S Hayes St, #400, Arlington VA 22202, USA

**McLaughlin, Audrey** — Government Official, Canada
410 Hoge St, Whitehorse, Yukon Y1A 1W2, Canada

**McLaughlin, Brian** — Actor
Brooks Murphy Stevens, 5619 N Lankershim Blvd, North Hollywood CA 91601 USA

**McLaughlin, Byron S** — Baseball Player
7030 Alamitos Ave, San Diego CA 92154, USA

**McLaughlin, David** — Association Executive
American Red Cross, 431 18th St NW, Washington DC 20006, USA

**McLaughlin, Emma** — Writer
Atria Books, 1230 Ave of Americas, New York NY 10020 USA

**McLaughlin, Jake** — Actor
Paradigm Agency, 360 N Crescent Dr, North Building, Beverly Hills CA 90210 USA

**McLaughlin, Jim** — Architect
McLaughlin Assoc, PO Box 479, Sun Valley ID 83353, USA

**McLaughlin, Joey R** — Baseball Player
1611 S Troost Ave, Tulsa OK 74120, USA

**McLaughlin, John** — Jazz Guitarist, Composer
Ted Kurland, 173 Brighton Ave, Boston MA 02134 USA

**McLaughlin, John E** — Government Official
Central Intelligence Agency, Deputy Director's Office, Washington DC 20505, USA

**McLaughlin, John J** — Commentator
McLaughlin Group, 1717 Rhode Island Ave NW, #640, Washington DC 20036, USA

**McLaughlin, Joseph J (Joe)** — Football Player
65 Pells Fishing Road, Brewster MA 02631, USA

**McLaughlin, Michael (Mike)** — Auto Racing Driver
PO Box 45, Waterloo NY 13165, USA

**McLaughlin, Michael D (Bo)** — Baseball Player
536 N Grand, Mesa AZ 85201, USA

**McLean, A J** — Singer (Backstreet Boys), Actor
Podwell Entertainment, 710 N Orlando Ave, #203, West Hollywood CA 90069, USA

**McLean, Don** — Singer, Songwriter
Paradise Artists, PO Box 1821, Ojai CA 93024 USA

**McLean, Greg** — Director, Writer
W M E Entertainment, 9601 Wilshire Blvd, #300, Beverly Hills CA 90210 USA

**McLean, Hayley** — Singer, Songwriter
Agency Group Ltd, 142 W 57th St, #600, New York NY 10019 USA

**McLean, Jane** — Actress
Oscars Abrams Zimel, 438 Queen St E, Toronto ON M5A 1T4, Canada

**McLean, Kirk** — Ice Hockey Player
Burnaby Express, 3676 Kensington Ave, Burnaby BC V5B 4Z6, Canada

**McLean, Michelle** — Beauty Queen
McLean Children's Trust, PO Box 97428, Maerua Mall, Windhoek, Namibia

**McLean, Rene** — Jazz Saxophonist, Flutist
Brad Simon Organization, 445 E 80th St, #4C, New York NY 10075 USA

**McLean, Sally** — Actress, Producer
Salmac Mgmt, PO Box 526, Mount Martha VIC 3934, Australia

**McLean-Ross, Lucella** — Baseball Player
401-5107 47th St, Lloydminster AB T9V 0G1, Canada

**McLeavy, Robin** — Actress
United Talent Agency, U T A Plaza, 9336 Civic Center Dr, Beverly Hills CA 90210 USA

**McLemore, Ben** — Basketball Player
Sacramento Kings, Arco Arena, 1 Sports Parkway, Sacramento CA 95834 USA

**McLemore, Dana** — Football Player
125 Seagate Dr, San Mateo CA 94403, USA

**McLemore, Elle** — Actress
Paradigm Agency, 360 N Crescent Dr, North Building, Beverly Hills CA 90210 USA

**McLemore, LaMonte** — Singer (Fifth Dimension)
Brokaw Co, 9255 W Sunset Blvd, #804, West Hollywood CA 90069 USA

**McLemore, Mark T** — Baseball Player
533 S White Chapel Blvd, Southlake TX 76092, USA

**McLendon-Covey, Wendi** — Actress, Producer, Writer
John Carrabino Management, 5900 Wilshire, #406, Los Angeles CA 90036, USA

**McLennan, Jamie** — Ice Hockey Player
Calgary Flames, PO Box 1540, Station M, Calgary AB T2P 3B9, Canada

**McLeod, Erin** — Soccer Player
Canadian Soccer, Place Soccer Canada, 237 Metcalfe St, Ottawa ON K2P 1R2, Canada

**McLeod, R J Jackie** — Ice Hockey Player
13 John Hair Court, Saskatoon SK S7J 2K6, Canada

**McLeod, Robert D (Bob)** — Football Player
600 Spring Creek Road, Brenham TX 77833, USA

**McLerie, Allyn Ann** — Actress, Dancer
3344 Campanil Dr, Santa Barbara CA 93109, USA

**McLish, Rachel** — Actress, Body Builder
Ron Samuels Entertainment, 100 Wilshire Blvd, #750, Santa Monica CA 90401, USA

**McLlwain, Dave** — Ice Hockey Player
Yacht Club Woods, Grand Bend ON N0M 1T0, Canada

**McLoughlin, Tom** — Director
Paradigm Agency, 360 N Crescent Dr, North Building, Beverly Hills CA 90210 USA

**McLouth, Nathan R (Nate)** — Baseball Player
6116 W Fieldstone Hills Dr SE, Caledonia MI 49316, USA

**McLure, Charles E, Jr** — Government Official
250 Yerba Santa Ana, Los Altos CA 94022, USA

**McMahan, Jack W** — Baseball Player
131 Forest View Circle, Hot Springs AR 71913, USA

**McMahon, Andrew R** — Singer, Pianist, Songwriter
A P A Talent/Literary Agency, 405 S Beverly Dr, #300, Beverly Hills CA 90212 USA

**McMahon, Donald A** — Businessman
63 W Wieuca Road NE, #1, Atlanta GA 30342, USA

**McMahon, James R (Jim)** — Football Player
22431 N Violetta Dr, Scottsdale AZ 85255, USA

**McMahon, Julian** — Actor
W M E Entertainment, 9601 Wilshire Blvd, #300, Beverly Hills CA 90210 USA

**McMahon, Michael E (Mike)** — Football Player
313 Oak Grove Court, Wexford PA 15090, USA

**McMahon, Stacy** — Model
White Tiger Modeling, PO Box 5298, South Melbourne VIC 3205, Australia

**McMahon, Vincent K, Jr** — Professional Wrestling Executive
World Wrestling Entertainment, Titan Towers, 1241 E Main St, Stamford CT 06902 USA

**McMakin, John G** — Football Player
608 Longview Ave, Anacortes WA 98221, USA

**McManus, James M (Jim)** — Baseball Player
2352 Hopkins Mill Road, Duluth GA 30096, USA

**McManus, Michaela** — Actress
United Talent Agency, U T A Plaza, 9336 Civic Center Dr, Beverly Hills CA 90210 USA

**McMartin, John** — Actor, Singer
Artists Agency, 9430 Olympic Blvd, Beverly Hills CA 90212 USA

**McMath, Jimmy L** — Baseball Player
3321 22nd St, Tuscaloosa AL 35401, USA

**McMenamin, Mark A S** — Geologist
Mount Holyoke College, Geology Dept, South Hadley MA 01075, USA

**McMichael, Gregory W (Greg)** — Baseball Player
240 Parkside Club Court, Duluth GA 30097, USA

**McMichael, Randy H** — Football Player
361 17th St NW, Atlanta GA 30363, USA

**McMichael, Steve D** — Football Player
1212 Santa Fe Road, #103, Romeoville IL 60446, USA

**McMillan, Caroline Pierce** — Golfer
7625 E Phantom Way, Scottsdale AZ 85255, USA

**McMillan, Ernest C (Ernie)** — Football Player
14816 Sycamore Manor Court, Chesterfield MO 63017, USA

**McMillan, Nathaniel (Nate)** — Basketball Player, Coach
217 Great Lake Dr, Cary NC 27519, USA

**McMillan, Terry L** — Writer
PO Box 378, Pasadena CA 91102, USA

**McMillan, Thomas E (Tommy)** — Baseball Player
712 Spring Lake Road, Thomasville GA 31792, USA

**McMillan, William (Bill)** — Marksman
1930 Sandstone Vista, Encinitas CA 92024, USA

**M**

McMillen, C Thomas (Tom) — Representative, MD; Basketball Player
Homeland Security Capital Corp, 1005 N Glebe Road, #550, Arlington VA 22201, USA
McMillen, Robert — Track Athlete
5708 Golden West Ave, Temple City CA 91780, USA
McMillian, Audray G — Football Player
1230 Hahlo St, Houston TX 77020, USA
McMillian, James M (Jim) — Basketball Player
4804 Tara Dr, Greensboro NC 27410, USA
McMillian, Michael — Actor
Innovative Artists, 1505 10th St, Santa Monica CA 90401 USA
McMillin, James R (Jim) — Football Player
7985 Westview Dr, Lakewood CO 80214, USA
McMillon, William (Billy) — Baseball Player
1516 Lost Creek Dr, Columbia SC 29212, USA
McMonagle, Donald R — Astronaut
7737 E Shadow Vista Court, Tucson AZ 85750, USA
McMorrow, James Vincent — Singer, Songwriter
Agency Group Ltd, 142 W 57th St, #600, New York NY 10019 USA
McMullen, Curtis T — Mathematician
Harvard University, Science Center, Cambridge MA 02138, USA
McMullen, Kenneth L (Ken) — Baseball Player
10 Estaban Dr, Camarillo CA 93010, USA
McMullian, Amos R — Businessman
Flowers Industries, 200 US Highway 19 S, Thomasville GA 31792, USA
McMullin, Ernan V — Philosopher
University of Notre Dame, Philosophy Dept, Notre Dame IN 46556, USA
McMurray, James C (Jamie) — Auto Racing Driver
211 Milford Circle, Mooresville NC 28117, USA
McMurtry, Gregory W (Greg) — Football Player
755 Oak Point Lane, Madison Heights MI 48071, USA
McMurtry, J Craig — Baseball Player
2835 Bottoms East Road, Troy TX 76579, USA
McMurtry, James — Singer, Songwriter
High Road Touring, 751 Bridgeway, #200, Sausalito CA 94965 USA
McMurtry, Larry — Writer
PO Box 552, Archer City TX 76351, USA
McMurtry, Tom — Test Pilot
PO Box 273, Edwards CA 93523, USA
McNab, Mercedes — Actress, Model
Stone Manners Salners, 9911 W Pico Blvd, #1400, Los Angeles CA 90035 USA
McNab, Peter M — Ice Hockey Player
10311 Rancho Montecito, Parker CO 80138, USA
McNabb, Donovan — Football Player
21800 Towncenter Plaza, #266A, Sterling VA 20164, USA
McNabb, Duncan J — Air Force General
Commander, US Transportation Command, Scott Air Force Base IL 62225, USA
McNairy, Scoot — Actor
Group Films, 800 S Robertson Blvd, #5, Los Angeles CA 90035, USA
McNally, Andrew, IV — Publisher
Rand McNally Co, 9855 Woods Dr, Skokie IL 60077, USA
McNally, David (Dave) — Director, Producer, Writer
W M E Entertainment, 9601 Wilshire Blvd, #300, Beverly Hills CA 90210 USA
McNally, Kevin — Actor
Hatton McEwan, 3 Chocolate Studios, 7 Shepherdess Place, London N1 7LJ, England
McNally, Shannon M — Singer, Songwriter
Impact Artists Mgmt, 356 W 123rd St, New York NY 10027, USA
McNally, Stephen (Ste) — Singer, Guitarist (BBMak)
Spirit Media, PO Box 43591, Phoenix AZ 85080, USA
McNally, Terrence — Writer, Actor
Gersh Agency, 9465 Wilshire Blvd, #600, Beverly Hills CA 90212 USA
McNamara, Brian — Actor
Talent Works, 3500 W Olive Ave, #1400, Burbank CA 91505 USA
McNamara, Eileen — Journalist
Boston Globe, Editorial Dept, 135 William Morrissey Blvd, Dorchester MA 02125 USA
McNamara, Gerry — Ice Hockey Player
213-350 Mill Road, Etobicoke ON M9C 5R7, Canada
McNamara, James P (Jim) — Baseball Player
15317 Surrey House Way, Centreville VA 20120, USA
McNamara, John F — Baseball Player, Manager
1206 Beech Hill Road, Brentwood TN 37027, USA
McNamara, Julianne L — Gymnast, Actress
Todd Zeile, 5445 Via Nicola, Newbury Park CA 91320, USA
McNamara, Mark R C — Basketball Player
PO Box 134, Strawberry CA 95375, USA
McNamara, Melissa — Golfer
7715 S Quebec Ave, Tulsa OK 74136, USA
McNamara, Robert M (Bob) — Baseball Player
4764 Dalea Place, Oceanside CA 92057, USA
McNamara, Sean — Director
A P A Talent/Literary Agency, 405 S Beverly Dr, #300, Beverly Hills CA 90212 USA
McNamara, William (Billy) — Actor
Venture I A B, 3211 Cahuenga Blvd W, #104, Los Angeles CA 90068, USA
McNamee, Jessica — Actress
United Talent Agency, U T A Plaza, 9336 Civic Center Dr, Beverly Hills CA 90210 USA
McNanie, Sean — Football Player
14915 Rancho Real, Del Mar CA 92014, USA
McNaught, Judith — Writer
Random House, 1745 Broadway, #1800, New York NY 10019 USA
McNaughton, John D — Director, Producer, Writer
Gersh Agency, 9465 Wilshire Blvd, #600, Beverly Hills CA 90212 USA
McNaughton, Robert F, Jr — Computer Scientist
2511 15th St, Troy NY 12180, USA
McNeal, Donald (Don) — Football Player
3311 Toledo Plaza, Coral Gables FL 33134, USA
McNealy, Scott G — Businessman
Sun Microsystems, 4150 Network Circle, Santa Clara CA 95054, USA

McMillen - McNealy

| | |
|---|---|
| **McNeely, Jeffrey L (Jeff)** | Baseball Player |
| 405 Everette St, Monroe NC 28112, USA | |
| **McNeil, Clifton A** | Football Player |
| 1001 Westbury Dr, #98, Mobile AL 36609, USA | |
| **McNeil, Freeman** | Football Player |
| PO Box 62, Greenlawn NY 11740, USA | |
| **McNeil, Kate** | Actress |
| 1743 N Dillon St, Los Angeles CA 90026, USA | |
| **McNeil, Lori** | Tennis Player |
| International Mangement Group, 1 Erieview Plaza, 1360 E 9th St, Cleveland OH 44114 USA | |
| **McNeil, Patrick (Pat)** | Football Player |
| 2117 US Highway 80 E, Mesquite TX 75150, USA | |
| **McNeil, Ryan D** | Football Player |
| 315 14th St NW, Atlanta GA 30318, USA | |
| **McNeill, Corbin A, Jr** | Businessman |
| P E C O Energy Co, 2301 Market St, Philadelphia PA 19103, USA | |
| **McNeill, Frederick A (Fred)** | Football Player |
| 3500 W Manchester Blvd, #320, Inglewood CA 90305, USA | |
| **McNeill, Robert Duncan** | Actor |
| Rothman Agency, 9250 Wilshire Blvd, #PH, Beverly Hills CA 90212, USA | |
| **McNeill, Robert J (Bob)** | Basketball Player |
| 1318 Wooded Way, Bryn Mawr PA 19010, USA | |
| **McNeill, Thomas G (Tom)** | Football Player |
| 31019 Torrey Road, Waller TX 77484, USA | |
| **McNeill, W Donald (Don)** | Tennis Player |
| 2165 15th Ave, Vero Beach FL 32960, USA | |
| **McNerney, W James, Jr** | Businessman |
| Boeing Co, 100 N Riverside, Chicago IL 60606, USA | |
| **McNertney, Gerald E (Jerry)** | Baseball Player |
| 1124 10th St, Nevada IA 50201, USA | |
| **McNichol, Kristy** | Actress |
| Good Guy Entertainment, 3733 Oakfield Dr, Sherman Oaks CA 91423, USA | |
| **McNish, Allan** | Auto Racing Driver |
| C S S Stellar Mgmt, 34-43 Russell St, London WC2B 5HA, England | |
| **McNiven, Julie** | Actress |
| Don Buchwald, 6500 Wilshire Blvd, #2200, Los Angeles CA 90048 USA | |
| **McNorton, Bruce E** | Football Player |
| PO Box 672, Bloomfield Hills MI 48303, USA | |
| **McNutt, Stephen F** | Cinematographer |
| Innovative Artists, 1505 10th St, Santa Monica CA 90401 USA | |
| **McOmie, Maggie** | Actress |
| Arthouse Talent, 107 SE Washington St, #156, Portland OR 97214, USA | |
| **M'Cormack, Adetokumboh** | Actor |
| Hofflund/Polone, 9465 Wilshire Blvd, #420, Beverly Hills CA 90212 USA | |
| **McPartlin, Anthony (Ant)** | Actor, Producer |
| B/W/R, 292 Madison Ave, #900, New York NY 10017, USA | |
| **McPartlin, Ryan** | Actor, Model |
| Evolution Entertainment, 901 N Highland Ave, Los Angeles CA 90038 USA | |
| **McPeak, Merrill A (Tony)** | Air Force General |
| 123 Furnace St, Lake Oswego OR 97034, USA | |
| **McPhee, John A** | Writer |
| 475 Drake's Corner Road, Princeton NJ 08540, USA | |
| **McPhee, Jonathan** | Conductor |
| PO Box 1425, Marblehead MA 01945, USA | |
| **McPhee, Katharine H** | Singer, Actress |
| Schiff Co, 9200 Sunset Blvd, #430, West Hollywood CA 90232 USA | |
| **McPhee, Kodi Smit** | Actor |
| I C M Partners, 10250 Constellation Blvd, #900, Los Angeles CA 90067 USA | |
| **McPhee, Martha** | Writer |
| Wylie Agency, 250 W 57th St, #2114, New York NY 10107 USA | |
| **McPhee, Mike** | Ice Hockey Player |
| 16 Brook Point Road, Tantallon NS B3Z 2R3, Canada | |
| **McPherson, Charles** | Jazz Saxophonist |
| Joel Chriss Co, 300 Mercer St, #3J, New York NY 10003 USA | |
| **McPherson, Dallas L** | Baseball Player |
| 219 Gold Crest Dr, Braselton GA 30517, USA | |
| **McPherson, Donald G (Don)** | Football Player |
| Sports Leadership Institute, Adelphi University, Garden City NY 11530, USA | |
| **McPherson, James A** | Writer |
| Little Brown, 3 Center Plaza, #100, Boston MA 02108 USA | |
| **McPherson, James M** | Historian |
| 15 Randall Road, Princeton NJ 08540, USA | |
| **McPherson, John** | Cartoonist (Close to Home) |
| Universal Press Syndicate, 4520 Main St, #700, Kansas City MO 64111 USA | |
| **McPherson, Kristy** | Golfer |
| Ladies Pro Golf Assn, 100 International Golf Dr, Daytona Beach FL 32124 USA | |
| **McQuarrie, Christopher** | Writer, Diector, Producer |
| Invisible Ink, 9696 Culver Blvd, #203, Culver City CA 90232, USA | |
| **McQuarters, Robert W (R W)** | Football Player |
| 1548 E 54th St N, Tulsa OK 74126, USA | |
| **McQueen, Chad** | Actor |
| 8306 Wilshire Blvd, #438, Beverly Hills CA 90211, USA | |
| **McQueen, Cozell** | Basketball Player |
| 100 E Charing Cross, Cary NC 27513, USA | |
| **McQueen, Michael R (Mike)** | Baseball Player |
| 6623 Lost Horizon Dr, Austin TX 78759, USA | |
| **McQueen, Steven R** | Actor |
| Schiff Co, 9200 Sunset Blvd, #430, West Hollywood CA 90232 USA | |
| **McQueen, Steven R (Steve)** | Artist, Director |
| Casorotto Ramsay, Waverley House, 7-12 Noel St, London W1F 8GQ, England | |
| **McQueen, Tanya** | Actress |
| Generate, 1545 26th St, #200, Santa Monica CA 90404, USA | |
| **McQuilken, Kim E** | Football Player |
| 360 Highgrove Dr, Fayetteville GA 30215, USA | |
| **McRae, Basil** | Ice Hockey Player |
| 759 Hyde Park Road, #252, London ON N6H 3S2, Canada | |

**McRae, Benjamin P (Bennie)** — Football Player
532 W 143rd St, #63, New York NY 10031, USA
**McRae, Harold O (Hal)** — Baseball Player, Manager
519 Sand Crane Court, Bradenton FL 34212, USA
**McRaney, Gerald** — Actor
217 Keller St, Bay Saint Louis MS 39520, USA
**McReynolds, Jesse L** — Singer, Mandolin Player (Jim & Jesse)
PO Box 304, Gallatin TN 37066, USA
**McReynolds, Lawrence J (Larry), III** — Sportscaster, Auto Racing Mechanic
123 Mystic Lake Loop, Mooresville NC 28117, USA
**McReynolds, W Kevin** — Baseball Player
2 Country Place, Roland AR 72135, USA
**McRobbie, Michael A** — Educator
Indiana University, President's Office, 107 S Indiana, Bloomington IN 47405, USA
**McRobbie, Peter** — Actor
Abrams Artists, 9200 W Sunset Blvd, #1125, West Hollywood CA 90069 USA
**McRoy, Spike** — Golfer
742 Mira Vista Dr SE, Huntsville AL 35802, USA
**McShane, Ian** — Actor
McShane Productions, 30 New Bridge St, London EC4V 6BJ, England
**McShera, Sophie** — Actress
Curtis Brown Group, 28-29 Haymarket St, #500, London SW1Y 4SP, England
**McSorley, Gerard** — Actor
Insight Mgmt, 1134 S Cloverdale Ave, Los Angeles CA 90019 USA
**McSorley, Marty** — Ice Hockey Player
3301 The Strand, Hermosa Beach CA 90254, USA
**McSwain, Rodney (Rod)** — Football Player
5393 Stonewood Dr, Hickory NC 28602, USA
**McTavish, Graham** — Actor
Stone Manners Salners, 9911 W Pico Blvd, #1400, Los Angeles CA 90035 USA
**McTeer, Janet** — Actress
Rights House, Drury House, 34-43 Russell St, London WC2B 5HA, England
**McTeigue, James** — Director
Creative Artists Agency, 2000 Ave of Stars, #100, Los Angeles CA 90067 USA
**McTiernan, John** — Director
Paradigm Agency, 360 N Crescent Dr, North Building, Beverly Hills CA 90210 USA
**McVey, Robert P** — Ice Hockey Player
3333 NE 34th St, #1522, Fort Lauderdale FL 33308, USA
**McVicar, Daniel** — Actor
1704 Oak St S, Santa Monica CA 90405, USA
**McVie, Christine** — Singer (Fleetwood Mac), Songwriter
406 Poplar Dr, Wilmette IL 60091, USA
**McVie, John** — Bassist (Fleetwood Mac), Songwriter
4224 Waialae Ave, Honolulu HI 96816, USA
**McVie, Tom** — Ice Hockey Coach
5713 Willow Springs Highway, Ferndale WA 98248, USA
**McWhirter, Jillian** — Actress
PO Box 6308, Beverly Hills CA 90212, USA
**McWilliams, Brian** — Labor Leader
Longshoremen/Warehousemen Union, 1188 Franklin St, San Francisco CA 94109, USA
**McWilliams, Fleming** — Singer
Michael Dixon Mgmt, 119 Pebble Creek Road, Franklin TN 37064, USA
**McWilliams, Johnny** — Football Player
4540 E Blue Spruce Lane, Gilbert AZ 85298, USA
**McWilliams, Larry D** — Baseball Player
4102 Beckley Court, Colleyville TX 76034, USA
**McWilliams-Franklin, Taj** — Basketball Player
Washington Mystics, Verizon Center, 401 9th St NW, #750, Washington DC 20004 USA
**Meacham, Jon** — Writer
Random House, 1745 Broadway, #1800, New York NY 10019 USA
**Meacham, Russell L (Rusty)** — Baseball Player
1906 Eden Glen Lane, Pearland TX 77581, USA
**Meachem, Robert** — Football Player
New Orleans Saints, 5800 Airline Highway, Metairie LA 70003 USA
**Mead, Chuck** — Guitarist (BR5-149)
Thirty Tigers, 1604 8th Ave S, #200, Nashville TN 37203, USA
**Mead, Courtland** — Actor
I C M Partners, 10250 Constellation Blvd, #900, Los Angeles CA 90067 USA
**Mead, Dana G** — Businessman
300 Boylston St, #1103, Boston MA 02116, USA
**Mead, Lee S** — Actor, Singer
Artist Rights Group, 4 Great Portland St, London W1W 8PA, England
**Mead, Shepherd** — Writer
53 Rivermead Court, London SW6 3RY, England
**Meade, Angela** — Opera Singer
I M G Artists, Hogarth Business Park, Chiswick, London W4 2TH, England
**Meade, Carl J** — Astronaut
15013 Live Oak Springs Canyon Road, Canyon Country CA 91387, USA
**Meador, Eddie D (Ed)** — Football Player
1135 Padgett Hill Road, Natural Bridge VA 24578, USA
**Meadows, Brian** — Baseball Player
917 Butter & Egg Road, Troy AL 36081, USA
**Meadows, Jayne** — Actress
16185 Woodvale Road, Encino CA 91436, USA
**Meadows, Michael R (Louie)** — Baseball Player
110 Heavens Lane, Maysville NC 28555, USA
**Meadows, Shane** — Director
Casorotto Ramsay, Waverley House, 7-12 Noel St, London W1F 8GQ, England
**Meadows, Stephen** — Actor
1760 Courtney Ave, Los Angeles CA 90046, USA
**Meadows, Tim** — Actor, Comedian
A P A Talent/Literary Agency, 405 S Beverly Dr, #300, Beverly Hills CA 90212 USA
**Meadows, William H** — Association Executive
Wilderness Society, President's Office, 1615 M St NW, Washington DC 20036, USA
**Meads, D Donald (Don)** — Baseball Player
3220 Cypress Way, Santa Rosa CA 95405, USA

**Meads, Johnny s** — Football Player
9419 Pine Lilly Court, Navarre FL 32566, USA
**Meagher, Mary T** — Swimmer
404 Vanderwall, Peachtree City GA 30269, USA
**Meagher, Rick** — Ice Hockey Player
2698 Innisfil Road, Mississauga ON L5M 4J2, Canada
**Mealing, Amanda** — Actress
Curtis Brown Group, 28-29 Haymarket St, #500, London SW1Y 4SP, England
**Meaney, Colm** — Actor
Innovative Artists, 1505 10th St, Santa Monica CA 90401 USA
**Meaney, Kevin** — Actor, Comedian, Writer
OmniPop Talent Group, 4605 Lankershim Blvd, #201, Toluca Lake CA 91602 USA
**Means, David** — Writer
Wylie Agency, 250 W 57th St, #2114, New York NY 10107 USA
**Means, Natrone J** — Football Player
14602 Greenpoint Lane, Huntersville NC 28078, USA
**Means, Winslow** — Basketball Player
1336 Arch St, Zanesville OH 43701, USA
**Meany, Colm** — Actor
Troika, 74 Clerkenwell Road, #300, London EC1M 5QA, England
**Meara, Anne** — Actress, Comedienne
118 Riverside Dr, #5A, New York NY 10024, USA
**Meares, Patrick J (Pat)** — Baseball Player
8405 E Bridlewood St, Wichita KS 67206, USA
**Mears, Casey J** — Auto Racing Driver
5020 Carmel Park Dr, Charlotte NC 28226, USA
**Mears, Derek** — Actor
Kazarian/Measures/Ruskin, 11969 Ventura Blvd, #300, Studio City CA 91604 USA
**Mears, F Gary** — Singer, Guitarist (Casuals)
12170 Country Road 215, Tyler TX 75707, USA
**Mears, Rick R** — Auto Racing Driver
1536 NW Buttonbush Circle, Palm City FL 34990, USA
**Mears, Roger, Sr** — Truck Racing Driver
PO Box 520, Terrell NC 28682, USA
**Mears, Walter R** — Journalist
Associated Press, Editorial Dept, 2021 K St NW, #600, Washington DC 20006, USA
**Meat Loaf** — Singer, Actor
Greene Assoc, 1901 Ave of Stars, #130, Los Angeles CA 90067 USA
**Mebane, Brandon J** — Football Player
2310 SE 2nd Court, Renton WA 98056, USA
**Mecchi, Irene** — Writer
Abrams Artists, 9200 W Sunset Blvd, #1125, West Hollywood CA 90069 USA
**Meche, Gilbert A (Gil)** — Baseball Player
6513 Ridge Road, Kansas City MO 64152, USA
**Mechem, Charles S, Jr** — Golf Executive, Businessman
United States Show, 1 Eastwood Dr, Cincinnati OH 45227, USA
**Mechler, Pia** — Actress
Stacey Castro Media, 4009 Leeward Ave, Los Angeles CA 90005 USA
**Mechlowicz, Scott** — Actor
Management 360, 9111 Wilshire Blvd, Beverly Hills CA 90210 USA
**Meciar, Vladimir** — Prime Minister, Slovakia
Urad Vlady SR, Nam Slobody 1, 81370 Bratislava, Slovakia
**Mecir, James M (Jim)** — Baseball Player
3679 Annis Circle, Pleasanton CA 94588, USA
**Mecklenburg, Karl B** — Football Player
6372 S Zenobia Court, Littleton CO 80123, USA
**Medak, Peter** — Director
Gersh Agency, 9465 Wilshire Blvd, #600, Beverly Hills CA 90212 USA
**Medavoy, Mike** — Businessman, Producer
Phoenix Pictures, 10203 Santa Monica Blvd, #400, Los Angeles CA 90067, USA
**Medders, Brandon E** — Baseball Player
9732 Charolais Dr, Tuscaloosa AL 35405, USA
**Meddick, Jim** — Cartoonist (Monty)
United Feature Syndicate, PO Box 5610, Cincinnati OH 45201 USA
**Medeiros, Glenn** — Singer
PO Box 8, Lawai HI 96765, USA
**Medford, Paul J** — Actor, Choreographer
Gavin Barker Assoc, 2D Wimpole St, London W1G 0EB, England
**Mediate, Rocco** — Golfer
2548 Medina Circle, Medina WA 98039, USA
**Medich, George F (Doc)** — Baseball Player
3007 Woodfield Dr, Aliquippa PA 15001, USA
**Medina Estevez, Jorge Arturo Cardinal** — Religious Leader
Congregation for Divine Worship, Piazza Pio XII 10, 00193 Rome, Italy
**Medina Sanchez, Dasnilo** — President, Dominican Republic
Palacio Nacional, Calle Moises Garcia, Ave Mexico, Santo Domingo, Dominican Republic
**Medlen, Kris** — Baseball Player
2161 Technology Place, Long Beach CA 90810, USA
**Medley, Bill** — Singer (Righteous Brothers)
Barry Rillera, 9841 Hot Springs Dr, Huntington Beach CA 92646, USA
**Medoff, Mark H** — Writer
PO Box 3072, Las Cruces NM 88003, USA
**Medved, Aleksandr V** — Freestyle Wrestler
Belarussian State Univeristy, Sports Excellence Dept, 220030 Minsk, Belarus
**Medved, Ronald G (Ron)** — Football Player
6615 239th Ave E, Buckley WA 98321, USA
**Medvedenko, Stanislav (Slava)** — Basketball Player
1700 Ruhland Ave, Manhattan Beach CA 90266, USA
**Medvedev, Andrei** — Tennis Player
Association of Tennis Professionals, 200 Tournament Road, Ponte Vedra Beach FL 32082 USA
**Medvedev, Dmitri A** — Prime Minister, Russia
Prime Minister's Office, Krasnopresneskaya Nab 2, 103274 Moscow, Russia
**Medvedev, Zhores A** — Biologist
4 Osborn Gardens, London NW7 1DY, England
**Medvin, Scott H** — Baseball Player
673 Lynbrook Ave, Tonawanda NY 14150, USA

Meads - Medvin

| | |
|---|---|
| **Medway, Heather** | Actress |
| A P A Talent/Literary Agency, 405 S Beverly Dr, #300, Beverly Hills CA 90212 USA | |
| **Medwin, Michael** | Actor |
| I C M Partners, Marlborough House, 10 Earlham St, #300, London WC2H 9LNP, England | |
| **Mee, L Darnell** | Basketball Player |
| 2005 Westland Dr SW, #1201, Cleveland TN 37311, USA | |
| **Meehan, Gerald M (Gerry)** | Ice Hockey Player |
| 2 Dafoe Court, Aurora ON L4G 7C8, Canada | |
| **Meehan, Martin T (Marty)** | Educator; Representative, MA |
| University of Massachusetts, Chancellor's Office, Lowell MA 01854, USA | |
| **Meeke, Brent** | Ice Hockey Player |
| 11331 Whitetail Run St NW, Bolivar OH 44612, USA | |
| **Meeker, Howie** | Ice Hockey Player, Coach, Sportscaster |
| 979 Dickinson Way, Parksville BC V9P 1Z7, Canada | |
| **Meeks, Robert E (Bob)** | Football Player |
| PO Box 29734, Denver CO 80229, USA | |
| **Meeler, C Philip (Phil)** | Baseball Player |
| 102 Pine Ln, Knightdale NC 27545, USA | |
| **Meena** | Actress |
| 58 2nd St, Venkatesh Nagar, Virugabakkam, Chennai TN 600092, India | |
| **Meents, Scott** | Basketball Player |
| 4231 155th Place SE, Bellevue WA 98006, USA | |
| **Meese, Edwin, III** | Attorney General |
| 1800 Old Meadow Road, #810, Mc Lean VA 22102, USA | |
| **Meester, Bradley R (Brad)** | Football Player |
| 7644 Chipwood Lane, Jacksonville FL 32256, USA | |
| **Meester, Leighton** | Actress, Singer |
| W M E Entertainment, 9601 Wilshire Blvd, #300, Beverly Hills CA 90210 USA | |
| **Meeuwsen, Terry A** | Beauty Queen, Singer, Entertainer |
| Pat Robertson's 700 Club, 977 Centerville Turnpike, Virginia Beach VA 23463, USA | |
| **Megaton, Olivier** | Director |
| W M E Entertainment, 9601 Wilshire Blvd, #300, Beverly Hills CA 90210 USA | |
| **Meggysey, David M (Dave)** | Football Player |
| 2528 Benvenue Ave, Berkeley CA 94704, USA | |
| **MeGrew, Mike** | Baseball Player |
| 25 Karen Dr, Hope Valley RI 02832, USA | |
| **Mehl, Lance A** | Football Player |
| 44920 Kacsmar Estates Dr, Saint Clairsville OH 43950, USA | |
| **Mehldau, Brad** | Jazz Pianist |
| International Music Network, 278 Main St, Gloucester MA 01930, USA | |
| **Mehra, Smirti** | Golfer |
| 4038 Greystone Dr, Clermont FL 34711, USA | |
| **Mehring, Sona** | Social Activist |
| CaringBridge, PO Box 6032, Albert Lea MN 56007, USA | |
| **Mehringer, David M** | Astronomer |
| University of Illinois, Astronomy Dept, Champaign IL 61820, USA | |
| **Mehta, Deepa** | Director, Writer |
| I C M Partners, 10250 Constellation Blvd, #900, Los Angeles CA 90067 USA | |
| **Mehta, Sujata** | Actress |
| 56 Dev Chhaya Tardeo Haji Ali Road, Tardeo, Mumbai MS 400034, India | |
| **Mehta, Ved P** | Writer |
| 139 E 79th St, New York NY 10075, USA | |
| **Mehta, Zubin** | Conductor |
| 27 Oakmont Dr, Los Angeles CA 90049, USA | |
| **Meidani, Rexhep** | President, Albania |
| Club de Madrid, C/Goya 5-7, Pasaje 2, 28001 Madrid, Spain | |
| **Meier, David K (Dave)** | Baseball Player |
| 523 W Stuart Ave, Fresno CA 93704, USA | |
| **Meier, Dieter** | Synthesizer Player (Yello) |
| Creative Artists Agency, 2000 Ave of Stars, #100, Los Angeles CA 90067 USA | |
| **Meier, Raymond** | Photographer |
| Raymond Meier Photography, 532 Broadway, #800, New York NY 10012, USA | |
| **Meier, Richard A** | Pritzker Architectural Laureate |
| Richard Meier Partners, 475 10th Ave, #600, New York NY 10018, USA | |
| **Meier, Robert J D (Rob)** | Football Player |
| 7551 Scarlet Ibis Lane, Jacksonville FL 32256, USA | |
| **Meier, Waltraud** | Opera Singer |
| Hilbert Artists Mgmt, Maximilanstr 22, 80539 Munich, Germany | |
| **Meieran, Andrew** | Director, Producer |
| W M E Entertainment, 9601 Wilshire Blvd, #300, Beverly Hills CA 90210 USA | |
| **Meiers, Shallan A** | Model |
| Playboy Promotions, 2706 Media Center Dr, Los Angeles CA 90065 USA | |
| **Meighan, Tom** | Singer (Kasabian) |
| International Talent Booking, Ariel House, 74A Charlotte St, #100 London W1T 4QJ, England | |
| **Meigs, Montgomery C** | Army General |
| Business Executives for National Security, 1030 15th NW, Washington DC 20005, USA | |
| **Meili, Launi** | Markswoman |
| 2001 Wagon Gap Trail, Monument CO 80132, USA | |
| **Meilinger, Steven F (Steve)** | Football Player |
| 719 Camino Road, Lexington KY 40502, USA | |
| **Meindl, James D** | Electrical Engineer |
| Georgia Institute of Technology, Microelectronics Center, Atlanta GA 30332, USA | |
| **Meine, Klaus** | Singer, Guitarist (Scorpions) |
| Und Verlags, Bohlenweg 8, 30835 Langenhagen, Germany | |
| **Meinwald, Jerrold** | Chemist |
| 429 Warren Road, Ithaca NY 14850, USA | |
| **Meirelles, Fernando** | Director |
| O2 Films, Rua Heliopolis 410, Vila Hamburguesa, Sao Paulo SP 05318 010, Brazil | |
| **Meisel, Stephen** | Photographer |
| 64 Wooster St, New York NY 10012, USA | |
| **Meiselas, Susan** | Photographer |
| 256 Mott St, New York NY 10012, USA | |
| **Meisner, Gregory P (Greg)** | Football Player |
| 229 Carr Dr, Ligonier PA 15658, USA | |
| **Meisner, Joachim Cardinal** | Religious Leader |
| Archbishop's Diocese, Marzellenstr 32, 50668 Cologne, Germany | |

**Meisner, Randy** — Bassist, Singer (Eagles, Poco)
Rick Alter Mgmt, 1018 17th Ave S, #12, Nashville TN 37212, USA
**Meister, Elisabeth** — Opera Singer
I M G Artists, Hogarth Business Park, Chiswick, London W4 2TH, England
**Meixler, Edward (Ed)** — Football Player
13812 Hastings Farm Road, Huntersville NC 28078, USA
**Meja** — Singer (Legacy of Sound), Composer
Basic Music Mgmt, Norrtullsgatan 51, 113 45 Stockholm, Sweden
**Mejia, Jorge Maria Cardinal** — Religious Leader
Biblioteca Apostolica Vaticina, 00120 Vatican City
**Mejia, Paul R** — Ballet Dancer, Choreographer
Fort Worth Ballet, 6848 Green Oaks Road, Fort Worth TX 76116, USA
**Mejias, Roman G** — Baseball Player
27325 Terrytown Road, Sun City CA 92586, USA
**Mekka, Eddie** — Actor
8217 San Ramon Dr, Las Vegas NV 89147, USA
**Mekki, Smail** — Actor
Cineart, 28 Rue Mogador, 78009 Paris, France
**Melamed, Lisa** — Producer
Paradigm Agency, 360 N Crescent Dr, North Building, Beverly Hills CA 90210 USA
**Melamid, Aleksander** — Artist
53 Lisspenard St, New York NY 10013, USA
**Melancon, Charles J (Charlie)** — Representative, LA
International Franchise Assn, 1501 K St NW, #350, Washington DC 20005, USA
**Melancon, Mei** — Actress
Intellectual Artists Mgmt, 10585 Santa Monica Blvd, #135, Los Angeles CA 90025, USA
**Melanie** — Singer, Guitarist, Songwriter
53 Baymont St, #5, Clearwater Beach FL 33767, USA
**Melano, Fabrizio** — Director
Columbia Artists Mgmt Inc, 1790 Broadway, #702, New York NY 10019 USA
**Melanson, Roland (Rollie)** — Ice Hockey Player
728 Rue Pierre Biard, Boucherville QC J4B 7R3, Canada
**Melcher, John** — Senator, MT
2519 Wylie Ave, Missoula MT 59802, USA
**Melchionni, Gary D** — Basketball Player
1040 Grandview Blvd, Lancaster PA 17601, USA
**Melchionni, William P (Bill)** — Basketball Player
115 Whitehall Blvd, Garden City NY 11530, USA
**Melchior, Ib** — Writer
8228 Marymount Lane, Los Angeles CA 90069, USA
**Mele, Sabath A (Sam)** — Baseball Player, Manager
340 Adams St, Quincy MA 02169, USA
**Mele-Mel** — Rap Artist
Groove Entertainment, 1005 N Alfred St, #2, West Hollywood CA 90069, USA
**Melendez, John (Stuttering)** — Actor, Comedian
Paradigm Agency, 360 N Crescent Dr, North Building, Beverly Hills CA 90210 USA
**Melendez, Lisette** — Singer
La' Entertainment Booking 2834 Rosemeade Dr, Monroe NC 28110, USA
**Melendez, Ron** — Actor
Jay D Schwartz Assoc, 3151 Cahuenga Blvd W, #220, Los Angeles CA 90068, USA
**Melhuse, Adam M** — Baseball Player
6940 Avila Valley Dr, San Luis Obispo CA 93405, USA
**Melinda** — Illusionist
Miracle Mile Shops, 3663 Las Vegas Blvd S, #900, Las Vegas NV 89109, USA
**Melini, Angela** — Model, Actress
Playboy Promotions, 2706 Media Center Dr, Los Angeles CA 90065 USA
**Mellanby, Scott** — Ice Hockey Player
2548 Town and Country Lane, Saint Louis MO 63131, USA
**Mellekas, John S** — Football Player
498 Broadway, Newport RI 02840, USA
**Mellencamp, John** — Singer, Songwriter
Belmont Mall Studio, 5087 Lower Schooner Road, Nashville IN 47448, USA
**Mello, Craig C** — Nobel Medicine Laureate
25 Fessenden Road, Barrington RI 02806, USA
**Mello, Tamara** — Actress
A P A Talent/Literary Agency, 405 S Beverly Dr, #300, Beverly Hills CA 90212 USA
**Mellons, Ken** — Singer, Guitarist, Songwriter
PO Box 8293, Hermitage TN 37076, USA
**Mellor, James R** — Businessman
23 Shreve Dr, Laguna Beach CA 92651, USA
**Mellor, Thomas R (Tom)** — Ice Hockey Player
63 Spoonhill Ave, Marlborough MA 01752, USA
**Melman, Jeffrey (Jeff)** — Director, Producer
I C M Partners, 10250 Constellation Blvd, #900, Los Angeles CA 90067 USA
**Melnick, Bruce E** — Astronaut
Boeing Aerospace, PO Box 21233, Kennedy Space Center, Orlando FL 32815, USA
**Melnick, Valeriya** — Model
Fashion Model Mgmt, Via Monterosa 80, 20149 Milan, Italy
**Melnyk, Larry** — Ice Hockey Player
1748 Sugarpine Court, Coquitlam BC V3E 3E4, Canada
**Melo, Brian** — Singer, Songwriter
Agency Group Ltd, 142 W 57th St, #600, New York NY 10019 USA
**Meloan, Jonathan M (Jon)** — Baseball Player
8017 Lichtenauer Dr, Lenexa KS 66219, USA
**Meloche, Gilles** — Ice Hockey Player
Pittsburgh Penguins, Consol Energy Center, 1001 5th Ave, Pittsburgh PA 15219 USA
**Meloni, Christopher** — Actor
Gersh Agency, 41 Madison Ave, #3301, New York NY 10010 USA
**Meloy, Colin P H** — Singer, Guitarist (Decemberists)
Big Hassle, 44 Wall St, #2200, New York NY 10005, USA
**Melrose, Barry J** — Ice Hockey Player, Coach
10 Windy Ridge, Glens Falls NY 12801, USA
**Melroy, Pamela A** — Astronaut
3605 14th St N, Arlington VA 22201, USA
**Melson, Sara** — Actress
Jerry Lembo Entertainment Group, 96 Linwood Plaza, #470, Fort Lee NJ 07024, USA

# M

**Melton, Barry** — Singer (Country Joe & the Fish)
PO Box 890983, Sacramento CA 95798, USA

**Melton, William E (Bill)** — Baseball Player
333 E 35th St, Chicago IL 60616, USA

**Meltzer, Allan L** — Economist
Carnegie Mellon University, Economics Dept, Pittsburgh PA 15260, USA

**Meltzer, Brad** — Writer
20533 Biscayne Blvd, #371, Aventura FL 33180, USA

**Melua, Katie** — Singer, Songwriter
Dramatico Ltd, PO Box 214, Farnham, Surrey GU10 5AL, England

**Meluskey, Mitchell W (Mitch)** — Baseball Player
26 Meadowbrooke Road, Yakima WA 98903, USA

**Melvill, Michael W (Mike)** — Astronaut, Test Pilot
24120 Jacaranda Dr, Tehachapi CA 93561, USA

**Melvin, Leland D** — Astronaut
N A S A, Johnson Space Center, 2101 NASA Road, Houston TX 77058 USA

**Melvin, Robert P (Bob)** — Baseball Player, Manager
5637 E Canyon Ridge North Dr, Cave Creek AZ 85331, USA

**Melvoin, Wendy** — Singer, Guitarist
Girl Brothers, 9454 Wilshire Blvd, #711, Beverly Hills CA 90212, USA

**Melzack, Ronald** — Psychologist
51 Banstead Road, Montreal QC H4X 1P1, Canada

**Memory, Thara** — Jazz Trumpeter
American Music Program, 116 NE 29th Ave, Portland OR 97232, USA

**Memphis Bleek** — Rap Artist
Green Light Talent Agency, PO Box 3172, Beverly Hills CA 90212 USA

**Mena, Maria V** — Singer, Songwriter
United Talent Agency, U T A Plaza, 9336 Civic Center Dr, Beverly Hills CA 90210 USA

**Menand, Louis** — Historian
New Yorker, Editorial Dept, 4 Times Square, Basement C1B, New York NY 10036 USA

**Menard, Paul** — Auto Racing Driver
T R G Motorsports, 292 Rolling Hill Road, Mooresville NC 28117, USA

**Menaul, Christopher S** — Director
United Agents, 12-26 Lexington St, London W1F 0LE, England

**Mench, Kevin F** — Baseball Player
1305 Danbury Parks Dr, Keller TX 76248, USA

**Menchaca, Penelope** — Entertainer
Telemundo Network Group, 2470 W 8th Ave, Hialeah FL 33010 USA

**Menchu Tum, Rigoberta** — Nobel Peace Laureate
Av Simeon Canas 4-04 Zona 2, Ciudad de Guatemala, Guatemala

**Mencia, Carlos** — Actor, Comedian, Writer
Brillstein Entertainment Partners, 9150 Wilshire Blvd, #350, Beverly Hills CA 90212 USA

**Menczer, Pauline** — Surfer
6 Burra Burra CL, Ocean Shores NSW 2483, Australia

**Mendel, Gilles** — Fashion Designer
J Mendel, 723 Madison Ave, New York, NY 10065 10065, USA

**Mendel, Nathan G (Nate)** — Bassist (Foo Fighters)
S A M, 722 Seward St, Los Angeles CA 90038, USA

**Mendelsohn, Ben** — Actor
United Management, 61 Marlborough St, #45, Level 4, Surry Hills NSW 2010, Australia , USA

**Mendelsohn, Carol** — Producer, Writer
W M E Entertainment, 9601 Wilshire Blvd, #300, Beverly Hills CA 90210 USA

**Mendenhall, John R** — Football Player
PO Box 532, Cullen LA 71021, USA

**Mendenhall, Ken E** — Football Player
1708 S Rankin St, Edmond OK 73013, USA

**Mendes, Eva** — Actress, Model
Management 360, 9111 Wilshire Blvd, Beverly Hills CA 90210 USA

**Mendes, Sam** — Director
Creative Artists Agency, 2000 Ave of Stars, #100, Los Angeles CA 90067 USA

**Mendes, Sergio** — Pianist
W M E Entertainment, 9601 Wilshire Blvd, #300, Beverly Hills CA 90210 USA

**Mendez, Akissa** — Singer (Allure)
Universal Attractions, 135 W 26th St, #1200, New York NY 10001 USA

**Mendler, Bridgit** — Actress
Gersh Agency, 9465 Wilshire Blvd, #600, Beverly Hills CA 90212 USA

**Mendoza Moncada, Dayana S** — Beauty Queen, Model
Trump Model Agency, 91 5th Ave, #300, New York NY 10003 USA

**Mendoza, Linda** — Director, Producer
A P A Talent/Literary Agency, 405 S Beverly Dr, #300, Beverly Hills CA 90212 USA

**Mendoza, Mark (Animal)** — Singer, Bassist (Twisted Sister)
Rebellion Entertainment, 2440 Broadway, #111, New York NY 10024, USA

**Mendoza, Martha** — Journalist
Associated Press, Editorial Dept, 450 W 33rd St, #1500, New York NY 10001 USA

**Mendoza, Michael J (Mike)** — Baseball Player
14207 S 20th St, Phoenix AZ 85048, USA

**Mendoza, Natalie J** — Actress, Singer
R G M Artist, 64-76 Kippax St, #202, Surry Hills NSW 2010, Australia

**Mendoza, Ramiro** — Baseball Player
PO Box 7027, Brandon FL 33508, USA

**Meneses, Alex** — Actress
Pakula/King, 9229 W Sunset Blvd, #315, West Hollywood CA 90069 USA

**Meneses, Antonio** — Concert Cellist
Concert/Spectacle Agency, 29 Rue Couloureniere, 1204 Geneva, Switzerland

**Meneve, Russ** — Actor, Comedian
C H Entertainment, 6 W 14th St, New York NY 10011, USA

**Menez, Bernard** — Actor, Singer
119 Blvd de Grenelle, 75015 Paris, France

**Menges, Chris** — Cinematographer, Director
Claire Best Assoc, 736 Seward St, Los Angeles CA 90038, USA

**Menhart, Paul G** — Baseball Player
725 Kelsall Dr, Richmond Hill GA 31324, USA

**Menichetti, Roberto** — Fashion Designer
Via Perugina 88, Gubbio (PG), Italy

**Menke, Denis J** — Baseball Player
1246 Berkshire Lane, Tarpon Springs FL 34688, USA

**Menken, Alan** — Composer
Mason Co, 1212 Ave of Americas, #1400, New York NY 10036, USA
**Mennell, Laura** — Actress
I C M Partners, 10250 Constellation Blvd, #900, Los Angeles CA 90067 USA
**Menon, Mambillikalathil G K** — Physicist
C63 Tarang Apts, Mother Dairy Road, Patparganj, Delhi 110092, India
**Menounos, Maria** — Actress, Model
W M E Entertainment, 9601 Wilshire Blvd, #300, Beverly Hills CA 90210 USA
**Mensah, Peter** — Actor
A V O Talent, 5670 Wilshire Blvd, #1930, Los Angeles CA 90036, USA
**Menshov, Vladimir V** — Actor, Director
3D Tverskaya-Yamskaya 52, #29, 125047 Moscow, Russia
**Mentzer, Ethan** — Bassist (Click Five)
Sharp & Focused Mgmt, 323 Broadway St, Cambridge MA 02139, USA
**Menuicucci, Pier Marino** — Co-Regent, San Marino
Co-Regent's Office, Government Palace, 47031 San Marino
**Menzel, Idina** — Actress, Singer
One Entertainment, 347 5th Ave, #1404, New York NY 10016 USA
**Menzel, Jiri** — Director
Divadlo na Vinchradech, Namesti Miru 7, 12000 Prague 2, Czech Republic
**Menzer, Ina** — Boxer
Spotlight Boxing, Am Stadtrand 27, 22047 Hamburg, Germany
**Menzies, Marvin** — Basketball Coach
New Mexico State University, Athletic Dept, Las Cruces NM 88003, USA
**Menzies, Peter G, Jr** — Cinematographer
903 Tahoe Blvd, #802, Incline Village NV 89451, USA
**Menzies, Tobias** — Actor
Paradigm Agency, 360 N Crescent Dr, North Building, Beverly Hills CA 90210 USA
**Menzies-Ulrich, Heather** — Actress
University of Michigan Comprehensive Cancer Center, Urich Sarcoma Research Fund, Ann Arbor MI 48109, USA
**Meola, Tony** — Soccer Player
488 Forest St, Kearny NJ 07032, USA
**Meoli, Rudolph B (Rudy)** — Baseball Player
1211 San Gabriel Ave, Henderson NV 89002, USA
**Meow, Meow** — Opera Singer
I M G Artists, Hogarth Business Park, Chiswick, London W4 2TH, England
**Meraz, Alex** — Actor
Innovative Artists, 1505 10th St, Santa Monica CA 90401 USA
**Merbold, Ulf** — Astronaut, Germany
Am Sonnenhang 4, 53721 Siegburg, Germany
**Mercader, Julio** — Archaeologist
University of Calgary, Archaeology Dept, Calgary AB T2N 1N4, Canada
**Mercado, Orlando L** — Baseball Player
12021 W Louise Court, Sun City AZ 85373, USA
**Merced Villaneuva, Orlando L** — Baseball Player
PO Box 190494, San Juan PR 00919, USA
**Mercein, Charles S (Chuck)** — Football Player
59 Club Pointe Dr, White Plains NY 10605, USA
**Mercer, James R** — Singer, Guitarist (Shins)
Nasty Little Man, 110 Greene St, #605, New York NY 10012 USA
**Mercer, Kelvin** — Rap Artist (De La Soul)
Richard Walters, PO Box 2789, Toluca Lake CA 91610 USA
**Mercer, Michael (Mike)** — Football Player
64463 McGrath Road, Bend OR 97701, USA
**Mercer, Robert E** — Businessman
11 Island Estates Parkway, Palm Coast FL 32137, USA
**Mercer, Toby** — Artist
Mercer Studios, 316 E Reserve Dr, Kalispell MT 59901, USA
**Merchant, Larry** — Boxing Sportscaster
470 20th St, Santa Monica CA 90402, USA
**Merchant, Natalie** — Singer, Songwriter
Creative Artists Agency, 2000 Ave of Stars, #100, Los Angeles CA 90067 USA
**Merchant, Stephen** — Producer, Comedian, Actor
W M E Entertainment, 9601 Wilshire Blvd, #300, Beverly Hills CA 90210 USA
**Mercier, Michele** — Actress
Residence Cape di Monte, 06400 Cannes, France
**Mercilus, Whitney** — Football Player
Houston Texans, 2 Reliant Park, Houston TX 77054 USA
**Mercker, Kent H** — Baseball Player
5340 Muirfield Court, Dublin OH 43017, USA
**Merckx, Eddy** — Cyclist
S'Herenweg 11, 1860 Meise, Belgium
**Mercurio, Jed** — Writer
Simon & Schuster, 1230 Ave of Americas, Concourse 1, New York NY 10020 USA
**Mercurio, Paul** — Actor, Singer
Beyond Films, 53-55 Brisbane St, Sunnyhills, Sydney NSW 2010, Australia
**Meredith, O Claiborne (Cla), III** — Baseball Player
3807 Kensington Ave, Richmond VA 23221, USA
**Meredith, Richard O (Dick)** — Ice Hockey Player
26580 Hickory Blvd, Bonita Springs FL 34134, USA
**Meridith, Ronald K (Ron)** — Baseball Player
308 Via Promesa, San Clemente CA 92673, USA
**Meriwether, Elizabeth (Liz)** — Writer, Producer
W M E Entertainment, 9601 Wilshire Blvd, #300, Beverly Hills CA 90210 USA
**Meriwether, Lee** — Actress, Beauty Queen
12139 Jeanette Place, Granada Hills CA 91344, USA
**Merkel, Angela D** — Chancellor, Germany
Bundeskanzlerant, Willy-Brandt-Str 1, 10557 Berlin, Germany
**Merkens, Guido A** — Football Player
8101 Research Forest Dr, Spring TX 77382, USA
**Merkerson, S Epatha** — Actress, Singer
I C M Partners, 10250 Constellation Blvd, #900, Los Angeles CA 90067 USA
**Merkosky, Glenn** — Ice Hockey Player
113 Farr Lane, Queensbury NY 12804, USA
**Merle-Pellet, Carole H** — Alpine Skier
Chalet La Calette, 04400 Super-Sauze, France

**M**

# M

| | |
|---|---|
| **Merletti, Lewis C** <br> Cleveland Browns, 76 Lou Groza Blvd, Berea OH 44017 USA | Law Enforcement Official |
| **Merlin, Jan** <br> 347 N California St, Burbank CA 91505, USA | Actor |
| **Merlo, James L (Jim)** <br> 1547 E Starpass Dr, Fresno CA 93730, USA | Football Player |
| **Merloni, Louis W (Lou)** <br> 29 Wild Hunter Road, Dennis MA 02638, USA | Baseball Player |
| **Mero, Rena (Sable)** <br> Rena Productions, 760 Valley Stream Dr, Geneva FL 32732, USA | Wrestler, Model, Actress |
| **Meron, Neil** <br> Storyline Entertainment, 8335 Sunset Blvd, #207, West Hollywood CA 90069, USA | Producer |
| **Merow, James F** <br> US Claims Court, 717 Madison Place NW, Washington DC 20439, USA | Judge |
| **Merrell, Barry** <br> 253 Raquette St, Winnipeg MB R3K 1M9, Canada | Ice Hockey Player |
| **Merrells, Jason** <br> QVoice, 8 Kings St, London WC2E 8HN, England | Actor |
| **Merrick, Doris** <br> 609 Desert West Dr, Rancho Mirage CA 92270, USA | Actress |
| **Merrick, Marge** <br> Professional Bowlers Assn, 719 2nd Ave, #701, Seattle WA 98104 USA | Bowler |
| **Merrick, Robert** <br> 470 Sea Meadow Dr, Portsmouth RI 02871, USA | Yachtsman |
| **Merrick, Wayne** <br> 68 Chesham Court, London ON N6G 3T4, Canada | Ice Hockey Player |
| **Merrill, Catherine** <br> Old Church Pottery, 1456 Florida St, San Francisco CA 94110, USA | Artist |
| **Merrill, Dina** <br> Talent Works, 3500 W Olive Ave, #1400, Burbank CA 91505 USA | Actress |
| **Merrill, Edward W** <br> 90 Somerset St, Belmont MA 02478, USA | Chemical Engineer |
| **Merrill, Mark C** <br> 782 Mimosa Lane, Saint Paul MN 55112, USA | Football Player |
| **Merrill, Robbie** <br> Front Line Mgmt, 1100 Glendon Ave, #2000, Los Angeles CA 90024 USA | Bassist (Godsmack, Everclear) |
| **Merrill, Stephen E (Steve)** <br> 562 Main St, Farmington NH 03835, USA | Governor, NH |
| **Merriman, Ryan** <br> W K T Public Relations, 9350 Wilshire Blvd, #450, Beverly Hills CA 90212 USA | Actor |
| **Merriman, Shawne D** <br> 27750 Cowdrey St, #105, Wesley Chapel FL 33544, USA | Football Player |
| **Merriott, Ronald** <br> 1271 McDole Dr, Sugar Grove IL 60554, USA | Diver |
| **Merritt, Chris** <br> Askonas Holt, Lincoln House, 300 High Holborn, London WC1V 7JH, England | Opera Singer |
| **Merritt, Courtney** <br> Coast to Coast Talent, 3350 Barham Blvd, Los Angeles CA 90068 USA | Actress |
| **Merritt, Gilbert S** <br> US Court of Appeals, US Courthouse, 701 Broadway, Nashville TN 37203, USA | Judge |
| **Merritt, Jack N** <br> US Army Assn, 2425 Wilson Blvd, #100, Arlington VA 22201, USA | Army General |
| **Merritt, James J (Jim)** <br> 2777 Blue Spruce Dr, Hemet CA 92545, USA | Baseball Player |
| **Merritt, Stephin R** <br> Sacks Co, 427 W 14th St, #300, New York NY 10014, USA | Singer (Magnetic Fields), Songwriter |
| **Merritt, Tift** <br> High Road, 751 Bridgeway, #200, Sausalito CA 94965, USA | Singer, Songwriter |
| **Merriweather, Daniel P** <br> Roc Nation, 1411 Broadway, #3800, New York NY 10018, USA | Singer, Songwriter |
| **Merriweather, Michael L (Mike)** <br> PO Box 8351, Stockton CA 95208, USA | Football Player |
| **Merrow, Jeffrey C (Jeff)** <br> 5989 Shadburn Ferry Road, Buford GA 30518, USA | Football Player |
| **Merrow, Susan** <br> Sierra Club, 85 2nd St, #200, San Francisco CA 94105, USA | Association Executive |
| **Merten, Alan G** <br> George Mason University, President's Office, 4400 University Dr, Fairfax VA 22030, USA | Educator |
| **Merten, Lauri** <br> 1010 Del Harbour Dr, Delray Beach FL 33483, USA | Golfer |
| **Mertens, Alan** <br> PacWest Racing Group, PO Box 1717, Bellevue WA 98009, USA | Auto Racing Executive |
| **Mertens, Francois** <br> 79 Bonnie Vue Lane, New Milford CT 06776, USA | Cyclist |
| **Mertens, Jerome W (Jerry)** <br> 465 Woodside Dr, Woodside CA 94062, USA | Football Player |
| **Merton, Robert C** <br> 75 Cambridge Parkway, #E1108, Cambridge MA 02142, USA | Nobel Economics Laureate |
| **Mertz, Edwin T** <br> 1504 Via Della Scala, Henderson NV 89052, USA | Biochemist |
| **Mertz, Francis J** <br> 54 Woodcrest Dr, Morristown NJ 07960, USA | Educator |
| **Merullo, Matthew B (Matt)** <br> 8 Fox Run Road, Madison CT 06443, USA | Baseball Player |
| **Merwin, John D** <br> PO Box 1029, Hudson OH 44236, USA | Governor, VI |
| **Merwin, William Stanley (W S)** <br> Steven Barclay Agency, 12 Western Ave, Petaluma CA 94952, USA | Writer |
| **Merz, Curtis (Curt)** <br> 1111 W Seminole St, Springfield MO 65807, USA | Football Player |
| **Merz, Suzanne (Sue)** <br> 5 Douglas Dr, Greenwich CT 06831, USA | Ice Hockey Player |
| **Mesa, Jose R N** <br> PO Box 112207, Miami FL 33111, USA | Baseball Player |
| **Meschery, Thomas N (Tom)** <br> 1216 Versailles Ave, Alameda CA 94501, USA | Basketball Player |

**Meselson, Matthew S** — Biochemist
Harvard University, Fairchild Biochemistry Laboratories, Cambridge MA 02138, USA
**Mesereau, Thomas D** — Attorney
1875 Century Park E, Los Angeles CA 90067, USA
**Mesguich, Daniel** — Actor, Director
Agence Monita Derrieux, 17-21 Rue Duret, 75116 Paris, France
**Mesina Stanley, Dianne** — Producer, Writer
Paradigm Agency, 360 N Crescent Dr, North Building, Beverly Hills CA 90210 USA
**Mesquida, Roxane** — Actress
Agence Elisabeth Simpson, 62 Boulevard Du Montparnasse, 75015 Paris, France
**Messenger, Randall J (Randy)** — Baseball Player
455 Market St, #2240, San Francisco CA 94105, USA
**Messer, L Dale** — Football Player
5449 N Brooks Ave, Fresno CA 93711, USA
**Messerschmid, Ernst** — Astronaut, Germany
Universitat Stuttgart, Pfaffenwaldring 31, 70569 Stuttgart, Germany
**Messerschmidt, J Alexander (Andy)** — Baseball Player
200 Lagunita Dr, Soquel CA 95073, USA
**Messi, Lionel A (Leo)** — Soccer Player
F C Barcelona, Aristides Maillo S/N, 08028 Barcelona, Spain
**Messier, Eric** — Ice Hockey Player
9671 Timber Hawk Circle, #22, Littleton CO 80126, USA
**Messier, Mark D** — Ice Hockey Player
45 Birchwood Dr, Greenwich CT 06831, USA
**Messina, Chris** — Actor
Brillstein Entertainment Partners, 9150 Wilshire Blvd, #350, Beverly Hills CA 90212 USA
**Messina, James M (Jim)** — Singer, Songwriter
Direct Management Group, 947 N La Cienega Blvd, #G, West Hollywood CA 90069, USA
**Messina, Jo Dee** — Singer, Songwriter
Sanctuary Mgmt, 15301 Ventura Blvd, Building B, Sherman Oaks CA 91403, USA
**Messing, Debra** — Actress
3 Arts Entertainment, 9460 Wilshire Blvd, #700, Beverly Hills CA 90212 USA
**Messinger, Rina** — Beauty Queen
Miss Universe Organization, 1370 Ave of Americas, #1600, New York NY 10019 USA
**Messner, Heinrich (Heini)** — Alpine Skier
Huebenweg 11, 6150 Steinach, Austria
**Messner, Johnny** — Actor
A P A Talent/Literary Agency, 405 S Beverly Dr, #300, Beverly Hills CA 90212 USA
**Messner, Reinhold** — Explorer, Mountaineer
Firmian, Sigmudskronerstr 53, 39100 Bozen, Italy
**Meszaros, Andrej** — Ice Hockey Player
Philadelphia Flyers, 1st Union Center, 3601 S Broad St, Philadelphia PA 19148 USA
**Meszaros, Marta** — Director
MalFilm Studio, Lumumba Utca 174, 1149 Budapest, Hungary
**Metcalf, Eric Q** — Football Player
6027 S Redwing St, Seattle WA 98118, USA
**Metcalf, John** — Writer
128 Lewis St, Ottawa ON K2P 0S7, Canada
**Metcalf, Laurie** — Actress
W M E Entertainment, 9601 Wilshire Blvd, #300, Beverly Hills CA 90210 USA
**Metcalf, Ryan** — Actor
Red Letter Entertainment, 437 W 48th St, #D, New York NY 10036, USA
**Metcalf, Terrance R (Terry)** — Football Player
5112 S Fountain St, Seattle WA 98178, USA
**Metcalf, Terrence O** — Football Player
1524 Jackson Ave E, #9, Oxford MS 38655, USA
**Metcalfe, Jesse** — Actor
Gersh Agency, 9465 Wilshire Blvd, #600, Beverly Hills CA 90212 USA
**Metcalfe, Robert M** — Inventor (Ethernet), Computer Scientist
Polaris Venture Partners, 1000 Winter St, #3350, Waltham MA 02451, USA
**Metcalf-Lindenburger, Dorothy M** — Astronaut
N A S A, Johnson Space Center, 2101 NASA Road, Houston TX 77058 USA
**Metheny, Patrick B (Pat)** — Jazz Guitarist, Composer
Ted Kurland, 173 Brighton Ave, Boston MA 02134 USA
**Method Man** — Rap Artist (Wu-Tang Clan), Actor
Smart Girl Productions, 8335 Sunset Blvd, #222, West Hollywood CA 90069, USA
**Metrano, Art** — Actor
C E S D, 10635 Santa Monica Blvd, #130, Los Angeles CA 90025 USA
**Metro, Charles (Charlie)** — Baseball Player, Manager
7890 Indiana St, Arvada CO 80007, USA
**Metropolit, Glen** — Ice Hockey Player
1070 Redwine Cove Road SW, Dalton GA 30720, USA
**Mette-Marit** — Princess, Norway
Det Kongelige, Slottet, Drammensvein 1, 0010 Oslo, Norway
**Mettifogo, Roberto** — Photographer
Via Montorio 54, 37131 Verona, Italy
**Metzelaars, Peter H (Pete)** — Football Player
10640 Pine Valley Path, Indianapolis IN 46234, USA
**Metzger, Clarence E (Butch)** — Baseball Player
641 Rivergate Way, Sacramento CA 95831, USA
**Metzger, Roger H** — Baseball Player
3560 Bluebonnet Blvd, Brenham TX 77833, USA
**Metzger, Stephane** — Actor
Agence Artiste Adequet, 108 Rue Reaumur, 75002 Paris, France
**Metzner, Raven** — Producer, Writer
W M E Entertainment, 9601 Wilshire Blvd, #300, Beverly Hills CA 90210 USA
**Meuli, Daniela** — Snowboard Athlete
Muehlstra 26, 7260 Davos Dorf, Switzerland
**Meunier-Lebouc, Patricia** — Golfer
110 Dalena Way, Palm Beach Gardens FL 33418, USA
**Mew** — Keyboardist (Elastica)
C E O Mgmt, Ransomes Dock, 35-37 Parkgate Road, London SW11 4NP, England
**Mewes, Jason** — Actor
C E S D, 10635 Santa Monica Blvd, #130, Los Angeles CA 90025 USA
**Mey, Uwe-Jens** — Speed Skater
Vulkanstr 22, 10367 Berlin, Germany

**Meyer Reyes, Deborah E (Debbie)** — Swimmer
PO Box 2076, Carmichael CA 95609, USA
**Meyer, Aaron** — Concert, Rock Violinist; Composer
PO Box 25486, Portland OR 97298, USA
**Meyer, Breckin** — Actor
I C M Partners, 10250 Constellation Blvd, #900, Los Angeles CA 90067 USA
**Meyer, Dakota L** — Afghanistan War Hero (CMH)
1384 Brockman Keltner Road, Greensburg KY 42743, USA
**Meyer, Daniel J** — Businessman
7655 Annesdale Dr, Cincinnati OH 45243, USA
**Meyer, Daniel L (Dan)** — Baseball Player
433 Cedar Lane, Mickleton NJ 08056, USA
**Meyer, Daniel T (Dan)** — Baseball Player
11540 Marsh Creek Road, Clayton CA 94517, USA
**Meyer, Dina** — Actress
Evolution Entertainment, 901 N Highland Ave, Los Angeles CA 90038 USA
**Meyer, Dirk** — Businessman
Advanced Micro Devices, 1 A M D Place, PO Box 3453, Sunnyvale CA 94088, USA
**Meyer, Don** — Basketball Coach
Northern State University, Athletic Dept, Aberdeen SD 57401, USA
**Meyer, Edgar** — Concert Double Bassist, Composer
I M G Artists, Carnegie Hall Tower, 152 W 57th St, #500, New York NY 10019 USA
**Meyer, Edward C** — Army General
1101 S Arlington Ridge Road, #1116, Arlington VA 22202, USA
**Meyer, John** — Architect
Meyer/Gifford/Jones, 270 Lafayette St, New York NY 10012, USA
**Meyer, Laurence H** — Economist, Government Official
Federal Reserve Board, 20th St & Constitution Ave NW, Washington DC 20551, USA
**Meyer, Loren H** — Basketball Player
3577 330th St, Ruthven IA 51358, USA
**Meyer, Nicholas** — Director, Writer
Creative Artists Agency, 2000 Ave of Stars, #100, Los Angeles CA 90067 USA
**Meyer, Ron** — Businessman
Universal Studios, 100 Universal City Plaza, Universal City CA 91608, USA
**Meyer, Stephenie** — Writer
Little Brown/Mysterious Press/Warner, 1271 Ave of Americas, New York NY 10020 USA
**Meyer, Urban** — Football Coach
8562 SW 12th Lane, Gainesville FL 32607, USA
**Meyer, Yves F** — Mathematician
Ecole Normale Superieure, 61 Ave President Wilson, 94235 Cachan, France
**Meyer-Landrut, Lena** — Singer, Songwriter
Brainpool, Schanzenstr 22, 51063 Cologne, Germany
**Meyerowitz, Joel** — Photographer
817 W End Ave, #11D, New York NY 10025, USA
**Meyerriecks, Jeffrey** — Concert Guitarist
Lindy Martin Mgmt, 1007 Lakewater Dr, Henrico VA 23229, USA
**Meyers Drysdale, Ann E** — Basketball Player, Sportscaster
235 W Main St, Los Gatos CA 95030, USA
**Meyers Tikalsky, Linda** — Skier
RR 5 Box 265T, Santa Fe NM 87506, USA
**Meyers, Anne Akiko** — Concert Violinist
Colbert Artists, 111 W 57th St, #1416, New York NY 10019 USA
**Meyers, Ari** — Actress
Holly Lebed Personal Mgmt, 10535 Wilshire Blvd, #808, Los Angeles CA 90024, USA
**Meyers, August (Augie)** — Singer, Organist (Sir Douglas Quintet)
Encore Talent, 6803 Crown Ridge, San Antonio TX 78239, USA
**Meyers, Chad W** — Baseball Player
7636 Leawood St, Papillion NE 68046, USA
**Meyers, David** — Director, Writer
Creative Artists Agency, 2000 Ave of Stars, #100, Los Angeles CA 90067 USA
**Meyers, David W (Dave)** — Basketball Player
40629 Carmelina Circle, Temecula CA 92591, USA
**Meyers, Josh** — Actor, Comedian
Paul Kohner, 9300 Wilshire Blvd, #555, Beverly Hills CA 90212 USA
**Meyers, Nancy** — Director, Producer
W M E Entertainment, 9601 Wilshire Blvd, #300, Beverly Hills CA 90210 USA
**Meyers, Seth** — Actor, Comedian
Brillstein Entertainment Partners, 9150 Wilshire Blvd, #350, Beverly Hills CA 90212 USA
**Meyfarth, Ulrike Nasse-** — Track Athlete
Buschweg 53, 51519 Odenthal, Germany
**Meyjes, Menno** — Director, Writer
Casorotto Ramsay, Waverley House, 7-12 Noel St, London W1F 8GQ, England
**Meyrowitz, Carol M** — Businesswoman
T J X Companies, 770 Conchituate Road, Framingham MA 01701, USA
**Meyssignac, Émmanuelle** — Actress
Artmedia, 20 Ave Rapp, 75007 Paris, France
**Meyyappan, Meyya** — Nanotechnologist
Ames Research Center, Nanotechnology Center, Moffett Field CA 94035, USA
**Mezentseva, Galina** — Ballerina
Kirov Ballet Theater, 1 Pl Iskusstr, 190000 Saint Petersburg, Russia
**Mezlekia, Nega** — Writer
Picador USA Books, 175 5th Ave, New York NY 10010, USA
**Mezzogiorno, Giovanna** — Actress
Media Art Mgmt, C/ Castelló 82, 2 Derecha, 28006 Madrid, Spain
**Mfume, Kweisi** — Association Executive
3000 Druid Park Dr, Baltimore MD 21215, USA
**MGMT** — Pop, Rock Music Duo
Paradigm Agency, 404 W Franklin St, Monterey CA 93940 USA
**Mhyre, Wencke S** — Singer, Actress
Im Vendia 22, 1315 Nesoya, Norway
**Mi Hyun Kim** — Golfer
Ladies Pro Golf Assn, 100 International Golf Dr, Daytona Beach FL 32124 USA
**Miano, Richard J (Rich)** — Football Player
Miano Sports Bar, 7168 Makaa St, Honolulu HI 96825, USA
**Miartusova, Nella** — Model
Club Nella, PO Box 25, 18200 Prague 8, Czech Republic

**Mica, Daniel L** — Representative, FL
Credit Union National Assn, 601 Pennsylvania NW, #600W, Washington DC 20004, USA
**Micarelli, Lucia** — Concert, Jazz Violinist
I M C, 1155 Boul Ree-Levesque Ouest, #2500, Montreal QC H3B 2K4, Canada
**Miceli, Daniel (Danny)** — Baseball Player
8520 Bowden Way, Windermere FL 34786, USA
**Miceli, Justine** — Actress
Paradigm Agency, 360 N Crescent Dr, North Building, Beverly Hills CA 90210 USA
**Michael** — King, Romania
Villa Serena, 77 Chemin Louis-Degallier, 1290 Versoix-Geneva, Switzerland
**Michael, Eugene R (Gene)** — Baseball Player, Manager, Executive
49 Union Ave, Upper Saddle River NJ 07458, USA
**Michael, George** — Singer, Guitarist, Songwriter
Lippman Entertainment, 23586 Calabasas Road, #208, Calabasas CA 91302, USA
**Michael, M Blane** — Judge
US Appeals Court, 300 Virginia St E, #7602, Charleston WV 25301, USA
**Michael, Ralph** — Actor
Michael Slessinger, 8730 W Sunset Blvd, #220W, West Hollywood CA 90069 USA
**Michael, Richard J (Rich)** — Football Player
957 S Van Ness Ave, San Francisco CA 94110, USA
**Michaell, Monnae** — Actress
Geddes Agency, 8430 Santa Monica Blvd, #201, West Hollywood CA 90069 USA
**Michaels, Alan R (Al)** — Sportscaster
401 S Bristol Ave, Los Angeles CA 90049, USA
**Michaels, Bret** — Singer (Poison)
Agency for Performing Arts, 405 S Beverly Dr, #500, Beverly Hills CA 90212, USA
**Michaels, Ellen** — Model, Photographer
PO Box 1757, New York NY 10021, USA
**Michaels, Fern** — Writer
9 David Court, Edison NJ 08820, USA
**Michaels, Jason D** — Baseball Player
5019 Avenue Avignon, Lutz FL 33558, USA
**Michaels, Julie** — Actress
PO Box 7304, #149, North Hollywood CA 91603, USA
**Michaels, Lorne** — Producer, Screenwriter
Broadway Video, 1619 Broadway, #900, New York NY 10019, USA
**Michaels, Louis A (Lou)** — Football Player
69 Grace St, Kingston PA 18704, USA
**Michaels, Marilyn** — Actress, Comedienne, Singer
Scotland/Kozak Artist Group, 157 E 57th St, #18B, New York NY 10022, USA
**Michaels, Walter (Walt)** — Football Player, Coach
12 Birch Ave, Wilkes Barre PA 18705, USA
**Michaelsen, Kari** — Actress
Silver Star AG Ltd, 3905 Auto Mall Dr, Westlake Village CA 91362, USA
**Michaels-Moore, Anthony** — Opera Singer
I M G Artists, Burlington Lane, Chiswick, London W4 2TH, England
**Michaelson, Ingrid** — Singer, Pianist/Songwriter
Paradigm Agency, 360 N Crescent Dr, North Building, Beverly Hills CA 90210 USA
**Michalak, Christian M (Chris)** — Baseball Player
1108 Mockingbird Lane, Keller TX 76248, USA
**Michaleczewski, Dariusz** — Boxer
Ul Rajska 4C, 80850 Gdansk, Poland
**Michalek, Zbynek** — Ice Hockey Player
3160 Annandale Dr, Presto PA 15142, USA
**Michalka, Alyson (Aly)** — Singer, Actress
Creative Artists Agency, 2000 Ave of Stars, #100, Los Angeles CA 90067 USA
**Michalka, Amanda J (A J)** — Singer, Actress, Songwriter
Prospect Park, 2049 Century Park E, #2550, Los Angeles CA 90067, USA
**Michals, Duane** — Photographer
109 E 19th St, New York NY 10003, USA
**Micheaux, Larry W** — Basketball Player
2914 Calendar Lake Dr, Missouri City TX 77459, USA
**Micheaux, Nikki** — Actress
Don Buchwald, 6500 Wilshire Blvd, #2200, Los Angeles CA 90048 USA
**Micheel, Shaun** — Golfer
1267 Dubray Lake Circle, Collierville TN 38017, USA
**Michel, F Curtis** — Astronaut
2101 University Blvd, Houston TX 77030, USA
**Michel, Hartmut** — Nobel Chemistry Laureate
Max Planck Biophysics Institute, 60438 Frankfurt am Main, Germany
**Michel, James A** — President, Seychelles
President's Office, State House, PO Box 655, Victoria, Mahe, Seychelles
**Michel, Jean-Louis** — Underwater Scientist
I F R E M E R, Center de Toulon, 83500 La Seyne dur Mer, Toulon, France
**Michel, Paul R** — Judge
US Court of Appeals, 717 Madison Place NW, Washington DC 20439, USA
**Michel, Pras** — Rap Artist, Actor
Blue Train Entertainment, 9333 Wilshire Blvd, G Level, Beverly Hills CA 90210 USA
**Michele, Chrisette** — Singer, Songwriter
I C M Partners, 10250 Constellation Blvd, #900, Los Angeles CA 90067 USA
**Michele, Michael** — Actress
Innovative Artists, 1505 10th St, Santa Monica CA 90401 USA
**Micheler, Elisabeth** — Canoeing Athlete
Gruntenstr 45, 86163 Augsburg, Germany
**Micheletti Bain, Roberto** — President, Honduras
Casa Presidencial, Blvd Juan Pablo II, Tegucigalpa MDC, Honduras
**Michell, Keith** — Actor
Chatto & Linnit, 123A King's Road, London SW3 4PL, England
**Michell, Roger** — Director
Independent Talent Group, 40 Whitfield St, London W1T 2RH, England
**Michelle** — Singer, Actress
Kunstlemanagement Uwe Kanthak, Hopfenmarkt 31, 20457 Hamburg, Germany
**Michelle, Candice** — Model, Wrestler, Actress
Abraxas Talent, 4260 Troost Ave, #1, Studio City CA 91604, USA
**Michels, John J** — Football Player
504 Matterhorn Dr, Gatlinburg TN 37738, USA

**M**

Michels, Stephanie — Actress
C E S D, 10635 Santa Monica Blvd, #130, Los Angeles CA 90025 USA
Michelson, Claudia — Actress
Agentur Hoestermann, Gneisenaustr 94, 10961 Berlin, Germany
Michie, David A R — Artist
17 Gilmour Road, Edinburgh EH16 5NS, England
Michiko — Empress, Japan
Imperial Palace, 1-1 Chiyoda, Chiyodaku, Tokyo 100 0001, Japan
Michod, David — Director
Blue-Tongue Films, PO Box 873, Darlinghurst, Sydney NSW 1300, Australia
Michos, Anastas N — Cinematographer
I C M Partners, 10250 Constellation Blvd, #900, Los Angeles CA 90067 USA
Mick — Drummer (Dave Dee Dozy Beaky Mick Tich)
Gerd Kehren Mgmt, Postfach 1408, 41804 Erkelenz, Germany
Mickell, Darren — Football Player
9250 Chelsea Dr, Miramar FL 33025, USA
Mickelson Cummins, Anna — Rowing Athlete
Cummins Chiropractic & Wellness, 4122 Factoria Blvd SE #202  Bellevue WA 98006, USA
Mickelson, Philip A (Phil) — Golfer
Gaylord Sports Mgmt, 13845 N Northsight Blvd, #200, Scottsdale AZ 85260, USA
Mickens, Terry K — Football Player
5725 Martin Road. #4268, Plano TX 75024, USA
Middendorf, Tracy — Actress
Bauman Redanty Shaul Agency, 5757 Wilshire Blvd, #473, Los Angeles CA 90036 USA
Middlebrooks, Willie F — Football Player
18775 SW 78th Court, Cutler Bay FL 33157, USA
Middleditch, Thomas — Actor
W M E Entertainment, 9601 Wilshire Blvd, #300, Beverly Hills CA 90210 USA
Middleton, Clark — Actor
CornerStone Talent Agency, 37 W 20th St, #1007, New York NY 10011, USA
Middleton, Darren — Guitarist (Powderfinger)
Secret Service, PO Box 401, Fortitude Valley QLD 4006, Australia
Middleton, Richard (Rick) — Ice Hockey Player
PO Box 1161, Hampton NH 03843, USA
Middleton, Terdell — Football Player
1893 Prospect St, Memphis TN 38106, USA
Middleton, Tuppence — Actress
United Talent Agency, U T A Plaza, 9336 Civic Center Dr, Beverly Hills CA 90210 USA
Midgley, John — Sound Mixer
Creative Media Mgmt, Ealing Studio, Ealing Green, London W5 5EP, England
Midkiff, Dale — Actor
Amsel Eisenstadt Frazier, 5055 Wilshire Blvd, #865, Los Angeles CA 90036 USA
Midler, Bette — Singer, Actress
Creative Artists Agency, 2000 Ave of Stars, #100, Los Angeles CA 90067 USA
Midori — Concert Violinist
Midori Foundation, 850 7th Ave, #705, New York NY 10019, USA
Miechur, Thomas F — Labor Leader
Cement & Allied Workers Union, 2500 Brickdale, Elk Grove Village IL 60007, USA
Miele, Rudolf — Businessman
Miele & Cie, Carl-Miele-Str 29, 33332 Guterslh, Germany
Mientkiewicz, Douglas A (Doug) — Baseball Player
810 Lugo Ave, Coral Gables FL 33156, USA
Miers, Harriet E — Government Official, Attorney
Locke Liddell Sapp, 901 15th St NW, #900, Washington DC 20005, USA
Mies, Richard W — Navy Admiral
Navy Mutual Aid Assn, Directors Board, 29 Carpenter Road, Arlington VA 22214, USA
Mieske, Matthew T (Matt) — Baseball Player
2199 E Bombay Road, Midland MI 48642, USA
Miettinen, Antti — Ice Hockey Player
Tampa Bay Lightning, 401 Channelside Dr, Tampa FL 33602 USA
Mifsud Bonnici, Ugo — President, Malta
18 Erin Serracino Inglott Road, Cospicua, Malta
Migay, Rudolph J (Rudy) — Ice Hockey Player
485 Belrose Road, Thunder Bay ON P7G 1K1, Canada
Migenes, Julia — Opera Singer
Rainbow High Entertainment, 3500 W Olive Ave, #300, Burbank CA 91505, USA
Miggins, Lawrence E (Larry) — Baseball Player
2405 Kingston St, Houston TX 77019, USA
Migliore, Richard — Thoroughbred Racing Jockey
48 Killearn Road, Millbrook NY 12545, USA
Mignola, Mike — Cartoonist (Hellboy)
Dark Horse Publishing, 10956 SE Main St, Portland OR 97222 USA
Miguel — Singer, Songwriter, Producer
Sony Records, 550 Madison Ave, #1000, New York NY 10022, USA
Miguel, Luis — Singer
Front Line Mgmt, 1100 Glendon Ave, #2000, Los Angeles CA 90024 USA
Mihm, Christopher S (Chris) — Basketball Player
4708 Peace Pipe Path, Austin TX 78746, USA
Mihok, Dash — Actor
Gersh Agency, 9465 Wilshire Blvd, #600, Beverly Hills CA 90212 USA
Mijares, Cristian — Boxer
DiBella Entertainment, 350 7th Ave, #800, New York NY 10001, USA
Mika — Singer, Songwriter
Champion Entertainment, 9 E 63rd St, New York NY 10065, USA
Mikan, G Lawrence (Larry) — Basketball Player
891 Carmona Court, Chula Vista CA 91910, USA
Mikati, Najib A — Prime Minister, Lebanon
Premier's Office, Serail, Place de l'Etoile, Beirut, Lebanon
Mike-Mayer, Istvan (Steve) — Football Player
681 Lincoln Ave, Glen Rock NJ 07452, USA
Mike-Mayer, Nicholas (Nick) — Football Player
681 Lincoln Ave, Glen Rock NJ 07452, USA
Mikhalchenko, Alla A — Ballerina
Malaya Gruzinskaya St 12/18, 123242 Moscow, Russia
Mikhalkov, Nikita S — Director
Maly Kozikhinsky Per 4, #16-17, 103001 Moscow, Russia

**Mikita, Stanley (Stan)** — Ice Hockey Player
57 Chesterfield Court, Burr Ridge IL 60527, USA
**Mikkelborg, Palle** — Jazz Trumpeter, Composer
Kjell Kalleklev Mgmt, Georgerne Verft 12, 5011 Bergen, Norway
**Mikkelsen, A Verner Å (Vern)** — Basketball Player, Golfer
17715 Breconville Road, Wayzata MN 55391, USA
**Mikkelsen, Lars** — Actor
Conway Van Gelder Grant, 8-12 Broadwick St, #300, London W1F 8HW, England
**Mikkelsen, Mads** — Actor
Arts Mgmt, Kronprinsensgade 9A, 1114 Copenhagen K, Denmark
**Mikkelson, Meaghan** — Ice Hockey Player
Ice Complex, Winter Park, 88 Canada Olympic Road SW, Calgary AB T3B 5R5, Canada
**Mikkelson, William R (Bill)** — Ice Hockey Player
47 Glen Meadow Crescent, Saint Aliber AB T8N 3A2, Canada
**Miko, Izabella** — Actress
Affirmative Entertainment, 425 N Robertson Blvd, Los Angeles CA 90048, USA
**Mikolaj, Aga** — Opera Singer
Künstleragentur Augstein & Hahn, Tal 28 80331 Munich, Germany
**Miksis, Alfonse K (Al)** — Basketball Player
522 E Algonquin Road, #203, Schaumburg IL 60173, USA
**Mikva, Abner J** — Judge
442 New Jersey Ave SE, Washington DC 20003, USA
**Milacki, Robert (Bob)** — Baseball Player
1873 Martinique Dr, Lake Havasu City AZ 86406, USA
**Milano, Alyssa** — Actress
Creative Artists Agency, 2000 Ave of Stars, #100, Los Angeles CA 90067 USA
**Milano, Dan** — Producer, Writer, Actor
Gersh Agency, 9465 Wilshire Blvd, #600, Beverly Hills CA 90212 USA
**Milanov, Rossen** — Conductor
Princeton Symphony Orchestra, 575 Ewing St, Princeton, NJ 08540, USA
**Milanovic, Zoran** — Prime Minister, Croatia
Prime Minister's Office, Radicev Trg 7, 41000 Zagreb, Croatia
**Milbern, David** — Actor
Regent Entertainment, 10940 Wilshire Blvd, #1600, Los Angeles CA 90024, USA
**Milbourne, Lawrence W (Larry)** — Baseball Player
747 Yale Terrace, Lake Havasu City AZ 86406, USA
**Milbrett, Tiffeny** — Soccer Player
1902 SW Broadleaf Dr, Portland OR 97219, USA
**Milburn, Brendan** — Pianist (GrooveLily), Songwriter
GrooveLily, PO Box 11570, Glendale CA 91226, USA
**Milburn, Glyn C** — Football Player
8815 S 2nd Ave, Inglewood CA 90305, USA
**Milburn, H Theodore** — Judge
440 Alexian Way, #37, Signal Mountain TN 37377, USA
**Milbury, Mike** — Ice Hockey Player, Coach
61 Edwardel Road, Needham MA 02492, USA
**Milch, David** — Producer, Writer
Red Board Productions, 3000 W Olympic Blvd, Building 4, Santa Monica CA 90404, USA
**Milchan, Arnon** — Producer
Regency Enterprises, 4000 Warner Blvd, #66, Burbank CA 91522, USA
**Miledi, Ricardo** — Neurobiologist
9 Gibbs Court, Irvine CA 92617, USA
**Miles, Aaron W** — Baseball Player
1716 San Jose Dr, Davenport IA 52807, USA
**Miles, Darius L** — Basketball Player
1906 Llewellyn Road, Bellevue IL 62223, USA
**Miles, Heather** — Singer, Songwriter
Rounder Records, 1 Rounder Way, Burlington MA 01803 USA
**Miles, Joanna** — Actress
Artists Agency, 9430 Olympic Blvd, Beverly Hills CA 90212 USA
**Miles, John R (Jack)** — Writer
3568 Mountain View Ave, Pasadena CA 91107, USA
**Miles, John W** — Geophysicist
1764 Overlook Lane, Santa Barbara CA 93103, USA
**Miles, Leslie E (Les)** — Football Coach
Lousiana State University, Athletic Dept, Baton Rouge LA 70803, USA
**Miles, Lynn** — Singer, Songwriter
LiveTourArtists, 1451 White Oaks Blvd, Oakville ON L6H 4R9, Canada
**Miles, Ron** — Jazz Trumpeter
Metropolitan State University, Jazz Studies Dept, 1201 5th St, Denver CO 80204, USA
**Miles, Sarah** — Actress
Chithurst Manor, Trotten near Petersfield, Hampshire GU31 5EU, England
**Miles, Sylvia** — Actress
A P A Talent/Literary Agency, 405 S Beverly Dr, #300, Beverly Hills CA 90212 USA
**Miles, Vera** — Actress
PO Box 1599, Palm Desert CA 92261, USA
**Miles-Clark, Jearl** — Track Athlete
J J Clark, University of Florida, Athletic Dept, Gainesville FL 32604, USA
**Milhazes, Beatriz** — Artist
Stephen Friedman Gallery, 25-28 Old Burlington St, London W1S 3AN, England
**Milhoan, Michael** — Actor
Talent Works, 3500 W Olive Ave, #1400, Burbank CA 91505 USA
**Mili, Itula** — Football Player
4468 Glenmoor Hills Dr, South Jordan UT 84095, USA
**Milian, Christina** — Singer, Actress, Songwriter
Milian Mgmt, 16830 Ventura Blvd, #501, Encino CA 91436, USA
**Miliband, David W** — Government Official, England
Foreign Secretary's Office, 11 Downing St, London SW1A 2AA, England
**Milicevic, Ivana** — Actress, Model
A P A Talent/Literary Agency, 405 S Beverly Dr, #300, Beverly Hills CA 90212 USA
**Milicic, Darko** — Basketball Player
5460 Whitehall Blvd, Oakland Township MI 48306, USA
**Milinchik, Joseph M (Joe)** — Football Player
653 Ryan Dr, Allentown PA 18103, USA
**Milinovich, Gia M** — Producer
Sue Rider Mgmt, PO Box 49175, London SW19 3WY, England

## M

**Milioti, Cristin** — Actress
Gersh Agency, 9465 Wilshire Blvd, #600, Beverly Hills CA 90212 USA
**Militello, Sam S** — Baseball Player
3217 W Saint John St, Tampa FL 33607, USA
**Militzok, Nathan (Nat)** — Basketball Player
78 Blue Lagoon, Laguna Beach CA 92651, USA
**Milius, John F** — Director, Writer
I C M Partners, 10250 Constellation Blvd, #900, Los Angeles CA 90067 USA
**Milk, Barry** — Educator
Bowdoin College, President's Office, Brunswick ME 04011, USA
**Milk, Chris** — Photographer
Anonymous Content, 3532 Hayden Ave, Culver City CA 90232 USA
**Milk, Mike** — DJ Dance Musician
Future Music, Bayerstr 77A, 80335 Munich, Germany
**Milken, Michael R** — Financier, Philanthropist
4543 Tara Dr, Encino CA 91436, USA
**Milla, Roger** — Soccer Player
Federation de Football, BP 1116, Yaounde, Cameroon
**Millan, Amy** — Singer, Guitarist
High Road Touring, 751 Bridgeway, #200, Sausalito CA 94965 USA
**Millan, Cesar** — Psychologist
Dog Psychology Center, PO Box 1130, Canyon Country CA 91386, USA
**Millan, Felix B** — Baseball Player
G16 Calle Camarero Parq Ecusetre, Carolina PR 00987, USA
**Millar, Ian** — Equestrian
Landmark Sport Group, 1 City Centre Dr, #605, Mississauga ON L5B 1M2, Canada
**Millar, Kevin C** — Baseball Player
14200 Flat Top Ranch Road, Austin TX 78732, USA
**Millar, Miles** — Producer, Writer
Millar/Gough Ink, 500 S Buena Vista St, Animations Building, Burbank CA 91521, USA
**Millar, Will** — Singer, Musician (Irish Rovers)
Lyon Group, PO Box 2428, Agoura Hills CA 91376, USA
**Millard, Bart** — Singer (MercyMe)
Brickhouse Entertainment, 106 Mission Court, #1202, Franklin TN 37067, USA
**Millard, Bryan J** — Football Player
507 Sabine St, #1001, Austin TX 78701, USA
**Millard, Keith** — Football Player
3739 Oakhurst Way, Dublin CA 94568, USA
**Millardet, Patricia** — Actress
Agents Associes, 201 Rue du Faubourg Saint Honore, 75008 Paris, France
**Milledge, Lastings D** — Baseball Player
11114 Sailbrooke Dr, Riverview FL 33579, USA
**Millegan, Eric** — Actor
Don Buchwald, 6500 Wilshire Blvd, #2200, Los Angeles CA 90048 USA
**Millen, Greg** — Ice Hockey Player
980 Orch, Bridgenorth ON K0L 1H0, Canada
**Millen, Hugh B** — Football Player
6836 Cascade Ave SE, Snoqualmie WA 98065, USA
**Millen, Matt G** — Football Player, Executive, Sportscaster
862 Durham Road, Riegelsville PA 18077, USA
**Miller, Aaron** — Ice Hockey Player
147 Appletree Point Road, Burlington VT 05408, USA
**Miller, Alan** — Journalist
Los Angeles Times, Editorial Dept, 202 W 1st St, Los Angeles CA 90012 USA
**Miller, Alan R** — Football Player
3118 Erie Dr, Orchard Lake MI 48324, USA
**Miller, Alice** — Golfer
2 Log Church Road, Wilmington DE 19807, USA
**Miller, Allison** — Actress
Beth Goldstein Mgmt, 4433 Colbath Ave, #34, Sherman Oaks CA 91423, USA
**Miller, Alyssa** — Model
Mous Model Mgmt, 117 N Robertson Blvd, Los Angeles CA 90048, USA
**Miller, Amara** — Actress
United Talent Agency, U T A Plaza, 9336 Civic Center Dr, Beverly Hills CA 90210 USA
**Miller, Andre L** — Basketball Player
Denver Nuggets, Pepsi Center, 1000 Chopper Circle, Denver CO 80204 USA
**Miller, Andrea** — Choreographer, Dance Executive
Gallim Dance, 304 W 75th St, New York NY 10023, USA
**Miller, Anthony** — Basketball Player
1083 Superior St, Benton Harbor MI 49022, USA
**Miller, Bebe** — Choreographer, Dancer
Bebe Miller Dance Co, 54 W 21st St, #502, New York NY 10010, USA
**Miller, Bennett** — Director
Creative Artists Agency, 2000 Ave of Stars, #100, Los Angeles CA 90067 USA
**Miller, Billy J** — Actor
Innovative Artists, 1505 10th St, Santa Monica CA 90401 USA
**Miller, Billy R** — Football Player
3957 Skelton Canyon Circle, Westlake Village CA 91362, USA
**Miller, Bode** — Alpine Skier
65 Easton Valley Road, Franconia, NH 03580, USA
**Miller, Bradley A (Brad)** — Basketball Player
2731 Marl Oak Dr, Highland Park IL 60035, USA
**Miller, Bruce** — Producer
Jackoway Tyerman Wertheimer, 1925 Century Park E, #2200, Los Angeles CA 90067 USA
**Miller, C Arden** — Pediatrician
350 Carolina Meadows Villa, Chapel Hill NC 27517, USA
**Miller, Carol** — Bowler
Professional Bowlers Assn, 719 2nd Ave, #701, Seattle WA 98104 USA
**Miller, Cheryl D** — Basketball Player, Coach
3206 Ellington Dr, Los Angeles CA 90068, USA
**Miller, Christa** — Actress
I C M Partners, 10250 Constellation Blvd, #900, Los Angeles CA 90067 USA
**Miller, Christine Cook** — Judge
US Claims Court, 717 Madison Place NW, Washington DC 20439, USA
**Miller, Christopher J (Chris)** — Football Player
701 W Hackberry Dr, Chandler AZ 85248, USA

**M**

| | |
|---|---|
| **Miller, Cleophus (Cleo), Jr** <br> 16613 Raymond St, Maple Heights OH 44137, USA | Football Player |
| **Miller, Colleen M (Coco)** <br> Los Angeles Sparks, 888 S Figueroa St, #2010, Los Angeles CA 90017 USA | Basketball Player |
| **Miller, Corky A P** <br> 1115 7th St, Calimesa CA 92320, USA | Baseball Player |
| **Miller, Damian D** <br> N1276 Wuensch Road, La Crosse WI 54601, USA | Baseball Player |
| **Miller, Dan** <br> J Records, 745 5th Ave, #600, New York NY 10151 USA | Singer (O-Town) |
| **Miller, Darrell K** <br> 21159 Via Alisa, Yorba Linda CA 92887, USA | Baseball Player |
| **Miller, David** <br> Back 40 Design, PO Box 7985, Edmond OK 73083, USA | Cartoonist (Dave) |
| **Miller, David Alan** <br> Opus 3 Artists, 470 Park Ave S, #900N, New York NY 10016 USA | Conductor |
| **Miller, Dennis** <br> Brillstein Entertainment Partners, 9150 Wilshire Blvd, #350, Beverly Hills CA 90212 USA | Actor, Comedian |
| **Miller, Denny** <br> 9612 Gavin Stone Ave, Las Vegas NV 89145, USA | Actor |
| **Miller, Derek** <br> Agency Group Ltd, 142 W 57th St, #600, New York NY 10019 USA | Guitarist, Singer (Sleigh Bells) |
| **Miller, Dyar K** <br> 8816 Admirals Bay Dr, Indianapolis IN 46236, USA | Baseball Player |
| **Miller, E Heath, Jr** <br> 1304 Hidden Canyon Court, Sewickley PA 15143, USA | Football Player |
| **Miller, Edward L (Eddie)** <br> 1819 Alfreda Blvd, San Pablo CA 94806, USA | Baseball Player |
| **Miller, Everett** <br> 13655 Ahwahnee Way, Poway CA 92064, USA | Hero |
| **Miller, Frank** <br> Shapiro-Lichtman, 8827 Beverly Blvd, Los Angeles CA 90048 USA | Actor, Writer |
| **Miller, Frank** <br> Dark Horse Publishing, 10956 SE Main St, Portland OR 97222 USA | Cartoonist (Sin City, Dark Knight) |
| **Miller, Fred D** <br> 4535 Black Rock Road, Upperco MD 21155, USA | Football Player |
| **Miller, Fred J** <br> 7143 Sawmill Trail, Houston TX 77040, USA | Football Player |
| **Miller, Gabrielle** <br> Oscars Abrams Zimel, 438 Queen St E, Toronto ON M5A 1T4, Canada | Actress |
| **Miller, George D** <br> 20 Phillips Pond South, Natick MA 01760, USA | Air Force General |
| **Miller, George T (Kennedy)** <br> 30 Orwell St, King's Cross, Sydney NSW 2011, Australia | Director, Producer |
| **Miller, Harland** <br> N9 Design, Century Quay, Sutton Harbour, Plymouth PL4 0EP, England | Artist, Writer |
| **Miller, Howard S** <br> Endurance Talent Mgmt, 2920 W Olive Ave, #202, Burbank CA 91505, USA | Actor |
| **Miller, James A** <br> 1822 Masters Lane, Madison WI 53719, USA | Oncologist |
| **Miller, James C, III** <br> Citizens for Sound Economy, 1250 H St NW, Washington DC 20005, USA | Government Official |
| **Miller, James D (Jim)** <br> 9916 King Road, Davisburg MI 48350, USA | Football Player |
| **Miller, James G (Jim)** <br> PO Box 863, Ripley MS 38663, USA | Football Player |
| **Miller, Jamir M** <br> 6717 E Meadowlark Lane, Paradise Valley AZ 85253, USA | Football Player |
| **Miller, Jeff** <br> Breen Agency, 25 Music Square W, Nashville TN 37203, USA | Bassist (Caedmon's Call) |
| **Miller, Jeremy** <br> Acumen Entertainment Partners, 15915 Ventura Blvd, #304, Encino CA 91436, USA | Actor |
| **Miller, Jerry** <br> Smithsonian Institution Press, 750 9th St NW, #4300, Washington DC 20560, USA | Navy Admiral |
| **Miller, Jody** <br> PO Box 413, Blanchard OK 73010, USA | Singer |
| **Miller, Joel McKinnon** <br> Greene Assoc, 1901 Ave of Stars, #130, Los Angeles CA 90067 USA | Actor |
| **Miller, John** <br> ABC-TV, News Dept, 77 W 66th St, New York NY 10023 USA | Commentator |
| **Miller, John A** <br> 5105 River Ave, #A, Newport Beach CA 92663, USA | Baseball Player |
| **Miller, John E** <br> 13443 Old Annapolis Road, Mount Airy MD 21771, USA | Baseball Player |
| **Miller, John L (Johnny)** <br> Johnny Miller Enterprises, PO Box 2260, Napa CA 94558, USA | Golfer, Sportscaster |
| **Miller, John W** <br> Central Connecticut State University, President's Office, New Britain CT 06050, USA | Educator |
| **Miller, Jon** <br> ESPN-TV, ESPN Plaza, 935 Middle St, Bristol CT 06010 USA | Sportscaster, Baseball Player |
| **Miller, Jonathan W** <br> Royce Carlton, 866 United Nations Plaza, New York NY 10017, USA | Director |
| **Miller, Jonny Lee** <br> Independent Talent Group, 40 Whitfield St, London W1T 2RH, England | Actor |
| **Miller, Joshua H (Josh)** <br> 572 Macleod Dr, Gibsonia PA 15044, USA | Football Player |
| **Miller, Joshua J (Josh)** <br> Gersh Agency, 9465 Wilshire Blvd, #600, Beverly Hills CA 90212 USA | Actor, Director, Writer |
| **Miller, Julie** <br> Vector Mgmt, PO Box 120479, Nashville TN 37212 USA | Singer, Songwriter |
| **Miller, Justin M** <br> Arizona Cardinals, PO Box 888, Phoenix AZ 85001 USA | Football Player |
| **Miller, Keith A** <br> 190 Water St, #2, Milford MI 48381, USA | Baseball Player |
| **Miller, Keith H** <br> 3705 Arctic Blvd, Anchorage AK 99503, USA | Governor, AK |

Miller - Miller

**M**

**Miller, Kelly** — Basketball Player
New York Liberty, Madison Square Garden, 2 Penn Plaza, New York NY 10121 USA
**Miller, Kelly D** — Ice Hockey Player
3783 Chippendale Circle, Okemos MI 48864, USA
**Miller, Kevin** — Drummer (Fuel)
Media Five Entertainment, 3005 Brodhead Road, #170, Bethlehem PA 18020, USA
**Miller, Kevin B** — Ice Hockey Player
4243 Redbud Trail, Williamston MI 48895, USA
**Miller, Kristen E** — Actress, Comedienne
Talent Works, 3500 W Olive Ave, #1400, Burbank CA 91505 USA
**Miller, Kurt E** — Baseball Player
1511 Iroquois Circle, Carrollton TX 75007, USA
**Miller, L Anthony** — Football Player
325 S San Dimas Canyon Road, #108, San Dimas CA 91773, USA
**Miller, Lajos** — Opera Singer
Hegyalja Utca 32, 3232 Matrafured, Hungary
**Miller, Larry** — Actor, Comedian
Brillstein Entertainment Partners, 9150 Wilshire Blvd, #350, Beverly Hills CA 90212 USA
**Miller, Lawrence J (Larry)** — Basketball Player
311 Mulberry St, Catasauqua PA 18032, USA
**Miller, Linda Lael** — Writer
Harlequin Enterprises, 225 Duncan Mill Road, Don Mills ON MJB JK9, Canada
**Miller, Marcus** — Jazz Bassist, Composer
I C M Partners, 10250 Constellation Blvd, #900, Los Angeles CA 90067 USA
**Miller, Marisa** — Actress, Model
Cartel Mgmt, 665 N Lillian Way, Los Angeles CA 90004, USA
**Miller, Mark** — Singer (Sawyer Brown)
O-Seven Artist Mgmt, PO Box 210586, Nashville TN 37221, USA
**Miller, Marlin** — Opera Singer
I M G Artists, Hogarth Business Park, Chiswick, London W4 2TH, England
**Miller, McKaley** — Actress
Osbrink Talent Agency, 4343 Lankershim Blvd, #100, North Hollywood CA 91602 USA
**Miller, Michael L (Mike)** — Basketball Player
2869 Ladbrook Way, Thousand Oaks CA 91361, USA
**Miller, Mildred** — Opera Singer
PO Box 110108, Pittsburgh PA 15232, USA
**Miller, N Keith** — Baseball Player
1831 W Alamosa Dr, Terrell TX 75160, USA
**Miller, Nancy (Ann)** — Writer, Producer
W M E Entertainment, 9601 Wilshire Blvd, #300, Beverly Hills CA 90210 USA
**Miller, Nate** — Boxer
1943 N Uber St, Philadelphia PA 19121, USA
**Miller, Nicole J** — Fashion Designer
780 Madison Ave, Front 1, New York NY 10065, USA
**Miller, Norman C (Norm)** — Baseball Player
43 Columbia Crest Place, Spring TX 77382, USA
**Miller, Oliver J** — Basketball Player
2912 S Meadow Dr, Fort Worth TX 76133, USA
**Miller, Omar Benson** — Actor
A P A Talent/Literary Agency, 405 S Beverly Dr, #300, Beverly Hills CA 90212 USA
**Miller, Paul** — Actor
Fountainhead Talent, 131 Davenport Road, Toronto ON M5R 1H8, Canada
**Miller, Paul D** — Navy Admiral, Businessman
Teledyne Technologies, 1049 Camino Dos Rios, Thousand Oaks CA 91360, USA
**Miller, Penelope Ann** — Actress
A P A Talent/Literary Agency, 405 S Beverly Dr, #300, Beverly Hills CA 90212 USA
**Miller, Peter North** — Businessman
Quinneys, Camilla Dr, Westhumble, Dorking, Surrey RH5 6BU, England
**Miller, Randall S (Randy)** — Baseball Player
22523 Oak Mist Lane, Katy TX 77494, USA
**Miller, Raymond R (Ray)** — Baseball Manager
PO Box 41, New Athens OH 43981, USA
**Miller, Rebecca** — Actress, Director, Writer
Creative Artists Agency, 2000 Ave of Stars, #100, Los Angeles CA 90067 USA
**Miller, Reginald W (Reggie)** — Basketball Player, Sportscaster
3785 Puerco Canyon Road, Malibu CA 90265, USA
**Miller, Rhett** — Singer (Old 97's), Songwriter
Paradigm Agency, 360 N Crescent Dr, North Building, Beverly Hills CA 90210 USA
**Miller, Richard A (Rick)** — Baseball Player
12790 Silverthorn Court, Bonita Springs FL 34135, USA
**Miller, Risa** — Writer
Saint Martin's Press, 175 5th Ave, #400, New York NY 10010 USA
**Miller, Robert (Steve)** — Businessman
Delphi Automotive Systems, 5725 Delphi Dr, Troy MI 48098, USA
**Miller, Robert Ellis** — Director
1901 Ave of Stars, #1040, Los Angeles CA 90067, USA
**Miller, Robert G** — Businessman
Albertsons, 250 E Parkcenter Blvd, Boise ID 83706, USA
**Miller, Robert G (Bob)** — Baseball Player
1702 Keim Trail, Saint Charles IL 60174, USA
**Miller, Robert J (Bob)** — Baseball Player
1202 Andover Circle, Commerce Township MI 48390, USA
**Miller, Robert J (Bob)** — Governor, NV
Jones Vargas, 3773 S Howard Hughes Parkway, #300S, Las Vegas NV 89169, USA
**Miller, Robert L** — Football Player
5403 Augusta Trail, Fort Collins CO 80528, USA
**Miller, Ryan** — Singer, Guitarist (Guster)
Nettwerk Mgmt, 345 7th Ave, #2400, New York NY 10001, USA
**Miller, Sam** — Director
Independent Talent Group, 40 Whitfield St, London W1T 2RH, England
**Miller, Scott P** — Football Player
1570 NW 128th Dr, #306, Sunrise FL 33323, USA
**Miller, Sean** — Basketball Coach
University of Arizona, Athletic Dept, Tucson AZ 85721, USA
**Miller, Selvia (Junior)** — Football Player
3051 Agate Court, Lincoln NE 68516, USA

**Miller - Miller**

**Miller, Shannon** — Gymnast
Shannon Miller Lifestyle, 4319 Salisbury Road, #4, Jacksonville FL 32218, USA
**Miller, Shawn V** — Football Player
3070 W Old Highway Road, Morgan UT 84050, USA
**Miller, Sienna A** — Actress, Model
United Agents, 12-26 Lexington St, London W1F 0LE, England
**Miller, Steve** — Singer, Songwriter, Orchestra Leader
Randex Communications, 906 Jonathan Lane, Marlton NJ 08053, USA
**Miller, Steven P (Buddy)** — Guitarist, Songwriter
Vector Mgmt, PO Box 120479, Nashville TN 37212 USA
**Miller, Stuart L (Stu)** — Baseball Player
3701 Ocaso Court, Cameron Park CA 95682, USA
**Miller, Susan** — Model, Actress
Playboy Promotions, 2706 Media Center Dr, Los Angeles CA 90065 USA
**Miller, Tangi** — Actress, Producer, Writer
Olivia Entertainment, PO Box 19398, Los Angeles CA 90019, USA
**Miller, Taylor** — Actress
Innovative Artists, 1505 10th St, Santa Monica CA 90401 USA
**Miller, Travis E** — Baseball Player
51 Whisper Way, Eaton OH 45320, USA
**Miller, Trever D** — Baseball Player
24155 Hideout Trail, Land O Lakes FL 34639, USA
**Miller, Troy** — Producer, Director
Dakota Pictures, 4133 Lankershim Blvd, North Hollywood CA 91602, USA
**Miller, Valerie Rae** — Actress
United Talent Agency, U T A Plaza, 9336 Civic Center Dr, Beverly Hills CA 90210 USA
**Miller, Von** — Football Player
Denver Broncos, 13655 E Broncos Parkway, Englewood CO 80112 USA
**Miller, Wade T** — Baseball Player
12 Woods Way, Reading PA 19610, USA
**Miller, Webb** — Biologist
Pennsylvania State University, Biology Dept, Wartik Laboratory, University Park PA 16802, USA
**Miller, Wentworth** — Actor
I C M Partners, 10250 Constellation Blvd, #900, Los Angeles CA 90067 USA
**Miller, Wiley** — Cartoonist (Non Sequitur/Us & Them)
8 Granite Heights Road, Kennebunkport ME 04046, USA
**Miller, William J (Bill)** — Football Player
701 Belden Court, Saint Augustine FL 32086, USA
**Miller, Willie T** — Football Player
6290 Walnut Dr, Pinson AL 35126, USA
**Miller, Zachary P (Zach)** — Football Player
Seattle Seahawks, 12 Seahawks Way, Renton WA 98056 USA
**Miller-Lawrence, Christa** — Actress
I C M Partners, 10250 Constellation Blvd, #900, Los Angeles CA 90067 USA
**Millett, Kate** — Women's Activist, Writer
20 Old Overlook Road, Poughkeepsie NY 12603, USA
**Millett, Terroon** — Boxer
6548 Whitney Ave, Saint Louis MO 63133, USA
**Millhauser, Steven** — Writer
235 Caroline St, Saratoga Springs NY 12866, USA
**Millican, Clay** — Auto Racing Driver
545 Watson Road, Atoka TN 38004, USA
**Milligan, Dustin** — Actor
Red Mgmt, 415 W Esplanade, #3, North Vancouver BC V7M 1A6, Canada
**Milligan, Joseph** — Guitarist (Anberlin)
Arson Media Group, 23 N Summerlin Ave, #200, Orlando FL 32801, USA
**Milligan, Randy A** — Baseball Player
6905 Real Princess Lane, Gwynn Oak MD 21207, USA
**Milliken, Angie** — Actress
Polaris Entertainment, 8048 W 3rd St, #300, Los Angeles CA 90048, USA
**Milliken, James B** — Educator
University of Nebraska, President's Office, Lincoln NE 68588, USA
**Million, Mike** — Director, Producer, Writer
Brucks/McDonald Entertainment, 1635 N Cahuenga Blvd, #400, Los Angeles CA 90028, USA
**Millman, Gabriel** — Actor
Harvest Talent Mgmt, 124 W 80th St, #1, New York NY 10024, USA
**Millner, F Ann** — Educator
Weber State University, President's Office, 3848 Harrison Blvd, Ogden UT 84408, USA
**Millns, James G (Jim), Jr** — Ice Dancer
7603 Dunbridge Dr, Odessa FL 33556, USA
**Millo, Aprile E** — Opera Singer
Columbia Artists Mgmt Inc, 1790 Broadway, #702, New York NY 10019 USA
**Milloy, Lawyer M** — Football Player
57 Chapman Loop, Steilacoom WA 98388, USA
**Mills, Alan B** — Baseball Player
1811 Bellgrove St, Lakeland FL 33805, USA
**Mills, Alley** — Actress
Stone Manners Salners, 9911 W Pico Blvd, #1400, Los Angeles CA 90035 USA
**Mills, Barry** — Educator
Bowdoin College, President's Office, Brunswick ME 04011, USA
**Mills, Christopher (Chris)** — Basketball Player
2223 Camden Ave, Los Angeles CA 90064, USA
**Mills, Crispian** — Singer, Guitarist (Kula Shakur)
Little Big Man, 39A Grammercy Park N, #1C, New York NY 10010, USA
**Mills, Donna** — Actress
Talent Works, 3500 W Olive Ave, #1400, Burbank CA 91505 USA
**Mills, Ernest L (Ernie)** — Football Player
PO Box 2435, Dunnellon FL 34430, USA
**Mills, Frank** — Pianist, Composer
Rocklands Entertainment, PO Box 48216, Saint Petersburg FL 33743, USA
**Mills, Hayley** — Actress, Singer
Chatto & Linnit, 123A King's Road, London SW3 4PL, England
**Mills, J Bradley (Brad)** — Baseball Player, Manager
4746 W Buena Vista Court, Visalia CA 93291, USA
**Mills, John Henry** — Football Player
755 Bahia Circle, Ocala FL 34472, USA

# M

| | |
|---|---|
| **Mills, Judson**<br>Dino May Mgmt, 11262 Ventura Blvd, #PH, Studio City CA 91604, USA | Actor |
| **Mills, Juliet**<br>Diamond Management, 31 Percy St, London W1T 2DD, England | Actress |
| **Mills, Mary**<br>310 S Ocean Blvd, #106, Boca Raton FL 33432, USA | Golfer |
| **Mills, Mary**<br>I M G Artists, Hogarth Business Park, Chiswick, London W4 2TH, England | Opera Singer |
| **Mills, Michael E (Mike)**<br>REM/Athens Ltd, PO Box 8032, Athens GA 30603, USA | Bassist (REM) |
| **Mills, Mike**<br>United Talent Agency, U T A Plaza, 9336 Civic Center Dr, Beverly Hills CA 90210 USA | Director |
| **Mills, Phoebe**<br>Harris Agency, 17814 Lillian St, Omaha NE 68136, USA | Gymnast |
| **Mills, Stephanie**<br>Wenig-LaMonica Assoc, 580 White Plains Road, #130, Tarrytown NY 10591, USA | Singer, Actress |
| **Mills, Terry R**<br>37840 Scott Pine Dr, New Boston MI 48164, USA | Basketball Player |
| **Mills, William H (Bill)**<br>4344 Commercial St, Port Charlotte FL 33953, USA | Baseball Player |
| **Mills, William M (Billy)**<br>7760 Winding Way, #722, Fair Oaks CA 95628, USA | Track Athlete |
| **Mills, Zach**<br>Paradigm Agency, 360 N Crescent Dr, North Building, Beverly Hills CA 90210 USA | Actor |
| **Millsap, Paul**<br>Atlanta Hawks, Centennial Tower, 101 Marietta St NW, #1900, Atlanta GA 30303 USA | Basketball Player |
| **Millwood, Kamla**<br>Impact Model Mgmt, 324-326 Regent St, #104, London W1B 3HH, England | Model |
| **Millwood, Kevin A**<br>1204 Suncast Lane, #2, El Dorado Hills CA 95762, USA | Baseball Player |
| **Milne, Brian F**<br>1411 Beacon St, Cincinnati OH 45230, USA | Football Player |
| **Milner, Anthony F D**<br>147 Heythorp St, Southfields, London SW18 5BT, England | Composer |
| **Milner, Edward J (Eddie)**<br>491 Stambaugh Ave, Columbus OH 43207, USA | Baseball Player |
| **Milner, Martin**<br>3106 Azahar St, Carlsbad CA 92009, USA | Actor |
| **Milnes, Sherrill E**<br>Herbert Barrett, 266 W 37th St, #2000, New York NY 10018 USA | Opera Singer |
| **Milnor, John W**<br>3 Laurel Lane, Setauket NY 11733, USA | Abel Mathematics Laureate |
| **Milos, Sofia**<br>Rogers & Cowan, 8687 Melrose Ave, #G700, West Hollywood CA 90069 USA | Actress |
| **Miloszewski, Steve**<br>David Levy Mgmt, 200 W 57th St, #308, New York NY 10019, USA | Guitarist (Reveille) |
| **Milot, Richard P (Rich)**<br>15840 Hunton Lane, Haymarket PA 20169, USA | Football Player |
| **Milsap, Ronnie**<br>Ronnie Milsap Enterprises, PO Box 40665, Nashville TN 37204, USA | Singer, Pianist, Songwriter |
| **Milsome, Douglas**<br>Gems, Studio Five, Stangate House, Stanwell Road, Penarth CF64 2AA, England | Cinematographer |
| **Milstead, Roderick L (Rod), Jr**<br>6674 Fenwick Road, Bryans Road MD 20616, USA | Football Player |
| **Milton, Eric R**<br>1133 Asquith Dr, Arnold MD 21012, USA | Baseball Player |
| **Milton, Peter W**<br>2 New Hampshire Turnpike S, Francestown NH 03043, USA | Artist |
| **Milton-Jones, DeLisha**<br>San Antonio Silver Stars, 1 AT&T Center, San Antonio TX 78219 USA | Basketball Player |
| **Mimbs, Michael R (Mike)**<br>2761 Mimbs Road, Alamo GA 30411, USA | Baseball Player |
| **Mimica-Gezzan, Sergio**<br>United Talent Agency, U T A Plaza, 9336 Civic Center Dr, Beverly Hills CA 90210 USA | Director, Producer |
| **Mimieux, Yvette**<br>Howard Ruby Photography, 2222 Corinth Ave, Los Angeles CA 90064, USA | Actress |
| **Mims-Flowers, Tairia**<br>Amateur Softball, 2801 NE 50th St, Oklahoma City OK 73111, USA | Softball Player |
| **Mina, Denise**<br>Little Brown, 3 Center Plaza, #100, Boston MA 02108 USA | Writer |
| **Minaj, Nicki**<br>Creative Artists Agency, 2000 Ave of Stars, #100, Los Angeles CA 90067 USA | Rap Artist, Singer, Songwriter |
| **Mincy, Charles A**<br>2227 W 24th St, #7, Los Angeles CA 90018, USA | Football Player |
| **Mindel, Lee F**<br>Shelton Mindel Assoc, 56 W 22nd St, #1200, New York NY 10010, USA | Architect |
| **Minear, Tim**<br>W M E Entertainment, 9601 Wilshire Blvd, #300, Beverly Hills CA 90210 USA | Writer, Producer |
| **Minenkov, Andrei**<br>Skating Federation, Luchnesksaia Nab 8, 119871 Moscow, Russia | Ice Dancer |
| **Miner, Rachel**<br>Untitled Entertainment, 350 S Beverly Dr, #200, Beverly Hills CA 90212 USA | Actress |
| **Miner, Steve**<br>Gersh Agency, 9465 Wilshire Blvd, #600, Beverly Hills CA 90212 USA | Director |
| **Ming Tsai**<br>Food Network, 1180 Ave of Americas, #1200, New York NY 10036 USA | Chef |
| **Mingenbach, Louise**<br>United Talent Agency, U T A Plaza, 9336 Civic Center Dr, Beverly Hills CA 90210 USA | Costume Designer |
| **Minghella, Max**<br>Creative Artists Agency, 2000 Ave of Stars, #100, Los Angeles CA 90067 USA | Actor |
| **Mingiedi, Mawangu**<br>Concerted Efforts, PO Box 440326, Somerville MA 02144 USA | Percussionist, Likembe Player |
| **Ming-Na Wen**<br>Gersh Agency, 9465 Wilshire Blvd, #600, Beverly Hills CA 90212 USA | Actress |
| **Mingo, Barkevious L**<br>Cleveland Browns, 76 Lou Groza Blvd, Berea OH 44017 USA | Football Player |

**Mills - Mingo**

**Mingo, Eugene L (Gene)** — Football Player
5701 E Colorado Ave, Denver CO 80224, USA
**Minh Tran** — Dancer, Choreographer
2014 NE 47th Ave, Portland OR 97213, USA
**Miniefield, Kevin L** — Football Player
11733 E Starflower Dr, Chandler AZ 85249, USA
**Minkoff, Rob** — Director, Producer, Animator
Oasis Media Group, 8730 W Sunset Blvd, #700, West Hollywood CA 90069, USA
**Minkowski, Marc** — Conductor
Deutsche Grammaphon Records, 810 7th Ave, New York NY 10019 USA
**Minnelli, Liza** — Actress, Singer
150 E 69th St, #21G, New York NY 10021, USA
**Minnette, Dylan** — Actor
C E S D, 10635 Santa Monica Blvd, #130, Los Angeles CA 90025 USA
**Minnick, Walter C (Walt)** — Representative, ID
The Majority Group LLP, 1701 Pennsylvania Ave NW, #300, Washington DC 20006, USA
**Minnifield, Dirk D** — Basketball Player
10902 Little Gap Court, Sugar Land TX 77498, USA
**Minnifield, Frank D** — Football Player
4809 Chaffey Lane, Lexington KY 40515, USA
**Minnillo, Vanessa** — Entertainer
B/W/R, 9100 Wilshire Blvd, #500W, Beverly Hills CA 90212 USA
**Minns, Martyn** — Religious Leader
Truro Church, Rector's Office, 10520 Main St, Fairfax VA 22030, USA
**Minogue, Danii** — Singer
PO Box 46824, London SW11 3WS, England
**Minogue, Kylie** — Singer, Actress
Primary Talent International, 10-11 Jockey's Fields, London WC1R 4BN, England
**Minor, Blas, Jr** — Baseball Player
7139 N Dean St, Winton CA 95388, USA
**Minor, Greg M** — Basketball Player
6543 Merrick Landing Blvd, Windermere FL 34786, USA
**Minor, Jerry** — Actor
United Talent Agency, U T A Plaza, 9336 Civic Center Dr, Beverly Hills CA 90210 USA
**Minor, Shane** — Singer
E S P Mgmt, 838 N Doheny Dr, #302, West Hollywood CA 90069, USA
**Minor, Travis D** — Football Player
PO Box 1635, Hallandale FL 33008, USA
**Minoso, Saturino O A A (Minnie)** — Baseball Player
3700 N Lake Shore Dr, #303, Chicago IL 60613, USA
**Minot, Eliza** — Writer
Knopf Publishers, 1745 Broadway, New York NY 10019 USA
**Minow, Newton N** — Government Official
179 E Lake Shore Dr, #15W, Chicago IL 60611, USA
**Minshall, James E (Jim)** — Baseball Player
615 Manatee Ave, Ellenton FL 34222, USA
**Minshew, Alicia** — Actress
Don Buchwald, 6500 Wilshire Blvd, #2200, Los Angeles CA 90048 USA
**Minsky, Charles D** — Cinematographer
202 Toro Canyon Road, Carpinteria CA 93013, USA
**Minsky, Marvin L** — Computer Scientist
Massachusetts Institute of Technology, Computer Science Dept, Cambridge MA 02139, USA
**Minter, Alan** — Boxer
Fighting Talk, 30 Peterborough Way, Fellgate, Jarrow NE32 4XD, Canada
**Minter, Barry A** — Football Player
2626 Garcitas Creek, Richmond TX 77406, USA
**Minter, Kristin** — Actress
Lovett Mgmt, 1327 Brinkley Ave, Los Angeles CA 90049, USA
**Minter, Michael C )Mike)** — Football Player
506 N East Ave, Kannapolis NC 28083, USA
**Minton, Gregory B (Greg)** — Baseball Player
690 N Muleshoe Road, Apache Junction AZ 85119, USA
**Minton, Yvonne F** — Opera Singer
Organisation International Artistique, 16 Ave F D Roosevelt, 75008 Paris, France
**Mintz, Beatrice** — Embryologist
Fox Chase Cancer Center, 333 Cottman Ave, Philadelphia PA 19111, USA
**Mintz, Daniel (Dan)** — Actor, Writer
Creative Artists Agency, 2000 Ave of Stars, #100, Los Angeles CA 90067 USA
**Mintz, Shlomo** — Concert Violinist, Conductor
Künstleragentur Raab & Bohm, Plankengasse 7, 1010 Vienna, Austria
**Mintz-Plasse, Christopher** — Actor
United Talent Agency, U T A Plaza, 9336 Civic Center Dr, Beverly Hills CA 90210 USA
**Minucci, Chieli** — Guitarist, Composer
Axis Artists Mgmt, 9715 Belmar Ave, Northridge CA 91324, USA
**Minutelli, Gino M** — Baseball
3305 Foxtrot Court, Spring Hill TX 76639, USA
**Mio, Eddie** — Ice Hockey Player
PO Box 252745, West Bloomfield MI 48325, USA
**Miou-Miou** — Actress
U B B A, 6 Rue de Braque, 75003 Paris, France
**Mir, Isabelle** — Alpine Skier
65170 Saint-Lary, France
**Mira, George** — Football Player
19225 SW 128th Court, Miami FL 33177, USA
**Mirabella, Erin** — Cyclist
914 N Idaho St, La Habra CA 90631, USA
**Mirabella, Grace** — Editor, Publisher
Mirabella, Editor's Office, 200 Madison Ave, New York NY 10016, USA
**Mirabella, Paul T** — Baseball Player
125 Jenks Road, Morristown NJ 07960, USA
**Mirabelli, Douglas A (Doug)** — Baseball Player
9788 Edgewood Ave, Traverse City MI 49685, USA
**Miraldi, Dean M** — Football Player
14015 Live Oak Lane, Grass Valley CA 95945, USA
**Miranda, Claudio** — Cinematographer
Dattner Disposto, 10635 Santa Monica Blvd, #165, Los Angeles CA 90025, USA

**Miranda, Lin-Manuel** — Lyricist, Actor, Singer
W M E Entertainment, 9601 Wilshire Blvd, #300, Beverly Hills CA 90210 USA
**Miranda, Pia** — Actress
United Mgmt, 61 Marlborough St, #400-45, Surry Hills NSW 2010, Australia
**Mirchoff, Beau** — Actor
A P A Talent/Literary Agency, 405 S Beverly Dr, #300, Beverly Hills CA 90212 USA
**Mirer, Rick F** — Football Player
820 Braxton Court, Goshen IN 46526, USA
**Mirich, Rex L** — Football Player
620 W Yaqui Dr, Tucson AZ 85704, USA
**Miricioiu, Nelly** — Opera Singer
53 Midhurst Ave, Muswell Hill, London N10 3EP, England
**Mirikitani, Janice** — Writer
Celestial Arts Press, 6001 Shellmound St, #400, Emeryville CA 94608, USA
**Mirisch, Walter M** — Producer
647 Warner Ave, Los Angeles CA 90024, USA
**Mirkin, David** — Director, Producer, Writer
Gersh Agency, 9465 Wilshire Blvd, #600, Beverly Hills CA 90212 USA
**Mirman, Eugene** — Actor
I C M Partners, 10250 Constellation Blvd, #900, Los Angeles CA 90067 USA
**Mirmira, Raghavendra G** — Biochemist, Molecular Biologist
University of Virginia Medical School, Endocrinology & Metabolism Dept, Charlottesville VA 22903, USA
**Mironov, Boris O** — Ice Hockey Player
2911 Bayview Ave, North York ON M2K 1E8, Canada
**Mironov, Dmitri O** — Ice Hockey Player
2911 Bayview Ave, North York ON M2K 1E8, Canada
**Mirren, Helen** — Actress
Stan Rosenfield Assoc, 2029 Century Park E, #1190, Los Angeles CA 90067 USA
**Mirrione, Stephen** — Editor
I C M Partners, 10250 Constellation Blvd, #900, Los Angeles CA 90067 USA
**Mirrlees, James A** — Nobel Economics Laureate
Trinity College, Economics Dept, Cambridge CB2 1TQ, England
**Mirziyoyev, Shavkat M** — Prime Minister, Uzbekistan
Prime Minister's Office, Mustarilik 5, 70008 Tashkent, Uzbekistan
**Miscavige, David** — Religious Leader
Scientology Religious Tech Center, 1710 Ivar St, #1100, Los Angeles CA 90028, USA
**Misch, Patrick T J** — Baseball Player
366 E Krista Way, Tempe AZ 85284, USA
**Mischak, Robert M (Bob)** — Football Player
73 Brookwood Road, #12, Orinda CA 94563, USA
**Mischer, Don** — Producer, Director, Writer
Don Mischer Productions, 8899 Beverly Blvd, #902, Los Angeles CA 90048, USA
**Mischka, James** — Fashion Designer
Badgley Mischka, 215 W 40th St, New York NY 10018, USA
**Misersky, Antje** — Biathlete
Grenzgraben 3A, 98714 Stutzerbach, Germany
**Mishkin, Frederic** — Government Official, Economist
Columbia University, Economics Dept, New York NY 10027, USA
**Misiano, Christopher (Chris)** — Director, Producer
Creative Artists Agency, 2000 Ave of Stars, #100, Los Angeles CA 90067 USA
**Misiano, Vincent** — Director
Creative Artists Agency, 2000 Ave of Stars, #100, Los Angeles CA 90067 USA
**Miskulin, Joey (Cowpolka King)** — Singer, Accordionist (Riders in the Sky)
New Frontier Mgmt, 1921 Broadway, Nashville TN 37203, USA
**Misner, Susan** — Actress
One Entertainment, 1321 7th St, #203, Santa Monica CA 90401 USA
**Misrach, Richard L** — Photographer
1420 45th St, Emeryville CA 94608, USA
**Missick, Dorian** — Actor
A P A Talent/Literary Agency, 405 S Beverly Dr, #300, Beverly Hills CA 90212 USA
**Mistry, Jimi** — Actor
Brillstein Entertainment Partners, 9150 Wilshire Blvd, #350, Beverly Hills CA 90212 USA
**Mistry, Kaizad** — Computer Chip Engineer
Intel Corp, 5200 NE Elam Parkway, Hillsboro OR 97124, USA
**Mitalipov, Shoukhrat** — Reproductive Biologist
3075 NW Overlook Dr, Hillsboro OR 97124, USA
**Mitchard, Jacquelyn** — Writer
Penguin Books, 375 Hudson St, Basement 1, New York NY 10014 USA
**Mitchell, Aidan D** — Actor
Stone Manners Salners, 9911 W Pico Blvd, #1400, Los Angeles CA 90035 USA
**Mitchell, Andrea** — Commentator
2710 Chain Bridge Road NW, Washington DC 20016, USA
**Mitchell, Augie** — Guitarist (Intruders)
Billy Paul Mgmt, 8215 Winthrop St, Philadelphia PA 19136, USA
**Mitchell, Betsy** — Swimmer
Laurel High School, Athletic Dept, 1 Lyman Circle, Beachwood OH 44122, USA
**Mitchell, Bobby** — Golfer
435 Wimbish Dr, Danville VA 24541, USA
**Mitchell, Brandon P** — Football Player
806 Schlessinger St, Abbeville LA 70510, USA
**Mitchell, Brian K** — Football Player
5435 Chandley Farm Circle, Centreville VA 20120, USA
**Mitchell, Brian Stokes** — Actor, Singer
Paradigm Agency, 360 N Crescent Dr, North Building, Beverly Hills CA 90210 USA
**Mitchell, Bruce D (Waddie)** — Singer, Guitarist, Writer
Scott O'Malley Assoc, 433 E Cuchamas St, Colorado Springs CO 80903, USA
**Mitchell, Daryl M (Chill)** — Actor
United Talent Agency, U T A Plaza, 9336 Civic Center Dr, Beverly Hills CA 90210 USA
**Mitchell, Donald R** — Football Player
5620 Minner Dr, Beaumont TX 77708, USA
**Mitchell, Dryden** — Bassist, Pianist (Alien Ant Farm)
Creative Artists Agency, 2000 Ave of Stars, #100, Los Angeles CA 90067 USA
**Mitchell, Edgar D** — Astronaut
PO Box 540037, Greenacres FL 33454, USA
**Mitchell, Elizabeth** — Actress
I F A Talent Agency, 8730 W Sunset Blvd, #490, West Hollywood CA 90069 USA

| | |
|---|---|
| **Mitchell, Elizabeth R (Liz)** | Singer (Boney M) |
| International Artists, PO Box 100334, 47563 Goch, Germany | |
| **Mitchell, Finesse** | Actor, Comedian |
| I C M Partners, 10250 Constellation Blvd, #900, Los Angeles CA 90067 USA | |
| **Mitchell, George** | Guitarist (Intruders) |
| Billy Paul Mgmt, 8215 Winthrop St, Philadelphia PA 19136, USA | |
| **Mitchell, George J** | Senator, ME |
| D L A Piper, 1251 Ave of Americas, #C2-75, New York NY 10020, USA | |
| **Mitchell, George P** | Businessman, Philanthropist |
| Mitchell Energy & Development, PO Box 4000, The Woodlands TX 77387, USA | |
| **Mitchell, James H (Jim)** | Football Player |
| 120 Twin Creek Terrace, Forest VA 24551, USA | |
| **Mitchell, Jessie J (Mitch)** | Baseball Player |
| 1964 Cherry Ave, Birmingham AL 35214, USA | |
| **Mitchell, John** | Baseball Player |
| 1708 Castleberry Way, Birmingham AL 35214, USA | |
| **Mitchell, John Cameron** | Actor, Director, Writer |
| Creative Artists Agency, 2000 Ave of Stars, #100, Los Angeles CA 90067 USA | |
| **Mitchell, John K** | Baseball Player |
| 5017 Hasty Dr, Nashville TN 37211, USA | |
| **Mitchell, Johnny** | Football Player |
| 7617 Courtyard Run W, Boca Raton FL 33433, USA | |
| **Mitchell, Joni** | Singer, Songwriter |
| 624 Funchal Road, Los Angeles CA 90077, USA | |
| **Mitchell, Kawika U** | Football Player |
| 971 N Lake Sybelia Dr, Maitland FL 32751, USA | |
| **Mitchell, Keith** | Actor |
| A P A Talent/Literary Agency, 405 S Beverly Dr, #300, Beverly Hills CA 90212 USA | |
| **Mitchell, Keith A** | Baseball Player |
| 731 S 42nd St, San Diego CA 92113, USA | |
| **Mitchell, Kenneth** | Actor |
| Innovative Artists, 1505 10th St, Santa Monica CA 90401 USA | |
| **Mitchell, Kevin D** | Baseball Player |
| 3869 Ocean View Blvd, San Diego CA 92113, USA | |
| **Mitchell, Kim** | Singer |
| 41 Britain St, #305, Toronto ON M5A 1R, Canada | |
| **Mitchell, Kirsty L** | Actress |
| Conway Van Gelder Grant, 8-12 Broadwick St, #300, London W1F 8HW, England | |
| **Mitchell, Leona** | Opera Singer |
| Columbia Artists Mgmt Inc, 1790 Broadway, #702, New York NY 10019 USA | |
| **Mitchell, Leroy** | Football Player |
| 6598 N Pinewood Dr, Parker CO 80134, USA | |
| **Mitchell, Lydell D** | Football Player |
| 702 Reservoir St, Baltimore MD 21217, USA | |
| **Mitchell, Lyvonia A (Stump)** | Football Player, Coach |
| 43091 Old Gallivan Terrace, Ashburn VA 20147, USA | |
| **Mitchell, Mack H** | Football Player |
| PO Box 741, Diboll TX 75941, USA | |
| **Mitchell, Maia** | Actress |
| EATON Management, 138 Cathedral St, Woolloomooloo, Sydney NSW 2011, Australia | |
| **Mitchell, Mike** | Director, Actor, Writer |
| Creative Artists Agency, 2000 Ave of Stars, #100, Los Angeles CA 90067 USA | |
| **Mitchell, Paul M** | Baseball Player |
| 23 Carr Road, Berlin MA 01503, USA | |
| **Mitchell, Penelope** | Actress |
| A P A Talent/Literary Agency, 405 S Beverly Dr, #300, Beverly Hills CA 90212 USA | |
| **Mitchell, Peter C (Pete)** | Football Player |
| 125 Sawbill Palm Dr, Ponte Vedra Beach FL 32082, USA | |
| **Mitchell, Radha** | Actress |
| Shanahan Mgmt, PO Box 1509, Darlinghurst NSW 1300, Australia | |
| **Mitchell, Robert** | Baseball Player |
| 2009 Elmwood Ave, Tampa FL 33605, USA | |
| **Mitchell, Robert C (Bobby)** | Football Player, Executive |
| 36 Hollyberry Court, Rockville MD 20852, USA | |
| **Mitchell, Robert Vance (Bobby)** | Baseball Player |
| 8697 Tiogawoods Dr, Sacramento CA 95828, USA | |
| **Mitchell, Roland E** | Football Player |
| PO Box 5701, Lake Charles LA 70606, USA | |
| **Mitchell, Roscoe E, Jr** | Jazz Reeds Player, Composer |
| S R O Artists, 6629 University Ave, #206, Middleton WI 53562, USA | |
| **Mitchell, Samuel E (Sam), Jr** | Basektball Player, Coach |
| 73 Smokerise Point, Peachtree City GA 30269, USA | |
| **Mitchell, Shareen** | Actress |
| Independent Artists Agency, 9601 Wilshire Blvd, #750, Beverly Hills CA 90210, USA | |
| **Mitchell, Sharmba** | Boxer |
| 819 Hayward Ave, Takoma Park MD 20912, USA | |
| **Mitchell, Shay** | Actress |
| A P A Talent/Literary Agency, 405 S Beverly Dr, #300, Beverly Hills CA 90212 USA | |
| **Mitchell, Silas Weir** | Actor |
| Greene Assoc, 1901 Ave of Stars, #130, Los Angeles CA 90067 USA | |
| **Mitchell, Steven Long (Steve)** | Writer, Producer, Director |
| Imagiquest Entertainment, 10200 Riverside Dr, #201, Toluca Lake CA 91602, USA | |
| **Mitchell, Thomas G (Tom)** | Football Player |
| 1421 SW 49th Terrace, Cape Coral FL 33914, USA | |
| **Mitchell, Todd** | Basketball Player |
| 4134 Emmajean Road, Toledo OH 43607, USA | |
| **Mitchell, Tony** | Cinematographer, Director |
| United Agents, 12-26 Lexington St, London W1F 0LE, England | |
| **Mitchell, Vernessa** | Singer |
| Higher Ground Ministries, PO Box 72651, Newnan, GA 30271, USA | |
| **Mitchell, W Scott** | Football Player |
| 2375 S State St, Springville UT 84663, USA | |
| **Mitchell, Warren** | Actor |
| Shanahan Mgmt, 91 Campbell St, #300, Surry Hills NSW 2010, Australia | |
| **Mitchell, William R (Willie)** | Ice Hockey Player |
| Los Angeles Kings, Staples Center, 1111 S Figueroa St, Los Angeles CA 90015 USA | |

| | |
|---|---|
| **Mitchell-Smith, Ilan** | Actor |
| 10460 Queens Blvd, #10C, Forest Hills NY 11375, USA | |
| **Mitchison, N Avrion** | Zoologist, Anatomist |
| 14 Belitha Villas, London N1 1PD, England | |
| **Miti, Carlotta** | Actress |
| Carol Levi Mgmt, Via Giuseppe Pisanelli 2, 00196 Rome, Italy | |
| **Mitra, Rhona** | Actress |
| Untitled Entertainment, 350 S Beverly Dr, #200, Beverly Hills CA 90212 USA | |
| **Mitre, Sergio A** | Baseball Player |
| 1707 Summer Sky St, Chula Vista CA 91915, USA | |
| **Mitsotakis, Konstantinos** | Prime Minister, Greece |
| 1 Aravantinou St, 106 74 Athens, Greece | |
| **Mittal, Lakshmi N** | Businessman |
| L N M Group, Hofplein 20, #1500, Rotterdam 3032, Netherlands | |
| **Mitte, R J** | Actor |
| Bauman Redanty Shaul Agency, 5757 Wilshire Blvd, #473, Los Angeles CA 90036 USA | |
| **Mittermaier-Neureuther, Rosemarie (Rosi)** | Alpine Skier |
| Winkelmoos-Alm, 83242 Reit Im Winkel, Germany | |
| **Mittermayer, Tatjana** | Freestyle Moguls Skier |
| Bucha 2A, 83661 Lenggries, Germany | |
| **Mitterrutzner, Martin** | Opera Singer |
| Kunstler Sekretariat am Gasteig, Rosenheimer Str 52, 81669 Munich, Germany | |
| **Mitterwald, George E** | Baseball Player |
| 1721 Murdock Blvd, Orlando FL 32825, USA | |
| **Mittleman, Steve** | Actor, Comedian |
| A K A Talent, 6310 San Vicente Blvd, #200, Los Angeles CA 90048 USA | |
| **Mitts, Heather** | Soccer Player, Sportscaster |
| Atlanta Beat, 1955 Vaughn Road, #209, Kennesaw GA 30144, USA | |
| **Mitz, Alonzo L** | Football Player |
| 2609 NE 4th St, #216, Renton WA 98056, USA | |
| **Mivelaz, Betty** | Bowler |
| 1543 Grand Ave, Medford OR 97504, USA | |
| **Mix, Bryant L** | Football Player |
| 37 Greenwood Plantation Road, Natchez MS 39120, USA | |
| **Mix, Ronald J (Ron)** | Football Player |
| 7840 Mission Center Court, #104, San Diego CA 92108, USA | |
| **Mix, Steven C (Steve)** | Basketball Player |
| 25743 Willowbend Road, Perrysburg OH 43551, USA | |
| **Mix, Timothy** | Opera Singer |
| I M G Artists, Hogarth Business Park, Chiswick, London W4 2TH, England | |
| **Mixon, Katy** | Actress |
| W M E Entertainment, 9601 Wilshire Blvd, #300, Beverly Hills CA 90210 USA | |
| **Mixon, Kenneth J (Kenny)** | Football Player |
| 175 Bayridge Lane, Weston FL 33326, USA | |
| **Mixson, J Wayne** | Governor, FL |
| 2219 Demeron Road, Tallahassee FL 32308, USA | |
| **Miyamoto, Shigeru** | Video Game Designer |
| Nintendo, 11-1 Kamitoba, Hokotatecho Minamiku, Kyoto 601 8501, Japan | |
| **Miyamura, Hiroshi H** | Korean War Army Hero (CMH) |
| 659 Kaimalino St, Kailua HI 96734, USA | |
| **Miyazaki, Hayao** | Animator |
| Studio Ghibli, 1-4-25 Kajinocho, Koganeishi 184 0002, Japan | |
| **Miyazato, Ai** | Golfer |
| Ladies Pro Golf Assn, 100 International Golf Dr, Daytona Beach FL 32124 USA | |
| **Miyori, Kim** | Actress |
| Susan Smith, 1344 N Wetherly Dr, Los Angeles CA 90069 USA | |
| **Mize, John D** | Vietnam War Air Force Hero |
| 112 Sunset Dr, Belmond IA 50421, USA | |
| **Mize, Larry** | Golfer |
| 106 Graystone Court, Columbus GA 31904, USA | |
| **Mize, Ola L** | Korean War Army Hero (CMH) |
| 211 Hartwood Dr, Gadsden AL 35901, USA | |
| **Mizerock, John J** | Baseball Player, Manager |
| 1189 Leasure Run Road, Rochester Mills PA 15771, USA | |
| **Mizota, Diane** | Actress |
| Paradise Group, PO Box 69451, West Hollywood CA 90069, USA | |
| **Mizrahi, Isaac** | Fashion Designer |
| 1516 S Canfield Ave, Los Angeles CA 90035, USA | |
| **Mleczko-Griswold, Allison J (A J)** | Ice Hockey Player |
| 3 Hinckley Lane, Nantucket MA 02554, USA | |
| **Mlicki, David J (Dave)** | Baseball Player |
| 5350 Reserve Dr, Dublin OH 43017, USA | |
| **Mnookin, Robert H** | Attorney, Educator |
| 10 Follen St, Cambridge MA 02138, USA | |
| **Mnouchkine, Ariane** | Director |
| Theatre du Soleil, Cartoucherie, 75012 Paris, France | |
| **Mo Yan** | Nobel Literature Laureate |
| Meutheun, 215 Vauxhall Bridge Road, London SW1V 1EJ, England | |
| **Moakes, Gordon P** | Guitarist (Bloc Party) |
| Coalition Mgmt, 12 Barley Mow Passage, London W4 4PH, England | |
| **Moakler, Shanna L** | Beauty Queen, Actress, Model |
| Global Artists Agency, 6253 Hollywood Blvd, #508, Los Angeles CA 90028 USA | |
| **Moalem, Sharon** | Writer |
| Harper Collins Publishers, 10 E 53rd St, Cellar 1, New York NY 10022 USA | |
| **Moates, David A (Dave)** | Baseball Player |
| 7924 24th Ave W, Bradenton FL 34209, USA | |
| **Moats, David** | Journalist |
| Rutland Herald, Editorial Dept, PO Box 668, Rutland VT 05702, USA | |
| **Moats, Sanford K** | Air Force General, WW II Hero |
| 59-635 Akanoho Place, Haleiwa HI 96712, USA | |
| **Mobley, Cuttino R** | Basketball Player |
| PO Box 11319, Beverly Hills CA 90213, USA | |
| **Mobley, John U** | Football Player |
| 3512 Legacy Hills Court, Longwood FL 32779, USA | |
| **Mobley, Mary Ann** | Actress, Beauty Queen |
| Corsa Agency, 11704 Wilshire Blvd, #204, Los Angeles CA 90025, USA | |

| | |
|---|---|
| **Mobley, Orson O** | Football Player |
| 400 S 24th Ave, Hattiesburg MS 39401, USA | |
| **Moby** | Singer, Guitarist |
| Deutsch-Ebgkuscge Freundschaft, 51 Lonsdale Road, London NW6 6RA, England | |
| **Moceanu, Dominique** | Gymnast |
| Medialine Communications, 7300 York Ave S, #204, Edina MN 55435, USA | |
| **Mochrie, Colin** | Actor, Comedian |
| 385 Adelaide St W, Toronto ON M5V 1S4, Canada | |
| **Mock Garrett** | Baseball Player |
| 13650 Maisemore Road, Houston TX 77015, USA | |
| **Mock, Geraldine F (Jerrie)** | Aviatrix |
| 343 E King St, Quincy FL 32351, USA | |
| **Mockett, Cathy** | Golfer |
| 1601 Antigua Way, Newport Beach CA 92660, USA | |
| **Mocumbi, Pascoal M** | Prime Minister, Mozambique |
| 1874 Ave Arnando Tivane, Maputo, Mozambique | |
| **Modano, Michael (Mike)** | Ice Hockey Player |
| 6424 Mimosa Lane, Dallas TX 75230, USA | |
| **Modell, Frank** | Cartoonist |
| 115 Three Mile Course, Guilford CT 06437, USA | |
| **Modin, Fredrik** | Ice Hockey Player |
| 8955 Dunn Curt, Dublin OH 43017, USA | |
| **Modine, Matthew** | Actor |
| Untitled Entertainment, 350 S Beverly Dr, #200, Beverly Hills CA 90212 USA | |
| **Modry, Jaroslav** | Ice Hockey Player |
| 1724 Malvern Hill Place, Duluth GA 30097, USA | |
| **Modrzejewski, Robert J** | Vietnam War Marine Corps Hero (CMH) |
| 4725 Oporto Court, San Diego CA 92124, USA | |
| **Modzelewski, Richard B (Dick)** | Football Player |
| 1357 Fox Run Dr, #105, Willoughby OH 44094, USA | |
| **Moe, Douglas E (Doug)** | Basketball Player, Coach |
| 13 Arnold Palmer, San Antonio TX 78257, USA | |
| **Moe, Thomas S (Tommy)** | Alpine Skier |
| 1556 Hidden Lane, Anchorage AK 99501, USA | |
| **Moegle, Richard L (Dicky)** | Football Player |
| 4207 DeForest Ridge Circle, Katy TX 77494, USA | |
| **Moehler, Brian M** | Baseball Player |
| 269 Woodlawn Dr NE, Marietta GA 30067, USA | |
| **Moehringer, J R** | Journalist |
| Los Angeles Times, Editorial Dept, 202 W 1st St, Los Angeles CA 90012 USA | |
| **Moe-Humphreys, Karen** | Swimmer, Swimming Coach |
| 505 Augusta Dr, Moraga CA 94556, USA | |
| **Moeller, Chad E** | Baseball Player |
| 11058 E Raintree Dr, Scottsdale AZ 85255, USA | |
| **Moeller, Chet** | Football Player |
| Wilson Price Information Technology, 3815 Interstate Court, Montgomery AL 36109, USA | |
| **Moeller, David** | Luge Athlete |
| Meet Success, Auf der Eierwiese 1, 82031 Gruenwald, Germany | |
| **Moeller, Dennis L** | Inventor |
| 147 Florence Dr, Jupiter FL 33458, USA | |
| **Moeller, Dennis M** | Baseball Player |
| 24979 Constitution Ave, #536, Valencia CA 91381, USA | |
| **Moeller, Edward** | Basketball Player |
| 1011 Kelton College Way, Morrisville NC 27560, USA | |
| **Moeller, Joseph D (Joe)** | Baseball Player |
| 1505 Avenida de Nogales, San Clemente CA 92672, USA | |
| **Moeller, Robert T** | Navy Admiral |
| Deputy Commander, Military Operations, US Africa Command, APO AE 09751, USA | |
| **Moellering, John H** | Army General |
| United Services Automobile Assn, USAA Building, 9800 Fredericksburg Road, San Antonio TX 78288, USA | |
| **Moen, John** | Drummer (Decemberists) |
| Big Hassle, 44 Wall St, #2200, New York NY 10005, USA | |
| **Moennig, Katherine** | Actress |
| Framework Entertainment, 9057 Nemo St, #C, West Hollywood CA 90069 USA | |
| **Moffatt, Henry K** | Mathematical Physicist |
| 6 Banhams Close, Cambridge CB4 1HX, England | |
| **Moffatt, Katy** | Singer, Guitarist, Songwriter |
| PO Box 334, O Fallon IL 62269, USA | |
| **Moffett, D W** | Actor |
| 3 Arts Entertainment, 9460 Wilshire Blvd, #700, Beverly Hills CA 90212 USA | |
| **Moffett, Donald** | Artist |
| Anthony Meier Fine Arts, 1969 California St, San Francisco CA 94109, USA | |
| **Moffitt, John** | Track Athlete |
| Vector Sports Mgmt, 417 Keller Parkway, Keller TX 76248, USA | |
| **Moffitt, Peggy** | Model, Actress |
| Browns, 23-27 S Moulton St, London W1K 5RD, England | |
| **Moffitt, Randall J (Randy)** | Baseball Player |
| 1725 Baltic Ave, Prescott AZ 86301, USA | |
| **Mofford, Rose** | Governor, AZ |
| 330 W Maryland Ave, #104, Phoenix AZ 85013, USA | |
| **Mogenburg, Dietmar** | Track Athlete |
| Alter Garfen 34, 51371 Leverkusen, Germany | |
| **Mogilny, Alexander G** | Ice Hockey Player |
| 10225 Collins Ave, #2202, Bal Harbour FL 33154, USA | |
| **Mogis, Michael R (Mike)** | Musician (Bright Eyes) |
| Press Here, 138 W 25th St, #700, New York NY 10001, USA | |
| **Mohacsi, Mary** | Bowler |
| 15445 Sunset St, Livonia MI 48154, USA | |
| **Mohamed Khouna, Cheikh El Avia Ould** | Prime Minister, Mauritania |
| Prime Minister's Office, Nouakchott, Mauritania | |
| **Mohammed VI** | King, Morocco |
| Royal Palais, Dar Al Mahkzen, Rabat, Morocco | |
| **Mohammed, Nazr T** | Basketball Player |
| Chicago Bulls, United Center, 1901 W Madison St, Chicago IL 60612 USA | |
| **Mohapatra, Bibhu** | Fashion Designer |
| 270 W 38th St, #1100, New York NY 10018, USA | |

**Mohler, Michael R (Mike)** — Baseball Player
1627 S Shirley Ave, Gonzales LA 70737, USA
**Mohoric, Dale R** — Baseball Player
15501 Rockside Road, Maple Heights OH 44137, USA
**Mohr, Christopher G (Chris)** — Football Player
3260 Surrey Road, Thomson GA 30824, USA
**Mohr, Dustan** — Baseball Player
103 Parkwood Dr, Hattiesburg MS 39402, USA
**Mohr, Jay** — Actor, Comedian
Giraffe Productions, 4406 Vantage Ave, Studio City CA 91604, USA
**Mohri, Mamoru** — Astronaut, Japan
Japanese Aerospace Exploration Agency, 2-1-1 Sengen, Tsukuba-shi, Ibaraki 305 8505, Japan
**Mohseni, Saad** — Businessman
Moby Group, 3 Street 12, Wazir Akbar Khan, District 10, Kabul, Afghanistan
**Mohyeldin, Ayman** — Journalist
Al Jazeera, PO Box 23127, Doha, Qatar
**Moio, Ashton** — Actor
Innovative Artists, 1505 10th St, Santa Monica CA 90401 USA
**Moir, Richard** — Actor
Shanahan Mgmt, PO Box 1509, Darlinghurst NSW 1300, Australia
**Moir, Scott** — Ice Skater
Ilderton Skating Club, Box 33, Ilderton, ON N0M 2A0, Canada
**Moiso, Jerome** — Basketball Player
Cleveland Cavaliers, Gund Arena, 1 Center Court, Cleveland OH 44115 USA
**Mojsiejenko, Ralf** — Football Player
11334 Baldwin Road, Bridgman MI 49106, USA
**Mok, Karen** — Actress
Creative Artists Agency, 2000 Ave of Stars, #100, Los Angeles CA 90067 USA
**Mokeski, Paul K** — Basketball Player
4004 Crestwood Dr, Carrolton TX 75007, USA
**Mokosak, Carl** — Ice Hockey Player
8073 Rum Creek Trail NE, Rockford MI 49341, USA
**Mokri, Amir M** — Cinematographer
Gersh Agency, 9465 Wilshire Blvd, #600, Beverly Hills CA 90212 USA
**Mol, Gretchen** — Actress
John Carrabino Mgmt, 5900 Wilshire Blvd, #406, Los Angeles CA 90036 USA
**Molale, Brandon** — Actor
Coolwaters Productions, 10061 Riverside Dr, Box 531, Toluca Lake CA 91602 USA
**Molaro, Sandrine** — Actress
TalentBox Cineart, 28 Rue de Mogador, 75009 Paris, France
**Molden, Alex M** — Football Player
2030 Wellington Dr, West Linn OR 97068, USA
**Moldovan, Diana** — Model
Yes Model Mgmt, 2 Bibescu Voda BL P5, #26, Bucharest, Romania
**Mole, Fenton L** — Baseball Player
738 Glen Eagle Court, Danville CA 94526, USA
**Molgg, Manfred** — Alpine Skier
Via Paracia 3/5, 39030 S Vigilio, Italy
**Molina Matta, Jose B** — Baseball Player
Tampa Bay Rays, 1 Tropicana Dr, Saint Petersburg FL 33705 USA
**Molina, Alfred** — Actor, Singer
Lou Coulson, 37 Berwick St, London W1V 3RF, England
**Molina, Angela** — Actress
Agents Associes, 201 Rue du Faubourg Saint Honore, 75008 Paris, France
**Molina, Benjamin J (Bengie)** — Baseball Player
6475 E Crantree Place, Yuma AZ 85365, USA
**Molina, Mario J** — Nobel Chemistry Laureate
PO Box 12406, La Jolla CA 92039, USA
**Molina, Yadier B** — Baseball Player
1005 Bluff Pointe Court, Caseyville IL 62232, USA
**Molinari, Anna** — Fashion Designer
Via G Ferraris 13/15/15/15A, 411012 Carpi (Modena), Italy
**Molinaro, Al** — Actor
1530 Arboles Dr, Glendale CA 91207, USA
**Molinaro, Robert J (Bob)** — Baseball Player
1 Harbourside Dr, #2312, Delray Beach FL 33483, USA
**Molitor, Paul L** — Baseball Player
6725 Iroquois Circle, Minneapolis MN 55439, USA
**Molko, Brian** — Singer, Guitarist (Placebo), Songwriter
Riverman Mgmt, George House, Brecon Road, London W6 8PY, England
**Moll, John L** — Electronics Engineer
4111 Old Trace Road, Palo Alto CA 94306, USA
**Moll, Kurt** — Opera Singer
Gross Theaterstr 34, 20354 Hamburg, Germany
**Moll, Richard** — Actor
Studio Talent Group, 1328 12th St, Santa Monica CA 90401, USA
**Molla, Jordi** — Actor
Paradigm Agency, 360 N Crescent Dr, North Building, Beverly Hills CA 90210 USA
**Moller, Paul** — Inventor (Sky Car), Engineer
Moller International, 1222 Research Park Dr, Davis CA 95618, USA
**Moller, Randy** — Ice Hockey Player
3950 NW 23rd Terrace, Boca Raton FL 33431, USA
**Moller-Gladisch, Silke** — Track Athlete
Lange Str 6, 18055 Rostock, Germany
**Mollo, John** — Costume Designer
Dower House, Church St, West Hanney, Wantage OX12 0LW, England
**Mollo-Christensen, Erik L** — Oceanographer
10 Barberry Road, Lexington MA 02421, USA
**Molloy, Irene** — Actress
Gersh Agency, 9465 Wilshire Blvd, #600, Beverly Hills CA 90212 USA
**Molloy, Matt** — Flutist (Chieftains)
Macklam/Feldman Mgmt, 1505 W 2nd Ave, #200, Vancouver BC V6H 3Y4, Canada
**Moloney, Janel** — Actress
Gersh Agency, 9465 Wilshire Blvd, #600, Beverly Hills CA 90212 USA
**Moloney, Paddy** — Singer (Chieftains)
Macklam/Feldman Mgmt, 1505 W 2nd Ave, #200, Vancouver BC V6H 3Y4, Canada

| | |
|---|---|
| **Moloney, Richard H (Rich)** | Baseball Player |
| 125 Mallard Way, Waltham MA 02452, USA | |
| **Moltmann, Jurgen** | Theologian |
| Liebermeister Str 12, 72076 Tubingen, Germany | |
| **Molyneux, Juan Pablo** | Architect |
| J P Molyneux Studio, 29 E 69th St, New York NY 10021, USA | |
| **Mom Rajawong Sirikit Kitiyarara** | Queen, Thailand |
| Royal Residence, Chitralada Villa, 9 Rama VI Road, Soi 30, Bangkok 10400, Thailand | |
| **Momaday, N Scott** | Writer |
| University of Arizona, English Dept, Tucson AZ 85721, USA | |
| **Momesso, Sergio** | Ice Hockey Player |
| Momesso Caffe, 3669 Boul St Jean, Dollard les Ormeaux QC H9G 1X2, Canada | |
| **Momoa, Jason** | Actor, Model |
| A P A Talent/Literary Agency, 405 S Beverly Dr, #300, Beverly Hills CA 90212 USA | |
| **Momsen, Taylor** | Actress |
| Das Communications, 83 Riverside Dr, New York NY 10024, USA | |
| **Monacelli, Amleto** | Bowler |
| Professional Bowlers Assn, 719 2nd Ave, #701, Seattle WA 98104 USA | |
| **Monaco, Kara** | Model |
| Dino May Mgmt, 11262 Ventura Blvd, #PH, Studio City CA 91604, USA | |
| **Monaco, Kelly M** | Actress, Model, Dancer |
| W M E Entertainment, 9601 Wilshire Blvd, #300, Beverly Hills CA 90210 USA | |
| **Monae, Janelle** | Singer |
| W M E Entertainment, 9601 Wilshire Blvd, #300, Beverly Hills CA 90210 USA | |
| **Monaghan, Cameron** | Actor |
| C E S D, 10635 Santa Monica Blvd, #130, Los Angeles CA 90025 USA | |
| **Monaghan, Dominic** | Actor |
| A P A Talent/Literary Agency, 405 S Beverly Dr, #300, Beverly Hills CA 90212 USA | |
| **Monaghan, Kris** | Golfer |
| 54 Golf Course Dr, Ranchos de Taos NM 87557, USA | |
| **Monaghan, Marjorie** | Actress |
| John Crosby Mgmt, 1310 N Spaulding Ave, Los Angeles CA 90046 USA | |
| **Monaghan, Michelle** | Actress |
| I C M Partners, 10250 Constellation Blvd, #900, Los Angeles CA 90067 USA | |
| **Monahan, Dan** | Actor |
| Cuzzings Mgmt, 1425 N Detroit St, #304, Los Angeles CA 90046, USA | |
| **Monahan, David H** | Actor, Director |
| Bauman Redanty Shaul Agency, 5757 Wilshire Blvd, #473, Los Angeles CA 90036 USA | |
| **Monahan, Garry** | Ice Hockey Player |
| 4665 Piccadilly N, West Vancouver BC V7W 1E3, Canada | |
| **Monahan, Gretchen (Gretta)** | Entertainer |
| Food Network, 1180 Ave of Americas, #1200, New York NY 10036 USA | |
| **Monahan, Pat** | Singer (Train) |
| Jon Landau, 150 Rowayton Ave, Norwalk CT 06853, USA | |
| **Monahan, William** | Writer, Director |
| W M E Entertainment, 9601 Wilshire Blvd, #300, Beverly Hills CA 90210 USA | |
| **Monastyrska, Liudmyla** | Opera Singer |
| I M G Artists, Hogarth Business Park, Chiswick, London W4 2TH, England | |
| **Monbouquette, William C (Bill)** | Baseball Player |
| 46 Doonan St, Medford MA 02155, USA | |
| **Moncrief, Sidney A** | Basketball Player |
| 9842 Audelia Road, #1109, Dallas TX 75238, USA | |
| **Moncrieff, Karen** | Actress, Director, Writer |
| Anonymous Content, 3532 Hayden Ave, Culver City CA 90232 USA | |
| **Mond, Josh** | Producer |
| United Talent Agency, U T A Plaza, 9336 Civic Center Dr, Beverly Hills CA 90210 USA | |
| **Mondale, Walter F** | Vice President; Senator, MN |
| Dorsey & Whitney, 50 S 6th St, #1500, Minneapolis MN 55402, USA | |
| **Monday, Kenneth D (Kenny)** | Freestyle Wrestler |
| 4119 W Deer Crossing Dr, Stillwater OK 74074, USA | |
| **Monday, Robert J (Rick)** | Baseball Player, Sportscaster |
| 811 Gayfeather Lane, Vero Beach FL 32963, USA | |
| **Mondey, Fawnia** | Actress, Model |
| 631 N Stephanie St, #162, Henderson NV 89014, USA | |
| **Mondlock, Buddy** | Singer, Guitarist, Songwriter |
| Stewart Mgmt, PO Box 27581, Denver CO 80227, USA | |
| **Mondou, Pierre** | Ice Hockey Player |
| 239 Rue Wildor Larochelle, Sorel Tracy QC J3P 6R2, Canada | |
| **Mone, Michelle** | Fashion Designer |
| M J M International, 8 Redwood Crescent, Peel Park, Glasgow G74 5PA, Scotland | |
| **Moneo, J Rafael** | Pritzker Architectural Laureate |
| Calle Mino 5, 28002 Madrid, Spain | |
| **Monet, Daniella** | Actress |
| Paradigm Agency, 360 N Crescent Dr, North Building, Beverly Hills CA 90210 USA | |
| **Money B** | Rap Music |
| L W 1, 9378 Wilshire Blvd, #310, Beverly Hills CA 90212, USA | |
| **Money, Eddie** | Singer |
| I C M Partners, 730 5th Ave, New York NY 10019 USA | |
| **Money, Eric V** | Basketball Player |
| 457 S Harvard Ave, Tucson AZ 85710, USA | |
| **Money, Ken** | Astronaut, Canada |
| D C I E M, 1133 Sheppard Ave W, #2000, Downsview ON M3M 3B9, Canada | |
| **Monger, Christopher** | Director |
| I C M Partners, 10250 Constellation Blvd, #900, Los Angeles CA 90067 USA | |
| **Monger, Matthew L (Matt)** | Football Player |
| 10219 S Canton Ave, Tulsa OK 74137, USA | |
| **Monheit, Jane** | Singer, Songwriter |
| American International Artists, 356 Pine Valley Road, Hoosick Falls NY 12090, USA | |
| **Monica** | Singer |
| Spirit Media, PO Box 43591, Phoenix AZ 85080, USA | |
| **Monifah** | Singer, Songwriter |
| Richard Walters, PO Box 2789, Toluca Lake CA 91610 USA | |
| **Mo'Nique** | Actress, Comedienne |
| Spectrum Talent Agency, 520 W 43rd St, New York NY 10036, USA | |
| **Moniz, Wendy** | Actress |
| Innovative Artists, 1505 10th St, Santa Monica CA 90401 USA | |

**M**

| | |
|---|---|
| **Monk, Arthur (Art)**<br>10896 Lake Windemere Dr, Great Falls VA 22066, USA | Football Player, Sportscaster |
| **Monk, Debra**<br>Gage Group, 450 7th Ave, #1809, New York NY 10123 USA | Actress, Singer |
| **Monk, Meredith J**<br>228 W Broadway, New York NY 10013, USA | Choreographer, Composer |
| **Monk, Sophie**<br>A P A Talent/Literary Agency, 405 S Beverly Dr, #300, Beverly Hills CA 90212 USA | Singer, Actress |
| **Monninger, Nikki**<br>Ink Tank Public Relations, 1825 W Sunset Blvd, #102, Los Angeles CA 90026, USA | Bassist, Singer (Silversun Pickups) |
| **Monoharova, Taitana**<br>I M G Artists, Hogarth Business Park, Chiswick, London W4 2TH, England | Opera Singer |
| **Monoson, Lawrence**<br>Ovation Mgmt, 12028 National Blvd, Los Angeles CA 90064, USA | Actor |
| **Monroe, Ashley**<br>Spalding Entertainment, 1025 16th Ave, #303, Nashville TN 30312, USA | Singer, Songwriter |
| **Monroe, Craig K**<br>4123 Lynn Dr, Texarkana TX 75503, USA | Baseball Player |
| **Monroe, Jordan**<br>Playboy Promotions, 2706 Media Center Dr, Los Angeles CA 90065 USA | Model |
| **Monroe, Kimber**<br>1230 N Horn, #728, West Hollywood CA 90069, USA | Actress |
| **Monroe, Lawrence J (Larry)**<br>725 N Hundley St, Hoffman Estates IL 60169, USA | Baseball Player |
| **Monroe, Maika**<br>W M E Entertainment, 9601 Wilshire Blvd, #300, Beverly Hills CA 90210 USA | Actress |
| **Monroe, Meredith**<br>Abrams Artists, 9200 W Sunset Blvd, #1125, West Hollywood CA 90069 USA | Actress |
| **Monroe, Mircea**<br>Innovative Artists, 1505 10th St, Santa Monica CA 90401 USA | Actress |
| **Monroe, Steve**<br>House of Representatives, 1434 6th St, #1, Santa Monica CA 90401 USA | Actor |
| **Monroe, V Earl (Pearl)**<br>1925 Adam Clayton Powell Jr Blvd, #6D, New York NY 10026, USA | Basketball Player |
| **Monroe, Zachary C (Zach)**<br>1 Sandalwood Lane, Bartonville IL 61607, USA | Baseball Player |
| **Monson, Dan**<br>California State University, Athletic Dept, Long Beach CA 90840, USA | Basketball Coach |
| **Monson, Thomas S**<br>Church of Latter-Day Saints, 47 E South Temple, Salt Lake City UT 84150, USA | Religious Leader |
| **Montador, Steve**<br>5857 NW 122nd Terrace, Coral Springs FL 33076, USA | Ice Hockey Player |
| **Montag, Heidi**<br>Innovator Mgmt, 8899 Beverly Blvd, #622, Los Angeles CA 90048, USA | Actress, Singer, Model |
| **Montagnier, Luc**<br>World AIDS Research Foundation, Castello 4930, 30122 Venice, Italy | Nobel Medicine Laureate |
| **Montague, Diana**<br>91 Saint Martin's Lane, London WC2, England | Opera Singer |
| **Montague, Emily**<br>Talent Works, 3500 W Olive Ave, #1400, Burbank CA 91505 USA | Actress |
| **Montague, John E**<br>52 Northshore Circle, Dadeville AL 36853, USA | Baseball Player |
| **Montaigne, Lawrence**<br>1827 Morganton Dr, Henderson NV 89052, USA | Actor |
| **Montalbano, Chuck**<br>4725 Farmdale Ave, North Hollywood CA 91602, USA | Golfer |
| **Montana, Claude**<br>131 Rue Saint-Denis, 75001 Paris, France | Fashion Designer |
| **Montana, Joseph C (Joe), Jr**<br>9010 Franz Valley Road, Calistoga CA 94515, USA | Football Player |
| **Montana, Manny**<br>S D B Partners, 1801 Ave of Stars, #902, Los Angeles CA 90067 USA | Actor |
| **Montanaro, Carlo**<br>I M G Artists, Hogarth Business Park, Chiswick, London W4 2TH, England | Conductor |
| **Montanez, Guillermo N (Willie)**<br>HC 5 Box 52020, Caguas PR 00725, USA | Baseball Player |
| **Montefusco, John J**<br>1 Oakdale Dr, Middletown NJ 07748, USA | Baseball Player |
| **Monteith, Hank**<br>35 William St, Stratford ON N5A 4X9, Canada | Ice Hockey Player |
| **Monteith, Kelly**<br>PO Box 11669, Knoxville TN 37939, USA | Actor, Comedian |
| **Montelone, Richard (Rich)**<br>441 Lucerne Ave, Tampa FL 33606, USA | Baseball Player |
| **Monterey, Judi**<br>Playboy Promotions, 2706 Media Center Dr, Los Angeles CA 90065 USA | Model |
| **Montero, Gabriela**<br>I M G Artists, Hogarth Business Park, Chiswick, London W4 2TH, England | Concert Pianist |
| **Montero, Miguel A**<br>Arizona Diamondbacks, Chase Field, 401 E Jefferson, Phoenix AZ 85003 USA | Baseball Player |
| **Montero, Pablo**<br>Apodaca Promotions, 7171 E Tidwell Road, Houston TX 77022, USA | Singer, Actor |
| **Montes, Marisa**<br>E M I Records, 150 5th Ave, #700, New York NY 10011 USA | Singer, Guitarist |
| **Montevecchi, Liliane**<br>Fifi Oscard, 110 W 40th St, #1601, New York NY 10018, USA | Singer, Actress, Dancer |
| **Monteverde, Alejandro Gomez**<br>Metanoia Films, 2950 Los Feliz Blvd, #204, Los Angeles CA 90039, USA | Writer, Director, Producer |
| **Montez, Chris**<br>Utopia Artists, PO Box 1569, Jupiter FL 33468, USA | Singer |
| **Montgomerie, Colin S**<br>International Mgmt Group, Pier House, Strand on the Green, London W4 3NN, England | Golfer |
| **Montgomery, Alton**<br>441 N 9th St, Griffin GA 30223, USA | Football Player |
| **Montgomery, Anne**<br>ESPN-TV, ESPN Plaza, 935 Middle St, Bristol CT 06010 USA | Sportscaster |

|  |  |
|------|-----------|
| **Montgomery, Belinda**<br>Epstein-Wyckoff, 280 S Beverly Dr, #400, Beverly Hills CA 90212 USA | Actress |
| **Montgomery, Chuck**<br>Don Buchwald, 6500 Wilshire Blvd, #2200, Los Angeles CA 90048 USA | Actor |
| **Montgomery, Cleotha (Cleo)**<br>1801 Crape Myrtle Circle, Irving TX 75063, USA | Football Player |
| **Montgomery, D Lamont (Monty)**<br>3011 Pecan Way Court, Richmond TX 77406, USA | Football Player |
| **Montgomery, Eddie**<br>Parallel Entertainment, 209 10th Ave S, #506, Nashville TN 37203, USA | Singer (Montgomery Gentry) |
| **Montgomery, Gregory H (Greg), Jr**<br>2112 Brentwood Dr, Baton Rouge LA 70809, USA | Football Player |
| **Montgomery, James P (Jim)**<br>1537 Bella Vista Dr, Dallas TX 75218, USA | Swimmer, Coach |
| **Montgomery, Janet**<br>Hamilton Hodell, 66-68 Margaret St, #500, London W1W 8SR, England | Actress |
| **Montgomery, Jeffrey T (Jeff)**<br>3701 W 140th St, Overland Park KS 66224, USA | Baseball Player |
| **Montgomery, Jim**<br>Rensselaer Polytechnic Institute, Athletic Dept, 110 8th St, Troy NY 12180, USA | Ice Hockey Player |
| **Montgomery, John Michael**<br>Hallmark Direction, 713 18th Ave S, Nashville TN 37203, USA | Singer |
| **Montgomery, Kevin**<br>Brooks Murphy Stevens, 5619 N Lankershim Blvd, North Hollywood CA 91601 USA | Actor |
| **Montgomery, Marvin J (Marv)**<br>1509 S Macon St, Aurora CO 80012, USA | Football Player |
| **Montgomery, Melba**<br>Fat City Artists, 1906 Chet Atkins Place, #502, Nashville TN 37212 USA | Singer |
| **Montgomery, Mike**<br>University of California, Athletic Dept, Berkeley CA 94720, USA | Basketball Coach |
| **Montgomery, Poppy**<br>United Talent Agency, U T A Plaza, 9336 Civic Center Dr, Beverly Hills CA 90210 USA | Actress |
| **Montgomery, Robert A**<br>Johns Hopkins University Medical Center, Transplantation Center, Baltimore MD 21218, USA | Surgeon |
| **Montgomery, Robert E (Bob)**<br>2 Parkway Dr, Saugus MA 01906, USA | Baseball Player |
| **Montgomery, Steven L (Steve)**<br>13731 Mercado Dr, Del Mar CA 92014, USA | Baseball Player |
| **Montgomery, Sy**<br>Ballatine Books, 1745 Broadway, New York NY 10019 USA | Writer |
| **Montgomery, Wilbert N**<br>5846 Pine Brook Farm Road, Sykesville MD 21784, USA | Football Player |
| **Montiel, Dito**<br>Underground Films & Mgmt, 447 S Highland Ave, Los Angeles CA 90036, USA | Director, Writer |
| **Montler, Michael R (Mike)**<br>479 Tiara Vista Dr, Grand Junction CO 81507, USA | Football Player |
| **Montminy, Marc R**<br>Salk Institute, 10100 N Torrey Pines Road, La Jolla CA 92037 USA | Neurochemist |
| **Montoya, Craig**<br>Pinnacle Entertainment, 30 Glenn St, White Plains NY 10603, USA | Bassist (Everclear) |
| **Montoya, Henry (Coco)**<br>J B Mgmt, PO Box 25703, Chicago IL 60625, USA | Guitarist |
| **Montoya, Juan**<br>330 E 59th St, #200, New York NY 10022, USA | Interior Designer |
| **Montoya, Juan Pablo**<br>Earnhardt Ganassi Racing, 8500 Westmoreland Dr, Concord NC 28027, USA | Auto Racing Driver |
| **Montoya, Max, Jr**<br>2110 Williams Road, Hebron KY 41048, USA | Football Player |
| **Montoyo, Jose Carlos (Charlie)**<br>438 Summer Sails Dr, Valrico FL 33594, USA | Baseball Player |
| **Montross, Eric S**<br>4668 S NC Highway 150, Lexington NC 27295, USA | Basketball Player |
| **Montsho Este**<br>Agency Group Ltd, 142 W 57th St, #600, New York NY 10019 USA | Rap Artist (Arrested Development) |
| **Montvidas, Edgaras**<br>Maxine Robertson Mgmt, 14 Forge Dr, Claygate KT1O 0HR, England | Opera Singer |
| **Montville, Leigh**<br>I C M Partners, 10250 Constellation Blvd, #900, Los Angeles CA 90067 USA | Sportswriter |
| **Monty, Peter C (Pete)**<br>PO Box 338, Wellington CO 80549, USA | Football Player |
| **Moock, Joseph G (Joe)**<br>12432 Pecos Ave, Greenwell Springs LA 70739, USA | Baseball Player |
| **Moodie, Janice**<br>19746 Woodchase Circle, Orlando FL 32836, USA | Golfer |
| **Moody, Eric**<br>336 Gleneagle Circle, Irmo SC 29063, USA | Baseball Player |
| **Moody, Ivan L (Ghost)**<br>10th Street Entertainment, 568 Broadway, #608, New York NY 10012, USA | Singer (Five Finger Death Punch) |
| **Moody, Keith M**<br>4632 Riverview Court, Tracy CA 95377, USA | Football Player |
| **Moody, Lynne**<br>Gersh Agency, 9465 Wilshire Blvd, #600, Beverly Hills CA 90212 USA | Actress |
| **Moody, Ron**<br>Ingleside, 41 The Green, Southgate, London N14, England | Actor |
| **Moody-Luckhurst, Teri**<br>103 Pierrepont Isle, Duluth GA 30097, USA | Golfer |
| **Moog, Andy**<br>530 Rolling Hills Road, Coppell TX 75019, USA | Ice Hockey Player |
| **Moomaw, Donn D**<br>3124 Corda Dr, Los Angeles CA 90049, USA | Football Player |
| **Moon, Elizabeth**<br>Jabberwocky Literary Agency, PO Box 4558, Sunnyside NY 11104, USA | Writer |
| **Moon, H Warren**<br>Seattle Seahawks, 12 Seahawks Way, Renton WA 98056 USA | Football Player |
| **Moon, Jamario R**<br>Charlotte Bobcats, 333 E Trade St, #A, Charlotte NC 28202 USA | Basketball Player |

**M**

**Moon, Philip** — Actor
Don Buchwald, 6500 Wilshire Blvd, #2200, Los Angeles CA 90048 USA
**Moon, Sheri** — Actress
Dimension Films, 345 Hudson St, #1300, New York NY 10014, USA
**Moon, Wallace W (Wally)** — Baseball Player
3801 E Crest Dr, #6401, Bryan TX 77802, USA
**Mooney, Beth E** — Businesswoman
KeyCorp, 127 Public Square, Cleveland OH 44114, USA
**Mooney, Debra** — Actress
Principal Entertainment, 9255 Sunset Blvd, #500, Los Angeles CA 90069 USA
**Mooney, Edward K (Ed)** — Football Player
4105 63rd St, Lubbock TX 79413, USA
**Mooney, John** — Singer, Guitarist
Intrepid Artists, Midtown Plaza, 1300 Baxter St, #405, Charlotte NC 28204, USA
**Mooney, John J** — Inventor (3-Way Catalytic Converter)
85 Colgate Ave, Wyckoff NJ 07481, USA
**Mooneyham, William C (Bill)** — Baseball Player
5731 White Crane Road, Atwater CA 95301, USA
**Moonves, Leslie** — Businessman, Producer
Columbia Broadcasting System Inc, 7800 Beverly Blvd, Los Angeles CA 90036, USA
**Moore, Abra** — Singer
Progressive Global Agency, PO Box 50294, Nashville TN 37205, USA
**Moore, Alan** — Cartoonist, Writer
Top Shelf, PO Box 1282, Marietta GA 30061, USA
**Moore, Alvin** — Football Player
1111 W Lark Dr, Chandler AZ 85286, USA
**Moore, Alvin E (Junior)** — Baseball Player
3728 Wall Ave, Richmond CA 94804, USA
**Moore, Andre M** — Basketball Player
12137 S Justine St, Chicago IL 60643, USA
**Moore, Angelo C** — Singer, Saxophonist (Fishbone)
Silverback Mgmt, 9469 Jefferson Blvd, #101, Culver City CA 90232, USA
**Moore, Ann S** — Publisher
Time-Life, Chairwoman's Office, Time-Life Building, New York NY 10020, USA
**Moore, Archie F** — Baseball Player
201 Courtland Road, Indiana PA 15701, USA
**Moore, Balor L** — Baseball Player
6301 Almeda Road, #717, Houston TX 77021, USA
**Moore, Barbara** — Actress, Model
Playboy Promotions, 2706 Media Center Dr, Los Angeles CA 90065 USA
**Moore, Benjamin P** — Artist
3123 39th Place S, Seattle WA 98144, USA
**Moore, Billie** — Basketball Coach
2247 Meadow Lane, Fullerton CA 92831, USA
**Moore, Bradley A (Brad)** — Baseball Player
3135 Challenger Point Dr, Loveland CO 80538, USA
**Moore, Brandon** — Football Player
Enter-Sports Mgmt, 5 Concourse Parkway, #3000, Atlanta GA 30328, USA
**Moore, Calvin C** — Mathematician
1408 Eagle Pointe Court, Lafayette CA 94549, USA
**Moore, Chante** — Singer, Songwriter
Mauldin Brand Agency, 1280 W Peachtree St, #300, Atlanta GA 30309, USA
**Moore, Charles W (Charlie)** — Baseball Player
342 County Road 276, Cullman AL 35057, USA
**Moore, Charles, Jr** — Track Athlete
10 Barclay St, #39C, New York NY 10007, USA
**Moore, Chris** — Producer, Director, Actor
Hansen Jacobson Teller, 450 N Roxbury Dr, #800, Beverly Hills CA 90210 USA
**Moore, Christina** — Actress
C E S D, 10635 Santa Monica Blvd, #130, Los Angeles CA 90025 USA
**Moore, Clinton R (Mikki)** — Basketball Player
Golden State Warriors, 1011 Broadway, Oakland CA 94605 USA
**Moore, Corey A** — Football Player
Cincinnati Bengals, 1 Paul Brown Stadium, Cincinnati OH 45202 USA
**Moore, Corwin** — Writer, Actor
Creative Artists Agency, 2000 Ave of Stars, #100, Los Angeles CA 90067 USA
**Moore, David E (Dave)** — Football Player
PO Box 174, Macon NC 27551, USA
**Moore, Demi** — Actress
Creative Artists Agency, 2000 Ave of Stars, #100, Los Angeles CA 90067 USA
**Moore, Dick** — Cartoonist (Our Gang)
Dick Moore Assoc, 1560 Broadway, New York NY 10036, USA
**Moore, Dorothy** — Singer
Betty of Troy, 100 Lincoln Ave, #12D, Mineola NY 11501, USA
**Moore, Dylan** — Actress
Stone Manners Salners, 9911 W Pico Blvd, #1400, Los Angeles CA 90035 USA
**Moore, E McNeil** — Football Player
1212 Woodlawn Dr, Center TX 75935, USA
**Moore, Eric P** — Football Player
2225 Lindsay Lane, Florissant MO 63031, USA
**Moore, Ezekiel (Zeke), Jr** — Football Player
3422 Prudence Court, Houston TX 77045, USA
**Moore, Gary D** — Baseball Player
7985 Roundrock Road, Dallas TX 75248, USA
**Moore, Geoff** — Singer, Songwriter
Breen Agency, 110 30th Ave N, #3, Nashville TN 37203, USA
**Moore, Gerald H (Jerry)** — Football Coach
Appalachian State University, Athletic Dept, Boone NC 28608, USA
**Moore, Harold G (Hal)** — Army General, Writer, Hero
585 Moores Mill Road, Auburn AL 36830, USA
**Moore, Herman J** — Football Player
3160 Fallen Oaks Court, #605, Rochester Hills MI 48309, USA
**Moore, Jackie** — Singer
T-Best Talent Agency, 508 Honey Lake Court, Danville CA 94506 USA
**Moore, Jackie S** — Baseball Player, Manager
2721 Laurel Valley Lane, Arlington TX 76006, USA

| | |
|---|---|
| **Moore, James** <br> 2624 Abner Place NW, Atlanta GA 30318, USA | Baseball Player |
| **Moore, James E, Jr** <br> 18940 Joaquin Court, Salinas CA 93908, USA | Army General |
| **Moore, Jason** <br> W M E Entertainment, 9601 Wilshire Blvd, #300, Beverly Hills CA 90210 USA | Director |
| **Moore, Joel David** <br> I C M Partners, 10250 Constellation Blvd, #900, Los Angeles CA 90067 USA | Actor |
| **Moore, Jonathan Patrick** <br> Management 360, 9111 Wilshire Blvd, Beverly Hills CA 90210 USA | Actor |
| **Moore, Josh** <br> Breen Agency, 25 Music Square W, Nashville TN 37203, USA | Keyboardist (Caedmon's Call) |
| **Moore, Joshua Logan** <br> Innovative Artists, 1505 10th St, Santa Monica CA 90401 USA | Actor |
| **Moore, Julianne** <br> Management 360, 9111 Wilshire Blvd, Beverly Hills CA 90210 USA | Actress, Model |
| **Moore, Kellen** <br> Detroit Lions, 222 Republic Dr, Allen Park MI 48101 USA | Football Player |
| **Moore, Kelvin O** <br> 75 Stoney Point Terrace, Covington GA 30014, USA | Baseball Player |
| **Moore, Langston** <br> 1022 W Estrella Dr, Chandler AZ 85224, USA | Football Player |
| **Moore, Leonard E (Lenny)** <br> 8815 Stonehaven Road, Randallstown MD 21133, USA | Football Player |
| **Moore, LeRoy M** <br> 24 Mary Day Ave, Pontiac MI 48341, USA | Football Player |
| **Moore, Loree** <br> New York Liberty, Madison Square Garden, 2 Penn Plaza, New York NY 10121 USA | Basketball Player |
| **Moore, Lorrie** <br> University of Wisconsin, English Dept, Madison WI 53706, USA | Writer |
| **Moore, Lucille** <br> 6450 Miami Circle, South Bend IN 46614, USA | Baseball Player |
| **Moore, Mandy** <br> Reinhard Agency, 2021 Arch St, #400, Philadelphia PA 19103, USA | Singer, Actress, Model |
| **Moore, Mary** <br> 4225 Lake Grove Court, White Lake MI 48383, USA | Baseball Player |
| **Moore, Mary Tyler** <br> 510 E 86th St, #21A, New York NY 10028, USA | Actress |
| **Moore, Maulty J** <br> 5781 S Sable Circle, Margate FL 33063, USA | Football Player |
| **Moore, Maya A** <br> Minnesota Lynx, Target Center, 600 1st Ave N, Minneapolis MN 55403 USA | Basketball Player |
| **Moore, Melanie Deanne** <br> James/Levy Mgmt, 3500 W Olive Ave, #1470, Burbank CA 91505 USA | Actress |
| **Moore, Melba** <br> Hanns Wolters International, 501 5th Ave, #2112A, New York NY 10017, USA | Singer, Actress |
| **Moore, Melissa Anne** <br> PO Box 55, Versailles KY 40383, USA | Actress |
| **Moore, Mewelde J C** <br> 6345 Riverine Dr, Baton Rouge LA 70820, USA | Football Player |
| **Moore, Michael (Mike)** <br> Attorney General's Office, PO Box 220, Jackson MS 39205, USA | Attorney |
| **Moore, Michael F** <br> Dog Eat Dog Films, 430 W 14th St, #401, New York NY 10014, USA | Director |
| **Moore, Michael W (Mike)** <br> 1472 E Calle de Caballos, Tempe AZ 85284, USA | Baseball Player |
| **Moore, Nathaniel (Nat)** <br> Nat Moore Assoc, 16911 NE 6th Ave, North Miami Beach FL 33162, USA | Football Player |
| **Moore, Patrick** <br> 4638 E Dartmouth St, Mesa AZ 85205, USA | Golfer |
| **Moore, R Barry** <br> 6702 Conifer Circle, Indian Trail NC 28079, USA | Baseball Player |
| **Moore, Red** <br> 2450 Perry Blvd NW, Atlanta GA 30318, USA | Baseball Player |
| **Moore, Richard W (Dickie)** <br> 4955 Chemin Saint Francois, Saint Laurent QC H4S 1P3, Canada | Ice Hockey Player |
| **Moore, Robert A** <br> 1906 E Gate Dr, Stone Mountain GA 30087, USA | Football Player |
| **Moore, Robert D (Bob)** <br> 1641 Chelsea Road, Palos Verdes Estates CA 90274, USA | Baseball Player |
| **Moore, Robert R (Bob)** <br> 20 Sally Ann Road, Orinda CA 94563, USA | Football Player |
| **Moore, Robert S (Rob)** <br> 14239 S 8th St, Phoenix AZ 85048, USA | Football Player |
| **Moore, Robert V (Bobby)** <br> 3703 Hyde Park Ave, Cincinnati OH 45209, USA | Baseball Player |
| **Moore, Roger** <br> Diamond Mgmt, 31 Percy St, London W1T 2DD, England | Actor |
| **Moore, Ronald L (Ron)** <br> 5730 N Oakwood St, Spencer TX 73084, USA | Football Player |
| **Moore, Samuel D (Sam)** <br> I'ma Da Wife Enterprises, 7119 E Shea Blvd, #109-436, Scottsdale AZ 85254, USA | Singer (Sam & Dave) |
| **Moore, Scott** <br> Creative Artists Agency, 2000 Ave of Stars, #100, Los Angeles CA 90067 USA | Director, Writer |
| **Moore, Scott A** <br> Baltimore Orioles, Oriole Park, 333 W Camden St, Baltimore MD 21201 USA | Baseball Player |
| **Moore, Shemar** <br> Innovative Artists, 1505 10th St, Santa Monica CA 90401 USA | Actor |
| **Moore, Stephen** <br> Markham Froggatt Irwin, Julian House, 4 Windmill St, London W1P 1HF, England | Actor |
| **Moore, Stephen Campbell** <br> Untitled Entertainment, 350 S Beverly Dr, #200, Beverly Hills CA 90212 USA | Actor |
| **Moore, Thomas** <br> Harper/Collins Publishers, 10 E 53rd St, Cellar 1, New York NY 10022, USA | Writer |
| **Moore, Thomas M (Tom)** <br> 1038 Forest Harbor Dr, Hendersonville TN 37075, USA | Football Player |

**M**

| | |
|---|---|
| **Moore, Thurston** | Singer, Guitarist (Sonic Youth) |
| Silva Artist Mgmt, 722 Seward St, Los Angeles CA 90038, USA | |
| **Moore, Tracy L** | Basketball Player |
| 12116 E 37th Place, Tulsa OK 74146, USA | |
| **Moore, Trevor P** | Actor, Comedian, Writer, Director |
| Creative Artists Agency, 2000 Ave of Stars, #100, Los Angeles CA 90067 USA | |
| **Moore, Warren N (Trey)** | Baseball Player |
| 5128 Bellerive Bend Dr, College Station TX 77845, USA | |
| **Moorehead, Aaron M** | Football Player |
| 1717 Trillium Lane, Blacksburg VA 24060, USA | |
| **Moorehead, Emery M** | Football Player |
| 1005 Sussex Dr, Northbrook IL 60062, USA | |
| **Moorehead, Kindal J** | Football Player |
| 10011 Montrose Dr, Charlotte NC 28269, USA | |
| **Moorer, Allison** | Singer, Songwriter, Actress |
| Gold Village Entertainment, 72 Madison Ave, #800, New York NY 10016, USA | |
| **Moore-Warner, Eleanor** | Baseball Player |
| 2172 Kinney Ave NW, Grand Rapids MI 49534, USA | |
| **Moore-Watkins, Pauline** | Actress |
| 4077 SW Sunset Dr, #202, Lake Oswego OR 97035, USA | |
| **Moorhouse, Jocelyn** | Director, Producer, Writer |
| Creative Artists Agency, 2000 Ave of Stars, #100, Los Angeles CA 90067 USA | |
| **Moorman, Brian D** | Football Player |
| 1035 Eagle Point Dr, Saint Augustine FL 32092, USA | |
| **Moorman, Maurice F (Mo), Jr** | Football Player |
| 9641 Shelbyville Road, Simpsonville KY 40067, USA | |
| **Mora Gramunt, Gabriel** | Architect |
| Mora-Sanvisens Arquitectes, 24 Herzegovina, Pal 1, 08006 Barcelona, Spain | |
| **Mora, Gene** | Cartoonist (Graffiti) |
| United Feature Syndicate, PO Box 5610, Cincinnati OH 45201 USA | |
| **Mora, James L (Jim), Jr** | Football Coach |
| University of California, Athletic Dept, Los Angeles CA 90024, USA | |
| **Mora, Melvin** | Baseball Player |
| 2316 Willow Vale Dr, Fallston MD 21047, USA | |
| **Mora, Naima** | Model |
| Ford Models Inc, 111 5th Ave, #900, New York NY 10003 USA | |
| **Morabito, Timothy R (Tim)** | Football Player |
| 98 Myrtle Ave, Edgewater NJ 07020, USA | |
| **Moraes, Adrian** | Rodeo Bull Rider |
| Professional Bull Riders Assn, 6 S Tejon St, #700, Colorado Springs CO 80903, USA | |
| **Moraga, David** | Baseball Player |
| 608 Peach Court, Fairfield CA 94534, USA | |
| **Morahan, Christopher T** | Director |
| Highcombe, Devil's Punchbowl, Thursley, Godalming, Surrey GU8 6NS, England | |
| **Morales Ayma, Juan Evo** | President, Bolivia |
| President's Office, Palacio de Gobierno, Plaza Murilla, La Paz, Bolivia | |
| **Morales Elvira, Erik I** | Boxer |
| Miguel Diaz, 9483 Bondeno St, Las Vegas NV 89123, USA | |
| **Morales Hernandez, Jose M** | Baseball Player |
| PO Box 770985, Winter Garden FL 34777, USA | |
| **Morales, Esai** | Actor |
| Innovative Artists, 1505 10th St, Santa Monica CA 90401 USA | |
| **Morales, Natalie** | Actress |
| United Talent Agency, U T A Plaza, 9336 Civic Center Dr, Beverly Hills CA 90210 USA | |
| **Morales, P Pablo** | Swimmer |
| University of Nebraska, Athletic Dept, Lincoln NE 68588, USA | |
| **Morales, Richard A (Rich)** | Baseball Player |
| 1650 Rosita Road, Pacifica CA 94044, USA | |
| **Morales-Rhodes, Natalie L** | Actress, Producer, Commentator |
| United Talent Agency, U T A Plaza, 9336 Civic Center Dr, Beverly Hills CA 90210 USA | |
| **Moran, Erin** | Actress |
| The Agency, 3711 Ocean Front Walk, #1, Marina del Rey CA 90292 USA | |
| **Moran, Ian P** | Ice Hockey Player |
| PO Box 1462, Duxbury MA 02331, USA | |
| **Moran, J Kevin** | Navy Admiral |
| Investor Relations Group, 11 Stone St, #300, New York NY 10003, USA | |
| **Moran, Jason** | Jazz Pianist |
| Vision Arts Mgmt, 16 Clint Finger Roads, Saugerties NY 12477, USA | |
| **Moran, Julie** | Sportscaster, Actress |
| Creative Artists Agency, 2000 Ave of Stars, #100, Los Angeles CA 90067 USA | |
| **Moran, Nick** | Actor, Director |
| Ken McReddie Assoc, 101 Finsbury Pavement, London EC2A 1RS, England | |
| **Moran, R Alan (Al)** | Baseball Player |
| 34134 Banbury St, Farmington Hills MI 48331, USA | |
| **Moran, Richard J (Rich)** | Football Player |
| 7252 Mimosa Dr, Carlsbad CA 92011, USA | |
| **Moran, Sean F** | Football Player |
| 13577 W 84th Dr, Arvada CO 80005, USA | |
| **Moran, Terry** | Commentator |
| ABC-TV, News Dept, 77 W 66th St, New York NY 10023 USA | |
| **Moran, Thomas L (Tommy)** | Producer, Writer |
| Creative Artists Agency, 2000 Ave of Stars, #100, Los Angeles CA 90067 USA | |
| **Moran, William N (Billy)** | Baseball Player |
| PO Box 82, Luthersville GA 30251, USA | |
| **Morandi, Piergiorgio** | Conductor |
| I M G Artists, Hogarth Business Park, Chiswick, London W4 2TH, England | |
| **Morandini, Michael R (Mickey)** | Baseball Player |
| 242 Crabapple Lane, Valparaiso IN 46383, USA | |
| **Moranis, Rick** | Actor, Comedian |
| Bailey Brand Mgmt, 506 Santa Monica Blvd, #327, Santa Monica CA 90401, USA | |
| **Morano Walker, Reed** | Cinematographer |
| Gersh Agency, 9465 Wilshire Blvd, #600, Beverly Hills CA 90212 USA | |
| **Morante, Laura** | Actress, Director, Writer |
| Voyez Mon Agent, 20 Ave Rapp, 75007 Paris, France | |
| **Morariu, Ana Caterina** | Actress |
| Cristiano Cucchini Mgmt, Lungotevere dei Mellini 10, 00193 Rome, Italy | |

*Moore - Morariu*

**Morath, Max** — Singer
Producers Inc, 11806 N 56th St, Tampa FL 33617 USA

**Moravcik, Jozef** — Prime Minister, Slovakia
Primacialne Ham 1, Box 192, 81422 Bratislava, Slovakia

**Moravec, Ivan** — Concert Pianist
Pod Vyhidkou 520, 16000 Prague 6, Czech Republic

**Morawetz, Cathleen S** — Mathematician
251 Mercer St, New York NY 10012, USA

**Morbito, Paul** — Guitarist (Chesterfield Kings)
Agency Group Ltd, 142 W 57th St, #600, New York NY 10019 USA

**Morceli, Noureddine** — Track Athlete
Youth & Sports Ministry, 3 Rue Mohamed Belouizdad, Algiers, Algeria

**Mordecai, Michael H (Mike)** — Baseball Player
10 Cross Creek Lane, Dothan AL 36303, USA

**Mordente, Tony** — Actor, Dancer, Choreographer
31 Bay Harbor Dr, Bigfork MT 59911, USA

**Mordkovitch, Lydia** — Concert Violinist
25B Belsize Ave, London NW3 3BL, England

**More, Camilla** — Actress
Sharon Kemp, 477 S Robertson Blvd, #204, Beverly Hills CA 90211 USA

**More, Jayson** — Ice Hockey Player
9532 Thoroughbred Way, Brentwood TN 37027, USA

**More, Michelle** — Volleyball Player, Model
Association of Volleyball Professionals, 960 Knox St, #A, Torrance CA 90502 USA

**Moreau, Ethan B** — Ice Hockey Player
Columbus Blue Jackets, Arena, 200 W Nationwide Blvd, #1, Columbus OH 43215 USA

**Moreau, Jeanne** — Actress
Artmedia, 20 Ave Rapp, 75007 Paris, France

**Moreh, Dror** — Director, Producer, Cinematographer
United Talent Agency, U T A Plaza, 9336 Civic Center Dr, Beverly Hills CA 90210 USA

**Morehead, David M (Dave)** — Baseball Player
13872 Glenmere Dr, Santa Ana CA 92705, USA

**Moreira, Airto** — Jazz Percussionist
A Train Entertainment, 401 Grand Ave, #300, Oakland CA 94610, USA

**Morel, Eric** — Boxer
7119 Tree Lane, Madison WI 53717, USA

**Morel, Francois** — Composer, Conductor, Concert Pianist
Laval University, 1055 Av du Seminaire, Quebec QC G1V 0A6, Canada

**Morel, Pierre** — Director, Cinematographer
Sentient Entertainment, 1617 Broadway, Mezzanine Suite, Santa Monica CA 90404, USA

**Moreland, B Keith** — Baseball Player
4209 Hidden Canyon Cove, Austin TX 78746, USA

**Morell, Michael J** — Government Official
Central Intelligence Agency, Director's Office, Washington DC 20505, USA

**Morello, Thomas B (Tom)** — Singer, Guitarist
G A S Entertainment, 722 Seward St, Los Angeles CA 90038, USA

**Moreno, Belita** — Actress
Paradigm Agency, 360 N Crescent Dr, North Building, Beverly Hills CA 90210 USA

**Moreno, Catalina Sandino** — Actress
Principal Entertainment, 9255 Sunset Blvd, #500, Los Angeles CA 90069 USA

**Moreno, Chino** — Singer, Guitarist (Deftones)
Velvet Hammer Music, 9911 W Pico Blvd, #350, Los Angeles CA 90035, USA

**Moreno, Ezekiel A (Zeke)** — Football Player
1881 Harris Mill Ave, Chula Vista CA 91913, USA

**Moreno, Jorge** — Singer
Rogers & Cowan, 8687 Melrose Ave, #G700, West Hollywood CA 90069 USA

**Moreno, Luis Alberto** — Financier, Government Official
Inter-America Development Bank, 1300 New York Ave NW, Washington DC 20577, USA

**Moreno, Mario** — Bassist (Los Tucanes de Tijuana)
Tucanes Inc, 6055 E Washington Blvd, #455, Commerce CA 90040, USA

**Moreno, Orber** — Baseball Player
4833 Kingston Circle, Kissimmee FL 34746, USA

**Moreno, Rita** — Actress, Singer
David Belenzon Mgmt, PO Box 5000, PO Box 67, Rancho Santa Fe CA 92067, USA

**Moreno, Roberto** — Auto Racing Driver
252 Montclaire Circle, Weston FL 33326, USA

**Moreno-Ocampo, Luis** — Attorney
International Criminal Court, Maanweg 174, 2516 The Hague AB, Netherlands

**Morenstein, Harley** — Actor, Comedian
Gersh Agency, 9465 Wilshire Blvd, #600, Beverly Hills CA 90212 USA

**Moresco, Robert (Bobby)** — Producer, Director, Writer, Actor
Moresco Productions, 4231 W National Ave, Burbank CA 91505, USA

**Moret, Rogelio (Roger)** — Baseball Player
HC 1 Box 5225, Guaynabo PR 00971, USA

**Moretti, Fabrizio** — Drummer (Strokes)
M V O Ltd, 370 7th Ave, #807, New York NY 10001, USA

**Moretz, Chloe Grace** — Actress
W M E Entertainment, 9601 Wilshire Blvd, #300, Beverly Hills CA 90210 USA

**Morey, Bill** — Actor
Kazarian/Measures/Ruskin, 11969 Ventura Blvd, #300, Studio City CA 91604 USA

**Morey, Sean J** — Football Player
63 McCosh Circle, Princeton NJ 8540, USA

**Morga, Tom** — Actor, Stuntman
Stuntmen Assn, 10660 Riverside Dr, #200E, Toluca Lake CA 91602, USA

**Morgan, Abi** — Writer
Creative Artists Agency, 2000 Ave of Stars, #100, Los Angeles CA 90067 USA

**Morgan, Alexandra P (Alex)** — Soccer Player
Wasserman Media Group, 10960 Wilshire Blvd, #2200, Los Angeles CA 90024, USA

**Morgan, Anthony E** — Football Player
10306 Reno Ave, Cleveland OH 44105, USA

**Morgan, Barbara R** — Astronaut
2996 S Rookery Lane, Boise ID 83706, USA

**Morgan, Chad** — Actor
S M S Talent, 8383 Wilshire Blvd, #230, Beverly Hills CA 90211 USA

**Morgan, Craig** — Singer, Guitarist, Songwriter
Vector Mgmt, PO Box 120479, Nashville TN 37212 USA

**M**

| | |
|---|---|
| **Morgan, Daniel T (Dan), Jr** | Football Player |
| 1915 Funny Cide Dr, Waxhaw NC 28173, USA | |
| **Morgan, Debbi** | Actress |
| Mitchell K Stubbs Assoc, 8695 W Washington Blvd, #204, Culver City CA 90232 USA | |
| **Morgan, Debelah** | Singer, Songwriter |
| D A S Communications, 83 Riverside Dr, New York NY 10024, USA | |
| **Morgan, Donald M** | Cinematographer |
| 15826 Mayall St, North Hills CA 91343, USA | |
| **Morgan, Gil** | Golfer |
| PO Box 806, Edmond OK 73083, USA | |
| **Morgan, Glen** | Director, Producer, Writer |
| Creative Artists Agency, 2000 Ave of Stars, #100, Los Angeles CA 90067 USA | |
| **Morgan, James N** | Economist |
| 1217 Bydding Road, Ann Arbor MI 48103, USA | |
| **Morgan, Jane** | Singer |
| 63 North St, Kennebunkport ME 04046, USA | |
| **Morgan, Jaye P** | Singer, Actress |
| 1185 La Grange Ave, Newbury Park CA 91320, USA | |
| **Morgan, Jeffrey Dean** | Actor |
| United Talent Agency, U T A Plaza, 9336 Civic Center Dr, Beverly Hills CA 90210 USA | |
| **Morgan, John G, Jr** | Navy Admiral |
| Deputy CNO, Operations/Plans/Strategy, HqUSN, Pentagon, Washington DC 20350 USA | |
| **Morgan, Joseph** | Actor |
| Richard Konigsberg Mgmt, 400 N Mansfield Ave, Los Angeles CA 90036, USA | |
| **Morgan, Joseph L (Joe)** | Baseball Player |
| 3523 Country Club Place, Danville CA 94506, USA | |
| **Morgan, Joseph M (Joe)** | Baseball Player, Manager |
| 15 Oak Hill Dr, Walpole MA 02081, USA | |
| **Morgan, Kevin L** | Baseball Player |
| 205 Yearling Road, #A, Duson LA 70529, USA | |
| **Morgan, Lorrie** | Singer |
| Webster Assoc, PO Box 23015, Nashville TN 37202, USA | |
| **Morgan, Marabel** | Writer |
| Total Woman Inc, 1300 NW 167th St, Miami FL 33169, USA | |
| **Morgan, Meli'sa** | Singer |
| Orpheus, 630 9th Ave, #1101, New York NY 10036, USA | |
| **Morgan, Michael** | Geneticist |
| Wellcome Trust, 183 Euston Road, London NW1 2BE, England | |
| **Morgan, Michele** | Actress, Singer |
| Agents Associes Claudie Nolte, 201 Rue du Faubourg Saint Honore, 75001 Paris, France | |
| **Morgan, Mike** | Baseball Player |
| PO Box 681130, Park City UT 84068, USA | |
| **Morgan, Mike** | Cartoonist (For Heaven's Sake) |
| Trinity United Methodist Church, 814 West Ave, Cartersville GA 30120, USA | |
| **Morgan, Peter** | Writer, Director |
| Independent Talent Group, 40 Whitfield St, London W1T 2RH, England | |
| **Morgan, Piers** | Commentator |
| CNN-TV, News Dept, 820 1st St NE, #1000, Washington DC 20002 USA | |
| **Morgan, Quincy D E** | Football Player |
| 2715 Taylorcrest, Missouri City TX 77459, USA | |
| **Morgan, Robert B** | Senator, NC |
| PO Box 377, Lillington NC 27546, USA | |
| **Morgan, Robert M (Bobby)** | Baseball Player |
| 3004 Stoneybrook Road, Oklahoma City OK 73120, USA | |
| **Morgan, Robin E** | Editor, Writer |
| Ms Magazine, Editorial Dept, 230 Park Ave, New York NY 10169, USA | |
| **Morgan, Stanley D** | Football Player |
| PO Box 383048, Germantown TN 38183, USA | |
| **Morgan, Thomas R** | Marine Corps General |
| 8105 Haddington Court, Fairfax Station VA 22039, USA | |
| **Morgan, Tim** | Auto Racing Executive |
| Morgan-McClure Motorsports, 26502 Newbanks Road, Abingdon VA 24210, USA | |
| **Morgan, Tracy** | Actor, Comedian |
| P M K-B N C, 8687 Melrose Ave, #800, Los Angeles CA 90069 USA | |
| **Morgan, Trevor** | Actor |
| I F A Talent Agency, 8730 W Sunset Blvd, #490, West Hollywood CA 90069 USA | |
| **Morgan, Walter** | Golfer |
| 15536 Fishermans Rest Court, Cornelius NC 28031, USA | |
| **Morgan, William N** | Architect |
| William Morgan Architects, 220 E Forsyth St, Jacksonville FL 32202, USA | |
| **Morganna** | Entertainer, Model |
| PO Box 20281, Columbus OH 43220, USA | |
| **Morgenson, Gretchen C** | Journalist |
| New York Times, Editorial Dept, 229 W 43rd St, New York NY 10036 USA | |
| **Morgenstern, Joe** | Journalist |
| Wall Street Journal, Editorial Dept, 1 World Financial Center, New York NY 10281 USA | |
| **Morgenstern, Julie** | Writer |
| Julie Morgenstern Enterprises, 850 7th Ave, New York NY 10019, USA | |
| **Morgenthau, Kramer** | Cinematographer |
| 1632 Maltman Ave, Los Angeles CA 90026, USA | |
| **Morgenthau, Robert M** | Attorney |
| 1085 Park Ave, New York NY 10128, USA | |
| **Morhardt, Meredith G (Moe)** | Baseball Player |
| 219 Spencer Hill Road, Winsted CT 06098, USA | |
| **Mori, Barbara** | Actress |
| Caliber Media, 9229 W Sunset Blvd, #705, West Hollywood CA 90069, USA | |
| **Mori, Emanuel (Manny)** | President, Micronesia |
| President's Office, Palikir, Kolonia, Pohnpei FM 96941, Micronesia | |
| **Mori, Hanae** | Fashion Designer |
| Veronique de Moussai, 5 Place de l'Alma, 75008 Paris, France | |
| **Mori, Riyo** | Beauty Queen |
| Miss Universe Organization, 1370 Ave of Americas, #1600, New York NY 10019 USA | |
| **Mori, Yoshiro** | Prime Minister, Japan |
| House of Representatives, 1-7-1 Nagatacho, Chiyodaku, Tokyo 100 0014, Japan | |
| **Morial, Marc H** | Social Activist; Mayor, New Orleans |
| National Urban League, 120 Wall St, #700, New York NY 10005, USA | |

**Morgan - Morial**

**Moriarty, Erin**
Jordan Gill Dornbaum, 1133 Broadway, #623, New York NY 10010, USA — Actress
**Moriarty, Laura**
University of Kansas, English Dept, Lawrence KS 66045, USA — Writer
**Moriarty, Michael**
Actor International, Via Fosso del Poggio 141, 00189 Rome, Italy — Actor
**Moriarty, Mike**
5 E Oleander Dr, Mount Laurel NJ 08054, USA — Baseball Player
**Moriarty, Thomas (Tom), Jr**
28800 Fairmount Blvd, Cleveland OH 44124, USA — Football Player
**Moriarty-Gentile, Cathy**
Liebman Entertainment, 235 Park Ave S, #1000, New York NY 10003, USA — Actress
**Moric, Nina**
New York Model Mgmt, 596 Broadway, #701, New York NY 10012 USA — Model, Singer
**Morillon, Philippe**
Ministere de la Defense, 14 Rue Saint-Dominique, 75700 Paris, France — Army General, France
**Morin, Catherine**
Artmedia, 20 Ave Rapp, 75007 Paris, France — Actress
**Morin, James C (Jim)**
Miami Herald, Editorial Dept, 1 Herald Plaza, Miami FL 33132 USA — Editorial Cartoonist
**Morin, Lee M E**
10 Marys Creek Lane, Friendswood TX 77546, USA — Astronaut
**Moringstar, Darren**
1515 W Ingomar Road, Pittsburgh PA 15237, USA — Basketball Player
**Morissette, Alanis**
Creative Artists Agency, 2000 Ave of Stars, #100, Los Angeles CA 90067 USA — Singer, Songwriter, Actress, Producer
**Moritz, Louisa**
405 S Cliftwood Ave, Los Angeles CA 90049, USA — Actress
**Moriyama, Raymond**
32 Davenport Road, Toronto ON M5R 1H3, Canada — Architect
**Mork, Truls**
Harrison/Parrott, 5-6 Albion Court, London W6 0QT, England — Concert Cellist
**Morkis, Dorothy**
17 Farm St, Dover MA 02030, USA — Equestrian
**Morlan, John G**
3290 Belgreen St, Grove City OH 43123, USA — Baseball Player
**Morland, David**
5531 Oxford Moor Blvd, Windermere FL 34786, USA — Golfer
**Morley, Joanne**
I M G, Pier House, Strand-on-the-Green, Chiswick, London W4 3NN England — Golfer
**Morley, Lawrence W**
90 Hemlock St, Saint Thomas ON N5R 1X9, Canada — Geophysicist
**Morley, Malcolm**
Sperone Westwater, 415 W 13th St, #200, New York NY 10014, USA — Artist, Sculptor
**Morman, Alvin**
117 Philadelphia Dr, Rockingham NC 28379, USA — Baseball Player
**Morman, Russell L (Russ)**
3209 S Mark Twain Ave, Blue Springs MO 64015, USA — Baseball Player
**Mornas, Pierre-Olivier**
Art 7, 11 Rue Du Bouloi, 75001 Paris, France — Actor
**Morneau, Justin E G**
1829 Forestview Lane N, Minneapolis MN 55441, USA — Baseball Player
**Moroder, Giorgio**
Soundtrack Music Assoc, 1460 4th St, #308, Santa Monica CA 90401 USA — Composer
**Moronko, Jeffrey R (Jeff)**
3903 Bartons Court, Sugar Land TX 77479, USA — Baseball Player
**Moroski, Michael H (Mike)**
1214 Pine Lane, Davis CA 95616, USA — Football Player
**Morozov, Akeksei A**
Pittsburgh Penguins, Consol Energy Center, 1001 5th Ave, Pittsburgh PA 15219 USA — Ice Hockey Player
**Morozov, Vladimir M**
Kirov Ballet Theater, 1 Pl Iskusstr, 190000 Saint Petersburg, Russia — Opera Singer
**Morrall, Earl E**
2751 68th St SW, Naples FL 34105, USA — Football Player
**Morrell, David**
United Talent Agency, U T A Plaza, 9336 Civic Center Dr, Beverly Hills CA 90210 USA — Writer, Producer
**Morricone, Andrea**
W M E Entertainment, 9601 Wilshire Blvd, #300, Beverly Hills CA 90210 USA — Composer
**Morricone, Ennio**
A R S Latina Film, Viale Pl Nervi, 04100 Latina, Italy — Composer
**Morris, Betty**
2169 Donovan Dr, Lincoln CA 95648, USA — Bowler
**Morris, Byron (Bam)**
251 NE 4th St, Cooper TX 75432, USA — Football Player
**Morris, Carol**
Miss Universe Organization, 1370 Ave of Americas, #1600, New York NY 10019 USA — Beauty Queen
**Morris, Christopher V (Chris)**
3097 Milford Chase SW, Marietta GA 30008, USA — Basketball Player
**Morris, Danny W**
802 E Main St, Petersburg IN 47567, USA — Baseball Player
**Morris, Derek**
9820 E Thompson Peak Parkway, #718, Scottsdale AZ 85255, USA — Ice Hockey Player
**Morris, Doug**
Universal Music Group, 100 Universal City Plaza, Universal City CA 91608, USA — Businessman
**Morris, Edmund**
222 Central Park S, #14A, New York NY 10019, USA — Writer, Educator
**Morris, Errol**
W M E Entertainment, 9601 Wilshire Blvd, #300, Beverly Hills CA 90210 USA — Director
**Morris, Eugene E (Mercury)**
11315 SW 243rd Terrace, Homestead FL 33032, USA — Football Player
**Morris, Garrett**
Global Artists Agency, 6253 Hollywood Blvd, #508, Los Angeles CA 90028 USA — Actor, Singer
**Morris, Gary**
Gurley Co, PO Box 150657, Nashville TN 37215 USA — Singer
**Morris, Heather E**
A K A Talent, 6310 San Vicente Blvd, #200, Los Angeles CA 90048 USA — Actress, Writer

**Morris, Iain** — Writer
Creative Artists Agency, 2000 Ave of Stars, #100, Los Angeles CA 90067 USA
**Morris, James P** — Opera Singer
Columbia Artists Mgmt Inc, 1790 Broadway, #702, New York NY 10019 USA
**Morris, James S (Jim)** — Baseball Player
2216 Rock Creek Dr, Kerrville TX 78028, USA
**Morris, James T** — Government Official
World Food Programme, Via Cesare Giulio Viola 68, 00148 Rome, Italy
**Morris, Jan** — Writer
Trefan Morys, Llanystumdwy, Criccieth, Gwymedd LL52 0LP, Wales
**Morris, Jason N** — Judo Athlete
575 Swaggertown Road, Schenectady NY 12302, USA
**Morris, Jay Hunter** — Opera Singer
I M G Artists, Carnegie Hall Tower, 152 W 57th St, #500, New York NY 10019 USA
**Morris, Jennifer P (Jenny)** — Singer
Harbour Agency, 135 Forbes St, Woolloomooloo NSW 2011, Australia
**Morris, Jessica** — Actress
Prestige Talent Agency, 9250 Wilshire Blvd, #208, Beverly Hills CA 90212, USA
**Morris, John** — Curling Athlete
Curling Assn, 1660 Vimont Court, Cumberland ON K4A 4J4, Canada
**Morris, John C** — Neurologist
Memory Diagnostic Center, 4488 Forest Park Ave, Saint Louis MO 63108, USA
**Morris, John D** — Baseball Player
2645 Elm Dr, North Bellmore NY 11710, USA
**Morris, John S (Jack)** — Baseball Player
7993 100th St N, Saint Paul MN 55110, USA
**Morris, Johnny E** — Football Player
753 Shoreline Road, Lake Barrington IL 60010, USA
**Morris, Jon** — Ice Hockey Player
16 Gail St, Chelmsford MA 01824, USA
**Morris, Jon N** — Football Player
10 Berkeley Court, Bluffton SC 29910, USA
**Morris, Joseph E (Joe)** — Football Player
307 Mark Twain Way, Mahway NJ 07430, USA
**Morris, Julian** — Actor
Brillstein Entertainment Partners, 9150 Wilshire Blvd, #350, Beverly Hills CA 90212 USA
**Morris, Kathryn** — Actress
Mosiac Media Group, 9200 W Sunset Blvd, #1000, Los Angeles CA 90069 USA
**Morris, Keith** — Singer (Black Flag, Circle Jerks)
Agency Group, 1880 Century Park E, #711, Los Angeles CA 90067, USA
**Morris, Larry** — Sculptor
105 N Union St, #4, Alexandria VA 22314, USA
**Morris, Mark W** — Choreographer, Dancer
Mark Morris Dance Group, 3 Lafayette Ave, #504, Brooklyn NY 11217, USA
**Morris, Matthew C (Matt)** — Baseball Player
397 Old Jupiter Beach Road, Jupiter FL 33477, USA
**Morris, Maurice A** — Football Player
772 Golden Eagle Dr, Conway SC 29527, USA
**Morris, Michael S (Mike)** — Football Player
5421 Oriole Dr, Farmington MN 55024, USA
**Morris, Nathan** — Singer (Boyz II Men)
Selverne Co, 3450 Cahuenga Blvd W, #906, Los Angeles CA 90068, USA
**Morris, Oswald (Ossie)** — Cinematographer
Holbrook, Church St, Fontmell Magna, Shaftesbury SP7 0NY, England
**Morris, Phil** — Actor
Innovative Artists, 1505 10th St, Santa Monica CA 90401 USA
**Morris, Raheem** — Football Coach
Washington Redskins, 21300 Redskin Park Dr, Ashburn VA 20147 USA
**Morris, Redmond** — Producer
Independent Talent Group, 40 Whitfield St, London W1T 2RH, England
**Morris, Reginald H** — Cinematographer
255 Bambaugh Circle, #308, Scarborough ON M1W 3T6, Canada
**Morris, Robert** — Sculptor
PO Box 100, Gardiner NY 12525, USA
**Morris, Ronald (Ron)** — Track Athlete
330 S Reese Place, Burbank CA 91506, USA
**Morris, Sarah Jane** — Actress, Producer
Gersh Agency, 9465 Wilshire Blvd, #600, Beverly Hills CA 90212 USA
**Morris, Shellee** — Singer (Twister Alley)
6117 Highway 135, Lake City AR 72437, USA
**Morris, Trevor** — Film Composer
Trevor Morris Studios, 1550 18th St, Santa Monica CA 90404, USA
**Morris, W Harold (Hal)** — Baseball Player
6138 Payne Stewart Dr, Windermere FL 34786, USA
**Morris, Warren R** — Baseball Player
1215 Wilshire Dr, Alexandria LA 71303, USA
**Morris, Wayna** — Singer (Boyz II Men)
Wright Entertainment Group, PO Box 590009, Orlando FL 32859, USA
**Morris, Wayne L** — Football Player
5715 Old Ox Road, Dallas TX 75241, USA
**Morrison, Adam J** — Basketball Player
7301 Vista del Mar, #11, Playa del Rey CA 90293, USA
**Morrison, Christopher W (Mink)** — Director, Writer
I C M Partners, 10250 Constellation Blvd, #900, Los Angeles CA 90067 USA
**Morrison, Denise M** — Businesswoman
Campbell Soup Co, 1 Campbell Place, Camden NJ 08103, USA
**Morrison, Denny** — Speed Skater
Agenda Sport Marketing, 119-9A St NE, Calgary AL T2E 9C5, Canada
**Morrison, Don A** — Football Player
10191 FM 512, Wolfe City TX 75496, USA
**Morrison, Fred L** — Football Player
38189 Greywalls Dr, Murrieta CA 92562, USA
**Morrison, Grant** — Cartoonist
I C M Partners, 10250 Constellation Blvd, #900, Los Angeles CA 90067 USA
**Morrison, Ian (Scotty)** — Ice Hockey Executive, Referee
Kenniss Lake, RR 1 PO Box 314, Haliburton ON K0M 1S0, Canada

**Morrison, James**  Singer, Songwriter
412 S Pueblo Ave, Ojai CA 93023, USA
**Morrison, James**  Actor, Producer, Director
Mitch Clem Mgmt, 2600 W Olive Ave, #500, Burbank CA 91505, USA
**Morrison, James F (Jim)**  Baseball Player
8715 11th Ave Place NW, Bradenton FL 34209, USA
**Morrison, Jennifer**  Actress
John Carrabino Mgmt, 5900 Wilshire Blvd, #406, Los Angeles CA 90036 USA
**Morrison, Jim**  Ice Hockey Player
1 Potts Lane, Port Hope ON L1A 0A4, Canada
**Morrison, Kathryn**  Model
Playboy Promotions, 2706 Media Center Dr, Los Angeles CA 90065 USA
**Morrison, Lew**  Ice Hockey Player
406 Souris St, Harntey MB R0M 0X0, Canada
**Morrison, Mark**  Singer
Atlantic Records, 1290 Ave of Americas, Concourse 3, New York NY 10104 USA
**Morrison, Matthew J**  Actor
Creative Artists Agency, 2000 Ave of Stars, #100, Los Angeles CA 90067 USA
**Morrison, Michael F (Mike)**  Basketball Player
113 Rivanna Lane, Greenville SC 29607, USA
**Morrison, Phil**  Director, Producer
Management 360, 9111 Wilshire Blvd, Beverly Hills CA 90210 USA
**Morrison, Shayne**  Bassist (Perfect Stranger)
Great American Talent, PO Box 2476, Hendersonville TN 37077, USA
**Morrison, Shelley**  Actress
Don Gerler, 3349 Cahuenga Blvd W, #1, Los Angeles CA 90068 USA
**Morrison, Steven C (Steve)**  Football Player
4485 Lake Forest Dr E, Ann Arbor MI 48108, USA
**Morrison, Temuera**  Actor
Robert Bruce Agency, 218 Richmond, Grey Lynn, Auckland 1021, New Zealand
**Morrison, Toni**  Nobel Literature Laureate
185 Nassau St, Princeton NJ 08542, USA
**Morrison, Van**  Singer, Guitarist, Songwriter
115A Glenthorne, Hammersmith, London W6 OLJ, England
**Morrison-Gamberdella, Esther**  Baseball Player
3179 Pleasant Creek Road, Rogue River OR 97537, USA
**Morriss, Guy W**  Football Player
3825 Cocanougher Road, Perryville KY 40468, USA
**Morrissey**  Singer, Songwriter
Paradigm Agency, 360 N Crescent Dr, North Building, Beverly Hills CA 90210 USA
**Morrissey, David**  Actor
Troika, 74 Clerkenwell Road, #300, London EC1M 5QA, England
**Morrissey, James M (Jim)**  Football Player
48 Fox Trail, Lincolnshire IL 60069, USA
**Morrissey, Neil**  Actor
Independent Talent Group, 40 Whitfield St, London W1T 2RH, England
**Morrone, Joe**  Soccer Coach
University of Connecticut, Athletic Dept, Storrs Mansfield CT 06269, USA
**Morrow, Bobby Joe**  Track Athlete
2022 Elmwood Dr, Harlingen TX 78550, USA
**Morrow, Brenden**  Ice Hockey Player
Pittsburgh Penguins, Consol Energy Center, 1001 5th Ave, Pittsburgh PA 15219 USA
**Morrow, Bruce (Cousin Brucie)**  Entertainer
CBS Radio Network, 51 W 52nd St, New York NY 10019, USA
**Morrow, Harold, Jr**  Football Player
126 Golden Isles Dr, #62A, Hallandale Beach FL 33009, USA
**Morrow, Joshua**  Actor
Marv Dauer Mgmt, 11661 San Vicente Blvd, #104, Los Angeles CA 90049, USA
**Morrow, Kenneth (Ken)**  Ice Hockey Player
6732 NW Monticello Dr, Kansas City MO 64152, USA
**Morrow, Mari**  Actress
C E S D, 10635 Santa Monica Blvd, #130, Los Angeles CA 90025 USA
**Morrow, Rob**  Actor
Hofflund/Polone, 9465 Wilshire Blvd, #420, Beverly Hills CA 90212 USA
**Morrow, Steve**  Soccer Coach
F C Dallas, 9200 World Cup Way, #202, Frisco TX 75034 USA
**Morse, C Jeremy**  Financier
102A Drayton Gardens, London SW10 9RJ, England
**Morse, Catherine C (Cathy)**  Golfer
6228 Celadon Circle, West Palm Beach FL 33418, USA
**Morse, David**  Guitarist (Air Supply)
PO Box 3367, Beverly Hills CA 90212, USA
**Morse, David**  Actor
United Talent Agency, U T A Plaza, 9336 Civic Center Dr, Beverly Hills CA 90210 USA
**Morse, David E**  Publisher
Christian Science Monitor, Publisher's Office, 1 Norway St, Boston MA 02136, USA
**Morse, F Bradford**  Representative, MA
411 E 53rd Ave, #18C, New York NY 10022, USA
**Morse, Helen**  Actress
International Casting Service, 218 Crown St, #2, Darlinghurst, NSW 2010, Australia
**Morse, John P**  Golfer
9291 17 Mile Road, Marshall MI 49068, USA
**Morse, Michael J (Mike)**  Baseball Player
417 NW 97th Ave, Plantation FL 33324, USA
**Morse, Robert**  Actor
Bauman Redanty Shaul Agency, 5757 Wilshire Blvd, #473, Los Angeles CA 90036 USA
**Morse, Steven J (Steve)**  Guitarist, Songwriter
Frank Solomon Mgmt, PO Box 639, Natick MA 01760, USA
**Mort, Cynthia**  Writer, Producer, Director
W M E Entertainment, 9601 Wilshire Blvd, #300, Beverly Hills CA 90210 USA
**Mortensen, Chris (Mort)**  Sportscaster
ESPN-TV, ESPN Plaza, 935 Middle St, Bristol CT 06010 USA
**Mortensen, Dale T**  Nobel Economics Laureate
Northwestern University, Economics Dept, Evanston IL 60208, USA
**Mortensen, Daniel E (Dan)**  Rodeo Saddle Bronc Rider
945 Noblewood Dr, Billings MT 59101, USA

# M

**Mortensen, Jesper (Junior)** — Singer, Guitarist (Junior Senior)
Festival Network Mgmt, 30 Irving Place, #600, New York NY 10003, USA
**Mortensen, Viggo** — Actor
Rawlings Co, 3933 Patrick Henry Place, Agoura Hills CA 91301, USA
**Mortier, Gerard** — Director
Kultur Ruhr, Leifhestr 35, 45886 Gelsenkirchen, Germany
**Mortier, Koen** — Director, Producer, Writer
New School Media, 9229 Sunset Blvd, #301, West Hollywood CA 90069, USA
**Mortimer Barrett, Angela** — Tennis Player
Oaks, Coombe Hill, Beverly Lane, Kingston on Thames, Surrey, England
**Mortimer, Emily** — Actress
Independent Talent Group, 40 Whitfield St, London W1T 2RH, England
**Morton, Bruce A** — Commentator
CNN-TV, News Dept, 820 1st St NE, #1000, Washington DC 20002 USA
**Morton, Chad A** — Football Player
50 State Route 120, East Rutherford NJ 07073, USA
**Morton, Euan** — Actor, Singer
Innovative Artists, 1505 10th St, Santa Monica CA 90401 USA
**Morton, Guy, Jr** — Baseball Player
567 Ferndale Ave, Vermillion OH 44089, USA
**Morton, Joe** — Actor
TalentWorks, 220 E 23rd St, #400, New York NY 10010, USA
**Morton, Johnnie J** — Football Player
2911 Oakwood Lane, Torrance CA 90505, USA
**Morton, Judee** — Actress
2386 Sunset Heights Dr, Los Angeles CA 90046, USA
**Morton, K Elaine** — Model, Actress
PO Box 965, Lahaina HI 96767, USA
**Morton, Kristopher (Colt)** — Baseball Player
3245 Santa Barbara Dr, Wellington FL 33414, USA
**Morton, L Craig** — Football Player
450 E Strawberry Dr, #1, Mill Valley CA 94941, USA
**Morton, Lewis** — Producer, Writer
Creative Artists Agency, 2000 Ave of Stars, #100, Los Angeles CA 90067 USA
**Morton, Margaret** — Curling Athlete
Curling Assn, 14 Donnelly Dr, Bedford, Bedfordshire MK4 9TU, England
**Morton, Mark** — Guitarist (Lamb of God)
Entertainment Services, 1000 Main Street Plaza, #303, Voorhees NJ 08043, USA
**Morton, Michael D** — Football Player
5254 Strike the Gold Lane, Wesley Chapel FL 33544, USA
**Morton, Richard** — Basketball Player
1111 Gilman Ave, San Francisco CA 94124, USA
**Morton, Samantha** — Actress
Principato-Young, 9465 Wilshire Blvd, #880, Beverly Hills CA 90212 USA
**Mortson, Gus** — Ice Hockey Player
Central Gas Ontario, PO Box 1456, Timmins ON P4N 7X4, Canada
**Morukov, Boris V** — Cosmonaut
Cosmonaut Training Center, Star City, 141160 Zvezdny Gorodok, Moscow Oblast, Russia
**Mos Def** — Rap Artist, Actor, Producer
Brookside Artists Mgmt, 250 W 57th St, #2303, New York NY 10107, USA
**Mosby, Bernice** — Basketball Player
Washington Mystics, Verizon Center, 401 9th St NW, #750, Washington DC 20004 USA
**Moschen, Michael** — Juggler
PO Box 178, Cornwall Bridge CT 06754, USA
**Moschenko, Sergei I** — Cosmonaut
Cosmonaut Training Center, Star City, 141160 Zvezdny Gorodok, Moscow Oblast, Russia
**Moschitto, Rosario A (Ross)** — Baseball Player
1633 SW Harbour Isles Circle, Port Saint Lucie FL 34986, USA
**Moscow, David** — Actor
Robert Stein Mgmt, PO Box 3797, Beverly Hills CA 90212, USA
**Mosebar, Donald H (Don)** — Football Player
1713 Walnut Ave, Manhattan Beach CA 90266, USA
**Moseby, Lloyd A** — Baseball Player
9140 Los Lagos Circle S, Granite Bay CA 95746, USA
**Moseley, Bill** — Actor
Judy Fox Mgmt, 1525 1/2 S Beverly Dr, Los Angeles CA 90035, USA
**Moseley, Dustin A** — Baseball Player
1602 Line Ferry Road, Texarkana AR 71854, USA
**Moseley, Jonny** — Freestyle Moguls Skier
167 Trinidad Dr, Belvedere Tiburon CA 94920, USA
**Moseley, Mark D** — Football Player
7250 Middle Road, Middletown VA 22645, USA
**Moseley, William** — Actor
A P A Talent/Literary Agency, 405 S Beverly Dr, #300, Beverly Hills CA 90212 USA
**Moseley-Braun, Carol** — Senator, IL
Ambassador Organics, 1634 E 53rd St, #200, Chicago IL 60615, USA
**Moser, Barry** — Illustrator
155 Pantry Road, North Hatfield MA 01066, USA
**Moser, Johannes** — Concert Cellist
I M G Artists, Hogarth Business Park, Chiswick, London W4 2TH, England
**Moser, Michele** — Curling Athlete
Curling Assn, PO Box 606, 3000 Bern, Switzerland
**Moser, Richard A (Rick)** — Football Player
24040 Camino del Avion, Dana Point CA 92629, USA
**Moses, Albert** — Actor
15 Overstone Road, Harpenden, Hertfordshire AL5 5PN, England
**Moses, Edwin C** — Track Athlete
1184 Daventry Way NE, Atlanta GA 30319, USA
**Moses, Gerald B (Jerry)** — Baseball Player
PO Box 2153, Wolfeboro NH 03894, USA
**Moses, Haven C** — Football Player
1140 Cherokee St, #604, Denver CO 80204, USA
**Moses, Mark** — Actor
Innovative Artists, 1505 10th St, Santa Monica CA 90401 USA
**Moses, Pablo** — Singer
Keep on Kicking Music, 330 84th St, #9, Miami Beach FL 33141, USA

**Moses, Rick** — Actor, Singer
Calder Agency, 19919 Redwing St, Woodland Hills CA 91364 USA
**Moses, Robert (Bob)** — Educator, Social Activist
99 Bishop Allen Dr, Cambridge MA 02139, USA
**Moses, William R** — Actor
Amsel Eisenstadt Frazier, 5055 Wilshire Blvd, #865, Los Angeles CA 90036 USA
**Moshe, Guy** — Director, Writer
Creative Artists Agency, 2000 Ave of Stars, #100, Los Angeles CA 90067 USA
**Mosher, Gregory D** — Director, Producer
I C M Partners, 730 5th Ave, New York NY 10019 USA
**Mosimann, Anton** — Chef
Mosimann's, 11B W Halkin St, London SW1X 8JL, England
**Mosisili, B Pakalitha** — Prime Minister, Lesotho
Chairman's Office, Military Council, PO Box 527, Maseru 100, Lesotho
**Moskau, Paul R** — Baseball Player
5041 N Apache Hills Trail, Tucson AZ 85750, USA
**Moskovitz, Dustin** — Businessman
Asana Inc, 3180 18th St, San Francisco CA 94110, USA
**Moskowitz, Robert S** — Artist
81 Leonard St, New York NY 10013, USA
**Mosley, Lacey N** — Singer (Flyleaf)
W M E Entertainment, 9601 Wilshire Blvd, #300, Beverly Hills CA 90210 USA
**Mosley, Max R** — Auto Racing Executive
International Automobile Federation, 8 Place de la Concorde, 75008 Paris, France
**Mosley, Roger E** — Actor
4470 W Sunset Blvd, #107-342, Los Angeles CA 90027, USA
**Mosley, Shane (Sugar)** — Boxer
Chrome Enterprise, PO Box 1924, Pomona CA 91769, USA
**Mosley, Walter** — Writer
37 Carmine St, #275, New York NY 10014, USA
**Mosquera, Julio A** — Baseball Player
1419 Stone Creek Dr, Tarpon Springs FL 34689, USA
**Moss, Cynthia** — Animal Conservationist
African Wildlife Foundation, Mara Road, PO Box 48177, Nairobi, Kenya
**Moss, Damian** — Baseball Player
1877 Georgia Highway 19 South, Dublin GA 31021, USA
**Moss, Eddie B** — Football Player
15404 Eagle Estates Lane, Florissant MO 63034, USA
**Moss, Elisabeth G** — Actress
Ribisi Entertainment Group, 3278 Wilshire Blvd, #702, Los Angeles CA 90010, USA
**Moss, Eric Owen** — Architect
8557 Higuera St, Culver City CA 90232, USA
**Moss, Geoffrey** — Cartoonist, Illustrator
315 E 68th St, New York NY 10065, USA
**Moss, J Lester (Les)** — Baseball Player
420 Tullis Ave, Longwood FL 32750, USA
**Moss, Kate** — Model
Colegrave House, 70 Berners St, London W1T 3NL, England
**Moss, P Buckley** — Artist
1 Popular Grove Lane, Mathews VA 23109, USA
**Moss, Paige** — Actress
Open Entertainment, 1051. N Cole Ave, #B, Los Angeles CA 90038, USA
**Moss, Perry** — Golfer
5660 S Lakeshore Dr, #505, Shreveport LA 71119, USA
**Moss, Perry L** — Football Player, Coach
420 Caddie Dr, Debary FL 32713, USA
**Moss, Perry V** — Basketball Player
165 Columbia Dr, Amherst MA 01002, USA
**Moss, Randy G** — Football Player
5030 Champion Blvd, #G6, Boca Raton FL 33496, USA
**Moss, Ronald M (Ronn)** — Actor, Bassist
Harbour Agency, 135 Forbes St, Woolloomooloo NSW 2011, Australia
**Moss, Santana T** — Football Player
7262 SW 123rd Place, Miami FL 33183, USA
**Moss, Shirley** — Sculptor
Moss Studios, PO Box 18104, Anaheim CA 92817, USA
**Moss, Stirling** — Auto Racing Driver
Stirling Moss Ltd, 46 Shephard St, Mayfair, London W1Y 8JN, England
**Moss, Winston N** — Football Player
937 Thornberry Creek Dr, Oneida WI 54155, USA
**Moss, Zefross P** — Football Player
126 Kensington Dr, Madison AL 35758, USA
**Moss-Bachrach, Ebon** — Actor
Innovative Artists, 1505 10th St, Santa Monica CA 90401 USA
**Mossbauer, Rudolf L** — Nobel Physics Laureate
Stumpflingstr 6A, 82031 Grunwald, Germany
**Mosser, Jonell** — Singer
A P A Talent/Literary Agency, 405 S Beverly Dr, #300, Beverly Hills CA 90212 USA
**Mosshart, Alison** — Singer, Guitarist (Kills), Songwriter
Third Man Records, 623 7th Ave S, Nashville TN 37203, USA
**Mossi, Donald L (Don)** — Baseball Player
23250 Canyon Lane, Caldwell ID 83607, USA
**Most, Donny** — Actor
28451 Foothill Dr, Agoura Hills CA 91301, USA
**Mostert, Dutch** — Artist
93696 Mallard Lane, North Bend OR 97459, USA
**Mostow, George D** — Mathematician
300 Audubon Court, New Haven CT 06510, USA
**Mostow, Jonathan** — Director
W M E Entertainment, 9601 Wilshire Blvd, #300, Beverly Hills CA 90210 USA
**Mota, Jose M** — Baseball Player
19058 E La Crosse St, Glendora CA 91741, USA
**Mota, Manuel R (Manny)** — Baseball Player
PO Box 2820, Toluca Lake CA 91610, USA
**Mota, Rosa** — Track Athlete
R Teatro 194 4 Esq, 4100 Porto, Portugal

# M

| | |
|---|---|
| **Mote, Bobby**<br>6510 SW King Lane, Culver OR 97734, USA | Rodeo Rider |
| **Mote, Kelley H**<br>75 Baldwin Ave, Point Lookout NY 11569, USA | Football Player |
| **Mothersbaugh, Mark A**<br>Mutato Muzika, 8760 W Sunset Blvd, West Hollywood CA 90069, USA | Singer, Keyboardist (Devo), Songwriter |
| **Motion, Andrew**<br>University of East Anglia, English Dept, Norwich NR4 7TJ, England | Writer |
| **Motlanthe, Kgalema P**<br>PO Box 61884, Marshalltown 2107, South Africa | President, South Africa |
| **Motley, Darryl D**<br>10800 W 65th St, Shawnee KS 66203, USA | Baseball Player |
| **Mott, Darwin**<br>11 Palenchuk Place, Meadow Lake SK S9X 1H2, Canada | Ice Hockey Player |
| **Mott, Morris K**<br>9 Elmdale Blvd, Brandon MB R7B 1B5, Canada | Ice Hockey Player |
| **Mott, W Stephen (Steve), III**<br>7108 N Highfield Dr, Birmingham AL 35242, USA | Football Player |
| **Mott, William I (Bill)**<br>WinStar Farms, 3301 Pisgah Pike, Versailles KY 40383, USA | Horse Tracing Trainer |
| **Motta, J Richard (Dick)**<br>423 Highway 89, Fish Haven ID 83287, USA | Basketball Coach |
| **Mottau, Mike**<br>57 Herring Weir Road, Duxbury MA 2332, USA | Ice Hockey Player |
| **Mottelson, Ben R**<br>Nordita, Blegdamsvej 17, 2100 Copenhagen 0, Denmark | Nobel Physics Laureate |
| **Mottola, Charles E (Chad)**<br>6479 Lake Pembroke Place, Orlando FL 32829, USA | Baseball Player |
| **Mottola, Greg**<br>United Talent Agency, U T A Plaza, 9336 Civic Center Dr, Beverly Hills CA 90210 USA | Director, Writer |
| **Mottola, Thomas D**<br>Casablanca Records, 8255 W Sunset Blvd, West Hollywood CA 90046, USA | Businessman |
| **Motz, Diana Gribbon**<br>US Appeals Court, 101 W Lombard St, #3625, Baltimore MD 21201, USA | Judge |
| **Mouawad, Jerry**<br>Imago Theater, PO Box 15182, Portland OR 97293, USA | Director |
| **Mouchawar, Alan**<br>1943 Port Trinity Place, Newport Beach CA 92660, USA | Water Polo Player |
| **Mouglalis, Anna**<br>Agents Associes, 201 Rue du Faubourg Saint Honore, 75008 Paris, France | Actress |
| **Moulay Hassan**<br>Royal Palace, Rabat, Morocco | Crown Prince, Morocco |
| **Mould, Robert A (Bob)**<br>Zeitgeist Artist Mgmt, 660 York Ave, #216, San Francisco CA`94110 | Singer, Guitarist, Songwriter |
| **Moulder-Brown, John**<br>Spotlight, 7 Leicester Place, London WC2H 7RJ, England | Actor |
| **Moulds, Eric S**<br>30 Brownstone Court, East Amherst NY 14051, USA | Football Player |
| **Mouli**<br>12 Srinivasa Ave, Chennai TN 600028, India | Actress |
| **Moulton, Sara**<br>Sara Moulton Enterprises, 130 W 24th St, #3B, New York NY 10011, USA | Chef |
| **Moultrie, Arnett N**<br>Philadelphia 76ers, 1st Union Center, 3601 S Broad St, Philadelphia PA 19148 USA | Basketball Player |
| **Mounce, Anthony D (Tony)**<br>237 Cotton Bayou Lane, Kenner LA 70065, USA | Baseball Player |
| **Mounsey, Tara**<br>22 Forge Pond, #B, Canton MA 02021, USA | Ice Hockey Player |
| **Mount, Anson**<br>Creative Artists Agency, 2000 Ave of Stars, #100, Los Angeles CA 90067 USA | Actor |
| **Mount, Richard C (Rick)**<br>904 Hopkins Road, Lebanon IN 46052, USA | Basketball Player |
| **Mountcastle, Vernon B, Jr**<br>6605 Walnutwood Circle, Baltimore MD 21212, USA | Neurophysiologist |
| **Moura, Wagner**<br>United Talent Agency, U T A Plaza, 9336 Civic Center Dr, Beverly Hills CA 90210 USA | Actor, Producer |
| **Mourinho, Jose**<br>F C Inter Milan, Via Durini 24, 20122 Milan, Italy | Soccer Player, Coach |
| **Mourning, Alonzo**<br>3525 Anchorage Way, Miami FL 33133, USA | Basketball Player |
| **Mouskouri, Nana J**<br>Les Visiteurs du Soir, 40 Rue De la Folie Regmault, 75011 Paris, France | Singer, Songwriter |
| **Moussa, Amre M**<br>Arab League, PO Box 11642, Tahrir Square, Cairo, Egypt | Government Official, Egypt |
| **Mouton, James R**<br>4710 Lakeside Meadow Court, Missouri City TX 77459, USA | Baseball Player |
| **Mouton, Lyle J**<br>4101 Auston Way, Palm Harbor FL 34685, USA | Baseball Player |
| **Movsessian-Lamoriello, Victoria (Viki)**<br>17 Webb St, Lexington MA 02420, USA | Ice Hockey Player |
| **Mowat, Farley M**<br>18 King St, Port Hope ON L1A 2R4, Canada | Writer, Naturalist |
| **Mowatt, Ezekial (Zeke)**<br>Mowatt Inc, 194 Passaic St, #2A, Hackensack NJ 07601, USA | Football Player |
| **Mowatt, Judy**<br>Judy M Music, 25 Wellington Dr, Kingston 6, Jamaica | Singer |
| **Mowers, Mark**<br>10 Pollock Dr, Middleton MA 01949, USA | Ice Hockey Player |
| **Mowerson, Robert**<br>2601 Kenzie Terrace, #324, Minneapolis MN 55418, USA | Swimmer |
| **Mowg**<br>W M E Entertainment, 9601 Wilshire Blvd, #300, Beverly Hills CA 90210 USA | Composer |
| **Mowins, Beth**<br>ESPN-TV, ESPN Plaza, 935 Middle St, Bristol CT 06010 USA | Sportscaster |
| **Mowrey, Caitlin**<br>Innovative Artists, 1505 10th St, Santa Monica CA 90401 USA | Actress |

**Mote - Mowrey**

**Mowrey, Dude** — Singer
Joe Taylor Artist Agency, 2802 Columbine Place, Nashville TN 37204 USA
**Mowry, Tahj D** — Actor
Felker Toczak Gellman, 10880 Wilshire Blvd, #2070, Los Angeles CA 90024 USA
**Mowry, Tia** — Actress
Kritzer Levine Wilkins Griffin, 11872 La Grange Ave, #100, Los Angeles CA 90025 USA
**Mowry-Housley, Tamera** — Actress
United Talent Agency, U T A Plaza, 9336 Civic Center Dr, Beverly Hills CA 90210 USA
**Moxey, Jim** — Ice Hockey Player
7 Blue Heron Dr, Orangeville ON L9W 5K6, Canada
**Moxey, John Llewellyn** — Director
Shapiro-Lichtman, 8827 Beverly Blvd, Los Angeles CA 90048 USA
**Moya, Carlos** — Tennis Player
Ave Diagonal 618 3D, 08021 Barcelona, Spain
**Moyer, Jamie** — Baseball Player
5500 34th St W, Badenton FL 34210, USA
**Moyer, Kenneth W (Ken)** — Football Player
3896 Magma Court, Mason OH 45040, USA
**Moyer, Paul S** — Football Player
9411 NE 32nd St, Clyde Hill WA 98004, USA
**Moyer, Stephen** — Actor, Director
United Agents, 12-26 Lexington St, London W1F 0LE, England
**Moyers, Bill D** — Commentator
151 Central Park W, #5N, New York NY 10023, USA
**Moyle, Allan** — Director, Writer
Becsey Wisdom Kalajian, 849 S Wooster St, #7, Los Angeles CA 90035, USA
**Moynahan, Bridget** — Actress, Model
Brillstein Entertainment Partners, 9150 Wilshire Blvd, #350, Beverly Hills CA 90212 USA
**Moynihan, Bobby** — Actor, Comedian
United Talent Agency, U T A Plaza, 9336 Civic Center Dr, Beverly Hills CA 90210 USA
**Moynihan, Christopher (Chris)** — Actor, Producer, Writer
Domain Talent, 9229 W Sunset Blvd, #710, West Hollywood CA 90069 USA
**Moynihan, Colin B** — Government Official, England
Crown Reach, 16 Grosvenor Road, London SW1V 3JV, England
**Moyse, Heather** — Bobsled Athlete
Alberta Bobsled, Niven Center, 140 Canada Olympic Road, Calgary AB T3B 5RS, Canada
**Mozilo, Angelo R** — Financier
Countrywide Credit Industries, 4500 Park Granada, Calabasas CA 91302, USA
**Mr Cheeks** — Rap Artist (Lost Boyz)
Agency Group Ltd, 142 W 57th St, #600, New York NY 10019 USA
**Mraz, Jason** — Singer, Songwriter
Bill Silva Mgmt, 8225 Santa Monica Blvd, West Hollywood CA 90046, USA
**Mrazovich, Chuck** — Basketball Player
7260 W 12th Ave, Hialeah FL 33014, USA
**Mroudjae, Ali** — Prime Minister, Comoros
BP 58, Rond Point Gobadjou, Moroni, Comoros
**Mrozik, Rick** — Ice Hockey Player
2234 Kelly Ave, Cloquet MN 55720, USA
**Mruczkowski, Scott A** — Football Player
10701 Mountview Ave, Cleveland OH 44125, USA
**Msamati, Lucian** — Actor
Diamond Mgmt, 31 Percy St, London W1T 2DD, England
**Mswati III, Makhosetive** — King, Swaziland
Lozitha Palace, PO Box 1, Mbabane, Swaziland
**Muccino, Gabriele** — Director
Creative Artists Agency, 2000 Ave of Stars, #100, Los Angeles CA 90067 USA
**Muckalt, Bill** — Ice Hockey Player
3001 Civic Center Circle NE, Rio Rancho NM 87144, USA
**Mucke, Manuela** — Canoeing Athlete
Charlottenstr 13, 10315 Berlin, Germany
**Muckensturm, Jerry R** — Football Player
4209 Hickory Lane, Jonesboro AR 72401, USA
**Muckler, John** — Ice Hockey Executive, Coach
387 Woods Acres Dr, East Amherst NY 14051, USA
**Mudd, Daniel** — Government Official, Financier
Federal National Mortgage Assn, 3900 Wisconsin Ave NW, Washington DC 20016, USA
**Mudd, Howard E** — Football Player, Coach
15933 Reserve Dr SE, North Bend WA 98045, USA
**Mudd, Roger H** — Commentator
7167 Old Dominion Dr, McLean VA 22101, USA
**Mudge, Jennifer** — Actress
Group Entertainment, 115 W 29th St, #1102, New York NY 10001, USA
**Mudra, Darrell** — Football Coach
424 Tiger Hammock Road, Crawfordville FL 32327, USA
**Muehe, Anna Maria** — Actress
Fitz & Skoglund, Linienstr 130, 10115 Berlin, Germany
**Mueller, Edward** — Businessman
Qwest Communications, 1801 California St, #5200, Denver CO 80202, USA
**Mueller, George E** — Electrical Engineer, Missile Scientist
Kistler Aerospace Corp, 3760 Carillon Point, Kirkland WA 98033, USA
**Mueller, Gerd** — Soccer Player
Neuestr 21, 81479 Munich, Germany
**Mueller, Leah Poulos** — Speed Skater
11455 N Mulberry Dr, Mequon WI 53092, USA
**Mueller, Lisel** — Writer
Louisiana State University Press, PO Box 25053, Baton Rouge LA 70894, USA
**Mueller, Niels** — Director
W M E Entertainment, 9601 Wilshire Blvd, #300, Beverly Hills CA 90210 USA
**Mueller, Vance A** — Football Player
8141 Damico Dr, El Dorado Hills CA 95762, USA
**Mueller, Willard L (Willie)** — Baseball Player
2320 Tolbert Lane, West Bend WI 53090, USA
**Mueller, William R (Bill)** — Baseball Player
570 W Canyon Way, Chandler AZ 85248, USA
**Mueller-Stahl, Armin** — Actor
I C M Partners, 10250 Constellation Blvd, #900, Los Angeles CA 90067 USA

# M

| | |
|---|---|
| **Muench, David** | Photographer |
| PO Box 30500, Santa Barbara CA 93130, USA | |
| **Mugabe, Robert G** | President, Zimbabwe |
| President's Office, Munhumutapa Bldg, Samora Machel Ave, Harare, Zimbabwe | |
| **Mugabi, John** | Boxer |
| PO Box 246, Main Beach, Gold Coast QLD, Australia | |
| **Mughelli, Ovie P** | Football Player |
| 3485 Moye Trail, Duluth GA 30097, USA | |
| **Mugler, Thierry** | Fashion Designer |
| Patrick Alaux, 4 Rue Faubourg Saint Honore, 75008 Paris, France | |
| **Muhammad, Eddie Mustafa** | Boxer |
| 9030 W Sahara Blvd, Las Vegas NV 89117, USA | |
| **Muhammad, Shabazz** | Basketball Player |
| Minnesota Timberwolves, Target Center, 600 1st Ave N, Minneapolis MN 55403 USA | |
| **Muhelsen, Muhammed** | Photojournalist |
| Associated Press, Editorial Dept, 450 W 33rd St, #1500, New York NY 10001 USA | |
| **Muhlbach, Donald L (Don), Jr** | Football Player |
| 711 Pinetree Lane, Lufkin TX 75904, USA | |
| **Muhtadee Billah al-** | Prince Heir Apparent, Brunei |
| Istana Nural Iman, Bandar Seri Begawan 1100, Brunei Darussalam, Brunei | |
| **Muirhead, Oliver** | Actor |
| Don Buchwald, 6500 Wilshire Blvd, #2200, Los Angeles CA 90048 USA | |
| **Mujica, Jose Pepe** | President, Uruguay |
| Chacra El Paso de la Arena, Montevideo, Uruguay | |
| **Mujurawar, Ali Mohammed** | Prime Minister, Republic of Yemen |
| Premier's Office, Street of 26th September, Sana'a, Yemen Arab Republic | |
| **Mukai, Chiaki Naito-** | Astronaut, Japan |
| 100 Cyberonics Blvd, #201, Houston TX 77058, USA | |
| **Mukherjee, Bharati** | Writer |
| 130 Rivoli St, San Francisco CA 94117, USA | |
| **Mukherjee, Pranab K** | President, India |
| President's Office, Bharat Ka, Rashtrapti Bhavan, New Delhi 110004, India | |
| **Mukherjee, Siddhartha** | Writer |
| Charles Scribner's Sons, 866 3rd Ave, New York NY 10022 USA | |
| **Mula, Inva** | Opera Singer |
| Columbia Artists Mgmt Inc, 1790 Broadway, #702, New York NY 10019 USA | |
| **Mulally, Alan R** | Businessman |
| Ford Motor Co, Dearborn Road, Dearborn MI 48121, USA | |
| **Mulari, Tarja** | Speed Skier |
| Motion Oy, Vanhan Mankkaantie 33, 02180 Espoo, Finland | |
| **Mularkey, Michael R (Mike)** | Football Player, Coach |
| 4411 Meadow Club Dr, Suwanee GA 30024, USA | |
| **Mulcahy, Kathleen** | Artist, Sculptor |
| 260 Whittengale Road, Oakdale PA 15071, USA | |
| **Mulcahy, Russell** | Director |
| A P A Talent/Literary Agency, 405 S Beverly Dr, #300, Beverly Hills CA 90212 USA | |
| **Muldaur, Diana** | Actress |
| 20 Cummings Way, Edgartown MA 02539, USA | |
| **Muldaur, Geoff** | Singer, Guitarist |
| Nancy Fly Agency, PO Box 90306, Austin TX 78709, USA | |
| **Muldaur, Maria** | Singer, Songwriter |
| Prime Time Entertainment, 2388 Research Dr, Livermore CA 94550, USA | |
| **Mulder, Karen** | Model |
| Metropolitan Modeling Agency, 5 Union Square W, #500, New York NY 10003, USA | |
| **Mulder, Mark** | Baseball Player |
| 10295 E Cholla St, Scottsdale AZ 85260, USA | |
| **Muldoon, Patrick** | Actor, Model |
| Eclectic Pictures, 7119 Sunset Blvd, #375, Los Angeles CA 90046, USA | |
| **Muldoon, Paul B** | Writer |
| Princeton University, Creative Writing Progam, Princeton NJ 08544, USA | |
| **Muldowney, Dominic J** | Composer |
| Carlin Music, 3 Bridge Approach, Chalk Farm, London NW1 8BD, England | |
| **Muldowney, Shirley** | Auto Racing Driver |
| 47803 Forbes St, Chesterfield MI 48047, USA | |
| **Mulgrew, Kate** | Actress |
| Innovative Artists, 1505 10th St, Santa Monica CA 90401 USA | |
| **Mulhern, Matt** | Actor |
| Don Buchwald, 6500 Wilshire Blvd, #2200, Los Angeles CA 90048 USA | |
| **Mulhern, Richard** | Ice Hockey Player |
| 397 Walpole Ave, Beaconsfield QC H9W 2G6, Canada | |
| **Mulhern, Ryan** | Ice Hockey Player |
| 42 Faculty Circle, Kingston RI 02881, USA | |
| **Mulhern, Sinead** | Opera Singer |
| Guy Barzilay Artists, 420 W 25th St, #4F, New York NY 10001, USA | |
| **Mulholland, John F** | Army General |
| Army Special Operations Command, 2929 Desert Storm Dr, Fort Bragg NC 28310, USA | |
| **Mulholland, Terence J (Terry)** | Baseball Player |
| 11655 N 18th Place, Phoenix AZ 85020, USA | |
| **Mulitalo, Edwin M** | Football Player |
| 12587 Moonlite Hill Court, Herriman UT 84096, USA | |
| **Mulkerin, Ted** | Writer |
| Creative Artists Agency, 2000 Ave of Stars, #100, Los Angeles CA 90067 USA | |
| **Mulkey, Chris** | Actor |
| Don Buchwald, 6500 Wilshire Blvd, #2200, Los Angeles CA 90048 USA | |
| **Mulkey-Robertson, Kim** | Basketball Player, Coach |
| Baylor University, Athletic Dept, Waco TX 76798, USA | |
| **Mull, Carter** | Photographer |
| Marc Foxx Gallery, 6150 Wilshire Blvd, #5, Los Angeles CA 90048, USA | |
| **Mull, Martin** | Actor |
| Anonymous Content, 3532 Hayden Ave, Culver City CA 90232 USA | |
| **Mullady, Thomas S (Tom)** | Football Player |
| 2855 Crooked Oak Dr, Germantown TN 38138, USA | |
| **Mullally, Megan** | Actress, Singer |
| United Talent Agency, U T A Plaza, 9336 Civic Center Dr, Beverly Hills CA 90210 USA | |
| **Mullan, Carrie** | Actress |
| United Agents, 12-26 Lexington St, London W1F 0LE, England | |

Muench - Mullan

**Mullan, Peter** — Actor, Director
Markham Froggatt Irwin, Julian House, 4 Windmill St, London W1P 1HF, England

**Mullane, Richard M (Mike)** — Astronaut
1301 Las Lomas Road NE, Albuquerque NM 87106, USA

**Mullaney, Mark A** — Football Player
17448 Frondell Court, Eden Prairie MN 55347, USA

**Mullavey, Greg** — Actor
31 Tiemann Place, #48, New York NY 10027, USA

**Mullen, Brian** — Ice Hockey Player
124 Berkeley Circle, Basking Ridge NJ 07920, USA

**Mullen, Joseph P (Joey)** — Ice Hockey Player
36 Friends Lane, South Dennis MA 02660, USA

**Mullen, Larry, Jr** — Drummer (U-2)
Principle Mgmt, 30-32 Sir John Rogerson Quay, Dublin 2, Ireland

**Mullen, M David** — Cinematographer
3930 Wade St, Los Angeles CA 90066, USA

**Mullen, Michael G (Mike)** — Navy Admiral
Chairman, Joint Chiefs of Staff, Pentagon, Washington DC 20318 USA

**Mullen, Nicole C** — Singer, Songwriter
Creative Artists Agency, 2000 Ave of Stars, #100, Los Angeles CA 90067 USA

**Mullen, Scott** — Baseball Player
73 Walling Grove Road, Beaufort SC 29907, USA

**Mullen, Thomas** — Writer
I C M Partners, 10250 Constellation Blvd, #900, Los Angeles CA 90067 USA

**Mullens, Byron J (B J)** — Basketball Player
Charlotte Bobcats, 333 E Trade St, #A, Charlotte NC 28202 USA

**Muller, Egon** — Motorcycle Racing Rider
Dorfstr 17, 24247 Rodenbek/Kiel, Germany

**Muller, Gerd** — Soccer Player
Heinrich-Vogel-Str 10A, 81479 Munich, Germany

**Muller, Ina** — Singer, Actress
105 Music, Hopfensack 20, 20457 Hamburg, Germany

**Muller, Jorg** — Auto Racing Driver
Insert Motorsport, Fassoldshof 1, 95336 Mainleus, Germany

**Muller, K Alex** — Nobel Physics Laureate
Haldenstr 54, 8909 Hedingen, Switzerland

**Muller, Kirk** — Ice Hockey Player, Coach
Calgary Flames, PO Box 1540, Station M, Calgary AB T2P 3B9, Canada

**Muller, Lillian** — Model, Actress
PO Box 20029-414, Encino CA 91416, USA

**Muller, Michel** — Actor
Artmedia, 20 Ave Rapp, 75007 Paris, France

**Muller, Peter** — Alpine Skier
Haldenstr 18, 8134 Adliswil, Switzerland

**Muller, Richard S** — Electrical, Microbiotics Engineer
University of California, Sensor/Actuator Center, Berkeley CA 94720, USA

**Muller-Brachmann, Hanno** — Opera Singer
Kunstler Sekretariat am Gasteig, Rosenheimer Str 52, 81669 Munich, Germany

**Muller-Schott, Daniel** — Concert Violist
Konzertdirektion Schmid, Konigstra 36, 30175 Hannover, Germany

**Muller-Westernhagen, Marius** — Singer, Actor
Motor Entertainment, Brunnenstr 24, 10119 Berlin, Germany

**Mulligan, Brian** — Opera Singer
I M G Artists, Hogarth Business Park, Chiswick, London W4 2TH, England

**Mulligan, Carey H** — Actress
Julian Belfrage Assoc, 9 Argyll St, #300, London W1F 7TG, England

**Mulligan, Deanna M** — Businesswoman
Guardian Life Insurance, 7 Hanover Square, New York NY 10004, USA

**Mulligan, Gerry** — Writer
3 Arts Entertainment, 9460 Wilshire Blvd, #700, Beverly Hills CA 90212 USA

**Mulligan, Richard C** — Molecular Biologist, Geneticist
Children's Hospital, Genetics Dept, 320 Longwood Ave, Boston MA 02115, USA

**Mulligan, Sean P** — Baseball Player
24474 Eastgate Dr, Diamond Bar CA 91765, USA

**Mulligan, Wayne E** — Football Player
2410 The Haul Over, Johns Island SC 29455, USA

**Mulliken, William (Bill)** — Swimmer
4216 N Keeler Ave, Chicago IL 60641, USA

**Mullin, Christopher P (Chris)** — Basketball Player
116 Laurelwood Dr, Danville CA 94506, USA

**Mullin, Reed D** — Drummer (Corrosion of Conformity)
Chipster, 100 Village Square Crossing, Palm Beach Gardens FL 33410 USA

**Mulliniks, S Rance** — Baseball Player
2614 S Peppertree St, Visalia CA 93277, USA

**Mullins, Aimee** — Model, Athlete
Authentic Talent/Literary Mgmt, 45 Main St, #1004, Brooklyn NY 11201, USA

**Mullins, Gerald B (Gerry)** — Football Player
PO Box 523, Saxonburg PA 16056, USA

**Mullins, Gregory E (Greg)** — Baseball Player
PO Box 443, Florahome FL 32140, USA

**Mullins, Jeffrey V (Jeff)** — Basketball Player, Coach
8866 N Sea Oaks Way, #202, Vero Beach FL 32963, USA

**Mullins, Melinda** — Actress
Access Talent Voice Overs, 171 Madison Ave, #910, New York NY 0016, USA

**Mullins, Shawn** — Singer, Songwriter
Russell Carter Artist Mgmt, 567 Ralph Mcgill Blvd NE, Atlanta GA 30312, USA

**Mullis, Kary B** — Nobel Chemistry Laureate
2743 Hillview Dr, Newport Beach CA 92660, USA

**Mullova, Viktoria Y** — Concert Violinist
Kunstler Sekretariat am Gasteig, Rosenheimer Str 52, 81669 Munich, Germany

**Mulloy, Gardner P** — Tennis Player
800 NW 9th Ave, Miami FL 33136, USA

**Muloin, Wayne** — Ice Hockey Player
2991 Hayes St, Avon OH 44011, USA

**Mulroney, Dermot** — Actor
W M E Entertainment, 9601 Wilshire Blvd, #300, Beverly Hills CA 90210 USA

**Mulroney, Kieran** — Actor, Writer
Management 360, 9111 Wilshire Blvd, Beverly Hills CA 90210 USA
**Mulroney, M Brian** — Prime Minister, Canada
47 Forden Crescent, Westmount QC H3Y 2Y5, Canada
**Mulrooney, Richard** — Soccer Player
Houston Dynamo, 1415 Louisiana, #3400, Houston TX 77002 USA
**Mulva, James J** — Businessman
ConocoPhillips Inc, 600 N Daisy Ashford, Houston TX 77079, USA
**Mulvey, Callan** — Actor
Creative Artists Agency, 2000 Ave of Stars, #100, Los Angeles CA 90067 USA
**Mulvey, Grant** — Ice Hockey Player
70 E Scott St, #706, Chicago IL 60610, USA
**Mulvey, Kevin** — Baseball Player
24 Eric Court, Parlin NJ 08859, USA
**Mulvey, Paul** — Ice Hockey Player
8009 Oak Hollow Lane, Fairfax Station VA 22039, USA
**Mulvihill, Robert** — Basketball Player
53 Pike Dr, #1C, Wayne NJ 07470, USA
**Mumba, Samantha** — Singer, Actress
Helter Skelter, 347-353 Chiswick High Road, London W4 4HS, England
**Mumford, Eloise** — Actress
Paradigm Agency, 360 N Crescent Dr, North Building, Beverly Hills CA 90210 USA
**Mumley, Nicholas (Nick)** — Football Player
1432 Audubon Dr, Columbus IN 47203, USA
**Mumphrey, Jerry W** — Baseball Player
7709 FM 850, Tyler TX 75705, USA
**Mumy, Billy** — Actor
PO Box 433, 11333 Moorpark St, North Hollywood CA 91603, USA
**Munchak, Michael A (Mike)** — Football Player, Coach
9155 Saddlebow Dr, Brentwood TN 37027, USA
**Muncrief, Kevin** — Golfer
939 S Flood Ave, Norman OK 73069, USA
**Mundae, Misty** — Actress
El Independent Cinema, PO Box 132, Butler NJ 07405, USA
**Mundell, Robert A** — Nobel Economics Laureate
35 Claremont Ave, New York NY 10027, USA
**Mundy, Carl E, Jr** — Marine Corps General
9308 Ludgate Dr, Alexandria VA 22309, USA
**Mundy, Chris** — Producer, Writer
United Talent Agency, U T A Plaza, 9336 Civic Center Dr, Beverly Hills CA 90210 USA
**Mundy, John H** — Historian
29 Claremont Ave, New York NY 10027, USA
**Mungle, Matthew W** — Make-Up Artist
Milton Agency, 6715 Hollywood Blvd, #206, Los Angeles CA 90028, USA
**Muni, Craig** — Ice Hockey Player
9291 Via Cimato Dr, Clarence Center NY 14032, USA
**Munitz, Barry** — Foundation Executive
J Paul Getty Trust, 1200 Getty Center Dr, #400, Los Angeles CA 90049, USA
**Muniz, Armando** — Boxer
6657 45th St, Riverside CA 92509, USA
**Muniz, Frankie** — Actor
Paradigm Agency, 360 N Crescent Dr, North Building, Beverly Hills CA 90210 USA
**Muniz, Vik** — Photographer
169 Bond St, Brooklyn NY 11217, USA
**Munk, Walter H** — Geophysicist
9530 La Jolla Shores Dr, La Jolla CA 92037, USA
**Munn, Allison** — Actress
Innovative Artists, 1505 10th St, Santa Monica CA 90401 USA
**Munninghoff, Scott A** — Baseball Player
866 Laverty Lane, Cincinnati OH 45230, USA
**Munns, Allen G** — Navy Admiral
Commander, Submarine Command Atlantic, 7958 Blandy Road, Norfolk VA 23511 USA
**Munoz, J Oscar** — Baseball Player
14161 Leaning Pine Dr, Hialeah FL 33014, USA
**Munoz, M Anthony** — Football Player, Sportscaster
7575 Rockeby Court, Cincinnati OH 45241, USA
**Munoz, Michael A (Mike)** — Baseball Player
1000 Carroll Meadows Court, Southlake TX 76092, USA
**Munoz, Ricardo J (Ricky)** — Singer, Accordian Player (Intocable)
Serca Music, 2020 W Houston Ave, McAllen TX 78501, USA
**Munoz, Roberto (Bobby)** — Baseball Player
9040 NW 20th St, Pembroke Pines FL 33024, USA
**Munro, Alice A** — Nobel Literature Laureate
PO Box 1133, Clinton ON N0M 1L0, Canada
**Munro, Caroline** — Actress
Jim Thompson Mgmt, Herricks, School Lane, West Sussex BN18 9DR, England
**Munro, Lochlyn** — Actor, Producer
Characters Talent Mgmt, 8 Elm St, Toronto ON M5G 1G7, Canada
**Munro, Peter D** — Baseball Player
4311 Westmoreland St, Little Neck NY 11363, USA
**Munroe, Odessa** — Actress
Carrier Talent Mgmt, 1080 Howe St, #705, Vancouver BC V6Z 2T1, Canada
**Munsel, Patrice** — Opera Singer
PO Box 472, Schroon Lake NY 12870, USA
**Munson, Eric W** — Baseball Player
2640 Becker Court, Dubuque IA 52001, USA
**Munson, John** — Bassist (Semisonic)
Monterey Peninsula Artists, 404 W Franklin St, Monterey CA 93940 USA
**Munter, Leilani** — Auto Racing Driver, Social Activist
PO Box 3355, Mooresville NC 38117, USA
**Munter, Scott** — Baseball Player
13024 Jessie Ave, Omaha NE 68164, USA
**Muntyan, Mikhail** — Opera Singer
16 N Iorga Str, #13, 277012 Chisnau, Moldova
**Mura, Stephen A (Steve)** — Baseball Player
31892 Old Oak Road, Trabuco Canyon CA 92679, USA

| | |
|---|---|
| **Murad, Ferid** | Nobel Medicine Laureate |
| 3409 Wilson Blvd, Arlington VA 22201, USA | |
| **Murakami, Haruki** | Writer |
| I C M Partners, 730 5th Ave, New York NY 10019 USA | |
| **Murakami, Masanori** | Baseball Player |
| 1-4-15-1506 Nisho Ohi Shinagawaku, Tokyo 140 0015, Japan | |
| **Murakami, Ryu** | Writer |
| Kodansha Books, 2-12-21 Otowa, Bunkyoku, Tokyo 112 8001, Japan | |
| **Murakami, Takashi** | Artist |
| Management 360, 9111 Wilshire Blvd, Beverly Hills CA 90210 USA | |
| **Murat, Bernard** | Actor, Director |
| Artmedia, 20 Ave Rapp, 75007 Paris, France | |
| **Murat, Stephanie** | Actress, Director, Writer |
| Artmedia, 20 Ave Rapp, 75007 Paris, France | |
| **Murayama, Makio** | Biochemist |
| 304 Midsummer Dr, Gaithersburg MD 20878, USA | |
| **Murayama, Tomiichi** | Prime Minister, Japan |
| 3-2-2 Chiyomachi, Oita, Oita 870, Japan | |
| **Murch, Walter** | Editor, Sound Effects Editor |
| Mirisch Agency, 8840 Wilshire Blvd, #100, Beverly Hills CA 90211 USA | |
| **Murchison, Ira** | Track Athlete |
| 10113 S Sangamon St, Chicago IL 60643, USA | |
| **Murciano, Enrique** | Actor |
| Untitled Entertainment, 350 S Beverly Dr, #200, Beverly Hills CA 90212 USA | |
| **Murcutt, Glenn** | Pritzker Architectural Laureate |
| Neeson Murcutt Architects, 71 York St, #500, Sydney NSW 2000, Australia | |
| **Murdoch, Don** | Ice Hockey Player |
| Hockey in the Rockies School, PO Box 383, Cranbrook BC V1C 4H9, Canada | |
| **Murdoch, K Rupert** | Publisher |
| News America Publishing, 1211 Ave of Americas, #500, New York NY 10036, USA | |
| **Murdoch, Robert (Bob)** | Ice Hockey Player |
| 410 11th Ave S, Cranbrook BC V1C 2P9, Canada | |
| **Murdoch, Robert J (Bob)** | Ice Hockey Player, Coach |
| 1330 Angelo Dr, Beverly Hills CA 90210, USA | |
| **Murdoch, Stuart L** | Singer, Songwriter (Belle & Sebastian) |
| Ground Control Touring, 20 Jay St, #826, Brooklyn NY 11201 USA | |
| **Murdoch, William W** | Population Ecologist |
| University of California, Ecology Evolution Marine Biology Dept, Santa Barbara CA 93106, USA | |
| **Murdock, David H** | Businessman |
| 10900 Wilshire Blvd, #1600, Los Angeles CA 90024, USA | |
| **Murdock, George P** | Anthropologist |
| 107 E Wynnewood Road, Wynnewood PA 19096, USA | |
| **Murdock, Shirley** | Singer |
| PO Box 26249, Dayton OH 45426, USA | |
| **Muresan, Gheorghe** | Basketball Player, Actor |
| 12250 Glen Road, Potomac MD 20854, USA | |
| **Muresan, Lucian Cardinal** | Religious Leader |
| Archdiocese, Fagaras & Alba Iulia, Str Petro Pavel Aron 2, 515 400 Blaj AB, Romania | |
| **Muriel, Xavier** | Drummer (Buckcherry) |
| 10th Street Mgmt, 700 N San Vicente Blvd, #G410, West Hollywood CA 90069, USA | |
| **Murino, Caterina** | Actress |
| Soli Assoc, Viale Dei Parioli 44, 00197 Rome, Italy | |
| **Muris, Timothy J** | Government Official |
| George Mason University, Law School, Fairfax VA 22030, USA | |
| **Murkoff, Heidi** | Writer |
| What To Expect Foundation, 211 W 80th St, Lower Level, New York, NY 10024, USA | |
| **Murley, Matt** | Ice Hockey Player |
| 32 Hialeah Dr, Troy NY 12182, USA | |
| **Muro, J Michael** | Cinematographer |
| Gersh Agency, 9465 Wilshire Blvd, #600, Beverly Hills CA 90212 USA | |
| **Murofushi, Koji A** | Track Athlete |
| World Athletics Mgmt, Untersperr 4A, 4644 Scharnstein, Austria | |
| **Murphey, Christopher** | Producer, Writer |
| Rothman Brecher Agency, 920 Wilshire Blvd, #PH, Beverly Hills CA 90212, USA | |
| **Murphey, Michael Martin** | Singer, Songwriter |
| Artra Artists, 130 S Canal St, #211, Chicago IL 60606, USA | |
| **Murphy, Ben** | Actor |
| 2690 Rambla Pacifico St, Malibu CA 90265, USA | |
| **Murphy, Bob** | Golfer |
| 12005 Dunes Road, Boynton Beach FL 33436, USA | |
| **Murphy, Calvin J** | Basketball Player, Executive |
| 8218 Cliffshire Court, Houston TX 77083, USA | |
| **Murphy, Carolyn** | Model, Actress |
| W M E Entertainment, 9601 Wilshire Blvd, #300, Beverly Hills CA 90210 USA | |
| **Murphy, Caryle M** | Journalist |
| Washington Post, Editorial Dept, 1150 15th St NW, Washington DC 20071, USA | |
| **Murphy, Charles S** | Government Official |
| 100 Bluff View Dr, #503C, Belleair Bluffs FL 33770, USA | |
| **Murphy, Charlie Q** | Actor, Comedian |
| I C M Partners, 10250 Constellation Blvd, #900, Los Angeles CA 90067 USA | |
| **Murphy, Cillian** | Actor |
| Lisa Richards Agency, 108 Upper Leeson St, Dublin 4, Ireland | |
| **Murphy, Dale B** | Baseball Player |
| 467 Aspen Ridge Lane, Alpine UT 84004, USA | |
| **Murphy, Daniel F (Danny)** | Baseball Player |
| 5030 Champion Blvd, #6226, Boca Raton FL 33496, USA | |
| **Murphy, Daniel T** | Baseball Player |
| 2878 Dickie Court, Jacksonville FL 32216, USA | |
| **Murphy, David Lee** | Singer |
| D Mgmt, PO Box 121682, Nashville TN 37212, USA | |
| **Murphy, David M** | Baseball Player |
| 3708 Sunrise Ranch Road, Southlake TX 76092, USA | |
| **Murphy, Diana E** | Judge |
| US Court of Appeals, 300 S 4th St, #11E, Minneapolis MN 55415, USA | |
| **Murphy, Donald** | Actor |
| PO Box 904, Ranchester WY 82839, USA | |

**M**

Murad - Murphy

**Murphy, Donald R (Donnie)** — Baseball Player
10211 Willow Bend Circle, #18, Charlotte NC 28210, USA

**Murphy, Donna** — Actress, Singer, Dancer
Brookside Artists Mgmt, 250 W 57th St, #2303, New York NY 10107, USA

**Murphy, Dwayne K** — Baseball Player
1811 S Karen Dr, Chandler AZ 85286, USA

**Murphy, Eddie** — Actor, Comedian
Eddie Murphy Productions, 9601 Wilshire Blvd, #300, Beverly Hills CA 90210, USA

**Murphy, Erin** — Actress
Commercial Talent, 9255 Sunset Blvd, #505, West Hollywood CA 90069, USA

**Murphy, Glenn** — Businessman
Gap Inc, 2 Folsom St, San Francisco CA 94105, USA

**Murphy, Gord** — Ice Hockey Player
10041 Cartgate Court, Dublin OH 43017, USA

**Murphy, Joe** — Ice Hockey Player
10292 Horton Road, Goodrich MI 48438, USA

**Murphy, Jonathan** — Actor
Innovative Artists, 1505 10th St, Santa Monica CA 90401 USA

**Murphy, Kevin** — Producer, Writer
W M E Entertainment, 9601 Wilshire Blvd, #300, Beverly Hills CA 90210 USA

**Murphy, Kim** — Journalist
Los Angeles Times, Editorial Dept, 202 W 1st St, Los Angeles CA 90012 USA

**Murphy, Lawrence T (Larry)** — Ice Hockey Player
1167 Connaught Dr, Ennismore ON K0L 1T0, Canada

**Murphy, Mark H** — Football Player
935 N Broadway, DePere WI 54115, USA

**Murphy, Mark H** — Singer
Janlyn Public Relations, 106 Cabrini Blvd, #4-I, New York NY 10033, USA

**Murphy, Mark S** — Football Player
3699 Myersville Road, Uniontown OH 44685, USA

**Murphy, Michael** — Actor
Paul Kohner, 9300 Wilshire Blvd, #555, Beverly Hills CA 90212 USA

**Murphy, Michael R** — Judge
US Court of Appeals, Federal Building, 125 S State St, Salt Lake City UT 84138, USA

**Murphy, Mike** — Ice Hockey Player, Coach
National Hockey League, 50 Bay St, #1100, Toronto ON M5J 2X8, Canada

**Murphy, Nate** — Paleontologist
Judith River Dinosaur Institute, PO Box 51177, Billings MT 59105, USA

**Murphy, Nick** — Director, Producer, Writer
Independent Talent Group, 40 Whitfield St, London W1T 2RH, England

**Murphy, Peter J** — Singer (Bauhaus)
C E C Mgmt, 520 E Ave, New York NY 10018, USA

**Murphy, Reg** — Editor, Publisher
National Geographic Society, 1145 17th St NW, Washington DC 20036, USA

**Murphy, Rob** — Ice Hockey Player
Hockey Stall, 35 Mika St, Stittsville ON K2S 1K8, Canada

**Murphy, Robert A (Rob)** — Baseball Player
44 S Sewalls Point Road, Stuart FL 34996, USA

**Murphy, Ron** — Ice Hockey Player
1 Valley Road, Nanticoke ON N0H 1L0, Canada

**Murphy, Ronald T (Ronnie)** — Basketball Player
14800 Hanover Pike, Upperco MD 21155, USA

**Murphy, Rosemary** — Actress
Don Buchwald, 6500 Wilshire Blvd, #2200, Los Angeles CA 90048 USA

**Murphy, Ryan** — Director, Producer, Writer
Creative Artists Agency, 2000 Ave of Stars, #100, Los Angeles CA 90067 USA

**Murphy, Sean P** — Golfer
1004 June Place, Lovington NM 88260, USA

**Murphy, Thomas (Tom)** — Writer
4 Garville Road, Dublin 6, County Dublin, Ireland

**Murphy, Thomas A (Tom)** — Baseball Player
26561 Via Sacramento, Capistrano Beach CA 92624, USA

**Murphy, Thomas F (Tommy)** — Baseball Player
1824 Dunsford Road, Jacksonville FL 32207, USA

**Murphy, Thomas S** — Businessman
Capital Cities/ABC, 77 W 66th St, New York NY 10023, USA

**Murphy, Tod J** — Basketball Player
23 Parsons Hill Road, Wenham MA 01984, USA

**Murphy, Troy B** — Basketball Player
Dallas Mavericks, Pavilion, 2909 Taylor St, Dallas TX 75226 USA

**Murphy, William E (Billy)** — Baseball Player
5309 66th Ave Court W, University Place WA 98467, USA

**Murphy, William P, Jr** — Inventor (Disposable Metal Trays)
25 SW 24th Road, Miami FL 33129, USA

**Murphy-O'Connor, Cormac Cardinal** — Religious Leader
Archbishop's House, Ambrosden Ave, London SW1P 1QJ, England

**Murray, Andrew (Andy)** — Tennis Player
Ace Group, 13 Harwood Road, London NW6 4QP, England

**Murray, Andy** — Ice Hockey Coach
5765 232nd St W, Faribault MN 55021, USA

**Murray, Ann** — Opera Singer
Augstein & Hahn, Tal 28, 80331 Munich, Germany

**Murray, Anne** — Singer
Box 69030, 12 Sainte Claire Ave E, Toronto, ON M4T 1KO, Canada

**Murray, Bill** — Actor, Comedian
Ziffren Brittenham Branca, 1801 Century Park W, #700, Los Angeles CA 90067 USA

**Murray, Brian** — Actor
Paradigm Agency, 360 Park Ave S, #1600, New York NY 10010 USA

**Murray, Brian Doyle** — Actor
Abrams Artists, 9200 W Sunset Blvd, #1125, West Hollywood CA 90069 USA

**Murray, Bryan C** — Ice Hockey Coach, Executive
2215 NE 32nd Ave, Fort Lauderdale FL 33305, USA

**Murray, Calvin D** — Baseball Player
17434 Courtney Pine Circle, Spring TX 77379, USA

**Murray, Chad Michael** — Actor, Model
Brillstein Entertainment Partners, 9150 Wilshire Blvd, #350, Beverly Hills CA 90212 USA

**Murray, Cherry A** — Physicist
Lucent Technologies, 700 Mountain Ave, New Providence NJ 07974, USA
**Murray, Chris** — Chemist
I B M Watson Research Center, PO Box 218, Yorktown Heights NY 10598 USA
**Murray, Dale A** — Baseball Player
5695 FM 2718, Yorktown TX 78164, USA
**Murray, Dave** — Guitarist (Iron Maiden)
Sanctuary Music Mgmt, 82 Bishop's Bridge Road, London W2 6BB, England
**Murray, David K** — Jazz Saxophonist, Orchestra Leader
Joel Chriss Co, 300 Mercer St, #3J, New York NY 10003 USA
**Murray, Devon** — Actor
PO Box 814, Maynooth, County Kildare, Ireland
**Murray, Don** — Actor
1201 La Patera Canyon Road, Goleta CA 93117, USA
**Murray, Doug** — Cartoonist ('Nam)
Marvel Comic Group, 10 E 40th St, #900, New York NY 10016, USA
**Murray, Eddie C** — Baseball Player
15609 Bronco Dr, Canyon Country CA 91387, USA
**Murray, Edward P (Eddie)** — Football Player
1070 Forest Bay Dr, Waterford MI 48328, USA
**Murray, Glen** — Ice Hockey Player
1320 10th St, Manhattan Beach CA 90266, USA
**Murray, Hannah** — Actress
Troika, 74 Clerkenwell Road, #300, London EC1M 5QA, England
**Murray, Iain** — Yachtsman
International Management Group, 75490 Fairway Dr, Indian Wells CA 92210, USA
**Murray, James D** — Biologist
University of Washington, Applied Mathematics Dept, PO Box 352420, Seattle WA 98195, USA
**Murray, Jennifer** — Aviatrix, Explorer
Polar First, Onslow Gardens, #2, London SW7 3LX, England
**Murray, Jim** — Ice Hockey Player
37 Viceroy Crescent, Brandon MB R7B 3R7, Canada
**Murray, Joel** — Actor
Abrams Artists, 9200 W Sunset Blvd, #1125, West Hollywood CA 90069 USA
**Murray, Jonathan** — Producer, Director, Writer
Bunim/Murray Productions, 6007 Sepulveda Blvd, Van Nuys CA 91411, USA
**Murray, Keith** — Rap Artist
Green Light Talent Agency, PO Box 3172, Beverly Hills CA 90212 USA
**Murray, Larry** — Baseball Player
3200 Round Hill Dr, Hayward CA 94542, USA
**Murray, Peg** — Actress
800 Light House Road, Southold NY 11971, USA
**Murray, Randy** — Ice Hockey Player
Royal Lepage Foothills, 50-805 5th Ave SW, Calgary AB T2P 0N6, Canada
**Murray, Rob** — Ice Hockey Player
Providence Bruins, 1 La Salle Square, Providence RI 02903, USA
**Murray, Robert (Bob)** — Ice Hockey Player, Executive
Anaheim Ducks, 2695 E Katella Ave, Anaheim CA 92806 USA
**Murray, Ronald (Flip)** — Basketball Player
Atlanta Hawks, Centennial Tower, 101 Marietta St NW, #1900, Atlanta GA 30303 USA
**Murray, Sean** — Actor
Unified Mgmt, 4231 National Ave, Burbank CA 91505, USA
**Murray, Stuart** — Architect
Stuart Murray Assoc, 144 High St, North Sydney NSW 2060, Australia
**Murray, Terence R (Terry)** — Ice Hockey Player, Coach
11 Kirkwood Road, Scarborough ME 04074, USA
**Murray, Terrence (Terry)** — Financier
Fleet Boston Corp, PO Box 55850, Boston MA 02205, USA
**Murray, Tracy L** — Basketball Player
2419 Tour Edition Dr, Henderson NV 89074, USA
**Murray, Troy** — Ice Hockey Player
Chicago Blackhawks, United Center, 1901 W Madison St, Chicago IL 60612, USA
**Murray, Ty** — Rodeo Rider
1660 Private Road 1213, Stephenville TX 76401, USA
**Murray-Leslie, Alex** — Singer (Chicks in Speed)
K Records, 924 Jefferson St SE, #101, Olympia WA 98501, USA
**Murrell, Adrian** — Football Player
17236 Green Dolphin Lane, Cornelius NC 28031, USA
**Murrett, Robert B** — Navy Admiral
National Geospatial Intelligence Agency, 7500 Geoint Dr, Springfield VA 22150 USA
**Murrey, Dorie S** — Basketball Player
230 NE 178th St, Shoreline WA 98155, USA
**Murro, Noam** — Director, Producer
Management 360, 9111 Wilshire Blvd, Beverly Hills CA 90210 USA
**Murtagh, Kate** — Actress
5104 Greenbush Ave, Sherman Oaks CA 91423, USA
**Murton, Matthew H (Matt)** — Baseball Player
2304 Silver Palm Dr, #302, Kissimmee FL 34747, USA
**Murzyn, Dana** — Ice Hockey Player
41 Sunset Way SE, Calgary AB T2X 3H6, Canada
**Musabayev, Talgat A** — Cosmonaut
Cosmonaut Training Center, Star City, 141160 Zvezdny Gorodok, Moscow Oblast, Russia
**Musante, Tony** — Actor
Fifi Oscard Agency, 110 W 40th St, #1600, New York NY 10018, USA
**Musburger, Brent W** — Sportscaster
286 Locha Dr, Jupiter FL 33458, USA
**Muse, Arizona** — Model, Actress
Next Model Mgmt, 23 Watts St, New York NY 10013 USA
**Muser, Anthony J (Tony)** — Baseball Player, Manager
1122 Martha Ann Dr, Los Alamitos CA 90720, USA
**Museveni, Yoweri K** — President, Uganda; Army General
President's Office, PO Box 7108, Kampala, Uganda
**Musgrave, F Story** — Astronaut
8572 Sweetwater Trail, Kissimmee FL 34747, USA
**Musgrave, Mandy** — Actress
Talent Works, 3500 W Olive Ave, #1400, Burbank CA 91505 USA

**M**

Murray - Musgrave

**M**

| | |
|---|---|
| **Musgrave, R Kenton** <br> US Court of International Trade, 1 Federal Plaza, New York NY 10278, USA | Judge |
| **Musgrave, Ted** <br> Ultra Motorsports, 22 Raceway Dr, Mooresville NC 28115, USA | Auto, Truck Racing Driver |
| **Musgrave, Thea** <br> Novello Co, 8/9 Firth St, London W1V 5TZ, England | Composer, Conductor |
| **Musgrave, William S (Bill)** <br> 4062 Leprechan Way, Duluth GA 30097, USA | Football Player |
| **Musil, Frantisek (Frank)** <br> Edmonton Oilers, 11230 110th St, Edmonton AB T5G 3H7, Canada | Ice Hockey Player |
| **Musiol, Bogdan** <br> Fitness-Studio, Talstr 50, 98544 Zella-Mehlis, Germany | Bobsled Athlete |
| **Musiq** <br> Island/Def Soul Records, 825 8th Ave, #2700, New York NY 10019, USA | Singer |
| **Musk, Elon** <br> SpaceX, 1 Rocket Road, Hawthorne CA 90250, USA | Businessman |
| **Musker, John** <br> Creative Artists Agency, 2000 Ave of Stars, #100, Los Angeles CA 90067 USA | Animator, Director, Writer |
| **Musselman, Jeffrey J (Jeff)** <br> 1842 Port Tiffin Place, Newport Beach CA 92660, USA | Baseball Player |
| **Musselwhite, Charlie** <br> Rosebud Agency, PO Box 170429, San Francisco CA 94117 USA | Singer, Harmonica Player, Guitarist |
| **Mussenden, Isis** <br> Messina Baker Entertainment, 955 Carrillo Dr, #100, Los Angeles CA 90048 USA | Costume Designer |
| **Mussina, Michael C (Mike)** <br> 737 White Church Road, Muncy PA 17756, USA | Baseball Player |
| **Musso, Mitchel T** <br> Principato-Young, 9465 Wilshire Blvd, #880, Beverly Hills CA 90212 USA | Actor |
| **Mustafaa, Najee** <br> 4265 Jailette Road, Atlanta GA 30349, USA | Football Player |
| **Mustaine, David S (Dave)** <br> E S P Mgmt, 838 N Doheny Dr, #302, West Hollywood CA 90069, USA | Guitarist (Metallica, Megadeth) |
| **Mustard, Chad A** <br> 6329 S 171st St, Omaha NE 68135, USA | Football Player |
| **Muster, Brad W** <br> 2017 Stony Oak Court, Santa Rosa CA 95403, USA | Football Player |
| **Muster, Thomas** <br> 370 Felter Ave, Hewlett NY 11557, USA | Tennis Player |
| **Mustin, Henry C** <br> 2347 S Rolfe St, Arlington VA 22202, USA | Navy Admiral |
| **Mustonen, Olli** <br> Hazard Chase, 25 City Road, Cambridge CB1 1DP, England | Concert Pianist, Conductor, Composer |
| **Mutchnick, Max** <br> W M E Entertainment, 9601 Wilshire Blvd, #300, Beverly Hills CA 90210, USA | Producer |
| **Mutebi II, Ronald Muwenda** <br> Mengo Palace, PO Box 58, Kampala, Uganda | King, Uganda |
| **Muth, Rene** <br> Pennsylvania State University, Athletic Dept, University Park PA 16802, USA | Basketball Coach |
| **Muti, Ornella** <br> Union Italy S R L, Piazzle di Porta Pia 116, 00198 Rome, Italy | Actress |
| **Muti, Riccardo** <br> Via Corti Alle Mura 25, 48100 Ravenna, Italy | Conductor |
| **Mutombo, Dikembe** <br> 4787 Northside Dr NW, Atlanta GA 30327, USA | Basketball Player |
| **Mutscheller, James F (Jim)** <br> 12350 Rosslare Ridge Road, #102, Lutherville Timonium MD 21093, USA | Football Player |
| **Mutter, Anne-Sophie** <br> Ebersberger Str 10, 81679 Munich, Germany | Concert Violinist |
| **Muxworthy, Jake** <br> Innovative Artists, 1505 10th St, Santa Monica CA 90401 USA | Actor |
| **Muzzatti, Jason** <br> 4581 Dunmorrow Dr, Okemos MI 48864, USA | Ice Hockey Player |
| **Mwampembwa, Godfrey (Gado)** <br> Sasa Serna Productions, PO Box 13956, Nairobi, Kenya | Editorial Cartoonist |
| **Mya** <br> Media Artists Group, 8222 Melrose Ave, #203, Los Angeles CA 90048 USA | Singer, Actress, Songwriter |
| **Myasnikovich, Mikhail U** <br> Prime Minister's Office, Karl Marx Str 38, 220016 Minsk, Belarus | Prime Minister, Belarus |
| **Myers, Barton** <br> 949 Toro Canyon Road, Santa Barbara CA 93108, USA | Architect |
| **Myers, Billie** <br> R J O Artist Relations & Mgmt, H S B C Bank, 101 W 14th St, New York NY 10011, USA | Singer, Actress |
| **Myers, Brett A** <br> 385 Summerset Dr, Saint Johns FL 32259, USA | Baseball Player |
| **Myers, Chris** <br> Fox-TV, Sports Dept, 205 W 67th St, New York NY 10065 USA | Sportscaster |
| **Myers, Dale D** <br> Dale Myers Assoc, 7835 Rush Rose Dr, #214, Carlsbad CA 92009, USA | Space Engineer |
| **Myers, Danny** <br> Childress Racing, PO Box 1189, Industrial Dr, Welcome NC 27374, USA | Auto Racing Driver |
| **Myers, Gregory J (Greg)** <br> 2915 S Deframe Way, Lakewood CO 80228, USA | Football Player |
| **Myers, Gregory R (Greg)** <br> 7917 Brasado Way, Riverside CA 92508, USA | Baseball Player |
| **Myers, Jack D** <br> 14 Prout Road, Freeport ME 04032, USA | Physician |
| **Myers, Joel Philip** <br> 151 W Market St, Marietta PA 17547, USA | Glass Artist |
| **Myers, John M (Jack)** <br> 25 Biltmore Lane, Menlo Park CA 94025, USA | Football Player |
| **Myers, Lisa** <br> NBC-TV, News Dept, 4001 Nebraska Ave NW, Washington DC 20016 USA | Commentator |
| **Myers, Margaret J (Dee Dee)** <br> Vanity Fair, Conde Nast Publications, 4 Times Square, New York NY 10036, USA | Government Official, Commentator |
| **Myers, Michael** <br> Opera et Concert, 37 Rue de la Chaussee d'Antin, 75009 Paris, France | Opera Singer |

**Musgrave - Myers**

**Myers, Michael S (Mike)**                                    Baseball Player
337 High Ridge Way, Castle Rock CO 80108, USA

**Myers, Mike**                                                Actor, Comedian
W M E Entertainment, 9601 Wilshire Blvd, #300, Beverly Hills CA 90210 USA
**Myers, Norman**                            Environmental Scientist, Conservationist
Upper Meadow, Old Road, Headington, Oxford OX3 8SZ, England
**Myers, Peter E (Pete)**                                      Basketball Player
19W011 13th St, Lombard IL 60148, USA
**Myers, Randall K (Randy)**                                   Baseball Player
15525 NE Caples Road, Brush Prairie WA 98606, USA
**Myers, Richard B (Dick)**                                    Air Force General
Kansas State University, History Dept, Manhattan KS 66506, USA
**Myers, Roderick D**                                          Baseball Player
1816 S 3rd St, Conroe TX 77301, USA
**Myers, Rodney L**                                            Baseball Player
229 E Tanya Road, Phoenix AZ 85086, USA
**Myers, Russell**                                        Cartoonist (Broom Hilda)
Tribune Media Services, 435 N Michigan Ave, #1500, Chicago IL 60611 USA
**Myers, Terry-Jo**                                            Golfer
11592 Timberline Circle, Fort Myers FL 33966, USA
**Myers, Thomas P (Tom)**                                      Football Player
6015 Rapid Creek Court, Kingwood TX 77345, USA
**Myers, Walter Dean**                                         Photographer
Miriam Altshuler Literary Agency, 53 Old Post Road N, Red Hook NY 12571, USA
**Myerson, Bess**                         Beauty Queen, Actress, Consumer Activist
453 7th St, Santa Monica CA 90402, USA
**Myerson, Mike**                                          Guitarist (Heartland)
Country Thunder Records, 1016 17th Ave S, Nashville TN 37212, USA
**Myerson, Roger B**                                    Nobel Economics Laureate
1219 Elmwood Ave, Wilmette IL 60091, USA
**Myers-Tikalsky, Linda**                                      Skier
RR 5 Box 2651, Santa Fe NM 87506, USA
**Myette, Aaron**                                              Baseball Player
14277 101A Ave, Surry BC V0B 2G2, Canada
**Mygind, Peter**                                              Actor
Elmer Dahl Agencies, Kanneworff Overgaard, Square 8B, 5600 Faabourg, Denmark
**Myhre, John**                             Art Director, Production Designer
Sandra Marsh & Associates, 9150 Wilshire Blvd, #220, Beverly Hills CA 90212, USA
**Myhrvold, Nathan**                                           Businessman
Intellectual Ventures, 3150 139th Ave SE, Building 4, Bellevue WA 98005, USA
**Myles, Alannah**                              Singer, Guitarist, Songwriter
Miracle Prestige, 1 Water Lane, Camden Town, London NW1 8N2, England
**Myles, Heather**                                             Singer
Heather Hotline, 5165 Brighton Dr, Riverside CA 92504, USA
**Myles, Sophia**                                              Actress
Gersh Agency, 9465 Wilshire Blvd, #600, Beverly Hills CA 90212 USA
**Mylnikov, Sergei A**                                  Ice Hockey Player
Kuzkin Cup Hockey, Ul Talalikkin VI 28, 109029 Moscow, Russia
**Myre, Philippe (Phil)**                               Ice Hockey Player
39270 Heatherbrook Dr, Farmington Hills MI 48331, USA
**Myrick, Daniel**                                             Director
Media Talent Group, 9200 W Sunset Blvd, #550, West Hollywood CA 90069 USA
**Myrtle, Charles J (Chip), Jr**                               Football Player
7500 E Quincy Ave, #E110, Denver CO 80237, USA
**Myslinski, Thomas J (Tom), Jr**                              Football Player
1762 Dickens Cove, Germantown TN 38139, USA
**Mystikal**                                                   Rap Artist
I C M Partners, 10250 Constellation Blvd, #900, Los Angeles CA 90067 USA

**N**

**Na Yeon Choi** — Golfer
Ladies Pro Golf Assn, 100 International Golf Dr, Daytona Beach FL 32124 USA
**Na, Kevin** — Golfer
Professional Golfer's Assn, PO Box 109601, Palm Beach Gardens FL 33410 USA
**Naacke, Lisa** — Actress
Z B F Agentur, Friedrichstr 39, 10969 Berlin, Germany
**Naber, John P** — Swimmer
PO Box 50107, Pasadena CA 91115, USA
**Nabholz, Christopher W (Chris)** — Baseball Player
1 Cottage Hill W, Pottsville PA 17901, USA
**Nabokov, Evgeni V** — Ice Hockey Player
5763 Poppy Hills Place, San Jose CA 95138, USA
**Nabors, Jim** — Actor, Singer
PO Box 10364, Honolulu HI 96816, USA
**Nachamkin, Boris A** — Basketball Player
350 E 62nd St, #5J, New York NY 10065, USA
**Nachbaur, Donald K (Don)** — Ice Hockey Player
671 Clermont Dr, Richland WA 99352, USA
**Nachmanoff, Jeffrey** — Director, Writer
Creative Artists Agency, 2000 Ave of Stars, #100, Los Angeles CA 90067 USA
**Nachtwey, James** — Photojournalist
First Run/Icarus Films, 32 Court St, #2007, Brooklyn NY 11201, USA
**Nadal, Rafael (Rafa)** — Tennis Player
International Management Group, Via Augusta 200, 08021 Barcelona, Spain
**Nadeau, Gary** — Director
First Wave, 319 E 85th St, #200, New York NY 10028, USA
**Nader, Laura** — Anthropologist
University of California, Anthropology Dept, Kroeber Hall, Berkeley CA 94720, USA
**Nader, Michael** — Actor
Paradigm Agency, 360 N Crescent Dr, North Building, Beverly Hills CA 90210 USA
**Nader, Ralph** — Consumer Activist
1600 20th St NW, Washington DC 20009, USA
**Nadig, Marie-Theres** — Alpine Skier
Haus Olympia, 8897 Flumserberg, Switzerland
**Nadingar, Emmanuel D** — Prime Minister, Chad
Prime Minister's Office, La Primature, Vale Royal, N'Djamena, Chad
**Nady, Xavier C, VI** — Baseball Player
11320 Wild Meadow Place, San Diego CA 92131, USA
**Naess, Leona K** — Singer, Songwriter
Paradigm Agency, 360 Park Ave S, #1600, New York NY 10010 USA
**Nafzger, Carl** — Thoroughbred Racing Trainer
General Delivery, Olton TX 79064, USA
**Nafziger, Dana A** — Football Player
251 El Dorado Way, Pismo Beach CA 93449, USA
**Nagalla, Srinivasa R** — Pediatrician
Oregon Health Science University, 3181 SW Jackson Park Dr, Portland OR 97239 USA
**Nagano, Kent G** — Conductor
Berkeley Symphony Orchestra, 1942 University Ave, #207, Berkeley CA 94704, USA
**Nagel, Sidney R** — Physicist
4913 S Kimbark Ave, Chicago IL 60615, USA
**Nagel, Steven R** — Astronaut
3801 Eagle View Court, Columbia MO 65203, USA
**Nagel, Thomas** — Philosopher
New York University, Law School, 40 Washington Square S, New York NY 10012, USA
**Nagler, R Gern** — Football Player
73595 Agave Lane, Palm Desert CA 92260, USA
**Nagra, Parminder** — Actress
Rights House, Drury House, 34-43 Russell St, London WC2B 5HA, England
**Nagy, Charles H** — Baseball Player
60 Robin Road, Westbury NY 11590, USA
**Nagy, Michael** — Opera Singer
Kunstler Sekretariat am Gasteig, Rosenheimer Str 52, 81669 Munich, Germany
**Nagy, Michael T (Mike)** — Baseball Player
8 Indian Trail, Bronx NY 10465, USA
**Naharin, Ohad** — Choreographer
Batsheva Dance Co, 6 Yechieli St, Tel-Aviv 65149, Israel
**Nahodha, Shamsi Vuai** — Chief Minister, Zanzibar
Chief Minister's Office, PO Box 239, Zanzibar, Tanzania
**Nahon, Chris** — Director
Hansen Jacobson Teller, 450 N Roxbury Dr, #800, Beverly Hills CA 90210, USA
**Nahorodny, William G (Bill)** — Baseball Player
1948 Rainbow Dr, Clearwater FL 33765, USA
**Nahyan, Khalifa bin Zayed Al** — President, United Arab Emirates
Manhal Palace, Abu Dhabi, United Arab Emirates
**Naidu, Ajay** — Actor, Director, Writer
Global Artists Agency, 6253 Hollywood Blvd, #508, Los Angeles CA 90028 USA
**Naidus, Alex** — Bassist (Pains of Being Pure at Heart)
Slumberland Records, PO Box 19029, Oakland CA 94619, USA
**Naifeh, Steven W** — Writer
335 Sumter St SE, Aiken SC 29801, USA
**Nail, David** — Singer
Universal Music Group, 401 Commerce St, #1100, Nashville TN 37219 USA
**Nail, Jimmy** — Actor
Independent Talent Group, 40 Whitfield St, London W1T 2RH, England
**Nailatikau, Epeli** — President, Fiji; Brigadier General
President's Office, Government House, Berkeley Crescent, PO Box 2513, Suva, Viti Levu, Fiji
**Nails, Jamie M** — Football Player
PO Box 667291, Pompano Beach FL 33066, USA
**Naim, Yael** — Singer, Pianist, Songwriter
Partisan Arts, PO Box 5085, Larkspur CA 94977, USA
**Naima** — Model
Ford Models Inc, 111 5th Ave, #900, New York NY 10003 USA
**Naimoli, Vincent** — Baseball Executive
16616 Villalenda de Avila, Tampa FL 33613, USA
**Naipaul, V S** — Nobel Literature Laureate
Gillon Aitken Ltd, 29 Fernshaw Road, London SW10 0TG, England

**Na Yeon Choi - Naipaul**

**Nair, Mira** — Director
Lavin Agency, 222 3rd St, #1130, Cambridge MA 02142, USA
**Nairne, Robert C (Rob)** — Football Player
2611 Colt Road, Rancho Palos Verdes CA 90275, USA
**Naisbitt, John** — Writer
Spittelauer Platz 5A3A, 1090 Vienna, Austria
**Naish, Bronwen** — Concert Double Bass Player
Moelfre, Cwm Pennant, Garndolbenmaen, Gwunedd, North Wales LL5 9AX, Wales
**Najee** — Jazz Saxophonist
Red Entertainment Agency, 505 8th Ave, #1004, New York NY 10018, USA
**Najiib Tun Razak** — Prime Minister, Malaysia
Prime Minister's Office, Jalan Dato Onn, 50502 Kuala Lumpur, Malaysia
**Najimy, Kathy** — Actress
Abrams Artists, 9200 W Sunset Blvd, #1125, West Hollywood CA 90069 USA
**Najita, Tetsuo** — Historian
University of Chicago, History Dept, 1126 E 59th St, Chicago IL 60637, USA
**Nakache, Olivier** — Director
Creative Artists Agency, 2000 Ave of Stars, #100, Los Angeles CA 90067 USA
**Nakajima, Tadashi** — Astronomer
California Institute of Technology, Astronomy Dept, Pasadena CA 91125, USA
**Nakajima, Tsuneyuki (Tommy)** — Golfer
International Management Group, 7-18-18 Roppongi, Minatoku, Tokyo 106 0032 Japan
**Nakama, Keo** — Swimmer
1344 9th Ave, Honolulu HI 96816, USA
**Nakamatsu, Jon** — Concert Pianist
Van Cliburn Foundation, 2525 Ridgmar Blvd, #307, Fort Worth TX 76116, USA
**Nakamura, Kuniwo** — President, Palau
Ta Belau Party, Olbiil Era Kelulau, Koror PW 96940, Palau
**Nakamura, Shuji** — Inventor (Blue & White LED Lasers)
University of California, Engineering College, Santa Barbara CA 93106, USA
**Nakamura, Suzy** — Actress
Innovative Artists, 1505 10th St, Santa Monica CA 90401 USA
**Nakanishi, Koji** — Chemist
560 Riverside Dr, New York NY 10027, USA
**Nakata, Hideo** — Director
I C M Partners, 10250 Constellation Blvd, #900, Los Angeles CA 90067 USA
**Nakata, Hidetoshi** — Soccer Player
A C Parma, Viale Partigiani d'Italia, 43100 Parma, Italy
**Nakatani, Corey** — Thoroughbred Racing Jockey
PO Box 7673, Louisville KY 40257, USA
**Naked, Bif** — Singer, Songwriter
Crazed Mgmt, PO Box 356, Jamison PA 18929, USA
**Nakhirunkanok, Porntip (Bui)** — Beauty Queen
Angels Wings Foundation, 1482 E Valley Road, #428, Montecito CA 93108, USA
**Nalbandian, David** — Tennis Player
Asociacion de Tenis, Avda San Juan 1307, 1148 Buenos Aires, Argentina
**Nalder, Eric C** — Journalist
Seattle Times, Editorial Dept, 1000 Denny Way, Seattle WA 98109 USA
**Nalen, Thomas A (Tom)** — Football Player
4081 Preserve Parkway N, Greenwood Village CO 80121, USA
**Nalick, Anna** — Singer, Songwriter
Boulevard Mgmt, 21731 Ventura Blvd, #300, Woodland Hills CA 91364, USA
**Nalin, David R** — Pharmacologist
100 Luck Hill Road, West Chester PA 19382, USA
**Nall, Benita** — Actress
C E S D, 10635 Santa Monica Blvd, #130, Los Angeles CA 90025 USA
**Nall, N Anita** — Swimmer
PO Box 872505, Tempe AZ 85287, USA
**Nalluri, Bharat** — Director
Independent Talent Group, 40 Whitfield St, London W1T 2RH, England
**Nam Tae-Hee** — Soccer Player
Football Assn, 1-131 Sinmunno, 2-Ga Jongno-Gu, Seoul 110 062, South Korea
**Nama, George A** — Artist, Sculptor
RR 1 Box 72, Montauk NY 11954, USA
**Namaliu, Rabbie L** — Prime Minister, Papua New Guinea
PO Box 6655, National Capital District, Boroko, Papua New Guinea
**Namath, Joseph W (Joe)** — Football Player, Actor
Namanco Productions, 300 E 51st St, #7D, New York NY 10022, USA
**Nambu, Yoichiro** — Nobel Physics Laureate
University of Chicago, Fermi Institute, 5640 S Ellis Ave, Chicago IL 60637, USA
**Nance, John J** — Writer
4512 8th Ave, Tacoma WA 98405, USA
**Nance, Todd** — Drummer (Widespread Panic)
Brown Cat Inc, 400 Foundry St, Athens GA 30601 USA
**Nanne, Louis V (Lou)** — Ice Hockey Player
6982 Tupa Dr, Minneapolis MN 55439, USA
**Nannini, Alessandro** — Auto Racing Driver
Via Massetana Romana 56, 53199 Siena, Italy
**Nannini, Gianna** — Singer, Songwriter
Cose di Musica, Via Plinio 15, 20129 Milan, Italy
**Nantis, Rich** — Ice Hockey Player
9585 Rue Jourdain, Quebec QC G2K 1K5, Canada
**Nanty, Isabelle** — Actress
Voyez Mon Agent, 20 Ave Rapp, 75007 Paris, France
**Nantz, James W (Jim), III** — Sportscaster
CBS-TV, Sports Dept, 51 W 52nd St, New York NY 10019 USA
**Napier, John** — Designer
M L R, Douglas House, 16-18 Douglas St, London SW1P 4PB, England
**Napier, Mark** — Ice Hockey Player, Executive
National Hockey League Alumni Assn, 170 Attwell Dr, #650, Toronto ON M9W 5Z5, Canada
**Napier, Wilfrid F Cardinal** — Religious Leader
Archbishop's House, 154 Gordon Road, Greyville 4023, South Africa
**Napoles, Jose A** — Boxer
Cerrada Tizapan 9-303 Ediciov, Codigo Postel, Mexico City DF 06080 , Mexico
**Napoli, Michael A (Mike)** — Baseball Player
2010 NW 118th Ave, Pembroke Pines FL 33026, USA

**Napolitano, Christopher** — Editor
Playboy, Editor's Office, 680 N Lake Shore Dr, Chicago IL 60611, USA
**Napolitano, Giorgio** — President, Italy
President's Office, Palazzo del Quirinale, Via Nazionale 190, 00184 Rome, Italy
**Napolitano, Janet** — Secretary, Homeland Security
University of California, President's Office, 1111 Franklin St, Oakland CA 9460, USA
**Napolitano, Johnette** — Singer (Concrete Blonde), Songwriter
Agency Group Ltd, 142 W 57th St, #600, New York NY 10019 USA
**Naragon, Harold R (Hal)** — Baseball Player
1521 Hagey Dr, Barberton OH 44203, USA
**Narain, Nicole** — Model, Actress
8033 W Sunset Blvd, #224, West Hollywood CA 90046, USA
**Naranjo, Gerardo** — Director
Creative Artists Agency, 2000 Ave of Stars, #100, Los Angeles CA 90067 USA
**Narayen, Shantanu** — Businessman
Adobe Systems, 345 Park Ave, San Jose CA 95110, USA
**Narcisse, Daniel** — Handball Player
T H W Kiel Handball, Ziegelteich 30, 24103 Kiel, Germany
**Nardelli, Robert L** — Businessman
Chrysler Corp, 100 Chrysler Dr, Auburn Hills MI 48326, USA
**Narducci, Kathrine** — Actress
Greene Assoc, 1901 Ave of Stars, #130, Los Angeles CA 90067 USA
**Narducci, Tim** — Singer, Guitarist (Systematic)
Artist Group International, 9560 Wilshire Blvd, #400, Beverly Hills CA 90212 USA
**Nares, James** — Artist
Paul Kasmin Gallery, 511 W 27th St, New York NY 10001, USA
**Narita, Hiro** — Cinematographer
2262 Magnolia Ave, Petaluma CA 94952, USA
**Narleski, Raymond E (Ray)** — Baseball Player
1183 Chews Landing Road, Clementon NJ 08021, USA
**Narron, Jerry A** — Baseball Player, Manager
106 W Seeboth St, #809, Milwaukee WI 53204, USA
**Naruhito** — Crown Prince, Japan
Imperial Palace, 1-1 Chiyoda, Chiyodaku, Tokyo 100 0001, Japan
**Narvekar, Prabhakar R** — Government Official, Financier
4701 Willard Ave, Chevy Chase MD 20815, USA
**Narveson, Christopher G (Chris)** — Baseball Player
1804 Kenwyck Manor Way, Raleigh NC 27612, USA
**Nasar, Sylvia** — Writer
Columbia University, 2950 Broadway, Front 1, New York NY 10027, USA
**Nascimento, Milton** — Singer, Songwriter
Feinstein Mgmt, 8560 W Sunset Blvd, West Hollywood CA 90069, USA
**Nash Whitaker, Keisha** — Fashion Designer
344 E 59th St, New York NY 10022, USA
**Nash, Charles F (Cotton)** — Basketball, Baseball Player
600 Summershade Circle, Lexington KY 40502, USA
**Nash, David** — Sculptor
Capel Rhiw, Blanau, Ffestiniog, Gwynedd Wales LL41 3NT, Wales
**Nash, Graham W** — Singer, Songwriter
Creative Artists Agency, 2000 Ave of Stars, #100, Los Angeles CA 90067 USA
**Nash, James E (Jim)** — Baseball Player
4383 White Surrey Dr NW, Kennesaw GA 30144, USA
**Nash, Jamia S** — Actress, Singer
Carson-Adler Agency, 250 W 57 St, #2030, New York NY 10107, USA
**Nash, John F, Jr** — Nobel Economics Laureate
Princeton University, Economics Dept, Fine Hall, Princeton NJ 08544, USA
**Nash, Johnny** — Singer, Songwriter
I C M Partners, 730 5th Ave, New York NY 10019 USA
**Nash, Joseph A (Joe)** — Football Player
15 Colgate Road, Wellesley MA 02482, USA
**Nash, Kate** — Singer, Songwriter
High Road Touring, 751 Bridgeway, #200, Sausalito CA 94965 USA
**Nash, Kenny** — Singer
1336 NE 16th Terrace, Fort Lauderdale FL 33304, USA
**Nash, Leigh** — Singer (Sixpence None the Richer)
Nettwerk Mgmt, 1545 Wilcox Ave, #200, Los Angeles CA 90028, USA
**Nash, Niecy** — Actress, Comedienne
Principato-Young, 9465 Wilshire Blvd, #880, Beverly Hills CA 90212 USA
**Nash, Noreen** — Actress
719 N Maple Dr, Beverly Hills CA 90210, USA
**Nash, Rick** — Ice Hockey Player
57 Deerfield Crescent, Brampton ON L6T 1K8, Canada
**Nash, Robert L (Bob)** — Basketball Player
659 Kahiau Loop, Honolulu HI 96821, USA
**Nash, Steven J (Steve)** — Basketball Player
6602 E Indian Bend Road, Paradise Valley AZ 85253, USA
**Nash, Tyson** — Ice Hockey Player
16895 SW 91st Ave, #17, Portland OR 97223, USA
**Naslund, Markus** — Ice Hockey Player
Mike Gillis Assoc, 154 Earl St, Kingston ON K7L 2H2, Canada
**Naslund, Mats T** — Ice Hockey Player
General Delivery, 6963 Pregassona, Switzerland
**Naslund, Ronald A (Ron)** — Ice Hockey Player
2600 Cheyenne Circle, Hopkins MN 55305, USA
**Nasr, Seyyed Hossein** — Theologian
George Washington University, Gelman Library, Washington DC 20052, USA
**Nastase, Ilie** — Tennis Player
Calea Plevnei 14, Bucharest, Hungary
**Natal, Robert M (Bob)** — Baseball Player
3913 Cockrill Dr, McKinney TX 75070, USA
**Natali, Vincenzo** — Director, Writer
Creative Artists Agency, 2000 Ave of Stars, #100, Los Angeles CA 90067 USA
**Natalicio, Diana S** — Educator
University of Texas, President's Office, El Paso TX 79968, USA
**Natalie** — Dancer, Choreographer, Singer
Supreme Entertainment Artists, PO Box 15601, Boston MA 02215, USA

**Natanson, Agathe** — Actress
Artmedia, 20 Ave Rapp, 75007 Paris, France
**Nater, Swen E** — Basketball Player
4125 248th Court SE, Issaquah WA 98029, USA
**Nathan, David G** — Physician
Dana-Farber Cancer Institute, 44 Binney St, Boston MA 02115, USA
**Nathan, Joseph A** — Businessman
Compuware Corp, 1 Campus Martius, Detroit MI 48226, USA
**Nathan, Joseph M (Joe)** — Baseball Player
19066 Vogel Farm Road, Eden Prairie MN 55347, USA
**Nathan, Sellapan Ramanathan (S R)** — President, Singapore
President's Office, Orchard Road, Istana, 238823 Singapore, Singapore
**Nathan, Tony C** — Football Player, Coach
15110 Dunbarton Place, Hialeah FL 33016, USA
**Nathaniel (Popp), Bishop** — Religious Leader
Romanian Orthodox Episcopate, 2522 Grey Tower Road, Jackson MI 49201, USA
**Nathanson, Jeff** — Director, Producer, Writer
United Talent Agency, U T A Plaza, 9336 Civic Center Dr, Beverly Hills CA 90210 USA
**Nathanson, Matt** — Singer, Songwriter
Zeitgeist Artist Mgmt, 660 York St, #216, San Francisco CA 94110, USA
**Nathman, John B** — Navy Admiral
Commander, Fleet Forces Command, 1562 Mitscher Ave, Norfolk VA 23551 USA
**Natonski, Richard F** — Marine Corps General
Commander, Marine Forces Command, 1468 Ingram St, Norfolk VA 23511 USA
**Natori, Josie C** — Fashion Designer
Natori Co, 40 E 34th St, New York NY 10016, USA
**Natsuki, Shizuko** — Writer
2-6-1 Ooile, Mini-amiku, Fukuokashi 815 0073, Japan
**Natt, Calvin L** — Basketball Player
25201 E Indore Dr, Aurora CO 80016, USA
**Natter, Robert J** — Navy Admiral
Robert J Natter Assoc, 507 Rutile Dr, Porte Vedre FL 32082, USA
**Nattiel, Ricky R** — Football Player
835 NW 119th St, Gainesville FL 32606, USA
**Nattress, Eric J (Ric)** — Ice Hockey Player
Stoney Creek Warriors, 467 Charlton Ave E, Hamilton ON L8W 2Z9, Canada
**Naughton, David** — Actor
14955 Dickens St, #208, Sherman Oaks CA 91403, USA
**Naughton, James** — Actor, Singer
Paradigm Agency, 360 N Crescent Dr, North Building, Beverly Hills CA 90210 USA
**Naughton, Naturi** — Singer (3LW), Actress
Innovative Artists, 1505 10th St, Santa Monica CA 90401 USA
**Naulls, William D (Willie)** — Basketball Player
511 S Carondelet St, #403, Los Angeles CA 90057, USA
**Nault, Marie-Eve** — Soccer Player
Canadian Soccer, Place Soccer Canada, 237 Metcalfe St, Ottawa ON K2P 1R2, Canada
**Nauman, Bruce L** — Sculptor, Artist
HC 75, Box 82, Galisteo NM 87540, USA
**Nause, Martha** — Golfer
13206 Patterson Trail, Minocqua WI 54548, USA
**Nauta, Katie** — Actress, Singer, Model
L A Talent, 7700 Sunset Blvd, Los Angeles CA 90046 USA
**Nava, Gregory** — Director
I C M Partners, 10250 Constellation Blvd, #900, Los Angeles CA 90067 USA
**Nava, Michael** — Writer
California Supreme Court, 350 McAllister St, San Francisco CA 94102, USA
**Navarrete, Ximena** — Beauty Queen, Model
Miss Universe Organization, 1370 Ave of Americas, #1600, New York NY 10019 USA
**Navarro Cintron, Jaime** — Baseball Player
8100 Oak Park Road, Orlando FL 32819, USA
**Navarro Vivas, Dioner F** — Baseball Player
13243 Pike Lake Dr, Riverview FL 33579, USA
**Navarro, Carlos** — Boxer
1722 W 59th Place, Los Angeles CA 90047, USA
**Navarro, David M (Dave)** — Guitarist, Pianist (Jane's Addiction)
Universal Media Artists, 8222 Melrose Ave, #203, Los Angeles CA 90048, USA
**Navarro, Guillermo J** — Cinematographer
Mirada, 4235 Redwood Ave, Los Angeles CA 90066, USA
**Navarro, Juan Carlos** — Basketball Player
19545 S Ashglen Circle, Collierville TN 38107, USA
**Navies, Hannibal C** — Football Player
2354 Gallard St, Lawrenceville GA 30043, USA
**Navka, Tatiana A** — Ice Dancer
Skating Federation, Luchnesksaia Nab 8, 119871 Moscow, Russia
**Navon, Itzhak** — President, Israel
39 Jabotinsky St, Jerusalem, Israel
**Navratilova, Martina** — Tennis Player
Women's Tennis Assn, 1 Progress Plaza, #1500, Saint Petersburg FL 33701 USA
**Naylor, Gloria** — Writer
One Way Productions, 638 2nd St, Brooklyn NY 11215, USA
**Naylor, Phyllis Reynolds** — Writer
401 Russell Ave, #713, Gaithersburg MD 20877, USA
**Naymark, Lola** — Actress
Agence Artiste Adequet, 108 Rue Reaumur, 75002 Paris, France
**Nayyar, Kunal** — Actor, Comedian
Innovative Artists, 1505 10th St, Santa Monica CA 90401 USA
**Nazarbayev, Nursultan A** — President, Kazakhstan
President's Office, 11 Beybitshilik St, 473000 Astana, Kazakhstan
**Nazario, Ednita** — Singer, Songwriter
Angelo Medina Enterprises, PO Box 8319, Santyrce PR 00910, USA
**Nazario, Sonia** — Journalist
Los Angeles Times, Editorial Dept, 202 W 1st St, Los Angeles CA 90012 USA
**NdegeOcello, Me'Shell** — Singer, Bassist, Songwriter
Rosebud Agency, PO Box 170429, San Francisco CA 94117 USA
**N'Dour, Youssou** — Singer
International Music Network, 278 Main St, #400, Gloucester MA 01930 USA

**Neagle, Dennis E (Denny), Jr** — Baseball Player
16254 Sandstone Dr, Morrison CO 80465, USA
**Neal, Blaine** — Baseball Player
256 Dowdy Dr, Gibbstown NJ 08027, USA
**Neal, Diane** — Actress
Socially Awkward Productions, 344 Grove St, #117, Jersey City NJ 07302, USA
**Neal, Dylan** — Actor
Metropolitan Talent Agency, 5405 Wilshire Blvd, #218, Los Angeles CA 90036 USA
**Neal, Elise** — Actress
A P A Talent/Literary Agency, 405 S Beverly Dr, #300, Beverly Hills CA 90212 USA
**Neal, Fred (Curly)** — Basketball Player
1639 Tiverton St, Winter Springs FL 32708, USA
**Neal, Lloyd** — Basketball Player
905 NE Mariners Loop, Portland OR 97211, USA
**Neal, Lorenzo L** — Football Player
10520 Waterbury Dr, Stockton CA 95209, USA
**Neal, Richard I** — Marine Corps General
Military Officers Assn, 201 N Washington St, Alexandria VA 22314, USA
**Neal, Stephen M (Steve)** — Football Player
126 Fales Road, North Attleboro MA 02760, USA
**Neal, T Daniel (Dan)** — Football Player
711 Homestead Blvd, Louisville KY 40207, USA
**Neale, Harry** — Ice Hockey Coach
224 Quail Hollow Lane, East Amherst NY 14051, USA
**Nealon, Kevin** — Actor, Comedian
Gersh Agency, 41 Madison Ave, #3301, New York NY 10010 USA
**Nealy, Eddie C (Ed)** — Basketball Player
702 Lightstone Dr, San Antonio TX 78258, USA
**Neame, Christopher** — Actor
Brady Brannon Rich, 5670 Wilshire Blvd, #820, Los Angeles CA 90036 USA
**Neame, Gareth** — Producer
Carnival Film & Television, 55 New Oxford St, London WC1A 1BS, England
**Near, Holly** — Singer, Songwriter, Actress
PO Box 236, Ukiah CA 95482, USA
**Neary, Martin G J** — Concert Organist, Conductor
71 Clancarty Road, Fulham, London SW6 3BB, England
**Neaton, Patrick (Pat)** — Ice Hockey Player
3519 Olde Dominion Dr, #2, Brighton MI 48114, USA
**Neblett, Carol** — Opera Singer
Sardos Artists, 180 W End Ave, New York NY 10023, USA
**Nebout, Claire** — Actress
Artmedia, 20 Ave Rapp, 75007 Paris, France
**Necas, Petr** — Prime Minister, Czech Republic
Premier's Office, Nabrezi Edvarda Benese 4, 11801 Prague 1, Czech Republic
**Necciai, Ronald A (Ron)** — Baseball Player
6261 Overlook Lane, Belle Vernon PA 15012, USA
**Nece, Ryan C** — Football Player
4401 W Kennedy Blvd, #300, Tampa FL 33609, USA
**Nechita, Alexandra** — Artist
Wentworth Gallery, 1118 NW 159th Dr, Miami FL 33169, USA
**Neckar, Stanislav (Stan)** — Ice Hockey Player
10255 Waterside Oaks Dr, Tampa FL 33647, USA
**Nederlander, James M** — Producer
Nederlander Organization, 1450 Broadway, #2000, New York NY 10018, USA
**Nedjari, Al** — Actor
Grantham-Hazekdune, 5 Blenheim St, London W1S 1LD, England
**Nedney, Joseph T (Joe)** — Football Player
121 Lauren Circle, Scotts Valley CA 95066, USA
**Nedomansky, Vaclav** — Ice Hockey Player
6600 Beachview Dr, #204, Rancho Palos Verdes CA 90275, USA
**Nedovic, Nemanja** — Basketball Player
Golden State Warriors, 1011 Broadway, Oakland CA 94605 USA
**Nedved, Pavel** — Soccer Player
F C Juventus, Corso Galilo Ferraris 32, 10128 Turin, Italy
**Nedved, Petr** — Ice Hockey Player
H C Bili Tygri Liberec, Tipsport Arena, Jeronymova 494/20, 46007 Liberec, Czech Republic
**Nee, Adam** — Actor
Brillstein Entertainment Partners, 9150 Wilshire Blvd, #350, Beverly Hills CA 90212 USA
**Needham, Connie** — Actress
26234 Kingsington Lane, Laguna Hills CA 92653, USA
**Needham, Tracey** — Actress
Stone Manners Salners, 9911 W Pico Blvd, #1400, Los Angeles CA 90035 USA
**Needleman, Herbert L** — Cardiologist, Pharmacologist
Pittsburgh University Medical School, 3811 O'Hara St, Pittsburgh PA 15213, USA
**Needleman, Jacob** — Philosopher
841 Wawona Ave, Oakland CA 94610, USA
**Neel, Troy L** — Baseball Player
PO Box 1582, El Campo TX 77437, USA
**Neely, Bob** — Ice Hockey Player
72 Squire Bakers Lane, Markham ON L3P 3H2, Canada
**Neely, Cam** — Ice Hockey Player, Executive
76 Davison Dr, Lincoln MA 01773, USA
**Neely, Mark E, Jr** — Historian
Oxford University Press, 198 Madison Ave, #800, New York NY 10016, USA
**Neely, Ralph E** — Football Player
6943 Sperry St, Dallas TX 75214, USA
**Neeman, Calvin A (Cal)** — Baseball Player
93 Champagne Dr, Lake Saint Louis MO 63367, USA
**Neeson, Liam** — Actor
Artist Rights Group, 4 Great Portland St, London W1W 8PA, England
**Nef, John U** — Historian
2726 N St NW, Washington DC 20007, USA
**Nef, Sonja** — Alpine Skier
Halten 345, 9035 Grub, Switzerland
**Neff, Garrett** — Model
Click Model Mgmt, 881 7th Ave, New York NY 10019 USA

| | |
|---|---|
| **Neff, Lucas** | Actor |
| Untitled Entertainment, 350 S Beverly Dr, #200, Beverly Hills CA 90212 USA | |
| **Neff, Steve** | Bowler |
| 3655 S Suncoast Blvd, Homosassa FL 34448, USA | |
| **Negahban, Navid** | Actor |
| House of Representatives, 1434 6th St, #1, Santa Monica CA 90401 USA | |
| **Negay, Notah** | Golfer |
| Professional Golfer's Assn, PO Box 109601, Palm Beach Gardens FL 33410 USA | |
| **Negray, Ronald A (Ron)** | Baseball Player |
| 587 W Nimisila Road, Akron OH 44319, USA | |
| **Negreanu, Daniel** | Poker Player |
| World Poker Tour Enterprises, 5700 Wilshire Blvd, #350, Los Angeles CA 90036 USA | |
| **Negri Sembilan, Yang Di-Pertuan Besar** | Ruler, Malaysia |
| Yang Di-Pertuan Agong's Residence, Serembam, Malaysia | |
| **Negron, Chuck** | Singer (Three Dog Night) |
| J-Bird Entertainment, 248 W Park Ave, #180, Long Beach NY 11561 USA | |
| **Negron, Taylor** | Actor |
| Stone Manners Salners, 9911 W Pico Blvd, #1400, Los Angeles CA 90035 USA | |
| **Negroponte, John D** | Government Official |
| Yale University, International Affairs Dept, New Haven CT 06520, USA | |
| **Negroponte, Nicholas** | Computer Engineer |
| 69 Mount Vernon St, Boston MA 02108, USA | |
| **Nehamas, Alexander** | Philosopher |
| Princeton University, Philosophy Dept, Princeton NJ 08544, USA | |
| **Nehberg, Rudiger** | Explorer, Adventurer |
| Grossenseer Str 1A, 22929 Rausdorf, Germany | |
| **Nehemiah, Renaldo** | Track Athlete, Football Player |
| 15515 Owens Glen Terrace, North Potomac MD 20878, USA | |
| **Neher, Erwin** | Nobel Medicine Laureate |
| Domane 11, 37120 Bovenden, Germany | |
| **Nehmer, Meinhard** | Bobsled Athlete |
| Varnkevitz, 18556 Altenkirchen, Germany | |
| **Nehy, Regine** | Actress |
| Innovative Artists, 1505 10th St, Santa Monica CA 90401 USA | |
| **Neibauer, Gary W** | Baseball Player |
| 146 Delta Ave, Bismarck ND 58504, USA | |
| **Neid, Silvia** | Soccer Player |
| Betramstr 18, 60320 Frankfurt/Main, Germany | |
| **Neidert, John T** | Football Player |
| 4731 Placid Circle, Sarasota FL 34231, USA | |
| **Neidich, Charles** | Conductor, Concert Clarinetist |
| Diane Saldick Mgmt, 225 E 36th St, New York NY 10016, USA | |
| **Neil, Andrew F** | Editor |
| Glenburn Enterprises, PO Box 584, London SW7 3QY, England | |
| **Neil, Dan** | Automobile Critic |
| Los Angeles Times, Editorial Dept, 202 W 1st St, Los Angeles CA 90012 USA | |
| **Neil, Deanna** | Writer, Actress |
| EcoSeekers, PO Box 637, Nyack NY 10960, USA | |
| **Neil, Hildegarde** | Actress |
| Associated International Mgmt, 7 Hatton Garden, #400, London EC1N 8AD, England | |
| **Neil, Vince** | Singer (Motley Crue) |
| Tenth Street Entertainment, 700 San Vicente Blvd, #G410, West Hollywood CA 90069, USA | |
| **Neill, Michael R (Mike)** | Baseball Player |
| 17 Cape May Point, Greensboro NC 27455, USA | |
| **Neill, Noel** | Actress |
| 2295 Belgrade Road, Metropolis IL 62960, USA | |
| **Neill, Sam** | Actor |
| Rights House, Drury House, 34-43 Russell St, London WC2B 5HA, England | |
| **Neils, Steven L (Steve)** | Football Player |
| 1329 Waterford Road, Saint Paul MN 55125, USA | |
| **Neilson, Jim** | Ice Hockey Player |
| 907-525 Sainte Mary Ave, Winnipeg MB R3C 3X3, Canada | |
| **Neilson-Bell, Sandra** | Swimmer |
| 3101 Mistyglen Circle, Austin TX 78746, USA | |
| **Neinas, Charles M (Chuck)** | Football Executive |
| 5344 Westridge Dr, Boulder CO 80301, USA | |
| **Nelligan, Kate** | Actress |
| Innovative Artists, 235 Park Ave S, #1000, New York NY 10003 USA | |
| **Nellis, M Duane** | Educator |
| University of Idaho, President's Office, Administration Building, Moscow ID 83844, USA | |
| **Nellis, William J** | Physicist |
| Lawrence Livermore Laboratory, 7000 East Ave, Livermore CA 94550, USA | |
| **Nelly** | Rap Artist (Saint Lunatics), Actor |
| ItGirl Public Relations, 5225 Wilshire Blvd, #718, Los Angeles CA 90036, USA | |
| **Nelsen, William K (Bill)** | Football Player |
| 13512 Dornoch Dr, Orlando FL 32828, USA | |
| **Nelson, Albert (Al)** | Football Player |
| 660 Boas St, #918, Harrisburg PA 17102, USA | |
| **Nelson, Alvin** | Rodeo Rider |
| 1441 W Beicegel Creek Road, Grassy Butte ND 58634, USA | |
| **Nelson, Azumah** | Boxer |
| Trustworthy Boxing, PO Box 939, Mamprobi, Accra, Ghana | |
| **Nelson, C Shane** | Football Player |
| 115 Knoll Trail, Sandia TX 78383, USA | |
| **Nelson, Cailin** | Astrophysicist |
| Lawrence Livermore Laboratory, 7000 East Ave, Livermore CA 94550, USA | |
| **Nelson, Charles L (Chuck)** | Football Player |
| 3028 162nd Place SE, Mill Creek WA 98012, USA | |
| **Nelson, Colette** | Model, Bodybuilder |
| PO Box 1122, Seaford NY 11783, USA | |
| **Nelson, Craig T** | Actor |
| Paradigm Agency, 360 N Crescent Dr, North Building, Beverly Hills CA 90210 USA | |
| **Nelson, Cynthia (Cindy)** | Alpine Skier |
| PO Box 1699, 0171 Larkspur Lane, Vail CO 81658, USA | |
| **Nelson, Darrin M** | Football Player |
| 9116 1/2 S Manhattan Place, Los Angeles CA 90047, USA | |

**Nelson, David A** — Judge
US Court of Appeals, Courthouse Building, 425 Walnut St, Cincinnati OH 45202, USA
**Nelson, David E (Dave)** — Baseball Player
12213 Clubhouse Dr, Bradenton FL 34202, USA
**Nelson, Deborah** — Journalist
Seattle Times, Editorial Dept, 1000 Denny Way, Seattle WA 98109 USA
**Nelson, Dennis R** — Football Player
612 East St S, Kewanee IL 61443, USA
**Nelson, Diane** — Curling Athlete
Curling Assn, 1660 Vimont Court, Cumberland ON K4A 4J4, Canada
**Nelson, Donald A (Nellie)** — Basketball Player, Coach, Executive
2284 S Kihei Road, Kihei HI 96753, USA
**Nelson, Dorothy W** — Judge
US Court of Appeals, 125 S Grand Ave, Pasadena CA 91105, USA
**Nelson, Edmund C (Ed)** — Football Player
1160 Billings Dr, Pittsburgh PA 15241, USA
**Nelson, Edwin S (Ed)** — Actor
4568 Peeples Road, Oak Ridge NC 27310, USA
**Nelson, George D** — Astronaut
A A A S Project, 1200 New York Ave NW, #100, Washington DC 20005, USA
**Nelson, Jameer** — Basketball Player
Orlando Magic, 8701 Maitland Summit Blvd, Orlando FL 32810 USA
**Nelson, James** — Singer (Celtic Tenors)
PO Box 32, Kells, County Meath, Ireland
**Nelson, James (Jim)** — Editor
Gentlemen's Quarterly, Editor's Office, 350 Madison Ave, New York NY 10017, USA
**Nelson, James E** — Religious Leader
Baha'i Faith, 536 Sheridan Road, Wilmette IL 60091, USA
**Nelson, Jeffrey A (Jeff)** — Baseball Player
8270 Stone Crop Dr, #N, Ellicott City MD 21043, USA
**Nelson, Jennifer Yuh** — Director, Animator
DreamWorks Animation, 1000 Flower St, Glendale CA 91201, USA
**Nelson, John** — Visual Effects Artist
I C M Partners, 10250 Constellation Blvd, #900, Los Angeles CA 90067 USA
**Nelson, John Allen** — Actor
4960 Fulton Ave, Sherman Oaks CA 91423, USA
**Nelson, John R** — Theologian
1111 Hermann Dr, #19A, Houston TX 77004, USA
**Nelson, Joseph G (Joe)** — Baseball Player
2407 Azure Circle, Highland CA 92346, USA
**Nelson, Judd** — Actor
Don Buchwald, 6500 Wilshire Blvd, #2200, Los Angeles CA 90048 USA
**Nelson, Judith** — Opera, Concert Singer
2600 Buena Vista Way, Berkeley CA 94708, USA
**Nelson, Keith E** — Guitarist (Buckcherry), Songwriter
10th Street Mgmt, 700 N San Vicente Blvd, #G410, West Hollywood CA 90069, USA
**Nelson, Larry** — Golfer
421 Oakmont Circle, Marietta GA 30067, USA
**Nelson, Lauren** — Beauty Queen
Miss America Organization, 1370 Ave of Americas, #1600, New York NY 10019 USA
**Nelson, Lee M** — Football Player
23 Lindley Ave NW, Marietta GA 30064, USA
**Nelson, Liza** — Writer
G P Putnam's Sons, 375 Hudson St, New York NY 10014 USA
**Nelson, Marilyn Carlson** — Businesswoman
Carlson Companies, Carlson Parkway, PO Box 59159, Minneapolis MN 55459, USA
**Nelson, Mark** — Actor
Talent Works, 3500 W Olive Ave, #1400, Burbank CA 91505 USA
**Nelson, Melvin F (Mel)** — Baseball Player
27420 Fisher St, Highland CA 92346, USA
**Nelson, Ralph A** — Nutritionist
Carle Foundation Hospital, 611 W Park St, #1, Urbana IL 61801, USA
**Nelson, Ricky L** — Baseball Player
2599 E Desert Broom Place, Chandler AZ 85286, USA
**Nelson, Robert A (Bob)** — Artist
125 Nelson, Lakeside OR 97449, USA
**Nelson, Roger E** — Baseball Player
4113 Limerick Dr, Lake Wales FL 33859, USA
**Nelson, Scott** — Baseball Umpire
800 Sara Dr, Coshocton OH 43812, USA
**Nelson, Sean C** — Singer, Keyboardist (Harvey Danger)
Barsuk Records, PO Box 22546, Seattle WA 98122, USA
**Nelson, Steven L (Steve)** — Football Player, Coach
143 Saddleworth Way, Middleboro MA 02346, USA
**Nelson, Terry L** — Football Player
3393 Highway 51 N, Arkadelphia AR 71923, USA
**Nelson, Tim Blake** — Actor, Director
Gateway Management, 860 Via de la Paz, #F10, Pacific Palisades CA 90272, USA
**Nelson, Todd** — Ice Hockey Player
Atlanta Thrashers, 101 Marietta St NW, #1900, Atlanta GA 30303 USA
**Nelson, Tracy** — Actress
Scott Carlson Entertainment, 5739 Bucknell Ave, Valley Village CA 91607, USA
**Nelson, W Eugene (Gene)** — Baseball Player
12476 Lombardy St, Spring Hill FL 34608, USA
**Nelson, William H (Bill)** — Football Player
PO Box 9235, Pahrump NV 89060, USA
**Nelson, Willie** — Singer, Guitarist, Songwriter
Creative Artists Agency, 2000 Ave of Stars, #100, Los Angeles CA 90067 USA
**Nelson, Yvette** — Actress, Model
International Talent Agency, Beverly Hills Triangle, 9701 Wilshire Blvd, Beverly Hills CA 90212, USA
**Nemchinov, Sergei L** — Ice Hockey Player
53 Walker Ave, Rye NY 10580, USA
**Nemcova, Petra** — Model, Actress
Innovative Artists, 1505 10th St, Santa Monica CA 90401 USA
**Nemec, Corin** — Actor
Abrams Artists, 9200 W Sunset Blvd, #1125, West Hollywood CA 90069 USA

| | |
|---|---|
| **Nemechek, Joseph F (Joe), III** | Auto, Truck Racing Driver |
| 128 S Iredell Industrial Park Road, Mooresville NC 28115, USA | |
| **Nemelka, Richard** | Basketball Player |
| 6108 S 1300 E, Salt Lake City UT 84121, USA | |
| **Nemeth, Miklos** | Prime Minister, Hungary |
| Keszi U 7, 1029 Budapest II, Hungary | |
| **Nemov, Alexei** | Gymnast |
| Gymnastics Federation, Lujnetskaya Nabereynaya 8, 119270 Moscow, Russia | |
| **Nen, Robert A (Robb)** | Baseball Player |
| 8 S View, Trabuco Canyon CA 92679, USA | |
| **Nepomniaschy, Alex** | Cinematographer |
| Innovative Artists, 1505 10th St, Santa Monica CA 90401 USA | |
| **Nerem, Robert M** | Mechanical Engineer |
| 9435 Creekside Trail, Stone Mountain GA 30087, USA | |
| **Neri Vela, Rodolfo** | Astronaut, Mexico |
| Playa Copacabana 131, Col Marte, Mexico City DF 08830, Mexico | |
| **Neri, Francesca** | Actress |
| Blue Train Entertainment, 798 Brooktree Road, Pacific Palisades CA 90272, USA | |
| **Neri, Manuel** | Sculptor |
| Charles Cowes Gallery, 210 11th Ave, #500, New York NY 10001, USA | |
| **Nerlove, Marc L** | Economist |
| University of Maryland, Economics Research Dept, College Park MD 20742, USA | |
| **Nero, Franco** | Actor |
| Muse Mgmt, 1541 Ocean Ave, #200, Santa Monica CA 90401, USA | |
| **Nero, Peter** | Pianist, Conductor |
| 202 Hidden Acres Lane, Media PA 19063, USA | |
| **Nerud, John** | Thoroughbred Racing Executive, Trainer |
| 19 Pound Hollow Road, Glen Head NY 11545, USA | |
| **Nesbitt, Christine** | Speed Skater |
| 13215 66th St NW, #36, Edmonton AB T5C 0B2, Canada | |
| **Nesbitt, James** | Actor |
| Artist Rights Group, 4 Great Portland St, London W1W 8PA, England | |
| **Nesbitt, Mairead** | Fiddler, Violinist (Celtic Woman) |
| W M E Entertainment, 9601 Wilshire Blvd, #300, Beverly Hills CA 90210 USA | |
| **Nesbo, Jo** | Writer |
| R W S G Agency, 1107 1/2 Glendon Ave, Los Angeles CA 90024 | |
| **Nesby, Ann** | Singer |
| Labor Force Mgmt, 1200 Highway 74 S, #103, Peachtree City GA 30269, USA | |
| **Nesher, Avi** | Director, Producer, Writer |
| Gersh Agency, 9465 Wilshire Blvd, #600, Beverly Hills CA 90212 USA | |
| **Nesic, Alex** | Actor |
| Principato-Young, 9465 Wilshire Blvd, #880, Beverly Hills CA 90212 USA | |
| **Nesmith, Michael (Mike)** | Singer, Guitarist (Monkees) |
| Videoranch, 1793 Catalina St, Seaside CA 93955, USA | |
| **Nespoli, Paolo A** | Astronaut, Italy |
| 2011 Dawn Crest Court, Kemah TX 77565, USA | |
| **Nespral, Jackie** | Commentator |
| NBC-TV, News Dept, 30 Rockefeller Plaza, #270E, New York NY 10112 USA | |
| **Ness, Michael J (Mike)** | Singer, Guitarist (Social Distortion) |
| Relentless Artist Mgmt, 1922 Placentia, #A, Costa Mesa CA 92627, USA | |
| **Ness, Rick** | Singer, Guitarist (Fig Dish) |
| Metropolitan Entertainment Group, 2 Penn Plaza, #1500, New York NY 10121, USA | |
| **Nessen, Ronald H (Ron)** | Government Official, Journalist |
| 6409 Walhonding Road, Bethesda MD 20816, USA | |
| **Nessler, Brad** | Sportscaster |
| ABC-TV, Sports Dept, 77 W 66th St, New York NY 10023 USA | |
| **Nesta, Alessandro** | Soccer Player |
| Lazio F C, Via di Santa Cornelia 14, 00060 Formello, Italy | |
| **Nester, Eugene W** | Microbiologist |
| Washington University, Microbiology Dept, Seattle WA 98195, USA | |
| **Nesterenko, Eric** | Ice Hockey Player |
| PO Box 1025, Vail CO 81658, USA | |
| **Nesterenko, Yevgeny Y** | Opera Singer |
| Fruzenskaya Nab 24 Korp 1, #178, 119146 Moscow, Russia | |
| **Nesterovic, Radoslav (Rasho)** | Basketball Player |
| 11 Sanctuary Dr, San Antonio TX 78248, USA | |
| **Nestico, Samuel A (Sammy)** | Composer, Arranger |
| 1731 Blackbird Circle, Carlsbad CA 92011, USA | |
| **Netanyahu, Benjamin** | Prime Minister, Israel |
| Prime Minister's Office, 3 Rehov Kaplan, Jerusalem 91919, Israel | |
| **Netherland, Joseph H** | Businessman |
| F M C Corp, 200 E Randolph Dr, Chicago IL 60601, USA | |
| **Netolicky, Robert (Bob)** | Basketball Player |
| PO Box 531, Carmel IN 46082, USA | |
| **Netravali, Arun N** | Engineer |
| 10 Byron Court, Westfield NJ 07090, USA | |
| **Netrebko, Anna Y** | Opera Singer |
| Centre Stage Artist Mgmt, Stralauer Allee 1, 10245 Berlin, Germany | |
| **Nettles, G Douglas (Doug)** | Football Player |
| 13105 Quail Creek Court, Silver Spring MD 20904, USA | |
| **Nettles, Graig** | Baseball Player |
| 11217 Carmel Creek Road, #2, San Diego CA 92130, USA | |
| **Nettles, James A (Jim)** | Football Player |
| 3817 Mandeville Canyon Road, Los Angeles CA 90049, USA | |
| **Nettles, James W (Jim)** | Baseball Player |
| 4632 N Darien Dr, Tacoma WA 98407, USA | |
| **Nettles, Jennifer** | Singer (Sugarland) |
| Supreme Entertainment Arists, PO Box 15601, Boston MA 02215, USA | |
| **Nettles, John** | Actor |
| Saraband Assoc, 265 Liverpool Road, London N1 1NL, England | |
| **Neu, Michael D (Mike)** | Baseball Player |
| 406 Fraga Court, Martinez CA 94553, USA | |
| **Neufeld, Elizabeth F** | Biochemist |
| University of California Medical School, Biology Dept, Los Angeles CA 90024, USA | |
| **Neufeld, Ray** | Ice Hockey Player |
| Selkirk Steelers, 1011 Manitoba Ave, Selkirk MB R1A 3T7, Canada | |

**Neufeld, Sarah** — Violinist (Arcade Fire)
Billions Corp, 3522 W Armitage Ave, Chicago IL 60647 USA
**Neugebauer, Gerry** — Astrophysicist
California Institute of Technology, Astrophysics Dept, Pasadena CA 91125, USA
**Neugebauer, Marcia** — Physicist
7519 S Elliot Lane, Tucson AZ 85747, USA
**Neugebauer, Nick** — Baseball Player
101 S Sahuaro Dr, Gilbert AZ 85233, USA
**Neuhauser, Duncan V B** — Epidemiologist
PO Box 932, Blue Hill ME 04614, USA
**Neuheisel, Richard (Rick)** — Football Player, Coach
3601 Winding Creek Road, Sacramento CA 95864, USA
**Neumann, Liselotte** — Golfer
11003 Muirfield Dr, Rancho Mirage CA 92270, USA
**Neumann, Randy** — Boxer, Referee
600 E Crescent Ave, #104, Upper Saddle River NJ 7458, USA
**Neumann, Wolfgang** — Opera Singer
Metropolitan Opera Assn, Lincoln Center Plaza, New York NY 10023 USA
**Neumannnova, Katerina** — Cross Country Skier
Svantlova 1803, 39701 Pisek, Czech Republic
**Neumark, Julie** — Actress, Singer, Songwriter
Sterling Artists Mgmt, 11054 Ventura Blvd, #285, Studio City CA 91604, USA
**Neumeier, Daniel G (Dan)** — Baseball Player
N2635 County Road V, Lodi WI 53555, USA
**Neumeier, John** — Choreographer
Hamburg Ballet, 54 Caspar-Voght-Str, 20535 Hamburg, Germany
**Neuner, Magdalena** — Biathlete
Postfach 1354, 82145 Planegg, Germany
**Neuvic, Thierry** — Actor
Artmedia, 20 Ave Rapp, 75007 Paris, France
**Neuwelt, Edward A** — Neurologist
Oregon Health Sciences University, 3181 SW Jackson Park Dr, Portland OR 97201, USA
**Neuwirth, Bebe** — Actress, Dancer, Singer
I C M Partners, 10250 Constellation Blvd, #900, Los Angeles CA 90067 USA
**Nevarez, Alfred** — Singer (All-4-One)
Universal Attractions, 135 W 26th St, #1200, New York NY 10001 USA
**Neveldine, Mark** — Director, Writer
United Talent Agency, U T A Plaza, 9336 Civic Center Dr, Beverly Hills CA 90210 USA
**Neves, Jose Maria P** — Prime Minister, Cape Verde
Prime Minister's Office, Varzea CP 304, Cidade da Praia, Ilha de Santiago, Cape Verde
**Neville, Aaron** — Singer
Elevation Group, 1408 Encinal Ave, #A, Alameda CA 94501, USA
**Neville, Arthel** — Entertainer
1840 Victory Blvd, Glendale CA 91201, USA
**Neville, Bill** — Cartoonist (Tiny Toons)
506 Oakdale Road, Jamestown NC 27282, USA
**Neville, Robert C** — Theologian
Boston University, Theology School, Boston MA 02215, USA
**Neville, Thomas O (Tom), Jr** — Football Player
PO Box 11175, Montgomery AL 36111, USA
**Nevin, Bob** — Ice Hockey Player
61 River Court Blvd, East York ON M4K 3A3, Canada
**Nevin, Brooke** — Actress
Talent Works, 3500 W Olive Ave, #1400, Burbank CA 91505 USA
**Nevin, Phil J** — Baseball Player
18795 Heritage Dr, Poway CA 92064, USA
**Nevins, David** — Producer, Writer
Showtime Networks, 10880 Wilshire Blvd, #1600, Los Angeles CA 90024, USA
**Nevinson, Nancy** — Actress
23 Mill Close, Fishbourne, Chichester, England
**Nevitt, Charles G (Chuck)** — Basketball Player
3124 Cartwright Dr, Raleigh NC 27612, USA
**Newacheck, Kyle** — Actor, Writer, Producer, Director
United Talent Agency, U T A Plaza, 9336 Civic Center Dr, Beverly Hills CA 90210 USA
**Newbern, George** — Actor
Leslie Allan-Rice Mgmt, 1007 Maybrook Dr, Beverly Hills CA 90210, USA
**Newberry, Jeremy D** — Football Player
1225 Almondwood Dr, Antioch VA 94509, USA
**Newberry, Thomas (Tom)** — Football Player
PO Box 9299, Tavernier FL 33070, USA
**Newborn, Ira** — Composer
Vangelos Mgmt, 15233 Ventura Blvd, #200, Sherman Oaks CA 91403 USA
**Newcombe, Donald (Don)** — Baseball Player
1448 Young St, #1108, Honolulu HI 96814, USA
**Newcombe, John D** — Tennis Player
Newcombe's Tennis Ranch, 325 Mission Valley Road, New Braunfels TX 78132, USA
**Newell, Catharine** — Sculptor
Bullseye Gallery, 300 NW 13th Ave, Portland OR 97209, USA
**Newell, Homer E** — Physicist
2567 Nicky Lane, Alexandria VA 22311, USA
**Newell, Mike** — Director, Producer, Actor
50 Canon Entertainment, Oxford House, 76 Oxford St, London W1D 1BS, England
**Newell, Thomas D (Tom)** — Baseball Player
9525 Cordoba Blvd, Sparks NV 89441, USA
**Newfield, Heidi** — Singer, Guitarist (Trick Pony)
McGhee Entertainment, 801 18th Ave S, Nashville TN 37203, USA
**Newfield, Marc A** — Baseball Player
5591 Selkirk Dr, Huntington Beach CA 92649, USA
**Newhart, Bob** — Actor, Comedian
420 Amapola Lane, Los Angeles CA 90077, USA
**Newhouse, Donald E** — Publisher
Advance Publications, 950 W Fingerboard Road, Staten Island NY 10305, USA
**Newhouse, Frederick (Fred)** — Track Athlete
3003 Pine Lake Trail, Houston TX 77068, USA
**Newhouse, Robert F** — Football Player
6847 Truxton Dr, Dallas TX 75231, USA

**Newhouse, Samuel I, Jr** — Publisher
Advance Publications, 950 W Fingerboard Road, Staten Island NY 10305, USA
**Newlin, Michael F (Mike)** — Basketball Player
1414 Horseshoe Dr, Sugar Land TX 77478, USA
**Newman, Alan C (A C)** — Singer (New Pornographers)
Billions Corp, 3522 W Armitage Ave, Chicago IL 60647 USA
**Newman, Albert D (Al)** — Baseball Player
1044 Laroda, Ontario CA 91762, USA
**Newman, Alec** — Actor
Markham Froggatt Irwin, Julian House, 4 Windmill St, London W1P 1HF, England
**Newman, Anthony** — Concert Harpsichordist, Conductor
Gami/Simonds, 42 County Road, Morris CT 06763, USA
**Newman, Barry** — Actor
N2N Entertainment, 1230 Montana Ave, #303, Santa Monica CA 90403 USA
**Newman, Dan** — Ice Hockey Player
192 E County Road 27, RR 1, Cottam ON N0R 1B0, Canada
**Newman, David** — Composer
First Artists Mgmt, 4764 Park Granada, #210, Calabasas CA 91302 USA
**Newman, Edward K (Ed)** — Football Player
10100 SW 140th St, Miami FL 33176, USA
**Newman, Jaime Ray** — Actress
Burstein Co, 15304 W Sunset Blvd, #208, Pacific Palisades CA 90272 USA
**Newman, James** — Actor
Cassell-Levy Talent Agency, 843 N Sycamore Ave, Los Angeles CA 90038, USA
**Newman, James H** — Astronaut
18583 Martinique Dr, Houston TX 77058, USA
**Newman, Jeffrey L (Jeff)** — Baseball Player, Manager
10133 N 103rd St, Scottsdale AZ 85258, USA
**Newman, Jimmy C** — Singer, Songwriter
Joe Taylor Artist Agency, 2802 Columbine Place, Nashville TN 37204 USA
**Newman, Jon O** — Judge
US Court of Appeals, 450 Main St, #218, Hartford CT 06103, USA
**Newman, Josh** — Baseball Player
5909 Canyon Creek Dr, Dublin OH 43016, USA
**Newman, Kevin** — Commentator
ABC-TV, News Dept, 77 W 66th St, New York NY 10023 USA
**Newman, Kyle** — Director, Producer
Fire Thief Films, 15260 Ventura Blvd, #2100, Sherman Oaks CA 91403, USA
**Newman, Laraine** — Actress, Comedienne
Talent Works, 3500 W Olive Ave, #1400, Burbank CA 91505 USA
**Newman, Nanette** — Actress
Seven Pines, Wentworth, Surrey GU25 4QP, England
**Newman, Oscar** — Architect, Urban Planner
Community Design Analysis Institute, 66 Clover Dr, Great Neck NY 11021, USA
**Newman, Pauline** — Judge
US Court of Appeals, 717 Madison Place NW, Washington DC 20439, USA
**Newman, Phyllis** — Actress, Singer
211 Central Park West, #19E, New York NY 10024, USA
**Newman, Randy** — Singer, Pianist, Composer
Cathy Kerr Mgmt, 9079 Nemo St, West Hollywood CA 90069, USA
**Newman, Ryan J** — Auto, Truck Racing Driver
Stewart-Haas Racing, 6001 Haas Way, Kannapolis NC 28081, USA
**Newman, Terence** — Football Player
2817 Park Bridge Court, Dallas TX 75219, USA
**Newman, Thomas M** — Composer
Gorfaine/Schwartz, 4111 W Alameda Ave, #509, Burbank CA 91505 USA
**Newman, Zeb** — Actor
Framework Entertainment, 9057 Nemo St, #C, West Hollywood CA 90069 USA
**Newmar, Julie** — Actress
204 S Carmelina Ave, Los Angeles CA 90049, USA
**Newmark, Craig A** — Businessman
Craigslist, PO Box 225159, San Francisco CA 94122, USA
**Newmark, Dave** — Basketball Player
545 Pierce St, #2301, Albany CA 94706, USA
**Newsom, David** — Actor
Thruline Entertainment, 9250 Wilshire Blvd, #100, Beverly Hills CA 90212 USA
**Newsom, Gavin E** — Mayor, San Francisco
Mayor's Office, 400 S Van Ness Ave, San Francisco CA 94103, USA
**Newsom, Joanna** — Singer, Harpist
Billions Corp, 3522 W Armitage Ave, Chicago IL 60647 USA
**Newsome, Craig** — Football Player
200 Johnson St, Holmen WI 54636, USA
**Newsome, Harry K, Jr** — Football Player
213 Hawthorne Lane, Cheraw SC 29520, USA
**Newsome, Ozzie** — Football Player, Executive
6 Padonia Woods Court, Cockeysville MD 21030, USA
**Newsome, Timothy A (Timmy)** — Football Player
7005 Quartermile Lane, Dallas TX 75248, USA
**Newsome, Vincent K (Vince)** — Football Player
5308 Woodnote Lane, Columbia MD 21044, USA
**Newsome, William R (Billy)** — Football Player
PO Box 2001, Shreveport LA 71166, USA
**Newson, Warren D** — Baseball Player
13232 Padre Ave, Keller TX 76244, USA
**Newsted, Jason** — Bassist (Metallica)
205 Alamo View Place, Walnut Creek CA 94595, USA
**Newton, Becki** — Actress
United Talent Agency, U T A Plaza, 9336 Civic Center Dr, Beverly Hills CA 90210 USA
**Newton, Bill R** — Basketball Player
15 Brixworth Lane, #6, Nashville TN 37205, USA
**Newton, C M** — Basketball Coach, Administrator
524 Currie Way, Birmingham AL 35209, USA
**Newton, Cameron J (Cam)** — Football Player
Carolina Panthers, Ericsson Stadium, 800 S Mint St, Charlotte NC 28202 USA
**Newton, Chris** — Cyclist
National Cycling Centre, Stuart St, Manchester M11 4DQ, England

**Newton, Christopher** — Director
22 Prideaux St, Niagara-on-the-Lake ON L0S 1J0, Canada
**Newton, Juice** — Singer, Guitarist, Songwriter
O J Mgmt, 4321 Reyes Dr, Tarzana CA 91356, USA
**Newton, Matthew** — Actor
Robyn Gardiner Mgmt, 397 Riley St, Surry Hills NSW 2010, Australia
**Newton, Nathaniel (Nate), Jr** — Football Player
1921 White Oak Clearing, Southlake TX 76092, USA
**Newton, Richard Y (Dick), III** — Air Force General
Deputy CofS, Manpower/Personnel, HqUSAF, Pentagon, Washington DC 20330, USA
**Newton, Robert L (Bob)** — Football Player
37701 Hollister Dr, Palm Desert CA 92211, USA
**Newton, Roger** — Medical Researcher
Esperion Therapeutics, 695 K M S Place, 3621 S State St, Ann Arbor MI 48108, USA
**Newton, Thandie** — Actress
Independent Talent Group, 40 Whitfield St, London W1T 2RH, England
**Newton, Thomas R (Tom)** — Football Player
169 Park Road, Rochester NY 14622, USA
**Newton, Wayne** — Singer, Actor
Wayne Newton Mgmt, 6730 S Pecos Road, Las Vegas NV 89120, USA
**Newton-John, Olivia** — Singer, Actress
104 Lighthouse Dr, Jupiter Inlet Colony FL 33469, USA
**Neyelova, Marina M** — Actress
Potapovsky Per 12, 117333 Moscow, Russia
**Neymar** — Soccer Player
Confederacion de Futebol, Rua Victor Civita 66, #1, Rio de Janeiro 22775 044, Brazil
**Ne-Yo** — Rap Artist, Singer, Songwriter
W M E Entertainment, 9601 Wilshire Blvd, #300, Beverly Hills CA 90210 USA
**Nezhat, Camran** — Endocrinologist
Fertility/Endocrinology Center, 5555 Peachtree Dunwoody Road NE, Atlanta GA 30342, USA
**Ngata, E Haloti** — Football Player
Baltimore Ravens, Ravens Stadium, 1 Winning Dr, Baltimore MD 21230 USA
**Nguyen Minh Triet** — President, Vietnam
President's Palace, 1 Hoang Hoa Tham, Hanoi, Vietnam
**Nguyen Tan Dung** — Prime Minister, Vietnam
State Bank of Vietnam, 47-49 Thai To, Hanoi, Vietnam
**Nguyen, Dat T** — Football Player
115 Edge Creek, Boerne TX 78006, USA
**Nguyen, Dustin** — Actor
1051 S Dunsmuir Ave, Los Angeles CA 90019, USA
**Nguyen, Marcel** — Gymnast
PO Box 1307, 82003 Unterhaching, Germany
**Nguyen, Navia** — Model
Don Buchwald, 10 E 44th St, New York NY 10017 USA
**Nhamadjo, Manuel Serifo** — Acting President, Guinea-Bissau
President's Office, Palacio Presidential, Bissau, Guinea-Bissau
**Niblett, Emma (Scout)** — Singer, Songwriter
Puschen, Schleisische Str 38, 10997 Berlin, Germany
**Niccol, Andrew** — Writer, Director, Producer
Creative Artists Agency, 2000 Ave of Stars, #100, Los Angeles CA 90067 USA
**Nichanian, Veronique** — Fashion Designer
Hermes, 24 Rue Faubourg Saint Honore, 75008 Paris, France
**Nichol, Gene R, Jr** — Educator
University of North Carolina, Law School, Chapel Hill NC 27599, USA
**Nichol, Scott B** — Ice Hockey Player
612 Ladyhawk Lane, Victor NY 14564, USA
**Nicholas, Alison** — Golfer
Pat Darby, Badgar Farm House, Badgar near Wolverhampton WV6 7LS, England
**Nicholas, Denise** — Actress
932 S Longwood Ave, Los Angeles CA 90019, USA
**Nicholas, Henry** — Labor Leader
Hospital & Health Care Union, 330 W 42nd St, #1905, New York NY 10036, USA
**Nicholas, J D** — Singer, Guitarist (Commodores)
Management Assoc, 1920 Benson Ave, Saint Paul MN 55116, USA
**Nicholas, Nicholas J, Jr** — Publisher
Pluggers Inc, 1000 SW Broadway, #1850, Portland OR 97205, USA
**Nicholas, Peter M** — Businessman
Boston Scientific Corp, 1 Boston Scientific Place, Natick MA 01760, USA
**Nicholas, Thomas Ian** — Actor
Innovative Artists, 1505 10th St, Santa Monica CA 90401 USA
**Nicholls, Bernie** — Ice Hockey Player
17101 Planters Row, Addison TX 75001, USA
**Nicholls, Craig** — Singer (Vines)
Winterman-Goldstein, 17 Holdsworth St, Newtown NSW 2042, Australia
**Nicholls, David A** — Writer
Curtis Brown Group, 28-29 Haymarket St, #500, London SW1Y 4SP, England
**Nichols, Austin** — Actor
United Talent Agency, U T A Plaza, 9336 Civic Center Dr, Beverly Hills CA 90210 USA
**Nichols, Carl E** — Baseball Player
901 E Artesia Blvd, Compton CA 90221, USA
**Nichols, David C, Jr** — Navy Admiral
Deputy Commander, US Central Command, MacDill Air Force Base, Tampa FL 33621, USA
**Nichols, Dorothy L** — Government Official, Financier
Farm Credit Administration, 1501 Farm Credit Dr, #3600, McLean VA 22102, USA
**Nichols, Gates** — Guitarist (Confederate Railroad)
Bobby Roberts, 3050 Business Park Circle, #303, Goodlettsville TN 37221 USA
**Nichols, Hamilton J, Jr** — Football Player
11015 Kirkmead Dr, Houston TX 77089, USA
**Nichols, Jeff** — Director, Producer, Writer
Creative Artists Agency, 2000 Ave of Stars, #100, Los Angeles CA 90067 USA
**Nichols, Joe** — Singer
Alliance Media Relations, 3805 Rolland Road, Nashville TN 37205, USA
**Nichols, John** — Writer
New Press, 38 Greene St, #400, New York NY 10013, USA
**Nichols, Kenwood C** — Businessman
Champion International Corp, 1 Champion Plaza, Stamford CT 06921, USA

**Nichols, Kyra** — Ballerina
Peter Diggins Assoc, 133 W 71st St, New York NY 10023, USA
**Nichols, Larry** — Rubik Cube Designer
Moleculon Research Corp, 139 Main St, Cambridge MA 02142, USA
**Nichols, Lorrie** — Bowler
1251 Lexington Dr, Algonquin IL 60102, USA
**Nichols, Marisol** — Actress
Paradigm Agency, 360 N Crescent Dr, North Building, Beverly Hills CA 90210 USA
**Nichols, Mark** — Curling Athlete
Curling Assn, 1660 Vimont Court, Cumberland ON K4A 4J4, Canada
**Nichols, Mark S** — Football Player
5905 Penn Station Lane, Bakersfield CA 93311, USA
**Nichols, Michael (Nick)** — Photographer
National Geographic, Editorial Dept, 1145 17th St NW, Washington DC 20036 USA
**Nichols, Mike** — Director, Comedian
Creative Artists Agency, 2000 Ave of Stars, #100, Los Angeles CA 90067 USA
**Nichols, Nichelle** — Actress
23281 Leonora Dr, Woodland Hills CA 91367, USA
**Nichols, Peter R** — Writer
Alan Brodie, 211 Piccadilly, London W1V 9LD, England
**Nichols, Rachel E** — Actress, Model, Producer
Management 360, 9111 Wilshire Blvd, Beverly Hills CA 90210 USA
**Nichols, Rachel M** — Sportscaster
CNN-TV, 190 Marietta Ave SW, Atlanta GA 30303 USA
**Nichols, Robert H (Bobby)** — Golfer
8681 Glenlyon Court, Fort Myers FL 33912, USA
**Nichols, Rodney L (Rod)** — Baseball Player
1570 Elk Trail, Helena MT 59601, USA
**Nichols, Stephen** — Actor
PO Box 82231, Athens GA 30608, USA
**Nichols, T Reid** — Baseball Player
5473 Wild Cherry Circle, Milwaukee WI 53214, USA
**Nicholson, Andrew** — Basketball Player
Orlando Magic, 8701 Maitland Summit Blvd, Orlando FL 32810 USA
**Nicholson, David L (Dave)** — Baseball Player
15316 Lakepoint Dr, Benton IL 62812, USA
**Nicholson, Jack** — Actor
Bresler Kelly Assoc, 11500 W Olympic Blvd, #400, Los Angeles CA 90064 USA
**Nicholson, Julianne** — Actress
Creative Artists Agency, 2000 Ave of Stars, #100, Los Angeles CA 90067 USA
**Nicholson, Scott** — Writer
1888 Bernard Bledsoe Lane, Todd NC 28684, USA
**Nichting, Christopher T (Chris)** — Baseball Player
7151 Gracely Dr, Cincinnati OH 45233, USA
**Nickel, Scott** — Cartoonist (Eek, Team Bob, His & Hers)
Paws Inc, 5440 E County Road 450, Albany IN 47320, USA
**Nickens, Tim** — Journalist
Tampa Bay Times, Editorial Dept, 490 1st Ave S, Saint Petersburg FL 33701, USA
**Nickerson, Donald A, Jr** — Religious Leader
Episcopal Church, 815 2nd Ave, Basement, New York NY 10017, USA
**Nickerson, Hardy O** — Football Player
1820 Melvin Road, Oakland CA 94602, USA
**Nickey, Donnie O** — Football Player
3491 General Hood Trail, Nashville TN 37204, USA
**Nicklaus, Jack W** — Golfer
Golf Podium, Infinity Sports, 5500 Military Trail, #22-294, Jupiter FL 33458, USA
**Nickle, Doug** — Baseball Player
19440 Victoria Court, #R2, Sonoma CA 95476, USA
**Nicks, Carl, Jr** — Football Player
Tampa Bay Buccaneers, 1 W Buccaneer Place, Tampa FL 33607 USA
**Nicks, Hakeem** — Football Player
New York Giants, Meadowlands Stadium, 102 Route 120, East Rutherford NJ 07073 USA
**Nicks, O Carl** — Basketball Player
10200 Yosemite Lane, Indianapolis IN 46234, USA
**Nicks, Regina** — Singer (Regina Regina)
Buddy Lee Attractions, 38 Music Square E, #300, Nashville TN 37203 USA
**Nicks, Stevie** — Singer, Songwriter
3929 E Clarendon Ave, Phoenix AZ 85018, USA
**Nickson, Julia** — Actress
Metropolitan Talent Agency, 5405 Wilshire Blvd, #218, Los Angeles CA 90036 USA
**Nickulas, Eric** — Ice Hockey Player
PO Box 507, West Barnstable MA 2668, USA
**Nicolaou, Kyriacos Costa** — Chemist
Scripps Research Institute, 10550 N Torrey Pines Road, La Jolla CA 92037 USA
**Nicole, Crista** — Model
Playboy Promotions, 2706 Media Center Dr, Los Angeles CA 90065 USA
**Nicole, Jasika** — Actress
Essay Management, 364 W 46th St, New York NY 10036, USA
**Nicole, Jayde** — Model
Playboy Promotions, 2706 Media Center Dr, Los Angeles CA 90065 USA
**Nicole, Kristen** — Model
Playboy Promotions, 2706 Media Center Dr, Los Angeles CA 90065 USA
**Nicolet, Danielle** — Actress
A P A Talent/Literary Agency, 405 S Beverly Dr, #300, Beverly Hills CA 90212 USA
**Nicol-Fox, Helen** — Baseball Player
432 E Cornell Dr, Tempe AZ 85283, USA
**Nicollier, Claude** — Astronaut, Switzerland
20 Leeward Lane, Houston TX 77058, USA
**Nicolodi, Daria** — Actress
Carol Levi Mgmt, Via Giuseppe Pisanelli 2, 00196 Rome, Italy
**Nicolson, Steve** — Actor
Ken McReddie Assoc, 101 Finsbury Pavement, London EC2A 1RS, England
**Nicora, Attilio Cardinal** — Religious Leader
Patrimony of Apostolic See, Palazzo Apostolico, 00120 Vatican City
**Nicosia, Steven R (Steve)** — Baseball Player
190 Northshore Crossing, Dallas GA 30157, USA

Nichols - Nicosia

## N

**Nidetch, Jean** — Businesswoman
Weight Watchers International, 3860 Crenshaw Blvd, Los Angeles CA 90008, USA
**Nie Haisheng** — Taikonaut
Satellite Launch Center, Jiuquan, Guangzhou Province, China
**Nieberg, Lars** — Equestrian
Gestit Waldershausen, 35315 Homberg, Germany
**Nied, David G** — Baseball Player
211 Masters Lane, Midlothian TX 76065, USA
**Niedenfuer, Thomas E (Tom)** — Baseball Player
3933 Losillias Dr, Sarasota FL 34238, USA
**Nieder, William H (Bill)** — Track Athlete
PO Box 310, Mountain Ranch CA 95246, USA
**Niederauer, Duncan** — Financier
N Y S E Euronext, 11 Wall St, New York NY 10005, USA
**Niederhoffer, Victor** — Squash Player
Niederhoffer Cross Zeckhauser, 757 3rd Ave, New York NY 10017, USA
**Niedermayer, Robert W (Rob)** — Ice Hockey Player
49 Belcourt Dr, Newport Beach CA 92660, USA
**Niedermayer, Scott** — Ice Hockey Player
49 Belcourt Dr, Newport Beach CA 92660, USA
**Niedernhuber, Barbara** — Luge Athlete
Schwarzeckstr 58, 83486 Ramsau, Germany
**Niehaus, Leonard (Lennie)** — Composer, Jazz Saxophonist
Soundtrack Music Assoc, 1460 4th St, #308, Santa Monica CA 90401 USA
**Niehoff, Robert T (Rob)** — Football Player
4874 Sandalwood Court, Mason OH 45040, USA
**Niekamp, Jim** — Ice Hockey Player
3511 E Cochise Dr, Phoenix AZ 85028, USA
**Niekro, Lance** — Baseball Player
3822 Cheverly Dr E, Lakeland FL 33813, USA
**Niekro, Philip H (Phil)** — Baseball Player
6382 Nichols Road, Flowery Branch GA 30542, USA
**Nields, Nerissa** — Singer
Bulletproof Artist Mgmt, 241 Main St, Easthampton MA 01027, USA
**Nielsen, Brian** — Boxer
Bettina Palle, 12 Skjulet, 2800 Bagsvend, Denmark
**Nielsen, Brigitte** — Actress, Model
Almond Talent Mgmt, 8217 Beverly Blvd, #8, West Hollywood CA 90048, USA
**Nielsen, Connie** — Actress
United Talent Agency, U T A Plaza, 9336 Civic Center Dr, Beverly Hills CA 90210 USA
**Nielsen, Gerald A (Jerry)** — Baseball Player
4631 Kewanee St, Fair Oaks CA 95628, USA
**Nielsen, Jeffrey M (Jeff)** — Ice Hockey Player
6113 Birchcrest Dr, Minneapolis MN 55436, USA
**Nielsen, Rick** — Singer, Guitarist (Cheap Trick)
Oakie Dokie Mgmt, 6090 Central Ave, Saint Petersburg FL 33707, USA
**Nielsen, S Gifford** — Football Player
10 Sarahs Cove, Sugar Land TX 77479, USA
**Nielsen, William Johnk** — Actor
Panorama Agency, ApS Ryesgade 103B, 2100 Copenhagen, Denmark
**Niemann, Jeffrey W (Jeff)** — Baseball Player
5922 Jason St, Houston TX 77074, USA
**Niemann, Randall H (Randy)** — Baseball Player
1585 SW Harbour Isles Circle, Port Saint Lucie FL 34986, USA
**Niemann, Richard W (Rich)** — Basketball Player
7911 Stanford Ave, Saint Louis MO 63130, USA
**Niemann-Stirnemann, Gunda** — Speed Skater
Postfach 503, 99010 Erfurt, Germany
**Niemeyer, Paul V** — Judge
US Court of Appeals, 101 W Lombard St, #3625, Baltimore MD 21201, USA
**Niemi Swayze, Lisa** — Actress
W K T Public Relations, 9350 Wilshire Blvd, #450, Beverly Hills CA 90212 USA
**Nieminen, Minna** — Rowing Athlete
Vuoksen Soutajat Ry, Koskenparras 10, 55100 Imatra, Finland
**Nieminen, Toni** — Ski Jumper
Landen Kanava 99, Vesijarvenkatu 74, 15140 Lahti, Finland
**Nieminen, Ville** — Ice Hockey Player
Saint Louis Blues, Scott Trade Center, 1401 Clark Ave, Saint Louis MO 63103 USA
**Nierman, Leonardo** — Artist, Sculptor
Amsterdam 43 PH, Mexico City 11 DF, Mexico
**Nies, Eric** — Actor, Model
Don Buchwald, 6500 Wilshire Blvd, #2200, Los Angeles CA 90048 USA
**Nieson, Charles B (Chuck)** — Baseball Player
8681 Carriage Hill Draw, Savage MN 55378, USA
**Nieto, Thomas A (Tom)** — Baseball Player
22446 Eagles Watch Dr, Land O Lakes FL 34639, USA
**Nieuwendyk, Joseph (Joe)** — Ice Hockey Player, Executive
3204 Drexel Dr, Dallas TX 75205, USA
**Nieuwenhuis, Hans** — Director
Columbia Artists Mgmt Inc, 1790 Broadway, #702, New York NY 10019 USA
**Nieves, Joe** — Actor
Kazarian/Measures/Ruskin, 11969 Ventura Blvd, #300, Studio City CA, USA
**Nieves, Melvin R (Mel)** — Baseball Player
6131 Seven Lakes W, West End NC 27376, USA
**Nigam, Anjul** — Actor, Writer, Producer
Brittany House Pictures, 1680 N Vine St, #326, Los Angeles CA 90028, USA
**Nigh, George P** — Governor, OK; Educator
University of Central Oklahoma, President's Office, Edmond OK 73034, USA
**Nightingale, Maxine** — Singer
Utopia Artists, PO Box 1821, Ojai CA 93024, USA
**Nighy, Bill** — Actor
W M E Entertainment, 9601 Wilshire Blvd, #300, Beverly Hills CA 90210 USA
**Nighy, Jo-Anne** — Actress
Associated International Mgmt, 7 Hatton Garden, #400, London EC1N 8AD, England
**Nigrelli, Ross F** — Pathologist
29 Barracuda Road, East Quogue NY 11942, USA

**Nidetch - Nigrelli**

| | |
|---|---|
| **Nihalani, Govind** | Director, Producer |
| 139 Aradhana, Bandra (E), Mumbai MS 400051, India | |
| **Niinimaa, Janne H** | Ice Hockey Player |
| 2200-201 Portage Ave, Winnipeg MB R3B 3L3, Canada | |
| **Niinisto, Sauli V** | President, Finland |
| President's Office, Mariankatu 2, 00170 Helsinki, Finland | |
| **Niittymaki, Antero** | Ice Hockey Player |
| 1751 Pinnacle Dr, #1500, McLean VA 22102, USA | |
| **Niklason, Laura E** | Tissue Engineer |
| Duke University, Medical School, Anesthesia Dept, Durham NC 27706, USA | |
| **Nikolas, Alexa** | Actress |
| Gersh Agency, 9465 Wilshire Blvd, #600, Beverly Hills CA 90212 USA | |
| **Nikolic, Tomislav** | Government Official, Serbia |
| President's Office, Nemanjina 11, 11000 Belgrade, Serbia | |
| **Nikolishin, Andrei I** | Ice Hockey Player |
| 105 Bloomfield Ave, Hartford CT 06105, USA | |
| **Niksic, Nermin** | Prime Minister, Bosnia-Herzegovia |
| Prime Minister's Office, Alipasina 1, 71000 Sarajevo, Bosnia & Herzegovina | |
| **Nilan, Christopher J (Chris)** | Ice Hockey Player |
| 577 Adams St, #D, Milton MA 02186, USA | |
| **Niland, John H** | Football Player |
| 16058 Chalfont Court, Dallas TX 75248, USA | |
| **Niles, Prescott** | Bassist (Knack) |
| Edge Mgmt, 10850 Wilshire Blvd, #300, Los Angeles CA 90024, USA | |
| **Nill, Jim** | Ice Hockey Player |
| 20837 Dundee Dr, Novi MI 48375, USA | |
| **Nilsen, John** | Composer, Pianist |
| Magic Wing Music, PO Box 222, West Linn OR 97068, USA | |
| **Nilsen, Kurt E** | Singer, Guitarist, Songwriter |
| Playroom, Sandakerveien 24D, #F2, 0473 Oslo, Norway | |
| **Nilsmark, Catrin** | Golfer |
| 187 Commodore Dr, Jupiter FL 33477, USA | |
| **Nilsson, David W (Dave)** | Baseball Player |
| 34 Lawnhill Road, Nelang QLD 4211, Australia | |
| **Nilsson, Kent** | Ice Hockey Player |
| 9034 Crichton Woods Dr, Orlando FL 32819, USA | |
| **Nilsson, Lennart** | Photographer |
| Engelbrektsgatan 18, 114 32 Stockholm, Sweden | |
| **Nilsson, Sandra** | Model |
| Playboy Promotions, 2706 Media Center Dr, Los Angeles CA 90065 USA | |
| **Nilsson, Ulf** | Ice Hockey Player |
| QBrick AB, Sodra Hamnvagen 22, Stockholm 11 541, Sweden | |
| **Nimmannitya, Suchitra** | Epidemiologist, Pediatrician |
| Children's Hospital, Rajvithee Road, Bangkok 10400, Thailand | |
| **Nimmo, Dirk** | Actor |
| Michael Whitehall, 125 Gloucester Road, London SW7 4TE, England | |
| **Nimoy, Leonard** | Actor, Director |
| Gersh Agency, 9465 Wilshire Blvd, #600, Beverly Hills CA 90212 USA | |
| **Nimphius, Kurt A** | Basketball Player |
| 750 Dry Creek Road, Sedona AZ 86336, USA | |
| **Nimri, Najwa** | Actress |
| Kuranda Mgmt, Santo Angel 84, 28043 Madrid, Spain | |
| **Ninowski, James (Jim), Jr** | Football Player |
| 2715 Melcombe Circle, #302, Troy MI 48084, USA | |
| **Nipar, Yvette** | Actress |
| Irv Schechter, 9460 Wilshire Blvd, #300, Beverly Hills CA 90212 USA | |
| **Nipon, Albert** | Fashion Designer |
| Leslie Faye Co, Albert Nipon Div, 1400 Broadway, #1600, New York NY 10018, USA | |
| **Nipper, Albert S (Al)** | Baseball Player |
| 401 White Birch Valley Court, Chesterfield MO 63017, USA | |
| **Nirenberg, Louis** | Mathematician |
| 221 W 82nd St, New York NY 10024, USA | |
| **Nirmala, Sister** | Religious Leader |
| Missionaries of Charity, 54A Lower Circular Road, Kolkata 700016, India | |
| **Nisbet, Robert A** | Historian, Sociologist |
| 6131 Purple Aster Lane NE, Albuquerque NM 87111, USA | |
| **Nisbett, Richard E** | Psychologist |
| University of Michigan, Culture & Cognition Program, Ann Arbor MI 48109, USA | |
| **Nischwitz, Ronald L (Ron)** | Baseball Player |
| 17 S Saint Clair St, #330, Dayton OH 45402, USA | |
| **Nishani, Bujar F** | President, Albania |
| President's Office, Bulevardi Deshmoret E Kombit, Tirana, Albania | |
| **Nishizawa, Junichi** | Electronics Engineer, Inventor |
| Semiconductor Research Institute, Kawauchi, Aobaku, Sendai 980 0862, Japan | |
| **Nishizawa, Ryue** | Pritzker Architect Laureate |
| Sanaa Ltd, 2-2-35-6B Higashi-Shinagawa, Tokyo 140 0002, Japan | |
| **Nishizuka, Yasutomi** | Biochemist, Pharmacologist |
| Kobe University Medical School, Pharmacology Dept, 650 0017 Kobe, Japan | |
| **Nishkian, Byron** | Skier |
| 150 4th St, #PH, San Francisco CA 94103, USA | |
| **Nispel, Marcus** | Director |
| Stone Soup, 12200 W Olympic Blvd, #140, Los Angeles CA 90064, USA | |
| **Nissalke, Thomas E (Tom)** | Basketball Coach |
| 3075 Kennedy Dr, #406, Salt Lake City UT 84108, USA | |
| **Nissen, Steven E (Steve)** | Cardiologist |
| 2200 Devonshire Dr, Cleveland OH 44106, USA | |
| **Nistico, Louis (Lou)** | Ice Hockey Player |
| 404 Westbury Crescent, Thunder Bay ON P7C 4N4, Canada | |
| **Nitkowski, Christopher J (C J)** | Baseball Player |
| 205 Townsend Lane, Alpharetta GA 30004, USA | |
| **Nittmann, David** | Artist |
| PO Box 19065, Boulder CO 80308, USA | |
| **Nitzkowski, Monte** | Swimming Coach |
| 7041 Seal Circle, Huntington Beach CA 92648, USA | |
| **Nivea** | Singer |
| I C M Partners, 10250 Constellation Blvd, #900, Los Angeles CA 90067 USA | |

**Nihalani - Nivea**

**Niven, David, Jr** — Actor, Businessman
1100 Alta Loma Road, #1004, West Hollywood CA 90069, USA
**Niven, Kip** — Actor
9000 W Sunset Blvd, #801, West Hollywood CA 90069, USA
**Niven, Laurence V (Larry)** — Writer
11874 Macoda Lane, Chatsworth CA 91311, USA
**Nivola, Alessandro** — Actor
Management 360, 9111 Wilshire Blvd, Beverly Hills CA 90210 USA
**Niwa, Gail** — Concert Pianist
Siegel Artist Mgmt, 1416 Hinman Ave, Evanston IL 60201, USA
**Niwano, Nikkyo** — Religious Leader
Rissho Kosei-kai, 2-11-1 Wada Suginamiku, Tokyo 166 8537, Japan
**Nix, A Kent** — Football Player
2732 Colonial Parkway, Fort Worth TX 76109, USA
**Nix, Jayson T** — Baseball Player
Toronto Blue Jays, Skydome, 1 Blue Jay Way, Toronto ON M5V 1J1, Canada
**Nix, Laynce M** — Baseball Player
1506 Princeton Ave, Midland TX 79701, USA
**Nix, Matthew E (Matt)** — Producer, Director, Writer
W M E Entertainment, 9601 Wilshire Blvd, #300, Beverly Hills CA 90210 USA
**Nix, Steve E** — Guitarist (Briefs)
Devil Dolls Booking, 3505 S Lamar Blvd, #1050, Austin TX 78704, USA
**Nix, William D** — Engineer
Stanford University, Materials Science/Engineering Dept, Stanford CA 94305, USA
**Nixo, Livinia H** — Actress
Laurel Bergman Mgmt, 389 Malvern Road, South Yarra VIC 3141, Australia
**Nixon, Agnes E** — Producer, Writer
774 Conestoga Road, Bryn Mawr PA 19010, USA
**Nixon, Amy** — Curling Athlete
Curling Assn, 1660 Vimont Court, Cumberland ON K4A 4J4, Canada
**Nixon, C Trotman (Trot)** — Baseball Player
1023 Ocean Ridge Dr, Wilmington NC 28405, USA
**Nixon, Cynthia** — Actress
Innovative Artists, 1505 10th St, Santa Monica CA 90401 USA
**Nixon, Kimberley** — Actress
United Talent Agency, U T A Plaza, 9336 Civic Center Dr, Beverly Hills CA 90210 USA
**Nixon, Marni** — Singer, Actress
Harden-Curtis, 850 7th Ave, #903, New York NY 10019, USA
**Nixon, Nicholas** — Photographer
25 Waverly St, Brookline MA 02445, USA
**Nixon, Norman E (Norm)** — Basketball Player
607 Marguerita Ave, Santa Monica CA 90402, USA
**Nixon, Otis J, Jr** — Baseball Player
400 Bass Way NW, Kennesaw GA 30144, USA
**Nixon, Russell E (Russ)** — Baseball Player, Manager
4265 Tee Pee Lane, Las Vegas NV 89129, USA
**Nixon, Torran B (Tory)** — Football Player
PO Box 308, Colfax CA 95713, USA
**Niznik, Stephanie** — Actress
Talent Works, 3500 W Olive Ave, #1400, Burbank CA 91505 USA
**Njue, John Cardinal** — Religious Leader
Archdiocese of Nairobi, PO Box 14231, Nairobi, Kenya
**Nkurunziza, Pierre** — President, Burundi
President's Office, Kiriri Presidential Palace, Bujumbura, Burundi
**Noah, Joakim** — Basketball Player
Chicago Bulls, United Center, 1901 W Madison St, Chicago IL 60612 USA
**Noah, John M** — Ice Hockey Player
3315 W Prairiewood Dr S, Fargo ND 58103, USA
**Noah, Max W** — Army General
552 Douty Hill Road, Sangerville ME 04479, USA
**Noah, Trevor** — Actor, Comedian, Writer
Levity Entertainment Group, 6701 Center Drive W, #1111, Los Angeles CA 90045, USA
**Noah, Yannick** — Tennis Player, Coach
20 Rue Billancourt, 92100 Boulogne, France
**Nobacon, Danbent** — Singer, Keyboardist (Chumbawamba)
Doug Smith Assoc, PO Box 1151, London W3 8ZJ, England
**Nobilo, Frank** — Golfer
10209 Atterbury Court, Orlando FL 32827, USA
**Nobis, Thomas H (Tommy), Jr** — Football Player, Executive
40 S Battery Place NE, Atlanta GA 30342, USA
**Noble** — Guitarist, Pianist (British Sea Power)
Agency Group Ltd, 361-373 City Road, London EC1V 1PQ, England
**Noble, Adrian K** — Director
Askonas Holt, Lincoln House, 300 High Holborn, London WC1V 7JH, England
**Noble, Brandon P** — Football Player
306 Lynne Place, Chester Springs PA 19425, USA
**Noble, Brian D** — Football Player
3664 Via Certaldo Ave, Henderson NV 89052, USA
**Noble, Charles E (Chuck)** — Basketball Player
3585 W Beechwood Ave, #106, Fresno CA 93711, USA
**Noble, Chelsea** — Actress
Insight Mgmt, 9818 Arkansas St, Bellflower CA 90706, USA
**Noble, Cheryl** — Curling Athlete
Curling Assn, 1660 Vimont Court, Cumberland ON K4A 4J4, Canada
**Noble, James** — Actor
Paradigm Agency, 360 Park Ave S, #1600, New York NY 10010 USA
**Noble, John** — Actor
Coast to Coast Talent, 3350 Barham Blvd, Los Angeles CA 90068 USA
**Noble, Richard** — Auto Speed Racing Driver
Richard Noble Consulting, Hunters, Headley Road, Grayshott, Surrey GU26 6DL, England
**Noblitt, Niles L** — Businessman
Biomet Inc, Airport Industrial Park, PO Box 587, Warsaw IN 46581, USA
**Nobu** — Chef, Restaurateur
Nobu's, 105 Hudson St, New York NY 10013, USA
**Noce, Paul D** — Baseball Player
913 W Maumee St, Adrian MI 49221, USA

**Nocera, Daniel G** — Chemist
Massachusetts Institute of Technology, Chemistry Dept, Cambridge MA 02139, USA

**Nochlin, Linda** — Art Historian
New York University, Fine Arts Institute, New York NY 10012, USA

**Nocioni, Andres** — Basketball Player
2281 Royal Ridge Dr, Northbrook IL 60062, USA

**Nock, George V** — Football Player
1025 Nine North Dr, #H, Alpharetta GA 30004, USA

**Noda, Yoshihiko** — Prime Minister, Japan
Democratic Party of Japan, 1-11-1 Nagatacho, Chiyoda, Tokyo 100 0014, Japan

**Noddle, Jeffrey** — Businessman
SuperValu Inc, 11840 Valley View Parkway, Eden Prairie MN 55344, USA

**Noe, Gaspar** — Director
W M E Entertainment, 9601 Wilshire Blvd, #300, Beverly Hills CA 90210 USA

**Noel, Chris** — Vietnam Radio Personality, Actress
291 NE 19th Ave, Boynton Beach FL 33435, USA

**Noel, Monique** — Model, Actress
Playboy Promotions, 2706 Media Center Dr, Los Angeles CA 90065 USA

**Noel, Nerlens** — Basketball Player
Philadelphia 76ers, 1st Union Center, 3601 S Broad St, Philadelphia PA 19148 USA

**Noel, Philip W** — Governor, RI
345 Channel View, #105, Warwick RI 02889, USA

**Noelle, Beyiana** — Model
Playboy Promotions, 2706 Media Center Dr, Los Angeles CA 90065 USA

**Noghaideli, Zurab** — Prime Minister, Georgia
Prime Minister's Office, Government House, Ingorokva 7, 380034 Tbilisi, Georgia

**Noguchi, Soichi** — Astronaut
N A S A, Johnson Space Center, 2101 NASA Road, Houston TX 77058 USA

**Noguchi, Thomas T** — Pathologist
1110 Avoca Ave, Pasadena CA 91105, USA

**Nogueira, Lucas** — Basketball Player
Boston Celtics, 226 Causeway St, #4, Boston MA 02114 USA

**Nogulich, Natalia** — Actress
Green Vision Artists Talent, 8981 Sunset Blvd, #101, Los Angeles CA 90069, USA

**Noiega Gomez, Eduardo** — Actor, Writer
U B B A, 6 Rue de Braque, 75003 Paris, France

**Nojima, Minoru** — Concert Pianist
John Gingrich Mgmt, PO Box 515, New York NY 10023, USA

**Nokelainen, Petteri** — Ice Hockey Player
Montreal Canadiens, 1275 Saint Antoine St W, Montreal QC H3C 5L2, Canada

**Nokes, Matthew D (Matt)** — Baseball Player
2255 Oxford Ave, Cardiff by the Sea CA 92007, USA

**Nokio** — Singer (Dru Hill)
I C M Partners, 10250 Constellation Blvd, #900, Los Angeles CA 90067 USA

**Noko** — Musician (Apollo440)
X L Talent, Reverb House, Bennett St, London W4 2AH, England

**Nola, Britany** — Model
Playboy Promotions, 2706 Media Center Dr, Los Angeles CA 90065 USA

**Nolan, Christopher** — Director, Writer
W M E Entertainment, 9601 Wilshire Blvd, #300, Beverly Hills CA 90210 USA

**Nolan, Faith** — Singer, Musician
PO Box 690, Station P, Toronto ON M5S 2Y4, Canada

**Nolan, Gary L** — Baseball Player
9025 Alpine Peaks Ave, Las Vegas NV 89147, USA

**Nolan, Graham** — Cartoonist
162 Godfrey Terrace, East Aurora NY 14052, USA

**Nolan, Jonathan** — Writer
W M E Entertainment, 9601 Wilshire Blvd, #300, Beverly Hills CA 90210 USA

**Nolan, Joseph W (Joe)** — Baseball Player
9515 Alix Dr, Saint Louis MO 63123, USA

**Nolan, Kathleen (Kathy)** — Actress
House of Representatives, 1434 6th St, #1, Santa Monica CA 90401 USA

**Nolan, Kenny** — Singer, Songwriter
Creative Artists Agency, 2000 Ave of Stars, #100, Los Angeles CA 90067 USA

**Nolan, Martin F** — Editor
Boston Globe, Editorial Dept, 135 W T Morrissey Blvd, Dorchester MA 02125, USA

**Nolan, Michelle** — Actress
Hofflund/Polone, 9465 Wilshire Blvd, #420, Beverly Hills CA 90212 USA

**Nolan, Mike** — Football Coach
Atlanta Falcons, 4400 Falcon Parkway, Flowery Branch GA 30542 USA

**Nolan, Norma B** — Beauty Queen
Miss Universe Organization, 1370 Ave of Americas, #1600, New York NY 10019 USA

**Nolan, Owen L** — Ice Hockey Player
3402 Crestmoor Dr, Saint Paul MN 55125, USA

**Nolan, Ted** — Ice Hockey Player, Coach
269 Queen St E, Sault Sainte Marie ON P6A 1Y9, Canada

**Nolan, Thomas B** — Geologist
2219 California St NW, Washington DC 20008, USA

**Nolan, Tom** — Actor
1335 N Ontario St, Burbank CA 91505, USA

**Noland, Robert L** — Businessman
5555 Eastlake Blvd, Washoe Valley NV 89704, USA

**Nolasco, Amaury** — Actor
Gersh Agency, 9465 Wilshire Blvd, #600, Beverly Hills CA 90212 USA

**Nolasco, C Enrique (Ricky)** — Baseball Player
824 Challenge Ave, Beaumont CA 92223, USA

**Noles, Dickie R** — Baseball Player
20 Dougherty Blvd, #I2, Glen Mills PA 19342, USA

**Nolet, Simon** — Ice Hockey Player
1342 Rue de la Belle Vue, Cap Rouge QC G1Y 2T1, Canada

**Nolfi, George** — Director, Producer, Writer
W M E Entertainment, 9601 Wilshire Blvd, #300, Beverly Hills CA 90210 USA

**Nolin, Gena Lee** — Actress, Model
Shandrew Public Relations, 1050 S Stanley Ave, Los Angeles CA 90019, USA

**Noll, Charles H (Chuck)** — Football Player, Coach
23680 Merano Court, #202, Bonita Springs FL 34134, USA

**Nolte, Claudia** — Government Official, Germany
Mulgarten 28, 98693 Ilmenau, Germany
**Nolte, Eric C** — Baseball Player
23885 Noelle Ave, Murrieta CA 92562, USA
**Nolte, Nick** — Actor
6714 Bonsall Dr, Malibu CA 90265, USA
**Nolting, Paul F** — Religious Leader
Church of Lutheran Confession, 620 E 50th St, Loveland CO 80538, USA
**Nomina, Thomas J (Tom)** — Football Player
20700 Park Place, Estero FL 33928, USA
**Nomura, Masayasu** — Molecular Biologist
74 Whitman Court, Irvine CA 92617, USA
**Nomvete, Pamela** — Actress
Ken McReddie Assoc, 101 Finsbury Pavement, London EC2A 1RS, England
**Nong Duc Manh** — General Secretary, Vietnam
General Secretary's Office, Hoang Hoa Tham St, Hanoi, Vietnam
**Nool, Erki** — Track Athlete
Regati 1, Tallinn 119871, Estonia
**Noonan, Brian** — Ice Hockey Player
262 W Eggleston Ave, Elmhurst IL 60126, USA
**Noonan, Chris** — Director
Creative Artists Agency, 2000 Ave of Stars, #100, Los Angeles CA 90067 USA
**Noonan, Daniel N (Danny)** — Football Player
19501 Woolworth Circle, Omaha NE 68130, USA
**Noonan, John T, Jr** — Judge
US Court of Appeals, Court Building, 95 7th St, San Francisco CA 94103, USA
**Noonan, Karl P** — Football Player
7149 Oxford Hunt Dr, Stanley NC 28164, USA
**Noonan, Pat** — Soccer Player
Los Angeles Galaxy, Home Depot Center, 18400 Avalon Blvd, Carson CA 90746 USA
**Noonan, Patrick F** — Association Executive, Conservationist
3553 Hamlet Place, Chevy Chase MD 20815, USA
**Noonan, Peggy** — Writer
Greater Talent Network, 437 5th Ave, #700, New York NY 10016, USA
**Noonan, Timothy J** — Businessman
Rite Aid Corp, 30 Hunter Lane, Camp Hill PA 17011, USA
**Noonan, Tom** — Actor
A K A Talent, 6310 San Vicente Blvd, #200, Los Angeles CA 90048 USA
**Noone, Kathleen** — Actress
130 W 42nd St, #1804, New York NY 10036, USA
**Noone, Nora Jane** — Actress
Gavin Barker Assoc, 2D Wimpole St, London W1G 0EB, England
**Noone, Peter** — Singer (Herman's Hermits), Actor
Creative Entertainment Assoc, 1950 Old Cuthbert Road, #J, Cherry Hill NJ 08034, USA
**Noor Al-Hussein** — Queen Mother, Jordan
Royal Hashemite Court, PO Box 5166, 11183 Amman, Jordan
**Nooteboom, Cees** — Writer
Suhrkamp Verlag, Linderstr 29, 60325 Frankfurt/Main, Germany
**Nooyi, Indra** — Businesswoman
PepsiCo, 700 Anderson Hill Road, Purchase NY 10577, USA
**Norberg, Anette** — Curling Athlete
Talaforum, Norr Malarstrand 6, 112 20 Stockholm, Sweden
**Norby, Caecilie** — Singer
Dansk Musikformidling, Tag Hammerskjolds Allee 42G, 2100 Copenhagen, Denmark
**Norcross, Clayton** — Actor
1327 Linda Way, Arcadia CA 91006, USA
**Nordenberg, Mark A** — Educator
University of Pittsburgh, Chancellor's Office, Pittsburgh PA 15261, USA
**Nordenstrom, Bjorn** — Cancer Radiologist
Karolinska Institute, Radiology Dept, 171 77 Stockholm, Sweden
**Nordhaus, William D** — Economist
Yale University, Economics Dept, New Haven CT 06520, USA
**Nordli, Odvar** — Prime Minister, Norway
Snarveien 4, 2312 Ottestad, Norway
**Nordling, Jeffrey** — Actor
A P A Talent/Literary Agency, 405 S Beverly Dr, #300, Beverly Hills CA 90212 USA
**Nordquist, Mark A** — Football Player
3495 Seacrest Dr, Carlsbad CA 92008, USA
**Nordqvist, Anna** — Golfer
Ladies Pro Golf Assn, 100 International Golf Dr, Daytona Beach FL 32124 USA
**Nordsieck, Kenneth H** — Astronomer
University of California, Astronomy Dept, Santa Cruz CA 95060, USA
**Nordstrom, John E** — Composer
Gorfaine/Schwartz, 4111 W Alameda Ave, #509, Burbank CA 91505 USA
**NORE** — Rap Artist
Don Buchwald, 6500 Wilshire Blvd, #2200, Los Angeles CA 90048 USA
**Noren, Irving A (Irv)** — Baseball, Basketball Player
3154 Camino Crest Dr, Oceanside CA 92056, USA
**Noren, Lars** — Writer
Ostermalmsgatan 33, 114 26 Stockholm, Sweden
**Norgard, Erik C** — Football Player
60 Harbor View Dr, Sugar Land TX 77479, USA
**Noriega, Carlos I** — Astronaut
4630 Silhouette Dr, Katy TX 77493, USA
**Noris, Joe** — Ice Hockey Player
1111 Via Carolina, La Jolla CA 92037, USA
**Norman, Christopher W (Chris)** — Singer, Songwriter, Producer
G I G Concerts, Schlossstr 20, 56566 Neuwied-Engers, Germany
**Norman, Daniel E (Dan)** — Baseball Player
430 McBroom Ave, Barstow CA 92311, USA
**Norman, Edie Jo** — Bowler
3544 Mariner Blvd, Spring Hill FL 34609, USA
**Norman, Gregory J (Greg)** — Golfer
Great White Shark Enterprises, 2041 Vista Parkway, #200, West Palm Beach FL 33411, USA
**Norman, Hayley Marie** — Actress
Underground Films & Mgmt, 447 S Highland Ave, Los Angeles CA 90036, USA

**Norman, Jessye** — Concert Singer
L'Orchidee, PO Box South, Crugers NY 10521, USA
**Norman, Kenneth D (Ken)** — Basketball Player
19020 Kedzie Ave, Homewood IL 60430, USA
**Norman, Marc** — Writer
I C M Partners, 10250 Constellation Blvd, #900, Los Angeles CA 90067 USA
**Norman, Marsha** — Writer
W M E Entertainment, 9601 Wilshire Blvd, #300, Beverly Hills CA 90210 USA
**Norman, Michael** — Astrophysicist
University of California, Astronomy Dept, La Jolla CA 90293, USA
**Norman, Monty** — Composer
P R S, 29/33 Berners St, London W1P 4AA, England
**Norman, Nelson A** — Baseball Player
6135 Long Key Lane, Boynton Beach FL 33472, USA
**Norman, Pettis B** — Football Player
1430 Bar Harbor Circle, Dallas TX 75232, USA
**Normandy, Jim** — Guitar Designer
Normandy Guitars, PO Box 3564, Salem OR 97302, USA
**Norodom Sihamoni** — King, Cambodia
Khemarind Palace, Phnom Penh, Cambodia
**Noronen, Mika** — Ice Hockey Player
65 S Autumn Dr, Rochester NY 14626, USA
**Norrena, Fredrik** — Ice Hockey Player
1750 Barrington Road, Columbus OH 43221, USA
**Norrington, Roger A C** — Conductor
Camerata Academica Salzburg, Bergstr 22, 5020 Salzburg, Austria
**Norrington, Stephen (Steve)** — Director
W M E Entertainment, 9601 Wilshire Blvd, #300, Beverly Hills CA 90210 USA
**Norris, Alan E** — Judge
US Court of Appeals, US Courthouse, 85 Marconi Blvd, Columbus OH 43215, USA
**Norris, Bruce** — Writer
Steppenwolf Theater, 758 W North Ave, #400, Chicago IL 60610, USA
**Norris, C Dwayne** — Ice Hockey Player
850 Eastlake Court, Oxford MI 48371, USA
**Norris, Carli** — Actress
Gavin Barker Assoc, 2D Wimpole St, London W1G 0EB, England
**Norris, Chuck** — Actor
Kritzer Levine Wilkins Griffin, 11872 La Grange Ave, #100, Los Angeles CA 90025 USA
**Norris, Daran** — Actor
I C M Partners, 10250 Constellation Blvd, #900, Los Angeles CA 90067 USA
**Norris, David Owen** — Concert Pianist
17 Manor Road, Andover, Hantsfordshire SP10 3JS, England
**Norris, Dean J** — Actor
Industry Entertainment, 955 Carillo Dr, #300, Los Angeles CA 90048 USA
**Norris, Elwood G (Woody)** — Inventor (Hypersonic Sound Technology)
American Technology Corp, 13112 Evening Creek Dr S, San Diego CA 92128, USA
**Norris, Hermione** — Actress
Artist Rights Group, 4 Great Portland St, London W1W 8PA, England
**Norris, Jack** — Ice Hockey Player
PO Box 332, Delisle SK S0L 0P0, Canada
**Norris, James F (Jim)** — Baseball Player
6375 Oak Hollow Dr, Burleson TX 76028, USA
**Norris, James R, Jr** — Chemist
University of Chicago, Chemistry Dept, 5735 S Ellis Ave, Chicago IL 60637, USA
**Norris, Lee** — Actor
Don Buchwald, 6500 Wilshire Blvd, #2200, Los Angeles CA 90048 USA
**Norris, Michael K (Mike)** — Baseball Player
6228 Ridgemont Dr, Oakland CA 94619, USA
**Norris, Michele** — Commentator
National Public Radio, 635 Massachusetts Ave NW, #1, Washington DC 20001, USA
**Norris, Patricia** — Costume Designer
Murtha Agency, 4240 Promenade Way, #232, Marina del Rey CA 90292, USA
**Norris, Paul J** — Businessman
W R Grace Co, 7500 Grace Dr, Columbia MD 21044, USA
**Norris, Terry** — Boxer
3668 Syracuse St, La Jolla CA 92122, USA
**Norris, Thomas R** — Vietnam War Navy Hero (CMH)
33593 E Hayden Lake Road, Hayden ID 83835, USA
**Norris, Tim** — Golfer
1604 Little Kitten Ave, Manhattan KS 66503, USA
**Norris, William A** — Judge
US Court of Appeals, 312 N Spring St, #G33, Los Angeles CA 90012, USA
**Norstrom, Mattias** — Ice Hockey Player
3516 Amherst Ave, Dallas TX 75225, USA
**Norsworthy, Lamar** — Businessman
2828 N Harwood St, #100, Dallas TX 75201, USA
**North, Andrew S (Andy)** — Golfer
3289 High Point Road, Madison WI 53719, USA
**North, Douglass C** — Nobel Economics Laureate
7569 Homestead Road, Benzonia MI 49616, USA
**North, Gary L** — Air Force General
Commander, Pacific Air Force, Hickam Air Force Base HI 96853 USA
**North, Jay** — Actor
290 NE 1st Ave, Lake Butler FL 32054, USA
**North, Nolan** — Actor, Comedian
Origin Talent, 4705 Laurel Canyon Blvd. #306, Studio City CA 91607, USA
**North, Oliver L** — Government Official, Marine Officer
Freedom Alliance, 22570 Markley Circle, #240, Sterling VA 20166, USA
**North, Peter** — Actor, Director, Producer
Vivid Entertainment, 3599 Cahuenga Blvd W, Los Angeles CA 90068, USA
**North, William A (Billy)** — Baseball Player
5523 106th Ave NE, Kirkland WA 98033, USA
**Northam, Jeremy** — Actor
Rights House, Drury House, 34-43 Russell St, London WC2B 5HA, England
**Northcutt, Dennis L** — Football Player
1 Park Plaza, #970, Irvine CA 92614, USA

**Northey, Scott R** — Baseball Player
9920 Bankside Dr, Roswell GA 30076, USA
**Northrop, Wayne** — Actor
37900 Road 800, Raymond CA 93653, USA
**Northrup, Anne M** — Representative, KY
Consumer Product Safety Commission, 4330 East West Highway, Bethesda MD 20814, USA
**Northway, Douglas (Doug)** — Swimmer
3239 E 3rd St, Tucson AZ 85716, USA
**Norton, Brad** — Ice Hockey Player
7 Great Road, Acton MA 01720, USA
**Norton, Edward** — Actor
W M E Entertainment, 9601 Wilshire Blvd, #300, Beverly Hills CA 90210 USA
**Norton, Graham** — Actor, Comedian
United Talent Agency, U T A Plaza, 9336 Civic Center Dr, Beverly Hills CA 90210 USA
**Norton, Gregory B (Greg)** — Baseball Player
11130 Eliot Court, Denver CO 80234, USA
**Norton, James A (Jim)** — Football Player
2550 S Ellsworth Road, #13, Mesa AZ 85209, USA
**Norton, Jeff** — Ice Hockey Player
285 Saint George St, Duxbury MA 02332, USA
**Norton, Jerry R** — Football Player
6901 Chevy Chase Ave, Dallas TX 75225, USA
**Norton, Kenneth H (Ken), Jr** — Football Player, Sportscaster
135 Union Jack Mall, Marina del Rey CA 90292, USA
**Norton, Peter** — Computer Software Designer
225 Arizona Ave, #200W, Santa Monica CA 90401, USA
**Norton, Thomas J (Tom)** — Baseball Player
4900 Southwood Dr, Sheffield Lake OH 44054, USA
**Norton, Virginia** — Bowler
11706 Mindanao St, Cypress CA 90630, USA
**Norton-Taylor, Judy** — Actress, Model
Tisherman Agency, 6767 Forest Lawn Dr, #101, Los Angeles CA 90068 USA
**Norville, Deborah** — Commentator
PO Box 426, Mill Neck NY 11765, USA
**Norwich, Craig R** — Ice Hockey Player
11448 Welters Way, Eden Prairie MN 55347, USA
**Norwood, Daron** — Singer
Texas Artist Group, 6999 E Highway 80, Odessa TX 79762, USA
**Norwood, Dorothy** — Singer, Songwriter
Universal Attractions, 135 W 26th St, #1200, New York NY 10001 USA
**Norwood, Lee C** — Ice Hockey Player
28876 Olson St, Livonia MI 48150, USA
**Norwood, Scott A** — Football Player
41955 Blue Flag Terrace, Stone Ridge VA 20105, USA
**Norwood, Willie B** — Basketball Player
414 W 122nd St, #B, Los Angeles CA 90061, USA
**Noseworthy, Jack** — Actor
Don Buchwald, 6500 Wilshire Blvd, #2200, Los Angeles CA 90048 USA
**Nossal, Gustav J V** — Immunologist, Pathologist
46 Fellows St, Kew VIC 3101, Australia
**Nosseck, Noel** — Director
1435 San Ysidro Dr, Beverly Hills CA 90210, USA
**Nossek, Joseph R (Joe)** — Baseball Player
630 Sunrise Dr, Amherst OH 44001, USA
**Nossiter, Jonathan** — Director, Producer, Writer
United Talent Agency, U T A Plaza, 9336 Civic Center Dr, Beverly Hills CA 90210 USA
**Notaro, Phyllis** — Bowler
11123 Maritime Court, Wellington FL 33449, USA
**Noth, Christopher** — Actor
Sanders/Armstrong/Caserta Mgmt, 2120 Colorado Ave, #120, Santa Monica CA 90404 USA
**Nothstein, Marty** — Cyclist
1019 Village Round, Allentown PA 18106, USA
**Notkin, Richard T** — Sculptor
PO Box 698, Helena MT 59624, USA
**Notkins, Abner L** — Virologist
National Institute of Dental Research, 9000 Rockville Pike, Bethesda MD 20892, USA
**Noto, Lucio A** — Businessman
Mobil Corp, 3225 Gallows Road, Fairfax VA 22037, USA
**Nott Cunningham, Tara** — Weightlifter
Olympic Training Center, 1 Olympic Plaza, Building 4, Colorado Springs CO 80909, USA
**Nott, John W F** — Government Official, England
31 Walpole St, London SW3 4QS, England
**Nottage, Lynn** — Writer
Gersh Agency, 9465 Wilshire Blvd, #600, Beverly Hills CA 90212 USA
**Nottebohm, Andreas** — Artist
17496 7th St E, Sonoma CA 95476, USA
**Nottingham, Donald R (Don)** — Football Player
5750 NE 36th Avenue Road, Ocala FL 34479, USA
**Nouri, Michael** — Actor
Burstein, 15304 W Sunset Blvd, #208, Pacific Palisades CA 90272, USA
**Noury, Alain** — Actor
Domaine de Hurlevents, 26400 Soyans Crest-Sud, France
**Nouvel, Jean** — Pritzker Architecture Laureate
Architectures Jean Nouvel, 10 Cite d'Angouleme, 75011 Paris, France
**Nova, Heather** — Singer
Free Trade Agency, 9 Chapel Place, Rivington St, London EC2A 3DQ, England
**Novacek, Jay M** — Football Player
PO Box 471490, Fort Worth TX 76147, USA
**Novack, K J** — Businessman
America Online, 22000 A O L Way, Sterling VA 20166, USA
**Novak Popper, Ilona** — Swimmer
Il Orso Utca 23, Budapest, Hungary
**Novak, Benjamin J (B J)** — Actor, Comedian, Writer
B/W/R, 9100 Wilshire Blvd, #500W, Beverly Hills CA 90212 USA
**Novak, John R** — Inventor (Air Cleaning Radiator)
Engelhard Corp, Automotive Emissions Systems, 101 Wood Ave, Iselin NJ 08830, USA

**Novak, Kim** — Actress
Cameron Enterprises, 10100 Santa Monica Blvd, #1060, Los Angeles CA 90067, USA
**Novak, Michael** — Theologian
5050 Ave Maria Blvd, Ave Maria FL 34142, USA
**Novakovic, Bojana** — Actress
Creative Artists Agency, 2000 Ave of Stars, #100, Los Angeles CA 90067 USA
**Novaro, Jean-Claude** — Sculptor
32 Chemin Hautes Vignasses, 06410 Biot, France
**Novello, Antonia C** — Physician, Government Official
1110 SW Ivanhoe Blvd, #14, Orlando FL 32804, USA
**Novello, Don (Father Guido Sarducci)** — Actor, Comedian
Elizabeth Rush Agency, 82 Cumberland Ave, Verona NJ 07044, USA
**Noveskey, Matt** — Bassist (Blue October)
Rainmaker Artists, PO Box 551665, Dallas TX 75355, USA
**Novitsky, Oleg** — Cosmonaut
Cosmonaut Training Center, Star City, 141160 Zvezdny Gorodok, Moscow Oblast, Russia
**Novoa, Rafael** — Actor
Univision, 605 3rd Ave, #1200, New York NY 10158 USA
**Novoa, Rafael A** — Baseball Player
3420 N 47th Way, Phoenix AZ 85018, USA
**Novotna, Jana** — Tennis Player
7834 Montvale Way, McLean VA 22102, USA
**Novotny, Dave** — Bassist (Saliva)
Helter Skelter, 347-353 Chiswick High Road, London W4 4HS, England
**Nowak, Piotr (Peter)** — Soccer Player, Coach
Philadelphia Union, Union Field, Seaport Dr, Chester PA 19013 USA
**Nowatzke, Thomas M (Tom)** — Football Player
4335 Diuble Road, Ann Arbor MI 48103, USA
**Nowell, Peter C** — Pathologist, Biologist
9 Foxcroft Lane, Media PA 19063, USA
**Nowicki, Tom** — Actor
Davis Mgmt, 4111 Lankershim Blvd, North Hollywood CA 91602, USA
**Nowitzki, Dirk** — Basketball Player
10735 Strait Lane, Dallas TX 75229, USA
**Nowra, Louis** — Writer
Level 18, Plaza 11, 500 Oxford St, Bondi Junction NSW 2011, Australia
**Nowrasteh, Cyrus** — Director, Writer
Creative Artists Agency, 2000 Ave of Stars, #100, Los Angeles CA 90067 USA
**Noxon, Marti** — Producer, Writer
W M E Entertainment, 9601 Wilshire Blvd, #300, Beverly Hills CA 90210 USA
**Noyce, Phillip** — Director
United Talent Agency, U T A Plaza, 9336 Civic Center Dr, Beverly Hills CA 90210 USA
**Noyori, Ryoji** — Nobel Chemistry Laureate
135-417 Shinden, Umemoricho, Nisshin, Aichi 470 0132, Japan
**Nozieres, Philippe P G F** — Physicist
15 Route de Saint Nizier, 38180 Seyssins, France
**Nozuka, Justin** — Singer, Songwriter
Coalition Entertainment Mgmt, 10271 Yonge St, #302, Richmond Hill ON L4C 3B5, Canada
**Nsibambi, Apolo** — Prime Minister, Uganda
Premier's Office, Parliament Building, PO Box 341, Kampala, Uganda
**Ntombi** — Queen Regent, Swaziland
Royal Residence, PO Box 1, Lobamba, Swaziland
**Nuami, Sheikh Humaid IV ibin Rashid, Al** — Ruler, Ajman
Royal Palace, PO Box 1, Ajman, United Arab Emirates
**Nubiola, Esther** — Actress
Cineart, 28 Rue Mogador, 78009 Paris, France
**Nucci, Danny** — Actor
Talent Works, 3500 W Olive Ave, #1400, Burbank CA 91505 USA
**Nucci, Leo** — Opera Singer
Opera Art, Via Isolalta Forette 11, 37068 Vigasio VR, Italy
**Nuce, Ted** — Rodeo Bull Rider
12606 Victory Ave, Oakdale CA 95361, USA
**Nugent, Alecia** — Singer
Keith Case Assoc, 1025 17th Ave S, #200, Nashville TN 37212 USA
**Nugent, Michael (Mike)** — Football Player
Cincinnati Bengals, 1 Paul Brown Stadium, Cincinnati OH 45202 USA
**Nugent, Nelle** — Producer
Foxboro Entertainment, 133 E 58th St, #301, New York NY 10022 USA
**Nugent, Theodore A (Ted)** — Singer, Guitarist, Songwriter
Madhouse Mgmt, PO Box 130109, Ann Arbor MI 48113, USA
**Nugent-Hopkins, Ryan J** — Ice Hockey Player
Edmonton Oilers, 11230 110th St, Edmonton AB T5G 3H7, Canada
**Null, Jason** — Guitarist (Saving Abel), Songwriter
Virgin Records, 338 N Foothill Road, Beverly Hills CA 90210 USA
**Numan, Gary** — Singer, Songwriter
Kras Artists, Leernseesteenweg 168, 9800 Deinze, Belgium
**Nu-Mark** — Rap Artist
Vision Entertainment Group, 1100 Glendon Ave, #1100, Los Angeles CA 90024, USA
**Numbers, Ronald L** — Historian
University of Wisconsin, History of Science & Health Dept, Madison WI 53706, USA
**Numminen, Teppo K** — Ice Hockey Player
5975 Tipperary Manor, Clarence Center NY 14032, USA
**Nunez, Edwin** — Baseball Player
2618 E Locust Dr, Chandler AZ 85286, USA
**Nunez, Joseph (Joe)** — Actor
Talent Works, 3500 W Olive Ave, #1400, Burbank CA 91505 USA
**Nunez, Victor** — Director
Gersh Agency, 9465 Wilshire Blvd, #600, Beverly Hills CA 90212 USA
**Nunley, Frank H** — Football Player
2131 Mulberry Circle, San Jose CA 95125, USA
**Nunn, Michael** — Boxer
314 E 13th St, #1, Davenport IA 52803, USA
**Nunn, Samuel A (Sam)** — Senator, GA
75 14th St NE, #4810, Atlanta GA 30309, USA
**Nunn, Terri** — Singer (Berlin)
M O B Agency, 6404 Wilshire Blvd, #505, Los Angeles CA 90048 USA

**Nunn, Trevor R** — Director
Royal National Theater, South Bank, London SE1 9PX, England
**Nunnally, Jonathan K (Jon)** — Baseball Player
36550 Chester Road, #504, Avon OH 44011, USA
**Nurse, Paul M** — Nobel Medicine Laureate
Clare Hall Laboratories, Cell Cycle Control Laboratory, Hertsfordshire EN6 3LD, England
**Nussbaum, Danny** — Actor
Conway Van Gelder Grant, 8-12 Broadwick St, #300, London W1F 8HW, England
**Nussbaum, Karen** — Labor Activist
9-5 National Working Women Assn, 231 W Wisconsin, #900, Milwaukee WI 53203, USA
**Nussbaum, Martha C** — Philosopher
University of Chicago, Law School, 111 E 60th St, Chicago IL 60637, USA
**Nussle, James A (Jim)** — Government Official, Representative, IA
PO Box 445, Marion IA 52302, USA
**Nusslein-Volhard, Christiane** — Nobel Medicine Laureate
Klosttermuhle 15, 72074 Tubingen, Germany
**Nutini, Paolo** — Singer
Atlantic Records, 1290 Ave of Americas, Concourse 3, New York NY 10104 USA
**Nutt, Amy Ellis** — Journalist
Newark Star-Ledger, Editorial Dept, 1 Star-Ledger Plaza, Newark NJ 07102, USA
**Nutt, Jim** — Artist
1035 Greenwood Ave, Wilmette IL 60091, USA
**Nuttall, Amy** — Actress, Singer
Merlin Elite, 37 Lower Belgrave St, London SW1W 0LS, England
**Nutten, Thomas R (Tom)** — Football Player
431 S Creek Dr, Osprey FL 34229, USA
**Nutter, Alice** — Singer, Percussionist (Chumbawamba)
Doug Smith Assoc, PO Box 1151, London W3 8ZJ, England
**Nutter, David** — Director
W M E Entertainment, 9601 Wilshire Blvd, #300, Beverly Hills CA 90210 USA
**Nutting, Wallace H** — Army General
6 Schooner Way, Saco ME 04072, USA
**Nutzle, Futzie** — Artist, Cartoonist
PO Box 325, Aromas CA 95004, USA
**Nuveman, Stacey** — Softball Player
USA Softball, 2801 NE 50th St, Oklahoma City OK 73111, USA
**Nuwer, Hank** — Writer, Journalist, Educator
Franklin College, Shirk Hall, 1100 Branigin Blvd, Franklin IN 46131, USA
**Nuyen, France** — Actress
1800 Franklin Canyon Terrace, Beverly Hills CA 90210, USA
**Nuzorewa, Abel Tendekayi** — Prime Minister, Zimbabwe
United African National Council, 40 Charter Road, Harare, Zimbabwe
**Nyad, Diana** — Swimmer, Sportscaster
870 5th Ave, Los Angeles CA 90005, USA
**Nyberg, Frederik** — Alpine Skier
Kaptensgatan 2C, 832 00 Froson, Sweden
**Nyberg, Karen L** — Astronaut
1848 Lake Landing Dr, League City TX 77573, USA
**Nyberg, Katarina** — Curling Athlete
Curling Assn, Idrottshuser, Marbackagatan 19, 123 43 Farsta, Sweden
**Nye, Bill** — Actor
W M E Entertainment, 9601 Wilshire Blvd, #300, Beverly Hills CA 90210 USA
**Nye, Blaine F** — Football Player
1200 Bay Laurel Dr, Menlo Park CA 94025, USA
**Nye, Erle A** — Businessman
6924 Desco, Dallas TX 75225, USA
**Nye, Robert** — Writer
Thornfield, Kingsland, Ballinghassig, County Cork, Ireland
**Nye, Ryan C** — Baseball Player
3319 Golf Course Dr, Alma AR 72921, USA
**Nyers, C Richard (Dick)** — Football Player
4055 N Riverside Dr, Columbus IN 47203, USA
**Nyers, Rezso** — Secretary General, Hungary
Ozgida Utca 22/A, 1025 Budapest, Hungary
**Nygaard, Richard L** — Judge
US Court of Appeals, 1st National Bank Building, 717 State St, Erie PA 16501, USA
**Nyland, William L** — Marine Corps General
2750 Semoran Circle, Pensacola FL 32503, USA
**Nylander, Michael** — Ice Hockey Player
8813 Mayberry Court, Potomac MD 20854, USA
**Nylund, Gary** — Ice Hockey Player
3504 154th St, Surry BC V3S 0R3, Canada
**Nyman, Michael L** — Composer, Pianist
Michael Nyman Ltd, PO Box 430, High Wycombe HP13 5QT, England
**Nyqvist, Michael** — Actor
W M E Entertainment, 9601 Wilshire Blvd, #300, Beverly Hills CA 90210 USA
**Nystedt, Knut** — Composer, Conductor
Det Norske Musikforlag A/S, Postbuks 1499 Bika, Oslo 0116, Norway
**Nystrom, Eric** — Ice Hockey Player
475 Berry Road, Syosset NY 11791, USA
**Nystrom, Joakim** — Tennis Player
Torsgatan 194, 931 00 Skelleftea, Sweden
**Nyswaner, Ronald L (Ron)** — Writer, Producer, Director
United Talent Agency, U T A Plaza, 9336 Civic Center Dr, Beverly Hills CA 90210 USA

**O, Karen** — Singer (Yeah Yeah Yeahs), Songwriter
Yeah Yeah Yeahs, 249 Metropolitan Ave, Brooklyn NY 11211, USA

**Oakenfold, Paul M** — DJ Musician
International Talent Booking, Ariel House, 74A Charlotte St, #100 London W1T 4QJ, England

**Oakes, W Warren** — Drummer (Against Me)
Boca Fiesta Restaurant, 232 SE 1st St, Gainesville FL 32601, USA

**Oakley, Charles** — Basketball Player
700 Park Regency Place NE, #1105, Atlanta GA 30326, USA

**Oates, Adam R** — Ice Hockey Player, Coach
53570 Del Gato Dr, La Quinta CA 92253, USA

**Oates, Bart S** — Football Player, Sportscaster
2 Silverbrook Road, Morristown NJ 07960, USA

**Oates, John** — Singer (Hall & Oates), Songwriter
Doyle-Kos Entertainment, 1 Penn Plaza, 2107, New York NY 10119, USA

**Oates, Joyce Carol** — Writer
McClelland & Stewart, 75 Sherbourne St, #500, Toronto ON M5A 2P9, Canada

**Oats, Carleton** — Football Player
10605 E Coralbell Ave, Mesa AZ 85208, USA

**Obama, Barack H, II** — President, United States; Nobel Laureate
White House, 1600 Pennsylvania Ave NW, Washington DC 20500 USA

**Obama, Michelle** — Wife of US President
White House, 1600 Pennsylvania Ave NW, Washington DC 20500 USA

**Obando Bravo, Miguel Cardinal** — Religious Leader
Arzobispado, Apartado 3058, Managua, Nicaragua

**O'Bannon, Edward C (Ed)** — Basketball Player
1397 Minuet St, Henderson NV 89052, USA

**Obasanjo, Olusegun** — President, Nigeria; Army General
Obasanjo Farms Nigeria, PO Box 90, Otta, Ogun State, Nigeria

**Obato, Gyo** — Architect
100 N Broadway, Saint Louis MO 63102, USA

**Obeid, Atef M** — Prime Minister, Egypt
Arab International Bank, 35 Abdel Khalek Sarwat St, Cairo, Egypt

**Obeidat, Ahmad Abdul-Majeed** — Prime Minister, Jordan
Law & Arbitration Center, PO Box 926544, Amman, Jordan

**Oben, Roman D** — Football Player
11476 Creekstone Lane, San Diego CA 92128, USA

**Oberg, Margo** — Surfer
Margo Oberg Surf School, Poipu Beach, Koloa HI 96756, USA

**Obergfoll, Christina** — Track Athlete
Alsfelder Str 27, 64289 Darnstadt, Germany

**Oberholser, Arron** — Golfer
5901 E Via Los Caballos, Paradise Valley AZ 85253, USA

**Oberkfell, Kenneth R (Ken)** — Baseball Player
1335 W Welsford Dr, Spring TX 77386, USA

**Obermeyer, Klaus F** — Fashion Designer
Sport Obermeyer, 115 Atlantic Ave, Aspen CO 81611, USA

**Obermueller, Wesley M (Wes)** — Baseball Player
7031 27th Ave, Newhall IA 52315, USA

**Oberoi, Vivek** — Actor
5 Krta Kunj Golden Beach, Ruia Park Juhu, Mumbai MS 400049, India

**O'Berry, Carl G** — Air Force General
Boeing Co, PO Box 4921, 3370 Miraloma Ave, Anaheim CA 92806, USA

**O'Berry, P Michael (Mike)** — Baseball Player
5977 S Fork Dr, Hoover AL 35244, USA

**Oberst, Conor M** — Singer, Guitarist (Bright Eyes)
Untitled Entertainment, 350 S Beverly Dr, #200, Beverly Hills CA 90212 USA

**Oberto, Fabricio R J** — Basketball Player
901 15th St, #1605, Arlington VA 22202, USA

**Obiang Nguema Mbasogo, Teodoro** — President, Equatorial Guinea
President's Office, Palacio de la Presidencia, Malabo, Equatorial Guinea

**O'Boyle, Maureen** — Entertainer
1600 Meadowood Lane, Charlotte NC 28211, USA

**Obradors, Jacqueline** — Actress
A P A Talent/Literary Agency, 405 S Beverly Dr, #300, Beverly Hills CA 90212 USA

**O'Bradovich, Edward (Ed)** — Football Player
235 N Smith St, #207, Palatine IL 60067, USA

**Obradovich, James R (Jim)** — Football Player
2601 Morningside Dr, Lomita CA 90717, USA

**Obraztsova, Elena V** — Opera Singer
Bolshoi Theater, Teatralnaya Pl 1, 103009 Moscow, Russia

**Obreht, Tea** — Writer
Random House, 1745 Broadway, #1800, New York NY 10019 USA

**O'Brian, Hugh** — Actor
O'Brian Youth Leadership, 31255 Cedar Valley, #327, Westlake Village CA 91362, USA

**O'Brien, Bill** — Football Coach
Pennsylvania State University, Athletic Dept, University Park PA 16802, USA

**O'Brien, Carl (Cubby)** — Actor
39919 NE 127th Court, Amboy WA 98601, USA

**O'Brien, Cathy** — Track Athlete
19 Foss Farm Road, Durham NH 03824, USA

**O'Brien, Charles H (Charlie)** — Baseball Player
4932 E 38th Place, Tulsa OK 74135, USA

**O'Brien, Conan** — Writer, Producer, Actor
W M E Entertainment, 9601 Wilshire Blvd, #300, Beverly Hills CA 90210 USA

**O'Brien, Dan** — Track Athlete
8390 E Via de Ventura, #110, Scottsdale AZ 85258, USA

**O'Brien, Dennis** — Ice Hockey Player
31 Hope St N, Port Hope ON L1A 2N4, Canada

**O'Brien, Edna** — Writer
David Godwin Assoc, 55 Monmouth St, London WC2H 9DG, England

**O'Brien, Edward J (Eddie)** — Baseball Player
522 Alder St, #101, Edmonds WA 98020, USA

**O'Brien, Edwin F Cardinal** — Religious Leader
Equestrian Order, 00120 Vatican City

**O'Brien, G Dennis** — Educator
PO Box 510, Middlebury VT 05753, USA

| | |
|---|---|
| **O'Brien, Jack** | Director, Choreographer |
| Gersh Agency, 9465 Wilshire Blvd, #600, Beverly Hills CA 90212 USA | |
| **O'Brien, Keith M P Cardinal** | Religious Leader |
| Archbishop's House, 42 Greenhill Gardens, Edinburgh EH10 4B5, Scotland | |
| **O'Brien, Kenneth J (Ken), Jr** | Football Player |
| 201 Manhattan Ave, Manhattan Beach CA 90266, USA | |
| **O'Brien, Margaret** | Actress |
| 14840 Valerio St, Van Nuys CA 91405, USA | |
| **O'Brien, Maureen** | Actress |
| United Agents, 12-26 Lexington St, London W1F 0LE, England | |
| **O'Brien, Michael** | Labor Leader |
| Transport Workers Union, 1700 Broadway, #200, New York NY 10019, USA | |
| **O'Brien, Pat** | Sportscaster, Entertainer |
| I C M Partners, 10250 Constellation Blvd, #900, Los Angeles CA 90067 USA | |
| **O'Brien, Peter M (Pete)** | Baseball Player |
| 5509 Montclair Dr, Colleyville TX 76034, USA | |
| **O'Brien, Richard** | Composer, Lyricist |
| TimeWarp, 1 Elm Grove, Hildenborough, Tonbridge Kent TN11 9HE, England | |
| **O'Brien, Ron** | Diving Coach |
| 80450 Overseas Highway, #401, Islamorada FL 33036, USA | |
| **O'Brien, Soledad** | Commentator |
| Al Jazeera America, Editorial Dept, 311 W 34th St, New York NY 10001 USA | |
| **O'Brien, Terrence L** | Judge |
| US Court of Appeals, 2120 Capitol Ave, #2131, Cheyenne WY 82001, USA | |
| **O'Brien, Tim** | Writer |
| Minnesota West Technical College, English Dept, Worthington MN 56187, USA | |
| **O'Brien, Tim** | Singer, Musician |
| W N S Group, 6 Rolyn Hills Dr, Orangeburg NY 10962, USA | |
| **O'Brien, Tina** | Actress |
| Shepherd Mgmt, 45 Maddox St, #400, London W1S 2PE, England | |
| **O'Brien, Tom** | Football Coach |
| North Carolina State University, Athletic Dept, Raleigh NC 27695, USA | |
| **O'Brien, Trever** | Actor |
| Luber Rocklin Entertainment, 8530 Wilshire Blvd, #555, Beverly Hills CA 90211 USA | |
| **O'Bryan, Sean** | Actor |
| Domain Talent, 9229 W Sunset Blvd, #710, West Hollywood CA 90069 USA | |
| **Obst, Lynda** | Producer, Writer |
| Lynda Obst Productions, 5555 Melrose Ave, Astaire Building, Los Angeles CA 90038, USA | |
| **O'Byrne, Brian F** | Actor |
| Lisa Richards Agency, 108 Upper Leeson St, Dublin 4, Ireland | |
| **O'Callaghan, Patricia M** | Singer |
| B C Fielder Mgmt, 53 Seton Park Road, Toronto ON M3C 3ZB, Canada | |
| **O'Callahan, John (Jack)** | Ice Hockey Player |
| 101 Linden Ave, Glencoe IL 60022, USA | |
| **Ocampo Uria, Adriana C** | Geologist, Planetary Scientist |
| National Aeronautics/Space Administration, 300 E St SW, Washington DC 20546, USA | |
| **Ocampo, Miguel** | Artist |
| Wood Street Gallery, 601 Wood St, Pittsburgh PA 15222, USA | |
| **O'Caroll, Sinead** | Singer (B*Witched) |
| Clintons, 55 Drury Lane, Covent Garden, London WC2B 5SQ, England | |
| **O'Carroll, Brendan** | Actor |
| Kaplan-Stahler Agency, 8383 Wilshire Blvd, #923, Beverly Hills CA 90211 USA | |
| **Ocasek, Ric** | Singer, Guitarist (Cars); Songwriter |
| Lookout Mgmt, 1460 4th St, #300, Santa Monica CA 90401 USA | |
| **Occhilupo, Mark** | Surfer |
| Billabong, 1 Billabong Place, Burleigh Heads QLD 4220, Australia | |
| **Ocean, Billy** | Singer, Songwriter |
| Universal Attractions, 135 W 26th St, #1200, New York NY 10001 USA | |
| **Ochiai, Masayuki** | Director |
| Director's Guild, Shibuya Goto Building, 3-2 Maruyama, #5, Shibuya, Tokyo 150 0044, Japan | |
| **Ochiltree, Dianne** | Writer |
| 716 Tropical Circle, Sarasota FL 34242, USA | |
| **Ochirbat, Punsalmaagiin** | President, Mongolia |
| Tengeriin Tsag Co, Olympic St 14, Ulan Bator, Mongolia | |
| **Ochman, Wieslaw** | Opera Singer |
| Ul Miaczynska 46B, 02-637 Warsaw, Poland | |
| **Ochoa, Alex** | Baseball Player |
| 14526 NW 83rd Passage, Hialeah FL 33016, USA | |
| **Ochoa, Ellen** | Astronaut |
| 4515 Sterling Wood Way, Houston TX 77059, USA | |
| **Ochoa, Lorena** | Golfer |
| Ladies Pro Golf Assn, 100 International Golf Dr, Daytona Beach FL 32124 USA | |
| **Ochowicz, James L (Jim)** | Cyclist |
| 945 Hutchinson Ave, Palo Alto CA 94301, USA | |
| **Ockels, Wubbo** | Astronaut, Netherlands |
| E S T E C, Postbus 299, 2200 Noordwijk AG, Netherlands | |
| **O'Connell, Brian** | Bassist |
| Junoon, Sidco Tower, #A-10/2, Strachen Road, Karachi 74200, Pakistan | |
| **O'Connell, Carol** | Writer |
| Berkley Publishing Group, 375 Hudson St, Basement 1, New York NY 10014 USA | |
| **O'Connell, Deirdre** | Actress |
| Innovative Artists, 1505 10th St, Santa Monica CA 90401 USA | |
| **O'Connell, Jack** | Actor |
| Conway Van Gelder Grant, 8-12 Broadwick St, #300, London W1F 8HW, England | |
| **O'Connell, Jerry** | Actor, Director |
| 3 Arts Entertainment, 9460 Wilshire Blvd, #700, Beverly Hills CA 90212 USA | |
| **O'Connell, Maura** | Singer |
| Rubin Media, PO Box 158161, Nashville TN 37215, USA | |
| **O'Connell, Mike** | Ice Hockey Player, Coach |
| 17 Border St, Cohasset MA 02025, USA | |
| **O'Connell, Robbie** | Singer, Songwriter |
| Producers Inc, 11806 N 56th St, Tampa FL 33617 USA | |
| **O'Connor, Brian** | Baseball Player |
| 3054 Inwood Dr, Cincinnati OH 45241, USA | |
| **O'Connor, Bryan D** | Astronaut |
| 1305 Lafayette Dr, Alexandria VA 22308, USA | |

|  |  |
|---|---|
| **O'Connor, Christy, Jr**<br>Gaylord Sports Mgmt, 13845 N Northsight Blvd, #200, Scottsdale AZ 85260 USA | Golfer |
| **O'Connor, Derrick**<br>Markham Froggatt Irwin, Julian House, 4 Windmill St, London W1P 1HF, England | Actor |
| **O'Connor, Edmund F**<br>1169 Ironsides Ave, Melbourne FL 32940, USA | Army General |
| **O'Connor, Erin**<br>2pm Model Mgmt, Norregade 2, 1165 Copenhagen K, Denmark | Model |
| **O'Connor, Frances**<br>Gersh Agency, 9465 Wilshire Blvd, #600, Beverly Hills CA 90212 USA | Actress |
| **O'Connor, Gavin**<br>Solaris, 12 Washington Blvd, #200, Venice CA 90292, USA | Actor, Director, Writer |
| **O'Connor, Glynnis**<br>Bauman Redanty Shaul Agency, 5757 Wilshire Blvd, #473, Los Angeles CA 90036 USA | Actress |
| **O'Connor, J Dennis**<br>Smithsonian Institution, Provost's Office, Washington DC 20560, USA | Educator |
| **O'Connor, Jack W**<br>PO Box 430, Yucca Valley CA 92286, USA | Baseball Player |
| **O'Connor, Jane**<br>Harper Collins Publishers, 10 E 53rd St, Cellar 1, New York NY 10022 USA | Writer |
| **O'Connor, Kelley**<br>I M G Artists, Hogarth Business Park, Chiswick, London W4 2TH, England | Opera Singer |
| **O'Connor, Kevin J**<br>Innovative Artists, 1505 10th St, Santa Monica CA 90401 USA | Actor |
| **O'Connor, Mark**<br>Columbia Artists Mgmt Inc, 1790 Broadway, #702, New York NY 10019 USA | Fiddler, Violinist |
| **O'Connor, Mary Anne**<br>60 Romanock Place, Fairfield CT 06825, USA | Basketball Player |
| **O'Connor, Michael**<br>Dench Arnold Agency, 10 Newburgh St, London W1F 7RN, England | Costume Designer |
| **O'Connor, Myles**<br>O'Connors Fine Footwear, 1415 1st St SW, Calgary AB T2R 0V9, Canada | Ice Hockey Player |
| **O'Connor, Patrick**<br>Paradigm Agency, 360 N Crescent Dr, North Building, Beverly Hills CA 90210 USA | Actor |
| **O'Connor, Patrick D (Pat)**<br>United Agents, 12-26 Lexington St, London W1F 0LE, England | Director, Writer |
| **O'Connor, Renee**<br>R O R Productions, 1601 N Sepulveda Blvd, #768, Manhattan Beach CA 90266, USA | Actress |
| **O'Connor, Sandra Day**<br>College of William & Mary, Chancellor's Office, Williamsburg VA 23187, USA | Supreme Court Justice, Educator |
| **O'Connor, Sinead**<br>Paradigm Agency, 360 N Crescent Dr, North Building, Beverly Hills CA 90210 USA | Singer, Songwriter |
| **O'Connor, Thom**<br>Moss Road, Voorheesville NY 12186, USA | Artist |
| **O'Connor, Timothy J (Tim)**<br>House of Representatives, 1434 6th St, #1, Santa Monica CA 90401 USA | Actor |
| **O'Connor, William F (Bill)**<br>1905-40 Richview Road, Toronto ON M9A 5C1, Canada | Football Player |
| **O'Conor, John**<br>Columbia Artists Mgmt Inc, 1790 Broadway, #702, New York NY 10019 USA | Concert Pianist |
| **Odadjian, Sharvarsh S (Shavo)**<br>Velmet Hammer Music, 9911 W Pico Blvd, #360W, Los Angeles CA 90035, USA | Bassist (System of a Down) |
| **Odar, Baran Bo**<br>United Talent Agency, U T A Plaza, 9336 Civic Center Dr, Beverly Hills CA 90210 USA | Director, Producer, Writer |
| **O'Dassey, Seregon**<br>G & G Talent, 926C Lincoln Ave, New York NY 11741, USA | Actress, Model, Producer |
| **O'Day, Aubrey M**<br>Bad Boy Entertainment, 1440 Broadway, #16, New York NY 10018 USA | Singer (Danity Kane), Songwriter, Model |
| **O'Day, George**<br>6 Turtle Lane, Dover MA 02030, USA | Yachtsman |
| **Oddleifson, Christopher R (Chris)**<br>1950 Westover Road, North Vancouver BC V7J 3J3, Canada | Ice Hockey Player |
| **Odelein, Lyle**<br>12569 Winding Hollow Lane, Frisco TX 75033, USA | Ice Hockey Player |
| **Odelein, Selmar**<br>Farm, Quill Lake SK S0A 3E0, Canada | Ice Hockey Player |
| **Odell, Bob H**<br>911 Stenton Place, Ocean City NJ 08226, USA | Football Player, Coach |
| **O'Dell, Nancy**<br>W M E Entertainment, 9601 Wilshire Blvd, #300, Beverly Hills CA 90210 USA | Actress |
| **O'Dell, Tony**<br>417 N Griffith Park Dr, Burbank CA 91506, USA | Actor |
| **O'Dell, William O (Billy)**<br>225 Odelll Road, Newberry SC 29108, USA | Baseball Player |
| **Oden, Gregory W (Greg), Jr**<br>Miami Heat, American Airlines Arena, 601 Biscayne Blvd, Miami FL 33132 USA | Basketball Player |
| **Oden, McDonald**<br>480 Chimneytop Dr, Antioch TN 37013, USA | Football Plater |
| **Oden, Robert**<br>PO Box 660, Aspen CO 81612, USA | Surgeon, Skiing Physician |
| **Oden, Robert A, Jr**<br>Carleton College, President's Office, 1 N College St, Northfield MN 55057, USA | Educator |
| **Odgers, Jeff**<br>Farm, Spy Hill SK S0A 3W0, Canada | Ice Hockey Player |
| **Odhiambo, David**<br>7 8th Ave, Lake Pleasant MA 01347, USA | Writer |
| **Odierno, Raymond T**<br>Chief of Staff, HqUSA, Pentagon, Washington DC 20310 USA | Army General |
| **Odjick, Gino**<br>Musquem Gold Academy, 3904 51st Ave W, Vancouver BC V6N 3W1, Canada | Ice Hockey Player |
| **Odjig, Daphne**<br>7841 Highway 97 North, #182, Kelowna BC V4V 1E7, Canada | Artist |
| **Odmark, Matthew T (Matt)**<br>Nettwerk Mgmt, 1650 W 2nd Ave, Vancouver BC V6J 4R3, Canada | Guitarist (Jars of Clay) |
| **Odom, Antwan**<br>4562 Raynor Court, Mason OH 45040, USA | Football Player |

O

**Odom, Clifton L (Cliff)** — Football Player
6708 Marthas Vineyard Dr, Arlington TX 76001, USA
**Odom, Johnny Lee (Blue Moon)** — Baseball Player
10343 Slater Ave, #204, Fountain Valley CA 92708, USA
**Odom, Lamar J** — Basketball Player
21731 Ventura Blvd, #300, Woodland Hills CA 91364, USA
**Odom, Stephen T (Steve)** — Football Player
1482 Lincoln St, Berkeley CA 94702, USA
**Odomes, Nathaniel B (Nate)** — Football Player
900 Quail Creek Dr, Columbus GA 31907, USA
**Odoms, Riley M** — Football Player
16731 Quail Park Dr, Missouri City TX 77489, USA
**O'Donnell, Andrew** — Basketball Player
3310 Lincoln Ave, Allentown PA 18103, USA
**O'Donnell, Annie** — Actress
Kazarian/Measures/Ruskin, 11969 Ventura Blvd, #300, Studio City CA 91604 USA
**O'Donnell, Chris** — Actor
W M E Entertainment, 9601 Wilshire Blvd, #300, Beverly Hills CA 90210 USA
**O'Donnell, Daniel** — Singer
Brockwell, 90B Lagan Road, Dublin Industrial Estate, Dublin 11, Ireland
**O'Donnell, Fred** — Ice Hockey Player
690 Carnaby St, Kingston ON K0H 2H0, Canada
**O'Donnell, Joseph R (Joe)** — Football Player
447 Bodley Crescent, Milan MI 48160, USA
**O'Donnell, Keir** — Actor
United Talent Agency, U T A Plaza, 9336 Civic Center Dr, Beverly Hills CA 90210 USA
**O'Donnell, Neil K** — Football Player
5329 Stanford Dr, Nashville TN 37215, USA
**O'Donnell, Rosie** — Actress
W M E Entertainment, 9601 Wilshire Blvd, #300, Beverly Hills CA 90210 USA
**O'Donnell, Sean** — Ice Hockey Player
1656 Manhattan Ave, Hermosa Beach CA 90254, USA
**O'Donnell, William (Bill)** — Harness Racing Driver
569 Penn Estate, East Stroudsburg PA 18301, USA
**O'Donoghue, Colin** — Actor
Alchemy Entertainment, 7024 Melrose Ave, #420, Los Angeles CA 90038 USA
**O'Donoghue, John E** — Baseball Player
5246 Far Oak Circle, Sarasota FL 34238, USA
**O'Donoghue, Neil** — Football Player
1118 Flushing Ave, Clearwater FL 33764, USA
**O'Donohue, John F** — Actor
Don Buchwald, 6500 Wilshire Blvd, #2200, Los Angeles CA 90048 USA
**O'Dowd, Chris** — Actor
United Talent Agency, U T A Plaza, 9336 Civic Center Dr, Beverly Hills CA 90210 USA
**Odrowski, Gerry** — Ice Hockey Player
PO Box 126, Trout Creek ON P0H 2L0, Canada
**Oduber, Nelson O** — Prime Minister, Aruba
Prime Minister's Office, L G Smith Blvd 76, Oranjestad, Aruba
**Oduye, Adepero** — Actress
Washington Square Arts, 1041 N Formosa Ave, Formosa Building, West Hollywood CA 90046, USA
**O'Dwyer, Billy** — Ice Hockey Player
11 Fox Hill Dr, Braintree MA 02184, USA
**Oe, Kenzaburo** — Nobel Literature Laureate
585 Seijo-Machi, Setagayaku, Tokyo, Japan
**Oedekerk, Steve** — Director
W M E Entertainment, 9601 Wilshire Blvd, #300, Beverly Hills CA 90210 USA
**Oefelein, William A** — Astronaut
Adventure Write, PO Box 113074, Anchorage AK 99511, USA
**Oelkers, Bryan A** — Baseball Player
3404 Taylor Ave, Bridgeton MO 63044, USA
**Oelze, Christiane** — Opera Singer
Augstein & Hahn, Tal 28, 80331 Munich, Germany
**Oester, Ronald J (Ron)** — Baseball Player
3760 Nine Mile-Tobasco Road, Cincinnati OH 45255, USA
**Oetiker, Phil** — Cinematographer
422 10th St, Brooklyn NY 11215, USA
**Oettinger, Anthony G** — Mathematician
65 Elizabeth Road, Belmont MA 02478, USA
**Offerdahl, John A** — Football Player
2749 NE 37th Dr, Fort Lauderdale FL 33308, USA
**Offerman, Jose A** — Baseball Player
10720 Moorpark St, North Hollywood CA 91602, USA
**Offerman, Nick** — Actor
United Talent Agency, U T A Plaza, 9336 Civic Center Dr, Beverly Hills CA 90210 USA
**Office, Rowland J (Rollie)** — Baseball Player
1028 Lake Glen Way, Sacramento CA 95822, USA
**Ofili, Chris** — Artist
Victoria Miro Gallery, 21 Cork St, London W1X 1HB, England
**O'Flaherty, Gerry** — Ice Hockey Player
5446 Cortez Crescent, North Vancouver BC V7R 4R4, Canada
**Ogando, Alexi** — Baseball Player
Texas Rangers, Ameriquest Field, 1000 Ballpark Way, #306, Arlington TX 76011 USA
**Ogato, Sadako** — Government Official, Japan
United Nations Office for Refugees, CP 2500, 1211 Geneva 2, Switzerland
**Ogbogu, Eric O** — Football Player
16814 Harbour Town Dr, Silver Spring MD 20905, USA
**Ogden, Carlos (Bud)** — Basketball Player
3324 S 4th St, Springfield IL 62703, USA
**Ogden, Jonathan P (Jon)** — Football Player
3330 Georgia Ave NW, Washington DC 20010, USA
**Ogden, Raymond D (Ray)** — Football Player
188 Anderson Dr, Brunswick GA 31520, USA
**Ogea, Chad W** — Baseball Player
3233 Plantation Court, Baton Rouge LA 70820, USA
**Ogi, Adolf** — President, Switzerland
United Nations, Palais des Nations, #C119, 1211 Geneva 10, Switzerland

| | |
|---|---|
| **Ogier, Bulle**<br>Artmedia, 20 Ave Rapp, 75007 Paris, France | Actress, Writer |
| **Ogilvie, Brian H**<br>4708 60th St, Red Deer AB T4N 7C7, Canada | Ice Hockey Player |
| **Ogilvie, Lana**<br>Company Models, 17 Little West 12th St, #333, New York NY 10014, USA | Model |
| **Ogilvie, N Joseph (Joe)**<br>10 Cicero Lane, Austin TX 78746, USA | Golfer |
| **Ogilvy, Geoff C**<br>8355 E Hartford Dr, #105, Scottsdale AZ 85255, USA | Golfer |
| **Ogilvy, Ian**<br>Julian Belfrage Assoc, 9 Argyll St, #300, London W1F 7TG, England | Actor |
| **Ogimi, Yuki Nagasato**<br>F F C Turbine Potsdam, Am Luftschiffhafen 2, #33, 14471 Potsdam, Germany | Soccer Player |
| **Ogio, Michel**<br>Governor General's Office, PO Box 79, Port Moresby 121, Papua New Guinea | Governor General, Papua New Guinea |
| **Ogle, Brett**<br>Advantage International, 1751 Pinnacle Dr, #1500, McLean VA 22102 USA | Golfer |
| **Oglivie, Benjamin A (Ben)**<br>1012 E Sandpiper Dr, Tempe AZ 85283, USA | Baseball Player |
| **O'Grady, Gail**<br>Shelter Entertainment, 9255 Sunset Blvd, #300, Los Angeles CA 90069 USA | Actress |
| **O'Grady, Sean**<br>5808 NW 117th Terrace, Oklahoma City OK 73162, USA | Boxer |
| **Ogren, Jayce**<br>I M G Artists, Carnegie Hall Tower, 152 W 57th St, #500, New York NY 10019 USA | Conductor |
| **Ogrin, David**<br>2321 Common St, #102, New Braunfels TX 78130, USA | Golfer |
| **Ogrodnick, John**<br>37034 Aldgate Court, Farmington Hills MI 48335, USA | Ice Hockey Player |
| **Ogunleye, Adewale**<br>19113 NW 23rd Court, Pembroke Pines FL 33029, USA | Football Player |
| **Ogwumike, Nnemkadi (Nnenka)**<br>Los Angeles Sparks, 888 S Figueroa St, #2010, Los Angeles CA 90017 USA | Basketball Player |
| **Oh Jae-Seok**<br>Football Assn, 1-131 Sinmunno, 2-Ga Jongno-Gu, Seoul 110 062, South Korea | Soccer Player |
| **Oh, Sadaharu**<br>Fukuoka Dome Daiei Hawks, 2-2-2 Jigyohama, Chuoku Fukuoka 810 0065, Japan | Baseball Player |
| **Oh, Sandra**<br>Principal Entertainment, 9255 Sunset Blvd, #500, Los Angeles CA 90069 USA | Actress |
| **Oh, Soon Teck**<br>Lee Assoc, 8961 W Sunset Blvd, #V, West Hollywood CA 90069, USA | Actor |
| **O'Hair, Sean**<br>PO Box 127, Pocopson PA 19366, USA | Golfer |
| **Ohakete, Ifeanyi**<br>11912 Crosswind Court, Reston VA 20194, USA | Football Player |
| **O'Hanlon, Francis B (Fran)**<br>27 W Wayne Ave, Easton PA 18042, USA | Basketball Player |
| **O'Hara, Catherine**<br>I C M Partners, 10250 Constellation Blvd, #900, Los Angeles CA 90067 USA | Actress, Comedienne |
| **O'Hara, Kelli**<br>Gersh Agency, 9465 Wilshire Blvd, #600, Beverly Hills CA 90212 USA | Actress, Singer |
| **O'Hara, M Kelley**<br>Soccer Federation, 1801 S Prairie Ave, Chicago IL 60616 USA | Soccer Player |
| **O'Hara, Maureen**<br>Artists Agency, 9430 Olympic Blvd, Beverly Hills CA 90212 USA | Actress |
| **O'Hare, Damian**<br>Innovative Artists, 1505 10th St, Santa Monica CA 90401 USA | Actor |
| **O'Hare, Denis**<br>Innovative Artists, 1505 10th St, Santa Monica CA 90401 USA | Actor, Singer |
| **O'Haver, Tommy**<br>Media Talent Group, 9200 W Sunset Blvd, #550, West Hollywood CA 90069 USA | Director, Writer, Actor |
| **O'Heir, Jim**<br>Stone Manners Salners, 9911 W Pico Blvd, #1400, Los Angeles CA 90035 USA | Actor |
| **Oher, Michael J**<br>Baltimore Ravens, Ravens Stadium, 1 Winning Dr, Baltimore MD 21230 USA | Football Player |
| **Ohl, Donald J (Don)**<br>2 E Lockhaven Court, Edwardsville IL 62025, USA | Basketball Player |
| **Ohlde, Nicole**<br>Tulsa Shock, B O K Center, 200 S Denver, Tulsa OK 74103 USA | Basketball Player |
| **Ohlendorf, C Ross**<br>2300 Barton Creek Blvd, #40, Austin TX 78735, USA | Baseball Player |
| **Ohlsson, Garrick**<br>Opus 3 Artists, 470 Park Ave S, #900N, New York NY 10016 USA | Concert Pianist |
| **Ohlund, K Mattias**<br>Tampa Bay Lightning, 401 Channelside Dr, Tampa FL 33602 USA | Ice Hockey Player |
| **Ohman, Jack**<br>Portland Oregonian, Editorial Dept, 1320 SW Broadway, Portland OR 97201, USA | Editorial Cartoonist (Mixed Media) |
| **Ohman, William M (Will)**<br>8939 E Norwood Circle, Mesa AZ 85207, USA | Baseball Player |
| **Ohme, Kevin A**<br>805 Starlifter Lane, Valrico FL 33594, USA | Baseball Player |
| **Ohnishi, Minoru**<br>Fuji Photo Film, 26-30 Nishiazabu, Minatoku, Tokyo 106 8620, Japan | Businessman |
| **Ohno, Apolo Anton**<br>Dreams Inc, 2 S University Dr, #325, Plantation FL 33324 USA | Speed Skater |
| **Ohno, Shinobu**<br>Football Assn, 3-10-15 Hongo, Bunkyoku, Tokyo 113 0033 Japan | Soccer Player |
| **Ohno, Yumiko**<br>W M E Entertainment, 9601 Wilshire Blvd, #300, Beverly Hills CA 90210 USA | Singer, Bassist (Buffalo Daughter) |
| **Ohr, Fred**<br>6401 Newburg Road, #211, Rockford IL 61108, USA | WW II Army Air Corps Hero |
| **Ohrner, Tommy (Tommi)**<br>Ortlinder 6, 81927 Munich, Germany | Actor |
| **Ohta, Tomoko**<br>20-20 Hatsunedai, Mishimashi, Shizuokaken 411 0018, Japan | Geneticist |

**O**

**Ohtani, Monshu Koshin** — Religious Leader
Horikawa-Dori, Hanayachosagaru, Shimogyoku, Kyoto 600 8501, Japan

**O'Hurley, John** — Actor
Marv Dauer Mgmt, 11661 San Vicente Blvd, #104, Los Angeles CA 90049, USA

**Ohuruogu, Christine I** — Track Athlete
N & E Beagles, 281 Prince Regent Lane, London E13 8SD, England

**Oistrakh, Igor D** — Concert Violinist
Novolesnaya Str 3, Korp 2, #10, Moscow, Russia

**Ojala, Kirt S** — Baseball Player
1902 Forest Lake Dr SE, Grand Rapids MI 49546, USA

**Ojeda, Eddie** — Singer, Guitarist (Twisted Sister)
Rebellion Entertainment, 2440 Broadway, #111, New York NY 10024, USA

**Ojeda, O Augie** — Baseball Player
5351 W Morgan Place, Chandler AZ 85226, USA

**Ojeda, Robert M (Bob)** — Baseball Player
20 Somerset Dr, Rumson NJ 07760, USA

**Oka, Masi** — Actor
United Talent Agency, U T A Plaza, 9336 Civic Center Dr, Beverly Hills CA 90210 USA

**Oka, Takeshi** — Chemist
1463 E Park Place, Chicago IL 60637, USA

**Okabe, Noriaki** — Engineer, Architect
Noriaki Okabe, Architecture Network, 1-14-19-1F Minato Chuohku, Tokyo 104 0043, Japan

**Okafor, Chukwuemeka N (Emeka)** — Basketball Player
840 Tchoupitoulas St, #102, New Orleans LA 70130, USA

**Okajima, Hideki** — Baseball Player
303 3rd St, #704, Cambridge MA 2142, USA

**Okamoto, Ayako** — Golfer
22627 Ladeene Ave, Torrance CA 90505, USA

**Okamoto, Tao** — Actress
I C M Partners, 10250 Constellation Blvd, #900, Los Angeles CA 90067 USA

**O'Kane, Deirdre** — Actress
Lisa Richards Agency, 33 Old Compton St, London W1D 5JT, England , USA

**Oke, Janette** — Writer
Baker Publishing Group, PO Box 6287, Grand Rapids MI 49516, USA

**Okeafor, Chikezie R (Chike)** — Football Player
8340 N Ridgeview Dr, Paradise Valley AZ 85253, USA

**O'Keefe, Jeremiah J, Sr** — WW II Marine Corps Air Force Hero
202 White Blvd, Ocean Springs MS 39564, USA

**O'Keefe, Jodie Lyn** — Actress
Vincent Cirrincione Assoc, 1516 N Fairfax Ave, Los Angeles CA 90046 USA

**O'Keefe, Laurence (Larry)** — Composer
I C M Partners, 10250 Constellation Blvd, #900, Los Angeles CA 90067 USA

**O'Keefe, Michael** — Actor
Paradigm Agency, 360 N Crescent Dr, North Building, Beverly Hills CA 90210 USA

**O'Keefe, Miles** — Actor
Sharp/Karrys, 117 N Orlando Ave, Los Angeles CA 90048, USA

**O'Keefe, Sean** — Educator, Governmemt Official
E A D S North America, 1616 N Fort Myer Dr, #1600, Arlington VA 22209, USA

**O'Keefe, Thomas V (Tommy)** — Basketball Player
1000 Potomac Lane, Alexandria VA 22308, USA

**Okeniyi, Dayo** — Actor
United Talent Agency, U T A Plaza, 9336 Civic Center Dr, Beverly Hills CA 90210 USA

**Okereke, Kelechukwu R (Kele)** — Singer, Guitarist (Bloc Party)
Coalition Mgmt, 12 Barley Mow Passage, London W4 4PH, England

**Okhotnikoff, Nikolai P** — Opera Singer
Canal Griboedova 109, #13, 190068 Saint Petersburg, Russia

**Okobi, Chukwunweze S (Chukky)** — Football Player
5516 Maple Heights Court, Pittsburgh PA 15232, USA

**Okogie, Anthony Olubunmi Cardinal** — Religious Leader
Archdiocese, PO Box 8, 19 Catholic Mission St, Lagos, Nigeria

**Okolowicz, Jeff** — Guitarist (Chesterfield Kings)
Agency Group Ltd, 142 W 57th St, #600, New York NY 10019 USA

**Okolowicz, Ted** — Guitarist (Chesterfield Kings)
Agency Group Ltd, 142 W 57th St, #600, New York NY 10019 USA

**Okonedo, Sophie** — Actress
Hamilton Hodell, 66-68 Margaret St, #500, London W1W 8SR, England

**Okoniewski, J Stephen (Steve)** — Football Player
222 S Oakland Ave, Oconto Falls WI 54154, USA

**O'Koren, Michael F (Mike)** — Basketball Player
109 Quaker Road, Mickleton NJ 08056, USA

**Okoye, Christian E** — Football Player
10082 Big Pine Dr, Rancho Cucamonga CA 91737, USA

**Okrie, Leonard J (Len)** — Baseball Player
2636 Burke Lane, Fayetteville NC 28306, USA

**Okumoto, Yuji** — Actor
Kono Kitchen, 8501 5th Ave NE, Seattle WA 98115, USA

**Okumura, Tomohiro** — Concert Violinist
Jecklin Assoc, 2717 Nichols Lane, Davenport IA 52803, USA

**Okun, Daniel A** — Environmental Engineer
204 Carol Woods, 750 Weaver Dairy Road, Chapel Hill NC 27514, USA

**Okur, Mehmet** — Basketball Player
1387 Perrys Hollow Road, Salt Lake City UT 84103, USA

**Oladipo, Victor** — Basketball Player
Orlando Magic, 8701 Maitland Summit Blvd, Orlando FL 32810 USA

**Olafsson, Olafur Darri** — Actor
A P A Talent/Literary Agency, 405 S Beverly Dr, #300, Beverly Hills CA 90212 USA

**Olagundoye, Toks** — Actress
Glick Agency, 1321 7th St, #203, Santa Monica CA 90401 USA

**Olah, George A** — Nobel Chemistry Laureate
2252 Gloaming Way, Beverly Hills CA 90210, USA

**Olajuwon, Hakeem A** — Basketball Player
1305 N Horseshoe Dr, Sugar Land TX 77478, USA

**Olander, Edwin (Ed)** — WW II Marine Corps Air Force Hero
85 N Maple St, Florence MA 01062, USA

**Olander, James B (Jim)** — Baseball Player
8421 S Triangle R Ranch Place, Vail AZ 85641, USA

**Olander, Jimmy** — Guitarist (Diamond Rio)
Modern Mgmt, 1625 Broadway, #600, Nashville TN 37203, USA
**Olandt, Ken** — Actor
3216 Allegheny Court, Westlake Village CA 91362, USA
**Olazabal, Jose Maria** — Golfer
Real Club Golf de San Sebastian, Baserritar Etorbidea 1, 20280 Hondarribia, Gipuzkoa, Spain
**Olberding, Mark A** — Basketball Player
4131 Cliff Oaks St, San Antonio TX 78229, USA
**Olbermann, Keith T** — Sportscaster, Commentator
I C M Partners, 10250 Constellation Blvd, #900, Los Angeles CA 90067 USA
**Olczyk, Ed** — Ice Hockey Player, Coach
4581 Pamela Court, Long Grove IL 60047, USA
**Olden, Paul** — Sportscaster
68 Dean St, #3F, Brooklyn NY 11201, USA
**Oldenburg, Brandon** — Animator
Moonbot Studios, 2031 Kings Highway, #102, Shreveport LA 71103, USA
**Oldenburg, Claes T** — Sculptor
556 Broome St, New York NY 10013, USA
**Oldenburg, Richard E** — Museum Executive
447 E 57th St, New York NY 10022, USA
**Olderman, Murray** — Sportswriter
28 La Costa Dr, Rancho Mirage CA 92270, USA
**Oldershaw, Kelsey** — Actress
Darren Goldberg Mgmt, 5225 Wilshire Blvd, #419, Los Angeles CA 90036, USA
**Oldfield, Bruce** — Fashion Designer
27 Beauchamp Place, London SW3 1 NJ, England
**Oldfield, Mike** — Singer, Songwriter
PO Box 2031, Blandford DT11 9YB, England
**Oldfield, Sally** — Singer
Global Artists Mgmt, Willy-Brandt-Str 39, 50374 Erftstadt, Germany
**Oldham, Christopher M (Chris)** — Football Player
8701 E Wilshire Dr, Scottsdale AZ 85257, USA
**Oldham, John H** — Baseball Player
1845 Anne Way, San Jose CA 95124, USA
**Oldham, John O (Johnny)** — Basketball Player, Coach
2127 Sycamore Dr, Bowling Green KY 42104, USA
**Oldham, Todd** — Fashion Designer
120 Wooster St, New York NY 10012, USA
**Oldis, Robert C (Bob)** — Baseball Player
7414 Pohick Road, Lorton VA 22079, USA
**Oldman, Gary** — Actor, Director
A P A Talent/Literary Agency, 405 S Beverly Dr, #300, Beverly Hills CA 90212 USA
**Oldring, Peter** — Actor, Comedian
Schumacher Mgmt, 10323 Santa Monica Blvd, #101, Los Angeles CA 90024, USA
**Olds, Gabriel** — Actor
Stone Manners Salners, 9911 W Pico Blvd, #1400, Los Angeles CA 90035 USA
**Olds, Sharon** — Writer
Knopf Publishers, 1745 Broadway, New York NY 10019 USA
**Oldstone, Michael B A** — Neuropharmacologist
Scripps Research Institute, Neuropharmacology Dept, La Jolla CA 92037, USA
**Olear, Doug** — Actor
Progressive Artists Agency, 9696 Culver Blvd, #110, Culver City CA 90232 USA
**O'Leary, Brian T** — Astronaut
Future Focus on Human Potential, 5136 E Karen Dr, Scottsdale AZ 85254, USA
**O'Leary, Hazel R** — Secretary, Energy; Educator
Fisk University, President's Office, 1000 17th Ave N, Nashville TN 37208, USA
**O'Leary, John** — Actor
Gage Group, 14724 Ventura Blvd, #505, Sherman Oaks CA 91403 USA
**O'Leary, Matthew** — Actor
I C M Partners, 10250 Constellation Blvd, #900, Los Angeles CA 90067 USA
**O'Leary, Michael** — Actor
38 Prospect Ave, Montclair NJ 07042, USA
**O'Leary, Troy F** — Baseball Player
1060 W Norwood St, Rialto CA 92377, USA
**Olejnik, Craig** — Actor
Robert Stein Mgmt, PO Box 3797, Beverly Hills CA 90212, USA
**Oleksy, Jozef** — Prime Minister, Poland
Sejm R P, Ul Wiejska 4/6/8, 00 902 Warsaw, Poland
**Ole-Moiyol, Onesmo** — Molecular Biologist, Immunologist
Insect Physiologist Centre, Nyayo Stadium, PO Box 30772, Nairobi, Kenya
**Olerud, John G** — Baseball Player
PO Box 606, Medina WA 98039, USA
**Olesz, Rostislav** — Ice Hockey Player
8687 Melrose Ave, #7, West Hollywood CA 90069, USA
**Olevsky, Julian** — Concert Violinist
68 Blue Hills Road, Amherst MA 01002, USA
**Oleynik, Larisa** — Actress
Savage Agency, 6212 Banner Ave, Los Angeles CA 90038 USA
**Olin, Ken** — Actor
Innovative Artists, 1505 10th St, Santa Monica CA 90401 USA
**Olin, Laurie** — Landscape Architect
227 S 6th St, Philadelphia PA 19106, USA
**Olin, Lena** — Actress
Paradigm Agency, 360 N Crescent Dr, North Building, Beverly Hills CA 90210 USA
**Oliphant, Patrick B (Pat)** — Editorial Cartoonist
Susan Conway Gallery, 1214 13th St, Washington DC 20005, USA
**Olitzky, Kerry M** — Religious Leader, Rabbi
Jewish Outreach Institute, 1270 Broadway, #609, New York NY 10001, USA
**Oliu, Ingrid** — Actress
Appletini Agency, 224 E Olive St, #209, Burbank CA 91502, USA
**Oliva, L Jay** — Educator
Skirball Performing Arts Center, 60 Washington Square S, New York NY 10012, USA
**Oliva, Pedro (Tony)** — Baseball Player
212 Spring Valley Dr, Minneapolis MN 55420, USA
**Olivares Palqu, Omar** — Baseball Player
PO Box 1328, San German PR 00683, USA

**O**

| | |
|---|---|
| **Olivares, Ruben**<br>Geno Productions, PO Box 113, Montebello CA 90640, USA | Boxer |
| **Olivas, John D**<br>595 36th St, Manhattan Beach CA 90266, USA | Astronaut |
| **Olive, Jason**<br>Liebman Entertainment, 12 E 46th St, #500, New York NY 10017, USA | Actor, Director, Producer |
| **Olive, John**<br>8652 Harjoan Ave, San Diego CA 92123, USA | Basketball Player |
| **Oliveira, Elmar**<br>C M Artists, 127 W 96th St, #13B, New York NY 10025 USA | Concert Violinist |
| **Oliver, Albert (Al)**<br>PO Box 1466, Portsmouth OH 45662, USA | Baseball Player |
| **Oliver, Brian**<br>Creative Artists Agency, 2000 Ave of Stars, #100, Los Angeles CA 90067 USA | Producer |
| **Oliver, Christian**<br>House of Representatives, 1434 6th St, #1, Santa Monica CA 90401 USA | Actor |
| **Oliver, Clarence H (Clancy)**<br>233 Springview, Irvine CA 92620, USA | Football Player |
| **Oliver, Daniel T**<br>318 Prince St, #6, Alexandria VA 22314, USA | Navy Admiral |
| **Oliver, Darren C**<br>1804 Larkspur Court, Southlake TX 76092, USA | Baseball Player |
| **Oliver, Dean**<br>21386 Notus Road, Greenleaf ID 83626, USA | Rodeo Rider |
| **Oliver, Hubert (Hubie)**<br>136 Blake St, Elyria OH 44035, USA | Football Player |
| **Oliver, Jamie**<br>PO Box 51372, London N1 7WX, England | Chef |
| **Oliver, John**<br>W M E Entertainment, 9601 Wilshire Blvd, #300, Beverly Hills CA 90210 USA | Actor, Writer, Producer |
| **Oliver, Joseph M (Joe)**<br>5223 Oak Island Road, Belle Isle FL 32809, USA | Baseball Player |
| **Oliver, Louis, III**<br>5082 SW 167th Ave, Miramar FL 33027, USA | Football Player |
| **Oliver, Mary**<br>Molly Malone Cook Agency, PO Box 1071, Sweet Briar VA 24595, USA | Writer |
| **Oliver, Murray C**<br>5505 McGuire Road, Minneapolis MN 55439, USA | Ice Hockey Player |
| **Oliver, Nancy**<br>United Talent Agency, U T A Plaza, 9336 Civic Center Dr, Beverly Hills CA 90210 USA | Producer, Writer |
| **Oliver, Nathaniel (Nate)**<br>4403 Oak Hill Road, Oakland CA 94605, USA | Baseball Player |
| **Oliver, Pam**<br>Ken Lindner Assoc, 2049 Century Park East, #1000, Los Angeles CA 90067, USA | Sportscaster |
| **Oliver, Robert L (Bob)**<br>1716 G St, Rio Linda CA 95673, USA | Baseball Player |
| **Oliver, Winslow P**<br>2027 Summerall Court, Richmond TX 77406, USA | Football Player |
| **Olivero, Chris**<br>Innovative Artists, 1505 10th St, Santa Monica CA 90401 USA | Actor |
| **Olivia**<br>Ozone Productions, PO Box 4153 Point Dume Station, Malibu CA 90265, USA | Artist, Illustrator |
| **Olivier, Philip**<br>Associated International Mgmt, 7 Hatton Garden, #400, London EC1N 8AD, England | Actor |
| **Olivieri, Dawn**<br>A P A Talent/Literary Agency, 405 S Beverly Dr, #300, Beverly Hills CA 90212 USA | Actress |
| **Olivo, America**<br>Northern Exposure Talent, 570 Granville St, #503, Vancouver BC V6C 3P1, Canada | Actress, Model |
| **Olivo, Joey**<br>9628 Poinciana St, Pico Rivera CA 90660, USA | Boxer |
| **Olivo, Karen**<br>Liebman Entertainment, 12 E 46th St, #500, New York NY 10017, USA | Actress, Dancer |
| **Olivo, Miguel E**<br>10004 Plaza de Oro Dr, Oakdale CA 95361, USA | Baseball Player |
| **Olivor, Jane**<br>Ed Keane, 32 Saint Edwards Road, Boston MA 02128, USA | Singer |
| **Oliwa, Krzystof**<br>4 Meeker Dr, Florham Park NJ 07932, USA | Ice Hockey Player |
| **Olkewicz, Neal T**<br>116 Topaz Dr, Gilbertsville PA 19525, USA | Football Player |
| **Olkewicz, Walter**<br>Commercial Talent, 9255 Sunset Blvd, #505, Los Angeles CA 90069, USA | Actor |
| **Ollie, Kevin J**<br>University of Connecticut, Athletic Dept, Storrs CT 06269, USA | Basketball Player, Coach |
| **Ollila, Jorma J**<br>Royal Dutch Shell, Carel v Bylandtlaan 16, 2596 The Haag HR, Netherlands | Businessman |
| **Ollom, James D (Jim)**<br>10916 27th Ave SE, Everett WA 98208, USA | Baseball Player |
| **Olmedo, Alex**<br>5067 Woodley Ave, Encino CA 91436, USA | Tennis Player |
| **Olmert, Ehud**<br>29 November Road, Jerusalem 92105, Israel | Prime Minister, Israel |
| **Olmi, Paolo**<br>I M G Artists, Hogarth Business Park, Chiswick, London W4 2TH, England | Conductor |
| **Olmo, Luis F R (Jibaro)**<br>620 Calle Jose Ramon Figueroa, San Juan PR 00907, USA | Baseball Player |
| **Olmos, Edward James**<br>Olmos Productions, 500 S Buena Vista St, Old Animation Building, Burbank CA 91521, USA | Actor |
| **Olmstead, Alan R (Al)**<br>1008 Pinecone Trail, Florissant MO 63031, USA | Baseball Player |
| **Olmstead, M Bert**<br>2-1512 High Country Dr NW, High River AB T1V 1V9, Canada | Ice Hockey Player, Coach |
| **Olmstead, Matt**<br>W M E Entertainment, 9601 Wilshire Blvd, #300, Beverly Hills CA 90210 USA | Producer |
| **Olney, Claude W**<br>Olney 'A' Seminars, PO Box 686, Scottsdale AZ 85252, USA | Educator |

**Olivares - Olney**

**Olney, David C** — Singer, Songwriter
Mary Sack Mgmt, PO Box 330911, Nashville TN 37203, USA
**Olofsson-Zidek, Anna Carin** — Biathlete
Margareta Silver, Jamtlandsgatan 8, 842 32 Sveg, Sweden
**Olojede, Dele** — Journalist
New York Newsday, Editorial Dept, 235 Pinelawn Road, Melville NY 11747 USA
**O'Loughlin, Gerald S** — Actor
23388 Mulholland Dr, #204, Woodland Hills CA 91364, USA
**O'Loughlin, Sean** — Conductor, Composer
I M G Artists, Carnegie Hall Tower, 152 W 57th St, #500, New York NY 10019 USA
**Olowokandi, Michael** — Basketball Player
10061 SW 60th Court, Miami FL 33156, USA
**Olsavsky, Jerome D (Jerry)** — Football Player
92 Lake Shore Dr, Youngstown OH 44511, USA
**Olsdal, Stefan A B** — Bassist, Guitarist (Placebo)
Riverman Records, George House, Brecon Road, London W6 8PY, England
**Olsen, Andrew H (Andy)** — Baseball Umpire
451 93rd Ave N, Saint Petersburg FL 33702, USA
**Olsen, Ashley** — Actress
DualStar Entertainment Group, 3760 Robertson Blvd, Los Angeles CA 90067, USA
**Olsen, Bud** — Basketball Player
1602 Gardiner Lane, #130, Louisville KY 40205, USA
**Olsen, Elizabeth** — Actress
Gersh Agency, 41 Madison Ave, #3301, New York NY 10010 USA
**Olsen, Eric Christian** — Actor
United Talent Agency, U T A Plaza, 9336 Civic Center Dr, Beverly Hills CA 90210 USA
**Olsen, Gregory (Greg)** — Tourist Cosmonaut
Sensors Unlimited, 3490 US Route 1, Building 12, Princeton NJ 08540, USA
**Olsen, Kevin** — Baseball Player
3353 Dales Dr, Norco CA 92860, USA
**Olsen, Kristina** — Singer, Songwriter
Emerging Music, Sarah's Cottage Horns Cross, Bideford, Devonshire EX39 5DW, England
**Olsen, Mark V** — Producer, Writer
Creative Artists Agency, 2000 Ave of Stars, #100, Los Angeles CA 90067 USA
**Olsen, Mary Kate** — Actress
DualStar Entertainment Group, 3760 Robertson Blvd, Los Angeles CA 90067, USA
**Olsen, Olaf** — Archaeologist
Strevelsjovedvej 2, Alro, 8300 Oder, Denmark
**Olsen, Paul E** — Geologist
Columbia University, Lamont-Doherty Geological Laboratory, New York NY 10027, USA
**Olsen, Phillip V (Phil)** — Football Player
112 Hitching Post Road, Bozeman MT 59715, USA
**Olsen, Scott M** — Baseball Player
2991 NE 185th St, #1701, Aventura FL 33180, USA
**Olsen, Stanford** — Opera Singer
Columbia Artists Mgmt Inc, 1790 Broadway, #702, New York NY 10019 USA
**Olshansky, Igor** — Football Player
PO Box 5000, Rancho Santa Fe CA 92067, USA
**Olshwanger, Ron** — Photojournalist
1447 Meadowside Dr, Saint Louis MO 63146, USA
**Olson, Allen I** — Governor, ND
631 Broken Arrow Road, Chanhassen MN 55317, USA
**Olson, Benjamin D (Benji)** — Football Player
2211 Old Natchez Trace, Franklin TN 37069, USA
**Olson, Candice** — Interior Designer
Fusion Television, 145 Front St E, #L1, Toronto ON M5A 1E3, Canada
**Olson, Dennis** — Ice Hockey Player
521 1st Ave S, Kenora ON P9N 1W6, Canada
**Olson, Eric T** — Navy Admiral
Commander, US Special Operations Command, MacDill Air Force Base FL 33621 USA
**Olson, Gale** — Model
Playboy Promotions, 2706 Media Center Dr, Los Angeles CA 90065 USA
**Olson, Greggory W (Gregg)** — Baseball Player
1996 Port Nelson Place, Newport Beach CA 92660, USA
**Olson, Gregory W (Greg)** — Baseball Player
18592 Saint Mellion Place, Eden Prairie MN 55347, USA
**Olson, Harold V** — Football Player
1012 Keystone Lane, Clemson SC 29631, USA
**Olson, Heather** — Actress
T C M Model & Talent, 2200 6th Ave, #530, Seattle WA 98121, USA
**Olson, Hope** — Model
Playboy Promotions, 2706 Media Center Dr, Los Angeles CA 90065 USA
**Olson, James** — Actor
29122 Cliffside Dr, Malibu CA 90265, USA
**Olson, Jeremy** — Journalist
Minneapolis Star Tribune, Editorial Dept, 425 Portland Ave S, Minneapolis MN 55488 USA
**Olson, Josh** — Writer, Director
BenderSpink, 8447 Wilshire Blvd, #250, Beverly Hills CA 90211 USA
**Olson, Kaitlin** — Actress
Creative Artists Agency, 2000 Ave of Stars, #100, Los Angeles CA 90067 USA
**Olson, Karl A** — Baseball Player
1417 Pin Oak Dr, Gardnerville NV 89410, USA
**Olson, Lisa** — Sportswriter
New York Daily News, Editorial Dept, 220 E 42nd St, New York NY 10017 USA
**Olson, Mancur** — Economist
4316 Claggett Pine Way, University Park MD 20782, USA
**Olson, Mark** — Singer, Songwriter (Jayhawks)
Red Ryder Entertainment, 1532 N Milwaukee Ave, #207, Chicago IL 60622, USA
**Olson, Mark W** — Government Official, Economist
Public Accounting Oversight Board, 1666 K St NW, #800, Washington DC 20006, USA
**Olson, Nancy** — Actress
945 N Alpine Dr, Beverly Hills CA 90210, USA
**Olson, Peter W** — Businessman, Publisher
Random House, 1745 Broadway, #1800, New York NY 10019 USA
**Olson, R Lute** — Basketball Coach
5831 E Finisterra, Tucson AZ 85750, USA

# O

**Olson, Theodore B** — Government Official
Gibson Dunn Crutcher, 1050 Connecticut Ave NW, #300, Washington DC 20036, USA
**Olson, Timothy L (Tim)** — Baseball Player
5416 Pebble Court, McKinney TX 75070, USA
**Olson, Weldon N (Weldy)** — Ice Hockey Player
2623 Goldenrod Lane, Findlay OH 45840, USA
**Olsson, Christian** — Track Athlete
F S D Internet Tjanster, Box 5026, 250 03 Helsinborg, Sweden
**Olsson, Curt G** — Financier
Skandinaviska Enskilda Banken, 106 40 Stockholm, Sweden
**Olsson, E Staffan** — Handball Player, Coach
Hammarby I F, Box 20056, 104 60 Stockholm, Sweden
**Olsson, Johan** — Cross Country Skier
Asarna Idrottsklubb, Box 79, 840 31 Asarna, Sweden
**Olsson, Paul J (P J)** — Singer, Songwriter
Good Times Music, 506 Shelden Ave, Houghton MI 49931, USA
**Olszewski, Jan F** — Prime Minister, Poland
Biuro Poselskie, Al Ujazdowskie 13, 00567 Warsaw, Poland
**Olwine, Edward R (Ed)** — Baseball Player
223 Spanish Lakes Dr, Nokomis FL 34275, USA
**Olynyk, Kelly** — Basketball Player
Boston Celtics, 226 Causeway St, #4, Boston MA 02114 USA
**Olyphant, Timothy** — Actor
Brillstein Entertainment Partners, 9150 Wilshire Blvd, #350, Beverly Hills CA 90212 USA
**O'Malley, Mike** — Actor
Creative Artists Agency, 2000 Ave of Stars, #100, Los Angeles CA 90067 USA
**O'Malley, Peter** — Baseball Executive
515 S Figueroa St, #1988, Los Angeles CA 90071, USA
**O'Malley, Robert E** — Vietnam War Marine Corps Hero (CMH)
PO Box 775, Goldthwaite TX 76844, USA
**O'Malley, Sean P Cardinal** — Religious Leader
Archdiocese of Boston, 66 Brooks Dr, Braintree MA 02184, USA
**O'Malley, Susan** — Basketball Executive
Washington Wizards, M C I Centre, 601 F St NW, Washington DC 20004 USA
**O'Malley, Thomas D** — Businessman
Tosco Corp, 1700 E Putnam Ave, #500, Old Greenwich CT 06870, USA
**O'Malley, Thomas P (Tom)** — Baseball Player
10 Carriage Square, Montoursville PA 17754, USA
**Omar, Don** — Singer
Relentless Agency, 261 E 134th St, #200, South Bronx NY 10454, USA
**O'Mara, Jason** — Actor
Independent Talent Group, 40 Whitfield St, London W1T 2RH, England
**O'Mara, Kate** — Actress
Michael Ladkin Mgmt, 1 Duchess St, #1, London W1N 3DE, England
**O'Mara, Mark** — Harness Racing Driver, Trainer
6882 NW 65th Terrace, Parkland FL 33067, USA
**Omarion** — Singer (B2K), Songwriter, Actor
Pyramid Entertainment Group, 377 Rector Place, #21A, New York NY 10280 USA
**O'Meara, Mark F** — Golfer
2000 Auburn Dr, #330, Beachwood OH 44122, USA
**O'Meara, Peter** — Actor
Roar Mgmt, 9701 Wilshire Blvd, #800, Beverly Hills CA 90212 USA
**Omeyer, Thierry** — Handball Player
T H W Kiel Handball, Ziegelteich 30, 24103 Kiel, Germany
**Omidyar, Pierre M** — Businessman
Omidyar Network, 2145 Hamilton Ave, San Jose CA 95125, USA
**Omundson, Timothy** — Actor
Innovative Artists, 1505 10th St, Santa Monica CA 90401 USA
**Omura, Satoshi** — Organic Chemist
Kitasato Institute, 9-1-5 Shirokane, Tokyo 108 8641, Japan
**Onaiyekan, John O** — Religious Leader
Archbishop's House, Area 3, Section 2, PO Box 286, Garki, Abuja FCT, Nigeria
**O'Nan, Stewart** — Writer
Viking Press, 375 Hudson St, New York NY 10014 USA
**Ondaatje, Michael** — Writer
Glendon College, English Dept, 2275 Bayview, Toronto ON M4N 3M6, Canada
**Ondricek, Miroslav** — Cinematographer
Nad Pomnikem 1, 15200 Prague 5 Smichow, Czech Republic
**O'Neal, Alexander** — Singer, Songwriter
Green Light Talent Agency, PO Box 3172, Beverly Hills CA 90212 USA
**O'Neal, Carlton (Carol)** — Model
Playboy Promotions, 2706 Media Center Dr, Los Angeles CA 90065 USA
**O'Neal, Deltha L, III** — Football Player
10225 Meadowknoll Dr, Loveland OH 45140, USA
**O'Neal, E Stanley** — Financier
Merrill Lynch Co, World Financial Center, 2 Vesey St, New York NY 10007, USA
**O'Neal, Griffin** — Actor
21368 Pacific Coast Highway, Malibu CA 90265, USA
**O'Neal, Jermaine** — Basketball Player
1500 Ocean Dr, #1206, Miami Beach FL 33139, USA
**O'Neal, Leslie C** — Football Player
8015 Hemingway Ave, San Diego CA 92120, USA
**O'Neal, Ralph T** — Chief Minister, British Virgin Islands
Chief Minister's Office, Road Town, Tortola, British Virgin Islands
**O'Neal, Randall J (Randy)** — Baseball Player
10015 Honey Tree Court, Orlando FL 32836, USA
**O'Neal, Ryan** — Actor
David Shapira Assoc, 193 N Robertson Blvd, Beverly Hills CA 90211 USA
**O'Neal, Shaquille R** — Basketball Player
9927 Giffin Court, Windermere FL 34786, USA
**O'Neal, Steve** — Football Player
2914 Coronado Dr, College Station TX 77845, USA
**O'Neal, Tatum** — Actress
Mavrick Artists Agency, 6100 Wilshire Blvd, #550, Los Angeles CA 90048, USA
**O'Neil, Edward W (Ed)** — Football Player
6691 Aiken Road, Lockport NY 14094, USA

**Olson - O'Neil**

**O'Neil, Lawrence** — Director
I C M Partners, 10250 Constellation Blvd, #900, Los Angeles CA 90067 USA

**O'Neil, Linda** — Actress, Model
C E S D, 10635 Santa Monica Blvd, #130, Los Angeles CA 90025 USA

**O'Neil, Melissa C** — Singer
19 Entertainment, 8560 W Sunset Blvd, #900, Los Angeles CA 90069 USA

**O'Neil, Robert M** — Educator
University of Virginia, Law School, Charlottesville VA 22903, USA

**O'Neil, Tricia** — Actress
David Shapira Assoc, 193 N Robertson Blvd, Beverly Hills CA 90211 USA

**O'Neill of Bengarve, O Sylvia** — Philosopher
Newham College, Philosophy Dept, Cambridge CB3 9DF, England

**O'Neill, Brian** — Ice Hockey Executive
2600-1800 McGill College Ave, Montreal QC H3A 3J6, Canada

**O'Neill, Dan** — Association Executive
Mercy Corps, 45 SW Ankeny St, Portland OR 97204, USA

**O'Neill, Dan** — Cartoonist (Odd Bodkins, O'Neill)
PO Box 1297, Nevada City CA 95959, USA

**O'Neill, Doug** — Thoroughbred Racing Trainer
Doug O'Neill Stable, Hollywood Park, 1050 S Prairie Ave, Inglewood CA 90301, USA

**O'Neill, Ed** — Actor
Paradigm Agency, 360 N Crescent Dr, North Building, Beverly Hills CA 90210 USA

**O'Neill, Eugene F** — Communications Engineer
394 Dogford Road, Etna NH 03750, USA

**O'Neill, Jennifer** — Actress, Model
Jennifer O'Neill Ministries, 30 Hillenglade Dr, Nashville TN 37207, USA

**O'Neill, Maggie** — Actress
Independent Talent Group, 40 Whitfield St, London W1T 2RH, England

**O'Neill, Michael E** — Financier
Citigroup Inc, 55 E 52nd St, New York NY 10055, USA

**O'Neill, Morgan** — Director, Writer, Actor
Paradigm Agency, 360 N Crescent Dr, North Building, Beverly Hills CA 90210 USA

**O'Neill, Paul A** — Baseball Player
7785 Hartford Hill Lane, Cincinnati OH 45242, USA

**O'Neill, Paul H** — Secretary, Treasury
3 Von Lent Place, Pittsburgh PA 15232, USA

**O'Neill, Susan (Susie)** — Swimmer
Elite Sports Properties, 326 Seaview Road, Henley Beach SA 5022, Australia

**Ong, John D** — Businessman, Diplomat
230 Aurora St, Hudson OH 44236, USA

**Onkotz, Dennis H** — Football Player
270 Walker Dr, State College PA 16801, USA

**Ono, Takashi** — Gymnast
Gymnastics Assn, Kishi Hall, 1-1 Jinnan Shibuyaku, Tokyo 150 8050, Japan

**Ono, Yoko** — Filmmaker, Singer, Artist
Dakota Hotel, 1 W 72nd St, #1, New York NY 10023, USA

**Onopka, Snejana** — Model
Women Model Mgmt, 199 Lafayette St, #700, New York NY 10012 USA

**O'Nora, Brian** — Baseball Umpire
5265 Nashua Dr, Youngstown OH 44515, USA

**Onorati, Peter** — Actor
Liberman-Zerman Mgmt, 252 N Larchmont Blvd, #200, Los Angeles CA 90004 USA

**Ontiveros, Steven (Steve)** — Baseball Player
9970 E Charter Oak Road, Scottsdale AZ 85260, USA

**Ontkean, Michael** — Actor
PO Box 51, Kilauea HI 96754, USA

**Onufriyenko, Yuri I** — Cosmonaut
Cosmonaut Training Center, Star City, 141160 Zvezdny Gorodok, Moscow Oblast, Russia

**Onweagba, Oluchi** — Model
D N A Model Mgmt, 555 W 25th St, #600, New York NY 10001 USA

**Onyali, Mary** — Track Athlete
Kurt Varricchio, 23861 El Toro Road, #700, Lake Forest CA 92630, USA

**Oosterhuis, Peter** — Golfer
2823 Providence Road, #182, Charlotte NC 28211, USA

**Opacic, Paul** — Actor
Associated International Mgmt, 7 Hatton Garden, #400, London EC1N 8AD, England

**Opasik, Jim** — Artist
1914 Beverly Road, Catonsville MD 21228, USA

**Opertti Baddan, Didier** — Government Official, Uruguay
A L A D I, Calle Cebollati 1461, Montevideo CP 11200, Uruguay

**Ophuls, Marcel** — Director
10 Rue Ernest Deloison, 92200 Neuilly-sur-Seine, France

**Opie, Alan** — Opera Singer
I M G Artists, Hogarth Business Park, Chiswick, London W4 2TH, England

**Opik, Ernst J** — Astronomer
University of Maryland, Physics & Astronomy Dept, College Park MD 20742, USA

**Oplev, Niels Arden** — Director
I C M Partners, 10250 Constellation Blvd, #900, Los Angeles CA 90067 USA

**Oppegard, Peter** — Figure Skater
East West Ice Palace, 11446 Artesia Blvd, Artesia CA 90701, USA

**Oppenheim, Irwin** — Chemical Physicist
140 Upland Road, Cambridge MA 02140, USA

**Oppenheim-Barnes of Gloucester, Sally** — Government Official, England
Quietways, Highlands, Painswick, Gloustershire GL6 6SL, England

**Oppenheimer, Alan** — Actor
1207 Beverly Green Dr, Beverly Hills CA 90212, USA

**Oppenheimer, Benjamin R** — Astronomer
Columbia University, Astronomy Dept, New York NY 10027, USA

**Oppenheimer, Deborah** — Producer, Writer
N B C Universal, 100 Universal City Plaza, Universal City CA 91608, USA

**Oppewall, Jeannine Claudia** — Art Director
Gersh Agency, 9465 Wilshire Blvd, #600, Beverly Hills CA 90212 USA

**Oquendo, Jose M R G** — Baseball Player
13219 Selma Road, De Soto MO 63020, USA

**O'Quinn, Terry** — Actor
I F A Talent Agency, 8730 W Sunset Blvd, #490, West Hollywood CA 90069 USA

**Oquist, Michael L (Mike)** — Baseball Player
1910 Raton Ave, La Junta CO 81050, USA
**Orakpo, Brian N** — Football Player
Washington Redskins, 21300 Redskin Park Dr, Ashburn VA 20147 USA
**Oram, Tara** — Actress, Singer
R G K Entertainment Group, 2B Minto St,#6, Toronto ON M4L 1B6, Canada
**Oram, Tara** — Singer
Agency Group Ltd, 142 W 57th St, #600, New York NY 10019 USA
**Oramo, Sakari M** — Conductor
Royal Stockholm Symphony Orchestra, Konserthus, Hotorget 8, Box 7083, 103 87 Stockholm, Sweden
**Orange, Walter (Clyde)** — Singer, Drummer (Commodores)
Management Assoc, 1920 Benson Ave, Saint Paul MN 55116, USA
**Orbach, Raymond L** — Educator
4004 Petra Path, Austin TX 78731, USA
**Orban, Viktor** — Prime Minister, Hungary
Prime Minister's Office, Kossuth Lajos Ter 1-3, 1055 Budapest, Hungary
**Orbit, William** — Keyboardist, Songwriter, Actor
Creative Artists Agency, 2000 Ave of Stars, #100, Los Angeles CA 90067 USA
**Ord, Robert L (Bob), III** — Army General
3020 Ribera Road, Carmel CA 93923, USA
**Ordonez, Magglio J** — Baseball Player
181 Nurmi Dr, Fort Lauderdale FL 33301, USA
**Ordonez, Pilar** — Actress
Hac de Pavones 169, 28030 Madrid, Spain
**Ordonez, Rey** — Baseball Player
16501 NW 84th Ave, Hialeah FL 33016, USA
**Ordway, Frederick I, III** — Writer
3423 Lookout Dr SE, Huntsville AL 35801, USA
**O'Ree, William E (Willie)** — Ice Hockey Player
7961 Anders Circle, La Mesa CA 91942, USA
**O'Reilly Werry, Heather A** — Soccer Player
Soccer Federation, 1801 S Prairie Ave, Chicago IL 60616 USA
**O'Reilly, Ahna** — Actress
W M E Entertainment, 9601 Wilshire Blvd, #300, Beverly Hills CA 90210 USA
**O'Reilly, Anthony J F** — Businessman, Publisher
H J Heinz Co, PO Box 57, Pittsburgh PA 15230, USA
**O'Reilly, Bill** — Commentator
O'Reilly Factor, Fox-TV, 1211 Ave of Americas, New York NY 10036, USA
**O'Reilly, David J** — Businessman
Chevron Corp, 6001 Bollinger Canyon Road, San Ramon CA 94583, USA
**O'Reilly, Genevieve** — Actress
PO Box 128, Surry Hills NSW 2010, Australia
**O'Reilly, Terry** — Ice Hockey Player
PO Box 5544, Salisbury MA 01952, USA
**O'Reilly, Tim** — Publisher, Businessman
O'Reilly Media, 1005 Gravenstein Highway N, Sebastopol CA 95472, USA
**Oremans, Miriam** — Tennis Player
Octagon Worldwide, 1751 Pinnacle Dr, #1500, McLean VA 22102 USA
**Orenstein, Andrew** — Producer, Writer
Paradigm Agency, 360 N Crescent Dr, North Building, Beverly Hills CA 90210 USA
**Oreskovich, Alesha** — Model
Playboy Promotions, 2706 Media Center Dr, Los Angeles CA 90065 USA
**Origliasso, Jessica** — Singer (Vernoicas), Actress
Harbour Agency, 135 Forbes St, Woolloomooloo NSW 2011, Australia
**Origliasso, Lisa** — Singer (Veronicas), Actress
Harbour Agency, 135 Forbes St, Woolloomooloo NSW 2011, Australia
**O'Riordan, Dolores M E** — Singer (Cranberries), Songwriter
Creative Artists Agency, 2000 Ave of Stars, #100, Los Angeles CA 90067 USA
**Oritz, John** — Actor
Gersh Agency, 9465 Wilshire Blvd, #600, Beverly Hills CA 90212 USA
**Orkin, Stuart H** — Pediatrician, Oncologist
Harvard Stem Cell Institute, Holyoke Center, #727W, 1350 Massachusetts Ave, Cambridge MA 02138, USA
**Orland, Frank J** — Oral Microbiologist, Dentist
519 Jackson Blvd, Forest Park IL 60130, USA
**Orlandi, Luca** — Fashion Designer
Luca Luca, 19 W 36th St, #400, New York NY 10018, USA
**Orlando, Gates** — Ice Hockey Player
252 Bennington Hills Court, West Henrietta NY 14586, USA
**Orlando, Tony** — Singer
Brokaw Co, 9255 W Sunset Blvd, #804, West Hollywood CA 90069 USA
**Orlean, Susan** — Writer
New Yorker, Editorial Dept, 4 Times Square, Basement C1B, New York NY 10036 USA
**Orleans, Joan** — Singer
PO Box 2596, New York NY 10009, USA
**Orloff, John** — Producer, Writer
Creative Artists Agency, 2000 Ave of Stars, #100, Los Angeles CA 90067 USA
**Orlovsky, Daniel J (Dan)** — Football Player
2 Reliant Park, Houston TX 77054, USA
**Orman, Suze** — Writer
Suze Orman Financial Group, 2000 Powell St, #1605, Emeryville CA 94608, USA
**Ormond, Julia** — Actress
Gersh Agency, 9465 Wilshire Blvd, #600, Beverly Hills CA 90212 USA
**Orms, Barry D** — Basketball Player
3 Loudon Dr, #8, Fishkill NY 12524, USA
**Ornish, Dean** — Cardiologist
Preventive Medicine Research Institute, 900 Bridgeway, #2, Sausalito CA 94965, USA
**Ornstein, Donald S** — Mathematician
857 Tolman Dr, Stanford CA 94305, USA
**Ornstein, Norman J** — Political Scientist
2212 Wyoming Ave NW, Washington DC 20008, USA
**Orosco, Jesse R** — Baseball Player
16242 Winecreek Road, San Diego CA 92127, USA
**O'Rourke, James P (Charlie)** — Baseball Player
15612 N Little Spokane Dr, Spokane WA 99208, USA
**O'Rourke, Tom** — Actor
Talent Works, 3500 W Olive Ave, #1400, Burbank CA 91505 USA

**Orozco, Gabriel** — Sculptor
Marian Goodman Gallery, 124 W 57th St, New York NY 10019, USA
**Orozco-Estrada, Andres** — Conductor
I M G Artists, Hogarth Business Park, Chiswick, London W4 2TH, England
**Orpik, R Brooks** — Ice Hockey Player
2396 Hilltop Road, Presto PA 15142, USA
**Orr, James F, III** — Businessman
U N U M Provident Corp, 2211 Congress St, Portland ME 04122, USA
**Orr, John M (Johnny)** — Basketball Coach, Administrator
5736 Gallery Court, West Des Moines IA 50266, USA
**Orr, Kay S** — Governor, NE
1425 H St, Lincoln NE 68508, USA
**Orr, Louis M** — Basketball Player, Coach
1333 Pine Valley Dr, Bowling Green OH 43402, USA
**Orr, Peterson T (Pete)** — Baseball Player
400 Rannie Road, Newmarket ON L3X 2N3, Canada
**Orr, Robert G (Bobby)** — Ice Hockey Player
Orr Hockey Group, PO Box 290836, Charlestown MA 02129, USA
**Orr, Shantee D** — Football Player
PO Box 20301, Houston TX 77225, USA
**Orr, Terrance F (Terry)** — Football Player
2710 Kellogg Ave, Dallas TX 75216, USA
**Orr, Terrence S** — Ballet Dancer, Executive
Pittsburgh Ballet Theater, 2900 Liberty Ave, Pittsburgh PA 15201, USA
**Orrall, Robert Ellis** — Singer
3 E 54th St, #1400, New York NY 10022, USA
**Orr-Cahall, Christina** — Museum Director
Museum & Library Service Institute, 1800 M St NW, #900, Washington DC 20036, USA
**Orrell, Thomas M** — Biologist
Smithsonian Natural History Museum, 10th & Constitution, Washington DC 20560, USA
**Orr-Ewing, Hamish** — Businessman
Fox Mill, Purton near Swindon, Wilts SN5 9EF, England
**Orrico, Stacie** — Singer, Actress
Creative Artists Agency, 2000 Ave of Stars, #100, Los Angeles CA 90067 USA
**Orser, Brian** — Figure Skater
I M G Canada, 175 Bloor St E, #400S, Toronto ON M4W 3R8, Canada
**Orser, Leland** — Actor
Gersh Agency, 9465 Wilshire Blvd, #600, Beverly Hills CA 90212 USA
**Orsini, Myrna J** — Sculptor
Orsini Studios, 4411 N 7th St, Tacoma WA 98406, USA
**Orsino, John J** — Baseball Player
6141 Terra Mere Circle, Boynton Beach FL 33437, USA
**Orsulak, Joseph M (Joe)** — Baseball Player
29 Keansburg Road, Parsippany NJ 07054, USA
**Orszag, Peter R** — Government Official
Office of Management/Budget, 1600 Pennsylvania Ave NW, Washington DC 20500, USA
**Orta, Jorge** — Baseball Player
1201 Heather Hill Crescent, Flossmoor IL 60422, USA
**Ortega Gaona, Amancio** — Businessman
Inditex SA, Avenida de la Diputacion, 15142 Arteixo, La Coruna, Spain
**Ortega Saavedra, J Daniel** — President, Nicaragua
President's Office, Casa de Gobierno, Barrio El Carmen, #2398, Managua, Nicaragua
**Ortega y Alamino, Jaime L Cardinal** — Religious Leader
Apartado 594, Calle Habana 152, Havana 10100, Cuba
**Ortega, Bill** — Baseball Player
4635 NW 95th Ave, Doral FL 33178, USA
**Ortega, Chico P (Chick)** — Actor
Artmedia, 20 Ave Rapp, 75007 Paris, France
**Ortega, Fernando** — Singer, Songwriter
Street Level Artist Agency, 107 E Centre St, Warsaw IN 46580, USA
**Ortega, Kenny** — Director, Choreographer
Paradigm Agency, 360 N Crescent Dr, North Building, Beverly Hills CA 90210 USA
**Ortega, Lindi** — Singer, Songwriter
Agency Group Ltd, 142 W 57th St, #600, New York NY 10019 USA
**Ortenberg, Arthur** — Businessman
Liz Claiborne Inc, 1441 Broadway, New York NY 10018, USA
**Ortenzio, Frank J** — Baseball Player
2357 Oak Forest St, Jacksonville FL 32250, USA
**Orth, Viviane** — Model
Louisa Models, Ebersbergerstr 9, 81679 Munich, Germany
**Orth, Zak** — Actor
Gersh Agency, 9465 Wilshire Blvd, #600, Beverly Hills CA 90212 USA
**Ortiz, Adalberto C (Junior)** — Baseball Player
296 Strayer St, Johnstown PA 15906, USA
**Ortiz, Ana** — Actress
G E F Entertainment, 122 N Clark Dr, #401, Los Angeles CA 90048, USA
**Ortiz, Carlos** — Boxer
2050 Seward Ave, #3L, Bronx NY 10473, USA
**Ortiz, Cristina** — Concert Pianist
Harrison/Parrott, 5-6 Albion Court, London W6 0QT, England
**Ortiz, David A** — Baseball Player
296 Strayer St, Johnstown PA 15906, USA
**Ortiz, Domingo** — Percussionist (Widespread Panic)
Brown Cat Inc, 400 Foundry St, Athens GA 30601 USA
**Ortiz, John** — Actor, Producer
Gersh Agency, 41 Madison Ave, #3301, New York NY 10010 USA
**Ortiz, Russell R (Russ)** — Baseball Player
4040 E McClellan Road, #13, Mesa AZ 85205, USA
**Ortiz, Shalim** — Actor
C E S D, 10635 Santa Monica Blvd, #130, Los Angeles CA 90025 USA
**Ortlieb, Patrick** — Alpine Skier
Hotel Montana, Oberlech 588, 6764 Lech, Austria
**Ortmeier, Dan** — Baseball Player
2121 Fairmont Dr, Flower Mound TX 75028, USA
**Ortmeyer, Jed** — Ice Hockey Player
1421 S 52nd St, Omaha NE 68106, USA

**Ortner, Bev** — Bowler
PO Box 436, Odebolt IA 51458, USA
**Orton, Beth** — Singer
Paradigm Agency, 360 Park Ave S, #1600, New York NY 10010 USA
**Orton, John A** — Baseball Player
2929 E Dublin St, Gilbert AZ 85295, USA
**Orton, Kyle R** — Football Player
3114 Coates Crossing, Baton Rouge LA 70810, USA
**Osborn, David V (Dave)** — Football Player
18067 Judicial Way N, Lakeville MN 55044, USA
**Osborn, John Jay, Jr** — Writer
14 Fair Oaks St, San Francisco CA 94110, USA
**Osborn, Kassidy** — Singer (SheDaisy)
L G B Media, 1228 Pineview Lane, Nashville TN 37211, USA
**Osborn, Kelsi** — Singer (SheDaisy)
L G B Media, 1228 Pineview Lane, Nashville TN 37211, USA
**Osborn, Kristyn** — Singer (SheDaisy), Songwriter
L G B Media, 1228 Pineview Lane, Nashville TN 37211, USA
**Osborne, Anders** — Singer, Guitarist, Songwriter
525 Worldwide Music, PO Box 957, Salem MA 01945, USA
**Osborne, Bobby** — Singer, Mandolinist (Osborne Brothers)
Lancer Agency, PO Box 160, Hendersonville TN 37077, USA
**Osborne, Donovan A** — Baseball Player
1851 Brightstone Court, Reno NV 89521, USA
**Osborne, James H (Jim)** — Football Player
4 Canyon Court, Algonquin IL 60102, USA
**Osborne, Jeffrey** — Singer, Songwriter
Wenig-LaMonica Associates, 580 White Plains Road, #130, Tarrytown NY 10591 USA
**Osborne, Joan** — Singer, Songwriter
Paradigm Agency, 360 N Crescent Dr, North Building, Beverly Hills CA 90210 USA
**Osborne, Keith** — Ice Hockey Player
Niagara Falls Hockey, 6570 Frederica St, Niagara Falls ON L2G 1C9, Canada
**Osborne, Kent** — Actor
Creative Management Entertainment Group, 2050 S Bundy Dr, #280, Los Angeles CA 90025, USA
**Osborne, Lawrence** — Writer
Farrar Straus Giroux, 18 W 18th St, #700, New York NY 10011 USA
**Osborne, Mark** — Ice Hockey Player
28 Princess Anne Crescent, Etobicoke ON M9A 2P1, Canada
**Osborne, Mark** — Director, Animator
W M E Entertainment, 9601 Wilshire Blvd, #300, Beverly Hills CA 90210 USA
**Osborne, Mary** — Surfer, Model
Patagonia, 8550 White Fir St, Reno NV 89523 USA
**Osborne, Mary Pope** — Writer
Random House, 1745 Broadway, #1800, New York NY 10019 USA
**Osborne, Thomas W (Tom)** — Football Coach; Representative, NE
5400 Trotter Road, Lincoln NE 68516, USA
**Osbourne, Jack** — Actor
W M E Entertainment, 9601 Wilshire Blvd, #300, Beverly Hills CA 90210 USA
**Osbourne, John M (Ozzy)** — Singer, Songwriter
Sharon Osbourne Mgmt, 8899 Beverly Blvd, #905, Los Angeles CA 90048, USA
**Osbourne, Kelly** — Singer, Actress
W M E Entertainment, 9601 Wilshire Blvd, #300, Beverly Hills CA 90210 USA
**Osbourne, Sharon** — Producer, Actress
Sharon Osbourne Mgmt, Regent House, 1 Pratt Mews, London NW1 0AD, England
**Osburn, Julie** — Actress
S M S Talent, 8383 Wilshire Blvd, #230, Beverly Hills CA 90211 USA
**Osburn, L Pat** — Baseball Player
208 64th Street Court NW, Bradenton FL 34209, USA
**Osby, Greg** — Jazz Saxophonist
Kavon Artist Mgmt, 295 E Swedesford Road, #161, Wayne PA 19087, USA
**O'Scannlain, Diarmuid F** — Judge
US Court of Appeals, Pioneer Courthouse, 555 SW Yamhill St, Portland OR 97204, USA
**Oscar, Carlos** — Actor, Comedian
Heidi Rotbart Management, 1810 Malcolm Ave, #207, Los Angeles CA 90025, USA
**Osgood, Charles** — Commentator
CBS-TV, News Dept, 524 W 57th St, New York NY 10019, USA
**Osgood, Charles E** — Psychologist
30 E Main St, Champaign IL 61820, USA
**Osgood, Chris** — Ice Hockey Player
1445 Penniman Ave, Plymouth MI 48170, USA
**Osgood, Kassim A** — Football Player, Actor
Gersh Agency, 9465 Wilshire Blvd, #600, Beverly Hills CA 90212 USA
**O'Shannon, Daniel T (Dan)** — Producer, Writer
Gendler & Kelly, 450 N Roxbury Dr, #1000, Beverly Hills CA 90210, USA
**O'Shea, Daniel P (Danny)** — Ice Hockey Player
7343 Colfax Ave S, Minneapolis MN 55423, USA
**O'Shea, Michael D** — Cinematographer
Murtha Agency, 1025 Colorado Ave, Santa Monica CA 90401, USA
**Osheroff, Douglas D** — Nobel Physics Laureate
75 Ranch Road, Woodside CA 94062, USA
**Oshima, Hiromi** — Model
Playboy Promotions, 2706 Media Center Dr, Los Angeles CA 90065 USA
**Osiecki, Mark** — Ice Hockey Player
7482 New Albany Links Dr, New Albany OH 43054, USA
**Osik, Keith R** — Baseball Player
5 Pal Court, Shoreham NY 11786, USA
**Osin, Roman** — Cinematographer
Independent Talent Group, 40 Whitfield St, London W1T 2RH, England
**Osinski, Daniel (Dan)** — Baseball Player
9723 W Amber Trail, Sun City AZ 85351, USA
**Oslin, K T** — Singer
Consortium, 49 Music Square W, #210, Nashville TN 37203, USA
**Osman, H P** — Marine Corps General
Deputy CofS, Manpower/Reserves, HqUSMC, 2 Navy St, Washington DC 20380, USA
**Osman, Mat** — Bassist (Suede)
Interceptor Enterprises, 98 White Lion St, London N1 9PF, England

**Oswald, Stephen S** — Astronaut, Admiral
N A S A, Johnson Space Center, 2101 NASA Road, Houston TX 77058 USA

**Oswalt, Roy E** — Baseball Player
107 Oakmont Road, Starkville MS 39759, USA

**Oszajca, John** — Singer
Interscope Records, 2220 Colorado Ave, Santa Monica CA 90404 USA

**Otanez, Willis A** — Baseball Player
7904 March Brown Ave, Las Vegas NV 89149, USA

**Otellini, Paul S** — Businessman
Intel Corp, 2200 Mission College Blvd, Santa Clara CA 95054, USA

**Oteri, Cheri** — Actress, Comedienne
Mavrick Artists Agency, 6100 Wilshire Blvd, #550, Los Angeles CA 90048, USA

**Othenin-Girard, Dominque** — Director
327 S Church Lane, Los Angeles CA 90049, USA

**Otis, Amos J** — Baseball Player
8930 Tiger Shale Way, Las Vegas NV 89123, USA

**Otis, Carre** — Actress, Model
Dash Group, 550 N Larchmont Blvd, #201, Los Angeles CA 90004, USA

**Otis, James L (Jim)** — Football Player
14795 Greenleaf Valley Dr, Chesterfield MO 63017, USA

**O'Toole, Annette** — Actress
I C M Partners, 10250 Constellation Blvd, #900, Los Angeles CA 90067 USA

**O'Toole, James J (Jim)** — Baseball Player
1010 Lanette Dr, Cincinnati OH 45230, USA

**O'Toole, Peter S** — Actor
Chartwell Ink Mgmt, 7319 Beverly Blvd, #10, Los Angeles CA 90036, USA

**O'Toole, Shane** — Architect
68 Irishtown Road, Dublin 4, Ireland

**Otstott, Charles P** — Army General
6152 Pohick Station Dr, Fairfax Station VA 22039, USA

**Otsuka, Akinori** — Baseball Player
891 Fairway Dr, Boulder City NV 89005, USA

**Ott, Alice Sara** — Concert Pianist
Harrison/Parrott, 5-6 Albion Court, London W6 0QT, England

**Ott, Mirjam** — Curling Athlete
Curling Assn, PO Box 606, 3000 Bern, Switzerland

**Ott, Mona Asuka** — Concert Pianist
Harrison/Parrott, 5-6 Albion Court, London W6 0QT, England

**Ott, Steve** — Ice Hockey Player
2758 Saint Clair, Pointe Aux Roches ON N0R 1N0, Canada

**Otten, James E (Jim)** — Baseball Player
1417 N Forest, Mesa AZ 85203, USA

**Ottenbrite, Anne** — Swimmer
Swimming Canada, 2197 Riverside Dr, #700, Ottawa ON K1H 7X3, Canada

**Ottey-Page, Merlene** — Track Athlete
Jamaican Olympic Committee, PO Box 544, Kingston 10, Jamaica

**Ottke, Sven** — Boxer
Anke Luetkenhorst, Maastricherstr 38, 80672 Cologne, Germany

**Otto, August J (Gus)** — Football Player
8705 Leeward Dr, Las Vegas NV 89117, USA

**Otto, Bjorn** — Track Athlete
Marc Osenberg Athletics, Altenbach 14, 42799 Leichlingen, Germany

**Otto, David A (Dave)** — Baseball Player
1383 Shady Lane, Wheaton IL 60187, USA

**Otto, Frei P** — Architect, Structural Engineer
Berghalde 19, 7250 Leonberg, 71229 Warmbroun, Germany

**Otto, Gotz** — Actor
Z B F Agentur, Friedrichstr 39, 10969 Berlin, Germany

**Otto, James** — Singer, Songwriter
Red Light Mgmt, PO Box 159310, Nashville TN 37215, USA

**Otto, James E (Jim)** — Football Player
00 Estates Dr, Auburn CA 95602, USA

**Otto, Joel** — Ice Hockey Player
7144 Sues Dr, Pequot Lakes MN 56472, USA

**Otto, John E** — Drummer (Limp Bizkot)
Flip/Interscope Records, 8733 Sunset Blvd, #205, West Hollywood CA 90069, USA

**Otto, Kristin** — Swimmer
Z D F Sportedaktion, Postfach 4040, 55100 Mainz, Germany

**Otto, Michael** — Businessman
Wandsbeker Str 3-7, 22179 Hamburg, Germany

**Otto, Miranda** — Actress
United Agents, 12-26 Lexington St, London W1F 0LE, England

**Otto, Sylke** — Luge Athlete
Egersdorfer Str 3, 90513 Zirndorf, Germany

**Otunbayeva, Roza I** — President, Kyrgyzstan
Social Democratic Party, Ul Shabdan Baatyr, #D4B, 720003 Bishkek, Kyrgyzstan

**Ouattara, Alassane D** — President, Cote d'Ivoire; Financier
International Monetary Fund, 700 19th St NW, #12-300H, Washington DC 20431, USA

**Oubre, Louis B, III** — Football Player
12345 I 10 Service Road, #2403, New Orleans LA 70128, USA

**Ouchi, William G** — Educator
University of California, Graduate Management School, Los Angeles CA 90024, USA

**Oue, Eiji** — Conductor
I M G Artists, Hogarth Business Park, Chiswick, London W4 2TH, England

**Ouedraogo, Gerard Kango** — Prime Minister, Burkina Faso
01 BP 347, Ouagadougou, Burkina Faso

**Ouedraogo, Idrissa** — Director
01 BP 2524, Ouagadougou, Burkina Faso

**Ouellet, Marc Cardinal** — Religious Leader
Archdiocese of Quebec, 2 Rue Port-Dauphin, Quebec QC G1R 4R6, Canada

**Ouellette, Caroline** — Ice Hockey Player
Team Canada, 2424 University Dr NW, Calgary AB T2N 3Y9, Canada

**Ouellette, Philip R (Phil)** — Baseball Player
7421 Poppy St, Corona CA 92881, USA

**Oukach, Zineb** — Actress
Anthony Assoc, PO Box 910, New York NY 10108, USA

| | |
|---|---|
| **Ouma, Kassim**<br>Peltz Boxing Promotions, 2501 Brown St, Philadelphia PA 19130, USA | Boxer |
| **Oumarou, Seyni**<br>Prime Minister's Office, State House, BP 353, Abuja, Niger | Prime Minister, Niger |
| **Oundjian, Peter**<br>Toronto Symphony Orchestra, 6-212 King St E, Toronto ON M58 1K5, Canada | Conductor |
| **Ousland, Borge**<br>Axel Huitfeldts V5, 1170 Oslo, Norway | Trans Polar Skier |
| **Ousset, Cecile**<br>Intermusica Artists Mgmt, 16 Duncan Terrace, London N1 8B7, England | Concert Pianist |
| **Outerbridge, Peter**<br>O A Z, 438 Queen St E, Toronto ON M5A 1T4, Canada | Actor |
| **Outhwaite, Tamzin**<br>Conway Van Gelder Grant, 8-12 Broadwick St, #300, London W1F 8HW, England | Actress |
| **Outlaw, Charles (Bo)**<br>Orlando Magic, 8701 Maitland Summit Blvd, Orlando FL 32810 USA | Basketball Player |
| **Outman, Joshua S (Josh)**<br>5273 Seasonbrooks Lane, Imperial MO 63052, USA | Baseball Player |
| **Outman, Tim**<br>2863 Lydick Way, Eugene OR 97401, USA | Sculptor |
| **Outtara, Alassane D**<br>President's Office, Presidential Palace, N'Gokro, Yamoussoukro, Cote d'Ivoire | President, Ivory Coast |
| **Ouyahia, Ahmed**<br>Prime Minister's Office, 32 Ave Souidani Boudiemad, Algiers, Algeria | Prime Minister, Algeria |
| **Ovadia, Moni**<br>Promo Music, Via Della Volto 21, 40131 Bologna (BO), Italy | Composer, Writer |
| **Ovchinikov, Vladimir P**<br>Manygate, 13 Cotswold Mews, 30 Battersea Square, London SW11 3RA, England | Concert Pianist |
| **Ovechkin, Alexander M**<br>6301 Osprey Terrace, Coconut Creek FL 33073, USA | Ice Hockey Player |
| **Overall, Park**<br>1374 Ripley Island Road, Afton TN 37616, USA | Actress |
| **Overath, Wolfgang**<br>Auf Dem Hummerich 5, 53721 Siegburg, Germany | Soccer Player |
| **Overbay, Lyle S**<br>107 Captain Lane, Centralia WA 98531, USA | Baseball Player |
| **Overbeck, Carla**<br>205 Zaoata Lane, Chapel Hill NC 27517, USA | Soccer Player |
| **Overbey, Kellie**<br>Stone Manners Salners, 9911 W Pico Blvd, #1400, Los Angeles CA 90035 USA | Actress |
| **Overend, Ned**<br>Boure Bicycle Clothing, 98 Everett St, Durango CO 81303, USA | Cyclist |
| **Overgard, Robert M**<br>Church of Lutheran Brethren, PO Box 655, Fergus Falls MN 56538, USA | Religious Leader |
| **Overhauser, Albert W**<br>236 Pawnee Dr, West Lafayette IN 47906, USA | Physicist |
| **Overman, Ion**<br>Don Buchwald, 6500 Wilshire Blvd, #2200, Los Angeles CA 90048 USA | Actress |
| **Overman, Larry E**<br>University of California, Chemistry Dept, Irvine CA 92717, USA | Chemist |
| **Overmyer, Eric**<br>Creative Artists Agency, 2000 Ave of Stars, #100, Los Angeles CA 90067 USA | Writer, Producer |
| **Overstreet, Chord**<br>W M E Entertainment, 9601 Wilshire Blvd, #300, Beverly Hills CA 90210 USA | Actor |
| **Overstreet, Tommy**<br>Capitol Mgmt Group, 1214 16th Ave S, Nashville TN 37212, USA | Singer, Songwriter |
| **Overton, David**<br>Cheesecake Factory Inc, 26901 Malibu Hills Road, Agoura Hills CA 91301, USA | Businessman, Restauranteur |
| **Overton, Kelly**<br>Management 360, 9111 Wilshire Blvd, Beverly Hills CA 90210 USA | Actress |
| **Overy, H Michael (Mike)**<br>3010 N 152nd Lane, Goodyear AZ 85395, USA | Baseball Player |
| **Ovitz, Michael S**<br>1234 Benedict Canyon Dr, Beverly Hills CA 90210, USA | Businessman |
| **Ovredal, Andre**<br>W M E Entertainment, 9601 Wilshire Blvd, #300, Beverly Hills CA 90210 USA | Director |
| **Ovsyannikov, Oleg**<br>Skating Assn, Luchnesksaia Nab 8, 119871 Moscow, Russia | Ice Dancer |
| **Owchar, Dennis**<br>154 Krieghoff Ave, Markham ON L3R 1W1, Canada | Ice Hockey Player |
| **Owchinko, Robert D (Bob)**<br>15111 N Hayden Road, #160-357, Scottsdale AZ 85260, USA | Baseball Player |
| **Owen, Beverly**<br>Tony Greco, 1435 Bellaire Place, Pittsburgh PA 15226, USA | Actress |
| **Owen, Chris**<br>J L A Talent Agency, 9151 Sunset Blvd, West Hollywood CA 90069, USA | Actor |
| **Owen, Clive**<br>42 West, 220 W 42nd St, #1200, New York NY 10036, USA | Actor |
| **Owen, Dave**<br>1921 FM 3136, Cleburne TX 76031, USA | Baseball Player |
| **Owen, David A L**<br>78 Narrow St, Limehouse, London E14 8BP, England | Government Official, Educator |
| **Owen, Gary**<br>I C M Partners, 10250 Constellation Blvd, #900, Los Angeles CA 90067 USA | Actor |
| **Owen, Joshua R (Jake)**<br>Morris Management Group, 818 19th Ave S, Nashville TN 37203, USA | Singer |
| **Owen, Lawrence T (Larry)**<br>804 White Pine St, New Carlisle OH 45344, USA | Baseball Player |
| **Owen, Lloyd**<br>Hamilton Hodell, 66-68 Margaret St, #500, London W1W 8SR, England | Actor |
| **Owen, Michael**<br>Liverpool F C, Anfield Road, Liverpool L4 0TH, England | Soccer Player |
| **Owen, Priscilla R**<br>US Court of Appeals, 903 San Jacinto Blvd, #400, Austin TX 78701, USA | Judge |
| **Owen, Randy Y**<br>Alabama Band Promotions, PO Box 680529, Fort Payne AL 35968, USA | Singer, Guitarist (Alabama) |

**O**

**Ouma - Owen**

**Owen, Spike D** — Baseball Player
11211 Musket Rim St, Austin TX 78738, USA
**Owen, W Thomas (Tom)** — Football Player
PO Box 3, Albany OK 74721, USA
**Owens, Billy E** — Basketball Player
608 Canary Dr, Carlisle PA 17013, USA
**Owens, C Burgess, Jr** — Football Player
1430 Telegraph Road, West Chester PA 19380, USA
**Owens, Daniel W (Dan)** — Football Player
280 Selkirk Lane, Duluth GA 30097, USA
**Owens, Edwin (Cotton)** — Auto Racing Driver, Owner
Cotton Owens Enterprises, 7921 Valley Falls Road, Spartanburg SC 29303, USA
**Owens, Eric B** — Baseball Player
22431 N 54th St, Phoenix AZ 85054, USA
**Owens, Gary** — Entertainer
I C M Partners, 10250 Constellation Blvd, #900, Los Angeles CA 90067 USA
**Owens, James P (Jim)** — Baseball Player
1426 Ramada Dr, Houston TX 77062, USA
**Owens, Loren E (Steve)** — Football Player
3700 W Robinson, #230, Norman OK 73072, USA
**Owens, Mel T** — Football Player
13603 Marina Pointe Dr, #A612, Marina del Rey CA 90292, USA
**Owens, Morris L** — Football Player
4156 W Michigan Ave, Glendale AZ 85308, USA
**Owens, Rena** — Actress, Model
Ken Belling, PO Box 300471, Casselberry FL 32730, USA
**Owens, Robert G, Jr** — WW II Marine Corps Air Force Hero
730 Amicus Ave, Newport Beach CA 92610, USA
**Owens, Terrell E** — Football Player
5207 Sandy Shores Court, Lithonia GA 30038, USA
**Owens, Thomas W (Tom)** — Basketball Player
19788 Wildwood Dr, West Linn OR 97068, USA
**Owens, Virginia L (Ginny)** — Singer
Street Level Artist Agency, 107 E Centre St, Warsaw IN 46580, USA
**Owings, Micah B** — Baseball Player
3208 Druid Hills Reserve Dr NE, Atlanta GA 30329, USA
**Owsley, Douglas** — Anthropologist
Smithsonian Institution, 17th & M Sts NW, Washington DC 20036, USA
**Oxenberg, Catherine** — Actress
Power Entertainment, 9100 Wilshire Blvd, Beverly Hills CA 90212, USA
**Oxford, Vern P** — Singer, Songwriter
Landmark Communications Group, 116 W Rockwood St, Rockwood TN 37854, USA
**Oxtoby, David W** — Educator
Pomona College, President's Office, 120 E Bonita, Claremont CA 91711, USA
**Oxy Moron, Monty** — Keyboardist (Damned)
Leave Home Booking, 10 W Broadway, #608, Salt Lake City UT 84101, USA
**Oyakawa, Yoshinobu (Yoshi)** — Swimmer
4171 Hutchinson Road, Cincinnati OH 45248, USA
**Oyaya, Mary** — Actress
Coolwaters Productions, 10061 Riverside Dr, Box 531, Toluca Lake CA 91602 USA
**Oyelowo, David O** — Actor
Hamilton Hodell, 66-68 Margaret St, #500, London W1W 8SR, England
**Oz, Amos** — Writer
Ben Gurion University, PO Box 653, 84105 Beersheva, Israel
**Oz, Frank R** — Puppeteer, Director
36 Herrick Road, Sharon CT 06069, USA
**Ozaki, Masashi** — Golfer
Bridgestone Sports, 14230 Lochridge Blvd, #G, Covington GA 30014, USA
**Ozaki, Satoshi** — Physicist
Brookhaven National Laboratory, Heavy Ion Collider, 2 Center St, Upton NY 11973, USA
**Ozawa, Ichiro** — Government Official, Japan
2-38 Fukuromachi, Mizusawashi, Iwateken 023-0814, Japan
**Ozawa, Seiji** — Conductor
Vienna State Opera, Opernrig 2, 1010 Vienna, Austria
**Ozbek, Rifat** — Fashion Designer
Ozbek Ltd, 18 Haunch of Venison Yard, London W1Y 1AF, England
**Ozick, Cynthia** — Writer
34 Soundview St, New Rochelle NY 10805, USA
**Ozio, David** — Bowler
6110 Barrington Ave, Beaumont TX 77706, USA
**Ozolinsh, Sandis** — Ice Hockey Player
701 Golf Club Dr, Castle Rock CO 80108, USA
**Ozon, Francois** — Director
Films Talents, 34 Rue Du Louvre, 75001 Paris, France , USA
**Ozuk, Charles, Jr** — WW II Army Air Corps Hero
5740 Churchill Lane, Libertyville IL 60048, USA
**Ozuna, Fritz** — Artist
6769 State Highway 27, Comfort TX 78013, USA
**Ozzie, Raymond (Ray)** — Computer Software Designer
50 Harbor St, Manchester MA 01944, USA

**Paabo, Svante** — Zoo Executive
Evolutionary Anthropology Institute, Deutscher Platz 6, 04103 Leipzig, Germany
**Paasikivi, Lilli** — Opera Singer
Harrison/Parrott, 5-6 Albion Court, London W6 0QT, England
**Paavo, Jarvi** — Conductor
Cincinnati Symphony Orchestra, 1241 Elm St, Cincinnati OH 45202, USA
**Pabo, Carl O** — Biologist
Protean Futures, 475 Gate 5 Road, #210A, Sausalito CA 94965, USA
**Pabst, Augie** — Auto Racing Driver
Race Legends, 5410 Highway 73, Marshall WI 53559, USA
**Pacar, Johnny** — Actor
Innovative Artists, 1505 10th St, Santa Monica CA 90401 USA
**Pace, Betty D** — Molecular Chemist
University of Texas Medical Center, 900 W Campbell Road, Richardson TX 75080, USA
**Pace, Calvin L** — Football Player
4044 Lyon Blvd SW, Atlanta GA 30331, USA
**Pace, Darrell O** — Archery Athlete
4394 Princeton Road, Hamilton OH 45011, USA
**Pace, Dominic** — Actor
Shapiro-Lichtman, 8827 Beverly Blvd, Los Angeles CA 90048 USA
**Pace, Judy** — Actress
4139 Cloverdale Ave, Los Angeles CA 90008, USA
**Pace, Lee** — Actor
Management 360, 9111 Wilshire Blvd, Beverly Hills CA 90210 USA
**Pace, Norman R, Jr** — Microbiologist
University of Colorado, Molecular Cellular Dept, Boulder CO 80309, USA
**Pace, Orlando L** — Football Player
939 Tucker Lane, Saint Louis MO 63131, USA
**Pace, Stanley C** — Businessman
16561 Merrill Court, Chagrin Falls OH 44023, USA
**Pacella, John L** — Baseball Player
1500 Abbotsford Green Dr, Powell OH 43065, USA
**Pacey, Steven** — Actor
Ken McReddie Assoc, 101 Finsbury Pavement, London EC2A 1RS, England
**Pachal, Clayton** — Ice Hockey Player
230 Laycoe Crescent, Saskatoon SK S7S 1H5, Canada
**Pachauri, Rajendra K** — Climatologist
Tata Energy Reseach Institute, Habitat Place, New Delhi 110003, India
**Pacheco, Ferdie** — Sportscaster
4151 Gate Lane, Miami FL 33137, USA
**Pacheco, Johnny** — Musician, Composer
Universal Attractions, 135 W 26th St, #1200, New York NY 10001 USA
**Pachulia, Zaur (Zaza)** — Basketball Player
Atlanta Hawks, Centennial Tower, 101 Marietta St NW, #1900, Atlanta GA 30303 USA
**Pacino, Al** — Actor
Creative Artists Agency, 2000 Ave of Stars, #100, Los Angeles CA 90067 USA
**Paciorek, James J (Jim)** — Baseball Player
9641 E Waters Edge Place, Tucson AZ 85749, USA
**Paciorek, Thomas M (Tom)** — Baseball Player
2389 Broad Creek Dr, Stone Mountain GA 30087, USA
**Packard, Kelly** — Actress, Model
21071 Placerita Canyon Road, Newhall CA 91321, USA
**Packer, A William (Billy)** — Sportscaster
Bazel Group, 115 Penn Warren Dr, #300, Brentwood TN 37027, USA
**Packer, Ann** — Writer
Random House, 1745 Broadway, #1800, New York NY 10019 USA
**Packer, David** — Actor
Creative Artists Agency, 2000 Ave of Stars, #100, Los Angeles CA 90067 USA
**Packham, Jenny** — Fashion Designer
Spectrum House, 32-34 Gordon House Road, #A, London NW5 1LP, England
**Packwood, Robert W (Bob)** — Senator, OR
Sunrise Research, 2201 Wisconsin Ave NW, #C120, Washington DC 20007, USA
**Pacquiano, Alberto D (Bobby)** — Boxer
Top Rank Inc, 3908 Howard Hughes Parkway, #580, Las Vegas NV 89169, USA
**Pacquiao, Emanuel D (Manny)** — Boxer
4th St, Seaview Heights, Lawaan, Talisay City, Cebu PH 6045, Philippines
**Pacula, Joanna** — Actress
Chuck Binder Mgmt, 1465 Lindacrest Dr, Beverly Hills CA 90210 USA
**Padalecki, Jared** — Actor
Industry Entertainment, 955 Carillo Dr, #300, Los Angeles CA 90048 USA
**Padalka, Gennady I** — Cosmonaut
Cosmonaut Training Center, Star City, 141160 Zvezdny Gorodok, Moscow Oblast, Russia
**Padbury, Wendy** — Actress
Evans & Reiss, 100 Fawe Park Road, London SW15 2EA, England
**Paddio, Gerald** — Basketball Player
2801 Crystal Bay Dr, Las Vegas NV 89117, USA
**Paddock, John** — Ice Hockey Player, Coach, Executive
Philadelphia Flyers, 1st Union Center, 3601 S Broad St, Philadelphia PA 19148 USA
**Padgett, Jason** — Actor
G V A Talent Agency, 8981 W Sunset Blvd, #101, West Hollywood CA 90069, USA
**Padilha, Jose** — Director, Producer, Writer
Creative Artists Agency, 2000 Ave of Stars, #100, Los Angeles CA 90067 USA
**Padilla, Douglas (Doug)** — Track Athlete
182 N 555 W, Orem UT 84057, USA
**Padilla, Vicente D** — Baseball Player
1816 O'Henry Court, Arlington TX 76006, USA
**Padjean, Gary A** — Football Player
9314 Tower Bridge Road, Indianapolis IN 46240, USA
**Padma-Nathan, Harin** — Urologist
1245 16th St, #312, Santa Monica CA 90404, USA
**Padmore, Mark** — Opera Singer
Maxine Robertson Mgmt, 14 Forge Dr, Claygate KT10 0HR, England
**Paek, Jim** — Ice Hockey Player
119 Alexander Dr, Elyria OH 44035, USA
**Paerson, Anja** — Alpine Skier
Bjorkvagen 9, 920 64 Tarnaby, Sweden

**P**

**Paabo - Paerson**

# P

| | |
|---|---|
| **Paetkau, David** <br> Precision Entertainment, 6338 Wilshire Blvd, Los Angeles CA 90048, USA | Actor |
| **Paetz, Robert** <br> 7203 Macy Court, Riverside CA 92503, USA | Space Scientist |
| **Paez, Jorge (Maromero)** <br> Call G 650-4, Col Nueva, Mexicali 21100 , Baja, Mexico | Boxer |
| **Paez, Richard A** <br> US Appellate Court, Court Building, 125 S Grand Ave, Pasadena CA 91105, USA | Judge |
| **Paez, Rodolfo (Fito)** <br> Sony Records, 550 Madison Ave, #600, New York NY 10022 USA | Pianist |
| **Pagac, Frederick (Fred)** <br> 10261 Normandy Crest, Eden Prairie MN 55347, USA | Football Player |
| **Pagan, David P (Dave)** <br> 504 10th Ave W, Nipawin SK S0E 1E0, Canada | Baseball Player |
| **Pagan, Michael J** <br> Innovative Artists, 1505 10th St, Santa Monica CA 90401 USA | Actor |
| **Pagano, Charles D (Chuck)** <br> Indianapolis Colts, 7001 W 56th St, Indianapolis IN 46254 USA | Football Coach |
| **Pagano, Lindsay** <br> Azoff Music, 1100 Glendon Ave, #2000, Los Angeles CA 90024, USA | Singer |
| **Pagano, Walter** <br> Artmedia, 20 Ave Rapp, 75007 Paris, France | Actor |
| **Page, Alan C** <br> Page Education Foundation, PO Box 581254, Minneapolis MN 55458, USA | Football Player, Judge |
| **Page, Anthony** <br> I C M Partners, 10250 Constellation Blvd, #900, Los Angeles CA 90067 USA | Director |
| **Page, Ashley** <br> Scottish Ballet, Tramway, 25 Albert Dr, Glasgow G41 2PE, Scotland | Ballet Dancer, Choreographer |
| **Page, David C** <br> Massachusetts Institute of Techonolgy, Genetics Dept, Cambridge MA 02139, USA | Geneticist |
| **Page, Ellen** <br> W M E Entertainment, 9601 Wilshire Blvd, #300, Beverly Hills CA 90210 USA | Actress |
| **Page, Frank S** <br> First Baptist Church, 200 W Main St, Taylors SC 29687, USA | Religious Leader |
| **Page, Genevieve** <br> 52 Rue de Vaugirard, 75006 Paris, France | Actress |
| **Page, Harrison** <br> S D B Partners, 1801 Ave of Stars, #902, Los Angeles CA 90067 USA | Actor |
| **Page, Jimmy** <br> International Talent Booking, Ariel House, 74A Charlotte St, #100 London W1T 4QJ, England | Singer (Yardbirds/Led Zeppelin) |
| **Page, Joanna** <br> Independent Talent Group, 40 Whitfield St, London W1T 2RH, England | Actress |
| **Page, Larry** <br> Google Inc, 1600 Amphitheatre Parkway, #41, Mountain View CA 94043, USA | Businessman, Computer Scientist |
| **Page, Michael** <br> PO Box 229, North Salem NY 10560, USA | Equestrian |
| **Page, Michael R (Mike)** <br> 599 Briarcliff Dr, Woodruff SC 29388, USA | Baseball Player |
| **Page, Michelle** <br> House of Representatives, 1434 6th St, #1, Santa Monica CA 90401 USA | Actress |
| **Page, Pierre** <br> Anaheim Ducks, 2695 E Katella Ave, Anaheim CA 92806 USA | Ice Hockey Coach |
| **Page, Sam** <br> Inphenate, 9701 Wilshire Blvd, #1000, Beverly Hills CA 90212 USA | Actor |
| **Page, Solomon** <br> 9302 Vista Circle, Irving TX 75063, USA | Football Player |
| **Page, Steven** <br> Paradigm Agency, 360 Park Ave S, #1600, New York NY 10010 USA | Singer, Guitarist (Barenaked Ladies) |
| **Page, Tim** <br> Washington Post, Editorial Dept, 1150 15th St NW, Washington DC 20071, USA | Journalist |
| **Pagel, Karl D** <br> 2698 N Ellis St, Chandler AZ 85224, USA | Baseball Player |
| **Pagel, Mike J** <br> 3263 Millstone Creek Road, Lancaster SC 29720, USA | Football Player |
| **Pagels, Elaine H** <br> Princeton University, Religion Dept, Princeton NJ 08544, USA | Theologian |
| **Pagett, Nicola** <br> Art Work Entertainment, 5900 Wilshire Blvd, #2900, Los Angeles CA 90036, USA | Actress |
| **Paglia, Camille** <br> University of the Arts, Humanities Dept, 320 S Broad St, Philadelphia PA 19102, USA | Writer, Educator |
| **Pagliarulo, Michael T (Mike)** <br> 11 Fieldstone Dr, Winchester MA 01890, USA | Baseball Player |
| **Pagonis, William G** <br> 202 Smalstig Road, Evans City PA 16033, USA | Army General |
| **Pahang** <br> Istana Abu Bakar, Pekan, Pahang, Malaysia | Sultan, Malaysia |
| **Pahlavi, Fara Diba** <br> Kambiz Atabai, PO Box 2931, New York NY 10185, USA | Empress, Iran |
| **Pahlsson, O Samuel (Sammy)** <br> 9429 Tartan Ridge Blvd, Dublin OH 43017, USA | Ice Hockey Player |
| **Pahud, Emmanuel** <br> Opus 3 Artists, 470 Park Ave S, #900N, New York NY 10016 USA | Concert Flutist |
| **Pahukoa, Jeff K** <br> 2612 79th Ave NE, Everett WA 98258, USA | Football Player |
| **Paich, David F** <br> Monterey International, 200 W Superior St, #202, Chicago IL 60654 USA | Singer, Keyboardist (Toto) |
| **Paiement, Rosaire W** <br> 3351 S Palm Aire Dr, #301, Pompano Beach FL 33069, USA | Ice Hockey Player |
| **Paiement, Wilf** <br> 1064 Streambank Dr, Mississauga ON L5H 3Z1, Canada | Ice Hockey Player |
| **Paige Kent, Heather** <br> Paradigm Agency, 360 N Crescent Dr, North Building, Beverly Hills CA 90210 USA | Actress |
| **Paige, Amanda** <br> Playboy Promotions, 2706 Media Center Dr, Los Angeles CA 90065 USA | Model |
| **Paige, Elaine** <br> Douglas Gorman Rothacker Wilhelm, 1501 Broadway, #703, New York NY 10036 USA | Singer, Actress |

| | |
|---|---|
| **Paige, Janis** | Actress |
| 1700 Rising Glen Road, Los Angeles CA 90069, USA | |
| **Paige, Jennifer** | Singer, Songwriter |
| Great Scott Productions, 4750 Lincoln Blvd, #229, Marina del Rey CA 90292, USA | |
| **Paige, Peter** | Actor |
| Creative Artists Agency, 2000 Ave of Stars, #100, Los Angeles CA 90067 USA | |
| **Paige, Stephone** | Football Player |
| 8293 N Paula Ave, Fresno CA 93720, USA | |
| **Paige, Tony** | Footbal Player |
| 208 Mowbray Road, Silver Spring MD 20904, USA | |
| **Paik Kun Woo** | Concert Pianist |
| Worldwide Artists, 12 Rosebery, Thornton Heath, Surrey CR7 8PT, England | |
| **Pailes, William A** | Astronaut |
| 411 S Cedar Ridge Circle, Robinson TX 76706, USA | |
| **Paine, John** | Singer, Guitarist (Brothers Four) |
| Bob Flick Productions, 300 Vine St, #14, Seattle WA 98121, USA | |
| **Painter, John Mark** | Musician (Fleming & John) |
| Michael Dixon Mgmt, 119 Pebblecreek Road, Franklin TN 37064, USA | |
| **Painter, Lance T** | Baseball Player |
| 2683 E Pinto Dr, Gilbert AZ 85296, USA | |
| **Pais, Josh** | Actor |
| Innovative Artists, 1505 10th St, Santa Monica CA 90401 USA | |
| **Paisley, Brad** | Singer |
| Schmidt Relations, 3012 Business Park Circle, #500, Goodlettsville TN 37072, USA | |
| **Paisley, David** | Actor |
| Associated International Mgmt, 7 Hatton Garden, #400, London EC1N 8AD, England | |
| **Paisley, Ian R K** | First Minister, Northern Ireland |
| Parsonage, 17 Cyprus Ave, Belfast BT5 5NT, Northern Ireland | |
| **Pak, Charles** | Medical Researcher |
| University of Texas Southwestern Medical Center, 5323 Harry Hines Blvd, Dallas TX 75390 USA | |
| **Pak, Se Ri** | Golfer |
| 7926 Versilia Dr, Orlando FL 32836, USA | |
| **Paksas, Rolandus** | President, Lithuania |
| Liberal Union, Radvilaites Srt 1, #210, 2000 Vilnius, Lithuania | |
| **Palahniuk, Chuck** | Writer, Actor |
| United Talent Agency, U T A Plaza, 9336 Civic Center Dr, Beverly Hills CA 90210 USA | |
| **Palance, Holly** | Actress |
| 98 Millstone Road, Brewster MA 02631, USA | |
| **Palast, Greg** | Writer |
| E P Dutton, 375 Hudson St, New York NY 10014 USA | |
| **Palastra, Joseph T, Jr** | Army General |
| RR 1 Box 267, Myrtle MO 65778, USA | |
| **Palatas, Cameron** | Actor |
| New Wave Entertainment, 2660 W Olive Ave, Burbank CA 91505 USA | |
| **Palau, Doug** | Producer, Writer |
| A P A Talent/Literary Agency, 405 S Beverly Dr, #300, Beverly Hills CA 90212 USA | |
| **Palau, Luis** | Evangelist |
| Luis Palau Evangelistic Assn, 1500 NW 167th Place, Beaverton OR 97006, USA | |
| **Palazzari, Doug** | Ice Hockey Player, Executive |
| 4370 Dynasty Dr, Colorado Springs CO 80918, USA | |
| **Palazzi, Togo A** | Basketball Player |
| 84 Framingham Road, Southborough MA 01772, USA | |
| **Palden Namgyal** | Prince, Sikkim |
| J P Morgan Chase, 270 Park Ave, #1200, New York NY 10017, USA | |
| **Paleczny, Piotr** | Concert Pianist |
| Chopin Music Academy, Ul Okolnik 2, 00 368 Warsaw, Poland | |
| **Palekar, Amol** | Actor, Director |
| Chire Bandee, 10th N S Road, J V P D Scheme, Mumbai MS 400049, India | |
| **Palelei, Si'ulagi J (Lonnie)** | Football Player |
| 1808 SW Chief Circle, Blue Springs MO 64015, USA | |
| **Palermaa, Osku** | Bowler |
| Storm Products, 165 S 8th W, Brigham City UT 84302, USA | |
| **Palermo, Stephen M (Steve)** | Baseball Umpire |
| 5102 W 143rd Terrace, Overland Park KS 66224, USA | |
| **Paley, Albert R** | Sculptor |
| Paley Studio, 25 N Washington St, Rochester NY 14614, USA | |
| **Paley, Michael** | Religious Leader, Rabbi |
| Jewish Resource Center, 130 E 59th St, New York NY 10022, USA | |
| **Palffy, Zigmund (Ziggy)** | Ice Hockey Player |
| H K 36 Skalica Clementisova 50, 90901 Skalica, Slovakia | |
| **Palicki, Adrianne** | Actress |
| United Talent Agency, U T A Plaza, 9336 Civic Center Dr, Beverly Hills CA 90210 USA | |
| **Palin, Michael E** | Actor, Comedian, Writer (Monty Python) |
| Gumby Corp, 34 Tavistock St, London WC2E 7PB, England | |
| **Palin, Sarah L H** | Governor, Alaska |
| Alive Communications, 7680 Goddard St, #200, Colorado Springs CO 80920, USA | |
| **Palis, Jacob** | Mathematician |
| Instituto Matematica, Estrada Castornina 110, Rio de Janeiro 22460 320 RJ, Brazil | |
| **Palkiewicz, Jacek** | Explorer |
| Via Filzi 18, 36022 Cassola Vicenza, Italy | |
| **Pall, Donn S** | Baseball Player |
| 8001 Waterford Lakes Dr, #2311, Charlotte NC 28210, USA | |
| **Pall, Olga Scarzezzini-** | Alpine Skier |
| Fahrenweg 28, 6060 Absam, Austria | |
| **Palladino, Aleksa** | Actress, Singer |
| Gersh Agency, 9465 Wilshire Blvd, #600, Beverly Hills CA 90212 USA | |
| **Palladino, Daniel** | Producer, Writer |
| Creative Artists Agency, 2000 Ave of Stars, #100, Los Angeles CA 90067 USA | |
| **Palladino, Erik** | Actor, Producer, Writer |
| Coronel Group, 1100 Glendon Ave, #1700, Los Angeles CA 90046, USA | |
| **Palladio, Sam** | Actor |
| W M E Entertainment, 9601 Wilshire Blvd, #300, Beverly Hills CA 90210 USA | |
| **Pallavi** | Actress |
| 14A Director Colony, Kodambakkam, Chennai TN 600024, India | |
| **Palleroni, Sergio** | Architect |
| University of Texas, Architecture School, Austin TX 78712, USA | |

# P

**Palli, Anne-Marie** — Golfer
7477 E Cannon Dr, Scottsdale AZ 85258, USA
**Pallone, David M (Dave)** — Baseball Umpire
1610 Little Raven St, #515, Denver CO 80202, USA
**Pally, Adam** — Actor
Creative Artists Agency, 2000 Ave of Stars, #100, Los Angeles CA 90067 USA
**Palm, Richard P (Mike)** — Baseball Player
21 Riverview Place, Scituate MA 02066, USA
**Palm, Siegfried** — Concert Cellist
Gerhild Baron Mgmt, Dornbacher Str 41/III/3, 1170 Vienna, Austria
**Palmade, Pierre** — Actor
Voyez Mon Agent, 20 Ave Rapp, 75007 Paris, France
**Palmateer, Mike** — Ice Hockey Player
30 Simmons Crescent, Aurora ON L4G 6B5, Canada
**Palmaz, Julio C** — Inventor (Intravascular Stent)
University of Texas Health & Science Center, 7703 Floyd Curl Dr, San Antonio TX 78229, USA
**Palmeiro Corrales, Rafael C** — Baseball Player
5216 Reims Court, Colleyville TX 76034, USA
**Palmeiro, Orlando** — Baseball Player
11991 SW 103rd Terrace, MIami FL 33186, USA
**Palmer, Amanda** — Singer, Songwriter
Agency Group Ltd, 1880 Century Park E, #711, Los Angeles CA 90067 USA
**Palmer, Arnold D** — Golfer
9007 Bay Hill Blvd, Orlando FL 32819, USA
**Palmer, Betsy** — Actress
3 Glen Hill Road, #304, Danbury CT 6811, USA
**Palmer, Brad** — Ice Hockey Player
Box 544, Lake Cowichan BC V0R 2G0, Canada
**Palmer, Carl** — Drummer (Emerson Lake & Palmer, Asia)
Talent Consultants International, 105 Shad Row, #B, Piermont NY 10968 USA
**Palmer, Carson** — Football Player
25052 Adelanto Dr, Laguna Niguel CA 92677, USA
**Palmer, Chris** — Football Player, Coach
Houston Texans, 2 Reliant Park, Houston TX 77054 USA
**Palmer, Dave R** — Army General, Educator
4531 Blue Ridge Dr, Belton TX 76513, USA
**Palmer, David L** — Football Player
PO Box 310871, Birmingham AL 35231, USA
**Palmer, David W** — Baseball Player
61 Sherman Ave, Glens Falls NY 12801, USA
**Palmer, Dean W** — Baseball Player
3864 W Millers Bridge Road, Tallahassee FL 32312, USA
**Palmer, Diana** — Writer
Harlequin Enterprises, 225 Duncan Mill Road, Don Mills ON MJB JK9, Canada
**Palmer, Geoffrey** — Actor
Marmont Mgmt, Langham House, 302/8 Regent St, London W1R 5AL, England
**Palmer, Geoffrey W R** — Prime Minister, New Zealand
63 Roxburgh St, Mount Victoria, Wellington 6011, New Zealand
**Palmer, Gregg** — Actor
5726 Graves Ave, Encino CA 91316, USA
**Palmer, James A (Jim)** — Baseball Player, Sportscaster
239 Sanford Ave, Palm Beach FL 33480, USA
**Palmer, Jesse J** — Football Player, Sportscaster
8052 Hopkins Lane, Indianapolis IN 46250, USA
**Palmer, Keke** — Actress
W M E Entertainment, 9601 Wilshire Blvd, #300, Beverly Hills CA 90210 USA
**Palmer, Patsy** — Actress
Qtalent, 161 Drury Lane, #300, London WC2B 5PN, England
**Palmer, Peter W** — Actor
PO Box 482, Simpsonville KY 40067, USA
**Palmer, Russell E** — Financier
Palmer Group, 3600 Market St, #530, Philadelphia PA 19104, USA
**Palmer, Ryan H** — Golfer
4909 Rockrimmon Court, Colleyville TX 76034, USA
**Palmer, Sandra** — Golfer
498 Peralta Ave, Long Beach CA 90803, USA
**Palmer, Teresa** — Actress
Management 360, 9111 Wilshire Blvd, Beverly Hills CA 90210 USA
**Palmer, Violet** — Basketball Referee
N B A Referees Assn, 1455 Pennsylvania Ave NW, #225, Washington DC 20004, USA
**Palmer, Walter** — Basketball Player
87 South St, Rockport MA 01966, USA
**Palmer, William R** — Publisher
Detroit News, Publisher's Office, 615 W Lafayette Blvd, Detroit MI 48226, USA
**Palmer, Zoie** — Actress
Characters Talent Mgmt, 8 Elm St, Toronto ON M5G 1G7, Canada
**Palmieri, Eddie** — Jazz Pianist, Singer
Universal Attractions, 135 W 26th St, #1200, New York NY 10001 USA
**Palminteri, Chazz** — Actor
W M E Entertainment, 1325 Ave of Americas, New York NY 10019 USA
**Palmisano, Samuel J** — Businessman
I B M Corp, 1 North Castle Dr, #2, Armonk NY 10504, USA
**Palombi, Ron** — Bowler
227 E 29th St, Erie PA 16504, USA
**Palomino, Carlos** — Boxer
4200 Longridge Ave, Studio City CA 91604, USA
**Palsson, Thorsteinn** — Prime Minister, Iceland
Hateigsvegur 40, 105 Reykjavik, Iceland
**Paltrow, Gwyneth** — Actress, Model, Singer
Brillstein Entertainment Partners, 9150 Wilshire Blvd, #350, Beverly Hills CA 90212 USA
**Paltrow, Jake** — Director
United Talent Agency, U T A Plaza, 9336 Civic Center Dr, Beverly Hills CA 90210 USA
**Palumba, Joseph C (Joe)** — Football Player
927 Old Garth Road, Charlottesville VA 22901, USA
**Pampling, Rodney (Rod)** — Golfer
9 Campbell Court, Lewisville TX 75077, USA

| | |
|---|---|
| **Pamuk, Orhan** | Nobel Literature Laureate |
| Purtelas Mah Beyoglu, Beyoglu Istanbul, Turkey | |
| **Pan Hong** | Actress |
| Omei Film Studio, Tonghui Menwai, Chengdu City, Sichuan Province, China | |
| **Panabaker, Danielle** | Actress |
| Management 360, 9111 Wilshire Blvd, Beverly Hills CA 90210 USA | |
| **Panabaker, Kay** | Actress |
| Sanders/Armstrong/Caserta Mgmt, 2120 Colorado Ave, #120, Santa Monica CA 90404 USA | |
| **Panafieu, Bernard L A Cardinal** | Religious Leader |
| Archdiocese, 14 Place du Colonel-Edon, 13284 Marseille Cedex 07, France | |
| **Pancake, Sam** | Actor |
| Pakula/King, 9229 W Sunset Blvd, #315, West Hollywood CA 90069 USA | |
| **Pandey, Chunky** | Actor |
| 1 A/B Monisha Apts, Saint Andrews Road, Bandra, Mumbai MS 400050, India | |
| **Pandolfo, Jay** | Ice Hockey Player |
| 3 Meadowcroft Road, Burlington MA 01803, USA | |
| **Pandor, Henk** | Artist |
| 3422 Harrison St SE, Portland OR 97214, USA | |
| **Panetta, Leon E** | Government Official; Representative, NY |
| Defense Department, Pentagon, Washington DC 20301 USA | |
| **Panettiere, Hayden** | Actress, Singer |
| Brookside Artists Mgmt, 250 W 57th St, #2303, New York NY 10107, USA | |
| **Panettiere, Jansen** | Actor |
| C E S D, 10635 Santa Monica Blvd, #130, Los Angeles CA 90025 USA | |
| **Pang Qing** | Figure Skater |
| Skating Assn, 56 Zhongguancun South St, Haidian, Beijing 100044, China | |
| **Pang, Darren R** | Ice Hockey Player |
| 7439 Washington Ave, Saint Louis MO 63130, USA | |
| **Panic, Milan** | Prime Minister, Yugoslavia; Businessman |
| I C N Pharmaceuticals, 3300 Hyland Ave, Costa Mesa CA 92626, USA | |
| **Panichas, George A** | Writer |
| PO Box AB, College Park MD 20741, USA | |
| **Panichgul, Thakoon** | Fashion Designer |
| 270 Lafayette St, #810, New York NY 10012, USA | |
| **Panikkar, Sean** | Opera Singer |
| I M G Artists, Hogarth Business Park, Chiswick, London W4 2TH, England | |
| **Panis, Olivier** | Auto Racing Driver |
| Bar Team, Box 5014, Brackley, Northhamptonshire NN13, England | |
| **Panish, Morton B** | Physical Chemist |
| 52 Baldwin Road, Freeport ME 04032, USA | |
| **Panjabi, Archana (Archie)** | Actress |
| Biscuit Boy Productions, PO Box 13467, London NW4 1WQ, England | |
| **Panke Reithofer, Norbert** | Businessman |
| Bayerische Motoren Werke, Petuelring 130, 80788 Munich, Germany | |
| **Pankey, Irvin L (Irv)** | Football Player |
| 348 Walker St, Aberdeen MD 21001, USA | |
| **Pankin, Stuart** | Actor |
| Abrams Artists, 9200 W Sunset Blvd, #1125, West Hollywood CA 90069 USA | |
| **Pankovits, James F (Jim)** | Baseball Player |
| 6014 Catalina Dr, #115, North Myrtle Beach SC 29582, USA | |
| **Pankow, James C** | Trombone Player (Chicago), Songwriter |
| 3826 Bowsprit Circle, Westlake Village CA 91361, USA | |
| **Pankow, John** | Actor |
| Gersh Agency, 9465 Wilshire Blvd, #600, Beverly Hills CA 90212 USA | |
| **Panni, Marcello** | Conductor, Composer |
| 3 Piazza Borghese, 00186 Rome, Italy | |
| **Panoff, Robert** | Nuclear Engineer |
| 1140 Connecticut Ave NW, Washington DC 20036, USA | |
| **Panos, Zois (Joe)** | Football Player |
| 360 Rustic Lane, Hartland WI 53029, USA | |
| **Panova, Elena** | Circus Aerialist |
| Cirque du Soleil, 8400 2nd Ave, Montreal QC H1Z 4M6, Canada | |
| **Panozzo, Chuck** | Bassist (Styx) |
| Alliance Artists, 1225 Northmeadow Parkway, #100, Roswell GA 30076, USA | |
| **Panteleev, Grigori** | Ice Hockey Player |
| 5 Commonwealth Road, Natick MA 01760, USA | |
| **Pantoliano, Joe** | Actor |
| Principal Entertainment, 130 W 42nd St, #614, New York NY 10036, USA | |
| **Panula, Jorma** | Conductor, Composer |
| Sibelius Academy, P Rautatiekatu 9, 00100 Helsinki 10, Finland | |
| **Paola** | Queen, Belgium |
| Koninklijk Palais, Rue de Brederode, 1000 Brussels, Belgium | |
| **Paoli, Cecile** | Actress |
| Agents Associes, 201 Rue du Faubourg Saint Honore, 75008 Paris, France | |
| **Paolini, Christopher** | Writer |
| Random House, 1745 Broadway, #1800, New York NY 10019 USA | |
| **Paolo, Connor** | Actor |
| Abrams Artists, 9200 W Sunset Blvd, #1125, West Hollywood CA 90069 USA | |
| **Papa, Bob** | Sportscaster |
| N F L Network, 10950 Washington Blvd, #100, Culver City CA 90232 USA | |
| **Papa, John P** | Baseball Player |
| 275 Mary Ave, Stratford CT 06614, USA | |
| **Papa, Tom** | Actor, Comedian |
| 3 Arts Entertainment, 9460 Wilshire Blvd, #700, Beverly Hills CA 90212 USA | |
| **Papamichael, Phedon M** | Cinematographer |
| Innovative Artists, 1505 10th St, Santa Monica CA 90401 USA | |
| **Papas, Irene** | Actress |
| Anne Alvares Correa, 34 Rue Jouffroy d'Abbans, 75017 Paris, France | |
| **Papazian, Marty** | Actor |
| Chasen Agency, 8899 Beverly Blvd, #405, Los Angeles CA 90048 USA | |
| **Pape, Rene** | Opera, Concert Singer, Actor |
| Artists Mgmt, Dahlmannstra 9, 10629 Berlin, Germany | |
| **Papert, Seymour S** | Mathematician |
| Learning Barn, PO Box 387, Blue Hill ME 04614, USA | |
| **Papi, Stanley G (Stan)** | Baseball Player |
| 1111 W Sierra Madre Ave, Fresno CA 93705, USA | |

**P**

**Pamuk - Papi**

| | |
|---|---|
| **Papis, Massimiliano (Max)**<br>10855 NW 33rd St, Miami FL 33172, USA | Auto Racing Driver |
| **Papo, Brandon**<br>C E S D, 10635 Santa Monica Blvd, #130, Los Angeles CA 90025 USA | Actor |
| **Papoulias, Karolos**<br>President's Office, Presidential Palace, Herodes Atticus St, 10674 Athens, Greece | President, Greece |
| **Papp, Robert J, Jr**<br>Commandant, US Coast Guard, 2100 2nd St SW, Washington DC 20593 USA | Coast Guard Admiral |
| **Pappalardi, Felix**<br>Skyline Music, 2270 Maiden Lane SW, Roanoke VA 24015, USA | Singer, Bassist (Mountain) |
| **Pappano, Antonio**<br>I M G Artists, Hogarth Business Park, Chiswick, London W4 2TH, England | Conductor |
| **Pappas, Deane**<br>4511 W Wyoming Dr, Fayetteville AR 72704, USA | Golfer |
| **Pappas, George**<br>21108 Blakely Shores Dr, Cornelius NC 28031, USA | Bowler |
| **Pappas, Milton S (Milt)**<br>319 Aspen Dr, Beecher IL 60401, USA | Baseball Player |
| **Pappin, James J (Jim)**<br>48947 Greasewood Lane, Palm Desert CA 92260, USA | Ice Hockey Player |
| **Paquette, Craig H**<br>16626 S Magenta Road, Phoenix AZ 85048, USA | Baseball Player |
| **Paquin, Anna**<br>W M E Entertainment, 9601 Wilshire Blvd, #300, Beverly Hills CA 90210 USA | Actress |
| **Paradis, Vanessa**<br>Agence Artiste Adequet, 108 Rue Reaumur, 75002 Paris, France | Model, Singer, Actress |
| **Paradise, Robert (Bob)**<br>1303 Beechwood Place, Saint Paul MN 55116, USA | Ice Hockey Player |
| **Parazaider, Walter**<br>Front Line Mgmt, 1100 Glendon Ave, #2000, Los Angeles CA 90024 USA | Woodwind Musician (Chicago) |
| **Parazynski, Scott E**<br>2015 Wroxton Road, Houston TX 77005, USA | Astronaut |
| **Parcells, Duane C (Bill)**<br>Miami Dolphins, 7500 SW 30th St, Davie FL 33314 USA | Football Coach, Executive |
| **Pardee, Arthur B**<br>987 Memorial Dr, #271, Cambridge MA 02138, USA | Biochemist |
| **Pardee, John**<br>Paradigm Agency, 360 N Crescent Dr, North Building, Beverly Hills CA 90210 USA | Producer |
| **Pardes, Herbert**<br>New York Presbyterian Hospital, 161 Fort Washington Ave, New York NY 10032, USA | Psychiatrist |
| **Pardo, Don**<br>NBC-TV, News Dept, 30 Rockefeller Plaza, #270E, New York NY 10112 USA | Commentator |
| **Pardo, Etela**<br>Gavin Barker Assoc, 2D Wimpole St, London W1G 0EB, England | Actress |
| **Pardo, J D**<br>Innovative Artists, 1505 10th St, Santa Monica CA 90401 USA | Actor |
| **Pardo, Jimmy**<br>Gersh Agency, 9465 Wilshire Blvd, #600, Beverly Hills CA 90212 USA | Actor, Comedian, Writer |
| **Pardue, Kip**<br>Roar Mgmt, 9701 Wilshire Blvd, #800, Beverly Hills CA 90212 USA | Actor |
| **Pardue, Mary-Lou**<br>Massachusetts Institute of Technology, Biology Dept, Cambridge MA 02139, USA | Biologist |
| **Pare, Jessica**<br>United Talent Agency, U T A Plaza, 9336 Civic Center Dr, Beverly Hills CA 90210 USA | Actress |
| **Pare, Michael**<br>Stolen Thunder Mgmt, 7950 W Sunset Blvd, #516, Los Angeles CA 90046, USA | Actor |
| **Pare, Richard**<br>43 Brunswick Road, Montclair NJ 07042, USA | Photographer |
| **Paredes, Marisa**<br>Alsire Garcia Maroto, Pl Espana 18, #15, 28008 Madrid, Spain | Actress |
| **Parekh, Asha**<br>Azad Road, Juhu, Mumbai MS 400049, India | Actress |
| **Paremski, Natasha**<br>I M G Artists, Hogarth Business Park, Chiswick, London W4 2TH, England | Concert Pianist |
| **Parent, Bernard M (Bernie)**<br>Schooner Island Marina, 5100 Lake Road, #H-01, Wildwood NJ 08260, USA | Ice Hockey Player |
| **Parent, Mark A**<br>8829 Midview Dr, Palo Cedro CA 96073, USA | Baseball Player |
| **Parent, Monique**<br>PO Box 3458, Ventura CA 93006, USA | Actress, Model |
| **Paret, Peter**<br>Institute for Advanced Studies, Historical Studies School, Princeton NJ 08540, USA | Historian |
| **Paretsky, Sara N**<br>5831 S Blackstone Ave, Chicago IL 60637, USA | Writer |
| **Parfit, Derek A**<br>All Souls College, Philosophy Dept, Oxford OX1 4AL, England | Philosopher |
| **Parfitt, Judy**<br>Conway Van Gelder Grant, 8-12 Broadwick St, #300, London W1F 8HW, England | Actress |
| **Pargo, Jannero**<br>3280 Timberwood Lane, Riverwoods IL 60015, USA | Basketball Player |
| **Parham, Lennon**<br>Mosiac Media Group, 9200 W Sunset Blvd, #1000, Los Angeles CA 90069 USA | Producer, Writer, Actress |
| **Parillaud, Anne**<br>Artmedia, 20 Ave Rapp, 75007 Paris, France | Actress |
| **Parilli, Vito (Babe)**<br>8060 E Girard Ave, #218, Denver CO 80231, USA | Football Player, Coach |
| **Paris, Jhevon**<br>Agency Group Ltd, 142 W 57th St, #600, New York NY 10019 USA | Singer, Songwriter |
| **Paris, Kelly J**<br>1515 Redwood Circle, Thousand Oaks NJ 91360, USA | Baseball Player |
| **Paris, Mica**<br>Richard Walters, PO Box 2789, Toluca Lake CA 91610 USA | Singer |
| **Paris, Myrna**<br>Columbia Artists Mgmt Inc, 1790 Broadway, #702, New York NY 10019 USA | Opera Singer |
| **Paris, Twila**<br>Proper Mgmt, PO Box 150867, Nashville TN 37215, USA | Singer, Songwriter |

**Paris, William (Bubba)** — Football Player
4096 Beacon Place, Discovery Bay CA 94505, USA
**Parise, Jean-Paul (J P)** — Ice Hockey Player
3814 Raspberry Ridge Road NW, Prior Lake MN 55372, USA
**Parise, Vanessa** — Actress
Lara Rosenstock Mgmt, 8371 Blackburn Ave, #1, Los Angeles CA 90048, USA
**Parise, Zachary J (Zach)** — Ice Hockey Player
78 Blackburne Terrace, West Orange NJ 07052, USA
**Parish, Diane** — Actress
C A M, 111 Shoreditch High St, #400, London E1 6JN, England
**Parish, Robert L** — Basketball Player
18730 Peninsula Circle Dr, Cornelius NC 28031, USA
**Parish, Sarah** — Actress
Another Tongue, 10-11 D'Arblay St, London W1F 8DS, England
**Parisi, Angelo** — Judo Athlete
Judo Institute, 21-25 Ave de la Porte de Chatillon, 75680 Paris, France
**Parisot, Dean** — Director, Producer, Writer
Creative Artists Agency, 2000 Ave of Stars, #100, Los Angeles CA 90067 USA
**Parisse, Annie** — Actress
Gersh Agency, 9465 Wilshire Blvd, #600, Beverly Hills CA 90212 USA
**Parizeau, Michel G** — Ice Hockey Player
250 Rue Chauveau, Drummondville QC J2C 6L2, Canada
**Park Chan-Wook** — Director
Moho Films, 3002 S K M CITY, 869 Janghang-Dong, Ilsandong-Gu, Gyeonggi-Do 410-839, South Korea
**Park Chu-Young** — Soccer Player
Football Assn, 1-131 Sinmunno, 2-Ga Jongno-Gu, Seoul 110 062, South Korea
**Park Hye-Won** — Speed Skater
Skating Union, 88 Bangyee-Dong, Songpaku, Seoul 138 749, South Korea
**Park Jong-Woo** — Soccer Player
Football Assn, 1-131 Sinmunno, 2-Ga Jongno-Gu, Seoul 110 062, South Korea
**Park, Chan Ho** — Baseball Player
10 Hallcrest Dr, Ladera Ranch CA 92694, USA
**Park, D Bradford (Brad)** — Ice Hockey Player
20 Stanley Road, Lynnfield MA 01940, USA
**Park, Ernest C (Ernie)** — Football Player
3160 Private Road 1101, Clyde TX 79510, USA
**Park, Grace** — Actress
Untitled Entertainment, 350 S Beverly Dr, #200, Beverly Hills CA 90212 USA
**Park, Grace** — Golfer
8298 E Tallfeather Dr, Scottsdale AZ 85255, USA
**Park, Inbee** — Golfer
Ladies Pro Golf Assn, 100 International Golf Dr, Daytona Beach FL 32124 USA
**Park, James T** — Microbiologist
11 Bradford Road, Weston MA 02493, USA
**Park, Linda** — Actress
Seven Summits, 8906 W Olympic Blvd, Beverly Hills CA 90211, USA
**Park, Megan** — Actress
Paradigm Agency, 360 N Crescent Dr, North Building, Beverly Hills CA 90210 USA
**Park, Merle F** — Ballerina
Royal Ballet School, 144 Talgarth Road, London W14 9DE, England
**Park, Michael** — Actor
Innovative Artists, 1505 10th St, Santa Monica CA 90401 USA
**Park, Nicholas W (Nick)** — Animator, Director
Aardvark Animation, Gas Ferry Road, Bristol B51 6UN, England
**Park, Ray** — Actor
Priluck Co, 1230 Montana Ave, Santa Monica CA 90403, USA
**Park, Richard** — Ice Hockey Player
6416 Vista Pacifica, Rancho Palos Verdes CA 90275, USA
**Park, Steve** — Auto Racing Driver
261 Indian Trail Road, Mooresville NC 28117, USA
**Park, Sydney** — Actress
3 Arts Entertainment, 9460 Wilshire Blvd, #700, Beverly Hills CA 90212 USA
**Parke, Dorothy** — Actress
A K A Talent Agency, 6310 San Vicente Blvd, #200, Los Angeles CA 90048, USA
**Parke, Evan** — Actor
Essential Talent, 6399 Wilshire Blvd, #400, Los Angeles CA 90048, USA
**Parkening, Christopher** — Concert Guitarist
I M G Artists, Carnegie Hall Tower, 152 W 57th St, #500, New York NY 10019 USA
**Parker Kennedy, Jessica** — Actress
Play Mgmt, 807 Powell St, #220, Vancouver BC V6A 1H7, Canada
**Parker, Alan W** — Director
United Talent Agency, U T A Plaza, 9336 Civic Center Dr, Beverly Hills CA 90210 USA
**Parker, Andrea** — Actress
A P A Talent/Literary Agency, 405 S Beverly Dr, #300, Beverly Hills CA 90212 USA
**Parker, B Frank** — Football Player
RR 4 Box 83-2, Broken Bow OK 74728, USA
**Parker, Barrington D, Jr** — Judge
US Court of Appeals, Moynihan Courthouse, 500 Pearl St, New York NY 10007, USA
**Parker, Candace** — Basketball Player
Los Angeles Sparks, 888 S Figueroa St, #2010, Los Angeles CA 90017 USA
**Parker, Caryl Mack** — Singer
Rancho Divine Productions , 9 Music Square S, #108, Nashville TN 37203, USA
**Parker, Christian** — Baseball Player
10101 Mesa Arriba Ave NE, Albuquerque NM 87111, USA
**Parker, Christopher** — Actor
I C M Partners, 10250 Constellation Blvd, #900, Los Angeles CA 90067 USA
**Parker, Craig** — Actor
Karen Kay Mgmt, PO Box 446, Auckland 1140, New Zealand
**Parker, David G (Dave)** — Baseball Player
Cobra Industries, 4038 Oak Tree Court, Loveland OH 45140, USA
**Parker, Denise** — Archery Athlete
131 W 4300 N, Ogden UT 84414, USA
**Parker, Eleanor** — Actress
2195 La Paz Way, Palm Springs CA 92264, USA
**Parker, Eugene N** — Physicist
1006 Gardner Road, Flossmoor IL 60422, USA

**Parker, Franklin** — Writer
Western Carolina University, Education & Psychology Dept, Cullowhee NC 28723, USA
**Parker, Glenn A** — Football Player, Sportscaster
5420 N Campbell Ave, Tucson AZ 85718, USA
**Parker, Graham** — Singer, Guitarist
Roots Agency, 177 Woodland Ave, Westwood NJ 07675, USA
**Parker, Harry W** — Baseball Player
7180 Ellerson Mill Circle, #B, Mechanicsville VA 23111, USA
**Parker, Jameson** — Actor
1604 N Vista Ave, Los Angeles CA 90046, USA
**Parker, Jamie** — Actor
Rights House, Drury House, 34-43 Russell St, London WC2B 5HA, England
**Parker, Jeff** — Editorial Cartoonist
Florida Today, Editorial Dept, 1 Gannett Plaza, Melbourne FL 32940, USA
**Parker, Jo Ellen Johnson** — Educator
Sweet Briar College, President's Office, Sweet Briar VA 24595, USA
**Parker, Jon Kimura** — Concert Pianist
Opus 3 Artists, 470 Park Ave S, #900N, New York NY 10016 USA
**Parker, Kelly** — Soccer Player
Canadian Soccer, Place Soccer Canada, 237 Metcalfe St, Ottawa ON K2P 1R2, Canada
**Parker, Kristal** — Golfer
5675 E Bent Tree Dr, Scottsdale AZ 85266, USA
**Parker, Lara** — Actress
PO Box 1254, Topanga CA 90290, USA
**Parker, Lucinda** — Artist
Laura Russo Gallery, 805 NW 21st St, Portland OR 97209, USA
**Parker, Maceo** — Jazz Saxophonist
Coda Agency, 229 Shoreditch High St, London E1 6PJ, England
**Parker, Mark** — Businessman
Nike Inc, 1 SW Bowerman Dr, Beaverton OR 97005, USA
**Parker, Mary-Louise** — Actress
W M E Entertainment, 1325 Ave of Americas, New York NY 10019 USA
**Parker, Molly** — Actress
Characters Talent Mgmt, 8 Elm St, Toronto ON M5G 1G7, Canada
**Parker, Nate** — Actor
Roar Mgmt, 9701 Wilshire Blvd, #800, Beverly Hills CA 90212 USA
**Parker, Nathaniel** — Actor
Independent Talent Group, 40 Whitfield St, London W1T 2RH, England
**Parker, Nicole Ari** — Actress
Gersh Agency, 41 Madison Ave, #3301, New York NY 10010 USA
**Parker, Noelle** — Actress
9300 Wilshire Blvd, #555, Beverly Hills CA 90212, USA
**Parker, Paula Jai** — Actress
Levity Entertainment, 6701 Center Drive W, #1111, Los Angeles CA 90045 USA
**Parker, Ray, Jr** — Singer, Guitarist
Paradise Artists, 2002 Hogback Road, Ann Arbor MI 48015, USA
**Parker, Richard A (Rick)** — Baseball Player
2641 NE 74th St, Kansas City MO 64119, USA
**Parker, Riddick T, Jr** — Football Player
11226 NE 68th St, #212B, Kirkland WA 98033, USA
**Parker, Robert** — Singer, Saxophonist
Jeff Hubbard, PO Box 26334, Indianapolis IN 46226, USA
**Parker, Robert A R** — Astronaut
N A S A, Johnson Space Center, 2101 NASA Road, Houston TX 77058 USA
**Parker, Sage** — Actress
Kazarian/Measures/Ruskin, 11969 Ventura Blvd, #300, Studio City CA 91604 USA
**Parker, Sarah Jessica** — Actress, Model
Pretty Matches Productions, 1100 Ave of Americas, #G26, New York NY 10026, USA
**Parker, Scott** — Ice Hockey Player
1950 W Wolfensberger Court, Castle Rock CO 80109, USA
**Parker, Scott** — Motorcyle Racing Rider
6096 Grand Blanc Road, Swartz Creek MI 48473, USA
**Parker, T Jefferson** — Writer
E P Dutton, 375 Hudson St, New York NY 10014 USA
**Parker, Thomas A (Tom)** — Singer, Guitarist (Wanted)
Industry Music Group, 128 Regent Road, Hanley Stoke, Trent ST1 3AY, England
**Parker, Trey, II** — Animator, Writer
Important Films, 12910 Culver Blvd, #A, Los Angeles CA 90066, USA
**Parker, Vaughn A** — Football Player
2500 6th Ave, #107, San Diego CA 92103, USA
**Parker, W Anthony (Tony)** — Basketball Player
11214 Anagua Springs, Boerne TX 78006, USA
**Parker, W Douglas (Doug)** — Businessman
America West Airlines, 4000 E Sky Harbor Blvd, Phoenix AZ 85034, USA
**Parker, William** — Surgeon
Duke University Medical School, Surgery Dept, 201 Trent Dr, Durham NC 27710, USA
**Parker, William N (Willie)** — Football Player
9327 Kai Dr, Beach City TX 77523, USA
**Parker, Willie E** — Football Player
Washington Redskins, 21300 Redskin Park Dr, Ashburn VA 20147 USA
**Parker-Bowles, Camilla** — Duchess of Cornwall, England
Buckingham Palace, London SW1A 1AA, England
**Parkhill, Barry** — Basketball Player
3429 Cesford Grange, Keswick VA 22947, USA
**Parkhurst, Carolyn** — Writer
Little Brown, 3 Center Plaza, #100, Boston MA 02108 USA
**Parkhurst, Heather-Elizabeth** — Actress
8491 W Sunset Blvd, #440, West Hollywood CA 90069, USA
**Parkins, Barbara** — Actress
Bis Mgmt, 12115 San Vicente Blvd, #109, Los Angeles CA 90049, USA
**Parkinson, Bradford W** — Businessman, Inventor
2360 Camino Edna, San Luis Obispo CA 93401, USA
**Parkinson, Dian** — Entertainer, Model
Jo-Ann Geffem, 3151 Cahuenga Blvd, #235, Los Angeles CA 90068, USA
**Parkinson, Mark V** — Governor, KS
American Health Care Assn, 1201 L St NW, Washington DC 20005, USA

**Parkinson, Robert L, Jr** — Businessman
Abbott Laboratories, 100 Abbott Park Road, North Chicago IL 60064, USA
**Parks, Cherokee B** — Basketball Player
PO Box 11525, Las Vegas NV 89111, USA
**Parks, David W (Dave)** — Football Player
12113 Palisades Parkway, Austin TX 78732, USA
**Parks, Francine** — Model
Playboy Promotions, 2706 Media Center Dr, Los Angeles CA 90065 USA
**Parks, Maxie** — Track Athlete
4545 E Norwich Ave, Fresno CA 93726, USA
**Parks, Michael** — Actor
1618 N Vine St, #614, Los Angeles CA 90028, USA
**Parks, Suzan-Lori** — Writer
Steven Barclay Agency, 12 Western Ave, Petaluma CA 94952, USA
**Parks, Van Dyke** — Singer, Composer
2141 Layton St, Pasadena CA 91104, USA
**Parks, Wole** — Actor
Abrams Artists, 9200 W Sunset Blvd, #1125, West Hollywood CA 90069 USA
**Parlow, Cindy** — Soccer Player
3911 Tamarron Circle, #101, Memphis TN 38125, USA
**Parmalee, Bernard A (Bernie)** — Football Player
9208 158th St, Overland Park KS 66221, USA
**Parmenter, Charles S** — Chemist
Indiana University, Chemistry Dept, Bloomington IN 47405, USA
**Parmet, Philip (Phil)** — Cinematographer
Paradigm Agency, 360 N Crescent Dr, North Building, Beverly Hills CA 90210 USA
**Parmitano, Luca** — Cosmonaut, Italy
European Space Center, Linder Hohe, Box 906096, 51127 Cologne, Germany
**Parnell, Bobby** — Baseball Player
2265 Barger Road, Salisbury NC 28146, USA
**Parnell, Chris** — Actor, Comedian
Mosiac Media Group, 24 Music Square W, #100, Nashville TN 37203, USA
**Parnell, Lee Roy** — Singer, Guitarist
A P A Talent/Literary Agency, 3017 Poston Ave, #200, Nashville TN 37203 USA
**Parnevik, Jesper** — Golfer
17553 SE Conch Bar Ave, Jupiter FL 33469, USA
**Parodi, Starr** — Composer
Evolution Music, 1680 Vine St, #500, Los Angeles CA 90028, USA
**Parol, Tina** — Singer, Songwriter
Motown Records, 6255 W Sunset Blvd, Los Angeles CA 90028 USA
**Parque, James V (Jim)** — Baseball Player
4109 Crystal Ridge Dr SE, Puyallup WA 98372, USA
**Parr, Carolyn Miller** — Judge
US Tax Court, 400 2nd St NW, Washington DC 20217, USA
**Parr, Robert G** — Chemist
701 Kenmore Road, Chapel Hill NC 27514, USA
**Parra, Derek** — Speed Skater
14927 Treseder St, Draper UT 84020, USA
**Parra, Manuel A (Manny)** — Baseball Player
3142 Halverson Way, Roseville CA 95661, USA
**Parrella, John L** — Football Player
8161 Regency Dr, Pleasanton CA 94588, USA
**Parrett, Jeffrey D (Jeff)** — Baseball Player
2765 Pinckard Pike, Versailles KY 40383, USA
**Parrett, William** — Businessman
Deloitte Touche Tohmatsu, 433 Country Club Road, New Canaan CT 06840, USA
**Parrilla, Lana** — Actress
I F A Talent Agency, 8730 W Sunset Blvd, #490, West Hollywood CA 90069 USA
**Parris, Fred** — Singer (Five Satins)
First Class Entertainment, 483 Ridgewood Road, Maplewood NJ 07040, USA
**Parris, Gary T** — Football Player
5170 9th St, Vero Beach FL 32966, USA
**Parris, Steven M (Steve)** — Baseball Player
403 Rookery Court, Joliet IL 60431, USA
**Parris, Teyonah** — Actress
A P A Talent/Literary Agency, 405 S Beverly Dr, #300, Beverly Hills CA 90212 USA
**Parrish, Bernard P (Bernie)** — Football Player
4129 NW 32nd St, Gainesville FL 32605, USA
**Parrish, Hunter** — Actor
Management 360, 9111 Wilshire Blvd, Beverly Hills CA 90210 USA
**Parrish, John H** — Baseball Player
325 Charles Road, Lancaster PA 17603, USA
**Parrish, Lance M** — Baseball Player
1101 Chateau Lane, Nashville TN 37215, USA
**Parrish, Larry A** — Baseball Player, Manager
234 Green Haven Lane W, Dundee FL 33838, USA
**Parrish, Lemar R** — Football Player
52 Brittany Way, Palmetto GA 30268, USA
**Parros, Peter** — Actor
Amsel Eisenstadt Frazier, 5055 Wilshire Blvd, #865, Los Angeles CA 90036 USA
**Parros, Rick U** — Football Player
15932 E Lehigh Circle, Aurora CO 80013, USA
**Parrott, Andrew H** — Conductor
Allied Artists, 42 Montpelier Square, London SW7 1JZ, England
**Parrott, Michael E A (Mike)** — Baseball Player
PO Box 1264, Lyons CO 80540, USA
**Parry, Craig** — Golfer
5139 Latrobe Dr, Windemere FL 34786, USA
**Parry, Edward (Ed)** — Basketball Player
6152 Benoit Road, Clay MI 48001, USA
**Parry, Richard Reed** — Musician (Arcade Fire)
Billions Corp, 3522 W Armitage Ave, Chicago IL 60647 USA
**Parry, Robert T** — Government Official, Financier
11362 Barranca Road, Santa Rosa Valley CA 93012, USA
**Parseghian, Ara R** — Football Coach, Sportscaster
51767 Oakbrook Court, Granger IN 46530, USA

| | |
|---|---|
| **Parshall, George W** | Chemist |
| 2401 Pennsylvania Ave, #714, Wilmington DE 19806, USA | |
| **Parsky, Gerald L** | Attorney |
| Aurora Capital Partners, 1800 Century Park East, Los Angeles CA 90067, USA | |
| **Parsley, Ambrosia** | Singer (Shivaree) |
| Zoe/Rounder Records, 1 Rounder Way, Burlington MA 01803, USA | |
| **Parsley, Clifford D (Cliff)** | Football Player |
| 7601 E 134th Terrace, Grandview MO 64030, USA | |
| **Parsons, Alan** | Musician |
| World Entertainment Assoc, 8815 Conroy Windemere Road, #407, Orlando FL 32835, USA | |
| **Parsons, Charles D** | Philosopher |
| 22 Hancock St, Cambridge MA 02139, USA | |
| **Parsons, David** | Choreographer |
| Parsons Dance Foundation, 476 Broadway, New York NY 10013, USA | |
| **Parsons, David (Dave)** | Bassist (Bush) |
| Front Line Mgmt, 1100 Glendon Ave, #2000, Los Angeles CA 90024 USA | |
| **Parsons, Estelle** | Actress |
| Paradigm Agency, 360 Park Ave S, #1600, New York NY 10010 USA | |
| **Parsons, Jim** | Actor, Comedian |
| Creative Artists Agency, 2000 Ave of Stars, #100, Los Angeles CA 90067, USA | |
| **Parsons, John T** | Inventor (Machine Numerical Control) |
| 1456 Brigadoon Court, Traverse City MI 49686, USA | |
| **Parsons, Karyn** | Actress |
| Lesher Entertainment, 1134 S Cloverdale Ave, Los Angeles CA 90019, USA | |
| **Parsons, Nicholas** | Actor |
| Diamond Mgmt, 31 Percy St, London W1T 2DD, England | |
| **Parsons, Phil** | Auto Racing Driver |
| 18801 Coveside Lane, Cornelius NC 28031, USA | |
| **Parsons, Robert H (Bob)** | Football Player |
| 1098 Stanton Road, Lake Zurich IL 60047, USA | |
| **Parsons, Robert K** | Astronaut |
| Jackson & Kelly, PO Box 553, Charleston,WV 25322, USA | |
| **Part, Arvo** | Composer |
| Universal Edition, 48 Great Marlborough St, London S1F 7BB, England | |
| **Partee, Barbara H** | Educator |
| 50 Hobart Lane, Amherst MA 01002, USA | |
| **Partee, Dennis F** | Football Player |
| 604 E Rusk St, Marshall TX 75670, USA | |
| **Parton, Dolly** | Singer, Actress, Songwriter |
| Dollywood Co, 2700 Dollywood Parks Blvd, Pigeon Forge TN 37863, USA | |
| **Parton, Stella** | Singer |
| Attic Entertainment, PO Box 120871, Nashville TN 37212, USA | |
| **Partridge, Alex** | Rowing Athlete |
| Leander Club, Henley on Thames, Leander RG9 2LP, England | |
| **Partridge, John A** | Architect |
| Cudham Court, Cudham near Sevenoaks, Kent TN14 7QF, England | |
| **Partridge, Leah** | Opera Singer |
| Columbia Artists Mgmt Inc, 1790 Broadway, #702, New York NY 10019 USA | |
| **Partridge, Richard B (Rick)** | Football Player |
| 707 Reeder Road, Paramus NJ 07652, USA | |
| **Partridge, Wendy** | Costume Designer |
| Paradigm Agency, 360 N Crescent Dr, North Building, Beverly Hills CA 90210 USA | |
| **Paruzzi, Gabriella** | Cross Country Skier |
| Via Cardorna 47, 33010 Fuzine UR, Italy | |
| **Pasanella, Giovanni** | Architect |
| Pasanella & Klein, 330 W 42nd St, New York NY 10036, USA | |
| **Pasanella, Marco** | Furniture Designer |
| Pasanella Co, 45 W 18th St, New York NY 10011, USA | |
| **Pasarell, Charles** | Tennis Player |
| 78200 Miles Ave, Indian Wells CA 92210, USA | |
| **Pascal, Adam** | Actor, Singer |
| Innovative Artists, 1505 10th St, Santa Monica CA 90401 USA | |
| **Pascal, Amy** | Businesswoman |
| Sony Pictures Entertainment, 10202 W Washington Blvd, Culver City CA 90232, USA | |
| **Pascal, Olivia** | Actress |
| Agentur Alexander, Lamonstr 9, 81679 Munich, Germany | |
| **Pascal, Pedro** | Actor |
| Innovative Artists, 235 Park Ave S, #1000, New York NY 10003 USA | |
| **Pascal-Trouillot, Ertha** | President, Haiti |
| Christ Roi 21, Port-au-Prince, Haiti | |
| **Paschall, William H (Bill)** | Baseball Player |
| 7926 Windspray Dr, Summerfield NC 27358, USA | |
| **Pasco, Richard** | Actor |
| Michael Whitehall, 125 Gloucester Road, London SW7 4TE, England | |
| **Pascoal, Hermeto** | Jazz Musician, Composer |
| Eye for Eye Talent, 1139 San Carlos Ave, #310, San Carlos CA 94070, USA | |
| **Pascual, Camilo A** | Baseball Player |
| 7741 SW 32nd St, Miami FL 33155, USA | |
| **Pascual, Luis** | Director |
| Theatre de l'Europe, 1 Place Paul Claudel, 75006 Paris, France | |
| **Pascual, Mercedes** | Ecologist, Evolutionary Biologist |
| University of Michigan, Ecology & Biology Dept, Ann Arbor MI 48109, USA | |
| **Pasdar, Adrian** | Actor |
| I C M Partners, 10250 Constellation Blvd, #900, Los Angeles CA 90067 USA | |
| **Pasek, Justine** | Beauty Queen, Model |
| Physical Modelos, Edificia Parque Uracaca Av, Balboa, Panama City, Panama | |
| **Pash, Jim** | Singer (Surfaris) |
| 624 Sistine St, Las Vegas NV 89144, USA | |
| **Pashnick, Larry J** | Baseball Player |
| 506 Highland St, Wyandotte MI 48192, USA | |
| **Pashos, Anthony G (Tony)** | Football Player |
| 23 30th Ave, Jacksonville Beach FL 32250, USA | |
| **Pasian, Karina** | Singer |
| Def Jam Records, 828 8th Ave, New York NY 10019 USA | |
| **Pasillas, Jose A, II** | Drummer (Incubus) |
| Variety Artists, 1924 Spring St, Paso Robles CA 93446 USA | |

| | |
|---|---|
| **Pasin, Dave** | Ice Hockey Player |
| 787 Holly Oak Dr, Palo Alto CA 94303, USA | |
| **Paskai, Laszlo Cardinal** | Religious Leader |
| Uri Utca 62, 1014 Budapest, Hungary | |
| **Paslawski, Greg** | Ice Hockey Player |
| 10 Topping Lane, Saint Louis MO 63131, USA | |
| **Pasqua, Daniel A (Dan)** | Baseball Player |
| 45 Silo Ridge Road E, Orland Park IL 60467, USA | |
| **Pasquale, Steven** | Actor |
| I C M Partners, 10250 Constellation Blvd, #900, Los Angeles CA 90067 USA | |
| **Pasqualino, Luke** | Actor |
| B W H Agency, 117 Shaftesbury Ave, London WC2H 8AD, England | |
| **Pasqualoni, Paul** | Football Coach |
| University of Connecticut, Athletic Dept, Storrs CT 06269, USA | |
| **Pasquette, Didier** | Circus Tightrope Walker |
| 15 Ave du Stade, 10400 Trainelfrance, France | |
| **Pasquin, John R** | Director, Producer |
| Paradox Productions, 801 Tarcuto Way, Los Angeles CA 90077, USA | |
| **Pass, Patrick D** | Football Player |
| 57 Revere Terrace, Attleboro MA 02703, USA | |
| **Passarelli, Pasquale** | Greco-Roman Wrestler |
| Pfalzer Waldweg 5, 68753 Waghausel, Germany | |
| **Passer, Ivan** | Director |
| Innovative Artists, 1505 10th St, Santa Monica CA 90401 USA | |
| **Passmore, John A** | Philosopher |
| 6 Jansz Crescent, Manuka ACT 2603, Australia | |
| **Passmore, Matt** | Actor |
| W M E Entertainment, 9601 Wilshire Blvd, #300, Beverly Hills CA 90210 USA | |
| **Passos Coelho, Pedro M M** | Prime Minister, Portugal |
| Prime Minister's Office, Rua du Imprensa a Estrela 8, 1249068 Lisbon, Portugal | |
| **Pastan, Linda** | Writer |
| 11710 Beall Mountain Road, Potomac MD 20854, USA | |
| **Pastides, Harris** | Educator |
| University of South Carolina, President's Office, Osborne Building, Columbia SC 29208, USA | |
| **Pastis, Stephan** | Cartoonist |
| 1 Snoopy Place, Santa Rosa CA 95403, USA | |
| **Pastner, Josh** | Basketball Coach |
| University of Memphis, Athletic Dept, 570 Normal St, Memphis TN 38152, USA | |
| **Pastore, Vincent** | Actor |
| PO Box 207, Bronx NY 10464, USA | |
| **Pastorini, Dante A (Dan), Jr** | Football Player |
| 2323 McCue Road, #1909, Houston TX 77056, USA | |
| **Pastrana, Al** | Football Player |
| 1628 Ridout Road, Annapolis MD 21409, USA | |
| **Patat, Frederic** | Spatinaut, France |
| Faculte de Medecine, 2 Bis Blvd Tonnelle, 37032 Tours Cedex, France | |
| **Patch, Karen** | Costume Designer |
| United Talent Agency, U T A Plaza, 9336 Civic Center Dr, Beverly Hills CA 90210 USA | |
| **Patchett, Ann** | Writer |
| Saint Martin's Press, 175 5th Ave, #400, New York NY 10010 USA | |
| **Pate, Jerome K (Jerry)** | Golfer |
| 5 Hyde Park Road, Pensacola FL 32503, USA | |
| **Pate, Jonas** | Director, Writer |
| W M E Entertainment, 9601 Wilshire Blvd, #300, Beverly Hills CA 90210 USA | |
| **Pate, Josh** | Director, Writer |
| W M E Entertainment, 9601 Wilshire Blvd, #300, Beverly Hills CA 90210 USA | |
| **Pate, Steve** | Golfer |
| 1034 Brookview Ave, Westlake Village CA 91361, USA | |
| **Patek, Frederick J (Freddie)** | Baseball Player |
| 5408 NE Wedgewood Lane, Lees Summit MO 64064, USA | |
| **Patekar, Nana** | Actor |
| 304 Sheetal Apna Ghar Soc, Samarth Nagar Andgeri, Mumbai MS 400058, India | |
| **Patel, C Kumar N** | Inventor (Carbon Dioxide Laser) |
| 1171 Roberto Lane, Los Angeles CA 90077, USA | |
| **Patel, Dev** | Actor |
| Curtis Brown Group, 28-29 Haymarket St, #500, London SW1Y 4SP, England | |
| **Pateman, Carole** | Political Scientist |
| University of California, Political Science Dept, Los Angeles CA 90024, USA | |
| **Patera, John A (Jack)** | Football Player, Coach |
| 82 Osprey Dr, Cle Elum WA 98922, USA | |
| **Patera, Ken** | Weightlifter |
| 6932 Stratford Road, Saint Paul MN 55125, USA | |
| **Paterson, Bill** | Actor |
| Gordon & French, 12-13 Poland St, London W1F 8QB, England | |
| **Paterson, D Rick** | Ice Hockey Player, Executive |
| Anaheim Ducks, 2695 E Katella Ave, Anaheim CA 92806 USA | |
| **Paterson, David A** | Governor, NY |
| WOR Radio, 111 Broadway, #300, New York NY 10006, USA | |
| **Paterson, Jodi Ann** | Model |
| Playboy Promotions, 2706 Media Center Dr, Los Angeles CA 90065 USA | |
| **Paterson, Joseph A (Joe)** | Ice Hockey Player |
| 49 Sullivan Place, Lake George NY 12845, USA | |
| **Paterson, Katherine** | Writer |
| 70 Wildersburg Common, Barre VT 05641, USA | |
| **Patey, Larry J** | Ice Hockey Player |
| 2713 Autumn Run Court, Chesterfield MO 63005, USA | |
| **Pathon, Jerome** | Football Player |
| 611 Carrotwood Terrace, Plantation FL 33324, USA | |
| **Patil, Pratibha** | President, India |
| President's Office, Bharat Ka, Rashtrapti Bhavan, New Delhi 110004, India | |
| **Patinkin, Mandy** | Actor, Singer |
| Paradigm Agency, 360 N Crescent Dr, North Building, Beverly Hills CA 90210 USA | |
| **Patitz, Tatjana** | Model, Actress |
| Trump Model Agency, 91 5th Ave, #300, New York NY 10003 USA | |
| **Patkau, John** | Architect |
| Patkau Architects, 560 Beaty St, #L110, Vancouver BC V6B 2L3, Canada | |

**Pato, Alexandre** — Soccer Player
F C Milan, Via Filippo Turati 3, 20121 Milan, Italy
**Patriarco, Earle** — Opera Singer
Askonas Holt, Lincoln House, 300 High Holborn, London WC1V 7JH, England
**Patric, Jason** — Actor
Creative Artists Agency, 2000 Ave of Stars, #100, Los Angeles CA 90067 USA
**Patrick, Bill** — Sportscaster
NBC-TV, Sports Dept, 30 Rockefeller Plaza, #270E, New York NY 10112 USA
**Patrick, Butch** — Actor
15701 Redington Dr, Redington Beach FL 33708, USA
**Patrick, Craig** — Ice Hockey Player
113 Royston Road, Pittsburgh PA 15238, USA
**Patrick, Danica** — Auto Racing Driver, Model
Danica Racing, PO Box 155, Roscoe IL 61073, USA
**Patrick, James** — Ice Hockey Player
5024 Red Tail Run, Buffalo NY 14221, USA
**Patrick, Kyle** — Singer, Guitarist (Click Five)
Sharp & Focused Mgmt, 323 Broadway St, Cambridge MA 02139, USA
**Patrick, Mike** — Sportscaster
ESPN-TV, ESPN Plaza, 935 Middle St, Bristol CT 06010 USA
**Patrick, Nicholas J M** — Astronaut
10811 Oak Creek St, Houston TX 77024, USA
**Patrick, Robert** — Actor
Coronel Group, 1100 Glendon Ave, #1700, Los Angeles CA 90046, USA
**Patrick, Thomas M** — Businessman
Peoples Energy Corp, 130 E Randolph Dr, #300, Chicago IL 60601, USA
**Patridge, Audrina** — Actress
I C M Partners, 10250 Constellation Blvd, #900, Los Angeles CA 90067 USA
**Patron, Javier** — Director
I C M Partners, 10250 Constellation Blvd, #900, Los Angeles CA 90067 USA
**Patten of Barnes, Christopher F** — Governor General, Hong Kong; Educator
Oxford University, Chancellor's Office, Oxford OX1 2JD, England
**Patten, Cassandra** — Swimmer
Stockport Metro, 12 Grand Central Square, Stockport SK1 3TA, England
**Patten, David** — Football Player
333 Oak Creek Circle, Columbia SC 29223, USA
**Patten, John L (Joel), II** — Football Player
13415 Marble Rock Dr, Chantilly VA 20151, USA
**Patterson, Berman** — Singer (Cleftones)
605 Universe Blvd, #T1212, Juno Beach FL 33408, USA
**Patterson, Carly** — Gymnast
3401 Therondunn Dr, Plano TX 75023, USA
**Patterson, Christian** — Actor
Ken McReddie Assoc, 101 Finsbury Pavement, London EC2A 1RS, England
**Patterson, Colin** — Ice Hockey Player
Just in Case Fire, 11979 40th St SE, Calgary AB T2Z 4M3, Canada
**Patterson, D Corey** — Baseball Player
1115 Gordon Combs Road NW, Marietta GA 30064, USA
**Patterson, Daryl A** — Baseball Player
20145 Tollhouse Road, Clovis CA 93619, USA
**Patterson, Elvis V** — Football Player
8915 Allman Road, Lenexa KS 66219, USA
**Patterson, Francine G (Penny)** — Animal Psychologist (Koko Trainer)
Gorilla Foundation, PO Box 620640, Redwood City CA 94062, USA
**Patterson, Gary** — Football Coach
Texas Christian University, Athletic Dept, Fort Worth TX 76129, USA
**Patterson, Gary** — Cartoonist
Patterson International, 25208 Malibu Road, Malibu CA 90265, USA
**Patterson, James** — Writer, Businessman
10 Red Horse Hill Road, Sharon CT 06069, USA
**Patterson, James T** — Historian
Brown University, History Dept, Providence RI 02912, USA
**Patterson, John H** — Baseball Player
2709 Country Club Dr, Orange TX 77630, USA
**Patterson, John M** — Governor, AL
Court of Judiciary, PO Box 30155, Montgomery AL 36103, USA
**Patterson, K Shawn** — Football Player
15711 E Avenida del Ville Court, Chandler AZ 85249, USA
**Patterson, Kenneth B (Ken)** — Baseball Player
1202 Maverick Trail, McGregor TX 76657, USA
**Patterson, Lorna** — Actress
23852 Pacific Coast Highway, #355, Malibu CA 90265, USA
**Patterson, Marnette** — Actress
Abrams Artists, 9200 W Sunset Blvd, #1125, West Hollywood CA 90069 USA
**Patterson, Merritt** — Actress
Play Management, 807 Powell St, #220, Vancouver BC V6A 1H7, Canada
**Patterson, Michael** — Financier
J P Morgan Chase, 270 Park Ave, #1200, New York NY 10017, USA
**Patterson, Richard North** — Writer
PO Box 183, West Tisbury MA 02575, USA
**Patterson, Robert C (Bob)** — Baseball Player
3106 47th Avenue Lane NE, Hickory NC 28601, USA
**Patterson, Robert M** — Vietnam War Army Air Hero (CMH)
907 Ironwood Dr, Henderson KY 42420, USA
**Patterson, Ross** — Actor
B/W/R, 9100 Wilshire Blvd, #500W, Beverly Hills CA 90212 USA
**Patterson, Scott** — Actor
Hofflund/Polone, 9465 Wilshire Blvd, #420, Beverly Hills CA 90212 USA
**Patterson, Scott R** — Baseball Player
148 Tall Maple Court, Freeburg IL 62243, USA
**Patti, Sandi** — Singer, Pianist
PO Box 6, Pendleton IN 46064, USA
**Patti, Thomas** — Artist
10 Federico Dr, Pittsfield MA 01201, USA
**Pattillo, Charles C** — Air Force General, WW II Hero
11514 Little Bay Harbor Way, Spotsylvania VA 22551, USA

**Pattillo, Linda** — Commentator
CNN-TV, News Dept, 820 1st St NE, #1000, Washington DC 20002 USA
**Pattin, Martin W (Marty)** — Baseball Player
3401 Sweetgrass Court, Lawrence KS 66049, USA
**Pattinson, Robert** — Actor
Curtis Brown Group, 28-29 Haymarket St, #500, London SW1Y 4SP, England
**Patton, Carl V** — Educator
Georgia State University, President's Office, Atlanta GA 30303, USA
**Patton, Marvcus R** — Football Player
110 Gallatin St NW, Washington DC 20011, USA
**Patton, Melvin (Mel)** — Track Athlete
2312 Via del Aguagate, Fallbrook CA 92028, USA
**Patton, Mike** — Singer (Faith No More)
Ipecac Records, PO Box 1778, Orinda CA 94563, USA
**Patton, Paula** — Actress
W M E Entertainment, 9601 Wilshire Blvd, #300, Beverly Hills CA 90210 USA
**Patton, Ricky R** — Football Player
1454 Brookline Court SE, Mableton GA 30126, USA
**Patton, Troy J** — Baseball Player
33635 W Decker Dr, Magnolia TX 77355, USA
**Patton, William C (Will)** — Actor
Paradigm Agency, 360 N Crescent Dr, North Building, Beverly Hills CA 90210 USA
**Patty, J Edward (Budge)** — Tennis Player
La Marne, 14 Ave de Jurigoz, 1006 Lausanne, Switzerland
**Patulski, Walter G (Walt)** — Football Player
420 Kimber Road, Syracuse NY 13224, USA
**Patzaichin, Ivan** — Canoeing Athlete
S C Sportiv Unirea Tricolor, Soseaua Stefan Cel Mare 9, 020121 Bucharest, Romania
**Patzakis, Michele** — Opera Singer
Prappas Co, 9201 Wilshire Blvd, #204, Beverly Hills CA 90210, USA
**Pau, Peter** — Cinematographer
Gersh Agency, 9465 Wilshire Blvd, #600, Beverly Hills CA 90212 USA
**Pauk, Gyorgy** — Concert Violinist
27 Armitage Road, London NW11 8QT, England
**Paul, Aaron M** — Actor
United Talent Agency, U T A Plaza, 9336 Civic Center Dr, Beverly Hills CA 90210 USA
**Paul, Adrian** — Actor
Filmblips, 4968 Yonge St, #2911, Toronto ON M2N 7G9, Canada
**Paul, Alexandra** — Actress
Forster Entertainment, 12533 Woodgreen St, Building B, Los Angeles CA 90036, USA
**Paul, Billy** — Singer
Billy Paul Mgmt, 8215 Winthrop St, Philadelphia PA 19136, USA
**Paul, Christi** — Commentator
CNN-TV, 190 Marietta Ave SW, Atlanta GA 30303 USA
**Paul, Christiane** — Actress
Players Agentur Mgmt, Sophienstr 21, 10178 Berlin-Mille, Germany
**Paul, Christopher E (Chris)** — Basketball Player
749 Fountain Brook Lane, Lewisville NC 27023, USA
**Paul, Dana** — Singer, Bassist (Cornerstone)
Dana Paul Productions, 9421 Live Oak Place, #101, Davie/Fort Lauderdale FL 33324, USA
**Paul, Don Michael** — Director, Writer, Actor
A P A Talent/Literary Agency, 405 S Beverly Dr, #300, Beverly Hills CA 90212 USA
**Paul, Ellis** — Singer, Songwriter
Ralph Jaccodine Mgmt, PO Box 381982, Cambridge MA 02238, USA
**Paul, Frankie** — Singer
Keep on Kicking Music, 330 84th St, #9, Miami Beach FL 33141, USA
**Paul, Henry** — Singer (BlackHawk), Songwriter
Debra McCloud Accounting, 1400 18th Ave S, #C3, Nashville TN 37212, USA
**Paul, Jarrad** — Actor, Writer
Principato-Young, 9465 Wilshire Blvd, #880, Beverly Hills CA 90212 USA
**Paul, Joshua W (Josh)** — Baseball Player
4126 Canoga Park Dr, Brandon FL 33511, USA
**Paul, Kevin** — Actor
Jana Luker Agency, 1923 1/2 Westwood Blvd, #3, Los Angeles CA 90025, USA
**Paul, Markus D** — Football Player
26 Reid Court, Mahwah NJ 07430, USA
**Paul, Michael G (Mike)** — Baseball Player
5121 N Circulo Sobrio, Tucson AZ 85718, USA
**Paul, Robert** — Figure Skater
10675 Rochester Ave, Los Angeles CA 90024, USA
**Paul, Sean** — Rap Artist (Youngbloodz)
Headline Entertainment, 8 Haughton Ave, Kingston 10, Jamaica
**Paul, Tito J** — Football Player
2394 Ness Court, Powell OH 43065, USA
**Paul, Tommy** — Boxer
3578 Village Green Dr, Sarasota FL 34239, USA
**Paul, Vinnie** — Drummer (Pantera)
Concrete Mgmt, 361 W Broadway, #200, New York NY 10013, USA
**Paul, Whitney** — Football Player
6802 Thornwild Road, Missouri City TX 77489, USA
**Paul, Wolfgang J** — Soccer Player
Postfach 1324, 59939 Olsberg-Bigge, Germany
**Paula, Alejandro F (Jandi)** — Prime Minister, Netherlands Antilles
Premier's Office, Fort Amsterdam 17, Willemstad, Netherlands Antilles
**Paulauskas, Arturas** — President, Lithuania
Seimas, Gedimino Pr 53, LT 2600 Vilnius, Lithuania
**Pauley, Jane** — Commentator
I C M Partners, 10250 Constellation Blvd, #900, Los Angeles CA 90067 USA
**Paulino, Ronny A** — Baseball Player
129 Cardinal Circle, Pittsburgh PA 15237, USA
**Pauls, Raymond** — Jazz Pianist, Composer
Veidenbaum Str 41/43, #26, 226001 Riga, Latvia
**Paulsen, Gary** — Writer
126 Bookout NE, Tularosa NM 88352, USA
**Paulsen, Robert (Rob)** — Actor
Sutton-Barth Vennari, 5900 Wilshire Blvd, #700, Los Angeles CA 90036 USA

**Paulsen, Tiffany** — Actress
Creative Artists Agency, 2000 Ave of Stars, #100, Los Angeles CA 90067 USA

**Paulson, Carl** — Golfer
8211 Tibet Butler Dr, Windermere FL 34786, USA

**Paulson, Dainard A** — Football Player
2904 Main St, Union Gap WA 98903, USA

**Paulson, Dennis J** — Golfer
1872 Shadetree Dr, San Marcos CA 92078, USA

**Paulson, Henry M (Hank), Jr** — Secretary, Treasury; Financier
401 N Michigan Ave, #3100, Chicago IL 60611, USA

**Paulson, Jay** — Actor
Ira Belgrade Mgmt, 5850E W 3rd St, Los Angeles CA 90036, USA

**Paulson, Kenneth** — Editor, Foundation Executive
Newseum, 555 Pennsylvania Ave NW, Washington DC 20001, USA

**Paulson, Richard L** — Businessman
Potlatch Corp, 601 W Riverside Ave, #1100, Spokane WA 99201, USA

**Paulson, Sarah** — Actress
United Talent Agency, U T A Plaza, 9336 Civic Center Dr, Beverly Hills CA 90210 USA

**Paultz, William E (Billy)** — Basketball Player
1914 Waters Edge Lane, Seabrook TX 77586, USA

**Paulus, Diane** — Director, Writer
Gersh Agency, 9465 Wilshire Blvd, #600, Beverly Hills CA 90212 USA

**Paulusma, Polly** — Singer, Guitarist, Songwriter
One Little Indian Records, 34 Trinity Crescent, London SW17 7AE, England

**Paup, Bryce E** — Football Player
4300 Oak Ridge Circle, De Pere WI 54115, USA

**Pausini, Laura** — Singer, Songwriter
Gente Mgmt, Via Palermo 8, 20121 Milan, Italy

**Pavan, Marisa** — Actress
4 Allee des Brouillards, 75018 Paris, France

**Pavan, Sarah L** — Volleyball Player
University of Nebraska, Athletic Dept, Lincoln NE 68588, USA

**Pavano, Carl A** — Baseball Player
PO Box 1307, Thomasville GA 31799, USA

**Pavelich, Mark T** — Ice Hockey Player
19 E Norwood Shores, Lutsen MN 55612, USA

**Pavelich, Martin N (Marty)** — Ice Hockey Player
1709 Forest Lane, Bloomfield Hills MI 48301, USA

**Pavese, James P (Jim)** — Ice Hockey Player
65 Whittier Dr, Kings Park NY 11754, USA

**Pavia, Ria** — Actress
Talent Works, 3500 W Olive Ave, #1400, Burbank CA 91505 USA

**Pavin, Corey** — Golfer
4332 Gilbert Ave, Dallas TX 75219, USA

**Pavlas, David L** — Baseball Player
PO Box 1224, Shiner TX 77984, USA

**Pavletich, Donald S (Don)** — Baseball Player
13645 Adelaide Lane, Brookfield WI 53005, USA

**Pavlik, Kelly (Ghost)** — Boxer
949 Cornell Ave, Youngstown OH 44502, USA

**Pavlik, Roger A** — Baseball Player
622 Beaver Bend Road, Houston TX 77037, USA

**Pavlo** — Guitar Player
Agency Group Ltd, 142 W 57th St, #600, New York NY 10019 USA

**Pavlovic, Aleksandar (Sasha)** — Basketball Player
Boston Celtics, 226 Causeway St, #4, Boston MA 02114 USA

**Pawelczyk, James A (Jim)** — Astronaut
N A S A, Johnson Space Center, 2101 NASA Road, Houston TX 77058 USA

**Pawlak, Waldemar** — Prime Minister, Poland
Zarzad Glowny ZOSP RP, Ul Obozna 1, 00 340 Warsaw, Poland

**Pawlenty, Timothy J (Tim)** — Governor, MN
Financial Services Roundtable, 1001 Pennsylvania Ave NW, #500 South, Washington DC 20004, USA

**Pawlikowski, Pawel** — Director
Creative Artists Agency, 2000 Ave of Stars, #100, Los Angeles CA 90067 USA

**Pawlowski, John** — Baseball Player
257 Mill Branch Way, North Augusta SC 29860, USA

**Pawson, John** — Architect
70-78 York Way, #B, London N1 9AG, England

**Paxon, L William (Bill)** — Representative, NY
Akin Gump Strauss Hauer, 1333 New Hampshire NW, #400, Washington DC 20036, USA

**Paxson, James E (Jim)** — Basketball Player
3225 Southdale Dr, #1, Dayton OH 45409, USA

**Paxson, John M** — Basketball Player, Executive
125 Boardman Court, Lake Bluff IL 60044, USA

**Paxton, Leonitas E (Lonie), III** — Football Player
2495 Oak Vista Court, Castle Rock CO 80104, USA

**Paxton, Michael D (Mike)** — Baseball Player
1145 S Indian Wells Dr, Collierville TN 38017, USA

**Paxton, Robert O** — Historian
460 Riverside Dr, #72, New York NY 10027, USA

**Paxton, Sara** — Actress
United Talent Agency, U T A Plaza, 9336 Civic Center Dr, Beverly Hills CA 90210 USA

**Paxton, Tom** — Singer, Songwriter
Fleming Artists, 543 N Main St, Ann Arbor MI 48104, USA

**Paxton, William A (Bill)** — Actor
W M E Entertainment, 9601 Wilshire Blvd, #300, Beverly Hills CA 90210 USA

**Payer, Serge** — Ice Hockey Player
2343 Lorraine St, RR 1, Rockland ON K4K 1K7, Canada

**Payette, Julie** — Astronaut, Canada
Space Agency, Rockliffe Base, Ottawa ON K1A 1A1, Canada

**Paymah, Karl** — Football Player
PO Box 4268, Culver City CA 90231, USA

**Paymer, David** — Actor
A P A Talent/Literary Agency, 405 S Beverly Dr, #300, Beverly Hills CA 90212 USA

**Payne, Alexander** — Director, Producer, Writer
Ad Hominem Enterprises, 506 Santa Monica Blvd, #400, Santa Monica CA 90401, USA

| | |
|---|---|
| **Payne, Allen** | Actor |
| Harrison Stokes, 8730 W Sunset Blvd, #270, West Hollywood CA 90069, USA | |
| **Payne, Anthony E** | Composer |
| 2 Wilton Square, London N1 3DL, England | |
| **Payne, Bruce** | Actor |
| Gilbertson Entertainment, 1334 3rd Street Promenade, #201, Santa Monica CA 90401 USA | |
| **Payne, C Ladell** | Educator |
| Randolph-Macon College, President's Office, Ashland VA 23005, USA | |
| **Payne, David N** | Optical Fiber Engineer |
| Southampton University, Electronics Dept, Highfield, Southampton SO17 1BJ, England | |
| **Payne, Dougie** | Bassist (Travis) |
| Wildlife Entertainment, 21 Heathmans Road, London SW6 4TJ, England | |
| **Payne, Freda** | Singer, Actress |
| Scott Stander Assoc, 4533 Van Nuys Blvd, #401, Sherman Oaks CA 91403 USA | |
| **Payne, Harry C** | Educator |
| Williams College, President's Office, Williamstown MA 01267, USA | |
| **Payne, Henry** | Editorial Cartoonist |
| Detroit News, Editorial Dept, 615 W Lafayette, Detroit MI 48226, USA | |
| **Payne, Julie** | Actress |
| Pakula/King, 9229 W Sunset Blvd, #315, West Hollywood CA 90069 USA | |
| **Payne, Keith** | Vietnam War Australian Army Hero (VC) |
| 2 Saint Bee's Ave, Bucasia QLD 4740, Australia | |
| **Payne, Keri-Anne** | Swimmer |
| Stockport Metro, 12 Grand Central Square, Stockport SK1 3TA, England | |
| **Payne, Roger S** | Biologist, Conservationist |
| 191 Western Road, Lincoln MA 01773, USA | |
| **Payne, Scherrie** | Singer |
| Starwil Talent, 433 N Camden Dr, #400, Beverly Hills CA 90210, USA | |
| **Payne, Seth C** | Football Player |
| 7908 Westwood Dr, Houston TX 77055, USA | |
| **Payne, Steven J (Steve)** | Ice Hockey Player |
| N6497 County Road N, Beldenville WI 54003, USA | |
| **Payne, Tom** | Actor |
| Paradigm Agency, 360 N Crescent Dr, North Building, Beverly Hills CA 90210 USA | |
| **Payne, Waylon** | Singer, Actor |
| Nine Yards Entertainment, 8530 Wilshire Blvd, #500, Beverly Hills CA 90211 USA | |
| **Pays, Amanda** | Actress |
| Origin Talent, 4705 Laurel Canyon Blvd, #306 , Studio City CA 91607, USA | |
| **Payton, Benjamin F** | Educator |
| 20200 Chapel Trace, Estero FL 33928, USA | |
| **Payton, Christian** | Actor |
| Grossman & Jack Talent,  33 W Grand Ave, #402, Chicago IL 60654, USA | |
| **Payton, Edward (Eddie)** | Football Player |
| 118 Woodland Hills Blvd, Madison MS 39110, USA | |
| **Payton, Gary D** | Basketball Player |
| 2745 S Monte Cristo Way, Las Vegas NV 89117, USA | |
| **Payton, Gary E** | Astronaut |
| 2367 Diamond Creek Dr, Colorado Springs CO 80921, USA | |
| **Payton, Jason L (Jay)** | Baseball Player |
| 3000 Cone Manor Lane, Raleigh NC 27613, USA | |
| **Payton, Nicholas** | Jazz Trumpeter |
| Management Ark, 116 Village Blvd, #200, Princeton NJ 08540, USA | |
| **Payton, Sean** | Football Player, Coach |
| 2006 Brazos Court, Westlake TX 76262, USA | |
| **Pazienza, Vinny** | Boxer |
| 54 Tivoli Court, Warwick RI 02886, USA | |
| **Peaches** | Singer, Songwriter |
| Butterscotch Castle, 535 Geary St, #612, San Francisco CA 94102, USA | |
| **Peacock, Alice** | Singer, Songwriter |
| Silverleaf Booking, 59 W 1st St, Boiling Springs PA 17007, USA | |
| **Peacock, Andrew S** | Government Official, Australia |
| 19 Queens Road, Melbourne VIC 3004, Australia | |
| **Peacock, James L, III** | Anthropologist |
| University of North Carolina, Anthropology Dept, 301 Alumni Building, Chapel Hill NC 27599, USA | |
| **Peake, Don** | Guitarist, Composer |
| Marcelli Co, 11333 Moorpark, #411, Studio City CA 91602, USA | |
| **Peake, Pat** | Ice Hockey Player |
| 327 Hecht Dr, Madison Heights MI 48071, USA | |
| **Peake, Ryan A** | Singer, Guitarist (Nickelback) |
| Union Entertainment Group, 17737 Ventura Blvd, #208, Encino CA 91316, USA | |
| **Peaker, E J** | Actress |
| 4935 Densmore Ave, Encino CA 91436, USA | |
| **Pear, David L (Dave)** | Football Player |
| 3126 199th Ave SE, Sammamish WA 98075, USA | |
| **Pearce, Guy** | Actor |
| Shanahan Mgmt, PO Box 1509, Darlinghurst NSW 1300, Australia | |
| **Pearce, Jacqueline** | Actress |
| Rhubarb Personal Mgmt, 6 Langley St, #41, London WC2H 9JA, England | |
| **Pearce, Oscar** | Actor |
| Ken McReddie Assoc, 101 Finsbury Pavement, London EC2A 1RS, England | |
| **Pearce, Reynold** | Fashion Designer |
| Pearce Fionda, Loft, 27 Horsell Road, Highbury, London N5 1XL, England | |
| **Pearce, Stephen** | Religious Leader, Rabbi |
| Congregation Emanuel, 2 Lake St, San Francisco CA 94118, USA | |
| **Pearce, Steven W (Steve)** | Baseball Player |
| 1928 E Gachet Blvd, Lakeland FL 33813, USA | |
| **Pearcy, Stephen** | Singer (Ratt) |
| Tom Vitorino Mgmt, 11606 Vimy Road, Granada Hills CA 91344, USA | |
| **Pearl, Barry** | Actor |
| Coolwaters Productions, 10061 Riverside Dr, Box 531, Toluca Lake CA 91602 USA | |
| **Pearl, Judea** | Computer Scientist, Statistician |
| University of California, Computer Science Dept, Los Angeles CA 90024, USA | |
| **Pearlstein, Philip** | Artist |
| 361 W 36th St, New York NY 10018, USA | |
| **Pearlstein, Randy** | Actor |
| Bleeker Street Entertainment, 853 Broadway, #1214, New York NY 10003, USA | |

# P

| | |
|---|---|
| **Pearlstein, Steven** | Journalist |
| Washington Post, Editorial Dept, 1150 15th St NW, Washington DC 20071 USA | |
| **Pearlstine, Norman** | Editor |
| Carlyle Group, 1000 Pennsylvania Ave NW, Washington DC 20003, USA | |
| **Pearman, F Alvin, Jr** | Football Player |
| 5601 Chadfort Lane, Charlotte NC 28226, USA | |
| **Pearson, Albert G (Albie)** | Baseball Player |
| 55473 Oakhill, La Quinta CA 92253, USA | |
| **Pearson, Allison** | Writer |
| Knopf Publishers, 1745 Broadway, New York NY 10019 USA | |
| **Pearson, Becky** | Golfer |
| 1630 SW 8th Ave, Boca Raton FL 33486, USA | |
| **Pearson, David G** | Auto Racing Driver |
| 290 Burnett Road, Boiling Springs SC 29316, USA | |
| **Pearson, Drew** | Football Player |
| 3721 Mount Vernon Way, Plano TX 75025, USA | |
| **Pearson, Jayice (J C)** | Football Player |
| 721 SW Winterhill Lane, Lees Summit MO 64081, USA | |
| **Pearson, Keir** | Writer, Editor, Producer |
| Management 360, 9111 Wilshire Blvd, Beverly Hills CA 90210 USA | |
| **Pearson, Larry** | Auto Racing Driver |
| Buckshot Racing, 182 Belue Road, Spartansburg SC 29303, USA | |
| **Pearson, Mike Parker** | Archaeologist |
| Sheffield University, Archaeology Dept, Sheffield S1 4ET, England | |
| **Pearson, Preston J** | Football Player |
| Pro Style Assoc, 9104 Moss Farm Lane, Dallas TX 75243, USA | |
| **Pearson, Ralph G** | Chemist |
| 715 Grove Lane, Santa Barbara CA 93105, USA | |
| **Pearson, Richard (Rick)** | Editor |
| I C M Partners, 10250 Constellation Blvd, #900, Los Angeles CA 90067 USA | |
| **Pearson, Ridley** | Writer |
| Dell Books, 1745 Broadway, New York NY 10019 USA | |
| **Pearson, Robert G** | Ice Hockey Player |
| Beyond the Point, 467 Meadow St, Oshawa ON L1L 1B9, Canada | |
| **Pearson, Scott** | Ice Hockey Player |
| Medassets Inc, 100 N Point Center E, #200, Alpharetta GA 30022, USA | |
| **Pearson, T R** | Writer |
| Crown Publishing Group, 1745 Broadway, #1300, New York NY 10019 USA | |
| **Peart, Neal** | Drummer (Rush) |
| S L Feldman Mgmt, 1505 W 2nd Ave, #200, Vancouver BC V6H 3Y4, Canada | |
| **Pease, Patsy** | Actress |
| 15432 Hartland St, Van Nuys CA 91406, USA | |
| **Peavy, Jacob E (Jake)** | Baseball Player |
| PO Box 346, Catherine AL 36728, USA | |
| **Peca, Michael A (Mike)** | Ice Hockey Player |
| 46 Golden Pheasant Dr, Getzville NY 14068, USA | |
| **Pechstein, Claudia** | Speed Skater |
| Powerplay Mgmt, Seepromenade 53, 14476 Gross, Germany | |
| **Peck, Austin** | Actor |
| Stone Manners Salners, 9911 W Pico Blvd, #1400, Los Angeles CA 90035 USA | |
| **Peck, Carolyn** | Basketball Player, Coach |
| University of Florida, Athletic Dept, Gainesville FL 32611, USA | |
| **Peck, Cecilia** | Actress |
| Cabin Creek Films, 270 Lafayette St, #710, New York NY 10012, USA | |
| **Peck, Ethan** | Actor |
| I C M Partners, 10250 Constellation Blvd, #900, Los Angeles CA 90067 USA | |
| **Peck, J Eddie** | Actor |
| Element Talent Agency, 120 S Vignes, #202, Los Angeles CA 90012, USA | |
| **Peck, Raoul** | Director, Producer, Writer |
| United Talent Agency, U T A Plaza, 9336 Civic Center Dr, Beverly Hills CA 90210 USA | |
| **Peck, Richard E** | Educator, Writer |
| 96 Homesteads Road, Placitas NM 87043, USA | |
| **Peck, Robert Newton** | Writer |
| 430 Village Place, #214, Longwood FL 32779, USA | |
| **Peck, Tom** | Auto Racing Driver |
| 417 E North St, McConnellsburg PA 17233, USA | |
| **Pecker, David J** | Publisher |
| American Media, 600 S East Coast Ave, Lantana FL 33462, USA | |
| **Pecker, Jean-Claude** | Astronomer |
| Pusat-Tasek, Les Corbeaux, 85350 L'lle d'Yeu, France | |
| **Peckovam Dagmar** | Opera Singer |
| Na Pankraci 101, 14000 Prague 4, Czech Republic | |
| **Pecota, William J (Bill)** | Baseball Player |
| 332 NE Warrington Court, Lees Summit MO 64064, USA | |
| **Pecqueur, Mario** | Actor |
| Artmedia, 20 Ave Rapp, 75007 Paris, France | |
| **Pedersen, Allen (Al)** | Ice Hockey Player |
| 2261 Fieldcrest Dr, Colorado Springs CO 80921, USA | |
| **Pedersen, William** | Architect |
| Kohn Pedersen Fox Assoc, 111 W 57th St, #300, New York NY 10019, USA | |
| **Pedersen-Bieri, Maya** | Skeleton Athlete |
| Saeter, 3818 Oyer, Norway | |
| **Pederson, Barry A** | Ice Hockey Player |
| 18 Cutting Road, Swampscott MA 01907, USA | |
| **Pederson, Denis E** | Ice Hockey Player |
| 74 Cummings Circle, West Orange NJ 07052, USA | |
| **Pederson, Douglas I (Doug)** | Football Player |
| 12 Gladwynne Terrace, Moorestown NJ 08057, USA | |
| **Pederson, Mark** | Ice Hockey Player |
| 151 Equestrian Lane, Kalispell MT 59901, USA | |
| **Pedrad, Nasim** | Actress, Comedian |
| Principato-Young, 9465 Wilshire Blvd, #880, Beverly Hills CA 90212 USA | |
| **Pedregon, Cruz** | Drag Racing Driver |
| Cruz Pedregon Racing, 462 South Point Circle, #A, Brownsburg IN 46112, USA | |
| **Pedregon, Frank** | Drag Racing Driver |
| Frank Pedregon Racing, 6174 Cabernet Place, Alta Loma CA 91766, USA | |

| | |
|---|---|
| **Pedretti, Adam** | Drummer (Killing Heidi) |
| Harbour Agency, 135 Forbes St, Woolloomooloo NSW 2011, Australia | |
| **Pedrique, Alfredo J (Al)** | Baseball Player |
| 10382 E Oakbrook St, Tucson AZ 85747, USA | |
| **Pedro, James A (Jimmy)** | Judo Athlete |
| 52 Valley St, Wakefield MA 01880, USA | |
| **Pedroía, Dustin L** | Baseball Player |
| 26425 S 116th St, Chandler AZ 85249, USA | |
| **Pedroni, Simone** | Concert Pianist |
| Pro Arte, Fosswinckelsgt 9, 5007 Bergen, Norway | |
| **Peebles, Ann** | Singer |
| Universal Attractions, 135 W 26th St, #1200, New York NY 10001 USA | |
| **Peebles, P James E** | Physicist, Educator |
| 24 Markham Road, Princeton NJ 08540, USA | |
| **Peek, Antwan M** | Football Player |
| 19555 E Kerry Place, Strongsville OH 44149, USA | |
| **Peeler, Anthony E** | Basketball Player |
| 4502 E 48th St, Kansas City MO 64130, USA | |
| **Peelle, Justin M** | Football Player |
| 14040 Iris Lane, Poway CA 92064, USA | |
| **Peeples, George** | Basketball Player |
| 1032 Loma Lisa Lane, Arcadia CA 91006, USA | |
| **Peeples, Lewis** | Singer (Five Satins) |
| Paramount Entertainment, PO Box 12, Far Hills NJ 07931 USA | |
| **Peeples, Nia** | Actress, Singer |
| Levity Entertainment Group, 6701 Center Drive W, #1111, Los Angeles CA 90045, USA | |
| **Peerce, Larry** | Director |
| 225 W 34th St, #1012, New York NY 10122, USA | |
| **Peers, Holly J** | Model |
| Samantha Bond Mgmt, Elysium Gate, 126-128 New Kings Road, London  SW6 4LZ, England | |
| **Peet, Amanda** | Actress |
| Management 360, 9111 Wilshire Blvd, Beverly Hills CA 90210 USA | |
| **Peete, Calvin** | Golfer |
| 128 Garden Gate Dr, Ponte Vedra Beach FL 32082, USA | |
| **Peete, Rodney** | Football Player |
| 11964 Crest Place, Beverly Hills CA 90210, USA | |
| **Peeters, Pete** | Ice Hockey Player |
| Peeters Farm, Namao AB T0A 2N0, Canada | |
| **Pegg, Simon** | Actor, Comedian, Writer |
| United Talent Agency, U T A Plaza, 9336 Civic Center Dr, Beverly Hills CA 90210 USA | |
| **Pegram, Erric D** | Football Player |
| 2030 Teagarden Lane, Naples FL 34110, USA | |
| **Pei, Ieoh Ming (I M)** | Pritzker Architectural Laureate |
| 11 Sutton Place, New York NY 10022, USA | |
| **Peinemann, Edith** | Concert Pianist |
| Pro Musicis, Ruetistr 38, 8032 Zurich, Switzerland | |
| **Peirce, Kimberly** | Director, Producer, Writer |
| Creative Artists Agency, 2000 Ave of Stars, #100, Los Angeles CA 90067 USA | |
| **Peirse, Sarah** | Actress |
| R G M Artist, 64-76 Kippax St, #202, Surry Hills NSW 2010, Australia | |
| **Peirsol, Aaron** | Swimmer |
| 1748 Plaza Del Norte, Newport Beach CA 92661, USA | |
| **Peirson, John** | Ice Hockey Player, Sportscaster |
| 3 Steepletree Lane, Wayland MA 01778, USA | |
| **Peizewat, Gwendal** | Ice Dancer |
| Sports de Glace Federation, 35 Rue Felicien David, 75016 Paris, France | |
| **Pejman, Bob** | Artist |
| Pejman Gallery, 509 Millburn Ave, Short Hills NJ 07078, USA | |
| **Pekarkova, Iva** | Writer |
| Farrar Straus Giroux, 18 W 18th St, #700, New York NY 10011 USA | |
| **Pekovic, Nikola** | Basketball Player |
| Minnesota Timberwolves, Target Center, 600 1st Ave N, Minneapolis MN 55403 USA | |
| **Peldon, Ashley** | Actress |
| Marshak/Zachary Co, 8840 Wilshire Blvd, #100, Beverly Hills CA 90211 USA | |
| **Peldon, Courtney** | Actress |
| Bartels Co, PO Box 57593, Sherman Oaks CA 91413, USA | |
| **Pele** | Soccer Player |
| Rua Riachuelo 121-3, Andar-Fones 34-1633/35, Santos SP 11010 911, Brazil | |
| **Pelecanos, George P** | Writer |
| Little Brown, 3 Center Plaza, #100, Boston MA 02108 USA | |
| **Pelen, Perrine** | Alpine Skier |
| 31 Ave de l'Eygala, 38700 Corens Mont Fleury, France | |
| **Pelfrey, Michael A (Mike)** | Baseball Player |
| 1204 Suncast Lane, #2, El Dorado Hills CA 95762, USA | |
| **Pelikan, Lisa** | Actress |
| Diamond Mgmt, 31 Percy St, London W1T 2DD, England | |
| **Pelini, Mark (Bo)** | Football Coach |
| University of Nebraska, Athletic Dept, Lincoln NE 68588, USA | |
| **Pell, George Cardinal** | Religious Leader |
| Archdiocese, Polding Centre, 133 Liverpool St, Sydney NSW 2000, Australia | |
| **Pell, Paula** | Writer |
| W M E Entertainment, 9601 Wilshire Blvd, #300, Beverly Hills CA 90210 USA | |
| **Pellea, Oana** | Actress |
| Ken McReddie Assoc, 101 Finsbury Pavement, London EC2A 1RS, England | |
| **Pellegrino, Edmund D** | Physician |
| 5610 Wisconsin Ave, Chevy Chase MD 20815, USA | |
| **Pellegrino, Mark** | Actor |
| Domain Talent, 9229 W Sunset Blvd, #710, West Hollywood CA 90069 USA | |
| **Pellerin, Scott** | Ice Hockey Player |
| 10 Dunraven Road, Windham NH 03087, USA | |
| **Pelletier, David J** | Ice Dancer |
| 12116 NW 128th St, Edmonton AB T5L 1C3, Canada | |
| **Pelletier, Marcel** | Ice Hockey Player |
| Boston Bruins, 100 Legends Way, #250, Boston MA 02114 USA | |
| **Pelletreau, Robert H, Jr** | Diplomat |
| State Department, 2201 C St NW, Washington DC 20520 USA | |

**P**

**Pelley - Penikett**

**Pelley, Scott** — Commentator
CBS-TV, News Dept, 51 W 52nd St, New York NY 10019 USA
**Pelli, Cesar A** — Architect
Cesar Pelli Assoc, 1056 Chapel St, New Haven CT 06510, USA
**Pellington, Mark** — Director
Creative Artists Agency, 2000 Ave of Stars, #100, Los Angeles CA 90067 USA
**Pelluer, Steven C (Steve)** — Football Player
2632 W Lake Sammamish Parkway NE, Redmond WA 98052, USA
**Pelphrey, John** — Basketball Coach
University of Arkansas, Athletic Dept, Fayetteville AR 72701, USA
**Peltason, Jack W** — Educator
18 Whistler Court, Irvine CA 92617, USA
**Pelton, M Lee** — Educator
Willamette University, President's Office, 900 State St, Salem OR 97301, USA
**Peltonen, Ville** — Ice Hockey Player
Dynamo Minsk, Minsk Arena, Pr Pobeditelei 111, 220116 Minsk, Belarus
**Peltz, J Russell** — Boxing Promoter
Peltz Boxing Promotions, 2501 Brown St, Philadelphia PA 19130, USA
**Peltz, Nelson** — Businessman
Trian Companies, 900 3rd Ave, New York NY 10022, USA
**Peluce, Meeno** — Actor
PO Box 3743, Glendale CA 91221, USA
**Peluso, Lisa** — Actress
Shauna Sickenger, PO Box 301, Ramona CA 92065, USA
**Peluso, Michael D (Mike)** — Ice Hockey Player
3616 W Fuller St, Edina, MN 55410, USA
**Pelyk, Michael J (Mike)** — Ice Hockey Player
56-385 East Mall, Toronto ON M9B 6J4, Canada
**Pelzer, Dave** — Writer
D-Esprit, PO Box 1846, Rancho Mirage CA 92270, USA
**Pemberton, Johnny** — Actor
Principato-Young, 9465 Wilshire Blvd, #880, Beverly Hills CA 90212 USA
**Pena Martinez, Geronimo** — Baseball Player
KM 17 7 Pista Duarte, Los Alcarrizzos, Dominican Republic
**Pena Nieto, Enrique** — President, Mexico
Palacio Nacional, Los Pinos, Puerto 1, 11850 Mexico City DF, Mexico
**Pena Padilla, Antonio F (Tony)** — Baseball Player, Manager
New York Yankees, Yankee Stadium, E 161st St & River Ave, Bronx NY 10451 USA
**Pena Vasquez, Alejandro** — Baseball Player
12635 Etris Road, Roswell GA 30075, USA
**Pena, Anthony** — Actor
Sha'Lin Talent Mgmt, PO Box 11411, Burbank CA 91510, USA
**Pena, Carlos F** — Baseball Player
4248 Cascada Circle, Hollywood FL 33024, USA
**Pena, Elizabeth** — Actress
Bauman Redanty Shaul Agency, 5757 Wilshire Blvd, #473, Los Angeles CA 90036 USA
**Pena, Federico F** — Secretary, Transportation, Energy
362 Detroit St, #A, Denver CO 80206, USA
**Pena, Jennifer M** — Singer
Apodaca Promotions, 717 E Tidwell Road, Houston TX 77022, USA
**Pena, Michael A** — Actor
Management 360, 9111 Wilshire Blvd, Beverly Hills CA 90210 USA
**Pena, Orlando G** — Baseball Player
1750 W 46th St, #416, Hialeah FL 33012, USA
**Pena, Paco** — Concert Guitarist, Composer
Wim Visser Ruysdaelkade 5, 1072 Amsterdam AG, Netherlands
**Pena, Wilfredo M (Wily Mo)** — Baseball Player
27250 Breakers Dr, Wesley Chapel FL 33544, USA
**Penacoli, Jerry** — Entertainer
I C M Partners, 10250 Constellation Blvd, #900, Los Angeles CA 90067 USA
**Penate, Jack** — Singer, Songwriter
United Agents, 12-26 Lexington St, London W1F 0LE, England
**Pence, Hunter A** — Baseball Player
10301 Wagon Road W, Austin TX 78736, USA
**Penchion, Robert E (Bob)** — Football Player
110 Elliott Ave, Muscle Shoals AL 35661, USA
**Pendatchanska, Alexandrina** — Opera Singer
Opera et Concert, 37 Rue de la Chaussee d'Antin, 75009 Paris, France
**Pender, Melvin (Mel)** — Track Athlete
2330 Goodwood Blvd SE, Smyrna GA 30080, USA
**Penderecki, Krzysztof E** — Composer, Conductor
Ul Cisowa 22, 30229 Cracow, Poland
**Pendergrass, Henry P** — Physician
Vanderbilt University Medical School, 1621 21st Ave S, Nashville TN 37212, USA
**Penders, Tom** — Basketball Coach
George Washington University, Athletic Dept, Washington DC 20052, USA
**Pendleton, Moses** — Dancer, Choreographer
Momix, PO Box 35, Washington CT 06794, USA
**Pendleton, Terry L** — Baseball Player
332 Grassmeade Way, Snellville GA 30078, USA
**Pendleton, Victoria** — Cyclist
Three60 Sports Mgmt, 158-160 N Gower St, London NW1 2ND, England
**Penghlis, Thaao** — Actor
Metropolitan Talent Agency, 5405 Wilshire Blvd, #218, Los Angeles CA 90036 USA
**Pengily, Kirk** — Guitarist, Saxophonist, Singer (INXS)
8 Hayes St, #1, Neutral Bay 20891 NSW, Australia
**Pengo, Polycarp Cardinal** — Religious Leader
PO Box 167, Dar-es-Salaam, Tanzania
**Penhall, Joe** — Director, Writer
Judy Daish Assoc, 2 Saint Charles Place, London W10 6EG, England
**Penicheiro, Ticha** — Basketball Player
Los Angeles Sparks, 888 S Figueroa St, #2010, Los Angeles CA 90017 USA
**Penick, Trevor** — Singer (O-Town)
Trans Continental Records, 127 W Church St, #350, Orlando FL 32801, USA
**Penikett, Tahmoh** — Actor
Gersh Agency, 9465 Wilshire Blvd, #600, Beverly Hills CA 90212 USA

**Peniston, Cecilia V (CeCe)** — Singer
250 W 57th St, #821, New York NY 10107, USA

**Penky, Joseph F** — Chemical Engineer
Purdue University, Chemical Engineering Dept, West Lafayette IN 47907, USA

**Penn, (Jillette)** — Comedian, Illusionist (Penn & Teller)
A P A Talent/Literary Agency, 405 S Beverly Dr, #300, Beverly Hills CA 90212 USA

**Penn, Christopher A (Chris)** — Football Player
PO Box 123, South Coffeyville OK 74072, USA

**Penn, Kal** — Actor
Gersh Agency, 9465 Wilshire Blvd, #600, Beverly Hills CA 90212 USA

**Penn, Michael** — Singer, Songwriter
Mark Spector, 100 5th Ave, #1100, New York NY 10011, USA

**Penn, Sean** — Actor, Director
Creative Artists Agency, 2000 Ave of Stars, #100, Los Angeles CA 90067 USA

**Penn, Zak** — Director, Producer, Writer, Actor
Zak Penn's Co, 6240 W 3rd St, #421, Los Angeles CA 90036, USA

**Pennacchio, Len A** — Geneticist
Stanford University, Human Genome Center, Stanford CA 94305, USA

**Penner, Dustin** — Ice Hockey Player
117 E Balboa Blvd, Newport Beach, CA 92661, USA

**Penner, Jonathan** — Actor
I C M Partners, 10250 Constellation Blvd, #900, Los Angeles CA 90067 USA

**Penner, Stanford S** — Aeronautical Engineer
5912 Avenida Chamnez, La Jolla CA 92037, USA

**Penney, Steve** — Ice Hockey Player
155 Rue Notre Dame, Saint Pereol des Neiges QC G0A 3R0, Canada

**Pennie, Collins** — Actor
Untitled Entertainment, 350 S Beverly Dr, #200, Beverly Hills CA 90212 USA

**Pennie, Michael W** — Sculptor
117 Bradford Road, Atworth, Melksham, Wiltshire SN12 8HY, England

**Pennington, Brad L** — Baseball Player
7220 E State Road 160, Salem IN 47167, USA

**Pennington, Clifford (Cliff)** — Ice Hockey Player
9960 5th St N, #203, Saint Petersburg FL 33702, USA

**Pennington, Clifton R (Cliff)** — Baseball Player
23603 Hartwick Lane, San Antonio TX 78259, USA

**Pennington, J Chad** — Football Player
2421 Dry Ridge Road, Versailles KY 40383, USA

**Pennington, Janice** — Model, Actress
PO Box 11402, Beverly Hills CA 90213, USA

**Pennington, Julia** — Actress
Judy Schoen, 606 N Larchmont Blvd, #309, Los Angeles CA 90004 USA

**Pennington, Michael** — Actor
41 Marlborough Hill, London NW8 0NG, England

**Pennington, Ty** — Actor
Agency S G H, 6525 Sunset Blvd, #900-PH, Los Angeles CA 90028, USA

**Pennison, Jay L** — Football Player
3007 W Autumn Run Circle, Sugar Land TX 77479, USA

**Pennock of Norton, Raymond** — Businessman
Morgan Grenfell Group, 23 Great Winchester St, London EC2P 2AX, England

**Pennock, Chris** — Actor
25150 1/2 Malibu Road, Malibu CA 90265, USA

**Penny, Bradley W (Brad)** — Baseball Player
25071 Abercrombie Lane, Calabasas CA 91302, USA

**Penny, Daniel** — Geoscientist
University of Sydney, Geoscience Dept, Sydney NSW 2006, Australia

**Penny, Joe** — Actor
Gage Group, 14724 Ventura Blvd, #505, Sherman Oaks CA 91403 USA

**Penny, Roger P** — Businessman
Bethlehem Steel, 1655 Valley Center Parkway, #200, Bethlehem PA 18017, USA

**Penny, Sydney** — Actress
Stone Manners Salners, 9911 W Pico Blvd, #1400, Los Angeles CA 90035 USA

**Pennyfeather, William N (Will)** — Baseball Player
333 Rector St, #6D, Perth Amboy NJ 08861, USA

**Penot, Jacques** — Actor
9 Rue de I'Isly, 75008 Paris, France

**Penrose, Patricia (Tricia)** — Actress, Singer
International Artists, 193-197 High Holborn, London WC1V 7BD, England

**Penry-Jones, Rupert** — Actor
Artist Rights Group, 4 Great Portland St, London W1W 8PA, England

**Penske, Jay** — Businessman
Penske Media Corporation, 16026 Royal Oak Rd, Encino CA 91436, USA

**Penske, Roger S** — Auto Racing Driver, Executive
Penske Racing, Penske Plaza, 366 Riverfront, Reading PA 19602, USA

**Pentecost, Del** — Actor
Paradigm Agency, 360 N Crescent Dr, North Building, Beverly Hills CA 90210 USA

**Pentland, Alex P** — Computer Scientist
Massachusetts Institute of Technology, Media Laboratory, Cambridge MA 02139, USA

**Penzias, Arno A** — Nobel Physics Laureate
New Enterprise Assoc, 2855 Sand Hill Road, Menlo Park CA 94025, USA

**Peoples, David** — Golfer
2545 Cedarwood Dr, Germantown TN 38138, USA

**Peoples, David Webb** — Director, Writer
Creative Artists Agency, 2000 Ave of Stars, #100, Los Angeles CA 90067 USA

**Peoples, John** — Physicist
Fermi National Acceleration Laboratory, C D F Collaboration, PO Box 500, Batavia IL 60510, USA

**Peper, Tim** — Actor
Paradigm Agency, 360 N Crescent Dr, North Building, Beverly Hills CA 90210 USA

**Pepitone, Joseph A (Joe)** — Baseball Player
27 Roosevelt Blvd, Massapequa NY 11758, USA

**Peplinski, Jim** — Ice Hockey Player
Peplinski Auto Leasing, 212 Meridian Road NE, Calgary AB T2A 2N6, Canada

**Peplowski, Ken** — Jazz Saxophonist, Clarinetist
Hot Jazz Mgmt, 116 E 27th St, New York NY 10016, USA

**Pepoy, Andrew** — Cartoonist (Annie)
Tribune Media Services, 435 N Michigan Ave, #1500, Chicago IL 60611 USA

**P**

| | |
|---|---|
| **Pepper Mochrie, Dorothy (Dottie)** | Golfer |
| PO Box 623, Saratoga Springs NY 12866, USA | |
| **Pepper, Barry** | Actor |
| Paul Kohner, 9300 Wilshire Blvd, #555, Beverly Hills CA 90212 USA | |
| **Pepper, Beverly** | Sculptor |
| Torre Gentile, 06059 Todi (PG), Italy | |
| **Pepper, Cynthia** | Actress |
| 219 Friendly Court, Henderson NV 89052, USA | |
| **Pepper, John E, Jr** | Businessman |
| Walt Disney Co, 500 S Buena Vista St, Burbank CA 91521, USA | |
| **Pepperberg, Irene M** | Writer |
| Harper Collins Publishers, 10 E 53rd St, Cellar 1, New York NY 10022 USA | |
| **Peppers, Julius F** | Football Player |
| 173 Rehoboth Lane, Mooresville NC 28117, USA | |
| **Peppler, Mary Jo** | Volleyball Player |
| Coast Volleyball Club, 11526 Sorrento Valley Road, San Diego CA 92121, USA | |
| **Pera, Renee Reijo** | Human Reproductive Biologist |
| University of California Medical Center, 505 Parnassus, San Francisco CA 94122, USA | |
| **Perabo, Piper** | Actress |
| United Talent Agency, U T A Plaza, 9336 Civic Center Dr, Beverly Hills CA 90210 USA | |
| **Perahia, Murray** | Concert Pianist |
| Askonas Holt, Lincoln House, 300 High Holborn, London WC1V 7JH, England | |
| **Peralta Fabi, Ricardo** | Astronaut, Mexico |
| Ciudad Universitaria, Instituto de Ingenieria, Circuito Escolar Sn, CP 04510, Mexico DF, Mexico | |
| **Peralta Morones, Oribe P** | Soccer Player |
| Federacion de Futbol, Colima 373 Colonia Roma, Delegacion Cuauhtemoc, Mexico City DF 06700, Mexico | |
| **Peralta, Jhonny A** | Baseball Player |
| 27940 Berringer Run, Westlake OH 44145, USA | |
| **Percival, Brian** | Director |
| Gotham Group, 9255 Sunset Blvd, #515, Los Angeles CA 90069, USA | |
| **Percival, Lance** | Actor |
| Rhubarb Agency, 1A Devonshire Road, #100, London W4 2EU, England | |
| **Percival, Mac L** | Football Player |
| 6710 Flowermound Dr, Sugar Land TX 77479, USA | |
| **Percival, Troy E** | Baseball Player |
| 1090 Coronet Dr, Riverside CA 92506, USA | |
| **Perconte, John P (Jack)** | Baseball Player |
| 6197 Hinterlong Court, Lisle IL 60532, USA | |
| **Perdue, William E (Will)** | Basketball Player |
| 6310 Innisbrook Dr, Prospect KY 40059, USA | |
| **Perec, Marie-Jose** | Track Athlete |
| H S International Sports Mgmt, 9871 Irvine Center Dr, Irvine CA 92618, USA | |
| **Peregrym, Missy** | Actress |
| Gersh Agency, 9465 Wilshire Blvd, #600, Beverly Hills CA 90212 USA | |
| **Pereira, Mike** | Football Executive, Sportscaster |
| National Football League, 280 Park Ave, #12W, New York NY 10017, USA | |
| **Perek, Lubos** | Astronomer |
| Kourimska 28, 13000 Prague 3, Czech Republic | |
| **Perelman, Ronald O** | Businessman |
| Revlon Group, 35 E 62nd St, New York NY 10065, USA | |
| **Perelman, Vadim** | Director, Writer |
| Rumble Media, 1620 Broadway, Santa Monica CA 90403, USA | |
| **Perenyi, Miklos** | Concert Violinist |
| Liszt Academy of Music, PO Box 206, Liszt Ter 8, 1391 Budapest, Hungary | |
| **Peres, Shimon** | Nobel Peace Laureate; President, Israel |
| President's Office, Beit Hanassi, 3 Hanassi St, Jerusalem 92188, Israel | |
| **Peress, Gilles** | Photographer |
| 48 Great Jones St, #2SE, New York NY 10012, USA | |
| **Peretokin, Mark** | Ballet Dancer |
| Bolshoi Theater, Teatralnaya Pl 1, 103009 Moscow, Russia | |
| **Peretz, Jesse** | Director |
| United Talent Agency, U T A Plaza, 9336 Civic Center Dr, Beverly Hills CA 90210 USA | |
| **Pereyra, Marianela** | Actress |
| Brady Brannon Rich, 5670 Wilshire Blvd, #820, Los Angeles CA 90036, USA | |
| **Perez Batista, Manuel M (Manny)** | Actor |
| Don Buchwald, 6500 Wilshire Blvd, #2200, Los Angeles CA 90048 USA | |
| **Perez de Cuellar, Javier** | Secretary General, United Nations |
| Avenida Aurelio Miro Quesada 1071, San Isifro, Lima 2, Peru | |
| **Perez Esquivel, Adolfo** | Nobel Peace Laureate |
| Servicio Paz y Justicia, Piedras 730, 1070 Buenos Aires, Argentina | |
| **Perez Fernandez, Pedro** | Government Official, Spain |
| Partido Socialista Obrero Espanol, Ferraz 68 y 70, 28008 Madrid, Spain | |
| **Perez Molina, Otto F** | President, Guatemala |
| President's Office, Palacio Nacional, 6 Avenida 419, Guatemala City, Guatemala | |
| **Perez, Amanda** | Singer, Songwriter |
| Paradigm Agency, 360 N Crescent Dr, North Building, Beverly Hills CA 90210 USA | |
| **Perez, Antonio M** | Businessman |
| Eastman Kodak Co, 343 State St, Rochester NY 14650, USA | |
| **Perez, Atanasio R (Tony)** | Baseball Player, Manager |
| 1717 N Bayshore Dr, #3246, Miami FL 33132, USA | |
| **Perez, Carmen** | Actress |
| Evolution Entertainment, 901 N Highland Ave, Los Angeles CA 90038 USA | |
| **Perez, Chris** | Guitarist, Orchestra Leader, Actor |
| Big F D Entertainment, 301 Arizona Ave, #200, Santa Monica CA 90401, USA | |
| **Perez, Eduardo A** | Baseball Player |
| 113 Calle Las Flores, San Juan PR 00911, USA | |
| **Perez, Hugo E** | Soccer Player |
| 22018 Newbridge Dr, Lake Forest CA 92630, USA | |
| **Perez, Jossie** | Opera Singer |
| Columbia Artists Mgmt Inc, 1790 Broadway, #702, New York NY 10019 USA | |
| **Perez, Luiz (Louie)** | Drummer, Singer (Los Lobos) |
| Gold Mountain, 3940 Laurel Canyon Blvd, #444, Studio City CA 91604 USA | |
| **Perez, Manny** | Actor |
| Don Buchwald, 6500 Wilshire Blvd, #2200, Los Angeles CA 90048 USA | |
| **Perez, Martin R (Marty), Jr** | Baseball Player |
| 30 Willowick Dr, Decatur GA 30034, USA | |

**Pepper Mochrie - Perez**

**Perez, Melido T G** — Baseball Player
Nigua KM 21 1/2, Santo Domingo, Dominican Republic
**Perez, Rosie** — Actress, Singer
Authentic Talent Mgmt, 45 Main St, #1000, Brooklyn NY 11201, USA
**Perez, Timothy Paul** — Actor
Three Moons Entertainment, 5441 E Beverly Blvd, #G, Los Angeles CA 90022, USA
**Perez, Vincent** — Actor, Director
United Agents, 12-26 Lexington St, London W1F 0LE, England
**Pergine, John S** — Football Player
5 Jody Dr, Plymouth Meeting PA 19462, USA
**Perillo, Gregory** — Artist
2 Blackwell Road, Nesconset NY 11767, USA
**Perine, Kelly** — Actor, Comedian
Mark Holder Mgmt, 5225 Wilshire Blvd, #600, Los Angeles CA 90036 USA
**Perisho, Matthew A (Matt)** — Baseball Player
1462 W Cardinal Way, Chandler AZ 85286, USA
**Perkin, J D** — Sculptor
Laura Russo Gallery, 805 NW 21st St, Portland OR 97209, USA
**Perkins, Broderick P** — Baseball Player
5367 San Vicente Blvd, #237, Los Angeles CA 90019, USA
**Perkins, Carl C** — Representative, KY
1401 15th St, Huntington WV 25701, USA
**Perkins, Courtland D** — Aeronautical Engineer
400 Hilltop Terrace, Alexandria VA 22301, USA
**Perkins, Donald A (Don)** — Football Player
808 Vassar Dr NE, Albuquerque NM 87106, USA
**Perkins, Edward J** — Diplomat
2801 New Mexico Ave NW, #1407, Washington DC 20007, USA
**Perkins, Elizabeth** — Actress
Gersh Agency, 9465 Wilshire Blvd, #600, Beverly Hills CA 90212 USA
**Perkins, Elvis** — Singer, Songwriter
Flatiron Borman Mgmt, 15 W 26th St, #1200, New York NY 10010, USA
**Perkins, Emily** — Actress
Wales University, Film Studies, Aberystwuth, Ceredigion SY23 3AJ, Wales
**Perkins, Glen W** — Baseball Player
19775 Jersey Ave, Lakeville MN 55044, USA
**Perkins, Gregory S (Tex)** — Singer, Songwriter
MajorBox Music, PO Box 1164, Windsor VIC 3181, Australia
**Perkins, Homer G** — Businessman
372 S Shore Road, Pascoag RI 02859, USA
**Perkins, Jack** — Commentator
A&E Network, 235 E 45th St, New York NY 10017, USA
**Perkins, John M** — Civil Rights Activist
1655 Saint Charles St, Jackson MS 39209, USA
**Perkins, Kathleen Rose** — Actress
Trademark Talent, 144 S Beverly Dr, #404, Beverly Hills CA 90212, USA
**Perkins, Kendrick** — Basketball Player
137 Fox Road, Waltham MA 02451, USA
**Perkins, Kieren** — Swimmer
GPO Box 232, Brisbane QED 4001, Australia
**Perkins, Lawrence B, Jr** — Architect
4 Rectory Lane, Scarsdale NY 10583, USA
**Perkins, Lucian** — Photojournalist
3103 17th St NW, Washington DC 20010, USA
**Perkins, Millie** — Actress
2511 Canyon Dr, Los Angeles CA 90068, USA
**Perkins, Oz** — Actor
Greene Assoc, 1901 Ave of Stars, #130, Los Angeles CA 90067 USA
**Perkins, Polly** — Actress
Associated International Mgmt, 7 Hatton Garden, #400, London EC1N 8AD, England
**Perkins, Samuel B (Sam)** — Basketball Player
14901 Bellbrook Dr, Dallas TX 75254, USA
**Perkins, Stephen A** — Drummer (Jane's Addiction), Songwriter
DeMann Entertainment, 9465 Wilshire Blvd, #426, Beverly Hills CA 90212, USA
**Perkins, Susan Y** — Beauty Queen
23 Winsor Way, Weston MA 02493, USA
**Perkins, Travis** — Actor
Abraxas Talent, 4260 Troost Ave, #1, Studio City CA 91604, USA
**Perkins, W Ray** — Football Player, Coach
57 Honors Lane, Hattiesburg MS 39402, USA
**Perkins, Warren C (Red)** — Basketball Player
717 Fairfield Ave, Gretna LA 70056, USA
**Perkowski, Harold W (Harry)** — Baseball Player
211 McGinnis St, Beckley WV 25801, USA
**Perks, Craig** — Golfer
321 Thibodeaux Dr, Lafayette LA 70503, USA
**Perl, Frank J** — Cinematographer
5020 Biloxi Ave, North Hollywood CA 91601, USA
**Perl, Martin L** — Nobel Physics Laureate
3737 El Centro Ave, Palo Alto CA 94306, USA
**Perlich, Max** — Actor
Anthem Entertainment, 5225 Wilshire Blvd, #615, Los Angeles CA 90036, USA
**Perlini, Fred** — Ice Hockey Player
409 Albert St W, Sault Sainte Marie ON P6A 1C2, Canada
**Perlman, Harvey** — Educator
University of Nebraska, Chancellor's Office, Lincoln NE 68588, USA
**Perlman, Itzhak** — Concert Violinist, Conductor
I M G Artists, Hogarth Business Park, Chiswick, London W4 2TH, England
**Perlman, Jonathan S (Jon)** — Baseball Player
3225 Bryn Mawr Dr, Dallas TX 75225, USA
**Perlman, Lawrence** — Businessman
Ceridian Corp, 3311 E Old Shakopee Road, Minneapolis MN 55425, USA
**Perlman, Navah** — Concert Pianist
I M G Artists, Hogarth Business Park, Chiswick, London W4 2TH, England
**Perlman, Rhea** — Actress
8665 Burton Way, #507, Los Angeles CA 90048, USA

| | |
|---|---|
| **Perlman, Ron** <br> Kritzer Levine Wilkins Griffin, 11872 La Grange Ave, #100, Los Angeles CA 90025 USA | Actor |
| **Perlmutter, Saul** <br> Lawrence Berkeley National Laboratory, 1 Cycloton Road, Berkeley CA 94720 USA | Nobel Physics Laureate |
| **Perlozzo, Samuel B (Sam)** <br> 18101 Emerald Bay St, Tampa FL 33647, USA | Baseball Player, Manager |
| **Perls, Tom** <br> 2 Harrington Lane, Weston MA 02493, USA | Physician |
| **Perman, Jay A** <br> University of Maryland, President's Office, 220 Arch St, Baltimore MD 21201, USA | Educator |
| **Pernel, Florence** <br> Artmedia, 20 Ave Rapp, 75007 Paris, France | Actress |
| **Pernice, Tom, Jr** <br> 38390 Shoal Creek Dr, Murrieta CA 92562, USA | Golfer |
| **Pero, Anthony J (A J)** <br> Rebellion Entertainment, 2440 Broadway, #111, New York NY 10024, USA | Singer, Drummer (Twisted Sister) |
| **Peron, Carlos** <br> Creative Artists Agency, 2000 Ave of Stars, #100, Los Angeles CA 90067 USA | Synthesizer Player (Yello) |
| **Perot, Edward J (Petey)** <br> 2401 Hillside Road, Ruston LA 71270, USA | Football Player |
| **Perot, H Ross** <br> Perot Systems, 2300 W Plano Parkway, Plano TX 75075, USA | Businessman, Presidential Candidate |
| **Perot, Henry Ross, Jr** <br> Perot Group, Lakeside Square, 12377 Merit Dr, #1700, Dallas TX 75251, USA | Aviator |
| **Perranoski, Ronald P (Ron)** <br> 3805 Indian River Dr, Vero Beach FL 32963, USA | Baseball Player |
| **Perrault, Dominique** <br> Perrault Architecte, 26 Rue Brunneseau, 75629 Paris Cedex 13, France | Architect |
| **Perreau, Gigi** <br> 18411 Hatteras St, #120, Tarzana CA 91356, USA | Actress |
| **Perreault, Annie** <br> Speed Skating Canada, 2781 Lancaster Road, #402, Ottawa ON K1B 1A7, Canada | Speed Skater |
| **Perreault, Gilbert (Gil)** <br> 4 Rue de la Serenite, Victoriaville QC G6S 1J4, Canada | Ice Hockey Player |
| **Perreault, Yanic** <br> 4303 E Cactus Road, #345, Phoenix AZ 85032, USA | Ice Hockey Player |
| **Perrella, James E** <br> Ingersoll-Rand Co, PO Box 6820, Piscataway NJ 08855, USA | Businessman |
| **Perren, Diego** <br> Curling Assn, PO Box 606, 3000 Bern, Switzerland | Curling Athlete |
| **Perret, Craig** <br> 825 Antioch Road, Shelbyville KY 40065, USA | Thoroughbred Racing Jockey |
| **Perretta, Ralph J** <br> 1305 Calle Scott, Encinitas CA 92024, USA | Football Player |
| **Perrette, Pauley** <br> S D B Partners, 1801 Ave of Stars, #902, Los Angeles CA 90067 USA | Actress |
| **Perri, Christina** <br> Atlantic Records, 9229 W Sunset Blvd, #900, West Hollywood CA 90069 USA | Singer, Songwriter |
| **Perrier, Mireille** <br> Jean-François Pignard de Marthod, 11 Rue Chanez, 75781 Paris Cedex 16, France | Actress |
| **Perriman, Brett R** <br> PO Box 83337, Conyers GA 30013, USA | Football Player |
| **Perrine, Valerie** <br> Bensky Entertainment, 15030 Ventura Blvd, #343, Sherman Oaks CA 91403, USA | Actress |
| **Perrineau, Harold, Jr** <br> A P A Talent/Literary Agency, 405 S Beverly Dr, #300, Beverly Hills CA 90212 USA | Actor |
| **Perrotta, Tom** <br> Saint Martin's Press, 175 5th Ave, #400, New York NY 10010 USA | Writer |
| **Perry, A Joseph (Joe)** <br> Front Line Mgmt, 1100 Glendon Ave, #2000, Los Angeles CA 90024 USA | Guitarist (Aerosmith), Songwriter |
| **Perry, Alex** <br> 104/106 The Strand, 412-414 George St, Sydney NSW 2000, Australia | Fashion Designer |
| **Perry, Anne** <br> Tyrn Vawr, Seafield, Portmahomack, Rosshire IV20 1RE, Scotland | Writer |
| **Perry, Barry W** <br> Engelhard Corp, 101 Wood Ave, Iselin NJ 08830, USA | Businessman |
| **Perry, Bradley Steven** <br> Coast to Coast Talent, 3350 Barham Blvd, Los Angeles CA 90068 USA | Actor |
| **Perry, Curtis R** <br> 1222 I St NE, Washington DC 20002, USA | Basketball Player |
| **Perry, Darren** <br> 801 Volvo Parkway, #109, Chesapeake VA 23320, USA | Football Player |
| **Perry, Edward L (Ed)** <br> 1583 SW 161st Ave, Pembroke Pines FL 33027, USA | Football Player |
| **Perry, Elliott L** <br> 3230 Scheibler Road, Memphis TN 38128, USA | Basketball Player |
| **Perry, Felton** <br> Hollywood Book, 6562 Hollywood Blvd, Los Angeles CA 90028, USA | Actor |
| **Perry, Gaylord J** <br> All Sports USA, PO Box 489, Spruce Pine NC 28777, USA | Baseball Player |
| **Perry, Gerald** <br> 2940 Dell Dr, Columbia SC 29209, USA | Football Player |
| **Perry, Gerald E** <br> 336 5th St, Manhattan Beach CA 90266, USA | Football Player |
| **Perry, Gerald J** <br> 1348 Waterford Green Close, Marietta GA 30068, USA | Baseball Player |
| **Perry, Herbert E (Herb), Jr** <br> 978 N Fletcher Ave, Mayo FL 32066, USA | Baseball Player |
| **Perry, J Christopher (Chris)** <br> 170 Valley Run Dr, Powell OH 43065, USA | Golfer |
| **Perry, J Kenneth (Kenny)** <br> 418 Quail Ridge Road, Franklin KY 42134, USA | Golfer |
| **Perry, James E (Jim)** <br> 155 Porters Glen, New London NC 28127, USA | Baseball Player |
| **Perry, Jeff** <br> Principal Entertainment, 9255 Sunset Blvd, #500, Los Angeles CA 90069 USA | Actor |

**Perlman - Perry**

**Perry, John Bennett** — Actor
Greene Assoc, 1901 Ave of Stars, #130, Los Angeles CA 90067 USA
**Perry, John R** — Philosopher
Stanford University, Language/Information Study Center, Stanford CA 94305, USA
**Perry, Katy** — Singer, Songwriter
Direct Management Group, 947 N La Cienega Blvd, #G, West Hollywood CA 90069, USA
**Perry, Keith** — Singer, Fiddler, Songwriter
Curb Records, 48 Music Square E, Nashville TN 37203 USA
**Perry, Lee (Scratch)** — Singer (Upsetters)
Agency Group Ltd, 142 W 57th St, #600, New York NY 10019 USA
**Perry, Linda** — Singer (Four Non Blondes), Songwriter
W M E Entertainment, 9601 Wilshire Blvd, #300, Beverly Hills CA 90210 USA
**Perry, Luke** — Actor
Himber Entertainment, PO Box 950, South Orange NJ 07079 USA
**Perry, Matthew** — Actor
Creative Artists Agency, 2000 Ave of Stars, #100, Los Angeles CA 90067 USA
**Perry, Melvin G (Bob)** — Baseball Player
445 Fox Chase Village, New Bern NC 28562, USA
**Perry, Michael Dean** — Football Player
1029 Sedgewood Circle, Charlotte NC 28211, USA
**Perry, Michael R** — Writer, Producer
United Talent Agency, U T A Plaza, 9336 Civic Center Dr, Beverly Hills CA 90210 USA
**Perry, Michelle** — Concert French Horn Player
Columbia Artists Mgmt Inc, 1790 Broadway, #702, New York NY 10019 USA
**Perry, Phil** — Singer
Morey Management Group, 1100 Glendon Ave, #1100, Los Angeles CA 90024, USA
**Perry, Rodney C (Rod)** — Football Player
40 E Bloomfield Lane, Westfield IN 46074, USA
**Perry, Scott E** — Football Player
2807 Graysby Ave, San Pedro CA 90732, USA
**Perry, Stephen H (Steve)** — Singer (Cherry Poppin Daddies)
Paradise Artists, PO Box 1821, Ojai CA 93024 USA
**Perry, Stephen P (Steve)** — Singer (Journey), Songwriter
Perry S Oretzky, 10880 Wilshire Blvd, #920, Los Angeles CA 90024, USA
**Perry, Steve** — Writer
959 E Cinnamon Dr, Lemoore CA 93245, USA
**Perry, Todd J** — Football Player
13805 Brittle Road, Alpharetta GA 30004, USA
**Perry, Troy D** — Religious Leader
Metropolitan Churches Fellowship, 5300 Santa Monica Blvd, Los Angeles CA 90029, USA
**Perry, Tyler** — Actor, Director, Writer
34th Street Films, 8200 Wilshire Blvd, #300, Beverly Hills CA 90211, USA
**Perry, Vernon, Jr** — Football Player
PO Box 842201, Houston TX 77284, USA
**Perry, W Patrick (Pat)** — Baseball Player
1115 W Franklin St, Taylorville IL 62568, USA
**Perry, William A (Refrigerator)** — Football Player
2885 Old Camp Long Road, Aiken SC 29805, USA
**Perry, William J** — Secretary, Defense
11210 Hooper Lane, Los Altos Hills CA 94024, USA
**Perryman, Jill** — Actress
4 Hillside Crescent, Gooseberry Hill WA 6076, Australia
**Perryman, Robert L (Bob)** — Football Player
PO Box 8543, Haverhill MA 01835, USA
**Persad-Bissessar, Kamla** — Prime Minister, Trinidad & Tobago
Prime Minister's Office, Whitehall, Maraval Road, Port of Spain, Trinidad & Tobago
**Persaud, Deborah** — Pediatrician, Surgeon, Virologist
Johns Hopkins Children's Hospital, Surgery Dept, 1800 Orleans St, Baltimore MD 21287, USA
**Persbrandt, Mikael** — Actor
I C M Partners, 10250 Constellation Blvd, #900, Los Angeles CA 90067 USA
**Pershing, Jennifer** — Model
Playboy Promotions, 2706 Media Center Dr, Los Angeles CA 90065 USA
**Persoff, Nehemiah** — Actor
5670 Moonstone Beach Dr, Cambria CA 93428, USA
**Person, Chuck C** — Basketball Player
2022 Ruhland Ave, Redondo Beach CA 90278, USA
**Person, Houston** — Jazz Saxophonist
Hot Jazz Mgmt, 116 E 27th St, New York NY 10016, USA
**Person, Robert A** — Baseball Player
25 Bellerive Acres, Saint Louis MO 63121, USA
**Person, Wesley L** — Basketball Player
PO Box 481, Brantley AL 36009, USA
**Personen, Richard M** — Football Player
765 Pine Hills Place, The Villages FL 32162, USA
**Persons, Peter** — Golfer
1153 Saint Andrews Dr, Macon GA 31210, USA
**Persson, Elisabeth** — Curling Athlete
Curling Assn, Idrottshuser, Marbackagatan 19, 123 43 Farsta, Sweden
**Persson, Jorgen** — Cinematographer
Rydbolundsvagen 7, 185 31 Vaxholm, Sweden
**Persson, Nina E** — Singer (Cardigans), Songwriter
Talent Trust, Kungsgatan 9C, 411 19 Gothenburg, Sweden
**Persson, Ricard** — Ice Hockey Player
2200-201 Portage Ave, Winnipeg MB R3B 3L3, Canada
**Persson, Stefan** — Businessman
Hennes & Mauritz AB, Sverigekontoret, 106 38 Stockholm, Sweden
**Persson, Torsten** — Economist
Stockholm University, International Economic Studies Institute, 106 91 Stockholm, Sweden
**Perzanowski, Stanley (Stan)** — Baseball Player
PO Box 133, New Park PA 17352, USA
**Pescatelli, Tammy** — Actress, Comedienne
Parallel Entertainment, 9420 Wilshire Blvd, #250, Beverly Hills CA 90212 USA
**Pesce, Gaetano** — Interior Designer
543 Broadway, #5, New York NY 10012, USA
**Pesch, Dorothee (Doro)** — Singer (Warlock)
Postfach 105313, 40044 Dusseldorf, Germany

# P

**Pesci, Joe** — Actor
Jay Julien Mgmt, 1501 Broadway, #2600, New York NY 10036, USA

**Pescia, Lisa** — Actress
Coast to Coast Talent, 3350 Barham Blvd, Los Angeles CA 90068 USA

**Pescucci, Gabriella** — Costume Designer
Sandra Marsh & Associates, 9150 Wilshire Blvd, #220, Beverly Hills CA 90212, USA

**Pesek, Libor** — Conductor
I M G Artists, Hogarth Business Park, Chiswick, London W4 2TH, England

**Pess, Katalin** — Model
Names Model Mgmt, Via Savona 53, 20144 Milan, Italy

**Pestka, Sidney** — Molecular Geneticist
Robert Wood Johnson Medical School, 675 Hoes Lane, Piscataway NJ 08854, USA

**Pestova, Daniela** — Model
Next Model Mgmt, 9 Boul de la Madeleine, 75001 Paris, France

**Pesut, George** — Ice Hockey Player
1008-415 Michigan St, Victoria BC V8V 1R8, Canada

**Petagine, Roberto A** — Baseball Player
1098 Hunting Lodge Dr, Miami Springs FL 33166, USA

**Peter, Valentine J** — Religious Leader, Social Worker
Father Flanagan's Boys Town, 14100 Crawford St, Boys Town NE 68010, USA

**Peterek, Jeffrey A (Jeff)** — Baseball Player
8073 Elm Valley Road, Three Oaks MI 49128, USA

**Peterle, Lozje** — Prime Minister, Slovenia
Slovenian Christian Democrats, Beethovnova 4, 1000 Ljubljana, Slovenia

**Peterman, D Brian** — Coast Guard Admiral
Commander, US Coast Guard Atlantic, 4131 Crawford St, Portsmouth VA 23704 USA

**Peterman, Melissa** — Actress
A P A Talent/Literary Agency, 405 S Beverly Dr, #300, Beverly Hills CA 90212 USA

**Peterman, Steven** — Producer
Jackoway Tyerman Wertheimer, 1925 Century Park E, #2200, Los Angeles CA 90067 USA

**Peters, Anthony L (Tony)** — Football Player
2402 Boston St, Muskogee OK 74401, USA

**Peters, Bernadette** — Singer, Actress
323 W 80th St, New York NY 10024, USA

**Peters, Bob** — Ice Hockey Coach
Bemidji State University, Athletic Dept, Bemidji MN 56601, USA

**Peters, Christopher M (Chris)** — Baseball Player
613 Chessbriar Dr, Three Oaks MI 49128, USA

**Peters, Clarke** — Actor
Stone Manners Salners, 9911 W Pico Blvd, #1400, Los Angeles CA 90035 USA

**Peters, Clayre** — Model
Playboy Promotions, 2706 Media Center Dr, Los Angeles CA 90065 USA

**Peters, Dan** — Drummer (Mudhoney)
Legends of 21st Century, 7 Trinity Row, Florence MA 01062, USA

**Peters, Devereaux** — Basketball Player
Minnesota Lynx, Target Center, 600 1st Ave N, Minneapolis MN 55403 USA

**Peters, Emmitt** — Dog Sled Racer
General Delivery, Ruby AK 99768, USA

**Peters, Evan** — Actor
Creative Artists Agency, 2000 Ave of Stars, #100, Los Angeles CA 90067 USA

**Peters, Garry** — Ice Hockey Player
3020 Eastview, Saskatoon SK S7J 3J2, Canada

**Peters, Gary C** — Baseball Player
7121 N Serenoa Dr, Sarasota FL 34241, USA

**Peters, Gretchen** — Singer, Songwriter
Val Denn Agency, 100 Congress Ave, #2000, Austin TX 78701, USA

**Peters, Jan** — Singer
959 7th St, Beaver PA 15009, USA

**Peters, Jason R** — Football Player
95 Stroughton Lane, Orchard Park NY 14127, USA

**Peters, Jim, Jr** — Ice Hockey Player
Vermont Academy, PO Box 500, Saxtons River VT 05154, USA

**Peters, Jon** — Producer
9941 Tower Lane, Beverly Hills CA 90210, USA

**Peters, Maria Liberia** — Prime Minister, Netherlands Antilles
Prime Minister's Office, Fort Amsterdam, Willemstad, Netherlands Antilles

**Peters, Mary** — Track Athlete
Willowtree Cottage, River Road, Dunmurray, Belfast, Northern Ireland

**Peters, Mike** — Editorial Cartoonist
PO Box 957, Bradenton FL 34206, USA

**Peters, Ralph** — Writer
Trident Media Group, 41 Madison Ave, #3600, New York NY 10010 USA

**Peters, Rick** — Actor
Talent Works, 3500 W Olive Ave, #1400, Burbank CA 91505 USA

**Peters, Roberta** — Opera Singer, Actress
19356 Cedar Glen Dr, Boca Raton FL 33434, USA

**Peters, Russell** — Actor, Comedian
Seven Summits Mgmt, 8906 W Olympic Blvd, Beverly Hills CA 90211 USA

**Peters, Scott** — Producer, Writer
Rothman Brecher Agency, 9465 Wilshire Blvd, #840, Beverly Hills CA 90212 USA

**Peters, Timothy** — Auto, Truck Racing Drivier
B H R, PO Box 1708, Mount Juliet TN 37121, USA

**Peters, Tom** — Writer, Management Consultant
Tom Peters Group, 555 Hamilton Ave, Palo Alto CA 94301, USA

**Peters, Vicki** — Model, Actress
Playboy Promotions, 2706 Media Center Dr, Los Angeles CA 90065 USA

**Peters, Volney M** — Football Player
325 Lancaster Road, Walnut Creek CA 94595, USA

**Petersen, Byron E** — Pathologist
University of Florida Medical School, PO Box 100275, Gainesville FL 32610, USA

**Petersen, Chris** — Football Coach
Boise State University, Athletic Dept, Boise ID 83725, USA

**Petersen, Christopher R (Chris)** — Baseball Player
242 Timberland Ave, Longwood FL 32750, USA

**Petersen, Cole** — Actor
Simmons & Scott, 7942 Mulholland Dr, Los Angeles CA 90046, USA

**Petersen, John D** — Educator
University of Tennessee, President's Office, Holt Tower, Knoxville TX 37996, USA
**Petersen, Kurt D** — Football Player
5520 Linmore Lane, Plano TX 75093, USA
**Petersen, Paul** — Actor, Singer
A Minor Consideration, 14530 Denker Ave, Gardena CA 90247, USA
**Petersen, Suzann** — Golfer
Gladengveien 3B, 0661 Oslo, Norway
**Petersen, Theodore H (Ted)** — Football Player
1195 N 17000E, Momence IL 60954, USA
**Petersen, Toby** — Ice Hockey Player
2529 Bryant Ave S, Minneapolis MN 55405, USA
**Petersen, William L** — Actor
High Horse Films, 100 Universal City Plaza, Building 2128, Universal City CA 91608, USA
**Petersen, Wolfgang** — Director
Paradigm Agency, 360 N Crescent Dr, North Building, Beverly Hills CA 90210 USA
**Peterson, Adam C** — Baseball Player
6401 NE 14th St, Vancouver WA 98665, USA
**Peterson, Adrian L** — Football Player
9212 Cold Stream Lane, Eden Prairie MN 55347, USA
**Peterson, Anthony W (Tony)** — Football Player
1124 Lakewood Circle, Naperville IL 60540, USA
**Peterson, Bob** — Writer
Pixar, 1200 Park Ave, Emeryville CA 94608, USA
**Peterson, Buzz** — Basketball Coach
University of Tennessee, Athletic Dept, Knoxville TN 37996, USA
**Peterson, Calvin E (Cal)** — Football Player
22646 Ingomar St, Canoga Park CA 91304, USA
**Peterson, Chase N** — Educator
910 S Donner Way, #201, Salt Lake City UT 84108, USA
**Peterson, David C** — Photojournalist
4805 Pinehurst Court, Pleasant Hill IA 50327, USA
**Peterson, Debbi** — Singer, Drummer (Bangles)
Russell Carter Artist Mgmt, 567 Ralph Mcgill Blvd, Atlanta GA 30312, USA
**Peterson, Donald H** — Astronaut
Aerospace Operations Consultants, 427 Pebblebrook Dr, Seabrook TX 77586, USA
**Peterson, Fred I (Fritz)** — Baseball Player
PO Box 137, East Dubuque IL 61025, USA
**Peterson, George P (Bud)** — Educator
Georgia Institute of Technology, President's Office, Atlanta GA 30332, USA
**Peterson, J Todd** — Football Player
135 Bellacree Road, Duluth GA 30097, USA
**Peterson, John** — Freestyle Wrestler
457 19th Ave, Comstock WI 54826, USA
**Peterson, Julian T** — Football Player
1750 Merton Road NE, Atlanta GA 30306, USA
**Peterson, Melvin L (Mel)** — Basketball Player
2896 Evergreen Lane, Aurora IL 60502, USA
**Peterson, Michael J** — Singer
Dennis Mgmt, 1002 18th Ave S, Nashville TN 37212, USA
**Peterson, Morris, Jr** — Basketball Player
909 Lafayette St, #12, New Orleans LA 70113, USA
**Peterson, Peter G** — Secretary of Commerce, Financier
Blackstone Group, 345 Park Ave, Basement LB4, New York NY 10154, USA
**Peterson, Steven** — Architect
Peterson/Littenberg Architecture, 131 E 66th St, #1B, New York NY 10065, USA
**Peterson, Sylvia** — Singer (Chiffons)
Lustig Talent, PO Box 770850, Orlando FL 32877 USA
**Peterson, Vicki** — Singer, Guitarist (Bangles)
Russell Carter Artist Mgmt, 567 Ralph Mcgill Blvd, Atlanta GA 30312, USA
**Peterson, William W (Bill)** — Football Player
13536 Mijo Lane, Lakeside CA 92040, USA
**Petersson, Tom** — Singer, Bassist (Cheap Trick, Swag)
Oakie Dokie Mgmt, 6090 Central Ave, Saint Petersburg FL 33707, USA
**Petey Pablo** — Rap Artist
Green Light Talent Agency, PO Box 3172, Beverly Hills CA 90212 USA
**Petit, Michel** — Ice Hockey Player
129 Latches Lane, Media PA 19063, USA
**Petit, Philippe** — High Wire Walker
Cathedral of Saint John the Devine, 1047 Amsterdam Ave, New York NY 10025, USA
**Petitbon, Richard A (Richie)** — Football Player, Coach
9628 Percussion Way, Vienna VA 22182, USA
**Petitgout, Lewis G (Luke)** — Football Player
5221 S Nichol St, Tampa FL 33611, USA
**Petke, Mike** — Soccer Player, Coach
Red Bulls New York, 600 Cape May St, Harrison, NJ 07029 USA
**Petkovic, Andrea** — Tennis Player
Tannenweg 24, 64347 Griesheim, Germany
**Peto, Richard** — Epidemiologist
Radcliffe Infirmary, Harkness Building, Oxford ON OX2 6HE, England
**Petra, Yvon** — Tennis Player
Residence du Prieure, 78100 Saint Germain-en-Laye, France
**Petraglia, John (Johnny)** — Bowler
25 Turnbridge Court, Jackson NJ 08527, USA
**Petralli, Eugene J (Geno)** — Baseball Player
119 Laser Lane, Weatherford TX 76087, USA
**Petrella, Robert (Bob)** — Football Player
116 Aberdeen Way, Rio Grande NJ 08242, USA
**Petrenko, Vasily** — Conductor
I M G Artists, Hogarth Business Park, Chiswick, London W4 2TH, England
**Petrenko, Viktor** — Figure Skater
Ice Vault Arena, 10 Nevins Road, Wayne NJ 07470, USA
**Petri, Michala** — Concert Recorder Player
Nordskraenten 3, 2980 Kokkedal, Denmark
**Petri, Nina** — Actress
Agentur Carola Studlar, Agnesstr 47, 80798 Munich, Germany

**Petrich, Robert M (Bob)** — Football Player
1391 Silverberry Court, El Cajon CA 92019, USA
**Petrick, Benjamin W (Ben)** — Baseball Player
1553 NE Jackson School Road, Hillsboro OR 97124, USA
**Petrie, Daniel M, Jr** — Director
Enderby Entertainment, 18034 Ventura Blvd, #445, Encino CA 91316, USA
**Petrie, Donald** — Director
Gersh Agency, 9465 Wilshire Blvd, #600, Beverly Hills CA 90212 USA
**Petrie, Geoff M** — Basketball Player, Executive
3675 Holly Hill Lane, Loomis CA 95650, USA
**Petrino, Paul** — Football Player, Coach
University of Idaho, Athletic Dept, Moscow ID 83844, USA
**Petro, Johan** — Basketball Player
Brooklyn Nets, 15 Metro Tech Center, #1100, Brooklyn NY 11201 USA
**Petrocelli, Americo P (Rico)** — Baseball Player
37 Green Heron Lane, Nashua NH 03062, USA
**Petrone, Shana** — Singer
Epic Records, 34 Music Square E, Nashville TN 37203, USA
**Petroni, Michael** — Director, Writer, Actor
W M E Entertainment, 9601 Wilshire Blvd, #300, Beverly Hills CA 90210 USA
**Petronio, Stephen** — Dancer, Choreographer
95 Saint Marks Place, New York NY 10009, USA
**Petroro, Marisa** — Actress
House of Representatives, 1434 6th St, #1, Santa Monica CA 90401 USA
**Petroske, John E (Jack)** — Ice Hockey Player
PO Box 366, Side Lake MN 55781, USA
**Petrov, Denis A** — Figure Skater
World Ice Arena, 1881th Bao'an Road, Luohu District, Shenzhen 518001, China
**Petrova, Nadia** — Tennis Player
Women's Tennis Assn, 1 Progress Plaza, #1500, Saint Petersburg FL 33701 USA
**Petrovic, Tim** — Golfer
11602 Turtle Lane, Austin TX 78726, USA
**Petrovicky, Ronald** — Ice Hockey Player
3236 Birkdale Ave, Duluth, GA 30097, USA
**Petrovics, Emil** — Composer
Attila Utca 29, 1013 Budapest, Hungary
**Petruska, Richard** — Basketball Player
4704 Pine Oak Park, #636, Houston TX 77081, USA
**Petry, Daniel J (Dan)** — Baseball Player
30715 Mystic Forest Dr, Farmington Hills MI 48331, USA
**Petry, Leroy A** — Afghanistan War Army Hero (CMH)
Public Affairs Office, PO Box 339500, Joint Base Lewis-McChord WA 98433, USA
**Petsko, Gregory A** — Chemist, Biochemist
51 Hampshire St, West Newton MA 02465, USA
**Pett, Joel** — Editorial Cartoonist
PO Box 174, Wilmore KY 40390, USA
**Pettengill, Gordon H** — Planetary Physicist
Massachusetts Institute of Technology, Space Research Center, Cambridge MA 02139, USA
**Pettersen, Suzann** — Golfer
R&A Group Services, Beach House, Golf Place, Saint Andrews Fife KY16 9JA, Scotland
**Pettersson, Carl** — Golfer
2208 Oak Lawn Way, Wake Forest NC 27587, USA
**Pettet, Joanna** — Actress
Paradigm Agency, 360 N Crescent Dr, North Building, Beverly Hills CA 90210 USA
**Pettie, Jim** — Ice Hockey Player
81 Kirk Road, Rochester NY 14612, USA
**Pettiford, Valerie** — Actress, Singer
Talent Works, 3500 W Olive Ave, #1400, Burbank CA 91505 USA
**Pettigrew, Gary L** — Football Player
2707 E 27th Ave, #2B, Spokane WA 99223, USA
**Pettigrew, L Eudora** — Educator
State University of New York, President's Office, Old Westbury NY 11568, USA
**Pettinger, Matt** — Ice Hockey Player
3075 Eastdowne Road, Victoria BC V8R 5S1, Canada
**Pettini, Joseph P (Joe)** — Baseball Player
112 Logan Court, Bethany WV 26032, USA
**Pettis, Gary G** — Baseball Player
3129 Crestline Court, Antioch CA 94531, USA
**Pettis, Madison** — Actress
Coast to Coast Talent, 3350 Barham Blvd, Los Angeles CA 90068 USA
**Pettit, Donald R** — Astronaut
2014 Country Ridge Dr, Houston TX 77062, USA
**Pettit, G W Paul** — Baseball Player
928 Sarazen St, Hemet CA 92543, USA
**Pettit, Robert E (Bob), Jr** — Basketball Player
7 Garden Lane, New Orleans LA 70124, USA
**Pettitte, Andrew E (Andy)** — Baseball Player
2222 W Lawther Dr, Deer Park TX 77536, USA
**Petty, J T** — Director, Writer
Creative Artists Agency, 2000 Ave of Stars, #100, Los Angeles CA 90067 USA
**Petty, Kyle E** — Auto Racing Driver
135 Longfield Dr, Mooresville NC 28115, USA
**Petty, Lori** — Actress
Intellectual Property Group, 10585 Santa Monica Blvd, #140, Los Angeles CA 90025, USA
**Petty, Richard L** — Auto Racing Driver
Richard Petty Motorsports, 7065 Zephyr Place, Concord NC 28027, USA
**Petty, Tom** — Singer, Guitarist, Songwriter
East End Mgmt, 13721 Ventura Blvd, #200, Sherman Oaks CA 91423, USA
**Pettyfer, Alex** — Actor
W M E Entertainment, 9601 Wilshire Blvd, #300, Beverly Hills CA 90210 USA
**Peugeot, Roland** — Businessman
170 Ave Victor Hugo, 75116 Paris, France
**Pevec, Katja** — Actress
Greene Assoc, 1901 Ave of Stars, #130, Los Angeles CA 90067 USA
**Peyroux, Madeleine** — Singer, Songwriter
American International Artists, 356 Pine Valley Road, Hoosick Falls NY 12090, USA

| | | |
|---|---|---|
| **Peyser, Penny**<br>22039 Alizondo Dr, Woodland Hills CA 91364, USA | Actress | |
| **Peyton, Brad**<br>Verve Talent & Literary Agency, 9696 Culver Blvd, #301, Culver City CA 90232, USA | Director | **P** |
| **Pfaff, Judy**<br>319 Greenwich St, #5L, New York NY 10013, USA | Sculptor | |
| **Pfahl, John**<br>Janet Borden, 560 Broadway, #601, New York NY 10012, USA | Photographer | |
| **Pfann, George R**<br>120 Warwick Place, Ithaca NY 14850, USA | Football Player, Coach | |
| **Pfeiffer, Meg**<br>Kuka, Bolschestr 20, 12587 Berlin, Germany | Singer | |
| **Pfeiffer, Michelle**<br>Management 360, 9111 Wilshire Blvd, Beverly Hills CA 90210 USA | Actress | |
| **Pfeiffer, Norman**<br>Hardy Holzman Pfeiffer, 811 W 7th St, #430, Los Angeles CA 90017, USA | Architect | |
| **Pfeil, Robert R (Bobby)**<br>2358 Pheasant Run Circle, Stockton CA 95207, USA | Baseball Player | |
| **Pfell, Mark**<br>2565 Chelsea Road, Palos Verdes Estates CA 90274, USA | Golfer | |
| **Pfister, Wally**<br>2500 Jupiter Dr, Los Angeles CA 90046, USA | Cinematographer | |
| **Pflug, Jo Ann**<br>PO Box 3292, Jupiter FL 33469, USA | Actress | |
| **Pfund, Leroy H (Lee)**<br>130 Windsor Park Dr, #C214, Carol Stream IL 60188, USA | Baseball Player | |
| **Pfund, Randy**<br>50 S Pointe Dr, #608, Miami Beach FL 33139, USA | Basketball Coach, Executive | |
| **Phair, Liz**<br>KillerMoxie Mgmt, 5890 W Jefferson Blvd, #J, Los Angeles CA 90016, USA | Singer, Songwriter, Actress | |
| **Pham Minh Man, Jean-Baptiste Cardinal**<br>Toa Tonggiam Muc, 180 Nguyen Dink Chieu, Thanh-Pho Ho Chi Minh, Vietnam | Religious Leader | |
| **Pham Tuan**<br>4C-1000-Soc Son, Hanoi, Vietnam | Cosmonaut, Vietnam | |
| **Phaneuf, Dion**<br>271 Heath Road NW, Edmonton AB T6R 1V3, Canada | Ice Hockey Player | |
| **Pharr, Tommy L**<br>314 Harrison Lane, Winder GA 30680, USA | Football Player | |
| **Phegley, Roger D**<br>43 Timberlane Dr, Morton IL 61550, USA | Basketball Player | |
| **Phelan, James J (Jim)**<br>16579 Old Emmitsburg Road, Emmitsburg MD 21727, USA | Basketball Player, Coach | |
| **Phelps, Doug**<br>Webster & Assoc Public Relations, PO Box 23015, Nashville TN 37202, USA | Singer, Bassist (Kentucky Headhunters) | |
| **Phelps, Edmund S**<br>45 E 89th St, #28B, New York NY 10128, USA | Nobel Economics Laureate | |
| **Phelps, James**<br>United Agents, 12-26 Lexington St, London W1F 0LE, England | Actor | |
| **Phelps, Jaycie**<br>1443 Persimmon Circle, Greenfield IN 46140, USA | Gymnast | |
| **Phelps, Kelly Joe**<br>Different Strings, 30 Eldon Terrace, Windmill Hill Bristol BS3 4PA, England | Singer, Guitarist, Songwriter | |
| **Phelps, Kenneth A (Ken)**<br>6030 E Foothill Dr N, Paradise Valley AZ 85253, USA | Baseball Player | |
| **Phelps, Michael E**<br>16720 Huerta Road, Encino CA 91436, USA | Neuroscientist, Inventor | |
| **Phelps, Michael F**<br>PO Box 65239, Baltimore MD 21209, USA | Swimmer | |
| **Phelps, Oliver**<br>United Agents, 12-26 Lexington St, London W1F 0LE, England | Actor | |
| **Phelps, Richard F (Digger)**<br>Lordly & Dane, 1344 Main St, Waltham MA 02451, USA | Basketball Coach, Sportscaster | |
| **Phelps, Ricky Lee**<br>Webster & Assoc Public Relations, PO Box 23015, Nashville TN 37202, USA | Singer, Musician (Kentucky Headhunters) | |
| **Phifer, Mekhi**<br>Facilitator Films, 4000 Warner Blvd, Building 17, Burbank CA 91522, USA | Actor | |
| **Philaret, Patriarch**<br>10 Osvobozdeniya St, 220004 Minsk, Belarus | Religious Leader | |
| **Philbin, Gerald J (Gerry)**<br>9976 Marsala Way, Delray Beach FL 33446, USA | Football Player | |
| **Philbin, Joseph (Joe)**<br>Miami Dolphins, 7500 SW 30th St, Davie FL 33314 USA | Football Coach | |
| **Philbin, Regis**<br>101 W 67th St, #51A, New York NY 10023, USA | Entertainer | |
| **Philbrick, Denise**<br>5364 Carnegie Loop, Livermore CA 94550, USA | Golfer | |
| **Philcox, Todd S**<br>1156 Creeks Edge Court, Ponte Vedra FL 32082, USA | Football Player | |
| **Philip**<br>Buckingham Palace, Westminster, London SW1A 1AA, England | Prince, England; Duke of Edinburgh | |
| **Philip, George M**<br>State University of New York, President's Office, 1400 Washington Ave, Albany NY 12222, USA | Educator | |
| **Philip, Primate**<br>Antiochian Orthodox Christian Church, 358 Mountain Road, Englewood NJ 07631, USA | Religious Leader | |
| **Philippe**<br>Koninklijk Palais, Rue de Brederode, 1000 Brussels, Belgium | King, Belgium | |
| **Philippoussis, Mark**<br>Octagon Worldwide, 1751 Pinnacle Dr, #1500, McLean VA 22102 USA | Tennis Player | |
| **Philipps, Busy**<br>I C M Partners, 10250 Constellation Blvd, #900, Los Angeles CA 90067 USA | Actress | |
| **Philips, Chuck**<br>Los Angeles Times, Editorial Dept, 202 W 1st St, Los Angeles CA 90012 USA | Journalist | |
| **Philips, Gina**<br>Kritzer Levine Wilkins Griffin, 11872 La Grange Ave, #100, Los Angeles CA 90025 USA | Actress | |
| **Phillipoff, Harold**<br>736 Georgia St SE, Albuquerque NM 87108, USA | Ice Hockey Player | |

# P

**Phillippe, Ryan** — Actor
Schiff Co, 9200 Sunset Blvd, #430, West Hollywood CA 90232 USA

**Phillips, Andre L P** — Track Athlete
Edison High School, 1425 Center St, Stockton CA 95206, USA

**Phillips, Anthony** — Guitarist (Genesis), Songwriter
Solo Agency, 53-55 Fulham High St, #200, London SW6 3JJ, England

**Phillips, Arianne** — Costume Designer
United Talent Agency, U T A Plaza, 9336 Civic Center Dr, Beverly Hills CA 90210 USA

**Phillips, Bijou** — Singer, Model, Actress
Untitled Entertainment, 350 S Beverly Dr, #200, Beverly Hills CA 90212 USA

**Phillips, Bill** — Physical Fitness Expert
Muscle Media, 444 Corporate Circle, Golden CO 80401, USA

**Phillips, Bobbie** — Actress
Kelly Agency, 3001 Heavenly Ridge St, Thousand Oaks CA 91362, USA

**Phillips, Brandon E** — Baseball Player
586 Rowland Road, Stone Mountain GA 30083, USA

**Phillips, Britta** — Bassist (Luna, Dean & Britta)
Don Buchwald, 6500 Wilshire Blvd, #2200, Los Angeles CA 90048 USA

**Phillips, Caryl** — Writer
A P Watt Ltd, 20 John St, London WC1N 2DR, England

**Phillips, Charles W** — Football Player
915 N Holliston Ave, Pasadena CA 91104, USA

**Phillips, Chynna** — Singer, Actress
D S W Entertainment, 116 E 16th St, #900, New York NY 10003, USA

**Phillips, Clarence G (J R)** — Baseball Player
12210 N Rio Vista Dr, Sun City AZ 85351, USA

**Phillips, D Eugene (Gene)** — Basketball Player
11606 Whisper Willow St, San Antonio TX 78230, USA

**Phillips, Derek** — Actor
Evolution Entertainment, 901 N Highland Ave, Los Angeles CA 90038 USA

**Phillips, Dwight** — Track Athlete
USA Track & Field, RCA Dome, PO Box 140, Indianapolis IN 46225 USA

**Phillips, Eddie L** — Basketball Player
800 McCary St SW, Birmingham AL 35211, USA

**Phillips, Emo** — Actor, Comedian
Harbour Agency, 63 William St, #300, East Sydney NSW 1022, Australia

**Phillips, Erin V** — Basketball Player
Indiana Fever, Conseco Fieldhouse, 125 S Pennsylvania, Indianapolis IN 46204 USA

**Phillips, Ethan** — Actor
Talent Works, 3500 W Olive Ave, #1400, Burbank CA 91505 USA

**Phillips, G Andrew (Andy)** — Baseball Player
12744 Frog Ridge Road, Buhl AL 35446, USA

**Phillips, Gersha** — Costume Designer
Paradigm Agency, 360 N Crescent Dr, North Building, Beverly Hills CA 90210 USA

**Phillips, Grant-Lee** — Singer, Guitarist, Songwriter, Actor
Umbrella Group, 20 West St, #30E, New York NY 10002, USA

**Phillips, J Dixon, Jr** — Judge
US Court of Appeals, 100 Europa Dr, Chapel Hill NC 27517, USA

**Phillips, James J (Red)** — Football Player
67 Lakeview Dr, #10D, Alexander City AL 35010, USA

**Phillips, Jason H** — Football Player
6350 W Mystic Meadow, Houston TX 77021, USA

**Phillips, Jason L** — Baseball Player
1777 Tara Way, San Marcos CA 92078, USA

**Phillips, Jay** — Actor
I C M Partners, 10250 Constellation Blvd, #900, Los Angeles CA 90067 USA

**Phillips, Jermaine** — Football Player
11802 Derbyshire Dr, Tampa FL 33626, USA

**Phillips, Jess W, Jr** — Football Player
2820 San Antonio St, Beaumont TX 77701, USA

**Phillips, John** — Basketball Coach
University of Tulsa, Athletic Dept, Tulsa OK 74104, USA

**Phillips, John L** — Astronaut
154 Canoe Cove Lane, Sandpoint ID 83864, USA

**Phillips, Joseph C** — Actor
Don Buchwald, 6500 Wilshire Blvd, #2200, Los Angeles CA 90048 USA

**Phillips, Joseph G (Joe)** — Football Player
4080 SE 39th Circle, Ocala FL 34480, USA

**Phillips, Judith** — Landscape Architect
1840 Zearing Ave NW, Albuquerque NM 87104, USA

**Phillips, Julianne** — Actress
3 Arts Entertainment, 9460 Wilshire Blvd, #700, Beverly Hills CA 90212 USA

**Phillips, K Anthony (Tony)** — Baseball Player
13341 E Cochise Road, Scottsdale AZ 85259, USA

**Phillips, Kate** — Writer
Houghton Mifflin Harcourt, 215 Park Ave S, #1200, New York NY 10003 USA

**Phillips, Kenneth (Kenny)** — Football Player
Philadelphia Eagles, 1 Novacare Way, Philadelphia PA 19145 USA

**Phillips, Kevin** — Actor
A P A Talent/Literary Agency, 405 S Beverly Dr, #300, Beverly Hills CA 90212 USA

**Phillips, Kevin P** — Political Analyst
Grand Central Publishing, 237 Park Ave, #1300, New York NY 10017, USA

**Phillips, Kimberly** — Model
Playboy Promotions, 2706 Media Center Dr, Los Angeles CA 90065 USA

**Phillips, Kristie** — Gymnast
610 1st Ave, Asbury Park NJ 07712, USA

**Phillips, Lawrence L** — Football Player
9527 Langdon Ave, North Hills CA 91343, USA

**Phillips, Leslie S** — Actor
78 Maida Vale, London W9 1PR, England

**Phillips, Lisa Ann** — Actress
Don Buchwald, 6500 Wilshire Blvd, #2200, Los Angeles CA 90048 USA

**Phillips, Lou Diamond** — Actor
Global Artists Agency, 6253 Hollywood Blvd, #508, Los Angeles CA 90028, USA

**Phillips, Loyd W** — Football Player
739 Sands Road, Cave Springs AR 72718, USA

**Phillippe - Phillips**

**Phillips, Mackenzie** — Actress
S D B Partners, 1801 Ave of Stars, #902, Los Angeles CA 90067 USA
**Phillips, Melvin (Mel), Jr** — Football Player
6368 Milk Wagon Lane, Hialeah FL 33014, USA
**Phillips, Michael D (Mike)** — Baseball Player
3322 Ridgefield St, Irving TX 75062, USA
**Phillips, Michelle** — Singer (Mamas & Papas), Actress
Rebel Entertainment Partners, 5700 Wilshire Blvd, #456, Los Angeles CA 90036, USA
**Phillips, Nathan** — Actor
Principato-Young, 9465 Wilshire Blvd, #880, Beverly Hills CA 90212 USA
**Phillips, Norma** — Social Activist
Mothers Against Drunk Driving, PO Box 819100, Dallas TX 75381, USA
**Phillips, Owen M** — Geophysical Engineer
462 Heron Point, Chestertown MD 21620, USA
**Phillips, Paul A** — Baseball Player
507 N Main Ave, Demopolis AL 36732, USA
**Phillips, Peter C B** — Economist
PO Box 208281, New Haven CT 06520, USA
**Phillips, Phil** — Singer, Songwriter
PO Box 105, Jennings LA 70546, USA
**Phillips, Preston T** — Architect
Preston T Phillips Architect, PO Box 3037, Bridgehampton NY 11932, USA
**Phillips, Reginald K** — Football Player
8300 W Airport Blvd, #906, Houston TX 77071, USA
**Phillips, Richard** — Captain, Maersk Alabama Cargo Ship
211 River Road, Underhill VT 05489, USA
**Phillips, Sam** — Singer, Songwriter
High Road Touring, 751 Bridgeway, #200, Sausalito CA 94965 USA
**Phillips, Sean** — Cartoonist
153 Petherton Road, Highbury, London N5 2RS, England
**Phillips, Sian** — Actress
Dalzell & Beresford, 26 Astwood Mews, London SW7 4DE, England
**Phillips, Susanna** — Opera Singer
I M G Artists, Hogarth Business Park, Chiswick, London W4 2TH, England
**Phillips, T Scott** — Drummer (Creed, Alter Bridge)
Wind-Up Records, 72 Madison Ave, #800, New York NY 10016 USA
**Phillips, Todd** — Director, Writer
Green Hat Productions, 4000 Warner Blvd, Building 66, Burbank CA 91522, USA
**Phillips, W Taylor (Tay)** — Baseball Player
594 Mein Mitchell Road, Hiram GA 30141, USA
**Phillips, Wade** — Football Coach
6115 Norway Road, Dallas TX 75230, USA
**Phillips, Warren H** — Publisher
Bridge Works Publications, PO Box 1798, Bridgehampton NY 11932, USA
**Phillips, Wendy** — Actress
Stone Manners Salners, 9911 W Pico Blvd, #1400, Los Angeles CA 90035 USA
**Phillips, William D** — Nobel Physics Laureate
13409 Chestnut Oak Dr, Gaithersburg MD 20878, USA
**Phillips, Zara A E** — Princess, England; Equestrian
Gatecombe Park, Hampton Fields, Minchinhampton, Gloucestershire GL6 9AT, England
**Phillipson, Don** — Soccer Executive
5014 Gladiola Way, Golden CO 80403, USA
**Philo, Phoebe** — Fashion Designer
Chloe, 54-56 Rue du Faubourg Saint Honore, 75008 Paris, France
**Philp, Tom** — Journalist
Sacramento Bee, Editorial Dept, 2100 Q St, Sacramento CA 95816 USA
**Phinney, Davis** — Cyclist, Sportscaster
470 Juniper Ave, Boulder CO 80304, USA
**Phipps, Michael E (Mike)** — Football Player
2748 NE 25th St, Lighthouse Point FL 33064, USA
**Phipps, William E** — Actor
Commercial Talent, 9255 Sunset Blvd, #505, Los Angeles CA 90069, USA
**Phoebus, Thomas H (Tom)** — Baseball Player
2822 SW Lakemont Place, Palm City FL 34990, USA
**Phoenix, Joaquin R** — Actor, Singer, Guitarist
Patricola Public Relations, 9171 Wilshire Blvd, #441, Beverly Hills CA 90210 USA
**Piano, Renzo** — Pritzker Architectural Laureate
Renzo Piano Building Workshop, Via Rubens 29, 16158 Genoa, Italy
**Piat, Jean** — Actor
Artmedia, 20 Ave Rapp, 75007 Paris, France
**Piatkowski, Eric T** — Basketball Player
2125 S 189th Circle, Omaha NE 68130, USA
**Piau, Sandrine** — Opera Singer
I M G Artists, Hogarth Business Park, Chiswick, London W4 2TH, England
**Piazza, Michale J (Mike)** — Baseball Player
1000 S Pointe Dr, #3101, Miami Beach FL 33139, USA
**Piazza, Rod** — Singer, Harmonica Player
Blue Mountain Artists, 810 Tyvola Road, #114, Charlotte NC 28217, USA
**Piazza, Vincent** — Actor
Gersh Agency, 9465 Wilshire Blvd, #600, Beverly Hills CA 90212 USA
**Picard, Geoffrey** — Rowing Athlete
2020 W Lake Blvd, Tahoe City CA 96145, USA
**Picard, J Noel** — Ice Hockey Player
3636 Wilmington Ave, Saint Louis MO 63116, USA
**Picard, Robert R J** — Ice Hockey Player
4718 Grand Cypress Circle N, Coconut Creek FL 33073, USA
**Picardo, Robert** — Actor
Sovereign Talent Group, 8421 Wilshire Blvd, #200, Beverly Hills CA 90211, USA
**Picasso, Paloma** — Jewelry Designer, Actress
Quintana Ron Ltd, 291A Brompton Road, London SW3 2DY, England
**Picatto, Alexandra** — Actress
Abrams Artists, 9200 W Sunset Blvd, #1125, West Hollywood CA 90069 USA
**Piccard, Bertrand** — Balloonist
Winds of Hope, Ave de Florimont 20, 1006 Lausanne, Switzerland
**Picciolo, Robert M (Rob)** — Baseball Player
11773 Invierno Dr, San Diego CA 92124, USA

**Piccoli, Michel** — Actor
11 Rue des Lions Saint Paul, 75004 Paris, France
**Piccolo, Ottavia** — Actress
Anne Alvares Correa, 34 Rue Jouffroy d'Abbans, 75017 Paris, France
**Piccolo, Rina** — Cartoonist (Six Chix, Tina's Groove)
King Features Syndicate, 300 W 57th St, #1500, New York NY 10019 USA
**Piccone, Louis J (Lou)** — Football Player
325 N Forest Road, Buffalo NY 14221, USA
**Piccone, Robin** — Fashion Designer
Piccone Apparel Corp, 1424 Washington Blvd, Venice CA 90291, USA
**Pichardo, Hipolito** — Baseball Player
21218 Saint Andrews Blvd, #305, Boca Raton FL 33433, USA
**Pichette, Dave** — Ice Hockey Player
4751 Rue Escoffier, Quebec QC G1Y 3J4, Canada
**Pick, Amelie** — Actress
Artmedia, 20 Ave Rapp, 75007 Paris, France
**Pickard, Nancy** — Writer
4020 W 94th Terrace, #211, Prairie Village KS 66207, USA
**Pickel, William G (Bill)** — Football Player
9 Autumn Ridge Road, South Salem NY 10590, USA
**Pickens, Carl M** — Football Player
3085 Sugarloaf Club Dr, Duluth GA 30097, USA
**Pickens, James, Jr** — Actor
Wright Entertainment, 3207 Winnier Dr, Los Angeles CA 90068, USA
**Pickens, Jo Ann** — Opera Singer
Norman McCann Artists, 56 Lawrie Park Gardens, London SE26 6XJ, England
**Pickens, T Boone, Jr** — Businessman
B P Capital, 8117 Preston Road, #260, Dallas TX 75225, USA
**Pickering, Jeff** — Cartoonist (Spats)
King Features Syndicate, 300 W 57th St, #1500, New York NY 10019 USA
**Pickering, Thomas R** — Diplomat, Businessman
2318 Kimbro St, Alexandria VA 22307, USA
**Pickett, Cecil L (Ricky)** — Baseball Player
1017 Wood Ridge Dr, Azle TX 76020, USA
**Pickett, Cindy** — Actress
Shelter Entertainment, 9255 Sunset Blvd, #300, Los Angeles CA 90069 USA
**Pickett, Rex** — Director, Writer
A P A Talent/Literary Agency, 405 S Beverly Dr, #300, Beverly Hills CA 90212 USA
**Pickett, Ryan L** — Football Player
Green Bay Packers, 1265 Lombardi Ave, Green Bay WI 54304 USA
**Pickford, Kevin P** — Baseball Player
6006 N Harcourt Dr, Coeur D'Alene ID 83815, USA
**Pickitt, John L** — Air Force General
38 Sunrise Point Road, Clover SC 29710, USA
**Pickler, Kellie** — Singer, Songwriter
Fitzgerald Hartley, 1908 Wedgewood Ave, Nashville TN 37212, USA
**Pickles, Christina** — Actress
Domain Talent, 9229 W Sunset Blvd, #710, West Hollywood CA 90069 USA
**Pickles, Vivian** — Actress
91 Regent St, London W1R 8RU, England
**Pickup, Ronald** — Actor
54 Crouch Hall Road, London N8 8HG, England
**Picolotti, Romina** — Social Activist
Human Rights Center, Gen Paz 186, 10 Mo Pisa A, Cordoba 5000, Argentina
**Picoult, Jodi** — Writer
PO Box 508, Etna NH 03750, USA
**Pictor, Bruce** — Drummer (Association)
Variety Artists, 1924 Spring St, Paso Robles CA 93446 USA
**Piddock, Jim** — Actor
Amsel Eisenstadt Frazier, 5055 Wilshire Blvd, #865, Los Angeles CA 90036 USA
**Pidgeon, Rebecca** — Actress, Singer
Ken McReddie Assoc, 101 Finsbury Pavement, London EC2A 1RS, England
**Pidhirny, Harry** — Ice Hockey Player
1880 Valley Farm Road, Pickering ON L1V 6B3, Canada
**Piech, Ferdinand** — Businessman
Volkswagenwerk AG, 38436 Wolfsburg, Germany
**Piedmont, Matt** — Director, Producer, Writer
Creative Artists Agency, 2000 Ave of Stars, #100, Los Angeles CA 90067 USA
**Piedra, Jorge** — Baseball Player
2208 Vaquero Estates Blvd, Westlake TX 76262, USA
**Pielmeier, John** — Writer, Actor, Producer
Creative Artists Agency, 2000 Ave of Stars, #100, Los Angeles CA 90067 USA
**Pienaar, Jacobus F** — Rugby Player
Rugby Football Union, PO Box 99, Newlands 7725, South Africa
**Piene, Otto** — Sculptor, Artist
383 Old Ayer Road, Groton MA 01450, USA
**Pier, Christina** — Opera Singer
I M G Artists, Hogarth Business Park, Chiswick, London W4 2TH, England
**Pierce, Allison** — Singer, Guitarist (Pierces)
Paradigm Agency, 360 N Crescent Dr, North Building, Beverly Hills CA 90210 USA
**Pierce, Catherine** — Singer (Pierces)
Paradigm Agency, 360 N Crescent Dr, North Building, Beverly Hills CA 90210 USA
**Pierce, Chester M** — Psychiatrist
17 Prince St, Jamaica Plain MA 02130, USA
**Pierce, David Hyde** — Actor, Singer
2400 Inverness Ave, Los Angeles CA 90027, USA
**Pierce, Donald R (Don)** — Thoroughbred Racing Jockey
340 Neptune Ave, Encinitas CA 92024, USA
**Pierce, Edward J (Ed)** — Baseball Player
702 E Laurel Ave, Glendora CA 91741, USA
**Pierce, Jeffrey** — Actor
Don Buchwald, 6500 Wilshire Blvd, #2200, Los Angeles CA 90048 USA
**Pierce, Jeffrey C (Jeff)** — Baseball Player
1046 Lantern Lanes, Circle Pines MN 55014, USA
**Pierce, Jill** — Actress
Extreme Team Productions, 15941 S Harlem, #319, Tinley Park IL 60477, USA

| | |
|---|---|
| **Pierce, Jonathan**<br>Bob Doyle Assoc, 1111 17th Ave S, Nashville TN 37212, USA | Singer |
| **Pierce, Kirstin**<br>Don Buchwald, 6500 Wilshire Blvd, #2200, Los Angeles CA 90048 USA | Actress |
| **Pierce, L Jack**<br>1002 Cortez St, Laredo TX 78040, USA | Baseball Player |
| **Pierce, Lincoln**<br>United Feature Syndicate, PO Box 5610, Cincinnati OH 45201 USA | Cartoonist (Big Nate) |
| **Pierce, Mary**<br>Women's Tennis Assn, 1 Progress Plaza, #1500, Saint Petersburg FL 33701 USA | Tennis Player |
| **Pierce, Paul A**<br>79 Winter St, Lincoln MA 01773, USA | Basketball Player |
| **Pierce, Randy**<br>178 Five Arches Dr, RR 2, Pakenham ON K0A 2X0, Canada | Ice Hockey Player |
| **Pierce, Ron**<br>PO Box 361, Clarksburg NJ 08510, USA | Harness Racing Driver |
| **Pierce, Tamora**<br>Random House, 1745 Broadway, #1800, New York NY 10019 USA | Writer |
| **Pierce, W William (Billy)**<br>1321 Baileys Crossing Dr, Lemont IL 60439, USA | Baseball Player |
| **Pierce, Wendell**<br>Paradigm Agency, 360 N Crescent Dr, North Building, Beverly Hills CA 90210 USA | Actor |
| **Pierce-Roberts, Tony**<br>1 Princes Gardens, London W5 1SD, England | Cinematographer |
| **Piercy, Marge**<br>PO Box 1473, Wellfleet MA 02667, USA | Writer |
| **Piercy, Scott**<br>Professional Golfer's Assn, PO Box 109601, Palm Beach Gardens FL 33410 USA | Golfer |
| **Pierpoint, Eric**<br>2199 Topanga Skyline Dr, Topanga CA 90290, USA | Actor |
| **Pierre, Juan D**<br>6148 NW 65th Terrace, Parkland FL 33067, USA | Baseball Player |
| **Pierre-Paul, Jason**<br>New York Giants, Meadowlands Stadium, 102 Route 120, East Rutherford NJ 07073 USA | Football Player |
| **Piers, Julie**<br>Ladies Pro Golf Assn, 100 International Golf Dr, Daytona Beach FL 32124 USA | Golfer |
| **Piersall, James A (Jimmy)**<br>1105 Oakview Dr, Wheaton IL 60187, USA | Baseball Player |
| **Pierson, Emma**<br>Independent Talent Group, 40 Whitfield St, London W1T 2RH, England | Actress |
| **Pierson, Geoffrey**<br>Stone Manners Salners, 9911 W Pico Blvd, #1400, Los Angeles CA 90035 USA | Actor |
| **Pierson, Jack**<br>Cheim & Read, 547 W 25th St, New York NY 10001, USA | Photographer, Sculptor |
| **Pierson, Kate**<br>Lazy Meadow Motel, 5191 Route 28, Mount Tremper NY 12457, USA | Singer, Organist (B-52's) |
| **Pierson, Markus**<br>OutWest, 7216 Washington St NE, #A, Albuquerque NM 87109, USA | Artist, Sculptor |
| **Pierson, Peter S (Pete)**<br>17646 Jamestown Way, #D, Lutz FL 33558, USA | Football Player |
| **Pierson, Plenette**<br>New York Liberty, Madison Square Garden, 2 Penn Plaza, New York NY 10121 USA | Basketball Player |
| **Pierson, Reggie L**<br>17566 Elderberry Circle, Carson CA 90746, USA | Football Player |
| **Pierzynski, Anthony J (A J)**<br>9313 Tibet Pointe Circle, Windermere FL 34786, USA | Baseball Player |
| **Pieterse, Sasha**<br>A P A Talent/Literary Agency, 405 S Beverly Dr, #300, Beverly Hills CA 90212 USA | Actress |
| **Pietkiewicz, Stanley T (Stan)**<br>2213 Venetian Way, Winter Park FL 32789, USA | Basketball Player |
| **Pietrangeli, Nicola (Nicky)**<br>Via Eustachio Manfredi 15, 00197 Rome, Italy | Tennis Player |
| **Pietrangelo, Frank**<br>6371 Moretta Dr, Niagara Falls ON L2E 4H7, Canada | Ice Hockey Player |
| **Pietrus, Mickael**<br>13420 Bonica Way, Windermere FL 34786, USA | Basketball Player |
| **Pietruski, John M, Jr**<br>27 E Corsica Court, Farmingdale NJ 07727, USA | Businessman |
| **Pietrzak, James M (Jim)**<br>8807 Citrus Village Dr, #108, Tampa FL 33626, USA | Football Player |
| **Pietrzykowski, Zbigniew**<br>Ul Gomicza 5, Bielsko-Biata 43 409, Poland | Boxer |
| **Pietz, Amy**<br>Innovative Artists, 1505 10th St, Santa Monica CA 90401 USA | Actress |
| **Pifferini, Robert M (Bob), Jr**<br>1731 Granite Hill Road, Placerville CA 95667, USA | Football Player |
| **Pigford, Eva**<br>Ford Models Inc, 111 5th Ave, #900, New York NY 10003 USA | Model, Actress |
| **Pigg, Landon**<br>R C A Records, 8750 Wilshire Blvd, Beverly Hills CA 90211 USA | Singer, Songwriter |
| **Piggott, Lester K**<br>Beech Tree House, Tostock, Bury Saint Edmonds, Suffolk 1P30 9NY, England | Thoroughbred Racing Jockey |
| **Piggott, Marcus**<br>Art Partner, 155 6th Ave, #1500, New York NY 10013, USA | Photographer |
| **Pignatano, Joseph B (Joe)**<br>150 78th St, Brooklyn NY 11209, USA | Baseball Player |
| **Pigott-Smith, Tim**<br>Conway Van Gelder Grant, 8-12 Broadwick St, #300, London W1F 8HW, England | Actor |
| **Pihlman, Tuomas**<br>105 Spit Brook Road, Nashua NH 03062, USA | Ice Hockey Player |
| **Pike, Gary**<br>10031 Benares Place, Sun Valley CA 91352, USA | Singer (Lettermen) |
| **Pike, Jim**<br>M P I Talent Agency, 1801 Ave of Stars, #1420, Los Angeles CA 90067, USA | Singer (Lettermen) |
| **Pike, Mike H (Mark)**<br>508 Marywood Court, Edgewood KY 41017, USA | Football Player |

V.I.P. Address Book

747

**P**

**Pierce - Pike**

# P

| | |
|---|---|
| **Pike, Nicholas** <br> First Artists Mgmt, 4764 Park Granada, #210, Calabasas CA 91302 USA | Composer |
| **Pike, Rosamund** <br> United Agents, 12-26 Lexington St, London W1F 0LE, England | Actress |
| **Pilarczyk, Daniel E** <br> 100 E 8th St, #800, Cincinnati OH 45202, USA | Religious Leader |
| **Pilati, Stefano** <br> Yves Saint Laurent, 7 Ave George V, 75008 Paris, France | Fashion Designer |
| **Pileggi, Mitch** <br> Pakula/King, 9229 W Sunset Blvd, #315, West Hollywood CA 90069 USA | Actor |
| **Pileggi, Nicholas** <br> Bloom Hergott Diemer, 150 S Rodeo Dr, #300, Beverly Hills CA 90212 USA | Writer, Producer |
| **Pilger, John R** <br> 57 Hambatt Road, London SW4 9EQ, England | Journalist, Filmmaker, Environmentalist |
| **Pilgrim, Evan B** <br> 1787 Cobblestone Dr, Provo UT 84604, USA | Football Player |
| **Piligian, Craig** <br> Pilgrim Films, 12020 Chandler Blvd, #200, North Hollywood CA 91607, USA | Producer |
| **Pilkington, Lorraine** <br> Another Tongue, 10-11 D'Arbay St, London W1F 8DS, England | Actress |
| **Pill, Alison** <br> Burstein Co, 15304 W Sunset Blvd, #208, Pacific Palisades CA 90272 USA | Actress |
| **Pilla, Anthony M** <br> Catholic Bishops National Conference, 3211 4th St, Washington DC 20017, USA | Religious Leader |
| **Pillari, Ross** <br> B P America Inc, 535 Madison Ave, #200, New York NY 10022, USA | Businessman |
| **Piller Cottrer, Pietro** <br> Borgo Gran Villa 76, 32047 Sappada, Italy | Cross Country Skier |
| **Piller, Zachery P (Zach)** <br> 23 Colonel Winstead Dr, Brentwood TN 37027, USA | Football Player |
| **Pillers, Lawrence D** <br> 140 David Clemons Road, Quincy FL 32352, USA | Football Player |
| **Pilliod, Charles J, Jr** <br> 49 Twin Oaks Road, #2, Akron OH 44313, USA | Diplomat, Businessman |
| **Pillitteri, Lynn J** <br> Western Washington University, Biology Dept, 516 High St, Bellingham WA 98225, USA | Biologist |
| **Pillow, Ray** <br> Joe Taylor Artist Agency, 2802 Columbine Place, Nashville TN 37204 USA | Singer, Songwriter |
| **Pilote, Pierre P** <br> PO Box 247, Wyevale ON L0L 2T0, Canada | Ice Hockey Player |
| **Pinault, Francois** <br> Artemis SA, 5 Blvd de Latour-Maubourg, 75007 Paris, France | Businessman |
| **Pincay, Laffit, Jr** <br> 719 Carriage House Dr, Arcadia CA 91006, USA | Thoroughbred Racing Jockey |
| **Pinchak, Jimmy (Jax)** <br> Stone Manners Salners, 9911 W Pico Blvd, #1400, Los Angeles CA 90035 USA | Actor |
| **Pinchot, Bronson** <br> Amsel Eisenstadt Frazier, 5055 Wilshire Blvd, #865, Los Angeles CA 90036 USA | Actor |
| **Pinckney, Edward L (Ed)** <br> 3350 SW 27th Ave, #1004, Miami FL 33133, USA | Basketball Player |
| **Pinckney, Sandra** <br> Food Network, 1180 Ave of Americas, #1200, New York NY 10036 USA | Chef |
| **Pincling, Andrew (Pinch)** <br> Leave Home Booking, 1400 S Foothill Dr, #34, Salt Lake City UT 84108, USA | Drummer (Damned) |
| **Pincus, Henry** <br> Principato-Young, 9465 Wilshire Blvd, #880, Beverly Hills CA 90212 USA | Director |
| **Pinda, Mizengo** <br> Prime Minister's Office, PO Box 980, Dodoma, Tanzania | Prime Minister, Tanzania |
| **Pinder, A Gerald (Gerry)** <br> 320 39th Ave SW, Calgary AB T2S 0W7, Canada | Ice Hockey Player |
| **Pinder, Cyril C** <br> 7137 S Luella Ave, Chicago IL 60649, USA | Football Player |
| **Pinder, Lucy K** <br> Girl Mgmt, 22 Noel St, London W1F 8GS, England | Model |
| **Pinder, Michael (Mike)** <br> Moody Blues, 53-55 High St, Cobham, Surrey KT11 3DP, England | Keyboardist (Moody Blues) |
| **Pine, Chris** <br> Creative Artists Agency, 2000 Ave of Stars, #100, Los Angeles CA 90067 USA | Actor |
| **Pine, Courtney** <br> Free Trade Agency, 20-22 Curtain Road, London EC2A 3NF, England , USA | Jazz Saxophonist |
| **Pine, Linda** <br> Abrams-Rubaloff Lawrence, 8075 W 3rd St, #303, Los Angeles CA 90048 USA | Actress |
| **Pine, Robert** <br> 4212 Ben Ave, Studio City CA 91604, USA | Actor |
| **Pineau-Valencienne, Didier** <br> 63 Rue de la Boetie, 75008 Paris, France | Businessman |
| **Pineda, Michael F** <br> New York Yankees, Yankee Stadium, E 161st St & River Ave, Bronx NY 10451 USA | Baseball Player |
| **Pineiro, Joel A** <br> 3410 Poinciana Ave, Miami FL 33133, USA | Baseball Player |
| **Piñera Echenique, M J Sebastian** <br> President's Office, Palacio de la Monedo, Santiago, Chile | President, Chile |
| **Pinera, Mike** <br> Neal Hollander Agency, 9966 Majorca Place, Boca Raton FL 33434 USA | Singer, Guitarist |
| **Pines, Alexander** <br> University of California, Chemistry Dept, Hildebrand Hall, Berkeley CA 94720, USA | Chemist |
| **Pinette, John** <br> Luber Rocklin Entertainment, 8530 Wilshire Blvd, #555, Beverly Hills CA 90211 USA | Actor, Comedian, Writer, Producer |
| **Pinger, Mark** <br> 5201 Orduna Dr, #6, Coral Gables FL 33146, USA | Swimmer |
| **Pini, Daniela** <br> I M G Artists, Hogarth Business Park, Chiswick, London W4 2TH, England | Opera Singer |
| **Piniella, Louis V (Lou)** <br> 1005 Taray de Avila, Tampa FL 33613, USA | Baseball Player, Manager |
| **Pink** <br> R D W M, 1158 26th St, #564, Santa Monica CA 90403, USA | Singer, Songwriter |

**Pike - Pink**

| | |
|---|---|
| **Pinkel, Donald P** | Pediatrician |
| 275 Marlene Dr, San Luis Obispo CA 93405, USA | |
| **Pinkel, Gary** | Football Coach |
| University of Missouri, Athletic Dept, Columbia MO 64211, USA | |
| **Pinker, Steven A** | Psychologist |
| Harvard University, Psychology Dept, Cambridge MA 01238, USA | |
| **Pinkett Smith, Jada** | Actress |
| Paradigm Agency, 360 N Crescent Dr, North Building, Beverly Hills CA 90210 USA | |
| **Pinkett, Allen J** | Football Player |
| 320 W 8th Place, Hobart IN 46342, USA | |
| **Pinkins, Tonya** | Actress, Singer |
| Warren Cowan, 8899 Beverly Blvd, #918, Los Angeles CA 90048 USA | |
| **Pinkney, V Reginald (Reggie)** | Football Player |
| 518 Rock Canyon Dr, Fayetteville NC 28303, USA | |
| **Pinkston, Rob** | Actor |
| Momentum Talent, 9401 Wilshire Blvd, #501, Beverly Hills CA 90212, USA | |
| **Pinkston, Ryan** | Actor |
| A P A Talent/Literary Agency, 405 S Beverly Dr, #300, Beverly Hills CA 90212 USA | |
| **Pinkwater, Julie** | Publisher |
| Ladies' Home Journal, Publisher's Office, 125 Park Ave, New York NY 10017, USA | |
| **Pinner, Artose D** | Football Player |
| 102 Big Blue Court, Hopkinsville KY 42240, USA | |
| **Pinney, Raymond E (Ray)** | Football Player |
| 6529 NE Windermere Road, #B, Seattle WA 98105, USA | |
| **Pinnock, Trevor** | Conductor, Concert Harpsichordist |
| 35 Gloucester Crescent, London NW1 7DL, England | |
| **Pino, Danny** | Actor |
| G E F Entertainment, 122 N Clark Dr, #401, Los Angeles CA 90048, USA | |
| **Pino, Mario** | Thoroughbred Racing Jockey |
| 8400 Serena Creek Ave, Boynton Beach FL 33473, USA | |
| **Pinol, Jacqueline** | Actress |
| Talent Works, 3500 W Olive Ave, #1400, Burbank CA 91505 USA | |
| **Pinon, Dominique** | Actor |
| Agence Artiste Adequet, 108 Rue Reaumur, 75002 Paris, France | |
| **Pinos, Carmen** | Architect |
| Av Diagonal 490, #3/2, 08026 Barcelona, Spain | |
| **Pinsent, Gordon E** | Actor |
| Noble Caplan Abrams, 1260 Yonge St, #200, Toronto ON M4T 1W6, Canada | |
| **Pinsent, Matthew** | Rowing Athlete |
| British International Rowing Office, 6 Lower Mall, London W6 9DJ, England | |
| **Pinsky, Drew** | Actor, Moive Producer |
| Dr Drew Productions, 14742 Ventura Blvd, #PH, Sherman Oaks CA 91403, USA | |
| **Pinsky, Robert N** | Writer |
| Boston University, Creative Writing Dept, 236 Bay State Road, Boston MA 02215, USA | |
| **Pinson, Bobby O** | Singer, Guitarist, Songwriter |
| Susan Niles Public Relations, 726 Bresslyn Road, Nashville TN 37205, USA | |
| **Pinson, Julie** | Actress |
| 13576 Cheltenham Dr, Sherman Oaks CA 91423, USA | |
| **Pintat Santolaria, Albert** | Head of Government, Andorra |
| President's Office, Casa de la Valle, Andorra la Vella, Andorra | |
| **Pintauro, Danny** | Actor |
| Preston Entertainment, 8033 Sunset Blvd, #2750, Los Angeles CA 90046, USA | |
| **Pinter, Mark** | Actor |
| Gage Group, 14724 Ventura Blvd, #505, Sherman Oaks CA 91403 USA | |
| **Pinto, Freida** | Actress, Model |
| Creative Artists Agency, 2000 Ave of Stars, #100, Los Angeles CA 90067 USA | |
| **Pinto, Inbal** | Dancer, Choreographer |
| Inbal Pinto Dance Co, 5 Yechley St, Neve Tzedek, Tel-Aviv 65149, Israel | |
| **Pinto, Mandie** | Singer |
| 27660 Heather Ridge Way, Canyon Country CA 91351, USA | |
| **Pinto, Maria** | Fashion Designer |
| 133 N Jefferson St, #600, Chicago IL 60601, USA | |
| **Pintscher, Matthias** | Composer, Conductor |
| Grenenau, Fischerweg 2, 34302 Guxhagen, Germany | |
| **Piollet, Marc** | Conductor |
| Kunstler Sekretariat am Gasteig, Rosenheimer Str 52, 81669 Munich, Germany | |
| **Piotrovsky, Mikhail B** | Museum Executive |
| State Hermitage Museum, 2 Dvortsovaya, 190000 Saint Petersburg, Russia | |
| **Piotrowski, Tom** | Basketball Player |
| 80 Clarks Landing Road, Port Republic, NJ 08241, USA | |
| **Piovanelli, Silvano Cardinal** | Religious Leader |
| Piazzi S Giovanni 3, 50129 Florence, Italy | |
| **Piovani, Nicola** | Composer |
| Via G Veroese 103, 00146 Rome, Italy | |
| **Piper, Billie P** | Singer, Actress |
| Rights House, Drury House, 34-43 Russell St, London WC2B 5HA, England | |
| **Piper, Cherie** | Ice Hockey Player |
| Team Canada, 2424 University Dr NW, Calgary AB T2N 3Y9, Canada | |
| **Piper, Jacki** | Actress |
| Rob Groves Mgmt, 33 Glasshouse St, Soho, London W1B 5DG, England | |
| **Piper, Roddy** | Professional Wrestler, Actor |
| Super Artists, 2910 Main St, #200, Santa Monica CA 90405, USA | |
| **Pipes, Leah** | Actress |
| Untitled Entertainment, 350 S Beverly Dr, #200, Beverly Hills CA 90212 USA | |
| **Pipes, R Byron** | Educator |
| 4509 Sugar Maple Dr, Lafayette IN 47905, USA | |
| **Pipkin, Joyce C (J C)** | Football Player |
| 1026 Stone Stack Dr, Bethlehem PA 18015, USA | |
| **Pippen, Scottie** | Basketball Player |
| 3393 Old Mill Road, Highland Park IL 60035, USA | |
| **Pippig, Uta** | Track Athlete |
| Take the Magic Step, 777 NW 51st St, #309, Boca Raton FL 33431, USA | |
| **Pippy, Katelyn** | Actress |
| A P A Talent/Literary Agency, 405 S Beverly Dr, #300, Beverly Hills CA 90212 USA | |
| **Piquet, Nelson** | Auto Racing Driver |
| Autodromo, SEN/CDPM, Rua da Gasolina #01, Brasilia DF 7007 400, Brazil | |

**Piraro, Dan** — Cartoonist (Bizarro)
534 Wilcox Ave, Los Angeles CA 90004, USA
**Pires de Miranda, Pedro** — Government Official, Portugal
Avenida da India 10, 1300 Lisbon, Portugal
**Pires do Nascimento, Alexandre** — Singer
E M I Records, 150 5th Ave, #700, New York NY 10011 USA
**Pires, Cleo** — Actress
Ascend Entertainment, 950 10th St, #A, Santa Monica CA 90403, USA
**Pires, Maria Joao** — Concert Pianist
Deutsche Grammaphon Records, 810 7th Ave, New York NY 10019 USA
**Pirkis, Max** — Actor
I C M Partners, 10250 Constellation Blvd, #900, Los Angeles CA 90067 USA
**Pirkl, Gregory D (Greg)** — Baseball Player
6822 Emerald Bay Lane, Indianapolis IN 46237, USA
**Pirner, Dave** — Singer (Soul Asylum), Songwriter
Monterey Peninsula Artists, 404 W Franklin St, Monterey CA 93940 USA
**Piro, Stephanie** — Cartoonist (Six Chix)
PO Box 605, Hampton NH 03843, USA
**Pirtie, Gerald E (Gerry)** — Baseball Player
30306 E 59th St, Broken Arrow OK 74014, USA
**Pirus, Alex** — Ice Hockey Player
15W222 Concord St, Elmhurst IL 60126, USA
**Pisapia, Joe** — Singer, Bassist (Guster)
Nettwerk Mgmt, 345 7th Ave, #2400, New York NY 10001, USA
**Pisarcik, Joseph A (Joe)** — Football Player
27 Compass Circle, Mount Laurel NJ 08054, USA
**Pisarev, Andrei** — Concert Pianist
I M G Artists, Hogarth Business Park, Chiswick, London W4 2TH, England
**Pischetsrider, Bernd** — Businessman
Volkswagen AG, Brieffach 1849, 38436 Wolfsburg, Germany
**Pisciotta, Marc G** — Baseball Player
867 Village Green NW, Marietta GA 30064, USA
**Piscitelli, Sabitino C (Sabby), Jr** — Football Player
500 NW 15th Court, Boca Raton FL 33486, USA
**Piscopo, Joe** — Actor, Comedian
Amsel Eisenstadt Frazier, 5055 Wilshire Blvd, #865, Los Angeles CA 90036 USA
**Pister, Karl S** — Educator
University of California, Chancellor's Office, Santa Cruz CA 95064, USA
**Pistone, Tom** — Auto Racing Driver
7858 Old Concord Road, Charlotte NC 28213, USA
**Pistor, Ludger** — Actor
Stacey Castro Media, 4009 Leeward Ave, Los Angeles CA 90005 USA
**Pitbull** — Rap Artist
Media Artists Group, 8255 Sunset Blvd, Los Angeles CA 90046, USA
**Pitchford, Dean** — Lyricist, Writer
8491 W Sunset Blvd, PO Box 111, West Hollywood CA 90069, USA
**Pitcock, Joan** — Golfer
341 E Lester Ave, Fresno CA 93720, USA
**Pitel, Piyush** — Businessman
Cabletron Systems, 35 Industrial Way, Rochester NY 14614, USA
**Pithart, Petr** — Government Official, Czech Republic
Drazickeho Nam 10/65, 11800 Prague 1, Czech Republic
**Pitillo, Maria** — Actress
Karen Foreman Mgmt, 17547 Ventura Blvd, Encino CA 91316, USA
**Pitino, Richard (Rick)** — Basketball Coach
200 Pepperbush Road, Louisville KY 40207, USA
**Pitkamaki, Tero** — Track Athlete
P L 42, 60511 Hyllykallo, Finland
**Pitkanen, Joni** — Ice Hockey Player
1214 Cobble Creek Circle, Cherry Hill NJ 08003, USA
**Pitko, Alexander (Alex)** — Baseball Player
2689 Sports Village Loop, #12, Pinetop AZ 85935, USA
**Pitlick, Lance** — Ice Hockey Player
5010 Shenandoah Lane N, Minneapolis MN 55446, USA
**Pitlock, Lee E (Skip)** — Baseball Player
215 Prospect St, Seguin TX 78155, USA
**Pitman, Jennifer S** — Thoroughbred Racing Trainer
Owls Barn, Kintbury, Hungerford, Berks RG17 9XS, England
**Pitof** — Director, Writer
A P A Talent/Literary Agency, 405 S Beverly Dr, #300, Beverly Hills CA 90212 USA
**Pitou Zimmerman, Penny** — Alpine Skier
560 Sanborn Road, Sanbornton NH 03269, USA
**Pitre, Louise** — Singer, Actress
Paquin Entertainment, 395 Notre Dame Ave, Winnipeg MB R3B 1R2, Canada
**Pitt, Brad** — Actor, Producer
Brillstein Entertainment Partners, 9150 Wilshire Blvd, #350, Beverly Hills CA 90212 USA
**Pitt, Eugene S** — Singer (Jive Five)
Neal Hollander Agency, 9966 Majorca Place, Boca Raton FL 33434 USA
**Pitt, Harvey L** — Government Official, Financier
Kalorama Partners, 1130 Connecticut Ave NW, #800, Washington DC 20036, USA
**Pitt, Michael** — Actor
W M E Entertainment, 9601 Wilshire Blvd, #300, Beverly Hills CA 90210 USA
**Pittaro, Christopher F (Chris)** — Baseball Player
42 Pintinalli Dr, Trenton NJ 08619, USA
**Pittas, Dimitri** — Opera Singer
Columbia Artists Mgmt Inc, 1790 Broadway, #702, New York NY 10019 USA
**Pittin, Alessandro** — Nordic Combined Skier
G S Fiamme Gialle, Via alle Coste 14, 38037 Predazzo (TN), Italy
**Pittman, Charles H** — Marine Corps General
Lexington Institute, 1600 Wilson Blvd, #900, Arlington VA 22209 USA
**Pittman, Danny R** — Football Player
2456 E Ficus Way, Gilbert AZ 85298, USA
**Pittman, James A, Jr** — Endocrinologist
5 Ridge Dr, Birmingham AL 35213, USA
**Pittman, Kavika C** — Football Player
3316 Mayfair Lane, Lewisville TX 75077, USA

| | |
|---|---|
| **Pittman, Michael** | Football Player |
| 24595 Town Center Dr, #3111, Valencia CA 91355, USA | |
| **Pittman, Richard A** | Vietnam War Marine Corps Hero (CMH) |
| 1217 Chaparral Way, Stockton CA 95209, USA | |
| **Pitts, Frank H** | Football Player |
| 8249 S Laredo Ave, Baton Rouge LA 70811, USA | |
| **Pitts, Gaylen R** | Baseball Player |
| 214 Rocky Bluff Lane, Mountain Home AR 72653, USA | |
| **Pitts, Greg** | Actor |
| Innovative Artists, 1505 10th St, Santa Monica CA 90401 USA | |
| **Pitts, Jacob** | Actor |
| A P A Talent/Literary Agency, 405 S Beverly Dr, #300, Beverly Hills CA 90212 USA | |
| **Pitts, John M** | Football Player |
| 3412 Stoneleigh Run Dr, Buford GA 30519, USA | |
| **Pitts, Leonard, Jr** | Columnist |
| Miami Herald, Editorial Dept, 1 Herald Plaza, Miami FL 33132 USA | |
| **Pitts, Robert (R C)** | Basketball Player |
| 12655 E Milburn Ave, Baton Rouge LA 70815, USA | |
| **Pitts, Ron** | Football Player, Sportscaster |
| 3811 Davids Road, Agoura Hills CA 91301, USA | |
| **Pittsley, James M (Jim)** | Baseball Player |
| 102 Dixon Ave, DuBois PA 15801, USA | |
| **Piven, Jeremy** | Actor |
| Creative Artists Agency, 2000 Ave of Stars, #100, Los Angeles CA 90067 USA | |
| **Pivonka, Michal** | Ice Hockey Player |
| 8312 Grand Estuary Trail, #102, Bradenton FL 34212, USA | |
| **Piznarski, Mark** | Director |
| W M E Entertainment, 9601 Wilshire Blvd, #300, Beverly Hills CA 90210 USA | |
| **Pizzarelli, John P (Bucky), Sr** | Jazz Guitarist |
| Abby Hoffer Enterprises, 223 1/2 E 48th St, New York NY 10017 USA | |
| **Pizzarelli, John, Jr** | Singer, Jazz Guitarist |
| Vector Mgmt, PO Box 120479, Nashville TN 37212 USA | |
| **Pizzaro, Juan C** | Baseball Player |
| 2262 Ave Borinquen, San Juan PR 00915, USA | |
| **Pizzorno, Sergio** | Guitarist (Kasabian), Songwriter |
| International Talent Booking, Ariel House, 74A Charlotte St, #100 London W1T 4QJ, England | |
| **Place, Marcella** | Field Hockey Player |
| 141 Meadow View Road, Orinda CA 94563, USA | |
| **Place, Mary Kay** | Actress |
| Gersh Agency, 9465 Wilshire Blvd, #600, Beverly Hills CA 90212 USA | |
| **Placido, Violante** | Actress, Singer |
| Via dela Farnesina 240, 00194 Rome, Italy | |
| **Pladson, Gordon C** | Baseball Player |
| 19087 87th Ave, Surrey BC V4N 3G5, Canada | |
| **Plager, Robert B (Bob)** | Ice Hockey Player |
| 362 Branchport Dr, Chesterfield MO 63017, USA | |
| **Plager, S Jay** | Judge |
| US Court of Appeals, 717 Madison Place NW, Washington DC 20439, USA | |
| **Plakson, Suzie** | Actress |
| 302 N La Brea Ave, #363, Los Angeles CA 90036, USA | |
| **Plamondon, Gerard (Gerry)** | Ice Hockey Player |
| 450 Rue de Montreal, Sherbrooke QC J1H 1E5, Canada | |
| **Plan B** | Rap Artist |
| 679 Artists, 21 Carnaby St, London W1F 7DA, England | |
| **Plana, Tony** | Actor |
| A P A Talent/Literary Agency, 405 S Beverly Dr, #300, Beverly Hills CA 90212 USA | |
| **Plank, Douglas M (Doug)** | Football Player |
| 12622 E Paradise Dr, Scottsdale AZ 85259, USA | |
| **Plank, Edward A (Eddie)** | Baseball Player |
| 1353 Leawood Road, Englewood FL 34223, USA | |
| **Plank, Julie** | Basketball Coach |
| Washington Mystics, Verizon Center, 401 9th St NW, #750, Washington DC 20004 USA | |
| **Plank, Raymond** | Businessman |
| Apache Corp, 2000 Post Oak Blvd, #100, Houston TX 77056, USA | |
| **Plano, Richard J** | Physicist |
| 10 Longwood Dr, #533, Westwood MA 02090, USA | |
| **Plant, Robert** | Singer, Songwriter |
| High Road Touring, 751 Bridgeway, #200, Sausalito CA 94965 USA | |
| **Plante, Bruce** | Editorial Cartoonist |
| Chattanooga Times, Editorial Dept, 100 E 11th St, #400, Chattanooga TN 37402, USA | |
| **Plante, Daniel L (Dan)** | Ice Hockey Player |
| 5 Gillingham Court, Algonquin IL 60102, USA | |
| **Plante, Derek J** | Ice Hockey Player |
| 6829 Meadow Grass Lane S, Cottage Grove MN 55016, USA | |
| **Plante, Pierre R** | Ice Hockey Player |
| 129 Rue Rapin, Salaberry-de-Valleyfield QC J6S 5M4, Canada | |
| **Plante, William M** | Commentator |
| CBS-TV, News Dept, 2020 M St NW, Washington DC 20036 USA | |
| **Plantenberg, Erik J** | Baseball Player |
| 1846 Creekside Dr NE, Owatonna MN 55060, USA | |
| **Plantier, Phillip A (Phil)** | Baseball Player |
| 16001 Martincoit Road, Poway CA 92064, USA | |
| **Plantu** | Editorial Cartoonist |
| Le Monde, Editorial Dept, 21 Bis Rue Claude Bernard, 75005 Paris, France | |
| **Plaskett, Thomas G** | Businessman |
| 5215 N O'Connor Blvd, #1070, Irving TX 75039, USA | |
| **Platanias, Dimitri** | Opera Singer |
| I M G Artists, Hogarth Business Park, Chiswick, London W4 2TH, England | |
| **Plater-Zyberk, Elizabeth M** | Architect |
| Duany & Plater-Zyberk Architects, 1023 SW 25th Ave, Miami FL 33135, USA | |
| **Platini, Michel** | Soccer Player |
| F I F A, Hitugweg 11, PO Box 85, 8030 Zurich 30, Switzerland | |
| **Platov, Evgeni** | Ice Dancer |
| Princeton Sports Center, PO Box 155, Blawenburg NJ 08504, USA | |
| **Platt, Campion A** | Architect |
| Campion A Platt Architect, 152 Madison Ave, #900, New York NY 10016, USA | |

**Platt, Howard** — Actor
Shirley Hamilton, 333 E Ontario, #302, Chicago IL 60611, USA
**Platt, Marc E** — Producer
Marc Platt Productions, 100 Universal City Plaza, Bungalow 5163, Universal City CA 91608, USA
**Platt, Oliver** — Actor
W M E Entertainment, 9601 Wilshire Blvd, #300, Beverly Hills CA 90210 USA
**Player, Gary J** — Golfer
Blair Atholl Farm, Lanseria, Fourways near Johannesburg, Gauteng 2068, South Africa
**Player, Scott D** — Football Player
115 Averley Way, Saint Johns FL 32259, USA
**Playfair, James (Jim)** — Ice Hockey Player, Coach
200-99 Station St, Saint John NB E2L 4X4, Canada
**Playfair, Larry** — Ice Hockey Player
724 Ransom Road, Grand Island NY 14072, USA
**Plaza, Aubrey** — Actress, Comedienne
Creative Artists Agency, 2000 Ave of Stars, #100, Los Angeles CA 90067 USA
**Pleasant, Anthony D** — Football Player
17249 Connor Quay Court, Cornelius NC 28031, USA
**Pleasant, Marquis A** — Football Player
3549 Rio Grande Circle, Dallas TX 75233, USA
**Pleau, Lawrence W (Larry)** — Ice Hockey Player, Executive
650 Spyglass Summit Dr, Chesterfield MO 63017, USA
**Plec, Julie** — Producer, Writer
W M E Entertainment, 9601 Wilshire Blvd, #300, Beverly Hills CA 90210 USA
**Pleis, William (Bill)** — Baseball Player
16744 4th Ave NE, Bradenton FL 34212, USA
**Plemons, Jesse** — Actor
Talent Works, 3500 W Olive Ave, #1400, Burbank CA 91505 USA
**Plesac, Daniel T (Dan)** — Baseball Player
245 White Thorne Lane, Valpariso IN 46383, USA
**Pleshette, John** — Actor, Director
Lynn Pleshette Literary Agency, 2700 N Beachwood Dr, Los Angeles CA 90068, USA
**Pless, Rance** — Baseball Player
5528 Asheville Highway, Greenville TN 37743, USA
**Pletcher, Eldon** — Editorial Cartoonist
210 Canberra Court, Slidell LA 70458, USA
**Pletcher, Todd A** — Thoroughbred Racing Trainer
Todd Pletcher Racing Stables, PO Box 30066, Elmont NY 11003, USA
**Pletnev, Mikhail V** — Conductor, Concert Pianist
Russian National Orchestra, Garibaldi 19, 117335 Moscow, Russia
**Plett, Willi** — Ice Hockey Player
Willi Plett Sports Park, 1248 Harris Commons Place, Roswell GA 30076, USA
**Plevneliev, Rosen A** — President, Bulgaria
President's Office, 2 Dondukov Blvd, 1123 Sofia, Bulgaria
**Plews, Herbert E (Herb)** — Baseball Player
350 Ponca Place, Boulder CO 80303, USA
**Pliego, Cesar** — Bassist (Kinky)
Marcella C Public Relations, 646 S Barrington Ave, #206, Brentwood CA 90049, USA
**Plies** — Rap Artist
Multi Entertainment, 4044 W Lake Mary Blvd, #104-324, Lake Mary FL 32746, USA
**Plimpton, Martha** — Actress
Innovative Artists, 1505 10th St, Santa Monica CA 90401 USA
**Plisetskaya, Maya M** — Ballerina
Tverskaya 25/9, #31, 103050 Moscow, Russia
**Pliska, Paul** — Opera Singer
George M Martynuk, 352 7th Ave, New York NY 10001, USA
**Plitmann, Hila** — Opera Singer
I M G Artists, Hogarth Business Park, Chiswick, London W4 2TH, England
**Plodinec, Timothy A (Tim)** — Baseball Player
23251 Gilmore St, West Hills CA 91307, USA
**Ploeger, Kurt A** — Football Player
6451 E Nance St, Mesa AZ 85215, USA
**Ploenchit, Saen Sor** — Boxer
Songchai Co, 71/23 Setsiri Rd, Sams Payathai, Bangkok 10400, Thailand
**Plotkin, Stanley A** — Virologist
3940 Delancey St, Philadelphia PA 19104, USA
**Plotnick, Jack** — Actor
Stone Manners Salners, 9911 W Pico Blvd, #1400, Los Angeles CA 90035 USA
**Plott, Charles R** — Economist
881 El Campo Dr, Pasadena CA 91107, USA
**Plowden, David** — Writer, Photographer
609 Cherry St, Winnetka IL 60093, USA
**Plowright, Joan A** — Actress
Malthouse, Horsham Road, Ashurst, Steyning, West Sussex BN44 3AR, England
**Plowright, Rosalind A** — Opera Singer
83 Saint Mark's Ave, Salisbury, Wiltshire SP1 3DW, England
**Pluhar, Erika** — Actress
Huschkgasse 5, 1190 Vienna, Austria
**Plum, Milton R (Milt)** — Football Player
1104 Oakside Court, Raleigh NC 27609, USA
**Plumb** — Singer
FlatRock Mgmt, 2021 21st Ave S, #B104, Nashville TN 37212, USA
**Plumb, C Henry** — Government Official
Dairy Farm, Maxstoke, Coleshill, Warwicks B46 2QJ, England
**Plumb, Eve** — Actress
Clear Talent Group, 325 W 38th St, #1203, New York NY 10018, USA
**Plumb, Ron** — Ice Hockey Player
975 Auden Park Dr, Kingston ON K7M 7T9, Canada
**Plumer, Patricia (PattiSue)** — Track Athlete
USA Track & Field, 4341 Starlight Dr, Indianapolis IN 46239 USA
**Plumlee, Mason A** — Basketball Player
Brooklyn Nets, 15 Metro Tech Center, #1100, Brooklyn NY 11201 USA
**Plumlee, Miles C** — Basketball Player
Phoenix Suns, 201 E Jefferson St, Phoenix AZ 85004 USA
**Plummer, Ahmed K** — Football Player
PO Box 30147, Columbus OH 43230, USA

**Plummer, Amanda** — Actress
Artist Group, 1650 Broadway, #1105, New York NY 10019 , USA
**Plummer, Bruce E** — Football Player
712 Fairmont Park Dr, Dacula GA 30019, USA
**Plummer, Christopher** — Actor, Singer
49 Wampum Hill Road, Weston CT 06883, USA
**Plummer, Gary L** — Football Player
10374 Rue Chamberry, San Diego CA 92131, USA
**Plummer, Glenn** — Actor
Innovative Artists, 1505 10th St, Santa Monica CA 90401 USA
**Plummer, Jason S (Jake)** — Football Player
282 Winterberry Way, Sandpoint ID 83864, USA
**Plummer, William F (Bill)** — Baseball Player, Manager
8504 Oak Terrace Lane, Millville CA 96062, USA
**Plunk, Eric V** — Baseball Player
9520 Pats Point Dr, Corona CA 92883, USA
**Plunkett, Arthur S (Art)** — Football Player
332 Santa Monica Dr, Henderson NV 89014, USA
**Plunkett, Gerard** — Actor
M A Mgmt, 1947 Pendrell St, #106, Vancouver BC V6G 1T5, Canada
**Plunkett, James W (Jim), Jr** — Football Player
51 Kilroy Way, Atherton CA 94027, USA
**Plunkett, Marcella** — Actress
Lisa Richards Agency, 108 Upper Leeson St, Dublin 4, Ireland
**Plunkett, Maryann** — Actress
Davis Spylios Mgmt, 244 W 54th St, #707, New York NY 10019, USA
**Plushenko, Evgeny** — Figure Skater
Flashlight Artists Agency, Via Enrico Fermi 18, 39100 Bolzano (BZ), Italy
**Ply, Robert V (Bobby)** — Football Player
8616 Ash Ave, Raytown MO 64138, USA
**Plympton, Jeffrey H (Jeff)** — Baseball Player
8 Robin St, Plainville MA 02762, USA
**Plyushch, Ivan S** — Head of State, Ukraine
Verkhovna Rada, M Hrushevskoho 5, 252019 Kiev, Ukraine
**P-Nut** — Bassist (311)
311 Hive, 8904 Florence Dr, Omaha NE 68147, USA
**Poapst, Steve** — Ice Hockey Player
502 Kelly Court, Lombard IL 60148, USA
**Pocklington, Peter H** — Ice Hockey Executive
Edmonton Oilers, 11230 110th St, Edmonton AB T5G 3H7, Canada
**Pocoroba, Biff B** — Baseball Player
3445 Broxton Mill Way, Snellville GA 30039, USA
**Pocza, Harvie** — Ice Hockey Player
135 Sun Harbour Close Road, Calgary AB T2X 3C4, Canada
**Podein, Shjon** — Ice Hockey Player
4350 Browndale Ave, Minneapolis MN 55424, USA
**Podell, Eyal** — Actor
Paul Kohner, 9300 Wilshire Blvd, #555, Beverly Hills CA 90212 USA
**Podesta, John D** — Government Official
3743 Brandywine St, Washington DC 20016, USA
**Podesta, Rossana** — Actress
Via Bartolomeo Ammanati 8, 00187 Rome, Italy
**Podeswa, Jeremy** — Director
Rebelfilms, 317 Manning Ave, Toronto ON M6J 2K8, Canada
**Podewell, Cathy** — Actress
17328 S Crest Dr, Los Angeles CA 90035, USA
**Podhoretz, Norman** — Editor, Writer
Commentary, Editor's Office, 165 E 56th St, New York NY 10022, USA
**Podlesh, Adam** — Football Player
1302 Hackberry Court, Libertyville IL 60048, USA
**Podloski, Ray** — Ice Hockey Player
13323 118th St NW, Edmonton AB T5E 5L6, Canada
**Podolak, Edward J (Ed)** — Football Player
2227 Emma Road, Basalt CO 81621, USA
**Podowski, Debbie** — Actress
Red Mgmt, Box 3, 415 W Esplanade, North Vancouver BC V7M 1A6, Canada
**Podsednik, Scott E** — Baseball Player
6613 Herbert Road, Colleyville TX 76034, USA
**Poe** — Singer, Songwriter
Nettwerk Mgmt, 1650 W 2nd Ave, Vancouver BC V6J 4R3, Canada
**Poe, Dontari** — Football Player
Kansas City Chiefs, 1 Arrowhead Dr, Kansas City KS 64129 USA
**Poe, Johnnie E** — Football Player
1102 Colas Ave, East Saint Louis IL 62207, USA
**Poehler, Amy** — Actress, Comedienne
W M E Entertainment, 9601 Wilshire Blvd, #300, Beverly Hills CA 90210 USA
**Poelvoorde, Benoit** — Actor
Voyez Mon Agent, 20 Ave Rapp, 75007 Paris, France
**Poepping, Michael H (Mike)** — Baseball Player
13791 250th Ave, Pierz MN 56364, USA
**Poesy, Clemence** — Actress
Agence Elizabeth Simpson, 62 Blvd du Montparnasse, 75015 Paris, France
**Poff, John W** — Baseball Player
2786 Mishler Road, Mio MI 48647, USA
**Poggioli, Sylvia** — Commentator
National Public Radio, 635 Massachusetts Ave NW, #1, Washington DC 20001, USA
**Pogorelich, Ivo** — Concert Pianist
Columbia Artists Mgmt Inc, 1790 Broadway, #702, New York NY 10019 USA
**Pogostkina, Alina** — Concert Violinist
Harrison/Parrott, 5-6 Albion Court, London W6 0QT, England
**Pogrebin, Letty Cottin** — Editor, Writer, Social Activist
33 W 67th St, New York NY 10023, USA
**Pogue, Donald W** — Judge
US Court of International Trade, 1 Federal Plaza, New York NY 10278, USA
**Pogue, William R** — Astronaut
1890 N Atlantic Ave, #A705, Cocoa Beach FL 32931, USA

| | |
|---|---|
| **Pohamba, Hifikepunye L** | President, Namibia |
| President's Office, State House, Mugabe Ave, Windhoek 9000, Namibia | |
| **Pohl, Don** | Golfer |
| 903 E Bellows St, Mount Pleasant MI 48858, USA | |
| **Pohl, John (Johnny)** | Ice Hockey Player |
| 2382 Clover Lane, Red Wing MN 55066, USA | |
| **Pohlman, Jenny** | Artist |
| 3824 SW Morgan St, Seattle WA 98126, USA | |
| **Poile, David R** | Ice Hockey Executive |
| Nashville Predators, 501 Broadway, Nashville TN 37203 USA | |
| **Poile, Don** | Ice Hockey Player |
| 165 Woodford Dr SW, Calgary AB T2W 4C2, Canada | |
| **Poinar, George O, Jr** | Entomologist |
| Oregon State University, Entomology Dept, Corvallis OR 97331, USA | |
| **Poindexter, Buster** | Singer |
| Agency Group Ltd, 142 W 57th St, #600, New York NY 10019 USA | |
| **Poindexter, John M** | Navy Admiral, Government Official |
| 10 Barrington Fare, Rockville MD 20850, USA | |
| **Poindexter, Larry** | Actor |
| Talent Works, 3500 W Olive Ave, #1400, Burbank CA 91505 USA | |
| **Pointer, Aaron E** | Baseball Player |
| 4902 N Scenic View Lane, Tacoma WA 98407, USA | |
| **Pointer, Anita** | Singer (Pointer Sisters) |
| 12060 Crest Court, Beverly Hills CA 90210, USA | |
| **Pointer, Bonnie** | Singer (Pointer Sisters) |
| T-Best Talent Agency, 508 Honey Lake Court, Danville CA 94506 USA | |
| **Pointer, Noel** | Jazz Violinist |
| Headline Talent, 1650 Broadway, #401, New York NY 10313 USA | |
| **Pointer, Priscilla** | Singer (Pointer Sisters) |
| 213 16th St, Santa Monica CA 90402, USA | |
| **Pointer, Ruth** | Singer (Pointer Sisters) |
| Morey Management Group, 1100 Glendon Ave, #1100, Los Angeles CA 90024 USA | |
| **Poirot, Pierre** | Actor |
| Artmedia, 20 Ave Rapp, 75007 Paris, France | |
| **Poisel, Philipp** | Singer |
| Holunder Records, Waldhornlestr 18, 72072 Tuebingen, Germany | |
| **Poison Ivy** | Bassist (Cramps), Songwriter |
| Leave Home Booking, 10 W Broadway, #608, Salt Lake City UT 84101, USA | |
| **Poitier, Sidney** | Actor |
| Creative Artists Agency, 2000 Ave of Stars, #100, Los Angeles CA 90067 USA | |
| **Poitier, Sydney Tamiia** | Actress |
| I C M Partners, 10250 Constellation Blvd, #900, Los Angeles CA 90067 USA | |
| **Polaha, Kristoffer** | Actor |
| Medavoy Mgmt, 10203 Santa Monica Blvd, #400, Los Angeles CA 90067 USA | |
| **Polamalu, Troy A** | Football Player |
| 1761 Colgate Circle, La Jolla CA 92037, USA | |
| **Polanco, Placido E** | Baseball Player |
| 8950 SW 63rd Court, Miami FL 33156, USA | |
| **Polanski, Roman** | Director, Writer |
| Chalet Milky Way, 3780 Gstaad, Switzerland | |
| **Polansky, Mark L** | Astronaut |
| 2010 Hillside Oak Lane, Houston TX 77062, USA | |
| **Polanyi, John C** | Nobel Chemistry Laureate |
| University of Toronto, Chemistry Dept, Toronto ON M5S 3H6, Canada | |
| **Polchinski, Joseph G** | Physicist |
| University of California, Physics Institute, Santa Barbara CA 93106, USA | |
| **Pole, Richard H (Dick)** | Baseball Player |
| 5124 Marsh Field Lane, Sarasota FL 34235, USA | |
| **Polee, Dwayne L** | Basketball Player |
| 1169 E 60th St, Los Angeles CA 90001, USA | |
| **Polegato, Brett** | Opera, Concert Singer |
| International Mgmt Group, Pier House, Strand on the Green, London W4 3NN, England | |
| **Polenzani, Matthew** | Opera Singer |
| I M G Artists, Hogarth Business Park, Chiswick, London W4 2TH, England | |
| **Polese, Kim** | Businesswoman |
| Marimba Inc, 440 Clyde Ave, Mountain View CA 94043, USA | |
| **Poleshchuk, Alexander F** | Cosmonaut |
| Cosmonaut Training Center, Star City, 141160 Zvezdny Gorodok, Moscow Oblast, Russia | |
| **Poletiek, Noah** | Actor |
| Don Buchwald, 6500 Wilshire Blvd, #2200, Los Angeles CA 90048 USA | |
| **Poletto, Severino Cardinal** | Religious Leader |
| Via Arcivescovado 12, 10121 Torino, Italy | |
| **Poleway, Christopher J** | Businessman |
| Fortune Group, Time & Life Building, Rockefeller Center, New York NY 10020, USA | |
| **Policarpo, Jose da Cruz Cardinal** | Religious Leader |
| Curia Parriarcal, Campo di Saint Clara, 1100 473 Lisbon, Portugal | |
| **Polich, Mike** | Ice Hockey Player |
| 825 3rd St NE, Osseo MN 55369, USA | |
| **Polinsky, Alexander** | Actor |
| C E S D, 10635 Santa Monica Blvd, #130, Los Angeles CA 90025 USA | |
| **Polish, Mark** | Actor, Producer, Writer |
| United Talent Agency, U T A Plaza, 9336 Civic Center Dr, Beverly Hills CA 90210 USA | |
| **Polish, Michael** | Director, Producer, Writer |
| Creative Artists Agency, 2000 Ave of Stars, #100, Los Angeles CA 90067 USA | |
| **Polito, Jon** | Actor |
| Domain Talent, 9229 W Sunset Blvd, #710, West Hollywood CA 90069 USA | |
| **Politte, Clifford A (Cliff)** | Baseball Player |
| 6306 Sprig Oak Court, #C, Saint Louis MO 63128, USA | |
| **Politzer, H David** | Nobel Physics Laurete |
| 1145 Linda Vista Ave, Pasadena CA 91103, USA | |
| **Polk, Carlos D** | Football Player |
| 922 Saint Germain Road, Chula Vista CA 91913, USA | |
| **Polk, DaShon L** | Football Player |
| 3503 Cornwall Court, Missouri City TX 77459, USA | |
| **Polk, Steven R** | Air Force General |
| Inspector General, HqUSAF, Pentagon, Washington DC 20330 USA | |

**Polkinghorne, John C** — Theologian, Templeton Laureate
Queen's College, Cambridge University, Cambridge CB3 9ET, England
**Poll, Jon** — Director, Producer
Gersh Agency, 9465 Wilshire Blvd, #600, Beverly Hills CA 90212 USA
**Polla, Dennis L** — Microbiotics Engineer
University of Minnesota, Electrical Engineering Dept, Minneapolis MN 55455, USA
**Pollack, Andrea** — Swimmer
S S V, Postfach 420140, 34070 Kassel, Germany
**Pollack, Daniel** — Concert Pianist
University of Southern California, Music Dept, Los Angeles CA 90089, USA
**Pollack, Frank** — Football Player
907 Hillcrest Trail, Southlake TX 76092, USA
**Pollack, Jeffrey N** — Poker Executive
Federated Sports & Gaming, Palms Casino & Resort, 4301 W Flamingo Road, Las Vegas NV 89103, USA
**Pollack, Kevin** — Actor
Don Buchwald, 6500 Wilshire Blvd, #2200, Los Angeles CA 90048 USA
**Pollak, Avshalom** — Dancer, Choreographer
Inbal Pinto Dance Co, 5 Yechley St, Neve Tzedek, Tel-Aviv 65149, Israel
**Pollak, Cheryl A** — Actress
PO Box 761460, Los Angeles CA 90076, USA
**Pollak, Kevin** — Actor, Comedian
Red Bird Cinema, 11601 Wilshire Blvd, #2200, Los Angeles CA 90025, USA
**Pollak, Lisa** — Journalist
Baltimore Sun, Editorial Dept, 501 N Calvert St, Baltimore MD 21278, USA
**Pollak, Michael D (Mike)** — Football Player
Carolina Panthers, Ericsson Stadium, 800 S Mint St, Charlotte NC 28202 USA
**Pollan, Tracy** — Actress
Gersh Agency, 9465 Wilshire Blvd, #600, Beverly Hills CA 90212 USA
**Pollard, Bernard K** — Football Player
5605 Fairhaven Ave, Woodland Hills CA 91367, USA
**Pollard, Frank D, Jr** — Football Player
113 L C R 474, Mexia TX 76667, USA
**Pollard, Marcus L** — Football Player
673 Meadow Lakes Dr, Pine Mountain GA 31822, USA
**Pollard, Michael J** — Actor
520 S Burnside Ave, #12A, Los Angeles CA 90036, USA
**Pollard, Robert** — Singer, Musician, Songwriter
Manage This, PO Box 256, Old Chelsea Station, New York NY 10113, USA
**Pollard, Robert L (Bob)** — Football Player
8987 Washington Blvd, Beaumont TX 77707, USA
**Pollard, Scot** — Basketball Player
10389 Windemere, Carmel IN 46032, USA
**Pollari, Joey** — Actor
United Talent Agency, U T A Plaza, 9336 Civic Center Dr, Beverly Hills CA 90210 USA
**Pollen, Arabella R H** — Fashion Designer
Canham Mews, #8, Canham Road, London W3 7SR, England
**Polley, Sarah** — Actress, Director
10 Mary St, #308, Toronto ON M4Y 1P9, Canada
**Pollini, Armando** — Fashion Designer
Via Gambolina 51/6, 27029 Vigevano (PV), Italy
**Pollini, Maurizio** — Concert Pianist
R E S I A, Via Manzoni 31, 20120 Milan, Italy
**Pollock, Alex J** — Government Official, Financier
Federal Home Loan Bank, 111 E Wacker Dr, #800, Chicago IL 60601, USA
**Pollock, David M** — Football Player
Cincinnati Bengals, 1 Paul Brown Stadium, Cincinnati OH 45202 USA
**Pollock, Griselda** — Artist
Leeds University, Fine Arts Dept, Leeds LS2 9JT, England
**Pollock, J C** — Writer
I C M Partners, 10250 Constellation Blvd, #900, Los Angeles CA 90067 USA
**Polo, Ana Maria** — Commentator
Telemundo Network Group, 2470 W 8th Ave, Hialeah FL 33010 USA
**Polo, Joseph (Joe)** — Curling Athlete
Curling Assn, 5525 Clem's Way, Stevens Point WI 54482 USA
**Polo, Teri** — Actress, Model
Gersh Agency, 9465 Wilshire Blvd, #600, Beverly Hills CA 90212 USA
**Polone, Gavin** — Actor, Producer
Pariah, 9229 W Sunset Blvd, #208, West Hollywood CA 90069, USA
**Poloni, John P** — Baseball Player
1714 Polo Club Dr, Tarpon Springs FL 34689, USA
**Polonich, Dennis** — Ice Hockey Player
70 Varsity Estates Close NW, Calgary AB T3B 5J1, Canada
**Poloujadoff, Michel E** — Electrical Engineer
8 Rue Roches, 77760 Buthiers, France
**Polshak, James Stewart** — Architect
Polshak Partnership, 320 W 134th St, #800, New York NY 10030, USA
**Polson, John** — Actor, Director, Producer
Creative Artists Agency, 2000 Ave of Stars, #100, Los Angeles CA 90067 USA
**Polson, Ralph M** — Basketball Player
3846 S Eagle Lane, Spokane WA 99206, USA
**Polyakov, Valeri V** — Cosmonaut
Health Ministry, Choroshevskoye Chaussee 76A, 123007 Moscow, Russia
**Polynice, Olden** — Basketball Player
PO Box 220339, Newhall CA 91322, USA
**Pomakov, Robert** — Opera Singer
I M G Artists, Hogarth Business Park, Chiswick, London W4 2TH, England
**Pomeroy, Earl R** — Representative, ND
Alston & Bird LLP, 950 F St NW, Washington DC 20004, USA
**Pomers, Scarlett** — Actress, Singer
D M G Talent, 4804 Laurel Canyon Blvd, Valley Village CA 91607, USA
**Pominville, Jason** — Ice Hockey Player
9123 Curry Lane, Clarence Center NY 14032, USA
**Pommier, Jean-Bernard** — Concert Pianist, Conductor
Musike Academies, 12 Rte Praz Gilliard, 1000 Lausanne, Switzerland
**Pomodora, Arnaldo** — Sculptor
Via Vigevano 5, 20144 Milan, Italy

# P

**Pompeo, Ellen** — Actress
John Carrabino Mgmt, 5900 Wilshire Blvd, #406, Los Angeles CA 90036 USA
**Pomplun, Raquel** — Model
PO Box 9235, Glendale CA 91226, USA
**Ponazecki, Joe** — Actor
Don Buchwald, 10 E 44th St, New York NY 10017 USA
**Ponce Enrile, Juan** — Government Official, Philippines
2305 Morado St, Dasmarinas Village, Makati, Metro Manila, Philippines
**Ponce, Carlos** — Singer, Actor
Luber Rocklin Entertainment, 8530 Wilshire Blvd, #555, Beverly Hills CA 90211 USA
**Ponce, Miguel A** — Soccer Player
Federacion de Futbol, Colima 373 Colonia Roma, Delegacion Cuauhtemoc, Mexico City DF 06700, Mexico
**Ponce, Walter** — Concert Pianist
University of California, Music Dept, Los Angeles CA 90024, USA
**Poncia, Vincent (Vinnie), Jr** — Singer, Songwriter
Joel Faden, 250 W 57th St, New York NY 10107, USA
**Ponder, David E (Dave)** — Football Player
1818 Sandalwood Lane, Grapevine TX 76051, USA
**Ponder, Moana** — Sculptor
Art Inc, 9401 San Pedro, San Antonio TX 78216, USA
**Pondexter, Cappie** — Basketball Player
New York Liberty, Madison Square Garden, 2 Penn Plaza, New York NY 10121 USA
**Pondexter, Clifton (Cliff)** — Basketball Player
1135 W Stuart Ave, Fresno CA 93711, USA
**Ponomarenko, Sergei V** — Ice Dancer
Sharks Ice, 1500 S 10th St, San Jose CA 95112, USA
**Pons, B Stanley** — Chemist
University of Utah, Chemistry Dept, Eyring Building, Salt Lake City UT 84112, USA
**Pons, Juan** — Opera Singer
Herbert Breslin, 119 W 57th St, #1505, New York NY 10019 USA
**Ponson, Sidney A** — Baseball Player
2541 NE 35th Dr, Fort Lauderdale FL 33308, USA
**Ponta, Victor-Viorel (Vic)** — Prime Minister, Romania
Prime Minister's Office, Piata Vicotriei 1, 71201 Bucharest, Romania
**Pontbriand, Ryan D** — Football Player
3044 Forest Lake Dr, Westlake OH 44145, USA
**Pontes, Marcos C** — Astronaut, Brazil
Cosmonaut Training Center, Star City, 141160 Zvezdny Gorodok, Moscow Oblast, Russia
**Ponti, Michael** — Concert Pianist
Heubergstr 32, 83565 Eschenlohe, Germany
**Pontius, Chris** — Actor
Untitled Entertainment, 350 S Beverly Dr, #200, Beverly Hills CA 90212 USA
**Pontois, Noella-Chantal** — Ballerina
25 Rue de Maubeuge, 75009 Paris, France
**Ponty, Jean-Luc** — Jazz Violinist, Composer
10340 Santa Monica Blvd, Los Angeles CA 90025, USA
**Pook, Christopher R (Chris)** — Auto Racing Executive
Championship Auto Racing, 5350 Lakeview Parkway S Dr, Indianapolis IN 46268 USA
**Pook, Jocelyn** — Composer
Kraft-Engel Mgmt, 15233 Ventura Blvd, #200, Sherman Oaks CA 91403 USA
**Pool, David A** — Football Player
8120 Walcot Lane, #D, Cincinnati OH 45249, USA
**Pool, James L** — Pharmacologist
Baylor Medical Center, 1200 Moursand Ave, Houston TX 77030 USA
**Pool, John L** — Cancer Surgeon
1011 Charles St, #C, Fredericksbrg VA 22401, USA
**Pool, Kenneth R (Bud)** — WW II Army Air Corps Hero
6840 Kilimanjaro Dr, Evergreen CO 80439, USA
**Poole, Brian** — Singer (Tremeloes)
Jason West Agency, Gables House, Saddlebow, Kings Lynn PE34 3AR, England
**Poole, David J** — Artist
Royal Portrait Painters Society, 17 Carlton House Terrace, London SW1Y 5BD, England
**Poole, James R (Jim)** — Baseball Player
605 Falls Lake Dr, Alpharetta GA 30022, USA
**Poole, Keith R S** — Football Player
4100 S Arizona Ave, #4, Chandler AZ 85248, USA
**Poole, Nathan L** — Football Player
8686 Longwood St, San Diego CA 92126, USA
**Poole, Tyrone** — Football Player
3415 Rivers Call Blvd, Atlanta GA 30339, USA
**Poole, William** — Government Official, Economist
Federal Reserve Bank, PO Box 442, Saint Louis MO 63166, USA
**Pooler, Rosemary S** — Judge
US Court of Appeals, Lee Courthouse, 100 S Clinton St, Syracuse NY 13202, USA
**Pooley, Don** — Golfer
5251 N Camino Sumo, Tucson AZ 85718, USA
**Pooley, Emma** — Cyclist
Bigla Cycling Team, Bahnhofstr 4, 3507 Biglen, Switzerland
**Poons, Larry** — Artist
Salander O'Reilly Galleries, 20 E 79th St, New York NY 10075, USA
**Poots, Imogen** — Actress
Independent Talent Group, 40 Whitfield St, London W1T 2RH, England
**Pop, Iggy** — Singer, Songwriter, Actor
Susan Blond Inc, 50 W 57th St, #1400, New York NY 10019 USA
**Popa Chubby** — Singer, Guitarist
Concerted Efforts, PO Box 440326, Somerville MA 02144 USA
**Popcorn, Faith** — Businesswoman
Brain Reserve, 1 Dag Hammarskjold Plaza, #1600, New York NY 10017, USA
**Pope, Carly** — Actress
Kritzer Levine Wilkins Griffin, 11872 La Grange Ave, #100, Los Angeles CA 90025 USA
**Pope, Charles (Charlies)** — Singer (Tams)
Richard De La Font Agency, 4845 S Sheridan Road, #505, Tulsa OK 74145 USA
**Pope, Clarence C, Jr** — Religious Leader
Fort Worth Episcopal Church Diocese, 6300 Ridlea Place, Fort Worth TX 76116, USA
**Pope, Dick** — Cinematographer
Independent Talent Group, 40 Whitfield St, London W1T 2RH, England

*Pompeo - Pope*

| | |
|---|---|
| **Pope, Edwin**<br>Miami Herald, Editorial Dept, 1 Herald Plaza, Miami FL 33132 USA | Sportswriter |
| **Pope, Manley**<br>Albewanin, 156 5th Ave, #904, New York NY 10010 10010, USA | Actor |
| **Pope, Marquez P**<br>PO Box 470487, San Francisco CA 94147, USA | Football Player |
| **Pope, Odeon**<br>MarsJazz Booking, 1006 Ashby Place, Charlottesville VA 22901, USA | Jazz Saxophonist, Orchestra Leader |
| **Pope, Tim**<br>I C M Partners, 10250 Constellation Blvd, #900, Los Angeles CA 90067 USA | Director |
| **Popein, Larry**<br>80-650 Harrington Road, Kamloops BC V2B 6T7, Canada | Ice Hockey Player |
| **Popiel, Jan V**<br>2501 Peppermill Ridge Dr, Chesterfield MO 63005, USA | Ice Hockey Player |
| **Popiel, Poul P**<br>2501 Peppermill Ridge Dr, Chesterfield MO 63005, USA | Ice Hockey Player |
| **Popoff, A Jay**<br>Sepeyts Entertainment, 5543 Edmondson Pike, #8A, Nashville TN 37211, USA | Singer (Lit) |
| **Popoff, Frank P**<br>Indiana University, Kelly Business School, 1309 East St, Bloomington IN 47405, USA | Businessman |
| **Popoff, Jeremy A**<br>Sepetys Entertainment, 5543 Edmondson Pike, #8A, Nashville TN 37211, USA | Guitarist (Lit) |
| **Popov, Aleksandr**<br>International Olympic Committee, Chateau de Vidy, 1007 Lausanne, Switzerland | Swimmer |
| **Popov, Dmytro**<br>I M G Artists, Hogarth Business Park, Chiswick, London W4 2TH, England | Opera Singer |
| **Popov, Leonid I**<br>Cosmonaut Training Center, Star City, 141160 Zvezdny Gorodok, Moscow Oblast, Russia | Cosmonaut |
| **Popovac, Gwynn**<br>17270 Robin Ridge, Sonora CA 95370, USA | Artist, Sculptor |
| **Popovic, Bojana Petrovic**<br>Z R K Buducnost T-Mobile, Ivan Milutinovic B B, 81000 Podgorica, Montenegro | Handball Player |
| **Popovic, Mark**<br>30 New Mountain Road, Stoney Creek ON L8G 2R7, Canada | Ice Hockey Player |
| **Popovich, Gregg**<br>41 Vineyard Dr, San Antonio TX 78257, USA | Basketball Executive, Coach |
| **Popovich, Gregory**<br>Planet Hollywood Theater Resort, 3667 Las Vegas Blvd S, Las Vegas NV 89109, USA | Animal Trainer, Comedian |
| **Popovich, Paul E**<br>2604 Woodlawn Road, Northbrook IL 60062, USA | Baseball Player |
| **Poppen, Christoph**<br>Deutsche Radio Philharmonie, Saint Johanner Markt 27, 66111 Saarbrücken, Germany | Conductor |
| **Popper, John**<br>Hard Head Productions, PO Box 651, New York NY 10014, USA | Singer, Musician (Blues Traveler) |
| **Popplewell, Anna**<br>I C M Partners, 10250 Constellation Blvd, #900, Los Angeles CA 90067 USA | Actress |
| **Popson, David G (Dave)**<br>82 Fall St, Ashley PA 18706, USA | Basketball Player |
| **Poquette, Benedict J (Ben)**<br>17917 N Shore Estates Road, Spring Lake MI 49456, USA | Basketball Player |
| **Poquette, Thomas A (Tom)**<br>3411 Ridgeway Dr, Eau Claire WI 54701, USA | Baseball Player |
| **Poranski, Jason**<br>Ba Da Bing Records, 181 Clermont Ave, #403, Brooklyn NY 11205, USA | Guitarist, Mandolin Player (Beirut) |
| **Porcaro, Steven M (Steve)**<br>13596 Contour Dr, Sherman Oaks CA 91423, USA | Composer, Keyboardist (Toto) |
| **Porcellino, John**<br>PO Box 881, Elgin IL 60121, USA | Cartoonist (King-Cat) |
| **Porcello, Frederick A (Rick), III**<br>PO Box 27, Oldwick NJ 08858, USA | Baseball Player |
| **Porch, Colleen**<br>Amsel Eisenstadt Frazier, 5055 Wilshire Blvd, #865, Los Angeles CA 90036 USA | Actress |
| **Porch, Michelle**<br>Vincent Cirrincione Assoc, 1516 N Fairfax Ave, Los Angeles CA 90046 USA | Actress |
| **Porcher, Robert**<br>PO Box 691464, Orlando FL 32869, USA | Football Player |
| **Porfilio, John C**<br>US Court of Appeals, 1919 Stout St, Denver CO 80294, USA | Judge |
| **Porizkova, Paulina**<br>One Entertainment, 347 5th Ave, #1404, New York NY 10016 USA | Model, Actress |
| **Porretta, Matthew**<br>A K A Talent, 6310 San Vicente Blvd, #200, Los Angeles CA 90048 USA | Actor |
| **Port, Christopher C (Chris)**<br>432 Walnut St, New Orleans LA 70118, USA | Football Player |
| **Port, Whitney**<br>Creative Artists Agency, 2000 Ave of Stars, #100, Los Angeles CA 90067 USA | Producer, Actress |
| **Portenoy, Russell K**<br>Beth Israel Medical Center, Pain Medicine Dept, 1st Ave & 16th St, New York NY 10003, USA | Neurologist |
| **Porter, Andrew (Andy)**<br>2502 W 117th St, Hawthorne CA 90250, USA | Baseball Player |
| **Porter, Billy**<br>Industry Entertainment, 955 Carillo Dr, #300, Los Angeles CA 90048 USA | Singer, Actor |
| **Porter, Charles W (Chuck)**<br>9321 Snyder Lane, Perry Hall MD 21128, USA | Baseball Player |
| **Porter, Daniel E (Dan)**<br>7360 Cowles Mountain Road, San Diego CA 92119, USA | Baseball Player |
| **Porter, Daryl M**<br>9053 W Sunrise Blvd, Plantation FL 33322, USA | Football Player |
| **Porter, David H**<br>Skidmore College, President's Office, Saratoga Springs NY 12866, USA | Educator |
| **Porter, Gary**<br>Milwaukee Journal Sentinel, Editorial Dept, PO Box 371, Milwaukee WI 53201 USA | Journalist |
| **Porter, Gayle**<br>Gaston-Porter Health Improvement Center, 8612 Timber Hill, Potomac MD 20854, USA | Psychologist, Social Activist |
| **Porter, Greg**<br>God's Katrina Kitchen, 554 Camp Ave, Gulfport MS 39501, USA | Social Activist |

**P**

**Pope - Porter**

V.I.P. Address Book

**Porter, J W (Jay)** — Baseball Player
9677 Heather Circle W, Palm Beach Gardens FL 33410, USA
**Porter, James W (Jim), II** — Association Executive
National Rifle Association, 11250 Waples Mill Road, Fairfax VA 22030, USA
**Porter, Jody** — Singer (Fountains of Wayne), Guitarist
Big Hassle, 157 Chambers St, #1200, New York NY 10007, USA
**Porter, John E** — Representative, IL
Hogan & Hartson, 555 13th Ave NW, #800E, Washington DC 20004, USA
**Porter, Joseph E (Joey)** — Football Player
9523 Laramie Ave, Bakersfield CA 93314, USA
**Porter, Kalan** — Singer, Songwriter
Agency Group Ltd, 142 W 57th St, #600, New York NY 10019 USA
**Porter, Kevin J** — Football Player
260 Mulberry Dr, Senoia GA 30276, USA
**Porter, Lee** — Golfer
1604 Birch Lane, Greensboro NC 27408, USA
**Porter, Lorena** — Singer (Klymaxx)
R D M J Entertainment Mgmt, 3619 Rose Ave, Long Beach CA 90807 USA
**Porter, Marquis D (Bo)** — Baseball Player
1226 N Teal Estates Circle, Fresno TX 77545, USA
**Porter, Otto, Jr** — Basketball Player
Washington Wizards, M C I Centre, 601 F St NW, Washington DC 20004 USA
**Porter, R Kalan** — Singer
B M G Canada, 190 Liberty St, #100, Toronto ON M6K 3L5, Canada
**Porter, Randy** — Auto Racing Driver
Laughlin Racing, 113 Pride Dr, Simpsonville SC 29681, USA
**Porter, Richard A (Ricky)** — Football Player
24 Wyegate Court, Owings Mills MD 21117, USA
**Porter, Robert L (Bob)** — Baseball Player
771 Pueblo Ave, Napa CA 94558, USA
**Porter, Ronald D (Ron)** — Football Player
3960 NW 99th Ave, Coral Springs FL 33065, USA
**Porter, Rufus** — Football Player
20403 Amberlight Lane, Katy TX 77450, USA
**Porter, Scott** — Actor
Brillstein Entertainment Partners, 9150 Wilshire Blvd, #350, Beverly Hills CA 90212 USA
**Porterfield, Ellary** — Actress
Gersh Agency, 9465 Wilshire Blvd, #600, Beverly Hills CA 90212 USA
**Porter-King, Mary Bea** — Golfer
6412 Kalama Road, Kapaa HI 96746, USA
**Portes, Alejandro** — Sociologist
Princeton University, Sociology Dept, Princeton NJ 08544, USA
**Portes, Andrea** — Writer
I C M Partners, 10250 Constellation Blvd, #900, Los Angeles CA 90067 USA
**Portes, Richard D** — Economist
London Business School, Regent's Park, London NW1 4SA, England
**Portillo, Michael D X** — Government Official, England
House of Commons, Westminster, London SW1A 0AA, England
**Portis, Charles** — Writer
7417 Kingwood Road, Little Rock AR 72207, USA
**Portis, Clinton E** — Football Player
3510 NE 156th Ave, Gainesville FL 32609, USA
**Portisch, Lajos** — Chess Player
Chess Federation, Nephadsereg Utca 10, 1055 Budapest, Hungary
**Portman, John C, Jr** — Architect
303 Peachtree Center Ave NE, #575, Atlanta GA 30303, USA
**Portman, Natalie** — Actress
Brillstein Entertainment Partners, 9150 Wilshire Blvd, #350, Beverly Hills CA 90212 USA
**Portman, Rachel** — Composer
Independent Talent Group, 40 Whitfield St, London W1T 2RH, England
**Portman, Robert M (Bob)** — Basketball Player
1412 Winter Sweet Place, Hillsborough NC 27278, USA
**Portnow, Richard** — Actor
Don Buchwald, 6500 Wilshire Blvd, #2200, Los Angeles CA 90048 USA
**Portnoy, Darin** — Association Executive, Physician
Doctors Without Borders, PO Box 5030, Hagerstown MD 21741, USA
**Porto, James** — Photographer
601 W 26th St, #1321, New York NY 10001, USA
**Portugal, Mark S** — Baseball Player
65 Serpentine Road, Warren RI 02885, USA
**Portwich, Ramona** — Canoeing Athlete
K C Limmer, Stockhardtweg 3, 30453 Hanover, Germany
**Porvari, Jukka** — Ice Hockey Player
Pohjola Vahinkovakuutus Oy Ostoreskonta E1, Pohjola 00013, Finland
**Poryes, Michael** — Producer
Paradigm Agency, 360 N Crescent Dr, North Building, Beverly Hills CA 90210 USA
**Porzio, L Michael (Mike)** — Baseball Player
PO Box 2242, Westport CT 06880, USA
**Posa, Victor** — Ice Hockey Player
162 Bonny Meadows Dr, Aurora ON L4G 6N1, Canada
**Posada Villeta, Jorge R** — Baseball Player
300 E 77th St, #11B, New York NY 10075, USA
**Posada, Leopold J (Leo)** — Baseball Player
8200 Grand Canal Dr, Miami FL 33144, USA
**Posavad, Mike** — Ice Hockey Player
Compass Flooring, 6390 Kestral Road, Mississauga ON L5T 1Z3, Canada
**Pose, Scott V** — Baseball Player
1216 Kintail Dr, Raleigh NC 27613, USA
**Posehn, Brian** — Actor, Comedian, Writer, Producer
Gersh Agency, 9465 Wilshire Blvd, #600, Beverly Hills CA 90212 USA
**Posen, Zac** — Fashion Designer
United Talent Agency, U T A Plaza, 9336 Civic Center Dr, Beverly Hills CA 90210 USA
**Poses, Frederic M** — Businessman
AlliedSignal Inc, PO Box 4000, Morristown NJ 07962, USA
**Posey, Gerald D (Buster), III** — Baseball Player
San Francisco Giants, AT&T Park, 24 Willie Mays Plaza, San Francisco CA 94107 USA

| | |
|---|---|
| **Posey, James M M** | Basketball Player |
| 3471 Main Highway, #515, Miami FL 33133, USA | |
| **Posey, Parker** | Actress |
| Untitled Entertainment, 350 S Beverly Dr, #200, Beverly Hills CA 90212 USA | |
| **Posin, Arie** | Director, Producer, Writer |
| W M E Entertainment, 9601 Wilshire Blvd, #300, Beverly Hills CA 90210 USA | |
| **Posluszny, Paul M** | Football Player |
| 12023 Wynnfield Lakes Circle, Jacksonville FL 32246, USA | |
| **Posner, David M** | Religious Leader, Rabbi |
| Temple Emanuel, 1 E 65th St, New York NY 10065, USA | |
| **Posner, Michael R H (Mike)** | Singer, Songwriter |
| Elitaste, 2029 Century Park E, #500, Los Angeles CA 90067, USA | |
| **Posner, Richard A** | Judge |
| US Court of Appeals, 219 S Dearborn St, #2302B, Chicago IL 60604, USA | |
| **Posokhin, Mikhail M** | Architect |
| Mosproyekt-2, 2 Brestskaya Str 5, 123056 Moscow, Russia | |
| **Post, Avery D** | Religious Leader |
| 80 Lyme Road, #246, Hanover NH 03755, USA | |
| **Post, Glen F, III** | Businessman |
| CenturyLink, 100 Century Tel Dr, Monroe LA 71203, USA | |
| **Post, Louise L** | Singer, Guitarist |
| S T C Entertainment, 5627 Sepulveda Blvd, #230, Van Nuys CA 91411, USA | |
| **Post, Markie** | Actress |
| Glick Agency, 1260 6th St, #100, Santa Monica CA 90401, USA | |
| **Post, Mike** | Composer |
| Mike Post Productions, 1007 W Olive Ave, Burbank CA 91506, USA | |
| **Post, Richard M (Dickie)** | Football Player |
| 1229 Seminole St, Los Alamos NM 87544, USA | |
| **Post, Ron** | Association Executive |
| Medical Teams International, 14150 SW Milton Court, Portland OR 97224, USA | |
| **Post, Sandra** | Golfer |
| Sandra Post Golf School, 15731 Regional Road 50, Cakedin ON L7E 3H9, Canada | |
| **Postell, Lavor** | Basketball Player |
| 2201 Lady Marion Lane, Albany GA 31707, USA | |
| **Postema, Pam** | Baseball Umpire |
| 8983 Norma Place, West Hollywood CA 90069, USA | |
| **Poster, Steven B (Steve)** | Cinematographer |
| W M E Entertainment, 9601 Wilshire Blvd, #300, Beverly Hills CA 90210 USA | |
| **Postlewait, Kathy** | Golfer |
| 111 Saint Johns Landing Dr, Winter Springs FL 32708, USA | |
| **Postman, Marc** | Astronomer |
| 3303 Lightfoot Dr, Pikesville MD 21208, USA | |
| **Poteat, Henry M (Hank), II** | Football Player |
| 19 Welsford Way, Mount Holly NJ 08060, USA | |
| **Potente, Franka** | Actress |
| Gersh Agency, 9465 Wilshire Blvd, #600, Beverly Hills CA 90212 USA | |
| **Pothier, Brian** | Ice Hockey Player |
| 1537 Morton Ave, New Bedford MA 02745, USA | |
| **Poti, Thomas E (Tom)** | Ice Hockey Player |
| 2 Honey Locust Lane, Sandwich MA 02563, USA | |
| **Potrykus, Ingo** | Plant Scientist |
| Eidgenossische Tech Hochshule, Plant Science Dept, 8093 Zurich, Switzerland | |
| **Potter, Carol** | Actress |
| Pakula/King, 9229 W Sunset Blvd, #315, West Hollywood CA 90069 USA | |
| **Potter, Chris** | Jazz Saxophonist |
| Vision Arts Mgmt, 16 Clint Fingers Road, Saugerties NY 12477, USA | |
| **Potter, Christopher J (Chris)** | Actor |
| 565 Orwell St, Missigauga ON L5A 2W4, Canada | |
| **Potter, Cynthia (Cindy)** | Diver, Sportscaster |
| 2628 Winding Lane NE, Atlanta GA 30319, USA | |
| **Potter, Dan M** | Religious Leader |
| 21 Forest Dr, Albany NY 12205, USA | |
| **Potter, Grace** | Singer (Nocturnals) |
| Measurement Arts, 214 Sullivan St, #400, New York NY 10012, USA | |
| **Potter, Huntington** | Molecular Biologist |
| Florida Alzheimer's Disease Research Center, 12901 Bruce Downs Blvd, Tampa, FL 33612, USA | |
| **Potter, John** | Government Official |
| US Postal Service, 475 L'Enfant Plaza SW, #3138, Washington DC 20260, USA | |
| **Potter, Madeleine** | Actress |
| Ken McReddie Assoc, 101 Finsbury Pavement, London EC2A 1RS, England | |
| **Potter, Martin** | Surfer |
| Gotcha International, 32 Journey, #250, Aliso Viejo CA 92656, USA | |
| **Potter, Michael G (Mike)** | Baseball Player |
| 21582 Archer Circle, Huntington Beach CA 92646, USA | |
| **Potter, Monica** | Actress |
| Schiff Co, 9200 Sunset Blvd, #430, West Hollywood CA 90232 USA | |
| **Potter, Philip A** | Religious Leader |
| Bishop Barbel Wartenberg-Potter, Plessenstr 5A, 24837 Schleswig, Germany | |
| **Potter, Richard** | Saxophonist (Eve Unbound) |
| United Talent Agency, U T A Plaza, 9336 Civic Center Dr, Beverly Hills CA 90210 USA | |
| **Potter, Ryan** | Actor |
| C E S D, 10635 Santa Monica Blvd, #130, Los Angeles CA 90025 USA | |
| **Potter, Sally** | Actress, Director, Writer |
| Creative Artists Agency, 2000 Ave of Stars, #100, Los Angeles CA 90067 USA | |
| **Potter, Ted, Jr** | Golfer |
| Professional Golfer's Assn, PO Box 109601, Palm Beach Gardens FL 33410 USA | |
| **Pottios, Myron J (Mike)** | Football Player |
| 4234 Hilaria Way, Newport Beach CA 92663, USA | |
| **Potts, Annie** | Actress |
| Innovative Artists, 1505 10th St, Santa Monica CA 90401 USA | |
| **Potts, Cliff** | Actor |
| PO Box 131, Topanga CA 90290, USA | |
| **Potts, Michael L (Mike)** | Baseball Player |
| 604 18th St, Butner NC 27509, USA | |
| **Potts, Paul R** | Opera Singer |
| Modest Mgmt, Matrix Complex, 91A Peterborough Road, London SW6 3BU, England | |

| | |
|---|---|
| **Potts, Roosevelt B** | Football Player |
| 113 Mounger Road, Rayville LA 71269, USA | |
| **Potvin, Denis** | Ice Hockey Player |
| 6820 NW 101st Terrace, Parkland FL 33076, USA | |
| **Potvin, Felix** | Ice Hockey Player |
| Les Cantonniers de Magog, 100 Saint-Alphones, Magoh QC J1X 3Y5, Canada | |
| **Potvin, Jean R** | Ice Hockey Player |
| 24 Longwood Dr, Huntington Station NY 11746, USA | |
| **Potzsch, Oliver** | Writer |
| Ullstein, Friedrichstr 126, 10117 Berlin, Germany | |
| **Poul, Alan** | Producer, Actor |
| Boku Films, 14545 Victory Blvd, Van Nuys CA 91411, USA | |
| **Poulin, Dave** | Ice Hockey Player, Coach |
| 46 E Cedar St, #1, Chicago IL 60611, USA | |
| **Poulin, Patrick** | Ice Hockey Player |
| Burger King, 415 25E Ave, Saint-Eustache QC J7P 4Y1, Canada | |
| **Poullain, Frankie** | Bassist (Darkness) |
| Whitehouse Mgmt, PO Box 43829, London NW6 3PJ, England | |
| **Poulos, Leah** | Speed Skater |
| 11455 B Mulberry Dr, Mequon WI 53092, USA | |
| **Poulsen, Ken S** | Baseball Player |
| PO Box 1699, Oakhurst CA 93644, USA | |
| **Pound, Richard W D** | Olympics Executive |
| 87 Arlington Ave, Westmount QC H3Y 2W5, Canada | |
| **Pounder, C C H** | Actress |
| Mitchell K Stubbs Assoc, 8695 W Washington Blvd, #204, Culver City CA 90232 USA | |
| **Pounder-O'Toole, Cheryl** | Ice Hockey Player |
| Team Canada, 2424 University Dr NW, Calgary AB T2N 3Y9, Canada | |
| **Pounds, Darryl L** | Football Player |
| 4613 Lambert Place, Alexandria VA 22311, USA | |
| **Poundstone, Paula** | Actress, Comedienne |
| W M E Entertainment, 9601 Wilshire Blvd, #300, Beverly Hills CA 90210 USA | |
| **Poupard, Paul Cardinal** | Religious Leader |
| Piazza San Calisto 16, 00120 Vatican City | |
| **Poupaud, Pierre** | Actor |
| Artmedia, 20 Ave Rapp, 75007 Paris, France | |
| **Pournelle, Jerry E** | Writer |
| 12051 Laurel Terrace, Studio City CA 91604, USA | |
| **Pousette, Lena** | Actress |
| Atkins Assoc, 8040 Ventura Canyon Ave, Panorama City CA 91402 USA | |
| **Poussaint, Alvin F** | Psychiatrist |
| Judge Baker Guidance Center, 53 Parker Hill Ave, Roxbury Crossing MA 02120, USA | |
| **Poust, Tracy** | Producer, Writer |
| W M E Entertainment, 9601 Wilshire Blvd, #300, Beverly Hills CA 90210 USA | |
| **Povenmire, Daniel K (Dan)** | Producer, Animator |
| Disney Channel, Phineas & Ferb Show, 500 S Buena Vista St, Burbank, CA 91521, USA | |
| **Povetkin, Aleksandr V** | Boxer |
| Sauerland Event, Hanns-Braun-Str, 14053 Berlin, Germany | |
| **Povich, Maury R** | Commentator, Entertainer |
| Creative Artists Agency, 2000 Ave of Stars, #100, Los Angeles CA 90067 USA | |
| **Povinelli, Mark** | Actor |
| Kazarian/Measures/Ruskin, 11969 Ventura Blvd, #300, Studio City CA 91604 USA | |
| **Powe, Leon, Jr** | Basketball Player |
| 45 Kings Way, Waltham MA 02451, USA | |
| **Powell, A J Philip** | Architect |
| 16 Little Boltons, London SW10 9LP, England | |
| **Powell, Alonzo S** | Baseball Player |
| 220 N Patterson Blvd, Dayton OH 45402, USA | |
| **Powell, Arthur L (Art)** | Football Player |
| 1304 City Lights Dr, Aliso Viejo CA 92656, USA | |
| **Powell, Brittney** | Actress, Model |
| Amsel Eisenstadt Frazier, 5055 Wilshire Blvd, #865, Los Angeles CA 90036 USA | |
| **Powell, Cecil** | Test Pilot |
| 220 Villa Verde Dr SE, Rio Rancho NM 87124, USA | |
| **Powell, Charles E (Charley)** | Football Player |
| 4119 Aralia Road, Altadena CA 91001, USA | |
| **Powell, Cincinnatus (Cincy)** | Basketball Player |
| 2541 Brookside Dr, Irving TX 75063, USA | |
| **Powell, Clifton** | Actor |
| Opus Entertainment, 5225 Wilshire Blvd, #905, Los Angeles CA 90036, USA | |
| **Powell, Colin L** | Army General, Secretary of State |
| 1317 Ballantrae Farm Dr, McLean VA 22101, USA | |
| **Powell, D Dwane, Jr** | Editorial Cartoonist |
| Raleigh News Observer, Editorial Dept, 215 S McDowell, Raleigh NC 27601, USA | |
| **Powell, Dennis C** | Baseball Player |
| 1743 Eastgate Ave, Upland CA 91784, USA | |
| **Powell, Donald D** | Interior Designer |
| Powell Kleinschmidt, PO Box 1130, Libertyville IL 60048, USA | |
| **Powell, Earl A (Rusty), III** | Museum Executive |
| National Gallery of Art, Constitution Ave & 4th St NW, Washington DC 20565, USA | |
| **Powell, Eric** | Cartoonist (Goon) |
| 2401 Cairo Bend Road, Lebanon TN 37087, USA | |
| **Powell, Esteban** | Actor, Producer |
| C E S D, 10635 Santa Monica Blvd, #130, Los Angeles CA 90025 USA | |
| **Powell, Glen** | Actor |
| Resolution, 1801 Century Park East, #2300, Los Angeles CA 90067 USA | |
| **Powell, Hosken** | Baseball Player |
| 1289 Tamara St, Pensacola FL 32504, USA | |
| **Powell, J Mac** | Singer, Guitarist (Third Day) |
| Creative Trust, 5141 Virginia Way, #320, Brentwood TN 37027, USA | |
| **Powell, James R** | Inventor (Magnetic Levitation Train) |
| Plus Ultra Technologies, 180 Harbor Road, Stony Brook NY 11790, USA | |
| **Powell, James W (Jay)** | Baseball Player |
| 155 Butler Dr, Ridgeland MS 39157, USA | |
| **Powell, Jane** | Singer, Actress |
| 150 W End Ave, #26C, New York NY 10023, USA | |

|  |  |
|---|---|
| **Powell, Jeremy R**<br>3022 W Summit Walk Court, Anthem AZ 85086, USA | Baseball Player |
| **Powell, Jerome (Jay)**<br>Federal Reserve System, 20th St & Constitution Ave NW, Washington DC 20551, USA | Government Leader, Financier |
| **Powell, Jesse**<br>Universal Attractions, 135 W 26th St, #1200, New York NY 10001 USA | Singer, Songwriter |
| **Powell, Jimmy**<br>49895 Lago Dr, La Quinta CA 92253, USA | Golfer |
| **Powell, John**<br>Kraft-Engel Mgmt, 15233 Ventura Blvd, #200, Sherman Oaks CA 91403 USA | Composer |
| **Powell, John G**<br>5545 Sobb Ave, Las Vegas NV 89118, USA | Track Athlete |
| **Powell, John W (Boog)**<br>Boog's Barbeque, 333 W Camden St, Baltimore MD 21201, USA | Baseball Player |
| **Powell, Josh**<br>Atlanta Hawks, Centennial Tower, 101 Marietta St NW, #1900, Atlanta GA 30303 USA | Basketball Player |
| **Powell, L Dante**<br>5715 W Walton St, Long Beach CA 90815, USA | Baseball Player |
| **Powell, Luke**<br>Indiana State University, Athletic Dept, 401 N 4th St, Terre Haute IN 47809, USA | Football Player |
| **Powell, Marvin, Jr**<br>5441 8th Ave, Los Angeles CA 90043, USA | Football Player |
| **Powell, Michael (Mike)**<br>7676 N Fresno St, #27, Fresno CA 93720, USA | Track Athlete |
| **Powell, Michael K**<br>College of William & Mary, PO Box 8795, Williamsburg VA 23187, USA | Government Official |
| **Powell, Monroe**<br>Personality Presents, 880 E Sahara Ave, #101, Las Vegas NV 89104, USA | Singer (Platters) |
| **Powell, Renee**<br>PO Box 30196, East Canton OH 44730, USA | Golfer |
| **Powell, Robert**<br>Diamond Mgmt, 31 Percy St, London W1T 2DD, England | Actor |
| **Powell, Sandy**<br>Independent Talent Group, 40 Whitfield St, London W1T 2RH, England | Costume Designer |
| **Powell, Susan**<br>6333 Bryn Mawr Dr, Los Angeles CA 90068, USA | Actress |
| **Power, Cat**<br>Ground Control, 108 E Main St, #8, Carrboro NC 27510, USA | Singer, Pianist, Guitarist |
| **Power, Dave**<br>Bauman Redanty & Shaul, 5757 Wilshire Blvd, #473, Los Angeles CA 90036, USA | Actor |
| **Power, J D (Dave)**<br>J D Power Associates, 2625 Townsgate Road, Westlake Village CA 91361, USA | Businessman |
| **Power, Lawrence**<br>Ingpen & Williams, 131 Putney Bridge Road, London SW15 2PA, England | Concert Viola Player |
| **Power, Samantha**<br>US Mission, United Nations Plaza, New York NY 10017, USA | Diplomat, Writer, Social Activist |
| **Power, Susan**<br>G P Putnam's Sons, 375 Hudson St, New York NY 10014 USA | Writer |
| **Power, Ted H**<br>1165 Tahiti Parkway, Sarasota FL 34236, USA | Baseball Player |
| **Power, Udana**<br>Iatia Well Inc, 1050 S Hayworth Ave, Los Angeles CA 90035, USA | Actress, Writer |
| **Power, Will**<br>Penske Racing, Penske Plaza, 366 Riverfront, Reading PA 19602, USA | Auto Racing Driver |
| **Power, Will**<br>I C M Partners, 10250 Constellation Blvd, #900, Los Angeles CA 90067 USA | Writer, Composer, Actor |
| **Powers, Clyde J**<br>6020 NW Williams Ave, Lawton OK 73505, USA | Football Player |
| **Powers, James B**<br>American Baptist Assn, 4605 N State Line, Texarkana TX 75503, USA | Religious Leader |
| **Powers, Richard**<br>University of Illinois, English Dept, Champaign IL 61820, USA | Writer |
| **Powers, Ross**<br>PO Box 186, Londonderry VT 05148, USA | Snowboard Skier |
| **Powers, Stefanie**<br>PO Box 5087, Sherman Oaks CA 91413, USA | Actress |
| **Powers, Warren A**<br>14742 Thornbird Manor Parkway, Chesterfield MO 63017, USA | Football Player |
| **Powers, Williams, Jr**<br>University of Texas, President's Office, Austin TX 78712, USA | Educator |
| **Powis, Lynn**<br>2669 S Columbine St, Denver CO 80210, USA | Ice Hockey Player |
| **Powter, Daniel P**<br>Gary Stamler Mgmt, 3055 Overland Ave, #200, Los Angeles CA 90034, USA | Singer, Pianist, Songwriter |
| **Powter, Susan**<br>Stop the Insanity, 6250 Ridgewood Road, Saint Cloud MN 56395, USA | Physical Fitness Expert, Writer |
| **Poynter, Dougie**<br>Helter Skelter, 347-353 Chiswick High Road, London W4 4HS, England | Bassist (McFly), Songwriter |
| **Poza, Jorge**<br>Televisa, Blvd A Lopez Mateos 232, Colonia San Angel, Mexico City DF 01060 CP, Mexico | Actor |
| **Pozsgay, Imre**<br>Parliament Buildings, Kossuth Lajos Ter 1, 1055 Budapest, Hungary | Government Official, Hungary |
| **Prabaya, Adrian**<br>Harrison/Parrott, 5-6 Albion Court, London W6 0QT, England | Conductor |
| **Prabhakar, Arati**<br>US Venture Partners, 2735 Sand Hill Road, Menlo Park CA 94025, USA | Financier |
| **Prada, Miuccia**<br>Galleria Vittorio Emanuele 60-65, 20121 Milan, Italy | Fashion Designer |
| **Prado, Edgar**<br>1519 Shoreline Way, Hollywood FL 33019, USA | Thoroughbred Racing Jockey |
| **Prado, Edward C**<br>US Court of Appeals, 755 E Mulberry Ave, San Antonio TX 78212, USA | Judge |
| **Prady, Bill**<br>Rothman Brecher Agency, 9250 Wilshire Blvd, #PH, Beverly Hills CA 90212, USA | Producer, Writer, Actor |
| **Prammanasudh, Stacy**<br>5016 S Toledo Ave, #18-O, Tulsa OK 74135, USA | Golfer |

**P**

**Powell - Prammanasudh**

**Prance, Ghillean T** — Botanist
Old Vicarage, Silver St, Lyme Regis, Dorset DT7 3HS, England
**Prantera, Amanda** — Writer
Bloomsbury Publishing, 50 Bedford Square, London WC1B 3DP, England
**Pras** — Rap Artist (Fugees)
I C M Partners, 10250 Constellation Blvd, #900, Los Angeles CA 90067 USA
**Prasad, Sunand** — Architect
Penoyre & Prasad, 28-42 Banner St, London EC1Y 8QE, England
**Prasad, Udayan** — Director, Actor
United Talent Agency, U T A Plaza, 9336 Civic Center Dr, Beverly Hills CA 90210 USA
**Prasong Tuchinda** — Pediatrician
Phya-Thai II Hospital, 943 Phaholythin, Phayatha Bangkok 10400, Thailand
**Pratchett, Terry** — Writer
Colin Smythe, PO Box 6, Gerrards Cross, Bucks SL9 8XA, England
**Prather, Joan** — Actress
31647 Sea Level Dr, Malibu CA 90265, USA
**Pratiwi Sudarmono P** — Astronaut, Indonesia
Universitas Indonesia, Microbiology Dept, Salemba Raya, Jakata 10430, Indonesia
**Pratt, Awadagin** — Concert Pianist
C M Artists, 127 W 96th St, #13B, New York NY 10025 USA
**Pratt, Chris** — Actor
Creative Artists Agency, 2000 Ave of Stars, #100, Los Angeles CA 90067 USA
**Pratt, Deborah** — Actress
Bruce Clute, 8205 Santa Monica Blvd, #1-299, West Hollywood CA 90046, USA
**Pratt, George C** — Judge
55 Sugar Tom Ridge, East Norwich NY 11732, USA
**Pratt, Judson** — Actor
2585 N Fountain Arbor Way, Orange CA 92867, USA
**Pratt, Kelly** — Ice Hockey Player
23 Lombard Crescent, Saint Albert AB T8N 3N1, Canada
**Pratt, Kelly** — Trumpeter (Beirut)
Ba Da Bing Records, 181 Clermont Ave, #403, Brooklyn NY 11205, USA
**Pratt, Keri Lynn** — Actress
Innovative Artists, 1505 10th St, Santa Monica CA 90401 USA
**Pratt, Michael P (Mike)** — Basketball Player
14603 Landon Court, Louisville KY 40245, USA
**Pratt, Robert H (Bob), Jr** — Football Player
4322 Monument Park, Richmond VA 23230, USA
**Pratt, Roger** — Cinematographer
10 Nightingale Lane, Hornsey, London N8 7QU, England
**Pratt, Todd A** — Baseball Player
5950 Dorset Bridge Road, Douglasville GA 30135, USA
**Pratt, Tracy** — Ice Hockey Player
1705-15038 101st Ave, Surrey BC V3R 0N2, Canada
**Pratt, Victoria** — Actress
Don Buchwald, 6500 Wilshire Blvd, #2200, Los Angeles CA 90048 USA
**Praver, Tori** — Model
I M G Models, 304 Park Ave S, #PH N, New York NY 10010 USA
**Preate, Ernest D, Jr** — Attorney, Government Official
Attorney General's Office, 4th & Walnut, Harrisburg PA 17120, USA
**Prebble, Lucy** — Producer, Writer
Rod Hall Agency, 7 Mallow St, London EC1Y 8RQ, England
**Precourt, Charles J** — Astronaut
1960 Shoshone Dr, Ogden UT 84403, USA
**Predock, Antoine** — Architect
Antoine Predock Architect, 300 12th St, Albuquerque NM 87102, USA
**Preece, Steven P (Steve)** — Football Player
2723 NW Monte Vista Terrace, Portland OR 97210, USA
**Pregerson, Harry** — Judge
US Court of Appeals, 21800 Oxnard St, Woodland Hills CA 91367, USA
**Preisler, Gary** — Director
I C M Partners, 10250 Constellation Blvd, #900, Los Angeles CA 90067 USA
**Preissing, Thomas J (Tom)** — Ice Hockey Player
1824 Anglers Dr, Steamboat Springs CO 80487, USA
**Prejean, Patrick** — Actor
Agence Babette Pouget, 36 Rue de Ponthieu, 75008 Paris, France
**Prejean, Sister Helen** — Social Activist, Writer
3009 Grand Route Saint John, #6, New Orleans LA 70119, USA
**Prelutsky, Jack** — Writer
PO Box 366, 7683 SE 27th St, Mercer Island WA 98040, USA
**Premji, Azim** — Businessman, Philanthropist
Wipro Ltd, Doddakannelli, Sarjapur Road, Bangalore 560035, India
**Prentice, Dean S** — Ice Hockey Player
350 Doon Valley Dr, Kitchener ON N2P 2M9, Canada
**Prepon, Laura** — Actress
Gersh Agency, 9465 Wilshire Blvd, #600, Beverly Hills CA 90212 USA
**Prescott, Edward C** — Nobel Economics Laureate
2308 Lake Place, Minneapolis MN 55405, USA
**Prescott, John L** — Government Official, England
365 Saltshouse Road, Sutton on Hull, North Humberside, England
**Prescott, Jon** — Actor
Abrams Artists, 9200 W Sunset Blvd, #1125, West Hollywood CA 90069 USA
**Prescott, Kathryn** — Actress
Curtis Brown Group, 28-29 Haymarket St, #500, London SW1Y 4SP, England
**Prescott, Robert T** — Actor
Innovative Artists, 1505 10th St, Santa Monica CA 90401 USA
**Presko, Joseph E (Joe)** — Baseball Player
1612 NE 77th Terrace, Kansas City MO 64118, USA
**Presle, Micheline** — Actress
6 Rue Antoine Dubois, 75006 Paris, France
**Presley, Angaleena** — Singer/Songwriter
Ten Ten Music Group, 33 Music Square W, #110, Nashville TN 37203, USA
**Presley, Brian** — Actor
I/D Public Relations, 7060 Hollywood Blvd, #800, Los Angeles CA 90028 USA
**Presley, James A (Jim)** — Baseball Player
2449 Bonanza Dr, Cantonment FL 32533, USA

**Presley, Lisa Marie**
International Talent Agency, Beverly Hills Triangle, 9701 Wilshire Blvd, Beverly Hills CA 90212, USA — Actress, Singer

**Presley, Priscilla**
1167 Summit Dr, Beverly Hills CA 90210, USA — Actress

**Presley, Richard**
W M E Entertainment, 9601 Wilshire Blvd, #300, Beverly Hills CA 90210 USA — Guitarist (Breeders)

**Presley, Wayne**
1339 Kingsway Dr, Highland MI 48356, USA — Ice Hockey Player

**Press, Bill**
CNN-TV, 190 Marietta Ave SW, Atlanta GA 30303 USA — Commentator

**Press, Frank**
2500 Virginia Ave, #616 South, Washington DC 20037, USA — Geophysicist

**Press, Natalie**
United Agents, 12-26 Lexington St, London W1F 0LE, England — Actress

**Pressel, Morgan**
3111 Clint Moore Road, #101, Boca Raton FL 33496, USA — Golfer

**Pressey, Paul M**
782 Haddonstone Circle, Lake Mary FL 32746, USA — Basketball Player, Coach

**Pressler, H Paul**
3711 San Felipe St, #9J, Houston TX 77027, USA — Attorney, Judge

**Pressler, Larry L**
1666 K St NW, #500, Washington DC 20006, USA — Senator, SD

**Pressler, Menahem M J**
Melvin Kaplan, 115 College St, #4, Burlington VT 05401, USA — Concert Pianist

**Pressley, Dominic I**
1406 Whooping Court, Upper Marlboro MD 20774, USA — Basketball Player

**Pressley, Harold**
6470 Matheny Way, Citrus Heights CA 95621, USA — Basketball Player

**Pressley, Robert**
6 Forestdale Dr, Asheville NC 28803, USA — Auto, Truck Racing Driver

**Pressman, Edward R**
Edward R Pressman Films, 1639 11th St, #251, Santa Monica CA 90404, USA — Producer

**Pressman, Lawrence**
15033 Encanto Dr, Sherman Oaks CA 91403, USA — Actor

**Pressman, Michael**
Glick Agency, 1321 7th St, #203, Santa Monica CA 90401 USA — Director

**Pressman, Sally**
United Talent Agency, U T A Plaza, 9336 Civic Center Dr, Beverly Hills CA 90210 USA — Actress

**Prestel, James F (Jim)**
6150 N Hurricane Court, Parker CO 80134, USA — Football Player

**Prestia, Francis (Rocco)**
Air Tight Mgmt, PO Box 113, Winchester Center CT 06094, USA — Bassist (Tower of Power)

**Preston, Carrie**
Innovative Artists, 1505 10th St, Santa Monica CA 90401 USA — Actress

**Preston, Douglas**
Editions L'Archipel, 34 Rue des Bourdonnais, 75001 Paris, France — Writer

**Preston, Duncan**
46 Hilltop House, Hornsey Lane, London N6 5NW, England — Actor

**Preston, J A**
Paradigm Agency, 360 N Crescent Dr, North Building, Beverly Hills CA 90210 USA — Actor

**Preston, Kelly**
Creative Artists Agency, 2000 Ave of Stars, #100, Los Angeles CA 90067 USA — Actress, Model

**Preston, Mike**
House of Representatives, 1434 6th St, #1, Santa Monica CA 90401 USA — Actor

**Preston, R David (Dave)**
PO Box 16511, Golden CO 80402, USA — Football Player

**Preston, Raymond N (Ray), Jr**
820 Regulo Place, #1811, Chula Vista CA 91910, USA — Football Player

**Preston, Simon J**
Little Hardwick, Langton Green, Tunbridge Wells, Kent TN3 0EY, England — Concert Organist, Choirmaster

**Preston, Steven C**
Small Business Administration, 409 3rd St SW, Washington DC 20024, USA — Secretary of Housing & Urban Development

**Prestridge, Luke E**
17802 Island Spring Lane, Tomball TX 77377, USA — Football Player

**Pretre, Georges**
Chateau de Vaudricourt, A Naves, 81100 Par Castres, France — Conductor

**Prettyman, Tristan**
High Road Touring, 751 Bridgeway, #200, Sausalito CA 94965 USA — Singer, Songwriter

**Preus, David W**
2481 Como Ave, Saint Paul MN 55108, USA — Religious Leader

**Previn, Andre G**
180 W 80th St, #206, New York NY 10024, USA — Conductor, Composer, Jazz Pianist

**Prevost, Greg**
Agency Group Ltd, 142 W 57th St, #600, New York NY 10019 USA — Singer, Musician (Chesterfield Kings)

**Prevost, Josette**
Levin Agency, 8484 Wilshire Blvd, #745, Beverly Hills CA 90211, USA — Actress

**Prew, William A**
30600 Telegraph Road, #3110, Bingham Farms MI 48025, USA — Swimmer, Businessman

**Preziosi, Alessandro**
Carol Levi Mgmt, Via Giuseppe Pisanelli 2, 00196 Rome, Italy — Actor

**Price, Alan**
Cromwell Mgmt, 20 Drayhorse Road, Ramsey, Cambridgeshire PE26 I5D, England — Singer, Organist (Animals), Songwriter

**Price, Antony**
17 Langton St, London SW10 0JL, England — Fashion Designer

**Price, Armintie A**
Atlanta Dream, 83 Walton St NW, #400, Atlanta, GA 30303 USA — Basketball Player

**Price, Bryan R**
Cincinnati Reds, Great American Ball Park, 100 Main St, Cincinnati OH 45202 USA — Baseball Manager

**Price, Elex D**
2833 J B Mance Ave, Jackson MS 39213, USA — Football Player

**Price, Frank**
Price Entertainment, 527 Spoleto Dr, Pacific Palisades CA 90272, USA — Film Executive

**Price, H Brent**
1111 W Wynona Ave, Enid OK 73703, USA — Basketball Player

**Price, Hilary**
221 Pine St, #414, Florence MA 01062, USA — Cartoonist (Rhymes with Orange)

| | |
|---|---|
| **Price, Jack**<br>39 Waterloo St S, Goderich ON N7A 3P1, Canada | Ice Hockey Player |
| **Price, James G**<br>12205 Mohawk Road, Leawood KS 66209, USA | Physician, Columnist |
| **Price, Jimmie W (Jim)**<br>57152 Willow Way, Washington MI 48094, USA | Baseball Player |
| **Price, Joseph W (Joe)**<br>1874 Arabian Court, Hebron KY 41048, USA | Baseball Player |
| **Price, Katie (Jordan)**<br>Volition, Raleigh Studios, 1600 Rosecrans Ave, #400, Manhattan Beach CA 90266, USA | Model, Singer |
| **Price, Kelly**<br>J L Entertainment, 18653 Ventura Blvd, #340, Tarzana CA 91356, USA | Singer |
| **Price, Larry C**<br>930 S Garfield St, Denver CO 80209, USA | Photojournalist |
| **Price, Lia Scott**<br>Lia Scott Price Productions, 4455 Torrance Blvd, #866, Torrance CA 90503, USA | Actress, Producer, Writer |
| **Price, Lindsay**<br>Management 360, 9111 Wilshire Blvd, Beverly Hills CA 90210 USA | Actress |
| **Price, Lloyd**<br>95 Horseshoe Hill Road, Pound Ridge NY 10576, USA | Singer, Pianist, Songwriter |
| **Price, M V Leontyne**<br>9 Vandam St, New York NY 10013, USA | Opera Singer |
| **Price, Marc**<br>8444 Magnolia Dr, Los Angeles CA 90046, USA | Actor |
| **Price, Megyn**<br>A P A Talent/Literary Agency, 405 S Beverly Dr, #300, Beverly Hills CA 90212 USA | Actress |
| **Price, Michael F**<br>Franklin Mutual Advisors, 57 John F Kennedy Parkway, Short Hills NJ 07078, USA | Financier |
| **Price, Mike**<br>4415 Thorleigh Dr, Indianapolis IN 46226, USA | Basketball Player |
| **Price, Mitchell L**<br>9944 Candlestick Lane, Pensacola FL 32514, USA | Football Player |
| **Price, Molly**<br>Gersh Agency, 9465 Wilshire Blvd, #600, Beverly Hills CA 90212 USA | Actress |
| **Price, Nichoas R L (Nick)**<br>Nick Price Group, 900 S US Highway 1, #105, Jupiter FL 33477, USA | Golfer |
| **Price, Noel**<br>21 Windeyer Crescent, Kanata ON K2K 2P6, Canada | Ice Hockey Player |
| **Price, Pat**<br>PO Box 3, Robson BC V0G 1X0, Canada | Ice Hockey Player |
| **Price, Paul B**<br>1056 Overlook Road, Berkeley CA 94708, USA | Physicist |
| **Price, Peerless L**<br>5658 Legends Club Circle, Braselton GA 30517, USA | Football Player |
| **Price, Phoebe**<br>P Mgmt, 11666 Montana Ave, Los Angeles CA 90049, USA | Actress |
| **Price, Ray**<br>Bobby Roberts, 3050 Business Park Circle, #303, Goodlettsville TN 37221 USA | Singer, Guitarist |
| **Price, Richard**<br>Creative Artists Agency, 2000 Ave of Stars, Los Angeles CA 90067, USA | Writer |
| **Price, Rick**<br>Harbour Agency, 135 Forbes St, Woolloomooloo NSW 2011, Australia | Singer, Musician, Songwriter |
| **Price, Willard D**<br>PO Box 2783, Laguna Hills CA 92654, USA | Explorer |
| **Priddy, Nancy**<br>11223 Sunshine Terrace, Studio City CA 91604, USA | Actress |
| **Priddy, Robert S (Bob)**<br>136 Shingiss St, #214, McKees Rocks PA 15136, USA | Baseball Player |
| **Pride, Charley**<br>Cecca Productions, PO Box 670507, Dallas TX 75367, USA | Singer, Guitarist, Baseball Player |
| **Pride, Curtis J**<br>Gallaudet University, Athletic Dept, 800 Florida Ave NE, Washington DC 20002, USA | Baseball Player |
| **Pride, Dicky**<br>4645 Cason Cove Dr, Windermere FL 34786, USA | Golfer |
| **Pridemore, L Thomas (Tom), Jr**<br>3935 Poplar Springs Road, Gainesville GA 30507, USA | Football Player |
| **Priesand, Sally J**<br>32 Fernwood Dr, Asbury Park NJ 07712, USA | Religious Leader |
| **Priest, Eddie Lee (Ed), Jr**<br>445 Ballard Road, Altoona AL 35952, USA | Baseball Player |
| **Priest, Maxi**<br>Virgin Records, 150 5th Ave, Front 3, New York NY 10011 USA | Singer |
| **Priest, Steve**<br>D C M International, 296 Nether St, Finchley, London N3 1RJ, England | Singer, Bassist (Sweet) |
| **Priestlay, Ken**<br>5438 Crescent Dr, Delta BC V4K 2C9, Canada | Ice Hockey Player |
| **Priestley, Jason**<br>A P A Talent/Literary Agency, 405 S Beverly Dr, #300, Beverly Hills CA 90212 USA | Actor |
| **Priestley, Thomas (Tom), Jr**<br>Paradigm Agency, 360 N Crescent Dr, North Building, Beverly Hills CA 90210 USA | Director |
| **Prieto, Ariel**<br>15325 SW 53rd St, Miami FL 33185, USA | Baseball Player |
| **Prieto, Rodrigo**<br>PO Box 3338, Beverly Hills CA 90212, USA | Cinematographer |
| **Prigioni, Pablo**<br>New York Knicks, Madison Square Garden, 2 Penn Plaza, New York, NY 10121 USA | Basketball Player |
| **Primack, Joel R**<br>University of California, Astronomy Dept, Santa Cruz CA 95064, USA | Astronomer |
| **Primakov, Yevgeny M**<br>Federation Chamber of Commerce, Ilyinka Str 6, 103684 Moscow, Russia | Prime Minister, Russia |
| **Primeau, Keith**<br>2 Danforth Dr, Voorhees NJ 08043, USA | Ice Hockey Player |
| **Primeau, Wayne**<br>Toronto Maple Leafs, AirCanada Center, 40 Bay St, Toronto ON M5J 2K2, Canada | Ice Hockey Player |
| **Primes, Robert**<br>Innovative Artists, 1505 10th St, Santa Monica CA 90401 USA | Cinematographer |

**Primrose, Neil** — Drummer (Travis)
Wildlife Entertainment, 21 Heathmans Road, London SW6 4TJ, England
**Prince** — Singer, Guitarist, Songwriter
Paisley Park Enterprises, 7801 Audubon Road, Chanhassen MN 55317, USA
**Prince Paul** — Rap Artist, DJ Musician, Producer
Agency Group Ltd, 142 W 57th St, #600, New York NY 10019 USA
**Prince, Bart** — Architect
3501 Monte Vista NE, Albuquerque NM 87106, USA
**Prince, Donald M (Don)** — Baseball Player
11143 James B White Highway S, Whiteville NC 28472, USA
**Prince, Faith** — Actress, Singer
Hart Mgmt, 1900 Ave of Stars, #1800, Los Angeles CA 90067, USA
**Prince, Harold S (Hal)** — Producer, Director
Directors Company, 311 W 43rd St, #307, New York NY 10036, USA
**Prince, Jonathan** — Actor, Producer, Writer
United Talent Agency, U T A Plaza, 9336 Civic Center Dr, Beverly Hills CA 90210 USA
**Prince, Larry L** — Businessman
Genuine Parts Co, 2999 Circle 75 Parkway, Atlanta GA 30339, USA
**Prince, Peter** — Writer
Bloomsbury Publishing, 50 Bedford Square, London WC1B 3DP, England
**Prince, Richard** — Artist, Photographer
Michael Kohn Gallery, 8071 Beverly Blvd, Los Angeles CA 90048, USA
**Prince, Tayshaun D** — Basketball Player
8866 Prestancia Cove S, Memphis TN 38125, USA
**Prince, Thomas A (Tom)** — Baseball Player
6816 10th Ave NW, Bradenton FL 34209, USA
**Prince-Bythewood, Gina** — Writer, Director, Producer
Creative Artists Agency, 2000 Ave of Stars, #100, Los Angeles CA 90067 USA
**Princess Superstar** — Rap Artist, Singer, Songwriter
SuperVision Management Group, 59-65 Worship St, London EC2A 2DU, England
**Principal, Victoria** — Actress
23852 Pacfic Coast Highway, #785, Malibu CA 90265, USA
**Principe, Joe** — Bassist (Rise Against)
Agency Group Ltd, 142 W 57th St, #600, New York NY 10019 USA
**Prine, Andrew** — Actor
3364 Longridge Ave, Sherman Oaks CA 91423, USA
**Prine, John** — Singer, Songwriter
Al Bunetta Mgmt, 33 Music Square W, #102B, Nashville TN 37203, USA
**Pringle, Joan** — Actress
Talent Works, 3500 W Olive Ave, #1400, Burbank CA 91505 USA
**Prinosil, David** — Tennis Player
T C Wolfsberg, Am Schanzl 3, 92224 Amberg, Germany
**Printup, Marcus** — Jazz Trumpeter
Universal Attractions, 135 W 26th St, #1200, New York NY 10001 USA
**Prinz, Bret R** — Baseball Player
15471 N 88th Ave, Peoria AZ 85382, USA
**Prinze, Freddie, Jr** — Actor
Brillstein Entertainment Partners, 9150 Wilshire Blvd, #350, Beverly Hills CA 90212 USA
**Prinzi, Frank** — Cinematographer
571 W 113th St, #24, New York NY 10025, USA
**Prioleau, Pierson O** — Football Player
2221 Santee River Road, Saint Stephen SC 29479, USA
**Prior of Brampton, James M L** — Government Official, England
36 Morpeth Mansions, London SW1P 1ER, England
**Prior, Anthony E** — Football Player
3529 Holding St, Riverside CA 92501, USA
**Prior, Madeleine E (Maddy)** — Singer
Park Promotions, PO Box 651, Park Road, Oxford OX2 9RB, England
**Prior, Mark W** — Baseball Player
10284 Waddell Circle, San Diego CA 92124, USA
**Prior, Michael R (Mike)** — Football Player
14511 Quail Pointe Dr, Carmel IN 46032, USA
**Prior, Susan** — Actress
Mollison Keightley Management, 139 Cathedral St, Woolloomooloo, Sydney NSW 2011, Australia
**Priory, Richard B** — Businessman
Duke Energy Co, 526 S Church St, Charlotte NC 28202, USA
**Pritchard, Barry** — Singer, Guitarist (Fortunes)
Lustig Talent, PO Box 770850, Orlando FL 32877 USA
**Pritchard, Connor** — Producer, Writer
I C M Partners, 10250 Constellation Blvd, #900, Los Angeles CA 90067 USA
**Pritchard, David E** — Physicist
Massachusetts Institute of Technology, Physics Dept, Cambridge MA 02139, USA
**Pritchard, Michael R (Mike)** — Football Player
PO Box 93114, Las Vegas NV 89193, USA
**Pritchard, Ronald D ((Ron)** — Football Player
495 E Coconino Dr, Chandler AZ 85249, USA
**Pritchett, Christopher D (Chris)** — Baseball Player
959 Fir Tree Place, Carlsbad CA 92011, USA
**Pritchett, Kelvin B** — Football Player
46679 Pinehurst Circle, Stone Mountain GA 30087, USA
**Pritchett, Matthew (Matt)** — Cartoonist (Matt)
London Daily Telegraph, 181 Marsh Wall, London E14 9SR, England
**Pritchett, Stanley J** — Football Player
523 Monteagle Trace, Stone Mountain GA 30087, USA
**Pritko, Steven (Steve)** — Football Player
328 Chanticlair Dr, Apex NC 27502, USA
**Probst, Jeff** — Producer, Director, Actor
W M E Entertainment, 9601 Wilshire Blvd, #300, Beverly Hills CA 90210 USA
**Probst, Lawrence F (Larry), III** — Businessman
US Olympic Committee, 1 Olympic Plaza, Building 6, Colorado Springs CO 80909 USA
**Prochaska, Andreas** — Director
Spielkind-Mattias Frik, Zimmerstr 11, 10969 Berlin, Germany
**Prochazka, Martin** — Ice Hockey Player
H C Kladno, Petra Bezruc 2531, 27280 Kladno, Czech Republic
**Prochnow, Jurgen** — Actor
Innovative Artists, 1505 10th St, Santa Monica CA 90401 USA

**P**

**Primrose - Prochnow**

**Prock, Markus** — Luge Athlete
Tyrolean Luge Assn, Olympia World, Olympiastr 10, 6020 Innsbruck, Austria
**Procter, Emily** — Actress, Model
Paradigm Agency, 360 N Crescent Dr, North Building, Beverly Hills CA 90210 USA
**Proctor, James A (Jim)** — Baseball Player
2 Westmoreland Place, Saint Louis MO 63108, USA
**Proctor, Phillip** — Actor
C E S D, 10635 Santa Monica Blvd, #130, Los Angeles CA 90025 USA
**Proctor, Robert N** — Scientific Historian
Stanford University, History Dept, Stanford CA 94305, USA
**Proctor, Scott C** — Baseball Player
428 NE Bayberry Lane, Jensen Beach FL 34957, USA
**Prodi, Romano** — Prime Minister, Italy
Prime Minister's Office, Palazzo Chigi, Piazza Colonna 370, 00187 Rome, Italy
**Proehl, Richard S (Ricky)** — Football Player
3504 Bromley Wood Lane, Greensboro NC 27410, USA
**Proenza, William (Bill)** — Climatologist, Government Official
US National Weather Service, 11691 SW 17th St, Miami FL 33165, USA
**Professor Griff** — Rap Artist (Public Enemy)
Brookes Co, 3710 S Robertson Blvd, #100, Culver City CA 90232, USA
**Prohgress** — Singer (Far East Movement)
Stampede Mgmt, 12530 Beatrice St, Los Angeles CA 90066, USA
**Prokop, Joseph M (Joe)** — Football Player
1042 N Mountain Ave, Upland CA 91786, USA
**Prokop, Matt** — Actor
Management 360, 9111 Wilshire Blvd, Beverly Hills CA 90210 USA
**Proly, Michael J (Mike)** — Baseball Player
21 Hollander Dr, Taylors SC 29687, USA
**Promuto, Vincent L (Vince)** — Football Player
9 Island Dr, Norwalk CT 06855, USA
**Pronger, Christopher R (Chris)** — Ice Hockey Player
345 S Hinchman Ave, Haddonfield NJ 08033, USA
**Pronger, Sean J** — Ice Hockey Player
1229 Firwood Dr, Pittsburgh PA 15243, USA
**Pronovost, Andre J A** — Ice Hockey Player
1412 46E Rue, Shawinigan QC G9N 5B8, Canada
**Pronovost, J Jean D** — Ice Hockey Player
Hockey Ministries, 1100 La Gauchetiere St W, Montreal QC H3B 2S2, Canada
**Pronovost, Peter** — Intensive Care Physician
Johns Hopkins University Medical Center, Baltimore MD 21218 USA
**Pronovost, R Marcel** — Ice Hockey Player, Coach
4620 Dali Court, Windsor ON N9G 2M8, Canada
**Propes, Duane** — Guitarist (Little Texas)
Splash Public Relations, 1520 16th Ave S, #2, Nashville TN 37212, USA
**Prophet, Billy** — Singer (Jive Five)
Paramount Entertainment, PO Box 12, Far Hills NJ 07931 USA
**Prophet, Ronald L V (Ronnie)** — Singer
1227 Saxon Dr, Nashville TN 37215, USA
**Propp, Brian** — Ice Hockey Player
2320 Riverton Road, Cinnaminson NJ 08077, USA
**Prose, Francine** — Writer
P E N American Center, 588 Broadway, #303, New York NY 10012, USA
**Prospal, Vaclav** — Ice Hockey Player
3908 Tarrington Lane, Columbus OH 43220, USA
**Prosser, James** — Singer
Refugee Mgmt, 209 10th Ave S, #347, Cummins Station, Nashville TN 37203, USA
**Prosser, Robert** — Religious Leader
Cumberland Presbyterian Church, 1978 Union Ave, Memphis TN 38104, USA
**Prost, Alain M P** — Auto Racing Driver
11 Ave de la Gare, 1260 Nyon, Switzerland
**Prost, Sharon** — Judge
US Court of Appeals, 717 Madison Place NW, Washington DC 20439, USA
**Protopopov, Oleg A** — Figure Skater
Chalet Hubel, 3818 Grindelwald, Switzerland
**Proulx, Brooklynn** — Actress
Global Creative, 1051 N Cole Ave, #B, Los Angeles CA 90038, USA
**Proulx, E Annie** — Writer
PO Box 789, Saratoga WY 82331, USA
**Prout, Brian** — Drummer (Diamond Rio)
Modern Mgmt, 1625 Broadway, #600, Nashville TN 37203, USA
**Prout, Kirsten** — Actress
Alchemy Entertainment, 7024 Melrose Ave, #420, Los Angeles CA 90038 USA
**Proval, David** — Actor
Glick Agency, 1260 6th St, #100, Santa Monica CA 90401, USA
**Provence, Andrew C** — Football Player
224 Providence Road, Fayetteville GA 30215, USA
**Provenza, Paul** — Actor, Director
Metropolitan Talent Agency, 5405 Wilshire Blvd, #218, Los Angeles CA 90036 USA
**Provost, Jon** — Actor
627 Montclair Ave, Santa Rosa CA 95409, USA
**Prowse, David** — Actor
Spotlight, 7 Leicester Place, London WC2H 7BP, England
**Proyas, Alex** — Director, Producer, Writer
Creative Artists Agency, 2000 Ave of Stars, #100, Los Angeles CA 90067 USA
**Prpic, Joel** — Ice Hockey Player
2586 S Shore Road, Sudbury ON P3G 1M3, Canada
**Prucha, Petr** — Ice Hockey Player
6122 S Cypress Point Dr, Chandler AZ 85249, USA
**Prudhomme, Christian** — Cycling Executive
A S O, 2 Rue Rouget de l'Isle, 92130 Issy Les Mouoimeaux, France
**Prudhomme, Don** — Drag Racing Driver
Don Prudhomme Racing, 1232 Distribution Way, Vista CA 92081, USA
**Prudhomme, Paul** — Chef
2424 Chartres St, New Orleans LA 70117, USA
**Pruett, Jeanne** — Singer, Songwriter
Joe Taylor Artist Agency, 2802 Columbine Place, Nashville TN 37204 USA

| | |
|---|---|
| **Pruett, Scott**<br>9743 W Bray Creek St, Star ID 83669, USA | Auto Racing Driver |
| **Pruetz, Jill**<br>Iowa State University, Anthropology Dept, Ames IA 50011, USA | Primatologist, Anthropologist |
| **Pruitt, Gregory D (Greg)**<br>13851 Larchmere Blvd, Cleveland OH 44120, USA | Football Player |
| **Pruitt, James B**<br>PO Box 244483, Boynton Beach FL 33424, USA | Football Player |
| **Pruitt, Jordan L**<br>Black Angel Records, PO Box 54, Fairview TN 37862, USA | Singer |
| **Pruitt, Michael L (Mike)**<br>20568 Kelsey Lane, Strongsville OH 44149, USA | Football Player |
| **Pruitt, Mickey A**<br>15647 Dante Dr, South Holland IL 60473, USA | Football Player |
| **Pruitt, Ronald R (Ron)**<br>3632 Turnberry Dr, Medina OH 44256, USA | Baseball Player |
| **Prunariu, Dumitru D**<br>Str Sf Spiridon 12, #4, 70231 Bucharest, Romania | Cosmonaut, Romania |
| **Prunskiene, Kazimiera D**<br>Kriviu 53A-13, 2007 Vilnius, Lithuania | Prime Minister, Lithuania |
| **Prusiner, Stanley B**<br>University of California, Biochemistry Dept, San Francisco CA 94143, USA | Nobel Medicine Laureate |
| **Pruzansky, Mark E**<br>975 Park Ave, New York NY 10028, USA | Orthopedic Surgeon |
| **Pryce, Jonathan**<br>Julian Belfrage Assoc, 9 Argyll St, #300, London W1F 7TG, England | Actor, Singer |
| **Pryce, Malcolm**<br>Bloomsbury Publishing, 50 Bedford Square, London WC1B 3DP, England | Writer |
| **Pryce, Trevor W**<br>12057 Open Run Road, Ellicott City MD 21042, USA | Football Player |
| **Prydz, Eric**<br>Ministry of Sound, 103 Gaunt St, London SE1 6DP, England | DJ Musician |
| **Prynoski, Chris**<br>Titmouse, 6616 Lexington Ave, Los Angeles CA 90038, USA | Animator, Producer |
| **Pryor, Aaron**<br>2964 High Forest Lane, #345, Cincinnati OH 45223, USA | Boxer |
| **Pryor, David H**<br>507 N 11th St, Paragould AR 72450, USA | Senator, Governor, AR |
| **Pryor, Gregory R (Greg)**<br>9726 W 115th Terrace, Overland Park KS 66210, USA | Baseball Player |
| **Pryor, Nicholas**<br>S D B Partners, 1801 Ave of Stars, #902, Los Angeles CA 90067 USA | Actor |
| **Przybilla, Joel A**<br>3815 N Brookfield Road, #104, Brookfield WI 53045, USA | Basketball Player |
| **Psycho Les**<br>Agency Group Ltd, 142 W 57th St, #600, New York NY 10019 USA | Rap Artist (Beatnuts) |
| **Ptacek, Louis J**<br>University of California Medical Center, Fu & Ptacek Laboratories, 1550 4th St, San Francisco CA 94158, USA | Geneticist |
| **Ptashne, Mark S**<br>Harvard University, Biochemistry Dept, Cambridge MA 02138, USA | Biochemist |
| **Pucci, Lou Taylor**<br>United Talent Agency, U T A Plaza, 9336 Civic Center Dr, Beverly Hills CA 90210 USA | Actor |
| **Pucillo, Michael (Mike)**<br>9402 Council Rock Court, Riverview FL 33578, USA | Football Player |
| **Puck, Wolfgang**<br>805 N Sierra Dr, Beverly Hills CA 90210, USA | Chef |
| **Puckett, Gary**<br>10710 Seminole Blvd, #3, Largo FL 33778, USA | Singer, Songwriter |
| **Pudi, Danny**<br>United Talent Agency, U T A Plaza, 9336 Civic Center Dr, Beverly Hills CA 90210 USA | Actor, Writer |
| **Puenzo, Luis A**<br>Cinematografia Nacional Instituto, Lima 319, 1073 Buenos Aires, Argentina | Director |
| **Puerta, Joe**<br>Lustig Talent, PO Box 770850, Orlando FL 32877 USA | Singer, Guitarist (Ambrosia) |
| **Puett, Tommy**<br>16621 Cerulean Court, Chino Hills CA 91709, USA | Actor |
| **Puetz, Garry S**<br>1779 Robinson Road, Dahlonega GA 30533, USA | Football Player |
| **Puffer, Brandon**<br>1546 Haynie Bend, Round Rock TX 78665, USA | Baseball Player |
| **Pugacheva, Alla B**<br>State Variety Theater, Bersenevskaya Nab 20/2, 109072 Moscow, Russia | Singer |
| **Puget, Jade E**<br>S A M, 722 Seward St, Los Angeles CA 90038, USA | Guitarist (AFI) |
| **Puget, Jean-Loup**<br>Institut d'Astrophysique Spatiale, Paris-Sud, 91898 Orsay Cedex, France | Astrophysicist |
| **Pugh, Gareth**<br>Mandi Lennard Publicity, 2 Hoxton St, London N1 6NG, England | Fashion Designer |
| **Pugh, Jethro, Jr**<br>Gifts Inc, 329 E Colorado Blvd, #505, Dallas TX 75203, USA | Football Player |
| **Pugh, Larry**<br>RR 4, New Castle PA 16101, USA | Football Player |
| **Pugh, Timothy D (Tim)**<br>8015 N 187th East Ave, Owasso OK 74055, USA | Baseball Player |
| **Pugsley, Don**<br>Gar Lester Agency, 4130 Cahuenga Blvd, #108, Universal City CA 91602, USA | Actor |
| **Puhl, Terrance S (Terry)**<br>918 Gondola St, Sugar Land TX 77478, USA | Baseball Player |
| **Pujats, Janis Cardinal**<br>Metropolijas Kurija, Maza Pils Iela 2/A, 1050 Riga, Latvia | Religious Leader |
| **Pujol, Laetitia**<br>Paris Opera Ballet, Place de l'Opera, 75009 Paris, France | Ballerina |
| **Pujols Alcantara, J Albert**<br>102 Grand Meridien Forest, Chesterfield MO 63005, USA | Baseball Player |
| **Pujols, Luis B**<br>3867 Jonathans Way, Boynton Beach FL 33436, USA | Baseball Player, Manager |

**Puleo, Charles M (Charlie)** — Baseball Player
3202 Miser Station Road, Louisville TN 37777, USA

**Puleston-Davies, Ian** — Actor
Ken McReddie Assoc, 101 Finsbury Pavement, London EC2A 1RS, England

**Pulford, Robert J (Bob)** — Ice Hockey Player, Coach
78 Coventry Road, Northfield IL 60093, USA

**Pulgram, William** — Interior Designer
3747 Peachtree Road NE, #1425, Atlanta GA 30319, USA

**Pulido, Roberto (Bobby), Jr** — Singer
Texas Sounds Entertainment, 957 NASA Parkway, #542, Houston TX 77058, USA

**Puljic, Vinko Cardinal** — Religious Leader
Nadbiskupski Ordinarijat, Kaptol 7, 71000 Sarajevo, Bosnia & Herzegovina

**Pulkkinen, David** — Ice Hockey Player
5095 Croatia Road, Sudbury ON P3G 1L5, Canada

**Pullen, Melanie Clark** — Actress
Julian Belfrage Assoc, 9 Argyll St, #300, London W1F 7TG, England

**Pulliam, Harvey J** — Baseball Player
2009 Mount Hamilton Dr, Antioch CA 94531, USA

**Pulliam, Keshia Knight** — Actress
A P A Talent/Literary Agency, 405 S Beverly Dr, #300, Beverly Hills CA 90212 USA

**Pullman, Bill** — Actor
I C M Partners, 10250 Constellation Blvd, #900, Los Angeles CA 90067 USA

**Pullman, Philip** — Writer
24 Templar Road, Oxford OX2 8LT, England

**Pulsford, K H Nigel** — Singer, Guitarist (Bush)
Front Line Mgmt, 1100 Glendon Ave, #2000, Los Angeles CA 90024 USA

**Pulsipher, Lindsay** — Actress
I C M Partners, 10250 Constellation Blvd, #900, Los Angeles CA 90067 USA

**Pulsipher, William T (Bill)** — Baseball Player
1986 SW Certosa Road, Port Saint Lucie FL 34953, USA

**Pulver, Lara** — Actress
Independent Talent Group, 40 Whitfield St, London W1T 2RH, England

**Pulver, Liselotte** — Actress
Villa Bip, Route Suisse 21, 1166 Perroy VD, Switzerland

**Pulz, Penny** — Golfer
10315 W Winninger Circle, Sun City AZ 85351, USA

**Puna, Henry T** — Prime Minister, Cook Islands
Prime Minister's Office, Avarua, Rarotonga, Cook Islands

**Punch, Lucy** — Actress
United Agents, 12-26 Lexington St, London W1F 0LE, England

**Punsalan Swallow, Elizabeth** — Ice Dancer, Coach
Detroit Skating Club, 888 Denison Court, Bloomfield Hills MI 48302, USA

**Punto, Nicholas P (Nick)** — Baseball Player
19550 N Grayhawk Dr, #1122, Scottsdale AZ 85255, USA

**Puppa, Daren** — Ice Hockey Player
4526 Cheval Blvd, Lutz FL 33558, USA

**Pupunu, Alfred S (Al)** — Football Player
415 Conestoga Road, Moscow ID 83843, USA

**Purcell, Dominic** — Actor
Untitled Entertainment, 350 S Beverly Dr, #200, Beverly Hills CA 90212 USA

**Purcell, James N** — Government Official
5113 W Running Brook Road, Columbia MD 21044, USA

**Purcell, Lee** — Actress
Coast to Coast Talent, 3350 Barham Blvd, Los Angeles CA 90068 USA

**Purcell, Patrick B** — Publisher
Boston Herald, Publisher's Office, 1 Herald St, Boston MA 02118, USA

**Purcell, Sarah** — Actress
4437 Alla Road, #6, Marina del Rey CA 90292, USA

**Purcell, William** — Astrophysicist
Northwestern University, Astrophysics Dept, Evanston IL 60208, USA

**Purdee, Nathan** — Actor
Irv Schechter, 9460 Wilshire Blvd, #300, Beverly Hills CA 90212 USA

**Purdie, Bernard (Pretty)** — Jazz Drummer
Benay Enterprises, 62 E Starrs Plain Road, Danbury CT 06810, USA

**Purdy, Alfred** — Writer
Harbour Publishing, PO Box 219, Madeira Park BC V0N 2H0, Canada

**Purdy, Joe** — Singer, Songwriter
Agency Group Ltd, 142 W 57th St, #600, New York NY 10019 USA

**Purdy, Jolene** — Actress
Innovative Artists, 1505 10th St, Santa Monica CA 90401 USA

**Purdy, Robert** — Actor
Associated International Mgmt, 7 Hatton Garden, #400, London EC1N 8AD, England

**Purdy, Ted** — Golfer
14259 N 2nd Ave, Phoenix AZ 85023, USA

**Purefoy, James** — Actor
Independent Talent Group, 40 Whitfield St, London W1T 2RH, England

**Puri, Om** — Actor
Conway Van Gelder Grant, 8-12 Broadwick St, #300, London W1F 8HW, England

**Purify, Robert L (Bobby)** — Singer
Conqueroo, 11271 Ventura Blvd, #522, Studio City CA 91604 USA

**Purim, Flora** — Singer
A Train Mgmt, 401 Grand Ave, #300, Oakland CA 94610, USA

**Purinton, Dale** — Ice Hockey Player
2045 Cowichan Bay Road, Cowichan Bay BC V0R 1N1, Canada

**Purl, Linda** — Actress
Momentum Talent Mgmt, 13935 Burbank Blvd, #102, Valley Glen CA 91401, USA

**Purtzer, Tom** — Golfer
10529 N 106th Place, Scottsdale AZ 85258, USA

**Purvanov, Georgi** — President, Bulgaria
President's Office, 2 Dondukov Blvd, 1123 Sofia, Bulgaria

**Purves, William** — Financier
100 Ebury Mews, London SW1 9NX, England

**Purvis, Jeffrey (Jeff)** — Auto Racing Driver
1157 Dunbar Cove Road, Clarksville TN 37043, USA

**Purvis, Neal** — Writer, Producer
United Talent Agency, U T A Plaza, 9336 Civic Center Dr, Beverly Hills CA 90210 USA

**Puryear, Martin** — Sculptor
Drysdale Gallery, 700 New Hampshire Ave NW, #917, Washington DC 20037, USA
**Puscau, Alina** — Model, Singer, Actress
I M G Models, 304 Park Ave S, #PH N, New York NY 10010 USA
**Pusch, Alexander** — Fencer
Lindenweg 39, 97941 Tauberbischofsheim, Germany
**Pusey, Chris** — Ice Hockey Player
287 Brantwood Park Road, Brantford ON N3P 1H6, Canada
**Pusha T** — Rap Artist (Clipse)
American Talent Agency, 26 Finney Farm Road, Croton on Hudson NY 10520, USA
**Pushelberg, Glenn** — Interior Designer
Yabu Pushelberg, 138 Spring St, #400, New York NY 10012, USA
**Pushor, Jamie** — Ice Hockey Player
29 Jay Road W, Lake George NY 12845, USA
**Puskaric, Ljubomir** — Opera Singer
I M G Artists, Hogarth Business Park, Chiswick, London W4 2TH, England
**Putch, John** — Actor
I C M Partners, 10250 Constellation Blvd, #900, Los Angeles CA 90067 USA
**Putilin, Nikolai G** — Opera Singer
Mariinsky Theater, Teatralnaya Square 1, 190000 Saint Petersburg, Russia
**Putin, Vladimir V** — President, Russia
President's Office, Kremlin, Staraya Pl 4, 103132 Moscow, Russia
**Putman, P Edward (Ed)** — Baseball Player
PO Box 3366, Mesquite NV 89024, USA
**Putnam, Ashley** — Opera Singer
Maurice Mayer, 201 W 54th St, #1C, New York NY 10019, USA
**Putnam, C Duane** — Football Player
1545 Magnolia Ave, Ontario CA 91762, USA
**Putnam, Hilary W** — Philosopher
31 Cleveland St, Arlington MA 02474, USA
**Putnam, Patrick E (Pat)** — Baseball Player
4040 Staley Road, Fort Myers FL 33905, USA
**Putterman, Seth J** — Physicist
University of California, Physics Dept, Los Angeles CA 90024, USA
**Puttnam, David T** — Producer
Enigma Productions, 29A Tufton St, London SW1P 3QL, England
**Putz, Joseph J (J J)** — Baseball Player
7818 N Sherri Lane, Paradise Valley AZ 85253, USA
**Putze, Martin** — Bobsled Athlete
B S R Rennsteig Oberhof, Alte Ohrdrufer Str 6, 98559 Oberhof, Germany
**Putzier, Jebediah L (Jeb)** — Football Player
2641 W 131st Terrace, Leawood KS 66209, USA
**Putzulu, Bruno** — Actor
Voyez Mon Agent, 20 Ave Rapp, 75007 Paris, France
**Puzzuoli, P David (Dave)** — Football Player
22214 Rock Creek Circle, Strongsville OH 44149, USA
**Pyatt, F Nelson** — Ice Hockey Player
1680 Arthur St W, Thunder Bay ON P7K 1A8, Canada
**Pyavko, Vladislav I** — Opera Singer
Bryusov Per 2/14, #27, 103009 Moscow, Russia
**Pye, R Edward (Eddie)** — Baseball Player
307 Polk St, Columbia TN 38401, USA
**Pyfrom, Shawn C** — Actor
Podwall Entertainment, 710 N Orlando Ave, #203, West Hollywood CA 90069, USA
**Pygram, Wayne** — Actor
Peachtree Services, 1805 134th Ave SE, #27, Bellevue WA 98005, USA
**Pyle, Andy** — Bassist (Kinks)
Larry Page, 29 Ruston Mews, London W11 1RB, England
**Pyle, Chuck** — Singer, Guitarist, Songwriter
Terri Stewart Management & Booking, PO Box 27581, Denver CO 80227, USA
**Pyle, Michael J (Mike)** — Football Player
2436 Saranac Court, Glenview IL 60026, USA
**Pyle, Missi** — Actress
McKeon-Myrones Mgmt, 3500 Olive Ave, #770, Burbank CA 91505 USA
**Pyle, Thomas D (Artimus)** — Drummer (Lynyrd Skynyrd)
Lustig Talent, PO Box 770850, Orlando FL 32877 USA
**Pyle, W Palmer** — Football Player
14808 N Olympic Way, Fountain Hills AZ 85268, USA
**Pynchon, Thomas** — Writer
Henry Holt, 175 5th Ave, #400, New York NY 10010 USA
**Pyne, Natasha** — Actress
Kate Feast, Primrose Hill Studios, Fitzroy Road, London NW1 8TR, England
**Pyne, Stephen J** — Historian
Arizona State University, History Dept, Tempe AZ 85287, USA
**Pysnarski, Timothy M (Tim)** — Baseball Player
10716 S Austin Ave, Chicago Ridge IL 60415, USA
**Pytka, Joseph (Joe)** — Director, Actor
United Talent Agency, U T A Plaza, 9336 Civic Center Dr, Beverly Hills CA 90210 USA

**Q**

| | |
|---|---|
| **Q** | Singer (112) |
| Def Jam Records, 828 8th Ave, New York NY 10019 USA | |
| **Q, Maggie** | Actress, Model |
| Creative Artists Agency, 2000 Ave of Stars, #100, Los Angeles CA 90067 USA | |
| **Qabus ibin Sa'id al Sa'id** | Sultan, Oman |
| Diwan, PO Box 632, Muscat 113, Oman | |
| **Qasimi, Sheikh Dr Sultan ibn Muhammad Al** | Ruler, Sharjah |
| Ruler's Palace, Sharjah, United Arab Emirates | |
| **Qasimi, Sheikh Saqr ibn Muhammad Al** | Ruler, Ras Al Khaimah |
| Ruler's Palace, Ras Al Khaimah, United Arab Emirates | |
| **Q-Tip** | Rap Artist |
| Creative Artists Agency, 2000 Ave of Stars, #100, Los Angeles CA 90067 USA | |
| **Quagmire, Joshua** | Cartoonist (Cutey Bunny) |
| PO Box 2221, Los Angeles CA 90078, USA | |
| **Quaid, Dennis** | Actor |
| W M E Entertainment, 9601 Wilshire Blvd, #300, Beverly Hills CA 90210 USA | |
| **Quaid, Jack** | Actor |
| United Talent Agency, U T A Plaza, 9336 Civic Center Dr, Beverly Hills CA 90210 USA | |
| **Quaid, Randy** | Actor, Producer |
| Quaid Films, Box 156 Station F, 50 Charles St, Toronto ON M4Y 2L5, Canada | |
| **Quaintance, Rachel** | Actress, Comedienne |
| Greater Visions Artists Talent Agency, 8981 W Sunset Blvd, #101, West Hollywood CA 90069 USA | |
| **Qualls, Chad M** | Baseball Player |
| 8416 Big View Dr, Austin TX 78730, USA | |
| **Qualls, D J** | Actor |
| Paul Kohner, 9300 Wilshire Blvd, #555, Beverly Hills CA 90212 USA | |
| **Qualls, James R (Jim)** | Baseball Player |
| 410 N Country Road 950, Sutter IL 62373, USA | |
| **Quance, Kristine** | Swimmer |
| 1320 Moncado Dr, Glendale CA 91207, USA | |
| **Quann Jendrick, Megan** | Swimmer |
| 11602 135th Street Court E, Puyallup WA 98374, USA | |
| **Quant, Mary** | Fashion Designer |
| Mary Quant Ltd, 7 Montpelier St, Knightsbridge, London SW7 1EX, England | |
| **Quantrill, Paul J** | Baseball Player |
| 334 E Lake Road, Palm Harbor FL 34685, USA | |
| **Quarles, Shelton E** | Football Player |
| 17019 Candeleda de Avila, Tampa FL 33613, USA | |
| **Quarrie, Donald (Don)** | Track Athlete |
| Jamaican Amateur Athletic Assn, PO Box 272, Kingston 5, Jamaica | |
| **Quasthoff, Thomas** | Concert Singer |
| C M Artists, 127 W 96th St, #13B, New York NY 10025 USA | |
| **Quatro, Suzi** | Singer, Songwriter, Actress |
| Cape Entertainment, 8432 NW 31st Court, Fort Lauderdale FL 33351, USA | |
| **Quaye, Finley** | Singer |
| Paquin Entertainment, 468 Stradbrook Ave, Winnipeg MB R3L 0J9, Canada | |
| **Quayle, Anna** | Actress |
| Caroline Dawson, 125 Gloucester Road, London SW7 4TE, England | |
| **Quayle, J Danforth (Dan)** | Vice President |
| Laura Mintner, 7001 N Scottsdale Road, Scottsdale AZ 85253, USA | |
| **Quayle, Steven** | Director |
| Gersh Agency, 9465 Wilshire Blvd, #600, Beverly Hills CA 90212 USA | |
| **Queen Ida** | Singer, Accordian Player |
| Traditional Arts Services, 3661 Albion Place N, #2, Seattle WA 98103, USA | |
| **Queen Latifah** | Rap Artist, Actress, Model |
| Flavor Unit Entertainment, 155 Morgan St, Jersey City NJ 07302, USA | |
| **Queen, Jeffrey R (Jeff)** | Football Player |
| 4765 Canterbury Court, Oceanside CA 92056, USA | |
| **Queffelec, Anne** | Concert Pianist |
| 15 Ave Corneille, 78600 Maisons-Laffitte, France | |
| **Queler, Eve** | Conductor |
| Opera Orchestra of New York, 344 E 63rd St, #B1, New York NY 10065, USA | |
| **Quenneville, Joel N** | Ice Hockey Player, Coach |
| 835 S Park Ave, Hinsdale IL 60521, USA | |
| **Querim, Molly** | Sportscaster |
| CBS-TV, Sports Dept, 51 W 52nd St, New York NY 10019 USA | |
| **Query, Jeff L** | Football Player |
| 93 Woodlily Place, Spring TX 77382, USA | |
| **Questlove** | Drummer (Roots), DJ |
| Paradigm Agency, 360 N Crescent Dr, North Building, Beverly Hills CA 90210 USA | |
| **Questrom, Allen I** | Businessman |
| J C Penney Co, 6501 Legacy Dr, Plano TX 75024, USA | |
| **Quezada, Milly** | Singer |
| Alpha Artists , 261 E 134th St, #200, Bronx NY 10454, USA | |
| **Quick, Diana** | Actress |
| Independent Talent Group, 40 Whitfield St, London W1T 2RH, England | |
| **Quick, James E (Jim)** | Baseball Umpire |
| 6061 Keeble Lane, Camino CA 95709, USA | |
| **Quick, Jonathan D (Jon)** | Ice Hockey Player |
| Los Angeles Kings, Staples Center, 1111 S Figueroa St, Los Angeles CA 90015 USA | |
| **Quick, Michael A (Mike)** | Football Player |
| 13 Slab Branch Road, Marlton NJ 08053, USA | |
| **Quie, Albert H (Al)** | Governor, MN |
| 4209 Christy Lane, Minnetonka MN 55345, USA | |
| **Quigley, Dana C** | Golfer |
| 2670 Tecumseh Dr, West Palm Beach FL 33409, USA | |
| **Quigley, Laura** | Singer, Bassist (Misty River) |
| 1111B NW 131st Way, Vancouver WA 98685, USA | |
| **Quigley, Linnea** | Actress |
| Purrfect Productions, PO Box 1771, Pompano Beach, FL 33061 USA | |
| **Quilici, Frank R** | Baseball Player, Manager |
| 3413 E 126th St, Burnsville MN 55337, USA | |
| **Quill, Timothy E** | Social Activist, Internist |
| University of Rochester, Medical & Dentistry School, Rochester NY 14642, USA | |
| **Quillan, Frederick D (Fred)** | Football Player |
| 2924 Bailey Lane, Eugene OR 97401, USA | |

**Q - Quillan**

| | |
|---|---|
| **Quin, Sara K** | Singer (Tegan & Sara), Songwriter |
| Paquin Entertainment, 468 Stradbrooke Ave, Winnipeg MB R3L 0J9, Canada | |
| **Quince, Dolvett** | Physical Fitness Instructor, Actor |
| Rogers & Cowan, 8687 Melrose Ave, #G700, West Hollywood CA 90069 USA | |
| **Quindlen, Anna M** | Columnist |
| I C M Partners, 10250 Constellation Blvd, #900, Los Angeles CA 90067 USA | |
| **Quinlan, Kathleen** | Actress |
| Mavrick Artists Agency, 6100 Wilshire Blvd, #550, Los Angeles CA 90048, USA | |
| **Quinlan, Maeve** | Actress |
| Beech Park Entertainment, 2934 Beverly Glen Circle, #333, Los Angeles CA 90077, USA | |
| **Quinlan, Thomas R (Tom)** | Baseball Player |
| 1061 Sterling St S, Saint Paul MN 55119, USA | |
| **Quinlan, William D (Bill)** | Football Player |
| 393 Mount Vernon St, Lawrence MA 01843, USA | |
| **Quinn, Aidan** | Actor |
| Paradigm Agency, 360 N Crescent Dr, North Building, Beverly Hills CA 90210 USA | |
| **Quinn, Aileen** | Actress |
| 12747 Riverside Dr, #208, Valley Village CA 91607, USA | |
| **Quinn, Brayden T (Brady)** | Football Player |
| 5889 Connolly Court, Dublin OH 43016, USA | |
| **Quinn, Brian** | Soccer Player, Coach |
| Brian Quinn Soccer School, 9606 Aero Dr, #3500, San Diego CA 92123, USA | |
| **Quinn, Carmel** | Singer |
| Producers Inc, 11806 N 56th St, Tampa FL 33617 USA | |
| **Quinn, Colin** | Actor, Comedian |
| Brillstein Entertainment Partners, 9150 Wilshire Blvd, #350, Beverly Hills CA 90212 USA | |
| **Quinn, Cynthia** | Dancer |
| Momix, PO Box 35, Washington CT 06794, USA | |
| **Quinn, DeClan** | Cinematographer |
| 22 Cherry Ave, Cornwall on Hudson NY 12520, USA | |
| **Quinn, Ed** | Actor |
| I C M Partners, 10250 Constellation Blvd, #900, Los Angeles CA 90067 USA | |
| **Quinn, J B Patrick (Pat)** | Ice Hockey Player, Coach |
| Edmonton Oilers, 11230 110th St, Edmonton AB T5G 3H7, Canada | |
| **Quinn, Jane Bryant** | Columnist |
| Newsweek, Editorial Dept, 251 W 57th St, New York NY 10019, USA | |
| **Quinn, Jonathan G (Jonny)** | Drummer (Snow Patrol) |
| Big Life Mgmt, 67-69 Charlton St, London NW1 1HY, England | |
| **Quinn, Jonathan R** | Football Player |
| 8409 W 145th Terrace, Overland Park KS 66223, USA | |
| **Quinn, Kimberly** | Actress |
| Don Buchwald, 6500 Wilshire Blvd, #2200, Los Angeles CA 90048 USA | |
| **Quinn, Marc** | Artist, Sculptor |
| Saatchi Gallery, Duke Of York's H Q, King's Road, London SW3 4RY, England | |
| **Quinn, Martha** | Actress, Model |
| Kazarian/Measures/Ruskin, 11969 Ventura Blvd, #300, Studio City CA 91604 USA | |
| **Quinn, Michael P (Mike)** | Football Player |
| 10703 Del Monte Dr, Houston TX 77042, USA | |
| **Quinn, Molly C** | Actress |
| Ellen Meyer Mgmt, 8899 Beverly Blvd, #612, West Hollywood CA 90048, USA | |
| **Quinn, Noelle** | Basketball Player |
| Washington Mystics, Verizon Center, 401 9th St NW, #750, Washington DC 20004 USA | |
| **Quinn, Patricia** | Actress |
| Jonathan Altaras Assoc, 11 Garrick St, London WC2E 9AR, England | |
| **Quinn, Sally** | Journalist |
| 3014 N St NW, Washington DC 20007, USA | |
| **Quinones August, Denise M** | Beauty Queen, Actress |
| Untitled Entertainment, 350 S Beverly Dr, #200, Beverly Hills CA 90212 USA | |
| **Quinones Torruellas, Luis R** | Baseball Player |
| 5821 Calle San Bruno Urb Santa Teresita, Ponce PR 00730, USA | |
| **Quinones, John** | Commentator |
| ABC-TV, News Dept, 77 W 66th St, New York NY 10023 USA | |
| **Quint, Deron T** | Ice Hockey Player |
| 13 Littlehale Road, Durham NH 03824, USA | |
| **Quintal, Stephane** | Ice Hockey Player |
| 1356A Rue La Fontaine, Montreal QC H2L 1T5, Canada | |
| **Quintana, Carlos** | Boxer |
| DiBella Entertainment, 350 7th Ave, #800, New York NY 10001, USA | |
| **Quinto, Zachary** | Actor |
| Creative Artists Agency, 2000 Ave of Stars, #100, Los Angeles CA 90067 USA | |
| **Quirk, James P (Jamie)** | Baseball Player |
| 310 W 123rd Terrace, Kansas City MO 64145, USA | |
| **Quirk, Matthew** | Writer |
| Hatchette Book Group, 3 Center Plaza, Boston MA 02108, USA | |
| **Quiroga, Elena** | Writer |
| Agencia Balcells, Diagonal 580, 08021 Barcelona, Spain | |
| **Quist, Janet** | Model |
| 13446 Poway Road, #239, Poway CA 92064, USA | |
| **Quivar, Florence** | Opera Singer |
| Columbia Artists Mgmt Inc, 1790 Broadway, #702, New York NY 10019 USA | |
| **Quivers, Robin O** | Entertainer |
| Sirius Satellite Radio, 1221 Ave of Americas, New York NY 10020, USA | |
| **Quock, Audrey** | Model, Actress |
| New York Model Mgmt, 596 Broadway, #701, New York NY 10012 USA | |
| **Quon, Xian** | Model |
| Otto Models, 2901 W Coast Highway, #350, Newport Beach CA 92663, USA | |
| **Qureshi, Aisam** | Tennis Player |
| Octagon Worldwide, 1751 Pinnacle Dr, #1500, McLean VA 22102 USA | |
| **Qvist, Trine** | Curling Athlete |
| Curling Assn, Idraettens Hus, 2605 Brondby, Denmark | |

**Q**

# R

|  |  |
|---|---|
| **Raab, Marc A** <br> 8500 Sea Pines Place, McKinney TX 75070, USA | Football Player |
| **Raabe, Brian C** <br> 38760 Kost Trail, North Branch MN 55056, USA | Baseball Player |
| **Raabe, Max** <br> Max Raabe & Partner, Meinekestr 6, 10719 Berlin, Germany | Opera Singer |
| **Raakhee** <br> Muktangan Sarojini, Naidu Road, Santacruz, Mumbai MS 400054, India | Actress |
| **Raba, Robert (Bob)** <br> 16066 Acre St, North Hills CA 91343, USA | Football Player |
| **Rabach, Casey E** <br> 5707 Bay Shore Dr, Sturgeon Bay WI 54235, USA | Football Player |
| **Rabal, Liberto** <br> Anne Alvares Correa, 34 Rue Jouffroy d'Abbans, 75017 Paris, France | Actor |
| **Raban, Jonathan** <br> Pantheon Books, 1745 Broadway, New York NY 10019, USA | Writer |
| **Rabe, Charles H (Charlie)** <br> 6059 E Sierra Blanca St, Mesa AZ 85215, USA | Baseball Player |
| **Rabe, David W** <br> Creative Artists Agency, 2000 Ave of Stars, #100, Los Angeles CA 90067 USA | Writer |
| **Rabe, Lily** <br> Framework Entertainment, 9057 Nemo St, #C, West Hollywood CA 90069 USA | Actress |
| **Rabe, Pamela** <br> Shanahan Mgmt, PO Box 1509, Darlinghurst NSW 1300, Australia | Actress |
| **Rabelo, Mike** <br> 5813 N 17th St, Tampa FL 33610, USA | Baseball Player |
| **Rabemananjara, Charles** <br> Premier's Office, BP 248, Mahazoarivo, 101 Antananarivo, Madagascar | Prime Minister, Madagascar |
| **Rabin, Trevor** <br> Kraft-Engel Mgmt, 15233 Ventura Blvd, #200, Sherman Oaks CA 91403 USA | Composer |
| **Rabinovitch, B Seymour** <br> 116 Fairview Ave N, #832, Seattle WA 98109, USA | Chemist |
| **Rabinowitz, Dorothy** <br> Wall Street Journal, Editorial Dept, 1 World Financial Center, New York NY 10281 USA | Journalist |
| **Rabinowitz, Jesse C** <br> University of California, Molecular & Cell Biology Dept, Berkeley CA 94720, USA | Biochemist |
| **Rabinyan, Dorit** <br> Bloomsbury Publishing, 50 Bedford Square, London WC1B 3DP, England | Writer |
| **Rabkin, Mitchell T** <br> Beth Israel Deaconess Medical Center, 330 Brookline Ave, Boston MA 02215, USA | Physician |
| **Raboteau, Albert J** <br> Princeton University, Religion School, Princeton NJ 08544, USA | Religious Historian |
| **Rabourdin, Olivier** <br> J F P M, 11 Rue Chavez, 75781 Paris Cedex 16, France | Actor |
| **Raboy, Marcus** <br> Modus Entertainment, 8730 W Sunset Blvd, #290, West Hollywood CA 90069, USA | Director |
| **Raburn, Ryan N** <br> 6612 Ike Smith Road, Plant City FL 33565, USA | Baseball Player |
| **Raby, Stuart** <br> Ohio State University, Physics Dept, Columbus OH 43210, USA | Physicist |
| **Racette, Patricia** <br> Opus 3 Artists, 470 Park Ave S, #900N, New York NY 10016 USA | Opera Singer |
| **Rachel, Allyn** <br> Creative Artists Agency, 2000 Ave of Stars, #100, Los Angeles CA 90067 USA | Actress |
| **Rachel, Leah** <br> W M E Entertainment, 9601 Wilshire Blvd, #300, Beverly Hills CA 90210 USA | Actress, Writer |
| **Rachins, Alan** <br> Talent Works, 3500 W Olive Ave, #1400, Burbank CA 91505 USA | Actor |
| **Rachlin, Julian** <br> Askonas Holt, Lincoln House, 300 High Holborn, London WC1V 7JH, England | Concert Violinist |
| **Racicot, Marc F** <br> 28013 Swan Cove Dr, Bigfork MT 59911, USA | Governor, MT |
| **Racine, Yves** <br> Arizona Capital Inc, 1515 Ave Saint Jean Baptiste, Quebec QC G2E 5E2, Canada | Ice Hockey Player |
| **Rackers, Neil W** <br> 12374 Whitworth Terrace Court, Saint Louis MO 63141, USA | Football Player |
| **Rackley, Derek L** <br> 2770 Shumard Oak Dr, Braselton GA 30517, USA | Football Player |
| **Rackley, Marvin E (Marv)** <br> 512 S Bibb St, Westminster SC 29693, USA | Baseball Player |
| **Raczka, Michael (Mike)** <br> 72 Foley St, Southington CT 06489, USA | Baseball Player |
| **Radachowsky, George J, Jr** <br> 63 Lake Place N, Danbury CT 06810, USA | Football Player |
| **Radcliffe, Daniel** <br> Artist Rights Group, 4 Great Portland St, London W1W 8PA, England | Actor |
| **Rade, John A** <br> 611 Deertrail Dr, Hailey ID 83333, USA | Football Player |
| **Rademacher, Ingo** <br> S D B Partners, 1801 Ave of Stars, #902, Los Angeles CA 90067 USA | Actor |
| **Rademacher, T Peter (Pete)** <br> 5585 River Styx Road, Medina OH 44256, USA | Boxer |
| **Rademacher, William S (Bill)** <br> 5409 Maple Ridge, Haslett MI 48840, USA | Football Player |
| **Rader, David M (Dave)** <br> 14413 Westdale Dr, Bakersfield CA 93314, USA | Baseball Player |
| **Rader, Dotson C** <br> Parade Magazine, Editorial Dept, 750 3rd Ave, New York NY 10017, USA | Writer |
| **Rader, Douglas L (Doug)** <br> 3332 SE Court Dr, Stuart FL 34997, USA | Baseball Player, Manager |
| **Rader, Paul A** <br> Ashbury College, President's Office, 1 Macklem Dr, Wilmore KY 40390, USA | Religious Leader, Educator |
| **Rader, Randall R** <br> US Appeals Court, 717 Madison Place NW, Washington DC 20439, USA | Judge |
| **Rader-Shieber, Chas** <br> Columbia Artists Mgmt Inc, 1790 Broadway, #702, New York NY 10019 USA | Director |

| | |
|---|---|
| **Radford, Mark J** | Basketball Player |
| 3423 NE 22nd Ave, Portland OR 97212, USA | |
| **Radford, Michael** | Director |
| Intellectual Artists Mgmt, 10585 Santa Monica Blvd, #135, Los Angeles CA 90025, USA | |
| **Radigan, Terry** | Singer, Songwriter |
| S C Entertainment, 360 W 22nd St, #9A, New York NY 10011, USA | |
| **Radin, Joshua** | Singer, Songwriter, Actor |
| Wilspro Mgmt, PO Box 9. Point Pleasant NJ 08742, USA | |
| **Radinsky, Scott D** | Baseball Player |
| 2974 Santiago St, Westlake Village CA 91362, USA | |
| **Radke, Brad W** | Baseball Player |
| 125 18th St, Belleair Beach FL 33786, USA | |
| **Radko, Christopher** | Artist |
| PO Box 536, Elmsford NY 10523, USA | |
| **Radmanovic, Nebojsa** | President, Bosnia & Herzegovina |
| President's Office, Marsala Titz 7, 71000 Sarajevo, Bosnia & Herzegovina | |
| **Radmanovic, Vladimir** | Basketball Player |
| Chicago Bulls, United Center, 1901 W Madison St, Chicago IL 60612 USA | |
| **Radner, Roy** | Economist |
| 30711 Overlook Run, Buena Vista CO 81211, USA | |
| **Radnor, Josh** | Actor |
| United Talent Agency, U T A Plaza, 9336 Civic Center Dr, Beverly Hills CA 90210 USA | |
| **Radojevic, Danilo** | Ballet Dancer |
| American Ballet Theatre, 890 Broadway, #300, New York NY 10003 USA | |
| **Radovich, Frank R** | Basketball Player |
| 121 Lakewood Dr, Statesboro GA 30458, USA | |
| **Radtke, Ed** | Director, Writer |
| Parseghian/Planco, 388 2nd Ave, #506, New York, NY 10010 USA | |
| **Radulov, Alexander** | Ice Hockey Player |
| 2600 Hillsboro Pike, #322, Nashville TN 37212, USA | |
| **Radvanovsky, Sondra** | Opera Singer |
| I M G Artists, Hogarth Business Park, Chiswick, London W4 2TH, England | |
| **Radwanska, Agnieszka** | Tennis Player, Model |
| Women's Tennis Assn, 1 Progress Plaza, #1500, Saint Petersburg FL 33701 USA | |
| **Rady, Michael** | Actor |
| Gersh Agency, 9465 Wilshire Blvd, #600, Beverly Hills CA 90212 USA | |
| **Rae, Brenda** | Opera Singer |
| Columbia Artists Mgmt Inc, 1790 Broadway, #702, New York NY 10019 USA | |
| **Rae, Cassidy** | Actress |
| 24708 Riverchase Dr, #B213, Valencia CA 91355, USA | |
| **Rae, Charlotte** | Actress |
| C E S D, 10635 Santa Monica Blvd, #130, Los Angeles CA 90025 USA | |
| **Rae, Corinne Bailey** | Singer, Songwriter |
| Creative Artists Agency, 2000 Ave of Stars, #100, Los Angeles CA 90067 USA | |
| **Rae, Patricia** | Actress |
| Rebel Entertainment Partners, 5701 Wilshire Blvd, #456, Los Angeles CA 90036, USA | |
| **Raether, Harold H (Hal)** | Baseball Player |
| 6105 Lincoln Dr, #133, Minneapolis MN 55436, USA | |
| **Rafalski, Brian C** | Ice Hockey Player |
| 615 Lighthouse Way, Sanibel FL 33957, USA | |
| **Rafelson, Bob** | Director |
| 1543 Dog Team Road, New Haven VT 05472, USA | |
| **Raffarin, Jean-Pierre** | Prime Minister, France |
| 7 Route de Saint-Georges, 86360 Chasseneuil-du-Poitou, France | |
| **Rafferty, Thomas M (Tom)** | Football Player |
| 1526 Mount Gilead Road, Roanoke TX 76262, USA | |
| **Rafikov, Mars Z** | Cosmonaut |
| Ul M Gorkova 59, KV 44, 480 002 Almaty, Kazakhstan | |
| **Rafsanjani, Hojatoleslam H** | President, Iran |
| Expediency Council of Islamic Order, Majilis, Teheran, Iran | |
| **Rafter, Patrick** | Tennis Player |
| Cherish the Children Foundation, 108 King William St, #800, Adelaide SA 5000, Australia | |
| **Ragan, David** | Auto Racing Driver |
| Roush Fenway Racing, 4600 Roush Place, Concord NC 28027, USA | |
| **Ragin, John S** | Actor |
| 5706 Briarcliff Road, Los Angeles CA 90068, USA | |
| **Raglan, Herb** | Ice Hockey Player |
| 335 King St, Peterborough ON K9J 2S8, Canada | |
| **Ragnarsson, Marcus** | Ice Hockey Player |
| Hallonstigen 2, Bjorklinge 74 030, Sweden | |
| **Rago, Joseph** | Journalist |
| Wall Street Journal, Editorial Dept, 1 World Financial Center, New York NY 10281 USA | |
| **Ragogna, Mike** | Singer, Guitarist, Songwriter |
| PO Box 2331, Fairfield IA 52556, USA | |
| **Ragonese, Isabella** | Actress |
| Officine Artistiche, Via Francesco Domenico Guerrazzi 7, 00152 Rome, Italy | |
| **Ragsdale, William** | Actor |
| Stone Manners Salners, 9911 W Pico Blvd, #1400, Los Angeles CA 90035 USA | |
| **Rahal, Robert W (Bobby)** | Auto Racing Driver, Owner |
| Team Rahal Racing, 4601 Lyman Dr, Hilliard OH 43026, USA | |
| **Rahim, Tahar** | Actor |
| A U R A Agency, 34/36 Rue du Louvre, 75001 Paris France | |
| **Rahlves, Daron** | Alpine Skier |
| 11655 Mount Rose View Dr, Truckee CA 96161, USA | |
| **Rahm, Kevin** | Actor |
| Gersh Agency, 9465 Wilshire Blvd, #600, Beverly Hills CA 90212 USA | |
| **Rahman Khan, Ataur** | Prime Minister, Bangladesh |
| Bangladesh Jatiya League, 500A Dhanmondi R/A, Road 7, Dhaka, Bangladesh | |
| **Rahman, Allah Rakkha (A R)** | Composer |
| Panchthan Recording Inn, 5 4th St, Dr Subbaraya Nagar, Kodambakkam, Chennai 24, India | |
| **Rahzel** | Rap Artist, Percussionist (Roots) |
| Agency Group Ltd, 142 W 57th St, #600, New York NY 10019 USA | |
| **Raible, Steve C** | Football Player |
| 18 W Raye St, Seattle WA 98119, USA | |
| **Raich, Eric J** | Baseball Player |
| 3963 Edward Dr, Brunswick OH 44212, USA | |

**Raichle, Marcus E** — Neurologist, Radiologist
Washington University Medical School, Radiology Dept, Saint Louis MO 63110, USA
**Raikkonen, Kimi** — Auto Racing Driver
Team Lotus, Hethel Industrial Estate, Potash Lane, Hethel, Norfolk NR14 8EY, England
**Railsback, Steve** — Actor
11684 Ventura Blvd, #581, Studio City CA 91604, USA
**Raimey, David E (Dave)** — Football Player
2212 W 2nd St, Dayton OH 45417, USA
**Raimi, Sam** — Director, Producer, Actor
Stars Road Entertainment, 10202 W Washington Blvd, Lean Building, Culver City CA 90232, USA
**Raimi, Ted** — Actor
Liberman-Zerman Mgmt, 252 N Larchmont Blvd, #200, Los Angeles CA 90004 USA
**Raimond, Jean-Bernard** — Government Official, France
12 Rue des Poissonniers, 92200 Neuilly-sur-Seine, France
**Raimondi, Ruggero** — Opera Singer
M Gromof, 140 Bis Rue Lecourbe, 75015 Paris, France
**Raine, Craig A** — Writer
New College, English Dept, Oxford OX1 3BN, England
**Rainer, Luise** — Actress
34 Eaton Mews North, London SW1 XAS, England
**Rainer, Wali R** — Football Player
8119 Braidstone Terrace, Chesterfield VA 23838, USA
**Raines, F Anthony (Tony)** — Auto, Truck Racing Driver
Front Row Motorsports, 3536 Denver Dr, Denver NC 28037, USA
**Raines, Shirley C** — Educator
University of Memphis, President's Office, Administration Building, Memphis TN 38152, USA
**Raines, Timothy (Tim)** — Baseball Player
1242 Saint Albans Loop, Lake Mary FL 32746, USA
**Rainey, Charles D (Chuck)** — Baseball Player
6484 Del Cerro Blvd, San Diego CA 92120, USA
**Rainey, James** — Pianist (Stamps Quartet)
PO Box 1471, Brentwood TN 37024, USA
**Rainey, Matt** — Photojournalist
Star-Ledger, Editorial Dept, 1 Star-Ledger Plaza, Newark NJ 07102, USA
**Rainford, Rob** — Chef
Agency Group, 9348 Civic Center Dr, #200, Beverly Hills CA 90210 USA
**Rains, Traver** — Fashion Designer
Heatherette, 111 E 7th St, New York NY 10009, USA
**Rainwater, Keech** — Drummer (Lonestar)
Borman Entertainment, 4322 Harding Pike, #429, Nashville TN 37205, USA
**Raiola, Dominic** — Football Player
7940 Barnsbury Ave, West Bloomfield MI 48324, USA
**Raisa, Francia** — Actress
Abrams Artists, 9200 W Sunset Blvd, #1125, West Hollywood CA 90069 USA
**Raisman, Alexandra R (Aly)** — Gymnast
Octagon Worldwide, 1751 Pinnacle Dr, #1500, McLean VA 22102 USA
**Raison, Miranda** — Actress
Ken McReddie Assoc, 101 Finsbury Pavement, London EC2A 1RS, England
**Raitt, Bonnie L** — Singer, Songwriter
Gold Mountain, 3940 Laurel Canyon Blvd, #444, Studio City CA 91604 USA
**Raja Permaisuri Agong XIII** — Sultana, Malaysia
Sultan's Palace, Istana Bukit Serene, 50502 Kuala Lumpur, Malaysia
**Rajapakse, Mahinda** — President, Sri Lanka
President's Office, Republic Square, Sri Jayewardenepura Kotte, Sri Lanka
**Rajasulochana** — Actress
70 G N Chetty Road, T Nagar, Chennai TN 600017, India
**Rajat, Kapoor** — Actor, Director
140 Andheri Indl Est, Andheri (W), Mumbai MS 400053, India
**Rajna, Thomas** — Concert Pianist, Composer
10 Wyndover Road, Claremont, Cape Town, West Cape 7708, South Africa
**Rajoelina, Audray** — President, Madagascar
President's Office, 11 Oktomvri BB, 101 Antananarivo, Madagascar
**Rajoy, Mariano** — Prime Minister, Spain
Prime Minister's Office, Complejo de las Moncloa, 28071 Madrid, Spain
**Rajskub, Mary Lynn** — Actress
Innovative Artists, 1505 10th St, Santa Monica CA 90401 USA
**Rakaa Iriscience** — Rap Artist (Dilated Peoples)
Zzonked, Stratford Workshops, Burford Road, London E15 2SP, England
**Rakers, Jason P** — Baseball Player
547 Hickory Hollow Dr, Canfield OH 44406, USA
**Rakhmonov, Imomali S** — President, Tajikistan
President's Office, Rudaki Prospect 80, 734051 Dusanabe, Tajikistan
**Rakim** — Rap Artist (Eric B & Rakim)
Padell Nadell Fine Wineberger, 59 Maiden Lane, #2700, New York NY 10038 USA
**Rakoczy, Gregg A** — Football Player
9031 Quail Creek Dr, Tampa FL 33647, USA
**Rakove, Jack N** — Historian, Writer
Stanford University, History Dept, Stanford CA 94305, USA
**Rales, Steven M** — Businessman
Danaher Corp, 1250 24th St NW, Washington DC 20037, USA
**Rall, J Edward** — Physician
9901 Longs Mill Road, Rocky Ridge MD 21778, USA
**Rall, Ted** — Editorial Cartoonist
Chronicle Features, 901 Mission St, San Francisco CA 94103 USA
**Ralph, Richard P** — Governor, Falkland Islands
Governor's Office, Government House, Stanley, Falkland Islands
**Ralph, Sheryl Lee** — Actress, Singer
S M S Talent, 8383 Wilshire Blvd, #230, Beverly Hills CA 90211 USA
**Ralston, Dennis** — Tennis Player
203 Wellwood Lane, Conroe TX 77304, USA
**Ralston, John R** — Football Player, Coach
8245 Claret Court, San Jose CA 95135, USA
**Ralston, Steve** — Soccer Player
New England Revolution, 1 Patriot Place, Foxboro MA 02035 USA
**Ram, C Venkata** — Physician
Texas Southwestern Medical Center, 5323 Harry Hines Blvd, Dallas TX 75390, USA

**Rama IX** King, Thailand
Chitralada Villa, Bangkok, Thailand
**Ramachandran, Vilayanur S** Neuroscientist
University of California San Diego, Brian/Cognition Center, 9500 Gilman Drive, La Jolla CA 92093, USA
**Ramage, Rob** Ice Hockey Player
16127 Wilson Manor Dr, Chesterfield MO 63005, USA
**Ramahatra, Victor** Prime Minister, Madagascar; Army General
PO Box 6004, 101 Antananarivo, Madagascar
**Ramakrishnan, Venkatraman** Nobel Chemistry Laureate
M R C Molecular Biology Laboratory, Hills Road, Cambridge CB2 0QH, England
**Ramamurthy, Sendhil** Actor
Levine Okwu Erickson, 6363 Wilshire Blvd, #300, Los Angeles CA 90048, USA
**Ramazzotti, Eros L W** Singer, Songwriter
Trident Mgmt, Corso Europa 13, 20122 Milan, Italy
**Rambahadur Limbu** Vietnam War Borneo Army Hero (VC)
Box 420, Bandar Seri Begawan, Negara Brunei Darussalam, Brunei
**Rambis, D Kurt** Basketball Player, Coach
20 Chatham, Manhattan Beach CA 90266, USA
**Ramenofsky Wingfield, Marilyn** Swimmer
1240 NW 116th St, Seattle WA 98177, USA
**Ramey, Samuel E** Opera Singer
320 Central Park West, New York NY 10025, USA
**Ramgoolam, Navinchandra** Prime Minister, Mauritius
Prime Minister's Office, Government Center, Port Louis, Mauritius
**Ramirez Vazquez, Pedro** Architect
Avenida de la Fuentes 170, Mexico City 01900 DF, Mexico
**Ramirez, Aramis N** Baseball Player
1440 N Lake Shore Dr, #10EG, Chicago IL 60610, USA
**Ramirez, Cear** Chef
Brooklyn Fare Restaurant, 200 Schermerhorn St, Brooklyn NY 11201, USA
**Ramirez, Cierra** Actress
Corsa Agency, 11704 Wilshire Blvd, #204, Los Angeles CA 90025, USA
**Ramirez, Dania** Actress
I C M Partners, 10250 Constellation Blvd, #900, Los Angeles CA 90067 USA
**Ramirez, Edgar** Actor
Creative Artists Agency, 2000 Ave of Stars, #100, Los Angeles CA 90067 USA
**Ramirez, Efren** Actor
Clear Talent Group, 10950 Ventura Blvd, Studio City, CA 91604, USA
**Ramirez, Hanley** Baseball Player
2903 Lake Ridge Lane, Weston FL 33332, USA
**Ramirez, Horacio** Baseball Player
6424 Queens Court Trace, Mableton GA 30126, USA
**Ramirez, Manuel A (Manny)** Baseball Player
13737 NW 18th Court, Pembroke Pines FL 33028, USA
**Ramirez, Marisa** Actress
Harrison Stokes, 8730 W Sunset Blvd, #270, West Hollywood CA 90069, USA
**Ramirez, Michael P (Mike)** Editorial Cartoonist
Investor's Business Daily, 19 W 44th St, #1804, New York NY 10036, USA
**Ramirez, Pedro J** Editor
El Mundo, Editor's Office, Calle Pradillo 42, 28002 Madrid, Spain
**Ramirez, Raul** Tennis Player
Avenida Ruiz, 65 Sur Ensenada, Baja California, Mexico
**Ramirez, Sara** Actress
Mitchell K Stubbs Assoc, 8695 W Washington Blvd, #204, Culver City CA 90232 USA
**Ramis, Harold A** Actor, Director, Writer
United Talent Agency, U T A Plaza, 9336 Civic Center Dr, Beverly Hills CA 90210 USA
**Ramo, Simon** Businessman
1221 Ocean Ave, #1003, Santa Monica CA 90401, USA
**Ramon, Haim** Government Official, Israel
Knesset, Kiryat Ben-Gurion, Jerusalem 91950, Israel
**Ramos Guerra, Pedro G (Pete)** Baseball Player
6637 W 22nd Lane, Hialeah FL 33016, USA
**Ramos Ricciardi, Tabare R (Tab)** Soccer Player
Tab Ramos Soccer Programs, 17 Blair Road, Aberdeen NJ 07747, USA
**Ramos, Constance (Connie)** Actress
Paradigm Agency, 360 N Crescent Dr, North Building, Beverly Hills CA 90210 USA
**Ramos, Del** Singer (Association)
Variety Artists, 1924 Spring St, Paso Robles CA 93446 USA
**Ramos, Domingo A** Baseball Player
Carr Duarte KM 8 1/2, Ucey al Medio, Santiago, Dominican Republic
**Ramos, Fidel V** President, Philippines; Army General
120 Maria Cristina St, AAVA Muntinlupa City, Philippines
**Ramos, Hilario (Larry), Jr** Singer, Guitarist (Association)
Variety Artists, 1924 Spring St, Paso Robles CA 93446 USA
**Ramos, Melvin J (Mel)** Artist
5941 Ocean View Dr, Oakland CA 94618, USA
**Ramos, Patrick** Drummer (Versus)
Ground Control Touring, 20 Jay St, #838, Brooklyn NY 11201, USA
**Ramos, Roberto (Bobby)** Baseball Player
8945 Lake Irma Point, Orlando FL 32817, USA
**Ramos, Rudy** Actor, Singer
Craig Wyckoff Mgmt, 11300 Ventura Blvd, #100, Studio City CA 91604, USA
**Ramos, Sarah** Actress, Director, Writer
I C M Partners, 10250 Constellation Blvd, #900, Los Angeles CA 90067 USA
**Ramos-Horta, Jose** Nobel Laureate; President, Timor-Leste
President's Office, Dili, Timor-Leste
**Ramotar, Donald** President, Guyana
President's Office, Brickham, New Garden & South Sts, Georgetown, Guyana
**Ramphele, Mamphela A** Educator
International Bank of Reconstruction/Development, 1818 H St NW, Washington DC 20433, USA
**Rampling, Charlotte** Actress
Diamond Mgmt, 31 Percy St, London W1T 2DD, England
**Ramsay, Anne** Actress
A P A Talent/Literary Agency, 405 S Beverly Dr, #300, Beverly Hills CA 90212 USA
**Ramsay, Craig** Ice Hockey Player, Coach
12205 Glenmore Dr, Coral Springs FL 33071, USA

# R

**Ramsay, Gordon** — Chef, Entertainer
One Potato Two Potato, 1950 Sawtelle Blvd, #346, Los Angeles CA 90025, USA
**Ramsay, John T (Jack)** — Basketball Coach, Executive
11118 Gulf Shore Dr, #904, Naples FL 34108, USA
**Ramsay, Laymon** — Baseball Player
2417 Princeton Ave SW, Birmingham AL 35211, USA
**Ramsay, Lynne** — Director, Writer
W M E Entertainment, 9601 Wilshire Blvd, #300, Beverly Hills CA 90210 USA
**Ramsay, Marshall** — Cartoonist
Copley News Service, 123 Camino de la Reina, San Diego CA 92108, USA
**Ramsey, Anessa** — Actress
Mitchell K Stubbs Assoc, 8695 W Washington Blvd, #204, Culver City CA 90232 USA
**Ramsey, Calvin (Cal)** — Basketball Player
New York University, Alumni Office, 181 Mercer St, New York NY 10012, USA
**Ramsey, David** — Actor
A P A Talent/Literary Agency, 405 S Beverly Dr, #300, Beverly Hills CA 90212 USA
**Ramsey, Derrick K** — Football Player
C M R 445 Box 23, APO AE 09046, USA
**Ramsey, Fernando D** — Baseball Player
2501 Sandy Trail, Keller TX 76248, USA
**Ramsey, Frank V, Jr** — Basketball Player, Coach
PO Box 363, Madisonville KY 42431, USA
**Ramsey, James R** — Educator
University of Louisville, President's Office, Louisville KY 40292, USA
**Ramsey, Laura** — Actress
Luber Rocklin Entertainment, 8530 Wilshire Blvd, #555, Beverly Hills CA 90211 USA
**Ramsey, Lowell W (Chuck), Jr** — Football Player
17519 Martel Road, Lenoir City TN 37772, USA
**Ramsey, Mary** — Singer (10000 Maniacs)
Geffen Records, 10900 Wilshire Blvd, #1000, Los Angeles CA 90024 USA
**Ramsey, Michael** — Attorney
2120 Welch St, Houston TX 77019, USA
**Ramsey, Michael (Mike)** — Ice Hockey Player
Ramsey's Gold Medal Sports, 445 W 79th St, Chanhassen MN 55317, USA
**Ramsey, Michael Jeffrey (Mike)** — Baseball Player
11564 92nd Way N, Largo FL 33773, USA
**Ramsey, Nathan L (Nate)** — Football Player
1938 Cambridge St, Philadelphia PA 19130, USA
**Ramsey, Wesley (Wes)** — Actor
Abrams Artists, 9200 W Sunset Blvd, #1125, West Hollywood CA 90069 USA
**Ramsey, William E** — Navy Admiral
825 Bayshore Dr, Pensacola FL 32507, USA
**Ramsfjell, Bent Aanund** — Curling Athlete
Curling Assn, Sognsveien 75, Serviceboks 1, 0840 Oslo, Norway
**Ramson, Eason L** — Football Player
3526 Bayberry Dr, Walnut Creek CA 94598, USA
**Ramstein, Marco** — Curling Athlete
Curling Assn, PO Box 606, 3000 Bern, Switzerland
**Ran, Shulamit** — Composer
University of Chicago, Music Dept, 5845 S Ellis Ave, Chicago IL 60637, USA
**Ranaldo, Lee** — Guitarist (Sonic Youth)
Silva Artist Mgmt, 722 Steward St, Los Angeles CA 90038, USA
**Rand Reese, Mary** — Track Athlete
6650 Los Gatos, Atascadero CA 93422, USA
**Rand, A Barry** — Association Executive, Businessman
American Association of Retired Persons, 601 E St NW, Washington DC 20049, USA
**Rand, Robert W** — Neurosurgeon, Educator
Good Samaritan Hospital, Neurosciences Institute, Los Angeles CA 90017, USA
**Randa, Joseph G (Joe)** — Baseball Player
6436 Ensley Lane, Mission Hills KS 66208, USA
**Randall, Alice** — Writer, Songwriter
McCormick & Williams, 37 W 20th St, New York NY 10011, USA
**Randall, Anne** — Actress, Model
10526 W Tropicana Circle, Sun City AZ 85351, USA
**Randall, Carolyn D** — Judge
US Court of Appeals, 515 Rusk St, #12015, Houston TX 77002, USA
**Randall, Claire** — Religious Leader
9965 W Royal Oak Road, #1214, Sun City AZ 85351, USA
**Randall, Frankie** — Boxer
1210 Ashwood Dr, Jefferson City TN 37760, USA
**Randall, James O (Sap)** — Baseball Player
158 Heather Lane, Ruston LA 71270, USA
**Randall, Jon** — Singer, Songwriter
Joe's Garage, 4405 Belmont Park Terrace, Nashville TN 37215, USA
**Randall, Josh** — Actor
I F A Talent Agency, 8730 W Sunset Blvd, #490, West Hollywood CA 90069 USA
**Randall, Lisa** — Physicist
Harvard University, Physics Dept, Cambridge MA 02138, USA
**Randall, Semeka C** — Basketball Player, Coach
Michigan State University, Athletic Dept, East Lansing MI 48824, USA
**Randazzo, Mike** — Actor
585 Gatewood Dr, Greenwood IN 46143, USA
**Randi, James** — Illusionist
201 SE 12th St, Fort Lauderdale FL 33316, USA
**Randle El, Antwaan** — Football Player
PO Box 3247, Leesburg VA 20177, USA
**Randle, E Tate** — Football Player
11116 Sea Hero Lane, Austin TX 78748, USA
**Randle, Ervin L** — Football Player
900 Spring Creek Dr, Grapevine TX 76051, USA
**Randle, John A** — Football Player
375 Calamus Circle, Hamel MN 55340, USA
**Randle, Leonard S (Lenny)** — Baseball Player
39461 Cozumel Court, Murrieta CA 92563, USA
**Randle, Theresa** — Actress
Agency Group, 9348 Civic Center Dr, #200, Beverly Hills CA 90210 USA

**Randle, Tom** — Opera Singer
I M G Artists, Hogarth Business Park, Chiswick, London W4 2TH, England

**Randolph, A Raymond** — Judge
US Court of Appeals, 333 Constitution NW, #4400, Washington DC 20001, USA

**Randolph, Alvin C (Al)** — Football Player
319 Roble Ave, Redwood City CA 94061, USA

**Randolph, Anthony E, Jr** — Basketball Player
Denver Nuggets, Pepsi Center, 1000 Chopper Circle, Denver CO 80204 USA

**Randolph, Carl** — Bassist (Reveille)
David Levin Mgmt, 200 W 57th St, #308, New York NY 10019, USA

**Randolph, Joyce** — Actress
295 Central Park West, #18A, New York NY 10024, USA

**Randolph, Leo** — Boxer
17020 20th Ave E, Spanaway WA 98387, USA

**Randolph, Robert** — Guitarist
Red Light Mgmt, 44 Wall St, #2200, New York NY 10005, USA

**Randolph, Sam** — Golfer
5285 Heightsview Lane E, #322, Fort Worth TX 76132, USA

**Randolph, Stephen** — Baseball Player
3706 Apache Forest Dr, Austin TX 78739, USA

**Randolph, Willie I** — Baseball Player, Manager
715 Jenney Trail, Franklin Lakes NJ 07417, USA

**Randolph, Zachary (Zach)** — Basketball Player
Memphis Grizzlies, 191 Beale St, Memphis TN 38103 USA

**Randrup, Michael** — Test Pilot
10 Fairlawn Road, Lythamst, Annes, Lancashire FY8 5PT, England

**Rands, Bernard** — Composer, Conductor
Harvard University, Music Dept, Cambridge MA 02138, USA

**Raney, Sue** — Singer
5114 Ranchito Ave, Sherman Oaks CA 91423, USA

**Ranford, William (Bill)** — Ice Hockey Player
670 Vista Lago Circle N, Palm Desert CA 92211, USA

**Ranglin, Ernest** — Guitarist, Composer
Universal Attractions, 135 W 26th St, #1200, New York NY 10001 USA

**Ranheim, Paul S** — Ice Hockey Player
12128 N Reflection Ridge Dr, Oro Valley AZ 85755, USA

**Rania al-Abdullah** — Queen, Jordan
Royal Palace, Royal Hashemite Court, Amman, Jordan

**Raniere, Sandro** — Soccer Player
Confederacion de Futebol, Rua Victor Civita 66, #1, Rio de Janeiro 22775 044, Brazil

**Ranieri, Luisa** — Actress
Media Art Mgmt, C/ Castelló 82, 2 Derecha, 28006 Madrid, Spain

**Ranken, Andrew** — Drummer (Pogues)
Agency Group Ltd, 361-373 City Road, London EC1V 1PQ, England

**Ranki, Dezso** — Concert Pianist
Ordogorom Lejto 11/B, 1112 Budapest, Hungary

**Rankin, Alfred M, Jr** — Businessman
N A C C O Industries, 5875 Landerbrook Dr, #300, Cleveland OH 44124, USA

**Rankin, Chris** — Actor
Marlowes Agency, HMS President, Victoria Embankment, Blackfriars, London EC4Y 0HJ, England

**Rankin, Judy** — Golfer
2715 Racquet Club Dr, Midland TX 79705, USA

**Rankin, Kevin** — Actor
Abrams Artists, 9200 W Sunset Blvd, #1125, West Hollywood CA 90069 USA

**Rankine, Terry** — Architect
Cambridge Seven Assoc, 1050 Massachusetts Ave, Cambridge MA 02138, USA

**Ranks, Shabba** — Singer
Sony Records, 2100 Colorado Ave, Santa Monica CA 90404 USA

**Rannazzisi, Stephen** — Actor
Brillstein Entertainment Partners, 9150 Wilshire Blvd, #350, Beverly Hills CA 90212 USA

**Ransey, Kelvin** — Basketball Player
3195 Monterey Dr, Tupelo MS 38801, USA

**Ransom, B Cody** — Baseball Player
3146 E Boston St, Gilbert AZ 85295, USA

**Ransom, Derrick W, Jr** — Football Player
505 Sawgrass Dr, Akron OH 44333, USA

**Ransom, Jeffrey D (Jeff)** — Baseball Player
2131 Curtis St, Berkeley CA 94702, USA

**Ransone, James (P J)** — Actor
Management 360, 9111 Wilshire Blvd, Beverly Hills CA 90210 USA

**Rao, C N Ramachandra** — Chemist
J N C President's House, Indian Science Institute, Bangalor 560012, India

**Rao, Calyampudi R** — Mathematician, Statistician
29 Old Orchard St, Buffalo NY 14221, USA

**Rao, Michael** — Educator
Virginia Commonwealth University, President's Office, Richmond VA 23284, USA

**Rapace, Noomi** — Actress
Agentfirman Planthaber/Kilden, Drottninggatan 55, 111 21 Stockholm, Sweden

**Rapada, Clayton A (Clay)** — Baseball Player
2737 Fenway Ave, Chesapeake VA 23323, USA

**Rapaport, Michael** — Actor
Paradigm Agency, 360 N Crescent Dr, North Building, Beverly Hills CA 90210 USA

**Raphael** — Singer, Actor
Los Rosales #7, Monteprincipe, 28668 Boadilla del Monte, Madrid, Spain

**Raphael, Fredric M** — Writer, Director
Steve Kenis Co, Royalty House, 72-74 Dean St, London WID 3SG, England

**Raphael, June** — Actress
United Talent Agency, U T A Plaza, 9336 Civic Center Dr, Beverly Hills CA 90210 USA

**Raphael, Sally Jessy** — Entertainer, Actress
249 Quaker Hill Road, Pawling NY 12564, USA

**Rapinoe, Megan A** — Soccer Player
Seattle Sounders, 12 Seahawks Way, Renton WA 98056 USA

**Rapoport, Ellen** — Writer, Producer
Management 360, 9111 Wilshire Blvd, Beverly Hills CA 90210 USA

**Rapp, Adam** — Writer, Director
United Talent Agency, U T A Plaza, 9336 Civic Center Dr, Beverly Hills CA 90210 USA

# R

**Rapp, Anthony D** — Actor, Singer
Untitled Entertainment, 435 Hudson St, #900, New York NY 10014 USA
**Rapp, Patrick L (Pat)** — Baseball Player
2554 Pete Seay Road, Sulphur LA 70663, USA
**Rapp, Vernon F (Vern)** — Baseball Player, Manager
1559 Redwing Lane, Broomfield CO 80020, USA
**Rappaport, Ben** — Actor
Gersh Agency, 9465 Wilshire Blvd, #600, Beverly Hills CA 90212 USA
**Rappeneau, Jean-Paul** — Director, Writer
24 Rue Henri Barbusse, 75005 Paris, France
**Rapping 4-Tay** — Rap Artist
Richard Walters, PO Box 2789, Toluca Lake CA 91610 USA
**Rarick, Cindy** — Golfer
PO Box 30001, Tucson AZ 85751, USA
**Rasby, Walter H** — Football Player
6413 Brookbury Court, Charlotte NC 28226, USA
**Rasche, David** — Actor
Innovative Artists, 1505 10th St, Santa Monica CA 90401 USA
**Rascoe, Robert B (Bobby)** — Basketball Player
523 Sumpter Ave, Bowling Green KY 42101, USA
**Rascon, Alfred V** — Vietnam War Army Hero (CMH)
10397 Derby Dr, Laurel MD 20723, USA
**Rash, Jim** — Actor, Writer
Creative Artists Agency, 2000 Ave of Stars, #100, Los Angeles CA 90067 USA
**Rash, Ron** — Writer
320 Princess Grace Ave, Clemson SC 29631, USA
**Rash, Steve** — Director
Gersh Agency, 9465 Wilshire Blvd, #600, Beverly Hills CA 90212 USA
**Rashad, Ahmad** — Football Player, Sportscaster
13220 Verdun Dr, Palm Beach Gardens FL 33410, USA
**Rashad, Phylicia** — Actress
Parseghian/Planco, 388 2nd Ave, #506, New York, NY 10010 USA
**Rasheeda** — Rap Artist
I C M Partners, 10250 Constellation Blvd, #900, Los Angeles CA 90067 USA
**Rasizade, Artur T** — Prime Minister, Azerbaijan
Prime Minister's Office, Lermontov Str 68, 370066 Baku, Azerbaijan
**Rask, Tuukka M** — Ice Hockey Player
Boston Bruins, 100 Legends Way, #250, Boston MA 02114 USA
**Raskin, Alex** — Journalist
Los Angeles Times, Editorial Dept, 202 W 1st St, Los Angeles CA 90012 USA
**Rasley, Rocky** — Football Player
1747 W Harbor Dr, Isleton CA 95641, USA
**Rasmussen, Anders Fogh** — Prime Minister, Denmark
N A T O Headquarters, Blvd Leopold III, 1110 Brussels, Belgium
**Rasmussen, Blair A** — Basketball Player
9810 SE 35th Place, Mercer Island WA 98040, USA
**Rasmussen, Dennis L** — Baseball Player
PO Box 547341, Orlando FL 32854, USA
**Rasmussen, Erik** — Ice Hockey Player
5124 Clear Spring Court, Minnetonka MN 55345, USA
**Rasmussen, Gerry B** — Cartoonist (Bub Slug, Betty)
10716 69th Ave NW, Edmonton AB T6H 2E1, Canada
**Rasmussen, Poul Nyrup** — Prime Minister, Denmark
Allegade 6A, 2000 Frederiksberg, Denmark
**Rasmussen, Randall L (Randy)** — Football Player
81 Grumman Hill Road, Wilton CT 06897, USA
**Rasmussen, Rie** — Actress, Director
McCue Sussmane Zapfel, 521 Fifth Ave, #2800, New York NY 10175, USA
**Rasmussen, Wayne F** — Football Player
PO Box 756, Brandon SD 57005, USA
**Raspberry, Larry** — Singer (Gentrys)
Craig Nowag Attractions, 2095 Exeter Road, Germantown TN 38138, USA
**Rasuk, Victor** — Actor
Gersh Agency, 9465 Wilshire Blvd, #600, Beverly Hills CA 90212 USA
**Ratajkowski, Emily** — Actress, Model
C E S D, 10635 Santa Monica Blvd, #130, Los Angeles CA 90025 USA
**Ratchford, Jeremy** — Actor
Fountainhead Talent, 131 Davenport Road, Toronto ON M5R 1H8, Canada
**Ratchuk, Peter** — Ice Hockey Player
218 Ruskin Road, Buffalo NY 14226, USA
**Ratcliffe, John A** — Radio Astronomer
193 Huntingdon Road, Cambridge CB3 0DL, England
**Ratelle, J G Y Jean** — Ice Hockey Player
1200 Salem St, #111, Lynnfield MA 01940, USA
**Rath, A Gary** — Baseball Player
202 James Dr, Long Beach MS 39560, USA
**Rath, Meaghan** — Actress
Rain Mgmt, 1800 Stanford St, Santa Monica CA 90404, USA
**Rathbone, Jackson** — Actor
Cutler Mgmt, 165 Little Park Lane, Los Angeles CA 90049, USA
**Rather, Dan** — Commentator
45 E 80th St, #26A, New York NY 10075, USA
**Rather, David E (Bo)** — Football Player
4050 W Centre Ave, #215, Portage MI 49024, USA
**Rathje, Mike** — Ice Hockey Player
14850 Blossom Hill Road, Los Gatos CA 95032, USA
**Rathke, Henrich K M H** — Religious Leader
Schleifmuhlenweg 11, 19061 Schwering, Germany
**Rathman, Thomas D (Tom)** — Football Player
2762 Bloomfield Crossing, Bloomfield Hills MI 48304, USA
**Ratleff, W Edward (Ed)** — Basketball Player
4202 Paseo de Oro, Cypress CA 90630, USA
**Ratley, Sarah Lee** — Astronaut Candidate
PO Box 6973, Leawood KS 66206, USA
**Ratliff, Jeremiah J (Jay)** — Football Player
Dallas Cowboys, 1 Cowboys Parkway, Irving TX 75063 USA

**Rapp - Ratliff**

**Ratliff, Paul H** — Baseball Player
78 Campton Place, Laguna Niguel CA 92677, USA
**Ratliff, Theo C** — Basketball Player
1180 Mount Paran Road NW, Atlanta GA 30327, USA
**Ratliffe, Lisa** — Model
New York Model Mgmt, 596 Broadway, #701, New York NY 10012 USA
**Ratner, Brett** — Director
Rat Entertainment, 100 Universal City Plaza, Bungalow 5196, Universal City CA 91608, USA
**Ratner, Marina** — Mathematician
University of California, Mathematics Dept, Berkeley CA 94720, USA
**Ratner, Mark A** — Chemist
615 Greenleaf Ave, Glencoe IL 60022, USA
**Ratser, Dmitri** — Concert Pianist
Naxim Gershunoff, 1401 NE 9th St, #38, Fort Lauderdale FL 33304, USA
**Rattay, Timothy F (Tim)** — Football Player
2556 W Princeville Dr, Anthem AZ 85086, USA
**Rattle, Simon D** — Conductor
Askonas Holt, Lincoln House, 300 High Holborn, London WC1V 7JH, England
**Ratushinskaya, Irina B** — Writer
Vargius Publishing House, Kazakova Str 18, 107005 Moscow, Russia
**Ratzenberger, John** — Actor
Management Squared, 10900 Wilshire Blvd, #1400, Los Angeles CA 90024, USA
**Rau, Douglas J (Doug)** — Baseball Player
RR 1 Box 154A, Columbus TX 78934, USA
**Rauch, Jasen** — Guitarist, Composer (Red)
Paradigm Agency, 404 W Franklin St, Monterey CA 93940 USA
**Rauch, Jon** — Baseball Player
14081 N Old Forest Trail, Oro Valley AZ 85755, USA
**Rauch, Melissa** — Actress
W M E Entertainment, 9601 Wilshire Blvd, #300, Beverly Hills CA 90210 USA
**Raup, David M** — Paleontologist
423 Johnson Dr, Washington Island WI 54246, USA
**Rausse, Errol** — Ice Hockey Player
338 Rossiare Dr, Arnold MD 21012, USA
**Rautins, Leo R** — Basketball Player
202 Litchfield Dr, Syracuse NY 13224, USA
**Rautzhan, Clarence G (Lance)** — Baseball Player
2472 Covington Dr, Myrtle Beach SC 29579, USA
**Ravali** — Actress
159 Thirupathi Nagar, Valasaravakkam, Chennai TN 600087, India
**Ravanello, Rick** — Actor
Greene Assoc, 1901 Ave of Stars, #130, Los Angeles CA 90067 USA
**Raven, Eddy** — Singer, Guitarist, Songwriter
Birds of a Feather, PO Box 2476, Hendersonville TN 37077, USA
**Raven, Marion** — Singer (M-2-M), Songwriter
10th Street Mgmt, 700 N San Vicente Blvd, #G410, West Hollywood CA 90069, USA
**Raven, Peter H** — Botanist
Missouri Botanical Garden, 4355 Shaw Blvd, Saint Louis MO 63110, USA
**Raven-Symone** — Actress, Singer
United Talent Agency, U T A Plaza, 9336 Civic Center Dr, Beverly Hills CA 90210 USA
**Raver, Kim** — Actress
Mosiac Media Group, 9200 W Sunset Blvd, #1000, Los Angeles CA 90069 USA
**Ravera, Gina** — Actress
Rookery, 8200 Wilshire Blvd, #100, Beverly Hills CA 90212, USA
**Ravich, Rand** — Director, Producer, Writer
Creative Artists Agency, 2000 Ave of Stars, #100, Los Angeles CA 90067 USA
**Ravitch, Diane S** — Historian
New York University, Press Building, Washington Place, New York NY 10003, USA
**Ravlich, Matt** — Ice Hockey Player
15 Appletree Lane, Dalton MA 01226, USA
**Ravony, Francisque** — Prime Minister, Madagascar
Union des Forces Vivas Democratiques, Antananarivo, Madagascar
**Rawat, Navi** — Actress
Innovative Artists, 1505 10th St, Santa Monica CA 90401 USA
**Rawi, Raad** — Actor
Ken McReddie Assoc, 101 Finsbury Pavement, London EC2A 1RS, England
**Rawles, James Wesley** — Writer
Trident Media Group, 41 Madison Ave, #3600, New York NY 10010 USA
**Rawley, Shane W** — Baseball Player
4587 Cherrybark Court, Sarasota FL 34241, USA
**Rawlings, Florence** — Singer, Songwriter
Agency Group Ltd, 361-373 City Road, London EC1V 1PQ, England
**Rawlins, Adrian** — Actor
Ken McReddie Assoc, 101 Finsbury Pavement, London EC2A 1RS, England
**Rawlinson, Johnnie B** — Judge
US Court of Appeals, US Courthouse, 333 Las Vegas Blvd S, Las Vegas NV 89101, USA
**Rawls, Elizabeth E (Betsy)** — Golfer
101 Lynthwaite Farm Lane, Wilmington DE 19803, USA
**Rawls, Sam** — Cartoonist (Pops Place)
King Features Syndicate, 300 W 57th St, #1500, New York NY 10019 USA
**Ray J** — Singer, Songwriter, Actor
Norwood & Norwood, 22817 Ventura Blvd, #432, Woodland Hills CA 91364, USA
**Ray, Amy** — Singer (Indigo Girls), Songwriter
Russell Carter Artist Mgmt, 567 Ralph Mcgill Blvd, Atlanta GA 30312, USA
**Ray, Billy** — Director, Writer
Management 360, 9111 Wilshire Blvd, Beverly Hills CA 90210 USA
**Ray, Chris** — Baseball Player
15311 Winding Creek Dr, Tampa FL 33613, USA
**Ray, Clifford (Cliff)** — Basketball Player, Coach
Boston Celtics, 226 Causeway St, #4, Boston MA 02114 USA
**Ray, Edward B (Eddie)** — Football Player
219 W Oak Lane, Lake Charles LA 70605, USA
**Ray, Edward J** — Educator
Oregon State University, President's Office, Corvallis OR 97331, USA
**Ray, J Earl** — Basketball Player
446 N Lowell St, Casper WY 82601, USA

# R

| | |
|---|---|
| **Ray, Jimmy** | Singer |
| Epic Records, 9830 Wilshire Blvd, Beverly Hills CA 90212 USA | |
| **Ray, John** | Fashion Designer |
| Gucci Group, 1 Amstelplein, 1096 HA Amsterdam, Netherlands | |
| **Ray, John C (Johnny)** | Baseball Player |
| 12470 S 432, Chouteau OK 74337, USA | |
| **Ray, Rachael** | Chef |
| W M E Entertainment, 1325 Ave of Americas, New York NY 10019 USA | |
| **Ray, Rob** | Ice Hockey Player |
| 289 Sausalito Dr, East Amherst NY 14051, USA | |
| **Ray, Robert D** | Governor, IA |
| Blue Cross/Blue Shield of Iowa, 636 Grand Ave, Des Moines IA 50309, USA | |
| **Ray, Ronald E** | Vietnam War Army Hero (CMH) |
| 2670 Saint Andrews Blvd, Tarpon Springs FL 34688, USA | |
| **Ray, Terry** | Football Player |
| 42559 Angel Wing Way, Ashburn WA 20148, USA | |
| **Raybon, Marty** | Singer, Songwriter |
| Bobby Roberts, 3050 Business Park Circle, #303, Goodlettsville TN 37221 USA | |
| **Raycroft, Andrew** | Ice Hockey Player |
| Vancouver Canucks, 800 Griffiths Way, Vancouver BC V6B 6G1, Canada | |
| **Raye, Collin** | Singer |
| Flood Bumstead McCready McCarthy, 16 W 22nd St, #200, New York NY 10010 USA | |
| **Rayford, Floyd K** | Baseball Player |
| 11701 Pointe Circle, Fort Myers FL 33908, USA | |
| **Rayl, James R (Jim)** | Basketball Player |
| 201 W Boulevard, Kokomo IN 46902, USA | |
| **Raymer, Cory G** | Football Player |
| 34900 Delia Court, Round Hill VA 20141, USA | |
| **Raymo, Maureen** | Geologist |
| Boston University, Geology Dept, Boston MA 02215, USA | |
| **Raymond, Corey** | Football Player |
| 106 Carter St, New Iberia LA 70560, USA | |
| **Raymond, J Claude** | Baseball Player |
| 3 De la Citiere, #911, Saint Luc QC J0J 2A0, Canada | |
| **Raymond, Janice** | Model |
| Playboy Promotions, 2706 Media Center Dr, Los Angeles CA 90065 USA | |
| **Raymond, Lisa** | Tennis Player |
| 5 Diemer Dr, Media PA 19063, USA | |
| **Raymond, Ralph** | Softball Coach |
| USA Softball, 1 Olympia Plaza, Colorado Springs CO 80909, USA | |
| **Raymonde, Tania** | Actress |
| A P A Talent/Literary Agency, 405 S Beverly Dr, #300, Beverly Hills CA 90212 USA | |
| **Raymond-James, Michael** | Actor |
| Talent Works, 3500 W Olive Ave, #1400, Burbank CA 91505 USA | |
| **Raymund, Monica** | Actress |
| Gersh Agency, 9465 Wilshire Blvd, #600, Beverly Hills CA 90212 USA | |
| **Raymund, Steven A** | Businessman |
| Tech Data Corp, 5350 Tech Data Dr, Clearwater FL 33760, USA | |
| **Raynaud, Jean-Pierre** | Sculptor |
| 12 Ave Rhin et Danube, 92250 La Gareene Colombes, France | |
| **Rayner, Adam** | Actor |
| Innovative Artists, 1505 10th St, Santa Monica CA 90401 USA | |
| **Raynor, Bruce** | Labor Leader |
| Unite, 275 7th Ave, #1100, New York NY 10001, USA | |
| **Raz, Joseph** | Philosopher |
| Oxford University, Balliol College, Oxford OX1 3BJ, England | |
| **Raz, Kavi** | Actor |
| Dale Garrick, 1017 N La Cienega Blvd, #109, West Hollywood CA 90069 USA | |
| **Razah** | Singer, Songwriter |
| Def Jam Records, 828 8th Ave, New York NY 10019 USA | |
| **Raz-B** | Singer (B2K) |
| Pyramid Entertainment Group, 377 Rector Place, #21A, New York NY 10280 USA | |
| **Razborov, A A** | Mathematician |
| Princeton University, Mathematics Dept, Princeton NJ 08540, USA | |
| **Raziano, Barry J** | Baseball Player |
| 1315 4th St, Kenner LA 70062, USA | |
| **Re, Giovanni Battisti Cardinal** | Religious Leader |
| Palazzina dell-Arciprete, 00120 Vatican City | |
| **Rea, Chris** | Singer, Guitarist, Songwriter |
| Richard De La Font Agency, 4845 S Sheridan Road, #505, Tulsa OK 74145 USA | |
| **Rea, Connie M** | Basketball Player |
| 13 Marina Dr, Winter Haven FL 33881, USA | |
| **Rea, Stephen** | Actor |
| Barking Dog Entertainment, 609 Greenwich St, #600, New York NY 10014, USA | |
| **Read, Dolly** | Model, Actress |
| 30765 Pacific Coast Highway, #103, Malibu CA 90265, USA | |
| **Read, James** | Actor |
| Pakula/King, 9229 W Sunset Blvd, #315, West Hollywood CA 90069 USA | |
| **Read, Richard** | Journalist |
| Portland Oregonian, Editorial Dept, 1320 SW Broadway, Portland OR 97201, USA | |
| **Read, Sister Joel** | Educator |
| Alverno College, President's Office, PO Box 343922, Milwaukee WI 53234, USA | |
| **Readdy, William F (Bill)** | Astronaut |
| N A S A, Johnson Space Center, 2101 NASA Road, Houston TX 77058 USA | |
| **Reader, Ted** | Chef |
| Agency Group, 9348 Civic Center Dr, #200, Beverly Hills CA 90210 USA | |
| **Readman, Andrew** | Actor |
| Ken McReddie Assoc, 101 Finsbury Pavement, London EC2A 1RS, England | |
| **Ready, Randy M** | Baseball Player |
| 4410 Enfield Dr, Dallas TX 75220, USA | |
| **Reagan, Nancy D** | Wife of US President, Actress |
| 10880 Wilshire Blvd, #870, Los Angeles CA 90024, USA | |
| **Reagon, Bernice Johnson** | Singer (Sweet Honey in the Rock) |
| American University, History Dept, Washington DC 20016, USA | |
| **Reagon, Toshi** | Singer, Guitarist |
| M R A Records, PO Box 8322, Silver Spring MD 20907, USA | |

**Ray - Reagon**

**Reagor, W Montae** — Football Player
2328 Sunset Ridge Circle, Cedar Hill TX 75104, USA
**Reale, Willie** — Writer, Lyricist
Creative Artists Agency, 2000 Ave of Stars, #100, Los Angeles CA 90067 USA
**Reality, Maxim** — Singer, Emcee (Prodigy)
Midi Mgmt, Jenkins Lane, Great Hallinsbury, Essex CM22 7QL, England
**Reardon, Jeffrey J (Jeff)** — Baseball Player
5 Marlwood Lane, Palm Beach Gardens FL 33418, USA
**Reaser, Elizabeth** — Actress
United Talent Agency, U T A Plaza, 9336 Civic Center Dr, Beverly Hills CA 90210 USA
**Reason, Rex** — Actor
Roadside Productions, 20105 Rhapsody Road, Walnut Creek CA 91789, USA
**Reasoner, Marty** — Ice Hockey Player
9427 Crystal Beach Road, Hammondsport NY 14840, USA
**Reasons, Gary P** — Football Player
805 Glendevon Dr, McKinney TX 75071, USA
**Reaume, Marc A** — Ice Hockey Player
299 Laurier Dr, LaSalle ON N9J 1L7, Canada
**Reaves, T Johnson (John)** — Football Player
4825 W San Miguel St, Tampa FL 33629, USA
**Reavie, Chez** — Golfer
Gaylord Sports Mgmt, 13845 N Northsight Blvd, #200, Scottsdale AZ 85260 USA
**Reavis, David C (Dave)** — Football Player
5495 S Newport Circle, Greenwich Village CO 80111, USA
**Reavley, Thomas M** — Judge
3830 Wickersham Lane, Houston TX 77027, USA
**Rebek, Julius, Jr** — Chemist
2330 Calle de Oro, La Jolla CA 92037, USA
**Rebekah** — Singer
International Talent Booking, Ariel House, 74A Charlotte St, #100 London W1T 4QJ, England
**Reberger, Frank B** — Baseball Player
439 Sunset View Lane, Hope ID 83836, USA
**Rebhorn, James** — Actor
S M S Talent, 8383 Wilshire Blvd, #230, Beverly Hills CA 90211 USA
**Reboulet, Jeffrey A (Jeff)** — Baseball Player
3776 Grand Oak Trail, Dayton OH 45440, USA
**Rebraca, Zeljko** — Basketball Player
1550 8th St, Manhattan Beach CA 90266, USA
**Recari, Beatriz** — Golfer
Ladies Pro Golf Assn, 100 International Golf Dr, Daytona Beach FL 32124 USA
**Recasner, Eldridge D** — Basketball Player
6159 164th Ave SE, Bellevue WA 98006, USA
**Recchi, Mark** — Ice Hockey Player
114 Fairway Lane, Pittsburgh PA 15238, USA
**Rechichar, Albert D (Bert)** — Football Player
141 W McClain Road, Belle Vernon PA 15012, USA
**Reckell, Peter** — Actor
Mattie Mgmt, 415 N Camden Dr, #203, Beverly Hills CA 90210, USA
**Reckermann, Jonas** — Volleyball Player
Vitesse Karcher GmbH, Karolingerstra 41, 70736 Fellbach, Germany , USA
**Rector, Jeff** — Actor
10748 Aqua Vista St, North Hollywood CA 91602, USA
**Redahl, Gordon (Gord)** — Ice Hockey Player
201 Milton St, Flin Flon MB R8A 0H8, Canada
**Redbone, Leon** — Singer, Guitarist
Pathfinder Mgmt, 1009 16th Ave S, Nashville TN 37212, USA
**Redd, Glenn H** — Football Player
4526 W 1500 N, Ogden UT 84404, USA
**Redd, Michael W** — Basketball Player
2 Crescent Pond, New Albany OH 43054, USA
**Redden, Barry D** — Football Player
PO Box 6501, Katy TX 77491, USA
**Redden, Wade** — Ice Hockey Player
Boston Bruins, 100 Legends Way, #250, Boston MA 02114 USA
**Reddick, Cat** — Soccer Player
2620 Altadena Road, Birmingham AL 35243, USA
**Reddick, Jaret R** — Singer, Guitarist (Bowling for Soup)
Rainmaker Artists, PO Box 551665, Dallas TX 75355, USA
**Reddick, Lance** — Actor
Innovative Artists, 1505 10th St, Santa Monica CA 90401 USA
**Redding, Cory B** — Football Player
Indianapolis Colts, 7001 W 56th St, Indianapolis IN 46254 USA
**Redding, Timothy J (Tim)** — Baseball Player
1801 E Palm Valley Blvd, Round Rock TX 78664, USA
**Reddout, Franklin P (Frank)** — Basketball Player
379 Niblick Circle, Winter Haven FL 33881, USA
**Reddy, D Raj** — Computer Scientist
Robotics Institute, Carnegie-Mellon University, Pittsburgh PA 15213, USA
**Reddy, Helen** — Singer, Actress
Stacey Testro International, 8265 W Sunset Blvd, #102, West Hollywood CA 90046, USA
**Redeker, Quinn** — Actor
8075 3rd Ave, #303, Los Angeles CA 90048, USA
**Redfern, Peter I (Pete)** — Baseball Player
12516 Haddon Ave, Sylmar CA 91342, USA
**Redford, Amy Hart** — Actress
Paradigm Agency, 360 N Crescent Dr, North Building, Beverly Hills CA 90210 USA
**Redford, J A C** — Composer
Gorfaine/Schwartz, 4111 W Alameda Ave, #509, Burbank CA 91505 USA
**Redford, Paul** — Writer, Producer
W M E Entertainment, 9601 Wilshire Blvd, #300, Beverly Hills CA 90210 USA
**Redford, Robert** — Actor, Director
Sundance Institute, 5900 Wilshire Blvd, #800, Los Angeles CA 90036, USA
**Redgrave, Jemma** — Actress
Conway Van Gelder Grant, 8-12 Broadwick St, #300, London W1F 8HW, England
**Redgrave, Steven G** — Rowing Athlete
Athole Still Mgmt, 25-27 Westow St, London SE19 3RY, England

**Redgrave, Vanessa** — Actress, Singer
Gavin Barker Assoc, 2D Wimpole St, London W1G 0EB, England
**Redick, Jonathan Clay (J J)** — Basketball Player
2919 Toro Canyon Road, Austin TX 78746, USA
**Reding, Juli** — Actress, Model
PO Box 1806, Beverly Hills CA 90213, USA
**Redman** — Rap Artist
One Entertainment, 347 5th Ave, #1404, New York NY 10016 USA
**Redman, Amanda** — Actress
Lip Service Casting, 60-66 Wardour St, London W1F 0TA, England
**Redman, Chris J** — Football Player
15410 Beckley Crossing Dr, Louisville KY 40245, USA
**Redman, Joshua** — Jazz Saxophonist, Composer
Wilkins Mgmt, 323 Broadway, Cambridge MA 02139, USA
**Redman, Mark A** — Baseball Player
6818 E 109th St, Tulsa OK 74133, USA
**Redman, Michele** — Golfer
3410 Queensland Lane N, Minneapolis MN 55447, USA
**Redman, Richard C (Rick)** — Football Player
8953 Windham Court NE, Lacey WA 98516, USA
**Redman, Susie** — Golfer
30442 Wayside Dr, Spanish Fort AL 36527, USA
**Redmann, Teal** — Actress
Innovative Artists, 1505 10th St, Santa Monica CA 90401 USA
**Redmayne, Eddie** — Actor
United Agents, 12-26 Lexington St, London W1F 0LE, England
**Redmond, H Wayne** — Baseball Player
18061 Sussex St, Detroit MI 48235, USA
**Redmond, Markus** — Actor
Stagecoach Entertainment, 1223 Wilshire Blvd, #1560, Santa Monica CA 90403, USA
**Redmond, Marlon B** — Basketball Player
441 Oak St, San Francisco CA 94102, USA
**Redmond, Michael E (Mickey)** — Ice Hockey Player
30699 Harlincin Court, Franklin MI 48025, USA
**Redmond, Michael P (Mike)** — Baseball Player
13506 S Bluegrouse Lane, Spokane WA 99224, USA
**RedOne** — Songwriter, Record Producer
Paradigm Agency, 360 N Crescent Dr, North Building, Beverly Hills CA 90210 USA
**Redpath, Jean** — Singer
Sunny Knowe, Promenade, Leven, Fife KY8 4DH, Scotland
**Redquest, Greg** — Ice Hockey Player
139 Springdale Dr, Barrie ON L4M 4Y1, Canada
**Redstone, Sumner M** — Businessman
98 Baldpate Hill Road, Newton MA 02459, USA
**Redus, Gary E** — Baseball Player
2202 Mallard Lane SE, Decatur AL 35601, USA
**Redzepi, Rene** — Chef, Restauranteur
Noma Restaurant, Strandgade 93, 1401 Copenhagen K, Denmark
**Reece, Beasley** — Football Player, Sportscaster
17 Stirling Way, Lumberton NJ 08048, USA
**Reece, Daniel L (Danny)** — Football Player
5519 S Corning Ave, Los Angeles CA 90056, USA
**Reece, Gabrielle (Gabby)** — Volleyball Player, Model
PO Box 2227, Malibu CA 90265, USA
**Reece, Maynard** — Artist
5315 Robertson Dr, Des Moines IA 50312, USA
**Reed Lorsch, Kira** — Actress, Producer, Writer
R H L 4401 Wilshire Blvd, #200, Los Angeles CA 90010, USA
**Reed, Alvin D** — Football Player
3910 Abbeywood Dr, Pearland TX 77584, USA
**Reed, Alyson** — Actress, Singer, Dancer
Opus Entertainment, 5225 Wilshire Blvd, #905, Los Angeles CA 90036, USA
**Reed, Andre D** — Football Player
3865 Torrey Hill Lane, San Diego CA 92130, USA
**Reed, Anthony W (Tony)** — Football Player
14068 Mount Tabor Road, Odessa MO 64076, USA
**Reed, Brandy** — Basketball Player
Los Angeles Sparks, 888 S Figueroa St, #2010, Los Angeles CA 90017 USA
**Reed, Brian** — Guitarist (EvinRudes), Songwriter
Turner Management Group, 9200 W Sunset Blvd, #600, West Hollywood CA 90069, USA
**Reed, Darren D** — Baseball Player
8101 Santa Ana Road, Ventura CA 93001, USA
**Reed, Edward E (Ed), Jr** — Football Player
4703 Avatar Lane, Owings Mills MD 21117, USA
**Reed, Eric** — Jazz Pianist
Ellora Mgmt, PO Box 755, Lakeville CT 06039, USA
**Reed, Frank R** — Football Player
6989 Windstone Lane, Stone Mountain GA 30087, USA
**Reed, Hubert F (Hub)** — Basketball Player
46601 Garretts Lake Road, Shawnee OK 74804, USA
**Reed, Ishmael S** — Writer
1446 6th St, #C, Berkeley CA 94710, USA
**Reed, Jeff S** — Baseball Player
259 Sunrise Dr, Elizabethton TN 37643, USA
**Reed, Jeffrey M (Jeff)** — Football Player
1702 S Shore Court, Pittsburgh PA 15203, USA
**Reed, Jerry M** — Baseball Player
13964 106th Ave, Largo FL 33774, USA
**Reed, Jody E** — Baseball Player
3539 Lake Padgett Dr, Land O'Lakes FL 34639, USA
**Reed, John Shedd** — Financier
Citigroup Inc, 55 E 52nd St, New York NY 10055, USA
**Reed, Johnny** — Singer (Orioles)
Jackson Artists, 7251 Lowell Dr, #200, Overland Park KS 66204, USA
**Reed, Joseph B (Joe)** — Football Player
106 Whitechapel Court, Cedar Park TX 78613, USA

**Reed, Mark A** — Physicist
Syracuse University, Engineering/Applied Science Dept, Syracuse NY 13244, USA
**Reed, Mitchell** — Bassist, Fiddle Player (BeauSoleil)
Rosebud Agency, PO Box 170429, San Francisco CA 94117 USA
**Reed, Nikki** — Actress, Writer
Thruline Entertainment, 9250 Wilshire Blvd, #100, Beverly Hills CA 90212 USA
**Reed, Oscar L** — Football Player
700 Elizabeth Lane, Minneapolis MN 55411, USA
**Reed, Pamela** — Actress
Innovative Artists, 1505 10th St, Santa Monica CA 90401 USA
**Reed, Patrick** — Director
White Pine Pictures, 822 Richmond St W, #301, Toronto ON M6J 1C9, Canada
**Reed, Patrick N** — Golfer
Professional Golfer's Assn, PO Box 109601, Palm Beach Gardens FL 33410 USA
**Reed, Peter (Pete)** — Rowing Athlete
Leander Club, Henley on Thames, Leander RG9 2LP, England
**Reed, Peyton** — Director, Producer, Writer, Actor
W M E Entertainment, 9601 Wilshire Blvd, #300, Beverly Hills CA 90210 USA
**Reed, Ralph** — Religious Leader
1801 Sarah Dr, #L, Chesapeake VA 23320, USA
**Reed, Rex T** — Film Critic
Dakota Hotel, 1 W 72nd St, #86, New York NY 10023, USA
**Reed, Richard A (Rick)** — Baseball Player
9604 County Road 107, #7, Proctorville OH 45669, USA
**Reed, Ronald L (Ron)** — Baseball, Basketball Player
2613 Cliffview Dr, Lilburn GA 30047, USA
**Reed, Shanna** — Actress
1327 Brinkley Ave, Los Angeles CA 90049, USA
**Reed, Stephen V (Steve)** — Baseball Player
5335 Pine Ridge Road, Golden CO 80403, USA
**Reed, Thomas C** — Government Official
Quaker Hill Development Corp, PO Box 2240, Healdsburg CA 95448, USA
**Reed, W Jake** — Football Player
PO Box 1848, Frisco TX 75034, USA
**Reed, Willis, Jr** — Basketball Player, Coach, Executive
PO Box 1779, Ruston LA 71273, USA
**Reeder, Serena** — Actress
Hess Entertainment, 250 S Beverly Dr, #201, Beverly Hills CA 90212, USA
**Reeds, Mark** — Ice Hockey Player
7823 Cardinal Ridge Court, Saint Louis MO 63119, USA
**Reedus, Norman** — Actor, Model
Brillstein Entertainment Partners, 9150 Wilshire Blvd, #350, Beverly Hills CA 90212 USA
**Reekie, Joe** — Ice Hockey Player
622 Sean Dr, Annapolis MD 21401, USA
**Reep, Jon** — Actor, Comedian
Gersh Agency, 9465 Wilshire Blvd, #600, Beverly Hills CA 90212 USA
**Rees, Andrew** — Opera Singer
Musichall Ltd, Vicarage Way, Ringmer BN8 5LA, England
**Rees, Clifford H (Ted), Jr** — Air Force General
1620 Mayflower Court, #B414, Winter Park FL 32792, USA
**Rees, Dai** — Fashion Designer
6 Blackstock Mews, Blackstock Road, London N4 2BT, England
**Rees, Eberhard** — Physicist
69 Revere Way, Huntsville AL 35801, USA
**Rees, Jed** — Musician, Actor
Paradigm Agency, 360 N Crescent Dr, North Building, Beverly Hills CA 90210 USA
**Rees, John W** — Bassist (Men at Work)
Fish Creek, Gippsland VIC 3959, Australia
**Rees, Martin J** — Astronomer
King's College, Astronomy Institute, Cambridge CB2 1ST, England
**Rees, Mina** — Mathematician
301 E 66th St, New York NY 10065, USA
**Rees, Roger** — Actor
Innovative Artists, 1505 10th St, Santa Monica CA 90401 USA
**Reese, Calvin (Pokey)** — Baseball Player
12416 Sylvan Oak Way, Charlotte NC 28273, USA
**Reese, Della** — Singer, Actress
Lett-Reese International Promotions, 1910 Bel Air Road, Los Angeles CA 90077, USA
**Reese, Izell** — Football Player
10270 Willeo Creek Trace, Roswell GA 30075, USA
**Reese, Jeffrey K (Jeff)** — Ice Hockey Player
856 Longwood Circle, Haddonfield NJ 08033, USA
**Reese, Kevin P** — Baseball Player
1221 Willow St, San Diego CA 92106, USA
**Reese, Mason** — Actor
Nowbar, 22 7th Ave S, New York NY 10014, USA
**Reese, Richard B (Rich)** — Baseball Player
PO Box 2339, Carefree AZ 85377, USA
**Reese, Tracy** — Fashion Designer
T R Designs, 260 W 39th St, #1900, New York NY 10018, USA
**Reeser, Autumn** — Actress
Kritzer Levine Wilkins Griffin, 11872 La Grange Ave, #100, Los Angeles CA 90025 USA
**Reeser, Morgan** — Yachtsman
1948 Coral Gardens Dr, Wilton Manors FL 33306, USA
**Reeves, Bryant** — Basketball Player
11648 S 4710 Road, Muldrow OK 74948, USA
**Reeves, Daniel E (Dan)** — Football Player, Coach; Sportscaster
785 W Conway Dr SW, Atlanta GA 30327, USA
**Reeves, Dianne** — Singer
Depth of Field Mgmt, 1501 Broadway, #1304, New York NY 10036, USA
**Reeves, Jacques D** — Football Player
619 Scenic Dr, Irving TX 75039, USA
**Reeves, Julie** — Singer
PO Box 300, Russell KY 41169, USA
**Reeves, Keanu** — Actor
3 Arts Entertainment, 9460 Wilshire Blvd, #700, Beverly Hills CA 90212 USA

| | |
|---|---|
| **Reeves, Khalid** <br> 11519 140th St, Jamaica NY 11436, USA | Basketball Player |
| **Reeves, Martha** <br> Ideal Entertainment, 1674 Broadway, #300, New York NY 10019, USA | Singer (Martha & the Vandellas) |
| **Reeves, Matt** <br> Creative Artists Agency, 2000 Ave of Stars, #100, Los Angeles CA 90067 USA | Director, Producer, Writer |
| **Reeves, Perrey** <br> Paradigm Agency, 360 N Crescent Dr, North Building, Beverly Hills CA 90210 USA | Actress |
| **Reeves, Richard** <br> Universal Press Syndicate, 4520 Main St, #700, Kansas City MO 64111 USA | Columnist |
| **Reeves, Robert (Bobby)** <br> Novi Entertainment, PO Box 17077, Beverly Hills CA 90209, USA | Singer (Adema) |
| **Reeves, Saskia** <br> Markham Froggatt Irwin, Julian House, 4 Windmill St, London W1P 1HF, England | Actress |
| **Reeves, Scott** <br> House of Representatives, 1434 6th St, #1, Santa Monica CA 90401 USA | Actor, Singer (Blue County) |
| **Reeves, Shirley Alston** <br> Universal Attractions, 135 W 26th St, #1200, New York NY 10001 USA | Singer |
| **Reeves, Walter J** <br> PO Box 16171, Fort Worth TX 76162, USA | Football Player |
| **Refaeli, Bar** <br> One Model Mgmt, 424 W Broadway, #200, New York NY 10012 USA | Model |
| **Refn, Nicolas Winding** <br> W M E Entertainment, 9601 Wilshire Blvd, #300, Beverly Hills CA 90210 USA | Director |
| **Regalado, Rudolph V (Rudy)** <br> PO Box 475, Borrego Springs CA 92004, USA | Baseball Player |
| **Regalado, Victor** <br> Tijuana Country Club, 2630 E Point Beyer Blvd, #106, San Ysidro CA 92703, USA | Golfer |
| **Regalbuto, Joe** <br> Stone Manners Salners, 9911 W Pico Blvd, #1400, Los Angeles CA 90035 USA | Actor |
| **Regan, Brian** <br> Gersh Agency, 9465 Wilshire Blvd, #600, Beverly Hills CA 90212 USA | Actor, Comedian, Writer, Producer |
| **Regan, Bridget** <br> Gersh Agency, 41 Madison Ave, #3301, New York NY 10010 USA | Actress |
| **Regan, Fionn** <br> Coalition Mgmt, 3A Brackenbury Road, London W6 0BE, England | Singer, Songwriter |
| **Regan, Judith** <br> New Enterprises, 1211 Ave of Americas, Lower C31, New York NY 10036, USA | Writer, Entertainer |
| **Regan, Philip R (Phil)** <br> 1375 108th St, Byron Center MI 49315, USA | Baseball Player, Manager |
| **Regat, Jacques** <br> 13830 Jarvi Dr, Anchorage AK 99515, USA | Sculptor |
| **Regat, Mary** <br> 13830 Jarvi Dr, Anchorage AK 99515, USA | Sculptor |
| **Regehr, Duncan P** <br> Oscars Abrams Zimel, 438 Queen St E, Toronto ON M5A 1T4, Canada | Actor |
| **Regen, Elizabeth** <br> Don Buchwald, 6500 Wilshire Blvd, #2200, Los Angeles CA 90048 USA | Actress |
| **Regen, Richard** <br> United Talent Agency, U T A Plaza, 9336 Civic Center Dr, Beverly Hills CA 90210 USA | Writer, Producer |
| **Reger, Nate** <br> I C M Partners, 10250 Constellation Blvd, #900, Los Angeles CA 90067 USA | Writer |
| **Regilio, Nicholas D (Nick)** <br> 6505 Raham Court, Port Orange FL 32128, USA | Baseball Player |
| **Regina Lee** <br> Brothers Management Assoc, 141 Dunbar Ave, Fords NJ 08863 USA | Singer |
| **Regis, John** <br> 67 Fairby Road, London SE12 8JP, England | Track Athlete |
| **Regner, Thomas E (Tom)** <br> 2231 Big Trail Circle, Reno NV 89521, USA | Football Player |
| **Regnier, Charles** <br> Neherstr 7, 81675 Munich, Germany | Actor, Director |
| **Rehberg, Scott J** <br> 1153 Thistle Lane, Lebanon OH 45036, USA | Football Player |
| **Reherman, Lee** <br> Ellis Talent Group, 4705 Laurel Canyon Blvd, #300, Valley Village CA 91607 91607, USA | Actor |
| **Rehm, Fred** <br> 19340 W Stonehedge Dr, #A, Brookfield WI 53045, USA | Basketball Player |
| **Rehm, Jack D** <br> 19 Neponset Ave, #9A, Old Saybrook CT 06475, USA | Publisher |
| **Rehr, Frank** <br> United Feature Syndicate, PO Box 5610, Cincinnati OH 45201 USA | Cartoonist (Ferd'nand) |
| **Reibsten, Janet** <br> Bloomsbury Publishing, 50 Bedford Square, London WC1B 3DP, England | Psychologist |
| **Reich, Charles A** <br> Crown Publishing Group, 1745 Broadway, #1300, New York NY 10019 USA | Attorney, Educator, Writer |
| **Reich, Frank M** <br> 7591 Pennycroft Dr, Indianapolis IN 46236, USA | Football Player |
| **Reich, Robert B** <br> 1230 Bonita Ave, Berkeley CA 94709, USA | Secretary, Labor |
| **Reich, Stephen M (Steve)** <br> Howard Stokar Mgmt, 870 W End Ave, New York NY 10025, USA | Composer |
| **Reichardt, Frederic C (Rick)** <br> 2404 NW 63rd Terrace, Gainesville FL 32606, USA | Baseball Player |
| **Reichardt, Louis F (Lou)** <br> University of California, Rock Hall, 1550 4th St, San Francisco, 94158, USA | Mountaineer, Physiologist |
| **Reichel, Robert** <br> Toronto Maple Leafs, AirCanada Center, 40 Bay St, Toronto ON M5J 2K2, Canada | Ice Hockey Player |
| **Reichenbach, J Michael (Mike)** <br> 2230 Cloverly Circle, Jamison PA 18929, USA | Football Player |
| **Reichert, Daniel R (Dan)** <br> 445 Cornell Dr, Turlock CA 95382, USA | Baseball Player |
| **Reichert, David G (Dave)** <br> PO Box 53322, Bellevue WA 98015, USA | Law Enforcement Official, Representative |
| **Reichert, Jack F** <br> 580 Douglas Dr, Lake Forest IL 60045, USA | Businessman, Bowling Executive |

| | |
|---|---|
| **Reichert, Tanja** | Actress |
| Pacific Artists, 1404-510 W Hastings St, Vancouver BC V6B 1L8, Canada | |
| **Reichl, Ruth M** | Editor, Columnist |
| Gourmet, Editorial Dept, 4 Times Square, New York NY 10036, USA | |
| **Reichle, Luke** | Costume Designer |
| Innovative Artists, 1505 10th St, Santa Monica CA 90401 USA | |
| **Reichman, Fred** | Artist |
| 1235 Stanyan St, San Francisco CA 94117, USA | |
| **Reichow, Garet N (Jerry)** | Football Player |
| 9 Meredith Dr, Santa Fe NM 87506, USA | |
| **Reichs, Kathleen (Kathy)** | Writer, Anthropologist |
| University of North Carolina, English Dept, Charlotte NC 28223, USA | |
| **Reid, Andrew W (Andy)** | Football Player, Coach |
| Kansas City Chiefs, 1 Arrowhead Dr, Kansas City KS 64129 USA | |
| **Reid, Clifford A** | Research Scientist, Businessman |
| Complete Genomics, 2071 Stierlin Court, Mountain View CA 94043, USA | |
| **Reid, Dale** | Golfer |
| Ladies European Tour, Denham Court Drive, Denham, Buckinghamshire UB9 5PG, England | |
| **Reid, Daphne Maxwell** | Actress, Producer |
| Tim Reid Productions, 1 New Millennium Dr, Petersburg VA 23805, USA | |
| **Reid, Dave** | Ice Hockey Player |
| 1522 Hawkswood Dr, RR 1, Ennismore ON K0L 1T0, Canada | |
| **Reid, Delroy (Junior)** | Singer (Black Uhuru) |
| Caribbean Entertainment, PO Box 1115, Miami FL 33160, USA | |
| **Reid, Don S** | Singer (Statler Brothers), Songwriter |
| American Major Talent, 8747 Highway 304, Hernando MS 38632, USA | |
| **Reid, Harold W** | Singer (Statler Brothers), Songwriter |
| American Major Talent, 8747 Highway 304, Hernando MS 38632, USA | |
| **Reid, Herman (J R)** | Basketball Player |
| 121 Cemetary St, Chester SC 29706, USA | |
| **Reid, Jim** | Singer, Guitarist (Jesus & Mary Chain) |
| Paradise Artists, PO Box 1821, Ojai CA 93024 USA | |
| **Reid, Michael B (Mike)** | Football Player, Composer |
| 825 Overton Lane, Nashville TN 37220, USA | |
| **Reid, Mike** | Golfer |
| 1220 Chadwick Dr, Westminster MD 21158, USA | |
| **Reid, Ogden R** | Journalist, Diplomat |
| Ophir Hill, Purchase NY 10577, USA | |
| **Reid, Richard** | Actor |
| Kritzer Levine Wilkins Griffin, 11872 La Grange Ave, #100, Los Angeles CA 90025 USA | |
| **Reid, Robert K** | Basketball Player, Coach |
| Washington Wizards, M C I Centre, 601 F St NW, Washington DC 20004 USA | |
| **Reid, Sebastian (Sam)** | Actor |
| Rights House, Drury House, 34-43 Russell St, London WC2B 5HA, England | |
| **Reid, Shauna** | Writer |
| Harper Collins Publishers, 10 E 53rd St, Cellar 1, New York NY 10022 USA | |
| **Reid, Tanya** | Actress |
| Edna Talent Mgmt, 318 Dundas St W, Toronto ON M5T 1G5, Canada | |
| **Reid, Tara** | Actress, Model |
| Glick Agency, 1321 7th St, #203, Santa Monica CA 90401 USA | |
| **Reid, Terry** | Singer |
| Geoffrey Blumenauer Artists, PO Box 343, Burbank CA 91503 USA | |
| **Reid, Tim** | Actor, Director, Producer |
| Tim Reid Productions, 1 New Millennium Dr, Petersburg VA 23805, USA | |
| **Reid, Tom** | Ice Hockey Player |
| 603 Hawthorne Woods Dr, Saint Paul MN 55123, USA | |
| **Reid, Vernon** | Guitarist (Living Colour) |
| Conqueroo, 11271 Ventura Blvd, #522, Studio City CA 91604 USA | |
| **Reid, William** | Singer, Guitarist (Jesus & Mary Chain) |
| Paradise Artists, PO Box 1821, Ojai CA 93024 USA | |
| **Reiff, Ethan** | Writer, Director |
| United Talent Agency, U T A Plaza, 9336 Civic Center Dr, Beverly Hills CA 90210 USA | |
| **Reifsnyder, Robert H (Bob)** | Football Player |
| 681 Ocean Parkway, Berlin MD 21811, USA | |
| **Reightler, Kenneth S, Jr** | Astronaut |
| 1602 Honeysuckle Ridge Court, Annapolis MD 21401, USA | |
| **Reihner, George A** | Football Player |
| 1010 Electric St, Scranton PA 18509, USA | |
| **Reilly, Gabrielle** | Model, Commentator |
| 14117 W 53rd Terrace, Shawnee KS 66216, USA | |
| **Reilly, James F, II** | Astronaut |
| 15903 Lake Lodge Dr, Houston TX 77062, USA | |
| **Reilly, John** | Actor |
| Sovereign Talent Group, 8421 Wilshire Blvd, #200, Beverly Hills CA 90211 USA | |
| **Reilly, John C** | Actor |
| Framework Entertainment, 9057 Nemo St, #C, West Hollywood CA 90069 USA | |
| **Reilly, Kelly** | Actress |
| I C M Partners, 10250 Constellation Blvd, #900, Los Angeles CA 90067 USA | |
| **Reilly, Michael E (Mike)** | Baseball Umpire |
| 131 Smithfield Road, Battle Creek MI 49015, USA | |
| **Reilly, William K** | Government Official |
| Stanford University, International Studies Institute, Stanford CA 94305, USA | |
| **Reimann, Aribert** | Composer, Concert Pianist |
| Hohenzollerndamm 97, 10717 Berlin, Germany | |
| **Reimer, Dennis J (Denny)** | Army General |
| 2602 N Brandywine St, Arlington VA 22207, USA | |
| **Reimers, Bruce M** | Football Player |
| 2206 W River Dr, Humboldt IA 50548, USA | |
| **Rein, Andrew** | Freestyle Wrestler |
| 31 Acorn Dr, Hawthorn Woods IL 60047, USA | |
| **Reina** | Singer, Songwriter |
| T-Best Talent Agency, 508 Honey Lake Court, Danville CA 94506 USA | |
| **Reinders, Kate** | Singer, Actress |
| Paradigm Agency, 360 N Crescent Dr, North Building, Beverly Hills CA 90210 USA | |
| **Reineck, Thomas** | Canoeing Athlete |
| Graf-Bernadotte-Str 4, 45133 Essen, Germany | |

**R**

**Reichert - Reineck**

| | |
|---|---|
| **Reineke, Chad** | Baseball Player |
| 1904 Tanglewood Dr, Defiance OH 43512, USA | |
| **Reinemund, Steven S** | Businessman |
| PepsiCo Inc, 700 Anderson Hill Road, Purchase NY 10577, USA | |
| **Reiner, Carl** | Actor, Writer, Director |
| 714 N Rodeo Dr, Beverly Hills CA 90210, USA | |
| **Reiner, Rob** | Director, Producer, Actor |
| Castle Rock Entertainment, 9169 W Sunset Blvd, West Hollywood CA 90069, USA | |
| **Reinert, Sean** | Drummer (Cynic) |
| Season of Mist Records, 111 Rt de la Valebtinell, 13011 Marseille, France | |
| **Reinfeldt, J Fredrik** | Prime Minister, Sweden |
| Prime Minister's Office, Rosenbad 4, 103 33 Stockholm, Sweden | |
| **Reinfeldt, Michael R (Mike)** | Football Player |
| 1204 Waterstone Blvd, Franklin TN 37069, USA | |
| **Reinhardt, John E** | Diplomat |
| 3154 Gracefield Road, #417, Silver Spring MD 20904, USA | |
| **Reinhardt, Nicole** | Canoeing Athlete |
| Agentur Koster, Alsterdorfer Str 208, 22297 Hamburg, Germany | |
| **Reinhardt, Stephen R** | Judge |
| US Court of Appeals, 312 N Spring St, #G33, Los Angeles CA 90012, USA | |
| **Reinhart, Gregory** | Opera Singer |
| I M G Artists, Hogarth Business Park, Chiswick, London W4 2TH, England | |
| **Reinhart, Haley** | Singer |
| 19 Entertainment, 8560 W Sunset Blvd, #900, Los Angeles CA 90069 USA | |
| **Reinhart, Paul** | Ice Hockey Player |
| 2911 Altamont Crescent, West Vancouver BC V7V 3B9, Canada | |
| **Reinharz, Jehuda** | Educator |
| 131 Sewall Ave, #71, Brookline MA 2446, USA | |
| **Reinhold, Judge** | Actor, Director |
| A K A Talent, 6310 San Vicente Blvd, #200, Los Angeles CA 90048 USA | |
| **Reinking, Ann** | Actress, Dancer, Choreographer, Director |
| 5912 E Sapphire Lane, Phoenix AZ 85253, USA | |
| **Reinprecht, Steven E** | Ice Hockey Player |
| 45 S Garfield St, Denver CO 80209, USA | |
| **Reirden, Todd** | Ice Hockey Player |
| 17 Herons Bill Dr, Bluffton SC 29909, USA | |
| **Reiser, Jerry** | Architect |
| 28 S Washington Ave, Dobbs Ferry NY 10522, USA | |
| **Reiser, Paul** | Actor, Writer |
| Nuance Productions, 4049 Radford Ave, Studio City CA 91604, USA | |
| **Reisman, Garrett E** | Astronaut |
| 1715 Hedgecroft Dr, Seabrook TX 77586, USA | |
| **Reiss, Albert J, Jr** | Sociologist |
| 600 Prospect St, #7A, New Haven CT 06511, USA | |
| **Reiss, Howard** | Chemist |
| 16656 Oldham St, Encino CA 91436, USA | |
| **Reiss, Tom** | Writer |
| Crown Publishing Group, 1745 Broadway, #1300, New York NY 10019 USA | |
| **Reisz, Michael** | Actor |
| Mosiac Media Group, 9200 W Sunset Blvd, #1000, Los Angeles CA 90069 USA | |
| **Reiter, Mario** | Alpine Skier |
| Hauselweg 5, 6830 Rankweil, Austria | |
| **Reiter, Sabrina** | Actress |
| Daniela Stibitz Mgmt, Himmelstr 11/6, 1190 Vienna, Austria | |
| **Reiter, Stanley** | Economist |
| 425 Davis St, #425, Evanston IL 60201, USA | |
| **Reiter, Thomas** | Astronaut, Germany |
| European Space Center, Linder Hohe, Box 906096, 51127 Cologne, Germany | |
| **Reitman, Ivan** | Director, Producer |
| 900 Cold Springs Road, Santa Barbara CA 93108, USA | |
| **Reitman, Jason** | Director, Writer |
| W M E Entertainment, 9601 Wilshire Blvd, #300, Beverly Hills CA 90210 USA | |
| **Reitman, Joseph D (Joe)** | Actor |
| Talent Works, 3500 W Olive Ave, #1400, Burbank CA 91505 USA | |
| **Reitsma, Chris** | Baseball Player |
| 6050 Jim Davis Road, Parrish FL 34219, USA | |
| **Reitz, Bruce A** | Cardiac Surgeon |
| Falk CV Research Center, 300 Pasteur Dr, Stanford CA 94305, USA | |
| **Reitz, Donald L** | Artist |
| PO Box 206, Clarkdale AZ 86324, USA | |
| **Reitz, Kenneth J (Ken)** | Baseball Player |
| 2833 Fairways Circle, Lutz FL 33558, USA | |
| **Reklow, Jesse** | Cartoonist (Slow Wave) |
| 2415 College Ave, #20, Berkeley CA 94704, USA | |
| **Relaford, Desmond L (Desi)** | Baseball Player |
| 12483 Highview Dr, Jacksonville FL 32225, USA | |
| **Rellford, Richard A** | Basketball Player |
| 28 Balfour Road W, Palm Beach Gardens FL 33418, USA | |
| **Relman, Arnold S** | Editor, Physician |
| New England Journal of Medicine, 860 Winter St, #2, Waltham MA 02451, USA | |
| **Relyea, John** | Singer |
| Opus 3 Artists, 470 Park Ave S, #900N, New York NY 10016 USA | |
| **Remar, James** | Actor |
| Gersh Agency, 9465 Wilshire Blvd, #600, Beverly Hills CA 90212 USA | |
| **Rembert, John L (Johnny)** | Football Player |
| 2564 Willow Creek Dr, Orange Park FL 32003, USA | |
| **Remedios, Alberto T** | Opera Singer |
| Stuart Trotter, 21 Lanhill Road, London W9 2BS, England | |
| **Remek, Vladimir** | Cosmonaut, Czech Republic |
| European Parliament, Batiment Altiero Spinelli, Rue Wiertz 60, 1047 Brussels, Belgium | |
| **Remigino, Lindy** | Track Athlete |
| 22 Paris Lane, Newington CT 06111, USA | |
| **Remini, Leah M** | Actress |
| A P A Talent/Literary Agency, 405 S Beverly Dr, #300, Beverly Hills CA 90212 USA | |
| **Remlinger, Michael J (Mike)** | Baseball Player |
| 18331 N 93rd Way, Scottsdale AZ 85255, USA | |

**Remnick, David J** — Writer, Editor
257 W 86th St, #11A, New York NY 10024, USA
**Rempe, Jim** — Billiards Player
60 George Dr, Jefferson Township PA 18436, USA
**Remy, Gerald P (Jerry)** — Baseball Player
1403 Wisteria Way, Wayland MA 01778, USA
**Renaud, Line** — Singer, Actress
5 Rue de Bois de Boulogne, 75016 Paris, France
**Renaud, Mark** — Ice Hockey Player
11788 Tecumseh Road E, Windsor ON N8N 1L7, Canada
**Renault, Dennis** — Editorial Cartoonist
Sacramento Bee, Editorial Dept, 21st & Q Sts, Sacramento CA 95852, USA
**Renbourn, John** — Guitarist (Pentangle), Songwriter
Folklore Inc, 1671 Appian Way, Santa Monica CA 90401, USA
**Rendall, Mark** — Actor
Talent Works, 3500 W Olive Ave, #1400, Burbank CA 91505 USA
**Rendell of Barbergh, Ruth B** — Writer
26 Cornwall Terrace Mews, London NW1 5LL, England
**Rendell, Edward G (Ed)** — Governor, PA
Ballard Spahr, 1755 Market St, #5100, Philadelphia PA 19103, USA
**Rendell, Marjorie O** — Judge
US Court of Appeals, US Courthouse, 601 Market St, Philadelphia PA 19106, USA
**Renee, Lyne** — Actress
Don Buchwald, 6500 Wilshire Blvd, #2200, Los Angeles CA 90048 USA
**Renes, Lawrence** — Conductor
Harrison/Parrott, 5-6 Albion Court, London W6 0QT, England
**Renfrew of Kaimsthorn, Andrew C** — Archaeologist
McDonald Archaeological Institute, Downing St, Cambridge CB2 3ER, England
**Renfro, Melvin L (Mel)** — Football Player
Renfro Bridge Foundation, 8211 Hunnicut Road, Dallas TX 75228, USA
**Renfro, Mike R** — Football Player
PO Box 93073, Southlake TX 76092, USA
**Renfroe, Cohen W (Laddie)** — Baseball Player
236 Hickory Lane, Batesville MS 38606, USA
**Renfroe, Jeff** — Director
Characters Talent Agency, 1505 W 2nd Ave, #200, Vancouver BC V6H 3Y4, Canada
**Renick, W Richard (Rick)** — Baseball Player
7320 Hawkins Road, Sarasota FL 34241, USA
**Renier, Jeremie** — Actor
A C T 1, 83 Rue Saint Honore, 75001 Paris, France
**Renko, Steven (Steve)** — Baseball Player
15812 W 136th St, Olathe KS 66062, USA
**Renne, Paul** — Geologist
Berkeley Geochronology Center, 2445 Ridge Road, Berkeley CA 94709, USA
**Renner, Jeremy** — Actor
Creative Artists Agency, 2000 Ave of Stars, #100, Los Angeles CA 90067 USA
**Rennert, Laurence H (Dutch)** — Baseball Umpire
2560 46th Road, Vero Beach FL 32966, USA
**Rennert, Wolfgang** — Conductor
Holbeinstr 58, 12203 Berlin, Germany
**Renney, Tom** — Ice Hockey Coach
Detroit Red Wings, Joe Louis Arena, 600 Civic Center Dr, Detroit MI 48226 USA
**Rennie, Callum Keith** — Actor
A P A Talent/Literary Agency, 405 S Beverly Dr, #300, Beverly Hills CA 90212 USA
**Reno, Janet** — Attorney General
11200 N Kendall Dr, Miami FL 33176, USA
**Reno, Jean** — Actor
I C M Partners, 10250 Constellation Blvd, #900, Los Angeles CA 90067 USA
**Reno, Loren M** — Air Force General
Deputy CofS, Logistics/Installations, HqUSAF, Pentagon, Washington DC 20330 USA
**Reno, William H** — Army General
2706 S Ives St, Arlington VA 22202, USA
**Renoth, Heidi** — Snowboard Skier
Lercheckerweg 23, 83471 Berchtesgaden, Germany
**Rensberger, Scott** — Journalist
914 7th St NE, Washington DC 20002, USA
**Rense Noland, Paige** — Editor
Architectural Digest, Editorial Dept, 5900 Wilshire Blvd, Los Angeles CA 90036, USA
**Renshaw, Jeannine** — Actress, Producer
I C M Partners, 10250 Constellation Blvd, #900, Los Angeles CA 90067 USA
**Renteria, Richard A (Rich)** — Baseball Player
43310 Calle Nacido, Temecula CA 92592, USA
**Rentmeester, Co** — Photographer
PO Box 1562, Westhampton Beach NY 11978, USA
**Renton of Mount Harry, R Timothy** — Government Official, England
Mount Harry House, Offham, Lewes, East Sussex BN7 3QW, England
**Rentzel, T Lance** — Football Player
12014 Monument Dr, #354, Fairfax VA 22033, USA
**Rentzepis, Peter M** — Chemist
University of California, Chemistry Dept, Irvine CA 92717, USA
**Renuart, V Eugene (Gene), Jr** — Air Force General
Commander, US Northern Command, Peterson Air Force Base CO 80914 USA
**Renzetti, Donato** — Conductor
Columbia Artists Mgmt Inc, 1790 Broadway, #702, New York NY 10019 USA
**Renzi, Andrea** — Actor
Carol Levi Mgmt, Via Giuseppe Pisanelli 2, 00196 Rome, Italy
**Renzulli, Frank** — Producer, Writer
Creative Artists Agency, 2000 Ave of Stars, #100, Los Angeles CA 90067 USA
**Repin, Vadim V** — Concert Violinist
Eckholdtweg 2A, 23566 Lubeck, Germany
**Repko, Jason E** — Baseball Player
93005 E Chelsea Road, Kennewick WA 99338, USA
**Requa, John** — Writer, Director
W M E Entertainment, 9601 Wilshire Blvd, #300, Beverly Hills CA 90210 USA
**Rerych, Stephen (Steve)** — Swimmer
1142 Ridgewood Dr, Point Pleasant WV 25550, USA

**R**

*Remnick - Rerych*

# R

**Res** — Singer
Padell Nadell Fine Wineberger, 59 Maiden Lane, #2700, New York NY 10038 USA
**Resch, Alexander** — Luge Athlete
Gesprachsstoff Marketing, Scholssstr 9B, 82140 Olching, Germany
**Resch, Glenn A (Chico)** — Ice Hockey Player
607 8th St, Lyndhurst NJ 07071, USA
**Rescher, Nicholas** — Philosopher
1033 Milton St, Pittsburgh PA 15218, USA
**Reske, Hans-Joachim** — Track Athlete
Sinshimer Str 18, 69226 Nussloch, Germany
**Reskin, Barbara** — Sociologist
University of Washington, Sociology Dept, Seattle WA 98195, USA
**Resnais, Alain** — Director
Intertalent, 16 Rue Henri Barbusse, 75005 Paris, France
**Resnick, Marcia** — Photographer
2 Grove St, #1F, New York NY 10014, USA
**Resop, Christopher P (Chris)** — Baseball Player
2152 Harlans Run, Naples FL 34105, USA
**Resor, Helen** — Ice Hockey Player
22 N Stanwich Road, Greenwich CT 06831, USA
**Ressler, Glenn E** — Football Player
1524 Woodcreek Dr, Mechanicsburg PA 17055, USA
**Restani, Jane A** — Judge
US Court of International Trade, 1 Federal Plaza, New York NY 10278, USA
**Restovich, Michael** — Baseball Player
710 11th St SW, Rochester MN 55902, USA
**Resweber, Carroll C** — Motorcycle Racing Rider
2440 Imhoff Ave, Port Arthur TX 77642, USA
**Reswick, James B** — Engineer
PO Box 549, Crozet VA 22932, USA
**Retondo, Mike** — Guitarist (Plain White T's)
One Moment Mgmt, PO Box 55156, Sherman Oaks CA 91413 USA
**Retore, Guy** — Theater Executive
Theatre de l'Est Parisien, 159 Ave Gambetta, 75020 Paris, France
**Rettenmund, Mervin W (Merv)** — Baseball Player
1860 San Carlos Ave, San Carlos CA 94070, USA
**Retton, Mary Lou** — Gymnast
110 Kennywood Dr, Fairmont WV 26554, USA
**Retzer, Kenneth L (Ken)** — Baseball Player
746 Harvard Dr, Edwardsville IL 62025, USA
**Retzer, Otto W** — Director
Justinus-Kerner-Str 10, 80686 Munich, Germany
**Retzlaff, Palmer (Pete)** — Football Player
669 New Road, Gilbertsville PA 19525, USA
**Reuben, David R** — Psychiatrist
Scott Meredith, 1675 Broadway, New York NY 10019, USA
**Reuben, Gloria** — Actress
Great Northern Artists, 350 Dupont St, Toronto ON M5R 1V9, Canada
**Reubens, Paul** — Comedian, Actor
W M E Entertainment, 9601 Wilshire Blvd, #300, Beverly Hills CA 90210 USA
**Reuschel, Paul R** — Baseball Player
1143 Stacy Lane, Macomb IL 61455, USA
**Reuschel, Ricky E (Rick)** — Baseball Player
PO Box 143, Renfrew PA 16053, USA
**Reuss, Jerry** — Baseball Player
1 Line Dr, Des Moines IA 50309, USA
**Reuten, Thekla** — Actress
Innovative Artists, 1505 10th St, Santa Monica CA 90401 USA
**Reutimann, David** — Auto Racing Driver
Tommy Baldwin Racing, 296 Cayuga Road, Mooresville NC 28117, USA
**Reutter, Katherine** — Speed Skater
Q Sports Marketing, 534 W Evergreen St, Wheaton IL 60187, USA
**Rev, Martin** — Synthesizer Player (Suicide)
International Booking Department, Bodenseestr 91, 81243 Munich, Germany
**Reveiz, Fuad Y** — Football Player
PO Box 22430, Knoxville TN 37933, USA
**Revell, Graeme** — Composer
Kraft-Engel Mgmt, 15233 Ventura Blvd, #200, Sherman Oaks CA 91403 USA
**Revere, Paul** — Pianist (Paul Revere & the Raiders)
Buddy Lee Attractions, 38 Music Square E, #300, Nashville TN 37203 USA
**Reverho, Christine** — Actress
Artmedia, 20 Ave Rapp, 75007 Paris, France
**Revering, David A (Dave)** — Baseball Player
1063 Crows Wing Way, Ivins UT 84738, USA
**Revill, Clive** — Actor
15029 Encanto Dr, Sherman Oaks CA 91403, USA
**Revin, Sergei N** — Cosmonaut
Cosmonaut Training Center, Star City, 141160 Zvezdny Gorodok, Moscow Oblast, Russia
**Rex, Simon** — Actor, Producer
Luber Rocklin Entertainment, 8530 Wilshire Blvd, #555, Beverly Hills CA 90211 USA
**Rey, Antonia** — Actress
Alvarado Rey Agency, 7906 Santa Monica Blvd, #205, West Hollywood CA 90046, USA
**Rey, Reynaldo** — Actor, Comedian, Writer
Starwil Talent Agency, 433 N Camden Dr, #400, Beverly Hills CA 90210, USA
**Reyes Rosales, Diego Antonio** — Soccer Player
Federacion de Futbol, Colima 373 Colonia Roma, Delegacion Cuauhtemoc, Mexico City DF 06700, Mexico
**Reyes, Carlos A** — Baseball Player
23811 Butterfly Landing Dr, Land O'Lakes FL 34638, USA
**Reyes, Eddie** — Guitarist
Helter Skelter, 347-353 Chiswick High Road, London W4 4HS, England
**Reyes, Jose B** — Baseball Player
24 Stone Hill Dr S, Manhasset NY 11030, USA
**Reyes, Judy** — Actress
Talent Works. 3500 W Olive Ave, #1400, Burbank CA 91505 USA
**Reynolds Booth, Nancy** — Skier
3197 Padaro Lane, Carpinteria CA 93013, USA

**Reynolds, Albert** — Prime Minister, Ireland
18 Nilesbury Road, Ballsbridge, Dublin 4, Ireland
**Reynolds, Anna** — Opera Singer
Peesten 9, 95359 Kasendorf, Germany
**Reynolds, Archie E** — Baseball Player
1828 Pinecrest Dr, Tyler TX 75701, USA
**Reynolds, Burt** — Actor
Kritzer Levine Wilkins Griffin, 11872 La Grange Ave, #100, Los Angeles CA 90025 USA
**Reynolds, Carolyn** — Artist
1440 Catalina, Laguna Beach CA 92651, USA
**Reynolds, Corey** — Actor
New Wave Entertainment, 2660 W Olive Ave, Burbank, CA 91505, USA
**Reynolds, Dean** — Commentator
ABC-TV, News Dept, 5010 Creston St, Hyattsville MD 20781 USA
**Reynolds, Debbie** — Actress, Singer
6514 Lankershim Blvd, North Hollywood CA 91606, USA
**Reynolds, Derrick S (Ricky)** — Football Player
37540 Church Ave, Dade City FL 33525, USA
**Reynolds, Donald E (Don)** — Baseball Player
6035 NE 35th Place, Portland OR 97211, USA
**Reynolds, Edward (Ed)** — Football Player
2387 Country Side Dr, Fleming Isle FL 32003, USA
**Reynolds, G Craig** — Baseball Player
4210 Hidden Links Court, Kingwood TX 77339, USA
**Reynolds, Gene** — Actor, Producer
2034 Castillian Dr, Los Angeles CA 90068, USA
**Reynolds, Glenn F** — Inventor (Proscar Drug)
242 Edgewood Ave, Westfield NJ 07090, USA
**Reynolds, Harold C** — Baseball Player, Sportscaster
2890 NW Angelica Dr, Corvallis OR 97330, USA
**Reynolds, James** — Actor
1925 Hanscom Dr, South Pasadena CA 91030, USA
**Reynolds, James N (Jim), IV** — Baseball Umpire
708 Highpoint Dr, Rocky Hill CT 06067, USA
**Reynolds, Jerry O** — Basketball Coach, Executive
Sacramento Kings, Arco Arena, 1 Sports Parkway, Sacramento CA 95834 USA
**Reynolds, John Brently** — Actor
Hansen Jacobson Teller, 450 N Roxbury Dr, #800, Beverly Hills CA 90210 USA
**Reynolds, John H** — Physicist, Educator
University of California, Physics Dept, Berkeley CA 94720, USA
**Reynolds, John S (Jack)** — Football Player
11480 SW 102nd St, Miami FL 33176, USA
**Reynolds, Kenneth L (Ken)** — Baseball Player
182 Greenwood St, Marlborough MA 01752, USA
**Reynolds, Kevin** — Director
W M E Entertainment, 9601 Wilshire Blvd, #300, Beverly Hills CA 90210 USA
**Reynolds, Patrick** — Actor, Social Activist
260 S Rodeo Dr, Beverly Hills CA 90212, USA
**Reynolds, R Shane** — Baseball Player
3540 Marantha Dr, Sugar Land TX 77479, USA
**Reynolds, Robert** — Bassist (Mavericks, Swag)
AristoMedia, 1620 16th Ave S, Nashville TN 37212, USA
**Reynolds, Robert A (Bob)** — Baseball Player
952 SW Campus Dr, #2603, Federal Way WA 98023, USA
**Reynolds, Roger L** — Composer
University of California, Music Department, La Jolla CA 92093, USA
**Reynolds, Ronn D** — Baseball Player
1410 N Armour St, Wichita KS 67206, USA
**Reynolds, Ryan** — Actor
Dark Trick Films, PO Box 10605, Beverly Hills CA 90213, USA
**Reynolds, Sheldon** — Guitarist (Earth Wind & Fire)
Great Scott Productions, 4750 Lincoln Blvd, #229, Marina del Rey CA 90292, USA
**Reynolds, Thomas A, Jr** — Attorney
Winston & Strawn, 1 First National Plaza, 45 W Wacker Dr, Chicago IL 60601, USA
**Reynolds, Thomas D (Tommie)** — Baseball Player
640 Jinks Crossing Road, Bainbridge GA 39819, USA
**Reynolds, Tim** — Instrumentalist
Blue Mountain Artists, 810 Tyvola Road, #114, Charlotte NC 28217, USA
**Reynolds, W Ann** — Educator
University of Alabama, Outreach Development Center, Birmingham AL 35294, USA
**Reynor, Jack** — Actor
W M E Entertainment, 9601 Wilshire Blvd, #300, Beverly Hills CA 90210 USA
**Reynoso, Armando R** — Baseball Player
PO Box 442, Scottsdale AZ 85252, USA
**Reza, Yasmina** — Writer, Actresss, Comedienne
Gersh Agency, 9465 Wilshire Blvd, #600, Beverly Hills CA 90212 USA
**Reznikoff, William S** — Biochemist
University of Wisconsin, Biochemistry Dept, 433 Babcock Dr, Madison WI 53706, USA
**Reznor, M Trent** — Singer (Nine Inch Nails)
W M E Entertainment, 9601 Wilshire Blvd, #300, Beverly Hills CA 90210 USA
**Rhames, Ving** — Actor
Innovative Artists, 1505 10th St, Santa Monica CA 90401 USA
**Rhea, Caroline** — Actress, Comedienne
Kipperman Mgmt, 420 W End Ave, #1G, New York NY 10024 USA
**Rheaume, Manon** — Ice Hockey Player
50499 Laurel Ridge Court, Northville MI 48168, USA
**Rhett, Errict U** — Football Player
6 NW 108th Terrace, Plantation FL 33324, USA
**Rhey, Ashley** — Actress, Model
1220 Airport Freeway, #G456, Bedford TX 76022, USA
**Rhimes, Shonda** — Writer, Producer
I C M Partners, 10250 Constellation Blvd, #900, Los Angeles CA 90067 USA
**Rhine, Kendall L, Sr** — Basketball Player
6240 State Route 127 N, Alto Pass IL 62905, USA
**Rhines, Peter B** — Oceanographer
5753 61st Ave NE, Seattle WA 98105, USA

**R**

**Reynolds - Rhines**

# R

**Rhoads, James B** — Archivist
1300 Fox Run Trail, Platte City MO 64079, USA
**Rhoads, Paul** — Football Coach
Iowa State University, Athletic Dept, Ames IA 50011, USA
**Rhoda, Hilary** — Model
I M G Models, 304 Park Ave S, #PH N, New York NY 10010 USA
**Rhoden, Richard A (Rick)** — Baseball Player
8009 Whisper Lake Lane E, Ponte Vedra FL 32082, USA
**Rhodes, Arthur L, Jr** — Baseball Player
14114 Phoenix Road, Phoenix MD 21131, USA
**Rhodes, Cynthia** — Actress, Dancer
15260 Ventura Blvd, #2100, Sherman Oaks CA 91403, USA
**Rhodes, Damian (Dusty)** — Ice Hockey Player
8595 Sanctuary Dr, Mentor OH 44060, USA
**Rhodes, Donnelly** — Actor
Northern Exposure Talent Management Group, 570 Granville St, Vancouver BC V6C 3P1, Canada
**Rhodes, Eugene S (Gene)** — Basketball Player
132 N Peterson Ave, #8, Louisville KY 40206, USA
**Rhodes, Frank H T** — Geologist, Educator
Cornell University, Geology Dept, Snee Hall, Ithaca NY 14853, USA
**Rhodes, Jewell Parker** — Writer
Arizona State University, English Dept, Tempe AZ 85287, USA
**Rhodes, Karl D (Dusty)** — Baseball Player
4230 Cedar Bend Dr, Missouri City TX 77459, USA
**Rhodes, Kerry** — Football Player
Arizona Cardinals, PO Box 888, Phoenix AZ 85001 USA
**Rhodes, Kim** — Actress
Glick Agency, 1321 7th St, #203, Santa Monica CA 90401 USA
**Rhodes, Nick** — Keyboardist (Duran Duran)
D D Productions, 93A Westbourne Park Villas, London W2 5ED, England
**Rhodes, Philip** — Drummer (Gin Blossoms, Pharaohs)
W M E Entertainment, 1600 Division St, #300, Nashville TN 37203 USA
**Rhodes, Ray** — Football Player, Coach
1507 Juliet Dr, Allen TX 75013, USA
**Rhodes, Richard L** — Writer
Janklow & Nesbit, 445 Park Ave, #1300, New York NY 10022, USA
**Rhodes, Robert** — Architect
Robert Rhodes Associates Architects, 330 W 42nd St, New York NY 10036, USA
**Rhodes, Rodrick** — Basketball Player
PO Box 17704, Sugar Land TX 77496, USA
**Rhodes, Tom** — Actor, Comedian
OmniPop Talent Group, 4605 Lankershim Blvd, #201, Toluca Lake CA 91602 USA
**Rhodes, Zandra L** — Fashion Designer
79-85 Bermondsey St, London SE1 3XF, England
**Rhodri, Steffan** — Actor
Ken McReddie Assoc, 101 Finsbury Pavement, London EC2A 1RS, England
**Rhomberg, Kevin J** — Baseball Player
9692 Executive Court, Mentor OH 44060, USA
**Rhome, Gerald B (Jerry)** — Football Player, Coach
3883 Morning Meadow Lane, Buford GA 30519, USA
**Rhone, Earnest C (Earnie)** — Football Player
3603 Potomac Ave, Texarkana TX 75503, USA
**Rhone, Sylvia** — Businesswoman
Epic Records, 9830 Wilshire Blvd, Beverly Hills CA 90212 USA
**Rhyan, Dick** — Golfer
111 Camp Dr, Georgetown TX 78633, USA
**Rhymes, Busta** — Rap Artist, Actor
T C A/Jed Root, 9220 Sunset Blvd, #315, Los Angeles CA 90069, USA
**Rhys Meyers, Jonathan** — Actor
Brillstein Entertainment Partners, 9150 Wilshire Blvd, #350, Beverly Hills CA 90212 USA
**Rhys, Phillip** — Actor
Independent Talent Group, 40 Whitfield St, London W1T 2RH, England
**Rhys-Davies, John** — Actor
Just Voices Agency, 140 Buckingham Palace Road, London SW1W 9SA, England
**Ribant, Dennis J** — Baseball Player
46 Sidra Cove, Newport Coast CA 92657, USA
**Ribble, Pat** — Ice Hockey Player
23 Cheyenne Court, Leamington ON N8H 5E2, Canada
**Ribbs, Willy T** — Auto Racing Driver
2343 Ribbs Lane, San Jose CA 95116, USA
**Ribeau, Sidney A** — Educator
Howard University, President's Office, Washington DC 20059, USA
**Ribeiro, Alfonso** — Actor
Creative Talent Group, 1900 Ave of Stars, #2475, Los Angeles CA 90067, USA
**Ribeiro, Ignacio** — Fashion Designer
Clements Ribeiro Ltd, 48 S Molton St, London W1X 1HE, England
**Ribeiro, Michael T (Mike)** — Ice Hockey Player
5609 Monterey Dr, Frisco TX 75034, USA
**Ribisi, Giovanni** — Actor
Management 360, 9111 Wilshire Blvd, Beverly Hills CA 90210 USA
**Ribisi, Marissa** — Actress
United Talent Agency, U T A Plaza, 9336 Civic Center Dr, Beverly Hills CA 90210 USA
**Ricard, Alan C** — Football Player
10306 Ripple Lake Dr, Houston TX 77065, USA
**Ricard, Jean-Pierre B Cardinal** — Religious Leader
Archdiocese of Bordeaux, 183 Cours de la Somme, 33034 Bordeaux, France
**Ricardo, Benito C (Benny)** — Football Player, Actor, Comedian
3012 Harding Way, Costa Mesa CA 92626, USA
**Ricci, Christina** — Actress
Management 360, 9111 Wilshire Blvd, Beverly Hills CA 90210 USA
**Ricci, Mike** — Ice Hockey Player
286 Mountain Laurel Lane, Los Gatos CA 95032, USA
**Rice, Andrew (Andy)** — Football Player
801 N Main St, Hallettsville TX 77964, USA
**Rice, Anne** — Writer
9 Monte Carlo Dr, Kenner LA 70065, USA

**Rice, Bobby G** — Singer
505 Canton Pass, Madison TN 37115, USA
**Rice, Buddy** — Auto Racing Driver
Panther Racing, 5740 Decatur Blvd, Indianapolis IN 46241, USA
**Rice, Chris** — Singer, Pianist, Songwriter
Hardly Entertainment, 1650 Murfreesboro Road, #133, Franklin TN 37067, USA
**Rice, Condoleezza** — Secretary, State
Stanford University, Hoover Institution, Stanford CA 94305, USA
**Rice, Damien** — Singer, Guitarist, Songwriter
13 Artists, 11-14 Kensington St, Brighton BN1 4AJ, England
**Rice, Gigi** — Actress
Bamboo Mgmt, 17 Buccaneer St, Marina Del Rey CA 90292, USA
**Rice, Glen A** — Basketball Player
8920 SW 162nd Terrace, Palmetto Bay FL 33157, USA
**Rice, James E (Jim)** — Baseball Player
35 Bobby Jones Dr, Andover MA 01810, USA
**Rice, James R** — Geophysicist
Harvard University, Applied Science Division, Cambridge MA 02138, USA
**Rice, Jerry L** — Football Player
3223 Paseo, Grand Prairie TX 75054, USA
**Rice, John L** — Baseball Umpire
2666 E 73rd St, #12W, Chicago IL 60649, USA
**Rice, Kenneth E (Ken)** — Football Player
10619 Big Canoe, Big Canoe GA 30143, USA
**Rice, Luanne** — Writer
I C M Partners, 10250 Constellation Blvd, #900, Los Angeles CA 90067 USA
**Rice, Raymell M (Ray)** — Football Player
Baltimore Ravens, Ravens Stadium, 1 Winning Dr, Baltimore MD 21230 USA
**Rice, Sidney R** — Football Player
Seattle Seahawks, 12 Seahawks Way, Renton WA 98056 USA
**Rice, Simeon J** — Football Player
371 Channelside Walkway, #301, Tampa FL 33602, USA
**Rice, Stephanie** — Swimmer
Saint Peters Swim Club, Box 598, Indooroopilly QLD 4068, Australia
**Rice, Steven (Steve)** — Ice Hockey Player
99 Duncairn Ave, Kitchener ON N2M 4S5, Canada
**Rice, Stuart A** — Chemist
5517 S Kimbark Ave, Chicago IL 60637, USA
**Rice, Susan E** — Government Official, Diplomat
US Mission, United Nations Plaza, New York NY 10017, USA
**Rice, Thomas M** — Theoretical Physicist
Theoretische Physik, ETH-Honggerberg, 8093 Zurich, Switzerland
**Rice, Timothy M B (Tim)** — Lyricist
Chilterns, France-Hill Dr, Camberley, Surrey GU153-30A, England
**Rich, Adam** — Actor
Jeff Ballard Public Relations 4814 Lemona Ave, Sherman Oaks CA 91403, USA
**Rich, Alexander** — Molecular Biologist
2 Walnut Ave, Cambridge MA 02140, USA
**Rich, Allan** — Actor
Greater Vision Agency, 9229 W Sunset Blvd, #320, West Hollywood CA 90069, USA
**Rich, David Lowell** — Director
721 Royal Anne Lane, #201, Raleigh NC 27615, USA
**Rich, Frank H** — Drama Critic, Columnist
New York Times, Editorial Dept, 229 W 43rd St, New York NY 10036 USA
**Rich, John** — Singer, Guitarist, Songwriter
Morris Management Group, 818 19th Ave S, Nashville TN 37203, USA
**Rich, Katie** — Actress
10100 Santa Monica Blvd, #2490, Los Angeles CA 90067, USA
**Rich, Tommy** — Basketball Player
1348 Clubview Court, Venice FL 34292, USA
**Rich, Tony** — Singer, Keyboardist, Songwriter
Prestige, 220 E 23rd St, #303, New York NY 10010, USA
**Richard of Ammanford, Ivor S** — Government Official, England
11 South Square, Gray's Inn, London WC1R 5EU, England
**Richard, Cecile** — Association Executive
Planned Parenthood Federation, 434 W 33rd St, New York NY 10001, USA
**Richard, Chris** — Baseball Player
11389 Ironwood Road, San Diego CA 92131, USA
**Richard, Cliff** — Singer
Harley House, Portsmouth Road, Box 46C, Esher, Surrey KT10 0RB, England
**Richard, Dawn** — Model, Actress
Playboy Promotions, 2706 Media Center Dr, Los Angeles CA 90065 USA
**Richard, Dawn A** — Singer (Danity Kane)
Bad Boy Entertainment, 1440 Broadway, #16, New York NY 10018 USA
**Richard, Deb** — Golfer
736 Port Charlotte Dr, Ponte Vedra FL 32081, USA
**Richard, Henri** — Ice Hockey Player
905-4300 Place de Cageux, Ile Paton Laval QC H7W 4Z3, Canada
**Richard, James Rodney (J R)** — Baseball Player
Mary Olive Baptist Church, 2804 McGowan St, Houston TX 77004, USA
**Richard, Nathalie** — Actress
Voyez Mon Agent, 20 Ave Rapp, 75007 Paris, France
**Richard, Pierre** — Actor
Artmedia, 20 Ave Rapp, 75007 Paris, France
**Richards, Ariana** — Actress
Don Buchwald, 6500 Wilshire Blvd, #2200, Los Angeles CA 90048 USA
**Richards, Bradley G (Brad)** — Ice Hockey Player
101 Warren St, #3150, New York NY 10007, USA
**Richards, Brooke** — Model
Playboy Promotions, 2706 Media Center Dr, Los Angeles CA 90065 USA
**Richards, Dakota Blue** — Actress
Artist Rights Group, 4 Great Portland St, London W1W 8PA, England
**Richards, David R (Dave)** — Football Player
4209 San Carlos St, Dallas TX 75205, USA
**Richards, Denise** — Actress, Model
Model Management Group, 1024 6th Ave, #201, New York NY 10018, USA

**Richards, Emilie** — Writer
PO Box 228, Chautauqua NY 14722, USA

**Richards, Eugene** — Photographer, Filmmaker
Many Voices, 472 13th St, Brooklyn NY 11215, USA

**Richards, George Maxwell** — President, Trinidad & Tobago
President's House, Botanical Garden Area, Port of Spain, Trinidad & Tobago

**Richards, J August (Jamie)** — Actor
Greenlight Mgmt, 13848 Valleyheart Dr, Sherman Oaks CA 91423, USA

**Richards, J Golden** — Football Player
7274 Winesap Court, Salt Lake City UT 84121, USA

**Richards, J R** — Singer (Dishwalla)
W M E Entertainment, 1325 Ave of Americas, New York NY 10019 USA

**Richards, Keith** — Singer (Rolling Stones), Songwriter
25 Walden Woods Lane, Weston CT 06883, USA

**Richards, Kim** — Actress
10326 Orton Ave, Los Angeles CA 90064, USA

**Richards, Lucille** — Baseball Player
17 Stonemeadow Dr, Bridgewater MA 2324, USA

**Richards, Mark** — Surfer
Mark Richards Surfboards, 755 Hunter St, Newcastle NSW 2302, Australia

**Richards, Michael** — Actor, Comedian
Abrams Artists, 275 7th Ave, #2600, New York NY 10001 USA

**Richards, Paul L** — Physicist
University of California, Physics Dept, LeConte Hall, Berkeley CA 94720, USA

**Richards, Paul W** — Astronaut
N A S A, Johnson Space Center, 2101 NASA Road, Houston TX 77058 USA

**Richards, Renee** — Tennis Player
1604 Union St, San Francisco CA 94123, USA

**Richards, Rex E** — Chemist
13 Woodstock Close, Oxford OX2 8DB, England

**Richards, Richard N** — Astronaut
N A S A, Johnson Space Center, 2101 NASA Road, Houston TX 77058 USA

**Richards, Robert E (Bob)** — Track Athlete
76782 Interstate 20, Gordon TX 76453, USA

**Richards, Robert G (Bobby)** — Football Player
2881 Fairplay Road, Rutledge GA 30663, USA

**Richards, Russell E (Rusty)** — Baseball Player
1193 Spring Sage St, Henderson NV 89011, USA

**Richards, Stephanie** — Actress
H David Moss, 733 Seward St, #PH, Los Angeles CA 90038 USA

**Richards, Todd M** — Ice Hockey Player, Coach
Columbus Blue Jackets, Arena, 200 W Nationwide Blvd, #1, Columbus OH 43215 USA

**Richards, Warren J** — Writer
9075 S 700 E, #109, Sandy UT 84070, USA

**Richardson, Alpette (Al)** — Football Player
PO Box 371105, Decatur GA 30037, USA

**Richardson, Ashley** — Model
Jason Weinberg Assoc, 451 Greenwich St, New York NY 10013, USA

**Richardson, Cameron** — Model, Actress
Paradigm Agency, 360 N Crescent Dr, North Building, Beverly Hills CA 90210 USA

**Richardson, Clint D** — Basketball Player
1207 9th Ave NW, Puyallup WA 98371, USA

**Richardson, Damien A** — Football Player
1300 E Cromwell Ave, Fresno CA 93720, USA

**Richardson, Dan** — Drummer (Stereo Mud)
Agency Group Ltd, 142 W 57th St, #600, New York NY 10019 USA

**Richardson, Dave** — Ice Hockey Player
62 Agassie Dr, Winnipeg MB R3T 2K7, Canada

**Richardson, Derek** — Actor
I C M Partners, 10250 Constellation Blvd, #900, Los Angeles CA 90067 USA

**Richardson, Donna** — Physical Fitness Expert
Anchor Bay Entertainment, 1699 Stutz Dr, Troy MI 48084, USA

**Richardson, Dorothy (Dot)** — Softball Player
1120 W Lakeshore Dr, Clermont FL 34711, USA

**Richardson, Emma** — Singer, Bassist (Band of Skulls)
Pias Entertainment Group, Trading Centre, 101 Farm Lane, #24, London SW6 1QJ, England

**Richardson, Gloster V** — Football Player
9143 S Euclid Ave, Chicago IL 60617, USA

**Richardson, Gordon C (Gordie)** — Baseball Player
23 Saint Paul Church Road, Colquitt GA 39837, USA

**Richardson, Greg** — Boxer
382 Camden Ave, Youngstown OH 44505, USA

**Richardson, Jack** — Artist
12171 Sunset Ave, Grass Valley CA 95945, USA

**Richardson, Jake** — Actor
Untitled Entertainment, 350 S Beverly Dr, #200, Beverly Hills CA 90212 USA

**Richardson, Jane S** — Biochemist
Duke University, Biochemistry Dept, Durham NC 27708, USA

**Richardson, Jason A** — Basketball Player
75 Dahlia St, Denver CO 80220, USA

**Richardson, Jeffrey S (Jeff)** — Baseball Player
11779 W Fordson Dr, Marana AZ 85653, USA

**Richardson, Jeremy T** — Basketball Player
Orlando Magic, 8701 Maitland Summit Blvd, Orlando FL 32810 USA

**Richardson, Jerome (Pooh)** — Basketball Player
23434 Sherman Way, West Hills CA 91307, USA

**Richardson, Jerome J (Jerry)** — Football Player, Executive
Carolina Panthers, Ericsson Stadium, 800 S Mint St, Charlotte NC 28202 USA

**Richardson, Joely** — Actress
Ken McReddie Assoc, 101 Finsbury Pavement, London EC2A 1RS, England

**Richardson, John E** — Football Player
3053 Eagles Claw Ave, Thousand Oaks CA 91362, USA

**Richardson, Ken** — Chemist, Inventor
Pfizer Laboratories, Ramsgate Road, Sandwich Kent CT13 9NJ, England

**Richardson, Ken** — Ice Hockey Player
Hockey Heritage, 400 Government Road W, Kirkland Lake ON P2N 3M6, Canada

**Richardson, Kevin Michael** — Actor
C E S D, 10635 Santa Monica Blvd, #130, Los Angeles CA 90025 USA
**Richardson, Kevin S** — Singer (Backstreet Boys)
Vox Inc, 6420 Wilshire Blvd, #1080, Los Angeles CA 90048 USA
**Richardson, Kyle D** — Football Player
3516 Balmar Mews Road, Baltimore MD 21211, USA
**Richardson, LaTanya** — Actress
Framework Entertainment, 9057 Nemo St, #C, West Hollywood CA 90069 USA
**Richardson, Linda** — Opera Singer
Musichall Ltd, Vicarage Way, Ringmer BN8 5LA, England
**Richardson, Mark** — Drummer (Skunk Anansie)
13 Artists, 11-14 Kensington St, Brighton BN1 4AJ, England
**Richardson, Michael C (Mike)** — Football Player
723 Owen Ave, #C, Huntington Beach CA 92648, USA
**Richardson, Micheal Ray** — Basketball Player
5012 SW Oxford Place, Lawton OK 73505, USA
**Richardson, Mike** — Publisher
Dark Horse Publishing, 10956 SE Main St, Portland OR 97222 USA
**Richardson, Miranda** — Actress
Independent Talent Group, 40 Whitfield St, London W1T 2RH, England
**Richardson, Nolan** — Basketball Coach
4057 N Hughmount Road, Fayetteville AR 72704, USA
**Richardson, Patricia** — Actress
Innovative Artists, 1505 10th St, Santa Monica CA 90401 USA
**Richardson, Robert B** — Cinematographer
Skouras Agency, 1149 3rd St, #300, Santa Monica CA 90403 USA
**Richardson, Robert C (Bobby)** — Baseball Player
47 Adams Ave, Sumter SC 29150, USA
**Richardson, Robert, Jr** — Auto Racing Driver
PO Box 523, McKinney TX 75070, USA
**Richardson, Sam** — Sculptor
4121 Sequoyah Road, Oakland CA 94605, USA
**Richardson, Terry** — Ice Hockey Player
3598 Rosemary Heights Crescent, Surrey BC V3S 0P2, Canada
**Richardson, Trent** — Football Player
Indianapolis Colts, 7001 W 56th St, Indianapolis IN 46254 USA
**Richardson, William B (Bill)** — Secretary, Energy; Governor, NM
A P C O Worldwide, Global Strategies Division, 700 12th St NW, #800, Washington DC 20005, USA
**Richardson, William C** — Foundation Executive, Educator
W K Kellogg Foundation, 1 Michigan Ave E, Battle Creek MI 49017, USA
**Richardson, William R** — Army General
8612 Dixie Place, McLean VA 22102, USA
**Richardson, Willie L** — Football Player
5928 Waverly Dr, Jackson MS 39206, USA
**Richardson-Whitfield, Salli** — Actress
Innovative Artists, 1505 10th St, Santa Monica CA 90401 USA
**Richards-Ross, Sanya (Sandie)** — Track Athlete
Octagon Worldwide, 1751 Pinnacle Dr, #1500, McLean VA 22102 USA
**Richen, John M** — Sculptor
Contemporary Fine Arts Gallery, 7946 Ivanhoe Ave, La Jolla CA 92037, USA
**Richer, Stephane** — Ice Hockey Player
Club de Golf Montpelier, 440 Ave S Richaer, Montpelier QC J0V 1M0, Canada
**Richert, Peter G (Pete)** — Baseball Player
80 La Cerra Dr, Rancho Mirage CA 92270, USA
**Richey, Cliff** — Tennis Player
2936 Cumberland Dr, San Angelo TX 76904, USA
**Richey, Jennifer** — Actress
C E S D, 10635 Santa Monica Blvd, #130, Los Angeles CA 90025 USA
**Richey, Kim** — Singer, Songwriter
Flood Bumstead McCready McCarthy, 1700 Hayes St, #304, Nashville TN 37203 USA
**Richey, Wade E** — Football Player
207 Bayonne Dr, Lafayette LA 70507, USA
**Richie, Lionel** — Singer, Songwriter
Creative Artists Agency, 2000 Ave of Stars, #100, Los Angeles CA 90067 USA
**Richie, Nicole** — Actress, Producer
Paradigm Agency, 360 N Crescent Dr, North Building, Beverly Hills CA 90210 USA
**Richie, Robert E (Bob)** — Baseball Player
1835 Meadowvale Way, Sparks NV 89431, USA
**Richie, Shane** — Singer, Actor
International Artistes, 193-197 High Holborn, London WC1V 7BD, England
**Richings, Julian** — Actor
Gary Goddard Agency, 10 St Mary's St, #305, Toronto ON M4Y 1P9, Canada
**Richling, Greg** — Singer, Bassist (Wallflowers)
B K Entertainment Group, 15300 Ventura Blvd, #203, Sherman Oaks CA 91403, USA
**Richman, Caryn** — Actress
1805 Via Arriba, Palos Verdes Estates CA 90274, USA
**Richman, Jason** — Producer, Writer
W M E Entertainment, 9601 Wilshire Blvd, #300, Beverly Hills CA 90210 USA
**Richman, Jonathan** — Singer, Guitarist (Modern Lovers), Actor
High Road Touring, 751 Bridgeway, #200, Sausalito CA 94965 USA
**Richman, Peter Mark** — Actor
5114 Del Moreno Dr, Woodland Hills CA 91364, USA
**Richmond, Anthony B** — Cinematograhper
United Talent Agency, U T A Plaza, 9336 Civic Center Dr, Beverly Hills CA 90210 USA
**Richmond, Branscombe** — Actor
PO Box 881095, Pukalani HI 96788, USA
**Richmond, Geri** — Chemist
University of Oregon, Chemistry Dept, Eugene OR 97403, USA
**Richmond, Mitchell J (Mitch)** — Basketball Player
25374 Prado de la Felicidad, Calabasas CA 91302, USA
**Richmond, Steve** — Ice Hockey Player
21290 W Pepper Dr, Lake Zurich IL 60047, USA
**Richt, Mark** — Football Coach
University of Georgia, Athletic Dept, PO Box 1472, Athens GA 30603, USA
**Richter, Allen G (Al)** — Baseball Player
3810 Atlantic Ave, #703, Virginia Beach VA 23451, USA

# R

**Richardson - Richter**

# R

**Richter, Andy** — Actor, Comedian
Creative Artists Agency, 2000 Ave of Stars, #100, Los Angeles CA 90067 USA

**Richter, Barry** — Ice Hockey Player
7202 Timberwood Dr, Madison WI 53719, USA

**Richter, Burton** — Nobel Physics Laureate
620 Sand Hill Road, #206C, Palo Alto CA 94304, USA

**Richter, Gerhard** — Artist
Bismarckstr 50, 50672 Cologne, Germany

**Richter, Jason James** — Actor
Aqua Talent, 9000 Sunset Blvd, #700, Los Angeles CA 90069, USA

**Richter, John F** — Basketball Player
2740 Narcissa Road, Plymouth Meeting PA 19462, USA

**Richter, Michael T (Mike)** — Ice Hockey Player
61 Cutler Road, Greenwich CT 06831, USA

**Richter, Pat V** — Football Player, Administrator
11111 Bardon Road, Woodruff WI 54568, USA

**Richwine, Maria** — Actress
Acme Talent Agency, 4727 Wilshire Blvd, #333, Los Angeles CA 90010 USA

**Rickard, Joe** — Drummer (Red)
Paradigm Agency, 404 W Franklin St, Monterey CA 93940 USA

**Rickard, Robbie** — Bowler
Professional Bowlers Assn, 719 2nd Ave, #701, Seattle WA 98104 USA

**Rickards, Ashley** — Actress
United Talent Agency, U T A Plaza, 9336 Civic Center Dr, Beverly Hills CA 90210 USA

**Rickards, Emily Bett** — Actress
Muse Artist Management, 708 Denman St, #200, Vancouver BC V6G 2L5, Canada

**Ricker, Maelle D** — Snowboarding Athlete
Agenda Sport Marketing, 318 11th Ave SE, #340, Calgary AB T2G 0Y2 Canada T2G

**Ricketts, Thomas G (Tom), Jr** — Football Player
720 Warrendale Bayne Road, Wexford PA 15090, USA

**Rickhards, Dominic** — Actor
Gavin Barker Assoc, 2D Wimpole St, London W1G 0EB, England

**Rickles, Don** — Actor, Comedian
10249 Century Woods Dr, Los Angeles CA 90067, USA

**Rickman, Alan** — Actor
Independent Talent Group, 40 Whitfield St, London W1T 2RH, England

**Ricks, Christopher B** — Writer, Educator
Lasborough Park near Tetbury, Gloucestershire GL8 8UF, England

**Ricks, Mikhael R** — Football Player
5024 Lincoln St, Hollywood FL 33021, USA

**Rickter, Alicia** — Model, Actress
Innovative Artists, 1505 10th St, Santa Monica CA 90401 USA

**Rico, Alfredo C (Fred)** — Baseball Player
7720 Ensign Ave, Sun Valley CA 91352, USA

**Rida, Flo** — Rap Artist
Susan Blond Inc, 50 W 57th St, #1400, New York NY 10019 USA

**Riddell, Derek** — Actor
Hamilton Hodell, 66-68 Margaret St, #500, London W1W 8SR, England

**Riddick, Frank A, Jr** — Physician
150 Broadway St, #709, New Orleans LA 70118, USA

**Riddick, Robbert L (Robb)** — Football Player
111 Lilli Lane, Woodstock GA 30188, USA

**Riddick, Steven (Steve)** — Track Athlete
PO Box 1892, Norfolk VA 23501, USA

**Riddiford, Lynn M** — Zoologist
40733 Manor House Road, Leesburg VA 20175, USA

**Riddleberger, Dennis M (Denny)** — Baseball Player
35785 Hunter Ave, Westland MI 48185, USA

**Riddles, Libby** — Dog Sled Racer
PO Box 15253, Fritz Creek AK 99603, USA

**Riddoch, Gregory L (Greg)** — Baseball Player, Manager
703 Windflower Dr, Longmont CO 80504, USA

**Rider, Isaiah (J R)** — Basketball Player
PO Box 121R, Montchanin DE 19710, USA

**Ridge, Thomas J (Tom)** — Secretary, Home Security; Governor, PA
Westwood Estate Dr, Erie PA 16506, USA

**Ridgeley, Andrew** — Singer, Guitarist (Wham!)
8800 W Sunset Blvd, #401, West Hollywood CA 90069, USA

**Ridgeway, Angie** — Golfer
419 Glen Crest Dr, Moore SC 29369, USA

**Ridgeway, Frank** — Cartoonist (Mr Abernathy)
King Features Syndicate, 300 W 57th St, #1500, New York NY 10019 USA

**Ridgway, Jeff** — Baseball Player
9041 Parlor Dr, Ladson SC 29456, USA

**Ridgway, Stanard (Stan)** — Singer, Songwriter
Conqueroo, 11271 Ventura Blvd, #522, Studio City CA 91604 USA

**Ridker, Paul** — Cardiologist
Brigham & Women's Hospital, 75 Francis St, Boston MA 02115, USA

**Ridley, John** — Writer, Director, Producer
Creative Artists Agency, 2000 Ave of Stars, #100, Los Angeles CA 90067 USA

**Ridley, Mike** — Ice Hockey Player
Home Run Sports, 1005 St Mary's Road, Winnipeg MB R2M 3S4, Canada

**Ridlon, James A (Jim)** — Football Player
4468 E Lake Road, Cazenovia NY 13035, USA

**Ridnour, Lukas R (Luke)** — Basketball Player
Milwaukee Bucks, Bradley Center, 1001 N 4th St, #2, Milwaukee WI 53203 USA

**Riedel, Lars** — Track Athlete
Trinitatis Str 20, 09130 Chemnitz, Germany

**Riedel, Oliver (Ollie)** — Bassist (Rammstein)
Pilgrim Mgmt, PO Box 540101, 10042 Berlin, Germany

**Riedlbauch, Vaclav** — Composer
Revolucni 6, 11000 Prague 1, Czech Republic

**Riedling, John** — Baseball Player
2118 Homestead Lane, Franklin TN 37064, USA

**Rieffel, Lisa** — Actress
A P A Talent/Literary Agency, 405 S Beverly Dr, #300, Beverly Hills CA 90212 USA

| | |
|---|---|
| **Riegert, Peter** | Actor |
| Don Buchwald, 10 E 44th St, New York NY 10017 USA | |
| **Riegger, John** | Golfer |
| 768 Tossa de Mar Ave, Henderson NV 89002, USA | |
| **Riegle, Gene** | Harness Racing Driver, Trainer |
| 818 Chestnut Circle, Greenville OH 45331, USA | |
| **Riehle, Richard** | Actor |
| Stone Manners Salners, 9911 W Pico Blvd, #1400, Los Angeles CA 90035 USA | |
| **Riemersma, A Jay** | Football Player |
| 3067 Regency Parkway, Zeeland MI 49464, USA | |
| **Riendeau, Vincent** | Ice Hockey Player |
| Harrington College, Che Riviere Rouge, Harrington QC JBG 2S7, Canada | |
| **Rienstra, John W** | Football Player |
| PO Box 2447, Frisco CO 80443, USA | |
| **Ries, Christopher D** | Artist |
| Keelersburg Road, Tunkhannock PA 18657, USA | |
| **Riesch, Maria Hoefl-** | Alpine Skier |
| Wildenauer Str 22, 82467 Garmisch-Partenkirchen, Germany | |
| **Riesco, Armando** | Actor |
| Liebman Entertainment, 12 E 46th St, #500, New York NY 10017, USA | |
| **Riesenberg, Douglas J (Doug)** | Football Player |
| 25068 Starr Creek Road, Corvallis OR 97333, USA | |
| **Riesgo, D Nikco** | Baseball Player |
| 29625 Bermuda Lane, Southfield MI 48076, USA | |
| **Riesgraf, Beth** | Actress, Director, Writer |
| Insight Entertainment, 1134 S Colverdale Ave, Los Angeles CA 90019, USA | |
| **Riess, Adam G** | Nobel Physics Laureate |
| Space Telescope Science Institute, 3700 San Martin Dr, Baltimore MD 21218, USA | |
| **Riessen, Marty** | Tennis Player |
| PO Box 5444, Santa Barbara CA 93150, USA | |
| **Rieu, Andre L M N** | Concert Violinist, Conductor, Composer |
| Andre Rieu Productions, Postfach 1329, 6201 Maastricht BH, Netherlands | |
| **Riffenburgh, Beau** | Historian |
| Bloomsbury Publishing, 50 Bedford Square, London WC1B 3DP, England | |
| **Rifkin, Arnold** | Producer |
| Cheyenne Enterprises, 406 Wilshire Blvd, Santa Monica CA 90401, USA | |
| **Rifkin, Jeremy** | Writer, Social Activist |
| 1660 L St NW, #216, Washington DC 20036, USA | |
| **Rifkin, Joshua** | Concert Pianist, Conductor |
| 100 Montgomery St, Cambridge MA 02140, USA | |
| **Rifkin, Ron** | Actor, Singer |
| Innovative Artists, 235 Park Ave S, #1000, New York NY 10003 USA | |
| **Rigazio, Donald** | Ice Hockey Player |
| 8514 Cheffield Dr, Louisville KY 40222, USA | |
| **Rigby McCoy, Cathleen R (Cathy)** | Gymnast, Actress |
| McCoy Rigby Entertainment, 22601 La Palma Ave, #105, Yorba Linda CA 92887, USA | |
| **Rigby, Amy** | Singer, Songwriter |
| Public Emily, 56 Main St, #206, Northampton MA 01060, USA | |
| **Rigby, Jean P** | Opera Singer |
| John Coast Mgmt, Manfield House, 3769 Strand, London WC1, England | |
| **Rigby, Randall L, Jr** | Army General |
| 869 Oak Hill Road, Lake Barrington IL 60010, USA | |
| **Rigg, Diana** | Actress |
| Artist Rights Group, 4 Great Portland St, London W1W 8PA, England | |
| **Riggi, Chris** | Actor |
| Gersh Agency, 9465 Wilshire Blvd, #600, Beverly Hills CA 90212 USA | |
| **Riggin, Patrick M (Pat)** | Ice Hockey Player |
| 112 Fairlane Ave, London ON N6K 3E6, Canada | |
| **Riggins, John** | Football Player, Sportscaster |
| 8000 Riverside Dr, Cabin John MD 20818, USA | |
| **Riggle, Rob** | Actor, Comedian |
| Principato-Young, 9465 Wilshire Blvd, #880, Beverly Hills CA 90212 USA | |
| **Riggleman, James D (Jim)** | Baseball Player, Manager |
| 14950 Gulf Blvd, #1003, Madeira Beach FL 33708, USA | |
| **Riggs, Adam D** | Baseball Player |
| 26 Pebble Hollow Court, Spring TX 77381, USA | |
| **Riggs, Chandler** | Actor |
| I C M Partners, 10250 Constellation Blvd, #900, Los Angeles CA 90067 USA | |
| **Riggs, Gerald** | Football Player |
| 2574 Bright Court, Decatur GA 30034, USA | |
| **Riggs, Lorrin A** | Psychologist |
| 80 Lyme Road, #104, Hanover NH 03755, USA | |
| **Riggs, R Scott** | Auto, Truck Racing Driver |
| 216 Preston Andrews Road, Bahama NC 27503, USA | |
| **Riggs, Ransom** | Writer |
| Paradigm Agency, 360 N Crescent Dr, North Building, Beverly Hills CA 90210 USA | |
| **Righetti, Amanda** | Actress |
| United Talent Agency, U T A Plaza, 9336 Civic Center Dr, Beverly Hills CA 90210 USA | |
| **Righetti, David A (Dave)** | Baseball Player |
| 552 Magdalena Ave, Los Altos Hills CA 94024, USA | |
| **Rigoni, Benito** | Bobsled Athlete |
| Olympic Committee, Foro Italico, Largo Lauro de Bosis 15, 00135 Rome, Italy | |
| **Rihanna** | Singer |
| Roc Nation, 1411 Broadway, #3800, New York NY 10018, USA | |
| **Riis, Bjarne L** | Cyclist |
| Riis Cycling, Firskowej 36, 2800 KGS Lyngby, Denmark | |
| **Rijker, Lucia** | Boxer, Kickboxer, Actress |
| Sports Placement Service, 6671 W Sunset Blvd, #1521, Los Angeles CA 90028, USA | |
| **Rijo, Jose A** | Baseball Player |
| 2127 Brickell Ave, #2101, Miami FL 33129, USA | |
| **Rikaart, Greg** | Actor |
| S D B Partners, 1801 Ave of Stars, #902, Los Angeles CA 90067 USA | |
| **Riker, Albert J** | Plant Pathologist |
| 2760 E 8th St, Tucson AZ 85716, USA | |
| **Riker, Robin** | Actress |
| Stone Manners Salners, 9911 W Pico Blvd, #1400, Los Angeles CA 90035 USA | |

**R**

**Riker, Thomas E (Tom)**  Basketball Player
600 Fines Creek Road, Clyde NC 28721, USA
**Riklis, Meshulam**  Businessman
Riklis Family Corp, 2901 Las Vegas Blvd S, Las Vegas NV 89109, USA
**Riles, Ernest**  Baseball Player
221 Asante Dr, Ellenwood GA 30294, USA
**Riley, Amber**  Actress
P M K-B N C, 8687 Melrose Ave, #800, Los Angeles CA 90069 USA
**Riley, Bridget L**  Artist
Karsten Schubert, 47 Lexington St, London W1R 3LG, England
**Riley, Chris J**  Golfer
2289 Surrey Meadows Ave, Henderson NV 89052, USA
**Riley, E Theodore (Teddy)**  Songwriter, Singer (Blackstreet)
Richard Walters, PO Box 2789, Toluca Lake CA 91610 USA
**Riley, Elaine**  Actress
405 N Bay Front, Newport Beach CA 92662, USA
**Riley, Eric**  Basketball Player
6601 Sands Point Dr, #4, Houston TX 77074, USA
**Riley, Gerald (Jerry)**  Dog Sled Racer
General Delivery, Nenana AK 99760, USA
**Riley, Jack**  Actor
C E S D, 10635 Santa Monica Blvd, #130, Los Angeles CA 90025 USA
**Riley, James C**  Army General
Commanding General, V Corps, APO AE 09079 USA
**Riley, James G (Jim)**  Football Player
2201 Cardinal Dr, Edmond OK 73013, USA
**Riley, Jeannie C**  Singer
906 Granville Road, Franklin TN 37064, USA
**Riley, John P (Jack), Jr**  Ice Hockey Player, Coach
PO Box 1302, Marstons Mills MA 02648, USA
**Riley, Kenneth J (Ken)**  Football Player
1035 Carver Ave, Bartow FL 33830, USA
**Riley, Madison**  Actress
Emerald Talent Group, 15260 Ventura Blvd, #1200, Sherman Oaks CA 91403, USA
**Riley, Matthew P (Matt)**  Baseball Player
17169 W Ironwood St, Surprise AZ 85388, USA
**Riley, Michael**  Actor
Gary Goodard Agency, 149 Chuch St, #200, Toronto ON M5B 1Y4, Canada
**Riley, Mike**  Football Coach
Oregon State University, Athletic Dept, Corvallis OR 97331, USA
**Riley, Patrick J (Pat)**  Basketball Player, Coach, Executive
180 Arvida Parkway, Miami FL 33156, USA
**Riley, Richard D**  Association Executive
16 Boathouse Road, Laconia NH 03246, USA
**Riley, Richard W**  Secretary, Education; Governor, SC
Nelson Mullins Riley Scarborough, 104 S Main St, #900, Greenville SC 29601, USA
**Riley, Ruth**  Basketball Player
Metis Sports Management, 132 N Old Woodward Ave, Birmingham MI 48009
**Riley, Sam**  Actor
Creative Artists Agency, 2000 Ave of Stars, #100, Los Angeles CA 90067 USA
**Riley, Steve B**  Football Player
7 Via Cancion, San Clemente CA 92673, USA
**Riley, Talulah**  Actress
Independent Talent Group, 40 Whitfield St, London W1T 2RH, England
**Riley, Tarrus**  Singer
Agency Group Ltd, 142 W 57th St, #600, New York NY 10019 USA
**Riley, Terry M**  Composer, Pianist
Shri Moonshine Ranch, 13699 Moonshine Road, Camptonville CA 95922, USA
**Riley, Tom**  Actor
I C M Partners, 10250 Constellation Blvd, #900, Los Angeles CA 90067 USA
**Riley, Victor A**  Football Player
1430 Bavand Circle, #107, Rock Hill SC 29732, USA
**Riley, Victor J, Jr**  Financier
100 Elm St, Williamstown MA 01267, USA
**Riley, William (Bill)**  Ice Hockey Player
286 Buckingham Ave, Riverview NB E1B 2P2, Canada
**Riley, William J**  Judge
US Court of Appeals, Federal Building, PO Box 307, Omaha NE 68101, USA
**Rilling, Helmuth**  Conductor, Concert Organist
Opus 3 Artists, 470 Park Ave S, #900N, New York NY 10016 USA
**Rimes, LeAnn**  Singer
PO Box 150667, Nashville TN 37215, USA
**Rimington, Dave B**  Football Player
125 W 110th St, #5A, New York NY 10026, USA
**Rimington, Stella**  Government Official, England
PO Box 1604, London SW1P 1XB, England
**Rimmel, James E**  Religious Leader
Evangelical Presbyterian Church, 26049 Five Mile Road, Redford MI 48239, USA
**Rinaldi, Kathy**  Tennis Player
Advantage International, 1025 Thomas Jefferson NW, #450, Washington DC 20007 USA
**Rinaldi, Richard P (Rich)**  Basketball Player
1117 Perry Lane, Collegeville PA 19426, USA
**Rinaldo, Benjamin**  Skier
Ski World, 2680 Buena Park Dr, Studio City CA 91604, USA
**Rincon, Juan M**  Baseball Player
5150 Lincoln Dr, Minneapolis MN 55436, USA
**Rinehart, Kenneth**  Chemist
University of Illinois, Chemistry Dept, Urbana IL 61801, USA
**Ring, R Royce**  Baseball Player
PO Box 2184, El Cajon CA 92021, USA
**Ring, Timothy M**  Businessman
C F Bard Co, 730 Central Ave, Murray Hill NJ 07974, USA
**Ringenberg, Jason**  Singer (Jason & the Scorchers)
Roughneck Music, 7553 Gannon Ave, Saint Louis MO 63130, USA
**Ringer, Jennifer**  Ballerina
New York City Ballet, Lincoln Center Plaza, New York NY 10023 USA

**Ringer, Noah** — Actor
Creative Artists Agency, 2000 Ave of Stars, #100, Los Angeles CA 90067 USA

**Ringgold, Faith** — Writer, Artist
Simon & Schuster, 1230 Ave of Americas, Concourse 1, New York NY 10020 USA

**Ringle, William M** — Anthropologist
Davidson College, Anthropolgy Dept, Chambers Hall, Davidson NC 28035, USA

**Ringwald, Molly** — Actress
Untitled Entertainment, 350 S Beverly Dr, #200, Beverly Hills CA 90212 USA

**Rinker, Laurie A** — Golfer
PO Box 550, Jensen Beach FL 34958, USA

**Rinker, Lee C** — Golfer
1151 Egret Circle S, #380, Jupiter FL 33458, USA

**Rinna, Lisa** — Actress, Model
Paradigm Agency, 360 N Crescent Dr, North Building, Beverly Hills CA 90210 USA

**Rinne, Pekka** — Ice Hockey Player
Nashville Predators, 501 Broadway, Nashville TN 37203 USA

**Rinsch, Carl** — Director, Producer, Writer
Brillstein Entertainment Partners, 9150 Wilshire Blvd, #350, Beverly Hills CA 90212 USA

**Rintoul, David** — Actor
Ken McReddie Assoc, 101 Finsbury Pavement, London EC2A 1RS, England

**Rintoul, Steve** — Golfer
17506 Osprey Manor Way, Lithia FL 33547, USA

**Rintzler, Marius A** — Opera Singer
Friedingstr 18, 40625 Dusseldorf, Germany

**Rinzler, Lisa** — Cinematographer
Gersh Agency, 9465 Wilshire Blvd, #600, Beverly Hills CA 90212 USA

**Riordan, Michael W (Mike)** — Basketball Player
140 Inwood Road, Stevensville MD 21666, USA

**Riordan, Richard J** — Mayor, Los Angeles
141 N Bristol Ave, Los Angeles CA 90049, USA

**Rios Montt, J Efrain** — President, Guatemala; Army General
6A Avenida A 3-18 Zona 1, Guatemela City, Guatemala

**Rios, Alberto** — Writer
Arizona State University, English Dept, Tempe AZ 85287, USA

**Rios, Armando** — Baseball Player
790 Ridenhour Circle, Orlando FL 32809, USA

**Rios, Brandon L** — Boxer
Top Rank Inc, 3908 Howard Hughes Parkway, #580, Las Vegas NV 89169 USA

**Rios, Daniel (Danny)** — Baseball Player
2523 W 9th Lane, Hialeah FL 33010, USA

**Rios, Emily** — Actress
Kass Management, 501 Santa Monica Blvd, #604, Los Angeles CA 90401, USA

**Rios, Marcelo** — Tennis Player
International Mgmt Group, Via Augusta 200, #400, 08021 Barcelona, Spain

**Rios, Mark** — Architect
Rios Clementi Hale Studios, 639 N Larchmont Blvd, #101, Los Angeles CA 90004, USA

**Rios, Susan** — Artist
Try Art Galleries, 3100 Porter St, Soquel CA 95073, USA

**Riotta, Vincent** — Actor
Untitled Entertainment, 350 S Beverly Dr, #200, Beverly Hills CA 90212 USA

**Rioux, Gerry** — Ice Hockey Player
213 Grosvenor, Ironquois Falls ON P0K 1G0, Canada

**Ripa, Kelly** — Actress, Model
Milojo Productions, 270 Lafayette St, #702, New York NY 10012, USA

**Ripert, Eric** — Chef
Le Bernardin, 787 7th Ave, Concourse 1, New York NY 10019, USA

**Ripken, Calvin E (Cal), Jr** — Baseball Player
1427 Clarkview Road, #100, Baltimore MD 21209, USA

**Ripken, William O (Bill)** — Baseball Player
900 Mount Soma Court, Fallston MD 21047, USA

**Ripley, Alice** — Actress, Singer
Thruline Entertainment, 9250 Wilshire Blvd, #100, Beverly Hills CA 90212 USA

**Ripley, Allen S** — Baseball Player
50 Dunham St, Attleboro MA 02703, USA

**Rippey, Rodney Allan** — Actor
3941 Veselich Ave, #4-251, Los Angeles CA 90039, USA

**Ripple, Kenneth F** — Judge
US Court of Appeals, 204 S Main St, South Bend IN 46601, USA

**Rippy, Leon** — Actor
Greene Assoc, 1901 Ave of Stars, #130, Los Angeles CA 90067 USA

**Rippy, Nicolas** — Model
Wilhelmina Models, 300 Park Ave S, #200, New York NY 10010 USA

**Ris, Hans** — Zoologist
2116 Madison St, Madison WI 53711, USA

**RisCassi, Robert W** — Army General
Spectrum Group, 11 Canal Center Plaza, #103, Alexandria VA 22314, USA

**Riseborough, Andrea** — Actress
Independent Talent Group, 40 Whitfield St, London W1T 2RH, England

**Riseborough, Douglas J (Doug)** — Ice Hockey Player, Coach
77928 Grey Wolf Trail, La Quinta CA 92253, USA

**Risen, James** — Journalist
New York Times, Editorial Dept, 229 W 43rd St, New York NY 10036 USA

**Risien, Cody L** — Football Player
505 Bulian Lane, Austin TX 78746, USA

**Riske, David R** — Baseball Player
2771 Culloden Ave, Henderson NV 89044, USA

**Risley, William C (Bill)** — Baseball Player
1160 Prim Rose Circle, Greenwood AR 72936, USA

**Rison, Andre P** — Football Player
6293 N Jennings Road, Mount Morris MI 48458, USA

**Rispoli, Michael** — Actor
Principal Entertainment, 130 W 42nd St, #614, New York NY 10036, USA

**Risser, Paul G** — Educator
Natural History Museum, Director's Office, PO Box 37012, Washington DC 20013, USA

**Rissling, Gary** — Ice Hockey Player
7905 Tilmont Ave, Parkville MD 21234, USA

**Riszdorfer, Michal** — Canoeing Athlete
Bratislava Ul M Scho SKP, Trnasvkeho 2/A, 84446 Bratislava, Slovakia
**Riszdorfer, Richard** — Canoeing Athlete
Bratislava Ul M Scho SKP, Trnasvkeno 2/A, 84446 Bratislava, Slovakia
**Ritcher, James A (Jim)** — Football Player
8620 Bournemouth Dr, Raleigh NC 27615, USA
**Ritchie, Brian** — Bassist (Violent Femmes)
Good Feelings Artist Mgmt, PO Box 6632, Minneapolis MN 55406, USA
**Ritchie, Darren** — Actor
A P A Talent/Literary Agency, 405 S Beverly Dr, #300, Beverly Hills CA 90212 USA
**Ritchie, Guy** — Director
Creative Artists Agency, 2000 Ave of Stars, #100, Los Angeles CA 90067 USA
**Ritchie, Ian** — Architect
110 Three Colt St, London E14 8A2, England
**Ritchie, Jay S** — Baseball Player
8275 Highway 52, Rockwell NC 28138, USA
**Ritchie, Jean** — Singer, Dulcimer Player, Songwriter
Music Tree Artist Mgmt, 1414 Philadelphia Ave, Pittsburgh PA 15233, USA
**Ritchie, Jill** — Actress
Wallman Public Relations, 10323 Santa Monica Blvd, #109, Los Angeles CA 90025, USA
**Ritchie, Jim** — Sculptor
Adelson Galleries, Mark Hotel, 19 E 82nd St, New York NY 10028, USA
**Ritchie, John H** — Architect
Mount, Heswall, Wirral L60 4RD, England
**Ritchie, Jon D** — Football Player
6135 Log Cabin Trail, Enola PA 17025, USA
**Ritchie, Todd E** — Baseball Player
114 Hulan Dr, Kerens TX 75144, USA
**Ritchson, Alan** — Actor
United Talent Agency, U T A Plaza, 9336 Civic Center Dr, Beverly Hills CA 90210 USA
**Ritenour, Lee M** — Jazz Guitarist, Singer, Composer
11808 Dorothy St, #108, Los Angeles CA 90049, USA
**Ritger, Dick** — Bowler
804 Valley View Dr, River Falls WI 54022, USA
**Ritson, Blake** — Actor
Curtis Brown Group, 28-29 Haymarket St, #500, London SW1Y 4SP, England
**Rittenhouse, Lenore** — Golfer
295 Bellhaven Dr, Carthage NC 28327, USA
**Ritter, C Dowd** — Financier
AmSouth Bancorp, AmSouth Sonat Tower, 1900 5th Ave N, Birmingham AL 35203, USA
**Ritter, Huntley** — Actor
Stafford Films, 9701 Wilshire Blvd, #1000, Beverly Hills CA 90212, USA
**Ritter, Jason** — Actor
I C M Partners, 730 5th Ave, New York NY 10019 USA
**Ritter, Josh** — Singer, Songwriter
Concerted Efforts, PO Box 440326, Somerville MA 02144 USA
**Ritter, Krysten** — Actress
Group Entertainment, 115 West 29th St, #1102, New York NY 10001, USA
**Ritter, Reggie B** — Baseball Player
1564 Estep Road, Donaldson AR 71941, USA
**Ritter, Tyson J** — Singer, Bassist (All-American Rejects)
Creative Artists Agency, 2000 Ave of Stars, #100, Los Angeles CA 90067 USA
**Rittinger, Al** — Ice Hockey Player
5423 Wallace Ave, Delta BC V4M 3V4, Canada
**Ritts, Jim** — Golf Executive
Ladies Pro Golf Assn, 100 International Golf Dr, Daytona Beach FL 32124 USA
**Ritz, Kevin D** — Baseball Player
68559 8th Street Road, Cambridge OH 43725, USA
**Ritzman, Alice** — Golfer
614 S Foys Lake Dr, Kalispell MT 59901, USA
**Riva, Diana-Maria** — Actress
Jonas Public Relations, 240 26th St, #3, Santa Monica CA 90402 USA
**Riva, Emmanuelle** — Actress
Anne Alvares Correa, 34 Rue Jouffroy d'Abbans, 75017 Paris, France
**Rivaldo** — Soccer Player
F C Milan, Via Filippo Turati 3, 20121 Milan, Italy
**Rivas, Daniel Louis** — Actor
A P A Talent/Literary Agency, 405 S Beverly Dr, #300, Beverly Hills CA 90212 USA
**Rivera Carrera, Norberto Cardinal** — Religious Leader
Curia Arzobispal, Aptdo Postal 24-4-33, Mexico City DF 06700, Mexico
**Rivera Mendoza, Zuleyka J** — Beauty Queen
Miss Universe Organization, 1370 Ave of Americas, #1600, New York NY 10019 USA
**Rivera Pedraza, Luis A** — Baseball Player
16 Calle Lazaro Ramos, Cidra PR 00739, USA
**Rivera, Ana Liz** — Actress
Televisa, Blvd A Lopez Mateos 232, Colonia San Angel, Mexico City DF 01060 CP, Mexico
**Rivera, Chita** — Actress, Singer, Dancer
Shopiro & Lobel, 220 W 42nd St, #1900, New York NY 10036, USA
**Rivera, Geraldo** — Entertainer
17 Annett Ave, Edgewater NJ 07020, USA
**Rivera, Jerry** — Singer
Alpha Artists International, 261 E 134th St, #200, Bronx NY 10454, USA
**Rivera, Jessica** — Opera Singer
I M G Artists, Hogarth Business Park, Chiswick, London W4 2TH, England
**Rivera, Jose** — Writer, Producer
I C M Partners, 10250 Constellation Blvd, #900, Los Angeles CA 90067 USA
**Rivera, Jose Antonio** — Boxer
7 Rodi Circle, Worcester MA 01603, USA
**Rivera, Manuel J (Jim)** — Baseball Player
2311 Abbey Dr, #7, Fort Wayne IN 46835, USA
**Rivera, Marco A** — Football Player
1854 Rue de Isabelle, Flower Mound TX 75022, USA
**Rivera, Mariano** — Baseball Player
147 Anderson Hill Road, Purchase NY 10577, USA
**Rivera, Michael** — Actor
Innovative Artists, 1505 10th St, Santa Monica CA 90401 USA

| | |
|---|---|
| **Rivera, Michael R (Mike)** | Baseball Player |
| 2814 Harwood Court, Kissimmee FL 34744, USA | |
| **Rivera, Robert** | Artist |
| 21 Sandia Lane, Placitas NM 87043, USA | |
| **Rivera, Ronald E (Ron)** | Football Player, Coach |
| 14420 Rancho del Prado Trail, San Diego CA 92127, USA | |
| **Rivero, Jorge** | Actor |
| H David Moss, 733 Seward St, #PH, Los Angeles CA 90038 USA | |
| **Rivers, Austin J** | Basketball Player |
| New Orleans Pelicans, 1250 Poydras St, #101, New Orleans LA 70113 USA | |
| **Rivers, David L** | Basketball Player |
| 10509 Greensprings Dr, Tampa FL 33626, USA | |
| **Rivers, Glenn A (Doc)** | Basketball Player, Coach |
| 5 Isle Of Sicily, Winter Park FL 32789, USA | |
| **Rivers, J Milton (Mickey)** | Baseball Player |
| 350 NW 48th St, Miami FL 33127, USA | |
| **Rivers, Jamie A** | Football Player |
| 40 Waterman Place, Saint Louis MO 63112, USA | |
| **Rivers, Joan** | Entertainer, Comedienne |
| Larry Thompson Organization, 9663 Santa Monica Blvd, #801, Beverly Hills CA 90210, USA | |
| **Rivers, Johnny** | Singer, Songwriter |
| 3141 Coldwater Canyon Lane, Beverly Hills CA 90210, USA | |
| **Rivers, Keith** | Football Player |
| Cincinnati Bengals, 1 Paul Brown Stadium, Cincinnati OH 45202 USA | |
| **Rivers, Marcellus** | Football Player |
| 12003 Eden Lane, Frisco TX 75034, USA | |
| **Rivers, Melissa** | Actress, Producer |
| Larry Thompson Organization, 9663 Santa Monica Blvd, #801, Beverly Hills CA 90210, USA | |
| **Rivers, Philip** | Football Player |
| San Diego Chargers, 4020 Murphy Canyon Road, San Diego CA 92123 USA | |
| **Rivers, Reginald C (Reggie)** | Football Player |
| 407 Corona St, Denver CO 80218, USA | |
| **Rivers, Samuel R (Sam)** | Bassist (Limp Bizkit) |
| Flip/Interscope Records, 8733 Sunset Blvd, #205, West Hollywood CA 90069, USA | |
| **Rivers, Wayne** | Ice Hockey Player |
| 7736 Cedar Lake Ave, San Diego CA 92119, USA | |
| **Rives, Donald E (Don)** | Football Player |
| 4910 Oldfield Dr, Arlington TX 76016, USA | |
| **Rivest, Ronald L** | Computer Scientist |
| Massachusetts Institute of Technology, Electrical Engineering Dept, Cambridge MA 02139, USA | |
| **Rivette, Jacques** | Director |
| Voyez Mon Agent, 20 Ave Rapp, 75007 Paris, France | |
| **Riviere, Jean-Max** | Composer |
| 6 Rue Choron, 75009 Paris, France | |
| **Rivlin, Alice M** | Government Official |
| 2842 Chesterfield Place, Washington DC 20008, USA | |
| **Rix, J Simon** | Bassist (Kaiser Chiefs) |
| Red Light Mgmt, 8439 Sunset Blvd, West Hollywood CA 90069, USA | |
| **Rizzi, Darren** | Football Player, Coach |
| University of Rhode Island, Athletic Dept, Kingston RI 02881, USA | |
| **Rizzo, Joseph V (Joe)** | Football Player |
| 6131 Dorsett Place, Wilmington NC 28403, USA | |
| **Rizzo, Michael (Mike)** | DJ Musician |
| T-Best Talent Agency, 508 Honey Lake Court, Danville CA 94506 USA | |
| **Rizzo, Patrice (Patti)** | Golfer |
| 1033 NE 17th Way, #2004, Fort Lauderdale FL 33304, USA | |
| **Rizzo, Pietro** | Conductor |
| I M G Artists, Hogarth Business Park, Chiswick, London W4 2TH, England | |
| **Rizzo, Todd M** | Baseball Player |
| 7 Williamsburg Court, Sewell NJ 08080, USA | |
| **Rizzo, Willy** | Photographer, Furniture Designer |
| Paul Smith Gallery, 9 Albermarle St, London W1S 4BL, England | |
| **Rizzotti, Jennifer** | Basketball Player, Coach |
| University of Hartford, Athletic Dept, West Hartford CT 06117, USA | |
| **Rizzuto, Garth** | Ice Hockey Player |
| 109 13th Ave S, Cranbrook BC B1C 2V6, Canada | |
| **Roa, Joseph R (Joe)** | Baseball Player |
| 677 E Brickley Ave, Hazel Park MI 48030, USA | |
| **Roach, Jason G** | Baseball Player |
| 6004 Delaval Lane, Raleigh NC 27614, USA | |
| **Roach, Jay** | Director |
| Everyman Pictures, 1512 16th St, #3, Santa Monica CA 90404, USA | |
| **Roach, John G** | Football Player |
| 4101 San Carlos St, Dallas TX 75205, USA | |
| **Roach, Melvin E (Mel)** | Baseball Player |
| 4131 Southhaven Road, Richmond VA 23235, USA | |
| **Roach, Steve** | Musician |
| Hearts of Space, PO Box 5916, Sausalito CA 94966, USA | |
| **Roache, Linus** | Actor |
| I C M Partners, 10250 Constellation Blvd, #900, Los Angeles CA 90067 USA | |
| **Roaches, Carl E** | Football Player |
| 1314 Twining Oaks Lane, Missouri City. TX 77489, USA | |
| **Roaf, William L (Willie)** | Football Player |
| 208 Cypress Bayou Lane, Kenner LA 70065, USA | |
| **Roan, Oscar B, III** | Football Player |
| 9 Pringle Lane, Rockwall TX 75087, USA | |
| **Roark, Terry P** | Educator |
| 1752 Edward Dr, Laramie WY 82072, USA | |
| **Roarke, Michael T (Mike)** | Baseball Player |
| 940 Quaker Lane, #2302, East Greenwich RI 02818, USA | |
| **Robards, Jake** | Actor |
| Don Buchwald, 10 E 44th St, New York NY 10017 USA | |
| **Robards, Karen** | Writer |
| Pocket Books, 1230 Ave of Americas, New York NY 10020 USA | |
| **Robards, Sam** | Actor |
| Paradigm Agency, 360 N Crescent Dr, North Building, Beverly Hills CA 90210 USA | |

**Robb, AnnaSophia** — Actress
Creative Artists Agency, 2000 Ave of Stars, #100, Los Angeles CA 90067 USA
**Robb, Charles S** — Governor, Senator, VA
George Mason University, Law School, 3301 N Fairfax Dr, Arlington VA 22201, USA
**Robb, David** — Actor
Hobson's International, 62 Chiswick High Road, London W4 1SY, England
**Robb, Douglas (Doug)** — Singer (Hoobastank)
Creative Artists Agency, 2000 Ave of Stars, #100, Los Angeles CA 90067 USA
**Robb, Peter** — Writer
Bloomsbury Publishing, 50 Bedford Square, London WC1B 3DP, England
**Robb, Walter L** — Businessman, Inventor
1358 Ruffner Road, Schenectady NY 12309, USA
**Robbie, Margot** — Actress
Creative Artists Agency, 2000 Ave of Stars, #100, Los Angeles CA 90067 USA
**Robbins, Austin D** — Football Player
4627 Hilltop Terrace SE, Washington DC 20019, USA
**Robbins, Barret G** — Football Player
21715 Don Gee Court, Santa Clarita CA 91350, USA
**Robbins, Brian** — Director, Producer, Actor
Varsity Pictures, 1040 N Las Palmas Ave, Building 2, Los Angeles CA 90038, USA
**Robbins, Deanna** — Actress
630 N Keystone St, Burbank CA 91506, USA
**Robbins, Jake** — Baseball Player
14208 Castle Abbey Lane, Charlotte NC 28277, USA
**Robbins, James E (Tootie)** — Football Player
3600 W Ray Road, #1031, Chandler AZ 85226, USA
**Robbins, Jane** — Actress
Scott Marshall Mgmt, 44 Perry Road, London W3 7NA, England
**Robbins, Kelly** — Golfer
1025 Lincoln Dr, Weidman MI 48893, USA
**Robbins, Randy** — Football Player
583 E Palo Verde St, Casa Grande AZ 85122, USA
**Robbins, Tim** — Actor, Director
Actor's Gang, 9070 Venice Blvd, Culver City CA 90232, USA
**Robbins, Tom** — Writer
PO Box 338, La Conner WA 98257, USA
**Robbins, Tony** — Writer
Jennifer Martinez, 9888 Carroll Centre Road, #100, San Diego CA 92126, USA
**Robelot, Jane** — Commentator
CBS-TV, News Dept, 51 W 52nd St, New York NY 10019 USA
**Roberge, Bertrand R (Bert)** — Baseball Player
267 Sunderland Dr, Auburn ME 04210, USA
**Roberge, Kalyna** — Speed Skater
Speed Skating Canada, 2781 Lancaster Road, #402, Ottawa ON K1B 1A7, Canada
**Roberson, Andre** — Basketball Player
Oklahoma City Thunder, 211 N Robinson Ave, #300, Oklahoma City OK 73102 USA
**Roberson, Antoinette** — Singer, Songwriter, Record Producer
Diva Central, 7510 W Sunset Blvd, #1445, Los Angeles CA 90046 USA
**Roberson, James W** — Cinematographer
PO Box 121013, Big Bear Lake CA 92315, USA
**Roberson, Rick** — Basketball Player
635 W West Ave, Fullerton CA 92832, USA
**Robert, Alain (Spiderman)** — Rock, Urban Climber
Maverick House Publishing, Dunboyne Business Park, Dunboyne, County Meath, Ireland
**Robert, Jacques F** — Attorney, Educator
14 Villa Saint-Georges, 92160 Antony, France
**Robert, Rene P** — Ice Hockey Player
8-5490 Glen Erin Dr, Mississauga ON L5M 5R4, Canada
**Roberto, Phillip J (Phil)** — Ice Hockey Player
5238 Ottawa Ave, Niagara Falls ON L2E 4Y8, Canada
**Roberts, Alfredo** — Football Player
4001 Tolbert Place, Carmel IN 46074, USA
**Roberts, Ashley** — Singer (Pussycat Dolls), Actress
A K A Talent, 6310 San Vicente Blvd, #200, Los Angeles CA 90048 USA
**Roberts, Bernard** — Concert Pianist
Uwchlaw'r Coed, Llanbedr, Gwynedd LL45 2NA, Wales
**Roberts, Bradley K (Brad)** — Singer, Guitarist (Crash Test Dummies)
Agency Group Ltd, 142 W 57th St, #600, New York NY 10019 USA
**Roberts, Brian L** — Businessman
Comcast Corp, 1500 Market St, #800W, Philadelphia PA 19102, USA
**Roberts, Brian M** — Baseball Player
11326 E Mimosa Dr, Scottsdale AZ 85262, USA
**Roberts, Bruce** — Singer, Songwriter
Gorfaine/Schwartz, 4111 W Alameda Ave, #509, Burbank CA 91505 USA
**Roberts, Cecil** — Labor Leader
United Mine Workers, 8315 Lee Highway, #500, Fairfax VA 22031, USA
**Roberts, Corrine (Cookie)** — Commentator
5315 Bradley Blvd, Bethesda MD 20814, USA
**Roberts, Craig** — Actor
W M E Entertainment, 9601 Wilshire Blvd, #300, Beverly Hills CA 90210 USA
**Roberts, Dallas** — Actor
United Talent Agency, U T A Plaza, 9336 Civic Center Dr, Beverly Hills CA 90210 USA
**Roberts, Dan** — Bassist (Crash Test Dummies)
Agency Group Ltd, 142 W 57th St, #600, New York NY 10019 USA
**Roberts, David (Dave)** — Track Athlete
14310 SW 73rd Ave, Archer FL 32618, USA
**Roberts, David L (Dave)** — Baseball Player
9705 Sam Bass Trail, Keller TX 76244, USA
**Roberts, David L (Dave)** — Ice Hockey Player
43690 Algonquin Dr, #26, Novi MI 48375, USA
**Roberts, David R (Dave)** — Baseball Player
1208 Crestview Dr, Cardiff by the Sea CA 92007, USA
**Roberts, David W (Dave)** — Baseball Player
6937 Laurel Valley Dr, Fort Worth TX 76132, USA
**Roberts, Dee** — Artist
2012 N 19th St, Boise ID 83702, USA

**Roberts, Doris** — Actress
6225 Quebec Dr, Los Angeles CA 90068, USA
**Roberts, Emma R** — Actress, Singer
Sweeney Entertainment, 6253 Hollywood Blvd, #201, Los Angeles CA 90028 90028, USA
**Roberts, Eric A** — Actor
Sovereign Talent Group, 8421 Wilshire Blvd, #200, Beverly Hills CA 90211, USA
**Roberts, Eugene L, Jr** — Editor
New York Times, Editorial Dept, 229 W 43rd St, New York NY 10036, USA
**Roberts, Frederick C (Fred)** — Basketball Player
463 Knight Circle, Alpine UT 84004, USA
**Roberts, Gary** — Ice Hockey Player
2095 Lake Shore Blvd, Toronto ON M8V 4G4, Canada
**Roberts, Gene** — Editor, Historian
University of Maryland, Journalism Dept, College Park MD 20742, USA
**Roberts, Gordon R** — Vietnam War Army Hero (CMH)
445 Ward-Koebel Road, Oregonia OH 45054, USA
**Roberts, Ian** — Actor
W M E Entertainment, 9601 Wilshire Blvd, #300, Beverly Hills CA 90210 USA
**Roberts, Jake (The Snake)** — Professional Wrestler
Prince Marketing Group, 18 Carillon Circle, Livingston NJ 07039 USA
**Roberts, James A (Jim)** — Ice Hockey Player, Coach
137 Ridgecrest Dr, Chesterfield MO 63017, USA
**Roberts, John** — Director
Creative Artists Agency, 2000 Ave of Stars, #100, Los Angeles CA 90067 USA
**Roberts, John** — Chief Justice, Supreme Court
US Supreme Court, 1st St NE, Washington DC 20543, USA
**Roberts, John** — Commentator
CBS-TV, News Dept, 51 W 52nd St, New York NY 10019 USA
**Roberts, John D** — Chemist
California Institute of Technology, Crellin Laboratory, Pasadena CA 91125, USA
**Roberts, John D (J D)** — Football Player, Coach
6708 Trevi Court, Oklahoma City OK 73116, USA
**Roberts, Jonathan** — Dancer
Abrams Artists, 9200 W Sunset Blvd, #1125, West Hollywood CA 90069 USA
**Roberts, Jordan** — Director, Writer, Actor
Creative Artists Agency, 2000 Ave of Stars, #100, Los Angeles CA 90067 USA
**Roberts, Joseph (Joe)** — Basketball Player
10975 Elvessa St, Oakland CA 94605, USA
**Roberts, Julia** — Actress
Creative Artists Agency, 2000 Ave of Stars, #100, Los Angeles CA 90067 USA
**Roberts, Julie** — Singer
Ron Shapiro Mgmt, 56 W 22nd St, #600S, New York NY 10010, USA
**Roberts, Kenny** — Motorcycle Racing Rider
K R Marketing, 419 Medina Road, Medina OH 44256, USA
**Roberts, Kevin J** — Businessman
Saatchi & Saatchi Worldwide, 375 Hudson St, Basement 3, New York NY 10014, USA
**Roberts, Larry** — Sculptor
PO Box 663, Bandon OR 97411, USA
**Roberts, Lawrence G** — Computer Scientist, Engineer
Caspian Networks, 170 Baytech Dr, San Jose CA 95134, USA
**Roberts, Leon J (Bip)** — Baseball Player
PO Box 170299, Arlington TX 76003, USA
**Roberts, Leon K** — Baseball Player
4711 Chapel Springs Court, Arlington TX 76017, USA
**Roberts, Leonard** — Actor
Luber Rocklin Entertainment, 8530 Wilshire Blvd, #555, Beverly Hills CA 90211 USA
**Roberts, Loren** — Golfer
8429 Orchard Hill Dr, Germantown TN 38138, USA
**Roberts, Lynn** — Singer, Actress
42 Vespers Way, Okatie SC 29909, USA
**Roberts, M Brigitte** — Writer
Gillon Atkin, 29 Fernshaw Road, London SW10 0TG, England
**Roberts, Marcus** — Jazz Pianist
R C A Records, 8750 Wilshire Blvd, Beverly Hills CA 90211 USA
**Roberts, Marvin J (Marv)** — Basketball Player
6202 Carriage Gate Lane SE, Mableton GA 30126, USA
**Roberts, Michele** — Writer
Henry Holt, 175 5th Ave, #400, New York NY 10010 USA
**Roberts, Nicola M** — Singer (Girls Aloud)
Concorde International, 101 Shepherds Bush Road, London W6 7LP, England
**Roberts, Nora** — Writer
19239 Burnside Bridge Road, Keedysville MD 21756, USA
**Roberts, Patricia (Trish)** — Basketball Player
218 Carver Dr, Monroe GA 30655, USA
**Roberts, Paul H** — Mathematician
PO Box 951567, Los Angeles CA 90095, USA
**Roberts, R Michael** — Animal Scientist
2213 Hominy Branch Court, Columbia MO 65201, USA
**Roberts, Richard J** — Nobel Medicine Laureate
New England Biolabs, 240 County Road, Ipswich MA 01938, USA
**Roberts, Richard L** — Educator
Oral Roberts University, President's Office, 7777 S Lewis Ave, Tulsa OK 74171, USA
**Roberts, Rick** — Actor
Gary Goddard Agency, 10 Sainte Mary's St, #305, Toronto ON M4Y 5QD, Canada
**Roberts, Robin** — Sportscaster, Commentator
ESPN-TV, ESPN Plaza, 935 Middle St, Bristol CT 06010 USA
**Roberts, Ryan A** — Baseball Player
6017 Avalon St, North Richland Hills TX 76180, USA
**Roberts, Sam** — Singer
Agency Group Ltd, 142 W 57th St, #600, New York NY 10019 USA
**Roberts, Shawn** — Actor
Gersh Agency, 9465 Wilshire Blvd, #600, Beverly Hills CA 90212 USA
**Roberts, Stanley C** — Basketball Player
1192 Congaree Road, Hopkins SC 29061, USA
**Roberts, Stephen** — Opera Singer
I M G Artists, Hogarth Business Park, Chiswick, London W4 2TH, England

| | |
|---|---|
| **Roberts, Tanya** | Actress |
| Good Guy Entertainment, 3733 Oakfield Dr, Sherman Oaks CA 91423, USA | |
| **Roberts, Tiffany** | Soccer Player |
| 2772 Ascot Dr, San Ramon CA 94583, USA | |
| **Roberts, Tony** | Actor |
| 970 Park Ave, #8N, New York NY 10028, USA | |
| **Roberts, Walter (Walt)** | Football Player |
| 268 Kenbrook Circle, San Jose CA 95111, USA | |
| **Roberts, William H (Bill)** | Football Player |
| 18520 NW 67th Ave, #141, Hialeah FL 33015, USA | |
| **Roberts, Willis A** | Baseball Player |
| 11501 Harts Road, Jacksonville FL 32218, USA | |
| **Roberts, Xavier** | Businessman, Doll Designer |
| PO Box 1438, Cleveland GA 30528, USA | |
| **Robertson of Port Ellen, George I M** | Government Official, England |
| House of Lords, Westminster, London SW1A 0PW, England | |
| **Robertson, Alvin C** | Basketball Player |
| 2919 Biering Peak, San Antonio TX 78247, USA | |
| **Robertson, Andre L** | Baseball Player |
| 2229 Cross Lane, Orange TX 77630, USA | |
| **Robertson, Belinda** | Fashion Designer |
| B R Cashmere, 22 Palmerston Place, Edinburgh EH12 5AL, Scotland | |
| **Robertson, Brittany (Britt)** | Actress |
| Innovative Artists, 1505 10th St, Santa Monica CA 90401 USA | |
| **Robertson, Daryl B** | Baseball Player |
| 52 Princeton Dr, Midvale UT 84047, USA | |
| **Robertson, David** | Conductor |
| Opus 3 Artists, 470 Park Ave S, #900N, New York NY 10016 USA | |
| **Robertson, David A** | Baseball Player |
| New York Yankees, Yankee Stadium, E 161st St & River Ave, Bronx NY 10451 USA | |
| **Robertson, Davis** | Dancer |
| Joffrey Ballet, 70 E Lake St, #1300, Chicago IL 60601, USA | |
| **Robertson, DeWayne** | Football Player |
| 26 Green St, Newbury MA 01951, USA | |
| **Robertson, Donald A (Don)** | Baseball Player |
| 5715 W Monte Vista Road, Phoenix AZ 85035, USA | |
| **Robertson, Ed** | Guitarist (Barenaked Ladies), Songwriter |
| Nettwerk Mgmt, 6525 W Sunset Blvd, #800, Los Angeles CA 90028 USA | |
| **Robertson, Finlay** | Actor |
| Independent Talent Group, 40 Whitfield St, London W1T 2RH, England | |
| **Robertson, Geordie** | Ice Hockey Player |
| 1 Scarborough Park, Rochester NY 14625, USA | |
| **Robertson, Isiah B** | Football Player |
| 906 Mill Spring Dr, Garland TX 75040, USA | |
| **Robertson, Jenny** | Actress |
| Shelter Entertainment, 9255 Sunset Blvd, #300, Los Angeles CA 90069 USA | |
| **Robertson, Joseph E, Jr** | Ophthalmologist, Educator |
| Oregon Health Science University, President's Office, Portland OR 97201, USA | |
| **Robertson, Kathleen** | Actress |
| Untitled Entertainment, 350 S Beverly Dr, #200, Beverly Hills CA 90212 USA | |
| **Robertson, Kimmy** | Actress |
| Innovative Artists, 1505 10th St, Santa Monica CA 90401 USA | |
| **Robertson, Leslie E** | Structural Engineer |
| 100 Riverside Blvd, #18D, New York NY 10069, USA | |
| **Robertson, M G (Pat)** | Evangelist |
| Christian Broadcast Network, 100 Centerville Turnpike, Virginia Beach VA 23463, USA | |
| **Robertson, Marcus A** | Football Player |
| 39534 Danielle Dr, Northville MI 48167, USA | |
| **Robertson, Mike** | Snowboarding Athlete |
| Snowboard Federation, 301-333 Terminal Ave, Vancouver BC V6A 4C1, Canada | |
| **Robertson, Nathan D (Nate)** | Baseball Player |
| 7918 W 53rd St N, Maize KS 67101, USA | |
| **Robertson, Oscar P** | Basketball Player |
| 621 Tusculum Ave, Cincinnati OH 45226, USA | |
| **Robertson, Richard P (Rich)** | Baseball Player |
| 1201 Crescent Terrace, Sunnyvale CA 94087, USA | |
| **Robertson, Richard W (Rich)** | Baseball Player |
| 32202 Sandwedge Dr, Waller TX 77484, USA | |
| **Robertson, Robbie** | Singer, Guitarist (Band); Songwriter |
| Special Artists Agency, 9200 Sunset Blvd, #410, West Hollywood CA 90069 USA | |
| **Robertson, Robert E (Bob)** | Baseball Player |
| 10015 Shinnamon Dr SW, Cumberland MD 21502, USA | |
| **Robertson, Ruth** | Artist, Photographer |
| 602 3rd St, Herndon VA 20170, USA | |
| **Robertson, Shirley A** | Yachtswoman |
| Lynx Sports Mgmt, Lymington Road, Lymington, Hampshire SO41 5S5, England | |
| **Roberts-Smith, Benjamin** | Afghanistan War Air Hero (VC) |
| Victoria Cross Assn, Old Admiralty Building, London SW1A 2BL, England | |
| **Robes, Ernest C (Bill)** | Ski Jumper |
| 3 Mile Road, Etna NH 03750, USA | |
| **Robey, Frederick R (Rick)** | Basketball Player |
| 2108 Club Vista Place, Louisville KY 40245, USA | |
| **Robidoux, William J (Billy Joe)** | Baseball Player |
| 2 King George Dr, Ware MA 01082, USA | |
| **Robillard, Michael J (Duke)** | Guitarist, Orchestra Leader |
| Rosebud Agency, PO Box 170429, San Francisco CA 94117 USA | |
| **Robin, Cynthia** | Archaeologist |
| Northwestern University, Anthropology Dept, 1812 Hillman, Evanston IL 60208, USA | |
| **Robin, Janet** | Singer, Guitarist |
| Little Sister Records, PO Box 351715, Los Angeles CA 90035, USA | |
| **Robin, Muriel** | Actress |
| Voyez Mon Agent, 20 Ave Rapp, 75007 Paris, France | |
| **Robins, Craig** | Businessman |
| Dacra Development Corp, 3841 NE 2nd Ave, #400, Miami FL 33137, USA | |
| **Robins, Laila** | Actress |
| Paradigm Agency, 360 N Crescent Dr, North Building, Beverly Hills CA 90210 USA | |

**Roberts - Robins**

| | |
|---|---|
| **Robinson Peete, Holly** | Actress |
| Innovative Artists, 1505 10th St, Santa Monica CA 90401 USA | |
| **Robinson, Alex J** | Singer, Songwriter |
| Agency Group Ltd, 142 W 57th St, #600, New York NY 10019 USA | |
| **Robinson, Alexia** | Actress |
| Heylee Winters Assoc, 8491 W Sunset Blvd, #268, West Hollywood CA 90069, USA | |
| **Robinson, Andrew J** | Actor |
| 2671 Byron Place, Los Angeles CA 90046, USA | |
| **Robinson, Ann** | Actress |
| 1357 Elysian Park Dr, Los Angeles CA 90026, USA | |
| **Robinson, Anne** | Entertainer |
| Penrose Media, 19 Victoria Grove, London W8 5RW, England | |
| **Robinson, Brooks C** | Baseball Player |
| 9210 Baltimore National Pike, Ellicot MD 21042, USA | |
| **Robinson, Bruce** | Writer, Actor, Director |
| Paradigm Agency, 360 N Crescent Dr, North Building, Beverly Hills CA 90210 USA | |
| **Robinson, Bruce P** | Baseball Player |
| 1310 Dellcrest Lane, La Jolla CA 92037, USA | |
| **Robinson, Bumper** | Actor |
| Mathews Management, 8730 Sunset Blvd, #200, Los Angeles CA 90069, USA | |
| **Robinson, Charles** | Actor |
| Stone Manners Salners, 9911 W Pico Blvd, #1400, Los Angeles CA 90035 USA | |
| **Robinson, Chip** | Auto Racing Driver |
| 3034 Lake Forest Dr, Augusta GA 30909, USA | |
| **Robinson, Chris** | Actor |
| Daniel Hoff Agency, 5455 Wilshire Blvd, #1100, Los Angeles CA 90036, USA | |
| **Robinson, Christopher M (Chris)** | Singer, Guitarist (Black Crowes) |
| Paradigm Agency, 404 W Franklin St, Monterey CA 93940, USA | |
| **Robinson, Clarence (Arnie)** | Track Athlete |
| 2904 Ocean View Blvd, San Diego CA 92113, USA | |
| **Robinson, Clifford R** | Basketball Player |
| 702 Sandia Place, Franklin Lakes NJ 07417, USA | |
| **Robinson, Clifford T (Cliff)** | Basketball Player |
| 98 S Bardsbrook Circle, Spring TX 77382, USA | |
| **Robinson, Craig** | Actor, Comedian |
| 3 Arts Entertainment, 9460 Wilshire Blvd, #700, Beverly Hills CA 90212 USA | |
| **Robinson, Craig G** | Baseball Player |
| 648 Picketts Mill Dr, Shreveport LA 71115, USA | |
| **Robinson, David M** | Basketball Player |
| PO Box 691207, San Antonio TX 78269, USA | |
| **Robinson, Dawn S** | Singer (En Vogue, Lucy Pearl) |
| Creative Artists Agency, 2000 Ave of Stars, #100, Los Angeles CA 90067 USA | |
| **Robinson, Don A** | Baseball Player |
| 1215 86th Court NW, Bradenton FL 34209, USA | |
| **Robinson, Doug** | Ice Hockey Player |
| 6 Tiffany Court, Saint Catherines ON L2M 7N3, Canada | |
| **Robinson, E Rafael** | Football Player |
| 4312 Forest Hill Circle, Forest Hill TX 76140, USA | |
| **Robinson, Eddie J** | Football Player |
| 6315 E Mystic Meadow, Houston TX 77021, USA | |
| **Robinson, Emily Erwin** | Singer (Dixie Chicks); Songwriter |
| Strategic Artists Mgmt, 1100 Glendon Ave, #1100, Los Angeles CA 90024, USA | |
| **Robinson, Fatima** | Dancer, Choreographer, Video Director |
| PO Box 833, 8306 Wilshire Blvd, Beverly Hills CA 90213, USA | |
| **Robinson, Floyd A** | Baseball Player |
| PO Box 152419, San Diego CA 92195, USA | |
| **Robinson, Frank** | Baseball Player, Manager |
| 15557 Aqua Verde Dr, Los Angeles CA 90077, USA | |
| **Robinson, Fred C** | Educator |
| Yale University, English Dept, New Haven CT 06520, USA | |
| **Robinson, Gerald** | Football Player |
| 4708 Scarborough Place, Stone Mountain GA 30087, USA | |
| **Robinson, Glenn** | Basketball Coach |
| Franklin & Marshall College, Athletic Dept, Lancaster PA 17604, USA | |
| **Robinson, Ivan** | Boxer |
| 140 W Roselyn St, Philadelphia PA 19120, USA | |
| **Robinson, Jackie** | Basketball Player |
| 130 W Harcourt St, Long Beach CA 90805, USA | |
| **Robinson, James P (Jimmy)** | Football Player |
| 4326 Fox Hollow Court, Oneida WI 54155, USA | |
| **Robinson, Janice** | Singer (Livin' Joy) |
| Nene Musik Productions, 1460 SW Santiago Ave, Port Saint Lucie FL 34953 USA | |
| **Robinson, Jeffrey D (Jeff)** | Baseball Player |
| 27 Weber Lane, Trabuco Canyon CA 92679, USA | |
| **Robinson, Jeffrey M (Jeff)** | Baseball Player |
| 2103 Monarch Ridge Dr, El Cajon CA 92019, USA | |
| **Robinson, Jeffrey W (Jeff)** | Football Player |
| 1020 W Ruffner St, Seattle WA 98119, USA | |
| **Robinson, Jerry D** | Football Player |
| 2398 Julio Lane, Santa Rosa CA 95401, USA | |
| **Robinson, John** | Actor |
| Paradigm Agency, 360 N Crescent Dr, North Building, Beverly Hills CA 90210 USA | |
| **Robinson, John A** | Football Coach |
| 1513 Village View Road, Encinitas CA 92024, USA | |
| **Robinson, Johnny N** | Football Player |
| 3209 S Grand St, Monroe LA 71202, USA | |
| **Robinson, Keith D** | Actor, Singer |
| A P A Talent/Literary Agency, 405 S Beverly Dr, #300, Beverly Hills CA 90212 USA | |
| **Robinson, Ken** | Educator |
| Washington Speakers Bureau, 1663 Prince St, Alexandria VA 22314, USA | |
| **Robinson, Kerry K** | Baseball Player |
| 133 Vlasis Dr, Ballwin MO 63011, USA | |
| **Robinson, Koren** | Football Player |
| 6735 Middleboro Dr, Raleigh NC 27612, USA | |
| **Robinson, Larry** | Ice Hockey Player, Coach |
| 10709 Winding Stream Way, Bradenton FL 34212, USA | |

Robinson Peete - Robinson

**Robinson, Laura** — Actress
Henderson/Hogan, 850 7th Ave, #1003, New York NY 10019 USA

**Robinson, Marcus A** — Football Player
PO Box 1924, Fort Valley GA 31030, USA

**Robinson, Marilynne** — Writer
University of Iowa, Iowa Writers' Workshop, Dey House, Iowa City IA 52242, USA

**Robinson, Mark L** — Football Player
303 Pennsylvania Ave, Palm Harbor FL 34683, USA

**Robinson, Mark R** — Singer, Guitarist (Unrest, Grenadine)
Go Ahead Booking, PO Box 5068, Hoboken NJ 07030, USA

**Robinson, Mary T W** — President, Ireland
Aras an Uachtarain, Phoenix Park, Dublin 8, Ireland

**Robinson, Matthew (Matt)** — Director, Producer
M C S Agency, 47 Dean St, London W1D 5BE, England

**Robinson, Matthew G (Matt)** — Football Player
12374 Mandarin Road, Jacksonville FL 32223, USA

**Robinson, Melvin D (Bo)** — Football Player
PO Box 2323, Coppell TX 75019, USA

**Robinson, Morris** — Singer
Opus 3 Artists, 470 Park Ave S, #900N, New York NY 10016 USA

**Robinson, Nathaniel C (Nate)** — Basketball Player
Chicago Bulls, United Center, 1901 W Madison St, Chicago IL 60612 USA

**Robinson, Nick** — Actor
Savage Agency, 6212 Banner Ave, Los Angeles CA 90038 USA

**Robinson, Nicole** — Actress
Stone Manners Salners, 9911 W Pico Blvd, #1400, Los Angeles CA 90035 USA

**Robinson, Oliver L** — Basketball Player
9640 Eastpointe Circle, Birmingham AL 35217, USA

**Robinson, Patrick** — Writer
Harper Collins Publishers, 10 E 53rd St, Cellar 1, New York NY 10022 USA

**Robinson, Patrick** — Fashion Designer
Gap Inc, 2 Folsom St, San Francisco CA 94105, USA

**Robinson, Paul H** — Football Player
1303 W 26th St, Safford AZ 85546, USA

**Robinson, Phil Alden** — Director, Writer
Academy of Motion Picture Arts & Sciences, 8949 Wilshire Blvd, Beverly Hills CA 90211, USA

**Robinson, R David (Dave)** — Football Player
406 S Rose Blvd, Akron OH 44320, USA

**Robinson, Randall** — Social Activist, Writer
African American Registry, PO Box 19441, Minneapolis MN 55419, USA

**Robinson, Rich** — Guitarist (Black Crowes), Songwriter
Paradigm, 404 W Franklin St, Monterey CA 93940, USA

**Robinson, Rob** — Ice Hockey Player
23466 Greening Dr, Novi MI 48375, USA

**Robinson, Ronald D (Ron)** — Baseball Player
3128 E Race Ave, Visalia CA 93292, USA

**Robinson, Ronnie** — Basketball Player
4169 S Germantown Road, Memphis TN 38125, USA

**Robinson, Shawna** — Auto, Truck Racing Driver
Performance One, 545 Pitts School Road NW, #C, Concord NC 28027, USA

**Robinson, Shelton D** — Football Player
18725 20th Dr SE, Bothell WA 98012, USA

**Robinson, Smokey** — Singer, Songwriter
Podwall Entertainment, 710 N Orlando Ave, #203, West Hollywood CA 90069, USA

**Robinson, Stephen K** — Astronaut
286 Cottage Circle, Davis CA 95616, USA

**Robinson, Thomas E** — Basketball Player
Portland Trail Blazers, Rose Garden, 1 N Center Court St, Portland OR 97227 USA

**Robinson, Todd** — Director, Producer, Writer
Paradigm Agency, 360 N Crescent Dr, North Building, Beverly Hills CA 90210 USA

**Robinson, Twyla** — Opera Singer
Columbia Artists Mgmt Inc, 1790 Broadway, #702, New York NY 10019 USA

**Robinson, V Gene** — Religious Leader
Diocesan House, 63 Green St, Concord NH 03301, USA

**Robinson, W Dunta** — Football Player
485 Vincent Dr, Athens GA 30607, USA

**Robinson, W Edward (Eddie)** — Baseball Player
6104 Cholla Dr, Fort Worth TX 76112, USA

**Robinson, Wayne L** — Football Player
2341 Main Highway, Breaux Bridge LA 70517, USA

**Robinson, Wendy Raquel** — Actress
Talent Works, 3500 W Olive Ave, #1400, Burbank CA 91505 USA

**Robinson, Zuleikha** — Actress
Gersh Agency, 41 Madison Ave, #3301, New York NY 10010 USA

**Robisch, David G (Dave)** — Basketball Player
1401 Guemes Court, Springfield IL 62702, USA

**Robiskie, Terry J** — Football Player, Coach
7000 Lanier Islands Parkway, Buford GA 30518, USA

**Robison, Bruce** — Singer, Songwriter
Crowley Artist Mgmt, 602 Wayside Dr, Wimberley TX 78676, USA

**Robison, Charles F (Charlie)** — Singer, Songwriter
S H O Artists, 864 Pinnacle Hill Road, Kingston Springs TN 37082, USA

**Robison, Paula** — Concert Flutist
Musicians Corporate Mgmt, PO Box 825, Highland NY 12528, USA

**Robitaille, Luc** — Ice Hockey Player, Executive
1750 14th St, #D, Santa Monica CA 90404, USA

**Robitaille, Mike** — Ice Hockey Player
121 Ransom Oaks Dr, East Amherst NY 14051, USA

**Robitaille, Pat** — Singer, Songwriter
Agency Group Ltd, 142 W 57th St, #600, New York NY 10019 USA

**Robitaille, Randy** — Ice Hockey Player
632 Seyton Dr, Nepean ON K2H 7X5, Canada

**Robles Ortega, Francisco Cardinal** — Religious Leader
Apartado 7, Zuazva 1100, Monterrey NL 64000, Mexico

**Robles, Marisa** — Concert Harpist
38 Luttrell Ave, London SW15 6PE, England

**Robles, Mike** — Actor, Comedian, Producer
I C M Partners, 10250 Constellation Blvd, #900, Los Angeles CA 90067 USA
**Robson, Bryan** — Soccer Player
Middlesbrough F C, Riverside Stadium, Middlebrough TS3 6RS, England
**Robson, Thomas J (Tom)** — Baseball Player
7331 W Morrow Dr, Glendale AZ 85308, USA
**Robuchon, Joel** — Chef
Societe de Gestion Culinaire, 67 Blvd Gen M Valin, 75015 Paris, France
**Robyn** — Singer
D E F Mgmt, 51 Lonsdale Road, Queens Park, London NW6 6RA, England
**Rocard, Michel L L** — Prime Minister, France
Hotel de Ville, 63 Rue M Berteaux, 78700 Conflans-Sainte-Honorine, France
**Rocca, Constantino** — Golfer
Golf Products International, 5719 Lake Lindero Dr, Agoura Hills CA 91301, USA
**Rocca, Maurice A (Mo)** — Actor, Comedian, Writer
Gersh Agency, 9465 Wilshire Blvd, #600, Beverly Hills CA 90212 USA
**Rocca, Patrick** — Actor
Artmedia, 20 Ave Rapp, 75007 Paris, France
**Rocca, Peter** — Swimmer
534 Hazel Ave, San Bruno CA 94066, USA
**Rocchigiani, Ralf** — Boxer
Rocky's Gym, Grabenstr 200A, 47057 Duisburg, Germany
**Rocco Yim** — Architect
38/F A I A Tower, 183 Electric Road, North Point, Hong Kong SAR, China
**Rocco, Alex** — Actor
Sovereign Talent Group, 10474 S Santa Monica Blvd, #301, Los Angeles CA 90025, USA
**Rocha, John** — Fashion Designer
12-13 Temple Lane, Dublin 2, Ireland
**Roche, Alden S, Jr** — Football Player
1082 Farragut St, New Orleans LA 70114, USA
**Roche, Anthony D (Tony)** — Tennis Player
5 Kapiti St, Saint Ives NSW 2075, Australia
**Roche, E Kevin** — Pritzker Architectural Laureate
Roche Dinkeloo Assoc, 20 Davis St, Hamden CT 06517, USA
**Roche, John M** — Basketball Player
191 Clayton Lane, #303, Denver CO 80206, USA
**Rochefort, Jean** — Actress
Le Chene Rogneaux, 078125 Grosvre, France
**Rochefort, Julien** — Actor
Artmedia, 20 Ave Rapp, 75007 Paris, France
**Rochefort, Leon J F** — Ice Hockey Player
1661 Rue Notre Dame, Sainte Marthe du Cap QC G8T 4J9, Canada
**Rochefort, Normand** — Ice Hockey Player
7704 Camminare Dr, Sarasota FL 34238, USA
**Rochelle, Michael D** — Army General
Deputy CofS Manpower & Personnel, HqUSA, Pentagon, Washington DC 20310, USA
**Rocher, Guy** — Sociologist
4911 Chemin de la Cote-des-Neiges, #409, Montreal QC H3V 1H7, Canada
**Rochester, Paul G** — Football Player
9209 Sweet Berry Dr, Jacksonville FL 32256, USA
**Rochford, Michael J (Mike)** — Baseball Player
5185 Cougars Prowl, Lake Worth FL 33449, USA
**Rochon, Lela** — Actress
Brillstein Entertainment Partners, 9150 Wilshire Blvd, #350, Beverly Hills CA 90212 USA
**Rock, Angela** — Volleyball Player
4771 Vista Lane, San Diego CA 92116, USA
**Rock, Antonio (Tony)** — Actor, Comedian
Bleu Entertainment, 4935 Whitsett Ave, #8, Valley Village CA 91607, USA
**Rock, Chris** — Actor, Comedian, Director
I C M Partners, 10250 Constellation Blvd, #900, Los Angeles CA 90067 USA
**Rock, Pete** — Rap Artist, DJ Musician
Agency Group Ltd, 142 W 57th St, #600, New York NY 10019 USA
**Rock, Walter W (Walt)** — Football Player
1030 Highams Court, Woodbridge VA 22191, USA
**Rockburne, Dorothea G** — Artist, Sculptor
140 Grand St, #2WF, New York NY 10013, USA
**Rockefeller, David** — Financier
1 Chase Manhattan Plaza, New York NY 10005, USA
**Rockefeller, James S** — Financier
425 Park Ave, New York NY 10022, USA
**Rockell** — Singer, Songwriter
T-Best Talent Agency, 508 Honey Lake Court, Danville CA 94506 USA
**Rocker, John L** — Baseball Player
1223 Manor Oaks Court, Atlanta GA 30338, USA
**Rocker, Lee** — Bassist (Stray Cats)
LiveTourArtists, 1451 White Oaks Blvd, Oakville ON L6H 4R9, Canada
**Rocker, Tracy Q** — Football Player
1792 Northumberland Dr, Brentwood TN 37027, USA
**Rockett, Patrick E (Pat)** — Baseball Player
17107 Eagle Hollow Dr, San Antonio TX 78248, USA
**Rockett, Richard A (Rikki)** — Drummer (Poison)
Front Line Mgmt, 1100 Glendon Ave, #2000, Los Angeles CA 90024 USA
**Rockette, Joannie** — Figure Skater
International Management Group, 767 5th Ave, #4500, New York NY 10153, USA
**Rockwell, David** — Architect
Rockwell Group, 5 Union Square W, New York NY 10003, USA
**Rockwell, Sam** — Actor
Arcieri Assoc, 305 Madison Ave, #2315, New York NY 10165 USA
**Rodan, Jay** — Actor
Entertainment Creative Interface, 9200 W Sunset Blvd, #434, West Hollywood CA 90069, USA
**Rodas, Richard M (Rick)** — Baseball Player
6877 Bergano Place, Rancho Cucamonga CA 91701, USA
**Rodat, Robert** — Producer, Writer
Gersh Agency, 9465 Wilshire Blvd, #600, Beverly Hills CA 90212 USA
**Roday, James** — Actor
Principal Entertainment, 9255 Sunset Blvd, #500, Los Angeles CA 90069 USA

# R

**Rodd, Marcia** — Actress
12315 Tiara St, Valley Village CA 91607, USA

**Roddam, Francis G (Franc)** — Director
Independent Talent Group, 40 Whitfield St, London W1T 2RH, England

**Roddick, Andrew S (Andy)** — Tennis Player
140 Shermans Mill Dr, Ingram TX 78025, USA

**Rode, Franc Cardinal** — Religious Leader
Consecrated Life Institutes, Piazza del Uffizio 11, 00193 Rome, Italy

**Rodenhauser, Mark T** — Football Player
1451 Charlotte Highway, York SC 29745, USA

**Rodenheiser, Richard P (Dick)** — Ice Hockey Player
186 State St, Framingham MA 01702, USA

**Roderick, Brande** — Model, Actress
Prince Marketing Group, 18 Carillon Circle, Livingston NJ 07039 USA

**Rodger, Kate** — Actress, Model
J K A Talent Agency, 12725 Ventura Blvd, #H, Studio City CA 91604, USA

**Rodgers of Quarry Bank, William T** — Government Official, England
43 North Road, London N6 4BE, England

**Rodgers, Aaron C** — Football Player
2360 Crown Pointe Blvd, Suamico WI 54173, USA

**Rodgers, Derrick A** — Football Player
15222 SW 52nd St, Miramar FL 33027, USA

**Rodgers, Jimmie** — Singer, Songwriter
42230 Sandy Bay Road, Bermuda Dunes CA 92203, USA

**Rodgers, Joan** — Opera Singer
113 Sotheby Road, London N5 2UT, England

**Rodgers, John S (Johnny)** — Football Player
PO Box 11172, Omaha NE 68111, USA

**Rodgers, Michael E** — Actor
Innovative Artists, 1505 10th St, Santa Monica CA 90401 USA

**Rodgers, Nile G** — Guitarist (Chic), Businessman
Lustig Talent, PO Box 770850, Orlando FL 32877 USA

**Rodgers, Paul** — Singer (Free, Bad Company), Songwriter
Work Hard, 19D Pinhold Road, London SW16 5GD, England

**Rodgers, Phil** — Golfer
Grand Del Mar, 5200 Grand Del Mar Way, San Diego CA 92130, USA

**Rodgers, Robert L (Buck)** — Baseball Player, Manager
5181 West Knoll Dr, Yorba Linda CA 92886, USA

**Rodgers, William H (Bill)** — Track Athlete
Bill Rodgers Running Center, 1 N Market St, #353, Boston MA 02109, USA

**Rodgers-Cromartie, Dominique R** — Football Player
Philadelphia Eagles, 1 Novacare Way, Philadelphia PA 19145 USA

**Roditi, Claudio** — Trumpeter
McClair Public Relations, PO Box 55, Radio Station, New York NY 10101, USA

**Rodl, Henrik** — Basketball Player
A L B A Berlin, Olympischer Platz 4, 14053 Berlin, Germany

**Rodman, Dennis K** — Basketball Player, Actor
Rodman Group, 4910 Campus Dr, Newport Beach CA 92660, USA

**Rodman, Howard A** — Writer, Producer, Director
University of Southern California, Cinematic Arts Dept, Los Angeles CA 90089, USA

**Rodney, Fernando** — Baseball Player
Tampa Bay Rays, 1 Tropicana Dr, Saint Petersburg FL 33705 USA

**Rodnina, Irina** — Figure Skater
7415 W 80th St, Los Angeles CA 90045, USA

**Rodrigue, George** — Artist
Rodrigue Studio, 1434 S College Road, Lafayette LA 70503, USA

**Rodrigue, George** — Journalist
Dallas News, Editorial Dept, 508 Young St, Dallas TX 75202, USA

**Rodrigues, Charlie** — Cartoonist (Charlie)
Tribune Media Services, 435 N Michigan Ave, #1500, Chicago IL 60611 USA

**Rodriguez** — Singer, Songwriter
Agency Group Ltd, 142 W 57th St, #600, New York NY 10019 USA

**Rodriguez Madariaga, Oscar A Cardinal** — Religious Leader
Conferencia Episcopal, Lavreles, Comayaguela 3121, Tegucigalpa, Honduras

**Rodriguez Romero, Jose Antonio** — Soccer Player
Federacion de Futbol, Colima 373 Colonia Roma, Delegacion Cuauhtemoc, Mexico City DF 06700, Mexico

**Rodriguez Zapatero, Jose Luis** — Prime Minister, Spain
Council of State, C/Mayor 79, 28013 Madrid, Spain

**Rodriguez, Adam** — Actor
Global Artists Agency, 1648 Wilcox Ave, #3, Los Angeles CA 90028, USA

**Rodriguez, Alexander E (Alex)** — Baseball Player
171 E Sunrise Ave, Coral Gables FL 33133, USA

**Rodriguez, Alfredo** — Concert Pianist
I M G Artists, Hogarth Business Park, Chiswick, London W4 2TH, England

**Rodriguez, Amy J** — Soccer Player
Philadelphia Independence, Union Field, Seaport Dr, Chester PA 19013 USA

**Rodriguez, Anthony** — Golfer
13602 Summer Glen Dr, San Antonio TX 78247, USA

**Rodriguez, Arturo S** — Labor Leader
United Farm Workers, 29700 Woodford Tehachapi Road, Keene CA 93531, USA

**Rodriguez, Carlos** — Baseball Player
10139 Snyder Church Road, Baltimore OH 43105, USA

**Rodriguez, Carrie** — Singer, Fiddle Player, Songwriter
Rosebud Agency, PO Box 170429, San Francisco CA 94117 USA

**Rodriguez, Daniel** — Opera Singer
Performers of the World, 5657 Wilshire Blvd, #280, Los Angeles CA 90036 USA

**Rodriguez, David M** — Army General
I S A Force, N A T O Hdqs, Blvd Leopold III, Brussells 1110, Belgium , USA

**Rodriguez, Davinia** — Opera Singer
I M G Artists, Hogarth Business Park, Chiswick, London W4 2TH, England

**Rodriguez, Edwin** — Baseball Player, Manager
7901 30th Ave N, Saint Petersburg FL 33710, USA

**Rodriguez, Freddy** — Actor
3 Arts Entertainment, 9460 Wilshire Blvd, #700, Beverly Hills CA 90212 USA

**Rodriguez, Genesis** — Actress
I C M Partners, 10250 Constellation Blvd, #900, Los Angeles CA 90067 USA

**Rodriguez, Gina** — Actress
A P A Talent/Literary Agency, 405 S Beverly Dr, #300, Beverly Hills CA 90212 USA
**Rodriguez, Ivan (Pudge)** — Baseball Player
15530 SW 70th Terrace, Miami FL 33193, USA
**Rodriguez, Jai** — Actor
Michael Einfeld Mgmt, 10630 Moorpark Ave, #101, Toluca Lake CA 91602, USA
**Rodriguez, Jennifer (Jen)** — Speed Skater
Q Sports Marketing, 534 W Evergreen St, Wheaton IL 60187 USA
**Rodriguez, Johnny** — Singer, Guitarist, Songwriter
240 S Wilson Blvd, Nashville TN 37205, USA
**Rodriguez, Jose Luis** — Actor
T G A Voice, 100 Lincoln Road, #928, Miami Beach FL 33178, USA
**Rodriguez, Juan (Chi Chi)** — Golfer
Chi Chi Rodriguez Academy, 3030 N McMullen Booth Road, Clearwater FL 33761, USA
**Rodriguez, Marco** — Actor
Ellis Talent Group, 4705 Laurel Canyon Blvd, #300 Valley Village CA 91607, USA
**Rodriguez, Michelle** — Actress
Untitled Entertainment, 350 S Beverly Dr, #200, Beverly Hills CA 90212 USA
**Rodriguez, Narciso** — Fashion Designer
50 Bond St, #700, New York NY 10012, USA
**Rodriguez, Paul** — Actor, Comedian, Producer
Rodriguez Entertainment, 3940 Laurel Canyon Blvd, #1159, Studio City CA 91604, USA
**Rodriguez, Ramon** — Actor
Maydew & Golenberg, 8383 Wilshire Blvd, #1050, Beverly Hills CA 90211, USA
**Rodriguez, Raul** — Float Designer
Fiesta Floats, 9362 Lower Azusa Road, Temple City CA 91780, USA
**Rodriguez, Richard A (Rich)** — Baseball Player
14578 Corkwood Dr, Moorpark CA 93021, USA
**Rodriguez, Richard A (Rich)** — Football Coach, Sportscaster
University of Arizona, Athletic Dept, Tucson AZ 85721, USA
**Rodriguez, Rico** — Actor
Clear Talent Group, 10950 Ventura Blvd, Studio City CA 91604, USA
**Rodriguez, Rita M** — Financier
Academy for Educational Development, 1825 Connecticut Ave NW, Washington DC 20006, USA
**Rodriguez, Robert** — Director
Trouble Maker Studios, 4900 Old Manor Road, Austin TX 78723, USA
**Rodriguez, Sergio** — Basketball Player
New York Knicks, Madison Square Garden, 2 Penn Plaza, New York, NY 10121 USA
**Rodriguez, Valente** — Actor
Talent Works, 3500 W Olive Ave, #1400, Burbank CA 91505 USA
**Rodriguez-Lopez, Omar** — Guitarist (Mars Volta), Composer
Agency Group Ltd, 142 W 57th St, #600, New York NY 10019 USA
**Roe, Alex** — Actor
Associated International Mgmt, 7 Hatton Garden, #400, London EC1N 8AD, England
**Roe, Allison P** — Track Athlete
34 Martin Crescent, Northcote, Auckland 0627, New Zealand
**Roe, John H** — Businessman
Bemis Co, Northstar Center, 222 S 9th St, Minneapolis MN 55402, USA
**Roe, Marty** — Singer, Guitarist (Diamond Rio)
Modern Mgmt, 1625 Broadway, #600, Nashville TN 37203, USA
**Roe, Tommy** — Singer, Songwriter
Horizon Talent Agency, PO Box 26037, Minneapolis MN 55426, USA
**Roebuck, Daniel** — Actor
Leslie Allen-Rice Mgmt, 1007 Maybrook Dr, Beverly Hills CA 90210, USA
**Roebuck, Edward J (Ed)** — Baseball Player
3434 Warwood Road, Lakewood CA 90712, USA
**Roeder, Robert G** — Biochemist
504 E 63rd St, #33P, New York NY 10065, USA
**Roeg, Nicolas J** — Director
Luc Roeg Artists, 32 Tavustick St, London WC2, England
**Roehm, Carolyn J** — Fashion Designer
Carolyn Roehm Inc, 257 W 39th St, #400, New York NY 10018, USA
**Roelandts, Willem P** — Businessman
Xilinx, PO Box 240010, San Jose CA 95154, USA
**Roelofs, Wendell L** — Biochemist, Entomologist
4 Crescence Dr, Geneva NY 14456, USA
**Roemer, John E** — Economist
University of California, Economics Dept, Davis CA 95616, USA
**Roemer, Sarah** — Actress
Luber Rocklin Entertainment, 8530 Wilshire Blvd, #555, Beverly Hills CA 90211 USA
**Roenick, Jeremy** — Ice Hockey Player
8525 E Dixileta Dr, Scottsdale AZ 85266, USA
**Roenicke, Gary S** — Baseball Player
11023 Rough and Ready Road, Rough and Ready CA 95975, USA
**Roenicke, Ronald J (Ron)** — Baseball Player, Manager
2212 Avenida Las Ramblas, Chino Hills CA 91709, USA
**Roenning, Joachim** — Director
Roenbergfilm, Pilestredet 75C, 0354 Oslo, Norway
**Roerig, Zach** — Actor
Innovative Artists, 1505 10th St, Santa Monica CA 90401 USA
**Roesch, Michael** — Biathlete
Im Kohlhau 6, 01773 Zinwald, Germany
**Roesky, Herbert W** — Chemist
Gottingen University, Inorganic Chemistry Dept, 37077 Gottingen, Germany
**Roethlisberger, Ben** — Football Player
200 Fernwood Dr, Clinton PA 15026, USA
**Roethlisberger, Nadia** — Curling Athlete
Curling Assn, PO Box 606, 3000 Bern, Switzerland
**Roffe-Steinrotter, Diann** — Alpine Skier
248 N 29th St, Camp Hill PA 17011, USA
**Rogan, Joe** — Actor, Comedian
W M E Entertainment, 9601 Wilshire Blvd, #300, Beverly Hills CA 90210 USA
**Roge, Pascal** — Concert Pianist
17 Ave des Cavaliers, 1224 Geneva, Switzerland
**Rogen, Seth** — Actor, Comedian, Writer
Principal Entertainment, 9255 Sunset Blvd, #500, Los Angeles CA 90069 USA

**Rogers of Riverside, Richard G** — Pritzker Architectural Laureate
Rogers Partnership, Thames Wharf, Rainville Road, London W6 9HA, England

**Rogers, Carlos C** — Football Player
San Francisco 49ers, 4949 Centennial Blvd, Santa Clara CA 95054 USA

**Rogers, Carlos D** — Basketball Player
Indiana Pacers, Conseco Fieldhouse, 125 S Pennsylvania, Indianapolis IN 46204 USA

**Rogers, Erik** — Singer (Stereo Mud)
Agency Group Ltd, 142 W 57th St, #600, New York NY 10019 USA

**Rogers, Garnet** — Singer, Songwriter, Guitarist
Fleming Artists, 543 N Main St, Ann Arbor MI 48104, USA

**Rogers, George W, Jr** — Football Player
1007 Lofty Pine Dr, Columbia SC 29212, USA

**Rogers, Gil** — Actor
Don Buchwald, 10 E 44th St, New York NY 10017 USA

**Rogers, Ingrid** — Actress
Flick Commercials, 9057 Nemo St, #A, West Hollywood, CA 90069, USA

**Rogers, James B (J B)** — Director
Reflection Pictures, 2001 Wilshire Blvd, #250, Santa Monica CA 90403, USA

**Rogers, James E** — Businessman
Duke Energy, 212 S Tryon St, #400, Charlotte NC 28281, USA

**Rogers, John M** — Judge
US Court of Appeals, US Courthouse, 100 E 5th St, #3100, Cincinnati OH 45202, USA

**Rogers, Judith W** — Judge
US Court of Appeals, 333 Constitution NW, #4400, Washington DC 20001, USA

**Rogers, June Scobee** — Writer
Challenger Center, 1250 N Pitt St, #1, Alexandria VA 22314, USA

**Rogers, Kenneth A (Kenny)** — Baseball Player
1730 Ottinger Road, Roanoke TX 76262, USA

**Rogers, Lynn L** — Wildlife Biologist, Ecologist
145 W Conan St, Ely MN 55731, USA

**Rogers, Melody** — Actress
C E S D, 10635 Santa Monica Blvd, #130, Los Angeles CA 90025 USA

**Rogers, Melvin N** — Football Player
3113 S Manitoba Dr, Santa Ana CA 92704, USA

**Rogers, Michele** — Model
Playboy Promotions, 2706 Media Center Dr, Los Angeles CA 90065 USA

**Rogers, Mimi** — Actress
Paradigm Agency, 360 N Crescent Dr, North Building, Beverly Hills CA 90210 USA

**Rogers, Nick** — Yachtsman
Royal Yachting Squadron, Castle Cowles, Isle of Wight PO31 7QT, England

**Rogers, Randy** — Singer, Band Leader
36D Mgmt, 36 Natta Circle, New Braunfels TX 78132, USA

**Rogers, Rob** — Editorial Cartoonist
Pittsburgh Post-Gazette, Editorial Dept, 23 Blvd Allies, Pittsburgh PA 15222, USA

**Rogers, Robert** — Architect
Rogers Marvel Architects, 145 Hudson St, #304, New York NY 10013, USA

**Rogers, Rodney R** — Basketball Player
Jazzie's Trucking LLC, 333 Shady Grove Dr, Timberlake NC 27583, USA

**Rogers, Rosemary** — Writer
Avon Books, 959 8th Ave, New York NY 10019, USA

**Rogers, Shaun C O** — Football Player
New York Giants, Meadowlands Stadium, 102 Route 120, East Rutherford NJ 07073 USA

**Rogers, Stephen D (Steve)** — Baseball Player
2 Lenape Lane, Princeton Junction NJ 08550, USA

**Rogers, Tracy D** — Football Player
1011 Tam O'Shanter Dr, Bakersfield CA 93309, USA

**Rogers, Tristan** — Actor
C E S D, 10635 Santa Monica Blvd, #130, Los Angeles CA 90025 USA

**Rogers, Wayne** — Actor
11828 La Grange Ave, Los Angeles CA 90025, USA

**Rogers, William C (Bill)** — Golfer
123 Eaton St, #104, San Antonio TX 78209, USA

**Roggenburk, Garry E** — Baseball Player
33550 Streamview Dr, Avon OH 44011, USA

**Rogoff, Ilan** — Concert Pianist
Apdo 1098, 07080 Palma de Mallorca, Spain

**Rogoff, Kenneth S** — Economist
11 Hillside Ave, Cambridge MA 02140, USA

**Rogombe, Rose Francine** — President, Gabon
Senate President's Office, BP 546, Libreville, Gabon

**Rohbock, Shauna** — Bobsled Athlete
Q Sports Marketing, 534 W Evergreen St, Wheaton IL 60187 USA

**Rohde, David** — Journalist
Christian Science Monitor, Editorial Dept, 1 Norway St, Boston MA 02136 USA

**Rohde, Hillary** — Fashion Designer
Hillary Rohde Cashmere, 22 Moray Place, Edinburgh EH3 6DB, Scotland

**Rohde, Leonard E (Len)** — Football Player
324 Alta Vista Ave, Los Altos Hills CA 94022, USA

**Rohde, Lisa** — Rowing Athlete
9807 Whitehorn Dr, Charlotte NC 28277, USA

**Rohlander, Uta** — Track Athlete
Liebigstr 9, 06237 Leuna, Germany

**Rohlf, F James** — Biometrician
State University of New York, Ecology & Evolution Dept, Stony Brook NY 11794, USA

**Rohm, Elisabeth** — Actress
A P A Talent/Literary Agency, 405 S Beverly Dr, #300, Beverly Hills CA 90212 USA

**Rohr, James E** — Financier
P N C Bank Corp, 1 P N C Plaza, 249 5th Ave, Pittsburgh PA 15222, USA

**Rohrer, Katherine** — Opera Singer
Columbia Artists Mgmt Inc, 1790 Broadway, #702, New York NY 10019 USA

**Roiphe, Anne** — Writer
Bloomsbury Publishing, 50 Bedford Square, London WC1B 3DP, England

**Roizman, Bernard** — Virologist
5555 S Everett Ave, Chicago IL 60637, USA

**Roizman, Owen** — Cinematographer
17533 Magnolia Blvd, Encino CA 91316, USA

Rojas Medrano, Melquiades (Mel)                                                    Baseball Player
15645 Collins Ave, #802, North Miami Beach FL 33160, USA
Rojas Rivas, Octavio R (Cookie)                                           Baseball Player, Manager
19195 Mystic Pointe Dr, #3002, Aventura FL 33180, USA
Rojas, Tito (El Gallo)                                                       Singer, Orchestra Leader
Alpha Artists International, 261 E 134th St, #200, Bronx NY 10454, USA
Rojcewicz, Susan (Sue)                                                              Basketball Player
16360 Blackie Road, Salinas CA 93907, USA
Rojeski, Shawn                                                                       Curling Athlete
510 11th St NW, Chisholm MN 55719, USA
Roker, Al                                                                               Entertainer
W M E Entertainment, 1325 Ave of Americas, New York NY 10019 USA
Rokke, Ervin J                                                                    Air Force General
810 Dolan Dr, Monument CO 80132, USA
Rokker, Heinz                                                              WW II German Luftwaffe Hero
Zietenstr 21, 26131 Oldenburg, Germany
Roland, Edgar E (Ed), Jr                                        Singer (Collective Soul), Songwriter
Creative Artists Agency, 2000 Ave of Stars, #100, Los Angeles CA 90067 USA
Roland, Johnny E                                                           Football Player, Coach
10339 Corbell Dr, #C, Saint Louis MO 63146, USA
Roland, M Dean                                         Guitarist, Keyboardist (Collective Soul)
Creative Artists Agency, 2000 Ave of Stars, #100, Los Angeles CA 90067 USA
Rolandi, Gianna                                                                       Opera Singer
New York City Opera, Lincoln Center Plaza, New York NY 10023, USA
Rolen, Scott B                                                                      Baseball Player
11711 N Pennsylvania St, #250, Carmel IN 46032, USA
Roles-Williams, Barbara                                                             Figure Skater
3790 Leisure Lane, Las Vegas NV 89103, USA
Rolfe Johnson, Anthony                                                             Opera Singer
Ulf Tornqvist, Sankt Eriksgatan 100, 113 31 Stockholm, Sweden
Rolfe, Dale                                                                    Ice Hockey Player
365 Hughson St, Gravenhurst ON P1P 1G8, Canada
Rolie, Gregg                                                    Singer, Keyboardist (Santana)
Tabletop Productions, PO Box 698, Carson City NV 89702, USA
Roll, Dean M                                                                             Wrestler
Shark Stuff, PO Box 752073, Dayton OH 45475, USA
Rolle                                                                        Musician (Fearless)
Helter Skelter, 347-353 Chiswick High Road, London W4 4HS, England
Rolle, Antrel R                                                                    Football Player
28232 SW 158th Court, Homestead FL 33033, USA
Rolle, Donald D (Butch)                                                           Football Player
17822 NW 15th St, Pembroke Pines FL 33029, USA
Rolle, Samari T                                                                    Football Player
16201 Quiet Vista Circle, Delray Beach FL 33446, USA
Roller, David E (Dave)                                                            Football Player
1110 Anthony Court, Suwanee GA 30024, USA
Rolling, Henry L                                                                   Football Player
8256 Garnet Canyon Lane, Las Vegas NV 89129, USA
Rollins, Edward J (Ed)                                                        Political Consultant
Dilenschneider Group, 200 Park Ave, MetLife Building, New York NY 10166, USA
Rollins, Henry                                                          Singer, Songwriter, Actor
Rollins Mgmt, 7510 Sunset Blvd, #602, Los Angeles CA 90046, USA
Rollins, James C (Jimmy)                                                          Baseball Player
120 Fox Chase Court, Swedesboro NJ 08085, USA
Rollins, John                                                                             Golfer
5501 Montclair Dr, Colleyville TX 76034, USA
Rollins, Richard J (Rich)                                                         Baseball Player
4146 Evergreen Lane, Richfield OH 44286, USA
Rollins, Theodore W (Sonny)                                        Jazz Saxophonist, Composer
Ted Kurland, 173 Brighton Ave, Boston MA 02134 USA
Rollins, Wayne M (Tree)                                                 Basketball Player, Coach
PO Box 681971, Orlando FL 32868, USA
Rolston, Brian                                                                Ice Hockey Player
9923 Kay Ray Road, Williamsburg MI 49690, USA
Rolston, Holmes III                                     Philosopher, Templeton Religion Laureate
1712 Concord Dr, Fort Collins CO 80526, USA
Rolston, Matthew                                                                      Photographer
United Talent Agency, U T A Plaza, 9336 Civic Center Dr, Beverly Hills CA 90210 USA
Roman, Freddie                                                                  Actor, Comedian
Dick Hall Productions, 889 S Brentwood Blvd, #201, Saint Louis MO 63105, USA
Roman, John G                                                                      Football Player
27 Duffryn Ave, Malvern PA 19355, USA
Roman, Lauren E                                                                         Actress
8330 Grand Ave NE, Bainbridge Island WA 98110, USA
Roman, Petre                                                            Prime Minister, Romania
Str Nikolai Gogol 2, Sector 1, 012017 Bucharest, Romania
Romanchych, Larry                                                            Ice Hockey Player
3989 206A St, Langley BC V3A 7A8, Canada
Romanek, Mark                                                                   Director, Writer
Creative Artists Agency, 2000 Ave of Stars, #100, Los Angeles CA 90067 USA
Romanenko, Roman Y                                                                     Cosmonaut
Cosmonaut Training Center, Star City, 141160 Zvezdny Gorodok, Moscow Oblast, Russia
Romanenko, Yuri V                                                                      Cosmonaut
Cosmonaut Training Center, Star City, 141160 Zvezdny Gorodok, Moscow Oblast, Russia
Romano, Chris                                                          Actor, Writer, Producer
United Talent Agency, U T A Plaza, 9336 Civic Center Dr, Beverly Hills CA 90210 USA
Romano, Christy Carlson                                                         Actress, Singer
Rebel Entertainment Partners, 5700 Wilshire Blvd, #456, Los Angeles CA 90036, USA
Romano, Jason A                                                                   Baseball Player
1411 Willow Oak Circle, Bradenton FL 34209, USA
Romano, John A (Johnny), Jr                                                       Baseball Player
160 W Pago Pago Dr, Naples FL 34113, USA
Romano, Larry                                                                             Actor
C E S D, 10635 Santa Monica Blvd, #130, Los Angeles CA 90025 USA
Romano, Pete                                                                        Cinematographer
HydroFlex Inc, 301 E El Segundo Blvd, El Segundo CA 90245, USA

**R**

Rojas Medrano - Romano

|  |  |
|---|---|
| **Romano, Ray** <br> I C M Partners, 10250 Constellation Blvd, #900, Los Angeles CA 90067 USA | Actor, Comedian, Producer |
| **Romano, Rino** <br> 6931 Paseo del Serra, Los Angeles CA 90068, USA | Actor |
| **Romano, Roberto** <br> 5865 Rue Brossard, Saint-Leonard QC H1T 3R6, Canada | Ice Hockey Player |
| **Romanov, Pyotr V** <br> Pr Mira 108, 660017 Krasnoyarsk, Russia | Government Official, Russia |
| **Romanov, Stephanie** <br> Untitled Entertainment, 350 S Beverly Dr, #200, Beverly Hills CA 90212 USA | Actress |
| **Romanowski, William T (Bill)** <br> 390 Hampton Road, Piedmont CA 94611, USA | Football Player |
| **Romans, Ben** <br> Soundtrack Music, 1460 4th St, #308, Santa Monica CA 90401, USA | Keyboardist (Click Five) |
| **Romanus, Richard** <br> 14011 Ventura Blvd, #213, Sherman Oaks CA 91403, USA | Actor |
| **Romar, Lorenzo** <br> 4408 164th Lane SE, Issaquah WA 98027, USA | Basketball Player, Coach |
| **Romario** <br> Adelaide F C, PO Box 620, Hindmarsh SA 5007, Australia | Soccer Player |
| **Romashin, Anatoliy V** <br> Vspolny Per 16 Korp 1, #60, 103101 Moscow, Russia | Actor |
| **Romatowski, Jenny** <br> 3116 Highlands Blvd, Palm Harbor FL 34684, USA | Softball, Baseball Player |
| **Romberg, Brett C** <br> Atlanta Falcons, 4400 Falcon Parkway, Flowery Branch GA 30542 USA | Football Player |
| **Rombolo, Tony** <br> Front Line Mgmt, 1100 Glendon Ave, #2000, Los Angeles CA 90024 USA | Guitarist (Godsmack) |
| **Rome, Jim** <br> Creative Artists Agency, 2000 Ave of Stars, #100, Los Angeles CA 90067 USA | Actor, Writer |
| **Rome, Sydne** <br> Isabella Gull Assoc, Vicolo del Buon Consiglio, 00184 Rome, Italy | Actress |
| **Romeike, Hinrich** <br> Moholzu, 24809 Nubbel, Germany | Equestrian |
| **Romensky, Anka** <br> PO Box 3897, Hallandale FL 33008, USA | Model |
| **Romeo** <br> Don Buchwald, 6500 Wilshire Blvd, #2200, Los Angeles CA 90048 USA | Singer (Immature), Actor |
| **Romeo, Paolo Cardinal** <br> Archdiocese of Palermo, Corso Vittorio Emanuel 461, 90134 Palermo, Italy | Religious Leader |
| **Romeo, Robin** <br> Professional Bowlers Assn, 719 2nd Ave, #701, Seattle WA 98104 USA | Bowler |
| **Romer, Christina D** <br> University of California, Economics Dept, Evans Hall, Berkeley CA 94720, USA | Government Official, Economist |
| **Romer, Roy R** <br> Los Angeles School District, 333 S Beaudry Ave, #209, Los Angeles CA 90017, USA | Governor, CO; Educator |
| **Romero, Anders** <br> Professional Golfer's Assn, PO Box 109601, Palm Beach Gardens FL 33410 USA | Golfer |
| **Romero, Angel** <br> Richard Gilkerson, 1737 Whitley Ave, #200, Los Angeles CA 90028, USA | Concert Guitarist |
| **Romero, Celino** <br> Columbia Artists Mgmt Inc, 1790 Broadway, #702, New York NY 10019 USA | Concert Guitarist |
| **Romero, Danny, Jr** <br> 800 Salida Sandia SW, Albuquerque NM 87105, USA | Boxer |
| **Romero, Edgardo (Ed)** <br> 1380 Wood Row Way, Wellington FL 33414, USA | Baseball Player |
| **Romero, George A** <br> Gersh Agency, 9465 Wilshire Blvd, #600, Beverly Hills CA 90212 USA | Director |
| **Romero, Ned** <br> 249 Vista Royale Circle W, Palm Desert CA 92211, USA | Actor |
| **Romero, Pepe** <br> Columbia Artists Mgmt Inc, 1790 Broadway, #702, New York NY 10019 USA | Concert Guitarist |
| **Romero, Randy P** <br> 7124 Louisiana Highway 343, Kaplan LA 70548, USA | Thoroughbred Racing Jockey |
| **Romero, Rebecca J** <br> National Cycling Centre, Stewart St, Manchester M11 4DQ, England | Cyclist, Rowing Athlete |
| **Rometty, Virginia M** <br> I B M Corp, 1 North Castle Dr, #2, Armonk NY 10504, USA | Businesswoman |
| **Romig, Joseph H (Joe)** <br> 1300 Plaza Court N, Lafayette CO 80026, USA | Football Player |
| **Romijn, Rebecca** <br> United Talent Agency, U T A Plaza, 9336 Civic Center Dr, Beverly Hills CA 90210 USA | Model, Actress |
| **Romine, Kevin A** <br> 8750 Rogue River Ave, Fountain Valley CA 92708, USA | Baseball Player |
| **Rominger, Kent V** <br> 2714 Bridgeport Ave, Salt Lake City UT 84121, USA | Astronaut |
| **Romney, Hervin A R** <br> 1556 San Benito Ave, Coral Gables FL 33134, USA | Architect |
| **Romo, Antonio R (Tony)** <br> Dallas Cowboys, 1 Cowboys Parkway, Irving TX 75063 USA | Football Player |
| **Romo, Daniela** <br> Televisa, Blvd A Lopez Mateos 232, Colonia San Angel, Mexico City DF 01060 CP, Mexico | Actress |
| **Romulo** <br> Confederacion de Futebol, Rua Victor Civita 66, #1, Rio de Janeiro 22775 044, Brazil | Soccer Player |
| **Rona, Jeff** <br> Rykodisc Records, 30 Irving Place, #300, New York NY 10003 USA | Composer |
| **Ronaldinho** <br> F C Milan, Via Filippo Turati 3, 20121 Milan, Italy | Soccer Player |
| **Ronaldo** <br> S C Corinthians Paulista, Rua Sao Jorge 777, Tatuape 03087 000, Sao Paulo SP, Brazil | Soccer Player |
| **Ronaldo, Christiano** <br> Gestifute, Oceans 3/15/02 #D, 2 Office, United Park, 1990-197 Lisbon, Portugal | Soccer Player |
| **Ronan, Edward (Ed)** <br> 70 Jefferson Road, Franklin MA 02038, USA | Ice Hockey Player |
| **Ronan, Saoirse** <br> Macfarlane Chard, 7 Adelaide St, Dun Laoghaire, County Dublin, Ireland | Actress |

**Ronan, William J** — Railway Engineer
525 S Flagler Dr, West Palm Beach FL 33401, USA
**Rondo, Rajon P** — Basketball Player
9 Fridolin Hill, Lincoln MA 01773, USA
**Roney, Wallace** — Jazz Trumpeter
BookArts Co, 6404 Wilshire Blvd, #1750, Los Angeles CA 90048, USA
**Ronney, Paul D** — Astronaut
613 Ranchito Road, Monrovia CA 91016, USA
**Ronning, Clifford J (Cliff)** — Ice Hockey Player
7130 Kitchener St, Burnaby BC V5A 1L3, Canada
**Ronning, Joachim** — Director
Roenbergfilm, Pilestredet 75C, 0354 Oslo, Norway
**Ronningen, Jon** — Greco-Roman Wrestler
Mellomasveien 132, 1414 Trollasen, Norway
**Rono, Peter** — Track Athlete
Mount Saint Mary's College, Athletic Dept, Emmitsburg MD 21727, USA
**Ronson, Leonard K (Len)** — Ice Hockey Player
2006 SW Eastwood Ave, Gresham OR 97080, USA
**Ronson, Samatha** — Singer, Songwriter
Creative Artists Agency, 2000 Ave of Stars, #100, Los Angeles CA 90067 USA
**Ronstadt, Linda M** — Singer
Trident Media Group, 41 Madison Ave, #3600, New York NY 10010, USA
**Ronty, Paul** — Ice Hockey Player
2300 Commonwealth Ave, #3-4, Auburndale MA 02466, USA
**Roof, Phillip A (Phil)** — Baseball Player
1301 Pillar Chase, Paducah KY 42001, USA
**Rook, Susan** — Commentator
CNN-TV, 190 Marietta Ave SW, Atlanta GA 30303 USA
**Rooker, James P (Jim)** — Baseball Player
2378 Windchime Dr, Jacksonville FL 32224, USA
**Rooker, Michael** — Actor
Kritzer Levine Wilkins Griffin, 11872 La Grange Ave, #100, Los Angeles CA 90025 USA
**Rooney** — Rock Music Group
Agency Group Ltd, 1880 Century Park E, #711, Los Angeles CA 90067 USA
**Rooney, Daniel M (Dan)** — Football Executive, Diplomat
940 N Lincoln Ave, Pittsburgh PA 15233, USA
**Rooney, Joe Don** — Singer, Guitarist (Rascal Flatts)
Turner & Nichols, 49 Music Square W, #500, Nashville TN 37203, USA
**Rooney, Kathleen** — Writer
University of Arkansas Press, 105 N McIlroy Ave, Fayetteville AR 72701, USA
**Rooney, Kevin** — Actor
Emptage Hallett, 14 Rathbone Place, London W1T 1HT, England
**Rooney, Mercy** — Model, Actress
Playboy Promotions, 2706 Media Center Dr, Los Angeles CA 90065 USA
**Rooney, Mickey** — Actor
741 S Garfield Ave, Alhambra CA 91801, USA
**Rooney, Patrick E (Pat)** — Baseball Player
4825 Lighthouse Dr, Racine WI 53402, USA
**Rooney, Steven P (Steve)** — Ice Hockey Player
5 Helen Dr, Canton MA 02021, USA
**Roos, Don** — Director, Writer
Is or Isn't Entertainment, 8391 Beverly Blvd, #125, Los Angeles CA 90048, USA
**Roos, Michael (Mike)** — Football Player
500 Madison Ave, #103, Nashville TN 37208, USA
**Root, Amanda** — Actress
I C M Partners, 10250 Constellation Blvd, #900, Los Angeles CA 90067 USA
**Root, Stephen** — Actor
Gersh Agency, 9465 Wilshire Blvd, #600, Beverly Hills CA 90212 USA
**Root, William J (Bill)** — Ice Hockey Player
33 Hamilton Hall Dr, Markham ON L3P 3L5, Canada
**Roper, Dee Dee (Spinderella)** — Rap Artist (Salt'N'Pepa)
Next Plateau Records, 1650 Broadway, #1103, New York NY 10019, USA
**Roper, John A** — Football Player
4213 Alice St, Houston TX 77021, USA
**Roponun, Riitta-Liise** — Cross Country Skier
Oulu Ski Club, Sammonkatu 6, 90570 Oulu, Finland
**Rorem, Ned** — Composer, Writer
PO Box 764, Nantucket MA 02554, USA
**Rosa, Angela Alvarado** — Actress
Marshak/Zachary Co, 8840 Wilshire Blvd, #100, Beverly Hills CA 90211 USA
**Rosa, John W, Jr** — Air Force General, Educator
Citadel, President's Office, Charleston SC 29409, USA
**Rosa, Robi Draco (Robby)** — Singer, Producer, Composer
Creative Artists Agency, 2000 Ave of Stars, #100, Los Angeles CA 90067 USA
**Rosado, Eduardo** — Opera Singer
Calle 3, Ave Cupules 112A, Col G Giberes, Menda, Yucatan 97070, Mexico
**Rosales, Gaudencio B Cardinal** — Religious Leader
Archdiocese of Manila, 121 Arzobispo St, 1099 Manila, Philippines
**Rosales, Jennifer (Jenny)** — Golfer
265 S Vine St, Anaheim CA 92805, USA
**Rosamilia, Alex** — Guitarist (Gaslight Anthem)
Esther Creative Group, 27 W 24th St, #404, New York NY 10010, USA
**Rosand, David** — Art Historian
560 Riverside Dr, New York NY 10027, USA
**Rosario** — Singer, Actress, Songwriter
Mega Music Productions, 16950 North Bay Road, #1706, Sunny Isles Beach FL 33160, USA
**Rosario, Joann** — Singer
Universal Attractions, 135 W 26th St, #1200, New York NY 10001 USA
**Rosas, Cesar** — Singer, Songwriter (Los Lobos)
Gold Mountain, 3940 Laurel Canyon Blvd, #444, Studio City CA 91604 USA
**Rosato, Genesia** — Ballerina
Royal Ballet, Covent Garden, Bow St, London WC2E 9DD, England
**Rosberg, Keke E** — Auto Racing Driver
7 Rue Gabian, 9800 Monte Carlo, Monaco
**Rosborough, Patty** — Actress, Comedienne
OmniPop Talent Group, 4605 Lankershim Blvd, #201, Toluca Lake CA 91602 USA

**Roschkov, Victor** — Editorial Cartoonist
Toronto Star, Editorial Dept, 1 Yonge St, Toronto ON M5E 1E5, Canada 90068, USA

**Rose Marie** — Actress, Singer
6916 Chisholm Ave, Van Nuys CA 91406, USA

**Rose, Adam** — Actor
Stone Manners Salners, 9911 W Pico Blvd, #1400, Los Angeles CA 90035 USA

**Rose, Andrew** — Composer
1620 Ashland Ave, Santa Monica CA 90405, USA

**Rose, Anika Noni** — Actress, Singer
David Williams Mgmt, 9614 Olympic Blvd, #F, Beverly Hills CA 90212, USA

**Rose, Axl** — Singer (Guns N' Roses), Songwriter
5055 Latigo Canyon Road, Malibu CA 90265, USA

**Rose, Bernard** — Director, Writer, Cinematographer
Casorotto Ramsay, Waverley House, 7-12 Noel St, London W1F 8GQ, England

**Rose, Brian** — Baseball Player
5 Ashland St, South Dartmouth MA 02748, USA

**Rose, Charles (Charlie)** — Commentator, Producer, Actor
Rose Communications, 499 Park Ave, #1500, New York NY 10022, USA

**Rose, Chris** — Sportscaster
Fox-TV, Sports Dept, PO Box 900, Beverly Hills CA 90213 USA

**Rose, Clarence** — Golfer
106 Harding Place, Goldsboro NC 27534, USA

**Rose, Cristine** — Actress
S M S Talent, 8383 Wilshire Blvd, #230, Beverly Hills CA 90211 USA

**Rose, Derrick M** — Basketball Player
Chicago Bulls, United Center, 1901 W Madison St, Chicago IL 60612 USA

**Rose, Donovan J** — Football Player
103 Lenox Court, Yorktown VA 23693, USA

**Rose, Irwin** — Nobel Chemistry Laureate
3 McClelland Farm Road, Deerfield MA 01342, USA

**Rose, Jalen** — Basketball Player
Three Tier Entertainment, 645 W 9th St, #406, Los Angeles CA 90015, USA

**Rose, Jamie** — Actress
Marshak/Zachary Co, 8840 Wilshire Blvd, #100, Beverly Hills CA 90211 USA

**Rose, Jessica** — Actress
Hirsch Wallerstein Hayum, 10100 Santa Monica Blvd, #1700, Los Angeles CA 90067 USA

**Rose, John** — Cartoonist (Snuffy Smith)
King Features Syndicate, 300 W 57th St, #1500, New York NY 10019 USA

**Rose, Joseph H (Joe)** — Football Player
3293 SW 138th Way, Davie FL 33330, USA

**Rose, Justin R** — Golfer
4sports & Entertainment, 8 Celbridge Mews, London W2 6EU, England

**Rose, Kenny F (Ken)** — Football Player
1736 Bronzewood Court, Newbury Park CA 91320, USA

**Rose, Lee** — Director, Producer
Broder Webb Chervin Silbermann, 9242 Beverly Blvd, Beverly Hills CA 90210 USA

**Rose, Lela** — Fashion Designer
224 W 30th St, #1400, New York NY 10001, USA

**Rose, Michael** — Singer (Black Uhuru)
Ultima Talent, 858 Westbourne Dr, #3, West Hollywood CA 90069, USA

**Rose, Pam** — Singer (Kennedy Rose)
PO Box 50362, Nashville TN 37205, USA

**Rose, Peter E (Pete)** — Baseball Player, Manager
13348 Chandler Blvd, Sherman Oaks CA 91401, USA

**Rose, Peter E (Pete), Jr** — Baseball Player
3921 Legendary Ridge Lane, Cleves OH 45002, USA

**Rose, Sherrie** — Actress, Model
1758 Laurel Canyon Blvd, Los Angeles CA 90046, USA

**Roseau, Maurice E D** — Mechanical Engineer
144 Bis Ave du General Leclerc, 92330 Sceaux, France

**Roselle, David P** — Educator
14 Laurel Ridge Road, Wilmington DE 19807, USA

**Rosellini, Anne** — Film Producer, Writer
Gersh Agency, 9465 Wilshire Blvd, #600, Beverly Hills CA 90212 USA

**Rosello Rodriguez, David (Dave)** — Baseball Player
HC 1 Box 8125, Hormigueros PR 00660, USA

**Rosemont, Romy** — Actress
Main Title Mgmt, 8383 Wilshire Blvd, #408, Beverly Hills CA 90211 USA

**Rosen, Albert L (Al)** — Baseball Player, Executive
15 Mayfair Dr, Rancho Mirage CA 92270, USA

**Rosen, Beatrice** — Actress
Cinetalent, 18 Rue Seguier, 75006 Paris, France , USA

**Rosen, Dan** — Director
Modus Entertainment, 8569 Holloway Dr, #1, West Hollywood CA 90069, USA

**Rosen, Harold A** — Engineer, Inventor
Rosen Electrical Equipment, 8401 Slauson Ave, Pico Rivera CA 90660, USA

**Rosen, Milton W** — Engineer, Physicist
5610 Alta Vista Road, Bethesda MD 20817, USA

**Rosen, Nathaniel** — Concert Cellist
3273 SW Avalon Way, #B, Seattle WA 98126, USA

**Rosenbaum, Edward E** — Physician
333 NW 23rd St, Portland OR 97210, USA

**Rosenbaum, Michael** — Actor
A P A Talent/Literary Agency, 405 S Beverly Dr, #300, Beverly Hills CA 90212 USA

**Rosenberg, Alan** — Actor
Innovative Artists, 1505 10th St, Santa Monica CA 90401 USA

**Rosenberg, Howard** — Music Critic
5859 Larboard Lane, Agoura Hills CA 91301, USA

**Rosenberg, Pierre M** — Museum Executive
Musee du Louvre, 34-36 Quai du Louvre, 75068 Paris, France

**Rosenberg, Scott** — Writer
W M E Entertainment, 9601 Wilshire Blvd, #300, Beverly Hills CA 90210 USA

**Rosenberg, Steven A** — Oncologist, Surgeon
National Cancer Institute, 31 Center Dr, Building 10, Bethesda MD 20892, USA

**Rosenberg, Tina** — Writer
New School for Social Research, World Policy Institute, New York NY 10011, USA

**Rosenblath, Marshall N** — Physicist
2311 Via Siena, La Jolla CA 92037, USA

**Rosenblatt, Dana** — Boxer
39 Cleveland Road, Chestnut Hill MA 02467, USA

**Rosenbluth, Leonard R (Lennie)** — Basketball Player
124 Meadowmont Village Circle, Chapel Hill NC 27517, USA

**Rosenburg, Saul A** — Oncologist
Stanford University Medical School, Oncology Division, 300 Pasteur Dr, Stanford CA 94305, USA

**Rosendahl, Heidemarie (Heide) Ecker-** — Track Athlete
Burscheider Str 426, 51381 Leverkusen, Germany

**Rosenfeld, Irene B** — Businesswoman
Kraft Foods, 3 Lakes Dr, Northfield IL 60093, USA

**Rosenfeld, Isadore** — Clinical Physician
Warner Books, 1271 Ave of Americas, New York NY 10020 USA

**Rosenfels, Sage J** — Football Player
19651 Hickory St, Omaha NE 68130, USA

**Rosenfelt, David** — Writer
Warner Books, 1271 Ave of Americas, New York NY 10020 USA

**Rosenfield, John Max** — Educator
1573 Cambridge St, #711, Cambridge MA 2138, USA

**Rosengrant, John** — Visual Effects Designer
Legacy Effects, 340 Parkside Dr, San Fernando CA 91340, USA

**Rosengren, Eric** — Government Official, Financier
Federal Reserve Bank, 500 Atlantic Ave, Boston MA 02210, USA

**Rosenquist, James A** — Artist
PO Box 4, 420 Broadway, Aripeka FL 34679, USA

**Rosenstein, Samuel M** — Judge
US Court of International Trade, 2200 S Ocean Lane, Fort Lauderdale FL 33316, USA

**Rosenthal, Amy Krouse** — Writer
Harper Collins Publishers, 10 E 53rd St, Cellar 1, New York NY 10022 USA

**Rosenthal, David S** — Director, Writer
W M E Entertainment, 9601 Wilshire Blvd, #300, Beverly Hills CA 90210 USA

**Rosenthal, Jacob (Jack)** — Journalist
New York Times, Editorial Dept, 229 W 43rd St, New York NY 10036, USA

**Rosenthal, Jody Anschutz** — Golfer
18938 E McDowell Mountain Dr, Rio Verde AZ 85263, USA

**Rosenthal, Mark D** — Director, Producer, Writer
Verve Talent, 9696 Culver Blvd, #301, Culver City CA 90232, USA

**Rosenthal, Philip** — Producer, Writer, Actor
Creative Artists Agency, 2000 Ave of Stars, #100, Los Angeles CA 90067 USA

**Rosenthal, Rachel** — Performance Artist
2847 S Robertson Blvd, Los Angeles CA 90034, USA

**Rosenthal, Rick** — Director
Whitewater Films, 11264 La Grange Ave, Los Angeles CA 90025, USA

**Rosenthal, Robert J** — Editor
Philadelphia Inquirer, Editorial Dept, 400 N Broad St, Philadelphia PA 19130, USA

**Rosenwinkel, Kurt** — Guitarist, Keyboardist
Word of Mouth Music, 235 E 22nd St, #9F, New York NY 10010, USA

**Rosenzweig, Barney** — Producer
2311 Fisher Island Dr, Miami Beach FL 33109, USA

**Rosenzweig, Robert M** — Educator
1462 Dana Ave, Palo Alto CA 94301, USA

**Roses, Allen D** — Neurologist
Glaxo Wellcome, 5 Moore Dr, Durham NC 27709, USA

**Rosewall, Ken** — Tennis Player
Turramurra, 111 Pentacost Ave, Sydney NSW 2074, Australia

**Roshan, Hrithik** — Actor
Filmkraft Mayur, Tilak Road, Santa Cruz (W), Mumbai MS 400054, India

**Roshan, Rakesh** — Director, Producer, Actor
Kavita 10th Road, J V P D Scheme, Mumbai MS 400049, India

**Rosin, Dino** — Sculptor
Arte Studio, Fondamento Manin 40, 30141 Murano, Italy

**Rosinski, Edward J** — Inventor (Zeolite Catalytic Cracking)
1308 Kellogg Ave, Utica NY 13502, USA

**Rosman, Mark** — Director
Paradigm Agency, 360 N Crescent Dr, North Building, Beverly Hills CA 90210 USA

**Rosner, Robert** — Astrophysicist
4950 S Greenwood Ave, Chicago IL 60615, USA

**Rosnes, Renee** — Jazz Pianist
Integrity Talent, 1 Westcroft Court, Cockeysville MD 21030 USA

**Rosovsky, Henry** — Economist
130 Mount Auburn St, #506, Cambridge MA 02138, USA

**Ross Fairbanks, Anne** — Swimmer
995 Lombardy Lane, Denver CO 80215, USA

**Ross Naess, Evan** — Actor
Kritzer Levine Wilkins Griffin, 11872 La Grange Ave, #100, Los Angeles CA 90025 USA

**Ross, Aaron J** — Football Player
13001 Bay Hill Dr, Beltsville MD 20705, USA

**Ross, Annie** — Actress, Singer
Abby Hoffer Enterprises, 223 1/2 E 48th St, New York NY 10017 USA

**Ross, Atticus** — Composer
Costa Communications, 8265 Sunset Blvd, #101, Los Angeles CA 90046, USA

**Ross, Ben** — Director
Brillstein Entertainment Partners, 9150 Wilshire Blvd, #350, Beverly Hills CA 90212 USA

**Ross, Betsy** — Sportscaster
ESPN-TV, ESPN Plaza, 935 Middle St, Bristol CT 06010 USA

**Ross, Charlotte** — Actress
Untitled Entertainment, 350 S Beverly Dr, #200, Beverly Hills CA 90212 USA

**Ross, Chris** — Bassist, Keyboardist (Wolfmother)
John Watson Mgmt, PO Box 281, Surry Hills NSW 2010, Australia

**Ross, Christopher** — Cinematographer
Independent Talent Group, 40 Whitfield St, London W1T 2RH, England

**Ross, Cody J** — Baseball Player
21469 N 83rd St, Scottsdale AZ 85255, USA

**Ross, David A** — Museum Director
Whitney Museum of American Art, 945 Madison Ave, New York NY 10021, USA

**Ross, David W (Dave)** — Baseball Player
2768 Millstone Plantation Road, Tallahassee FL 32312, USA
**Ross, Diana** — Singer, Actress
Sunshine Sachs Assoc, 149 5th Ave, #700, New York NY 10010, USA
**Ross, Don** — Body Builder
PO Box 981, Venice CA 90294, USA
**Ross, Donald R** — Judge
US Court of Appeals, Federal Building, PO Box 307, Omaha NE 68101, USA
**Ross, Evan** — Actor
Kritzer Levine Wilkins Griffin, 11872 La Grange Ave, #100, Los Angeles CA 90025 USA
**Ross, F Robert (Bob)** — Baseball Player
862 Bergamo Ave, San Jacinto CA 92583, USA
**Ross, Gary** — Director, Writer
Creative Artists Agency, 2000 Ave of Stars, #100, Los Angeles CA 90067 USA
**Ross, Gary D** — Baseball Player
1729 Cuadro Vista, San Marcus CA 92078, USA
**Ross, Jeffrey (Jeff)** — Actor, Comedian
Thruline Entertainment, 9250 Wilshire Blvd, #100, Beverly Hills CA 90212 USA
**Ross, Jerry L** — Astronaut
N A S A, Johnson Space Center, 2101 NASA Road, Houston TX 77058 USA
**Ross, John** — Chemist
620 Sand Hill Road, #402B, Palo Alto CA 94304, USA
**Ross, Jonathan** — Actor
Off the Kerb Productions, 22 Thornhill Crescent, London N1 1BJ, England
**Ross, Karie** — Sportscaster
ESPN-TV, ESPN Plaza, 935 Middle St, Bristol CT 06010 USA
**Ross, Katharine** — Actress
33050 Pacific Coast Highway, Malibu CA 90265, USA
**Ross, Kevin L** — Football Player
537 Beacon St, Camden NJ 08105, USA
**Ross, Kyla B** — Gymnast
Gym-Max Academy, 2969 Century Place, Costa Mesa CA 92626, USA
**Ross, Liberty** — Model
Storm Model Agency, 5 Jubilee Place, Chelsea, London SW3 3TD, England
**Ross, Lonny** — Actor, Comedian
Thruline Entertainment, 9250 Wilshire Blvd, #100, Beverly Hills CA 90212 USA
**Ross, Marion** — Actress
C E S D, 10635 Santa Monica Blvd, #130, Los Angeles CA 90025 USA
**Ross, Mark J** — Baseball Player
1747 N Wild Hyacinth Dr, Tucson AZ 85715, USA
**Ross, Marv** — Guitarist (Quarterflash)
Pacific Talent Agency, PO Box 19145, Portland OR 97280, USA
**Ross, Matt** — Actor
I C M Partners, 10250 Constellation Blvd, #900, Los Angeles CA 90067 USA
**Ross, Rick** — Rap Artist, Songwriter
Multi Entertainment Group, 4044 W Lake Mary Blvd, #104-324, Lake Mary FL 32746, USA
**Ross, Ricky** — Singer (Deacon Blue)
Impressive Public Relations, 9 Jeffreys Place, London NW1 9PP, England
**Ross, Rindy** — Singer, Saxophonist (Quarterflash)
Pacific Talent Agency, PO Box 19145, Portland OR 97280, USA
**Ross, Terrence** — Basketball Player
Toronto Raptors, Air Canada Center, 20 Bay St, Toronto ON M5J 2N8, Canada
**Ross, Thomas W, Sr** — Educator
University of North Carolina, President's Office, 910 Raleigh Road, Chapel Hill NC 27514, USA
**Ross, Tracee Ellis** — Actress
I C M Partners, 10250 Constellation Blvd, #900, Los Angeles CA 90067 USA
**Ross, Wilburn K** — WW II Army Hero (CMH)
819 Haskell St, Dupont WA 98327, USA
**Ross, William** — Composer
Gorfaine/Schwartz, 4111 W Alameda Ave, #509, Burbank CA 91505 USA
**Rossant, Colette** — Writer
Bloomsbury Publishing, 50 Bedford Square, London WC1B 3DP, England
**Rossdale, Gavin M** — Singer, Songwriter (Bush); Actor
Creative Artists Agency, 2000 Ave of Stars, #100, Los Angeles CA 90067 USA
**Rosselli, Joe** — Baseball Player
6231 Le Sage Ave, Woodland Hills CA 91367, USA
**Rossellini, Isabella** — Model, Actress
Ancieri Assoc, 305 Madison Ave, #2315, New York NY 10165, USA
**Rossen, Carol** — Actress
15450 Longbow Dr, Sherman Oaks CA 91403, USA
**Rosser, Ronald E** — WW II Army Hero (CMH)
36 James St, Roseville OH 43777, USA
**Rosset, Marc** — Tennis Player
Michel Rosset, Rue Albert Gos 16, 1206 Geneva, Switzerland
**Rossi, Anni** — Violist
Agency Group Ltd, 142 W 57th St, #600, New York NY 10019 USA
**Rossi, Derrick J** — Pathologist
Harvard University, Stem Cell Institute, 124 Mount Auburn St, Cambridge MA 02138, USA
**Rossi, Paolo** — Soccer Player
F C Juventus, Corso Galilo Ferraris 32, 10128 Turin, Italy
**Rossi, Theo** — Actor
Greene Assoc, 1901 Ave of Stars, #130, Los Angeles CA 90067 USA
**Rossi, Valentino** — Motorcycle Racing Rider
Via C Basti 5/A, 61010 Tavullia (PU), Italy
**Rossier, Bernard** — Pharmacologist
University of Lausanne, Biology Dept, Rue du Bugnon 27, 1005 Lausanne, Switzerland
**Rossington, Gary R** — Guitarist (Lynyrd Skynyrd)
Vector Mgmt, PO Box 120479, Nashville TN 37212 USA
**Rossini, Bianca** — Actress
Arlene Thornton, 12001 Ventura Blvd, #201, Studio City CA 91604, USA
**Rossio, Terry** — Writer, Producer
Creative Artists Agency, 2000 Ave of Stars, #100, Los Angeles CA 90067 USA
**Rossiter, Martin** — Singer, Pianist (Gene)
Agency Group Ltd, 361-373 City Road, London EC1V 1PQ, England
**Rossiter, Robert E** — Businessman
Lear Corp, 21557 Telegraph Road, Southfield MI 48033, USA

| | |
|---|---|
| **Rosskopf, Joerg** | Table Tennis Player |
| Tischtennisbund, Otto-Fleck-Schneise 12A, 60528 Frankfurt/Maim, Germany | |
| **Rossman, Michael G** | Biochemist |
| 1208 Wiley Dr, West Lafayette IN 47906, USA | |
| **Rosso, Louis T** | Businessman |
| 4300 N Harbor Blvd, Fullerton CA 92835, USA | |
| **Rossouw, Jacques** | Physician |
| National Institutes of Health, Women's Health Initiative, 6701 Rockledge Dr, Bethesda MD 20817, USA | |
| **Rossovich, Rick** | Actor |
| Schumacher Mgmt, 10323 Santa Monica Blvd, #101, Los Angeles CA 90024, USA | |
| **Rossovich, Timothy J (Tim)** | Football Player, Actor |
| 19811 Wildwood West Dr, Penn Valley CA 95946, USA | |
| **Rossum, Allen B L** | Football Player |
| 5669 Legends Club Circle, Braselton GA 30517, USA | |
| **Rossum, Emmy** | Actress, Singer |
| Schiff Co, 9200 Sunset Blvd, #430, West Hollywood CA 90232 USA | |
| **Rossy, Elam J (Rico)** | Baseball Player |
| A7 Calle Atenas, Repto Flamingo, Ext Forest Hills, Bayamon PR 00959, USA | |
| **Rost, Andrea** | Opera Singer |
| Nefelejes U 27, Budaors 2040, Hungary | |
| **Roszak, Thomas** | Architect |
| Roszak/A D C, PO Box 8528, Northfield IL 60093, USA | |
| **Rota, Darcy** | Ice Hockey Player |
| 2510 Ashurst Ave, Coquitlam BC V3K 5T4, Canada | |
| **Rotas, Nikiphoros G** | Composer |
| 15 Astydamantos St, Athens 116 34, Greece | |
| **Roth, Andrea** | Actress |
| Domain Talent, 9229 W Sunset Blvd, #710, West Hollywood CA 90069 USA | |
| **Roth, Ann** | Costume Designer |
| Road 3, Box 3124, Bangor PA 18013, USA | |
| **Roth, Arnold** | Cartoonist (Poor Arnold's Almanac) |
| National Cartoonists Society, 9 Ebony Court, Brooklyn NY 11229, USA | |
| **Roth, David Lee** | Singer (Van Halen), Songwriter |
| Rhino Entertainment, 3400 W Olive Ave, Burbank CA 91505, USA | |
| **Roth, Doug** | Basketball Player |
| 9975 Spillway Circle, #201, Cordova TN 38016, USA | |
| **Roth, Eli** | Actor, Director, Writer |
| Creative Artists Agency, 2000 Ave of Stars, #100, Los Angeles CA 90067 USA | |
| **Roth, Eric** | Writer |
| Creative Artists Agency, 2000 Ave of Stars, #100, Los Angeles CA 90067 USA | |
| **Roth, Jack A** | Molecular Biologist |
| M D Anderson Medical Center, 1515 Holcombe Blvd, #207, Houston TX 77030 USA | |
| **Roth, Jane R** | Judge |
| US Court of Appeals, 333 Constitution Ave NW, #3128, Washington DC 20001, USA | |
| **Roth, Jesse** | Endocrinologist |
| National Institute of Arthritis, 9000 Rockville Pike, Bethesda MD 20892, USA | |
| **Roth, Joe** | Businessman |
| Creative Artists Agency, 2000 Ave of Stars, #100, Los Angeles CA 90067 USA | |
| **Roth, John A** | Businessman |
| Nortel Networks Corp, 8200 Dixie Road, Brampton ON L6T 5P6, Canada | |
| **Roth, Klaus F** | Mathematician |
| Colbost, 16A Drummond Road, Iverness IV2 4NB, Scotland | |
| **Roth, Mark S** | Bowler |
| 13 Wellesley Road, Montclair NJ 07043, USA | |
| **Roth, Matt** | Actor |
| Bauman Redanty Shaul Agency, 5757 Wilshire Blvd, #473, Los Angeles CA 90036 USA | |
| **Roth, Matthew M (Matt)** | Football Player |
| 14081 SW 54th St, Miramar FL 33027, USA | |
| **Roth, Michael S** | Educator |
| Wesleyan University, President's Office, Wesleyan Station, Middletown CT 06459, USA | |
| **Roth, Philip** | Writer |
| Wylie Agency, 250 W 57th St, #2114, New York NY 10107, USA | |
| **Roth, Rachel** | Actress |
| Amsel Eisenstadt Frazier, 5055 Wilshire Blvd, #865, Los Angeles CA 90036 USA | |
| **Roth, Tim** | Actor, Director |
| Markham Froggatt Irwin, Julian House, 4 Windmill St, London W1P 1HF, England | |
| **Rothberg, Patti** | Singer, Songwriter |
| Marquee Mgmt, 240 Madison Ave, #800, New York NY 10016, USA | |
| **Rothenberg, Adam** | Actor |
| United Talent Agency, U T A Plaza, 9336 Civic Center Dr, Beverly Hills CA 90210 USA | |
| **Rothenberg, Andres** | Actor |
| Global Artists Agency, 6253 Hollywood Blvd, #508, Los Angeles CA 90028 USA | |
| **Rothhaar, Will** | Actor |
| Innovative Artists, 1505 10th St, Santa Monica CA 90401 USA | |
| **Rothman, James E** | Nobel Medicine Laureate |
| Yale University Medical School, Cell Biology Dept, New Haven CT 06520, USA | |
| **Rothman, John** | Actor |
| Don Buchwald, 10 E 44th St, New York NY 10017 USA | |
| **Rothman, Les** | Basketball Player |
| 11854 Fountainside Circle, Boynton Beach FL 33437, USA | |
| **Rothman, Stephanie** | Director |
| 11925 Mayfield Ave, #4, Los Angeles CA 90049, USA | |
| **Rothrock, Cynthia** | Actress |
| 20670 Callon Dr, Topanga CA 90290, USA | |
| **Rothschild, Lawrence L (Larry)** | Baseball Player, Manager |
| 4508 W Culbreath Ave, Tampa FL 33609, USA | |
| **Rothstein, Ronald (Ron)** | Basketball Coach |
| 60 Edgewater Dr, #4E, Coral Gables FL 33133, USA | |
| **Rotimi** | Singer, Songwriter, Actor |
| W M E Entertainment, 9601 Wilshire Blvd, #300, Beverly Hills CA 90210 USA | |
| **Rottenberg, Linda** | Non-Profit Executive |
| Endeavor Global, 900 Broadway, #301, New York NY 10003, USA | |
| **Rotter, Stephen A** | Editor |
| Paradigm Agency, 360 N Crescent Dr, North Building, Beverly Hills CA 90210 USA | |
| **Rottet, Lauren** | Interior Designer |
| D M J M/Rottet, 515 S Flower St, 800, Los Angeles CA 90071, USA | |

**R**

**Rosskopf - Rottet**

# R

| | |
|---|---|
| **Rottino, Vincent A (Vinny)**<br>4939 Crystal Spring, Racine WI 53406, USA | Baseball Player |
| **Rottner, Marvin (Mickey)**<br>5757 N Sheridan Road, #88, Chicago IL 60660, USA | Basketball Player |
| **Rouco Varela, Antonio Maria Cardinal**<br>Arzobispado, Called San Justo 2, 28071 Madrid, Spain | Religious Leader |
| **Rouen, Thomas F (Tom), Jr**<br>20343 N Hayden Road, #105, Scottsdale AZ 85255, USA | Football Player |
| **Roughead, Gary**<br>Chief of Naval Operations, HqUSN, Pentagon, Washington DC 20350 USA | Navy Admiral |
| **Rouleau, Joseph-Alfred**<br>32 Lakeshore Road, Beaconsfield QC H9W 4H3, England | Opera Singer |
| **Roulston, Tom**<br>6814 E 25th St, #N, Wichita KS 67226, USA | Ice Hockey Player |
| **Roundtree, Raleigh C**<br>2001 Roosevelt Dr, Augusta GA 30904, USA | Football Player |
| **Roundtree, Richard**<br>4441 Cahuenga Blvd, #A, Toluca Lake CA 91602, USA | Actor |
| **Roundtree, Saudia**<br>University of Central Florida, Athletic Dept, 4000 Central Florida Blvd, Orlando FL 32816, USA | Basketball Player, Coach |
| **Rounsaville, V Gene**<br>537 Red Rome Lane, Brentwood CA 94513, USA | Baseball Player |
| **Rourke, James P (Jim)**<br>466 Plymouth St, Abington MA 02351, USA | Football Player |
| **Rourke, Mickey**<br>Edelstein Laird Sobel, 9255 W Sunset Blvd, #800, Los Angeles CA 90069 USA | Actor |
| **Rouse, Bob**<br>19135 74th Ave, RR 15, Surrey BC V4N 3G5, Canada | Ice Hockey Player |
| **Rouse, Christopher**<br>University of Rochester, Eastman Music School, 26 Gibbs St, Rochester NY 14604, USA | Composer |
| **Rouse, Christopher**<br>W M E Entertainment, 9601 Wilshire Blvd, #300, Beverly Hills CA 90210 USA | Editor |
| **Rouse, Irving**<br>509 Rockavon Road, Narberth PA 19072, USA | Anthropologist |
| **Rouse, Jeffrey (Jeff)**<br>600 Sharon Park Dr, #B208, Menlo Park CA 94025, USA | Swimmer |
| **Rouse, Mitch**<br>Paradigm Agency, 360 N Crescent Dr, North Building, Beverly Hills CA 90210 USA | Actor, Director, Writer |
| **Rousey, Ronda J (Rowdy)**<br>Hayastan M M A Academy, 7229 Atoll Ave, North Hollywood CA 91601, USA | Judo Athlete |
| **Roush, Jack**<br>Roush Racing, 4600 Roush Place, Concord NC 28027, USA | Auto Racing Executive |
| **Rouson, C Lee**<br>20 Main St, Flanders NJ 07836, USA | Football Player |
| **Rousseau, J J Robert (Bobby)**<br>Golf Club, PO Box 222 Suc Bureau Chef, Louiseville QC J5V 2L6, Canada | Ice Hockey Player |
| **Rousseff, Dilma V**<br>Palacio do Planalto, Praca dos 3 Poderas, 70 150 Brasilia DF, Brazil | President, Brazil |
| **Roussel, Dominic**<br>Success Hockey, 1717 Rue Fleetwood, Laval QC H7N 4B2, Canada | Ice Hockey Player |
| **Roussel, Nathalie**<br>Artmedia, 20 Ave Rapp, 75007 Paris, France | Actress |
| **Roussel, Thomas J (Tom)**<br>13 Heron Lane, Mandeville LA 70471, USA | Football Player |
| **Rousselot, Philippe**<br>Gersh Agency, 9465 Wilshire Blvd, #600, Beverly Hills CA 90212 USA | Cinematographer |
| **Route, Ronald A**<br>Inspector General, HqUSN, Pentagon, Washington DC 20350 USA | Navy Admiral |
| **Routh, Brandon**<br>Main Title Mgmt, 8383 Wilshire Blvd, #408, Beverly Hills CA 90211 USA | Actor |
| **Routledge, Alison**<br>Marmont Mgmt, Langham House, 302/8 Regent St, London W1R 5AL, England | Actress |
| **Routledge, Patricia**<br>Marmont Mgmt, Langham House, 302/8 Regent St, London W1R 5AL, England | Actress |
| **Routt, Stanford B**<br>Kansas City Chiefs, 1 Arrowhead Dr, Kansas City KS 64129 USA | Football Player |
| **Rouvali, Santtu-Matias**<br>Tapiola Sinfonietta, PO Box 3262, 02070 City of Espoo, Finland | Conductor |
| **Rouve, Jean-Paul**<br>U B B A, 6 Rue de Braque, 75003 Paris, France | Actor |
| **Rouvel, Catherine**<br>Artmedia, 20 Ave Rapp, 75007 Paris, France | Actress |
| **Rouviere, Koby**<br>C E S D, 10635 Santa Monica Blvd, #130, Los Angeles CA 90025 USA | Actor |
| **Roux, Albert H**<br>Le Gavroche, 43 Upper Brook St, London W1Y 1PF, England | Chef, Restaurateur |
| **Roux, Jean-Louis**<br>4145 Blueridge Crescent, #2, Montreal QC H3H 1S7, Canada | Director, Actor |
| **Roux, Michel A, Sr**<br>Waterside Inn, Ferry Road, Bray, Berkshire SL6 2AT, England | Chef, Restaurateur |
| **Rove, Karl C**<br>1333 New Hampshire Ave NW, #600, Washington DC 20036, USA | Government Official |
| **Rovero, Jennifer**<br>Playboy Promotions, 2706 Media Center Dr, Los Angeles CA 90065 USA | Model |
| **Rovner, Ilana D**<br>US Court of Appeals, 219 S Dearborn St, Chicago IL 60604, USA | Judge |
| **Rovner, Michael**<br>640 Broadway, #7E, New York NY 10012, USA | Photographer, Artist |
| **Rowan, Kelly**<br>Untitled Entertainment, 350 S Beverly Dr, #200, Beverly Hills CA 90212 USA | Actress |
| **Rowan, Peter**<br>A-Train Entertainment, 401 Grand Ave, #300, Oakland CA 94610, USA | Singer, Guitarist |
| **Rowand, Aaron R**<br>34 Meadowhawk Lane, Las Vegas NV 89135, USA | Baseball Player |
| **Rowbotham, Stephen**<br>Leander Club, Henley on Thames, Leander RG9 2LP, England | Rowing Athlete |

**Rowden, William H** — Navy Admiral
55 Pinewood Court, Lancaster VA 22503, USA
**Rowdon, Wade L** — Baseball Player
230 Crooked Tree Trail, Deland FL 32724, USA
**Rowe, Brad** — Actor
Domain Talent, 9229 W Sunset Blvd, #710, West Hollywood CA 90069 USA
**Rowe, Charlie** — Actor
United Talent Agency, U T A Plaza, 9336 Civic Center Dr, Beverly Hills CA 90210 USA
**Rowe, David H (Dave)** — Football Player
980 Sherwood Ave, Asheboro NC 27205, USA
**Rowe, Jack** — Writer
Pocket Books, 1230 Ave of Americas, New York NY 10020 USA
**Rowe, John W** — Businessman
Exelon Corp, 10 S Dearborn St, #4800, Chicago IL 60603, USA
**Rowe, Misty** — Actress, Model
2193 River Road, Egg Harbor Cay NJ 08215, USA
**Rowe, Nicholas** — Actor
Julian Belfrage Assoc, 9 Argyll St, #300, London W1F 7TG, England
**Rowe, Robert B (Bob)** — Football Player
1754 Highview Circle Court, Ballwin MO 63021, USA
**Rowe, Sandra M** — Editor
Portland Oregonian, Editorial Dept, 1320 SW Broadway, Portland OR 97201, USA
**Rowe, Thomas J (Tom)** — Ice Hockey Player
1121 Park West Blvd, Mount Pleasant SC 29466, USA
**Rowell, Victoria** — Actress
Third Hill Entertainment, 195 S Beverly Dr, #400, Beverly Hills CA 90212, USA
**Rowland, Dave** — Singer (Dave & Sugar)
PO Box 121089, Nashville TN 37212, USA
**Rowland, Derrick** — Basketball Player
3 Island View Road, Cohoes NY 12047, USA
**Rowland, J David** — Businessman
6 Danbury St, London N1 8JU, England
**Rowland, James Anthony** — Governor General, Australia; Marshal
17 Pindari Ave, Mosman NSW 2088, Australia
**Rowland, Kelly** — Singer (Destiny's Child), Actress
I C M Partners, 10250 Constellation Blvd, #900, Los Angeles CA 90067 USA
**Rowland, Landon H** — Businessman
Kansas City Southern, PO Box 219335, Kansas City MO 64121, USA
**Rowland, Mark** — Track Athlete, Coach
Oregon Track Club, PO Box 11364, Eugene OR 97440, USA
**Rowland, Richard G (Rich)** — Baseball Player
593 E 1st St, Cloverdale CA 95425, USA
**Rowlands, Gena** — Actress
7917 Woodrow Wilson Dr, Los Angeles CA 90046, USA
**Rowlands, Tom** — Singer, Musician (Chemical Brothers)
9PR, 65-69 White Lion St, London N1 9PR, England
**Rowley, Cynthia** — Fashion Designer
W M E Entertainment, 9601 Wilshire Blvd, #300, Beverly Hills CA 90210 USA
**Rowley, Janet D** — Physician
5310 S University Ave, Chicago IL 60615, USA
**Rowling, J K (Jo)** — Writer
PO Box 27036, Edinburgh EH10 5WB, Scotland
**Rowlinson, John S** — Chemist
12 Pullens Field, Headington OX3 0BU, England
**Rowny, Edward L** — Army General
6200 Oregon Ave NW, #345, Washington DC 20015, USA
**Rowser, John F** — Football Player
17564 Alta Vista Dr, Southfield MI 48075, USA
**Roxburgh, Richard** — Actor
United Agents, 12-26 Lexington St, London W1F 0LE, England
**Roy** — Animal Illusionist (Siegfried & Roy)
Kirvin Doak Communications, 7935 W Sahara Ave, #201, Las Vegas NV 89117, USA
**Roy C** — Singer, Songwriter
Carolina Record Distributors, 229 Augusta Highway, Allendale SC 29810, USA
**Roy, Alfred** — Songwriter, Lyricist
2708 Range Road, Los Angeles CA 90065, USA
**Roy, Andre** — Ice Hockey Player
Calgary Flames, PO Box 1540, Station M, Calgary AB T2P 3B9, Canada
**Roy, Aruna** — Political, Social Activist
Mazdoor Kisan Shakti Sangathan, Village Devdoongri, Post Brar, Rajsamand, Rajasthan, India
**Roy, Arundhati** — Writer
India Ink Publishing, C1 Soami Nagar, New Delhi 110 017, India
**Roy, Brandon** — Basketball Player
19807 183rd Way SE, Renton WA 98058, USA
**Roy, Derek** — Ice Hockey Player
100 Rivermist Dr, Buffalo NY 14202, USA
**Roy, Drew** — Actor
United Talent Agency, U T A Plaza, 9336 Civic Center Dr, Beverly Hills CA 90210 USA
**Roy, Jean-Pierre** — Baseball Player
407 Rue des Harfangs, Saint-Nicolas QC G7A 3H4, Canada
**Roy, John** — Actor, Comedian
Galloways One, 15 Lexham Mews, London W8 6JW, England
**Roy, Jonathan** — Singer
Agency Group Ltd, 142 W 57th St, #600, New York NY 10019 USA
**Roy, Lesley** — Singer
Jive Records, 137-39 W 25th St, #1100, New York NY 10001 USA
**Roy, Loriene** — Association Executive, Librarian
American Library Assn, 50 E Huron, Chicago IL 60611, USA
**Roy, Patrick** — Ice Hockey Player
201 Chemin de la Plage Saint Laurent, Quebec QC G1Y 1W6, Canada
**Roy, Rachel** — Fashion Designer
Mavrick Artists Agency, 6100 Wilshire Blvd, #550, Los Angeles CA 90048, USA
**Roy, Reena** — Actress
Pam Villa D'Monte Park Road, Bandra, Mumbai MS 400050, India
**Royal, Bert V** — Producer, Writer
Paradigm Agency, 360 N Crescent Dr, North Building, Beverly Hills CA 90210 USA

**R**

| | |
|---|---|
| **Royal, Billy Joe**<br>Bobby Roberts, 3050 Business Park Circle, #303, Goodlettsville TN 37221 USA | Singer; Songwriter |
| **Royal, Lauren**<br>PO Box 52932, Irvine CA 92619, USA | Writer |
| **Royal, Segolene**<br>Parti Socialiste, 10 Rue de Solferino, 75333 Paris, France | Government Official, France |
| **Royals, Mark A**<br>4035 Courtside Way, Tampa FL 33618, USA | Football Player |
| **Royce Da 5'9"**<br>I C M Partners, 10250 Constellation Blvd, #900, Los Angeles CA 90067 USA | Rap Artist |
| **Roye, Orpheus M**<br>12955 NW 18th Manor, Pembroke Pines FL 33028, USA | Football Player |
| **Royer, Stanley D (Stan)**<br>9301 Christopher Lake Dr, Columbia IL 62236, USA | Baseball |
| **Royo Sanchez, Aristides**<br>Morgan & Morgan, PO Box 1824, Panama City 1, Panama | President, Panama |
| **Royo, Andre**<br>Don Buchwald, 6500 Wilshire Blvd, #2200, Los Angeles CA 90048 USA | Actor |
| **Royo, Jose**<br>Triad Art Group, 44 E Belmont Dr, Romeoville IL 60446, USA | Artist |
| **Royo-Torres, Rafael**<br>Teruel-Dinopolis Museum, Poligono de los Planos, 44002 Teruel, Spain | Paleontologist |
| **Royster, Jeron K (Jerry)**<br>1 Brewers Way, Milwaukee WI 53214, USA | Baseball Player, Manager |
| **Royster, Willie A**<br>229 55th St NE, Washington DC 20019, USA | Baseball Player |
| **Rozalla**<br>Mission Control, City Business Center, Lower Road, London SE16 2XB, England | Singer |
| **Rozanov, Evgeny G**<br>International Architecture Academy, 2nd Brestskaya Str 4, 103104 Moscow, Russia | Architect |
| **Rozbruch, S Robert**<br>Cornell University Weill Medical College, 519 E 72nd St, New York NY 10021, USA | Orthopedic Surgeon |
| **Rozema, David S (Dave)**<br>1560 N Renaud Road, Grosse Pointe Woods MI 48236, USA | Baseball Player |
| **Rozema, Patricia**<br>Creative Artists Agency, 2000 Ave of Stars, #100, Los Angeles CA 90067 USA | Director |
| **Rozhdestvensky, Gennady N**<br>Victor Hochhauser Ltd, 4 Oak Hill Way, London NW3, England | Conductor |
| **Rozier, Clifford G**<br>PO Box 1194, Palmetto FL 34220, USA | Basketball Player |
| **Rozier, Michael M (Mike)**<br>9 Hidden Hollow Lane, Sicklerville NJ 08081, USA | Football Player |
| **Roznovsky, Victor S (Vic)**<br>266 W Bluff Ave, Fresno CA 93711, USA | Baseball Player |
| **Rozsival, Michal**<br>6751 N Sunset Blvd, Glendale AZ 85305, USA | Ice Hockey Player |
| **Ruah, Daniela**<br>Gersh Agency, 9465 Wilshire Blvd, #600, Beverly Hills CA 90212 USA | Actress |
| **Ruano Pascual, Virginia**<br>Women's Tennis Assn, 1 Progress Plaza, #1500, Saint Petersburg FL 33701 USA | Tennis Player |
| **Rubalcaba, Gonzalo**<br>Joel Chriss Co, 300 Mercer St, #3J, New York NY 10003 USA | Jazz Pianist, Composer |
| **Rubbia, Carlo**<br>C E R N, Particle Physics Laboratory, 1211 Geneva 23, Switzerland | Nobel Physics Laureate |
| **Ruben, Joseph P (Joe)**<br>Paradigm Agency, 360 N Crescent Dr, North Building, Beverly Hills CA 90210 USA | Director |
| **Rubens, Sibylla**<br>Kunstler Sekretariat am Gasteig, Rosenheimer Str 52, 81669 Munich, Germany | Opera Singer |
| **Rubenstein, Ann**<br>NBC-TV, News Dept, 30 Rockefeller Plaza, #270E, New York NY 10112 USA | Commentator |
| **Rubenstein, Edward**<br>Stanford University Medical School, Surgery Dept, Stanford CA 94305, USA | Physician |
| **Ruberto, John E (Sonny)**<br>207 Ambridge Court, #204, Chesterfield MO 63017, USA | Baseball Player |
| **Rubiano Saenz, Pedro Cardinal**<br>Arzubispado, Carrera 7 N 10-20, Santa Fe de Bogota DC 1, Colombia | Religious Leader |
| **Rubick, Robin J (Rob)**<br>PO Box 63, Curtis MI 49820, USA | Football Player |
| **Rubik, Erno**<br>Rubik Studio, Varosmajor Utca 74, 1122 Budapest, Hungary | Inventor (Rubik Cube) |
| **Rubin, Amy**<br>Hervey/Grimes Talent, 10561 Missouri Ave, #2, Los Angeles CA 90025 USA | Actress |
| **Rubin, Chandra**<br>708 S Saint Antoine St, Lafayette LA 70501, USA | Tennis Player |
| **Rubin, Gloria**<br>I C M Partners, 10250 Constellation Blvd, #900, Los Angeles CA 90067 USA | Actress |
| **Rubin, Harry**<br>University of California, Molecular Biology Dept, Berkeley CA 94720, USA | Biologist |
| **Rubin, Jennifer**<br>Charles Riley Public Relations, 7122 Beverly Blvd, #F, Los Angeles CA 90036, USA | Actress, Model |
| **Rubin, Leigh**<br>Creators Syndicate, 737 3rd St, Hermosa Beach CA 90254 USA | Cartoonist (Rubes) |
| **Rubin, Richard**<br>Metropolitan Talent Agency, 5405 Wilshire Blvd, #218, Los Angeles CA 90036 USA | Actor, Musician |
| **Rubin, Robert**<br>Massachusetts General Hospital, 32 Fruit St, Boston MA 02114, USA | Medical Researcher |
| **Rubin, Robert E**<br>Citigroup Inc, 55 E 52nd St, New York NY 10055, USA | Secretary, Treasury; Financier |
| **Rubin, Tibor (Ted)**<br>5442 Marietta Ave, Garden Grove CA 92845, USA | Korean War Army Hero (CMH) |
| **Rubin, Vanessa**<br>Joel Chriss Co, 300 Mercer St, #3J, New York NY 10003 USA | Singer |
| **Rubin, Vera C**<br>Carnegie Institution, 5241 Broad Branch Road NW, Washington DC 20015, USA | Astronomer |
| **Rubinek, Saul**<br>Great Northern Artists Mgmt, 350 Dupont St, Toronto ON M5R 1V9, Canada | Actor, Director, Producer |

**Royal - Rubinek**

| | |
|---|---|
| **Rubino, Frank A** | Attorney |
| 1001 Brickell Bay Dr, #2206, Miami FL 33131, USA | |
| **Rubinoff, Ira** | Biologist |
| Smithsonian Tropical Research Institute, Unit 0848, APO AA 34002, USA | |
| **Rubinstein, John A** | Actor |
| 4417 Leydon Ave, Woodland Hills CA 91364, USA | |
| **Rubinstein, Jonathan J (Jon)** | Businessman, Computer Scientist |
| Palm Inc, 950 W Maude Ave, Sunnyvale CA 94085, USA | |
| **Rubinstein, Peter J** | Religious Leader, Rabbi |
| Central Synagogue, 123 E 55th St, New York NY 10022, USA | |
| **Rubin-Vega, Daphne** | Actress, Singer |
| Paradigm Agency, 360 N Crescent Dr, North Building, Beverly Hills CA 90210 USA | |
| **Rubio, Paulina** | Singer |
| Sanctuary Artist Management, 15301 Ventura Blvd, #400 Bldg B, Sherman Oaks CA 91403, USA | |
| **Rubio, Ricard (Ricky)** | Basketball Player |
| Minnesota Timberwolves, Target Center, 600 1st Ave N, Minneapolis MN 55403 USA | |
| **Ruby, Sterling** | Artist |
| Xavier Hufkens, 6-8 Rue Saint-Georges, 1050 Brussels, Belgium | |
| **Rucchin, Steve** | Ice Hockey Player |
| 614 Acacia Ave, Corona del Mar CA 92625, USA | |
| **Rucci, Ralph** | Fashion Designer, Artist |
| Chado Ralph Rucci, 536 Broadway, #6, New York NY 10012, USA | |
| **Rucci, Todd L** | Football Player |
| 5 Southview Lane, Lititz PA 17543, USA | |
| **Ruccolo, Richard** | Actor |
| A P A Talent/Literary Agency, 405 S Beverly Dr, #300, Beverly Hills CA 90212 USA | |
| **Rucinski, Artur** | Opera Singer |
| I M G Artists, Hogarth Business Park, Chiswick, London W4 2TH, England | |
| **Rucinsky, Martin** | Ice Hockey Player |
| 8025 Bonhomme Ave, Saint Louis MO 63105, USA | |
| **Ruck, Alan** | Actor |
| Innovative Artists, 1505 10th St, Santa Monica CA 90401 USA | |
| **Ruckelshaus, William D** | Businessman, Government Official |
| Pugent Sound Partnership, PO Box 47500, Olympia WA 98504, USA | |
| **Ruckenstein, Eli** | Chemical Engineer |
| 755 Renaissance Dr, #203, Buffalo NY 14221, USA | |
| **Rucker, Anja** | Track Athlete |
| T U S Jena, Wollnitzer Str 42, 07749 Jena, Germany | |
| **Rucker, Darius** | Singer (Hootie & the Blowfish) |
| McGhee Entertainment, 801 18th Ave S, Nashville TN 37203, USA | |
| **Rucker, David M (Dave)** | Baseball Player |
| 18602 Piper Place, Yorba Linda CA 92886, USA | |
| **Rucker, Michael D (Mike)** | Football Player |
| 5971 Rolling Ridge Dr, Kannapolis NC 28081, USA | |
| **Rucker, Reginald J (Reggie)** | Football Player |
| 4517 Saint Germain Blvd, Cleveland OH 44128, USA | |
| **Rudakova, Natalya** | Actress |
| Don Buchwald, 10 E 44th St, New York NY 10017 USA | |
| **Rudbottom, Roy R, Jr** | Diplomat |
| 7831 Park Lane, #213A, Dallas TX 75225, USA | |
| **Rudd, Delaney** | Basketball Player |
| 422 Chesham Dr, Kernersville NC 27284, USA | |
| **Rudd, Dwayne D** | Football Player |
| 22 Williams Road, Trenton SC 29847, USA | |
| **Rudd, John** | Basketball Player |
| 4440 Sweet Bay Dr, Lake Charles LA 70611, USA | |
| **Rudd, Paul** | Actor |
| United Talent Agency, U T A Plaza, 9336 Civic Center Dr, Beverly Hills CA 90210 USA | |
| **Rudd, Phillip H N (Phil)** | Drummer (AC/DC) |
| Alberts Music, 9 Rangers Road, Neutral Bay, Sydney NSW 2089, Australia | |
| **Rudd, Ricky** | Auto Racing Driver |
| Entertainment Marketing, 124 Summerville Dr, Mooresville NC 28115, USA | |
| **Rudd, Xavier** | Singer, Songwriter |
| Creative Artists Agency, 1 Beadon Road, #400 London W6 0EA, England , USA | |
| **Ruddy, Timothy D (Tim)** | Football Player |
| 3885 Vale View Lane, Mead CO 80542, USA | |
| **Rudel, Julius** | Conductor |
| 101 Central Park West, #11A, New York NY 10023, USA | |
| **Rudenstine, Neil L** | Educator |
| A W Mellon Foundation, 140 E 62nd St, New York NY 10065, USA | |
| **Rudi, Joseph O (Joe)** | Baseball Player |
| 17667 Deer Park Loop, Baker City OR 97814, USA | |
| **Rudin, Scott** | Producer |
| Scott Rudin Productions, 120 W 45th St, #1001, New York NY 10036, USA | |
| **Rudisha, David L** | Track Athlete |
| Saint Patrick's High School, PO Box 310, 30700 Iten, Keiyo District, Rift Valley Province, Kenya | |
| **Rudnay, John C (Jack)** | Football Player |
| 7219 Whipperwill Road, Versailles MO 65084, USA | |
| **Rudner, Rita** | Actress, Comedienne, Writer |
| 2877 Paradise Dr, #1605, Los Angeles CA 90032, USA | |
| **Rudnick, Paul** | Writer |
| Creative Artists Agency, 2000 Ave of Stars, #100, Los Angeles CA 90067 USA | |
| **Rudolf, Kevin** | Singer, Musician, Songwriter |
| Cash Money/Motown Records, 6255 W Sunset Blvd, Los Angeles CA 90028, USA | |
| **Rudolph, Alan S** | Director |
| William J Goldstein, 15760 Ventura Blvd, #1600, Encino CA 91436, USA | |
| **Rudolph, Benjamin (Ben)** | Football Player |
| 561 E General Gorgas Dr, Mobile AL 36617, USA | |
| **Rudolph, Council, Jr** | Football Player |
| 8310 Lago Vista Dr, Tampa FL 33614, USA | |
| **Rudolph, John L (Jack)** | Football Player |
| 2211 Glynndale Dr, Valdosta GA 31602, USA | |
| **Rudolph, Kenneth V (Ken)** | Baseball Player |
| 9969 E Bayview Dr, Scottsdale AZ 85258, USA | |
| **Rudolph, Lars** | Actor |
| Gunda Kniggendorff Mgmt, Postfach 440414, 12004 Berlin, Germany | |

# R

**Rudolph, Maya** — Actress, Comedienne
3 Arts Entertainment, 9460 Wilshire Blvd, #700, Beverly Hills CA 90212 USA
**Rudometkin, John** — Basketball Player
6181 Wise Road, Newcastle CA 95658, USA
**Rudorfler, Erich** — German Air Force Hero
Bismarkstr 3A, 23677 Bad Schwarteau, Germany
**Rudzinski, Witold** — Composer
Ul Narbutta 50 m 6, 02541 Warsaw, Poland
**Rue, Sara** — Actress, Comedienne
Alan David Mgmt, 8840 Wilshire Blvd, #200, Beverly Hills CA 90211, USA
**Ruebell, Matthew A (Matt)** — Baseball Player
7509 W Augusta Blvd, Yorktown IN 47396, USA
**Ruegamer, C Grey** — Football Player
7380 E Eastern Ave, #124, Las Vegas NV 89123, USA
**Ruehl, Mercedes** — Actress
Innovative Artists, 1505 10th St, Santa Monica CA 90401 USA
**Ruel, Claude** — Ice Hockey Coach
102-1450 Rue Beauhamois, Longueuil QC J4M 1X2, Canada
**Ruelas, Gabriel (Gabe)** — Boxer
1119 S Hudson Ave, Los Angeles CA 90019, USA
**Ruell, Aaron** — Actor, Director, Writer
Universal Media Artists, 8222 Melrose Ave, #203, Los Angeles CA 90048, USA
**Ruelle, David P** — Mathematician
1 Ave Charles-Comar, 91440 Bures-sur-Yvette, France
**Ruess, Nathaniel J (Nate)** — Singer (Fun, Format), Songwriter
Nettwerk Management Group, 1650 W 2nd Ave, Vancouver BC V6J 4R3, Canada
**Rueter, Kirk W** — Baseball Player
46 Pheasant Ridge Court, Nashville IL 62263, USA
**Ruether, Mike A** — Football Player
23014 Gardner Dr, Alpharetta GA 30009, USA
**Ruether, Rosemary R** — Theologian
530 Mayflower Road, Claremont CA 91711, USA
**Ruettgers, Kenneth F (Ken)** — Football Player
16897 Golden Stone Dr, Sisters OR 97759, USA
**Ruettiger, Daniel E (Rudy)** — Football Player
293 Goldstar St, Henderson NV 89012, USA
**Ruff, Howard J** — Financial Analyst, Writer
PO Box 441, Orem UT 84059, USA
**Ruff, Lindy** — Ice Hockey Player, Coach
5006 Winding Lane, Clarence NY 14031, USA
**Ruff, Matt** — Writer
Harper Collins Publishers, 10 E 53rd St, Cellar 1, New York NY 10022 USA
**Ruff, Orlando B** — Football Player
202 S Raymond Ave, #304, Pasadena CA 91105, USA
**Ruffalo, Mark** — Actor
Brillstein Entertainment Partners, 9150 Wilshire Blvd, #350, Beverly Hills CA 90212 USA
**Ruffcorn, Scott P** — Baseball Player
2137 Barton Hills Dr, Austin TX 78704, USA
**Ruffin, Bruce W** — Baseball Player
4808 Pyrenees Pass, Austin TX 78738, USA
**Ruffin, Jimmy** — Singer
Universal Attractions, 135 W 26th St, #1200, New York NY 10001 USA
**Ruffin, Johnny R** — Baseball Player
4229 Trumpworth Court, Valrico FL 33596, USA
**Ruffner, Paul** — Basketball Player
3352 N 100 E, #210, Provo UT 84604, USA
**Ruge, John A** — Cartoonist
240 Bronxville Road, #B4, Bronxville NY 10708, USA
**Rugers, Martin** — Astronomer
University of Washington, Astronomy Dept, Seattle WA 98195, USA
**Ruggiano, Justin M** — Baseball Player
8711 Tallwood Dr, Austin TX 78759, USA
**Ruggiero, Angela** — Ice Hockey Player
196 Old Military Road, Lake Placid NY 12946, USA
**Ruhe, Martin** — Cinematographer
Independent Talent Group, 40 Whitfield St, London W1T 2RH, England
**Ruhl, Sarah** — Writer
Bret Adams Artists Agency, 448 W 44th St, New York NY 10036, USA
**Ruhnke, Kent** — Ice Hockey Player
Felsenrainstr 11, Zurich 8052, Switzerland
**Ruhsam, John W** — WW II Marine Corps Air Force Hero
1010 American Eagle Blvd, #346, Sun City Center FL 33573, USA
**Ruini, Camillo Cardinal** — Religious Leader
Vicar of Rome, 00120 Vatican City
**Ruivivar, Anthony M** — Actor
Gersh Agency, 9465 Wilshire Blvd, #600, Beverly Hills CA 90212 USA
**Ruiz Anchia, Juan** — Cinematographer
Gersh Agency, 9465 Wilshire Blvd, #600, Beverly Hills CA 90212 USA
**Ruiz, Hector** — Businessman
Advanced Micro Devices, 1 A M D Place, PO Box 3453, Sunnyvale CA 94088, USA
**Ruiz, John** — Boxer
11009 Salford Dr, Las Vegas NV 89144, USA
**Ruiz, Manuel (Chico)** — Baseball Player
267 Calle Tapia, San Juan PR 00912, USA
**Ruiz-Corforte, Tracie L** — Synchronized Swimmer
B T O Foundation, 312 Sweet Cherry Court, Hollidaysburg PA 16648, USA
**Rukeyser, William S** — Publisher
1509 Rudder Lane, Knoxville TN 37919, USA
**Rule, Ann** — Writer
PO Box 98846, Seattle WA 98198, USA
**Rule, Bobby F (Bob)** — Basketball Player
4303 Kansas Ave, Riverside CA 92507, USA
**Ruley, Amy** — Basketball Coach
North Dakota State University, Athletic Dept, Fargo ND 58105, USA
**Rulin, Olesya** — Actress
Paul Kohner, 9300 Wilshire Blvd, #555, Beverly Hills CA 90212 USA

**Rudolph - Rulin**

| | |
|---|---|
| **Rullo, Gerenoso C (Jerry)** | Basketball Player |
| 300 Brookline Blvd, Havertown PA 19083, USA | |
| **Rumer** | Singer, Songwriter |
| Agency Group Ltd, 361-373 City Road, London EC1V 1PQ, England | |
| **Rummells, Dave** | Golfer |
| 1820 Harbor Blvd, Kissimmee FL 34744, USA | |
| **Rummenigge, Karl-Heinz** | Soccer Player |
| Eichleite 4, 80231 Grunwald, Germany | |
| **Rumph, Michael J (Mike)** | Football Player |
| 4686 SW 179th Way, Miramar FL 33029, USA | |
| **Rumsfeld, Donald H** | Secretary, Defense; Businessman |
| 1718 M St NW, #366, Washington DC 20036, USA | |
| **Runager, Max C** | Football Player |
| 109 Roger Smith, Williamsburg VA 23185, USA | |
| **Runcie, James** | Writer |
| David Godwin Assoc, 55 Monument St, London WC2H 9DG, England | |
| **Runco, Mario, Jr** | Astronaut |
| 207 Lakeshore Dr, Seabrook TX 77586, USA | |
| **Rundgren, Todd** | Singer, Songwriter |
| Panacea Entertainment, 13587 Andalusia Dr, Santa Rosa Valley CA 93102, USA | |
| **Runge, Brian** | Baseball Umpire |
| 8225 E County Dr, El Cajon CA 92021, USA | |
| **Runge, Paul W** | Baseball Player |
| 1719 W Community Dr, Jupiter FL 33458, USA | |
| **Runnells, Thomas W (Tom)** | Baseball Player, Manager |
| 6045 Settlers Ridge Circle, Sylvania OH 43560, USA | |
| **Runnicles, Donald** | Conductor |
| Opus 3 Artists, 470 Park Ave S, #900N, New York NY 10016 USA | |
| **Running, Steve** | Ecologist |
| 1419 Khanabad Dr, Missoula MT 59802, USA | |
| **Runyan, Joe** | Dog Sled Racer |
| Rt 1, 314.5 Parks Highway, Nenana AK 99760, USA | |
| **Runyan, Jon D** | Football Player |
| 262 Mount Laurel Road, #1, Mount Laurel NJ 08054, USA | |
| **Runyan, Marla** | Track Athlete |
| 5135 Center Way, Eugene OR 97405, USA | |
| **Runyan, Sean D** | Baseball Player |
| 1958 Bermuda Pointe Dr, Haines City FL 33844, USA | |
| **Runyon, Edwin** | Religious Leader |
| General Baptists Assn, 100 Stinson Dr, Poplar Bluff MO 63901, USA | |
| **Ruotsalainen, Reijo J** | Ice Hockey Player |
| Jukurit Mikkeli Raviradantie 1, 50100 Mikkeli, Finland | |
| **RuPaul** | Actor, Producer, Singer |
| RuCo, 332 Bleeker St, #F22, New York NY 10014, USA | |
| **Rupe, Joshua M (Josh)** | Baseball Player |
| 225 Arrowfield Road, Virginia Beach VA 23454, USA | |
| **Rupe, Ryan K** | Baseball Player |
| 2 Windflower Place, Spring TX 77381, USA | |
| **Rupert, Michael** | Actor, Composer, Director |
| Don Buchwald, 10 E 44th St, New York NY 10017 USA | |
| **Rupp, Debra Jo** | Actress |
| Stone Manners Salners, 9911 W Pico Blvd, #1400, Los Angeles CA 90035 USA | |
| **Rupp, Duane** | Ice Hockey Player |
| 2446 McMonagle Ave, Pittsburgh PA 15216, USA | |
| **Rupp, Michael (Mike)** | Ice Hockey Player |
| 3936 Medford Square, Hilliard OH 43026, USA | |
| **Ruppel, Adam** | Guitarist (Systematic) |
| Artist Group International, 9560 Wilshire Blvd, #400, Beverly Hills CA 90212 USA | |
| **Ruprecht, Tom** | Writer |
| United Talent Agency, U T A Plaza, 9336 Civic Center Dr, Beverly Hills CA 90210 USA | |
| **Rusby, Kate A** | Singer, Songwriter |
| Pure Records & Mgmt, PO Box 174, Penistone S36 8XB, England | |
| **Rusch, Glendon J** | Baseball Player |
| 6428 Chaffee St, Tujunga CA 91042, USA | |
| **Rusch, Kristine Kathryn** | Writer |
| PO Box 479, Lincoln City OR 97367, USA | |
| **Ruscha, Edward J** | Artist |
| 5920-24 Blackwelder St, Culver City CA 90232, USA | |
| **Ruscio, Kenneth** | Educator |
| Washington & Lee University, President's Office, Lexington VA 24450, USA | |
| **Ruse, Michael** | Philosopher |
| 651 E 6th Ave, Tallahassee FL 32303, USA | |
| **Rusedski, Greg** | Tennis Player |
| Association of Tennis Professionals, 200 Tournament Road, Ponte Vedra Beach FL 32082 USA | |
| **Rusesabagina, Paul** | Humanitarian |
| Baron Albert d'Huartlaan 124, 1950 Kraainem, Belgium | |
| **Rush, Barbara** | Actress |
| House of Representatives, 1434 6th St, #1, Santa Monica CA 90401 USA | |
| **Rush, Bobby** | Singer, Musician, Songwriter |
| Wenig-LaMonica Associates, 580 White Plains Rd, #130, Tarrytown NY 10591, USA | |
| **Rush, Brandon L** | Basketball Player |
| Utah Jazz, Energy Solutions Arena, 301 W South Temple, Salt Lake City UT 84101 USA | |
| **Rush, Deborah** | Actress |
| Gersh Agency, 9465 Wilshire Blvd, #600, Beverly Hills CA 90212 USA | |
| **Rush, Geoffrey** | Actor |
| Shanahan Mgmt, Berman House, 91 Campbell St, #300, Surry Hills NSW 2010, Australia | |
| **Rush, Gerald M (Jerry)** | Football Player |
| 17536 Oak Dr, Detroit MI 48221, USA | |
| **Rush, Jennifer** | Singer |
| Michow Concerts, Postfach 20264, 29216 Hamburg, Germany | |
| **Rush, Kareem L** | Basketball Player |
| 2805 E 62nd St, Kansas City MO 64130, USA | |
| **Rush, Merrilee** | Singer, Songwriter |
| Cape Entertainment, 4799 Coconut Creek Parkway, #258, Coconut Creek FL 33063 USA | |
| **Rush, Otis** | Singer, Guitarist |
| J W Entertainment, PO Box 78904, Atlanta GA 30357 USA | |

**R**

Rullo - Rush

| | |
|---|---|
| **Rush, Richard W** | Director, Producer |
| 821 Stradella Road, Los Angeles CA 90077, USA | |
| **Rush, Robert J (Bob)** | Football Player |
| 420 Mary Lane, Auburn AL 36830, USA | |
| **Rush, Robert R (Bob)** | Baseball Player |
| 444 S Higley Road, #116, Mesa AZ 85206, USA | |
| **Rushbrook, Claire** | Actress |
| Troika, 74 Clerkenwell Road, #300, London EC1M 5QA, England | |
| **Rushdie, A Salman** | Writer |
| United Talent Agency, U T A Plaza, 9336 Civic Center Dr, Beverly Hills CA 90210 USA | |
| **Rushen, Patrice L** | Singer, Songwriter |
| Groove Entertainment, 1005 N Alfred St, #2, West Hollywood CA 90069, USA | |
| **Rushlow, Timothy A (Tim)** | Singer, Guitarist (Rushlow Harris) |
| K M G Records, 3631 W End Ave, Nashville TN 37205, USA | |
| **Ruskin, Joseph** | Actor |
| 13840 Kittridge St, Van Nuys CA 91405, USA | |
| **Ruskowski, Terry** | Ice Hockey Player |
| 2542 Silent Shore Court, Richmond TX 77406, USA | |
| **Russ, Tim** | Actor |
| C E S D, 10635 Santa Monica Blvd, #130, Los Angeles CA 90025 USA | |
| **Russ, William** | Actor |
| 26500 Agoura Road, Calabasas CA 91302, USA | |
| **Russell Beale, Simon** | Actor |
| Richard Stone Partnership, De Walden Court, 85 New Cavendish St, London W1W 6XD, England | |
| **Russell, Adam W** | Baseball Player |
| 627 Mariner Village, Huron OH 44839, USA | |
| **Russell, Allison** | Singer (Po' Girl) |
| Emerging Music, Horns Cross, Bidesford, Devon EX39 5DW, England | |
| **Russell, Betsy** | Actress |
| Marshak/Zachary Co, 8840 Wilshire Blvd, #100, Beverly Hills CA 90211 USA | |
| **Russell, Brenda** | Singer, Songwriter, Keyboardist |
| S K M Artist Mgmt, PO Box 25906, Los Angeles CA 90025, USA | |
| **Russell, Bryon D** | Basketball Player |
| 22451 Cass Ave, Woodland Hills CA 91364, USA | |
| **Russell, C Andrew (Andy)** | Football Player |
| 230 Glen Abbey Court, Presto PA 15142, USA | |
| **Russell, Catherine** | Actress |
| Rights House, Drury House, 34-43 Russell St, London WC2B 5HA, England | |
| **Russell, Cazzie L** | Basketball Player |
| Savannah College of Art & Design, Athletic Dept, Savannah GA 31402, USA | |
| **Russell, Charles O (Chuck)** | Director |
| Gersh Agency, 9465 Wilshire Blvd, #600, Beverly Hills CA 90212 USA | |
| **Russell, Christopher T** | Geophysicist |
| University of California, Institute of Geophysics & Planetary Physics, Los Angeles CA 90024, USA | |
| **Russell, Clive** | Actor |
| Shepherd Mgmt, 45 Maddox St, #400, London W1S 2PC, England | |
| **Russell, Craig** | Actor, Writer, Producer |
| Langford Assoc, 17 Westfields Ave, Barnes, London SW13 0AT, England | |
| **Russell, David O** | Director, Writer |
| Creative Artists Agency, 2000 Ave of Stars, #100, Los Angeles CA 90067 USA | |
| **Russell, Graham C** | Singer (Air Supply) |
| PO Box 3367, Beverly Hills CA 90212, USA | |
| **Russell, Hugh** | Opera Singer |
| Columbia Artists Mgmt Inc, 1790 Broadway, #702, New York NY 10019 USA | |
| **Russell, JaMarcus** | Football Player |
| 13111 Skyline Road, Oakland CA 94619, USA | |
| **Russell, James T** | Inventor |
| 14589 51st St, Bellevue WA 98006, USA | |
| **Russell, Jay** | Director |
| A P A Talent/Literary Agency, 405 S Beverly Dr, #300, Beverly Hills CA 90212 USA | |
| **Russell, Jeffrey L (Jeff)** | Baseball Player |
| 2325 Oak Knoll Dr, Colleyville TX 76034, USA | |
| **Russell, Jena** | Actress, Singer |
| United Agents, 12-26 Lexington St, London W1F 0LE, England | |
| **Russell, John W** | Baseball Player, Manager |
| 1709 NE Woodland Shores Court, Lees Summit MO 64086, USA | |
| **Russell, Keri** | Actress, Model |
| Burstein Co, 15304 W Sunset Blvd, #208, Pacific Palisades CA 90272 USA | |
| **Russell, Kimberly** | Actress |
| 14622 Ventura Blvd, Sherman Oaks CA 91403, USA | |
| **Russell, Kurt** | Actor |
| 1417 Capri Dr, Pacific Palisades CA 90272, USA | |
| **Russell, Leon** | Singer, Pianist, Songwriter |
| PO Box 24455, New Orleans LA 70184, USA | |
| **Russell, Liane B** | Geneticist |
| 130 Tabor Road, Oak Ridge TN 37830, USA | |
| **Russell, Lucy** | Actress, Model |
| Hamilton Hodell, 66-68 Margaret St, #500, London W1W 8SR, England | |
| **Russell, M Campanella (Campy)** | Basketball Player |
| 66 Earlmoor Blvd, Pontiac MI 48341, USA | |
| **Russell, Margaret A** | Editor |
| Architectural Digest, Editorial Dept, 5900 Wilshire Blvd, Los Angeles CA 90036, USA | |
| **Russell, Mark** | Actor, Comedian |
| PO Box 9904, Washington DC 20016, USA | |
| **Russell, Phil** | Ice Hockey Player |
| 590 Wind Drift Lane, Spring Lake MI 49456, USA | |
| **Russell, Sharman Apt** | Writer |
| Western New Mexico State University, English Dept, Silver City NM 88062, USA | |
| **Russell, Theresa** | Actress |
| Scott Zimmerman Mgmt, 1644 Courtney Ave, Los Angeles CA 90046, USA | |
| **Russell, Tom** | Singer, Songwriter |
| Val Denn Agency, 100 Congress Ave, #2000, Austin TX 78701, USA | |
| **Russell, Twan S** | Football Player |
| 212 Lakeside Circle, Sunrise FL 33326, USA | |
| **Russell, William E (Bill)** | Baseball Player, Manager |
| 27982 Red Pine Court, Valencia CA 91354, USA | |

| | |
|---|---|
| **Russell, William F (Bill)** | Basketball Player, Coach |
| 9415 SE 52nd St, Mercer Island WA 98040, USA | |
| **Russell, Willy** | Writer |
| Casorotto Ramsay, Waverley House, 7-12 Noel St, London W1F 8GQ, England | |
| **Russi, Bernhard** | Alpine Skier |
| Postfach 107, 5620 Bremgarten, Switzerland | |
| **Russo Adamo, Pat** | Model |
| Playboy Promotions, 2706 Media Center Dr, Los Angeles CA 90065 USA | |
| **Russo, Daniel** | Actor |
| Agents Associes, 201 Rue du Faubourg Saint Honore, 75008 Paris, France | |
| **Russo, David** | Director, Writer, Actor |
| Rugolo Entertainment, 195 S Beverly Drive, #400, Beverly Hills CA 90212, USA | |
| **Russo, Dominic** | Producer, Writer |
| I C M Partners, 10250 Constellation Blvd, #900, Los Angeles CA 90067 USA | |
| **Russo, Gianni** | Actor |
| Sanders Agency, 9014 Melrose Ave, West Hollywood CA 90069, USA | |
| **Russo, James** | Actor, Writer |
| 8306 Wilshire Blvd, #438, Beverly Hills CA 90211, USA | |
| **Russo, John** | Writer |
| 216 Euclid Ave, Glassport PA 15045, USA | |
| **Russo, Martin A** | Representative, IL |
| Cassidy & Assoc, 700 13th Ave NW, #400, Washington DC 20005, USA | |
| **Russo, Rene** | Actress, Model |
| John Crosby Mgmt, 1310 N Spaulding Ave, Los Angeles CA 90046 USA | |
| **Russo, Richard** | Writer |
| Knopf Publishers, 1745 Broadway, New York NY 10019 USA | |
| **Rut, Tomasz** | Artist |
| 1909 Tigertail Blvd, Dania Beach FL 33004, USA | |
| **Rutan, Elbert L (Burt)** | Airplane Designer |
| 14329 Rutan Road, Mojave CA 93501, USA | |
| **Rutan, Richard G (Dick)** | Experimental Airplane Pilot, Designer |
| 2833 Delmar Ave, Mojave CA 93501, USA | |
| **Rutgens, Joseph C (Joe)** | Football Player |
| 227 W Devlin St, Spring Valley IL 61362, USA | |
| **Ruth, Daniel** | Journalist |
| Tampa Bay Times, Editorial Dept, 490 1st Ave S, Saint Petersburg FL 33701, USA | |
| **Ruth, Lauren** | Cartoonist |
| PO Box 200206, New Haven CT 06520, USA | |
| **Ruth, Michael J (Mike)** | Football Player |
| 8222 Kirkbride Dr, Danvers MA 01923, USA | |
| **Rutherford, Emily** | Actress |
| Paradigm Agency, 360 N Crescent Dr, North Building, Beverly Hills CA 90210 USA | |
| **Rutherford, James E (Jim)** | Ice Hockey Player |
| 2542 Village Manor Way, Raleigh NC 27614, USA | |
| **Rutherford, John S (Johnny), III** | Auto Racing Driver |
| 4919 Black Oak Lane, River Oaks TX 76114, USA | |
| **Rutherford, Kelly** | Actress |
| Luber Rocklin Entertainment, 8530 Wilshire Blvd, #555, Beverly Hills CA 90211 USA | |
| **Rutherford, Mike** | Guitarist (Genesis) |
| Solo Agency, 53-55 Fulham High St, #200, London SW6 3JJ, England | |
| **Rutherfurd, Emily** | Actress |
| Paradigm Agency, 360 N Crescent Dr, North Building, Beverly Hills CA 90210 USA | |
| **Ruthven, Richard D (Dick)** | Baseball Player |
| 13480 Providence Lake Dr, Alpharetta GA 30004, USA | |
| **Rutigliano, Sam** | Football Coach |
| 9671 Metcalf Road, Willoughby OH 44094, USA | |
| **Rutkowski, Edward J A (Ed)** | Football Player |
| 47 Brenton Lane, Hamburg NY 14075, USA | |
| **Rutland, Robert A** | Historian |
| Tulsa University, History Dept, Tulsa OK 74101, USA | |
| **Rutledge, Jeffrey R (Jeff)** | Football Player, Coach |
| 6102 W Gary Dr, Chandler AZ 85226, USA | |
| **Rutledge, Johnny B, Jr** | Football Player |
| 756 SW 10th St, Belle Glade FL 33430, USA | |
| **Rutledge, Justin** | Singer, Songwriter |
| Six Shooter Mgmt, PO Box 98038, 970 Queen St E, Toronto ON M5V 1V2, Canada | |
| **Rutledge, Roderick A (Rod)** | Football Player |
| 1254 4th Way, Pleasant Grove AL 35127, USA | |
| **Rutsala, Vern A** | Writer |
| 2494 NE 24th St, Portland OR 97212, USA | |
| **Rutschman, Adolph (Ad)** | Football Coach |
| 2142 NW Pinehurst Dr, McMinnville OR 97128, USA | |
| **Rutschow-Stomporowski, Katrin** | Rowing Athlete |
| Rosenthaler Str 34-35, 10178 Berlin, Germany | |
| **Ruttan, Susan** | Actress |
| Talent Works, 3500 W Olive Ave, #1400, Burbank CA 91505 USA | |
| **Rutter, John M** | Composer, Conductor |
| Old Lacey's, Saint John's St, Duxford, Cambridge CB2 4RA, England | |
| **Ruud, Barrett J** | Football Player |
| 1821 S 33rd St, Lincoln NE 68506, USA | |
| **Ruud, Thomas R (Tom)** | Football Player |
| 1821 S 33rd St, Lincoln NE 68506, USA | |
| **Ruuska Percy, Sylvia** | Swimmer |
| 4216 College View Way, Carmichael CA 95608, USA | |
| **Ruusuvuori, Aarno E** | Architect |
| Annankatu 15 B 10, 00120 Helsinki 12, Finland | |
| **Ruuttu, Christian** | Ice Hockey Player |
| Phoenix Coyotes, 6751 N Sunset Blvd, #200, Glendale AZ 85305 USA | |
| **Ruutu, Jarko** | Ice Hockey Player |
| Ottawa Senators, Scotia Bank Place, Kanata ON K2V 1A5, Canada | |
| **Ruutu, Tuomo I** | Ice Hockey Player |
| Carolina Hurricanes, R B C Center, 1400 Edwards Mills Road, Raleigh NC 27607 USA | |
| **Rux, Carl Hancock** | Rap Artist |
| Music & Art Mgmt, 9 W Walnut St, #2D, Asheville NC 28801, USA | |
| **Ruzek, Roger B** | Football Player |
| 6404 Penina Trail, Denton TX 76210, USA | |

# R

## Russell - Ruzek

# R

**Ruzowitsky, Stefan** — Director
United Agents, 12-26 Lexington St, London W1F 0LE, England

**Ryal, Mark D** — Baseball Player
PO Box 266, Prague OK 74864, USA

**Ryan, Amy** — Actress
Gersh Agency, 9465 Wilshire Blvd, #600, Beverly Hills CA 90212 USA

**Ryan, Bob** — Sportswriter
Boston Globe, Editorial Dept, 135 William Morrissey Blvd, Dorchester MA 02125 USA

**Ryan, Cathy Cahlin** — Actress
Sovereign Talent Group, 8421 Wilshire Blvd, #200, Beverly Hills CA 90211 USA

**Ryan, Debbie** — Basketball Coach
University of Virginia, Athletic Dept, PO Box 400827, Charlottesville VA 22904, USA

**Ryan, Ed** — Harness Racing Executive
PO Box 6249, Freehold NJ 07728, USA

**Ryan, Frank B** — Football Player
PO Box 185, Grafton VT 05146, USA

**Ryan, Heather** — Model
Playboy Promotions, 2706 Media Center Dr, Los Angeles CA 90065 USA

**Ryan, James D (Buddy)** — Football Coach
819 Abingdon Lane, Shelbyville KY 40065, USA

**Ryan, James J (Jim)** — Football Player
1726 C St NE, Washington DC 20002, USA

**Ryan, James L** — Judge
US Court of Appeals, US Courthouse, 231 W Lafayette Blvd, Detroit MI 48226, USA

**Ryan, Jay** — Actor
United Talent Agency, U T A Plaza, 9336 Civic Center Dr, Beverly Hills CA 90210 USA

**Ryan, Jeri L** — Actress
I C M Partners, 10250 Constellation Blvd, #900, Los Angeles CA 90067 USA

**Ryan, Kay** — Writer
College of Marin, English Dept, 835 College Ave, Kentfield CA 94904, USA

**Ryan, Kenneth E (Ken)** — Baseball Player
45 Tanager Road, Seekonk MA 02771, USA

**Ryan, Kevin** — Actor
I C M Partners, 10250 Constellation Blvd, #900, Los Angeles CA 90067 USA

**Ryan, Kwame** — Conductor
Orchestre National Bordeaux Aquataine, Place de Comédie, BP 90095, 33025 Bordeaux Cedex, France

**Ryan, L Nolan, Jr** — Baseball Player
237 Escalara Parkway, Georgetown TX 78628, USA

**Ryan, Lee** — Singer, Songwriter, Actor
Independent Talent Group, 40 Whitfield St, London W1T 2RH, England

**Ryan, Lisa Dean** — Actress
1327 Brinkley Ave, Los Angeles CA 90049, USA

**Ryan, Matt** — Actor
W M E Entertainment, 9601 Wilshire Blvd, #300, Beverly Hills CA 90210 USA

**Ryan, Matthew T (Matt)** — Football Player
3268 Bransley Way, Duluth GA 30097, USA

**Ryan, Max** — Actor, Producer
Kritzer Levine Wilkins Griffin, 11872 La Grange Ave, #100, Los Angeles CA 90025 USA

**Ryan, Meg** — Actress
I C M Partners, 10250 Constellation Blvd, #900, Los Angeles CA 90067 USA

**Ryan, Michael E (Mike)** — Air Force General
United Services Automobile Assn, 9800 Fredericksburg Road, San Antonio TX 78288, USA

**Ryan, Michael J (Mike)** — Baseball Player
592 Stoneham Road, Wolfeboro NH 03894, USA

**Ryan, Michael S** — Baseball Player
521 Water St, Indiana PA 15701, USA

**Ryan, Michelle** — Actress
Independent Talent Group, 40 Whitfield St, London W1T 2RH, England

**Ryan, Mitchell** — Actor
C E S D, 10635 Santa Monica Blvd, #130, Los Angeles CA 90025 USA

**Ryan, Norbert R, Jr** — Navy Admiral
Military Officers Assn, 201 N Washington St, Alexandria VA 22314, USA

**Ryan, Patrick L (Pat)** — Football Player
6930 Old Kent Dr, Knoxville TN 37919, USA

**Ryan, Rebecca** — Model, Actress
United Agents, 12-26 Lexington St, London W1F 0LE, England

**Ryan, Rex** — Football Coach
New York Jets, 1 Jets Dr, Florham Park NJ 07932 USA

**Ryan, Robert V (B J), Jr** — Baseball Player
1211 Perdenalas Trail, Westlake TX 76262, USA

**Ryan, Roz** — Actress
Gage Group, 450 7th Ave, #1809, New York NY 10123 USA

**Ryan, Shawn** — Producer, Writer
MiddKid Productions, 10201 W Pico Blvd, Los Angeles CA 90035, USA

**Ryan, Thomas M** — Businessman
C V S/Caremark Corp, 1 C V S/Caremark Dr, Woonsocket RI 02895, USA

**Ryan, Tim** — Actor
S M S Talent, 8383 Wilshire Blvd, #230, Beverly Hills CA 90211 USA

**Ryan, Tom K** — Cartoonist (Tumbleweeds)
North American Syndicate, 235 E 45th St, New York NY 10017 USA

**Ryans, DeMeco** — Football Player
Philadelphia Eagles, 1 Novacare Way, Philadelphia PA 19145 USA

**Ryazanov, Eldar A** — Director
Bolshoi Tishinski Per 12, #70, 123557 Moscow, Russia

**Rybczynski, Witold** — Writer
Charles Scribner's Sons, 866 3rd Ave, New York NY 10022 USA

**Rybkin, Ivan P** — Government Official, Russia
Administration of President, Staraya Pl 4, 103132 Moscow, Russia

**Rychel, Warren** — Ice Hockey Player
Windsor Spitfires, 334 Wyandotte St E, Windsor ON N9A 3H6, Canada

**Rychlec, Thomas R (Tom)** — Football Player
71 Round Hill Road, Southington CT 06489, USA

**Rycroft Strickland, Melissa K** — Actress
W M E Entertainment, 9601 Wilshire Blvd, #300, Beverly Hills CA 90210 USA

**Rycroft, Carter** — Curling Athlete
Curling Assn, 1660 Vimont Court, Cumberland ON K4A 4J4, Canada

**Ryczek, Daniel S (Dan)** — Football Player
3714 Monitor Place, Olney MD 20832, USA
**Ryczek, Paul A** — Football Player
9335 Scott Road, Roswell GA 30076, USA
**Rydal, Emma** — Actress
Rights House, Drury House, 34-43 Russell St, London WC2B 5HA, England
**Rydalch, Ronald J (Ron)** — Football Player
500 E Durfee St, Grantsville UT 84029, USA
**Rydell, Bobby** — Singer, Actor
917 Bryn Mawr Ave, Penn Valley PA 19072, USA
**Rydell, Christopher** — Actor
911 N Sweetzer, #C, West Hollywood CA 90069, USA
**Rydell, Mark** — Director
Concourse Productions, 435 N Oakhurst Dr, #602, Beverly Hills CA 90210, USA
**Ryder, Lisa** — Actress
Red Mgmt, 415 W Esplanade, Box 3, North Vancouver BC V7M 1A6, Canada
**Ryder, Mitch** — Singer, Guitarist, Band Leader
Utopia Artists, 108 E Matilja St, #1821, Ojai CA 93023, USA
**Ryder, Norman B** — Sociologist
Princeton University, Sociology Dept, Princeton NJ 08544, USA
**Ryder, Thomas O** — Publisher
Reader's Digest Assn, Publisher's Office, PO Box 100, Pleasantville NY 10570, USA
**Ryder, Winona** — Actress
Gersh Agency, 9465 Wilshire Blvd, #600, Beverly Hills CA 90212 USA
**Ryding, Yvonne A** — Beauty Queen
Anderzson Care, PO Box 160, SE 271 24 Ystad, Sweden
**Rydze, Richard** — Diver
383 Kane Blvd, Pittsburgh PA 15243, USA
**Ryerson, Ann** — Actress
Abrams Artists, 9200 W Sunset Blvd, #1125, West Hollywood CA 90069 USA
**Rykiel, Sonia F** — Fashion Designer
175 Blvd Saint Germain, 75006 Paris, France
**Rylance, Georgina** — Actress
Markham Froggatt Irwin, Julian House, 4 Windmill St, London W1P 1HF, England
**Rylance, Mark** — Director, Actor
Hamilton Hodell, 66-68 Margaret St, #500, London W1W 8SR, England
**Rylko, Stanislaw Cardinal** — Religious Leader
Pontifical Council for Laity, Piazza S Calisto 16, 00153 Rome, Italy
**Ryman, Robert T** — Artist
17 W 16th St, New York NY 10011, USA
**Rymer, Charlie** — Golfer, Sportscaster
11721 Camden Park Dr, Windermere FL 34786, USA
**Rynkiewicz, Mariusz** — Sculptor
12401 Alexander Road, Everett WA 98204, USA
**Rypdal, Terje** — Guitarist, Flutist, Composer
Kjell Kalleklev Mgmt, Georgemes Verft 12, 5011 Bergen, Norway
**Rypien, Mark R** — Football Player
8817 N Warren St, Spokane WA 99208, USA
**Ryu So-Yeon** — Golfer
Ladies Pro Golf Assn, 100 International Golf Dr, Daytona Beach FL 32124 USA
**Ryumin, Valery V** — Cosmonaut
Cosmonaut Training Center, Star City, 141160 Zvezdny Gorodok, Moscow Oblast, Russia
**Ryun, James R (Jim)** — Track Athlete; Representative, KS
132 D St SE, Washington DC 20003, USA
**Ryzhkov, Nikolai I** — Premier, Russia
Federation Council, Bolshaya Dmitrovka Str 26, 103009 Moscow, Russia
**RZA** — Rap Artist (Wu-Tang Clan), Actor
Creative Artists Agency, 2000 Ave of Stars, #100, Los Angeles CA 90067 USA

**Saadiq, Raphael** — Singer, Songwriter
Universal Attractions, 135 W 26th St, #1200, New York NY 10001 USA

**Saar, Bettye** — Artist
8074 Willow Glen Road, Los Angeles CA 90046, USA

**Saar, Eric** — Writer
Penguin Books, 375 Hudson St, Basement 1, New York NY 10014 USA

**Saarinen, Aino-Kalsa** — Cross Country Skier
Suomen Hiihtoliitto, Radiokatu 20, 00093 Slu, Finland

**Saarinen, Tero** — Dancer, Choreographer
Tero Saarinen Co, Bulevardi 23-27, 00180 Helsinki, Finland

**Saarloos, Kirk C** — Baseball Player
2518 Stadium Dr, Fort Worth TX 76109, USA

**Saatchi, Charles** — Businessman
36 Golden Square, London W1R 4EE, England

**Saatchi, Maurice** — Businessman
36 Golden Square, London W1R 4EE, England

**Sabah IV, Sheikh Ahmad Jabar al-Sabah** — Emir, Kuwait
Darwa Salwa Palace, Amiry Diwan, Kuwait City, Kuwait

**Sabah, Sheikh Nasser Al Mohammed al-** — Prime Minister, Kuwait
Prime Minister's Office, PO Box 4, Safat 13001, Kuwait City, Kuwait

**Saban, Louis H (Lou)** — Football Player, Coach
2087 Appalachee Circle, Tavares FL 32778, USA

**Saban, Nick** — Football Coach
University of Alabama, Athletic Dept, Tuscaloosa AL 35487, USA

**Sabara, Daryl** — Actor
A P A Talent/Literary Agency, 405 S Beverly Dr, #300, Beverly Hills CA 90212 USA

**Sabates, Felix** — Auto Racing Executive
Ganassi Racing, 600 E Laburnum Ave, Richmond VA 23222, USA

**Sabathia, Carsten C (C C)** — Baseball Player
PO Box 30, Alpine NJ 07620, USA

**Sabatini, David D** — Cell Biologist, Biochemist
New York University, Cell Biology/Biochemistry Dept, New York NY 10012, USA

**Sabatini, Gabriela** — Tennis Player
35/35 Grosvenor St, London W1K 4QX, England

**Sabatino, Michael** — Actor
13538 Valleyheart Dr, Sherman Oaks CA 91423, USA

**Sabato, Antonio, Jr** — Actor, Model
Global Artists Agency, 6253 Hollywood Blvd, #508, Los Angeles CA 90028 USA

**Sabbah, Sam** — Actor
Premier Talent Group, 4370 Tujunga Ave, #110, Studio City CA 91604, USA

**Sabbatini, Rory** — Golfer
2939 Crockett St, #348, Fort Worth TX 76107, USA

**Sabelle** — Singer, Songwriter
Sarmast Entertainment, 241 W 36th St, #2R, New York NY 10018, USA

**Saberhagen, Bret W** — Baseball Player
Make a Difference Foundation, 6520 Platt Ave, #566, West Hills CA 91307, USA

**Sabo, Christopher A (Chris)** — Baseball Player
7455 Stonemeadow Lane, Cincinnati OH 45242, USA

**Sabol, Edward E (Ed)** — Producer, Filmmaker
N F L Films, 330 Fellowship Road, Mount Laurel NJ 08054, USA

**Sabourin, Gary B** — Ice Hockey Player
54 Holland Ave, Chatham ON N7M 2C7, Canada

**Saca Gonzalez, E Antonio (Tony)** — President, El Salvador
Casa Presidencial, Calle Dario Gonzales 806, San Salvador, El Salvador

**Sacca, Anthony J (Tony)** — Football Player
11 Heather Glen Lane, Riverside NJ 08075, USA

**Sacco, Joe** — Cartoonist
305 SE Ankeny St, Portland OR 97233, USA

**Sacco, Joe W** — Ice Hockey Player, Coach
1001 Southbury Place, Littleton CO 80129, USA

**Saccone, Viviana** — Actress
Telefe, Pavon 2444, (C1248AAT) Buenos Aires, Argentina

**Sachar, Louis** — Writer
Delacorte Press, 1540 Broadway, New York NY 10036 USA

**Sacharuk, Lawrence W (Larry)** — Ice Hockey Player
HG Tiroler Wasserkraft, Olumpiastr 10, 6020 Innsbruck, Austria

**Sachdev, Asha** — Actress
18B Sunset Heights, 59 Pali Hill Bandra, Mumbai MS 400050, India

**Sachenbacher-Stehle, Evi** — Cross Country Skier
Birnbacher Str 1, 83242 Reit im Winkl, Germany

**Sachs, Ira** — Director, Writer
Marie Therese Guirgis Mgmt, 125 Riverside Dr, #8C, New York NY 10024, USA

**Sachs, Jeffrey D** — Economist
Harvard University, International Development Institute, Cambridge MA 02138, USA

**Sack, Kevin** — Journalist
Los Angeles Times, Editorial Dept, 202 W 1st St, Los Angeles CA 90012 USA

**Sack, Robert D** — Judge
US Court of Appeals, Moynihan Courthouse, 500 Pearl St, New York NY 10007, USA

**Sack, Steve** — Editorial Cartoonist
Minneapolis Star-Tribune, 425 Portland Ave, Minneapolis MN 55488, USA

**Sackheim, Daniel** — Director
Creative Artists Agency, 2000 Ave of Stars, #100, Los Angeles CA 90067 USA

**Sackhoff, Katee** — Actress
Bleu Entertainment, 5225 Wilshire Blvd, #336, Los Angeles CA 90036, USA

**Sacko, Soumana** — Prime Minister, Mali
Villa 14 Bis 48, Sema Gexco, Bamako, Mali

**Sacks, Greg** — Auto Racing Driver
6092 Sabal Creek Blvd, Port Orange FL 32128, USA

**Sacks, Jonathan H** — Religious Leader
735 High Road, London N12 0US, England

**Sacks, Oliver W** — Writer, Physician, Neurologist
2 Horatio St, #3G, New York NY 10014, USA

**Sacramone, Alicia M** — Gymnast
Frederick Sacramone, 41 Hastings Road, Winchester MA 01890, USA

**Sadat, Jehan El-** — Social Activist
University of Maryland, International Development Center, College Park MD 20742, USA

**Sade** — Singer, Songwriter
Marshall Arts, Utopia Village, 7 Chalcot Road, London NW1 8LH, England

**Sadecki, Raymond M (Ray)** — Baseball Player
4237 E Clovis Ave, Mesa AZ 85206, USA

**Sadek, Michael G (Mike)** — Baseball Player
6741 Quartz Mine Road, Mountain Ranch CA 95246, USA

**Sadier, Laetitia** — Singer, Musician (Stereolab)
Duophonic Records, PO Box 3787, London SE22 9DZ, England

**Sadik, Nafis** — Government Official, Pakistan
300 E 56th St, #9J, New York NY 10022, USA

**Sadiq Al-Mahedi** — Prime Minister, Sudan
Club de Madrid, C/Goya 5-7, Pasaje 2, 28001 Madrid, Spain

**Sadler, Donnie L** — Baseball Player
802 Sadler Road, Valley Mills TX 76689, USA

**Sadler, Elliott W B** — Auto, Truck Racing Driver
108 Conway Court, Mooresville NC 28117, USA

**Sadler, Herman M (Hermie), III** — Auto Racing Driver
PO Box 32, Emporia VA 23847, USA

**Sadoski, Thomas** — Actor
United Talent Agency, U T A Plaza, 9336 Civic Center Dr, Beverly Hills CA 90210 USA

**Sadoyan, Isabelle** — Actress
Artmedia, 20 Ave Rapp, 75007 Paris, France

**Saenz, Olmedo** — Baseball Player
4300 W Ford City Dr, #1002, Chicago IL 60652, USA

**Saez Conde, Inez L** — Beauty Queen
Miss Universe Organization, 1370 Ave of Americas, #1600, New York NY 10019 USA

**Safdie, Moshe** — Architect
100 Rev Nazareno Properzi Way, Somerville MA 02143, USA

**Safer, Morley** — Commentator
CBS-TV, News Dept, 524 W 57th St, New York NY 10019, USA

**Saffiotti, Umberto** — Pathologist
5114 Wissioming Road, Bethesda MD 20816, USA

**Saffo, Paul** — Non-Profit Executive, Journalist
Institute for the Future, 27740 Sand Hill Road, Menlo Park CA 94025, USA

**Safin, Marat M** — Tennis Player
T C Weiden am Postkeller, Schirmitzer Weg, 92637 Weiden, Germany

**Safina, Carl** — Marine Biologist
Blue Spring Institute, 250 Lawrence Hill Road, Cold Spring Harbor NY 11724, USA

**Safina, Dinara M** — Tennis Player
Women's Tennis Assn, 1 Progress Plaza, #1500, Saint Petersburg FL 33701 USA

**Safiq, Ahmed M** — Prime Minister, Egypt
Prime Minister's Office, PO Box 191, 1 Majlis El-Shaab St, Cairo CA104, Egypt

**Safire** — Rap Artist
Brothers Management Assoc, 141 Dunbar Ave, Fords NJ 08863 USA

**Safran, Joshua** — Director, Writer
United Talent Agency, U T A Plaza, 9336 Civic Center Dr, Beverly Hills CA 90210 USA

**Safuto, Dominick (Randy)** — Singer (Randy & the Rainbows)
Brothers Management Assoc, 141 Dunbar Ave, Fords NJ 08863 USA

**Safuto, Frank** — Singer (Randy & the Rainbows)
Brothers Management Assoc, 141 Dunbar Ave, Fords NJ 08863 USA

**Sagal, Katey** — Actress
B & B Mgmt, 1041 N Formosa Ave, West Hollywood CA 90046, USA

**Saganiuk, Rocky** — Ice Hockey Player
13252 Lake Mary Dr, Plainfield IL 60585, USA

**Sagdeev, Roald Z** — Physicist
University of Maryland, East-West Space Center, College Park MD 20742, USA

**Sage, Bill** — Actor
Don Buchwald, 6500 Wilshire Blvd, #2200, Los Angeles CA 90048 USA

**Sage, Halston** — Actress
Creative Artists Agency, 2000 Ave of Stars, #100, Los Angeles CA 90067 USA

**Sage, William (Bill)** — Actor
Don Buchwald, 6500 Wilshire Blvd, #2200, Los Angeles CA 90048 USA

**Sagebrecht, Marianne** — Actress
Postfach 1454, 80539 Munich, Germany

**Sagemiller, Melissa** — Actress
Paradigm Agency, 360 N Crescent Dr, North Building, Beverly Hills CA 90210 USA

**Sager, Anthony J (A J)** — Baseball Player
10310 Belmont Meadows Lane, Perrysburg OH 43551, USA

**Sager, Carole Bayer** — Singer, Songwriter
10779 Bellagio Road, Los Angeles CA 90077, USA

**Sager, Craig** — Sportscaster
Jock Jill & Frankie's Sports Grill, 5600 Roswell Road NE, #M3, Atlanta GA 30342, USA

**Saget, Robert L (Bob)** — Actor, Comedian
Brillstein Entertainment Partners, 9150 Wilshire Blvd, #350, Beverly Hills CA 90212 USA

**Sagnier, Ludivine** — Actress
Agence Elisabeth Simpson, 62 Blvd du Montparnasse, 75015 Paris, France

**Sagripanti, Giacomo** — Conductor
I M G Artists, Hogarth Business Park, Chiswick, London W4 2TH, England

**Sahagun, Elena** — Actress
Artists Agency, 9430 Olympic Blvd, Beverly Hills CA 90212 USA

**Sahakyan, Bako** — President, Nagorno-Karabakh
President's Office, Nagorno-Karabakh, Stepanakert, Nahorni, Azerbaijan

**Sahanaja, Darian** — Keyboardist (Wondermints)
Paradise Artists, PO Box 1821, Ojai CA 93024 USA

**Sahay, Vikram (Vik)** — Actor
Don Buchwald, 6500 Wilshire Blvd, #2200, Los Angeles CA 90048 USA

**Sahl, Mort** — Actor, Comedian
1441 3rd Ave, #12C, New York NY 10028, USA

**Said, Ali Ahmad (Adonis)** — Writer
Green Inter Books, 6022 Wilshire Blvd, #200A, Los Angeles CA 90036, USA

**Said, Boris** — Auto, Truck Racing Driver
15 Avalon Road, Martin GA 30557, USA

**Sailors, Kenneth L (Ken)** — Basketball Player
2119 E Grand Ave, #6, Laramie WY 82070, USA

**Saini, Rajiv** — Architect, Interior Designer
Rajiv Saini Assoc, 9 Jer Mansion, Bandra (W), Mumbai 400050, India

| | |
|---|---|
| **Sainsbury of Preston Candover, John D** | Businessman |
| J Sainsbury PLC, 33 Holborn, London EC1N 2HT, England | |
| **Sainsbury of Turville, David J** | Businessman |
| Eagle House, 110 Jermyn St, London SW1Y 6EE, England | |
| **Sainsbury, R Mark** | Philosopher |
| King's College, Philosophy Dept, London WC2R 2LS, England | |
| **Saint Claire, Randy A** | Baseball Player |
| 7117 State Route 8, Brant Lake NY 12815, USA | |
| **Saint James, Susan** | Actress |
| 174 West St, #54, Litchfield CT 06759, USA | |
| **Saint, Crosbie E** | Army General |
| 1116 N Pitt St, Alexandria VA 22314, USA | |
| **Saint, Eva Marie** | Actress |
| I C M Partners, 10250 Constellation Blvd, #900, Los Angeles CA 90067 USA | |
| **Sainte-Marie, Buffy** | Singer, Guitarist, Songwriter |
| RR 1 Box 368, Kapaa HI 96746, USA | |
| **Saint-Subber, Arnold** | Producer |
| 116 E 64th St, New York NY 10065, USA | |
| **Sainz Gall de Perez, Ines** | Journalist |
| TV Azteca, Periferico 4121, Colonia Fuentes Pedregal, DF CP 14141, Mexico | |
| **Sainz, Salvador** | Actor, Director |
| Ave Prat de la Riba 43, 43201 Reus (Tarragona), Spain | |
| **Saipe, Mike E** | Baseball Player |
| 4191 Combe Way, San Diego CA 92122, USA | |
| **Sajak, Pat** | Entertainer |
| Wheel of Fortune Show, 3400 Riverside Dr, #201, Burbank CA 91505, USA | |
| **Sajko, Kristina** | Model |
| D N A Model Mgmt, 555 W 25th St, #600, New York NY 10001 USA | |
| **Sakaguchi, Mizuho** | Soccer Player |
| Football Assn, 3-10-15 Hongo, Bunkyoku, Tokyo 113 0033 Japan | |
| **Sakamoto, Ryoichi** | Composer, Musician |
| K A B America, 302A W 12th St, #181, New York NY 10014, USA | |
| **Sakamura, Ken** | Computer Scientist, Inventor |
| University of Tokyo, Information Science Dept, 7-3-1 Hongo, Bunkyoku, Tokyo 113 0033, Japan | |
| **Sakata, Lenn H** | Baseball Player |
| 2490 2nd Ave, Merced CA 95340, USA | |
| **Sakato, George T** | WW II Army Hero (CMH) |
| 8369 Katherine Way, Denver CO 80221, USA | |
| **Sakharov, Alik** | Cinematographer |
| Global Artists Agency, 6253 Hollywood Blvd, #508, Los Angeles CA 90028 USA | |
| **Sakic, Joseph S (Joe)** | Ice Hockey Player |
| 4785 S Franklin St, Englewood CO 80113, USA | |
| **Sakmann, Bert** | Nobel Medicine Laureate |
| Max Planck Institute, Jahnstr 39, 69120 Heidelberg, Germany | |
| **Saks, Gene** | Director, Actor |
| I C M Partners, 730 5th Ave, New York NY 10019 USA | |
| **Sakshaug, Eugene C** | Electrical Engineer |
| 18 Grove Ave, Pittsfield MA 01201, USA | |
| **Sala, Edoardo** | Actor |
| Agenzia Paola Bonelli, Via Parioli 50, 00197 Rome, Italy | |
| **Sala, Richard** | Cartoonist (Peculia) |
| 3131 College Ave, Berkeley CA 94705, USA | |
| **Sala, Sharon** | Writer |
| Mira/Harlequin, 225 Duncan Mill Road, Don Mills ON MJB JK9, CA | |
| **Salaam, Rashaan I** | Football Player |
| 8132 Brookhaven Road, San Diego CA 92114, USA | |
| **Saladino, John F** | Interior Designer |
| Saladino Group, 200 Lexington Ave, #1600, New York NY 10016, USA | |
| **Salans, Lester B** | Physician |
| Sandoz Research Institute, RR 10, East Hanover NJ 07936, USA | |
| **Salas, Mark B** | Baseball Player |
| 1302 6th St SE, Ruskin FL 33570, USA | |
| **Salazar, Alberto** | Track Athlete |
| Nike Inc, 1 SW Bowerman Dr, Beaverton OR 97005, USA | |
| **Salazar, Angel** | Actor, Comedian |
| Roger Paul, 1650 Broadway, #304, New York NY 10019, USA | |
| **Salazar, Kenneth L (Ken)** | Secretary, Interior; Senator, CO |
| Interior Department, 1849 C St NW, Washington DC 20240 USA | |
| **Salazar, Luis E** | Baseball Player |
| 20808 Cabrillo Way, Boca Raton FL 33428, USA | |
| **Salcido Flores, Carlos A** | Soccer Player |
| Federacion de Futbol, Colima 373 Colonia Roma, Delegacion Cuauhtemoc, Mexico City DF 06700, Mexico | |
| **Saldana, Theresa** | Actress |
| I C M Partners, 10250 Constellation Blvd, #900, Los Angeles CA 90067 USA | |
| **Saldana, Zoe** | Actress |
| I C M Partners, 10250 Constellation Blvd, #900, Los Angeles CA 90067 USA | |
| **Saldanha, Carlos** | Animator, Director |
| W M E Entertainment, 9601 Wilshire Blvd, #300, Beverly Hills CA 90210 USA | |
| **Saldi, J Jay, IV** | Football Player |
| 303 Donley Court, Southlake TX 76092, USA | |
| **Saldivar, Lou** | Graphic Artist |
| Milwaukee Journal Sentinel, Editorial Dept, PO Box 371, Milwaukee WI 53201 USA | |
| **Sale, Jamie R** | Ice Dancer |
| 12116 NW 128th St, Edmonton AB T5L 1C3, Canada | |
| **Saleaumua, R Daniel (Dan)** | Football Player |
| 1603 Morning Breeze Lane, National City CA 91950, USA | |
| **Saleh, Karim** | Actor |
| Ken McReddie Assoc, 101 Finsbury Pavement, London EC2A 1RS, England | |
| **Salem, Dahlia** | Actress |
| Precision Entertainment, 6338 Wilshire Blvd, Los Angeles CA 90048, USA | |
| **Salem, Harvey M** | Football Player |
| 25 Menlo Place, Berkeley CA 94707, USA | |
| **Salem, Kario** | Writer, Actor |
| Creative Artists Agency, 2000 Ave of Stars, #100, Los Angeles CA 90067 USA | |
| **Salenger, Meredith** | Actress |
| Genesis Entertainment Partners, 4145 Garden Ave, Los Angeles CA 90039, USA | |

**Salerno-Sonnenberg, Nadja** — Concert Violinist
Opus 3 Artists, 470 Park Ave S, #900N, New York NY 10016 USA
**Sales, Nykesha** — Basketball Player
Connecticut Sun, 1 Mohegan Sun Blvd, Uncasville CT 06382 USA
**Saleski, Don** — Ice Hockey Player
1800 N Ridley Creek Road, Media PA 19063, USA
**Salfati, Pierre-Henri** — Actor, Director, Writer
Artmedia, 20 Ave Rapp, 75007 Paris, France
**Salgado, Curtis** — Singer, Harmonica Player
Pacific Talent, PO Box 19145, Portland OR 97280, USA
**Salgado, Michael** — Singer, Accordionist
Management Plus, PO Box 132, Seguin TX 78155, USA
**Salgado, Sebastiano R, Jr** — Photographer
Instituto Terra, Bulcao Farm Land Institute, PO Box 005, 35200 000 Aimores MG, Brazil
**Saliers, Emily** — Singer (Indigo Girls), Songwriter
Russell Carter Artist Mgmt, 567 Ralph Mcgill Blvd, Atlanta GA 30312, USA
**Salim, Salim Ahmed** — Prime Minister, Tanzania
Organization of African Unity, PO Box 3243, Addis Ababa, Ethiopia
**Salinas, Carmen** — Actress
T G A Voice, 100 Lincoln Road, #928, Miami Beach FL 33178, USA
**Salinger, Matt** — Actor
Bresler Kelly Assoc, 11500 W Olympic Blvd, #400, Los Angeles CA 90064 USA
**Salisbury, Laney** — Writer
Random House, 1745 Broadway, #1800, New York NY 10019 USA
**Salisbury, R Sean** — Football Player
5823 Brushy Creek Trail, Dallas TX 75252, USA
**Salkeld, Roger W** — Baseball Player
27834 Ridgegrove Dr, Santa Clarita CA 91350, USA
**Sall, Macky** — Prime Minister, Senegal
President's Office, Ave Roume, BP 168, Dakar, Senegal
**Sallah, Michael D** — Journalist
Toledo Blade, Editorial Dept, 541 N Superior St, Toledo OH 43660, USA
**Salle, David** — Artist
Deitch-Boone Gallery, 541 W 24th St, New York NY 10011, USA
**Salle, Jerome** — Director, Writer
U B B A, 6 Rue de Braque, 75003 Paris, France
**Salles, Walter, Jr** — Director
VideoFilmes, Rua Do Russel 270 - Gloria, Rio de Janeiro RJ 22210 110, Brazil
**Salley, John T** — Basketball Player, Sportscaster, Actor
4619 Caritina Dr, Tarzana CA 91356, USA
**Sallinen, Aulis H** — Composer
Teosto, Lauttasaarentie 1, 00200 Helsinki 20, Finland
**Salling, Mark** — Actor
Momentum Talent, 9401 Wilshire Blvd, #501, Beverly Hills CA 90212, USA
**Sallis, Peter** — Actor
Jonathan Altaras Assoc, 11 Garrick St, London WC2E 9AR, England
**Sally, Jerome E** — Football Player
4107 Roxbury Court, Columbia MO 65203, USA
**Salminen, Matti** — Opera Singer
Mariedi Anders Artists, 3030 Baker St, San Francisco CA 94123 USA
**Salming, Borje** — Ice Hockey Player
Box 45438, 104 31 Stockholm, Sweden
**Salmoiraghi, Franco** — Photographer
PO Box 61708, Honolulu HI 96839, USA
**Salmon, Timothy J (Tim)** — Baseball Player
6061 E Sunnside Dr, Scottsdale AZ 85254, USA
**Salmons, John R** — Basketball Player
909 Waverly Road, Bryn Mawr PA 19010, USA
**Salmons, Stephen (Steve)** — Volleyball Player
1717 N El Dorado Ave, Ontario CA 91764, USA
**Salo, Mika J** — Auto Racing Driver
Sauber Racing, Wildbachstr 9, 8340 Hinwil, Switzerland
**Salo, Ola** — Singer, Guitarist, Pianist (The Ark)
Live Nation, Linnegatan 89, Box 21451, 104 51 Stockholm, Sweden
**Salo, Sami** — Ice Hockey Player
Vancouver Canucks, 800 Griffiths Way, Vancouver BC V6B 6G1, Canada
**Salo, Teemu** — Curling Athlete
Curling Assn, Kalatorppa 2A62, 02230 Espoo, Finland
**Salo, Tommy M** — Ice Hockey Player
Lefksands I F, Box 118, 793 23 Leksand, Sweden
**Salome, Jean-Paul** — Director
Voyez Mon Agent, 20 Ave Rapp, 75007 Paris, France
**Salomon, Leon E (Lee)** — Army General
2795 Kipps Colony Dr S, Saint Petersburg FL 33707, USA
**Salomon, Mikael** — Director, Cinematographer
Creative Artists Agency, 2000 Ave of Stars, #100, Los Angeles CA 90067 USA
**Salonen, Esa-Pekka** — Conductor, Composer
Cathy Nelson, Court House, Dorstone, Herefordshire HR3 6AW, England
**Salonga, Lea** — Singer, Actress
David Belenzon Mgmt, PO Box 5000, PMB 67, Rancho Santa Fe CA 92067, USA
**Salopek, Paul** — Journalist
Chicago Tribune, Editorial Dept, 350 N Orleans St, Chicago IL 60654 USA
**Salt, Charlotte** — Actress
Seven Summits Mgmt, 8906 W Olympic Blvd, Beverly Hills CA 90211 USA
**Salt, Jennifer** — Actress
3742 Sheridge Dr, Sherman Oaks CA 91403, USA
**Saltalamacchia, Jarrod S** — Baseball Player
12688 Headwater Circle, Wellington FL 33414, USA
**Salter, Bryant J** — Football Player
16810 SW 88th Court, Village of Palmetto Bay FL 33157, USA
**Salter, James** — Writer
Knopf Publishers, 1745 Broadway, New York NY 10019 USA
**Salter, Russell D** — Immunologist
University of Pittsburgh Medical School, Immunology Dept, Pittsburgh PA 15260, USA
**Saltykov, Aleksey A** — Director
Institute Mosfilmovsky Per 4A, #104, 119285 Moscow, Russia

**Saltykov, Boris G** — Economist; Government Official, Russia
Russian Technologies, Bryusov Per 11, 103009 Moscow, Russia
**Salva, Victor** — Director
Resolution, 1801 Century Park East, #2300, Los Angeles CA 90067 USA
**Salvador, Bryce** — Ice Hockey Player
422 Lenox Ave, Westfield NJ 07090, USA
**Salvadori, Al** — Basketball Player
1204 Lenox Dr, Bethel Park PA 15102, USA
**Salvatore, Diane J** — Editor
Ladies' Home Journal, Editor's Office, 125 Park Ave, New York NY 10017, USA
**Salvatore, Robert A (R A)** — Writer
Tom Doherty Assoc, 175 5th Ave, New York NY 10010, USA
**Salvay, Bennett** — Composer
Gorfaine/Schwartz, 4111 W Alameda Ave, #509, Burbank CA 91505 USA
**Salvino, Carmen** — Bowler
65 Stevens Dr, Schaumburg IL 60173, USA
**Salwen, Hal** — Director
Gersh Agency, 9465 Wilshire Blvd, #600, Beverly Hills CA 90212 USA
**Salzman, Mark** — Writer
Random House, 1745 Broadway, #1800, New York NY 10019 USA
**Sam the Sham** — Singer
6123 Old Brunswick Road, Arlington TN 38002, USA
**Samaras, Antonis** — Prime Minister, Greece
Prime Minister's Office, Maximos Mansion, 19 Irodou Attikou St, 10674 Athens, Greece
**Samaras, Lucas** — Sculptor, Photographer
Pace Wildenstein Gallery, 32 E 57th St, #400, New York NY 10022, USA
**Samardzija, Jeff** — Baseball Player
3351 N Southport Ave, Chicago IL 60657, USA
**Samberg, Andy** — Actor
United Talent Agency, U T A Plaza, 9336 Civic Center Dr, Beverly Hills CA 90210 USA
**Samberg, D Andrew (Andy)** — Actor, Comedian
Mosiac Media Group, 9200 W Sunset Blvd, #1000, Los Angeles CA 90069 USA
**Sambito, Joseph C (Joe)** — Baseball Player
23 Modesto, Irvine CA 92602, USA
**Sambora, Richard S (Richie)** — Singer, Songwriter (Bon Jovi)
Bon Jovi Mgmt, 809 Elder Circle, Austin TX 78733, USA
**Samcoff, Edward W (Ed)** — Baseball Player
8153 Maderia Port Lane, Fair Oaks CA 95628, USA
**Sameshima, Aya** — Soccer Player
Football Assn, 3-10-15 Hongo, Bunkyoku, Tokyo 113 0033 Japan
**Samet, Jonathan M** — Epidemiologist
Johns Hopkins University, Bloomberg Public Health School, Baltimore MD 21205, USA
**Samford, Ronald E (Ron)** — Baseball Player
2174 Kessler Court, Dallas TX 75208, USA
**Samie, Catherine** — Actress
Artmedia, 20 Ave Rapp, 75007 Paris, France
**Samios, Nicholas P** — Science Administrator, Physicist
Brookhaven National Laboratory, Director's Office, 2 Center St, Upton NY 11973, USA
**Sammons, Clint** — Baseball Player
732 King Sword Court SE, Mableton GA 30126, USA
**Sammons, Mary F** — Businesswoman
Rite Aid Corp, 30 Hunter Lane, Camp Hill PA 17011, USA
**Samms, Emma** — Actress
2934 1/2 N Beverly Glen Circle, #417, Los Angeles CA 90077, USA
**Samoilova, Tatiana Y** — Actress
Spiridonyevsky Per 8/11, 103104 Moscow, Russia
**Samokutyaev, Alexander M** — Cosmonaut
Cosmonaut Training Center, Star City, 141160 Zvezdny Gorodok, Moscow Oblast, Russia
**Sampen, William A (Bill)** — Baseball Player
11 Carnaby Court, Brownsburg IN 46112, USA
**Sampey, Angelle** — Motorcycle Racing Rider, Auto Driver
Star Racing, PO Box 1241, Americus GA 31709, USA
**Sample, Joseph L (Joe)** — Jazz Pianist
Patrick Rains Assoc, 1255 5th Ave, #7J, New York NY 10029, USA
**Sample, Steven B** — Educator
211 S Orange Grove Blvd, #14, Pasadena CA 91105, USA
**Sample, William A (Billy)** — Baseball Player
10 Pascack Road, Township of Washington NJ 07676, USA
**Sampler, Philece** — Actress
Vox Inc, 6420 Wilshire Blvd, #1080, Los Angeles CA 90048 USA
**Samples, Keith** — Writer
Characters Talent Mgmt, 8 Elm St, Toronto ON M5G 1G7, Canada
**Sampleton, Lawrence** — Football Player
2900 Bunny Run, Austin TX 78746, USA
**Sampras, Peter (Pete)** — Tennis Player
2552 Via Anita, Palos Verdes Estates CA 90274, USA
**Sampson, Benjamin D (Benji)** — Baseball Player
8312 Flat Rock Court, North Richland Hills TX 76182, USA
**Sampson, Gary** — Ice Hockey Player
Alaska Sportsman's Lodge, PO Box 231985, Anchorage AK 99523, USA
**Sampson, Kelvin** — Basketball Coach
Milwaukee Bucks, Bradley Center, 1001 N 4th St, #2, Milwaukee WI 53203 USA
**Sampson, R Gregory (Greg)** — Football Player
3286 Highland Dr, Carlsbad CA 92008, USA
**Sampson, Ralph L, Jr** — Basketball Player, Coach
530 Myrtle St, Harrisonburg VA 22802, USA
**Sams, Dean** — Keyboardist (Lonestar)
Borman Entertainment, 4322 Harding Pike, #429, Nashville TN 37205, USA
**Sams, Jeremy** — Composer
Faber Music, 3 Queen Square, London WC1N 3AU, England
**Sams, Judy** — Golfer
2603 Wells Ave, Sarasota FL 34232, USA
**Sams, Russell** — Actor
Talent Works, 3500 W Olive Ave, #1400, Burbank CA 91505 USA
**Samsonov, Sergei V** — Ice Hockey Player
2896 Croftshire Court, Rochester MI 48306, USA

**Samuel, Amado R** — Baseball Player
1931 Yale Dr, Louisville KY 40205, USA
**Samuel, Asante T** — Football Player
4130 Triple Crown Court, Davie FL 33330, USA
**Samuel, Juan M** — Baseball Player
777 S Eden St, Baltimore MD 21231, USA
**Samuel, Xavier** — Actor
Shanahan Mgmt, Berman House, 91 Campbell St, #300, Surry Hills NSW 2010, Australia
**Samuell, Yann** — Director, Writer
Films Talents, 34 Rue Du Louvre, 75001 Paris, France
**Samuels, Chris** — Football Player
8415 Fredericksburg Road, #906, San Antonio TX 78229, USA
**Samuels, Roger N** — Baseball Player
4865 Tampico Way, San Jose CA 95118, USA
**Samuelsson, Bengt I** — Nobel Medicine Laureate
Karolinska Institute, Chemistry Dept, 171 77 Stockholm, Sweden
**Samuelsson, K Mikael** — Ice Hockey Player
44751 Roundview Dr, Novi MI 48375, USA
**Samuelsson, Kjell** — Ice Hockey Player
5 Simsbury Dr, Voorhees NJ 08043, USA
**Samuelsson, Ulf** — Ice Hockey Player, Coach
19175 N 95th Place, Scottsdale AZ 85255, USA
**Sanada, Hiroyuki** — Actor
Lighthouse Entertainment, 9220 W Sunset Blvd, #200, West Hollywood CA 90069 USA
**Sanborn, David** — Jazz Saxophonist, Composer
Patrick Rains Assoc, 1255 5th Ave, #7J, New York NY 10029, USA
**Sanches, Brian L** — Baseball Player
9020 Taylor Circle, Orange TX 77630, USA
**Sanches, Stacy** — Model, Actress
Playboy Promotions, 2706 Media Center Dr, Los Angeles CA 90065 USA
**Sanchez Azuara, Rocio** — Actress
TV Azteca, Periferico 4121, Colonia Fuentes Pedregal, DF CP 14141, Mexico
**Sanchez Vicario, Arantxa** — Tennis Player
Sabino de Arana 28, #6-1A, 08028 Barcelona, Spain
**Sanchez Vicario, Emilio A** — Tennis Player
Sabino de Arana 28, #6-1A, 08028 Barcelona, Spain
**Sanchez, Alejandro A (Alex)** — Baseball Player
1400 Mellissa Circle, Antioch CA 94509, USA
**Sanchez, Ana Maria** — Opera Singer
Opera et Concert, 37 Rue de la Chaussee d'Antin, 75009 Paris, France
**Sanchez, Ashlyn** — Actress
Osbrink Talent Agency, 4343 Lankershim Blvd, #100, North Hollywood CA 91602 USA
**Sanchez, David** — Saxophonist
Addeo Music International, 37 W 26th St, #315, New York NY 10010, USA
**Sanchez, Duaner** — Baseball Player
56748 Eastvue Dr, Osceola IN 46561, USA
**Sanchez, Eduardo** — Director, Producer, Writer
Haxan Films, PO Box 261370, Encino CA 91426, USA
**Sanchez, Frederick P (Freddy), Jr** — Baseball Player
2494 E Cloud Dr, Chandler AZ 85249, USA
**Sanchez, Keram Malicki** — Actor
Nine Yards Entertainment, 8530 Wilshire Blvd, #500, Beverly Hills CA 90211 USA
**Sanchez, Kiele** — Actress
Industry Entertainment, 955 Carillo Dr, #300, Los Angeles CA 90048 USA
**Sanchez, Marco** — Actor
Stone Manners Salners, 9911 W Pico Blvd, #1400, Los Angeles CA 90035 USA
**Sanchez, Mark D** — Football Player
New York Jets, 1 Jets Dr, Florham Park NJ 07932 USA
**Sanchez, Pedro** — Soil Scientist
Columbia University, Earth Institute, New York NY 10027, USA
**Sanchez, Poncho** — Jazz Drummer
Regime Mgmt, 150 W Alameda Ave, #230, Burbank CA 91502, USA
**Sanchez, Roselyn** — Actress
A P A Talent/Literary Agency, 405 S Beverly Dr, #300, Beverly Hills CA 90212 USA
**Sanchez, Samuel** — Cyclist
Euskadi-Fundacio Ciolista, C/Iparragirre 46-1, 48010 Bilboa, Spain
**Sanchez, Sergio G** — Writer
United Talent Agency, U T A Plaza, 9336 Civic Center Dr, Beverly Hills CA 90210 USA
**Sanchez-Gijon, Aitana** — Actress
Alsira Garcia Maroto, Gran Via 63, #3 Izda, 28013 Madrid, Spain
**Sanchez-Vilella, Roberto** — Governor, Puerto Rico
414 Ave Munoz Rivera, #7A, Stop 31-1/2, San Juan PR 00918, USA
**Sand, Paul** — Actor
Paradigm Agency, 360 N Crescent Dr, North Building, Beverly Hills CA 90210 USA
**Sand, Todd** — Figure Skater
2973 Harbor Blvd, #468, Costa Mesa CA 92626, USA
**Sanda, Dominique** — Actress
Agence Metropolitan Paris, 23 Blvd des Capucines, 75002 Paris, France
**Sandberg of Passfield, Michael G R** — Financier
Waterside, Passfield, Liphook, Hants GU30 7RT, England
**Sandberg, Espen** — Director
Roenbergfilm, Pilestredet 75C, 0354 Oslo, Norway
**Sandberg, Ryne D** — Baseball Player, Manager
26 Biltmore Estates, Phoenix AZ 85016, USA
**Sande, Emeli** — Singer, Musician, Songwriter
Virgin Records, Kensal House, 533-79 Harrow Road, London W10 4RH, England
**Sandelin, Scott** — Ice Hockey Player, Coach
4880 Adrian Lane, Hermantown MN 55811, USA
**Sandeman, William S (Bill)** — Football Player
PO Box 203, Homewood CA 96141, USA
**Sandeno, Kaitlin** — Swimmer
78 Townsend, Irvine CA 92620, USA
**Sander, Anne** — Golfer
1261 Parkside Dr E, Seattle WA 98112, USA
**Sander, Casey** — Actor
Leavitt Talent Group, 11500 W Olympic Blvd, #400, Los Angeles CA 90064, USA

**S**

**Samuel - Sander**

| | |
|---|---|
| **Sander, Ian** | Producer, Director, Actor |
| Sander/Moses Productions, 500 S Buena Vista St, Burbank CA 91521, USA | |
| **Sander, Jil** | Fashion Designer |
| Osterfeldstr 32-34, 22529 Hamburg, Germany | |
| **Sander, Judith M** | Artist |
| 25218 Oak Lane, Philomath OR 97370, USA | |
| **Sanders, Anthony M** | Baseball Player |
| 7881 E McGee Mountain Road, Tucson AZ 85750, USA | |
| **Sanders, Barry D** | Football Player |
| PO Box 81336, Rochester MI 48308, USA | |
| **Sanders, Beverly** | Actress |
| 12218 Morrison St, Valley Village CA 91607, USA | |
| **Sanders, Bill** | Cartoonist |
| PO Box 661, Milwaukee WI 53201, USA | |
| **Sanders, C J** | Actor |
| Abrams Artists, 9200 W Sunset Blvd, #1125, West Hollywood CA 90069 USA | |
| **Sanders, Charles A (Charlie)** | Football Player, Coach |
| 3418 Palm Aire Court, Rochester Hills MI 48309, USA | |
| **Sanders, Chris** | Director, Actor |
| W M E Entertainment, 9601 Wilshire Blvd, #300, Beverly Hills CA 90210 USA | |
| **Sanders, David A** | Baseball Player |
| 10411 S Ellen St, Mulvane KS 67110, USA | |
| **Sanders, Deion L** | Football, Baseball Player, Sportscaster |
| 1280 N Preston Road, Prosper TX 75078, USA | |
| **Sanders, Doug** | Golfer |
| 1311 Nantucket Dr, Houston TX 77057, USA | |
| **Sanders, Eric D** | Football Player |
| 9325 Tailey Circle, Duluth GA 30097, USA | |
| **Sanders, Erin** | Actress |
| C E S D, 10635 Santa Monica Blvd, #130, Los Angeles CA 90025 USA | |
| **Sanders, Frank V** | Football Player |
| 4551 E Desert Trumpet Road, Phoenix AZ 85044, USA | |
| **Sanders, Franklyn B (Frank)** | Ice Hockey Player |
| 613 Lake View Dr, Saint Paul MN 55129, USA | |
| **Sanders, James B** | Football Player |
| Arizona Cardinals, PO Box 888, Phoenix AZ 85001 USA | |
| **Sanders, Jay O** | Actor |
| Innovative Artists, 1505 10th St, Santa Monica CA 90401 USA | |
| **Sanders, Jeff** | Basketball Player |
| PO Box 374, South Holland IL 60473, USA | |
| **Sanders, John F** | Baseball Player |
| 3004 Cheshire Court, Woodstock GA 30189, USA | |
| **Sanders, Jonathan (Jon)** | Yachtsman |
| Riverview Gardens, 20 Dean St, #95, Claremont, Perth WA 6010, Australia | |
| **Sanders, Kenneth G (Ken)** | Baseball Player |
| 12141 Parkview Lane, Hales Corners WI 53130, USA | |
| **Sanders, Kenneth R (Ken)** | Football Player |
| 3067 FM 217, Valley Mills TX 76689, USA | |
| **Sanders, Marlene** | Commentator |
| 175 Riverside Dr, New York NY 10024, USA | |
| **Sanders, Pharoah** | Jazz Saxophonist |
| Joel Chriss Co, 300 Mercer St, #3J, New York NY 10003 USA | |
| **Sanders, Reginald L (Reggie)** | Baseball Player |
| 122 Vista Del Mar Lane, #102, Myrtle Beach SC 29572, USA | |
| **Sanders, Richard** | Actor |
| 4954 Strohm Ave, North Hollywood CA 91601, USA | |
| **Sanders, Ricky W** | Football Player |
| 4822 Rockwood Dr, Houston TX 77004, USA | |
| **Sanders, Scott G** | Baseball Player |
| 315 Belmont Dr, Thibodaux LA 70301, USA | |
| **Sanders, Summer** | Swimmer, Sportscaster |
| 731 Martingale Lane, Park City UT 84098, USA | |
| **Sanders, Susan (Sue)** | Golfer |
| 3888 Cheyenne Place, Sedalia CO 80135, USA | |
| **Sanders, Thomas D** | Football Player |
| 2030 Appleton Dr, Missouri City TX 77489, USA | |
| **Sanders, Thomas E (Satch)** | Basketball Player, Executive |
| 114 Fenway, Boston MA 02115, USA | |
| **Sanders, Troy** | Singer, Bassist (Mastodon) |
| Pinnacle Entertainment, 30 Glenn St, White Plains NY 10603, USA | |
| **Sanders, W J (Jerry), III** | Businessman |
| Advanced Micro Devices, 1 A M D Place, PO Box 3453, Sunnyvale CA 94088, USA | |
| **Sanderson, Cael S** | Freestyle Wrestler |
| Pennsylvania State University, Athletic Dept, University Park PA 16802, USA | |
| **Sanderson, Derek M** | Ice Hockey Player |
| Howland Capital Mgmt, 75 Federal St, Boston MA 02110, USA | |
| **Sanderson, Geoff M** | Ice Hockey Player |
| Philadelphia Flyers, 1st Union Center, 3601 S Broad St, Philadelphia PA 19148 USA | |
| **Sanderson, Peter** | Artist |
| 1105 Shell Gate Plaza, Alameda CA 94501, USA | |
| **Sanderson, Scott D** | Baseball Player |
| 945 Newcastle Dr, Lake Forest IL 60045, USA | |
| **Sanderson, Theresa (Tessa)** | Track Athlete |
| Performing Artistes, 24A High St, Cobham KT11 3EB, England | |
| **Sanderson, William** | Actor |
| Talent Works, 3500 W Olive Ave, #1400, Burbank CA 91505 USA | |
| **Sandeson, William S** | Editorial Cartoonist |
| 2230 Muskoday Pass, Fort Wayne IN 46809, USA | |
| **Sandford, Ed** | Ice Hockey Player |
| 18 Clearwater Road, Winchester MA 01890, USA | |
| **Sandford, John** | Writer, Journalist |
| G P Putnam's Sons, 375 Hudson St, New York NY 10014 USA | |
| **Sandiford, L Erskine** | Prime Minister, Barbados |
| Hillvista, Porters, Saint James, Barbados | |
| **Sandin, Daniel J** | Inventor (Cave Electronic Visualization) |
| University of Illinois, Electronic Visualization Laboratory, 842 W Taylor St, Chicago IL 60607, USA | |

| | |
|---|---|
| **Sandlak, Jim** | Ice Hockey Player |
| 74 Green Hedge Lane, London ON N6H 5A6, Canada | |
| **Sandler, Adam** | Actor, Comedian |
| Brillstein Entertainment Partners, 9150 Wilshire Blvd, #350, Beverly Hills CA 90212 USA | |
| **Sandler, Herbert M** | Financier |
| Sandler Foundation, 121 Steuart St, San Francisco CA 94105, USA | |
| **Sandler, Tony** | Singer (Sandler & Young) |
| Producers Inc, 11806 N 56th St, Tampa FL 33617 USA | |
| **Sandlock, Michael J (Mike)** | Baseball Player |
| 81 Bible St, Cos Cob CT 06807, USA | |
| **Sandlund, Debra** | Actress |
| Innovative Artists, 1505 10th St, Santa Monica CA 90401 USA | |
| **Sandoval Iniguez, Juan Cardinal** | Religious Leader |
| Arzobispado, Liceo 17, #1-331, 44100 Guadalajara, Mexico | |
| **Sandoval, Arturo** | Jazz Trumpeter, Pianist |
| PO Box 143936, Coral Gables FL 33114, USA | |
| **Sandoval, Eugene** | Architect |
| Zimmer Gunner Frasca Partnership, 320 SW Oak St, #500, Portland OR 97204, USA | |
| **Sandoval, Hope** | Singer (Mazzy Star, Going Home) |
| High Road Touring, 751 Bridgeway, #200, Sausalito CA 94965 USA | |
| **Sandoval, Miguel** | Actor |
| Innovative Artists, 1505 10th St, Santa Monica CA 90401 USA | |
| **Sandoval, Sonny** | Singer (POD) |
| Atlantic Records, 9229 W Sunset Blvd, #900, West Hollywood CA 90069 USA | |
| **Sandow, Nicholas J (Nick)** | Actor |
| Stone Manners Salners, 9911 W Pico Blvd, #1400, Los Angeles CA 90035 USA | |
| **Sandrelli, Stefania** | Actress |
| T N A, Viale Parioli 41, 00197 Rome, Italy | |
| **Sandri, Leonardo Cardinal** | Religious Leader |
| Oriental Churches Congregation, Palazzo del Bramante, 00193 Rome, Italy | |
| **Sandrich, Jay H** | Director |
| Creative Artists Agency, 2000 Ave of Stars, #100, Los Angeles CA 90067 USA | |
| **Sands, Charles D (Charlie)** | Baseball Player |
| 28940 Bermuda Pointe Circle, #103, Bonita Springs FL 34134, USA | |
| **Sands, Julian** | Actor |
| S D B Partners, 1801 Ave of Stars, #902, Los Angeles CA 90067 USA | |
| **Sands, Stark** | Actor |
| Management 360, 9111 Wilshire Blvd, Beverly Hills CA 90210 USA | |
| **Sands, Terdell D** | Football Player |
| PO Box 2217, Chattanooga TN 37409, USA | |
| **Sands, Tommy** | Singer, Actor |
| Lustig Talent, PO Box 770850, Orlando FL 32877 USA | |
| **Sandt, Thomas J (Tom)** | Baseball Player |
| 15265 Boones Way, Lake Oswego OR 97035, USA | |
| **Sandusky, Alexander B (Alex)** | Football Player |
| 22 Floral Ave, Key West FL 33040, USA | |
| **Sandvig, Jake** | Actor |
| Innovative Artists, 1505 10th St, Santa Monica CA 90401 USA | |
| **Sandy B** | Singer |
| T-Best Talent Agency, 508 Honey Lake Court, Danville CA 94506 USA | |
| **Sandy, Gary** | Actor |
| PO Box 818, Cynthiana KY 41031, USA | |
| **Sane, Justin** | Singer, Songwriter |
| Agency Group Ltd, 142 W 57th St, #600, New York NY 10019 USA | |
| **Sanejouand, Jean Michel** | Artist |
| Belle-Ville, 49150 Vaulandry, France | |
| **Sanford, Arlene** | Director, Producer, Writer |
| Anonymous Content, 3532 Hayden Ave, Culver City CA 90232 USA | |
| **Sanford, Chance S** | Baseball Player |
| 15028 Bardwell Lane, Frisco TX 75035, USA | |
| **Sanford, Ed** | Ice Hockey Player |
| 18 Clearwater Road, Winchester MA 01890, USA | |
| **Sanford, J Frederick (Fred)** | Baseball Player |
| 1046 W 600 N, Salt Lake City UT 84116, USA | |
| **Sanford, Lucius M** | Football Player |
| 1350 Allegheny St SW, Atlanta GA 30310, USA | |
| **Sanford, Meredith L (Mo)** | Baseball Player |
| 2800 Highway 389, Starkville MS 39759, USA | |
| **Sanford, O Leo** | Football Player |
| 3044 Gorton Road, Columbia MD 21046, USA | |
| **Sanford, Richard M (Rick)** | Football Player |
| 110 Oak Park Dr, #B, Irmo SC 29063, USA | |
| **Sanford, Ron** | Basketball Player |
| 3129 Santana Lane, Plano TX 75023, USA | |
| **Sang Hun Choe** | Journalist |
| Associated Press, Editorial Dept, 450 W 33rd St, #1500, New York NY 10001 USA | |
| **Sangare, Oumou** | Singer |
| Concerted Efforts, PO Box 440326, Somerville MA 02144 USA | |
| **Sangay, Lonsang** | Prime Minister, Tibet Exile Government |
| Tibet Government in Exile, Kashag, Dharmsala 176205 H P, India | |
| **Sanger, Frederick** | Nobel Chemistry Laureate |
| Far Leys, Fen Lane, Swaffham Bulbeck, Cambridge CB5 0NJ, England | |
| **Sangheli, Andrei** | Prime Minister, Moldova |
| Parliament House, Prosp 105, 277073 Kishinnew, Moldova | |
| **SanGiacomo, Laura** | Actress |
| I C M Partners, 10250 Constellation Blvd, #900, Los Angeles CA 90067 USA | |
| **Sangster, Thomas** | Actor |
| Curtis Brown Group, 28-29 Haymarket St, #500, London SW1Y 4SP, England | |
| **Sanguillen, Manny** | Baseball Player |
| 2838 SW 4th St, Boynton Beach FL 33435, USA | |
| **Sanguinetti Coirolo, Julio Maria** | President, Uruguay |
| Partido Colorado, Andres Martinez Trueba 1271, Montevideo, Uruguay | |
| **SanMiguel, Renay** | Commentator |
| CNN-TV, 190 Marietta Ave SW, Atlanta GA 30303 USA | |
| **Sano, Roy I** | Religious Leader |
| United Methodist Church, 100 Maryland Ave NE, #300, Washington DC 20002, USA | |

## S

| | |
|---|---|
| **Sansa, Maya**<br>Markham Froggatt Irwin, Julian House, 4 Windmill St, London W1P 1HF, England | Actress |
| **Sansom, Chip**<br>204 Long Beach Road, Centerville MA 02632, USA | Cartoonist (Born Loser) |
| **Sansweet, Steven J**<br>PO Box 2009, San Rafael CA 94912, USA | Writer |
| **Sant, Alfred**<br>National Labor Center, Mills End Road, Hanrum, Malta | Prime Minister, Malta |
| **Santa Rosa, Gilberto**<br>Universal Attractions, 135 W 26th St, #1200, New York NY 10001 USA | Singer |
| **Santana Araque, Johan A**<br>10471 Via Lombardia Court, Miromar Lakes FL 33913, USA | Baseball Player |
| **Santana de la Cruz, Rafael F**<br>3220 SE 1st Ave, Cape Coral FL 33904, USA | Baseball Player |
| **Santana, Carlos**<br>Santana Mgmt, 121 Jordan St, San Rafael CA 94901, USA | Guitarist, Singer, Songwriter |
| **Santana, Ervin R**<br>Kansas City Royals, Kauffman Stadium, 1 Royal Way, Kansas City MO 64129 USA | Baseball Player |
| **Santana, Manuel**<br>International Tennis Hall of Fame, 194 Bellevue Ave, Newport RI 02840, USA | Tennis Player |
| **Santaolalla, Gustavo**<br>First Artists, 4764 Park Granada, #210, Calabasas CA 91302 USA | Guitarist, Composer |
| **Santer, Jacques**<br>69 Rue J P Huberty, 1742 Luxembourg-Ville, Luxembourg | Prime Minister, Luxembourg |
| **Santiago, Benito R**<br>PO Box 5759, Lighthouse Point FL 33074, USA | Baseball Player |
| **Santiago, Christina L**<br>Playboy Promotions, 2706 Media Center Dr, Los Angeles CA 90065 USA | Model |
| **Santiago, Eddie**<br>Pozo International Promotions, 170 E 116th St, New York NY 10029, USA | Singer |
| **Santiago, Jose**<br>690 Calle Cesar Gonzalez, #2108, San Juan PR 00918, USA | Baseball Player |
| **Santiago, Joseph A (Joey)**<br>X-Ray Touring, 77-79 Great Eastern St, #A, London EC2A 3HU, England | Guitarist (Pixies) |
| **Santiago, Lina**<br>Richard Walters, PO Box 2789, Toluca Lake CA 91610 USA | Singer |
| **Santiago, Otis J (O J)**<br>8780 NW 37th Place, Hollywood FL 33024, USA | Football Player |
| **Santiago, Ray**<br>Innovative Artists, 1505 10th St, Santa Monica CA 90401 USA | Actor |
| **Santiago, Saundra**<br>C E S D, 257 Park Ave S, #950, New York NY 10010 USA | Actress |
| **Santiago-Hudson, Ruben**<br>Vincent Cirrincione Assoc, 1516 N Fairfax Ave, Los Angeles CA 90046 USA | Actor |
| **Santigold**<br>Roc Nation Mgmt, 1411 Broadway New York NY 10018, USA | Singer, Songwriter |
| **Santilli, Ivana D**<br>The Agency Group, 2 Berkeley St, #202, Toronto ON M5A 4J5, Canada | Singer, Songwriter, Keyboardist |
| **SantoDomingo, Rafael**<br>PO Box 21, Orocovis PR 00720, USA | Baseball Player |
| **Santoni, Reni**<br>Geddes Agency, 8430 Santa Monica Blvd, #201, West Hollywood CA 90069 USA | Actor |
| **Santora, Nick**<br>W M E Entertainment, 9601 Wilshire Blvd, #300, Beverly Hills CA 90210 USA | Producer |
| **Santorelli, Frank**<br>Bleecker Street Entertainment, 853 Broadway, #1214, New York NY 10003, USA | Actor |
| **Santorini, Alan J (Al)**<br>100 Wescott Dr, Clemson SC 29631, USA | Baseball Player |
| **Santoro, Rodrigo**<br>I C M Partners, 10250 Constellation Blvd, #900, Los Angeles CA 90067 USA | Actor |
| **Santos Ordonez, Elvin E**<br>Casa Presidencial, Blvd Juan Pablo II, Tegucigalpa MDC, Honduras | President, Honduras |
| **Santos, Anthony (Romeo)**<br>Sony Music Miami, 605 Lincoln Road Road, #700, Miami Beach FL 33139 USA | Singer, Songwriter |
| **Santos, Joe**<br>Amsel Eisenstadt Frazier, 5055 Wilshire Blvd, #865, Los Angeles CA 90036 USA | Actor |
| **Santos, Jose**<br>620 SW 99th Ave, Pembroke Pines FL 33025, USA | Thoroughbred Racing Jockey |
| **Santos, Juan Manuel**<br>Palacio de Narino, Plaza de Bolivar, Santa Fe, Bogota DE, Colombia | President, Colombia |
| **Santos, Rick**<br>S&S Automotive, 14127 Washington Ave, San Leandro CA 94578, USA | Drag Racing Driver |
| **SantosDeOliveira, Alessandra**<br>Washington Mystics, Verizon Center, 401 9th St NW, #750, Washington DC 20004 USA | Basketball Player |
| **Santovenia, Nelson D**<br>14642 SW 141st Court, Miami FL 33186, USA | Baseball Player |
| **Sanz, Alejandro**<br>R L M International, Puerto de Santa Maria 65, 28043 Madrid, Spain | Singer, Songwriter |
| **Sanz, Horatio**<br>United Talent Agency, U T A Plaza, 9336 Civic Center Dr, Beverly Hills CA 90210 USA | Actor, Comedian |
| **Saperstein, David**<br>Religious Action Center, 2027 Massachusetts Ave NW, Washington DC 20036, USA | Religious Leader, Rabbi, Writer |
| **Sapienza, Al**<br>S D B Partners, 1801 Ave of Stars, #902, Los Angeles CA 90067 USA | Actor |
| **Sapolu, M Jesse**<br>1123 Buckingham Dr, #B, Costa Mesa CA 92626, USA | Football Player |
| **Sapp, Gerome D**<br>4654 Riverstone Dr, Owings Mills MD 21117, USA | Football Player |
| **Sapp, Marvin**<br>Sony Records, 2100 Colorado Ave, Santa Monica CA 90404 USA | Singer |
| **Sapp, Theron C**<br>892 N Belair Road, Augusta GA 30909, USA | Football Player |
| **Sapp, Warren H**<br>PO Box 585, Windermere FL 34786, USA | Football Player, Sportscaster |
| **Sapphire**<br>Viking Press, 375 Hudson St, New York NY 10014 USA | Writer |

| | |
|---|---|
| **Saprykin, Oleg V** | Ice Hockey Player |
| 15802 N 71st St, #451, Scottsdale AZ 85254, USA | |
| **Sara, Mia** | Actress |
| Gersh Agency, 9465 Wilshire Blvd, #600, Beverly Hills CA 90212 USA | |
| **Sarafyan, Angela** | Actress |
| Innovative Artists, 1505 10th St, Santa Monica CA 90401 USA | |
| **Saraiva Martins, Jose Cardinal** | Religious Leader |
| Palazzo delle Congregazioni, Piazzo Pio XII, 00193 Rome, Italy | |
| **Saralegui, Cristina** | Commentator |
| T G A Voice, 100 Lincoln Road, #928, Miami Beach FL 33178, USA | |
| **Sarandon, Chris** | Actor |
| Stone Manners Salners, 9911 W Pico Blvd, #1400, Los Angeles CA 90035 USA | |
| **Sarandon, Susan** | Actress, Model |
| I C M Partners, 10250 Constellation Blvd, #900, Los Angeles CA 90067 USA | |
| **Saraste, Jukka-Pekka** | Conductor |
| Columbia Artists Mgmt Inc, 1790 Broadway, #702, New York NY 10019 USA | |
| **Sarasvuo, Virpi Kuitunen** | Cross Country Skier |
| Ilmarisentie 26B, 03100 Nummela, Finland | |
| **Sarbanes, Paul S** | Senator, MD |
| 320 Suffolk Road, Baltimore MD 21218, USA | |
| **Sardinha, Dane** | Baseball Player |
| 156 Kuuhei Road, Kailua HI 96734, USA | |
| **Sardo, Michael** | Producer, Writer |
| Creative Artists Agency, 2000 Ave of Stars, #100, Los Angeles CA 90067 USA | |
| **Sardou, Michel** | Singer |
| Artmedia, 20 Ave Rapp, 75007 Paris, France | |
| **Sarelle, Leilani** | Actress |
| Affinity Artists Agency, 5724 W 3rd St, #511, Los Angeles CA 90036, USA | |
| **Sarfati, Alain** | Architect |
| 43 Rue Maurice Ripoche, 75014 Paris, France | |
| **Sargent, Ben** | Editorial Cartoonist |
| Austin American-Statesman, 166 E Riverside Dr, Austin TX 78704, USA | |
| **Sargent, Joseph D** | Producer, Director |
| 27432 Latigo Bay View Dr, Malibu CA 90265, USA | |
| **Sargsyan, Serzh A** | President, Armenia |
| President's Office, Marshal Bagramian Prosp 19, 375010 Yerevan, Armenia | |
| **Sargysan, Tigran** | Prime Minister, Armenia |
| Prime Minister's Office, Ul Nalbandyyrna 32, 375010 Yerevan, Armenia | |
| **Sarich, Cory** | Ice Hockey Player |
| 19322 Autumn Woods Ave, Tampa FL 33647, USA | |
| **Sarkisian, Steve** | Football Player, Coach |
| University of Washington, Athletic Dept, Seattle WA 98195, USA | |
| **Sarne, Tanya** | Fashion Designer |
| Ghost Ltd, The Chapel, 263 Kensal Road, London W10 5DB, England | |
| **Sarner, Craig B** | Ice Hockey Player |
| 1375 Brown Road S, Wayzata MN 55391, USA | |
| **Sarno, Joe** | Writer |
| 5941 W Irving Park Road, Chicago IL 60634, USA | |
| **Sarnoff, Elizabeth (Liz)** | Producer, Writer |
| W M E Entertainment, 9601 Wilshire Blvd, #300, Beverly Hills CA 90210 USA | |
| **Sarr, Theodore-Adrien Cardinal** | Religious Leader |
| Archevech, BP 1908, Avenue Jean XXIII, Dakar, Senegal | |
| **Sarsgaard, Peter** | Actor |
| Creative Artists Agency, 2000 Ave of Stars, #100, Los Angeles CA 90067 USA | |
| **Sartain, Dan** | Singer, Songwriter |
| Agency Group Ltd, 142 W 57th St, #600, New York NY 10019 USA | |
| **Sasaki, Kazuhiro** | Baseball Player |
| Seattle Mariners, Safeco Field, PO Box 4100, Seattle WA 98194 USA | |
| **Sasha** | DJ Msician |
| Red Light Mgmt, PO Box 1467, Charlottesville VA 22902, USA | |
| **Saskamoose, Fred** | Ice Hockey Player |
| PO Box 225, Shell Lake SK S0J 2G0, Canada | |
| **Sasse, Joshua** | Actor |
| Olivia Bell Management, 193 Wardour St, London W1F 8ZF, England | |
| **Sasselov, Dimitar** | Astronomer |
| Harvard-Smithsonian Astrophysics Center, 60 Garden St, Cambridge MA 02138, USA | |
| **Sasser, Clarence E** | Vietnam War Army Hero (CMH) |
| 13414 FM 521, Rosharon TX 77583, USA | |
| **Sasser, Grant** | Ice Hockey Player |
| 1949 SE Orient Dr, Gresham OR 97080, USA | |
| **Sasser, James R (Jim)** | Senator, TN; Diplomat |
| 601 Mainstream Dr, Nashville TN 37228, USA | |
| **Sasser, Mack D (Mackey)** | Baseball Player |
| 19 Harrington Lane, Dothan AL 36305, USA | |
| **Sasso, Will** | Actor, Comedian |
| Paradigm Agency, 360 N Crescent Dr, North Building, Beverly Hills CA 90210 USA | |
| **Sasson, Deborah** | Opera, Pop Singer |
| Erlenhaupstr 10, 64625 Bensheim, Germany | |
| **Sassoon, Beverly** | Model |
| 2533 Benedict Canyon Dr, Beverly Hills CA 90210, USA | |
| **Sassoon, David** | Fashion Designer |
| Bellville Sassoon, 18 Culford Gardens, London SW3 2ST, England | |
| **Sassou-Nguesso, Denis** | President, Congo People's Republic |
| Palais du Peuple, Quartier Plateau, Brazzaville, Congo Republic | |
| **Sastre Candil, Carlos** | Cyclist |
| Team Geox, Via Feltrina Centro 16, 31044 Biadene de Montebelluna, Italy | |
| **Sastre, Ines** | Model, Actress |
| Paradigm Agency, 360 N Crescent Dr, North Building, Beverly Hills CA 90210 USA | |
| **Sata, Michael C** | President, Zambia |
| President's Office, State House, PO Box 30208, Lusaka, Zambia | |
| **Satan, Miroslav** | Ice Hockey Player |
| 46 Kettlepond Road, Jericho NY 11753, USA | |
| **Satcher, David M** | Navy Admiral, Government Official |
| Morehouse College, Medical School, Atlanta GA 30314, USA | |
| **Satcher, Robert L (Bobby), Jr** | Astronaut |
| N A S A, Johnson Space Center, 2101 NASA Road, Houston TX 77058 USA | |

**S**

**Sater, Steven** — Lyricist, Writer, Producer
Creative Artists Agency, 2000 Ave of Stars, #100, Los Angeles CA 90067 USA

**Sather, Glen C** — Ice Hockey Player, Executive
77380 Vista Rosa, La Quinta CA 92253, USA

**Satine, Elena** — Actress
I C M Partners, 10250 Constellation Blvd, #900, Los Angeles CA 90067 USA

**Sato, Kazuo** — Economist
300 E 71st St, #15H, New York NY 10021, USA

**Sato, Yuka** — Figure Skater
Detroit Figure Skating Club, 888 Denison Court, Bloomfield Hills MI 48302, USA

**Satra, Sonia** — Actress
C E S D, 257 Park Ave S, #950, New York NY 10010 USA

**Satrapi, Marjane** — Writer, Director, Actress
United Talent Agency, U T A Plaza, 9336 Civic Center Dr, Beverly Hills CA 90210 USA

**Satriani, Joe** — Singer, Guitarist
Entourage Talent Assoc, 236 W 27th St, #800, New York NY 10001, USA

**Satriano, Thomas V (Tom)** — Baseball Player
5320 Otis Ave, Tarzana CA 91356, USA

**Satterfield, Paul** — Actor
8323 W 1st St, Los Angeles CA 90048, USA

**Sattler, John F** — Marine Corps General
Director, Strategic Plans/Policy, Joint Staff, Pentagon, Washington DC 20310 USA

**Saturday, Jeffrey B (Jeff)** — Football Player
2437 Londonberry Blvd, Carmel IN 46032, USA

**Saturno, William** — Archaeologist
University of New Hampshire, Anthropology Dept, Durham NH 03824, USA

**Saturova, Simona** — Opera Singer
Kunstler Sekretariat am Gasteig, Rosenheimer Str 52, 81669 Munich, Germany

**Saucier, Kevin A** — Baseball Player
2316 Silversides Loop, Pensacola FL 32526, USA

**Saud, Prince Sultan Bin Abdulaziz al** — Government Official, Saudi Arabia
Defense Ministry, PO Box 26731, Airport Road, Riyadh 11165, Saudi Arabia

**Saudek, Jan** — Photographer
Blodkova 6, 13000 Prague 3, Czech Republic

**Sauer, Craig C** — Football Player
6926 Pagenkopf Road, Maple Plain MN 55359, USA

**Sauer, Louis** — Architect
3472 Marlowe St, Montreal QC H4A 3L7, Canada

**Sauer, Richard J** — Educator, Association Executive
National 4-H Council, 7100 Connecticut Ave, Chevy Chase MD 20815, USA

**Sauerbeck, Scott W** — Baseball Player
1818 4th St W, Palmetto FL 34221, USA

**Sauerbrun, Todd S** — Football Player
8201 N Oleander Ave, Niles IL 60714, USA

**Sauerbrunn, Rebecca E (Becky)** — Soccer Player
D C United, R F K Stadium, 2400 E Capitol St SE, Washington DC 20003 USA

**Sauerlander, Willibald P W** — Art Historian
Victoriastr II, 80803 Munich, Germany

**Sauers, Gene** — Golfer
9 Judsons Court, Savannah GA 31410, USA

**Saul, David J** — Prime Minister, Bermuda
Rocky Ledge, 18 Devonshire Bay Road, DV 07, Bermuda

**Saul, John W, III** — Writer
Grade A Entertainment, 149 S Barrington Ave, #719, Los Angeles CA 90049, USA

**Saul, Ralph S** — Businessman
1400 Waverly Road, #B037, Gladwyne PA 19035, USA

**Saul, Ronald R (Ron)** — Football Player
78 Sleepy Hollow Circle, Charles Town WV 25414, USA

**Saul, Stephanie** — Journalist
Newsday, Editorial Dept, 235 Pinelawn Road, Melville NY 11747, USA

**Saulters, Glynn** — Basketball Player
240 Country Lane, Quitman LA 71268, USA

**Saum, Sherri M** — Actress
Abrams Artists, 9200 W Sunset Blvd, #1125, West Hollywood CA 90069 USA

**Saunders, Bernie** — Ice Hockey Player
150 Pinecrest Dr, Hastings on Hudson NY 10706, USA

**Saunders, George** — Writer
Random House, 1745 Broadway, #1800, New York NY 10019 USA

**Saunders, Jennifer** — Actress
United Agents, 12-26 Lexington St, London W1F 0LE, England

**Saunders, John** — Sportscaster
ESPN-TV, ESPN Plaza, 935 Middle St, Bristol CT 06010 USA

**Saunders, John R** — Auto Racing Executive
Watkins Glen Speedway, PO Box 500F, Watkins Glen NY 14891, USA

**Saunders, Joseph F (Joe)** — Baseball Player
1415 E Grand Canyon Dr, Chandler AZ 85249, USA

**Saunders, Pamela** — Model, Actress
Playboy Promotions, 2706 Media Center Dr, Los Angeles CA 90065 USA

**Saunders, Phillip (Flip)** — Basketball Coach
Washington Wizards, M C I Centre, 601 F St NW, Washington DC 20004 USA

**Saunders, Tony** — Baseball Player
PO Box 434, Severna Park MD 21146, USA

**Saunders, Townsend** — Freestyle Wrestler
733 Chantilly Dr, Sierra Vista AZ 85635, USA

**Saura, Carlos** — Director
Antonio Duran, Calle Arturo Soria 52, #Edif 2, 1-5A, 28027 Madrid, Spain

**Sauter, Johnathan J (Johnny)** — Auto, Truck Racing Driver
779 S Washburn St, #8, Oshkosh WI 54904, USA

**Sauve, Robert (Bob)** — Ice Hockey Player
Jandec Inc, 803-3080 Boul le Carrefour, Laval QC H7T 2R5, Canada

**Sauveur, Richard D (Rich)** — Baseball Player
3312 47th Ave E, Bradenton FL 34203, USA

**Savage, Ben** — Actor
Abrams Artists, 9200 W Sunset Blvd, #1125, West Hollywood CA 90069 USA

**Savage, Chantay** — Singer
Universal Attractions, 135 W 26th St, #1200, New York NY 10001 USA

**Savage, Charlie** — Journalist
Boston Globe, Editorial Dept, 135 William Morrissey Blvd, Dorchester MA 02125 USA
**Savage, Don** — Basketball Player
53 Park Edge, #1E, Berkeley Heights NJ 07922, USA
**Savage, Fred** — Actor, Director
Creative Artists Agency, 2000 Ave of Stars, #100, Los Angeles CA 90067 USA
**Savage, John** — Actor
5584 Bonneville Road, Hidden Hills CA 91302, USA
**Savage, John J (Jack)** — Baseball Player
9920 White Blossom Blvd, Louisville KY 40241, USA
**Savage, Martin** — Actor
United Agents, 12-26 Lexington St, London W1F 0LE, England
**Savage, Michael (Mike)** — Actor, Writer
Hilda Phisick Agency, 78 Temple Sheen Road, London SW14 7RR, England
**Savage, Paul** — Curling Athlete
Curling Assn, 1660 Vimont Court, Cumberland ON K4A 4J4, Canada
**Savage, Rick** — Bassist (Def Leppard)
Front Line Mgmt, 1100 Glendon Ave, #2000, Los Angeles CA 90024 USA
**Savage, Stephanie** — Producer
W M E Entertainment, 9601 Wilshire Blvd, #300, Beverly Hills CA 90210 USA
**Savage, Theodore E (Ted)** — Baseball Player
1510 Mallard Landing Court, Chesterfield MO 63017, USA
**Savage-Rumbaugh, Susan** — Primatologist
Great Ape Trust, 4200 SE 44th Ave, Des Moines IA 50320, USA
**Saval, Dany** — Actress
131 Rue de l'Universite, 75007 Paris, France
**Savant, Doug** — Actor
Paradigm Agency, 360 N Crescent Dr, North Building, Beverly Hills CA 90210 USA
**Savard, Andre** — Ice Hockey Player
Pittsburgh Penguins, Consol Energy Center, 1001 5th Ave, Pittsburgh PA 15219 USA
**Savard, Denis** — Ice Hockey Player, Coach
8307 Regency Court, Willow Springs IL 60480, USA
**Savard, Marc** — Ice Hockey Player
197 8th St, #511, Charlestown MA 02129, USA
**Savard, Serge A** — Ice Hockey Player, Executive
1790 Champs du Golf, RR 1, Saint Bruno QC J3V 4P6, Canada
**Savary, Jerome** — Director
Opera Comique, 5 Rue Favart, 75002 Paris, France
**Savchenko, Aliona** — Figure Skater
Eisstadion Ingo Steuer, Wittgensdorfer Str 2A, 09114 Chemnitz, Germany
**Savchenko, Arkadiy M** — Opera Singer
8-358 Storozhovskaya Str, 220002 Minsk, Belarus
**Saverine, Robert P (Bob)** — Baseball Player
228 Slice Dr, Stamford CT 06907, USA
**Savery, Uffe** — Percussion Musician (Safri Duo)
P D H Music, Dag Hammarskjold Alle 42 G, 2100 Copenhagen 0, Denmark
**Savic, Maja** — Handball Player
Z R K Buducnost T-Mobile, Ivan Milutinovic B B, 81000 Podgorica, Montenegro
**Savident, John** — Actor
Granada Television, Quay St, Manchester M60 9EA, England
**Savidge, Jennifer** — Actress
Talent Works, 3500 W Olive Ave, #1400, Burbank CA 91505 USA
**Saville, Curtis** — Long Distance Rower, Explorer
RFD Box 44, West Charleston VT 05872, USA
**Saville, Kathleen** — Long Distance Rower, Explorer
RFD Box 44, West Charleston VT 05872, USA
**Savini, Tom** — Actor, Special Effects Artist
311 Taylor St, Pittsburgh PA 15224, USA
**Savinykh, Viktor P** — Cosmonaut
Moscow State University, Aerophotogrammetry Institute, Gorokhovskiy 4, 103064 Moscow, Russia
**Saviola, Camille** — Actress
Kazarian/Measures/Ruskin, 11969 Ventura Blvd, #300, Studio City CA 91604 USA
**Savitskaya, Svetlana Y** — Cosmonaut
Russian Association, Khovanskaya Str 3, 129515 Moscow, Russia
**Savitt, Richard (Dick)** — Tennis Player
19 E 80th St, New York NY 10075, USA
**Savoy, Guy** — Chef
101 Blvd Pereire, 75017 Paris, France
**Savransky, Morris (Moe)** — Baseball Player
128 Dorset Dr, Boca Raton FL 33434, USA
**Savre, Danielle** — Actress, Singer
Talent Works, 3500 W Olive Ave, #1400, Burbank CA 91505 USA
**Sawa, Devon** — Actor
Gersh Agency, 9465 Wilshire Blvd, #600, Beverly Hills CA 90212 USA
**Sawa, Homare** — Soccer Player
Football Assn, 3-10-15 Hongo, Bunkyoku, Tokyo 113 0033 Japan
**Sawalha, Julia** — Actress
Ken McReddie Assoc, 101 Finsbury Pavement, London EC2A 1RS, England
**Sawalha, Nadia** — Actress
B B C, Broadcasting House, Portland Place, London W1A 1AA, England
**Sawalha, Nadim** — Actor
Associated International Mgmt, 7 Hatton Garden, #400, London EC1N 8AD, England
**Sawallisch, Wolfgang** — Conductor, Concert Pianist
Hinterm Bichl 2, 83224 Grassau, Germany
**Sawyer, Alan L** — Basketball Player
117 San Juan Dr, Sequim WA 98382, USA
**Sawyer, Diane** — Commentator
147 Columbus Ave, #300, New York NY 10023, USA
**Sawyer, Forrest** — Commentator
NBC-TV, News Dept, 30 Rockefeller Plaza, #270E, New York NY 10112 USA
**Sawyer, John W** — Football Player
23637 Sunnyside Lane, Zachary LA 70791, USA
**Sawyer, Kevin** — Ice Hockey Player
5118 N Ivy Court, Spokane Valley WA 99206, USA
**Sawyer, Ray** — Singer, Guitarist (Dr Hook)
Artists International Mgmt, 9850 Sandalfoot Blvd, #458, Boca Raton FL 33428, USA

**Sawyer, Talance M** — Football Player
6150 Brookhaven Dr, Bastrop LA 71220, USA
**Sax, David J (Dave)** — Baseball Player
3352 Eaton Dr, Roseville CA 95661, USA
**Sax, Geoffrey** — Director
I C M Partners, 10250 Constellation Blvd, #900, Los Angeles CA 90067 USA
**Sax, Stephen L (Steve)** — Baseball Player
201 Wesley Court, Roseville CA 95661, USA
**Saxe, Adrian A** — Artist
4835 N Figueroa St, Los Angeles CA 90042, USA
**Saxon, Edward** — Producer
Edward Saxon Productions, 1526 14th St, #105, Santa Monica CA 90404, USA
**Saxon, James E** — Football Player
28500 Fox Hollow Dr, Hayward CA 94542, USA
**Saxon, John** — Actor
Beacon Talent, 9250 Sunset Blvd, #727, Los Angeles CA 90069, USA
**Saxon, Michael E (Mike)** — Football Player
211 Winding Hollow Lane, Coppell TX 75019, USA
**Saxton, Charlie** — Actor
Creative Artists Agency, 2000 Ave of Stars, #100, Los Angeles CA 90067 USA
**Saxton, James E (Jimmy)** — Football Player
5000 Mission Oaks Blvd, #52, Austin TX 78735, USA
**Sayako** — Princess, Japan
Imperial Palace, 1-1 Chiyoda, Chiyodaku, Tokyo 100, Japan
**Sayalero Fernandez, Maritza** — Beauty Queen
Aveida Ruiz, 65 Sun Ensenada, Baja California, Mexico
**Sayed, Mostafa Amr El** — Chemist
579 Westover Dr NW, Atlanta GA 30305, USA
**Sayer, Leo** — Singer, Songwriter
Harbour Agency, 135 Forbes St, Woolloomooloo NSW 2011, Australia
**Sayers, Gale E** — Football Player
1313 N Ritchie Court, #407, Chicago IL 60610, USA
**Saykally, Richard J** — Chemist
University of California, Chemistry Dept, Latimer Hall, Berkeley CA 94720, USA
**Sayles, John T** — Director
210 13th St, Hoboken NJ 07030, USA
**Saylor, Edward J** — WW II Army Air Corps Hero
41802 207th Ave SE, Enumclaw WA 98022, USA
**Saylor, Morgan** — Actress
United Talent Agency, U T A Plaza, 9336 Civic Center Dr, Beverly Hills CA 90210 USA
**Scacchi, Greta** — Actress
Shanahan Mgmt, Berman House, 91 Campbell St, Surry Hills NSW 2010, Australia
**Scaggs, William R (Boz)** — Singer, Songwriter
Front Line Mgmt, 1100 Glendon Ave, #2000, Los Angeles CA 90024 USA
**Scaglione, Josefina** — Actress, Singer
Untitled Entertainment, 350 S Beverly Dr, #200, Beverly Hills CA 90212 USA
**Scagliotti, Allison** — Actress
Schiff Co, 9200 Sunset Blvd, #430, West Hollywood CA 90232 USA
**Scaife, Oliver L (Bo), III** — Football Player
6505 Banbury Crossing, Brentwood TN 37027, USA
**Scala, Tina** — Actress
Jack Scagneti Talent, 5118 Vineland Ave, #101, North Hollywood CA 91601, USA
**Scalabrine, Brian** — Basketball Player
1513 Griffin Ave, Enumclaw WA 98022, USA
**Scalapino, Douglas J** — Physicist
University of California, Physics Dept, Santa Barbara CA 93106, USA
**Scales, Charles A (Charley)** — Football Player
4035 Vistaview St, West Mifflin PA 15122, USA
**Scales, Dwight A** — Football Player
6112 Roosevelt Circle NW, Huntsville AL 35810, USA
**Scales, Prunella M** — Actress
Conway Van Gelder Grant, 8-12 Broadwick St, #300, London W1F 8HW, England
**Scalia, Antonin** — Supreme Court Justice
US Supreme Court, 1 1st St NE, Washington DC 20543 USA
**Scalia, Jack** — Actor
16260 Ventura Blvd, Encino CA 91436, USA
**Scallions, Bret** — Singer, Guitarist (Fuel)
Media Five Entertainment, 3005 Brodhead Road, #170, Bethlehem PA 18020, USA
**Scalzo, Tony** — Singer, Bassist (Fastball)
Russell Carter Artists, 315 Ponce de Leon Blvd, #755, Decatur GA 30030, USA
**Scamarcio, Riccardo** — Actor
Cineart, 28 Rue Mogador, 78009 Paris, France
**Scaminace, Joseph M** — Businessman
Sherwin-Williams Co, 101 W Prospect Ave, #1020, Cleveland OH 44115, USA
**Scamurra, Peter (Pete)** — Ice Hockey Player
15 Guinevere Court, Getzville NY 14068, USA
**Scancarelli, Jim** — Cartoonist (Gasoline Alley)
Mark J Cohen, PO Box 1892, Santa Rosa CA 95402, USA
**Scandiuzzi, Roberto** — Opera Singer
Atelier Fedelli, Via Casekke 76, 40068 San Lazzaro Savena (Bo), Italy
**Scanlan, Robert G (Bob). Jr** — Baseball Player
12400 Montecito Road, #315, Seal Beach CA 90740, USA
**Scanlan, Teresa** — Beauty Queen
Miss America Organization, 1370 Ave of Americas, #1600, New York NY 10019 USA
**Scanlon, J Patrick (Pat)** — Baseball Player
7400 Portland Ave S, Minneapolis MN 55423, USA
**Scanlon, Thomas M, Jr** — Philosopher
Harvard University, Philosophy Dept, Cambridge MA 02138, USA
**Scannell, Susan** — Actress
247 S Beverly Dr, #102, Beverly Hills CA 90212, USA
**Scaparrotti, Curtis M (Mike)** — Army General
Director, Joint Staff, Pentagon, Washington DC 20340, USA
**Scarabelli, Michele** — Actress
Characters Talent Agency, 8 Elm St, Toronto ON M5G 1G7, Canada
**Scarbath, John C (Jack)** — Football Player
736 Calvert Road, Rising Sun MD 21911, USA

**Scarbery, Randy J** — Baseball Player
5010 E Lewis Ave, Fresno CA 93727, USA

**Scarborough, C Joseph (Joe)** — Commentator; Representative, FL
MSNBC-TV, 900 Sylvan Ave, Englewood Cliffs NJ 07632, USA

**Scarce, G McCurdy (Mac)** — Baseball Player
1010 Richmond Glen Circle, Alpharetta GA 30004, USA

**Scardapane, Dario** — Producer, Writer
Management 360, 9111 Wilshire Blvd, Beverly Hills CA 90210 USA

**Scardelletti, Robert A** — Labor Leader
Transportation Communications Union, 3 Research Place, Rockville MD 20850, USA

**Scardino, Don** — Director
Creative Artists Agency, 2000 Ave of Stars, #100, Los Angeles CA 90067 USA

**Scarf, Herbert E** — Economist
200 Leeder Hill Dr, #2711, Hamden CT 06517, USA

**Scarface** — Rap Artist (Geto Boys)
J L Entertainment, 18653 Ventura Blvd, #340, Los Angeles CA 91356 USA

**Scarfe, Gerald A** — Cartoonist
Jane Asher Party Cakes, 22-24 Cale St, London SW3 3QU, England

**Scarfe, Jonathan** — Actor
Gary Goddard Agency, 10 Saint Mary's St, #305, Toronto ON M4Y 1P9, Canada

**Scargill, Arthur** — Labor Leader
National Union of Mineworkers, 2 Huddersfield Road, Barnsley, England

**Scarimbolo, Adam** — Actor
C E S D, 10635 Santa Monica Blvd, #130, Los Angeles CA 90025 USA

**Scarpitto, Robert F (Bob)** — Football Player
117 White Oaks Lane, Carmel Valley CA 93924, USA

**Scarr, Sandra W** — Psychologist
77-6222 Kaunmakumalu Dr, Holualoa HI 96725, USA

**Scarry, Elaine** — Educator
Harvard University, English Dept, Cambridge MA 02138, USA

**Scarsone, Steven W (Steve)** — Baseball Player
3935 E Rough Rider Road, #1158, Phoenix AZ 85050, USA

**Scarwid, Diana E** — Actress
Committed Artists Entertainment, 2600 W Olive Ave, #500, Burbank CA 91505, USA

**Scatchard, Dave** — Ice Hockey Player
8312 N 50th St, Paradise Valley AZ 85253, USA

**Scates, Allen E** — Volleyball Coach
8433 Apple Hill Court, Las Vegas NV 89128, USA

**Scattini, Monica** — Actress
Carol Levi Mgmt, Via Giuseppe Pisanelli 2, 00196 Rome, Italy

**Scelzi, Gary** — Drag Racing Driver
Alan Johnson Racing, 2772 S Cherry Ave, Fresno CA 93706, USA

**Scerbo, Cassie** — Actress
Strong Management, 9350 Wilshire Blvd. #224, Beverly Hills CA 90212, USA

**Schaaf-Behle, Petra** — Biathlete
Am Rodeland 22, 34508 Willingen, Germany

**Schaal, Kristen** — Actress, Writer
Avalon Mgmt, 4A Exmoor St, London W10 6BD, England

**Schaal, Paul** — Baseball Player
68-1962 Puu Nui St, Waikoloa HI 96738, USA

**Schaal, Richard** — Actor
612 Gulf Blvd, #9, Indian Rocks Beach FL 33785, USA

**Schaal, Wendy** — Actress
Gage Group, 14724 Ventura Blvd, #505, Sherman Oaks CA 91403 USA

**Schacher, Mel** — Bassist (Grand Funk Railroad)
Lustig Talent, PO Box 770850, Orlando FL 32877 USA

**Schachman, Howard K** — Molecular Biochemist
University of California, Molecular Biology Dept, Berkeley CA 94720, USA

**Schacht, Henry B** — Businessman
Lucent Technologies Inc, 600 Mountain Ave, New Providence NJ 07974, USA

**Schachter-Shalomi, Zalman** — Religious Leader, Rabbi
Yesod Foundation, PO Box 48, Boulder CO 80306, USA

**Schacker, Harold (Hal)** — Baseball Player
4609 N Matanzas Ave, Tampa FL 33614, USA

**Schacter, Beth** — Director, Writer
Anonymous Content, 3532 Hayden Ave, Culver City CA 90232 USA

**Schacter-Shalomi, Zalman** — Religious Leader
Spiritual Eldering Institute, 535 W S Boulder Road, Lafayette CO 80026, USA

**Schade, Frank** — Basketball Player
826 Nicolet Ave, Oshkosh WI 54901, USA

**Schaden, Rick** — Businessman
Quiznos, 1975 Lawrence St, Denver CO 80202, USA

**Schadler, Bernard R (Ben)** — Basketball Player
808 Bauer Dr, San Carlos CA 94070, USA

**Schadler, Jay** — Commentator
ABC-TV, News Dept, 77 W 66th St, New York NY 10023 USA

**Schaech, Jonathan** — Actor
A P A Talent/Literary Agency, 405 S Beverly Dr, #300, Beverly Hills CA 90212 USA

**Schaefer, Henry F, III** — Chemist
University of Georgia, Computational Quantum Chemistry Center, Athens GA 30602, USA

**Schaefer, Jeffrey S (Jeff)** — Baseball Player
2110 Woodbend Trail, Fort Mill SC 29708, USA

**Schaefer, Roberto** — Cinematographer
Innovative Artists, 1505 10th St, Santa Monica CA 90401 USA

**Schaeffer, Eric** — Actor, Director, Producer
Paradigm Agency, 360 N Crescent Dr, North Building, Beverly Hills CA 90210 USA

**Schaeffer, Frank** — Writer
Carroll & Graf, 245 W 17th St, #1100, New York NY 10011, USA

**Schaeffer, Leonard** — Businessman
WellPoint Health Networks, 1 Wellpoint Way, Westlake Village CA 91362, USA

**Schaeffer, Mark P** — Baseball Player
18261 Parthenia St, Northridge CA 91325, USA

**Schaeffer, William** — Hero
1865 Paseo de Oro, Colorado Springs CO 80904, USA

**Schaetzel, John R** — Writer
3050 Military Road NW, #555, Washington DC 20015, USA

**Schafer, Christine** — Opera Singer
Columbia Artists Mgmt Inc, 1790 Broadway, #702, New York NY 10019 USA
**Schafer, Edward T (Ed)** — Secretary, Agriculture; Governor, ND
1131 N 4th St, Bismarck ND 58501, USA
**Schafer, Hans** — Soccer Player
D F B, Postfach 710265, 60492 Frankfurt, Germany
**Schafer, Jordan J** — Baseball Player
80 Pine Forest Dr, Haines City FL 33844, USA
**Schafer, Susanne** — Actress
Agentur Carola Studlar, Agnesstr 47, 80798 Munich, Germany
**Schaffel, Maria** — Actress
Stone Manners Salners, 9911 W Pico Blvd, #1400, Los Angeles CA 90035 USA
**Schaffer, Eric** — Concert Executive
Kennedy Center for Performing Arts, 2700 F St NW, Washington DC 20566, USA
**Schaffer, Jimmie R (Jim)** — Baseball Player
655 Birch Terrace, Coopersburg PA 18036, USA
**Schafrath, Richard P (Dick)** — Football Player
704 Ashland Road, Mansfield OH 44905, USA
**Schaible, Michael** — Interior Designer
Bray-Schnaible Design, 80 W 40th St, #800, New York NY 10018, USA
**Schaitber, Harold A** — Labor Leader
International Fire Fighters, 1750 New York Ave NW, #300, Washington DC 20006, USA
**Schajris Rodriguez, Noel** — Singer, Guitarist (Sin Bandera)
Westwood Mgmt, Maria de Teresa 250, San Angel, Mexico City 01040, Mexico
**Schall, Alvin A** — Judge
US Appeals Court, 717 Madison Place NW, Washington DC 20439, USA
**Schaller, George B** — Zoologist
90 Sentry Hill Road, Roxbury CT 06783, USA
**Schaller, Willie** — Soccer Player
3283 S Indiana St, Lakewood CO 80228, USA
**Schallert, William** — Actor
14920 Ramos Place, Pacific Palisades CA 90272, USA
**Schallock, Arthur L (Art)** — Baseball Player
749 Crocus Dr, Sonoma CA 95476, USA
**Schally, Andrew V** — Nobel Medicine Laureate
3801 Collins Ave, Miami Beach FL 33140, USA
**Schama, Simon M** — Historian, Writer
Columbia University, Art History Dept, Fairweather Hall, Cambridge MA 02138, USA
**Schamehorn, Kevin** — Ice Hockey Player
5536 Stoney Brook Road, Kalamazoo MI 49009, USA
**Schamus, James** — Director, Producer
Creative Artists Agency, 2000 Ave of Stars, #100, Los Angeles CA 90067 USA
**Schanberg, Sydney H** — Journalist
PO Box 236, Rifton NY 12471, USA
**Schankweiler, Scott B** — Football Player
11 Bartley Court, Nottingham MD 21236, USA
**Schanley, Tom** — Actor
Maverick Artists, 6100 Wilshire Blvd, #550, Los Angeles CA 90048, USA
**Schapiro, Mary L** — Financier, Government Official
Promontory Financial Group, 801 17th St NW, #1100, Washington DC 20006, USA
**Schapker, Alison** — Producer, Writer
W M E Entertainment, 9601 Wilshire Blvd, #300, Beverly Hills CA 90210 USA
**Schapp, Dick** — Sportscaster
ESPN-TV, ESPN Plaza, 935 Middle St, Bristol CT 06010 USA
**Scharansky, Natan** — Social Activist, Computer Scientist
Shalem Center, 13 Yehoshua Bin-Nun St, Jersalem 93145, Israel
**Scharer, Erich** — Bobsled Athlete
Grutstra 63, 8074 Herrliberg, Switzerland
**Scharping, Rudolf** — Government Official, Germany
Wilhelmstr 5, 56112 Lahnstein, Germany
**Schattinger, Jeffrey C (Jeff)** — Baseball Player
PO Box 134, Lake Arrowhead CA 92352, USA
**Schatz, Howard** — Photographer
435 W Broadway, #200, New York NY 10012, USA
**Schatz, Mark** — Bassist (Nickel Creek)
Q-Prime South, 131 S 11th St, Nashville TN 37206 USA
**Schatzeder, Daniel E (Dan)** — Baseball Player
186 River Mist Dr, Oswego IL 60543, USA
**Schatzman, Evry** — Astrophysicist
11 Rue de l'Eglise, Dompierre, 60420 Maignelay-Montigny, France
**Schaub, Matthew R (Matt)** — Football Player
3300 Irvine Ave, #300, Newport Beach CA 92660, USA
**Schaudt, Martin** — Equestrian
Gerhardstr 10/2, 72461 Albstadt, Germany
**Schauer, Frederick F** — Attorney, Educator
Harvard University, Kennedy Government School, Cambridge MA 02138, USA
**Schaufuss, Peter** — Ballet Dancer, Director
Papoutsis Representation, 18 Sundial Ave, London SE25 4BX, England
**Schaukowith, Carl** — Football Player
11700 Bishops Content Road, Bowie MD 20721, USA
**Schayes, Adolph (Dolph)** — Basketball Player, Coach
PO Box 156, Syracuse NY 13214, USA
**Schayes, Daniel L (Danny)** — Basketball Player
8586 E Krail St, Scottsdale AZ 85250, USA
**Schazad, Graziella** — Singer
Warner Music Group, Alter Wandraham 14, 20457 Hamburg, Germany , USA
**Schechtman, Daniel** — Nobel Chemistry Laureate
Technion Institute of Technology, Haifa 32000, Israel
**Scheck, Barry** — Attorney, Educator
Yeshiva University, Law School, 55 5th Ave, #600, New York NY 10003, USA
**Scheckter, Jody D** — Auto Racing Driver
Home Farm, Laverstoke Park, Overton, Hampshire RG25 3DR, England
**Schedeen, Anne** — Actress
Metropolitan Talent Agency, 5405 Wilshire Blvd, #218, Los Angeles CA 90036 USA
**Schedwill, Sybille J** — Actress
Funke & Stertz, Schulterblatt 58, 20357 Hamburg, Germany

**Scheer, Paul** — Actor, Comedian, Writer
Principato-Young, 9465 Wilshire Blvd, #880, Beverly Hills CA 90212 USA
**Scheffer, Will** — Producer, Writer
Creative Artists Agency, 2000 Ave of Stars, #100, Los Angeles CA 90067 USA
**Schefter, Adam** — Sportscaster
ESPN-TV, ESPN Plaza, 935 Middle St, Bristol CT 06010 USA
**Scheib, Carl A** — Baseball Player
2922 Old Ranch Road, San Antonio TX 78217, USA
**Scheibel, Arnold B** — Psychiatrist
100 Bay Place, #804, Oakland CA 94610, USA
**Scheid, Eusebio Oscar Cardinal** — Religious Leader
Archdiocese, Rua Benjamin Constant 23/502, 20241 Rio de Janeiro, Brazil
**Scheinblum, Richard A (Richie)** — Baseball Player
1308 Woodstock Dr, Palm Harbor FL 34684, USA
**Schekman, Randy W** — Nobel Medicine Laureate
University of California Medical School, Cell Biology Dept, Berkeley CA
**Schell, Catherine** — Actress
Postfach 800504, 51005 Cologne, Germany
**Schell, Maximilian** — Actor
Baumbauer Actors, Hanfelderstr 32, 82319 Starnberg, Germany
**Schellhase, David G (Dave)** — Basketball Player
862 Walnut Ridge E, Logansport IN 46947, USA
**Schelling, Thomas C** — Nobel Economics Laureate
4506 Wetherill Road, Bethesda MD 20816, USA
**Schellman, John A** — Chemist
65 W 30th Ave, #508, Eugene OR 97405, USA
**Schelmerding, Kirk** — Auto Racing Mechanic
Childress Racing, PO Box 1189, Industrial Dr, Welcome NC 27374, USA
**Schelotto, Guillermo Barros** — Soccer Player
Columbus Crew, 1 Black & Gold Blvd, Columbus OH 43211 USA
**Schemansky, Norbert** — Weightlifter
24826 New York St, Dearborn MI 48124, USA
**Schenker, Michael** — Guitarist (UFO, Scorpions)
Artists Worldwide, 3921 Wilshire Blvd, #619, Los Angeles CA 90010, USA
**Schenker, Rudolf** — Guitarist (Scorpions)
Und Verlags, Bohlenweg 8, 30835, Germany
**Schenkkan, Robert F, Jr** — Writer, Actor
W M E Entertainment, 9601 Wilshire Blvd, #300, Beverly Hills CA 90210 USA
**Schenkman, Eric** — Musician (Spin Doctors)
D A S Communications, 83 Riverside Dr, New York NY 10024 USA
**Schepisi, Frederic A (Fred)** — Director
Echo Lake Productions, 421 S Beverly Dr, #800, Beverly Hills CA 90212, USA
**Scheraga, Harold A** — Chemist
223 Savage Farm Dr, Ithaca NY 14850, USA
**Scherbachenko, Ekaterina** — Opera Singer
I M G Artists, Hogarth Business Park, Chiswick, London W4 2TH, England
**Scherbo, Vitali** — Gymnast
8308 Aqua Spray Ave, Las Vegas NV 89128, USA
**Scherer, Frederic M** — Economist
53 Standish St, #2, Cambridge MA 02138, USA
**Scherer, Odilo P Cardinal** — Religious Leader
Avenida Higienopolis 890, 02138-908 Sao Paulo SP, Brazil
**Scherman, Frederick J (Fred)** — Baseball Player
7454 S Tipp Cowlesville Road, Tipp City OH 45371, USA
**Scherman, Nossom** — Religious Leader, Rabbi, Editor
ArtScroll/Mesorah Publications, 4514 11th Ave, Brooklyn NY 11219, USA
**Scherrer, Tom** — Golfer
2608 Drommore Lane, Raleigh NC 27614, USA
**Scherrer, William J (Bill)** — Baseball Player
222 Fareway Lane, Grand Island NY 14072, USA
**Scherza, Chuck** — Ice Hockey Player
51 Manistee St, Pawtucket RI 02861, USA
**Scherzinger, Nicole** — Singer (Eden's Crush, Pussycat Dolls)
W M E Entertainment, 9601 Wilshire Blvd, #300, Beverly Hills CA 90210 USA
**Scheuer, Paul J** — Chemist
3217 Melemele Place, Honolulu HI 96822, USA
**Schiano, Gregory E (Greg)** — Football Coach
Tampa Bay Buccaneers, 1 W Buccaneer Place, Tampa FL 33607 USA
**Schiavo, Mary** — Government Official, Social Activist
Ohio State University, Public Policy Dept, Columbus OH 43210, USA
**Schiavo, Richard J** — Thoroughbred Racing Executive
I E A H Stables, 595 Stewart Ave, #450, Garden City NY 11530, USA
**Schiavone, Francesca** — Tennis Player
Via Teano 21, 20161 Milan, Italy
**Schickel, Richard** — Writer, Film Critic
9051 Dicks St, West Hollywood CA 90069, USA
**Schickele, Peter** — Composer, Comedian
Opus 3 Artists, 470 Park Ave S, #900N, New York NY 10016 USA
**Schiebold, Hans** — Artist
13705 SW 118th Court, Portland OR 97223, USA
**Schieffer, Bob** — Commentator
CBS-TV, News Dept, 2020 M St NW, Washington DC 20036 USA
**Schierholtz, Nathan J (Nate)** — Baseball Player
7500 E Deer Valley Road, #118, Scottsdale AZ 85255, USA
**Schiff, Andras** — Concert Pianist
Terry Harrison Mgmt, Market St, Charlbury, Oxfordshire OX7 3PJ, England
**Schiff, Heinrich** — Concert Cellist, Conductor
Astrid Schoerke, Monckegergallee 41, 30453 Hanover, Germany
**Schiff, Mark** — Actor, Comedian
Gail Stocker Presents, 1025 N Kings Road, #113, West Hollywood CA 90069, USA
**Schiff, Richard** — Actor
I F A Talent Agency, 8730 W Sunset Blvd, #490, West Hollywood CA 90069 USA
**Schiff, Stacy** — Writer
Little Brown, 1271 Ave of Americas, New York NY 10020, USA
**Schiffer, Claudia** — Model, Actress
Aussenwall 94, 47495 Rheinberg, Germany

**Schiffer, Michael** — Writer, Producer
Ballpark Pictures, PO Box 508, Venice CA 90294, USA
**Schiffman, Guillaume** — Cinematographer
20 Rue Saulnier, 75009 Paris, France
**Schiffman, Mark** — Physician, Epidemiologist
National Cancer Institute, 6120 Executive Blvd, Bethesda MD 20892, USA
**Schiffman, Michael** — Actor
Harvest Mgmt, PO Box 279, Jefferson Valley NY 10535, USA
**Schiffrin, Andre** — Publisher
New Press, 450 W 41st St, New York NY 10036, USA
**Schifrin, Lalo** — Composer
710 N Hillcrest Road, Beverly Hills CA 90210, USA
**Schild, Marlies** — Alpine Skier
Weikersbach 9, 5760 Saalfelden, Austria
**Schiller, Lawrence J** — Producer, Director, Writer
60 W 57th St, #19B, New York NY 10019, USA
**Schiller, Rob** — Director
Evolution Entertainment, 901 N Highland Ave, Los Angeles CA 90038 USA
**Schiller, Robert J** — Nobel Economics Laureate
Cowles Foundation, Box 208281, New Haven CT 06511, USA
**Schilling, Curtis M (Curt)** — Baseball Player
7 Woodridge Road, Medfield MA 02052, USA
**Schilling, Taylor** — Actress
Gersh Agency, 9465 Wilshire Blvd, #600, Beverly Hills CA 90212 USA
**Schimberni, Mario** — Businessman
Armando Curcio Editore SpA, Via IV Novembre, 00187 Rome, Italy
**Schimmel, Paul R** — Biologist, Biochemist
Scripps Research Institute, 10550 N Torrey Pines Road, La Jolla CA 92037, USA
**Schindelholz, Lorenz** — Bobsled Athlete
Hardstr 184, 4715 Herbetswil, Switzerland
**Schinkel, Kenneth (Ken)** — Ice Hockey Player
19927 Beaulieu Court, Fort Myers FL 33908, USA
**Schipper, Jessicah** — Swimmer
Swimming Australia, 12/7 Beissel St, Belconnen ACT 2617, Australia
**Schirripa, Steve R** — Actor
Innovative Artists, 1505 10th St, Santa Monica CA 90401 USA
**Schisgal, Murray J** — Writer
I C M Partners, 730 5th Ave, New York NY 10019 USA
**Schissler, Les** — Bowler
3060 E Bridge St, #20, Brighton CO 80601, USA
**Schlafly, Phyllis S** — Women's Activist
68 Fairmount Ave, Alton IL 62002, USA
**Schlamme, Thomas (Tommy)** — Director
Creative Artists Agency, 2000 Ave of Stars, #100, Los Angeles CA 90067 USA
**Schlatter, Charlie** — Actor
Sutton-Barth Vennari, 5900 Wilshire Blvd, #700, Los Angeles CA 90036 USA
**Schleeh, Russ** — Test Pilot
21634 Paseo Maravia, Mission Viejo CA 92692, USA
**Schlegel, Hans W** — Astronaut, Germany
European Space Center, Linder Hohe, Box 906096, 51127 Cologne, Germany
**Schlegel, Sylvester** — Drummer (The Ark)
Live Nation, Linnegatan 89, Box 21451, 104 51 Stockholm, Sweden
**Schlereth, Mark F** — Football Player
9479 S Shadow Hill Circle, Lone Tree CO 80124, USA
**Schlesinger, Adam** — Singer (Fountains of Wayne), Songwriter
Big Hassle, 157 Chambers St, #1200, New York NY 10007, USA
**Schlesinger, Cory M** — Football Player
36 Bradford Court, Dearborn MI 48126, USA
**Schlesinger, James R** — Secretary, Defense; Energy
Georgetown University, 1800 K St NW, #400, Washington DC 20006, USA
**Schlessinger, Laura** — Radio Psychologist, Physiologist
3201 Campanil Dr, Santa Barbara CA 93109, USA
**Schlichtmann, Jan** — Attorney
359 Hale St, Beverly Farms MA 01915, USA
**Schlink, Bernhard** — Writer
Heilbronner Str 3, 10779 Berlin, Germany
**Schlitt, John W** — Singer (Petra, Head East)
112 Glen Haven Lane, Franklin TN 37069, USA
**Schlondorff, Volker O** — Director
Studio Babelsberg, Postfach 900361, 14439 Potsdam, Germany
**Schloredt, Robert S (Bob)** — Football Player
Nestle-Beich, 1827 N 167th St, Shoreline WA 98133, USA
**Schlossberg, Hayden** — Director, Writer
Creative Artists Agency, 2000 Ave of Stars, #100, Los Angeles CA 90067 USA
**Schlueter, Dale W** — Basketball Player
15555 SW Harcourt Terrace, Portland OR 97224, USA
**Schluter, Poul H** — Prime Minister, Denmark
Frederiksborg Allee 66, 1820 Frederiksberg C, Denmark
**Schmautz, Robert J (Bobby)** — Ice Hockey Player
19866 N 90th Ave, Peoria AZ 85382, USA
**Schmeichel, Peter** — Soccer Player
Aston Villa, Villa Park, Trinity Road, Birmingham B6 6HE, England
**Schmelz, Alan G (Al)** — Baseball Player
7406 E Camino Rayo de Luz, Scottsdale AZ 85266, USA
**Schmemann, Serge** — Journalist
New York Times, Editorial Dept, 229 W 43rd St, New York NY 10036, USA
**Schmid, Benjamin** — Concert, Jazz Violinist
Harrison/Parrott, Lucile-Grahn-Stra 37, 81675 Munich, Germany
**Schmid, Daniel J (Dan)** — Bassist (Cherry Poppin' Daddies)
Paradise Artists, PO Box 1821, Ojai CA 93024 USA
**Schmid, Harald** — Track Athlete
Schulstr 11, 63594 Hasselroth, Germany
**Schmid, Kyle** — Actor
Glick Agency, 1321 7th St, #203, Santa Monica CA 90401 USA
**Schmid, Sigi** — Soccer Coach
Seattle Sounders, 12 Seahawks Way, Renton WA 98056 USA

| | |
|---|---|
| **Schmidgall-Potter, Jennifer L** | Ice Hockey Player |
| 3640 Wooddale Ave S, #103, Minneapolis MN 55416, USA | |
| **Schmidly, David J** | Educator |
| University of New Mexico, President's Office, Albuquerque NM 87131, USA | |
| **Schmidt, Andreas** | Opera Singer |
| Fossredder 51, 22359 Hamburg, Germany | |
| **Schmidt, Benno C, Jr** | Educator |
| Edison Project, 375 Park Ave, New York NY 10152, USA | |
| **Schmidt, Brian P** | Nobel Physics Laureate |
| Australian National University, Mount Stromlo Observatory, Canberra ACT 0200, Australia | |
| **Schmidt, David J (Dave)** | Baseball Player |
| 7172 N Serenoa Dr, Sarasota FL 34241, USA | |
| **Schmidt, Eric E** | Businessman, Computer Engineer |
| Google Inc, 1600 Amphitheatre Parkway, #41, Mountain View CA 94043, USA | |
| **Schmidt, Helmut** | Chancellor, West Germany |
| Neuberger Weg 80, 22419 Hamburg, Germany | |
| **Schmidt, Henry J (Hank)** | Football Player |
| 4641 Mission Bell Lane, La Mesa CA 91941, USA | |
| **Schmidt, Jason D** | Baseball Player |
| 6539 E Cheney Dr, Paradise Valley AZ 85253, USA | |
| **Schmidt, Joseph P (Joe)** | Football Player |
| 226 Norcliff Dr, Bloomfield Hills MI 48302, USA | |
| **Schmidt, Kathryn (Kate)** | Track Athlete |
| 1008 Dexter St, Los Angeles CA 90042, USA | |
| **Schmidt, Kenneth** | Actor |
| Coast to Coast Talent, 3350 Barham Blvd, Los Angeles CA 90068 USA | |
| **Schmidt, Klaus** | Archeologist |
| German Archaeological Institute, Inonu Caddesi 10, 34437 Istanbul, Turkey | |
| **Schmidt, Maarten** | Astronomer |
| California Institute of Technology, Astronomy Dept, Pasadena CA 91125, USA | |
| **Schmidt, Michael J (Mike)** | Baseball Player |
| 373 Eagle Dr, Jupiter FL 33477, USA | |
| **Schmidt, Milton C (Milt)** | Ice Hockey Player |
| 10 Longwood Dr, #376, Westwood MA 02090, USA | |
| **Schmidt, Richard** | Surgeon |
| University of Pennsylvania Hospital, 3400 Spruce St, Philadelphia PA 19104, USA | |
| **Schmidt, Rob** | Director |
| Gersh Agency, 9465 Wilshire Blvd, #600, Beverly Hills CA 90212 USA | |
| **Schmidt, Robert M (Bob)** | Football Player |
| 10005 Sky View Way, #2106, Fort Myers FL 33913, USA | |
| **Schmidt, Sam** | Auto Racing Driver |
| Sam Schmidt Racing, 6803 Coffman Road, Indianapolis IN 46208, USA | |
| **Schmidt, Sophie** | Soccer Player |
| Canadian Soccer, Place Soccer Canada, 237 Metcalfe St, Ottawa ON K2P 1R2, Canada | |
| **Schmidt, Susan** | Journalist |
| Washington Post, Editorial Dept, 1150 15th St NW, Washington DC 20071 USA | |
| **Schmidt, Terry R** | Football Player |
| 2 Stone River Dr, Asheville NC 28804, USA | |
| **Schmidt, William (Bill)** | Track Athlete |
| 1809 Devonwood Court, Knoxville TN 37922, USA | |
| **Schmidt, Wolfgang** | Track Athlete |
| Birkheckenstr 116B, 70599 Stuttgart, Germany | |
| **Schmidt, Wrenn** | Actress |
| I C M Partners, 10250 Constellation Blvd, #900, Los Angeles CA 90067 USA | |
| **Schmiegel, Klaus K** | Inventor (Prozac) |
| 4507 Staughton Dr, Indianapolis IN 46226, USA | |
| **Schmiesing, Joseph F (Joe)** | Football Player |
| 19460 County Road 2, Sauk Centre MN 56378, USA | |
| **Schmirler, Sandra** | Curling Athlete |
| Curling Assn, 1660 Vimont Court, Cumberland ON K4A 4J4, Canada | |
| **Schmit, Timothy B** | Singer, Bassist (Eagles) |
| W M E Entertainment, 1325 Ave of Americas, New York NY 10019 USA | |
| **Schmitt, Arnd** | Fencer |
| Rheinuferweg 59B, 47495 Bornheim, Germany | |
| **Schmitt, Harrison H (Jack)** | Senator, NM; Astronaut |
| PO Box 90730, Albuquerque NM 87199, USA | |
| **Schmitt, Janis** | Model |
| Playboy Promotions, 2706 Media Center Dr, Los Angeles CA 90065 USA | |
| **Schmitt, John C** | Football Player |
| 2 Mayflower Road, Glen Head NY 11545, USA | |
| **Schmitt, Martin** | Ski Jumper |
| W W P Group, Lustenauerstra 64, 6850 Dornbirn, Austria | |
| **Schmitt, Maximilian** | Opera Singer |
| Kunstler Sekretariat am Gasteig, Rosenheimer Str 52, 81669 Munich, Germany | |
| **Schmitz, Oliver** | Director, Writer |
| Above the Line, Wielandstr 5, 10625 Berlin, Germany | |
| **Schmock, Jonathan** | Actor, Director |
| A P A Talent/Literary Agency, 405 S Beverly Dr, #300, Beverly Hills CA 90212 USA | |
| **Schmoeller, David** | Director |
| 3910 Woodhill Ave, Las Vegas NV 89121, USA | |
| **Schmoll, Steve** | Baseball Player |
| 4758 Chastain Dr, Melbourne FL 32940, USA | |
| **Schmolzer, August** | Actor, Writer |
| Agentur Carola Studlar, Agnesstr 47, 80798 Munich, Germany | |
| **Schnabel, Julian** | Artist, Director |
| Cinetic Mgmt, 555 W 25th St, #400, New York NY 10001 USA | |
| **Schnackenberg, Roy L** | Artist, Sculptor |
| 180 E Pearson St, Chicago IL 60611, USA | |
| **Schnarre, Monika** | Model, Actress |
| Alex Stevens, 137 N Larchmont, #259, Los Angeles CA 90004, USA | |
| **Schnebel, Dieter** | Composer |
| Hektorstr 15, 10711 Berlin, Germany | |
| **Schnebli, Dolf** | Architect |
| Sudstr 45, 8008 Zurich, Switzerland | |
| **Schneck, David L (Dave)** | Baseball Player |
| 3891 Lehigh Dr, Northampton PA 18067, USA | |

| | |
|---|---|
| **Schneck, Michael L (Mike)** | Football Player |
| 2006 Condor Lane, Gibsonia PA 15044, USA | |
| **Schneeberger, Gisela** | Actress |
| Agentur Carola Studlar, Agnesstr 47, 80798 Munich, Germany | |
| **Schneerson, Rachel** | Immunologist |
| National Institutes of Health, 9000 Rockville Pike, Bethesda MD 20892, USA | |
| **Schneider, Aaron** | Cinematographer |
| Anonymous Content, 3532 Hayden Ave, Culver City CA 90232 USA | |
| **Schneider, Bob** | Singer, Songwriter |
| Agency Group Ltd, 142 W 57th St, #600, New York NY 10019 USA | |
| **Schneider, Brian D** | Baseball Player |
| 130 Playa Rienta Way, Palm Beach Gardens FL 33418, USA | |
| **Schneider, Christoph (Doom)** | Drummer (Rammstein) |
| Pilgrim Mgmt, PO Box 54101, 10042 Berlin, Germany | |
| **Schneider, Cory** | Ice Hockey Player |
| Vancouver Canucks, 800 Griffiths Way, Vancouver BC V6B 6G1, Canada | |
| **Schneider, Daniel J (Dan)** | Actor, Director, Producer |
| W M E Entertainment, 9601 Wilshire Blvd, #300, Beverly Hills CA 90210 USA | |
| **Schneider, Daniel L (Dan)** | Baseball Player |
| PO Box 30940, Tucson AZ 85751, USA | |
| **Schneider, Eliza** | Actress |
| W M E Entertainment, 9601 Wilshire Blvd, #300, Beverly Hills CA 90210 USA | |
| **Schneider, Fred** | Singer, Songwriter (B-52s) |
| Direct Management Group, 947 N La Cienega Blvd, #G, West Hollywood CA 90069, USA | |
| **Schneider, Jeffrey T (Jeff)** | Baseball Player |
| 268 Pin Oak Dr, Geneseo IL 61254, USA | |
| **Schneider, John** | Actor, Singer |
| Trail's End, 4607 Lakeview Canyon Road, #569, Westlake Village CA 91361, USA | |
| **Schneider, Lew** | Producer, Writer, Actor |
| United Talent Agency, U T A Plaza, 9336 Civic Center Dr, Beverly Hills CA 90210 USA | |
| **Schneider, Mathieu** | Ice Hockey Player |
| 1311 6th St, Manhattan Beach CA 90266, USA | |
| **Schneider, Max** | Actor |
| W M E Entertainment, 9601 Wilshire Blvd, #300, Beverly Hills CA 90210 USA | |
| **Schneider, Paul** | Writer |
| MacMillan, 175 5th Ave, New York NY 10010 USA | |
| **Schneider, Paul A** | Actor |
| Creative Artists Agency, 2000 Ave of Stars, #100, Los Angeles CA 90067 USA | |
| **Schneider, Rob** | Actor, Comedian |
| Gersh Agency, 9465 Wilshire Blvd, #600, Beverly Hills CA 90212 USA | |
| **Schneider, Robert** | Singer, Guitarist (Apples in Stereo) |
| Billions Corp, 3522 W Armitage Ave, Chicago IL 60647 USA | |
| **Schneider, Verena (Vreni)** | Alpine Skier |
| An der Matt, 8767 Elm, Switzerland | |
| **Schneider, William C (Buzz)** | Ice Hockey Player |
| 5656 Turtle Lake Road, Saint Paul MN 55126, USA | |
| **Schneiderman, David A** | Publisher, Editor |
| I C M Partners, 10250 Constellation Blvd, #900, Los Angeles CA 90067 USA | |
| **Schneier, Arthur** | Religious Leader, Association Executive |
| Appeal of Conscience Foundation, 119 W 57th St, #820, New York NY 10019, USA | |
| **Schnelker, Robert B (Bob)** | Football Player |
| 85 Silver Oaks Circle, Naples FL 34119, USA | |
| **Schnelldorfer, Manfred** | Figure Skater |
| Seydlitzstr 55, 80993 Munich, Germany | |
| **Schnellenberger, Howard** | Football Coach |
| 118 SE 25th Ave, Boynton Beach FL 33435, USA | |
| **Schnetzer, Stephen** | Actor |
| Liebman Entertainment, 25 E 21st St, #PH, New York NY 10010, USA | |
| **Schnieders, Richard** | Businessman |
| Sysco Corp, 1390 Enclave Parkway, Houston TX 77077, USA | |
| **Schnitker, J Michael (Mike)** | Football Player |
| PO Box 968, Conifer CO 80433, USA | |
| **Schnittker, Richard D (Dick)** | Basketball Player |
| 2303 E Las Granadas, Green Valley AZ 85614, USA | |
| **Schnitzer, Morris** | Organic Chemist |
| 6035 Murray St, Niagara Falls ON L2G 2K4, Canada | |
| **Schobel, Aaron R** | Football Player |
| 1024 Yaupon Creek Estuary, Columbus TX 78934, USA | |
| **Schobel, Frank** | Singer |
| Artist Management Uwe Kanthak, Postfach 113124, 20431 Hamburg, Germany | |
| **Schobel, Matthew T (Matt)** | Football Player |
| PO Box 1276, Columbus TX 78934, USA | |
| **Schoch, Philipp** | Snowboarding Athlete |
| Waldheim, 8496 Steg, Switzerland | |
| **Schochet, Bob** | Cartoonist |
| 6 Sunset Road, Highland Mills NY 10930, USA | |
| **Schock, Gina** | Singer, Drummer (Go-Go's) |
| Direct Managment Group, 947 N La Cienega Blvd, #G, West Hollywood CA 90069, USA | |
| **Schock, Ron** | Ice Hockey Player |
| 1360 Whalen Road, Penfield NY 14526, USA | |
| **Schockemohle, Alwin** | Equestrian |
| Kreis Diepholz/Niedersachsen, 49453 Muhlen, Germany | |
| **Schoeller, Pierre** | Director, Writer |
| Agence Associes, 82 Rue de Rennes, 75006 Paris, France | |
| **Schoen, Gerald T (Gerry)** | Baseball Player |
| 110 Mark Twain Dr, #21, New Orleans LA 70123, USA | |
| **Schoen, Max H** | Dentist |
| 123 Wellfleet Circle, Folsom CA 95630, USA | |
| **Schoenaerts, Matthias** | Actor |
| Lisa Richards Agency, 108 Upper Leeson St, Dublin 4, Ireland | |
| **Schoenbaechler, Andreas** | Aerials Skier |
| Muhlrutistr 2, 8910 Affoltern a A, Switzerland | |
| **Schoenborn, Christoph Cardinal** | Religious Leader |
| Wollzeile 2, 1010 Vienna, Austria | |
| **Schoendienst, Albert F (Red)** | Baseball Player, Manager |
| 1105 Jo Carr Dr, Town and Country MO 63017, USA | |

**Schoene, Russ** — Basketball Player
1136 205th Ave NE, Sammamish WA 98074, USA
**Schoeneweis, Scott D** — Baseball Player
14420 E Kern Court, Fountain Hills AZ 85268, USA
**Schoenfeld, Jim** — Ice Hockey Player, Coach
45 W 60th St, #18D, New York NY 10023, USA
**Schoenfield, Al** — Swimming Executive
75 Santa Rosa St, San Luis Obispo CA 93405, USA
**Schoenke, Raymond F (Ray), Jr** — Football Player
21151 Woodfield Road, Gaithersburg MD 20882, USA
**Schofield, David** — Actor
Ken McReddie Assoc, 101 Finsbury Pavement, London EC2A 1RS, England
**Schofield, Dwight** — Ice Hockey Player
9024 Cardinal Terrace, Saint Louis MO 63144, USA
**Schofield, J Richard (Dick)** — Baseball Player
138 Circle Dr, Springfield IL 62703, USA
**Schofield, John** — Jazz Guitarist, Composer
International Music Network, 278 Main St, Gloucester MA 01930, USA
**Schofield, Oscar** — Oceanographer
Marine Biology/Ocean Optics Center, 71 Dudley Road, New Brunswick NJ 08901, USA
**Schofield, Richard C (Dick)** — Baseball Player
17703 Gardenview Place Court, Glencoe MO 63038, USA
**Scholes, Myron S** — Nobel Economics Laureate
34 Stern Lane, Atherton CA 94027, USA
**Scholl, Andreas** — Opera Singer
I M G Artists, Hogarth Business Park, Chiswick, London W4 2TH, England
**Schollander, Donald A (Don)** — Swimmer
3576 Lakeview Blvd, Lake Oswego OR 97035, USA
**Scholten, Jim** — Singer, Bassist (Sawyer Brown)
O-Seven Artist Mgmt, PO Box 210586, Nashville TN 37221, USA
**Scholtz, Bruce D** — Football Player
6636 W William Cannon Dr, #834, Austin TX 78735, USA
**Schomberg, A Thomas** — Sculptor
4923 S Snowberry Lane, Evergreen CO 80439, USA
**Schon, Jan Hendrik** — Inventor (Molecule Transistor)
Lucent Technology Bell Laboratory, 600 Mountain Ave, New Providence NJ 07974, USA
**Schon, Kyra** — Actress
930 N Sheridan Ave, Pittsburgh PA 15206, USA
**Schon, Neal J** — Guitarist (Journey)
Front Line Mgmt, 1100 Glendon Ave, #2000, Los Angeles CA 90024 USA
**Schonberg, Claude-Michel** — Composer
Cameron Mackintosh Ltd, 1 Bedford Square, London WC1B 3RA, England
**Schonert, Turk L** — Football Player
7 Sugar Mill Court, Lancaster NY 14086, USA
**Schonherr, Ivonne** — Actress
Sascha Wunsch Artists Mgmt, Stubenrauchstr 57, 12161 Berlin, Germany
**Schonhuber, Franz** — Commentator
Europaburo, Fraunhoferstr 23, 80469 Munich, Germany
**Schoofs, Mark** — Journalist
Village Voice, Editorial Dept, 32 Cooper Square, New York NY 10003, USA
**Schooler, Michael R (Mike)** — Baseball Player
519 N Buttonwood St, Anaheim CA 92805, USA
**Schoolnik, Gary** — Microbiologist
Stanford University Medical School, Microbiology Dept, Stanford CA 94305, USA
**Schools, Dave** — Bassist (Widespread Panic)
Brown Cat Inc, 400 Foundry St, Athens GA 30601 USA
**Schoomaker, Peter J (Pete)** — Army General
Special Operations Warrior Foundation, PO Box 13483, Tampa FL 33681, USA
**Schopf, J William** — Paleobiologist
University of California, Study of Evolution Center, Los Angeles CA 90024, USA
**Schorer, Jane** — Journalist
Des Moines Register, Editorial Dept, PO Box 957, Des Moines IA 50306, USA
**Schorr, Bill** — Cartoonist (Phoebe's Place, Grizzwells)
Cagle Cartoons, PO Box 22342, Santa Barbara CA 93121 USA
**Schorske, Carl E** — Historian, Writer
112 Sunnyside Road, Silver Spring MD 20910, USA
**Schott, Ben** — Photographer, Writer
Rogers Coleridge White, 20 Powis Mews, London W11 1JN, England
**Schottenheimer, Martin E (Marty)** — Football Coach, Sportscaster
19825 Northcove Road, #B, Cornelius NC 28031, USA
**Schourek, Peter A (Pete)** — Baseball Player
13761 Balmoral Greens Ave, Clifton VA 20124, USA
**Schrade, Brad** — Journalist
Minneapolis Star Tribune, Editorial Dept, 425 Portland Ave S, Minneapolis MN 55488 USA
**Schrader, Kenneth (Ken)** — Auto, Truck Racing Driver
Ken Schrader Racing, 4403 Stough Road, Concord NC 28027, USA
**Schrader, Maria** — Actress
Davien Littlefield Mgmt, 477 Madison Ave, New York NY 10022, USA
**Schrader, Paul J** — Director, Writer
Parseghian/Planco, 388 2nd Ave, #506, New York, NY 10010 USA
**Schrag, Ariel** — Writer
Peikoff Law Office, 173 E Broadway, #C1, New York NY 10002 USA
**Schram, Jessica (Jessy)** — Actress
C E S D, 10635 Santa Monica Blvd, #130, Los Angeles CA 90025 USA
**Schramka, Paul E** — Baseball Player
W180N9923 Riversbend Circle W, Germantown WI 53022, USA
**Schramm, David** — Actor
Gersh Agency, 9465 Wilshire Blvd, #600, Beverly Hills CA 90212 USA
**Schranz, Karl** — Alpine Skier
Hotel Gami, 6580 Saint Anton, Austria
**Schreiber, Adam B** — Football Player
PO Box 27085, Panama City FL 32411, USA
**Schreiber, Liev** — Actor, Director
Creative Artists Agency, 2000 Ave of Stars, #100, Los Angeles CA 90067 USA
**Schreiber, Martin J** — Governor, WI
2700 S Shore Dr, #B, Milwaukee WI 53207, USA

**Schreiber, Pablo** — Actor
I C M Partners, 10250 Constellation Blvd, #900, Los Angeles CA 90067 USA
**Schreiber, Stuart L** — Chemist
Harvard University, Chemistry Dept, Cambridge MA 02138, USA
**Schreiber, Theodore H (Ted)** — Baseball Player
116 Nantucket Isle, Centerville GA 31028, USA
**Schreier, Peter** — Opera Singer, Conductor
Peter McCann Ltd, 56 Lawrie Park Gardens, London SE26 6XY, England
**Schremp, Rob** — Ice Hockey Player
303 Phillips St, Fulton NY 13069, USA
**Schrempf, Detlef** — Basketball Player
9735 NE 1st St, Bellevue WA 98004, USA
**Schrempp, Jurgen E** — Businessman
Daimler-Chrysler AG, Plieningerstra, 70546 Stuttgart, Germany
**Schreyer, Cynthia (Cindy)** — Golfer
208 Brushy Hill Road, Danbury CT 06810, USA
**Schreyer, Edward R** — Governor General, Canada
250 Wellington Crescent, #401, Winnipeg MB R3M 0B3, Canada
**Schrieffer, John R** — Nobel Physics Laureate
22465 Tuna Place, Boca Raton FL 33428, USA
**Schrimshaw, Nevin S** — Nutritionist
Sandwich Notch Farm, Thornton NH 03223, USA
**Schrock, Richard R** — Nobel Chemistry Laureate
15 Cabot St, Winchester MA 01890, USA
**Schroder, Ernst A** — Actor
Podere Montalto, Castellina In Chianti, 53011 Siena, Italy
**Schroder, Rick** — Actor, Director
Hofflund/Polone, 9465 Wilshire Blvd, #420, Beverly Hills CA 90212 USA
**Schroeder, A William (Bill)** — Baseball Player
4760 S Providence Dr, New Berlin WI 53146, USA
**Schroeder, Barbet G** — Director, Producer
Creative Artists Agency, 2000 Ave of Stars, #100, Los Angeles CA 90067 USA
**Schroeder, Carly** — Actress
Innovative Artists, 1505 10th St, Santa Monica CA 90401 USA
**Schroeder, Dennis** — Basketball Player
Atlanta Hawks, Centennial Tower, 101 Marietta St NW, #1900, Atlanta GA 30303 USA
**Schroeder, Eugene W (Gene)** — Football Player
918 Aaron Court, Crown Point IN 46307, USA
**Schroeder, Gerhard** — Chancellor, Germany
Buro Bundeskanzler, Unter den Linden 50, 10117 Berlin, Germany
**Schroeder, Jay B** — Football Player
502 Hampton Road, Burbank CA 91504, USA
**Schroeder, Jim** — Bowler
3 Greenhaven Terrace, Tonawanda NY 14150, USA
**Schroeder, John H** — Educator
University of Wisconsin, Chancellor's Office, Milwaukee WI 53211, USA
**Schroeder, Manfred R** — Physicist
Rieswartenweg 8, 37077 Gottingen, Germany
**Schroeder, Mary M** — Judge
US Court of Appeals, 230 N 1st Ave, #101, Phoenix AZ 85003, USA
**Schroeder, Patricia S** — Representative, CO
621 Nadina Place, Kissimmee FL 34747, USA
**Schroeder, Paul W** — Historian
604 S Western Ave, Champaign IL 61821, USA
**Schroeder, Steven A** — Foundation Executive, Physician
10 Paseo Mirasol, Belvedere Tiburon CA 94920, USA
**Schroeder, Terry** — Water Polo Player, Coach
North Ranch Chiropractic, 31225 La Baya Dr, #206, Westlake Village CA 91362, USA
**Schroeder, William F (Bill)** — Football Player
2176 Shady Lane, Green Bay WI 54313, USA
**Schrom, Kenneth M (Ken)** — Baseball Player
1002 Black Diamond Court, Portland TX 78374, USA
**Schroy, Kenneth M (Ken)** — Football Player
79 Russell Road, Garden City NY 11530, USA
**Schroyer, Heath** — Basketball Coach
University of Wyoming, Athletic Dept, Laramie WY 82071, USA
**Schruefer, John J** — Gynecologist
3800 Reservoir Road NW, Washington DC 20007, USA
**Schu, Richard S (Rick)** — Baseball Player
2013 Driftwood Circle, El Dorado Hills CA 95762, USA
**Schuba, Beatrice (Trixi)** — Figure Skater
Giorgengasse 2/1/8, Vienna 1190, Austria
**Schubert, Christoph** — Ice Hockey Player
Atlanta Thrashers, 101 Marietta St NW, #1900, Atlanta GA 30303 USA
**Schubert, Richard F** — Association Executive
6615 Madison-McLean Dr, McLean VA 22101, USA
**Schubert, Steven W (Steve)** — Football Player
7 Douglas Dr, Candia NH 03034, USA
**Schuck, Anett** — Canoeing Athlete
Defoestry 6A, 04159 Leipzig, Germany
**Schuck, John** — Actor
Douglas Gorman Rothacker Wilhelm, 1501 Broadway, #703, New York NY 10036, USA
**Schuck, Walter** — WW II German Luftwaffe Hero
Tekstr 55, 66424 Homburg/Saar, Germany
**Schueler, Ronald R (Ron)** — Baseball Player
3201 E Camino Sin Nombre, Paradise Valley AZ 85253, USA
**Schuffenhauer, Bill** — Bobsled Athlete
2888 Marilyn Dr, Ogden UT 84403, USA
**Schuh, Jeffrey J (Jeff)** — Football Player
5550 Vagabond Lane N, Minneapolis MN 55446, USA
**Schuhl, Jean Jacques** — Writer
Editions Gallimard, 5 Rue Sebastien Bottin, 75007 Paris, France
**Schul, Robert (Bob)** — Track Athlete
320 Wisteria Dr, Dayton OH 45419, USA
**Schuldt, Travis** — Actor
Stone Manners Salners, 9911 W Pico Blvd, #1400, Los Angeles CA 90035 USA

**Schuler, Carolyn J** — Swimmer
26552 Via del Sol, Mission Viejo CA 92691, USA
**Schull, Amanda** — Ballerina, Actress
San Francisco Ballet, 455 Franklin St, San Francisco CA 94102, USA
**Schull, Rebecca** — Actress
9300 Wilshire Blvd, #410, Beverly Hills CA 90212, USA
**Schuller, Grete** — Sculptor
8 Barstow Road, #7G, Great Neck NY 11021, USA
**Schuller, Gunther** — Composer, Conductor
Margun Music, 167 Dudley Road, Newton Center MA 02459, USA
**Schuller, Robert H** — Evangelist
464 S Esplanade St, Orange CA 92869, USA
**Schult, Arthur W (Art)** — Baseball Player
9255 SW 90th St, Ocala FL 34481, USA
**Schult, Jurgen** — Track Athlete
Drosselweg 6, 19069 Leuna, Germany
**Schulters, Lance A** — Football Player
594 Grant Ave, Roselle NJ 07203, USA
**Schultz, C Budd (Buddy)** — Baseball Player
785 Northwood Loop, Prescott AZ 86303, USA
**Schultz, Carl** — Director
I C M Partners, 10250 Constellation Blvd, #900, Los Angeles CA 90067 USA
**Schultz, Connie** — Journalist
Cleveland Plain Dealer, Editorial Dept, 801 Superior Ave, Cleveland OH 44113 USA
**Schultz, Dave** — Ice Hockey Player
1001 Harbour Cove, Somers Point NJ 08244, USA
**Schultz, Dean** — Government Official, Financier
Federal Home Loan Bank, 1079 Hutchinson Road, Walnut Creek CA 94598, USA
**Schultz, Dwight** — Actor
Media Partners, 8306 Wilshire Blvd, #337, Beverly Hills CA 90211, USA
**Schultz, George W (Barney)** — Baseball Player
400 Fern Brook Lane, #218, Mount Laurel NJ 08054, USA
**Schultz, Howard** — Businessman
Starbucks Corp, 2401 Utah Ave S, #800, Seattle WA 98134, USA
**Schultz, John** — Director, Producer, Writer
Creative Artists Agency, 2000 Ave of Stars, #100, Los Angeles CA 90067 USA
**Schultz, Mark** — Singer
Lucid Artists Mgmt, 54 Music Square E, #200, Nashville TN 37203, USA
**Schultz, Michael A** — Director
Chrystalite Productions, PO Box 1940, Santa Monica CA 90406, USA
**Schultz, Nick** — Ice Hockey Player
201 Downey St, Strasbourg SK S9G 4V0, Canada
**Schultz, Peter C** — Inventor (Silica Optical Waveguide)
Heraeus Amersil Inc, 3473 Satellite Blvd, #300, Duluth GA 30096, USA
**Schultz, Peter G** — Chemist
Salk Research Institute, 10550 N Torrey Pine Road, La Jolla CA 92037, USA
**Schultz, Philip** — Writer
Houghton Mifflin Harcourt, 215 Park Ave S, #1200, New York NY 10003 USA
**Schultz, Richard D** — Association Executive
US Olympic Committee, 1 Olympic Plaza, Building 6, Colorado Springs CO 80909 USA
**Schultz, Stanley G** — Physiologist
4955 Heatherglen Dr, Houston TX 77096, USA
**Schultz, William (Bill)** — Football Player
9954 Hidden Falls Circle, Fishers IN 46037, USA
**Schultze, Charles L** — Government Official, Economist
5520 33rd St NW, Washington DC 20015, USA
**Schulweis, Harold M** — Religious Leader, Rabbi
Congregation Valley Beth Shalom, 15739 Ventura Blvd, Encino CA 91436, USA
**Schulz, Axel** — Boxer
Bliss Media, Nuhrenstr 23, 15234 Frankfurt, Germany
**Schulz, Jeffrey A (Jeff)** — Baseball Player
1167 N Stockwell Road, Evansville IN 47715, USA
**Schulz, Kurt E** — Football Player
5075 Rockledge Dr, Clarence NY 14031, USA
**Schulz, Ted** — Golfer
94 Persimmon Ridge Dr, Louisville KY 40245, USA
**Schulze, Donald A (Don)** — Baseball Player
20558 Geer Ave, Hilmar CA 95324, USA
**Schulze, Paul** — Actor
Kyle Friz Mgmt, 6325 Heather Dr, Los Angeles CA 90068, USA
**Schulze, Richard M** — Businessman
Best Buy Co, 7601 Penn Ave S, Minneapolis MN 55423, USA
**Schumacher, Joel** — Director
Joel Schumacher Productions, 10960 Wilshire Blvd, #1900, Los Angeles CA 90024, USA
**Schumacher, Michael** — Auto Racing Driver
Postfach 308, 1234 Vufflens-le-Chateau, Switzerland
**Schumacher, Ralf** — Auto Racing Driver
Williams B M W, Grove Wantage, Oxfordshire OX12 0DQ, England
**Schumacher, Tony** — Drag Racing Driver
Schumacher Racing, 1681 E Northfield Dr, #A, Brownsburg IN 46112, USA
**Schumacher, William (Billy)** — Boat Racing Driver
U-37 Racing Team, 2819 20th Ave W, Seattle, WA 98199, USA
**Schumaker, Jared M (Skip)** — Baseball Player
8877 Tulare Dr, #310B, Huntington Beach CA 92646, USA
**Schumann, Jochen** — Yachtsman
Birkenstr 88, 48336 Penzberg, Germany
**Schumann, Ralf** — Marksman
Steomach 22, 97640 Stockheim, Germany
**Schumer, Amy** — Actress, Comedienne, Writer, Producer
Mosiac Media Group, 9200 W Sunset Blvd, #1000, Los Angeles CA 90069 USA
**Schur, Michael** — Producer, Writer, Actor
United Talent Agency, U T A Plaza, 9336 Civic Center Dr, Beverly Hills CA 90210 USA
**Schurman, Maynard F** — Ice Hockey Player
301 Beaver St, Summerside PE C1N 2A2, Canada
**Schurmann, Petra** — Swimmer
Max-Emanuel-Str 7, 82319 Starnberg, Germany

**Schurr, Harry W** — Vietnam War Air Force Hero
1178 Davis Dr, Fairborn OH 45324, USA

**Schurr, Wayne A** — Baseball Player
10030 W 500 S, Hudson IN 46747, USA

**Schussler Fiorenza, Elisabeth** — Writer, Theologian
Notre Dame University, Theology Dept, Notre Dame IN 46556, USA

**Schutz, Carl J** — Baseball Player
PO Box 162, French Settlement LA 70733, USA

**Schutz, Dana** — Artist
Friedrich Petzel Gallery, 537 W 22nd St, New York NY 10011, USA

**Schutz, Susan Polis** — Writer
Blue Mountain Arts Inc, PO Box 4549, Boulder CO 80306, USA

**Schutz, William N (Bill)** — Football Player
9954 Hidden Falls Circle, Fishers IN 46037, USA

**Schutze, Jim** — Writer, Journalist
Avon Books, 1350 Ave of Americas, New York NY 10019, USA

**Schuur, Diane** — Singer
Stiletto Entertainment, 8295 S La Cienega Blvd, Inglewood CA 90301, USA

**Schwab, Charles R** — Financier
Charles Schwab Co, 101 Montgomery St, #200, San Francisco CA 94104, USA

**Schwab, Corey** — Ice Hockey Player
20633 76th Ave SE, Snohomish WA 98296, USA

**Schwabe, Michael S (Mike)** — Baseball Player
304 36th St, Newport Beach CA 92663, USA

**Schwahn, Mark** — Producer, Writer
W M E Entertainment, 9601 Wilshire Blvd, #300, Beverly Hills CA 90210 USA

**Schwall, Donald B (Don)** — Baseball Player
2000 Lake Marshall Dr, Gibsonia PA 15044, USA

**Schwaller, Andreas** — Curling Athlete
Curling Assn, PO Box 606, 3000 Bern, Switzerland

**Schwaller, Christof** — Curling Athlete
Curling Assn, PO Box 606, 3000 Bern, Switzerland

**Schwantz, James W (Jim)** — Football Player
1047 W Chatham Dr, Palatine IL 60067, USA

**Schwantz, Kevin** — Motorcycle Racing Rider
Kevin Schwantz School, 3446 Winder Highway, #M234, Flowery Branch GA 30542, USA

**Schwarthoff, Florian** — Track Athlete
Fischweiher 51, 64646 Heppenheim, Germany

**Schwartz, Alan** — Financier
Bear Stearns Co, 383 Madison Ave, New York NY 10179, USA

**Schwartz, Ben** — Actor, Comedian, Writer
W M E Entertainment, 9601 Wilshire Blvd, #300, Beverly Hills CA 90210 USA

**Schwartz, Bryan L** — Football Player
14805 Silver Feather Circle, Broomfield CO 80023, USA

**Schwartz, D Randall (Randy)** — Baseball Player
757 El Rancho Dr, El Cajon CA 92019, USA

**Schwartz, Jim** — Football Coach
Detroit Lions, 222 Republic Dr, Allen Park MI 48101 USA

**Schwartz, Josh** — Writer, Producer
W M E Entertainment, 9601 Wilshire Blvd, #300, Beverly Hills CA 90210 USA

**Schwartz, Lloyd** — Journalist
27 Pennsylvania Ave, Somerville MA 02145, USA

**Schwartz, Maite** — Actress
Talent Works, 3500 W Olive Ave, #1400, Burbank CA 91505 USA

**Schwartz, Martha** — Landscape Architect
Martha Schwartz Partners, 147 Sherman St, #200A, Cambridge MA 02140, USA

**Schwartz, Maxime** — Medical Administrator
Institut Pasteur, 25-28 Rue du Docteur-Roux, 75724 Paris Cedex 15, France

**Schwartz, Neena B** — Endocrinologist
450 Davis St, Evanston IL 60201, USA

**Schwartz, Norton A** — Air Force General
Chief of Staff, HqUSAF, Pentagon, Washington DC 20330 USA

**Schwartz, Scott** — Actor
19111 Arminta St, Reseda CA 91335, USA

**Schwartz, Stephen L** — Composer, Lyricist, Singer
Andrew Freedman Public Relations, 9127 Thrasher Ave, Los Angeles CA 90069, USA

**Schwartz, Thomas A** — Army General
Military Child Education Coalition, PO Box 2519, Harker Heights TX 76548, USA

**Schwartzbach, Gerald** — Attorney
655 Redwood Highway, #277, Mill Valley CA 94941, USA

**Schwartzel, Charl A J L** — Golfer
International Sports Mgmt, Cherry Tree Farm, Rostherne, Cheshire WA14 3RZ, England

**Schwartzman, John** — Cinematographer, Director
Murtha Agency, 1025 Colorado Ave, Santa Monica CA 90401, USA

**Schwartzman, Robert** — Actor
I C M Partners, 10250 Constellation Blvd, #900, Los Angeles CA 90067 USA

**Schwary, Ronald L** — Actor, Producer, Director
W M E Entertainment, 9601 Wilshire Blvd, #300, Beverly Hills CA 90210 USA

**Schwarz, Gerard R** — Conductor
Royal Liverpool Orchestra, Hope St, Liverpool L1 9BP, England

**Schwarz, Hanna** — Opera Singer
Opera et Concert, 37 Rue de la Chaussee d'Antin, 75009 Paris, France

**Schwarz, Julian** — Concert Cellist
C M Artists, 127 W 96th St, #13B, New York NY 10025 USA

**Schwarzbein, Diana** — Physician, Writer
Health Communications, 3201 SW 15th St, Deerfield Beach FL 33442, USA

**Schwarzenegger, Arnold A** — Body Builder, Actor; Governor, CA
Creative Artists Agency, 2000 Ave of Stars, #100, Los Angeles CA 90067 USA

**Schwarzman, Stephen A** — Financier
Blackstone Group, 345 Park Ave, Basement Lobby B4, New York NY 10154, USA

**Schwarz-Schilling, Christian** — Government Official, Germany
Am Dohlberg 10, 63564 Budingen, Germany

**Schweickart, Russell L** — Astronaut
B612 Foundation, 2440 W El Camino Real, #300, Mountain View CA 94040, USA

**Schweiger, Til** — Actor
Barefoot Films, Saarbrueckerstra 36, 10405 Berlin, Germany

**Schweigert, Stuart E** — Football Player
4825 Gratiot Road, Saginaw MI 48638, USA
**Schweiker, Richard S (Dick)** — Secretary, Health & Human Services
8890 Windy Ridge Way, McLean VA 22102, USA
**Schweikher, Paul** — Architect
3222 E Missouri Ave, Phoenix AZ 85018, USA
**Schweitz, John E** — Basketball Player
813 Smith Dr, Florence SC 29501, USA
**Schwentke, Robert** — Director
Creative Artists Agency, 2000 Ave of Stars, #100, Los Angeles CA 90067 USA
**Schwer, William (Billy)** — Boxer
5 Grange Ave, Luton LU4 9AS, England
**Schwertsik, Kurt** — Composer
Penzinger Str 26, 1140 Vienna, Austria
**Schwery, Henri Cardinal** — Religious Leader
CP 2334, 1950 Sion 2, Switzerland
**Schwimmer, David** — Actor, Director
Creative Artists Agency, 2000 Ave of Stars, #100, Los Angeles CA 90067 USA
**Schwimmer, Rusty** — Actress
Meghan Schumacher Mgmt, 13351D Riverside Dr, #387, Sherman Oaks CA 91423, USA
**Schwinden, Ted** — Governor, MT
401 N Fee St, Helena MT 59601, USA
**Schwitters, Roy F** — Physicist
1718 Cromwell Hill, Austin TX 78703, USA
**Schygulla, Hanna** — Actress
Agents Associes Marie Chen, 201 Rue Faubourg Saint Honore, 75008 Paris, France
**Schypinski, Gerald A (Jerry)** — Baseball Player
28014 Shadowwood Lane, Harrison Township MI 48045, USA
**Scialfa, Patty** — Singer (E Street Band)
1224 Benedict Canyon, Beverly Hills CA 90210, USA
**Sciarra, John M** — Football Player
404 Morning Star Lane, Newport Beach CA 92660, USA
**Scio, Yvonne** — Actress, Model
Artmedia, 20 Ave Rapp, 75007 Paris, France
**Scioli, Brad E** — Football Player
106 Steinbright Dr, Collegeville PA 19426, USA
**Sciorra, Annabella** — Actress
A P A Talent/Literary Agency, 405 S Beverly Dr, #300, Beverly Hills CA 90212 USA
**Scioscia, Michael L (Mike)** — Baseball Player, Manager
1915 Falling Star Ave, Westlake Village CA 91362, USA
**Scirica, Anthony J** — Judge
US Court of Appeals, 601 Market St, #22614, Philadelphia PA 19106, USA
**Sclisizzi, Enio** — Ice Hockey Player
100 Millside Dr, Milton ON L9T 5E2, Canada
**Scob, Edith** — Actress
Agence Artistes Cinetea, 15 Rue Chapon, 75003 Paris, France
**Scobee, Joshua T (Josh)** — Football Player
11686 Blackstone River Dr, Jacksonville FL 32256, USA
**Scobey, Josh** — Football Player
1372 E Mead Dr, Chandler AZ 85249, USA
**Scodelario, Kaya** — Actress
Curtis Brown Group, 28-29 Haymarket St, #500, London SW1Y 4SP, England
**Scofidio, Ricardo** — Architect
Diller Scofidio Renfro, 601 W 26th St, #1815, New York NY 10001, USA
**Scofield, John** — Jazz Guitarist
International Music Network, 278 Main St, Gloucester MA 01930, USA
**Scofield, Richard M (Dick)** — Air Force General
3251 Country Club Parkway, Castle Rock CO 80108, USA
**Scoggins, Matt** — Diving Coach
4900 Calhoun Canyon Loop, Austin TX 78735, USA
**Scoggins, Tracy** — Actress
Metropolitan Talent Agency, 5405 Wilshire Blvd, #218, Los Angeles CA 90036 USA
**Scola Balvoa, Luis A** — Basketball Player
11801 Sea Shadow Bend, Pearland TX 77584, USA
**Scola, Angelo Cardinal** — Religious Leader
Archdiocese, S Marco 320/A, 30124 Venice, Italy
**Scola, Ettore** — Director
Via Bertoloni 1/E, 00197 Rome, Italy
**Scolari, Peter** — Actor
C E S D, 10635 Santa Monica Blvd, #130, Los Angeles CA 90025 USA
**Scolnick, Edward M** — Geneticist, Virologist
1201 Magnolia Dr, Wayland MA 01778, USA
**Sconiers, Daryl A** — Baseball Player
16775 S Paine St, #1, Fontana CA 92336, USA
**Scorcio, Michael (Mike)** — WW II Army Air Corps Hero
10360 SE Waverly Court, #405, Portland OR 97222, USA
**Score, Michael (Mike)** — Singer, Keyboardist (Flock of Seagulls)
Lustig Talent, PO Box 770850, Orlando FL 32877 USA
**Scorpio** — Rap Artist (Furious Five)
Universal Attractions, 135 W 26th St, #1200, New York NY 10001, USA
**Scorsese, Martin** — Director
Sikelia Productions, 110 W 57th St, #500, New York NY 10019, USA
**Scorupco, Izabella** — Actress, Singer, Model
Mikas Stockholm, Bredgrand 2, 111 30 Stockholm, Sweden
**Scott Brown, Denise** — Architect
Venturi Scott Brown Assoc, 4236 Main St, Philadelphia PA 19127, USA
**Scott Thomas, Kristin A** — Actress
Agence Artiste Adequet, 108 Rue Reaumur, 75002 Paris, France
**Scott, A David (Dave)** — Football Player
3151 Robindale Road, Decatur GA 30034, USA
**Scott, Adam** — Golfer
Professional Golfer's Assn, PO Box 109601, Palm Beach Gardens FL 33410 USA
**Scott, Adam** — Actor
W M E Entertainment, 9601 Wilshire Blvd, #300, Beverly Hills CA 90210 USA
**Scott, Alvin L** — Basketball Player
5786 W Townley Ave, Glendale AZ 85302, USA

**Scott, Andy** — Guitarist (Sweet)
D C M International, 296 Nether St, Finchley, London N3 1RJ, England
**Scott, Anthony (Tony)** — Baseball Player
120 Seay St, Spartanburg SC 29306, USA
**Scott, April** — Actress
C E S D, 10635 Santa Monica Blvd, #130, Los Angeles CA 90025 USA
**Scott, B James** — Football Player
10127 Chisholm Trail, Dallas TX 75243, USA
**Scott, Bartholomew E (Bart)** — Football Player
6 Kings Court, Morristown NJ 07960, USA
**Scott, Brian** — Truck Racing Driver
Joe Gibbs Racing, 6001 Haas Way, Kannapolis NC 28127, USA
**Scott, Byron A** — Basketball Player, Coach
7505 Hannum Ave, Culver City CA 90230, USA
**Scott, Camilla** — Actress
Characters Talent Mgmt, 8 Elm St, Toronto ON M5G 1G7, Canada
**Scott, Campbell** — Actor, Producer, Director
Paradigm Agency, 360 N Crescent Dr, North Building, Beverly Hills CA 90210 USA
**Scott, Chad O** — Football Player
18526 Reliant Dr, Gaithersburg MD 20879, USA
**Scott, Charles T (Charlie)** — Basketball Player
300 Chastain Manor Dr, Norcross GA 30071, USA
**Scott, Clarence R, Jr** — Football Player
216 Sisson Ave NE, Atlanta GA 30317, USA
**Scott, Clyde L (Smackover)** — Football Player, Track Athlete
12840 Rivercrest Dr, Little Rock AR 72212, USA
**Scott, Darnay** — Football Player
18551 Patton St, Detroit MI 48219, USA
**Scott, Darrell** — Singer, Songwriter
New Frontier Touring, 1503 17th Ave S, Nashville TN 37212, USA
**Scott, Dave** — Triathlete, Coach
3080 Valmont Road, #242, Boulder CO 80301, USA
**Scott, David R** — Astronaut
Merces, V C Johnson, 30 Hackamore Lane, #1, Bell Canyon CA 91307, USA
**Scott, Deborah Lynn** — Costume Designer
Innovative Artists, 1505 10th St, Santa Monica CA 90401 USA
**Scott, Dennis E** — Basketball Player
5425 Palm Lake Circle, Orlando FL 32819, USA
**Scott, DeQuincy** — Football Player
PO Box 5746, Pearl MS 39288, USA
**Scott, Desiree R M** — Soccer Player
Canadian Soccer, Place Soccer Canada, 237 Metcalfe St, Ottawa ON K2P 1R2, Canada
**Scott, Donald M (Donnie)** — Baseball Player
6042 114th Terrace N, Pinellas Park FL 33782, USA
**Scott, Donovan** — Actor
Judy Fox Mgmt, 1525 1/2 S Beverly Dr, Los Angeles CA 90035, USA
**Scott, Doug** — Mountaineer
Warwick Mill Center, Weck Bridge, Carlisle Cumbria CA4 8RR, England
**Scott, Dougray** — Actor
W M E Entertainment, 9601 Wilshire Blvd, #300, Beverly Hills CA 90210 USA
**Scott, E C** — Singer
Jay Reil Assoc, 3430 Bayberry Dr, Northbrook IL 60062, USA
**Scott, Freddie L** — Football Player
PO Box 197, Coahoma MS 38617, USA
**Scott, Gary T** — Baseball Player
25 W Elm St, #47, Greenwich CT 06830, USA
**Scott, Gloria Dean Randle** — Educator
Bennett College, President's Office, Greensboro NC 27401, USA
**Scott, Herbert C, Jr** — Football Player
605 Rawhide Court, Plano TX 75023, USA
**Scott, Hillary** — Singer, Songwriter (Lady Antebellum)
Capitol Records, 810 7th Ave, New York NY 10019 USA
**Scott, Irene F** — Judge
US Tax Court, 400 2nd St NW, Washington DC 20217, USA
**Scott, J Raymond (Ray)** — Basketball Player, Coach
5318 Indian Trail, Ypsilanti MI 48197, USA
**Scott, Jack** — Singer, Songwriter
34039 Coachwood Dr, Sterling Heights MI 48312, USA
**Scott, Jacob E (Jake), Jr** — Football Player
32 Seaside South Court, Key West FL 33040, USA
**Scott, Jacqueline** — Actress
Lichtman/Salners, 15865 Royal Haven Place, Sherman Oaks CA 91403 USA
**Scott, Jake** — Singer, Guitarist
PO Box 18106, Encino CA 91416, USA
**Scott, Jake** — Director
Black Dog Films, 42-44 Beak St, London W1F 9RH, England
**Scott, Janette** — Actress
Old Loft, 21 Leinster Mews, Lancaster Gate, London W2 3EX, England
**Scott, Jason Shane** — Actor
Commercial Talent, 9255 Sunset Blvd, #505, Los Angeles CA 90069, USA
**Scott, Jean Bruce** — Actress
Autry National Center, 4700 Western Heritage Way, Los Angeles CA 90027, USA
**Scott, Jerry** — Cartoonist (Baby Blues, Zits)
Creators Syndicate, 737 3rd St, Hermosa Beach CA 90254 USA
**Scott, Jill** — Singer, Songwriter, Actress
Creative Artists Agency, 2000 Ave of Stars, #100, Los Angeles CA 90067, USA
**Scott, Jimmy** — Singer
Maurice Montoya Music Agency, 1133 Broadway, #1608, New York NY 10010, USA
**Scott, Jonathan R** — Football Player
Chicago Bears, 1000 Football Dr, Lake Forest IL 60045 USA
**Scott, Josey** — Singer (Saliva)
Helter Skelter, 347-353 Chiswick High Road, London W4 4HS, England
**Scott, Kathryn Leigh** — Actress
3236 Bennett Dr, Los Angeles CA 90068, USA
**Scott, Klea** — Actress
Sovereign Talent Group, 8421 Wilshire Blvd, #200, Beverly Hills CA 90211, USA

| | |
|---|---|
| **Scott, LaToucha** | Singer (Xscape) |
| Richard Walters, PO Box 2789, Toluca Lake CA 91610 USA | |
| **Scott, Lizabeth** | Actress |
| 8277 Hollywood Blvd, Los Angeles CA 90069, USA | |
| **Scott, Lorna** | Actress |
| Tyler Kjar, 10153 1/2 Riverside Dr, #255, Toluca Lake CA 91602 USA | |
| **Scott, Luke B** | Baseball Player |
| 1111 Saxon Blvd, Orange City FL 32763, USA | |
| **Scott, Manda** | Writer |
| Delacorte Press, 1540 Broadway, New York NY 10036 USA | |
| **Scott, Mark (Gus)** | Drummer (Trixter) |
| Global Star Productions, 103 Godwin Ave, #225, Midland Park NJ 07432, USA | |
| **Scott, Melody Thomas** | Actress |
| 12068 Crest Court, Beverly Hills CA 90210, USA | |
| **Scott, Michael W (Mike)** | Baseball Player |
| 28355 Chat Dr, Laguna Niguel CA 92677, USA | |
| **Scott, Mike** | Singer (Waterboys), Songwriter |
| Agency Group Ltd, 142 W 57th St, #600, New York NY 10019 USA | |
| **Scott, Pippa** | Actress |
| 10 Ocean Park Blvd, #1, Santa Monica CA 90405, USA | |
| **Scott, Randolph C (Randy)** | Football Player |
| 1440 Woodland Lake Dr, Snellville GA 30078, USA | |
| **Scott, Ray** | Singer |
| Hallmark Direction, 713 18th Ave S, Nashville TN 37203, USA | |
| **Scott, Reid** | Actor |
| Impression Entertainment, 9229 W Sunset Blvd, #700, Los Angeles CA 90069, USA | |
| **Scott, Richard U (Dick)** | Football Player |
| 3369 Upland Court, Adamstown MD 21710, USA | |
| **Scott, Ridley** | Director |
| 632 N La Peer Dr, West Hollywood CA 90069, USA | |
| **Scott, Robert B (Bobby)** | Football Player |
| 801 McKinley Pointe Lane, Knoxville TN 37934, USA | |
| **Scott, Rodney** | Actor |
| Domain Talent, 9229 W Sunset Blvd, #710, West Hollywood CA 90069 USA | |
| **Scott, Rodney D** | Baseball Player |
| 4206 Priscilla Ave, Indianapolis IN 46226, USA | |
| **Scott, Seann William** | Actor |
| Elephant Pictures, 200 N Elizabeth St, #200C, Chicago IL 60607, USA | |
| **Scott, Sherie Rene** | Actress, Singer |
| Principal Entertainment, 9255 Sunset Blvd, #500, Los Angeles CA 90069 USA | |
| **Scott, Spencer** | Model |
| PO Box 461177, Los Angeles CA 90046, USA | |
| **Scott, Stephen** | Jazz Pianist |
| Bridge Agency, 35 Clark St, #A5, Brooklyn Heights NY 11201, USA | |
| **Scott, Stuart** | Sportscaster |
| ESPN-TV, ESPN Plaza, 935 Middle St, Bristol CT 06010 USA | |
| **Scott, Tamika** | Singer (Xscape) |
| Richard Walters, PO Box 2789, Toluca Lake CA 91610 USA | |
| **Scott, Thomas C (Tom)** | Football Player |
| 3259 Kirkwood Court, Keswick VA 22947, USA | |
| **Scott, Timothy** | Sculptor |
| 50 Clare Court, Judd St, London WC1H 9QW, England | |
| **Scott, Timothy D (Tim)** | Baseball Player |
| 956 W Julia Way, Hanford CA 93230, USA | |
| **Scott, Todd C** | Football Player |
| 5605 Avenue P, Galveston TX 77551, USA | |
| **Scott, Tom** | Jazz Saxophonist, Composer |
| Performers of the World, 5657 Wilshire Blvd, #280, Los Angeles CA 90036 USA | |
| **Scott, Tom Everett** | Actor |
| Paradigm Agency, 360 N Crescent Dr, North Building, Beverly Hills CA 90210 USA | |
| **Scott, Walter B** | Football Player |
| 1991 Edgefield Road, Trenton SC 29847, USA | |
| **Scott, Willard H, Jr** | Entertainer |
| NBC-TV, News Dept, 30 Rockefeller Plaza, #270E, New York NY 10112 USA | |
| **Scott, Willie L, Jr** | Football Player |
| 1123 Long St, Newberry SC 29108, USA | |
| **Scott, Winston E** | Astronaut |
| PO Box 1192, Cape Canaveral FL 32920, USA | |
| **Scotti, Benjamin J (Ben)** | Football Player |
| 715 N Beverly Dr, Beverly Hills CA 90210, USA | |
| **Scotti, Nick** | Actor, Singer |
| Untitled Entertainment, 350 S Beverly Dr, #200, Beverly Hills CA 90212 USA | |
| **Scotto, Renata** | Opera Singer |
| 3 Stone Hallow Way, Armonk NY 10504, USA | |
| **Scottoline, Lisa** | Writer |
| Harper Collins Publishers, 10 E 53rd St, Cellar 1, New York NY 10022 USA | |
| **Scotty, Ludwig** | President, Nauru |
| President's Office, Government Offices, Yaren, Nauru | |
| **Scovell, Nell** | Producer |
| Paradigm Agency, 360 N Crescent Dr, North Building, Beverly Hills CA 90210 USA | |
| **Scowcroft, Brent** | Government Official, Air Force General |
| 900 17th St NW, #500, Washington DC 20006, USA | |
| **Scrafford, Kirk T** | Football Player |
| 19400 US Highway 93 N, Florence MT 59833, USA | |
| **Scranton, James D (Jim)** | Baseball Player |
| 27519 Hammack Ave, Perris CA 92570, USA | |
| **Scranton, Nancy** | Golfer |
| 1816 Forest Glen Way, Saint Augustine FL 32092, USA | |
| **Scribner, William C (Bucky)** | Football Player |
| 246 Porter Mill Bend Dr, Camdenton MO 65020, USA | |
| **Scrimm, Angus** | Actor |
| PO Box 5193, North Hollywood CA 91616, USA | |
| **Scrivener, Wayne A (Chuck)** | Baseball Player |
| 1766 Hazel St, Birmingham AL 48009, USA | |
| **Scroggins, Tracy L** | Football Player |
| 6001 N Ocean Dr, #707, Hollywood FL 33019, USA | |

**S**

Scott - Scroggins

**Scruggs, Anthony R (Tony)** — Baseball Player
11621 Braddock Dr, #17, Culver City CA 90230, USA
**Scruggs, Randy** — Singer, Songwriter
Creative Artists Agency, 3310 W End Ave, #500, Nashville TN 37203 USA
**Scudamore, Peter** — Steeplechase Racing Jockey
Mucky Cottage, Grangehill, Naunton, Cheltenham, Glos GL54 3AY, England
**Scudder, W Scott** — Baseball Player
943 Farm Road 1499, Paris TX 75460, USA
**Scuderi, Robert J (Rob)** — Ice Hockey Player
16 Old Colony Dr, Dover MA 02030, USA
**Scudero, Joseph A (Joe)** — Football Player
2534 N Railroad Way, Hemando FL 34442, USA
**Scullion, Mary** — Social Activist
Project Home, 1515 Fairmount Ave, Philadelphia PA 19130, USA
**Scully, John F, Jr** — Football Player
3500 Bankview Dr, Joliet IL 60431, USA
**Scully, Sean P** — Artist
Brooke Alexander Gallery, 59 Wooster St, New York NY 10012, USA
**Scully, Vincent E (Vin)** — Sportscaster
25090 Jim Bridger Road, Hidden Hills CA 91302, USA
**Scully-Power, Paul D** — Astronaut
US Navy Underwater Systems Laboratory, 33A Code, New London CT 06320, USA
**Sculthorpe, Peter J** — Composer
91 Holdsworth St, Woollahra, NSW 2025, Australia
**Scurlock, Clifton T (Kliph)** — Drummer (Flaming Lips)
World's Fair Mgmt, 1208 Chowing Ave, Edmond OK 73034, USA
**Scurry, Briana** — Soccer Player
11610 137th Ave N, Dayton MN 55327, USA
**Scurti, John** — Actor
Gersh Agency, 41 Madison Ave, #3301, New York NY 10010 USA
**Scutaro, Marcos H (Marco)** — Baseball Player
19877 E Country Club Dr, #3503, Miami FL 33180, USA
**Sea, Daniela** — Actress
Mange-ment, 1103 1/2 Glendon Ave, Los Angeles CA 90024, USA
**Seacrest, Ryan** — Entertainer
Creative Artists Agency, 2000 Ave of Stars, #100, Los Angeles CA 90067 USA
**Seaforth-Hayes, Susan** — Actress
Hayforth Enterprises, 11333 Moorpark St, #368, Studio City CA 91602, USA
**Seaga, Edward P G** — Prime Minister, Jamaica
24-26 Grenada Crescent, New Kingston, Kingston 5, Jamaica
**Seagal, Steven** — Actor
9325 E Brahma Road, Scottsdale AZ 85262, USA
**Seagrave, Jocelyn** — Actress
Perspective Film, 15030 Ventura Blvd, Sherman Oaks CA 91403, USA
**Seagren, Robert L (Bob)** — Track Athlete, Actor
24710 Palermo Dr, Calabasas CA 91302, USA
**Seagrove, Jenny** — Actress
Rights House, Drury House, 34-43 Russell St, London WC2B 5HA, England
**Seal** — Singer, Songwriter
Creative Artists Agency, 2000 Ave of Stars, #100, Los Angeles CA 90067 USA
**Seal, Mark** — Writer
Viking Press, 375 Hudson St, New York NY 10014 USA
**Seal, Paul N** — Football Player
21599 Hidden Rivers Dr N, Southfield MI 48075, USA
**Seale, Bobby** — Political Activist (Black Panthers)
Cafe Society, 302 W Chelton Ave, Philadelphia PA 19144, USA
**Seale, John C** — Cinematographer
Mirisch Agency, 1801 Century Park E, Los Angeles CA 90067, USA
**Seale, Samuel R (Sam)** — Football Player
1818 Da Gama Court, Escondido CA 92026, USA
**Seals, George E** — Football Player
1101 1st St, #204, Coronado CA 92118, USA
**Seals, James** — Singer, Songwriter (Seals & Crofts)
Star Entertainment, 1675 York Ave, #32C, New York NY 10128, USA
**Seals, Raymond B (Ray)** — Football Player
664 NW Shaw Glen, Lake City FL 32055, USA
**Seaman, Christopher** — Conductor
Symphony Australia, 1 Oxford Street, #5-2, Darlinghurst NSW 2010, Australia
**Seaman, David** — Soccer Player
Arsenal London, Avenell Road, Highbury, London N5 1BU, England
**Seanez, Rudy C** — Baseball Player
1422 McCabe Cove Road, El Centro CA 92243, USA
**Searage, Raymond M (Ray)** — Baseball Player
9737 Pine Lake Trail, Saint Petersburg FL 33708, USA
**Searcy, Leon, Jr** — Football Player
3841 Biggin Church Road, Jacksonville FL 32224, USA
**Searcy, Nick** — Actor
Abrams Artists, 275 7th Ave, #2600, New York NY 10001, USA
**Searcy, W Stephen (Steve)** — Baseball Player
5112 Gouffon Road, Knoxville TN 37918, USA
**Searfoss, Richard A** — Astronaut
24480 Silver Creek Way, Tehachapi CA 93561, USA
**Sears, Joe** — Actor
Gersh Agency, 9465 Wilshire Blvd, #600, Beverly Hills CA 90212 USA
**Sears, Kenneth R (Ken)** — Basketball Player
40 Cutter Dr, Watsonville CA 95076, USA
**Sears, Paul B** — Ecologist
17 Las Milpas, Taos NM 87571, USA
**Seasick Steve** — Singer, Songwriter
Agency Group Ltd, 1880 Century Park E, #711, Los Angeles CA 90067 USA
**Seaver, G Thomas (Tom)** — Baseball Player
1761 Diamond Mountain Road, Calistoga CA 94515, USA
**Seavey, David** — Editorial Cartoonist
USA Today, Editorial Dept, 1000 Wilson Blvd, Arlington VA 22209, USA
**Seay, Robert M (Bobby)** — Baseball Player
1591 Oak Circle N, Sarasota FL 34232, USA

**Sebastian, Cuthbert M** — Governor General, Saint Kitts & Nevis
Governor General's House, 6 Canyon St, Basseterre, Saint Kitts & Nevis
**Sebastian, John** — Singer, Songwriter
2431 Briarcrest Road, Beverly Hills CA 90210, USA
**Sebastiani, Sergio Cardinal** — Religious Leader
Palazzo delle Congregazioni, Lardo del Colonnato 3, 00193 Rome, Italy
**Sebelius, Kathleen G** — Secretary, Health; Governor, KS
Health/Human Services Dept, 200 Independence Ave SW, Washington DC 20201 USA
**Sebestyen, Marta** — Singer, Flutist
Konzertagentur Berthold Seliger, Nonnengasse 15, 36037 Fulda, Germany
**Sebold, Alice** — Writer
Dunow Carlson Lerner Literary Agency, 27 W 20th St, #1107, New York NY 10011, USA
**Sebra, Robert B (Bob)** — Baseball Player
20 Misners Trail, Ormond Beach FL 32174, USA
**Secada, Jon** — Singer, Songwriter
Bridge Mgmt, 427 NE 107th St, Miami FL 33161, USA
**Seckel, Danny** — Actor, Comedian
OmniPop Talent Group, 4605 Lankershim Blvd, #201, Toluca Lake CA 91602 USA
**Secor, Kyle** — Actor
Brillstein Entertainment Partners, 9150 Wilshire Blvd, #350, Beverly Hills CA 90212 USA
**Secord, Al** — Ice Hockey Player
950 Ginger Court, Southlake TX 76092, USA
**Secord, John** — Singer, Guitarist, Songwriter
Making Texas Music, Old Putnam Bank Building, PO Box 1013, Putnam TX 76469, USA
**Secord, Richard V** — Army General
Computerized Thermal Imaging, 1719 W 2800 S, Ogden UT 84401, USA
**Secrest, Meryle** — Writer
Bloomsbury Publishing, 50 Bedford Square, London WC1B 3DP, England
**Secrest, Wayne** — Bassist (Confederate Railroad)
Bobby Roberts, 3050 Business Park Circle, #303, Goodlettsville TN 37221 USA
**Seda, Jon** — Actor
I C M Partners, 10250 Constellation Blvd, #900, Los Angeles CA 90067 USA
**Sedaka, Neil** — Singer, Pianist, Songwriter
Neal Sedaka Music, 730 5th Ave, #950, New York NY 10019, USA
**Sedaris, Amy** — Actress, Comedienne
Paradigm Agency, 360 N Crescent Dr, North Building, Beverly Hills CA 90210 USA
**Sedaris, David** — Writer
64 Thompson St, New York NY 10012, USA
**Seddon, Margaret Rhea** — Astronaut
1709 Shagbark Trail, Murfreesboro TN 37130, USA
**Sedelmaier, J Josef (Joe)** — Director; Animator
Sedelmaier Film Productions, 858 W Armitage Ave, #267, Chicago IL 60614, USA
**Sedgman, Frank A** — Tennis Player
28 Bolton Ave, Hampton VIC 3188, Australia
**Sedgwick, Kyra** — Actress
United Talent Agency, U T A Plaza, 9336 Civic Center Dr, Beverly Hills CA 90210 USA
**Sedin, Daniel** — Ice Hockey Player
1233 Nanton Ave, Vancouver BC V6H 2C7, Canada
**Sedin, Henrik** — Ice Hockey Player
C A A Hockey, 822 11th Ave SW, #204, Calgary AB T2R 0E5, Canada
**Sedlbauer, Ronald A (Ron)** — Ice Hockey Player
4231 Lakeshore Road, Burlington ON L7L 1A5, Canada
**Sedney, Jules** — Prime Minister, Suriname
May St 34, Paramaribo, Suriname
**Sedykh, Yuri G** — Track Athlete
Light Athletics Federation, Luzhnetskaya Nab 8, 119270 Moscow, Russia
**See, Carolyn** — Writer
930 3rd St, #203, Santa Monica CA 90403, USA
**See, Lisa** — Writer
El Pueblo Monument Authority, 125 Paseo de Plaza, #400, Los Angeles CA 90012, USA
**See, Marshall** — Basketball Player
1138 S Canal Circle, Camp Verde AZ 86322, USA
**See, R Laurence (Larry)** — Baseball Player
1913 W Remington Dr, Chandler AZ 85286, USA
**Seear, Beatrice N S** — Government Official, England
189B Kennington Road, London SE11 6ST, England
**Seear, Noot** — Model, Actress
Innovative Artists, 1505 10th St, Santa Monica CA 90401 USA
**Seedorf, Clarence** — Soccer Player
F C Milan, Via Filippo Turati 3, 20121 Milan, Italy
**Seeger, Anthony** — Ethnomusicologist
University of California, Music Dept, Los Angeles CA 90024, USA
**Seeger, Peggy** — Singer, Songwriter
Real People Music, 520 S Clinton Ave, Oak Park IL 60304, USA
**Seeger, Pete** — Singer, Banjoist, Songwriter
PO Box 431, Dutchess Junction, Beacon NY 12508, USA
**Seehofer, Horst L** — President, Germany
Bundeskanzlerant, Schlossplatz 1, 10178 Berlin, Germany
**Seehorn, Rhea** — Actress
Untitled Entertainment, 350 S Beverly Dr, #200, Beverly Hills CA 90212 USA
**Seelbach, Charles F (Chuck)** — Baseball Player
13800 Fairhill Road, #501, Cleveland OH 44120, USA
**Seeler, Uwe** — Soccer Player
H S V, Rothenbaumchaussee 125, 20149 Hamburg, Germany
**Seeley, Andrew M E (Drew)** — Actor, Singer, Songwriter
PO Box 250, 522 S Hunt Club Blvd, Apopka FL 32704, USA
**Seeley, Thomas D** — Biologist
Cornell University, Biological Sciences Division, Ithaca NY 14853, USA
**Seeling, Angelle** — Motorcycle Racing Rider
G Smith Motorsports, 10567 Airline Dr, Saint Rose LA 70087, USA
**Seely, Jeannie** — Singer, Songwriter
Tessier-Marsh Talent, 2825 Blue Book Dr, Nashville TN 37214 USA
**Seeman, Nadrian C (Ned)** — Chemist, Nanotechnologist
New York University, Chemistry Dept, New York NY 10003, USA
**Seezer, Maurice** — Singer, Composer
Bloomsbury Publishing, 50 Bedford Square, London WC1B 3DP, England

**S**

**Sefcki, Kevin J** — Baseball Player
16921 Steeplechase Parkway, Orland Park IL 60467, USA

**Seffrin, John R** — Association Executive
American Cancer Society, 1599 Clifton Road NE, Atlanta GA 30329, USA

**Sefolosha, Thabo** — Basketball Player
910 Colony Dr, Salisbury MD 21804, USA

**Sega, Ronald M** — Astronaut, Electrical Engineer
711A Massey Lane, Alexandria VA 22314, USA

**Segal, Fred** — Fashion Designer
Fred Segal Jeans, 8100 Melrose Ave, Los Angeles CA 90046, USA

**Segal, George** — Actor
A Mgmt, 12001 Ventura Place, #340, Studio City CA 91604 USA

**Segal, Michael** — Actor
27 Cyprus Ave, Finchley, London N3 1SS, England

**Segal, Peter** — Director, Producer, Writer
Creative Artists Agency, 2000 Ave of Stars, #100, Los Angeles CA 90067 USA

**Segal, Uri** — Conductor
M A Artists Mgmt, 28 Sheffield Terrace, London W8 7NA, England

**Segan, Noah** — Actor, Producer
United Talent Agency, U T A Plaza, 9336 Civic Center Dr, Beverly Hills CA 90210 USA

**Segel, Jason** — Actor
W M E Entertainment, 9601 Wilshire Blvd, #300, Beverly Hills CA 90210 USA

**Seger, Bob** — Singer, Songwriter
3841 LaPlaya Lane, Orchard Lake MI 48324, USA

**Seger, Shea** — Singer
Helter Skelter, 347-353 Chiswick High Road, London W4 4HS, England

**Segerstam, Leif S** — Composer, Conductor
Garvey & Ivor, 59 Lansdowne Place, Hove BN3 1FL, England

**Segui, David V** — Baseball Player
13421 Leavenworth Road, Kansas City KS 66109, USA

**Segui, Diego P** — Baseball Player
7520 King St, #J, Overland Park KS 66214, USA

**Segura, Francisco (Pancho)** — Tennis Player
Rancho La Costa Hotel & Spa, 7690 Camino Real, Carlsbad CA 92009, USA

**Seguso, Robert** — Tennis Player
3405 54th Dr W, Bradenton FL 34210, USA

**Sehorn, Jason H** — Football Player, Sportscaster
1901 Wild Holly Lane, Charlotte NC 28226, USA

**Seibel, Anne** — Production Designer, Art Director
Sheldon Prosnit Agency, 800 S Robertson Blvd, #6, Los Angeles CA 90035, USA

**Seibert, Kurt E** — Baseball Player
95 Amberwood Circle, Irmo SC 29063, USA

**Seidel, Guenter** — Equestrian
2108 Oxford Ave, Cardiff-by-the-Sea CA 92007, USA

**Seidel, Martie** — Singer (Dixie Chicks)
Strategic Artists Mgmt, 1100 Glendon Ave, #1100, Los Angeles CA 90024, USA

**Seidelman, Susan** — Director
Michael Shedler, 350 5th Ave, New York NY 10118, USA

**Seidenberg, Dennis** — Ice Hockey Player
20073 N 85th Place, Scottsdale AZ 85255, USA

**Seidenberg, Ivan G** — Businessman
Verizon Communications, 1095 Ave of Americas, New York NY 10036, USA

**Seidler, David** — Writer
Independent Talent Group, 40 Whitfield St, London W1T 2RH, England

**Seidler, Helga** — Track Athlete
Bersarinstr 42, 09130 Chemnitz, Germany

**Seifert, George G** — Football Coach, Sportscaster
1276 Estate Dr, Los Altos Hills CA 94024, USA

**Seiffert, Lisa** — Model
Elite Model Mgmt, 404 Park Ave S, #900, New York NY 10016 USA

**Seigenthaler, John M** — Commentator
Al Jazeera America, Editorial Dept, 311 W 34th St, New York NY 10001 USA

**Seigner, Emmanuelle** — Actress
Agence Artiste Adequet, 108 Rue Reaumur, 75002 Paris, France

**Seigner, Mathilde** — Actress
Artmedia, 20 Ave Rapp, 75007 Paris, France

**Seikaly, Ronald F (Rony)** — Basketball Player
2060 N Bay Road, Miami Beach FL 33140, USA

**Seilacher, Adolf** — Geologist, Geophysicist
Yale University, Geology/Geophysics Laboratory, New Haven CT 06520, USA

**Seiling, Richard J (Ric)** — Ice Hockey Player
71 Christina Dr, North Chili NY 14514, USA

**Seiling, Rodney A (Rod)** — Ice Hockey Player
Toronto Hotel Assn, 590-207 Queens Quay W, Toronto ON M5J 1A7, Canada

**Seimetz, Amy** — Actress
One Entertainment, 347 5th Ave, #1404, New York NY 10016 USA

**Seinfeld, Evan** — Actor, Director, Writer
Larger Than Life Mgmt, 12119 Morrison St, Valley Village CA 91607, USA

**Seinfeld, Jerry** — Actor, Comedian
Shapiro/West Assoc, 141 El Camino, #205, Beverly Hills CA 90212, USA

**Seinfeld, John H** — Chemical Engineer
363 Patrician Way, Pasadena CA 91105, USA

**Seiple, Larry R** — Football Player
1361 W Golfview Dr, Pembroke Pines FL 33026, USA

**Seipp, Michelle** — Actress
Chateau/Billings Talent Agency, 8489 W 3rd St, #1032, Los Angeles CA 90048, USA

**Seitzer, Kevin L** — Baseball Player
2845 W 137th Terrace, Overland Park KS 66224, USA

**Seiwald, Robert J** — Inventor (Fluorescent Dye)
59 Burnside Ave, San Francisco CA 94131, USA

**Seixas, E Victor (Vic), Jr** — Tennis Player
8 Harbor Point Dr, #207, Mill Valley CA 94941, USA

**Seizinger, Katja** — Alpine Skier
Rudolf-Epp-Str 48, 69412 Eberbach, Germany

**Sejima, Kazuyo** — Pritzker Architect Laureate
Sanaa Ltd, 2-2-35-6B Higashi-Shinagawa, 140 0002 Tokyo, Japan

**Seki, Syuzo** — Chemist
Osaka University, Chemistry Dept, 1-1 Yamadaoka, Suitashi, Osaka 565-0871, Japan

**Sekler, Eduard F** — Educator, Architect
Harvard University, Graduate Design School, Gund Hall, Cambridge MA 02138, USA

**Sela, Michael** — Immunologist, Chemist
Weizmann Science Institute, Immunology Dept, Rehovot 76100, Israel

**Selander, Robert K** — Biologist
Pennsylvania State University, Biology Dept, University Park PA 16802, USA

**Selanne, Teemu I** — Ice Hockey Player
31731 Madre Selva Lane, Trabuco Canyon CA 92679, USA

**Selby, David** — Actor
S M S Talent, 8383 Wilshire Blvd, #230, Beverly Hills CA 90211 USA

**Selby, Hubert, Jr** — Writer
Bloomsbury Publishing, 50 Bedford Square, London WC1B 3DP, England

**Selby, R Briton (Brit)** — Ice Hockey Player
174 Divadale Dr, East York ON M4G 2P6, Canada

**Selby, William F (Bill)** — Baseball Player
4468 Misty Oaks Lane, Nesbit MS 38651, USA

**Seldes, Marian** — Actress
Paradigm Agency, 360 Park Ave S, #1600, New York NY 10010 USA

**Seldin, Donald W** — Physician
Texas Southwestern Medical Center, 5323 Harry Hines Blvd, Dallas TX 75390, USA

**Seldon, Bruce** — Boxer
Rocco DePersia, 35 Kings Highway E, #102, Haddonfield NJ 08033, USA

**Sele, Aaron H** — Baseball Player
4 Oak Tree Dr, Newport Beach CA 92660, USA

**Seles, Monica** — Tennis Player
2895 Dick Wilson Dr, Sarasota FL 34240, USA

**Self, Bill** — Basketball Coach
University of Kansas, Athletic Dept, Allen Fieldhouse, Lawrence KS 66045, USA

**Self, Clarence E** — Football Player
43W689 Willow Creek Court, Elburn IL 60119, USA

**Self, Todd** — Baseball Player
10238 Cardiff Dr, Keithville LA 71047, USA

**Selfridge, Andrew P (Andy)** — Football Player
3400 Dunscroft Court, Keswick VA 22947, USA

**Selick, Henry** — Director
Laika Entertainment, 1400 NW 22nd Ave, Portland OR 97210, USA

**Selig, Allan H (Bud)** — Baseball Executive
Commissioner's Office, 777 E Wisconsin Ave, #3060, Milwaukee WI 53202, USA

**Selig, Franz-Josef** — Opera Singer
I M G Artists, Hogarth Business Park, Chiswick, London W4 2TH, England

**Selim, Ali** — Director, Writer
I C M Partners, 10250 Constellation Blvd, #900, Los Angeles CA 90067 USA

**Selivanov, Alexander** — Ice Hockey Player
4003 W Tacon St, Tampa FL 33629, USA

**Sellar JoAnne** — Producer
United Talent Agency, U T A Plaza, 9336 Civic Center Dr, Beverly Hills CA 90210 USA

**Sellars, Peter** — Director
American National Theater, Kennedy Center, 2700 F St NW, Washington DC 20566, USA

**Selldorf, Annabelle** — Architect
Selldorf Architects, 860 Broadway, #200, New York NY 10003, USA

**Selleca, Connie** — Actress
Binder Assoc, 1465 Lindacrest Dr, Beverly Hills CA 90210, USA

**Selleck, Tom** — Actor
PO Box 1029, Penrose CO 81240, USA

**Seller, Peg** — Synchronized Swimmer, Coach
72 Monkswood Crescent, Newmarket ON L3Y 2K1, Canada

**Sellers, Bradley D (Brad)** — Basketball Player
682 Arbor Way, Aurora OH 44202, USA

**Sellers, Franklin** — Religious Leader
Reformed Episcopal Church, 2001 Frederick Road, Catonsville MD 21228, USA

**Sellers, Jeffrey D (Jeff)** — Baseball Player
266 Raines Road, Easley NC 29640, USA

**Sellers, Piers J** — Astronaut
16011 Craighurst Dr, Houston TX 77059, USA

**Sellers, Ron F** — Football Player
1111 Green Bayberry Dr, Palm Beach Gardens FL 33418, USA

**Sellers, Rosabell Laurenti** — Actress
Studio Emme, Via Leonardo Greppi 130, 00149 Rome, Italy

**Sells, David W (Dave)** — Baseball Player
700 Blue Ridge Lane, Vacaville CA 95688, USA

**Selmon, Dewey W** — Football Player
2725 S Berry Road, Norman OK 73072, USA

**Selten, Reinhard** — Nobel Economics Laureate
Hardtweg 23, 53639 Konigswinter, Germany

**Seltmann, Sally** — Singer, Songwriter
Agency Group Ltd, 142 W 57th St, #600, New York NY 10019 USA

**Seltz, Rolland A** — Basketball Player
3328 Oswego Heights Road, Saint Paul MN 55126, USA

**Seltzer, David** — Director, Writer
I C M Partners, 10250 Constellation Blvd, #900, Los Angeles CA 90067 USA

**Selverstone, Katy** — Actress
Agency Group, 9348 Civic Center Dr, #200, Beverly Hills CA 90210 USA

**Selvie, George** — Football Player
Dallas Cowboys, 1 Cowboys Parkway, Irving TX 75063 USA

**Selvy, Franklin D (Frank)** — Basketball Player
18 Oglethorpe Lane, Hilton Head SC 29926, USA

**Selway, Philip J (Phil)** — Drummer (Radiohead)
Courtyard, 21 Nursery, Sutton Courtenay, Abingdon, Oxon OX14 4UA, England

**Selwood, Brad** — Ice Hockey Player
77 Colonel Wayling Blvd, Sharon ON L0G 1V0, Canada

**Selya, Bruce M** — Judge
US Court of Appeals, US Courthouse, Pastore Building, Kennedy Plaza, Providence RI 02903, USA

**Selznick, Brian** — Writer, Illustrator
Scholastic Press, 555 Broadway, New York NY 10012 USA

| | |
|---|---|
| **Semak, Michael W**<br>1796 Spruce Hill Road, Pickering ON L1V 1S4, Canada | Photographer |
| **Sember, Michael D (Mike)**<br>285 S Country Club Blvd, Boca Raton FL 33487, USA | Baseball Player |
| **Semel, David**<br>W M E Entertainment, 9601 Wilshire Blvd, #300, Beverly Hills CA 90210 USA | Director, Producer |
| **Semel, Terry S**<br>Windsor Media Investments, 10877 Wilshire Blvd, Los Angeles CA 90024, USA | Businessman |
| **Semenchuk, Ekaterina**<br>I M G Artists, Hogarth Business Park, Chiswick, London W4 2TH, England | Opera Singer |
| **Semenov, Anatoli A**<br>4015 Royal Vista Circle, Corona CA 92881, USA | Ice Hockey Player |
| **Semenova, Juliana**<br>Zalalela 4-35, Riga 1010, Latvia | Basketball Player |
| **Seminara, Frank P**<br>8029 Harbor View Terrace, Brooklyn NY 11209, USA | Baseball Player |
| **Semiz, Teata**<br>27 Burnside Place, Haskell NJ 07420, USA | Bowler |
| **Semizorova, Nina L**<br>2 Zhukovskaya St, #8, Moscow, Russia | Ballerina |
| **Semkow, Jerzy G**<br>Opus 3 Artists, 470 Park Ave S, #900N, New York NY 10016 USA | Conductor |
| **Semler, Dean**<br>4260 Arcola Ave, Toluca Lake CA 91602, USA | Cinematographer, Director |
| **Sempe, Jean-Jacques**<br>4 Rue du Moulin-Vert, 75014 Paris, France | Cartoonist |
| **Semple Thompson, Carol**<br>2045 Henry Road, Sewickley PA 15143, USA | Golfer |
| **Semple, Maria**<br>Little Brown, 3 Center Plaza, #100, Boston MA 02108 USA | Writer, Producer |
| **Semple, Robert B, Jr**<br>New York Times, Editorial Dept, 229 W 43rd St, New York NY 10036 USA | Journalist |
| **Semproch, Roman A (Ray)**<br>4220 Buechner Ave, Cleveland OH 44109, USA | Baseball Player |
| **Semyonov, Vladilen G**<br>15/17-504 Roubinshteina St, 191002 Saint Petersburg, Russia | Ballet Dancer |
| **Sen, Amartya K**<br>Trinity College, Economics Dept, Cambridge CB2 1TQ, England | Nobel Economics Laureate |
| **Sen, Mrinal**<br>C501 Talkatora Road, New Delhi 110 01, India | Director |
| **Sen, Nandana**<br>Prinicipal Entertainment,130 W 42nd St, #614, New York NY 10036, USA | Actress |
| **Sen, Riya**<br>62B Ruia Park, Huhu, Mumbai MS 400049, India | Actress, Model |
| **Sen, Sushmita**<br>Beach Queen, #600 Rd, Versova Andheri (W), Mumbai MS 400061, India | Beauty Queen, Actress |
| **Sena, Dominic**<br>W M E Entertainment, 9601 Wilshire Blvd, #300, Beverly Hills CA 90210 USA | Director |
| **Sendel, Peter**<br>Zallaer Str 9, 98599 Oberhof, Germany | Biathlete |
| **Senderens, Alain**<br>Restaurant Lucas Carton, 9 Place de la Madeleine, 75008 Paris, France | Chef |
| **Sendlein, Robin B**<br>5645 Friars Road, #379, San Diego CA 92110, USA | Football Player |
| **Senior, Peter**<br>International Mangement Group, 1 Erieview Plaza, 1360 E 9th St, Cleveland OH 44114 USA | Golfer |
| **Senna, Bruno**<br>Williams F1, Grove, Wantage, Oxfordshire OX12 0DQ, England | Auto Racing Driver |
| **Sennewald, Robert W**<br>311 S Lee St, Alexandria VA 22314, USA | Army General |
| **Sensabaugh, Gerald L**<br>12251 Heron Cove Court, Jacksonville FL 32218, USA | Football Player |
| **Sensibaugh, J Michael (Mike)**<br>18414 Woodlands Terrace Dr, Glencoe MO 63038, USA | Football Player |
| **Sentelle, David B**<br>US Court of Appeals, 333 Constitution Ave NW, #4400, Washington DC 20001, USA | Judge |
| **Seoane, Manuel M (Manny)**<br>4703 N Rome Ave, Tampa FL 33603, USA | Baseball Player |
| **Seon Hwa Lee**<br>Ladies Pro Golf Assn, 100 International Golf Dr, Daytona Beach FL 32124 USA | Golfer |
| **Sepe, Crescenzio Cardinal**<br>Villa Betania, Via Urbans VIII 16, 00165 Rome, Italy | Religious Leader |
| **Septimus, Jacob (Jake)**<br>Creative Artists Agency, 2000 Ave of Stars, #100, Los Angeles CA 90067 USA | Producer, Director, Writer |
| **Sepulveda, Charlie**<br>Ralph Mercado Mgmt, 568 Broadway, #608, New York NY 10012, USA | Jazz Trumpeter |
| **Sepulveda, Daniel W**<br>Pittsburgh Steelers, 3400 S Water St, Pittsburgh PA 15203 USA | Football Player |
| **Serafini, Daniel J (Dan)**<br>4380 Garratt Circle, Sparks NV 89436, USA | Baseball Player |
| **Serafinowicz, Peter**<br>Troika, 74 Clerkenwell Road, #300, London EC1M 5QA, England | Actor, Comedian |
| **Seraphine, Oliver J**<br>44 Green's Lane, Goodwill, Dominica | Prime Minister, Dominica |
| **Serbedzija, Rade**<br>United Agents, 12-26 Lexington St, London W1F 0LE, England | Actor |
| **Serebrier, Jose**<br>20 Queensgate Gardens, London SW7 5LZ, England | Conductor, Composer |
| **Seredova, Alena**<br>Riccardo Gay Model Mgmt, Corso Vercelli 40, 20145 Milan, Italy | Model, Actress |
| **Sereno, Paul**<br>University of Chicago, Paleontology Dept, Chicago IL 60537, USA | Paleontologist |
| **Seres, Fiona**<br>Independent Talent Group, 40 Whitfield St, London W1T 2RH, England | Writer, Actress |
| **Seresin, Michael**<br>59 N Wharf Road, London W2 1LA, England | Cinematographer |

**Sereys, Jacques** — Actor
84 Blvd Malesherbes, 75008 Paris, France

**Sergeant, Peta** — Actress, Director, Writer
Principato-Young, 9465 Wilshire Blvd, #880, Beverly Hills CA 90212 USA

**Sergei, Ivan** — Actor
McKeon-Myrones Mgmt, 3500 Olive Ave, #770, Burbank CA 90505, USA

**Serig, Jennifer** — Fashion Designer
Perception Public Relations, 13333 Ventura Blvd, #203, Sherman Oaks CA 91423, USA

**Serkin, Peter A** — Concert Pianist
C M Artists, 127 W 96th St, #13B, New York NY 10025 USA

**Serkis, Andy** — Actor
Lou Coulson Assoc, 37 Berwick St, London W1V 8RS, England

**Serlemitsos, Peter J** — Astronomer
B B X R T Project, Goddard Space Flight Center, Greenbelt MD 20771, USA

**Serlenga, Nikki** — Soccer Player
1489 Hawthorne Ave NW, Atlanta GA 30309, USA

**Sermet, Huseyin** — Composer, Concert Pianist
Harrison/Parrott, 5-6 Albion Court, London W6 0QT, England

**Sermon, Erick** — Rap Artist (EPMD)
I C M Partners, 10250 Constellation Blvd, #900, Los Angeles CA 90067 USA

**Serna, Assumpta** — Actress
8306 Wilshire Blvd, #438, Beverly Hills CA 90211, USA

**Serna, Pepe** — Actor
Vox Inc, 6420 Wilshire Blvd, #1080, Los Angeles CA 90048 USA

**Serna, Pepe** — Actor
Jeffrey Leavitt Agency, 11500 West Olympic Blvd, #400, Los Angeles CA 90064, USA

**Serniz, Teata** — Bowler
Professional Bowlers Assn, 719 2nd Ave, #701, Seattle WA 98104 USA

**Serota, Nicholas A** — Museum Executive
Tate Britain, Millbank, London SW1P 4RG, England

**Serowik, Jeff** — Ice Hockey Player
371 Davisville Road, East Falmouth MA 02536, USA

**Serpico, Terry** — Actor
Don Buchwald, 6500 Wilshire Blvd, #2200, Los Angeles CA 90048 USA

**Serra, Eduardo** — Cinematographer
United Agents, 12-26 Lexington St, London W1F 0LE, England

**Serra, Richard** — Sculptor
173 Duane St, New York NY 10013, USA

**Serralles, Jeanine** — Actress
Don Buchwald, 6500 Wilshire Blvd, #2200, Los Angeles CA 90048 USA

**Serrano, Jimmy** — Baseball Player
2943 E Erika Court, Grand Junction CO 81504, USA

**Serrano, Nestor** — Actor
D2 Mgmt, 9255 Sunset Blvd, #600, West Hollywood CA 90069, USA

**Serratos, Christian** — Actress
Global Artists Agency, 6253 Hollywood Blvd, #508, Los Angeles CA 90028 USA

**Serre, Jean-Pierre** — Abel Mathematics Laureate
6 Ave de Montespan, 75116 Paris, France

**Serres, Jacques** — Actor
Artmedia, 20 Ave Rapp, 75007 Paris, France

**Servais, Scott D** — Baseball Player
4409 Triple Eagle Trail, Larkspur CO 80118, USA

**Servan-Schreiber, Jean-Claude** — Journalist
147 Bis Rue d'Alesia, 75014 Paris, France

**Server, Josh** — Actor
Amsel Eisenstadt Frazier, 5055 Wilshire Blvd, #865, Los Angeles CA 90036 USA

**Service, Scott D** — Baseball Player
9920 Prechtel Road, Cincinnati OH 45252, USA

**Servis, John C** — Thoroughbred Racing Trainer
2649 Woodsview Dr, Bensalem PA 19020, USA

**Servitto, Matt** — Actor
Abrams Artists, 275 7th Ave, #2600, New York NY 10001 USA

**Sesselmann, Lauren** — Soccer Player
Canadian Soccer, Place Soccer Canada, 237 Metcalfe St, Ottawa ON K2P 1R2, Canada

**Sessions, John** — Actor, Writer
Markham Froggatt Irwin, Julian House, 4 Windmill St, London W1P 1HF, England

**Sessions, Ramon** — Basketball Player
Charlotte Bobcats, 333 E Trade St, #A, Charlotte NC 28202 USA

**Sessions, Ronnie** — Singer, Guitarist, Songwriter
PO Box 242, Horseshoe Bend AR 72536, USA

**Sessions, William S** — Law Enforcement Official, Judge
112 E Pecan St, #2900, San Antonio TX 78205, USA

**Sessler, Gerhard M** — Inventor (Telephone Microphone)
Fichtenstra 30B, 64285 Darmstadt, Germany

**Seth, Vikram** — Writer
Curtis Brown, 37 Queensferry St, Edinburgh EH2 4QS, Scotland

**Settani, Sandra** — Model
Playboy Promotions, 2706 Media Center Dr, Los Angeles CA 90065 USA

**Settle, Matthew** — Actor
A P A Talent/Literary Agency, 405 S Beverly Dr, #300, Beverly Hills CA 90212 USA

**Setzer, Brian** — Singer, Guitarist
W M E Entertainment, 9601 Wilshire Blvd, #300, Beverly Hills CA 90210 USA

**Setzer, Dennis** — Auto, Truck Racing Driver
Saint Paul's Church Road, #47A, Asheville NC 28803, USA

**Setzer, Philip** — Violinist (Emerson String Quartet)
I M G Artists, Burlington Lane, Chiswick, London W4 2TH, England

**Setziol-Phillips, Monica** — Sculptor
542 NE Hill St, Sheridan OR 97378, USA

**Seubert, Richard A (Rich)** — Football Player
35 Oak Lane, Wayne NJ 07470, USA

**Sevcik, Jaroslav** — Ice Hockey Player
Dalhousie Memorial Arena, 6185 South St, Halifax NS B3H 1T7, Canada

**Sevele, Feleti V** — Prime Minister, Tonga
Prime Minister's Office, PO Box 62, Taufa'ahau Road, Nuku'alofa, Tonga

**Severance, Joan** — Model, Actress
PO Box 282, Carbondale CO 81623, USA

**Severin, G Timothy (Tim)** — Explorer
Inchybridge, Timoleague, County Cork, Ireland
**Severinsen, Carl H (Doc)** — Jazz Trumpeter, Conductor
11812 San Vicente Blvd, #200, Los Angeles CA 90049, USA
**Severinson, Albert H (Al)** — Baseball Player
133 Warren Ave, Mystic CT 06355, USA
**Severson, Jeffrey K (Jeff)** — Football Player
216 College Park Dr, Seal Beach CA 90740, USA
**Severson, John** — Publisher
PO Box 10699, Lahaina, Maui HI 96761, USA
**Severson, Kimberly (Kim)** — Equestrian
631 Dobby Creek Road, Scottsville VA 24590, USA
**Severson, Richard A (Rich)** — Baseball Player
1036 N 145th Circle, Omaha NE 68154, USA
**Severyn, Brent** — Ice Hockey Player
4521 Avebury Dr, Plano TX 75024, USA
**Sevier, Corey** — Actor
Innovative Artists, 1505 10th St, Santa Monica CA 90401 USA
**Sevigny, Chloe** — Actress
W M E Entertainment, 9601 Wilshire Blvd, #300, Beverly Hills CA 90210 USA
**Seward, Adam H** — Football Player
8905 Coast Walk Circle, Las Vegas NV 89117, USA
**Sewell, Rufus** — Actor
Julian Belfrage Assoc, 9 Argyll St, #300, London W1F 7TG, England
**Sewell, Steven E (Steve)** — Football Player
15918 E Crestridge Place, Centennial CO 80015, USA
**Seweryn, Andrzej** — Actor
Comedie Francaise, Place Colette, 75001 Paris, France
**Sexsmith, Ron** — Singer, Songwriter
S L Feldman Mgmt, 1505 W 2nd Ave, #200, Vancouver BC V6H 3Y4, Canada
**Sexson, Richmond L (Richie)** — Baseball Player
2828 NW Lakemont Dr, Bend OR 97701, USA
**Sexton, Brendan, III** — Actor
Innovative Artists, 1505 10th St, Santa Monica CA 90401 USA
**Sexton, Chad R** — Drummer (311)
311 Hive, 8904 Florence Dr, Omaha NE 68147, USA
**Sexton, Charlie** — Actor
Don Buchwald, 6500 Wilshire Blvd, #2200, Los Angeles CA 90048 USA
**Sexton, Jimmy D** — Baseball Player
2680 Baxter Road, Wilmer AL 36587, USA
**Sexton, John** — Educator
New York University, President's Office, Washington Square, New York NY 10012, USA
**Sexton, John W** — Photographer
2217 Miner St, Costa Mesa CA 92627, USA
**Sexton, Martin** — Singer, Songwriter
Red Light Mgmt, 925 W 7th Ave, Denver CO 80204, USA
**Sexton, Michael R (Mike)** — Poker Player
World Poker Tour Enterprises, 1920 Main St, #1150, Irvine CA 92615, USA
**Seydoux, Geraldine** — Molecular Biologist, Geneticist
Johns Hopkins University, Molecular Biology Dept, Baltimore MD 21218, USA
**Seydoux, Lea** — Actress
Creative Artists Agency, 2000 Ave of Stars, #100, Los Angeles CA 90067 USA
**Seyferth, Dietmar** — Chemist
Massachusetts Institute of Technology, Chemistry Dept, Cambridge MA 02139, USA
**Seyfried, Amanda** — Actress
Innovative Artists, 1505 10th St, Santa Monica CA 90401 USA
**Seyfried, Gordon C** — Baseball Player
56428 Lowe Ave, Yucca Valley CA 92284, USA
**Seymour, Jane** — Actress
Catfish Productions, 22631 Pacific Coast Highway, #313, Malibu CA 90265, USA
**Seymour, John** — Senator, CA
239 S Helix Ave, #26, Solana Beach CA 92075, USA
**Seymour, Lynn** — Ballerina
Artistes in Action, 16 Balderton St, London W1Y 1TF, England
**Seymour, Mark** — Singer, Songwriter
Loud & Clear Mgmt, PO Box 276, Albert Park VIC 3206, Australia
**Seymour, Paul C** — Football Player
4188 Shoals Dr, Okemos MI 48864, USA
**Seymour, Richard V** — Football Player
862 Chattooga Trace, Suwanee GA 30024, USA
**Seymour, Stephanie** — Model
4180 Ruffin Road, #235, San Diego CA 92123, USA
**Seymour, Stephanie K** — Judge
US Court of Appeals, US Courthouse, 333 W 4th St, #411, Tulsa OK 74103, USA
**Sezer, Ahmet Necdet** — President, Turkey
Milli Savunma Bakanligi, 06100 Ankara, Turkey
**Sfeir, Nasrallah Pierre Cardinal** — Religious Leader
Patriarcat Maronite, Bkerke, Lebanon
**Sgouros, Dimitris** — Concert Pianist
Tompazi 28 Str, Piraeus 18537, Greece
**Shaara, Jeff** — Writer
Ballatine Books, 1745 Broadway, New York NY 10019 USA
**Shaback, Nicholas (Nick)** — Basketball Player
3019 49th St, Astoria NY 11103, USA
**Shabala, Adam** — Baseball Player
2800 W North Ave, #303, Chicago IL 60647, USA
**Shack, Edward S P (Eddie)** — Ice Hockey Player
508 Fairlawn Ave, North York ON M5M 1V2, Canada
**Shackelford, Ted** — Actor
12305 Valley Heart Dr, Studio City CA 91604, USA
**Shackleford, Charles E** — Basketball Player
107 E Peyton Ave, Kinston NC 28501, USA
**Shadyac, Tom** — Director
W M E Entertainment, 9601 Wilshire Blvd, #300, Beverly Hills CA 90210 USA
**Shafer, Martin** — Producer, Writer
Castle Rock Entertainment, 9169 W Sunset Blvd, West Hollywood CA 90069, USA

**Shaffer, Atticus** — Actor
Osbrink Talent Agency, 4343 Lankershim Blvd, #100, North Hollywood CA 91602 USA
**Shaffer, Kevin C** — Football Player
5779 Legends Club Circle, Braselton GA 30517, USA
**Shaffer, Lee P, II** — Basketball Player
3822 Nottaway Road, Durham NC 27707, USA
**Shaffer, Paul** — Orchestra Leader, Keyboardist
Panacea Entertainment, 13587 Andalusia Dr E, Camarillo CA 93012, USA
**Shaffer, Peter L** — Writer
Lantz, 888 7th Ave, #2500, New York NY 10106, USA
**Shagan, Steve** — Writer
10375 Wilshire Blvd, #10E, Los Angeles CA 90024, USA
**Shagari, A Shehu U A** — President, Nigeria
22 Shehu Crescent, PO Box 162, Adarawa, Sokoto State, Nigeria
**Shaggy** — Singer
Scikron Entertainment, PO Box 297350, Pembroke Pines FL 33029, USA
**Shagimuratova, Albina** — Opera Singer
I M G Artists, Hogarth Business Park, Chiswick, London W4 2TH, England
**Shaguch, Marina** — Opera, Concert Singer
Columbia Artists Mgmt Inc, 1790 Broadway, #702, New York NY 10019 USA
**Shah, Idries** — Writer
A P Watt Ltd, 26/28 Bedford Row, London WC1R 4HL, England
**Shah, Satish** — Actor, Comedian
30A Anand Nagar, Forjeet St, Mumbai MS 400036, India
**Shah, Sonal** — Actress, Singer
Don Buchwald, 6500 Wilshire Blvd, #2200, Los Angeles CA 90048 USA
**Shaham, Gil** — Concert Violinist
Canary Classics, Knifedge Ltd, 4 Margaret St, London W1W 8RF, England
**Shaham, Orli** — Concert Pianist
Opus 3 Artists, 470 Park Ave S, #900N, New York NY 10016 USA
**Shahi, Sarah** — Actress, Model
McKeon-Myones Mgmt, 3500 W Olive Ave, #770, Burbank CA 91505, USA
**Shaiman, Marc** — Composer, Lyricist
8476 Brier Dr, Los Angeles CA 90046, USA
**Shake, Christi** — Model
Starr Entertainment, 2518 Lodge Forest Dr, Sparrows Point MD 21219, USA
**Shakes, Paul** — Ice Hockey Player
RR 4 PO, Slayner ON L0M 1S0, Canada
**Shakespeare, Frank J, Jr** — Businessman, Diplomat
303 Coast Blvd, La Jolla CA 92037, USA
**Shakin' Stevens** — Singer, Songwriter
Agency Group Ltd, 142 W 57th St, #600, New York NY 10019 USA
**Shakira** — Singer, Songwriter
Creative Artists Agency, 2000 Ave of Stars, #100, Los Angeles CA 90067 USA
**Shakman, Matt** — Actor, Director
W M E Entertainment, 9601 Wilshire Blvd, #300, Beverly Hills CA 90210 USA
**Shakur, Mustafa** — Basketball Player
Washington Wizards, M C I Centre, 601 F St NW, Washington DC 20004 USA
**Shalala, Donna E** — Secretary, Health & Human Services
University of Miami, President's Office, Coral Gables FL 33124, USA
**Shales, Thomas W** — Journalist
Washington Post, Editorial Dept, 1150 15th St NW, Washington DC 20071, USA
**Shalhoub, Tony** — Actor
I C M Partners, 10250 Constellation Blvd, #900, Los Angeles CA 90067 USA
**Shalit, Gene** — Film Critic
NBC-TV, News Dept, 30 Rockefeller Plaza, #270E, New York NY 10112 USA
**Sham, Brad M** — Sportscaster
Dallas Cowboys, 1 Cowboys Parkway, Irving TX 75063 USA
**Shamblin, Allen** — Songwriter
Built On Rock Music, PO Box 417, Franklin TN 37065, USA
**Shamsky, Art** — Baseball Player
PO Box 1400, New York NY 10163, USA
**Shanahan, Brendan F** — Ice Hockey Player
47 Saquatucket Bluffs Road, Harwich Port MA 02646, USA
**Shanahan, Mike** — Football Coach
20 Cherry Hills Farm Dr, Englewood CO 80113, USA
**Shand, David (Dave)** — Ice Hockey Player
307 N Harris St, Saline MI 48176, USA
**Shand, Remy** — Singer, Songwriter
S L Feldman Mgmt, 1505 W 2nd Ave, #200, Vancouver BC V6H 3Y4, Canada
**Shandling, Garry** — Actor, Comedian
Creative Artists Agency, 2000 Ave of Stars, #100, Los Angeles CA 90067 USA
**Shandrowsky, Alex** — Labor Leader
Marine Engineer Beneficial Assn, 444 N Capitol St NW, Washington DC 20001, USA
**Shane, Bob** — Singer (Kingston Trio)
Fuji Productions, PO Box 34397, San Diego CA 92163, USA
**Shange, Ntozake** — Writer
Saint Martin's Press, 175 5th Ave, #400, New York NY 10010, USA
**Shanice** — Singer, Songwriter
Performers of the World, 5657 Wilshire Blvd, #280, Los Angeles CA 90036 USA
**Shankar, Anoushka** — Sitar Player, Singer, Composer
Opus 3 Artists, 470 Park Ave S, #900N, New York NY 10016 USA
**Shankar, Naren** — Producer, Writer
Rothman Brecher Agency, 9465 Wilshire Blvd, #840, Beverly Hills CA 90212, USA
**Shankle, Joel** — Track Athlete
16181 Berryvale Lane, Culpepper VA 22701, USA
**Shankman, Adam** — Director
United Talent Agency, U T A Plaza, 9336 Civic Center Dr, Beverly Hills CA 90210 USA
**Shanks, Michael** — Actor, Writer, Director
Don Buchwald, 6500 Wilshire Blvd, #2200, Los Angeles CA 90048 USA
**Shanle, Scott** — Football Player
3736 Loyola Dr, #263, Kenner LA 70065, USA
**Shanley, John Patrick** — Writer
Creative Artists Agency, 2000 Ave of Stars, #100, Los Angeles CA 90067 USA
**Shannon, Carver B** — Football Player
6005 S La Cienega Blvd, Los Angeles CA 90056, USA

**Shannon, Colleen** — Model
Identity Talent Agency, 9107 Wilshire Blvd, #450, Beverly Hills CA 90210 USA

**Shannon, Darrin A** — Ice Hockey Player
Clarica, 23 Victoria St W, Alliston ON L9R 1S9, Canada

**Shannon, Darryl** — Ice Hockey Player
18 Landings Dr, Buffalo NY 14228, USA

**Shannon, Howard P (Howie)** — Basketball Player, Coach
4009 Valdez Court, Plano TX 75074, USA

**Shannon, Karissa** — Model
Playboy Promotions, 2706 Media Center Dr, Los Angeles CA 90065 USA

**Shannon, Kristina** — Model
Playboy Promotions, 2706 Media Center Dr, Los Angeles CA 90065 USA

**Shannon, Mem** — Singer, Guitarist, Songwriter
Miasma Mgmt, 1048 Hesper Ave, Metairie LA 70005, USA

**Shannon, Michael** — Actor
Creative Artists Agency, 2000 Ave of Stars, #100, Los Angeles CA 90067 USA

**Shannon, Molly** — Actress, Comedienne
United Talent Agency, U T A Plaza, 9336 Civic Center Dr, Beverly Hills CA 90210 USA

**Shannon, Polly** — Actress
Noble Caplan Abrams, 1260 Yonge St, #200, Toronto ON M4T 1W6, Canada

**Shannon, Randy L** — Football Player, Coach
7420 SW 107th Ave, #7-207, Miami FL 33173, USA

**Shannon, T Michael (Mike)** — Baseball Player, Sportscaster
3104 Southwick Dr, Saint Charles MO 63301, USA

**Shannon, Vicellous Reon** — Actor
Don Buchwald, 6500 Wilshire Blvd, #2200, Los Angeles CA 90048 USA

**Shanteau, Eric L** — Swimmer
Premier Management Group, 115 Crescent Commons, Cary, NC 27518 USA

**Shantz, Robert C (Bobby)** — Baseball Player
152 E Mount Pleasant Ave, Ambler PA 19002, USA

**Shao, En** — Conductor
I M G Artists, Hogarth Business Park, Chiswick, London W4 2TH, England

**Shapiro, Alan** — Director, Producer, Writer
Gersh Agency, 9465 Wilshire Blvd, #600, Beverly Hills CA 90212 USA

**Shapiro, Anna D** — Director
Abrams Artists, 9200 W Sunset Blvd, #1125, West Hollywood CA 90069 USA

**Shapiro, Harold T** — Educator
10 Campbelton Circle, Princeton NJ 08540, USA

**Shapiro, Irwin I** — Physicist
17 Lantern Lane, Lexington MA 02421, USA

**Shapiro, Joel E** — Sculptor
Pace Wildenstein Gallery, 32 E 57th St, #400, New York NY 10022, USA

**Shapiro, Maurice M** — Astrophysicist
5225 Pooks Hill Road, #1122S, Bethesda MD 20814, USA

**Shapiro, Paul** — Director, Producer, Writer
A P A Talent/Literary Agency, 405 S Beverly Dr, #300, Beverly Hills CA 90212 USA

**Shapiro, Robert B** — Businessman
Monsanto Co, 800 N Lindbergh Blvd, Saint Louis MO 63167, USA

**Shapiro, Robert L** — Attorney
2224 Century Hill, Los Angeles CA 90067, USA

**Sharaf, Essam A** — Prime Minister, Egypt
Prime Minister's Office, PO Box 191, 1 Majlis El-Shaab St, Cairo CA104, Egypt

**Sharapova, Maria Y** — Tennis Player
I M G Academies, 5500 34th St W, Bradenton FL 34210, USA

**Sharbino, Saxon** — Actress
W M E Entertainment, 9601 Wilshire Blvd, #300, Beverly Hills CA 90210 USA

**Share, Charles E (Charlie)** — Basketball Player
12922 Twin Meadows Court, Saint Louis MO 63146, USA

**Sharer, Kevin W** — Businessman
Amgen Inc, 1 Amgen Center Dr, Newbury Park CA 91320, USA

**Shargin, Yuri G** — Cosmonaut
Cosmonaut Training Center, Star City, 141160 Zvezdny Gorodok, Moscow Oblast, Russia

**Sharian, John** — Actor
Industry Entertainment, 955 Carillo Dr, #300, Los Angeles CA 90048 USA

**Sharif, Omar** — Actor
Steve Kenis Co, Royalty House, 72-74 Dean St, London WID 3SG, England

**Sharipov, Salizhan S** — Cosmonaut
Cosmonaut Training Center, Star City, 141160 Zvezdny Gorodok, Moscow Oblast, Russia

**Sharissa** — Singer
Virgin Records, 150 5th Ave, Front 3, New York NY 10011 USA

**Sharkey, Edward J (Ed)** — Football Player
3615 Russell Road, Centralia WA 98531, USA

**Sharkey, Jack** — Writer
39927 Chippewa Circle, Murrieta CA 92562, USA

**Sharma, Barbara** — Actress
PO Box 29125, Los Angeles CA 90029, USA

**Sharma, Madhav** — Actor
Ken McReddie Assoc, 101 Finsbury Pavement, London EC2A 1RS, England

**Sharma, Rakesh** — Cosmonaut, India
Hindustan Aeronautics, Bangalore 560037, India

**Sharma, Suraj** — Actor
Creative Artists Agency, 2000 Ave of Stars, #100, Los Angeles CA 90067 USA

**Sharman, Helen P** — Cosmonaut, England
National Physical Laboratory, Hampton Road, Teddington, Middlesex TW11 0L, England

**Sharman, Jim** — Director
M&L, 49 Daringhurst St, Kings Cross NSW 2100, Australia

**Sharockman, Edward C (Ed)** — Football Player
8955 Thomas Lane, Saint Paul MN 55125, USA

**Sharon, Richard L (Dick)** — Baseball Player
PO Box 325, Dillon MT 59725, USA

**Sharp, Dee Dee** — Singer
Cape Entertainment, 8432 NW 31st Court, Sunrise FL 33351, USA

**Sharp, Doug** — Bobsled Athlete
US Bobsled & Skeleton Federation, 1631 Mesa Ave, #A, Colorado Springs CO 80906 USA

**Sharp, Gene** — Peace Activist
Albert Einstein Institution, PO Box 455, East Boston MA 02128, USA

**Sharp, Isadore** — Businessman
Four Seasons Hotels, 1165 Leslie St, Toronto ON M3C 2K8, Canada
**Sharp, Keesha** — Actress, Director
Gartner/Green Entertainment, 5225 Wilshire Blvd, #1200, Los Angeles CA 90036, USA
**Sharp, Kevin** — Singer
Red Ridge Entertainment, 1208 16th Ave S, Lower Lobby, Nashville TN 37212, USA
**Sharp, Leslie** — Actress
I C M Partners, 10250 Constellation Blvd, #900, Los Angeles CA 90067 USA
**Sharp, Linda K** — Basketball Coach
Phoenix Mercury, American West Arena, 201 E Jefferson St, Phoenix AZ 85004 USA
**Sharp, Marsha** — Basketball Coach
Texas Tech University, Athletic Dept, Lubbock TX 79409, USA
**Sharp, Phillip A** — Nobel Medicine Laureate
36 Fairmont Ave, Newton MA 02458, USA
**Sharp, Scott** — Auto Racing Driver
Extreme Speed Motorsports, 7782 Jack James Drive, Stuart FL 34997, USA
**Sharp, Timm** — Actor
United Talent Agency, U T A Plaza, 9336 Civic Center Dr, Beverly Hills CA 90210 USA
**Sharp, Walter L** — Army General
Commander, UN Command & US Forces Korea, Unit 15327, APO AP 96218, USA
**Sharp, William H (Bill)** — Baseball Player
2244 Thornwood Ave, Wilmette IL 60091, USA
**Sharpe, Luis E, Jr** — Football Player
19188 Beaverland St, Detroit MI 48219, USA
**Sharpe, Rochelle P** — Journalist
94 Dudley St, #2, Brookline MA 02445, USA
**Sharpe, Shannon** — Football Player, Sportscaster
867 Carlton Ridge NE, Atlanta GA 30342, USA
**Sharpe, Sterling** — Football Player, Sportscaster
81 Running Fox Road, Columbia SC 29223, USA
**Sharpe, William F** — Nobel Economics Laureate
PO Box 610, Los Altos CA 94023, USA
**Sharper, Darren M** — Football Player
100 S Pointe Dr, #2808, Miami Beach FL 33139, USA
**Sharper, H James (Jamie), Jr** — Football Player
11613 Heverley Court, Glen Allen VA 23059, USA
**Sharpless, Josh** — Baseball Player
206 Mountain Dr, Carnegie PA 15106, USA
**Sharpless, K Barry** — Nobel Chemistry Laureate
Scripps Research Institute, 10550 Torrey Pines Road, La Jolla CA 92037, USA
**Sharpley, Glen** — Ice Hockey Player
Sharpley Sports, 536 Highland St, Haliburton ON K0M 1S0, Canada
**Sharpton, Al** — Social Activist, Religious Leader
104 W 145th St, New York NY 10039, USA
**Sharqi, Sheikh Hamad ibn Muhammad Ash** — Ruler, Fujairah
Royal Palace, Emiri Court, PO Box 1, Fujairah, United Arab Emirates
**Shatalov, Valdimir A** — Cosmonaut
Cosmonaut Training Center, Star City, 141160 Zvezdny Gorodok, Moscow Oblast, Russia
**Shatkin, Aaron J** — Molecular Biologist
1381 Rahway Road, Scotch Plains NJ 07076, USA
**Shatner, William** — Actor
Le Big Boss Productions, Paramount Studios, 5555 Melrose Ave, Hollywood CA 90038, USA
**Shattuck, Kim** — Singer, Guitarist (Muffs)
I C M Partners, 730 5th Ave, New York NY 10019 USA
**Shaud, Grant** — Actor
Innovative Artists, 1505 10th St, Santa Monica CA 90401 USA
**Shaud, John A** — Air Force General, Association Executive
Air Force Aid Society, 241 18th St S, #202, Arlington VA 22202, USA
**Shaughnessy, Charles** — Actor
Stone Manners Salners, 9911 W Pico Blvd, #1400, Los Angeles CA 90035 USA
**Shaunessy, Scott** — Ice Hockey Player
1 Treetop Lane, Duxbury MA 02332, USA
**Shave, Jonathan T (Jon)** — Baseball Player
1801 Park Way Dr, Fernandina Beach FL 32034, USA
**Shaver, Billy Joe** — Singer, Songwriter
Class Act Entertainment, PO Box 160236, Nashville TN 37216, USA
**Shaver, Helen** — Actress, Director
Forward Entertainment, 9255 Sunset Blvd, #805, Los Angeles CA 90069, USA
**Shaver, Jeffrey T (Jeff)** — Baseball Player
9651 E Clinton St, Scottsdale AZ 85260, USA
**Shavers, Ernie** — Boxer
2275 Linley Court, Denver CO 80219, USA
**Shaw, Amanda** — Singer, Fiddle Player
Poorman Mayfield Music Group, 5500 Prytania St, #625, New Orleans LA 70115, USA
**Shaw, Bernard** — Commentator
5801 Nicholson Lane, #1516, Rockville MD 20852, USA
**Shaw, Bernard L** — Chemist
14 Monkbridge Road, Leeds, West Yorkshire LS6 4DX, England
**Shaw, Bradley W (Brad)** — Hockey Player, Coach
8782 Lawn Ave, Saint Louis MO 63144, USA
**Shaw, Brewster H, Jr** — Astronaut
3519 Rice Blvd, Houston TX 77005, USA
**Shaw, Brian K** — Basketball Player
540 Brickell Key Dr, #1513, Miami FL 33131, USA
**Shaw, Bryony** — Yachtswoman
Lynx Sports Mgmt, Lymington Road, Lymington, Hampshire SO41 5S5, England
**Shaw, Caroline** — Composer, Singer, Violinist
Roomful of Teeth, New Amsterdam Records, 98A Van Dyke St, Brooklyn, NY 11231, USA
**Shaw, David** — Ice Hockey Player
6920 Plainfield Road, Columbia SC 29206, USA
**Shaw, David** — Football Coach
Stanford University, Athletic Dept, Stanford CA 94305, USA
**Shaw, Dennis W** — Football Player
14844 Priscilla St, San Diego CA 92129, USA
**Shaw, Donald W (Don)** — Baseball Player
857 Waterford Villas Dr, Lake Saint Louis MO 63367, USA

**Shaw, Fiona** — Actress
I C M Partners, 10250 Constellation Blvd, #900, Los Angeles CA 90067 USA

**Shaw, Hannah** — Model
Why Not Model Agency, Via Zenale 9, 20123 Milan, Italy

**Shaw, Ivan** — Actor
Innovative Artists, 1505 10th St, Santa Monica CA 90401 USA

**Shaw, Jane** — Businesswoman
Intel Corp, 2200 Mission College Blvd, Santa Clara CA 95054, USA

**Shaw, Jason** — Actor, Model
Innovative Artists, 1505 10th St, Santa Monica CA 90401 USA

**Shaw, Jeffrey L (Jeff)** — Baseball Player
1215 Storybrook Dr, Washington Court House OH 43160, USA

**Shaw, Joe** — Actor
Ken McReddie Assoc, 101 Finsbury Pavement, London EC2A 1RS, England

**Shaw, John H** — Geophysicist
Harvard University, Geophysics Dept, Cambridge MA 02138, USA

**Shaw, Kenneth E (Pete)** — Football Player
699 14th St, #356, San Diego CA 92101, USA

**Shaw, Lindsey** — Actress
Paradigm Agency, 360 N Crescent Dr, North Building, Beverly Hills CA 90210 USA

**Shaw, Marlena** — Singer
100 Redstone St, Las Vegas NV 89145, USA

**Shaw, Martin** — Actor
Ken McReddie Assoc, 101 Finsbury Pavement, London EC2A 1RS, England

**Shaw, Rick** — Singer (Brandywine Singers)
Cuzin Richard Entertainment Services, PO Box 4585, Portsmouth NH 03802, USA

**Shaw, Ron** — Singer (Brandywine Singers)
Cuzin Richard Entertainment Services, PO Box 4585, Portsmouth NH 03802, USA

**Shaw, Run Run** — Producer
Shaw House, Lot 220 Clear Water Bay Road, Kowloon, Hong Kong, China

**Shaw, Ryan** — Singer
Monterey International, 200 W Superior St, #202, Chicago IL 60654 USA

**Shaw, Scott** — Photojournalist
20771 Lake Road, Rocky River OH 44116, USA

**Shaw, Stan** — Actor
Metropolitan Talent Agency, 5405 Wilshire Blvd, #218, Los Angeles CA 90036 USA

**Shaw, Terrance B (Terry)** — Football Player
PO Box 701645, Dallas TX 75370, USA

**Shaw, Thomas R (Tommy)** — Singer, Guitarist (Styx); Songwriter
Alliance Artists, 1825 Lockeway Dr, #204, Alpharetta GA 30004, USA

**Shaw, Timothy A (Tim)** — Swimmer, Water Polo Player
5315 River Ave, Newport Beach CA 92663, USA

**Shaw, Victoria** — Singer, Songwriter
V L S Mgmt, PO Box 58175, Nashville TN 37205, USA

**Shaw, Vinessa** — Actress, Model
I C M Partners, 10250 Constellation Blvd, #900, Los Angeles CA 90067 USA

**Shaw, William L (Billy)** — Football Player
573 Old Rothell Road, Toccoa GA 30577, USA

**Shawanda, Crystal** — Singer, Guitarist
W M E Entertainment, 1600 Division St, #300, Nashville TN 37203 USA

**Shawkat, Alia** — Actress
Basra Entertainment, 8-444 Perez Road, #O, Cathedral City CA 92234, USA

**Shawn Jay** — Rap Artist (Field Mob)
Geffen Records, 10900 Wilshire Blvd, #1000, Los Angeles CA 90024 USA

**Shawn, Wallace** — Actor, Writer
Stone Manners Salners, 9911 W Pico Blvd, #1400, Los Angeles CA 90035 USA

**Shay, Jerome P (Jerry)** — Football Player
81 E Shasta St, Chula Vista CA 91910, USA

**Shaye, Lin** — Actress
Don Buchwald, 6500 Wilshire Blvd, #2200, Los Angeles CA 90048 USA

**Shaye, Robert K** — Businessman
New Line Cinema, 116 N Robertson Blvd, #400, Los Angeles CA 90048, USA

**Shaye, Skyler** — Actress
Artists Only Mgmt, 10203 Santa Monica Blvd, Los Angeles CA 90067, USA

**Shayk, Irina** — Model
Women Model Mgmt, 199 Lafayette St, #700, New York NY 10012 USA

**Shaykh, Hanan al-** — Writer
Rogers Coleridge White, 20 Powis Mews, London W11 1JN, England

**Shchedrin, Rodion K** — Composer
25/9 Tverskaya St, #31, 103050 Moscow, Russia

**Shea, Aaron T** — Football Player
2992 Waterfall Way, Westlake OH 44145, USA

**Shea, Charity** — Actress
B/W/R, 9100 Wilshire Blvd, #500W, Beverly Hills CA 90212 USA

**Shea, John** — Actor
S M S Talent, 8383 Wilshire Blvd, #230, Beverly Hills CA 90211 USA

**Shea, Judith** — Artist, Sculptor
124 Chambers St, New York NY 10007, USA

**Shea, Katt** — Actress
I C M Partners, 10250 Constellation Blvd, #900, Los Angeles CA 90067 USA

**Shea, Pat** — Singer, Songwriter
P B S Records, PO Box 991, Orchard Park NY 14127, USA

**Shea, Robert M** — Marine Corps General
Director, Command Control Communications, HqUSMC, Washington DC 20380, USA

**Shea, Terry** — Football Coach
Miami Dolphins, 7500 SW 30th St, Davie FL 33314 USA

**Sheaffer, Danny T** — Baseball Player
165 Savannah Lane, Mount Airy NC 27030, USA

**Shealy, Ryan N** — Baseball Player
2168 NE 63rd Court, Fort Lauderdale FL 33308, USA

**Shear, Jules** — Singer, Songwriter
Concerted Efforts, PO Box 440326, Somerville MA 02144 USA

**Shear, Rhonda** — Actress, Comedienne, Model
J Cast Productions, 2550 Greenvalley Road, Los Angeles CA 90046, USA

**Sheard, Kierra (Kiki)** — Singer
E M I Gospel, PO Box 5085, Brentwood TN 37024, USA

| | |
|---|---|
| **Shearer, Al** | Actor |
| Safran Co, 8748 Holloway Dr, West Hollywood CA 90069, USA | |
| **Shearer, Alan** | Soccer Player |
| Newcastle United F C, Saint James Park, Newcastle-Tyne NE1 4ST, England | |
| **Shearer, Bob** | Golfer |
| International Management Group, 281 Clarence St, Sydney NSW 2000, Australia | |
| **Shearer, Harry J** | Actor, Comedian |
| Affirmative Entertainment, 425 N Robertson Blvd, Los Angeles CA 90048, USA | |
| **Shearer, Peter M** | Geophysicist |
| Scripps Oceanographic Institute, Geophysics Dept, La Jolla CA 92093, USA | |
| **Shearer, S Bradford (Brad)** | Football Player |
| 1909 Lakeshore Dr, #B, Austin TX 78746, USA | |
| **Shearn, Tom** | Baseball Player |
| 20429 Rita Blanca Circle, Pflugerville TX 78660, USA | |
| **Shears, Jake** | Singer (Scissors Sisters) |
| Girlie Action, 59 W 19th St, #4B, New York NY 10011 USA | |
| **Shearsmith, Reece** | Actor |
| Independent Talent Group, 40 Whitfield St, London W1T 2RH, England | |
| **Sheckler, Ryan A** | Skateboarder, Actor |
| 927 Calle Negocio, #K, San Clemente CA 92673, USA | |
| **Shectman, Stephen A** | Astronomer |
| Carniegie Observatories, 813 Santa Barbara St, Pasadena CA 91101, USA | |
| **Shedd, Kendrick D (Kenny)** | Football Player |
| 1928 Tioga Pass Way, Antioch CA 94531, USA | |
| **Sheedy, Ally** | Actress |
| Innovative Artists, 1505 10th St, Santa Monica CA 90401 USA | |
| **Sheehan, Doug** | Actor |
| Judy Schoen, 606 N Larchmont Blvd, #309, Los Angeles CA 90004 USA | |
| **Sheehan, Neil** | Journalist |
| 4505 Klingle St NW, Washington DC 20016, USA | |
| **Sheehan, Patricia A (Patty)** | Golfer |
| 8395 Panorama Dr, Reno NV 89511, USA | |
| **Sheehan, Robert** | Actor |
| United Talent Agency, U T A Plaza, 9336 Civic Center Dr, Beverly Hills CA 90210 USA | |
| **Sheehan, Susan** | Writer |
| 4505 Klingle St NW, Washington DC 20016, USA | |
| **Sheehy, Gail H** | Writer |
| 300 E 57th St, #18D, New York NY 10022, USA | |
| **Sheehy, Neil K** | Ice Hockey Player |
| 7760 France Ave S, #1100, Minneapolis MN 55435, USA | |
| **Sheehy, Timothy K (Tim)** | Ice Hockey Player |
| Sheehy Hockey, 4 Boswell Lane, Southborough MA 01772, USA | |
| **Sheeler, Jim** | Journalist |
| Rocky Mountain News, Editorial Dept, 101 W Colfax Ave, #500, Denver CO 80202, USA | |
| **Sheen, Charles (Charlie)** | Actor |
| Evolution Entertainment, 901 N Highland Ave, Los Angeles CA 90038 USA | |
| **Sheen, Jacqueline** | Actress, Model |
| Playboy Promotions, 2706 Media Center Dr, Los Angeles CA 90065 USA | |
| **Sheen, Martin** | Actor |
| 29351 Bluewater Road, Malibu CA 90265, USA | |
| **Sheen, Michael** | Actor |
| Roxanne Vacca Mgmt, 73 Bleak St, London W1R 3LF, England | |
| **Sheeran, Josette** | Government Official, Journalist |
| UN World Food Program, Cesare Giulio Viola 68/70, 00148 Rome, Italy | |
| **Sheets, Andrew M (Andy)** | Baseball Player |
| 104 Villaggio Dr, Lafayette LA 70508, USA | |
| **Sheets, Ben M** | Baseball Player |
| 105 E Shore Road, Monroe LA 71203, USA | |
| **Sheets, Larry K** | Baseball Player |
| 1411 Chippendale Road, Luther Timonium MD 21093, USA | |
| **Sheffer, Craig** | Actor |
| Innovative Artists, 1505 10th St, Santa Monica CA 90401 USA | |
| **Sheffield, Frederick J (Fred)** | Basketball Player |
| 11664 McDougall, Tustin CA 92782, USA | |
| **Sheffield, Gary A** | Baseball Player |
| 6754 Ralston Beach Circle, Tampa FL 33614, USA | |
| **Sheffield, William J (Bill)** | Governor, AK |
| PO Box 91476, Anchorage AK 99509, USA | |
| **Sheik, Duncan** | Singer, Songwriter |
| Sweet180, 141 W 28th St, #300, New York NY 10001, USA | |
| **Sheil, Kate Lyn** | Actress |
| One Entertainment, 347 5th Ave, #1404, New York NY 10016 USA | |
| **Sheila E** | Singer, Drummer |
| Universal Attractions, 135 W 26th St, #1200, New York NY 10001 USA | |
| **Sheindlin, Judy (Judge)** | Entertainer, Judge |
| Big Ticket Television, 5842 W Sunset Blvd, #303, Los Angeles CA 90028, USA | |
| **Sheinkin, Rachel** | Writer, Lyricist |
| New York University, Graduate Musical Theater Writing Program, New York NY 10012, USA | |
| **Shelby, John T** | Baseball Player |
| 2232 Broadhead Lane, Lexington KY 40515, USA | |
| **Shelby, Mark** | Jazz Bassist, Composer |
| Thomas Cassidy, PO Box 1311, Tucson AZ 85702 USA | |
| **Sheldon, Roland F (Rollie)** | Baseball Player |
| 614 NE Coronado St, Lees Summit MO 64063, USA | |
| **Sheldon, Scott P** | Baseball Player |
| 5202 Blue Cypress Lane, League City TX 77573, USA | |
| **Shell, Arthur (Art)** | Football Player, Coach |
| 419 Rilea Way, Oakland CA 94605, USA | |
| **Shell, Donnie** | Football Player |
| 2945 Shandon Road, Rock Hill SC 29730, USA | |
| **Shellenback, James P (Jim)** | Baseball Player |
| 10627 Dreamy Lane, Parker AZ 85344, USA | |
| **Shelley, Barbara** | Actress |
| Ken McReddie Assoc, 101 Finsbury Pavement, London EC2A 1RS, England | |
| **Shelley, Carole** | Actress, Singer |
| CornerStone Talent Agency, 37 W 20th St, #1107, New York NY 10011, USA | |

**Shelley, Howard G** — Concert Pianist, Conductor
Caroline Baird Artists, Farmoor Eynsham, Oxfordshire OX29 4DA, England

**Shelley, Jody** — Ice Hockey Player
16169 State Route 374, Laurelville OH 43135, USA

**Shelley, Pete** — Singer, Guitarist (Buzzcocks)
Free Trade Agency, Chapel Place, Rivington St, London EC2A 3DQ, England

**Shelley, Rachel** — Actress
Independent Talent Group, 40 Whitfield St, London W1T 2RH, England

**Shelley, Steve** — Drummer (Sonic Youth)
Silva Artist Mgmt, 722 Seward St, Los Angeles CA 90038, USA

**Shelmerdine, Kirk** — Auto Racing Engineer
Kirk Shelmerdine Racing, PO Box 1133, Welcome NC 27374, USA

**Shelton, Abigail** — Actress
Dale Garrick, 1017 N La Cienega Blvd, #109, West Hollywood CA 90069 USA

**Shelton, Blake T** — Singer, Songwriter
W M E Entertainment, 1600 Division St, #300, Nashville TN 37203 USA

**Shelton, Chris** — Baseball Player
6382 Shady Grove Circle, Salt Lake City UT 84121, USA

**Shelton, Daimon** — Football Player
9069 Quail Feather Way, Elk Grove CA 95624, USA

**Shelton, Deborah** — Actress, Beauty Queen
2265 Westwood Blvd, #251, Los Angeles CA 90064, USA

**Shelton, Lonnie J** — Basketball Player
3883 Union Ave, #5, Bakersfield CA 93305, USA

**Shelton, Lonnie J (L J)** — Football Player
6034 W Trovita Place, Chandler AZ 85226, USA

**Shelton, Lynn** — Director
United Talent Agency, U T A Plaza, 9336 Civic Center Dr, Beverly Hills CA 90210 USA

**Shelton, Marley C** — Actress
Untitled Entertainment, 350 S Beverly Dr, #200, Beverly Hills CA 90212 USA

**Shelton, Richard E** — Football Player
6367 Raw Hyde Trail N, Jacksonville FL 32210, USA

**Shelton, Ricky Van** — Singer, Guitarist, Songwriter
PO Box 111, Woodlawn VA 24381, USA

**Shelton, Robert N** — Educator
University of Arizona, President's Office, Tucson AZ 85721, USA

**Shelton, Ronald W (Ron)** — Director
Oasis Media Group, 8730 W Sunset Blvd, #PHW, Los Angeles CA 90069, USA

**Shelton, Samantha** — Actress
Untitled Entertainment, 350 S Beverly Dr, #200, Beverly Hills CA 90212 USA

**Shelton, Uriah** — Actor
Coast to Coast Talent, 3350 Barham Blvd, Los Angeles CA 90068 USA

**Shemi, Calman** — Artist
Jacques Soussana Graphics, 37 Pierre Koenig St, Jerusalem 91401, Israel

**Shen Wei** — Choreographer
Shen Wei Dance Arts, 520 8th Ave, #303, New York NY 10018, USA

**Shen Xue** — Figure Skater
Skating Assn, 56 Zhongguancun South St, Haidian, Beijing 100044, China

**Shen, Parry** — Actor
Stone Manners Salners, 9911 W Pico Blvd, #1400, Los Angeles CA 90035 USA

**Shenandoh, Joanne** — Singer, Songwriter, Actress
Oneida Nation Territory, PO Box 450, Oneida NY 13421, USA

**Shengelaia, Eldar N** — Director, Writer
Ioseliani St 37, #58, 380091 Tbilisi, Georgia

**Shengelaia, Georgy N** — Director
Kekelidze St 16, #12, 380091 Tbilisi, Georgia

**Shenk, Thomas E** — Molecular Biologist
Princeton University, Molecular Biology Dept, Princeton NJ 08544, USA

**Shenkman, Ben** — Actor
Suskin Mgmt, 2 Charlton St, #5K, New York NY 10014, USA

**Shenton, Ann** — Synthesizer Player (Add N to X)
Kork Agency, 1880 Century Park E, #711, Los Angeles CA 90067 USA

**Shepard, Dax** — Actor
Creative Artists Agency, 2000 Ave of Stars, #100, Los Angeles CA 90067 USA

**Shepard, Devon** — Writer, Producer
I C M Partners, 10250 Constellation Blvd, #900, Los Angeles CA 90067 USA

**Shepard, Jean** — Singer
Midnight Special Productions, PO Box 916, Hendersonville TN 37077, USA

**Shepard, Jewel** — Actress, Model
A P A Talent/Literary Agency, 405 S Beverly Dr, #300, Beverly Hills CA 90212 USA

**Shepard, Jules** — Social Activist
7120 Minstrel Way, #206, Columbia MD 21045, USA

**Shepard, Richard** — Director, Writer
W M E Entertainment, 9601 Wilshire Blvd, #300, Beverly Hills CA 90210 USA

**Shepard, Roger N** — Psychologist
6041 Fair Oaks Blvd, Carmichael CA 95608, USA

**Shepard, Samuel K (Sam)** — Writer, Actor
I C M Partners, 730 5th Ave, New York NY 10019 USA

**Shepard, Vonda** — Singer, Songwriter
Marleah Leslie Assoc, 1645 Vine St, #712, Los Angeles CA 90028, USA

**Shepherd, Ben** — Bassist (Soundgarden)
Susan Silver Mgmt, 6523 California Ave SW, #348, Seattle WA 98136, USA

**Shepherd, Cybill** — Actress, Model
Don Buchwald, 6500 Wilshire Blvd, #2200, Los Angeles CA 90048 USA

**Shepherd, Elizabeth** — Actress
London Mgmt, 2-4 Noel St, London W1V 3RB, England

**Shepherd, Kenny Wayne** — Guitarist
Shepherd Entertainment, 1085 Crouch Road, Benton LA 71006, USA

**Shepherd, Morgan** — Auto, Truck Racing Driver
Shepherd Racing Ventures, 4905 Jeffrey Lane, Conover NC 28613, USA

**Shepherd, Neferteri** — Model
Amsel Eisenstadt Frazier, 5055 Wilshire Blvd, #865, Los Angeles CA 90036 USA

**Shepherd, Ronald W (Ron)** — Baseball Player
5821 FM 349, Kilgore TX 75662, USA

**Shepherd, Sherri** — Actress
Creative Artists Agency, 2000 Ave of Stars, #100, Los Angeles CA 90067 USA

**Shepherd, Sherrie** — Cartoonist (Francie)
United Feature Syndicate, PO Box 5610, Cincinnati OH 45201 USA

**Shepherd, William M** — Astronaut
18623 Prince William Lane, Houston TX 77058, USA

**Sheppard, Anna** — Costume Designer
I C M Partners, 10250 Constellation Blvd, #900, Los Angeles CA 90067 USA

**Sheppard, Delia** — Actress, Model
Kazarian/Measures/Ruskin, 11969 Ventura Blvd, #300, Studio City CA 91604 USA

**Sheppard, Gregg** — Ice Hockey Player
2521 Blue Jay Crescent, North Battleford SK S9A 3Z3, Canada

**Sheppard, Henry F, Jr** — Football Player
313 Waterstone, Victoria TX 77901, USA

**Sheppard, Jonathan E** — Steeplechase Racing Trainer
287 Lamborn Town Road, West Grove PA 19390, USA

**Sheppard, Lito D** — Football Player
268 Clearwater Dr, Ponte Vedra Beach FL 32082, USA

**Sheppard, Mark** — Actor
Ken McReddie Assoc, 101 Finsbury Pavement, London EC2A 1RS, England

**Sheppard, Ray** — Ice Hockey Player
19110 Fox Landing Dr, Boca Raton FL 33434, USA

**Sheppard, T G** — Singer, Guitarist
R J Kaltenbach Personal Mgmt, PO Box 550, Harvard IL 60033, USA

**Sher, Antony** — Actor
I C M Partners, Marlborough House, 10 Earlham St, #300, London WC2H 9LNP, England

**Sher, Bartlett** — Director
Creative Artists Agency, 2000 Ave of Stars, #100, Los Angeles CA 90067 USA

**Sher, Eden** — Actress
Innovative Artists, 1505 10th St, Santa Monica CA 90401 USA

**Sher, Stacey** — Producer
Double Feature Films, 9320 Wilshire Blvd, #200, Beverly Hills CA 90212, USA

**Shera, Mark** — Actor
PO Box 15717, Beverly Hills CA 90209, USA

**Sherbedgia, Rade** — Actor
United Agents, 12-26 Lexington St, London W1F 0LE, England

**Sherffius, John** — Editorial Cartoonist
Saint Louis Post Dispatch, Editorial Dept, 900 N Tucker, Saint Louis MO 63101, USA

**Sheridan, Bonnie Bramlett** — Singer (Delaney & Bonnie), Actress
18011 Martha St, Encino CA 91316, USA

**Sheridan, Dave** — Actor
David Shapira Assoc, 193 N Robertson Blvd, Beverly Hills CA 90211 USA

**Sheridan, Howard M** — Radiologist, Businessman
4020 Sheridan St, #B, Hollywood FL 33021, USA

**Sheridan, James P (Jamey)** — Actor
Brillstein Entertainment Partners, 9150 Wilshire Blvd, #350, Beverly Hills CA 90212 USA

**Sheridan, Jim** — Director, Producer
Hell's Kitchen International, 21 Mespil Road, Dublin 4, Ireland

**Sheridan, Lisa** — Actress
Landrum Arts, 712 Milam St, #103, Shreveport LA 71101, USA

**Sheridan, Nicolette** — Actress
B/W/R, 9100 Wilshire Blvd, #500W, Beverly Hills CA 90212 USA

**Sheridan, Patrick A (Pat)** — Baseball Player
31654 Taft St, Wayne MI 48184, USA

**Sheridan, Tayler** — Actress
Evolution Entertainment, 901 N Highland Ave, Los Angeles CA 90038 USA

**Sheridan, Tye** — Actor
Mosiac Media Group, 9200 W Sunset Blvd, #1000, Los Angeles CA 90069 USA

**Sherk, Jerry M** — Football Player
1518 Orangeview Dr, Encinitas CA 92024, USA

**Sherk, Kathy** — Golfer
1333 Dorval Dr, Oakville ON L6M 4G2, Canada

**Sherlock, Nancy J** — Astronaut
N A S A, Johnson Space Center, 2101 NASA Road, Houston TX 77058 USA

**Sherman, Alex (Allie)** — Football Player, Coach
136 E 55th St, #12H, New York NY 10022, USA

**Sherman, Bobby** — Singer, Actor
1870 Sunset Plaza Dr, Los Angeles CA 90069, USA

**Sherman, Cindy M** — Photographer
9 Debrosses St, #520A, New York NY 10032, USA

**Sherman, Heath B** — Football Player
PO Box 54, Glen Flora TX 77443, USA

**Sherman, Michael (Mickey)** — Attorney
Sherman & Richichi, 27 5th St, Stamford CT 06905, USA

**Sherman, Michael F (Mike)** — Football Coach
3337 Arapaho Ridge Dr, College Station TX 77845, USA

**Sherman, Patsy O** — Chemist, Inventor (Scotchgard)
1451 Highview Ave, Saint Paul MN 55121, USA

**Sherman, Richard M** — Composer, Lyricist
Cowans DeBaets Abrahams, 41 Madison Ave, 3400, New York NY 10010, USA

**Sherman, Rodney J (Rod)** — Football Player
PO Box 4551, Incline Village NV 89450, USA

**Sherman-Palladino, Amy** — Producer, Director, Writer
Creative Artists Agency, 2000 Ave of Stars, #100, Los Angeles CA 90067 USA

**Sherod, Edmund (Ed)** — Basketball Player
519 Montvale Ave, Richmond VA 23222, USA

**Sherrard, Michael W (Mike)** — Football Player
PO Box 992, Agoura Hills CA 91376, USA

**Sherrill, Betty** — Interior Designer
McMillen Inc, 155 E 56th St, #500, New York NY 10022, USA

**Sherrill, George F** — Baseball Player
2092 Lee Place, Memphis TN 38104, USA

**Sherrington, Georgina** — Actress
J G M, 15 Lexham Mews, London W8 6JW, England

**Sherry, Fionnuala** — Violinist (Secret Garden)
Thranesgate 2B, Oslo 473, Norway

**Sherry, Norman B (Norm)** — Baseball Player, Manager
4383 Nobel Dr, #89, San Diego CA 92122, USA

**Sherven, Gord** — Ice Hockey Player
184 Hampshire Grove NW, Calgary AB T3A 5B3, Canada

**Sherwin, Timothy T (Tim)** — Football Player
6 Mill Road, Latham NY 12110, USA

**Sherwood, Alison** — Journalist
Milwaukee Journal Sentinel, Editorial Dept, PO Box 371, Milwaukee WI 53201 USA

**Sherwood, Brad** — Actor, Comedian
C E S D, 10635 Santa Monica Blvd, #130, Los Angeles CA 90025 USA

**Shesol, Jeff** — Cartoonist (Thatch)
Creators Syndicate, 737 3rd St, Hermosa Beach CA 90254 USA

**Sheth, Sheetal** — Actress
Defining Artists Agency, 10 Universal City Plaza, #2000, Universal City CA 91608, USA

**Shetty, Reshma** — Actress
Station 3 Entertainment, 300 W 55th St, #5L, New York NY 10019, USA

**Shetty, Shilpa** — Actress
12 Dev Darshan, 262 Saint Anthony Road, Chembur, Mumbai 400071, India

**Shetty, Sunil** — Actor
18/B Prithvi Apartments, Altamont Road, Mumbai MS 400026, India

**Shevchenki, Andriy** — Soccer Player
F C Milan, Via Filippo Turati 3, 20121 Milan, Italy

**Shi, David E** — Educator
Furman University, President's Office, Greenville SC 29613, USA

**Shiancoe, Visanthe** — Football Player
2316 City Place, Edgewater NJ 07020, USA

**Shicoff, Neil** — Opera Singer
Opera et Concert, 37 Rue de la Chaussee d'Antin, 75009 Paris, France

**Shields, Ashley** — Basketball Player
Atlanta Dream, 83 Walton St NW, #400, Atlanta, GA 30303 USA

**Shields, Ben** — Actor
Abrams Artists, 9200 W Sunset Blvd, #1125, West Hollywood CA 90069 USA

**Shields, Blake** — Actor
Pakula/King, 9229 W Sunset Blvd, #315, West Hollywood CA 90069 USA

**Shields, Brooke** — Model, Actress
United Talent Agency, U T A Plaza, 9336 Civic Center Dr, Beverly Hills CA 90210 USA

**Shields, Perry** — Judge
US Tax Court, 400 2nd St NW, Washington DC 20217, USA

**Shields, R Scot** — Baseball Player
16139 Pine Valley Dr, Northville MI 48168, USA

**Shields, Robert** — Mime (Shields & Yarnell), Artist
Robert Shields Designs, PO Box 3161, Cottonwood AZ 86326, USA

**Shields, Stephen C (Steve)** — Ice Hockey Player
123 E Balboa Blvd, Newport Beach CA 92661, USA

**Shields, Stephen M (Steve)** — Baseball Player
4969 Leonard Dr, Gadsden AL 35903, USA

**Shields, Will H** — Football Player
13125 W 127th Place, Overland Park KS 66213, USA

**Shields, William D (Billy)** — Football Player
12701 Treeridge Terrace, Poway CA 92064, USA

**Shields, Willow** — Actress
I C M Partners, 10250 Constellation Blvd, #900, Los Angeles CA 90067 USA

**Shifflett, Steven E (Steve)** — Baseball Player
24004 E 172nd St, Pleasant Hill MO 64080, USA

**Shiflett, Chris** — Guitarist (Foo Fighters, Dead Peasants)
Silva Artists Mgmt, 722 Seward St, Los Angeles CA 90038, USA

**Shifrin, David** — Concert Clarinetist
C M Artists, 127 W 96th St, #13B, New York NY 10025 USA

**Shifty Shellshock** — Rap Artist, Lyricist (Crazy Town)
Q Prime, 729 7th Ave, #1600, New York NY 10019, USA

**Shigeta, James** — Actor
C E S D, 10635 Santa Monica Blvd, #130, Los Angeles CA 90025 USA

**Shikler, Aaron** — Artist
Meredith Long Co, 2323 San Felipe St, Houston TX 77019, USA

**Shiller, Robert J** — Economist
Yale University, Cowles Foundation, PO Box 208281, New Haven CT 06520, USA

**Shima, Masatoshi** — Electronics Engineer
Shima Co, 260 Tsurumaki, Omika Haramachishi, Fukushima 975 0049, Japan

**Shimabukuro, Jake** — Singer, Ukulele Player
A P A Talent/Literary Agency, 405 S Beverly Dr, #300, Beverly Hills CA 90212 USA

**Shimell, William** — Opera Singer
I M G Artists, Hogarth Business Park, Chiswick, London W4 2TH, England

**Shimer, Brian** — Bobsled Athlete
2613 Lakeview Dr, Naples FL 34112, USA

**Shimerman, Armin** — Actor
Stone Manners Salners, 9911 W Pico Blvd, #1400, Los Angeles CA 90035 USA

**Shimizu, Jenny** — Model, Actress
Elite Model Mgmt, 404 Park Ave S, #900, New York NY 10016 USA

**Shimizu, Takashi** — Director
Media Complex, 7-6-52-408 Akasaka, Minatoku, Tokyo 107-0052, Japan

**Shimkus, Joanna** — Actress
Creative Artists Agency, 2000 Ave of Stars, #100, Los Angeles CA 90067 USA

**Shimomura, Osamu** — Nobel Chemistry Laureate
324 Sippewissett Road, Falmouth MA 02540, USA

**Shimono, Sab** — Actor
12711 Ventura Blvd, #440, Studio City CA 91604, USA

**Shimony, Abner E** — Physicist
16 Claflin Road, #2, Brookline MA 02445, USA

**Shin Sang-Ho** — Sculptor
Hong-ik University, Sangsu Dong, Ma Po Gu, Seoul 121 791, South Korea

**Shin Yong-Moon** — Geneticist
National University, Sillimdong, Gwanakgu, Seoul 151 742, South Korea

**Shin, Jiyai** — Golfer
Ladies Pro Golf Assn, 100 International Golf Dr, Daytona Beach FL 32124 USA

**Shinabarger, Tim** — Sculptor
Legacy Gallery, 75 N Cache Ave, Box 4977, Jackson WY 83001, USA

**Shinall, Zakary S (Zak)** — Baseball Player
16605 Sell Circle, Huntington Beach CA 92649, USA

**Shindle, Katherine (Kate)** — Beauty Queen, Actress
Gage Group, 14724 Ventura Blvd, #505, Sherman Oaks CA 91403 USA
**Shine, Michael (Mike)** — Track Athlete
508 Royal Road, State College PA 16801, USA
**Shiner, Richard E (Dick), Jr** — Football Player
19 Fox Trail, Gettysburg PA 17325, USA
**Shinners, J John T** — Football Player
N120W14985 Freistadt Road, Germantown WI 53022, USA
**Shinoda, Mike** — Singer (Linkin Park)
Gorfaine/Schwartz, 4111 W Alameda Ave, #509, Burbank CA 91505 USA
**Shinseki, Eric K (Ric)** — Secretary, Veterans Affairs; General
Veteran Affairs Department, 810 Vermont Ave NW, Washington DC 20420 USA
**Shinya, Hiromi** — Gastroenterologist
Beth Israel Medical Center, Endoscopy Unit, 1st Ave & 16th St, New York NY 10461, USA
**Shipka, Kiernan** — Actress
42 West, 11400 W Olympic Blvd, #1100, Los Angeles CA 90064 USA
**Shipler, David K** — Journalist
4005 Thornapple St, Chevy Chase MD 20815, USA
**Shipley, Craig B** — Baseball Player
Boston Red Sox, Fenway Park, 4 Yawkey Way, Boston MA 02215 USA
**Shipley, Jennifer M** — Prime Minister, New Zealand
Club de Madrid, C/Goya 5-7, Pasaje 2, 28001 Madrid, Spain
**Shipley, Walter V** — Financier
Chase Manhattan Corp, 270 Park Ave, New York NY 10017, USA
**Shipman, Claire** — Commentator
ABC-TV, News Dept, 77 W 66th St, New York NY 10023 USA
**Shipp, E R** — Columnist
New York Daily News, Editorial Dept, 220 E 42nd St, New York NY 10017, USA
**Shipp, Jerry** — Basketball Player
PO Box 370, Kingston OK 73439, USA
**Shipp, John Wesley** — Actor
Stewart Talent, 318 W 53rd St, #201, New York NY 10019, USA
**Shirakawa, Hideki** — Nobel Chemistry Laureate
University of Tsukuba, Chemistry Dept, Sakura-Mura, Ibaraki 000 305, Japan
**Shiraki, Ryan** — Director, Writer, Actor
A P A Talent/Literary Agency, 405 S Beverly Dr, #300, Beverly Hills CA 90212 USA
**Shire, David L** — Composer
250 Piermont Ave, Piermont NY 10968, USA
**Shire, Talia** — Actress, Director
10730 Bellagio Road, Los Angeles CA 90077, USA
**Shirk, Gary L** — Football Player
PO Box 287, Laporte PA 18626, USA
**Shirley, Barton A (Bart)** — Baseball Player
6538 Orangetip Dr, Corpus Christi TX 78414, USA
**Shirley, Danny** — Singer (Confederate Railroad)
Bobby Roberts, 3050 Business Park Circle, #303, Goodlettsville TN 37221 USA
**Shirley, George I** — Opera Singer
University of Michigan, Music School, Ann Arbor MI 48109, USA
**Shirley, John** — Writer
Tarcher/Penguin Press, 375 Hudson St, Basement 3, New York NY 10014, USA
**Shirley, Robert C (Bob)** — Baseball Player
761 W 13th St, Tulsa OK 74127, USA
**Shirley-Quirk, John S** — Opera Singer
2932 Huntingdon Ave, Baltimore MD 21211, USA
**Shirreffs, John A** — Thoroughbred Racing Trainer
Hollywood Park Race Track, Barn 55 S, PO Box 369, Inglewood CA 90306, USA
**Shiver, Sanders T** — Football Player
16507 Ariel Court, Bowie MD 20716, USA
**Shivers, Chris** — Rodeo Bull Rider
192 Shivers Road, Jonesville LA 71343, USA
**Shivers, Roy L** — Football Player
2067 Hidden Hollow Lane, Henderson NV 89012, USA
**Shkaplerov, Anton N** — Cosmonaut
Cosmonaut Training Center, Star City, 141160 Zvezdny Gorodok, Moscow Oblast, Russia
**Shoals, Roger R** — Football Player
365 Righters Mill Road, Gladwyne PA 19035, USA
**Shobert, Don W (Bubba)** — Motorcycle Racing Rider
8905 153rd St, Wolfforth TX 79382, USA
**Shock G** — Rap Artist, Producer
Entertainment Artists, 2409 21st Ave S, #100, Nashville TN 10019 USA
**Shocked, Michelle** — Singer, Guitarist, Songwriter
Conqueroo, 11271 Ventura Blvd, #522, Studio City CA 91604 USA
**Shockley, J Costen** — Baseball Player
493 Wilson St, Georgetown DE 19947, USA
**Shockley, Jeremy C** — Football Player
1330 West Ave, #3601, Miami Beach FL 33139, USA
**Shockley, William** — Actor
JKA Talent Agency, 12725 Ventura Blvd, #H, Studio City CA 91604, USA
**Shoebottom, Bruce** — Ice Hockey Player
40 Woodfield Dr, Scarborough ME 04074, USA
**Shoecraft, John A** — Balloonist
Shoecraft Contracting Co, 7430 E Stetson Dr, Scottsdale AZ 85251, USA
**Shoemaker, Carolyn S** — Geologist, Astronomer
US Geological Survey, 2255 N Gemini Dr, Flagstaff AZ 86001, USA
**Shoemaker, Craig** — Actor, Comedian
Levity Entertainment Group, 6701 Center Drive W, #1111, Los Angeles CA 90045, USA
**Shoemaker, Robert M** — Army General
PO Box 768, Belton TX 76513, USA
**Shofner, Delbert M (Del)** — Football Player
1665 Del Mar Ave, San Marino CA 91108, USA
**Shofner, James (Jim)** — Football Player, Coach
9620 Champions Dr, Granbury TX 76049, USA
**Shoji, Dave** — Volleyball Coach
University of Hawaii, Athletic Dept, Hilo HI 96720, USA
**Shoji, Tadashi** — Fashion Designer
Tadashi Shoji Assoc, 3016 E 44th St, Vernon CA 90058, USA

**Shonekan, Ernest A O** — President, Nigeria
12 Alexander Ave, Ikoyi, Lagos, Nigeria

**Shonin, Georgi S** — Cosmonaut, Air Force General
Cosmonaut Training Center, Star City, 141160 Zvezdny Gorodok, Moscow Oblast, Russia

**Shonta, Charles J (Chuck)** — Football Player
17435 Ava Court, New Boston MI 48164, USA

**Shooter, Eric M** — Neurobiologist
370 Golden Oak Dr, Portola Valley CA 94028, USA

**Shopay, Thomas M (Tom)** — Baseball Player
10145 NW 19th St, Doral FL 33172, USA

**Shope, Allan** — Architect
Shope Reno Wharton, 18 Marshall St, #114, Norwalk CT 06854, USA

**Shoppach, Kelly B** — Baseball Player
6117 Forest River Dr, Fort Worth TX 76112, USA

**Shor, Miriam** — Actress
Impression Entertainment, 9229 W Sunset Blvd, #700, Los Angeles CA 90069, USA

**Shor, Peter W** — Applied Mathematician
47 Manor Ave, Wellesley MA 02482, USA

**Shore, David** — Writer, Producer
Shore Z Productions, 9100 Wilshire Blvd, #400W, Beverly Hills CA 90212, USA

**Shore, Gary** — Director, Producer
Anonymous Content, 3532 Hayden Ave, Culver City CA 90232 USA

**Shore, Howard** — Composer
Columbia Artists Mgmt Inc, 1790 Broadway, #702, New York NY 10019 USA

**Shore, Pauly** — Actor, Comedian
Innovative Artists, 1505 10th St, Santa Monica CA 90401 USA

**Shore, Roberta** — Actress
PO Box 71639, Salt Lake City UT 84171, USA

**Shore, Stephen** — Photographer
Bard College, Photography Dept, Annandale-on-Hudson NY 12504, USA

**Shores, Del** — Producer, Writer
Del Shores Productions, 8581 Santa Monica Blvd, #560, West Hollywood CA 90069, USA

**Shorr, Lonnie** — Actor, Comedian
W B A Entertainment, PO Box 281802, Nashville TN 37229, USA

**Short, Brandon D** — Football Player
6700 Fairview Road, #430, Charlotte NC 28210, USA

**Short, Columbus** — Actor
Brillstein Entertainment Partners, 9150 Wilshire Blvd, #350, Beverly Hills CA 90212 USA

**Short, Eugene** — Basketball Player
8111 Fondren Lake Dr, Houston TX 77071, USA

**Short, Margaret E** — Artist
105 Garibaldi St, Lake Oswego OR 97035, USA

**Short, Martin** — Actor, Comedian, Singer
Brillstein Entertainment Partners, 9150 Wilshire Blvd, #350, Beverly Hills CA 90212 USA

**Short, Purvis** — Basketball Player
8111 Fondren Lake Dr, Houston TX 77071, USA

**Short, Rick** — Baseball Player
3021 Forsythe Court, Peoria IL 61614, USA

**Short, Roger V** — Biologist
18 Gwingana Crescent, Glen Waverley VIC 3150, Australia

**Short, Wes** — Golfer
11128 Sea Hero Lane, Austin TX 78748, USA

**Short, William R (Bill)** — Baseball Player
2975 57th St, Sarasota FL 34243, USA

**Shorter, Frank** — Track Athlete
558 Utica Court, Boulder CO 80304, USA

**Shorter, Wayne** — Jazz Saxophonist, Composer
Universal Attractions, 135 W 26th St, #1200, New York NY 10001 USA

**Shorthill, Richard W** — Engineer
University of Utah, Mechanical Engineering Dept, Salt Lake City UT 84112, USA

**Shortland, Cate** — Director, Writer
H L A Management, PO Box 1536, Strawberry Hills, NSW 2012, Australia

**Shortridge, George** — Golfer
13896 Ironstone Trail NW, Anoka MN 55303, USA

**Shortridge, Kennedy F** — Microbiologist
University of Auckland, Medical Dept, PB 92019, Auckland, New Zealand

**Shortridge, Stephen C** — Actor, Artist
223 E Sherman Ave, Coeur D'Alene ID 83814, USA

**Shortz, Will** — Columnist
New York Times, Editorial Dept, 229 W 43rd St, New York NY 10036 USA

**Shostakovich, Maxim D** — Conductor, Concert Pianist
Columbia Artists Mgmt Inc, 1790 Broadway, #702, New York NY 10019 USA

**Shouse, Brian D** — Baseball Player
3121 W Summerbend Court, Peoria IL 61615, USA

**Shouse, Dexter** — Basketball Player
4523 E Rhonda Dr, Phoenix AZ 85018, USA

**Show, Grant** — Actor
Innovative Artists, 1505 10th St, Santa Monica CA 90401 USA

**Showalter, Michael** — Actor, Producer, Writer
United Talent Agency, U T A Plaza, 9336 Civic Center Dr, Beverly Hills CA 90210 USA

**Showalter, William N (Buck), III** — Baseball Manager
9736 Hathaway St, Dallas TX 75220, USA

**Shower, Kathy** — Model, Actress
Playboy Promotions, 2706 Media Center Dr, Los Angeles CA 90065 USA

**Shreve, Anita** — Writer
Little Brown, 3 Center Plaza, #100, Boston MA 02108 USA

**Shreve, Susan R** — Writer
3506 35th St NW, Washington DC 20016, USA

**Shribman, David M** — Journalist, Cartoonist
Boston Globe, Editorial Dept, 1130 Connecticut NW, #520, Washington DC 20036, USA

**Shrider, Richard G (Dick)** — Basketball Player
6666 Morning Sun Road, Oxford OH 45056, USA

**Shrimpton, Jean** — Model, Actress
Abbey Hotel, Penzance, Cornwall TR18 4AR, England

**Shriner, Kin** — Actor
63 Cavalry Road, Weston CT 06883, USA

| | |
|---|---|
| **Shriner, Wil** | Entertainer, Director |
| 5313 Quakertown Ave, Woodland Hills CA 91364, USA | |
| **Shriver, Loren J** | Astronaut |
| 2513 Nimbus Dr, Estes Park CO 80517, USA | |
| **Shriver, Maria O** | Commentator |
| Hyperion Books, 114 5th Ave, New York NY 10011 USA | |
| **Shriver, Pamela H (Pam)** | Tennis Player |
| 8743 Mylander Lane, #R, Towson MD 21286, USA | |
| **Shroff, Jackie** | Actor |
| 1302 Le Pepeyon, Mount Mary Road, Bandra, Mumbai MS 400050, India | |
| **Shrontz, Frank A** | Businessman |
| 2949 81st Place, #P, Mercer Island WA 98040, USA | |
| **Shtalenkov, Mikhail A** | Ice Hockey Player |
| 7 Faenza, Newport Coast CA 92657, USA | |
| **Shtokolov, Boris T** | Opera Singer |
| Kirov Ballet Theater, 1 Pl Iskusstr, 190000 Saint Petersburg, Russia | |
| **Shu Qi** | Actress, Model |
| I M G Models, 8 Rue Danielle Casanova, 75002 Paris, France | |
| **Shu, Yiqian** | Artist |
| 30 SW 167th Ave, Beaverton OR 97006, USA | |
| **Shuba, George T** | Baseball Player |
| 3421 Bentwillow Lane, Youngstown OH 44511, USA | |
| **Shuchuk, Gary** | Ice Hockey Player |
| 5713 Lancashier Court, Fitchburg WI 53711, USA | |
| **Shue, Andrew** | Actor |
| Creative Artists Agency, 2000 Ave of Stars, #100, Los Angeles CA 90067 USA | |
| **Shue, Elisabeth** | Actress |
| Management 360, 9111 Wilshire Blvd, Beverly Hills CA 90210 USA | |
| **Shue, Eugene W (Gene)** | Basketball Coach, Executive |
| 4338 Redwood Ave, #303, Marina del Rey CA 90292, USA | |
| **Shuey, Paul K** | Baseball Player |
| 5252 Mill Dam Road, Wake Forest NC 27587, USA | |
| **Shuffield, Joey** | Drummer (Fastball) |
| Russell Carter Artists, 567 Ralph Mcgill Blvd NE, Atlanta GA 30312, USA | |
| **Shui, Lan** | Conductor |
| Singapore Symphony, 4 Battery Road #20-01, 049908 Singapore | |
| **Shukor, Sheikh Muszaphar** | Cosmonaut |
| Cosmonaut Training Center, Star City, 141160 Zvezdny Gorodok, Moscow Oblast, Russia | |
| **Shula, David D (Dave)** | Football Coach |
| 10805 Indian Trail, Cooper City FL 33328, USA | |
| **Shula, Donald F (Don)** | Football Player, Coach |
| 16 Indian Creek Island Road, Indian Creek Village FL 33154, USA | |
| **Shula, Mike** | Football Player, Coach |
| 19140 Peninsula Club Dr, Cornelius NC 28031, USA | |
| **Shuler, Ellie G (Buck), Jr** | Air Force General |
| 32 Willow Way W, Alexander City AL 35010, USA | |
| **Shuler, Mickey C, Sr** | Football Player |
| 332 Belle Vista Dr, Marysville PA 17053, USA | |
| **Shulgin, Alexander** | Chemist |
| 1483 Shulgin Road, Lafayette CA 94549, USA | |
| **Shulman, Douglas H** | Government Official |
| Internal Revenue Service, 1111 Constitution Ave NW, Washington DC 20224, USA | |
| **Shulman, Julius** | Interior Designer |
| 314 E Arrellaga St, Santa Barbara CA 93101, USA | |
| **Shultz, George P** | Secretary, State, Treasury & Labor |
| 776 Dolores St, Stanford CA 94305, USA | |
| **Shum, Harry, Jr** | Actor, Dancer |
| Innovative Artists, 1505 10th St, Santa Monica CA 90401 USA | |
| **Shumate, John H** | Basketball Player, Coach |
| 16406 S 12th Place, Phoenix AZ 85048, USA | |
| **Shumeyko Hegre, Luba** | Model |
| Ocinum, Rua das Hortas, 9050-024 Funchal Madeira, Portugal | |
| **Shumpert, Terrance D (Terry)** | Baseball Player |
| 8432 Fairview Court, Lone Tree CO 80124, USA | |
| **Shure, Aaron** | Writer, Producer |
| Katz Golden Sullivan Rosenman, 2001 Wilshire Blvd, #400, Santa Monica CA 90403, USA | |
| **Shuster, John** | Curling Athlete |
| Curling Assn, 5525 Clem's Way, Stevens Point WI 54482 USA | |
| **Shutler, Philip D** | Marine Corps General |
| 8917 Braeburn Dr, Annandale VA 22003, USA | |
| **Shutt, Stephen J (Steve)** | Ice Hockey Player |
| 7814 Heritage Grand Place, Bradenton FL 34212, USA | |
| **Shuttleworth, Mark** | Tourist Cosmonaut |
| H B D Venture Capital,  PO Box 1159, Durbanville 7551, South Africa | |
| **Shvachka, Anzhelina** | Opera Singer |
| I M G Artists, Hogarth Business Park, Chiswick, London W4 2TH, England | |
| **Shved, Alexey V** | Basketball Player |
| Minnesota Timberwolves, Target Center, 600 1st Ave N, Minneapolis MN 55403 USA | |
| **Shy, Leslie F (Les)** | Football Player |
| 512 N McClurg Court, #3611, Chicago IL 60611, USA | |
| **Shyamalan, M Night** | Director, Writer |
| W M E Entertainment, 9601 Wilshire Blvd, #300, Beverly Hills CA 90210 USA | |
| **Shyne** | Rap Artist |
| Entertainment Artists, 2409 21st Ave S, #100, Nashville TN 10019 USA | |
| **Sia, Beau** | Actor |
| Creative Artists Agency, 2000 Ave of Stars, #100, Los Angeles CA 90067 USA | |
| **Siana** | Model |
| 2113 Cocoa Circle, Virginia Beach VA 23454, USA | |
| **Siani, Michael J (Mike)** | Football Player |
| 3601 W Broadway, #25-102, Columbia MO 65203, USA | |
| **Siaosi Tupov V** | King, Tonga |
| Royal Palace, PO Box 6, Nuku'alofa, Tonga | |
| **Sibbett, Jane** | Actress |
| John Carrabino Mgmt, 5900 Wilshire Blvd, #406, Los Angeles CA 90036 USA | |
| **Siberry, Jane** | Singer, Songwriter |
| Sheeba Records, 238 Davenport Road, #291, Toronto ON M5R 1J6, Canada | |

**Sibley, Antoinette** — Ballerina
Royal Dancing Academy, 36 Battersea Square, London SW11 3LT, England

**Sichting, Jerry L** — Basketball Player, Executive
3190 Country Club Road, Martinsville IN 46151, USA

**Siddall, Joseph C (Joe)** — Baseball Player
2785 Sierra Dr, Windsor ON N9E 2Y9, Canada

**Siddig, Alexander** — Actor
Markham Froggatt Irwin, Julian House, 4 Windmill St, London W1P 1HF, England

**Siddons, Anne R** — Writer
767 Vermont Road, Atlanta GA 30319, USA

**Sidibe, Gabourey** — Actress
Principal Entertainment, 130 W 42nd St, New York NY 10036, USA

**Sidibe, Modibo** — Prime Minister, Mali
Prime Minister's Office, BP 97, Bamako, Mali

**Sidlin, Murray** — Conductor
Catholic University, Music School, Washington DC 20064, USA

**Sidney, Dainon T** — Football Player
605 Lakemeade Point, Old Hickory TN 37138, USA

**Sidora, Drew** — Actress
I C M Partners, 10250 Constellation Blvd, #900, Los Angeles CA 90067 USA

**Sidorenko, Wladimir** — Boxer
Universum Boxing Promotion, Am Stadtrand 27, 22047 Hamburg, Germany

**Sidorkiewicz, Peter** — Ice Hockey Player
1056 Swiss Heights, Oshawa ON L1K 3B4, Canada

**Sidorski, Sergei S** — Prime Minister, Belarus
Prime Minister's Office, Pl Nezavisimosti, 220010 Minsk, Belarus

**Sidran, Ben** — Jazz Entertainer, Composer
Blue Moon/Go Jazz Records, PO Box 2023, Madison WI 53701, USA

**Siebel Newsom, Jennifer** — Actress
Don Buchwald, 6500 Wilshire Blvd, #2200, Los Angeles CA 90048 USA

**Siebels, Jonathan L (Jon)** — Guitarist (Eve 6)
Agency Group Ltd, 1880 Century Park E, #711, Los Angeles CA 90067 USA

**Siebern, Norman L (Norm)** — Baseball Player
4181 5th Ave NW, Naples FL 34119, USA

**Siebert, Paul E** — Baseball Player
1711 Acker St, Orlando FL 32837, USA

**Siebert, Wilfred C (Sonny)** — Baseball Player
2583 Brush Creek Road, Saint Louis MO 63129, USA

**Siebler, Dwight L** — Baseball Player
11565 S 204th St, Gretna NE 68028, USA

**Sieg, Derek** — Director, Writer
United Agents, 12-26 Lexington St, London W1F 0LE, England

**Siega, Marcos** — Director
Creative Artists Agency, 2000 Ave of Stars, #100, Los Angeles CA 90067 USA

**Siegal, John W (Johnny)** — Football Player
PO Box 47, Harvey's Lake PA 18618, USA

**Siegel, Barry** — Journalist
Los Angeles Times, Editorial Dept, 202 W 1st St, Los Angeles CA 90012 USA

**Siegel, Bernard S (Bernie)** — Surgeon, Writer
61 Oxbow Lane, Woodbridge CT 06525, USA

**Siegel, Dan** — Pianist, Composer
Central Entertainment Group, 251 W 39th St, New York NY 10018, USA

**Siegel, David** — Director, Producer, Writer
W M E Entertainment, 9601 Wilshire Blvd, #300, Beverly Hills CA 90210 USA

**Siegel, Eric** — Actor
I C M Partners, 10250 Constellation Blvd, #900, Los Angeles CA 90067 USA

**Siegel, Herbert J** — Businessman
Chris-Craft Industries, 55 E 59th St, #22B, New York NY 10022, USA

**Siegel, Janis** — Singer (Manhattan Transfer)
I C M Partners, 730 5th Ave, New York NY 10019 USA

**Siegel, Jay** — Singer, Guitarist (Tokens)
Brothers Management Assoc, 141 Dunbar Ave, Fords NJ 08863 USA

**Siegel, Mike** — Actor, Comedian
Parallel Entertainment, 9420 Wilshire Blvd, #250, Beverly Hills CA 90212 USA

**Siegel, Randolph** — Publisher
Parade, Publisher's Office, 711 3rd Ave, New York NY 10017, USA

**Siegel, Robert** — Architect
Gwathmey-Siegel Architects, 475 10th Ave, #300, New York NY 10018, USA

**Siegel, Robert C** — Commentator
National Public Radio, 635 Massachusetts Ave NW, #1, Washington DC 20001, USA

**Siegfried** — Animal Illusionist (Siegfried & Roy)
Kirvin Doak Communications, 7935 W Sahara Ave, #201, Las Vegas NV 89117, USA

**Siekevitz, Philip** — Cell Biologist
290 W End Ave, New York NY 10023, USA

**Siemaszko, Casey** — Actor
Abrams Artists, 9200 W Sunset Blvd, #1125, West Hollywood CA 90069 USA

**Siemaszko, Nina** — Actress
Vanguard Management Group, 8060 Melrose Ave, #400, Los Angeles CA 90046, USA

**Sieminski, Charles L (Chuck)** — Football Player
5000 Village Way, #406, Marcus Hook PA 19061, USA

**Siemionow, Maria** — Reconstructive Surgeon
Cleveland Clinic, 9500 Euclid Ave, Cleveland OH 44195 USA

**Siemon, Jeffrey G (Jeff)** — Football Player
5401 Londonderry Road, Minneapolis MN 55436, USA

**Siena, James** — Artist
83 Canal St, #508, New York NY 10002, USA

**Siering, Laura G (Lauri)** — Swimmer
PO Box 1352, Tres Pinos CA 95075, USA

**Sierra, Gregory** — Actor
3374 Punta Alta, #C, Laguna Woods CA 92637, USA

**Sierra, Ruben A** — Baseball Player
12355 SW 51st St, Miami Fl 33175, USA

**Siers, Kevin** — Editorial Cartoonist
Charlotte Observer, Editorial Dept, 600 S Tryon St, Charlotte NC 28202, USA

**Sievers, Eric** — Football Player
11550 Great Falls Way, Great Falls VA 22066, USA

**Sievers, Roy E** — Baseball Player
11505 Bellefontaine Road, Saint Louis MO 63138, USA
**Sievwright, Ebe** — Actor
Associated International Mgmt, 7 Hatton Garden, #400, London EC1N 8AD, England
**Siew, Vincent C** — Prime Minister, Taiwan
Kuomintang, #232-234, Sec 2, BaDe Road, Zhongshan District, Taipei, Taiwan
**Siff, Maggie** — Actress
Paradigm Agency, 360 N Crescent Dr, North Building, Beverly Hills CA 90210 USA
**Sifford, Charlie** — Golfer
7540 Sanctuary Circle, Brecksville OH 44141, USA
**Sigel, Beanie** — Rap Artist, Actor, Composer
Big Bloc Entertainment, 2 Bala Plaza, #300, Bala Cynwyd PA 19004, USA
**Sigel, Jay** — Golfer
1284 Farm Road, Berwyn PA 19312, USA
**Sigel, N Thomas (Tom)** — Cinematographer
I C M Partners, 10250 Constellation Blvd, #900, Los Angeles CA 90067 USA
**Sights, Shay** — Actress
15030 Ventura Blvd, #556, Sherman Oaks CA 91403, USA
**Siglar, Ricky A** — Football Player
13901 Newton St, #406, Overland Park KS 66223, USA
**Sigler, Jamie-Lynn** — Actress, Singer
Paradigm Agency, 360 N Crescent Dr, North Building, Beverly Hills CA 90210 USA
**Sigler, John C** — Association Executive
National Rifle Association, 11250 Waples Mill Road, Fairfax VA 22030, USA
**Sigman, Stan** — Businessman
Cingular Wireless, 5565 Glenridge Connector, Atlanta GA 30342, USA
**Sigman, Stephanie** — Actress
I C M Partners, 10250 Constellation Blvd, #900, Los Angeles CA 90067 USA
**Sigwart, Ulrich** — Heart Surgeon
Centre Hospitalier Universitaire Vaudois, 1011 Lausanne, Switzerland
**Sihol, Caroline** — Actress
Artmedia, 20 Ave Rapp, 75007 Paris, France
**Siilasvuo, Ensio** — Army General, Finland
Castrenikatu 6A17, 00530 Helsinki 53, Finland
**Siimann, Mart** — Prime Minister, Estonia
Riigikugu, Lossi Plats 1A, Tallinn 0100, Estonia
**Sikahema, Vai** — Football Player
28 Abington Road, Mount Laurel NJ 08054, USA
**Sikander, Shahzia** — Artist
Deitch Projs, 76 Grand St, New York NY 10013, USA
**Sikes, Cynthia** — Actress
Defining Artists Agency, 4370 Tujunga Ave, #120, Studio City CA 91604, USA
**Sikharulidze, Anton T** — Figure Skater
Skating Federation, Luznetskaya Nab 8, 119871 Moscow, Russia
**Sikking, James B** — Actor
258 S Carmelina Ave, Los Angeles CA 90049, USA
**Sikma, Jack W** — Basketball Player
9125 NE 21st Place, Clyde Hill WA 98004, USA
**Sikorski, Brian** — Baseball Player
17930 Wexford St, Roseville MI 48066, USA
**Sikovetsky, Dimitry** — Conductor, Concert Violinist
I M G Artists, Hogarth Business Park, Chiswick, London W4 2TH, England
**Silajdzic, Haris** — Co-Prime Minister, Bosnia & Herzegovina
President's Office, Marsala Titz 7, 71000 Sarajevo, Bosnia & Herzegovina
**Silas, James E** — Basketball Player
6800 Thistle Hill Way, Austin TX 78754, USA
**Silas, Paul T** — Basketball Player, Coach
2463 Peninsula Shores Court, Denver NC 28037, USA
**Silas, Samuel L (Sam)** — Football Player
PO Box 308, Hawthorne NJ 07507, USA
**Silatolu, Ratu Timoci** — Prime Minister, Fiji
Prime Minister's Office, New Government Buildings, 6 Berkeley Crescent, Suva, Viti Levu, Fiji
**Silberling, Bradley (Brad)** — Director, Writer
United Talent Agency, U T A Plaza, 9336 Civic Center Dr, Beverly Hills CA 90210 USA
**Silberman, Laurence H** — Judge, Diplomat
US Court of Appeals, 333 Constitution Ave NW, #4400, Washington DC 20001, USA
**Silberstein, Diane Wichard** — Publisher
Playboy, Publisher's Office, 680 N Lake Shore Dr, Chicago IL 60611, USA
**Silbey, Robert J** — Chemist
Massachusetts Institute of Technology, Chemistry Dept, Cambridge MA 02139, USA
**Siler, Eugene E, Jr** — Judge
403 Sycamore St, #1, Williamsburg KY 40769, USA
**Silja, Anja** — Opera Singer
Artists Mgmt, Rutistr 52, 8044 Zurich, Switzerland
**Silk, Alexandria** — Exotic Dancer, Model
396 Bethany St, Thousand Oaks CA 91360, USA
**Silk, Anna** — Actress
K G Talent, 55-1/2 Sumach St, Toronto, ON M5A 3J6, Canada
**Silk, David M (Dave)** — Ice Hockey Player
PO Box 130, Minot MA 02055, USA
**Sill, Aleta** — Bowler
Professional Bowlers Assn, 719 2nd Ave, #701, Seattle WA 98104 USA
**Silla, Felix** — Actor
5313 Magenta Court, Las Vegas NV 89108, USA
**Sillas, Karen** — Actress
PO Box 725, Wading River NY 11792, USA
**Silliman, Ron** — Writer
262 Orchard Road, Paoli PA 19301, USA
**Sillinger, Mike** — Ice Hockey Player, Executive
Edmonton Oilers, 11230 110th St, Edmonton AB T5G 3H7, Canada
**Sillman, Amy** — Artist
705 Driggs Ave, Brooklyn NY 11211, USA
**Sills, Douglas (Doug)** — Actor, Singer
Talent Works, 3500 W Olive Ave, #1400, Burbank CA 91505 USA
**Sills, Stephen** — Architect, Interior Designer
Sills Huniford Assoc, 30 E 67th St, #300, New York NY 10065, USA

**S**

**Silpa, Mitch** — Actor, Comedian
OmniPop Talent Group, 4605 Lankershim Blvd, #201, Toluca Lake CA 91602 USA
**Siltala, Michael (Mike)** — Ice Hockey Player
1693 Ruscombe Close, Mississauga ON L5J 1Y4, Canada
**Silva, Alan Jones** — Circus Tightrope Walker
Cirque du Soleil, 8400 2nd Ave, Montreal QC H1Z 4M6, Canada
**Silva, Anibal Antonio Cavaco** — President, Portugal
President's Office, Palacio de Belem, Calcada da Ajuda 11, 1349022 Lisbon, Portugal
**Silva, Carlos** — Baseball Player
280 Bergamot Dr, Hamel MN 55340, USA
**Silva, Daniel** — Writer
3512 Winfield Lane NW, Washington DC 20007, USA
**Silva, Henry** — Actor
8747 Clifton Way, #305, Beverly Hills CA 90211, USA
**Silva, Jose L** — Baseball Player
401 Pappan Dr, Imperial PA 15126, USA
**Silva, Thiago E** — Soccer Player
Confederacion de Futebol, Rua Victor Civita 66, #1, Rio de Janeiro 22775 044, Brazil
**Silver, Horace** — Jazz Pianist, Composer
Bridge Agency, 35 Clark St, #A5, Brooklyn NY 11201, USA
**Silver, Jeffrey** — Producer
United Talent Agency, U T A Plaza, 9336 Civic Center Dr, Beverly Hills CA 90210 USA
**Silver, Joan Micklin** — Director, Producer, Writer
Silverfilm Productions, 510 Park Ave, #9B, New York NY 10022, USA
**Silver, Joel** — Producer
Silver Pictures, 4000 Warner Blvd, Burbank CA 91522, USA
**Silver, Joshua D** — Inventor (Adjustable Corrective Glasses)
Clarendon Laboratory, Parks Road, Oxford OX1 3PU, England
**Silver, Nathaniel A (Nate)** — Statistician
New York Times, FiveThirtyEight, Editorial Dept, 229 W 43rd St, New York NY 10036, USA
**Silver, Nicky** — Writer
W M E Entertainment, 9601 Wilshire Blvd, #300, Beverly Hills CA 90210 USA
**Silver, Scott** — Director, Writer
Creative Artists Agency, 2000 Ave of Stars, #100, Los Angeles CA 90067 USA
**Silvera, Charles A R (Charlie)** — Baseball Player
1240 Manzanita Dr, Millbrae CA 94030, USA
**Silverberg, Robert** — Writer
PO Box 13160, Station E, Oakland CA 94661, USA
**Silveri, Scott** — Producer, Writer
W M E Entertainment, 9601 Wilshire Blvd, #300, Beverly Hills CA 90210 USA
**Silverio, Luis P** — Baseball Player
9600 NW 58th Court, Parkland FL 33076, USA
**Silverman, Barry G** — Judge
US Court of Appeals, 230 N 1st St, Phoenix AZ 85004, USA
**Silverman, Henry R** — Businessman
Cendant Corp, 9 W 57th St, New York NY 10019, USA
**Silverman, Jonathan** — Actor
Untitled Entertainment, 350 S Beverly Dr, #200, Beverly Hills CA 90212 USA
**Silverman, Kenneth E** — Writer, Educator
New York University, English Dept, 19 University Place, New York NY 10003, USA
**Silverman, Peter** — Writer
Paradigm Agency, 360 N Crescent Dr, North Building, Beverly Hills CA 90210 USA
**Silverman, Sarah** — Actress, Comedienne, Producer
Creative Artists Agency, 2000 Ave of Stars, #100, Los Angeles CA 90067 USA
**Silvers, Robert** — Artist
Henry Holt, 175 5th Ave, #400, New York NY 10010 USA
**Silverstein, Craig** — Producer, Writer
W M E Entertainment, 9601 Wilshire Blvd, #300, Beverly Hills CA 90210 USA
**Silverstein, Joseph H** — Conductor, Concert Violinist
Utah Symphony Orchestra, 123 W South Temple, Salt Lake City UT 84101, USA
**Silverstone, Alicia** — Actress
United Talent Agency, U T A Plaza, 9336 Civic Center Dr, Beverly Hills CA 90210 USA
**Silvestri, Alan A** — Composer
Gorfaine/Schwartz, 4111 W Alameda Ave, #509, Burbank CA 91505 USA
**Silvestri, David J (Dave)** — Baseball Player
15511 Country Mill Court, Chesterfield MO 63017, USA
**Silvestrini, Achille Cardinal** — Religious Leader
Oriental Churches Congregation, Via Conciliazione 34, 00193 Rome, Italy
**Silvetti, Jorge** — Architect
Machado & Silvetti, 500 Harrison Ave, Boston MA 02118, USA
**Silvia** — Queen Consort, Sweden
Kungliga Slottet, Stottsbacken, 111 30 Stockholm, Sweden
**Silvstedt, Victoria** — Model, Actress
Abrams Artists, 9200 W Sunset Blvd, #1125, West Hollywood CA 90069 USA
**Sim, Jonathan (Jon)** — Ice Hockey Player
104 Willow Ave, New Glasgow NS B2H 1Z5, Canada
**Sim, Keong** — Actor
Omnipop Talent Group, 4605 Lankershim Blvd, #201, Toluca Lake CA 91602 91602, USA
**Sima, Raymond Ndong** — Prime Minister, Gabon
Prime Minister's Office, BP 91, Immeuble du 2 Decembre, Libreville, Gabon
**Simanek, Robert E** — Korean War Marine Corps Hero (CMH)
25194 Westmoreland Dr, Farmington Hills MI 48336, USA
**Simas, William A (Bill)** — Baseball Player
6084 Millerton Road, Friant CA 93626, USA
**Simbomana, Adrien** — Prime Minister, Burundi
PO Box 2251, Vugizo, Bujumbura, Burundi
**Sime, David W (Dave)** — Track Athlete, Physician
9140 Bay Dr, Surfside FL 33154, USA
**Simeone, Diane M** — Oncologist
University of Michigan Comprehensive Cancer Center, 1500 E Medical Center Dr, Ann Arbor MI 48109, USA
**Simeoni, Sara** — Track Athlete
Via di Castello, Veronese 32, 37010 Rivoli Verona, Italy
**Simes, John W (Jack), II** — Cyclist
7753 Probst Hill Road, New Tripoli PA 18066, USA
**Simic, Charles** — Writer
PO Box 192, Strafford NH 03884, USA

**Simien, Tracy A** — Football Player
409 N Martin Luther King St, Sweeny TX 77480, USA
**Simitis, Konstantinos (Kostas)** — Prime Minister, Greece
Maximus Mansion, Herodou Atticou 19, 10674 Athens, Greece
**Simmer, Charlie** — Ice Hockey Player
70 Coulee View SW, Calgary AB T3H 5J6, Canada
**Simmonds, Kennedy A** — Prime Minister, Saint Kitts & Nevis
PO Box 167, Earle Morne Development, Basseterre, Saint Kitts & Nevis
**Simmonds, Kim** — Guitarist (Savoy Brown)
Ozark Talent, 718 Schwarz Road, Lawrence KS 66049, USA
**Simmons, Adele S** — Foundation Executive, Educator
Catherine T MacArthur Foundation, 140 S Dearborn St, #1000, Chicago IL 60603, USA
**Simmons, Bill** — Sportscaster
ESPN-TV, ESPN Plaza, 935 Middle St, Bristol CT 06010 USA
**Simmons, Brian E** — Football Player
6417 Lake Burden View Dr, Windermere FL 34786, USA
**Simmons, Brian L** — Baseball Player
226 Village Dr, Canonsburg PA 15317, USA
**Simmons, Chelan** — Actress
Intellectual Artists Mgmt, 10585 Santa Monica Blvd, #135, Los Angeles CA 90025, USA
**Simmons, Clyde, Jr** — Football Player
3948 3rd St S, #344, Jacksonville Beach FL 32250, USA
**Simmons, Curtis T (Curt)** — Baseball Player
200 Park Road, Ambler PA 19002, USA
**Simmons, Dan** — Writer
Little Brown, 3 Center Plaza, #100, Boston MA 02108 USA
**Simmons, Don** — Ice Hockey Player
4998 Skerkston Road, RR 1, Ridgway ON L0S 1N9, Canada
**Simmons, Gene** — Singer, Bassist (Kiss)
Gene Simmons Co, PO Box 16075, Beverly Hills CA 90209, USA
**Simmons, H A Kendall** — Football Player
1725 Altamont Court, Auburn AL 36830, USA
**Simmons, Harris H** — Financier
Zions Bancorp, 1 S Main St, Salt Lake City UT 84133, USA
**Simmons, Henry** — Actor
Principato-Young, 9465 Wilshire Blvd, #880, Beverly Hills CA 90212 USA
**Simmons, J K** — Actor
Gersh Agency, 41 Madison Ave, #3301, New York NY 10010 USA
**Simmons, Jaason** — Actor
Gilbertson Entertainment, 1334 3rd Street Promenade, #201, Santa Monica CA 90401 USA
**Simmons, Jason L** — Football Player
10002 Ivy Mill Court, Missouri City TX 77459, USA
**Simmons, Jerry B** — Football Player
30227 Avenida Selecta, Rancho Palos Verdes CA 90275, USA
**Simmons, Johnny** — Actor
W M E Entertainment, 9601 Wilshire Blvd, #300, Beverly Hills CA 90210 USA
**Simmons, Joseph** — Rap Artist (Run-DMC)
Richard Walters, PO Box 2789, Toluca Lake CA 91610 USA
**Simmons, Kimora Lee** — Model, Fashion Designer
Phat Fashions, 512 Fashion Ave, #4300, New York NY 10018, USA
**Simmons, Lionel J** — Basketball Player
108 Wellesley Court, Mount Laurel NJ 08054, USA
**Simmons, Nelson B** — Baseball Player
4445 Rosebud Lane, #B, La Mesa CA 91941, USA
**Simmons, Richard** — Physical Fitness Instructor, Producer
Celebrities Plus, 8899 Beverly Blvd, #811, Los Angeles CA 90048, USA
**Simmons, Robert G (Bob)** — Football Player
16040 Chalfont Circle, Dallas TX 75248, USA
**Simmons, Rudd** — Producer
Claire Best Assoc, 736 Seward St, Los Angeles CA 90038, USA
**Simmons, Russell** — Music Producer, Fashion Designer
Simmons-Lathan Media Group, 6100 Wilshire Blvd, #1111, Los Angeles CA 90048, USA
**Simmons, Ruth J** — Educator
Brown University, President's Office, Providence RI 02912, USA
**Simmons, Tabitha** — Stylist, Shoe Designer
Tabitha Simmons Accessories, 601 West 26th St, #309, New York, NY 10001, USA
**Simmons, Ted L** — Baseball Player
PO Box 26, Chesterfield MO 63006, USA
**Simms, Christopher D (Chris)** — Football Player
811 Lynnbrook Road, Nashville TN 37215, USA
**Simms, Larry** — Actor
3441 Lewis Ave, Long Beach CA 90807, USA
**Simms, Michael E (Mike)** — Baseball Player
PO Box 96011, Southlake TX 76092, USA
**Simms, Philip (Phil)** — Football Player, Sportscaster
930 Old Mill Road, Franklin Lakes NJ 07417, USA
**Simms, Travis** — Boxer
28 Martin Luther King, #43, South Norwalk CT 06854, USA
**Simollardes, Drew** — Singer (Reveille)
David Levin Mgmt, 200 W 57th St, #308, New York NY 10019, USA
**Simon, Bob** — Commentator
CBS-TV, News Dept, 2020 M St NW, Washington DC 20036 USA
**Simon, Carly** — Singer, Songwriter
Ciancia Mgmt, 1 William Morris Place, Beverly Hills CA 90212, USA
**Simon, Chris** — Ice Hockey Player
PO Box 1, Wawa ON P0S 1K0, Canada
**Simon, Corey J** — Football Player
6089 Leigh Read Road, Tallahassee FL 32309, USA
**Simon, David** — Producer, Writer, Actor
Creative Artists Agency, 2000 Ave of Stars, #100, Los Angeles CA 90067 USA
**Simon, Dick** — Auto Racing Executive
24896 SeaCrest Dr, Dana Point CA 92829, USA
**Simon, George W** — Astronaut
PO Box 62, Sunspot NM 88349, USA
**Simon, Hugh** — Actor
Ken McReddie Assoc, 101 Finsbury Pavement, London EC2A 1RS, England

**Simon, James E (Jim)** — Football Player
8501 SW 103rd Ave, Gainesville FL 32608, USA
**Simon, John I** — Film, Drama Critic
New York Magazine, Editorial Dept, 444 Madison Ave, #1400, New York NY 10022, USA
**Simon, Josette** — Actress
Conway Van Gelder Grant, 8-12 Broadwick St, #300, London W1F 8HW, England
**Simon, Leon M** — Mathematician
Stanford University, Mathematics Dept, Stanford CA 94305, USA
**Simon, Lou Anna** — Educator
Michigan State University, President's Office, East Lansing MI 48824, USA
**Simon, Melvin I** — Biologist
California Institute of Technology, Biology Dept, Pasadena CA 91125, USA
**Simon, Neil** — Writer
350 Park Ave, #1600, New York NY 10022, USA
**Simon, Paul** — Singer, Guitarist, Songwriter
Paul Simon Music, 1619 Broadway, #500, New York NY 10019, USA
**Simon, Sam** — Producer, Writer, Animator
Paradigm Agency, 360 N Crescent Dr, North Building, Beverly Hills CA 90210 USA
**Simon, Scott** — Commentator, Writer
NBC-TV, News Dept, 30 Rockefeller Plaza, #270E, New York NY 10112 USA
**Simonds, Charles F** — Sculptor, Architect
26 E 22nd St, New York NY 10010, USA
**Simone, Hannah** — Actress
Gersh Agency, 9465 Wilshire Blvd, #600, Beverly Hills CA 90212 USA
**Simoneau, Mark L** — Football Player
1018 Park Ave, Rose Hill KS 67133, USA
**Simoneau, Yves** — Director
W M E Entertainment, 9601 Wilshire Blvd, #300, Beverly Hills CA 90210 USA
**Simonini, Edward C (Ed)** — Football Player
3825 E 66th St, Tulsa OK 74136, USA
**Simonis, Adrianus J Cardinal** — Religious Leader
Aartsbisdom, BP 14019, Maliebaan, 3508 Utrecht SB, Netherlands
**Simonischek, Maximilian** — Actor
Agentur Carola Studlar, Agnesstr 47, 80798 Munich, Germany
**Simonov, Yuriy I** — Conductor
Moscow Symphony Orchestra, Gorky Park, 9 Krymsky Val, 119049 Moscow, Russia
**Simons, Douglas E (Doug)** — Baseball Player
1988 Mount Olive Road, Lookout Mountain GA 30750, USA
**Simons, Ed** — Singer, Musician (Chemical Brothers)
9PR, 65-69 White Lion St, London N1 9PR, England
**Simons, Elwyn L** — Anthropologist
Duke University, Primate Center, 3705 Erwin Road, Durham NC 27705, USA
**Simons, Kai L** — Biochemist
Max-Planck-Molekulare Zellbiologie-Institut, 01307 Dresden, Germany
**Simons, Raf** — Fashion Designer
House of Dior, 30 Ave Montaigne, 75008 Paris, France
**Simons, Timothy (Tim)** — Actor
United Talent Agency, U T A Plaza, 9336 Civic Center Dr, Beverly Hills CA 90210 USA
**Simontacchi, Jason** — Baseball Player
6924 Birdie Lane, Saint Louis MO 63129, USA
**Simonyan, Mikhail** — Concert Violinist
I M G Artists, Carnegie Hall Tower, 152 W 57th St, #500, New York NY 10019 USA
**Simonyi, Charles** — Tourist Cosmonaut
International Software Corp, 2821 Northup Way, #250, Bellevue WA 98004, USA
**Simpkins, L Dixon (Dickey)** — Basketball Player
6104 Saint Andrews Way, Hixson TN 37343, USA
**Simpson, Alan** — Educator
Yellow Gate Farm, Little Compton RI 02837, USA
**Simpson, Alan K** — Senator, WY
1201 Sunshine Ave, PO Box 270, Cody WY 82414, USA
**Simpson, Ashlee** — Singer, Songwriter, Actress
Creative Artists Agency, 2000 Ave of Stars, #100, Los Angeles CA 90067 USA
**Simpson, Bill** — Auto Racing Executive
Simpson Performance Products, 328 FM 306, New Braunfels TX 78130, USA
**Simpson, Bobby** — Ice Hockey Player
4779 Limestone Lane NW, Acworth GA 30102, USA
**Simpson, Carl W** — Football Player
2507 Brentwood Road, Decatur GA 30032, USA
**Simpson, Carole** — Commentator
ABC-TV, News Dept, 77 W 66th St, New York NY 10023 USA
**Simpson, Charles R** — Judge
US Tax Court, 400 2nd St NW, Washington DC 20217, USA
**Simpson, Claire** — Film Editor
Independent Talent Group, 40 Whitfield St, London W1T 2RH, England
**Simpson, Cody** — Singer, Songwriter
PO Box 1766, Studio City CA 91614, USA
**Simpson, Craig** — Ice Hockey Player
CBC-TV, PO Box 500, Station A, Toronto ON M5W 1E6, Canada
**Simpson, Daryl** — Singer (Celtic Tenors)
PO Box 32, Kells, County Meath, Ireland
**Simpson, Derrick (Duckie)** — Singer (Black Uhuru)
Agency Group, 9348 Civic Center Dr, #200, Beverly Hills CA 90210 USA
**Simpson, Geoffrey** — Cinematographer
PO Box 3194, Bellevue Hills NSW 2023, Australia
**Simpson, J F Webb** — Golfer
Professional Golfer's Assn, PO Box 109601, Palm Beach Gardens FL 33410 USA
**Simpson, Jessica** — Singer, Songwriter, Actress, Model
Sony Pictures Entertainment, 10202 W Washington Blvd, Culver City CA 90232, USA
**Simpson, Jimmi** — Actor
W M E Entertainment, 9601 Wilshire Blvd, #300, Beverly Hills CA 90210 USA
**Simpson, Joe A** — Baseball Player
4681 Jefferson Township Lane, Marietta GA 30066, USA
**Simpson, Josh** — Artist
Frank Williams Road, Shelburne Falls MA 01370, USA
**Simpson, Juliene Brazinski** — Basketball Player
PO Box 1267, Stroudsburg PA 18360, USA

**Simpson, Martin** — Guitarist
Moneypenny Agency, Stables, Main St, North Dalton, Driffield East Yorkshire YO25 9XA, England
**Simpson, Orenthal James (O J)** — Football Player, Actor, Sportscaster
Lovelock Correctional Center, #1027820, 1200 Prison Road, Lovelock NV 89419, USA
**Simpson, Ralph D** — Basketball Player
7578 S Duquesne Way, Aurora CO 80016, USA
**Simpson, Richard C (Dick)** — Baseball Player
PO Box 3593, Culver City CA 90231, USA
**Simpson, Scott** — Golfer
15778 Paseo Hermosa, Poway CA 92064, USA
**Simpson, Suzi** — Model, Actress
24338 El Toro Road, #E315, Laguna Woods CA 92637, USA
**Simpson, Tim** — Golfer
1061 Spy Glass Hill, Greensboro GA 30642, USA
**Simpson, Tom** — Keyboardist (Snow Patrol)
Big Life Mgmt, 67-69 Charlton St, London NW1 1HY, England
**Simpson, Valerie** — Singer (Ashford & Simpson), Songwriter
Spirit Media, PO Box 43591, Phoenix AZ 85080, USA
**Simpson, Wayne K** — Baseball Player
330 E Collamer Dr, Carson CA 90746, USA
**Simpson, William T (Bill)** — Football Player
5732 Huntley Ave, Garden Grove CA 92845, USA
**Simpson-Miller, Portia L** — Prime Minister, Jamaica
Prime Minister's Office, 1 Devon Road, PO Box 272, Kingston 6, Jamaica
**Sims, Allan E (Al)** — Ice Hockey Player
4215 Winding Way Dr, Fort Wayne IN 46835, USA
**Sims, Barry A** — Football Player
369 Golden Grass Dr, Alamo CA 94507, USA
**Sims, Billy R** — Football Player
PO Box 3147, Coppell TX 75019, USA
**Sims, Christopher A (Chris)** — Economist
Princeton University, Economics Dept, Princeton NJ 08544, USA
**Sims, Duane B (Duke)** — Baseball Player
10509 Shoalhaven Dr, Las Vegas NV 89134, USA
**Sims, Ernie, III** — Football Player
Indianapolis Colts, 7001 W 56th St, Indianapolis IN 46254 USA
**Sims, Jocko** — Actor
Benedetti Management, 13101 W Washington Blvd, #234, Culver City CA 90066, USA
**Sims, Keith A** — Football Player
1522 SW 37th St, Fort Lauderdale FL 33312, USA
**Sims, Kenneth W (Ken)** — Football Player
PO Box 236, Kosse TX 76653, USA
**Sims, Molly** — Model, Actress
W M E Entertainment, 9601 Wilshire Blvd, #300, Beverly Hills CA 90210 USA
**Sims, Neil** — Drummer (Catherine Wheel)
Paradigm Agency, 360 Park Ave, #1600, New York NY 10022 USA
**Sims, Robert A (Bob)** — Basketball Player
915 Highland Ave, #3, Duarte CA 91010, USA
**Sims, Ryan O** — Football Player
311 Yellow Poplar Terrace, Spartanburg SC 29306, USA
**Sinatra, Christina (Tina)** — Actress, Writer
30966 Broach Beach Road, Malibu CA 90265, USA
**Sinatra, Frank, Jr** — Singer, Actor
Universal Attractions, 135 W 26th St, #1200, New York NY 10001 USA
**Sinatra, Nancy** — Singer, Actress
Universal Attractions, 135 W 26th St, #1200, New York NY 10001 USA
**Sinatro, Matthew S (Matt)** — Baseball Player
2619 239th Ave SE, Sammamish WA 98075, USA
**Sinbad** — Actor, Comedian
A P A Talent/Literary Agency, 405 S Beverly Dr, #300, Beverly Hills CA 90212 USA
**Sinclair, Christine M** — Soccer Player
Western New York Flash, Sahlen Sports Park, 7070 Seneca St, Elma NY 14059, USA
**Sinclair, Claire** — Model, Actress
Playboy Promotions, 2706 Media Center Dr, Los Angeles CA 90065 USA
**Sinclair, Clive M** — Inventor (Pocket Calculator)
Sinclair Research, 7 York Central, 70 York Way, London N1 9AG, England
**Sinclair, Michael G (Mike)** — Football Player
1914 Pannell St, Houston TX 77020, USA
**Sinclair, Nancy** — Actress
Studio Talent Group, 1328 12th St, Santa Monica CA 90401, USA
**Sindelar, Joey** — Golfer
18 Prospect Ridge, Horseheads NY 14845, USA
**Sinden, Donald A** — Actor
Rats Castle, Isle of Oxney, Kent TN30 7HX, England
**Sinden, Harold J (Harry)** — Ice Hockey Player, Coach, Executive
9 Olde Village Dr, Winchester MA 01890, USA
**Sinegal, James D** — Businessman
Costco Wholesale Corp, 999 Lake Dr, #200, Issaquah WA 98027, USA
**Singer, Bryan** — Director, Producer
Bad Hat Productions, 10201 W Pico Blvd, Building 50, Los Angeles CA 90064, USA
**Singer, Eric W** — Drummer (Kiss, Alice Cooper)
E D M Productions, 11684 Ventura Blvd, #408, Studio City CA 91604, USA
**Singer, Isadore M** — Abel Mathematics Laureate
Massachusetts Institute of Technology, Mathematics Dept, Cambridge MA 02139, USA
**Singer, Jerome L** — Psychologist
Yale University, Zigler Center, New Haven CT 06520, USA
**Singer, Lori** — Actress
Jackoway Tyerman Wertheimer, 1925 Century Park E, #2200, Los Angeles CA 90067 USA
**Singer, Marc** — Actor
David Shapira Assoc, 193 N Robertson Blvd, Beverly Hills CA 90211 USA
**Singer, Maxine F** — Educator, Molecular Biochemist
5410 39th St NW, Washington DC 20015, USA
**Singer, Peter A D** — Philosopher, Ethicist
Princeton University, Human Values Center, Princeton NJ 08544, USA
**Singer, Rachel** — Actress
Bauman Assoc, 250 W 57th St, #2223, New York NY 10107 USA

**Singer, William R (Bill)** — Baseball Player
1119 Mallard Marsh Dr, Osprey FL 34229, USA
**Singh, Amrita** — Actress
Lokhandwala Complex, #5, Andheri Link Road, Mumbai MS 400058, India
**Singh, Bipin** — Dancer, Choreographer
Manipuri Nartanalaya, 15A Bipin Pal Road, Kolkata 700026, India
**Singh, Tjinder** — Singer (Cornershop)
Zzonked Public Relations, Burford Road, London E15 2SP, England
**Singh, Vijay** — Golfer
210 N Serenata Dr, #532, Ponte Vedra Beach FL 32082, USA
**Singler, Kyle E** — Basketball Player
Detroit Pistons, Palace, 4 Championship Dr, Auburn Hills MI 48326 USA
**Singletary, Daryle** — Singer
Bobby Roberts, 3050 Business Park Circle, #303, Goodlettsville TN 37221 USA
**Singletary, Michael (Mike)** — Football Player, Coach
18411 Nicklaus Way, Eden Prairie MN 55347, USA
**Singletary, Tony** — Director
A P A Talent/Literary Agency, 405 S Beverly Dr, #300, Beverly Hills CA 90212 USA
**Singleton, Alshermond G (Al)** — Football Player
8 Cromwell Dr, Chester NJ 07930, USA
**Singleton, Chris** — Football Player
4700 S Fulton Ranch Blvd, #63, Chandler AZ 85248, USA
**Singleton, Christopher V (Chris)** — Baseball Player
2038 Town Manor Court, Dacula GA 30019, USA
**Singleton, Isaac** — Actor
Coolwaters Productions, 10061 Riverside Dr, Box 531, Toluca Lake CA 91602 USA
**Singleton, Kenneth W (Kenny)** — Baseball Player
10 Sparks Farm Road, Sparks MD 21152, USA
**Singleton, Margie** — Singer
Country Music Spectacular, PO Box 567, Hendersonville TN 37077, USA
**Singleton, William D** — Publisher
MediaNews Group, 101 W Colfax Ave, Denver CO 80202, USA
**Sinha, Mala** — Actress
8 Turner Road, Bandra, Mumbai MS 400050, India
**Sinha, Shatrughan** — Actor
104 Green Star Apts, Sherly Rajan Road, Bandra, Mumbai MS 400050, India
**Sinisalo, Ikka** — Ice Hockey Player
6221 Main St, Voorhees NJ 08043, USA
**Sinise, Gary** — Actor
Polaris Productions, 8135 W 4th St, #200, Los Angeles CA 90048, USA
**Sinise, Moira** — Actress
Creative Artists Agency, 2000 Ave of Stars, #100, Los Angeles CA 90067 USA
**Sinkford, William** — Religious Leader
Unitarian Universalist Assn, President's Office, 25 Beacon St, Boston MA 02108, USA
**Sinn, Pearl** — Golfer
132 21st Place, Manhattan Beach CA 90266, USA
**Sinner, George A** — Governor, ND
101 3rd St N, Moorhead MN 56560, USA
**Sinsheimer, Robert L** — Biologist, Educator
4606 Via Cavente, Santa Barbara CA 93110, USA
**Sinyavskaya, Tamara I** — Opera Singer
Kunstleragentur Raab & Bohm, Plankengasse 7, 1010 Vienna, Austria
**Siorpaes, Gildo** — Bobsled Athlete
Olympic Committee, Foro Italico, Largo Lauro de Bosis 15, 00135 Rome, Italy
**Siouxsie Sioux** — Singer (Siouxsie & the Banshees)
Helter Skelter, 347-353 Chiswick High Road, London W4 4HS, England
**Sipchen, Bob** — Journalist
Los Angeles Times, Editorial Dept, 202 W 1st St, Los Angeles CA 90012 USA
**Sipe, Brian W** — Football Player
1630 Luneta Dr, Del Mar CA 92014, USA
**Sipinen, Arto K** — Architect
Munkkiniemenranta 39, 00330 Helsinki, Finland
**Sipos, Shaun** — Actor
Innovative Artists, 1505 10th St, Santa Monica CA 90401 USA
**Sir Mix-A-Lot** — Rap Artist
Entertainment Artists, 2409 21st Ave S, #100, Nashville TN 10019 USA
**Siraguso, Tony** — Football Player, Sportscaster
15 Annabelle Lane, Florham Park NJ 07932, USA
**Sircar, Tiya** — Actress
John Carrabino Mgmt, 5900 Wilshire Blvd, #406, Los Angeles CA 90036, USA
**Siren, Heikki** — Architect
Tiirasaarentie 35, 00200 Helsinki, Finland
**Siren, Katri A H** — Architect
Tiirasaarentie 35, 00200 Helsinki, Finland
**Siren, Ville** — Ice Hockey Player
Saint Louis Blues, Scott Trade Center, 1401 Clark Ave, Saint Louis MO 63103 USA
**Sirgo, Otto** — Actor, Director
Televisa, Blvd A Lopez Mateos 232, Colonia San Angel, Mexico City DF 01060 CP, Mexico
**Siri Singh Sahib** — Religious Leader
Sikh, PO Box 351149, Los Angeles CA 90035, USA
**Sirico, Tony** — Actor
McGowan Mgmt, 8733 W Sunset Blvd, #103, West Hollywood CA 90069 USA
**Sirikit** — Queen, Thailand
Royal Residence, Chitralada Villa, 9 Rama VI Road, Soi 30, Bangkok 10400, Thailand
**Sirindhorn** — Princess, Thailand
Royal Residence, Chitralada Villa, 9 Rama VI Road, Soi 30, Bangkok 10400, Thailand
**Sirleaf, Ellen Johnson** — President, Liberia; Nobel Peace Laureate
President's Office, Executive Mansion, Capitol Hill, Monrovia, Liberia
**Sirmon, Peter A** — Football Player
5729 Sterling Oaks Dr, Brentwood TN 37027, USA
**Sirola, Joseph A** — Actor
T G M D Talent, 6767 Forest Lawn Dr, #101, Los Angeles CA 90068, USA
**Sirtis, Marina** — Actress
Polaris Entertainment, 8048 W 3rd St, #300, Los Angeles CA 90048 USA
**Sisemore, Jerald G (Jerry)** — Football Player
17301 Whippoorwill Trail, Leander TX 78645, USA

**Sisk, Douglas R (Doug)** — Baseball Player
3610 42nd Ave NE, Tacoma WA 98422, USA
**Sisk, Tommie W** — Baseball Player
164 E 4635 N, Provo UT 84604, USA
**Siska, Adam T** — Bassist (Academy Is)
Decaydance Records, 9229 W Sunset Blvd, #900, West Hollywood CA 90069, USA
**Siskin, Paul** — Interior Designer
Siskin Valls Inc, 21 W 58th St, #2B, New York NY 10019, USA
**Sislen, Myrna** — Concert Guitarist
Lindy Martin Mgmt, 1007 Lakewater Dr, Henrico VA 23229, USA
**Sisley, Tomer** — Actor, Director, Writer
Cineart, 28 Rue Mogador, 78009 Paris, France
**Sisqo** — Singer (Dru Hill)
Davis Shapiro Lewit Hayes, 150 S Rodeo Dr, #200, Beverly Hills CA 90212, USA
**Sissel** — Singer
Continental A/s, PO Box 143, 2051 Jessheim, Norway
**Sister Bliss** — Musician (Faithless)
Helter Skelter, 347-353 Chiswick High Road, London W4 4HS, England
**Sister Max** — Fashion Designer
Mount Everest Centre for Buddhist Studies, Katmandu, Nepal
**Sisto, Jeremy** — Actor
Gersh Agency, 9465 Wilshire Blvd, #600, Beverly Hills CA 90212 USA
**Sistrunk, Manuel (Manny)** — Football Player
3856 Williams Road, Montgomery AL 36110, USA
**Sistrunk, Otis** — Football Player
PO Box 372, Dupont WA 98327, USA
**Sitbon, Martine** — Fashion Designer
6 Rue de Braque, 75003 Paris, France
**Sites, Brian** — Actor
Innovative Artists, 1505 10th St, Santa Monica CA 90401 USA
**Sitkovetsky, Dmitry** — Concert Violinist, Conductor
Kunstleragentur Raab & Bohm, Plankengasse 7, 1010 Vienna, Austria
**Sittenfeld, Curtis** — Writer
Random House, 1745 Broadway, #1800, New York NY 10019 USA
**Sittler, Darryl G** — Ice Hockey Player
18 Jedburgh Road, Toronto ON M5M 3J6, Canada
**Sittler, Walter** — Actor
Agentur Heppeler, Seinstr 54, 81667 Munich, Germany
**Sitton, Charles E (Charlie)** — Basketball Player
3035 SW Homesteader Road, West Linn OR 97068, USA
**Sivad, Darryl** — Actor
Commercial Talent, 9255 Sunset Blvd, #505, Los Angeles CA 90069, USA
**Siwy, James G (Jim)** — Baseball Player
6919 April Wind Ave, Las Vegas NV 89131, USA
**Sixx, Nikki** — Singer, Bassist, Drummer (Motley Crue)
936 Vista Ridge Lane, Westlake Village CA 91362, USA
**Siza, Alvaro** — Pritzker Architectural Laureate
Oporto University, Architecture School, 4150 755 Oporto, Portugal
**Sizemore, Grady, III** — Baseball Player
1951 W 26th St, #512, Cleveland OH 44113, USA
**Sizemore, Ted C** — Baseball Player
14030 Conway Road, Chesterfield MO 63017, USA
**Sizemore, Tom** — Actor
Global Artists Agency, 6253 Hollywood Blvd, #508, Los Angeles CA 90028 USA
**Sizova, Alla I** — Ballerina
Universal Ballet School, 4301 Harewood Road NE, Washington DC 20017, USA
**Sjoberg, Patrik** — Track Athlete
Hokegatan 17, 416 66 Goteberg, Sweden
**Sjoland, Patrik** — Golfer
PGA European Tour, Wentworth Drive, Virginia Water Surrey GU25 4LX, England
**Sjooblom, Lenna** — Model
Playboy Promotions, 2706 Media Center Dr, Los Angeles CA 90065 USA
**Sjostrom, Fredrik** — Ice Hockey Player
18362 N 94th Place, Scottsdale AZ 85255, USA
**Skabo, Paul** — Test Pilot
18 Wisteria Court, Novato CA 94945, USA
**Skaggs, David L (Dave)** — Baseball Player
11131 Arlington Ave, Riverside CA 92505, USA
**Skaggs, James L (Jimmie)** — Football Player
421 Falcon Ridge Road, Ellensburg WA 98926, USA
**Skaggs, Ricky** — Singer, Guitarist
380 Forest Retreat, Hendersonville TN 37075, USA
**Skah, Khalid** — Track Athlete
Boite Postale 2577, Fez, Morocco
**Skalde, Jarrod** — Ice Hockey Player
305 1/2 E Front St, Bloomington IL 61701, USA
**Skalski, Joseph D (Joe)** — Baseball Player
15546 Drexel Ave, Dolton IL 60419, USA
**Skansi, Paul A** — Football Player
23795 Brixton Place, Poulsbo WA 98370, USA
**Skarda, Randy** — Ice Hockey Player
26885 Noble Road, Excelsior MN 55331, USA
**Skaricic, Marija** — Actress
Croatian Audiovisual Center, Nova Ves 18, 10 000 Zacreb, Croatia
**Skarmeta, Antonio** — Writer
Mohrenstr 42, 10117 Berlin, Germany
**Skarsgard, Alexander J H** — Actor
Creative Artists Agency, 2000 Ave of Stars, #100, Los Angeles CA 90067 USA
**Skarsgard, Bill** — Actor
Agentfirman Planthaber/Kildén, Drottninggatan 55, 111 21 Stockholm, Sweden
**Skarsten, Rachel** — Actress
Creative Drive Artists, 66 King St E, #400, Toronto ON M5A 1J3, Canada
**Skaugstad, David W (Dave)** — Baseball Player
16222 Monterey Lane, #274, Huntington Beach CA 92649, USA
**Skeggs, Leonard T, Jr** — Biochemist
10212 Blair Lane, Willoughby OH 44094, USA

# S

**Skelly, James** — Singer (Coral)
S J M Mgmt, St Matthews, Liverpool Road, Manchester M3 4NQ, England

**Skelton, Byron G** — Judge
US Court of Appeals, 717 Madison Ave NW, Washington DC 20439, USA

**Skelton, Richard K (Rich), Jr** — Rodeo Rider
1139 County Road 312, Llano TX 78643, USA

**Skelton, Stuart** — Opera Singer
I M G Artists, Hogarth Business Park, Chiswick, London W4 2TH, England

**Skerrit, Roosevelt** — Prime Minister, Dominica
Premier's Office, Government Headquarters, Kennedy Ave, Roseau, Dominica

**Skerritt, Tom** — Actor
Pitt Group, 9465 Wilshire Blvd, #420, Beverly Hills CA 90212, USA

**Skiba, Matthew T (Matt)** — Singer, Guitarist (Alkaline Trio)
X-Ray Touring, 77-79 Great Eastern St, London EC2A 3HU, England

**Skibbie, Lawrence F** — Army General
2309 S Queen St, Arlington VA 22202, USA

**Skidmore, R Roe** — Baseball Player
964 E Martin Dr, Decature IL 62521, USA

**Skiles, Scott A** — Basketball Player, Coach
3975 S Inverness Farm Road, Bloomington IN 47401, USA

**Skillings, Muzz** — Bassist (Living Colour)
Entertainment Artists, 2409 21st Ave S, #100, Nashville TN 10019 USA

**Skin** — Singer (Skunk Anansie)
13 Artists, 11-14 Kensington St, Brighton BN1 4AJ, England

**Skinner, Albert L (Al)** — Basketball Player, Coach
145 Great Plain Ave, Wellesley MA 02482, USA

**Skinner, Claire** — Actress
Markham Froggatt Irwin, Julian House, 4 Windmill St, London W1P 1HF, England

**Skinner, Joel P** — Baseball Player
275 Pamilla Circle, Avon Lake OH 44012, USA

**Skinner, John A (Jonty)** — Swimmer, Coach
University of Alabama, Athletic Dept, Tuscaloosa AL 35487, USA

**Skinner, Julie** — Curling Athlete
Curling Assn, 1660 Vimont Court, Cumberland ON K4A 4J4, Canada

**Skinner, Mike** — Auto, Truck Racing Driver
Mike Skinner Enterprises, 201 Cessna Blvd, #4, Port Orange FL 32128, USA

**Skinner, Robert R (Bob)** — Baseball Player, Manager
1576 Diamond St, San Diego CA 92109, USA

**Skinner, Samuel K** — Secretary, Transportation; Businessman
Commonwealth Edison, 1 First National Plaza, PO Box 767, Chicago IL 60690, USA

**Skinner, Sonny** — Golfer
114 Northlake Dr, Sylvester GA 31791, USA

**Skinner, Val** — Golfer
44 Bridge Ave, Bay Head NJ 08742, USA

**Skizas, Louis P (Lou)** — Baseball Player
2101 W White St, #118, Champaign IL 61821, USA

**Skjelbreid, Ann-Elen** — Biathlete
5640 Eikelandsosen, Norway

**Skjvorecky, Josef** — Writer
Erindale College, English Dept, Toronto ON M5S 1A5, Canada

**Skladany, Thomas E (Tom)** — Football Player
6666 Highland Lakes Place, Westerville OH 43082, USA

**Skloff, Michael** — Composer
Gorfaine/Schwartz, 4111 W Alameda Ave, #509, Burbank CA 91505 USA

**Skoglund, Sandy** — Photographer, Sculptor
Janet Borden, 560 Broadway, #601, New York NY 10012, USA

**Skok, Craig R** — Baseball Player
981 Slash Pine Way, Lawrenceville GA 30043, USA

**Skolimowski, Jerzy** — Director, Actor
Film Polski, Ul Mazowiecka 6/8, 00048 Warsaw, Poland

**Skolnick, Mark H** — Geneticist
University of Utah Medical Center, Genetics Dept, Salt Lake City UT 84112, USA

**Skolnikoff, Eugene B** — Political Scientist
1010 Waltham St, #542, Lexington MA 2421, USA

**Skoog, Meyer U (Whitey)** — Basketball Player, Coach
1302 W Traverse Road, #203, Saint Peter MN 56082, USA

**Skorodenski, Warren** — Ice Hockey Player
161 MacEwan Ridge Circle NW, Calgary AB T3K 3W3, Canada

**Skoronski, Robert F (Bob)** — Football Player
3807 Signature Dr, Middletown WI 53562, USA

**Skorton, David J** — Educator
Cornell University, President's Office, Ithaca NY 14853, USA

**Skorupan, John P** — Football Player
142 Crossing Ridge Trail, Cranberry Township PA 16066, USA

**Skotheim, Robert A** — Museum Executive
2120 Place Road, Port Angeles WA 98363, USA

**Skou, Jens C** — Nobel Chemistry Laureate
Rislundvej 9, Risskov 8240, Denmark

**Skoula, Martin** — Ice Hockey Player
2441 Sheridan Ave S, Minneapolis MN 55405, USA

**Skouras, Thanos** — Economist
8 Chlois St, 14562 Athens, Greece

**Skovhus, Bo** — Opera Singer
Balmer & Dixon Mgmt, Granitweg 2, 8006 Zurich, Switzerland

**Skow, James J (Jim)** — Football Player
748 Knollview Blvd, Ormond Beach FL 32174, USA

**Skream** — Electronic Musician (Magnetic Man)
Columbia Records, 9 Derry St, London W8 5HY, England

**Skrebneski, Victor** — Photographer
1350 N LaSalle Dr, Chicago IL 60610, USA

**Skrepenak, Gregory A (Greg)** — Football Player
Hyders Total Fitness Center, 400 Middle Road, Nanticoke PA 18634, USA

**Skride, Baiba** — Concert Violinist
Konzertdirektion Schmid, Konigstra 36, 30175 Hannover, Germany

**Skriko, Petri** — Ice Hockey Player
Kirjatyontekijankatu 4 A 3, 00170 Helsinki, Finland

**Skripochka, Oleg I** — Cosmonaut
Cosmonaut Training Center, Star City, 141160 Zvezdny Gorodok, Moscow Oblast, Russia

**Skrmetta, Matt** — Baseball Player
827 Poinsetta Dr, Indian Harbour Beach FL 32937, USA

**Skrovan, Steve** — Actor, Comedian, Producer
W M E Entertainment, 9601 Wilshire Blvd, #300, Beverly Hills CA 90210 USA

**Skrowaczewski, Stanislaw** — Conductor, Composer
Minnesota Symphony, 1111 Nicollet Mall, Minneapolis MN 55403, USA

**Skrudland, Brian** — Ice Hockey Player
Argo Sales, 717 7th Ave SW, #1300, Calgary AB T2P 0Z3, Canada

**Skube, Robert J (Bob)** — Baseball Player
4153 W Charlotte Dr, Glendale AZ 85310, USA

**Skvortsov, Alexander A** — Cosmonaut
Cosmonaut Training Center, Star City, 141160 Zvezdny Gorodok, Moscow Oblast, Russia

**Sky, Alison** — Environmental Artist
60 Greene St, New York NY 10012, USA

**Sky, Amy** — Singer, Songwriter
LiveTourArtists, 1451 White Oaks Blvd, Oakville ON L6H 4R9, Canada

**Sky, Jennifer** — Actress
Dunham Literary, 110 William St, #2202, New York NY 10038 10038, USA

**Sky, Patrick** — Singer, Songwriter
Ossian Records, 118 Beck Road, Loudon NH 03307, USA

**Skye, Azura** — Actress
B/W/R, 9100 Wilshire Blvd, #500W, Beverly Hills CA 90212 USA

**Skye, Ione** — Actress
Concrete Entertainment, 468 N Camden Dr, #200, Beverly Hills CA 90210, USA

**Skyrms, Brian** — Philosopher
University of California, Philosophy Dept, Irvine CA 92697, USA

**Slack, Reggie** — Football Player
5973 Queen St, Milton FL 32570, USA

**Slade, Bernard N** — Writer
345 N Saltair Ave, Los Angeles CA 90049, USA

**Slade, Chris** — Drummer (AC/DC)
11 Leominster Road, Morden, Surrey SA4 6HN, England

**Slade, Christopher C (Chris)** — Football Player
4163 Onslow Place SE, Smyrna GA 30080, USA

**Slade, David** — Actor, Comedian, Director
Anonymous Content, 3532 Hayden Ave, Culver City CA 90232 USA

**Slade, Isaac** — Singer, Pianist (Fray)
A2 Mgmt, 624 Davis St, #200, Evanston IL 60201, USA

**Slade, Jeff** — Basketball Player
5354 Farmington Road, Toledo OH 43623, USA

**Slade, Mark** — Actor
38 Joppa Road, Worcester MA 01602, USA

**Slade, Roy** — Artist, Museum Executive
31 Island Way, #801, Clearwater FL 33767, USA

**Slagle, James R** — Computer Scientist
Massachusetts Institute of Technology, Mathematics Dept, Cambridge MA 02139, USA

**Slagle, Roger L** — Baseball Player
536 W 3rd St, Larned KS 67550, USA

**Slaney, John** — Ice Hockey Player
96 Mullen Dr, Sicklerville NJ 08081, USA

**Slaney, Mary Decker** — Track Athlete
87141 Kellmore St, Eugene OR 97402, USA

**Slash** — Singer, Guitarist (Guns N' Roses)
First Artists Mgmt, 4764 Park Granada, #210, Calabasas CA 91302 USA

**Slate, Jenny** — Actress, Comedianne
W M E Entertainment, 9601 Wilshire Blvd, #300, Beverly Hills CA 90210 USA

**Slaten, Douglas (Doug)** — Baseball Player
233 Rennie Ave, Venice CA 90291, USA

**Slater, Christian** — Actor
United Talent Agency, U T A Plaza, 9336 Civic Center Dr, Beverly Hills CA 90210 USA

**Slater, Helen** — Actress
DeSante Frank Co, 10061 Riverside Dr, #377, Toluca Lake CA 91602, USA

**Slater, Jackie R** — Football Player
PO Box 6411, Orange CA 92863, USA

**Slater, Kelly** — Surfer, Actor
Quicksilver, 15202 Graham St, Huntington Beach CA 92649, USA

**Slater, Mark W** — Football Player
10545 Rome Ave, Young America MN 55397, USA

**Slater, Reggie** — Basketball Player
8 Saint Christopher Court, Sugar Land TX 77479, USA

**Slater, Rodney E** — Secretary, Transportation
Paton Boggs, 2050 M St NW, Washington DC 20036, USA

**Slatkin, Leonard E** — Conductor
Detroit Symphony, 3711 Woodward Ave, Detroit MI 48201, USA

**Slaton, Anthony T (Tony)** — Football Player
122 E Childs Ave, Merced CA 95341, USA

**Slaton, James M (Jim)** — Baseball Player
4082 N Arbor Lane, Buckeye AZ 85396, USA

**Slattery, Anthony D J (Tony)** — Actor
Belfield & Ward, 80-81 Saint Martin's Lane, London WC2N 4AA, England

**Slattery, John M, Jr** — Actor
Gersh Agency, 9465 Wilshire Blvd, #600, Beverly Hills CA 90212 USA

**Slattvik, Simon** — Nordic Combined Athlete
Bankgata 22, 2600 Lillehammer, Norway

**Slaught, Donald M (Don)** — Baseball Player
27 Middleridge Lane S, Rolling Hills CA 90274, USA

**Slaughter, Alvin** — Singer, Songwriter
Alvin Slaughter Ministries, 3221 Southwestern Blvd, #311, Orchard Park NY 14127, USA

**Slaughter, Karin** — Writer
Delacorte Press, 1540 Broadway, New York NY 10036 USA

**Slaughter, Tavaris J (T J)** — Football Player
2035 Pinehurst Dr, Gardendale AL 35071, USA

**Slaughter, Webster M** — Football Player
3706 Rory Court, Missouri City TX 77459, USA

**Slavin, Jonathan** — Actor
Coronel Group, 1100 Glendon Ave, #1700, Los Angeles CA 90046, USA
**Slavin, Neal** — Photographer
62 Green St, New York NY 10012, USA
**Slavitt, David R** — Writer
35 West St, #5, Cambridge MA 02139, USA
**Slay, Brandon** — Freestyle Wrestler
6155 Lehman Dr, Colorado Springs CO 80918, USA
**Slayback, William G (Bill)** — Baseball Player
25710 Armstrong Circle, #E, Stevenson Ranch CA 91381, USA
**Slayton, Maurice W** — Financier
Conning Corp, City Place II, 185 Asylum St, #1500, Hartford CT 06103, USA
**Slean, Sarah** — Singer, Songwriter
Agency Group, 2 Berkeley St, #202, Toronto ON M5A 4J5, Canada
**Sledge, Joni** — Singer (Sister Sledge)
Nationwide Entertainment, 2756 N Green Valley Parkway, Henderson NV 89014 USA
**Sledge, Kathy** — Singer (Sister Sledge)
491 York Road, Jenkintown PA 19046, USA
**Sledge, Percy** — Singer
PO Box 220082, Great Neck NY 11022, USA
**Sleiman, Haaz** — Actor
Gersh Agency, 9465 Wilshire Blvd, #600, Beverly Hills CA 90212 USA
**Slezak, Erika** — Actress
I C M Partners, 730 5th Ave, New York NY 10019 USA
**Slichter, Charles P** — Physicist
61 Chestnut Court, Champaign IL 61822, USA
**Slick Rick** — Rap Artist
Entertainment Artists, 2409 21st Ave S, #100, Nashville TN 10019 USA
**Slick, Grace** — Singer (Jefferson Airplane), Songwriter
Mission Control, 15030 Ventura Blvd, #541, Sherman Oaks CA 91403, USA
**Slim Helu, Carlos** — Businessman
Telmex, Porque Via 198, Cuauhtemoc CP, 06599 Mexico City DF, Mexico
**Sliwinska, Edyta** — Dancer
Bloc Talent Agency, 5651 Wilshire Blvd, #C, Los Angeles CA 90036, USA
**Sloan, Bridget** — Gymnast
USA Gymnastics, 201 S Capital Ave, #300, Indianapolis IN 46275 USA
**Sloan, David L** — Football Player
2711 Nottingham St, Houston TX 77005, USA
**Sloan, Edward J (Ed)** — Singer, Guitarist (Crossfade)
216 Lincoln St, West Columbia SC 29170, USA
**Sloan, Eliot** — Singer (Blessid Union of Souls)
Union Artists Group, 214 Woodhavens, Union SC 29379, USA
**Sloan, Gerald E (Jerry)** — Basketball Player, Coach
5583 W 13680 S, Herriman UT 84096, USA
**Sloan, John** — Actor
Innovative Artists, 1505 10th St, Santa Monica CA 90401 USA
**Sloan, P F** — Singer, Songwriter
All the Best, PO Box 164, Cedarhurst NY 11516, USA
**Sloan, Stephen C (Steve)** — Football Player, Coach, Administrator
6312 Masters Blvd, Orlando FL 32819, USA
**Sloan, Tod** — Ice Hockey Player
11 Hedge Road, RR 2, Sutton West ON L0E 1R0, Canada
**Sloane, Carol** — Singer
Bennett Morgan, 1022 RR 376, #3, Wappinger Falls NY 12590 USA
**Sloane, Lindsay** — Actress
Gersh Agency, 9465 Wilshire Blvd, #600, Beverly Hills CA 90212 USA
**Slocombe, Douglas** — Cinematographer
London Mgmt, 2-4 Noel St, London W1V 3RB, England
**Slocum, Heath** — Golfer
5640 Keystone Road, Pensacola FL 32504, USA
**Slocum, Matt** — Instrumentalist (Sixpence), Songwriter
Nettwerk Mgmt, 1201 Villa Place, #206, Nashville TN 37212 USA
**Slocumb, Heathcliff (Heath)** — Baseball Player
1045 Arthur St, Uniondale NY 11553, USA
**Slon, Steven** — Editor
Saturday Evening Post, 1100 Waterway Blvd, Indianapolis IN 46202, USA
**Slonimski, Piotr** — Biologist
Le Haut Chantemesle, 72150 Courdemanche, France
**Slonimsky, Sergey M** — Composer
9 Kanal Griboedova, #97, 191186 Saint Petersburg, Russia
**Slotnick, Joey** — Actor
Gersh Agency, 9465 Wilshire Blvd, #600, Beverly Hills CA 90212 USA
**Slotnick, Mortimer H** — Artist
43 Amherst Dr, New Rochelle NY 10804, USA
**Sloves, Marvin** — Businessman
31 San Juan Ranch Road, Santa Fe NM 87506, USA
**Sloviter, Dolores K** — Judge
US Court of Appeals, Courthouse, 601 Market St, #18614, Philadelphia PA 19106, USA
**Slowery, Kevin M** — Baseball Player
1478 Quigg Dr, Pittsburgh PA 15241, USA
**Sloyan, James** — Actor
920 Kagawa St, Pacific Palisades CA 90272, USA
**Sluby, Tom** — Basketball Player
39 Poplar St, Ramsey NJ 07446, USA
**Slug** — Drummer (Marvelous 3)
Progressive Global Agency, 103 W Tyne Dr, Nashville TN 37205, USA
**Sluman, Jeffrey G (Jeff)** — Golfer
939 Cleveland Road, Hinsdale IL 60521, USA
**Slusarski, Joseph A (Joe)** — Baseball Player
11 Rodelle Woods Dr, Weldon Spring MO 63304, USA
**Slutskaya, Irina E** — Figure Skater
Skating Federation, Luznetskaya Nabererhnya 8, 11987 Moscow, Russia
**Smail, Doug** — Ice Hockey Player
PO Box 573, Blum TX 76627, USA
**Smajstria, Craig L** — Baseball Player
4606 Honey Creek Court, Pearland TX 77584, USA

**Smale, Stephen** — Mathematician
68 Highgate Road, Kensington CA 94707, USA

**Small, Aaron J** — Baseball Player
775 Loudon Road, Loudon TN 37774, USA

**Small, Mary** — Writer, Illustrator
PO Box 765, Rozelle NSW 2039, Australia

**Small, Marya** — Actress
CLInc, 843 N Sycamore Ave, Los Angeles CA 90038 USA

**Small, Torrance R** — Football Player
66 Chateau Mouton Dr, Kenner LA 70065, USA

**Small, William N** — Navy Admiral
1605 Bluecher Court, Virginia Beach VA 23454, USA

**Smalley, Roy F, III** — Baseball Player
6319 Timber Trail, Minneapolis MN 55439, USA

**Smallwood, Dwana** — Dancer
Alvin Ailey American Dance Foundation, 405 W 55th St, New York NY 10019, USA

**Smallwood, Richard** — Singer, Composer
Sierra Mgmt, 1035 Bates Court, Hendersonville TN 37075, USA

**Smart, Amy** — Actress
Gersh Agency, 9465 Wilshire Blvd, #600, Beverly Hills CA 90212 USA

**Smart, Erinn** — Fencer
49 W 85th St, #1D, New York NY 10024, USA

**Smart, J Keith** — Basketball Player, Coach
5306 Asterwood Dr, Dublin CA 94568, USA

**Smart, Jean** — Actress
17351 Rancho St, Encino CA 91316, USA

**Smart, Keeth** — Fencer
15 Washington Place, #1F, New York NY 10003, USA

**Smart, Shaka** — Basketball Coach
Virginia Commonwealth, Athletic Dept, Richmond VA 23284, USA

**Smatresek, Neal J** — Educator
University of Nevada, President's Office, 4505 S Maryland Parkway, Las Vegas NV 89154, USA

**Smeal, Eleanor C** — Women's Activist
Feminist Majority Foundation, 1600 Wilson Blvd, #8014, Arlington VA 22209, USA

**Smedile, Anthony** — Drummer (Dig)
Overland Productions, 156 W 56th St, #500, New York NY 10019, USA

**Smedsmo, Dale** — Ice Hockey Player
609 3rd St NE, Roseau MN 56751, USA

**Smedvig, Rolf** — Concert Trumpeter
Columbia Artists Mgmt Inc, 1790 Broadway, #702, New York NY 10019 USA

**Smee, Sebastian** — Journalist
Boston Globe, Editorial Dept, 135 William Morrissey Blvd, Dorchester MA 02125 USA

**Smehlik, Richard** — Ice Hockey Player
8824 Hearthstone Dr, East Amherst NY 14051, USA

**Smerek, Donald F (Don)** — Football Player
1298 Valhalla Dr, Denver NC 28037, USA

**Smerlas, Frederick C (Fred)** — Football Player
23 Farwell St, Newtonville MA 02460, USA

**Smigel, Robert** — Actor, Comedian
Creative Artists Agency, 2000 Ave of Stars, #100, Los Angeles CA 90067 USA

**Smigelsky, David W (Dave)** — Football Player
4332 Nesting Place, Oakwood GA 30566, USA

**Smiley, Jane G** — Writer
235 El Caminto Road, Carmel Valley CA 93924, USA

**Smiley, John P** — Baseball Player
208 W 3rd Ave, Collegeville PA 19426, USA

**Smiley, Justin** — Football Player
721 Baldwin Palm Ave, Plantation FL 33324, USA

**Smiley, Tava** — Actress
P M K-B N C, 8687 Melrose Ave, #800, Los Angeles CA 90069 USA

**Smiley, Tavis** — Entertainer
Smiley Group, 4434 Crenshaw Blvd, Los Angeles CA 90043, USA

**Smirnoff, Karina** — Dancer
Karina Smirnoff Dance, 21270 Ventura Blvd, Woodland Hills CA 91364, USA

**Smirnoff, Yakov** — Actor, Comedian
Comrade Entertainment, 3750 W 76 Country Blvd, Branson MO 65616, USA

**Smirnov, Igor N** — President, Transnistria
President's Office, 25 October Str, Tiraspol, Transnistria, Moldova

**Smisek, Jeff** — Businessman
United-Continental Airlines, 77 W Wacker Dr, Mezzanine, Chicago IL 60601, USA

**Smit, Johannes H M (Jantje)** — Singer
Postbus 100, 1130 Vollendamm AC, Netherlands

**Smith Court, Margaret** — Tennis Player
21 Lowanna Way, City Beach, Perth WA 6010, Australia

**Smith, Aaron D** — Football Player
4900 S Ulster St, #8-106, Denver CO 80237, USA

**Smith, Adrian D** — Architect
1100 W Summerfield Dr, Lake Forest IL 60045, USA

**Smith, Adrian F** — Guitarist (Iron Maiden)
Chipster, 100 Village Square Crossing, Palm Beach Gardens FL 33410 USA

**Smith, Adrian H** — Basketball Player
2829 Saddleback Dr, Cincinnati OH 45244, USA

**Smith, Al F** — Football Player
15 Pembroke St, Sugar Land TX 77479, USA

**Smith, Alan E** — Molecular Biologist
Genzyme Corp, 500 Kendall St, Cambridge MA 02142, USA

**Smith, Alexander D (Alex)** — Football Player
4665 Gaviota Court, Bonita CA 91902, USA

**Smith, Alexander McCall** — Writer
Pantheon Books, 1745 Broadway, New York NY 10019 USA

**Smith, Alexis** — Artist
1625 Shell Ave, Venice CA 90291, USA

**Smith, Allison** — Actress
Barry Freed, 2040 Ave of Stars, #400, Los Angeles CA 90067 USA

**Smith, Amber** — Model, Actress
Elite Model Mgmt, 119 Washington Ave, #501, Miami Beach FL 33139, USA

| | |
|---|---|
| **Smith, Andre D, Jr** | Football Player |
| Cincinnati Bengals, 1 Paul Brown Stadium, Cincinnati OH 45202 USA | |
| **Smith, Andrea B** | Artist |
| 1590 Lokia St, Lahaina HI 96761, USA | |
| **Smith, Anna Deavere** | Actress |
| Creative Artists Agency, 2000 Ave of Stars, #100, Los Angeles CA 90067 USA | |
| **Smith, Anne** | Tennis Player |
| Bew Ravs, 3737 Cole Ave, #110, Dallas TX 75204, USA | |
| **Smith, Anthony B** | Football Player |
| 2724 Hunters Point Dr, Wexford PA 15090, USA | |
| **Smith, Anthony W** | Football Player |
| PO Box 573, Fontana CA 92334, USA | |
| **Smith, Antonio D** | Football Player |
| 2015 Grand River Dr, Richmond TX 77406, USA | |
| **Smith, Antonique** | Actress, Singer |
| P M K-B N C, 8687 Melrose Ave, #800, Los Angeles CA 90069 USA | |
| **Smith, Antowain D** | Football Player |
| 2121 Hepburn St, #917, Houston TX 77054, USA | |
| **Smith, April** | Writer |
| 427 7th St, Santa Monica CA 90402, USA | |
| **Smith, Arlene** | Singer (Chantels) |
| Veta Gardner, 1661 SE Goucho Ave, Port Saint Lucie FL 34952, USA | |
| **Smith, Arthur** | Guitarist, Songwriter |
| PO Box 11715, Charlotte NC 28220, USA | |
| **Smith, Arthur K, Jr** | Educator |
| 45 Wexford Club Dr, Hilton Head SC 29928, USA | |
| **Smith, Artie E** | Football Player |
| 3809 W 68th St, Stillwater OK 74074, USA | |
| **Smith, B** | Model, Publisher, Restauranteur |
| B Smith with Style, 168 Park Ave, Harrison NY 10528, USA | |
| **Smith, Barbara Herrnstein** | Educator |
| Duke University, Science & Cultural Theory Center, Durham NC 27708, USA | |
| **Smith, Barry** | Synthesizer Player (Add N to X) |
| Kork Agency, 1880 Century Park E, #711, Los Angeles CA 90067 USA | |
| **Smith, Barton E (Barty)** | Football Player |
| 2290 Dabney Road, Richmond VA 23230, USA | |
| **Smith, Beau** | Cartoonist |
| Flying Fist Ranch, PO Box 706, Ceredo WV 25507, USA | |
| **Smith, Ben** | Ice Hockey Coach |
| 47 Norwood Heights, Gloucester MA 01930, USA | |
| **Smith, Ben** | Cartoonist (Ratz) |
| King Features Syndicate, 300 W 57th St, #1500, New York NY 10019 USA | |
| **Smith, Benjamin J (Ben)** | Football Player |
| 211 Cobblestone Trail, Avondale Estates GA 30002, USA | |
| **Smith, Billy E** | Baseball Player |
| 9246 Mare Country, San Antonio TX 78254, USA | |
| **Smith, Billy Ray, Jr** | Football Player |
| 14755 Caminito Porta Delgada, Del Mar CA 92014, USA | |
| **Smith, Blake** | Guitarist (Fig Dish) |
| Metropolitan Entertainment Group, 2 Penn Plaza, #1500, New York NY 10121, USA | |
| **Smith, Bob** | Golfer |
| PO Box 6511, Ventura CA 93006, USA | |
| **Smith, Bobby** | Ice Hockey Player |
| 10800 E Cactus Road, #46, Scottsdale AZ 85259, USA | |
| **Smith, Bobby Gene** | Baseball Player |
| 1267 Tucker Road, #15, Hood River OR 97031, USA | |
| **Smith, Brad** | Astronomer |
| Jet Propulsion Laboratory, 4800 Oak Grove Dr, Pasadena CA 91109 USA | |
| **Smith, Brad** | Ice Hockey Player |
| Colorado Avalanche, Pepsi Center, 1000 Chopper Circle, Denver CO 80204 USA | |
| **Smith, Brady** | Actor |
| Schachter Entertainment, 1157 S Beverly Dr, #200, Los Angeles CA 90035 USA | |
| **Smith, Brady M** | Football Player |
| 3555 Moye Trail, Duluth GA 30097, USA | |
| **Smith, Brent M** | Football Player |
| 258 Ridgewood Dr, Pontotoc MS 38863, USA | |
| **Smith, Bruce A** | Businessman |
| Tesoro Petroleum Corp, 300 Concord Plaza Dr, San Antonio TX 78216, USA | |
| **Smith, Bruce B** | Football Player |
| 1640 Spring House Trail, Virginia Beach VA 23455, USA | |
| **Smith, Byther** | Singer, Guitarist, Bassist |
| J Reil Assoc, 3430 Bayberry Dr, Northbrook IL 60062, USA | |
| **Smith, C Douglas (Doug)** | Football Player |
| 25661 Pacific Crest Dr, Mission Viejo CA 92692, USA | |
| **Smith, C Reginald (Reggie)** | Baseball Player |
| Reggie Smith Baseball Center, 16161 Ventura Blvd, #775, Encino CA 91436, USA | |
| **Smith, Calvin** | Track Athlete |
| 16703 Sheffield Park Rd, Lutz FL 33549, USA | |
| **Smith, Carl R** | Air Force General |
| 2345 S Queen St, Arlington VA 22202, USA | |
| **Smith, Carter** | Director |
| Cinetic Mgmt, 555 W 25th St, #400, New York NY 10001 USA | |
| **Smith, Cedric D** | Football Player |
| 14808 Benson St, Overland Park KS 66221, USA | |
| **Smith, Chadwick G (Chad)** | Drummer (Red Hot Chili Peppers) |
| Q Prime, 729 7th Ave, #1600, New York NY 10019 USA | |
| **Smith, Charles D** | Basketball Player |
| PO Box 190, Cedar Grove NJ 07009, USA | |
| **Smith, Charles E (Charlie)** | Football Player |
| 1906 Crescent Dr, Monroe LA 71202, USA | |
| **Smith, Charles H (Charlie)** | Football Player |
| 14074 Skyline Blvd, Oakland CA 94619, USA | |
| **Smith, Charles H (Chuck)** | Football Player |
| 8819 Steeplechase Dr, Knoxville TN 37922, USA | |
| **Smith, Charles Martin** | Actor, Director |
| A P A Talent/Literary Agency, 405 S Beverly Dr, #300, Beverly Hills CA 90212 USA | |

**Smith, Chelsi** — Beauty Queen, Singer, Actress
335 E San Augustine St, Deer Park TX 77536, USA
**Smith, Chris** — Golfer
208 S Bellerive Dr, Peru IN 46970, USA
**Smith, Christina** — Model
Playboy Promotions, 2706 Media Center Dr, Los Angeles CA 90065 USA
**Smith, Christine** — Model
Playboy Promotions, 2706 Media Center Dr, Los Angeles CA 90065 USA
**Smith, Christoper W (Chris)** — Baseball Player
4206 Dawn Lane, Oceanside CA 92056, USA
**Smith, Christopher** — Director, Writer
United Agents, 12-26 Lexington St, London W1F 0LE, England
**Smith, Christopher** — Physiologist, Pharmacologist
King's College, Strand, London WC2R 2LS, England
**Smith, Chuck** — Baseball Player
1300 Saint Charles Place, #810, Pembroke Pines FL 33026, USA
**Smith, Clifford V, Jr** — Educator, Foundation Executive
1205 NW Kline Place, Corvallis OR 97330, USA
**Smith, Colin** — Rowing Athlete
Leander Club, Henley on Thames, Leander RG9 2LP, England
**Smith, Connie** — Singer
TG2 Artists, 201 Rainbow Dr, Carrboro NC 27510, USA
**Smith, Cotter** — Actor
Innovative Artists, 1505 10th St, Santa Monica CA 90401 USA
**Smith, D Brooks** — Judge
US Court of Appeals, Allegheny Center, Old Route 22 W, Duncansville PA 16635, USA
**Smith, Dallas** — Ice Hockey Player
4390 SW 107th Ave, #4, Beaverton OR 97005, USA
**Smith, Dan F** — Businessman
Lyondell Petrochemical Co, 1221 McKinney St, #700, Houston TX 77010, USA
**Smith, Daniel C (Dan), Jr** — Baseball Player
4411 Adonis Dr, Salt Lake City UT 84124, USA
**Smith, Danny** — Actor, Producer, Writer
Roger A Pliakas, 9720 Wilshire Blvd, #700, Beverly Hills CA 90212, USA
**Smith, Darden** — Singer, Guitarist, Songwriter
Eastern Star Productions, 2625 Alcatraz Ave, #302, Berkeley CA 94705, USA
**Smith, Darrin A** — Football Player
7274 NW 19th Court, Pembroke Pines FL 33024, USA
**Smith, Daryl C** — Baseball Player
3 Sunny Hills Court, Randallstown MD 21133, USA
**Smith, David Lee** — Actor
Chaotic Mgmt, 4221 Wilshire Blvd, #395, Los Angeles CA 90010, USA
**Smith, David R** — Electrical Engineer
Duke University, Electrical Engineering Dept, Durham NC 27708, USA
**Smith, David W (Dave)** — Football Player
3709 E Meadowview Dr, Gilbert AZ 85298, USA
**Smith, Dean E** — Basketball Coach
University of North Carolina, Athletic Dept, PO Box 2126, Chapel Hill NC 27515, USA
**Smith, Dennis** — Football Player
2450 Achilles Dr, Los Angeles CA 90046, USA
**Smith, Derek** — Ice Hockey Player
201 Bramblewood Lane, East Amherst NY 14051, USA
**Smith, Derek M** — Football Player
3352 Adams Run, Encinitas CA 92024, USA
**Smith, Derrick** — Ice Hockey Player
Durham Fury, 595 Wentworth St E, Oshawa ON L1H 3V8, Canada
**Smith, Detron N** — Football Player
6390 Saddle Rock Trail S, Aurora CO 80016, USA
**Smith, Dick** — Diving Coach
PO Box 1831, Dewey AZ 86327, USA
**Smith, Donald L (Don)** — Football Player
3338 Pineview Dr, Holiday FL 34691, USA
**Smith, Donna** — Model, Actress
Playboy Promotions, 2706 Media Center Dr, Los Angeles CA 90065 USA
**Smith, Doug** — Football Player, Coach
25661 Pacifc Crest Dr, Mission Viejo CA 92692, USA
**Smith, Douglas (Doug)** — Basketball Player
25482 Pennsylvania Ave, Novi MI 48375, USA
**Smith, Douglas (Doug)** — Actor
Medavoy Mgmt, 10203 Santa Monica Blvd, #400, Los Angeles CA 90067 USA
**Smith, Dylan** — Actor
Talent Works, 3500 W Olive Ave, #1400, Burbank CA 91505 USA
**Smith, E Alexander (Alex)** — Football Player
9604 Gretna Green Dr, Tampa FL 33626, USA
**Smith, E Perry** — Football Player
14251 E Wyoming Place, Aurora CO 80012, USA
**Smith, E Z** — Photographer
2036 N Farris Ave, Fresno CA 93704, USA
**Smith, Earl C** — Baseball Player
2764 N Leonard Ave, Fresno CA 93737, USA
**Smith, Earl J (J R), III** — Basketball Player
New York Knicks, Madison Square Garden, 2 Penn Plaza, New York, NY 10121 USA
**Smith, Elliott A** — Football Player
850 N Jefferson St, #A205, Jackson MS 39202, USA
**Smith, Elmore** — Basketball Player
PO Box 241475, Cleveland OH 44124, USA
**Smith, Emmitt J, III** — Football Player, Sportscaster
15001 Winnwood Road, Dallas TX 75254, USA
**Smith, Erik Scott** — Actor, Singer
Leverage Mgmt, 3030 Pennsylvania Ave, Santa Monica CA 90404 USA
**Smith, F Dean** — Track Athlete
PO Box 71, Breckenridge TX 76424, USA
**Smith, Faryl** — Singer
Agency Group Ltd, 361-373 City Road, London EC1V 1PQ, England
**Smith, Floyd** — Ice Hockey Player
138 Stonehenge Dr, Orchard Park NY 14127, USA

**Smith - Smith**

| | |
|---|---|
| **Smith, Frankie L**<br>620 N Grayson St, Groesbeck TX 76642, USA | Football Player |
| **Smith, Frederick W**<br>F D X Corp, 942 S Shady Grove Road, Memphis TN 38120, USA | Businessman |
| **Smith, G Seth**<br>76 Sunline Dr, Brandon MS 39042, USA | Baseball Player |
| **Smith, Gary**<br>Colorado Rapids, 1000 Chopper Circle, Denver CO 80204 USA | Soccer Coach |
| **Smith, Geoff**<br>42-1525 Westside Road S, Kelowna BC V1Z 3Y3, Canada | Ice Hockey Player |
| **Smith, George**<br>Universal Press Syndicate, 4520 Main St, #700, Kansas City MO 64111 USA | Cartoonist (Smith Family) |
| **Smith, George E**<br>Bell Laboratories, 600 Mountain Ave, Murray Hill NJ 07974, USA | Nobel Physics Laureate |
| **Smith, George E (G E)**<br>Boston Event Works, PO Box 180, Medford MA 02155, USA | Guitarist/Orchestra Leader |
| **Smith, Gerard**<br>World Tennis Assn, 133 1st St NE, Saint Petersburg FL 33701, USA | Publisher, Tennis Executive |
| **Smith, Gordon C**<br>14227 Kellywood Lane, Houston TX 77079, USA | Football Player |
| **Smith, Gordon H**<br>116 S Main St, #3, Pendleton OR 97801, USA | Senator, OR |
| **Smith, Gordon J (Gord)**<br>6 Carriage Dr, West Haven CT 06516, USA | Ice Hockey Player |
| **Smith, Gregory**<br>Paradigm Agency, 360 N Crescent Dr, North Building, Beverly Hills CA 90210 USA | Actor |
| **Smith, Gregory D (Greg)**<br>9930 SW Lumbee Lane, Tualatin OR 97062, USA | Basketball Player |
| **Smith, Gregory White**<br>129 1st Ave SW, Aiken SC 29801, USA | Writer |
| **Smith, Hamilton O**<br>13607 Hanover Pike, Reisterstown MD 21136, USA | Nobel Medicine Laureate |
| **Smith, Harold R (Hal)**<br>9514 Londonderry Court, Fort Smith AR 72908, USA | Baseball Player |
| **Smith, Harold W (Hal)**<br>637 Houston St, Columbus TX 78934, USA | Baseball Player |
| **Smith, Harrison**<br>Minnesota Vikings, 9520 Viking Dr, Eden Prairie MN 55344 USA | Football Player |
| **Smith, Harry**<br>CBS-TV, News Dept, 51 W 52nd St, New York NY 10019 USA | Commentator |
| **Smith, Harry**<br>580 E Cuyahoga Falls Ave, Akron OH 44310, USA | Bowler |
| **Smith, Hedrick L**<br>6935 Wisconsin Ave, #208, Chevy Chase MD 20815, USA | Journalist |
| **Smith, Hunter D**<br>9601 E 300 S, Zionesville IN 46077, USA | Football Player |
| **Smith, Ian Michael**<br>C E S D, 10635 Santa Monica Blvd, #130, Los Angeles CA 90025 USA | Actor |
| **Smith, Irvin M (Irv)**<br>11552 W Green Dr, Youngstown AZ 85363, USA | Football Player |
| **Smith, J D, Jr**<br>3332 Florida St, Oakland CA 94602, USA | Football Player |
| **Smith, J Dwight**<br>PO Box 98, Varnville SC 29944, USA | Baseball Player |
| **Smith, Jackie L**<br>1566 Walpole Dr, Chesterfield MO 63017, USA | Football Player |
| **Smith, Jaclyn**<br>10398 Sunset Blvd, #1200, Los Angeles CA 90077, USA | Actress |
| **Smith, Jaden**<br>W M E Entertainment, 9601 Wilshire Blvd, #300, Beverly Hills CA 90210 USA | Actor |
| **Smith, James (Bonecrusher)**<br>6850 Blue Heron Blvd, #302, Myrtle Beach SC 29588, USA | Boxer |
| **Smith, James A (Jim)**<br>3805 Chimney Rock Dr, Flower Mound TX 75022, USA | Football Player |
| **Smith, James L (Jimmy)**<br>1730 S Arroyo Lane, Gilbert AZ 85295, USA | Baseball Player |
| **Smith, James Ray (Jim Ray)**<br>7049 Cliffbrook Dr, Dallas TX 75254, USA | Football Player |
| **Smith, Jason M**<br>Pro-Rep Entertainment, 113-276 Midpark Way SE, Calgary AB T2X 1J6, Canada | Ice Hockey Player |
| **Smith, Jason Matthew**<br>Greene Assoc, 1901 Ave of Stars, #130, Los Angeles CA 90067 USA | Actor |
| **Smith, Jason V**<br>New Orleans Pelicans, 1250 Poydras St, #101, New Orleans LA 70113 USA | Basketball Player |
| **Smith, Jason W**<br>6350 Golden Acres Dr, Cottondale AL 35453, USA | Baseball Player |
| **Smith, Jean Kennedy**<br>4 Sutton Place, New York NY 10022, USA | Diplomat, Foundation Executive |
| **Smith, Jerry E**<br>US Court of Appeals, 515 Rusk Ave, #12015, Houston TX 77002, USA | Judge |
| **Smith, Jimmy Lee, Jr**<br>105 Long Leaf Place, Madison MS 39110, USA | Football Player |
| **Smith, John F (Jack), Jr**<br>Delta Airlines, Board of Directors, PO Box 20706, Atlanta GA 30320, USA | Businessman |
| **Smith, John M**<br>184 Centre St, Dover MA 02030, USA | Football Player |
| **Smith, John Thomas (J T)**<br>1904 Chasewood Circle, Arlington TX 76011, USA | Football Player |
| **Smith, John W**<br>5315 S Sangre Road, Stillwater OK 74074, USA | Freestyle Wrestler, Coach |
| **Smith, Jonathan Z**<br>University of Chicago, History of Religion Dept, Chicago IL 60637, USA | Historian, Religion Educator |
| **Smith, Joseph L (Joe)**<br>7639 Leafwood Dr, Norfolk VA 23518, USA | Basketball Player |
| **Smith, Joshua (Josh)**<br>Detroit Pistons, Palace, 4 Championship Dr, Auburn Hills MI 48326 USA | Basketball Player |

**Smith, Justin** — Football Player
2222 Terra Nova Lane, San Jose CA 95121, USA

**Smith, K Akili M** — Football Player
PO Box 95, Jamul CA 91935, USA

**Smith, Kathy** — Physical Fitness Instructor
42080 State St, Palm Desert CA 92211, USA

**Smith, Katie** — Basketball Player
2494 Farleigh Road, Columbus OH 43231, USA

**Smith, Keely Shaye** — Entertainer, Writer
W M E Entertainment, 9601 Wilshire Blvd, #300, Beverly Hills CA 90210 USA

**Smith, Keith L** — Baseball Player
5823 13th St E, Bradenton FL 34203, USA

**Smith, Kellita** — Actress
Stone Manners Salners, 9911 W Pico Blvd, #1400, Los Angeles CA 90035 USA

**Smith, Ken** — Landscape Architect
80 Warren St, #28, New York NY 10007, USA

**Smith, Kenneth (Kenny)** — Basketball Player, Sportscaster
Octagon Worldwide, 1751 Pinnacle Dr, #1500, McLean VA 22102 USA

**Smith, Kenneth E (Ken)** — Baseball Player
100 Lansdowne Blvd, Youngstown OH 44506, USA

**Smith, Kerr** — Actor
Gersh Agency, 9465 Wilshire Blvd, #600, Beverly Hills CA 90212 USA

**Smith, Kevin** — Director, Writer
View Askew Productions, PO Box 93339, Los Angeles CA 90093, USA

**Smith, Kevin Max (see Kevin Max)** — Singer (DC Talk), Songwriter
True Artist Mgmt, 227 3rd Ave N, Franklin TN 37064, USA

**Smith, Kurtwood L** — Actor
Progressive Artists Agency, 9696 Culver Blvd, #110, Culver City CA 90232 USA

**Smith, Lacey B** — Historian
Northwestern University, History Dept, Evanston IL 60208, USA

**Smith, Lance** — Football Player
4600 Nobility Court, Charlotte NC 28269, USA

**Smith, Lanty L** — Financier
Wachovia Corp, 301 S College St, #4000, Charlotte NC 28202, USA

**Smith, Larry** — Basketball Player
1767 Lakeside Dr, Vicksburg MS 39180, USA

**Smith, Lauren Lee** — Actress
Gersh Agency, 9465 Wilshire Blvd, #600, Beverly Hills CA 90212 USA

**Smith, Lavay** — Singer
Berkeley Agency, 2608 9th St, #301, Berkeley CA 94710 USA

**Smith, Lavenski R** — Judge
11 Twin Pine Place, Little Rock AR 72210, USA

**Smith, Lee** — Writer
219 N Churton St, Hillsborough NC 27278, USA

**Smith, Lee** — Editor
Gersh Agency, 9465 Wilshire Blvd, #600, Beverly Hills CA 90212 USA

**Smith, Lee A** — Baseball Player
PO Box 399, Castor LA 71016, USA

**Smith, Leroy P (Roy)** — Baseball Player
472 Gramatan Ave, #G2, Mount Vernon NY 10552, USA

**Smith, Leslie C** — WW II Army Air Corps Hero
1700 Tice Valley Blvd, #221, Walnut Creek CA 94595, USA

**Smith, Lois** — Actress
A K A Talent, 6310 San Vicente Blvd, #200, Los Angeles CA 90048 USA

**Smith, Lonnie** — Baseball Player
145 Wesley Forest Dr, Fayetteville GA 30214, USA

**Smith, Lonnie Liston, Jr** — Jazz Keyboardist
Universal Attractions, 135 W 26th St, #1200, New York NY 10001 USA

**Smith, Louis** — Gymnast
Huntingdon Gymnastic Club, Claytons Way, Huntingdon PE29 1UT, England

**Smith, M Elizabeth (Liz)** — Columnist
160 E 38th St, #33C, New York NY 10016, USA

**Smith, Madeline** — Actress
Joan Gray, Sunbury Island, Sunbury on Thames, Middlesex, England

**Smith, Maggie** — Actress
Independent Talent Group, 40 Whitfield St, London W1T 2RH, England

**Smith, Margo** — Singer, Songwriter
Tri-Star Enterprises, PO Box 3367 Brentwood, TN 37024

**Smith, Marilynn** — Golfer
3784 N 162nd Lane, Goodyear AZ 85395, USA

**Smith, Mark E** — Baseball Player
1312 Elmhurst Lane, Flower Mound TX 75028, USA

**Smith, Marquis T** — Football Player
843 51st St, San Diego CA 92114, USA

**Smith, Martha** — Actress, Model
Maggie Smith Management, 3365 Paseo Del Sol, Calabasas CA 91302, USA

**Smith, Marvel A** — Football Player
30 Waterfront Dr, Pittsburgh PA 15222, USA

**Smith, Marvin (Smitty)** — Jazz Drummer
Joel Chriss Co, 300 Mercer St, #3J, New York NY 10003 USA

**Smith, Matt** — Actor
Troika, 74 Clerkenwell Road, #300, London EC1M 5QA, England

**Smith, Michael** — Singer, Songwriter
Artists of Note, PO Box 11, Kaneville IL 60144, USA

**Smith, Michael A (Mike)** — Baseball Player
3226 Livingston Road, Jackson MS 39213, USA

**Smith, Michael W** — Singer, Keyboardist, Songwriter
Creative Artists Agency, 2000 Ave of Stars, #100, Los Angeles CA 90067 USA

**Smith, Michael W (Mike)** — Football Player, Coach
619 Feamster Dr, Houston TX 77022, USA

**Smith, Mike** — Editorial Cartoonist
Las Vegas Sun, Editorial Dept, 2275 Corporate Circle, #300, Henderson NV 89074, USA

**Smith, Mike** — Thoroughbred Racing Jockey
3445 NE 210th St, Miami FL 33180, USA

**Smith, Mike** — Football Player, Coach
Atlanta Falcons, 4400 Falcon Parkway, Flowery Branch GA 30542 USA

**Smith, Mindy** — Singer, Songwriter
Monterey International, 200 W Superior St, #202, Chicago IL 60654 USA

**Smith, Musa** — Football Player
229 Anniversary Lane, Acworth GA 30102, USA

**Smith, Nathaniel B (Nate)** — Baseball Player
6365 Tahoe Dr, Atlanta GA 30349, USA

**Smith, Neal** — Drummer (Alice Cooper)
Maxine Harvard, 7942 W Bell Road, #C5, Glendale AZ 85308 USA

**Smith, Neil** — Football Player
9423 Nall Ave, Overland Park KS 66207, USA

**Smith, Nicholas** — Actor
Michelle Braidman, 10/11 Lower John St, London W1R 3PE, England

**Smith, Nolan D** — Basketball Player
Portland Trail Blazers, Rose Garden, 1 N Center Court St, Portland OR 97227 USA

**Smith, O Guinn** — Track Athlete
2 Hawthorne Place, #3P, Boston MA 02114, USA

**Smith, Onterrio P** — Football Player
PO Box 38252, Sacramento CA 95838, USA

**Smith, Orlando (Tubby)** — Basketball Coach
Texas Tech University, Athletic Dept, Lubbock TX 79409, USA

**Smith, Osborne E (Ozzie)** — Baseball Player, Sportscaster
201 Kendall Bluff Court, Chesterfield MO 63017, USA

**Smith, Otis F** — Basketball Player
607 Applewood Ave, Altamonte Springs Fl 32714, USA

**Smith, Parrish** — Rap Artist (EPMD)
I C M Partners, 10250 Constellation Blvd, #900, Los Angeles CA 90067 USA

**Smith, Patti** — Singer, Songwriter
High Road Touring, 751 Bridgeway, #200, Sausalito CA 94965 USA

**Smith, Peter J (Pete)** — Baseball Player
10030 Halstead Dr, Suwanee GA 30024, USA

**Smith, Peter L (Pete)** — Baseball Player
3512 Dixon Lane, The Villages FL 32162, USA

**Smith, R Jackson** — Diver
122 Palmers Hill Road, #3101, Stamford CT 06902, USA

**Smith, R Jeffrey** — Journalist
Washington Post, Editorial Dept, 1150 15th St NW, Washington DC 20071 USA

**Smith, Ralph A** — Football Player
PO Box 1406, McComb MS 39649, USA

**Smith, Raonall A** — Football Player
1609 119th Street Court NW, Gig Harbor WA 98332, USA

**Smith, Raymond E (Ray)** — Baseball Player
17183 Poblado Court, San Diego CA 92127, USA

**Smith, Renee Felice** — Actress
Don Buchwald, 6500 Wilshire Blvd, #2200, Los Angeles CA 90048 USA

**Smith, Rex** — Actor
Re/Max Realtors, 6695 E Pacific Coast Highway, #150, Long Beach CA 90803, USA

**Smith, Richard H (Dick)** — Baseball Player
1926 Norwood Lane, State College PA 16803, USA

**Smith, Rick** — Ice Hockey Player
RR 1, Perth Road Village ON K0H 2L0, Canada

**Smith, Riley** — Actor
Innovative Artists, 1505 10th St, Santa Monica CA 90401 USA

**Smith, Robaire F** — Football Player
4002 Silver Ridge Blvd, Missouri City TX 77459, USA

**Smith, Robert** — Singer, Guitarist (Cure)
Primary Talent International, 10-11 Jockey's Fields, London WC1R 4BN, England

**Smith, Robert C (Bob)** — Senator, NH
9012 Rocky Lake Court, Sarasota FL 34238, USA

**Smith, Robert E (Bobby)** — Baseball Player
2822 60th Ave, Oakland CA 94605, USA

**Smith, Robert Gray (Graysmith)** — Editorial Cartoonist
San Francisco Chronicle, 901 Mission St, San Francisco CA 94103, USA

**Smith, Robert H** — Financier
1277 Parkview Ave, Pasadena CA 91103, USA

**Smith, Robert Lee** — Singer (Tams)
Speer Entertainment Services, PO Box 2620, McDonough GA 30253, USA

**Smith, Robert S** — Football Player
25601 Thistle Valley Court, Porter TX 77365, USA

**Smith, Robyn** — Thoroughbred Racing Jockey
1155 San Ysidro Dr, Beverly Hills CA 90210, USA

**Smith, Roderick (Rod)** — Football Player
6304 Charrington Dr, Englewood CO 80111, USA

**Smith, Roger** — Actor
2707 Benedict Canyon Dr, Beverly Hills CA 90210, USA

**Smith, Roger Guenveur** — Actor
Don Buchwald, 6500 Wilshire Blvd, #2200, Los Angeles CA 90048 USA

**Smith, Rolland** — Commentator
CBS-TV, News Dept, 524 W 57th St, New York NY 10019, USA

**Smith, Ron** — Drag Racing Driver
14933 165th Place SE, Renton WA 98059, USA

**Smith, Russell** — Singer (Amazing Rhythm Aces), Songwriter
Gen-X Entertainment, PO Box 128164, Nashville TN 37212, USA

**Smith, Sam** — Basketball Player
246 Calvary Colony Road, Memphis TN 38127, USA

**Smith, Scott B** — Writer
Lynne Pleshette Agency, 2700 N Beachwood Dr, Los Angeles CA 90068, USA

**Smith, Shawnee** — Actress
Kritzer Levine Wilkins Griffin, 11872 La Grange Ave, #100, Los Angeles CA 90025 USA

**Smith, Shelley** — Actress, Model
4184 Colfax Ave, Studio City CA 91604, USA

**Smith, Sheridan** — Actress
Independent Talent Group, 40 Whitfield St, London W1T 2RH, England

**Smith, Sherman L** — Football Player
1032 N 41st Place, Renton WA 98056, USA

**Smith, Sinjin** — Volleyball Player, Model
Beach Volleyball Camps, PO Box 1714, Pacific Palisades CA 90272, USA

| | |
|---|---|
| **Smith, Stanley R (Stan)** | Tennis Player |
| 2 Widewater Road, Hilton Head SC 29926, USA | |
| **Smith, Stephanie** | Singer |
| Select Artist Group, PO Box 1418, La Vergne TN 37086, USA | |
| **Smith, Stephen C (Steve)** | Football Player |
| 1104 Lake Shore Dr, Barrington IL 60010, USA | |
| **Smith, Steve** | Basketball Coach |
| Oak Hill Academy, Athletic Dept, 2635 Oak Hill Road, Mouth of Wilson VA 24363, USA | |
| **Smith, Steve (T J Tatters)** | Clown |
| Big Apple Circus, 505 8th Ave, #1900, New York NY 10018 USA | |
| **Smith, Steven** | Labor Leader |
| National Rural Letter Carriers Assn, 1630 Duke St, #200, Alexandria VA 22314, USA | |
| **Smith, Steven A (Steve)** | Football Player |
| 2717 Millwood Dr, Richardson TX 75082, USA | |
| **Smith, Steven D (Steve)** | Basketball Player |
| 755 Heards Ferry Road NW, Atlanta GA 30328, USA | |
| **Smith, Steven L** | Astronaut |
| N A S A, Johnson Space Center, 2101 NASA Road, Houston TX 77058 USA | |
| **Smith, Stevronne L (Steve)** | Football Player |
| Tampa Bay Buccaneers, 1 W Buccaneer Place, Tampa FL 33607 USA | |
| **Smith, Susan M** | Model |
| Playboy Promotions, 2706 Media Center Dr, Los Angeles CA 90065 USA | |
| **Smith, Tangela N** | Basketball Player |
| San Antonio Silver Stars, 1 AT&T Center, San Antonio TX 78219 USA | |
| **Smith, Taran Noah** | Actor |
| Full Circle Mgmt, 12665 Kling St, Studio City CA 91604, USA | |
| **Smith, Tasha** | Actress |
| A P A Talent/Literary Agency, 405 S Beverly Dr, #300, Beverly Hills CA 90212 USA | |
| **Smith, Taylor** | Golfer |
| 1157 Sandlake Road, Saint Augustine FL 32092, USA | |
| **Smith, Thomas L, Jr** | Football Player |
| 360 N C Highway 37 N, Gates NC 27937, USA | |
| **Smith, Tommie** | Track Athlete, Football Player |
| 1800 Lilburn Stone Mountain Road, Stone Mountain GA 30087, USA | |
| **Smith, Tony** | Basketball Player |
| 2645 N 40th St, Milwaukee WI 53210, USA | |
| **Smith, Travian D** | Football Player |
| 13841 County Road 2167D, Tatum TX 75691, USA | |
| **Smith, Travis W** | Baseball Player |
| 1865 Cherry St, Clarkston WA 99403, USA | |
| **Smith, Troy** | Football Player |
| Baltimore Ravens, Ravens Stadium, 1 Winning Dr, Baltimore MD 21230 USA | |
| **Smith, Vernice C** | Football Player |
| 4347 Arajo Court, Orlando FL 32812, USA | |
| **Smith, Vernon L** | Nobel Economics Laureate |
| 336 N Lemon St, Orange CA 92866, USA | |
| **Smith, Vince** | Singer, Songwriter |
| Process Talent Mgmt, 439 Wiley Ave, Franklin PA 16323, USA | |
| **Smith, Vinson R** | Football Player |
| 807 Alexander St, #807, Statesville NC 28677, USA | |
| **Smith, Wadada Leo** | Jazz Trumpeter, Composer |
| California Institute of the Arts, Music Dept, 24700 McBean Parkway, Valencia CA 91355, USA | |
| **Smith, Walter** | Computer Software Designer |
| Microsoft Corp, 1 Microsoft Way, Redmond WA 98052, USA | |
| **Smith, Walter H F** | Oceanographer, Cartologist |
| National Oceanic/Atmospheric Admin, 14th St & Constitution Ave, Washington DC 20230, USA | |
| **Smith, Wayne L** | Football Player |
| 7730 S Bishop St, Chicago IL 60620, USA | |
| **Smith, Wendy** | Singer, Guitarist (Prefab Sprout) |
| Paradigm Agency, 360 N Crescent Dr, North Building, Beverly Hills CA 90210 USA | |
| **Smith, Wilbur A** | Writer |
| Charles Pick Consultancy, 21 Dagmar Terrace, London N1 2BN, England | |
| **Smith, Will** | Actor, Singer, Rap Artist |
| Overbrook Entertainment, 10202 W Washington Blvd, Poitier Building, Culver City CA 90232, USA | |
| **Smith, William** | Actor |
| Spotlight, 7 Leicester Place, London WC2H 7RJ, England | |
| **Smith, William (Bill), Jr** | Swimmer |
| 45-090 Namoku St, #E2, Kaneohe HI 96744, USA | |
| **Smith, William (Billy)** | Ice Hockey Player |
| NY Islanders Alumni Assn, 1535 Old Country Road, #1, Plainview NY 11803, USA | |
| **Smith, William D** | Navy Admiral |
| 7025 Fairway Oaks, Fayetteville PA 17222, USA | |
| **Smith, William J (Billy)** | Ice Hockey Player |
| 8356 Quail Meadow Way, West Palm Beach FL 33412, USA | |
| **Smith, William Jay** | Writer |
| 62 Luther Shaw Road, RR 1 Box 151, Cummington MA 01026, USA | |
| **Smith, William Y** | Army General |
| 6541 Brooks Place, Falls Church VA 22044, USA | |
| **Smith, Willie E** | Baseball Player |
| 1330 E 68th St, Savannah GA 31404, USA | |
| **Smith, Willow** | Actress, Singer |
| Overbrook Entertainment, 450 N Roxbury Dr, #400, Beverly Hills CA 90210, USA | |
| **Smith, Wyatt** | Actor |
| Coast to Coast Talent, 3350 Barham Blvd, Los Angeles CA 90068 USA | |
| **Smith, Yeardley** | Actress |
| A P A Talent/Literary Agency, 405 S Beverly Dr, #300, Beverly Hills CA 90212 USA | |
| **Smith, Zadie** | Writer |
| A P Watt, 20 John St, London WC1N 2DR, England | |
| **Smith, Zane W** | Baseball Player |
| 420 Windship Place NW, Atlanta GA 30327, USA | |
| **Smith-Cameron, J** | Actress |
| Gersh Agency, 9465 Wilshire Blvd, #600, Beverly Hills CA 90212 USA | |
| **Smither, Chris** | Singer, Guitarist, Songwriter |
| Young/Hunter Mgmt, PO Box 3219, Amherst MA 01004, USA | |
| **Smitherman, Stephen** | Baseball Player |
| PO Box 1890, McAlester OK 74502, USA | |

**S**

| | | |
|---|---|---|
| **Smithers, William** | | Actor |
| 2202 Anacapa St, Santa Barbara CA 93105, USA | | |
| **Smithies, Oliver** | | Nobel Medicine Laureate |
| 318 Umstead Dr, Chapel Hill NC 27516, USA | | |
| **Smithson, W Michael (Mike)** | | Baseball Player |
| 25405 Swan Creek Road, Centerville TN 37033, USA | | |
| **Smit-McPhee, Kodi** | | Actor |
| I C M Partners, 10250 Constellation Blvd, #900, Los Angeles CA 90067 USA | | |
| **Smit-McPhee, Sianoa** | | Actress |
| Intellectual Artists Mgmt, 10585 Santa Monica Blvd, #135, Los Angeles CA 90025, USA | | |
| **Smitrovich, Bill** | | Actor |
| 3512 Crownridge Dr, Sherman Oaks CA 91403, USA | | |
| **Smits, Jimmy** | | Actor |
| United Talent Agency, U T A Plaza, 9336 Civic Center Dr, Beverly Hills CA 90210 USA | | |
| **Smits, Rik** | | Basketball Player |
| 8346 E 550 S, Zionsville IN 46077, USA | | |
| **Smiun, Dick** | | Basketball Player |
| 2073 Donegal Circle, Salt Lake City UT 84109, USA | | |
| **Smoke** | | Rap Artist (Field Mob) |
| Geffen Records, 10900 Wilshire Blvd, #1000, Los Angeles CA 90024, USA | | |
| **Smolan, Rick** | | Photographer |
| Workman Publishers, 225 Varick St, #900, New York NY 10014, USA | | |
| **Smolinski, Bryan A** | | Ice Hockey Player |
| 4869 Stoneleigh Road, Bloomfield Hills MI 48302, USA | | |
| **Smolinski, Mark W** | | Football Player |
| 3300 Country Club Road, Petoskey MI 49770, USA | | |
| **Smolka, James W** | | Test Pilot |
| PO Box 2123, Lancaster CA 93539, USA | | |
| **Smolla, Rodney A** | | Educator |
| Furman University, President's Office, 3300 Poinsetta Highway, Greenville SC 29613, USA | | |
| **Smollett, Jurnee** | | Actress |
| I C M Partners, 10250 Constellation Blvd, #900, Los Angeles CA 90067 USA | | |
| **Smoltz, John A** | | Baseball Player |
| 700 Foxhollow Run, Alpharetta GA 30004, USA | | |
| **Smoot, George F, III** | | Nobel Physics Laureate |
| Lawrence Berkeley Laboratory, 1 Cyclotron Road, Berkeley CA 94720, USA | | |
| **Smoove, J B** | | Actor, Comedian, Writer |
| W M E Entertainment, 9601 Wilshire Blvd, #300, Beverly Hills CA 90210 USA | | |
| **Smothers, Dick** | | Actor, Comedian (Smothers Brothers) |
| Smothers Winery, PO Box 219, Kenwood CA 95452, USA | | |
| **Smothers, Tom** | | Actor, Comedian (Smothers Brothers) |
| Smothers Winery, PO Box 219, Kenwood CA 95452, USA | | |
| **Smulders, Cobie** | | Actress |
| United Talent Agency, U T A Plaza, 9336 Civic Center Dr, Beverly Hills CA 90210 USA | | |
| **Smurfit, Victoria** | | Actress |
| United Agents, 12-26 Lexington St, London W1F 0LE, England | | |
| **Smyl, Stanley P (Stan)** | | Ice Hockey Player |
| Vancouver Canucks, 800 Griffiths Way, Vancouver BC V6B 6G1, Canada | | |
| **Smyth, Greg** | | Ice Hockey Player |
| 62 Carrick Dr, Saint John's NF A1A 4N7, Canada | | |
| **Smyth, Joe** | | Singer, Drummer (Sawyer Brown) |
| O-Seven Artist Mgmt, PO Box 210586, Nashville TN 37221, USA | | |
| **Smyth, Patty** | | Singer, Songwriter |
| 23712 Malibu Colony Road, Malibu CA 90265, USA | | |
| **Smyth, Randy** | | Yachtsman |
| 17136 Bluewater Lane, Huntington Beach CA 92649, USA | | |
| **Smyth, Ryan A G** | | Ice Hockey Player |
| Chance Restaurant, 2550-10155 102nd St NW, Edmonton ON T5J 4G8, Canada | | |
| **Smyth, Steve** | | Baseball Player |
| 44005 Northgate Ave, Temecula CA 92592, USA | | |
| **Smythe, Danny** | | Singer, Drummer (Box Tops) |
| Horizon Mgmt, PO Box 8770, Endwell NY 13762, USA | | |
| **Snead, Esix** | | Baseball Player |
| 1332 42nd St, Orlando FL 32839, USA | | |
| **Snead, Jesse Caryle (J C)** | | Golfer |
| 11815 SE Plandome Dr, Hobe Sound FL 33455, USA | | |
| **Snead, Norman B (Norm)** | | Football Player |
| 6311 Courthouse Road, Providence Forge VA 23140, USA | | |
| **Snead, W T, Sr** | | Religious Leader |
| Baptist Convention Missionary, PO Box 1602, Los Angeles CA 90001, USA | | |
| **Snedden, Stephen** | | Actor |
| Marshak/Zachary Co, 8840 Wilshire Blvd, #100, Beverly Hills CA 90211 USA | | |
| **Snedeker, Brandt** | | Golfer |
| 2509 Iron Gate Court, Franklin TN 37069, USA | | |
| **Snee, Christopher (Chris)** | | Football Player |
| 1049 Clark Road, Franklin Lake NJ 07417, USA | | |
| **Sneed, Ed** | | Golfer |
| 4155 Nottinghill Gate Road, Columbus OH 43220, USA | | |
| **Sneed, Floyd** | | Drummer (Three Dog Night) |
| Creative Artists Agency, 2000 Ave of Stars, #100, Los Angeles CA 90067 USA | | |
| **Snegur, Mircea Ion** | | President, Moldova |
| 62A Puschin Str, Chsinev, Moldova | | |
| **Snell, Esmond E** | | Biochemist |
| 819 Tempted Ways Dr, Longmont CO 80504, USA | | |
| **Snell, Ian D** | | Baseball Player |
| 15612 Lemon Fish Dr, Bradenton FL 34202, USA | | |
| **Snell, Matthews (Matt)** | | Football Player |
| Snell Construction, 175 Clendenny Ave, Jersey City NJ 07304, USA | | |
| **Snell, Nathaniel (Nate)** | | Baseball Player |
| 272 Hampton Dr, Orangeburg SC 29118, USA | | |
| **Snell, Peter** | | Track Athlete |
| 6452 Dunston Lane, Dallas TX 75214, USA | | |
| **Snell, Ray M** | | Football Player |
| 1411 W Linebaugh Ave, Tampa FL 33612, USA | | |
| **Snell, Tony** | | Basketball Player |
| Chicago Bulls, United Center, 1901 W Madison St, Chicago IL 60612 USA | | |

**Smithers - Snell**

| | |
|---|---|
| **Snelling, Chris** | Baseball Player |
| PO Box 184, Sumner WA 98390, USA | |
| **Snelson, Kenneth D** | Sculptor, Artist |
| 37 W 12th St, New York NY 10011, USA | |
| **Snepsts, Harold** | Ice Hockey Player |
| 5623 Highfield Dr, Burnaby BC V5B 1E4, Canada | |
| **Sneva, Tom** | Auto Racing Driver |
| 3301 E Valley Vista Lane, Paradise Valley AZ 85253, USA | |
| **Sniadecki, James B (Jim)** | Football Player |
| 3267 Congressional Circle, Fairfield CA 94534, USA | |
| **Snicket, Lemony** | Writer |
| Harper Collins Publishers, 10 E 53rd St, Cellar 1, New York NY 10022 USA | |
| **Snider, David D (Dee)** | Singer (Twisted Sister) |
| Coallier Entertainment, 48 W 56th St, #5A, New York NY 10019, USA | |
| **Snider, Edward M (Ed)** | Ice Hockey Executive |
| PO Box 25088, Philadelphia PA 19147, USA | |
| **Snider, Malcolm P** | Football Player |
| 3997 Orchard Heights Road NW, Salem OR 97304, USA | |
| **Snider, Mike** | Banjo Player, Comedian |
| PO Box 610, Gleason TN 38229, USA | |
| **Snider, R Michael** | Medical Researcher |
| Pfizer Pharmaceuticals, Eastern Point Road, Groton CT 06340, USA | |
| **Snider, Todd** | Singer, Songwriter |
| Gold Mountain, 3940 Laurel Canyon Blvd, #444, Studio City CA 91604 USA | |
| **Snider, Van V** | Baseball Player |
| 1615 Windsor Dr, Cleveland OH 44124, USA | |
| **Snipes, Wesley** | Actor |
| Snell & Wilmer, 600 Anton Ave, #1400, Costa Mesa CA 92626, USA | |
| **Snitzler, Larry** | Concert Guitarist |
| Lindy Martin Mgmt, 1007 Lakewater Dr, Henrico VA 23229, USA | |
| **Snook, Frank W** | Baseball Player |
| 2580 Elysium Ave, Eugene OR 97401, USA | |
| **Snook, Sarah** | Actress |
| United Talent Agency, U T A Plaza, 9336 Civic Center Dr, Beverly Hills CA 90210 USA | |
| **Snoop Dogg-Lion** | Rap Artist |
| Stampede Mgmt, 12530 Beatrice St, Los Angeles CA 90066, USA | |
| **Snopek, Christopher S (Chris)** | Baseball Player |
| 101 Ashton Park Blvd, Madison WS 39110, USA | |
| **Snow** | Singer, Songwriter |
| Agency Group Ltd, 142 W 57th St, #600, New York NY 10019 USA | |
| **Snow, Brittany** | Actress |
| I C M Partners, 10250 Constellation Blvd, #900, Los Angeles CA 90067 USA | |
| **Snow, D J (Michelle)** | Basketball Player |
| Washington Mystics, Verizon Center, 401 9th St NW, #750, Washington DC 20004 USA | |
| **Snow, Eric** | Basketball Player |
| 3115 Manor Bridge Dr, Alpharetta GA 30004, USA | |
| **Snow, Garth** | Ice Hockey Player |
| 4 Weeping Willow Court, Glen Head NY 11545, USA | |
| **Snow, Gene** | Drag Racing Driver |
| Snowman Racing, 5719 Airport Freeway, Haltom City TX 76117, USA | |
| **Snow, Jack T (J T)** | Baseball Player |
| 750 W California Way, Woodside CA 94062, USA | |
| **Snow, John W** | Secretary, Treasury; Businessman |
| Cerberus Capital Mgmt, 299 Park Ave, #2300, New York NY 10171, USA | |
| **Snow, Justin W** | Football Player |
| 1826 Milford St, Carmel IN 46032, USA | |
| **Snow, Mark** | Composer |
| Robert Urband Assoc, 8981 W Sunset Blvd, #311, West Hollywood CA 90069, USA | |
| **Snowden, James J (Jim)** | Football Player |
| 8647 Point of Woods Dr, Manassas VA 20110, USA | |
| **Snowden, M L** | Sculptor |
| Masterpiece Publishing, 5 Watson, Irvine CA 92618, USA | |
| **Snowdon, Earl of (A C R Armstrong-Jones)** | Photographer |
| 22 Launceston Place, London W8 5RL, England | |
| **Snowdon, Lisa** | Model, Actress |
| Money Mgmt, 42A Berwick St, London W1F 8RZ, England | |
| **Snuggerud, Dave** | Ice Hockey Player |
| 4529 Saddlewood Dr, Minnetonka MN 55345, USA | |
| **Snyder, Allan W** | Optical Scientist |
| National University, Optical Science Center, Canberra ACT 2601, Australia | |
| **Snyder, Barbara** | Educator |
| Case Western University, President's Office, Aldebert Hall, Cleveland OH 44106, USA | |
| **Snyder, Bill** | Football Coach |
| Kansas State University, Athletic Dept, Manhattan KS 66506, USA | |
| **Snyder, Christoper R (Chris)** | Baseball Player |
| 4921 W Electra Lane, Glendale AZ 85310, USA | |
| **Snyder, Evan** | Neurologist |
| Harvard Medical School, 25 Shattuck St, Boston MA 02115, USA | |
| **Snyder, Gary S** | Writer |
| 18442 MacNab Cypress Road, Nevada City CA 95959, USA | |
| **Snyder, Gerald G (Jerry)** | Baseball Player |
| 2553 Wild Oak Forest Lane, Seabrook TX 77586, USA | |
| **Snyder, J Cory** | Baseball Player |
| 468 N Loafer Dr, Payson UT 84651, USA | |
| **Snyder, James R (Jimmy)** | Baseball Player, Manager |
| 7516 Dunbridge Dr, Odessa FL 33556, USA | |
| **Snyder, Joey, III** | Golfer |
| 8811 E Riviera Dr, Scottsdale AZ 85260, USA | |
| **Snyder, Kirk P** | Basketball Player |
| Minnesota Timberwolves, Target Center, 600 1st Ave N, Minneapolis MN 55403 USA | |
| **Snyder, Kyle E** | Baseball Player |
| 1869 Upper Cove Terrace, Sarasota FL 34231, USA | |
| **Snyder, Liza** | Actress |
| Susan Smith, 1344 N Wetherly Dr, Los Angeles CA 90069 USA | |
| **Snyder, Richard J (Dick)** | Basketball Player |
| 4621 E Mockingbird Lane, Paradise Valley AZ 85253, USA | |

**Snyder, Russell H (Russ)** — Baseball Player
PO Box 264, Nelson NE 68961, USA
**Snyder, Solomon H** — Psychiatrist, Pharmacologist
3801 Canterbury Road, #1001, Baltimore MD 21218, USA
**Snyder, Suzanne** — Actress
Premiere Artists Agency, 1875 Century Park E, #2250, Los Angeles CA 90067 USA
**Snyder, William D** — Photojournalist
Rochester Institute of Technology, Photojournalism Dept, Rochester NY 14623, USA
**Snyder, Zack** — Director, Writer
Cruel & Unusual Films, 4000 Warner Blvd, Building 90, Burbank CA 91522, USA
**Snyderman, Nancy** — Surgeon, Entertainer
ABC-TV, News Dept, 77 W 66th St, New York NY 10023 USA
**So Ywon Ryu** — Golfer
Ladies Pro Golf Assn, 100 International Golf Dr, Daytona Beach FL 32124 USA
**So, Perry** — Conductor
Harrison/Parrott, 5-6 Albion Court, London W6 0QT, England
**Soares, Mario A N L** — President, Portugal
Rua Dr Joao Soares #2-3, 1600 Lisbon, Portugal
**Sobchuk, Dennis J** — Ice Hockey Player
PO Box 2541, Carefree AZ 85377, USA
**Sobel, Dava** — Writer
Walker Co, 435 Hudson St, New York NY 10014, USA
**Sobers, Ricky B** — Basketball Player
6530 Annie Oakley Dr, #1414, Henderson NV 89014, USA
**Sobieski, Leelee** — Actress
Mosiac Media Group, 9200 W Sunset Blvd, #1000, Los Angeles CA 90069 USA
**Sobrero Markgraf, Kate** — Soccer Player
5055 N Cumberland Blvd, Milwaukee WI 53217, USA
**Sobrino-Stearns, Michelle** — Publisher
Variety, 5900 Wilshire Blvd, #3100, Los Angeles CA 90036, USA
**Sobule, Jill** — Singer, Songwriter
Fleming Artists, 543 N Main St, Ann Arbor MI 48104, USA
**Sochor, James (Jim)** — Football Coach
1018 Kent Dr, Davis CA 95616, USA
**Sodano, Angelo Cardinal** — Religious Leader
Office of Secretary of State, Plaza Apostolico, 00120 Vatican City
**Soderbergh, Steven A** — Director
Anonymous Content, 3532 Hayden Ave, Culver City CA 90232 USA
**Soderholm, Eric T** — Baseball Player
10S360 Hampshire Lane W, Willowbrook IL 60527, USA
**Soderqvist, Johan** — Composer
First Artists, 4764 Park Granada, #210, Calabasas CA 91302 USA
**Sodowski, Clint R** — Baseball Player
351 Whippoorwill Road, Ponca City OK 74604, USA
**Soedergren, Anders** — Cross Country Skier
Hinderstigen 4, 831 32 Ostersund, Sweden
**Soell, Stefan** — Photographer
Fotodesign Stefan Soell, Gewerbepark, Fallenbrunner 17, 88045 Friedrichshafen, Germany
**Soetaert, Douglas H (Doug)** — Ice Hockey Player
13006 66th Ave SE, Snohomish WA 98296, USA
**Sofaer, Abraham D** — Attorney
1200 Bryant St, Palo Alto CA 94301, USA
**Sofer, Rena** — Actress
Framework Entertainment, 9057 Nemo St, #C, West Hollywood CA 90069 USA
**Soffer, Jesse Lee** — Actor
Innovative Artists, 1505 10th St, Santa Monica CA 90401 USA
**Sofield, William** — Interior Designer, Artist
Studio Sofield, 380 Lafayette St, #300, New York NY 10003, USA
**Softley, Iain** — Director
32A Carnaby St, London W1V 1PA, England
**Sogaard, Ole S** — Epidemiologist
Aarhus Universiy Hospital, Skejby, Brendstrupgardsvej 100, 8000 Aarhus N, Denmark
**Sogliuzzo, Andre** — Actor
W M E Entertainment, 9601 Wilshire Blvd, #300, Beverly Hills CA 90210 USA
**Sohn, Kurt F** — Football Player
6 Paine Commons, Yaphank NY 11980, USA
**Sohn, Sonja** — Actress
A P A Talent/Literary Agency, 250 W 57th St, #1701, New York NY 10107 USA
**Sojo, Luis B** — Baseball Player
19250 Wood Sage Dr, Tampa FL 33647, USA
**Soklosky, Bing** — Cinematographer
4654 Cartwright Ave, North Hollywood CA 91602, USA
**Soko** — Singer, Actress
Agence Artiste Adequat, 108 Rue Reaumur, 75002 Paris, France
**Sokoloff, Marla** — Actress
A P A Talent/Literary Agency, 405 S Beverly Dr, #300, Beverly Hills CA 90212 USA
**Sokolov, Grigory L** — Concert Pianist
Konzertdirektion Schmid, Konigstra 36, 30175 Hannover, Germany
**Sokolov, Valeriy** — Concert Violinist
Harrison/Parrott, 5-6 Albion Court, London W6 0QT, England
**Sokomanu, A George** — President, Vanuatu
Mele Village, PO Box 1319, Port Vila, Vanuatu
**Sokurov, Alexander N** — Director
Smolenskaya Nab 4, #222, 199048 Saint Petersburg, Russia
**Solana Madariaga, Javier** — Government Official, Spain
European Union Foreign Office, Rue de la Loi, 1048 Brussels, Belgium
**Solberg, Magnar** — Biathlete
Stabellvn 60, 7000 Trondheim, Norway
**Soleil, Stella** — Singer
Kurfirst/Blackwell, 601 W 26th St, #11, New York NY 10001, USA
**Soles, P J** — Actress
Paradigm Agency, 360 N Crescent Dr, North Building, Beverly Hills CA 90210 USA
**Solh, Rashid el-** — Prime Minister, Lebanon
Chambre de Deputes, Place de l'Etoile, Beirut, Lebanon
**Solich, Frank** — Football Coach
Ohio University, Athletic Dept, Athens OH 45701, USA

**Solinger, Bob** — Ice Hockey Player
65-101 Grove Dr, Spruce Grove AB T7X 3H7, Canada
**Solis, Alex** — Thoroughbred Racing Jockey
2241 Redwood Dr, Glendora CA 91741, USA
**Soljacic, Marin** — Physicist
Massachusetts Institute of Technology, Physics Dept, Cambridge MA 02139, USA
**Sollee, Ben** — Cellist, Singer, Songwriter
High Road Touring, 751 Bridgeway, #200, Sausalito CA 94965 USA
**Sollett, Peter** — Director
W M E Entertainment, 9601 Wilshire Blvd, #300, Beverly Hills CA 90210 USA
**Sollscher, Goran** — Concert Guitarist
Herbert Barrett, 266 W 37th St, #2000, New York NY 10018 USA
**Solo, Ksenia** — Actress
Abrams Artists, 9200 W Sunset Blvd, #1125, West Hollywood CA 90069 USA
**Soloff, Lew** — Trumpeter (Blood Sweat & Tears)
Abby Hoffer Enterprises, 223 1/2 E 48th St, New York NY 10017 USA
**Soloman, Sean C** — Space Scientist
Carnegie Institution, Terrestrial Magnetism Dept, Washington DC 20015, USA
**Solomon, Ariel E** — Football Player
5045 51st St, Boulder CO 80301, USA
**Solomon, Bruce** — Actor
Hollander, 14011 Ventura Blvd, #202W, Sherman Oaks CA 91423, USA
**Solomon, Jesse W** — Football Player
401 SW Bunker St, Madison FL 32340, USA
**Solomon, Robert** — Economist
8502 W Howell Road, Bethesda MD 20817, USA
**Solomon, Susan** — Atmospheric Chemist
National Oceanic/Atmospheric Admin, 325 Broadway, Boulder CO 80305, USA
**Solondz, Todd** — Director, Writer
W M E Entertainment, 9601 Wilshire Blvd, #300, Beverly Hills CA 90210 USA
**Solovay, Robert M** — Mathematician
University of California, Mathematics Dept, Berkeley CA 94720, USA
**Soloviyev, Vladimir A** — Cosmonaut
Khovanskaya Ul D 3, Kv 28, 129515 Moscow, Russia
**Solovyev, Anatoly Y** — Cosmonaut
Cosmonaut Training Center, Star City, 141160 Zvezdny Gorodok, Moscow Oblast, Russia
**Solovyev, Sergei A** — Director, Writer
Akademika Pilyugina Str 8, Korp 1, #330, 117393 Moscow, Russia
**Solow, Robert M** — Nobel Economics Laureate
1010 Waltham St, #328, Lexington MA 02421, USA
**Solt, Ronald M (Ron)** — Football Player
1200 Thornhurst Road, Bear Creek Township PA 18702, USA
**Soltan, Jerzy** — Architect
148 Boylston St, Watertown MA 02472, USA
**Soltau, Gordon L (Gordy)** — Football Player
1290 Sharon Park Dr, #50, Menlo Park CA 94025, USA
**Solvay, Jacques E** — Businessman
Solvay & Cie SA, Rue du Prince Albert 33, 1050 Brussels, Belgium
**Solzhenitsyn, Ignat** — Concert Pianist
Columbia Artists Mgmt Inc, 1790 Broadway, #702, New York NY 10019 USA
**Som, Peter** — Fashion Designer
Peter Som Inc, 215 W 40th St, New York NY 10018, USA
**Somare, Michael T** — Prime Minister, Papua New Guinea
Prime Minister's Office, Parliament House, Waigani 131 N D, Papua New Guinea
**Somerhalder, Ian** — Actor
I C M Partners, 10250 Constellation Blvd, #900, Los Angeles CA 90067 USA
**Somers, Gwen** — Actress, Model
Alice Fries Agency, 1927 Vista Del Mar Ave, Los Angeles CA 90068, USA
**Somers, Suzanne** — Actress
Port Carling Productions, 23961 Craftsman Road, Calabasas CA 91302, USA
**Somerset, Williard F (Willie)** — Basketball Player
6441 Oak View Dr, Harrisburg PA 17112, USA
**Somerville, Bonnie** — Actress, Singer
McKeon-Myrones Mgmt, 3500 Olive Ave, #770, Burbank CA 91505 USA
**Somerville, David (Dave)** — Singer (Diamonds)
10061 Riverside Dr, #114, Toluca Lake CA 91602, USA
**Somerville, Robert E** — Religion Educator
Columbia University, Religion Dept, Claremont Hall, New York NY 10027, USA
**Sommaruga, Cornelio** — Association Executive
16 Chemin des Crets-de-Champel, 1206 Geneva, Switzerland
**Sommer, Alfred** — Epidemiologist
Johns Hopkins University, Hygiene/Public Health School, Baltimore MD 21218, USA
**Sommer, Elke** — Actress, Model
Literature Unlimited, 1850 N Whitley Ave, #1020, Los Angeles CA 90028, USA
**Sommer, Josef** — Actor
Don Buchwald, 6500 Wilshire Blvd, #2200, Los Angeles CA 90048 USA
**Sommer, Richard O (Rich), II** — Actor
A P A Talent/Literary Agency, 405 S Beverly Dr, #300, Beverly Hills CA 90212 USA
**Sommer, Ron** — Businessman
Deutsche Telekom, Friedrich-Ebert-Allee 140, 53113 Bonn, Germany
**Sommer, Roy** — Ice Hockey Player
65 Roman Dr, Shrewsbury MA 01545, USA
**Sommer-Bodenbu, Angela** — Writer, Artist
PO Box 834, Silver City NM 88062, USA
**Sommers, Joanie** — Singer
Xentel, 101 NE 3rd Ave, #203, Fort Lauderdale FL 33301, USA
**Sommers, Stephen** — Director
Sommers Co, 204 Santa Monica Blvd, #A, Santa Monica CA 90401, USA
**Sommore, Laura Rambough** — Actress, Comedienne
Universal Attractions, 135 W 26th St, #1200, New York NY 10001 USA
**Somorjai, Gabor A** — Chemist
665 San Luis Road, Berkeley CA 94707, USA
**Son, Masayoshi** — Inventor (Pocket Electronic Translator)
24-1 Nihonbash, Hakozakicho, Chuoku, Tokyo 103 8501, Japan
**Sondeckis, Saulis** — Conductor
Saint Petersburg Hermitage Orchestra, Mikhailovskaya Str 2, 191186 Saint Petersburg, Russia

**S**

Solinger - Sondeckis

**Sondheim, Stephen J** — Composer, Lyricist
265 Wollaton Vale, Wollato, Nottingham NG8 2PX, England
**Sonefeld, Jim** — Drummer (Hootie & the Blowfish)
FishCo Mgmt, 2519 Devine Street  Columbia SC 29205, USA
**Song, Brenda** — Actress
United Talent Agency, U T A Plaza, 9336 Civic Center Dr, Beverly Hills CA 90210 USA
**Songaila, Antoinette** — Astronomer
University of Hawaii, Astronomy Dept, Honolulu HI 96822, USA
**Songaila, Darius** — Basketball Player
141 S Longfellow Lane, Mooresville NC 28117, USA
**Soni, Karan** — Actor
Michael Zanuck's Agency, 28035 Dorothy Dr, #120, Agoura Hills CA 91301, USA
**Soni, Rebecca** — Swimmer
University of Southern California, Trojan Swim Club, Athletic Dept, Los Angeles CA 90089, USA
**Sonique** — Singer, Synthesizer Player
Ultra D J Mgmt, 2 City Business Centre, Lower Road, London SE16 2XB, England
**Sonja** — Queen, Norway
Det Kongelige Slott, Drammensveien 1, 0010 Oslo, Norway
**Sonnanstine, Andrews M (Andy)** — Baseball Player
526 Reimer Road, Wadsworth OH 44281, USA
**Sonnenfeld, Barry** — Director
W M E Entertainment, 9601 Wilshire Blvd, #300, Beverly Hills CA 90210 USA
**Sonnenschein, Hugo F** — Educator, Economist
1126 E 59th St, Chicago IL 60637, USA
**Sonnichsen, Matt** — Volleyball Player
Newberry College, Athletic Dept, Newberry SC 29108, USA
**Sonnier, Jo-El** — Singer, Guitarist
Fat City Artists, 1906 Chet Atkins Place, #502, Nashville TN 37212 USA
**Sonzero, Jim** — Director, Writer
United Talent Agency, U T A Plaza, 9336 Civic Center Dr, Beverly Hills CA 90210 USA
**Soo Yun Kang** — Golfer
Ladies Pro Golf Assn, 100 International Golf Dr, Daytona Beach FL 32124 USA
**Soomekh, Bahar** — Actress
McClure Assoc, 5225 Wilshire Blvd, #909, Los Angeles CA 90036, USA
**Sope Mautamata, Barak T** — Prime Minister, Vanuatu
Melanesian Progressive Pati (MPP), PO Box 39, Port Vila, Vanuatu
**Sophia** — Queen Consort, Spain
Palacio de la Zarzuela, 28071 Madrid, Spain
**Sophie** — Hereditary Princess, Liechtenstein
Heriditary Princess's Residence, Schloss Vaduz, 9490 Vaduz, Liechtenstein
**Sorbo, Kevin** — Actor
914 Westwood Blvd, #584, Los Angeles CA 90024, USA
**Sorel, Edward** — Artist, Illustrator
156 Franklin St, New York NY 10013, USA
**Sorel, Jean** — Actor
Agents Associes, 201 Rue du Faubourg Saint Honore, 75008 Paris, France
**Sorel, Louise** — Actress
20 E 74th St, #3F, New York NY 10021, USA
**Sorensen, Andrew A** — Educator
Greenville Hospital System, 701 Grove Road, Greenville SC 29605, USA
**Sorensen, Holly B** — Producer, Writer, Actress
United Talent Agency, U T A Plaza, 9336 Civic Center Dr, Beverly Hills CA 90210 USA
**Sorensen, Jacki F** — Physical Fitness Expert
Jacki's Inc, 129 1/2 N Woodland Blvd, #5, Deland FL 32720, USA
**Sorensen, Lary A** — Baseball Player
42515 Northville Place Dr, #406, Northville MI 48167, USA
**Sorensen, Nicholas C (Nick)** — Football Player
305 Grandview Dr, Blacksburg VA 24060, USA
**Sorenson, B Reed** — Auto Racing Driver
4623 Rivers Edge Village, #6508, Ponce Inlet FL 32127, USA
**Sorenson, Garrett** — Opera Singer
I M G Artists, Hogarth Business Park, Chiswick, London W4 2TH, England
**Sorenstam, Annika** — Golfer
International Mangement Group, 1 Erieview Plaza, 1360 E 9th St, Cleveland OH 44114 USA
**Sorenstam, Charlotta** — Golfer
1411 W Whitman Court, Anthem AZ 85086, USA
**Sorey, Revie C, II** — Football Player
10 E Delaware Place, #31C, Chicago IL 60611, USA
**Sorgi, James (Jim)** — Football Player
1316 Greenstone Dr, Danville IN 46122, USA
**Soriano, Alfonso G** — Baseball Player
21 E Huron St, #3301, Chicago IL 60611, USA
**Soriano, Edward** — Army General
Northrop Grumman, 1840 Century Park E, Los Angeles CA 90067, USA
**Soriano, Rafael** — Baseball Player
7601 60th Dr NE, #A, Marysville WA 98270, USA
**Sorkin, Aaron B** — Producer, Writer
W M E Entertainment, 9601 Wilshire Blvd, #300, Beverly Hills CA 90210 USA
**Sorkin, Andrew Ross** — Actor
Creative Artists Agency, 2000 Ave of Stars, #100, Los Angeles CA 90067 USA
**Sorkin, Arleen** — Actress
Creative Artists Agency, 2000 Ave of Stars, #100, Los Angeles CA 90067 USA
**Sorlie, Donald M** — Test Pilot
6947 Wagner Way NW, #A, Gig Harbor WA 98335, USA
**Sorokin, Peter P** — Physicist
5 Ashwood Road, South Salem NY 10590, USA
**Soros, George** — Financier
Soros Fund Mgmt, 888 7th Ave, #2900, New York NY 10106, USA
**Sorrell, Henry T** — Football Player
404 Oak St, Talladega AL 35160, USA
**Sorrell, John W** — Fashion Designer
Lawns, 16 South Grove, London N6 6BJ, England
**Sorrell, Martin** — Businessman
Ogilvy & Mather Worldwide, 1 Soldiers Field Park, #413, Boston MA 02163, USA
**Sorrento, Paul A** — Baseball Player
5918 Mont Blance Place NW, Issaquah WA 98027, USA

**Sortun, Henrik M (Rick)** — Football Player
6708 16th Ave NW, Seattle WA 98117, USA

**Sorum, Matt** — Drummer (Velvet Revolver)
Sanctuary Mgmt, 15301 Ventura Blvd, Building B, Sherman Oaks CA 91403, USA

**Sorvino, Mira K** — Actress
Untitled Entertainment, 350 S Beverly Dr, #200, Beverly Hills CA 90212 USA

**Sorvino, Paul** — Actor
Innovative Artists, 1505 10th St, Santa Monica CA 90401 USA

**Sosa, Elias M** — Baseball Player
333 Red Barn Trail, Matthews NC 28104, USA

**Sosa, Ernest** — Philosopher
Brown University, Philosophy Dept, Providence RI 02912, USA

**Sosa, Samuel (Sammy)** — Baseball Player
505 N Lake Shore Dr, #5500, Chicago IL 60611, USA

**Sosnovska, Olga** — Actress
Innovative Artists, 1505 10th St, Santa Monica CA 90401 USA

**Sossamon, Shannyn** — Actress
A P A Talent/Literary Agency, 405 S Beverly Dr, #300, Beverly Hills CA 90212 USA

**Sostorics, Colleen** — Ice Hockey Player
Team Canada, 2424 University Dr NW, Calgary AB T2N 3Y9, Canada

**Sotillo, Nolan A** — Actor
United Talent Agency, U T A Plaza, 9336 Civic Center Dr, Beverly Hills CA 90210 USA

**Sotin, Hans** — Opera Singer
Schulheide 10, 21227 Bendestorf, Germany

**Sotkilava, Zurab L** — Opera Singer
Bolshoi Theater, Teatralnaya Pl 1, 103009 Moscow, Russia

**Soto, Blanca** — Actress
Latin World Entertainment, 3470 NW 82nd Ave, #670, Miami FL 33122, USA

**Soto, Geovany** — Baseball Player
6319 Perch Creek Dr, Houston TX 77049, USA

**Soto, Jock** — Ballet Dancer
New York City Ballet, Lincoln Center Plaza, New York NY 10023 USA

**Soto, Mario M** — Baseball Player
Cincinnati Reds, Great American Ball Park, 100 Main St, Cincinnati OH 45202 USA

**Soto, Talisa** — Actress, Model
Framework Entertainment, 9057 Nemo St, #C, West Hollywood CA 90069 USA

**Sotomayor Sanabria, Javier** — Track Athlete
International Mangement Group, 1 Erieview Plaza, 1360 E 9th St, Cleveland OH 44114 USA

**Sotomayor, Antonio** — Artist
3 LeRoy Place, San Francisco CA 94109, USA

**Sotomayor, Sonia M** — Supreme Court Justice
US Supreme Court, 1 1st St NE, Washington DC 20543 USA

**Soualem, Zinedine** — Actor
Voyez Mon Agent, 20 Ave Rapp, 75007 Paris, France

**Souare, Ahmed Tidiane** — Prime Minister, Guinea
Prime Minister's Office, PO Box 5141, Cite des Nations, Conakry, Guinea

**Souchon, Alain** — Singer
Voyez Mon Agent, 20 Ave Rapp, 75007 Paris, France

**Soukupova, Hana** — Model
Mega Model Agency, Kaiser-Wilhelm-Str 93, 20355 Hamburg, Germany

**Soul, David** — Actor, Singer
Diamond Mgmt, 31 Percy St, London W1T 2DD, England

**Soulja Boy** — Rap Artist
Soulja Boy Music, 113 Shadow Lane, Batesville MS 38606, USA

**Soumare, Cheikh Hadjibou** — Prime Minister, Senegal
Prime Minister's Office, Ave Leopold Sedar Senghor, Dakar, Senegal

**Soumyanath, Amala** — Neurologist
Oregon Health Science University, 3181 SW Jackson Park Dr, Portland OR 97239 USA

**Souray, Sheldon S** — Ice Hockey Player
4124 Madella Ave, Sherman Oaks CA 91403, USA

**Sourouzian, Hourig** — Archaeologist
31 Abu El Reda, 11211 Cairo-Zamalek, Egypt

**Soutar, Dave** — Bowler
6910 Chickasaw Bayou Road, Bradenton FL 34203, USA

**Soutar, Judy** — Bowler
6910 Chickasaw Bayou Road, Bradenton FL 34203, USA

**Soutendijk, Renee** — Actress
Agentur Dirk Fehrecke, Ludwigkirchplatz 2, 10719 Berlin, Germany , USA

**Souter, David H** — Supreme Court Justice
214 Hopkins Green Road, Contoocook NH 03229, USA

**Southam, James** — Cross Counry Skier
18230 Norway Dr, Anchorage AK 99516, USA

**Souther, J D** — Singer, Guitarist, Songwriter
Paul Hanan Mgmt, 7775 Sunset Blvd, #118, Los Angeles CA 90046, USA

**Southern, Edwin M** — Biochemist
Oxford University, Wellington Square, Oxford OX1 2JD, England

**Southern, Silas (Eddie)** — Track Athlete
2006 Custer Parkway, Richardson TX 75080, USA

**Southern, Taryn** — Actress, Singer
I C M Partners, 10250 Constellation Blvd, #900, Los Angeles CA 90067 USA

**Southwick, Leslie H** — Judge
US Court of Appeals, Eastland Courthouse, 245 E Capitol St, Jackson MS 39201, USA

**Southworth, William F (Bill)** — Baseball Player
320 Dobbins Road, Saint Louis MO 63119, USA

**Souto de Moura, Eduardo** — Pritzker Architectual Laureate
University of Oporto, Architecture Faculty, Praca Gomes Teixeira, 4099 002 Oporto, Portugal

**Souza, K Mark** — Baseball Player
1120 Dumas Way, Roseville CA 95747, USA

**Souza, Luciana** — Singer, Composer
Vision Arts Mgmt, 16 Clint Fingers Road, Saugerties NY 12477, USA

**Sova, Peter M** — Cinematographer
1492 Roses Brook Road, South Kortright NY 13842, USA

**Sovern, Michael I** — Educator, Attorney
Columbia University, Law School, 435 W 116th St, New York NY 10027, USA

**Sovran, Gino** — Basketball Player
2669 Cheswick Dr, Troy MI 48084, USA

## S

| Name | Address | Profession |
|---|---|---|
| **Sowell, Arnold (Arnie)** | 1647 Waterstone Lane, #1, Charlotte NC 28262, USA | Track Athlete |
| **Sowell, Jerald M** | 201 Stockton Dr, Southlake TX 76092, USA | Football Player |
| **Sowell, Thomas** | Stanford University, Hoover Institution, Stanford CA 94305, USA | Economist |
| **Sowells, Richard A (Rich)** | 16718 Chewton Glen St, Tomball TX 77377, USA | Football Player |
| **Soyer, Ferdi Sabit** | Prime Minister's Office, Via Mersin 10, Lefkosa, Turkish Northern Cypress | Prime Minister, Turkish Northern Cypress |
| **Soyinka, Wole** | University of Nevada, Creative Writing Dept, Las Vegas NV 89154, USA | Nobel Literature Laureate |
| **Soyster, Harry E** | 56 Lakeview Ave, #14, New Canaan CT 06840, USA | Army General |
| **Sozzi, Sebastian** | Harvest Talent Mgmt, 121 W 80th St, #1, New York NY 10024, USA | Actor |
| **Spaak, Ruth** | 20 Sandfield Road, Stratford upon Avon, Warwickshire CV37 9AG, England | Artist |
| **Spacek, Jaroslav** | 5944 Corinne Lane, Clarence Center NY 14032, USA | Ice Hockey Player |
| **Spacek, Sissy** | PO Box 22, #640, Cobham VA 22947, USA | Actress |
| **Spacey, Kevin** | Joanne Horowitz Mgmt, 9350 Wilshire Blvd, #224, Beverly Hills CA 90212, USA | Actor |
| **Spacks, Patricia M** | 249 E Jefferson St, Charlottesville VA 22902, USA | Educator |
| **Spade, David** | W M E Entertainment, 9601 Wilshire Blvd, #300, Beverly Hills CA 90210 USA | Actor, Comedian |
| **Spade, Kate** | 48 W 25th St, #400, New York NY 10010, USA | Fashion Designer |
| **Spader, James** | I C M Partners, 10250 Constellation Blvd, #900, Los Angeles CA 90067 USA | Actor |
| **Spaelty, Valeria** | Curling Assn, PO Box 606, 3000 Bern, Switzerland | Curling Athlete |
| **Spagnola, John S** | 414 Hillbrook Road, Bryn Mawr PA 19010, USA | Football Player |
| **Spagnuolo, Steve J** | New Orleans Saints, 5800 Airline Highway, Metairie LA 70003 USA | Football Coach |
| **Spain, Douglas** | Kritzer Levine Wilkins Griffin, 11872 La Grange Ave, #100, Los Angeles CA 90025 USA | Actor |
| **Spalding, Esperanza** | Montuno Producciones, Calle Rosello 246, #5-2, 08008 Barcelona, Spain | Singer, Bassist, Composer |
| **Spalding, Leslie** | 1055 O'Malley Dr, Billings MT 59102, USA | Golfer |
| **Spall, Rafe** | Troika, 74 Clerkenwell Road, #300, London EC1M 5QA, England | Actor |
| **Spall, Timothy** | Markham Froggatt Irwin, Julian House, 4 Windmill St, London W1P 1HF, England | Actor |
| **Spampinato, Joey** | Skyline Music, 2270 Maiden Lane SW, Roanoke VA 24015, USA | Bassist (NRBQ) |
| **Spampinato, Johnny** | Skyline Music, 2270 Maiden Lane SW, Roanoke VA 24015, USA | Guitarist (NRBQ) |
| **Span, K Denard** | Washington Nationals, 1500 S Capitol St SE, Washington DC 20003 USA | Baseball Player |
| **Spanbauer, Tom** | Houghton Mifflin Harcourt, 215 Park Ave S, #1200, New York NY 10003 USA | Writer |
| **Spander, Art** | San Francisco Examiner, Editorial Dept, 110 5th Ave, San Francisco CA 94118, USA | Sportswriter |
| **Spangler, Albert D (Al)** | 27202 Afton Way, Huffman TX 77336, USA | Baseball Player |
| **Spani, Gary L** | 3920 NE Sequoia St, Lees Summit MO 64064, USA | Football Player |
| **Spano, Joe** | Sutton-Barth Vennari, 5900 Wilshire Blvd, #700, Los Angeles CA 90036 USA | Actor |
| **Spano, Robert** | Opus 3 Artists, 470 Park Ave S, #900N, New York NY 10016 USA | Conductor |
| **Spano, Vincent** | Kincaid Mgmt, 849 S Broadway, #902, Los Angeles CA 90014, USA | Actor |
| **Spanswick, Willaim H (Bill)** | 1200 Commonwealth Circle, #202, Naples FL 34116, USA | Baseball Player |
| **Sparks, Dana** | Regenerate Films, 1408 E Thousand Oaks Blvd, Thousand Oaks CA 91362, USA | Actress |
| **Sparks, Daniel E (Dan)** | 2396 N Bruceville Road, Vincennes IN 47591, USA | Basketball Player, Coach |
| **Sparks, Hal** | Innovative Artists, 1505 10th St, Santa Monica CA 90401 USA | Actor, Singer, Comedian |
| **Sparks, J Jeffrey (Jeff)** | 714 W 42nd St, Houston TX 77018, USA | Baseball Player |
| **Sparks, Jordin** | Varela Media, 14 E 77th St, #3F, New York NY 10075, USA | Singer, Actress |
| **Sparks, Larry** | Larry Sparks Show, PO Box 505, Greensburg IN 47240, USA | Singer |
| **Sparks, Nicholas C** | United Talent Agency, U T A Plaza, 9336 Civic Center Dr, Beverly Hills CA 90210 USA | Writer |
| **Sparks, Paul** | Gersh Agency, 41 Madison Ave, #3301, New York NY 10010 USA | Actor |
| **Sparks, Phillippi D** | 4812 W Avenida del Rey, Phoenix AZ 85083, USA | Football Player |
| **Sparks, Stephanie** | 48 Redwood Lane, Wheeling WV 26003, USA | Golfer |
| **Sparks, Steven W (Steve)** | 4019 Colony Oaks Dr, Sugar Land TX 77479, USA | Baseball Player |
| **Sparrow, Rory D** | 111 Valley Road, Montclair NJ 07042, USA | Basketball Player |
| **Sparv, Camila** | 1460 Ocean Dr, #311, Miami Beach FL 33139, USA | Actress |

**Sowell - Sparv**

| | |
|---|---|
| **Sparxxx, Bubba**<br>Esterman Entertainment, 12333 Pretoria Dr, Silver Spring MD 20904 USA | Rap Artist |
| **Speake, Robert C (Bob)**<br>4742 SW Urish Road, Topeka KS 66610, USA | Baseball Player |
| **Speakes, Stephen M**<br>Deputy CofStaff, Resourcing/Programs, HqUSA, Pentagon, Washington DC 20310, USA | Army General |
| **Speakman-Pitt, William**<br>Victoria Cross Assn, Old Admiralty Building, London SW1A 2BL, England | Korean War South African Army Hero (VC) |
| **Spear, Laurinda H**<br>Arquitectonica International, 801 Brickell Ave, #1100, Miami FL 33131, USA | Architect |
| **Spearin, Charles**<br>Agency Group Ltd, 142 W 57th St, #600, New York NY 10019 USA | Musician |
| **Spearritt, Hannah**<br>Curtis Brown Group, 28-29 Haymarket St, #500, London SW1Y 4SP, England | Actress, Singer, Model |
| **Spears, Abigail M**<br>15552 Cool Valley Road, Valley Center CA 92082, USA | Tennis Player |
| **Spears, Aries**<br>J K A Talent, 12725 Ventura Blvd, #H, Studio City CA 91604, USA | Actor, Comedian, Writer, Producer |
| **Spears, Britney**<br>Creative Artists Agency, 2000 Ave of Stars, #100, Los Angeles CA 90067 USA | Singer, Actress, Model |
| **Spears, Eddie**<br>N A S S Talent Management, 2212 Lea Ave, Bozeman MT 59715, USA | Actor |
| **Spears, Glen F**<br>Commander, 12th Air Force, Davis-Monthan Air Force Base AZ 85707 USA | Air Force General |
| **Spears, Jamie Lynn**<br>Tri Star Sports & Entertainment, 450 N Roxbury Dr, #602, Beverly Hills CA 90210, USA | Actress |
| **Spears, Marcus D**<br>18634 Cypress Lake Village Dr, Cypress TX 77429, USA | Football Player |
| **Spears, Marcus R**<br>3649 Shady Creek Court, Frisco TX 75033, USA | Football Player |
| **Spears, Stephen**<br>2021 County Road 33, Fair Hope AL 36532, USA | Sculptor |
| **Special Ed**<br>Entertainment Artists, 2409 21st Ave S, #100, Nashville TN 10019 USA | Rap Artist |
| **Speck, Fred**<br>2165 Country Club Dr, #23, Burlington ON L7M 4H4, Canada | Ice Hockey Player |
| **Speck, R Clifford (Cliff)**<br>823 S Nueva Vista Dr, Palm Springs CA 92264, USA | Baseball Player |
| **Speck, Will**<br>Management 360, 9111 Wilshire Blvd, Beverly Hills CA 90210 USA | Director |
| **Specter, Rachel**<br>Kritzer Levine Wilkins Griffin, 11872 La Grange Ave, #100, Los Angeles CA 90025 USA | Actress |
| **Spector, Ronnie**<br>Universal Attractions, 135 W 26th St, #1200, New York NY 10001 USA | Singer |
| **Speech**<br>Agency Group Ltd, 142 W 57th St, #600, New York NY 10019 USA | Rap Artist (Arrested Development) |
| **Speeckaert, Glynn**<br>Dattner Dispoto, 10635 Santa Monica Blvd, #165, Los Angeles CA 90025, USA | Cinematographer |
| **Speed, Horace A**<br>6821 State Boulevard Extension, Meridian MS 39305, USA | Baseball Player |
| **Speed, Lake C**<br>Bud Moore Engineering, 400 N Fairview St, Spartanburg SC 29303, USA | Auto Racing Driver |
| **Speed, Scott A**<br>Red Bull Racing, 136 Knob Hill Road, Mooresville NC 28117, USA | Auto, Truck Racing Driver |
| **Speed, U Grant**<br>139 S 400 E, Lindon UT 84042, USA | Sculptor |
| **Speedman, Scott**<br>Gary Goddard Agency, 10 Sainte Mary St, #305, Toronto, ON M4Y 1P9, Canada | Actor |
| **Speer, Hugo**<br>Independent Talent Group, 40 Whitfield St, London W1T 2RH, England | Actor |
| **Speers, Ted**<br>61515 Brookway Dr, South Lyon MI 48178, USA | Ice Hockey Player |
| **Spehr, Timothy J (Tim)**<br>8524 Briargrove Dr, Woodway TX 76712, USA | Baseball Player |
| **Speier, Chris E**<br>3614 El Encarto Dr, Calabasas CA 91302, USA | Baseball Player |
| **Speight, Lester (Rasta)**<br>T C A/Jed Root, 9220 Sunset Blvd, #315, Los Angeles CA 90069, USA | Actor, Producer |
| **Speights, Marresse**<br>Memphis Grizzlies, 191 Beale St, Memphis TN 38103 USA | Basketball Player |
| **Speigner, Levale**<br>1041 Bond St, Thomasville GA 31757, USA | Baseball Player |
| **Speir, Dona**<br>Playboy Promotions, 2706 Media Center Dr, Los Angeles CA 90065 USA | Model, Actress |
| **Speiser, Jerry**<br>T P A, PO Box 124, Round Corner NSW, Australia | Drummer (Men at Work) |
| **Spektor, Regina**<br>Ron Shapiro Mgmt, 56 W 22nd St, #601, New York NY 10010, USA | Singer, Pianist, Songwriter |
| **Spelke, Elizabeth S**<br>Harvard University, Psychology Dept, Cambridge MA 02138, USA | Psychologist |
| **Spelling, Randy**<br>United Talent Agency, U T A Plaza, 9336 Civic Center Dr, Beverly Hills CA 90210 USA | Actor |
| **Spelling, Tori**<br>594 S Mapleton Dr, Los Angeles CA 90024, USA | Actress |
| **Spellman, Alonzo R**<br>1201 W Queen St, Tulsa OK 74127, USA | Football Player |
| **Spellman, John D**<br>7048 51st Ave NE, Seattle WA 98115, USA | Governor, WA |
| **Spence, A Michael**<br>768 Mayfield Ave, Stanford CA 94305, USA | Nobel Economics Laureate |
| **Spence, Bruce**<br>Johnson & Laird Management, PO Box 78340, Grey Lynn Auckland 1245, New Zealand | Actor |
| **Spence, Gerry**<br>3325 N University Ave, #200B, Provo UT 84604, USA | Attorney |
| **Spence, J Robert (Bob)**<br>3081 Bonita Woods Dr, Bonita CA 91902, USA | Baseball Player |

**S**

# S

**Spence, Nicky** — Opera Singer
I M G Artists, Carnegie Hall Tower, 152 W 57th St, #500, New York NY 10019 USA

**Spence, Sebastian** — Actor
Kirk Talent Agencies, 196 W 3rd Ave, #102, Vancouver BC V5Y 1E9, Canada

**Spencer, Abigail** — Actress
I C M Partners, 10250 Constellation Blvd, #900, Los Angeles CA 90067 USA

**Spencer, Andre** — Basketball Player
1315 W Gage Ave, Los Angeles CA 90044, USA

**Spencer, Baldwin** — Prime Minister, Antigua & Barbuda
Prime Minister's Office, Factory Road, Saint John's, Antigua & Barbuda

**Spencer, Bud** — Actor
Smile Productions, Via Cortina d'Ampezzo 156, 00135 Rome, Italy

**Spencer, Chaske** — Actor
Josselyne Herman Assoc, 345 E 56th St, #3B, New York NY 10022, USA

**Spencer, Chris** — Actor, Comedian
Parallel Entertainment, 9420 Wilshire Blvd, #250, Beverly Hills CA 90212 USA

**Spencer, Daryl D** — Baseball Player
2740 S Larkin St, Wichita KS 67216, USA

**Spencer, Des** — Artist
Sheraton Mirage, Davidson St, Port Douglas 4871 QLD, Australia

**Spencer, Elizabeth** — Writer
402 Longleaf Dr, Chapel Hill NC 27517, USA

**Spencer, Elmore** — Basketball Player
2770 Foxlair Trail, Atlanta GA 30349, USA

**Spencer, Felton L** — Basketball Player
4102 Nicholas Roy Court, Prospect KY 40059, USA

**Spencer, Freddie** — Motorcycle Racing Rider
7055 Speedway Blvd, #E106, Las Vegas NV 89115, USA

**Spencer, George E** — Baseball Player
8160 Hickory Ave, Galena OH 43021, USA

**Spencer, J Robert** — Actor, Singer
Polaris Entertainment, 8048 W 3rd St, #300, Los Angeles CA 90048, USA

**Spencer, James A (Jimmy), Jr** — Football Player, Coach
5331 Talavero Place, Parker CO 80134, USA

**Spencer, Jeremy** — Drummer (Five Finger Death Punch)
10th Street Entertainment, 568 Broadway, #608, New York NY 10012, USA

**Spencer, Jesse** — Actor, Musician
Management 360, 9111 Wilshire Blvd, Beverly Hills CA 90210 USA

**Spencer, Jimmy** — Auto Racing Driver
597 Kenway Loop, Mooresville NC 28117, USA

**Spencer, Jon** — Singer, Guitarist (Pussy Galore)
Rascoff/Zysblat Organization, 250 W 57th St, New York NY 10107 USA

**Spencer, Lara** — Actress
W M E Entertainment, 9601 Wilshire Blvd, #300, Beverly Hills CA 90210 USA

**Spencer, LaVryle** — Writer
Berkley Publishing Group, 375 Hudson St, Basement 1, New York NY 10014 USA

**Spencer, M Shane** — Baseball Player
2858 Manzanita View Road, Alpine CA 91901, USA

**Spencer, Octavia** — Actress
W M E Entertainment, 9601 Wilshire Blvd, #300, Beverly Hills CA 90210 USA

**Spencer, Scott** — Writer
Harper Collins Publishers, 10 E 53rd St, Cellar 1, New York NY 10022 USA

**Spencer, Sean** — Baseball Player
3584 E Calistoga Court, Port Orchard WA 98366, USA

**Spencer, Shawntae** — Football Player
3714 Henley Dr, Pittsburgh PA 15235, USA

**Spencer, Sidney** — Basketball Player
New York Liberty, Madison Square Garden, 2 Penn Plaza, New York NY 10121 USA

**Spencer, Stanley R (Stan)** — Baseball Player
3100 NE 188th St, Ridgefield WA 98642, USA

**Spencer, Timothy A (Tim)** — Football Player
1675 N Pebble Beach Way, Vernon Hills IL 60061, USA

**Spencer, Tracie** — Singer
Richard Walters, PO Box 2789, Toluca Lake CA 91610 USA

**Spencer-Devlin, Muffin** — Golfer
1278 Glenneyre St, #155, Laguna Beach CA 92651, USA

**Spenn, Frederick C (Fred)** — Baseball Umpire
105 Heather Lane, Parrish FL 34219, USA

**Sperber Carter, Paula** — Bowler
10331 SW 102nd Ave, Miami FL 33176, USA

**Sperl, Natalie Denise** — Actress
C E S D, 10635 Santa Monica Blvd, #130, Los Angeles CA 90025 USA

**Sperring, Robert W (Rob)** — Baseball Player
13302 Chriswood Dr, Cypress TX 77429, USA

**Speth, James G** — Government Official
986 Forest Road, New Haven CT 06515, USA

**Spezialy, Tom** — Producer, Writer
Jackoway Tyerman Wertheimer, 1925 Century Park E, #2200, Los Angeles CA 90067 USA

**Spheeris, Penelope** — Director
Spheeris Films, 3940 Laurel Canyon Blvd, #18, Studio City CA 91604, USA

**Spice 1** — Rap Artist
Richard Walters, PO Box 2789, Toluca Lake CA 91610 USA

**Spicer, Kimberly** — Model
Playboy Promotions, 2706 Media Center Dr, Los Angeles CA 90065 USA

**Spicer, Paul** — Football Player
136 Greenbriar Estates Dr, Saint Johns FL 32259, USA

**Spicer, Robert O (Bob)** — Baseball Player
423 McPhee Dr, Fayetteville NC 28305, USA

**Spicer, William E, III** — Physicist
620 Sand Hill Road, #305E, Palo Alto CA 94304, USA

**Spiegel, Scott** — Director
A P A Talent/Literary Agency, 405 S Beverly Dr, #300, Beverly Hills CA 90212 USA

**Spiegelman, Art** — Illustrator, Writer
Raw Books & Graphics, 27 Greene St, New York NY 10013, USA

**Spielberg, David** — Actor
10537 Cushdon Ave, Los Angeles CA 90064, USA

**Spielberg, Robin** — Pianist, Composer
Roots Agency, 108 Glenray Court, New Freedom PA 17349, USA

**Spielberg, Steven** — Director
Amblin Entertainment, 100 Universal City Plaza, #477, Universal City CA 91608, USA

**Spielman, C Christopher (Chris)** — Football Player, Sportscaster
2094 Edgemont Road, Columbus OH 43212, USA

**Spielmann, Gotz** — Director, Writer
I C M Partners, 10250 Constellation Blvd, #900, Los Angeles CA 90067 USA

**Spierig, Michael** — Director
W M E Entertainment, 9601 Wilshire Blvd, #300, Beverly Hills CA 90210 USA

**Spierig, Peter** — Director
W M E Entertainment, 9601 Wilshire Blvd, #300, Beverly Hills CA 90210 USA

**Spiers, Ronald I** — Diplomat
1329 Middletown Road, South Londonderry VT 05155, USA

**Spiers, William J (Bill)** — Baseball Player
9233 Old State Road, Cameron SC 29030, USA

**Spieth, Jordan** — Golfer
Professional Golfer's Assn, PO Box 109601, Palm Beach Gardens FL 33410 USA

**Spiezio, Edward W (Ed)** — Baseball Player
2027 Taller Road, Morris IL 60450, USA

**Spiezio, Scott E** — Baseball Player
7615 Saratoga Road, Morris IL 60450, USA

**Spikes, Cameron W** — Football Player
35 Raven Dr, Bryan TX 77808, USA

**Spikes, Jack E** — Football Player
9537 Highland View Dr, Dallas TX 75238, USA

**Spikes, L Charles (Charlie)** — Baseball Player
531 N Border Dr, Bogalusa LA 70427, USA

**Spikes, Takeo G** — Football Player
5005 Heatherwood Court, Roswell GA 30075, USA

**Spilborghs, Ryan A** — Baseball Player
1204 Suncast Lane, #2, El Dorado Hills CA 95762, USA

**Spiller, Michael A** — Cinematographer
2418 Roscomare Road, Los Angeles CA 90077, USA

**Spillner, Daniel R (Dan)** — Baseball Player
18505 SE Newport Way, #C113, Issaquah WA 98027, USA

**Spilman, W Harry** — Baseball Player
4423 S Saint Phillips Road, Mount Vernon IN 47620, USA

**Spindler, Marc R** — Football Player
6993 Bond Trail, Clarkston MI 48348, USA

**Spindt, Capp** — Inventor (Field Emission Display Screen)
S R I International, 333 Ravenswood Ave, Menlo Park CA 94025, USA

**Spinella, Stephen** — Actor
Innovative Artists, 1505 10th St, Santa Monica CA 90401 USA

**Spinelli, Jerry** — Writer
331 Melvin Road, Phoenixville PA 19460, USA

**Spiner, Brent** — Actor
Innovative Artists, 1505 10th St, Santa Monica CA 90401 USA

**Spinetta, Jean-Cyril** — Businessman
Groupe Air France, 45 Rue de Paris, 95747 Roissy CDG Cedex, France

**Spinks, Cory** — Boxer
6167 Tennessee St, Saint Louis MO 63111, USA

**Spinks, Leon** — Boxer
209 Jones St, Hollister MO 65672, USA

**Spinks, Michael** — Boxer
925 Centre Road, Wilmington DE 19807, USA

**Spinks, Scipio R** — Baseball Player
11422 Rock Bridge Lane, Sugar Land TX 77498, USA

**Spinotti, Dante** — Cinematographer
334 14th St, Santa Monica CA 90402, USA

**Spires, Gregory T (Greg)** — Football Player
26202 Ridgefield Park Lane, Cypress TX 77433, USA

**Spiridakos, Tracy** — Actress
Gersh Agency, 9465 Wilshire Blvd, #600, Beverly Hills CA 90212 USA

**Spiro, Jordana** — Actress
I C M Partners, 10250 Constellation Blvd, #900, Los Angeles CA 90067 USA

**Spirtas, Kevin** — Actor
Stone Manners Salners, 9911 W Pico Blvd, #1400, Los Angeles CA 90035 USA

**Spitz, Mark A** — Swimmer
Premier Management Group, 115 Crescent Commons, Cary, NC 27518 USA

**Spitz, Sabine** — Cyclist
Sabine Spitz Sport Pro, Ralf Schaeuble, Diegeringerstr 17, 79730 Murg, Germany

**Spitzer, Eliot L** — Governor, NY
Current TV, Viewpoint Show, 435 Hudson St, #400, New York NY 10014, USA

**Spitzer, Robert** — Psychiatrist
Columbia University, Psychiatry School, New York NY 10027, USA

**Spitzer, Toby** — Religious Leader, Rabbi
Congregation Dorshei Tzedek, 60 Highland St, West Newton MA 02465, USA

**Spivakov, Vladimir T** — Conductor, Concert Violinist
Kosmodamianskaya Embankment 52, #301, 115054 Moscow, Russia

**Spivey, Ernest L (Junior), Jr** — Baseball Player
4140 S Ambrosia Dr, Chandler AZ 85248, USA

**Spizzirri, Angelo** — Actor
Don Buchwald, 6500 Wilshire Blvd, #2200, Los Angeles CA 90048 USA

**Splatt, Rachelle** — Drag Racing Driver
Rachelle Splatt Racing, 37 MacQuarie Drive, Thomastown VIC 3074, Australia

**Spoelstra, Erik** — Basketball Coach
Miami Heat, American Airlines Arena, 601 Biscayne Blvd, Miami FL 33132 USA

**Spoljaric, Paul N** — Baseball Player
545 Gramiak Road, Kelowna BC V1X 1K4, Canada

**Spong, John S** — Religious Leader
24 Puddingstone Lane, Morris Plains NJ 07950, USA

**Spooneybarger, Tim** — Baseball Player
7815 Eight Mile Creek Road, Pensacola FL 32526, USA

**Spork, Shirley** — Golfer
73010 Somera Road, Palm Desert CA 92260, USA

**Sporkin, Stanley** — Government Official, Judge
US District Court, Courthouse, 3rd St & Constitution Ave NW, Washington DC 20001, USA

**Sporleder, Gregory** — Actor
Brian Wilkins Mgmt, 10585 Santa Monica Blvd, #120, Los Angeles CA 90025, USA

**Sposa, Mike** — Golfer
11678 Sunrise View Lane, Wellington FL 33449, USA

**Spose** — Rap Artist
Agency Group Ltd, 142 W 57th St, #600, New York NY 10019 USA

**Spotakova, Barbora** — Track Athlete
A S C Dukla Prague, Oddil Aletiky, PS 59, 16044 Prague 6, Czech Republic

**Spottiswoode, Roger** — Director
9696 Culver Blvd, #203, Culver City CA 90232, USA

**Spound, Michael** — Actor
Kazarian/Measures/Ruskin, 11969 Ventura Blvd, #300, Studio City CA 91604 USA

**Spradlin, Danny R** — Football Player
1011 Laurie St, Maryville TN 37803, USA

**Spradlin, Jerry C** — Baseball Player
25208 Pennsylvania Ave, Lomita CA 90717, USA

**Spragan, Donald (Donnie), Jr** — Football Player
312 Riviera Dr, Union City CA 94587, USA

**Sprague, Edward N (Ed), Jr** — Baseball Player
4677 Pine Valley Circle, Stockton CA 95219, USA

**Sprague, Edward N (Ed), Sr** — Baseball Player
19015 N Davis Road, Lodi CA 95242, USA

**Sprague, Jack** — Truck Racing Driver
X-Press Motorsports, 610 Performance Road, Mooresville NC 28117, USA

**Spratlan, Lewis** — Composer
Amherst College, Music Dept, Amherst MA 01002, USA

**Sprayberry, Dylan** — Actor
United Talent Agency, U T A Plaza, 9336 Civic Center Dr, Beverly Hills CA 90210 USA

**Sprayberry, James M** — Vietnam War Army Hero
426 Holiday Dr, Titus AL 36080, USA

**Sprecher, Jill** — Director, Producer, Writer
Paradigm Agency, 360 N Crescent Dr, North Building, Beverly Hills CA 90210 USA

**Sprecher, Karen** — Director, Producer, Writer
Paradigm Agency, 360 N Crescent Dr, North Building, Beverly Hills CA 90210 USA

**Spreitler, Taylor** — Actress
Coast to Coast Talent, 3350 Barham Blvd, Los Angeles CA 90068 USA

**Sprewell, Latrell F** — Basketball Player
1120 E Pleasant St, Milwaukee WI 53202, USA

**Spriggs, George H** — Baseball Player
77A W Bay Front Road, Lothian MD 20711, USA

**Spriggs, Larry M** — Basketball Player
23900 Cancuna Court, Huson MT 59846, USA

**Spring, Frank** — Ice Hockey Player
638 Upper Ottawa St, Hamilton ON L8T 3T5, Canada

**Spring, Jack R** — Baseball Player
PO Box 118, Colbert WA 99005, USA

**Spring, Justin E** — Gymnast
University of Illinois, Athletic Dept, Champaign IL 61820, USA

**Spring, Sherwood C** — Astronaut
2116 McDonough Lane, San Diego CA 92106, USA

**Springer, Dennis L** — Baseball Player
1060 W Windsor Court, Hanford CA 93230, USA

**Springer, Jerry** — Entertainer; Mayor, Cincinnati
Coast to Coast Talent, 3350 Barham Blvd, Los Angeles CA 90068 USA

**Springer, Michael (Mike)** — Golfer
1482 E Forest Oaks Dr, Fresno CA 93730, USA

**Springer, Robert C** — Astronaut
202 Village Circle, Sheffield AL 35660, USA

**Springer, Russell P (Russ)** — Baseball Player
PO Box 185, 4357 Highway 8, Pollock LA 71467, USA

**Springer, Steven M (Steve)** — Baseball Player
6962 Carla Circle, Huntington Beach CA 92647, USA

**Springfield, Rick** — Singer, Actor
Doyle-Kos Entertainment, 1 Penn Plaza, #2107, New York NY 10119, USA

**Springs, Alice** — Photographer
Residence Saint-Roman, 7 Ave Saint-Ramon, #T1008, Monte Carlo, Monaco

**Springs, Kirk E** — Football Player
10091 Thoroughbred Lane, Cincinnati OH 45231, USA

**Springs, Shawn** — Football Player
19892 Naples Lakes Terrace, Ashburn VA 20147, USA

**Springsteen, Bruce** — Singer, Songwriter
2 Cross Road, Colts Neck NJ 07722, USA

**Springsteen, Jay R** — Motorcycle Racing Rider
3774 S Shore Dr, Lapeer MI 48446, USA

**Sprinkle, Edward A (Ed)** — Football Player
13340 Edinburgh Dr, Palos Heights IL 60463, USA

**Sproles, Darren L** — Football Player
New Orleans Saints, 5800 Airline Highway, Metairie LA 70003 USA

**Sprouse, Cole** — Actor
I/D Public Relations, 7060 Hollywood Blvd, #800, Los Angeles CA 90028 USA

**Sprouse, Dylan** — Actor
I/D Public Relations, 7060 Hollywood Blvd, #800, Los Angeles CA 90028 USA

**Sprout, Robert S (Bob)** — Baseball Player
1609 Cypress Point, Lady Lake FL 32159, USA

**Sprowl, Robert J (Bobby)** — Baseball Player
4711 Leeward Ave, Northport AL 35473, USA

**Spruce, Andrew (Andy)** — Ice Hockey Player
1223 Kantora Road, Lively ON P3Y 1H8, Canada

**Spurgeon, Jay** — Baseball Player
212 Hartsdale Road, Rochester NY 14622, USA

**Spurlock, Morgan** — Actor, Director
Arlook Group, 205 S Beverly Dr, #209, Beverly Hills CA 90212, USA

**Spurrier, Stephen O (Steve)** — Football Player, Coach
126 Beaver Ridge Dr, Elgin SC 29045, USA

**Spuzich, Sandra** — Golfer
Ladies Pro Golf Assn, 100 International Golf Dr, Daytona Beach FL 32124 USA

**Squibb, June** — Actress
Gage Group, 14724 Ventura Blvd, #505, Sherman Oaks CA 91403 USA

**Squier, Billy** — Singer, Guitarist, Songwriter
Paradise Artists, PO Box 1821, Ojai CA 93024 USA

**Squier, Ken** — Sportscaster
Ken Squier Productions, 9 Stowe St, Waterbury VT 05676, USA

**Squire, Chris** — Bassist (Yes)
Sun Artists, 9 Hillgate St, London W8 7SP, England

**Squirek, Jack S** — Football Player
4051 Vezbar Dr, Seven Hills OH 44131, USA

**Squires, Michael L (Mike)** — Baseball Player
9548 Autumnwood Circle, Kalamazoo MI 49009, USA

**Squyres, Steven W** — Space Scientist
Cornell University, Planetary Science Dept, Ithaca NY 14853, USA

**Srinivasan, Rangaswamy** — Inventor (Excimer Laser)
UVTech Assoc, 98 Cedar Lane, Ossining NY 10562, USA

**Srinivasan, Skikanth (Sri)** — Judge
US Court of Appeals, 333 Constitution Ave NW, #4400, Washington DC 20001, USA

**St Clair, Jessica** — Actress, Comedienne
Creative Artists Agency, 2000 Ave of Stars, #100, Los Angeles CA 90067 USA

**St Clair, R Michael (Mike)** — Football Player
1606 Birchwood Ave, Cincinnati OH 45224, USA

**St Clair, Robert B (Bob)** — Football Player
3312 Parker Hill Road, Santa Rosa CA 95404, USA

**St Croix, Rick** — Ice Hockey Player
27 Brigantine Bay, Winnipeg MB R3P 1R1, Canada

**St Esprit, Patrick** — Actor
Abrams Artists, 9200 W Sunset Blvd, #1125, West Hollywood CA 90069 USA

**St George, William R** — Navy Admiral
862 San Antonio Place, San Diego CA 92106, USA

**St James, Lyn** — Auto Racing Driver
L S J Racing, 57 Gasoline Alley, #D, Indianapolis IN 46222, USA

**St James, Rebecca** — Singer
Smallbone Mgmt, PO Box 1524, Franklin TN 37065, USA

**St Jean, Leonard W (Len).** — Football Player
32 Ledgebrook Ave, Stoughton MA 02072, USA

**St John, Jill** — Actress
Borinstein Oreck Bogart, 3172 Dona Susana Dr, Studio City CA 91604 USA

**St John, Kristoff** — Actor, Producer
21781 Ventura Blvd, Woodland Hills CA 91364, USA

**St John, Lara** — Concert Violinist
Barrett Vantage Artists, 505 8th Ave, #601, New York NY 10018, USA

**St John, Paige** — Journalist
Sarasota Herald-Tribune, Editorial Dept, 1741 Main St, Sarasota FL 34236, USA

**St John, Scott** — Concert Violinist, Viola Player
Frank Salomon, 121 W 27th St, #703, New York NY 10001 USA

**St John, Trevor** — Actor
Innovative Artists, 1505 10th St, Santa Monica CA 90401 USA

**St Laurent, Andre** — Ice Hockey Player
947 Rue Riverview, Otterburn Park QC J3H 1Z1, Canada

**St Laurent, Dollard H** — Ice Hockey Player
Les Tour Angrignons, 1500 Angrignon Blvd, LaSalle QC H8N 3H8, Canada

**St Louis, Frantz** — Actor
Artists Agency, 9430 Olympic Blvd, Beverly Hills CA 90212 USA

**St Louis, Martin** — Ice Hockey Player
18145 Longwater Run Dr, Tampa FL 33647, USA

**St Marseille, Francis L (Frank)** — Ice Hockey Player
RR 4, Ashton ON 0A 1B0, Canada

**St Patrick, Mathew** — Actor
Ace Media, 9200 W Sunset Blvd, #1000, Los Angeles CA 90069, USA

**St Pier, Natasha** — Singer
Guy Cloutier, 446 Blvd Saint Lautenbur 900, Montreal QC H2W 1Z5, Canada

**St Pierre, Brian** — Football Player
Carolina Panthers, Ericsson Stadium, 800 S Mint St, Charlotte NC 28202 USA

**St Pierre, Monique** — Model, Actress
Playboy Promotions, 2706 Media Center Dr, Los Angeles CA 90065 USA

**Staab, Rebecca** — Actress
Stone Manners Salners, 9911 W Pico Blvd, #1400, Los Angeles CA 90035 USA

**Staal, Eric C** — Ice Hockey Player
6009 Over Hadden Court, Raleigh NC 27614, USA

**Staal, Jordan** — Ice Hockey Player
Candy Mountain Road, RR 6, Thunder Bay ON P7C 5N5, Canada

**Stabile, Nick** — Actor
Raw Talent Mgmt, 9615 Brighton Way, #300, Beverly Hills CA 90210 USA

**Stabiner, Karen** — Writer
Voice/Hyperion Books, 77 W 66th St, #1100, New York NY 10023, USA

**Stablein, Brian P** — Football Player
2023 Woodland Hall Dr, Delaware OH 43015, USA

**Stablein, George C** — Baseball Player
2903 Penman, Tustin CA 92782, USA

**Stabler, Ken M (Kenny)** — Football Player
7311 Bay Road, #A, Mobile AL 36605, USA

**Stacey Q** — Singer, Actress, Songwriter
641 S Palm St, #D, La Habra CA 90631, USA

**Stacey, John** — Actor
Gavin Barker Assoc, 2D Wimpole St, London W1G 0EB, England

**Stackhouse, Jerry D** — Basketball Player
5266 Settles Bridge Road, Suwanee GA 30024, USA

**Stackhouse, Ron** — Ice Hockey Player
RR 2, Haliburton ON K0M 1S0, Canada

**Stackpole, H C (Hank)** — Marine Corps General
Asia-Pacific Security Studies Center, 2058 Maluhia Road, Honolulu HI 96815, USA

**Stackpole, Michael A** — Writer
PO Box 60333, Phoenix AZ 85082, USA

**Stacomb, Kevin M** — Basketball Player
14 Florida Ave, Jamestown RI 02835, USA

**Stacy, Billy M** — Football Player
400 Colonial Circle, Starkville MS 39759, USA

**Stacy, Hollis** — Golfer
405 74th St, Holmes Beach FL 34217, USA

**Stacy, Peter (Spider)** — Singer (Pogues)
Agency Group Ltd, 361-373 City Road, London EC1V 1PQ, England

**Stadlen, Lewis J** — Actor
Gage Group, 450 7th Ave, #1809, New York NY 10123 USA

**Stadler, Craig R** — Golfer
113 Elk Crossing, Evergreen CO 80439, USA

**Stadler, Sergei V** — Concert Violinist, Conductor
Kaiserstr 43, 80801 Munich, Germany

**Stadtman, Thressa C** — Biochemist
16907 Redland Road, Derwood MD 20855, USA

**Staehle, Marvin G (Marv)** — Baseball Player
19421 Cromwell Court, #208, Fort Myers FL 33912, USA

**Stafford, J Matthew** — Football Player
Detroit Lions, 222 Republic Dr, Allen Park MI 48101 USA

**Stafford, James Francis Cardinal** — Religious Leader
Pontifical Council for the Laity, Piazza S Calisto 16, 00153 Rome, Italy

**Stafford, James W (Jim)** — Singer, Songwriter
Dick Hall Productions, 1767 Lakewood Ranch Blvd, Bradenton FL 34211, USA

**Stafford, Jimmy** — Guitarist (Train)
Jon Landau, 150 Rowayton Ave, Norwalk CT 06853, USA

**Stafford, Michelle** — Actress
Glick Agency, 1250 6th St, #100, Santa Monica CA 90401, USA

**Stafford, Nancy** — Actress
PO Box 3353, Westlake Village CA 91359, USA

**Stafford, Thomas P** — Astronaut, Air Force General
A V D, PO Box 604, Glenn Dale MD 20769, USA

**Stafford-Clark, Max** — Director, Actor
Royal Court Theatre, Sloane Square, London SW1 8AS, England

**Stager, Gus** — Swimming Coach
University of Michigan, Athletic Dept, Ann Arbor MI 48104, USA

**Staggers, Jonathan L (Jon), Jr** — Football Player
3835 Oakes Dr, Hayward CA 94542, USA

**Staggs, Jeffrey H (Jeff)** — Football Player
4641 Jeri Way, El Cajon CA 92020, USA

**Stahl, Georgia** — Actress
Sokoll & Friends Eventmanagement, Im Husarenlager 12A, 76187 Karlsruhe, Germany

**Stahl, Larry F** — Baseball Player
1506 E Main St, #A, Belleville IL 62221, USA

**Stahl, Lesley R** — Commentator
CBS-TV, News Dept, 51 W 52nd St, New York NY 10019 USA

**Stahl, Lisa** — Actress
Peak Models & Talent, 25852 McBean Parkway, #190, Valencia CA 91355, USA

**Stahl, Nick** — Actor
I C M Partners, 10250 Constellation Blvd, #900, Los Angeles CA 90067 USA

**Stahl, Norman H** — Judge
US Court of Appeals, 1 Courthouse Way, Boston MA 02210, USA

**Stahl-David, Michael** — Actor
B/W/R, 9100 Wilshire Blvd, #500W, Beverly Hills CA 90212 USA

**Stahle, Louise** — Golfer
Gaylord Sports Mgmt, 13845 N Northsight Blvd, #200, Scottsdale AZ 85260 USA

**Stahler, Jeff** — Editorial Cartoonist
United Feature Syndicate, PO Box 5610, Cincinnati OH 45201 USA

**Stahoviak, Scott E** — Baseball Player
507 Balmoral Court, Grayslake IL 60030, USA

**Stai, Brenden M** — Football Player
5333 New Castle Road, Lincoln NE 68516, USA

**Staiano-Coico, Lisa** — Educator
City College of New York, President's Office, 160 Convent Ave, New York NY 10031, USA

**Staiger, Roy J** — Baseball Player
1233 Tyler Dr, Lebanon MO 65536, USA

**Staios, Steve** — Ice Hockey Player
1213 Newbridge Trace NE, Atlanta GA 30319, USA

**Stairs, Matthew W (Matt)** — Baseball Player
79 Skyline Road, Bangor ME 04401, USA

**Staite, Jewel** — Actress
Elements Entertainment, 1635 N Cahuenga Blvd, #500, Los Angeles CA 90028, USA

**Stajan, Matthew (Matt)** — Ice Hockey Player
1369 Victor Ave, Mississauga ON L5G 3A2, Canada

**Stalder, Keith J** — Marine Corps General
Commanding General, 2nd Marine Expeditionary Force, Camp Lejeune NC 28542 USA

**Staley, Dawn M** — Basketball Player, Coach
Dawn Staley Foundation, 1224 Glenwood Road, Columbia SC 29204, USA

**Staley, Duce** — Football Player
150 N 9th St, West Columbia SC 29169, USA

**Staley, Joan** — Actress, Model
24516 Windsor Dr, #B, Valencia CA 91355, USA

**Staley, William P (Bill)** — Football Player
9210 Todd Road, Potter Valley CA 95469, USA

**Stallard, E Tracy** — Baseball Player
PO Box 905, Wise VA 24293, USA

**Stallard, Tom** — Rowing Athlete
Leander Club, Henley on Thames, Leander RG9 2LP, England

**Stallings, Eugene C (Gene), Jr** — Football Coach
6508 County Road 43200, Powderly TX 75473, USA

**Stallings, George** — Religious Leader
African American Catholic Congregation, 1015 I St NE, Washington DC 20002, USA

**Stallings, Larry J** — Football Player
555 Town Hall Court, Saint Louis MO 63141, USA

**Stallone, Frank** — Actor, Singer, Songwriter
W M E Entertainment, 9601 Wilshire Blvd, #300, Beverly Hills CA 90210 USA

**Stallone, Sylvester** — Actor, Director, Writer
W M E Entertainment, 9601 Wilshire Blvd, #300, Beverly Hills CA 90210 USA
**Stalls, David M** — Football Player
2800 Forest St, Denver CO 80207, USA
**Stallworth, David A (Dave)** — Basketball Player
4400 N Rushwood St, Wichita KS 67226, USA
**Stallworth, Donte' L** — Football Player
6601 53rd St, Sacramento CA 95823, USA
**Stallworth, Issac (Bud)** — Basketball Player
14 Westwood Road, Lawrence KS 66044, USA
**Stallworth, Johnny L (John)** — Football Player
302 Osman Dr, Madison AL 35756, USA
**Stam, Jessica** — Model
International Model Mgmt, 25 Dunlop St E, Barrie ON L4M 1A2, Canada
**Stam, Katie** — Beauty Queen
Miss America Organization, 1370 Ave of Americas, #1600, New York NY 10019 USA
**Stamberg, Josh** — Actor
Abrams Artists, 9200 W Sunset Blvd, #1125, West Hollywood CA 90069 USA
**Stamberg, Peter** — Interior Designer
Stamberg Aferiat Architecture, 126 5th Ave, #13A, New York NY 10011, USA
**Stamer, Joshua L (Josh)** — Football Player
202 Oxford Creek Road, Cary NC 27519, USA
**Stamey, Christopher C (Chris)** — Singer, Guitarist, Songwriter
Conqueroo, 11271 Ventura Blvd, #522, Studio City CA 91604 USA
**Stamile, Lauren** — Actress
Schumacher Mgmt, 10323 Santa Monica Blvd, #101, Los Angeles CA 90024, USA
**Stamkos, Steven** — Ice Hockey Player
Tampa Bay Lightning, 401 Channelside Dr, Tampa FL 33602 USA
**Stamler, Lorne** — Ice Hockey Player
2806 Marie Court, Clearwater FL 33761, USA
**Stamm, Daniel** — Director, Writer
Creative Artists Agency, 2000 Ave of Stars, #100, Los Angeles CA 90067 USA
**Stamm, Michael E (Mike)** — Swimmer
3929 Everett Ave, Oakland CA 94602, USA
**Stamos, John** — Actor
Brillstein Entertainment Partners, 9150 Wilshire Blvd, #350, Beverly Hills CA 90212 USA
**Stamp, Terence** — Actor
Untitled Entertainment, 350 S Beverly Dr, #200, Beverly Hills CA 90212 USA
**Stampley, Joe** — Singer, Songwriter
Joe Taylor Artist Agency, 2802 Columbine Place, Nashville TN 37204 USA
**Stamps, Sylvester** — Football Player
1831 Eisenhower Dr, Vicksburg MS 39180, USA
**Stams, Frank M** — Football Player
2870 Marcia Blvd, Cuyahoga Falls OH 44223, USA
**Stan, Sebastian** — Actor
W M E Entertainment, 9601 Wilshire Blvd, #300, Beverly Hills CA 90210 USA
**Stanat, Dug** — Sculptor, Animator
46828 Bradley St, Fremont CA 94539, USA
**Stanback, Haskell L** — Football Player
1523 Windward Dr, Locust Grove GA 30248, USA
**Stanbury, John B** — Pharmacologist
10 Longwood Dr, #106, Westwood MA 02090, USA
**Stanchfield, Darby** — Actress
Principal Entertainment, 9255 Sunset Blvd, #500, Los Angeles CA 90069 USA
**Standhardt, Kenneth** — Artist
4875 Garnet St, Eugene OR 97405, USA
**Standiford, Les** — Writer
Harper/Collins, 10 E 53rd St, Cellar 1, New York NY 10022, USA
**Standing, George** — Ice Hockey Player
34 Cliff Ave, Huntsville ON P1H 1G1, Canada
**Standing, John** — Actor
United Agents, 12-26 Lexington St, London W1F 0LE, England
**Standridge, Jason** — Baseball Player
6228 Cardinal Dr, Pinson AL 35126, USA
**Stanek, Al** — Baseball Player
96 Allyn St, Holyoke MA 01040, USA
**Stanfel, Richard (Dick)** — Football Player, Coach
1104 Juniper Parkway, Libertyville IL 60048, USA
**Stanfield, Frederic W (Fred)** — Ice Hockey Player
59 Cheshire Lane, East Amherst NY 14051, USA
**Stanfield, Kevin B** — Baseball Player
7565 Newcomb St, San Bernardino CA 92410, USA
**Stanfill, William T (Bill)** — Football Player
3117 Wisteria Court, Albany GA 31721, USA
**Stanford, Aaron** — Actor
Management 360, 9111 Wilshire Blvd, Beverly Hills CA 90210 USA
**Stanford, Angela** — Golfer
6225 Pecan Orchard Court, Fort Worth TX 76179, USA
**Stanford, Jason** — Baseball Player
4505 W Mesquital del Oro, Tucson AZ 85742, USA
**Stang, Peter J** — Organic Chemist
University of Utah, Chemistry Dept, Salt Lake City UT 84112, USA
**Stangassinger, Thomas** — Alpine Skier
Hofgasse 19, 5422 Durenberg-Hallein, Austria
**Stange, A Lee** — Baseball Player
436 Dolphin St, Melbourne Beach FL 32951, USA
**Stange, Maya** — Actress
L M C M, 99 Spring St, #100, Bondi Junction NSW 2022, Australia
**Stanhope, Douglas G (Doug)** — Actor, Comedian
Gersh Agency, 9465 Wilshire Blvd, #600, Beverly Hills CA 90212 USA
**Stanhouse, Donald J (Don)** — Baseball Player
4 Creekmere Dr, Roanoke TX 76262, USA
**Stanich, George** — Track Athlete, Basketball Player
15816 Marigold Ave, Gardena CA 90249, USA
**Stanifer, Rob** — Baseball Player
13547 Las Palmas Dr, Largo FL 33774, USA

**Stanka, Joe D** — Baseball Player
32718 Weymouth Court, Fulshear TX 77441, USA

**Stankalla, Stefan** — Alpine Skier
Furstenstr 14, 82467 Garmisch-Partenkirchen, Germany

**Stankiewicz, Andrew N (Andy)** — Baseball Player
9729 Wren Bluff Dr, San Diego CA 92127, USA

**Stankiewicz, Myron** — Ice Hockey Player
53 Tynedale Ave, London ON N6H 5P6, Canada

**Stankovic, Borislav (Boris)** — Basketball Executive
PO Box 7005, 81479 Munich, Germany

**Stankowski, Paul** — Golfer
4713 Rangewood Dr, Flower Mound TX 75028, USA

**Stanley, B Chadwick (Chad)** — Football Player
21451 Merlot Lane, Tyler TX 75703, USA

**Stanley, Christopher** — Actor
A P A Talent/Literary Agency, 405 S Beverly Dr, #300, Beverly Hills CA 90212 USA

**Stanley, Daryl** — Ice Hockey Player
PO Box 164, Balmoral MB R0C 0H0, Canada

**Stanley, Frederick B (Fred)** — Baseball Player
2109 Winthrop Hill Road, Argyle TX 76226, USA

**Stanley, James C (Jim)** — Producer, Writer
Paradigm Agency, 360 N Crescent Dr, North Building, Beverly Hills CA 90210 USA

**Stanley, Marianne Crawford** — Basketball Coach
Los Angeles Sparks, 888 S Figueroa St, #2010, Los Angeles CA 90017 USA

**Stanley, Mitchell J (Mickey)** — Baseball Player
6370 Cunningham Lake Road, Brighton MI 48116, USA

**Stanley, P Stephen** — Navy Admiral
Director, Force Structure Resources, Joint Staff, Pentagon, Washington DC 20318 USA

**Stanley, Paul** — Singer, Guitarist (Kiss)
McGhee Entertainment, 8730 W Sunset Blvd, #200, West Hollywood CA 90069, USA

**Stanley, R Michael (Mike)** — Baseball Player
1108 NE 10th Ave, Fort Lauderdale FL 33304, USA

**Stanley, Ralph** — Guitarist, Singer
7455 Dr Ralph Stanley Highway, Coeburn WA 24230, USA

**Stanley, Ralph, II** — Singer, Guitarist
Class Act Entertainment, PO Box 160236, Nashville TN 37216, USA

**Stanley, Robert W (Bob)** — Baseball Player
30 Tansy Ave, Stratham NH 03885, USA

**Stanley, Samuel L, Jr** — Educator
State University of New York, President's Office, Stony Brook NY 11784, USA

**Stanley, Steven M** — Paleobiologist
4308 Folly Quarter Road, Ellicott City MD 21042, USA

**Stanley, Walter** — Football Player
23977 E Alamo Place, Aurora CO 80016, USA

**Stanowski, Wally** — Ice Hockey Player
227 Mill Road, Toronto ON M9C 1Y3, Canada

**Stansfield Smith, Colin** — Architect
Three Ministers House, 76 High St, Winchester, Hantforshire SO23 8UL, England

**Stansfield, Lisa** — Singer, Songwriter
PO Box 59, Ashwell, Hertsfordshire SG7 5NG, England

**Stansky, Peter D L** — Historian
375 Pinehill Road, Hillsborough CA 94010, USA

**Stantis, Scott** — Editorial Cartoonist (Buckets)
Birmingham News, Editorial Dept, 2200 4th Ave N, Birmingham AL 35203, USA

**Stanton, Andrew** — Animator, Director, Writer
Pixar Animation, 1200 Park Ave, Emeryville CA 94608, USA

**Stanton, Doug** — Writer
Charles Scribner's Sons, 866 3rd Ave, New York NY 10022 USA

**Stanton, Harry Dean** — Actor
14527 Mulholland Dr, Los Angeles CA 90077, USA

**Stanton, Jeff** — Motorcycle Racing Rider
1137 Athens Road, Sherwood MI 49089, USA

**Stanton, Leroy B** — Baseball Player
1751 N Norwood Lane, Florence SC 29506, USA

**Stanton, Michael T (Mike)** — Baseball Player
PO Box 1154, Woodinville WA 98072, USA

**Stanton, Molly** — Actress
Gersh Agency, 9465 Wilshire Blvd, #600, Beverly Hills CA 90212 USA

**Stanton, Paul** — Ice Hockey Player
2150 Sheepshead Dr, Naples FL 34102, USA

**Stanton, Phil** — Entertainer (Blue Man Group)
Blue Man Group Productions, 411 Lafayette St, #300, New York NY 10003, USA

**Stanton, W Michael (Mike)** — Baseball Player
19602 Indigo Lake Dr, Magnolia TX 77355, USA

**Stanton-Ogulnick, Alysa** — Religious Leader, Rabbi
Congregation Bayt Shalom, 4351 E 10th St, Greenville NC 27858, USA

**Stanzler, Wendey** — Director, Producer
Verve Talent/Literary Agency, 9696 Culver Blvd, #301, Culver City CA 90232 USA

**Stapinski, Helene** — Writer
Saint Martin's Press, 175 5th Ave, #400, New York NY 10010 USA

**Staple, Neville E** — Singer, Percussionist (Specials)
1st 4 UK Artists, 4 Spencer Walk, Tilbury RM18 8XJ, England

**Staples, Mavis** — Singer (Staple Singers)
PO Box 498360, Chicago IL 60649, USA

**Stapleton, David L** — Baseball Player
51 N Bayview Ave, Fairhope AL 36532, USA

**Stapleton, Kevin** — Actor
Roth Assoc, 250 W 85th St, New York NY 10024, USA

**Stapleton, Mike** — Ice Hockey Player
7719 Cottage Dr, Bellaire MI 49615, USA

**Stapleton, Oliver** — Cinematographer
Independent Talent Group, 40 Whitfield St, London W1T 2RH, England

**Stapleton, Pat** — Ice Hockey Player
623 Saulsberry St, Strathroy ON N7G 3R4, Canada

**Stapleton, Sullivan** — Actor
W M E Entertainment, 9601 Wilshire Blvd, #300, Beverly Hills CA 90210 USA

**Stapleton, Walter K** — Judge
US Court of Appeals, Federal Building, 844 N King St, Wilmington DE 19801, USA

**Stapp, Scott** — Singer (Creed), Lyricist
W M E Entertainment, 9601 Wilshire Blvd, #300, Beverly Hills CA 90210 USA

**Star, Darren W** — Director, Producer
Darren Star Productions, 9200 Sunset Blvd, #430, Los Angeles CA 90069, USA

**Star, Ryan** — Singer, Songwriter
Creative Artists Agency, 2000 Ave of Stars, #100, Los Angeles CA 90067 USA

**Starbird, Kate** — Basketball Player
Indiana Fever, Conseco Fieldhouse, 125 S Pennsylvania, Indianapolis IN 46204 USA

**Starbuck, Jo Jo** — Figure Skater
33 Pomeroy Road, Madison NJ 07940, USA

**Starck, Philippe** — Architect, Industrial Designer
Starck-Ubix, 27 Rue Pierre Poli, 92130 Issey-le-Mooulineaux, France

**Stardust, Alvin** — Singer, Guitarist, Actor
Shout Promotions, PO Box 42, Manchester M46 0WX, England

**Starfield, Barbara H** — Physician
Johns Hopkins University, Hygiene School, 624 N Broadway, Baltimore MD 21205, USA

**Stargell, Tony L** — Football Player
131 Jenny Road, Grantville GA 30220, USA

**Starikov, Sergei V** — Ice Hockey Player
209 Greenbrook Road, Green Brook NJ 08812, USA

**Stark, Dennis J (Denny)** — Baseball Player
213 N Elm St, Edgerton OH 43517, USA

**Stark, Don** — Actor
Premier Talent Group, 4370 Tujunda Ave, #110, Studio City CA 91604, USA

**Stark, Jonathan** — Tennis Player
11593 NW Blackhawk Dr, Portland OR 97229, USA

**Stark, Koo** — Actress
Rebecca Blond, 69A King's Road, London SW3 4NX, England

**Stark, Matthew S (Matt)** — Baseball Player
3203 E Birchwood Place, Chandler AZ 85249, USA

**Stark, Melissa** — Sportscaster, Commentator
NBC-TV, News Dept, 30 Rockefeller Plaza, #270E, New York NY 10112 USA

**Stark, Nathan J** — Attorney
4000 Cathedral Ave NW, #132, Washington DC 20016, USA

**Stark, Rohn T** — Football Player
PO Box 10067, Lahaina HI 96761, USA

**Starke, Anthony** — Actor
Geddes Agency, 8430 Santa Monica Blvd, #201, West Hollywood CA 90069 USA

**Starke, George L** — Football Player
1406 Corcoran St NW, #A, Washington DC 20009, USA

**Starks, Duane L** — Football Player
12495 Stoneway Court, Davie FL 33330, USA

**Starks, John L** — Basketball Player
PO Box 8146, Stamford CT 06905, USA

**Starks, Maximillian W (Max), IV** — Football Player
11247 San Jose Blvd, #108, Jacksonville FL 32223, USA

**Starks, Randolph (Randy), Jr** — Football Player
2535 SW 105th Terrace, Davie FL 33324, USA

**Starks, Scott D** — Football Player
12774 Oxford Crossing Dr, Jacksonville FL 32224, USA

**Starkweather, Gary K** — Optical Engineer
10274 Parkwood Dr, #7, Cupertino CA 95014, USA

**Starling, H Denby** — Navy Admiral
Commander, Naval Cyber Command, 2465 Guadalcanal, Little Creek VA 23521, USA

**Starling, James D** — Army General
3581 Joshua Road, Shingle Springs CA 95682, USA

**Starling, John** — Singer, Guitarist
M Hitchcock Mgmt, 1204 Talon Way, Franklin TN 37069, USA

**Starling, Marlon** — Boxer
235 Main St, #9C1, West Hartford CT 06106, USA

**Starn, Douglas** — Photographer
Stux Gallery, 163 Mercer St, #1, New York NY 10012, USA

**Starn, Mike** — Photographer
Stux Gallery, 163 Mercer St, #1, New York NY 10012, USA

**Starner, Shelby** — Singer
Morebarn Music, 30 Hillcrest Ave, Morristown NJ 07960, USA

**Starnes, James R** — WW II Army Air Corps Hero
16001 Lakeshore Villa Dr, #330, Tampa FL 33613, USA

**Starnes, Vaughn A** — Cardiac, Lung Surgeon
Stanford University Medical Center, Heart/Lung Transplant Dept, Stanford CA 94305, USA

**Starr, Albert** — Cardiac Surgeon
1792 SW Montgomery Dr, Portland OR 97201, USA

**Starr, B Bartlett (Bart)** — Football Player, Coach
2065 Royal Fern Lane, Birmingham AL 35244, USA

**Starr, Blaze** — Exotic Dancer
HC 70, Box 1477, Wilsonville WV 25699, USA

**Starr, Brenda K** — Singer
Brothers Management Assoc, 141 Dunbar Ave, Fords NJ 08863 USA

**Starr, David** — Auto, Truck Racing Driver
Boys Will Be Boys Racing, 610 Performance Road, Mooresville NC 28115, USA

**Starr, Kay** — Singer
Ira Okun Entertainment, 1459 Lauren Court, Encinitas CA 92024, USA

**Starr, Kenneth W** — Government Official, Judge
Baylor University, President's Office, Waco TX 76798, USA

**Starr, Martin** — Actor
United Talent Agency, U T A Plaza, 9336 Civic Center Dr, Beverly Hills CA 90210 USA

**Starr, Paul E** — Sociologist
Princeton University, Sociology Dept, Green Hall, Princeton NJ 08544, USA

**Starr, Randy** — Singer (Insiders), Songwriter
D D S, 230 Park Ave, New York NY 10169, USA

**Starr, Richard E (Dick)** — Baseball Player
613 N Crescent Dr, Kittanning PA 16201, USA

**Starr, Ringo** — Singer, Drummer (Beatles)
Rocca Bella, 90 Jermyn St, #100, London SW1Y 6JD, England

**Starrette, Herman P (Herm)** — Baseball Player
103 Howard Pond Loop, Statesville NC 28625, USA
**Starring, Stephen D** — Football Player
9035 S Tenaya Way, Las Vegas NV 89113, USA
**Starzewski, Tomasz** — Fashion Designer
House of Tomasz Starzewski, 15-17 Pont St, London SW1X 9EH, England
**Starzl, Thomas E** — Surgeon
University of Pittsburgh Medical School, Surgery Dept, Pittsburgh PA 15261, USA
**Stashower, Daniel** — Writer
E P Dutton, 375 Hudson St, New York NY 10014 USA
**Stashwick, Todd** — Actor
A P A Talent/Literary Agency, 405 S Beverly Dr, #300, Beverly Hills CA 90212 USA
**Stasiuk, Victor J (Vic)** — Ice Hockey Player
7 Canyon Gardens W, Leftbridge AB T1K 6V1, Canada
**Stassforth, Bowen** — Swimmer
26203 Birchfield Ave, Rancho Palos Verdes CA 90275, USA
**Stastny, Anton** — Ice Hockey Player
Route de Broye 45, 1008 Prilli, Swtizerland
**Stastny, Paul** — Ice Hockey Player
Colorado Avalanche, Pepsi Center, 1000 Chopper Circle, Denver CO 80204 USA
**Stastny, Peter** — Ice Hockey Player
465 S Mason Road, Saint Louis MO 63141, USA
**Staszak, Ray** — Ice Hockey Player
8273 96th Court S, Boynton Beach FL 33472, USA
**Staten, Vince** — Writer
9323 Loch Lea Lane, Louisville KY 40291, USA
**Statham, Harry** — Basketball Coach
McKendree College, Athletic Dept, Lebanon IL 62254, USA
**Statham, Jason** — Actor
Current Entertainment, 9378 Wilshire Blvd, #210, Beverly Hills CA 90212, USA
**Static, Wayne** — Vocalist, Guitarist (Static-X), Actor
United Talent Agency, U T A Plaza, 9336 Civic Center Dr, Beverly Hills CA 90210 USA
**Station, Larry W, Jr** — Football Player
PO Box 471, Seale AL 36875, USA
**Statman, Andy** — Mandolinist
C M Mgmt, 5749 Larryan Dr, Woodland Hills CA 91367, USA
**Staton, Aaron** — Actor
I C M Partners, 10250 Constellation Blvd, #900, Los Angeles CA 90067 USA
**Staton, Candi** — Singer
Celebrity Talent Agency, 111 E 14th St, #249, New York NY 10003, USA
**Staub, Daniel J (Rusty)** — Baseball Player
403 S Sapodilla Ave, #214, West Palm Beach FL 33401, USA
**Staubach, Roger T** — Football Player
5242 Ravine Dr, Dallas TX 75220, USA
**Stauber, Liz** — Actress
Blue Ridge, 535 W 23rd St, #S10A, New York NY 10011, USA
**Stauber, Robb** — Ice Hockey Player
Stauber's Goal Crease, 7401A Washington Ave S, Minneapolis MN 55439, USA
**Stauffer, Timothy J (Tim)** — Baseball Player
1464 Summit Ave, Cardiff CA 92007, USA
**Stauffer, William A (Bill)** — Basketball Player
13808 Sheridan Ave, Urbandale IA 50323, USA
**Staunton, Imelda** — Actress
Conway Van Gelder Grant, 8-12 Broadwick St, #300, London W1F 8HW, England
**Staurovsky, Jason C** — Football Player
4822 E 87th Place, Tulsa OK 74137, USA
**Staveley, William D M** — Navy Admiral, England
Thames Health Authority, 40 Eastbourne Terrace, London W3 2QR, England
**Stavridis, James G** — Navy Admiral
Commander, US European Command, Stuttgart, Unit 30400, APO AE 09128 USA
**Stayskal, Wayne** — Editorial Cartoonist
Tampa Tribune, Editorial Dept, 200 S Parker St, Tampa FL 33606, USA
**Staysniak, Joseph A (Joe)** — Football Player
4094 Forest Dr, Brownsburg IN 46112, USA
**Stead, Erin E** — Illustrator
MacMillan, 175 5th Ave, New York NY 10010 USA
**Stead, Philip** — Writer
MacMillan, 175 5th Ave, New York NY 10010 USA
**Steadman, Alison** — Actress
Artist Rights Group, 4 Great Portland St, London W1W 8PA, England
**Steadman, J Richard** — Sports Orthopedic Surgeon
Steadman Hawkins Clinic, 181 W Meadows Dr, #400, Vail CO 81657, USA
**Steadman, Mark** — Writer
450 Pin-du-Lac Dr, Central SC 29630, USA
**Steadman, Ralph I** — Cartoonist, Illustrator
Old Loose Court, Loose Valley, Maidstone, Kent ME15 9SE, England
**Steadman, Robert L** — Cinematographer
15925 Temecula St, Pacific Palisades CA 90272, USA
**Steagall, Russell (Red)** — Singer, Guitarist
PO Box 136639, Fort Worth TX 76136, USA
**Stearns, Cheryl** — Skydiver
613 Saddlebred Lane, Raeford NC 28376, USA
**Stearns, Jeff** — Actor
Abrams Artists, 9200 W Sunset Blvd, #1125, West Hollywood CA 90069 USA
**Stearns, John H** — Baseball Player
2251 Shell Beach Road, #36, Pismo Beach CA 93449, USA
**Stebbins, Richard V** — Track Athlete
9305 Bahia Track Way, Ocala FL 34472, USA
**Stebbins, Theodore Ellis, Jr** — Art Historian
Harvard University, Fogg Art Museum, Cambridge MA 02138, USA
**Steber, Christopher L** — Actor
Gavin Barker Assoc, 2D Wimpole St, London W1G 0EB, England
**Stecher, Mario** — Nordic Combined Skier
Leins 103, 6471 Arzi im Pitztal, Austria
**Stecher, Renate Meissner-** — Track Athlete
Haydnstr 11, #526/38, 07749 Jena, Germany

| | |
|---|---|
| **Stecher, Theodore P** | Astronomer |
| U I T Project, Goddard Space Flight Center, Greenbelt MD 20771, USA | |
| **Stechschulte, Gene** | Baseball Player |
| 206 Wellington Place, Findlay OH 45840, USA | |
| **Steckel, Les** | Football Player, Coach |
| 195 Blew Court, East Brunswick NJ 08816, USA | |
| **Stecker, Aaron** | Football Player |
| 26 Vernal Spring, Irvine CA 92603, USA | |
| **Ste-Croix, Gilles** | Circus Executive |
| Cirque du Soleil, 8400 2nd Ave, Montreal QC H1Z 4M6, Canada | |
| **Steding, Katy** | Basketball Player, Coach |
| 21625 SW 100th Dr, Tualatin OR 97062, USA | |
| **Steed, Joel E** | Football Player |
| 12607 Blanco Terrace Lane, Houston TX 77041, USA | |
| **Steel of Aikwood, David M S** | Government Official, England |
| Aikwood Tower, Ettrick Bridge, Selkirkshire Sel TD7 5HJ, Scotland | |
| **Steel, Amy** | Actress |
| Imperium 7 Artists, 5455 Wilshire Blvd, #1706, Los Angeles CA 90036 USA | |
| **Steel, Danielle F** | Writer |
| PO Box 470130, San Francisco CA 94147, USA | |
| **Steel, John** | Drummer (Animals) |
| Lustig Talent, PO Box 770850, Orlando FL 32877 USA | |
| **Steele, Allan M, Jr** | Writer |
| 1640 S Sepulveda Blvd, #218, Los Angeles CA 90025, USA | |
| **Steele, Barbara** | Actress |
| 2460 Benedict Canyon Dr, Beverly Hills CA 90210, USA | |
| **Steele, Dan** | Bobsled Athlete |
| US Bobsled & Skeleton Federation, 1631 Mesa Ave, #A, Colorado Springs CO 80906 USA | |
| **Steele, George (Animal)** | Professional Wrestler, Actor |
| PO Box 321343, Cocoa Beach FL 32932, USA | |
| **Steele, J Lendale (Glen), Jr** | Football Player |
| 188 Marshdale Ave SW, Concord NC 28025, USA | |
| **Steele, Jeffrey** | Singer, Songwriter |
| Lofton Creek Records, 13751 Lebanon Road, Old Hickory TN 37138, USA | |
| **Steele, Larry N** | Basketball Player |
| PO Box 372, Vernonia OR 97064, USA | |
| **Steele, Michael** | Singer, Bassist (Bangles) |
| Bangles Mall, PO Box 180, 1341 W Fullerton Ave, Chicago IL 60614, USA | |
| **Steele, Richard** | Boxing Referee |
| 2438 Antler Point Dr, Henderson NV 89074, USA | |
| **Steele, Sarah** | Actress |
| Gersh Agency, 41 Madison Ave, #3301, New York NY 10010 USA | |
| **Steele, Shelby** | Writer |
| San Jose State University, English Dept, San Jose CA 95192, USA | |
| **Steele, Tim** | Auto Racing Driver |
| 11433 24th Ave, Marne MI 49435, USA | |
| **Steele, Tommy** | Singer, Actor |
| International Management Group, 3 Burlington Lane, London W4 2TH, England | |
| **Steele-Perkins, Christopher H** | Photographer |
| 49 Saint Francis Road, London SE22 8DE, England | |
| **Steels, James E (Jim)** | Baseball Player |
| 1654 Via Rico, Santa Maria CA 93454, USA | |
| **Steen, Anders** | Ice Hockey Player |
| Farjestadsvagen 85, Karlstad 85 465, Sweden | |
| **Steen, Jessica** | Actress |
| Bauman Redanty Shaul Agency, 5757 Wilshire Blvd, #473, Los Angeles CA 90036 USA | |
| **Steen, Paprika** | Actress |
| Paradigm Agency, 360 N Crescent Dr, North Building, Beverly Hills CA 90210 USA | |
| **Steenburgen, Mary** | Actress |
| Management 360, 9111 Wilshire Blvd, Beverly Hills CA 90210 USA | |
| **Steenland, Douglas** | Businessman |
| Northwest Airlines, 2700 Lone Oak Parkway, Saint Paul MN 55121, USA | |
| **Steenstra, Kenneth G (Ken)** | Baseball Player |
| 1228 Pheasant Court, Liberty MO 64068, USA | |
| **Steeples, Eddie** | Actor |
| Innovative Artists, 1505 10th St, Santa Monica CA 90401 USA | |
| **Steers, Burr** | Director |
| Creative Artists Agency, 2000 Ave of Stars, #100, Los Angeles CA 90067 USA | |
| **Steevens, Morris D (Morrie)** | Baseball Player |
| 14465 Cadillac Dr, San Antonio TX 78248, USA | |
| **Stefan, Gregory S** | Ice Hockey Player |
| 11243 Maplecroft Court, Raleigh NC 27617, USA | |
| **Stefan, Patrik** | Ice Hockey Player |
| 1450 Bluebird Canyon Dr, Laguna Beach CA 92651, USA | |
| **Stefani, Gwen** | Singer (No Doubt), Songwriter |
| Schiff Co, 9200 Sunset Blvd, #430, West Hollywood CA 90232 USA | |
| **Stefanich, Jim** | Bowler |
| 1444 Coral Bell Dr, Joliet IL 60435, USA | |
| **Stefanik, Mike** | Auto Racing Driver |
| 106 Pierremount Ave, New Britain CT 06053 | |
| **Stefaniuk, Robert** | Actor, Director |
| Loeb & Loeb, 10100 Santa Monica Blvd, #2200, Los Angeles CA 90067 USA | |
| **Stefanovich, Tamara** | Concert Pianist |
| Harrison/Parrott, 5-6 Albion Court, London W6 0QT, England | |
| **Stefanski, Bud** | Ice Hockey Player |
| RR 1, Buckhorn ON K0L 1J0, Canada | |
| **Stefanson, Leslie** | Actress |
| I C M Partners, 10250 Constellation Blvd, #900, Los Angeles CA 90067 USA | |
| **Stefanyshyn-Piper, Heidemarie M** | Astronaut |
| 3722 W Pine Brook Way, Houston TX 77059, USA | |
| **Stefecekova, Zuzana** | Markswoman |
| Jurkovicova 1, 94911 Nitra, Slovakia | |
| **Stefero, John R** | Baseball Player |
| 6239 Chestnut Oak Lane, Linthicum Heights MD 21090, USA | |
| **Steffen, Britta** | Swimmer |
| Regine Eichhorn, Bizestr 1, 13088 Berlin, Germany | |

**S**

Stecher - Steffen

| | |
|---|---|
| **Steffen, James W (Jim)** | Football Player |
| 1440 Westway, Arnold MD 21012, USA | |
| **Steffes, Kent** | Volleyball Player |
| 14675 Titus St, Panorama City CA 91402, USA | |
| **Steger, Charles W** | Educator |
| Virginia Polytechnic Institute, President's Office, Blacksburg VA 24061, USA | |
| **Steger, Michael** | Actor |
| Stone Manners Salners, 9911 W Pico Blvd, #1400, Los Angeles CA 90035 USA | |
| **Stegman, David W (Dave)** | Baseball Player |
| 3234 Simmons Dr, Grove City OH 43123, USA | |
| **Steiger, Ueli** | Cinematographer |
| 2222 Kenilworth Ave, Los Angeles CA 90039, USA | |
| **Steigerwalt, Gary** | Concert Pianist |
| Pro Musicus Foundation, 1351 Ocean Front Walk, #203, Santa Monica CA 90401, USA | |
| **Steilen, Mark** | Director, Writer |
| I C M Partners, 10250 Constellation Blvd, #900, Los Angeles CA 90067 USA | |
| **Stein, Ben** | Actor, Comedian |
| Innovative Artists, 1505 10th St, Santa Monica CA 90401 USA | |
| **Stein, Chris** | Guitarist (Blondie) |
| Agency Group Ltd, 142 W 57th St, #600, New York NY 10019 USA | |
| **Stein, Ed** | Editorial Cartoonist |
| Rocky Mountain News, Editorial Dept, 101 W Colfax Ave, #500, Denver CO 80202, USA | |
| **Stein, Elias M** | Mathematician |
| 132 Dodds Lane, Princeton NJ 08540, USA | |
| **Stein, Gilbert (Gil)** | Ice Hockey Executive |
| National Hockey League, 650 5th Ave, #3300, New York NY 10019, USA | |
| **Stein, Jeremy C** | Government Leader, Economist |
| Federal Reserve System, 20th St & Constitution Ave NW, Washington DC 20551, USA | |
| **Stein, Mark** | Singer, Organist (Vanilla Fudge) |
| Future Vision, 280 Riverside Dr, #12L, New York NY 10025, USA | |
| **Stein, Robert** | Editor |
| McCall's, Editor's Office, 375 Lexington Ave, New York NY 10017, USA | |
| **Stein, W Blake** | Baseball Player |
| 115 Bonne Vie Dr, Brandon MS 39047, USA | |
| **Stein, William A (Bill)** | Baseball Player |
| 10421 Grayhawk Lane, Fort Worth TX 76244, USA | |
| **Steinbach, Alice** | Journalist |
| Baltimore Sun, Editorial Dept, 501 N Calvert St, Baltimore MD 21278, USA | |
| **Steinbach, Eric** | Football Player |
| 2043 W Fletcher St, Chicago IL 60618, USA | |
| **Steinbach, Terry L** | Baseball Player |
| Terry Steinbach Scholarship Fund, PO Box 181, Hamel MN 55340, USA | |
| **Steinbacher, Arabella** | Concert Violinist |
| I M G Artists, Bandelstrasse 35, 30171 Hannover, Germany | |
| **Steinbauer, Ben** | Director, Producer |
| United Talent Agency, U T A Plaza, 9336 Civic Center Dr, Beverly Hills CA 90210 USA | |
| **Steinberg, Daniel** | Physician |
| University of California Medical School, 9500 Gilman Dr, La Jolla CA 92093, USA | |
| **Steinberg, David** | Actor, Comedian, Director |
| Coolwaters Productions, 10061 Riverside Dr, Box 531, Toluca Lake CA 91602 USA | |
| **Steinberg, Jon** | Producer, Writer |
| W M E Entertainment, 9601 Wilshire Blvd, #300, Beverly Hills CA 90210 USA | |
| **Steinberg, Mark** | Concert Violinist |
| Mannes College of Music, 150 W 85th St, New York NY 10024, USA | |
| **Steinberg, Paul** | Cartoonist |
| New Yorker, Editorial Dept, 4 Times Square, Basement C1B, New York NY 10036 USA | |
| **Steinberg, William (Billy)** | Lyricist |
| McDaniel Entertainment, 1311 Broadway, Santa Monica CA 90404, USA | |
| **Steinberger, Jack** | Nobel Physics Laureate |
| 25 Chemin des Merles, 1213 Onex, Geneva, Switzerland | |
| **Steindorff, Scott** | Producer, Writer |
| Stone Village, 1036 Carol Dr, West Hollywood CA 90069, USA | |
| **Steinem, Gloria** | Women's Activist, Editor |
| 118 E 73rd St, New York NY 10021, USA | |
| **Steiner, F George** | Writer |
| 32 Barrow Road, Cambridge, England | |
| **Steiner, Melvin J (Mel)** | Baseball Umpire |
| 27217 White Alder Court, Murrieta CA 92562, USA | |
| **Steiner, Michael** | Sculptor, Artist |
| 704 Broadway, New York NY 10003, USA | |
| **Steiner, Paul** | Editorial Cartoonist |
| Washington Times, Editorial Dept, 3600 New York Ave NE, Washington DC 20002, USA | |
| **Steiner, Peter** | Cartoonist |
| New Yorker, Editorial Dept, 4 Times Square, Basement C1B, New York NY 10036 USA | |
| **Steiner, Tommy Shane** | Singer |
| Collinsworth Bright, 209 10th Ave S, #216, Nashville TN 37203, USA | |
| **Steinfeld, Hailee** | Actress |
| I C M Partners, 10250 Constellation Blvd, #900, Los Angeles CA 90067 USA | |
| **Steinfeld, Jake** | Actor, Body Builder |
| 622 Toyopa Dr, Pacific Palisades CA 90272, USA | |
| **Steinfort, Frederick W (Fred)** | Football Player |
| PO Box 24981, Denver CO 80224, USA | |
| **Steinhafel, Gregg W** | Businessman |
| Target Corp, 1000 Nicollet Mall, Minneapolis MN 55403, USA | |
| **Steinhardt, Arnold** | Violinist (Guarneri String Quartet) |
| Herbert Barrett, 266 W 37th St, #2000, New York NY 10018 USA | |
| **Steinhardt, Paul J** | Physicist |
| 1000 Cedargrove Road, Wynnewood PA 19096, USA | |
| **Steinhardt, Richard** | Biologist |
| University of California, Biology Dept, Berkeley CA 94720, USA | |
| **Steinhauer, Sherri** | Golfer |
| 5010 Hammersley Road, Madison WI 53711, USA | |
| **Steinkraus, William (Bill)** | Equestrian |
| 40 Great Island, Darien CT 06820, USA | |
| **Steinkuhler, Dean E** | Football Player |
| 8041 S 37th St, Lincoln NE 68516, USA | |

| | |
|---|---|
| **Steinman, James R (Jim)** | Composer, Songwriter |
| D A S Communications, 83 Riverside Dr, New York NY 10024, USA | |
| **Steinmetz, Richard** | Actor |
| Melanie Greene Mgmt, 425 N Robertson Blvd, West Hollywood CA 90048 USA | |
| **Steinseifer Bates, Carolyn L (Carrie)** | Swimmer |
| 9309 Benzon Dr, Pleasanton CA 94588, USA | |
| **Steinwedell, Nicole** | Actress |
| I C M Partners, 10250 Constellation Blvd, #900, Los Angeles CA 90067 USA | |
| **Steir, Pat** | Artist |
| 601 W 26th St, #1207, New York NY 10001, USA | |
| **Steirer, Ricky F** | Baseball Player |
| 1015 Haverhill Road, Baltimore MD 21229, USA | |
| **Steitz, Joan A** | Biochemist |
| 45 Prospect Hill Road, Branford CT 06405, USA | |
| **Steitz, Thomas A** | Nobel Chemistry Laureate |
| Yale University, Molecular Biophysics Dept, New Haven CT 06520, USA | |
| **Stelfox, Shirley** | Actress |
| Associated International Mgmt, 7 Hatton Garden, #400, London EC1N 8AD, England | |
| **Stella, Frank P** | Artist, Sculptor |
| 17 Jones St, New York NY 10014, USA | |
| **Stelle, Kellogg S** | Physicist |
| Imperial College, Prince Consort Road, London SW7 2BZ, England | |
| **Stemkowski, Peter D (Pete)** | Ice Hockey Player |
| 146 Albany Blvd, #21C, Atlantic Beach NY 11509, USA | |
| **Stempniak, Lee** | Ice Hockey Player |
| 4469 Clinton St, Buffalo NY 14224, USA | |
| **Stemrick, Gregory E (Greg), Sr** | Football Player |
| 1012 Matthews Dr, Cincinnati OH 45215, USA | |
| **Sten, Sanna** | Rowing Athlete |
| Helsingin Soutuklubi Ry, Kousatie 17 E 10, 00430 Helsinki, Finland | |
| **Stenerud, Jan** | Football Player |
| 6955 Overhill Road, Mission Hills KS 66208, USA | |
| **Stengade, Stine** | Actress |
| Jonathan Arun, 2.06 Clerkenwell Workshops, 31 Clerkenwell Close, London EC1R 0AU, England | |
| **Stenger, Brian F** | Football Player |
| 7921 Kellogg Creek Dr, Mentor OH 44060, USA | |
| **Stenhouse, Michael S (Mike)** | Baseball Player |
| 70 Woodbury Road, Cranston RI 02905, USA | |
| **Stenmark, Ingemar** | Alpine Skier |
| Karlsuddsvagen 58B, 185 93 Vaxholm, Sweden | |
| **Stenner, Charles E, Jr** | Air Force General |
| Chief, Air Force Reserve, HqUSAF, Pentagon, Washington DC 20310 USA | |
| **Stennett, Renaldo A (Rennie)** | Baseball Player |
| 6519 Boticelli Dr, Lake Worth FL 33467, USA | |
| **Stensrud, Michael I (Mike)** | Football Player |
| 304 S Winnebago St, Lake Mills IA 50450, USA | |
| **Stepanek, Ondrej** | Canoeing Athlete |
| S K Neumanna 386, 25001 Brandy's Nad Labem, Tschenchien, Czech Republic | |
| **Stepanova, Maria** | Basketball Player |
| Phoenix Mercury, American West Arena, 201 E Jefferson St, Phoenix AZ 85004 USA | |
| **Stepanovich, Aleksandar (Alex)** | Football Player |
| 939 W 29th St, Lorain OH 44052, USA | |
| **Stepashin, Sergei V** | Prime Minister, Russia; Army General |
| Accounts Chamber, Zubovskaya Pl 2, 119992 Moscow, Russia | |
| **Stephanie** | Princess, Monaco |
| Palais Grimaldi, 2 Blvd du Moulins, 98015 Monte Carlo, Monaco | |
| **Stephanopoulos, George R** | Journalist, Government Official |
| ABC-TV, News Dept, 5010 Creston St, Hyattsville MD 20781 USA | |
| **Stephanopoulos, George R** | Journalist, Government Official |
| 474 W 238th St, #2B, Bronx NY 10463, USA | |
| **Stephanson, Ken** | Ice Hockey Player |
| 6 Heron Road, Box 1491, Siglavik MB R0C 1B0, Canada | |
| **Stephen, Louis R (Buzz)** | Baseball Player |
| 15512 Sycamore St, Porterville CA 93257, USA | |
| **Stephen, Marcus** | President, Nauru |
| President's Office, Government Offices, Yaren, Nauru | |
| **Stephen, Scott D** | Football Player |
| 4132 Palm Tree Court, La Mesa CA 91941, USA | |
| **Stephens, Aaron** | Actor |
| Michael Bruno Group, 13576 Cheltenham Dr, Sherman Oaks CA 91423, USA | |
| **Stephens, Bret L** | Journalist |
| Wall Street Journal, Editorial Dept, 1 World Financial Center, New York NY 10281 USA | |
| **Stephens, G Eugene (Gene)** | Baseball Player |
| 602 Erin Ave, Monroe LA 71201, USA | |
| **Stephens, Jamain** | Football Player |
| 105 W 6th St, Tabor City NC 28463, USA | |
| **Stephens, John M** | Baseball Player |
| 1325 Oak Point Court, Venice FL 34292, USA | |
| **Stephens, Louanne** | Actress |
| Mary Collins Agency, 2909 Cole Ave, #250, Dallas TX 75204, USA | |
| **Stephens, Stanley G (Stan)** | Governor, MT |
| 4 Capitol Court, Helena MT 59601, USA | |
| **Stephens, Thomas G (Tom)** | Football Player |
| 69 Orchard Road, Swampscott MA 01907, USA | |
| **Stephens, Toby** | Actor |
| United Agents, 12-26 Lexington St, London W1F 0LE, England | |
| **Stephenson, Bob** | Ice Hockey Player |
| 8 Tufts Crescent, Outlook SK S0L 2N0, Canada | |
| **Stephenson, C Earl** | Baseball Player |
| 4043 Zacks Mill Road, Angier NC 27501, USA | |
| **Stephenson, Debra** | Actress, Comedienne |
| Independent Talent Group, 40 Whitfield St, London W1T 2RH, England | |
| **Stephenson, Dwight E** | Football Player |
| 6241 N Dixie Highway, Fort Lauderdale FL 33334, USA | |
| **Stephenson, Garrett C** | Baseball Player |
| 947 W State St, Eagle ID 83616, USA | |

**Stephenson, Gordon** — Architect
55/14 Albert St, Claremont WA 6010, Australia
**Stephenson, Jan L** — Golfer
500 Rugby St, Orlando FL 32804, USA
**Stephenson, John H (Johnny)** — Baseball Player
7 Mauroner Dr, Hammond LA 70401, USA
**Stephenson, Neal T** — Writer
Avon Books, 1350 Ave of Americas, New York NY 10019 USA
**Stephenson, Phillip R (Phil)** — Baseball Player
1307 Hancock St, Dodge City KS 67801, USA
**Stephenson, Randall** — Businessman
A T & T Inc, 175 E Houston St, San Antonio TX 78205, USA
**Stephenson, Robert L (Bobby)** — Baseball Player
1518 Brookhaven Blvd, Norman OK 73072, USA
**Stephens-Tysland, Kelly** — Ice Hockey Player
Experience Momentum, 4720 200th St SW, Lynnwood WA 98036, USA
**Stepnoski, Mark M** — Football Player
1131 Meadow Creek Dr, #C1108, Irving TX 75038, USA
**Steppe, M Holbrook (Brook)** — Basketball Player
3486 Clare Cottage Terrace, Palm Desert CA 92211, USA
**Steranka, Joe** — Golf Executive
Professional Golfer's Assn, PO Box 109601, Palm Beach Gardens FL 33410 USA
**Steranko, Jim** — Cartoonist
PO Box 974, Reading PA 19603, USA
**Sterban, Richard A** — Singer (Oak Ridge Boys)
329 Rockland Road, Hendersonville TN 37075, USA
**Sterkel, Jill** — Swimmer
2206 Heritage Well Lane, Pflugerville TX 78660, USA
**Sterling, Annette** — Singer (Martha & Vandellas)
Soundedge Personal Mgmt, 332 Southdown Road, Huntington NY 11743, USA
**Sterling, Maury** — Actor
Innovative Artists, 1505 10th St, Santa Monica CA 90401 USA
**Sterling, Mindy** — Actress
Groundlings, 7307 Melrose Ave, Los Angeles CA 90046, USA
**Sterling, Randall W (Randy)** — Baseball Player
2516 Linda Ave, Key West FL 33040, USA
**Sterling, Tisha** — Actress
PO Box 235, Ketchum ID 83340, USA
**Stern, Daniel** — Actor
C E S D, 10635 Santa Monica Blvd, #130, Los Angeles CA 90025 USA
**Stern, David** — Religious Leader, Rabbi
8500 Hillcrest Ave, Dallas TX 75225, USA
**Stern, David J** — Basketball Executive
National Basketball Assn, 645 5th Ave, #1800, New York NY 10022 USA
**Stern, David J** — Conductor
I M G Artists, Hogarth Business Park, Chiswick, London W4 2TH, England
**Stern, Fritz R** — Historian
15 Claremont Ave, New York NY 10027, USA
**Stern, Gardner** — Writer, Producer
Paradigm Agency, 360 N Crescent Dr, North Building, Beverly Hills CA 90210 USA
**Stern, Gary H** — Government Official, Financier
Federal Reserve Bank, PO Box 291, Minneapolis MN 55480, USA
**Stern, Gerald** — Writer
W W Norton, 500 5th Ave, #600, New York NY 10110 USA
**Stern, Howard A** — Entertainer
Don Buchwald, 10 E 44th St, New York NY 10017 USA
**Stern, Joseph** — Actor, Producer
Creative Artists Agency, 2000 Ave of Stars, #100, Los Angeles CA 90067 USA
**Stern, Marcus** — Journalist
San Diego Union-Tribune, Editorial Dept, 350 Camino Reina, San Diego CA 92108 USA
**Stern, Melvin E** — Oceanographer
Florida State University, Oceanography Dept, Tallahassee FL 32306, USA
**Stern, Michael (Mike)** — Jazz Guitarist
Universal Attractions, 135 W 26th St, #1200, New York NY 10001 USA
**Stern, Robert A M** — Architect
Robert A M Stern Architects, 460 W 34th St, #1800, New York NY 10001, USA
**Stern, Ronnie** — Ice Hockey Player
224 Oakwood Blvd, Hustisford WI 53034, USA
**Stern, Shoshannah** — Actress
C E S D, 257 Park Ave S, #950, New York NY 10010 USA
**Stern, Thomas E (Tom)** — Cinematographer
I C M Partners, 10250 Constellation Blvd, #900, Los Angeles CA 90067 USA
**Sternberg, Robert J** — Psychologist
4321 S Western Road, Stillwater OK 74074, USA
**Sternberg, Sigmund** — Religous Leader, Templeton Laureate
80 East End Road, London N3 2SY, England
**Sternberg, Thomas** — Businessman
Staples Inc, PO Box 9265, Framingham MA 01701, USA
**Sternecky, Neal** — Cartoonist (Pogo)
52 Bluebird Lane, Naperville IL 60565, USA
**Sternhagen, Frances** — Actress
152 Sutton Manor Road, New Rochelle NY 10801, USA
**Sternin, Joshua** — Producer, Writer
Morris Yorn Barnes, 2000 Ave of Stars, #300N, Los Angeles CA 90067 USA
**Sternlicht, Barry** — Interior Designer
Starwood Capital Group, 591 W Putnam Ave, Greenwich CT 06830, USA
**Sterrett, Samuel B** — Judge
US Tax Court, 400 2nd St NW, Washington DC 20217, USA
**Stetter, Karl O** — Microbiologist
Universtat Regensburg, Universitats Str 31, 93053 Regensburg, Germany
**Stetter, Mitch B** — Baseball Player
4237 N Osceola Ave, Norridge IL 60706, USA
**Stettner, Louis** — Photographer
172 W 79th St, #6G, New York NY 10024, USA
**Stettner, Patrick** — Director
United Talent Agency, U T A Plaza, 9336 Civic Center Dr, Beverly Hills CA 90210 USA

| | |
|---|---|
| **Steuer, Ingo** | Figure Skater |
| Liebigstr 9, 09113 Chemnitz, Germany | |
| **Steussie, Todd E** | Football Player |
| 59 Clermont Lane, Saint Louis MO 63124, USA | |
| **Stevenin, Robinson** | Actor |
| Artmedia, 20 Ave Rapp, 75007 Paris, France | |
| **Stevens, Amber** | Actress |
| I C M Partners, 10250 Constellation Blvd, #900, Los Angeles CA 90067 USA | |
| **Stevens, Andrew** | Actor |
| CineTel Films, 8255 Sunset Blvd, Los Angeles CA 90046, USA | |
| **Stevens, April** | Singer |
| 19530 Superior St, Northridge CA 91324, USA | |
| **Stevens, Brad** | Basketball Coach |
| Boston Celtics, 226 Causeway St, #4, Boston MA 02114 USA | |
| **Stevens, Brinke** | Actress |
| PO Box 7112, Van Nuys CA 91409, USA | |
| **Stevens, Carrie** | Model, Actress |
| C A Talent, 25 Palatine, #437, Irvine CA 92612, USA | |
| **Stevens, Charles A (Chuck)** | Baseball Player |
| 12591 George Reyburn Road, Garden Grove CA 92845, USA | |
| **Stevens, Chuck** | Photographer |
| PO Box 422782, San Francisco CA 94142, USA | |
| **Stevens, Connie** | Singer, Actress |
| Brogan Agency, 1517 Park Row Dr, Venice CA 90291, USA | |
| **Stevens, D Lee** | Baseball Player |
| 940 Graland Place, Highlands Ranch CO 80126, USA | |
| **Stevens, Dan** | Actor |
| Julian Belfrage Assoc, 9 Argyll St, #300, London W1F 7TG, England | |
| **Stevens, Dana** | Director, Writer, Actress |
| United Talent Agency, U T A Plaza, 9336 Civic Center Dr, Beverly Hills CA 90210 USA | |
| **Stevens, David J (Dave)** | Baseball Player |
| 2630 Candlewood Way, La Habra CA 90631, USA | |
| **Stevens, Dorit** | Actress, Model |
| 22425 Ventura Blvd, #118, Woodland Hills CA 91364, USA | |
| **Stevens, Eileen** | Social Activist |
| 126 Marion St, Sayville NY 11782, USA | |
| **Stevens, Eric Sheffer** | Actor |
| A P A Talent/Literary Agency, 405 S Beverly Dr, #300, Beverly Hills CA 90212 USA | |
| **Stevens, Fisher** | Actor |
| Paradigm Agency, 360 N Crescent Dr, North Building, Beverly Hills CA 90210 USA | |
| **Stevens, Gary** | Thoroughbred Racing Jockey |
| 136 W Carter Ave, Sierra Madre CA 91024, USA | |
| **Stevens, George, Jr** | Producer |
| C E S D, 10635 Santa Monica Blvd, #130, Los Angeles CA 90025 USA | |
| **Stevens, Howard M, Jr** | Football Player |
| 235 Cedarhurst Lane, Franklinton NC 27525, USA | |
| **Stevens, Jan** | Composer |
| Gorfaine/Schwartz, 4111 W Alameda Ave, #509, Burbank CA 91505 USA | |
| **Stevens, Jeffrey A (Jeff)** | Baseball Player |
| Chicago Cubs, Wrigley Field, 1060 W Addison St, Chicago IL 60613 USA | |
| **Stevens, Jerramy** | Football Player |
| 10047 Main St, #515, Bellevue WA 98004, USA | |
| **Stevens, John A** | Ice Hockey Player, Coach |
| Los Angeles Kings, Staples Center, 1111 S Figueroa St, Los Angeles CA 90015 USA | |
| **Stevens, John Paul** | Supreme Court Justice |
| US Supreme Court, 1 1st St NE, Washington DC 20543 USA | |
| **Stevens, Kenneth N** | Electrical Engineer |
| 15298 SE Oregon Trail Dr, Clackamas OR 97015, USA | |
| **Stevens, Kevin M** | Ice Hockey Player |
| 36 Saint George St, Duxbury MA 02332, USA | |
| **Stevens, Louis D** | Inventor (Disk Storage Device) |
| 421 Coates Dr, Aptos CA 95003, USA | |
| **Stevens, Mark** | Writer |
| New York Times, Editorial Dept, 229 W 43rd St, New York NY 10036 USA | |
| **Stevens, Mick** | Cartoonist |
| New Yorker, Editorial Dept, 4 Times Square, Basement C1B, New York NY 10036 USA | |
| **Stevens, Rachel L** | Actress, Singer (S Club 7), Model |
| Artist Rights Group, 4 Great Portland St, London W1W 8PA, England | |
| **Stevens, Ray** | Singer, Songwriter |
| Bobby Roberts Co, PO Box 1547, Goodlettsville TN 37070, USA | |
| **Stevens, Richard G (Dick)** | Football Player |
| 4100 Cimmaron Trail, Granbury TX 76049, USA | |
| **Stevens, Robert J** | Businessman |
| Lockheed Martin Corp, 6801 Rockledge Dr, Bethesda MD 20817, USA | |
| **Stevens, Robert M** | Cinematographer |
| 1920 S Beverly Glen Blvd, #106, Los Angeles CA 90025, USA | |
| **Stevens, Rogers** | Guitarist (Blind Melon) |
| Shapiro Co, 9229 W Sunset Blvd, #607, West Hollywood CA 90069 USA | |
| **Stevens, Scott** | Ice Hockey Player |
| 280 Spook Hollow Road, Far Hills NJ 07931, USA | |
| **Stevens, Shadoe** | Actor, Entertainer |
| James Kellem Assoc, 8033 Sunset Blvd, #115, Los Angeles CA 90046, USA | |
| **Stevens, Shakin'** | Singer, Songwriter |
| Mgmt Gerd Kehren, Postfach 1455, 41804 Erkelenz, Germany | |
| **Stevens, Stella** | Actress, Model |
| 2180 Coldwater Canyon Dr, Beverly Hills CA 90210, USA | |
| **Stevens, Sufjan** | Singer, Songwriter |
| Billions Corp, 3522 W Armitage Ave, Chicago IL 60647 USA | |
| **Stevens, Taylor** | Writer |
| Crown Publishing Group, 1745 Broadway, #1300, New York NY 10019 USA | |
| **Stevens, Tony** | Bassist (Foghat) |
| J-Bird Entertainment, 248 W Park Ave, #180, Long Beach NY 11561 USA | |
| **Stevenson, Adlai E, III** | Senator, IL |
| 20 N Clark St, #750, Chicago IL 60602, USA | |
| **Stevenson, DeShawn** | Basketball Player |
| 1348 Lake Whitney Dr, Windermere FL 34786, USA | |

**Stevenson, G Raymond (Ray)** — Actor
Conway Van Gelder Grant, 8-12 Broadway St, #300, London W1F 8HW, England

**Stevenson, Jeremy** — Ice Hockey Player
7899 W 6 Mile Road, Brimley MI 49715, USA

**Stevenson, John** — Animator
I/D Public Relations, 7060 Hollywood Blvd, #800, Los Angeles CA 90028 USA

**Stevenson, Juliet** — Actress
68 Pall Mall, London SW1Y 5ES, England

**Stevenson, Miriam J** — Beauty Queen
Miss Universe Organization, 1370 Ave of Americas, #1600, New York NY 10019 USA

**Stevenson, Parker** — Actor
A K A Talent, 6310 San Vicente Blvd, #200, Los Angeles CA 90048 USA

**Stevenson, Turner** — Ice Hockey Player
4530 251st Way NE, Redmond WA 98053, USA

**Stevenson, Venetia** — Actress
4827 Riverton Ave, North Hollywood CA 91601, USA

**Steverson, Todd A** — Baseball Player
109 W Glenhaven Dr, Phoenix AZ 85045, USA

**Stevie B** — Singer, Songwriter
Paramount Entertainment, PO Box 12, Far Hills NJ 07931 USA

**Stew** — Singer, Songwriter, Actor
Paradigm Agency, 360 Park Ave S, #1600, New York NY 10010 USA

**Steward, John** — Drummer (Fishbone)
Silverback Mgmt, 9469 Jefferson Blvd, #101, Culver City CA 90232, USA

**Stewart, Al** — Singer, Guitarist, Songwriter
Chapman & Co Mgmt, 14011 Ventura Blvd, #405, Sherman Oaks CA 91423, USA

**Stewart, Alana** — Actress
Boulevard Mgmt, 21731 Ventura Blvd, #300, Woodland Hills CA 91364, USA

**Stewart, Alec** — Cricketer
Surrey County Cricket Club, Kennington Oval, London SE11 5SS, England

**Stewart, Amy** — Actress
Amsel Eisenstadt Frazier, 5055 Wilshire Blvd, #865, Los Angeles CA 90036 USA

**Stewart, Andrew D (Andy)** — Baseball Player
641 Geddes St, Wilmington DE 19805, USA

**Stewart, Anthony W (Tony)** — Auto Racing Driver
Stewart-Haas Racing, 6001 Haas Way, Kannapolis NC 28081, USA

**Stewart, Bill** — Jazz Drummer
Blue Note Records, 6920 W Sunset Blvd, Los Angeles CA 90028 USA

**Stewart, Blair J** — Ice Hockey Player
1604 Cottenham Lane, Virginia Beach VA 23454, USA

**Stewart, Cameron G (Cam)** — Ice Hockey Player
2929 Buffalo Speedway, #218, Houston TX 77098, USA

**Stewart, Carl E** — Judge
US Court of Appeals, 300 Fannin St, Shreveport LA 71101, USA

**Stewart, Catherine Mary** — Actress
Don Buchwald, 6500 Wilshire Blvd, #2200, Los Angeles CA 90048 USA

**Stewart, Charlotte** — Actress
E J C Mgmt, 6562 Hollywood Blvd, Los Angeles CA 90028, USA

**Stewart, Chelsea** — Soccer Player
Canadian Soccer, Place Soccer Canada, 237 Metcalfe St, Ottawa ON K2P 1R2, Canada

**Stewart, David A (Dave)** — Keyboardist, Guitarist (Eurythmics)
I C M Partners, 10250 Constellation Blvd, #900, Los Angeles CA 90067 USA

**Stewart, David A (Dave)** — Composer
Weapons of Mass Entertainment, 6253 Hollywood Blvd, #1104, Los Angeles CA 90028, USA

**Stewart, David K (Dave)** — Baseball Player
17762 Vineyard Lane, Poway CA 92064, USA

**Stewart, Donald L (Don)** — Televangelist
Don Stewart Ministries, PO Box 2960, Phoenix AZ 85062, USA

**Stewart, Eve** — Art Director, Production Designer
Dattner Dispoto, 10635 Santa Monica Blvd, #165, Los Angeles CA 90025, USA

**Stewart, French** — Actor
Innovative Artists, 1505 10th St, Santa Monica CA 90401 USA

**Stewart, Garry** — Dancer
Australian Dance Theatre, 126 Belair Road, Hawthorn SA 5062 Australia

**Stewart, Ian** — Government Official, England
House of Commons, Westminster, London SW1A 0AA, England

**Stewart, Ian K** — Baseball Player
125 Rainbow Lane, Candler NC 28715, USA

**Stewart, James B** — Journalist
Wall Street Journal, Editorial Dept, 1 World Financial Center, New York NY 10281, USA

**Stewart, James O** — Football Player
4610 34th Ave, Vero Beach FL 32967, USA

**Stewart, Jason** — Actor
Brillstein Entertainment Partners, 9150 Wilshire Blvd, #350, Beverly Hills CA 90212 USA

**Stewart, Jermaine** — Singer
Richard Walters, PO Box 2789, Toluca Lake CA 91610 USA

**Stewart, Jim** — Ice Hockey Player
57 Lincoln St, Spencer MA 01562, USA

**Stewart, John Y (Jackie)** — Auto Racing Driver
Clayton House, Butler Cross, Ellesborough, Bucks HP17 0UR, England

**Stewart, Jon** — Actor, Comedian, Writer
I C M Partners, 10250 Constellation Blvd, #900, Los Angeles CA 90067 USA

**Stewart, Kimberly** — Actress, Model, Producer
Amsel Eisenstadt Frazier, 5055 Wilshire Blvd, #865, Los Angeles CA 90036 USA

**Stewart, Kordell** — Football Player
Robinson Griege Theole, 5950 Sherry Lane, #700, Dallas TX 75225, USA

**Stewart, Kristen** — Actress
Gersh Agency, 9465 Wilshire Blvd, #600, Beverly Hills CA 90212 USA

**Stewart, Larry** — Singer, Guitarist
Fitzgerald-Hartley, 1908 Wedgewood Ave, Nashville TN 37212, USA

**Stewart, Lisa** — Singer
Friedman & LaRosa, 1344 Lexington Ave, New York NY 10128, USA

**Stewart, Martha H** — Businesswoman, Entertainer, Publisher
Martha Stewart Living Omnimedia, 11 W 42nd St, #2500, New York NY 10036, USA

**Stewart, Mary** — Writer
House of Letterawe, Lock Awe, Argyll PA33 1AH, Scotland

| | |
|---|---|
| **Stewart, Matt** | Football Player |
| 4389 Village Club Dr, Powell OH 43065, USA | |
| **Stewart, Melvin, Jr** | Swimmer |
| 7308 Seneca Falls Loop, Austin TX 78739, USA | |
| **Stewart, Michael A** | Football Player |
| 103 Los Padres Dr, Thousand Oaks CA 91361, USA | |
| **Stewart, Natalie** | Singer (Floetry), Songwriter |
| DreamWorks Records, 1000 Flower St, Glendale CA 91201 USA | |
| **Stewart, Patrick** | Actor |
| Independent Talent Group, 40 Whitfield St, London W1T 2RH, England | |
| **Stewart, Paul** | Ice Hockey Player |
| 16 Bridgeview Circle, Walpole MA 02081, USA | |
| **Stewart, Pete** | Singer, Guitarist (Tait) |
| True Artist Mgmt, 227 3rd Ave N, Franklin TN 37064, USA | |
| **Stewart, Philip J** | Ecologist |
| Oxford University, Plant Sciences Dept, Oxford OX1 2JD, England | |
| **Stewart, Potter** | Judge |
| US Court of Appeals, US Courthouse, 100 E 5th St, #317, Cincinnati OH 45202, USA | |
| **Stewart, R J** | Writer, Producer |
| A P A Talent/Literary Agency, 405 S Beverly Dr, #300, Beverly Hills CA 90212 USA | |
| **Stewart, Ralph** | Ice Hockey Player |
| 175 Sherwood Dr, Thunder Bay ON P7B 6L1, Canada | |
| **Stewart, Ray** | Golfer |
| 2777 DeHavilland Place, Abbotsford BC V2T 5E2, Canada | |
| **Stewart, Robert H (Bob)** | Ice Hockey Player |
| 16756 Kehrs Mill Estates Dr, Chesterfield MO 63005, USA | |
| **Stewart, Robert L** | Astronaut, Army General |
| 2864 S Circle Dr, #800, Colorado Springs CO 80906, USA | |
| **Stewart, Roderick D (Rod)** | Singer, Songwriter |
| Artists Group International, 150 E 58th, New York NY 10155, USA | |
| **Stewart, Ryan E** | Football Player |
| 2715 Owens Ave SW, Marietta GA 30064, USA | |
| **Stewart, Scott** | Baseball Player |
| 5243 Hickory Knoll Lane, Mount Holly NC 28120, USA | |
| **Stewart, Shannon H** | Baseball Player |
| 14348 SW 156th Ave, Miami FL 33196, USA | |
| **Stewart, Tommy** | Drummer (Godsmack) |
| Front Line Mgmt, 1100 Glendon Ave, #2000, Los Angeles CA 90024 USA | |
| **Stewart, Tonea** | Actress |
| Alabama State University, Theater Arts Dept, Montgomery AL 36101, USA | |
| **Stewart, Tyler** | Drummer (Barenaked Ladies) |
| Nettwerk Mgmt, 6525 W Sunset Blvd, #800, Los Angeles CA 90028 USA | |
| **Stewart, Will Foster** | Actor |
| 8730 Santa Monica Blvd, #1, West Hollywood CA 90069, USA | |
| **Stewart, William W (Bill)** | Baseball Player |
| 44842 Aspen Ridge Dr, Northville MI 48168, USA | |
| **Stezer, Philip** | Violinist (Emerson String Quartet) |
| I M G Artists, Burlington Lane, Chiswick, London W4 2TH, England | |
| **Stice, Eric** | Psychologist |
| Oregon Research Institute, 1715 Franklin Blvd, Eugene OR 97403, USA | |
| **Stich, Michael** | Tennis Player |
| Ernst-Barlach-Str 44, 25336 Elmshorn, Germany | |
| **Stich, Stephen P** | Philosopher |
| 55 Liberty St, #8A, New York NY 10005, USA | |
| **Sticht, J Paul** | Businessman |
| 11732 Lake House Court, North Palm Beach FL 33408, USA | |
| **Stickel, Fred A** | Publisher |
| Portland Oregonian, 1320 SW Broadway, Portland OR 97201, USA | |
| **Stickles, Edward (Ted)** | Swimmer |
| 1142 Sharynwood Dr, Baton Rouge LA 70808, USA | |
| **Stickney, Timothy D** | Actor |
| Talent Works, 3500 W Olive Ave, #1400, Burbank CA 91505 USA | |
| **Sticky Fingaz** | Rap Artist (Onyx), Actor |
| I C M Partners, 10250 Constellation Blvd, #900, Los Angeles CA 90067 USA | |
| **Stieb, David A (Dave)** | Baseball Player |
| 3375 Cory Dr, Reno NV 89509, USA | |
| **Stieber, Tamar** | Journalist |
| Albuquerque Journal, Editorial Dept, 7777 Jefferson NE, Albuquerque NM 87109, USA | |
| **Stiefel, Ethan** | Ballet Dancer |
| American Ballet Theatre, 890 Broadway, #300, New York NY 10003 USA | |
| **Stiegler, Josef (Pepi)** | Alpine Skier |
| PO Box 290, Teton Village WY 83025, USA | |
| **Stielike, Ulrich (Uli)** | Soccer Player, Manager |
| Casa Postale 78, 2000 Neuchatel, Switzerland | |
| **Stienburg, Trevor** | Ice Hockey Player |
| 2376 Connaught Ave, Halifax NS B3L 2Z4, Canada | |
| **Stienke, James L (Jim)** | Football Player |
| 4707 Interlachen Lane, Austin TX 78747, USA | |
| **Stiers, David Ogden** | Actor |
| Mitchell K Stubbs Assoc, 8695 W Washington Blvd, #204, Culver City CA 90232 USA | |
| **Stieve, Terry A** | Football Player |
| 1407 Vail Place, Saint Louis MO 63104, USA | |
| **Stigers, Curtis** | Singer, Saxophonist |
| Bennett Morgan, 1022 RR 376, #3, Wappinger Falls NY 12590 USA | |
| **Stiglitz, Joseph E** | Nobel Economics Laureate |
| Columbia University, Economics Dept, New York NY 10027, USA | |
| **Stigman, Richard L (Dick)** | Baseball Player |
| 12914 5th Ave S, Burnsville MN 55337, USA | |
| **Stigwood, Robert C** | Producer |
| Barton Manor, Whippingham, East Cowes, PO32 6LB, Isle of Wight, England | |
| **Stiles, Darron** | Golfer |
| 130 Wild Turkey Run, Pinehurst NC 28374, USA | |
| **Stiles, Jackie** | Basketball Player |
| Patrick J Stiles, 115 E Hamilton, Claflin KS 67525, USA | |
| **Stiles, Julia** | Actress |
| Untitled Entertainment, 350 S Beverly Dr, #200, Beverly Hills CA 90212 USA | |

**Stiles, Ryan** — Actor, Comedian
A P A Talent/Literary Agency, 405 S Beverly Dr, #300, Beverly Hills CA 90212 USA

**Stilgoe, Richard** — Lyricist
Noel Gray Artists, 24 Denmark St, London WC2H 8NJ, England

**Still, Arthur B (Art)** — Football Player
9813 Betsy Ross Court, Liberty MO 64068, USA

**Still, Ken** — Golfer
1210 Princeton St, Fircrest WA 98466, USA

**Still, Ray** — Concert Oboist, Conductor
PO Box 504, Saxtons River VT 05154, USA

**Still, Susan L** — Astronaut
N A S A, Johnson Space Center, 2101 NASA Road, Houston TX 77058 USA

**Still, Valerie** — Basketball Player
Valerie Still Foundation, PO Box 452, Powell OH 43065, USA

**Still, William C, Jr** — Chemist
Columbia University, Chemistry Dept, New York NY 10027, USA

**Stiller, Ben** — Actor, Comedian, Director
Red Hour Films, 629 N La Brea Ave, Los Angeles CA 90036, USA

**Stiller, Jerry** — Actor, Comedian
118 Riverside Dr, #5A, New York NY 10024, USA

**Stillman, Cory** — Ice Hockey Player
397 Sweet Bay Ave, Plantation FL 33324, USA

**Stillman, Royle E** — Baseball Player
580 J B Court, Glenwood Springs CO 81601, USA

**Stillman, Whit** — Director
Mosiac Media Group, 9200 W Sunset Blvd, #1000, Los Angeles CA 90069 USA

**Stills, Kenneth L (Ken)** — Football Player
647 Michael St, Oceanside CA 92057, USA

**Stills, Stephen** — Singer, Guitarist (Crosby Stills Nash)
I C M Partners, 10250 Constellation Blvd, #900, Los Angeles CA 90067 USA

**Stillwagon, Jim R** — Football Player
3999 Parkway Lane, Hilliard OH 43026, USA

**Stillwell, Kurt A** — Baseball Player
1105 Lassen View Dr, Westwood CA 96137, USA

**Stilwell, Richard D** — Opera Singer
Columbia Artists Mgmt Inc, 1790 Broadway, #702, New York NY 10019 USA

**Stilwell, Victoria** — Actress
W M E Entertainment, Centrepoint Tower, 103 New Oxford St, London WC1A 1DD, England

**Stinchcomb, Jonathan (Jon)** — Football Player
1010 Chateau Lafitte Dr W, Kenner LA 70065, USA

**Stinchcomb, Matthew D (Matt)** — Football Player
301 Anderson Road, Alameda CA 94502, USA

**Stine, Richard** — Editorial Cartoonist
PO Box 348, Hansville WA 98340, USA

**Stine, Robert L (R L)** — Writer
225 W 71st St, New York NY 10023, USA

**Stiner, Carl W** — Army General
Special Operations Warrior Foundation, PO Box 13483, Tampa FL 33681, USA

**Sting** — Singer, Actor, Bassist, Songwriter
Kathryn Shenker Mgmt, 1776 Broadway, #2205, New York NY 10019, USA

**Stinnett, Kelly L** — Baseball Player
845 N Harris Dr, Mesa AZ 85203, USA

**Stinson, G Robert (Bob)** — Baseball Player
1309 Bando Lane, The Villages FL 32162, USA

**Stinson, Lemuel D** — Football Player
7629 Grassland Dr, Fort Worth TX 76133, USA

**Stinson, Thomas E (Tommy)** — Bassist (Replacement, Guns 'N' Roses)
Agency Group Ltd, 142 W 57th St, #600, New York NY 10019 USA

**Stipanovich, Stephen E (Steve)** — Basketball Player
14 Ridgecreek, Saint Louis MO 63141, USA

**Stipe, J Michael** — Singer (REM), Songwriter
REM/Athens Ltd, 170 College Ave, Athens GA 30601, USA

**Stirling, Rachel** — Actress
United Agents, 12-26 Lexington St, London W1F 0LE, England

**Stirratt, John** — Bassist (Uncle Tupelo, Wilco)
Tom Margherita Mgmt, 2200 W Foster Ave, #2, Chicago IL 60625, USA

**Stitch, Stephen P** — Philosopher
Rutgers University, Philosophy Dept, New Brunswick NJ 08901, USA

**Stith, Bryant L** — Basketball Player
20697 Governor Harrison Parkway, Freeman VA 23856, USA

**Stits, William D (Bill)** — Football Player
1177 Eolus Ave, Encinitas CA 92024, USA

**Stivrins, Alex F** — Basketball Player
11330 Sundown Dr, Scottsdale AZ 85260, USA

**Stix-Brunell, Beatriz** — Ballerina
Morphoses/Wheeldon Co, 800 5th Ave, #18F, New York NY 10065, USA

**Stock, Barbara** — Actress
7329 Capistrano Ave, West Hills CA 91307, USA

**Stock, Mark A** — Football Player
16549 Levade Dr, Leesburg VA 20176, USA

**Stock, P J** — Ice Hockey Player
Team 990, 1310 Greene Ave, #300, Montreal QC H3Z 2B5, Canada

**Stock, Wesley G (Wes)** — Baseball Player
PO Box 1309, Allyn WA 98524, USA

**Stockard, Aaron** — Writer
W M E Entertainment, 9601 Wilshire Blvd, #300, Beverly Hills CA 90210 USA

**Stockdale, Andrew** — Singer, Guitarist (Wolfmother)
John Watson Mgmt, PO Box 281, Surry Hills NSW 2010, Australia

**Stockdale, Gretchen** — Actress
Don Buchwald, 6500 Wilshire Blvd, #2200, Los Angeles CA 90048 USA

**Stocker, Kevin D** — Baseball Player
1204 N Murray Lane, Liberty Lake WA 99019, USA

**Stockett, Kathryn** — Writer
Don Congdon Assoc, 110 William St, New York NY 10038, USA

**Stockman, Shawn** — Singer (Boyz II Men)
Creative Talent Management Group, 433 N Camden Dr, #600, Beverly Hills CA 90210, USA

| | |
|---|---|
| **Stockmayer, Walter H**<br>Willey Hill, Norwich VT 05055, USA | Physical Chemist |
| **Stockton, Dave K**<br>30378 Copper Hill Court, Redlands CA 92373, USA | Golfer |
| **Stockton, David**<br>Dattner Disposto, 10635 Santa Monica Blvd, #165, Los Angeles CA 90025, USA | Cinematographer |
| **Stockton, David, Jr**<br>10 Carrera Dr, Redlands CA 92373, USA | Golfer |
| **Stockton, Dick**<br>5781 NW 24th Ave, #901, Boca Raton FL 33496, USA | Sportscaster |
| **Stockton, John H**<br>538 W Sumner Ave, Spokane WA 99204, USA | Basketball Player |
| **Stockton, Richard L (Dick)**<br>715 Stadium Dr, San Antonio TX 78212, USA | Tennis Player |
| **Stockwell, Dean**<br>Abrams Artists, 9200 W Sunset Blvd, #1125, West Hollywood CA 90069 USA | Actor |
| **Stockwell, Jeff**<br>United Talent Agency, U T A Plaza, 9336 Civic Center Dr, Beverly Hills CA 90210 USA | Writer, Producer |
| **Stockwell, John**<br>I C M Partners, 10250 Constellation Blvd, #900, Los Angeles CA 90067 USA | Actor, Director |
| **Stoddard, Jack**<br>27-4275 Millcroft Park Dr, Burlington ON L7M 4L9, Canada | Ice Hockey Player |
| **Stoddard, Robert L (Bob)**<br>15760 Sunnyside Ave, Morgan Hill CA 95037, USA | Baseball Player |
| **Stoddard, Timothy P (Tim)**<br>4545 Gettysburg Dr, Rolling Meadows IL 60008, USA | Baseball Player |
| **Stoermer, Mark**<br>W M E Entertainment, 9601 Wilshire Blvd, #300, Beverly Hills CA 90210 USA | Bassist (Killers) |
| **Stofa, John C**<br>7344 Jefferson Meadows Dr, Blacklick OH 43004, USA | Football Player |
| **Stogner, Patrick**<br>C E S D, 10635 Santa Monica Blvd, #130, Los Angeles CA 90025 USA | Actor |
| **Stoicheff, Boris P**<br>66 Collier St, #6B, Toronto ON M4W 1L9, Canada | Physicist |
| **Stojakovic, Predrag (Peja)**<br>501 Gibson Dr, #424, Roseville CA 95678, USA | Basketball Player |
| **Stojko, Elvis**<br>Mentor Marketing, 2 Saint Clair Ave E, Toronto ON M4T 2T, Canada | Figure Skater |
| **Stok, Barbara**<br>PO Box 1012, 9701 BA Groningen, Netherlands | Cartoonist (Barbaraal) |
| **Stoker, Michael G P**<br>3 Barrington House, Southacre Dr, Cambridge CB2 2TY, England | Virologist |
| **Stoker, Richard**<br>Ricordi Co, 210 New King's Road, London SW6 4NZ, England | Composer |
| **Stokes, Brian**<br>12140 66th Ave, Seminole FL 33772, USA | Baseball Player |
| **Stokes, Gregory L (Greg)**<br>2505 Plymouth St, Marion IA 52302, USA | Basketball Player |
| **Stokes, John**<br>351 Windermere Blvd, #411, Alexandria LA 71303, USA | WW II Navy Air Force Hero |
| **Stokes, L Fred**<br>2132 Alameda St, Orlando FL 32804, USA | Football Player |
| **Stokes, Patrick T**<br>Anheuser-Busch Co, 1 Busch Place, Saint Louis MO 63118, USA | Businessman |
| **Stokkan, Bill**<br>Championship Auto Racing, 5350 Lakeview Parkway S Dr, Indianapolis IN 46268 USA | Auto Racing Executive |
| **Stokley, Brandon**<br>1029 Anaconda Dr, Castle Rock CO 80108, USA | Football Player |
| **Stoklos, Randy**<br>Beach Volleyball Camps, PO Box 1714, Pacific Palisades CA 90272, USA | Volleyball Player |
| **Stole, Mink**<br>635 Colorado Ave, #3B, Baltimore MD 21210, USA | Actress |
| **Stolhanske, Eric**<br>United Talent Agency, U T A Plaza, 9336 Civic Center Dr, Beverly Hills CA 90210 USA | Actor, Comedian, Writer, Producer |
| **Stoll, Corey**<br>Suskin Mgmt, 2 Charlton St, #5K, New York NY 10014, USA | Actor |
| **Stolle, Frederick S**<br>Turnberry Isle Yacht & Racquet Club, 19735 Turnberry Way, Miami FL 33180, USA | Tennis Player |
| **Stoller, Fred**<br>Amsel Eisenstadt Frazier, 5055 Wilshire Blvd, #865, Los Angeles CA 90036 USA | Actor |
| **Stoller, Mike**<br>Leiber/Stoller Entertainment, 9000 W Sunset Blvd, #720, West Hollywood CA 90069, USA | Composer |
| **Stolley, Paul D**<br>10205 Wincopin Circle, #312, Columbia MD 21044, USA | Epidemiologist, Pharmacologist |
| **Stolper, Pinchas**<br>Orthodox Jewish Congregations Union, 11 Broadway, New York NY 10004, USA | Religious Leader |
| **Stoltenberg, Jens**<br>Prime Minister's Office, Akersgaten 42, Ploensgt 8, 0030 Oslo, Norway | Prime Minister, Norway |
| **Stoltz, Eric**<br>United Talent Agency, U T A Plaza, 9336 Civic Center Dr, Beverly Hills CA 90210 USA | Actor, Director, Producer |
| **Stoltz, Kelley**<br>Goldstar Public Relations, PO Box 130, Ross on Wye HR9 6WY, England | Singer, Songwriter |
| **Stoltz, Roland**<br>Lilgatan 16, Skelleftea 93 154, Sweden | Ice Hockey Player |
| **Stoltzman, Richard L**<br>Frank Salomon, 121 W 27th St, #703, New York NY 10001 USA | Concert Clarinetist |
| **Stolze, Lena**<br>Agentur Carola Studlar, Neuroeder str 1C, 82152 Planegg, Germany | Actress |
| **Stone, Angie**<br>J Erving Group, 154 Krog St, #130, Atlanta GA 30307, USA | Singer, Songwriter |
| **Stone, Charles, III**<br>United Talent Agency, U T A Plaza, 9336 Civic Center Dr, Beverly Hills CA 90210 USA | Director, Actor |
| **Stone, Curtis**<br>W M E Entertainment, 9601 Wilshire Blvd, #300, Beverly Hills CA 90210 USA | Chef |
| **Stone, D Dean**<br>1451 20th Ave, #204, East Moline IL 61244, USA | Baseball Player |

**Stone, Doug** — Singer, Songwriter
PO Box 943, Springfield TN 37172, USA

**Stone, Dwight** — Football Player
1128 Deep Hollow Court, Waxhaw NC 28173, USA

**Stone, E Donald (Donnie)** — Football Player
101 W H St, Jenks OK 74037, USA

**Stone, Edward C, Jr** — Space Scientist, Physicist
PO Box 40747, Pasadena CA 91114, USA

**Stone, Emma** — Actress
Anonymous Content, 3532 Hayden Ave, Culver City CA 90232 USA

**Stone, Eugene D (Gene)** — Baseball Player
6897 Highway 262 SE, Othello WA 99344, USA

**Stone, Fred** — Artist
Equinart Inc, 5911 Colodny Dr, Agoura Hills CA 91301, USA

**Stone, George H** — Baseball Player
1206 Eastland Ave, Ruston LA 71270, USA

**Stone, H Ronald (Ron)** — Baseball Player
11720 NW Lovejoy St, Portland OR 97229, USA

**Stone, Isaac (Biz)** — Businessman
Twitter Inc, 795 Folsom St, #600, San Francisco CA 94107, USA

**Stone, Jeffrey G (Jeff)** — Baseball Player
RR 1 Box 392, Portageville MO 63873, USA

**Stone, Jennifer** — Actress
United Talent Agency, U T A Plaza, 9336 Civic Center Dr, Beverly Hills CA 90210 USA

**Stone, Jessica** — Actress
Paradigm Agency, 360 N Crescent Dr, North Building, Beverly Hills CA 90210 USA

**Stone, Joss** — Singer, Songwriter, Actress
Mavrick Artists Agency, 6100 Wilshire Blvd, #550, Los Angeles CA 90048, USA

**Stone, Kenneth B (Ken), Jr** — Football Player
16 W Riverside Dr, Jupiter FL 33469, USA

**Stone, Lara C** — Model
I M G Models, 304 Park Ave S, #PH N, New York NY 10010 USA

**Stone, Matt** — Animator, Writer
Morris Yorn Barnes, 2000 Ave of Stars, #300N, Los Angeles CA 90067 USA

**Stone, Michael A** — Football Player
23162 Coventry Woods Lane, Southfield MI 48034, USA

**Stone, Nicole L (Nikki)** — Freestyle Aerials Skier
5272 Heather Lane, Park City UT 84098, USA

**Stone, Oliver W** — Director, Writer
Ixtlan Corp, 12233 W Olympic Blvd, #322, Los Angeles CA 90064, USA

**Stone, Ricky** — Baseball Player
6494 Lakeview Court, Hamilton OH 45011, USA

**Stone, Robert A** — Writer
PO Box 967, Block Island RI 02807, USA

**Stone, Sharon** — Actress, Model
Chuck Binder Mgmt, 1465 Lindacrest Dr, Beverly Hills CA 90210 USA

**Stone, Skyler** — Actor, Comedian
Justice & Ponder, PO Box 480033, Los Angeles CA 90048 90048, USA

**Stone, Sly** — Singer, Keyboardist, Songwriter
Richard Walters, PO Box 2789, Toluca Lake CA 91610 USA

**Stone, Steven M (Steve)** — Baseball Player, Sportscaster
9261 N 128th Way, Scottsdale AZ 85259, USA

**Stonebarger, Suzanne** — Volleyball Player, Model
Association of Volleyball Professionals, 960 Knox St, #A, Torrance CA 90502 USA

**Stoneman, William H (Bill)** — Baseball Player, Executive
2519 N San Miguel Dr, Orange CA 92867, USA

**Stoner, Alyson R** — Actress, Dancer
Paradigm Agency, 360 N Crescent Dr, North Building, Beverly Hills CA 90210 USA

**Stoner, Casey** — Motorcycle Racing Rider
Ducati Moto G P, Via C Ducati 3, 40132 Bologna, Italy

**Stones, Dwight E** — Track Athlete
4790 Irvine Blvd, #105, Irvine CA 92620, USA

**Stonesipher, Donald H (Don)** — Football Player
1502 Canberry Court, Wheeling IL 60090, USA

**Stonestreet, Eric** — Actor
I C M Partners, 10250 Constellation Blvd, #900, Los Angeles CA 90067 USA

**Stookey, Paul** — Singer (Peter Paul & Mary), Songwriter
Fritz/Byers Mgmt, 1455 N Doheny Dr, Los Angeles CA 90069, USA

**Stoops, Robert A (Bob)** — Football Coach
University of Oklahoma, Athletic Dept, 108 E Brooks St, Norman OK 73069, USA

**Stoppard, Tom S** — Writer
United Agents, 12-26 Lexington St, London W1F 0LE, England

**Storaro, Vittorio** — Cinematographer
Via Divino Amore 2, 00040 Frattocchie Merino, Italy

**Storch, Larry** — Actor, Comedian
330 W End Ave, #17F, New York NY 10023, USA

**Storey, Awvee** — Basketball Player
Edge Sports Int'l, 3649 W Chase St, #100, Skokie IL 60076, USA

**Storey, David M** — Writer
2 Lyndhurst Gardens, London NW3, England

**Stork, Jeffrey (Jeff)** — Volleyball Player
Pepperdine University, Athletic Dept, 24255 Pacific Coast Highway, Malibu CA 90263, USA

**Storke, Adam** — Actor
Don Buchwald, 6500 Wilshire Blvd, #2200, Los Angeles CA 90048 USA

**Storm, Gregory** — Actor
Paradigm Agency, 360 N Crescent Dr, North Building, Beverly Hills CA 90210 USA

**Storm, Hannah** — Commentator, Sportscaster
ESPN-TV, ESPN Plaza, 935 Middle St, Bristol CT 06010 USA

**Storm, Jim** — Ice Hockey Player
2609 Harvest Hills Dr, Brighton MI 48114, USA

**Storm, Tempest** — Exotic Dancer
3905 Cambridge St, #3, Las Vegas NV 89119, USA

**Stormare, Peter** — Actor
Silver Lining Entertainment, 421 S Beverly Drive, #700, Beverly Hills CA 90212 USA

**Stormer, Horst L** — Nobel Physics Laureate
20 E 9th St, #14P, New York NY 10003, USA

**Storms, Kirsten** — Actress
Paradigm Agency, 360 N Crescent Dr, North Building, Beverly Hills CA 90210 USA

**Storr, Jamie** — Ice Hockey Player
Jamie Storr Goalie School, 650 N Sepulveda Blvd, Los Angeles CA 90049, USA

**Story, Karl** — Illustrator (Nightwing)
D C Comics, 1700 Broadway, #400, New York NY 10019 USA

**Story, Liz** — Pianist, Songwriter
S R O Artists, PO Box 9532, Madison WI 53715, USA

**Story, Tim** — Director, Producer
United Talent Agency, U T A Plaza, 9336 Civic Center Dr, Beverly Hills CA 90210 USA

**Stossel, John** — Commentator
Beresford Apartments, 211 Central Park West, #15K, New York NY 10024, USA

**Stosur, Samatha J (Sam)** — Tennis Player
Tennis Australia, Melbourne Park, Batman Avenue, Melbourne VIC 3121, Australia

**Stothers, Mike** — Ice Hockey Player
Grand Rapids Griffins, 130 Fulton St W, #111, Grand Rapids MI 49503, USA

**Stott, Kathryn L** — Concert Pianist
Jane Ward, 38 Townfield, Rickmansworth, Hertfordshire WD3 2DD, England

**Stott, Ken** — Actor
Rights House, Drury House, 34-43 Russell St, London WC2B 5HA, England

**Stott, Nicole M P** — Astronaut
N A S A, Johnson Space Center, 2101 NASA Road, Houston TX 77058 USA

**Stottlemyre, Melvin L (Mel)** — Baseball Player
26004 SE 27th St, Sammamish WA 98075, USA

**Stottlemyre, Todd V** — Baseball Player
10839 E Gold Dust Ave, Scottsdale AZ 85259, USA

**Stotts, Terry** — Basketball Coach
Portland Trail Blazers, Rose Garden, 1 N Center Court St, Portland OR 97227 USA

**Stoudamire, Damon L** — Basketball Player
8325 Broadway St, #202, Pearland TX 77581, USA

**Stoudemire, Amar'e** — Basketball Player
346 E Tuckey Lane, Phoenix AZ 85012, USA

**Stouder, Sharon M** — Swimmer
144 Loucks Ave, Los Altos CA 94022, USA

**Stoudt, Bud** — Bowler
431 Lehman St, Lebanon PA 17046, USA

**Stoudt, Clifford L (Cliff)** — Football Player
5348 Drumcally Lane, Dublin OH 43017, USA

**Stouffer, Kelly W** — Football Player
7430 370th Trail, Rushville NE 69360, USA

**Stoughton, Blaine** — Ice Hockey Player
267th Ave SW, Dauphin MB R7N 1W5, Canada

**Stoutmire, Omar A** — Football Player
PO Box 85, Prosper TX 75078, USA

**Stovall, Dale E** — Vietnam War Air Force Hero
7440 Arroyo Lane, Missoula MT 59808, USA

**Stovall, DaRond** — Baseball Player
1107 Goelz Dr, East Saint Louis IL 62203, USA

**Stovall, Jerry L** — Football Player
7948 Wrenwood Blvd, #C, Baton Rouge LA 70809, USA

**Stovall, Maurice A, Jr** — Football Player
4406 Kendal Court, Valrico FL 33596, USA

**Stover Irwin Russ, Juno** — Diver
512 Lanai Circle, Union City CA 94587, USA

**Stover, George** — Actor
PO Box 10005, Baltimore MD 21285, USA

**Stover, J Matthew (Matt)** — Football Player
15 Ivy Reach Court, Cockeysville MD 21030, USA

**Stover, Jeffrey O (Jeff)** — Football Player
260 Cohasset Road, #190, Chico CA 95926, USA

**Stover, Stewart L (Smokey)** — Football Player
140 Ridgela Circle, Duson LA 70529, USA

**Stowe, David H, Jr** — Businessman
435 L'Ambiance Dr, #308 Longboat Key FL 34228, USA

**Stowe, Harold R (Hal)** — Baseball Player
1361 Union New Hope Road, Gastonia NC 28056, USA

**Stowe, Madeleine** — Actress
Brillstein Entertainment Partners, 9150 Wilshire Blvd, #350, Beverly Hills CA 90212 USA

**Stowe, Tyronne K** — Football Player
PO Box 164, Chandler AZ 85244, USA

**Stowell, Austin** — Actor
Creative Artists Agency, 2000 Ave of Stars, #100, Los Angeles CA 90067 USA

**Stowers, Christopher J (Chris)** — Baseball Player
3773 Wakefield Hall Square SE, Smyrna GA 30080, USA

**Stowers, Saleisha** — Model
Elite Model Mgmt, 404 Park Ave S, #900, New York NY 10016 USA

**Stoya** — Actress
Media Artists Group, 333 E 43rd St, #115, New York NY 10017, USA

**Stoyanov, Krasimir M** — Cosmonaut, Bulgaria
Cosmonaut Training Center, Star City, 141160 Zvezdny Gorodok, Moscow Oblast, Russia

**Stoyanovich, Peter (Pete)** — Football Player
18185 Parkshore Dr, Northville MI 48168, USA

**St-Pierre, Kim** — Ice Hockey Player
Team Canada, 2424 University Dr NW, Calgary AB T2N 3Y9, Canada

**Stracey, John H** — Boxer
8 Serpentine Road, Wallasey CH44 0AX, England

**Strachan, Michael D (Mike)** — Football Player
105 Yellowstone St, Kenner LA 70065, USA

**Strachan, Rodney (Rod)** — Swimmer
3250 Cabrillo Highway, Harmony CA 93435, USA

**Strachan, Stephen M (Steve)** — Football Player
161 Old Post Road, Mooresville NC 28117, USA

**Strader, Cam** — Auto Racing Driver
J R Motorsports, 349 Cayuga Dr, Mooresville NC 28117, USA

**Stradford, Troy E** — Football Player
James Crystal Radio Group, 6600 N Andrews Ave, #160, Fort Lauderdale FL 33309, USA

| | |
|---|---|
| **Stradlin, Izzy** | Guitarist (Guns N' Roses) |
| Front Line Mgmt, 1100 Glendon Ave, #2000, Los Angeles CA 90024 USA | |
| **Stradling, Harry A, Jr** | Cinematographer |
| 3664 Avenida Callada, Calabasas CA 91302, USA | |
| **Strahan, Michael A** | Football Player, Actor, Sportscaster |
| 23679 Calabasas Road, Calabasas CA 91302, USA | |
| **Strahler, Michael W (Mike)** | Baseball Player |
| 8 Canyon Draw, Alamogordo NM 88310, USA | |
| **Strahovski, Yvonne** | Actress |
| McKeon-Myrones Mgmt, 3500 Olive Ave, #770, Burbank CA 91505 USA | |
| **Straight, Susan** | Writer |
| Hyperion Books, 114 5th Ave, New York NY 10011 USA | |
| **Strain, Joseph A (Joe)** | Baseball Player |
| 8668 E Otero Circle, Centennial CO 80112, USA | |
| **Strain, Julie** | Actress, Model |
| J S Inc, 8491 Sunset Blvd, #1850, West Hollywood CA 90069, USA | |
| **Strain, Sammy** | Singer (O'Jays) |
| Associated Booking Corp, 501 Madison Ave, #501, New York NY 10022 USA | |
| **Strait, Donald** | WW II Army Air Corps Hero |
| 6 Burning Tree Place, Jackson Springs NC 27281, USA | |
| **Strait, George** | Singer, Guitarist |
| Erv Woolsey Co, 1000 18th Ave S, Nashville TN 37212, USA | |
| **Strait, Steven** | Actor, Singer |
| 3 Arts Entertainment, 9460 Wilshire Blvd, #700, Beverly Hills CA 90212 USA | |
| **Straka, Martin** | Ice Hockey Player |
| HC Pizen Stefanikovo, Namesti 1, 30133 Pizen, Czech Republic | |
| **Strampe, Bob** | Bowler |
| 31029 Louise Court, Warren MI 48088, USA | |
| **Strampe, Robert E (Bob)** | Baseball Player |
| 19210 W Lance Hill Road, Cheney WA 99004, USA | |
| **Strand, Mark** | Writer |
| 5825 S Dorchester Ave, #9W, Chicago IL 60637, USA | |
| **Strand, Robin** | Actor |
| 4083 Camellia Ave, Studio City CA 91604, USA | |
| **Strane, John** | WW II Navy Air Force Hero |
| 18230 Mirasol Dr, San Diego CA 92128, USA | |
| **Strang, Deborah** | Actress |
| McCabe Group, 3211 Cahuenga Blvd W, #104, Los Angeles CA 90068, USA | |
| **Strang, William G** | Mathematician |
| 7 Southgate Road, Wellesley MA 02482, USA | |
| **Strange, Curtis N** | Golfer, Sportscaster |
| 147 S Spooners St, Morehead City NC 28557, USA | |
| **Strange, J Douglas (Doug)** | Baseball Player |
| 435 Heights Dr, Gibsonia PA 15044, USA | |
| **Strange, Pat** | Baseball Player |
| 156 Mill St, Springfield MA 01108, USA | |
| **Strange, Sarah** | Actress |
| Elizabeth Hodgson Mgmt, 1536 W 12th Ave, #5, Vancouver BC V6J 2E1, Canada | |
| **Strassen, Volker** | Mathematician |
| Oskar-Pletsch-Str 12, 01324 Dresden, Germany | |
| **Strasser, Robin** | Actress |
| Innovative Artists, 235 Park Ave S, #1000, New York NY 10003 USA | |
| **Strasser, Teresa** | Actress, Comedienne |
| Renaissance Mgmt, P O Box 17379, Beverly Hills CA 90209, USA | |
| **Strasser, Todd** | Writer |
| PO Box 859, Larchmont NY 10538, USA | |
| **Strassman, Marcia** | Actress |
| Geddes Agency, 8430 Santa Monica Blvd, #201, West Hollywood CA 90069 USA | |
| **Stratas, Teresa** | Opera Singer |
| Vincent Farrell Assoc, 481 8th Ave, #340, New York NY 10001, USA | |
| **Strathairn, David** | Actor |
| I C M Partners, 10250 Constellation Blvd, #900, Los Angeles CA 90067 USA | |
| **Stratham, Jason** | Actor |
| Creative Artists Agency, 2000 Ave of Stars, #100, Los Angeles CA 90067 USA | |
| **Stratton, Arthur (Art)** | Ice Hockey Player |
| General Delivery, Succ Main, Saint Adolphie MB R5A 1A3, Canada | |
| **Stratton, Charlie** | Actor |
| Judi Farkas Mgmt, 116 N Mansfield Ave, Los Angeles CA 90036, USA | |
| **Stratton, D Michael (Mike)** | Football Player |
| 2611 Shore Lane Dr, Knoxville TN 37932, USA | |
| **Stratton, Dennis** | Guitarist (Iron Maiden) |
| Sanctuary Music Mgmt, 82 Bishop's Bridge Road, London W2 6BB, England | |
| **Straub, Chester J** | Judge |
| US Court of Appeals, Moynihan Courthouse, 500 Pearl St, New York NY 10007, USA | |
| **Straub, Peter F** | Writer |
| 53 W 85th St, New York NY 10024, USA | |
| **Straughan, Peter** | Writer |
| Casorotto Ramsay, Waverley House, 7-12 Noel St, London W1F 8GQ, England | |
| **Strause, Colin** | Visual Effects Producer, Director |
| Hydraulx, 1447 2nd St, #200, Santa Monica CA 90401, USA | |
| **Strause, Greg** | Visual Effects Producer, Director |
| Hydraulx, 1447 2nd St, #200, Santa Monica CA 90401, USA | |
| **Strauss, Neil** | Writer |
| Anderson Group Public Relations, 8060 Melrose Ave, #400, Los Angeles CA 90046, USA | |
| **Strauss, Peter** | Actor |
| Stone Manners Salners, 9911 W Pico Blvd, #1400, Los Angeles CA 90035 USA | |
| **Strauss, Robert S** | Political Executive, Diplomat |
| Akin Gump Strauss, 1333 New Hampshire Ave NW, #400, Washington DC 20036, USA | |
| **Straw, John W (Jack)** | Government Official, England |
| House of Commons, Westminster, London SW1A 0AA, England | |
| **Strawberry, Darryl E** | Baseball Player |
| 1802 Sterling Oaks Dr, Saint Peters MO 63376, USA | |
| **Strawbridge, George W, Jr** | Throughbred, Steeplechase Racing Owner |
| Augustin Stables, Greenlawn Road, Cochranville PA 19330, USA | |
| **Strawder, Joe** | Basketball Player |
| 3037 SW Taylors Ferry Road, Portland OR 97219, USA | |

| | |
|---|---|
| **Streck, Ron**<br>7527 S 84th East Ave, Tulsa OK 74133, USA | Golfer |
| **Streck, Ronald J**<br>Healthcare Distribution Mgmt Assn, 1821 Michael Faraday Dr, Reston VA 20190, USA | Association Executive |
| **Streep, Meryl**<br>Creative Artists Agency, 2000 Ave of Stars, #100, Los Angeles CA 90067 USA | Actress |
| **Street, Elliott**<br>Atlanta Models & Talent, 309 Maple Dr, #201, Atlanta GA 30354, USA | Actor |
| **Street, Huston L**<br>8300 Big View Dr, Austin TX 78730, USA | Baseball Player |
| **Street, Picabo**<br>Park City Ski Resort, Director of Skiing, 1345 Lowell Ave, Park City UT 84060, USA | Alpine Skier |
| **Street, Rebecca**<br>255 Cabrini Blvd, #7G, New York NY 10040, USA | Actress |
| **Streets, Tai**<br>16134 Hillcrest Circle, Orland Park IL 60467, USA | Football Player |
| **Streets, The**<br>Coalition Mgmt, 12 Barley Mow Passage, London W4 4PH, England | Rap Artist |
| **Streisand, Barbra**<br>160 W 96th St, New York NY 10025, USA | Singer, Actress, Director |
| **Streit, Kurt**<br>I M G Artists, Hogarth Business Park, Chiswick, London W4 2TH, England | Opera Singer |
| **Streitenfeld, Marc**<br>First Artists, 4764 Park Granada, #210, Calabasas CA 91302 USA | Composer |
| **Strekalov, Gennady M**<br>Federation Peace Committee, 36 Mira Prospekt, 129090 Moscow, Russia | Cosmonaut |
| **Strel, Martin**<br>Marathon Swim Mgmt Group, 227 H St, #207, Salt Lake City UT 84103, USA | Swimmer |
| **Strenger, Richard G (Rich)**<br>1064 Arborak Way, Lake Orion MI 48362, USA | Football Player |
| **Stresi, Alexia**<br>Artmedia, 20 Ave Rapp, 75007 Paris, France | Actress |
| **Streuli, Walter H (Walt)**<br>1107 Westminster Dr, Greensboro NC 27410, USA | Baseball Player |
| **Strianese, Michael**<br>L-3 Communications, 600 3rd Ave, New York NY 10016, USA | Businessman |
| **Stricker, Steven C (Steve)**<br>5804 N Sherman Ave, Madison WI 53704, USA | Golfer |
| **Stricker, Williams L (Bill)**<br>2930 Driftwood Place, #70, Stockton CA 95219, USA | Basketball Player |
| **Strickland, Donald D**<br>1110 Gilman Ave, San Francisco CA 94124, USA | Football Player |
| **Strickland, Gail**<br>14732 Oracle Place, Pacific Palisades CA 90272, USA | Actress |
| **Strickland, James M (Jim)**<br>2139 Equestrian Road, Paso Robles CA 93446, USA | Baseball Player |
| **Strickland, KaDee**<br>Anonymous Content, 3532 Hayden Ave, Culver City CA 90232 USA | Actress |
| **Strickland, Keith**<br>Direct Management Group, 947 N La Cienega Blvd, #G, West Hollywood CA 90069, USA | Drummer (B-52's) |
| **Strickland, Rodney (Rod)**<br>3120 Hemingway Lane, Lexington KY 40513, USA | Basketball Player |
| **Strickland, Scott M**<br>415 Enchanted River Dr, Spring TX 77388, USA | Baseball Player |
| **Strickland, Ted, III**<br>Midwest Gateway Partners, 35 N 4th St, #340, Columbus OH 43215, USA | Governor, Representative, OH |
| **Strickson, Mark**<br>Evans & Reiss, 100 Fawe Park Road, London SW15 2EA, England | Actor |
| **Strider, Marjorie V**<br>170 Clint Finger Lane, Saugerties NY 12477, USA | Artist, Sculptor |
| **Strieber, Whitney**<br>Gersh Agency, 9465 Wilshire Blvd, #600, Beverly Hills CA 90212 USA | Writer, Producer, Actor |
| **Strief, Zachary D (Zach)**<br>5480 Carterway Dr, Milford OH 45150, USA | Football Player |
| **Strigl, Dennis F (Denny)**<br>Verizon Communications, 140 West St, New York NY 10007, USA | Businessman |
| **Strik, Reshad**<br>B/W/R, 9100 Wilshire Blvd, #500W, Beverly Hills CA 90212 USA | Actor |
| **Striker, Gisela**<br>Harvard University, Philosophy Dept, Cambridge MA 02138, USA | Philosopher |
| **Stringer, Arthur (Art)**<br>12680 Royal Shores Dr, Conroe TX 77303, USA | Football Player |
| **Stringer, C Vivian**<br>Rutgers University, Athletic Dept, New Brunswick NJ 08903, USA | Basketball Coach |
| **Stringer, Howard**<br>186 Riverside Dr, New York NY 10024, USA | Businessman |
| **Stringert, Harold L (Hal)**<br>1711 Dole St, #603, Honolulu HI 96822, USA | Football Player |
| **Stringfellow, Ken**<br>Entourage Talent Assoc, 236 W 27th St, #800, New York NY 10001, USA | Musician (Posies), Songwriter |
| **Stringfield, Sherry**<br>John Carrabino Mgmt, 5900 Wilshire Blvd, #406, Los Angeles CA 90036 USA | Actress |
| **Stritch, Elaine**<br>Carlyle Hotel, 35 E 76th St, New York NY 10021, USA | Singer, Actress |
| **Strittmatter, Mark A**<br>6533 Dutch Creek St, Littleton CO 80130, USA | Baseball Player |
| **Strobel, Eric M**<br>6617 129th St W, Saint Paul MN 55124, USA | Ice Hockey Player |
| **Strobel, Heidi**<br>RR 1 Box 274A, Long Lane MO 65590, USA | Illusionist, Model |
| **Stroble, Bobby**<br>526 W 2nd Ave, Albany GA 31701, USA | Golfer |
| **Strock, Donald J (Don)**<br>1512 Passion Vine Circle, Weston FL 33326, USA | Football Player, Coach |
| **Strode, Haley**<br>Paradigm Agency, 360 N Crescent Dr, North Building, Beverly Hills CA 90210 USA | Actress |

**Strohmayer, John E** — Baseball Player
1825 Crosby Lane, Redding CA 96003, USA
**Strohmayer, Tod** — Astronomer
Goddard Space Flight Center, NASA/GSFC, Greenbelt MD 20771, USA
**Strollsteimer, Jason E** — Singer, Guitarist (VonBondies)
Tsunami Entertainment, 2525 Hyperion Ave, Los Angeles CA 90027, USA
**Strolz, Hubert** — Alpine Skier
6767 Warth 19, Austria
**Strom, Brent T** — Baseball Player
2202 N Catalina Vista Loop, Tucson AZ 85749, USA
**Strom, Brock T** — Football Player
4301 W 110th St, Leawood KS 66211, USA
**Strom, Richard J (Rick)** — Football Player
8905 Moor Park Run, Duluth GA 30097, USA
**Strom, Sally** — Artist
2388 SW Vermont St, #36, Portland OR 97219, USA
**Stroman, Susan** — Choreographer, Director
42 West, 220 W 42nd St, #1200, New York NY 10036 USA
**Stromberg, Robert** — Art Director, Production Designer
United Talent Agency, U T A Plaza, 9336 Civic Center Dr, Beverly Hills CA 90210 USA
**Strominger, Jack L** — Biochemist
Dana Faber Cancer Institute, Biochemistry Dept, 44 Binney St, Boston MA 02115, USA
**Strong, Barrett** — Singer, Songwriter
Motown Records, 6255 W Sunset Blvd, Los Angeles CA 90028 USA
**Strong, Brenda** — Actress
Liberman-Zerman Mgmt, 252 N Larchmont Blvd, #200, Los Angeles CA 90004 USA
**Strong, Daniel W (Danny)** — Actor, Writer
Sweeney Entertainment, 6253 Hollywood Blvd, #201, Los Angeles CA 90028, USA
**Strong, Joe** — Baseball Player
1340 Corcoran Ave, Vallejo CA 94589, USA
**Strong, Ken** — Ice Hockey Player
1773 Grosvenor Place, Mississauga ON L5L 3V8, Canada
**Strong, Mack C** — Football Player
14343 SE 92nd St, Newcastle WA 98059, USA
**Strong, Mark** — Actor
Markham Froggatt Irwin, Julian House, 4 Windmill St, London W1P 1HF, England
**Strong, Mary** — Sportscaster
N F L Network, 10950 Washington Blvd, #100, Culver City CA 90232 USA
**Strong, Maurice F** — Government Official, Canada
S3 Holdings, 150 Isabella St, #100, Ottawa ON K15 1V7, Canada
**Strong, Rider** — Actor
United Talent Agency, U T A Plaza, 9336 Civic Center Dr, Beverly Hills CA 90210 USA
**Stroock, Daniel W** — Mathematician
55 Frost St, Cambridge MA 02140, USA
**Strossen, Nadine** — Attorney, Association Executive
450 Riverside Dr, #51, New York NY 10027, USA
**Stroucken, Albert** — Businessman
Owens-Illinois Inc, 1 Michael Owens Way, Perrysburg OH 43551, USA
**Stroud, Don** — Actor
500 Lunalilo Home Road, #16A, Honolulu HI 96825, USA
**Stroud, Edwin M (Ed)** — Baseball Player
1696 Oak St SW, Warren OH 44485, USA
**Stroud, Marcus L** — Football Player
964 Detroit St, Jacksonville FL 32254, USA
**Stroughter, Stephen L (Steve)** — Baseball Player
323 NE 2nd Ave, Visalia CA 93291, USA
**Stroup, Jessica** — Actress
I C M Partners, 10250 Constellation Blvd, #900, Los Angeles CA 90067 USA
**Stroup, Theodore G (Ted), Jr** — Army General
2085 Hopewood Dr, Falls Church VA 22043, USA
**Strouse, Charles** — Composer
171 W 57th St, New York NY 10019, USA
**Strout, Elizabeth** — Writer
Random House, 1745 Broadway, #1800, New York NY 10019 USA
**Strube, Juergen F** — Businessman
B A S F Corp, Aktiengesellschaft, 67056 Ludwigshafen, Germany
**Strudwick, Suzanne** — Golfer
5525 Crestwood Dr, Knoxville TN 37914, USA
**Struever, Stuart M** — Anthropologist
2000 Sheridan Road, Evanston IL 60208, USA
**Strug, Kerri** — Gymnast
2611 N Santa Lucia Dr, Tucson AZ 85715, USA
**Struth, Thomas** — Photographer
Achenbachstr 74, 40237 Dusseldorf, Germany
**Struthers, Sally** — Actress
Vincent Cirrincione Assoc, 1516 N Fairfax Ave, Los Angeles CA 90046 USA
**Struve, Nicolas** — Actor
Artmedia, 20 Ave Rapp, 75007 Paris, France
**Struycken, Carel** — Actor
PO Box 1365, Avalon CA 90704, USA
**Strykert, Ron** — Guitarist (Men at Work)
T P A, PO Box 124, Round Corner NSW 2158, Australia
**Stuart, Bradley (Brad)** — Ice Hockey Player
131 Pinta Court, Los Gatos CA 95030, USA
**Stuart, Freundel J** — Prime Minister, Barbados
Prime Minister's Office, Bay St, Saint Michael, Bridgetown, Barbados
**Stuart, James Patrick** — Actor
Brillstein Entertainment Partners, 9150 Wilshire Blvd, #350, Beverly Hills CA 90212 USA
**Stuart, Jason** — Actor, Comedian
Ideal Talent Agency, 10806 Ventura Blvd, #2, Studio City CA 91604, USA
**Stuart, Jill** — Fashion Designer
550 Fashion Ave, #2400, New York NY 10018, USA
**Stuart, Katie** — Actress
Pacific Artists Mgmt, 1285 W Broadway, #685, Vancouver BC V6H 3X8, Canada
**Stuart, Marty** — Singer, Mandolin Player, Songwriter
Green Room, 1100 16th Ave S, Nashville TN 37212, USA

**Stubblefield, Dana W** — Football Player
5226 Pisa Court, San Jose CA 95138, USA
**Stubblefield, Mickey** — Baseball Player
4870 Seldon Way SE, Smyrna GA 30080, USA
**Stubbs, Franklin L** — Baseball Player
PO Box 325, Goshen KY 40026, USA
**Stubbs, Imogen M** — Actress
Nick Hern Books, Glasshouse, 49A Goldhawk Road, London W12 8QP, England
**Stubing, Lawrence G (Moose)** — Baseball Player, Manager
10821 Laconia Dr, Villa Park CA 92861, USA
**Stucchio, Emil** — Singer
LaGuardia Associates Entertainment, 271 Grove Ave, #E, Verona NJ 07044, USA
**Stuck, Hans-Joachim** — Auto Racing Driver
Harmstatt 3, 6352 Ellmau/Tirol, Austria
**Stuckey, Henry L** — Football Player
3615 Winchester Ave, Atlantic City NJ 08401, USA
**Stuckey, James D (Jim)** — Football Player
1314 Headquarters Plantation Dr, Johns Island SC 29455, USA
**Stuckey, Rodney N** — Basketball Player
2740 Castlemartin Court, Oakland Township MI 48306, USA
**Studdard, David D (Dave)** — Football Player
4490 S Clarkson St, Englewood CO 80113, USA
**Studdard, Ruben** — Singer
19 Music & Mgmt, 35-37 Parkgate Road, London SW11 4NP, England
**Studer, Cheryl** — Opera Singer
International Performing Artists, 125 Crowfield Dr, Knoxville TN 37922, USA
**Studin, Jan** — Publisher
Better Homes & Gardens, Publisher's Office, 1716 Locust, Des Moines IA 50309, USA
**Studney, Dan** — Actor
Paradigm Agency, 360 N Crescent Dr, North Building, Beverly Hills CA 90210 USA
**Studstill, Patrick L (Pat)** — Football Player
2235 Linda Flora Dr, Los Angeles CA 90077, USA
**Studt, Amy** — Singer, Pianist
19 Music & Mgmt, 35-37 Parkgate Road, London SW11 4NP, England
**Studwell, J Scott** — Football Player
10415 Brown Farm Circle, Eden Prairie MN 55347, USA
**Stufflebeem, John** — Navy Admiral
Director, Navy Staff, HqUSN, Pentagon, Washington DC 20350 USA
**Stuhlbarg, Michael** — Actor
Viking Entertainment, 445 W 23rd St, #1A, New York NY 10011, USA
**Stuhr, Jerzy** — Actor, Director
Graffiti Ltd, Ul SW Gertrudy 5, 31107 Cracow, Poland
**Stukes, Charles (Charlie)** — Football Player
4020 Cedar Grove Crest, Chesapeake VA 23321, USA
**Stulce, Michael D (Mike)** — Track Athlete
5711 Hunters Chase Court, Lithonia GA 30038, USA
**Stults, Eric W** — Baseball Player
13810 Ranier Dr, Middlebury, IN 46540, USA
**Stults, George S** — Actor, Model
Bleu Entertainment, 5225 Wilshire Blvd, #401, Los Angeles CA 90036, USA
**Stultz, Geoffrey S (Geoff)** — Actor
United Talent Agency, U T A Plaza, 9336 Civic Center Dr, Beverly Hills CA 90210 USA
**Stultz, Jack C** — Army General
Chief, Army Reserve, HqUSA, Pentagon, Washington DC 20310, USA
**Stump, David** — Cinematographer
H F W D Creative Representation, 394 E Glaucus St, Encinitas CA 92024, USA
**Stump, James G (Jim)** — Baseball Player
7432 Creekside Dr, Lansing MI 48917, USA
**Stump, Patrick** — Singer, Guitarist (Fall Out Boy)
PO Box 219, 1187 Wilmette Ave, Wilmette IL 60091, USA
**Stumpel, Jozef** — Ice Hockey Player
6301 Osprey Terrace, Coconut Creek FL 33073, USA
**Stumpf, John** — Financier
Wells Fargo, 420 Montgomery St, San Francisco CA 94104, USA
**Stumpf, Kenneth E** — Vietnam War Army Hero (CMH)
16528 State Highway 131, Tomah WI 54660, USA
**Stumpf, Paul K** — Biochemist
1515 Shasta Dr, #2219, Davis CA 95616, USA
**Stunyo-Korpak, Jeanne G** — Diver
1435 Almagre Peak Dr, Colorado Springs CO 80921, USA
**Stuper, John A** — Baseball Player
38 Lake St, Hamden CT 06517, USA
**Stupnitsky, Gene** — Actor, Comedian, Writer
W M E Entertainment, 9601 Wilshire Blvd, #300, Beverly Hills CA 90210 USA
**Stupp, Samuel I** — Engineer
Northwestern University, Engineering Dept, Evanston IL 60208, USA
**Stupples, Karen L** — Golfer
9736 Covent Garden Dr, Orlando FL 32827, USA
**Sturckow, Frederick W (Rick)** — Astronaut
RR 2 Box 14, Dickinson TX 77539, USA
**Sturgeon, Peter** — Ice Hockey Player
23 Millwood Road, Erin ON N0B 1T0, Canada
**Sturges, Shannon** — Actress
Precision Entertainment, 6338 Wilshire Blvd, Los Angeles CA 90048, USA
**Sturgess, Jim** — Actor
Garricks, Angel House, 76 Mallinson Road, London SW11 1BN, England
**Sturm, Felix** — Boxer
Universum Boxing Promotion, Am Stadtrand 27, 22047 Hamburg, Germany
**Sturm, Jerry G** — Football Player
1900 E Girard Place, #1503, Englewood CO 80113, USA
**Sturm, Marco J** — Ice Hockey Player
500 Atlantic Ave, #14P, Boston MA 02210, USA
**Sturm, Yfke** — Model
I M G Models, 304 Park Ave S, #PH N, New York NY 10010 USA
**Sturman, Eugene** — Sculptor, Artist
190 Loma Metisse St, Malibu CA 90265, USA

| | |
|---|---|
| **Sturr, James W (Jimmy), Jr**<br>United Polka Artists, PO Box 1, Florida NY 10921, USA | Orchestra Leader |
| **Sturridge, Charles**<br>United Agents, 12-26 Lexington St, London W1F 0LE, England | Director |
| **Sturt, Frederick N (Fred)**<br>120 N Berkey Southern Road, Swanton OH 43558, USA | Football Player |
| **Sturtze, Tanyon J**<br>501 Knights Run Ave, #2316, Tampa FL 33602, USA | Baseball Player |
| **Sturzaker, David**<br>Ken McReddie Assoc, 101 Finsbury Pavement, London EC2A 1RS, England | Actor |
| **Styler, Trudie**<br>Maven Pictures, 380 Lafayette St, #202, New York NY 10003, USA | Actress, Producer |
| **Styles P**<br>J Erving Group, 154 Krog St, #130, Atlanta GA 30307, USA | Rap Artist (Lox) |
| **Styles, Lorenzo C**<br>10276 Oxford Dr, Lewiston ID 83501, USA | Football Player |
| **Stynes, Christopher D (Chris)**<br>1980 NE 7th St, #106, Deerfield Beach FL 33441, USA | Baseball Player |
| **Styron, Alexandra**<br>Little Brown, 3 Center Plaza, #100, Boston MA 02108 USA | Writer |
| **Suarez Gonzalez, Adolfo**<br>Antonio Maura 4, 28014 Madrid, Spain | Prime Minister, Spain |
| **Suarez Navarro, Carla**<br>Saragossa 145, 08006 Barcelona, Spain | Tennis Player |
| **Suarez, Anne**<br>U B B A, 6 Rue de Braque, 75003 Paris, France | Actress |
| **Suarez, Jeremy**<br>Innovative Artists, 1505 10th St, Santa Monica CA 90401 USA | Actor |
| **Suarez, Kenneth R (Ken)**<br>6000 Forest Lane, Fort Worth TX 76112, USA | Baseball Player |
| **Suau, Anthony**<br>Denver Post, Editorial Dept, PO Box 1709, Denver CO 80201, USA | Photojournalist |
| **Subkoff, Tara**<br>I C M Partners, 10250 Constellation Blvd, #900, Los Angeles CA 90067 USA | Actress |
| **Subotnick, Morton L**<br>25 Minetta Lane, #4B, New York NY 10012, USA | Composer |
| **Substance, Markee**<br>Moksha Mgmt, PO Box 102, London E15 2HH, England | Keyboardist (Kosheen) |
| **Such, Richard S (Dick)**<br>7614 Divot Dr, Sanford NC 27332, USA | Baseball Player |
| **Sucharetza, Marla**<br>Abrams Artists, 9200 W Sunset Blvd, #1125, West Hollywood CA 90069 USA | Actress |
| **Suchecka, Rysia**<br>N B B J Architecture/Design, 111 S Jackson St, Seattle WA 98104, USA | Interior Designer |
| **Suchet, David**<br>Ken McReddie Assoc, 101 Finsbury Pavement, London EC2A 1RS, England | Actor |
| **Suchocka, Hanna**<br>Urzad Rady Ministrow, Al Ujazdowskie 1/3, 00567 Warsaw, Poland | Prime Minister, Poland |
| **Suchy, Radoslav**<br>7801 N 54th St, Paradise Valley AZ 85253, USA | Ice Hockey Player |
| **Sud, Veena**<br>Felker Toczak Gellman, 10880 Wilshire Blvd, #2070, Los Angeles CA 90024 USA | Producer |
| **Sudakis, William P (Bill)**<br>44054 Elkhorn Trail, Indian Wells CA 92210, USA | Baseball Player |
| **Sudan, Madhu**<br>81 Benton Road, Somerville MA 02143, USA | Computer Scientist |
| **Sudano, Brooklyn**<br>A P A Talent/Literary Agency, 405 S Beverly Dr, #300, Beverly Hills CA 90212 USA | Actress, Singer |
| **Sudduth, Skipp**<br>One Entertainment, 347 5th Ave, #1404, New York NY 10016 USA | Actor, Director |
| **Sudduth-Smith, Jill**<br>9917 Calabasas Ave, Las Vegas NV 89117, USA | Synchronized Swimmer |
| **Sudeikis, Jason**<br>Creative Artists Agency, 2000 Ave of Stars, #100, Los Angeles CA 90067 USA | Actor, Comedian |
| **Suedhof, Thomas C**<br>Stanford University Medical School, Molecular Physiology Dept, Stanford CA 94305, USA | Nobel Medicine Laureate |
| **Sugar, Leo T**<br>7161 Golden Eagle Court, #1012, Fort Myers FL 33912, USA | Football Player |
| **Sugar, Steve**<br>Future Music, Bayerstr 77A, 80335 Munich, Germany | DJ Musician (Mike & Sugar) |
| **Sugarman, Burt**<br>Giant Group, 9440 Santa Monica Blvd, #407, Beverly Hills CA 90210, USA | Producer |
| **Sugg, B Alan**<br>University of Arkansas, President's Office, Fayetteville AR 72701, USA | Educator |
| **Sugg, Diana K**<br>Baltimore Sun, Editorial Dept, 501 N Calvert St, Baltimore MD 21278, USA | Journalist |
| **Suggs, M Louise**<br>424 Royal Crescent Court, Saint Augustine FL 32092, USA | Golfer |
| **Suggs, Shafer L**<br>12849 Barrow Lane, Plainfield IL 60585, USA | Football Player |
| **Suggs, Terrell R**<br>281 N Brookside St, Chandler AZ 85225, USA | Football Player |
| **Suggs, W Walter (Walt), Jr**<br>11105 Bradyville Pike, Readyville TN 37149, USA | Football Player |
| **Suh, Yeree**<br>I M G Artists, Hogarth Business Park, Chiswick, London W4 2TH, England | Opera Singer |
| **Suhey, Matthew J (Matt)**<br>550 Carriage Way, Deerfield IL 60015, USA | Football Player |
| **Suhl, Harry**<br>University of California, Physics Dept, 9500 Gilman Dr, La Jolla CA 92093, USA | Physicist |
| **Suhonen, Alpo**<br>Chicago Blackhawks, United Center, 1901 W Madison St, Chicago IL 60612 USA | Ice Hockey Coach |
| **Suhr, Jennifer Stuczynski (Jenn)**<br>730 Jenkins Road, Churchville NY 14428, USA | Track Athlete |
| **Suhrheinrich, Richard F**<br>US Court of Appeals, 315 W Allegan St, #210, Lansing MI 48933, USA | Judge |

**Suhrstedt, Timothy (Tim)** — Cinematographer
Innovative Artists, 1505 10th St, Santa Monica CA 90401 USA
**Sui, Anna** — Fashion Designer
113 Greene St, Front A, New York NY 10012, USA
**Suits, Julia** — Editorial Cartoonist
Creators Syndicate, 737 3rd St, Hermosa Beach CA 90254 USA
**Sukarnoputri, D F Megawati** — President, Indonesia
Dewan Perwakilan Rakyat, Jalan Gatot Subroto 16, Jakarta, Indonesia
**Sukla, Edward A (Ed)** — Baseball Player
16 Perch, Irvine CA 92604, USA
**Sukova, Helena** — Tennis Player
1 Ave Grande Bretagne, Monte Carlo, Monaco
**Sukowa, Barbara** — Actress
Artmedia, 20 Ave Rapp, 75007 Paris, France
**Sularz, Guy P** — Baseball Player
10818 N 83rd St, Scottsdale AZ 85260, USA
**Suleiman, Michel** — President, Lebanon; General
President's Office, Palais de Baebda, Beirut, Lebanon
**Sulfsted, Alex F** — Football Player
8140 Shawnee Run Road, Cincinnati OH 45243, USA
**Suliman, Ali** — Actor
Paradigm Agency, 360 N Crescent Dr, North Building, Beverly Hills CA 90210 USA
**Sulkin, Gregg** — Actor
D2 Mgmt, 9255 Sunset Blvd, #600, West Hollywood CA 90069, USA
**Sullanmaa, Jani** — Curling Athlete
Curling Assn, Kalatorppa 2A62, 02230 Espoo, Finland
**Sullenberger, Chesley B (Sully)** — Airline Pilot Hero
General Delivery, Danville CA 94526, USA
**Sulliman, S Douglas (Doug)** — Ice Hockey Player
PO Box 28964, Scottsdale AZ 85255, USA
**Sullinger, Jared** — Basketball Player
Boston Celtics, 226 Causeway St, #4, Boston MA 02114 USA
**Sullivan, Brian** — Ice Hockey Player
392 E Beach Road, Charlestown RI 02813, USA
**Sullivan, Camille** — Actress
Red Mgmt, Box 3, 415 W Esplanade, North Vancouver BC V7M 1A6, Canada
**Sullivan, Chip** — Golfer
49 Homestead Circle, Troutville VA 24175, USA
**Sullivan, Christopher P (Chris)** — Football Player
64 Wagon Wheel Road, North Attleboro MA 02760, USA
**Sullivan, Cory** — Baseball Player
405 Overlook Court, Evanston WY 82930, USA
**Sullivan, Daniel J (Dan)** — Football Player
25 Algonquin Ave, Andover MA 01810, USA
**Sullivan, Danny** — Auto Racing Driver
PO Box 34290, Louisville KY 40232, USA
**Sullivan, David** — Actor
Intellectual Artists Mgmt, 10585 Santa Monica Blvd, #135, Los Angeles CA 90025, USA
**Sullivan, Erik Per** — Actor
Suzanne Smith, 451 Greenwich St, #500, New York NY 10103, USA
**Sullivan, Franklin L (Frank)** — Baseball Player
2715 Apapane St, Lihue HI 96766, USA
**Sullivan, George (Red)** — Ice Hockey Player
RR 2, Indian River ON K0L 2B0, Canada
**Sullivan, Gordon R** — Army General
Strategic Studies Institute, War College, 122 Forbes Ave, Carlisle PA 17013, USA
**Sullivan, Jazmine** — Singer, Songwriter
Creative Artists Agency, 2000 Ave of Stars, #100, Los Angeles CA 90067 USA
**Sullivan, Kathryn D** — Astronaut
795 Old Oak Trace, Columbus OH 43235, USA
**Sullivan, Kevin** — Journalist
Washington Post, Editorial Dept, 1150 15th St NW, Washington DC 20071 USA
**Sullivan, Kevin J** — Air Force General
Deputy CofS, Logistics/Installations, HqUSAF, Pentagon, Washington DC 20330 USA
**Sullivan, Kyle R** — Actor
Abrams Artists, 9200 W Sunset Blvd, #1125, West Hollywood CA 90069 USA
**Sullivan, Liam K** — Actor, Comedian
Kazarian/Measures/Ruskin, 11969 Ventura Blvd, #300, Studio City CA 91604 USA
**Sullivan, Louis W** — Secretary, Health & Human Services
223 Chestnut St, Atlanta GA 30314, USA
**Sullivan, Marc C** — Baseball Player
2038 W 1st S, #100, Fort Myers FL 33901, USA
**Sullivan, Michael J (Mike)** — Governor, WY; Diplomat
1124 S Durbin St, Casper WY 82601, USA
**Sullivan, Michael J (Mike)** — Golfer
Mike Sullivan Golf School, 5715 Fayetteville Road, Raleigh NC 27603, USA
**Sullivan, Mike** — Ice Hockey Player, Coach
275 Elm St, Duxbury MA 02332, USA
**Sullivan, Nicole** — Actress
Innovative Artists, 1505 10th St, Santa Monica CA 90401 USA
**Sullivan, Patrick J (Pat)** — Football Player, Coach
1717 Indian Creek Dr, Birmingham AL 35243, USA
**Sullivan, Paul E** — Navy Admiral
Commander, Naval Sea Systems, 1333 Isaac Hull Ave SE, Washington Navy Yard DC 20376 USA
**Sullivan, Peter** — Ice Hockey Player
316 Fairway Road, Regina SK S4Y 1J5, Canada
**Sullivan, Russell G M (Russ)** — Baseball Player
1701 Hill 'n' Dale St, Fredericksburg VA 22405, USA
**Sullivan, Sean** — Actor
Caldwell Jeffrey, 943 Queen St E, #200, Toronto ON M4M 1J6, Canada
**Sullivan, Stacy** — Actress
Cassell Levy Talent Agency, 843 N Sycamore Ave, Los Angeles CA 90038, USA
**Sullivan, Steve** — Ice Hockey Player
5536 Iron Gate Dr, Franklin TN 37069, USA
**Sullivan, Susan** — Actress
15355 Mulholland Dr, Los Angeles CA 90077, USA

**Sullivan, Tom** — Actor
Paradigm Agency, 360 N Crescent Dr, North Building, Beverly Hills CA 90210 USA
**Sullivan, W Scott** — Baseball Player
1649 Mayfair Court, Auburn AL 36830, USA
**Sullivan, William D** — Navy Admiral
US Representative, NATO Military Committee, PSC 80, Box 300, APO AE 09724 USA
**Sulston, John E** — Nobel Medicine Laureate
39 Mingle Lane, Stapleford, Cambridge CB2 5BG, England
**Sultan Salman Abdulaziz Al-Saud** — Astronaut, Saudi Arabia
Tourism/Antiquities Commission, PO Box 66680, Riyadh 11586, Saudi Arabia
**Sultan, Altoon** — Artist
PO Box 2, Groton VT 05046, USA
**Sultan, Donald K** — Artist
19 E 70th St, New York NY 10021, USA
**Sulzberger, Arthur O, Jr** — Publisher, Businessman
New York Times Co, Publisher's Office, 229 W 43rd St, New York NY 10036, USA
**Sumika, Aya** — Actress
I C M Partners, 10250 Constellation Blvd, #900, Los Angeles CA 90067 USA
**Sumino, Naoko** — Astronaut
NASDA, Tsukuba Space Center, 2-1-1 Sengen, Tukubashi, Ibaraki 305, Japan
**Sumlin, Kevin** — Football Coach
Texas A&M University, Athletic Dept, College Station TX 77843, USA
**Summar, Trent** — Singer (New Row Mob)
Grassroots Media, 1005 S Orlando Ave, Los Angeles CA 90035, USA
**Summe, Gregory L** — Businessman
PerkinElmer Inc, 45 William St, Wellesley MA 02481, USA
**Summer, Cree** — Actress, Singer
W M E Entertainment, 9601 Wilshire Blvd, #300, Beverly Hills CA 90210 USA
**Summerhays, Bruce P** — Golfer
2 Condie Circle, Farmington UT 84025, USA
**Summers, Andrew (Andy)** — Singer, Guitarist (Police)
21A Noel St, London W1V 3PD, England
**Summers, Carol** — Artist
2817 Smith Grade, Santa Cruz CA 95060, USA
**Summers, Dana** — Cartoonist (Lug Nuts, Bound & Gagged)
Orlando Sentinel, Editorial Dept, 633 N Orange Ave, Lobby, Orlando FL 32801, USA
**Summers, Jerry** — Singer (Dovells)
American Promotions, 2011 Ferry Ave, #U19, Camden NJ 08104, USA
**Summers, Lawrence H (Larry)** — Educator; Secretary, Treasury
National Economic Council, 1600 Pennsylvania Ave NW, Washington DC 20502, USA
**Summers, Linda** — Model
Playboy Promotions, 2706 Media Center Dr, Los Angeles CA 90065 USA
**Summers, Marc** — Entertainer
Rebel Entertainment Partners, 5700 Wilshire Blvd, #456, Los Angeles CA 90036, USA
**Summers, Tara** — Actress
I C M Partners, 10250 Constellation Blvd, #900, Los Angeles CA 90067 USA
**Summerville, Trish** — Costume Designer
Costume Designers Guild, 11969 Ventura Blvd, #100, Studio City CA 91604, USA
**Summitt, Pat S Head** — Basketball Player, Coach
3720 River Trace Lane, Knoxville TN 37920, USA
**Sumner, Charles (Charlie)** — Football Player, Coach
PO Box 11621, Lahaina HI 96761, USA
**Sumner, Mickey** — Actress
I C M Partners, 10250 Constellation Blvd, #900, Los Angeles CA 90067 USA
**Sumner, Peter** — Actor
Morrissey Mgmt, 77 Glebe Point Road, Glebe NSW 2037, Australia
**Sumner, Walter H (Walt)** — Football Player
PO Box 112, Ocilla GA 31774, USA
**Sumners, Rosalyn D** — Figure Skater
13314 NE 86th Place, Redmond WA 98052, USA
**Sumpter, Jeremy** — Actor
Innovative Artists, 1505 10th St, Santa Monica CA 90401 USA
**Sumpter, Tika** — Actress
C E S D, 10635 Santa Monica Blvd, #130, Los Angeles CA 90025 USA
**Sun Dandan** — Speed Skater
Skating Assn, 56 Zhongguancun South St, Haidian, Beijing 100044, China
**Sundaresh, S (Sundi)** — Businessman
Adeptec Inc, 691 S Milpitas Blvd, Milpitas CA 95035, USA
**Sunday, Gabriel** — Actor
Abrams Artists, 9200 W Sunset Blvd, #1125, West Hollywood CA 90069 USA
**Sundberg, James H (Jim)** — Baseball Player
2308 Newforest Court, Arlington TX 76017, USA
**Sunde, Milton J (Milt)** — Football Player
6008 W 104th St, Minneapolis MN 55438, USA
**Sundhage, Pia** — Soccer Player, Coach
US Women's Soccer, 1801 S Prairie Ave, Chicago IL 60616, USA
**Sundin, Gordon V (Gordie)** — Baseball Player
15600 Old 41 N, Naples FL 34110, USA
**Sundin, Mats J** — Ice Hockey Player
International Management Group, 801 6th St SW, Calgary AB T2P 3V8, Canada
**Sundvold, Jon T** — Basketball Player
2700 Westbrook Way, Columbia MO 65203, USA
**Sung Kang** — Actor
W M E Entertainment, 9601 Wilshire Blvd, #300, Beverly Hills CA 90210 USA
**Sung, Elizabeth** — Actress
G V A Talent, 9229 W Sunset Blvd, #320, West Hollywood CA 90069, USA
**Sung, Shi Yeon** — Conductor
I M G Artists, Hogarth Business Park, Chiswick, London W4 2TH, England
**Sunjata, Daniel** — Actor
United Talent Agency, U T A Plaza, 9336 Civic Center Dr, Beverly Hills CA 90210 USA
**Sunny, Tehmina** — Actress
Don Buchwald, 6500 Wilshire Blvd, #2200, Los Angeles CA 90048 USA
**Sunohara, Vicky** — Ice Hockey Player
Team Canada, 2424 University Dr NW, Calgary AB T2N 3Y9, Canada
**Sununu, John H** — Governor, NH; Government Official
49 Linden Road, Hampton Falls NH 03844, USA

**Sunyayev, Rashid A** — Astronomer
Space Studies Institute, Profsoyuznaya Str 84/32, 117910 Moscow, Russia
**Supernaw, Douglas A (Doug)** — Singer, Songwriter
Maximus Entertainment Booking, PO Box 27517, Austin TX 78755, USA
**Suplee, Ethan** — Actor
Don Buchwald, 6500 Wilshire Blvd, #2200, Los Angeles CA 90048 USA
**Suppan, Jeffrey S (Jeff)** — Baseball Player
17836 Sidwell St, Granada Hills CA 91344, USA
**Suraev, Maxim V** — Cosmonaut
Cosmonaut Training Center, Star City, 141160 Zvezdny Gorodok, Moscow Oblast, Russia
**Sure!, Al B** — Singer, Songwriter
I C M Partners, 10250 Constellation Blvd, #900, Los Angeles CA 90067 USA
**Surhoff, William J (B J)** — Baseball Player
5 Fenton St, Rye NY 10580, USA
**Surin, Bruny** — Track Athlete
PO Box 2, Succ Saint Michel, Montreal QC H2A 3L8, Canada
**Surmelis, Angelo** — Actor
Paradise Group, PO Box 69451, West Hollywood CA 90069, USA
**Surnow, Joel** — Producer
Paradigm Agency, 360 N Crescent Dr, North Building, Beverly Hills CA 90210 USA
**Surovy, Nicolas** — Actor
Hartig-Hilepo Agency, 54 W 21st St, #610, New York NY 10010 USA
**Sursok, Tammin** — Actress
Charlie Baby Productions, 8391 Beverly Blvd, #283, Los Angeles CA 90048, USA
**Surtain, Patrick F** — Football Player
2704 Boot Lane, Weston FL 33331, USA
**Surtees, John** — Auto Racing Driver
Team Surtees, Fircroft Way, Edenbridge, Kent TN8 6EJ, England
**Susa, Conrad** — Composer
433 Eureka St, San Francisco CA 94114, USA
**Suschitzky, J Peter** — Cinematographer
13 Priory Road, London NW6 4NN, England
**Suschitzky, Wolfgang** — Cinematographer
Douglas House, 6 Maida Ave, #11, London W2 1TG, England
**Susi, Carol Ann** — Actress
846 N Sweetzer Ave, West Hollywood CA 90069, USA
**Susi, Lolly** — Actress
Actual Management, 7 Great Russell St, London WC1B 3NH, England
**Suskind, Patrick** — Writer
Diogenes Verlag AG, Sprecherstr 8, 8032 Zurich, Switzerland
**Suslick, Kenneth S** — Chemist
University of Illinois, Chemistry Dept, Champaign IL 61820, USA
**Susman, Todd** — Actor
Luedtke Agency, 1674 Broadway, #7A, New York NY 10019, USA
**Susser, Craig** — Actor
I C M Partners, 10250 Constellation Blvd, #900, Los Angeles CA 90067 USA
**Sussman, Adam** — Writer, Producer
Brian Lutz Mgmt, 6464 Sunset Blvd, #860, Los Angeles CA 90028, USA
**Sussman, Kevin** — Actor
C E S D, 257 Park Ave S, #950, New York NY 10010 USA
**Sussman, Susan** — Writer
A P A Talent/Literary Agency, 405 S Beverly Dr, #300, Beverly Hills CA 90212 USA
**Sutcliffe, David** — Actor
Noble-Caplan Agency, 1260 Yonge St, #200, Toronto ON M4T 1W6, Canada
**Sutcliffe, Richard L (Rick)** — Baseball Player
616 NE Seabrook Court, Lees Summit MO 64064, USA
**Suter, Gary** — Ice Hockey Player
2128 County Road D, Lac du Flambu WI 54538, USA
**Suter, Robert A (Rob)** — Ice Hockey Player
4332 McConnell St, Fitchburg WI 53711, USA
**Suter, Ryan** — Ice Hockey Player
1554 Shining Ore Dr, Brentwood TN 37027, USA
**Sutherland, David** — Golfer
5431 Tree Side Dr, Carmichael CA 95608, USA
**Sutherland, Donald** — Actor
Creative Artists Agency, 2000 Ave of Stars, #100, Los Angeles CA 90067 USA
**Sutherland, Douglas A (Doug)** — Football Player
511 Kenilworth Ave, Duluth MN 55803, USA
**Sutherland, Gary L** — Baseball Player
338 Oakcliff Road, Monrovia CA 91016, USA
**Sutherland, Ivan E** — Computer Scientist
California Institute of Technology, Computer Science Dept, Pasadena CA 91125, USA
**Sutherland, Kevin** — Golfer
1230 Carter Road, Sacramento CA 95864, USA
**Sutherland, Kiefer** — Actor
Management 360, 9111 Wilshire Blvd, Beverly Hills CA 90210 USA
**Sutherland, Kristine** — Actress
S M S Talent, 8383 Wilshire Blvd, #230, Beverly Hills CA 90211 USA
**Sutherland, Leonardo C (Leo)** — Baseball Player
12082 Nieta Dr, Garden Grove CA 92840, USA
**Sutherland, Peter D** — Government Official, Ireland
68 Eglinton Road, Dublin 4, Ireland
**Sutherland, Sarah** — Actress
Gersh Agency, 9465 Wilshire Blvd, #600, Beverly Hills CA 90212 USA
**Sutherland, William F (Bill)** — Ice Hockey Player
305-2425 Main St, Winnipeg MB R2V 3N4, Canada
**Sutko, Glenn E** — Baseball Player
1403 River Green Dr NW, Atlanta GA 30327, USA
**Sutley, Nancy** — Government Official
White House, 1600 Pennsylvania Ave NW, Washington DC 20500, USA
**Sutor, George** — Basketball Player
29840 State Highway 27, Holcombe WI 54745, USA
**Sutorius, James** — Actor
Gage Group, 14724 Ventura Blvd, #505, Sherman Oaks CA 91403 USA
**Sutta, Jessica** — Singer (Pussycat Dolls), Actress
Almond Talent Agency, 8217 Beverly Blvd, #8, West Hollywood CA 90048, USA

**Sutter, Brent** — Ice Hockey Player, Coach
PO Box 545, Viking AB T0B 4N0, Canada
**Sutter, Brian** — Ice Hockey Player, Coach
Red Deer Rebels, C-4847 19th St, Red Deer AB T4R 2N7, Canada
**Sutter, Duane** — Ice Hockey Player, Coach
Calgary Flames, PO Box 1540, Station M, Calgary AB T2P 3B9, Canada
**Sutter, Edward L (Eddie)** — Football Player
5104 N Bevalon Place, Peoria IL 61614, USA
**Sutter, H Bruce** — Baseball Player
59 Waterside Dr SE, Cartersville GA 30121, USA
**Sutter, Kurt** — Producer, Writer
I C M Partners, 10250 Constellation Blvd, #900, Los Angeles CA 90067 USA
**Sutter, Richard G (Rich)** — Ice Hockey Player
Sutter Ice, 1920 17th St, Cooldale AB T1M 1M1, Canada
**Sutter, Ronald (Ron)** — Ice Hockey Player
44 Chaparral Cove SE, Calgary AB T2X 3L4, Canada
**Suttle, Dane L** — Basketball Player
138 W 69th St, Los Angeles CA 90003, USA
**Sutton, Donald H (Don)** — Baseball Player, Sportscaster
120 Calle de las Rosas, Rancho Mirage CA 92270, USA
**Sutton, Greg** — Basketball Player
PO Box 8101, Edmond OK 73083, USA
**Sutton, Hal E** — Golfer
40 Duck Haven Point, Bossier City LA 71111, USA
**Sutton, Larry J** — Baseball Player
14209 Woodward St, Overland Park KS 66223, USA
**Sutton, Michael** — Actor
Somers Teitelbaum David, 8840 Wilshire Blvd, #200, Beverly Hills CA 90211 USA
**Sutton, Tierney** — Singer
Terry M Hill, 41910 Boardwalk, #A2, Palm Desert CA 92211 USA
**Suvadova, Silvia** — Actress
Boris Rajek, 1228 Cabrillo Ave, Venice CA 90291, USA
**Suvalatsumi** — Actress
39 M G Chakrapani St, Sathya Garden, Saligrammam, Chennai TN 600093, India
**Suvari, Mena A** — Actress
Alchemy Entertainment, 7024 Melrose Ave, #420, Los Angeles CA 90038 USA
**Suwa, Gen** — Anthropologist
University of California, Human Evolutionary Science Laboratory, Berkeley CA 94720, USA
**Suwanai, Akiko** — Concert Violinist
Harrison/Parrott, 5-6 Albion Court, London W6 0QT, England
**Suyderhoud, Mike** — Water Skier
PO Box 492052, Redding CA 96049, USA
**Suzman, Janet** — Actress
Steve Kenis Co, Royalty House, 72-74 Dean St, London WID 3SG, England
**Suzor, Mark J** — Ice Hockey Player
1639 Hillcrest Dr, Sheridan WY 82801, USA
**Suzuki, David T** — Commentator, Geneticist, Enviromentalist
David Suzuki Foundation, 2221 W 4th Ave, Vancouver BC V6K 4S2, Canada
**Suzuki, Ichiro** — Baseball Player
New York Yankees, Yankee Stadium, E 161st St & River Ave, Bronx NY 10451 USA
**Suzuki, Kurt K** — Baseball Player
Washington Nationals, 1500 S Capitol St SE, Washington DC 20003 USA
**Suzuki, Masaaki** — Concert Organist, Harpsichord Player
Frank Salomon, 121 W 27th St, #703, New York NY 10001 USA
**Suzuki, Pat** — Actress, Singer
343 E 30th St, New York NY 10016, USA
**Suzuki, Robert** — Educator
California State University, President's Office, Bakersfield CA 93311, USA
**Suzy** — Columnist
18 E 68th St, #1B, New York NY 10065, USA
**Svala** — Singer, Songwriter
Tonaljos Music, Box 520, Rejkavikurvegur 38, Hafnafjordur 220, Iceland
**Svankmajer, Jan** — Director
Cerninska 5, 11800 Prague 1, Czech Republic
**Svare, Harland** — Football Player, Coach
6127 Paseo Jaquita, Carlsbad CA 92009, USA
**Svehla, Robert** — Ice Hockey Player
Dukla Trencin Hockey, Povaszka 34, 91101 Trencin, Slovakia
**Svenden, Birgitta** — Concert Singer
Ulf Tornqvist, Sankt Eriksgatan 100, 113 31 Stockholm, Sweden
**Svendsen, Louise A** — Museum Executive
16 Park Ave, New York NY 10016, USA
**Sveningsson, Magnus J** — Bassist (Cardigans)
Talent Trust, Kungsgatan 9C, 411 19 Gothenburg, Sweden
**Svenson, Bo** — Actor
Feldman Bailey Mgmt, 21781 Ventura Blvd, Woodland Hills CA 91364, USA
**Svensson, Leif** — Ice Hockey Player
Lisselbyvagan 39, 793 33 Leksand, Sweden
**Sverak, Jan** — Director
PO Box 33, 15500 Prague 515, Czech Republic
**Sveum, Dale C** — Baseball Player
13483 E Estrella Ave, Scottsdale AZ 85259, USA
**Svihus, Robert C (Bob)** — Football Player
23000 Guidotti Dr, Salinas CA 93908, USA
**Svoboda, Jiri** — Director
Performing Arts Academy, Malostranske Nam 12, 11800 Prague 1, Czech Republic
**Svoboda, Petr** — Ice Hockey Player
Sportrust Assoc, 818 18th St, #F, Santa Monica CA 90403, USA
**Swaby, Donn** — Actor
C E S D, 10635 Santa Monica Blvd, #130, Los Angeles CA 90025 USA
**Swados, Elizabeth A** — Writer, Composer
360 Central Park West, #16G, New York NY 10025, USA
**Swagerty, Jane** — Swimmer
9128 N 70th St, Paradise Valley AZ 85253, USA
**Swagerty, Keith M** — Basketball Player
22232 17th Ave SE, #205, Bothell WA 98021, USA

**Swaggart, Jimmy L** — Evangelist
PO Box 262550, Baton Rouge LA 70826, USA
**Swaggerty, William D (Bill)** — Baseball Player
116 S Forney Ave, Hanover PA 17331, USA
**Swail, Julie** — Water Polo Player, Coach
University of California, Athletic Dept, Irvine CA 92697, USA
**Swain, Chelse E A** — Actress
inMomemtum Mgmt, 14622 Ventura Blvd, #778, Sherman Oaks CA 91403, USA
**Swain, Dominique** — Actress
Don Buchwald, 6500 Wilshire Blvd, #2200, Los Angeles CA 90048 USA
**Swain, Garry** — Ice Hockey Player
PO Box 729, West Simsbury CT 06092, USA
**Swain, John W** — Football Player
409 E 135th St, Burnsville MN 55337, USA
**Swain, Michael L (Mike)** — Judo Athlete
128 W Campbell Ave, Campbell CA 95008, USA
**Swallow, Jerod** — Ice Dancer, Coach
Detroit Skating Club, 888 Denison Court, Bloomfield Hills MI 48302, USA
**Swaminathan, Monkombu S** — Geneticist
M S Swaminathan Foundation, 3 Cross St, Taramani, Madras 600113, India
**Swan, Billy** — Singer, Songwriter
Geoffrey Blumenauer Artists, PO Box 343, Burbank CA 91503 USA
**Swan, Craig S** — Baseball Player
296 Sound Beach Ave, Old Greenwich CT 06870, USA
**Swan, John W D** — Prime Minister, Bermuda
11 Grape Bay Dr, Paget PG 06, Bermuda
**Swan, Michael** — Actor
13576 Cheltenham Dr, Sherman Oaks CA 91423, USA
**Swan, Richard G** — Mathematician
700 Melrose Ave, #M3, Winter Park FL 32789, USA
**Swan, Robert** — Explorer
2041, 561 Keystone Ave, PM Box 640, Reno NV 89503, USA
**Swan, Serinda** — Actress
United Talent Agency, U T A Plaza, 9336 Civic Center Dr, Beverly Hills CA 90210 USA
**Swanberg, Joe** — Director, Actor
Creative Artists Agency, 2000 Ave of Stars, #100, Los Angeles CA 90067 USA
**Swanepoel, Candice** — Model
I M G Models, 304 Park Ave S, #PH N, New York NY 10010 USA
**Swank, Hilary** — Actress
2 S Films, 10390 Santa Monica Blvd, #210, Los Angeles CA 90025, USA
**Swanke, Karl V** — Football Player
4 Butternut Court, Essex Junction VT 05452, USA
**Swann, Charles D** — Football Player
5815 Vinings Retreat Court SW, Mableton GA 30126, USA
**Swann, Eric J** — Football Player
2321 Carex Court, Elk Grove CA 95757, USA
**Swann, Lynn C** — Football Player, Sportscaster
506 Hegner Way, #2, Sewickley PA 15143, USA
**Swanson, Arthur L (Red)** — Baseball Player
1139 Chippenham Dr, Baton Rouge LA 70808, USA
**Swanson, August G** — Physician
3146 Portage Bay Place E, #H, Seattle WA 98102, USA
**Swanson, Jackie** — Actress
15155 Albright St. Pacific Palisades CA 90272, USA
**Swanson, Judith** — Actress
Persona Mgmt, 40 E 9th St, New York NY 10003, USA
**Swanson, Kristy** — Actress, Model
Inphenate, 9701 Wilshire Blvd, #1000, Beverly Hills CA 90212 USA
**Swanson, Stanley L (Stan)** — Baseball Player
1705 E Whaley St, Longview TX 75601, USA
**Swanson, Steven R** — Astronaut
1414 Blueberry Lane, Friendswood TX 77546, USA
**Swanson, William H** — Businessman
Raytheon Co, 870 Winter St, Waltham MA 02451, USA
**Swaray, Estelle** — Singer, Rap Artist
Atlantic Records, 1290 Ave of Americas, Concourse 4, New York NY 10104, USA
**Sward, Anne** — Actress
Talent Management Group, 339 E 3900 S, #210, Salt Lake City UT 84107, USA
**Swardson, Nick** — Actor, Comedian, Writer, Producer
Brillstein Entertainment Partners, 9150 Wilshire Blvd, #350, Beverly Hills CA 90212 USA
**Swartzbaugh, David T (Dave)** — Baseball Player
113 Orchard St, Middletown OH 45044, USA
**Swatek, Barret** — Actress
Harrison Stokes, 8730 W Sunset Blvd, #270, West Hollywood CA 90069, USA
**Sway** — Entertainer
Bloom Effect, 112 S Portland Ave, #3A, Brooklyn NY 11217, USA
**Swayne, Harry V** — Football Player
2702 Baubitz Road, Reistertown MD 21136, USA
**Swayze, Don** — Actor
Baron Entertainment, 13848 Ventura Blvd, #A, Sherman Oaks CA 91423, USA
**Swead, Stephen** — Government Official
Fannie Mae, 3900 Wisconsin Ave NW, Washington DC 20016, USA
**Sweat, Keith** — Singer, Songwriter
Red Entertainment Agency, 505 8th Ave, #1004, New York NY 10018, USA
**Sweat, Lynn** — Artist
17 Good Hill Road, Weston CT 06883, USA
**Swedberg, Heidi** — Actress
Frontline Mgmt, 8265 Sunset Blvd, #209, West Hollywood CA 90046, USA
**Swedberg, Jaclyn** — Model, Actress
Playboy Promotions, 2706 Media Center Dr, Los Angeles CA 90065 USA
**Swedlin, Rosalie** — Producer
Anonymous Content, 3532 Hayden Ave, Culver City CA 90232 USA
**Sweeney, Alison** — Actress
United Talent Agency, U T A Plaza, 9336 Civic Center Dr, Beverly Hills CA 90210 USA
**Sweeney, Bob** — Ice Hockey Player
110 Brookview Dr, North Andover MA 01845, USA

**Sweeney, Brian E** — Baseball Player
199 Morsemere Ave, Yonkers NY 10703, USA

**Sweeney, Calvin E** — Football Player
4120 Olympiad Dr, Los Angeles CA 90043, USA

**Sweeney, D B** — Actor
Rain Management Group, 1631 21st St, Santa Monica CA 90404, USA

**Sweeney, Donald C (Don)** — Ice Hockey Player, Executive
5 Shady Nook Lane, Lynnfield MA 01940, USA

**Sweeney, I Anne** — Businesswoman
Disney Media Network, 3800 W Alameda Ave, #B, Burbank CA 91505, USA

**Sweeney, James J (Jim)** — Football Player
119 Justabout Road, Venetia PA 15367, USA

**Sweeney, John E** — Representative, NY
5 Plantation Crescent, Clifton Park NY 12065, USA

**Sweeney, John J** — Labor Leader
AFL-CIO, 1750 New York Ave NW, Lobby 1, Washington DC 20006, USA

**Sweeney, Julia** — Actress, Comedienne
W M E Entertainment, 9601 Wilshire Blvd, #300, Beverly Hills CA 90210 USA

**Sweeney, Mark P** — Baseball Player
6394 W Dublin Lane, Chandler AZ 85226, USA

**Sweeney, Michael J (Mike)** — Baseball Player
PO Box 1193, Rancho Santa Fe CA 92067, USA

**Sweeney, Pepper** — Actor
Gage Group, 14724 Ventura Blvd, #505, Sherman Oaks CA 91403 USA

**Sweeney, Ryan J** — Baseball Player
6941 Waterview Dr SW, Cedar Rapids IA 52404, USA

**Sweeney, Sunny M** — Singer, Songwriter, Guitarist
Republic Nashville Records, 1219 16th Ave S, Nashville TN 37212, USA

**Sweeney, Terry** — Actress, Comedienne
Creative Artists Agency, 2000 Ave of Stars, #100, Los Angeles CA 90067 USA

**Sweeney, Tim** — Ice Hockey Player
47 Ledgewood Dr, Hanover MA 02339, USA

**Sweet, Joseph L (Joe)** — Football Player
1530 NE 89th Court, Vancouver WA 98664, USA

**Sweet, Matthew** — Singer, Songwriter
Russell Carter Artists Mgmt, 567 Ralph Mcgill Blvd NE, Atlanta GA 30312, USA

**Sweet, Richard J (Rick)** — Baseball Player
1503 NE 89th Court, Vancouver WA 98664, USA

**Sweet, Sharon** — Opera Singer
Kunstleragentur Raab & Bohm, Plankengasse 7, 1010 Vienna, Austria

**Sweeten, Madylin** — Actress
Innovative Artists, 1505 10th St, Santa Monica CA 90401 USA

**Sweetland, Brad** — Animator
Pixar Animation, 1200 Park Ave, Emeryville CA 94608, USA

**Sweetnam, Skye** — Singer, Songwriter
Creative Artists Agency, 3310 W End Ave, #500, Nashville TN 37203 USA

**Swensen, Joseph A** — Conductor, Composer
Malmo Opera, Ronneholmsv 20, 200 10 Malmo, Sweden

**Swenson, Inga** — Actress, Singer
3351 Halderman St, Los Angeles CA 90066, USA

**Swenson, Jesse** — Actor
Innovative Artists, 1505 10th St, Santa Monica CA 90401 USA

**Swenson, Rick** — Dog Sled Racer
PO Box 16205, Two Rivers AK 99716, USA

**Swenson, Robert C (Bob)** — Football Player
PO Box 403, Erie CO 80516, USA

**Swenson, Ruth Ann** — Opera Singer
Metropolitan Opera Assn, Lincoln Center Plaza, New York NY 10023 USA

**Swenson, William D** — Afghanistan War Army Hero (CMH)
1818 E Denny Way, #101, Seattle WA 98122, USA

**Swensson, Earl S** — Architect
Earl Swensson Assoc, 2100 W End Ave, #1200, Nashville TN 37203, USA

**Swiczinsky, Helmut** — Architect
Coop Himmelblau, Seilerstatte 16/11A, 1010 Vienna, Austria

**Swienton, Gregory T** — Businessman
Ryder System Inc, 11690 NW 105th St, Medley FL 33178, USA

**Swift** — Rap Artist (D-12)
Coast to Coast Talent, 3350 Barham Blvd, Los Angeles CA 90068 USA

**Swift, Clive** — Actor
Roxane Vacca Mgmt, 8 Silver Place, London W1R 3LJ, England

**Swift, Douglas A (Doug)** — Football Player
265 S 25th St, Philadelphia PA 19103, USA

**Swift, Graham C** — Writer
A P Watt, 20 John St, London WC1N 2DR, England

**Swift, Harley E (Skeeter)** — Basketball Player
4987 Highway 11 W, Kingsport TN 37660, USA

**Swift, Hewson H** — Biologist
University of Chicago, Cell Biology Dept, Chicago IL 60637, USA

**Swift, Jeremy** — Actor
Independent Talent Group, 40 Whitfield St, London W1T 2RH, England

**Swift, Scott H** — Navy Admiral
Commander, 7th Fleet Yokosuka Japan, FPO AP 96601 USA

**Swift, Stephen J** — Judge
US Tax Court, 400 2nd St NW, Washington DC 20217, USA

**Swift, Stromile** — Basketball Player
3256 S Silverwind Cove, Memphis TN 38125, USA

**Swift, Taylor** — Singer, Guitarist, Songwriter
Taylor Swift Enterprises, 242 W Main St, PM Box 412, Hendersonville TN 37075, USA

**Swift, William C (Bill)** — Baseball Player
5880 E Sapphire Lane, Paradise Valley AZ 85253, USA

**Swilley, Dennis N** — Football Player
1020 Gruene River Dr, New Braunfels TX 78132, USA

**Swilling, Patrick T (Pat)** — Football Player
4425 Plum Orchard Ave, New Orleans LA 70126, USA

**Swinburne, Clare** — Actress
Associated International Mgmt, 7 Hatton Garden, #400, London EC1N 8AD, England

**Swindells, William, Jr** — Businessman
Willamette Industries, 1300 SW 5th Ave, #500, Portland OR 97201, USA
**Swindle, Orson** — Government Official
500 University Ave, #309, Honolulu HI 96826, USA
**Swindoll, Charles R** — Evangelist, Writer
Insight for Living, 211 Imperial Highway, Fullerton CA 92835, USA
**Swingle, Paul C** — Baseball Player
6844 S Whetstone Place, Chandler AZ 85249, USA
**Swingley, Douglas L (Doug)** — Dog Sled Racer
PO Box 672, Lincoln MT 59639, USA
**Swink, James E (Jim)** — Football Player
723 Euclid Ave, Rusk TX 75785, USA
**Swinny, Wayne** — Guitarist (Saliva)
Helter Skelter, 347-353 Chiswick High Road, London W4 4HS, England
**Swinson, Aaron** — Basketball Player
1004 Longley Cove, Heathrow FL 32746, USA
**Swinton, Reginald T (Reggie)** — Football Player
14200 Wimbledon Loop, Little Rock AR 72210, USA
**Swinton, Tilda** — Actress
Hamilton Hodell, 66-68 Margaret St, #500, London W1W 8SR, England
**Swisher, Carl C** — Anthropologist
Institute of Human Origins, 1288 9th St, Berkeley CA 94710, USA
**Swisher, Nicholas T (Nick)** — Baseball Player
6803 E Main St, #6601, Scottsdale AZ 85251, USA
**Swisher, Steven E (Steve)** — Baseball Player
432 60th St, Vienna WV 26105, USA
**Swisten, Amanda** — Actress
Xposure Public Relations, 8271 Melrose Ave, #110, Los Angeles CA 90046, USA
**Swit, Loretta** — Actress
Malibu Business/Shipping Center, 23852 Pacific Coast Highway, Malibu CA 90265, USA
**Switzer, Barry** — Football Player, Coach
700 W Timberdell Road, Norman OK 73072, USA
**Switzer, Jon M** — Baseball Player
1109 Elder Circle, Austin TX 78733, USA
**Switzer, Louis** — Interior Designer
Switzer Group, 535 5th Ave, #1100, New York NY 10017, USA
**Swizz Beatz** — Rap Artist, Music Producer
5W Public Relations, 888 7th Ave, #1200, New York NY 10106, USA
**Swoboda, Ronald A (Ron)** — Baseball Player
315 Alonzo St, New Orleans LA 70115, USA
**Swoopes, Sheryl** — Basketball Player
2020 Eldridge Parkway, #4605, Houston TX 77077, USA
**Sy, Omar** — Actor
Agence Artiste Adequet, 108 Rue Reaumur, 75002 Paris, France
**Syal, Meera** — Actress, Comedienne, Writer
United Agents, 12-26 Lexington St, London W1F 0LE, England
**Syberberg, Hans-Jurgen** — Director
Genter Str 15A, 80805 Munich, Germany
**Sybil** — Singer
Tony Denton Promotions, Charter House, 157-159 High St, London N14 6BP, England
**Sydney, Harry F** — Football Player
1558 Cardinal Lane, Green Bay WI 54313, USA
**Sydnor, Charles W, Jr** — Businessman, Educator
Commonwealth Public Broadcasting Corp, 23 Sesame St, Richmond VA 23235, USA
**Sydor, Darryl** — Ice Hockey Player
3358 Windmill Curve, Saint Paul MN 55129, USA
**Syed Sirajuddin Syed Putra Jamalullail** — Head of State, Malaysia
Sultan's Palace, Istana Bukit Serene, 50502 Kuala Lumpur, Malaysia
**Sykes, Eugene C (Gene)** — Football Player
15809 Council Ave, Baton Rouge LA 70817, USA
**Sykes, Jesse** — Singer, Songwriter
Barsuk Records, PO Box 22546, Seattle WA 98122, USA
**Sykes, Lynn R** — Geologist
100 Washington Spring Road, RR 1 Box 248, Palisades NY 10964, USA
**Sykes, Nathan J** — Singer (Wanted)
Industry Music Group, 128 Regent Road, Hanley Stoke, Trent ST1 3AY, England
**Sykes, Peter** — Director
International Talent Booking, Ariel House, 74A Charlotte St, #100 London W1T 4QJ, England
**Sykes, Phil** — Ice Hockey Player
1486 Brooke Court, Hastings MN 55033, USA
**Sykes, Richard B** — Businessman, Microbiologist
Imperial College, Exhibition Road, London SW7 2AZ, England
**Sykes, Robert J (Bob)** — Baseball
1451 County Road 900 E, Carmi IL 62821, USA
**Sykes, Wanda** — Actress, Comedienne
W M E Entertainment, 9601 Wilshire Blvd, #300, Beverly Hills CA 90210 USA
**Sykora, Petr** — Ice Hockey Player
2548 Appletree Dr, Pittsburgh PA 15241, USA
**Sylbert, Anthea** — Costume Designer
13949 Ventura Blvd, #309, Sherman Oaks CA 91423, USA
**Sylvester, Charles (Chuck)** — Harness Racing Trainer
PO Box 1066, Williamstown NJ 08094, USA
**Sylvester, Dean** — Ice Hockey Player
51 Upland Road, Plympton MA 02367, USA
**Sylvester, George H** — Air Force General
4571 Coniceville Road, Mount Jackson VA 22842, USA
**Sylvester, Harold** — Actor
Gage Group, 14724 Ventura Blvd, #505, Sherman Oaks CA 91403 USA
**Sylvester, Michael** — Opera Singer
Columbia Artists Mgmt Inc, 1790 Broadway, #702, New York NY 10019 USA
**Sylvester, Steven P (Steve)** — Football Player
10425 Londonderry Court, Cincinnati OH 45242, USA
**Sylvestri, Don** — Ice Hockey Player
1610 Redfern St, Sudbury ON P3A 3S9, Canada
**Sylvian, David** — Singer, Guitarist (Japan)
Opium Arts, 49 Portland Road, London W11 4LJ, England

**Symington, J Fife, III** — Governor, AZ
1700 W Washington St, Phoenix AZ 85007, USA

**Symms, Steven D** — Senator, ID
127 S Fairfax St, #137, Alexandria VA 22314, USA

**Symon, Michael** — Chef, Restauranteur
Lola Restaurant, 2058 E 4th St, Cleveland OH 44115, USA

**Symone, Raven** — Actress, Singer
United Talent Agency, U T A Plaza, 9336 Civic Center Dr, Beverly Hills CA 90210 USA

**Syms, Sylvia** — Actress
Barry Brown, 47 West Square, London SE11 4SP, England

**Synek, Ondrej** — Rowing Athlete
A S C Dukla Prague, Oddil Aletiky, PS 59, 16044 Prague 6, Czech Republic

**Sypek, Richard** — Actor
Paradigm Agency, 360 N Crescent Dr, North Building, Beverly Hills CA 90210 USA

**Syracuse, Joe** — Writer, Actor, Director
United Talent Agency, U T A Plaza, 9336 Civic Center Dr, Beverly Hills CA 90210 USA

**Syron, Richard F** — Financier, Government Official
Federal Home Loan Mortgage, 8200 Jones Branch Dr, McLean VA 22102, USA

**Szabados, Shannon** — Ice Hockey Player
Team Canada, 2424 University Dr NW, Calgary AB T2N 3Y9, Canada

**Szabo, Istvan** — Director
Vaci 6, 1132 Budapest, Hungary

**Szaro, Richard J (Rich)** — Football Player
171 Metropolitan Ave, Brooklyn NY 11211, USA

**Szczerbiak, Walter R (Wally)** — Basketball Player, Sportscaster
26 Peabody Road, Cold Spring Harbor NY 11724, USA

**Szekely, Eva** — Swimmer
Szepvolgyi Utca 4/B, 1025 Budapest, Hungary

**Szekessy, Karen** — Photographer
Haynstr 2, 20249 Hamburg, Germany

**Szemborski, Stanley R** — Navy Admiral
Director, Program Analysis/Evaluation, HqUSN, Pentagon, Washington DC 20350, USA

**Szemeredi, Endre** — Mathematician
Rutgers State University, Mathematics Dept, New Brunswick NJ 08903, USA

**Szep, Paul M** — Editorial Cartoonist
10610 Andrew Lane, Seminole FL 33777, USA

**Szewczenko, Tanja** — Figure Skater, Model, Actress
D E U, Betzenweg 34, 81247 Munich, Germany

**Szigmond, Vilmos** — Cinematographer
PO Box 2230, Los Angeles CA 90078, USA

**Szmanda, Eric** — Actor
A P A Talent/Literary Agency, 405 S Beverly Dr, #300, Beverly Hills CA 90212 USA

**Szohr, Jessica** — Actress
I C M Partners, 10250 Constellation Blvd, #900, Los Angeles CA 90067 USA

**Szoka, Edmund C Cardinal** — Religious Leader
Prefecture for Economic Affairs, 00120 Vatican City

**Szolkowy, Robin** — Figure Skater
Eisstadion Ingo Steuer, Wittgensdorfner Str 2A, 09114 Chemnitz, Germany

**Szostak, Jack W** — Nobel Medicine Laureate
Simches Research Center, 185 Cambridge St, Boston MA 02114, USA

**Szot, Paulo** — Actor, Opera Singer
Opera et Concert, 37 Rue de la Chaussee d'Antin, 75009 Paris, France

**Szott, David A (Dave)** — Football Player
11 Manor Dr, Morristown NJ 07960, USA

**Szulc, Radoslaw** — Conductor
Harrison/Parrott, 5-6 Albion Court, London W6 0QT, England

**Szuminski, Jason E** — Baseball Player
680 Serra St, #W402, Stanford CA 94305, USA

**Szymanski, James P (Jim)** — Football Player
541 Riverwalk Dr, Mason MI 48854, USA

**Szymanski, Richard F (Dick)** — Football Player
5270 Forest Edge Court, Sanford FL 32771, USA

**T Hooft, Gerardus** — Nobel Physics Laureate
Leuvenlaan 4, Postbus 80.195, 3508 Utrecht TD, Netherlands

**T I** — Rap Artist, Actor
J L Entertainment, 18653 Ventura Blvd, #340, Los Angeles CA 91356 USA

**T, Mr** — Actor
15203 La Maida St, Sherman Oaks CA 91403, USA

**Tabachnik, Michel** — Composer, Conductor
Garvey & Ivor, 59 Lansdowne Place, Hove BN3 1FL, England

**Tabackin, Lewis B (Lew)** — Jazz Flutist, Saxophonist
38 W 94th St, New York NY 10025, USA

**Tabai, Ieremia T** — President, Kiribati
Foreign Affairs Ministry, PO Box 68, Bairiki, Tarawa, Kiribati

**Tabak, Zan** — Basketball Player
230 W Superior St, #510, Chicago IL 60654, USA

**Tabaka, Jeffrey J (Jeff)** — Baseball Player
1481 Norview Dr, Clinton OH 44216, USA

**Tabaksblat, Morris** — Businessman
Reed Elsevier, Sara Burgerhartstr 25, 1055 Amsterdam KV, Netherlands

**Tabaracci, Rick** — Ice Hockey Player
PO Box 982001, Park City UT 84098, USA

**Tabata, Maki** — Speed Skater
Skating Federation, 1-1-1 Jinnan, #414, Shibuyaku, Tokyo 150 8050, Japan

**Tabin, Clifford S** — Geneticist, Molecular Biologist
Harvard Medical School, 240 Longwood Ave, Boston MA 02115, USA

**Tabitha 'Masentle** — Princess, Lesotho
Royal Palace, PO Box 524, Maseru, Lesotho

**Tabler, Patrick S (Pat)** — Baseball Player
8715 Blome Road, Cincinnati OH 45243, USA

**Tabor, June** — Singer
Headline Agency, 39 Churchffields, Milltown, Dublin 14, Ireland

**Tabor, Philip M (Phil)** — Football Player
519 E Harrison Ave, Wheaton IL 60187, USA

**Tabora, Roy Gonzalez** — Artist
Tabora Gallery, 2005 Kalia Road, Honolulu HI 96815, USA

**Tabori, Kristoffer** — Actor
International Artistes, 235 Regent St, London W1R 8AX, England

**Tabori, Laszlo** — Track Athlete
2221 W Olive Ave, Burbank CA 91506, USA

**Tacha, Deanell R** — Judge
US Court of Appeals, 4830 W 15th St, Lawrence KS 66049, USA

**Tadic, Boris** — President, Serbia
President's Office, Nemanjina 11, 11000 Belgrade, Serbia

**Taff, Russ** — Singer
Glickman Entertainment Group, PO Box 570815, Tarzana CA 91357, USA

**Taffe, Jeff** — Ice Hockey Player
1455 Truax Circle, Hastings MN 55033, USA

**Taffoni, Joseph A (Joe)** — Football Player
605 Golf Links Court, Chapin SC 29036, USA

**Tafoya, Joseph P (Joe)** — Football Player
14341 189th Way NE, Woodinville WA 98072, USA

**Tafoya, Michele** — Sportscaster
NBC-TV, Sports Dept, 30 Rockefeller Plaza, #270E, New York NY 10112 USA

**Taft, John** — Ice Hockey Player
5224 Oaklawn Ave, Minneapolis MN 55424, USA

**Taft, William H, IV** — Diplomat
Fried Frank Assoc, 1001 Pennsylvania Ave NW, #800, Washington DC 20004, USA

**Tagawa, Cary-Hiroyuki** — Actor
Abrams Artists, 9200 W Sunset Blvd, #1125, West Hollywood CA 90069 USA

**Tagg, Barclay** — Thoroughbred Racing Trainer
86 Geranium Ave, Floral Park NY 11001, USA

**Taghmaoui, Said** — Actor
Innovative Artists, 1505 10th St, Santa Monica CA 90401 USA

**Tagle, Luis Antonio G** — Religious Leader
Archdiocese, 121 Arzobispo St, Intramuros, PO Box 132, 1099 Manila, Philippines

**Tagliabue, Paul J** — Football Executive
4149 Parkglen Court NW, Washington DC 20007, USA

**Taglianetti, Peter A** — Ice Hockey Player
PO Box 120, Lawrence PA 15055, USA

**Taglioni, Alice** — Actress
Artmedia, 20 Ave Rapp, 75007 Paris, France

**Taguchi, So** — Baseball Player
12931 Twin Meadows Court, Saint Louis MO 63146, USA

**Tahir, Faran** — Actor
Greene Assoc, 1901 Ave of Stars, #130, Los Angeles CA 90067 USA

**Taillibert, Roger R** — Architect
163 Rue de la Pompe, 75116 Paris, France

**Taimak** — Actor
Media Artists Group, 8222 Melrose Ave, #203, Los Angeles CA 90048 USA

**Tait, John B** — Football Player
3408 Echo Springs Road, Lafayette CA 94549, USA

**Tait, Michael D** — Singer (DC Talk, Tait, Newsboys)
True Artist Mgmt, 227 3rd Ave N, Franklin TN 37064, USA

**Taittinger, Claude** — Businessman
9 Place Saint-Nicaise, BP 2741, 51061 Reims Cedex, France

**Tajbert, Vitali** — Boxer
Spotlight Boxing, Am Stadtrand 27, 22047 Hamburg, Germany

**Takac, Robby** — Bassist (Goo Goo Dolls)
Atlas/Third Rail Entertainment, 9200 W Sunset Blvd, West Hollywood CA 90069, USA

**Takacs, Tibor** — Director
A P A Talent/Literary Agency, 405 S Beverly Dr, #300, Beverly Hills CA 90212 USA

**Takacs-Nagy, Gabor** — Concert Violinist
Case Postale 186, 1245 Collonge-Bellerive, Switzerland

**Takagi, Toranosuke** — Auto Racing Driver
Nakajima Planning, 1-3-10 Higushi, Shivuyaku, Tokyo 150 0011, Japan

**Takahashi, Daisuke** — Figure Skater
Kansai University Skate Club, 3-3-35 Yamatecho, Suitashi, Osaka 564 8680 Japan

Takahashi, Joseph S — Neuroscientist
Northwestern University, Neurobiology Dept, 2153 Campus Dr, Evanston IL 60208, USA
Takahashi, Michiaki — Immunologist
Osaka University, Microbe Diseases Institute, Osaka 565 0871, Japan
Takahashi, Naoko — Track Athlete
Sekisui Chemical Co, 4-4-2 Nishintenma, Kitaku, Osaka 530 8565, Japan
Takase, Megumi — Soccer Player
Football Assn, 3-10-15 Hongo, Bunkyoku, Tokyo 113 0033 Japan
Takei, George — Actor
Hosato Enterprises, 419 N Larchmont Blvd, #41, Los Angeles CA 90004, USA
Takezawa, Kyoko — Concert Violinist
Opus 3 Artists, 470 Park Ave S, #900N, New York NY 10016 USA
Takko, Kari — Ice Hockey Player
Dallas Stars, 2601 Ave of Stars, #100, Frisco TX 75034 USA
Tal, Alona — Actress
Innovative Artists, 1505 10th St, Santa Monica CA 90401 USA
Tal, Shiraz — Model
Women Mgmt, 199 Lafayette St, New York NY 10012, USA
Talaba, Marian — Opera Singer
I M G Artists, Hogarth Business Park, Chiswick, London W4 2TH, England
Talafous, Dean — Ice Hockey Player
2418 Foxglove Circle, Hudson WI 54016, USA
Talagi, Toke T — Premier, Niue
Premier's Office, PO Box 40, Alofi, Niue Island
Talalay, Paul — Pharmacologist
5512 Boxhill Lane, Baltimore MD 21210, USA
Talalay, Rachel — Director
A P A Talent/Literary Agency, 405 S Beverly Dr, #300, Beverly Hills CA 90212 USA
Talamini, Robert G (Bob) — Football Player
3577 Cave Creek Manor, Las Cruces NM 88011, USA
Talancon, Ana Claudia — Actress
Gold Levin, 8424-A Santa Monica Blvd, #706, Los Angeles CA 90069, USA
Talat, Mehmet Ali — President, Turkish Northern Cyprus
President's Office, Turkish North Cypress, Via Mersin 10, Lefkosa, Turkey
Talavera, Tracee — Gymnast
106 Mandala Court, Walnut Creek CA 94596, USA
Talbert, David E — Director, Producer, Writer
Brillstein Entertainment Partners, 9150 Wilshire Blvd, #350, Beverly Hills CA 90212 USA
Talbert, Diron V — Football Player
PO Box 388, Rosenberg TX 77471, USA
Talbert, Don L — Football Player
PO Box 261, 3027 Highway 123, Richmond TX 77406, USA
Talbot, Don — Swimming Coach
Sports Federation, 333 River Road, Vanier, Ottawa ON K1L 8B9, Canada
Talbot, Frederick L (Fred) — Baseball Player
7701 Lunceford Lane, Falls Church VA 22043, USA
Talbot, Jena-Guy — Ice Hockey Player
4248 Notre Dame Quest St, Trois-Rivieres QC G9A 4Z5, Canada
Talbot, Maxime — Ice Hockey Player
111 Bellevue Ave, Pittsburgh PA 15229, USA
Talbot, Nita — Actress
3420 Merrimac Road, Los Angeles CA 90049, USA
Talbot, Stephen H — Actor, Producer
University of California, Graduate Journalism School, Berkeley CA 94720, USA
Talbot, Susan — Actress
Media Artists Group, 8222 Melrose Ave, #203, Los Angeles CA 90048 USA
Talbott, Michael — Actor, Director
231A Tano Road, Santa Fe NM 87506, USA
Talbott, N Strobridge (Strobe), III — Journalist, Association Executive
Brookings Institution, 1775 Massachusetts Ave NW, Washington DC 20036, USA
Talese, Gay — Writer
154 E Atlantic Blvd, Ocean City NJ 08226, USA
Tali, Anu — Conductor
Tali Management, Kohtu 3, 10130 Tallinn, Estonia
Taliaferro, George — Football Player
2708 Olcott Blvd, Bloomington IN 47401, USA
Taliaferro, Myron E (Mike) — Football Player
7332 Oakbluff Dr, Dallas TX 75254, USA
Tallas, Rob — Ice Hockey Player
1884 Classic Dr, Coral Springs FL 33071, USA
Tallet, Brian C — Baseball Player
3167 McClendon Court, Baton Rouge LA 70810, USA
Talley, Darryl V — Football Player
8713 Lake Tibet Court, Orlando FL 32836, USA
Talley, Gary — Singer, Guitarist (Box Tops)
Horizon Mgmt, PO Box 8770, Endwell NJ 13762, USA
Talley, Joel E — Vietnam War Air Force Hero
20 Lakeshore Dr, Shalimar FL 32579, USA
Tallman, Bob — Rodeo Sportscaster
3401 Lone Star Road, Poolville TX 76487, USA
Tallman, Patricia — Actress
Innovative Artists, 1505 10th St, Santa Monica CA 90401 USA
Tallman, Richard C — Judge
US Court of Appeals, US Courthouse, 1010 5th Ave, Seattle WA 98104, USA
Tallon, Dale — Ice Hockey Player
1533 W Everett Road, Lake Forest IL 60045, USA
Tally, Ted — Writer
Creative Artists Agency, 2000 Ave of Stars, #100, Los Angeles CA 90067 USA
Talon, Amelia — Model
Playboy Promotions, 2706 Media Center Dr, Los Angeles CA 90065 USA
Talton, Marion L (Tim) — Baseball Player
130 Hardy Talton Road, Pikeville NC 27863, USA
Talwalkar, Abhijit Y — Businessman
L S I Logic Corp, 1621 Barber Lane, Milpitas CA 95035, USA
Tam, Jeffrey E (Jeff) — Baseball Player
5255 Pina Vista Dr, Melbourne FL 32934, USA

**Tam, Vivienne** — Fashion Designer
550 Fashion Ave, #2000, New York NY 10018, USA

**Tamahori, Lee** — Director
W M E Entertainment, 9601 Wilshire Blvd, #300, Beverly Hills CA 90210 USA

**Tamaian, Ion** — Artist
Sibiu, Str Stadionului, 557260 Selimbar, Romania

**Tamargo, John F** — Baseball Player
19018 Fern Meadow Loop, Lutz FL 33558, USA

**Tamaro, Janet** — Producer, Writer
Creative Artists Agency, 2000 Ave of Stars, #100, Los Angeles CA 90067 USA

**Tamaryn** — Singer
Agency Group Ltd, 142 W 57th St, #600, New York NY 10019 USA

**Tamayo Mendez, Arnaldo** — Cosmonaut, Cuba
Calle 16, #504, C/5A y 7MA, Miramar, Ciudad Havana 11300, Cuba

**Tambellini, Roger** — Golfer
32513 N Scottsdale Road, #105, Scottsdale AZ 85266, USA

**Tambellini, Steve** — Ice Hockey Player
9 Laurel Place, Port Moody BC 33H 4N1, Canada

**Tambiah, Stanley J** — Anthropologist
Harvard University, Anthropology Dept, Cambridge MA 02138, USA

**Tamblyn, Amber** — Actress
United Talent Agency, U T A Plaza, 9336 Civic Center Dr, Beverly Hills CA 90210 USA

**Tamblyn, Russell I (Russ)** — Actor, Dancer
Hyler Mgmt, 20 Ocean Park Blvd, #25, Santa Monica CA 90405 USA

**Tambor, Jeffrey** — Actor
Burstein Co, 15304 W Sunset Blvd, #208, Pacific Palisades CA 90272 USA

**Tamburello, Benjamin A (Ben), Jr** — Football Player
4385 Milner Road W, Birmingham AL 35242, USA

**Tamer, Chris** — Ice Hockey Player
4215 Cornwell Lane, Whitmore Lake MI 48189, USA

**Tamia** — Singer, Songwriter, Actress
Chris Smith Mgmt, 21 Camden St, #500, Toronto ON M5V 1V2, Canada

**Tamm, Ralph E** — Football Player
942 Lake Gulch Road, Castle Rock CO 80104, USA

**Tamme, Jacob** — Football Player
Denver Broncos, 13655 E Broncos Parkway, Englewood CO 80112 USA

**Tan Dun** — Composer
Columbia Artists Mgmt Inc, 1790 Broadway, #702, New York NY 10019 USA

**Tan, Amy R** — Writer
I C M Partners, 10250 Constellation Blvd, #900, Los Angeles CA 90067 USA

**Tan, Melvyn** — Concert Pianist
Valerie Barber Mgmt, 4 Winsley St, #305, London W1N 7AR, England

**Tanabe, David** — Ice Hockey Player
2321 Fieldstone Curve, Saint Paul MN 55129, USA

**Tanaka, Asuna** — Soccer Player
Football Assn, 3-10-15 Hongo, Bunkyoku, Tokyo 113 0033 Japan

**Tanaka, Koichi** — Nobel Chemistry Laureate
Shimadzu Corp, 1 Nishinokyo-Kuwabaracho, Nakagoku, Kyoto 604 8511, Japan

**Tanaka, Shoji** — Physicist
Superconductivity Laboratory, 1-10-13 Shinonome, Kotoku, Tokyo 135 0062, Japan

**Tanana, Frank D** — Baseball Player
28492 S Harwich Dr, Farmington Hills MI 48334, USA

**Tancill, Chris** — Ice Hockey Player
14 Kingswood Circle, Verona WI 53593, USA

**Tancredi, Melissa P J** — Soccer Player
Canadian Soccer, Place Soccer Canada, 237 Metcalfe St, Ottawa ON K2P 1R2, Canada

**Tandja, Mamadou** — President, Niger
President's Office, State House, Aso Villa, Abuja, Niger

**Tanen, Sloane** — Writer
Bloomsbury Publishing, 50 Bedford Square, London WC1B 3DP, England

**Tanenbaum, Robert K** — Writer
Robert K Tanenbaum Law Offices, 708 N Roxbury Dr, Beverly Hills CA 90210, USA

**Tang Fei** — Prime Minister, Taiwan
Kuomintang, 11 Chang Shan South Road, Taipei 100, Taiwan

**Tang, David** — Fashion Designer
Shanghai Tang, 148 Connaught Road Central, #2300, Hong Kong, China

**Tang, Muhai** — Conductor
I M G Artists, Hogarth Business Park, Chiswick, London W4 2TH, England

**Tanguay, Alex** — Ice Hockey Player
78 Jackson St, #1, Denver CO 80206, USA

**Tani, Daniel M** — Astronaut
PO Box 1453, Great Falls VA 22066, USA

**Taniguchi, Tadatsugu** — Molecular Biologist
University of Tokyo Medical Center, 7-3-1, Hongo, Bunkyoku, Tokyo 113 0033 Japan

**Tank** — Singer, Songwriter
J L Entertainment, 511 Ave of Americas, #230, New York NY 10011, USA

**Tankersley, Taylor M** — Baseball Player
853 Chartier Court, Asheboro NC 27205, USA

**Tankian, Serj** — Singer, Musician (System of a Down)
Velvet Hammer Music, 9014 Melrose Ave, West Hollywood CA 90069, USA

**Tanksley, Rick** — Singer
Teerajay Music, PO Box 183, White House TN 37188, USA

**Tanksley, Steven D** — Plant Geneticist
Cornell University, Plant Genetics Dept, Emerson Hall, Ithaca NY 14853, USA

**Tannahill, Don** — Ice Hockey Player
10113 Lakeview Dr, Rancho Mirage CA 92270, USA

**Tannehill, Ryan T** — Football Player
Miami Dolphins, 7500 SW 30th St, Davie FL 33314 USA

**Tannen, Deborah F** — Writer
Georgetown University, Linguistics Dept, Washington DC 20057, USA

**Tannen, Steven O (Steve)** — Football Player
735 N Niagara St, Burbank CA 91505, USA

**Tannenwald, Theodore, Jr** — Judge
US Tax Court, 400 2nd St NW, Washington DC 20217, USA

**Tanner, Alain** — Director
Chemin Point-du-Jour 12, 1202 Geneva, Switzerland

**Tanner, Antwon** — Actor
Talent Works, 3500 W Olive Ave, #1400, Burbank CA 91505 USA

**Tanner, Barron K** — Football Player
7556 W Oregon Ave, Glendale AZ 85303, USA

**Tanner, Bruce M** — Baseball Player
324 Hearthstone Dr, New Castle PA 16105, USA

**Tanner, John P** — Ice Hockey Player
Hewlett Packard, 5150 Spectrum Way, Mississauga ON L4W 5G1, Canada

**Tanner, John S** — Representative, TN
Prime Policy Group LLP, 1110 Vermont Ave NW, #1000, Washington DC 20005, USA

**Tanner, Joseph R (Joe)** — Astronaut
800 Nelson Park Lane, Longmont CO 80503, USA

**Tanner, Roscoe** — Tennis Player
1109 Gnome Trail, Lookout Mountain TN 37350, USA

**Tannous, Afif I** — Government Official
6912 Oak Court, Annandale VA 22003, USA

**Tanon Ortiz, Olga T** — Singer, Composer
Universal Attractions, 135 W 26th St, #1200, New York NY 10001 USA

**Tanti, Tony** — Ice Hockey Player
Tanti Interiors, 121-2323 Boundray Road, Vancouver BC V5M 4V8, Canada

**Tanuja** — Actress
14 Usha Kiran 15, M L Dhahanukar Marg, Mumbai MS 400026, India

**Tanuvasa, Maa J** — Football Player
PO Box 893309, Mililani HI 96789, USA

**Tanzi, Vito** — Economist
5912 Walhondine Road, Bethesda MD 20816, USA

**Tao, Conrad** — Concert Pianist
I M G Artists, Hogarth Business Park, Chiswick, London W4 2TH, England

**Tao, Terence** — Mathematician
University of California, Mathematics Dept, Los Angeles CA 90024, USA

**Taormina, Sheila** — Swimmer, Triathlete
172 Nautica Mile Dr, Clermont FL 34711, USA

**Tapani, Kevin R** — Baseball Player
781 Ferndale Road N, Wayzata MN 55391, USA

**Tape, Gerald F** — Physicist
90 Camino Espejo, Santa Fe NM 87507, USA

**Tapert, Robert G** — Producer, Director, Writer
Senator International, 8750 Wilshire Blvd, Beverly Hills CA 90211, USA

**Taplitz, Daniel** — Director
United Talent Agency, U T A Plaza, 9336 Civic Center Dr, Beverly Hills CA 90210 USA

**Tapp, Darryl A** — Football Player
42742 Mirror Pond Place, Ashburn VA 20148, USA

**Tapper, Zoe** — Actress
Independent Talent Group, 40 Whitfield St, London W1T 2RH, England

**Tapping, Amanda** — Actress, Producer, Director
Play Mgmt, 220-807 Powell St, Vancouver BC V6A 1H7, Canada

**Tarabay, Nick E** — Actor
Medavoy Mgmt, 10203 Santa Monica Blvd, #400, Los Angeles CA 90067, USA

**Tarand, Andres** — Prime Minister
Riigikogu, Lossi Plats 1A, Tallinn 10130, Estonia

**Tarantino, Quentin** — Director
W M E Entertainment, 9601 Wilshire Blvd, #300, Beverly Hills CA 90210 USA

**Taranu, Cornel** — Composer, Conductor
Gh Dima Music Academy, IIC Bratianu Str 25, 3400 Cluj, Romania

**Tarasco, Anthony G (Tony)** — Baseball Player
3528 Maplewood Ave, Los Angeles CA 90066, USA

**Tarasova, Tatiana** — Figure Skating Coach
Connecticut Skating Center, 300 Alumni Road, Newington CT 06111, USA

**Tarasovic, George K** — Football Player
1503 Michael Dr, Pittsburgh PA 15227, USA

**Tarbuck, Jimmy (Tarby)** — Actor, Comedian
118 Beaufort St, London SW3 6BU, England

**Tardif, Marc** — Ice Hockey Player
Charlesbourg Toyota, 16070 Henri-Bourassa, Charlesbourg QC G1G 3Z8, Canada

**Tardio, Chris** — Actor
Framework Entertainment, 9057 Nemo St, #C, West Hollywood CA 90069 USA

**Tarelkin, Yevgeny I** — Cosmonaut
Cosmonaut Training Center, Star City, 141160 Zvezdny Gorodok, Moscow Oblast, Russia

**Tarjan, Robert E** — Mathematician
4 Constitution Hill E, Princeton NJ 08540, USA

**Tarkan** — Singer
International Creative Talent Agency, Mualim Cad 17, Orta Koy, 2007 Istanbul, Turkey

**Tarkanian, Jerry** — Basketball Coach
4767 Ocean Blvd, #1005, San Diego CA 92109, USA

**Tarkenton, Francis A (Fran)** — Football Player, Businessman
Tarkenton Co, 3340 Peachtree Road NE, #2570, Atlanta GA 30326, USA

**Tarpley, Roy J** — Basketball Player
819 Foxridge Dr, Arlington TX 76017, USA

**Tarr, Juraj** — Canoeing Athlete
Topolova 7, 94501 Komarno, Slovakia

**Tarses, Jamie** — Producer
W M E Entertainment, 9601 Wilshire Blvd, #300, Beverly Hills CA 90210 USA

**Tarses, Matt** — Producer, Writer
W M E Entertainment, 9601 Wilshire Blvd, #300, Beverly Hills CA 90210 USA

**Tartabull Guzman, Jose M** — Baseball Player
1658 W 72nd St, Hialeah FL 33014, USA

**Tartabull Mora, Danilio (Danny)** — Baseball Player
27337 Garza Dr, Santa Clarita CA 91350, USA

**Tartaglia, Antonio** — Bobsled Athlete
Olympic Committee, Foro Italico, Largo Lauro de Bosis 15, 00135 Rome, Italy

**Tartakovsky, Genndy** — Producer, Director
W M E Entertainment, 9601 Wilshire Blvd, #300, Beverly Hills CA 90210 USA

**Tarter, Jill** — Astrophysicist
Seti Institute Research Center, 2035 Mountain View, Mountain View CA 94043, USA

**Tartt, Donna** — Writer
Rogers Coleridge White, 20 Powis Mews, London W11 1JN, England

| | |
|---|---|
| **Tarver, Antonio D**<br>4701 Rue Bordeaux, Lutz FL 33558, USA | Boxer |
| **Tarzier, Carol**<br>1217 32nd St, Emeryville CA 94608, USA | Sculptor |
| **Tasby, Willie, Jr**<br>1210 E Renfro St, Plant City FL 33563, USA | Baseball Player |
| **Taschner, Jack G**<br>2170 Hidden Creek Road, Neenah WI 54956, USA | Baseball Player |
| **Tash**<br>Likwit Entertainment, PO Box 360713, Los Angeles CA 90036, USA | Rap Artist |
| **Tashian, Barry**<br>Tashian Music, PO Box 150921, Nashville TN 37215, USA | Singer, Guitarist, Songwriter |
| **Tashima, A Wallace**<br>US Court of Appeals, 125 S Grand Ave, Pasadena CA 91105, USA | Judge |
| **Tasker, Steven J (Steve)**<br>16 Gypsy Lane, East Aurora NY 14052, USA | Football Player, Sportscaster |
| **Tatarek, Robert F (Bob)**<br>5829 Southhall Road, Birmingham AL 35213, USA | Football Player |
| **Tataryn, Dave**<br>27 Fairway Court, Horseshoe Valley ON L0K 1N0, Canada | Ice Hockey Player |
| **Tataurangi, Phillip M (Phil)**<br>PO Box 15325, Irvine CA 92623, USA | Golfer |
| **Tate, Bruce**<br>David Harris Enterprises, 24210 E Fork Road, #9, Azusa CA 91702, USA | Singer (Penguins) |
| **Tate, Catherine**<br>United Talent Agency, U T A Plaza, 9336 Civic Center Dr, Beverly Hills CA 90210 USA | Actress |
| **Tate, David F**<br>3481 S Blackhawk Way, Aurora CO 80014, USA | Football Player |
| **Tate, Frank**<br>9560 Deering Dr, #18, Houston TX 77036, USA | Boxer |
| **Tate, Geoffrey W (Geoff)**<br>Monterey International, 200 W Superior St, #202, Chicago IL 60654 USA | Singer (Queensryche), Songwriter |
| **Tate, Grady**<br>Abby Hoffer Enterprises, 223 1/2 E 48th St, New York NY 10017 USA | Jazz Drummer, Singer |
| **Tate, James V**<br>PO Box 9668, North Amherst MA 01059, USA | Writer |
| **Tate, Jeffrey P**<br>Columbia Artists Mgmt Inc, 1790 Broadway, #702, New York NY 10019 USA | Conductor |
| **Tate, Larenz**<br>A P A Talent/Literary Agency, 405 S Beverly Dr, #300, Beverly Hills CA 90212 USA | Actor |
| **Tate, Randy**<br>Christian Coalition, 100 Centerville Turnpike, Virginia Beach VA 23463, USA | Religious Leader, Representative, WA |
| **Tate, Stuart D (Stu)**<br>695 Liberty Hill Road, Toney AL 35773, USA | Baseball Player |
| **Tatel, David S**<br>US Court of Appeals, 333 Constitution Ave NW, #4400, Washington DC 20001, USA | Judge |
| **Tatham, Chuck**<br>Collective, 8383 Wilshire Blvd, #1050, Beverly Hills CA 90211 USA | Actor, Writer |
| **Tatopolous, Patrick**<br>I C M Partners, 10250 Constellation Blvd, #900, Los Angeles CA 90067 USA | Special Effects Director |
| **Tattersall, David**<br>Lucasfilm, PO Box 2459, San Rafael CA 94912, USA | Cinematographer |
| **Tatulli, Mark**<br>Universal Press Syndicate, 4520 Main St, #700, Kansas City MO 64111 USA | Cartoonist (Heart of the City) |
| **Tatum, Bradford**<br>Brad Warshaw Mgmt, 8228 Sunset Blvd, Los Angeles CA 90046, USA | Actor |
| **Tatum, Channing**<br>Management 360, 9111 Wilshire Blvd, Beverly Hills CA 90210 USA | Actor, Model |
| **Tatum, Kenneth R (Ken)**<br>19 Oakdale Dr, Montevallo AL 35115, USA | Baseball Player |
| **Tatum, W Earl**<br>2300 W Skyline Road, Milwaukee WI 53209, USA | Basketball Player |
| **Tatupu, M Mea'alofa (Lofa)**<br>PO Box 1053, Bellevue WA 98009, USA | Football Player |
| **Taubensee, Edward K (Eddie)**<br>2582 S Maguire Road, #287, Ocoee FL 34761, USA | Baseball Player |
| **Taubman, A Alfred**<br>Taubman Co, 200 E Long Lake Road, #300, Bloomfield Hills MI 48304, USA | Businessman |
| **Taubman, Anatole**<br>United Agents, 12-26 Lexington St, London W1F 0LE, England | Actor |
| **Taubman, Anatole**<br>Agentur Charade Kunstler, Joseph-Hayden-Str 1, 10557 Berlin, Germany | Actor, Producer |
| **Taubman, William**<br>Amherst College, Political Science Dept, Amherst MA 01002, USA | Writer |
| **Taupin, Bernie**<br>2905 Roundup Road, Santa Ynez CA 93460, USA | Singer, Songwriter |
| **Tauran, Jean-Louis Cardinal**<br>Palazzo Apostolico, 00120 Vatican City | Religious Leader |
| **Taurasi, Diana**<br>Phoenix Mercury, American West Arena, 201 E Jefferson St, Phoenix AZ 85004 USA | Basketball Player |
| **Tauriello, Dena**<br>W Mgmt, 266 Elizabeth St, #1A, New York NY 10012, USA | Drummer (Antigone Rising) |
| **Tausch, Terry W**<br>2804 Ryder Court, Plano TX 75093, USA | Football Player |
| **Tauscher, Hansjorg**<br>Schwand 7, 87561 Oberstdorf, Germany | Alpine Skier |
| **Tauscher, Mark G**<br>2964 Nessie Lane, Sun Prairie WI 53590, USA | Football Player |
| **Taussig, Donald F (Don)**<br>1111 Ocean Dunes Circle, Jupiter FL 33477, USA | Baseball Player |
| **Tautolo, Terry L**<br>5713 E Huntdale St, Long Beach CA 90808, USA | Football Player |
| **Tautou, Audrey**<br>Artmedia, 20 Ave Rapp, 75007 Paris, France | Actress |
| **Tauziat, Nathalie**<br>Federation de Tennis, 1 Ave Gordon Bennett, 75016 Paris, France | Tennis Player |

**T**

**Tarver - Tauziat**

**Tauzin, Wilbert J (Billy)** — Association Official; Representative, LA
Pharmaceutical Research, 1100 15th St NW, #900, Washington DC 20005, USA
**Tavare, Jay** — Actor
Paul Greenstone, 3008 Sorrelwood Dr, San Ramon CA 94582, USA
**Tavares, John** — Lacrosse Player
Buffalo Bandits, H S B C Arena, 1 Knox Place, Buffalo NY 14216, USA
**Tavares, Sara** — Singer, Songwriter
Columbia Artists Mgmt Inc, 1790 Broadway, #702, New York NY 10019 USA
**Tavarez Carmen, Julian** — Baseball Player
1108 Fireside Trail, Broadview Heights OH 44147, USA
**Taveras Fabian, Franklin C (Frank)** — Baseball Player
Calle 31, #16 Los Colinos, Santiago, Dominican Republic
**Taveras, Willy** — Baseball Player
5535 Memorial Dr, #F, Houston TX 77007, USA
**Taverner, Sonia** — Ballerina
PO Box 2039, Stony Plain AB T7Z 1X6, Canada
**Tavernier, Bertrand R M** — Director
I C M Partners, Marlborough House, 10 Earlham St, #300, London WC2H 9LNP, England
**Tawan, Serria** — Model
Playboy Promotions, 2706 Media Center Dr, Los Angeles CA 90065 USA
**Taye, John** — Sculptor
1412 E Jefferson St, Boise ID 83712, USA
**Taylor, Aaron** — Actor
W M E Entertainment, 9601 Wilshire Blvd, #300, Beverly Hills CA 90210 USA
**Taylor, Aaron M** — Football Player
278 Black Amber Way, Brentwood CA 94513, USA
**Taylor, Andy** — Guitarist (Duran Duran)
D D Productions, 93A Westbourne Park Villas, London W2 5ED, England
**Taylor, Angel** — Singer, Songwriter
A2 Mgmt, 2336 W Belmont Ave, Chicago IL 60618, USA
**Taylor, Angelo F** — Track Athlete
Vector Sports Mgmt, 417 Keller Parkway, Keller TX 76248, USA
**Taylor, Anna Diggs** — Judge
US District Court, US Courthouse, 231 W Lafayette Blvd, #827, Detroit MI 48226, USA
**Taylor, Anthony P** — Basketball Player
5300 Parkview Dr, #1093, Lake Oswego OR 97035, USA
**Taylor, Antonio (Tony)** — Baseball Player
8415 NW 165th Terrace, Hialeah FL 33016, USA
**Taylor, April** — Singer
Thompson Entertainment Group, 1300 Division St, #207, Nashville TN 37203, USA
**Taylor, Ben** — Singer, Songwriter
W M E Entertainment, 9601 Wilshire Blvd, #300, Beverly Hills CA 90210 USA
**Taylor, Benedict** — Actor
Rhubarb, 1a Devonshire Road, Chiswick, London W4 2EU, England
**Taylor, Bobby (Chief)** — Ice Hockey Player
3912 Americana Dr, Tampa FL 33634, USA
**Taylor, Brian** — Director, Writer
United Talent Agency, U T A Plaza, 9336 Civic Center Dr, Beverly Hills CA 90210 USA
**Taylor, Brian D** — Basketball Player
3622 Green Vista Dr, Encino CA 91436, USA
**Taylor, Bruce B** — Baseball Player
8 Highland Park Road, Rutland MA 01543, USA
**Taylor, Bruce L** — Football Player
10324 Pontofino Circle, Trinity FL 34655, USA
**Taylor, Buck** — Actor
Linda McAlister Talent, 30 N Raymond, #409, Pasadena CA 91103, USA
**Taylor, Cecil P** — Jazz Pianist, Composer
Abby Hoffer Enterprises, 223 1/2 E 48th St, New York NY 10017 USA
**Taylor, Charles** — Philosopher, Templeton Religion Laureate
6603 Jeanne Mance, Montreal QC H2V 4LI, Canada
**Taylor, Charles G (Chuck)** — Baseball Player
1535 Georgetown Lane, Murfreesboro TN 37129, USA
**Taylor, Charles R (Charley)** — Football Player, Executive
12032 Canter Lane, Reston VA 20191, USA
**Taylor, Chester L** — Football Player
29006 Burning Tree Lane, Romulus MI 48174, USA
**Taylor, Christian M** — Producer, Director, Writer
Creative Artists Agency, 2000 Ave of Stars, #100, Los Angeles CA 90067 USA
**Taylor, Christine** — Actress
United Talent Agency, U T A Plaza, 9336 Civic Center Dr, Beverly Hills CA 90210 USA
**Taylor, Christy** — Actress
10990 Massachusetts Ave, #3, Los Angeles CA 90024, USA
**Taylor, Daren** — Drummer (Airborne Toxic Event)
Island Def Jam Records, 8920 W Sunset Blvd, #200, West Hollywood CA 90069 USA
**Taylor, Dave** — Ice Hockey Player, Executive
Dallas Stars, 2601 Ave of Stars, #100, Frisco TX 75034 USA
**Taylor, David M** — Football Player
82 Manchester St, Glen Rock PA 17327, USA
**Taylor, Doris A** — Cardiovascular Repair Researcher
University of Minnesota Medical School, Stem Cell Dept, Minneapolis MN 55455, USA
**Taylor, Dwight B** — Baseball Player
5163 Queen Mary Lane, Jackson MS 39209, USA
**Taylor, Dylan** — Actor
Thruline Entertainment, 9250 Wilshire Blvd, #100, Beverly Hills CA 90212 USA
**Taylor, Edwin W** — Biophysicist, Molecular Geneticist
University of Chicago, Biophysics Dept, 920 E 58th St, Chicago IL 60637, USA
**Taylor, Eric** — Bassist (Saving Abel)
Virgin Records, 338 N Foothill Road, Beverly Hills CA 90210 USA
**Taylor, Everett E (Ed)** — Football Player
2901 Clarke Road, Memphis TN 38115, USA
**Taylor, Femi** — Actress, Dancer
Coolwaters Productions, 10061 Riverside Dr, Box 531, Toluca Lake CA 91602 USA
**Taylor, Finn** — Director, Writer, Actor
Creative Artists Agency, 2000 Ave of Stars, #100, Los Angeles CA 90067 USA
**Taylor, Frederick** — Writer
Jane Turnbull Agency, 58 Elgin Crescent, London W11 2JJ, England

| | |
|---|---|
| **Taylor, Gwendoline**<br>Auckland Actors, P O Box 56460, Dominion Road, Auckland 1446, New Zealand , USA | Actress |
| **Taylor, Harry E**<br>2125 Cooks Lane, Fort Worth TX 76120, USA | Baseball Player |
| **Taylor, Henry S**<br>1120 Aqua Vista Dr NW, Gig Harbor WA 98335, USA | Writer |
| **Taylor, Holland**<br>Gersh Agency, 9465 Wilshire Blvd, #600, Beverly Hills CA 90212 USA | Actress |
| **Taylor, Ivan (Ike)**<br>4206 Lenox Oval, Pittsburgh PA 15237, USA | Football Player |
| **Taylor, J Herbert**<br>110 Wood Road, #H210, Los Gatos CA 95030, USA | Botanist |
| **Taylor, James**<br>2238 Dundas St W, PO Box 59039, Toronto ON, M6R 3B5, Canada | Singer, Songwriter |
| **Taylor, James**<br>Kunstler Sekretariat am Gasteig, Rosenheimer Str 52, 81669 Munich, Germany | Opera Singer |
| **Taylor, James (J T)**<br>Brothers Management Assoc, 141 Dunbar Ave, Fords NJ 08863 USA | Singer (Kool & the Gang) |
| **Taylor, James A**<br>PO Box 284, Trinity Center CA 96091, USA | Vietnam War Army Hero (CMH) |
| **Taylor, James Arnold**<br>19360 Rinaldi St, #501, Porter Ranch CA 91326, USA | Actor |
| **Taylor, James C (Jim)**<br>7840 Walden Road, Baton Rouge LA 70808, USA | Football Player |
| **Taylor, Jason P**<br>2980 Paddock Road, Weston FL 33331, USA | Football Player |
| **Taylor, Jennifer B**<br>Stewart Talent, 58 W Huron, Chicago IL 60654, USA | Model, Actress |
| **Taylor, Jermaine**<br>PO Box 3456, Little Rock AR 72203, USA | Boxer |
| **Taylor, Jill**<br>Playboy Promotions, 2706 Media Center Dr, Los Angeles CA 90065 USA | Model |
| **Taylor, Jill Bolte**<br>University of Indiana Medical School, Neuroanatomy Dept, Bloomington IN 47405, USA | Neuroanatomist |
| **Taylor, Jim**<br>Ad Hominem Enterprises, 506 Santa Monica Blvd, #400, Santa Monica CA 90401, USA | Producer |
| **Taylor, John**<br>D D Productions, 93A Westbourne Park Villas, London W2 5ED, England | Bassist (Duran Duran) |
| **Taylor, John G**<br>PO Box 326, Fresno CA 93708, USA | Football Player |
| **Taylor, Jonathan**<br>I C M Partners, 10250 Constellation Blvd, #900, Los Angeles CA 90067 USA | Producer, Director |
| **Taylor, Joseph H, Jr**<br>272 Hartley St, Princeton NJ 08540, USA | Nobel Physics Laureate |
| **Taylor, Kathleen**<br>Four Seasons Hotels, 1165 Leslie St, Toronto ON M3C 2K8, Canada | Businesswoman |
| **Taylor, Keith G**<br>PO Box 12324, Chandler AZ 85248, USA | Football Player |
| **Taylor, Kitrick L**<br>25975 Hacienda Court, Moreno Valley CA 92551, USA | Football Player |
| **Taylor, Lawrence J**<br>5796 Devon St, Port Orange FL 32127, USA | Football Player |
| **Taylor, Lili**<br>A P A Talent/Literary Agency, 405 S Beverly Dr, #300, Beverly Hills CA 90212 USA | Actress |
| **Taylor, Lionel**<br>201 Pinnacle Dr SE, #3614, Rio Rancho NM 87124, USA | Football Player, Coach |
| **Taylor, Livingston**<br>Producers Inc, 11806 N 56th St, Tampa FL 33617 USA | Singer, Songwriter |
| **Taylor, Louise**<br>Signature Sounds, PO Box 106, Whately MA 01093, USA | Singer, Songwriter |
| **Taylor, Marianne**<br>Harve Bennett Productions, PO Box 825, Culver City CA 90232, USA | Actress |
| **Taylor, Mark C**<br>Cyclone Taylor Hockey, 10386 Nordel Court, Delta BC V4G 1J7, Canada | Ice Hockey Player |
| **Taylor, Mark L**<br>S D B Partners, 1801 Ave of Stars, #902, Los Angeles CA 90067 USA | Actor |
| **Taylor, Martin**<br>P3 Music, Seabraes, 2 Perth Road, Dundee DD! 4LA, Scotand | Jazz Guitarist |
| **Taylor, Meldrick**<br>2917 N 4th St, Philadelphia PA 19133, USA | Boxer |
| **Taylor, Meshach**<br>Gilbertson Entertainment, 1334 3rd Street Promenade, #201, Santa Monica CA 90401 USA | Actor |
| **Taylor, Mick**<br>Jacobson & Colin, 60 Madison Ave, #1026, New York NY 10010, USA | Guitarist (Rolling Stones) |
| **Taylor, Nicole R (Niki)**<br>Tri Star Sports/Entertainment Group, 215 Ward Circle, #200, Brentwood TN 37027, USA | Model |
| **Taylor, Noah**<br>Linsten Morris Mgmt, 3 Gladstone St, #301, Newtown NSW 2042, Australia | Actor |
| **Taylor, Otis**<br>Conqueroo, 11271 Ventura Blvd, #522, Studio City CA 91604 USA | Singer, Musician |
| **Taylor, Otis, Jr**<br>6608 Woodson Road, Raytown MO 64133, USA | Football Player |
| **Taylor, Paul B**<br>Paul Taylor Dance Co, 551 Grand St, Lobby A, New York NY 10002, USA | Dancer, Choreographer |
| **Taylor, Penny**<br>Phoenix Mercury, American West Arena, 201 E Jefferson St, Phoenix AZ 85004 USA | Basketball Player |
| **Taylor, R Scott**<br>925 Indian Bridge Lane, Defiance OH 43512, USA | Baseball Player |
| **Taylor, Rachael**<br>Marquee Mgmt, Gate House, 188 Oxford St, Paddington NSW 2021, Australia | Actress |
| **Taylor, Reggie**<br>828 Havird St, Newberry SC 29108, USA | Baseball Player |
| **Taylor, Regina**<br>Innovative Artists, 1505 10th St, Santa Monica CA 90401 USA | Actress |
| **Taylor, Renee**<br>C E S D, 10635 Santa Monica Blvd, #130, Los Angeles CA 90025 USA | Actress |

**Taylor, Richard C (Dick)** — Guitarist (Pretty Things)
Talent Consultants International, 105 Shad Row, #B, Piermont NY 10968 USA
**Taylor, Richard E** — Nobel Physics Laureate
757 Mayfield Ave, Stanford CA 94305, USA
**Taylor, Richard L** — Costume & Special Effects Designer
Weta Workshop, PO Box 15208, Miramar, Wellington, New Zealand
**Taylor, Rip** — Actor, Comedian
1133 N Clark Dr, Los Angeles CA 90035, USA
**Taylor, Robert** — Actor
Marquee Mgmt, The Gatehouse, 188 Oxford St, #B, Paddington NSW 2021, Australia
**Taylor, Robert D (Hawk)** — Baseball Player
136 Skyway Dr, Murray KY 42071, USA
**Taylor, Robert E (Rob)** — Football Player
1820 Rebecca Road, Lutz FL 33548, USA
**Taylor, Robert L (Bob)** — Baseball Player
27 Sunnybrook Road, Springfield MA 01119, USA
**Taylor, Robert W** — Computer Engineer
1 Stadler Dr, Woodside CA 94062, USA
**Taylor, Rod** — Actor
Contemporary Artists, 610 Santa Monica Blvd, #202, Santa Monica CA 90401 USA
**Taylor, Roger** — Tennis Player
Salterswell Farm, Moreton-in-the-Marsh, Gloucester GL53 7HN, England
**Taylor, Roger A** — Drummer (Duran Duran)
D D Productions, 93A Westbourne Park Villas, London W2 5ED, England
**Taylor, Roger M** — Drummer (Queen)
Neal Levin, 15260 Ventura Blvd, #1700, Sherman Oaks CA 91403, USA
**Taylor, Roland M (Fatty)** — Basketball Player
3812 Homewood Ave, Ashtabula OH 44004, USA
**Taylor, Ronald W (Ron)** — Baseball Player
19 Alvin Ave, Toronto ON M4T 2A7, Canada
**Taylor, Roosevelt (Rosey)** — Football Player
7331 Ebbtide Dr, New Orleans LA 70126, USA
**Taylor, Samuel D (Sammy)** — Baseball Player
PO Box 152, Woodruff SC 29388, USA
**Taylor, Sandra** — Actress, Model
I P A Network, 231 E Alessandro Blvd, #A355, Riverside CA 92508, USA
**Taylor, Shane** — Actor
Emptage Hallett, 14 Rathbone Place, London W1T 1HT, England
**Taylor, Tamara** — Actress
Greene Assoc, 1901 Ave of Stars, #130, Los Angeles CA 90067 USA
**Taylor, Tate** — Actor, Director
W M E Entertainment, 9601 Wilshire Blvd, #300, Beverly Hills CA 90210 USA
**Taylor, Ted** — Ice Hockey Player
PO Box 244, Oak Lake MB R0M 1P0, Canada
**Taylor, Teresa** — Drummer (Butthole Surfers)
Kork Agency, 1880 Century Park E, #711, Los Angeles CA 90067, USA
**Taylor, Terry D** — Baseball Player
743 W Walnut Ave, Crestview FL 32536, USA
**Taylor, Teyana** — Rap Artist
Star Trak/Interscope Records, 2220 Colorado Ave, Santa Monica CA 90404, USA
**Taylor, Tiffany** — Model, Actress
PO Box 4511, West Hills CA 91308, USA
**Taylor, Tim** — Ice Hockey Player
9119 Woodridge Run Dr, Tampa FL 33647, USA
**Taylor, Travis L** — Football Player
13114 Tom Morris Dr, Jacksonville FL 32224, USA
**Taylor, Vanessa** — Actress, Model
Management 360, 9111 Wilshire Blvd, Beverly Hills CA 90210 USA
**Taylor, Vaughn** — Golfer
2536 Queens Court, Grovetown GA 30813, USA
**Taylor, William H (Billy)** — Baseball Player
201 Washington Place, Thomasville GA 31792, USA
**Taylor, William M (Bill)** — Baseball Player
PO Box 146, Acton CA 93510, USA
**Taylor, William T (Billy)** — Football Player
3 Greenwich Dr, #86, Jersey City NJ 07305, USA
**Taylor-Capps, Nancy** — Golfer
3205 Tallia Court, Charlotte NC 28269, USA
**Taylor-Compton, Scout** — Actress
Gersh Agency, 9465 Wilshire Blvd, #600, Beverly Hills CA 90212 USA
**Taylor-Gordon, Hannah** — Actress
Independent Talent Group, 40 Whitfield St, London W1T 2RH, England
**Taylor-Klaus, Bex** — Actress
Corsa Agency, 11704 Wilshire Blvd, #204, Los Angeles CA 90025, USA
**Taylor-Taylor, Courtney** — Singer, Guitarist (Dandy Warhols)
Monqui Records, PO Box 5908, Portland OR 97228, USA
**Taylor-Young, Leigh** — Actress
11300 W Olympic Blvd, #610, Los Angeles CA 90064, USA
**Taymor, Julie** — Director, Lyricist
Cinetic Mgmt, 555 W 25th St, #400, New York NY 10001 USA
**TaZEL, Erica** — Actress
Peter Strain, 5455 Wilshire Blvd, #1812, Los Angeles CA 90036 USA
**Tazoi, Jim Y** — WW II Army Hero
13360 N 600 W, Garland UT 84312, USA
**Tcherezov, Ivan Y** — Biathlete
Biathlon Union, Luzhnetskaja Nab 8, 119270 Moscow, Russia
**Tchongo Domingos, Salvador** — Government Official, Guinea-Bisseau
Assembleia Nacional Popular, Bisseau, Guinea-Bisseau
**Tchoudov, Maxim A** — Biathlete
Biathlon Union, Luzhnetskaja Nab 8, 119270 Moscow, Russia
**Te Kanawa, Kiri** — Opera Singer
Michael Storrs Music, 211 Piccadilly, London W1J 9HF, England
**Teacher, Brian D** — Tennis Player
Tennis Academy, Arroyo Seco Racquet Club, 920 Lohman Lane, South Pasadena CA 91030, USA
**Teachout, John** — Body Builder
202 Cambridge Farms Dr, Hoschton GA 30548, USA

| | |
|---|---|
| **Teaff, Grant G**<br>8265 Forest Ridge Dr, Waco TX 76712, USA | Football Coach, Executive |
| **Teagarden, Taylor H**<br>2007 Blestem Lane, Carrollton TX 75007, USA | Baseball Player |
| **Teagle, Terry M**<br>2111 Heatherwood Dr, Missouri City TX 77489, USA | Basketball Player |
| **Teague, Fred E (Trey), III**<br>862 Ashport Road, Jackson TN 38305, USA | Football Player |
| **Teague, George T**<br>6561 Meadow Lark Dr, Montgomery AL 36116, USA | Football Player |
| **Teague, Jeffrey D (Jeff)**<br>Atlanta Hawks, Centennial Tower, 101 Marietta St NW, #1900, Atlanta GA 30303 USA | Basketball Player |
| **Teague, Lewis**<br>Gersh Agency, 9465 Wilshire Blvd, #600, Beverly Hills CA 90212 USA | Director |
| **Teague, Marquis**<br>Chicago Bulls, United Center, 1901 W Madison St, Chicago IL 60612 USA | Basketball Player |
| **Teague, Marshall**<br>Geddes Agency, 8430 Santa Monica Blvd, #201, West Hollywood CA 90069 USA | Actor |
| **Teahen, Mark T**<br>8610 E Via Del Sol Dr, Scottsdale AZ 85255, USA | Baseball Player |
| **Teal, Clare**<br>Agency Group Ltd, 142 W 57th St, #600, New York NY 10019 USA | Singer |
| **Teal, Willie, Jr**<br>1322 Westchester Dr, Baton Rouge LA 70810, USA | Football Player |
| **Teale, Owen**<br>Markham Froggatt Irwin, Julian House, 4 Windmill St, London W1P 1HF, England | Actor |
| **Teasdale, Joseph P**<br>Commerce Tower, 911 Main St, #1210, Kansas City MO 64105, USA | Governor, MO |
| **Teasley, Nikki**<br>Tulsa Shock, B O K Center, 200 S Denver, Tulsa OK 74103 USA | Basketball Player |
| **Teasley, Ronald (Ron)**<br>19317 Coyle St, Detroit MI 48235, USA | Baseball Player |
| **Tebbit of Chingford, Norman B**<br>House of Lords, Westminster, London SW1A 0PW, England | Government Official, England |
| **Tebow, Timothy R (Tim)**<br>W M E Entertainment, 9601 Wilshire Blvd, #300, Beverly Hills CA 90210 USA | Football Player |
| **Tech N9ne**<br>Strange Music, PO Box 1114, Blue Springs MO 64013, USA | Rap Artist |
| **Tedeschi, David**<br>Innovative Artists, 1505 10th St, Santa Monica CA 90401 USA | Editor |
| **Tedeschi, Susan**<br>S L Feldman Mgmt, 1505 W 2nd Ave, #200, Vancouver BC V6H 3Y4, Canada | Singer |
| **Tee, Brian**<br>Bauman Redanty Shaul Agency, 5757 Wilshire Blvd, #473, Los Angeles CA 90036 USA | Actor |
| **Tee, Hayden**<br>Lambert House Enterprises, PO Box 226, Collaroy Beach NSW 2097, Australia | Actor, Singer |
| **Teegarden, Aimee**<br>Innovative Artists, 1505 10th St, Santa Monica CA 90401 USA | Actress |
| **Teevens, Eugene F (Buddy)**<br>Dartmouth College, Athletic Dept, Hanover NH 03755, USA | Football Coach |
| **Tefkin, Blair**<br>Bossyroots Records, 8033 W Sunset Blvd, #850, Los Angeles CA 90046, USA | Actress, Singer, Songwriter |
| **Teich, Malvin C**<br>Boston University, Electrical/Computer Engineering Dept, Boston MA 02215, USA | Electrical Engineer |
| **Teichman, Axel**<br>Neue Str 8, 98559 Oberhof, Germany | Cross Country Skier |
| **Teitel, Robert**<br>Creative Artists Agency, 2000 Ave of Stars, #100, Los Angeles CA 90067 USA | Actor, Producer |
| **Teitelbaum, Bill**<br>Tribune Media Services, 435 N Michigan Ave, #1500, Chicago IL 60611 USA | Cartoonist (Bottom Liners) |
| **Teitelbaum, Eric**<br>Tribune Media Services, 435 N Michigan Ave, #1500, Chicago IL 60611 USA | Cartoonist (Bottom Liners) |
| **Teitelbaum, Zalman**<br>Satmar Hasidic, 87 Morton St, Brooklyn NY 11211, USA | Religious Leader, Rabbi |
| **Teitell, Conrad L**<br>Cummings & Lockwood, 6 Landmark Square, Stamford CT 06901, USA | Attorney |
| **Teixeira, Mark C (Tex)**<br>2220 King Fisher Dr, Westlake TX 76262, USA | Baseball Player |
| **Tejada, Miguel O M**<br>3013 NE 20th Court, Fort Lauderdale FL 33305, USA | Baseball Player |
| **Tekulve, Kenton C (Kent)**<br>1531 Sequoia Dr, Pittsburgh PA 15241, USA | Baseball Player |
| **Tela**<br>American Talent Agency, 26 Finney Farm Road, Croton on Hudson NY 10520, USA | Rap Artist |
| **Telavi, Willy**<br>Prime Minister's Office, Vaiaku, Funafuti, Tuvalu | Prime Minister, Tuvalu |
| **Telfair, Sebastian**<br>Toronto Raptors, Air Canada Center, 20 Bay St, Toronto ON M5J 2N8, Canada | Basketball Player |
| **Telfer, Paul**<br>Don Buchwald, 6500 Wilshire Blvd, #2200, Los Angeles CA 90048 USA | Actor |
| **Telford, Anthony C**<br>9109 Cypress Keep Lane, Odessa FL 33556, USA | Baseball Player |
| **Telgheder, David W**<br>50 Orchard Crest Dr, Westtown NY 10998, USA | Baseball Player |
| **Telito, Filoimea**<br>Governor General's Office, Government House, Vaiaku, Funafuti, Tuvalu | Governor General, Tuvalu |
| **Tellefsen, Christopher**<br>Claire Best Assoc, 736 Seward St, Los Angeles CA 90038, USA | Editor |
| **Teller**<br>A P A Talent/Literary Agency, 405 S Beverly Dr, #300, Beverly Hills CA 90212 USA | Comedian, Illusionist (Penn & Teller) |
| **Teller, Juergen**<br>1 Telford Road, London W10 5SH, England | Photographer |
| **Teller, Miles**<br>Creative Artists Agency, 2000 Ave of Stars, #100, Los Angeles CA 90067 USA | Actor |
| **Tellmann, Thomas J (Tom)**<br>1021 Yankee Bush Road, Warren PA 16365, USA | Baseball Player |

**Tellqvist, K Mikael** — Ice Hockey Player
7932 E Feathersong Lane, Scottsdale AZ 85255, USA

**Telnaes, Ann C** — Editorial Cartoonist
Tribune Media Services, 435 N Michigan Ave, #1500, Chicago IL 60611 USA

**Teltscher, Eliot** — Tennis Player, Coach
Pepperdine University, Athletic Dept, Malibu CA 90265, USA

**Teltscher, Kate** — Historian
Bloomsbury Publishing, 50 Bedford Square, London WC1B 3DP, England

**Telushkin, Joseph** — Religious Leader, Rabbi, Writer
Center for Learning & Leadership, 440 Park Ave S, #400, New York NY 10016, USA

**Temchen, Sybil** — Actress
Untitled Entertainment, 350 S Beverly Dr, #200, Beverly Hills CA 90212 USA

**Temerlin, J Liener** — Businessman
201 E John Carpenter Freeway, Irving TX 75062, USA

**Temesvari, Andrea** — Tennis Player
ProServe, 1101 Woodrow Wilson Blvd, #1800, Arlington VA 22209 USA

**Temirkanov, Yuri K** — Conductor
State Philharmonia, Mikhailovskaya 2, 191186 Saint Petersburg, Russia

**Temple, Collis** — Basketball Player
2614 Dalrymple Dr, Baton Rouge LA 70808, USA

**Temple, Juno V** — Actress
United Talent Agency, U T A Plaza, 9336 Civic Center Dr, Beverly Hills CA 90210 USA

**Templeman, Simon** — Actor
A P A Talent/Literary Agency, 405 S Beverly Dr, #300, Beverly Hills CA 90212 USA

**Templeton, Ben** — Cartoonist (Motley's Crew)
Tribune Media Services, 2 Perry St, Cortlandt Manor NY 10567, USA

**Templeton, Garry L** — Baseball Player
13552 Del Poniente Road, Poway CA 92064, USA

**Tena, Natalia** — Actress
Curtis Brown Group, 28-29 Haymarket, #500, London SW1Y 4SP, England , USA

**Tenace, F Gene** — Baseball Player, Manager
2650 Cliff Hawk Court, Redmond OR 97756, USA

**Tenet, George J** — Government Official
Allen & Co, 711 5th Ave, New York NY 10022, USA

**Teng, Vienna** — Singer, Pianist, Songwriter
Deep South Entertainment, PO Box 17737, Raleigh NC 27619, USA

**Tenison, Renee** — Model, Actress
Tenison Group, 171 Pier Ave, #403, Santa Monica CA 90405, USA

**Tennant, Andy** — Director, Writer
Creative Artists Agency, 2000 Ave of Stars, #100, Los Angeles CA 90067 USA

**Tennant, David** — Actor, Director
Independent Talent Group, 40 Whitfield St, London W1T 2RH, England

**Tennant, Neil F** — Singer (Pet Shop Boys)
W M E Entertainment, 9601 Wilshire Blvd, #300, Beverly Hills CA 90210 USA

**Tennant, Scott** — Guitarist (LAGQ)
University of Southern California, Thornton Music School, Los Angeles CA 90089, USA

**Tennant, Stella** — Model
Select Model Mgmt, 17 Ferdinand St, London NW1 8EU, England

**Tennant, Veronica** — Ballerina
National Ballet of Canada, 157 King St E, Toronto ON M5C 1G9, Canada

**Tennant, Victoria** — Actress
Glick Agency, 1321 7th St, #203, Santa Monica CA 90401 USA

**Tenneson, Joyce** — Photographer
PO Box 228, Rockport ME 04856, USA

**Tenney, Jon** — Actor
Kritzer Levine Wilkins Griffin, 11872 La Grange Ave, #100, Los Angeles CA 90025 USA

**Tennille, Toni** — Singer (Captain & Tennille)
1040 Sun Wood Dr, Las Vegas NV 89145, USA

**Tennison, Chalee** — Singer
Buddy Lee Attractions, 38 Music Square E, #300, Nashville TN 37203 USA

**Tensi, Stephen M (Steve)** — Football Player
300 Flannery Fork Road, Blowing Rock NC 28605, USA

**Tent, Kevin** — Editor
Eastern Talent Agency, 849 S Broadway, #811, Los Angeles CA 90014, USA

**Tenuta, Judy** — Actress, Comedienne
13504 Contour Dr, Sherman Oaks CA 91423, USA

**Tepedino, Frank R** — Baseball Player
2 Pear Court, Saint James NY 11780, USA

**Tequila, Tila** — Singer, Model
8033 Sunset Blvd, #1029, West Hollywood CA 90046, USA

**Teraoka, Masami** — Artist
41-048 Kaulu St, Waimanalo HI 96795, USA

**Terbenche, Paul F** — Ice Hockey Player
238 Victoria St N, Port Hope ON L1A 3N4, Canada

**Terborgh, John W** — Ecologist, Environmentalist
Duke University, Tropical Conservation Center, PO Box 90381, Durham NC 27708, USA

**Terebey, Susan** — Astronomer
California State University, Physics & Astronomy Dept, Los Angeles CA 90032, USA

**Terentieva, Nina N** — Opera Singer
Bolshoi Theater, Teatralnaya Pl 1, 103009 Moscow, Russia

**Tereshchenko, Sergei A** — Prime Minister, Kazakhstan
121-18 Kounaev Str, 480100 Almaty, Kazakhstan

**Tereshkova, Valentina V** — Cosmonaut
Int'l Co-operation Assn, Vozdvizhenka Str 14-18, 103885 Moscow, Russia

**Terfel Jones, Bryn** — Opera Singer
Harlequin Agency, 203 Fidlas Road, Cardiff CF4 5NA, Wales

**Tergesen, Lee** — Actor
Industry Entertainment, 955 Carillo Dr, #300, Los Angeles CA 90048 USA

**Terminator X** — Rap Artist (Public Enemy)
Brookes Co, 8223 Gulana Ave, Playa del Rey CA 90293, USA

**Ter-Petrossian, Levon A** — President, Armenia
Marshal Baghramian Prospect 19, 375016 Yerevan, Armenia

**Terra, Scott** — Actor
Abrams Artists, 9200 W Sunset Blvd, #1125, West Hollywood CA 90069 USA

**Terracciano, Anthony P** — Financier
S L M Corp, 12061 Bluemont Way, Reston VA 20190, USA

| | |
|---|---|
| **Terrace, Herbert S**<br>17 Campfire Road, Chappaqua NY 10514, USA | Anthropologist, Primatologist |
| **Terranova, Joe**<br>Joe Taylor Artist Agency, 2802 Columbine Place, Nashville TN 37204 USA | Singer (Danny and the Juniors) |
| **Terrasson, Jacques-Laurent (Jacky)**<br>Joel Chriss Co, 300 Mercer St, #3J, New York NY 10003 USA | Jazz Pianist |
| **Terrazas Sandoval, Julio Cardinal**<br>Arzobispado, Casilla 25, Calle Ingavi 49, Santa Cruz de la Sierra, Bolivia | Religious Leader |
| **Terrell, C Walter (Walt)**<br>1304 Oxley Court, Union KY 41091, USA | Baseball Player |
| **Terrell, David W (Dave)**<br>43628 Cather Court, Ashburn VA 20147, USA | Football Player |
| **Terrell, Ernie**<br>11136 S Parnell, Chicago IL 60628, USA | Boxer |
| **Terrell, Patrick C (Pat)**<br>2490 Madrid Way S, Saint Petersburg FL 33712, USA | Football Player |
| **Terreri, Christopher A (Chris)**<br>120 Lake Dr, Mountain Lakes NJ 07046, USA | Ice Hockey Player |
| **Terrile, Richard**<br>2121 E Woodlyn Road, Pasadena CA 91104, USA | Astronomer |
| **Terrio, Christopher (Chris)**<br>Creative Artists Agency, 2000 Ave of Stars, #100, Los Angeles CA 90067 USA | Writer |
| **Terrion, Greg**<br>Terrion Esso Service, PO Box 428, Marmoro ON K0K 2M0, Canada | Ice Hockey Player |
| **Terris, Malcolm**<br>14 England's Lane, London NW3, England | Actor |
| **Terry, Christopher A (Chris)**<br>8209 Marshall Brae Dr, Raleigh NC 27616, USA | Football Player |
| **Terry, Clark**<br>4720 S Beech St, Pine Bluff AR 71603, USA | Jazz Trumpeter, Singer |
| **Terry, Jason E**<br>105 Kingston Minor NE, Atlanta GA 30342, USA | Basketball Player |
| **Terry, John**<br>Chelsea F C, Stamford Bridge, Fulham Road, London SW6 1HS, England | Soccer Player |
| **Terry, John**<br>1 Mgmt, 9000 W Sunset Blvd, #1550, Los Angeles CA 90069 USA | Actor |
| **Terry, John Q**<br>Old Exchange, Dedham, Colchester, Essex CO7 6HA, England | Architect |
| **Terry, Megan D**<br>2309 Hanscom Blvd, Omaha NE 68105, USA | Writer |
| **Terry, Nigel**<br>PO Box 1116, Belfast BT2 7AJ, Northern Ireland | Actor |
| **Terry, Ralph W**<br>801 Park St, Larned KS 67550, USA | Baseball Player |
| **Terry, Randall A**<br>Operation Rescue National, PO Box 360221, Melbourne FL 32936, USA | Social Activist |
| **Terry, Ruth**<br>622 Hospitality Dr, Rancho Mirage CA 92270, USA | Singer, Actress |
| **Terry, Scott R**<br>4943 Montford Dr, Saint Louis MO 63128, USA | Baseball Player |
| **Terry, Tony**<br>Green Light Talent Agency, PO Box 3172, Beverly Hills CA 90212 USA | Singer |
| **Terwilliger, W Wayne**<br>1909 Clear Creek Dr, Weatherford TX 76087, USA | Baseball Player |
| **Terzic, Adnan**<br>Prime Minister's Office, Alipasina 1, 71000 Sarajevo, Bosnia & Herzegovina | Prime Minister, Bosnia & Herzegovina |
| **Terzopoulos, Dmitri**<br>University of California, Computer Science Dept, Los Angeles CA 90024, USA | Computer Scientist |
| **Tesh, John**<br>TeshMedia Group, 13245 Riverside Dr, #305, Sherman Oaks CA 91423, USA | Composer, Pianist, Entertainer |
| **Teske, Rachel**<br>Gaylord Sports Mgmt, 13845 N Northsight Blvd, #200, Scottsdale AZ 85260 USA | Golfer |
| **Tesori, Jeanine**<br>W M E Entertainment, 9601 Wilshire Blvd, #300, Beverly Hills CA 90210 USA | Composer |
| **Tessaro, Kathleen**<br>William Morrow, 1350 Ave of Americas, New York NY 10019, USA | Writer |
| **Tessier, John**<br>I M G Artists, Hogarth Business Park, Chiswick, London W4 2TH, England | Opera Singer |
| **Tessier, Orval**<br>411 McDonell Crescent, Cornwall ON K6H 5N7, Canada | Ice Hockey Player |
| **Tessier-Lavigne, Marc**<br>255 Selby Lane, Atherton CA 94027, USA | Neurobiologist |
| **Tessmer, Jay W**<br>7861 Red Mahogany Road, Boynton Beach FL 33437, USA | Baseball Player |
| **Testa, Franco**<br>Via Calvi 15, 32021 Mogliano, Italy | Cyclist |
| **Testa, Mary**<br>Gage Group, 450 7th Ave, #1809, New York NY 10123 USA | Actress, Singer |
| **Testa, Sylvio**<br>Les Jardines du Golf, 06210 Mandelieu, Alpes Maritimes, France | Photographer |
| **Testaverde, Vincent F (Vinny)**<br>17122 Gunn Highway, Odessa FL 33556, USA | Football Player |
| **Testi, Fabio**<br>Via Siacci 38, 00197 Rome, Italy | Actor |
| **Testino, Mario**<br>National Portrait Gallery, Saint Martins Place, London WC2H 0HE, England | Photographer |
| **Teteak, Deral D**<br>8067 Palomino Dr, Naples FL 34113, USA | Football Player |
| **Teter, Hannah**<br>1554 Plumas Circle, South Lake Tahoe CA 96150, USA | Snowboard Athlete, Model |
| **Teton, John**<br>Earthlight Pictures, 791 4th St, Lake Oswego OR 97034, USA | Social Activist |
| **Tetriani, Lina**<br>I M G Artists, Hogarth Business Park, Chiswick, London W4 2TH, England | Opera Singer |
| **Tettamanzi, Dionigi Cardinal**<br>Arcivescovado, Piazza Matteotti 4, 16123 Genoa, Italy | Religious Leader |

**T**

Terrace - Tettamanzi

# T

| | |
|---|---|
| **Tettleton, Mickey L**<br>3500 Hollister Trail, Norman OK 73071, USA | Baseball Player |
| **Tetzlaff, Christian**<br>Shuman Assoc, 120 W 58th St, #8D, New York NY 10019, USA | Concert Violinist |
| **Teufel, Timothy S (Tim)**<br>PO Box 3517, Jupiter FL 33469, USA | Baseball Player, Manager |
| **Teukolsky, Saul A**<br>Cornell University, Physics/Astronomy Dept, Ithaca NY 14853, USA | Astrophysicist |
| **Teut, Nate**<br>2010 Sugar Creek Dr, Waukee IA 50263, USA | Baseball Player |
| **Tewell, Doug**<br>15216 Fairview Farm Road, Edmond OK 73013, USA | Golfer |
| **Tewes, Lauren**<br>Actor's Group Agency, 3400 Beacon Ave S, Seattle WA 98144, USA | Actress |
| **Tewkesbury, Joan F**<br>Creative Artists Agency, 2000 Ave of Stars, #100, Los Angeles CA 90067 USA | Director, Writer |
| **Tewksbury, Robert A (Bob)**<br>63 Ridge Road, Concord NH 03301, USA | Baseball Player |
| **Tews, Andreas**<br>Pflaumenbaum, Brunnenstr 32, 19053 Schwerin, Germany | Boxer |
| **Texada, Tia**<br>Power & Twersky Business Mgmt, 13801 Ventura Blvd, Sherman Oaks CA 91423, USA | Actress |
| **Thabeet, Hasheem**<br>Oklahoma City Thunder, 211 N Robinson Ave, #300, Oklahoma City OK 73102 USA | Basketball Player |
| **Thaborik, Marian**<br>301 Kenwood Parkway, #401, Minneapolis MN 55403, USA | Ice Hockey Player |
| **Thaci, Hashim**<br>Prime Minister's Office, Assembly, Mother Theresa St, 10000 Pristina, Kosovo | Prime Minister, Kosovo |
| **Thacker, Brian M**<br>11413 Monterey Dr, Silver Spring MD 20902, USA | Vietnam War Army Hero (CMH) |
| **Thacker, Charles P**<br>543 Tennyson Ave, Palo Alto CA 94301, USA | Computer Engineer |
| **Thacker, Thomas P (Tom)**<br>3655 Dogwood Lane, Cincinnati OH 45213, USA | Basketball Player |
| **Thackery, Jimmy**<br>Thunderbird Management Group, 133 Industrial Park Road, Larose LA 70373, USA | Singer, Guitarist (Nighthawks) |
| **Thagard, Norman E**<br>502 N Ride, Tallahassee FL 32303, USA | Astronaut, Physician |
| **Thain, John A**<br>C I T Group, 505 5th Ave, New York NY 10017, USA | Financier |
| **Thaler, Richard H**<br>University of Chicago, Booth Business School, Chicago IL 60637, USA | Economist |
| **Thalia**<br>Doyle-Kos Entertainment, 1 Penn Plaza, #2107, New York NY 10119, USA | Singer, Actress |
| **Thalmann, Melchior**<br>Kreuzbuhlstr 43, 8600 Dubendorf, Switzerland | Gymnast |
| **Thames, Marcus M**<br>101 Mount Moriah Circle, Louisville MS 39339, USA | Baseball Player |
| **Thani, Abdullah Nasser Khalifa al-**<br>Prime Minister's Office, PO Box 923, Dohar, Qatar | Prime Minister, Qatar |
| **Thani, Tamim bin Hamad al-**<br>Royal Palace, PO Box 923, Doha, Qatar | Emir, Qatar |
| **Thapa, Surya Bahadur**<br>Tangal, Kathmandu, Bagmati 44601, Nepal | Prime Minister, Nepal |
| **Tharp, Twyla**<br>Twyla Tharp Productions, 336 Central Park West, #17B, New York NY 10025, USA | Dancer, Choreographer |
| **Tharpe, Larry J**<br>3665 Greenbriar Road E, Macon GA 31204, USA | Football Player |
| **Thatcher, David J**<br>440 Dearborn Ave, Missoula MT 59801, USA | WW II Army Air Corps Hero |
| **Thatcher, Joseph (Joe)**<br>310 Ruddell Dr, Kokomo IN 46901, USA | Baseball Player |
| **Thatcher, Karen**<br>USA Hockey, 1775 Bob Johnson Dr, Colorado Springs CO 80906 USA | Ice Hockey Player |
| **Thatcher, Roland C, IV**<br>18 Floweruff Court, Spring TX 77380, USA | Golfer |
| **Thaxton, James I (Jim)**<br>4319 Deergrove Road, Memphis TN 38141, USA | Football Player |
| **Thayer, Bill**<br>PO Box 233, Snohomish WA 98291, USA | Explorer |
| **Thayer, Brynn**<br>PO Box 15006, Beverly Hills CA 90209, USA | Actress |
| **Thayer, Gregory A (Greg)**<br>1000 3rd St N, Sauk Rapids MN 56379, USA | Baseball Player |
| **Thayer, Helen**<br>PO Box 233, Snohomish WA 98291, USA | Explorer, Skier |
| **Thayer, Maria**<br>A P A Talent/Literary Agency, 405 S Beverly Dr, #300, Beverly Hills CA 90212 USA | Actress |
| **Thayer, Thomas A (Tom)**<br>50 Nohea Kai Dr, #I303, Lahaina HI 96761, USA | Football Player |
| **Thayer, W Paul**<br>10200 Hollow Way, Dallas TX 75229, USA | Government Official, Businessman |
| **Theberge, Greg**<br>31 Edgar, Sundridge ON P0A 1Z0, Canada | Ice Hockey Player |
| **Theile, David**<br>84 Woodville St, Hendea, Brisbane QLD 4011, Australia | Swimmer |
| **Thein Sein**<br>President's Office, Zaw Gyi St, Mayangon Tsp, Yangon, Myanmar | President, Myanmar; General |
| **Theismann, Joseph R (Joe)**<br>PO Box 186, Leesburg VA 20178, USA | Football Player, Sportscaster |
| **Theiss, Brooke**<br>Characters Talent Agency, 8 Elm St, Toronto ON M5G 1G7, Canada | Actress |
| **Theiss, Duane C**<br>66 Juniper Ave, Westerville OH 43081, USA | Baseball Player |
| **Thelan, Jodi**<br>8428 Melrose Place, #C, West Hollywood CA 90069, USA | Actress |

**Tettleton - Thelan**

| | |
|---|---|
| **Theler, Derek** | Actor |
| Paradigm Agency, 360 N Crescent Dr, North Building, Beverly Hills CA 90210 USA | |
| **Theobald, Ronald M (Ron)** | Baseball Player |
| 319 Jacaranda Place, Fullerton CA 92832, USA | |
| **Theodorakis, Mikis** | Composer |
| Epifanous 1, Akropolis, Athens, Greece | |
| **Theodore, Jose** | Ice Hockey Player |
| 238 S Maya Palm Dr, Boca Raton FL 33432, USA | |
| **Theodorescu, Monica** | Equestrian |
| Gestit Lindenhof, 48336 Sassenberg, Germany | |
| **Theodosakis, Jason** | Physician, Writer |
| Saint Martin's Press, 175 5th Ave, #400, New York NY 10010 USA | |
| **Theodosius, Primate Metropolitan** | Religious Leader |
| Orthodox Church in America, PO Box 675 RR 25A, Syosset NY 11791, USA | |
| **Therien, Christopher B (Chris)** | Ice Hockey Player |
| 15 Milford Dr, Marlton NJ 08053, USA | |
| **Theriot, Ryan S** | Baseball Player |
| 241 Granville Court, Baton Rouge LA 70810, USA | |
| **Theron, Charlize** | Actress, Model |
| W M E Entertainment, 9601 Wilshire Blvd, #300, Beverly Hills CA 90210 USA | |
| **Theroux, Justin** | Actor, Director |
| Creative Artists Agency, 2000 Ave of Stars, #100, Los Angeles CA 90067 USA | |
| **Theroux, Paul E** | Writer |
| 35 Elsynge Road, London SW18 2NR, England | |
| **Therrien, Michel** | Ice Hockey Player, Coach |
| 118 Carriage Dr, McKnight PA 15237, USA | |
| **Theus, Reggie W** | Basketball Player, Coach |
| 4259 Enoro Dr, Los Angeles CA 90008, USA | |
| **Theusner, Ulrike** | Model |
| Take 2 Model Mgmt, 6 Willow St, London EC2 4BH, England | |
| **Thewlis, David** | Actor |
| Ken McReddie Assoc, 101 Finsbury Pavement, London EC2A 1RS, England | |
| **Theys, Didier** | Auto Racing Driver |
| 5773 N 78th Place, Scottsdale AZ 85259, USA | |
| **Thibaudet, Jean-Yves** | Concert Pianist |
| M L Falcone, 55 W 68th St, #1114, New York NY 10023, USA | |
| **Thibault, Charles** | Physiologist |
| 4 Place Jussieu, 75005 Paris, France | |
| **Thibault, Jocelyn** | Ice Hockey Player |
| 550 Ch du Domaine, RR 5, Saint-Denis-de-Brompton QC J0B 2P0, Canada | |
| **Thibault, Mike F** | Basketball Coach |
| Washington Mystics, Verizon Center, 401 9th St NW, #750, Washington DC 20004 USA | |
| **Thibiant, Aída** | Fashion Consultant |
| Institut de Beaute, 449 N Canon Dr, Beverly Hills CA 90210, USA | |
| **Thibodeaux, Keith** | Actor |
| 5372 Jamaica Dr, Jackson MS 39211, USA | |
| **Thich Quang Do** | Religious Activist |
| Thanh Zinh Zen Monastery, Ho Chi Minh City, Vietnam | |
| **Thicke, Alan** | Actor |
| 7110 Gobernador Canyon Road, Carpinteria CA 93013, USA | |
| **Thicke, Chris** | Mandolin Player |
| Nonesuch Records, 75 Rockefeller Plaza, #800, New York NY 10019 USA | |
| **Thicke, Robin A** | Singer |
| Creative Artists Agency, 2000 Ave of Stars, #100, Los Angeles CA 90067 USA | |
| **Thiedemann, Fritz** | Equestrian |
| Ostreherweg 28, 25746 Heide, Germany | |
| **Thiele, Gerhard P J** | Astronaut, Germany |
| European Space Center, Linder Hohe, Box 906096, 51127 Cologne, Germany | |
| **Thielemann, Ray C (R C)** | Football Player |
| 210 Rose Meadow Lane, Alpharetta GA 30005, USA | |
| **Thielemans, Jean B (Toots)** | Jazz Harmonica Player, Guitarist |
| Uncle Jazz Productions, Fluitberg St 66, #5, 2900 Schoten, Belgium | |
| **Thielen, Gunter** | Businessman |
| Bertelsmann AG, Carl-Bertelsmann-Str 270, 33311 Guetersloh, Germany | |
| **Thiemens, Mark H** | Chemist |
| University of California, Chemistry Dept, 9500 Gilman Dr, La Jolla CA 92093, USA | |
| **Thieriot, Max** | Actor |
| Gersh Agency, 9465 Wilshire Blvd, #600, Beverly Hills CA 90212 USA | |
| **Thierry, John F** | Football Player |
| 6884 Arias Way, Painesville OH 44077, USA | |
| **Thiessen, Tiffani** | Actress |
| Paradigm Agency, 360 N Crescent Dr, North Building, Beverly Hills CA 90210 USA | |
| **Thiffault, Leo** | Ice Hockey Player |
| 1340 Marble Dr, Columbus OH 43227, USA | |
| **Thigpen, Curtis B** | Baseball Player |
| 1405 W 51st St, Austin TX 78756, USA | |
| **Thigpen, Robert T (Bobby)** | Baseball Player |
| 1857 Brightwaters Blvd NE, Saint Petersburg FL 33704, USA | |
| **Thigpen, Yancey D** | Football Player |
| 7210 Yellowhorn Trail, Waxhaw NC 28173, USA | |
| **Thile, Christopher S (Chris)** | Mandolinist, Guitarist (Nickel Creek) |
| Creative Artists Agency, 2000 Ave of Stars, #100, Los Angeles CA 90067 USA | |
| **Thinnes, Roy** | Actor |
| 163 Amsterdam Ave, #307, New York NY 10023, USA | |
| **Thirlby, Olivia** | Actress |
| Management 360, 9111 Wilshire Blvd, Beverly Hills CA 90210 USA | |
| **Thirlwell, J G** | Singer, Songwriter |
| Agency Group Ltd, 142 W 57th St, #600, New York NY 10019 USA | |
| **Thirsk, Robert B (Bob)** | Astronaut, Canada |
| N A S A, Johnson Space Center, 2101 NASA Road, Houston TX 77058 USA | |
| **Thistlethwaite, Anthony** | Musician (Waterboys) |
| Agency Group Ltd, 142 W 57th St, #600, New York NY 10019 USA | |
| **Thobele, Dingaan B** | Boxer |
| 1202 Chiwelo, PO Chiwelo, Soweto 1818, South Africa | |
| **Thoen, Skip** | Basketball Player |
| 330 Buckland Trace, Louisville KY 40245, USA | |

**T**

**Theler - Thoen**

**T**

**Thoenen, Richard C (Dick)** — Baseball Player
862 Smith St, Harrisburg OR 97446, USA
**Thom, Bing W** — Architect
1430 Burrad St, Vancouver BC V6Z 2A3, Canada
**Thoma, Georg** — Nordic Combined Athlete
Bisten 6, 79856 Hinterzarten, Germany
**Thomas, Aaron N** — Football Player
3793 NW Sparrow Place, Corvallis OR 97330, USA
**Thomas, Adalius D** — Football Player
195 Highway 9, Kellyton AL 35089, USA
**Thomas, Andrew S W (Andy)** — Astronaut
N A S A, Johnson Space Center, 2101 NASA Road, Houston TX 77058 USA
**Thomas, Aurelius** — Football Player
PO Box 91157, Columbus OH 43209, USA
**Thomas, B Clendon** — Football Player
7508 Rumsey Road, Oklahoma City OK 73132, USA
**Thomas, B J** — Singer, Songwriter
Honeyman Music, PO Box 120003, Arlington TX 76012, USA
**Thomas, Barbara S** — Government Official
News International, 1 Virginia St, London E1 9XY, England
**Thomas, Benjamin (Ben), Jr** — Football Player
2155 Herndon St, Auburn AL 36830, USA
**Thomas, Betty** — Actress, Director
Dominant Pictures, 1438 N Gower St, Building 35, Los Angeles CA 90028, USA
**Thomas, Billy M** — Army General
626 Sweetbrush, San Antonio TX 78258, USA
**Thomas, Blair L** — Football Player
401 Gulph Ridge Dr, King of Prussia PA 19406, USA
**Thomas, Broderick L** — Football Player
12004 Opal Creek Dr, Pearland TX 77584, USA
**Thomas, Cal** — Actor
Creative Artists Agency, 2000 Ave of Stars, #100, Los Angeles CA 90067 USA
**Thomas, Calvin L** — Football Player
908 Manchester Ave, Westchester IL 60154, USA
**Thomas, Carl** — Singer (Faith Evans)
Universal Attractions, 135 W 26th St, #1200, New York NY 10001 USA
**Thomas, Carla** — Singer
Rodgers Redding, PO Box 4603, Macon GA 31208 USA
**Thomas, Charles** — Baseball Player
137 Black Oak Dr, Asheville NC 28804, USA
**Thomas, Charles G (Chuck)** — Football Player
2201 Purple Majesty Court, Las Vegas NV 89117, USA
**Thomas, Clarence** — Supreme Court Justice
US Supreme Court, 1 1st St NE, Washington DC 20543 USA
**Thomas, Craig** — Actor, Producer
United Talent Agency, U T A Plaza, 9336 Civic Center Dr, Beverly Hills CA 90210 USA
**Thomas, D Etan** — Basketball Player
2147 Vittoria Court, Bowie MD 20721, USA
**Thomas, Damien** — Actor
Curtis Brown Group, 28-29 Haymarket St, #500, London SW1Y 4SP, England
**Thomas, Dave G** — Football Player
2115 Salt Myrtle Lane, Orange Park FL 32003, USA
**Thomas, David** — Concert Singer
Allied Artists, 42 Montpelier Square, London SE10 8HP, England
**Thomas, David (Dave)** — Actor, Comedian
M B S T Entertainment, 345 N Maple Dr, #200, Beverly Hills CA 90210 USA
**Thomas, David Clayton** — Singer (Blood Sweat & Tears)
Music Avenue Inc, 43 Washington St, Groveland MA 01834, USA
**Thomas, David L** — Singer (Pere Ubu)
Billions Corp, 3522 W Armitage Ave, Chicago IL 60647 USA
**Thomas, Debra J (Debi)** — Figure Skater
2601 Windward Blvd, Champaign IL 61821, USA
**Thomas, Dennis (Dee Tee)** — Saxophonist (Kool & the Gang)
Spirit Media, PO Box 43591, Phoenix AZ 85080 USA
**Thomas, Derrel O** — Baseball Player
112 Juniperhill Lane, Riverside CA 92506, USA
**Thomas, Donald A** — Astronaut
1029 Hart Road, Towson MD 21286, USA
**Thomas, Donald Michael (D M)** — Writer
Coach House, Rashleigh Vale, Tregolls Road, Truro, Cornwall TR1 1TJ, England
**Thomas, Earlie B** — Football Player
PO Box 1445, Laporte CO 80535, USA
**Thomas, Eddie Kaye** — Actor
Gersh Agency, 9465 Wilshire Blvd, #600, Beverly Hills CA 90212 USA
**Thomas, Elizabeth Marshall** — Anthropologist, Environmentalist, Writer
80 E Mountain Road, Peterborough NH 03458, USA
**Thomas, Emma** — Producer
Bloom Hergott Diemer, 150 S Rodeo Dr, #300, Beverly Hills CA 90212 USA
**Thomas, Emmitt E** — Football Player, Coach
4603 NE Dick Howser Circle, Lees Summit MO 64064, USA
**Thomas, Frank E** — Baseball Player
1540 Villa Rica Dr, Henderson NV 89052, USA
**Thomas, Frank J** — Baseball Player
118 Doray Dr, Pittsburgh PA 15237, USA
**Thomas, Gareth** — Actor
Emptage Hall, 14 Rathbone Place, London W1T 1HT, England
**Thomas, Gareth** — Engineer
University of California, Materials Science Dept, Berkeley CA 94720, USA
**Thomas, George E, Jr** — Baseball Player
5804 Ivrea Dr, Sarasota FL 34238, USA
**Thomas, Geraint** — Cyclist
Team Barolworld, Trav Via Provinciale 1/C, 25030 Adro (BS), Italy
**Thomas, Heather** — Actress
Innovative Artists, 1505 10th St, Santa Monica CA 90401 USA
**Thomas, Heidi** — Actress
Lichtman/Salners, 15865 Royal Haven Place, Sherman Oaks CA 91403 USA

Thoenen - Thomas

| | |
|---|---|
| **Thomas, Henry** | Actor |
| Brillstein Entertainment Partners, 9150 Wilshire Blvd, #350, Beverly Hills CA 90212 USA | |
| **Thomas, Henry L, Jr** | Football Player |
| 16811 Southern Oaks Dr, Houston TX 77068, USA | |
| **Thomas, Henry W** | Writer |
| 3214 Warder St NW, Washington DC 20010, USA | |
| **Thomas, Hollis** | Baseball Player |
| 9163 SE 48th Court Road, Ocala FL 34480, USA | |
| **Thomas, Hollis, Jr** | Football Player |
| 5957 McLeod Dr, Las Vegas NV 89120, USA | |
| **Thomas, Ian** | Singer, Songwriter |
| Anthem Entertainment, 189 Carlton St, Toronto ON M5A 2K7, Canada | |
| **Thomas, Irma** | Singer |
| Irma Thomas Inc, PO Box 26126, New Orleans LA 70186, USA | |
| **Thomas, Irving** | Basketball Player |
| 5117 Lakosee Court, Orlando FL 32818, USA | |
| **Thomas, Isiah L, III** | Basketball Player, Executive, Coach |
| Florida International University, Athletic Dept, Miami FL 33199, USA | |
| **Thomas, J Gorman** | Baseball Player |
| 5 Reef Club, Hilton Head Island SC 29926, USA | |
| **Thomas, J Leroy (Lee)** | Baseball Player |
| 14260 Manderleigh Woods Dr, Chesterfield MO 63017, USA | |
| **Thomas, J Michael (Mickey)** | Singer (Starship) |
| That's Entertainment International, PO Box 2230, Folsom CA 95763, USA | |
| **Thomas, Jake** | Actor |
| Stan Rogow Productions, 3000 Olympic Blvd, Santa Monica CA 90404, USA | |
| **Thomas, James (J T)** | Football Player |
| 408 Arden Dr, Monroeville PA 15146, USA | |
| **Thomas, James E (Jim), Jr** | Basketball Player |
| 4499 Willow Hill Road, Portal GA 30450, USA | |
| **Thomas, Jay** | Actor |
| Don Buchwald, 6500 Wilshire Blvd, #2200, Los Angeles CA 90048 USA | |
| **Thomas, Joe** | Football Player |
| 2276 Stones Throw, Westlake OH 44145, USA | |
| **Thomas, John M** | Chemist |
| Royal Institution, 21 Albemarle St, London W1X 4BS, England | |
| **Thomas, John T (Bud)** | Baseball Player |
| 2475 Woodland Dr, Sedalia MO 65301, USA | |
| **Thomas, Johnny, Jr** | Football Player |
| 1818 Darby Lane, Fresno TX 77545, USA | |
| **Thomas, Jonathan Taylor** | Actor |
| Innovative Artists, 1505 10th St, Santa Monica CA 90401 USA | |
| **Thomas, Julian** | Archaeologist |
| Manchester University, Archaeology Dept, Manchester M13 9PL, England | |
| **Thomas, Keith V** | Historian |
| Broad Gate, Broad St, Ludlow, Shropshire SY8 1NJ, England | |
| **Thomas, Keni** | Singer, Songwriter |
| W M E Entertainment, 1600 Division St, #300, Nashville TN 37203 USA | |
| **Thomas, Kenny** | Singer, Songwriter |
| Lou Coulson Assoc, 37 Berwick St, London W1V 8RS, England | |
| **Thomas, Khleo** | Actor |
| Creative Partners Group, 1522 2nd St, Santa Monica CA 90401, USA | |
| **Thomas, Kiwaukee S** | Football Player |
| 901 W Pinedale Dr, Plant City FL 33563, USA | |
| **Thomas, Kurt** | Gymnast |
| 4421 Hidden Hill Road, Norman OK 73072, USA | |
| **Thomas, Kurt V** | Basketball Player |
| 1826 Brook Terrace Trail, Dallas TX 75232, USA | |
| **Thomas, Lamar N** | Football Player |
| 10524 NW 13th Lane, Gainesville FL 32606, USA | |
| **Thomas, Larry** | Actor, Director |
| Synergy Talent, 13251 Ventura Blvd, Studio City CA 91604, USA | |
| **Thomas, Larry W** | Baseball Player |
| 3825 Graham Lane, Eight Mile AL 36613, USA | |
| **Thomas, Lavale A** | Football Player |
| 7602 Antlers Lane, Charlotte NC 28210, USA | |
| **Thomas, Linn** | Model, Actress |
| 80 5th Avenue, #908, Box 21, New York NY 10011, USA | |
| **Thomas, Mark A** | Football Player |
| 556 Hillsboro St, Monticello GA 31064, USA | |
| **Thomas, Marlo** | Actress |
| 420 E 54th St, #28G, New York NY 10022, USA | |
| **Thomas, Mary** | Singer (Crystals) |
| American Mgmt, 19948 Mayall St, Chatsworth CA 91311, USA | |
| **Thomas, Michael Tilson** | Conductor, Concert Pianist |
| San Francisco Symphony, Davies Symphony Hall, San Francisco CA 94102, USA | |
| **Thomas, Norris L** | Football Player |
| 3202 Boston Ave, Pascagoula MS 39581, USA | |
| **Thomas, Orlando P** | Football Player |
| 330 Mill Pond Dr, Youngsville LA 70592, USA | |
| **Thomas, Patrick S (Pat)** | Football Player |
| 612 Middle Cove Dr, Plano TX 75023, USA | |
| **Thomas, Patrick W (Pat)** | Football Player |
| PO Box 17622, Jacksonville FL 32245, USA | |
| **Thomas, Peter** | Composer |
| Via Riviera 28, 6976 Castagnola/Lugano, Switzerland | |
| **Thomas, Philip Michael** | Actor |
| PO Box 23714, Brooklyn NY 11202, USA | |
| **Thomas, Pinklon** | Boxer |
| 2045 Wild Tamarind Blvd, Orlando FL 32828, USA | |
| **Thomas, Randy** | Football Player |
| 2254 Nelms Dr SW, Atlanta GA 30315, USA | |
| **Thomas, Ray** | Flutist, Singer (Moody Blues) |
| Insight Mgmt, 1222 16th Ave S, #300, Nashville TN 37212, USA | |
| **Thomas, Rebecca** | Director |
| Paradigm Agency, 360 N Crescent Dr, North Building, Beverly Hills CA 90210 USA | |

**Thomas, Reg** — Ice Hockey Player
7245 Colonel Talbot Road, London ON N6L 1H9, Canada

**Thomas, Richard** — Actor
2027 Kentucky Route 825, Hagerhill KY 41222, USA

**Thomas, Rob** — Singer (Matchbox 20), Songwriter
Lippman Entertainment, 23586 Calabasas Road, #208, Calabasas CA 91302, USA

**Thomas, Robb W** — Football Player
179 NW Outlook Vista Dr, Bend OR 97701, USA

**Thomas, Robert D** — Publisher
223 Mariomi Road, New Canaan, CT 06840

**Thomas, Robert R (Bob)** — Football Player
259 Linden St, Glen Ellyn IL 60137, USA

**Thomas, Robin** — Actor
Marshak/Zachary Co, 8840 Wilshire Blvd, #100, Beverly Hills CA 90211 USA

**Thomas, Rodney D** — Football Player
PO Box 664, Groveton TX 75845, USA

**Thomas, Roy J** — Baseball Player
6881 SW 167th Place, Beaverton OR 97007, USA

**Thomas, Rozonda (Chilli)** — Rap Artist (TLC), Actress
Diggit Entertainment, 6 W 18th St, #800, New York NY 10011, USA

**Thomas, Scott** — Ice Hockey Player
49 Redspire Way, East Amherst NY 14051, USA

**Thomas, Sean** — Writer
Bloomsbury Publishing, 50 Bedford Square, London WC1B 3DP, England

**Thomas, Sean Patrick** — Actor
Innovative Artists, 1505 10th St, Santa Monica CA 90401 USA

**Thomas, Serena Scott** — Actress
S M S Talent, 8383 Wilshire Blvd, #230, Beverly Hills CA 90211 USA

**Thomas, Sidney R** — Judge
US Court of Appeals, 316 N 26th St, #5405, Billings MT 59101, USA

**Thomas, Stanley B (Stan)** — Baseball Player
10827 159th Court NE, Redmond WA 98052, USA

**Thomas, Steve** — Entertainer
'This Old House' Show, PO Box 2284, South Burlington VT 05407, USA

**Thomas, Steve** — Ice Hockey Player
Plain & Simple, 289 Bering Ave, Toronto ON M8Z 3A5, Canada

**Thomas, Tamara Craig** — Actress
Independent Artists Agency, 9601 Wilshire Blvd, #750, Beverly Hills CA 90210, USA

**Thomas, Thurman L** — Football Player
7562 Eddy Road, Colden NY 14033, USA

**Thomas, Tillman J** — Prime Minister, Grenada
Prime Minister's Office, Botanical Gardens, Tanteen, Saint George's, Grenada

**Thomas, Timothy J (Tim), Jr** — Ice Hockey Player
29 James Ave, Middleton MA 01949, USA

**Thomas, Timothy M (Tim)** — Basketball Player
Dallas Mavericks, Pavilion, 2909 Taylor St, Dallas TX 75226 USA

**Thomas, Tommy** — Singer
Ivett Stone Agency, W292N6910 Dorn Road, Hartland WI 53029, USA

**Thomas, Tony** — Producer, Writer, Actor
Creative Artists Agency, 2000 Ave of Stars, #100, Los Angeles CA 90067 USA

**Thomas, Wayne** — Ice Hockey Player
San Jose Sharks, San Jose Arena, 525 W Santa Clara St, San Jose CA 95113 USA

**Thomas, William (Tra), III** — Football Player
17 Elderberry Dr, Medford NJ 08055, USA

**Thomas, William H, Jr** — Football Player
2401 Echo Dr, Amarillo TX 79107, USA

**Thomas, Zachary M (Zach)** — Football Player
PO Box 491631, Charlotte NC 28269, USA

**Thomas-Graham, Pamela** — Businesswoman
Liz Claiborne Inc, 1441 Broadway, New York NY 10018, USA

**Thomason, C J** — Actor
Peter Strain, 5455 Wilshire Blvd, #1812, Los Angeles CA 90036 USA

**Thomason, Harry Z** — Producer
10732 Riverside Dr, North Hollywood CA 91602, USA

**Thomason, Marsha** — Actress
Artist Rights Group, 4 Great Portland St, London W1W 8PA, England

**Thomassin, Florence** — Actress
Artmedia, 20 Ave Rapp, 75007 Paris, France

**Thomassin, Gerald** — Actor
Artmedia, 20 Ave Rapp, 75007 Paris, France

**Thomasson, Gary L** — Baseball Player
8300 N 53rd St, Paradise Valley AZ 85253, USA

**Thome, James H (Jim)** — Baseball Player
125 E 8th St, Hinsdale IL 60521, USA

**Thomerson, Tim** — Actor
Innovative Artists, 1505 10th St, Santa Monica CA 90401 USA

**Thomese, P F** — Writer
Bloomsbury Publishing, 50 Bedford Square, London WC1B 3DP, England

**Thomopoulos, Anthony D** — Businessman
5357 Long Shadow Court, Westlake Village CA 91362, USA

**Thompkins, Russell, Jr** — Singer (Stylistics)
Wenig-LaMonica Associates, 580 White Plains Road, #130, Tarrytown NY 10591 USA

**Thompson, Al** — Actor, Producer, Director
S M S Talent, 8383 Wilshire Blvd, #230, Beverly Hills CA 90211 USA

**Thompson, Alexis (Lexi)** — Golfer
Ladies Pro Golf Assn, 100 International Golf Dr, Daytona Beach FL 32124 USA

**Thompson, Andrea** — Actress
Sovereign Talent Group, 8421 Wilshire Blvd, #200, Beverly Hills CA 90211 USA

**Thompson, Andrew J (Andy)** — Baseball Player
1405 Bayshore Blvd, Tampa FL 33606, USA

**Thompson, Anthony** — Football Player, Coach
5035 E DeAnn Dr, Bloomington IN 47404, USA

**Thompson, April Yvette** — Actress
SimonSez Entertainment, 12 Desbrosses St, New York NY 10013, USA

**Thompson, Arland L** — Football Player
6692 S Routt St, Littleton CO 80127, USA

| | |
|---|---|
| **Thompson, Aundra** | Football Player |
| 12060 Galva Dr, Dallas TX 75243, USA | |
| **Thompson, Barbara** | Baseball Player |
| 1721 Edgebrook Dr, Rockford IL 61107, USA | |
| **Thompson, Bennie** | Football Player |
| 10157 Placid Lake Court, Columbia MD 21044, USA | |
| **Thompson, Bobb'e J** | Rap Artist, Actor |
| I C M Partners, 10250 Constellation Blvd, #900, Los Angeles CA 90067 USA | |
| **Thompson, Bobby L** | Baseball Player |
| 7006 Hunters Glen Dr, Charlotte NC 28214, USA | |
| **Thompson, Brent K** | Ice Hockey Player |
| New York Islanders, 1255 Hempstead Turnpike, Uniondale NY 11553 USA | |
| **Thompson, Brian** | Actor, Director, Writer |
| David Shapira Assoc, 193 N Robertson Blvd, Beverly Hills CA 90211 USA | |
| **Thompson, Brooke** | Actress |
| 10515 Mersham Hill Dr, Bakersfield CA 93311, USA | |
| **Thompson, Brooks J** | Basketball Player |
| 29222 Oakview Ridge, Boerne TX 78015, USA | |
| **Thompson, Caroline W** | Writer, Director |
| I C M Partners, 10250 Constellation Blvd, #900, Los Angeles CA 90067 USA | |
| **Thompson, Charissa** | Sportscaster |
| Fox-TV, Sports Dept, 205 W 67th St, New York NY 10065 USA | |
| **Thompson, Charles L (Tim)** | Baseball Player |
| 536 Summit Dr, Lewistown PA 17044, USA | |
| **Thompson, Chaun T** | Football Player |
| 10514 Huffines Dr, Rowlett TX 75089, USA | |
| **Thompson, Chris** | Producer, Writer |
| Rothman Brecher Agency, 9465 Wilshire Blvd, #840, Beverly Hills CA 90212 USA | |
| **Thompson, Christopher** | Astrophysicist |
| University of North Carolina, Astrophysics Dept, Chapel Hill NC 27599, USA | |
| **Thompson, Christopher** | Actor |
| Artmedia, 20 Ave Rapp, 75007 Paris, France | |
| **Thompson, Cornelius A (Corny)** | Basketball Player |
| 207 Lamentation Dr, Berlin CT 06037, USA | |
| **Thompson, Darrell A** | Football Player |
| 4220 Oakview Lane N, Minneapolis MN 55442, USA | |
| **Thompson, David O** | Basketball Player, Executive |
| 5114 Berkeley Creek Lane, Charlotte NC 28277, USA | |
| **Thompson, David W** | Space Scientist, Businessman |
| Orbital Science Corp, 21839 Atlantic Blvd, Dulles VA 20166, USA | |
| **Thompson, Derek** | Baseball Player |
| 3212 Pine Shadow Dr, Land O'Lakes FL 34639, USA | |
| **Thompson, Derrius D** | Football Player |
| 3810 Vitruvian Way, #504, Addison TX 75001, USA | |
| **Thompson, Don** | Businessman |
| McDonald's Corp, McDonald's Plaza, 1 Kroc Dr, Oak Brook IL 60523, USA | |
| **Thompson, Edward K** | Editor |
| 300 Riverside Dr, #10E, New York NY 10025, USA | |
| **Thompson, Edward T** | Editor |
| 11 Cotswold Dr, North Salem NY 10560, USA | |
| **Thompson, Emma** | Actress |
| Hamilton Hodell, 66-68 Margaret St, #500, London W1W 8SR, England | |
| **Thompson, Ernest** | Writer |
| RR 1 Box 3240, Ashland NH 03217, USA | |
| **Thompson, Errol** | Ice Hockey Player |
| PO Box 58, Station Main, Summerside PE C1N 4P6, Canada | |
| **Thompson, F M (Daley)** | Track Athlete |
| Olympic Assn, 1 Wadsworth Plain, London SW18 1EH, England | |
| **Thompson, Fred Dalton** | Senator, TN; Actor |
| Paradigm Agency, 360 Park Ave S, #1600, New York NY 10010 USA | |
| **Thompson, G Ralph** | Religious Leader |
| Seventh-Day Adventists, 12501 Old Columbia Pike, Silver Spring MD 20904, USA | |
| **Thompson, Gary** | Basketball Player |
| 2531 Park Vista Circle, Ames IA 50014, USA | |
| **Thompson, Gary Scott** | Writer, Producer |
| W M E Entertainment, 9601 Wilshire Blvd, #300, Beverly Hills CA 90210 USA | |
| **Thompson, Gerald** | Opera Singer |
| I M G Artists, Hogarth Business Park, Chiswick, London W4 2TH, England | |
| **Thompson, Gina** | Singer |
| Richard Walters, PO Box 2789, Toluca Lake CA 91610 USA | |
| **Thompson, Gordon** | Actor |
| Gage Group, 14724 Ventura Blvd, #505, Sherman Oaks CA 91403 USA | |
| **Thompson, Hilary** | Actress |
| 13202 Weddington St, Sherman Oaks CA 91401, USA | |
| **Thompson, Hugh D (Rocky)** | Golfer |
| 2608 Chamberlain Dr, Plano TX 75023, USA | |
| **Thompson, Hugh L** | Educator |
| 752 Bayside Dr, #402, Cape Canaveral FL 32920, USA | |
| **Thompson, Ian** | Landscape Architect |
| Bloomsbury Publishing, 50 Bedford Square, London WC1B 3DP, England | |
| **Thompson, Jack** | Actor |
| June Cann Mgmt, 118 Oxford St, Woollahra NSW 2025, Australia | |
| **Thompson, Jack B** | Football Player |
| 10439 7th Ave SW, Seattle WA 98146, USA | |
| **Thompson, James** | Writer |
| G P Putnam's Sons, 375 Hudson St, New York NY 10014 USA | |
| **Thompson, James B, Jr** | Geologist |
| 1010 Waltham St, #1, Lexington MA 02421, USA | |
| **Thompson, James R (Jim), Jr** | Governor, IL |
| Winston & Strawn, 35 W Wacker Dr, #2800, Chicago IL 60601, USA | |
| **Thompson, James R, Jr** | Space Administrator |
| 5046 Somerby Dr SE, Huntsville AL 35802, USA | |
| **Thompson, Jason** | Basketball Player |
| Sacramento Kings, Arco Arena, 1 Sports Parkway, Sacramento CA 95834 USA | |
| **Thompson, Jason C** | Actor |
| Wishlab, 2225 Hyperion Ave, #A, Los Angeles CA 90027, USA | |

**Thompson, Jason D**     Baseball Player
4056 Summerfield Dr, Troy MI 48085, USA
**Thompson, Jason M**     Baseball Player
10359 Trillium Dr, Las Vegas NV 89135, USA
**Thompson, Jennifer (Jenny)**     Swimmer
6 Evans Dr, Dover NH 03820, USA
**Thompson, Jill**     Cartoonist
D C Comics, 1700 Broadway, #400, New York NY 10019 USA
**Thompson, Jody**     Actress
Characters Talent, 200-1505 W 2nd Ave, Vancouver BC V6H 3Y4, Canada
**Thompson, John Griggs**     Abel Mathematics Laureate
University of Florida, Mathematics Dept, PO Box 118105, Gainesville FL 32611, USA
**Thompson, John R**     Basketball Player, Coach, Sportscaster
3636 16th St NW, #B1161, Washington DC 20010, USA
**Thompson, Justin W**     Baseball Player
37111 Edgewater Dr, Pinehurst TX 77362, USA
**Thompson, Kenan**     Actor
United Talent Agency, U T A Plaza, 9336 Civic Center Dr, Beverly Hills CA 90210 USA
**Thompson, Kenneth L**     Computer Scientist
A T & T Bell Lucent Laboratory, 600 Mountain Ave, New Providence NJ 07974 USA
**Thompson, Klay A**     Basketball Player
Golden State Warriors, 1011 Broadway, Oakland CA 94605 USA
**Thompson, L Donnell**     Football Player
7503 Kepley Road, Chapel Hill NC 27517, USA
**Thompson, Lamont D**     Football Player
1320 Wildwing Lane, Vallejo CA 94591, USA
**Thompson, Larry D**     Government Official
PepsiCo, 700 Anderson Hill Road, Purchase NY 10577, USA
**Thompson, LaSalle**     Basketball Player
3805 Northcliff Lane, Roseville CA 95747, USA
**Thompson, Lea**     Actress
Innovative Artists, 1505 10th St, Santa Monica CA 90401 USA
**Thompson, Lee (Kix)**     Singer, Saxophonist (Madness)
I T F, Ariel House, 74A Charlotte St, London W1T 4QJ, England
**Thompson, Leonard I**     Football Player
5534 W Glenrosa Ave, Phoenix AZ 85031, USA
**Thompson, Leonard S**     Golfer
9010 Marsh View Court, Ponte Vedra FL 32082, USA
**Thompson, Linda**     Actress, Songwriter
6342 Sycamore Meadows Dr, Malibu CA 90265, USA
**Thompson, Linda**     Singer, Songwriter
Shore Fire Media, 32 Court St, #1600, Brooklyn NY 11201 USA
**Thompson, Lonnie**     Glaciologist
Ohio State University, Geology Dept, Columbus OH 43210, USA
**Thompson, Mark R**     Baseball Player
1122 Lord Murphy Way, Bowling Green KY 42104, USA
**Thompson, Mike**     Editorial Cartoonist
Detroit Free Press, Editorial Dept, 600 W Fort St, Detroit MI 48226 USA
**Thompson, Milton B (Milt)**     Baseball Player
PO Box 663, Williamstown NJ 08094, USA
**Thompson, Mychal G**     Basketball Player
11 Paverstone Lane, Laderna Ranch CA 92694, USA
**Thompson, Norman J (Norm)**     Football Player
PO Box 4552, Hayward CA 94540, USA
**Thompson, Obadele**     Track Athlete
Amateur Athletics Assn, PO Box 46, Bridgetown, Barbados
**Thompson, Paul R J N**     Drummer (Franz Ferdinand)
M A M A Group, 57-65 Worship Ave, London EC2A 2DU, England
**Thompson, Paul S**     Basketball Player
3422 N 40th St, Milwaukee WI 53216, USA
**Thompson, Reece**     Actor
Play Mgmt, 807 Powell St, #220, Vancouver BC V6A 1H7, Canada
**Thompson, Reyna O**     Football Player
1502 NW 183rd Terrace, Pembroke Pines FL 33029, USA
**Thompson, Richard**     Cartoonist (Cul de Sac)
Universal Press Syndicate, 4520 Main St, #700, Kansas City MO 64111 USA
**Thompson, Richard**     Singer, Songwriter, Guitarist
High Road Touring, 751 Bridgeway, #200, Sausalito CA 94965 USA
**Thompson, Richard G**     Baseball Player
Oakland Athletics, McAfee Coliseum, 7000 Coliseum Way, #3, Oakland CA 94621 USA
**Thompson, Richard N (Rich)**     Baseball Player
7 Chambers Court, Huntington Station NY 11746, USA
**Thompson, Ricky D**     Football Player
1277 Brazos Bluff Dr, China Spring TX 76633, USA
**Thompson, Robert L (Bobby)**     Football Player
10712 S 7th Ave, Inglewood CA 90303, USA
**Thompson, Robert R (Robby)**     Baseball Player
4438 Gun Club Road, West Palm Beach FL 33406, USA
**Thompson, Rocky L**     Ice Hockey Player
Oklahoma City Barons, 501 N Walker, #140, Oklahoma City OK 73102, USA
**Thompson, Ryan O**     Baseball Player
2153 Fullerton Dr, Indianapolis IN 46214, USA
**Thompson, Sarah**     Actress
Brillstein Entertainment Partners, 9150 Wilshire Blvd, #350, Beverly Hills CA 90212 USA
**Thompson, Scott**     Businessman
ShopRunner, 225 Washington St, #300, Conshohocken PA 19428, USA
**Thompson, Scott**     Actor, Singer, Writer, Producer
Glickman Talent Mgmt, 204 Saint George St, #20, Toronto ON M5R 2N6, Canada , USA
**Thompson, Scottie**     Actress
M P G Mgmt, 1136 Roxbury Drive, Los Angeles CA 90035, USA
**Thompson, Sophie**     Actress
Saint James Mgmt, 22 Groom Place, London SW1, England
**Thompson, Steve M**     Football Player
Victory Foursquare Gospel Church, 11911 State Ave, Marysville WA 98271, USA
**Thompson, Sue**     Singer, Guitarist
Curb Entertainment, 3907 W Alameda Ave, #200, Burbank CA 91505, USA

**Thompson, Susanna** — Actress
Paradigm Agency, 360 N Crescent Dr, North Building, Beverly Hills CA 90210 USA
**Thompson, Taylor Ann** — Actress
A P A Talent/Literary Agency, 405 S Beverly Dr, #300, Beverly Hills CA 90212 USA
**Thompson, Ted C** — Football Player
222 Nicolet Place, De Pere WI 54115, USA
**Thompson, Teddy** — Singer, Songwriter
Gold Village Entertainment, 72 Madison Ave, #800, New York NY 10016, USA
**Thompson, Teri** — Actress
Red Talent, 9595 Wilshire Blvd, #900, Beverly Hills CA 90212, USA
**Thompson, Tessa** — Actress
Greene Assoc, 1901 Ave of Stars, #130, Los Angeles CA 90067 USA
**Thompson, Tina M** — Basketball Player
Los Angeles Sparks, 888 S Figueroa St, #2010, Los Angeles CA 90017 USA
**Thompson, Tommy G** — Secretary, Health & Human Services
1313 Manassas Trail, Madison WI 53718, USA
**Thompson, Tristan T J** — Basketball Player
Cleveland Cavaliers, Gund Arena, 1 Center Court, Cleveland OH 44115 USA
**Thompson, U Leroy** — Football Player
5005 Princess Anne Court, Knoxville TN 37918, USA
**Thompson, V Scot** — Baseball Player
330 Dodds Road, Butler PA 16002, USA
**Thompson, Verlon** — Singer, Guitarist, Songwriter
V N S Records, 9 Music Square S, #148, Nashville TN 37203, USA
**Thompson, Wilbur (Moose)** — Track Athlete
1111 Stevely Ave, Long Beach CA 90815, USA
**Thompson, William A (Billy)** — Football Player
6522 Jackson Court, Littleton CO 80130, USA
**Thompson, William T (Billy)** — Basketball Player
19678 Palm Spring Dr, Boca Raton FL 33428, USA
**Thompson, Willis H (Weegie)** — Football Player
14501 Felbridge Way, Midlothian VA 23113, USA
**Thoms, Arthur W (Art), Jr** — Football Player
90 Goodfellow Dr, Moraga CA 94556, USA
**Thoms, Tracie** — Actress
Gersh Agency, 41 Madison Ave, #3301, New York NY 10010 USA
**Thomsen, Cecile** — Actress
Art Mgmt, Kronprinsensgade 9A, Copenhagen K, CPH 114, Denmark
**Thomsen, Martha E** — Actress, Model
Playboy Promotions, 2706 Media Center Dr, Los Angeles CA 90065 USA
**Thomsen, Ulrich** — Actor
Greene Assoc, 1901 Ave of Stars, #130, Los Angeles CA 90067 USA
**Thomson of Fleet, David** — Businessman
Thomson Newspapers, 65 Queen St W, Toronto ON M5H 2M8, Canada
**Thomson, Brian E** — Designer
5 Little Dowling St, Paddington NSW 2021, Australia
**Thomson, Erik** — Actor
R G M Artist, 64-76 Kippax St, #202, Surry Hills NSW 2010, Australia
**Thomson, Floyd** — Ice Hockey Player
General Delivery, Dunchurch ON P0A 1G0, Canada
**Thomson, Gordon** — Actor
Gage Group, 14724 Ventura Blvd, #505, Sherman Oaks CA 91403 USA
**Thomson, H C (Hank)** — Harness Racing Official
PO Box 38, Mullett Lake MI 49761, USA
**Thomson, James A** — Biologist
University of Wisconsin, Morgridge Research Institute, Madison WI 53706, USA
**Thomson, John C** — Baseball Player
1414 E Kent St, Sulphur LA 70663, USA
**Thomson, Judith J** — Philosopher, Metaphysician
Massachusetts Institute of Technology, Philosophy Dept, Cambridge MA 02139, USA
**Thomson, June** — Commentator
KNBC-TV, News Dept, 3000 W Alameda Ave, Burbank CA 91523, USA
**Thomson, Kim** — Actress
Caroline Dawson, 125 Gloucester Road, London SW7 4TE, England
**Thomson, Kristen** — Actress
LaFeaver Talent Mgmt, 162 John St, #300, Toronto ON M5V 2E5, Canada
**Thomson, Peter W** — Golfer
Carmel House, 44 Mathoura Road, Toorak VIC 3142, Australia
**Thomson, Rupert** — Writer
Bloomsbury Publishing, 50 Bedford Square, London WC1B 3DP, England
**Thon, Olaf** — Soccer Player
Rosenthaler Str 40-41, Hackesche Hofe, 10178 Berlin, Germany
**Thon, Richard W (Dickie)** — Baseball Player
C17 Calle Lirio del Mar, Urb Dorado del Mar, Dorado PR 00646, USA
**Thone, Charles** — Governor, NE
Erickson & Sederstrom, 301 S 13th St, #400, Lincoln NE 68508, USA
**Thoni, Gustav** — Alpine Skier, Coach
39026 Prato Allo Stelvio-Prao BZ, Italy
**Thor, Brad** — Writer
Pocket Books, 1230 Ave of Americas, New York NY 10020 USA
**Thora** — Actress
C E S D, 10635 Santa Monica Blvd, #130, Los Angeles CA 90025 USA
**Thorburn, Clifford C D (Cliff)** — Snooker Player
31 West Side Dr, Markham ON L3P 7J5, Canada
**Thorell, Clarke** — Actor
Paradigm Agency, 360 N Crescent Dr, North Building, Beverly Hills CA 90210 USA
**Thoresen, Jan** — Curling Athlete
Curling Assn, Sognsveien 75, Serviceboks 1, 0840 Oslo, Norway
**Thorin, Donald E, Sr** — Cinematographer
15260 Ventura Blvd, #1040, Sherman Oaks CA 91403, USA
**Thormodsgard, Paul G** — Baseball Player
7752 E Rose Lane, Scottsdale AZ 85250, USA
**Thorn, Christopher** — Guitarist (Blind Melon)
Shapiro Co, 9229 W Sunset Blvd, #607, West Hollywood CA 90069 USA
**Thorn, Erin** — Basketball Player
Indiana Fever, Conseco Fieldhouse, 125 S Pennsylvania, Indianapolis IN 46204 USA

**Thorn, Paul** — Singer, Songwriter
New Frontier Touring, 1503 17th Ave S, Nashville TN 37212, USA

**Thorn, Rodney K (Rod)** — Basketball Player, Executive
17008 Treviso Way, Naples FL 34110, USA

**Thorn, Tracey** — Singer (Everything But the Girl)
J F D Mgmt, Acklam Workshops, 10 Acklam Road, London W10 5QZ, England

**Thornburgh, Richard L (Dick)** — Attorney General; Governor, PA
Kirkpatrick & Lockhart, 210 6th Ave, #1100, Pittsburgh PA 15222, USA

**Thorne, Bella** — Actress
W M E Entertainment, 9601 Wilshire Blvd, #300, Beverly Hills CA 90210 USA

**Thorne, Callie** — Actress
Gersh Agency, 41 Madison Ave, #3301, New York NY 10010 USA

**Thorne, Frank** — Cartoonist (Moonshine McJuggs)
1967 Grenville Road, Scotch Plains NJ 07076, USA

**Thorne, Gary** — Commentator
55 W Chops Point Road, Bath ME 04530, USA

**Thorne, Kip S** — Physicist
California Institute of Technology, Physics Dept, Pasadena CA 91125, USA

**Thornell, Jack R** — Photojournalist
3421 Tennessee Ave, Kenner LA 70065, USA

**Thorne-Smith, Courtney** — Actress, Model
W M E Entertainment, 9601 Wilshire Blvd, #300, Beverly Hills CA 90210 USA

**Thornhill, Lisa** — Actress
Glick Agency, 1321 7th St, #203, Santa Monica CA 90401 USA

**Thorning-Schmidt, Helle** — Prime Minister, Denmark
Christiansborg Palace, Prins Jorgens Gard 11, 1218 Copenhagen K, Denmark

**Thornton, Al** — Basketball Player
Golden State Warriors, 1011 Broadway, Oakland CA 94605 USA

**Thornton, Billy Bob** — Actor, Director, Writer
Media Talent Group, 9200 W Sunset Blvd, #550, West Hollywood CA 90069 USA

**Thornton, James M** — Football Player
1010 Fuller Road, Gurnee IL 60031, USA

**Thornton, Joseph E (Joe)** — Ice Hockey Player
20121 Hill Ave, Saratoga CA 95070, USA

**Thornton, Kathryn C** — Astronaut
100 Bedford Place, Charlottesville VA 22903, USA

**Thornton, Kevin** — Singer (Color Me Badd)
J-Bird Entertainment, 4905 S Atlantic Ave, Ponce Inlet FL 32127 USA

**Thornton, Louis (Lou)** — Baseball Player
725 Henderson Road, Hope Hull AL 36043, USA

**Thornton, Matthew J (Matt)** — Baseball Player
9820 W Eagle Talon Trail, Peoria AZ 85383, USA

**Thornton, Melody** — Singer (Pussycat Dolls), Actress
J H Mgmt, 420 Lexington Ave, #331, New York NY 10170 USA

**Thornton, Michael E** — Vietnam War Navy Air Hero (CMH)
17040 W FM 1097 Road, #6101, Montgomery TX 77356, USA

**Thornton, Otis B** — Baseball Player
4312 Ave L, Birmingham AL 35208, USA

**Thornton, Robert G (Bob)** — Basketball Player
27865 Espinoza, Mission Viejo CA 92692, USA

**Thornton, Scott C** — Ice Hockey Player
624 30th St, Manhattan Beach CA 90266, USA

**Thornton, Shawn** — Ice Hockey Player
12 Sackville St, #2, Charlestown MA 02129, USA

**Thornton, Sidney** — Football Player
8537 Parkdale Dr, Shreveport LA 71108, USA

**Thornton, Sigrid** — Actress
Australian Film Institute, 236 Dorcas St, South Melbourne VIC 3205, Australia

**Thornton, Tiffany** — Actress
C E S D, 10635 Santa Monica Blvd, #130, Los Angeles CA 90025 USA

**Thornton, William E** — Astronaut
7640 Pimilco Lane, Boerne TX 78015, USA

**Thornton, Zach** — Soccer Player
Club Deportivo Chivas, 18400 Avalon Blvd, #500, Carson CA 90746 USA

**Thorogood, George** — Singer, Guitarist
Monterey International, 200 W Superior St, #202, Chicago IL 60654 USA

**Thorp, H Holden** — Educator
University of North Carolina, Chancellor's Office, South Building, Chapel Hill NC 27599, USA

**Thorpe, Harriet** — Actress
Gavin Barker Assoc, 2D Wimpole St, London W1G 0EB, England

**Thorpe, Ian** — Swimmer
Sports & Entertainment, 243 Liverpool St, #300, East Sydney NSW 2010, Australia

**Thorpe, J Jeremy** — Government Official, England
2 Orme Square, Bayswater, London W2 4RS, England

**Thorpe, Jimmy L (Jim)** — Golfer
1612 Kersley Circle, Lake Mary FL 32746, USA

**Thorpe, Otis H** — Basketball Player
PO Box 400, Canfield OH 44406, USA

**Thorsness, Leo K** — Vietnam Air Force Hero (CMH)
239 Watterson Way, Madison AL 35756, USA

**Thorson, Linda** — Actress
Noble Caplan Abrams, 1260 Yonge St, #200, Toronto ON M4T 1W6, Canada

**Thost, Nicola** — Snowboard Skier
German Competitors Assn, Kuppenheimstr 15, 75179 Pforzheim, Germany

**Thouless, David James** — Physicist
University of Washington, Physics Dept, Seattle WA 98195, USA

**Thrash, James** — Football Player
16005 Hampton Road, Hamilton VA 20158, USA

**Thrash, William G** — Marine Corps General
8 Hadley Lane, Hilton Head Island SC 29926, USA

**Threadgill, Henry L** — Jazz Saxophonist, Composer
Joel Chriss Co, 300 Mercer St, #3J, New York NY 10003 USA

**Threatt, Sedale E** — Basketball Player
PO Box 1085, Alabaster AL 35007, USA

**Threets, Erick** — Baseball Player
2080 Vintage Lane, Livermore CA 94550, USA

**Threlfall, David** — Actor
James Sharkey, 34 Kingly Court, London W1R 5LE, England
**Thrift, Clifford R (Cliff)** — Football Player
705 Trisha Lane, Norman OK 73072, USA
**Throop, George L** — Baseball Player
239 Windwood Lane, Sierra Madre CA 91024, USA
**Thrower, James M (Jim)** — Football Player
17421 Pontchartrain Blvd, Detroit MI 48203, USA
**Thuillier, Luc** — Actor
Artmedia, 20 Ave Rapp, 75007 Paris, France
**Thumann, Chad** — Writer, Actor
United Talent Agency, U T A Plaza, 9336 Civic Center Dr, Beverly Hills CA 90210 USA
**Thun, Matteo** — Interior Designer
9 Via Appiani, 20121 Milan, Italy
**Thune, Nick** — Actor, Comedian
3 Arts Entertainment, 9460 Wilshire Blvd, #700, Beverly Hills CA 90212 USA
**Thunman, Nils R** — Navy Admiral
1516 S Willemore Ave, Springfield IL 62704, USA
**Thuot, Pierre J** — Astronaut
22897 Thornbury Dr, Hollywood MD 20636, USA
**Thurber, Rawson Marshall** — Director, Writer, Actor
Creative Artists Agency, 2000 Ave of Stars, #100, Los Angeles CA 90067 USA
**Thurier, Blaine** — Singer, Director
Skrzyniarz & Mallean, 9229 Sunset Blvd, #525, Los Angeles CA 90069, USA
**Thurlow, Stephen C (Steve)** — Football Player
198 Shore Road, Old Greenwich CT 06870, USA
**Thurman, Dennis L** — Football Player
New York Jets, 1 Jets Dr, Florham Park NJ 07932, USA
**Thurman, Gary M** — Baseball Player
225 W 32nd St, Indianapolis IN 46208, USA
**Thurman, James D** — Army General
Commander, UN Command & US Forces Korea, Unit 15327, APO AP 96218 USA
**Thurman, Michael R (Mike)** — Baseball Player
1360 7th St, West Linn OR 97068, USA
**Thurman, Uma** — Actress, Model
Untitled Entertainment, 350 S Beverly Dr, #200, Beverly Hills CA 90212 USA
**Thurman, William E** — Air Force General
10 Firestone Dr, Pinehurst NC 28374, USA
**Thurmond, Mark A** — Baseball Player
1614 Kings Castle Dr, Katy TX 77450, USA
**Thurmond, Nathaniel (Nate)** — Basketball Player, Executive
5094 Diamond Heights Blvd, #B, San Francisco CA 94131, USA
**Thurow, Lester C** — Economist
Massachusetts Institute of Technology, Economics Dept, Cambridge MA 02139, USA
**Thurston, Frederick C (Fuzzy)** — Football Player
E1462 Grandview Road, Waupaca WI 54981, USA
**Thurston, Joseph W (Joe)** — Baseball Player
9024 Paso Robles Way, Elk Grove CA 95758, USA
**Thwaites, Brenton** — Actor
W M E Entertainment, 9601 Wilshire Blvd, #300, Beverly Hills CA 90210 USA
**Thyer, Mario** — Ice Hockey Player
170 Silver Road, Bangor ME 04401, USA
**Thyne, T J** — Actor
Greene Assoc, 1901 Ave of Stars, #130, Los Angeles CA 90067 USA
**Thyssen, Greta** — Actress
444 E 82nd St, New York NY 10028, USA
**Tian, Valerie** — Actress
Greene Assoc, 1901 Ave of Stars, #130, Los Angeles CA 90067 USA
**Tiant, Luis C** — Baseball Player
11998 Hidden Links Dr, Fort Myers FL 33913, USA
**Tiao, Luc-Adolphe** — Prime Minister, Burkina Faso
Prime Minister's Office, 03 BP 7027, Ouagadougou 03, Burkina Faso
**Tibbetts, Billy** — Ice Hockey Player
79 Jericho Road, Scituate MA 02066, USA
**Tibbs, Jay L** — Baseball Player
1100 Stonebrook Lane, Oneonta AL 35121, USA
**Ticci, Stefano** — Bobsled Athlete
Olympic Committee, Foro Italico, Largo Lauro de Bosis 15, 00135 Rome, Italy
**Tice, George A** — Photographer
581 Kings Highway E, Atlantic Hills NJ 07716, USA
**Tice, John K** — Football Player
1004 Bartlett Loop, West Point NY 10996, USA
**Tice, Michael P (Mike)** — Football Player, Coach
1213 Ashbury Lane, Libertyville IL 60048, USA
**Tich** — Musician (Dave Dee Dozy Beaky Mick Tich)
Gerd Kehren Mgmt, Postfach 1408, 41804 Erkelenz, Germany
**Tichy, Milan** — Ice Hockey Player
2413 NW 7th St, Boynton Beach FL 33426, USA
**Tickner, Charles (Charlie)** — Figure Skater
5410 Sunset Dr, Littleton CO 80123, USA
**Ticotin, Rachel** — Actress
Stone Manners Salners, 9911 W Pico Blvd, #1400, Los Angeles CA 90035 USA
**Tidrow, Richard W (Dick)** — Baseball Player
324 NE Warrington Court, Lees Summit MO 64064, USA
**Tidwell, Moody R, III** — Judge
US Claims Court, 717 Madison Place NW, Washington DC 20439, USA
**Tiefenthaler, Verle M** — Baseball Player
1852 Quint Ave, Carroll IA 51401, USA
**Tiegs, Cheryl** — Model
809 Nimes, Los Angeles CA 90077, USA
**Tierney, Garrett** — Bassist (Brand New)
Stunt Company Media, 20 Jay St, #208, Brooklyn NY 11201, USA
**Tierney, Maura** — Actress
United Talent Agency, U T A Plaza, 9336 Civic Center Dr, Beverly Hills CA 90210 USA
**Tierney, William (Bill)** — Lacrosse Coach
Denver University, Athletic Dept, Peter Barton Stadium, Denver CO 80210, USA

**Tiffany** — Singer, Model
Almond Talent Agency, 8217 Beverly Blvd, #8, West Hollywood CA 90048, USA
**Tiffany, John** — Director
Casorotto Ramsay, Waverley House, 7-12 Noel St, London W1F 8GQ, England
**Tiffee, Terry R** — Baseball Player
4 Epernay Circle, Little Rock AR 72223, USA
**Tiffin, Pamela** — Actress
15 W 67th St, New York NY 10023, USA
**Tigah** — Rap Artist
Columbia Records, 9830 Wilshire Blvd, Beverly Hills CA 90212 USA
**Tigar, Kenneth** — Actor
Gage Group, 14724 Ventura Blvd, #505, Sherman Oaks CA 91403 USA
**Tigelaar, Liz** — Producer, Writer
W M E Entertainment, 9601 Wilshire Blvd, #300, Beverly Hills CA 90210 USA
**Tiger, Lionel** — Anthropologist, Social Scientist
248 W 23rd St, #400, New York NY 10011, USA
**Tigerman, Stanley** — Architect
910 N Lakeshore Dr, #2916, Chicago IL 60611, USA
**Tighe, Kevin** — Actor
Domain Talent, 9229 W Sunset Blvd, #710, West Hollywood CA 90069 USA
**Tijan, Robert** — Biochemist, Molecular Biologist
Howard Hughes Medical Institution, 4000 Jones Bridge Road, Chevy Chase MD 20815, USA
**Tikaram, Ramon** — Actor
Curtis Brown Group, 28-29 Haymarket St, #500, London SW1Y 4SP, England
**Tilbrook, Glenn** — Singer, Guitarist (Squeeze)
Quioxtic Records/Stress Mgmt, PO Box 27947, London SE7 8WN, England
**Tilelli, John H, Jr** — Army General
Stanford University, International Studies Dept, Stanford CA 94305, USA
**Tilghman, Kelly** — Sportscaster
Golf Channel, 7580 Commerce Center Dr, Orlando FL 32819, USA
**Tilghman, Shirley M C** — Educator, Molecular Biologist
Princeton University, President's Office, Princeton NJ 08544, USA
**Tiliakos, Dimitris** — Opera Singer
I M G Artists, Hogarth Business Park, Chiswick, London W4 2TH, England
**Till, James E** — Biophysicist, Cell Biologist
182 Briar Hill Ave, Toronto ON M4R 1H9, Canada
**Tilleman, Michael J (Mike)** — Football Player
180 Country Road 800 NW, Havre MT 59501, USA
**Tiller, Nadja** — Actress
Via Tamporiva 26, 6976 Castagnola, Switzerland
**Tillerson, Rex W** — Businessman
ExxonMobil Corp, 5959 Las Colinas Blvd, Irving TX 75039, USA
**Tillery, Linda** — Singer, Percussionist (Loading Zone)
Berkeley Agency, 2608 9th St, #301, Berkeley CA 94710 USA
**Tilley, Patrick L (Pat)** — Football Player, Coach
PO Box 4523, Shreveport LA 71134, USA
**Tilley, Tom** — Ice Hockey Player
14724 Maple St, Overland Park KS 66223, USA
**Tilling, Camilla** — Opera, Concert Singer
Harrison/Parrott, 5-6 Albion Court, London W6 0QT, England
**Tillis, Mel** — Singer, Guitarist, Songwriter
Mel Tillis Enterprises, PO Box 305, Silver Springs FL 34489, USA
**Tillis, Pam** — Singer, Songwriter
PO Box 128575, Nashville TN 37212, USA
**Tillman, Charles** — Football Player
31227 Sage Court, Libertyville IL 60048, USA
**Tillman, George, Jr** — Director, Producer, Writer
State Street Pictures, 9255 W Sunset Blvd, #528, Los Angeles CA 90069, USA
**Tillman, Kerry J (Rusty)** — Baseball Player
8711 Newton Road, #61, Jacksonville FL 32216, USA
**Tillman, Lewis D** — Football Player
PO Box 166, Madison MS 39130, USA
**Tillman, Robert L** — Businessman
Lowe's Companies, 1605 Curtis Bridge Road, Wilkesboro NC 28697, USA
**Tillman, Spencer A** — Football Player
19 Lake Mist Court, Sugar Land TX 77479, USA
**Tillman, Travares A** — Football Player
3720 Tanglewood Dr SE, Atlanta GA 30339, USA
**Tillmans, Wolfgang** — Artist, Photographer
Maureen Paley Interim Art, 21 Herald St, London E 6JT, England
**Tillotson, Johnny** — Singer
American Mgmt, 19948 Mayall St, Chatsworth CA 91311, USA
**Tilly, Jennifer** — Actress
Innovative Artists, 1505 10th St, Santa Monica CA 90401 USA
**Tilly, Meg** — Actress
I F A Talent Agency, 8730 W Sunset Blvd, #490, West Hollywood CA 90069 USA
**Tilson, Joseph (Joe)** — Artist
2 Brook Street Mansions, 41 Davies St, London W1Y 1FJ, England
**Tilton, Charlene** — Actress, Model
Premier Talent Group, 4370 Tujunga Ave, #110, Studio City CA 91604, USA
**Tilton, Robert** — Evangelist
Robert Tilton Ministries, PO Box 819000, Dallas TX 75381, USA
**Timbaland** — Rap Artist, Music Producer
W M E Entertainment, 9601 Wilshire Blvd, #300, Beverly Hills CA 90210 USA
**Timberlake, Gary D** — Baseball Player
14016 Waters Edge Dr, Louisville KY 40245, USA
**Timberlake, Justin** — Singer ('N Sync), Actor
W M E Entertainment, 9601 Wilshire Blvd, #300, Beverly Hills CA 90210 USA
**Timchal, Cindy** — Lacrosse Coach
University of Maryland, Athletic Dept, College Park MD 20742, USA
**Timken, William R, Jr** — Businessman, Diplomat
State Department, 2201 C St NW, Washington DC 20520 USA
**Timko, Brittany** — Soccer Player
Vancouver Whitecaps, The Landing, 375 Water St, Vancouver BC V6B 5C6, Canada
**Timlin, Addison** — Actress
Gersh Agency, 9465 Wilshire Blvd, #600, Beverly Hills CA 90212 USA

**Timlin, Michael A (Mike)** — Baseball Player
355 High Ridge Way, Castle Rock CO 80108, USA
**Timmer, Marianne** — Speed Skater
K N S B, Postbus 1120, 3800 Amersfoort BC, Netherlands
**Timmerman, Adam L** — Football Player
1635 585th St, Cherokee IA 51012, USA
**Timmermann, Thomas H (Tom)** — Baseball Player
197 Coyote Court, Pinckney MI 48169, USA
**Timmermann, Ulf** — Track Athlete
Conrad Blenkle Str 34, 13055 Berlin, Germany
**Timmins, Margo** — Singer (Cowboy Junkies)
S L Feldman Mgmt, 1505 W 2nd Ave, #200, Vancouver BC V6H 3Y4, Canada
**Timmins, Michael** — Guitarist (Cowboy Junkies), Songwriter
S L Feldman Mgmt, 1505 W 2nd Ave, #200, Vancouver BC V6H 3Y4, Canada
**Timmins, Peter** — Drummer (Cowboy Junkies)
S L Feldman Mgmt, 1505 W 2nd Ave, #200, Vancouver BC V6H 3Y4, Canada
**Timmons, Jeffrey B (Jeff)** — Singer (98 Degrees)
Marsellie Mgmt, 6228 Fallbrook Ave, Woodland Hills CA 91367, USA
**Timmons, Osborne L (Ozzie)** — Baseball Player
4901 S 83rd St, Tampa FL 33619, USA
**Timms, Michele** — Basketball Player
Phoenix Mercury, American West Arena, 201 E Jefferson St, Phoenix AZ 85004 USA
**Timms, Sally** — Singer (Pine Valley Cosmonauts)
Billions Corp, 3522 W Armitage Ave, Chicago IL 60647 USA
**Timmy T** — Singer, Rap Artist, Musician
Richard Walters, PO Box 2789, Toluca Lake CA 91610 USA
**Timofeyeva, Nina V** — Ballerina
Bolshoi Theater, Teatralnaya Pl 1, 103009 Moscow, Russia
**Timofti, Nicolae** — President, Moldova
Presidential Palace, 23 Nicolae Iorge Str, 227033 Chishinev, Moldova
**Timonen, Kimmo S (Kime)** — Ice Hockey Player
125 Upland Way, Haddonfield NJ 08033, USA
**Timoney, John F** — Law Enforcement Official
Miami Police Department, 400 NW 2nd Ave, Miami FL 33128, USA
**Timpson, Michael D** — Football Player
1823 Derby Glen Dr, Orlando FL 32837, USA
**Timsit, Patrick** — Actor
Artmedia, 20 Ave Rapp, 75007 Paris, France
**Tindemans, Leonard C (Leo)** — Prime Minister, Belgium
Jan Verbertlei 24, 2650 Edegem, Belgium
**Tindle, David** — Artist
Via Giovanni Pacchini 118B, S Maria del Giudice, 55058 Lucca, Italy
**Ting, Alice** — Chemist
Massachusetts Institute of Technology, Chemistry Dept, Cambridge MA 02139, USA
**Ting, Samuel C C** — Nobel Physics Laureate
2 Eliot Place, Jamaica Plain MA 02130, USA
**Tinglehoff, H Michael (Mick)** — Football Player
20517 Kalmeadow Court, Lakeview MN 55044, USA
**Tingley, Ronald I (Ron)** — Baseball Player
349 Omni Dr, Sparks NV 89441, USA
**Tinker, Grant A** — Businessman
541 Perugia Way, Los Angeles CA 90077, USA
**Tinkham, Michael** — Physicist
6126 SE Grant St, Portland OR 97215, USA
**Tinoisamoa, Pisa D** — Football Player
4384 Austin Pass Dr, Saint Charles MO 63304, USA
**Tinordi, Mark** — Ice Hockey Player
545 Devonshire Court, Severna Park MD 21146, USA
**Tinsley, Bruce** — Editorial Cartoonist
King Features Syndicate, 300 W 57th St, #1500, New York NY 10019 USA
**Tinsley, Jackson B (Jack)** — Editor
Fort Worth Star-Telegram, Editorial Dept, 808 Throckmorton St, Fort Worth TX 76102 USA
**Tinsley, Jamaal L** — Basketball Player
12122 Ellingwood Dr, Auburndale FL 33823, USA
**Tinsley, Jeremy** — Poker Player
World Poker Tour, 1041 N Formosa Blvd, #PH 2, West Hollywood CA 90046, USA
**Tinsley, Lee O** — Baseball Player
237 Tenor St, Shelbyville KY 40065, USA
**Tippett, Andre B** — Football Player
17 Knob Hill St, Sharon MA 02067, USA
**Tippett, David (Dave)** — Ice Hockey Player, Coach, Executive
10287 E Diamond Rim Dr, Scottsdale AZ 85255, USA
**Tippett, Phil** — Animator
Tippett Studio, 2741 10th St, Berkeley CA 94710, USA
**Tippin, Aaron** — Singer, Songwriter
Tip Top Entertainment, PO Box 41689, Nashville TN 37204, USA
**Tippins, Kenny (Ken)** — Football Player
524 Renaissance Way, Conyers GA 30012, USA
**Tipton, Analeigh** — Actress
Creative Artists Agency, 2000 Ave of Stars, #100, Los Angeles CA 90067 USA
**Tipton, Dave L** — Football Player, Coach
915 Bonneville Ave, Sunnyvale CA 94087, USA
**Tipton, Glenn R** — Guitarist (Judist Priest)
Trinfold Mgmt, 12 Oval Road, #300, Camden, London NW1 7D4, England
**Tiriac, Ion** — Tennis Player, Coach
Ion Tiriac/T V Enterprises, 251 E 49th St, New York NY 10017, USA
**Tirico, Michael J (Mike)** — Sportscaster
ESPN-TV, ESPN Plaza, 935 Middle St, Bristol CT 06010 USA
**Tirimo, Martino** — Concert Pianist, Conductor
1 Romeyn Road, London SW16 2NU, England
**Tirio, Dave** — Guitarist (Plain White T's)
One Moment Mgmt, PO Box 55156, Sherman Oaks CA 91413 USA
**Tisby, Dexter** — Singer (Penguins)
David Harris Enterprises, 24210 E Fork Road, #9, Azusa CA 91702, USA
**Tisch, James S** — Businessman
Loews Corp, 667 Madison Ave, #700, New York NY 10065, USA

**Tisch, Steve** — Writer
1162 Tower Road, Beverly Hills CA 90210, USA
**Tischinski, Thomas A (Tom)** — Baseball Player
9905 N Donnelly Ave, Kansas City MO 64157, USA
**Tisdale, Ashley** — Actress, Singer, Songwriter
Blondie Girl Productions, 1040 N Las Palmas, Building 40, Los Angeles CA 90038, USA
**Tishby, Noa** — Actress
Burstein Co, 15304 W Sunset Blvd, #208, Pacific Palisades CA 90272 USA
**Titanic, Morris** — Ice Hockey Player
146 Delta Road, Buffalo NY 14226, USA
**Titensor, Glen W** — Football Player
729 Montrose Court, Flower Mound TX 75022, USA
**Title, Stacy** — Director
I C M Partners, 10250 Constellation Blvd, #900, Los Angeles CA 90067 USA
**Titmuss, Abi** — Model, Entertainer
Money Mgmt, 42A Berwick St, London W1F 8RE, England
**Tito, Dennis A** — Tourist Cosmonaut
1800 Alta Mura Road, Pacific Palisades CA 90272, USA
**Titov, German M** — Ice Hockey Player
9 Aspen Ridge Gate SW, Calgary AB T3H 5V4, Canada
**Titov, Vladimir G** — Cosmonaut
3 Hovanskaya Str 8, 129515 Moscow, Russia
**Titov, Yuri E** — Gymnast
Kolokolnikov Per 6, #19, 103045 Moscow, Russia
**Tits, Jacques L** — Abel Mathematics Laureate
12 Rue du Moulin des Pres, 75013 Paris, France
**Tittle, Yelberton A (Y A)** — Football Player
168 Elana Ave, Atherton CA 94027, USA
**Titus, Christopher** — Actor, Comedian, Writer
Gersh Agency, 9465 Wilshire Blvd, #600, Beverly Hills CA 90212 USA
**Tizard, Catherine A** — Governor General, New Zealand
1/12A Wallace St, Herne Bay, Auckland 1011, New Zealand
**Tizon, Albert** — Journalist
Seattle Times, Editorial Dept, 1000 Denny Way, Seattle WA 98109 USA
**Tjarnqvist, C Daniel** — Ice Hockey Player
Colorado Avalanche, Pepsi Center, 1000 Chopper Circle, Denver CO 80204 USA
**Tjeknavorian, Loris-Zare** — Composer, Conductor
State Philharmonia, Mashtots Prospekt 46, 0002 Yerevan, Armenia
**Tjoflat, Gerald B** — Judge
US Court of Appeals, 311 W Monroe St, Jacksonville FL 32202, USA
**Tkachuk, Keith** — Ice Hockey Player
11243 Hunters Pond Road, Saint Louis MO 63141, USA
**Tkaczuk, Walter R (Walt)** — Ice Hockey Player
River Valley Golf & Country Club, RR 3, Sainte Mary's ON N0M 2G0, Canada
**To, Johnnie** — Director
Milky Way Image, Milky Way Building, #1F, 77 Hung To Road, Kwun Tong, Hong Kong, China
**Toback, James** — Director, Writer
Resolution, 1801 Century Park E, #2300, Los Angeles CA 90067, USA
**Tobeck, Robert L (Robbie)** — Football Player
6620 320th St E, Eatonville WA 98328, USA
**Tober, Barbara D** — Editor
620 Park Ave, New York NY 10065, USA
**Tobey, James** — Actor
Paradigm Agency, 360 N Crescent Dr, North Building, Beverly Hills CA 90210 USA
**Tobian, Gary M** — Diver
9171 Belted Kingfisher Road, Blaine WA 98230, USA
**Tobias, Andrew** — Writer, Columnist
146 Central Park W, New York NY 10023, USA
**Tobias, Oliver** — Actor
Agentur Lentz, Barestr 48, 80799 Munich, Germany
**Tobias, Randall L** — Businessman, Diplomat
State Department, 2201 C St NW, Washington DC 20520 USA
**Tobias, Robert M** — Labor Leader
American University, Public Affairs School, Washington DC 20057, USA
**Tobik, David V (Dave)** — Baseball Player
848 Chancellor Heights Dr, Ballwin MO 63011, USA
**Tobin, Don** — Cartoonist (Little Woman)
12312 Ranchwood Road, Santa Ana CA 92705, USA
**Tobin, James R** — Businessman
Baxter Scientific, 1 Boston Scientific Place, Natick MA 01760, USA
**Tobin, Robert G** — Businessman
Ahold USA, 1385 Hancock St, Quincy MA 02169, USA
**Tobin, Vince** — Football Coach
15997 W Monterey Way, Goodyear AZ 85395, USA
**Tobolowsky, Stephen** — Actor
Innovative Artists, 1505 10th St, Santa Monica CA 90401 USA
**TobyMac** — Singer, Rap Artist (DC Talk)
True Artist Mgmt, 227 3rd Ave B, Franklin TN 37064, USA
**Toca, Jorge L** — Baseball Player
7940 NW 167th Terrace, Hialeah FL 33016, USA
**Tocchet, Rick** — Ice Hockey Player, Coach
PO Box 13563, Pittsburgh PA 15243, USA
**Tochi, Brian** — Actor
247 S Beverly Dr, #102, Beverly Hills CA 90212, USA
**Toczyska, Stefania** — Opera Singer
Stafford Law, 6 Barham Close, Weybridge, Surrey KT13 9PR, England
**Todd, Ann E** — Actress
2419 Oregon St, Berkeley CA 94705, USA
**Todd, C Richard** — Football Player
PO Box 478, Florence AL 35631, USA
**Todd, Hallie** — Actress
In-House Media, 13636 Ventura Blvd, #298, Sherman Oaks CA 91423, USA
**Todd, Harry W** — Businessman
Carlisle Enterprises, 777 Fay Ave, La Jolla CA 92037, USA
**Todd, James R (Jim), Jr** — Baseball Player
21639 Hill Gail Way, Parker CO 80138, USA

**Todd, Josh** — Singer (Buckcherry)
Agency Group Ltd, 142 W 57th St, #600, New York NY 10019 USA

**Todd, Kevin** — Ice Hockey Player
15 Narla Lane, Utica NY 13501, USA

**Todd, Lani** — Model
Playboy Promotions, 2706 Media Center Dr, Los Angeles CA 90065 USA

**Todd, Lee** — Educator
University of Kentucky, President's Office, Lexington KY 40506, USA

**Todd, Mark J** — Equestrian
PO Box 507, Cambridge, New Zealand

**Todd, Mia Doi** — Singer, Guitarist, Songwriter
Fanatic Promotion, 322 Bleecker St, #G7, New York NY 10014, USA

**Todd, Tony** — Actor
Innovative Artists, 1505 10th St, Santa Monica CA 90401 USA

**Todd, Virgil H** — Religious Leader, Educator
3095 E Glengarry Road, Memphis TN 38128, USA

**Toennies, Jan Peter** — Physicist
Ewaldstr 7, 37075 Gottingen, Germany

**Toews, Jeffrey M (Jeff)** — Football Player
11924 Silver Oak Dr, Davie FL 33330, USA

**Toews, Jonathan B** — Ice Hockey Player
Chicago Blackhawks, United Center, 1901 W Madison St, Chicago IL 60612 USA

**Toews, Loren J** — Football Player
165 Hawthorne Ave, Los Altos Hills CA 94022, USA

**Tofani, Loretta A** — Journalist
Philadelphia Inquirer, Editorial Dept, 400 N Broad St, Philadelphia PA 19130, USA

**Toffler, Alvin** — Writer, Futurist
Random House, 1745 Broadway, #1800, New York NY 10019 USA

**Toft, Rod** — Bowler
11350 12th St N, Lake Elmo MN 55042, USA

**Tognini, Michel** — Cosmonaut, France; Air Force General
European Space Center, Linder Hohe, Box 906096, 51127 Cologne, Germany

**Tognoni, Gina** — Actress
Innovative Artists, 1505 10th St, Santa Monica CA 90401 USA

**Togo, Jonathan** — Actor
C E S D, 10635 Santa Monica Blvd, #130, Los Angeles CA 90025 USA

**Togunde, Victor** — Actor
Greater Visions Artists Talent Agency, 8981 W Sunset Blvd, #101, West Hollywood CA 90069 USA

**Toibin, Colm** — Writer
23 Carnew St, Arbour Hill, Dublin 7, County Dublin, Ireland

**Tokarev, Valery I** — Cosmonaut
Cosmonaut Training Center, Star City, 141160 Zvezdny Gorodok, Moscow Oblast, Russia

**Tokes, Laszlo** — Religious Leader, Political Activist
Craivei Str 1, 3700 Oradea, Romania

**Tokody, Ilona** — Opera Singer
Hungarian State Opera, Andrassy Utca 22, 1062 Budapest, Hungary

**Tokombayeva, Aysulu A** — Ballerina
Usenbaev Str 37, #33, 720021 Bishkek, Kyrgystan

**Tolan, Peter** — Actor, Director, Producer
Fedora Entertainment, 15300 Ventura Blvd, Sherman Oaks CA 91403, USA

**Tolan, Robert (Bobby)** — Baseball Player
804 Woodstock St, Bellaire TX 77401, USA

**Tolbert, B Thomas (Tom)** — Basketball Player
368 Creedon Circle, Alameda CA 94502, USA

**Tolbert, Berlinda** — Actress
Pallas Mgmt, 12535 Chandler Blvd, #1, Valley Village CA 91607, USA

**Tolbert, L James (Jim)** — Football Player
2435 Corinna Court, San Diego CA 92105, USA

**Tolbert, Mike** — Football Player
Carolina Panthers, Ericsson Stadium, 800 S Mint St, Charlotte NC 28202 USA

**Tolbert, Raymond L (Ray)** — Basketball Player
2205 Crestwood Dr, Anderson IN 46016, USA

**Tolbert, Tony L** — Football Player
475 S White Chapel Blvd, Southlake TX 76092, USA

**Tolcher, Michael** — Singer, Guitarist, Songwriter
Elevation Group, 1408 Encinal Ave, #A, Alameda CA 94501, USA

**Toledano, Eric** — Director
Creative Artists Agency, 2000 Ave of Stars, #100, Los Angeles CA 90067 USA

**Toledo, Esteban** — Golfer
61 Rockport, Irvine CA 92602, USA

**Toledo, Francisco** — Artist
Vorpal Gallery, 1 Front St, #1550, San Francisco CA 94111, USA

**Toledo, Isabel** — Fashion Designer
277 5th Ave, New York NY 10016, USA

**Toledo, Rafael** — Actor
Culbertson Group, 8430 Santa Monica Blvd, #210, West Hollywood CA 90069, USA

**Tolentino, Jose F** — Baseball Player
26711 Caceres Circle, Mission Viejo CA 92691, USA

**Toles, Thomas G (Tom)** — Editorial Cartoonist
4625 46th St NW, Washington DC 20016, USA

**Tolhurst, Lol** — Drummer (Cure)
Primary Talent Int'l, 10-11 Jockey's Fields, London WC1R 4BN, England

**Toliver, Freddie L (Fred)** — Baseball Player
674 Medical Center Dr, San Bernardino CA 92411, USA

**Toliver, Kristi** — Basketball Player
Chicago Sky, 20 W Kinzie St, #1010, Chicago IL 60654 USA

**Tolkan, James** — Actor
Paradigm Agency, 360 N Crescent Dr, North Building, Beverly Hills CA 90210 USA

**Toll, Joanne** — Producer
W M E Entertainment, 9601 Wilshire Blvd, #300, Beverly Hills CA 90210 USA

**Toll, Robert I** — Businessman
Toll Brothers, 250 Gibraltar Road, Horsham PA 19044, USA

**Tollberg, Brian** — Baseball Player
2104 39th St W, Bradenton FL 34205, USA

**Tollefson, Dave** — Football Player
Oakland Raiders, 1220 Harbor Bay Parkway, Alameda CA 94502 USA

# T

| | |
|---|---|
| **Tolles, Tommy**<br>233 Park Dr, Hendersonville NC 28739, USA | Golfer |
| **Tolleson, J Wayne**<br>313 Mossycup Oak Court, Spartanburg SC 29306, USA | Baseball Player |
| **Tolliver, Billy Joe**<br>9837 Neesonwood Dr, Shreveport LA 71106, USA | Football Player |
| **Tolman, Timothy L (Tim)**<br>11425 N Ingot Loop, Tucson AZ 85737, USA | Baseball Player |
| **Tolsky, Susan**<br>10815 Acama St, North Hollywood CA 91602, USA | Actress |
| **Tom, Heather**<br>Luedtke Agency, 1674 Broadway, #7A, New York NY 10019, USA | Actress |
| **Tom, Kiana**<br>PO Box 1111, Sunset Beach CA 90742, USA | Physical Fitness Expert, Model |
| **Tom, Lauren**<br>Pop Art Mgmt, PO Box 55363, Sherman Oaks CA 91413, USA | Actress |
| **Tom, Logan M L**<br>2001 E 21st St, #136, Signal Hill CA 90755, USA | Volleyball Player |
| **Tom, Nicholle**<br>Talent Works, 3500 W Olive Ave, #1400, Burbank CA 91505 USA | Actress |
| **Toma, David**<br>PO Box 854, Rahway NJ 07065, USA | Writer |
| **Tomalty, Glenn**<br>5423 Boomerang Way, RR 6, Fernie BC V0B 1M6, Canada | Ice Hockey Player |
| **Tomanek, Richard C (Dick)**<br>165 Duff Dr, Avon Lake OH 44012, USA | Baseball Player |
| **Tomasevicz, Curtis (Curt)**<br>Team Holcomb, PO Box 118, Oakley UT 84055, USA | Bobsled Athlete |
| **Tomasson, Helgi**<br>San Francisco Ballet, 455 Franklin St, San Francisco CA 94102, USA | Ballet Dancer, Director |
| **Tomba, Alberto**<br>Via Pambarola 7, 40068 S Lazzaro Di Savana, Italy | Alpine Skier |
| **Tomberlin, Andy L**<br>7411 Crooked Creek Church Road, Monroe NC 28110, USA | Baseball Player |
| **Tombs, Tina M**<br>5502 E Rockridge Road, Phoenix AZ 85018, USA | Golfer |
| **Tomczak, Michael J (Mike)**<br>139 Witherow Road, Sewickley PA 15143, USA | Football Player |
| **Tomei, Concetta**<br>Innovative Artists, 1505 10th St, Santa Monica CA 90401 USA | Actress |
| **Tomei, Marisa**<br>Creative Artists Agency, 2000 Ave of Stars, #100, Los Angeles CA 90067 USA | Actress |
| **Tomi, Vicente Ehate**<br>Prime Minister's Office, Malabo, Equatorial Guinea | Prime Minister, Equatorial Guinea |
| **Tomich, Jared J**<br>2222 Red River Dr, Schererville IN 46375, USA | Football Player |
| **Tomita, Stan**<br>2439 Saint Louis Dr, Honolulu HI 96816, USA | Photographer |
| **Tomita, Tamlyn**<br>Geddes Agency, 8430 Santa Monica Blvd, #201, West Hollywood CA 90069 USA | Actress |
| **Tomjanovich, Rudolph (Rudy)**<br>19 West Lane, Houston TX 77019, USA | Basketball Player, Coach |
| **Tomko, Brett D**<br>14008 Lake Poway Road, Poway CA 92064, USA | Baseball Player |
| **Tomko, Jozef Cardinal**<br>Villa Betania, Via Urbano VIII-16, 00165 Rome, Italy | Religious Leader |
| **Tomlak, Mike**<br>2200 Bordeaux Crescent, Thunder Bay ON P7K 1C2, Canada | Ice Hockey Player |
| **Tomlin, Chris**<br>Creative Artists Agency, 2000 Ave of Stars, #100, Los Angeles CA 90067 USA | Singer, Songwriter |
| **Tomlin, David A (Dave)**<br>2020 Clayton Pike, Manchester OH 45144, USA | Baseball Player |
| **Tomlin, Lily**<br>W M E Entertainment, 9601 Wilshire Blvd, #300, Beverly Hills CA 90210 USA | Actress, Comedienne |
| **Tomlin, Mike**<br>1224 Shady Ave, Pittsburgh PA 15232, USA | Football Coach |
| **Tomlin, Randy L**<br>153 Ridgeview Lane, Madison Heights VA 24572, USA | Baseball Player |
| **Tomlinson, Charles**<br>Bristol University, English Dept, Bristol BS8 1TH, England | Writer |
| **Tomlinson, Derek J (Ray)**<br>B B & N Technologies, 10 Moulton St, Cambridge MA 02138, USA | Computer Scientist, Inventor |
| **Tomlinson, Eleanor**<br>Conway Van Gelder Grant, 8-12 Broadwick St, #300, London W1F 8HW, England | Actress |
| **Tomlinson, John**<br>Music International, 13 Ardilaun Road, Highbury, London N5 2QR, England | Opera Singer |
| **Tomlinson, LaDainian**<br>18755 Heritage Dr, Poway CA 92064, USA | Football Player |
| **Tomlinson, Mel A**<br>790 Riverside Dr, #6B, New York NY 10032, USA | Ballet Dancer |
| **Tompkins, Paul F**<br>Avalon Mgmt, 4a Exmoor St, London W10 6BD, England | Actor |
| **Tompkins, Ronald E (Ron)**<br>25072 Leucadia St, #G, Laguna Niguel CA 92677, USA | Baseball Player |
| **Tompkins, Susie**<br>2500 Steiner St, #PH, San Francisco CA 94115, USA | Fashion Designer |
| **Toms, David**<br>6606 Gilbert Dr, Shreveport LA 71106, USA | Golfer |
| **Toms, Thomas H (Tommy)**<br>126 Leadbetter Road, Wayne ME 04284, USA | Baseball Player |
| **Tomsco, George**<br>Fireballs Entertainment, 1224 Cottonwood, Raton NM 87740, USA | Musician (Fireballs) |
| **Tomsic, Dubravka**<br>Hazard Chase, Richmond House, 16-20 Regent St, Cambridge BB2 1DB, England | Concert Pianist |
| **Tomsic, Ronald (Ron)**<br>22 Twilight Bluff, Newport Beach CA 92657, USA | Basketball Player |

**Tolles - Tomsic**

**Tomson, Shaun** — Surfer
Solitude Clothing, 1206 Coast Village Circle, Santa Barbara CA 93108, USA
**Tonchi, Stefano** — Editor
W, Editorial Dept, 1166 Ave of Americas, #1500, New York NY 10036, USA
**Toneff, Robert (Bob)** — Football Player
18 Dutch Valley Lane, San Anselmo CA 94960, USA
**Tonegawa, Susumu** — Nobel Medicine Laureate
101 Chestnut Hill Road, Chestnut Hill MA 02467, USA
**Tonelli, John** — Ice Hockey Player
4 Vincent Lane, Armonk NY 10504, USA
**Toner, Mike** — Journalist
Atlanta Journal-Constitution, Editorial Dept, 223 Perimeter Center Parkway, Atlanta GA 30346, USA
**Toney, Andrew** — Basketball Player
1613 14th Ave N, Birmingham AL 35204, USA
**Toney, Anthony** — Football Player
632 Donner Way, Salinas CA 93906, USA
**Toney, Sedric A** — Basketball Player
3831 Sweetwater Dr, Brecksville OH 44141, USA
**Tong Jian** — Figure Skater
Skating Assn, 56 Zhongguancun South St, Haidian, Beijing 100044, China
**Tong, Anote** — President, Kiribati
President's Office, PO Box 68, Bairiki, Tarawa Atoll, Kiribati
**Tong, Matthew C H (Matt)** — Drummer (Bloc Party)
Coalition Mgmt, 12 Barley Mow Passage, London W4 4PH, England
**Tong, Stanley** — Director
Innovative Artists, 1505 10th St, Santa Monica CA 90401 USA
**Tongue, Reginal C (Reggie)** — Football Player
1353 Saint Albans Dr, Baton Rouge LA 70810, USA
**Tonioli, Bruno** — Dance Judge
Independent Talent Group, 40 Whitfield St, London W1T 2RH, England
**Tonis, Mike** — Baseball Player
9231 Bella Vista Place, Elk Grove CA 95624, USA
**Tonkin, Peter F** — Architect
Tonkin Zulaikha Greer, 2 Liverpool Lane, East Sydney NSW 2010, Australia
**Tonkin, Phoebe** — Actress
I C M Partners, 10250 Constellation Blvd, #900, Los Angeles CA 90067 USA
**Tonnesen, Bill** — Landscape Architect
105 E 15th St, Tempe AZ 85281, USA
**Tookey, Tim** — Ice Hockey Player
21008 W Ridge Road, Buckeye AZ 85396, USA
**Toolson, Andrew K (Andy)** — Basketball Player
722 Ranch Circle, Alpine UT 84004, USA
**Toom, Tanel** — Director
W M E Entertainment, 9601 Wilshire Blvd, #300, Beverly Hills CA 90210 USA
**Toomay, Patrick J (Pat)** — Football Player
221 Tornasol Lane NE, Albuquerque NM 87113, USA
**Toomer, Amani A** — Football Player
25 Regency Place, Weehawken NJ 07086, USA
**Toomey, Sean** — Ice Hockey Player
1741 Saunders Ave, Saint Paul MN 55116, USA
**Toomey, William A (Bill)** — Track Athlete
4360 Park Terrace Dr, #160, Westlake Village CA 91361, USA
**Toomin, Amy** — Writer, Producer
United Talent Agency, U T A Plaza, 9336 Civic Center Dr, Beverly Hills CA 90210 USA
**Toon, Al L, Jr** — Football Player
PO Box 620770, Middleton WI 53562, USA
**Tootoo, Jordin J K** — Ice Hockey Player
2600 Hillsboro Pike, #359, Nashville TN 37212, USA
**Toparovsky, Simon** — Sculptor
5760 W Adams Blvd, Los Angeles CA 90016, USA
**Topol, Chaim** — Actor
22 Vale Court, Maidville, London W9 1RT, England
**Topol, Richard** — Actor
Bret Adams Agency, 448 W 44th St, New York NY 10036, USA
**Topolsky, Ken** — Director
A P A Talent/Literary Agency, 405 S Beverly Dr, #300, Beverly Hills CA 90212 USA
**Topper, John** — Singer (Blues Traveler)
Monterey Peninsula Artists, 404 W Franklin St, Monterey CA 93940 USA
**Toppin, Ruperto (Rupe)** — Baseball Player
PO Box 25724, Miami FL 33102, USA
**Toppo, Telesphore P Cardinal** — Religious Leader
Archdiocese, PO Box 5, Purulia Road, Ranchi 834001 Jharkland, India
**Toradze, Alexander** — Concert Pianist
Columbia Artists Mgmt Inc, 1790 Broadway, #702, New York NY 10019 USA
**Torbert, Stephanie** — Photographer
3824 Harriet Ave, Minneapolis MN 55409, USA
**Torborg, Jeffrey A (Jeff)** — Baseball Player, Manager
47 Railroad Ave, Manahawkin NJ 08050, USA
**Torcato, Anthony D (Tony)** — Baseball Player
1547 SW Clay St, Dallas OR 97338, USA
**Torchetti, John** — Ice Hockey Coach
14 Crows Nest Lane, Marshfield MA 2050, USA
**Torczon, Laverne J** — Football Player
6472 Country Club Dr, Columbus NE 68601, USA
**Torenstra, Waldemar** — Actor
Mover Shaker, De Lairessestraat 141, Amsterdam 1075 HJ, Netherlands
**Torgeson, LaVern E** — Football Player
17672 Gainsford Lane, Huntington Beach CA 92649, USA
**Torii, Keiko U** — Biologist
Washington University, Torii Laboratory, Biology Dept, Box 355325, Seattle WA 98195, USA
**Tork, Peter** — Singer, Bassist (Monkees)
Alan Cottam Agency, 19 Charles St, Lancashire Wigan WN1 2BP, England
**Torke, Michael** — Composer
Columbia Artists Mgmt Inc, 1790 Broadway, #702, New York NY 10019 USA
**Torkelson, Eric G** — Football Player
1196 Pleasant Valley Dr, Oneida WI 54155, USA

T

Tomson - Torkelson

**T**

**Tormis, Veljo** — Composer
Estonian Academy of Music, Ravala Pst 16, Tallinn 10143, Estonia

**Tormohlen, Gene** — Basketball Player
2248 Walker Dr, Lawrenceville GA 30043, USA

**Torn, Rip** — Actor
Sovereign Talent Group, 8421 Wilshire Blvd, #200, Beverly Hills CA 90211 USA

**Torng, Hwa C** — Inventor (Computer Processor)
Cornell University, Electrical Engineering Dept, Ithaca NY 14853, USA

**Torok, Mitchell** — Singer, Guitarist, Songwriter
5100 Weaver Road, #702, Lake Charles LA 70605, USA

**Torp, Niels A** — Architect
Industrigaten 59, PO Box 5387, 0304 Oslo, Norway

**Torrance, Ingrid** — Actress
Lucas Talent, 100 W Pender St, #700, Vancouver BC V6B 1RB, Canada

**Torrance, Sam** — Golfer
Parallel Murray Mgmt, 56 Ennismore Gardens, London SW7 1AJ, England

**Torre, Frank J** — Baseball Player
13901 Palm Grove Place, West Palm Beach FL 33418, USA

**Torre, Joseph P (Joe)** — Baseball Player, Manager
20 Lawrence Lane, Harrison NY 10528, USA

**Torrealba, Yorvit A** — Baseball Player
3801 S Ocean Dr, #15F, Hollywood FL 33019, USA

**Torrence, Dean** — Singer (Jan & Dean), Songwriter
18932 Gregory Lane, Huntington Beach CA 92646, USA

**Torrence, Gwendolyn (Gwen)** — Track Athlete
Gold Medal Mgmt, 1750 14th St, Boulder CO 80302, USA

**Torrence, Nate** — Actor
Messina Baker Entertainment, 955 Carrillo Dr, #100, Los Angeles CA 90048 USA

**Torres Delgado, Dayanara** — Beauty Queen, Actress
Univision, 605 3rd Ave, #1200, New York NY 10158 USA

**Torres, Dara** — Swimmer, Model
47 Wilsondale St, Dover MA 02030, USA

**Torres, Diego** — Singer
Mega Music Productions, 16950 North Bay Road, #1706, Sunny Isles Beach FL 33160, USA

**Torres, Eve** — Dancer, Model, Wrestler
World Wrestling Entertainment, Titan Towers, 1241 E Main St, Stamford CT 06902 USA

**Torres, Felix** — Baseball Player
HC 1 Box 6424, Santa Isabel PR 00757, USA

**Torres, Fina** — Director
I C M Partners, 10250 Constellation Blvd, #900, Los Angeles CA 90067 USA

**Torres, Gina** — Actress
Framework Entertainment, 9057 Nemo St, #C, West Hollywood CA 90069 USA

**Torres, Harold** — Singer (Crests)
PO Box 5357, Spring Hill FL 34611, USA

**Torres, Hector E** — Baseball Player
662 Lexington St, Dunedin FL 34698, USA

**Torres, Hector S J (Tico)** — Drummer (Bon Jovi)
Bon Jovi Mgmt, 809 Elder Circle, Austin TX 78733, USA

**Torres, Oscar Orlando** — Actor, Writer, Producer
Caliber Media, 9229 W Sunset Blvd, #705, West Hollywood CA 90069, USA

**Torres, Raffi** — Ice Hockey Player
118 Church St, Markham ON L3P 2M4, Canada

**Torres, Rosendo (Rusty)** — Baseball Player
250 N Cedar St, Massapequa NY 11758, USA

**Torres, Salomon R** — Baseball Player
101 Crimson Dr, Pittsburgh PA 15237, USA

**Torres, Tommy** — Singer, Songwriter
A-PR Media, 8334 Lefferts Blvd, #3C, Kew Gardens NY 11415, USA

**Torressani, Alessandra** — Actress
United Talent Agency, U T A Plaza, 9336 Civic Center Dr, Beverly Hills CA 90210 USA

**Torreton, Philippe** — Actor
Artmedia, 20 Ave Rapp, 75007 Paris, France

**Torretta, Gino L** — Football Player
7830 SW 48th Court, Miami FL 33143, USA

**Torrey, Bill** — Ice Hockey Player, Executive
2740 Clubhouse Pointe, West Palm Beach FL 33409, USA

**Torrey, Rich** — Cartoonist (Hartland)
King Features Syndicate, 300 W 57th St, #1500, New York NY 10019 USA

**Torrez, Michael A (Mike)** — Baseball Player
1015 Frances Court, Naperville IL 60563, USA

**Torriero, Talan** — Actor
I C M Partners, 10250 Constellation Blvd, #900, Los Angeles CA 90067 USA

**Torrijos Espino, Martin E** — President, Panama
Palacio Presidencial, Valija 50, Panama City 1, Panama

**Torrini, Emiliana** — Singer, Songwriter
International Talent Booking, Ariel House, 74A Charlotte St, #100 London W1T 4QJ, England

**Torrissen, Birger** — Nordic Skier
PO Box 216, Lakeville CT 06039, USA

**Torruella, Juan R** — Judge
US Court of Appeals, 150 Ave Carlos Chardon, #119, San Juan PR 00918, USA

**Torry, Guy** — Actor, Comedian
Barry Katz Entertainment, 10100 Santa Monica Blvd, #2400, Los Angeles CA 90067, USA

**Torry, Joe** — Actor, Comedian
Proclaim Talent Agency, PO Box 23158, New Orleans LA 70183, USA

**Tortelier, Yan Pascal** — Conductor, Concert Violinist
M A de Valmalete, Building Gaceau, 11 Ave Delcasse, 75635 Paris, France

**Torti, Robert** — Actor
Big House Studios, 4420 Lankershim Blvd, North Hollywood CA 91602, USA

**Tortorella, John** — Ice Hockey Coach
108 3rd Ave, Saint Pete Beach FL 33706, USA

**Tortorella, Nico** — Actor
Gersh Agency, 9465 Wilshire Blvd, #600, Beverly Hills CA 90212 USA

**Torv, Anna** — Actress
United Mgmt, Marlborough House, 61 Marlborough St, #400-45, Surry Hills NSW 2010, Australia

**Torvalds, Linus** — Computer Software Designer
Open Source Development Laboratories, 12725 SW Millikan Way, Beaverton OR 97005, USA

**Torvbraaten, Tore** — Curling Athlete
Curling Assn, Sognsveien 75, Serviceboks 1, 0840 Oslo, Norway
**Torve, Kelvin C** — Baseball Player
18701 Hammock Lane, Davidson NC 28036, USA
**Torvill, Jayne** — Ice Dancer
Sue Young, PO Box 32, Heathfield, East Sussex TN21 0BW, England
**Tory, Anna** — Actress
Conway Van Gelder Grant, 8-12 Broadwick St, #300, London W1F 8HW, England
**Tosca, Carlos** — Baseball Manager
PO Box 3623, Brandon FL 33509, USA
**Toscano, Harry** — Golfer
231 Rose Hill Dr, New Castle PA 16105, USA
**Tosh, Daniel** — Actor, Comedian
W M E Entertainment, 9601 Wilshire Blvd, #300, Beverly Hills CA 90210 USA
**Toskala, Vesa** — Ice Hockey Player
Calgary Flames, PO Box 1540, Station M, Calgary AB T2P 3B9, Canada
**Toski, Bob** — Golfer
20914 Hamaca Court, Boca Raton FL 33433, USA
**Totenberg, Nina** — Commentator
National Public Radio, 635 Massachusetts Ave NW, #1, Washington DC 20001, USA
**Toth, Melissa** — Costume Designer
Gersh Agency, 9465 Wilshire Blvd, #600, Beverly Hills CA 90212 USA
**Toth, Thomas J (Tom)** — Football Player
13723 Lindsay Dr, Orland Park IL 60462, USA
**Totmianina, Tatiana** — Figure Skater
Skating Federation, Luznetskaya Nabererhnya 8, 119871 Moscow, Russia
**Totten, Robert** — Director
PO Box 7180, Big Bear Lake CA 92315, USA
**Totter, Audrey** — Actress
Motion Picture Country Home, 23388 Mulholland Dr, Woodland Hills CA 91364, USA
**Totushek, John B** — Navy Admiral
Military Officers Assn, 201 N Washington St, Alexandria VA 22314, USA
**Tough, Kelly** — Model, Actress
Playboy Promotions, 2706 Media Center Dr, Los Angeles CA 90065 USA
**Toulouse, Gerard** — Physicist
Laboratoire de Physique d'E N S, 24 Rue Lhomond, 75231 Paris, France
**Tountas, Pete** — Bowler
10100 N Calle del Carnero, Tucson AZ 85737, USA
**Toups, Fontaine** — Bassist, Guitarist, Singer (Versus)
Ground Control Touring, 20 Jay St, #838, Brooklyn NY 11201, USA
**Touraine, Jean-Louis** — Immunologist
Edouard-Herriot Hopital, Place d'Arsonval, 69437 Lyons Cedex 03, France
**Toure, Daby** — Singer, Songwriter
Rosebud Agency, PO Box 170429, San Francisco CA 94117 USA
**Toure, Younoussi** — Prime Minister, Mali
Union Economique/Monetaire, 01 BP 543, Ouagadougou 01, Burkina Faso
**Tournet, Scott** — Guitarist (Grace Potter & Nocturnals)
Paradigm Agency, 404 W Franklin St, Monterey CA 93940 USA
**Tournier, Michel** — Writer
Le Presbytere, Choisel, 78460 Chevreuse, France
**Toussaint, Allen** — Jazz Singer, Pianist, Composer
272 Abalon Court, New Orleans LA 70114, USA
**Toussaint, Beth** — Actress
Innovative Artists, 1505 10th St, Santa Monica CA 90401 USA
**Toussaint, Lorraine** — Actress
Innovative Artists, 1505 10th St, Santa Monica CA 90401 USA
**Tovar, Steven E (Steve)** — Football Player
5607 Wagstaff Dr, Lawrence KS 66049, USA
**Tovey, Bramwell** — Conductor
I M G Artists, Hogarth Business Park, Chiswick, London W4 2TH, England
**Tovey, Russell** — Actor
Independent Talent Group, 40 Whitfield St, London W1T 2RH, England
**Tovoli, Luciano** — Cinematographer
United Talent Agency, U T A Plaza, 9336 Civic Center Dr, Beverly Hills CA 90210 USA
**Towe, Monte C** — Basketball Player, Coach
1517 Stratford Hall Circle, Murfreesboro TN 37130, USA
**Tower, Joan P** — Composer
Bard College, Music Dept, Annandale on Hudson NY 12504, USA
**Tower, Keith R** — Basketball Player
12530 Aldershot Lane, Windermere FL 34786, USA
**Towers, Constance** — Actress
Cassell-Levy, 843 N Sycamore Ave, Los Angeles CA 90038, USA
**Towers, Joshua E (Josh)** — Baseball Player
1033 Crescent Falls St, Henderson NV 89011, USA
**Towery, William C (Blackie)** — Basketball Player
314 W Carlisle St, Marion KY 42064, USA
**Towle, Stephen R (Steve)** — Football Player
609 NE Lake Pointe Dr, Lees Summit MO 64064, USA
**Towles, Justin R (J R)** — Baseball Player
13806 Lowell Ave, Tomball TX 77377, USA
**Towne, Robert** — Director, Writer
1417 San Remo Dr, Pacific Palisades CA 90272, USA
**Townend, Peter** — Surfer, Publisher
820 Geneva Ave, #A, Huntington Beach CA 92648, USA
**Towner, Ralph N** — Jazz Guitarist, Pianist
Ted Kurland, 173 Brighton Ave, Boston MA 02134 USA
**Townes, Charles H** — Nobel Physics, Templeton Prize Laureate
5016 Wallingford Ave N, Seattle WA 98103, USA
**Townes, Linton R** — Basketball Player
PO Box 254, Luray VA 22835, USA
**Towns, Lester, III** — Football Player
2225 Hawkins St, #131, Charlotte NC 28203, USA
**Towns, Morris M** — Football Player
7102 Rusting Oaks Dr, Richmond TX 77469, USA
**Townsell, Joseph R (Jo Jo)** — Football Player
PO Box 606, Gardnerville NV 89410, USA

**Townsend, Andre** — Football Player
6206 Providence Club Dr, Mableton GA 30126, USA

**Townsend, Colleen** — Actress
National Presbyterian Church, 4101 Nebraska Ave NW, Washington DC 20016, USA

**Townsend, Heath** — Model
I M G Models, 304 Park Ave S, #PH N, New York NY 10010 USA

**Townsend, Jill Perry** — Artist, Sculptor
Skob Knob Studios, 1936 NE 63rd St, Lincoln City OR 97367, USA

**Townsend, John W, Jr** — Space Scientist
6532 79th St, Cabin John MD 20818, USA

**Townsend, Milon** — Artist
Blue Moon Press, 262 Moul Road, Hilton NY 14468, USA

**Townsend, Raymond** — Basketball Player
5160 Cribari Knolls, San Jose CA 95135, USA

**Townsend, Robert** — Actor, Director
A P A Talent/Literary Agency, 405 S Beverly Dr, #300, Beverly Hills CA 90212 USA

**Townsend, T Deshea** — Football Player
3208 Lenox Oval, Pittsburgh PA 15237, USA

**Townsend, Tammy** — Actress, Singer
Abrams Artists, 275 7th Ave, #2600, New York NY 10001 USA

**Townshend, Graeme S** — Ice Hockey Player
PO Box 1231, Saco ME 04072, USA

**Townshend, Peter D B** — Singer, Guitarist (Who), Songwriter
4 Friars Lane, Richmond, Surrey TW9 1NL, England

**Toy, Camden** — Actor
Coolwaters Productions, 10061 Riverside Dr, Box 531, Toluca Lake CA 91602 USA

**Toynton, Ian** — Director, Producer
Creative Artists Agency, 2000 Ave of Stars, #100, Los Angeles CA 90067 USA

**Toyoda, Akio** — Businessman
Toyota Motor Corp, 1 Toyotacho, Toyota City, Aichi Pref 471 8701, Japan

**Toyoda, Shoichiro** — Businessman
Keidanren Kaikan Building, 1-9-4 Ohtemachi, Chuyodaku, Tokyo 100 8188, Japan

**Tozer, Faye L** — Singer, Actress
Concorde International Artistes, 101 Shepherds Bush Road, London W6 7LP, England

**Tozzi, Umberto** — Singer, Songwriter
Momy Records, Le Vallespir, 25 Blvd Du, 98000 Monaco, Monaco

**T-Pain** — Singer, Rap Artist, Songwriter, Actor
American Talent Agency, 248 W 35th St, # 501  New York NY 10001, USA

**Traa** — Bassist (POD)
Atlantic Records, 9229 W Sunset Blvd, #900, West Hollywood CA 90069 USA

**Traber, William H (Billy), Jr** — Baseball Player
836 Lomita St, El Segundo CA 90245, USA

**Trabert, M Anthony (Tony)** — Tennis Player
115 Knotty Pine Trail, Ponte Vedra Beach FL 32082, USA

**Tracewski, Richard J (Dick)** — Baseball Player, Manager
5 Flora Dr, Peckville PA 18452, USA

**Trachsel, Stephen P (Steve)** — Baseball Player
18750 Heritage Dr, Poway CA 92064, USA

**Trachta, Jeff** — Actor
590 S Indian Trail, Palm Springs CA 92264, USA

**Trachtenberg, Michelle** — Actress
United Talent Agency, U T A Plaza, 9336 Civic Center Dr, Beverly Hills CA 90210 USA

**Tracy, Andrew M (Andy)** — Baseball Player
2226 Park Circle, Lewis Center OH 43035, USA

**Tracy, Chad A** — Baseball Player
9422 Sir Huon Lane, Waxhaw NC 28173, USA

**Tracy, James E (Jim)** — Baseball Player, Manager
7112 Woodhall Court, Presto PA 15142, USA

**Tracy, Jeanie** — Singer
T-Best Talent Agency, 508 Honey Lake Court, Danville CA 94506 USA

**Tracy, Keegan Connor** — Actress
S M S Talent, 8383 Wilshire Blvd, #230, Beverly Hills CA 90211 USA

**Tracy, Paul** — Auto Racing Driver
10524 Allthorn Ave, Las Vegas NV 89144, USA

**Trager, Milton** — Physical Therapist
Trager Institute, 3800 Park East Dr, #100, Beachwood OH 44122, USA

**Trahan, Donald R (D J), Jr** — Golfer
32 Eastlake Road, Mount Pleasant SC 29464, USA

**Train, Harry D, II** — Navy Admiral
401 College Place, #10, Norfolk VA 23510, USA

**Train, Kristina** — Singer, Songwriter
Michael Hausman Artist Mgmt, 511 Ave of Americas, #197, New York NY 10011, USA

**Trainor, Bernard E** — Marine Corps General
46874 Grissom St, Sterling VA 20165, USA

**Trainor, Jerry** — Actor
I C M Partners, 10250 Constellation Blvd, #900, Los Angeles CA 90067 USA

**Trainor, Kevin** — Actor
Ken McReddie Assoc, 101 Finsbury Pavement, London EC2A 1RS, England

**Trainor, Saxon** — Actress
Sager Mgmt, 260 S Beverly Dr, #205, Beverly Hills CA 90212, USA

**Trammell, Alan S** — Baseball Player, Manager
191 22nd St, Del Mar CA 92014, USA

**Trammell, Sam** — Actor
Innovative Artists, 1505 10th St, Santa Monica CA 90401 USA

**Trammell, Terry** — Sports Orthopedic Surgeon
Orthopedics-Indianapolis, 1801 N Senate Blvd, #200, Indianapolis IN 46202, USA

**Trammell, Thomas J (Bubba)** — Baseball Player
4672 NW 114th St, #310, Doral FL 33178, USA

**Transtromer, Tomas G** — Nobel Literature Laureate
Stadahuset, 421 87 Vasteras, Sweden

**Traore, Diouncounda** — Acting President, Mali
President's Office, BP 1463, Bamako, Mali

**Trapp, John Q** — Basketball Player
4785 Primavera St, Las Vegas NV 89122, USA

**Traub, Charles H** — Photographer
39 E 10th St, New York NY 10003, USA

| | |
|---|---|
| **Traub, Sophie** | Actress |
| Characters Talent Mgmt, 8 Elm St, Toronto ON M5G 1G7, Canada | |
| **Traub, Yaron** | Conductor |
| Opus 3 Artists, 470 Park Ave S, #900N, New York NY 10016 USA | |
| **Traue, Antje** | Actress |
| United Talent Agency, U T A Plaza, 9336 Civic Center Dr, Beverly Hills CA 90210 USA | |
| **Trautmann, Richard** | Judo Athlete |
| Horemansstr 29, 80636 Munich, Germany | |
| **Trautwig, Al** | Sportscaster |
| NBC-TV, Sports Dept, 30 Rockefeller Plaza, #270E, New York NY 10112 USA | |
| **Travanti, Daniel J** | Actor |
| 1077 Melody Road, Lake Forest IL 60045, USA | |
| **Travers, Patrick H (Pat)** | Singer, Guitarist |
| Hook Entertainment, 26033 Mulholland Highway, Malibu CA 91302, USA | |
| **Travers, William E (Bill)** | Baseball Player |
| 10 Shoreline Dr, Foxboro MA 02035, USA | |
| **Travis, Dale** | Opera Singer |
| Columbia Artists Mgmt Inc, 1790 Broadway, #702, New York NY 10019 USA | |
| **Travis, Kylie** | Model, Actress |
| Hartig-Hilepo Agency, 54 W 21st St, #610, New York NY 10010 USA | |
| **Travis, Nancy** | Actress |
| A P A Talent/Literary Agency, 405 S Beverly Dr, #300, Beverly Hills CA 90212 USA | |
| **Travis, Pete** | Director |
| W M E Entertainment, 9601 Wilshire Blvd, #300, Beverly Hills CA 90210 USA | |
| **Travis, Randy** | Singer, Guitarist, Songwriter |
| Pure Fix Entertainment, 15333 N Pima Road, #145, Scottsdale AZ 85258, USA | |
| **Travis, Scott** | Drummer (Judas Priest) |
| Trinifold Mgmt, 12 Oval Road, #300, Camden, London NW1 7DH, England | |
| **Travis, Stacey** | Actress |
| Essential Talent Mgmt, 6399 Wilshire Blvd, #400, Los Angeles CA 90048, USA | |
| **Traviss, Karen** | Writer |
| Scovil Chichak Galen, 276 5th Ave, #708, New York NY 10001, USA | |
| **Travolta, Ellen** | Actress |
| 6470 E Sunnyside Road, Coeur D'Alene ID 83814, USA | |
| **Travolta, Joey** | Singer, Director |
| 23634 Tiara St, Woodland Hills CA 91367, USA | |
| **Travolta, John** | Actor |
| 1504 Live Oak Lane, Santa Barbara CA 93105, USA | |
| **Traxler, William B, Jr** | Judge |
| US Court of Appeals, Powell Courthouse, 1100 E Main St, Richmond VA 23219, USA | |
| **Traya, Misti** | Actress |
| Abrams Artists, 9200 W Sunset Blvd, #1125, West Hollywood CA 90069 USA | |
| **Traylor, B Keith** | Football Player |
| 508 E Shreveport St, Broken Arrow OK 74011, USA | |
| **Traylor, Susan** | Actress |
| Abrams Artists, 275 7th Ave, #2600, New York NY 10001 USA | |
| **Traynor, J Michael** | Attorney |
| 3131 Eton Ave, Berkeley CA 94705, USA | |
| **Traynor, John (Jay)** | Singer (Jay & the Americans) |
| Jet Music, 17 Pauline Court, Rensselaer NY 12144, USA | |
| **Traynowicz, Mark J** | Football Player |
| 1668 Sioux St, Lincoln NE 68502, USA | |
| **Trcic, Michael** | Sculptor |
| 175 Goodrow Lane, Sedona AZ 86336, USA | |
| **Treach** | Rap Artist (Naughty By Nature) |
| Don Buchwald, 6500 Wilshire Blvd, #2200, Los Angeles CA 90048 USA | |
| **Treacy, Philip** | Fashion Designer |
| Philip Treacy Ltd, 69 Elizabeth St, London SW1W 9PJ, England | |
| **Treadaway, Harry** | Actor |
| United Agents, 12-26 Lexington St, London W1F 0LE, England | |
| **Treadaway, Luke** | Actor |
| Hamilton Hodell, 66-68 Margaret St, #500, London W1W 8SR, England | |
| **Treadell, Victoria M (Vicki)** | High Commissioner, New Zealand |
| High Commissioner's Office, 44 Hill St, Wellington 6011, New Zealand | |
| **Treadway, H Jeffrey (Jeff)** | Baseball Player |
| 8812 Estes Road, Macon GA 31220, USA | |
| **Treadway, James C, Jr** | Government Official |
| Laurel Ledge Farm, Croton Lake Road, RR 4, Mount Kisco NY 10549, USA | |
| **Treadwell, David M** | Football Player |
| 553 Rita Place, Castle Pines CO 80108, USA | |
| **Treanor, Matthew A (Matt)** | Baseball Player |
| 460 NW 115th Way, Coral Springs FL 33071, USA | |
| **Trebek, Alex** | Entertainer |
| 3405 Fryman Road, Studio City CA 91604, USA | |
| **Trebelhorn, Thomas L (Tom)** | Baseball Player, Manager |
| 7753 E Montebello Ave, Scottsdale AZ 85250, USA | |
| **Trebil, Dan** | Ice Hockey Player |
| 8551 Big Woods Lane, Eden Prairie MN 55347, USA | |
| **Trebunskaya, Anna** | Dancer |
| Abrams Artists, 9200 W Sunset Blvd, #1125, West Hollywood CA 90069 USA | |
| **Tree, Michael** | Violist (Guarneri String Quartet) |
| 45 E 89th St, New York NY 10128, USA | |
| **Tregear, Lucy** | Actress |
| Gavin Barker Assoc, 2D Wimpole St, London W1G 0EB, England | |
| **Treisman, Anne M** | Psychologist |
| Princeton University, Psychology Dept, Princeton NJ 08544, USA | |
| **Treitler, Leo** | Musicologist |
| City University of New York, Graduate Center, 365 5th Ave, #8204, New York NY 10016, USA | |
| **Trejo, Danny** | Actor |
| Amsel Eisenstadt Frazier, 5055 Wilshire Blvd, #865, Los Angeles CA 90036 USA | |
| **Trelford, Donald G** | Editor |
| 15 Fowler Road, London N1 2EA, England | |
| **Tremblay, Francois-Louis** | Speed Skater |
| C P V Quebec, Arena Duberger, Duberger Park, 3050 Boul Central, Quebec QC G1P3N9, Canada | |
| **Tremblay, Gilles** | Ice Hockey Player |
| 104-218 Rue Notre-Dame, Repentigny QC P1B 7R5, Canada | |

# T

**Tremblay, Mario** — Ice Hockey Player, Coach
743 Passaic Ave, #412, Clifton NJ 07012, USA
**Tremblay, Michel** — Writer
294 Carre Saint Louis, #5E, Montreal QC H2X 1A4, Canada
**Tremblay, Yannick** — Ice Hockey Player
9911 Carrington Lane, Alpharetta GA 30022, USA
**Tremel, William L (Bill)** — Baseball Player
315 E 23rd Ace, Altoona PA 16601, USA
**Tremie, Christopher J (Chris)** — Baseball Player
484 Marion Lane, New Waverly TX 77358, USA
**Tremonti, Mark T** — Guitarist (Creed, Alter Bridge)
Agency Group, 1776 Broadway, #430, New York NY 10019, USA
**Trenary, Jill** — Figure Skater
4445 Governors Point, Colorado Springs CO 80906, USA
**Trent, Gary D** — Basketball Player
1150 Northwood Circle, New Albany OH 43054, USA
**Trentini, Caroline** — Model
Why Not Model Mgmt, Via Zenale 9, 20123 Milan, Italy
**Trento, Joseph** — Writer
Public Education Center, 1830 Connecticut Ave NW, #3, Washington DC 20009, USA
**Trepagnier, Jeffrey (Jeff)** — Basketball Player
1414 N McDivitt Ave, Compton CA 90221, USA
**Treschev, Sergei Y** — Cosmonaut
Cosmonaut Training Center, Star City, 141160 Zvezdny Gorodok, Moscow Oblast, Russia
**Tress, Arthur** — Photographer
2705 Marlborough Lane, Cambria CA 93428, USA
**Tressel, James P (Jim)** — Football Coach
Indianapolis Colts, 7001 W 56th St, Indianapolis IN 46254 USA
**Tresvant, John B** — Basketball Player
14814 61st Dr SE, Snohomish WA 98296, USA
**Trethewey, Natasha** — Writer
Emory University, Creative Writing Program, 201 Dowman Drive, Atlanta GA 30322, USA
**Tretiak, Vladislav** — Ice Hockey Player
Hockey Federation, Luzhnetskaia Naberezhnaia 8, 119992 Moscow, Russia
**Tretiakov, Alexander V** — Skeleton Athlete
Ski Assn, Luzhnetskaya Nab 8, 119270 Moscow, Russia
**Tretyakov, Victor V** — Concert Violinist
Berlin Konzeragentur Monika Ott, Dramburger Str 46, 12683 Berlin, Germany
**Treu, Adam R** — Football Player
3176 NW Shevlin Meadows Dr, Bend OR 97701, USA
**Trever, John** — Editorial Cartoonist
Albuquerque Journal, Editorial Dept, 717 Silver Ave SW, Albuquerque NM 87102, USA
**Trevi, Gloria** — Singer, Songwriter, Actress
Westwood Entertainment, J M de Teresa 250, Col Tlacopc San Miguel, Mexico City 01040, Mexico
**Trevino, Alejandro (Alex)** — Baseball Player
PO Box 288, Houston TX 77001, USA
**Trevino, Lee B** — Golfer
4906 Park Lane, Dallas TX 75220, USA
**Trevino, Michael** — Actor
Greene Assoc, 1901 Ave of Stars, #130, Los Angeles CA 90067 USA
**Trevino, Rick** — Singer
Texas Boogie Productions, 1 Bis Chemin Aman, 64370 Orthez, France
**Trevor, William** — Writer
Viking Press, 375 Hudson St, New York NY 10014, USA
**Trevorrow, Colin** — Director, Writer
3 Arts Entertainment, 9460 Wilshire Blvd, #700, Beverly Hills CA 90212 USA
**Trey Songz** — Singer, Songwriter
Atlantic Records, 1290 Ave of Americas, Concourse 3, New York NY 10104 USA
**Trezeguet, David N** — Soccer Player
F C Juventus, Corso Galilo Ferrarsi 32, 10128 Turin, Italy
**Triano, Jay** — Basketball Coach
Toronto Raptors, Air Canada Center, 20 Bay St, Toronto ON M5J 2N8, Canada
**Trias, Jasmine S** — Singer
Universal Records, 70 Universal City Plaza, Universal City CA 91608 USA
**Tribbett, Greg (Gurgg)** — Guitarist (Mudvayne)
Agency Group Ltd, 142 W 57th St, #600, New York NY 10019 USA
**Tribe, Laurence H** — Attorney, Educator
Harvard University, Law School, Griswold Hall, Cambridge MA 02138, USA
**Trible, Paul S, Jr** — Senator, VA; Educator
Christopher Newport University, President's Office, 50 University Place, Newport News VA 23606, USA
**Trice, Obie** — Rap Artist
J L Entertainment, 18653 Ventura Blvd, #340, Los Angeles CA 91356 USA
**Trichet, Jean-Claude** — Financier
5 Rue de Beaujolais, 75001 Paris, France
**Trick Daddy** — Rap Artist
Nene Musik Productions, 1460 SW Santiago Ave, Port Saint Lucie FL 34953 USA
**Trickett, Lisbeth (Libby) C** — Swimmer
Swimming Australia, 12/7 Beissel St, Bekonnen ACT 2617, Australia
**Tricky** — Rap Artist, Songwriter
Crown Music, Matrix Complex, 91 Peterborough Road, London SW6 3BU, England
**Trier, Joachim** — Director
Casorotto Ramsay, Waverley House, 7-12 Noel St, London W1F 8GQ, England
**Triffle, Carol** — Director
Imago Theater, PO Box 15182, Portland OR 97293, USA
**Trigger, Sarah** — Actress
Forward Entertainment, 9255 Sunset Blvd, #805, Los Angeles CA 90069, USA
**Triggs Hodge, Andrew** — Rowing Athlete
Molesey Boat Club, Barge Walk, East Molesey, Surrey KT8 9AJ, England
**Trillin, Calvin M** — Writer
New Yorker, Editorial Dept, 4 Times Square, Basement C1B, New York NY 10036 USA
**Trillo, J Manuel (Manny)** — Baseball Player
7309 W Coyle Ave, Chicago IL 60631, USA
**Trimble, David W** — Nobel Peace Laureate
2 Queen St, Lurgen, County Armagh BT66 8BQ, Northern Ireland
**Trimble, Vance H** — Editor
25 Oakhurst Ave, Wewoka OK 74884, USA

**Trimble, Vivian** — Keyboardist (Luscious Jackson)
Metropolitan Entertainment, 2 Penn Plaza, #2600, New York NY 10121, USA
**Trimmer, H William** — Macrobiotics Engineer
1345 McLaurin Road, Siler City NC 27344, USA
**Trimper, Tim** — Ice Hockey Player
1028 Broughton Lane, Newmarket ON L3X 2L7, Canada
**Trina** — Rap Artist
Pyramid Entertainment Group, 377 Rector Place, #21A, New York NY 10280 USA
**Trinh, Eugene** — Astronaut
N A S A Headquarters, 300 E St SW, Washington DC 20546, USA
**Trinidad, Felix (Tito)** — Boxer
RR 6 Box 11479, San Juan PR 00926, USA
**Trinkaus, Erik** — Paleontologist
Washington University, Paleontolgy Dept, PO Box 1214, Saint Louis MO 63188, USA
**Trinneer, Connor** — Actor
Abrams Artists, 9200 W Sunset Blvd, #1125, West Hollywood CA 90069 USA
**Trintignant, Jean-Louis** — Actor
Artmedia, 20 Ave Rapp, 75007 Paris, France
**Triplett, Kirk** — Golfer
4527 N 61st Place, Scottsdale AZ 85251, USA
**Triplett, William C (Bill)** — Football Player
222 Beechwood Dr, Youngstown OH 44506, USA
**Trippe, Thomas G** — Physicist
Lawrence Livermore Laboratory, 7000 East Ave, Livermore CA 94550 USA
**Trippi, Charles L (Charlie)** — Football Player
125 Riverhill Court, Athens GA 30606, USA
**Tripplehorn, Jeanne** — Actress
Gersh Agency, 9465 Wilshire Blvd, #600, Beverly Hills CA 90212 USA
**Tripplett, Larry C J** — Football Player
4065 Ambergate Place, Dublin CA 94568, USA
**Tripucka, P Kelly** — Basketball Player
14 Devon Road, Boonton NJ 07005, USA
**Trischka, Tony** — Banjoist
Blue Mountain Artists, 810 Tyvola Road, #114, Charlotte NC 28217, USA
**Tristan, Dorothy** — Actress
Film Acres, 2622 E 850 N, La Porte IN 46350, USA
**Trlicek, Richard A (Ricky)** — Baseball Player
PO Box 1109, La Grange TX 78945, USA
**Troccoli, Kathleen C (Kathy)** — Singer, Songwriter
K T Designs, 5543 Edmondson Pike, #7A, Nashville TN 37211, USA
**Troche, Celeste** — Golfer
560 Perry St, #108, Auburn AL 36830, USA
**Troche, Rose** — Actress, Writer, Director, Producer
Gersh Agency, 9465 Wilshire Blvd, #600, Beverly Hills CA 90212 USA
**Trocheck, Kathy H** — Writer
Harper Collins Publishers, 10 E 53rd St, Cellar 1, New York NY 10022 USA
**Troe, Jurgen** — Chemist
Universitat Gottingen, Tammannstr 6, 37077 Gottingen, Germany
**Troedson, Richard L (Rich)** — Baseball Player
899 Bowen Ave, San Jose CA 95123, USA
**Troger, Christian-Alexander** — Swimmer
I Muncher Swim Club, Josefstr 26, 82941 Deisenhofen, Germany
**Trohman, Joe** — Guitarist (Fall Out Boy)
PO Box 219, 1187 Wilmette Ave, Wilmette IL 60091, USA
**Troisgros, Pierre E R** — Chef, Restauranteur
20 Route de Commelle, 42120 Le Coteau, France
**Trollope, Joanna** — Writer
Crossworld Publishing, 61-63 Uxbridge Road, London W5 5SA, England
**Trombetta, Monica** — Actress
I C M Partners, 730 5th Ave, New York NY 10019 USA
**Trombley, Michael S (Mike)** — Baseball Player
2 Hilltop Park, Wilbraham MA 01095, USA
**Trombone Shorty** — Jazz Trombonist, Band Leader
Rosebud Agency, PO Box 170429, San Francisco CA 94117 USA
**Tronnier, Ellen** — Baseball Player
328 Anemone Ave, Palmyra WI 53156, USA
**Troost, Ernest** — Singer, Songwriter
First Artists Mgmt, 4764 Park Granada, #210, Calabasas CA 91302 USA
**Troska, Zdenek** — Director
Hostice u Volyne 77, 38701 Volyne, Czech Republic
**Trosper, Jennifer Harris** — Space Scientist
Jet Propulsion Laboratory, 4800 Oak Grove Dr, Pasadena CA 91109 USA
**Trost, Barry M** — Chemist
24510 Amigos Court, Los Altos Hills CA 94024, USA
**Trost, Carlisle A H** — Navy Admiral
7101 River Crescent Dr, Annapolis MD 21401, USA
**Trott, Stephen S** — Judge, Singer (Highwaymen)
US Court of Appeals, US Courthouse, 550 W Fort St, Boise ID 83724, USA
**Trotter, De'Hashia T (Deedee)** — Track Athlete
9900 Brannigan Circle, Knoxville TN 37923, USA
**Trotter, Jeremiah** — Football Player
6863 F M 1398, Parkton MD 21120, USA
**Trottier, Bryan J** — Ice Hockey Player, Coach
504 Bluegrass Dr, Canonsburg PA 15317, USA
**Trottier, Guy** — Ice Hockey Player
1003 Hazel Ave, Englewood OH 45322, USA
**Trotz, Barry** — Ice Hockey Coach
9001 Demery Court, Brentwood TN 37027, USA
**Trouble Valli** — Guitarist (Crazy Town)
Q Prime, 729 7th Ave, #1600, New York NY 10019, USA
**Troughton, Sam** — Actor
Markham Froggatt Irwin, Julian House, 4 Windmill St, London W1P 1HF, England
**Trounson, Alan** — Biologist
Monash University, Immunology/Stem Cell Laboratory, Monash VIC 3800, Australia
**Troup, P William (Bill), III** — Football Player
4 Quail Wood Court, Parkton MD 21120, USA

**T**

Trimble - Troup

**Troupe, Benjamin L (Ben)** — Football Player
1105 Rannoch Place, Nashville TN 37220, USA
**Troupe, Tom** — Actor, Writer
8829 Ashcroft Ave, West Hollywood CA 90048, USA
**Trout, Steven R (Steve)** — Baseball Player
PO Box 1155, Tinley Park IL 60477, USA
**Trout, Walter** — Singer, Guitarist, Songwriter
Fish-Net Productions, 5840 W Craig Road, #120-228, Las Vegas NV 89130, USA
**Trower, Robin** — Singer, Guitarist (Procol Harum)
Stardust Enterprises, 4600 Franklin Ave, Los Angeles CA 90027, USA
**Troxel, Gary** — Singer (Fleetwoods)
11471 Earle Dr, Mount Vernon WA 98273, USA
**Troxel, Melanie** — Auto Racing Driver
PO Box 637, Brownsburg IN 46112, USA
**Troy, Michael F (Mike)** — Swimmer
21187 E Alyssa Road, Queen Creek AZ 85142, USA
**Troyer, Verne** — Actor
12400 Ventura Blvd, #630, Studio City CA 91604, USA
**Trpceski, Simon** — Concert Pianist
Kirshbaum Demler Assoc, 711 W End Avenue, #5KN, New York, NY 10025, USA
**Truax, William F (Billy)** — Football Player
735 Ruth Ave, Gulfport MS 39501, USA
**Truby, Chris** — Baseball Player
12244 Silverado Dr, Fishers IN 46037, USA
**Trucco, Michael** — Actor, Director
McKeon-Myrones Mgmt, 3500 Olive Ave, #770, Burbank CA 91505 USA
**Trucks, Derek** — Orchestra Leader, Guitarist
Monterey International, 200 W Superior St, #202, Chicago IL 60654 USA
**Trucks, Toni** — Actress
Greene Assoc, 1901 Ave of Stars, #130, Los Angeles CA 90067 USA
**Trudeau, Garry B** — Cartoonist (Doonesbury)
459 Columbus Ave, #200, New York NY 10024, USA
**Trudeau, Jack F** — Football Player
PO Box 375, Zionsville IN 46077, USA
**True, Rachel** — Actress
Kritzer Levine Wilkins Griffin, 11872 La Grange Ave, #100, Los Angeles CA 90025 USA
**Trueba, Fernando** — Animator, Producer, Writer
Creative Artists Agency, 2000 Ave of Stars, #100, Los Angeles CA 90067 USA
**Trueblood, Jeremy T** — Football Player
10603 Keswick Place, Tampa FL 33626, USA
**Truesdale, Yanic** — Actor
Nancy Iannios Public Relations, PO Box 430, Signal Mountain TN 37377 USA
**Truex, Lambertson** — Fashion Designer
I C Insight Communications, Piazzale Baiamonti 4, 20154 Milan, Italy
**Truex, Martin L, Jr** — Auto Racing Driver
172 Tennessee Circle, Mooresville NC 28117, USA
**Trufant, Desmond** — Football Player
Atlanta Falcons, 4400 Falcon Parkway, Flowery Branch GA 30542 USA
**Trufant, Marcus L** — Football Player
15504 SE 79th Place, Newcastle WA 98059, USA
**Truglio, Joe Lo** — Actor
United Talent Agency, U T A Plaza, 9336 Civic Center Dr, Beverly Hills CA 90210 USA
**Truhill, Geraldine Sloan (Jerri)** — Astronaut Candidate
1431 Lamp Post Lane, Richardson TX 75080, USA
**Truitt, Olanda R** — Football Player
1901 16th Way N, Bessemer AL 35020, USA
**Trujillo, Chadwick** — Astronomer
California Institute of Technology, Astronomy Dept, Pasadena CA 91125, USA
**Trujillo, Michael A (Mike)** — Baseball Player
16373 6475 Road, Montrose CO 81403, USA
**Trujillo, Robert** — Bassist (Ozzy Osborne, Metallica)
Q Prime, 729 7th Ave, #1600, New York NY 10019 USA
**Trujillo, Solomon D** — Businessman
Qwest Communications, 700 Qwest Tower, 1801 California St, Denver CO 80202, USA
**Trull, Donald D (Don)** — Football Player
8706 Bloomfield Turn, Missouri City TX 77459, USA
**Trulli, Jarno** — Auto Racing Driver
Casa del Muschna, 7513 Silvaplana, Switzerland
**Trulsen, Paal** — Curling Athlete
Curling Assn, Sognsveien 75, Serviceboks 1, 0840 Oslo, Norway
**Truluck, R-Kal K** — Football Player
418 McDonough St, Saint Charles MO 63301, USA
**Truly, Richard H** — Astronaut, Space Administrator, Admiral
2340 Juniper Court, Golden CO 80401, USA
**Truman, Dan** — Pianist, Keyboardist (Diamond Rio)
Modern Mgmt, 1625 Broadway, #600, Nashville TN 37203, USA
**Truman, James** — Editor
Conde Nast Publications, Editorial Office, 4 Times Square, New York NY 10036, USA
**Trumka, Richard L** — Labor Leader
AFL-CIO, 1750 New York Ave NW, Lobby 1, Washington DC 20006, USA
**Trump, Donald J** — Businessman, Actor
Trump Organization, 725 5th Ave, Basement, New York NY 10022, USA
**Trump, Ivana** — Businesswoman, Model
10 E 64th St, New York NY 10065, USA
**Trump, Ivanka** — Model
W M E Entertainment, 9601 Wilshire Blvd, #300, Beverly Hills CA 90210 USA
**Trumpy, Robert T (Bob), Jr** — Football Player, Sportscaster
75 Oak St, Cincinnati OH 45246, USA
**Trundy, Natalie** — Actress
2109 S Wilbur Ave, Walla Walla WA 99362, USA
**Truscott, Lucian K, IV** — Writer
Avon/William Morrow, 1350 Ave of Americas, #200, New York NY 10019 USA
**Trusnik, Jason** — Football Player
Cleveland Browns, 76 Lou Groza Blvd, Berea OH 44017 USA
**Truth Hurts** — Singer, Songwriter, Actress
Aftermath/Interscope Records, 2220 Colorado Ave, Santa Monica CA 90404, USA

**Tryba, Ted** — Golfer
6321 Cheryl St, Orlando FL 32819, USA

**Tryggvason, Bjarni V** — Astronaut, Canada
Space Agency, 6767 Route de Aeroport, Saint Hubert QC J3Y 8Y9, Canada

**Trynin, Jennifer** — Singer, Songwriter, Guitarist
Vector Mgmt, PO Box 120479, Nashville TN 37212 USA

**Tryon, W Augustus (Ty), IV** — Golfer
8713 Esplanade, #1, Orlando FL 32836, USA

**Tsakalidis, Iakovos (Jake)** — Basketball Player
6940 E Doubletree Ranch Road, Paradise Valley AZ 85253, USA

**Tsallagova, Elena** — Opera Singer
I M G Artists, Hogarth Business Park, Chiswick, London W4 2TH, England

**Tsamis, George A** — Baseball Player
12 Sweetbriar Court, Colchester CT 06415, USA

**Tsantiris, Len** — Soccer Coach
University of Connecticut, Athletic Dept, Storrs CT 06239, USA

**Tsao, I Fu** — Chemical Engineer
University of Michigan, Chemical Engineering Dept, Ann Arbor MI 48109, USA

**Tscharnke, Tim** — Cross Country Skier
Ulf Tscharnke, Simmersbergstra 55, 98666 Masserberg Ortsteil Schnett, Germany

**Tschetter, Kris** — Golfer
13 Culpepper St, Warrenton VA 20186, USA

**Tschogi, John M** — Basketball Player
295 Shirley St, Chula Vista CA 91910, USA

**Tschumi, Bernard** — Architect
7 Rue Pecquay, 75004 Paris, France

**Tschutscher, Klaus** — Prime Minister, Liechtenstein
Prime Minister's Office, Peter-Kaiser-Platz 1, 9490 Vaduz, Liechtenstein

**Tsereteli, Zurab K** — Sculptor
21 Prechistenka St, 119034 Moscow, Russia

**Tsia, Ming** — Chef
Blue Ginger, 583 Washington St, Wellesley MA 02482, USA

**Tsibliyev, Vasili V** — Cosmonaut
Cosmonaut Training Center, Star City, 141160 Zvezdny Gorodok, Moscow Oblast, Russia

**Tsien, Billie** — Interior Designer
Tod Williams Billie Tsien Architects, 222 Central Park S, New York NY 10019, USA

**Tsien, Richard W** — Neurobiologist
29 Washington Square W, #15A, New York NY 10011, USA

**Tsien, Roger Y** — Nobel Chemistry Laureate
University of California, Chemistry Dept, 9500 Gilman Dr, La Jolla CA 92093, USA

**Tsitouris, John P** — Baseball Player
5207 Austin Road, Monroe NC 28112, USA

**Tsonga, Jo-Wilfried** — Tennis Player
Association of Tennis Professionals, 200 Tournament Road, Ponte Vedra Beach FL 32082 USA

**Tsopei, Kiriaki (Corinna)** — Beauty Queen, Actress
Miss Universe Organization, 1370 Ave of Americas, #1600, New York NY 10019 USA

**Tsou, Cece** — Actress, Producer, Writer
C E S D, 10635 Santa Monica Blvd, #130, Los Angeles CA 90025 USA

**Tsoucalas, Nicholas** — Judge
US Court of International Trade, 1 Federal Plaza, New York NY 10278, USA

**Tsu, Irene** — Actress
House of Representatives, 1434 6th St, #1, Santa Monica CA 90401 USA

**Tsui, Daniel C** — Nobel Physics Laureate
53 College Road W, Princeton NJ 08540, USA

**Tsui, Lap-Chee** — Molecular Geneticist, Educator
Hong Kong University, Vice Chancellor's Office, Pokfulam Road, Hong Kong, China

**Tsujihara, Kevin** — Businessman
Warner Bros, 4000 Warner Blvd, Burbank CA 91522, USA

**Tsujii, Nobuyuki** — Concert Pianist
I M G Artists, Hogarth Business Park, Chiswick, London W4 2TH, England

**Tsuno, Yoshikazu** — Prime Minister, Japan
Imperial Palace, 1-1 Chiyoda, Chiyodaku, Tokyo 100 0001, Japan

**Tsvangirai, Morgan R** — Prime Minister, Zimbabwe
Prime Minister's Office, Private Bag 7700, Causeway, Harare, Zimbabwe

**Tua, David** — Boxer
Gotham Boxing, 1414 Ave of Americas, #404, New York NY 10019, USA

**Tuan, Nguyen** — Sculptor
Masterpiece Publishing, 5 Watson, Irvine CA 92618, USA

**Tuan, Yi-Fu** — Humanistic Geographer
University of Wisconsin, Geography Dept, Madison WI 53706, USA

**Tubbs, Gregory A (Greg)** — Baseball Player
833 Clay Ave, Cookeville TN 38501, USA

**Tubbs, Tony** — Boxer
913 Alcorn Lane, Muscatine IA 52761, USA

**Tubbs, Winfred O** — Football Player
4212 Debbie Dr, Grand Prairie TX 75052, USA

**Tuberville, Thomas H (Tommy)** — Football Coach
Cincinnati University, Athletic Dept, 2600 Clifton Ave, Cincinnati OH 45221, USA

**Tucci, Michael** — Actor
1425 Irving Ave, Glendale CA 91201, USA

**Tucci, Roberto Cardinal** — Religious Leader
Palazzo Pio, Piazza Pia 3, 00193 Rome, Italy

**Tucci, Stanley** — Actor, Director
Olive Productions, 161 Ave of Americas, #1100, New York NY 10013, USA

**Tuccillo, Liz** — Writer, Producer
United Talent Agency, U T A Plaza, 9336 Civic Center Dr, Beverly Hills CA 90210 USA

**Tuchman, Maurice** — Museum Curator
150 E 57th St, #PH 1A, New York NY 10022, USA

**Tuck, Jessica** — Actress
Greene Assoc, 1901 Ave of Stars, #130, Los Angeles CA 90067 USA

**Tuck, Justin L** — Football Player
New York Giants, Meadowlands Stadium, 102 Route 120, East Rutherford NJ 07073 USA

**Tucker, Anand** — Director
United Talent Agency, U T A Plaza, 9336 Civic Center Dr, Beverly Hills CA 90210 USA

**Tucker, Barbara** — Singer
Nene Musik Productions, 1460 SW Santiago Ave, Port Saint Lucie FL 34953 USA

**Tucker, Bill** — Bowler
26126 Meadowcrest Blvd, Huntington Woods MI 48070, USA

**Tucker, Chad** — Actor
W M E Entertainment, 9601 Wilshire Blvd, #300, Beverly Hills CA 90210 USA

**Tucker, Chris** — Actor, Comedian
W M E Entertainment, 9601 Wilshire Blvd, #300, Beverly Hills CA 90210 USA

**Tucker, Darcy** — Ice Hockey Player
8754 Crooked Stick Court, Lone Tree CO 80124, USA

**Tucker, Duncan** — Director, Writer
Brillstein Entertainment Partners, 9150 Wilshire Blvd, #350, Beverly Hills CA 90212 USA

**Tucker, John** — Ice Hockey Player
19833 Michigan Ave, Odessa FL 33556, USA

**Tucker, Jonathan** — Actor
United Talent Agency, U T A Plaza, 9336 Civic Center Dr, Beverly Hills CA 90210 USA

**Tucker, Lisa** — Actress, Singer
Creative Artists Agency, 2000 Ave of Stars, #100, Los Angeles CA 90067 USA

**Tucker, Michael** — Fertility Biologist
Reproductive Biology, 5505 Peachtree Dunwoody Road NE, Atlanta GA 30342, USA

**Tucker, Michael** — Actor
Stone Manners Salners, 9911 W Pico Blvd, #1400, Los Angeles CA 90035 USA

**Tucker, Michael A** — Baseball Player
407 Maple Ave N, Lehigh Acres FL 33972, USA

**Tucker, Rex T** — Football Player
2300 Culpepper Dr, Midland TX 79705, USA

**Tucker, Robert L (Bob), Jr** — Football Player
8 Hunter Road, Hazleton PA 18201, USA

**Tucker, Ryan H** — Football Player
24752 Eagle Pointe, Columbia Station OH 44028, USA

**Tucker, Tanya** — Singer
A P A Talent/Literary Agency, 405 S Beverly Dr, #300, Beverly Hills CA 90212 USA

**Tucker, Thomas J (T J)** — Baseball Player
6616 Ridge Top Dr, New Port Richey FL 34655, USA

**Tucker, Tony** — Boxer
Club Prana, 1619 7th Ave, Ybor City, Tampa FL 33605, USA

**Tucker, Trent** — Basketball Player
433 River St, Minneapolis MN 55401, USA

**Tucker, Y Arnold** — Football Player
PO Box 514, Hilbert WI 54129, USA

**Tuckwell, Barry E** — Concert French Horn Player, Conductor
Gallo & Giordano, 76 W 86th St, New York NY 10024, USA

**Tudor, John T** — Baseball Player
5 Nathan Lane, Middleton MA 01949, USA

**Tudor, Rob A** — Ice Hockey Player
69 Cimarron Meadows Way, Okotoks AB T1S 1V9, Canada

**Tudyk, Alan** — Actor
Gersh Agency, 9465 Wilshire Blvd, #600, Beverly Hills CA 90212 USA

**Tuer, Al** — Ice Hockey Player
Calgary Flames, PO Box 1540, Station M, Calgary AB T2P 3B9, Canada

**Tueting, Sarah** — Ice Hockey Player
488 Ash St, Winnetka IL 60093, USA

**Tufts, Robert M (Bob)** — Baseball Player
6738 108th St, #A27, Forest Hills NY 11375, USA

**Tufuga Efi, Tupuola Taisi** — Head of State, Samoa
Head of State's Office, Government House, Vailima, Apia, Samoa

**Tuggle, Anthony I** — Football Player
12345 Plymouth Dr, Baton Rouge LA 70807, USA

**Tuggle, Jessie L** — Football Player
540 Avala Court, Alpharetta GA 30022, USA

**Tugnutt, Ronald F B (Ron)** — Ice Hockey Player
10 Beech Grove Gardens, Stittsville ON K2S 1W5, Canada

**Tuiasosopo, Manu A** — Football Player
14616 NE 184th Place, Woodinville WA 98072, USA

**Tuilaepa Sailele Maljelegaio** — Prime Minister, Samoa
Prime Minister's Office, PO Box 193, Apia, Samoa

**Tuitert, Mark** — Speed Skater
Mauritslaan 34, 8448 Heerenveen PE, Netherlands

**Tu'ivakano, Lord** — Prime Minister, Tonga
Prime Minister's Office, PO Box 62, Taufa'ahau Road, Nuku'alofa, Tonga

**Tuke, Blair** — Yachtsman
Kerikeri Cruising Club, 346 Opito Bay Road, R D 1, Kerikeri 0294, Bay of Islands, New Zealand

**Tukur, Ulrich** — Actor
Anne Alvares Correa, 34 Rue Jouffroy d'Abbans, 75017 Paris, France

**Tulafono, Togiola T A** — Governor, AS
Governor's Office, Executive Office Building, #300, Pago Pago AS 96799 USA

**Tullis, William J (Willie)** — Football Player
10018 Knoboak Dr, #4, Houston TX 77080, USA

**Tulloch, Elizabeth (Bitsie)** — Actress
W M E Entertainment, 9601 Wilshire Blvd, #300, Beverly Hills CA 90210 USA

**Tulloch, Stephen M** — Football Player
629 Palisades Court, Brentwood TN 37027, USA

**Tully, Caitlin** — Concert Violinist
I M G Artists, Hogarth Business Park, Chiswick, London W4 2TH, England

**Tulowitzki, Troy T** — Baseball Player
Colorado Rockies Foundation, 2001 Blake St, Denver CO 80205, USA

**Tulving, Endel** — Psychologist
45 Baby Point Crescent, York ON M6S 2B7, Canada

**Tuman, Jerame D** — Football Player
1303 Hidden Canyon Court, Sewickley PA 15143, USA

**Tumi, Christian W Cardinal** — Religious Leader
Archveche, BP 179, Douala, Cameroon

**Tune, Thomas J (Tommy)** — Dancer, Actor, Choreographer
I C M Partners, 10250 Constellation Blvd, #900, Los Angeles CA 90067 USA

**Tung Chee Hwa** — Chief Executive, Hong Kong
Emeritus Chief Executive's Office, 28 Kennedy Road, Hong Kong, China

**Tunie, Tamara** — Actress
Paradigm Agency, 360 N Crescent Dr, North Building, Beverly Hills CA 90210 USA

**Tunnell, B Lee**
6000 Kingsbridge Dr, Oklahoma City OK 73162, USA
Baseball Player

**Tunney, Jim**
PO Box 1440, Pebble Beach CA 93953, USA
Football Referee

**Tunney, John V**
304 Chautauqua Blvd, Pacific Palisades CA 90272, USA
Senator, CA

**Tunney, Robin**
Creative Artists Agency, 2000 Ave of Stars, #100, Los Angeles CA 90067 USA
Actress

**Tunnicliffe, Anna**
New York Yacht Club, 37 W 44th St, New York NY 10036, USA
Yachtswoman

**Tunstall, Kate V (K T)**
Creative Artists Agency, 2000 Ave of Stars, #100, Los Angeles CA 90067 USA
Singer, Guitarist, Songwriter

**Tuohy, Kat**
OmniPop Talent Group, 4605 Lankershim Blvd, #201, Toluca Lake CA 91602 USA
Actress, Comedienne

**Tupa, Thomas J (Tom)**
6761 Rivercrest Dr, Brecksville OH 44141, USA
Football Player

**Tupman, Matt**
3 Lincoln St, Concord NH 03301, USA
Baseball Player

**Tupov VI**
Royal Palace, PO Box 6, Nuku'alofa, Tonga
King, Tonga

**Tupper, James**
I C M Partners, 10250 Constellation Blvd, #900, Los Angeles CA 90067 USA
Actor

**Tur, Arlene**
Gersh Agency, 9465 Wilshire Blvd, #600, Beverly Hills CA 90212 USA
Actress, Comedienne

**Turang, Brian C**
3014 McNab Ave, Long Beach CA 90808, USA
Baseball Player

**Turco, Marty**
3616 N Wayne Ave, Chicago IL 60613, USA
Ice Hockey Player

**Turco, Paige**
Gersh Agency, 9465 Wilshire Blvd, #600, Beverly Hills CA 90212 USA
Actress

**Turcotte, Alfie**
816 Hawk Dr, Wolverine Lake MI 48390, USA
Ice Hockey Player

**Turcotte, Darren**
North Bay Skyhawks, 100 Chippewa W, North Bay ON P1B 6G2, Canada
Ice Hockey Player

**Turcotte, Donald L (Don)**
27104 Middle Golf Dr, El Macero CA 95618, USA
Geophysicist

**Turcotte, Jean-Claude Cardinal**
1071 Rue de la Cathedrale, Montreal QC H2B 2V4, Canada
Religious Leader

**Turcotte, Mathieu**
Speed Skating Canada, 2781 Lancaster Road, #402, Ottawa ON K1B 1A7, Canada
Speed Skater

**Turcotte, Ron J M**
82 Seattle Slew Dr, Howell NJ 07731, USA
Thoroughbred Racing Jockey

**Turek, Roman**
Sports Corp, 10088 102nd Ave, Edmonton AB T5J 2Z1, Canada
Ice Hockey Player

**Turgeon, Mark**
University of Maryland, Athletic Dept, College Park MD 20742, USA
Basketball Coach

**Turgeon, Pierre**
1075 E Oxford Lane, Englewood CO 80113, USA
Ice Hockey Player

**Turgoose, Thomas**
Troika, 74 Clerkenwell Road, #300, London EC1M 5QA, England
Actor

**Turk, Danilo**
President's Office, Erjavcena 17, 61000 Ljubljana, Slovenia
President, Slovenia

**Turk, Matt E**
5114 Evergreen St, Bellaire TX 77401, USA
Football Player

**Turkel, Ann**
10701 Wilshire Blvd, #2001, Los Angeles CA 90024, USA
Actress, Model

**Turkoglu, Hidayet (Hedo)**
322 E Central Blvd, #1203, Orlando FL 32801, USA
Basketball Player

**Turkson, Peter K A Cardinal**
Archdiocese, PO Box 112, Cape Coast, Ghana
Religious Leader

**Turley, Kyle D**
1715 Championship Blvd, Franklin TN 37064, USA
Football Player

**Turlington, Christy**
United Talent Agency, U T A Plaza, 9336 Civic Center Dr, Beverly Hills CA 90210 USA
Model, Director

**Turman, Glynn R**
Elkins Mgmt, 8306 Wilshire Blvd, #3643, Beverly Hills CA 90211, USA
Actor

**Turnage, Mark-Anthony**
Cathy Nelson, Court Place, Dorstone, Herefordshire HR3 6AW, England
Composer

**Turnball, Ian**
23930 Ocean Ave, #154, Torrance CA 90505, USA
Ice Hockey Player

**Turnbloom, Lucas**
Southern Cross, Editorial Dept, 3888 Paducah Dr, San Diego CA 92117, USA
Editorial Cartoonist

**Turnbow, T Derrick**
2224 Brienz Valley Dr, Franklin TN 37064, USA
Baseball Player

**Turnbull, Perry**
2186 Cedar Forest Court, Chesterfield MO 63017, USA
Ice Hockey Player

**Turnbull, Renaldo A**
9507 Chanson Place, Matthews NC 28105, USA
Football Player

**Turnbull, Wendy**
822 Boylston Dt, #203, Chestnut Hill MA 02467, USA
Tennis Player

**Turner, Aidan**
Creative Artists Agency, 2000 Ave of Stars, #100, Los Angeles CA 90067 USA
Actor

**Turner, Alexander D (Alex)**
Wildlife Entertainment, 21 Heathman's Road, London SW6 4TJ, England
Singer, Guitarist (Arctic Monkeys)

**Turner, Andy**
Windish Agency, 1658 N Milwaukee Ave, #211, Chicago IL 60647, USA
Musician (Plaid)

**Turner, Brad**
A P A Talent/Literary Agency, 405 S Beverly Dr, #300, Beverly Hills CA 90212 USA
Director, Producer

**Turner, Bree**
Brillstein Entertainment Partners, 9150 Wilshire Blvd, #350, Beverly Hills CA 90212 USA
Actress

**Turner, Cathy**
251 East Ave, Hilton NY 14468, USA
Speed Skater

**Turner, Cecil A**
2717 Dog Leg Trail, McKinney TX 75069, USA
Football Player

**Turner, Christopher W (Chris)**
28553 N Quarry Dr, Elberta AL 36530, USA
Baseball Player

**Turner, Craig**
Hardin-Simmons University, President's Office, Abilene TX 79698, USA — Educator

**Turner, Dean**
26900 Captains Lane, Franklin MI 48025, USA — Ice Hockey Player

**Turner, Dylan**
Hatton McEwan, 3 Chocolate Studios, 7 Shepherdess Place, London N1 7LJ, England — Actor

**Turner, Edwin L**
Princeton University, Astrophysical Sciences Dept, Princeton NJ 08544, USA — Astrophysicist

**Turner, Elston H**
23 Commanders Cove, Missouri City TX 77459, USA — Basketball Player

**Turner, Floyd, Jr**
9626 Garden Row Dr, Sugar Land TX 77498, USA — Football Player

**Turner, Gideon**
Ken McReddie Assoc, 101 Finsbury Pavement, London EC2A 1RS, England — Actor

**Turner, Guinevere**
Jaret Entertainment, 6973 Birdview Ave, Malibu CA 90265, USA — Actress

**Turner, James A (Jim)**
14155 W 59th Place, Arvada CO 80004, USA — Football Player

**Turner, James T**
US Claims Court, 717 Madison Place NW, Washington DC 20439, USA — Judge

**Turner, James, Jr**
General Dynamics, 2941 Fairview Park Dr, #100, Falls Church VA 22042, USA — Businessman

**Turner, Janine**
Linda McAlister Talent, 530 S Lake Ave, #435, Pasadena CA 91101, USA — Actress, Model

**Turner, Jeffrey S (Jeff)**
1590 Woodland Ave, Winter Park FL 32789, USA — Basketball Player

**Turner, John N W**
59 Oriole Road, Toronto ON M4V 2E9, Canada — Prime Minister, Canada

**Turner, John W (Jerry)**
1935 18th St, #B, Santa Monica CA 90404, USA — Baseball Player

**Turner, John, Jr**
3217 Cedar Ave S, Minneapolis MN 55407, USA — Football Player

**Turner, Josh**
Modern Mgmt, 1625 Broadway, #600, Nashville TN 37203, USA — Singer, Guitarist

**Turner, Karri**
Premiere Artists Agency, 1875 Century Park E, #2250, Los Angeles CA 90067 USA — Actress

**Turner, Kathleen**
Don Buchwald, 6500 Wilshire Blvd, #2200, Los Angeles CA 90048, USA — Actress

**Turner, Keena**
8200 W Erb Way, Tracy CA 95304, USA — Football Player, Coach

**Turner, Kevin**
Microsoft Corp, 1 Microsoft Way, Redmond WA 98052, USA — Businessman

**Turner, Michael**
912 Chattanooga Trace, Suwanee GA 30024, USA — Football Player

**Turner, Morgan**
I C M Partners, 10250 Constellation Blvd, #900, Los Angeles CA 90067 USA — Actress

**Turner, Morris (Morrie)**
PO Box 3004, Berkeley CA 94703, USA — Cartoonist (Wee Pals)

**Turner, Nicholas (Nik)**
Money Talks Mgmt, PO Box 5, Whitland Dyfed SA34 0WA, Wales — Singer, Saxophonist (Hawkwind)

**Turner, Norv**
PO Box 400, Del Mar CA 92014, USA — Football Coach

**Turner, Odessa**
177 Cortland Terrace, Teaneck NJ 07666, USA — Football Player

**Turner, P Kevin**
215 Liberty Lake Dr, Vestavia AL 35242, USA — Football Player

**Turner, R E (Ted), III**
Turner Foundation, 133 Luckie St NW, #200, Atlanta GA 30303, USA — Sports Executive, Yachtsman, Businessman

**Turner, R Gerald**
Southern Methodist University, President's Office, Dallas TX 75275, USA — Educator

**Turner, Robert H (Bake)**
PO Box 277, Alpine TX 79831, USA — Football Player

**Turner, Ronald L**
Ceridian Corp, 3311 E Old Shakopee Road, Minneapolis MN 55425, USA — Businessman

**Turner, Shane L**
3032 Van Reed Road, Reading PA 19608, USA — Baseball Player

**Turner, Sherri**
5 Alpine St, Carbondale CO 81623, USA — Golfer

**Turner, Sophie**
Independent Talent Group, 40 Whitfield St, London W1T 2RH, England — Actress

**Turner, Stansfield**
600 New Hampshire Ave NW, #800, Washington DC 20037, USA — Navy Admiral, Government Official

**Turner, Steve**
Legends of 21st Century, 7 Trinity Row, Florence MA 01062, USA — Guitarist (Green River, Mudhoney)

**Turner, Tina**
L M A Productions, 998C Old Country Road, #409, Plainview NY 11803, USA — Singer, Actress

**Turner, Tyrin**
Williams Talent Agency, 1438 N Gower St, Building 35, Los Angeles CA 90028, USA — Actor

**Turner, Vernon M**
86 Crosshill St, Staten Island NY 10301, USA — Football Player

**Turner, W Matthew (Matt)**
829 Della Dr, Lexington KY 40504, USA — Baseball Player

**Turner, William (Bill)**
3271 Wisteria Tree St, Las Vegas NV 89135, USA — Basketball Player

**Turner, William H (Billy), Jr**
230 Nassau Blvd, Garden City NY 11530, USA — Thoroughbred Racing Trainer

**Turnesa, Marc**
Professional Golfer's Assn, PO Box 109601, Palm Beach Gardens FL 33410 USA — Golfer

**Turnley, David C**
34 Rue des Frances Bourgeois, 75003 Paris, France — Photojournalist

**Turnovsky, Martin**
Gerhild Baron, Dornbacher Str 41/III/2, 1170 Vienna, Austria — Conductor

**Turow, Scott F**
233 S Wacker Dr, #8000, Chicago IL 60606, USA — Writer

**Turre, Steve**
Brad Simon Organization, 445 E 80th St, #4C, New York NY 10075 USA — Jazz Trombonist

| | |
|---|---|
| **Turrell, James A**<br>Skystone Foundation, PO Box 220, Flagstaff AZ 86002, USA | Artist |
| **Turteltaub, Jon**<br>Junction Entertainment, 500 S Buena Vista St, Animation Building, Burbank CA 91521, USA | Director |
| **Turturro, Aida**<br>Framework Entertainment, 9057 Nemo St, #C, West Hollywood CA 90069 USA | Actress |
| **Turturro, John**<br>I C M Partners, 10250 Constellation Blvd, #900, Los Angeles CA 90067 USA | Actor, Director |
| **Turturro, Nicholas**<br>Kritzer Levine Wilkins Griffin, 11872 La Grange Ave, #100, Los Angeles CA 90025 USA | Actor, Director |
| **Turunen, Tarja**<br>N E M S Enterprises, Av Rivadavia 4686, 14 Capital Federal, Argentina | Singer, Songwriter |
| **Tushingham, Rita**<br>Lip Service, 4 Kingly St, London W1R 5LF, England | Actress |
| **Tusk, Donald F**<br>Ul Ursad Rady Ministrow, Ul Wiejska 4/8, 00583 Warsaw, Poland | Prime Minister, Poland |
| **Tuten, Melvin E, Jr**<br>13779 Mottlestone Dr, Pickerington OH 43147, USA | Football Player |
| **Tuten, Richard L (Rick)**<br>1146 SE 15th St, Ocala FL 34471, USA | Football Player |
| **Tutone, Tommy**<br>Hook Entertainment, 26033 Mulholland Highway, Malibu CA 91302, USA | Singer, Dancer |
| **Tutor, Ronald N**<br>Tutor Perini Corp, 15901 Olden St, Sylmar CA 91342, USA | Producer, Businessman |
| **Tuttle, Jerry O**<br>J O T Enterprises, 5875 Trinity Parkway, #130, Centreville VA 20120, USA | Navy Admiral |
| **Tuttle, Steve**<br>928 Belfair Road, Bellevue WA 98004, USA | Ice Hockey Player |
| **Tuttle, William G T, Jr**<br>9707 Ceralene Dr, Fairfax VA 22032, USA | Army General |
| **Tutu, Desmond M**<br>PO Box 1092, Milnerton, 7435 Cape Town, South Africa | Nobel Peace Laureate, Religious Leader |
| **Tuur, Regilio**<br>New York Boxing Club, 1616 Whitestone Expressway, Whitestone NY 11357, USA | Boxer |
| **Tuzzolino, Tony**<br>75 Chasewood Lane, East Amherst NY 14051, USA | Ice Hockey Player |
| **Tveit, Aaron**<br>Creative Artists Agency, 2000 Ave of Stars, #100, Los Angeles CA 90067 USA | Actor |
| **Tverdovsky, Oleg I**<br>8850 E Garden View Dr, Anaheim CA 92808, USA | Ice Hockey Player |
| **Twaalfhoven, Merlijn**<br>La Vie Sur Terre, Palamedesstr 9-1, 1054 Amsterdam HS, Netherlands | Composer |
| **Twain, Shania**<br>Special Artists Agency, 9200 Sunset Blvd, #410, West Hollywood CA 90069 USA | Singer, Songwriter, Model |
| **Twardzik, Dave J**<br>1670 Balmy Beach Dr, Apopka FL 32703, USA | Basketball Player, Executive |
| **Tway, Bob**<br>6300 Oak Heritage Trail, Edmond OK 73025, USA | Golfer |
| **Tweed, Shannon**<br>Characters Talent Mgmt, 8 Elm St, Toronto ON M5G 1G7, Canada | Actress, Model |
| **Tweedy, Cheryl**<br>Polydor Records, 364-366 Kensington High St, London W14 8NS, England | Singer (Girls Aloud) |
| **Tweedy, Jeff S**<br>Tom Margherita Mgmt, 2200 W Foster Ave, #2, Chicago IL 60625, USA | Singer, Guitarist (Uncle Tupelo, Wilco) |
| **Tweet**<br>Creative Artists Agency, 2000 Ave of Stars, #100, Los Angeles CA 90067 USA | Singer, Songwriter |
| **Twellman, Taylor**<br>ESPN-TV, ESPN Plaza, 935 Middle St, Bristol CT 06010 USA | Soccer Player, Sportscaster |
| **Twigg, Rebecca**<br>7001 Old Redmond Road, #E318, Redmond WA 98052, USA | Cyclist |
| **Twiggs, Gregory W (Greg)**<br>PO Box 5293, Carefree AZ 85377, USA | Golfer |
| **Twiggy**<br>4 Saint Georges House, Hanover Square, London W1R 9AJ, England | Model, Actress |
| **Twilley, Dwight**<br>Paramour Group, 10002 Hewlett St, Neillsville WI 54456, USA | Singer, Keyboardist, Songwriter |
| **Twilley, Howard J, Jr**<br>7040 Hill Forest Dr, Dallas TX 75230, USA | Football Player |
| **Twist, Tony**<br>63 Nordic Lane, Defiance MO 63341, USA | Ice Hockey Player |
| **Twista**<br>Courtney Barnes Group, 1680 N Vine St, #1119, Los Angeles CA 90028, USA | Rap Artist |
| **Twitty, Howard**<br>8007 E Mercer Lane, Scottsdale AZ 85260, USA | Golfer |
| **Twitty, Jeffrey D (Jeff)**<br>812 Willow Cove Road, Chapin SC 29036, USA | Baseball Player |
| **Twohy, David**<br>603 Ocean Ave, #3, Santa Monica CA 90402, USA | Director |
| **Twohy, Mike**<br>605 Beloit Ave, Kensington CA 94708, USA | Cartoonist |
| **Twohy, Robert**<br>New Yorker, Editorial Dept, 4 Times Square, Basement C1B, New York NY 10036 USA | Cartoonist |
| **Twomey, Steve**<br>City University of New York, Graduate Journalism School, 219 W 40th St, New York NY 10018, USA | Journalist |
| **Tydings, Joseph D**<br>2705 Pocock Road, Monkton MD 21111, USA | Senator, MD |
| **Tye, Larry**<br>Random House, 1745 Broadway, #1800, New York NY 10019 USA | Writer |
| **Tyers, Kathy**<br>Martha Millard Agency, 204 Park Ave, Madison NJ 07940, USA | Writer |
| **Tykwer, Tom**<br>Herbstfilm Produktion, Hufelandstr 33, 10407 Berlin, Germany | Director, Writer, Actor |
| **Tyler, Aisha**<br>United Talent Agency, U T A Plaza, 9336 Civic Center Dr, Beverly Hills CA 90210 USA | Actress, Comedienne |
| **Tyler, Anne**<br>8 Roland Gardens, Baltimore MD 21210, USA | Writer |

**T**

**Turrell - Tyler**

**Tyler, Bonnie**
I C M Partners, 10250 Constellation Blvd, #900, Los Angeles CA 90067 USA — Singer, Songwriter

**Tyler, Brian**
Chasen Agency, 8899 Beverly Blvd, #405, Los Angeles CA 90048 USA — Composer

**Tyler, James Michael**
A K A Talent, 6310 San Vicente Blvd, #200, Los Angeles CA 90048, USA — Actor

**Tyler, Judy**
Playboy Promotions, 2706 Media Center Dr, Los Angeles CA 90065 USA — Model

**Tyler, Liv**
Untitled Entertainment, 350 S Beverly Dr, #200, Beverly Hills CA 90212 USA — Actress, Model

**Tyler, Maurice M**
7066 Whitfield Dr, Riverdale GA 30296, USA — Football Player

**Tyler, Richard**
Richard Tyler Couture, 727 Washington St, New York NY 10014, USA — Fashion Designer

**Tyler, Robert**
Don Buchwald, 10 E 44th St, New York NY 10017 USA — Actor

**Tyler, Steven V**
Front Line Mgmt, 1100 Glendon Ave, #2000, Los Angeles CA 90024 USA — Singer (Aerosmith), Songwriter

**Tyler, Terry C**
6500 Tauton Road NW, Albuquerque NM 87120, USA — Basketball Player

**Tyler, Wendell A**
44143 20th St W, Lancaster CA 93534, USA — Football Player

**Tylo, Hunter**
11684 Ventura Blvd, #910, Studio City CA 91604, USA — Actress, Model

**Tylo, Michael**
11684 Ventura Blvd, #910, Studio City CA 91604, USA — Actor

**Tylor, Jud**
Talent Works, 3500 W Olive Ave, #1400, Burbank CA 91505 USA — Director

**Tylski, Richard L (Rich)**
5456 Tierra Verde Lane, Jacksonville FL 32258, USA — Football Player

**Tyminski, Daniel J (Dan)**
Keith Case Assoc, 1025 17th Ave S, #200, Nashville TN 37212 USA — Singer, Guitarist (Union Station)

**Tyner, Jason R**
5535 Sul Ross, Beaumont TX 77706, USA — Baseball Player

**Tyner, McCoy**
Blue Note Management Group, 131 W 3rd St, New York NY 10012, USA — Jazz Pianist, Composer

**Tynes, Lawrence J H**
11410 W 163rd Court, Olathe KS 66062, USA — Football Player

**Tyree, David M**
38 Poplar Road, Piscataway NJ 08854, USA — Football Player

**Tyrell, Steve**
Oscar Music Agency, 14 Inchmurrin Dr, Glasgow G73 5RT, Scotland — Singer

**Tyrrell, Timothy G (Tim)**
17 Fallstone Dr, Streamwood IL 60107, USA — Football Player

**Tyson, Cicely**
315 W 70th St, New York NY 10023, USA — Actress

**Tyson, Ian**
Richard Flohil Assoc, 60 McGill St, Toronto ON M5B 1H2, Canada — Singer, Songwriter

**Tyson, John H**
Tyson Foods Inc, 2200 W Don Tyson Parkway, Springdale AR 72762, USA — Businessman

**Tyson, Laura D**
London Business School Sussex Place, Regent Park, London NW1 4SA, England — Government Official, Economist

**Tyson, Michael G (Mike)**
Krupp Kommunications, 636 Ave of Americas, #4C, New York NY 10011, USA — Boxer

**Tyson, Michael R (Mike)**
479 Thunderhead Canyon Dr, Ballwin MO 63011, USA — Baseball Player

**Tyson, Neil de Grasse**
Hayden Planetarium, 81 Central Park W, New York NY 10024, USA — Astrophysicist

**Tyson, Richard**
C E S D, 10635 Santa Monica Blvd, #130, Los Angeles CA 90025 USA — Actor

**Tyson, Sylvia**
Jensen Music International, PO Box 3445, Charlottetown PE C1A 8W5, Canada — Singer, Songwriter

**Tyurin, Mikhail**
Cosmonaut Training Center, Star City, 141160 Zvezdny Gorodok, Moscow Oblast, Russia — Cosmonaut

| | |
|---|---|
| **Ubach, Alanna** | Actress |
| Margrit Polak Mgmt, 1920 Hillhurst, #405, Los Angeles CA 90027 90027, USA | |
| **Uchan, Philippe** | Actor, Director |
| Artmedia, 20 Ave Rapp, 75007 Paris, France | |
| **Uchida, Mitsuko** | Concert Pianist |
| Victoria Rowsell Artist Mgmt, 34 Addington Square, London SE5 7LB, England | |
| **Udenio, Fabiana** | Actress |
| House of Representatives, 1434 6th St, #1, Santa Monica CA 90401 USA | |
| **Uderzo, Albert** | Cartoonist |
| Les Editions Albert Rene, 26 Ave Victor Hugo, 75016 Paris, France | |
| **Udoka, Ime S** | Basketball Player |
| PO Box 40802, Portland OR 97240, USA | |
| **Udovenko, Hennadiy Y** | Government Official, Ukraine |
| Desyatynna Str 10, #2, 01025 Kiev, Ukraine | |
| **Udrih, Beno** | Basketball Player |
| 46 Arnold Palmer, San Antonio TX 78257, USA | |
| **Udvar-Hazy, Steven F** | Businessman, Philanthropist |
| 67 Beverly Park, Beverly Hills CA 90210, USA | |
| **Udvari, Frank** | Ice Hockey Referee |
| 6 Willow St, Waterloo ON N2J 2S3, Canada | |
| **Udy, Helene** | Actress |
| Society Entertainment, 15303 Ventura Blvd, Building C, Sherman Oaks CA 91403, USA | |
| **Ueberroth, Peter V** | Baseball, Olympics Executive |
| 184 Emerald Bay, Laguna Beach CA 92651, USA | |
| **Uecker, Gunther** | Artist |
| Kaiserstr 10, 40221 Dusseldorf, Germany | |
| **Uecker, R Keith** | Football Player |
| 169 Dorchester Road, Akron OH 44313, USA | |
| **Uecker, Robert G (Bob)** | Actor, Baseball Player, Sportscaster |
| W131N7867 N Country Club Court, Menomonee Falls WI 53051, USA | |
| **Uelses, John** | Track Athlete |
| 30660 Rolling Hills Dr, Valley Center CA 92082, USA | |
| **Uelsmann, Jerry N** | Photographer |
| 5701 SW 17th Dr, Gainesville FL 32608, USA | |
| **Ufland, Len** | Actor, Director |
| 16900 NE 19th Ave, North Miami Beach FL 33162, USA | |
| **Uggams, Leslie** | Singer, Actress |
| Gage Group, 450 7th Ave, #1809, New York NY 10123 USA | |
| **Uggla, Dan** | Baseball Player |
| 2004 Lincoln Road, Spring Hill TN 37174, USA | |
| **Ughi, Uto** | Concert Violinist |
| Cannareggio 4990/E, 30121 Venice, Italy | |
| **U-God** | Rap Artist (Wu-Tang Clan) |
| A&M Entertainment, 13280 NE Freeway, #F328, Houston TX 77040, USA | |
| **Ugueto, Luis E** | Baseball Player |
| 6009 188th Lane NE, #201, Redmond WA 98052, USA | |
| **Uhalt, Alfred H** | Astronaut |
| 2533 Shalmar Dr, Colorado Springs CO 80915, USA | |
| **Uhl, George R** | Geneticist |
| Johns Hopkins University Medical Center, Genetics Dept, Baltimore MD 21218, USA | |
| **Uhl, Petr** | Human Rights Activist |
| Pravo, Slezska 13, 12150 Prague, Czech Republic | |
| **Uhlenbeck, Karen K** | Mathematician |
| University of Texas, Mathematics Dept, Austin TX 78712, USA | |
| **Uhlenhake, Jeffrey A (Jeff)** | Football Player |
| 1304 Normandy Dr, Newark OH 43055, USA | |
| **Uhrmann, Michael** | Ski Jumper |
| Harslemstr 2, 94139 Breitenberg, Germany | |
| **Uhry, Alfred F** | Writer |
| Marshall Purdy, 226 W 47th St, #900, New York NY 10036, USA | |
| **Ulbrich, Jeffrey W (Jeff)** | Football Player |
| 2316 88th Place NE, Clyde Hill WA 98004, USA | |
| **Ulene, Arthur L** | Physician, Entertainer |
| 6511 Moore Dr, Los Angeles CA 90048, USA | |
| **Ulevich, Neal H** | Photojournalist |
| 11954 Glencoe Dr, Denver CO 80233, USA | |
| **Ulion-Silverman, Gretchen** | Ice Hockey Player |
| 640 Pleasant St, Framingham MA 01701, USA | |
| **Ullman, Myron E, III** | Businessman |
| Jackson Hole Group, 100 Spear St, #935, San Francisco CA 94105, USA | |
| **Ullman, Norman V A (Norm)** | Ice Hockey Player |
| 819-25 Austin Dr, Markham ON L3R 8H4, Canada | |
| **Ullman, Ricky** | Actor |
| Gersh Agency, 41 Madison Ave, #3301, New York NY 10010 USA | |
| **Ullman, Tracey** | Actress, Comedienne, Singer |
| Special Artists Agency, 9200 Sunset Blvd, #410, West Hollywood CA 90069 USA | |
| **Ullmann, Liv J** | Actress |
| Diamond Management, 31 Percy St, London W1T 2DD, England | |
| **Ullrich, Jan** | Cyclist |
| Burgunderweg 10, 79291 Merdingen, Germany | |
| **Ulmer, C Arthur (Artie)** | Football Player |
| 2200 Enclave Mill Dr, Dacula GA 30019, USA | |
| **Ulmer, Frances (Fran)** | Educator |
| University of Alaska, Chancellor's Office, 3211 Providence Dr, Anchorage AK 99508, USA | |
| **Ulmer, James (Blood)** | Jazz Guitarist, Singer |
| J W Entertainment, PO Box 78904, Atlanta GA 30357 USA | |
| **Ulmer, Kristen** | Extreme Athlete |
| 3734 Thousand Oaks Circle, Salt Lake City UT 84124, USA | |
| **Ulrich, Lars** | Drummer (Metallica) |
| Q Prime, 729 7th Ave, #1600, New York NY 10019 USA | |
| **Ulrich, Skeet** | Actor |
| Brillstein Entertainment Partners, 9150 Wilshire Blvd, #350, Beverly Hills CA 90212 USA | |
| **Ulrich, Thomas** | Boxer |
| Brunsbutteler Damm 29, 13581 Berlin, Germany | |
| **Ultra Nate** | Singer |
| Peach Bisquit, 963 Kent Ave, Brooklyn NY 11205, USA | |

# U

**Ulvaeus, Bjorn** — Singer (ABBA), Composer
Mono Music, Sodra Brobanken 41A, Skeppsjolmen, 111 49 Stockholm, Sweden

**Ulvang, Vegard** — Cross Country Skier
Fjellveien 53, 9900 Kirkenes, Norway

**Umbarger, James H (Jim)** — Baseball Player
3909 W Harmont Dr, Phoenix AZ 85051, USA

**Umberger, R J** — Ice Hockey Player
835 Rose Mary Hill Dr, Pittsburgh PA 15239, USA

**Umbers, Mark** — Actor
Paradigm Agency, 360 N Crescent Dr, North Building, Beverly Hills CA 90210 USA

**Umemoto, Nanako** — Architect
118 E 59th St, #402, New York NY 10022, USA

**Umhoefer, David** — Journalist
Journal Sentinal, Editorial Dept, 6525 W Bluemound Road, Milwaukee WI 53213, USA

**Umphlett, Thomas M (Tommy)** — Baseball Player
104 Berkley Road, Ahoskie NC 27910, USA

**Unanue, Emil R** — Immunopathologist
Washington University Medical School, Pathology Dept, Saint Louis MO 63110, USA

**Underwood, Blair** — Actor
I C M Partners, 10250 Constellation Blvd, #900, Los Angeles CA 90067 USA

**Underwood, Carrie** — Singer, Songwriter
8 Wentworth Place, Brentwood TN 37027, USA

**Underwood, Jacob** — Singer (O-Town)
Trans Continental Records, 127 W Church St, #350, Orlando FL 32801, USA

**Underwood, Jay** — Actor
6100 Wilshire Blvd, #1170, Los Angeles CA 90048, USA

**Underwood, Olen U** — Football Player
PO Box 2514, Conroe TX 77305, USA

**Underwood, Patrick J (Pat)** — Baseball Player
708 Riverview Dr, Kokomo IN 46901, USA

**Underwood, Sara Jean** — Model, Actress
I A G Entertainment, 5189 Argonne Court, San Diego CA 92117, USA

**Underwood, Scott** — Drummer (Train)
Jon Landau, 150 Rowayton Ave, Norwalk CT 06853, USA

**Unel, Birol** — Actor
Agentur Drews, Schumannstr 16, 10117 Berlin, Germany

**Uner, Idil** — Actress
Neue Schonhauser Str 16, 10178 Berlin, Germany

**Ungar, Jay** — Musician, Songwriter
Mike Greene Assoc, 339 E Liberty St, #220, Ann Arbor MI 48104, USA

**Ungaro, Emanuel M** — Fashion Designer
2 Ave Montaigne, 75008 Paris, France

**Unger, Brian** — Actor, Producer
Global Artists Agency, 6253 Hollywood Blvd, #508, Los Angeles CA 90028 USA

**Unger, Deborah Kara** — Actress
Seven Summits Mgmt, 8906 W Olympic Blvd, Beverly Hills CA 90211 USA

**Unger, Garry D** — Ice Hockey Player
Banff Hockey Academy, Box 2422, Banff AB T1L 1B9, Canada

**Unger, Joe** — Actor
718 N Kings, #30, West Hollywood CA 90069, USA

**Unger, Kay** — Fashion Designer
Saint Gillian Sportswear, 498 Fashion Ave, New York NY 10018, USA

**Unger, Roger H** — Internist
Texas Southwestern Medical Center, 5323 Harry Hines Blvd, Dallas TX 75390, USA

**Union, Gabrielle** — Actress
Intellectual Artists Mgmt, 10585 Santa Monica Blvd, #135, Los Angeles CA 90025, USA

**Unroe, Timothy Brian (Tim)** — Baseball Player
2719 S Joplin, Mesa AZ 85209, USA

**Unruh, James A** — Businessman
5426 E Morrison Lane, Paradise Valley AZ 85253, USA

**Unseld, Westley S (Wes)** — Basketball Player, Coach, Executive
2210 Cedar Circle Dr, Catonsville MD 21228, USA

**Unser, Alfred (Al), Jr** — Auto Racing Driver
PO Box 56696, Albuquerque NM 87187, USA

**Unser, Alfred (Al), Sr** — Auto Racing Driver
7625 Central Ave NW, Albuquerque NM 87121, USA

**Unser, Delbert E (Del)** — Baseball Player
33516 N 79th Way, Scottsdale AZ 85266, USA

**Unser, Robbie** — Auto Racing Driver
806 Laguayra Dr NE, Albuquerque NM 87108, USA

**Unser, Robert W (Bobby)** — Auto Racing Driver
7617 Frederick Lane SW, Albuquerque NM 87121, USA

**Unutoa, Morris T** — Football Player
829 S Jordan Way, Lehi UT 84043, USA

**Upatnieks, Juris** — Optical Engineer
Applied Optics, 2662 Valley Dr, Ann Arbor MI 48103, USA

**Upchurch, Richard (Rick)** — Football Player
4104 SE 20th Place, #B2, Cape Coral FL 33904, USA

**Upham, John L** — Baseball Player
1502 Pierre Ave, Windsor ON N9C 2K7, Canada

**Upham, Misty A** — Actress
Kerner Management Associates, 311 N Robertson Blvd, #288, Beverly Hills CA 90211, USA

**Uphoff-Becker, Nicole** — Equestrian
Freiherr-von-Lanen-Str 15, 48231 Warendorf, Germany

**Upshaw, Dawn** — Opera Singer
Nonesuch Records, 75 Rockefeller Plaza, #800, New York NY 10019 USA

**Upshaw, Marvin A (Marv)** — Football Player
3851 Madrone Ave, Oakland CA 94619, USA

**Upshaw, Regan C** — Football Player
746 Walker Road, #16, Great Falls VA 22066, USA

**Upshaw, Willie C** — Baseball Player
74 James St, Fairfield CT 06824, USA

**Upton, Kate** — Model, Actress
I M G Models, 304 Park Ave S, #PH N, New York NY 10010 USA

**Upton, Melvin E (B J)** — Baseball Player
1428 Harbour Walk Road, Tampa FL 33602, USA

**Ulvaeus - Upton**

**Upton, Pat** — Singer (Spiral Staircase)
Lustig Talent, PO Box 770850, Orlando FL 32877 USA

**Urango, Juan** — Boxer
Groupe Yvon Michel, 10172 Saint-Laurent, Montreal QC H3L 2N8, Canada

**Urb, Johann** — Model, Actor
Innovative Artists, 1505 10th St, Santa Monica CA 90401 USA

**Urb, Johann** — Actor
A P A Talent/Literary Agency, 405 S Beverly Dr, #300, Beverly Hills CA 90212 USA

**Urban, Jerheme W** — Football Player
217 Fleetwood Dr, San Antonio TX 78232, USA

**Urban, Karl L** — Actor
Principato-Young, 9465 Wilshire Blvd, #880, Beverly Hills CA 90212 USA

**Urban, Keith** — Singer
Borman Entertainment, 1222 16th Ave S, #23, Nashville TN 37212, USA

**Urbano, Michael (Mike)** — Drummer (Smash Mouth)
Creative Artists Agency, 2000 Ave of Stars, #100, Los Angeles CA 90067 USA

**Urbanski, Douglas** — Producer, Writer
Douglas Management Group, PO Box 691763, West Hollywood CA 90069, USA

**Urbanski, Krzystof** — Conductor
Indianapolis Symphony, 32 E. Washington St., #600, Indianapolis, IN 46204, USA

**Urdang, Leslie** — Producer
Olympus Pictures, 12424 Wilshire Blvd, #1120, Los Angeles CA 90025, USA

**Ure, Midge** — Singer, Guitarist
Tony Denton Promotions, Charter House, 157-159 High St, London N14 6BP, England

**Uresti, Omar** — Golfer
2503 Pebble Beach Dr, Austin TX 78747, USA

**Uribe, Juan C** — Baseball Player
425 Shoreline Road, Lake Barrington IL 60010, USA

**Urich, Justin** — Actor
Talent Group, 5670 Wilshire Blvd, #820, Los Angeles CA 90036, USA

**Urie, Brendon B** — Singer, Guitarist (Panic at the Disco)
Crush Music Mgmt, 60-62 E 11th St, #700, New York NY 10002, USA

**Urie, Michael** — Actor
Paradigm Agency, 360 N Crescent Dr, North Building, Beverly Hills CA 90210 USA

**Urin, Vladimir** — Ballet Executive
Bolshoi Theater, Teatralnaya Pl 1, 103009 Moscow, Russia

**Urkal, Oktay** — Boxer
Frank Bleydorn, Goethestr 25, 12207 Berlin, Germany

**Urlacher, Brian K** — Football Player
15044 W Little Saint Marys Road, Libertyville IL 60048, USA

**Urmanov, Aleksei** — Figure Skater
Union of Skaters, Luzhnetskaya Nab 8, 119871 Moscow, Russia

**Urosa Savino, Jorge L Cardinal** — Religious Leader
Archdiocese of Caracas, Plaza Bolivar, Apt 954, Caracas 1010A, Venezuela

**Urquhart, Brian E** — Diplomat
Howard Farms, Jerusalem Road, Tyringham MA 01264, USA

**Urseth, Bonnie** — Actress
Gage Group, 14724 Ventura Blvd, #505, Sherman Oaks CA 91403 USA

**Usachyov, Yury V** — Cosmonaut
Cosmonaut Training Center, Star City, 141160 Zvezdny Gorodok, Moscow Oblast, Russia

**Usery, Willie J, Jr** — Secretary, Labor
1101 S Arlington Ridge Road, Arlington VA 22202, USA

**Usher** — Rap Artist, Actor
W M E Entertainment, 9601 Wilshire Blvd, #300, Beverly Hills CA 90210 USA

**Usher, Robert R (Bob)** — Baseball Player
1022 N 5th St, San Jose CA 95112, USA

**Usher, Thomas J** — Businessman
U S X Corp, 600 Grant St, #450, Pittsburgh PA 15219, USA

**Usova, Maya** — Ice Dancer
Igloo Skating Rink, 3033 Fostertown, Mount Laurel NJ 08054, USA

**Ut, Nick** — Photographer
Associated Press, Photo Dept, 221 S Figueroa St, #300, Los Angeles CA 90012, USA

**Utay, William** — Actor
Arlene Thornton, 12711 Ventura Blvd, #490, Studio City CA 91604, USA

**Utkina, Sveta** — Model
I M G Models, 304 Park Ave S, #PH N, New York NY 10010 USA

**Utley, Garrick** — Commentator
ABC-TV, News Dept, 8 Carburton St, London W1P 7DT, England

**Utley, Michel G (Mike)** — Football Player
PO Box 349, Orondo WA 98843, USA

**Utt, Benjamin M (Ben)** — Football Player
143 Blackland Road NW, Atlanta GA 30342, USA

**Uvarov, Andrei I** — Ballet Dancer
Bolshoi Theater, Teatralnaya Pl 1, 103009 Moscow, Russia

**Uvini, Bruno** — Soccer Player
Confederacion de Futebol, Rua Victor Civita 66, #1, Rio de Janeiro 22775 044, Brazil

**Uzawa, Hirofumi** — Economist
Kamiyamacho 20-23, Shibuya, Tokyo 150 0047, Japan

**Uzumcu, Ahmet** — Government Official, Turkey
Prohibition of Chemical Weapons Organization, Johan de Wittlaan 32, 2517 Hague JR, Netherlands

# V

**V, Bobby** — Singer, Songwriter, Pianist
Agency for Artists, 244 5th Ave, #H230, New York NY 10001, USA

**Vaananen, Ossi** — Ice Hockey Player
Jokerit, Helsinki Halli Oy Areenankuja 1, 00240 Helsinki, Finland

**Vacano, Jost** — Cinematographer
Leoprechtingstr 18, 81739 Munich, Germany

**Vacanti, Charles A** — Surgeon
Massachusetts University Medical Center, Anesthesiology Dept, Worcester MA 02139, USA

**Vacariou, Nicolae** — President, Romania
Romanian Senate, Piata Revolutiei, 71243 Bucharest, Romania

**Vaccaro, Brenda** — Actress
I C M Partners, 10250 Constellation Blvd, #900, Los Angeles CA 90067 USA

**Vachon, Rogatien R (Rogie)** — Ice Hockey Player
648 Oxford Ave, Venice CA 90291, USA

**Vachss, Andrew H** — Writer
106-23 Metro Ave, Forest Hills NY 11375, USA

**Vactor, Theodore F (Ted)** — Football Player
11504 Channing Dr, Silver Spring MD 20902, USA

**Vadim, Christian** — Actor
Artmedia, 20 Ave Rapp, 75007 Paris, France

**Vadnais, Carol** — Ice Hockey Player
Prouix Vadnais, 955 Rue Bergar, Laval QC H7L 4Z6, Canada

**Vaduva, Leontina** — Opera Singer
Stafford Law, 6 Barham Close, Weybridge, Surrey KT13 9PR, England

**Vagelos, P Roy** — Businessman, Biochemist
82 Mosle Road, Far Hills NJ 07931, USA

**Vagnorius, Gediminas** — Prime Minister, Lithuania
Parliament, Prospekt Gedimino 53, 2002 Vilnius, Lithuania

**Vago, Constant** — Pathologist
Chemin Serre de Laurian, 30100 Ales, France

**Vagt, Robert F** — Foundation Executive, Educator
Heinz Endowments, 30 Dominion Tower, 625 Liberty Ave, Pittsburgh PA 15222, USA

**Vahala, Elina** — Concert Violinist
Sublime Music Agency, Ruusulankatu 14, 00250 Helsinki, Finland

**Vahi, Tiit** — Prime Minister, Estonia
Coalition Eesti Koonderakond, Raekoja Plats 16, 10146 Tallinn, Estonia

**Vai, Steve** — Guitarist (Alcatrazz, Whitesnake)
Septys Entertainment Group, 5543 Edmondson Park, #8A, Nashville TN 37211, USA

**Vail Evans, Justina** — Actress
651 N Kilkea Dr, Los Angeles CA 90048, USA

**Vail, Eric** — Ice Hockey Player
10055 Piney Ridge Walk, Alpharetta GA 30022, USA

**Vail, Michael L (Mike)** — Baseball Player
7946 San Jose Road, El Paso TX 79915, USA

**Vail, Thomas** — Editor
29225 Chagrin Blvd, #200, Beachwood OH 44122, USA

**Vaillancourt, Sarah M** — Ice Hockey Player
Team Canada, 2424 University Dr NW, Calgary AB T2N 3Y9, Canada

**Vaive, Richard C (Rick)** — Ice Hockey Player
Toronto Maple Leafs, AirCanada Center, 40 Bay St, Toronto ON M5J 2K2, Canada

**Vajiralongkorn** — Crown Prince, Thailand
Royal Residence, Chitralada Villa, 9 Rama VI Road, Soi 30, Bangkok 10400, Thailand

**Vajna, Andrew G** — Producer
Cinergi Productions, 2308 Broadway, Santa Monica CA 90404, USA

**Vajpayee, Atal Behari** — Prime Minister, India
7 Race Course Road, New Delhi 110011, India

**Valabik, Boris** — Ice Hockey Player
Boston Bruins, 100 Legends Way, #250, Boston MA 02114 USA

**Valance, Holly** — Singer, Actress
Jon Fowler Mgmt, 60A Highgate High St, London N6 5HX, England

**Valanciunas, Jonas** — Basketball Player
Toronto Raptors, Air Canada Center, 20 Bay St, Toronto ON M5J 2N8, Canada

**Valandrey, Charlotte** — Actress
Artmedia, 20 Ave Rapp, 75007 Paris, France

**Valar, Paul** — Skier
34 Hubertus Ring, Franconia NH 03580, USA

**Valbusa, Fulvio** — Cross Country Skier
Biancaneve 7, 37021 Bosco Chiesanuova, Italy

**Valderrama, Carlos** — Soccer Player
Colorado Rapids, 1000 Chopper Circle, Denver CO 80204 USA

**Valderrama, Wilmer** — Actor
United Talent Agency, U T A Plaza, 9336 Civic Center Dr, Beverly Hills CA 90210 USA

**Valdes, Ismael V** — Baseball Player
4001 26th St, Vero Beach FL 32960, USA

**Valdes, Jesus (Chucho)** — Jazz Pianist
D L Media, 124 N Highland Ave, Bala Cynwyd PA 19004 USA

**Valdes, Marc C** — Baseball Player
7519 Paula Dr, Tampa FL 33615, USA

**Valdes, Maximiano** — Conductor
C M Artists, 127 W 96th St, #13B, New York NY 10025 USA

**Valdespino, Hilario (Sandy)** — Baseball Player
3937 Lilac Haze St, Las Vegas NV 89147, USA

**Valdez, Luis** — Writer
El Teatro Capesino, 705 4th St, San Juan Bautista CA 95045, USA

**Valdivielso Lopez, Jose L** — Baseball Player
14 Rita Dr, Mount Sinai NY 11766, USA

**Valdivieso Sarmiento, Alfonso** — Government Official, Colombia
Foreign Affairs Ministry, Palacio San Carlos, Santa Fe, Bogota, Colombia

**Vale, Jerry** — Singer, Actor
40960 Glenmore Dr, Palm Desert CA 92260, USA

**Valek, Vladimir** — Conductor
Cesky Rozhlas, Vinohradska 12, 12000 Prague 2, Czech Republic

**Valen, Nancy** — Actress
Commercial Talent, 9255 Sunset Blvd, #505, West Hollywood CA 90069, USA

**Valensi, Nick** — Guitarist (Strokes)
M V O Ltd, 370 7th Ave, #807, New York NY 10001, USA

**V - Valensi**

| | |
|---|---|
| **Valente, Benita** | Opera Singer |
| Maurice Mayer, 201 W 54th St, #1C, New York NY 10019, USA | |
| **Valente, Catarina** | Singer, Guitarist, Actress |
| Villa Corallo, Via ai Ronci 12, 6816 Bissone, Switzerland | |
| **Valenti, James** | Opera Singer |
| I M G Artists, Hogarth Business Park, Chiswick, London W4 2TH, England | |
| **Valentin Rosario, Jose A** | Baseball Player |
| 3714 E Park Ave, Phoenix AZ 85044, USA | |
| **Valentin, Dave** | Jazz Flutist |
| Abby Hoffer Enterprises, 223 1/2 E 48th St, New York NY 10017 USA | |
| **Valentin, John W** | Baseball Player |
| 37 Golden Lane, Hazlet NJ 07730, USA | |
| **Valentin, Jose A** | Baseball Player |
| 3714 E Park Ave, Stamford CT 06903, USA | |
| **Valentine, Amber** | Singer, Guitarist (Jucifer) |
| Vamp Music Source, 902 W Franklin Ave, #15, Minneapolis MN 55405, USA | |
| **Valentine, Brooke** | Singer, Songwriter, Model, Actress |
| Virgin Records, 338 N Foothill Road, Beverly Hills CA 90210 USA | |
| **Valentine, Christopher W (Chris)** | Ice Hockey Player |
| Bell Sensplex, 1565 Maple Grove Road, Kanata ON K2V 1A3, Canada | |
| **Valentine, Dan** | Businessman |
| C-Cube Microsystems, 1551 McCarthy Blvd, Milpitas CA 95035, USA | |
| **Valentine, Darnell T** | Basketball Player |
| 7546 SW Ashford St, Portland OR 97224, USA | |
| **Valentine, Dean** | Businessman |
| Symbolic Action, 11601 Wilshire Blvd, #750, Los Angeles CA 90025, USA | |
| **Valentine, DeWain** | Artist |
| 17921 S Western Ave, Gardena CA 90248, USA | |
| **Valentine, Ellis C** | Baseball Player |
| 2708 Bridgemarker Dr, Grand Prairie TX 75054, USA | |
| **Valentine, Fred L** | Baseball Player |
| 4838 Blagden Ave NW, Washington DC 20011, USA | |
| **Valentine, Gary** | Actor, Comedian |
| Legacy Talent, 1300 Baxter St, #100A, Charlotte NC 28204, USA | |
| **Valentine, Greg** | Professional Wrestler |
| 13045 Farmington Trail, Seminole FL 33776, USA | |
| **Valentine, Hilton** | Guitarist (Animals) |
| Lustig Talent, PO Box 770850, Orlando FL 32877 USA | |
| **Valentine, Jacqui** | Singer, Bassist (Civet) |
| Kirky Organization, 9200 Sunset Blvd, #600, Los Angeles CA 90069, USA | |
| **Valentine, James** | Guitarist (Maroon 5) |
| J Records, 745 5th Ave, #600, New York NY 10151 USA | |
| **Valentine, James W** | Paleobiologist |
| 1351 Glendale Ave, Berkeley CA 94708, USA | |
| **Valentine, Joseph J (Joe)** | Baseball Player |
| 4168 Chiffon Lane, North Port FL 34287, USA | |
| **Valentine, Karen** | Actress |
| PO Box 1295, Washington CT 06793, USA | |
| **Valentine, Kathy** | Singer, Guitarist, Bassist (Go-Go's) |
| Rajiworld Tour Consultants, 800 W 3rd St, #2306, Austin TX 78701, USA | |
| **Valentine, Raymond C** | Agronomist |
| University of California, Plant Growth Laboratory, Davis CA 95616, USA | |
| **Valentine, Robert J (Bobby)** | Baseball Player, Manager, Sportscaster |
| 71 Wynnewood Lane, Stamford CT 06903, USA | |
| **Valentine, Scott E** | Actor |
| David Shapira Assoc, 193 N Robertson Blvd, Beverly Hills CA 90211 USA | |
| **Valentine, Steve** | Actor, Writer, Producer |
| Greater Visions Artists Talent Agency, 8981 W Sunset Blvd, #101, West Hollywood CA 90069 USA | |
| **Valentine, William N** | Physician |
| 2128 Quail Point Circle, Medford OR 97504, USA | |
| **Valentine, Zachary B (Zack)** | Football Player |
| 162 Harvest Road, Swedesboro NJ 08085, USA | |
| **Valentinetti, Vito J** | Baseball Player |
| 271 Summit Ave, Mount Vernon NY 10552, USA | |
| **Valentino** | Fashion Designer |
| Palazzo Mignanelli, Piazza Mignanelli 22, 00187 Rome, Italy | |
| **Valentino, Jim** | Cartoonist |
| Image Comics, 1071 N Batavia St, #A, Orange CA 92867, USA | |
| **Valentino, Victoria** | Model |
| Playboy Promotions, 2706 Media Center Dr, Los Angeles CA 90065 USA | |
| **Valenza, Tasia** | Actress |
| Danis Panaro Nist, 9201 W Olympic Blvd, Beverly Hills CA 90212, USA | |
| **Valenzuela, Fernando** | Baseball Player |
| 2123 N Beachwood Dr, Los Angeles CA 90068, USA | |
| **Valeriani, Richard G** | Commentator |
| 23 Island View Dr, Sherman CT 06784, USA | |
| **Valiant, Leslie G** | Computer Scientist |
| 50 Tyler Road, Belmont MA 02478, USA | |
| **Valk, Garry** | Ice Hockey Player |
| 681 Baycrest Dr, North Vancouver BC V7G 1N7, Canada | |
| **Vall, Ely Ould Mohamed** | President, Mauritania; Army Officer |
| President's Office, Cabinet Building, PO Box 2, Majuro, Marshall Islands | |
| **Valle, David (Dave)** | Baseball Player |
| 2260 95th Ave NE, Clyde Hill WA 98004, USA | |
| **Vallee, Roy** | Businessman |
| Avnet Inc, 2211 S 47th St, Phoenix AZ 85034, USA | |
| **Vallely, James (Jim)** | Writer |
| Brillstein Entertainment Partners, 9150 Wilshire Blvd, #350, Beverly Hills CA 90212 USA | |
| **Vallely, John S** | Basketball Player |
| 2042 Commodore Road, Newport Beach CA 92660, USA | |
| **Valletta, Amber E** | Model, Actress |
| Creative Artists Agency, 2000 Ave of Stars, #100, Los Angeles CA 90067 USA | |
| **Valley, Mark** | Actor |
| Vox Inc, 6420 Wilshire Blvd, #1080, Los Angeles CA 90048 USA | |
| **Valli, Frankie** | Singer, Guitarist |
| I C M Partners, 10250 Constellation Blvd, #900, Los Angeles CA 90067 USA | |

**Valli, Giambattista** — Fashion Designer
30 Rue Boissy de'Anglais, 75008 Paris, France

**Vallien, Bertil** — Artist
Roleks Vall, 621 93 Visby, Sweden

**Vallini, Agostino Cardinal** — Religious Leader
Apolstolic Signatura, Palazzo della Cancelleria, 00186 Rome, Italy

**Valmon, Andrew** — Track Athlete
16403 Danforth Circle, Rockville MD 20853, USA

**Valory, Ross L** — Bassist (Journey)
Front Line Mgmt, 1100 Glendon Ave, #2000, Los Angeles CA 90024 USA

**Valuev, Nikolai** — Boxer
Box-Way, Zaharyevskaya Ul 12, 191123 Saint Petersburg, Russia

**Valverde, Maria** — Actress
Tavistock Wood Mgmt, 45 Conduit St, London W1S 2YN, England

**Van, Lindsey** — Ski Jumper
1600 Pinebrook Blvd, #H3, Park City UT 84098, USA

**VanAcker, Drew** — Actor
Greene Assoc, 1901 Ave of Stars, #130, Los Angeles CA 90067 USA

**VanAllsburg, Chris** — Artist, Writer
Scholastic Press, 555 Broadway, New York NY 10012 USA

**VanAlmsick, Franziska (Franzi)** — Swimmer
FvA, Pf 1280, 68755 Hockenheim, Germany

**VanAmerongen, Jerry** — Cartoonist (Neighborhood)
10926 Owensmouth Ave, Chatsworth CA 91311, USA

**VanAmstel, Louis** — Dancer, Choreographer
Jay D Schwartz Assoc, 3151 Cahuenga Blvd, #220, Los Angeles CA 90068, USA

**VanArk, Joan** — Actress
Don Buchwald, 6500 Wilshire Blvd, #2200, Los Angeles CA 90048 USA

**VanArsdale, Richard A (Dick)** — Basketball Player, Executive
5434 E Lincoln Dr, Paradise Valley AZ 85253, USA

**VanArsdale, Thomas A (Tom)** — Basketball Player
7510 N Eucalyptus Dr, Paradise Valley AZ 85253, USA

**Vanasse, Karine** — Actress
W M E Entertainment, 9601 Wilshire Blvd, #300, Beverly Hills CA 90210 USA

**VanBenschoten, John** — Baseball Player
5918 Milburne Dr, Milford OH 45150, USA

**VanBerg, John C (Jack)** — Thoroughbred Racing Trainer
420 Fair Hill Dr, #1, Elkton MD 21921, USA

**VanBerkel, Bernard F (Ben)** — Architect
U N Studio, Stradhouderskade 113, 1073 AX Amsterdam NH, Netherlands

**Vanbiesbrouck, John** — Ice Hockey Player
67960 Campground Road, Washington MI 48095, USA

**VanBoxmeer, John M** — Ice Hockey Player
8033 E Santa Cruz Ave, Orange CA 92869, USA

**VanBrabant, C Oscar (Ozzie)** — Baseball Player
5389 William Dr, Lexington MI 48450, USA

**VanBreda Kolff, Jan M** — Basketball Player, Coach
1102 French Town Lane, Franklin TN 37067, USA

**VanCamp, Emily** — Actress
Thruline Entertainment, 9250 Wilshire Blvd, #100, Beverly Hills CA 90212 USA

**Vance, Courtney B** — Actor
Lighthouse Entertainment, 9220 Sunset Blvd, #200, West Hollywood CA 90069, USA

**Vance, Eric D** — Football Player
17613 Archland Pass Road, Lutz FL 33558, USA

**Vance, G Christopher (Chris)** — Actor
Paradigm Agency, 360 N Crescent Dr, North Building, Beverly Hills CA 90210 USA

**Vance, Gene C (Sandy)** — Baseball Player
5863 Chelton Dr, Oakland CA 94611, USA

**Vance, Kenny** — Singer (Jay & the Americans)
Perfect Impressions Entertainment, 154 Seminole Dr, Springfield IL 62704, USA

**VanCitters, Robert L** — Physiologist, Biophysicist
University of Washington Medical School, Physiology Dept, Seattle WA 98815, USA

**VanClief, D G** — Thoroughbred Racing Executive
Breeders' Cup Ltd, 2525 Harrodsburg Road, #500, Lexington KY 40504, USA

**Van-Culin, Samuel** — Religious Leader
16A Burgate, Canterbury CT1 2HG, England

**VanDam, Jose** — Opera Singer
Zurich Artists, Rutistr 52, 8044 Zurich-Gockhausen, Switzerland

**VandeBerg, Edward J (Ed)** — Baseball Player
4903 S Meadows Place, Chandler AZ 85248, USA

**VandenBerg, Lodewijk** — Astronaut
Constellation Technology Corp, 7887 Bryan Dairy Road, #100, Seminole FL 33777, USA

**VandenBergh, Maarten A** — Businessman
Lloyds T S B Group, 71 Lombard St, London EC3P 3BS, England

**VandenBosch, Kyle D** — Football Player
2331 E Cedar Place, Chandler AZ 85249, USA

**Vandenbussche, Ryan** — Ice Hockey Player
RE/Max Erie Shores Realty, 103 Queensway East, Simco ON N3Y 4M5, Canada

**VanDenHeuvel, Carlien** — Field Hockey Player
Stichtsche Cricket-en Hockeyclub, Postbus 72, 3720 Bilthoven BA, Netherlands

**VanDenHoogenband, Pieter** — Swimmer
PO Box 302, 6800 Arnhem AH, Netherlands

**Vander, Musetta** — Actress
David Shapira Assoc, 193 N Robertson Blvd, Beverly Hills CA 90211 USA

**VanderArk, Brad** — Bassist (Verve Pipe)
Artist in Mind, 14100 Dickens St, #2, Sherman Oaks CA 91423, USA

**VanderArk, Brian** — Singer, Guitarist (Verve Pipe)
Artist in Mind, 14100 Dickens St, #2, Sherman Oaks CA 91423, USA

**VanDerBeek, James** — Actor
Paradigm Agency, 360 N Crescent Dr, North Building, Beverly Hills CA 90210 USA

**Vanderbeek, Matthew J (Matt)** — Football Player
54 Endless Vista, Aliso Viejo CA 92656, USA

**Vanderberg Shaw, Helen** — Synchronized Swimming Coach
Heaven's Fitness, 301 14th St NW, Calgary AB T2N 2A1, Canada

**VanderBerge, Camille** — Sculptor
Solomon Dubnick Gallery, 1017 25th St, Sacramento CA 95816, USA

| | |
|---|---|
| **Vanderbundt, William G (Skip)**<br>4225 Los Coches Way, Sacramento CA 95864, USA | Football Player |
| **Vanderham, Joanna**<br>W M E Entertainment, 9601 Wilshire Blvd, #300, Beverly Hills CA 90210 USA | Actress |
| **VanDerham, Katarina**<br>PO Box 64666, Los Angeles CA 90064, USA | Model |
| **Vanderhoef, Larry N**<br>615 Francisco Place, Davis CA 95616, USA | Educator |
| **Vanderjagt, Michael J (Mike)**<br>631 Lewis Court, Marco Island FL 34145, USA | Football Player |
| **Vanderkaay, Peter**<br>5787 Bewster Road, Rochester MI 48306, USA | Swimmer |
| **Vanderkelen, Ronald (Ron)**<br>5300 Vernon Ave S, #307, Minneapolis MN 55436, USA | Football Player |
| **Vanderloo, Mark**<br>Wilhelmina Models, 300 Park Ave S, #200, New York NY 10010 USA | Model |
| **Vandermeersch, Bernard**<br>University of Bordeaux, Anthropology Dept, Bordeaux, France | Anthropologist |
| **VanderPoel, J Mark**<br>14760 Ave 208, Tulare CA 93274, USA | Football Player |
| **VanDerPol, Anneliese**<br>Gage Group, 14724 Ventura Blvd, #505, Sherman Oaks CA 91403 USA | Actress |
| **Vanderpool, Clare**<br>Random House, 1745 Broadway, #1800, New York NY 10019 USA | Writer |
| **VanDerRym, Sim**<br>Ecological Design Institute, PO Box 858, Inverness CA 94937, USA | Architect, Designer |
| **Vanderveen, Loet**<br>Lime Creek 5, Big Sur CA 93920, USA | Sculptor |
| **VanDerveer, Tara**<br>1036 Cascade Dr, Menlo Park CA 94025, USA | Basketball Coach |
| **VanDerWal, Frederique**<br>Innovative Artists, 1505 10th St, Santa Monica CA 90401 USA | Model |
| **VanderWal, John H**<br>5142 Abbeydale Dr SW, Grand Rapids MI 49546, USA | Baseball Player |
| **VanDerWee, Herman F A**<br>Ettingenstraat 10, 9170 Saint-Pauwels, Belgium | Historian |
| **Vanderzalm, Bas**<br>Medical Teams International, 14150 SW Milton Court, Portland OR 97224, USA | Association Executive |
| **VandeSande, Theo A**<br>Innovative Artists, 1505 10th St, Santa Monica CA 90401 USA | Cinematographer |
| **VandeVen, Monique**<br>9255 W Sunset Blvd, #505, West Hollywood CA 90069, USA | Actress, Director |
| **VandeWeghe, Albert**<br>7712 W Skyline Dr, Tulsa OK 74107, USA | Swimmer |
| **Vandeweghe, Ernest E (Ernie)**<br>PO Box 3006, Englewood CO 80155, USA | Basketball Player, Physician |
| **Vandeweghe, Ernest M (Kiki)**<br>PO Box 3006, Englewood CO 80155, USA | Basketball Player, Coach, Executive |
| **VandeWetering, John E**<br>29 Brickstone Circle, Rochester NY 14620, USA | Educator |
| **VanDien, Casper**<br>A P A Talent/Literary Agency, 405 S Beverly Dr, #300, Beverly Hills CA 90212 USA | Actor |
| **VanDoren, Mamie**<br>3419 Via Lido, #184, Newport Beach CA 92663, USA | Actress, Dancer, Model |
| **VanDorp, Wayne**<br>380 Laurentian Crescent, Coquitlam BC V3K 1Y5, Canada | Ice Hockey Player |
| **VanDusen, Frederick W (Fred)**<br>331 Gillette Dr, Franklin TN 37069, USA | Baseball Player |
| **VanDusen, Granville**<br>10974 Alta View Dr, Studio City CA 91604, USA | Actor |
| **VanDuyne, Robert S (Bob)**<br>1810 Douglas Ave, Clearwater FL 33755, USA | Football Player |
| **VanDyke, Bruce R**<br>143 Lakeview Dr, Canonsburg PA 15317, USA | Football Player |
| **VanDyke, Dick**<br>23215 Mariposa de Oro, Malibu CA 90265, USA | Actor |
| **VanDyke, F Alexander (Alex)**<br>8338 Sea Island Court, Elk Grove CA 95758, USA | Football Player |
| **VanDyke, Jerry**<br>J Cast Productions, 2550 Greenvalley Road, Los Angeles CA 90046, USA | Actor, Comedian |
| **VanDyke, Leroy F**<br>Leroy Van Dyke Enterprises, 29000 Highway V, Smithton MO 65350, USA | Singer |
| **VanDyke, Milton D**<br>Stanford University, Applied Mechanics Dept, Stanford CA 94305, USA | Aeronautical Engineer |
| **VanDyke, Philip**<br>1464 Madera Road, #108N, Simi Valley CA 93065, USA | Actor |
| **VanDyke, William G**<br>Donaldson Co, 1400 W 94th St, Minneapolis MN 55431, USA | Businessman |
| **VanDyken Rouen, Amy**<br>20343 N Hayden Road, #105, Scottsdale AZ 85255, USA | Swimmer, Sportscaster |
| **VanEeghen, Mark K**<br>90 Woodstock Lane, Cranston RI 02920, USA | Football Player |
| **VanEgmond, Timothy L (Tim)**<br>8839 Callaway Road, Gay GA 30218, USA | Baseball Player |
| **Vanek, John**<br>9th St, RD 1, Nesquehoning PA 18240, USA | Basketball Referee |
| **Vanek, Thomas**<br>9131 Curry Lane, Clarence Center NY 14032, USA | Ice Hockey Player |
| **Vaness, Carol**<br>I C M Artists, 40 W 57th St, #1800, New York NY 10019 USA | Opera Singer |
| **Vanessa-Mae**<br>PO Box 363, Bournmouth, Dorset BH7 6LA, England | Singer, Concert Violinist |
| **VanEvery, John**<br>555 Dixon Dr, Brandon MS 39047, USA | Baseball Player |
| **VanExcel, Nicky M (Nick)**<br>3102 Noble Lakes Lane, Houston TX 77082, USA | Basketball Player |

**V**

Vanderbundt - VanExcel

# V

**VanFraasen, Bastiaan C** — Philosopher
1347 Curtis St, Berkeley CA 94702, USA

**VanGaalen, Chad** — Musician
Agency Group Ltd, 142 W 57th St, #600, New York NY 10019 USA

**Vangelis** — Composer
Robert Urband Assoc, 8981 W Sunset Blvd, #311, West Hollywood CA 90069, USA

**Vangen, Scott D** — Astronaut
N A S A, Johnson Space Center, 2101 NASA Road, Houston TX 77058 USA

**Vangorder, David T (Dave)** — Baseball Player
212 Black Eagle Ave, Henderson NV 89002, USA

**VanGorp, Michele** — Basketball Player
Minnesota Lynx, Target Center, 600 1st Ave N, Minneapolis MN 55403 USA

**VanGrunsven, Theodora E G (Anky)** — Equestrian
Bonengang 1, 5421 BZ Gemert, Netherlands

**Vangsness, Kirsten** — Actress
Abrams Artists, 9200 W Sunset Blvd, #1125, West Hollywood CA 90069 USA

**VanGundy, Jeff** — Basketball Coach, Sportscaster
W M E Entertainment, 9601 Wilshire Blvd, #300, Beverly Hills CA 90210 USA

**VanGundy, Stan** — Basketball Coach
Orlando Magic, 8701 Maitland Summit Blvd, Orlando FL 32810 USA

**VanHalen, Alex** — Drummer (Van Halen)
12024 Summit Circle, Beverly Hills CA 90210, USA

**VanHalen, Eddie** — Singer, Guitarist (Van Halen)
20411 Chapter Dr, Woodland Hills CA 91364, USA

**VanHalen, Wolfgang** — Singer, Guitarist
Jackoway Tyerman Wertheimer, 1925 Century Park E, #2200, Los Angeles CA 90067 USA

**VanHamel, Martine** — Ballerina
290 Riverside Dr, New York NY 10025, USA

**VanHeek, Margaret** — Chemist
Schering-Plough Research, 2000 Galloping Hill Road, Kenilworth NJ 07033, USA

**VanHelden, Armand** — Music Producer
Ministry of Sound, 103 Grant St, London SE1 6DP, England

**VanHellmond, Andy** — Ice Hockey Referee
71 Hyde Road, Stratford ON N5A 7Z3, Canada

**VanHeusen, William P (Billy)** — Football Player
835 Hudson St, Denver CO 80220, USA

**VanHoften, James C D A** — Astronaut
Bechtel National Inc, 50 Beale St, San Francisco CA 94105, USA

**VanHolde, Kensal E** — Biochemist
229 NW 32nd St, Corvallis OR 97330, USA

**VanHolt, Brian** — Actor
Paradigm Agency, 360 N Crescent Dr, North Building, Beverly Hills CA 90210 USA

**VanHorn, Buddy** — Director
4409 Ponca Ave, Toluca Lake CA 91602, USA

**VanHorn, Christian** — Opera Singer
Opus 3 Artists, 470 Park Ave S, #900N, New York NY 10016 USA

**VanHorn, Douglas C (Doug)** — Football Player
149 Feronia Way, Rutherford NJ 07070, USA

**VanHorn, Patrick** — Actor
Brillstein Entertainment Partners, 9150 Wilshire Blvd, #350, Beverly Hills CA 90212 USA

**VanHorne, Keith** — Football Player
680 Thornmeadow Road, Riverwoods IL 60015, USA

**VanHouten, Carice** — Actress
Troika, 74 Clerkenwell Road, #300, London EC1M 5QA, England

**VanHoy, Jay** — Producer
Parts & Labor, 177 N 10th St, #F, Brooklyn NY 11211, USA

**Vanhoye, Albert Cardinal** — Religious Leader
Biblical Commission, Borgo S Spirito 4, CP 6139, 00195 Roma-Prati, Italy

**Vanian, David (Dave)** — Singer (Damned)
Leave Home Booking, 10 W Broadway, #608, Salt Lake City UT 84101, USA

**Vanilla Ice** — Rap Artist, Actor
T Q Mgmt, 2412 Piedra Dr, Plano TX 75023, USA

**VanImpe, Ed C** — Ice Hockey Player
849 Streams Dr, West Chester PA 19382, USA

**Vanity** — Singer, Actress, Model
39279 Paseo Padre Parkway, #214, Fremont CA 94538, USA

**VanKooten, Katie** — Opera Singer
I M G Artists, Hogarth Business Park, Chiswick, London W4 2TH, England

**VanLandingham, William J** — Baseball Player
3023 Old Hillsboro Road, Franklin TN 37064, USA

**VanLiere, Donna** — Writer
Saint Martin's Press, 175 5th Ave, #400, New York NY 10010 USA

**VanLyck, Henry** — Actor
Z B F Agentur, Friedrichstr 39, 10969 Berlin, Germany

**Vannelli, Gino** — Singer, Songwriter
McLachland Management International, 2821 Bransford Ave, Nashville TN 37204, USA

**VanNistelrooy, Ruud** — Soccer Player
F C Real Madrid, Avda Concha Espana 1, 28036 Madrid, Spain

**Vannoni, Dina Marue** — Model
PO Box 473, Chino CA 91708, USA

**VanNote, Jeffrey A (Jeff)** — Football Player
345 Hollyberry Dr, Roswell GA 30076, USA

**Vannucci, Ronnie, Jr** — Drummer (Killers)
W M E Entertainment, 9601 Wilshire Blvd, #300, Beverly Hills CA 90210 USA

**Vanocur, Sander** — Commentator
C E S D, 10635 Santa Monica Blvd, #130, Los Angeles CA 90025 USA

**Vanous, Lucky** — Model, Actor
28345 La Calenta, Mission Viejo CA 92692, USA

**VanOuten, Denise** — Actress
Artist Rights Group, 4 Great Portland St, London W1W 8PA, England

**Vanover, Larry W** — Baseball Umpire
3037 Sterling Court, Owensboro KY 42303, USA

**Vanover, Tamarick T** — Football Player
703 NW Wilson St, Lake City FL 32055, USA

**VanPatten, Dick** — Actor
13920 Magnolia Blvd, Sherman Oaks CA 91423, USA

**V**

|  |  |
|------|-----------|
| **VanPatten, Joyce** | Actress |
| S M S Talent, 8383 Wilshire Blvd, #230, Beverly Hills CA 90211 USA | |
| **VanPatten, Nels** | Actor |
| 12439 Magnolia Blvd, #197, Valley Village CA 91607, USA | |
| **VanPatten, Timothy** | Actor, Director |
| Creative Artists Agency, 2000 Ave of Stars, #100, Los Angeles CA 90067 USA | |
| **VanPatten, Vincent** | Actor |
| Michael Slessinger, 8730 W Sunset Blvd, #220W, West Hollywood CA 90069 USA | |
| **VanPeebles, Mario** | Actor, Director |
| Don Buchwald, 6500 Wilshire Blvd, #2200, Los Angeles CA 90048 USA | |
| **VanPeebles, Melvin** | Director, Writer |
| 353 W 56th St, #10F, New York NY 10019, USA | |
| **VanPelt, Bo** | Golfer |
| 3025 Backmeyer Road, Richmond IN 47374, USA | |
| **VanPelt, G Alexander (Alex)** | Football Player |
| 120 Ford City Road, Freeport PA 16229, USA | |
| **VanPoppel, Todd M** | Baseball Player |
| 340 Springfield Bend, Argyle TX 76226, USA | |
| **VanPraagh, James** | Actor, Producer |
| Special Artists Agency, 9200 Sunset Blvd, #410, West Hollywood CA 90069 USA | |
| **VanRensselaer, Miles** | Artist |
| 1352-54 River Road, Lopatcong NJ 08865, USA | |
| **VanRiper, Paul K** | Marine Corps General |
| Marine Corps Heritage Foundation, PO Box 998, 307 5th Ave, Quantico VA 22134, USA | |
| **VanRompuy, Herman A** | Prime Minister, Belgium |
| European Council, Rue de la Loi 175, 1048 Brussels, Belgium | |
| **VanRyn, Benjamin A (Ben)** | Baseball Player |
| 8911 Saddle Trail, San Antonio TX 78255, USA | |
| **VanRyn, Mike** | Ice Hockey Player |
| 17681 SW 54th St, Southwest Ranches FL 33331, USA | |
| **VanSant, Gus G, Jr** | Director |
| W M E Entertainment, 9601 Wilshire Blvd, #300, Beverly Hills CA 90210 USA | |
| **VanSanten, Shantel** | Actress, Model |
| Leverage Mgmt, 3030 Pennsylvania Ave, Santa Monica CA 90404 USA | |
| **VanScott, Eugene J** | Dermatologist |
| 3 Hidden Lane, Abington PA 19001, USA | |
| **VanSickle, Craig W** | Writer, Producer, Director |
| Paradigm Agency, 360 N Crescent Dr, North Building, Beverly Hills CA 90210 USA | |
| **Vanska, Osmo** | Conductor |
| Minnesota Symphony, Orchestra Hall, 1111 Nicollet Mall, Minneapolis MN 55403, USA | |
| **VanSlyke, Andrew J (Andy)** | Baseball Player |
| 710 S Price Road, Saint Louis MO 63124, USA | |
| **Vanstone, Ellen** | Producer |
| Alpern Group, 15645 Royal Oak Road, Encino CA 91436, USA | |
| **VanSusteren, Greta** | Commentator |
| Fox-TV, News Dept, 5151 Wisconsin Ave NW, #100, Washington DC 20016 USA | |
| **VanUmmerson, Claire A** | Educator |
| Cleveland State University, President's Office, Cleveland OH 44115, USA | |
| **VanValkenburgh, Deborah** | Actress |
| Beth Stein Assoc, 920 Abbot Kinney Blvd, Venice CA 90291, USA | |
| **VanVooren, Monique** | Actress |
| 165 E 66th St, New York NY 10065, USA | |
| **VanWachem, Loedwijk C** | Businessman |
| Royal Dutch Petroleum, 30 Van Bylandtaan, 2596 The Hague HR, Netherlands | |
| **VanWageningen, Yorick** | Actor |
| Conway Van Gelder Grant, 8-12 Broadwick St, #300, London W1F 8HW, England | |
| **VanWagner, James P (Jimmy)** | Football Player |
| 5246 N Royal Dr, Traverse City MI 49684, USA | |
| **VanWormer, Steve** | Actor |
| Vox Inc, 6420 Wilshire Blvd, #1080, Los Angeles CA 90048 USA | |
| **VanWyngarden, Andrew** | Singer, Guitarist, Pianist (MGMT) |
| Paradigm Agency, 404 W Franklin St, Monterey CA 93940 USA | |
| **VanZandt, Steven** | Guitarist, Actor |
| Renegade Nation Holdings, 434 Ave of Americas, #6R, New York NY 10011, USA | |
| **VanZant, Donnie** | Singer (Lynyrd Skynyrd, .38 Special) |
| Vector Mgmt, PO Box 120479, Nashville TN 37212 USA | |
| **VanZant, Johnny** | Singer (Lynyrd Skynyrd), Songwriter |
| Vector Mgmt, PO Box 120479, Nashville TN 37212 USA | |
| **VanZweden, Jaap** | Conductor |
| I M G Artists, Hogarth Business Park, Chiswick, London W4 2TH, England | |
| **Varad'a, Vaclav** | Ice Hockey Player |
| 9042 Stonebriar Dr, Clarence Center NY 14032, USA | |
| **Varadhan, Srinivasa S R** | Abel Mathematics Laureate |
| New York University, Courant Institute, 251 Mercer St, New York NY 10012, USA | |
| **Varady, Julia** | Opera Singer |
| Hanns Eisler Musik Hochschule, Charlottenstra 55, 10117 Berlin, Germany | |
| **Varda, Agnes** | Director |
| Cine-Tamaris, 86-88 Rue Daguerre, 75014 Paris, France | |
| **Vardalos, Nia** | Actress, Writer |
| Untitled Entertainment, 350 S Beverly Dr, #200, Beverly Hills CA 90212 USA | |
| **Vardell, Thomas A (Tommy)** | Football Player |
| 2424 E Ruby Hill Dr, Pleasanton CA 94566, USA | |
| **Varejao, Anderson F** | Basketball Player |
| Cleveland Cavaliers, Gund Arena, 1 Center Court, Cleveland OH 44115 USA | |
| **Varekova, Veronica** | Model |
| Next Model Mgmt, 9 Boul de la Madeleine, 75001 Paris, France | |
| **Varela, Fernando** | Singer |
| Mascioli Entertainment, 2202 Curry Ford Road, #E, Orlando FL 32806, USA | |
| **Varela, Leonor** | Actress |
| Kritzer Levine Wilkins Griffin, 11872 La Grange Ave, #100, Los Angeles CA 90025 USA | |
| **Varga, Imre** | Sculptor |
| Bartha Utca 1, 1126 Budapest XII, Hungary | |
| **Vargas Llosa, Mario** | Nobel Literature Laureate |
| Las Magnolias 295, 6 Piso, Barranco, Lima 4, Peru | |
| **Vargas, Devin** | Boxer |
| Star Boxing, 991 Morris Park Ave, Bronx NY 10462, USA | |

**VanPatten - Vargas**

# V

**Vargas, Elizabeth** — Commentator
ABC-TV, News Dept, 77 W 66th St, New York NY 10023 USA

**Vargas, Fernando** — Boxer
1695 Mesa Verde Ave, #220, Ventura CA 93003, USA

**Vargas, Ieda Maria** — Beauty Queen
Miss Universe Organization, 1370 Ave of Americas, #1600, New York NY 10019 USA

**Vargas, Jacob** — Actor
Paradigm Agency, 360 N Crescent Dr, North Building, Beverly Hills CA 90210 USA

**Vargas, Jason M** — Baseball Player
14775 Keota Lane, Apple Valley CA 92307, USA

**Vargas, Jay R** — Vietnam War Marine Corps Hero (CMH)
12466 Thornbush Court, San Diego CA 92131, USA

**Vargo, Tim** — Businessman
AutoZone Inc, 123 S Front St, Memphis TN 38103, USA

**Varitek, Jason A** — Baseball Player
PO Box 669, Suwanee GA 30024, USA

**Varlamarv, Sergei** — Ice Hockey Player
213 Germain St, Saint John NB E2L 2G5, Canada

**Varma, Indira** — Actress
Gordon & French, 12-13 Poland St, London W1F 8QB, England

**Varmus, Harold E** — Nobel Medicine Laureate
1 Gracie Square, #1E, New York NY 10028, USA

**Varney, Carleton B, Jr** — Interior Designer
Dorothy Draper Co, 60 E 56th St, #1000, New York NY 10022, USA

**Varney, Richard F (Pete)** — Baseball Player
14 Juniper Ridge Road, Acton MA 01720, USA

**Varon, Lisa Marie** — Model
131 Promenade Court, Louisville KY 40223, USA

**Varrela, Leonor** — Actress
Kritzer Levine Wilkins Griffin, 11872 La Grange Ave, #100, Los Angeles CA 90025 USA

**Varrichone, Frank J** — Football Player
26 Coffin Brook Road, Alton NH 03809, USA

**Varshavsky, Alexander** — Cell Biologist
California Institute of Technology, Cell Biology Dept, Pasadena CA 91125, USA

**Varsho, Gary A** — Baseball Player, Manager
11921 Starr Road, Chili WI 54420, USA

**Vartan, Michael** — Actor
Thruline Entertainment, 9250 Wilshire Blvd, #100, Beverly Hills CA 90212 USA

**Vartan, Sylvie** — Singer
Artmedia, 20 Ave Rapp, 75007 Paris, France

**Varty, Keith** — Fashion Designer
Bosco di San Francesco #6, 60020 Sirolo, Italy

**Varvatos, John** — Fashion Designer
Soho New York, 149 Mercer St, New York NY 10012, USA

**Varvel, Gary** — Editorial Cartoonist
PO Box 1121, Brownsburg IN 46112, USA

**Vasary, Tamas** — Concert Pianist, Conductor
Magyar Radio Zenekari Iroda, Brody Sandor Utica 5, 1800 Budapest, Hungary

**Vasconcellos Ferreira, Gabriel** — Soccer Player
F C Milan, Via Filippo Turati 3, 20121 Milan, Italy

**Vasconcellos, Martha M C** — Beauty Queen
2 Oak Terrace, #4, Somerville MA 02143, USA

**Vasgersian, Matt** — Sportscaster
7211 Eads Ave, La Jolla CA 92037, USA

**Vasher, Nathaniel D (Nathan)** — Football Player
1850 N Sawgrass St, Vernon Hills IL 60061, USA

**Vasilyev, Vladimir V** — Ballet Dancer, Executive
Smolenskaya Naberezhnaya 5/13 62, 121099 Moscow, Russia

**Vaske, Dennis J** — Ice Hockey Player
9750 Crescent Park Circle, #119, Orland Park IL 60462, USA

**Vasquez Rana, Mario** — Publisher
El Sol de Mexico, Guillermo Prieto 7, Cuauhtemoc DF 06470, Mexico

**Vasquez Rodríguez, Greivis J** — Basketball Player
Sacramento Kings, Arco Arena, 1 Sports Parkway, Sacramento CA 95834 USA

**Vasquez, Jacinto** — Thoroughbred Racing Jockey
4449 18th Terrace, Ocala FL 34479, USA

**Vasquez, Junior** — DJ Musician
Coast II Coast Entertainment, 3350 Wilshire Blvd, #1200, Los Angeles CA 90010, USA

**Vasquez, Wilfredo** — Boxer
Call 1 D-3, Urb San Fernando, Bayamon PR 00957, USA

**Vassar, Phil** — Singer, Songwriter
Red Light Mgmt, PO Box 159310, Nashville TN 37215, USA

**Vasser, Jimmy** — Auto Racing Driver
8605 Robinson Ridge Dr, Las Vegas NV 89117, USA

**Vassiliev, Oleg** — Artist
Neil K Rector, 172 E State St, #305, Columbus OH 43215, USA

**Vassilieva, Sofia** — Actress
Brillstein Entertainment Partners, 9150 Wilshire Blvd, #350, Beverly Hills CA 90212 USA

**Vassiliou, George V** — President, Cyprus
PO Box 874, 21 Academiou Ave, Aglandjia, Nicosia, Cyprus

**Vasyuchenko, Yuri** — Ballet Dancer
Bolshoi Theater, Teatralnaya Pl 1, 103009 Moscow, Russia

**Vasyutin, Vladimir V** — Cosmonaut
Cosmonaut Training Center, Star City, 141160 Zvezdny Gorodok, Moscow Oblast, Russia

**Vataha, Randel E (Randy)** — Football Player
36 Longmeadow Road, Lincoln MA 01773, USA

**Vatcher, James E (Jim)** — Baseball Player
16039 Northfield St, Pacific Palisades CA 90272, USA

**Vatchkov, Deyan** — Opera Singer
I M G Artists, Hogarth Business Park, Chiswick, London W4 2TH, England

**Vaughan, Greg** — Actor
Abrams Artists, 9200 W Sunset Blvd, #1125, West Hollywood CA 90069 USA

**Vaughan, Jimmie L** — Guitarist (Fabulous Thunderbirds)
Luther Wolf Agency, PO Box 685138, Austin TX 78768, USA

**Vaughan, Martha** — Biochemist
11351 Woodglen Dr, #501, Rockville MD 20852, USA

**Vargas - Vaughan**

**Vaughan, Peter** — Actor
Independent Talent Group, 40 Whitfield St, London W1T 2RH, England
**Vaughan, Tom** — Director, Writer
United Agents, 12-26 Lexington St, London W1F 0LE, England
**Vaughn, Ben** — Singer, Songwriter, Guitarist
Cross Road Mgmt, 45 W 11th St, #7B, New York NY 10011, USA
**Vaughn, Bruce** — Golfer
5615 N Monroe St, Hutchinson KS 67502, USA
**Vaughn, Clyde** — Army General
Director, Army National Guard, HqUSA, Pentagon, Washington DC 20310, USA
**Vaughn, Gregory L (Greg)** — Baseball Player
10830 Sheldon Woods Way, Elk Grove CA 95624, USA
**Vaughn, Jacque** — Basketball Player, Coach
715 Coving Court, Lawrence KS 66049, USA
**Vaughn, Jimmie** — Guitarist
Artemis Records, 130 5th Ave, #7, New York NY 10011, USA
**Vaughn, Matthew** — Director, Producer, Actor
Independent Talent Group, 40 Whitfield St, London W1T 2RH, England
**Vaughn, Maurice John** — Singer, Guitarist, Saxophonist
Jay Reil Assoc, 3430 Bayberry Dr, Northbrook IL 60062, USA
**Vaughn, Maurice S (Mo)** — Baseball Player
5455 Rings Road, #100, Dublin OH 43017, USA
**Vaughn, Robert** — Actor
68 Salem View Dr, Ridgefield CT 06877, USA
**Vaughn, Thomas R (Tom)** — Football Player
860 E Linda Lane, Gilbert AZ 85234, USA
**Vaughn, Tichina** — Opera Singer
I M G Artists, Hogarth Business Park, Chiswick, London W4 2TH, England
**Vaughn, Vince** — Actor
Wild West Picture Show Productions, 1210 N La Brea Ave, West Hollywood CA 90038, USA
**Vaught, Loy S** — Basketball Player
838 Andover Court SE, Grand Rapids MI 49508, USA
**Vaugier, Emmanuelle** — Actress
A P A Talent/Literary Agency, 405 S Beverly Dr, #300, Beverly Hills CA 90212 USA
**Vaupen, Drew** — Producer, Writer
I C M Partners, 10250 Constellation Blvd, #900, Los Angeles CA 90067 USA
**Vavakin, Leonid V** — Architect
Academy of Architecture, Dmitrova Str 24, 103874 Moscow, Russia
**Vavasseur, Sophie** — Actress
Troika, 74 Clerkenwell Road, #300, London EC1M 5QA, England
**Vayda, Brandon Michael** — Actor
Stone Manners Salners, 9911 W Pico Blvd, #1400, Los Angeles CA 90035 USA
**Vaydik, Gregory (Greg)** — Ice Hockey Player
6041 Village Bend Dr, #1007, Dallas TX 75206, USA
**Vazquez Rosas, Tabare R** — President, Uruguay
Chacra El Paso de la Arena, Montevideo, Uruguay
**Vazquez, Javier C** — Baseball Player
1441 S Prairie Ave, Chicago IL 60605, USA
**Veal, Orville I (Coot)** — Baseball Player
238 Stone Gables Dr, Gray GA 31032, USA
**Veale, Robert A (Bob)** — Baseball Player
2833 Bush Blvd, Birmingham AL 35208, USA
**Veals, Elton A** — Football Player
2981 Joyce Dr, Baton Rouge LA 70814, USA
**Veasey, Josephine** — Opera Singer
5 Meadow View, Whitechurch, Hantsfordshire RG28 7BL, England
**Veasley, Gerald** — Jazz Guitarist
Universal Attractions, 135 W 26th St, #1200, New York NY 10001 USA
**Veber, Francis P** — Director
Artmedia, 20 Ave Rapp, 75007 Paris, France
**Vecchione, Mike** — Marine Scientist
National Oceanic/Atmospheric Admin, 14th St & Constitution Ave, Washington DC 20230, USA
**Vecsei, Eva H** — Architect
4417 Circle Road, Montreal QC H3W 1Y6, Canada
**Vecsey, George S** — Sportswriter
New York Times, Editorial Dept, 229 W 43rd St, New York NY 10036, USA
**Vedder, Ed (Eddie)** — Singer (Pearl Jam), Songwriter
Curtis Mgmt, 1900 S Corgiat Dr, Seattle WA 98108, USA
**Vedernikov, Alexander** — Conductor
Askonas Holt, Lincoln House, 300 High Holborn, London WC1V 7JH, England
**Vee, Bobby** — Singer, Songwriter
Rockhouse Mgmt, PO Box 757, Saint Joseph MN 56374, USA
**Vega Polanco, Amelia** — Beauty Queen, Actress
Trump Model Agency, 91 5th Ave, #300, New York NY 10003 USA
**Vega, Alan** — Singer (Suicide)
International Booking Dept, Bodenseestr 91, 81243 Munich, Germany
**Vega, Alexa** — Actress
John Carrabino Mgmt, 5900 Wilshire Blvd, #406, Los Angeles CA 90036 USA
**Vega, Laura P** — Actress
Jaime Ferrar Agency, 4741 Laurel Canyon Blvd, #110, Valley Village CA 91607, USA
**Vega, Paz** — Actress
B/W/R, 9100 Wilshire Blvd, #500W, Beverly Hills CA 90212 USA
**Vega, Suzanne N** — Singer, Songwriter
Michael Hausman Artists Mgmt, 511 Ave of Americas, #197, New York NY 10011, USA
**Vega, Tata** — Singer
Universal Attractions, 135 W 26th St, #1200, New York NY 10001 USA
**Vegas, Jhonattan** — Golfer
Professional Golfer's Assn, PO Box 109601, Palm Beach Gardens FL 33410 USA
**Veglio, Antonio M Cardinal** — Religious Leader
Pastorial Care of Migrants & Itinerant People, Piazza S Calisto 16, 00120 Vatican City
**Veiga, Carlos A Wahnon de C** — Prime Minister, Cape Verde
W V Consultants, CP43A Praia, Santiago, Cape Verde
**Veigel, Allen F (Al)** — Baseball Player
1907 Dover Ave, Dover OH 44622, USA
**Veihmeyer, John B** — Businessman
K P M G, 345 Park Ave, New York NY 10154, USA

**Veil, Simone** — Government Official, France
11 Place Vauban, 75007 Paris, France
**Veingard, Allen S** — Football Player
1940 NW 180th Way, Pembroke Pines FL 33029, USA
**Veirs, Laura** — Singer, Songwriter
Primary Talent International, 10-11 Jockey's Fields, London WC1R 4BN, England
**Veisor, Michael D (Mike)** — Ice Hockey Player
16091 W Lakepoint Court, Prairieville LA 70769, USA
**Veitch, Darren W** — Ice Hockey Player
3410 Maricopa Highway, Ojai CA 93023, USA
**Veitch, John M** — Thoroughbred Racing Trainer
Kentucky Horse Racing Authority, 4063 Ironwood Turnpike, Lexington KY 40511, USA
**Veitch, Tom** — Writer
PO Box 479, Lincoln City OR 97367, USA
**Vejar, Chico** — Boxer
8103 N Hollow, #313, San Antonio TX 78240, USA
**Vejtasa, Stanley W (Swede)** — WW II Navy Air Force Hero
1649 Summit Lane, Escondido CA 92025, USA
**Velan, Chris** — Singer, Songwriter
Agency Group Ltd, 142 W 57th St, #600, New York NY 10019 USA
**Velard, Julian** — Singer, Songwriter, Pianist
Agency Group Ltd, 142 W 57th St, #600, New York NY 10019 USA
**Velarde, Randy L** — Baseball Player
4902 Thames Court, Midland TX 79705, USA
**Velasquez, Jacquelyn D (Jaci)** — Singer
Breen Agency, 110 30th Ave N, #3, Nashville TN 37203, USA
**Velasquez, Jorge L, Jr** — Thoroughbred Racing Jockey
2701 Valentine Ave, #407, Bronx NY 14058, USA
**Velasquez, Patricia** — Model, Actress
A P A Talent/Literary Agency, 405 S Beverly Dr, #300, Beverly Hills CA 90212 USA
**Velazquez, Frederico A (Freddie)** — Baseball Player
Jose Amado Solier #70, Santo Domingo, Dominican Republic
**Velazquez, Nadine** — Actress
Kritzer Levine Wilkins Griffin, 11872 La Grange Ave, #100, Los Angeles CA 90025 USA
**Veldhuis, Magdalena J M (Marleen)** — Swimmer
Eiffel Swimming PSV, Het Lover 40, 5501 Veldhoven CR, Netherlands
**Velez, Eddie** — Actor
Stone Manners Salners, 9911 W Pico Blvd, #1400, Los Angeles CA 90035 USA
**Velez, Lauren** — Actress
T M T Entertainment Group, 648 Broadway, #1002, New York NY 10012, USA
**Velez, Natalia** — Model
Mega Models Miami, 420 Lincoln Road, Miami Beach FL 33139, USA
**Velgos, Alicia** — Actress
Advance L A, 77904 Santa Monica Blvd, #200, Los Angeles CA 90046, USA
**Velikhov, Yevgeni P** — Physicist
Kurchatovskiy Institute, Kurchatova Pl 1, 123182 Moscow, Russia
**Velischek, Randy** — Ice Hockey Player
22 Hemlock Lane, Kinnelon NJ 07405, USA
**Veljohnson, Reginald** — Actor, Writer
22309 Haynes St, Woodland Hills CA 91303, USA
**Vella, John A** — Football Player
1890 Saint George Road, Danville CA 94526, USA
**Vellucci, Mike** — Ice Hockey Player
17302 Cameron Dr, Northville MI 48168, USA
**Veloso, Caetano** — Singer, Guitarist, Songwriter
International Music Network, 278 Main St, #400, Gloucester MA 01930 USA
**Veloso, Moreno** — Singer, Songwriter
Luaka Bop, 195 Chrystie St, #901F, New York NY 10002, USA
**Veloz, David** — Director, Producer, Writer
Creative Artists Agency, 2000 Ave of Stars, #100, Los Angeles CA 90067 USA
**Velten, Andreas** — Optical Physicist
Morgridge Research Institute, PO Box 7667, Madison WI 53707, USA
**Veltman, Jim (Scoop)** — Lacrosse Player
Agincort Collegiate Institute, Athletic Dept, Toronto ON M1S 1R6, Canada
**Veltman, Martinus J G** — Nobel Physics Laureate
University of Michigan, Randall Laboratory, Ann Arbor MI 48109, USA
**Veltri, Rachel** — Actress, Model
Luber Rocklin Entertainment, 8530 Wilshire Blvd, #555, Beverly Hills CA 90211 USA
**Venable, W McKinley (Mac)** — Baseball Player
107 Clark St, San Rafael CA 94901, USA
**Venables, Terry F** — Soccer Coach
Terry Venables Holdings, 213 Putney Bridge Road, London SW15 2NY, England
**Venafro, Michael R (Mike)** — Baseball Player
15151 Whimbrel Court, Fort Myers FL 33908, USA
**Venasky, Vic** — Ice Hockey Player
4307 W 234th Place, Torrance CA 90505, USA
**Vendela** — Model
T R Management Group, 11740 Wilshire Blvd, #A2109, Los Angeles CA 90025, USA
**Vendler, Helen H** — Educator, Writer
54 Trowbridge St, #2, Cambridge MA 02138, USA
**Vendt, Erik** — Swimmer
17 Amberwood Court, Buzzards Bay MA 02532, USA
**Venegas, Julieta** — Singer, Songwriter, Actress
United Talent Agency, U T A Plaza, 9336 Civic Center Dr, Beverly Hills CA 90210 USA
**Veneruzzo, Gary** — Ice Hockey Player
185 Fanshaw St, Thunder Bay ON P7C 5T7, Canada
**Venet, Bernar** — Sculptor, Artist
145 Ave of Americas, #5C, New York NY 10013, USA
**Venetiaan, R Ronald** — President, Suriname
Presidential Palace, Onafhankelikheidsplein 1, Paramaribo, Suriname
**Vengerov, Maxim** — Concert Violinist
Columbia Artists Mgmt Inc, 1790 Broadway, #702, New York NY 10019 USA
**Venito, Lenny** — Actor
Paradigm Agency, 360 N Crescent Dr, North Building, Beverly Hills CA 90210 USA
**Venlet, David J** — Navy Admiral
Commander, Naval Air Systems Command, Patuxent River MD 20670 USA

**Venora, Diane** — Actress
Don Buchwald, 6500 Wilshire Blvd, #2200, Los Angeles CA 90048 USA
**Venter, J Craig** — Molecular Biologist
11210 S Glen Road, Potomac MD 20854, USA
**Venters, Jonathan W (Jonny)** — Baseball Player
Atlanta Braves, Turner Field, 755 Hank Aaron Dr, Atlanta GA 30315 USA
**Ventimiglia, John** — Actor
Paul Kohner, 9300 Wilshire Blvd, #555, Beverly Hills CA 90212 USA
**Ventimiglia, Milo** — Actor
Creative Artists Agency, 2000 Ave of Stars, #100, Los Angeles CA 90067 USA
**Ventresca, Vincent** — Actor
Thruline Entertainment, 9250 Wilshire Blvd, #100, Beverly Hills CA 90212 USA
**Ventura, Robin M** — Baseball Player
1088 Newsom Springs Road, Arroyo Grande CA 93420, USA
**Ventura-Merkel, Catherine** — Publisher
A A R P Magazine, Publisher's Office, 601 E St NW, Washington DC 20049, USA
**Venturella, Michelle** — Softball Player
Iowa University, 219 Carver Hawkeye Arena, Iowa City IA 52242, USA
**Venturi, Rick** — Football Coach
910 Banbury Road, Noblesville IN 46062, USA
**Venturi, Robert** — Pritzker Architectural Laureate
Venturi Scott Brown Assoc, 4236 Main St, Philadelphia PA 19127, USA
**Venturini, Tisha** — Soccer Player
7101 Del Rio Ave, Modesto CA 95356, USA
**Venzago, Mario** — Conductor
Indianapolis Symphony, 32 E Washington St, #600, Indianapolis IN 46204, USA
**Vera, Billy** — Singer, Songwriter, Actor
Sutton-Barth Vennari, 5900 Wilshire Blvd, #700, Los Angeles CA 90036 USA
**Veras, Jose E** — Baseball Player
Detroit Tigers, Comerica Park, 2100 Woodward Ave, Detroit MI 48201 USA
**Verba, Ross R** — Football Player
3066 Arden Place, Saint Paul MN 55129, USA
**Verbeek, Lotte** — Actress
Innovative Artists, 1505 10th St, Santa Monica CA 90401 USA
**Verbeek, Pat** — Ice Hockey Player
Verbeek Farm, RR 1, Wyoming ON N0N 1T0, Canada
**Verbinski, Gregor (Gore)** — Director, Writer, Animator
Anonymous Content, 3532 Hayden Ave, Culver City CA 90232 USA
**Verchota, Philip J (Phil)** — Ice Hockey Player
PO Box 1181, Bemidji MN 56619, USA
**Verdi, Bob** — Sportswriter
Chicago Tribune, Editorial Dept, 435 N Michigan Ave, #1, Chicago IL 60611, USA
**Verdi, Maria** — Actress
Artmedia, 20 Ave Rapp, 75007 Paris, France
**Verdin, Clarence** — Football Player
6221 Eastover Dr, New Orleans LA 70128, USA
**Verdugo, Elena** — Actress
PO Box 2048, Chula Vista CA 91912, USA
**Verdy, Violette** — Ballerina
2000 Broadway, #2B, New York NY 10023, USA
**Vereen, Ben** — Actor, Dancer, Singer
Talent Works, 3500 W Olive Ave, #1400, Burbank CA 91505 USA
**Veres, David S (Dave)** — Baseball Player
871 Diamond Ridge Circle, Castle Rock CO 80108, USA
**Vergara, Sofia** — Singer, Actress, Model
Creative Artists Agency, 2000 Ave of Stars, #100, Los Angeles CA 90067 USA
**Verghese, Abraham** — Writer
United Talent Agency, U T A Plaza, 9336 Civic Center Dr, Beverly Hills CA 90210 USA
**Verhagen, Eduard** — Pediatrician
Groningen University Medical Center, Pediatrics Dept, Hanzeplein 1, 9700 Groningen RB, Netherlands
**Verheiden, Mark** — Producer, Writer
Creative Artists Agency, 2000 Ave of Stars, #100, Los Angeles CA 90067 USA
**Verhoeven, Lis** — Actress
Agentur Doris Mattes, 14 Merzstr, 81679 Munich, Germany
**Verhoeven, Paul** — Director
Marion Rosenberg, PO Box 69826, West Hollywood CA 90069 USA
**Verhoeven, Peter G (Pete)** — Basketball Player
12722 Fargo Ave, Hanford CA 93230, USA
**Verica, Tom** — Actor
20 Ironsides St, #18, Marina del Rey CA 90292, USA
**Veris, Garin L** — Football Player
2 Christine Dr, Atkinson NH 03811, USA
**Verkaik, Petra** — Actress, Model
Playboy Promotions, 2706 Media Center Dr, Los Angeles CA 90065 USA
**Verlaine, Tom** — Singer, Bassist (Television)
High Road Touring, 751 Bridgeway, #200, Sausalito CA 94965 USA
**Verlander, Justin B** — Baseball Player
3928 Fairfax Dr, Troy MI 48083, USA
**Verma, Inder M** — Molecular Biologist
Salk Institute, 10100 N Torrey Pines Road, La Jolla CA 92037, USA
**Vermeij, Geerat J** — Evolutionary Biologist, Paleontologist
University of California, Geology Dept, Davis CA 95616, USA
**Vermeil, Richard A (Dick)** — Football Coach, Sportscaster
775 Fairview Road, Coatesville PA 19320, USA
**Vermes, Peter** — Soccer Player, Manager
Sporting Kansas City, 210 W 19th Terrace, #200, Kansas City MO 64108 USA
**Vermilyea, Jamie** — Baseball Player
7051 E Calle Arandas, Tucson AZ 85750, USA
**Vernarsky, Kris** — Ice Hockey Player
13192 Hunt Road, Riley MI 48041, USA
**Vernes, Edith** — Actress
Voyez Mon Agent, 20 Ave Rapp, 75007 Paris, France
**Vernon, Annie** — Rowing Athlete
Marlow Rowing Club, 17 Elizabeth Road, Marlow SL7 1RH, England
**Vernon, Conrad** — Director, Writer, Actor
United Talent Agency, U T A Plaza, 9336 Civic Center Dr, Beverly Hills CA 90210 USA

**V**

**Vernon, Kate** — Actress
Shelter Entertainment, 9255 Sunset Blvd, #300, Los Angeles CA 90069 USA

**Vernon, Mike** — Ice Hockey Player
Bear Mountain, 208-2800 Bryn Mawr Road, Victoria BC V9B 3T4, Canada

**Vernonesi, Alberto** — Conductor
I M G Artists, Hogarth Business Park, Chiswick, London W4 2TH, England

**Veroni, Craig** — Actor
Muse Artists, 401-207 W Hastings St, Vancouver BC V6B 1H7, Canada

**Veronica** — Singer, Actress
Nene Musik Productions, 1460 SW Santiago Ave, Port Saint Lucie FL 34953 USA

**Veronica, Mayra** — Model, Beauty Queen
Parallel Entertainment, 9420 Wilshire Blvd, #250, Beverly Hills CA 90212 USA

**Veronis, John J, Jr** — Publisher
Veronis Suhler Stevenson, 350 Park Ave, New York NY 10022, USA

**Verplank, Scott** — Golfer
1850 W Waterloo Road, Edmond OK 73025, USA

**Verraros, James C (Jim)** — Singer, Actor
Stiletto Entertainment, 8295 S La Cienega Blvd, Inglewood CA 90301, USA

**Verrell, Cec** — Actress
Michael Slessinger, 8730 W Sunset Blvd, #220W, West Hollywood CA 90069 USA

**Versace, Dick** — Basketball Coach
Memphis Grizzlies, 191 Beale St, Memphis TN 38103 USA

**Versace, Donatella** — Fashion Designer
Gianni Versace SpA, Via Manzoni 38, 20121 Milan, Italy

**Versaldi, Giuseppe Cardinal** — Religious Leader
Palazzo della Congregazioni, Largo del Colonnato 3, 00193 Rome, Italy

**Verser, David** — Football Player
21 Bellemonte Ave, Lakeside Park KY 41017, USA

**Versini, Marie** — Actress
23 Residence Elysses, 78170 La Celle-Saint Cloud, France

**Verveen, Arie** — Actor
Global Artists Agency, 6253 Hollywood Blvd, #508, Los Angeles CA 90028, USA

**Ververgaert, Dennis A** — Ice Hockey Player
34484 Stoneleigh Ave, Abbotsford BC V2S 8N5, Canada

**Verwaayen, Ben** — Businessman
Alcatel-Lucent, 54 Rue le Boetie, 75006 Paris, France

**Verwey, Bob** — Golfer
International Mangement Group, 1 Erieview Plaza, 1360 E 9th St, Cleveland OH 44114 USA

**Very, Charlotte** — Actress
Cineart, 28 Rue Mogador, 78009 Paris, France

**Veryzer, Thomas M (Tom)** — Baseball Player
41 Union Ave, Islip NY 11751, USA

**Vesely, Jan** — Baskeball Player
Washington Wizards, M C I Centre, 601 F St NW, Washington DC 20004 USA

**Vesey, Jim** — Ice Hockey Player
11 Ellwood St, Charlestown MA 02129, USA

**Vesser, Dale A** — Army General
1313 Merchant Lane, McLean VA 22101, USA

**Vessey, John W, Jr** — Army General
27650 Little Whitefish Road, Garrison MN 56450, USA

**Vessey, Tricia** — Actress, Director, Producer
Jackoway Tyerman Wertheimer, 1925 Century Park E, #2200, Los Angeles CA 90067 USA

**Vest, Jake** — Cartoonist (That's Jake)
PO Box 350757, Grand Island FL 32735, USA

**Vesterbacka, Peter** — Video Game Designer
Rovio Mobile Ltd, Keilaranta 17, 02150 Espoo, Finland

**Vestiel, Franck** — Director, Writer
Paradigm Agency, 360 N Crescent Dr, North Building, Beverly Hills CA 90210 USA

**Vetri, Victoria** — Actress
610 N Van Ness Ave, Los Angeles CA 90004, USA

**Vetrov, Aleksandr** — Ballet Dancer
Bolshoi Theater, Teatralnaya Pl 1, 103009 Moscow, Russia

**Vettel, Sebastian** — Auto Racing Driver
Red Bull Racing, Bradbourne Drive, Tilbrook, Milton Keynes, MK7 8BJ, England

**Vettori, Ernst** — Ski Jumper
Fohrenweg 1, 6060 Absam-Eichat, Austria

**Vevers, Stuart** — Fashion Designer
Mulberry Ltd, Kilver Court, Shepton Mallet, Somerset BA4 5NF, England

**Veysey, Sid** — Ice Hockey Player
178 Ridgevale Dr, Bedford NS B4A 3S7, Canada

**Vezzoli, Francesco** — Artist
Gagosian Gallery, 980 Madison Ave, New York NY 10075 USA

**Viator, John A** — Biological Engineer
University of Missouri, Life Sciences Center, Columbia MO 65211, USA

**Vicent, Tania** — Speed Skater
Speed Skating Canada, 2781 Lancaster Road, #402, Ottawa ON K1B 1A7, Canada

**Vicius, Nicole** — Actress
Innovative Artists, 1505 10th St, Santa Monica CA 90401 USA

**Vick, Michael D** — Football Player
21 Haywagon Trail, Hampton VA 23669, USA

**Vickaryous, Jake** — Chemist
University of Oregon, Chemistry Dept, Eugene OR 97403, USA

**Vickers, Brian L** — Auto Racing Driver
27 High Tech Blvd, Thomasville NC 27360, USA

**Vickers, Jonathan S (Jon)** — Opera Singer
Collingtree, 18 Riddells Bay Road, Warwick WK 04, Bermuda

**Vickers, Kipp E** — Football Player
PO Box 78365, Indianapolis IN 46278, USA

**Vickers, Mike** — Guitarist (Manfred Mann)
E M I Records, 43 Brook Green, London W6 7EF, England

**Vickers, Steve** — Ice Hockey Player
238 Zokol Dr, Aurora ON L4G 0C2, Canada

**Vickrey, Dan** — Singer, Guitarist (Counting Crowes)
Creative Artists Agency, 2000 Ave of Stars, #100, Los Angeles CA 90067 USA

**Vico C** — Rap, Reggae Artist
A R Entertainment, 3400 Coral Way, #404, Miami FL 33145, USA

| | |
|---|---|
| **Victor, James** | Actor |
| H David Moss, 733 Seward St, #PH, Los Angeles CA 90038 USA | |
| **Victor, Renee** | Actress |
| Independent Artists, 9601 Wilshire Blvd, #750, Beverly Hills CA 90210, USA | |
| **Victoria** | Crown Princess, Sweden |
| Royal Palace, Kung Slottet, Stottsbacken, 111 30 Stockholm, Sweden | |
| **Victorino, Shane P** | Baseball Player |
| 1997 Alcova Ridge Dr, Las Vegas NV 89135, USA | |
| **Vidal, Cesar** | Singer, Guitarist (Caesars) |
| Paradigm Agency, 360 Park Ave, #1600, New York NY 10022 USA | |
| **Vidal, Christina** | Actress |
| McGowan Mgmt, 8733 W Sunset Blvd, #103, West Hollywood CA 90069 USA | |
| **Vidal, Deborah** | Golfer |
| 2033 Paramount Dr, Los Angeles CA 90068, USA | |
| **Vidal, Jean-Pierre** | Alpine Skier |
| Ski Federation, 50 Rue de Marquisats, BP 51, 74011 Annecy Cedex, France | |
| **Vidal, Lisa** | Actress |
| Paul Kohner, 9300 Wilshire Blvd, #555, Beverly Hills CA 90212 USA | |
| **Vidal, Ricardo J Cardinal** | Religious Leader |
| Chancery, D Jakosalem Str, PO Box 52, Cebu City 6000, Philippines | |
| **Vidal, Tanya** | Actress |
| McGowan Mgmt, 8733 W Sunset Blvd, #103, West Hollywood CA 90069 USA | |
| **Vidmar, Peter** | Gymnast |
| 455 Camino Flora Vista, San Clemente CA 92673, USA | |
| **Vidrio Serrano, Nestor V** | Soccer Player |
| Federacion de Futbol, Colima 373 Colonia Roma, Delegacion Cuauhtemoc, Mexico City DF 06700, Mexico | |
| **Vidro, Jose A C** | Baseball Player |
| 159 Wentworth Ave, Brockton MA 02301, USA | |
| **Viehboeck, Franz A** | Cosmonaut, Austria |
| Hauptstr 102/Top 3, 1140 Vienna, Austria | |
| **Vieillard, Roger** | Artist |
| 7 Rue de l'Estrapade, 75005 Paris, France | |
| **Vieira, Jelon** | Choreographer |
| Pentocle/Danceworks, 246 W 38th St, #800, New York NY 10018, USA | |
| **Vieira, Marcelo** | Soccer Player |
| F C Real Madrid, Avda Concha Espana 1, 28036 Madrid, Spain | |
| **Vieira, Meredith** | Commentator |
| Meredith Vieira Productions, 888 7th Ave, #503, New York NY 10106, USA | |
| **Vieira, Patrick** | Soccer Player |
| F C Juventus, Corso Galilo Ferraris 32, 10128 Turin, Italy | |
| **Viellard, Eric** | Actor |
| Artmedia, 20 Ave Rapp, 75007 Paris, France | |
| **Vieluf, Vince** | Actor, Writer, Director |
| Station3, 1051 N Cole Ave, #B, Los Angeles CA 90038, USA | |
| **Viener, John** | Actor, Writer |
| United Talent Agency, U T A Plaza, 9336 Civic Center Dr, Beverly Hills CA 90210 USA | |
| **Viesturs, Ed** | Mountaineer |
| 4462 NE Mill Heights Circle, Bainbridge Island WA 98110, USA | |
| **Vieth, Michelle** | Actress, Model |
| Televisa, Blvd A Lopez Mateos 232, Colonia San Angel, Mexico City DF 01060 CP, Mexico | |
| **Vig, Butch** | Drummer (Garbage), Record Producer |
| Creative Artists Agency, 2000 Ave of Stars, #100, Los Angeles CA 90067 USA | |
| **Vigil, Frederico** | Artist |
| National Hispanic Cultural Center, 1701 4th St SW, Albuquerque NM 87102, USA | |
| **Vigman, Gillian** | Actress, Comedienne |
| Brillstein Entertainment Partners, 9150 Wilshire Blvd, #350, Beverly Hills CA 90212 USA | |
| **Vigna, Marino** | Cyclist |
| Via Bruno Buozzi 130, 20089 Rozzano, Italy | |
| **Vigneault, Alain** | Ice Hockey Player, Coach |
| New York Rangers, Madison Square Garden, 2 Penn Plaza, New York NY 10121 USA | |
| **Vignelli, Lella** | Interior Designer |
| Vignelli Assoc, 130 E 67th St, New York NY 10065, USA | |
| **Vignelli, Massimo** | Interior Designer |
| Vignelli Assoc, 130 E 67th St, New York NY 10065, USA | |
| **Vigneron, Thierry** | Track Athlete |
| Adidas USA, 685 Cedar Crest Road, Spartanburg SC 29301, USA | |
| **Vigoda, Abe** | Actor |
| 3 Zircon Way, #D1, Woodland Park NJ 07424, USA | |
| **Vigoda, Valerie** | Singer, Violinist (GrooveLily) |
| GrooveLily, PO Box 11570, Glendale CA 91226, USA | |
| **Vikander, Alicia** | Actress |
| Actors in Scandanavia, Jaakarinkatu 10, 00150 Helsinki, Finland | |
| **Viktorenko, Aleksandr S** | Cosmonaut |
| Cosmonaut Training Center, Star City, 141160 Zvezdny Gorodok, Moscow Oblast, Russia | |
| **Vila, Bob** | Entertainer, Writer |
| 115 Kingston St, #300, Boston MA 02111, USA | |
| **Vilanch, Bruce** | Actor, Comedian, Writer |
| Hyler Mgmt, 20 Ocean Park Blvd, #25, Santa Monica CA 90405, USA | |
| **Vilar, Tracy** | Actress |
| Raw Talent Mgmt, 9615 Brighton Way, #300, Beverly Hills CA 90210 USA | |
| **Vilaro, Eduardo** | Dancer, Choreographer |
| Ballet Hispanico, 167 W 89th St, New York NY 10024, USA | |
| **Vilas, Guillermo** | Tennis Player |
| Ave Foch 86, 75016 Paris, France | |
| **Vilasuso, Jordi** | Actor |
| Artistry Mgmt, 340 N Camden Dr, #302, Beverly Hills CA 90210, USA | |
| **Vilenkin, Alex** | Physicist, Astronomer |
| Tufts University, Physics & Astronomy Dept, Medford MA 02155, USA | |
| **Villa, Carlos** | Artist |
| San Francisco Art Institute, 800 Chestnut St, San Francisco CA 94133, USA | |
| **Villafuerte, Brandon** | Baseball Player |
| PO Box 188, North Bridgton ME 04057, USA | |
| **Villanueva, Charlie** | Basketball Player |
| Detroit Pistons, Palace, 4 Championship Dr, Auburn Hills MI 48326 USA | |
| **Villanueva, Daniel D (Danny)** | Football Player |
| PO Box 258, Somis CA 93066, USA | |

**Victor - Villanueva**

**Villapiano, Philip J (Phil)** — Football Player
21 Riverside Dr, Rumson NJ 07760, USA
**Villaraigosa, Antonio** — Mayor, Los Angeles
Mayor's Office, City Hall, 200 N Spring St, Los Angeles CA 90012, USA
**Villari, Guy** — Singer (Regents)
293 Airport Road, Liberty NY 12754, USA
**Villarrial, Christopher H (Chris)** — Football Player
7234 Bibbs Road, Little Valley NY 14755, USA
**Villarroel, Vernoica** — Opera Singer
Columbia Artists Mgmt Inc, 1790 Broadway, #702, New York NY 10019 USA
**Villasenor, Diego** — Architect
Gob Tiburcio Montiel 96, Col S M Chapultepec, Mexico City DF 11850, Mexico
**Villazon, Rolando** — Opera Singer
Centre Stage Artist Mgmt, Stralauer Allee 1, 10245 Berlin, Gerany
**Villegas, Camilo** — Golfer
318 W Riverside Dr, Tequesta FL 33469, USA
**Villella, Edward J** — Ballet Dancer, Choreographer
Miami City Ballet, Roca Center, 2200 Liberty Ave, Miami Beach FL 33139, USA
**Villeneuve, Denis** — Director, Writer
Claude Girard, 5230 Boul Saint-Laurent, Montreal QC H2T 1S1, Canada
**Villeneuve, Gilles** — Ice Hockey Player
38 Grey Lane, Levittown NY 11756, USA
**Villeneuve, Jacques** — Auto Racing Driver
B A R Team, PO Box 5014, Brackley, Northamptonshire NN13 7YY, England
**Villiers, Christopher** — Actor
Hillman Trelfall, 33 Brookfield, Highgate W Hill, London N6 6AT, England
**Villone, Ronald T (Ron), Jr** — Baseball Player
855 NE Mulberry Dr, Boca Raton FL 33487, USA
**Vilma, Jonathan P** — Football Player
1331 Brickell Bay Dr, #2709, Miami FL 33131, USA
**Viloria, Brian** — Boxer
Gary Gittlesohn, 14372 Mulholland Dr, Los Angeles CA 90077, USA
**Vilsack, Thomas (Tom)** — Secretary, Agriculture; Governor, IA
Agriculture Department, 14th St & Independence Ave SW, Washington DC 20250 USA
**Vimond, Paul M** — Architect
91 Ave Niel, 75017 Paris, France
**Vin Rock** — Rap Artist (Naughty By Nature)
Evolution Talent Agency, 1501 Broadway, #1301, New York NY 10036 USA
**Vina, Fernando** — Baseball Player
9464 Clementine Way, Elk Grove CA 95758, USA
**Vinatieri, Adam M** — Football Player
11595 Ditch Road, Carmel IN 46032, USA
**Vince, Pruitt Taylor** — Actor
Burstein Co, 15304 Sunset Blvd, #208, Pacific Palisades CA 90272, USA
**Vincelette, Dan** — Ice Hockey Player
1345 Rue Bernier, RR 3, Acton Vale QC J0H 1A0, Canada
**Vincent, Amy** — Cinematographer
5932 Graciosa Dr, Los Angeles CA 90068, USA
**Vincent, Brian** — Actor
Imperium 7, 5455 Wilshire Blvd, #1706, Los Angeles CA 90036, USA
**Vincent, Cerina** — Actress
Brillstein Entertainment Partners, 9150 Wilshire Blvd, #350, Beverly Hills CA 90212 USA
**Vincent, Francis T (Fay), Jr** — Baseball Executive
290 Harbor Dr, Stamford CT 06902, USA
**Vincent, J Samuel (Sam)** — Basketball Player, Coach
PO Box 27459, Lansing MI 48909, USA
**Vincent, James F (Jim), Jr** — Choreographer, Dance Executive
Netherlands Dance Theater, Schedeldoekshaven 60, 2501 The Haag CH, Netherlands
**Vincent, Jan-Michael** — Actor
Freeman & Sutton, 8961 W Sunset Blvd, #200, West Hollywood CA 90069, USA
**Vincent, Jay F** — Basketball Player
PO Box 27459, Lansing MI 48909, USA
**Vincent, Keydrick T** — Football Player
1769 Derby Glen Dr, Orlando FL 32837, USA
**Vincent, Rhonda** — Singer
Upper Mgmt, 1036 Tulip Grove Road, Nashville TN 37076, USA
**Vincent, Richard F** — Army Field Marshal, England
House of Lords, Westminster, London SW1A 0PW, England
**Vincent, Rick** — Singer, Songwriter
Carter Career Mgmt, 1028 18th Ave S, #B, Nashville TN 37212 USA
**Vincent, Troy D** — Football Player
18900 Longhouse Place, Leesburg VA 20176, USA
**Vincent, Virginia** — Actress
4738 Works Place, San Diego CA 92116, USA
**Vincentelli, Francois** — Actor
Artmedia, 20 Ave Rapp, 75007 Paris, France
**Vincenzi, Penny** — Writer
Overlook Press, 141 Wooster St, #4B, New York NY 10012, USA
**Vinci, Roberta** — Tennis Player
Via Taranto 89, 74015 Martina Franca (TA), Italy
**Vincz, Melanie** — Actress
2212 Earle Court, Redondo Beach CA 90278, USA
**Vineyard, David K (Dave)** — Baseball Player
1850 Tariff Road, Left Hand WV 25251, USA
**Vingt-Trois, Andre A Cardinal** — Religious Leader
Ordinary of France, 7 Rue Saint Vincent, 75018 Paris Cedex 08, France
**Vining, David** — Gastroenterologist
2210 Bellefontaine St, #D, Houston TX 77030, USA
**Vinogradov, Pavel V** — Cosmonaut
Cosmonaut Training Center, Star City, 141160 Zvezdny Gorodok, Moscow Oblast, Russia
**Vinoly, Rafael** — Architect
50 Vandam St, New York NY 10013, USA
**Vinson, Charles A (Charlie)** — Baseball Player
3821 Walters Lane, District Heights MD 20747, USA
**Vinson, Sharni** — Actress, Model, Dancer
Flutie Entertainment, 9320 Wilshire Blvd, #202, Beverly Hills CA 90212 USA

**Vint, Jesse Lee, III**      Actor
Film Artists, 13563 1/2 Ventura Blvd, #200, Sherman Oaks CA 91423 USA
**Vinterberg, Thomas**      Director
Nimbus Film Productions, Hauchsvej 17, Frederiksberg 1825, Denmark
**Vinton, Bobby**      Singer
M P I Talent Agency, 9255 W Sunset Blvd, #407, West Hollywood CA 90069, USA
**Vinton, Will**      Animator, Director, Producer
Creative Artists Agency, 2000 Ave of Stars, #100, Los Angeles CA 90067 USA
**Viola, Bill**      Sculptor, Video Artist
282 Granada Ave, Long Beach CA 90803, USA
**Viola, Frank J, Jr**      Baseball Player
9868 Kilgore Road, Orlando FL 32836, USA
**Viola, Lisa**      Dancer
Paul Taylor Dance Co, 551 Grand St, Lobby A, New York NY 10002, USA
**Violette, Banks**      Artist
Blum & Poe Gallery, 2727 S La Cienega Blvd, Los Angeles CA 90034, USA
**Virata, Cesar E**      Prime Minister, Philippines
63 E Maya Dr, Quezon City, Philippines
**Virden, Claude**      Basketball Player
337 Fernwood Dr, Akron OH 44320, USA
**Virdon, William C (Bill)**      Baseball Player, Manager
1311 E River Road, Springfield MO 65804, USA
**Viren, Lasse**      Track Athlete
Suomen Urheilulitto Ry, Box 25202, 00250 Helsinki 25, Finland
**Virgil, Osvaldo J (Ozzie), Jr**      Baseball Player
5444 W Credance Blvd, Glendale AZ 85310, USA
**Virgil, Osvaldo J (Ozzie), Sr**      Baseball Player
4316 W Mescal St, Glendale AZ 85304, USA
**Virsaladze, Eliso K**      Concert Pianist
Moscow Conservatory, Bolshaya Nikitskaya Str 13/6, 125009 Moscow, Russia
**Virts, Terry W, Jr**      Astronaut
1904 Edgewater Court, Friendswood TX 77546, USA
**Virtue, Tom**      Actor
C E S D, 10635 Santa Monica Blvd, #130, Los Angeles CA 90025 USA
**Visconti, Tony**      Music Producer
Star Mangement Group, 1311 Mamaroneck Ave, #220, White Plains NY 10605, USA
**Viscuso, Sal**      Actor
Imperium 7 Talent, 5455 Wilshire Blvd, #1706, Los Angeles CA 90036, USA
**Vise, David A**      Journalist
Washington Post, Editorial Dept, 1150 15th St NW, Washington DC 20071, USA
**Vishnevski, Vitaly**      Ice Hockey Player
Internatioanl Sports Advisors, 878 Ridge View Way, Franklin Lakes NJ 07417, USA
**Vishnyova, Diana V**      Ballerina
Mariinsky Theater, Teatralnaya Square 1, 190000 Saint Petersburg, Russia
**Visitor, Nana**      Actress
Pantheon Talent, 1801 Century Park E, #1910, Los Angeles CA 90067, USA
**Visnjic, Goran**      Actor
Management 360, 9111 Wilshire Blvd, Beverly Hills CA 90210 USA
**Visnovsky, Lubomir**      Ice Hockey Player
1531 9th St, Manhattan Beach CA 90266, USA
**Viso, Michel**      Spatinaut, France
7 Domaine Chateau-Gaillard, 94700 Maisons-d'Alfort, France
**Visser, Angela**      Beauty Queen, Actress
4127 Crisp Canyon Road, Sherman Oaks CA 91403, USA
**Visser, Douwe**      Religious Leader
World Reformed Churches, 150 Rt de Ferney, 1211 Geneva 2, Switzerland
**Visser, Lesley**      Sportscaster
CBS-TV, Sports Dept, 51 W 52nd St, New York NY 10019 USA
**Vissi, Anna**      Singer
Confidential Talent Agency, 745 5th Ave, #800, New York NY 10151, USA
**Vitale, Dick**      Sportscaster, Basketball Coach
7810 Mathern Court, Bradenton FL 34202, USA
**Vitali, Massimo**      Photographer
Brancolini Grimaldi Gallery, 43-44 Albemarle St, London W1S 4JJ, England
**Vitamin C**      Singer, Actress
I C M Partners, 10250 Constellation Blvd, #900, Los Angeles CA 90067 USA
**Vitez, Michael**      Journalist
Philadelphia Inquirer, Editorial Dept, 400 N Broad St, Philadelphia PA 19130, USA
**Vitiello, Joseph D (Joe)**      Baseball Player
13615 Old El Camino Real, San Diego CA 92130, USA
**Vitko, Joseph J (Joe)**      Baseball Player
1853 Frankstown Road, #1, Johnstown PA 15902, USA
**Vito, Robert D**      Actor
Strong Management, 9350 Wilshire Blvd, #224, Beverly Hills CA 90212, USA
**Vitolo, Dennis**      Auto Racing Driver
2130 Intracoastal Dr, Fort Lauderdale FL 33305, USA
**Vitorgan, Emmanuil**      Actor; Director
Maly Kislovsky Per 7, #26, 103009 Moscow, Russia
**Vitousek, Peter M**      Botanist, Ecologist
Stanford University, Biological Science Dept, Stanford CT 94305, USA
**Vittadini, Adrienne**      Fashion Designer
Adrienne Vittadini Inc, 575 Fashion Ave, New York NY 10018, USA
**Vitti, Monica**      Actress
I P C, Via Francesco Siacci 38, 00197 Rome, Italy
**Vittori, Roberto**      Astronaut
European Space Center, Linder Hohe, Box 906096, 51127 Cologne, Germany
**Vitukhnovskaya, Alina A**      Writer
Leningradskoye Shosse 80, #89, 125565 Moscow, Russia
**Vivas, Miguel A**      Director, Writer, Actor
United Talent Agency, U T A Plaza, 9336 Civic Center Dr, Beverly Hills CA 90210 USA
**Vivek**      Actor, Comedian
9 Subhiksha Apts, 5 Tank St, U I Colony, Chennai TN 600024, India
**Vivian, Cody T (C T)**      Religious Leader, Writer, Activist
C T Vivian Leadership Institute, 355 Dix-Lee-On Drive, Fairburn GA 30213, USA
**Viviani, Gabriele**      Opera Singer
I M G Artists, Hogarth Business Park, Chiswick, London W4 2TH, England

**Vizcaino Arias, J Luis** — Baseball Player
5876 Germaine Lane, La Jolla CA 92037, USA
**Vizquel Gonzalez, Omar E** — Baseball Player
2704 212th Ave SE, Sammamish WA 98075, USA
**Vlady, Marina** — Actress
10 Ave de Marivaux, 78800 Mission Lafitte, France
**Vlasic, Blanka** — Track Athlete
Hrvatski Atletski Savez, Krizaniceva 5, 10000 Zagreb, Croatia
**Vlk, Miloslav Cardinal** — Religious Leader
Arcibiskupstvi, Hradcanske Nam 16/56, 11902 Prague 1, Czech Republic
**Voda, Jan K** — Surgeon
608 NW 9th St, Oklahoma City OK 73102, USA
**Vodianova, Natalia** — Model
D N A Model Mgmt, 555 W 25th St, #600, New York NY 10001 USA
**Vodopyanova, Natalia** — Basketball Player
Seattle Storm, Key Arena, 351 Elliott Ave W, #500, Seattle WA 98119 USA
**Voegele, Kate** — Singer, Songwriter, Actress
Wilspro Mgmt, PO Box 9, Point Pleasant NJ 08742, USA
**Voelker, Sabine** — Speed Skater
Rube Marketing, Maximilian-Welsch Str 7, 99084 Erfurt, Germany
**Voevodsky, Vladimir** — Mathematician
35 Stonehouse Dr, Princeton NJ 08540, USA
**Vogel, Darlene** — Actress
Venture I A B, 3211 Cahuenga Blvd W, #104, Los Angeles CA 90068, USA
**Vogel, Frank** — Basketball Coach
Indiana Pacers, Conseco Fieldhouse, 125 S Pennsylvania, Indianapolis IN 46204 USA
**Vogel, Mike** — Actor
W M E Entertainment, 9601 Wilshire Blvd, #300, Beverly Hills CA 90210 USA
**Vogel, Mitch** — Actor
3335 Honeysuckle Ave, Palmdale CA 93550, USA
**Vogel, Paula** — Writer
Gersh Agency, 9465 Wilshire Blvd, #600, Beverly Hills CA 90212 USA
**Vogel, Robert L (Bob)** — Football Player
2065 N Galena Road, Sunbury OH 43074, USA
**Vogelsong, Ryan A** — Baseball Player
637 W Jardin Dr, Casa Grande AZ 85122, USA
**Vogelstein, Bert** — Geneticist, Oncologist
Johns Hopkins University Medical School, Oncology Center, Baltimore MD 21218, USA
**Vogler, Jan** — Concert Cellist
Moira Johnson Consulting, 180 Metcalfe St, #404, Ottawa ON K2P 1P5, Canada
**Vogler, Timothy (Tim)** — Football Player
6710 Woodland Dr, Hamburg NY 14075, USA
**Vogt, Peter K** — Virologist
Scripps Institute, Oncovirology Dept, 10550 N Torrey Pines, La Jolla CA 92037, USA
**Vogts, Hans-Hubert (Berti)** — Soccer Player
Football Assoc, 2208 Nobel Ave, 1025 Baku, Azerbaijan
**Vohor, Serge** — Prime Minister, Vanuatu
Moderate Parties Union, PO Box 698, Port Via, Vanuatu
**Voie, Angelica** — Opera Singer
Harrison/Parrott, 5-6 Albion Court, London W6 0QT, England
**Voight, Jon** — Actor
Artists Only Management, 10203 Santa Monica Blvd, #500, Los Angeles CA 90067, USA
**Voight, Karen** — Physical Fitness Expert
Entertaining Fitness, 827 Chautauqua Blvd, Pacific Palisades CA 90272, USA
**Voight, Stuart A (Stu)** — Football Player
8832 Hunters Way, Saint Paul MN 55124, USA
**Voigt, Deborah** — Opera Singer
Columbia Artists Mgmt Inc, 1790 Broadway, #702, New York NY 10019 USA
**Voigt, John D (Jack)** — Baseball Player
1759 Bayshore Road, Nokomis FL 34275, USA
**Voisine, Roch** — Singer, Songwriter
Don Jones Productions, 550 Wellington St, London ON N6A 3P9, Canada
**Vokoun, Tomas** — Ice Hockey Player
6685 NW 122nd Ave, Parkland FL 33076, USA
**Volberding, Paul A** — Oncologist
General Hospital, AIDS Activities Dept, 995 Protrero, San Francisco CA 94110, USA
**Volchenkov, Anton** — Ice Hockey Player
New Jersey Devils, Arena, 50 State Route 120, East Rutherford NJ 07073 USA
**Volcker, Paul A** — Government Official, Financier
151 E 79th St, New York NY 10075, USA
**Volek, David** — Ice Hockey Player
5 Blue Sky Court, Huntington NY 11743, USA
**Volek, J William (Billy)** — Football Player
12487 Valley Vista Lane, Fresno CA 93730, USA
**Volf, Jaroslav** — Canoeing Athlete
S K Neumanna 386, 25001 Brandys Nad Labem, Czech Republic
**Volibracht, Michaele** — Fashion Designer, Artist
Bill Blass Ltd, 236 5th Ave, #800, New York NY 10001, USA
**Volk, Igor P** — Cosmonaut
G N C-R F L II, Zhukovskiy 2, 140160 Moscow, Russia
**Volk, Patricia** — Writer
Gloria Loomis, 133 E 35th St, New York NY 10016, USA
**Volk, Richard R (Rick)** — Football Player
15860 Irish Ave, Monkton MD 21111, USA
**Volkaert, Redd** — Guitarist (Twangbangers)
Nancy Fly Agency, PO Box 90306, Austin TX 78709, USA
**Volkert, Stephan** — Rowing Athlete
Semmelweisstr 42, 51061 Cologne, Germany
**Volkmann, Elisabeth** — Opera Singer
Sonnenstr 20, 80331 Munich, Germany
**Volkov, Aleksandr A** — Cosmonaut
Cosmonaut Training Center, Star City, 141160 Zvezdny Gorodok, Moscow Oblast, Russia
**Volkov, Alexander** — Basketball Player
1413 Waterford Green Dr, Mariette GA 30068, USA
**Volkov, Sergei A** — Cosmonaut
Cosmonaut Training Center, Star City, 141160 Zvezdny Gorodok, Moscow Oblast, Russia

**Volkow, Nora D** — Physician
National Drug Abuse Institute, 6001 Executive Blvd, Bethesda MD 20892, USA
**Vollbracht, Michaele** — Fashion Designer, Artist
General Delivery, Safety Harbor FL 34695, USA
**Volle, Michael** — Opera Singer
I M G Artists, Hogarth Business Park, Chiswick, London W4 2TH, England
**Vollenweider, Andreas** — Concert Harpist
Sempacher Str 16, 8032 Zurich, Switzerland
**Vollman, William T** — Writer
2090 8th Ave, Sacramento CA 95818, USA
**Vollmer, Dana W** — Swimmer
4002 Laramie Dr, Granbury TX 76049, USA
**Volmar, Douglas (Doug)** — Ice Hockey Player
120 Royal Oak Dr, #L, Bel Air MD 21015, USA
**Volmer, Arvo** — Conductor
Estonia National Opera, Estonia Ave 4, 10148 Tallinn, Estonia
**Volodos, Arcadi** — Concert Pianist
Columbia Artists Mgmt Inc, 1790 Broadway, #702, New York NY 10019 USA
**Voloshin, Valeri** — Cosmonaut
Cosmonaut Training Center, Star City, 141160 Zvezdny Gorodok, Moscow Oblast, Russia
**Volstad, Christopher K (Chris)** — Baseball Player
11774 Hemlock St, Palm Beach Gardens FL 33410, USA
**Volynov, Boris V** — Cosmonaut
Cosmonaut Training Center, Star City, 141160 Zvezdny Gorodok, Moscow Oblast, Russia
**VonAroldingen, Karin** — Ballerina
New York City Ballet, Lincoln Center Plaza, New York NY 10023 USA
**VonD, Kat** — Entertainer, Tattoo Artist
Creative Artists Agency, 2000 Ave of Stars, #100, Los Angeles CA 90067 USA
**VonDaniken, Erich** — Writer
Postfach, 3803 Beatenberg, Switzerland
**VonDetten, Erik T** — Actor
Innovative Artists, 1505 10th St, Santa Monica CA 90401 USA
**VonDohnanyi, Christoph** — Conductor
Cleveland Orchestra, Severance Hall, Cleveland OH 44106, USA
**VonDonnersmarck, Florian H** — Director
United Talent Agency, U T A Plaza, 9336 Civic Center Dr, Beverly Hills CA 90210 USA
**Vondracek, Lukas** — Concert Pianist
Harrison/Parrott, Lucile-Grahn-Str 37, 81675 Munich, Germany
**VonEschenbach, Andrew** — Surgeon, Government Official
US Food & Drug Administration, 5600 Fishers Lane, Rockville MD 20857, USA
**VonEsmarch, Nick** — Actor
Talent Works, 3500 W Olive Ave, #1400, Burbank CA 91505 USA
**VonFurstenberg, Betsy** — Actress
230 Central Park West, #16A, New York NY 10024, USA
**VonFurstenberg, Diane** — Fashion Designer
444 W 14th St, New York NY 10014, USA
**VonGarnier, Katja** — Director, Writer
Above the Line, Theresienstr 31, 80333 Munich, Germany
**Vongerichten, Jean-Georges** — Chef
Jean-Georges Restaurant, 19 Greene St, New York NY 10013, USA
**VonGerkan, Manon** — Model
Trump Model Mgmt, 91 5th Ave, #300, New York NY 10003, USA
**VonGrunigen, Michael** — Alpine Skier
Chalet Sunneblick, 3778 Schonried, Switzerland
**VonHagens, Gunther** — Anatomist
Institute for Plastination, Rathausstr 11, 69126 Heidelberg, Germany
**VonHippel, Peter H** — Chemist
1900 Crest Dr, Eugene OR 97405, USA
**VonHoff, Bruce F** — Baseball Player
423 S River Hills Dr, Tampa FL 33617, USA
**VonHohenzollern, Furst** — Heir, House of Hohenzollern-Sigmaringen
Landhaus Josefslust, 72488 Sigmaringen, Germany
**VonKlitzing, Klaus** — Nobel Physics Laureate
Max Planck Institute, Heisenbergstr 1, 70506 Stuttgart, Germany
**Vonn, Lindsey K** — Alpine Skier
International Management Group, 767 5th Ave, New York NY 10153, USA
**VonOelhoffen, Kimo K** — Football Player
402 Adams St, Richland WA 99352, USA
**VonOhlen, David (Dave)** — Baseball Player
653 Windmill Ave, West Babylon NY 11704, USA
**VonOtter, Anne Sofie** — Opera Singer
Opus 3 Artists, 470 Park Ave S, #900N, New York NY 10016 USA
**VonQuast, Veronika** — Actress
Agentur Ebisch, Schellingstra 124, 80798 Munich, Germany
**VonRingelheim, Paul H** — Sculptor
9 Great Jones St, New York NY 10012, USA
**VonRydingsvard, Ursula** — Sculptor
78 Ingraham St, Brooklyn NY 11237, USA
**VonSaltza Olmstead, S Christine (Chris)** — Swimmer
520 Crocker Road, Sacramento CA 95864, USA
**VonSchamann, Uwe D W** — Football Player
1236 Loma Dr, Norman OK 73072, USA
**VonStade, Frederica** — Opera Singer
333 Kennedy St, Oakland CA 94606, USA
**VonSydow, Max** — Actor
Diamond Mgmt, 31 Percy St, London W1T 2DD, England
**VonTeese, Dita** — Model, Actress, Dancer
Dishell Multimedia Group, 8306 Wilshire Blvd, #833, Beverly Hills CA 90211, USA
**VonTrier, Lars** — Director
Zentropa Entertainments, Filmbyen 22, 2650 Hvidovre, Denmark
**VonTrotta, Margarethe** — Director
Above The Line, Wielandstr 5, 10625 Berlin, Germany
**VonWeizsacker, Richard** — President, Germany
Am Kupfergraben 7, 10117 Berlin, Germany
**Voog, Ana** — Singer, Songwriter
M C A Records, 1755 Broadway, New York NY 10019 USA

**Voorhees, John J** — Dermatologist
3965 Waldenwood Dr, Ann Arbor MI 48105, USA

**Voorhies, Lark** — Actress
Cyrus & Cyrus, 9935 S Santa Monica Blvd, Beverly Hills CA 90212, USA

**Voorman, Klaus** — Artist
K & K Galleries, Grindelalla 182, 20144 Hamburg, Germany

**Vorgan, Gigi** — Actress
3637 Stone Canyon, Sherman Oaks CA 91403, USA

**Voris, Cyrus** — Writer, Producer, Actor
United Talent Agency, U T A Plaza, 9336 Civic Center Dr, Beverly Hills CA 90210 USA

**Voronin, Vladimir N** — President, Moldova
Presidential Palace, 23 Nicolae lorge Str, 227033 Chishinev, Moldova

**Vorontsov, Nikolai N** — Geneticist, Zoologist
Koltsov Biology Institute, Vavilova Str 26, 117334 Moscow, Russia

**Voros, Christina** — Director, Cinematographer
Gersh Agency, 9465 Wilshire Blvd, #600, Beverly Hills CA 90212 USA

**Voroshilo, Aleksander S** — Opera Singer
Bolshoi Theater, Teatralnaya Pl 1, 103009 Moscow, Russia

**Vosberg, Edward J (Ed)** — Baseball Player
7839 E Marquise Dr, Tucson AZ 85715, USA

**Vosloo, Arnold** — Actor
A P A Talent/Literary Agency, 405 S Beverly Dr, #300, Beverly Hills CA 90212 USA

**Voss, Brian** — Bowler
6115 Abbotts Bridge Road, #111, Duluth GA 30097, USA

**Voss, James S** — Astronaut
4207 Indian Sunrise Court, Houston TX 77059, USA

**Voss, John** — Biochemist
University of California, Biochemistry Dept, Davis CA 95616, USA

**Voss, Torsten** — Track Athlete
Dunkirchener Str 74, 47839 Krefeld, Germany

**Voss, William E (Bill)** — Baseball Player
10625 E Oak Creek Trail, Cornville AZ 86325, USA

**VosSavant, Marilyn** — Writer
Parade Publications, 711 3rd Ave, New York NY 10017, USA

**Vostell, Wolf** — Video Artist
Giesebrechstr 12, 10629 Berlin, Germany

**Votaw, Ty** — Golf Executive
Ladies Pro Golf Assn, 100 International Golf Dr, Daytona Beach FL 32124 USA

**Votolato, Rocky** — Singer, Guitarist
Undertow Music Collective, 1124 W Daniel, Champaign IL 61822, USA

**Votsis, Gloria** — Actress
T M T Entertainment Group, 648 Broadway, #912, New York, NY 10012, USA

**Votto, Joseph D (Joey)** — Baseball Player
4 Nantucket Crescent, Brampton ON L6S 3X5, Canada

**Voyagis, Yorgo** — Actor
Anne Alvares Correa, 34 Rue Jouffroy d'Abbans, 75017 Paris, France

**Voyles, Brad** — Baseball Player
314 East Ave, Casco WI 54205, USA

**Vraa, Sanna** — Model, Actress
Irv Schechter, 9460 Wilshire Blvd, #300, Beverly Hills CA 90212 USA

**Vrabel, Michael G (Mike)** — Football Player
777 W Orange Road, Delaware OH 43015, USA

**Vraciu, Alexander (Alex)** — WW II Navy Air Force Hero
309 Merrilee Place, Danville CA 94526, USA

**Vranes, Daniel L (Danny)** — Basketball Player
6480 Canyon Ranch Road, Salt Lake City UT 84121, USA

**Vratogna, Marco** — Opera Singer
I M G Artists, Hogarth Business Park, Chiswick, London W4 2TH, England

**Vuarnet, Jean** — Alpine Skier
Chalet Squaw Peak, 74110 Auoriaz, France

**Vucevic, Nikola** — Basketball Player
Orlando Magic, 8701 Maitland Summit Blvd, Orlando FL 32810 USA

**Vuckovich, Peter D (Pete)** — Baseball Player
86 Leonard St, Johnstown PA 15902, USA

**Vujanovic, Filip** — President, Montenegro
Presidential Palace, Cetinje, Montenegro

**Vukoto, Mick** — Ice Hockey Player
PO Box 3213, 7 Peases Point Road, Edgartown MA 02539, USA

**Vukovich, George S** — Baseball Player
305 W Calle Gota, Sahuarita AZ 85629, USA

**Vuolo, Lindsey** — Model
Playboy Promotions, 2706 Media Center Dr, Los Angeles CA 90065 USA

**Vuono, Carl E** — Army General
5796 Westchester St, Alexandria VA 22310, USA

**Vyborny, David** — Ice Hockey Player
4075 Blendon Grove Way, Columbus OH 43230, USA

**Vyent, Louise** — Model, Photographer
Louise Vyent Photography, 13 Mountainview Place, Montclair NJ 07042, USA

**Waakataar-Savoy, Paul** — Singer, Guitarist (A-Ha), Songwriter
Agency Group Ltd, 361-373 City Road, London EC1V 1PQ, England
**Waalkes, Otto** — Actor, Comedian
Papenhuder Str 61, 22087 Hamburg, Germany
**Wachowski, Andy** — Director
Circle of Confusion, 107-23 71st Road, #300, Forest Hills NY 11375, USA
**Wachowski, Laurence (Lana)** — Director
Circle of Confusion, 107-23 71st Road, #300, Forest Hills NY 11375, USA
**Wachs, Caitlin** — Actress
I C M Partners, 10250 Constellation Blvd, #900, Los Angeles CA 90067 USA
**Wachtel, Christine** — Track Athlete
Rostock Sports Club, Rostock, 17033 Mecklenburg-Vorpommoern, Germany
**Wachter, Anita** — Alpine Skier
Gantschierstr 579, 6780 Schruns, Austria
**Wackerman, Brooks** — Drummer (Bad Religion)
Goldstar Mgmt, PO Box 130, Ross on Wye HR9 6WY, England
**Wada, Tsuyoshi** — Baseball Player
Baltimore Orioles, Oriole Park, 333 W Camden St, Baltimore MD 21201 USA
**Waddell, Chris** — Model, Skier
Athletes for Hope, 3 Bethesda Metro Center, #450, Bethesda MD 20814, USA
**Waddell, Ernest** — Actor
Stone Manners Salners, 9911 W Pico Blvd, #1400, Los Angeles CA 90035 USA
**Waddell, John Henry** — Artist
10050 E Waddell Road, Cornville AZ 86325, USA
**Waddell, Justine** — Actress
United Agents, 12-26 Lexington St, London W1F 0LE, England
**Waddell, Thomas D (Tom)** — Baseball Player
10171 E Achi St, Tucson AZ 85748, USA
**Waddington of Read, David** — Governor General, Bermuda
39 Chester Way, #4, London SE11 4UR, England
**Waddington, Steven** — Actor
Julian Belfrage Assoc, 9 Argyll St, #300, London W1F 7TG, England
**Waddle, Thomas (Tom)** — Football Player, Sportscaster
8190 Tollbridge Dr, West Chester OH 45069, USA
**Waddy, William D (Billy)** — Football Player
2838 Highway 88, Minneapolis MN 55418, USA
**Wade, Adam** — Singer
C E S D, 257 Park Ave S, #950, New York NY 10010 USA
**Wade, Chrissie** — Musician (Alien Sex Fiend)
Mission Control, City Business Center, Lower Road, London SE16 2XB, England
**Wade, Dwyane T** — Basketball Player
9330 SW 59th Place, Miami FL 33156, USA
**Wade, Jason M** — Singer, Guitarist (Lifehouse)
Universal/Geffen Records, 2220 Colorado Ave, Santa Monica CA 90404, USA
**Wade, Justin** — Actor
Talent Works, 3500 W Olive Ave, #1400, Burbank CA 91505 USA
**Wade, Nik** — Musician (Alien Sex Fiend)
Mission Control, City Business Center, Lower Road, London SE16 2XB, England
**Wade, R John** — Football Player
3540 Traveler Road, Harrisonburg VA 22801, USA
**Wade, S Virginia** — Tennis Player
International Mangement Group, Pier House, Chiswick, London W4M 3NN, England
**Wade, William J (Bill), Jr** — Football Player
PO Box 210124, Nashville TN 37221, USA
**Wadham, Julian** — Actor
Ken McReddie Assoc, 101 Finsbury Pavement, London EC2A 1RS, England
**Wadhams, Wayne** — Singer, Keyboardist (Fifth Estate)
73 Hemenway, Boston MA 02115, USA
**Wadkins, Bobby** — Golfer
204 Kinloch Road, Manakin Sabot VA 23103, USA
**Wadkins, Lanny** — Golfer, Sportscaster
6002 Kettering Court, Dallas TX 75248, USA
**Wadlow, Jeff** — Director, Writer
Tower of Babbel Entertainment, 854 N Spaulding Ave, Los Angeles CA 90046, USA
**Wadsworth, Charles W** — Concert Pianist
PO Box 157, Charleston SC 29402, USA
**Wadsworth, Fred** — Golfer
823 Bryon Road, Columbia SC 29205, USA
**Waechter, Douglas M (Doug)** — Baseball Player
4590 13th Way NE, Saint Petersburg FL 33703, USA
**Waena, Nathaniel** — Governor General, Solomon Islands
Governor General's House, Box 252, Honiara, Guadacanal, Solomon Islands
**Wafer, Vakeaton Q (Von)** — Basketball Player
2503 Dallas St, Houston TX 77003, USA
**Wages, Harmon L** — Football Player
1846 Margaret St, #3C, Jacksonville FL 32204, USA
**Wages, William** — Cinematographer
Innovative Artists, 1505 10th St, Santa Monica CA 90401 USA
**Waggoner, Brooke** — Singer, Songwriter
Agency Group Ltd, 142 W 57th St, #600, New York NY 10019 USA
**Waggoner, Lyle** — Actor
1124 Oak Mirage Place, Westlake Village CA 91362, USA
**Waggoner, Paul E** — Agronomist
100 Crockett St, #312, Seattle WA 98109, USA
**Wagner, Allison** — Swimmer
912 NW 45th Terrace, Gainesville FL 32605, USA
**Wagner, Amber** — Opera Singer
I M G Artists, Hogarth Business Park, Chiswick, London W4 2TH, England
**Wagner, Barbara A** — Figure Skater
Alpharetta Family Skate Center, 10800 Davis Dr, Alpharetta GA 30009, USA
**Wagner, Bruce** — Writer, Producer, Actor
United Talent Agency, U T A Plaza, 9336 Civic Center Dr, Beverly Hills CA 90210 USA
**Wagner, Bryan J** — Football Player
6020 Arlyne Lane, Medina OH 44256, USA
**Wagner, Catherine** — Photographer
308 Precita Ave, San Francisco CA 94110, USA

**W**

| | |
|---|---|
| **Wagner, Chuck**<br>1200 Maldonado Dr, Pensacola Beach FL 32561, USA | Actor, Singer |
| **Wagner, Dajuan M**<br>Golden State Warriors, 1011 Broadway, Oakland CA 94605 USA | Basketball Player |
| **Wagner, Fred**<br>King Features Syndicate, 300 W 57th St, #1500, New York NY 10019 USA | Cartoonist (Grin & Bear It) |
| **Wagner, Gary E**<br>1707 Northbrook Court, Seymour IN 47274, USA | Baseball Player |
| **Wagner, Harold A**<br>4031 Savannah Trail, Santa Rosa CA 95404, USA | Businessman |
| **Wagner, Jill**<br>United Talent Agency, U T A Plaza, 9336 Civic Center Dr, Beverly Hills CA 90210 USA | Model, Actress |
| **Wagner, Johnson**<br>Professional Golfer's Assn, PO Box 109601, Palm Beach Gardens FL 33410 USA | Golfer |
| **Wagner, Katie**<br>Creative Managment Entertainment, 2050 S Bundy Dr, #280, Los Angeles CA 90025, USA | Actress |
| **Wagner, Kristina**<br>PO Box 491035, Los Angeles CA 90049, USA | Actress |
| **Wagner, Kurt**<br>High Road Touring, 751 Bridgeway, #200, Sausalito CA 94965 USA | Singer (Lambchop) |
| **Wagner, Lindsay**<br>Playboy Promotions, 2706 Media Center Dr, Los Angeles CA 90065 USA | Model |
| **Wagner, Lindsay**<br>22817 Ventura Blvd, #888, Woodland Hills CA 91364, USA | Actress |
| **Wagner, Lisa**<br>Professional Bowlers Assn, 719 2nd Ave, #701, Seattle WA 98104 USA | Bowler |
| **Wagner, Lou**<br>Amsel Eisenstadt Frazier, 5055 Wilshire Blvd, #865, Los Angeles CA 90036 USA | Actor |
| **Wagner, Louis C, Jr**<br>6336 Manchester Way, Alexandria VA 22304, USA | Army General |
| **Wagner, Mark D**<br>1838 Willow Arms Dr, Ashtabula OH 44004, USA | Baseball Player |
| **Wagner, Matthew (Matt)**<br>4340 Horton Road, West Linn OR 97068, USA | Cartoonist |
| **Wagner, Melinda**<br>Theodore Presser, 588 N Gulph Road, #B, King of Prussia PA 19406, USA | Composer |
| **Wagner, Michael R (Mike)**<br>203 E Wild Cherry Dr, Mars PA 16046, USA | Football Player |
| **Wagner, Paul A**<br>27081 State Highway 3, Kirksville MO 63501, USA | Baseball Player |
| **Wagner, Philip M**<br>32 Montgomery St, Boston MA 02116, USA | Columnist |
| **Wagner, Robert**<br>Chuck Binder Mgmt, 1465 Lindacrest Dr, Beverly Hills CA 90210 USA | Actor |
| **Wagner, Robert W**<br>Commander, Joint Forces Command, Norfolk VA 23551, USA | Army General |
| **Wagner, Robin S A**<br>Robin Wagner Studio, 890 Broadway, New York NY 10003, USA | Stage, Set Designer |
| **Wagner, Ryan S**<br>59 County Road 311, Yoakum TX 77995, USA | Baseball Player |
| **Wagner, Sune Rose**<br>Orchard, 100 Park Ave, #200, New York NY 10017, USA | Singer, Guitarist (Ravenonettes) |
| **Wagner, William E (Billy)**<br>5066 Jones Mill Road, Crozet VA 22932, USA | Baseball Player |
| **Wagner-Augustin, Katrin**<br>Kaastaienallee 35, 14471 Potsdam, Germany | Canoeing Athlete |
| **Wagoner, Dan**<br>Contemporary Dance Theater, 17 Duke's Road, London WC1H 9AB, England | Dancer, Choreographer |
| **Wagoner, David R**<br>5416 154th Place SW, Edmonds WA 98026, USA | Writer |
| **Wagoner, Harold E**<br>331 Lindsey Dr, Berwyn PA 19312, USA | Architect |
| **Wahl, Ken**<br>9654 W 131st St, #206, Palos Park IL 60464, USA | Actor |
| **Wahlberg, Donnie**<br>16815 Bircher St, Granada Hills CA 91344, USA | Singer, Actor |
| **Wahlberg, Mark**<br>W M E Entertainment, 9601 Wilshire Blvd, #300, Beverly Hills CA 90210 USA | Actor, Singer, Model |
| **Wahle, Michael J (Mike)**<br>6210 Avenida Cresta, La Jolla CA 92037, USA | Football Player |
| **Wahlgren, Olof G C**<br>Nicoloviusgatan 5B, 217 57 Malmo, Sweden | Editor |
| **Wahlstrom, Jarl H**<br>Borgstrominkuja 1A10, 00840 Helsinki 84, Finland | Religious Leader |
| **Waigel, Theodor**<br>Oberrohr, 86513 Ursberg, Germany | Government Official, Germany |
| **Waihee, John D, III**<br>745 Fort Street Mall, #600, Honolulu HI 96813, USA | Governor, HI |
| **Wailer, Bunny**<br>Wenig-LaMonica Associates, 580 White Plains Road, #130, Tarrytown NY 10591 USA | Singer (Bob Marley & the Wailers) |
| **Wain, Bea**<br>Society of Singers, 15456 Ventura Blvd, #304, Sherman Oaks CA 91403, USA | Singer |
| **Wain, David B**<br>Principato-Young, 9465 Wilshire Blvd, #880, Beverly Hills CA 90212 USA | Director |
| **Wainwright, Adam P**<br>2100 Brook Hill Court, Chesterfield MO 63017, USA | Baseball Player |
| **Wainwright, Angel M**<br>Amatruda Benson Assoc, 9107 Wilshire Blvd, #500, Beverly Hills CA 90210, USA | Actress |
| **Wainwright, Loudon, III**<br>Rosebud Agency, PO Box 170429, San Francisco CA 94117 USA | Singer, Songwriter |
| **Wainwright, Martha**<br>Agency Group, 2 Berkeley St, #202, Toronto ON M5A 4J5, Canada | Singer, Songwriter |
| **Wainwright, Rufus M**<br>M C T Mgmt, 520 8th Ave, #2001, New York NY 10018, USA | Singer, Songwriter |
| **Wainwright, Rupert**<br>Luber Rocklin Entertainment, 8530 Wilshire Blvd, #555, Beverly Hills CA 90211 USA | Director, Actor, Writer |

**Wagner - Wainwright**

**Waite, Alison** — Model
Playboy Promotions, 2706 Media Center Dr, Los Angeles CA 90065 USA
**Waite, Grant** — Golfer
1615 SE 73rd Place, Ocala FL 34480, USA
**Waite, John** — Singer (Babys, Bad English), Songwriter
Rounder Records, 1 Rounder Way, Burlington MA 01803 USA
**Waite, Ralph** — Actor
Marshak/Zachary Co, 8840 Wilshire Blvd, #100, Beverly Hills CA 90211 USA
**Waite, Terence H (Terry)** — Religious Leader
Wheelrights, Green Harvest, Bury Saint Edmunds, Suffolk IP29 4DH, England
**Waiters, Granville S** — Basketball Player
PO Box 91361, Columbus OH 43209, USA
**Waiters, Van A** — Football Player
6021 NW 201st Lane, Hialeah FL 33015, USA
**Waits, M Richard (Rick)** — Baseball Player
PO Box 1001, Patagonia AZ 85624, USA
**Waits, Tom** — Singer, Pianist, Songwriter
W M E Entertainment, 9601 Wilshire Blvd, #300, Beverly Hills CA 90210 USA
**Waitt, Theodore W (Ted)** — Businessman
Gateway Inc, 7565 Irvine Center Dr, Irvine CA 92618, USA
**Waitz, Richard H** — Cinematographer
405 Zenith Ave, Lafayette CO 80026, USA
**Wajda, Andrzej** — Director
Japanese/Technology Center, Ul Konopnickiej 26, 30 302 Cracow, Poland
**Wakamatsu, W Donald (Don)** — Baseball Player, Manager
8740 Ramblewood Court, Keller TX 76248, USA
**Wakata, Koichi** — Astronaut, Japan
Japanese Aerospace Exploration Agency, 2-1-1 Sengen, Tsukuba-shi, Ibaraki 305 8505, Japan
**Waked, Amr** — Actor
Ken McReddie Assoc, 101 Finsbury Pavement, London EC2A 1RS, England
**Wakefield, Charity** — Actress
I C M Partners, 10250 Constellation Blvd, #900, Los Angeles CA 90067 USA
**Wakefield, Rhys** — Actor
R G M Artist, 64-76 Kippax St, #202, Surry Hills NSW 2010, Australia
**Wakefield, Timothy S (Tim)** — Baseball Player
241 Lansing Island Dr, Indian Harbour Beach FL 32937, USA
**Wakeham of Maldon, John** — Government Official, England
House of Lords, Westminster, London SW1A 0PW, England
**Wakeland, Chris** — Baseball Player
60997 Luttrell Lane, Saint Helens OR 97051, USA
**Wakeley, Amanda** — Fashion Designer
7 Old Park Lane, London W1K 1QR, England
**Wakelin, Cara** — Model, Actress
Playboy Promotions, 2706 Media Center Dr, Los Angeles CA 90065 USA
**Wakeling, Dave** — Singer (General Public, English Beat)
Arcadia Group Mgmt, 11400 W Olympic Blvd, #200, Los Angeles CA 90064, USA
**Wakely, Ernie** — Ice Hockey Player
11052 E Roundup Dr, Dewey AZ 86327, USA
**Wakeman, Rick** — Keyboardist, Songwriter
I C M Partners, Marlborough House, 10 Earlham St, #300, London WC2H 9LNP, England
**Wakoski, Diane** — Writer
607 Division St, East Lansing MI 48823, USA
**Walbeck, Matthew L (Matt)** — Baseball Player
8216 Olive Ave, Fair Oaks CA 95628, USA
**Walchuk, Don** — Curling Athlete
Curling Assn, 1660 Vimont Court, Cumberland ON K4A 4J4, Canada
**Walcott, Derek A** — Nobel Literature Laureate
PO Box GM 926, Castries, Saint Lucia, West Indies
**Walcott, Gregory** — Actor
22246 Saticoy St, Canoga Park CA 91303, USA
**Walcott, Jennifer** — Model, Actress
O'Grady Entertainment Group, 4550 Via Marina, #305, Marina del Rey CA 90292, USA
**Walcutt, John** — Actor
Defining Artists Agency, 10 Universal City Plaza, #2000, Universal City CA 91608, USA
**Wald, Patricia M** — Judge
US Court of Appeals, 3rd & Constitution NW, Washington DC 20001, USA
**Waldau, Nicolaj Coster** — Actor
Lindberg Mgmt, Lavendelstre De 5-7, Baghuset 4 Sal, 1462 Copenhagen K, Denmark
**Waldegrave of North Hill, William** — Government Official, England
66 Palace Gardens Terrace, London W8 4RR, England
**Waldemore, Stanley A (Stan)** — Football Player
PO Box 611, New Vernon NJ 07976, USA
**Walden, Jordan C** — Baseball Player
Los Angeles Angels, Angel Stadium, 2000 E Gene Autry Way, Anaheim CA 92806 USA
**Walden, Lynette** — Actress
Metropolitan Talent Agency, 5405 Wilshire Blvd, #218, Los Angeles CA 90036 USA
**Walden, Robert** — Actor, Director, Writer
Bret Adams Agency, 448 W 44th St, New York NY 10036, USA
**Walden, Robert E (Bobby)** — Football Player
107 Springfield Dr, Bainbridge GA 39819, USA
**Walden, W G (Snuffy)** — Composer
Gorfaine/Schwartz, 4111 W Alameda Ave, #509, Burbank CA 91505 USA
**Waldhauser, Thomas D** — Marine Corps General
Commander, Central Command, 7115 S Boundary, MacDill Air Force Base FL 33621 USA
**Waldie, Marc R** — Volleyball Player
14020 E Ayesbury Circle, Wichita KS 67228, USA
**Waldner, Jan-Ove** — Table Tennis Player
Banda, Skjulstagatan 10, 632 29 Eskilstuna, Sweden
**Waldo, Janet** — Actress
C E S D, 10635 Santa Monica Blvd, #130, Los Angeles CA 90025 USA
**Waldorf, James J (Duffy), Jr** — Golfer
18510 Brymer St, Porter Ranch CA 91326, USA
**Waldron, Jeffrey** — Cinematographer
United Talent Agency, U T A Plaza, 9336 Civic Center Dr, Beverly Hills CA 90210 USA
**Waldron, Jeremy J** — Educator, Attorney
1061 Keith Ave, Berkeley CA 94708, USA

**Waldrop, Alex** — Thoroughbred Racing Executive
National Thoroughbred Racing, 2525 Harrodsburg Road, #500, Lexington KY 40504, USA
**Wales, Jimmy D (Jimbo)** — Internet Encyclopedia Designer
Wikipedia Foundation, 200 2nd Ave S, #358, Saint Petersburg FL 33701, USA
**Wales, Ross** — Swimmer
2233 Eastern Ave, #1B, Cincinnati OH 45202, USA
**Walesa, Lech** — Nobel Peace Laureate; President, Poland
Ul Dlugi Targ 24, 80828 Gdansk, Poland
**Walewander, James (Jim)** — Baseball Player
5023 Albridal Way, San Ramon CA 94582, USA
**Walger, Sonya** — Actress
Gersh Agency, 9465 Wilshire Blvd, #600, Beverly Hills CA 90212 USA
**Walheim, Rex J** — Astronaut
142 Hidden Lake Dr, League City TX 77573, USA
**Walia, Sonu** — Actress
20 Anchorage, Juhu-Versova Link Road, Andheri (W), Mumbai MS 400058, India
**Walk, Neal** — Basketball Player
6030 N 11th Ave, Phoenix AZ 85013, USA
**Walk, Robert V (Bob)** — Baseball Player
2494 Shadowbrook Dr, Wexford PA 15090, USA
**Walken, Christopher** — Actor
I C M Partners, 10250 Constellation Blvd, #900, Los Angeles CA 90067 USA
**Walker, Adam C** — Football Player
923 Bucknell Ave, Johnstown PA 15905, USA
**Walker, Alan C** — Anthropologist
Pennsylvania State University, Anthropology Dept, Pittsburgh PA 16802, USA
**Walker, Alice M** — Writer, Social Activist
PO Box 378, Philo CA 95466, USA
**Walker, Ally** — Actress
Luber Rocklin Entertainment, 8530 Wilshire Blvd, #555, Beverly Hills CA 90211 USA
**Walker, Andrew Kevin** — Actor, Writer
Kennedy/Miller Productions, 30 Orwell St, Sydney NSW 2011, Australia
**Walker, Andrew W** — Actor
Amanda Rosenthal Talent, 1255 University St, #502, Montreal QC H3B 3V8, Canada
**Walker, Anthony B (Tony)** — Baseball Player
2724 Morgan Dr, San Ramon CA 94583, USA
**Walker, Antoine D** — Basketball Player
450 W Huron St, Chicago IL 60654, USA
**Walker, Arnetia** — Actress
1040 4th St, #406, Santa Monica CA 90403, USA
**Walker, Benjamin** — Actor
Inspire Entertainment, 2332 Cotner Ave, #302. Los Angeles CA 90064, USA
**Walker, Bill** — Basketball Player
New York Knicks, Madison Square Garden, 2 Penn Plaza, New York, NY 10121 USA
**Walker, Bracy W** — Football Player
5683 Notting Hill Road, Gurnee IL 60031, USA
**Walker, Bradley G (Butch)** — Singer, Guitarist (Marvelous 3)
Crush Mgmt, 60-62 E 11th St, #700, New York NY 10003 USA
**Walker, Brian** — Cartoonist (Hi & Lois)
King Features Syndicate, 300 W 57th St, #1500, New York NY 10019 USA
**Walker, Bruce R** — Football Player
279 Eastlawn St, Detroit MI 48215, USA
**Walker, Charles D** — Astronaut
Boeing Co, 1200 Wilson Blvd, MC RS00, Arlington VA 22209, USA
**Walker, Charles D (Chuck)** — Football Player
1613 Tradd Court, Chesterfield MO 63017, USA
**Walker, Charls E** — Economist
19207 Racine Court, Montgomery Village MD 20886, USA
**Walker, Chester (Chet)** — Basketball Player
124 Fleet St, Marina del Rey CA 90292, USA
**Walker, Chris** — Actor
Rolf Kruger, 121 Gloucester Place, London W1H 3PJ, England
**Walker, Clay** — Singer
W M E Entertainment, 1600 Division St, #300, Nashville TN 37203 USA
**Walker, Cleotha (Chico)** — Baseball Player
450 W Huron St, Chicago IL 60654, USA
**Walker, Clint** — Actor
101 W McKnight Way, #B303, Grass Valley CA 95949, USA
**Walker, Darnell R** — Football Player
501 N 44th St, Muskogee OK 74401, USA
**Walker, Darrell** — Basketball Player, Coach
16122 Patriot Dr, Little Rock AR 72212, USA
**Walker, David M** — Government Official
Comeback America Initiative, 211 State St, #401, Bridgeport CT 06604, USA
**Walker, Denard A** — Football Player
17214 Lechlade Lane, Dallas TX 75252, USA
**Walker, Derek** — Architect
2 General Sage Dr, Santa Fe NM 87505, USA
**Walker, Derrick** — Auto Racing Executive
Walker Racing, 4035 Championship Dr, Indianapolis IN 46268, USA
**Walker, DeWayne** — Football Coach
New Mexico State University, Athletic Dept, Box 30001, Las Cruces NM 88003, USA
**Walker, Dreama** — Actress
Gersh Agency, 9465 Wilshire Blvd, #600, Beverly Hills CA 90212 USA
**Walker, Duane A** — Baseball Player
2509 Georgia Ave, Deer Park TX 77536, USA
**Walker, Eamonn** — Actor
I C M Partners, 10250 Constellation Blvd, #900, Los Angeles CA 90067 USA
**Walker, Fiona** — Actress
13 Despard Road, London N19 5NP, England
**Walker, G Mickey** — Football Player
22828 S Maple Point Road, Pickford MI 49774, USA
**Walker, Gary L** — Football Player
PO Box 138, Lavonia GA 30553, USA
**Walker, George T, Jr** — Composer
323 Grove St, Montclair NJ 07042, USA

**Walker, Greg** — Cartoonist (Hi & Lois)
King Features Syndicate, 300 W 57th St, #1500, New York NY 10019 USA

**Walker, Greg T** — Singer, Bassist (Blackfoot)
Artists International Mgmt, 9850 Sandalfoot Blvd, #458, Boca Raton FL 33428 USA

**Walker, Gregory L (Greg)** — Baseball Player
530 N Lake Shore Dr, #1009, Chicago IL 60611, USA

**Walker, Herschel J** — Football Player
2210 King Fisher Dr, Westlake TX 76262, USA

**Walker, Hezekiah X, Jr** — Singer, Choir Director, Religious Leader
Love Fellowship Tabernacle, 464 Liberty Ave, Brooklyn NY 11207, USA

**Walker, I Kenyatta** — Football Player
14813 Tudor Chase Dr, Tampa FL 33626, USA

**Walker, James T (Jamie)** — Baseball Player
11450 W 187th St, Spring Hill KS 66083, USA

**Walker, Javon L** — Football Player
7375 Talon Trail, Parker CO 80138, USA

**Walker, Jerry A** — Baseball Player
2015 Collins Blvd, Ada OK 74820, USA

**Walker, Jerry Jeff** — Singer, Guitarist, Songwriter
Goodknight Music, PO Box 39, Austin TX 78767, USA

**Walker, Jimmie (J J)** — Actor, Comedian
Roger Paul, 1650 Broadway, New York NY 10019, USA

**Walker, Joe Louis** — Singer, Guitarist
Oceanside Talent, 124 Virginia Place, #3, Costa Mesa CA 92627, USA

**Walker, John E** — Nobel Chemistry Laureate
M R C Molecular Biology Laboratory, Hills Road, Cambridge CB2 2QH, England

**Walker, John G** — Track Athlete
Jeffs Road, RD Papatoetoe, Aukland 2016, New Zealand

**Walker, John M, Jr** — Judge
US Court of Appeals, Moynihan Courthouse, 500 Pearl St, New York NY 10007, USA

**Walker, Jon Patrick** — Actor
Paradigm Agency, 360 N Crescent Dr, North Building, Beverly Hills CA 90210 USA

**Walker, Kelly** — Artist
5931 Glenoak Ave, Baltimore MD 21214, USA

**Walker, Kemba H** — Basketball Player
Charlotte Bobcats, 333 E Trade St, #A, Charlotte NC 28202 USA

**Walker, Kenneth (Kenny)** — Basketball Player
2252 Terrace Woods Park, Lexington KY 40513, USA

**Walker, Kenneth H** — Interior Designer
Future Brand, 300 Park Ave S, #700, New York NY 10010, USA

**Walker, Kevin (Geordie)** — Guitarist (Killing Joke)
Agency Group, 9348 Civic Center Dr, #200, Beverly Hills CA 90210 USA

**Walker, Kevin M** — Baseball Player
759 Chestnut Ave, Holtville CA 92250, USA

**Walker, Kurt** — Ice Hockey Player
1951 N Wesley Chapel Road, Eatonton GA 31024, USA

**Walker, Langston B** — Football Player
1281 Alder Creek Circle, San Leandro CA 94577, USA

**Walker, Larry K R** — Baseball Player
1667 Flagler Parkway, West Palm Beach FL 33411, USA

**Walker, Leonore** — Psychologist
Nova Southeastern University, Psychology Dept, Fort Lauderdale FL 33308, USA

**Walker, Little Toby** — Singer
PO Box 219, Wantagh NY 11793, USA

**Walker, Liza** — Actress
Jonathan Altaras Assoc, 11 Garrick St, London WC2E 9AR, England

**Walker, Lucy** — Director, Producer, Actress
Circle of Confusion, 8548 Washington Blvd, Culver City CA 90232, USA

**Walker, Mack** — Historian
Johns Hopkins University, History Dept, Baltimore MD 21218, USA

**Walker, Malcolm E, Jr** — Football Player
7140 Winterwood Lane, Dallas TX 75248, USA

**Walker, Marcy** — Actress
Leslie Bader, 2686 Lakewood Place, Westlake Village CA 91361, USA

**Walker, Marquis R** — Football Player
11576 Cherrylawn St, Detroit MI 48221, USA

**Walker, Michael C (Mike)** — Baseball Player
23195 Tankerley Road, Brooksville FL 34601, USA

**Walker, Michael Patrick** — Composer, Lyricist
W M E Entertainment, 1325 Ave of Americas, New York NY 10019 USA

**Walker, Mort** — Cartoonist (Beetle Bailey, Sarge)
61 Studio Road, Stamford CT 06903, USA

**Walker, Paul** — Actor
United Talent Agency, U T A Plaza, 9336 Civic Center Dr, Beverly Hills CA 90210 USA

**Walker, Peter** — Landscape Architect
Peter Walker Partners, 739 Allston Way, Berkeley CA 94710, USA

**Walker, Peter** — Director
23 Bentinck St, London W1U 2E8, England

**Walker, Peter B (Pete)** — Baseball Player
2 White Oak Lane, Quaker Hill CT 06375, USA

**Walker, Phillip (Phil) B** — Basketball Player
720 E Phil Ellena St, Philadelphia PA 19119, USA

**Walker, Polly** — Actress
Hamilton Hodell, 66-68 Margaret St, #500, London W1W 8SR, England

**Walker, R Thomas (Tom)** — Baseball Player
817 Whippoorwill Hill Road, Gibsonia PA 15044, USA

**Walker, Rebecca** — Writer
W M E Entertainment, 9601 Wilshire Blvd, #300, Beverly Hills CA 90210 USA

**Walker, Rick** — Football Player
906 Winstead St, Great Falls VA 22066, USA

**Walker, Sandra** — Opera Singer
Columbia Artists Mgmt Inc, 1790 Broadway, #702, New York NY 10019 USA

**Walker, Sarah E B** — Opera Singer
152 Inchmery Road, London SE6 1DF, England

**Walker, Scott** — Ice Hockey Player
301 Bailey Ridge Dr, Morrisville NC 27560, USA

**Walker, Scott** — Singer
Negus-Fancy Co, 78 Portland Road, London W11 4LQ, England
**Walker, Tim** — Photographer
Art & Commerce, 531 W 25th St, #400, New York NY 10001, USA
**Walker, Tonja** — Actress
Tonja Walker Productions, 404 E 76th St, #15C, New York NY 10021, USA
**Walker, Tyler L** — Baseball Player
45 Via del Sol, Nicasio CA 94946, USA
**Walker, Val J** — Football Player
3857 S Versailles Ave, Dallas TX 75209, USA
**Walker, Walter F (Wally)** — Basketball Player
154 Lombard St, #58, San Francisco CA 94111, USA
**Walker, Wayne H** — Football Player
2033 S White Pine Lane, Boise ID 83706, USA
**Wall, Angus** — Editor
Creative Artists Agency, 2000 Ave of Stars, #100, Los Angeles CA 90067 USA
**Wall, Brian A** — Sculptor
306 Lombard St, San Francisco CA 94133, USA
**Wall, Donnell L (Donne)** — Baseball Player
116 River Breeze Way, Saint Louis MO 63129, USA
**Wall, Erin** — Opera Singer
Columbia Artists Mgmt Inc, 1790 Broadway, #702, New York NY 10019 USA
**Wall, Frederick T** — Physical Chemist
2044 Kerwood Ave, Los Angeles CA 90025, USA
**Wall, John F** — Army General
507 Hanover St, Fredericksburg VA 22401, USA
**Wall, Lyndsay** — Ice Hockey Player
USA Hockey, 1775 Bob Johnson Dr, Colorado Springs CO 80906 USA
**Wall, M Danny** — Financier
1031 Chartwell Court, Salt Lake City UT 84103, USA
**Wall, Stanley A (Stan)** — Baseball Player
9907 E 80th St, Raytown MO 64138, USA
**Walla, Christopher (Chris)** — Singer, Guitarist (Death Cab for Cutie)
Zeitgeist Artist Mgmt, 660 York St, #216, San Francisco CA 94110, USA
**Wallace, Aaron J** — Football Player
9327 Edinburgh Lane, Frisco TX 75035, USA
**Wallace, Andy** — Auto Racing Driver
Childress-Howard Motorsports, PO Box 889, Denver NC 28037, USA
**Wallace, B Steven (Steve)** — Football Player
PO Box 76096, Atlanta GA 30358, USA
**Wallace, Ben** — Basketball Player
Phoenix Suns, 201 E Jefferson St, Phoenix AZ 85004 USA
**Wallace, Bruce** — Geneticist
940 McBryde Dr, Blacksburg VA 24060, USA
**Wallace, Christopher (Chris)** — Commentator
Fox-TV, News Dept, 205 E 67th St, New York NY 10065 USA
**Wallace, Craig K** — Physician
National Institutes of Health, 9000 Rockville Pike, Bethesda MD 20892, USA
**Wallace, Dee** — Actress
Amsel Eisenstadt Frazier, 5055 Wilshire Blvd, #865, Los Angeles CA 90036 USA
**Wallace, Don** — Actor
S M S Talent, 8383 Wilshire Blvd, #230, Beverly Hills CA 90211 USA
**Wallace, Gerald J** — Basketball Player
8381 Providence Road, Charlotte NC 28277, USA
**Wallace, J Clifford** — Judge
US Court of Appeals, 940 Front St, #5140, San Diego CA 92101, USA
**Wallace, Jane** — Entertainer
Cosgrove-Meurer Productions, 4303 W Verdugo Ave, Burbank CA 91505, USA
**Wallace, Jeffrey A (Jeff)** — Baseball Player
2904 Federal Ave, Alliance OH 44601, USA
**Wallace, Julie T** — Actress
Annette Stone, 9 Newburgh St, London W1V 1LH, England
**Wallace, Kenny** — Auto Racing Driver
8995 Harris Road, Concord NC 28027, USA
**Wallace, Marilyn** — Writer
Random House, 1745 Broadway, #1800, New York NY 10019 USA
**Wallace, Michael S (Mike)** — Baseball Player
12483 Elk Run Road, Midland VA 22728, USA
**Wallace, Mike** — Auto Racing Driver
Morgan-McClure Racing, 26502 Newbanks Road, Abington VA 24210, USA
**Wallace, Nayo** — Actress
Visionary Artists, 7162 Beverly Blvd, #324, Los Angeles CA 90036, USA
**Wallace, Randall** — Director
Media Talent Group, 9200 Sunset Blvd, #550, West Hollywood CA 90069, USA
**Wallace, Rasheed A** — Basketball Player
1979 Arthurs Way, Rochester Hills MI 48306, USA
**Wallace, Rheagan** — Actress
Creative Management Group, 8522 National Blvd, #108, Culver City CA 90232 USA
**Wallace, Robert C (Bob)** — Football Player
44111 N 43rd Dr, New River AZ 85087, USA
**Wallace, Robert Glenn** — Businessman
PO Box 10003, College Station TX 77842, USA
**Wallace, Russell W (Rusty), Jr** — Auto Racing Driver
16229 Jettson Road, Cornelius NC 28031, USA
**Wallach, Eli** — Actor
90 Riverside Dr, #6B, New York NY 10024, USA
**Wallach, Evan J** — Judge
US International Trade Court, 1 Federal Plaza, New York NY 10278, USA
**Wallach, Timothy C (Tim)** — Baseball Player
21750 Deveron Cove, Yorba Linda CA 92887, USA
**Wallack, Melissa** — Writer
I C M Partners, 10250 Constellation Blvd, #900, Los Angeles CA 90067 USA
**Wallberg, Heinz** — Conductor
Stocksiepen, 45133 Essen, Germany
**Wallem, Linda** — Producer
Jackoway Tyerman Wertheimer, 1925 Century Park E, #2200, Los Angeles CA 90067 USA

| | |
|---|---|
| **Wallenda, Delilah**<br>3650 Henrietta Place, Sarasota FL 34234, USA | Circus Tightrope Walker |
| **Wallenda, Nikolas (Nik)**<br>Wallenda Enterprises, PO Box 52551, Sarasota FL 34232, USA | Circus Tightrope Walker |
| **Wallenda, Tino**<br>3650 Henrietta Place, Sarasota FL 34234, USA | Circus Tightrope Walker |
| **Wallenstein, Andrew**<br>Variety, 5900 Wilshire Blvd, #3100, Los Angeles CA 90036, USA | Editor |
| **Waller, Anthony**<br>Seven Arts Pictures, 6121 W Sunset Blvd, #512, Los Angeles CA 90028, USA | Director |
| **Waller, Robert James**<br>12 Old Harper Road, Harper TX 78631, USA | Writer |
| **Waller, Ronald B (Ron)**<br>8773 Concord Road, Seaford DE 19973, USA | Football Player |
| **Wallerstein, Ralph G**<br>3447 Clay St, San Francisco CA 94118, USA | Hematologist |
| **Wallfisch, Raphael**<br>Ikon Artists Mgmt, 52 Upper St, #111B, London N1 0QH, England | Concert Cellist |
| **Walliams, David**<br>Troika, 74 Clekrenwell St, London EC1M 5QA, England | Actor |
| **Wallin, Niclas**<br>244 Johnson Ave, Los Gatos CA 95030, USA | Ice Hockey Player |
| **Walling, Camryn**<br>Abrams Artists, 9200 W Sunset Blvd, #1125, West Hollywood CA 90069 USA | Actor |
| **Walling, Dennis (Denny)**<br>PO Box 1312, Waynesboro VA 22980, USA | Baseball Player |
| **Wallinger, Karl**<br>Agency Group Ltd, 142 W 57th St, #600, New York NY 10019 USA | Keyboardist, Songwriter |
| **Wallis, Annabelle**<br>I C M Partners, 10250 Constellation Blvd, #900, Los Angeles CA 90067 USA | Actress |
| **Wallis, H Joseph (Joe)**<br>PO Box 659, Chesterfield MO 63006, USA | Baseball Player |
| **Wallis, Michael**<br>Perfect Impressions, 154 Seminole Dr, Springfield IL 62704, USA | Writer |
| **Wallis, Shani**<br>2119 Via Puerta, #Q, Laguna Woods CA 92637, USA | Actress, Singer |
| **Walliser, Maria**<br>Selfwingert, 7208 Malans, Switzerland | Alpine Skier |
| **Walls, C Wesley**<br>8711 Lake Challis Lane, Charlotte NC 28226, USA | Football Player |
| **Walls, Denise (Nee-C)**<br>2113 South Ave, Youngstown OH 44502, USA | Singer (Annointed), Songwriter |
| **Walls, Everson C**<br>4812 Portrait Lane, Plano TX 75024, USA | Football Player |
| **Walls, Jeannette**<br>Charles Scribner's Sons, 866 3rd Ave, New York NY 10022 USA | Writer |
| **Walls, Lenny B**<br>2800 Bush St, San Francisco CA 94115, USA | Football Player |
| **Walmsley, Jon**<br>Howard Talent West, 10657 Riverside Dr, Toluca Lake CA 91602, USA | Actor |
| **Walsch, Neale Donald**<br>Trident Media Group, 41 Madison Ave, #3600, New York NY 10010 USA | Writer |
| **Walser, Derrick**<br>592 Lorne St, New Glasgow NS B2H 4L3, Canada | Ice Hockey Player |
| **Walser, Martin**<br>Zum Hecht 36, 88662 Uberlingen-Nussdorf, Germany | Writer |
| **Walsh Jennings, Kerri L**<br>PO Box 33053, Los Gatos CA 95031, USA | Volleyball Player |
| **Walsh, Amanda**<br>I C M Partners, 10250 Constellation Blvd, #900, Los Angeles CA 90067 USA | Actress |
| **Walsh, Baillie**<br>Independent Talent Group, 40 Whitfield St, London W1T 2RH, England | Director |
| **Walsh, David M**<br>Gersh Agency, 9465 Wilshire Blvd, #600, Beverly Hills CA 90212 USA | Cinematographer |
| **Walsh, David P (Dave)**<br>500 Concord Lane, Edmond OK 73003, USA | Baseball Player |
| **Walsh, Diana Chapman**<br>Wellesley College, President's Office, Wellesley MA 02181, USA | Educator |
| **Walsh, Don**<br>International Maritime Inc, 14758 Sitkum Lane, Myrtle Point OR 97458, USA | Underwater Explorer |
| **Walsh, Donnie**<br>Indiana Pacers, Conseco Fieldhouse, 125 S Pennsylvania, Indianapolis IN 46204 USA | Basketball Coach, Executive |
| **Walsh, Dylan**<br>Gersh Agency, 9465 Wilshire Blvd, #600, Beverly Hills CA 90212 USA | Actor |
| **Walsh, Gwynyth**<br>Allman/Rea Mgmt, 141 Barrington Ave, Los Angeles CA 90049, USA | Actress |
| **Walsh, Joe**<br>Front Line Mgmt, 1100 Glendon Ave, #2000, Los Angeles CA 90024 USA | Singer, Guitarist (Eagles); Songwriter |
| **Walsh, John**<br>3111 S Dixie Highway, #244, West Palm Beach FL 33405, USA | Producer, Director, Actor |
| **Walsh, John, Jr**<br>J Paul Getty Museum, Getty Center, 1200 Getty Center Dr, Los Angeles CA 90049, USA | Museum Executive |
| **Walsh, Kate**<br>Creative Artists Agency, 2000 Ave of Stars, #100, Los Angeles CA 90067 USA | Actress |
| **Walsh, Kimberly J**<br>Concorde International, 101 Shepherds Bush Road, London W6 7LP, England | Singer (Girls Aloud) |
| **Walsh, Lawrence E**<br>1902 Bedford St, Nichols Hills OK 73116, USA | Government Official, Attorney |
| **Walsh, M Emmet**<br>S L J Mgmt, 833 N Edinburgh Ave, PH 11, Los Angeles CA 90046, USA | Actor |
| **Walsh, Maiara**<br>A P A Talent/Literary Agency, 405 S Beverly Dr, #300, Beverly Hills CA 90212 USA | Actress |
| **Walsh, Martin**<br>National Organization on Disability, 910 16th NW, #400, Washington DC 20006, USA | Association Executive |
| **Walsh, Martin**<br>Independent Talent Group, 40 Whitfield St, London W1T 2RH, England | Editor |

| | |
|---|---|
| **Walsh, Matt** | Actor, Comedian, Producer |
| Principato-Young, 9465 Wilshire Blvd, #880, Beverly Hills CA 90212 USA | |
| **Walsh, Patrick C** | Urologist |
| Johns Hopkins University, Brady Urological Institute, Baltimore MD 21205, USA | |
| **Walsh, Peter** | Actor |
| Paradigm Agency, 360 N Crescent Dr, North Building, Beverly Hills CA 90210 USA | |
| **Walsh, Stephen J (Steve)** | Football Player |
| 8801 Wellington View Dr, West Palm Beach FL 33411, USA | |
| **Walsh, Sydney** | Actress |
| Connor Ankrum Assoc, 1680 Vine St, #1016, Los Angeles CA 90028, USA | |
| **Walsh, Tom** | Sculptor |
| PO Box 133, Philomath OR 97370, USA | |
| **Walsh, Willie** | Businessman |
| British Airways, Waterside, PO Box 365, Harmondsworth UB7 0GB, England | |
| **Walsman, Leanna** | Actress |
| I C M Partners, 10250 Constellation Blvd, #900, Los Angeles CA 90067 USA | |
| **Walter, Gene W** | Baseball Player |
| 1901 Fairway Dr, LaGrange KY 40031, USA | |
| **Walter, Jessica** | Actress |
| Innovative Artists, 1505 10th St, Santa Monica CA 90401 USA | |
| **Walter, Joseph F (Joe), Jr** | Football Player |
| 4136 Binley Dr, Richardson TX 75082, USA | |
| **Walter, Lisa Ann** | Actress, Comedienne, Writer, Producer |
| Abrams Artists, 9200 W Sunset Blvd, #1125, West Hollywood CA 90069 USA | |
| **Walter, Michael D (Mike)** | Football Player |
| 6900 SW Knollwood St, Tualatin OR 97062, USA | |
| **Walter, Robert D** | Businessman |
| Cardinal Health, 7000 Cardinal Place, Dublin OH 43017, USA | |
| **Walter, Ryan** | Ice Hockey Player |
| Vancouver Canucks, 800 Griffiths Way, Vancouver BC V6B 6G1, Canada | |
| **Walter, Tracey** | Actress |
| Stone Manners Salners, 9911 W Pico Blvd, #1400, Los Angeles CA 90035 USA | |
| **Walter, Ulrich** | Astronaut, Germany |
| I B M Germany, Schonaicherstr 220, 71032 Boblingen, Germany | |
| **Walters, Barbara** | Commentator |
| 944 5th Ave, #6, New York NY 10021, USA | |
| **Walters, Charles L (Charlie)** | Baseball Player |
| 1717 Sutton Lane, Saint Paul MN 55118, USA | |
| **Walters, Dale** | Boxer |
| Ringside Fitness, 4 Bentall Centre, #49271, Vancouver BC V5Y 1C7, Canada | |
| **Walters, David** | Swimmer |
| Premier Management Group, 115 Crescent Commons, Cary, NC 27518 USA | |
| **Walters, David L** | Governor, OK |
| RR 2, Watts OK 74964, USA | |
| **Walters, Harry N** | Government Official |
| D H C Holdings Corp, 125 Thomas Dale, Williamsburg VA 23185, USA | |
| **Walters, Jamie** | Actor, Singer |
| Atlantic Records, 9229 W Sunset Blvd, #900, West Hollywood CA 90069 USA | |
| **Walters, Julie** | Actress |
| I C M Partners, 10250 Constellation Blvd, #900, Los Angeles CA 90067 USA | |
| **Walters, Kirk** | Editorial Cartoonist |
| Toledo Blade, Editorial Dept, 541 N Superior St, Toledo OH 43660, USA | |
| **Walters, Lisa** | Golfer |
| 211 S Westland Ave, #2, Tampa FL 33606, USA | |
| **Walters, Melora** | Actress |
| Medavoy Mgmt, 10203 Santa Monica Blvd, #400, Los Angeles CA 90067 USA | |
| **Walters, Michael C (Mike)** | Baseball Player |
| 79070 Desert Stream Dr, La Quinta CA 92253, USA | |
| **Walters, Minette** | Writer |
| Panmacmillan, 20 New Wharf Road, London N1 9RR, England | |
| **Walters, Peter I** | Businessman |
| 22 Hill St, London W1X 7FU, England | |
| **Walters, Rex A** | Basketball Player |
| 690 45th Ave, San Francisco CA 94121, USA | |
| **Walters, Ron** | Ice Hockey Player |
| 8 Garrison Crescent, Sherwood Park AB T8A 2S8, Canada | |
| **Walters, Stanley P (Stan)** | Football Player |
| 2021 W Wesley Road NW, Atlanta GA 30327, USA | |
| **Walters, Susan** | Actress |
| Allman/Rea Mgmt, 9255 Sunset Blvd, #600, Los Angeles CA 90069, USA | |
| **Walters, Troy M** | Football Player |
| 2843 Prado, Grand Prairie TX 75054, USA | |
| **Walthall, Romy** | Actress |
| Defining Artists, 10 Universal City Plaza, #2000, Universal City CA 91608 USA | |
| **Walthan, John** | Baseball Manager |
| 1354 NE Todd George Road, Lees Summit MO 64086, USA | |
| **Walther, Herbert** | Physicist |
| Egenhoferstr 7A, 81243 Munich, Germany | |
| **Walther, Paul G** | Basketball Player |
| 6555 Riverside Dr NW, Atlanta GA 30328, USA | |
| **Walther, Philip** | Physicist |
| University of Vienna, Physics Dept, Boltzmanngasse 5, 1090 Vienna, Austria | |
| **Walton, Anthony J (Tony)** | Costume, Set Designer |
| Costume Design Guild, 11969 Ventura Blvd, #100, Studio City CA 91604 USA | |
| **Walton, Anthony J (Tony)** | Scenic Designer, Illustrator |
| I C M Partners, 730 5th Ave, New York NY 10019 USA | |
| **Walton, Bruce K** | Baseball Player |
| 10704 Sunset Canyon Dr, Bakersfield CA 93311, USA | |
| **Walton, Christy R** | Businesswoman |
| Wal-Mart Stores, 702 SW 8th St, Bentonville AR 72712, USA | |
| **Walton, Daniel J (Danny)** | Baseball Player |
| PO Box 296, Huntsville UT 84317, USA | |
| **Walton, David** | Actor |
| One Set One Rep Productions, 839 N Gardner St, Los Angeles CA 90046, USA | |
| **Walton, Jim C** | Businessman |
| CNN-TV, 190 Marietta Ave SW, Atlanta GA 30303 USA | |

**Walton, Joseph (Joe)** — Football Player, Coach
8 Windycrest Dr, Beaver Falls PA 15010, USA
**Walton, Kendall L** — Philosopher
University of Michigan, Philosophy Dept, Ann Arbor MI 48109, USA
**Walton, Lawrence J (Larry)** — Football Player
PO Box 32204, Phoenix AZ 85064, USA
**Walton, Luke T** — Basketball Player
1613 Gates Ave, Manhattan Beach CA 90266, USA
**Walton, Mike** — Ice Hockey Player
Re/Max Professionals, 200-270 Kingsway, Etobicoke ON M9A 3T7, Canada
**Walton, S Robson (Rob)** — Businessman
Wal-Mart Stores, 702 SW 8th St, Bentonville AR 72716, USA
**Walton, William T (Bill), III** — Basketball Player, Sportscaster
1010 Myrtle Way, San Diego CA 92103, USA
**Waltrip, Darrell L** — Auto, Truck Racing Driver
Michael Waltrip Racing, 20310 Chartwell Center Dr, Cornelius NC 28031, USA
**Waltrip, Michael C (Mike)** — Auto Racing Driver
Michael Waltrip Racing, 20310 Chartwell Center Dr, Cornelius NC 28031, USA
**Waltz, Christoph** — Actor
Players Agentur Mgmt, Sophienstra 21, 10178 Berlin-Mitte, Germany
**Waltz, Lisa** — Actress
Stone Manners Salners, 9911 W Pico Blvd, #1400, Los Angeles CA 90035 USA
**Waluska, Nick** — Guitarist (Wondermints)
Paradise Artists, PO Box 1821, Ojai CA 93024 USA
**Walz, Carl E** — Astronaut
15506 Eagle Tavern Lane, Centreville VA 20120, USA
**Walz, Wesley (Wes)** — Ice Hockey Player
10435 Raleigh Road, Saint Paul MN 55129, USA
**Wamala, Emmanuel Cardinal** — Religious Leader
PO Box 14125, Mengo, Kampala, Uganda
**Wambach, M Abigail (Abby)** — Soccer Player
Powerplay Consultants, 1600 Parkwood Circle SE, #600, Atlanta GA 30339, USA
**Wambaugh, Joseph** — Writer
3520 Kellogg Way, San Diego CA 92106, USA
**Wamsley, Rick** — Ice Hockey Player
Saint Louis Blues, Scott Trade Center, 1401 Clark Ave, Saint Louis MO 63103 USA
**Wan Li** — Government Official, China
State Council, People's Congress, Tiananmen Square, Beijing 100006, China
**Wanamaker, Zoe** — Actress
Conway Van Gelder Grant, 8-12 Broadwick St, #300, London W1F 8HW, England
**Wand, Seth P** — Football Player
5515 NW 93rd St, Kansas City MO 64154, USA
**Wandmacher, Michael** — Composer
First Artists Mgmt, 4764 Park Granada, #210, Calabasas CA 91302 USA
**Wang Chunlu** — Speed Skater
Skating Assn, 56 Zhongguancun South St, Haidian, Beijing 100044, China
**Wang Jida** — Sculptor
7612 35th Ave, #3E, Jackson Heights NY 11372, USA
**Wang Jin** — Artist
Chinese Contemporary Gallery, Studio House, 7/9 Edith Grove, London SW 10 0JZ, England
**Wang Junxia** — Track Athlete
Athletic Assn, 9 Tiyuguan Road, Chongwen District, Beijing 100061, China
**Wang Meng** — Speed Skater
Skating Assn, 56 Zhongguancun South St, Haidian, Beijing 100044, China
**Wang Tian Ren** — Sculptor
Shaanxi Sculpture Institute, Longshoucun, Xi'am, Shaanxi 710016, China
**Wang Zhi Zhi** — Basketball Player
Miami Heat, American Airlines Arena, 601 Biscayne Blvd, Miami FL 33132 USA
**Wang, Chien-Ming** — Baseball Player
New York Yankees, Yankee Stadium, E 161st St & River Ave, Bronx NY 10451 USA
**Wang, Garrett** — Actor
501 E Del Mar Blvd, #310, Pasadena CA 91101, USA
**Wang, Henry Y** — Chemical Engineer
University of Michigan, Chemical Engineering Dept, Ann Arbor MI 48109, USA
**Wang, Peggy** — Singer (Pains of Being Pure at Heart)
Slumberland Records, PO Box 19029, Oakland CA 94619, USA
**Wang, Taylor G** — Astronaut, Physicist
1224 Arno Dr, Sierra Madre CA 91024, USA
**Wang, Vera** — Fashion Designer
Vera Wang Bridal House, 225 W 39th St, #900, New York NY 10018, USA
**Wang, Wayne** — Director
I C M Partners, 10250 Constellation Blvd, #900, Los Angeles CA 90067 USA
**Wang, Zhong L** — Nanotechnologist
Georgia Institute of Technology, Nanostructure Center, Atlanta GA 30332, USA
**Wangchuck, Jigme Khesar Namgyal** — King, Bhutan
Royal Palace, Tashichhodzong, Thimphu, Bhutan
**Wangchuck, Lyonpo Khandu** — Prime Minister, Bhutan
Jangsa, Shari Geog, Paro, Bhutan
**Wangchuk, Jigme Singye** — King, Bhutan
Royal Palace, Tashichhodzong, Thimphu, Bhutan
**Wanner, H Eric** — Foundation Executive
Russell Sage Foundation, 112 E 64th St, New York NY 10065, USA
**Wannstedt, David R (Dave)** — Football Coach
151 Rock Haven Lane, Pittsburgh PA 15228, USA
**Wansel, Dexter G** — Keyboardist, Pianist
Walt Reeder Productions, 93 Old Yorke Road, #1-604, Jenkintown PA 19046, USA
**Wanzer, Robert F (Bobby)** — Basketball Player
28 Greenwood Park, Pittsford NY 14534, USA
**Waples, Keith** — Harness Racing Driver
PO Box 632, Durham ON N0G 1R0, Canada
**Waples, Ronald (Ron)** — Harness Racing Driver, Trainer
7 Mill Run W, Hightstown NJ 08520, USA
**Wapner, Joseph A** — Entertainer, Judge
C E S D, 10635 Santa Monica Blvd, #130, Los Angeles CA 90025 USA
**Wapnick, Steven L (Steve)** — Baseball Player
5934 Woodcliffe Dr, Windsor CO 80550, USA

# W

**Wappel, Gord** — Ice Hockey Player
5544 Kartusch Place, Regina SK S4X 4K1, Canada
**Warbeck, Stephen** — Composer
United Agents, 12-26 Lexington St, London W1F 0LE, England
**Warburton, Patrick** — Actor
Sutton-Barth Vennari, 5900 Wilshire Blvd, #700, Los Angeles CA 90036 USA
**Warby, Kenneth P (Ken)** — Boat Racing Driver
7432 State Route 128, Miamitown OH 45041, USA
**Warchus, Matthew** — Director
Hamilton Hodell, 66-68 Margaret St, #500, London W1W 8SR, England
**Ward, Aaron** — Ice Hockey Player
112 Ronsard Lane, Cary NC 27511, USA
**Ward, Andre** — Jazz Saxophonist
Celebrity Talent Agency, 111 E 14th St, #249, New York NY 10003 USA
**Ward, Andre** — Boxer
Prince Boxing Gym, 3030 Jensen Dr, Houston TX 77026, USA
**Ward, Anita** — Singer
Richard Walters, PO Box 2789, Toluca Lake CA 91610 USA
**Ward, Bryan A** — Baseball Player
140 Bannock Court, East Dundee IL 60118, USA
**Ward, Burt** — Actor
Gentle Giants & Adoptions, PO Box 6005, Norco CA 92860, USA
**Ward, Burton** — Auto Racing Driver
Bill Davis Racing, 301 Old Thomasville Road, Winston Salem NC 27107, USA
**Ward, Cameron (Cam)** — Ice Hockey Player
1608 Shambrook Court, Raleigh NC 27614, USA
**Ward, Carlos N** — Jazz Saxophonist (B T Express)
Star-Vest Mgmt, 102 Ryders Lane, East Brunswick NJ 08816, USA
**Ward, Charlie** — Football, Basketball Player
3717 Drake St, Houston TX 77005, USA
**Ward, Christian** — Artist
Max Wigram Gallery, 106 New Bond St, London W1S 1DN, England
**Ward, Christopher L J (Chris)** — Football Player
PO Box 1365, Inglewood CA 90308, USA
**Ward, Colin N** — Baseball Player
PO Box 21413, Mesa AZ 85277, USA
**Ward, Dale** — Singer (Crescendo)
A Crosse the World, PO Box 23066, London W11 3FR, England
**Ward, David** — Opera Singer
1 Kennedy Crescent, Lake Wanaka, New Zealand
**Ward, David S** — Director, Writer
I C M Partners, 10250 Constellation Blvd, #900, Los Angeles CA 90067 USA
**Ward, Dedric L** — Football Player
3435 N 45th St, Phoenix AZ 85018, USA
**Ward, Dixon** — Ice Hockey Player
Okanagan Hockey School, 201-851 Eckhardt W, Penticton BC V2A 9C4, Canada
**Ward, Douglas Turner** — Actor, Writer
Negro Ensemble Co, 303 W 42nd St, #501, New York NY 10036, USA
**Ward, Edward J (Ed)** — Ice Hockey Player
9150 Weathervane Trail, Galesburg MI 49053, USA
**Ward, Fred** — Actor
A P A Talent/Literary Agency, 405 S Beverly Dr, #300, Beverly Hills CA 90212 USA
**Ward, Gemma** — Model
Creative Artists Agency, 2000 Ave of Stars, #100, Los Angeles CA 90067 USA
**Ward, Hines E, Jr** — Football Player
155 Fairfax Road, Pittsburgh PA 15221, USA
**Ward, Jacky** — Singer
821 19th Ave S, Nashville TN 37203, USA
**Ward, Jeff** — Motorcycle Racing Rider
Speed Technologies, 9716 S Virginia St, Reno NV 89511, USA
**Ward, JoAnn** — Actress, Producer
Creative Artists Agency, 2000 Ave of Stars, #100, Los Angeles CA 90067 USA
**Ward, John T, Jr** — Thoroughbred Racing Trainer
573 Clay Kiser Road, Paris KY 40361, USA
**Ward, Jonathan** — Actor
Auckland Actors, PO Box 56460, Dominion Road, Auckland 1030, New Zealand
**Ward, Kevin M** — Baseball Player
160 F Ave, Coronado CA 92118, USA
**Ward, Lauren** — Actress
Gavin Barker Assoc, 2D Wimpole St, London W1G 0EB, England
**Ward, M** — Singer (She & Him), Songwriter
Ground Control Touring, 420 W Main St, Carrboro NC 27510, USA
**Ward, Mickey (Irish)** — Boxer
132 Upham St, Lowell MA 01851, USA
**Ward, Pam** — Sportscaster
ESPN-TV, ESPN Plaza, 935 Middle St, Bristol CT 06010 USA
**Ward, Preston M** — Baseball Player
4371 De Silva Place, Las Vegas NV 89121, USA
**Ward, R Duane** — Baseball Player
1723 Letsche St, #90, Pittsburgh PA 15212, USA
**Ward, Rachel** — Actress, Director
Himber Entertainment, PO Box 950, South Orange NJ 07079 USA
**Ward, Rebecca** — Fencer
Oregon Fencing Alliance, 4840 SW Western Ave, #80, Beaverton OR 97005, USA
**Ward, Robert R (Bob)** — Football Player
515 N Academy St, Greensboro MD 21639, USA
**Ward, Ronald (Scooter)** — Singer (Cold)
Front Line Mgmt, 1100 Glendon Ave, #2000, Los Angeles CA 90024 USA
**Ward, Ronald L (Ron)** — Ice Hockey Player
3178 W 140th St, Cleveland OH 44111, USA
**Ward, Sela** — Actress
Management 360, 9111 Wilshire Blvd, Beverly Hills CA 90210 USA
**Ward, Susan** — Actress, Model
Pakula/King, 9229 W Sunset Blvd, #315, West Hollywood CA 90069 USA
**Ward, Tom** — Actor
Independent Talent Group, 40 Whitfield St, London W1T 2RH, England

**Ward, Turner M** — Baseball Player
232 Autumn Dr, Saraland AL 36571, USA
**Ward, Vincent** — Director, Writer, Actor
United Talent Agency, U T A Plaza, 9336 Civic Center Dr, Beverly Hills CA 90210 USA
**Ward, Wendy** — Golfer
12850 Sassin Station Road N, Edwall WA 99008, USA
**Ward, William T (Bill)** — Singer, Drummer (Black Sabbath)
Sharon Osborne Mgmt, 8899 Beverly Blvd, #905, West Hollywood CA 90048, USA
**Ward, Zach** — Actor
Diverse Talent Group, 9911 W Pico Blvd, #350W, Los Angeles CA 90035, USA
**Warden, John** — Attorney
Sullivan & Cromwell 125 Broad St, New York NY 10004, USA
**Warden, Jonathan E (Jon)** — Baseball Player
6575 Oasis Dr, Loveland OH 45140, USA
**Warden, Rick** — Actor
Independent Talent Group, 40 Whitfield St, London W1T 2RH, England
**Wardlaw, Kim McLane** — Judge
US Court of Appeals, 125 S Grand Ave, Pasadena CA 91105, USA
**Wardle, Curtis J (Curt)** — Baseball Player
13900 Pheasant Knoll Lane, Moreno Valley CA 92553, USA
**Ware, Andre** — Football Player, Sportscaster
3910 Wood Park, Sugar Land TX 77479, USA
**Ware, Billy** — Percussionist (BeauSoleil)
Rosebud Agency, PO Box 170429, San Francisco CA 94117 USA
**Ware, Chris** — Cartoonist
Fantagraphics Books, 7563 Lake City Way NE, Seattle WA 98115, USA
**Ware, DeMarcus** — Football Player
690 Rockingham Court, Colleyville TX 76034, USA
**Ware, Jeffrey A (Jeff)** — Baseball Player
2560 Mulberry Loop, Virginia Beach VA 23456, USA
**Ware, Justin** — Writer, Actor
Gersh Agency, 9465 Wilshire Blvd, #600, Beverly Hills CA 90212 USA
**Warfield, Paul D** — Football Player
16 Normandy Way, Rancho Mirage CA 92270, USA
**Warfield, Sonja** — Writer
Creative Artists Agency, 2000 Ave of Stars, #100, Los Angeles CA 90067 USA
**Wargo, Tom** — Golfer
2801 Putter Dr, Centralia IL 62801, USA
**Warhola, James** — Writer, Illustrator
56 Walkers Hill, Tivoli NY 12583, USA
**Wariner, Steve** — Singer, Guitarist, Songwriter
Steve Wariner Productions, PO Box 1647, Franklin TN 37065, USA
**Waring, Todd** — Actor
145 W 45th St, #1204, New York NY 10036, USA
**Warkentin, Thomas (Tom)** — Cartoonist (Flash Gordon)
King Features Syndicate, 300 W 57th St, #1500, New York NY 10019 USA
**Warlock, Billy** — Actor
Abrams Artists, 9200 W Sunset Blvd, #1125, West Hollywood CA 90069 USA
**Warmack, Chance** — Football Player
Tennessee Titans, 460 Great Circle Road, Nashville TN 37228 USA
**Warmenhoven, Daniel J** — Businessman
Network Appliance Inc, 495 E Java Dr, Sunnyvale CA 94089, USA
**Warnecke, Mark** — Swimmer
Am Schichtmeister 100, 58453 Witten, Germany
**Warner, Amelia** — Actress
Authentic Talent Mgmt, 20 Jay St, #M17, Brooklyn NY 11201 USA
**Warner, Chris** — Cartoonist (Black Cross)
Dark Horse Publishing, 10956 SE Main St, Portland OR 97222 USA
**Warner, Cornell** — Basketball Player
2479 Glen Meadow Lane, Escondido CA 92027, USA
**Warner, Curtis E (Curt)** — Football Player
Curt Warner Chevrolet, 10811 SE Mill Plain Blvd, Vancouver WA 98664, USA
**Warner, David** — Actor
Julian Belfrage Assoc, 9 Argyll St, #300, London W1F 7TG, England
**Warner, Douglas A, III** — Financier
J P Morgan Chase, 270 Park Ave, #1200, New York NY 10017, USA
**Warner, Jack D** — Baseball Player
5938 W Calle Lejos, Glendale AZ 85310, USA
**Warner, Jack Lionel** — Architect
Warner Group Architects, 1250 Coast Village Road, #J, Santa Barbara CA 93108, USA
**Warner, Jane** — Model
166 Ditching Road, Brighton Essex BN1 6JA, England
**Warner, Jim** — Ice Hockey Player
2011 Upper Saint Dennis Road, Saint Paul MN 55116, USA
**Warner, John J (Jackie)** — Baseball Player
19136 Highway 18 N, Apple Valley CA 92307, USA
**Warner, John W** — Senator, VA
Atoka Farm, PO Box 1320, Middleburg VA 20118, USA
**Warner, Julie** — Actress
Innovative Artists, 1505 10th St, Santa Monica CA 90401 USA
**Warner, Kurtis E (Kurt)** — Football Player
6712 E Cheney Dr, Paradise Valley AZ 85253, USA
**Warner, Malcolm-Jamal** — Actor
Abrams Artists, 9200 W Sunset Blvd, #1125, West Hollywood CA 90069 USA
**Warner, Margaret** — Commentator
News Hour Show, 2700 S Quincy St, #250, Arlington VA 22206, USA
**Warner, T C** — Actress
S D B Partners, 1801 Ave of Stars, #902, Los Angeles CA 90067 USA
**Warner, Todd** — Sculptor
155 NW 11th St, Boca Raton FL 33432, USA
**Warner, Tom** — Producer
Carsey-Warner Productions, 4024 Radford Ave, Building 3, Studio City CA 91604, USA
**Warner, Ty** — Toy Designer
Ty Inc, PO Box 5377, Hinsdale IL 60522, USA
**Warnes, Jennifer** — Singer, Songwriter
Donald Miller, 12746 Kling St, Studio City CA 91604, USA

| | |
|---|---|
| **Warnock, John E**<br>Adobe Systems, 375 Park Ave, San Jose CA 95110, USA | Businessman |
| **Warren G**<br>Progressive Global Agency, PO Box 50294, Nashville TN 37025, USA | Rap Artist |
| **Warren, Christoper (Chris), Jr**<br>Innovative Artists, 1505 10th St, Santa Monica CA 90401 USA | Actor |
| **Warren, Christopher C (Chris), Jr**<br>13707 Black Spruce Way, Chantilly VA 20151, USA | Football Player |
| **Warren, Cicero**<br>119 Brookwood St, East Orange NJ 07018, USA | Baseball Player |
| **Warren, Diane**<br>1896 Rising Glen Road, Los Angeles CA 90069, USA | Songwriter |
| **Warren, Donald J (Don)**<br>13507 Wilder Court, Clifton VA 20124, USA | Football Player |
| **Warren, Estella**<br>Don Buchwald, 6500 Wilshire Blvd, #2200, Los Angeles CA 90048 USA | Model, Actress |
| **Warren, Frederick M**<br>65 Cambridge Terrace, Christchurch 80013, New Zealand | Architect |
| **Warren, Gerard T**<br>13786 NE 222nd Place, Raiford FL 32083, USA | Football Player |
| **Warren, Gloria**<br>16872 Bosque Dr, Encino CA 91436, USA | Singer, Actress |
| **Warren, Gregory R (Greg)**<br>14 S 18th St, Pittsburgh PA 15203, USA | Football Player |
| **Warren, J Robin**<br>178 Lake St, Perth WA 6000, Australia | Nobel Medicine Laureate |
| **Warren, Jennifer**<br>1675 Old Oak Road, Los Angeles CA 90049, USA | Actress |
| **Warren, Kenneth S**<br>Picower Medical Research Institute, 350 Community Dr, Manhasset NY 11030, USA | Immunologist |
| **Warren, Kiersten**<br>Mitchell K Stubbs Assoc, 8695 W Washington Blvd, #204, Culver City CA 90232 USA | Actress |
| **Warren, Lamont A**<br>17735 Sorrel Ridge Dr, Spring TX 77388, USA | Football Player |
| **Warren, Lesley Ann**<br>Innovative Artists, 1505 10th St, Santa Monica CA 90401 USA | Actress |
| **Warren, Marc**<br>Ken McReddie Assoc, 101 Finsbury Pavement, London EC2A 1RS, England | Actor |
| **Warren, Michael (Mike)**<br>21216 Escondido St, Woodland Hills CA 91364, USA | Actor, Basketball Player |
| **Warren, Richard D (Rick)**<br>Saddleback Church, 1 Saddleback Parkway, Lake Forest CA 92630, USA | Evangelist, Writer |
| **Warren, Robert G (Bobby)**<br>989 Hardin Wadesboro Road, Hardin KY 42048, USA | Basketball Player |
| **Warren, Ron**<br>4025 Paddock Road, #401, Cincinnati OH 45229, USA | Baseball Player |
| **Warren, Rosanna**<br>11 Robinwood Ave, Needham MA 02492, USA | Writer |
| **Warren, Thomas L**<br>National Wildlife Federation, 11100 Wildlife Center Dr, Reston VA 20190, USA | Association Executive |
| **Warren, Tom**<br>2393 La Marque St, San Diego CA 92109, USA | Triathlete |
| **Warren, Ty'ron M (Ty)**<br>22 Ronald C Meyer Dr, North Attleboro MA 02760, USA | Football Player |
| **Warren, William M, Jr**<br>Energen Corp, 605 Richard Arrington Jr Blvd N, Birmingham AL 35203, USA | Businessman |
| **Warrener, Rhett**<br>761 W Ferry St, Buffalo NY 14222, USA | Ice Hockey Player |
| **Warren-Green, Christopher**<br>Charlotte Symphony Orchestra, 301 S Tryon St, #1700, Charlotte, NC 28282, USA | Conductor, Concert Violinist |
| **Warrick, Hakim H**<br>Orlando Magic, 8701 Maitland Summit Blvd, Orlando FL 32810 USA | Basketball Player |
| **Warrick, Peter**<br>1508 11th Ave E, Palmetto FL 34221, USA | Football Player |
| **Warshel, Arieh**<br>University of Southern California, Chemistry Dept, Los Angeles CA 90089, USA | Nobel Chemistry Laureate |
| **Warwick, Carl W**<br>14102 Bonney Brier Circle, Houston TX 77069, USA | Baseball Player |
| **Warwick, Dionne**<br>Red Entertainment Agency, 505 8th Ave, #1004, New York NY 10018, USA | Singer |
| **Warwick, Lonnie P**<br>828 Main St, Mount Hope WV 25880, USA | Football Player |
| **Wasdin, John T**<br>2676 Riverport Dr S, Jacksonville FL 32223, USA | Baseball Player |
| **Wash, Martha**<br>Mike Church Entertainment, 1100 Osborn Road, #335, Phoenix AZ 85014, USA | Singer |
| **Washburn, Abigail**<br>A C Entertainment, 507 S Gay St, Knoxville TN 37902, USA | Banjo Player, Singer |
| **Washburn, Barbara**<br>1010 Waltham St, #D327, Lexington MA 02421, USA | Cartographer |
| **Washburn, Beverly**<br>2561 Olivia Heights Ave, Henderson NV 89052, USA | Actress |
| **Washburn, Jarrod M**<br>10003 Olinger Road, Webster WI 54893, USA | Baseball Player |
| **Washburn, Ray C**<br>1103 N 49th St, Seattle WA 98103, USA | Baseball Player |
| **Washed Out**<br>Constant Artists, 3780 Wilshire Blvd, #500, Los Angeles CA 90010, USA | Electronica Musician |
| **Washington Tashiana**<br>Shirley Grant Management, 1333 Wellington Ave, Teaneck NJ 07666, USA | Actress |
| **Washington, Alonzo**<br>Omega 7, PO Box 171046, Kansas City KS 66117, USA | Cartoonist (Omega Man) |
| **Washington, Christopher (Chris)**<br>PO Box 17823, San Diego CA 92177, USA | Football Player |
| **Washington, Claudell**<br>4081 Clayton Road, #227, Concord CA 94521, USA | Baseball Player |

**Washington, Denzel** — Actor
Rogers & Cowan, 8687 Melrose Ave, #G700, West Hollywood CA 90069 USA

**Washington, DeWayne N** — Football Player
6205 Rocky Creek Way, Wake Forest NC 27587, USA

**Washington, Eugene (Gene)** — Football Player
2725 N Jewell Lane, Minneapolis MN 55447, USA

**Washington, Gene A** — Football Player
10521 Bellagio Road, Los Angeles CA 90077, USA

**Washington, Hayma** — Producer
A P A Talent/Literary Agency, 405 S Beverly Dr, #300, Beverly Hills CA 90212 USA

**Washington, Herbert (Herb) L** — Baseball Player
640 Saddlebrook Dr, Youngstown OH 44512, USA

**Washington, Isaiah** — Actor
Vincent Cirrincione Assoc, 1516 N Fairfax Ave, Los Angeles CA 90046 USA

**Washington, James H (Jim)** — Basketball Player
1108 Cardinal Way SW, Atlanta GA 30311, USA

**Washington, Joe D** — Football Player
Meadow Lark, 4 Treadwell Court, Lutherville Timonium MD 21093, USA

**Washington, Justin (Baby)** — Singer, Pianist
Headline Talent, 1650 Broadway, #401, New York NY 10313 USA

**Washington, Keith** — Singer
Associated Booking Corp, 501 Madison Ave, #501, New York NY 10022 USA

**Washington, Keith L** — Football Player
548 Parkview Dr, Grand Prairie TX 75052, USA

**Washington, Kermit A** — Basketball Player
7208 NE Hazel Dell Ave, Vancouver WA 98665, USA

**Washington, Kerry** — Actress
Creative Artists Agency, 2000 Ave of Stars, #100, Los Angeles CA 90067 USA

**Washington, Larue** — Baseball Player
6323 Reseda Blvd, #16, Tarzana CA 91335, USA

**Washington, Leon (Neon)** — Football Player
Seattle Seahawks, 12 Seahawks Way, Renton WA 98056 USA

**Washington, Lionel** — Football Player
5 Gleneagles Dr, La Place LA 70068, USA

**Washington, MaliVai** — Tennis Player
5 S Roscoe Blvd, Ponte Vedra Beach FL 32082, USA

**Washington, Marvin A** — Football Player
3616 Cripple Creek Dr, Dallas TX 75224, USA

**Washington, Mike L** — Football Player
366 Ridge Water Dr, Pike Road AL 36064, USA

**Washington, Richard L** — Basketball Player
4606 SE Logus Road, Portland OR 97222, USA

**Washington, Rico** — Baseball Player
2050 Old Clinton Road, Macon GA 31211, USA

**Washington, Ronald (Ron)** — Baseball Player, Manager
1400 S Clearview Parkway, New Orleans LA 70123, USA

**Washington, Russell E (Russ)** — Football Player
4375 Florida St, #4, San Diego CA 92104, USA

**Washington, Theodore (Ted), Jr** — Football Player
2715 Joust St, North Las Vegas NV 89030, USA

**Washington, Todd P** — Football Player
211 Glyndon Meadow Road, Reisterstown MD 21136, USA

**Washington, U L** — Baseball Player
PO Box 164, Stringtown OK 74569, USA

**Washington, Wilson** — Basketball Player
2625 Mapleton Ave, Norfolk VA 23504, USA

**Wasif, Imaad** — Singer, Songwriter
Agency Group Ltd, 142 W 57th St, #600, New York NY 10019 USA

**Wasikowska, Mia** — Actress
W M E Entertainment, 9601 Wilshire Blvd, #300, Beverly Hills CA 90210 USA

**Waslewski, Gary L** — Baseball Player
1799 E Terrestrial Place, Tucson AZ 85737, USA

**Wasmeier, Markus** — Alpine Skier
Breitensteinstr 14D, 83727 Schliersee-Neuhaus, Germany

**Wasmuth, Conny** — Canoing Athlete
S C Magdeburg, Friedrich-Ebert-Str 68, 39114 Magdeburg, Germany

**Wass, Ted** — Actor, Director, Producer
I C M Partners, 10250 Constellation Blvd, #900, Los Angeles CA 90067 USA

**Wasserburg, Gerald J** — Geophysicist
PO Box 2959, Florence OR 97439, USA

**Wasserman, Dan** — Editorial Cartoonist
Boston Globe, Editorial Dept, 135 William Morrissey Blvd, Dorchester MA 02125, USA

**Wasserman, Robert H** — Physiologist, Veterinarian
358 Savage Farm Dr, Ithaca NY 14850, USA

**Wasson, Erin** — Model
I M G Models, 304 Park Ave S, #PH N, New York NY 10010 USA

**Watanabe, Gedde** — Actor
Talent Works, 3500 W Olive Ave, #1400, Burbank CA 91505 USA

**Watanabe, Katsuaki** — Businessman
Toyota Motor Corp, 1 Toyotacho, Toyota City, Aichi Pref 471 8701, Japan

**Watanabe, Kazuhide** — Businessman
Mazda Motor Co, 3-1 Shinchi, Fuchucho, Akigun, Hiroshima 730 8670, Japan

**Watanabe, Ken** — Actor, Producer, Director
K-Dash (I), 2-7-10-5F Higashi, Shibuya, Tokyo 150 0011, Japan

**Watanabe, Sadao** — Jazz Saxophonist
International Music Network, 278 Main St, #400, Gloucester MA 01930 USA

**Watanabe, Shigeo** — Businessman
Bridgestone Corp, 10-1-1 Kyobashi, Chuoku, Tokyo 104 8340, Japan

**Waterbury, Steven C (Steve)** — Baseball Player
710 N Garfield St, Marion IL 62959, USA

**Waterhouse, Gabriel M (Gai)** — Thoroughbred Racing Trainer
Gai Waterhouse Racing, PO Box 834, Kensington NSW 1465, Australia

**Waterman, Dennis** — Actor
Associated International Mgmt, 7 Hatton Garden, #400, London EC1N 8AD, England

**Waterman, Felicity** — Actress
PO Box 234, Elk CA 95432, USA

**Waterman, Michael S** — Mathematician
University of Southern California, Mathematics Dept, Los Angeles CA 90089, USA

**Waterman, Pete** — Actor
Fremantle Media, 2700 Colorado Ave, #450, Santa Monica CA 90404 USA

**Waterman, Robert H** — Writer
Enterprise Media, 91 Harvey St, Cambridge MA 02140, USA

**Waters, Alice** — Chef
Chez Panisse, 1517 Shattuck Ave, Berkeley CA 94709, USA

**Waters, Brian D** — Football Player
6911 W 138th Terrace, Overland Park KS 66223, USA

**Waters, Charles T (Charlie)** — Football Player, Coach
9305 Moss Trail, Dallas TX 75231, USA

**Waters, Crystal** — Singer
AM/PM Entertainment Concepts, 415 63rd St, #200, Brooklyn NY 11220, USA

**Waters, Derek** — Actor
United Talent Agency, U T A Plaza, 9336 Civic Center Dr, Beverly Hills CA 90210 USA

**Waters, Dina** — Actress
Gersh Agency, 9465 Wilshire Blvd, #600, Beverly Hills CA 90212 USA

**Waters, Drew** — Actor, Model
A P A Talent/Literary Agency, 405 S Beverly Dr, #300, Beverly Hills CA 90212 USA

**Waters, John** — Director, Writer, Actor
United Talent Agency, U T A Plaza, 9336 Civic Center Dr, Beverly Hills CA 90210 USA

**Waters, John B** — Government Official
405 Burridge Waters Edge, Sevierville TN 37862, USA

**Waters, Lou** — Commentator
CNN-TV, 190 Marietta Ave SW, Atlanta GA 30303 USA

**Waters, Mark** — Director, Producer, Writer
Creative Artists Agency, 2000 Ave of Stars, #100, Los Angeles CA 90067 USA

**Waters, Richard** — Publisher
13919 Woods Run Court, Centreville VA 20121, USA

**Waters, Roger** — Singer, Bassist (Pink Floyd)
One Fifteen, Globe House, Middle Lane Mews, London N8 8PN, England

**Waterston, Katherine** — Actress
United Talent Agency, U T A Plaza, 9336 Civic Center Dr, Beverly Hills CA 90210 USA

**Waterston, Sam** — Actor
Gersh Agency, 9465 Wilshire Blvd, #600, Beverly Hills CA 90212 USA

**Wathan, John D** — Baseball Player, Manager
1354 NE Todd George Road, Lees Summit MO 64086, USA

**Watkins, Calvert W** — Educator
University of California, Classics Dept, Los Angeles CA 90024, USA

**Watkins, Carlene** — Actress
Bresler Kelly Assoc, 11500 W Olympic Blvd, #400, Los Angeles CA 90064 USA

**Watkins, David R (Dave)** — Baseball Player
506 Ridgewood Road, Louisville KY 40207, USA

**Watkins, Dean A** — Inventor (Electron Tubes), Businessman
Watkins-Johnson Co, 401 River Oaks Parkway, San Jose CA 95134, USA

**Watkins, Hays T, Jr** — Businessman
2111 Cedarfield Lane, Henrico VA 23233, USA

**Watkins, Michael W** — Director, Producer
A P A Talent/Literary Agency, 405 S Beverly Dr, #300, Beverly Hills CA 90212 USA

**Watkins, Michelle** — Actress
Capital Artists, 6404 Wilshire Blvd, #950, Los Angeles CA 90048, USA

**Watkins, Robert C (Bob)** — Baseball Player
4417 W 58th Place, Los Angeles CA 90043, USA

**Watkins, Robert L (Bobby)** — Football Player
1112 Devonshire Dr, DeSoto TX 75115, USA

**Watkins, Sara U** — Singer, Fiddler (Nickel Creek)
Nonesuch Records, 75 Rockefeller Plaza, #800, New York NY 10019 USA

**Watkins, Scott A** — Baseball Player
14660 W 18th St, Sand Springs OK 74063, USA

**Watkins, Sean C** — Guitarist (Nickel Creek)
Q-Prime South, 131 S 11th St, Nashville TN 37206 USA

**Watkins, Simon C** — Immunologist
University of Pittsburgh Medical School, Immunology Dept, Pittsburgh PA 15260, USA

**Watkins, Steve** — Baseball Player
3408 Evanston Ave, Lubbock TX 79407, USA

**Watkins, Tionne (T-Boz)** — Rap Artist (TLC)
Venture I A B, 3211 Cahuenga Blvd W, #104, Los Angeles CA 90068, USA

**Watkins, Tuc** — Actor
Stone Manners Salners, 9911 W Pico Blvd, #1400, Los Angeles CA 90035 USA

**Watley, Jody** — Singer
T C I, 1560 Broadway, #1308, New York NY 10036, USA

**Watling, Leonor** — Actress
A6 Cinema, Almirante 4, #3B, 28004 Madrid, Spain

**Watlington, J Neal** — Baseball Player
PO Box 418, Yanceyville NC 27379, USA

**Watney, Nicholas A (Nick)** — Golfer
816 Veramar Court, Henderson NV 89052, USA

**Watrous, Cynthia** — Actress
Principal Entertainment, 9255 Sunset Blvd, #500, Los Angeles CA 90069 USA

**Watrous, William R (Bill), Jr** — Jazz Trombonist
Thomas Cassidy, PO Box 1311, Tucson AZ 85702 USA

**Watson Richardson, Lillian (Pokey)** — Swimmer
4960 Maunalani Circle, Honolulu HI 96816, USA

**Watson, A J** — Auto Racing Engineer
5420 Crawfordsville Road, Indianapolis IN 46224, USA

**Watson, Adrienne** — Actress, Comedienne
OmniPop Talent Group, 4605 Lankershim Blvd, #201, Toluca Lake CA 91602 USA

**Watson, Albert M** — Photographer
44 Laight St, #1A, New York NY 10013, USA

**Watson, Alberta** — Actress
Gary Goddard Assoc, 10 Saint Mary St, #305, Toronto ON M4Y 1P9, Canada

**Watson, Alexander F** — Diplomat
Nature Conservancy International, 4245 Fairfax Dr, #100, Arlington VA 22203, USA

**Watson, Allen K** — Baseball Player
6144 65th St, Middle Village NY 11379, USA

**Watson, Barry** — Actor
Innovative Artists, 1505 10th St, Santa Monica CA 90401 USA
**Watson, Benjamin Charles** — Actor
Play Management, 807 Powell St, #220, Vancouver BC V6A 1H7, Canada , USA
**Watson, Benjamin S (Ben)** — Football Player
12397 Steeplechase Lane, Strongsville OH 44149, USA
**Watson, Bryan J** — Ice Hockey Player
400 Madison St, Alexandria VA 22314, USA
**Watson, Cecil J** — Physician
Abbott Northwestern Hospital, 2727 Chicago Ave, Minneapolis MN 55407, USA
**Watson, Dale** — Singer
Davis McLarty Agency, 708 S Lamar Blvd, #D, Austin TX 78704, USA
**Watson, Debbie** — Singer
PO Box 1570, Goodlettsville TN 37070, USA
**Watson, E Bruce** — Environmentalist
Rensselaer Polytechnic Institute, Earth & Environmental Dept, Troy NY 12180, USA
**Watson, Earl J** — Basketball Player
4310 N Holly Court, Kansas City MO 64116, USA
**Watson, Elizabeth M** — Law Enforcement Official
Houston Police Department, Chief's Office, 1200 Travis St, Houston TX 77002, USA
**Watson, Emily** — Actress
Independent Talent Group, 40 Whitfield St, London W1T 2RH, England
**Watson, Emma** — Actress, Model
Markham Froggatt Irwin, Julian House, 4 Windmill St, London W1P 1HF, England
**Watson, Gene** — Singer, Guitarist
Lytle Management Group, PO Box 128228, Nashville TN 37212, USA
**Watson, George L (Bubba), Jr** — Golfer
Professional Golfer's Assn, PO Box 109601, Palm Beach Gardens FL 33410 USA
**Watson, Jack H, Jr** — Government Official
Long Aldridge Norman, 1900 K St NW, Washington DC 20006, USA
**Watson, James A (Jim)** — Ice Hockey Player
1702 Coventry Lane, Glen Mills PA 19342, USA
**Watson, James D** — Nobel Medicine Laureate
Bungtown Road, Cold Spring Harbor NY 11724, USA
**Watson, Jamie L** — Basketball Player
PO Box 761, Elm City NC 27822, USA
**Watson, Jill** — Figure Skater
Desert Schools Coyote Center, 15829 N 83rd Ave, Peoria AZ 85382, USA
**Watson, Kenneth M** — Physicist, Oceanographer
8515 Costa Verde Blvd, #2008, San Diego CA 92122, USA
**Watson, Lillian** — Opera Singer
I M G Artists, Hogarth Business Park, Chiswick, London W4 2TH, England
**Watson, Mark** — Baseball Player
555 Spender Trace, Atlanta GA 30350, USA
**Watson, Martha** — Track Athlete
5509 Royal Vista Lane, Las Vegas NV 89149, USA
**Watson, Mills** — Actor
PO Box 600, Talent OR 97540, USA
**Watson, Patrick** — Singer, Songwriter
Agency Group, 2 Berkeley St, #202, Toronto ON M5A 4J5, Canada
**Watson, Patty Jo** — Anthropologist
Washington University, Anthropology Dept, PO Box 1114, Saint Louis MO 63188, USA
**Watson, Paul** — Environmental Activist
Sea Shepherd Conservation Society, PO Box 2670, Malibu CA 90265, USA
**Watson, Paul** — Photojournalist
Toronto Star, Editorial Dept, 1 Yonge St, Toronto ON M5E 1E6, Canada
**Watson, Richard Jesse** — Illustrator
2305 Ivy St, Port Townsend WA 98368, USA
**Watson, Robert E (Bobby)** — Basketball Player
1625 Sherwood Dr, Owensboro KY 42301, USA
**Watson, Robert J (Bob)** — Baseball Player
18103 Darling Point Court, Cypress TX 77429, USA
**Watson, Robert M (Bobby), Jr** — Jazz Saxophonist
Hot Jazz Mgmt, 328 W 43rd St, #4FW, New York NY 10036, USA
**Watson, Russell** — Singer
Sanctuary Artist Mgmt, 45-53 Sinclair Road, London W14 0NS, England , USA
**Watson, Stephen E** — Businessman
Dayton Hudson, 1000 Nicollet Mall, Minneapolis MN 55403, USA
**Watson, Stephen R (Steve)** — Football Player
4675 S Vine Way, Englewood CO 80113, USA
**Watson, Thomas S (Tom)** — Golfer
16104 Riggs Road, Stilwell KS 66085, USA
**Watson, Tuc** — Actor, Producer
Stone Manners Salners, 9911 W Pico Blvd, #1400, Los Angeles CA 90035 USA
**Watson, Wayne** — Singer
T B A Artist Mgmt, 300 10th Ave S, Nashville TN 37203, USA
**Watson, William C (Bill)** — Ice Hockey Player
1725 Vermillon Road, Duluth MN 55803, USA
**Watson-Johnson, Vernee** — Actress
C E S D, 10635 Santa Monica Blvd, #130, Los Angeles CA 90025 USA
**Watt, Ben** — Guitarist, Singer, Songwriter
J F D Mgmt, Acklam Workshops, 10 Acklam Road, London W10 5QZ, England
**Watt, Edward D (Eddie)** — Baseball Player
940 Locust St, North Bend NE 68649, USA
**Watt, James G** — Secretary, Interior
PO Box 3705, Jackson Hole WY 83001, USA
**Watt, Michael D (Mike)** — Singer, Bassist (Porno for Pyros)
Agency Group Ltd, 142 W 57th St, #600, New York NY 10019 USA
**Watt, Tom** — Ice Hockey Coach
Calgary Flames, PO Box 1540, Station M, Calgary AB T2P 3B9, Canada
**Watt-Cloutier, Sheila** — Social Activist
Inuit Circumpolar, 170 Laurier Ave, #504, Ottawa ON K1P 5V5, Canada
**Wattelet, Frank L** — Football Player
4 Deer Run Dr, Joplin MO 64804, USA
**Wattenberg, Ben J** — Demographer
American Enterprise Institute, 1150 17th St NW, Washington DC 20036, USA

**W**

| | |
|---|---|
| **Watters, Mark**<br>Air Edel, 9100 Wilshire Blvd, #350E, Beverly Hills CA 90212 USA | Composer, Conductor |
| **Watters, Richard J (Rickie)**<br>6263 Cypress Chase Dr, Windermere FL 34786, USA | Football Player |
| **Watters, Sam**<br>J-Bird Entertainment, 4905 S Atlantic Ave, Ponce Inlet FL 32127 USA | Singer (Color Me Badd) |
| **Watters, Tim**<br>2390 E Camelback Road, #100, Phoenix AZ 85016, USA | Ice Hockey Player |
| **Wattleton, A Faye**<br>Center for Advancement of Women, 165 W 46th St, #512, New York NY 10036, USA | Association Executive |
| **Watts, Andre**<br>C M Artists, 127 W 96th St, #13B, New York NY 10025 USA | Concert Pianist |
| **Watts, Charles R (Charlie)**<br>Rosebud Agency, PO Box 170429, San Francisco CA 94117 USA | Drummer (Rolling Stones) |
| **Watts, Daniele**<br>Anonymous Content, 3532 Hayden Ave, Culver City CA 90232 USA | Actress |
| **Watts, Donald E (Slick)**<br>5015 256th Ave NE, Redmond WA 98053, USA | Basketball Player |
| **Watts, Elizabeth**<br>Ingpen & Williams, 131 Putney Bridge Road, London SW15 2PA, England | Opera Singer |
| **Watts, Ernest J (Ernie)**<br>Bates Meyer, PO Box 2821, Big Bear Lake CA 92315, USA | Jazz Saxophonist |
| **Watts, Ernie**<br>I C M Partners, 730 5th Ave, New York NY 10019 USA | Art Director, Stage Designer |
| **Watts, Heather**<br>New York City Ballet, Lincoln Center Plaza, New York NY 10023 USA | Ballerina |
| **Watts, Julius Caesar (J C), Jr**<br>J C Watts Companies, 600 13th St NW, #790, Washington DC 20005, USA | Representative, OK; Football Player |
| **Watts, Lou**<br>Doug Smith Assoc, PO Box 1151, London W3 8ZJ, England | Singer (Chumbawamba) |
| **Watts, Naomi**<br>Untitled Entertainment, 350 S Beverly Dr, #200, Beverly Hills CA 90212 USA | Actress |
| **Watts, Quincy**<br>H S International Sports Mgmt, 9871 Irvine Center Dr, Irvine CA 92618, USA | Track Athlete |
| **Watts, Ronald M (Ron)**<br>875 Grace St, #101, Herndon VA 20170, USA | Basketball Player |
| **Waugh, John S**<br>60 Conant Road, Lincoln MA 01773, USA | Chemist |
| **Waugh, Scott**<br>I C M Partners, 10250 Constellation Blvd, #900, Los Angeles CA 90067 USA | Director |
| **Waugh, Stephen R (Steve)**<br>Team-Duet, 3 Winnie St, Cremone NSW 2090, Australia | Cricketer |
| **Wauters, Ann H W**<br>Seattle Storm, Key Arena, 351 Elliott Ave W, #500, Seattle WA 98119 USA | Basketball Player |
| **Wax, Ruby**<br>United Agents, 12-26 Lexington St, London W1F 0LE, England | Actress, Comedienne |
| **Waxman, Seth P**<br>Wilmer Hale, 1875 Pennsylvania Ave NW, Washington DC 20006, USA | Government Official, Attorney |
| **Wayans, Damon**<br>I C M Partners, 10250 Constellation Blvd, #900, Los Angeles CA 90067 USA | Actor, Comedian, Writer, Producer |
| **Wayans, Damon, Jr**<br>Mosiac Media Group, 9200 W Sunset Blvd, #1000, Los Angeles CA 90069 USA | Actor |
| **Wayans, Dwayne**<br>16405 Mulholland Dr, Los Angeles CA 90049, USA | Actor |
| **Wayans, Keenen Ivory**<br>Wayans Brothers Entertainment, 8730 W Sunset Blvd, #290, Los Angeles CA 90069, USA | Actor, Director |
| **Wayans, Kim**<br>A P A Talent/Literary Agency, 405 S Beverly Dr, #300, Beverly Hills CA 90212 USA | Actress, Writer, Director |
| **Wayans, Marlon**<br>Wayans Brothers Entertainment, 8730 W Sunset Blvd, #290, Los Angeles CA 90069, USA | Actor, Comedian |
| **Wayans, Shawn**<br>Modus Entertainment, 8730 W Sunset Blvd, #290, West Hollywood CA 90069, USA | Actor |
| **Wayda, Stephen**<br>Celebrity Pictures, 5757 Wilshire Blvd, Beverly Hills CA 90210, USA | Photographer |
| **Wayne, Gary A**<br>5762 W Ashbury Place, Lakewood CO 80227, USA | Baseball Player |
| **Wayne, Jimmy**<br>W M E Entertainment, 1600 Division St, #300, Nashville TN 37203 USA | Singer, Songwriter |
| **Wayne, John Ethan**<br>Wayne Enterprises, 210 62nd St, Newport Beach CA 92663, USA | Actor |
| **Wayne, Nathaniel (Nate), Jr**<br>2878 Grey Moss Pass, Duluth GA 30097, USA | Football Player |
| **Wayne, Patrick J**<br>10502 Whipple St, Toluca Lake CA 91602, USA | Actor |
| **Wayne, Reggie**<br>17000 Berkshire Court, Southwest Ranches FL 33331, USA | Football Player |
| **Wearing, Gillian**<br>Maureen Paley Interim Art, 21 Herald St, London E2 6JT, England | Artist |
| **Weary, J Fredrick (Fred)**<br>11315 Sailwing Creek Court, Pearland TX 77584, USA | Football Player |
| **Weatherall, David J**<br>8 Cumnor Rise Road, Cumnor Hill, Oxford OX2 9HD, England | Hematologist |
| **Weatherly, Michael**<br>Anonymous Content, 3532 Hayden Ave, Culver City CA 90232 USA | Actor |
| **Weatherly, Shawn N**<br>Connor Ankrum Assoc, 1680 Vine St, #1016, Los Angeles CA 90028, USA | Actress, Beauty Queen |
| **Weatherman, Woodroe (Woody)**<br>Chipster, 100 Village Square Crossing, Palm Beach Gardens FL 33410 USA | Guitarist (Corrosion of Conformity) |
| **Weathers, Carl**<br>2228 Walnut Ave, Venice CA 90291, USA | Actor, Football Player |
| **Weathers, J David (Dave)**<br>979 Lexington Highway, Loretto TN 38469, USA | Baseball Player |
| **Weatherspoon, Clarence**<br>PO Box 117, Crawford MS 39743, USA | Basketball Player |
| **Weatherspoon, Teresa G**<br>Los Angeles Sparks, 888 S Figueroa St, #2010, Los Angeles CA 90017 USA | Basketball Player |

**Watters - Weatherspoon**

**Weatherston, Katie** — Ice Hockey Player
Team Canada, 2424 University Dr NW, Calgary AB T2N 3Y9, Canada

**Weaver, Al** — Actor
Julian Belfrage Assoc, 9 Argyll St, #300, London W1F 7TG, England

**Weaver, Charles E (Charlie)** — Football Player
309 W Muncie Ave, Fresno CA 93711, USA

**Weaver, DeWitt** — Golfer
Weaver Golf Solutions, 5640 Golf Club Dr, Braselton GA 30517, USA

**Weaver, Fritz** — Actor
161 W 75th St, #15A, New York NY 10023, USA

**Weaver, Gary L** — Football Player
3496 Arden Road, Hayward CA 94545, USA

**Weaver, J Eric** — Baseball Player
2641 Weaver Road, Illiopolis IL 62539, USA

**Weaver, James** — Cartoonist
3438 Admiralty Lane, Indianapolis IN 46240, USA

**Weaver, Jason** — Actor
Luber Rocklin Entertainment, 8530 Wilshire Blvd, #555, Beverly Hills CA 90211 USA

**Weaver, Jeffrey C (Jeff)** — Baseball Player
1740 Classic Rose Court, Westlake Village CA 91362, USA

**Weaver, Jered D** — Baseball Player
1204 Suncast Lane, #2, El Dorado Hills CA 95762, USA

**Weaver, Leonard** — Football Player
Philadelphia Eagles, 1 Novacare Way, Philadelphia PA 19145 USA

**Weaver, Michael** — Actor
Brillstein Entertainment Partners, 9150 Wilshire Blvd, #350, Beverly Hills CA 90212 USA

**Weaver, Reg** — Labor Leader
National Education Assn, 1201 16th St NW, Washington DC 20036, USA

**Weaver, Roger E** — Baseball Player
65 Moyer St, Canajoharie NY 13317, USA

**Weaver, Sigourney** — Actress
Arcieri Assoc, 305 Madison Ave, #2315, New York NY 10165 USA

**Weaver, W Herman** — Football Player
8105 Hamilton Mill Dr, Chattanooga TN 37421, USA

**Weaver, Warren E** — Chemist
7607 Horsepen Road, Richmond VA 23229, USA

**Weaving, Hugo** — Actor
Shanahan Mgmt, 91 Campbell St, #300, Surry Hills NSW 2010, Australia

**Webb, Alexander D (Alex)** — Photographer
151 W 25th St, New York NY 10001, USA

**Webb, Anthony J (Spud)** — Basketball Player
1453 Mosslake Dr, DeSoto TX 75115, USA

**Webb, Brandon T** — Baseball Player
8814 E Ann Way, Scottsdale AZ 85260, USA

**Webb, Chloe** — Actress
PO Box 2824, Venice CA 90294, USA

**Webb, Christiaan** — Singer, Musician, Songwriter
SuperVision Mgmt, 109B Regents Park Road, London NW1 8UR, England

**Webb, Derek W** — Singer, Guitarist (Caedmon's Call)
Dryve Artist Mgmt, 510A E Iris Dr, Nashville TN 37204, USA

**Webb, Donald W (Don)** — Football Player
906 Roland Court, Jefferson City MO 65101, USA

**Webb, Henry G (Hank)** — Baseball Player
4527 Lake Valencia Blvd W, Palm Harbor FL 34684, USA

**Webb, James R (Jimmy)** — Football Player
1319 S Prairie Flower Road, Turlock CA 95380, USA

**Webb, Jimmy** — Singer, Songwriter
1560 N Laurel Ave, #109, Los Angeles CA 90046, USA

**Webb, Justin** — Singer, Musician, Songwriter
SuperVision Mgmt, 109B Regents Park Road, London NW1 8UR, England

**Webb, Karrie** — Golfer
725 Presidential Dr, Boynton Beach FL 33435, USA

**Webb, Lardarius** — Football Playee
Baltimore Ravens, Ravens Stadium, 1 Winning Dr, Baltimore MD 21230 USA

**Webb, Lee** — Evangelist, Commentator
700 Club, 977 Centerville Turnpike, Virginia Beach VA 23463, USA

**Webb, Marc** — Director
Creative Artists Agency, 2000 Ave of Stars, #100, Los Angeles CA 90067 USA

**Webb, Richmond J** — Football Player
4120 Humphrey Dr, Dallas TX 75216, USA

**Webb, Russell (Russ)** — Water Polo Player
611 Knob Hill Ave, Redondo Beach CA 90277, USA

**Webb, Sarah K** — Yachtswoman
Lynx Sports Mgmt, Lymington Road, Lymington, Hampshire SO41 5S5, England

**Webb, Steve** — Ice Hockey Player
27 Barberry Lane, Center Moriches NY 11934, USA

**Webb, Tamilee** — Physical Fitness Instructor
1770 Haydn Dr, Cardiff By The Sea CA 92007, USA

**Webb, Veronica** — Model, Actress
Don Buchwald, 10 E 44th St, New York NY 10017 USA

**Webb, Watt W** — Applied Physicist
Cornell University, BioPhysics Program, Ithaca NY 14853, USA

**Webb, Wayne** — Bowler
5850 Freeport Blvd, Sacramento CA 95822, USA

**Webber, Julian Lloyd** — Concert Cellist
I M G Artists, Hogarth Business Park, Chiswick, London W4 2TH, England

**Webber, Mark** — Actor
Innovative Artists, 1505 10th St, Santa Monica CA 90401 USA

**Webber, Mark A** — Auto Racing Driver
Octagon, 166 William Dr, Woolloomooloo NSW 2011, Australia

**Webber, Peter** — Director
United Agents, 12-26 Lexington St, London W1F 0LE, England

**Webber, Tristan** — Fashion Designer
Brower Lewis Public Relations, 74 Gloucester Place, London W1H 3HN, England

**Weber, Arnold R** — Educator
Northwestern University, Chancellor's Office, Evanston IL 60208, USA

# W

**Weber, Ben**
5550 Baird St, Groves TX 77619, USA — Baseball Player

**Weber, Ben, Jr**
King Features Syndicate, 300 W 57th St, #1500, New York NY 10019 USA — Cartoonist

**Weber, Bernard**
New7Wonders Foundation, PO Box 1212, 8034 Zurich, Switzerland — Explorer, Filmmaker

**Weber, Bruce**
Little Bear, 135 Watts St, #5, New York NY 10013, USA — Photographer

**Weber, Bruce**
University of Illinois, Athletic Dept, Assembly Hall, Champaign IL 61820, USA — Basketball Coach

**Weber, Charles F (Chuck), Jr**
12740 Cobblestone Creek Road, Poway CA 92064, USA — Football Player

**Weber, Charlie**
Warren Cowan Assoc, 8899 Beverly Blvd, #918, Los Angeles CA 90048, USA — Actor

**Weber, Eberhard**
Ted Kurland, 173 Brighton Ave, Boston MA 02134 USA — Jazz Bassist, Cellist, Composer

**Weber, Emmanuelle**
Artmedia, 20 Ave Rapp, 75007 Paris, France — Actress

**Weber, George B**
Chemin Moise-Duboule 19, 1209 Geneva, Switzerland — Association Executive

**Weber, J Vincent (Vin)**
Clark & Weinstock, 601 13th St NW, #410S, Washington DC 20005, USA — Representative, MN

**Weber, Jacques**
U B B A, 6 Rue de Braque, 75003 Paris, France — Actor, Director, Writer

**Weber, Jake**
Paradigm Agency, 360 N Crescent Dr, North Building, Beverly Hills CA 90210 USA — Actor

**Weber, Joseph F**
Commanding General, 3rd Marine Expeditionary Force Okinawa, FPO AP 96602 USA — Marine Corps General

**Weber, Mary E**
14 Hawkview St, Portola Valley CA 94028, USA — Astronaut

**Weber, Neil A**
1 Morning View, Irvine CA 92603, USA — Baseball Player

**Weber, Peter D (Pete)**
10500 Saint Xavier Lane, Saint Ann MO 63074, USA — Bowler

**Weber, Robert M (Bob)**
New Yorker, Editorial Dept, 4 Times Square, Basement C1B, New York NY 10036 USA — Cartoonist

**Weber, Shea M**
4527 Yancey Dr, Nashville TN 37215, USA — Ice Hockey Player

**Weber, Stephen L**
San Diego State University, President's Office, San Diego CA 92182, USA — Educator

**Weber, Steven**
Brillstein Entertainment Partners, 9150 Wilshire Blvd, #350, Beverly Hills CA 90212 USA — Actor

**Webre, Septime**
Washington Ballet, 3515 Wisconsin Ave NW, Washington DC 20016, USA — Choreographer

**Webster, Corey J**
66 Mallard Place, Secaucus NJ 07094, USA — Football Player

**Webster, James**
Cornell University, Music Dept, Ithaca NY 14853, USA — Musicologist

**Webster, Jeffrey T (Jeff)**
10405 SE 15th St, Oklahoma City OK 73130, USA — Basketball Player

**Webster, Larry M, Jr**
12 Oakridge Court, Elkton MD 21921, USA — Football Player

**Webster, Leonard N (Lenny)**
6211 Bridgeport Dr, Charlotte NC 28215, USA — Baseball Player

**Webster, Martell**
Washington Wizards, M C I Centre, 601 F St NW, Washington DC 20004 USA — Basketball Player

**Webster, Mitchell D (Mitch)**
3120 NE 91st Terrace, Kansas City MO 64156, USA — Baseball Player

**Webster, Robert D (Bob)**
269 Hacienda Carmel, Carmel CA 93923, USA — Diver

**Webster, Tom**
1750 Longfellow Dr, Canton MI 48187, USA — Ice Hockey Player

**Webster, Victor**
Innovative Artists, 1505 10th St, Santa Monica CA 90401 USA — Actor

**Webster, William G**
Commander, Army Central, Camp Arifjan Kuwait, APO AE 09306, USA — Army General

**Webster, William H**
4777 Dexter St NW, Washington DC 20007, USA — Law Enforcement Official

**Wecker, Andreas**
Am Dorfplatz 1, 16766 Klein-Ziethen, Germany — Gymnast

**Wecker, Kendra**
San Antonio Silver Stars, 1 AT&T Center, San Antonio TX 78219 USA — Basketball Player

**Weddington, Michael W (Mike)**
237 Sycamore Grove St, Simi Valley CA 93065, USA — Football Player

**Weddington, Sarah R**
Weddington Center, 709 W 14th St, Austin TX 78701, USA — Attorney

**Wedel, Dieter**
Nibelungenfestspiele, Von-Steuben-Str 5, 67549 Worms, Germany — Director

**Wedge, Chris**
Blue Sky Studios, 1 American Lane, Greenwich CT 06831, USA — Animator, Director, Producer

**Wedge, Eric M**
8285 SE 82nd St, Mercer Island WA 98040, USA — Baseball Player, Manager

**Wedgeworth, Ann**
70 Riverside Dr, New York NY 10024, USA — Actress

**Wedman, Scott D**
7912 NW Scenic Dr, Kansas City MO 64152, USA — Basketball Player

**Weed, Maurice James**
308 Overlook Road, #55, Asheville NC 28803, USA — Composer

**Weeden, Brandon K**
Cleveland Browns, 76 Lou Groza Blvd, Berea OH 44017 USA — Football Player

**Weekes, Kevin**
9251 Yonge St, #8-887, Richmond Hill ON L4C 9T3, Canada — Ice Hockey Player

**Weekes, Stephen K (Steve)**
2883 Thurleston Lane, Duluth GA 30097, USA — Ice Hockey Player

**Weekley, Thomas B (Boo)**
2555 New York St, Jay FL 32565, USA — Golfer

**Weeks, Ed**    Actor
W M E Entertainment, 9601 Wilshire Blvd, #300, Beverly Hills CA 90210 USA
**Weeks, Honeysuckle**    Actress
Ken McReddie Assoc, 101 Finsbury Pavement, London EC2A 1RS, England
**Weeks, Jared**    Singer (Saving Abel), Songwriter
Virgin Records, 338 N Foothill Road, Beverly Hills CA 90210 USA
**Weeks, John D**    Chemist
15301 Watergate Road, Silver Spring MD 20905, USA
**Weeks, John R**    Architect
39 Jackson's Lane, Highgate, London N6 5SR, England
**Weeks, Kent R**    Archaeologist
American University, 113 Kar El Aini St, Cairo 11511, Egypt
**Weeks, Perdita**    Actress
Troika, 74 Clerkenwell Road, #300, London EC1M 5QA, England
**Weeks, Rickie D**    Baseball Player
7473 Park Springs Circle, Orlando FL 32835, USA
**Weeks, Wendell**    Businessman
Corning Inc, Houghton Park, Corning NY 14931, USA
**Ween, Dean**    Singer, Guitarist (Ween)
High Road Touring, 751 Bridgeway, #200, Sausalito CA 94965 USA
**Ween, Gene**    Singer, Guitarst (Ween)
High Road Touring, 751 Bridgeway, #200, Sausalito CA 94965 USA
**Weese, Miranda**    Ballerina
New York City Ballet, Lincoln Center Plaza, New York NY 10023 USA
**Weger, Michael R (Mike)**    Football Player
825 Markwood Dr, Oxford MS 38655, USA
**Wegman, William E (Bill)**    Baseball Player
20521 Heather Court, Lawrenceburg IN 47025, USA
**Wegman, William G**    Artist, Photographer
239 W 18th St, New York NY 10011, USA
**Wegner, Paul D**    Sculptor
PO Box 603, Prather CA 93651, USA
**Wegryn Gross, Halley**    Actress
Innovative Artists, 1505 10th St, Santa Monica CA 90401 USA
**Wehling, Ulrich**    Nordic Combined Athlete
Skiverband, Hubertusstr 1, 81477 Munich, Germany
**Wehner, John P**    Baseball Player
105 Avery's Way, Cranberry Township PA 16066, USA
**Wehrli, Roger R**    Football Player
204 Fox Haven Court, O'Fallon MO 63368, USA
**Wehrmeister, David T (Dave)**    Baseball Player
115 Sharene Lane, #20, Walnut Creek CA 94596, USA
**Wei Hui**    Writer
Pocket Books, 1230 Ave of Americas, New York NY 10020 USA
**Wei, James**    Chemical Engineer
571 Lake St, Princeton NJ 08540, USA
**Weibel, Ewald R**    Biologist
University of Berne, Biology Dept, Hochshulstr 4, 3012 Berne, Switzerland
**Weibel, Robert**    Pediatrician
University of Pennsylvania Medical School, Pediatrics Dept, Philadelphia PA 19104, USA
**Weibring, D A**    Golfer
5865 Versailles Ave, Frisco TX 75034, USA
**Weicker, Lowell P, Jr**    Governor, Senator, CT
PO Box 877, Old Lyme CT 06371, USA
**Weida, Johnny A**    Air Force General, Educator
Deputy Chief of Staff, Operations Plans, HqUSA, Pentagon, Washington DC 20310 USA
**Weide, Robert B**    Director, Writer
Whyaduck Productions, 4804 Laurel Canyon Blvd, PMB 502, North Hollywood CA 91607, USA
**Weidenbaum, Murray L**    Government Official, Economist
6231 Rosebury Ave, Saint Louis MO 63105, USA
**Weidinger, Christine**    Opera Singer
Robert Lombardo Assoc, Harkness Plaza, 61 W 62nd St, #6F, New York NY 10023 USA
**Weidner, Bert J**    Football Player
517 NW 106th Ave, Plantation FL 33324, USA
**Weidner, Brant**    Basketball Player
1111 Colfax St, Evanston IL 60201, USA
**Weigand, Cary Lathan**    Artist
1666 China Gulch Road, Jacksonville OR 97530, USA
**Weigel, Teri**    Actress, Model
6433 Topanga Canyon Blvd, #103, Woodland Hills CA 91303, USA
**Weigert, Robin**    Actress
Innovative Artists, 1505 10th St, Santa Monica CA 90401 USA
**Weight, Douglas D (Doug)**    Ice Hockey Player
72 Feeks Lane, Locust Valley NY 11560, USA
**Weihenmayer, Erik**    Mountaineer
682 Partridge Circle, Golden CO 80403, USA
**Weikl, Bernd**    Opera Singer
Opera et Concert, 37 Rue de la Chaussee d'Antin, 75009 Paris, France
**Weil, Andrew**    Physician
1670 N Kolb Road, #240, Tucson AZ 85715, USA
**Weil, Bruno**    Conductor, Composer
Ingpen & Williams, 131 Putney Bridge Road, London SW15 2PA, England
**Weil, Cynthia**    Songwriter
Gorfaine/Schwartz, 4111 W Alameda Ave, #509, Burbank CA 91505 USA
**Weil, Frank A**    Association Executive
Smithsonian Institution, 900 Jefferson Dr SW, Washington DC 20560, USA
**Weil, Liza**    Actress
Principal Entertainment, 9255 Sunset Blvd, #500, Los Angeles CA 90069 USA
**Weiland, John H**    Businessman
C F Bard Co, 730 Central Ave, Murray Hill NJ 07974, USA
**Weiland, Paul**    Director
I C M Partners, 10250 Constellation Blvd, #900, Los Angeles CA 90067 USA
**Weiland, Scott**    Singer (Stone Temple Pilots), Songwriter
Brillstein Entertainment Partners, 9150 Wilshire Blvd, #350, Beverly Hills CA 90212 USA
**Weilerstein, Alisa**    Concert Cellist
Opus 3 Artists, 470 Park Ave S, #900N, New York NY 10016 USA

**W**

**Weeks - Weilerstein**

# W

**Weill, David (Dave)**
120 Mountain Spring Ave, San Francisco CA 94114, USA — Track Athlete

**Weill, Sanford I (Sandy)**
Citigroup Inc, 55 E 52nd St, New York NY 10055, USA — Businessman

**Wein, George**
Festival Productions, 30 Irving Place, #600, New York NY 10003, USA — Musical Producer

**Weinbach, Lawrence A**
Unisys Corp, Unisys Way, Blue Bell PA 19424, USA — Businessman

**Weinberg, Gerhard L**
1416 Mount Willing Road, Efland NC 27243, USA — Historian

**Weinberg, Max**
1612 34th St NW, Washington DC 20007, USA — Drummer (E-Street Band)

**Weinberg, Mike**
Innovative Artists, 1505 10th St, Santa Monica CA 90401 USA — Actor

**Weinberg, Robert A**
Whitehead Institute, 9 Cambridge Center, Cambridge MA 02142, USA — Cancer Researcher, Biochemist

**Weinberg, Steven**
University of Texas, Physics Dept, 2613 Wichita St, Austin TX 78712, USA — Nobel Physics Laureate

**Weinbrecht, Donna**
177 High Crest Dr, West Milford NJ 07480, USA — Freestyle Moguls Skier

**Weiner, Art E**
404 Kimberly Dr, Greensboro NC 27408, USA — Football Player

**Weiner, Erik**
Bleeker Street Entertainment, 853 Broadway, #1214, New York NY 10003, USA — Writer, Producer, Commentator

**Weiner, Gerald (Gerry)**
40 Fredmir St, Dollard-des-Ormeaux QC H9A 2R3, Canada — Government Official, Canada

**Weiner, Jennifer**
BenderSpink, 8447 Wilshire Blvd, #250, Beverly Hills CA 90211 USA — Writer

**Weiner, Matthew**
Creative Artists Agency, 2000 Ave of Stars, #100, Los Angeles CA 90067 USA — Producer, Writer

**Weiner, Mel**
Silverlake Mosaics, 1809 San Jacinto St, Los Angeles CA 90026, USA — Artist

**Weiner, Michael**
Major League Baseball Players Assn, 803 3rd St, New York NY 10022, USA — Baseball Executive, Labor Leader

**Weiner, Timothy E (Tim)**
New York Times, Editorial Dept, 1627 I St NW, #700, Washington DC 20006, USA — Journalist

**Weingarten, David M**
332 2nd St, Oakland CA 94607, USA — Architect

**Weingarten, Gene**
Washington Post, Editorial Dept, 1150 15th St NW, Washington DC 20071 USA — Journalist

**Weingarten, Randi**
American Federation of Teachers, 555 New Jersey Ave NW, Washington DC 20001, USA — Labor Leader, Educator

**Weingarten, Reid H**
Steptoe & Johnson, 1330 Connecticut Ave NW, Washington DC 20036, USA — Attorney

**Weinger, Scott**
W M E Entertainment, 9601 Wilshire Blvd, #300, Beverly Hills CA 90210 USA — Actor, Producer, Writer

**Weinhold, Matt**
OmniPop Talent Group, 4605 Lankersheim Blvd, #201, Toluca Lake CA 91602 USA — Actor, Comedian

**Weinke, Christopher J (Chris)**
12504 Portmarnock Court, Charlotte NC 28277, USA — Football Player

**Weinman, Rosalyn (Roz)**
United Talent Agency, U T A Plaza, 9336 Civic Center Dr, Beverly Hills CA 90210 USA — Producer, Writer

**Weinrich, Eric J**
337 Sea Meadows Lane, Yarmouth ME 04096, USA — Ice Hockey Player

**Weinstein, Diane Gilbert**
US Court of Claims, 717 Madison Place NW, Washington DC 20439, USA — Judge

**Weinstein, Harvey**
Weinstein Company, 345 Hudson St, #1300, New York NY 10014, USA — Producer

**Weinstein, Jack B**
US District Court, US Courthouse, 225 Cadman Plaza E, Brooklyn NY 11201, USA — Judge

**Weintraub, Jerry**
Jerry Weintraub Productions, 190 N Canon Dr, #204, Beverly Hills CA 90210, USA — Producer

**Weir, Alex**
Green Light Talent Agency, PO Box 3172, Beverly Hills CA 90212 USA — Guitarist (Brothers Johnson)

**Weir, Gillian C**
Denny Lyster Artists, PO Box 155, Stanmore HA1 3WF, England — Concert Organist, Harpsichordist

**Weir, John G (Johnny)**
Global Artists Agency, 6253 Hollywood Blvd, #508, Los Angeles CA 90028 USA — Figure Skater

**Weir, Judith**
Chester Music, 14-15 Berners St, London W1T 3LJ, England — Composer

**Weir, Mike**
2960 Oberland Road, Sandy UT 84092, USA — Golfer

**Weir, Peter L**
Australian Director's Guild, PO Box 211, Rozelle, Sydney NSW 2039, Australia — Director, Writer

**Weir, Stephnie C**
United Talent Agency, U T A Plaza, 9336 Civic Center Dr, Beverly Hills CA 90210 USA — Actress, Comedienne

**Weir, Wally**
448 Lakeshore Road, Beaconsfield QC H9W 4J5, Canada — Ice Hockey Player

**Weir, William F (Bill)**
CNN-TV, News Dept, 820 1st St NE, #1000, Washington DC 20002 USA — Commentator

**Weis, Albert J (Al)**
902 S Poplar Ave, Elmhurst IL 60126, USA — Baseball Player

**Weis, Charles J (Charlie)**
University of Kansas, Athletic Dept, Lawrence KS 66045, USA — Football Coach

**Weis, Joseph F, Jr**
US Court of Appeals, US Courthouse, 700 Grant St, #2270, Pittsburgh PA 15219, USA — Judge

**Weisacosky, Edward L (Ed)**
3291 2nd Ave SE, Naples FL 34117, USA — Football Player

**Weisberg, Ruth E**
11452 W Washington Blvd, Los Angeles CA 90066, USA — Artist

**Weisberger, Lauren**
Simon & Schuster, 1230 Ave of Americas, Concourse 1, New York NY 10020 USA — Writer, Actress

**Weisel, Heidi**
Heidi Weisel Inc, 420 W 14th St, #4SE, New York NY 10014, USA — Fashion Designer

**Weishoff, Paula**
20021 Colgate Circle, Huntington Beach CA 92646, USA — Volleyball Player

## Weill - Weishoff

**Weishuhn, Clayton C (Clay)** — Football Player
4521 Kropala Road, San Angelo TX 76905, USA
**Weiskopf, Tom** — Golfer
Weiskopf Designs, 20875 N Pima Road, #C4-173, Scottsdale AZ 85255, USA
**Weiskrantz, Lawrence** — Psychologist
Oxford University, Experimental Psychology Dept, Oxford OX1 3UD, England
**Weisman, Annie** — Actress, Producer, Writer
Gersh Agency, 9465 Wilshire Blvd, #600, Beverly Hills CA 90212 USA
**Weisman, Sam** — Actor, Director, Producer
United Talent Agency, U T A Plaza, 9336 Civic Center Dr, Beverly Hills CA 90210 USA
**Weiss, Avi** — Religious Leader, Rabbi
Hebrew Institute of Riverdale, 3700 Henry Hudson Parkway, Bronx NY 10463, USA
**Weiss, Brian L** — Psychotherapist, Writer
Weiss Institute, PO Box 560788, Miami FL 33256, USA
**Weiss, Cole Evan** — Actor
Greene Assoc, 1901 Ave of Stars, #130, Los Angeles CA 90067 USA
**Weiss, Daniel B (D B)** — Producer, Writer
Creative Artists Agency, 2000 Ave of Stars, #100, Los Angeles CA 90067 USA
**Weiss, David (David Was)** — Musician (Was Not Was), Songwriter
United Talent Agency, U T A Plaza, 9336 Civic Center Dr, Beverly Hills CA 90210 USA
**Weiss, Janet** — Singer, Drummer (Sleater-Kinney)
High Road Touring, 751 Bridgeway, #200, Sausalito CA 94965 USA
**Weiss, Julie** — Costume Designer
I C M Partners, 10250 Constellation Blvd, #900, Los Angeles CA 90067 USA
**Weiss, Kenneth R** — Journalist
Los Angeles Times, Editorial Dept, 202 W 1st St, Los Angeles CA 90012 USA
**Weiss, Margaret** — Writer
T S R, PO Box 707, Renton WA 98057, USA
**Weiss, Marion** — Architect, Sculptor
Weiss/Manfredi, 130 W 29th St, #1200, New York NY 10001, USA
**Weiss, Mary** — Singer (Shangri-Las)
Norton Records, PO Box 646, Cooper Station, New York NY 10276, USA
**Weiss, Michael** — Figure Skater
5301 Wisconsin Ave NW, #425, Washington DC 20015, USA
**Weiss, Michael T** — Actor, Director
Robert Stein Mgmt, 1180 S Beverly Drive, #304, Los Angeles CA 90035, USA
**Weiss, Mitch** — Journalist
Toledo Blade, 541 N Superior St, Toledo OH 43660 USA
**Weiss, Orion** — Concert Pianist
I M G Artists, Hogarth Business Park, Chiswick, London W4 2TH, England
**Weiss, Rob** — Producer, Writer, Actor
United Talent Agency, U T A Plaza, 9336 Civic Center Dr, Beverly Hills CA 90210 USA
**Weiss, Robert W (Bob)** — Basketball Player, Coach
3309 E Saint Andrews Way, Seattle WA 98112, USA
**Weiss, Stephen** — Ice Hockey Player
899 NW 123rd Dr, Coral Springs FL 33071, USA
**Weiss, Walter W** — Baseball Player, Manager
1275 Castle Point Dr, Castle Rock CO 80104, USA
**Weissenbach, Jean** — Geneticist
Genoscope, 2 Rue Gaston Cremieur, 91006 Evry Cedex, France
**Weissensteiner, Gerda** — Luge, Bobsled Athlete
Olympic Committee, Foro Italico, Largo Lauro de Bosis 15, 00135 Rome, Italy
**Weissflog, Jens** — Ski Jumper
Markt 2, 09484 Kurort Oberwiesenthal, Germany
**Weissman, Irving L** — Cancer Biologist, Pathologist
Stanford University, Pathology Dept, Beckman Center, Stanford CA 94305, USA
**Weissman, Robert** — Businessman
I M S Health Inc, 1499 Post Road, #12, Fairfield CT 06824, USA
**Weisz, Rachel** — Actress
Independent Talent Group, 40 Whitfield St, London W1T 2RH, England
**Weithaas, Antje** — Concert Violinist
C L B Mgmt, 28 Earlswood Road, London NW10 5QB, England
**Weithorn, Michael J** — Director, Writer
I C M Partners, 10250 Constellation Blvd, #900, Los Angeles CA 90067 USA
**Weitz, Bruce** — Actor
18826 Erwin St, Tarzana CA 91335, USA
**Weitz, Patricia** — Writer
Riverhead/Penguin Books, 375 Hudson St, Basement 1, New York NY 10014, USA
**Weitz, Paul** — Director, Producer, Actor
Depth of Field, 1724 Whitley Ave, Los Angeles CA
**Weitz, Paul J** — Astronaut
3086 N Tam O'Shanter Dr, Flagstaff AZ 86004, USA
**Weitzman, Howard L** — Attorney
2049 Central Park East, #1400, Los Angeles CA 90067, USA
**Weitzman, Matt** — Producer, Writer, Actor
Creative Artists Agency, 2000 Ave of Stars, #100, Los Angeles CA 90067 USA
**Weitzman, Richard L (Rick)** — Basketball Player
76 Birch St, Peabody MA 01960, USA
**Weitzman, Susan** — Writer, Psychotherapist
25 E Washington St, #2005, Chicago IL 60602, USA
**Weixler, Jess** — Actress, Writer
Gersh Agency, 9465 Wilshire Blvd, #600, Beverly Hills CA 90212 USA
**Weizenbaum, Zoe** — Actress
Innovative Artists, 1505 10th St, Santa Monica CA 90401 USA
**Welbourn, John R** — Football Player
3301 Palos Verdes Dr N, Palos Verdes Estates CA 90274, USA
**Welch, Florence** — Singer (Florence & the Machine)
Universal-Island Records, 22 Saint Peters Square, London W6 9NW, England
**Welch, Gillian** — Singer
Q Prime, 729 7th Ave, #1600, New York NY 10019 USA
**Welch, Herbert D (Herb), Jr** — Football Player
999 La Senda, Santa Barbara CA 93105, USA
**Welch, Jack** — Astronomer
University of California, Electrical Engineering Dept, Berkeley CA 94720, USA
**Welch, John F, Jr** — Businessman
3135 Easton Turnpike, Fairfield CT 06828, USA

**Welch, Justin** — Drummer (Elastica)
C M O Mgmt, Ransomes Dock, 35-37 Parkgate Road, London SW11 4NP, England

**Welch, Kevin** — Singer, Songwriter
Rob Hall Acoustic Music, PO Box 2105, Ringwood North VIC 3134, Australia , USA

**Welch, Larry D** — Air Force General
Henry L Stimson Center, 1111 19th St NW, #1200, Washington DC 20036, USA

**Welch, Lenny** — Singer
Lustig Talent, PO Box 770850, Orlando FL 32877 USA

**Welch, Lisa** — Model
Playboy Promotions, 2706 Media Center Dr, Los Angeles CA 90065 USA

**Welch, Michael** — Actor
Curtis Talent Mgmt, 9607 Arby Dr, Beverly HIlls CA 90210, USA

**Welch, Raquel** — Actress
Innovative Artists, 1505 10th St, Santa Monica CA 90401 USA

**Welch, Robert L (Bob)** — Baseball Player
11055 E Gold Dust Ave, Scottsdale AZ 85259, USA

**Welch, Robert W (Bo), III** — Production Designer, Director
United Talent Agency, U T A Plaza, 9336 Civic Center Dr, Beverly Hills CA 90210 USA

**Welch, Tahnee** — Actress, Model
John Doherity Mgmt, 125 Christopher St, #6C, New York NY 10014, USA

**Weld, Tuesday K** — Actress
711 W End Ave, #5KN, New York NY 10025, USA

**Weld, William F** — Governor, MA
Hale & Dorr, 60 State St, #25, Boston MA 02109, USA

**Weldon, Fay** — Writer
Casorotto Ramsay, Waverley House, 7-12 Noel St, London W1F 8GQ, England

**Weldon, Joan** — Actress
67 E 78th St, New York NY 10075, USA

**Weldon, W Casey** — Football Player
380 Castleton Ave, #5, Tallahassee FL 32312, USA

**Weldon, William C** — Businessman
Johnson & Johnson, 1 Johnson & Johnson Plaza, New Bruswick NJ 08933, USA

**Welker, Frank** — Actor
C E S D, 10635 Santa Monica Blvd, #130, Los Angeles CA 90025 USA

**Welker, Wesley C (Wes)** — Football Player
42 Commonwealth Ave, #5, Boston MA 02116, USA

**Welland, Colin** — Actor, Writer
United Agents, 12-26 Lexington St, London W1F 0LE, England

**Wellber, Omer Meir** — Conductor
I M G Artists, Hogarth Business Park, Chiswick, London W4 2TH, England

**Wellemeyer, Todd A** — Baseball Player
8402 Westover Dr, Prospect KY 40059, USA

**Weller, Freddy** — Singer, Songwriter
Ace Productions, PO Box 428, Portland TN 37148, USA

**Weller, Frederick (Fred)** — Actor, Writer, Director
Gersh Agency, 9465 Wilshire Blvd, #600, Beverly Hills CA 90212 USA

**Weller, Josh** — Singer, Songwriter
Agency Group Ltd, 142 W 57th St, #600, New York NY 10019 USA

**Weller, Michael** — Writer
Gersh Agency, 9465 Wilshire Blvd, #600, Beverly Hills CA 90212 USA

**Weller, Paul** — Singer, Musician (Jam), Songwriter
High Road Touring, 751 Bridgeway, #200, Sausalito CA 94965 USA

**Weller, Peter** — Actor
A P A Talent/Literary Agency, 405 S Beverly Dr, #300, Beverly Hills CA 90212 USA

**Weller, Walter** — Conductor, Concert Violinist
Harrison/Parrott, 5-6 Albion Court, London W6 0QT, England

**Welles, Terri** — Model, Actress
PO Box 2549, Del Mar CA 92014, USA

**Wellford, Harry W** — Judge
US Court of Appeals, Federal Building, 167 N Main St, Memphis TN 38103, USA

**Welling, Tom** — Actor, Model
Tom Welling Productions, 9350 Wilshire Blvd, #250, Beverly Hills CA 90212, USA

**Welliver, Titus** — Actor
Leverage Mgmt, 3030 Pennsylvania Ave, Santa Monica CA 90404, USA

**Wellman, Brad E** — Baseball Player
733 Graham Court, Danville CA 94526, USA

**Wellman, Gary J** — Football Player
1638 Wellington Place, Westlake Village CA 91361, USA

**Wellman, Mac** — Writer
Brooklyn College, Play Writing Dept, Brooklyn NY 11210, USA

**Wellman, William, Jr** — Actor
Angel City Talent, 8318 Kirkwood Drive, Los Angeles CA 90046, USA

**Wells, Albert P** — WW II Marine Corps Air Force Hero
903 Park Lane, Santa Barbara CA 93108, USA

**Wells, Annie** — Photojournalist
Press Democrat, Editorial Dept, 427 Mendocino Ave, Santa Rosa CA 95401, USA

**Wells, Audrey** — Writer, Director, Producer
Creative Artists Agency, 2000 Ave of Stars, #100, Los Angeles CA 90067 USA

**Wells, Chris** — Ice Hockey Player
7228 Ridge Way, Park City UT 84098, USA

**Wells, Cory** — Singer (Three Dog Night)
PO Box 96597, Las Vegas NV 89193, USA

**Wells, D Dean** — Football Player
1146 Copperfield Dr, Georgetown IN 47122, USA

**Wells, David L (Dave)** — Baseball Player
PO Box 8107, Rancho Santa Fe CA 92067, USA

**Wells, Dawn** — Actress
Scott Stander Assoc, 4533 Van Nuys Blvd, #401, Sherman Oaks CA 91403 USA

**Wells, Gawen D (Bonzi)** — Basketball Player
6416 N Bobtail Dr, Muncie IN 47304, USA

**Wells, Jay** — Ice Hockey Player
Hockey School, 990 Keg Lane, RR 22, Paris ON N3L 3E2, Canada

**Wells, Joel W** — Football Player
11 Flicker Point, Greenville SC 29609, USA

**Wells, John** — Producer, Director
John Wells Productions, 4000 Warner Blvd, Building 1, Burbank CA 91522, USA

| | |
|---|---|
| **Wells, Kerry Anne** | Beauty Queen |
| Miss Universe Organization, 1370 Ave of Americas, #1600, New York NY 10019 USA | |
| **Wells, Llewellyn** | Producer, Director |
| United Talent Agency, U T A Plaza, 9336 Civic Center Dr, Beverly Hills CA 90210 USA | |
| **Wells, Mark R** | Ice Hockey Player |
| 2341 Union Road, #132, West Seneca NY 14224, USA | |
| **Wells, Matthew** | Rowing Athlete |
| Leander Club, Henley on Thames, Leander RG9 2LP, England | |
| **Wells, Patricia** | Journalist |
| Harper Collins Publishers, 10 E 53rd St, Cellar 1, New York NY 10022 USA | |
| **Wells, R Kip** | Baseball Player |
| 12891 Westbrook Dr, Tyler TX 75704, USA | |
| **Wells, Reggie A** | Football Player |
| 2569 E Cherrywood Place, Chandler AZ 85249, USA | |
| **Wells, Robert L (Bob)** | Baseball Player |
| 154 Wilcox Road, Cowiche WA 98923, USA | |
| **Wells, Simon** | Director |
| Todd Smith Assoc, 11835 W Olympic Blvd, #640, Los Angeles CA 90064, USA | |
| **Wells, Stephen G** | Educator |
| University of Nevada Reno, President's Office, Reno NV 89511, USA | |
| **Wells, Theodore V, Jr** | Attorney |
| Paul Weiss Rifkind Warton Garrison, 1285 Ave of Americas, New York NY 10019, USA | |
| **Wells, Thomas B** | Judge |
| US Tax Court, 400 2nd St NW, Washington DC 20217, USA | |
| **Wells, Vernon, III** | Baseball Player |
| 2251 King Fisher Dr, Westlake TX 76262, USA | |
| **Wells, Warren** | Football Player |
| 1399 Pipkin St, Beaumont TX 77705, USA | |
| **Wells, Wayne A** | Freestyle Wrestler |
| 2010 S Broadway, Edmond OK 73013, USA | |
| **Welp, Christian (Chris)** | Basketball Player |
| 20618 38th Dr SE, Bothell WA 98021, USA | |
| **Welser-Most, Franz** | Conductor |
| Cleveland Symphony, Severance Hall, 11001 Euclid Ave, Cleveland OH 44106, USA | |
| **Welsh, Christopher C (Chris)** | Baseball Player |
| 12640 Huey Lane, Walton KY 41094, USA | |
| **Welsh, Darrell G** | Hero |
| 102 El Rancho Way, San Antonio TX 78209, USA | |
| **Welsh, David (Dave)** | Guitarist (Fray) |
| A2 Mgmt, 624 Davis St, #200, Evanston IL 60201, USA | |
| **Welsh, Irvine** | Writer |
| Independent Talent Group, 40 Whitfield St, London W1T 2RH, England | |
| **Welsh, Moray M** | Concert Cellist |
| 28 Somerfield Ave, Queens Park, London NW6 6JY, England | |
| **Welsh, Stephanie** | Photojournalist |
| PO Box 277, Wayne ME 04284, USA | |
| **Welsman, Carol** | Singer, Pianist |
| Bennett Morgan, 1022 RR 376, #3, Wappinger Falls NY 12590 USA | |
| **Welsome-Martin, Eileen** | Journalist |
| 2040 Locust St, Denver CO 80207, USA | |
| **Welteroth, Richard J (Dick)** | Baseball Player |
| 122 Eldred St, Williamsport PA 17701, USA | |
| **Wen Jiabao** | Premier, China |
| Premier's Office, Zhonganahai, Beijing 100017, China | |
| **Wen, Ming-Na** | Actress |
| Innovative Artists, 1505 10th St, Santa Monica CA 90401 USA | |
| **Wendell, Krissy** | Ice Hockey Player |
| 325 9th St SE, Minneapolis MN 55414, USA | |
| **Wendell, Steven J (Turk)** | Baseball Player |
| 227 Hidden Valley Lane, Castle Rock CO 80108, USA | |
| **Wendelstedt, H Hunter, III** | Baseball Umpire |
| 3044 SW 98th Way, Gainesville FL 32608, USA | |
| **Wenden, Michael** | Swimmer |
| Palm Beach Currumbin Center, Thrower Dr, Palm Beach Queens, Australia | |
| **Wenders, E Wilhelm (Wim)** | Director |
| Neue Road Movies, Ackerstr 14/15, #4HH, 10115 Berlin, Germany | |
| **Wendkos, Gina** | Writer |
| Industry Entertainment, 955 Carillo Dr, #300, Los Angeles CA 90048 USA | |
| **Wendl, Ingrid Turkovic-** | Figure Skater |
| Parliament, Innere Stadt, Dr Karl-Renner Ring 3, 2004 Vienna, Austria | |
| **Wendt, George** | Actor |
| Gage Group, 14724 Ventura Blvd, #505, Sherman Oaks CA 91403 USA | |
| **Wendt, Henry, III** | Businessman |
| 560 Warbass Way, Friday Harbor WA 98250, USA | |
| **Wengert, Donald P (Don)** | Baseball Player |
| 13100 Cedarwood Ave, Clive IA 50325, USA | |
| **Wengren, Mike** | Drummer (Disturbed) |
| Mitch Schneider Organization, 14724 Ventura Blvd, #500, Sherman Oaks CA 91403 USA | |
| **Wenham, David** | Actor |
| Markham Froggatt Irwin, Julian House, 4 Windmill St, London W1P 1HF, England | |
| **Wenner, Jann S** | Publisher, Producer |
| 37 W 70th St, New York NY 10023, USA | |
| **Wennington, William P (Bill)** | Basketball Player |
| 1985 Oak Grove Lane, Lake Forest IL 60045, USA | |
| **Wensink, John** | Ice Hockey Player |
| 29311 Bidwell Creek Road, Fredericktown MO 63645, USA | |
| **Wenstrom, Matt** | Basketball Player |
| 15714 Blanco Trails Lane, Cypress TX 77429, USA | |
| **Went, Joseph J** | Marine Corps General |
| 9204 Kristin Lane, Fairfax VA 22032, USA | |
| **Wentworth, Alexandra** | Actress, Comedienne, Writer |
| Gersh Agency, 9465 Wilshire Blvd, #600, Beverly Hills CA 90212 USA | |
| **Wentz, Pete** | Bassist (Fall Out Boy), Lyricist |
| PO Box 219, 1187 Wilmette Ave, Wilmette IL 60091, USA | |
| **Wenz, Otto** | Cycling Executive |
| 14230 W Armour Ave, New Berlin WI 53151, USA | |

W

Wells - Wenz

**W**

**Wenzel, Andreas** — Alpine Skier
Oberhul 151, Piechtenstein-Gampin, Liechtenstein

**Wenzel, Hanni Weirather-** — Alpine Skier
Fanalwegle 4, 9494 Schaan, Liechtenstein

**Wenzel, Kurt** — Writer
Random House, 1745 Broadway, #1800, New York NY 10019 USA

**Wepner, Chuck** — Boxer
153 Ave E, Bayonne NJ 07002, USA

**Wepper, Fritz** — Actor
N D F, Joseph-Dollinger-Bogen 26, 80807 Munich, Germany

**Werbach, Adam** — Environmentalist
Sierra Club, 85 2nd St, #200, San Francisco CA 94105, USA

**Werbowy, Daria** — Model
I M G Models, 304 Park Ave S, #PH N, New York NY 10010 USA

**Werdann, Robert** — Basketball Player
4739 40th St, #5F, Sunnyside NY 11104, USA

**Werenka, Bradley J (Brad)** — Ice Hockey Player
PO Box 92030, Edgemont RPO, Calgary AB T3A 6L9, Canada

**Werkheiser, Devon** — Actor
Coast to Coast Talent, 3350 Barham Blvd, Los Angeles CA 90068, USA

**Werley, George W** — Baseball Player
15415 Elk Ridge Lane, Chesterfield MO 63017, USA

**Werner, Anna** — Commentator
KHOU-TV, News Department, 1945 Allan Parkway, Houston TX 77019, USA

**Werner, Bjoern** — Football Player
Indianapolis Colts, 7001 W 56th St, Indianapolis IN 46254 USA

**Werner, Carla** — Singer, Songwriter
PO Box 3241, Tamarama NSW 2026, Australia

**Werner, Clyde L** — Football Player
3009 Islandview Court, Gig Harbor WA 98335, USA

**Werner, Donald P (Don)** — Baseball Player
2204 Briarwood Blvd, Arlington TX 76013, USA

**Werner, Marianne** — Track Athlete
Gauseland 2A, 44227 Dortmund, Germany

**Werner, Peter** — Director
Paradigm Agency, 360 N Crescent Dr, North Building, Beverly Hills CA 90210 USA

**Werner, Roger L, Jr** — Businessman
Prime Sports Ventures, 10000 Santa Monica Blvd, Los Angeles CA 90067, USA

**Werner, Susan** — Singer, Songwriter
Roots Agency, 177 Woodland Ave, Westwood NJ 07675, USA

**Werner, Tom** — Producer
Good Humor Television, 9255 W Sunset Blvd, #1040, West Hollywood CA 90069, USA

**Wernick, Pete** — Singer, Banjoist (Hot Rize)
Keith Case Assoc, 1025 17th Ave S, #200, Nashville TN 37212 USA

**Wersching, Annie** — Actress
S M S Talent, 8383 Wilshire Blvd, #230, Beverly Hills CA 90211 USA

**Wersching, Raimund (Ray)** — Football Player
18 Buttercup Lane, San Carlos CA 94070, USA

**Wert, Donald R (Don)** — Baseball Player
341 Smithville Road, New Providence PA 17560, USA

**Werth, Isabell** — Equestrian
Winterswicker Feld 4, 47495 Rheinberg, Germany

**Werth, Jayson R** — Baseball Player
PO Box 13457, Springfield IL 62791, USA

**Wertheim, Jorge** — Association Executive
UNESCO, Director's Office, UN Plaza, New York NY 10017, USA

**Wertheimer, Fredric M** — Public Policy Activist
3502 Macomb St NW, Washington DC 20016, USA

**Wertheimer, Linda** — Commentator
National Public Radio, 635 Massachusetts Ave NW, #1, Washington DC 20001, USA

**Wertmuller, Lina** — Director
Piazza Clotilde, 00196 Rome, Italy

**Wertmuller, Massimo** — Actor
Carol Levi Mgmt, Via Giuseppe Pisanelli 2, 00196 Rome, Italy

**Wertz, Matt** — Singer, Songwriter
Nettwerk Music Group, 1201 Villa Place, #206, Nashville TN 37212, USA

**Wertz, William C (Bill)** — Baseball Player
26514 Mingo Dr, Perrysburg OH 43551, USA

**Wescott, Seth B** — Snowboarding Athlete
Octagon Worldwide, 2 Union St, #300, Portland ME 04101 USA

**Wesker, Arnold** — Writer
Hay on Wye, Hereford HR3 5RJ, England

**Wesley, Dante J** — Football Player
104 Fawn Cove, White Hall AR 71602, USA

**Wesley, David B** — Basketball Player
6117 West End Blvd, New Orleans LA 70124, USA

**Wesley, Fred** — Jazz Trombonist
Universal Attractions, 135 W 26th St, #1200, New York NY 10001 USA

**Wesley, Glen E** — Ice Hockey Player
5305 Newstead Manor Lane, Raleigh NC 27606, USA

**Wesley, Gregory L (Greg)** — Football Player
9752 Sunset Circle, Lenexa KS 66220, USA

**Wesley, Norman H** — Businessman
Fortune Brands Inc, 520 Lake Cook Road, Deerfield IL 60015, USA

**Wesley, Paul** — Actor, Producer
I C M Partners, 10250 Constellation Blvd, #900, Los Angeles CA 90067 USA

**Wesley, Rutina** — Actress
Inspire Entertainment, 2332 Cotner Ave, #302, Los Angeles CA 90064, USA

**Wesley, Trevor (Blake)** — Ice Hockey Player
Okanagan Hockey School, 101-697 Wade W, Penticton BC V2A 1V6, Canada

**Wesley, Walter (Walt)** — Basketball Player
6417 Scott Lane, Fort Myers FL 33966, USA

**Wessel, Henry, Jr** — Photographer
PO Box 475, Richmond CA 94807, USA

**Wesson, Barry** — Baseball Player
36 Shore Dr NE, Brookhaven MS 39601, USA

| | |
|---|---|
| **West, Adam**<br>Kazarian/Measures/Ruskin, 11969 Ventura Blvd, #300, Studio City CA 91604 USA | Actor |
| **West, Chandra**<br>Characters Talent Mgmt, 8 Elm St, Toronto ON M5G 1G7, Canada | Actress |
| **West, Charles (Charlie)**<br>184 Laurel Ridge, South Salem NY 10590, USA | Football Player |
| **West, Cornel**<br>Princeton University, Afro American Studies Program, Princeton NJ 08544, USA | Theologian, Sociologist |
| **West, David J**<br>Hershey Co, 100 Crystal A Dr, PO Box 810, Hershey PA 17033, USA | Businessman |
| **West, David L**<br>1242 SW Seahawk Way, Palm City FL 34990, USA | Baseball Player |
| **West, David M**<br>Indiana Pacers, Conseco Fieldhouse, 125 S Pennsylvania, Indianapolis IN 46204 USA | Basketball Player |
| **West, Delonte**<br>8805 Charm Court, Brandywine MD 20613, USA | Basketball Player |
| **West, Dominic**<br>W M E Entertainment, 9601 Wilshire Blvd, #300, Beverly Hills CA 90210 USA | Actor |
| **West, Edward L (Ed), Jr**<br>1930 Ma Lee Dr, Moody AL 35004, USA | Football Player |
| **West, Ernest E**<br>912 Adams Ave, Greenup KY 41144, USA | Korean War Army Hero (CMH) |
| **West, Geoffrey**<br>Santa Fe Institute, 1399 Hyde Park Road, Santa Fe NM 87501, USA | Theoretical Physicist |
| **West, J Douglas (Doug)**<br>1131 Meridian Dr, Presto PA 15142, USA | Basketball Player |
| **West, Jacqueline**<br>Gersh Agency, 9465 Wilshire Blvd, #600, Beverly Hills CA 90212 USA | Costume Designer |
| **West, James E**<br>724 Berkeley Ave, Plainfield NJ 07062, USA | Inventor (Telephone Microphone) |
| **West, Jason**<br>Respawn Entertainment, 5990 Sepulveda Blvd, Van Nuys CA 91411, USA | Video Games Developer |
| **West, Jeffrey H (Jeff)**<br>12376 Adair Creek Way NE, Redmond WA 98053, USA | Football Player |
| **West, Jerome A (Jerry)**<br>Golden State Warriors, 1011 Broadway, Oakland CA 94605 USA | Basketball Player, Coach, Executive |
| **West, Joel**<br>Don Carroll Mgmt, 14211 Hatteras St, Sherman Oaks CA 91401, USA | Model, Actor |
| **West, Joseph H (Joe)**<br>17531 Cobblestone Lane, Clermont FL 34711, USA | Baseball Umpire |
| **West, Josh**<br>22 Cherwell St, Oxford OX 41BG, England | Rowing Athlete |
| **West, Kanye**<br>3200 Cherry Creek South Dr, #620, Denver CO 80209, USA | Rap Artist, Music Producer |
| **West, Keith**<br>Country Thunder Records, 1016 17th Ave S, Nashville TN 37212, USA | Bassist, Singer (Heartland) |
| **West, Leslie**<br>Survival Mgmt, 30765 Pacific Coast Highway, #325, Malibu CA 90265, USA | Singer, Guitarist (Mountain) |
| **West, Lizzie**<br>Warner Bros Records, 3300 Warner Blvd, Burbank CA 91505 USA | Singer |
| **West, Mark A**<br>644 Old Wagner Road, Petersburg VA 23805, USA | Basketball Player |
| **West, Martin**<br>427 N Canon Dr, Beverly Hills CA 90210, USA | Actor |
| **West, Maura**<br>Innovative Artists, 1505 10th St, Santa Monica CA 90401 USA | Actress |
| **West, Nathan**<br>United Talent Agency, U T A Plaza, 9336 Civic Center Dr, Beverly Hills CA 90210 USA | Actor |
| **West, Paul**<br>Elaine Markson Agency, 44 Greenwich Ave, #300, New York NY 10011, USA | Writer |
| **West, Roland D**<br>7464 Shaker Run Lane, West Chester OH 45069, USA | Basketball Player |
| **West, Shane**<br>Luber Rocklin Entertainment, 8530 Wilshire Blvd, #555, Beverly Hills CA 90211 USA | Actor |
| **West, Shelly**<br>Acts Nashville Talent, 1103 Bell Grimes Lane, Nashville TN 37207, USA | Singer |
| **West, Simon**<br>Simon West Productions, 3450 Cahuenga Blvd W, Building 510, Los Angeles CA 90068, USA | Director, Producer, Writer |
| **West, Stu**<br>Leave Home Booking, 10 W Broadway, #608, Salt Lake City UT 84101, USA | Bassist (Damned) |
| **West, Timothy L**<br>Gavin Barker Assoc, 2D Wimpole St, London W1G 0EB, England | Actor |
| **West, Togo D, Jr**<br>922 N Cameron Ave, Winston Salem NC 27101, USA | Secretary, Veterans Affairs |
| **West, Willie T**<br>PO Box 50430, Eugene OR 97405, USA | Football Player |
| **Westbrook, Brian C**<br>6204 Blue Sage Lane, Upper Marlboro MD 20772, USA | Football Player |
| **Westbrook, Bryant A**<br>28017 N 17th Dr, Phoenix AZ 85085, USA | Football Player |
| **Westbrook, Dexter**<br>200 E Church Lane, #405, Philadelphia PA 19144, USA | Basketball Player |
| **Westbrook, Jacob C (Jake)**<br>PO Box 574, Danielsville GA 30633, USA | Baseball Player |
| **Westbrook, Michael D**<br>2797 E Teakwood Place, Chandler AZ 85249, USA | Football Player |
| **Westbrook, Peter**<br>15 Washington Place, #1F, New York NY 10003, USA | Fencer |
| **Westbrook, Russell**<br>Oklahoma City Thunder, 211 N Robinson Ave, #300, Oklahoma City OK 73102 USA | Basketball Player |
| **Westbrooks, Gregory M (Greg)**<br>3832 10th Avenue Place, Moline IL 61265, USA | Football Player |
| **Westenhiser, Jamie**<br>Playboy Promotions, 2706 Media Center Dr, Los Angeles CA 90065 USA | Model |
| **Westenhofer, Bill**<br>Rhythm & Hues Studio, 2100 E Grand Ave, El Segundo CA 90245 90245, USA | Visual Effects Designer |

**W**

# W

**Westenra, Hayley** — Singer
Bandana Mgmt, 160 New Kings Road, London SW6 4LZ, England

**Westerberg, Paul** — Singer, Guitarist, Songwriter
Mitch Schneider Organization, 14724 Ventura Blvd, #500, Sherman Oaks CA 91403 USA

**Westfall, V Edward (Ed)** — Ice Hockey Player
699 Hillside Ave, New Hyde Park NY 11040, USA

**Westfeldt, Jennifer** — Actress
Innovative Artists, 1505 10th St, Santa Monica CA 90401 USA

**Westhead, Paul W** — Basketball Coach
University of Oregon, Athletic Dept, Eugene OR 97403, USA

**Westheimer, Gerald** — Optometrist
582 Santa Barbara Road, Berkeley CA 94707, USA

**Westheimer, Ruth S** — Sex Therapist, Psychologist, Producer
C E S D, 10635 Santa Monica Blvd, #130, Los Angeles CA 90025 USA

**Westin, Av** — Businessman, Journalist
King World Productions, 1700 Broadway, #3200, New York NY 10019, USA

**Westlake, Waldon T (Wally)** — Baseball Player
3800 61st St, Sacramento CA 95820, USA

**Westling, Jon** — Educator
285 Goddard Ave, Brookline MA 02445, USA

**Westmore, McKenzie K** — Actress, Singer
W M E Entertainment, 9601 Wilshire Blvd, #300, Beverly Hills CA 90210 USA

**Westmoreland, James** — Actor
52940 Avenida Navarro, La Quinta CA 92253, USA

**Westmoreland, Richard C (Dick)** — Football Player
5601 Sea Reef Place, San Diego CA 92154, USA

**Weston, Celia** — Actress
Innovative Artists, 235 Park Ave S, #1000, New York NY 10003 USA

**Weston, Ken** — Sound Mixer
I C M Partners, 10250 Constellation Blvd, #900, Los Angeles CA 90067 USA

**Weston, Kim** — Singer
Powerplay, PO Box 533, 5434 W Sample Road, Margate FL 33073, USA

**Weston, Michael** — Actor
Paradigm Agency, 360 N Crescent Dr, North Building, Beverly Hills CA 90210, USA

**Weston, Michael L (Mickey)** — Baseball Player
2702 Eisenhower Ave, Valparaiso IN 46383, USA

**Weston, Randolph (Randy)** — Jazz Pianist
PO Box 749, Maplewood NJ 07040, USA

**Weston, Stan** — Businessman
Leisure Concepts, 1414 Ave of Americas, New York NY 10019, USA

**Weston-Jones, Tom** — Actor
Markham Froggatt Irwin, Julian House, 4 Windmill St, London W1P 1HF, England

**Westphal, Paul D** — Basketball Player, Coach
1424 Granvia Altamira, Palos Verdes Estates CA 90274, USA

**Westwick, Edward G (Ed)** — Actor, Singer
Emptage Hallett, 14 Rathbone Place, London W1T 1HT, England

**Westwood, Joey** — Bassist (Red Jumpsuit Apparatus)
Virgin Records, 338 N Foothill Road, Beverly Hills CA 90210 USA

**Westwood, Vivienne** — Fashion Designer
Lanterns #3, Old School House, Bridge Lane, London SW11 3AD, England

**Wetherbee, James D (Jim)** — Astronaut
3818 Trailstone Lane, Katy TX 77494, USA

**Wetherby, Jeffrey B (Jeff)** — Baseball Player
28410 Great Bend Place, Fresno CA 93710, USA

**Wethington, Charles T, Jr** — Educator
2926 Four Pines Dr, Lexington KY 40502, USA

**Wetoska, Robert S (Bob)** — Football Player
1295 Forest Glen Dr S, Winnetka IL 60093, USA

**Wetteland, John K** — Baseball Player
1229 Kentucky Derby Dr, Argyle TX 76226, USA

**Wetter, Friedrich Cardinal** — Religious Leader
Erziozese Munich, Postfach 100551, 80079 Munich, Germany

**Wetterich, Brett** — Golfer
149 Morning Dew Circle, Jupiter FL 33458, USA

**Wettig, Patricia** — Actress
Innovative Artists, 1505 10th St, Santa Monica CA 90401 USA

**Wetton, John** — Singer, Bassist (Asia, UK)
Entourage Talent Assoc, 236 W 27th St, #800, New York NY 10001, USA

**Wetzel, Carl** — Ice Hockey Player
9401 James Ave S, #11, Minneapolis MN 55431, USA

**Wetzel, Donald C (Don)** — Inventor (Automated Teller Machine)
5706 Trail Meadow Dr, Dallas TX 75230, USA

**Wetzel, Gary G** — Vietnam War Army Hero (CMH)
PO Box 84, Oak Creek WI 53154, USA

**Wetzel, John F** — Basketball Player, Coach
13011 N Sunrise Canyon Lane, Marana AZ 85658, USA

**Wetzel, Robert G** — Botanist
16 Dunbrook, Tuscaloosa AL 35406, USA

**Wetzel, Robert L** — Army General
1425 Dartmouth Road, Columbus GA 31904, USA

**Wever, Merritt** — Actress
Innovative Artists, 1505 10th St, Santa Monica CA 90401 USA

**Wever, Stefan M** — Baseball Player
7 Corte Los Sombras, Greenbrae CA 94904, USA

**Wexler, Haskell** — Cinematographer
1247 Lincoln Blvd, #585, Santa Monica CA 90401 USA

**Wexler, Nancy S** — Clinical Psychologist
Hereditary Disease Foundation, 3960 Broadway, New York NY 10032, USA

**Wexler, Robert** — Religious Leader, Rabbi, Educator
Brandeis-Bardin, 1101 Peppertree, Brandeis CA 93064, USA

**Wexler, Robert F** — Representative, FL
Middle East Peace Center, 633 Pennsylvania NW, #500, Washington DC 20004, USA

**Weyerhaeuser, George** — Businessman
Weyerhaeuser Co, 33663 32nd Ave S, Federal Way WA 98023, USA

**Weymouth, Tina** — Bassist (Talking Heads, Tom Tom Club)
Premier Talent, 3 E 54th St, #1100, New York NY 10022 USA

**Whalen, Laurence J** — Judge
US Tax Court, 400 2nd St NW, Washington DC 20217, USA

**Whalen, Lindsay M** — Basketball Player
Minnesota Lynx, Target Center, 600 1st Ave N, Minneapolis MN 55403 USA

**Whalen, Sara** — Soccer Player
10 Francis Dr, Greenlawn NY 11740, USA

**Whaley, Frank** — Actor
A P A Talent/Literary Agency, 405 S Beverly Dr, #300, Beverly Hills CA 90212 USA

**Whaley, Suzi** — Golfer
15 Whitehall Place, Farmington CT 06032, USA

**Whalin, Justin G** — Actor
Deborah Miller, 9454 Wilshire Blvd, #715, Beverly Hills CA 90212, USA

**Whalley, Joanne** — Actress
Lou Coulson Assoc, 37 Berwick St, London W1V 8RS, England

**Whalum, Kirk** — Jazz Saxophonist
Cole Classic Mgmt, PO Box 231, Canoga Park CA 91305, USA

**Whang, Suzanne** — Actress
I C M Partners, 10250 Constellation Blvd, #900, Los Angeles CA 90067 USA

**Whannell, Leigh** — Actor
Paradigm Agency, 360 N Crescent Dr, North Building, Beverly Hills CA 90210 USA

**Wharram, Ken** — Ice Hockey Player
382 Aubrey St W, North Bay ON P1B 6H9, Canada

**Wharton, Bernard** — Architect
Shope Reno Wharton, 18 Marshall St, #114, Norwalk CT 06854, USA

**Wharton, G Travelle** — Football Player
111 Stenhouse Road, Simpsonville SC 29680, USA

**Whatley, Ennis** — Basketball Player
42 Brinkwood Road, Brookeville MD 20833, USA

**Whatmore, Sarah L** — Singer
Fremantle Media, 2700 Colorado Ave, #450, Santa Monica CA 90404 USA

**Wheatcroft, Georgina** — Curling Athlete
Curling Assn, 1660 Vimont Court, Cumberland ON K4A 4J4, Canada

**Wheatley, Ben** — Director
W M E Entertainment, 9601 Wilshire Blvd, #300, Beverly Hills CA 90210 USA

**Wheatley, Kevin** — Actor
Seven Summits Mgmt, 8906 W Olympic Blvd, Beverly Hills CA 90211 USA

**Wheatley, Tyrone A** — Football Player
5500 Sandstone Way, Fayetteville NY 13066, USA

**Wheaton, David** — Tennis Player
PO Box 401, Tonka Bay MN 55331, USA

**Wheaton, Wil** — Actor
Opus Entertainment, 5225 Wilshire Blvd, #905, Los Angeles CA 90036, USA

**Whedon, Joseph H (Joss)** — Actor, Director, Producer
Creative Artists Agency, 2000 Ave of Stars, #100, Los Angeles CA 90067 USA

**Wheeldon, Christopher** — Choreographer, Ballet Dancer
Morphoses/Wheeldon Co, 800 5th Ave, #18F, New York NY 10065, USA

**Wheeler, Adam** — Greco-Roman Wrestler
4854 Jedediah Smith Road, Colorado Springs CO 80922, USA

**Wheeler, Cheryl** — Singer, Songwriter
Morningstar Mgmt, PO Box 1770, Hendersonville TN 37077, USA

**Wheeler, Clinton** — Basketball Player
199 Scenic View Lane, Stone Mountain GA 30087, USA

**Wheeler, Daniel M (Dan)** — Baseball Player
215 Harrison Ave, Belleair Beach FL 33786, USA

**Wheeler, Dwight** — Football Player
2012 Sunnyslope Lane, Goodlettsville TN 37072, USA

**Wheeler, Gary** — Interior Designer
Perkins & Will, 330 N Wabash Ave, #3600, Chicago IL 60611, USA

**Wheeler, H Anthony** — Architect
South Inverleith Manor, 31/6 Kinnear Road, Edinburgh EH3 5PG, Scotland

**Wheeler, Howard A (Humpy)** — Auto Racing Executive
Wheeler Co, PO Box 1327, Cornelius NC 28031, USA

**Wheeler, John A** — Actor
414 Troy Court, Claremont CA 91711, USA

**Wheeler, Maggie** — Actress
Affirmative Entertainment, 425 N Robertson Blvd, Los Angeles CA 90048 USA

**Wheeler, Mark A** — Football Player
101 Meadowridge Cove, San Marcos TX 78666, USA

**Wheeler, Nicholas D (Nick)** — Singer, Guitarist (All-American Rejects)
Creative Artists Agency, 2000 Ave of Stars, #100, Los Angeles CA 90067 USA

**Wheeler-Nicholson, Dana** — Actress
Glick Agency, 1321 7th St, #203, Santa Monica CA 90401 USA

**Wheelock, Douglas H** — Astronaut
PO Box 580408, Houston TX 77258, USA

**Wheelock, Gary R** — Baseball Player
3354 N Park St, Buckeye AZ 85396, USA

**Whelan, Bill** — Composer
Sony Records, 2100 Colorado Ave, Santa Monica CA 90404 USA

**Whelan, Gary** — Actor
Ken McReddie Assoc, 101 Finsbury Pavement, London EC2A 1RS, England

**Whelan, Nicky** — Actress, Model
United Talent Agency, U T A Plaza, 9336 Civic Center Dr, Beverly Hills CA 90210 USA

**Whelan, Peter** — Writer
Lemon Unna Durbridge, Holland Park, 24 Pottery Lane, London W11 4LZ, England

**Whelan, Wendy** — Ballerina
New York City Ballet, Lincoln Center Plaza, New York NY 10023 USA

**Whelchel, Lisa** — Actress
Arcieri Assoc, 305 Madison Ave, #2315, New York NY 10165 USA

**Wheless, Jamy** — Animator
405 Fair St, Petaluma CA 94952, USA

**Whicker, Alan D** — Commentator
Trinity, Jersey JE3 5BA, Channel Islands, England

**Whigham, Larry J** — Football Player
33 Collins Road, Hattiesburg MS 39401, USA

**Whigham, Shea** — Actor
Principal Entertainment, 9255 Sunset Blvd, #500, Los Angeles CA 90069 USA

**Whillock, Jack F** — Baseball Player
2118 River Ridge Road, Arlington TX 76017, USA

**Whimper, Guy** — Football Player
1010 Main St, New Bern NC 28560, USA

**Whirry, Shannon** — Actress
Ford/Robert Black Agency, 4032 N Miller Road, #104, Scottsdale AZ 95251, USA

**Whisenant, Matthew M (Matt)** — Baseball Player
1035 Fairview Dr, La Canada Flintridge CA 91011, USA

**Whisenhunt, Ken** — Football Player, Coach
6286 E Cheney Dr, Paradise Valley AZ 85253, USA

**Whishaw, Anthony** — Artist
7A Albert Place, Victoria Road, London W8 5PD, England

**Whishaw, Ben** — Actor
Hamilton Hodell, 66-68 Margaret St, #500, London W1W 8SR, England

**Whisler, J Steven** — Businessman
Phelps Dodge Corp, 1 N Central Ave, #100, Phoenix AZ 85004, USA

**Whiston, Donald (Don)** — Ice Hockey Player
2 Jeffreys Neck Road, Ipswich MA 01938, USA

**Whitacre, Edward E, Jr** — Businessman
General Motors Corp, 100 Renaissance Center, Detroit MI 48243, USA

**Whitaker, Denzel** — Actor
Luber Rocklin Entertainment, 8530 Wilshire Blvd, #555, Beverly Hills CA 90211 USA

**Whitaker, Forest** — Actor, Director
Spirit Dance Entertainment, 1023 N Orange Dr, Los Angeles CA 90038, USA

**Whitaker, Jack** — Golfer
International Golf Partners, 3300 PGA Blvd, #820, Palm Beach Gardens FL 33410, USA

**Whitaker, Jack** — Sportscaster
500 Berwyn Baptist Road, Devon PA 19333, USA

**Whitaker, Louis R (Lou), Jr** — Baseball Player
17 Brownstone Lane, Greensboro NC 27410, USA

**Whitaker, Meade** — Judge
US Tax Court, 400 2nd St NW, Washington DC 20217, USA

**Whitaker, Pernell** — Boxer
310 Nottawat Court, Chesapeake VA 23320, USA

**Whitaker, Steve E** — Baseball Player
900 SE 6th Court, Fort Lauderdale FL 33301, USA

**Whitbread, Fatima** — Track Athlete
Javel-Inn, Mill Hill, Shenfield, Brentwood, Essex CM15 8EU, England

**Whitby, William E (Bill)** — Baseball Player
13926 Huntersville Concord Road, Huntersville NC 28078, USA

**Whitcomb, Bob** — Auto Racing Executive
Whitcomb Racing, 9201 Garrison Road, Charlotte NC 28278, USA

**Whitcomb, Edgar D** — Governor, IN
15415 Rome Road, Rome IN 47574, USA

**Whitcomb, Ian** — Singer, Songwriter
PO Box 451, Altadena CA 91003, USA

**White, Adrian D** — Football Player
688 Allen Lane, Orange Park FL 32073, USA

**White, Alan, III** — Drummer (Yes, Oasis)
Ignition Mgmt, 54 Linhope St, London NW1 6HL, England

**White, Andrew N, III** — Jazz Saxophonist
Vezco Productions, 163 Main St, Odessa ON K0H 2H0, Canada

**White, Andrew R (Whitey)** — Guitarist (Kaiser Chiefs)
Red Light Mgmt, 8439 Sunset Blvd, West Hollywood CA 90069, USA

**White, Artie** — Singer
C A I Entertainment Agency, PO Box 9267, Jackson MS 39286, USA

**White, Betty M** — Actress, Comedienne
PO Box 491965, Los Angeles CA 90049, USA

**White, Brian** — Ice Hockey Player
3 Gedick Road, Burlington MA 01803, USA

**White, Brian J, Jr** — Actor
Paradigm Agency, 360 N Crescent Dr, North Building, Beverly Hills CA 90210 USA

**White, Brian J, Jr** — Actor
United Talent Agency, U T A Plaza, 9336 Civic Center Dr, Beverly Hills CA 90210 USA

**White, Brooke** — Singer, Songwriter, Actress
Glick Agency, 1321 7th St, #203, Santa Monica CA 90401 USA

**White, Bryan** — Singer, Songwriter
Loudmouth Public Relations, PO Box 128192, Nashville TN 37212, USA

**White, Charles R** — Football Player, Administrator
31841 Via Faisan, Trabuco Canyon CA 92679, USA

**White, Charlie** — Ice Dancer
Arctic Edge Skating Club, 46615 Michigan Ave, Canton MI 48188, USA

**White, Chris** — Bassist (Zombies)
Lustig Talent, PO Box 770850, Orlando FL 32877 USA

**White, Devon M** — Baseball Player
6440 E Sierra Vista Dr, Paradise Valley AZ 85253, USA

**White, Dewayne (D J), Jr** — Basketball Player
Charlotte Bobcats, 333 E Trade St, #A, Charlotte NC 28202 USA

**White, Donna** — Golfer
200 Caribe Court, Greenacres FL 33413, USA

**White, Dwayne A** — Football Player
2117 Pinehurst Way, Coral Springs FL 33071, USA

**White, Edmund V** — Writer
I C M Partners, 10250 Constellation Blvd, #900, Los Angeles CA 90067 USA

**White, Edward A (Ed)** — Football Player
PO Box 1437, Julian CA 92036, USA

**White, Eugene** — Baseball Player
4166 Lockhart Dr N, Jacksonville FL 32209, USA

**White, G Edward** — Educator, Attorney
University of Virginia, Law School, Charlottesville VA 22903, USA

**White, Gabriel A (Gabe)** — Baseball Player
1571 Lakeview Dr, Sebring FL 33870, USA

**White, Gary C** — Biologist
Water.org, 920 Main St, #1800, Kansas City MO 64105, USA

**White, Harvey D** — Cardiologist
Green Lane Hospital, Cardioloy Dept, PB 92189, Auckland 1030, New Zealand

**White, Hubert L (Hubie)** — Basketball Player
101 E Gowen Ave, Philadelphia PA 19119, USA
**White, J Colin** — Ice Hockey Player
81 Western Ave, Morristown NJ 07960, USA
**White, J Michael (Mike)** — Baseball Player
26438 S Jardin Dr, Sun Lakes AZ 85248, USA
**White, Jack** — Singer, Guitarist (White Stripes)
Monotone Mgmt, 820 Seward St, Los Angeles CA 90038, USA
**White, Jaleel** — Actor
Pantheon Talent, 1801 Century Park E, #1910, Los Angeles CA 90067, USA
**White, James C (Jim)** — Football Player
14430 Andrea Way Lane, Houston TX 77083, USA
**White, James L** — Writer
I C M Partners, 10250 Constellation Blvd, #900, Los Angeles CA 90067 USA
**White, James W, IV** — Basketball Player
New York Knicks, Madison Square Garden, 2 Penn Plaza, New York, NY 10121 USA
**White, Jason** — Football Player
3203 Stone Dr, Tuttle OK 73089, USA
**White, Jeordie O** — Bassist (Marilyn Manson, Perfect Circle)
Coast II Coast Entertainment, 8671 Wilshire Blvd, Beverly Hills CA 90211, USA
**White, Jeris J** — Football Player
15 N Wisner St, Frederick MD 21701, USA
**White, Jerome C (Jerry)** — Baseball Player
343 N Wildwood, Hercules CA 94547, USA
**White, Jessica** — Model
Elite Model Mgmt, 345 N Maple Dr, #176, Beverly Hills CA 90210 USA
**White, John H** — Photojournalist
Chicago Sun-Times, Editorial Dept, 401 N Wabash Ave, Chicago IL 60611 USA
**White, John Patrick** — Actor
C E S D, 10635 Santa Monica Blvd, #130, Los Angeles CA 90025 USA
**White, Joseph H (Jo Jo)** — Basketball Player
2 Mansfield Road, Middleton MA 01949, USA
**White, Josh, Jr** — Singer, Songwriter
23625 Ripple Creek, Novi MI 48375, USA
**White, Julie** — Actress, Singer
Himber Entertainment, PO Box 950, South Orange NJ 07079 USA
**White, Karyn** — Singer
Cavaleri Assoc, 178 S Victory Blvd, #205, Burbank CA 91502, USA
**White, Katie** — Singer, Guitarist (Ting Tings)
Paradigm Agency, 404 W Franklin St, Monterey CA 93940 USA
**White, Lari** — Singer, Songwriter
R C A Records, 1400 18th Ave S, Nashville TN 37212 USA
**White, Lee A** — Football Player
600 Langtry Dr, Las Vegas NV 89107, USA
**White, Lenny, III** — Jazz Drummer
Universal Attractions, 135 W 26th St, #1200, New York NY 10001 USA
**White, Lillias** — Actress
Talent Works, 3500 W Olive Ave, #1400, Burbank CA 91505 USA
**White, Lorenzo M** — Football Player
2860 Somerset Dr, #111, Lauderdale Lakes FL 33311, USA
**White, Marco P** — Chef
The Restaurant, 66 Knightsbridge, London SW1X 7LA, England
**White, Marilyn** — Track Athlete
9605 6th Ave, Inglewood CA 90305, USA
**White, Mark** — Musician (Spin Doctors)
D A S Communications, 83 Riverside Dr, New York NY 10024 USA
**White, Mary Anne** — Chemist
30 Burnt Log Crescent, Etobicoke ON M9C 2J8, Canada
**White, Matthew J (Matt)** — Baseball Player
1853 Old Route 9, Windsor MA 01270, USA
**White, Maurice** — Singer (Earth Wind & Fire), Songwriter
Spirit Media, PO Box 43591, Phoenix AZ 85080, USA
**White, Meg** — Singer, Drummer (White Stripes)
Monotone Mgmt, 820 Seward St, Los Angeles CA 90038, USA
**White, Michael D** — Businessman
DirecTV, 2230 E Imperial Hwy, El Segundo CA 90245, USA
**White, Michael Jai** — Actor, Producer
24602 Garland Dr, Valencia CA 91355, USA
**White, Michael R** — Mayor, Cleveland
11655 Blue Ridge Road, Newcomerstown OH 43832, USA
**White, Michael S** — Producer
48 Dean St, London W1V 5HL, England
**White, Mike** — Actor, Director, Writer
United Talent Agency, U T A Plaza, 9336 Civic Center Dr, Beverly Hills CA 90210 USA
**White, Mike** — Football Coach
115 Grand Canal, Newport Beach CA 92662, USA
**White, Miles D** — Businessman
Abbott Laboratories, 100 Abbott Park Road, North Chicago IL 60064, USA
**White, Myron A** — Baseball Player
3201 S Deegan Dr, Santa Ana CA 92704, USA
**White, Nera D** — Basketball Player
RR 3 Box 165, Lafayette TN 37083, USA
**White, Persia** — Singer, Songwriter, Actress
Stone Manners Salners, 9911 W Pico Blvd, #1400, Los Angeles CA 90035 USA
**White, Peter** — Jazz Guitarist
Chapman & Co Mgmt, 14011 Ventura Blvd, #405, Sherman Oaks CA 91423, USA
**White, Randy L** — Football Player
1360 E Frontier Parkway, Prosper TX 75078, USA
**White, Raymond P, Jr** — Oral Surgeon
1506 Velma Road, Chapel Hill NC 27514, USA
**White, Rex** — Auto Racing Driver
187 Rivers Road, #222, Fayetteville GA 30214, USA
**White, Richard A (Rick)** — Baseball Player
2860 Windy Ridge Dr, Springfield OH 45502, USA
**White, Robert** — Artist
380 Millwood Ave, Winchester VA 22601, USA

**White, Robert M** — Meteorologist
Somerset House II, 5610 Wisconsin Ave, #1506, Chevy Chase MD 20815, USA
**White, Ron** — Actor, Writer, Producer
A P A Talent/Literary Agency, 405 S Beverly Dr, #300, Beverly Hills CA 90212 USA
**White, Rondell B** — Baseball Player
407 Creekside Dr, Gray GA 31032, USA
**White, Rory W** — Basketball Player
5303 32nd St S, Fargo ND 58104, USA
**White, Roy H** — Baseball Player
534 Mill Pond Way, Eatontown NJ 07724, USA
**White, Royce A** — Basketball Player
Houston Rockets, 1730 Jefferson St, Houston TX 77003 USA
**White, Samuel (Sammy)** — Football Player
102 Margaret Dr, Monroe LA 71203, USA
**White, Shaun** — Snowboard, Skateboard Athlete
Burton Snowboards, 80 Industrial Parkway, Burlington VT 05401, USA
**White, Sherman E (Sherm)** — Football Player
2710 Summerland Road, Aromas CA 95004, USA
**White, Stanley R (Stan)** — Football Player
10716 Pot Spring Road, Cockeysville MD 21030, USA
**White, Steven A** — Navy Admiral, Businessman
Stone & Webster Engineering, 4 Mount Royal Ave, #420, Marlboro MA 01752, USA
**White, Susanna** — Director
United Talent Agency, U T A Plaza, 9336 Civic Center Dr, Beverly Hills CA 90210 USA
**White, Sylvain** — Director
United Talent Agency, U T A Plaza, 9336 Civic Center Dr, Beverly Hills CA 90210 USA
**White, Timothy D** — Anthropologist
University of California, Human Evolutionary Studies Laboratory, Berkeley CA 94720, USA
**White, Timothy P** — Educator
University of California, Chancellor's Office, 900 University Ave, Riverside CA 92521, USA
**White, Tony Joe** — Singer, Songwriter
Tony Joe White Music, PO Box 1292, Franklin TN 37065, USA
**White, Vanna** — Entertainer, Actress, Model
'Wheel of Fortune' Show, 10202 W Washington Blvd, #2000, Culver City CA 90232, USA
**White, Verdine** — Bassist (Earth Wind & Fire), Songwriter
Spirit Media, PO Box 43591, Phoenix AZ 85080, USA
**White, W Daniel (Danny)** — Football Player
902 E San Angelo Ave, Gilbert AZ 85234, USA
**White, Willard W** — Opera Singer
10 Montague Ave, London SE4 1YP, England
**White, William B (Bill)** — Baseball Player, Executive
8517 Barn Owl, San Antonio TX 78255, USA
**White, William E** — Football Player
2323 Woodland Hall Dr, Powell OH 43065, USA
**Whited, Edward M (Ed)** — Baseball Player
PO Box 34, Carmel IN 46082, USA
**Whitehead, Axle** — Actor
United Talent Agency, U T A Plaza, 9336 Civic Center Dr, Beverly Hills CA 90210 USA
**Whitehead, Barb** — Golfer
9820 E Thompson Peak Parkway, #707, Scottsdale AZ 85255, USA
**Whitehead, Colson** — Writer
Doubleday Press, 1745 Broadway, New York NY 10019 USA
**Whitehead, Geoffrey** — Actor
Bryan Drew, Quadrant House, 80-82 Regent St, London W1B 5AU, England
**Whitehead, Jerome C** — Basketball Player
PO Box 5932, Playa Del Rey CA 90296, USA
**Whitehead, John A** — Physical Oceanographer
Woods Hole Oceanographic Institution, Physical Oceanography Dept, Woods Hole MA 02543, USA
**Whitehead, John C** — Foundation Executive, Financier
Goldman Sachs Foundation, 85 Broad St, Building 85, New York NY 10004, USA
**Whitehead, Lorne A** — Inventor (Prism Light Guide System)
T I R Systems, 77 Riverfront Gate, Burnaby BC V5J 5M4, Canada
**Whitehead, Nicole** — Model
Playboy Promotions, 2706 Media Center Dr, Los Angeles CA 90065 USA
**Whitehead, Paxton** — Actor
Gary Goddard Agency, 10 Saint Mary's St, Toronto ON M4Y 1P9, Canada
**Whitehead, Rachel** — Sculptor
Luhring Augustine Gallery, 531 W 24th St, New York NY 10011, USA
**Whitehead, Richard F** — Navy Admiral
American Cage & Machine Co, 135 S LaSalle St, Chicago IL 60603, USA
**Whitehead, Ruben A (Bud)** — Football Player
5438 N Brooks Ave, Fresno CA 93711, USA
**Whitehurst, Walter R (Wally)** — Baseball Player
102 Beverly Dr, Bay Saint Louis MS 39520, USA
**Whitelaw, Billie** — Actress
Rose Cottage, Plum St, Glensford, Suffolk C010 7PX, England
**Whiteman, Andrew** — Guitarist (Apostle of Hustle)
High Road Touring, 751 Bridgeway, #200, Sausalito CA 94965 USA
**Whitemore, Hugh** — Writer
Creative Artists Agency, 2000 Ave of Stars, #100, Los Angeles CA 90067 USA
**Whitemore, Willet F, Jr** — Cancer Researcher
2 Hawthorne Lane, Manhasset NY 11030, USA
**Whiten, Mark A** — Baseball Player
5810 Jefferson Park Dr, Tampa FL 33625, USA
**Whiteread, Rachel** — Sculptor
Anthony D'Offay, 22 Dering St, London W1R 9AA, England
**Whitesell, Emily** — Writer, Producer, Actress
Rain Management Group, 1631 21st St, Santa Monica CA 90404, USA
**Whitesell, John P** — Director
Sloane Offer Weber, 9601 Wilshire Blvd, #500, Beverly Hills CA 90210 USA
**Whitesell, Sean** — Actor, Producer, Writer
United Talent Agency, U T A Plaza, 9336 Civic Center Dr, Beverly Hills CA 90210 USA
**Whiteside, Matthew C (Matt)** — Baseball Player
255 Palisades Ridge Court, Eureka MO 63025, USA
**Whitesides, George M** — Chemist
124 Grasmere St, Newton MA 02458, USA

**Whitfield, Charles Malik** — Actor
Paradigm Agency, 360 N Crescent Dr, North Building, Beverly Hills CA 90210 USA

**Whitfield, Dondre** — Actor
Paul Kohner, 9300 Wilshire Blvd, #555, Beverly Hills CA 90212 USA

**Whitfield, Fred** — Rodeo Rider
17915 Becker Road, Hockley TX 77447, USA

**Whitfield, Lynn** — Actress
Allman/Rea Mgmt, 9355 Sunset Blvd, #600, Los Angeles CA 90069, USA

**Whitfield, Malvin G (Mal)** — Track Athlete
1322 28th St SE, Washington DC 20020, USA

**Whitfield, Mark** — Guitarist
Joel Chriss Co, 300 Mercer St, #3J, New York NY 10003 USA

**Whitfield, Simon** — Triathlete
Triathlon Canada, 4050 Wheelwright Crest, Mississauga ON L5L 2X5, Canada

**Whitfield, Terry B** — Baseball Player
849 Clearfield Dr, Millbrae CA 94030, USA

**Whitfield, Trent** — Ice Hockey Player
8781 Piney Orchard Parkway, Odenton MD 21113, USA

**Whitford, Bradley E (Brad)** — Guitarist (Aerosmith)
Front Line Mgmt, 1100 Glendon Ave, #2000, Los Angeles CA 90024 USA

**Whitham, Gerald B** — Mathematician
California Institute of Technology, Mathematics Dept, Pasadena CA 91125, USA

**Whiting, Lynn S** — Thoroughbred Racing Trainer
Lynn S Whiting Stable, 700 Central Ave, Louisville KY 40208, USA

**Whitlam, E Gough** — Prime Minister, Australia
Westfield Towers, 100 William St, Sydney NSW 2011, Australia

**Whitley, Kym** — Actress
Innovative Artists, 1505 10th St, Santa Monica CA 90401 USA

**Whitlock, Isiah, Jr** — Actor
Liebman Entertainment, 25 E 21st St, #PH, New York NY 10010 USA

**Whitlow, Robert E (Bob)** — Football Player
2005 S Rogers St, #41, Bloomington IN 47403, USA

**Whitman, Kari** — Actress, Model
House of Representatives, 1434 6th St, #1, Santa Monica CA 90401 USA

**Whitman, Mae** — Actress
I C M Partners, 10250 Constellation Blvd, #900, Los Angeles CA 90067 USA

**Whitman, Margaret C (Meg)** — Businesswoman
Hewlett Packard Co, 3000 Hanover St, Palo Alto CA 94304, USA

**Whitman, Marina Von Neumann** — Economist, Government Official
University of Michigan, Public Policy School, Ann Arbor MI 48109, USA

**Whitman, Stuart** — Actor
749 San Ysidro Road, Santa Barbara CA 93108, USA

**Whitmore, James, Jr** — Actor
1284 La Brea St, Thousand Oaks CA 91362, USA

**Whitmore, Jon** — Educator
Texas Tech University, President's Office, Lubbock TX 79409, USA

**Whitmore, Kay** — Ice Hockey Player
National Hockey League, 50 Bay St, #1100, Toronto ON M5J 2X8, Canada

**Whitmore, Tamika** — Basketball Player
Connecticut Sun, 1 Mohegan Sun Blvd, Uncasville CT 06382 USA

**Whitner, Donte** — Football Player
San Francisco 49ers, 4949 Centennial Blvd, Santa Clara CA 95054 USA

**Whitney, Ashley A** — Swimmer
124 Hearthstone Manor Circle, Brentwood TN 37027, USA

**Whitney, CeCe** — Actress
16857 San Fernando Mission Blvd, #46, Granada Hills CA 91344, USA

**Whitney, David** — Basketball Coach, Baseball Player
2178 Popps Ferry Road, Biloxi MS 39532, USA

**Whitney, Grace Lee** — Actress
PO Box 1869, Coarsegold CA 93614, USA

**Whitney, Raymond D (Ray)** — Ice Hockey Player
2908 Spaldwick Court, Raleigh NC 27613, USA

**Whitney, Ryan** — Ice Hockey Player
7 Stone Ave, Scituate MA 02066, USA

**Whitson, Eddie L (Ed)** — Baseball Player
10473 Mackenzie Way, Dublin OH 43017, USA

**Whitson, Elizabeth** — Actress
Sweeney Entertainment, 6253 Hollywood Blvd, #201, Los Angeles CA 90028, USA

**Whitson, Peggy A** — Astronaut
306 Lakeview Circle, Seabrook TX 77586, USA

**Whitt, Ernest L (Ernie)** — Baseball Player
37370 Moravian Dr, Clinton Township MI 48036, USA

**Whittaker, James (Jim)** — Mountaineer
2023 E Sims Way, #277, Port Townsend WA 98368, USA

**Whittaker, Jodie** — Actress
Independent Talent Group, 40 Whitfield St, London W1T 2RH, England

**Whittaker, Roger** — Singer, Songwriter
Howard Elson Promotions, 16 Penn Ave, Chesham Buckinghamshire HP5 2HS, England

**Whittingham, Charles A** — Publisher
1 E 66th St, #13D, New York NY 10065, USA

**Whittington, Arthur L (Art)** — Football Player
6709 La Tijera Blvd, #190, Los Angeles CA 90045, USA

**Whittington, Bill** — Auto Racing Driver
1881 W State Road 84, Fort Lauderdale FL 33315, USA

**Whittington, Reginald (Don)** — Auto Racing Driver
1881 W State Road 54, Fort Lauderdale FL 33315, USA

**Whittle, Jason** — Football Player
PO Box 1980, Osage Beach MO 65065, USA

**Whittle, Ricky** — Actor
True Public Relations, 6725 Sunset Blvd, #470, Los Angeles CA 90028, USA

**Whitton, Margaret** — Actress, Producer, Director
Tashtego Films, 11 W 10th St, New York NY

**Whitwam, David R** — Businessman
Whirlpool Corp, 2000 N State St, RR 63, Benton Harbor MI 49022, USA

**Whitworth, Andrew J** — Football Player
903 Adams Crossing, #110, Cincinnati OH 45202, USA

Whitfield - Whitworth

# W

**Whitworth, Johnny** — Actor, Producer
Greene Assoc, 1901 Ave of Stars, #130, Los Angeles CA 90067 USA

**Whitworth, Kathrynne A (Kathy)** — Golfer
1735 Mistletoe Dr, Flower Mound TX 75022, USA

**Whyte, Sandra** — Ice Hockey Player
81 Golden Hills Road, Saugus MA 01906, USA

**Whyte, Sean** — Ice Hockey Player
14315 W Desert Hills Dr, Surprise AZ 85379, USA

**Wi, Charlie** — Golfer
9400 Burnet Ave, #109, North Hills CA 91343, USA

**Wiberg, Kenneth B** — Chemist
160 Carmalt Road, Hamden CT 06517, USA

**Wiberg, Pernilla** — Alpine Skier
Margaretha Wiberg, Katterumsv 32, 602 10 Norrkoping, Sweden

**Wickander, Kevin D** — Baseball Player
4319 W Banff Lane, Glendale AZ 85306, USA

**Wickenheiser, Hayley** — Ice Hockey Player
Team Canada, 2424 University Dr NW, Calgary AB T2N 3Y9, Canada

**Wickersham, David C (Dave)** — Baseball Player
9118 W 104th Terrace, Overland Park KS 66212, USA

**Wickersham, Emily** — Actress
I C M Partners, 10250 Constellation Blvd, #900, Los Angeles CA 90067 USA

**Wickham, John A, Jr** — Army General
13500 N Rancho Vistoso Blvd, #519, Tucson AZ 85755, USA

**Wickham, Madeleine** — Writer
Thomas Dunne/Saint Martin's Press, 175 5th Ave, #400, New York NY 10010, USA

**Wicki-Fink, Agnes** — Actress
Weisgerberstr 2, 80805 Munich, Germany

**Wickman, Robert J (Bob)** — Baseball Player
6568 Cheyenne Dr, Abrams WI 54101, USA

**Wickner, Reed B** — Geneticist
National Institutes of Health, 9000 Rockville Pike, Bethesda MD 20892, USA

**Wickner, Sue H** — Molecular Biolgist
N C I Molecular Biology Laboratory, 37 Convent Dr, Bethesda MN 20892, USA

**Wicks, Ben** — Editorial Cartoonist
38 Yorkville Ave, Toronto ON M4W 1L5, Canada

**Wicks, Chuck** — Singer, Songwriter
W M E Entertainment, 1600 Division St, #300, Nashville TN 37203 USA

**Wicks, Ron** — Ice Hockey Referee
4 McLaughlin Road S, Brampton ON L6Y 3B2, Canada

**Wicks, Sidney** — Basketball Player
8650 Cashio St, #5, Los Angeles CA 90035, USA

**Wickwire, Jim** — Mountaineer
1416 W Roy St, Seattle WA 98112, USA

**Wickwire, Maria** — Sculptor
PO Box 2911, Battle Creek WA 97604, USA

**Wicoff, Erika** — Golfer
7815 Four Leaf Dr, Greenville IN 47124, USA

**Widby, G Ronald (Ron)** — Football, Basketball Player
542 Mahler Road, Wichita Falls TX 76310, USA

**Widdoes, Jamie** — Director, Producer, Actor
United Talent Agency, U T A Plaza, 9336 Civic Center Dr, Beverly Hills CA 90210 USA

**Widdoes, Kathleen** — Actress
24 E 11th St, New York NY 10003, USA

**Widdrington, Peter N T** — Businessman
Laidlaw Inc, 3221 N Service Road, Burlington ON L7R 3Y8, Canada

**Widell, David H (Dave)** — Football Player
13050 Wexford Hollow Road N, Jacksonville FL 32224, USA

**Widell, Douglas J (Doug)** — Football Player
4638 Pebble Brook Dr, Jacksonville FL 32224, USA

**Wideman, John Edgar** — Writer
University of Massachusetts, English Dept, Amherst MA 01003, USA

**Widger, Christopher J (Chris)** — Baseball Player
95 Fort Mott Road, Pennsville NJ 08070, USA

**Widman, Herbert (Herb)** — Water Polo Player
844 Monarch Circle, San Jose CA 95138, USA

**Widmann, Jorg** — Concert Clarinetist, Composer
Schott Music, Weihergarten 5, 55116 Mainz, Germany

**Widmer, Corey E** — Football Player
PO Box 1201, Manhattan MT 59741, USA

**Widmer-Schlumpf, Eveline** — President, Switzerland
Federal Chancellery, Bundeshaus-W, Bundesgasse, 3033 Berne, Switzerland

**Widom, Benjamin** — Chemist
204 The Parkway, Ithaca NY 14850, USA

**Wie, Michelle** — Golfer
17217 Leal Ave, Cerritos CA 90703, USA

**Wiebe, Susanne** — Fashion Designer
Amalienstr 39, 80799 Munich, Germany

**Wiegert, Zachary A (Zach)** — Football Player
919 N 264th St, Waterloo NE 68069, USA

**Wieghaus, Thomas R (Tom)** — Baseball Player
9724 E 8000 Road, #N, Grant Park IL 60940, USA

**Wiegmann, Casey P** — Football Player
21010 W 60th Terrace, Shawnee KS 66218, USA

**Wiehl, Christopher** — Actor
A P A Talent/Literary Agency, 405 S Beverly Dr, #300, Beverly Hills CA 90212 USA

**Wielicki, Krzysztof J** — Mountaineer
Ul A Frycza Modrzewskiego 21, 43100 Tychy, Poland

**Wieman, Carl E** — Nobel Physics Laureate
University of Colorado, Physics Dept, Campus Box 440, Boulder CO 80309, USA

**Wiemer, Jason** — Ice Hockey Player
428-5201 Dalhousie Dr NW, Calgary AB T3A 5Y7, Canada

**Wiener, Jacques L, Jr** — Judge
US Court of Appeals, 600 Camp St, New Orleans LA 70130, USA

**Wier, Murray N** — Basketball Player, Coach
118 Goodwater St, Georgetown TX 78633, USA

**Wiercinski, Francis** — Army General
Deputy Commander in Chief, Army Pacific Command, Honolulu HI 96861 USA
**Wieringa, Jeffrey A** — Navy Admiral
Director, Defense Security Cooperation Agency, Pentagon, Washington DC 20301, USA
**Wieschaus, Eric F** — Nobel Medicine Laureate
11 Pelham St, Boston MA 02118, USA
**Wiese, John P** — Judge
US Claims Court, 717 Madison Place NW, Washington DC 20439, USA
**Wiesel, Elie** — Writer, Nobel Peace Laureate
10155 Collins Ave, #1502, Bal Harbor FL 33154, USA
**Wiesenhahn, Robert B (Bob)** — Basketball Player
3315 Hickorycreek Dr, Cincinnati OH 45244, USA
**Wiesler, Robert G (Bob)** — Baseball Player
2325 Indiancup Dr, Florissant MO 63033, USA
**Wiesner, Kenneth (Ken)** — Track Athlete
3601 Meta Lake Road, Eagle River WI 54521, USA
**Wiest, Dianne** — Actress
I C M Partners, 730 5th Ave, New York NY 10019 USA
**Wiggin, Paul** — Football Player, Coach
5013 Ridge Road, Minneapolis MN 55436, USA
**Wiggin, Tom** — Actor
Don Buchwald, 6500 Wilshire Blvd, #2200, Los Angeles CA 90048 USA
**Wiggins, Audrey** — Singer
PO Box 121196, Nashville TN 37212, USA
**Wiggins, Bradley M** — Cyclist
Team High Road, 425 O'Connor Way, San Luis Obispo CA 93405, USA
**Wiggins, Jennifer** — Actress
D P N Talent, 9201 W Olympic Blvd, Beverly Hills CA 90212, USA
**Wiggins, Jermaine** — Football Player
111 Boston St, Topsfield MA 1983, USA
**Wiggins, John** — Singer
W M E Entertainment, 1600 Division St, #300, Nashville TN 37203 USA
**Wiggins, Laura Slade** — Actress
Don Buchwald, 6500 Wilshire Blvd, #2200, Los Angeles CA 90048 USA
**Wiggins, Mitchell L** — Basketball Player
PO Box 5072, Kinston NC 28503, USA
**Wiggins, Phil** — Singer, Harmonica Player, Songwriter
Blue Mountain Artists, 810 Tyvola Road, #114, Charlotte NC 28217, USA
**Wigginton, Ty A** — Baseball Player
120 Manitoba Lane, Mooresville NC 28117, USA
**Wigglesworth, Marian McKean** — Alpine Skier
General Delivery, Wilson WY 83014, USA
**Wigglesworth, Mark** — Conductor
C M Artists, 127 W 96th St, #13B, New York NY 10025 USA
**Wigglesworth, Ryan** — Composer, Conductor
Konzertdirektion Schmid, Konigstra 36, 30175 Hannover, Germany
**Wiggs, Susan** — Writer
PO Box 4469, Rolling Bay WA 98061, USA
**Wightman, Arthur S** — Mathematician, Physicist
16 Balsam Lane, Princeton NJ 08540, USA
**Wihtol, Alexander A (Sandy)** — Baseball Player
1889 Anthony Court, Mountain View CA 94040, USA
**Wiig, Kristen C** — Actress, Comedienne, Writer
United Talent Agency, U T A Plaza, 9336 Civic Center Dr, Beverly Hills CA 90210 USA
**Wiik, Sven** — Skier
PO Box 774484, Steamboat Springs CO 80477, USA
**Wiita, Carrie** — Actress
OmniPop Talent Group, 4605 Lankershim Blvd, #201, Toluca Lake CA 91602 USA
**Wilander, Mats** — Tennis Player
104 Cove Creek Road, Hailey ID 83333, USA
**Wilbraham, John H G** — Concert Cornetist, Trumpeter
9 Cuthbert St, Wells, Somerset BA5 2AW, England
**Wilbur, Delbert Q (Del)** — Baseball Player
4378 Autumn Lane, Lewiston NY 14092, USA
**Wilbur, Richard C** — Judge
US Tax Court, 400 2nd St NW, Washington DC 20217, USA
**Wilbur, Richard P** — Writer
87 Dodswell Road, Cummington MA 01026, USA
**Wilbur, Richard S** — Physician, Association Executive
985 Hawthorne Place, Lake Forest IL 60045, USA
**Wilburn, Johnnie R (J R), Jr** — Football Player
2211 Chalkwell Dr, Midlothian VA 23113, USA
**Wilburn, Ken** — Basketball Player
17 E Meyran Ave, Somers Point NJ 08244, USA
**Wilby, James** — Actor
Artist Rights Group, 4 Great Portland St, London W1W 8PA, England
**Wilcher, Mary** — Actress
Levine Mgmt, 9028 W Sunset Blvd, #PH1, West Hollywood CA 90069, USA
**Wilcher, Michael D (Mike)** — Football Player
1501 Fairlakes Place, Bowie MD 20721, USA
**Wilcox, Barry** — Ice Hockey Player
18859 86th Ave, Surrey BC V4N 3G5, Canada
**Wilcox, Chris R** — Basketball Player
Boston Celtics, 226 Causeway St, #4, Boston MA 02114 USA
**Wilcox, Daniel** — Football Player
4119 Old Washington Blvd, Halethorpe MD 21227, USA
**Wilcox, David** — Singer, Songwriter, Guitarist
Concerted Efforts, PO Box 440326, Somerville MA 02144 USA
**Wilcox, David (Dave)** — Football Player
94471 Willamette Dr, Junction City OR 97448, USA
**Wilcox, Larry** — Actor
10 Appaloosa Lane, Bell Canyon CA 91307, USA
**Wilcox, Lisa** — Actress
Stone Manners Salners, 9911 W Pico Blvd, #1400, Los Angeles CA 90035 USA
**Wilcox, Milton E (Milt)** — Baseball Player
1630 Lakeview Dr, Wolverine Lake MI 48390, USA

# W

Wilcox, Shannon — Actress
20518 Pacific Coast Highway, Malibu CA 90265, USA
Wilcutt, Terence W (Terry) — Astronaut
N A S A, Johnson Space Center, 2101 NASA Road, Houston TX 77058 USA
Wilczek, Frank A — Nobel Physics Laureate
4 Wyman Road, Cambridge MA 02138, USA
Wild, John P — Astronomer
1 Grant Crescent, #4, Griffith ACT 2603, Australia
Wilde, Gabriella — Actress
I C M Partners, 10250 Constellation Blvd, #900, Los Angeles CA 90067 USA
Wilde, Kim — Singer, Songwriter
Marty Wilde, Thatched Rest, Queen Hoo Lane, Tewin, Hertfordshire AL6 0LT, England
Wilde, Olivia — Actress
Hamilton Hodell, 66-68 Margaret St, #500, London W1W 8SR, England
Wilde, Patricia — Ballerina, Artistic Director
Pittsburgh Ballet Theater, 2900 Liberty Ave, Pittsburgh PA 15201, USA
Wilder, Alan C — Synthesizer Musician (Depeche Mode)
Creative Artists Agency, 2000 Ave of Stars, #100, Los Angeles CA 90067 USA
Wilder, Don — Cartoonist (Crock)
North American Syndicate, 235 E 45th St, New York NY 10017 USA
Wilder, Gene — Actor, Director
476 Scofieldtown Road, Stamford CT 06903, USA
Wilder, James — Actor
Chasen Agency, 8899 Beverly Blvd, #405, Los Angeles CA 90048 USA
Wilder, James C — Football Player
49 S Shirley St, Pontiac MI 48342, USA
Wilder, L Douglas — Governor, VA; Educator
Mayor's Office, City Hall, 900 E Broad St, Richmond VA 23219, USA
Wildes, Kevin W — Educator
Loyola University, President's Office, 6363 Saint Charles Ave, New Orleans LA 70118, USA
Wildman, George — Cartoonist (Popeye)
601 N Atlantic Ave, #603, New Smyrna FL 32169, USA
Wildman, Valerie — Actress
Scott Hart Mgmt, 14622 Ventura Blvd, #746, Sherman Oaks CA 91403, USA
Wildmon, Donald — Social Activist
National Federation of Decency, PO Box 1398, Tupelo MS 38802, USA
Wilds, Tristan — Actor
I C M Partners, 10250 Constellation Blvd, #900, Los Angeles CA 90067 USA
Wiles, Andrew J — Mathematician
Princeton University, Mathematics Dept, Princeton NJ 08544, USA
Wiles, Jason — Actor
Brillstein Entertainment Partners, 9150 Wilshire Blvd, #350, Beverly Hills CA 90212 USA
Wiles, Randall E (Randy) — Baseball Player
3716 Lake Catherine Dr, Harvey LA 70058, USA
Wiley, John F (Jack) — Football Player
1330 India Hook Road, #306, Rock Hill SC 29732, USA
Wiley, Lee — Singer
Country Crossroads, 7787 Monterey St, Gilroy CA 95020, USA
Wiley, Marcellus V — Football Player
5132 S Garth Ave, Los Angeles CA 90056, USA
Wiley, Morlon D — Basketball Player
2521 Fallview Lane, Carrollton TX 75007, USA
Wiley, Richard E — Government Official
Wiley Rein, 1776 K St NW, #1100, Washington DC 20006, USA
Wiley, William T — Artist
PO Box 661, Forest Knolls CA 94933, USA
Wilfong, Robert D (Rob) — Baseball Player
126 Maverick Dr, San Dimas CA 91773, USA
Wilford, Ernest L, Jr — Football Player
1516 Chatham Court, Saint Augustine FL 32092, USA
Wilford, John Noble, Jr — Journalist
232 W 10th St, New York NY 10014, USA
Wilfork, Vince L — Football Player
11 White Dove Road, Franklin MA 02038, USA
Wilhelm, David C — WW II Army Air Corps Hero
3333 E Florida Ave, #113, Denver CO 80210, USA
Wilhelm, Erik B — Football Player
PO Box 1602, Clackamas OR 97015, USA
Wilhelm, James W (Jim) — Baseball Player
348 Laurel Way, Mill Valley CA 94941, USA
Wilhelm, John W — Labor Leader
Hotel & Restaurant Employees Union, 1219 28th St NW, Washington DC 20007, USA
Wilhelm, Kati — Biathlete
Sport Marketing, Schaumainkai 91, 60596 Frankfurt am Main, Germany
Wilhelm, Matthew (Matt) — Football Player
14944 Huntington Gate Dr, Poway CA 92064, USA
Wilhoite, Kathleen — Actress
Gersh Agency, 9465 Wilshire Blvd, #600, Beverly Hills CA 90212 USA
Wilk, Vic — Golfer
1350 N Town Center Dr, #2082, Las Vegas NV 89144, USA
Wilkening, Laurel L — Educator
University of California, Chancellor's Office, Irvine CA 92717, USA
Wilkens, Leonard R (Lenny), Jr — Basketball Player, Coach, Executive
3429 Evergreen Point Road, Medina WA 98039, USA
Wilker, Greg — Photographer
3601 NW Adriatic Lane, Jensen Beach FL 34957, USA
Wilkerson, Bruce A — Football Player
2013 Breakers Point, Knoxville TN 37922, USA
Wilkerson, Curtis V — Baseball Player
PO Box 182993, Arlington TX 76096, USA
Wilkerson, Douglas (Doug) — Football Player
PO Box 7090, Rancho Santa Fe CA 92067, USA
Wilkerson, Isabel — Journalist
New York Times, Editorial Dept, 229 W 43rd St, New York NY 10036, USA
Wilkerson, Robert L (Bob) — Basketball Player
PO Box 7453, Upper Marlboro MD 20792, USA

**Wilkerson, S Bradley (Brad)** — Baseball Player
326 Griffith Ave, Owensboro KY 42301, USA
**Wilkerson, Tim** — Drag Racing Driver
Demand Flow Racing, 2901 Stevenson Dr, Springfield IL 62703, USA
**Wilkes, Debbi** — Figure Skater
Skate Canada, 865 Shefford Road, Ottawa ON K1J 1H9, Canada
**Wilkes, Jamaal A** — Basketball Player
7846 W 81st St, Playa del Rey CA 90293, USA
**Wilkes, Reggie W** — Football Player
6912 Wissahickon Ave, Philadelphia PA 19119, USA
**Wilkie, Bob** — Ice Hockey Player
303 S Forge Road, Palmyra PA 17078, USA
**Wilkie, Chris** — Guitarist (Dubstar)
Primary Talent Int'l, 2-12 Petonville Road, London N1 9PL, England
**Wilkie, David** — Ice Hockey Player
8919 N 159th Ave, Bennington NE 68007, USA
**Wilkie, David A** — Swimmer
Oaklands, Queens Hill, Ascot, Berkshire SL5 7JF, England
**Wilkin, Richard E** — Religious Leader
Winebrenner Theological Seminary, 950 N Main St, Findlay OH 45840, USA
**Wilkins Perez, Laisha** — Actress
Televisa, Blvd A Lopez Mateos 232, Colonia San Angel, Mexico City DF 01060 CP, Mexico
**Wilkins, Barry** — Ice Hockey Player
2230 W Monroe St, Chandler AZ 85224, USA
**Wilkins, Eric L** — Baseball Player
1650 W Joshua Lane, Meridian ID 83642, USA
**Wilkins, J Dominique** — Basketball Player
4415 Felix Way SE, Smyrna GA 30082, USA
**Wilkins, Jeffrey A (Jeff)** — Football Player
8288 S Raccoon Road, Canfield OH 44406, USA
**Wilkins, Marc A** — Baseball Player
1636 State Route 314 N, Mansfield OH 44903, USA
**Wilkins, Maurice (Mac)** — Track Athlete
1915 NW Columbine Lane, Portland OR 97229, USA
**Wilkins, Richard D (Rick)** — Baseball Player
12766 Longview Dr W, Jacksonville FL 32223, USA
**Wilkins, William W, Jr** — Judge
US Court of Appeals, PO Box 10648, Greenville SC 29603, USA
**Wilkinson, Adrienne** — Actress
Greater Visions Artists Talent Agency, 8981 W Sunset Blvd, #101, West Hollywood CA 90069 USA
**Wilkinson, Amanda** — Singer (Wilkinsons)
Bobby Roberts, 3050 Business Park Circle, #303, Goodlettsville TN 37221 USA
**Wilkinson, Clive** — Interior Designer, Architect
Clive Wilkinson Architect, 6116 Washington Blvd, Culver City CA 90232, USA
**Wilkinson, Dale W** — Basketball Player
3045 Goldfield Dr, Pocatello ID 83201, USA
**Wilkinson, Daniel R (Dan)** — Football Player
222 Republic Dr, Allen Park MI 48101, USA
**Wilkinson, J Harvie, III** — Judge
US Court of Appeals, 255 W Main St, Charlottesville VA 22902, USA
**Wilkinson, Joseph B, Jr** — Navy Admiral
340 Chesapeake Dr, Great Falls VA 22066, USA
**Wilkinson, June** — Model, Actress
4060 E Grenora Way, Long Beach CA 90815, USA
**Wilkinson, Kendra** — Actress, Model
A P A Talent/Literary Agency, 405 S Beverly Dr, #300, Beverly Hills CA 90212 USA
**Wilkinson, Laura** — Diver
PO Box 131961, Spring TX 77393, USA
**Wilkinson, Leon** — Bassist (Lynyrd Skynyrd)
Alliance Artists, 6025 Comers Parkway, #202, Norcross GA 30092, USA
**Wilkinson, Neil** — Ice Hockey Player
PO Box 57, Sherwood OR 97140, USA
**Wilkinson, Rhian** — Soccer Player
Canadian Soccer, Place Soccer Canada, 237 Metcalfe St, Ottawa ON K2P 1R2, Canada
**Wilkinson, Signe** — Editorial Cartoonist
Philadelphia Daily News, Editorial Dept, 400 N Broad, Philadelphia PA 19130, USA
**Wilkinson, Steve** — Singer (Wilkinsons)
Fitzgerald Hartley, 1908 Wedgewood Ave, Nashville TN 37212, USA
**Wilkinson, Tom** — Actor
Lou Coulson Assoc, 37 Berwick St, London W1V 8RS, England
**Wilkinson, Tyler** — Singer (Wilkinsons)
Fitzgerald Hartley, 1908 Wedgewood Ave, Nashville TN 37212, USA
**Wilks, Jimmy R (Jim)** — Football Player
4314 Leaflock Lane, Katy TX 77450, USA
**Will, George F** — Columnist
9 Grafton St, Chevy Chase MD 20815, USA
**Will, Robert L (Bob)** — Baseball Player
3417 S Country Club Road, Woodstock IL 60098, USA
**Will.I.Am** — Rap Artist (Elephunk, Black Eyed Peas)
Susan Blond Inc, 50 W 57th St, #1400, New York NY 10019 USA
**Willard, Fred C** — Actor, Comedian
Amsel Eisenstadt Frazier, 5055 Wilshire Blvd, #865, Los Angeles CA 90036 USA
**Willard, Gerald D (Jerry)** — Baseball Player
1421 Kumquat Place, Oxnard CA 93036, USA
**Willard, Kenneth H (Ken)** — Football Player
3071 Vistapoint Road, Midlothian VA 23113, USA
**Willard, Rod** — Ice Hockey Player
18 Overlook Dr, Wilbraham MA 01095, USA
**Willcocks, David V** — Concert Organist, Conductor
13 Grange Road, Cambridge CB3 9AS, England
**Willcuts, Lori** — Singer
Willcutts, 1102 N Springbrook Road, Newberg OR 97132, USA
**Willem-Alexander** — King, Netherlands
Binnenhof 19, 2513 The Hague AA, Netherlands
**Willet, E Crosby** — Glass Artist
Willet Stained Glass Studios, 811 E Cayuga St, Philadelphia PA 19124, USA

| | |
|---|---|
| **Willett, Chad** | Actor |
| Storylab Productions, 440 W 17th Ave, Vancouver BC V5Y2A2, Canada | |
| **Willett, Malcolm** | Cartoonist (Tight Corner) |
| Universal Press Syndicate, 4520 Main St, #700, Kansas City MO 64111 USA | |
| **Willette, JoAnn** | Actress |
| I C M Partners, 10250 Constellation Blvd, #900, Los Angeles CA 90067 USA | |
| **Will-Halpin, Maggie** | Golfer |
| 12423 Camoustie Lane, Richmond VA 23236, USA | |
| **Willhite, Gerald W** | Football Player |
| 10464 Iliff Court, Rancho Cordova CA 95670, USA | |
| **William** | Prince, England |
| Clarence House, Stable Yard Gate, London SW1A 1BA, England | |
| **Williams of Crosby, Shirley V T B** | Government Official, England |
| House of Lords, Westminster, London SW1A 0PW, England | |
| **Williams, Aeneas D** | Football Player |
| PO Box 16291, Saint Louis MO 63105, USA | |
| **Williams, Alfred H** | Football Player |
| Sports Radio 104.3, 7800 E Orchard Road, Greenwood Village CO 80111, USA | |
| **Williams, Allison** | Actress |
| Creative Artists Agency, 2000 Ave of Stars, #100, Los Angeles CA 90067 USA | |
| **Williams, Alvin L** | Basketball Player |
| Toronto Raptors, Air Canada Center, 20 Bay St, Toronto ON M5J 2N8, Canada | |
| **Williams, Andy** | Drummer (Doves) |
| C E S D, 10635 Santa Monica Blvd, #130, Los Angeles CA 90025 USA | |
| **Williams, Ann Claire** | Judge |
| US Court of Appeals, 219 S Dearborn St, Chicago IL 60604, USA | |
| **Williams, Anson** | Actor |
| 24612 Skyline View Dr, Malibu CA 90265, USA | |
| **Williams, Anthony D (Tony)** | Football Player |
| 1918 Bridgewater Dr, Lake Mary FL 32746, USA | |
| **Williams, Ashley** | Actress |
| Gersh Agency, 9465 Wilshire Blvd, #600, Beverly Hills CA 90212 USA | |
| **Williams, Ashley C** | Actress, Producer |
| Tug of War Productions, 8924 Blakeney Professional Drive, Charlotte NC 28277, USA | |
| **Williams, Austin** | Actor |
| Gersh Agency, 9465 Wilshire Blvd, #600, Beverly Hills CA 90212 USA | |
| **Williams, Barbara** | Actress |
| S M S Talent, 8383 Wilshire Blvd, #230, Beverly Hills CA 90211 USA | |
| **Williams, Barry** | Actor, Singer |
| Amsel Eisenstadt Frazier, 5055 Wilshire Blvd, #865, Los Angeles CA 90036 USA | |
| **Williams, Bernabe F (Bernie)** | Baseball Player, Guitarist, Composer |
| Scott Boras, 3 San Joaquin Plaza, #100, Newport Beach CA 92660, USA | |
| **Williams, Bernard (Bernie)** | Baseball Player |
| 6851 Arthur St, Oakland CA 94605, USA | |
| **Williams, Beth** | Model |
| Playboy Promotions, 2706 Media Center Dr, Los Angeles CA 90065 USA | |
| **Williams, Betty** | Nobel Peace Laureate |
| Knock Inverin, County Galway, Ireland | |
| **Williams, Billy** | Cinematographer |
| Coach House, Hawkshill Place, Esher, Surrey KT10 9HY, England | |
| **Williams, Billy Dee** | Actor |
| Coolwaters Productions, 10061 Riverside Dr, Box 531, Toluca Lake CA 91602 USA | |
| **Williams, Billy L** | Baseball Player |
| 586 Prince Edward Road, Glen Ellyn IL 60137, USA | |
| **Williams, Brian** | Football Player |
| 8704 Shady Hill Court, Colfax NC 27235, USA | |
| **Williams, Brian** | Commentator |
| NBC-TV, News Dept, 30 Rockefeller Plaza, #270E, New York NY 10112 USA | |
| **Williams, Brian M** | Football Player |
| 1133 Ashington Place, DeSoto TX 75115, USA | |
| **Williams, Brian O** | Baseball Player |
| 2409 Colt Lane, Crowley TX 76036, USA | |
| **Williams, Brian S** | Football Player |
| 1725 Charleston Lane, Waconia MN 55387, USA | |
| **Williams, Brooks** | Guitarist, Songwriter |
| Eastern Star Productions, 2625 Alcatraz Ave, #302, Berkeley CA 94705, USA | |
| **Williams, Bunny** | Interior Designer |
| 306 E 61st St, #500, New York NY 10065, USA | |
| **Williams, C K** | Writer |
| Princeton University, English Dept, Princeton NJ 08544, USA | |
| **Williams, Calvin J, Jr** | Football Player |
| 5032 Yellowood Ave, Baltimore MD 21209, USA | |
| **Williams, Cara** | Actress |
| 9903 Santa Monica Blvd, #606, Beverly Hills CA 90212, USA | |
| **Williams, Carnell L (Cadillac)** | Football Player |
| 6127 Parkside Meadow Dr, Tampa FL 33625, USA | |
| **Williams, Caroline** | Actress |
| International Talent Agency, 10 NBC Universal Studios Plaza, #2000, Universal City CA 91608, USA | |
| **Williams, Cecil** | Religious Leader, Social Activist |
| Glide Memorial United Methodist Church, 330 Ellis St, San Francisco CA 94102, USA | |
| **Williams, Charles E (Charlie)** | Basketball Player |
| 18675 Parkland Pl, #409, Shaker Heights OH 44122, USA | |
| **Williams, Charles L (Buck)** | Basketball Player |
| 9219 Fox Meadow Lane, Potomac MD 20854, USA | |
| **Williams, Charles P (Charlie)** | Baseball Player |
| 44 Frederick Ave, Port Orange FL 32127, USA | |
| **Williams, Charlie U** | Football Player |
| 3052 England Parkway, Grand Prairie TX 75054, USA | |
| **Williams, Christine** | Model |
| Playboy Promotions, 2706 Media Center Dr, Los Angeles CA 90065 USA | |
| **Williams, Christopher J (Chris)** | Actor |
| Artist Mgmt, 1119 Colorado Ave, #12, Santa Monica CA 90401, USA | |
| **Williams, Christy** | Artist |
| 2745 NE 89th St, Seattle WA 98115, USA | |
| **Williams, Cindy** | Actress |
| Cindy Williams Productions, 499 Canon Dr, #216, Beverly Hills CA 90210, USA | |

| | |
|---|---|
| **Williams, Clarence**<br>Los Angeles Times, Editorial Dept, 145 S Spring St, Los Angeles CA 90012, USA | Photojournalist |
| **Williams, Clarence, III**<br>Framework Entertainment, 9057 Nemo St, #C, West Hollywood CA 90069 USA | Actor |
| **Williams, Clevan (Tank)**<br>4053 Alexis Dr, Antioch TN 37013, USA | Football Player |
| **Williams, Clifford (Cliff)**<br>Alberts Music, 9 Rangers Road, Neutral Bay, Sydney NSW 2089, Australia | Bassist (AC/DC) |
| **Williams, Clyde A**<br>9754 Highway 79, Bethany LA 71007, USA | Football Player |
| **Williams, Colleen**<br>KNBC-TV, News Dept, 3000 W Alameda Ave, Burbank CA 91523, USA | Commentator |
| **Williams, Cress**<br>Abrams Artists, 275 7th Ave, #2600, New York NY 10001 USA | Actor |
| **Williams, Curtis**<br>David Harris Enterprises, 24210 E Fork Road, #9, Azusa CA 91702, USA | Singer (Penguins) |
| **Williams, D Keith**<br>1756 N Avignon Lane, Clovis CA 93619, USA | Baseball Player |
| **Williams, Dafydd R (David)**<br>N A S A, Johnson Space Center, 2101 NASA Road, Houston TX 77058 USA | Astronaut |
| **Williams, Dan, II**<br>4731 Corina Place NE, Roswell GA 30075, USA | Football Player |
| **Williams, Dana**<br>Modern Mgmt, 1625 Broadway, #600, Nashville TN 37203, USA | Bassist, Drummer (Diamond Rio) |
| **Williams, Dana L**<br>121 Arlene Dr, North Versailles PA 15137, USA | Baseball Player |
| **Williams, Dar**<br>R F Entertainment, 29 Haines Road, Bedford Hills NY 10507, USA | Singer, Songwriter |
| **Williams, Darnell (J D)**<br>Don Buchwald, 6500 Wilshire Blvd, #2200, Los Angeles CA 90048 USA | Actor |
| **Williams, Darryl E**<br>2841 NW 82nd Way, Pembroke Pines FL 33024, USA | Football Player |
| **Williams, Dave (Tiger)**<br>Pacific Rodera Energy, 1100-550 6th Ave SW, Calgary AB T2P 0S2, Canada | Ice Hockey Player |
| **Williams, David L**<br>15816 Crest Lane, Gardena CA 90249, USA | Football Player |
| **Williams, David W**<br>650 Flying Hawk Trail, Waynesville NC 28786, USA | Football Player |
| **Williams, Dean E**<br>309 Carlyle Lake Dr, Saint Louis MO 63141, USA | Businessman |
| **Williams, Delvin, Jr**<br>173 Sierra Vista Ave, #11, Mountain View CA 94043, USA | Football Player |
| **Williams, Demorrio D**<br>San Diego Chargers, 4020 Murphy Canyon Road, San Diego CA 92123 USA | Football Player |
| **Williams, Deniece**<br>Green Light Talent Agency, PO Box 3172, Beverly Hills CA 90212 USA | Singer |
| **Williams, Deron M**<br>PO Box 270, Draper UT 84020, USA | Basketball Player |
| **Williams, Don**<br>Chimes International Entertainment, PO Box 26312, Glasgow G76 7WX, Scotland | Singer, Guitarist, Songwriter |
| **Williams, Don**<br>6109 Rosedale Dr, Hyattsville MD 20782, USA | Basketball Player |
| **Williams, Donald E**<br>Science Applications International, 2200 Space Park Dr, #200, Houston TX 77058, USA | Astronaut |
| **Williams, Doug**<br>J K A Talent Agency, 12725 Ventura Blvd, #H, Studio City CA 91604, USA | Actor, Comedian, Writer, Producer |
| **Williams, Douglas L (Doug)**<br>10546 Greensprings Dr, Tampa FL 33626, USA | Football Player, Coach |
| **Williams, Dudley**<br>Alvin Ailey American Dance Foundation, 405 W 55th St, New York NY 10019, USA | Dancer |
| **Williams, E Virginia**<br>Boston Ballet, 19 Clarendon St, Boston MA 02116, USA | Artistic Director, Choreographer |
| **Williams, Easy**<br>Judy Schoen, 606 N Larchmont Blvd, #309, Los Angeles CA 90004 USA | Actor |
| **Williams, Edward L (Eddie)**<br>6229 Meadowgrass Lane, Las Vegas NV 89103, USA | Baseball Player |
| **Williams, Edy**<br>PO Box 6325, Woodland Hills CA 91365, USA | Actress, Model |
| **Williams, Elmo**<br>1249 Iris St, Brookings OR 97415, USA | Director, Producer |
| **Williams, Eric D**<br>4529 Dakota Trail, Saint Charles MO 63304, USA | Football Player |
| **Williams, Eric M**<br>11147 Corsicana Dr, Frisco TX 75035, USA | Football Player |
| **Williams, Eric T**<br>215 Haywood St, Garner NC 27529, USA | Football Player |
| **Williams, Erik G**<br>1 Wortham Court, Bear DE 19701, USA | Football Player |
| **Williams, Errick L (Ricky), Jr**<br>2307 Castilla Isle, Fort Lauderdale FL 33301, USA | Football Player |
| **Williams, Evan**<br>Twitter Inc, 795 Folsom St, #600, San Francisco CA 94107, USA | Businessman |
| **Williams, Frederick B (Freedom)**<br>Richard Walters, PO Box 2789, Toluca Lake CA 91610 USA | Rap Artist (C & C Music Factory) |
| **Williams, Freeman**<br>450 W 41st Place, Los Angeles CA 90037, USA | Basketball Player |
| **Williams, Gary Anthony**<br>Coast to Coast Talent, 3350 Barham Blvd, Los Angeles CA 90068 USA | Actor |
| **Williams, Gary B**<br>University of Maryland, Athletic Dept, College Park MD 20742, USA | Basketball Player, Coach |
| **Williams, George E**<br>606 Paden Dr, Cedar Park TX 78613, USA | Baseball Player |
| **Williams, Gerald**<br>9613 Callis Court, Harrisburg NC 28075, USA | Football Player |
| **Williams, Gerald F**<br>17011 Candeleda de Avila, Tampa FL 33613, USA | Baseball Player |

**W**

Williams - Williams

**W**

**Williams, Gregory** — Educator
University of Cincinnati, President's Office, 2600 Clifton Ave, Cincinnati OH 45221, USA
**Williams, Gregory S (Woody)** — Baseball Player
5110 Newpoint Dr, Fresno TX 77545, USA
**Williams, Gus** — Basketball Player
290 Collins Ave, #9H, Mount Vernon NY 10552, USA
**Williams, Hal** — Actor
Halmarter Enterprise, PO Box 14405, Palm Desert CA 92255, USA
**Williams, Hank, III** — Singer, Songwriter
Rider Mgmt, 931 Hilldale Ave, West Hollywood CA 90069, USA
**Williams, Hank, Jr** — Singer, Guitarist, Songwriter
W M E Entertainment, 1600 Division St, #300, Nashville TN 37203 USA
**Williams, Harland** — Actor, Comedian, Writer, Director
Gersh Agency, 9465 Wilshire Blvd, #600, Beverly Hills CA 90212 USA
**Williams, Harold M** — Museum Executive
J Paul Getty Museum, Getty Center, 1200 Getty Center Dr, Los Angeles CA 90049, USA
**Williams, Harvey L** — Football Player
16815 Southern Oaks Dr, Houston TX 77068, USA
**Williams, Hayley N** — Singer, Keyboardist (Paramore)
Big Hassle, 44 Wall St, #2200, New York NY 10005, USA
**Williams, Herbert L (Herb)** — Basketball Player, Coach
New York Knicks, Madison Square Garden, 2 Penn Plaza, New York, NY 10121 USA
**Williams, Hershel W** — WW II Marine Corps Hero (CMH)
3450 Wire Branch Road, Ona WV 25545, USA
**Williams, Holly** — Singer, Guitarist, Songwriter
Three Ring Projects, 111 Westwood Plaza, #101, Brentwood TN 37027, USA
**Williams, Howard E (Howie)** — Basketball Player
1940 Hamilton Lane, Carmel CA 46032, USA
**Williams, Howard L (Howie)** — Football Player
4731 Proctor Ave, Oakland CA 94618, USA
**Williams, Hype** — Director, Producer, Writer
Creative Artists Agency, 2000 Ave of Stars, #100, Los Angeles CA 90067 USA
**Williams, Ivy** — Writer
Mediachase, 834 N Harper Ave, Los Angeles CA 90046, USA
**Williams, Jaimie** — Actress
1019 Kane Concourse, #202, Bay Harbour Islands FL 33154, USA
**Williams, Jamal** — Football Player
7710 Hazard Center Dr, #E, San Diego CA 92108, USA
**Williams, James (Fly)** — Basketball Player
682 Ralph Ave, #2E, Brooklyn NY 11212, USA
**Williams, James A** — Labor Leader
Painters & Allied Trades, 1750 New York Ave NW, #501, Washington DC 20006, USA
**Williams, James A** — Army General
8928 Maurice Lane, Annandale VA 22003, USA
**Williams, James A (Froggy)** — Football Player
296 Sugarberry Circle, Houston TX 77024, USA
**Williams, James D** — Navy Admiral
20 Johnson Lane, Westport Island ME 04578, USA
**Williams, James F (Jimy)** — Baseball Player, Manager
1401 Olde Post Road, Palm Harbor FL 34683, USA
**Williams, James H (Jimmy)** — Football Player
54 Pennington Court, Buffalo NY 14228, USA
**Williams, James O** — Football Player
330 S Western Ave, Lake Forest IL 60045, USA
**Williams, Jason C** — Basketball Player
6103 Louise Cove Dr, Windermere FL 34786, USA
**Williams, Jay** — Football Player
1306 Roxanna Road NW, Washington DC 20012, USA
**Williams, Jayson** — Basketball Player, Sportscaster
NBC-TV, Sports Dept, 30 Rockefeller Plaza, #270E, New York NY 10112 USA
**Williams, Jeffrey N** — Astronaut
4918 Cross Creek Lane, League City TX 77573, USA
**Williams, Jerrol L** — Football Player
2562 Mizzoni Circle, Henderson NV 89052, USA
**Williams, Jesse** — Actor
W M E Entertainment, 9601 Wilshire Blvd, #300, Beverly Hills CA 90210 USA
**Williams, Jessica** — Jazz Pianist
T-Best Talent Agency, 508 Honey Lake Court, Danville CA 94506 USA
**Williams, Jett** — Singer
AddJet Productions, PO Box 177, Hartsville TN 37074, USA
**Williams, JoBeth** — Actress
Innovative Artists, 1505 10th St, Santa Monica CA 90401 USA
**Williams, Jody** — Nobel Peace Laureate
663 Lancaster St, Fredericksburg VA 22405, USA
**Williams, John A** — Writer
693 Forest Ave, Teaneck NJ 07666, USA
**Williams, John C** — Archery Athlete
833 Cordova Ave, Ormond Beach FL 32174, USA
**Williams, John C** — Concert Guitarist, Composer
Askonas Holt, Lincoln House, 300 High Holborn, London WC1V 7JH, England
**Williams, John L** — Football Player
1709 Husson Ave, Palatka FL 32177, USA
**Williams, John T** — Conductor, Composer
333 Loring Ave, Los Angeles CA 90024, USA
**Williams, Johnny** — Football Player
31921 Camino Capistrano, #13, San Juan Capistrano CA 92675, USA
**Williams, Joseph** — Composer
Gorfaine/Schwartz, 4111 W Alameda Ave, #509, Burbank CA 91505 USA
**Williams, Josh** — Singer, Guitarist, Mandola Player
Keith Case Assoc, 1025 17th Ave S, #200, Nashville TN 37212 USA
**Williams, Juan** — Writer
Fox-TV, News Dept, 205 E 67th St, New York NY 10065 USA
**Williams, Kameelah** — Rap Artist (702)
Richard Walters, PO Box 2789, Toluca Lake CA 91610 USA
**Williams, Karl D** — Football Player
2153 McKenzie Road, Mesquite TX 75181, USA

**Williams - Williams**

**Williams, Kate** — Actress
I C M Partners, 10250 Constellation Blvd, #900, Los Angeles CA 90067 USA

**Williams, Keller** — Singer, Songwriter, Guitarist
Madison House, 2060 Broadway, #225, Boulder CO 80302, USA

**Williams, Kelli** — Actress, Singer
I C M Partners, 10250 Constellation Blvd, #900, Los Angeles CA 90067 USA

**Williams, Kenneth R (Ken)** — Baseball Player
6430 E Sierra Vista Dr, Paradise Valley AZ 85253, USA

**Williams, Kevin E** — Basketball Player
1102 Blake Ave, #2, Brooklyn NY 11208, USA

**Williams, Kiely A** — Actress, Singer (Cheetah Girls)
W M E Entertainment, 9601 Wilshire Blvd, #300, Beverly Hills CA 90210 USA

**Williams, Lee E** — Football Player
11651 NW 4th St, Plantation FL 33325, USA

**Williams, Lenae T** — Basketball Player
A A I Sports, 16000 Dallas Parkway, #300, Dallas TX 75248, USA

**Williams, Linda** — Singer, Songwriter
Music Tree Artist Mgmt, 1414 Pennsylvania Ave, Pittsburgh PA 15233, USA

**Williams, Lorenzo** — Basketball Player
6001 Palm Trace Landings Dr, #318, Davie FL 33314, USA

**Williams, Lucinda** — Singer, Songwriter
High Road Touring, 751 Bridgeway, #300, Sausalito CA 94965, USA

**Williams, Lynn R** — Labor Leader
Harvard University, Politics Institute, 79 Kennedy St, Cambridge MA 02138, USA

**Williams, Madieu M** — Football Player
PO Box 96503, Washington DC 20090, USA

**Williams, Maisie** — Actress
Louise Johnson Mgmt, Arle Court, Cheltenham, Gloucestershire GL51 6PN, England

**Williams, Maiya** — Producer, Writer
A P A Talent/Literary Agency, 405 S Beverly Dr, #300, Beverly Hills CA 90212 USA

**Williams, Maizie U** — Singer (Boney M)
International Artists, PO Box 10034, 47563 Goch, Germany

**Williams, Malinda** — Actress
Inspire Entertainment, 9800 Wilshire Blvd, Beverly Hills CA 90212, USA

**Williams, Mario J** — Football Player
701 W Friar Tuck Lane, Houston TX 77024, USA

**Williams, Mark** — Bowler
Professional Bowlers Assn, 719 2nd Ave, #701, Seattle WA 98104 USA

**Williams, Mark W** — Baseball Player
1453 Trumansburg Road, Ithaca NY 14850, USA

**Williams, Marvin G** — Basketball Player
Utah Jazz, Energy Solutions Arena, 301 W South Temple, Salt Lake City UT 84101 USA

**Williams, Mary Alice** — Commentator
'Daily Rounds', Discovery Channel, 7700 Wisconsin Ave, Bethesda MD 20814, USA

**Williams, Mason** — Singer, Guitarist, Composer
PO Box 5105, Eugene OR 97405, USA

**Williams, Matt** — Writer, Director, Producer
Wind Dancer Productions, 200 W 57th St, #601, New York NY 10019, USA

**Williams, Matthew D (Matt)** — Baseball Player, Manager
4400 N Scottsdale Road, #381, Scottsdale AZ 85251, USA

**Williams, Maurice** — Singer, Songwriter
Cape Entertainment, 4799 Coconut Creek Parkway, #258, Coconut Creek FL 33063 USA

**Williams, Maurice (Mo)** — Basketball Player
Portland Trail Blazers, Rose Garden, 1 N Center Court St, Portland OR 97227 USA

**Williams, Maurice C** — Football Player
3653 Eastbury Dr, Jacksonville FL 32224, USA

**Williams, Maurice J** — Association Executive
Overseas Development Council, 1875 Connecticut Ave NW, Washington DC 20009, USA

**Williams, Maurice J (Moe)** — Football Player
10801 SW Fox Brown Road, Indiantown FL 34956, USA

**Williams, Meadow** — Actress, Producer, Writer
GruntWorks Entertainment, 548 Broadhollow Road, Melville NY 11747, USA

**Williams, Melvin G (Mel), Jr** — Navy Admiral
Commander, 2nd Fleet, FPO AE 09506 USA

**Williams, Merriwether** — Writer, Producer
Collective, 8383 Wilshire Blvd, #1050, Beverly Hills CA 90211 USA

**Williams, Michael D (Mike)** — Football Player
Jacksonville Jaguars, 1 AllTel Stadium Place, Jacksonville FL 32202 USA

**Williams, Michael D (Mike)** — Baseball Player
240 Horseshoe Farm Road, Pembroke VA 24136, USA

**Williams, Michael J (Mike)** — Football Player
2152 NW 74th Ave, Hollywood FL 33024, USA

**Williams, Michael Kenneth** — Actor
Imperium 7 Artists, 5455 Wilshire Blvd, #1706, Los Angeles CA 90036 USA

**Williams, Micheal D** — Basketball Player
1005 Lakeridge Court, Colleyville TX 76034, USA

**Williams, Michelle** — Singer (Destiny's Child)
I C M Partners, 10250 Constellation Blvd, #900, Los Angeles CA 90067 USA

**Williams, Michelle** — Actress
Creative Artists Agency, 2000 Ave of Stars, #100, Los Angeles CA 90067 USA

**Williams, Mitchell S (Mitch)** — Baseball Player
67 Highbridge Blvd, Medford NJ 08055, USA

**Williams, Montel** — Entertainer, Talk Show Host
Mountain Movers, 433 W 53rd St, New York NY 10019, USA

**Williams, Nathaniel R (Nate)** — Basketball Player
132 Stanmore Circle, Vallejo CA 94591, USA

**Williams, Nigel** — Writer, Producer
Judy Daish Assoc, 2 Saint Charles Place, London W10 6EG, England

**Williams, Olivia** — Actress
Independent Talent Group, 40 Whitfield St, London W1T 2RH, England

**Williams, Otis** — Singer (Temptations)
Barry Pollock Assoc, 9255 Sunset Blvd, #404, West Hollywood CA 90069, USA

**Williams, Pamela** — Jazz Saxophonist, Songwriter
Universal Attractions, 135 W 26th St, #1200, New York NY 10001 USA

**Williams, Patrick (Pat)** — Football Player
2839 Wilds Lane NW, Prior Lake MN 55372, USA

**W**

**Williams - Williams**

| | |
|---|---|
| **Williams, Patrick M**<br>3156 Mandeville Canyon Road, Los Angeles CA 90049, USA | Composer |
| **Williams, Paul (Punisher)**<br>Goossen Tutor Promotions, 15300 Ventura Blvd, #400, Sherman Oaks CA 91403 USA | Boxer |
| **Williams, Paul Andrew**<br>United Agents, 12-26 Lexington St, London W1F 0LE, England | Actor, Director, Writer |
| **Williams, Paul H**<br>8491 W Sunset Blvd, #1150, West Hollywood CA 90069, USA | Songwriter, Actor |
| **Williams, Perry L**<br>273 Old Laurinberg Road, Hamlet NC 28345, USA | Football Player |
| **Williams, Pharrell**<br>42 West, 220 W 42nd St, #1200, New York NY 10036 USA | Singer, Rap Artist (NERD), Songwriter |
| **Williams, Rachel**<br>Berzon Talent Agency, 23 Seton Road, Irvine CA 92612, USA | Model, Actress |
| **Williams, Randall D (Randy)**<br>11410 F M 586 S, Brookesmith TX 76827, USA | Baseball Player |
| **Williams, Randy**<br>5655 N Marty Ave, #204, Fresno CA 93711, USA | Track Athlete |
| **Williams, Redford B, Jr**<br>Duke University Medical School, Box 3708, Durham NC 27706, USA | Internist |
| **Williams, Reggie**<br>2016 Calloway St, Temple Hills MD 20748, USA | Basketball Player |
| **Williams, Reginald (Reggie)**<br>10 N Summerlin Ave, #53, Orlando FL 32801, USA | Football Player |
| **Williams, Richard E**<br>138 Royal College St, London NW1 0TA, England | Animator, Cartoonist (Pink Panther) |
| **Williams, Robbie**<br>I E Music, 111 Frithville Gardens, London W12 7JQ, England | Singer |
| **Williams, Robert A (Bobby)**<br>602 Stone Barn Road, Towson MD 21286, USA | Football Player |
| **Williams, Robert J (Ben)**<br>5961 Huntview Dr, Jackson MS 39206, USA | Football Player |
| **Williams, Robert Walter**<br>University of Washington, Physics Dept, Seattle WA 98195, USA | Physicist |
| **Williams, Robin**<br>1 Blackfield Dr, #409, Belvedere-Tiburon CA 94920, USA | Actor, Comedian |
| **Williams, Robin**<br>Music Tree Artist Mgmt, 1414 Pennsylvania Ave, Pittsburgh PA 15233, USA | Singer, Songwriter |
| **Williams, Roderick**<br>Ingpen & Williams, 131 Putney Bridge Road, London SW15 2PA, England | Opera Singer |
| **Williams, Roland L**<br>5671 Wrenwyck Place, Weldon Spring MO 63304, USA | Football Player |
| **Williams, Ronald A**<br>Aetna Inc, 151 Farmington Ave, Hartford CT 06156, USA | Businessman |
| **Williams, Roshumba**<br>Innovative Artists, 1505 10th St, Santa Monica CA 90401 USA | Model, Actress |
| **Williams, Rowan D**<br>Lambert Palace, London SE1 9JU, England | Religious Leader |
| **Williams, Roy**<br>University of North Carolina, Athletic Dept, PO Box 2126, Chapel Hill NC 27515, USA | Basketball Coach |
| **Williams, Roy E, Jr**<br>Chicago Bears, 1000 Football Dr, Lake Forest IL 60045 USA | Football Player |
| **Williams, Roy L**<br>4100 Buckingham Place, Colleyville TX 76034, USA | Football Player |
| **Williams, Ryan Piers**<br>Peikoff Law Office, 173 E Broadway, #C1, New York NY 10002 USA | Director, Producer, Writer |
| **Williams, Saul S**<br>Creative Artists Agency, 2000 Ave of Stars, #100, Los Angeles CA 90067 USA | Rap Artist |
| **Williams, Serena J**<br>6466 Emerald Dunes Dr, #105, West Palm Beach FL 33411, USA | Tennis Player |
| **Williams, Shad C**<br>4682 E Cornell Ave, Fresno CA 93703, USA | Baseball Player |
| **Williams, Shaun L**<br>11738 Gruen St, Sylmar CA 91342, USA | Football Player |
| **Williams, Shelden**<br>Brooklyn Nets, 15 Metro Tech Center, #1100, Brooklyn NY 11201 USA | Basketball Player |
| **Williams, Sherman C**<br>119 Patricia Ave, Mobile AL 36610, USA | Football Player |
| **Williams, Sidney (Sid)**<br>1044 W 82nd St, Los Angeles CA 90044, USA | Football Player |
| **Williams, Simon**<br>Dalzell & Beresford, 26 Astwood Mews, London SW7 4DE, England | Actor |
| **Williams, Speed**<br>9550 Tradewind St, Amarillo TX 79118, USA | Rodeo Rider |
| **Williams, Stanley W (Stan)**<br>4702 Hayter Ave, Lakewood CA 90712, USA | Baseball Player |
| **Williams, Stephanie E**<br>S M S Talent, 8383 Wilshire Blvd, #230, Beverly Hills CA 90211 USA | Actress |
| **Williams, Stephen**<br>1017 Foothills Trail, Santa Fe NM 87505, USA | Anthropologist |
| **Williams, Stephen F**<br>US Court of Appeals, 333 Constitution Ave NW, #4400, Washington DC 20001, USA | Judge |
| **Williams, Steve**<br>Leander Club, Henley on Thames, Leander RG9 2LP, England | Rowing Athlete |
| **Williams, Steven**<br>Stone Manners Salners, 9911 W Pico Blvd, #1400, Los Angeles CA 90035 USA | Actor |
| **Williams, Sunita L**<br>1522 Festival Dr, Houston TX 77062, USA | Astronaut |
| **Williams, Tamika**<br>Minnesota Lynx, Target Center, 600 1st Ave N, Minneapolis MN 55403 USA | Basketball Player |
| **Williams, Tavares (Monty)**<br>316 Dorrington Blvd, Metairie LA 70005, USA | Basketball Player, Coach |
| **Williams, Terrence**<br>Sacramento Kings, Arco Arena, 1 Sports Parkway, Sacramento CA 95834 USA | Basketball Player |
| **Williams, Terrie**<br>University of California, Biology Dept, Santa Cruz CA 95064, USA | Biologist |

| | |
|---|---|
| **Williams, Terry**<br>Damage Mgmt, 16 Lambton Place, London W11 2SH, England | Drummer (Dire Straits) |
| **Williams, Thomas S Cardinal**<br>Viard, 21 Eccleston Hill, PO Box 1937, Wellington 6015, New Zealand | Religious Leader |
| **Williams, Tod**<br>Tod Williams Billie Tsien Architects, 222 Central Park S, New York NY 10019, USA | Architect |
| **Williams, Tod**<br>United Talent Agency, U T A Plaza, 9336 Civic Center Dr, Beverly Hills CA 90210 USA | Director, Producer, Writer |
| **Williams, Todd**<br>Sanders/Armstrong/Caserta Mgmt, 2120 Colorado Ave, #120, Santa Monica CA 90404 USA | Actor |
| **Williams, Todd M**<br>16707 Whispering Glen Dr, Lutz FL 33558, USA | Baseball Player |
| **Williams, Tom**<br>2411 Princess Ave, Windsor ON N8T 1V2, Canada | Ice Hockey Player |
| **Williams, Tonya Lee**<br>Artists Agency, 9430 Olympic Blvd, Beverly Hills CA 90212 USA | Actress |
| **Williams, Treat**<br>A P A Talent/Literary Agency, 405 S Beverly Dr, #300, Beverly Hills CA 90212 USA | Actor |
| **Williams, U Tyrone**<br>6939 Westchester Circle, Bradenton FL 34202, USA | Football Player |
| **Williams, Ulis**<br>2511 29th St, Santa Monica CA 90405, USA | Track Athlete |
| **Williams, Vanessa A**<br>Shadow, 10 Universal City Plaza, #2000, Universal City CA 91608, USA | Actress, Producer |
| **Williams, Vanessa L**<br>United Talent Agency, U T A Plaza, 9336 Civic Center Dr, Beverly Hills CA 90210 USA | Actress, Singer, Beauty Queen |
| **Williams, Venus E S**<br>6466 Emerald Dunes Dr, #105, West Palm Beach FL 33411, USA | Tennis Player |
| **Williams, Victor**<br>Imperium 7, 5455 Wilshire Blvd, #1706, Los Angeles CA 90036, USA | Actor |
| **Williams, Victoria**<br>High Road Touring, 751 Bridgeway, #200, Sausalito CA 94965 USA | Singer, Guitarist, Songwriter |
| **Williams, Virginia**<br>Paul Kohner, 9300 Wilshire Blvd, #555, Beverly Hills CA 90212 USA | Actress |
| **Williams, Wade**<br>S M S Talent, 8383 Wilshire Blvd, #230, Beverly Hills CA 90211 USA | Actor |
| **Williams, Walter (Buddy)**<br>15700 Good Hope Road, Silver Spring MD 20905, USA | Baseball Player |
| **Williams, Walter A (Walt)**<br>2417 Monterey St, Brownwood TX 76801, USA | Baseball Player |
| **Williams, Walter A (Walt)**<br>3240 Beaumont St, Temple Hills MD 20748, USA | Basketball Player |
| **Williams, Walter F**<br>RR 4, Saucon Valley Road, Bethlehem PA 18015, USA | Businessman |
| **Williams, Walter Ray, Jr**<br>7903 SE 12th Circle, Ocala FL 34480, USA | Bowler |
| **Williams, Walter, Sr**<br>Associated Booking Corp, 501 Madison Ave, #501, New York NY 10022 USA | Singer (O'Jays) |
| **Williams, Warren, Jr**<br>1203 Gerald Ave, West Hempstead NY 11552, USA | Football Player |
| **Williams, Wendy**<br>A P A Talent/Literary Agency, 405 S Beverly Dr, #300, Beverly Hills CA 90212 USA | Actress |
| **Williams, William (Curly)**<br>2729 20th St, Sarasota FL 34234, USA | Baseball Player |
| **Williams, William A**<br>Environmental Protection Agency, 200 SW 35th St, Corvallis OR 97333, USA | Astronaut |
| **Williams, William G (Billy)**<br>RR 2 Box 822, Coconut Creek FL 33073, USA | Baseball Umpire |
| **Williams, Willie A**<br>PO Box 871445, Mesquite TX 75187, USA | Football Player |
| **Williamson, Carlton**<br>300 White Springs Lane, Peachtree City GA 30269, USA | Football Player |
| **Williamson, Corliss M**<br>Arkansas Baptist College, Athletic Dept, 1621 King Dr, Little Rock AR 72202, USA | Basketball Player |
| **Williamson, Frederick R (Fred)**<br>H David Moss, 733 Seward St, #PH, Los Angeles CA 90038, USA | Actor, Football Player |
| **Williamson, Jama**<br>Talent Works, 3500 W Olive Ave, #1400, Burbank CA 91505 USA | Actress |
| **Williamson, Jay**<br>24 Clemont Lane, Saint Louis MO 63124, USA | Golfer |
| **Williamson, Kevin**<br>W M E Entertainment, 9601 Wilshire Blvd, #300, Beverly Hills CA 90210 USA | Director, Producer, Writer |
| **Williamson, Marianne**<br>Los Angeles Center for Living, 8265 W Sunset Blvd, West Hollywood CA 90046, USA | Psychotherapist |
| **Williamson, Mark A**<br>1260 Hidden Mountain Dr, El Cajon CA 92019, USA | Baseball Player |
| **Williamson, Matthew**<br>37 Percy St, London W1P 2DJ, England | Fashion Designer |
| **Williamson, Michael**<br>Washington Post, Editorial Dept, 1150 15th St NW, Washington DC 20071 USA | Photojournalist |
| **Williamson, Michael**<br>10400 Hutting Place, Silver Spring MD 20902, USA | Writer |
| **Williamson, Mykelti T**<br>Innovative Artists, 1505 10th St, Santa Monica CA 90401 USA | Actor |
| **Williamson, Oliver E**<br>University of California, Economics Dept, Berkeley CA 94720, USA | Nobel Economics Laureate |
| **Williamson, Richard**<br>5137 Morrowick Road, Charlotte NC 28226, USA | Football Coach |
| **Williamson, Samuel R, Jr**<br>University of the South, President's Office, Sewanee TN 37375, USA | Educator |
| **Williamson, Scott R**<br>2623 Foran Dr, Cincinnati OH 45238, USA | Baseball Player |
| **Williamson, Troy**<br>Jacksonville Jaguars, 1 AllTel Stadium Place, Jacksonville FL 32202 USA | Football Player |
| **Williams-Paisley, Kimberly**<br>Kritzer Levine Wilkins Griffin, 11872 La Grange Ave, #100, Los Angeles CA 90025 USA | Actress |

**W**

*Williams - Williams-Paisley*

## W

| | |
|---|---|
| **Willie D**<br>Entertainment Artists, 2409 21st Ave S, #100, Nashville TN 10019 USA | Rap Artist (Geto Boys) |
| **Williford, D Vann**<br>4455 Fair Oaks Lane, High Point NC 27265, USA | Basketball Player |
| **Willig, Matthew J (Matt)**<br>4241 Prado de los Pajaros, Calabasas CA 91302, USA | Football Player |
| **Willimon, Beau**<br>Creative Artists Agency, 2000 Ave of Stars, #100, Los Angeles CA 90067 USA | Writer |
| **Willing, Nick**<br>Independent Talent Group, 40 Whitfield St, London W1T 2RH, England | Director |
| **Willingham, Joshua D (Josh)**<br>108 Cascade Dr, Florence AL 35633, USA | Baseball Player |
| **Willingham, Tyrone**<br>Octagon Worldwide, 1751 Pinnacle Dr, #1500, McLean VA 22102 USA | Football Coach |
| **Willis, Alicia Leigh**<br>Innovative Artists, 1505 10th St, Santa Monica CA 90401 USA | Actress |
| **Willis, Brian Davis**<br>Pacific Talent Agency, PO Box 19145, Portland OR 97280, USA | Drummer (Quarterflash) |
| **Willis, Bruce W**<br>Creative Artists Agency, 2000 Ave of Stars, #100, Los Angeles CA 90067 USA | Actor |
| **Willis, Carl B**<br>6811 Lipscomb Dr, Durham NC 27712, USA | Baseball Player |
| **Willis, Dave**<br>Brillstein Entertainment Partners, 9150 Wilshire Blvd, #350, Beverly Hills CA 90212 USA | Writer, Producer, Actor |
| **Willis, Dinah**<br>Playboy Promotions, 2706 Media Center Dr, Los Angeles CA 90065 USA | Model |
| **Willis, Dontrelle**<br>9820 E Thompson Peak Parkway, #726, Scottsdale AZ 85255, USA | Baseball Player |
| **Willis, Frederick F (Fred), III**<br>PO Box 558, Swampscott MA 01907, USA | Football Player |
| **Willis, Garrett**<br>528 Mountain Pass Lane, Knoxville TN 37923, USA | Golfer |
| **Willis, Gordon**<br>I C M Partners, 10250 Constellation Blvd, #900, Los Angeles CA 90067 USA | Cinematographer |
| **Willis, James G (Jim)**<br>PO Box 35, Boyce LA 71409, USA | Baseball Player |
| **Willis, Keith**<br>116 Coffeeberry Court, Garner NC 27529, USA | Football Player |
| **Willis, Kelly**<br>Davis McLarty Agency, 708 S Lamar Blvd, #D, Austin TX 78704, USA | Singer, Songwriter |
| **Willis, Kevin A**<br>1481 Jones Road, Roswell GA 30075, USA | Basketball Player |
| **Willis, Michael H (Mike)**<br>6234 Taggart St, Houston TX 77007, USA | Baseball Player |
| **Willis, Patrick L**<br>San Francisco 49ers, 4949 Centennial Blvd, Santa Clara CA 95054 USA | Football Player |
| **Willis, Ray**<br>8200 Poole Road, Knightdale NC 27545, USA | Football Player |
| **Willis, Rumer**<br>Untitled Entertainment, 350 S Beverly Dr, #200, Beverly Hills CA 90212 USA | Actress |
| **Willison, Mike**<br>Metropolitan Entertainment Group, 2 Penn Plaza, #1500, New York NY 10121, USA | Bassist (Fig Dish) |
| **Willits, Reggie G**<br>Los Angeles Angels, Angel Stadium, 2000 E Gene Autry Way, Anaheim CA 92806 USA | Baseball Player |
| **Willman, David**<br>Los Angeles Times, Editorial Dept, 202 W 1st St, Los Angeles CA 90012 USA | Journalist |
| **Willmon, Trent**<br>Hallmark Direction, 713 18th Ave S, Nashville TN 37203, USA | Singer, Songwriter |
| **Willms, Andre**<br>Rennebogen 94, 39130 Magdeburg, Germany | Rowing Athlete |
| **Willoch, Kare I**<br>Blokkaveien 6B, 0282 Oslo, Norway | Prime Minister, Norway |
| **Willoughby, James A (Jim)**<br>PO Box 707, Eufaula OK 74432, USA | Baseball Player |
| **Willoughby, William W (Bill)**<br>350 W Englewood Ave, Englewood NJ 07631, USA | Basketball Player |
| **Wills, Elliott T (Bump)**<br>1802 Briar Meadow Dr, Arlington TX 76014, USA | Baseball Player |
| **Wills, Garry**<br>Northwestern University, History Dept, Evanston IL 60201, USA | Historian |
| **Wills, Mark**<br>Scott Welch Mgmt, 1515 Harding Place, Nashville TN 37215, USA | Singer, Songwriter |
| **Wills, Maurice M (Maury)**<br>M & R Sports, 5 Dalton Valley Dr, Saint Peters MO 63376, USA | Baseball Player, Manager |
| **Wills, Rick**<br>Hard to Handle Mgmt, 16501 Ventura Blvd, #602, Encino CA 91436, USA | Bassist (Foreigner) |
| **Wills, Theodore C (Ted)**<br>10585 E Duckpoint Way, Clovis CA 93619, USA | Baseball Player |
| **Willsie, Brian**<br>45 Meadowbrook Road, Randolph NJ 07869, USA | Ice Hockey Player |
| **Willson-Piper, Marty**<br>Entourage Talent, 236 W 27th St, #800, New York NY 10001, USA | Guitarist (Church) |
| **Wilmarth, Christopher**<br>Betty Cunningham, 541 W 25th St, Front 2, New York NY 10001, USA | Artist, Sculptor |
| **Wilmarth, Dick**<br>1111 F St, Anchorage AK 99501, USA | Dog Sled Racer |
| **Wilmer, Douglas**<br>Julian Belfrage Assoc, 9 Argyll St, #300, London W1F 7TG, England | Actor |
| **Wilmer, Harry A**<br>Texas Health Science Center, Psychiatric Dept, San Antonio TX 78284, USA | Psychiatrist |
| **Wilmet, Paul R**<br>PO Box 330074, Nashville TN 37203, USA | Baseball Player |
| **Wilmore, Barry E (Butch)**<br>3002 Bryant Lane, Webster TX 77598, USA | Astronaut |
| **Wilmore, Larry**<br>United Talent Agency, U T A Plaza, 9336 Civic Center Dr, Beverly Hills CA 90210 USA | Actor, Comedian, Writer |

| | |
|---|---|
| **Wilmot, David** | Actor |
| Macfarlane Chard, 7 Adelaide St, Dun Laoghaire, County Dublin, Ireland | |
| **Wilms, Andre** | Actor |
| Voyez Mon Agent, 20 Ave Rapp, 75007 Paris, France | |
| **Wilmsmeyer, Klaus, Jr** | Football Player |
| 8209 Paddington Dr, Louisville KY 40222, USA | |
| **Wilmut, Ian** | Geneticist, Embryologist |
| Roslin Institute, Roslin Bio Centre, Midlothian EH25 9PS, Scotland | |
| **Wilpon, Fred** | Baseball Executive |
| 100 Sheep Lane, Locust Valley NY 11560, USA | |
| **Wilson of Tillyorn, David C** | Government Official, England; Diplomat |
| House of Lords, Westminster, London SW1A 0PW, England | |
| **Wilson, Adrian L** | Football Player |
| 10104 E Shangri La Road, Scottsdale AZ 85260, USA | |
| **Wilson, Aldra K (Al)** | Football Player |
| 11561 Warrington Court, Parker CO 80138, USA | |
| **Wilson, Alexander G (Sandy)** | Composer, Writer |
| 2 Southwell Gardens, #4, London SW7 4SB, England | |
| **Wilson, Alexandra** | Actress |
| Greater Visions Artists Talent Agency, 8981 W Sunset Blvd, #101, West Hollywood CA 90069 USA | |
| **Wilson, Allan B** | Molecular Biologist |
| University of California, Molecular Biology Dept, Berkeley CA 94724, USA | |
| **Wilson, Andrew** | Actor |
| United Talent Agency, U T A Plaza, 9336 Civic Center Dr, Beverly Hills CA 90210 USA | |
| **Wilson, Andrew N (A N)** | Writer |
| 21 Arlington Road, London NW1 7ER, England | |
| **Wilson, Ann D** | Singer (Heart) |
| H K Mgmt, 9200 W Sunset Blvd, #530, West Hollywood CA 90069 USA | |
| **Wilson, Ben** | Keyboardist (Blues Traveler) |
| C3 Presents, 98 San Jacinto Blvd, #400, Austin TX 78701, USA | |
| **Wilson, Blaine** | Gymnast |
| 7441 Murrayfield Dr, Columbus OH 43085, USA | |
| **Wilson, Blenda J** | Educator |
| California State University, President's Office, Northridge CA 91330, USA | |
| **Wilson, Brenard K** | Football Player |
| 1246 Dalemere Dr, Nashville TN 37207, USA | |
| **Wilson, Brian Anthony** | Actor, Producer |
| A D S Mgmt, 269 S Beverly Drive, #441, Beverly Hills CA 90212, USA | |
| **Wilson, Brian D** | Singer (Beach Boys), Songwriter |
| Lippin Group, 6100 Wilshire Blvd, #400, Los Angeles CA 90048, USA | |
| **Wilson, Brian P** | Baseball Player |
| 741 S Banning Circle, Mesa AZ 85206, USA | |
| **Wilson, C A S John** | Architect |
| John Wilson Assoc, 27 Horsell Road, London N5 1XL, England | |
| **Wilson, C Richard (Ricky)** | Singer (Kaiser Chiefs) |
| Red Light Mgmt, 8439 Sunset Blvd, West Hollywood CA | |
| **Wilson, C Wade** | Football Player |
| 6126 Mimosa Lane, Dallas TX 75230, USA | |
| **Wilson, Carey** | Ice Hockey Player |
| 85 Jean Louis Road, Winnipeg MB R2N 4A9, Canada | |
| **Wilson, Carnie** | Singer (Wilson Phillips, Wilsons) |
| 19528 Ventura Blvd, #624, Tarzana CA 91356, USA | |
| **Wilson, Casey R** | Actress, Writer |
| United Talent Agency, U T A Plaza, 9336 Civic Center Dr, Beverly Hills CA 90210 USA | |
| **Wilson, Cassandra** | Singer |
| Front Row Productions, 215 S 4th St, Forest City IA 50436, USA | |
| **Wilson, Cedrick** | Football Player |
| 380 N Island Dr, #312, Memphis TN 38103, USA | |
| **Wilson, Chandra** | Actress |
| Abrams Artists, 275 7th Ave, #2600, New York NY 10001 USA | |
| **Wilson, Charles J** | Football Player |
| 5444 Calder Dr, Tallahassee FL 32317, USA | |
| **Wilson, Charles K (Charlie)** | Singer (Gap Band), Songwriter |
| Universal Attractions, 135 W 26th St, #1200, New York NY 10001 USA | |
| **Wilson, Charles R** | Judge |
| US Court of Appeals, 801 N Florida Ave, #200, Tampa FL 33602, USA | |
| **Wilson, Chris** | Football Player |
| Washington Redskins, 21300 Redskin Park Dr, Ashburn VA 20147 USA | |
| **Wilson, Christopher J (C J)** | Baseball Player |
| Los Angeles Angels, Angel Stadium, 2000 E Gene Autry Way, Anaheim CA 92806 USA | |
| **Wilson, Cindy** | Singer, Guitarist (B-52's) |
| Direct Management Group, 947 N La Cienega Blvd, #G, West Hollywood CA 90069, USA | |
| **Wilson, Colin H** | Writer |
| Tetherdown, Trewallock Lane, Gorran Haven, Cornwall PL26 6NT, England | |
| **Wilson, Craig** | Water Polo Player |
| 1423 Lake Blvd, Davis CA 95616, USA | |
| **Wilson, Craig** | Baseball Player |
| 8241 Drybank Dr, Huntington Beach CA 92646, USA | |
| **Wilson, Craig F** | Baseball Player |
| 3427 E Tere St, Phoenix AZ 85044, USA | |
| **Wilson, Dan** | Singer, Guitarist, Songwriter |
| Monterey Peninsula Artists, 404 W Franklin St, Monterey CA 93940 USA | |
| **Wilson, Daniel A (Dan)** | Baseball Player |
| 2161 E Interlaken Blvd, Seattle WA 98112, USA | |
| **Wilson, Darnell** | Boxer |
| 1917 E Foxmoor Lane, Lafayette IN 47905, USA | |
| **Wilson, David** | Educator |
| Morgan State University, President's Office, Baltimore MD 21239, USA | |
| **Wilson, David C (Dave)** | Football Player |
| 2247 Farolito Ave, Long Beach CA 90815, USA | |
| **Wilson, David Mackenzie** | Museum Executive |
| Lifeboat House, Castletown IM9 1LD, Isle of Man, England | |
| **Wilson, Dean** | Golfer |
| 10914 Iris Canyon Lane, Las Vegas NV 89135, USA | |
| **Wilson, Desi B** | Baseball Player |
| 8 Janet Lane, Glen Cove NY 11542, USA | |

| | |
|---|---|
| **Wilson, Desire** <br> 4197 Serenade Road, Castle Rock CO 80104, USA | Auto Racing Driver |
| **Wilson, Doug** <br> 5620 Country Club Parkway, San Jose CA 95138, USA | Ice Hockey Player |
| **Wilson, Edward O** <br> 1010 Waltham St, #A208, Lexington MA 02421, USA | Writer, Zoologist |
| **Wilson, Elizabeth** <br> Paradigm Agency, 360 N Crescent Dr, North Building, Beverly Hills CA 90210 USA | Actress |
| **Wilson, F Paul** <br> 1933 State Route 35, #337, Wall Township NJ 07719, USA | Writer |
| **Wilson, F Perry** <br> 225 N 56th St, #217, Lincoln NE 68504, USA | Chemical Engineer |
| **Wilson, Frank** <br> North Carolina Motor Speedway, PO Box 2801, Daytona Beach FL 32120, USA | Auto Racing Executive |
| **Wilson, Gahan** <br> New Yorker, Editorial Dept, 4 Times Square, Basement C1B, New York NY 10036 USA | Cartoonist, Writer |
| **Wilson, George (Jiff)** <br> 151 Twin Lakes Dr, Fairfield OH 45014, USA | Basketball Player |
| **Wilson, Gerald S** <br> 4625 Brynhurst Ave, Los Angeles CA 90043, USA | Jazz Trumpeter, Composer |
| **Wilson, Gibril D** <br> 20 10th St NW, #2302, Atlanta GA 30309, USA | Football Player |
| **Wilson, Glenn D** <br> 300 Tara Park, Conroe TX 77302, USA | Baseball Player |
| **Wilson, Gretchen** <br> Morris Management Group, 818 19th Ave S, Nashville TN 37203, USA | Singer, Guitarist |
| **Wilson, Hugh** <br> I C M Partners, 10250 Constellation Blvd, #900, Los Angeles CA 90067 USA | Director |
| **Wilson, Ian A** <br> Scripps Research Institute, 10550 N Torrey Pines Road, La Jolla CA 92037, USA | Biologist |
| **Wilson, Jack E** <br> 12467 San Sebastian Court, Santa Rosa Valley CA 93012, USA | Baseball Player |
| **Wilson, Jack M** <br> University of Massachusetts, President's Office, 225 Franklin St, #3300, Boston MA 02110, USA | Educator |
| **Wilson, Jacquelyn** <br> Transworld Publishers, 61-63 Uxbridge Road, London W5 5SA, England | Writer |
| **Wilson, James (J C)** <br> 4785 Young Road, Waldorf MD 20601, USA | Football Player |
| **Wilson, James M** <br> University of Pennsylvania Medical Center, Genetics Dept, Philadelphia PA 19104, USA | Geneticist |
| **Wilson, Jane** <br> 317 W 83rd St, #2E, New York NY 10024, USA | Artist |
| **Wilson, Jean D** <br> Texas Southwestern Medical Center, 5323 Harry Hines Blvd, Dallas TX 75390, USA | Endocrinologist |
| **Wilson, Jeannie** <br> 4330 Talofa Ave, Toluca Lake CA 91602, USA | Actress |
| **Wilson, Jennifer** <br> I M G Artists, The Light Box, 111 Power Road, London W4 5PY, England | Opera, Concert Singer |
| **Wilson, Jerry L** <br> 19814 Moss Bark Trail, Richmond TX 77407, USA | Football Player |
| **Wilson, Jessica** <br> OmniPop Talent Group, 4605 Lankershim Blvd, #201, Toluca Lake CA 91602 USA | Actress, Comedienne |
| **Wilson, John (Johnny), Sr** <br> 8 Hillcrest Dr, Lock Haven PA 17745, USA | Baseball Player |
| **Wilson, Johnnie E** <br> Dimensions International, 2800 Eisenhower Ave, #300, Alexandria VA 22314, USA | Army General |
| **Wilson, Josh** <br> 2304 Cramden Road, Pittsburgh, PA MI 15241, USA | Baseball Player |
| **Wilson, Joshua (Josh)** <br> 515 Quincy Ave NE, Renton WA 98059, USA | Football Player |
| **Wilson, Julie** <br> Scott Stander Assoc, 4533 Van Nuys Blvd, #401, Sherman Oaks CA 91403 USA | Singer, Actress |
| **Wilson, Justin** <br> David Levin Mgmt, 200 W 57th St, #308, New York NY 10019, USA | Drummer (Reveille) |
| **Wilson, Keri-Lynn** <br> I M G Artists, Hogarth Business Park, Chiswick, London W4 2TH, England | Conductor |
| **Wilson, Kim** <br> Two Goats Entertainment, 5001 W Placita de los Vientos, Tucson AZ 85745, USA | Singer, Musician (Fabulous Thunderbird) |
| **Wilson, Kris** <br> PO Box 15, Chillicothe MO 64601, USA | Baseball Player |
| **Wilson, Kristen** <br> Craig Wyckoff & Associates, 13952 Runnymede St, Van Nuys CA 91405, USA | Actress |
| **Wilson, Lambert** <br> Rights House, Drury House, 34-43 Russell St, London WC2B 5HA, England | Actor |
| **Wilson, Landon** <br> 127 Tennyson Place, Coppell TX 75019, USA | Ice Hockey Player |
| **Wilson, Lawrence F (Larry)** <br> 11834 N Blackheath Road, Scottsdale AZ 85254, USA | Football Player, Executive |
| **Wilson, Linda S** <br> 26 Honey Locust Dr, Topsham ME 04086, USA | Educator |
| **Wilson, Luke** <br> I/D Public Relations, 7060 Hollywood Blvd, #800, Los Angeles CA 90028 USA | Actor |
| **Wilson, Mara** <br> Harry Gold Assoc, 3500 W Olive Ave, #1400, Burbank CA 91505, USA | Actress |
| **Wilson, Marc D** <br> 10820 157th Ave NE, Woodinville WA 98072, USA | Football Player |
| **Wilson, Marie** <br> Michael Bruno Group, 13576 Cheltenham Dr, Sherman Oaks CA 91423, USA | Actress |
| **Wilson, Mark J** <br> N41W27751 Ishnala Trail, Pewaukee WI 53072, USA | Golfer |
| **Wilson, Mary** <br> 2654 W Horizon Ridge Parkway, #B5, Henderson NV 89052, USA | Singer (Supremes) |
| **Wilson, Melanie** <br> Irv Schechter, 9460 Wilshire Blvd, #300, Beverly Hills CA 90212 USA | Actress |
| **Wilson, Michael (Tack)** <br> 1623 Schnell Dr, Arabi LA 70032, USA | Baseball Player |

Wilson - Wilson

**Wilson, Mike** — Ice Hockey Player
4647 Lake Charles Dr, Independence OH 44131, USA

**Wilson, Mike R** — Football Player
2908 N Poinsettia Ave, Manhattan Beach CA 90266, USA

**Wilson, Murray** — Ice Hockey Player
Wilson Consulting, 432-410 Bank St, Ottawa ON K2P 1Y8, Canada

**Wilson, Nancy** — Singer
Wenig-LaMonica Associates, 580 White Plains Road, #130, Tarrytown NY 10591 USA

**Wilson, Nancy L** — Singer (Heart)
Peters Mgmt, PO Box 1710, Topanga CA 90290, USA

**Wilson, Nemiah** — Football Player
11000 E Idaho Place, Aurora CO 80012, USA

**Wilson, Nigel E** — Baseball Player
35 Sabbe Crescent, Ajax ON L1T 4E3, Canada

**Wilson, Olin C** — Astronomer
1508 Circa del Lago, B110, San Marcos CA 92078, USA

**Wilson, Otis R** — Football Player
426 W Shadow Creek Dr, Vernon Hills IL 60061, USA

**Wilson, Owen C** — Actor
United Talent Agency, U T A Plaza, 9336 Civic Center Dr, Beverly Hills CA 90210 USA

**Wilson, Patrick** — Singer, Actor
Anonymous Content, 3532 Hayden Ave, Culver City CA 90232 USA

**Wilson, Patrick** — Immunologist
Oklahoma Medical Research Foundation, 825 NE 13th St, Oklahoma City OK 73104, USA

**Wilson, Paul** — Bassist, Pianist (Snow Patrol)
Big Life Mgmt, 67-69 Charlton St, London NW1 1HY, England

**Wilson, Paul A** — Baseball Player
949 Lenmore Court, Orlando FL 32812, USA

**Wilson, Peta** — Actress, Model
I C M Partners, 10250 Constellation Blvd, #900, Los Angeles CA 90067 USA

**Wilson, Peter L** — Architect
Architekturburo Bolles & Wilson, Alter Steinweg 17, 48143 Munster, Germany

**Wilson, Philippa C (Pippa)** — Yachtswoman
Lynx Sports Mgmt, Lymington Road, Lymington, Hampshire SO41 5S5, England

**Wilson, Preston J R** — Baseball Player
136 Paloma Dr, Coral Gables FL 33143, USA

**Wilson, Rainn** — Actor, Comedian
W M E Entertainment, 9601 Wilshire Blvd, #300, Beverly Hills CA 90210 USA

**Wilson, Ralph C, Jr** — Football Executive
99 Kercheval Ave, Grosse Pointe Farms MI 48236, USA

**Wilson, Rebel** — Actress
W M E Entertainment, 9601 Wilshire Blvd, #300, Beverly Hills CA 90210 USA

**Wilson, Reno** — Actor
Medavoy Mgmt, 10203 Santa Monica Blvd, #400, Los Angeles CA 90067 USA

**Wilson, Richard (Rick)** — Basketball Player
535 E Ormsby Ave, Louisville KY 40203, USA

**Wilson, Richard G (Rick)** — Ice Hockey Player
1624 Reno Run, Lewisville TX 75077, USA

**Wilson, Richard K** — Geneticist
Genome Sequencing Center, 4444 Forest Park Ave, Saint Louis MO 63108, USA

**Wilson, Ricky** — Basketball Player
8007 Oak Ridge Court, Bowie MD 20715, USA

**Wilson, Rik** — Ice Hockey Player
12076 Manchester Road, Saint Louis MO 63131, USA

**Wilson, Rita** — Actress, Singer
Creative Artists Agency, 2000 Ave of Stars, #100, Los Angeles CA 90067 USA

**Wilson, Robert Charles** — Writer
Bantam Books, 1745 Broadway, New York NY 10019 USA

**Wilson, Robert J (Red)** — Baseball Player
806 Cabot Lane, Madison WI 53711, USA

**Wilson, Robert M** — Actor
R W Work Ltd, 55 Washington St, #216, Brooklyn NY 11201, USA

**Wilson, Robert W** — Nobel Physics Laureate
38 Cole Court, Dumont NJ 07628, USA

**Wilson, Robin** — Singer (Gin Blossoms, Pharaohs)
Stone Manners Salners, 9911 W Pico Blvd, #1400, Los Angeles CA 90035 USA

**Wilson, Ronald L (Ron)** — Ice Hockey Player, Coach
17 Middleton Gardens Place, Bluffton SC 29910, USA

**Wilson, Ronald L (Ron)** — Ice Hockey Player
Hamilton Bulldogs, 101 York Blvd, Hamilton ON L8R 3L4, Canada

**Wilson, Roy** — Educator
University of Colorado, President's Office, Denver CO 80217, USA

**Wilson, Ruth** — Actress
Troika, 74 Clerkenwell Road, #300, London EC1M 5QA, England

**Wilson, S O'Neil (Neil)** — Baseball Player
4300 Highway 412 W, Lexington TN 38351, USA

**Wilson, Samuel W** — Army General, Educator
Hampden-Sydney College, President's Office, Hampden-Sydney VA 23943, USA

**Wilson, Scott** — Actor
Andrew Freedman Personal Mgmt, 20 Ironsides Street, #18, Marina del Rey CA 90292, USA

**Wilson, Sheree J** — Actress
Metropolitan Talent Agency, 5405 Wilshire Blvd, #218, Los Angeles CA 90036 USA

**Wilson, Stacy E** — Ice Hockey Player
Bowdoin College, Athletic Dept, Brunswick ME 04011, USA

**Wilson, Stanley W (Stan)** — Baseball Player
4701 Hayter St, Lakewood CA 90712, USA

**Wilson, Stephanie D** — Astronaut
N A S A, Johnson Space Center, 2101 NASA Road, Houston TX 77058 USA

**Wilson, Stephen D (Steve)** — Baseball Player
23-1041 Comox St, Vancouver BC V6E 1K1, Canada

**Wilson, Stephen E (Steve)** — Basketball Player
West Jefferson Middle School, 9449 Barnes Ave, Conifer CO 80433, USA

**Wilson, Steve A** — Football Player
3706 Village Estates Place, Tampa FL 33618, USA

**Wilson, Steven A (Steve)** — Football Player
8516 Doughton Dr, Bahama NC 27503, USA

# W

**Wilson, Steven J** — Singer, Guitarist (Porcupine Tree)
Agency Group Ltd, 361-373 City Road, London EC1V 1PQ, England

**Wilson, Stuart** — Actor
Curtis Brown Group, 28-29 Haymarket St, #500, London SW1Y 4SP, England

**Wilson, Thomas F** — Actor
Dusty Tuba Entertainment, PO Box 18106, Encino CA 91416, USA

**Wilson, Tom** — Baseball Player
2679 Tanglewood Court, Lake Havasu City AZ 86403, USA

**Wilson, Torrie** — Professional Wrestler, Model
Diverse Talent Group, 9911 Pico Blvd, #350W, Los Angeles CA 90035 USA

**Wilson, Tracy** — Ice Dancer, Sportscaster
CTV-TV, PO Box 9, Station O, Scarborough ON M4A 2M9, Canada

**Wilson, Trevor** — Basketball Player
824 15th St, Hermosa Beach CA 90254, USA

**Wilson, Trevor K** — Baseball Player
5173 Woodcrest Lane, Lake Oswego OR 97035, USA

**Wilson, Trisha** — Interior Designer
Wilson Assoc, 3811 Turtle Creek Dr, #1500, Dallas TX 75219, USA

**Wilson, Vance A** — Baseball Player
6368 Elizabeth Ave, Springdale AR 72762, USA

**Wilson, Wayne M** — Football Player
183 Willowdale Dr, Shepherdstown WV 25443, USA

**Wilson, William** — Basketball Player
130 Belmont St, Englewood NJ 07631, USA

**Wilson, William H (Mookie)** — Baseball Player
1111 Heyward Wilson Road, Eastover SC 29044, USA

**Wilson, William J** — Sociologist
Harvard University, Kennedy School of Government, Cambridge MA 02138, USA

**Wilson, Willie J** — Baseball Player
18 Vianney Ave, Scarborough ON M1L 4V4, Canada

**Wilson, Woody** — Cartoonist (Rex Morgan MD)
King Features Syndicate, 300 W 57th St, #1500, New York NY 10019 USA

**Wilson-Johnson, David R** — Opera Singer
28 Englefield Road, London N1 4ET, England

**Wilson-Sampras, Bridgette L** — Actress, Singer
Abrams Artists, 9200 W Sunset Blvd, #1125, West Hollywood CA 90069 USA

**Wilton, Penelope** — Actress
I C M Partners, 10250 Constellation Blvd, #900, Los Angeles CA 90067 USA

**Wiltsie, Jennifer** — Actress
Gavin Barker Assoc, 2D Wimpole St, London W1G 0EB, England

**Wimbley, Kamerion** — Football Player
17400 Sawgrass Circle, North Royalton OH 44133, USA

**Wimmer, Brian** — Actor
Integrated Mgmt, 1041 N Formosa Ave, West Hollywood CA 90046, USA

**Wimmer, Kurt** — Director
Creative Artists Agency, 2000 Ave of Stars, #100, Los Angeles CA 90067 USA

**Wimmer, Scott** — Auto Racing Driver
Richard Childress Racing, 425 Industrial Dr, Welcome NC 27374, USA

**Winans, BeBe** — Singer
Creative Artists Agency, 2000 Ave of Stars, #100, Los Angeles CA 90067 USA

**Winans, CeCe** — Singer
C W Entertainment, 115 Penn Warren Dr, #300-377, Brentwood TN

**Winans, Jeff D** — Football Player
272 Madeira Circle, Saint Petersburg FL 33715, USA

**Winans, Mario** — Singer
Bad Boy Entertainment, 1440 Broadway, #16, New York NY 10018 USA

**Winans, Matthew** — Baseball Umpire
21 Saint George Place, Sandy Hook CT 06482, USA

**Winans, Vicki** — Singer
Groove Entertainment, 1005 N Alfred St, #2, West Hollywood CA 90069, USA

**Winant, Scott** — Producer, Director
Hansen Jacobson Teller, 450 N Roxbury Dr, #800, Beverly Hills CA 90210 USA

**Winborne, Hughes** — Editor
I C M Partners, 10250 Constellation Blvd, #900, Los Angeles CA 90067 USA

**Winborne, Jamie L** — Football Player
195 Roscoe Lee Circle, Wetumpka AL 36092, USA

**Winbush, Angela** — Singer, Songwriter
Joyce Agency, 370 Harrison Ave, Harrison NY 10528, USA

**Winbush, Camille** — Actress
Stone Manners Salners, 9911 W Pico Blvd, #1400, Los Angeles CA 90035 USA

**Winbush, Troy** — Actor
A P A Talent/Literary Agency, 405 S Beverly Dr, #300, Beverly Hills CA 90212 USA

**Winceniak, Edward J (Ed)** — Baseball Player
10828 S Ave O, Chicago IL 60617, USA

**Wincer, Simon G** — Director
Creative Artists Agency, 2000 Ave of Stars, #100, Los Angeles CA 90067 USA

**Winchester, Jesse** — Singer, Pianist, Songwriter
Keith Case Assoc, 1025 17th Ave S, #200, Nashville TN 37212 USA

**Winchester, Philip** — Actor
Independent Talent Group, 40 Whitfield St, London W1T 2RH, England

**Winchester, Scott J** — Baseball Player
4705 Oakridge Dr, Midland MI 48640, USA

**Winchester, Simon** — Writer
Harper Collins Publishers, 10 E 53rd St, Cellar 1, New York NY 10022 USA

**Wincott, Michael** — Actor
Edith Grove Inc, 5900 Wilshire Blvd, #2250, Los Angeles CA 90036, USA

**Wind, Sabrina** — Producer
Paradigm Agency, 360 N Crescent Dr, North Building, Beverly Hills CA 90210 USA

**Winder, Sammy** — Football Player
Winder Construction Co, 4823 Green Crossing Road, Jackson MS 39213, USA

**Windhorn, Gordon R (Gordie)** — Baseball Player
145 Bent Creek Road, Danville VA 24540, USA

**Windis, Tony J** — Basketball Player
404 1st St, Rawlins WY 82301, USA

**Windon, Stephen F** — Cinematographer
PO Box 659, Northbridge, Sydney NSW 2063, Australia

**Wilson - Windon**

| | |
|---|---|
| **Windsor, Barbara** | Actress, Comedienne |
| 104 Crouch Hill, London NB 9EA, England | |
| **Windsor, David** | Baseball Player |
| 23972 Dublin St, Lake Forest CA 92630, USA | |
| **Windsor, Robert E (Bob)** | Football Player |
| 2625 Legends Way, Ellicott City MD 21042, USA | |
| **Wine, Robert P (Bobbie), Sr** | Baseball Player, Manager |
| 2614 Woodland Ave, Eagleville PA 19403, USA | |
| **Winegardner, Mark** | Writer |
| Florida State University, English Dept, Tallahassee FL 32306, USA | |
| **Wineland, David J** | Nobel Physics Laureate |
| National Institute of Standards & Technology, 325 Broadway, Boulder CO 80305, USA | |
| **Winfield, Antoine D** | Football Player |
| 10451 White Tail Crossing, Eden Prairie MN 55347, USA | |
| **Winfield, David M (Dave)** | Baseball Player |
| 2235 Stratford Circle, Los Angeles CA 90077, USA | |
| **Winfield, Leroy (Lee)** | Basketball Player |
| 7638 Forest View Dr, Saint Louis MO 63121, USA | |
| **Winfield, Rodney M** | Artist |
| 3483 Ocean Ave, Carmel CA 93923, USA | |
| **Winfrey, Oprah** | Entertainer, Actress |
| Harpo Productions, 110 N Carpenter St, Chicago IL 60607, USA | |
| **Winfrey, Roy** | Baseball Player |
| 2903 Renfro Dr NW, Atlanta GA 30318, USA | |
| **Wing, Andrea** | Photographer |
| Crown Bay Marina, #310, PM Box 10, Saint Thomas VI 00802, USA | |
| **Wing, Sean** | Actor |
| Innovative Artists, 1505 10th St, Santa Monica CA 90401 USA | |
| **Wingate, David G S** | Basketball Player |
| 11404 Glaetzer Lane, Charlotte NC 28270, USA | |
| **Winger, Debra** | Actress |
| I C M Partners, 10250 Constellation Blvd, #900, Los Angeles CA 90067 USA | |
| **Wingti, Paias** | Prime Minister, Papua New Guinea |
| Marea Haus, Waigani, PO Box 6605, Port Moresby, Boroko, Papua New Guinea | |
| **Wink, Chris** | Entertainer (Blue Man Group) |
| Blue Man Productions, 411 Lafayette St, #300, New York NY 10003, USA | |
| **Winkelried, Jon** | Financier |
| Goldman Sachs Co, 85 Broad St, Building 85, New York NY 10004, USA | |
| **Winkler, Angela** | Actress |
| Erna Baumbauer Mgmt, Kaplerstr 2, 81679 Munich, Germany | |
| **Winkler, Hans-Gunter** | Equestrian |
| Dr Rau Allee 48, 48231 Warendorf, Germany | |
| **Winkler, Henry** | Actor, Producer |
| PO Box 49914, Los Angeles CA 90049, USA | |
| **Winkler, Irwin** | Director, Producer |
| Irwin Winkler Productions, 211 S Beverly Dr, #220, Beverly Hills CA 90212, USA | |
| **Winkler, Max** | Actor, Writer, Producer |
| Creative Artists Agency, 2000 Ave of Stars, #100, Los Angeles CA 90067 USA | |
| **Winkles, Bobby B** | Baseball Manager |
| 78452 Calle Huerta, La Quinta CA 92253, USA | |
| **Winn, D Randolph (Randy)** | Baseball Player |
| 59 Leeds Court E, Danville CA 94526, USA | |
| **Winn, James F (Jim)** | Baseball Player |
| 3440 S Delaware Ave, #123, Springfield MO 65804, USA | |
| **Winnefeld, James A (Sandy), Jr** | Navy Admiral |
| Vice Chairman, Joint Chiefs of Staff, Pentagon, Washington DC 20318 USA | |
| **Winnick, Katheryn** | Actress |
| Gersh Agency, 9465 Wilshire Blvd, #600, Beverly Hills CA 90212 USA | |
| **Winningham, Herman S (Herm)** | Baseball Player |
| 1542 Belleville Road, Orangeburg SC 29115, USA | |
| **Winningham, Mare** | Actress |
| I F A Talent Agency, 8730 W Sunset Blvd, #490, West Hollywood CA 90069 USA | |
| **Winslet, Kate** | Actress |
| United Agents, 12-26 Lexington St, London W1F 0LE, England | |
| **Winslow, Dan** | Singer, Guitarist (Trashmen) |
| H T M/Headline Talent Mgmt, 39398 Moonlight Bay Trail, Pelican Rapids MN 56572 USA | |
| **Winslow, Kellen B, II** | Football Player |
| 2431 Cornerstone, Westlake OH 44145, USA | |
| **Winslow, Kellen B, Sr** | Football Player, Administrator |
| Central State University, Athletic Dept, PO Box 1004, Wilberforce OH 45384, USA | |
| **Winslow, Michael** | Actor, Comedian |
| Venture I A B, 3211 Cahuenga Blvd W, #104, Los Angeles CA 90068, USA | |
| **Winstead, Mary Elizabeth** | Actress |
| Creative Artists Agency, 2000 Ave of Stars, #100, Los Angeles CA 90067 USA | |
| **Winston, Charlie** | Singer, Songwriter |
| Agency Group Ltd, 142 W 57th St, #600, New York NY 10019 USA | |
| **Winston, Eric J** | Football Player |
| 4811 Palmetto St, Bellaire, TX 77401, USA | |
| **Winston, George** | Pianist, Composer |
| High Road Touring, 751 Bridgeway, #200, Sausalito CA 94965 USA | |
| **Winston, Roy C** | Football Player |
| 708 Highway 401, Napoleonville LA 70390, USA | |
| **Winstone, Ray** | Actor |
| C A M, 111 Shoreditch High St, #400, London E1 6JN, England | |
| **Winter, Blaise** | Football Player |
| 3520 Rose Mallow Loop, Oviedo FL 32766, USA | |
| **Winter, Donald** | Government Official |
| Navy Department, Secretary's Office, Pentagon, Washington DC 20350, USA | |
| **Winter, Edgar** | Singer, Guitarist, Keyboardist |
| Hook Entertainment, 26033 Mulholland Highway, Malibu CA 91302, USA | |
| **Winter, Edward D** | Actor |
| 32070 Waterside Lane, Westlake Village CA 91361, USA | |
| **Winter, Eric** | Actor |
| United Talent Agency, U T A Plaza, 9336 Civic Center Dr, Beverly Hills CA 90210 USA | |
| **Winter, Fred (Tex)** | Basketball Coach |
| Los Angeles Lakers, Staples Center, 1111 S Figueroa St, Los Angeles CA 90015 USA | |

**W**

**Windsor - Winter**

| | |
|---|---|
| **Winter, Johnny** <br> Bullseye Mgmt, PO Box 3207, Stamford CT 06905, USA | Singer, Guitarist |
| **Winter, Olaf** <br> An der Pirschheide 28, 14471 Potsdam, Germany | Canoeing Athlete |
| **Winter, Paul T** <br> Living Music Records, PO Box 72, Litchfield CT 06759, USA | Jazz, New Age Musician |
| **Winter, Ralph K, Jr** <br> US Court of Appeals, 141 Church St, New Haven CT 06510, USA | Judge |
| **Winter, Terence P** <br> Creative Artists Agency, 2000 Ave of Stars, #100, Los Angeles CA 90067 USA | Writer, Producer |
| **Winter, William F** <br> 633 N State St, Jackson MS 39202, USA | Governor, MS |
| **Winterbottom, Michael** <br> Independent Talent Group, 40 Whitfield St, London W1T 2RH, England | Director, Producer |
| **Winterhart, Paul** <br> Little Big Man, 39A Grammercy Park N, #1C, New York NY 10010, USA | Drummer (Kula Shaker) |
| **Winters, Abby** <br> PO Box 343, Fitzroy VIC 3065, Australia | Photographer |
| **Winters, Brian J** <br> 10111 Inverness Main St, #207, Englewood CO 80112, USA | Basketball Player, Coach |
| **Winters, Dean** <br> United Talent Agency, U T A Plaza, 9336 Civic Center Dr, Beverly Hills CA 90210 USA | Actor |
| **Winters, Edward G, III** <br> Commander, Special Warfare Command, 2000 Trident Way, Coronado CA 92155 USA | Navy Admiral |
| **Winters, Frank M** <br> 820 17th St, Union City NJ 07087, USA | Football Player |
| **Winters, Lisa** <br> Playboy Promotions, 2706 Media Center Dr, Los Angeles CA 90065 USA | Model |
| **Winters, Michael** <br> Mitchell K Stubbs Assoc, 8695 W Washington Blvd, #204, Culver City CA 90232 USA | Actor |
| **Winters, Michael J (Mike)** <br> 13644 Boquita Dr, Del Mar CA 92014, USA | Baseball Umpire |
| **Winters, Mickey** <br> Playboy Promotions, 2706 Media Center Dr, Los Angeles CA 90065 USA | Model |
| **Winther, Peter** <br> Gersh Agency, 9465 Wilshire Blvd, #600, Beverly Hills CA 90212 USA | Director, Producer, Writer |
| **Wintour, Anna** <br> Vogue, Editor's Office, 4 Times Square, #1200, New York NY 10036, USA | Editor |
| **Winwood, Stephen L (Steve)** <br> Trinley Cottage, Trinley, Gloucester GL19 4EU, England | Singer, Musician (Traffic); Songwriter |
| **Wire, Coy M** <br> 586 Park Dr NE, Atlanta GA 30306, USA | Football Player |
| **Wire, William S, II** <br> 706 Overton Park, Nashville TN 37215, USA | Businessman |
| **Wirth, Billy** <br> Arete Talent Agency, 454 N Robertson Blvd, Los Angeles CA 90048, USA | Actor, Director |
| **Wirth, Timothy E** <br> United Nations Foundation, 1225 Connecticut Ave NW, Washington DC 20036, USA | Senator, CO |
| **Wise, L DeWayne** <br> 709 Old Lexington Highway, Chapin SC 29036, USA | Baseball Player |
| **Wise, Phillip V (Phil)** <br> 11511 Poppy St NW, Minneapolis MN 55433, USA | Football Player |
| **Wise, Phyllis M** <br> University of Washington, President's Office, Gerberding Hall, Seattle WA 98195, USA | Neurobiologist, Educator |
| **Wise, Ray** <br> Abrams Artists, 9200 W Sunset Blvd, #1125, West Hollywood CA 90069 USA | Actor |
| **Wise, Richard C (Rick)** <br> 15160 NW Oakhills Dr, Beaverton OR 97006, USA | Baseball Player |
| **Wise, Willie M** <br> 2320 185th Place NE, Redmond WA 98052, USA | Basketball Player |
| **Wiseman, Brian** <br> 5917 Delores St, #B, Houston TX 77057, USA | Ice Hockey Player |
| **Wiseman, Frederick** <br> Zipporah Films, 1 Richdale Ave, #4, Cambridge MA 02140, USA | Producer |
| **Wiseman, Len R** <br> Creative Artists Agency, 2000 Ave of Stars, #100, Los Angeles CA 90067 USA | Director, Producer, Writer |
| **Wiseman, Mac** <br> PO Box 17028, Nashville TN 37217, USA | Singer |
| **Wish Bone** <br> Life Entertainment, 15441 Red Hill Ave, #G, Tustin CA 92780, USA | Rap Artist (Bone Thugs-N-Harmony) |
| **Wishart, Leonard P, III** <br> 19360 Magnolia Grove Square, #315, Leesburg VA 20176, USA | Army General |
| **Wisniewski, Andreas** <br> Gregory David Mayo, Reinhardtstra 35, 10117 Berlin, Germany | Actor |
| **Wisniewski, Stephen A (Steve)** <br> 36 El Alamo Court, Danville CA 94526, USA | Football Player |
| **Wisniewski, Tom** <br> W M E Entertainment, 9601 Wilshire Blvd, #300, Beverly Hills CA 90210 USA | Guitarist (MxPx) |
| **Wisocky, Rebecca** <br> Connor Ankrum Assoc, 1680 Vine St, #1016, Los Angeles CA 90028, USA | Actress |
| **Wisoff, Peter J K (Jeff)** <br> 4268 Brindisi Place, Pleasanton CA 94566, USA | Astronaut |
| **Wissman, David A (Dave)** <br> PO Box 38, Derby VT 05829, USA | Baseball Player |
| **Wiste, Jim** <br> 701 S University Blvd, Denver CO 80209, USA | Ice Hockey Player |
| **Wistert, Albert A (Ox)** <br> 1411 NE Olson Dr, Grants Pass OR 97526, USA | Football Player |
| **Wistrom, Grant A** <br> 1625 E Delmar St, Springfield MO 65804, USA | Football Player |
| **Witasick, Gerald A (Jay)** <br> 200 Wellington Court, Bel Air MD 21014, USA | Baseball Player |
| **Witcher, Richard V (Dick)** <br> 2031 E Taxidea Way, Phoenix AZ 85048, USA | Football Player |
| **Withem, Shannon B** <br> 39668 Dorchester Circle, Canton MI 48188, USA | Baseball Player |

**Withers, Bill** — Singer, Songwriter
Mattie Music Group, PO Box 16698, Beverly Hills CA 90209, USA
**Withers, Jane** — Actress
Keller & Vanderneth Business Mgmt, 1133 Broadway, #911, New York NY 10010, USA
**Withers, Pick** — Drummer (Dire Straits)
Damage Mgmt, 16 Lambton Place, London W11 2SH, England
**Witherspoon, John** — Actor, Comedian, Producer
Levity Entertainment, 6701 Center Drive W, #1111, Los Angeles CA 90045 USA
**Witherspoon, Reese** — Actress
Creative Artists Agency, 2000 Ave of Stars, #100, Los Angeles CA 90067 USA
**Witherspoon, Tim** — Boxer
Shuler Memorial Boxing Gym, 750 N Brooklyn St, Philadelphia PA 19104, USA
**Witherspoon, William C (Will)** — Football Player
4535 Wayland Dr, Nashville TN 37215, USA
**Witiuk, Doris** — Baseball Player
11821 N Hemlock St, Spokane WA 99218, USA
**Witiuk, Steve** — Ice Hockey Player
6 Leacock Ave, Winnipeg MB R3K 0G2, Canada
**Witkin, Jerome** — Artist
201 Whitestone Dr, Syracuse NY 13215, USA
**Witkin, Joel-Peter** — Photographer
1707 Five Points Road SW, Albuquerque NM 87105, USA
**Witkop, Bernhard** — Chemist
3807 Montrose Driveway, Chevy Chase MD 20815, USA
**Witman, Jon D** — Football Player
568 Woodsview Lane, Hellam PA 17406, USA
**Witmer, Tamara** — Model
Playboy Promotions, 2706 Media Center Dr, Los Angeles CA 90065 USA
**Witmeyer, Ronald H (Ron)** — Baseball Player
PO Box 763, Rancho Santa Fe CA 92067, USA
**Witt, Alicia** — Actress
Brillstein Entertainment Partners, 9150 Wilshire Blvd, #350, Beverly Hills CA 90212 USA
**Witt, Brendan** — Ice Hockey Player
691 Park Ave, Huntington NY 11743, USA
**Witt, George A** — Baseball Player
2209 Catalina St, Laguna Beach CA 92651, USA
**Witt, Howard** — Actor
Gage Group, 450 7th Ave, #1809, New York NY 10123 USA
**Witt, Katarina** — Figure Skater, Model
Gottmann GmbH, Schwalbacher Str 48, 65760 Eschborn, Germany
**Witt, Kevin J** — Baseball Player
6350 Concho Bay Dr, Houston TX 77041, USA
**Witt, Michael A (Mike)** — Baseball Player
37 Poppy Hills Road, Laguna Nigel CA 92677, USA
**Witt, Paul Junger** — Writer, Producer, Director
16032 Valley Vista Blvd, Encino CA 91436, USA
**Witt, Robert A (Bobby)** — Baseball Player
4601 Winewood Court, Colleyville TX 76034, USA
**Witt, Robert E** — Educator
University of Alabama, President's Office, PO Box 870100, Tuscaloosa AL 35487, USA
**Witt, Vicki** — Model
Playboy Promotions, 2706 Media Center Dr, Los Angeles CA 90065 USA
**Witte, Luke** — Basketball Player
3223 Arbor Pointe Dr, Charlotte NC 28210, USA
**Witten, C Jason** — Football Player
501 King Ranch Road, Southlake TX 76092, USA
**Witten, Edward** — Theoretical Physicist, Mathematician
Institute for Advanced Study, Einstein Lane, Princeton NJ 08540 USA
**Witter, Cherie** — Model, Actress
Playboy Promotions, 2706 Media Center Dr, Los Angeles CA 90065 USA
**Witter, Junior** — Boxer
Cybersportsbox, 23 Minna Road, Sheffield, South York S3 9AZ, England
**Witter, Karen** — Actress, Model
H/H/M, 247 S Beverly Dr, #102, Beverly Hills CA 90212, USA
**Witting, Steve** — Actor
Paradigm Agency, 360 N Crescent Dr, North Building, Beverly Hills CA 90210 USA
**Wittman, Randy S** — Basketball Player, Coach
8646 French Curve, Eden Prairie MN 55347, USA
**Witty, Chris** — Speed Skater
2644 E 2940 S, Salt Lake City UT 84109, USA
**Witucki, Casimir L (Cas)** — Football Player
3909 Spring Terrace, #248, Temple Hills MD 20748, USA
**Wlaschiha, Tom** — Actor
Agentur Hubchen, Pariser Str 20, 10707 Berlin, Germany
**Wobble, Jah** — Bassist (Public Image Limited)
Billions Corp, 3522 W Armitage Ave, Chicago IL 60647 USA
**Wockel-Eckert, Barbel** — Track Athlete
Im Bangert 61, 64750 Lutzelbach, Germany
**Wockenfuss, John B** — Baseball Player
26 Wallamsey Lane, Chesapeake City MD 21915, USA
**Woelki, Rainer M Cardinal** — Religious Leader
Archdiocese, Niederwallstr 8-9, 10017 Berlin, Germany
**Woerner, Scott A** — Football Player
6570 Highway 356, Sautee Nacoochee GA 30571, USA
**Woerth, Douglas** — Labor Leader
Airline Pilots Union, 535 Herndon Parkway, Herndon VA 20170, USA
**Woertz, Patricia** — Businesswoman
Archer Daniels Midland Co, 4666 Faries Parkway, #1, Decatur IL 62526, USA
**Wofford, Harris L** — Senator, PA
955 26th St NW, #501, Washington DC 20037, USA
**Woggon, Bill** — Cartoonist (Katy Keene)
2724 Cabot Court, Thousand Oaks CA 91360, USA
**Wohl, Bess** — Actress, Writer
Untitled Entertainment, 350 S Beverly Dr, #200, Beverly Hills CA 90212 USA
**Wohl, David B (Dave)** — Basketball Player, Coach, Executive
137 Morley Circle, Melville NY 11747, USA

**W**

**Wohlberg, Jeffrey** — Religious Leader, Rabbi
Adas Israel Congregation, 565 Broadway, Passaic NJ 07055, USA
**Wohlers, Mark E** — Baseball Player
135 Old Cedar Lane, Alpharetta GA 30004, USA
**Wohlford, James E (Jim)** — Baseball Player
24186 Lomitas Dr, Woodlake CA 93286, USA
**Wohlhuter, Richard C (Rick)** — Track Athlete
175 Dickinson Dr, Wheaton IL 60189, USA
**Wohlwender-Fricker, Marian** — Baseball Player
15210 Portside Dr, #401, Fort Myers FL 33908, USA
**Woit, Benedict F (Benny)** — Ice Hockey Player
607-20 Harding Blvd W, Richmond Hill ON L4C 9S4, Canada
**Woiwode, Larry** — Writer
State University of New York, English Dept, Binghamton NY 13901, USA
**Wojciechowski, John S** — Football Player
13317 Clyde Road, Holly MI 48442, USA
**Wojtowicz, R P** — Labor Leader
Railway Carmen Union, 3 Research Place, Rockville MD 20850, USA
**Wolanin, Craig** — Ice Hockey Player
4891 Gallagher Road, Rochester MI 48306, USA
**Wolcott, Gregory** — Actor
PO Box 622, Canoga Park CA 91305, USA
**Wolcott, Robert W (Bob)** — Baseball Player
3323 Bryson Way, Medford OR 97504, USA
**Wolczanski, Peter T** — Chemist
Cornell University, Chemistry Dept, Ithaca NY 14853, USA
**Wolde-Giorgis Lucha, Girma** — President, Ethiopia
President's Office, Presidential Palace, PO Box 1362, Addis Ababa, Ethiopia
**Wolf, Dale E** — Governor, DE
4830 Kennett Pike, #3221, Wilmington DE 19807, USA
**Wolf, David A** — Astronaut
Indianapolis Children's Museum, 3000 N Meridian St, Indianapolis IN 46208, USA
**Wolf, Dick** — Producer
W M E Entertainment, 9601 Wilshire Blvd, #300, Beverly Hills CA 90210 USA
**Wolf, James (Jim)** — Baseball Umpire
1507 E Glenhaven Dr, Phoenix AZ 85048, USA
**Wolf, Joseph F (Joe)** — Football Player
2324 Lehigh Parkway N, Allentown PA 18103, USA
**Wolf, Josh** — Actor, Comedian, Writer
Parallel Entertainment, 9420 Wilshire Blvd, #250, Beverly Hills CA 90212 USA
**Wolf, Naomi** — Writer
Royce Carlton Inc, 866 United Nations Plaza, #587, New York NY 10017, USA
**Wolf, Peter** — Singer (J Geils Band)
Front Line Mgmt, 1100 Glendon Ave, #2000, Los Angeles CA 90024 USA
**Wolf, Randall C (Randy)** — Baseball Player
8054 Royer Ave, Canoga Park CA 91304, USA
**Wolf, Sally** — Opera Singer
Columbia Artists Mgmt Inc, 1790 Broadway, #702, New York NY 10019 USA
**Wolf, Scott** — Actor
Innovative Artists, 1505 10th St, Santa Monica CA 90401 USA
**Wolf, Sigrid** — Alpine Skier
6652 Elbigenalp 45A, Austria
**Wolf, Vicente** — Interior Designer
Vicente Wolf Assoc, 333 W 39th St, New York NY 10018, USA
**Wolf, Walter B (Wally)** — Baseball Player
18580 Corte Fresco, Rancho Santa Fe CA 92091, USA
**Wolfe, Art** — Photographer
520 1st Ave S, Seattle WA 98104, USA
**Wolfe, Bernard (Bernie)** — Ice Hockey Player
8012 Glenbrook Road, Bethesda MD 20814, USA
**Wolfe, Brian** — Baseball Player
32524 Sprucewood Way, Lake Elsinore CA 92532, USA
**Wolfe, Collette** — Actress
Gersh Agency, 9465 Wilshire Blvd, #600, Beverly Hills CA 90212 USA
**Wolfe, George C** — Director
Loeb & Loeb, 10100 Santa Monica Blvd, #2200, Los Angeles CA 90067 USA
**Wolfe, James** — Sculptor
35 Cobe Road, Northport ME 04849, USA
**Wolfe, Laurence A (Larry)** — Baseball Player
5200 Blossomwood Court, Fair Oaks CA 95628, USA
**Wolfe, Nathan D** — Virologist
Global Viral Forcasting Initiative, 1 Sutter, #600, San Francisco CA 94104, USA
**Wolfe, Ralph S** — Microbiologist
University of Illinois, Microbiology Dept, Burrill Hall, Urbana IL 61801, USA
**Wolfe, Robert H** — Producer, Writer
I C M Partners, 10250 Constellation Blvd, #900, Los Angeles CA 90067 USA
**Wolfe, Sterling** — Actor
2609 Wyoming Ave, #A, Burbank CA 91505, USA
**Wolfe, Thad A** — Air Force General
4790 Longwood Point, Colorado Springs CO 80906, USA
**Wolfe, Thomas K (Tom), Jr** — Writer
Felker Toczak Gellman, 10880 Wilshire Blvd, #2070, Los Angeles CA 90024 USA
**Wolfenden of Westcott, John F** — Educator
White House, Guildford Road, Westcott near Dorking, Surrey, England
**Wolfensohn, James D** — Financier
James D Wolfensohn Co, 599 Lexington Ave, New York NY 10022, USA
**Wolfenstein, Lincoln** — Physicist
Carnegie-Mellon University, Physics Dept, 5000 Forbes, Pittsburgh PA 15213, USA
**Wolfermann, Klaus** — Track Athlete
Puma Sportschu, Postfach 1420, 91074 Herzogenaurach, Germany
**Wolfe-Simon, Felisa** — Biogeochemist
N A S A Astrobiology, Harvard University, 20 Oxford St Cambridge MA 02138, USA
**Wolff, Alexander D (Alex)** — Actor, Singer (Naked Brothers Band)
Creative Artists Agency, 2000 Ave of Stars, #100, Los Angeles CA 90067 USA
**Wolff, Bob** — Sportscaster
3 Salisbury Point, #2E, Nyack NY 10960, USA

**Wohlberg - Wolff**

| | |
|---|---|
| **Wolff, Christian** | Composer |
| Agentur Alexander, Lamontstr 9, 81679 Munich, Germany | |
| **Wolff, Christoph J** | Educator |
| 182 Washington St, Belmont MA 02478, USA | |
| **Wolff, Hugh** | Conductor |
| Van Walsum Mgmt, Tower Building, 11 York Road, London SE1 7NX, England | |
| **Wolff, Nathaniel M (Nat)** | Singer (Naked Brothers Band), Songwriter |
| Creative Artists Agency, 2000 Ave of Stars, #100, Los Angeles CA 90067 USA | |
| **Wolff, Sanford I** | Labor Leader |
| 8141 Broadway, New York NY 10023, USA | |
| **Wolff, Tobias J A** | Writer |
| Stanford University, English Dept, Stanford CA 94305, USA | |
| **Wolff, Torben** | Biologist, Zoologist |
| Hesseltoften 12, 2900 Hellerup, Denmark | |
| **Wolfley, Ronald P (Ron)** | Football Player |
| 17612 N 41st Place, Phoenix AZ 85032, USA | |
| **Wolford, William C (Will)** | Football Player |
| 205 Waterleaf Way, Louisville KY 40207, USA | |
| **Wolfowitz, Paul D** | Financier, Government Official |
| American Express Institute, 1150 17th St NW, Washington DC 20036, USA | |
| **Wolfram, Lea** | Actress |
| Casting-Agentur Schubert, Suarezstr 27, 14057 Berlin, Germany | |
| **Wolk, James** | Actor |
| W M E Entertainment, 9601 Wilshire Blvd, #300, Beverly Hills CA 90210 USA | |
| **Woll, Deborah Ann** | Actress |
| Creative Artists Agency, 2000 Ave of Stars, #100, Los Angeles CA 90067 USA | |
| **Wollack, Brad** | Actor, Writer, Producer |
| Creative Artists Agency, 2000 Ave of Stars, #100, Los Angeles CA 90067 USA | |
| **Wollman, Harvey L** | Governor, SD |
| RR 1 Box 43, Hitchcock SD 57348, USA | |
| **Wollman, Roger L** | Judge |
| US Court of Appeals, Federal Building, 400 S Phillips, Sioux Falls SD 57104, USA | |
| **Wolodarsky, Wallace (Wally)** | Producer, Writer |
| I C M Partners, 10250 Constellation Blvd, #900, Los Angeles CA 90067 USA | |
| **Wolpe, David** | Religious Leader, Rabbi |
| Sinai Temple, 10400 Wilshire Blvd, Los Angeles CA 90024, USA | |
| **Wolpe, Lenny** | Actor |
| Gage Group, 450 7th Ave, #1809, New York NY 10123 USA | |
| **Wolski, Wojciech (Wojtek)** | Ice Hockey Player |
| Washington Capitals, 627 N Glebe Road, #850, Arlington VA 22203 USA | |
| **Wolstenholme, Christopher T (Chris)** | Bassist (Muse) |
| Hall or Nothing P R, 35-37 Parkgate Road, London SW11 4NP, England | |
| **Wolters, Kara** | Basketball Player |
| 137 Westfield Dr, Holliston MA 01746, USA | |
| **Woltman, Rhea A** | Astronaut |
| 17 Polo Circle, Colorado Springs CO 80906, USA | |
| **Womack, Anthony D (Tony)** | Baseball Player |
| 8301 Marcliffe Court, Waxhaw NC 28173, USA | |
| **Womack, Floyd S** | Football Player |
| 105 Grandview Circle, Brandon MS 39047, USA | |
| **Womack, Horace G (Dooley)** | Baseball Player |
| 209 Weeping Cherry Lane, Columbia SC 29212, USA | |
| **Womack, James E** | Biologist, Agricultural Researcher |
| 2105 Farley, College Station TX 77845, USA | |
| **Womack, Lee Ann** | Singer |
| Erv Woolsey, 1000 18th Ave S, Nashville TN 37212, USA | |
| **Womack, Robert D (Bobby)** | Singer, Guitarist, Songwriter |
| Backstreet Booking, PO Box 18, Cincinnati OH 45203, USA | |
| **Womble, Royce C** | Football Player |
| 6350 Newt Patterson Road, Mansfield TX 76063, USA | |
| **Won Hye-Kyung** | Speed Skater |
| Skating Union, 88 Bangyee-Dong, Songpaku, Seoul 138 749, South Korea | |
| **Wonder, Stevie** | Singer, Songwriter |
| Steveland Morris Music, 4616 W Magnolia Blvd, Burbank CA 91505, USA | |
| **Wonder, Wayne** | Singer, Songwriter |
| Headline Entertainment, 8 Haughton Ave, Kingston 10, Jamaica | |
| **Wonders, Rich** | Bowler |
| 720 Augusta St, Racine WI 53402, USA | |
| **Wondolowski, Christopher E (Chris)** | Soccer Player |
| San Jose Earthquakes, 451 El Camino Real, #220, Santa Clara CA 95050 USA | |
| **Wong Kar Wai** | Director |
| Creative Artists Agency, 2000 Ave of Stars, #100, Los Angeles CA 90067 USA | |
| **Wong, Bradley D (B D)** | Actor |
| Gersh Agency, 9465 Wilshire Blvd, #600, Beverly Hills CA 90212 USA | |
| **Wong, James** | Director, Producer, Writer |
| W M E Entertainment, 9601 Wilshire Blvd, #300, Beverly Hills CA 90210 USA | |
| **Wong, Kailee W** | Football Player |
| 5410 Valerie St, Bellaire TX 77401, USA | |
| **Wong, Kirk** | Actor, Director |
| Global Artists Agency, 6253 Hollywood Blvd, #508, Los Angeles CA 90028, USA | |
| **Wong, Russell** | Actor |
| Innovative Artists, 1505 10th St, Santa Monica CA 90401 USA | |
| **Wong, Sue** | Fashion Designer |
| 3030 W 6th St, Los Angeles CA 90020, USA | |
| **Wong-Staal, Flossie** | Molecular Biologist |
| University of California, Molecular Biology Dept, La Jolla CA 92093, USA | |
| **Wonsley, George I** | Football Player |
| 2875 Spring Meadow Court, Indianapolis IN 46268, USA | |
| **Woo, John** | Director, Producer |
| Lion Rock Productions, 5100 Goldleaf Circle, #230, Los Angeles CA 90056, USA | |
| **Wood** | Drummer (British Sea Power) |
| Agency Group Ltd, 361-373 City Road, London EC1V 1PQ, England | |
| **Wood, Adam K C** | Lieutenant Governor, Isle of Man |
| Lieutenant Governor's Office, Government House, Onchan, Isle of Man | |
| **Wood, Annie** | Actress |
| Amsel Eisenstadt Frazier, 5055 Wilshire Blvd, #865, Los Angeles CA 90036 USA | |

**W**

**Wolff - Wood**

**Wood, Anthony** — Businessman
Roku Co, 12980 Saratoga Ave, #D, Saratoga CA 95070, USA

**Wood, Barbara** — Writer
1450 University Ave, #F161, Riverside CA 92507, USA

**Wood, Brenton** — Singer
Groove Entertainment, 1005 N Alfred St, #2, West Hollywood CA 90069, USA

**Wood, C Norman** — Air Force General
214 Lower Field Road, Dunnsville VA 22454, USA

**Wood, Carolyn** — Swimmer
4380 SW 86th Ave, Portland OR 97225, USA

**Wood, Carri** — Golfer
2001 Sabal Ridge Court, #H, Palm Beach Gardens FL 33418, USA

**Wood, Charles G** — Writer
Gordon Dickinson, 2 Crescent Grove, London SW4 7AH, England

**Wood, David L** — Basketball Player
585 White Quartz Dr, Reno NV 89511, USA

**Wood, Diane P** — Judge
US Court of Appeals, 219 S Dearborn St, Chicago IL 60604, USA

**Wood, Duane S** — Football Player
PO Box 601, Wilburton OK 74578, USA

**Wood, Elijah** — Actor
W M E Entertainment, 9601 Wilshire Blvd, #300, Beverly Hills CA 90210 USA

**Wood, Evan Rachel** — Actress
Creative Artists Agency, 2000 Ave of Stars, #100, Los Angeles CA 90067 USA

**Wood, Glen** — Auto Racing Executive
57 Rhody Creek Loop, Stuart VA 24171, USA

**Wood, Gordon S** — Historian
77 Keene St, Providence RI 02906, USA

**Wood, Jacob (Jake), Jr** — Baseball Player
9129 Daytona Dr, Pensacola FL 32506, USA

**Wood, Janet** — Actress
Acme Talent, 4727 Wilshire Blvd, #333, Los Angeles CA 90010, USA

**Wood, Jason W** — Baseball Player
9899 N Cascade Dr, Fresno CA 93730, USA

**Wood, John A** — Astrophysicist, Geologist
1716 Cambridge St, #16, Cambridge MA 02138, USA

**Wood, Kerry L** — Baseball Player
6838 E Chey Dr, Paradise Valley AZ 85253, USA

**Wood, Kimba M** — Judge
US District Court House, 40 Foley Square, #104, New York NY 10007, USA

**Wood, Lana** — Actress
1131 Oriole Circle, Fillmore CA 93015, USA

**Wood, Laurie J** — Model, Actress
Playboy Promotions, 2706 Media Center Dr, Los Angeles CA 90065 USA

**Wood, Leonard** — Auto Racing Driver
Wood Brothers Racing, 21 Performance Dr, Stuart VA 24171, USA

**Wood, M Richard (Dick)** — Football Player
41 Audubon Place, Newnan GA 30265, USA

**Wood, Maurice** — Physician
RR 2 Box 543B, Hot Springs VA 24445, USA

**Wood, Michael B (Mike)** — Baseball Player
1199 Cherlynn Terrace, West Palm Beach FL 33406, USA

**Wood, Michael S (Mike)** — Football Player
630 N Geyer Road, Saint Louis MO 63122, USA

**Wood, Nigel K** — Astronaut, England
Boscome Down Royal Air Force Base, Amesbury, Wiltshire SP4 0JF, England

**Wood, O Leon** — Basketball Player
3602 Brayton Ave, Long Beach CA 90807, USA

**Wood, Oliver** — Cinematographer
1549 N Gardner St, Los Angeles CA 90046, USA

**Wood, R Brandon** — Baseball Player
5936 E Saint John Road, Scottsdale AZ 85254, USA

**Wood, Rachel Hurd** — Actress
Troika, 74 Clerkenwell Road, #300, London EC1M 5QA, England

**Wood, Randolph B (Randy)** — Ice Hockey Player
2 Bridge St, Manchester MA 01944, USA

**Wood, Richard M** — Football Player, Coach
5413 Windbrush Dr, Tampa FL 33625, USA

**Wood, Robert J** — Astronaut
McDonnell Douglas Corp, PO Box 516, Saint Louis MO 63166, USA

**Wood, Ronald (Ron)** — Guitarist (Rolling Stones)
Monroe Sounds, 5 Church Row, Wandsworth Plain, London SW18 1ES, England

**Wood, Wilbur F, Jr** — Baseball Player
3 Elmbrook Road, Bedford MA 01730, USA

**Wood, William V (Willie)** — Football Player
Willie Wood Mechanical Systems, 7941 16th St NW, Washington DC 20012, USA

**Woodall, D Bradley (Brad)** — Baseball Player
3539 John Muir Dr, Middleton WI 53562, USA

**Woodall, F Alley (Al)** — Football Player
131 Field Crest Road, New Canaan CT 06840, USA

**Woodall, Jerry M** — Electrical Engineer, Inventor
Yale University, Microelectronic Center, 105 Wall St, New Haven CT 06511, USA

**Woodall, Lee A** — Football Player
63 Sleepy Hollow Dr, Detroit MI 48227, USA

**Woodall, Trinny** — Actress
Artist Rights Group, 4 Great Portland St, London W1W 8PA, England

**Woodard, Alfre** — Actress
I C M Partners, 10250 Constellation Blvd, #900, Los Angeles CA 90067 USA

**Woodard, Charlayne** — Actress, Writer
Sovereign Talent Group, 8421 Wilshire Blvd, #200, Beverly Hills CA 90211, USA

**Woodard, Kenneth E (Ken)** — Football Player
15389 Steel St, #201, Detroit MI 48227, USA

**Woodard, Lynette** — Basketball Player
4807 Pin Oak Park, #3210, Houston TX 77081, USA

**Woodard, Michael C (Mike)** — Baseball Player
PO Box 35, Maywood IL 60153, USA

**Wood - Woodard**

**Woodard, Rickey** — Jazz Saxophonist
J V C Music, 3800 Barham Blvd, #409, Los Angeles CA 90068, USA

**Woodard, Ronald B** — Businessman
MagnaDrive Inc, 600 108th Ave NE, #1014, Bellevue WA 98004, USA

**Woodard, Shannon** — Actress
Untitled Entertainment, 350 S Beverly Dr, #200, Beverly Hills CA 90212 USA

**Woodard, Steven L (Steve)** — Baseball Player
800 Frost Court SW, Hartselle AL 35640, USA

**Woodbine, Bokeem** — Actor
Gersh Agency, 9465 Wilshire Blvd, #600, Beverly Hills CA 90212 USA

**Woodbridge, Todd** — Tennis Player
Advantage International, PO Box 3297, North Burnley, VIC 3121, Australia

**Woodburn, Danny** — Actor
Artists Group, 3345 Wilshire Blvd, #915, Los Angeles CA 90010, USA

**Wooden, Shawn A** — Football Player
17741 SW 12th St, Pembroke Pines FL 33029, USA

**Woodeshick, Thomas (Tom)** — Football Player
PO Box 716, Blakeslee PA 18610, USA

**Woodforde, Mark** — Tennis Player
Octagon Worldwide, 1751 Pinnacle Dr, #1500, McLean VA 22102 USA

**Woodgate, Daniel (Woody)** — Drummer (Madness)
I T F, Ariel House, 74A Charlotte St, London W1T 4QJ, England

**Woodgette, Wanita D** — Singer (Danity Kane)
Bad Boy Entertainment, 1440 Broadway, #16, New York NY 10018 USA

**Woodhall, Richard (Richie)** — Boxer
Tony Clayman, 58/60 Kensington Church St, London W8 4DB, England

**Woodhead, Cynthia** — Swimmer
PO Box 1193, Riverside CA 92502, USA

**Woodhead, Danny** — Football Player
New England Patriots, 1 Patriot Place, Foxboro MA 02035 USA

**Woodland, Gary** — Golfer
Professional Golfer's Assn, PO Box 109601, Palm Beach Gardens FL 33410 USA

**Woodland, Lauren** — Actress
Michael Bruno Group, 13576 Cheltenham Dr, Sherman Oaks CA 91423, USA

**Woodley, Arthur** — Singer
Opus 3 Artists, 470 Park Ave S, #900N, New York NY 10016 USA

**Woodley, Dan** — Ice Hockey Player
6347 S Yukon Court, Littleton CO 80123, USA

**Woodley, LaMarr D** — Football Player
1635 Heritage Dr, Pittsburgh PA 15237, USA

**Woodley, Shailene** — Actress
Savage Agency, 6212 Banner Ave, Los Angeles CA 90038 USA

**Woodlief, Douglas E (Doug)** — Football Player
4953 Santa Evinita Dr, Fort Mohave AZ 86426, USA

**Woodmansee, John W, Jr** — Army General
23 Cattail Pond Dr, Frisco TX 75034, USA

**Woodruff, Blake** — Actor
Amsel Eisenstadt Frazier, 5055 Wilshire Blvd, #865, Los Angeles CA 90036 USA

**Woodruff, Bob** — Singer, Songwriter
Jim Della Croce Mgmt, 1229 17th Ave S, Nashville TN 37212, USA

**Woodruff, Bob** — Commentator
ABC-TV, News Dept, 77 W 66th St, New York NY 10023 USA

**Woodruff, Dwayne D** — Football Player
10382 Grubbs Road, Wexford PA 15090, USA

**Woodruff, Judy C** — Commentator
CNN-TV, News Dept, 820 1st St NE, #1000, Washington DC 20002 USA

**Woods, Alvis (Al)** — Baseball Player
2600 San Leandro Blvd, #1004, San Leandro CA 94578, USA

**Woods, Barbara Alyn** — Actress
Stone Manners Salners, 9911 W Pico Blvd, #1400, Los Angeles CA 90035 USA

**Woods, Christine** — Actress
Gersh Agency, 9465 Wilshire Blvd, #600, Beverly Hills CA 90212 USA

**Woods, Donald R (Don)** — Football Player
6340 Calle Tesoro NW, Albuquerque NM 87114, USA

**Woods, Elbert (Ickey)** — Football Player
505 E Sharon Road, #A, Cincinnati OH 45246, USA

**Woods, Eldrick T (Tiger)** — Golfer
E T W Corp, 501 N Highway A1A, Jupiter FL 33477, USA

**Woods, Gary L** — Baseball Player
PO Box 151, Solvang CA 93464, USA

**Woods, George** — Track Athlete
7631 Green Hedge Road, Edwardsville IL 62025, USA

**Woods, James** — Actor
Gersh Agency, 9465 Wilshire Blvd, #600, Beverly Hills CA 90212 USA

**Woods, James J (Jim)** — Baseball Player
4509 Gardenia Ave, Keyes CA 95328, USA

**Woods, Larry D** — Football Player
8906 Covent Garden St, Houston TX 77031, USA

**Woods, LeVar** — Football Player
570 Auburn Hills Dr, Coralville IA 52241, USA

**Woods, Michael** — Actor
Premier Taalent Mgmt, 1529 W 6th Ave, #206, Vancouver BC V6J 1R1, Canada

**Woods, Nan** — Actress
Geddes Agency, 8430 Santa Monica Blvd, #201, West Hollywood CA 90069 USA

**Woods, Paul** — Ice Hockey Player
4276 S Shore St, Waterford MA 48328, USA

**Woods, Philip W (Phil)** — Jazz Clarinetist, Saxophonist, Composer
PO Box 278, Delaware Water Gap PA 18327, USA

**Woods, Rick L** — Football Player
1567 76th Ave N, Saint Petersburg FL 33702, USA

**Woods, Robert E** — Football Player
4922 Devonshire Ave, Memphis TN 38117, USA

**Woods, Robert S** — Actor
PO Box 492, Kinderhook NY 12106, USA

**Woods, Ronald L (Ron)** — Baseball Player
5209 Desert Star Dr, Las Vegas NV 89130, USA

**W**

| | |
|---|---|
| **Woods, S Anthony (Tony)**<br>9 Sanford Ave, Belleville NJ 07109, USA | Football Player |
| **Woods, Simon**<br>Independent Talent Group, 40 Whitfield St, London W1T 2RH, England | Actor |
| **Woods, Skip**<br>Creative Artists Agency, 2000 Ave of Stars, #100, Los Angeles CA 90067 USA | Director, Producer, Writer |
| **Woods, Stuart**<br>G P Putnam's Sons, 375 Hudson St, New York NY 10014 USA | Writer |
| **Woods, Susan**<br>28164 Sloan Canyon Road, #A, Castaic CA 91384, USA | Actress |
| **Woods, Zach**<br>Innovative Artists, 1505 10th St, Santa Monica CA 90401 USA | Actor |
| **Woodside, D B**<br>Don Buchwald, 6500 Wilshire Blvd, #2200, Los Angeles CA 90048 USA | Actor |
| **Woodson, Abraham B (Abe)**<br>3680 Waynesvill St, Las Vegas NV 89122, USA | Football Player |
| **Woodson, Charles**<br>10010 Tavistock Road, Orlando FL 32827, USA | Football Player |
| **Woodson, Herbert H**<br>1034 Liberty Park Dr, Austin TX 78746, USA | Electrical Engineer |
| **Woodson, Jacqueline**<br>Bantam Books, 1745 Broadway, New York NY 10019 USA | Writer |
| **Woodson, Marvin L (Marv)**<br>3050 Redmond Dr, #2207, Dallas TX 75211, USA | Football Player |
| **Woodson, Michael D (Mike)**<br>New York Knicks, Madison Square Garden, 2 Penn Plaza, New York, NY 10121 USA | Basketball Player, Coach |
| **Woodson, Richard L (Dick)**<br>27879 Panorama Hills Dr, Menifee CA 92584, USA | Baseball Player |
| **Woodson, Robert L, Sr**<br>National Neighborhood Enterprise Center, 1424 16th St NW, Washington DC 20036, USA | Urban Activist |
| **Woodson, Roderick K (Rod)**<br>3304 Medallion Court, Pleasanton CA 94588, USA | Football Player, Sportscaster |
| **Woodson, Tracy M**<br>1559 Byfield Parkway, Valparaiso IN 46385, USA | Baseball Player |
| **Woodson, Warren V**<br>12680 Hillcrest Road, #1106, Dallas TX 75230, USA | Football Coach |
| **Woodson, William R**<br>North Carolina State University, Chancellor's Office, Peele Hall, Raleigh NC 27695, USA | Educator |
| **Woodville, Kate**<br>20141 S Sweetbriar Road, West Linn OR 97068, USA | Actress |
| **Woodward, Christopher M (Chris)**<br>15049 Howelhurst Dr, Baldwin Park CA 91706, USA | Baseball Player |
| **Woodward, Joanne G**<br>I C M Partners, 10250 Constellation Blvd, #900, Los Angeles CA 90067 USA | Actress |
| **Woodward, Kirsten**<br>Kirsten Woodward Hats, 26 Portobello Green Arcade, London W10, England | Fashion Designer |
| **Woodward, Margaret H (Maggie)**<br>Commander 17th Air Force, Ramstein Air Force Base, Unit 3300, APO AE 09094 , USA | Air Force General |
| **Woodward, Morgan**<br>2111 Rockledge Road, Los Angeles CA 90068, USA | Actor |
| **Woodward, Neil W, III**<br>1935 Edgemont Place W, Seattle WA 98199, USA | Astronaut |
| **Woodward, Robert J (Rob)**<br>58 Eastman Hill Road, Lebanon NH 03766, USA | Baseball Player |
| **Woodward, Robert U (Bob)**<br>3305 Old Point Road, Edgewater MD 21037, USA | Journalist |
| **Woodward, Roger R**<br>L H Productions, 2/37 Hendy Ave, Coogee NSW 2034, Australia | Concert Pianist, Conductor, Composer |
| **Woodward, Shannon**<br>Untitled Entertainment, 350 S Beverly Dr, #200, Beverly Hills CA 90212 USA | Actress |
| **Woodward, William F (Woody)**<br>10 San Marco Court, Palm Coast FL 32137, USA | Baseball Player |
| **Woody**<br>Mercury Records, 11150 Santa Monica Blvd, #1000, Los Angeles CA 90025 USA | Singer (Dru Hill) |
| **Woody, Damien M**<br>3 Roconan Dr, Mendham NJ 7945, USA | Football Player |
| **Wool, Christopher**<br>Luhring Augustine Gallery, 531 W 24th St, New York NY 10011, USA | Artist |
| **Wooldridge, Floyd L**<br>214 Barber St, Greenfield MO 65661, USA | Baseball Player |
| **Woolery, Chuck**<br>Western Creative, 26135 Plymouth Road, Redford MI 48239, USA | Actor |
| **Woolfolk, Harold E (Butch)**<br>4519 Magnolia Lane, Sugar Lane TX 77478, USA | Football Player |
| **Woolford, Donnell**<br>725 Lumber Lane, Charlotte NC 28214, USA | Football Player |
| **Woolgar, Fenella**<br>Independent Talent Group, 40 Whitfield St, London W1T 2RH, England | Actress |
| **Woollard, Robert G (Bob)**<br>RR 1 Box 456, Hamptonville NC 27020, USA | Basketball Player |
| **Woolley, Bennie L (Chip), Jr**<br>135 Road 5018, Bloomfield NM 87413, USA | Thoroughbred Racing Trainer |
| **Woolley, Jason D**<br>4019 Quarton Road, Bloomfield MI 48302, USA | Ice Hockey Player |
| **Woolley, Kenneth F**<br>790 George St, #500, Sydney NSW 2000, Australia | Architect |
| **Woolsey, Elizabeth D**<br>Trail Creek Ranch, 7100 West Trail Creek Road, Wilson WY 83014, USA | Alpine Skier, Executive |
| **Woolsey, R James**<br>Shea & Gardner, 901 New York Ave NW, Washington DC 20001, USA | Government Official |
| **Woolsey, Ralph A**<br>23388 Mulholland Dr, #109, Woodland Hills CA 91364, USA | Cinematographer |
| **Woolsey, William T**<br>1032 Seascape Circle, Rodeo CA 94572, USA | Swimmer |
| **Woolstenhulme, Rick, Jr**<br>Untitled Entertainment, 350 S Beverly Dr, #200, Beverly Hills CA 90212 USA | Drummer (Lifehouse) |

**Woods - Woolstenhulme**

| | |
|---|---|
| **Woolvett, Jaimz** | Actor |
| Noble Caplan Abrams, 1260 Yonge St, #200, Toronto ON M4T 1W6, Canada | |
| **Woomble, Roddy** | Singer (Idlewild) |
| Agency Group Ltd, 361-373 City Road, London EC1V 1PQ, England | |
| **Woosnam, Ian H** | Golfer |
| Dyffryn, Morda Road, Oswestry, Shropshire SY11 2AY, Wales | |
| **Woosnam, Phil** | Soccer Executive |
| 2211 Mainsail Dr, Marietta GA 30062, USA | |
| **Wooten, Hubert (Daddy), Jr** | Baseball Player |
| 120 Sandy Dr, Goldsboro NC 27534, USA | |
| **Wooten, Jim** | Commentator |
| ABC-TV, News Dept, 5010 Creston St, Hyattsville MD 20781 USA | |
| **Wooten, John B** | Football Player |
| 3760 Paradise Hills Dr, #2601, Euless TX 76040, USA | |
| **Wooten, Nicholas** | Producer, Writer |
| W M E Entertainment, 9601 Wilshire Blvd, #300, Beverly Hills CA 90210 USA | |
| **Wooten, Ronald J (Ron)** | Football Player |
| 2401 Lewis Grove Lane, Raleigh NC 27608, USA | |
| **Wooten, Victor L** | Jazz Bassist, Composer |
| Skyline Music, 563 Willow Hollow Dr NE, Atlanta GA 30328, USA | |
| **Wooten, W Shawn** | Baseball Player |
| 765 Ali Lane, Santa Monica CA 90402, USA | |
| **Wootten, Morgan** | Basketball Coach |
| 6912 Wells Parkway, University Park MD 20782, USA | |
| **Wopat, Tom** | Actor, Singer |
| Innovative Artists, 1505 10th St, Santa Monica CA 90401 USA | |
| **Word, Barry Q** | Football Player |
| 5746 Janneys Mill Circle, Haymarket VA 20169, USA | |
| **Word, Weldon R** | Engineer (Paveway Smart Bomb) |
| 626 Hurst Dr, Tyler TX 75703, USA | |
| **Worden, Alfred M** | Astronaut |
| PO Box 8065, Vero Beach FL 32963, USA | |
| **Wordsworth, Barry** | Conductor |
| I M G Artists, Hogarth Business Park, Chiswick, London W4 2TH, England | |
| **Workman, A K (Hank)** | Baseball Player |
| 307 19th St, Santa Monica CA 90402, USA | |
| **Workman, Haywoode W** | Basketball Player |
| 13711 Inoma St, #104, Tampa FL 33613, USA | |
| **Workman, Vincent I (Vince), Jr** | Football Player |
| 98 Southfield Ave, #605, Stamford CT 06902, USA | |
| **World Peace, Metta** | Basketball Player |
| Tri Star Sports & Entertainment, 1222 16th Ave S, #300, Nashville TN 37212, USA | |
| **Worley, Brian** | Singer (Stamps Quartet) |
| PO Box 1471, Brentwood TN 37024, USA | |
| **Worley, Darryl** | Singer |
| Rendy Lovelady Mgmt, 24 Middleton St, Nashville TN 37210, USA | |
| **Worley, Jo Anne** | Actress, Comedienne |
| Mavrick Artists, 6100 Wilshire Blvd, #550, Los Angeles CA 90048, USA | |
| **Worley, Timothy A (Tim)** | Football Player |
| Worley Global Enterprises, PO Box 14477, Huntsville AL 35815, USA | |
| **Worndl, Frank** | Alpine Skier |
| Burgsiedlung 19C, 87527 Sonthofen, Germany | |
| **Woronov, Mary** | Actress |
| Studio Talent Group, 1328 12th St, Santa Monica CA 90401, USA | |
| **Worrell, Bernie** | Singer, Musician (Parliament-Funkadelic) |
| Blue Mountain Artists, 810 Tyvola Road, #114, Charlotte NC 28217, USA | |
| **Worrell, Cameron J** | Football Player |
| 2829 E Christopher Dr, Fresno CA 93720, USA | |
| **Worrell, Peter** | Ice Hockey Player |
| 3560 Aladdin Ave, Boynton Beach FL 33436, USA | |
| **Worrell, Timothy H (Tim)** | Baseball Player |
| 4719 W El Cortez Place, Phoenix AZ 85083, USA | |
| **Worrell, Todd R** | Baseball Player |
| 810 Simmons Ave, Saint Louis MO 63122, USA | |
| **Worsham, Del** | Drag Racing Driver |
| PO Box 1329, Chino Hills CA 91709, USA | |
| **Worth, Maurice** | Businessman |
| Delta Air Lines, Hartsfield International Airport, Atlanta GA 30320, USA | |
| **Wortham, Barron W** | Football Player |
| 8608 Busch Gardens Dr, Fort Worth TX 76123, USA | |
| **Wortham, Richard C (Rich)** | Baseball Player |
| 1708 Mira Vista, Leander TX 78641, USA | |
| **Worthington, Allan F (Al)** | Baseball Player |
| 12070 Highway 55, Sterrett AL 35147, USA | |
| **Worthington, Craig R** | Baseball Player |
| 10019 Mattock Ave, Downey CA 90240, USA | |
| **Worthington, Sam** | Actor |
| Anonymous Content, 3532 Hayden Ave, Culver City CA 90232 USA | |
| **Worthy, James A** | Basketball Player, Sportscaster |
| 5750 Corbett St, Los Angeles CA 90016, USA | |
| **Worthy, Richard (Rick)** | Actor |
| S M S Talent, 8383 Wilshire Blvd, #230, Beverly Hills CA 90211 USA | |
| **Wortman, Keith D** | Football Player |
| 421 Bordeaux Way, Saint Peters MO 63376, USA | |
| **Wortman, Kevin** | Ice Hockey Player |
| 42 David Dr, Saugus MA 01906, USA | |
| **Wosner, Shai** | Concert Pianist |
| Opus 3 Artists, 470 Park Ave S, #900N, New York NY 10016 USA | |
| **Wottle, David J (Dave)** | Track Athlete |
| 9245 Forest Hill Lane, Germantown TN 38139, USA | |
| **Wotton, Mark** | Ice Hockey Player |
| Pro-Rep Entertainment, 113-276 Midpark Way SE, Calgary AB T2X 1J6, Canada | |
| **Wotus, Ronald A (Ron)** | Baseball Player |
| 6 Monteria Lane, Martinez CA 94553, USA | |
| **Wotzel, Mandy** | Figure Skater |
| Olympic Ice Rink, 1080 Centre Road, Melbourne VIC 3167, Australia | |

| | |
|---|---|
| **Wouk, Herman** | Writer |
| 303 W Crestview Dr, Palm Springs CA 92264, USA | |
| **Woywitka, Jeff** | Ice Hockey Player |
| RR 1, Mannville AB T0B 2W0, Canada | |
| **Wozniacki, Caroline** | Tennis Player |
| Noru Sports Group, Fredericksborggade 5A2, 1360 Copenhagen K, Denmark | |
| **Wozniak, Steve** | Computer Designer, Inventor |
| 16400 Blackberry Hill Road, Los Gatos CA 95030, USA | |
| **Wozniewski, Andrew (Andy)** | Ice Hockey Player |
| 322 Lakeview Dr, Buffalo Grove IL 60089, USA | |
| **Wragg, John** | Sculptor |
| 6 Castle Lane, Devizes, Wiltshire SN10 1HJ, England | |
| **Wray, Gordon R** | Engineer, Designer |
| Stonestack, Rempstone, Loughborough, Leicestershire LE12 6RH, England | |
| **Wray, Margaret Jane** | Opera Singer |
| Columbia Artists Mgmt Inc, 1790 Broadway, #702, New York NY 10019 USA | |
| **Wregget, Ken** | Ice Hockey Player |
| 176 Fieldgate Dr, Pittsburgh PA 15241, USA | |
| **Wrenn, Peter** | Harness Racing Driver |
| 5215 Wren Court, Carmel IN 46033, USA | |
| **Wrenn, Robert (Bob)** | Golfer |
| 8908 Watlington Road, Henrico VA 23229, USA | |
| **Wrighster, George F, III** | Football Player |
| 3014 Summit Place, Birmingham AL 35243, USA | |
| **Wright Shapiro, Elizabeth** | Actress |
| United Talent Agency, U T A Plaza, 9336 Civic Center Dr, Beverly Hills CA 90210 USA | |
| **Wright, Adam** | Singer, Guitarist (Wrights) |
| Third Coast Artists Mgmt, 2021 21st Ave S, #220, Nashville TN 37212, USA | |
| **Wright, Alex** | Actress |
| A P A Talent/Literary Agency, 405 S Beverly Dr, #300, Beverly Hills CA 90212 USA | |
| **Wright, Alexander** | Football Player |
| 501 S Mississippi St, Amarillo TX 79106, USA | |
| **Wright, Angela** | Actress |
| Commercial Talent, 9255 Sunset Blvd, #505, Los Angeles CA 90069, USA | |
| **Wright, Ben** | Sportscaster |
| CBS-TV, Sports Dept, 51 W 52nd St, New York NY 10019 USA | |
| **Wright, Betty** | Singer |
| Rodgers Redding, PO Box 4603, Macon GA 31208 USA | |
| **Wright, Beverly** | Environmental Activist, Sociologist |
| Deep South Environment Justice Center, 2601 Gentilly Blvd, New Orleans LA 70122, USA | |
| **Wright, Bonnie** | Actress |
| United Agents, 12-26 Lexington St, London W1F 0LE, England | |
| **Wright, Bradford N (Brad)** | Basketball Player |
| 1050 S Cloverdale Ave, Los Angeles CA 90019, USA | |
| **Wright, Bryant** | Religious Leader |
| Johnson Ferry Baptist Church, 955 Johnson Ferry Road, Marietta GA 30068, USA | |
| **Wright, Charles J** | Football Player |
| 2698 Wakefield Lane, Westlake OH 44145, USA | |
| **Wright, Charles P, Jr** | Writer |
| 940 Locust Ave, Charlottesville VA 22901, USA | |
| **Wright, Chely** | Singer, Actress |
| Creative Artists Agency, 2000 Ave of Stars, #100, Los Angeles CA 90067 USA | |
| **Wright, Clyde** | Baseball Player |
| 528 S Jeanine St, Anaheim CA 92806, USA | |
| **Wright, Craig M** | Architect |
| C M Wright Inc, 722 N La Cienega Blvd, West Hollywood CA 90069, USA | |
| **Wright, Danny** | Pianist |
| Engine Entertainment, 116 NE 136th Ave, Portland OR 97230, USA | |
| **Wright, David A** | Baseball Player |
| 1105 Hillston Court, Chesapeake VA 23322, USA | |
| **Wright, Dick** | Editorial Cartoonist |
| Columbus Dispatch, Editorial Dept, 34 S 3rd St, Columbus OH 43215, USA | |
| **Wright, Donald C (Don)** | Editorial Cartoonist |
| PO Box 1176, Palm Beach FL 33480, USA | |
| **Wright, Dorell L** | Basketball Player |
| 158 Twin Peaks Dr, Walnut Creek CA 94595, USA | |
| **Wright, Doug** | Writer |
| I C M Partners, 730 5th Ave, New York NY 10019 USA | |
| **Wright, Edgar** | Director, Writer |
| Independent Talent Group, 40 Whitfield St, London W1T 2RH, England | |
| **Wright, Elmo** | Football Player |
| 11419 Olympia Dr, Houston TX 77077, USA | |
| **Wright, Eric A** | Football Player |
| San Francisco 49ers, 4949 Centennial Blvd, Santa Clara CA 95054 USA | |
| **Wright, Felix C** | Football Player |
| 2698 Wakefield Lane, Westlake OH 44145, USA | |
| **Wright, Gary** | Singer, Songwriter |
| Air Tight Mgmt, 115 West Road, Winsted CT 06098, USA | |
| **Wright, George D** | Baseball Player |
| 4228 NE 18th St, Oklahoma City OK 73121, USA | |
| **Wright, Heather** | Actress |
| 1 Sunnyside, Wimbledon, London SW19, England | |
| **Wright, J Richard (Ricky)** | Baseball Player |
| 2502 Clark Lane, Paris TX 75460, USA | |
| **Wright, Jaguar** | Singer |
| Richard De La Font Agency, 4845 S Sheridan Road, #505, Tulsa OK 74145 USA | |
| **Wright, James C (Jim), Jr** | Representative, TX; Speaker |
| Texas Christian University, Political Science Dept, Fort Worth TX 76129, USA | |
| **Wright, James E** | Historian |
| 7 Quail Dr, Etna NH 03750, USA | |
| **Wright, Jamey A** | Baseball Player |
| 4325 Fairfax Ave, Dallas TX 75205, USA | |
| **Wright, Jaret** | Baseball Player |
| 3816 Vista Azul, San Clemente CA 92672, USA | |
| **Wright, Jay** | Basketball Coach |
| Villanova University, Athletic Dept, Villanova PA 19085, USA | |

| | |
|---|---|
| **Wright, Jay** | Writer |
| General Delivery, Piermont NH 03779, USA | |
| **Wright, Jeff D** | Football Player |
| 23426 N 21st Place, Phoenix AZ 85024, USA | |
| **Wright, Jeffrey** | Actor |
| Creative Artists Agency, 2000 Ave of Stars, #100, Los Angeles CA 90067 USA | |
| **Wright, Jeffrey R (Jeff)** | Football Player |
| 420 W Bluejay Dr, Chandler AZ 85286, USA | |
| **Wright, Joe** | Director, Producer, Actor |
| Shoebox Films, 82 Berwick St, London W1F 8TP, England | |
| **Wright, John** | Ice Hockey Player |
| 116 Hillsdale Ave, Toronto ON M5P 1G5, Canada | |
| **Wright, John M, Jr** | Army General |
| 5195 Cottingham Place, Alexandria VA 22304, USA | |
| **Wright, Judith A** | Writer |
| 17 Devonport St, #1, Lyons ACT 2060, Australia | |
| **Wright, Julian** | Basketball Player |
| 50 Pinehurst Dr, New Orleans LA 70131, USA | |
| **Wright, Kendall** | Football Player |
| Tennessee Titans, 460 Great Circle Road, Nashville TN 37228 USA | |
| **Wright, Kenneth W (Ken)** | Baseball Player |
| 1651 Ora Dr, Pensacola FL 32506, USA | |
| **Wright, L Rayfield** | Football Player |
| PO Box 2833, Weatherford TX 76086, USA | |
| **Wright, Larry** | Ice Hockey Player |
| Regina Fire Dept, PO Box 1790, Regina SK S4P 3C8, Canada | |
| **Wright, Lawrence** | Writer |
| Wylie Agency, 250 W 57th St, #2114, New York NY 10107 USA | |
| **Wright, Lawrence A** | Judge |
| US Tax Court, 400 2nd St NW, Washington DC 20217, USA | |
| **Wright, Lizz** | Singer |
| Direct Management Group, 947 N La Cienega Blvd, #G, West Hollywood CA 90069, USA | |
| **Wright, Louis D** | Football Player |
| 2263 S Quentin Way, #F301, Aurora CO 80014, USA | |
| **Wright, Mary K (Mickey)** | Golfer |
| 2972 SE Treasure Island Road, Port Saint Lucie FL 34952, USA | |
| **Wright, Max** | Actor |
| Bresler Kelly Assoc, 11500 W Olympic Blvd, #400, Los Angeles CA 90064 USA | |
| **Wright, Michael** | Actor |
| Don Buchwald, 6500 Wilshire Blvd, #2200, Los Angeles CA 90048 USA | |
| **Wright, Michelle** | Singer |
| Savannah Music, 205 Powell Place, #214, Brentwood TN 37027, USA | |
| **Wright, Nathaniel (Nate)** | Football Player |
| 11247 Zorita Court, San Diego CA 92124, USA | |
| **Wright, Pat** | Singer (Crystals) |
| Lustig Talent, PO Box 770850, Orlando FL 32877 USA | |
| **Wright, Peter** | WW II Army Air Corps Hero |
| 29 Devon Ave, Croton on Hudson NY 10520, USA | |
| **Wright, Peter R** | Ballet Dancer, Choreographer |
| 10 Chiswick Wharf, London W4 2SR, England | |
| **Wright, Petra** | Actress |
| Hartig-Hilepo Agency, 54 W 21st St, #610, New York NY 10010 USA | |
| **Wright, Randall S (Randy)** | Football Player |
| 2890 Commerce Park Dr, Fitchburg WI 53719, USA | |
| **Wright, Robin** | Actress, Model |
| Creative Artists Agency, 2000 Ave of Stars, #100, Los Angeles CA 90067 USA | |
| **Wright, Ronald L (Winky)** | Boxer |
| 2800 52nd St N, Saint Petersburg, FL 33710, USA | |
| **Wright, Ronald W (Ron)** | Baseball Player |
| 310 S 2100 E, Saint George UT 84790, USA | |
| **Wright, Sarah** | Actress |
| I C M Partners, 10250 Constellation Blvd, #900, Los Angeles CA 90067 USA | |
| **Wright, Shannon** | Singer (Wrights), Songwriter |
| Third Coast Artists Mgmt, 2021 21st Ave S, #220, Nashville TN 37212, USA | |
| **Wright, Sharone A** | Basketball Player |
| 6080 Lakeview Road, #3504, Warner Robins GA 31088, USA | |
| **Wright, Stephen** | Writer |
| Knopf Publishers, 1745 Broadway, New York NY 10019 USA | |
| **Wright, Stephen (Steve)** | Actor |
| Conway Van Gelder Grant, 8-12 Broadwick St, #300, London W1F 8HW, England | |
| **Wright, Stephen H (Steve)** | Football Player |
| 14 Conifer Square, Augusta GA 30909, USA | |
| **Wright, Steve T** | Football Player |
| 14 Conifer Square, Augusta GA 30909, USA | |
| **Wright, Steven** | Actor, Comedian |
| Brillstein Entertainment Partners, 9150 Wilshire Blvd, #350, Beverly Hills CA 90212 USA | |
| **Wright, Tanisha L** | Basketball Player |
| Seattle Storm, Key Arena, 351 Elliott Ave W, #500, Seattle WA 98119 USA | |
| **Wright, Thomas** | Actor |
| W M E Entertainment, 9601 Wilshire Blvd, #300, Beverly Hills CA 90210 USA | |
| **Wright, Thomas S (Tom)** | Baseball Player |
| 1116 Poplar Springs Church Road, Shelby NC 28152, USA | |
| **Wright, Toby L** | Football Player |
| 1602 E Winston Dr, Phoenix AZ 85042, USA | |
| **Wright, Trevor** | Actor |
| Evolution Entertainment, 901 N Highland Ave, Los Angeles CA 90038 USA | |
| **Wright, Tyler** | Ice Hockey Player |
| 1982 Chatfield Road, Columbus OH 43221, USA | |
| **Wright, Will** | Video Game Designer, Producer, Writer |
| Stupid Fun Club, 721 Channing Way, Berkeley CA 94720, USA | |
| **Wrightman, Timothy J (Tim)** | Football Player |
| 612 Unity Lane, Weiser ID 83672, USA | |
| **Wrightson, Bernard (Bernie)** | Diver |
| 924 Birch Ave, Escondido CA 92027, USA | |
| **Wrigley, William, Jr** | Businessman |
| William Wrigley Jr Co, 410 N Michigan Ave, Lower Level, Chicago IL 60611, USA | |

**W**

**Wright - Wrigley**

# W

**Wroblewski, David** — Writer
Ecco/Harper Collins Publishers, 10 E 53rd St, Cellar 1, New York NY 10022, USA

**Wrona, Richard J (Rick)** — Baseball Player
2946 E 57th St, Tulsa OK 74105, USA

**Wrubel, Bill** — Writer, Producer
Creative Artists Agency, 2000 Ave of Stars, #100, Los Angeles CA 90067 USA

**Wryn, Rhiannon Leigh** — Actress
B/W/R, 9100 Wilshire Blvd, #500W, Beverly Hills CA 90212 USA

**Wu Man** — Pipa Player
Opus 3 Artists, 470 Park Ave S, #900N, New York NY 10016 USA

**Wu, Alice** — Director, Writer
Creative Artists Agency, 2000 Ave of Stars, #100, Los Angeles CA 90067 USA

**Wu, Daniel** — Actor, Director, Writer
Creative Artists Agency, 2000 Ave of Stars, #100, Los Angeles CA 90067 USA

**Wu, Jason** — Fashion Designer
240 W 35th St, #1100, New York NY 10001, USA

**Wu, Sau Lan** — Physicist
29 Oxford St, Cambridge MA 02138, USA

**Wu, Tai Tsun** — Physicist
Harvard University, Physics Dept, Pierce Hall, 29 Oxford St, Cambridge MA 02138, USA

**Wu, Vivian** — Actress
S M S Talent, 8383 Wilshire Blvd, #230, Beverly Hills CA 90211 USA

**WuDunn, Sheryl** — Journalist
New York Times, Editorial Dept, 229 W 43rd St, New York NY 10036, USA

**Wuerffel, Daniel C (Danny)** — Football Player
424 Mimosa Dr, Decatur GA 30030, USA

**Wuerl, Donald W Cardinal** — Religious Leader
5001 Eastern Ave, Hyattsville MD 20782, USA

**Wuertz, Michael J** — Baseball Player
15209 N Thompson Peak Parkway, #B111, Scottsdale AZ 85260, USA

**Wuethrich, Kurt** — Nobel Chemistry Laureate
Federal Technology Institute, E T H Hvnggerberg, 8093 Zurich, Switzerland

**Wuhl, Robert** — Actor
C E S D, 10635 Santa Monica Blvd, #130, Los Angeles CA 90025 USA

**Wuhrer, Kari** — Actress
Innovative Artists, 1505 10th St, Santa Monica CA 90401 USA

**Wullbrandt, John** — Artist
PO Box 246, Carpinteria CA 93014, USA

**Wunder, Ingolf** — Concert Pianist
I M G Artists, Hogarth Business Park, Chiswick, London W4 2TH, England

**Wunderlich, Claudia** — Handball Player
Dt Handballbund, Strobelallee 56, 44139 Dortmund, Germany

**Wunderlich, Paul** — Artist
Haynstr 2, 20249 Hamburg, Germany

**Wunsch, Carl I** — Oceanographer
78 Washington Ave, Cambridge MA 02140, USA

**Wunsch, Gerald (Jerry)** — Football Player
2601 Red Maple Road, Wausau WI 54401, USA

**Wunsch, Kelly D** — Baseball Player
332 Palo Alto Way, Austin TX 78732, USA

**Wuorinen, Charles P** — Composer
Howard Stokar Mgmt, 870 W End Ave, New York NY 10025, USA

**Wurlitzer, Rudolph** — Writer
Two Dollar Radio Publishing, 141 E Town St, #200, Columbus OH 43215, USA

**Wurster, Charles D** — Coast Guard Admiral
Commander, US Coast Guard Pacific, Coast Guard Island, Alameda CA 94501 USA

**Wurster, Donald C** — Air Force General
Commander, Special Operations Command, Hurlburt Field FL 32544 USA

**Wurz, Alexander** — Auto Racing Driver
Benetton-Mecachrome, Enstone, Chipping Norton, Oxfordshire OX7 4EE, England

**Wust, Ireen** — Speed Skater
Spoorbaan 7, 5051 Goirle ET, Netherlands

**Wuycik, Dennis M** — Basketball Player
31 Rogerson Dr, Chapel Hill NC 27517, USA

**Wyatt, Greg A** — Sculptor
320 W 86th St, PH South, New York NY 10024, USA

**Wyatt, Harry M, III** — Air Force General
Director, Air National Guard, HqUSAF, Pentagon, Washington DC 20330 USA

**Wyatt, Helen** — Baseball Player
7714 Deerfield Road, Loves Park IL 61111, USA

**Wyatt, J Douglas (Doug)** — Football Player
4055 Hogan Dr, #301, Tyler TX 75709, USA

**Wyatt, Jennifer** — Golfer
Carolina Group, 2321 Devine St, #A, Columbia SC 29205, USA

**Wyatt, Keke** — Singer
Universal Attractions, 135 W 26th St, #1200, New York NY 10001 USA

**Wyatt, Kimberly** — Singer (Pussycat Dolls)
Creative Artists Agency, 2000 Ave of Stars, #100, Los Angeles CA 90067 USA

**Wyatt, Leslie** — Educator
Arkansas State University, President's Office, State University AR 72467, USA

**Wyatt, Shannon** — Actress
8949 Falling Creek Court, Annandale VA 22003, USA

**Wyatt, Sharon** — Actress
16830 Ventura Blvd, #300, Encino CA 91436, USA

**Wyche, Samuel D (Sam)** — Football Coach, Sportscaster
1138 Walhalla Highway, Pickens SC 29671, USA

**Wyeth, James Browning** — Artist
Lookout Farm, 701 Smiths Bridge Road, Wilmington DE 19807, USA

**Wyland** — Artist
Wyland Studios, 6 Mason, Irvine CA 92618, USA

**Wylde, Chris** — Actor, Writer, Producer
Stone Manners Salners, 9911 W Pico Blvd, #1400, Los Angeles CA 90035 USA

**Wylde, Peter** — Equestrian
247 Wood Dale Dr, Wellington FL 33414, USA

**Wylde, Zakk** — Singer, Guitarist, Songwriter
Survival Mgmt, 30765 Pacific Coast Highway, #325, Malibu CA 90265, USA

**Wroblewski - Wylde**

**Wyle, Noah** — Actor
Brillstein Entertainment Partners, 9150 Wilshire Blvd, #350, Beverly Hills CA 90212 USA
**Wylenzek, Thomasz** — Canoeing Athlete
Alfred Krupp Str 47, 45131 Essen, Germany
**Wylie, Adam** — Actor
Management 101, 11271 Ventura Blvd, #102, Studio City CA 91604 USA
**Wylie, Paul** — Figure Skater
9819 Deer Brook Lane, Charlotte NC 28210, USA
**Wyludda, Ilke** — Track Athlete
Liebigstr 9, 09113 Chemnitz, Germany
**Wyman, David M** — Football Player
20918 NE Redmond Fall City Road, Redmond WA 98053, USA
**Wyman, James T** — Businessman
1185 Ferndale Road W, Wayzata MN 55391, USA
**Wyman, William G (Bill)** — Bassist (Rolling Stones)
Ripple Productions, 344 Kings Road, London SW3 5UR, England
**Wymore, Patrice** — Actress
Port Antonio, Jamaica, British West Indies
**Wyms, Ellis R** — Football Player
15706 Tremout Hollow Lane, Houston TX 77044, USA
**Wynalda, Eric** — Soccer Player
2313 Stormcroft Court, Westlake Village CA 91361, USA
**Wyn-Davies, Geraint** — Actor
Innovative Artists, 1505 10th St, Santa Monica CA 90401 USA
**Wynder, A J** — Basketball Player
1 Cardenti Court, Newark DE 19702, USA
**Wyndham, Alex** — Actor
Finch & Partners, 29-37 Heddon St, London W1B 4BR, England
**Wyndham, Victoria** — Actress
Don Buchwald, 6500 Wilshire Blvd, #2200, Los Angeles CA 90048 USA
**Wynegar, Harold D (Butch)** — Baseball Player
PO Box 915811, Longwood FL 32791, USA
**Wyner, George** — Actor
3450 Laurie Place, Studio City CA 91604, USA
**Wyner, Yehudi** — Composer
Brandeis University, Music Dept, Waltham MA 02454, USA
**Wyngarde, Peter** — Actor
4 Acre Lane, Clock Face, Sainte Helen's, Lancashire WA9 4DZ, England
**Wynn, Bob** — Golfer
78455 Calle Orense, La Quinta CA 92253, USA
**Wynn, James S (Jimmy)** — Baseball Player
5507 Sandy Field Court, Rosharon TX 77583, USA
**Wynn, Renaldo L** — Football Player
9504 Empire Rock St, Las Vegas NV 89143, USA
**Wynn, Stephen A** — Businessman
Desert Inn Hotel, 3245 Las Vegas Blvd S, Las Vegas NV 89109, USA
**Wynne, Billy V** — Baseball Player
7722 Greenwich Court W, Jacksonville FL 32277, USA
**Wynne, Marvell** — Baseball Player
39640 Del Val Dr, Murrieta CA 92562, USA
**Wynott, Ryan** — Actor
Savage Agency, 6212 Banner Ave, Los Angeles CA 90038 USA
**Wynter, Sarah** — Actress
Paradigm Agency, 360 N Crescent Dr, North Building, Beverly Hills CA 90210 USA
**Wyrozub, Randy** — Ice Hockey Player
6717 Westminster Dr, East Amherst NY 14051, USA
**Wysocki, Benjamin J (Ben)** — Drummer (Fray)
A2 Mgmt, 624 Davis St, #200, Evanston IL 60201, USA
**Wysocki, Jacob** — Actor
Echo Lake Management, 421 S Beverly Dr, #800, Beverly Hills CA 90212, USA

**W**

Wyle - Wysocki

**Xanic von Bertrab - Yang di-Pertuan Agong XIII**

**Xanic von Bertrab, Alejandra** — Journalist
New York Times, Editorial Dept, 229 W 43rd St, New York NY 10036 USA

**Xhelilaj, Nik** — Actor
Cinematography National Center, Blvd Aleksander Mojsiu 77, 1012 Tirana, Albania

**Xiahui Fan** — Cosmologist
University of Arizona, Astronomy Dept, Tucson AZ 85721, USA

**Xiang Jing** — Sculptor
Saatchi Gallery, Duke Of York's H Q, King's Road, London SW3 4RY, England

**Xiang Liu** — Track Athlete
Global Athletes & Marketing, 437 Boylston St, Boston MA 02116, USA

**Xiao, Xiangming** — Biologist
University of New Hampshire, Earth Oceans Space Institute, Durham NH 03824, USA

**Xie Bingxin** — Writer
Central Nationalities Institute, Residential Qtrs, Beijing 100081, China

**Xie Tieli** — Director
Beijing Film Studio, 19 Beihuan Xilu Road, Beijing 100088, China

**Xu Bing** — Artist
540 Metropolitan Ave, #A, Brooklyn NY 11211, USA

**Xu Xing** — Geologist
Academy of Sciences, 52 Sanlihe Road, Beijing 100864, China

**Xue Wei** — Concert Violinist
134 Sheaveshill Ave, London NW9 6RY, England

**Xuereb, Salvator** — Actor
Kazarian/Measures/Ruskin, 11969 Ventura Blvd, #300, Studio City CA 91604 USA

**Xzibit** — Rap Artist, Actor
Management 360, 9111 Wilshire Blvd, Beverly Hills CA 90210 USA

**Ya'alon, Moshe** — Army General, Israel
Chief of Staff, Israeli Defense Forces, Kaplan St, Tel Aviv 67659, Israel

**Yablans, Frank** — Producer
88 Bull Path, East Hampton NY 11937, USA

**Yachmenev, Vitali A** — Ice Hockey Player
182 Silver Lady Lane, North Bay ON P1B 8G4, Canada

**Yacoub, Magdi H** — Surgeon
National Heart & Lung Institute, Dovehouse St, London SW3 6LY, England

**Yager, Faye** — Social Activist
Children of the Underground, 902 Curlew Court NW, Atlanta GA 30327, USA

**Yager, Rick** — Cartoonist (Buck Rogers)
King Features Syndicate, 300 W 57th St, #1500, New York NY 10019 USA

**Yagudin, Alexei** — Figure Skater
Connecticut Skating Center, 300 Alumni Road, Newington CT 06111, USA

**Yaitanes, Gregory C (Greg)** — Director, Producer
Creative Artists Agency, 2000 Ave of Stars, #100, Los Angeles CA 90067 USA

**Yake, Terry** — Ice Hockey Player
26 Mockingbird Lane, Tiverton RI 02878, USA

**Yakin, Boaz** — Director, Producer, Writer
Cinetic Mgmt, 555 W 25th St, #400, New York NY 10001 USA

**Yakupov, Nail R** — Ice Hockey Player
Edmonton Oilers, 11230 110th St, Edmonton AB T5G 3H7, Canada

**Yamagata, Hiro** — Artist
1050 Ave D, Redondo Beach CA 90277, USA

**Yamagata, Rachael** — Singer, Pianist, Songwriter
Paradigm Agency, 360 Park Ave, #1600, New York NY 10022 USA

**Yamaguchi, Kristi T** — Figure Skater
290 Las Quebradas Lane, Alamo CA 94507, USA

**Yamaguchi, Roy** — Restauranteur
Roy's Restaurant, Kai Plaza, 6600 Kalaniaole Highway, Honolulu HI 96825, USA

**Yamame, Marlene Mitsuko** — Actress
Herb Tannen, 10801 National Blvd, #101, Los Angeles CA 90064 USA

**Yamamoto, Kansai** — Fashion Designer
103 Grand St, New York NY 10013, USA

**Yamamoto, Yohji** — Fashion Designer
Yamamoto Europe, 155 Rue Saint-Martin, 75003 Paris, France

**Yamanaka, Shinya** — Nobel Medicine Laureate
Kyoto University, 53 Kawaharacho, Shogoin Yoshida, Sakyoku, Kyoto 606-8507, Japan

**Yamanaka, Tsuyoshi** — Swimmer
6-10-33 Akasaka, Minatoku, Tokyo 107 0052 Japan

**Yamani, Sheikh Ahmed Zaki** — Government Official, Saudi Arabia
PO Box 14850, Jeddah 21434, Saudi Arabia

**Yamano, Hiroshi** — Artist
Galleria Silecchia, 20 S Palm Ave, Sarasota FL 34236, USA

**Yamasaki, Taro M** — Photojournalist
People, Editorial Dept, Time-Life Building, New York NY 10020, USA

**Yamashita, Iris** — Writer
Circle of Confusion, 8548 Washington Blvd, Culver City CA 90232, USA

**Yamashita, Yasuhiro** — Judo Athlete, Coach
1117 Kitakaname, Hitatsuka Kanagawa 259 1207, Japan

**Yamassoum, Negoum** — Prime Minister, Chad
PO Box 43121, N'Djamena, Moursal, Chad

**Yamazaki, Naoko** — Astronaut, Japan
Japanese Aerospace Exploration Agency, 2-1-1 Sengen, Tsukuba-shi, Ibaraki 305 8505, Japan

**Yamin, Elliott** — Singer
Three Ring Projects, 111 Westwood Plaza, #101, Brentwood TN 37027, USA

**Yan** — Singer, Guitarist (British Sea Power)
Agency Group Ltd, 361-373 City Road, London EC1V 1PQ, England

**Yan, Liangkun** — Conductor
Central Philharmonic Society, 11-1 Hepingjie, Beijing 100013, China

**Yanagimachi, Ryuzo** — Biologist
University of Hawaii, Biology Dept, 1960 East-West Road, Honolulu HI 96822, USA

**Yancy, Emily** — Actress
Geddes Agency, 8430 Santa Monica Blvd, #201, West Hollywood CA 90069 USA

**Yanda, Marshall J** — Football Player
Baltimore Ravens, Ravens Stadium, 1 Winning Dr, Baltimore MD 21230 USA

**Yanez, Eduardo** — Actor
Independent Group, 8444 Wilshire Blvd, #500, Beverly Hills CA 90211, USA

**Yang di-Pertuan Agong XIII** — Sultan, Malaysia
Sultan's Palace, Istana Bukit Serene, 50502 Kuala Lumpur, Malaysia

**Yang Liwei**
Satellite Launch Center, Jiuquan, Guangzhou Province, China — Taikonaut, China

**Yang, Chen Ning**
8 Dorfer Lane, Nesconset NY 11767, USA — Nobel Physics Laureate

**Yang, Jerry**
Asian Pacific Fund, 225 Bush St, #590, San Francisco CA 94104, USA — Businessman, Computer Programmer

**Yang, Philemon Y**
Prime Minister's Office, BP 1057, Yaounde, Cameroon — Prime Minister, Cameroon

**Yang, Shang-Fa**
118 Villanova Dr, Davis CA 95616, USA — Biochemist

**Yang, Xao (Jerry)**
30380 River Estate Dr, Madera CA 93636, USA — Poker Player

**Yang, Young Eun (Y E)**
Professional Golfer's Assn, PO Box 109601, Palm Beach Gardens FL 33410 USA — Golfer

**Yang, Zhiguang**
Guangzhou Fine Art Institute, 257 Chang Gang Dong Lu St, Guangzhou 510260, China — Artist

**Yani Tseng**
9713 Chiltern Garden Dr, Orlando FL 32827, USA — Golfer

**Yankelovich, Daniel**
Public Agenda Foundation, 6 E 39th St, #900, New York NY 10016, USA — Social Scientist

**Yankovic, Al (Weird Al)**
14 E Mountain Road, Katonah NY 10536, USA — Actor, Comedian, Singer, Songwriter

**Yankowski, Ronald W (Ron)**
1318 Wulfert Road, Sanibel FL 33957, USA — Football Player

**Yannas, I V**
Massachusetts Institute of Technology, Engineering School, Cambridge MA 02139, USA — Polymer Scientist, Mechanical Engineer

**Yanni**
10563 Arcole Court, Wellington FL 33449, USA — Keyboardist, Songwriter

**Yano, Kyoko**
Football Assn, 3-10-15 Hongo, Bunkyoku, Tokyo 113 0033 Japan — Soccer Player

**Yanofsky, Charles**
725 Mayfield Ave, Stanford CA 94305, USA — Biologist

**Yanofsky, Nicole (Nikki)**
A440 Entertainment, 3500 de Maisonneuve W, #800, Montreal QC H3Z 3C1, Canada — Singer, Songwriter

**Yanukovych, Viktor F**
President's Office, Bankova Str 11, 01220 Kiev, Ukraine — Prime Minister, Ukraine

**Yao Ming**
18923 Crescent Bay Dr, Houston TX 77094, USA — Basketball Player

**Yao, Andrew C C**
Princeton University, Mathematics Dept, Princeton NJ 08544, USA — Mathematician

**Yapo, Mennan**
Spielkind, Zimmerstr 11, 10969 Berlin, Germany — Director

**Yarborough, W Caleb (Cale)**
Yarborough Racing, 2723 W Palmetto St, #8, Florence SC 29501, USA — Auto Racing Driver

**Yarbrough, Glenn**
PO Box 331368, Nashville TN 37203, USA — Singer, Songwriter (Limeliters)

**Yardley, Jim**
New York Times, Editorial Dept, 229 W 43rd St, New York NY 10036 USA — Journalist

**Yardley, Jonathan**
223 Hawthorne Road, Baltimore MD 21210, USA — Journalist, Critic

**Yared, Gabriel**
V2 Scandinavia, Bondegatan 64C, 116 33 Stockholm, Sweden — Composer

**Yarnall, Celeste**
2899 Agoura Road, #315, Westlake CA 91361, USA — Actress

**Yarno, George A**
1081 White Pine Flats Road, Troy ID 83871, USA — Football Player

**Yarno, John R**
10535 158th Ave NE, Redmond WA 98052, USA — Football Player

**Yaro, Boris**
17042 Calahan St, Northridge CA 91325, USA — Photojournalist

**Yarrow, Noel Peter**
27 W 67th St, #5E, New York NY 10023, USA — Singer (Peter Paul & Mary), Songwriter

**Yary, A Ronald (Ron)**
38886 Calle de Companero, Murrieta CA 92562, USA — Football Player

**Yasbeck, Amy**
Innovative Artists, 1505 10th St, Santa Monica CA 90401 USA — Actress

**Yashin, Aleksei**
6 Polo Dr, Old Westbury NY 11568, USA — Ice Hockey Player

**Yastrzemski, Carl M**
22 Lakeshore Road, Boxford MA 01921, USA — Baseball Player

**Yasutake, Patti**
145 S Fairfax Ave, #310, Los Angeles CA 90036, USA — Actress

**Yates, Bill**
King Features Syndicate, 300 W 57th St, #1500, New York NY 10019 USA — Cartoonist (Redeye)

**Yates, Billy**
Red Ridge Entertainment, 1208 16th Ave S, Loer Lobby 1, Nashville TN 37212, USA — Singer, Songwriter

**Yates, David**
Casorotto Ramsay, Waverley House, 7-12 Noel St, London W1F 8GQ, England — Director

**Yates, Dorian A M**
Mr Olympia Corner, 21100 Erwin St, Woodland Hills CA 91367, USA — Body Builder

**Yates, Erica Lyndzey**
OmniPop Talent Group, 4605 Lankershim Blvd, #201, Toluca Lake CA 91602 USA — Actress, Comedienne

**Yates, J D**
1235 Lane 30 1/4, Pueblo CO 81006, USA — Rodeo Rider

**Yates, Jim**
Jim Yates Racing, 2725B Old Washington Road, Waldorf MD 20601, USA — Drag Racing Driver

**Yates, Robert**
18923 Cove Side Lane, Cornelius NC 28031, USA — Auto Racing Executive

**Yates, Ronald W (Ron)**
525 Silhouette Way, Monument CO 80132, USA — Air Force General

**Yates, Tyler K**
3718 Omao Road, Koloa HI 96756, USA — Baseball Player

**Yau, Alan**
Wagamama Ltd, Waverley House, 7-12 Noel St, London W1F 8GQ, England — Restauranteur, Chef

**Yau, Shing-Tung**
Harvard University, Mathematics Dept, 1 Oxford St, Cambridge MA 02138, USA — Mathematician

# Y

**Yawer, Sheik Ghazi Mashal Ajil al-** — President, Iraq
Al-Sijound Majalis, Karradat Mariam, Baghdad, Iraq

**Ybarra y Churruca, Emilio de** — Financier
Banco Bilbao-Vizcaya, Paseo de la Castellana 81, 28046 Madrid, Spain

**Ye, Xiaogang** — Composer
Central Music Conservatory, 43 Baojia St, Xicheng District, Beijing 100031 P R, China

**Yeager, Andrea** — Tennis Player
PO Box 11720, 155 Nighthawk Dr, Aspen CO 81612, USA

**Yeager, Bunny** — Photographer, Model
585 NE 92nd St, Miami Shores FL 33138, USA

**Yeager, Charles E (Chuck)** — Test Pilot, Air Force General
PO Box 1507, Penn Valley CA 95946, USA

**Yeager, Jeana** — Experimental Airplane Pilot
302 Chaparral Dr, Sunnyvale TX 75182, USA

**Yeager, Stephen W (Steve)** — Baseball Player
PO Box 34184, Granada Hills CA 91394, USA

**Yeagley, Jerry** — Soccer Coach
1418 S Sare Road, Bloomington IN 47401, USA

**Yeakel, G Scott** — Astronaut
14224 E Kalil Dr, Scottsdale AZ 85259, USA

**Yearwood, Trisha** — Singer
Trisha Yearwood Inc, 3310 W End Ave , #400, Nashville TN 37203, USA

**Yeates, Jeffrey L (Jeff)** — Football Player
3793 Club Dr NE, Atlanta GA 30319, USA

**Yelchin, Anton** — Actor
Creative Artists Agency, 2000 Ave of Stars, #100, Los Angeles CA 90067 USA

**Yelding, Eric G** — Baseball Player
PO Box 325, Montrose AL 36559, USA

**Yeley, Christopher B H (J J)** — Auto, Truck Racing Driver
Mayfield Motorsports, 2220 Highway 49 N, Harrisburg NC 28075, USA

**Yeliseyev, Aleksei S** — Cosmonaut
Bauman Higher Technical School, Baumanskaya Ul 5, 107005 Moscow, Russia

**Yelle** — Singer, Songwriter
E M I Records, 150 5th Ave, #700, New York NY 10011 USA

**Yelle, Staphane** — Ice Hockey Player
212 Maplehurst Point, Littleton CO 80126, USA

**Yellen, Janet L** — Government Official, Financier
3933 Highwood Court NW, Washington DC 20007, USA

**Yellen, Linda B** — Producer, Director
Keckins Projects, 3 Sheridan Square, New York NY 10014, USA

**Yellowbird, Shane** — Singer, Songwriter
Agency Group Ltd, 142 W 57th St, #600, New York NY 10019 USA

**Yelvington, Richard J (Dick), Jr** — Football Player
2105 Barbe St, Lake Charles LA 70601, USA

**Yen, Donnie** — Actor
Paradigm Agency, 360 N Crescent Dr, North Building, Beverly Hills CA 90210 USA

**Yeo, Mike** — Hockey Coach
Minnesota Wild, XCel Energy Arena, 1275 Saint Antoine W, Saint Paul MN 55104 USA

**Yeoh, Michelle** — Actress
Gotham Group, 9255 Sunset Blvd, #515, Los Angeles CA 90069, USA

**Yeohlee** — Fashion Designer
Yeohlee Designs, 225 W 35th St, #1600, New York NY 10001, USA

**Yeoman, Owain** — Actor
Safran Co, 2000 Ave of Stars, #600N Los Angeles CA 90067, USA

**Yeoman, Robert D** — Cinematographer
2931 Washington Ave, Santa Monica CA 90403, USA

**Yeoman, William F (Bill)** — Football Player, Coach
3030 Country Club Blvd, Sugar Land TX 77478, USA

**Yepremian, Garabed S (Garo)** — Football Player
200 W Harmony Road, West Grove PA 19390, USA

**Yergin, Daniel H** — Writer
Cambridge Energy Research Assoc, 55 Cambridge Parkway, Cambridge MA 02142, USA

**Yerman, Jack** — Track Athlete
753 Camellia Dr, Paradise CA 95969, USA

**Yershov, Valery** — Artist
Rima Fine Art, 7130 E Main St, Scottsdale AZ 85251, USA

**Yes, Phyllis A** — Artist, Sculptor
23 SW Boundary St, Portland OR 97239, USA

**Yespica, Aida** — Model, Actress
Lela Mora Mgmt, Viale Monza 9, 20125 Milan, Italy

**Yester, Jim** — Singer, Guitarist (Association)
Variety Artists, 1924 Spring St, Paso Robles CA 93446 USA

**Yeston, Maury** — Composer
Yale University, Music Dept, New Haven CT 06520, USA

**Yett, Richard M (Rich)** — Baseball Player
5840 E Fairbrook Circle, Mesa AZ 85205, USA

**Yeun, Steven** — Actor
S D B Partners, 1801 Ave of Stars, #902, Los Angeles CA 90067 USA

**Yeutter, Clayton K** — Secretary, Agriculture
10955 Martingale Court, Potomac MD 20854, USA

**Yevtushenko, Yevgeny A** — Writer
Kutuzovski Prospekt 2/1, #101, 121248 Moscow, Russia

**Yewcic, Thomas J (Tom)** — Football, Baseball Player
31 Cherokee Road, Arlington MA 02474, USA

**Yi Jianlian** — Basketball Player
Dallas Mavericks, Pavilion, 2909 Taylor St, Dallas TX 75226 USA

**Yi Mun Yol** — Writer
Wylie Agency, 250 W 57th St, #2114, New York NY 10107 USA

**Yi So Yeon** — Cosmonaut, South Korea
Advanced Science/Technology Institute, Yuseong, Daejeon, South Korea

**Yi, Charlyne** — Actress, Comedienne
Mosiac Media Group, 9200 W Sunset Blvd, #1000, Los Angeles CA 90069 USA

**Yildiz, Rifat** — Greco-Roman Wrestler
Karl-Heeg Str 13C, 63773 Goldbach, Germany

**Yin Jun** — Artist
Soemo Fine Arts, 66 Xiaopunanjie, Songzhuang Tongzhou District, Beijing, China

## Yawer - Yin Jun

**Ying Huang** — Actress, Opera Singer
Columbia Artists Mgmt Inc, 1790 Broadway, #702, New York NY 10019 USA
**Yingluck Shinawatra** — Prime Minister, Thailand
Prime Minister's Office, Thanon Nakhon Patnom, Bangkok 10300, Thailand
**Yoakam, Dwight** — Singer, Guitarist, Songwriter
Bluebird House, 10153 1/2 Riverside Drive, #419, Universal City CA 91602, USA
**Yoav** — Singer, Songwriter
Creative Artists Agency, 2000 Ave of Stars, #100, Los Angeles CA 90067 USA
**Yoba, Malik** — Actor
Innovative Artists, 1505 10th St, Santa Monica CA 90401 USA
**Yoccoz, Jean-Christophe** — Mathematician
University of Paris-Sud (Orsey), 91405 Orsay-Cedex-Bait 425, France
**Yock, Robert J** — Judge
US Claims Court, 717 Madison Place NW, Washington DC 20439, USA
**Yocum, Matt** — Sportscaster
9910 Devonshire Dr, Huntsville NC 28078, USA
**Yoffie, Eric** — Religious Leader, Rabbi
Union for Reform Judaism, 633 3rd Ave, #700, New York NY 10017, USA
**Yoken, Mel B** — Writer
261 Carroll St, New Bedford MA 02740, USA
**Yonath, Ada** — Nobel Chemistry Laureate
Weizmann Science Institute, PO Box 26, Rehovot 76100, Israel
**Yong, Cao** — Artist
Pierside Hunt Gallery, 300 Pacific Coast Highway, Huntington Beach CA 92648, USA
**Yoo, Aaron** — Actor
Blue Ridge Entertainment, 535 W 23rd St, #S10A, New York NY 10011, USA
**Yoon, Bora** — Composer
I M G Artists, Hogarth Business Park, Chiswick, London W4 2TH, England
**Yorio, Kimberly** — Writer
Y C Media, 145 W 28th St, #1200, New York NY 10001, USA
**York, Francine** — Actress
PO Box 55008, Sherman Oaks CA 91413, USA
**York, Glen P** — Vietnam War Air Force Hero
1620 E Driftwood Dr, Tempe AZ 85283, USA
**York, James H (Jim)** — Baseball Player
31262 Via del Verde, San Juan Capistrano CA 92675, USA
**York, John J** — Actor
Stone Manners Salners, 9911 W Pico Blvd, #1400, Los Angeles CA 90035 USA
**York, Kathleen (Bird)** — Actress, Singer, Songwriter
Bauman Redanty Shaul Agency, 5757 Wilshire Blvd, #473, Los Angeles CA 90036 USA
**York, Lila** — Choreographer
Paul Taylor Dancer Co, 551 Grand St, Lobby A, New York NY 10002, USA
**York, Marty** — Actor
24616 Town Center Dr, #4207, Valencia CA 91355, USA
**York, Michael** — Actor
Peter Strain, 5455 Wilshire Blvd, #1812, Los Angeles CA 90036 USA
**York, Michael (Mike)** — Ice Hockey Player
6105 W Longview Dr, East Lansing MI 48823, USA
**York, Michael M** — Journalist
Lexington Herald-Leader, Editorial Dept, Main & Midland, Lexington KY 40507, USA
**York, Rachel** — Actress
Stone Manners Salners, 9911 W Pico Blvd, #1400, Los Angeles CA 90035 USA
**York, Raymond** — Thoroughbred Racing Jockey
27918 Taft Highway, Taft CA 93268, USA
**York, Taylor** — Guitarist (Paramore), Songwriter
Big Hassle, 44 Wall St, #2200, New York NY 10005, USA
**Yorke, Thom** — Singer (Radiohead)
Courtyard, 21 Nursery, Sutton Courteney, Abingdon, Oxford OX14 4UA, England
**Yorkin, Alan (Bud)** — Producer, Director
Bud Yorkin Productions, 250 Delfern Dr, Los Angeles CA 90077, USA
**Yorkin, Peg** — Women's Activist
Fund for Feminist Majority, 1600 Wilson Blvd, #704, Arlington VA 22209, USA
**Yorn, Peter (Pete)** — Singer, Songwriter
Trampoline Records, 8581 Santa Monica Blvd, #511, West Hollywood CA 90069, USA
**Yorzyk, William A (Bill)** — Swimmer
162 W Sturbridge Road, #7, East Brookfield MA 01515, USA
**Yost, E Frederick (Ned), III** — Baseball Player, Manager
108 Victoria Dr, La Grange GA 30240, USA
**Yost, Graham J** — Actor, Producer, Writer
Creative Artists Agency, 2000 Ave of Stars, #100, Los Angeles CA 90067 USA
**Yost, Paul A, Jr** — Coast Guard Admiral
James Madison Memorial Foundation, 200 K St NW, Washington DC 20001, USA
**Yothers, Tina** — Actress, Singer
12368 Apple Dr, Chino CA 91710, USA
**Youk Chhang** — Social Activist
Documentation Center, 66 Preah Sihanouok Blvd, Phnom Penh, Cambodia
**Youkilis, Kevin E** — Baseball Player
19475 N Grayhawk Dr, #1083, Scottsdale AZ 85255, USA
**Youmans, Maurice E (Maury)** — Football Player
300 Beach Dr NE, #2104, Saint Petersburg FL 33701, USA
**Young Buck** — Rap Artist (G-Unit)
Emmel Commuications, 36 W 25th St, #200, New York NY 10010, USA
**Young Jeezy** — Rap Artist
I C M Partners, 10250 Constellation Blvd, #900, Los Angeles CA 90067 USA
**Young MC** — Rap Artist
Entertainment Artists, 2409 21st Ave S, #100, Nashville TN 10019 USA
**Young, Adam** — Singer/Songwriter/Musician (Owl City)
Foundations Artist Mgmt, 628 Broadway, #503, New York NY 10012, USA
**Young, Aden** — Actor
Shanahan Mgmt, PO Box 1509, Darlinghurst NSW 1300, Australia
**Young, Adrian** — Drummer (No Doubt)
Rebel Waltz, 31652 2nd Ave, Laguna Beach CA 92651, USA
**Young, Alan** — Actor
T G M D Talent Agency, 6767 Forest Lawn Dr, #101, Los Angeles CA 90068, USA
**Young, Andrew** — Diplomat; Mayor, Atlanta
National Council of Churches, 523 Spring Oaks Blvd, Altamonte Springs FL 32714, USA

# Y

**Young, Angus M** — Guitarist (AC/DC), Songwriter
Alberts Music, 9 Rangers Road, Neutral Bay, Sydney NSW 2089, Australia

**Young, Archie (Dropo)** — Baseball Player
1804 Ethel Ave SW, Birmingham AL 35211, USA

**Young, B Asa (Ace)** — Singer, Songwriter, Actor
Creative Artists Agency, 2000 Ave of Stars, #100, Los Angeles CA 90067 USA

**Young, Barbara** — Baseball Player
5078 Edinboro Lane, Wilmington NC 28409, USA

**Young, Bellamy** — Actress
Framework Entertainment, 9057 Nemo St, #C, West Hollywood CA 90069 USA

**Young, Bob** — Cartoonist (Tim Tyler's Luck)
King Features Syndicate, 300 W 57th St, #1500, New York NY 10019 USA

**Young, Bob** — Producer
I C M Partners, 10250 Constellation Blvd, #900, Los Angeles CA 90067 USA

**Young, Brian** — Singer, Drummer (Fountains of Wayne)
Big Hassle, 157 Chambers St, #1200, New York NY 10007, USA

**Young, Bryant C** — Football Player
8454 NW 64th Lane, Gainesville FL 32653, USA

**Young, Burt** — Actor
Higgins Harte Int'l, 11 Pioneer Blvd, #F, Mequite NV 89027, USA

**Young, Charle E** — Football Player
PO Box 1276, Woodinville WA 98072, USA

**Young, Christopher** — Composer
Costa Communications, 8265 Sunset Blvd, #101, Los Angeles CA 90046, USA

**Young, Christopher A (Chris)** — Singer
Ron Shapiro Mgmt, 56 W 22nd St, #601, New York NY 10010, USA

**Young, Christopher B (Chris)** — Baseball Player
Arizona Diamondbacks, Chase Field, 401 E Jefferson, Phoenix AZ 85003 USA

**Young, Christopher R (Chris)** — Baseball Player
966 Muirlands Vista Way, La Jolla CA 92037, USA

**Young, Cliff** — Singer, Guitarist (Caedmon's Call)
Breen Agency, 25 Music Square W, Nashville TN 37203, USA

**Young, Colville N** — Governor General, Belize
Governor General's Office, Belize House, Belnopan, Belize

**Young, Curtis A (Curt)** — Baseball Player
10800 E Cactus Road, #2, Scottsdale AZ 85259, USA

**Young, Cyrus (Cy)** — Track Athlete
518 Grimes Ave, Modesto CA 95358, USA

**Young, Danielle** — Singer, Guitarist (Caedmon's Call)
Breen Agency, 25 Music Square W, Nashville TN 37203, USA

**Young, Dean** — Cartoonist (Blondie)
King Features Syndicate, 300 W 57th St, #1500, New York NY 10019 USA

**Young, Delmon D** — Baseball Player
3922 E Northridge Circle, Mesa AZ 85215, USA

**Young, Delwyn R** — Baseball Player
2212 Radcourt Dr, Hacienda Heights CA 91745, USA

**Young, Dmitri D** — Baseball Player
Washington Nationals, 1500 S Capitol St SE, Washington DC 20003 USA

**Young, Earl** — Singer (Trammps)
Atlantic/Buddah Records, 1290 Ave of Americas, Concourse 3, New York NY 10104, USA

**Young, Earl V** — Track Athlete
4344 Livingston Ave, Dallas TX 75205, USA

**Young, Eric O** — Baseball Player
120 Brewster Ave, Piscataway NJ 08854, USA

**Young, Ernest W (Ernie)** — Baseball Player
8995 E Palm Ridge Dr, Scottsdale AZ 85260, USA

**Young, Fred** — Singer, Drummer (Kentucky Headhunters)
Webster & Assoc PR, PO Box 23015, Nashville TN 37202, USA

**Young, Frederick K (Fredd)** — Football Player
4200 Real del Sur, Las Cruces NM 88011, USA

**Young, George L** — Track Athlete
8926 N Cox Road, Casa Grande AZ 85194, USA

**Young, Gerald A** — Baseball Player
10014 Rain Cloud Dr, Houston TX 77095, USA

**Young, Guard** — Gymnast
4000 Worthington Dr, Norman OK 73072, USA

**Young, Heather Rae** — Model
Playboy Promotions, 2706 Media Center Dr, Los Angeles CA 90065 USA

**Young, Howard (Howie)** — Ice Hockey Player
5527 N 22nd Dr, Phoenix AZ 85015, USA

**Young, J Steven (Steve)** — Football Player, Sportscaster
Forever Young Foundation, 21952 S Brandon St, Farmington Hills MI 48336, USA

**Young, Jacob** — Actor
Community Entertainment, 12100 Wilshire Blvd, #1135, Los Angeles CA 90025, USA

**Young, James** — Guitarist (Eli Young Band)
Triple 8 Mgmt, 1611 W 6th St, Austin TX 78703, USA

**Young, Jesse Colin** — Singer, Guitarist, Bassist, Songwriter
Maximus Entertainment Booking, 2 Professional Dr, #240, Gaithersburg MD 20879, USA

**Young, Jim** — Football Coach
US Military Academy, Athletic Dept, West Point NY 10966, USA

**Young, John Lloyd** — Actor, Singer
I C M Partners, 10250 Constellation Blvd, #900, Los Angeles CA 90067 USA

**Young, John Paul** — Singer, Songwriter
Teamwork Productions, PO Box 302, Dulwich Hill, NSW 2303, Australia

**Young, John T** — Baseball Player
124 W 57th St, Los Angeles CA 90037, USA

**Young, John W** — Astronaut
N A S A, Johnson Space Center, 2101 NASA Road, Houston TX 77058 USA

**Young, Kathryn** — Golfer
323 Date Ave, Imperial Beach CA 91932, USA

**Young, Kathy** — Singer
Cape Entertainment, 4799 Coconut Creek Parkway, #258, Coconut Creek FL 33063, USA

**Young, Keone** — Actor
Gage Group, 14724 Ventura Blvd, #505, Sherman Oaks CA 91403 USA

**Young, Kevin** — Track Athlete
H S International Sports Mgmt, 9871 Irvine Center Dr, Irvine CA 92618, USA

**Young, Kevin S** — Baseball Player
832 E Taurus Place, Chandler AZ 85249, USA

**Young, Laurence Retman** — Astronaut
217 Thorndike St, #108, Cambridge MA 02141, USA

**Young, Lonnie R** — Football Player
16699 W Papago St, Goodyear AZ 85338, USA

**Young, Malcolm M** — Guitarist (AC/DC), Songwriter
Alberts Music, 9 Rangers Road, Neutral Bay, Sydney NSW 2089, Australia

**Young, Matthew J (Matt)** — Baseball Player
471 Maylin St, Pasadena CA 91105, USA

**Young, Michael** — Actor, Director, Producer
Media Four, 10100 Santa Monica Blvd, #2300, Los Angeles CA 90067, USA

**Young, Michael B** — Baseball Player
3508 Bryn Mawr Dr, Dallas TX 75225, USA

**Young, Michael D (Mike)** — Football Player
275 S Arroyo Parkway, #717, Pasadena CA 91105, USA

**Young, Michael K** — Educator
808 36th Ave E, Seattle WA 98112, USA

**Young, Mighty Joe** — Singer, Guitarist
Jay Reil, 3430 Bayberry Dr, Northbrook IL 60062, USA

**Young, Neil** — Singer, Songwriter
I C M Partners, 730 5th Ave, New York NY 10019 USA

**Young, Nick** — Basketball Player
Philadelphia 76ers, 1st Union Center, 3601 S Broad St, Philadelphia PA 19148 USA

**Young, Paul A** — Singer
Mission Control, 44 Alexander, Meole Brace, Shrewsbury SY3 9HS, England

**Young, R Gilchrist I (Chris)** — Composer
First Artists Mgmt, 4764 Park Granada, #210, Calabasas CA 91302 USA

**Young, Richard** — Singer, Guitarist (Kentucky Headhunters)
Webster & Assoc PR, PO Box 23015, Nashville TN 37202, USA

**Young, Richard S** — Space Scientist
137 Saint Croix Ave, Cocoa Beach FL 32931, USA

**Young, Richard S** — Photographer
110 Highlever Road, London W10 6PL, England

**Young, Rickey D** — Football Player
2438 Grenadier Ave N, Saint Paul MN 55128, USA

**Young, Robert (Nat)** — Surfer
8 Bay St, Angourie NSW 2464, Australia

**Young, Robert E** — Football Player
159 Boyd Lane, Carthage MS 39051, USA

**Young, Roger** — Director
Freedman Broder & Company, 10100 Santa Monica Blvd, Los Angeles CA 90067, USA

**Young, Roynell** — Football Player
11823 Beinhorn Dr, Houston TX 77065, USA

**Young, Rusty** — Pedal Steel Musician (Poco)
Rick Alter Mgmt, 1018 17th Ave S, #12, Nashville TN 37212, USA

**Young, S Ulysses** — Baseball Player
4023 W 60th St, Los Angeles CA 90043, USA

**Young, Samuel D (Sam)** — Basketball Player
Philadelphia 76ers, 1st Union Center, 3601 S Broad St, Philadelphia PA 19148 USA

**Young, Scott A** — Ice Hockey Player
17 Sandy Ridge Road, Sterling MA 01564, USA

**Young, Sean** — Actress
Gregg Edwards Mgmt, 6072 Franklin Ave, #304, Los Angeles CA 90028, USA

**Young, Simone** — Conductor
Hamburgische Staatsoper, Grosse Theaterstr 25, 20354 Hamburg, Germany

**Young, Sophie** — Basketball Player
San Antonio Silver Stars, 1 AT&T Center, San Antonio TX 78219 USA

**Young, Steve** — Singer, Guitarist, Songwriter
Rob Hall Acoustic Music, PO Box 2105, Ringwood North VIC 3134, Australia

**Young, Tata** — Singer
Tata Entertainment, 317 Komol Sukosol Building, Silom Road, Bangkok 10500, Thailand

**Young, Thaddeus C** — Basketball Player
Philadelphia 76ers, 1st Union Center, 3601 S Broad St, Philadelphia PA 19148 USA

**Young, Tim** — Ice Hockey Player
15808 Park Terrace Dr, Eden Prairie MN 55346, USA

**Young, Timothy R (Tim)** — Baseball Player
20730 SE Sherry Ave, Blountstown FL 32424, USA

**Young, Tom** — Basketball Coach
Washington Wizards, M C I Centre, 601 F St NW, Washington DC 20004 USA

**Young, Valerie D** — Actress
Bobby Ball Agency, 4116 W Magnolia Blvd, #205, Burbank CA 91505, USA

**Young, Vince P, Jr** — Football Player
12006 Legend Manor Dr, Houston TX 77082, USA

**Young, Vincent** — Actor
Bohemia Group, 8170 Beverly Blvd, #102, Los Angeles CA 90048, USA

**Young, Warren H** — Ice Hockey Player
5960 Murray Ave, Bethel Park PA 15102, USA

**Young, Wendell E** — Ice Hockey Player
1616 E Campbell St, Arlington Heights IL 60004, USA

**Young, Wilbur E, Jr** — Football Player
119 Hartford Court, Charlottesville VA 22902, USA

**Young, William** — Labor Leader
National Assn of Letter Carriers, 100 Indiana NW, #709, Washington DC 20001, USA

**Young, William Allen** — Actor
Sovereign Talent Group, 8421 Wilshire Blvd, #200, Beverly Hills CA 90211, USA

**Young, William J L (Willie)** — Football Player
PO Box 426, Grambling LA 71245, USA

**Young, William R (Will)** — Singer, Actor
19 Music & Mgmt, 35-37 Parkgate Road, London SW11 4NP, England

**Young, Wise** — Neuroscientist
Rutgers University, Collaborative Neuroscience Center, New Brunswick NJ 08901, USA

**Youngberg, Renae** — Baseball Player
2001 Gasparilla Road, #A25, Placida FL 33946, USA

**Youngblood, H Jackson (Jack)** — Football Player, Sportscaster
4377 Steed Terrace, Winter Park FL 32792, USA

| | |
|---|---|
| **Youngblood, Jimmy L (Jim)**<br>1000 Kilgore Bridge Road, Woodruff SC 29388, USA | Football Player |
| **Youngblood, Joel R**<br>4446 E Camelback Road, #113, Phoenix AZ 85018, USA | Baseball Player |
| **Youngblood, Mary**<br>Silver Wave Records, PO Box 7943, Boulder CO 80306, USA | Flutist, Composer |
| **Youngen, Lois J**<br>45 Prall Lane, Eugene OR 97405, USA | Baseball Player |
| **Younger, Ben**<br>Brillstein Entertainment Partners, 9150 Wilshire Blvd, #350, Beverly Hills CA 90212 USA | Director, Producer, Writer |
| **Youngerman, Jack**<br>PO Box 508, Bridgehampton NY 11932, USA | Artist, Sculptor |
| **Younghans, Tom**<br>52 Douglas St, # 3, Saint Paul MN 55102, USA | Ice Hockey Player |
| **Young-Ochowicz, Sheila G**<br>945 Hutchinson Ave, Palo Alto CA 94301, USA | Speed Skater, Cyclist |
| **Youngs, Elaine**<br>Q Sports Marketing, 534 W Evergreen St, Wheaton IL 60187 USA | Volleyball Player |
| **Younis, Waqar**<br>Surrey County Cricket Club, Kennington Oval, London SE11 5SS, England | Cricketer |
| **Yount, Robin R**<br>5040 E Shea Blvd, #254, Scottsdale AZ 85254, USA | Baseball Player |
| **Youso, Frank M**<br>PO Box 1046, International Falls MN 56649, USA | Football Player |
| **Yowarsky, Walter (Walt)**<br>395 Dogwood Place NW, Cleveland TN 37312, USA | Football Player |
| **Yo-Yo**<br>Bridge & Tunnel Communications, 9157 Sunset Blvd, #205, West Hollywood CA 90069, USA | Singer, Actress |
| **Ysebaert, Paul R**<br>10 Harbor Blvd, #W528, Destin FL 32541, USA | Ice Hockey Player |
| **Yu Panglin**<br>Super 8 Hotel, 4 Shang Meilin Kaifeng Road, Shenzhen 518001, China | Businessman, Philanthropist |
| **Yu, Jessica**<br>Anonymous Content, 3532 Hayden Ave, Culver City CA 90232 USA | Director, Producer, Writer |
| **Yuan, Ron**<br>I C M Partners, 10250 Constellation Blvd, #900, Los Angeles CA 90067 USA | Actor |
| **Yuasa, Joji**<br>1517 Shields Ave, Encinitas CA 92024, USA | Composer |
| **Yudashkin, Valentin A**<br>Valentin Yudashkin Fashion House, Kutuzovsky Pr 19, 121151 Moscow, Russia | Fashion Designer |
| **Yudhoyono, Susilo Bambang**<br>President's Office, 15 Jalam Merdeka Utara, Jarkata, Indonesia | President, Indonesia; Army General |
| **Yue Jingyu**<br>Physical Culture/Sports Bureau, 9 Tiyuguan Road, Beijing 100763, China | Swimmer |
| **Yuen Woo-Ping**<br>Creative Artists Agency, 2000 Ave of Stars, #100, Los Angeles CA 90067 USA | Director, Choreographer |
| **Yukmouth**<br>Entertainment Artists, 2409 21st Ave S, #100, Nashville TN 10019 USA | Rap Musician |
| **Yulin, Harris**<br>Parseghian Planco, 322 8th Ave, #601, New York NY 10001, USA | Actor |
| **Yun Suk-Young**<br>Football Assn, 1-131 Sinmunno, 2-Ga Jongno-Gu, Seoul 110 062, South Korea | Soccer Player |
| **Yune, Rick**<br>Creative Artists Agency, 2000 Ave of Stars, #100, Los Angeles CA 90067 USA | Actor |
| **Yung Joc**<br>Brass Artists, 9025 Wilshire Blvd, #400, Beverly Hills CA 90211, USA | Rap Artist |
| **Yunis, Jorge J**<br>Thomas Jefferson University, Jefferson Medical College, Philadelphia PA 19107, USA | Geneticist, Pathologist |
| **Yunus, Muhammad**<br>Grameen Bank Bhavan, Mirpur 1, Dhaka 1216, Bangladesh | Nobel Peace Laureate |
| **Yurchikhin, Fyodor N**<br>N A S A, Johnson Space Center, 2101 NASA Road, Houston TX 77058 USA | Cosmonaut |
| **Yushkevich, Dmitri S**<br>International Sports Advisors, 878 Ridge View Way, Franklin Lakes NJ 07417, USA | Ice Hockey Player |
| **Yuspa, Cathy**<br>I C M Partners, 10250 Constellation Blvd, #900, Los Angeles CA 90067 USA | Producer |
| **Yustman, Odette**<br>Evolution Entertainment, 901 N Highland Ave, Los Angeles CA 90038 USA | Actress, Model |
| **Yusuf**<br>Creative Artists Agency, 2000 Ave of Stars, #100, Los Angeles CA 90067 USA | Singer, Songwriter |
| **Yusupova, Lidia**<br>Memorial Library, Malyy Karetnyy Pereulok 12, 127051 Moscow, Russia | Social Activist |
| **Yzaguirre, Raul**<br>National Council of La Raza, 1111 19th St NW, #1000, Washington DC 20036, USA | Social Activist |
| **Yzerman, Stephen G (Steve)**<br>PO Box 488, Bloomfield Hills MI 48303, USA | Ice Hockey Player, Executive |

| | |
|---|---|
| **Zaa, Charlie**<br>A-PR Media, 8334 Lefferts Blvd, #3C, Kew Gardens NY 11415, USA | Singer |
| **Zabaleta, Nicanor**<br>Villa Izar, Aldapeta, 20009 San Sebasatian, Spain | Concert Harpist |
| **Zabel, Mark**<br>Grosse Fischerei 18A, 39240 Calbe/Saale, Germany | Canoeing Athlete |
| **Zabel, Steven G (Steve)**<br>6000 Oak Tree Road, Edmond OK 73025, USA | Football Player |
| **Zabransky, Libor**<br>Rybarska Specialka Zabransky Koliste 59, Brno 60200, Czech Republic | Ice Hockey Player |
| **Zabriski, Bruce**<br>6228 Winding Lake Dr, Jupiter FL 33458, USA | Golfer |
| **Zabriskie, Grace**<br>Innovative Artists, 1505 10th St, Santa Monica CA 90401 USA | Actress |
| **Zachara, Jan**<br>Sladkovicova 13, 018 51 Nova Dubnica, Czech Republic | Boxer |
| **Zacharias, Christian**<br>I M G Artists, Hogarth Business Park, Chiswick, London W4 2TH, England | Concert Pianist, Conductor |
| **Zachry, Patrick P (Pat)**<br>7611 Bosque Blvd, Woodway TX 76712, USA | Baseball Player |
| **Zackham, Justin**<br>Two Tons Films, 375 Greenwich St, New York NY 10013, USA | Producer, Director, Writer |
| **Zadan, Craig**<br>Creative Artists Agency, 2000 Ave of Stars, #100, Los Angeles CA 90067 USA | Producer |
| **Zadeh, Lofti A**<br>904 Mendocino Ave, Berkeley CA 94707, USA | Computer Scientist (Fuzzy Logic) |
| **Zadel, C William**<br>Millipore Corp, 75 Wiggins Ave, Bedford MA 01730, USA | Businessman |
| **Zadora, Pia**<br>Marseille Company Mgmt, 6228 Fallbrook Ave, Woodland Hills CA 91367, USA | Actress, Singer, Model |
| **Zaentz, Saul**<br>Saul Zaentz Co, 2600 10th St, Berkeley CA 94710, USA | Producer |
| **Zaffaroni, Alejandro C**<br>Alza Corp, 6500 Paseo Padre Parkway, Fremont CA 94555, USA | Biochemist |
| **Zagorin, Perez**<br>1015 33rd St NW, #606, Washington DC 20007, USA | Historian |
| **Zagrosek, Lothar**<br>Kunstler Sekretariat am Gasteig, Rosenheimer Str 52, 81669 Munich, Germany | Conductor |
| **Zagunis, Mariel**<br>Robert F Zagunis, 20235 SW Gassner Road, Beaverton OR 97007, USA | Fencer |
| **Zahn, Geoffrey C (Geof)**<br>6536 Walsh Road, Dexter MI 48130, USA | Baseball Player |
| **Zahn, Paula A**<br>188 E 76th St, New York NY 10021, USA | Commentator |
| **Zahn, Steve**<br>W M E Entertainment, 9601 Wilshire Blvd, #300, Beverly Hills CA 90210 USA | Actor |
| **Zahn, Timothy**<br>PO Box 1755, Coos Bay OR 97420, USA | Writer |
| **Zahn, Wayne**<br>5018 S Barley Court, Gilbert AZ 85298, USA | Bowler |
| **Zaillian, Steven**<br>Film Rights, 159 S Beverly Dr, Beverly Hills CA 90212, USA | Director, Writer |
| **Zaine, Rod**<br>64 Drouin St, Ottawa ON K1K 2A7, Canada | Ice Hockey Player |
| **Zakarin, Mark**<br>Gersh Agency, 9465 Wilshire Blvd, #600, Beverly Hills CA 90212 USA | Writer, Producer |
| **Zaks, Jerry**<br>Helen Merrill, 825 8th Ave, #2600, New York NY 10019, USA | Director |
| **Zal, Roxana**<br>8265 W Sunset Blvd, #101, West Hollywood CA 90046, USA | Actress |
| **Zalapski, Zarley B**<br>Eishockey Club Olten, Postfach 523, 4601 Olten, Switzerland | Ice Hockey Player |
| **Zalesky, Jim**<br>University of Iowa, Athletic Dept, Iowa City IA 52242, USA | Freestyle Wrestler, Coach |
| **Zaletin, Sergei**<br>Cosmonaut Training Center, Star City, 141160 Zvezdny Gorodok, Moscow Oblast, Russia | Cosmonaut |
| **Zalyotin, Sergei V**<br>Cosmonaut Training Center, Star City, 141160 Zvezdny Gorodok, Moscow Oblast, Russia | Cosmonaut |
| **Zamba, Frieda**<br>2706 S Central Ave, Flagler Beach FL 32136, USA | Surfer |
| **Zambarloukos, Haris**<br>United Agents, 12-26 Lexington St, London W1F 0LE, England | Cinematographer |
| **Zambello, Francesca**<br>Opus 3 Artists, 470 Park Ave S, #900N, New York NY 10016 USA | Director |
| **Zametkin, Alan J**<br>National Mental Health Institute, 9000 Rockville Pike, Bethesda MD 20892, USA | Psychiatrist |
| **Zamfir, Gheorghe**<br>Lenhartzstr 15, 20249 Hamburg, Germany | Concert Pan-Pipes Player, Conductor |
| **Zamka, George D**<br>1936 Mandy Lane, League City TX 77573, USA | Astronaut |
| **Zampella, Vince**<br>Respawn Entertainment, PO Box 5650, Sherman Oaks CA 91413, USA | Video Game Developer |
| **Zamuner, Robert F (Rob)**<br>4317 Beau Rivage Circle, Lutz FL 33558, USA | Ice Hockey Player |
| **Zanardi, Alessandro (Alex)**<br>Via B Bordone 12, 35134 Padova, Italy | Auto Racing Driver |
| **Zander, Carl A**<br>2536 W Palomino Dr, Chandler AZ 85224, USA | Football Player |
| **Zander, Robin**<br>Oakie Dokie Mgmt, 6090 Central Ave, Saint Petersburg FL 33707, USA | Singer, Guitarist (Cheap Trick) |
| **Zander, Thomas**<br>Grundfeldstr 23, 73432 Aalen, Germany | Greco-Roman Wrestler |
| **Zanders, Emmanuel**<br>11015 Goodwood Blvd, Baton Rouge LA 70815, USA | Football Player |
| **Zandonella, Roberto**<br>Olympic Committee, Foro Italico, Largo Lauro de Bosis 15, 00135 Rome, Italy | Bobsled Athlete |

**Z**

**Zaa - Zandonella**

**Zane, Billy** — Actor
Paradigm Agency, 360 N Crescent Dr, North Building, Beverly Hills CA 90210 USA

**Zane, Frank** — Body Builder
PO Box 1090, La Mesa CA 91944, USA

**Zane, Lisa** — Actress
505 N Lake Shore Dr, #5407, Chicago IL 60611, USA

**Zanes, Dan** — Singer, Songwriter
Pomegranate Arts, 1140 Broadway, #305, New York NY 10001, USA

**Zanetti, Eugenio** — Actor, Director, Production Designer
Sandra Marsh Assoc, 9150 Wilshire Blvd, #220, Beverly Hills CA 90212 USA

**Zanetti, Massimo** — Conductor
I M G Artists, Hogarth Business Park, Chiswick, London W4 2TH, England

**Zanier, Michael (Mike)** — Ice Hockey Player
306 Rossland Ave, Trail BC V1R 3M8, Canada

**Zanni, Dominick T (Dom)** — Baseball Player
7 Sussex Ave, Massapequa NY 11758, USA

**Zano, Nick** — Actor
United Talent Agency, U T A Plaza, 9336 Civic Center Dr, Beverly Hills CA 90210 USA

**Zanotto, Kendra** — Synchronized Swimmer
18834 Lakeview Court, Los Gatos CA 95033, USA

**Zanova Steindler, Alena (Aja)** — Figure Skater
Wollman Skating Rink, 830 5th Ave, New York NY 10065, USA

**Zanuck, Lili Fini** — Producer, Director
Zanuck Co, 1600 Summitridge Dr, Beverly Hills CA 90210, USA

**Zanussi, Krzysztof** — Director, Producer, Writer
Ul Kaniowska 114, 01529, Warsaw, Poland

**Zanussi, Ronald K (Ron)** — Ice Hockey Player
PO Box 11326, Saint Paul MN 55111, USA

**Zapata, Carmen** — Actress
C E S D, 10635 Santa Monica Blvd, #130, Los Angeles CA 90025 USA

**Zapf, Hermann** — Book, Type Designer
2 Hammarskjold Plaza, New York NY 10017, USA

**Zapiro** — Editorial Cartoonist
Double Storey Books, PO Box 24299, Lansdowne 7779, South Africa

**Zapp, James (Jim)** — Baseball Player
820 Youngs Lane, Nashville TN 37207, USA

**Zappa, Ahmet** — Actor, Writer, Producer
I C M Partners, 10250 Constellation Blvd, #900, Los Angeles CA 90067 USA

**Zappa, Diva** — Actress
J K A Talent Agency, 12725 Ventura Blvd, #H, Studio City CA 91604, USA

**Zappa, Dweezil** — Singer, Guitarist, Actor
7885 Woodrow Wilson Dr, Los Angeles CA 90046, USA

**Zappa, Moon Unit** — Singer, Actress
J K A Talent Agency, 12725 Ventura Blvd, #H, Studio City CA 91604, USA

**Zarate Serna, Carlos** — Boxer
Gene Aguilera, PO Box 113, Montebello CA 90640, USA

**Zasada, Sobieslaw** — Auto Racing Driver
Zasada S A, Ul Omulewska 27, 04128 Warsaw, Poland

**Zaslav, David M** — Businessman
Discovery Communications Inc, One Discovery Place, Silver Spring MD 20910, USA

**Zatkoff, Roger** — Football Player
882 Hidden Ravines Court, Birmingham MI 48009, USA

**Zatopkova, Dana** — Track Athlete
Nad Kazankov 3, 17100 Prague 7, Czech Republic

**Zaun, Gregory O (Gregg)** — Baseball Player
26 E 6th St, #701, Cincinnati OH 45202, USA

**Zaveri, Anjala** — Actress
604 Jupiter Apts, Yari Road, Andheri, Mumbai MS 400058, India

**Zavisha, Brad** — Ice Hockey Player
General Delivery, Hines Creek AB T0H 2A0, Canada

**Zavos, Panos M** — Biologist
181 Collins Lane, Lexington KY 40503, USA

**Zayas, David** — Actor
Innovative Artists, 1505 10th St, Santa Monica CA 90401 USA

**Zayas, Victor Hugo** — Artist
Brewery Art Complex, 2100 N Main St, #A10, Los Angeles CA 90031, USA

**Zaz** — Singer
Sony Music, Neumarkter Str 28, 81673 Munich, Germany

**Zazzo, Lawrence** — Opera Singer
Harrison/Parrott, 5-6 Albion Court, London W6 0QT, England

**Zdrok, Victoria N** — Model, Actress, Dancer
PO Box 332, Pompton Lakes NJ 07442, USA

**Zea, Natalie** — Actress
True Mgmt, 8964 W 25th St, Los Angeles CA 90034, USA

**Zech, Lando W, Jr** — Navy Admiral, Government Official
1 White Flint N, 11555 Rockville Pike, Rockville MD 20852, USA

**Zeckendorf, William, Jr** — Businessman
502 Park Ave, New York NY 10022, USA

**Zeckhauser, Richard J** — Economist
138 Irving St, Cambridge MA 02138, USA

**Zedda, Alberto** — Conductor, Composer
Academia Rossiniana, Via Rossini 1, 61100 Pesaro, Italy

**Zedillo Ponce de Leon, Ernesto** — President, Mexico
Institutional Revolutionary, Insurges N 61, Mexico City 06350 DF, Mexico

**Zedlitz, Jean** — Golfer
4587 Gatetree Circle, Pleasanton CA 94566, USA

**Zednik, Richard** — Ice Hockey Player
4401 N Federal Highway, Boca Raton FL 33431, USA

**Zeffirelli, G Franco** — Director
Via Lucio Volumnio 37, 00178 Rome, Italy

**Zegen, Michael (Mike)** — Actor
United Talent Agency, U T A Plaza, 9336 Civic Center Dr, Beverly Hills CA 90210 USA

**Zegers, Kevin** — Actor
I C M Partners, 10250 Constellation Blvd, #900, Los Angeles CA 90067 USA

**Zeglis, John D** — Businessman
A T & T Wireless Group, 7277 164th Ave NE, Redmond WA 98052, USA

**Zehetner, Nora** — Actress
A P A Talent/Literary Agency, 405 S Beverly Dr, #300, Beverly Hills CA 90212 USA

**Zehr, Joey** — Actor, Drummer (Click Five)
Creative Artists Agency, 2000 Ave of Stars, #100, Los Angeles CA 90067 USA

**Zehringer, Rick** — Singer, Guitarist (McCoys)
Brothers Management Assoc, 141 Dunbar Ave, Fords NJ 08863 USA

**Zehrt, Monika Landgraf-** — Track Athlete
Stormstr 42, 15827 Blankenfelde, Germany

**Zeidan, Ali** — Prime Minister, Libya
Prime Minister's Office, Ghabat Al Nasr Convention Centre, Tripoli, Libya , USA

**Zeidel, Lazarus (Larry)** — Ice Hockey Player
6663 Erdrick St, Philadelphia PA 19135, USA

**Zeidler, Eberard H** — Architect, Designer
Zeidler Grinnell Partnership, 315 Queen St W, Toronto ON M5V 2X2, Canada

**Zeier, Eric R** — Football Player
PO Box 327, Nashville GA 31639, USA

**Zeifman, Jerome** — Attorney
57 North St, #105, Danbury CT 06810, USA

**Zeigler, C Dustin (Dusty)** — Football Player
440 Hodgeville Road, Guyton GA 31312, USA

**Zeigler, Marie** — Baseball Player
2502 N 22nd Ave, Phoenix AZ 85009, USA

**Zeile, Todd E** — Baseball Player
2324 Crombie Court, Thousand Oaks CA 91361, USA

**Zeitler, Kevin** — Football Player
Cincinnati Bengals, 1 Paul Brown Stadium, Cincinnati OH 45202 USA

**Zeitlin, Benh** — Director, Writer
W M E Entertainment, 9601 Wilshire Blvd, #300, Beverly Hills CA 90210 USA

**Zelenka, Joseph J (Joe)** — Football Player
12572 Highview Dr, Jacksonville FL 32225, USA

**Zelenskaya, Yelena E** — Opera Singer
Bolshoi Theater, Teatralnaya Pl 1, 103009 Moscow, Russia

**Zelepukin, Valeri M** — Ice Hockey Player
9595 Collins Ave, #610, Surfside FL 33154, USA

**Zelezny, Jan** — Track Athlete
Rue Armady 683, 29301 Boleslav, Czech Republic

**Zeliaeva, Valentina** — Model
Women Model Mgmt, 199 Lafayette St, #700, New York NY 10012 USA

**Zeller, Cody A** — Basketball Player
Charlotte Bobcats, 333 E Trade St, #A, Charlotte NC 28202 USA

**Zellner, Hunndens G (Peppi)** — Football Player
31 Dew Place, Forsyth GA 31029, USA

**Zellweger, Renee** — Actress
John Carrabino Mgmt, 5900 Wilshire Blvd, #406, Los Angeles CA 90036 USA

**Zelman, Aaron** — Writer, Producer
3 Arts Entertainment, 9460 Wilshire Blvd, #700, Beverly Hills CA 90212 USA

**Zelman, Daniel** — Producer, Writer, Actor
Stone Meyer Genow, 9665 Wilshire Blvd, #510, Beverly Hills CA 90212 USA

**Zelmani, Sophie** — Singer
United Stage Artists, PO Box 11029, 100 61 Stockholm, Sweden

**Zem, Roschdy** — Actor, Director
Artmedia, 20 Ave Rapp, 75007 Paris, France

**Zeman, E Robert (Bob)** — Football Player
4427 Maple Dr, Eagle River WI 54521, USA

**Zeman, Milos** — Prime Minister, Czech Republic
President's Office, Prague Castle, Prazsky Hrad, Hradecek, 11908 Prague 1, Czech Republic

**Zembriski, Walter** — Golfer
6507 Doubletrace Lane, Orlando FL 32819, USA

**Zemeckis, Robert L** — Director
ImageMovers, 100 Universal City, Bungalow 5170, Los Angeles CA 91608, USA

**Zen Ze Kiun, Joseph Cardinal** — Religious Leader
Diocese of Hong Kong, 16 Caine Road, #12F, Hong Kong, China

**Zendaya** — Actress
Monster Talent Mgmt, 6333 W 3rd St, #912, Los Angeles CA 90036, USA

**Zendejas, Anthony G (Tony)** — Football Player
24430 Avendia de Marcia, Yorba Linda CA 92887, USA

**Zender Meier, Gladys** — Beauty Queen
Miss Universe Organization, 1370 Ave of Americas, #1600, New York NY 10019 USA

**Zender, J W Hans** — Conductor, Composer
Horbener Str 28, 79100 Freiburg, Germany

**Zender, Stuart P J** — Bassist (Jamiroquai)
Nettwerk Mgmt, 6525 W Sunset Blvd, #800, Los Angeles CA 90028 USA

**Zent, Jason** — Ice Hockey Player
271 Dartmouth St, #4G, Boston MA 02116, USA

**Zentilli, Patricia** — Actress
Characters Talent Agency, 8 Elm St, Toronto ON M5G 1G7, Canada

**Zentmyer, George A, Jr** — Plant Pathologist
955 S El Camino Real, #216, San Mateo CA 94402, USA

**Zerbe, Anthony** — Actor
1175 High Road, Santa Barbara CA 93108, USA

**Zereoue, Amos L** — Football Player
226 Westside Ave, #B, Freeport NY 11520, USA

**Zerhouni, Elias A** — Government Official, Physician
National Institutes of Health, 9000 Rockville Pike, Bethesda MD 20892, USA

**Zero, Mark** — Singer (Randy & the Rainbows)
PO Box 656507, Fresh Meadows NY 11365, USA

**Zervas, Nicholas T** — Neurosurgeon
100 Canton Ave, Milton MA 02186, USA

**Zeta-Jones, Catherine** — Actress, Model
Independent Talent Group, 40 Whitfield St, London W1T 2RH, England

**Zetsche, Dieter** — Businessman
Daimler-Chrysler AG, Plieningerstr, 70546 Stuttgart, Germany

**Zetterberg, C Henrik** — Ice Hockey Player
1780 Hammond Court, Bloomfield Hills MI 48304, USA

**Zetterlund Bush, Yoko** — Volleyball Player
4055 Crystal Dawn Lane, #205, San Diego CA 92122, USA

**Zetumer, Joshua (Josh)**
United Talent Agency, U T A Plaza, 9336 Civic Center Dr, Beverly Hills CA 90210 USA — Writer, Producer
**Zewail, Ahmed H**
871 Winston Ave, San Marino CA 91108, USA — Nobel Chemist Laureate
**Zezelj, Danijel**
D C Comics, 1700 Broadway, #400, New York NY 10019, USA — Cartoonist, Writer
**Zgonina, Jeffrey M (Jeff)**
5418 Lampasas St, Houston TX 77056, USA — Football Player
**Zhai Zhigang**
Satellite Launch Center, Jiuquan, Guangzhou Province, China — Taikonaut, China
**Zhamnov, Alexei Y**
1950 N Orchard St, Chicago IL 60614, USA — Ice Hockey Player
**Zhang Dan**
Skating Assn, 56 Zhonguachun South St, Beijing 100044, China — Figure Skater
**Zhang Hao**
Skating Assn, 56 Zhonguachun South St, Beijing 100044, China — Figure Skater
**Zhang Jie**
501 Qian-Men Xi Da Jie, #97, Beijing 100031, China — Writer
**Zhang Xianliang**
Ningxia Writers' Assn, Yinchuan City, China — Writer
**Zhang Yimou**
Edko Films, 1212 Tiwer 2, Admiralty Centre, Hong Kong, China — Director
**Zhang Ziyi**
Flying Box Co, 1-4-20 Nishi Azabu, Minato, Tokyo 106 0031, Japan — Actress
**Zhang, Haochen**
I M G Artists, Hogarth Business Park, Chiswick, London W4 2TH, England — Concert Pianist
**Zhang, Liping**
I C M Artists, 40 W 57th St, #1800, New York NY 10019 USA — Opera Singer
**Zhang, Xian**
Coro Sinfonico di Milano Giuseppe Verdi, Via Clerici 3, 20121 Milan, Italy — Conductor
**Zhao Hongbo**
Skating Assn, 56 Zhonguanchun South St, Beijing 100044, China — Figure Skater
**Zhao Yanxia**
24 Xusubai 2nd Lane, Beijing 100034, China — Opera Singer
**Zhe Xi Lo**
Carnegie Natural History Museum, 4400 Forbes Ave, Pittsburgh PA 15213, USA — Anthropologist
**Zhen Haixia**
Physical Culture Bureau, 9 Tiyuguan Lu, Beijing 100061, China — Basketball Player
**Zhenan Bao**
A T & T Bell Lucent Laboratory, 600 Mountain Ave, New Providence NJ 07974 USA — Chemist, Inventor (Molecule Transistor)
**Zheng, Wei**
Johns Hopkins University, Astronomy Dept, Baltimore MD 21218, USA — Astronomer
**Zhirinovsky, Vladimir V**
State Duma, Okhotny Ryad 1, 103009 Moscow, Russia — Government Leader, Russia
**Zhislin, Grigory Y**
25 Whitehall Gardens, London W3 9RD, England — Concert Violinist
**Zhitnik, Alexei N**
8 Boxwood Way, Manhasset NY 11030, USA — Ice Hockey Player
**Zholobov, Vitali M**
Ul Yanvarskovo Vostaniya D 12, 252010 Kiev, Ukraine — Cosmonaut
**Zhou Long**
University of Missouri, Music Dept, Kansas City MO 64110, USA — Composer
**Zhudov, Vyacheslav D**
Cosmonaut Training Center, Star City, 141160 Zvezdny Gorodok, Moscow Oblast, Russia — Cosmonaut
**Zhulin, Alexsander V (Sasha)**
Skating Federation, Luchnekskaia Nab 8, 119871 Moscow, Russia — Ice Dancer
**Zhvanetsky, Mikhail M**
Lesnaya Str 4, #63, 125047 Moscow, Russia — Writer, Actor
**Zia, Begum Khaleda**
Bangladesh National Party, 29 Minto Road, Dhaka, Bangladesh — Prime Minister, Bangladesh
**Ziblijew, Wassili**
Cosmonaut Training Center, Star City, 141160 Zvezdny Gorodok, Moscow Oblast, Russia — Cosmonaut
**Zich, Denise**
Management Goldschmidt, Damaschkestr 33, 10711 Berlin, Germany — Actress
**Zicherman, Stu**
W M E Entertainment, 9601 Wilshire Blvd, #300, Beverly Hills CA 90210 USA — Producer, Writer
**Zickel, Mather**
Abrams Artists, 9200 W Sunset Blvd, #1125, West Hollywood CA 90069 USA — Actor
**Zidan, Ali**
Prime Minister's Office, Monrovia, Liberia — Prime Minister, Libya
**Zidane, Zinedine**
F C Real Madrid, Avda Concha Espana 1, 28036 Madrid, Spain — Soccer Player
**Zidek, Jiri (George)**
551 Landfair Ave, Los Angeles CA 90024, USA — Basketball Player
**Zidi, Malik**
Agence Artiste Adequet, 108 Rue Reaumur, 75002 Paris, France — Actor
**Zidlicky, Marek**
2006 Sweetbriar Ave, Nashville TN 37212, USA — Ice Hockey Player
**Ziegelmeyer, Nicole (Nikki)**
5912 Mastodon Pines Dr, Imperial MO 63052, USA — Speed Skater
**Ziegler, Alma**
403 Gold St, Auburn CA 95603, USA — Baseball Player
**Ziegler, Bill**
King Features Syndicate, 300 W 57th St, #1500, New York NY 10019 USA — Cartoonist
**Ziegler, Dolores**
Lynda Kay, 2702 Crestworth Lane, Buford GA 30519, USA — Opera Singer
**Ziegler, Jack**
New Yorker, Editorial Dept, 4 Times Square, Basement C1B, New York NY 10036 USA — Cartoonist
**Ziegler, John A, Jr**
3 Club Dr, Jupiter FL 33469, USA — Ice Hockey Player
**Ziegler, John L**
University of California Cancer Center, 2340 Sutter St, San Francisco CA 94115, USA — Oncologist
**Ziegler, Kate**
George Mason University, Athletic Dept, Fairfax VA 22030, USA — Swimmer
**Ziegler, Larry**
10315 Luton Court, Orlando FL 32836, USA — Golfer

**Ziegler, Marie**
6739 W Polk St, Phoenix AZ 85043, USA — Baseball Player

**Zielcke, Marie**
Kings Mgmt, Kaiserswerther Markt 29, 40489 Dusseldorf, Germany — Actress

**Zielenbach, Jen**
W Mgmt, 266 Elizabeth St, #1A, New York NY 10012, USA — Bassist (Antigone Rising)

**Ziem, Steven G (Steve)**
1309 Avalon Ave, Beaumont CA 92223, USA — Baseball Player

**Ziemann, Sonja**
Via del Alp Dorf, 7500 Saint Moritz, Switzerland — Actress

**Ziemba, Karen**
Talent Works, 3500 W Olive Ave, #1400, Burbank CA 91505 USA — Singer, Actress, Dancer

**Zien, Chip**
Innovative Artists, 1505 10th St, Santa Monica CA 90401 USA — Actor

**Zien, Sam (Cooking Guy)**
Discovery Channel, 7700 Wisconsin Ave, Bethesda MD 20814 USA — Chef

**Zierden, Don**
Washington Wizards, M C I Centre, 601 F St NW, Washington DC 20004 USA — Basketball Coach

**Ziering, Ian**
Ellis Talent Group, 4705 Laurel Canyon Blvd, #300, Valley Village CA 91607, USA — Actor

**Ziesak, Ruth**
Kunstler Sekretariat am Gasteig, Rosenheimer Str 52, 81669 Munich, Germany — Opera Singer

**Ziffren, Kenneth**
Ziffren Brittenham Branca, 1801 Century Park W, #700, Los Angeles CA 90067, USA — Attorney

**Zigler, Edward F**
Yale University, Bush Child Development Center, New Haven CT 06520, USA — Psychologist, Educator

**Zikes, Les**
424 S Stuart Lane, Palatine IL 60067, USA — Bowler

**Zilinskas, Annette**
Creative Artists Agency, 2000 Ave of Stars, #100, Los Angeles CA 90067 USA — Bassist (Bangles, Ringling Sisters)

**Zillmer, Ruth**
PO Box 709, Walworth WI 53184, USA — Baseball Player

**Zils, John**
N1513 Shore Haven Dr, Fontana WI 53125, USA — Structural Engineer

**Zim Zum**
Mitch Schneider Organization, 14724 Ventura Blvd, #500, Sherman Oaks CA 91403 USA — Guitarist (Marilyn Manson); Songwriter

**Zima, Madeline**
United Talent Agency, U T A Plaza, 9336 Civic Center Dr, Beverly Hills CA 90210 USA — Actress

**Zimbalist, Efrem, Jr**
1448 Holsted Dr, Solvang CA 93463, USA — Actor

**Zimbalist, Stephanie**
Franchot Mgmt, PO Box 48890A, Los Angeles CA 90048, USA — Actress

**Zimerman, Krystian**
Kernmatterstr 8B, 4102 Binningen, Switzerland — Concert Pianist

**Zimm, Bruno H**
3762 Dupont St, San Diego CA 92106, USA — Chemist

**Zimmer, Constance**
United Talent Agency, U T A Plaza, 9336 Civic Center Dr, Beverly Hills CA 90210 USA — Actress

**Zimmer, Donald W (Don)**
7069 Key Haven Road, #201, Seminole FL 33777, USA — Baseball Player, Manager

**Zimmer, Hans F**
Remote Control Productions, 1547 14th St, Santa Monica CA 90404, USA — Composer

**Zimmer, Kim**
Innovative Artists, 1505 10th St, Santa Monica CA 90401 USA — Actress

**Zimmer, Robert**
University of Chicago, President's Office, Chicago IL 60637, USA — Educator

**Zimmerer, Wolfgang**
Schwaigangerstr 22, 82418 Murnau, Germany — Bobsled Athlete

**Zimmerman, Daniel H E (Dan)**
United Talent Agency, U T A Plaza, 9336 Civic Center Dr, Beverly Hills CA 90210 USA — Drummer (Gamma Ray)

**Zimmerman, Gary W**
17450 Skylines Road, Bend OR 97701, USA — Football Player

**Zimmerman, Howard E**
7813 Westchester Dr, Middleton WI 53562, USA — Chemist

**Zimmerman, Jeffrey R (Jeff)**
2416 Chippendale Road, West Vancouver BC V7S 3J2, Canada — Baseball Player

**Zimmerman, Joey**
PO Box 450802, Kissimmee FL 34745, USA — Actor

**Zimmerman, Mary Beth**
6452 Century Park Place SE, Mableton GA 30126, USA — Golfer

**Zimmerman, Philip (Phil)**
Network Assoc, 4677 Old Ironside Dr, Santa Clara CA 95054, USA — Computer Software Designer

**Zimmerman, Ryan W**
3301 Washington Blvd, Arlington VA 22201, USA — Baseball Player

**Zimmermann, Egon**
Hotel Kristberg, Lech 316, 6764 Lech Am Arlberg, Austria — Alpine Skier

**Zimmermann, Frank Peter**
Kunstler Sekretariat am Gasteig, Rosenheimer Str 52, 81669 Munich, Germany — Concert Violinist

**Zimmermann, Jordan**
Washington Nationals, 1500 S Capitol St SE, Washington DC 20003 USA — Baseball Player

**Zimmermann, Markus**
Waldhauserstr 51-53, 83471 Schonau am Konigsee, Germany — Bobsled Athlete

**Zimmermann, Raquel**
D N A Model Mgmt, 555 W 25th St, #600, New York NY 10001 USA — Model

**Zimmermann, Serge**
Kunstler Sekretariat am Gasteig, Rosenheimer Str 52, 81669 Munich, Germany — Concert Violinist

**Zimmermann, Udo**
Operhaus Leipzig, Augustusplatz, 04109 Leipzig, Germany — Composer

**Zimpher, Nancy**
Cincinnati University, President's Office, Cincinnati OH 45221, USA — Educator

**Zingaretti, Luca**
Carol Levi Mgmt, Via Giuseppe Pisanelli 2, 00196 Rome, Italy — Actor

**Zinke, Olaf**
Johannes Bobrowski Str 22, 12627 Berlin, Germany — Speed Skater

**Zinkernagel, Rolf M**
Rebhusstr 47, 8126 Zumikon, Switzerland — Nobel Medicine Laureate

**Zinman, David J**
Aspen Music Festival, 2 Music School Road, Aspen CO 81611, USA — Conductor

**Zinner, Nicholas J (Nick)**
Yeah Yeah Yeahs, 249 Metropolitan Ave, Brooklyn NY 11211, USA — Guitarist, Songwriter (Yeah Yeah Yeahs)

**Zinni, Anthony C (Tony)**
139 Shady Creek Lane, Fredericksburg VA 22406, USA — Marine Corps General

**Zinszer, Pamela**
Playboy Promotions, 2706 Media Center Dr, Los Angeles CA 90065 USA — Actress, Model

**Zinta, Preity**
C10/A Ranwar Wadora Road, Off Hill Road, Bandra (W), Mumbai MS 400050, India — Actress, Model, Writer, Producer

**Zippel, David**
Kraft-Engel Mgmt, 15233 Ventura Blvd, #200, Sherman Oaks CA 91403 USA — Lyricist

**Zirner, Johannes**
Die Agenten, Ackerstr 11B, 10115 Berlin, Germany — Actor

**Zischler, Hanns**
Anne Alvares Correa, 34 Rue Jouffroy d'Abbans, 75017 Paris, France — Actor

**Zisk, Craig**
United Talent Agency, U T A Plaza, 9336 Civic Center Dr, Beverly Hills CA 90210 USA — Director, Producer

**Zisk, Randall (Randy)**
Creative Artists Agency, 2000 Ave of Stars, #100, Los Angeles CA 90067 USA — Director

**Zisk, Richard W (Richie)**
4231 NE 26th Terrace, Lighthouse Point FL 33064, USA — Baseball Player

**Zito, Barry W**
16627 Gilmore St, Van Nuys CA 91406, USA — Baseball Player

**Zito, Chuck**
Prince Marketing Group, 18 Carillon Circle, Livingston NJ 07039 USA — Actor, Model

**Zittel, Harry**
Innovative Artists, 1505 10th St, Santa Monica CA 90401 USA — Actor

**Zlatoper, Ronald J (Zap)**
1001 Kamokila Blvd, Kapolei HI 96707, USA — Navy Admiral

**Zlokovic, Berislav V**
University of Rochester, Medical Center, 601 Elmwood Ave, Rochester NY 14642, USA — Neurologist

**Zmed, Adrian**
Vincent Cirrincione Assoc, 1516 N Fairfax Ave, Los Angeles CA 90046 USA — Actor

**Zmievskaya Petrenko, Galina Y (Nina)**
Ice Vault Arena, 10 Nevins Road, Wayne NJ 07470, USA — Figure Skating Coach

**Zmolek, Doug**
537 Frederichs Dr SW, Rochester MN 55901, USA — Ice Hockey Player

**Znaider, Nikolaj**
I M G Artists, Hogarth Business Park, Chiswick, London W4 2TH, England — Conductor, Concert Violinist

**Zobrist, Benjamin T (Ben)**
545 Overview Lane, Franklin TN 37064, USA — Baseball Player

**Zoch, Jacqueline**
3421 Charing Wood Lane, Birmingham AL 35242, USA — Rowing Athlete

**Zockler, Billie**
Agentur Lentz, Herzogstr 66, 80469 Munich, Germany — Actress

**Zoe, Rachel**
Bravo-TV, 3000 N Alameda Ave, #250, Burbank CA 91523 USA — Fashion Designer, Stylist

**Zoeller, Frank (Fuzzy)**
418 Deer Run Trace, Floyds Knobs IN 47119, USA — Golfer

**Zoellick, Robert B**
Peterson Institute, 1750 Massachusetts Ave NW, Washington DC 20036, USA — Government Official, Financier

**Zoff, Dino**
F C Juventus, Corso Galilo Ferraris 32, 10128 Turin, Italy — Soccer Player

**Zokol, Richard F (Dick)**
Contemporary Communications, 1663 7th Ave W, Vancouver BC V6J 1S4, Canada — Golfer

**Zolak, Scott D**
40 Comstock Dr, Wrentham MA 02093, USA — Football Player

**Zoli, Winter Eve**
Melanie Greene Mgmt, 425 N Robertson Blvd, West Hollywood CA 90048 USA — Actress

**Zollar, Jawole Willa Jo**
Urban Bush Women, 138 S Oxford St, 4B, Brooklyn, NY 11217, USA — Dancer, Dance Executive

**Zoloth, Laurie**
Northwestern University, Medical School, Bioethics Center, Evanston IL 60208, USA — Educator

**Zombie, Rob**
Vision Entertainment Group, 8484 Wilshire Blvd, #425, Beverly Hills CA 90211, USA — Singer (White Zombie), Director

**Zombo, Rick**
2918 Ossenfort Road, Glencoe MO 63038, USA — Ice Hockey Player

**Zonderland, Epke**
PO Box 197, 8 530 Lemmer AD, Netherlands — Gymnast

**Zook, John E**
4302 N Spyglass Circle, Wichita KS 67226, USA — Football Player

**Zoran**
67 Hudson St, New York NY 10013, USA — Fashion Designer

**Zordich, Michael E (Mike)**
373 S Hazelwood Ave, Youngstown OH 44509, USA — Football Player

**Zore, Edward**
Northwestern Mutual Financial Network, 720 E Wisconsin, Milwaukee WI 53202, USA — Businessman

**Zorich, Christopher R (Chris)**
1231 W 33rd Place, Chicago IL 60608, USA — Football Player

**Zorich, Louis**
Don Buchwald, 6500 Wilshire Blvd, #2200, Los Angeles CA 90048 USA — Actor

**Zorn, James A (Jim)**
2006 W Mercer Way, Mercer Island WA 98040, USA — Football Player, Coach

**Zou Shiming**
Top Rank Inc, 3908 Howard Hughes Parkway, #580, Las Vegas NV 89169 USA — Boxer

**Zsigmond, Vilmos**
Skouras Agency, 1149 3rd St, #300, Santa Monica CA 90403 USA — Cinematographer

**Zubak, Kresimir**
Presidency, Marsala Titz 7A, 71000 Sarajevo, Bosnia-Herzegovina — Co-President, Bosnia-Herzegovina

**Zubeir Wako, Gabriel Cardinal**
Archdiocese, PO Box 49, Khartoum, Sudan — Religious Leader

**Zuber, Maria T**
Massachusetts Institute of Technology, Geophysics Dept, Cambridge MA 02139, USA — Geophysicist

**Zubov, Sergei M**
3916 Marquette St, Dallas TX 75225, USA — Ice Hockey Player

**Zubrus, Dainius G** — Ice Hockey Player
92 Union St, Montclair NJ 07042, USA
**Zucchero** — Singer, Guitarist
Studio Legale Costa, Via Azzo Gardino 54, 40122 Bologna, Italy
**Zucker, Arianne** — Actress, Model
Kritzer Levine Wilkins Griffin, 11872 La Grange Ave, #100, Los Angeles CA 90025 USA
**Zucker, David** — Director, Producer
Scott Free Productions, 42-44 Beak St, London W1F 9RH, England
**Zucker, Jerry** — Director, Producer
Zucker Productions, 1250 6th St, #201, Santa Monica CA 90401, USA
**Zuckerberg, Mark** — Businessman
Facebook, 156 University Ave, #200, Palo Alto CA 94301, USA
**Zuckerman, Harriet A** — Sociologist, Foundation Executive
Andrew W Mellon Foundation, 140 E 62nd St, New York NY 10065, USA
**Zuckerman, Joshua R (Josh)** — Actor
Gersh Agency, 9465 Wilshire Blvd, #600, Beverly Hills CA 90212 USA
**Zuckerman, Mortimer B** — Publisher
Boston Properties, 599 Lexington Ave, #1800, New York NY 10022, USA
**Zuckermann, Ariel** — Conductor, Concert Flutist
Georgian Chamber Orchestra, Hohe-Schul-Stra 4, 85049 Ingolstadt, Germany
**Zuhdi, Nazih** — Surgeon
3300 NW Expressway, Oklahoma City OK 73112, USA
**Zuiker, Anthony E** — Producer, Writer, Actor
Brillstein Entertainment Partners, 9150 Wilshire Blvd, #350, Beverly Hills CA 90212 USA
**Zuke, Michael (Mike)** — Ice Hockey Player
430 Norman Gate Dr, Ballwin MO 63011, USA
**Zuker, Danny** — Producer, Writer
Creative Artists Agency, 2000 Ave of Stars, #100, Los Angeles CA 90067 USA
**Zukerman, Eugenia** — Concert Flutist
Brooklyn College of Music, Bedford & H Aves, Brooklyn NY 11210, USA
**Zukerman, Pinchas** — Concert Violinist, Conductor
Kirshbaum Demler Assoc, 711 W End Ave, #5KN, New York NY 10025, USA
**Zullo, Alan** — Cartoonist (Hall of Shame)
Tribune Media Services, 435 N Michigan Ave, #1500, Chicago IL 60611 USA
**Zuluaga, Luz Marina** — Beauty Queen
Miss Universe Organization, 1370 Ave of Americas, #1600, New York NY 10019 USA
**Zuma, Jacob G** — President, South Africa
President's Office, Union Buildings, Pretoria 0001, South Africa
**Zumthor, Peter** — Architect
Suesswinggel 20, 7023 Haldenstein, Switzerland
**Zuniga, Daphne** — Actress
Bauman Redanty Shaul Agency, 5757 Wilshire Blvd, #473, Los Angeles CA 90036 USA
**Zuniga, Jose** — Actor
A P A Talent/Literary Agency, 405 S Beverly Dr, #300, Beverly Hills CA 90212 USA
**Zuniga, Miles** — Singer, Guitarist (Fastball)
Russell Carter Artists, 567 Ralph Mcgill Blvd NE, Atlanta GA 30312, USA
**Zupko, Ramon** — Composer
Western Michigan University, Music Dept, Kalamazoo MI 49008, USA
**Zurbriggen, Pirmin** — Alpine Skier
Hotel Larchenhof, 3905 Saas-Almagell, Switzerland
**Zurer, Ayelet Z** — Actress
Independent Artists, 9601 Wilshire Blvd, #750, Beverly Hills CA 90210 USA
**ZurHausen, Harald** — Nobel Medicine Laureate
Tumorvirus-C A T, Im Neuenheimer Feld 242, 69120 Heidelberg, Germany
**Zurkowski-Holmes, Agnes** — Baseball Player
206-2339 Lorne St, Regina SK S4P 2N2, Canada
**Zurrer, Emily** — Soccer Player
Canadian Soccer, Place Soccer Canada, 237 Metcalfe St, Ottawa ON K2P 1R2, Canada
**Zusi, Graham** — Soccer Player
Sporting Kansas City, 210 W 19th Terrace, #200, Kansas City MO 64108 USA
**Zuvella, Paul** — Baseball Player
2040 Canyon Crest Ave, San Ramon CA 94582, USA
**Zvereva, Natalia** — Tennis Player
Women's Tennis Assn, 1 Progress Plaza, #1500, Saint Petersburg FL 33701 USA
**Zvonareva, Vera I** — Tennis Player
S F X Sports, 846 Lincoln Road, #500, Miami Beach Fl 33139 USA
**Zwanzig, Robert W** — Chemical Physicist
8300 Burdette Road, #423, Bethesda MD 20817, USA
**Zweig, George** — Theoretical Physicist
Los Alamos National Laboratory, PO Box 1663, Los Alamos NM 87544, USA
**Zweig, Stefanie** — Writer
Rothschildallee 9, 60389 Frankfurt/Main, Germany
**Zwerling, Darrell** — Actor
CLInc Talent, 843 N Sycamore Ave, Los Angeles CA 90038, USA
**Zwick, Alyse Jean** — Actress, Comedienne, Model
OmniPop Talent Group, 4605 Lankershim Blvd, #201, Toluca Lake CA 91602 USA
**Zwick, Edward M (Ed)** — Director, Producer
Creative Artists Agency, 2000 Ave of Stars, #100, Los Angeles CA 90067 USA
**Zwick, Joel** — Director
Irv Schechter Agency, 9460 Wilshire Blvd, #300, Beverly Hills CA 90212 USA
**Zwigoff, Terry** — Director, Producer, Writer
W M E Entertainment, 9601 Wilshire Blvd, #300, Beverly Hills CA 90210 USA
**Zwilich, Ellen Taaffe** — Composer
Music Associates of America, 224 King St, Englewood NJ 07631, USA
**Zwonitzer, Mark** — Producer, Director, Writer
Simon & Schuster, 1230 Ave of Americas, Concourse 1, New York NY 10020 USA
**Zylberstein, Elsa** — Actress
Agence Artiste Adequet, 108 Rue Reaumur, 75002 Paris, France
**Zylis-Gara, Teresa** — Opera Singer
16A Blvd de Belgique, Monaco-Ville, Monaco
**Zylka, Chris** — Actor
W M E Entertainment, 9601 Wilshire Blvd, #300, Beverly Hills CA 90210 USA

# NECROLOGY

Listees of previous editions of the V.I.P. Address Book and the V.I.P. Address Book Update whose deaths have been reported prior to close of the compilation are listed below.

|  |  |
| --- | --- |
| Abelson, Alan | Editor, Columnist |
| Achebe, Chinua | Writer |
| Adams, Kenneth S (Bud) | Football Executive |
| Adams, Scott A | Football Player |
| Agnew, Harold M | Physicist |
| Ahmed, Iajuddin | President, Bangladesh |
| Aihara, Nobuyuki | Gymnast |
| Akens, Jewel | Singer, Producer |
| Alain, Marie-Claire | Concert Organist |
| Albul, Anatoly | Freestyle Wrestler |
| Allbritton, Joseph L (Joe) | Financier |
| Allen, Grady L | Football Player |
| Allison, Herbert M, Jr | Businessman |
| Alvarez, Rogelio | Baseball Player |
| Amphlett, Christina (Chrissy) | Singer (Divinyls) |
| Andersen, Hjalmar (Hjallis) | Speed Skater |
| Anderson, Gerry | Director, Puppeteer |
| Anderson, James W (Jim) | Ice Hockey Coach |
| Andreotti, Giulio | Prime Minister, Italy |
| Andrews, Inez | Singer |
| Andrews, Patricia (Patty) | Singer (Andrews Sisters) |
| Ansara, Michael | Actor, Producer, Director |
| Antonakos, Stephen | Sculptor |
| Antonetti, Lorenzo Cardinal | Religious Leader |
| Arbus, Alan | Actor |
| Arentzen, Willard P | Navy Admiral |
| Arfons, Walter C (Walt) | Auto Racing Driver, Builder |
| Arnold, Murray | Basketball Coach |
| Artschwager, Richard E | Artist |
| Aston, Peter G | Composer |
| Astroth, Joseph H (Joe) | Baseball Player |
| Auldridge, Mike | Dobra Player |
| Austin, William L (Bill) | Football Player |
| Ayers, Kevin | Guitarist (Soft Machine), Songwriter |
| Bain, Conrad | Actor |
| Baker, Mickey | Guitarist, Songwriter |
| Bakulin, Vladimir | Greco-Roman Wrestler |
| Bank, Frank | Actor |
| Barber, Miller | Golfer |
| Barnet, Will | Artist, Educator |
| Bartoletti, Bruno | Conductor |
| Bartolucci, Domenico Cardinal | Religious Leader |
| Bass, Fontella | Singer, Keyboardist |
| Batts, Matthew D (Matt) | Baseball Player |
| Beal, Jack | Artist |
| Bearer, Paul | Professional Wrestler |
| Beaty, Zelmo | Basketball Player |
| Beitz, Berthold | Businessman |
| Belcher, Jovan A | Football Player |
| Bell, Wallace R (Wally) | Baseball Umpire |
| Bellah, Robert N | Sociologist |
| Bellamy, Walter J (Walt) | Basketball Player |
| Bellany, John | Artist |
| Belov, Sergei | Basketball Player |
| Benerito, Ruth R | Inventor |
| Benjamin, Satima Bea | Singer, Social Activist |
| Bennett, Carl B | Basketball Executive |
| Bennett, Richard Rodney | Composer |
| Bennett, Todd | Track Athlete |
| Bernardi, Mario | Conductor, Concet Pianist |
| Berry, Sidney B | Army General |
| Bibbia, Nino | Luge Athlete |
| Bieler, Alfred (Fredy) | Ice Hockey Player |
| Bierwirth, John C | Businessman |
| Bignotti, George | Auto Racing Mechanic |
| Bird, Antonia | Director |
| Bischoff, Sabine | Fencer |
| Black, Karen | Actress |
| Blah, Moses | President, Liberia |
| Blair, Wren | Ice Hockey Coach |
| Bland, Bobby (Blue) | Singer |
| Blank, Les | Director, Producer, Cinematographer |
| Bob, Hans-Ekkehard | WW II German Luftwaffe Hero |
| Boerwinkle, Thomas F (Tom) | Basketball Player |
| Boggs, M Corinne M C (Lindy) | Representative, LA; Diplomat |
| Bolling, Milton J (Milt) | Baseball Player |
| Boreyko, Valentin | Rowing Athlete |
| Borico, Miguel Abia Biteo | Prime Minister, Equatorial Guinea |
| Bork, Robert H | Government Official, Judge |
| Born, Bertram H | Basketball Player |
| Bose, Amar G | Inventor (Audio Waveguide) |
| Bouchee, Edward F (Ed) | Baseball Player |
| Boussard, Herve | Cyclist |
| Bowen, Otis R | Secretary, Health & Human Services |
| Bowman, Don | Singer, Actor, Songwriter |
| Brennan, Eileen | Actress |
| Briers, Richard | Actor, Comedian |
| Brill, Yvonne M | Space Scientist |
| Brodeur, Denis | Ice Hockey Player, Photographer |
| Brooker, Richard | Actor |
| Brookes, Jacqueline | Actress |
| Brookes, Jon | Drummer (Charlatans) |
| Brooks, Jack B | Representative, TX |
| Brothers, Joyce D | Psychologist, Actress |
| Brown, Roy, Jr | Automobile Designer, Engineer |
| Brown, William J (Gates) | Baseball Player |
| Brubeck, David W (Dave) | Jazz Pianist |
| Buchanan, James M | Nobel Economics Laureate |
| Buchel, Markus | Head of Government, Liechtenstein |
| Burke, Clarence, Jr | Singer (Five Stairsteps) |
| Burkley, Dennis | Actor |
| Burr, Shawn | Ice Hockey Player |
| Buss, Gerald H (Jerry) | Basketball, Hockey Executive |
| Butler, John B (Jack) | Football Player |
| Byrd, Donaldson T L (Donald), II | Jazz Trumpeter |
| Byrd, Harry F, Jr | Senator, VA |
| Byrne, Anthony (Tony) | Boxer |
| Byrne, John J | Businessman |
| Caldwell, Philip | Businessman |
| Caldwell, William B, III | Army General |
| Cale, J J | Singer, Guitarist, Songwriter |
| Camp, Rick L | Baseball Player |
| Campbell, Helen Hannah | Baseball Executive |
| Campbell, William C | Golf Executive |
| Carey, Harry, Jr | Actor, Writer, Producer |
| Cargo, David F | Governor, NM |
| Caro, Anthony A | Sculptor |
| Carpenter, M Scott | Astronaut |
| Carroll, Earl (Speedo) | Singer (Cadillacs, Coasters) |
| Casablancas, John | Model Agency Executive |
| Casares, Ricardo (Rick) | Football Player |
| Cassatt, Chris | Cartoonist |
| Cassidy, Ed | Drummer (Spirit) |
| Castillo, Frank A | Baseball Player |
| Castillo, Jesus (Chucho) | Boxer |
| Cecil, Henry R A | Thoroughbred Racing Trainer |
| Cellucci, A Paul | Governor, MA; Diplomat |
| Chapman, Ernest | Rowing Athlete |
| Charlesworth, Sarah E | Photographer, Artist |
| Chavez, Hugo R | President, Venezuela |
| Cheli, Giovanni Cardinal | Religious Leader |
| Chereau, Patrice | Director |
| Chrisley, B O'Neil (Neil) | Baseball Player |
| Christensen, Todd J | Football Player, Sportscaster |
| Christy, Robert F | Physicist |
| Cisar, Cestmir | Council Chairman, Czechoslovakia |
| Clancy, Thomas J (Tom) | Writer |
| Clark, Kenneth R (Ken) | Football Player |
| Clark, William P | Secretary, Interior |
| Clarke, Bob | Cartoonist |
| Claudius, Leslie | Field Hockey Player |
| Clausen, Alden W (Tom) | Financier |
| Cliburn, Van | Concert Pianist |
| Coase, Ronald H | Nobel Economics Laureate |
| Cochrane, Jay | Aerialist |
| Coia, Angelo A | Football Player |
| Collings, Charles L | Businessman |
| Collins, Cardiss R | Representative, IL |
| Collins, Ray | Singer (Mothers of Invention) |
| Colombo, Emilio | Prime Minister, Italy |
| Colville, Alexander | Artist |
| Conley, Joe | Actor |
| Connell, Evan S, Jr | Writer |
| Connell, Jane | Singer, Actress |
| Conrad, Barnaby | Writer, Artist, Restauranteur |
| Cooper, Jeanne | Actress |
| Cosman, James H (Jim) | Baseball Player |
| Costa, David J (Dave) | Football Player |
| Costello, Diosa | Singer, Actress |
| Covington, Joey | Drummer (Jefferson Airplane) |

# NECROLOGY

|  | |
|---|---|
| Coyne, William J | Representative, PA |
| Cramer, Richard Ben | Journalist, Writer |
| Crandall, Richard | Mathematician |
| Crespino, Robert (Bob) | Football Player |
| Crispin, Ann C (A C) | Writer |
| Cullerton, William J | WW II Army Air Corps Hero |
| Cumming-Bruce, Francis E | Governor, Bahamas |
| Curran, Jack | Basketball, Baseball Coach |
| Curtis, Wesley E (Mac), Jr | Singer |
| Damiani, Damiano | Director |
| Dancer, Rachel L | Harness Racing Executive |
| Daniels, H Jack | Baseball Player |
| Danto, Arthur C | Philosopher, Art Critic |
| Davalillo Romero, Pompeyo A (Yo Yo) | Baseball Player |
| Davenport, Nigel | Actor |
| Davis, Colin R | Conductor |
| Davis, John J (Jack) | Football Player |
| Day, George E (Bud) | Vietnam War Air Force Hero (CMH) |
| Deal, Ellis F (Cot) | Baseball Player |
| DeBeus, A M Bernadette (Det) | Field Hockey Player |
| DeDuve, Christian R | Nobel Medicine Laureate |
| DellaCasa-Debeljevic, Lisa | Opera Singer |
| Dement, Kenneth | Football Player |
| DePreist, James A | Conductor |
| Detweiler, Robert S (Ducky) | Baseball Player |
| DeVilliers, Gerard | Writer |
| Diamandis, Peter G | Publisher |
| Diering, Charles E A (Chuck) | Baseball Player |
| Dietzel, Paul F | Football Player, Coach |
| Diffrient, Niels | Industrial Designer |
| Dixon, Jane Holmes | Religious Leader |
| Dodgson, Stephen C V | Composer |
| Dog, Tim | Rap Artist |
| Dolby, Raymond M (Ray) | Inventor, Sound Engineer |
| Donovan, Arthur J (Art), Jr | Football Player |
| Dorman, Lee | Bassist (Captain Beyond, Iron Butterfly) |
| Dowling, Vincent | Director, Writer |
| Drew, Urban | WW II Army Air Corps Hero |
| Drewes, Martin | German WW II Luftwaffe Hero |
| Dubzinski, Walter J (Walt) | Football Player |
| Duke, George | Jazz Keyboardist, Songwriter |
| Durbin, Deanna | Actress, Singer |
| Durning, Charles | Actor |
| Dutilleux, Henri | Composer |
| Duval, Daniel | Actor |
| Dworkin, Ronald M | Attorney, Philosopher |
| Easley, Walter E (Walt) | Football Player |
| Ebert, Roger J | Film Critic |
| Edgar, Robert W (Bob) | Religious Leader; Representative, PA |
| Edwards, Robert G | Nobel Medicine Laureate |
| Ehlers, Edwin S (Eddie) | Basketball Player |
| Elliott, Lloyd Hartman | Educator |
| Elliott, Peter R (Pete) | Football Player, Coach |
| Ellis, Allan D | Football Player |
| Ellis, David R | Director |
| Elshtain, Jean B | Ethicist, Educator, Philosopher |
| Eppridge, Bill | Photographer |
| Estes, Billie Sol | Businessman |
| Evey, Dick | Football Player |
| Fairbanks, Charles L (Chuck) | Football Coach |
| Falkanger, Torbjorn | Ski Jumper |
| Farina, Dennis | Actor |
| Faris, Mildred | Rodeo Executive, Barrel Racer |
| Farman, Joseph C | Geophysicist |
| Fay, Martin | Fiddler (Chieftains) |
| Felt, Richard G (Dick) | Football Player |
| Fishman, Jerald G | Businessman |
| Fitzgerald, Edmund B | Businessman |
| Flynn, Vince | Writer |
| Fogel, Robert W | Nobel Economics Laureate |
| Foley, Thomas S | Representative, WA; Speaker; Diplomat |
| Forbes, Bryan | Director, Writer |
| Forman, Denis | Businessman |
| Forrest, Steve | Actor |
| Forster, Joseph M | WW II Army Air Corps Hero |
| Fouce, Frank | Businessman |
| Frankenheimer, Leslie | Set Designer |
| Franklin, Bonnie | Actress |
| Franklin, Freddie | Ballet Dancer, Choreographer |
| Frasconi, Antonio | Artist |
| Freel, Ryan P | Baseball Player |
| Freese, Eugene L (Gene) | Baseball Player |
| Frei, Emil, III | Oncologist |
| French, Bob | Jazz Drummer |
| Fritz, Albert J (Al) | Bicycle Executive, Inventor |
| Frost, David P | Producer, Writer, Commentator |
| Fukuda, Keiko | Judo Athlete |
| Fullerton, C Gordon | Astronaut, Test Pilot |
| Funicello, Annette J | Actress, Singer |
| Gandolfini, James | Actor |
| Gann, Dodie Post | Alpine Skier |
| Gardner, W Booth | Governor, WA |
| Garfinkel, Jack (Dutch) | Basketball Player |
| Gaumont, Philippe | Cyclist |
| Gayle, Gordon D | WW II Marine Corps Hero, General |
| Gaze, F Anthony O (Tony) | WW II RAF Hero |
| German, Aleksei G | Director |
| Germond, Jack W | Journalist |
| Gershenz, Murray | Actor |
| Giannatos, Michael | Actor |
| Gilhooly, David J, III | Sculptor |
| Gilligan, John J | Governor, OH |
| Gilmar | Soccer Player |
| Glaser, Donald A | Nobel Physics Laureate |
| Glaser, Thomas P (Tompall) | Singer |
| Glasser, William | Psychiatrist |
| Glemp, Jozef Cardinal | Religious Leader |
| Goddard, John | Explorer |
| Goldberg, Gary David | Actor, Director, Producer |
| Goldie, Michael | Actor |
| Gorme, Eydie | Singer |
| Graca, Carlos Da | Prime Minister, Sao Tome & Principe |
| Grams, Rodney D (Rod) | Senator, MN |
| Granville, Joseph | Financier, Writer |
| Gravelle, Leo | Ice Hockey Player |
| Gray, Devin A | Basketball Player |
| Gray, Richard B (Dick) | Baseball Player |
| Gray, William H, III | Association Leader; Representative, PA |
| Greeley, Andrew M (Andy) | Writer, Sociologist |
| Greene, Jack | Singer, Guitarist, Drummer |
| Greenwood, L C Henderson (L C) | Football Player |
| Greig, Anthony W (Tony) | Cricket Player, Broadcaster |
| Griffin, Thomas C | WW II Army Air Corps Hero |
| Griffith, Emile A | Boxer |
| Griffiths, Richard | Actor |
| Grisanti, Susan | Classical Guitarist |
| Gruntz, George P | Jazz Pianist, Composer |
| Grut, William (Willie) | Modern Pentathlete |
| Gujral, Inder Kumar | Prime Minister, India |
| Gund, George, III | Basketball, Ice Hockey Executive |
| Gurics, Gyorgy | Freestyle Wrestler |
| Guy, William L | Governor, ND |
| Gyarmati, Dezso | Water Polo Player, Coach |
| Haddon, Laurence | Actor |
| Haji | Actress |
| Hamerow, Theodore S | Historian |
| Hanlon, Jack | Actor |
| Hanneman, Jeff | Guitarist (Slayer) |
| Hardwick, William B (Billy) | Bowler |
| Harris, B Gail | Baseball Player |
| Harris, Damon | Singer (Temptations) |
| Harris, Julie | Actress |
| Harrison, Noel | Actor, Singer |
| Harryhausen, Ray F | Director/Animator |
| Harshman, Marvel K (Marv) | Basketball Player, Coach |
| Hartley, Donna | Track Athlete |
| Hartstein, Bernd | Marksman |
| Harvey, Jonathan D | Composer |
| Hathaway, William D | Senator, ME |
| Hatton, Grady E | Baseball Player, Manager |
| Havens, Richie | Singer, Guitarist, Songwriter |
| Hawk, John D | WW II Army Hero (CMH) |
| Hawke, Hazel | Social Activist |
| Haycock, Peter | Guitarist (Climax Blues Band) |
| Hazan, Marcella | Chef |
| Hazewood, Drungo L | Baseball Player |
| Heaney, Seamus J | Nobel Literature Laureate |
| Heffner, Ray L | Educator |
| Heil, Gail | Singer, Fiddler |
| Heiniger, Patrick | Businessman |
| Herbig, George H | Astronomer |
| Herman, Jimmy | Actor |
| Hernandez, Enzo O | Baseball Player |
| Hernandez, Noe | Track Athlete |
| Hersh, Earl W | Baseball Player |
| Herzog, Maurice | Mountaineer, Explorer |

# NECROLOGY

| | |
|---|---|
| Heyman, Abigail | Photographer |
| Hietamies-Etelapaa, Mirja K | Nordic Skier |
| Hightower, Jack English | Representative, TX |
| Hightower, John B | Museum Director |
| Hijuelos, Oscar | Writer |
| Hill, Harlon | Football Player |
| Hill, Simmie, Jr | Basketball Player |
| Hilten, Heinz H | Space Scientist |
| Hinton, Charles E (Chuck), Jr | Baseball Player |
| Hirschman, Albert O | Economist |
| Hodgson, James D | Secretary, Labor |
| Hoffman, Daniel G | Writer |
| Hogan, J Paul | Inventor (Crystalline Polypropylene) |
| Holding, Robert E | Businessman |
| Hollander, John | Writer |
| Holmes, D Brainerd | Space Engineer, Businessman |
| Holshouser, James E, Jr | Governor, NC |
| Holt, John S | Football Player |
| Honore, Jean M Cardinal | Religious Leader |
| Hood, Clarence (Hooker) | Auto Racing Driver |
| Hood, Ted | Yachtsman |
| Hopkins, Michael | Sound Editor |
| Hormander, Lars V | Mathematician |
| Horn, Gyula | Prime Minister, Hungary |
| Hornig, Donald F | Chemist, Educator |
| Horsfall, Bernard | Actor |
| Hoskyns, Henry (Bill) | Fencer |
| Houghton, Edith | Baseball Player |
| House, William F | Physician, Otologist |
| Howser, Huell B | Producer |
| Hubel, David H | Nobel Medicine Laureate |
| Hudson, James C (Jim) | Football Player |
| Hurnik, Ilja | Concert Pianist, Composer |
| Huxley, Richard (Rick) | Guitarist (Dave Clark Five) |
| Huxtable, Ada Louise | Architectural Critic |
| Iliev, Konstantin | Composer |
| Inouye, Daniel K | Senator, HI; WW II Army Hero (CMH) |
| Jackson, George H | Singer, Songwriter |
| Jackson, Ronald Shannon | Jazz Drummer |
| Jackson, Thomas Penfield | Judge |
| Jacob, Francois | Nobel Medicine Laureate |
| Jakobson, Max | Journalist; Government Official, Finland |
| James, Don | Football Coach |
| Jenkins, Paul | Actor |
| Jennings, David T (Dave) | Football Player |
| Jens, Walter | Writer |
| Jensen, Elwood V | Biochemist |
| Jeremiah, David E | Navy Admiral |
| Jernstedt, Ken, Sr | WW II Marine Corps Hero |
| Jhabvala, Ruth Prawer | Writer |
| Jimenez Mendivil, Soraya | Weightlifter |
| Johansen, Arne | Speed Skater |
| Johnson, Haynes B | Journalist |
| Johnson, Virginia E | Sex Therapist, Psychologist |
| Jones, David (Deacon) | Football Player, Executive |
| Jones, David C | Air Force General |
| Jones, George | Singer, Guitarist, Songwriter |
| Jowdy, John | Bowling Journalist, Coach |
| Junior, Marvin | Singer (Dells) |
| Jurkovic, Mirko | Football Player |
| Kafi, Ali | President, Algeria |
| Kampelman, Max M | Diplomat |
| Kanin, Fay | Writer |
| Kaplow, Herbert E | Commentator |
| Karle, Jerome | Nobel Chemistry Laureate |
| Karmi, Ram | Architect |
| Karnow, Stanley | Historian |
| Karpov, Nikolay | Ice Hockey Player |
| Kasai, Masae | Volleyball Player |
| Kasha, Michael | Biophysicist |
| Kastenman, Petrus | Equestrian |
| Katz, Fred | Composer, Cellist |
| Kazmaier, Richard W (Dick), Jr | Football Player |
| Keilis-Borok, Vladimir I | Geophysicist, Mathematician |
| Kelly, Chris (Mac Daddy) | Rap Artist (Kris Kross) |
| Kelly, Jim | Actor |
| Kelly, Lisa Robin | Actress, Producer |
| Kelly, Thomas J (Tom) | Thoroughbred Racing Trainer |
| Kelso, Frank B, II | Navy Admiral |
| Kerr, John G | Actor |
| Keulen-Deelstra, Atje | Speed Skater |
| Kieschnick, William F | Businessman |
| King, Claude | Singer, Guitarist |
| King, Larry L | Writer |
| Kirk, Walton (Walt), Jr | Basketball Player |
| Klein, Lawrence R | Nobel Economics Laureate |
| Kloimstein, Josef | Rowing Athlete |
| Klugman, Jack | Actor |
| Kment, Petr | Greco-Roman Wrestler |
| Koch, Edward I | Mayor, New York City |
| Kocourek, David A | Football Player |
| Kolev, Todor | Actor |
| Koprowski, Hilary | Microbiologist |
| Koste, Klaus | Gymnast |
| Kravitz, Daniel (Danny) | Baseball Player |
| Krivak, Joe | Football Coach |
| Kucks, John C (Johnny) | Baseball Player |
| Kudelski, Stefan | Inventor (Portable Recorder) |
| Kuehnemund, Jan | Guitarist (Vixen) |
| Kulbacki, Joseph V (Joe) | Football Player |
| Kulikov, Viktor G | Army Marshal, Russia |
| Kump, Ernest J | Architect |
| Kurland, Robert A (Bob) | Basketball Player |
| Kurys, Sophie M | Baseball Player |
| Kustinskaya, Natalya | Actress |
| Lafont, Bernadette | Actress |
| LaMontaine, John | Composer |
| Lance, T Bert | Government Official |
| Landau, Saul | Writer, Director |
| Landes, David S | Historian |
| Langley, Neva Jane | Beauty Queen |
| Lanier, Allen | Musician (Blue Oyster Cult) |
| LaPierre, Camille A (Cam) | Ice Hockey Player |
| LaRoca, Pete | Jazz Drummer |
| Larsen, Arthur D (Art) | Tennis Player |
| Lautenberg, Frank R | Senator, NJ; Businessman |
| Lauter, Ed | Actor |
| Lawrence, Francis Leo | Educator |
| Lawrence, Larry W | Football Player |
| Leader, George M | Governor, PA |
| Leaf, Alexander | Physician |
| Lee, Alvin | Singer, Guitarist (Ten Years After) |
| Leech, Faith | Swimmer |
| Leffler, Jason | Auto, Truck Racing Driver |
| Leggett, W David (Dave) | Football Player |
| Leonard, Elmore | Writer |
| LeParmentier, Richard | Actor |
| Lerner, Gerda | Historian |
| Lesley, Bradley J (Brad) | Baseball Player |
| Lessing, Doris M | Nobel Literature Laureate |
| Levi-Montalcini, Rita | Nobel Medicine Laureate |
| Lewis, Anthony | Columnist |
| Lewis, Garrett | Set Decorator, Actor |
| Lewis, Leo | Football Player |
| Lewis, Lester | Producer, Writer |
| Libran, Frankie | Baseball Player |
| Lin, Chia-Chiao | Applied Mathematician |
| Linhart, Anton H (Toni) | Football Player |
| Lip, Tony | Actor |
| Lipkin-Shahak, Amnon | Army General, Israel |
| Lizalde, Enrique | Actor, Director |
| Logan, John (Johnny) | Baseball Player |
| Lokoloko, Tore | Governor General, Papua New Guinea |
| Lowe, William C | Businessman |
| Lucas, Cornel | Photographer |
| Luna, J J Bigas | Director |
| Lund, Pentti | Ice Hockey Player |
| Lyles, A C | Producer |
| Lynde, Stan | Cartoonist (Rick O'Shay) |
| Lynne, Gloria | Singer |
| Lytle, Marshall | Guitarist, Bassist |
| Machado, Mario | Commentator, Actor |
| MacNeil, Rita | Singer |
| Magic Slim | Singer, Guitarist |
| Magill, Frank J | Judge |
| Maier, Pauline R | Historian |
| Majerus, Rick | Basketball Coach, Sportscaster |
| Mako, C Gene | Tennis Player |
| Malone, Thomas F | Geophysicist |
| Mansouri, Lotfi | Opera Director |
| Mantee, Paul | Actor |
| Manzarek, Ray | Keyboardist (Doors) |
| March, Lori | Actress |
| Mariategui Chiappe, Sandro | Prime Minister, Peru |
| Markin, David R | Businessman |
| Martens, Wilfried | Prime Minister, Belgium |

# NECROLOGY

Martin, Boris M (Babe) — Baseball Player
Martin, David O'Brien — Representative, NY
Martinescu, Nicolae — Greco-Roman Wrestler
Matheson, Richard — Writer
Mauroy, Pierre — Prime Minister, France
May, Edgar — Journalist
Mazer, Bill — Sportscaster
Mazombwe, Medardo Joseph Cardinal — Religious Leader
Mazowiecki, Tadeusz — Prime Minister, Poland
McAlister, Maurice L — Financier
McCollister, John Y — US Representative, NE
McCord, Darris P — Football Player
McCracklin, Jimmy — Singer, Pianist, Harmonica Player
McCrary, Gregory A (Greg) — Football Player
McCready, Malinda G (Mindy) — Singer
McGarity, Vernon — WW II Army Hero (CMH)
McKeever, Ian — Mountaineer
McLaughlin, Joseph M — Judge
McMillan, David — Football Player
McMillan, Stephenie — Set Decorator
McPartland, Marian M — Jazz Pianist
McRae, Floyd (Buddy) — Singer (Chords)
McRoberts, Briony — Actress
McWilliams, Robert H, Jr — Judge
Meely, Cliff — Basketball Player
Meineke, Donald E (Don) — Basketball Player
Meistrell, Bob — Wetsuit Designer
Melato, Mariangela — Actress
Meminger, Dean P — Basketball Player
Mendelenyi-Agoston, Judit — Fencer
Mennea, Pietro — Track Athlete
Meriweather, Joe C — Basketball Player
Mertz, Barbara — Writer
Mesa, Arnaldo — Boxer
Messer, Thomas M — Museum Executive
Miles, John (Mule) — Baseball Player
Millar, Jeffrey L (Jeff) — Cartoonist (Tank McNamara)
Miller, Harry — Basketball Player, Coach
Miller, Justin M — Baseball Player
Miller, Mulgrew — Jazz Pianist
Miller, Scott — Singer, Songwriter (Game Theory)
Miller, Wayne F — Photographer
Mimoun, Alain — Track Athlete
Minarcin, Rudy A — Baseball Player
Mishra, Veer Bhadra — Environmentalist, Engineer
Missoni, Ottavio — Fashion Designer
Mitchell, George P — Businessman
Mitchell, Jack — Photographer
Mitchell, Leland — Basketball Player
Mitchell, Murray C — Basketball Player
Monteith, Cory — Actor
Moore, Patrick — Astronomer, Writer
Moran, Gertrude A (Gussie) — Tennis Player
Morgan, Edmund S — Historian
Morgan, Elaine — Writer
Moroi, Makoto — Composer
Morris, John W — Army General
Morris, Lawrence C (Larry) — Football Player
Morris, Lawrence D (Butch) — Jazz Cornetist, Composer
Morrison, Tommy — Boxer
Morwood, Michael J — Archaeologist
Mosson, Cordell (Boogie), Jr — Bassist (Parliament-Funkadelic)
Most, Samuel (Sam) — Jazz Saxophonist, Flutist
Motley, Ronald L — Attorney
Moulton, Alexander E — Bicycle Engineer
Moustaki, Georges — Singer, Songwriter
Muir, Karen — Swimmer
Mullen, Ford P (Moon) — Baseball Player
Muller, Steven — Educator
Muncie, Harry V (Chuck) — Football Player
Muri, James — WW II Army Air Corps Hero
Murphy, Gerard — Actor
Murray, Albert L — Writer
Murray, Bruce C — Planetary Scientist, Geologist
Murray, Joseph E — Nobel Medicine Laureate
Musial, Stanley F (Stan) — Baseball Player
Mussill, Bernard J (Barney) — Baseball Player
Myers, Lou — Actor
Nabrit, James M, Jr — Attorney, Educator
Nagy, Imre — Modern Pentathlete
Nagy, Stanislaw Cardinal — Religious Leader
Nakajima, Hiroshi — Physician, Government Official
Naugle, John — Space Scientist

Needham, Hal — Director
Nelis, Andre — Yachtsman
Nemec, Josef — Boxer
Nethercott, Acer — Rowing Athlete
Neuharth, Allen H — Publisher
Nguyen Khanh — Prime Minister, South Vietnam; General
Nicely, Jonnie — Model
Niemeyer, Oscar S F — Pritzker Architecture Laureate
Norton, Kenneth H (Ken) — Boxer, Actor
Norton, Richard E (Rick) — Football Player
O'Connor, Bridget — Writer
O'Day, Alan — Singer, Songwriter
Oliva, Sergio — Body Builder
Olley, Margaret — Artist
O'Neill, Jimmy — Actor
Oresko, Nicholas — WW II Army Hero (CMH)
O'Shea, Milo — Actor
Oshima, Nagisa — Director
Osmond, Cliff — Actor, Director
Otis, Glenn K — Army General
Owens, Major R O — Representative, NY
Pafko, Andrew (Andy) — Baseball Player
Page, Frank — Radio Broadcaster
Page, Patti — Singer, Actress
Paire-Davis, Lavonne (Pepper) — Baseball Player
Pall, Gloria — Entertainer, Actress
Palmer, James G (Jim) — Basketball Player
Palmer, John S — Commentator
Palmer, John S (Bud) — Basketball Player, Sportscaster
Palmer, Michael — Writer
Pardee, John P (Jack) — Football Player, Coach
Parker, Clarence M (Ace) — Football, Baseball Player
Parker, Harry — Rowing Athlete, Coach
Parr, Ralph S — Korean & Vietnam War Air Force Hero
Pastore, Frank E — Baseball Player
Patrick, Ruth — Educator
Patterson, Eugene C — Journalist
Pawson, Anthony J — Microbiologist
Peay, Francis — Football Player, Coach
Pellegrini, Margaret — Actress
Pepelyaev, Vevgeny G — Korean War Air Force Hero, Russia
Perry, Robert P — Molecular Biologist
Pert, Candace — Neuroscientist
Pertwee, Bill — Actor
Pfaff, Dieter — Actor
Phillips, Howard J — Public Policy Analyst
Phillips, Lloyd — Producer
Phillips, Oail Andres (Bum) — Football Coach, Sportscaster
Pierce, Tony M — Baseball Player
Pimenta, Simon Ignatius Cardinal — Religious Leader
Pinegin, Timir A — Yachtsman
Plummer, James W — Engineer
Pohl, Frederick G, Jr — Writer
Polic, Henry, II — Actor
Ponce, Ponciano (Poncie) — Actor
Post, Ted — Director
Potter, Michael — Molecular Biologist
Pran — Actor
Prentice, William C H — Educator
Presley, Reg — Singer (Troggs), Songwriter
Price, Marvin D — Baseball Player
Prudencio, Nelson — Track Athlete
Prystai, Dymtro (Metro) — Ice Hockey Player
Pulli, Frank V — Baseball Umpire
Puyana, Rafael — Concert Harpsichordist
Quezada Toruno, Rodolfo Cardinal — Religious Leader
Quintana, John — Rodeo Rider
Raffin, Deborah — Actress
Rahman, Mohammed Zillur — President, Bangladesh
Raines, Richard — Guitarist (Perfect Stranger)
Rainwater, Marvin — Singer
Ramirez, Mario — Baseball Player
Ramone, Philip (Phil) — Businessman, Songwriter
Ranis, Gustav — Economist
Rankin, Robert J — WW II Army Air Corps Hero
Reed, Lou — Singer (Velvet Undergound), Songwriter
Reems, Harry — Adult Film Actor
Reger, John G — Football Player
Reid, Elliott — Actor
Remini, Robert V — Historian
Renaud, Albert R (Ab) — Ice Hockey Player
Renfrew, Malcolm M — Chemist, Inventor
Resnik, Regina — Opera Singer

# NECROLOGY

| | |
|---|---|
| Rich, Marc | Businessman |
| Richards, Deke | Songwriter |
| Richardson, Midge T | Editor |
| Richardson, Robert C | Nobel Physics Laureate |
| Richbourg, Eli | Producer |
| Riegel, J P Hans | Businessman |
| Ries, Julien Cardinal | Religious Leader |
| Riopelle, Howard | Ice Hockey Player |
| Risner, J Robinson | Korean War Air Force Hero |
| Roberts, George A | Businessman |
| Robertson, Dale | Actor |
| Robinson, Flynn J | Basketball Player |
| Robinson, Jay | Actor |
| Rogers, Gregory | Writer, Illustrator |
| Rogers, Paul | Actor |
| Rogers, Reginald O (Reggie) | Football Player |
| Rogers, Robert E (Bobby) | Singer (Miracles), Songwriter |
| Rohrer, Heinrich | Nobel Physics Laureate |
| Romishevsky, Igor A | Ice Hockey Player |
| Rosa, Henrique | President, Guinea-Bissau |
| Rosen, Charles W | Concert Pianist, Writer |
| Ross, Ian M | Electrical Engineer |
| Rotblatt, Marvin (Marv) | Baseball Player |
| Rouse, Curtis L | Football Player |
| Royer, William H | Representative, CA |
| Rubin, Roy | Basketball Coach |
| Rubitsky, David | WW II Army Hero |
| Ruddle, Francis H | Biologist, Geneticist |
| Rudman, Warren B | Senator, NH |
| Ruscio, Al | Actor |
| Rushing, Marion G | Football Player |
| Saimes, George | Football Player, Executive |
| Sams, Ferrol A, Jr | Writer |
| Santos, Djalma | Soccer Player |
| Sarafian, Richard | Director, Actor, Writer |
| Sauer, George H, Jr | Football Player |
| Savage, J Robert (Bob) | Baseball Player |
| Savoldi, Angelo | Professional Wrestler |
| Schectman, Oscar B (Ossie) | Basketball Player |
| Schellenberg, August | Actor |
| Scherrer, Jean-Louis | Fashion Designer |
| Schmidt, Frederick A (Freddy) | Baseball Player |
| Schneider, Othmar | Alpine Skier |
| Schnitger, Henri C W (Hans) | Field Hockey Player |
| Schuh, Harry F | Football Player |
| Schutz, Klaus | Mayor, Berlin; Government Official |
| Schwarzkopf, H Norman | Army General |
| Scoon, Paul | Governor General, Grenada |
| Scott, Donald (Don) | Boxer |
| Scott, George | Baseball Player |
| Scott, Joe B | Baseball Player |
| Scranton, William W | Governor, PA; Ambassador to UN |
| Scrimshaw, Nevin S | Nutritionist |
| Seitz, Richard J (Dick) | Army General |
| Serebrov, Alexander A | Cosmonaut |
| Shane, Paul | Actor |
| Shankar, Ravi | Concert Sitar Player, Composer |
| Shapero, Harold S | Composer |
| Sharman, William W (Bill) | Basketball Player, Coach, Executive |
| Sharp, Alan | Writer |
| Sharpe, Thomas R (Tom) | Writer |
| Shaughnessy, Ed | Drummer |
| Shaw, E Clay, Jr | Representative, FL |
| Shea, George Beverly | Singer |
| Sheridan, Dinah | Actress |
| Sheridan, Tony | Singer |
| Shirley, Don | Jazz Pianist |
| Shrestha, Marich Man Singh | Prime Minister, Nepal |
| Simoncelli, Stefano | Fencer |
| Simpson, Andrew J | Yachtsman |
| Sincere, Jean | Actress |
| Skelton, Isaac Newton (Ike), IV | Representative, MO |
| Skov, Glen | Ice Hockey Player |
| Sleater, Louis M (Lou) | Baseball Player |
| Small, John K | Football Player |
| Smith, Bobbie | Singer (Spinners) |
| Smith, Cal | Singer |
| Smith, Harry E (Blackjack) | Football Player, Coach |
| Smith, Keith A | Marine Corps General |
| Smith, Lawrence Leighton | Conductor |
| Smith, Mel | Actor, Comedian |
| Smith, Paul T | Jazz Pianist |
| Smith, Ronald (Ron) | Football Player |
| Smith, Ronnie Ray | Track Athlete |
| Soldatenkov, Alexander | Aerospace Engineer, Rocket Designer |
| Soleri, Paolo | Architect, Sculptor |
| Solomon, David H | Endocrinologist, Geriatrician |
| Sombrotto, Vincent R | Labor Leader |
| Sonnenfeldt, Helmut | Businessman, Educator |
| Sow, Abdoulaye Sekou | Prime Minister, Mali |
| Speck, Christa | Model |
| Stanley, Allan H | Ice Hockey Player |
| Staples, Cleotha | Singer (Staple Singers) |
| Stapleton, Jean | Actress |
| Stark, Bruce | Cartoonist (Stark Impressions) |
| Stark, Graham | Actor |
| Starker, Janos | Concert Cellist |
| Steger, Joseph A | Educator |
| Steinberg, Saul P | Businessman |
| Steinmann, Daniel | Director |
| Stepashkin, Stanislav | Boxer |
| Stern, Bert | Photographer |
| Stern, Richard G | Writer |
| Stevens, Rise | Opera Singer |
| Stewart, James F (Jimmy) | Baseball Player |
| Stoker, Gordon | Singer (Jordanaires) |
| Stoltenberg, Brian D | Football Player |
| Stranahan, Frank | Golfer |
| Street, James | Football Player |
| Street, Richard | Singer (Temptations) |
| Stretton, Ronald | Cyclist |
| Strong, James | Businessman |
| Stuart, Maxine | Actress |
| Stuart, Roy J | Football Player |
| Sullivan, William H | Diplomat |
| Summerall, George A (Pat) | Football Player, Sportscaster |
| Sweeney, James (Jim) | Football Coach |
| Sweeney, Walter F (Walt) | Football Player |
| Sykes, Harry | Basketball Player |
| Szozda, Stanislaw | Cyclist |
| Tallchief, Maria | Ballerina |
| Tarr, Curtis W | Government Official, Businessman |
| Tavener, John K | Composer |
| Taylor, Gilbert | Cinematographer |
| Temes, Judit | Swimmer |
| Temp, James A (Jim) | Football Player |
| Tereshinski, Joseph P (Joe), Sr | Football Player |
| Thatcher of Lincolnshire, Margaret H | Prime Minister, England |
| Thomas, Gerald W | Educator |
| Thomas, Helen A | Journalist |
| Thomas, John C | Track Athlete |
| Thomas, Larri | Actress |
| Thomason, Robert L (Bobby) | Football Player |
| Thornton, Frank | Actor |
| Thorp, Richard | Actor |
| Throne, Malachi | Actor |
| Todorovsky, Piotr Y | Director |
| Tonini, Ersilio Cardinal | Religious Leader |
| Triandos, C Gus | Baseball Player |
| Trickle, Richard (Dick) | Auto Racing Driver |
| Tripucka, Francis J (Frank) | Football Player |
| Trucks, Virgil O (Fire) | Baseball Player |
| Tsybulenko, Viktor | Track Athlete |
| Turley, Robert L (Bob) | Baseball Player |
| Turnbull, William | Artist |
| Turner, Fred L | Businessman |
| Turro, Nicholas J | Chemist |
| Uchida, Irene A | Geneticist |
| Valdes, Alberto | Equestrian |
| Valdes, Ramon E (Bebo) | Jazz Pianist, Bandleader, Composer |
| VanBuren, Abigail | Columnist (Dear Abby) |
| Vance, John H (Jack) | Writer |
| Vasile, Radu | Prime Minister, Romania |
| Vaughn, Charles (Chico) | Basketball Player |
| Venturi, Ken | Golfer |
| Vickers, Stanley (Stan) | Track Athlete |
| Videla, Jorge Rafael | President, Argentina; Army General |
| Vikulov, Vladimir I | Ice Hockey Player |
| Villanueva del Campo, Armando | Prime Minister, Peru |
| Vishnevskaya, Galina P | Opera Singer |
| Vlad, Roman | Composer, Writer |
| Vlahos, Petro | Visual Effects |
| Vo Nguyen Giap | Army General, Vietnam |
| VonPuttkammer, Jesco F | Space Scientist |
| Vucanovich, Barbara F | Representative, NV |
| Wagner, Berny | Track Coach |

# NECROLOGY

| | | | |
|---|---|---|---|
| Walker, Colleen | Golfer | Williams, Esther | Swimmer, Actress |
| Wall, David | Ballet Dancer | Williams, Phillip L | Publisher |
| Wallace, Marcia | Actress | Williams, Samuel F (Sam) | Football Player |
| Walton, Cedar A, Jr | Jazz Pianist | Williams, T Ray | Basketball Player |
| Waltz, Kenneth N | Political Scientist | Williams, William (Billy) | Baseball Player |
| Ward, John H | Football Player | Wilson, Charles A (Charlie) | Representative, OH |
| Ward, Robert | Composer | Wilson, Kenneth G | Nobel Physics Laureate |
| Warlick, Ernest (Ernie) | Football Player | Winner, Michael R | Director, Producer |
| Warner, Bill | Motocycle Rider | Winters, Jonathan | Actor, Comedian |
| Warner, Rawleigh, Jr | Businessman | Woese, Carl R | Microbiologist |
| Warren, Fran | Singer | Womack, Cecil | Singer (Womack & Womack), Songwriter |
| Weaver, Earl S | Baseball Player, Manager | Woodland, N Joseph | Inventor, Bar Coding Scanner |
| Weaver, Ronald L (Ron) | Producer | Woods, Aubrey | Actress |
| Webster, Howard C (Shoat) | Rodeo Rider | Woodward, John F (Sandy) | Navy Admiral, England |
| Weege, Reinhold | Producer | Worthington, Cal | Businessman |
| Weider, Josef E (Joe) | Publisher, Body Building Executive | Yamauchi, Hiroshi | Businessman |
| Wertimer, Ned | Actor | Yates, Robert E (Bob) | Football Player |
| Wess, Frank W | Jazz Flutist, Saxophonist | Yochim, Leonard J (Len) | Baseball Player |
| Westering, Forrest (Frosty) | Football Coach | Young, Charles W (Bill) | Representative, FL |
| Wettstone, Gene | Gymnastics Coach | Young, Lee Thompson | Actor |
| Whalen, James F (Jim), Jr | Football Player | Zao Wou-ki | Artist |
| White, Wilford P (Whizzer) | Football Player | Zerbo, Saye | Prime Minister, Upper Volta; General |
| Whitfield, Fred D | Baseball Player | Ziglar, Hilary H (Zig) | Businessman, Writer |
| Whitfield, Willis | Inventor (Clean Room) | Zinger, Viktor A | Ice Hockey Player |
| Whitman, Slim | Singer, Guitarist | Zizic, Zoran | Prime Minister, Yugoslavia |
| Williams, Earl C | Baseball Player | Zweig, Martin E | Financier |

# UNITED STATES SENATE

The men and women below are current members of the US Senate. They can be reached by writing them in care of **US Senate, Washington, DC 20510**.

Letters should be addressed:

The Honorable Jane/John Doe
US Senator from _____

Salutations in letters should be:

Dear Mr/Ms Senator

| | | | |
|---|---|---|---|
| Alabama | Sessions, Jeff | Maryland | Mikulski, Barbara A |
| Alabama | Shelby, Richard C | Massachusetts | Markey, Edward J |
| Alaska | Begich, Mark P | Massachusetts | Warren, Elizabeth |
| Alaska | Murkowski, Lisa | Michigan | Levin, Carl M |
| Arizona | Flake, Jeffry L (Jeff) | Michigan | Stabenow, Deborah A (Debbie) |
| Arizona | McCain, John S, III | Minnesota | Franken, Al |
| Arkansas | Boozman, John N | Minnesota | Klobuchar, Amy J |
| Arkansas | Pryor, Mark L | Mississippi | Cochran, W Thad |
| California | Boxer, Barbara L | Mississippi | Wicker, Roger F |
| California | Feinstein, Dianne G B | Missouri | Blunt, Roy D |
| Colorado | Bennet, Michael | Missouri | McCaskill, Claire |
| Colorado | Udall, Mark E | Montana | Baucus, Max S |
| Connecticut | Blumenthal, Richard M | Montana | Tester, Jon |
| Connecticut | Murphy, Christopher S (Chris) | Nebraska | Fischer, Debra S (Deb) |
| Delaware | Carper, Thomas R. (Tom) | Nebraska | Johanns, Michael O (Mike) |
| Delaware | Coons, Christopher A (Chris) | Nevada | Heller, Dean |
| Florida | Nelson, William (Bill) | Nevada | Reid, Harry M |
| Florida | Rubio, Marco | New Hampshire | Ayotte, Kelly A |
| Georgia | Chambliss, C Saxby | New Hampshire | Shaheen, Jeanne |
| Georgia | Isakson, John H (Johnny) | New Jersey | Booker, Cory A |
| Hawaii | Hirono, Mazie K | New Jersey | Menendez, Robert (Bob) |
| Hawaii | Schatz, Brian E | New Mexico | Heinrich, Martin T |
| Idaho | Crapo, Michael D | New Mexico | Udall, Thomas S (Tom) |
| Idaho | Risch, James E (Jim) | New York | Gillibrand, Kirsten E R |
| Illinois | Durbin, Richard J (Dick) | New York | Schumer, Charles E (Chuck) |
| Illinois | Kirk, Mark S | North Carolina | Burr, Richard M |
| Indiana | Coats, Daniel R (Dan) | North Carolina | Hagan, Kay |
| Indiana | Donnelly, Joseph S (Joe), Sr | North Dakota | Heitkamp, Mary K (Heidi) |
| Iowa | Grassley, Charles E (Chuck) | North Dakota | Hoeven, John H, III |
| Iowa | Harkin, Thomas R (Tom) | Ohio | Brown, Sherrod C |
| Kansas | Moran, Gerald W (Jerry) | Ohio | Portman, Robert J (Rob) |
| Kansas | Roberts, C Patrick (Pat) | Oklahoma | Coburn, Thomas A (Tom) |
| Kentucky | McConnell, A Mitchell (Mitch), Jr | Oklahoma | Inhofe, James M (Jim) |
| Kentucky | Paul, Randall H (Rand) | Oregon | Merkley, Jeffrey A (Jeff) |
| Louisiana | Landrieu, Mary L | Oregon | Wyden, Ronald L (Ron) |
| Louisiana | Vitter, David B | Pennsylvania | Casey, Robert P (Bob), Jr |
| Maine | Collins, Susan M | Pennsylvania | Toomey, Patrick J (Pat) |
| Maine | King, Angus S, Jr | Rhode Island | Reed, John F (Jack) |
| Maryland | Cardin, Benjamin L (Ben) | Rhode Island | Whitehouse, Sheldon |

# UNITED STATES SENATE

| | | | |
|---|---|---|---|
| South Carolina | Graham, Linsey O | Vermont | Sanders, Bernard (Bernie) |
| South Carolina | Scott, Timothy E (Tim) | Virginia | Kaine, Timothy M (Tim) |
| South Dakota | Johnson, Timothy P (Tim) | Virginia | Warner, Mark R |
| South Dakota | Thune, John, III | Washington | Cantwell, Maria E |
| Tennessee | Alexander, A Lamar | Washington | Murray, Patricia L (Patty) |
| Tennessee | Corker, Robert P (Bob), Jr | West Virginia | Manchin, Joseph (Joe), III |
| Texas | Cornyn, John, III | West Virginia | Rockefeller, John D, IV |
| Texas | Cruz, R Edward (Ted) | Wisconsin | Baldwin, Tammy S G |
| Utah | Hatch, Orrin G | Wisconsin | Johnson, Ron |
| Utah | Lee, Michael S (Mike) | Wyoming | Barrasso, John A |
| Vermont | Leahy, Patrick J | Wyoming | Enzi, Michael B (Mike) |

# UNITED STATES HOUSE OF REPRESENTATIVES

The men and women below are current members of the US House of Representatives. They can be reached by writing them in care of **US House of Representatives, Washington, DC 20515**.

Letters should be addressed:  The Honorable Jane/John Doe
US Representative from _____

Salutations in letters should be:  Dear Mr/Ms Representative _____

| | | | |
|---|---|---|---|
| Alabama | Aderholt, Robert B | California | McKeon, Howard P (Buck) |
| Alabama | Bachus, Spencer T, III | California | McNearey, Jerry |
| Alabama | Brooks, Morris J (Mo) | California | Miller, Gary G |
| Alabama | Roby, Martha | California | Miller, George, III |
| Alabama | Rogers, Michael D (Mike) | California | Napolitano, Grace F |
| Alabama | Sewell, Terri | California | Negrete McLeod, Gloria |
| Alaska | Young, Donald E (Don) | California | Nunes, Devin |
| American Samoa | Faleomavaega, Eni F H | California | Pelosi, Nancy P D |
| Arkansas | Cotton, Thomas (Tom) | California | Peters, Scott H |
| Arkansas | Crawford, Rick | California | Rohrabacher, Dana |
| Arkansas | Griffin, J Timothy (Tim) | California | Roybal-Allard, Lucille |
| Arkansas | Womack, Stephen A (Steve) | California | Royce, Edward R (Ed) |
| Arizona | Barber, Ron | California | Ruiz, Raul |
| Arizona | Franks, Trent | California | Sanchez, Linda T |
| Arizona | Gosar, Paul | California | Sanchez, Loretta |
| Arizona | Grijalva, Raul M | California | Schiff, Adam B |
| Arizona | Kirkpatrick, Ann | California | Sherman, Bradley J (Brad) |
| Arizona | Pastor, Edward L (Ed) | California | Speier, Karen L (Jackie) |
| Arizona | Salmon, Matthew J (Matt) | California | Swalwell, Eric, Jr |
| Arizona | Schweikert, David | California | Takano, Mark A |
| Arizona | Sinema, Kyrsten | California | Thompson, Michael C (Mike) |
| California | Bass, Karen | California | Valadao, David |
| California | Becerra, Xavier | California | Vargas, Juan C |
| California | Bera, Amerish (Ami) | California | Waters, Maxine C |
| California | Brownley, Julia | California | Waxman, Henry A |
| California | Calvert, Kenneth S (Ken) | Colorado | Coffman, Michael |
| California | Campbell, John B T, Jr. | Colorado | DeGette, Diana L |
| California | Capps, Lois G | Colorado | Gardener, Cory |
| California | Cardenas, Tony | Colorado | Lamborn, Doug |
| California | Chu, Judy | Colorado | Perlmutter, Edwin G (Ed) |
| California | Cook, Paul | Colorado | Polis, Jared S (Jare) |
| California | Costa, James M (Jim) | Colorado | Tipton, Scott R |
| California | Davis, Susan A | Connecticut | Courtney, Joseph (Joe) |
| California | Denham, Jeffrey (Jeff) | Connecticut | DeLauro, Rosa L |
| California | Eshoo, Anna G | Connecticut | Esty, Elizabeth H |
| California | Farr, Samuel S (Sam) | Connecticut | Himes, James A (Jim) |
| California | Garamendi, John | Connecticut | Larson, John B |
| California | Hahn, Janice | Delaware | Carney, John C, Jr |
| California | Honda, Michael M (Mike) | District/Columbia | Norton, Eleanor Holmes |
| California | Huffman, Jared | Florida | Bilirakis, Gus M |
| California | Hunter, Duncan D | Florida | Brown, Corrine |
| California | Issa, Darrell E | Florida | Buchanan, Vernon G (Vern) |
| California | LaMalfa, Doug | Florida | Castor, Kathlerine A (Kathy) |
| California | Lee, Barbara J | Florida | Crenshaw, Ander |
| California | Lofgren, Sue (Zoe) | Florida | DeSantis, Ron |
| California | Lowenthal, Alan S | Florida | Deutch, Theodore (Ted) |
| California | Matsui, Doris O | Florida | Diaz-Balart, Mario R |
| California | McCarthy, Kevin | Florida | Frankel, Lois J |
| California | McClintock, Thomas M (Tom) | Florida | Garcia, Jose A (Joe) |

| | | | |
|---|---|---|---|
| Florida | Grayson, Alan M | Kentucky | Guthrie, Steven B (Brett) |
| Florida | Hastings, Alcee L | Kentucky | Massie, Thomas H |
| Florida | Mica, John L | Kentucky | Rogers, Harold D (Hal) |
| Florida | Miller, Jefferson B (Jeff) | Kentucky | Whitfield, Edward (Ed) |
| Florida | Murphy, Patrick E | Kentucky | Yarmuth, John |
| Florida | Nugent, Richard B | Louisiana | Boustany, Charles V, Jr |
| Florida | Posey, William (Bill) | Louisiana | Cassidy, William (Bill) |
| Florida | Radel, Henry J (Trey) | Louisiana | Fleming, John |
| Florida | Rooney, Thomas J (Tom) | Louisiana | Richmond, Cedric L |
| Florida | Ros-Lehtinen, Ileana | Louisiana | Scalise, Stephen J (Steve) |
| Florida | Ross, Dennis B | Maine | Michaud, Michael H (Mike) |
| Florida | Southerland, Stephen E (Steve) | Maine | Pingree, Chellie M |
| Florida | Wasserman Schultz, Debbie | Maryland | Cummings, Elijah E |
| Florida | Webster, Daniel | Maryland | Delaney, John K |
| Florida | Wilson, Frederica | Maryland | Edwards, Donna F |
| Florida | Yoho, Theodore S (Ted) | Maryland | Harris, Andrew P (Andy) |
| Florida | Young, C W (Bill) | Maryland | Hoyer, Steny H |
| Georgia | Barrow, John J | Maryland | Ruppersberger, C A (Dutch) |
| Georgia | Bishop, Sanford D, Jr | Maryland | Sarbanes, John P S |
| Georgia | Broun, Paul C, Jr | Maryland | Van Hollen, Chris |
| Georgia | Collins, Doug | Massachusetts | Capuano, Michael E (Mike) |
| Georgia | Gingrey, J Phillip (Phil) | Massachusetts | Keating, William R (Bill) |
| Georgia | Graves, J Thomas (Tom) | Massachusetts | Kennedy, Joseph P (Joe), III |
| Georgia | Johnson, Henry (Hank), Jr | Massachusetts | Lynch, Stephen F |
| Georgia | Kingston, John H (Jack) | Massachusetts | McGovern, James P (Jim) |
| Georgia | Lewis, John R | Massachusetts | Neal, Richard E |
| Georgia | Price, Thomas E (Tom) | Massachusetts | Tierney, John F |
| Georgia | Scott, J Austin | Massachusetts | Tsongas, Nicola S (Niki) |
| Georgia | Scott, David A | Michigan | Amash, Justin |
| Georgia | Westmoreland, Lynn A | Michigan | Benishek, Daniel J (Dan) |
| Georgia | Woodall, Robert (Rob) | Michigan | Bentivolio, Kerry |
| Guam | Bordallo, Madeleine | Michigan | Camp, David L (Dave) |
| Hawaii | Gabbard, Tulsi | Michigan | Conyers, John, Jr |
| Hawaii | Hanabusa, Colleen | Michigan | Dingell, John D, Jr |
| Idaho | Labrador, Raul R | Michigan | Huizenga, William P (Bill) |
| Idaho | Simpson, Michael K (Mike) | Michigan | Kildee, Daniel T (Dan) |
| Illinois | Callahan-Bustos, Cheryl L (Cheri) | Michigan | Levin, Sander M |
| Illinois | Davis, Daniel K (Danny) | Michigan | Miller, Candice S |
| Illinois | Davis, Rodney L | Michigan | Peters, Gray |
| Illinois | Duckworth, L Tammy | Michigan | Rogers, Michael J (Mike) |
| Illinois | Enyart, William L (Bill), Jr | Michigan | Upton, Frederick S (Fred) |
| Illinois | Foster, G William (Bill) | Michigan | Walberg, Timothy L (Tim) |
| Illinois | Gutierrez, Luis V | Minnesota | Bachmann, Michele M |
| Illinois | Hultgren, Randall M (Randy) | Minnesota | Ellison, Keith M |
| Illinois | Kelly, Robin L | Minnesota | Kline, John P |
| Illinois | Kinzinger, Adam A | Minnesota | McCollum, Betty L |
| Illinois | Lipinski, Daniel W (Dan) | Minnesota | Nolan, Richard M (Rick) |
| Illinois | Quigley, Michael (Mike) | Minnesota | Paulsen, Erik |
| Illinois | Roskam, Peter J | Minnesota | Peterson, Collin C |
| Illinois | Rush, Bobby L | Minnesota | Walz, Timothy J (Tim) |
| Illinois | Schakowsky, Janice D (Jan) | Mississippi | Harper, Gregg |
| Illinois | Schneider, Bradley S (Brad) | Mississippi | Nunnelee, P Alan |
| Illinois | Schock, Aaron | Mississippi | Palazzo, Steven M |
| Illinois | Shimkus, John M | Mississippi | Thompson, Bennie G |
| Indiana | Brooks, Susan W | Missouri | Clay, William L (Lacy), Jr |
| Indiana | Bucshon, Larry D | Missouri | Cleaver, Emanuel, II |
| Indiana | Carson, Andre D | Missouri | Graves, Samuel B (Sam) |
| Indiana | Messer, A Lucas (Luke) | Missouri | Hartzler, Vicky J |
| Indiana | Rokita, Theodore E (Todd) | Missouri | Long, William H (Billy) |
| Indiana | Stutzman, Marlin A | Missouri | Luetkemeyer, Blaine |
| Indiana | Visclosky, Peter J | Missouri | Smith, Jason T |
| Indiana | Walorski, Jackie | Missouri | Wagner, Ann |
| Indiana | Young, Todd C | Montana | Daines, Steven (Steve) |
| Iowa | Braley, Bruce | Nebraska | Fortenberry, Jeffrey L (Jeff) |
| Iowa | King, Steven A (Steve) | Nebraska | Smith, Adrian M |
| Iowa | Latham, Thomas (Tom) | Nebraska | Terry, Lee R |
| Iowa | Loebsack, David | Nevada | Amodei, Mark E |
| Kansas | Huelskamp, Timothy A (Tim) | Nevada | Heck, Joseph J (Joe) |
| Kansas | Jenkins, Lynn | Nevada | Horsford, Steven |
| Kansas | Pompeo, Michael R (Mike) | Nevada | Titus, Alice C (Dina) |
| Kansas | Yoder, Kevin | New Hampshire | McLane Kuster, Ann (Annie) |
| Kentucky | Barr, Garland H (Andy) | New Hampshire | Shea-Porter, Carol |

## UNITED STATES HOUSE OF REPRESENTATIVES

| | | | |
|---|---|---|---|
| New Jersey | Andrews, Robert E (Rob) | Ohio | Wenstrup, Brad |
| New Jersey | Frelinghuysen, Rodney P | Oklahoma | Bridenstine, James F (Jim) |
| New Jersey | Garrett, E Scott | Oklahoma | Cole, Thomas J (Tom) |
| New Jersey | Holt, Rush D, Jr | Oklahoma | Lankford, James |
| New Jersey | Lance, Leonard | Oklahoma | Lucas, Frank D |
| New Jersey | LoBiondo, Frank A | Oklahoma | Mullin, Markwayne |
| New Jersey | Pallone, Frank, Jr | Oregon | Blumenauer, Earl |
| New Jersey | Pascrell, William J (Bill), Jr | Oregon | Bonamici, Suzanne |
| New Jersey | Payne, Donald M | Oregon | DeFazio, Peter A (Pete) |
| New Jersey | Runyon, Jon D | Oregon | Schrader, Kurt |
| New Jersey | Sires, Albio | Oregon | Walden, Gregory (Greg) |
| New Jersey | Smith, Christopher H (Chris) | Pennsylvania | Barletta, Louis J (Lou) |
| New Mexico | Lujan, Ben R, Jr | Pennsylvania | Brady, Robert A (Bob) |
| New Mexico | Lujan Grisham, Michelle | Pennsylvania | Cartwright, Matthew A (Matt) |
| New Mexico | Pearce, Stevan E (Steve) | Pennsylvania | Dent, Charles W (Charlie) |
| New York | Bishop, Timothy H (Tim) | Pennsylvania | Doyle, Michael F (Mike) |
| New York | Clarke, Yvette D | Pennsylvania | Fattah, Chaka |
| New York | Collins, Christopher C (Chris) | Pennsylvania | Fitzpatrick, Michael G (Mike) |
| New York | Crowley, Joseph | Pennsylvania | Gerlach, James (Jim) |
| New York | Engel, Eliot L | Pennsylvania | Kelly, Michael (Mike) |
| New York | Gibson, Christopher P (Chris) | Pennsylvania | Marino, A Thomas (Tom) |
| New York | Grimm, Michael (Mike) | Pennsylvania | Meehan, Patrick L (Pat) |
| New York | Hanna, Richard | Pennsylvania | Murphy, Timothy F (Tim) |
| New York | Higgins, Brian | Pennsylvania | Perry, Scott G |
| New York | Israel, Steve | Pennsylvania | Pitts, Joseph R (Joe) |
| New York | Jeffries, Hakeem S | Pennsylvania | Rothfus, Keith J |
| New York | King, Peter T | Pennsylvania | Schwartz, Allyson Y |
| New York | Lowey, Nita M | Pennsylvania | Shuster, William (Bill) |
| New York | Maffei, Daniel B (Dan) | Pennsylvania | Thompson, Glenn |
| New York | Maloney, Carolyn B | Puerto Rico | Pierluisi, Pedro |
| New York | Maloney, Sean P | Rhode Island | Cicilline, David N |
| New York | McCarthy, Carolyn | Rhode Island | Langevin, James R |
| New York | Meeks, Gregory W | South Carolina | Clyburn, James E (Jim) |
| New York | Meng, Grace | South Carolina | Duncan, Jeffrey D (Jeff) |
| New York | Nadler, Jerrold L (Jerry) | South Carolina | Gowdy, Howard W (Trey), III |
| New York | Owens, William (Bill) | South Carolina | Mulvaney, John M (Mick) |
| New York | Rangel, Charles B | South Carolina | Rice, Hugh T (Tom) |
| New York | Reed, Thomas | South Carolina | Sanford, Mark |
| New York | Serrano, José E | South Carolina | Wilson, Addison G (Joe), Sr |
| New York | Slaughter, Louise M | South Dakota | Noem, Kristi L A |
| New York | Tonko, Paul D | Tennessee | Black, Diane L |
| New York | Velazquez, Nydia M | Tennessee | Blackburn, Marsha |
| North Carolina | Butterfield, George K (G K), Jr | Tennessee | Cohen, Stephen J (Steve) |
| North Carolina | Coble, J Howard | Tennessee | Cooper, James H S (Jim) |
| North Carolina | Ellmers, Renee J | Tennessee | DesJarlais, Scott E |
| North Carolina | Foxx, Virginia A | Tennessee | Duncan, John J (Jimmy), Jr |
| North Carolina | Holding, George E B | Tennessee | Fincher, Stephen |
| North Carolina | Hudson, Richard | Tennessee | Fleischmann, Charles J (Chuck) |
| North Carolina | Jones, Walter B, Jr | Tennessee | Roe, David P (Phil) |
| North Carolina | McHenry, Patrick T | Texas | Barton, Joseph L (Joe) |
| North Carolina | McIntyre, Douglas C (Mike), II | Texas | Brady, Kevin P |
| North Carolina | Meadows, Mark R | Texas | Burgess, Michael C |
| North Carolina | Pittenger, Robert | Texas | Carter, John R |
| North Carolina | Price, David E | Texas | Castro, Joaquin |
| North Carolina | Watt, Melvin L (Mel) | Texas | Conaway, Michael K (Mike) |
| North Dakota | Cramer, Kevin | Texas | Cuellar, Henry R |
| North Mariana Islands | Sablan, Gregorio K C | Texas | Culberson, John A |
| Ohio | Beatty, Joyce | Texas | Doggett, Lloyd A, II |
| Ohio | Boehner, John A | Texas | Farenthold, R Blake |
| Ohio | Chabot, Steven J (Steve) | Texas | Flores, William H (Bill) |
| Ohio | Fudge, Marcia L | Texas | Gallego, Pete P |
| Ohio | Gibbs, Robert B (Bob) | Texas | Gohmert, Louis B (Louie), Jr |
| Ohio | Johnson, William L (Bill) | Texas | Granger, Kay |
| Ohio | Jordan, James D (Jim) | Texas | Green, Alexander N (Al) |
| Ohio | Joyce, David P | Texas | Green, R Eugene (Gene) |
| Ohio | Kaptur, Marcia C (Marcy) | Texas | Hall, Ralph M |
| Ohio | Latta, Robert E (Bob) | Texas | Hensarling, Jeb |
| Ohio | Renacci, James B (Jim) | Texas | Hinojosa, Ruben E |
| Ohio | Ryan, Timothy J (Tim) | Texas | Jackson-Lee, Sheila |
| Ohio | Stivers, Stephen E (Steve) | Texas | Johnson, Eddie Bernice |
| Ohio | Tiberi, Patrick J (Pat) | Texas | Johnson, Samuel R (Sam) |
| Ohio | Turner, Michael R (Mike) | Texas | Marchant, Kenneth (Kenny) |

## UNITED STATES HOUSE OF REPRESENTATIVES

| | | | |
|---|---|---|---|
| Texas | McCaul, Michael T (Mike) | Virginia | Rigell, E Scott |
| Texas | Neugebauer, R Randolph (Randy) | Virginia | Scott, Robert C (Bobby) |
| Texas | O'Rourke, Robert F (Beto) | Virginia | Wittman, Robert J (Rob) |
| Texas | Olson, Peter G (Pete) | Virginia | Wolf, Frank R |
| Texas | Poe, Lloyd (Ted) | Washington | DelBene, Suzan K |
| Texas | Sessions, Peter A (Pete) | Washington | Hastings, Richard N (Doc) |
| Texas | Smith, Lamar S | Washington | Heck, Dennis (Denny) |
| Texas | Stockman, Stephen E (Steve) | Washington | Herrera Beutler, Jaime |
| Texas | Thornberry, William M (Mac) | Washington | Kilmer, Derek |
| Texas | Veasey, Marc | Washington | Larsen, Richard R (Rick) |
| Texas | Vela, Filemon B, Jr | Washington | McDermott, James A (Jim) |
| Texas | Weber, Randy | Washington | McMorris Rogers, Cathy |
| Texas | Williams, JRoger | Washington | Reichert, David G (Dave) |
| Utah | Bishop, Robert W (Rob) | Washington | Smith, D Adam |
| Utah | Chaffetz, Jason | West Virginia | Capito, Shelly Moore |
| Utah | Matheson, James D (Jim) | West Virginia | McKinley, David |
| Utah | Stewart, Christopher D (Chris) | West Virginia | Rahall, Nick Joe, II |
| Vermont | Welch, Peter F | Wisconsin | Duffy, Sean P |
| Virgin Islands | Christian-Christensen, Donna M | Wisconsin | Kind, Ronald J (Ron) |
| Virginia | Cantor, Eric I | Wisconsin | Moore, Gwendolynne S (Gwen) |
| Virginia | Connolly, Gerald E | Wisconsin | Petri, Thomas E (Tom) |
| Virginia | Forbes, J Randy | Wisconsin | Pocan, Mark |
| Virginia | Goodlatte, Robert W (Bob) | Wisconsin | Ribble, Reid J |
| Virginia | Griffith, H Morgan | Wisconsin | Ryan, Paul D, Jr |
| Virginia | Hurt, Robert | Wisconsin | Sensenbrenner, F James, Jr (Jim) |
| Virginia | Moran, James P (Jim), Jr | Wyoming | Lummis, Cynthia |

## UNITED STATES GOVERNORS

The men and women below are current US Governors. They can be reached by writing them in care of **Governor's Office** at the addresses listed below.

Letters should be addressed:     The Honorable Jane/John Doe
                                          Governor from _____

Salutations in letters should be:     Dear Mr/Ms Governor _____

| | | |
|---|---|---|
| Alabama | Bentley, Robert J | State Capitol, 600 Dexter Ave, Montgomery AL 36130, USA |
| Alaska | Parnell, Sean R | State Capitol Building, PO Box 110001, Juneau AK 99811, USA |
| American Samoa | Moliga Lolo M | Executive Office Building, #300, Utulei, Pago Pago, AS 96799 |
| Arizona | Brewer, Janice K (Jan) | State Capitol, 1700 W Washington St, Phoenix AZ 85007, USA |
| Arkansas | Beebe, Michael D | State Capitol, #250, Little Rock AR 72201, USA |
| California | Brown, Edmund G (Jerry) | State Capital, #100, Sacramento CA 95814, USA |
| Colorado | Hickenlooper, John W | 136 State Capitol, Denver CO 80203, USA |
| Connecticut | Malloy, Dan | State Capitol, 210 Capitol Ave, Hartford CT 06106, USA |
| Delaware | Markell, Jack A | Legislative Hall, Dover DE 19902, USA |
| Florida | Scott, Richard L (Rick) | PL 05 The Capitol, 400 S Monroe St, Tallahassee FL 32399, USA |
| Georgia | Deal, John N (Nathan) | State Capitol, #203, Atlanta GA 30334, USA |
| Guam | Calvo, Eddie Baza | Executive Chamber, PO Box 2950, Agana, GU 96932 |
| Hawaii | Abercrombie, Neil | Executive Chambers, #500, Honolulu HI 96813, USA |
| Idaho | Otter, C L (Butch) | State Capitol, 700 W Jefferson, #200, Boise ID 83702, USA |
| Illinois | Quinn, Patrick J | State House, 207 Statehouse, Springfield IL 62706, USA |
| Indiana | Pence, Michael R (Mike) | State House, #206, Indianapolis IN 46204, USA |
| Iowa | Brandstad, Terry E | State Capitol, Des Moines IA 50319, USA |
| Kansas | Brownback, Samuel D (Sam) | Capitol, 300 SW 10th Ave, #212S, Topeka KS 66612, USA |
| Kentucky | Beshear, Steven L (Steve) | State Capitol, 700 Capitol Ave, #100, Frankfort KY 40601, USA |
| Louisiana | Jindal, Piyosh (Bobby) | State Capitol, PO Box 94004, Baton Rouge LA 70804, USA |
| Maine | LePage, Paul R | Blaine House, 1 State House Station, Augusta ME 04333, USA |
| Maryland | O'Malley, Martin J | State House, 100 State Circle, Annapolis MD 21401, USA |
| Massachusetts | Patrick, Deval L | State House, #360, Boston MA 02133, USA |
| Michigan | Snyder, Richard D (Rick) | State Capitol, PO Box 30013, Lansing MI 48909, USA |
| Minnesota | Dayton, Mark B | 130 State Capitol, 75 Rev Dr MLK Jr Blvd, Saint Paul MN 55155, USA |
| Mississippi | Bryant, D Phillip (Phil) | State Capitol, PO Box 139, Jackson MS 39205, USA |
| Missouri | Nixon, Jeremiah W (Jay) | State Capitol, #218, PO Box 720, Jefferson City MO 65102, USA |
| Montana | Bullock, Steve | State Capitol, PO Box 0801, Helena MT 59620, USA |
| Nebraska | Heineman, David E (Dave) | State Capitol, PO Box 94848, Lincoln NE 68509, USA |
| Nevada | Sandoval, Brian E | State Capitol, 101 N Carson St, Carson City NV 89701, USA |
| New Hampshire | Hassan, Maggie | 25 Capitol St, #212,  Concord NH 03301, USA |
| New Jersey | Christie, Chris | State House, 125 W State St, PO Box 001, Trenton NJ 08625, USA |
| New Mexico | Martinez, Susana | State Capitol, #400, Santa Fe NM 87300, USA |
| New York | Cuomo, Andrew | State Capitol, Albany NY 12224, USA |
| North Carolina | McCrory, Patrick L (Pat) | State Capitol, 20301 Mail Service Center, Raleigh NC 27699, USA |
| North Dakota | Dalrymple, John (Jack) | State Capitol, 600 E Boulevard Ave, #101, Bismarck ND 58505, USA |
| Northern Marianas | Inos, Eloy | Governor's Office, Caller Box 10007, Saipan, MP 96950 |

## UNITED STATES GOVERNORS

| | | |
|---|---|---|
| Ohio | Kasich, John R | State House, 77 S High St, #3000, Columbus OH 43215, USA |
| Oklahoma | Fallin, Mary | State Capitol, 2300 N Lincoln Blvd, #212, Oklahoma City OK 73105, USA |
| Oregon | Kitzhaber, John A | State Capitol, 900 Court St, #160, Salem OR 97301, USA |
| Pennsylvania | Corbett, Thomas (Tom) | Main Capitol, #225, Harrisburg PA 17120, USA |
| Puerto Rico | Garcia Padilla, Alejandro J | La Fortaleza, PO Box 9020082, San Juan, PR 00902 |
| Rhode Island | Chafee, Lincoln D | State House, Providence RI 02903, USA |
| South Carolina | Haley, Nimrata R (Nikki) | State Capitol, PO Box 11829, Columbia SC 29211, USA |
| South Dakota | Daugaard, Dennis M | State Capitol, 500 E Capitol Ave Pierre, SD 57501, USA |
| Tennessee | Haslam, William E (Bill) | State Capitol, Nashville TN 37243, USA |
| Texas | Perry, James R (Rick) | State Capitol, PO Box 12428, Austin TX 78711, USA |
| Utah | Herbert, Gary R | State Capitol, #200, Salt Lake City UT 84114, USA |
| Vermont | Shumlin, Peter S | Pavilion Building, 109 State St, Montpelier VT 05609, USA |
| Virginia | McDonnell, Robert F (Bob) | State Capitol, #300, Richmond VA 23219, USA |
| Virgin Islands | deJongh, John, Jr | Gov't House, 21-22 Kongens Gade, Charlotte Amalie, St. Thomas, VI 00802 |
| Washington | Inselee, Jay R | State Capitol, PO Box 40002, Olympia WA 98504, USA |
| West Virginia | Tomblin, Earl R | 1900 Kanawha St, Charleston WV 25305, USA |
| Wisconsin | Walker, Scott K | 115 E State Capitol, Madison WI 53707, USA |
| Wyoming | Mead, Matthew H (Matt) | State Capitol, #124, Cheyenne WY 82002, USA |

## AGENCY ADDRESSES

| | | |
|---|---|---|
| 42 West | 11400 W Olympic Blvd, #1100 | Los Angeles CA 90064, USA |
| Abrams Artists & Associates | 9200 Sunset Blvd, #1125 | West Hollywood CA 90069, USA |
| Abrams-Rubaloff & Lawrence | 8075 W 3rd St | Los Angeles CA 90048, USA |
| A P A | 405 S Beverly Dr, #405 | Beverly Hills CA 90212, USA |
| A P A | 250 W 57th St, #1701 | New York NY 10107 USA |
| Agency Group | 9348 Civic Center Dr, #200 | Beverly Hills CA 90210, USA |
| Agency Group | 142 W 57th St, #600 | New York NY 10019, USA |
| Agency, The | 3711 Ocean Front Walk, #1 | Marina del Rey CA 90292, USA |
| Agents Associes Beaume | 201 rue du Faubourg Saint Honore | 75008 Paris, France |
| Agentur Killer | 54 Harthauser Str | 81545 Munich, Germany |
| Agentur DorisMattes | 14 Merzstr | 81679 Munich, Germany |
| Air Edel | 9100 Wilshire Blvd, #350E | Beverly Hills CA 90212, USA |
| Altaras, Jonathan | 11 Garrick St | London WC1V 2QA, England |
| Ambrosio/Mortimer & Associates | 165 W 45th St | New York NY USA |
| Amsel Eisenstadt & Frazier | 5055 Wilshire Blvd, #865 | Los Angeles CA 90036, USA |
| Artists Agency | 9430 Olympic Blvd | Beverly Hills CA 90212, USA |
| Artmedia | 20 Av Rapp | 75007 Paris, France |
| Askonas Holt | Lincoln House, 300 High Holborn | London WC1V 7JH England |
| Associated Booking Agency | PO Box 2055 | New York NY 10021, USA |
| Associated Talent International | 1320 Armacost Ave, #2 | Beverly Hills, CA 90212, USA |
| B/W/R Public Relations | 9100 Wilshire Blvd, #500W | Los Angeles CA 90036, USA |
| Bauman Redanty & Shaul | 5757 Wilshire Blvd, #473 | Los Angeles CA 90036, USA |
| Belfrage, Julian | 14 New Burlington St | London W1S 3DQ, England |
| Blake Agency | 23441 Malibu Canyon Road | Malibu CA 90265, USA |
| Blanchard, Enterprises Nina | 8826 Burton Way | Beverly Hills CA 90211, USA |
| Borinstein Oreck Bogart Agency | 3172 Dona Susana Dr | Studio City CA 91604, USA |
| Boss Models | 80 8th Ave | New York NY 10011, USA |
| Bragman, Nyman & Cafarelli | 8687 Melrose Ave, #800 | West Hollywood CA 90069, USA |
| Bresler Kelly & Associates | 11500 W Olympic Blvd, #352 | Los Angeles CA 90064, USA |
| Breslin, Herbert | 333 E 57th St | New York NY 10022, USA |
| Brillstein Entertainment Partners | 9150 Wilshire Blvd, #350 | Beverly Hills CA 90212, USA |
| Buchwald & Associates, Don | 6500 Wilshire Blvd, #2200 | Los Angeles CA 90048, USA |
| Burton Agency, Iris | 10100 Santa Monica Blvd, #1300 | Los Angeles CA 90067, USA |
| Camden ITG Talent Agency | 1501 Main St, #204 | Venice CA 90291, USA |
| Carroll Agency, William | 12811 Garden Grove Blvd, #209 | Garden Grove CA 92843, USA |
| Cassidy Inc, Thomas | P O 1311 | Tucson AZ 85702, USA |
| Cavaleri & Associates | 178 S Victory Blvd, #205 | Burbank CA 91502, USA |
| Century Artists | PO Box 59747 | Santa Barbara CA 93150, USA |
| CESD | 10635 Santa Monica Blvd, #130 | Los Angeles CA 90025, USA |
| Chasin Agency | 8899 Beverly Blvd, #716 | Los Angeles CA 90048, USA |
| Chatto & Linnit | 123A King's Road | London SW3 4PL, England |
| Circle Talent Associates | 433 N Camden Dr, #400 | Beverly Hills CA 90210, USA |
| Click Model Management | 881 7th Ave | New York NY 10019, USA |
| CLInc Talent Agency | 843 N Sycamore Ave | Los Angeles CA 90038, USA |
| C N A & Associates | 1875 Century Park E, #2250 | Los Angeles CA 90067, USA |
| Coast to Coast Talent Group | 3350 Barham Blvd | Los Angeles CA 90068, USA |
| Columbia Artists Management | 1790 Broadway, #702 | New York NY 10019, USA |
| Commercials Unlimited | 190 N Canon Drive, #202 | Beverly Hills CA 90210, USA |
| Conner Agency, Hall | 9169 Sunset Blvd | West Hollywood CA 90069, USA |
| Contemporary Artists | 610 Santa Monica Blvd, #202 | Santa Monica CA 90401, USA |

# AGENCY ADDRESSES

| | | |
|---|---|---|
| Cosden Agency, Robert | 3518 Cahuenga Blvd W, #200 | Los Angeles CA 90068, USA |
| Cramer/Marder Artists | 127 W 96th St, #13B | New York NY 10025, USA |
| Creative Artists Agency | 2000 Avenue of Stars | Los Angeles CA 90067, USA |
| Creative Entertainment Associates | 1950 Old Cuthbert Road, #J | Cherry Hill NJ, 08034, USA |
| Daish Associates, Judy | 2 Saint Charles Place | London M10 6EG, England |
| D H Talent Agency | 1800 N Highland Ave, #300 | Los Angeles CA 90028, USA |
| Domain Talent | 9229 Sunset Blvd, #710 | Los Angeles CA 90069, USA |
| Elite Model Management | 404 Park Ave S, #900 | New York NY 10016, USA |
| Entertainment Talent Agency | 9225 W Sunset Blvd, #805 | West Hollywood CA 90069, USA |
| Epstein-Wyckoff & Associates | 280 S Beverly Dr, #400 | Beverly Hills CA 90212, USA |
| Famous Artists Agency | 250 W 57th St | New York NY 10107, USA |
| Film Artists Associates | 13563 1/2 Ventura Blvd, #200 | Sherman Oaks CA 91423, USA |
| First Artists Agency | 4764 Park Granada, #210 | Calabasas, CA 91302, USA |
| Flick East-West Talents | 9057 Nemo St, #A | West Hollywood CA 90069, USA |
| Ford Model Agency | 111 5th Ave, #900 | New York NY 10003, USA |
| Front Line Management | 1100 Glendon Ave | Los Angeles CA 90024, USA |
| Gage Group | 14724 Ventura Blvd, #505 | Sherman Oaks CA 91403, USA |
| Geddes Agency | 8430 Santa Monica Blvd, #201 | West Hollywood CA 90069, USA |
| Gersh Agency | 9465 Wilshire Blvd, #600 | Beverly Hills CA 90212, USA |
| Gordon & Associates, Michelle | 260 S Beverly Dr, #308 | Beverly Hills CA 90212, USA |
| Gorfaine/Schwarz | 4111 W Alameda Ave #509 | Burbank CA 91505, USA |
| Grady Agency, Mary | 269 S Beverly Dr, #1088 | Beverly Hills CA 91212, USA |
| Greene & Associates | 190 N Canon Dr, #200 | Beverly Hills CA 90210, USA |
| Halliday & Associates, Buzz | 8899 Beverly Blvd, #715 | Los Angeles CA 90048, USA |
| Hallmark Entertainment | 8033 Sunset Blvd, #1000 | Los Angeles CA 90046, USA |
| Halpern & Associates | PO Box 5597 | Santa Monica, CA 90409, USA |
| Handprint Entertainment | 450 N Roxbury Dr, #602 | Beverly Hills CA 90210, USA |
| HarrisonParrott | 5-6 Albion Place | London W6 0QT, England |
| Henderson/Hogan Agency | 9255 W Sunset Blvd, #803 | West Hollywood CA 90069, USA |
| Hervey/Grimes Talent Agency | 10561 Missouri, #2 | Los Angeles CA 90025, USA |
| House of Representatives | 1434 6th St, #1 | Santa Monica CA 90401, USA |
| H T M/Headliner Talent Mgmt | 39398 Moonlight Bay Trail | Pelican Rapids MN 56572, USA |
| Hyler Mgmt | 3000 W Olympic Blvd, Bldg 5 | Santa Monica CA 90404, USA |
| Hyphenate | 1180 S Beverly Dr, #601 | Beverly Hills CA 90212, USA |
| I/D Public Relations | 7060 Hollywood Blvd | Los Angeles CA 90028, USA |
| I F A Talent Agency | 8730 Sunset Blvd, #490 | West Hollywood CA 90069, USA |
| Imagine Entertainment | 9465 Wilshire Blvd, #700 | Beverly Hills CA 90212, USA |
| I M G Models | 304 Park Ave S, #1200 | New York NY 10010, USA |
| Independent Talent Group | 40 Whitfield St | London W1T 2RH, England |
| Innovative Artists | 1505 10th Street | Santa Monica CA 91401, USA |
| ICM Partners | 10250 Constellation Blvd, #700 | Los Angeles CA 90067, USA |
| ICM Partners | 730 5th Ave | New York NY 10019, USA |
| ICM Partners | Marlborough House, 10 Earlham St, #300 | London WC2H 9LN, England |
| International Management Group | 1360 E 9th St, #1300 | Cleveland OH 44114, USA |
| International Talent Group | 40 Whitfield St | London W1T 2RH, England |
| Joyce Agency | 370 Harrison Ave | Harrison NY 10528, USA |
| Karg/Weissenbach Associates | 9255 Sunset Blvd, #1115 | Los Angeles CA 90065, USA |
| Katz Enterprises, Raymond | 345 N Maple Dr, #205 | Beverly Hills CA 90210, USA |
| Kazarian/Measures/Ruskin Agency | 11969 Ventura Blvd, #3 | Studio City CA 91604, USA |
| Kohner Inc, Paul | 9300 Wilshire Blvd, #555 | Beverly Hills CA 90212, USA |
| Kosden Agency, Robert | 7135 Hollywood Blvd, #PH2 | Los Angeles CA 90046, USA |
| Kraft-Benjamin-Engel | 9200 Sunset Blvd, #321 | Los Angeles CA 90069, USA |
| Kritzer Levine Wilkins | 11872 LaGrange Ave, #100 | Los Angeles CA 90025, USA |
| Kurland Associates, Ted | 173 Brighton Ave | Allston MA 02134, USA |
| L A Talent | 7700 Sunset Blvd, #200 | Los Angeles CA 90046, USA |
| Lee Attractions, Buddy | 38 Music Square E, #200 | Nashville TN 37203, USA |
| Light, Robert | 6404 Wilshire Blvd | Los Angeles CA 90048, USA |
| Lighthouse Entertainment | 9220 W Sunset Blvd, #200 | West Hollywood CA 90069, USA |
| London Management | 2-4 Noel St | London W1V 3RB, England |
| Lovell Associates | 7095 Hollywood Blvd, #1006 | Los Angeles CA 90028, USA |
| Luber Rocklin Entertainment | 8530 Wilshire Blvd, #555 | Beverly Hills CA 90211, USA |
| Main Title Entertainment | 8383 Wilshire Blvd, #408 | Beverly Hills CA 90211, USA |
| Management Javonovic | 24 Kathi-Kobus-Str | 80797 Munich, Germany |
| Markham & Froggatt | Julian House, 4 Windmill St | London W1P 1HF, England |
| Marshak Wycoff Associates | 280 S Beverly Dr, #400 | Beverly Hills CA 90212, USA |
| Marsh-Best Associates | 9150 Wilshire Blvd, #220 | Beverly Hills CA 90212, USA |
| M A X Agency | 166 N Canon Dr | Beverly Hills CA 90212, USA |
| M C A Concerts | 100 Universal City Plaza | Universal City CA 91608, USA |
| McKeon-Myrones Mgmt | 3500 Olive Ave, #770 | Burbank CA 91505, USA |
| Media Artists Group | 8255 W Sunset Blvd | Los Angeles CA 90046, USA |

# AGENCY ADDRESSES

| | | |
|---|---|---|
| Metropolitan Talent Agency | 7020 La Presa Dr | Los Angeles CA 90048, USA |
| M E W Inc | 8489 W 3rd St, #1100 | Los Angeles CA 90048, USA |
| Miskin Agency | 2355 Benedict Canyon | Beverly Hills CA 90210, USA |
| Monterey Peninsula Artists | 404 W Franklin St | Monterey CA 93940, USA |
| Morris Yorn Barnes | 2000 Avenue of Stars, #300N | Los Angeles CA 90067, USA |
| Moss Agency, Burton | 8827 Beverly Blvd, #L | Los Angeles CA 90048, USA |
| Nathe & Associates, Susan | 8281 Melrose Ave, #200 | Los Angeles CA 90046, USA |
| Nationwide Entertainment | 2756 N Green Valley Pkwy, #449 | Henderson NV 89014, USA |
| Next Model Management | 23 Watts St | New York NY 10013, USA |
| Octagon | 1751 Pinnacle Dr, #1500 | McLean VA 22102, USA |
| Opera et Concert | 37 Rue de la Chaussee d'Autin | 75009 Paris, France |
| Pakula/King & Associates | 9229 Sunset Blvd, #315 | West Hollywood CA 90069, USA |
| Paradigm Agency | 360 N Crescent Dr, North Building | Beverly Hills CA 90210, USA |
| Parseghian Planco | 388 2nd Ave, #506 | New York NY 10010, USA |
| Pauline's Talent Corp | 379 W Broadway, #502 | New York NY 10012, USA |
| Peters Fraser Dunlop | Drury House, 34-43 Russell St | London WC2B 5HA, England |
| P M K-B N C | 8687 Melrose Ave, #8 | Los Angeles CA 90069, USA |
| Premier Artists Agency | 1611 S Robertson Blvd | Los Angeles CA 90035, USA |
| Premier Talent Agency | 3 E 54th St, #1100 | New York NY 10022, USA |
| Principal Entertainment | 9255 Sunset Blvd, #500 | Los Angeles CA 90069, USA |
| Progressive Artists Agency | 1041 N Formosa Ave | West Hollywood CA 90046, USA |
| Rascoff/Zysblat Organization | 2500 57th St | New York NY 10107, USA |
| Redway Associates, John | 5 Denmark St | London WC2H 8LP, England |
| Reid Entertainment, John | Singes House, 32 Galena Road | London W6 0LT, England |
| Rich Management, Elaine | 2400 Whitman Place | Los Angeles CA 90068, USA |
| Rogers & Cowan Agency | 8687 Melrose Ave, #G700 | West Hollywood CA 90069, USA |
| Rollins Joffe Morra Brezner | 10201 Pico Blvd, #58 | Los Angeles CA 90064, USA |
| Rothberg, Arlyne | 349 S Linden Dr, #C | Beverly Hills CA 90212, USA |
| Rozon Mercer Mgmt | 201 N Robertson Blvd, #F | Beverly Hills CA 90211, USA |
| Ruffalo Management, Joseph | 9655 Wilshire Blvd, #850 | Beverly Hills CA 90212, USA |
| Rush Artists Management | 1600 Varick St | New York NY 10013, USA |
| Russo, Lynne | 3624 Mound View Ave | Studio City CA 91604, USA |
| Sanford-Beckett-Skouras | 1015 Gayley Ave, #300 | Los Angeles CA 90024, USA |
| Savage Agency | 6212 Banner Ave | Los Angeles CA 90038, USA |
| Schechter Co, Irv | 9460 Wilshire Blvd, #300 | Beverly Hills CA 90212, USA |
| Schiowitz/Clay | 1680 Vine St, #614 | Los Angeles CA 90028, USA |
| Schoen & Associates, Judy | 606 N Larchmont Blvd, #309 | Los Angeles CA 90004, USA |
| Schultz Agency, Kathleen | 6442 Coldwater Canyon Ave, #206 | Valley Glen CA 91606, USA |
| Schwartz Associates, Don | PO Box 3628 | Los Angeles CA 90078, USA |
| S D B Partners, Inc | 1801 Ave of Stars, #902 | Los Angeles CA 90067, USA |
| Sekura/A Talent Agency | PO Box 931779 | Los Angeles CA 90093, USA |
| Selected Artists Agency | 3900 W Alameda Ave, #345 | Burbank CA 91505, USA |
| Shapira & Associates, David | 193 N Robertson Blvd | Beverly Hills CA 90211, USA |
| Shapiro-Lichtman Agency | 8827 Beverly Blvd | Los Angeles CA 90048, USA |
| Sharkey Associates, James | 34 Kingly Court | London W1R 4LE, England |
| Shelter Entertainment | 9454 Wilshire Blvd, #715 | Beverly Hills CA 90212, USA |
| Sherrell Agency, Lew | 937 N Sinova | Mesa AZ 85205, USA |
| Shriver Public Relations, Evelyn | 830 E Hillview Dr | Brentwood TN 37027, USA |
| Silver Massetti & Szatmary | 8730 Sunset Blvd, #440 | West Hollywood CA 90069, USA |
| Sindell & Associates, Richard | 1910 Holmby Ave, #1 | Los Angeles, CA 90025, USA |
| Slessinger & Associates, Michael | 8730 Sunset Blvd, #270 | West Hollywood CA 90069, USA |
| Smith & Associates, Susan | 1344 N Wetherly Dr | Los Angeles CA 90069, USA |
| Smith/Gosnell/Nicholson | PO Box 1156 | Studio City CA 91614, USA |
| Somers Teitelbaum David | 8840 Wilshire Blvd, #200 | Beverly Hills CA 90211, USA |
| Special Artists Agency | 9200 Sunset Blvd, #410 | West Hollywood CA 90069, USA |
| Starwil Talent | 433 N Camden Dr, #400 | Beverly Hills CA 90210, USA |
| Sterling/Winters | 2029 Century Park E, #1400 | Los Angeles CA 90067, USA |
| Stone Manners Salners Agency | 9911 W Pico Blvd #1400 | Los Angeles CA 90035, USA |
| Strain & Associates, Peter | 5455 Wilshire Blvd, #1812 | Los Angeles CA 90036, USA |
| Talent Entertainment Group | 9111 Wilshire Blvd | Beverly Hills CA 90210, USA |
| TalentWorks | 3500 W Olive Ave, #1400 | Burbank, CA 91505, USA |
| Tannen & Associates, Herb | 10801 National Blvd, #101 | Los Angeles CA 90064, USA |
| Thomas Agency, Robert | 42350 Niagra Dr | Sterling Heights MI 48313, USA |
| Tisherman Agency | 6767 Forest Lawn Dr, #101 | Los Angeles CA 90068, USA |
| Twentieth Century Artists | 19528 Ventura Blvd | Tarzana CA 91356, USA |
| United Agents | 12-26 Lexington St | London W1F 0L#, England |
| United Talent Agency | 9336 Civic Center Dr | Beverly Hills CA 90210, USA |
| Untitled Entertainment | 350 S Beverly Dr, #200 | Beverly Hills CA 90212, USA |
| Variety Artists International | 1924 Spring St | Paso Robles CA 93446, USA |
| Webb Enterprises, Ruth | 7095 Hollywood Blvd | Los Angeles CA 90028, USA |

## AGENCY ADDRESSES

| | | |
|---|---|---|
| Wilder Agency | 3151 Cahuenga Blvd W, #310 | Los Angeles CA 90068, USA |
| Wilhelmina Artists | 8383 Wilshire Blvd, #650 | Beverly Hills CA 90211, USA |
| W K T Public Relations | 335 N Maple Dr, #351 | Beverly Hills CA 90210, USA |
| W M E Entertainment | 9601 Wilshire Blvd | Beverly Hills CA 90210, USA |
| Wolfman Jack Entertainment | 105 Rivershore Dr | Hertford NC 27944, USA |
| Z B F Agentur | Friedrichstr 39 | 10969 Berlin, Germany |
| Vox Inc | 5670 Wilshire Blvd, #820 | Los Angeles CA 90036, USA |

## SYNDICATE ADDRESSES

| | | |
|---|---|---|
| Associated Press | 450 W 33rd St, #1500 | New York NY 10001, USA |
| Creators Syndicate | 5777 W Century Blvd, #700 | Los Angeles CA 90045, USA |
| King Features Syndicate | 300 W 57th St, #1500 | New York NY 10019, USA |
| North American Syndicate | 235 E 45th St | New York NY 10017, USA |
| Times-Mirror Syndicate | Times-Mirror Square | Los Angeles CA 90053, USA |
| Tribune Media Services | 435 N Michigan Ave, #1500 | Chicago IL 60611, USA |
| United Feature Syndicate | 200 Madison Ave | New York NY 10016, USA |
| United Media Syndicate | 200 Park Ave, #400 | New York NY 10016, USA |
| United Press International | 2 Pennsylvania Plaza, #1800 | New York NY 10121, USA |
| Universal Press Syndicate | 4520 Main St, #700 | Kansas City MO 64111, USA |

## MAJOR TELEVISION STATION ADDRESSES

### American Broadcasting Company

| | | |
|---|---|---|
| ABC-LA | 500 S Buena Vista St | Burbank CA 91521, USA |
| ABC-NY | 77 W 66th St | New York NY 10023, USA |
| KABC-TV | 4151 Prospect Ave | Los Angeles CA 90027, USA |
| KGO-TV | 900 Front St | San Francisco CA 94111, USA |
| KTRK-TV | 3310 Bissonnet Dr | Houston TX 77005, USA |
| WABC-TV | 7 Lincoln Square | New York NY 10023, USA |
| WCVB-TV (Boston) | 5 TV Place | Needham MA 02194, USA |
| WFAA-TV | 606 Young St | Dallas TX 75202, USA |
| WJLA-TV | 3007 Tilden St NW | Washington DC 20008, USA |
| WLS-TV | 190 N State St | Chicago IL 60601, USA |
| WPIV-TV | 4100 City Line Ave | Philadelphia PA 19131, USA |
| WPLG-TV | 3900 Biscayne Blvd | Miami FL 33137, USA |
| WSB-TV | 1801 W Peachtree St NE | Atlanta GA 30309, USA |
| WVUE-TV | 1025 S Jefferson Davis Parkway | New Orleans LA 70125, USA |
| WXYZ-TV (Detroit) | 20777 W Ten-Mile Road | Southfield MI 48037, USA |

### Columbia Broadcasting System

| | | |
|---|---|---|
| CBS-LA | 7800 Beverly Blvd | Los Angeles CA 90036, USA |
| CBS-NY | 51 W 52nd St | New York NY 10019, USA |
| KCBS-TV | 6121 Sunset Blvd | Los Angeles CA 90028, USA |
| KHOU-TV | 1945 Allen Parkway | Houston TX 77019, USA |
| KPIX-TV | 855 Battery St | San Francisco CA 94111, USA |
| KYW-TV | 101 S Independence Mall E | Philadelphia PA 19106, USA |
| WBBM-TV | 630 N McClurg Court | Chicago IL 60611, USA |
| WBZ-TV | 1170 Soldiers Field Road | Boston MA 02134, USA |
| WCBS-TV | 524 W 57th St | New York NY 10019, USA |
| WCIX-TV | 8900 NW 18th Terrace | Miami FL 33172, USA |
| WUSA-TV | 4100 Wisconsin Ave NW | Washington DC 20016, USA |
| WWL-TV | 1024 N Rampart St | New Orleans LA 70116, USA |

### Fox Television

| | | |
|---|---|---|
| Fox-TV | 10201 W Pico Blvd | Los Angeles CA 90035, USA |
| KDFW-TV | 400 N Griffin St | Dallas TX 75202, USA |
| KRIV-TV | 3935 Westheimer Road | Houston TX 77027, USA |
| KTTV-TV | 5746 W Sunset Blvd | Los Angeles CA 90028, USA |
| KTVU-TV (San Francisco) | PO Box 22222 | Oakland CA 94623, USA |
| WAGA-TV | 1551 Briarcliff Road NE | Atlanta GA 30306, USA |
| WFLD-TV | 205 N Michigan Ave | Chicago IL 60601, USA |
| WFXT-TV (Boston) | 1000 Providence Highway | Dedham MA 02026, USA |
| WJBK-TV (Detroit) | 16550 W Nine-Mile Road | Southfield MI 48075, USA |
| WNOL-TV | 1661 Canal St | New Orleans LA 70112, USA |
| WNYW-TV | 205 E 67th St | New York NY 10021, USA |
| WSVN-TV | 1401 79th St Causeway | Miami FL 33141, USA |
| WTTG-TV | 5151 Wisconsin Ave NW, #100 | Washington DC 20016, USA |
| WTXF-TV | 330 Market St | Philadelphia PA 19106, USA |

### National Broadcasting Company

| | | |
|---|---|---|
| KNBC-TV (Los Angeles) | 3000 W Alameda Ave | Burbank CA 91523, USA |
| KPRC-TV | 8181 Southwest Freeway | Houston TX 77074, USA |

# MAJOR TELEVISION STATION ADDRESSES

## National Broadcasting Company

| | | |
|---|---|---|
| KNBC-TV (Los Angeles) | 3000 W Alameda Ave | Burbank CA 91523, USA |
| KPRC-TV | 8181 Southwest Freeway | Houston TX 77074, USA |
| KRON-TV | 1001 Van Ness Ave | San Francisco CA 94109, USA |
| KXAS-TV | 3900 Barnett St | Fort Worth TX 76103, USA |
| WDIV-TV | 550 W Lafayette Blvd | Detroit MI 48231, USA |
| WDSU-TV | 520 Royal St | New Orleans LA 70130, USA |
| WMAG-TV | 454 N Columbus Dr | Chicago IL 60611, USA |
| WMGM-TV (Philadelphia) | 1601 New Road | Linwood NJ 08221, USA |
| WNBC-TV | 30 Rockefeller Plaza, #207E | New York NY 10112, USA |
| WRC-TV | 4001 Nebraska Ave NW | Washington DC 20016, USA |
| WTVJ-TV | 316 N Miami Ave | Miami FL 33128, USA |
| WXIA-TV | 1611 W Peachtree St NE | Atlanta GA 30309, USA |

## CABLE TELEVISION CHANNEL ADDRESSES

| | | |
|---|---|---|
| American Christian Television | 6350 West Freeway | Fort Worth TX 76150, USA |
| American Movie Classics | 150 Crossways Park W | Woodbury NY 11797, USA |
| Arts & Entertainment | 235 E 45th St, #9 | New York NY 10017, USA |
| Black Entertainment Network | One BET Plaza, 1900 W Place NE | Washington DC 20018, USA |
| British Broadcasting Company | Wood Lane | London W12 8Q, England |
| Cable News Network (CNN) | 820 1st St NE, #1000 | Washington DC 20002, USA |
| Canadian Broadcasting Company | 1500 Bronson Ave | Ottawa ON K1G 3J5, Canada |
| Canadian Television Network | 42 Charles St E | Toronto ON M4Y 1T5, Canada |
| Capital Cities/ABC | 77 W 66th St | New York NY 10023, USA |
| Cartoon Network | 1050 Techwood Dr NW | Atlanta GA 30318, USA |
| Christian Broadcasting Network | 1000 Centerville Turnpike | Virginia Beach VA 23463, USA |
| Cinemax | 1100 6th Ave | New York NY 10036, USA |
| Columbia Broadcasting System | 51 W 52nd St | New York NY 10019, USA |
| Comedy Central | 345 Hudson St, #300 | New York NY 10014, USA |
| Consumer News & Business | 2200 Fletcher Ave | Fort Lee NJ 07024, USA |
| Country Music Television | 2806 Opryland Dr | Nashville TN 37214, USA |
| Court TV | 600 Third Ave | New York NY 10016, USA |
| C-SPAN | 400 N Capitol St NW, #650 | Washington DC 20001, USA |
| CW Television Network | 4000 Warner Blvd | Burbank CA 91522, USA |
| Discovery Channel | 7700 Wisconsin Ave | Bethesda MD 20814, USA |
| Disney Channel | 3800 W Alameda Ave | Burbank CA 91505, USA |
| E! (Entertainment Television) | 5750 Wilshire Blvd | Los Angeles CA 90036, USA |
| ESPN (Entertainment & Sports) | ESPN Plaza, 935 Middle St | Bristol CT 06010, USA |
| Family Channel | PO Box 64549 | Virginia Beach VA 23467, USA |
| Food Network | 1180 Ave of Americas, #1200 | New York NY 10036, USA |
| FX (Fox Net) | PO Box 900 | Beverly Hills CA 90213, USA |
| Game Show Network | 10202 W Washington Blvd | Culver City CA 90232, USA |
| Granada Television | 36 Golden Square | London W1R 2AX, England |
| HGTV (Home & Garden TV) | PO Box 50970 | Knoxville TN 37950, USA |
| History Channel | 235 E 45th St, #9 | New York NY 10017, USA |
| Home Box Office (HBO) | 1100 Ave of Americas | New York NY 10036, USA |
| Home Shopping Network | PO Box 9090 | Clearwater FL 34618, USA |
| Independent Film Channel | 150 Crossways Park W | Woodbury NY 11797, USA |
| Learning Channel | 7700 Wisconsin Ave | Bethesda MD 20814, USA |
| Lifetime | 111 8th St | New York NY 10011, USA |
| Madison Square Garden Network | 2 Pennsylvania Plaza | New York NY 10001, USA |
| Movie Channel (TMC) | 1633 Broadway | New York NY 10019, USA |
| MTV (Music Television) | 1515 Broadway | New York NY 10036, USA |
| National Broadcasting Company | 30 Rockefeller Plaza | New York NY 10112, USA |
| Nickelodeon | 1515 Broadway | New York NY 10036, USA |
| Oxygen | 75 9th Avenue | New York NY 10011, USA |
| PBS (Public Broadcasting System) | 1320 Braddock Place | Alexandria VA 22314, USA |
| Playboy Channel | 9242 Beverly Blvd | Beverly Hills CA 90210, USA |
| Prime Ticket Network | 10000 Santa Monica Blvd | Los Angeles CA 90067, USA |
| QVC Inc | 1365 Enterprise Dr | West Chester PA 19380, USA |
| Sci-Fi Channel | 1230 Ave of Americas | New York NY 10020, USA |
| Showtime Network | 1633 Broadway | New York NY 10019, USA |
| TBN (Trinity Broadcast Network) | PO Box A | Tustin CA 92711, USA |
| TBS (Turner Broadcasting System) | 1 CNN Center, PO Box 105366 | Atlanta GA 30348, USA |
| Telemundo Group | 1740 Broadway | New York NY 10019, USA |
| TNN (The Nashville Network) | 2806 Opryland Dr | Nashville TN 37214, USA |
| TNT (Turner Network Television) | 1050 Techwood Dr NW | Atlanta GA 30318, USA |
| TVA | 1600 de Maisonneuve Blvd E | Montreal QC H2L 4P2, Canada |
| Univision Network | 605 3rd Ave, #1200 | New York NY 10158, USA |
| USA Cable Network | 1230 Ave of Americas | New York NY 10020, USA |
| VH-1 (Video Hits One) | 1515 Broadway | New York NY 10036, USA |

## CABLE TELEVISION CHANNEL ADDRESSES

| | | |
|---|---|---|
| Viewer's Choice | 909 3rd Ave | New York NY 10022, USA |
| Warner Bros | 4000 Warner Blvd | Burbank CA 91522, USA |
| Weather Channel | 2600 Cumberland Parkway NW | Atlanta GA 30339, USA |

## RECORD COMPANY ADDRESSES

| | | |
|---|---|---|
| A&M Records | 70 University City Plaza | Universal City CA 91608, USA |
| Angel Records | 1750 N Vine St | Los Angeles CA 90028, USA |
| Angel Records | 150 5th Ave | New York NY 10011, USA |
| Arista Records | 8750 Wilshire Blvd, #300 | Beverly Hills CA 90211, USA |
| Arista Records | 745 5th Ave, #600 | New York NY 10151, USA |
| Asylum Records | 9229 Sunset Blvd, #718 | West Hollywood CA 90069, USA |
| Asylum Records | 75 Rockefeller Plaza | New York NY 10019, USA |
| Atlantic Records | 9229 Sunset Blvd, #900 | West Hollywood CA 90069, USA |
| Atlantic Records | 1290 Ave of Americas, Concourse 3 | New York NY 10104, USA |
| Blue Note Records | 6920 Sunset Blvd | Los Angeles CA 90028, USA |
| Capitol Records | 1750 N Vine St | Los Angeles CA 90028, USA |
| Capitol Records | 810 7th Ave | New York NY 10019, USA |
| Chrysalis Records | 8730 Sunset Blvd | West Hollywood CA 90069, USA |
| Chrysalis Records | 810 7th Ave, #4 | New York NY 10019, USA |
| Deutsche Grammaphon Records | 810 7th Ave | New York NY 10019, USA |
| Dreamwork Records | 1000 Flower St | Glendale CA 91201, USA |
| Elektra Records | 75 Rockefeller Plaza | New York NY 10019, USA |
| E M I America Records | 6920 Sunset Blvd | Los Angeles CA 90028, USA |
| E M I America Records | 150 5th Ave, #700 | New York NY 10011, USA |
| Epic Records | 1211 S Highland Ave | Los Angeles CA 90019, USA |
| Epic Records | 350 Madison Ave, #600 | New York NY 10022, USA |
| Geffen Records | 10900 Wilshire Blvd, #1000 | Los Angeles CA 90024, USA |
| Geffen Records | 1755 Broadway, #600 | New York NY 10019, USA |
| Island Def Jam Records | 8920 Sunset Blvd, #200 | West Hollywood CA 90069, USA |
| Island Def Jam Records | 925 8th St | New York NY 10019, USA |
| LaFace Records | 3350 Peach Tree Road | Atlanta GA 30319, USA |
| London Records | 810 7th Ave | New York NY 10019, USA |
| M C A Records | 70 Universal City Plaza | Universal City CA 91608, USA |
| M C A Records | 1755 Broadway | New York NY 10019, USA |
| Mercury Records | 54 Music Square E, #300 | Nashville TN 37203, USA |
| Motown Records | 6255 Sunset Blvd | Los Angeles CA 90028, USA |
| Nonesuch Records | 75 Rockefeller Plaza | New York NY 10019, USA |
| Phillips Records | 810 7th Ave | New York NY 10019, USA |
| Polydor Records | 70 Universal City Plaza | Universal City CA 91608, USA |
| Polydor Records | 810 7th Ave | New York NY 10019, USA |
| Polygram Records | 3800 W Alameda Ave, #1500 | Burbank CA 91505, USA |
| Polygram Records | Worldwide Plaza, 825 8th Ave | New York NY 10019, USA |
| R C A Records | 6363 Sunset Blvd, #429 | Los Angeles CA 90028, USA |
| R C A Records | 1540 Broadway, #3500 | New York NY 10036, USA |
| Reprise Records | 3300 Warner Blvd | Burbank CA 91505, USA |
| Reprise Records | 75 Rockefeller Plaza | New York NY 10019, USA |
| Rhino Records | 10635 Santa Monica Blvd | Los Angeles CA 90025, USA |
| Sire Records | 3300 Warner Blvd | Burbank CA 91505, USA |
| Sire Records | 75 Rockefeller Plaza | New York NY 10019, USA |
| Sony/Columbia/CBS Records | 2100 Colorado Ave | Santa Monica CA 90404, USA |
| Sony/Columbia/CBS Records | 550 Madison Ave, #600 | New York NY 10022, USA |
| Verve Records | 1755 Broadway, #600 | New York NY 10019, USA |
| Virgin Records | 338 N Foothill Road | Beverly Hills CA 90210, USA |
| Virgin Records | 150 5th Ave, #700 | New York NY 10011, USA |
| Warner Bros Records | 3300 Warner Blvd | Burbank CA 91505, USA |
| Warner Bros Records | 75 Rockefeller Plaza | New York NY 10019, USA |
| Windham Hill Records | PO Box 5501 | Beverly Hills CA 90209, USA |

## PUBLISHER ADDRESSES

| | | |
|---|---|---|
| Atheneum Publishers | 866 3rd Ave | New York NY10022, USA |
| Avon Books | 1350 Ave of Americas | New York NY 10019, USA |
| Berkley Publishing | 375 Hudson St, Basement 1 | New York NY 10014, USA |
| Chronicle Books | 680 2nd St | San Francisco CA 94107, USA |
| Crown Publishers | 201 E. 50th St | New York NY 10022, USA |
| Delacorte/Bantam/Dell/Doubleday | 1745 Broadway | New York NY 10019, USA |
| Dodd Mead | 6 Ram Ridge Road | Spring Valley NY 10977, USA |
| Dutton, EP/Penguin | 375 Hudson St, Basement 1 | New York NY 10014, USA |
| Farrar Straus Giroux | 18 W 18th St, #700 | New York NY 10011, USA |
| Grove Press | 841 Broadway | New York NY 10003, USA |
| Harcourt Brace | 525 B St | San Diego CA 92101, USA |
| Harper Collins | 10 E 53rd St, Cellar 1 | New York NY10022, USA |

## PUBLISHER ADDRESSES

| | | |
|---|---|---|
| Henry Holt | 175 5th Ave, #400 | New York NY 10010, USA |
| Houghton Mifflin | 215 Park Ave S, #1200 | New York NY 10003, USA |
| Hyperion Books | 114 5th Ave | New York NY 10011, USA |
| Knopf/Ballatine/Fawcett | 201 E 50th St | New York NY 10022, USA |
| Little Brown | 1271 Ave of Americas | New York NY 10020, USA |
| Little Brown | 3 Center Plaza, #100 | Boston MA 02108, USA |
| McGraw Hill | 1221 Ave of Americas, #C3A | New York NY 10020, USA |
| MacMillan | 1177 Ave of Americas, #1965 | New York NY 10036, USA |
| Morrow, William | 1350 Ave of Americas, #200 | New York NY 10019, USA |
| Mysterious Press/Warner Books | 1271 6th Ave | New York NY 10020, USA |
| New American Library | 1633 Broadway | New York NY 10019, USA |
| Norton, WW | 500 5th Ave, #600 | New York NY 10110, USA |
| Oxford University Press | 198 Madison Ave, #800 | New York NY 10016, USA |
| Pocket Books | 1230 Ave of Americas | New York NY 10020, USA |
| Prentice-Hall | RR 9W | Englewood Cliffs NJ 07632, USA |
| Putnam's Sons, GP | 375 Hudson St, Basement | New York NY 10014, USA |
| Random House | 1745 Broadway, #B1 | New York NY 10019, USA |
| Scholastic Press | 555 Broadway | New York NY 10012, USA |
| Scribner's Sons, Charles | 866 3rd Ave | New York NY 10022, USA |
| Simon & Schuster | 1230 Ave of Americas, Concourse 1 | New York NY 10020, USA |
| Saint Martin's Press | 175 5th Ave, #400 | New York NY 10010, USA |
| Viking Press | 375 Hudson St, Basement 1 | New York NY 10014, USA |

## PROFESSIONAL SPORTS TEAMS ADDRESSES

### Baseball

| | | |
|---|---|---|
| Arizona Diamondbacks | Chase Field, 401 E Jefferson | Phoenix AZ 85003, USA |
| Atlanta Braves | Turner Field, 755 Hank Aaron Drive | Atlanta GA 30315, USA |
| Baltimore Orioles | Oriole Park, 333 W Camden St | Baltimore MD 21201, USA |
| Boston Red Sox | Fenway Park, 4 Yawkey Way | Boston MA 02215, USA |
| Chicago Cubs | Wrigley Field, 1060 W Addison St | Chicago IL 60613, USA |
| Chicago White Sox | US Cellular Field, 333 W 35th St | Chicago IL 60616, USA |
| Cincinnati Reds | Great American Ball Park, 100 Main St | Cincinnati OH 45202, USA |
| Cleveland Indians | Jacobs Field, 2401 Ontario St | Cleveland OH 44115, USA |
| Colorado Rockies | Coors Field, 2001 Blake St | Denver CO 80205, USA |
| Detroit Tigers | Comerica Park, 2100 Woodward Ave | Detroit MI 48201, USA |
| Houston Astros | Minute Maid Field, 501 Crawford St | Houston TX 77002, USA |
| Kansas City Royals | Kauffman Stadium, 1 Royal Way | Kansas City MO 64129, USA |
| Los Angeles Angels of Anaheim | Angel Stadium, 2000 Gene Autry Way | Anaheim CA 92806, USA |
| Los Angeles Dodgers | Dodger Stadium, 1000 Elysian Park Ave | Los Angeles CA 90090, USA |
| Miami Marlins | 501 Marlins Way | Miami FL 33125, USA |
| Milwaukee Brewers | Miller Park, 1 Brewers Way | Milwaukee WI 53214, USA |
| Minnesota Twins | Metrodome, 34 Kirby Punkett Place | Minneapolis MN 55415, USA |
| New York Mets | Shea Stadium, 12301 Roosevelt Ave | Flushing NY 11368, USA |
| New York Yankees | Yankee Stadium, E 161st & River Ave | Bronx NY 10451, USA |
| Oakland Athletics | McAfee Coliseum, 7000 Coliseum Way, #3 | Oakland CA 94621, USA |
| Philadelphia Phillies | Citizens Bank Park, 1 Citizens Bank Way | Philadelphia PA 19148, USA |
| Pittsburgh Pirates | PNC Park, 115 Federal St, #115B | Pittsburgh PA 15212, USA |
| San Diego Padres | Petco Park, 100 Park Blvd | San Diego CA 92101, USA |
| San Francisco Giants | AT&T Park, 24 Willie Mays Plaza | San Francisco CA 94107, USA |
| Seattle Mariners | Safeco Field, PO Box 4100 | Seattle WA 98194, USA |
| Saint Louis Cardinals | Busch Stadium, 250 Stadium Plaza | Saint Louis MO 63102, USA |
| Tampa Bay Rays | Tropicana Field, 1 Tropicana Dr | Saint Petersburg FL 33705, USA |
| Texas Rangers | Ameriquest Field, 1000 Ballpark Way, #306 | Arlington TX 76011, USA |
| Toronto Blue Jays | Skydome, 1 Blue Jay Way, #3200 | Toronto ON M5V 1J1, Canada |
| Washington Nationals | 1500 S Capital St SE | Washington DC 20003, USA |

### Men's Basketball

| | | |
|---|---|---|
| Atlanta Hawks | 101 Marietta St NW, #1900 | Atlanta GA 30303, USA |
| Boston Celtics | 226 Causeway St, #400 | Boston MA 02114, USA |
| Brooklyn Nets | 15 MetroTech Center, #1100 | Brooklyn NY 11201, USA |
| Charlotte Bobcats | 333 E Trade St. #A | Charlotte NC 28202, USA |
| Chicago Bulls | United Center, 1901 W Madison St | Chicago IL 60612, USA |
| Cleveland Cavaliers | Gund Arena, 1 Center Court | Cleveland OH 44115, USA |
| Dallas Mavericks | 2500 Victory Ave | Dallas TX 75219, USA |
| Denver Nuggets | Pepsi Center, 1000 Chopper Circle | Denver CO 80204, USA |
| Detroit Pistons | Palace, 4 Championship Dr | Auburn Hills MI 48326, USA |
| Golden State Warriors | 1011 Broadway | Oakland CA 94605, USA |
| Houston Rockets | 1510 Polk St | Houston TX 77002, USA |
| Indiana Pacers | 125 S Pennsylvania St | Indianapolis IN 46204, USA |
| Los Angeles Clippers | Staples Center, 1111 S Figueroa St | Los Angeles CA 90015, USA |

# PROFESSIONAL SPORTS TEAMS ADDRESSES

## Men's Basketball

| | | |
|---|---|---|
| Los Angeles Lakers | Staples Center, 1111 S Figueroa St | Los Angeles CA 90015, USA |
| Memphis Grizzlies | 191 Beale St | Memphis TN 38103, USA |
| Miami Heat | 601 Biscayne Blvd | Miami FL 33132, USA |
| Milwaukee Bucks | 1001 N 4th St, #200 | Milwaukee WI 53203, USA |
| Minnesota Timberwolves | Target Center, 600 1st Ave N | Minneapolis MN 55403, USA |
| New Orleans Pelicans | 1250 Poydras St, #101 | New Orleans LA 70113, USA |
| New York Knicks | Madison Square Garden, 4 Penn Plaza | New York NY 10121, USA |
| Oklahoma City Thunder | 211 N Robinson Ave, #300 | Oklahoma City OK 73102, USA |
| Orlando Magic | 8701 Maitland Summit Blvd | Orlando FL 32810, USA |
| Philadelphia 76ers | 3601 S Broad St, #400 | Philadelphia PA 19148, USA |
| Phoenix Suns | 201 E Jefferson St | Phoenix AZ 85004, USA |
| Portland Trail Blazers | 1 N Center Court St, #200, Rose Garden | Portland OR 97227, USA |
| Sacramento Kings | Arco, Arena, 1 Sports Parkway | Sacramento CA 95834, USA |
| San Antonio Spurs | Key Arena, 1 AT&T Center | San Antonio TX 78219, USA |
| Seattle Supersonics | 1201 3rd Ave, #1000 | Seattle WA 98101, USA |
| Toronto Raptors | 20 Bay St, #1702 | Toronto ON M5J 2N8, Canada |
| Utah Jazz | 301 W South Temple | Salt Lake City UT 84101, USA |
| Washington Wizards | 601 F St NW | Washington DC 20004, USA |

## Women's Basketball (WNBA)

| | | |
|---|---|---|
| Atlanta Dream | 83 Walton St NW, #400 | Atlanta GA 30303, USA |
| Chicago Sky | 20 W Kinzie St, #1010 | Chicago IL 60654, USA |
| Connecticut Sun | 1 Mohegan Sun Blvd | Uncasville CT 06382, USA |
| Indiana Fever | 125 S Pennsylvania St | Indianapolis IN 46204, USA |
| Los Angeles Sparks | 888 S Figueroa St, #2010 | Los Angeles CA 90017, USA |
| Minnesota Lynx | 600 1st Ave N | Minneapolis MN 55403, USA |
| New York Liberty | 2 Penn Plaza, #1400 | New York NY 10121, USA |
| Phoenix Mercury | 201 E Jefferson St | Phoenix AZ 85004, USA |
| Sacramento Monarchs | Arco Arena, 1 Sports Parkway | Sacramento CA 95834, USA |
| San Antonio Silver Stars | 1 AT&T Center | San Antonio TX 78219, USA |
| Seattle Storm | 351 Elliott Ave W, #500 | Seattle WA 98119, USA |
| Tulsa Shock | BOK Center, 200 S Denver | Tulsa OK 74103, USA |
| Washington Mystics | Verizon Center, 401 9th St NW, #750 | Washington DC 20004, USA |

## Football

| | | |
|---|---|---|
| Arizona Cardinals | PO Box 888 | Phoenix AZ 85001, USA |
| Atlanta Falcons | 4400 Falcon Parkway | Flowery Branch GA 30542, USA |
| Baltimore Ravens | Ravens Stadium, 1 Winning Dr | Owings Mills MD 21117, USA |
| Buffalo Bills | 1 Bills Dr | Orchard Park NY 14127, USA |
| Carolina Panthers | Ericsson Stadium, 800 S Mint St | Charlotte NC 28202, USA |
| Chicago Bears | 1000 Football Dr | Lake Forest IL 60045, USA |
| Cincinnati Bengals | 1 Paul Brown Stadium | Cincinnati OH 45202, USA |
| Cleveland Browns | 76 Lou Groza Blvd | Berea OH 44017, USA |
| Dallas Cowboys | 1 Cowboys Parkway | Irving TX 75063, USA |
| Denver Broncos | 13655 Broncos Parkway | Englewood, CO 80112, USA |
| Detroit Lions | 222 Republic Drive | Allen Park MI 48101, USA |
| Green Bay Packers | 1265 Lombardi Ave | Green Bay WI 54304, USA |
| Houston Texans | 2 Reliant Park | Houston TX 77054, USA |
| Indianapolis Colts | 7001 W 56th St | Indianapolis IN 46254, USA |
| Jacksonville Jaguars | 1 AllTel Stadium Place | Jacksonville FL 32202, USA |
| Kansas City Chiefs | 1 Arrowhead Dr | Kansas City KS 64129, USA |
| Miami Dolphins | 7500 SW 30th St | Davie FL 33314, USA |
| Minnesota Vikings | 9520 Viking Dr | Eden Prairie MN 55344, USA |
| New England Patriots | 1 Patriot Place | Foxboro, MA 02035, USA |
| New Orleans Saints | 5800 Airline Highway | Metairie LA 70003, USA |
| New York Giants | Meadowlands Stadium, 102 Route 120 | East Rutherford NJ 07073, USA |
| New York Jets | 1 Jets Dr | Florham Park NJ 07932, USA |
| Oakland Raiders | 1220 Harbor Bay Parkway | Alameda CA 94502, USA |
| Philadelphia Eagles | 1 NovaCare Way | Philadelphia PA 19145, USA |
| Pittsburgh Steelers | 3400 S Water St | Pittsburgh PA 15203, USA |
| Saint Louis Rams | 901 N Broadway | Saint Louis MO 63101, USA |
| San Diego Chargers | 4020 Murphy Canyon Rd | San Diego CA 92123, USA |
| San Francisco 49ers | 4949 Centennial Blvd | Santa Clara CA 95054, USA |
| Seattle Seahawks | 12 Seahawks Way | Renton WA 98056, USA |
| Tennessee Titans | 460 Great Circle Road | Nashville TN 37228, USA |
| Tampa Bay Buccaneers | 1 W Buccaneer Place | Tampa FL 33607, USA |
| Washington Redskins | 21300 Redskin Park Dr | Ashburn VA 20147, USA |

# PROFESSIONAL SPORTS TEAMS ADDRESSES

## Ice Hockey

| | | |
|---|---|---|
| Anaheim Ducks | 2695 E Katella Ave | Anaheim CA 92806, USA |
| Boston Bruins | 100 Legends Way, #250 | Boston MA 02114, USA |
| Buffalo Sabres | 1 Seymour Knox Plaza | Buffalo NY 14203, USA |
| Calgary Flames | PO Box 1540, Station M | Calgary AB T2P 3B9, Canada |
| Carolina Hurricanes | RBC Center, 1400 Edwards Mill Road | Raleigh NC 27607, USA |
| Chicago Blackhawks | United Center, 1901 W Madison St | Chicago IL 60612, USA |
| Colorado Avalanche | Pepsi Center, 1000 Chopper Circle | Denver CO 80204, USA |
| Columbus Blue Jackets | 200 W Nationwide Blvd, Unit 1 | Columbus OH 43215, USA |
| Dallas Stars | 2601 Avenue of Stars | Frisco TX 75034, USA |
| Detroit Red Wings | Joe Louis Arena, 600 Civic Center Dr | Detroit MI 48226, USA |
| Edmonton Oilers | Edmonton Coliseum, 11230 110 St | Edmonton AB T5G 3G8, Canada |
| Florida Panthers | 1 Panthers Parkway | Sunrise FL 33323, USA |
| Hartford Whalers | Coliseum, 242 Trumbull St, #800 | Hartford CT 06103, USA |
| Los Angeles Kings | Staples Center, 1111 S Figueroa St | Los Angeles CA 90015, USA |
| Minnesota Wild | Xcel Energy Center, 1275 W Kellogg Blvd | Saint Paul MN 55104, USA |
| Montreal Canadiens | 1275 Saint Antoine St W | Montreal QC H3C 5L2, Canada |
| Nashville Predators | 501 Broadway | Nashville TN 37203, USA |
| New Jersey Devils | 165 Mulberry St | Newark NJ 07102, USA |
| New York Islanders | 1255 Hempstead Turnpike | Uniondale NY 11553, USA |
| New York Rangers | Madison Square Garden, 2 Penn Plaza | New York NY 10121, USA |
| Ottawa Senators | ScotiaBank Place, 1000 Palladium Dr | Kanata ON K2V 1A5, Canada |
| Philadelphia Flyers | 1st Union Center, 3601 S Broad St | Philadelphia PA 19148, USA |
| Phoenix Coyotes | 6751 N Sunset Blvd, #200 | Glendale AZ 85305, USA |
| Pittsburgh Penguins | Consol Energy Center, 1001 5th Ave | Pittsburgh PA 15219, USA |
| Saint Louis Blues | ScottTrade Center, 1401 Clark Ave | Saint Louis MO 63103, USA |
| San Jose Sharks | 525 W Santa Clara St | San Jose CA 95113, USA |
| Tampa Bay Lightning | 401 Channelside Dr | Tampa FL 33602, USA |
| Toronto Maple Leafs | AirCanada Center, 40 Bay St, #400 | Toronto ON M5J 2X2, Canada |
| Vancouver Canucks | 800 Griffiths Way | Vancouver BC V6B 6G1, Canada |
| Washington Capitals | 627 N Glebe Road | Arlington VA 22203, USA |
| Winnipeg Jets | 260 Hargrave St | Winnipeg MB R3C 5S5, Canada |

## Men's Soccer

| | | |
|---|---|---|
| A S Rome Spa | Piazzale Dino Viola | 00128 Rome, Italy |
| Chicago Fire | 7000 S Harlem Ave | Bridgeview IL 60455, USA |
| Club Deportivo Chivas | Home Depot Center, 18400 Avalon Blvd | Carson CA 90746, USA |
| Colorado Rapids | 1000 Chopper Circle | Denver CO 80204, USA |
| Columbus Crew | 1 Black & Gold Blvd | Columbus OH 43211, USA |
| D C United | RFK Stadium, 2400 E Capitol St SE | Washington DC 20003 USA |
| F C Dallas | 9200 World Cup Way, #202 | Frisco TX 75034, USA |
| Houston Dynamo | 1415 Louisiana, #3400 | Houston TX 77002, USA |
| Kansas City Wizards | 8900 State Line Road | Leawood MO 66206, USA |
| Los Angeles Galaxy | Home Depot Center, 18400 Avalon Blvd | Carson CA 90746, USA |
| New England Revolution | 1 Patriot Place | Foxboro MA 02035, USA |
| Portland Timbers | 1844 SW Morrison | Portland OR 97205, USA |
| Real Salt Lake | 9256 S State St | Sandy UT 84070, USA |
| Red Bull New York | 600 Cape May St | Harrison NJ 07029, USA |
| San Jose Earthquakes | 451 El Camino Real, #220 | Santa Clara CA 95050, USA |
| Seattle Sounders | 12 Seahawks Way | Renton WA 98056, USA |
| Toronto F C | Maple Leaf Sports, 40 Bay St, #400 | Toronto ON M5J 2X2, Canada |
| Vancouver Whitecaps | 375 Water St, #550 | Vancouver BC V6B 5C6, Canada |
| Montreal Impact | 4750 Sherbrooke Est | Montreal QB H1V 3S8, Canada |

## Women's Soccer

| | | |
|---|---|---|
| Atlanta Beat | 1955 Vaughn Road, #209 | Kennesaw GA 30144, USA |
| Boston Breakers | 400 Blue Hill Dr, #302 | Westwood MA 02090, USA |
| FC Kansas City | 5366 W 95th St | Prairie Village KS 66207, USA |
| Philadelphia Independence | Union Field, Seaport Dr | Chester, PA 19013, USA |
| Sky Blue F C | 80 Cottontail Lane, #400 | Somerset NJ 08873, USA |
| Western New York Flash | Sahlen Sports Park, 7070 Seneca St | Elma NY 14059 USA |

## OTHER SPORTS ORGANIZATION ADDRESSES

| | | |
|---|---|---|
| Amateur Athletic Union | PO Box 10000 | Lake Buena Vista FL 32830, USA |
| Amateur Softball Association | 2801 NE 50th St | Oklahoma City OK 73111, USA |
| American Bicycle Association | 1645 W Sunrise Blvd | Gilbert AZ 85233, USA |
| American Bowling Congress | 5301 S 76th St | Greendale WI 53129, USA |

# OTHER SPORTS ORGANIZATION ADDRESSES

| | | |
|---|---|---|
| American Horse Show Association | 220 E 42nd St | New York NY 10017, USA |
| American Hot Rod Association | 111 N Hayford Road | Spokane WA 99224, USA |
| American Kennel Club | 260 Madison Ave | New York NY 10016, USA |
| American League Baseball | 350 Park Ave, #1800 | New York NY 10022, USA |
| American Motorcycle Association | 13515 Yarmouth Dr | Pickerington OH 43147, USA |
| American Power Boat Association | 17640 E Nine Mile Road | East Detroit MI 48021, USA |
| American Pro Soccer League | 122 C St, NW | Washington DC 20001, USA |
| American Water Ski Association | 799 Overlook Dr | Winter Haven FL 33884, USA |
| Association of Int'l Amateur Boxing | Postamt Volkrdstr, Postlagernd | 10319 Berlin, Germany |
| Assn/Int'l Marathon/Road Races | 20 Trongate | Glasgow G1 5ES, England |
| Association of Ski Racing Pros | 148 Porters Point Road | Colchester VT 05446, USA |
| Association of Surfing Pros | 16691 Gothard St | Huntington Beach CA 92648, USA |
| Association of Tennis Pros | 200 Tournament Road | Ponte Vedra Beach FL 32082, USA |
| Association of Volleyball Pros | 6100 Center Dr, #900 | Los Angeles CA 90045, USA |
| Canadian Football League | 110 Eglinton Ave | Toronto, ON M4R 1A3, Canada |
| Canadian Nat'l Sports/Recreation | 1600 James Naismith Dr | Gloucestor ON KJB 5N4, Canada |
| Federation de International Hockey | Avenue des Arts 1 (bte 5) | 1040 Brussels, Belgium |
| Federation de International Ski | Worbstr 210, 3073 Gumligen B | Berne, Switzerland |
| Federation International de Canoe | G Massaia 59 | 50134 Florence, Italy |
| Federation Int'l de Football Assn | PO Box 85, Hitzigweg 11 | 8030 Zurich, Switzerland |
| Federation Int'l de Gymnastics | Juraweg 12 | 8250 Lyss, Switzerland |
| Federation Int'l I de Tir a l'Arc | Via Cerva 30 | 20122 Milan, Italy |
| Federation of Int'l Volleyball | Ave de la Gare 12 | 1001 Lausanne, Switzerland |
| Federation of Int'l Amateur Cycling | Via Cassia N 490 | 00198 Rome, Italy |
| Federation of Int'l Basketball | PO Box 700607, Kistlerhofstr 168 | 81379 Munich, Germany |
| Fedn of Int'l Bobsleigh/Toboggan | Via Piranesi 44/b | 20137 Milan, Italy |
| Fedn of Int'l du Sport Automobiles | 8 Place de la Concorde | 75008 Paris, France |
| Fedn of International Equestrian | PO Box 3000, Bolligenstr 54 | 32 Berne, Switzerland |
| FIFA Women's Football Assn | 37 Sussex Road, Ickenham | Middx UB10 8PN, England |
| Formula One Driver's Association | 2 Rue Jean Jaures | 1836 Luxembourg |
| Indy Racing League | 4565 W 16th St | Indianapolis IN 46222, USA |
| International Badminton Federation | 24 Winchcombe House | Cheltenham, Glos GL52 2NA, England |
| International Baseball Association | 201 S Capitol Ave, #490 | Indianapolis IN 46225, USA |
| International Boxing Federation | 134 Evergreen Place | East Orange NJ 07018, USA |
| International Cricket Council | Lord's Cricket Ground | London NW8 8QN, England |
| International Curling Federation | 2 Coates Crescent | Edinburgh EH3 7AN, England |
| International Game Fish Assn | 1301 E Atlantic Blvd | Pompano Beach FL 33060, USA |
| International Hot Rod Association | Highway 11E | Bristol TN 37620, USA |
| International Ice Hockey Fedn | Bellevuestr 8 | 1190 Vienna, Austria |
| International Jai Alai Association | 5 Calle Aldamar | San Sebastian 3, Spain |
| International Judo Federation | Avenida del Trabajo 2666 | CP 1406, Buenos Aires, Argentina |
| International Luge Federation | Olympiadestr 168 | 8786 Rottenmann, Austria |
| International Motor Sports Assoc | 1394 Broadway Ave | Braselton GA 30517, USA |
| International Olympic Committee | Chateau de Vidy | 1007 Lausanne, Switzerland |
| International Roller Skating Fefn | 1500 S 70th St | Lincoln NE 68506, USA |
| International Rugby Football Board | PO Box 902 | Auckland, New Zealand |
| International Skating Union | Promenade 73 | 7270 Davos-Platz, Switzerland |
| Int'l Sled Dog Racing Association | PO Box 446 | Nordman ID 83848, USA |
| International Softball Federation | 2801 NE 59th St | Oklahoma City OK 73111, USA |
| International Sport Automobile Fed | 8 Rue de la Concorde | 70008-E Paris, France |
| International Surfing Association | 5580 La Jolla Blvd. #145 | La Jolla CA 92037, USA |
| International Table Tennis Fedn | 53 London Rd, St Leonards-on-Sea | East Sussex TN37 6AY, England |
| International Tennis Federation | Palliser Road, Barons Court | London W14 9EN, England |
| International Volleyball Federation | Ave de la Gare 12 | 1003 Lausanne, Switzerland |
| International Weightlifting Fefn | Rosemberg Hp U1 | 1374 Budapest PF 614, Hungary |
| International Yacht Racing Union | 60 Knightsbridge, Westminster | London SWEX 7JX, England |
| Ladies Professional Bowlers Tour | 7171 Cherryvales Blvd | Rockford IL 61112, USA |
| Ladies Professional Golf Assn | 100 International Golf Dr | Daytona Beach FL 32124, USA |
| Little League Baseball | PO Box 3485 | Williamsport PA 17701, USA |
| Major Indoor Lacrosse League | 2310 W 75th St | Shawnee Mission KS 66208, USA |
| Major League Baseball | 350 Park Ave | New York NY 10022, USA |
| National Archery Association | 1 Olympic Plaza | Colorado Springs CO 80909, USA |
| National Assn of Stock Car Racing | 1801 Speedway Blvd | Daytona Beach FL 32015, USA |
| Nat'l Assn/Intercollegiate Athletics | 1221 Baltimore Ave | Kansas City MO 64105, USA |
| National Basketball Association | 645 5th Ave, Fl 19 | New York NY 10022, USA |
| National Collegiate Athletic Assn | 70 W Washington St | Indianapolis IN 46204, USA |
| National Football League | 280 Park Ave, Fl 12W | New York NY 10017, USA |
| National Hockey League | 1251 Ave of Americas | New York NY 10020, USA |
| National Hot Rod Association | 2023 Financial Way | Glendora CA 91741, USA |
| National League Baseball | 350 Park Ave, #1800 | New York NY 10022, USA |

## OTHER SPORTS ORGANIZATION ADDRESSES

| | | |
|---|---|---|
| National Pro Soccer League | 229 3rd St NW | Canton OH 44702, USA |
| National Rifle Association | 11250 Waples Mill Road | Fairfax VA 22030, USA |
| National Tractor Pullers Assn | 6155 Huntley Road, #B | Columbus OH 43229, USA |
| P G A Seniors Tour | 112 PGA Tour Blvd | Ponte Vedra Beach FL 32082, USA |
| Professional Bowlers Association | 1720 Merriman Road | Akron OH 44313, USA |
| Professional Golfers Association | 100 Ave of Champions | Palm Beach Gardens FL 33410, USA |
| Professional Rodeo Cowboys | 101 Pro Rodeo Dr | Colorado Springs CA 80919, USA |
| Professional Sports Car Racing | 1394 Broadway Ave | Braselton GA 30517, USA |
| Special Olympics | 1325 G St NW, #500 | Washington DC 20005, USA |
| Thoroughbred Racing Association | 420 Fair Hill Dr, #1 | Elkton MD 21921, USA |
| Union International de Tir (Rifle) | Bavariaring 21 | 80336 Munich, Germany |
| United Sys of Independent Soccer | 14497 N Dale Mabry Hwy, #2011 | Tampa FL 33618, USA |
| US Auto Club | 1720 Ruskin St | South Bend IN 46604, USA |
| US Bobsled Federation | 421 Old Military Road | Lake Placid NY 12946, USA |
| US Cycling Federation | 1 Olympic Plaza, Bldg 4 | Colorado Springs CO 80909, USA |
| US Figure Skating Association | 20 1st St | Colorado Springs CO 80906, USA |
| US Luge Association | 35 Church St | Lake Placid NY 12946, USA |
| US Olympic Committee | 1 Olympic Plaza, Bldg 6 | Colorado Springs CO 80909, USA |
| US Polo Association | 4059 Iron Works Pike | Lexington KY 40511, USA |
| US Skiing Association | 1500 Kearns Blvd, #F100 | Park City UT 84060, USA |
| US Soccer Federation | 1801 S Prairie Ave, #11 | Chicago IL 60616, USA |
| US Tennis Association | Flushing Meadow | Flushing NY 11368, USA |
| US Trotting Association | 750 Michigan Ave | Columbus OH 43215, USA |
| US Youth Soccer Association | PO Box 18404 | Memphis TN 38181, USA |
| USA Rugby | 3595 E Fountain Blvd, #M2 | Colorado Springs CO 80910, USA |
| USA Track & Field | 4341 Starlight Dr | Indianapolis IN 46239, USA |
| Virginia Slims Women's Tennis | 3135 Texas Commerce Tower | Houston TX 77002, USA |
| Women's Basketball Association | 4011 N Bennington | Kansas City MO 64117, USA |
| Women's Int'l Bowling Congress | 5301 S 76th St | Greendale WI 53129, USA |
| Women's Int'l Surfing Association | PO Box 512 | San Juan Capistrano CA 92675, USA |
| Women's Pro Volleyball Assn | 840 Apollo St, #204 | El Segundo CA 90245, USA |
| Women's Tennis Association | 1 Progress Plaza, #1500 | Saint Petersburg FL 33701, USA |
| World Boardsailing Association | Feldafinger Platz 2 | 81477 Munich, Germany |
| World Boxing Association | Rodrigo Sazagy, Apartado | 4070 Panama City, Panama |
| World Boxing Council | Genova 33, Colonia Juarez | Cuahtemoc 0660, Mexico |
| World Taekwondo Federation | San 76 Yuksam-Dong | Kangnam-Ku, Seoul, Korea |
| World Team Tennis | 445 N Wells St | Chicago IL 60610, USA |
| World Union of Karate Orgs | 1-15-16 Toranomon, Minato-ku | Tokyo 105, Japan |
| World Wrestling Entertainment | 1241 E Main St, Titan Towers | Stamford CT 06902, USA |

## HALLS OF FAME ADDRESSES

| | | |
|---|---|---|
| Academy of Sports | 4 Rue de Teheran | 75008 Paris, France |
| Amateur Athletic Foundation of LA | 2141 W Adams Blvd | Los Angeles CA 90018, USA |
| American Water Ski | 799 Overlook Dr SE | Winter Park FL 33884, USA |
| Auto Racing | 4790 W 16th St | Speedway IN 46224, USA |
| Classical Music | 4 E 4th St | Cincinnati OH 45202, USA |
| College Football | 1111 S Saint Joseph | South Bend IN 46601, USA |
| Hockey | 30 Yonge St | Toronto ON M5E 1X8, Canada |
| International Boxing | PO Box 425 | Canastota NY 13032, USA |
| International Gymnastics | 227 Brooks St | Oceanside CA 92054, USA |
| International Motor Sports | PO Box 1018 | Talladega AL 35160, USA |
| International Surfing | 5580 La Jolla Blvd, #373 | La Jolla CA 92037, USA |
| International Swimming | 1 Hall of Fame Dr | Fort Lauderdale FL 33316, USA |
| International Tennis | 194 Bellevue Ave | Newport RI 02840, USA |
| International Volleyball | PO Box 1895, 444 Dwight St | Hyoke MA 01040, USA |
| International Women's Sports | 342 Madison Ave, #728 | New York NY 10173, USA |
| Lacrosse Foundation | White Athletic Center, Homewood | Baltimore MD 21218, USA |
| Lawn Tennis Museum | All England Lawn Tennis Club | Wimbledon England |
| Ladies Professional Golf Assoc | 2570 Volusia Ave | Daytona Beach FL 32114, USA |
| Naismith Basketball | 1150 W Columbus Ave | Springfield MA 01105, USA |
| National Baseball | PO Box 590 | Cooperstown NY 13326, USA |
| National Bowling Museum | 111 Stadium Plaza | Saint Louis MO 63102, USA |
| National Cowboy | Heritage Center, 1700 NE 63rd St | Oklahoma City OK 73111, USA |
| National Cowgirl | 111 W 4th St, #300 | Fort Worth TX 76102, USA |
| Nat'l Football Foundation | 1865 Palmer Ave | Larchmont NY 10538, USA |
| Nat'l Museum of Racing | Union Ave | Saratoga Springs NY 128662 USA |
| Nat'l Ski | PO Box 191, Poplar & Mather | Ishpeming MI 49849, USA |
| Nat'l Softball | 2801 NE 50th St | Oklahoma City OK 73111, USA |
| Nat'l Sportscaster/Sportswriter | 322 E Innes St | Salisbury NC 28144, USA |
| Nat'l Sprint Car | 1402 N Lincoln Ave | Knoxville IA 50138, USA |

## HALLS OF FAME ADDRESSES

| | | |
|---|---|---|
| Nat'l Track & Field | 200 S Capital Ave | Indianapolis IN 46225, USA |
| Nat'l Wrestling | 405 W Hall of Fame Ave | Stillwater OK 74074, USA |
| PGA Tour | 112 Tournament Players Club Blvd | Ponte Vedra FL 32082, USA |
| PGA World Golf | PGA Blvd, PO Box 1908 | Pinehurst NC 28374, USA |
| Pro Football | 2121 George Halas Dr, NW | Canton OH 44708, USA |
| Pro Rodeo Hall of Champions | 101 Pro Rodeo Dr | Colorado Springs CO 80919, USA |
| Professional Bowlers Assn | 1720 Merriman Road | Akron OH 44313, USA |
| Professional Golfers Assn | PO Box 109601 | Palm Beach Gardens FL 33410, USA |
| Trapshooting | 601 W Vandalia Road | Vandalia OH 45377, USA |
| Trotter Horse Museum | PO Box 590 | Goshen NY 10924, USA |
| US Bicycling | 145 W Main St | Somerville NJ 08876, USA |
| US Figure Skating Assn | 20 1st St | Colorado Springs CO 80906, USA |
| US Golf Museum | Golf House | Far Hills NJ 07931, USA |
| US Hockey | PO Box 657, Hat Trick Ave | Eveleth MN 55734, USA |
| US Olympic Committee | 1750 E Boulder St | Colorado Springs CO 80909, USA |
| Women's Bowling | 5301 S 76th St | Greendale WI 53129, USA |
| Yachting | PO Box 129 | Newport RI 02840, USA |

## BIBLIOGRAPHY

Academy Players Directory, Academy of Motion Picture Arts/Sciences, 8949 Wilshire Blvd, Beverly Hills CA 90211, USA
African Who's Who, African Journal Ltd, 54-A Tottenham Court Rd, London W1P 08T, England
Biographical Dictionary of Governors of the US, Meckler Publishing, Ferry Lane W, Westport CT 06880, USA
Biographical Dictionary of US Executive Branch, Greenwood Press, 51 Riverside Ave, Westport CT 06880, USA
Congressional Directory, Superintendent of Documents, US Government Printing Office, Washington DC 20402, USA
Contemporary Architects, St Martin's Press, 175 5th Ave, New York NY 10010, USA
Contemporary Designers, Gale Research Co, Book Tower, Detroit MI 48226, USA
Contemporary Theatre, Film & Television, Gale Research Co, Book Tower, Detroit MI 48226, USA
Corporate 1000, Washington Monitor, 1301 Pennsylvania Ave NW, Washington DC 20004, USA
Editor & Publisher International Yearbook, 575 Lexington Ave, New York NY 10022, USA
International Directory of Films & Filmmakers, St James Press, 175 5th Ave, New York NY 10010, USA
International Who's Who, Europa Publications Ltd, 18 Bedford Square, London WC1B 3JN, England
International Who's Who in Music, Biddles Ltd, Walnut Tree House, Guildford, Surrey GU1 1DA, England
Kraks BlaBog, Nytorv 17, 1450 Copenhagen K, Denmark
Major Companies of the Far East, Graham & Trotman Ltd, 66 Wilton Road, London SW1V 1DE, England
Major Companies of Europe, Graham & Trotman Ltd, 66 Wilton Road, London SW1V 1DE, England
Martindale-Hubbell Law Directory, Reed Publishing, Summit NJ 07902, USA
Moody's International Manual, Moody's Investors Service, 99 Church St, New York NY 10007, USA
Notable Australians, Paul Hamlyn Pty Ltd, 31 176 S Creek Road, Dee Why, WA 2099, Australia
Notable New Zealanders, Paul Hamlyn Pty Ltd, 31 Airedale St, Auckland, New Zealand
Prominent Personalities in USSR, Scarecrow Press, Metuchen NJ 08840, USA
US Court Directory, Government Printing Office, Washington DC 20401, USA
US Government Manual, National Archives & Records Service, General Services Administration, Washington DC 20408, USA
Who's Who, A & C Black Ltd, St Martin's Press, 175 5th Ave, New York NY 10010, USA
Who's Who in America, Marquis Who's Who, 200 E Ohio St, Chicago IL 60611, USA
Who's Who in American Art, R R Bowker Co, 1180 Ave of Americas, New York NY 1003, USA
Who's Who in American Politics, R R Bowker Co, 1180 Ave of Americas, New York NY 10036, USA
Who's Who in Canada, Global Press, 164 Commanden Blvd, Agincourt ON M1S 3C7, Canada
Who's Who in France, Editions Jacques Lafitte SA, 75008 Paris, France
Who's Who in Germany, Verlag AG Zurich, Germany
Who's Who in Israel, Bronfman Publishers Ltd, 82 Levinsky St, Tel Aviv 61010, Israel
Who's Who in Poland, Graphica Comense Srl, 22038 Taverreiro, Italy
Who's Who in Scandinavia, A Sutter Druckerei GmbH, 4300 Essen, Germany
Who's Who in Switzerland, Nagel Publishers, 5-5 bis de l'Orangeris, Geneva, Switzerland
Who's Who in the Theatre, Pitman Press, 39 Parker St, London WC2B 5PB, England
Who's Who in Washington, Tiber Reference Press, 4340 East-West Highway, Bethesda MD 20814, USA
Writer's Directory, St James Press, 213 W Institute Place, Chicago IL 60610, USA

**Book design by Lee Ann Nelson.**
**Cover logo is Corvinus Skyline, Body type is Arial Narrow.**
**Production by Nelson Design, 9 Ridgeview Court, San Ramon, California 94583, USA**

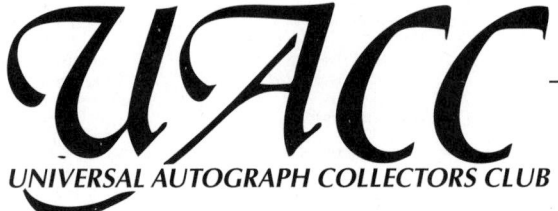

# "Best list of addresses available....

*... Top percentage of replies at minimum cost per name." —Jack Hilton, Collector*

# "Rates a 'best buy'...

*...worthwhile investment...other directories pale in comparison." —William L. Butts, Autograph Collector Magazine*

# "The format is excellent...

*...for easy consultation. Libraries will find it a great addition to their collection." —American Reference Books Annual*

"A **valuable resource** for many types of business. Researchers, publicists, fund raisers and marketing specialists are just a few of the professions that would benefit from owning this book."
—Rainbo Electronic Reviews

**SAVE $10.00!** Order the mid-August Update at the same time you order the V.I.P. ADDRESS BOOK and take $10 off your order!

### 60,000 essential V.I.P. addresses — at a cost of only a penny for every 10 addresses!

No matter what your need, you'll find virtually any address you may be looking for. Many of the names and addresses are not available in any other publication. That's why the Publisher's Marketing Association voted the V.I.P. Address Book the Benjamin Franklin Award for Directory of the Year.

## V.I.P. ADDRESS BOOK

Addresses of musicians, entertainers, government leaders, athletes, scientists, business leaders, artists, military leaders, publishers, activists and more...

# $94.95

5½"x8½"  LCCN 89-656029
*(Foreign orders add $21.00 postage)*

## V.I.P. ADDRESS UPDATE

The perfect complement to the V.I.P. ADDRESS BOOK. The Bureau of Statistics says 20% of people move each year. The mid-August UPDATE keeps you abreast of address changes and also adds new addresses to the basic volume.

# $24.95

5½"x8½"  LCCN 89-30776
*(Foreign orders add $4.00 postage)*

---

## Order toll-free 800-258-0615 or for more information 541-764-4233

To order by mail, complete this coupon and return with check, money order or credit card information (no C.O.D. orders) to:

**V.I.P. Address Book**
c/o Associated Media Companies
P.O. Box 489
Gleneden Beach, OR 97388 USA
Web site: www.vipaddress.com
Email: info@vipaddress.com

**Save $10.00!**
Order book
AND update for
ONLY $109.90
*(Foreign orders add postage: $25.00 for Book/Update)*

☐ Yes, please send _____ copies of the
**V.I.P. ADDRESS BOOK** at $94.95 each.
• Foreign orders add $21.00 per copy for postage.

☐ Yes, please send _____ copies of the
**V.I.P. ADDRESS BOOK UPDATE** at $24.95 each.
• Foreign orders add $4.00 for postage.

Charge: ☐ VISA ☐ MasterCard ☐ DISCOVER ☐ ▆▆

Account Number:
☐☐☐☐-☐☐☐☐-☐☐☐☐-☐☐☐☐

Expiration date: ☐☐-☐☐

Cardholder phone number ( _____ ) _____

Cardholder signature _____

Name _____

Address_____

City_____State _____Zip_____

Country _____

Library P.O. # _____

*Multiple copy discounts available! Call or write for details.*

# Have you visited our web page?

It's a great place to learn more about how the V.I.P. Address Book is compiled, read more about what people think of the book and even place your order conveniently online.

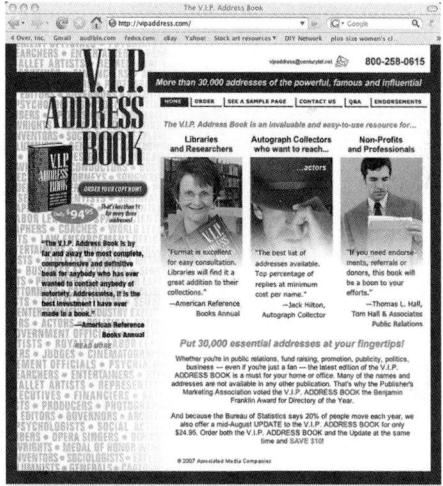

# www.VIPaddress.com

# Introducing a powerful new way to find those essential addresses you need RIGHT NOW:

# VIP Address File Database Lookup!

Now you can use the internet to access more than 230,000 VIP Addresses, including many unpublished addresses and alternate addresses. Execute custom searches, bookmark your favorite celebrities, email profiles to friends—it's the easiest and most flexible way to find and manage contact information.

## Only $9<sup>95</sup> per month

*No long-term contract to sign— you may cancel your subscription at any time!*

# To subscribe, visit:
# http://lookup.vipaddress.com

Call 541-764-4233 for more information

# A rare opportunity...

**...to browse & purchase more than 13,000 authentically autographed items from a private collection**

The **Wiggins Collection** boasts thousands of autographed photos, letters and cards from well-known artists, actors, politicians and world leaders from every corner of the globe. This massive, private collection has been carefully gathered over decades, and is now available for public purchase.

Use the convenient online search engine to browse the collection for your favorite celebrities, or to find the perfect pieces to complete your own collection.

Noteworthy items in the Wiggins Collection include autographed photographs from **Fred Astaire, Chet Atkins, James Brown, Michelle Pfeiffer, Alec Guiness, James Taylor, Marilyn Monroe, Franklin D. Roosevelt, Bing Crosby** and many, many others.

## *Shop today for the best selection!*

*To shop for autographed items, visit:*
# http://store.vipaddress.com

# Here's what people are saying...

"Celebrity hounds may find much to peruse in this directory..."
—*Chronicle of Philanthropy*

"Best list of addresses available. Top percentage of replies at minimum cost per name."
—*Jack Hilton, Collector*

"Absolutely indispensable for enterprising professional journalists."
—*Larry Meyer, Author, Editor, Educator*

"Not only is it an invaluable source for business inquiries, political and charitable activities, it's fun to leaf through."
—*Mike Wagner, Private Investor*

"The book is the writer-researcher's best friend. This is a resource tool I can't afford to be without."
—*Hank Nuwer, Author, Reporter, Educator*

"The book ranks high for accuracy especially compared to other reference works. Ideally suited for organizations and media."
—*Pam Keyes, Miami News-Record*

"By far and away the most complete, comprehensive and definitive book for anybody who has ever wanted to contact anybody of notoriety."
—*Christopher Snowden, Collector*

"The best source I've ever seen in my 30 years of writing!!"
—*Henry Jake Bommer, Collector*

"A valuable reference for anyone desirous of reaching people who daily appear on the national or international scene. An excellent addition to any library."
—*Anne Thompson, Rocky Ford Daily Gazette*

"The Benjamin Franklin Award winner as Directory of the Year!"
—*Independent Book Publishers Association*